EXTRA! EXTRA! FREE MEMBERS CAN NOW SUBMIT!

Plus, paid CGC members save up to 20% on grading and comic book pressing services!

CGC is the world's largest and most trusted third-party grading service for pop culture collectibles, including comics, magazines, TCGs, sports cards, video games, home video and concert posters with more than 15 million collectibles certified since 2000.

FREE

Access to
Online Resources

Free Grader Notes for
Comics When Available

Full Submission
Privileges to CGC

ASSOCIATE

Full Access to
Online Resources

Free Grader Notes for
Comics When Available

Full Submission Privileges
to CGC, NGC & PMG

10% Off CGC Grading
Tiers, Comic Book
Pressing & Fast Track

$15 CGC Shipping
Kit Voucher for
New Members

PREMIUM

Full Access to
Online Resources

Free Grader Notes for
Comics When Available

Full Submission Privileges
to CGC, NGC & PMG

10% Off CGC Grading
Tiers, Comic Book
Pressing & Fast Track

$20 CGC Shipping
Kit Voucher for
New Members

$150 Credit with CGC

ELITE

Full Access to
Online Resources

Free Grader Notes for
Comics When Available

Full Submission Privileges
to CGC, NGC & PMG

20% Off CGC Grading
Tiers, Comic Book
Pressing & Fast Track

$20 CGC Shipping
Kit Voucher for
New Members

$150 Credit with CGC

Scan the QR code to Join Today!

7

THE OVERSTREET® COMIC BOOK PRICE GUIDE

54TH EDITION

**COMICS FROM THE 1500s–PRESENT INCLUDED
FULLY ILLUSTRATED CATALOGUE
& EVALUATION GUIDE**

by ROBERT M. OVERSTREET
with YOLANDA RAMIREZ

GEMSTONE PUBLISHING

Stephen A. Geppi, Chief Executive Officer
J.C. Vaughn, President
Mark Huesman, Editor - Print
Amanda Sheriff, Editor - Digital
Yolanda Ramirez, Pricing Editor
Shawn Sippel, Digital Strategy Director
Liesa Yopp, Warehouse Operations
Tom Garey, Kathy Weaver, Brett Canby, Angela Phillips-Mills, Accounting Services

SPECIAL CONTRIBUTORS TO THIS EDITION

Julia Chiquete • Jon B. Cooke • Brendon & Brian Fraim • Dawn Guzzo
Mark Huesman • Mindy Lopkin • Joel Meadows • Brian Miller
Amanda Sheriff • Shawn Sippel • J.C. Vaughn • Carrie Wood

SPECIAL ADVISORS TO THIS EDITION

Bill Alexander • David T. Alexander • Tyler Alexander • Lon Allen • Dave Anderson
David J. Anderson, DDS • Matt Ballesteros • Peter Barbella • L.E. Becker • Jim Berry • Mike Bollinger • Steve Borock
Scott Braden • Russ Bright • Shawn Caffrey • John Chruscinski • Paul Clairmont • Art Cloos • Bill Cole
Ashley Cotter-Cairns • Jesse James Criscione • Brock Dickinson • Gary Dolgoff • John Dolmayan • Walter Durajlija
Ken Dyber • Daniel Ertle • D'Arcy Farrell • Bill Fidyk • Paul M. Figura • Joseph Fiore • Stephen Fishler
Dan Fogel • Kevin Forbes • Eric Fournier • Dan Gallo • Stephen Gentner • Josh Geppi • Steve Geppi
Douglas Gillock • Sean Goodrich • Tom Gordon III • Andy Greenham • Eric J. Groves • Jay Halstead • Terry Hoknes
Greg Holland • Steven Houston • Robert Isaac • Dr. Steven Kahn • Nick Katradis • Ivan Kocmarek • Timothy Kupin
Ben Labonog • Ben Lichtenstein • Stephen Lipson • Paul Litch • Doug Mabry • Brian Marcus • Will Mason
Jim McCallum • Todd McDevitt • Steve Mortensen • Josh Nathanson • Tom Nelson • Jamie Newbold • Karen O'Brien
Terry O'Neill • Michael Pavlic • Bill Ponseti • Sean Prosje • Tom Raupp • Mick Rabin • Alex Reece • Austin Reece
Stephen Ritter • Barry Sandoval • Buddy Saunders • Conan Saunders • Alika Seki • Todd Sheffer
Brian Sheppard • Frank Simmons • Marc Sims • Lauren Sisselman • Tony Starks • West Stephan • Al Stoltz
Doug Sulipa • Maggie Thompson • Michael Tierney • Ted VanLiew • Frank Verzyl
John Verzyl II • Rose Verzyl • Lon Webb • Mike Wilbur • Harley Yee • Vincent Zurzolo, Jr.

See a full list of Overstreet Advisors on pages 1100-1104

Teenage Mutant Ninja Turtles: Art by Kevin Eastman. ©2024 Viacom. All Rights Reserved.

Lady Death: Art by William Tucci. Lady Death ©2024 Lady Death, LLC.

Shi: Art by William Tucci. Shi ©2024 William Tucci.

The Shadow: Art by Michael Wm. Kaluta. The Shadow ©2024 Advance Magazine Publications. All rights reserved.

Big, Big Edition: Phantom Lady: Art by Aaron Lopresti.

Big, Big Edition: Golden Age Team-Up: Art by Dean Haspiel.

Teenage Mutant Ninja Turtles Hardcover Edition ISBN: 978-1-60360-634-9
Teenage Mutant Ninja Turtles Soft Cover Edition ISBN: 978-1-60360-633-2
Teenage Mutant Ninja Turtles - Advisors/Advertisers Hardcover Edition ISBN: 978-1-60360-632-5

Lady Death Hardcover Edition ISBN: 978-1-60360-636-3
Lady Death Soft Cover Edition ISBN: 978-1-60360-635-9

Shi Hardcover Edition ISBN: 978-1-60360-638-7
Shi Soft Cover Edition ISBN: 978-1-60360-637-0

The Shadow Hardcover Edition ISBN: 978-1-60360-640-0
The Shadow Soft Cover Edition ISBN: 978-1-60360-639-4

Phantom Lady - Big, Big Edition ISBN: 978-1-60360-643-1

Golden Age Team-Up - Big, Big Edition ISBN: 978-1-60360-644-8

Printed in Canada.

10 9 8 7 6 5 4 3 2 1

Fifty-fourth Edition: July 2024

Comic*Link*
AUCTIONS AND EXCHANGE
SINCE 1996

WE'LL FIND THE HIDDEN GEMS IN YOUR COLLECTION!

You likely know about the value of major keys like *Incredible Hulk* #181, *Amazing Spider-Man* #129 and *Giant-size X-Men* #1, but did you know that books like *Amazing Spider-Man* #114, *Sub-Mariner* #46 and *Detective Comics* #407 have sold for over $5,000 at auction? "Keys" are just the tip of the iceberg when it comes to valuable comics from the late 60s, 70s and 80s. Many common books in high-grade can sell for hundreds or even thousands of dollars more than reflected in this guide. Let us identify the hidden nuggets in your collection, advance your grading fees and maximize your return when selling! Check out these recent sales from our auctions to see what we mean:

$5,276
RESULT
Top Guide: $125

$42,000
RESULT
Top Guide: $260

$5,200
RESULT
Top Guide: $255

$5,285
RESULT
Top Guide: $18

$7,601
RESULT
Top Guide: $300

$7,700
RESULT
Top Guide: $400

$4,450
RESULT
Top Guide: $65

$5,101
RESULT
Top Guide: $95

Guide prices provided based on 2022-2023
Overstreet Price Guide NM- price

TO SELL, VISIT
ComicLink.com
buysell@comiclink.com
(617) 517-0062
M-F 8:30am to 5:30pm ET

LET US MAXIMIZE YOUR NET RETURN!
ATTAINING RECORD SALES SINCE 1996!
SELL IN OUR NEXT AUCTION!

TABLE OF CONTENTS

ACKNOWLEDGEMENTS

Teenage Mutant Ninja Turtles co-creator Kevin Eastman turned his guys loose on our cover and the result was magic. Not to be outdone, Billy Tucci (and colorist Wes Hartman) commemorated the 30th anniversaries of both Brian Pulido's *Lady Death* and his own *Shi* with two covers that connect to form one larger image. In comics we say "legend" too easily, but Michael Wm. Kaluta proved he is one with his return to The Shadow (with colors by Alex Sinclair). On the Big, Big edition, Aaron Lopresti brought us a beautiful Phantom Lady, and Dean Haspiel provided the inspired Golden Age team-up of Fantomah, Wonder Man and The Human Bomb.

Special thanks to Gemstone's own Yolanda Ramirez, Mark Huesman, Shawn Sippel, Amanda Sheriff, and J.C. Vaughn.

Special Thanks to the Overstreet Advisors who contributed to this edition, including Darren Adams, Bill Alexander, David T. Alexander, Tyler Alexander, Lon Allen, Dave Anderson, David J. Anderson, DDS, Matt Ballesteros, Peter Barbella, L.E. Becker, Jim Berry, Peter Bilelis, Esq., Steve Borock, Scott Braden, Russ Bright, Shawn Caffrey, John Chruscinski, Paul Clairmont, Art Cloos, Bill Cole, Ashley Cotter-Cairns, Jesse James Criscione, Brock Dickinson, Gary Dolgoff, John Dolmayan, Walter Durajlija, Ken Dyber, Jon Engel, Daniel Ertle, D'Arcy Farrell, Bill Fidyk, Paul M. Figura, Joseph Fiore, Stephen Fishler, Dan Fogel, Kevin Forbes, Eric Fournier, Brent Frankenhoff, Dan Gallo, Stephen Gentner, Josh Geppi, Steve Geppi, Douglas Gillock, Sean Goodrich, Tom Gordon III, Andy Greenham, Eric J. Groves, Jim Halperin, Jay Halstead, Rick Hirsch, Terry Hoknes, Greg Holland, Steven Houston, Robert Isaac, Matt Joaquin, Dr. Steven Kahn, Nick Katradis, Ivan Kocmarek, Timothy Kupin, Ben Labonog, Ben Lichtenstein, Stephen Lipson, Paul Litch, Doug Mabry, Brian Marcus, Will Mason, Jim McCallum, Todd McDevitt, Brent Moeshlin, Steve Mortensen, Marc Nathan, Josh Nathanson, Tom Nelson, Jamie Newbold, Karen O'Brien, Terry O'Neill, Michael Pavlic, Bill Ponseti, Bo Pritts, Mike Rabin, Tom Raupp, Alex Reece, Austin Reece, Stephen & Sharon Ritter, Barry Sandoval, Buddy Saunders, Conan Saunders, Alika Seki, Todd Sheffer, Brian Sheppard, Frank Simmons, Marc Sims, Lauren Sisselman, Tony Starks, West Stephan, Al Stoltz, Doug Sulipa, Maggie Thompson, Michael Tierney, Anthony Tincani, Tom Tunnicliff, Ted VanLiew, Frank Verzyl, John Verzyl II, Rose Verzyl, Lon Webb, Eddie Wendt, Mike Wilbur, Harley Yee, and Vincent Zurzolo, Jr., as well as to our additional contributors, including Stephen Baer, Dr. Jonathan Calure, Dawn Guzzo, and Kevin Poling. Without their active participation, this project would not have been possible.

Additionally, I would like to personally extend my thanks to all of those who encouraged and supported first the creation of and then subsequently the expansion of the *Guide* over the past five decades. While it's impossible in this brief space to individually acknowledge every individual, mention is certainly due to Lon Allen (Golden Age data), Mark Arnold (Harvey data), Larry Bigman (Frazetta-Williamson data), Bill Blackbeard (Platinum Age cover photos), Steve Borock and Mark Haspel (Grading), Glenn Bray (Kurtzman data), Gary M. Carter (DC data), J.B. Clifford Jr. (EC data), Gary Coddington (Superman data), Gary Colabuono (Golden Age ashcan data), Wilt Conine (Fawcett data), Chris Cormier (Miracleman data), Dr. S.M. Davidson (Cupples & Leon data), Al Dellinges (Kubert data), Stephen Fishler (10-Point Grading system), Chris Friesen (Glossary additions), David Gerstein (Walt Disney Comics data), Kevin Hancer (Tarzan data), Charles Heffelfinger and Jim Ivey (March of Comics listing), R.C. Holland and Ron Pussell (*Seduction* and *Parade of Pleasure* data), Grant Irwin (Quality data), Richard Kravitz (Kelly data), Phil Levine (giveaway data), Paul Litch (Copper & Modern Age data), Dan Malan & Charles Heffelfinger (Classic Comics data), Jon McClure (Whitman data), Fred Nardelli (Frazetta data), Marc Nathan (FCBD issues), Michelle Nolan (Love comics), Mike Nolan (MLJ, Timely, Nedor data), George Olshevsky (Timely data), Dr. Richard Olson (Grading and Yellow Kid info), Chris Pedrin (DC War data), Scott Pell ('50s data), Greg Robertson (National data), Don Rosa (Late 1940s to 1950s data), Matt Schiffman (Bronze Age data), Frank Scigliano (Little Lulu data), Gene Seger (Buck Rogers data), Rick Sloane (Archie data), David R. Smith, Archivist, Walt Disney Productions (Disney data), Bill Spicer and Zetta DeVoe (Western Publishing Co. data), Tony Starks (Silver and Bronze Age data), Al Stoltz (Golden Age & Promo data), Doug Sulipa (Bronze Age data), Don and Maggie Thompson (Four Color listing), Mike Tiefenbacher & Jerry Sinkovec (Atlas and National data), Raymond True & Philip J. Gaudino (Classic Comics data), Jim Vadeboncoeur Jr. (Williamson and Atlas data), Richard Samuel West (Victorian Age and Platinum Age data), Kim Weston (Disney and Barks data), Cat Yronwode (Spirit data), Andrew Zerbe and Gary Behymer (M. E. data).

A special thanks, as always, to my wife Caroline, for her encouragement and support on such a tremendous project, and to all who placed ads in this edition.

15

A NEW CHAPTER IN COLLECTING HISTORY IS HERE...

CGC is now grading pulps!

CGC is thrilled to announce that pulp grading has officially begun. Closely related to comic books, pulps have been seriously collected, researched and written about for many decades. They were one of the primary forms of entertainment during the first half of the 20th century, impacting American pop culture by influencing movies, radio, comic books and eventually television.

Maximize the potential of your books with

△△CGC® | PRESSING

CGC Pressing, formally known as CCS, is the best way to enhance the appearance of your collectibles. Our multi-step process has been modified and honed through thousands of hours of research and development. We've pressed hundreds of thousands of comics, many of them regarded as the most valuable in the hobby. Our experienced pressing team has been entrusted with Pedigree collections, key issues, modern comics, CGC Signature Series submissions, atypical comics and abnormal defects, all with expert results.

BEFORE

AFTER

Some of the non-color breaking defects that can be pressed, are:

- ✔ Bends
- ✔ Crunches
- ✔ Spine rolls
- ✔ Dents & indentations
- ✔ Ripples
- ✔ Warping

Scan the QR code to learn more about CGC Pressing!

CHILD is BORN

MOUNTS
TORTOLINI
SPARACIO
TUCCI

BASED ON THE GOSPELS ACCORDING TO
MATTHEW & LUKE

AMERICAN MYTHOLOGY PRESENTS

RETURN of THE LIVING DEAD ™

COMING SOON TO

AMERICANMYTHOLOGY
P R O D U C T I O N S

AMERICANMYTHOLOGY.COM

 @AMERICANMYTHOLOGYCOMICS @AMERICANMYTHO

AMERICAN MYTHOLOGY PRESENTS

RETURN of THE LIVING DEAD ™

COMING SOON TO

AMERICANMYTHOLOGY
PRODUCTIONS

AMERICANMYTHOLOGY.COM

 @AMERICANMYTHOLOGYCOMICS   @AMERICANMYTHO

COMICS ARE FOR EVERYONE

FREE COMIC BOOK DAY
May 3, 2025
freecomicbookday.com

Jusko Celebrates Kubert!

Acclaimed ERB Cover Artist Joe Jusko Recreates Joe Kubert's *Overstreet* #5 Cover For Its 50th Anniversary!

On Sale July 2025

ISSUE NO.
292
JUNE
JUL/AUG PRE-ORDER

GTM
GAME TRADE MAGAZINE

CELEBRATING 20 YEARS OF GAME TRADE MAGAZINE

$3.99 US $3.72 CAN

36006

6 03259 23905 6

PRINTED IN CANADA

IN THIS ISSUE:

- BATTLE ACROSS HISTORY WITH *DC HEROCLIX: MASTERS OF TIME* FROM WIZKIDS!
- OVER 150 ELEMENTAL MONSTERS JOIN THE FIGHT IN ROLL FOR COMBAT'S *BATTLEZOO ELDAMON!*

BATTLETECH
CATALYST

43

THE GOOD, THE BAD *and* HUGHES

William Hughes' Vintage Collectibles

P.O. Box 270244
Flower Mound, TX 75027

Office: 972-539-9190
Mobile: 973-432-4070

Whether you are buying or selling any Fine Vintage Collectibles, I'd like to get acquainted with you to discuss your options. I'm Bill Hughes.

I have been instrumental in the buying and selling of many of the largest, most valuable and noteworthy collections and individual collectibles to ever surface in the comic book, trading card and movie poster marketplaces. From the finest certified copies of **Marvel Comics #1, Action Comics #1, Superman #1, Detective Comics #27** and **Batman #1** to the only known copy of the super-rare **Dracula Style A original one sheet movie poster**, to the **Original Artwork for the entire book of X-Men #1** to the first "Gem Mint 10" certified **Mickey Mantle rookie baseball card**. With over **50 Years of experience I have Seen and Done it ALL!**

Whether you are looking to Buy, Sell or Consign your collectibles, please give me a call. **With 30,000+ Active Buying Customers, I can Afford to Pay the Most because I Get the Most for Top Quality Items.** So Why Wait? If you want a **Few Dollars More**, give me a call right away to discuss what you have to offer, or, more importantly, what I have to offer you!

There is No One Quicker on the draw with Fast Cash! You will come away with a smile on your face and **A Fistful of Dollars**. I want all dealings to have a Win-Win outcome, so try me. You'll be happy you did!

Senior Advisor
Overstreet
Price Guide

CGC
Comics Guaranty, LLC
CHARTER
MEMBER DEALER

ebay: comic-warehouse • whughes199@yahoo.com

PROTECT AND DISPLAY YOUR COLLECTION WITH OUR HAND-CRAFTED ACRYLIC CASES.

Features and Highlights:

- **HIGHEST QUALITY –** CGA uses only the highest quality acrylic with a minimum thickness of 1/8 " (3.2mm).
- **UNOBSTRUCTED VIEW –** Our cases are crystal clear acrylic, so that your item can be clearly viewed from all sides.
- **CUSTOM FIT –** We custom design our cases for every item's specific measurements with an added 1/8" to each dimension to allow the collectible to be inserted and removed without interior rubbing.
- **ROUNDED EDGES –** Every edge, inside and out, is flame-polished to perfection by our master acrylic craftsman.

10% OFF YOUR NEXT SUBMISSION

Use coupon code: CGA_TC2024

One per customer - Expires 12/31/2024

JOIN OUR NEW PREMIUM MEMBERSHIP!

Earn 5% back on all purchases PLUS enjoy exclusive discounts!

POPULATION REPORTS NOW AVAILABLE!

cgagrading.com   f 🖸 /cgagrading

WANTED

THE GREATEST COMICS OF ALL TIME!

I WANT THESE BACK!

I'm looking for all those great comics you saw on the previous page, and for many others as well! Some people thought when I donated a major collection to the Library of Congress that I stopped collecting. Nothing could be further from the truth!

I'm buying all the time! Are you in the market to sell your Pre-1965 comics? Send me your list!

Steve

Steve Geppi
gsteve@diamondcomics.com

The Inside
COLLECTOR

July/
August 1991
Volume 2
Number 2

$3.95
Canada
$4.95

Scandal Rocks
Toy World

Comics King
Steve Geppi

Jewels by Jumeau

Fireworks!!

Claymation Art

10150 York Road, Suite 300
Hunt Valley, MD 21030
410.598.1773

NOT FINAL ART

DEALERS • PUBLISHERS • COLLECTORS

ADVERTISE IN OVERSTREET®

54 YEARS OF REACHING SERIOUS COMIC BOOK FANS!

FOR MORE INFORMATION, EMAIL US AT

FEEDBACK@GEMSTONEPUB.COM

WWW.GEMSTONEPUB.COM

MARVEL

1/7 SCALE RESIN MINI-BUSTS

ALSO AVAILABLE:

GREEN GOBLIN

Get 20% off with code OVERSTREET
at diamondselecttoys.com

Gold Membership
$9.00/month *or* $90.00/year (two months free!)

- Access to browse comic database and basic data, as well as meta data about publishers, titles, issues, story arcs, characters, and contributors
- View Overstreet Pricing information
- Access to special editorial content
- Access to collection management (5 Collections)

- Unlimited issues
- Add issues to Want List
- Automatically create your Gap List
- Access to the Mobile App
- Ability to add Preferred Retailers

Annual Price Before Discount Applied

Silver Membership
$5.00/month *or* $50.00/year (two months free!)

- Access to browse comic database and basic data, as well as meta data about publishers, titles, issues, story arcs, characters, and contributors
- View Overstreet Pricing information
- Access to special editorial content
- Access to collection management (1 Collection)

- Up to 5000 issues
- Add issues to Want List
- Automatically create your Gap List
- Access to the Mobile App
- Ability to add Preferred Retailers

Annual Price Before Discount Applied

Bronze Membership
$3.00/month *or* $30.00/year (two months free!)

- Access to browse comic database and view basic data, as well as meta data about publishers, titles, issues, story arcs, characters, and contributors

- View Overstreet Pricing information
- Access to special editorial content

Annual Price Before Discount Applied

OverstreetAccess.com

Everyone knows the days of keeping unbagged comic books lying around are long gone – bags and boards are a forgone conclusion in this modern world of collecting. But what about when a bag and board aren't enough? Do you want to lie awake all night worrying that your comic is developing irreversible stresses that will reduce its value a thousandfold? You need something a little tougher to keep that comic safe, and Ironguard Supplies has just the thing. In addition to a full range of bags and boards in all sizes, Ironguard now offers comic toploaders, rigid sleeves that will keep your comic protected from even the most unforgiving longbox. Sleep easy, my friend.

Get 20& off with code OVERSTREET

See the full line at ironguardsupplies.com

f ⓘ /ironguardsupplies

HERITAGE®
COMICS & COMIC ART AUCTIONS

QUESTIONS TO ASK YOUR PROSPECTIVE AUCTIONEER

"IN ONE FORM OR ANOTHER, COMIC BOOKS HAVE BEEN AROUND SINCE THE 1800S."

"WELL BEFORE THE BIRTH OF THE SUPERHEROES, THERE WERE COMIC BOOKS."

THESE DAYS, THERE ARE COMICS FOR JUST ABOUT EVERY TASTE...

AND IT'S ALWAYS A GOOD TIME TO DISCOVER THE CLASSICS!

THERE'S USUALLY A REASON THAT CERTAIN COMICS HAVE STOOD THE TEST OF TIME...

AND THE WHOLE REASON THAT *THE OVERSTREET COMIC BOOK PRICE GUIDE* EXISTS IS THAT MANY COMICS HAVE GONE UP IN VALUE SINCE THEY WERE PUBLISHED!

WHILE MANY COMICS ARE VERY AFFORDABLE TO EVEN THE NEWEST FANS, SEVERAL ISSUES HAVE SOLD FOR MORE THAN *$1 MILLION!*

BACK ISSUE COMICS RANGE FROM LESS THAN COVER PRICE TO $6 MILLION!

CAN YOU BELIEVE THAT? PERHAPS I SHOULD STEAL ONE OF THEM...

HA HA HA HA HA!

JUST KIDDING, OF COURSE.

THE FIRST COMIC TO HIT $1 MILLION WAS *ACTION COMICS #1*, THE FIRST APPEARANCE OF SUPERMAN, BY THE WAY.

IN 15 MONTHS FROM LATE 2020 TO EARLY 2022, THE **TOTAL NUMBER** OF COMICS THAT HAVE SOLD FOR $1 MILLION OR HIGHER **MORE THAN DOUBLED!**

THE **GRADE** AND **SCARCITY** OF THE ISSUES HAVE A LOT TO DO WITH THAT. WE'LL GET INTO THAT IN JUST A BIT.

BUT LIKE I SAID **BEFORE,** OUR ADVICE WILL ALWAYS BE "COLLECT WHAT YOU LOVE AND YOU'LL **NEVER GO WRONG.**"

IT ALL STARTED WITH OUR FIRST EDITION BACK IN 1970, AND IT QUICKLY BECAME AN ANNUAL EVENT!

OVERSTREET PRICING AND GRADING STANDARDS ARE THE ACCEPTED FOUNDATION OF THE COMIC BOOK MARKETPLACE.

COMICS ARE LISTED ALPHABETICALLY BY TITLE, REGARDLESS OF PUBLISHER. THE MAIN SECTION LISTS COMICS FROM 1934 TO THE PRESENT.

THIS BOOK ALSO INCLUDES...

BIG LITTLE BOOKS
PROMOTIONAL COMICS
PIONEER AGE COMICS
VICTORIAN AGE COMICS
PLATINUM AGE COMICS

FANTASTIC FOUR (See Volume Three for issues #500-611)
Marvel Comics Group: Nov, 1961 - No. 416, Sept. 1996 (Created by Stan Lee & Jack Kirby)

1-Origin & 1st app. The Fantastic Four (Reed Richards: Mr. Fantastic, Johnny Storm: The Human Torch, Sue Storm: The Invisible Girl, & Ben Grimm: The Thing–Marvel's 1st super-hero group since the G.A.; 1st app. S.A. Human Torch); origin/1st app. The Mole Man.

7800	15,600	31,200	78,000	214,000	350,000

1-Golden Record Comic Set Reprint (1966)-cover not identical to original

46	92	138	340	770	1200

with Golden Record

59	118	177	472	1061	1650

2-Vs. The Skrulls (last 10¢ issue); (should have a pin-up of The Thing which many copies are missing)

630	1260	1890	5200	13,100	21,000

3-Fantastic Four don costumes & establish Headquarters; brief 1pg. origin; intro. The Fantasti-Car; Human Torch drawn w/two left hands on-c

660	1320	1980	5450	13,725	22,000

4-1st S. A. Sub-Mariner app. (5/62)

720	1440	2160	5950	14,975	24,000

5-Origin & 1st app. Doctor Doom

3280	6560	9840	26,200	54,100	82,000

6-Sub-Mariner, Dr. Doom team up; 1st Marvel villain team-up (2nd S.A. Sub-Mariner app.

367	734	1100	3120	7060	11,000

7,9,10: 7-1st app. Kurrgo. 9-3rd Sub-Mariner app. 10-Stan Lee & Jack Kirby app. in story

169	338	507	1394	3147	4900
179	358	537	1477	3339	5200
172	344	516	1419	3210	5000

* Many of the comic books are listed in groups such as 11-20, 21-30, 31-50, and so on.
* The prices listed along with such groupings represent the value of each issue in that group, not the group as a whole.
* It's difficult to overstate how much accurate grading plays into getting a good price for your sales or purchases.

ISN'T THE BEST PART OF COLLECTING THAT THERE ARE SO MANY DIFFERENT WAYS TO COLLECT?

YOU BET! YOU CAN CHOOSE TO FOLLOW INDIVIDUAL WRITERS, ARTISTS, PUBLISHERS, OR CHARACTERS...

YOU CAN COLLECT SUPERHEROES, WAR COMICS, WESTERNS, ROMANCE COMICS, OR WHATEVER YOU LIKE!

YOU CAN CHOOSE #1 ISSUES, FIRST APPEARANCES, CROSSOVERS, OR MANY OTHER VARIATIONS.

SO YOU'RE SAYING IT'S TRULY ABOUT COLLECTING WHAT YOU LIKE AND NOT WHAT SOMEONE ELSE LIKES?

WHETHER IT'S SPIDER-MAN OR EVERY COMIC BOOK APPEARANCE OF JAMES BOND, MAKE YOUR OWN PLAN. THEN GO TO IT!

THANKS TO OUR INCREDIBLE NETWORK OF OVERSTREET ADVISORS, WE NEVER STOP WORKING ON THIS STUFF!

AND AFTER MORE THAN 50 YEARS, WE'RE JUST GETTING WARMED UP!

Written by J.C. VAUGHN
Illustrated by BRENDON & BRIAN FRAIM
Colored by Hi-Fi's BRIAN MILLER
Lettered by MINDY LOPKIN
Edited by MARK HUESMAN

IT MAY SOUND CORNY, BUT THE BEST IS YET TO COME!

MULTIPLE COPIES OF KEY GOLDEN AGE BOOKS SOLD IN 2023-24

MARKET REPORT 2024 • Robert M. Overstreet

I'd like to personally extend my thanks to everyone who has supported *The Overstreet Comic Book Price Guide* over the years.

Bill Alexander reported, "Sales prices dropped big time on books of all ages, especially Copper and Modern Age books in certified 9.8 grade."

David Alexander stated, "The demand for collectible comics has not decreased. Our economy has been in the pits since the Covid money has dried up. During the Covid era when government money was flowing freely many comic prices were rising daily. When the money flow decreased, so did many comic book prices. In particular pre-Code Horror books spearheaded by the EC titles have seen not only constantly increasing demand but also rising prices."

Dave Anderson stated, "The comic market remains strong. The passion with which collectors fuel the market is always present and will continue to keep the hobby healthy."

Peter Barbella wrote, "Golden Age, of course, remains strong, and pre-Code Horror is on fire. Golden Age keys and classic covers (especially World War II covers) continue to dominate the market."

Lauren Becker noted, "The market is simply correcting itself from the Covid era. A CGC graded 7.0 *Hulk* #181 went from being an average $3,000 comic in 2019 to $6,000 by 2021, and then back to a respectful $4,500 by 2023."

Jim Berry reported, "2023 will also be remembered as a year that continued the post-Covid trend with values of comics remaining down and flat overall."

Russ Bright stated, "Prices are down but purchases are plentiful. Buyers are out there for almost any book."

Paul Clairmont wrote, "This year saw a return to normal market conditions and regular sales. As prices return to normal, I see more collectors emerging as books

#1 $6 million

#1 $810,000

#1 $2.3 million

become affordable."

Art Cloos noted, "Overall 2023 saw prices of Silver and Bronze Age Marvel keys continue their 2022 drop into 2023."

Gary Dolgoff stated, "Golden Age are generally rock-solid, yet most don't go up in *The Guide* yearly."

Walter Durajlija & Jay Halstead reported, "The comic book collecting and investing hobby has gone through a major correction over the past 18 months with comic book values giving back all their Covid era gains."

Ken Dyber wrote, "Simply put, people are buying less, and the ones that are buying, are focusing mostly on lower risk and/or lower ticket items. Golden Age is the one area of the market that has been more stable."

D'Arcy Farrell reported, "With Covid mostly gone, markets came back to 100% operations which included conventions and instore sales."

Bill Fidyk revealed, "2023 was a good year for the back issue magazine market despite market corrections that have caused sales prices to dip. Overall, prices seemed to fall slightly, but did not drastically decline."

Joseph Fiore reported, "A *re-holder scam* has been reported on the CGC forums where it is believed an eBay seller has seemingly figured out a way to get a lower grade comic into a higher grade slab." (See his market report.)

Kevin Forbes noted, "For the most part, comic book prices continued to gradually slide down a bit more most of the 2023 year."

Eric Fournier stated, "The market was putting on serious brakes. Our shows to follow were not the numbers both in attendance or sales."

Steve Gentner reported, "The explosion of prices of pre-Code Horror books was, and is Homeric!! Big prices for all manner of this segment just took off."

Eric Groves noted, "Golden Age books persist as the anchor of the hobby."

Greg Holland reported, "The CGC Census increased from 8,771,445 in December 2022 to 10,167,318 in December 2023."

Steven Houston & John Dolmayan wrote, "There is still money in our hobby, it's just all chasing the same books. Everything else is just dead wood right now."

Robert Isaac reported, "The one era of books that still holds strong is the Golden Age Heroes. Horror, Sci-fi and Romance from this era seem to be untouched by the radical waves."

Ben Labonog noted, "There was a big market re-correction on most keys that started around October 2022 and went through most of 2023."

Ben Lichtenstein stated, "Golden Age demand is as strong as ever with prices on average stable or increasing after the Covid Boom. There is still a very healthy interest in collecting comics, and there are plenty of new buyers who came back in 2020/2021."

Doug Mabry reported, "We noticed a slight softening in the market for average Golden age books."

Jim McCallum stated, "We've been offered more collections in the last six months than we ever have."

Todd McDevitt reported, "The big question is... can values rebound? Are there enough future collectors on the horizon to bolster demand for key issues?"

Bo Pritts added, "This year's current state of the comic market is down even more this year than it was last year."

Brent Moeshlin noted, "As the year went on, it became clear that comic valuations were not going to recover anytime soon."

Steve Mortensen stated, "Superhero and pre-Code Horror comics remain hot."

Josh Nathanson & Rick Hirsch reported, "Despite the overall collectibles market adjustment following the pandemic bubble, the high end comic book market remained very solid in 2023."

Jamie Newbold w/Matt Joaquin reported, "I enjoy seeing the resurgence in Golden Age comics collecting. My revered ECs act as though they exploded upon the scene."

Karen O'Brien noted, "After a market correction in the back half of 2022 that persisted into 2023, Golden Age books unsurprisingly held their luster."

Terry O'Neill wrote, "On a positive note, the convention scene for 2023 was quite good

#73 $114,000

#12 $204,000

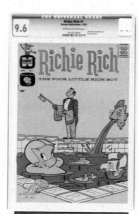

#1 $108,000

for selling comics, especially Golden Age and Atom Age."

Bill Ponseti noted, "2023 was the first year where our in-store year-over-year gross revenue remained flat."

Alex & Austin Reece reported, "Things in the comic industry this year were rocky at best. Comics across a variety of ages were decreasing in value month over month."

Buddy & Conan Saunders noted, "Golden Age was the safest buy during the past 3 years."

Alika Seki reported, "The Lahaina and Kula fires of August 8th have destroyed much of Maui. If you want to help the people of Maui with your donations, we recommend "Maui Rapid Response."

Todd Sheffer stated, "Sales and prices were still strong in all major categories. Comic book sales show values still rising for key books from the Golden, Silver and Bronze Age. Early DC and Timely superhero titles have a continued following. EC and other pre-Code Horror have been running strong when they come to market."

Marc Sims noted, "Golden Age comics, while not entirely immune to the downward pressures in the market, have performed exceedingly well all year."

Tony Starks reported, "The last 15 months have seen a significant pullback in prices paid for books/titles most commonly bought and sold. But pre-Code Horror is on fire. Romance? Napalm. Crime Comics? Where there is smoke... Better Archie comics (double entendre or sexy covers) have been desirable for years now. Good Girl art, Frazetta Dells 1960s Gold Key first issues as well. Demand for Romance is way up. Lots of love for Matt Baker covers/art. The Fox and St. John Giants are 3x *Guide* as they are very hard to find, even in low grade. ACG, St. John, Atlas/Timely, ECs and DC Romance are in high demand."

Karen O'Brien pointed out, "As the pandemic ages into an endemic state, comic shops resumed regular business hours."

West Stephan noted, "With an economic downturn and a potential recession looming, everyone is more selective as to what they are purchasing. These downward turns are typically short-lived as collectors realize putting money into the hobby is still a solid investment. "

Doug Sulipa reported, "2023 was a

year of market correction. Back issue prices jumped too fast in the hysteria of 2020-2021, they started to drop off in 2022, and in 2023 we saw prices fall even on the top keys like *Hulk* #181 and *Amazing Fantasy* #15. By the end of the year, prices leveled off and the market was stabilizing and getting back to normal. The strongest trend of the year is the rise in demand for Horror comics. Charlton Horror comics of the 1968-1984 era are very under-valued in the *Guide*. All the Marvel Horror comics are up in demand."

Ted VanLiew stated, "Golden Age and Atom Age books have held their value best, presumably because they're by far the scarcest issues."

Harley Yee wrote, "Golden Age books have held their prices better than the others. These books are rarer and I still see new collectors going straight into Golden Age. With many collectors moving into Golden Age, this market should see growth in 2024."

Vincent Zurzulo & Peter Barbella reported, "With Golden Age comics, we have seen stability and oftentimes increases in prices for comics from the 1930s-'50s. Blue chip titles like *Action*, *Detective*, *Captain America* and *Marvel Mystery* have done very well, along with many categories such as pre-Code Horror, Sci-fi, and Romance."

Golden Age Sales:
Action Comics #1 CGC 8.5 Kansas City Pedigree $6,000,000, CGC 6.0 $3,180,000, CGC 0.5 $408,000, page 1 $57,600
Action Comics #7 CGC 5.0 $156,000
Action Comics #20 CGC 7.0 $18,000
All Select Comics #1, CGC 4.0 $19,200
All Star Comics #8 CGC 9.4 $1,500,000, CGC 8.0 $180,000
Archie Comics #1 CGC 5.5 $66,000
Astonishing #30 CGC 9.2 Bethlehem Pedigree $36,000
Batman #1 CGC 9.4 $2,220,000, CGC 8.0 $1,220,000, CGC 7.0 $660,000, $630,000, CGC 6.0 $552,000, CGC 1.8 $144,000, $138,000,
Batman #37 CGC 9.6 Promise Collection Pedigree $48,000
Batman #59 CGC 9.6 $66,000
Batman #69 CGC 9.6 $24,000
Black Cat Mystery #50 CGC 6.5 $21,600
Captain America Comics #1 CGC 9.4 $3,120,000, CGC 9.2 $810,000, CGC 3.0 $126,000
Chamber of Chills #23 CGC 9.0 $22,800

#2 $31,200

#1 $1.38 million

#4 $900,000

Crime SuspenStories #22 CGC 9.0 $72,000, CGC 9.2 Gaines File Pedigree $72,000
Daredevil #1 CGC 9.0 $18,600
Detective Comics #27 CGC 6.0, $1,740,000
Detective Comics #29 CGC 5.5 Brittle $81,000
Detective Comics #30 CGC 5.5 $14,600
Detective Comics #33, CGC 6.5 $288,000
Detective Comics #58 Cover Art $270,000
Detective Comics #62, CGC 7.0 $18,600
Detective Comics #114 Double Cover, $84,000
Detective Comics #140 CGC 9.6 $360,000
Detective Comics #168, CGC 6.0 $20,400
Eerie Comics #1, CGC 9.2 $108,000, CGC 8.0 $28,800
Famous Funnies #214, CGC 8.5 $18,000
Flash Comics #1, CGC 5.0 $192,000
Front Page Comic Book #1, CGC 9.6 File Copy $26,400
Ghost #6, CGC 9.0 $33,600
Green Hornet #1, CGC 9.4 $31,200
Haunt of Fear #27 Cover Original Art $78,000
Leading Comics #1 Cover Original art, 1941 $150,000
Little Dot #1, CGC 9.6 $78,000
Marvel Comics #1, CGC 7.5 $675,000, CBCS Restored 2.5 $144,000
Marvel Mystery Comics #2, CGC 4.5 $26,400
Marvel Mystery Comics #3, CGC 2.5 $24,000
Marvel Mystery Comics #46 ,CGC 7.5 $45,600, CGC 6.0 $38,400
Mask Comics #1, The Promise Collection Pedigree CC 8.5 $144,000
More Fun Comics #55, CGC 9.6 Mile High Pedigree $264,000
More Fun Comics #72, CGC 1.5 $40,800
More Fun Comics #73, CGC 6.5 $120,000, CGC 7.0 $114,000
Prize Comics #13, Mile High Pedigree CGC 9.8 $24,000
Punch Comics #12, Crowley copy Pedigree CGC 8.0 $204,000
Richie Rich #1 CGC 9.$96,000, 108,000
Sensation Comics #1, CGC 7.0 $90,000, CGC 6.5 $84,000
Seven Seas Comics #4, CGC 9.2 Crippen ("D" copy 81,000
The Shadow #11 Cover Original Art, 1973 "The Arrival" $72,000
Shock SuspenStories #6 cover art, 1952 $840,000
Sub-Mariner #1, CGC 6.0 $31,200

Superman #1, CGC 7.0 $2,340.000, CGC 3.0 $360,000, CGC 5.0 $675,000, CGC 1.0 $108,000, CGC 1.5 $174,000
Wonder Woman #1, CGC 3.0 $27,600
World's Best Comics #1, CGC 8.0 $31,200
Zip Comics #7, CGC 9.8 Mile High $63,000

Silver Age: Ken Dyber reported, "This year has really crushed this time period in value more than any other period. An example from last year to this year would be *X-Men* #1 in 6.0 was $25k and is now $16k. *Hulk* #181 in 6.0 was $5,000 is now $3,300.

Ben Labonog noted, "Silver and Bronze Age keys were down anywhere from 30-50%."

Tom Tunnicliff pointed out, "This year's current state of the comic market is, I believe, down even more this year than it was last year."

Steve Mortensen reported, "Silver Age may be the most disappointing sector of the market, with large declines in key books."

Josh Nathanson stated, "The Silver Age continues to be one of the most popular segments of the hobby, with the superhero genre dominating the activity within this category."

Tom Nelson reported, "It's been mostly a soft year for Silver Age through Modern comics including high-grade CGC books."

Karen O'Brien noted, "Silver Age titles remain desirable in all conditions."

Terry O'Neill reported, "Silver Age comics cooled down quite a bit over the past two years."

Bill Ponseti wrote, "2023 was a strange year that saw tremendous price drops across the board for Silver, Bronze, Copper and Modern Age Comics."

Todd Sheffer reported, "Marvel continues to be the desired choice in Silver Age."

Marc Sims noted, "The market correction on Silver/Bronze/Copper that began midway through 2022 only accelerated in 2023."

Michael Tierney stated, "The sales lull that began before the 2022 election continued well into the next year."

Ted VanLiew noted, "Some really great Silver Age books have come down in price."

John Verzyl II & Rose Verzyl reported, "Because of a series of baffling decisions, the looming threat of comic book values being un-tied from the movies has come to fruition."

Harley Yee wrote, "The market in Silver, Bronze, Copper and Modern is in correction

#260 $26,400

#87 $210,000

#27 $78,000

territory."

Vincent Zurzolo & Peter Barbella noted, "We have seen downward corrections on prices ranging from 25-50% in value from the heights of the pandemic years."

Peter Barbella added, "Silver and Bronze Age continue to restabilize after the Covid boom of 2021-2022."

Silver Age through Modern Age Sales:
Adventure Comics #260 CGC 9.4 $26,400
Amazing Fantasy #15, CGC 9.6 $3,600,000, CGC 5.0 $69,601.20, CGC 5.5 $66,000, CGC 6.0 $66,000, $75,000, CGC 6.5 $96,000, CGC 7.0 $126,000, CGC 7.5 $117,000, CGC 8.0 $312,000, CGC 8.5 $552,000, CGC 9.2 $810,000
Amazing Spider-Man #1, CGC 9.8 Curator Pedigree $1,380,000, CGC 9.4 $264,000, CGC 8.5 $66,000
Amazing Spider-Man #3, CGC 9.0 $24,000
Amazing Spider-Man #9, CGC 9.8 $126,000
Amazing Spider-Man #14, CGC 9.4 $25,230
Amazing Spider-Man #22, page 7 original art, 1965 $96,000
Amazing Spider-Man #87 cover original art $210,000
Amazing Spider-Man #116 Original Cover art $132,000
Avengers #1, CGC 9.4 $120,000, CGC 9.2 $66,000
Avengers #4, CGC 9.8 $108,000, $132,000
Avengers #161 cover art $288,000
Brave and the Bold #28, CGC 9.6 $810,000
Brave and the Bold #54 CGC 9.6 $33,600
Daredevil #185 cover art $225,000
Detective Comics #404 Cover Original Art $90,000
Doctor Strange #5 cover Original Art, $84,000
Fantastic Four #1, CGC 9.2 $1,500,000, CGC 6.5 $42,000, CGC 8.5 $117,000
Fantastic Four #5, CGC 8.0 $22,800
Fantastic Four #48 CGC 9.8 $81,000, $93,000, $96,000
Fantastic Four #184 Cover Original art $120,000
Giant-Size X-Men #1, CGC 9.8 $25,200
House of Secrets #92, CGC 9.8 $84,000
Incredible Hulk #181, CGC 9.8 $66,000, $69,000, $72,000, $78,000, CGC 9.6 $18,600, CGC 8.0 $138,000, CGC 7.5 $84,000, CGC 6.0

$33,000

Iron Man Special #1 Cover Original Art $90,000

Journey Into Mystery #83, CGC 9.0 $80,265

Marvel Super Heroes Secret Wars #7 cover Original art $132,000

Nintendo Power #1, 1988 CGC 9.8 $108,000

Richie Rich #1 CGC 9.6 $96,000, $108,000

Showcase #4, CGC 9.6 $900,000, CGC 6.0 $37,200, CGC 8.0 81,000, $132,000

Silver Surfer #1 CGC 9.8 $132,000

Silver Surfer #4 CGC 9.8 $66,000

Star Wars #5 Cover Original Art 1977 $102,000

Tales of Suspense #39, CGC 9.2 $108,000, CGC 8.5 $69,000

Tales of Suspense #50, 13-pg. story original art "The Hands of the Mandarin" $210,000

Teenage Mutant Ninja Turtles #1 CGC 9.8 $156,000, $132,000, $120,000, CGC 9.2 $16,800, CGC 9.4 $22,200

Teenage Mutant Ninja Turtles #1 File Copy-Signature Series CGC 9.6 $38,400

Teenage Mutant Ninja Turtles #8 Cover Original Art 1986 $78,000

Tomb of Dracula #10 CGC 9.8 $28,800

Uncanny X-Men #177 Cover Original Art, 1984 $84,000

Vampirella #1 CGC 9.8 $78,000

What If #11 Cover Original Art, 1978 $63,000

X-Men #1 CGC 8.0 $102,000, $72,000, $66,000, CGC 8.5 $78,000, CGC 7.5 $78,000, $66,000, CGC 9.2 $186,000, CGC 9.2 $204,000, CGC 9.0 $108,000, CGC 7.0 $22,800

X-Men #3 CGC 9.8 Pacific Coast Pedigree $75,000

X-Men #26 Original cover art, $132,000

X-Men #94, CGC 9.8 $46,800

Bronze Age: Gary Dolgoff reported, "Bronze Age Marvels are solid sellers, and there are a number of Bronze keys that sell for over *Guide,* such as *Amazing Spider-Man* #129 (1st Punisher), #194 (1st Black Cat), #258 (1st Hobgoblin), *Daredevil* #131 (1st Bullseye), #168 (1st Elektra), *Tomb of Dracula* #10 (1st Blade), *Werewolf By Night* #32 (1st Moon Knight) and others.

#92 $84,000

#39 $215,000

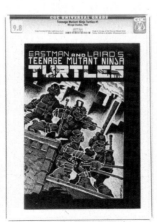

#1 $132,000

Ken Dyber added, "Another period showing declines in value and in people collecting."

Dan Gallo stated, "Marvels have been brutal. The super key issue books that we all thought were invincible proved otherwise. *Amazing Fantasy* #15 and *X-Men* #1, the two most popular books of the era had previously experienced massive increases so naturally when things got soft, they had the furthest to fall."

Dr. Steven Kahn wrote, "Almost all graded Silver and Bronze keys are down from between 30 to 50 percent."

Josh Nathanson & Rick Hirsch reported, "Record prices were achieved for Bronze Age keys in pristine condition, many of which sold for sums unimaginable to those of us who remember plunking down 20 or 25 cents for some of these comics in our youth."

Karen O'Brien stated, "Bronze Age titles are killing it at auction houses, eBay, and social media live "Claim sales" are all netting solid results for these books.

Terry O'Neill noted, "While demand is high, it's been increasingly difficult to acquire collections of this material, especially Marvel comics. As always, *Amazing Spider-Man* and *X-Men* are the most collected.

Alika Seki, PE. reported, "After a huge pandemic/crypto fueled boom in the collectibles market, a period of cooling has set in."

Al Stoltz stated, "Even big Marvel keys in lower grades that sold for nutty money and now have tumbled back."

The following market reports were submitted from some of our many advisors and are publish-ed here for your information. The opinions in these reports belong to each contributor and do not necessarily reflect the vews of the publisher or the staff of *The Overstreet Comic Book Price Guide* or Gemstone Publishing.

See you next year!

Robert M. Overstreet

THE
JOHN VERZYL
OVERSTREET® ADVISOR
AWARD

The John Verzyl Overstreet Advisor Award, named in honor
of our friend and longtime contributor John Verzyl,
is presented annually to an Advisor or Advisors
whose knowledge, contributions, ethics and reputation
are held in the highest esteem by his or her peers.

Nominations may be made by any Overstreet Advisor in good standing by
sending the nominee's name and description of why he or she represents the
positive attributes that John embodied for our hobby. To make a nomination,
email Gemstone Publishing's Mark Huesman at humark@gemstonepub.com.

MICHAEL EURY

Following a distinguished career as an editor for Comico, DC, and Dark Horse, it is MICHAEL EURY's second act that commends him as a recipient of The John Verzyl Overstreet Advisor Award for 2024.

Through his tireless efforts as the editor of *Back Issue* magazine, he has elevated the appreciation, documentation, and exaltation of comic books from the Bronze Age (and even more recent periods), a previously under-reported era. He has produced a lengthy run of issues of a periodical of insight, opinion, and history.

His work to share this information with the comics community at large exemplifies our criteria of a willingness to share his experience with collectors, dealers, historians, and the readership of *The Overstreet Comic Book Price Guide*.

OVERSTREET COVER SUBJECTS
FIRST APPEARANCES

TEENAGE MUTANT NINJA TURTLES
Teenage Mutant Ninja Turtles #1
1984
2024 NM- PRICE: $23,000

THE SHADOW
Shadow Comics #1
March 1940
2024 NM- PRICE: $20,000

LADY DEATH
Evil Ernie #1
December 1991
2024 NM- PRICE: $400

SHI
Razor Annual #1
December 1993
2024 NM- PRICE: $100

HUMAN BOMB
Police Comics #1
August 1941
2024 NM- PRICE: $35,000

FANTOMAH
Jungle Comics #2
February 1940
2024 NM- PRICE: $4,000

WONDER MAN
Mystery Comics #4
1944
2024 NM- PRICE: $2,200

PHANTOM LADY
Phantom Lady #13
August 1947
2024 NM- PRICE: $11,500

BILL ALEXANDER
COLLECTOR

My overall view of the comic book market for this year 2023: sales prices dropped big time on books of all ages especially Copper and Modern Age books in certified 9.8 grade.

The year 2023 was one of plummeting sales for 1980s Canadian price variants as well as non-Canadian price variant newsstand editions and direct edition comic books in the hobby. Books that skyrocketed up in value between January 2020 and January 2021 came crashing down in 2023 just as fast as they went up.

Take *Amazing Spider-Man* #238 for example. Just 4 years ago in 2020 as a direct edition in certified 9.8 grade, that key book was selling for over $3,000 and people amazingly were paying that much, but in late 2023 the book began selling for about half that price at about $1,500 in certified 9.8 grade.

In reality, all sales prices appear to be returning to what they once were in January of 2020 right before sales prices went nuts in the hobby doubling and tripling for no apparent reason. Many people lost a huge amount of money on 1980s-on-up books, especially key books in certified 9.8 that they way overpaid for, and today with the current market being as it is, cannot resell them without taking a big loss in money.

One Canadian price variant sale that stood out in September 2023 on ComicLink was *Wolverine* #4 CGC 9.9 (mini-series) selling for an amazing $9,377.00, the second highest known sale of a Canadian price variant to date.

Happy collecting to everyone, and always remember to collect what you love, not what people tell you to collect.

DAVID T. ALEXANDER, TYLER ALEXANDER AND EDDIE WENDT
DTACOLLECTIBLES.COM
CULTUREANDTHRILLS.COM

One thing is for certain. The demand for collectible comics has not decreased. Our economy has been in the pits since the COVID money has dried up. During the COVID era when government money was flowing freely many comic prices were rising daily.

When the money flow decreased so did many comic book prices. A lot of collectors got badly burned. It might be decades until prices reach the COVID levels again. What do you do with books you paid too much for? If you love the books hang on to them. If they mean enough to you it does not matter how much you paid for them. If you were looking for a long term investment, hang on to them. If you were looking for a quick turn profit then sell and start over. Many prices have come down particularly for books from the Silver and Bronze Ages. There is still a lot of energy in the hobby but the money is no longer pouring in.

People still want, love, respect and appreciate old comics. As Silver and Bronze era prices have seen decreases many collectors are now chasing books from the Golden and Platinum Ages. Although there have been some drops in the prices of expensive 1930s & 1940s, books most from that time period have retained their values and even increased in value. In particular pre-Code Horror books spearheaded by the EC titles have seen not only constantly increasing demand but also rising prices. When we think about pre-Code Horror titles we need to remember that this genre had a short lifespan as most of these came out between 1950 and early 1955. Actually some of the publishers were giving up on these titles in mid-1954. Demand has never wavered for early Timely and DC titles and Fawcett, Fox, MLJ & Fiction House are just a step behind.

In addition to Horror, all pre-Code titles are in demand including Romance, Sci-fi, Crime and War. Western comics have had strong sales during the last eight months. Pre-Code titles are going out by the box-load. If you have trouble selling yours, please contact us as we will take them. Romance issues have been the most popular with issues containing art by Matt Baker or Jack Kirby having massive popularity, and there are loads of other issues almost as desirable. This area has a big appeal to completists as most titles are available without having to sell your car.

Pulps are continuing to find homes with collectors who were previously only interested in comic books. There is just too much crossover activity with these two formats to not go after both. *The Spider* is currently the most in demand hero pulp, recently knocking *The Shadow* off that perch. For decades the top selling hero pulp title has rotated between the *Spider, Shadow* and *Doc Savage*. All the horror, spicy, weird and mystery titles are strong sellers. Even the facsimile reprints published in the last 5-10 years are in demand at premium prices. Most of these had short print runs. The first issue of *Weird Tales* introduced readers to terror and horror fiction and remains as one of the top pulps. Conan first appeared in this title and remains as one of the most popular characters in American fiction. Pulps began their standard format in the late 1800s after evolving from the dime novel style that was popular since the Civil War days. Basically the pulps died in the mid-1950s as TV became the popular form of entertainment.

The Platinum Age of Comics is an area where we have seen a lot of interest. This time period is considered to be from the late 1800s until the modern comic book format became standard in 1937-1938. The title most requested is *Judge Magazine* which was first published in 1881. This *Guide* has listings in both the Victorian and Platinum Age sections but has no content or pricing information. Collectors have been curious about this title and its influence on comics and comic art. We have processed several want lists for this series. The title is unique in that it constantly changed the size, location and font of its logo. Obviously this concept worked as the series ran for about 3000 issues ending in 1947 with a short revival in 1953. This might be a world record for the longest running satire, humor and comic art magazine in history. Interest is placed on some of the top comic and cartoon artists who appeared over the title's lifetime. Many pulp style good girl art covers appeared. Top artists to appear include: Carl Barks, Bill Holman, George Herriman, C.D. Russell, Norman Rockwell, Dr. Seuss, Carl Anderson, Ernie Bushmiller, Percy Crosby, John Held Jr, Jack Farr, Milt Gross, Rube Goldberg, Fontaine Fox, Gluyas Williams, Art Helfant, Jefferson Machamer, Fred Neher, Chon Day, Vernon Grant, Otto Soglow, James Montgomery Flagg, Paul Stahr, Enoch Bolles, R. B. Fuller, Crawford Young, Nate Collier and others. Most of these artists did extensive work in the comic and pulp fields. Some of the famous comic characters who appeared include: Krazy Kat and Ignatz, Skippy (who appeared in the first single character comic book), Pete the Tramp, Smokey Stover, Toonerville Trolley and others.

Prices for vintage *Judge* magazines range from $50 to $400 and appear to be on the rise. The standard that *Judge* set for satire, humor and comic magazines was unparalleled and paved the way for *Mad* magazine and other similar titles.

Good Girl Art cover by Enoch Bolles

Comic art cover by Nate Collier

Notable Sales:
Journey Into Mystery #1 3.0 $3,820.00
Amazing Spider-Man #194 9.8 $3,024.00
Blue Beetle #52 7.5 $3,020.00
Wonderworld #3 FR/G $2,000.00
Detective Comics #359 7.0 $1,830.00
Mystery Tales Pulp June 1938 VG $1,495.00
War Fury #1 VG $1,275.00
Witchcraft #6 6.5 $1,000.00
Wings #11 7.0 $950.00

DAVE ANDERSON, DDS
COLLECTOR

Despite higher interest rates and inflation, the comic market remains strong. The passion with which collectors fuel the market is ever present and will continue to keep the hobby healthy. Those who are only in it for investment purposes don't have the same passion for the comic books themselves, but do have the passion for making money. This continues to drive prices higher and higher on high end material. It seems that no matter what price is paid for books such as *Action Comics* #1 or *Detective Comics* #27, six months to a year later, the same book will sell for more. Investors recognize this and keep these prices high. Because of this, these high prices are preventing collectors from acquiring the high end books and forcing them to often settle for "parts" of them. Recently a front cover to *Detective* #27 with a married book cover sold for over $200,000, and a brittle page from *Action* #1 sold for $57,600. So there appears to be something for everyone at all levels.

Golden Age books remain very strong in all grades, and Silver Age books were steady but with some downturn in prices for mid and low grade copies.

LAUREN BECKER
COMIC*POP COLLECTIBLES

Pssst...Did you hear? Comics are dead! Nobody is buying anything, and the market is either collapsing or imploding (depending on who you talk to)! The apocalypse is coming! The end is near! The dead are rising from the grave! Dogs and cats, living together...MASS HYSTERIA!

Or...is the market simply correcting itself from the Covid era?

Let's think a moment. The collectibles market took off. Supply was simply not there, and the demand for comics/toys/cards took off. The only outlet was the internet to get anything for months. Even after places were finally opening up, the demand was still very high. So why did everything start to cool? Many people say it's because the "free money" stopped coming in. That's a partial truth. Yes, the free money helped, but it wasn't the main reason.

Once everything opened back up: 1) People had more options on where to spend their money (ie: concerts, sporting events, vacations, etc), and 2) Supply started to outstrip demand once the stores and comic cons started up again. A CGC graded 7.0 *Hulk* #181 went from being an average

$3,000 comic in 2019 to $6,000 by 2021, and then back to a respectful $4,500 by 2023. Everything rose during the hype (like all things normally do) and then fell back down to reality before the end of 2023. So what DID go up and practically stayed up?

Golden Age and Original art: Most Golden Age was difficult to find regardless, and as time continues onward, and Golden Age is getting older, so too is the rarity of many books. Most esoteric Golden Age (especially in higher grade) has become ever increasingly difficult to locate. We had a copy of *Spotlight Comics* #1 (CGC 4.0) that went for $525. A copy of the same book, almost 20 years prior, graded at an 8.5 sold for the same amount. A graded 4.5 sold for $312 only NINE MONTHS earlier.

This isn't to say that mainstream Golden Age titles aren't rising also. We had a copy of *Superman* #10 that we sold for $700, which was a 1.0 (raw) at best (front and back covers were torn off at the spine). A graded copy sold for $425 in March of 2023. Ours sold September of the same year for more. Golden Age is a very hot commodity right now, with prices fluctuating all over the spectrum.

Original art also seems to have no real ceiling. Pieces that you wouldn't dream of reaching 4-5 figures are doing that, and HIGHER! We sent in a Bernie Wrightson 2 page painted double spread from *Spider-Man: Hooky* to Heritage Auctions. At the end of the auction, the piece went for almost TWICE the amount we paid for it 2 years prior! Original art is climbing higher every single day with almost no signs of stopping!

Variant comics seem to be the bane of many store owners, especially exclusive covers that stores or companies produce in partnership with the publishers. Last year, Hustl did an exclusive *Spider-Man* #1 variant cover with Eminem front and center, facing Spidey in a rap off. The book sold out within an hour. Today, it is STILL a highly sought after variant that people shell out a LOT of money for.

We took a page out of Hustl/Eminem's book and did an exclusive cover with AEW wrestling star Danhausen for a reprint of *Batman* #251. We were able to have Bill Morrison (from *The Simpsons*...who Danhausen is a huge fan of) do the cover and not only did the final product come out great, it sold exceptionally well. The market for this book was better than both Danhausen and I expected. We debuted the exclusive live at Baltimore Comic Con with an exclusive foil edition for NYCC. Both did exceedingly well...so much so that C.M. Punk was interested in doing one with myself and Danhausen (unfortunately, Punk was fired from AEW and we couldnt do it, as DC and AEW are parts of Warner Bros).

The market is not dying as it's correcting itself and evolving.

Anyways, here are some 2023 CGC sales to show how items are doing. This is by NO means a full list of what was sold, but a sampling of what did...

Teenage Mutant Ninja Turtles #3 error edition CGC 9.2 $2,800
Batman Adventures #12 CGC 9.8 $2,226
Wonder Comics #14 CBCS 5.5 $1,400

Ghost Rider #1 CGC 6.5 $600
DC Comics Presents #26 CGC Sig. Series Marv Wolfman 9.4 $500
Space Ghost #1 (Gold Key) CGC 5.5 $300
Dixie Dugan #1 CGC 6.0 $300
Hansi the Girl Who Loved the Swastika CGC 5.5 $160
Captain Marvel Story Book #1 CGC 4.0 $225
Omega Men #3 CGC Sig. Series Keith Giffen (Lobo sketch) 9.6 $500
New Gods #1 CBCS signature verified Jack Kirby (on the cover) 7.5 $1,700
Captain America Comics #13 CGC 0.5 $2,250
Amazing Spider-Man #300 CGC 9.8 $4,800
Amazing Spider-Man chromium cover #300 CGC 9.8 $1,500
Amazing Spider-Man #33 CGC 9.0 $1,000
Superboy #1 CGC 2.0 $1,400
Marvel Mystery Comics #61 CGC 4.5 $1,200
Web of Spider-Man #1 CGC ss (LaRocque & Vess sketches) 9.4 $330
Ghostly Weird-Stories #120 CGC 4.0 $600
Chamber of Chills #25 CGC 2.0 $400
Weird Science Fantasy #29 CGC 4.5 $950
Silver Surfer #4 CGC 3.0 $580
Marvel Boy (1950) #1 CGC 4.5 $1,200
Tomb of Terror #15 CGC 2.5 $4,900

JIM BERRY
COLLECTOR

Greetings from Portland, Oregon. I am a collector and part-time dealer interested, primarily, in Golden Age comics. I've collected, dealt and traded since the early 1980s and I currently maintain a small eBay store as JB233 where I list mostly high grade books along with some random vintage odds and ends from my mom's hoard of possessions.

As a collector, I actively seek books from the 1940s and '50s with a focus on pre-Code Horror, Science Fiction, Romance and Crime featuring sex, drugs, bondage, exploding heads, atomic bomb mushroom clouds, headlights, injury to the eyes, and, of course, monkey brains - the good stuff! I pair these interests with a love of classic comic art by such masters as Wolverton, Schomburg, Baily, Ditko, Frazetta, L.B. Cole, Feldstein, Wood, The King and so many others.

2023 was a very interesting year for old comics here in Portland as we had reports of many stolen collections, one of which garnered national attention after a man's home was raided following his death. James Strand died in his house at the age of 88 and, after his body was removed, his empty home was ransacked and his treasure trove of incredibly rare comics and books was stolen by homeless squatters and drug addicts who quickly sold them across the city. Google "James Strand stolen comics" and you'll see the stories. Heritage created a list of books he'd purchased over the years and it was a jaw dropping collection of high grade pedigree books from the early 1940s with many Mile High copies. If you're into Golden Age books his collection will make you weep. . . God only knows what books and pieces of original art ended up in the hands of people who couldn't care less and used that old paper to start their campfires.

2023 will also be remembered as a year that continued the post-Covid trend with values of comics remaining down and flat overall. Yes, there are exceptions like - as of this writing - X-Men #130, the 1st Dazzler thanks to speculation that Taylor Swift might appear in the Deadpool 3 movie as the mutant crooner. But, clearly, that type of bubble-inflation based on movie speculation is stumbling as the interest in Marvel movies has flagged and the quality of those movies diluted with over-production and a general lack of thoughtful filmmaking.

This was the year I tried pressing and cleaning and found it to be quite a revelation. After doing some research, I decided to give Matt Christein of Excelsior Comic Book Pressing (improveyourcomics.com) a try with a handful of old books that had spine rolls and stains. Matt's work was incredible and he runs his business like a pro - great communication, packing, customer service - I am a True Believer!

I'd also like to shout out Shave Ahlvers of Sir Lonebuck's House Of Comics And Geekery in Woodinville, Washington. Shane's shop focuses on an extensive display of new issue books, graphic novels, and a selection of curated toys, accessories and local art. Last year, Shane and I partnered to review collections of his customers and it's been great fun. We've only had a couple of collections work out this year but hope springs eternal in 2024.

As always, thank you, Bob Overstreet and the skilled team at Gemstone for another great edition of The Guide. You guys are the best!

RUSS BRIGHT
MILL GEEK COMICS

This is one of the most difficult essays I have had to write. While the market has been strong, prices have been lower than in the past few years. People were paying record prices for everything in 2021 and 2022 and we seem to have a regression to the norm. The drop in prices has caused many people to wonder, "Is the sky falling?"

I believe not. Prices are down but purchasers are plentiful. Buyers are out there for almost any book and while they may want to purchase at lower prices, it doesn't signify the collapse of the industry. As we saw at the beginning of pandemic, people were liquidating books because of financial uncertainties. Then as things settled, people found themselves with more time for hobbies and more money while working from home. This caused many books, especially Copper and Modern Age keys, to rise in price.

The number of collectors increased as we saw a return to innocence. Collectors from the '90s rediscovered the warm nostalgia of their favorite books and as such we saw many impulse purchases that were higher than market norms. This has only recently slowed down and we're seeing a much more tempered view of the market.

A perennial favorite, New Mutants #98 saw heights

of OVER $2,800 in 2021 and has now returned to a more reasonable $1,400 average by the end of 2023. The perfect storm of people returning to work and having a decreased budget for comics as well as an increased number of graded copies has made this book trend downwards. We may see the price creep higher when the Deadpool 3 movie is released, but as a perpetually relevant book, it will never be unvaluable. It's a book that has many available copies but is always easy to sell.

My parting advice; HAVE PATIENCE. Nobody is forcing you to buy or sell in any market. People who panic lose. My advice has always been to collect what you love, and you'll always love your collection. This holds true more than ever this year and in this market.

"As always, Geek Responsibly!" - The Comic Sensei

JOHN CHRUSCINSKI
TROPIC COMICS

It's been a very interesting year for collectibles like video games and original art, and of course comic books. With most collectible markets cooling down, some like video games had the bottom drop out, while others like original art kept bring record prices. Even though the economy is not where it was a few years ago, the passion for collecting and investing in comics is still strong. Sales are still strong but at the now readjusted market prices. The movie- and TV show-driven market has cooled off because of so/so quality of most Disney/Marvel movies as they tend to revamp and change heroes into non recognizable characters for what they believe the other markets want to see abandoning their core market which has hurt the comics.

Now would seem to be the time to buy what was unaffordable a few years ago and can be gotten for a much more a reasonable price with room to grow in the future. We just helped one of our clients get a few books he has wanted for his collection for years, but at a much lower price than in the past. A CGC graded 9.8 Giant-Size X-Men #1 for $20,000. In the past they have sold at $50,000 and even higher. Strange Tales #110 in 4.5 for $2,000, X-Men #1 in 4.0 raw with minor glue for under $5000, Hulk #181 in CGC 6.5 for under $4,000. I believe these will all have a lot of growth when the market rebounds. Just like successful traders on the stock market do, when stock prices go down, they buy more knowing in time they will make a lot of profit.

Remember to collect what you like, and not what someone or website tells you should collect, and you will never lose in the true enjoyment of our wonderful hobby.

PAUL CLAIRMONT
PNJ COMICS

This year saw a return to normal market conditions and regular sales. Unaffected by large scale speculation and a flood of new buyers spending too much money in an area that they largely were not knowledgeable about. The disappearance of these types of buyers saw a major decrease in volume and prices attained in most areas of comic book

back issue sales. We alone saw back issue sales dip year over year by 70%. This would normally be cause for alarm but as I said earlier, it was simply a return to "normal" yearly sales, and it was business as usual.

I welcomed the normal pace as it was impossible to have a quality balance of personal life and business during those hectic years of the pandemic with its record sales and endless online buyers. The biggest positive was that it fast-forwarded my succession plan of early semi-retirement. I no longer work long hours or on weekends and have more time to be with my wife and children. That has always been the goal and I can say that 2023 was my best year ever because of the balance.

I really pulled back from buying collections or unnecessary inventory during this year. I had always been holding back many books throughout the years as I focused my attention selling on heavy speculation type of comics that the Marvel movies had once fueled. With the dilution of the quality of the movies and shows, we have seen that there isn't such a FOMO (Fear Of Missing Out) in that area anymore. Comics that fell into that category began to drop in value by 70-80% of their all-time highs. A good example of price correction is *Star Wars* #43. It's considered by some as the 1st appearance of Lando Calrissian. I had 17 CGC 9.8 Newsstand copies of this book during the pandemic. I've since sold all of them but in 2021 we were getting nearly $1,000 USD per copy and only 2 short years later I see the book is under $300 USD.

There were a lot of people looking to sell collections that had decreased so much in value that they were feeling a little stunned at what the offers were. I found myself not interested in buying the books because it was a lot of speculative type material.

I changed gears back to something I said in my first *Overstreet* report about ten years ago and that was being "First to Market." It still brings some of the best returns when you do your research. In short, you can still realize the best profit margins by looking for inefficiencies in the marketplace and being the supplier. It is a great way to change that $5.00 comic into a $200 to $300 encased collectible very quickly.

Having more time to focus on researching the market and working on projects such as being "First to Market", without the hectic and feverish sales pace, has led me to enjoy the hobby again as I'm able to reconnect with some of the books that made me become a collector in my childhood. I love the old Horror and Sci-Fi titles from the early '70s with their 20¢ cover prices. Looking for great covers from Adams, Wrightson, Kaluta and Brunner to name just a few. These books are actually very hard to find in great condition: titles such as *House of Mystery* and *House of Secrets* to other great ones such as *Vault of Evil* and *Where Monsters Dwell*. To me, these were

the types of books that packed a punch, and I would consider quality books. It was refreshing to flip through the pages and see the stuff that captured my imagination over 40 years ago. I was able to find my appreciation for the hobby again as I wasn't just a worker bee endlessly filling orders for books that didn't get me excited, those pesky speculation books filled with 1st appearances of D-class characters. One example is The Spot, who first appeared in *Spectacular Spider-Man* #97. During the pandemic, a book like this would fly off the shelf without blinking an eye. Nowadays, there isn't exactly a line up of buyers suddenly needing the 1st appearance of The Spot for their so called "collection".

This was the first time I finally saw Newsstand Editions starting to bring higher premiums than Canadian Price Variants. Although the Canadian Price Variants are much scarcer in high grade during the '80s there was a shift in buyer requests to the Newsstand Editions of the late '90s and early 2000s. I guess one could argue that it's comparing apples and oranges due to the eras, but each niche did command some hefty premiums at differing times. I had advocated for Newsstands about a decade ago saying they would be tougher to find in higher grade, especially around the 2000s, and it appears that prediction has started to come to light more this year than any previous. Not all issues bring premiums.

If you listed the only available copy for sale on a platform like eBay, it would usually sell for your asking price or close to it. It's not necessarily all about supply and demand either. It started to become content driven or needs a great cover to boot. It seemed the buying had more of a collector mentality again. Maybe completionists are looking to fill holes now that prices aren't so ridiculously overhyped from the pandemic age.

I also saw more buyers looking at purchasing raw books. This tells me that collectors are returning and that they are also wanting a deal on high grade books knowing they can trust a dealer that can grade accurately. As a veteran seller of comics, you begin to develop a keen sense of who is buying because they appreciate the stories and art and those who would be buying to try to flip for profits. I saw the needle sway to the appreciative collector and not a person who thought they were making savvy investments. I have to say, it was refreshing as I saw more and more people disappearing that had only entered basing their decision on greed and trying their damnedest to chase the money.

I'm once again optimistic about the future of back issue comic books. As prices return to normal, I see more collectors emerging as books become affordable. Now that the hobby has emerged from the pandemic there is a feeling of calm that allows me to embark in this hobby and the business with renewed energy knowing that I will work at my own pace and be more present with my family as I have nothing I need to achieve or prove. So, if I don't answer the phone or answer an email you can rest assured, I'm probably at the lake with my family.

As always, thank you to my family for all your love, support and trust which has allowed me to take risks and grow this business over the past 11 years. It's a team effort and I know I wouldn't be where I am today without you.

ART CLOOS
COLLECTOR

It's December 2023 and its time for the Overstreet Advisor reports to be handed in so here we go. First the upside.

In March the spring Big Apple show led off the 2023 convention scene in the tri-state area and with a nice amount of 1940s books on dealer's walls. In particular I was impressed by the sale of a beautiful *Marvel Mystery* #51 to a buyer who was beaming after he completed his purchase. There was of course a lot of Silver Age for sale and a DC Comics highlight was a high grade copy of the Silver Age Hal Jordan *Green Lantern* #1. A Silver Age Marvel stand out was a 9.4 CGC *Hulk* #1. In talking to dealers several noted that DC Silver and Bronze were becoming more interesting price wise for buyers as the price of Marvel keys had climbed so high over the last several years.

Then the Garden State Comic Con kicked off the summer circuit. As Allie and I made the rounds of the two dealer rooms virtually every comic dealer we spoke to was very pleased with their sales with one saying it was the best show he ever had and there was a strong selection to buy from. This was reflected at the dealers' booths with some DC keys that showed up on dealer walls for the first time in years. Sales did seem to be brisk, and I suspect that most dealers were happy with their sales for the two days of the show. Allie and I found a few things to take home and we were happy with what we found.

In August it was time for TerrifiCon and I was impressed by the number of comic dealers set up in the dealer's room. That validated the con's reputation as a show focused on comics. There was a strong mix of Golden to Modern books on display with key issues as well, and I am pleased to say that I brought home a bunch of Gold and Silver Age books and Allie brought home a bunch of Bronze Age books too. Most (but not all) of the dealers Allie and I spoke to were pleased with their sales and for some TerrifiCon is the main show that they do each year. One highlight showed that attic

finds can still be found as I met a couple who showed me four Golden Age comics *All-Flash* #1, *Superman* #2, *Batman* #15 and #17. The lady's brother got the comics from a friend and her brother put them in their father's attic where they remained for many years until her dad's death when they were rediscovered. A comic collector volunteered to help her sell the books. This is what brought them to TerrifiCon where they met me. I examined them and they were not high grade at all. I suggested the lady have the books graded and slabbed for sale which she did.

NYCC in October is always the highlight show on the east coast and we noticed that the crowd was much bigger than it was in 2022, something dealers and I talked about. Most dealers reported they were pleased with sales though there were a few that were not. As with Garden State one dealer I see every year told me it was the best show he ever had and there was a good range on dealers' walls of comics from the mid-1930s to the current hot books of today. With that rising interest in vintage DC there was a noticeable increase of those books on dealer walls.

Now the down side. The really big paradox here is despite the above positive comments from some of the shows we attended this year, others were not so positive. Overall 2023 saw prices of Silver and Bronze age Marvel keys continue their 2022 drop into 2023. In some cases by a lot. This was also reflected in GPA and auction results, especially late in the year. Some dealers who who had invested heavily in Silver Age Marvel now were finding it hard to move those books unless they adjusted their prices. Some did, some didn't. Mid and lower grade books were hit the worst though while most but not all high grade books had their moments. The truth is though, a correction in prices should have been expected. The market just got too far ahead of itself. It didn't help Marvel or DC that their 2023 movie slates were not received with the enthusiasm of previous years. Silver Age DCs more or less held their own as a still cheaper alternative to Marvel and more and more of them were showing up on dealers' walls. Golden Age remained basically steady and the Golden Age titles that Allie and I follow such as *All-American*, *All Star*, *Sensation*, *Wonder Woman*, *Captain Marvel* (Fawcett), *Batman* and *Detective* mostly did continue to sell okay along with an increasing interest in some of the more esoteric publishers.

As to what will happen with the market in 2024, only time will tell, but a couple of movies from the big two that are well received really couldn't hurt especially since Jim Lee says sales of DC comics have tripled since James Gunn took over. Take care and I will see you in 2025.

Confirmed 2023 sales: *Adventure Comics* #416 VG+ $20, #461 VF $25, #463 NM, $30; *All-American Comics* #96 VF $1,250; *All Star Comics* #6 VG $1200, #23 (4.5) $759.95; *Amazing Spider-Man* #113 VF $110; *Aquaman* (#4 VF-, #5 FN, #16 VF- $120 total), #20 FN+ $80, #35 FN+ $40, #47 FN $55; *Atom* #18 VF $25; *Batman* #169 VF $180, #345 VF+ $20; *Batman Family* #9 VF- $30, #15 VF+ $20; *Detective Comics* #328 FN+ $79, #330 VF- $68, #330 VF- $77.22; *Fantastic Four* #23 VF+ $425; *Flash* #120 (8.0) $625, #124 FN $55, #126 FN $55, #128 FN+ $60, #132 VF $50, #139 (7.0) $850; #143 FN $65, #157 VF- $55, #161 FN $45, #155 FN $60, #145 VF $150; *Journey Into Mystery* #91 VF+ Fantast Collection $900, #92 6.5 $540; *Justice League of America* V1 #70 VF $20; *Mystery In Space* #53 (4.0) $220; *Showcase* #16 FN- $90, #21 FN $75; *Strange Tales* #103 FN $120; *Tales To Astonish* #101 VF $75; *Wonder Woman* #79 (7.0) $600; *World's Finest* #75 6.0 FN $350, #77 6.5 FN $350, #82 6.5 FN+ $200, #78 5.0 $150, #83 5.0 $125, #85 6.5 $175, #86 5.5 $170, #89 5.5 $140, #91 8.0 $450, #93 5.5 $250, #111 8.5 $300, #112 8.5 $200, #244 VF $10, #245 VF $15, #246 $10, #247 VF $15, #248 VF $5, #249 VF $5, #250 FN $12, #252 FN- $12; *X-Men* first series #6 (7.0) $500.

ASHLEY COTTER-CAIRNS & SEAN GOODRICH
COLLECTORS

Our first full year as co-heads of comic books for Goldin has flown past! So much has happened this year that it's difficult to know where to begin.

For those of you who missed last year's report, Goldin acquired us in September 2022.

We had to drink from the fire hose for a while, as making the adjustment of going from being our own bosses to being employees was challenging, coming with all kinds of new tools and systems to learn, seemingly endless meetings and reports to write.

On the other side of the coin, we had joined goldin.com, a world-class auction company with its own Netflix series, *King of Collectibles: The Goldin Touch*, and consignments among the top tier of the hobby, including an *Action Comics* #1, *Detective Comics* #27 and multiple copies of *Superman* #1, a *Pep Comics* #22, *All-American* #16 and so much more.

We also changed our entire approach to the business of comic books, going from buying collections outright to a pure consignment model. This made for some challenging conversations with existing customers, who were accustomed to fast decisions and immediate cash payment.

In early 2023, we oversaw the launch of comic books on the Goldin marketplace, also their weekly auctions, and curated four Elite sales in Spring, Summer, Fall and Winter — and then an additional December Elite at short notice!

The Elite sales have since been rebranded as Pop Culture Elites, with particular strength in TCG, music collectibles and comic art as well as comic books.

One of my most memorable consignments of 2023 was an original owner Golden Age collection. The consignor's mother discovered her late husband's collection amongst his personal effects, and Goldin brought it to market for the first time since they were purchased off the newsstands.

The highlights included *All Star Comics* #8, *Daring Mystery Comics* #1, *Detective Comics* #25 and #37, *Adventure Comics* #37 (exceptionally rare!), *Marvel Mystery Comics* #6 and #12, *Stuntman Comics* #1, *U.S. Jones* #1, *Amazing Adventure Funnies* #1 and *Cow Puncher* #1. Such a cool find!

Most graded in the VG-FN+ range. *Adventure* #37 was a 6.5, tied for the highest graded to date and set a new record for this book.

Here are some of the many impressive sales Goldin achieved this year:

2000 A.D. #2 CGC 9.0 $5,820
Action Comics #1 CGC 3.0 $1.5M
Action Comics #6 CGC 7.0 $18,000
Adventure Comics #37 CGC 6.5 $10,187
All-American Comics #16 CGC 1.5 $72,000
All Star Comics #8 CGC 2.5 $22,275
Amazing Fantasy #15 CGC 7.5 $122,400
Amazing Fantasy #15 CGC 6.5 $74,400
Amazing Spider-Man #1 CGC 8.0 $54,000
Batman #8 CGC 8.5 $17,400
Captain America Comics #1 CGC 3.0 $146,400
Daring Mystery Comics #1 CGC 6.0 $35,380
Detective Comics #25 CGC 6.5 $10,525
Fantastic Four #1 CGC 7.5 $84,000
Incredible Hulk #1 CGC 8.0 $96,120
Incredible Hulk #1 CGC 6.0 $36,240
Mister Mystery #6 CGC 5.0 $7,200
Pep Comics #22 CGC 6.5 $180,000
Seven Seas Comics #4 CGC 6.0 $15,860
Silver Surfer #4 CGC 9.8 $51,600
Spider-Man #1 Gold UPC variant CGC 9.8 Signature Series Lee, McFarlane $3,660
Startling Terror Tales #11 CGC 3.0 $7,860
Superman #1 CGC 7.0 $1.620M
Superman #1 CGC 1.5 $134,400
Superman #1 CGC 0.5 $61,200
Superman #100 CGC 9.0 $12,300
Tales of Suspense #39 CGC 9.0 $80,520
X-Men #1 CGC 9.2 $168,600
X-Men #1 CGC 8.0 $62,220

Check out series two of the Netflix show *King of Collectibles*. Sean Goodrich and I are at your service and will give you the best deal and the most visibility when it's time to sell your collectibles. Have a great year!

JESSE JAMES CRISCIONE
JESSE JAMES COMICS

The challenges the comic book industry had in 2023 were extremely overwhelming. Not only did we pivot our platforms, we had to adjust our vision and strategy almost monthly. We saw a huge drop off in new issue sales and a huge increase in Back Issue sales as a whole. Not only was

Facebook live streaming continuing its upward audience participation, we saw eBay Live join the comic book community

Crowdfunding is still a great source for both consumer, publisher and creator. It's also brought in a fresh new group of collectors who are seeking new story lines and art. We have had to use our social media more than ever to attract those new collectors to the store. We also have started to get a bigger footprint at conventions in 2023, without actually going to them. In 2024 we will be attending conventions that are relevant to our online base and live streaming opportunities that might arise.

In 2024 we will continue to see more sellers online and at conventions and less Comic Book Stores worldwide. LCS's are very costly, and ROI is tighter than just an Average Joe selling out of their basement and almost zero overhead. The numbers are staggering (how many non LCS owners, there are) and a LCS owners will need to make tough decisions when their leases are up.

Exclusives continue to bring in new customers and will be even bigger in 2024.

Stores did start selling other genres, including trading card games, Funko Pops, plushies and other collectibles to increase their sales and draw new customers in. Though this has always been something we do through the years. The % in the store is much closer than its ever been to comic books.

Most of the LCS owners are hoping for a tighter industry in 2023. Publishers and distributors are having tighter requirements in 2024, such as not allowing just anybody to open an account or do an exclusive. If not the LCS will become the minority in the comic book industry by 2024 year's end. Some might say this has already happened.

For our brand, we are looking to build more market shares in the livestreaming world and will invest more time and money into virtual sales. Social networking will be the key to reaching a new audience and improving our customer base under 30 years old. We are very excited to see what 2024 brings us in the comic book world. We are ready to pivot daily.

BROCK DICKINSON
COLLECTOR

In last year's report, I described the 2022 comic market as a kind of intense hangover from the exuberances of the booming Covid-era. As sometimes happens after a hangover, the 2023 market might best be described as listless, weary and somewhat confused. Outside the comic world, the global economy was strong, and after big declines in 2022 stock markets rose by more than 20%. Historic workforce shortages meant that jobs were plentiful, unemployment was low, and wages were rising quickly. Investment in new manufacturing facilities in the United States reached unprecedented levels. And yet high inflation, global conflict and economic uncertainty all contributed to a growing sense of precariousness. In this nervous environment, collectibles like comic books

sometimes seemed like an irresponsible luxury, and the market was somewhat sluggish.

Traditionally in times of inflation, collectibles have been seen as a kind of hedge against inflationary pressures. However, one of the real impacts of the post-Covid hangover era has been the exit of many of the more extreme speculator voices from the market. As the easy money has evaporated, so have many of the "crypto bros" and YouTube influencers touting the next hot comic. This has shrunk the market to a significant degree, with the biggest impacts being felt in the FOMO-driven volatility of superhero keys related to movie hype and speculation. And while a shrinking market is not good for prices, it does suggest a bit of a return to fundamentals, which may benefit the market in the longer run. The rapid exit of the most extreme speculators has allowed the development of a more value-driven marketplace, with a few trends emerging to suggest where future growth may lie.

As, always, I'm focused mostly on the more modern end of the market, from the Bronze Age to the present. While this segment of the market doesn't always get the most press, it is the biggest portion of the hobby.

One of the key trends in 2023 has been the rapid emergence of Bronze Age Horror comics as a hot market, particularly with mid-1970s books from DC Comics like *House of Mystery* and *House of Secrets*. These books have been on the radar for awhile because of the work of popular artists of the period, including Bernie Wrightson, Neal Adams and Michael Kaluta, among many others. This initial interest has led collectors to realize how difficult it is to find many of these books in higher grades, and price growth in this portion of the market accelerated in 2023. This has grown to affect a range of DC Horror titles, including *Dark Mansion of Forbidden Love/Forbidden Tales of the Dark Mansion*, *Ghosts*, *Secrets of Haunted House*, *Sinister House of Secret Love*, *Swamp Thing*, *Weird Mystery Tales*, etc.

Also of note in this instance is *Elvira's House of Mystery*, a Copper Age anthology that ran from 1986 to 1987, illustrating how the "Bronze DC horror" trend is bleeding out in other directions and eras. There is some increased interest in Bronze Charlton Horror books, based primarily on the overlooked work of prominent artists, and to a lesser extent on Marvel Horror books. However, the rapid rise in prices for titles like *House of Mystery* and *House of Secrets* has started to make the long-neglected Silver Age issues of these titles look like a huge bargain. Prices are not yet rising significantly on these Silver Age issues, but demand is up.

This hunt for overlooked value has also led to increased interest in other neglected areas of the market. Bronze Age Romance is heating up, with collectors again realizing how prices in this portion of the market lag those of more mainstream books. Grade, scarcity, popular artists, and psychedelic or risqué covers have become key drivers of this trend.

Alongside Romance and Horror, however, Gold Key comics are being recognized as substantially undervalued in the marketplace. This trend may be attributed in part to the rapid rise in price for *Scooby-Doo* #1 over the past few years, with high grade copies now routinely commanding more than $10,000, and to smaller but still significant increases for *Star Trek* #1. The market has woken up to how tough many Gold Key issues are to find, especially in higher grades, and how many of them relate to intellectual property that continues to be culturally significant. Books like *Addams Family*, *Battle of the Planets*, *Doc Savage*, *Flintstones*, *Green Hornet*, *Jetsons*, *Jonny Quest*, *Munsters*, *Peanuts*, *The Phantom* and *Space Ghost* are all heating up, and commanding record prices in higher grades.

This focus on brands and properties originating outside of comics was itself a trend in 2023. Perhaps because of the poor performance of movies from both Marvel and DC and the collapse of the movie speculation bubble, the market distinctly shifted to an interest in other kinds of properties. By far the biggest example of this trend is the dramatic rise in prices for many comics based on video games. Leading this trend were the Nintendo books produced by Valiant Comics in the early 1990s. *The Legend of Zelda* #1 ($200 raw, over $1,300 for a graded 9.8) is perhaps the best example, but titles including *Adventures of Super Mario Bros.*, *Captain N*, *Nintendo Comics System*, and *Super Mario Bros.* all rose significantly in price. Virtually every major publisher has dabbled in this space, but the distribution of these books was often spotty, and they were typically not collected or saved in our superhero-centric hobby. This has led to substantial price spikes for a number of relatively obscure books, including Marvel's 1996 *Resident Evil* giveaway ($200), many issues of Archie's *Sonic the Hedgehog*, and even recent books like DC's 2008 *Gears of War* #1 ($40) or its 2012 *Uncharted* #1 ($30 for the regular cover, or $500 for the scarcer Adam Hughes variant). I've remarked on this video game trend in the past two or three market reports, and I continue see this as a major signal about where the market is headed in the future.

In a similar vein, the 2023 market saw increased interest in a number of toy-related comic properties. In the new issue market, Image Comics and Skybound launched a hugely successful surprise revival of G.I. Joe and Transformers, which has driven interest in the 1980s books featuring these characters. Marvel reacquired the licenses for both ROM and the Micronauts, spurring some back issue interest in those titles, and Masters of the Universe books from a range of publishers continued to rise in popularity. Several movie studios have continued to make noise about the possible development of shared movie universes involving multiple toy lines, so this is also an area of the market to keep an eye on.

In general, the retreat from superhero movie speculation in the market has allowed a renewed focus on the hobby's fundamentals, and revealed the emergence of some undervalued areas of the market. Most emblematic of this trend in my mind has been the rising prices for comics from the late artist and writer Dave Stevens, whose limited number of books have risen significantly again this year. With the speculative hype gone, collectors are turning to the overlooked gems of the hobby – to the titles, creators and properties that have long been celebrated by the hobby and the broader culture, but until recently have been obscured by hype-driven "investment' mentalities. This bodes well for the health of the market in the longer run.

GARY DOLGOFF
GARY DOLGOFF COMICS

2023: The year of, "Should I Stay, or Should I Go?"

As we age, us folks in Comics Fandom are still very reluctant to let go of our 'lifetime of love,' those funnybooks that we've accumulated and enjoyed for such a long time.

Some are ready to consider selling, and we try to make sure that we find these collections a good home, by not just cherry-picking the best and most desired comics and leaving the collector with the rest. We have our enthusiasm for purchasing on display, by buying and enjoying the **entire** collection.

Buying Collections - A Few Recent Field Examples:

One example was this collection (1940s-2020s) in upstate NY. This group of comics was owned by a long-running store owner and private collector. He had passed away and his family inherited the estate. This included his large personal home-collection, which in time, his family opted to sell. After the family consulted with a fellow comic dealer on who to contact, they suggested Gary Dolgoff. The thinking being that I could handle the large volume while being fair. In addition to a nice compact group of Timelys (which included a low-grade *Captain America* #1), there were a plethora of pre-superhero Marvels (I get a bit over *Guide* for these late 1950s and early 1960s, with great Kirby and Ditko art, and crazy monsters!), as well as some runs of *Daredevil*, *Fantastic Four* (missing a few of the very earliest issues), *Amazing Spider-Man*, *Strange Tales*, and others. And to round it all out, there was nearly a 15-foot truck full of 1970s through recent years, which included some of valuable newer comics. Some examples: *Edge Of Spider-Verse* #2, *Adam: Legends of the Blue Marvel*, *Batman Adventures* #12, *Goon* #1, *Invincible* #1, *NYX* #3, *Chew* #1, *Amazing Spider-Man* #300, *Albedo* #2, and *Batman Beyond* to name a few). In addition to running a super-gamut of years and decades - the collection had a much better than usual large group of interesting hardcovers and some softcovers, with some worth good money.

Regarding the older books, included was an interesting *Captain America* #1. In addition to having restoration and being somewhat brittle, a third of the front cover had been replaced with "phony" pieces to look as much like the original as possible. Still, being a *Captain America* #1, it sold for over $30,000. In summation, this was truly a "variety is the spice of life"- type collection.

Collection 2 - Another cool collection, this time with EC Horror, Sci-Fi, and Silver-Age Superhero, I purchased from a rock 'n roll fellow in good ol' New York City, "land of my birth." It was a somewhat compact collection to get, just several boxes, but withsome nice stuff to own. I kept the near-complete runs of EC Science Fiction comics (love the stories and art!). I sold the runs of *Frontline Combat, Two-Fisted Tales, Mad* #2-#23, & *Shock SuspenseStories* (which I already have in my personal collection). I also obtained his *Amazing Spider-Man* #1-100 (mostly GD to VG shape) which are always a perennial solid mover ('You can't go wrong with good ol' Spidey).

Collection 3 - DC Golden Age Superhero (brittle but still beautiful). The "parade-winner" was a low-grade *Superman* #1 (which I kept). Additionally, there were *Superman* #3, #5, and #6 along with *Batman* #3-#6 (which I also kept). Many of these copies had fragile pages unfortunately, but we were happy to pay good money for them considering. We always love these issues in ANY condition!

Evaluation of the Present Comic Market

Golden Age (1938-1955): Generally rock-solid, yet most don't go up in *Guide* yearly much if at all these days, but some are worth over *Guide*, or at least *Guide*.

DC Golden Age 1940s *Batman* and *Detective* are rising in value (especially *Batman* #1 and *Detective* #27-#38). And of course, *More Fun* with The Spectre is a perennial favorite! *Action Comics* #1 and *Superman* #1 are worth well over *Guide* in all grades. *All-American* #16 (Green Lantern) is an over-*Guide* comic as well. I haven't had one in so long but would love to get it in for my collection! Wonder Woman comics are generally worth somewhat over-Guide (especially *All Star* #8 which has extra pages to feature WW's 1st appearance!). I personally enjoy *All Star* comics with the Justice Society (the only consistent 1940's Superhero team!) and one of my favorite covers is #33 with Solomon Grundy, of which I proudly own a copy! When I was a teenager, I reveled in reading Jerry Bails' *All Star Index*, which gave you a few lines of description of each issue!)

Timely Golden Age are my favorites! From when I was a teen comics fan and onward, it's such a joy to have these. I got a couple of collections in the last years before the pandemic began, and they both contained a plethora of Timely comics, lucky me! I will pay a high price for them. So it gave me a major boost to my Timely collection. I now have like 41 G.A. *Captain America* issues, plus other Timelys, and I want more of them. They sell well for over *Guide*, by various amounts, with *Captain America* basically leading the pack.

Other Golden Age Centaurs almost always sell for over *Guide* by various amounts (I proudly own a *Man of*

War #1; great cover!) and MLJs (the predecessor to Archie Publications) are solid sellers. *Planet Comics* have been getting better and better in sales. Captain Marvel does not sell nearly as well as many other Golden Age, but those dynamic Mac Raboy *Master Comics*, with those WWII Captain Marvel Jr. covers always sell! (I have a number of them in my collection). The miniature early '40s *Speed Comics* are tough to get! ECs sell well across the board. Pre-Code late '40s/early '50s Horror comics sell great. I desire a collection of those, some of which I would keep!

Silver Age (1956-1969): Marvel Silver Age is still the bread-winner of comics collecting. They sell as good as, or better than, ever, with me getting over *Guide* for *Amazing Spider-Man* and *X-Men* for the most part (and paying, accordingly.) I can't keep in stock the first issues and first appearances, no matter what the grade. Sure, the prices have been fluctuating as of late, but they are still a good deal higher value than they were before the pandemic.

DC Silver Age *Batman* is by far the best of the DCs, followed by *Detective. Flash* moves pretty well… *Green Lantern* moves 'fair to middling', but the Neal Adams issues (#76 thru 89), still have their popularity. Unfortunately, Superman titles (*Action, Adventure,* 80-pg Giant, *Superboy, Superman, Lois Lane, Jimmy Olsen,* and *World's Finest*), don't move very well, and I find myself often selling them for well under *Guide*.

Bronze Age (1970-1983): Marvel and DC follow suit with their Silver Age counterparts. The Kirby DC comics are decent sellers (original, cool, "hippy-ish", they are) especially solid, is the title *Demon*, and the 15-issue Kirby run, of *Jimmy Olsen*! Runs of *Marvel Premiere/Spotlight, Batman, Detective, The Joker, Wonder Woman, Ghost Rider, Amazing Spider-Man,* and *X-Men* amongst others always sell - and that makes me even more of an "avid buyer" of Bronze!

Copper/Modern Ages (1984-Now): We love to buy newer stuff, too (comics, toys, hardcovers and softcovers, etc.). Plenty of these comics have real good "upshotter values" (*Chew, Goon, Invincible, NYX,* various Spider-Man & Batman issues, to name a few.)

I'm so happy that I chose buying and selling comics as my lifetime pursuit, and I say, 'Why stop now?'

WALTER DURAJLIJA AND JAY HALSTEAD BIG B COMICS/INTERNATIONAL COMIC EXCHANGE (ICE)

Walter Durajlija, Big B Comics, Hamilton Ontario and Niagara Falls Ontario

A heartfelt congratulations to Bob Overstreet, Mark Huesman, JC Vaughn and the whole Price Guide team on their continued commitment to this indispensable hobby resource that is *The Overstreet Comic Book Price Guide*.

We've seen less traffic this past year at our Big B Comics shop in Hamilton, ON. Poor support and performance from superhero movie franchises has led to less interest in our product mix from the general population, but our core hobbyists are still coming in. What is missing is all the casual visitors that the TV and film popular culture was pushing into the shop. I'm not sure what the answer is for getting more casual shoppers back into the comic store. Free Comic Book Day always helps and local initiatives driven by us, like Comics for Grades, help too but it's looking like we will need that pop culture boost again. Let's hope Disney and Warner and all the others can get their formulas working, let's hope they start producing engaging and entertaining films and TV shows, and let's hope this all carries over into more and more comic shop visits.

Comic shops have to continue to reinvent themselves as well. We're victims of our own success, as items we were the exclusive sellers for a decade ago can now be found at drug stores, dollar stores, bookstores, big box stores and on. We need to excel at unique product lines, we need to offer those unique services, and we need to create a growing loyal customer base for our shops. Easy to say, hard to do but this still needs to be done. For now our weekly new comic buyers are carrying the torch as best they can. We will not be able to just sit and wait for the cavalry to arrive, so we'll have to figure out ways to generate demand on our own.

The comic book collecting and investing hobby has gone through a major correction over the past 18 months with comic book values giving back all their Covid era gains. Actually, it's a little more nuanced than that, as some collecting stains in our hobby have shown resilience and have kept all their gains and even added to them during this period but those were a select grouping of books. Some comics are settling back to their pre-pandemic values while still other comic prices have collapsed and sunk well below their pre-pandemic values. For this last group of books, with the biggest value losses, it is more a supply side issue as the number of available graded copies shot up so drastically while their values made it economical to incur the cost of grading, price levels would have retreated to pre-pandemic levels had the supply remained relatively the same but the effect of the supply increasing by multiples has cause the prices to drop through the floor. It's my view that this correction was needed, so let's look at the strong but sustainable growth comic values were seeing in the 2010s, this growth was demand driven through the growth of the number of participants in the hobby. The Covid price surges ended up not being sustainable, what we are seeing now is a retrenching, a much needed one. It would be a mistake to assume that things will settle back to where they were pre-pandemic, too much has changed both on the demand and supply side. New patterns will emerge with some sectors of the hobby poised for future growth while other sectors of the hobby will suffer and languish further.

A growth sector in the hobby, for us anyway, is the Canadiana collectibles, we expanded our annual Canadiana icecollectibles eBay auction to twice a year because of the strong demand and strong prices we were getting for the WECA era (Canadian Whites) and FECA era (late '40s / early '50s Canadian Editions). These books are so scarce, let's

hope we can continue to source more.

We still see an active collecting market, with sales of raw comics in the $5 to $50 range doing very well here at the local level. Our sales of $500 comics are very slow at the Big B Comics shop on Upper James, but we're having a hard time keeping up and replenishing the $10 and $20 bins. It looks like the bulk of the collectors are still active in the hobby, they're just more active in the shallow end, so once they feel the waters heating up a bit in the deep end, I think we'll see more and more of them diving back in.

We noticed a stabilizing of some prices at the end of 2023. Our icecollectibles weekly eBay auctions were good barometers of price trends, and by the end of last year we were having enough sales results that were not below the last recorded sale to assume that there was a levelling off in the price drops. Some notable sales through our icecollectibles eBay auctions included *Amazing Spider-Man* #129 CGC 9.6 - $8,334, *Journey into Mystery* #85 CGC 6.5 - $4,400, *Batman* #237 CGC 9.6 - $1,901.07, *Triumph Comics* #6 (Canadian White) CGC 3.0 Restored - $1,806, *Super Mario Bros* #1 CGC 9.8 - $2,850.

I'd like to end the report with a special thanks to the Big B Comics and ICE Collectibles team for all their hard work and diligence. Please go out and support your local comic book shop.

JAY HALSTEAD - ICOMICEXCHANGE.COM

The year of 2023 will go down in history, as the 'do you remember when' year, there's no doubt. We all knew the fall was coming, but no one, and I mean no one, could have predicted how hard and how fast.

I'm going to keep my report relatively short this year, because for the first time in many decades, I can honestly say I don't know how to properly gauge the market. If you don't mind, as this is a bit personal, I have felt off this entire year. It's one thing to be someone who buys comics, whether it's for enjoyment or as part of your investment platform. But me, nope, I'm one of those guys who is and has been all-in for many decades. I have a giant personal collection as well as nearly a complete run of all the '82-'86 Canadian price variants (CPV), yes even the incredibly coveted *Arak* and *Amethyst* comics. For years I would tell anyone who would listen that if you have expendable income (not money you can't afford to lose of course), to buy old comics. I know a lot of people did well with my advice, including myself. But now, when many are over their heads deep in the mud with multiple copies of name-your-key that sell for half (or less), of what they were selling for last year, I find myself not knowing what to tell that investor. Should he hold and wait for the market to rebound? Or should he sell now to try to still get something while he can? I'm honestly at a loss. Where we go from here is anyone's guess. I just hope that some of the collectors that purchased comics for ultra high prices through 2021 and 2022 come back, or even stay and enjoy the discounts.

Speaking of discounts, as most of these reports are going

to repeat a lot of the same doom and gloom, I figured I'd just pile on. I figured I'd feature a few, 'can you believe that tanking' sales data from 2023. Here are my favorites.

We had a customer bring in a *Shazam!* #28 wherein we had sold a 9.4 the previous year for somewhere in the $1k range. Now I know this one was mainly movie-driven, and The Rock apparently wasn't well received as Black Adam, but I couldn't believe this tanking. Without checking GPA I decided to send the book in, which look like an easy 9.6, and low and behold it came back 9.6. So here's the data folks. The 2021 average was north of $1,500 for a 9.6. The 2022 average was almost identical however once the movie came and went (with little fanfare), the twelve-month average was $520 and the last sale was $350. Now that's a tanking!!! Be careful of that movie speculation gang!

And I'd be remiss not to add one of what was a super heavyweight modern, the Djurdjevic variant for *Ultimate Fall-out #4* in 9.8, the first appearance of Miles Morales. You want to talk about tanking? This book had multiple sales in the $40k range throughout 2022, and then unceremoniously hit $13k just a few months ago. Youch! That's a $25k bath. If that's not a tanking, I don't know what is!!!

Now being a Canadian price variant (CPV) guy this report would not be complete without a few CPVs. Here at ICE Collectibles we haven't had the pleasure of anyone bringing us a 9.8 *Amazing Spider-Man* #238, but I do follow the market quite closely. There's another book where I can calmly say, "Can you believe that tanking?" So in 2022 the first copy came to market, with incredible pent up demand. And because of that, it went for over $8k. Since then, another copy beat that record. It's the last sale that really makes you scratch you head though, almost half ($4,850), of the previous two $8k+ sales. Personally I believe that to be a great buy, but sadly right now, that has to be filed under "Can you believe that tanking?"

We were very fortunate though to get to run the first *Batman* #404 CPV that has come to market in an auction. And although we did well (over $2k), many in the industry felt like it was the sale was a little light. There are few who don't agree but had the book come to market in 2021 or 2022, we might have been looking at double what it ended up going for. Again, another terrific buy, but that's really the market in a nutshell.

So it's a turbulent market out there, be careful, do your homework, think things through and start taking advantage of some of the bargains that are now out there!

Ken Dyber
Tasteecat Comics

Hello comic friends. I own Tasteecat Comics, which has a brick-and-mortar store in Portland, OR that's been open for 9 years now. I've also been selling online and at conventions around the country for around two decades. You can shop direct at: www.tasteecatcomics.com or follow me on eBay & Social Media at: @Tasteecatcomics. The website is mobile friendly and easy to use with our shopping cart and

Advanced Search, where one can shop by time period, genre, price and/or publisher even. Our brick-and-mortar store is open 11-7 daily and has 4 great employees that help me run it, so a big shout out to Stephen, Duncan, Michael & Moises.

Well, let's start off with my big reminder... The business rebranded last year to our new name. Without going into all the details of the reasons why, I can let you know, the name and logo are after my late 22-year-old black cat Tastee (R.I.P.), who was rescued from a pool table in a bar in Chicago. My personal eBay ID is Tasteecat, so it seemed like an obvious choice.

This year's report, unlike previous ones, is going to focus on general aspects of the market, and not as specifically on certain areas/time periods. There are many things happening in the comic market place at present, but mostly this past year can be summed up with two words: MARKET CORRECTIONS.

However, there are a lot of variables contributing to this, some are comic market specific, like additional price hikes by publishers of new comics, the continued marginalization of Diamond Comic Distributors, a reduced interest in comic book movies, and the value of many collectibles dramatically decreasing to name just a few.

There are also many external forces such as the overall economy, housing market, inflation, global instability and I hate to say it, but even politics. People are frustrated, confused, scared, and generally lacking confidence on a variety of levels that are all contributing to their decision-making process.

The overall economy is actually not as bad as our sensationalized media has made it out to be. Unemployment is at a historic low, housing prices are relatively stable (although interest rates have put many buyers on pause mode), inflation has slowed considerably, and it seems the dreaded 'recession' word may not come to fruition. Add in such other concerns as, growing climate instability, along with two wars happening, and what will probably be a wild upcoming presidential election, the average human being at present is well... pretty stressed out. Let's not kid ourselves, so far, the 2020's (which started off with Covid) have the makings of possibly being one of the most stressful decades in history at the rate things are going.

This is some pretty heavy stuff that people are having to process. Throw in the increased access to information, and then trying to determine if it's valid, it's pretty easy for your brains synapse to accelerate into overdrive. You are wondering, how does this relate to comic books (yes, this is a 'Market Report')? Great question!

Simply put, people are buying less, and the ones that are buying, are focusing mostly on lower risk and/or lower ticket items as their confidence level is greatly diminished. This is something that is happening in all aspects of the comic market at present, new comics, trades, cards, vintage books, etc...

As a comic book store retailer, I've lost about 10% of my box/subscription customers. Some can't afford the extra monthly outgoing, others are moving back home for a bit to save money by living with their family, and others are moving out of the city that has become increasingly expensive to live in to make their dollar go farther in rural areas where cost of living is less. Customers who would regularly come in and buy TPBs/Manga are gone. New comic customers are still coming in regularly, but they are buying less, and cancelling titles faster. Magic and Pokémon card sales have really slowed as well. The collector (adult) customers are buying less or not at all, and the kids who come in with their parents are now just getting 1 pack instead of 2 or 3.

As for back issues in the shop, the people that regularly came in to dig through long boxes in the last couple years have mostly stopped coming in, or now just wait until our next sale. This isn't as alarming, as back issue sales of non-key books (ie: box stuff), had slowed down for years, so this has just returned to pre-Covid market in that regard. As for more expensive back issues, like wall/case books, key issues, etc... those are still moving, but the prices they are selling for have come WAY down from the last few years, and are now selling for close to what they were selling at in 2019.

This aspect is most obvious in the Silver – Copper Age key issue market. Books like *Hulk* #181, *New Mutants* #98, *Amazing Spider-Man* #361, *Thor* #337, *Tales of Suspense* #39, *X-Men* #1, *Fantastic Four* #5, etc. have all gone down in value in all grades a lot. Many by around 50%. A specific example would be *New Mutants* #98 in graded 9.8. Peak price in 2022 $2,800, current price $1,400. Personally, I think at $1,400, this book is pretty undervalued, and should probably be somewhere around $2,000, but buyers are concerned that the next sale will be lower than their buy price, so they're either waiting, or they're low-balling with an offer, that many times now that offer is being accepted, as the seller overpaid for the book, and needs to get some money back to pay bills.

This aspect has stabilized considerably towards the end of 2023, as I think we may be at, or at least near the bottom of this major market correction. You simply need to just take out the Covid time period pricing as that was a bubble market for a variety of reasons previously discussed at length in past *Guide* reports. If you are still working your same job, making the same amount of money, and do not have too much in the way of increased outgoing expenditures such as food, clothing, insurance, etc... NOW is a great time to be buying, if, and I say if, you can buy and hold. If you have to resell relatively quickly, or hoping for that quick bump, good luck with that.

I by all means do not have a crystal ball, but as some things change, some remain the same. I look back to my market report from 2009, and I said in that report "Now is the time to buy *Hulk* #181 in graded 9.8", as that book bottomed out at $9,000 (yeah, $9k for a 9.8!). Even in today's current uncertain market, that's still a $30-$50k book, so your $9k investment increased 4-5 times in today's soft market. So, buy and hold on key books now if you can afford it.

Conventions: I did a few this year, and attendance was good, and for the most part, buying and selling was also pretty good. What was interesting to me, was that my selling to other dealers this year almost didn't happen at all. The dealers were much less aggressive at acquiring new inventory than previous years from me. I think this was mostly due to them being focused on selling their existing inventory as a means to reduce outgoing expenditures. Another reason is typically dealer margins are better when buying collections or doing larger size purchases (buy more = getting a better discount), so unless a dealer had time to this, buying for them at a con wasn't happening.

My customer sales were good through, as long as my prices were in line with the current market. I spent half a day in my hotel room before the Baltimore convention repricing my inventory, lowering them to be priced at the new market prices, and this resulted in my best Baltimore show as far as me selling to the general public.

Buying for me at cons this year was quite good, if I found the right dealers, because as mentioned, some hadn't adjusted their prices yet, but others who had, or were willing to deal, or who had bought a new collection and priced it at current levels, there was a lot of great stuff to be found at reasonable prices.

Golden Age: This is the one area of the market that has been more stable. The customer base in this segment tends to be older age wise, and have more disposable income. These are also rarer books, and rarer items that you do not see as often tend to hold their value more. I noticed a bit of increased interest in War books (many still pretty affordable) and Sci-Fi books (Avon and Fiction House in particular), and a decrease in interest in Romance and Pre-Code Horror. The PCH books do seem to be holding their value pretty well (maybe a 10/15% drop but nothing too crazy), but many of these have gotten to be pretty expensive, so some people in the market at getting priced out now. ECs are selling quite strong at present, which is a bit odd, as they are always in demand, but I actually have seen a fair amount of them go up in value this past year, thus defying the rest of the market.

Super-hero books here are doing fine, a little regression or flat. Captain Marvels are selling quite fast for me. These are great reads, and so affordable (many in VF go for $200/$300, where a *Cap* or *Superman* would go for $1/$2k from the same year if not more). Overall, still a safe place to put your money, especially if it's for the longer term.

Silver Age: This year has really crushed this time period in value more than any other period. The Bronze and Copper Age key books have gone down the same percentage in many cases, but the Silver Age values were higher, so the dollar loss is greater. Any example from last year to this year would be *X-Men* #1 in 6.0 was $25k and is now $16k. *Hulk* #181 in 6.0 was $5,000 is now $3,300. The *X-Men* #1 is down 36%. *Hulk* #181 is down 34%. The dollar loss though is $9,000 on the *X-Men* #1 & $1,700 on the *Hulk* #181. Both are tough, but the *X-Men* #1 is much more difficult to stomach from an investment standpoint.

Now is a really great time to work on a run as 6.0-8.0 books on *Amazing Spider-Man*, *X-Men*, *Iron Man*, *Fantastic Four*, etc. have come down 40-60% in many instances.

Bronze Age: Also, many market corrections, but often the percentage decrease is less than the Silver Age. Horror titles are still selling quite fast like *House of Mystery, House of Secrets, Witching Hour, Ghosts, Tomb of Dracula* and *Werewolf By Night*. Sure, the key books are down, but the characters and genre overall are still doing well.

Romance comics from this period all need to go up in *Guide* a decent bit. I'd say 25-50% across the board, and double in 9.0 & 9.2. Charlton Romance has started to sell quite well, but certain titles and covers do better than others such as Greytone and the more psychedelic covers. Much of the interior artwork in these is OK, and the inking can be quite spotty, but they are a ton of fun to read and sell quickly. The Marvel Romance books like *Our Love Story* have some killer interior artwork by the likes of Colan, Heck and Giacoia to name a few. Many of these have 0-4 graded copies on the census, and some have very strong GPA sales like 9.0s going for $150 range which is 4x *Guide*, granted it's graded, but that would have me pricing it around $90, which is double *Guide*, and thus my suggested price point.

Horror Magazines from this period are selling like crazy for me! This has been my single hottest segment of the market. I bought a collection from my friend Travis, and have almost sold every single book from it. These are still pretty affordable, and very tough to find in 8.0 or better, so a market segment to keep our eye on.

Copper Age/Modern Age: Demand has really dropped off here in many areas. A lot of these collectors are in their 30's/40's age wise, and I think are being affected by the current economic climate a bit more than others, as they still have children to feed and put through school, so they're having to take a break on buying or just buy less and at lower prices. *TMNT*'s have really come back down, but *Spawn*s are selling like crazy at present. Think the new *Spawn* movie has a lot of people pretty excited.

Renaissance Age: This is the period I call the current comics (everything post *Walking Dead* #1), and for the most

is doing OK. *Something is Killing The Children* has settled down finally, *Saga* is actually not doing that great (which is shocking). IDW is finally starting to put out their own stuff, and a lot of it is pretty good. BOOM! is doing fairly well, and Image is finally starting to regress a bit as many of their flagship titles have ended or seem to be on hold forever (*Bitch Planet, Snotgirl, Black Monday Murders*).

Thanks to everyone for their support and it was great meeting many of you at conventions (especially so many of our new Instagram customers). I look forward to meeting more of you in the coming years. Happy collecting!

DANIEL ERTLE
CBCS - MANGA SPECIALIST

My report is going to be a bit different than normal this year. I have spent much of 2023 helping to develop an industry first for us in the grading and encapsulation business. By the time this comes out I'm sure most of you will have heard about this new venture and are as excited as we are about it. Of course, I am talking about manga grading.

Most of the people reading these reports are probably aware of the popularity and growth of manga in the comic book industry. The numbers coming out the last couple of years have shown that manga is the leading form of sequential art, and not by a small margin. With this popularity we have seen books increase in value and desirability. A few things affect the collectability of books and drive desirability and sales. One of the biggest drives are books being out of print (oop). These are books that were published years ago, sometimes by publishers that are no longer around, and for whatever reason these books only received that run of prints. Now, years later people are seeking out these books and prices have driven up in those instances. Another reason for a book's higher demand is a well-received anime adaptation. Anime has four seasons a year, accompanied with an announcement/speculation period before every new season. This causes first appearances to increase in price and can drive sales at brick-and-mortar shops for those specific titles. Also, more recently, variant covers in manga are appearing with greater frequency. Convention exclusives, or book shop exclusives are starting to become a trend in this space and we all know exclusivity increases the desirability of collecting a book.

Some people are probably asking "who or why would they want those graded?", and I can certainly understand the sentiment because we saw the same thing when people started grading floppies. Well, the manga team and I are all passionate about the hobby of collecting, and we felt this was a service that was really lacking in this space. People are often asking if their books are legitimate, are getting their tankobon (standalone book) signed by voice actors, and are spending hundreds of dollars, and in some cases thousands, without any kind of guarantee of the condition of the book. Several books have sold for over $500 on auction sites recently, including first Japanese printings of *One Piece* tankobon and several of the limited to 5000 editions of *One*

106

Piece, Dragon Ball, and *Naruto.* As this hobby grows, and not just in the U.S., we believe this service will help to protect buyers and sellers and prevent people from being defrauded or spending more on a lower quality book.

As I mentioned before, Beckett Manga is the first manga specific grading service in the world, and this truly is an international product. This format has really taken over the world in terms of comic book reading. A few things serve to make these stories more digestible for newer readers and people wanting things that you just can't readily get with comics. These stories are mostly self-contained and usually have a consistent creative team that is with the story from the beginning to the end. Speaking of end, many of these stories have definitive endings. So it's possible to collect an entire story fairly easily.

As far as the books that we will be grading, currently it's the tankobon sized books. These are the smaller square-bound books you can find in bookstores and comic shops around the world. These are the most accessible and easily collectable books in regards to manga currently. With this being the most popular format for most of the world, we decided to start there and developed a truly industry-leading case and inner-wells that protect books and display amazingly. These books honestly look great in a short box or on the shelf.

I know this is probably a new area for the market reports to cover but as the comic hobby grows and evolves, these books will continue to be part of the conversation. I hope to continue to provide insights to this budding market and collectors space and grow with it as collectors realize the potential and value that these books hold.

D'ARCY FARRELL
PENDRAGON COMICS

2023 was a tumultuous year in the world and our industry.

With Covid mostly gone, markets came back to 100% operations which included conventions and in store sales. The big surge of 2020-22 for back issue sales plummeted (mostly online). I did see a change in purchasing from big and moderate keys, to lower value runs. Buyers became more cautious.

What I did see as positive was a return to completing runs. Best runs we sold were anything Horror, especially Marvel of the 1970s. Not just the obvious *Werewolf by Night, Tomb of Dracula, Moon Knight,* but even the reprints. DC has its fair share of great Horror titles, led by *House of Secrets.* Other genres that perked up a bit were non super-hero companies such as Harvey, Archie, Gold Key, Disneys and the like.

Marvel movies won't see a return to greatness until I see *Blade.* The politically correct machine at Marvel/Disney just cant help ruin the great potential that Kirby, Simon and Ditko created. Will the Fantastic Four actually come out as Kirby evolved this historic franchise as intended? Or the X-Men (new) and all its glory that started with *Giant-Size X-Men* #1 and *X-Men* #94-143 with the genius of Claremont? I hope so. *Deadpool 3* with Jackman reprising Wolverine one last time

will be an amazing blip of success among so many flat-liners.

We are about to see if *Aquaman 2* can even be half as successful as the first installment. Again I hope so, but it's unlikely. *The Flash* I did enjoy, *Blue Beetle* was refreshing in some ways and I liked the casting, but it was too simple and obvious.

Smart Investing Advice: Ask yourself. What is better? To buy important keys or runs, such as *Amazing Spider-Man, X-Men, Batman* during this time of a lower market, or wait for the next big surge like what we saw 1-2 years ago and buy at its highest point? Do collectors really think an *Amazing Spider-Man* #129 can go any lower or *Daredevil* #168 or *Detective* #359 and the like? Have we hit the plateau and values have calmed? The answer is obvious. Always buy at the lowest time. Guess what, that's now. The smart collectors should be buying now.

The smart investors back in 1929 when the stock market crashed, stayed calm, held onto their investments, bought at the lowest point, and held off for the rebound.

Our market will get that rebound. It's always cyclical like any investment.

BILL FIDYK
COLLECTOR

2023 was a good year for the back issue magazine market despite market corrections that have caused sales prices to dip. Overall, prices seemed to fall slightly but did not drastically plummet from the previous year. Even key issues were not immune to this price decline, and it seems that the comic magazine back issue market is reflecting trends seen in the comic book back issue market as well as with collectibles in general. Inflation and a turbulent economy have made collectors more aware of a comic's price tag and made them more reluctant to drive up the bidding in the final minutes (or seconds) of an auction listing. Only high grade copies of magazines (9.6 and 9.8) or high grade examples pre-1966 (9.0 and above) seemed to have been immune to these price drops.

Here is a list of comic magazine key issues that were highly sought after in 2023:

Warren's *Eerie* #1: This was an ashcan edition rapidly put together by Warren to gain the rights to the *Eerie* title. Most collectors consider issue two to be the start of the run, but this mindset seems to be changing. This issue has had multiple prints with an authentic first print being difficult to verify making collector's hesitant to purchase a true first edition. However, CBCS has begun grading this issue and authenticating a true first copy (CGC still refuses to grade these). Several copies came to market in 2023 with CBCS copies seeing the highest prices realized.

Frazetta Covers: This has been a subset of Warren key issues that continues to gain popularity and high prices. 9.6 and 9.8 copies seem to break records whenever they come to market with *Eerie* #23 being the breakout "key" Frazetta cover issue.

Famous Monsters: I am always amazed at prices realized for high grade copies of issues one through twenty. In addition, several early issues have regional variants that are near impossible to find in high grade (or any grade at all) and go for multiples of what their regular issue counterparts sell for.

Blazing Combat: Issue one above an 8.0 is highly sought after with record breaking prices realized each time they do come to market. The black cover adds to the scarcity of this book in high grade as well.

Prices for high grade copies of *Vampirella* issue one have leveled off and have even dropped a bit to pre-2020 prices (even for 9.2 and above copies). This issue is still in high demand and a true Warren key.

Marvel: Marvel/Curtis titles are plentiful in all grades. Most prices for all issues slightly dipped from the previous year. However, "keys" in each run maintained or topped last year's realized prices when offered in any grade as opposed to issues that come before or after them in their respective runs.

Break out issues that realized high prices in 2023 for popular Marvel/Curtis runs include: *Savage Tales* #1 (first Man-Thing), *Vampire Tales* #2 (first Satana), *Deadly Hands of Kung Fu* #19 and #22, *Dracula Lives* #2 (first Marvel origin of Dracula, a book that is vastly underappreciated), *Monsters Unleashed* #1 (early Werewolf by Night appearance) and #10 (early Tigra appearance).

For *Marvel Preview*, it seems that issue #7 is surfacing as the top key of the run. Issue #4 has cooled off a bit. One main reason is that issue #7 has added appeal to horror collectors due to the early Satana appearance.

Marvel Super Special: Issue #1 is understandable due to the early KISS appearance in comics and the fact that it is the first issue in the run. The issue #6 (*Jaws 2* movie adaptation) must be a low print issue and has proven difficult to find above a 9.0. This magazine goes for multiples of *Guide* in high grade when it rarely comes to market.

Legion of Monsters one shot commands high prices and multiples of *Guide* everytime it is offered. Having a gorgeous Neal Adams cover helps its appeal. It's the first appearance of the Legion of Monsters in magazine format.

Skywald/Eerie publications: *Guide* prices are irrelevant when high grade copies (9.2 or higher) come to market for any issue of these two publishers. This is always the case and 2023 offered no new evidence that warehouse copies exist (like some of the Warrens or Marvels) or will ever be unearthed. Any high grade copies that exist are still locked away in private collections.

A MARVEL COMICS SUPER SPECIAL!

KISS

Forty pages of full-color comics. Plus never-before-published photos and features. Printed in real KISS blood.

PAUL FIGURA
CBCS - MODERN AND VINTAGE GRADER

Another year passes, and another convention year is in the books. As a team, we worked more shows, brought in more books, and never felt more achy and tired after each day than in previous years. Could the rumors really be true? We thought we were becoming the elder statesmen, but it seems more like the Crypt Keepers of numerous tomes of tales and artistic wonders. As true as the elder statesman comment might be, comic conventions are back in full swing with glorious, overcrowded halls and aggressive pricing.

For me, this year started at Fan Expo Dallas in June, then moved east of the Mississippi to MegaCon for the rest of the shows that I could fit in my schedule. It finally ended at the Rhode Island Comic Con in November. Attendance across the board at the conventions increased tremendously from the past few years, notably at Fan Expo Chicago. That show had the biggest increase in attendance since the old Wizard World Chicago days. It was so amazing to see! Sunday, the last day of New York Comic Con, the crowd just kept coming and coming! The show closed at 5:00 PM, and at 4:30 PM the show floor was as packed as it was at noon. It was just an incredible experience to be a part of!

The pure comic book shows had a great mix of vendors. The shows that were celebrity and pop culture oriented had just a few comic book creators there, but those few managed some impressive set ups. Pricing varied. New and Modern books were priced within reason with the hot books and the numerous variants fetching a premium price. However, a few of the Silver and Golden Age books I found were priced rather aggressively. But the cost of doing business at conventions can be rather expensive, which of course will be reflected in the pricing. I am also guessing that the pandemic was still in the back of a few people's minds.

Artist Alley and the celebrity sections of the convention halls were the most crowded. Convention goers flocked to meet and get pictures and autographs of their favorite comic creators, actors, voice actors, as well as writers and directors. I have mentioned in past reports the number of people wanting these signatures. It was never more evident as this past year showed us. Long lines for comic creators such as Al Milgrom, Chris Claremont, Simon Bisley and Walt and Louise Simonson, and many others. All the creators went above and beyond with each fan, talking and telling stories to each and every one, giving them a true fan experience to remember and talk about for years to come. The actors were no different. They didn't just sign autographs and move fans along, they took the time to thank them for coming to see them and visit a little bit. Spending that brief time with them is all it takes to make the waiting in line worth it for the fans.

To sum up the past year, it was great for comic conventions! The fans are returning to the shows, vendors are making sales, and creators, as well as celebrities, are meeting their admirers. It is a great time to be in attendance and sharing again in the experience!

Happy collecting!

JOSEPH FIORE
COMICWIZ.COM

This past year marks some milestones for me in my collecting journey. I'd decided to again temporarily hibernate my selling activities, and focus on several key areas where my time was being most utilized. The first being the appraisal work I do, and I've been extremely fortunate to assist several estates in valuing, and procuring strategies to help sell off their collections. One of them was a fantastic collection spanning multiple categories, which included a massive comic collection, but also a beautiful collection of toys that had been amassed from the 1960s to the late 1980s. The estate downsizing trend became more pronounced from my observations, and at least from where I'm located geographically. The tough economy left many people I knew in less than ideal financial circumstances, and several appraisals were for the purpose of selling to offset situations where they stood to otherwise lose their homes. This was not an easy thing to have to witness, and I began to notice some of the signs as early as when my oldest son began volunteering at the food bank, and learning from him that people with paying jobs were using it because they weren't able to stretch their earnings enough to put food on the table.

This precarious situation which is often described as an "affordability crisis" has trickled into our hobbies, as speculative activities have seemingly all but dwindled, very likely due to soaring interest rates, and any disposable income that might have been used in the past toward hobbying activities, is now needed for higher priority everyday essentials. The oft-repeated belief that a tough economy might allow collectors a ripened opportunity to get better deals is a misstated one. While markets have cooled significantly in comparison to consumer expenditures during COVID, due in large part to global economic circumstances, it isn't always the case that your ability to acquire items is guaranteed to be lower in a depressed market. This relates to a phenomenon I call a "supply choke", where items acquired during peak markets are not going to be easy to buy or wriggle loose at the expense of someone taking a loss on it for another person's benefit or gain, unless it's a duress sale situation. Situations may differ depending on the item, and a person's access to supply, but generally, this will apply more generally from collector to collector trading, even if that collector occasionally sells or buys/sells

mainly to upgrade pieces in their collection.

I began offering digital appraisals, available through QR code and/or serial number for easy online lookup on a computer or smartphone for toys (ToyVerify.com) and comics as well as comic art (ComicVerify.com). This has been a great way to transition into doing smaller scale and single item appraisals, which I was not able to do as often, because larger scale estate appraisals were requiring a lot more of my time to deliver a report format. The latter were often ordered by agents of insurance companies, lawyers and/or for more complex procedures such as probate or divorce. The amount of areas where appraisals are useful range from post-loss damage during shipping, to helping people who haven't been involved in hobbies for a very long time, who suddenly find themselves clearing out their attics or their parents homes, and need to gain an understanding on what the items are worth before deciding what to do next with them. This exposure has been a great way to remain dialed-in on markets, as well as developing relationships with people who continue to turn to me for hobby advice and assistance, even if it sometimes falls outside the scope of my appraisal assignments. Something I see as further validation to the reasons why I got into appraising in the first place, and that was because I saw a great need as a collector to help navigate the often difficult themes and topics of ownership, and how to better manage heirlooms and/or inheritances.

This segues nicely into the more memorable marker I passed in my collecting journey this year. One of the signs of aging that kind of creeps up on you is realizing online resources you once were able to use have disappeared. As our hobbying evolves to different social media sites, we realize that fragmentation creates more difficulty for us to search out information. This is particularly the case when I'm finding myself having to more often do my research using the Wayback machine, because those resources I have relied on for all these years have suddenly vanished. For all the advantages digital provides, this conundrum really speaks to one of the many reasons I feel the advisor's contributions in our market reporting is critical, particularly as a point of reference in print that gives the researcher greater control over access to data that isn't under the threat of disappearing or being purged. About 15% of my appraisals in the toy hobby are related to resources that have disappeared, and collectors not knowing how to chase that information down any longer. The other side of this is the perpetuation and spread of false information, and how bad actors see this absence of critical research vanishing as an opportunity to deceive.

On this same split path for a long-haul journeyman, where a collector's reward is dependent on the path you choose, there is this memorable moment to share from this past year. The story takes us back to the summer of 2005, when I attended my last San Diego Comic-Con, and it was during the convention that I ran into a friend of the Bob Montana family. For those unfamiliar with the name, Bob Montana was one of the first, if not the first, artist to draw Archie. He first drew Archie in 1941, and then went on to draw the syndicated Archie strip, both dailies and Sunday strips, and managed to hold onto almost all of his original art. A pretty amazing feat considering the relative scarcity of original art from the Golden Age of comics and newspaper strips.

He continued to illustrate the syndicated strip until he passed away in 1975, and he is without question on my Mount Rushmore of comic art greats right beside Jack Kirby, with Bob Montana being one of the longest serving artists on a single title. The Montana family wisely held onto the original art, thousands of pages and strips, only releasing the occasional page into the marketplace, but retaining the bulk to ensure that the collection remained relatively intact. This caused a demand for Bob Montana Archie art, as there wasn't that much of it to go around.

The happenstance occasion of making a connection to the family from an encounter at SDCC in 2005 marked the beginning of my attempts to acquire some original art from the Montana estate. After establishing contact back then, I was made aware that the family wanted the late Jerry Weist to appraise the collection, which I thought to be a smart move. After a year had passed, I began to catch word that Steve Geppi had made an offer to buy out the Montana OA, and if this had been the way things ended, I would have been happy with that outcome, despite losing out on an opportunity to own some of the art myself. After all, Steve Geppi had just opened a Museum at the time, and it seemed on the surface to be the right place for the art to end up, if for no other reason than the fact it could be displayed and enjoyed by visitors of the museum. Instead, what happened was the deal didn't materialize the way it was originally intended. The Montana family were understandably reluctant to discuss any matters concerning the sale of any art after this happened, and it appeared it just wasn't in the cards for me to add any Montana art to my collection of Archie OA.

In 2014, I started an Archie OA group on Facebook. Not expecting more than running the group to share some of my Archie comic art with other like minded collectors, I began seeing some interesting developments. Particularly, with the family of artists and creators of Archie Publications who began to join the group and participate in discussion and share stories of their families and the artwork produced during their time working at Archie Comics.

Earlier this year, I noticed one of the heirs of the Montana family posting in the group, and I hesitatingly reached out. It was an arduous process with long lags in communication, but I eventually did manage to finally rehash some of the discussions I'd begun 18 years ago to acquire some art from the Montana estate. As I write that number, I can't believe I had to wait that long. Perhaps this is yet another example of the downsides of aging, but I guess the old saying good things come to those who wait would apply here.

Below is my first share from that long overdue process to acquire art from the Montana family.

An *Archie* daily strip from July 13, 1953, by the late, great Bob Montana, acquired directly from the Bob Montana estate. It's incredible to think this strip turned 70 years old

this past summer! I'm thankful for having had the opportunity to work with the heirs, and while I haven't yet had an opportunity to scan all the pages and post them on CAF to share with the OA community, I hope to get to that at some point in the New Year, as well as continue the relationship I've formed with those who have helped make this all possible. It definitely took a village, and it's moments like these that remind us why we collect, and that with any goals we set, patience, persistence and eventual attainment are possible.

Before I conclude, it should be noted that at the time of writing this report, I am both following and assisting with research endeavors on a newly emerging issue that has been identified on the CGC forums. The discovery is being referred to as a "reholder scam" where it is believed an eBay seller has seemingly figured out a way to get a lower grade comic into a higher grade slab. I've now been involved in identifying six separate instances where a qualified (green label) CGC graded Incredible Hulk 181, ended-up in a similar or higher grade universal (blue label) CGC slab. In all instances, the comic had the Marvel Value Stamp (MVS) missing. In several instances, the entire page was missing. This means an INCOMPLETE comic found a way to sell as a universal blue label slab on six different occassions. The situation has also blown-up on YouTube, Facebook and Instagram. It is already beginning to raise considerable alarm within the collecting community, and I will continue to play a small part to provide as much assistance as my time affords me.

I involve myself in such unpaid, thankless tasks of trying to gather as much information to at least understand the extent of this seller's activities, and to expose the deception and fraud with as much evidence as I can gather, because I have the knowledge, and experience to assist in this way. The time factor is always the reason that dictates how much assisting I can do, but when you consider that as this scandal is unfolding, there are YouTubers who are "lifting" other people's detective work and claiming it as theirs to flex for likes and subscriptions, as well as Facebook groups which are deleting posts when members are found asking questions about this scandal. As you might imagine, it can frustrate even the most well-intentioned, while making it seem like it's more trouble than it is worth in getting involved.

From my perspective, collecting has always been the lynchpin to areas of interest like research, and networking, as well as forming long-standing friendships. In order for the confluence of these to function in tandem requires collaboration, cooperation and unity to truly benefit the individual, as well as the greater collecting community. We have all seen how tracking market growth by record sales and volume of sales stimulates spend in peak markets. It even makes for great YouTube content when you can show those record sales, sometimes not more than a few days, weeks or months apart. These all help reinforce those cool custom video thumbnails showing big yellow arrows graphing an upward trajectory. As entertaining as that may be for content, it isn't versed in any reality of the current state of the market. We've reached a period where a long-time contributor of the CGC forums using the alias MasterChief recently revealed through lists, graphs and charts, that since 2021, 290 Promise Collection "Pedigree" comic books have been sold/resold for a loss of over $1M, not including the $240k loss from the Nov 16th Heritage sales of *Batman* #37 and *Detective Comics* #146. It's when markets begin to trend in a downward or corrective manner that it also becomes important to keep a watchful eye for deceptive activities. It is no surprise to learn of this recent "reholder" and "swapping" scandal and the discoveries the community is still making, absent any response yet from CGC. The preservation of consumer confidence becomes inextricably tied to overall market health, and we all play a role in some way, shape or manner in achieving stability. As we find ourselves in a situation with tough economic and uncertain times ahead, where collectors may be concerned about unscrupulous and deceptive practices being used to game third-party grading, it's important we work together to overcome these challenging times. Rust never sleeps, but working together, we can overcome any challenge.

DAN FOGEL
HIPPY COMIX

This past year I chose to skip selling at conventions and stick to mail-order buying and selling wholesaling to retailers, as my main gig remains writing and publishing the next edition of *Fogel's Underground Comix Price Guide*. Although I mostly needed to grade and price UGs and Indies, the recent collections I purchased had mainstream titles as well, so my trusty *Overstreet* got its usual workout and I was able to squirrel away in my collection Dell, Gold Key, Whitman, Charlton, and *Classics Illustrated* goodies along with a few DC and Marvels to recover my youth.

2023 Sales Highlights: I must have been spray-on tanned in my sleep because Bronze and Copper won Gold Medals in my sales!

Bronze Age
Marvel: A *Marvel Comics Super Special* #4, "The Beatles Story" F+ $30, and various mid- to low-grade but lovable copies of *War is Hell*, *Weird Wonder Tales*, *Marvel Double Feature*, and *Captain America*.

Archie: *Chilling Adventures in Sorcery* and *Madhouse* were spookily in demand.

Pacific: *Starslayer*, *Alien Worlds*, *Berni Wrightson*, *Master of the Macabre*, and *Twisted Tales* shambled out the door.

First: *Warp* spaced out in a good way.

Eclipse: *Tales of Terror*, *Eclipse Graphic Album*, and *Alien Encounters* were visible in daylight.

Copper Age
Marvel: The Epic imprint had the most demand in decades as I moved *Dr. Zero*, *Critical Mass*, *St. George*, *Powerline*, *Metropol*, *The One*, *Plastic Forks*, *Interface*, *The Light and Darkness War*, and the Epic perfect-bound series.

Dark Horse: Comics' Greatest World imprint proved Nineties nostalgia is real, as I sold *Will to Power* and *Out of the Vortex*.

Kitchen Sink Press: *Death Rattle* Volumes 2 and 3 are frequently in demand but easy to restock.

As always, my perennial and heartfelt gratitude and admiration for the fine folks at Gemstone Publishing for letting me be a Special Advisor since 1987: Bob Overstreet, Steve Geppi, J.C. Vaughn, Mark Huesman, Amanda Sheriff, Yolanda Ramirez, and Mike Wilbur. Let's break some records in 2024-25!

KEVIN FORBES
COMIC INTERLUDE

Hello and Happy 4th of July, 2024! It's actually a little more than a week before Christmas 2023 here in Lexington, Kentucky as I write this market report for your reading pleasure. I'd love to tell you 2023 was a spectacular year for comic books, and everything comic related was amazing....but it just wasn't meant to be. Not yet at least. For the most part, comic book prices for 2023 were sort of a continuation of 2022. Across the board, comic book prices continued to gradually slide down a bit more most the year. More of a settling, than falling really. I had felt early 2023 prices were stabilizing, and maybe 5-10% did, but the vast majority of comic books continued to drop in price over the course of the year. Now in December, I honestly feel the ground floor for prices is pretty solid now, though we're still going to see falling prices in non-hot keys and lesser keys moving forward in 2024. For the next few years supply most likely will outweigh demand on 80% of books, in part because so many new investors to the hobby in 2020/2021 got burned so badly by the falling prices when the bubble burst. I'm optimistic though, with prices down on so many great books from the Golden Age all the way up to the Modern Age, I feel new collectors, seasoned collectors, and speculators alike will all help make 2024 a solid, stable year for comic books.

2024 will make 28 years for my retail store, Comic Interlude, and it will also my last. I'll either sell, or close my store this coming spring. You will still be able to find me on eBay, my seller ID is comicinterlude. It's been a great run, but retail is a younger persons game, and I'm looking forward to relaxing more and focusing on my online sales, conventions, and growing my pressing/cleaning clientele. I appreciate all my wonderful and loyal customers, many of whom are very close friends, I'm happy to say. It's pretty cool how many have been with me the whole time. Owning a store is like having an extended family, and it's been amazing seeing long-time customers kids go from babies to successful, well-rounded, gainfully employed men and women, now many with babies of their own!

Current/Modern Comics: Demand for new, weekly comics, from all the different publishers is solid. While I can't say I'm happy with what Marvel is doing with most of their comic book storylines, I do feel DC, Image, Dark Horse, BOOM! and quite a few smaller independents (Titan, DSTLRY, AWA) are really putting out some great books. I've always prided myself in having a good selection of independent titles in the store, and I think it's essential for getting new readers

111

into the hobby. As for demand for the Modern keys, they were one of the areas that took a pretty good beating all of 2023. Constantly fluctuating prices, usually slightly downward, and plentiful supply keep them unstable for the near future. If you're buying and plan on holding for 10-20 years from now, sure you try to get the best price possible, but don't be too concerned with the market fluctuations over the next few years. Buy and hold comic book investing has rarely NOT worked out, especially if you're buying a mix of genres and eras. The Dark Horse *Star Wars* titles are way down the past year, along with keys like *New Mutants* #98, *Batman Adventures* #12, and even *Amazing Spider-Man* #300...to the tune of 25-30%. Some of my 2023 current/modern sales: *Spawn* #1 CGC 9.6 Newsstand $189, *The Boys* #1 CGC 9.8 $375, *The Boys* #1 CGC 9.6 $195, *Battle Chasers* #1 CGC 9.8 $150, *All-New Marvel Now Point One* #1 CGC 9.8 $395, *Strange Academy* #1 CGC 9.6 Opena 1:50 Variant $575, *Star Wars: The Clone Wars* #2 CGC 9.8 $275, *Teen Titans Go!* #23 CGC 9.8 $775, *Walking Dead* #1 CGC 9.6 $1,500, *Star Wars: The Clone Wars* #1 CGC 9.8 $2,095, *Venom* #3 CGC 9.8 $230, and *Wolverine* #8 CGC 9.8 $335.

Bronze Age Comics: I've said it time and again, ever since I was writing market reports for *Overstreet Fan* magazine back in the '90s, Bronze Age is by far my favorite era of comic books! So many great stories, so many great covers, so many new characters, 1st appearances, deaths, and origins. Truly something for everyone, and will always be very popular and sought after by seasoned collectors, dealers, speculators, and new collectors getting into the hobby too. High grade issues, hard to find issues, they've all taken their hits the past 2 years now. Many keys from this time period are down by as much as 40%, with the highest grades down 15-20%. Make no mistake though, these books always have been and always will be very collectible! There are still so many popular and also unknown characters (to the general public), that made their first appearances in titles from this era who have NOT yet appeared in a movie or tv show. I feel investments in Bronze Age keys will pay off long term, and by that I mean 10 years or longer. Take advantage of the down market, it will not last forever.

Some of my Bronze Age sales from 2023: *Batman* #244 CGC 9.2 $775, *Batman* #244 CGC 9.4 $950, *Batman* #234 CGC 8.0 $595, *Black Panther* #1 CGC 9.8 $825, *Black Panther* #1 CGC 9.6 $299, *Daredevil* #131 CGC 9.8 $5,195, *Star Wars* #1 CGC 9.8 $3,850, *Star Wars* #2 CGC 9.6 Newsstand $415, *Tomb of Dracula* #1 CGC 7.5 $440, *X-Men* #129 CGC 9.8 Newsstand $2,900, and *Giant-Size X-Men* #1 CGC 6.5 $2,395.

Silver Age Comics: Interestingly, one of the hardest hit segments over the past year and a half. Key issues and higher grade issues from this age have always been very desirable

among collectors, and not easy to come by. Yet surprisingly, prices on quite a few Marvel key issues from very popular titles like *Amazing Spider-Man*, *Fantastic Four*, and *X-Men* are down as much as 50% recently. DC titles have done a much better of maintaining their prices. DC titles haven't had anywhere near the volatility that Marvel titles have had the past few years. DC titles have held onto most of their gains from the past few years, and most only being down in the 10-15% range. Unfortunately any movie key issues from this time period, regardless of being Marvel. DC or other (Gold Key, Dell, Charlton), are all down substantially. Nice medium grade books (5.5-7.5) from all these titles, including a lot of key issues, regularly sell in the $100-$200 range already graded, which is absolutely amazing. Bigger keys in lower grades are selling graded (2.0-3.5) in the $150-$300 range. Great jumping on point for newer and/or younger collectors.

Prices aren't jumping up and around as much as needed to get the flippers and speculators back in at this point, but even they can find some books to pick up and sit on at these prices. I was surprised to see prices staying down all year, and I still expect to see more consistent upward moving prices later on in 2024 and into 2025, especially with *Fantastic Four* and *X-Men* books. In a few years when the new movies start getting attention, many of these books will rebound at least in the upward direction of 2021 prices. The only books I feel will possibly fully rebound would be the first 5-10 issues of *Fantastic Four* and *X-Men*. Some of my Silver Age sales from 2023: *Action Comics* #252 CGC 2.0 $1,325, *Amazing Spider-Man* CGC 3.0 $650, *Amazing Spider-Man* #7 CGC 6.5 $1,400, *Amazing Spider-Man* #23 CGC 5.0 $250, *Amazing Spider-Man* #54 CGC 9.0 $299, *Amazing Spider-Man* #1 CBCS 4.5 (Restored) $7,900, *Aquaman* #29 CGC 8.0 $399, *Batman* #155 CGC 7.0 $1,225, *Detective Comics* #276 CGC 6.5 $519, *Detective Comics* #298 CGC 6.0 $1,250, *Fantastic Four* #6 CGC 2.5 $675, *Four Color* #878 (Dell) CGC 5.5 $575, *Journey Into Mystery* #103 CGC 5.0 $660, *Wonder Woman* #115 CGC 7.0 $295, and *Green Lantern* #1 CGC 4.0 $1,350.

Golden Age Comics: No big changes here, except with the highest grade. All the major keys from this era have maintained well, with some common issues and lesser keys dropping 10-15%, but in higher grades record setting prices are common. Most books from this era are hard to find in most any grade, so it's not surprising the high grades continue to set records. This age has attracted a whole new group of investors, and even investment groups offering you a stake in a big book, with both competing with longtime, deep pocket collectors. Again, easy to understand the record setting prices, and textbook example of supply and demand in the collecting market. I was lucky enough to pick up a nice collection of lower and mid-grade books this past year, as well as a handful that came into my store, and another small stack bought from a friend/collector at the Fan Expo show in Chicago. Timelys, early DC and Fawcetts, and of course pre-Code Horror lead the way. Some of my Golden Age sales in 2023: *Crime Mysteries* #15 CGC 4.5 $519, *Adventures into Weird Worlds* #9 CGC 3.5 $210, *Battle Report* #6 CGC 6.0 $495, *Batman* #52 CGC 4.0 $1,420, and *Captian Midnight* #65 CGC 6.0 $179.

In Closing: While I do see less demand, especially the 2nd half of this year, I feel optimistic about our hobby and confident things will remain fairly stable moving forward. The biggest drops this year have been in more Modern keys, and to be honest knowing what print runs are, it's kind of amazing they go as high as they do. But in fairness, it's a testament to the popularity of an individual character. When I think of a book like *New Mutants* #98, 1st app. of Deadpool, and someone tells me it's rare...it's impossible to not laugh. There are over 28,000 graded copies, and almost 5,000 are graded CGC 9.8. How a book like this even remotely approaches $3,000 at one time is, regardless of popularity, is almost unbelievable.... and I do this for a living! The fact it's still a $1,400 book in 9.8 now still blows me away, when I know what $1,400 will buy in this hobby. Bottom line, people buy what they want, and demand drives prices. I might not agree with it, and I would never recommend buying the book as an investment, but if someone wants it and is willing to pay market prices for it, then it is what it is. If you buy what you like, then it's not all about investing, so you can enjoy it for what it is. Have a great 2024, and talk to you again in 2025!

ERIC FOURNIER
GUARDIAN COMICS

Well another year is in the books, and it's time for a look back on 2023. I guess we start at the beginning and work forward like all good reports do. We started the year off like most years, weekend shows buying and selling books, but they weren't quite as strong as the last few years. We noticed on both sides of the coin, buyers were looking for deals and sellers were looking for all time highs. It lead to a bit of a tug-o-war. This wasn't the first time we've seen something like this as the housing market did this in 2022 and continued in 2023 and heck even the stock markets were doing similar dances. Despite all of this we had a very good start to the year. We finalized the sale of a *Batman* #1 you know the nice banana 10c cover from 1940, ya that one! A long time customer finally pulled the trigger on it and even though I protested us even selling it we decided this was a home worth letting it go to. We also picked up a few raw collections over the course of the year with some nice highlights in them being an *X-Men* #1, *Hulk* #181, *Amazing Spider-Man* #129. It wasn't until about July that we really noticed a bigger drop in the market. We were still moving slabs and raw books well but after that it seemed like the market was putting on serious brakes. Our shows to follow were not the numbers both in attendance or sales we were used to. Customers were just looking at the dis-

count bins and not so much interested in the bigger books.

We seemed to get calls and emails for more collections, when discussing pricing with these sellers it seemed they'd heard about the great gains of the last few years but hadn't followed close enough to know that those highs were not the same anymore. We unfortunately passed on more collections than we have ever had to as sellers just had too high of expectations and we also were being more cautious than normal given that it seemed week over week books were declining. Now that we are past most of the Covid restrictions and it seems like business is back to normal, there does seem to be lighter crowds at events. I don't believe this to be from Covid but rather from a combination of burn out, funds and decreasing prices. In regards to burn out it seemed like only yesterday each time a Marvel, DC or Indy project was green lit or hitting theatres or appearing on TV, books would explode that had relevance to that. However it seems like fans just don't care anymore. Did they get burnt buying into "white Vision" or another similar book that went from dollar bins to hundreds of dollars and seemingly in a month back to dollar bins? Do they not enjoy the hero films like they once did? Did the writers strike hurt the momentum the studios had? Or likely all of these issues. Funds certainly seem to be discussed more and more each day. Interest rates! Yikes! Inflation at the grocery store! Yikes! These also take away from the hobby as everyone has to decide what to spend their income on which means less spending and less shows.

Decreasing prices always hurt an industry. When everyone is making money everyone is happy, when only a select few are making money people move on. Until the last few years there was never a shortage of the buyer who was digging at a show finding books underpriced to sell online or at a smaller show. However when prices are constantly dropping they don't want to take a risk buying a book and being buried with it, which hurts the full time dealers, which hurts the venue promoters, which hurts the guests and artists it's a giant negative loop. Where does it stop? Well here is time for my prediction corner. As of writing this in mid Dec we've seen the stock market slowly creep up the last few weeks, we've heard rumblings of rate drops coming several times in 2024 both of these likely excite people. Keys are starting to look mighty attractive again as their prices have dropped so much from their all time highs. Once the keys start gaining steam it brings up the rest! I'm thinking late 2024 if you haven't bought that big book you've been waiting for you will have missed the bottom.

We had some smoking sales this year despite all the negativity the market has shown. These include ultra high grade Spidey 2 & 4. Multiple key other spidey books like 3, 5, 9, but non of them top the ASM 129 9.8 we sold in the summer! Talk about a stunner. Already mentioned the *Batman* #1, however we also sold an *Amazing Spider-Man* #1, *X-Men* #1, *Avengers* #1, *Walking Dead* #1. As I've mentioned in other reports I enjoy buying way more than selling - is that a bad thing. We picked up some really fun books including an ultra high grade *Werewolf By Night* #32, *Showcase* #22, *Fantastic Four* #5, *Hulk* #181, *X-Men* #1 and many many more. It always amazes me the stories some collectors have. One of the ones we bought this year he'd been keep the books for 50+ years now. When he was younger he would staple the stories together (so the *Fantastic Four*#48,49,50) all had staple holes in them. When we were going through the books and brought his attention to it, he blushed and said man you guys are good you caught that but yes I stapled them together 50+ years ago and then learned it was a bad thing to do so I removed them! He was bummed to learn of this childhood mistake but he was able to take his wife on a very nice extended vacation after we were done with him. To finish the year off we purchased a decent collection of all raw Silver/Bronze run books. I haven't had much of a chance to dig through the collection but I'm pretty sure we are going to have a really good "boxing day" show to give 2023 a nice send off!

I hope all your favourite stores were able to weather the 2023 storm as we know it's been tough for some and we hope to see everyone excited in 2024!

DAN GALLO
DEALER

As I sit here writing this report, Thanksgiving was just two weeks ago and a lot can happen between now and the time you read this. This time last year I wrote that 2022 was a mixed bag; the first half was strong while the second half saw things turn for the worse. Prices softened and demand waned, most notably for Marvel Silver, Bronze and Copper Age keys. Unfortunately, in 2023, not much has changed.

The focus of my business has always been CGC graded key issues, mainly Marvels. I dabbled in other areas, but in most recent years it was Marvel books that made up 90% of my operation. Given the changing landscape I had to make adjustments. Over the last 18 months I did more DCs, Golden Age and original art, lanes that weren't volatile, to mitigate the risk that Marvel books presented. I still dealt in Marvels but I had to be on the cautious side.

The feeling I get from others in the hobby, (dealers, collectors and investors), is that the market is soft. I would push back on that a bit. Some segments are soft while others are not just strong but are thriving. So, to the doom and gloom crowd…take a breath. Let's break it down:

Golden Age: I was never a Golden Age guy. Sure, I would fall into one every now and then, but I never really focused on them. Now I do, specifically Timelys such as *Caps*, *Marvel Mystery*, *All Winners* and *All-Select*. The war covers are fantastic and I wish I would have discovered them earlier. They are very challenging to buy as they never seem to go cheap. They are widely collected, and the supply is nonexistent. I sleep well at night knowing I have some of them. To say that the market is strong for this would be an understatement. Also worth considering are the Wonder Woman books, (*All Star* #8, *Sensation* #1, and *Wonder Woman* #1), and the early *Detective* Batman covers, (#29, 31, 33, 35 and 38).

Silver Age: Marvels have been a problem. Just about all of the top Marvel Silver Age books started to slide at the back end of 2022 and continued through 2023, (even

though we had some good moments along the way), with super key issues having been hit the hardest. As I mentioned earlier, I still buy Marvels but I really pick my spots and I recommend that you do as well. You have a gut so listen to it and don't worry if you buy something and the next one goes for a little less. Much of the fat has already been cut out so we should be very near the bottom, (at least that is what my gut tells me). I like *Fantastic Four* #5 and early *Amazing Spider-Man* issues in high grade.

Continuing my trend from last year, I am still actively looking for DC keys. Anytime I had a nice clean DC key in higher grade it sold pretty quickly whereas with a similar Marvel book people would take a wait-and-see approach. Unlike Marvels, I never really saw DC prices go down, (which I attribute to DC prices already having bottomed out years ago while everyone was Marvel crazy). I saw an uptick in demand as some buyers turned their attention towards DCs which were already at bargain levels. Also, DC Studios offers a glimmer of hope that their productions will deliver. I like *Detective* #359, *Batman* #181, *Showcase* #8 and *Action* #252.

Bronze Age: Bronze Age Marvel keys have had a rough year with just about all the keys taking a hit. Funny thing is that the demand is still strong for the big ones, *Amazing Spider-Man* #129, *Hulk* #181, *Giant-Size X-Men* #1 and *Marvel Spotlight* #5, but they just sell at lower levels. As for DC, I absolutely love *House of Secrets* #92. *Batman* #232 is another favorite of mine and there may be no book that is more under the radar than *All Star Western* #10 in super high grade.

Original Art: This is a segment that keeps chugging along and I bought even more art in 2023 than I did in 2022, (and that was a record!). I have been ramping up my art activity as one way to combat the Marvel volatility that we've been living with over the last 18 months. And I'm glad that I have, because to be honest, I like dealing in the art just a little bit more than I do the books. If you have never purchased a piece of original comic book art, I strongly recommend that you do. It doesn't have to be an overly expensive piece; just buy something that you think looks cool and hang it on your wall. Do it once and you just might be hooked!

Marvel Cinematic Universe: The brand is completely shot. They went from doing no wrong to having no clue. They have clearly forgotten who their audience is. They have taken us for granted and we are not having any of it.

Auctions: Good books auctioned off on eBay are getting crushed. I understand the convenience that eBay affords those who want a quick cash out, as well as those whose business model is predicated on the eBay auction, but there's nothing that lowers the bar more than what is happening here. As a seller, you're much better off going to a major auction house, and if you're a buyer, you can get some absolute steals here.

Conclusion: You could sum up 2023 like this: original comic art, Timelys, and DC keys have all performed well while Marvel keys have not. If you don't have the stomach for the Marvel volatility, you have other lanes that won't keep you up at night. That being said, there are real opportunities right now to pick up Marvel keys, some up to 50% off their apex, if you can live with some short-term risk. And remember, just because I am hesitant on some books doesn't mean that you should be as well. I have to buy for now while you will be buying for a longer-term.

In speaking with fellow dealers, as well as high-end investors and collectors, I've come across a similar sentiment: There's a lot of money out there that's just waiting to come back in. That time will come. The question is will you get there first?

STEPHEN GENTNER
GOLDEN AGE SPECIALIST

Greetings Comic Collectors!! Again I am honored to share with you my thoughts and experiences this past year as an Advisor to this *Guide*. *The Overstreet Comic Book Price Guide* continues to be a handy resource for wonderful comic content, data, and titles information! This has been an especially busy year for me in comics! After the Covid Bump crashed on the comic market, an amazing thing happened. The number and quality of books coming on to the Market went wild. I haven't seen this level of beautiful books being offered for decades. Is it because people were trying to get out? Was it from older collector's books suddenly appearing? Was it to sell nice books to seek NICER books? Probably all of that!

Starting early in 2023, I filled in my favorite Good Girl *Blue Beetle*s by Jack Kamen. I had sold my first copies except issue #54 in the early 2000s. One after another they appeared in nice shape on My Comic Shop, eBay, and Instagram. Surprisingly at prices that were fair. Of course, Good Girl from the Golden Age is one of my favorite genres. But the explosion of prices of Pre-Code Horror books was,

and is, Homeric!! Big prices for all manner of this segment just took off, and continues even today. It is my feeling that the number of dedicated, moneyed Collectors chasing these Horror gems will eventually hit the ceiling. Supply isn't enormous, and demand certainly has risen and continues to rise. I feel eventually these collectors will not be able to attain the books they want, and will shift to a different genre.

In my mind, I feel that Golden Age Good Girl will be a target for them. In particular, Matt Baker books. Baker is truly the King of Good Girl amongst many wonderful artists, like Jack Kamen, Al Feldstein, Maurice Whitman, Joe Doolin, Bob Lubbers, Wally Wood, Ken Bald, L.B. Cole, Alex Schomburg and others. In March, I was chasing a *Cindy* comic by Ken Bald from an Instagram follower, which he

said NO to. But he then offered me *Diary Secrets* #16 by Matt Baker instead! He made such a good deal for me, so I bought it (and he sold me the *Cindy* three weeks later!) This crystalized Matt Baker books from St. John Publishing as my target! Such amazing art! I then had the same bounty of supply fall into my lap! Again in nice shape and so much more reasonably priced compared to Pre-Code Horror. I probably shot myself in the foot by buying so many examples out of the supply being offered that sellers started raising their prices! Titles like *Teenage Romances*, *Wartime Romances*, *Pictorial Romances*, *Cinderella Love*, *Diary Secrets*, *Teenage Confessions*, and so many other titles!! Matt Baker created a wealth of truly beautiful covers and interior stories!

Writer Dana Dutch had a knack for creating seamy, icky plot lines for Matt to illustrate. Their Pre-Code team up gave each of them the opportunity to really showcase betrayal, heartbreak, infidelity, revenge, and all manner of sexy situations! Dana would conjure up the nasty plots, and Matt would embrace them in his sexy, pulchritudinous art!! Clever panel construction spilled headlights, cabooses, sexual postures, and sexy legs akimbo into our laps each month! St. John's president was Archer St. John, and he and Matt Baker were very good friends. It was a green light for ALL these topics and art after Baker left The Iger House of Art. My Instagram Wall @ collecto6 shows a raft of these St. John beauties, both covers and interiors where possible. Swing by and scroll, won't you?

Just now in November, some Pre-Code Horror books I have been exposed to just fell into my lap. I wasn't looking, somehow they found me...! *The Dead Who Walk* nn, *Dark Mysteries* #10, and *Dark Mysteries* #19. All of these Blue Chips were not TOO expensive. Both those *Dark Mysteries* are true exemplars of the PCH Genre...especially issue #10. The rotting corpse boy torching three witches in red dresses in a forgotten graveyard is chilling. Hy Fleishman's art here is troubling. VERY!! I sent some big raw books in to CGC for the full treatment after owning them for so many years. *Seven Seas* #4 came back a 6.5, *Seven Seas* #6 came back a 7.5, and *Exciting Comics* #39, the candy-bar cover came back a 7.0. I also found a copy of *True To Life Romances* #11 by Star Comics, featuring a classic L.B. Cole romance cover. Cole's PCH covers are very sought after now! His extravagant color palette, almost "black light" vivid in execution, is phenomenal. But his good girl work showcases his wonderful artistic excellence, relying more on superlative art than coloring tricks. Again, swing by the Instagram and say hello! I hope all of you had a great collecting year!!

Tom Gordon III
Monumental Holdings LLC

This past year has been of a corrective nature to the past few years in comics. While comics are down in many cases from their Covid era market highs, many are above the pre-Covid values if we remove the Covid era sales data.

The collectibles markets overall were incredibly on fire the past few years with countless record sales in comic books, original comic art, vintage watches, vintage action figures, movie props, Pokémon cards, and many other categories. As the market has cooled to previous levels, we've witnessed many who jumped in quickly leaving these markets and in some cases at a significant financial loss. While investing in collectibles can be profitable, it's always wise to research anything you invest in.

The Golden Age market is a strong consistent seller with key issues and classic covers leading the way. We've observed collectors switching from Silver Age keys and buying more Golden Age for a variety of reasons. These include scarcity and also the classic historic World War II era covers.

We continue to have requests for Archie and related titles which sell easily for well over *Guide* as collectors are happy to locate those needed issues. Fawcett key issues and classic covers are seeing strong demand as collectors are paying more attention. DC and Timely are easy sellers with the only resistance to prices being some of the lesser DC titles like *Boy Commandos*, *Star Spangled Comics*, and the like. We are also seeing serious interest in the obscure and rare smaller publishers when these types of comics are available.

Pre-Code Horror is still a strong part of the marketplace, with availability unable to keep up with demand. Key issues are always desired in any grade for collectors and we've seen repeated inquiries for *Eerie* #12, the first Dracula with Wally Wood art. High demand issues include *Punch Comics* #12, *Chamber of Chills* #19, *Crime SuspenStories* #22, *Black Cat Mystery* #50, *Tomb of Terror* #15, *Mister Mystery* #6 and #12, and *Haunted Thrills* #6 to highlight a few.

Silver Age comics especially keys continue to have strong demand, but prices have adjusted on many after the strong run-ups of the past few years. I believe over time we will see some of these values gradually rebound on some level. Requests for Marvel keys still continue to far out strip availability. DC Silver Age in many cases are significantly harder to find in high grade condition compared to their Marvel counterparts.

Bronze Age keys are a constant seller with buyers continuing to purchase the big keys including *Amazing Spider-Man* #129, *Giant-Size X-Men* #1, *House of Secrets* #92, *Incredible Hulk* #181, *Werewolf By Night* #32, and numerous others. These books have seen an adjustment in the prices of the past years which should see collectors have a better opportunity to acquire more comics for their cash.

We are still seeing serious interest in international editions of American comics from a wide array of collectors. Canadian Price Variant editions or CPV's are still of interest given their scarcity and difficulty to many collectors. Time will tell how this market plays out, but we continue to have requests for these and modern newsstand editions of comics.

The entertainment industry and news media has seen numerous headlines and articles claiming the fall of the comic book movie and the superhero genre. I believe noted author Mark Twain said it best, "The reports of my death are greatly exaggerated." We have witnessed the film genre stumble and have countless missteps and even sadly Marvel Studios and Disney which has been the gold standard suffer in the recent past. The biggest challenge in my opinion is that they got away from quality stories and longstanding characters and deviated from what made Marvel Studios great and successful. The overall stumble of the entertainment genre has had a ripple effect on the comic market in regards to people speculating on comics and characters motivated by movie appearances or online streaming channel appearances. It wasn't uncommon for individuals to be up at midnight or at the launch of the latest episode and then attempt to acquire multiple copies searching eBay and numerous online comic retailers in the attempt to make a profit through comic book arbitrage. The entertainment industry has also suffered from this past year's strike which lasted 148 days, is one of the longest in the industries history and had a profound effect on the lives of those who work in the industry. Marvel and DC both will only be releasing one movie each in 2024 with *Deadpool 3* and *Joker: Folie à Deux*. We can only hope that the studios are regrouping to get back to what has made this entertainment genre a success.

With 2024 beginning, we will see if the comic book market that has weathered the economic storm of the Covid era market explosion. The market overall will continue to regain a better position of overall health and stability in the New Year and beyond.

Eric J. Groves
The Comic Art Foundation

Golden Age books persist as the anchor of the hobby. There are good reasons for this phenomenon. First, the artistic beauty of many comics produced between 1940-1945 is astonishing. The use of primary colors, combined with superlative artwork and a new breed of hero, resulted in eye appeal unrivaled to this day. Visualize the DC and Timely covers of that time, especially those by Simon and Kirby. Second, the very feel, the heft, of these books likewise stimulated the senses in a way only a lover of comics can grasp.(You can't experience this sensation today with a slabbed book.) Third, the Golden Age comic set the model for thousands of books to come, among other things, by developing the concept of the heroic alter ego. Bruce Wayne by day, Batman at night. Finally, there will always be another example of any Silver Age book, usually in any condition desired, but this cannot be said for Golden Age comics. Time and the paper drives of

WWII have seen to that.

Values attributable to Golden Age comics have steadily increased over the decades. This is not investment advice, but it does lend confidence when buying Golden Age books. Golden Age comics are genuine American artifacts, truly emblematic of the time and place they were published.

As things stand now, we perceive that collectors are purchasing Golden Age comics largely because the supply is diminishing as never before. The number of surviving copies is finite. We also observe that titles and imprints overlooked in past years now enjoy renewed attention, with good reason. Early Quality comics like *Military*, *Police*, *Plastic Man* and *Uncle Sam* not only look great, but they read well. The same may be said of Fiction House titles, particularly *Wings*, with its covers combining aviation and good girl art. The hunt is still on for MLJ, Centaur, Nedor and similar publishers. Even Fawcett titles, traditionally somewhat slow, are moving out, and why not? *Captain Marvel Adventures*, *Captain Marvel Jr.*, *Marvel Family* and *Whiz* are pure fun and always have been. Mr. Tawny, the talking tiger? Those titles sold extraordinarily well in their day. There are still a sufficient number of copies around, albeit not so much with lower numbers of *Whiz*.

As to the Atom Age, we have long characterized this as a period of experimentation. The proliferation of genres and new titles established that comics could be about much more than superheroes. Now, more than ever before, collectors are picking up a wide variety of Atom Age titles, especially pre-Code Horror. Atlas comics sell best.

We are inclined to think the Silver Age market will take care of itself. There will always be market corrections. We are confident that the inherent value of early Silver Age titles, particularly Marvels, will do well over the long haul.

Finally we sometimes ask, "How did all this get started?" Herewith, our suggested answer. Little boys always saved comic books. Remember the emblem on the cover of the 1940s *Supersnipe* comic proclaiming the McFadden kid as "the boy with the most comic books in America"? Back in the day, the original objective was to complete runs of particular titles. We were not greatly concerned with "keys" or superior condition. We could scarcely have anticipated slabbing comics much less selling them internationally for astronomical prices. In 1952, or thereabouts, I came upon a copy of *Boy Comics* #61, with a spectacular cover featuring Iron Jaw, one of the most vicious Golden Age Nazi villains. I wanted to know more about him and what went before, so I set out to put together a complete run of *Boy Comics*, which eventually I did. Yes, little boys collect comic books. Nowadays, it is the big boys who slab comic books and trade in them for prices in the millions. I often wonder if we are any better off for all this.

TERRY HOKNES
WWW.TERRYHOKNES.COM

After the peaks of Covid, much of the modern comic market has crashed back down. Way fewer buyers in general this year resulting in lower prices on most modern key books. Some drastic examples of key books that fell drastically include *Ultimate Fallout* #4 CGC 9.6 2nd printing (2011) copies fell from sales of $450 in 2021 to $95.00 in late 2023. Of course there are always the latest hot books that have their big moment and many movie/tv tie-in books will still have quick jumps. The safest market this past year was Golden and Platinum Age books - the long term collectors are reliable and continue to build their collections and appreciate the rarity of these early books. Whether it was early superhero books, popular crime & horror covers, or scarce Platinum Age books, these popular fields of collecting saw their prices held or increasing.

There is a dedicated group of comic book collectors who help the collecting community every single day with insightful articles about comics called CBSI. I joined the team a few years ago and help promote comic book collecting. Thousands of articles are posted every year at www.comicbookinvest.com. You can also join discussions with 17,000 collectors on the CBSI Facebook group. I also publish my own series of books on comic book history and investing at www.TerryHoknes.com. I have also published 10,000 articles on comic books at my website. You can also find me at Facebook at Terry Hoknes Comics.

Congrats to *Overstreet* for another great year of documenting comic history and collecting info and happy 85th birthday to Batman and Marvel Comics !

GREG HOLLAND
SLABDATA.COM

The CGC Census increased from 8,771,445 in December 2022 to 10,167,418 in December 2023. This 15.9% increase in a single year is significantly lower than last year, when a 27.5% increase was seen between December 2021 and December 2022. *Amazing Spider-Man* #300 is still the most-submitted comic book, now at 35,600 graded copies. *Spawn* #1 moved up to 2nd place this year, with *Amazing Spider-Man* #361 in 3rd place. *Marvel Super Heroes Secret Wars* #8 is now 4th place, and *New Mutants* #98 is now 5th.

The most submitted comic from DC Comics is *Batman: The Killing Joke* in 28th place overall. *Batman: The Killing Joke* was in 27th place last year and 21st place the year before. None of the Top 100 books submitted to CGC most often are from a publisher other than Marvel, DC, or Image. CGC has now graded almost 320,000 different titles and issues, but the Top 100 most-submitted books to CGC represent almost 11% of all CGC graded comics. One in every nine CGC slabs comes from a short list of just 100 comics (see cgcdata.com for the full list). Approximately one in every three CGC slabs (34%) contains a comic book dated 2010 to present, demonstrating a continued demand for immediate CGC grading upon publication. Only a few comic books are in both the Top 100 submitted and printed since 2010 with *Ultimate Fallout* #4, *Amazing Spider-Man* #4 (2014), *Darth Vader* #3, *Edge of*

Spider-Verse #2, *Venom* #3, and *Batman* #1 (2011) as the most prominent.

CGC Census Counts by Comic Decade (as of mid-December 2023):

1930s = 11,554 (0.11%) –
1940s = 215,865 (2.12%) –
1950s = 243,189 (2.4%) –
1960s = 1,181,047 (11.6%) –
1970s = 1,323,578 (13.0%) –
1980s = 1,578,934 (15.5%) –
1990s = 1,323,282 (13.0%) –
2000s = 830,666 (8.2%) –
2010s = 1,954,866 (19.2%) –
2020s = 1,495,317 (14.7%) –
Others = 9,120 (0.09%) – ("Others" includes undated books)
Total = 10,167,418.

CGC "Worthiness": There are now more CGC graded comic books printed between 2020 and 2023 than all of CGC graded comics from any decade apart from the 1980s and the 2010s. Is it accurate to say that more comics printed in the last four years are "CGC Worthy" than any of the decades prior to the 1980s? I doubt many would agree with this statement. The question of CGC "Worthiness" is more complex than the counts on the CGC Census. The fees associated with CGC grading are lower for recent comics versus comics from pre-1975. Secondly, there are already 350,000 signature series comics for four years from 2020 to 2023, but less than 200,000 signature series for any decade prior to the 2010s. A third factor is the "newness" factor. Initial demand coincides with CGC grading for comic books printed today, while CGC did not exist at the time of publication for most decades of comic books. Another factor is the high grades of recently printed comics, which are often purchased for protected collections, compared to comics which have had 25 to 90 years pass since publication. There are many other factors which influence whether a comic is sent to CGC for grading, but the bottom line is that there are now more CGC slabbed comics from 2020 to 2023 than nearly any complete decade prior. The only decades with more CGC graded comics are the 1980s and the 2010s.

Accidental Demand: One aspect of the market that continually pops up in my research and analysis is the concept of "accidental demand". When we look at the origins of the comic book market, it really is "accidental demand" from the start. *Action Comics* #1 and *Detective Comics* #27 were successful, but disposable products, and the demand for copies of those issues years later could not be matched by remaining supplies.

While comic books were always intended to entertain, it was a complete accident that an entire industry and market for out-of-print comic books would be created. By the time of the Silver Age, the basic concept of comic book collecting was known, but the tales of carefully cultivated Silver Age collections being thrown away by parents or teenagers deciding they were unsuitable for "grown-ups" still populate message boards today.

The first few decades of the comic book market are almost entirely the result of the "accidental demand" many years later for products which were only intended to survive a few months. It's important to note that this "accidental demand" was always in opposition to the prevailing view of the day that there was no reason to hold onto those particular comic books. By the time the market was established in spite of the majority view, it was too late to save those comics which had been discarded decades earlier.

There have been particular instances of "accidental demand" in every decade since the Silver Age. One example is the 30-cent and 35-cent cover price test markets from Marvel in 1976 and 1977. Comic book prices were increased by five cents in select geographies to determine how the sales would be impacted by the price increase. Marvel did not intend to create a limited cover price variant for the back issue market. It was accidental demand which created the price variant market, many years after the original intention of the publisher, and despite many retailers and collectors who would have insisted for decades that there should be no market difference for otherwise identical books.

Canadian Price Variants and U.K. pence editions of comic books are other examples of "accidental demand" decades later. It would not take a majority of collectors to desire pence or Canadian variants for the market to shift from discounts to premiums. The supply of those issues is low enough that the interest of only a few collectors could shift the market from disdain to greater demand. Many collectors still believe that U.K. pence editions are reprints, however, it is now understood that they were printed at the same time as the U.S. editions of those comics. Decades of discounts or disparaging of U.K. pence editions would end quickly if only a small amount of collectors began to seek U.K. pence editions. Information about survival rates for these comics is still being discovered, but it will eventually become common knowledge as 30 cent and 35 cent price variants are now much better understood.

It is fascinating how much "accidental demand" has changed and shaped the comic book industry. We know the same is true in other popular collectible markets, whether it was old coins being melted down, baseball cards in bicycle spokes, or action figures ripped from their packaging. "Accidental demand" seems like the best description looking back, and in each case, the majority of people (even the experts) would have argued against collecting, protecting, and securing those items for the future. As always, collect what you enjoy, and if some (experts) insist that your favorite collectible isn't anything special, see if they'll sell you all of theirs at a discount. Odds are, those frequent discouragers don't even have any of what you want, but they may have several variant comics from the past four years in CGC slabs as an alternative. Time will tell which collectibles would have been better choices.

STEVEN HOUSTON & JOHN DOLMAYAN TORPEDO COMICS
STEVEN HOUSTON

Welcome to the Torpedo Comics annual market report, covering sales information and a description of current market conditions from August 2022 to December 2023.

Torpedo Comics news: In a rather bold move, John forged ahead with opening a further two stores in California, one in Topanga and the other in Glendale. Thus giving the company four stores total in California (including Irvine and Orange Country) as well as our signature store in Las Vegas, for a grand total of five. John also decided upon a new warehouse location, while also liquidating a large amount of dead bulk product. A busy few months indeed. To facilitate all this logistical work, we had to cut down on our convention appearances, setting up at WonderCon, the Shortboxed show, TorpedoCon and of course ComicCon: San Diego in 2023. All four shows were more successful than in recent years, not because of sales, but rather our attention to efficiency in regards to what product we brought, how many booths we purchased and how many staff were utilized. On a personal note, both the Shortboxed event and our own TorpedoCon were highly successful. In case you are unaware, TorpedoCon is a throwback show, mainly comics only, low costs and a true comic fans dream, an idea John had many years ago, a convention model Terry O'Neill has used successfully for years.

The Current Market (new issues): With Torpedo opening up more and more new stores, it has become imperative that the two major comic companies (Marvel & DC) publish enough high selling product to keep 'new issue day' as something special. Unfortunately, both companies are under attack, one assault being from outside forces, such as a dreadful economy, the other being internal, as it seems that editorial and management from both companies seem determined to commit financial suicide. The comic book industry is at the mercy of the wider economy, not just the US economy, but the world economy which has been in a major slump since the end of the lockdowns and the pandemic. As for new issue sales, the decline we have seen for the last couple of years continues at a pace, seemingly ignored by the 'powers that be'. Confusion seems to reign unrestrained at this time as questions are being asked by many as to why Manga sales have been going through the roof, while American super-hero comics are being left on the shelf as print runs drop and drop.

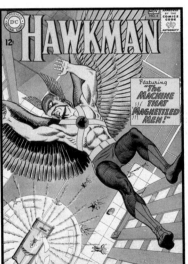

Actual sales figures for comics are almost impossible to come by these days, as publishers are holding onto that information for dear life, while the sales from book stores is very transparent and show a steep decline in sales from both Marvel and DC. In this writer's opinion, the current trend of creative and editorial staff to try to appeal to a smaller section of the populace has begun to erode sales, with people currently working at both companies who actually don't like many of the characters that populate their individual universes. They seem to feel the need to change the characters for the perceived better. The results have been startling as the product being produced has alienated long-time readers leading to former fanatical fans dropping books. Insulated from outside financial forces, creators and editors can try to drive the comics they think readers HAVE to read to market, leading to constant reboots and a multitude of variant editions as each new volume number #1 is released. One would need reams of pages to fully explain the reasons for new issue sales declines, but for now, all one has to know is, if a creator has disdain for what they are working on, its chances of being liked or loved by long-time readers is zero.

Regarding important sales from this era, the drop off in terms of sales and return on speculator investments has been devastating. Being honest here for a moment, the ONLY thing keeping the modern industry alive right now is sales of the hundreds of thousands of variant editions being published each year. A massive secondary market has opened up these past few years where anyone who has the time and the money can purchase variant after variant, send them into be graded and then if the book hits the magic 9.8 grade, flip them on eBay. Thus, publishers, especially Marvel and DC can keep coming out with rebooted titles, unleash a hundred variant copies, with various ratios, be it, 1/10, 1/100, 1/1000 or even 1/5000 and the books will sell. Thousands of 'new collectors' flowed into the hobby during the pandemic, purchasing variants by the boatload and flipping them for enormous profits. That gravy train is well and truly dead as I write this report, with hundreds of thousands of CGC variant copies languishing in storage locations or in the back rooms of the few comic stores still around. Many of the super hot variants from this era have lost two thirds of their value, creating a huge sucking sound, as an army of speculators leave the hobby to lick their wounds. If this continues, comic stores may be in real danger if they rely on new issues sales at all. As soon as people stop picking up multiples of the variants, the publishers will cancel titles, while at the same time, hundreds of comic shops will be closed and the stock blown out to the few dealers who still have money.

Vintage Sales: The various eras of collecting have not been immune to the ravages of the economy. I have seen the collecting of regular non key 'filler' issues slow to a crawl, especially DC titles which have become almost unsellable, unless discounted to obscene levels. Be it Silver of Bronze, DC only has a handful of books that are seemingly in demand. *House of Secrets* #92 (Swamp Thing), *Hawkman* #4 (Zatanna), *Detective* #459 (Batgirl), *Batman* #227 (Neal

Adams cover), *Batman* #232 (Ra's al Ghul), *Batman* #234 (Two-Face), *Batman* #251 (Joker cover). Other keys are stuck, even books like *Brave and the Bold* #28 (JLA) or *Showcase* #22 (Green Lantern) are slowing, unless discounted! Even pre-hero and pre-Code Horror books have slowed for us, books that were breaking all sorts of sales records in 2021. The rest of DC's Silver and Bronze catalog is a wasteland of despair. *Justice League of America*, *Teen Titans*, *Flash* and *Green Lantern*, except *Green Lantern* #76 , 85 and 87, are all proverbial fossils belonging to long extinct universes.

As for Marvel, even the mighty Marvel zombies have pulled in their purse strings, focusing on certain books, the usual suspects being *Incredible Hulk* #181, *Giant-Size X-Men* #1, *Star Wars* #1 (35-cent variant) even books such as *Fantastic Four* #1 and *Incredible Hulk* #1 have stalled in price. The big keys will always hold their value more, obviously the collectors able to afford such high end rare comics are unfazed by inflation and high gas costs. However, I do know of many dealers who are holding their big keys back, in the hopes of those unbelievable prices seen in 2021 returning. They will of course, but not for a few years. As for common filler issues, *Amazing Spider-Man* is still the Marvel king, followed by the *X-Men*, while titles such as *Thor*, *Avengers*, *Iron Man* and *Captain America* have slowed, unless in super-high grade or discounted at horrendous levels. Even once 'too hot to touch' books like *Marvel Spotlight* #5 (Ghost Rider) and *Werewolf by Night* #32 (Moon Knight) seem to have leveled off. *Tomb of Dracula* #10 (Blade) still has some heat, as the movie is still a ways away and speculators are hoping for big things.

In conclusion: There is still money in our hobby, it's just all chasing the same books. Everything else is just dead wood right now. The big dealers are playing a waiting game holding their big books back, while believe it or not, collectors are not selling their collections right now, scared away by the current market conditions that force potential purchasers to offer extremely low offers, compared with 2021. The Golden Era of superhero movies seems to be over, as the latest Marvel super-hero offering *The Marvels* has bombed at the box office and some are beginning to repeat the same line "super-hero fatigue". Can it be true, can the Golden Era of modern super-hero movies which began in 2005, finally be over? Or will the film companies learn from their mistakes and prove us all wrong and reignite the world of super-heroes on the big screen? One thing is clear at this time, the current financial woes of the US are not going away soon, it may be half way through 2026, when the economy turns around. Even the unstoppable CGC may suffer a downturn if these market conditions remain or get worse. I'm reminded of a scene from a movie from 1977, *The White Buffalo*, starring Charles Bronson in the context of all those CGC's languishing unsold in peoples homes, store back rooms and storage locations. In the movie, Charles Bronson arrives in a frontier town by train to be shocked by piles of buffalo bones or "spikes" piled up hundreds of feet beside the train tracks. Millions upon millions of buffalo reduced to nothing but bones, a scene that affected me greatly as a child. Now transpose those buffalo bones for CGCs, mostly modern books, many not worth the plastic used to encapsulate them, piled hundreds of feet high, signifying golden times past, and now a reminder of speculation gone wild.

ROBERT ISAAC
RED HOOD COMICS

If there will be a buyer's market during a time when comic books are as actively bought, sold and collected as they have been the last 15 years, then that time is now. The 2023 year continued to see market correction from the inflation of COVID, and the awful films and streaming shows spewing from studios like Disney aren't helping to slow the crash. While Golden Age books maintain immunity to the deflation of COVID prices, comics and key issues from other eras aren't as strong.

The Golden Immunity: With all the crashing of prices in 2023, the one era of books that still holds strong is the Golden Age. Heroes, Horror, Sci-fi and Romance from this era seem to be untouched by the radical waves caused by many factors that affect the Silver, Bronze and Modern eras and it's for a number of reasons:

• The Scarcity. Let's pull this into the light. The thrill of collecting is the hunt and the ecstasy of collecting is the find. The "uncommon" factor always rewards in value and in intimacy with collectors. When attending conventions, you'll find *Secret Wars* #8 at every booth at the show including the dweebs selling plastic lightsabers. But at how many booths will you find *Cap* Timely's or ANY of the 73 issues of *Planet Comics* available? These days, maybe at one or two, unless at a comic-only show when everyone has left the fluff behind to bring out the real books.

• The Covers. We are gravitationally pulled to the classic art and appeal as if history is a force, or the ghostly hand made of scent that develops in cartoons when a freshly-baked pie is placed on a window sill. You are hypnotized by them. A Golden Age cover is far more recognizable than a virgin sketch cover second printing facsimile edition newsstand variant.

• The Movies. At this point, just be grateful for the decade of Marvel movies we were treated to from 2008-2018, and leave it at that. They did their job. Theatrical movies and shows from streaming services that once served as catalysts for the comic book collector market have now become anchors, focusing more on sending messages to serve the woke world and fulfill agendas rather than focus on the storytelling and character development that the Avengers Infinity Saga did so well. But when you associate comic books with Hollywood productions, it only affects books from Silver to Modern.

With the crashing prices of Marvel and DC Silver and Bronze Age keys, Golden Age collecting and dealing feels more intimate than with the other eras that we see an abundance of just from being in the hobby, and the love is absolutely much more real.

The Numbers: Let's get a couple of disappointments out of the way first. *Headline Comics* #8 in 9.0 sold for $48,000, a book I felt would command a stronger value, even at auction. It was upgraded from a 7.5 through CGC, and while I made money, I would have loved to have kept it at that price if I could only see the future. Another disappointment was the 8.0 *Detective Comics* #168 Crippen Pedigree copy, the highest pedigree copy of this book known, selling for $38,400 only for a 7.5 at the end of the year sell for almost the same. I sold a *Prize Comics* #13 CGC 9.8 from the Edgar Church (Mile High) collection through Heritage Auctions for nearly $20,000 above its highest-recorded sale of a 9.6 copy. I sold a *Prize Comics* #7, featuring the origin and first appearance of Frankenstein and the first appearance of the Green Llama, a book with only 12 copies on the CGC Census, for $20,000, which possibly could have even done more at auction. I sold a *Venus* #19 CGC 8.5, one of the few higher grades out there, for $76,000 through ComicConnect, which was $24,000 more than what it sold for in 2021, during COVID. *Teenage Mutant Ninja Turtles* #1 in 9.8 has taken quite the dive. First off, it's always been a book I believed to be worth far more than it was (in 9.8 grade) than what it would sell for over the years. Then it passed the $100,000 mark. Then it passed the $200,000 mark. And now it's calmed to the lower $100,000s, which is what mine sold for at a little over $130,000. But my most successful win of the year in sales, has to be the sale of what became the third *Daredevil* #1 9.8. Unfortunately I can't kiss and tell on this one, but it strongly helped acquire what you'll read about in the next paragraph.

The Acquisition of The Grail: My prize acquisition this year, and for all years I should say, is finally achieving MY grail of grails, the cover art (and part splash) to *Detective Comics* #168, through the help of Vincent Zurzolo of ComicConnect. I've branded my business around this book, and after a four-year pursuit, last year it became a reality and I was able to pay it off last September, to unveil it a month later at New York Comic Con and close a five-year chapter in my book. The text scroll on the art was moved to the splash upon publishing along with a similar image and layout as the cover, and the cape was reversed. But the notes attached to the top of the art are so amazing to read, as what has developed so many years later with the massive popularity of one of comics' greatest villains (if not THE greatest), along with the Red Hood identity and as often as it's referenced, that him being referred to as "Large Hooded Figure" really mystifies an uncertainty and disconnect from the surprise future that they couldn't have predicted at the time.

It's been quite a rollercoaster for comics the past few years, but the growing interest in original art from the hobby and community alike and amongst the new collectors, well I would expect that market to flourish more in 2024, even if the value in books does not.

DR. STEVEN KAHN
INNER CHILD COMICS AND COLLECTIBLES

THE UGLY: The malaise that began infecting virtually all areas of collectibles in 2022 continued to express itself throughout 2023 and as the year wound down, it appeared to have not yet reached its nadir. Collectors who desperately sought relief and hope for a future found little or none.

It was a year in which it was difficult to find any reliable resource to accurately predict the future. The click baiters who created large online followings by blasting comics as a no-brain source of guaranteed future wealth were suddenly found to be eating their words. In order to maintain a hold on their followers, they conveniently flipped and become nattering nabobs of negativity.

The perfect storm that occurred during Covid had long passed. Even though 70 percent of the population continued to earn during this period almost everyone was socially locked in their homes with nowhere to spend their paychecks. Compounding that was the influx of free money from the government (to both individuals and clever businesses). People had time on their hands and interest in nostalgia and collectibles exploded.

But that ultimately came at a cost and the repercussions have continued to reverberate to this day. In addition, people who filled the market with new cash and drove it to heretofore unimaginable and unsustainable prices had just as quickly disappeared and unlikely to ever re-enter the marketplace. The sell off has continued and we have yet to see an end. All of it brought back the memories of the '90s collecting collapse and then some.

When I submitted my report last year, I said that the lows

were still comfortably above pre-Covid levels, but as we have rebooted our data a different picture has emerged.

With very few exceptions, the market has crashed and the current numbers you see do not reflect true values. Inflation has devalued the purchasing power of our dollars. Anyone who has gone shopping has seen how inflation has affected virtually everything. The incessant printing of money by our government has meant that today's dollar will give you about 75 to 80 cents of purchasing power when compared to the days before Covid. Purchasing power lost through inflation is permanent and will never be recaptured and these changes need to be factored when you assess the value of your collectibles. Today, $1,000 has become $750-800.

THE BAD: It was extremely difficult to find comics that were bulletproof and holding value. Even the bluest of the blue chips suffered the pain. *Amazing Fantasy* #15 in grades at 4.0 and below was down between 35% to 60% from the 2021 highs.

Superman #1 offered a teachable moment. This book had historically high demand and extremely short supply. At the Covid peak, a 3.0 copy sold for $780,000. Six months ago, a 3.0 copy sold for just $360,000 and as I am writing this report, the exact same copy just sold again for $300,000. That translated to over a 60 percent drop in a couple of years. More than that, a 7.0 copy which was the third highest graded book in the entire census went from $2.6 million to $1.4 million, a 40-plus percent drop.

Many Silver and Bronze Age keys performed far worse. The insane prices realized for even obscure Marvel characters associated in the rapidly collapsing Marvel movie franchises dropped in some cases over 90 percent and will likely never recover. DC keys suffered less because they had never reached the lofty peaks of the Marvels. More significantly, when you factor in the inflation effect as I described, true values nearly across the board have dipped below pre-Covid levels.

Over the last several years I predicted that public would finally tire of the unending repetition in the superhero movies and it seems that we have now passed that point. In addition, changes in Disney management brought in all the issues associated with the so-called Social Justice Warriors, 'Inclusionists', Cancel Culture, Wokeness, and the like dictating how movies should be made. It seems that the public has finally said that it has had enough and even if changes are made, it is is likely to be too little, too late.

If you are a seller, I want to reinforce the importance of finding transparency when choosing where to sell your books. If selling through an auction house, you need to be able to easily check and track how that auction house has been performing with like graded books. Do not focus or rely on record breaking sales alone. Try to see as many previous auctions as you can within a reasonable time frame and see if patterns emerge. If selling an *Amazing Fantasy* #15, I would want to see confirmed sales for the last few years of that book.

If the auction house typically includes multiple copies of the your book with many grades close to yours in the same auction, I would proceed with extra caution. Finally, as with stock market advice and as noted in the *Superman* example

above, remember that 'past performance is neither an indicator or guarantee of future results'.

...AND THE GOOD!: So, what's good??? If we have or are close to bottoming out, this could be a great buying opportunity. Newly burned investors are selling in large numbers. Many dealers with brick and mortar stores need cash in order to stay in business and must sell. And prices haven't been this low in years. Many areas of comic collecting have little or no interest and if the dealers ever bring them out, you can fill your runs again. Magazine size books are extremely cheap. And the list goes on.

The one shining light that I saw consistently in comic sales in 2023 was a mix of rare and desirable '40s and '50s books. These included Golden and Atomic Age books with "interesting covers." If a woman was in bondage, if acid was being poured over a melting face or if Nazis were involved, you probably had a winner. EC Horror covers were doing well and the more gruesome the better. Matt Baker Romance covers were strong as well. Rarity and eye appeal were the driving forces at work here. Books like *Captain America Comics* #3 had an insatiable demand and I still dream of finding some of those great books to add to my collection.

This last year and a half has been a real test. I still love collecting as much as ever. Even as I am growing older with each passing year, I still don't see an end to feeding this passion. Collecting what you love may ultimately be the saving grace for the true collector.

I am currently processing a hundred boxes filled with graphic novels and more recent books (those heavy, heavy boxes) that I hope one day will find a home. Since I've never had any employees, I still do all the heavy lifting myself and moving 65 pound boxes while precariously perched on a ladder is not as easy as it used to be. Nevertheless, I am still hungry and long to see a few more collections before I'm done.

As always, please do not hesitate to give me a call if you have any questions or need advice about your collection. My phone and text number is (847-971-1223) and my email is Stevenkahn47@gmail.com. If you know of anyone selling any cool stuff relating to Pop Culture, let me know as well. My store has survived riots, burglaries, and many floods over the last decade and a half and I hope to be doing this for a bit more time.

Finally, in spite of all the bumps in the road, all that needs to show up at the store is one short box of books or a tub of toys that I've never seen before and the years peel away. I am as excited as I was in 1956 after spending my weekly 25 cent allowance for 5 packs of baseball cards and sitting on the stoop outside the drugstore as soon as I left the store.

With the sun beating down on my head, I open each pack slowly, carefully, never revealing the next card and filling my mouth with a piece of tooth rotting pink bubble gum with each new pack. Looking for Mickey Mantle, but instead finding 5 Sandy Koufax cards resting inside my last pack. As I begin to walk home, the clouds slide over the sun and a gentle breeze cools my neck. The huge wad of gum has begun to lose its sweetness, which is now filling my insides and as I am in this reverie, my Inner Child begins to smile.........Not a bad day. Not a bad day at all!

NICK KATRADIS
COLLECTOR

As I sit behind my computer this final week of December 2023, I am starting my market report with the record sale of Frank Frazetta's *Dark Kingdom* oil painting, which sold in June 2023 for $6 million, eclipsing Frazetta's *Egyptian Queen* sale in 2019 of $5.4 million. Outside of this mind-numbing sale though, the most notable observation was that there were very few other parabolic sales of comic art in 2023. Maybe the market has finally cooled off? or maybe it's just taking a breather? We will see.

The next closest notable sale of comic art in 2023 was a *Dark Knight Returns* #3 double page spread, which sold for $550k in October 2023. And the next highest sale after that was the *X-Men* #98 cover by Dave Cockrum, which sold for $432k in January 2023. Also, in November 2023, a page from *Tales of Suspense* #39, 1st appearance of Iron Man issue, sold for $336k. And finally, the Golden Age cover to *Detective Comics* #58, from 1941, sold for $270k.

These results may suggest that we may have hit a top in 2022. Judging by the lackluster top comic art sales of 2023, it's quite possible.

In the world of comics, a *Detective Comics* #27 in CGC 6.0 sold for $1.74 million in March 2023. And the same month, a *Batman* #1 in CGC 8.0 sold for $1.11 million. A *Captain America* #1 in CGC 9.2 sold for $810k in June 2023, and an *Amazing Fantasy* #15 in 9.2 sold for $810,000 in the beginning of the year. A *Batman* #1 in CGC 7.0 sold in March 2023 for $660k. And a *Superman* #1 Pedigree in CGC 5.0 sold for $675k in January 2023. Another *Batman* #1 in CGC 6.0 sold in January 2023 for $552k.

The jury is still out on the health of the comic market, judging from the above results, and only time will tell if prices stay in this current plateau range or if they may actually pull back in 2024. The current state of the comic and comic art market currently seems to be in a static state with most collectors unsure if sales will stagnate and fall or if they will rebound. Many collectors I spoke to feel that it would only take a few high-end weak sales in 2024 to possibly spur a rush for the exits.

I believe that demographics are starting to have an impact. As more collectors enter their golden years, especially those in their 70s and some in their 80s, I'm sure most are starting to think about succession, basically if/when they should consider selling some or all of their collections and not placing the burden of the task on their families. After all, they can probably better "dispose" of their collectables in their lifetimes, than their family can. Since the wives and children of most collectors do not share their passion for comics and comic art, it's more prudent to lighten up or downsize their collections in their lifetimes.

I'm sure some collectors will do nothing and just leave instructions to their family to put up their lifelong accumulations in auction, if they pass away. But most other collectors, many holding seven figure collections, will begin to consider selling some or all of their collections at some point. It seems that 2024 will be a pivotal year, as many old timers will reassess their collections and determine what they want to sell.

The past few years, we have seen a large quantity of art coming to market and more recently, the trend has been more obvious across all price ranges. It would not be difficult or far-fetched to believe that a perfect storm can occur, and selling can accelerate past the point where the market can absorb a glut of comics and art, if it becomes available.

In speaking with some fellow older collectors the past year at conventions I have attended, I'm hearing more and more often "I can't buy much anymore, so I'm happy with what I have." And many others have bluntly told me, "I'm selling everything over the next few years." So the question is are there more new collectors entering the hobby as more older players are exiting. And if they are, will they fill the gap at the high end sandbox or deep end of the hobby pool? Even if a new collector has deep pockets, usually they enter slowly into the hobby before they venture into the 5 and 6 figure price range of collecting.

I have also spoken to many younger collectors this year, to get an idea what their collecting strategy is. Most of the new "players" in comic art have indicated that everything they buy is with a keen eye toward exiting if values sour. And most consider every purchase as a smart decision when questioned if they worry about overpaying. And most of them forecast that prices of their collections will continue to rise into perpetuity. This is quite shocking and actually scary.

In conclusion, the consensus by many younger collectors of comic art is that they can approach the hobby as an opportunity to make money over time. Not necessarily because they love comics. And I venture to say that most of them consider their collections as retirement vehicles. That is not a healthy harbinger for the hobby. All are perpetual bulls, and there are no bears in sight. Another bad sign. I have not met a single young collector that entered the hobby since 2016, that is worried about ever losing value on any of their purchases. Basically, this is a "can't lose" mentality. Is that a sound logic? Only time will tell.

I have been a collector of comics and comic art for over 51 years of my life. I continue to be very bullish about vintage art and comics, as long as they are in the hands of passionate collectors. But what I am witnessing more and more is that the younger collector base is different in that they are passionate, but in a different way. Their passion is about "what they paid" and "what it's worth". Most younger collectors don't buy runs of comics like the older collectors did; instead, they only buy the KEYS, evidence that they are not collectors, rather speculators. This has created a younger collector base that is not defined by strong hands. Their passion is more and more based on value, so when the market does pull back, many will run for the exits. Which is the recipe for a bloodbath in the making. And if a stampede happens, as in any other asset class, it won't be pretty. But what do I know.

IVAN KOCMAREK
COLLECTOR

This past year the comic world received a stark fiscal haircut, perhaps in preparation for the coming year and a new phase in its continuing evolution. The few of us who have been around since before the first issue of the *Overstreet Guide* don't see this as a calamity but just another stage in the long run of the growth of this "hobby" (I choose this word intentionally.). Those speculators moving around in the shallow shoals and rock pools of 9.8 modern slabs are finding that the waters are drying up and they cannot even recover their slabbing costs anymore. I wonder if repercussions from this will even impact the recent expansion of CGC. We have to wait and see how the hobby evolves from this point.

My little corner of this hobby is Canadian Golden Age comics, that is the old war time (WECA comics from 1941-46) and the reprints or FECA comics that came after (roughly 1947-55). These books, in my estimation, are still, perhaps due to their comparative rarity and scarcity of coming onto the market, much sought after by collectors who are willing to pay healthy money for them and money that generally continues to grow each year.

Here are the strongest results I've been able to put together from this past year:

WECA Comics (1941-46)

Title	Grade	Sold by	Sale Price
Better Comics Vol. 1 #2	7.0	Heritage	$15,600
Atomic Comics #1	9.0	Heritage	$2,880
Commando Comics #12	VG+	Heritage	$2,640
Triumph-Adventure #1	NG	eBay (Blissard)	$2,025
Triumph-Adventure #6	3.0R	eBay (icecollectibles)	$1,806
Speed Savage nn	Fair	Heritage	$1,680
Triumph Comics #22	VG-FN	Heritage	$1,320
Triumph Comics #21	GD-VG	Heritage	$1,320
Dime Comics #9	4.0	Heritage	$1,320
Your New World #1	VG	Heritage	$1,320
Canadian Heroes #1	FN+	Heritage	$1,000
Commando Comics #13	FN+	eBay	$1,000

Remember that finding these war time Canadian comics in proper FN (6.0) and up is uncommon, so I would expect the value of WECA comics in grade to only keep going up. The other thing to notice is that the most lucrative place to sell WECA comics seems to be Heritage with 75% of the top dozen results coming from there.

FECA Comics (Canadian Reprint Comics 1947-55)

Title	Grade	Sold by	Sale Price
Strange Mysteries #13	7.5	Heritage	$9,600
Weird Suspense Stories #1	4.5	eBay (icecollectibles)	$6,433
Tales of Horror #2	8.5	Heritage	$4,800
Marvel Tales #96	8.0	Heritage	$4,560
Superboy #1	5.0	eBay	$4,000
Reform School Girl nn	2.0	Heritage	$3,626
Marvel Tales Annual #1	9.2	eBay (icecollectibles)	$3,451
Reform School Girl nn	5.0 R	Heritage	$3,000
Strange Mysteries #1	9.2	eBay (icecollectibles)	$2,654
Mysteries #1	6.5	Heritage	$1,560
Journey into Fear #3	9.0	Heritage	$1,440
Blonde Phantom #19	8.0	eBay (icecollectibles)	$1,325
Superman #53	VG-FN	eBay (icecollectibles)	$1,201
Marvel Mystery Comics #88	5.0	Heritage	$1,200
Colossal Comics #1	VG-FN	Heritage	$1,020
My Desire #34	VG+	eBay (icecollectibles)	$912

There are 16 comics on this list. Heritage has 9 of them or 56% and eBay's Icecollectibles has 6 or 38%, together accounting for 94% of these best sales results for FECA comics. So if you are looking for comics like these for your collection, these seem to be the best places to look or to sell if you are looking to sell comics like these. Notice that some of these comics are Superior titles that had US distribution and appear in *Overstreet*. The one true "hybrid" Canadian reprint comic, that is one with a new title and masthead that doesn't reprint a US comic directly is *Colossal Comics* #1 which is second from bottom on the list.

The results for these comics remain healthy and gradually rising. Let's see what the new year brings for them.

TIMOTHY KUPIN
KOOPS COMICS

For the fifth year in a row, I am honored to be given an opportunity to contribute to *The Overstreet Comic Book Price Guide*. It's been another busy year that has gone by far too quickly. I've setup at 19 different shows in 12 different states including a few new ones.

I'm now up to 35 states in which I've done a comic con. I did a show in Gasdsen, Alabama in May, Des Moines, Iowa in early June, Capser, Wyoming in late June, Columbia, Missouri in mid August and Topeka, Kansas in mid November. Some were better than others. As usual I did some buying. Sales in Iowa, Missouri and Kansas were pretty decent.

As far as the regular shows I do, the 'Old Man Con' in Scottsdale is always good. The Torpedo show in Glendale, CA was a far cry from the one in 2021 but a solid show. Comic Con was a blast and we did well there. PulpFest was a lot of fun. That was my first one but I'll keep going back. I did two shows in Houston and did well at both.

I had my best ever OAFCON in September. If you've never been to this Oklahoma show, you should give it a try. It's one of the oldest comic cons in the USA.

Living in Oklahoma spares me from cross-country trips.

Instead I have long West Coast trips and long East Coast trips. In 2023 I've driven West five times for the Cal Comic Con, the one day Tucson show, two Scottsdale shows and of course the 13 day trip for the Torpedo show and Comic-Con International. I've also driven East four times to pick up old wooden display racks from Eide's, PulpFest, Virginia Vintage Comic Con and finally the Big Apple Con just weeks ago.

Bear in mind most of these trips are multi-purpose and not just for the show. For example, both PulpFest and Big Apple centered around me picking up collections in Pittsburgh. The first two West Coast trips allowed me to empty my storage in Tucson.

The bad news is that my store is still not open. I did manage to double my space when the opportunity presented itself. I now have the unit directly behind me. We have to install a doorway and a 2 hour fire door and then it will be connected. Trust me when I tell you I'm filling them both up with books and comics.

Next year's report will include some news from Koops Comics brick-n-mortar. Bottom line, I spent too much time on the road in 2023 buying and selling comics. 2023 was a lot of fun. 2024 will be even better.

BEN LABONOG
PRIMETIME COMICS

There was a big market re-correction on most keys that started around Oct. 2022 and went through most of 2023. Silver and Bronze Age keys were down anywhere from 30% - 50%. Even some choice Golden Age keys were not immune to slight price resistance. There was concern on buying keys at current fair market value fearing continued re-correction, but nonetheless, there hasn't been a better time to acquire major keys at significant discounts. Some notable observations that were made during 2023: 1) An increase in private deals (hotel rooms/lobbies) at shows and private geek get-togethers. 2) Burnout from common Silver Age keys and high prices. 3) Raw books are generally a safe bet from long time collectors.

A highlighted event for me in 2023 was a surprise zoom call with two of Alex Schomburg's granddaughters who wanted to learn more about their grandfather's comic book work. It was quite a pleasure meeting them remotely with a few other collectors! We shared with them some of Alex's highly prized covers, and impressed upon them that their grandfather was a major contributer to pulp and comic book cover art. In addition, Marc Newman (House of Comics) was able to get long time fanzine editor Gary Carter to set up at the August 2023 Berkeley Con. It was a treat to see Gary and talk with him at length about all the great *Comic Book*

Marketplace magazines he was a part of in the '90s.

In June 2023, I began a personal adventure into the world of pulps by accident. I was at a local show and decided to purchase two slabbed books. The dealer and I were a few hundred dollars apart on a price so he offered to let me pick out a handful of pulps from the long boxes at his booth. I pulled out an Alex Schomburg 1953 Sci-Fi/UFO pulp titled *Fantastic Story Magazine*. I grabbed seven other covers that grabbed my eye and that sent me on a six month journey into pulps. There are many fascinating covers and new artists to explore in the pulp world, and it is like studying the *Gerber Photo Journals* all over again. Many pulps are very affordable (compared to comic books) and are sitting in an untapped market. Spicey/skull/bondage covers appear to be in high demand. Quite a number of Golden Age comic covers and interior panels were swiped from pulps. Comic book artists used films, pulp magazines, and newspaper strips to gather ideas. In fact, pulps are considered the precursors to comic books. Richard Evans (Bedrock City) had this to say on pulps: "They are the last, affordable vintage collectible." With CGC set to start grading pulps in December 2023, I foresee many Golden Age collectors coming into the pulp market. A few notable observations from my pulp experience so far: 1) A must have for Alex Schomburg fans is to pair *Startling Stories* (Sept., 1939) with *Daring Mystery Comics* #1 (Oct, 1939) which are Schomburg's 1st Sci-Fi pulp cover and 1st cover for Timely Comics, respectively. 2) Masked Raider (Rider) and Ka-Zar were actually the first Marvel/Timely characters published by Martin Goodman. The Masked Raider was initially called the Masked Rider and was introduced in his own pulp title in 1934. Ka-Zar was really a Tarzan swipe that Goodman published in *Ka-Zar* #1 (Oct, 1936). Both characters made their first comic book appearances in *Marvel Comics* #1 (1939), and proved to be worthy carryovers from the pulps. 3) There are at least four (possibly 7) pulps which contain house ads for *Marvel Comics* #1 (Oct/Nov, 1939). This is a key moment for Martin Goodman as he was a very successful pulp publisher who took a risk in comic book publishing. Goodman wisely chose to place house ads in select pulps to generate interest. Apparently, the ads worked, as the October print of *Marvel Comics* #1 sold out its initial test run of 80,000 copies within a week.

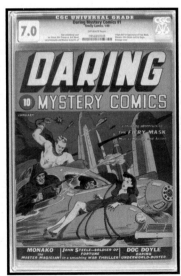

A massive trade involving three major collectors took place at a collectors' convention early in 2023. Involved in the deal was a *Detective Comics* #31 CGC 2.5 that traded hands at $120k. Other books involved was a *Fantastic Comics* #3 CGC 1.5, *Mystic Comics* #8 CGC 1.8, and a big ticket Timely book in *Marvel Mystery Comics* #9 CGC 1.5. These books all went to new, satisfied owners. Other major books trading hands privately throughout the year included a

Sub-Mariner Comics #1 CGC 2.5, *Marvel Mystery Comics* #8 CGC 3.0, *Superman* #3 CGC 4.0, and two copies of *Suspense Comics* #3 CGC .5 (incomplete) each in the $50k range. Cartoon and funny animal comics had renewed interest. Key books like *Terry Toons* #38 (Timely, 1945 - 1st App. Mighty Mouse), *Richie Rich* #1 (Harvey, 1960), and *Scooby-Doo* #1 (Gold Key, 1970) saw increased demand.

For 2024, I anticipate buying to be conservative with common Silver Age and Bronze Age keys. Scarcer Golden Age comics in any condition should continue to have little to no price point boundaries and steady demand due to difficult supply and availability. Pulps and their fabulously painted covers will be the newest primetime product to blaze across the comic book trail in the form of CGC holders. May your collection truly be "Primetime" in 2024!

BEN LICHTENSTEIN
ZAPP COMICS

What a Long Strange (Round) Trip It's Been: I'm back with a brief market report. My shops celebrated 30 years in business and 2023 was a volatile year indeed! After the insane Covid boom in 2021, prices on most back issues corrected hard and continue to slide. Most keys are down 25% to 60% from Covid peak prices, with some Modern keys down a whopping 80%. As my opening line says, prices look like they are on the way to round trip to 2019 prices. I continue to purchase collections and key issues, but being careful to leave a margin of safety.

Whatnot is a major established new channel. It's the Wild West on there, with some great deals and great sellers as well some dubious grading/prices/sales strategies. *Caveat emptor*.

We tested Whatnot, but decided it was not the right fit for us.

As the red arrows on gpanalysis.com continue month after month, I've been steadily buying quality keys since the beginning of the year. However, I'm leaving dry powder to spend in 2024 because it feels like things will stay bumpy for a while. Many customers who purchased during the craze of 2021 are still coping with massive losses on their purchases. This, along with inflation and a drying up of free government money has resulted in a contraction in purchasing. Some buyers are simply out of money and the other buyers that do have money are being more cautious.

The market is not completely frozen, however. The usual keys will sell, but just have to priced very sharp. So, every time I get a *Giant-Size X-Men* #1, *Amazing Spider-Man* keys, Neal Adams *Batman* issues, etc. they sell quickly because I'm pricing at current market with tight grading.

I returned to New York Comic Con this year. While the show continues to focus more on Anime and Pop culture, we had a successful show overall. The energy was fairly positive among comics fans, and we sold lots of books. Any Golden Age moves well and Silver to Bronze is very strong. Again,

books have to be priced and graded carefully, as the customer is more cautious these days.

Brick and mortar shops on average are seeing a difficult time unless highly diversified. Many shops closed down in 2023 as sales on new books and superhero TPBs have softened. Also, collectible card games, Funkos, and sports cards have cooled. They are far from dead, but now returning to normal.

New comic sales unfortunately reached a new nadir. Marvel and DC appear to lack a cohesive editorial plan and independents are, with a few bright spots, very risky to carry at this time. There are still plenty of great stories being made, but readers are really pulling back. High prices and better entertainment options remain a major challenge for the new books market. I'm hopeful that a possible revamp can turn things around, but who knows really?

Manga is the bright spot for us and we continue to expand that category. Mainstream graphic novel sales are quite rocky for us, besides the very top perennial sellers.

All is not lost however in the world of funny books.

Golden Age demand is as strong as ever with prices on average stable or increasing after the Covid Boom. There is still a very healthy interest in collecting comics and there are plenty of new buyers who came back in 2020/2021 and are sticking around.

"Bin" books are selling fine, particularly pre-1985. Keys will sell if priced realistically. Marvel is still king, but when it comes to Silver/Bronze, there are buyers for literally every genre. Even Gold Keys and Charltons actually move just fine when priced well. There is still strong organic demand for comic collecting, albeit with a smaller budget.

We are resisting selling a few books that we feel are getting punished too much in this environment, but overall just adjusting to reality and doing fine. I'm always looking for collections that include runs going back to Silver and Bronze. Modern-only collections are purchased as well, but most of it in bulk, as we get offered Moderns quite often.

If you or someone you know has a large collection to sell, please let me know!

In the short to intermediate term, I remain very optimistic about this hobby of ours. I want to thank all of our many customers and my staff for their support. Looking forward to many more years slingin' back issues! See ya at the shop (or convention).

STEPHEN LIPSON
COLLECTOR

2023 was a resounding success for me. Although not many copies of the Canada Golden Age comics from 1941-1946 surfaced, I was able to obtain a complete run of the Canadian *Classics Illustrated* series in high grade. I was also successful in acquiring a complete run of the *Classic Comics/Classics Illustrated* first editions published in the United States from #1-169 as well.

One book of note that I was able to acquire after almost 2 decades of searching was the elusive *Triumph Comics* #10, featuring Nelvana of the Northern Lights. This allowed me to finally complete my collection of every appearance of Nelvana in print.

My area of collecting and focus is the Canadian Golden Age era. In 2023, I have sold several books this year to collectors and I see an upswing in prices realized:

Sampling of 2023 Personal Sales of note:

Colossal Comics Bell Features Giant Uncertified $2,000

Rocket Comics Vol 4 #3 CGC 2.5 $1,500

Joke Comics #22 Uncertified 4.0 $1,500

Better Comics Volume 3 #7 Uncertified 3.0 $1,500

Triumph Comics #14 Uncertified 2.5 $1,200

Wow Comics #1 Uncertified 2.5 $1,600

There still appears to be a dearth of availability of the Canadian Golden Age World War II era books from 1941-1946, due to low print runs, and the fact that comics were meant to be read and thrown away. The paper drives of the Second World War also had contributed to the scarcity as well.

DOUG MABRY
THE GREAT ESCAPE

Greetings from Tennessee and Kentucky! It's been another interesting year for us. We've had several larger collections offered to us this year, but all from older collectors. This may be a trend that continues as we start to see folks who began collecting in the '60s and '70s start to reach the age where they move their collections on to new homes.

One of the changes we noticed was a slight softening in the market for average Golden Age books. Some certainly still demand many multiples of *Guide*, but many issues are back to *Guide* prices or slightly over. Timelys and MLJs, classic covers, and hot artists still command a premium, but books like the Quality and Fawcett books have slowed considerably from their 2020 highs. One collection we bought was several hundred DC/All American books. The *Batman* and *Flash Comics* flew out of the store at between 10 and 30% over *Guide*. *Sensation, Wonder Woman, Action*, and *Superman* sold strongly at around *Guide*. We were surprised that some of the Green Arrow cover *More Fun* issues sat for quite awhile even at *Guide* prices. But even at *Guide* price (and even through a few sales) the Superboy *Adventure Comics* and the *World's Finest* books have just not moved well. On the other hand, we had a group of coverless/incomplete Timely books that brought quite a bit over *Guide* at auction.

Silver Age Marvels are still very strong, but Silver Age DC (except *Batman*) just don't seem to move. This has been a trend that's been going on for around 20 years now and I don't see any sign of it changing.

An interesting trend that we're seeing more and more of is that of collecting individual pages from books. This seems to be a growing area of interest for many folks who feel that they'll never be able to own complete copies of some of these books. But the interesting thing is that we're starting to see people interested in buying pages from non-key Golden Age books. Interesting pages from a *Captain America* or *Detective* can sell relatively easily. I do have to admit, though, that I don't understand why someone would want to have an individual page graded. You already know what grade it's going to get, so save the time and money and slap that sucker in a mylar bag.

Bronze Age remains strong for the major Marvel characters, although secondary series are slower.

BRIAN MARCUS
CAVALIER COMICS

Greetings from the mountains of Southwest Virginia. It's been another good year for the store overall but, and that's a big but, new comic sales have been very flat. The direction of Marvel and DC has turned off most of the regular customers and hasn't brought in any new ones. The quality of the art and storytelling just isn't there anymore. Graphic Novel sales of newer stuff have fallen off too but once again, the classic collected stories still sell.

Back issues have been steady, and I've had a problem keeping them in stock. People are still looking for the classic storylines and runs of their favorite characters. Even the newer collectors are bypassing the newer comics for the older stuff.

Manga sales have been way up and we've been expanding that selection every month. Seems to me that's where a lot of the readers are going to.

Key sales of books in the past year include *Amazing Spider-Man* #300 CGC 9.4 $700, *Tomb of Dracula* #1 CGC 5.5 $250, *Iron Man* #128 CGC 8.5 $100, *Amazing Spider-Man* #4 (1st Silk) CGC 9.6 $150, *Edge of the Spider-Verse* #2 CGC 9.2 $375.

WILL MASON
DAVE & ADAM'S

Hello and thank you for stopping and taking the time to read this. As I sit here, I just witnessed one of the single highest sales in the history of comic books. Reflecting back on this as well as last year, it's amazing just how wide of a spectrum our hobby spans in regards to what it offers to customers of all backgrounds in terms of both interest and affordability.

The back half of 2022 posed some real challenges for the comic book marketplace to say the least. While we all reaped the benefits of red hot sales for about 2 years, many were caught holding inventory that they had paid pandemic level prices for, only to find themselves upside down. Many choose to hold, and stash books away, hoping for a future return on their investment. We made the decision to take the opposite approach, choosing to move a lot of this inventory through new and emerging selling platforms.

In March of 2023 we decided to dive into the deep end in the online streaming pool, and it's arguably one of the best decisions we ever made. Inventory that would often sit dormant was now incredibly viable and selling at a brisk pace. What started as a way to sell low dollar items, quickly turned into bigger key issues to go along with the quick moving "bulk" books that we had acquired over the years. It has, for the better, dramatically improved and changed our strategies regarding not only sales, but acquiring inventory as well as a reduction in operating costs. Graded signed books by writers, artists, and celebrities have become arguably some of our best sellers, leading us to increase our participation in signings both in person and via mail-away.

We also saw a significant increase around the middle of the year in regards to large original owner collections being offered to us and the rest of the market as a whole. With the amount of healthy competition in the marketplace, I ask myself fairly often, "How many more of these can there actually be out there?", but lo and behold the phone continues to ring and e-mails fill my inbox and off we go, more often than not returning with a large truck filled with boxes of books. This coupled with new strategies in regards to purchasing has led to a significant rebound from the end of 2022.

The summer convention season was a smash hit and we recorded our best SDCC ever in July. This was refreshing in the sense that as convention operating costs, like almost everything else, have continued to grow year over year. While we've trimmed down our show schedule by being more selective, the appeal of the 1-day comic focused con has only continued to grow with events like the Little Giant Old School Show, Shortboxed Live, and the Collector's Summit all becoming must attend events.

In the end and looking forward to the future, our goal relates back to what I said in regards to the wide spectrum of comic collectors. Try to acquire as much diverse inventory to be able to appeal to all of them. Whether it be in our daily streams helping people fill in holes in their runs, or large auction house worthy purchases, our goal is to serve all of them as best as possible by offering a wide variety of books.

JIM McCALLUM
GUARDIAN COMICS

Where did everybody go? 2023 had to have been the wildest ride for the comic book collecting community in quite some time, if not ever. Full of ups and downs, highs and lows and everything in between. It's been a tough navigation to survive it one piece, but we did our best.

The market is definitely strong enough, as we sold two of our biggest books in 2023, including a *Batman* #1 4.0 (Moderate B-3) and an *Amazing Spider-Man* #129 9.8 white pager in May and June of this year. The buyers are out there, but just in smaller numbers it seems.

The real question is to try an examine what has happened in the marketplace? First off, the comic hobby isn't the only collectible market suffering from a downturn, it has affected the sports card hobby, the trading card game market, even the vintage toy hobby as a whole is in a lull. So, this softening is across the board in most other markets, and nobody is immune.

Have we suffered superhero fatigue? It does look like that is a possibility. I remember the times before *Infinity War*, when every Marvel movie was an "event" and if you didn't see the latest feature at the theatre on opening night, you felt as if you were missing out. You rearranged your entire schedule to make sure you weren't. Then for the next week or two, those same customers would come into the shop and discuss how amazing the movie was, and discussed all the finest nuances of the film to anybody who would listen. Nowadays those same collectors haven't even seen the latest films, nor really have any desire to, nor feel like they have missed out on anything. Is that Marvel's fault, for putting out lesser product out than we are used to, or have collectors lost interest in seeing their favourite heroes on the big screen, as they have been doing it on almost a "religious" basis since Iron Man in 2008 till *Endgame* in 2019. That's an amazing 11 year run that collectively captured our imaginations as a community and never let go...well until now.

Inflation, a subject that nobody enjoys talking about but let's face it, purchasing power for the entire western world has been affected by it. Our wages and salaries haven't kept up with the rates of inflation and a dollar isn't worth what it was just a few short years ago. Have many hobbyists pulled back for a while and make sure the necessities like food and shelter are taken care of first and luxuries like comic books are taking a temporary back seat? Most likely.

The convention season has been a head scratcher as well. In March for the Toronto ComicCon which attracts about 50,000 attendees for the weekend, even though it was absolutely jam packed, shoulder to shoulder, comic book sales were the weakest we have ever witnessed. Not only at our booth, but every other dealer we spoke with. If you needed a reprieve from the crowds, you could have just stood in front of a comic dealers booth, and you would have had plenty of room to yourself. The opposite could be said for our biggest show of the year, Fan Expo in August with 135,000 total in attendance, comic book sales were as brisk as we had ever seen, and a record setting show for us. What was missing though was the top-quality comic book dealers. Dealers whom had been staples at the show for twenty plus years, getting away from these large Pop Culture Events. The presence of the traditional comic book dealer has been waning at these types of shows for years now and 2023 one really took notice. Perhaps lack of competition was the reason for our windfall at the show.

Another trend we've noticed is the lack of attendees at the local one day, strictly comics focussed shows. In October, the once jam-packed mecca of Comic Book Shows in the Greater Toronto Area was a shadow of its former self as at any given time, you could throw bowling balls down the aisles and not hit a single person. It was a very sad sight to behold, and our least successful show in over seven years now.

I know this market uncertainty has had a profound impact on the way many local comicbook stores in our metropolitan area do business, including a few permanent closures. Some stores have scaled back their hours and/or closed three or four days a week now to cut down on overhead. A local store that had the most beautiful store front in the city, scaled their operation back into a less glamorous but much more comic focussed location. We've been approached to buy out a couple of stores, or at least their inventory.

Speaking of inventory, that's the one thing that HASN'T been an issue this year. We've been offered more collections in the last six months than we ever have. At least every other day somebody is emailing us to sell some keys, or even their whole collections that they've been amassing for twenty, thirty and even fifty years in one particular case. Why are people selling? One large collection we purchased was because the owner was coming onto his 50th anniversary and wanted to go around the world instead of leaving the collection as burden to his children and enjoy the proceeds from the labour of his love. Another collector was leaving the city and built his dream home. Although he still loved the books, he had no interest in moving dozens of long boxes to his new home taking up valuable space on the moving truck. Aging and shifting priorities have always brought new material to the market, so the phenomenon isn't new, but I'm not sure we are seeing new collectors to the market to gobble these gems into their collections. They sell in a heartbeat still, with our diehard customer base dropping everything to get first crack at fresh stock.

How long will this last? Collectors are collectors, and once the collecting gene is inside of you it's almost impossible to keep dormant. So, although the market and world may seem a little gloomy today, it's not going to last forever. It might take a few years to get back to where we would all like it to be, but slow and steady has always been the mantra for a healthy market. If you bought your Silver Age keys in 2021 and 2022, on paper right now it doesn't look very pretty but hopefully you bought what you liked (as one always should) and when the market rebounds you'll have nothing to worry about and will be glad you rode out the storm. Remember collecting should never be about a quick flip, or Instagram likes, it should always be about the love you have for the artform and those four colour pieces of newsprint we all cherish and adore.

TODD MCDEVITT
NEW DIMENSION COMICS

Greetings from Western Pennsylvania! And Ohio! I've been lucky enough to be in the comic book business since 1986 and have 5 stores in the Pittsburgh region and one in Ohio. Plus, I host the 3 Rivers Comicon in Pittsburgh. Lots of insights!

Just when I thought the comic book industry couldn't get any more dynamic, it just keeps on changing! That is probably true for all aspects, but I'm speaking from my perspective that is mostly vintage material. The stimulation of the Covid era has fallen off. We thought there was no end in sight for escalating prices on some of the most sought-after books. But, all good things... I really thought the best books would ride it out: *Amazing Fantasy* #15, *Hulk* #181, and *Amazing Spider-Man* #129. All books I scored in 2023, but had to buy, and price, conservatively as I watched the sales trends fall. And even with that balancing act, they sat, or are still sitting, longer than I have ever seen. All this really makes me wonder about the future. Prices are set high. Maybe collectors got what they wanted, many holy grails included. Supply is flowing well as many collectors part with there collections, or they are offered as an estate scenario. Sorry to point out that last part, but it's a reality. So, more supply, less demand. I think I learned what happens next in college. And it hit in 2023.

So, the big question is ... can values rebound? Are there enough future collectors on the horizon to bolster demand for key issues? Or, has it played out that well? A major player in creating demand has been films. Well, it seems all the top picks for that have been flushed out and now (as I write this) the hobby rests on the hotness of Madame Web. I have to think your money is better spent on blue chip caliber books like 1st appearances of characters that have been around for decades. Lots of decades. While they have dipped, they aren't going anywhere and, like real estate, they aren't making more.

I'm lucky to have a lot of great people working with me to keep New Dimension Comics cruising along! I always asked them to help me with insight and hears what they had to say.

ANTHONY TINCANI, MANAGER AT NEW DIMENSION COMICS BUTLER, PA

It seems like there is a bit of a post-movie craze hangover in terms of what people are looking for these days in comics. There is less of a demand for things that tie into the latest theatrical release or the newest season of something adapted from comics (*Invincible* very much being an exception). This sounds like it would be a bad thing, but with it, what is left are people who have developed a true appreciation for collecting and/or investing.

Some of these folks have been in the market for years, but quite a few are returning from long hiatuses, and even some are experiencing it as new comers. The veterans definitely make the vintage side of things interesting, always on the hunt for those last few books that will round out their collections. That can be anything from Silver Age *Adventure Comics*, pre-Iron Man *Tales of Suspense*, or Frank Miller's run of *Daredevil*. Returning collectors love digging through our back issues to get caught up with the stories they missed. I'm always needing more *Spider-Man*s! An interesting one is the newer crew of comic fans. All of them have their own tastes and styles for what they look after. Some are kids who love things like Spider-Gwen or Young Justice and want as much stuff as they can get from those properties. Others can be adults with kids of their own who follow specific writers or artists. But as they collect, their taste broadens, as they take in what the medium has to offer.

2023 certainly has been an interesting year, as our need for vintage and back issues seems to constantly be growing. We are looking forward to what the coming year brings to the table.

TOM TUNNICLIFF, ELLWOOD CITY, PA LOCATION

Any quick internet search will tell you that the comic market will grow between 4.8% - 10.5% annually over the next few years or even the next decade, depending on the report you read. This is plausible to me considering the Earth's population only took 14 years to go from seven billion to eight and, as these earthlings come of age and start reading and become interested in comics (and/or others rediscover them!), I see nothing but growth. On the other side of the coin, the problems I do see that might hinder or slow growth are not insurmountable or even real obstacles.

The publishing end of the industry leads the charge with variant covers numbering in the double digits for some issues, short lived runs (why does a character have a 12 issue run that ends, just to restart the following month? I mean what volume of *Punisher* are we up to..? 20? 25?), and cash grab events and crossovers that spread to every title they publish trying once again to milk our wallets while the proverbial iron was hot, something that most of our customers know is a publisher strategy that they will not fall for. Counting for the rest of the impediments to growth are tired plot devices, overall story fatigue, (multiple) multiverses... (Who can tell me how many there are now? And I am sure there will be a couple more by the time this publishes!) Last, but definitely not the least, just how many times can a character, world, or even universe die just to reset things as a new jumping on point?

The tactics and plot devices are tiresome to some, but for the many fans that tire of them, just as many are continuously getting into the hobby, either reading, collecting, or both. Though we may lament just how many Civil Wars or Crises need to happen, I look forward to this projected growth and hope that, with a little innovative storytelling and fresh ideas, the growth will be towards to higher end of the predictions.

BO PRITTS, MANAGER NEW DIMENSION COMICS, OHIO

This year's current state of the comic market is, I believe, down even more this year than it was last year. New comic book prices and the quantity of books releasing continue to increase. However, interest and the current economic climate have people taking a step back from collecting. The comic industry for years has relied on the Marvel cinematic universe and the DC cinematic universe to drive interest. Marvel has ruled that aspect of the industry, and Marvel has been responsible for flop after flop at the box office and on their streaming service. The comic industry seems more interested in pushing their political agendas and diversity instead of writing/producing quality and compelling stories. Maybe one day they will learn from their mistakes and fix things, but at this time I highly doubt that will happen.

BRENT MOESHLIN
QUALITY COMIX

2023 started off very strong continuing the incredible Holiday season of 2022. As the year went on, it became clear that comic valuations were not going to recover anytime soon. That realization by collectors and dealers resulted in slowing purchases, especially on Silver thru Modern Age keys over $1,000. Everything has to be priced right at market in order to sell them in a reasonable amount of time. Since Golden Age comics are in low supply, they have been much more resilient to price declines. The good news is that prices over the last 3 - 4 months have appeared to stabilize and we expect a more stable market in 2024. Here are some key sales that Quality Comix made on QualityComix.com in 2023:

Action Comics #16 CGC VG 4.0 $4,460
Amazing Fantasy #15 CGC GD- 1.8 $22,290
Amazing Fantasy #15 CGC GD+ 2.5 $25,990
Amazing Fantasy #15 CGC VG 4.0 $37,500
Amazing Fantasy #15 CGC VG/FN 5.0 $58,990
Avengers #1 CGC VG+ 4.5 $5,740
Batman #121 CGC VG- 3.5 $2,190
Fantastic Four #1 CGC VG+ 4.5 $22,000
Fantastic Four #53 CGC NM+ 9.6 $2,050
Green Lantern #40 CGC NM+ 9.6 $4,000
Green Lantern #76 CGC NM- 9.2 $2,675
Incredible Hulk #1 CGC VG+ 4.5 $29,790
Incredible Hulk #180 CGC NM 9.4 $3,190
Journey Into Mystery #83 CGC VF- 7.5 $54,000
X-Men #1 CGC FA 1.0 $4,300
X-Men #1 CGC VG/FN 5.0 $13,700

STEVE MORTENSEN
MIRACLE COMICS

2023 was rough for certain sectors of the comic book market, yet a banner year for other segments. In all, we saw the resilience of the hobby as well as its attachment to Hollywood and to the economy. As U.S. interest rates hit a 20+ year high, money became tight. And with high inflation, collectors had less to spend. In the 2021 peak, prices soared following Hollywood news, But the 2023 writers' and actors' strikes slowed demand for many key books. We saw *Incredible Hulk* #181 in CGC 8.0 go from near $10,000 in 2021 to around $5,000 now, as of this writing. On the flip side, Golden Age superhero books continue to surge, as well as rare pre-Code Horror. Most other books remained flat in 2023.

Let's look at the different sectors of the market:

Golden Age: Superhero and pre-Code Horror comics remain hot. All issues of G.A. Batman, Superman, and Captain America are selling well; in my opinion, these are the blue-chip investment books to put money into if you are looking to diversify from stocks. VG copies are relatively affordable at around $500-2,000 each for a common issue. Make sure you buy from a reputable dealer to ensure grading accuracy and restoration checks.

Silver Age: This may be the most disappointing sector of the market, with large declines in key books. At its height, a CGC 4.0 of *Amazing Fantasy* #15 fetched $75,000. It is now selling regularly in the $38,000 range. *Incredible Hulk* #1 CGC 4.0 at its peak was selling for $38,000 and is now selling for around $24,000. *X-Men* #1 in CGC 4.0 sold at its high for $24,000 and the last sale in November of 2023 was for $9,000. Ouch. As Disney begins producing more movies and content, I suspect these prices will rise again. You can already see it in comics like *Journey Into Mystery* #85 (1st Loki). The prices have risen since season two came out.

Bronze Age: Horror comics of all ages are selling well, particularly the DC issues of *House of Mystery* and *House of Secrets*; and for Marvel the *Dead of Night, Vault of Evil, Marvel Chillers,* and *Crypt of Shadows*.

Copper Age: Common Copper Age issues remain affordable and have been holding their value. A collector can purchase a CGC 9.8 of common issues for between $50-100 (Copper Age issues are now about 40 years old). I have also noticed demand for CGC 9.4 and CGC 9.6s; the price point is lower on those, but they do move.

Modern Age: Gold standards such as *TMNT* #1 have held their value well, but the common modern comic has suffered under the post-Covid market. Even keys such as *New Mutants* #98 (1st Deadpool) have declined. At its peak, it was selling for $3,000 in 2021 but now hovers around $1,400. The Newsstand Edition had a peak price of $5,200 in 2021 but now sells for $2,500. It is still one of the great Modern books for investors. I expect over time it will regain most, if not all, of its value.

It may take years (a decade?) for some of the comic drops to regain their past value. And for some of the modern books, the best prices may be behind them. I believe *Incredible Hulk* #181 CGC 8.0 will reach the $10,000 mark again, but it may take a few more movies and quite a bit more time. In the meantime, sellers may have to take signifi-

cant losses to move books. Collectors will have to realize that dealers' buying points will be much lower than they used to. But the hobby is solid as a new generation emerges that will take the mantle and grow the hobby; that is the hope for collectors and dealers alike.

I think 2024 will be an improvement as we head into an election year, which tends to be better on the economy. With the Hollywood strikes over, there will be ample content for all of us to consume next year – which should fuel a comic turnaround.

JOSH NATHANSON & RICK HIRSCH COMICLINK

For nearly 30 years ComicLink.com has been a leading consignment and auction firm for comic books and related artwork. We were the first online comic book and comic art consignment website, serving buyers and sellers of comic books and related original artwork since 1996. We have facilitated the sale of just about every valuable comic book that exists in a multitude of conditions.

If you have valuable comic books or related original artwork or other collectibles, we invite you to visit ComicLink. com, CertifiedLink.com and to reach out to us if you have interest in selling. We'll work with you to optimize the value of your collection. We assist with everything including evaluating your collection for certification, processing, pricing, marketing and selling your material. We do all this work, and offer upfront cash advances, for a very minimal commission rate. All you have to do is ship us your comics or artwork or drop off the material at one of our offices or a major convention.

Despite the overall collectibles market adjustment following the pandemic bubble, the high end comic book market remained very solid in 2023 and ComicLink achieved many very strong prices including a **significant number of record results for the sale of both certified comic books and related artwork**. Record prices were most common among Golden Age offerings, but were also achieved for select Silver, Bronze, Copper and Modern Age certified comic books. Generally, prices appear stabilized well above pre-pandemic levels.

Below are just a small sample of the strong prices achieved on ComicLink between January and December of 2023.

Golden Age (1933-1955): The Golden Age market remained quite healthy throughout 2023, with many of the trends from previous years continuing. Market growth is driven by first appearance and origin issues, early appearances of popular heroes and villains, Pre-Code Horror, Good Girl Art and classic covers by the likes of Schomburg, Baker, L.B. Cole and Frazetta. Sample prices:

Action Comics #6 5.0 $10,740, #12 5.0 $29,250 and 4.0 $26,039 and #15 7.5 $37,205

Adventure Comics #40 3.5 $31,000, #42 7.0 $8,555 and #48 8.0 $21,990

All Winners Comics #1 8.0 $16,500

All-American Comics #17 8.5 $18,250

Archie Comics #1 3.5 $33,000

Atomic Comics #1 (Green Publications) 9.8 $22,512

Batman #11 8.5 $37,000

Black Cat Mystery #50 9.4 $65,000 and 8.5 $35,557

Captain America Comics #3 4.0 $35,310, #13 9.0 $44,500, 8.5 $29,000 and #37 3.5 $11,609

Chamber of Chills #19 6.5 $18,703

Detective Comics #27 NG (married front and back covers only) $221,777 and #359 9.4 $35,500

Double Action Comics #2 Untrimmed Cover Proof NG $10,250

Four Color #178 9.2 $14,100

Hangman Comics #3 8.0 $29,138

Haunted Thrills #5 8.0 $14,500

Human Torch #12 6.5 $16,075

Marvel Mystery Comics #4 2.5 $38,333, #7 8.0, #8 7.5, #9 4.0 $64,600, #11 9.0 $11,555 and #40 7.5 $20,065

Mask Comics #1 6.0 $27,761 and #2 5.5 $23,138

More Fun Comics #55 3.0 $13,258

Science Comics #2 7.5 $32,000

Silver Streak Comics #7 6.0 $11,250

Superman #2 3.0 $14,656, #15 9.0 $24,772, #48 9.6 $14,250, #53 9.0 $13,011 and #76 9.6 $18,451

Suspense Comics #4 7.5 $21,250 and #11 8.0 $25,250

Weird Science-Fantasy #29 9.2 $9,678

Young Allies #1 8.5 $20,251

Silver Age (1956-1969): The Silver Age continues to be one of the most popular segments of the hobby, with the superhero genre dominating the activity within this category. *Amazing Fantasy* #15 remains the leading "Holy Grail" of the era and *Amazing Spider-Man* the most collected title.

Note: All comic book examples in this report are certified by CGC unless otherwise mentioned.

Amazing Fantasy #15 7.5 $175,000, 4.0 $64,000, 3.5 $37,000 and 2.5 $26,750

Amazing Spider-Man #1 4.5 $16,500, #3 9.4 $50,888, #5 9.6 $23,251, #6 9.4 $18,250, #7 9.4 $12,000, #11 9.4 $21,250, #12 9.8 $25,801, #13 9.2 $11,805, #14 9.6 $42,000, #16 9.8 $33,000, #17 9.6 $10,916, #23 9.6 $13,050, #28 9.4 $16,916, #129 9.8 $39,000 and #300 9.8 Newsstand $13,251

Avengers #1 7.5 $15,500, #7 9.6 $11,250 and #48 9.8 $15,677

Captain America #100 9.8 $12,750 and #117 9.8 $60,000

Daredevil #7 9.6 $31,000

Fantastic Four #5 8.0 $28,750, #7 9.4 $25,000, #9 9.8 $38,777, #12 9.6 $45,700, #46 9.8 $20,251 and #48 9.8 $100,000

Incredible Hulk #6 9.6 $25,806, #102 9.8 $12,500 and #181 9.6 $24,027 and Annual #1 9.8 $11,550

Journey Into Mystery #84 9.4 $72,001

Showcase #4 5.5 $35,000

Silver Surfer #4 9.6 $18,200 and #10 9.8 $12,305

Star Trek #1 (1967) 9.4 $11,651

Strange Tales #135 9.8 $32,000 and #169 9.8 $23,801

Tales of Suspense #39 6.5 $26,090

Thor #128 9.8 $13,195

X-Men #4 9.4 $25,050 and #14 9.6 $17,750

Bronze Age (1970-1979): Record prices were achieved for Bronze Age keys in pristine condition. With the early Bronze Age comics now over 50 years old, the era has gained full recognition and major keys from the era in high grade are recognized as true blue chip collectibles.

Conan the Barbarian #1 9.8 $8,000

Deadly Hands of Kung Fu #19 9.9 $13,250

House of Secrets #92 9.8 $125,000

Marvel Feature Vol. 1 #1 9.8 $15,250

Marvel Spotlight #5 9.4 $18,250

Savage Tales #1 9.8 $13,250

X-Men #94 9.8 $53,000 and #137 9.9 $7,600

Modern Age: 1980-Present

With the Modern Age designation now covering a 40+ year period, there are numerous examples of high value comic books from the era.

Batman: The Dark Knight Returns #1 9.9 $25,429

DC Comics Presents #26 9.9 $30,002

Ultimate Fallout #4 9.8 Variant $33,000

Venom: Lethal Protector #1 9.8 Black Cover/Printing Error $12,245

Walking Dead #1 (2003) 9.9 $14,001

Wolverine Limited Series #1 CGC 9.9 $15,250

Original Artwork: 2023 was a strong year for ComicLink in terms of original artwork sales.

Jack Kirby *Incredible Hulk* #3 page 1 title splash $290,000; *Avengers* #3 page $81,000; Fantastic Four #28 page $38,888

Dave Cockrum *X-Men* #122 cover $250,000

John Romita *Amazing Spider-Man* #71 cover $220,000

Johnny Craig *Vault of Horror* #35 cover $183,333

Jim Starlin *Thanos Quest* #1 cover $140,144

Wally Wood *Daredevil* #5 page 1 title splash $110,000

Mike Dringenberg *The Sandman* #8 page $100,500

Mike Parobeck *Batman Adventures* #12 Harley Quinn page $97,756

Rich Buckler and Joe Sinnott *Fantastic Four* #169 cover $83,888

Barry Windsor-Smith *Conan the Barbarian* #5 cover $70,000

Marshall Rogers and Terry Austin *Doctor Strange* #49 cover $50,999

Dale Keown *Incredible Hulk* #369 cover $50,000

Boris Vallejo *Red Sonja* #3 *When Hell Laughs* paperback cover $47,555

Jim Lee *X-Men* #5 Double Page Splash $36,552

Mark Bagley Spider-Man Fleer Trading Card art $35,500, *Amazing Spider-Man* #374 splash $34,000

Don Heck *Tales of Suspense* #52 page $34,877

Travis Charest *Batman* #489 cover $33,000

John Buscema *Thor* #192 cover $32,050
Bill Sienkiewicz *Moon Knight* #14 cover $29,138
Jim Starlin and Joe Sinnott *Marvel Feature* #11 page 1
  title splash $28,027
Sal Buscema *Daredevil* #89 cover $27,951

TOM NELSON
TOP NOTCH COMICS

It's December 2023 and I am giving you my *Overstreet* market report. It's been mostly a soft year for Silver Age through Modern comics including high-grade CGC books. Even some of the low print independent and scarcer Marvel and DC were still soft in prices. It seems like the most popular Movie Marvel titles which had large run ups in 2021 and 2022 ended up with the largest losses bringing their values closer to 2019 prices. A larger portion of Silver and Bronze DC didn't balloon increase during the Covid bubble, and their prices have been more consistent to even moderate increases. There are also many bright areas for price increases. The Bronze Age Horror books saw solid interest and price increases, this primarily includes DC Horror in all conditions, not just high grade. The late Silver and Bronze Warren horror magazines like *Eerie, Creepy* and the flagship *Vampirella* runs saw an increased interest, as there are many classic covers by the likes of Frazetta tucked away throughout the runs. The Silver Age Gold Key #1s first editions had solid sales above *Guide*, titles like *Jonny Quest, Magnus the Robot Fighter, Green Hornet, Doctor Solar, Astro Boy, Star Trek, Scooby Doo* 1970, *Munsters, Space Ghost, Space Family Robinson*, and *Scarecrow of Romney Marsh*.

The Superhero run for collectors is still dominated by the *Amazing Spider-Man, X-Men* and *Batman*. The Modern era run collectors are *Spawn, Invincible* and the *Amazing Spider-Man*.

I'd like to do my top 10 DC Silver Age books in very fine, which is a 8.0 grade again this year. Due to their scarcity and volatility in prices many of these books do not sell publicly every year in 8.0 grade or above.

Showcase #4	$125,000
Showcase #22	$50,000
Brave and the Bold #28	$22,000
Action Comics #242	$22,000
Our Army at War #83	$20,000
Adventure Comics #247	$18,000
Batman #121	$15,000
Showcase #8	$12,000
Flash #105	$12,000

The top 10 chart still has *Showcase* #4 first Flash by a wide margin over *Showcase* #22 which is first appearance of Green Lantern. The third book is *Brave and the Bold* #28 the first Justice League, fourth book is *Action* #242 first Brainiac, the highest value War book *Our Army at War* #83 first Sergeant Rock, *Adventure* #247 first Legion of the Super-Heroes, *Action* #252 first Supergirl, *Batman* #121 first Mr. Freeze, *Showcase* #8 first Captain Cold and *Flash* #105 in the tenth spot.

The next top 10 are the Independents from the Modern era in near mint- 9.2 condition, excluding variants and mail air additions. Some of these values were down also from their previous highs.

Teenage Mutant Ninja Turtles #1 1st print	$17,500
Albedo #2	$8,000
Bone #1	$2,500
Teenage Mutant Ninja Turtles #1 2nd print	$2,500
The Crow #1	$1,000
Teenage Mutant Ninja Turtles #1 3rd print	$1,000
Walking Dead #1	$850
Primer #2	$800
Invincible #1	$800
Batman Adventures #12	$650

My third group of books in Near Mint- 9.2 condition comic books that feature crossover games and video game first appearances. Prices of these books were down also even though they are scarcer independents.

Nintendo Sneak Preview	
1990 *Comics Buyers' Guide* promotional	$500
Maximum Carnage #1 promotional	$500
Blip #1983 first Donkey Kong and Mario	$300
Dragon Ball sneak Preview Viz 1998	$300
Dragon Ball #1 1998 Viz	$250
Legends of Zelda #1 1990 Valiant	$200
Sonic Hedgehog #1 1991 promotional	$200
Super Mario Brothers #1 1993 Valiant	$200
Dragon Ball Z #1 1998 Viz	$200
Pokemon: Electric Tale of Pikachu #1	
1999 promotional	$200

The back issue market is still strong with the number of books being sold almost equal to the same number of units we sold last year. Some highlights from the past year all in CGC grades. *Conan* #58 9.8 $600, *Daredevil* #131 9.4 $650, *Darkwing Duck* #1 9.8 $300, *Dazzler* #1 9.8 $200, *Dragon Ball* #1 9.6 $400, *Exciting* #51 4.0 $950, *Fantastic Four* #52 8.0 $2,400, *Fantastic Four* #52 6.0 $750, *Fantastic Four* #244 9.6 $150, *Fantasy Quarterly* #1 9.8 $1,425, *Hot Wheels* #1 9.0 $300, *House of Secrets* #92 5.0 $1,250, *Incredible Hulk* #2 3.0 $1,800, *John Carter Warlord* #18 9.8 $500, *Marvel Spotlight* #2 8.0 $560, *Predator* #1 9.8 $500, *Rom* #1 9.8 $250, *Sandman* #8 9.8 $600, *Silver Surfer* #14 9.0 $330, *Spawn* #1 9.8 newsstand $850, *Spider-Man 2099* #1 9.8 newsstand #1 $475, *Spider-Man and his Amazing Friends* #1 9.8 newsstand $400, *Star Wars* #5 9.8 multi-pack 9.8 $450, and *Star Wars* #6 multi-pack 9.8 $500.

JAMIE NEWBOLD WITH MATT JOAQUIN
SOUTHERN CALIFORNIA COMICS

Greetings! If you are holding this copy there's a good chance you are at Comic-Con International and Mark Huesman delivered it to you with the help of one of my people. Or, you bought it from us out of one of many boxes we order for sales at our booth at the Con. I harbor no shame for this plug!

First a round-up of the previous two San Diego Cons. We were all rescued from the pandemic "tie-down" when SDCC 2022 brought us all together. This was our second best show over a span of shows going back to the early 1970s. Everything sold to previously-repressed buyers still giddy with new-found freedom and money to spend. The internet/social network of buying had whetted appetites for in-person shopping. Big books sold and stacks of comics left our two booths.

SDCC 2023 was a slightly different matter. Our show saw the stepping-back of the Hollywood presence and the crowds that always seems to weigh down the other end of the exhibitor's hall like an unbalanced seesaw. The entire week brought back-issue dealers a wealth of people who seemed ready to explore since Hollywood bailed. But this crowd seemed more interested in exploring comics rather than shelling out for more expensive keys. We did about half the sales of 2022, but on the backs of quantities of cheaper comics. The Post-Covid Hangover had set in.

One look at GPA told me that the back-issue market was sliding backward. Armchair speculators shopped with plans to invest and sell while various state governments kept us locked down. When we were set free and it was time to go back to work, it also seemed time to unload those investments. The 'net was fat with the same comics, graded or not, all going up for auction or on internet stores. Our physical store here in San Diego watched an increase in disinterested parties scanning our comics with the overt opinion they "can get it cheaper on eBay." Last year's prices were not necessarily this year's prices. On the flip-side we've never been approached with collections in the quantities we saw over a year's time.

"Can I ask why you're selling?", I plumbed:

1- "I bought all this stuff 'cause I thought I could make money on it."

2- "I guess I got involved when the market was hot."

3- "I thought I got a good deal on these comics but didn't really know anything about them."

4- "I had fun buying on eBay and figured if I needed to sell them they'd probably be worth more."

5- "Is grading still a thing? The comics I bought looked pretty good to me."

Some of these comments were a tad facetious and yet they encompassed the price-drops for so many comics that carried huge demand. We altered some our business model: pay less for purchases and sell for less cost. Otherwise we just held the line on prices deciding to wait out the market and see what happens.

I saw a lot of new faces in our store exploring our vintage old comics. I spoke to some as they rolled their index fingers down the screens of their phones. They'd entered the comic book market as a result of the Covid seclusions, some began again during the pandemic). Either way, eBay was their price control for choices they wished to purchase. Everything they knew about buying comics came from eBay.

I come from the generation that formed comic book grading, honed its degrees of quality and then attached values. Evolution has brought collectors forward where grade should matter more than ever but it doesn't for all. Collecting enters a quagmire when the price looks right without understanding grading until its submission time. As I said above, collections have been arriving in good amounts. That includes graded comics, mostly from CGC and then CBCS. The one-two punch of buy online and then submit online has hammered more than a few people. Now, they are in the hole for money and the grades they got, for reasons they can't fathom, won't allow them to cash in. I explain where they went wrong in order to lessen the blows of my purchase prices, which were percentages of current retail. They bought a NM raw and got a 7.0 in the mail. Of course, some "blame the messenger." I can't help that but most grudgingly accept the truth they went into collecting with eyes wide-shut.

I only want to inform and teach to make them wary and better educated.

One other aspect of business is the subscriber. Our subscription list has taken a hit from customers who have exited California or just inhaled too much inflation. Every comic book store can sympathize with subscribers who bail. We tried various methods to hold them accountable. The sage advice to hold their credit card numbers back-fired when one customer filed a chargeback against us for use of his card. The credit card company reversed the charge and we were out money.

I enjoy seeing the resurgence in Golden Age comics collecting. My revered ECs act as though they just exploded upon the scene. Unlike Silver Age activity, GA comics show less pricing downturns in the market. I figure it's generational, as well as pandemic originated. People just gotta buy something. Silver to current keys flood retail sites while GA's scarcity helps the push.

San Diego hosts several comic and/or toy conventions. Sadly, two of them are on hiatus. I don't know if they are coming back as of December 2023. I know the promoters, but I don't butt into their business. One fault definitely lays in the venue costs. A promoter cautious of over head will find costs just too high for a show that needs a couple of thousand attendees to be profitable. Both shows attract a lot of customers and yet, not enough to remain solvent. There is the other venue issue: venues in town are constantly being remodeled, sold-off, or replaced as San Diego continues to build high-density housing.

Never have my store manager Matt Joaquin or I studied posts on social networks about the sales of new comics as much as we do now. The sour news mirrors our back issue sales dilemma. My problems are every other retailer's problems. I'm not going to belabor the obvious.

The distribution of new comics added competition when Lunar Distribution forced Diamond to relinquish DC Comics. More followed. The biggest gripes from us involve shortages and damaged products. Diamond presented us with both constantly and still does. Lunar came out of the gate with less-to-none. Diamond's packaging leaves us with clumps of comic books separated and not together by title. Lunar keeps the titles together. Lunar has shown recent deficiencies as they absorb new publishers and grow their inventory.

Adding to the comments I wrote about acquired walk-in collections, I'm in awe of how often original, vintage comic collections keep surfacing. We see them once or twice a month. By vintage I mean pre-1980 stuff. Original owners and/or their descendents are in enough abundance to make me believe there are almost infinite quantities of undiscovered comics to be had. One collection was contained in the most classic of carriers: seven steamer trunks adorned with old stickers identifying the owner's travels in the US Navy. At some point, the guy bought packs of used polyurethane comic book bags. All the comics survived in high grade without the benefit of comic backing boards. A few graded higher with pressing which raised the level of quality to Outstanding. The comics ranged from the mid-1960s to the 1980s. But, the 1980s comics are the "new" 1960s Silver Age for many of my customers. Ya gotta keep up with the times!

I am finishing the saga of the actor/thief from last year's *Guide*. Ray Buffer, renowned in the *New York Post* and on TMZ for stealing from comic book stores, met his fate. The Court forced him to accept probation after serving one day in jail and paying me for my loss. As comic book thievery remains rampant it's comforting to know there is justice out there.

KAREN O'BRIEN
COMICS JOURNALIST

If this year's "weekend warrior" small comics shows were any indication, the back issue market is healthy. As we celebrated the return of audiences to the large comics conventions in 2022, it wasn't until 2023 that the smaller comics shows returned to form. Many of these smaller shows changed dates or venues (or both) since 2019, and organizers I spoke with were grateful to be up and running again. Plowing through a long box and looking down the table at the seven others you still had to go through was a thrill mostly absent during the pandemic. But the persistent crowds I encountered at three local shows this year were spending up for higher condition grades and enjoying good values on bulk purchases from dealmaking vendors.

E-commerce via eBay and other auction options and social media updates via Facebook, Instagram, and other venues became accepted practices by savvy comic shops during the pandemic—and it seems those digital commitments are here to stay. Augmenting brick-and-mortar stores

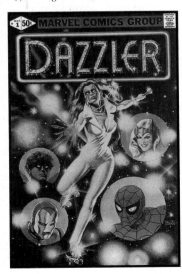

with e-commerce efforts can be time consuming but profitable. Everything from weekly new release updates to Free Comic Book Day festivities appear on the social media feeds now, and I welcome all the info my local comics shop shares.

How are your collecting projects coming along? I've nearly finished the Modern run I was working on (thanks to those local shows!), and I'm plugging away at my Bronze Age run. I picked up a couple of books for this run in lower grades than I'd like and stored them with notes to upgrade as soon as I can. Do you do that, too? The organization project is also moving along nicely, and it would go a lot faster if I didn't stop to read so many of the books I'm supposed to be organizing! I know this happens to you, too. Collectors.

My observations on the comics marketplace for 2023:

After a market correction in the back half of 2022 that persisted into 2023, Golden Age books unsurprisingly held their luster.

Atomic Age space titles and pre-Code Horror books are always in demand, with rising prices for lesser conditions. Desire for the 1950s Westerns was flat, and prices are friendly in lower grades—this might be the time to "trade up" to higher grades or start collecting a run.

Silver Age titles remain desirable in all conditions, with prices in the lower grades showing movement this year. Military and Romance titles show signs of life. Patience and homework are essential if you're working on Silver Age runs, as books are available but opportunities for bargains are few, so verify condition on potential acquisitions. (Before you pay "up" for a book, remove it from the bag and verify the back cover condition. I've talked to more than one collector this year who would have passed on a book if they had taken the time for that step.)

Bronze Age titles are doing well at auctions. Notable auction houses, eBay, and social media live "claim sales" continue to achieve solid results with increasing demand. Most sword & sorcery books were flat, but *Conan the Barbarian* #1 remains a hot key. Don't ignore Romance titles (especially series carried over from the Silver Age) in higher grades. Military and Westerns fizzle during the Bronze Age, but interest in *All-Star Western* #10 (1972, first appearance of Johah Hex) is still strong. Speculation on the potential casting of singer Taylor Swift as Dazzler in the upcoming *Deadpool 3* film has fueled the fire for two titles: *Uncanny X-Men* #130 (1980, first appearance of Dazzler) and *Dazzler* #1 (1981, ongoing series). Super hero titles rule this era on valuation and demand, however, so if you're working on runs, budget accordingly and practice patience.

Increasing interest in key issues has seeped into the Copper Age books, which remain affordable and relatively easy to find in high grades. The 2023 SAG-AFTRA strike slowed down production of *Deadpool 3* but ramped up its hype, and that could cause a spike in demand for Deadpool-related and Wolverine-related titles. Noteworthy this year are *Batman* #423 (1988, Todd McFarlane cover art), *Wolverine* #1 (1988, first solo series), New Mutants #81 (1991, first appearance of Deadpool, a perpetual favorite), *Wonder Woman* #1 (1987), *Uncanny X-Men* #244 (first appearance of Jubilee), *Spider-Man* #1 (1990), and *Sandman* #1 (1989).

Modern Age demand is driven by popular characters, good genre books, some carryover interest from films and television series, slabbed book speculators, and variants. *Batman*, with its string of topnotch creative teams, remains a top pick. This is also the age of the creator-owned comic, with titles like *Saga* and *Monstress* from Image Comics perpetually on "best of" lists. Modern horror has found an enthusiastic modern audience, as have sci-fi and fantasy titles. Publishers like Image, IDW, Dark Horse, Oni Press, BOOM! Studios, Ahoy Comics, Scout Comics, and Vault Comics are fearlessly releasing miniseries-length and ongoing titles that may well have collecting potential, including *Sirens of the City, W0rldtr33, Something Epic, Under the Influence, Dwellings, The Hunger & The Dusk, Lovesick, The Nasty, Damn Them All, Black Cloak*, and more.

As I do with every edition, I'll end this report with a call to encourage the next generation of collectors. Your knowledge of this hobby and approach to collecting can inspire others, so reach out when you can. Opportunities exist through local libraries to display collections or lead discussions on hobby topics (donate this book to your local library immediately!), and the reference librarian is an excellent resource. Speaking to groups of adults, including the Rotary, Kiwanis, or Lion's Club, in your hometown can prompt members to introduce the hobby to the young people in their lives. And speaking of young people, the Boy Scouts of America offers a "Collections" merit badge. Comic book collecting certainly fits the criteria for the badge, so contact your local scout troop and volunteer for a short presentation. While the Girl Scouts of the USA doesn't have a "Collections" option, it does offer a merit badge for Cadettes (grades 6-8) in "Comic Artist," and the artists among us might be of assistance.

Collect what you enjoy, and enjoy your collection!

TERRY O'NEILL
TERRY'S OLD SCHOOL COMICS/
CALCOMICCON/
NATIONWIDE COMICS

This 2022-2023 report is my first true post-pandemic report. My primary focus is selling vintage comics at conventions. I also have a website that is infrequently updated; however, if you find something there of interest, you can call or e-mail me and I'll sell it to you if I have it.

For the past 25 years I published a paper catalog that was also available in PDF format. Unfortunately, 2023 was the first year I was unable to get my inventory verified in time for printing, (usually completed by mid-January), and I had to move on to convention-season planning.

As for the convention scene, we did more conventions than originally planned: February CalComicCon then March, with two shows in SoCal. In April, we traveled to AZ for a store show at Fantastic Worlds, then on to NH for the Little Giant Old School show, followed by Windy City Pulp and Paperback show. No shows were planned for May, but we were invited to Shortboxed Live and were offered a booth at the Comicon Revolution. In June, out to Denver for Rocky Mountain Con and then up to Puyallup, WA for Summer Con. In July we headed south to Torpedo show, August we drove out to the Pulpfest in Pittsburgh, then to Illinois for the Fan Expo. We exhibited at OAFCON in September, and in Portland, OR and Bellingham WA shows in October. Our final 2023 convention was the Old-Man-Con in Scottsdale, AZ.

On a positive note, the Convention scene for 2023 was quite good for selling comics, especially Golden Age and Atom Age. We did well at most shows mentioned, possibly because we have a large inventory of comics prior to 1960 in just about every title, publisher, and genre.

There were a lot of Silver, Bronze, and Modern Age at every convention. Competition was fierce as the prices had dropped the previous couple of years, especially effecting dealers offering only that type of inventory. I eventually put a up a sign that I would match Internet prices to help move my Silver and Bronze Age comics. For price-matching, we used GPAnalysis and Go-Collect as well as eBay and auction sites. As a result, I often sold books for less than I paid in order to price-match.

That said, prices are stabilizing, and I've noticed increased demand for some DC Comics, especially the keys, compared to a year or two ago. Hopefully, we've seen the bottom of that market. On the other hand, Bronze Age comics are not doing as well, prices have dropped, and they may not recover as quickly; there's plenty available, (mostly in higher grades), and they're not really that rare. The 2023 *Overstreet Price Guide* shows some of them actually went negative.

Golden Age (1938-1945): I specialize in this era and buy mostly from long-time customers who still call me to buy their comics for one reason or another (marriage, divorce, new car, no longer collect, new house, college tuition etc.). Most Golden Age comics are superhero titles such as *Superman, Batman, Captain America, Human Torch, Wonder Woman, Captain Marvel, Blue Beetle*, and *Fighting Yank*, along with a host of other characters. There are a few other genres like Disney (*Four Color*) and Science Fiction/Adventure such as Fiction House titles. Sales of note: *Captain America Comics* #13 1.5 $4200; *Batman* #13 3.5 $1800 & #6 2.0 $1500; *Detective* #72 6.0 $950; *Spotlight* #2 6.0 $1000; *Marvel Mystery* #43 1.0 $900; *Real Life Comics* #3 1.0 $3500; *Speed Comics* #1 CGC 3.5 Qualified $2400; *Military*

Comics #5, CGC 4.5 $350; *Master Comics* #31 CGC 0.5 $250; *Young Allies* #2 CGC 2.0 $2000 and *Speed Comics* #31 CBCS 2.0 Trimmed $2500.

Atom Age (1946-1955): The titles sold were so many that it's easier to say what did not sell. I stopped bringing Westerns such as *Roy Rogers*, *Classics Illustrated*, and Kid's Humor such as *Casper* to shows. Crime such as *Murder Inc.*, War such as *Combat Casey*, Horror such as *Witches Tales*, Sci-fi such as *Strange Worlds*, Teen Humor such as *Kilroy's*, Romance such as *My Confessions*, Humor such as *Dizzy Dames*, and of course Superhero such as *Wonder Woman* all sold well, especially in very good or better condition. Sales of note: *Authentic Police Cases* #8 5.0 $550; *Strange Worlds* #4 CGC 4.0 $1200; *Witchcraft* #5 CGC 3.5 $655; *Blue Bolt Weird* #115 3.0 $1500; *Weird Science* #12 (1st) $1500; *Jo-Jo* (#8) #9 CGC 4.0 $1400; *Phantom Lady* #21 1.6 $1200; *Foxhole* #3 3.0 $700; *Crimes by Women* #6 5.0 $650; *Tomb of Terror* #12 4.5 $550; *Vault of Horror* #23 5.0 $550 and *Zoot* #14 5.0 $500.

Silver Age (1956-1970): As previously noted, Silver Age comics cooled down quite a bit over the past two years to the point that certain items are selling for less than they cost back in 2020/2021. Overall, collectors are looking for deals on items that look better than the actual grade. Many collectors had phones in hand checking grades while shopping for comics. Most common non-key comics from runs sell well if priced around the *Guide*. Early *Spider-Man*, *Batman*, *Avengers*, *Fantastic Four*, *Flash*, and most pre-1965 comics have held or increased in value. Common non-key issues in lower grade need to be discounted to sell. Sales of note: *Amazing Spider-Man* #6 5.0 $2000 & #33 9.0 $1500; *Action* #252 3.0 $1400 Gos; *Avengers* #64 9.6 $400; *Daredevil* #38 9.0 $400; *Brave & the Bold* #28 4.0 $4700; *Incredible Hulk* #102 9.0 $85; *Justice League of America* #1 1.5 $700 WsRs; *Journey into Mystery Annual* #1 4.0 $550; *Strange Tales* #110 3.5 $3500; *Superman's Girlfriend Lois Lane* #106 6.5 $400; *Tales to Astonish* #25 6.5 $400 and *X-Men* #6 6.5 $500.

Bronze Age (1971-1985): As previously noted, Bronze Age has cooled down and competition among dealers is fierce as the marketplace realigns. Collectors are looking for these items at current market prices, while dealers often have older inventory still stickered at the previous higher prices. Sales of note: *Conan the Barbarian* #1 7.0 $450, #23 8.5 $350, & #24 9.0 $500; *Daredevil* #168 7.0 $300; *House of Secrets* #92 CGC 6.0 $1000; *Iron Man* #128 9.4 $300; *Tomb of Dracula* #25 9.4 $400 and *X-Men* #94 8.5 $2500.

Magazines (All): I only bring a few magazines to shows these days, mostly keys and other high-demand magazines. That said, *Savage Tales* #1 in high grade is a sought-after magazine. Some sales of note: *Savage Tales* #1 3.5 $500; *Marvel Comics Super Special* #1 9.6 $250 and *American Splendor* #1 6.5 $250.

Copper Age & Independents (1981-Now): Far from being an expert in this area, they do help pay the bills. Those who read this era as teens are still nostalgic; Spider-Man

is always in demand followed by Batman titles. TMNT is often asked for but rarely available. Sales of note: *Amazing Spider-Man* #252 8.0 $250; *Batman Adventures: Mad Love* 9.6 $250; *Marvel Super-Heroes Secret Wars* #8 9.0 $250; *Twisted Tales* #2 9.6 $45; *Legends of Zelda* #3 9.4 $150 and *Invincible* #50 9.6 $100.

Graded Books: We mostly sell graded books at conventions and a few through auction houses such as Heritage, ComicLink, ComicConnect and Shortboxed. Some sales of note: *Journey into Mystery* #11 CGC 5.0 $1200; *Marvel Mystery* #8 CGC 1.0 resto $2169; *Rangers* #28 CGC 3.0 $788 and *Sunny* #12 CGC 2.5 $280.

Internet Sales: Most of our inventory is at www.ter-ryscomics.com . We update our website about three or four times a year.

In conclusion, as I write this report for the *Overstreet Comic Book Price Guide*, I'm reminded of a discussion on Facebook about the relevance of the *Guide*. Some commented they don't use it while others questioned the accuracy of prices. I, as well as others, pointed out that the word "Guide" is the intention and that's exactly what makes it so useful to any person involved in the comic collecting world. It is not intended to reflect daily fluctuations or sudden spikes or drops in the marketplace. I use it to price 90+ percent of the items I offer for sale and believe that those who say it is not useful do not understand the comic collecting industry.

MICHAEL PAVLIC
PURPLE GORILLA COMICS

Pay attention comic collectors, we need to discuss a touchy but important subject: death. Now, I hope we all will have a long, good life and have all our affairs managed perfectly but the sad reality is that some of us are going to die, soon and unexpectedly. If your loved ones don't have the slightest interest in comics and you've not left specific instructions for the collection then you've just added an additional burden on your grieving family. While they may have no connection to the comics themselves, those books are a link to you. For those you leave behind, selling your collection is like losing another piece of you. It's a very hard thing to do, especially with all the other important tasks that settling an estate entails.

This past year I've dealt with a few widows who were trying to sell their husband's books. It's heartbreaking. With everything else they have to deal with, both financially and emotionally, trying to navigate the comic market is stressful. They have no clue of the "fair market value" of the comics, they have no idea which potential buyers are being truthful or those who are trying to rip them off. I'm rather sure that most people would not want to research the value of those 15 long boxes that sit in your basement.

So, dear comic collector, it's up to you to make it as easy as possible for your loved ones to deal with your comics. You know the value. You know who the good eggs are and you know who to avoid. You probably have a pal or two who

137

are into the hobby. You might have a favourite comic store that's staffed by decent, honest people. Your loved ones need to know this. The hardest part of selling comics is knowing where to start and who to deal with.

Another important part is being realistic about the value of the books. Sure, according to *Overstreet* or eBay or whatever metric you use to determine value, your comics are worth "something." Selling to a private collector will probably get the family more than selling to a store, but again, that depends on the character of the buyer. Telling those you leave behind to get full value for the collection is most likely unrealistic, especially if they deal with a comic store. Don't tell them to "throw it on eBay" if they don't know the market. Your collection might have some real fancy books, but I'll bet there's plenty of books that aren't that big of a deal. To expect these books to fetch *Guide* prices is a mistake. Ain't happening.

How do you, dear collector, bring up this touchy subject? No one wants to talk about death. It's hard, but it's harder still for those you love after you're gone. Help them NOW. If you can't talk about it, then leave a note with your collection, maybe write the important information on a box lid telling them who to talk to, who to potentially sell to and update this info as necessary. Knowledge is power, give your family that power! I've seen firsthand how devastating that this can be for a family, so anything you can do to make their lives easier is the right thing to do.

As always, I need to thank *Overstreet* for the opportunity to have this platform to speak to y'all. Thanks also to Ben and Martin at Phoenix Comics here in Calgary and Dave at Amazing Fantasy in Red Deer for all the help and support. And to Doyle, it will always be your fault!!

BILL PONSETI
FANTASTIC WORLDS COMICS

Greetings comic fans! Well, 2023 has come to a close and I, for one, am glad to see it go in many ways. By all accounts it was a very strange year, that saw tremendous price drops across the board for Silver, Bronze, Copper, and Modern Age comics. While there were some price reductions in the bigger Golden Age keys, it wasn't to the degree or as sweeping as it was for all the other ages of comics. It was almost with trepidation that I would check current fair market value before heading out to a show with my inventory, as I would then have to spend many hours pricing my books down as much as 50% by years end.

2023 was also the first year where our in-store year-over-year gross revenue remained flat. Many of my fellow comic shop owners relayed similar results for their shops. However, the comic convention and show season for me was terrific! Every show we set up at in 2023 was very successful for selling. As long as comics were priced in alignment with the current market conditions, collectors were happy to add them to their collections. Our online sales with Shortboxed and eBay did pretty well for us this year too. To end the year we held our first live claim sale on Instagram and it really out performed my expectations.

Much of the speculation and speculators that drove prices to an unsustainable level in 2021 seemed to be, thankfully, absent for the most part. The "movie effect" seemed to dwindle as well, which is also probably not a terrible thing.

In terms of demand by era, collectors avidly sought out Timelys (no surprise there) Fawcetts (pleasant surprise), EC comics and pre-Code Horror comics led the way in Golden Age. Marvel remained king in Silver, Bronze and Copper ages, with *Amazing Spider-Man* back issues still outpacing all other titles. DC collectors still can't get enough *Batman* back issues, and we struggled to source enough supply to meet the demand. *Batman* keys are an easy sell, but run fillers still were buying non-key *Batman* comics.

As it relates to condition, we observed that high grade keys and non-keys didn't move as well the second half of the year as they did in the first half. Conversely we had much greater success selling low to mid-grade copies of these books. Certainly price played a huge role in this change in strategy for collectors. The old adage that low grade is better than no grade became the mantra for many collectors we dealt with.

On a positive note, 2023 marked another year of younger folks and kids coming in and buying, and starting to collect new comics and back issues. The new comic publishers need to do a better job of targeting this demographic, not just with *Sonic* and *My Little Pony* for the early readers, but solid super-hero stories for all ages.

I wasn't as active this year in the original comic artwork area as I normally would have been, but I did see some price reductions there as well. But premium art still brought premium prices.

Here's to hoping 2024 is a year of normal growth and lots of fun. I think it will be.

Until next year, keep buying what you love and you always win.

TOM RAUPP
POP CULTURE PLAYGROUND

I'm Thomas Raupp and I handle the convention part of POP Culture Playground. We set up at 20 to 30 shows in a year. Some are one day events others are 2 to 4 day events. We sell Silver Age to current comic books and comic related magazines, fanzines, treasury sized comics and promo comics. At times we will have original art for sale as well as comic related games, toys and action figures. We also deal in records, posters and other collectibles.

Sales in 2023 were good, just not as strong as 2022. The market is adjusting as some keys did not hold their value at shows or online. I was surprised at the prices of treasury sized comics online and found that at the shows they sold for over *Guide* in high grade, some at 20% to 40% more. At the shows, we sell a lot of magazines. *Creepy* and *Vampirella* and the top sellers. Many of the Eerie publication mags and the Skywall ones sell in any grade. *Savage Tales* #1 magazine was our hot seller as I buy it any time I can. That one does not last more then a show or two before it is gone. We bought and sold five copies of *Savage Tales* #1 in 2023.

Dells, Gold Key and Charlton comics do well in the Carolinas. Photo covers and TV related titles sell best. Marvel and DC Horror did well at the shows for us this year. DC War comics were a good seller as well. *Sgt. Rock* was the main title along with *Our Army at War*.

The bigger conventions have turned into more of a Pop culture related event. They seem more focus on media guest. Higher booth fees and parking fees have us rethinking many of the events we set up at. Small to mid size shows that focus on comic books and toys are a better fit for us.

I picked up my first *Overstreet* in late 1976. A few of the kids I was hanging with, the ones that traded comics, liked that they could find a value for the comics they treasured. I have made sure to get an *Overstreet* every year since. Yes there are a few apps for those who like to look up prices and see the going trend. I still like to read all the market reports, and look at the prices of books and see what is up or down in the top 100 comics. The *Guide* is great for pricing

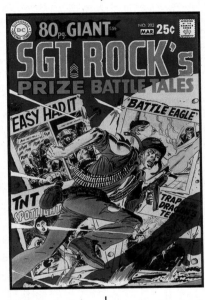

about 90% of the books we deal with. There is that 10% that is always up and down. We check eBay sold prices, and also what books sell for at the shows.

The best advice I can give is to buy what you like. When you see a book that you hardly ever see, you might want to buy it as it may not be there when you come back around.

ALEX & AUSTIN REECE
REECE'S RARE COMICS
AUSTIN REECE

Hello all, I am honored to once again be writing a report for the Overstreet Price Guide! For those of you who don't know me, my brother Alex and I are co-owners of Reece's Rare Comics. We have been running our company together full time for the past 5 years, and were employees of our dad for some time before that. Over the years, we have built and operated 3 different websites, completed thousands of transactions across multiple platforms, and attended many of our industries largest trade shows throughout the country. We currently operate www.reececomics.com, where we specialize in selling vintage comics from the 1930s-1990s and have an inventory of more than 18,000 books for sale.

The years continue to fly by, and I am excited to share some insights from our little corner of the market in 2023.

As I'm sure will be made apparent by the time you get to my Market Report, things in the comic industry this year

were rocky at best. Comics across a variety of ages were decreasing in value month over month for the full year. As of this writing, we are still witnessing corrections on some books, while others are beginning to stabilize slightly. As I wrote in my report last year, I expected most books to fall back to their 2019 levels, and for the most part that has held true. However, some books still have some room to fall, while others have moved into overcorrection territory. Rising interest rates, uncertainty in the economy, and a complete lackluster MCU lineup certainly didn't help any, but at the end of the day we were still dealing with fallout from the meteoric rise of prices from Covid, and finally saw the majority of books fall back to earth. I do think this has created an opportunity in the market for books that have slipped below 2019 levels, and gives you an idea of which books I may still be staying away from, from an investment perspective.

That's not to say we didn't sell any books this year, but had to overcome the new challenges posed in this market. While it may seem obvious, one of our biggest hurdles of the year was keeping inventory priced at current market level throughout the year. Repricing books throughout the year allowed us to sell books quickly and move that money into new inventory at the new market price. You may be thinking that this is a "duh" moment, but with only 4 total employees, the act of repricing an inventory of 15,000+ books was a difficult and time consuming task as we tried to maintain the normal flow of the rest of our business. The difficulty lay in the rate at which prices were falling, as books that were repriced in June were soon overpriced again in August. These quick price corrections were a challenge to us on the buying side as well, as we had to approach buying new collections with the understanding that the collection may decrease by 10-15% from when we agreed to purchase it until we were able to process and list the items for sale.

While you may think that the price corrections from this year would lead to less in person sales, we had a very strong convention season and noticed increased attendance across the board at nearly every Con we attended. Despite what you may read online, there is still something great about getting a group of your friends together to attend a convention and bond over a shared love of comic books. I recommend to everyone- try to get out and attend a show sometime this year, as the best part of comic books is the relationships you build year in and year out and seeing our friends and customers across the country is something we look forward to every year. I highly recommend Heroes Con in Charlotte, North Carolina, Baltimore Comic Con, and Megacon down in Orlando, Florida.

Regarding in person sales, we noticed that the price correction from Covid peaks led to a lot of retail customers re-entering the market as the books they were interested in purchasing were back within budget. This created what we called the "reverse sticker shock", where customers were surprised by how much certain keys had fallen, and secured some of the books that were previously unobtainable.

Our main business is selling books online, and we were pleased with the strength of our online business and continued to push more inventory onto our website and eBay. Unfortunately, eBay is still a big part of our business, but I encourage you to shop direct from us on our website, where all of the same books are listed for a discount and includes a number of tools built with the collector in mind.

As of this writing, we are working to integrate our inventory on the Shortboxed platform to provide another option for our customers to shop with us, and are also participating in twice a week Whatnot auctions. These auctions have allowed us to process a backlog of vintage inventory, while also allowing us another avenue to engage with our customers and sell some books quickly and fairly.

This is all to say that we are constantly evolving as a company to expand our market reach and are always willing to try new things. While these ideas may not pan out long-term, I don't think we can rely on the convention and eBay model to sustain our business as we look 5 and 10 years into the future.

I think that by the time you read this, the worst of the price corrections will be behind us, and we should be looking at a much more stable market come Summertime. That isn't to say I think books are going to see massive leaps like we had the past few years, but that we are shifting back to the slow and steady growth of the previous decade, rather than the massive swings we saw from 2020-2023.

Ultimately, the collectors are the ones who are the backbone of this market, and the trends I saw in 2023 were that more collectors were able to reenter the market, and we had less speculation than ever before. The hype on movie books is down, and collectors are still buying what they like. We saw a surge of interest in pre-Code Horror and pulps, while Golden Age keys continued to sell well throughout the year. There was still a ton of interest in acquiring Silver Age keys, but only if you were priced at or slightly below market price. The same was true for Bronze Age books, but there was a massive amount of inventory available for any of those books, so you needed to be willing to sell under market if you wanted to move out of a book quickly.

In my opinion, having comic collectors reenter the market is the most important predictor of long-term growth and stability, as collectors are the ones that are going to hold the supply even when demand surges. Most collectors I know are only selling because they have moved on from the hobby, or out of necessity. Which leads me to this: if you buy what you like and can afford, you will have a good time. There are infinite ways to enjoy this hobby, and whether that means you only buy Silver Age Marvel keys, pre-Code Horror, or cool covers from different eras, you will be served well by sticking with what you enjoy. I still believe in the long-term growth of Silver Age keys and iconic Golden Age titles, and am interested to see what books break out in 2024.

With that said, I look forward to another year of participating in this wonderful hobby, and the opportunities that will provide. I hope to see some of you around at a show, speak to you on the phone, or chat by email in the coming year!

ALEX REECE

Hello all! I hope everyone has had a great start to 2024. 2023 was an interesting year, so let's get right into it. You will read about the downturn in the market in all of the other reports so I will spend my time writing about some different subjects.

Firstly, while it in incontrovertible that we are well off of COVID highs for many books, this has actually had some positive benefits from a dealer/buyer perspective, first and foremost being that true collectors can afford sought after key issues again. It is no secret that the COVID bubble attracted investment money into the comic book hobby, and while it started to pull out in 2022, we saw a more dramatic withdrawal in 2023. A great benchmark book is *Amazing Fantasy* #15. This book was indicative of many Silver Age keys during the pandemic, shooting up to stratospheric heights and getting well out of range for the average buyer. 2.0s at one point were trading in the $35k range, and I cannot tell you how many people came up to me at shows and said that they thought *Amazing Fantasy* #15 was forever out of their budget at those price points. Flash forward to the end of 2023 and the price has corrected significantly, with a copy in 2.0 most recently selling for $15k in October of 2023. This is marginally above 2019 prices, and slightly above 2019 price points is true almost across the board for most grades of the book. While this is still a hefty amount of money, it dramatically increases the buyer pool that is able to afford an *Amazing Fantasy* #15.

True collectors acquiring and keeping key books is the backbone of our hobby, and with the fall in price of these books so many more people are able to purchase keys. *AF #15* is just one book, but I believe it is representative of most of the Silver Age.

Secondly, when prices were going up month over month, we routinely had people who could not believe the price of books. Take an *X-Men #1*, for example. In the early part of 2023, after 2 years after wild price increases, people had expectations of high prices built in. When they would come up to me at a show, they would sigh and ask the price of that same *X-Men #1*, internally assuming they would not be able to afford it. When I quoted them current market value, their eyes would light up, and often a sale would occur. In their minds, if they had it pegged as a $7,500 book and I told them it was $5,000, they felt like they were getting value. We sold a ton of books thanks to this and it helped keep our inventory moving and fresh. Obviously, there were also plenty of books that did not sell and appeared overpriced, but when a reasonable buyer came in with an offer that was close to FMV, we were happy to take it, and also repriced our inventory a few times in 2023.

Next, let's talk about Golden Age. You will likely read in other reports about how Golden Age was the one resilient sector of the market, and by and large that remained true in 2023. Hard to find and sought after GA routinely set sales records and was a buttress against downward pressure in the rest of the market. I am not sure if that tailwind can continue into 2024, so I would not advise jumping onto that bandwagon just for the sake of investment. Buy Gold if you like it, since last year proved that even books perceived as unassailable were capable of massive correction, and Gold may prove to be susceptible to that as well in the future.

Lastly, I wanted to touch on some of our purchases for the year. We bought everything from single issues to 15,000 book collections in 2023. It definitely was more of a buyer's market, but it did come with its own set of challenges. While most people were reasonable and understood that the market was in correction territory, a small segment of sellers were stuck on what their comics had previously been worth, instead of focusing on what they were worth at the moment. The former group of people were usually easy to work with and we got a deal done, while the latter group saw our success rate of purchasing material plummet to near zero. The other challenge was that buying a large group of comics in a falling market is a risky proposition. If you buy a book at 70-80% of FMV, it only takes a few bad sales comps before you are hoping to break even, and this happened to us a few times in 2023. While we were aggressively buying material, it did make it more difficult to come to an agreement with potential sellers. Thankfully the market has equalized a bit and during the last few months of 2023 it was much easier to come to terms and purchase collections.

The premiere collection we bought this year contained 100 short boxes of slabs and 50 long boxes of raw comics, containing deep runs of Silver Age and Bronze Age comics. It was the second (and final) part of the Key City collection, the first section of which we initially rolled out in 2022. The remainder was sold to us in the summer of 2023, and kept us busy for most of that season. We bought several other smaller collections ranging in size from 5 long boxes to 20, and bought single issues of high grade and or key books as well. We are always looking to purchase quality material, so please reach to me or Austin if you have anything you are thinking of selling.

The comic market has been hard to predict the last few years, so I will sign off with our usual mantra, which rings more important than ever these days: Buy what you like and buy the best you can afford! If you follow those tenants, you will be sure to have a rewarding and satisfying collecting journey. Many well wishes to all of our customers and friends who continue to make this hobby such a joy, and I hope to see many of you at a show in 2024. Cheers!

STEPHEN & SHARON RITTER WORLDWIDE COMICS

Our 2024 *Overstreet* report for the 2023 comic market results began with one big question: Was the comic market going to experience the classic "What goes up must come down" after the galactic year 2021 was for the comic market. In other words, was the "Pandemic" surge we saw going to keep prices at their going levels or were we going to see a waterfall collapse?

For those not familiar with us, WorldWide Comics is primarily an internet business specializing in vintage comics, catering to all ends of the collector base in both grades and material. We offer comics from the Golden to the Copper Age with over 10,000 third party (CGC) graded comics on our website and about 50,000 non-third party graded comics. We are fixtures at many major comic conventions each year and participate in all major auction houses around the country.

Due to the massive increases we saw in the comic market due to the "Pandemic" surge of 2020-2021, we are first going to review what we saw in this period and how it shaped the 2023 market, a year that saw the world recovering from the COVID-19 restrictions that caused world chaos in every market.

2020 – The Surge (First Full Year of the Pandemic): The surge for the comic market actually began at the end of 2020 when COVID restrictions were just put in place nationwide and comic sales began a once-in-a-life time climb never seen before. During the last quarter of 2020, the Pandemic was still causing most people to be shut in at home, giving collectors with a steady flow of income more time than ever to shop on-line.

2021 – The Plateau (Post-Pandemic Year): In the first half of 2021, prices on comics kept soaring, it was almost a race for buyers to purchase as quickly and as frequently as they could. Each month was more chaotic than the previous, it was a feeding frenzy of collectors and dealers, each spending as often and as fast as they could. By the middle of the year, the nation was almost fully back to work but beginning to experience economic difficulties which eventually began to impact the comic market. In July, we saw the absolute peak of the year-long bubble as prices began to dip but just slightly throughout the rest of the year.

2022 – The Continuous Fall (World Opening Up After the Pandemic): The year began with a steadying of the market with only slight drops on Silver to Modern keys but mostly a plateau for all other comics from these eras. But, by March of 2022, most all Silver to Modern comics began a slow steady decay in prices. Although the market was sagging, sells remained high as conventions were now ramping up to their pre-Pandemic days. By the middle of the year, most comics (Golden Age comics seemed immune to this drop) were now selling well below the peak we saw in 2021 and it was hard to determine when it was going to bottom out and steady out. Most investors were no longer buying by the end of the year and collectors were apprehensive to buy big value books not knowing if the comic would hold its value in the next few months much less in the next year. This fear kept prices dropping into 2023.

2023 – The Bottom Out (World Returns to Normal): Our estimate is the lowest dip in the Silver to Modern Age comic market hit around March/April of 2023. With the beginning of convention summer season, we began seeing purchases from the investor type clients again and prices seen in auctions were no longer falling. Auctions, which had a glut of material in 2022 due to the number of people that were still trying to capitalize before the huge market swing was over, were now starting to cut back on the volume of material offered every month. This huge volume likely led in part to the continuous fall of prices as too much material was still being auctioned off when no one was buying. Throughout our description of the market in this report, Golden Age comics seem to be the exception to the rule. Although they did see large increases when the market was surging, they did not excessively soar in 2021 like Silver to Modern Age comics did. At the same time, they did not see any sort of a lag much less a crash that the other eras saw. It is safe to say that Golden Age was the safest buy during the past 3 years. By the middle of 2023, we were now aggressively pursuing Silver Age keys which we had not been able to do with confidence over the previous year. At the end of 2023, we are seeing a market that is much more stable than any time in the previous three years with sells at the normal clip. The only part of the market that we view with a bit of uncertainty is still the Silver to Modern key issues. Sales have steadied on them, but they do not sell as quickly as they had before.

The big picture over the past few years is that comics are selling well above what they were prior to the large "Pandemic" surge of 2021, but it was one wild rollercoaster ride to get here. Our last three Overstreet reports were all breaking out this topsy-turvy ride we have been on due to how unique it was for our market. We suspect things are now settled down and next year we will go back to providing a market report more focused on the year as a whole and not a month-by-month blow. Let's hope 2024 continues to bring more confidence for all types of buyers which will only strengthen the comic market. Good hunting!!

CONAN SAUNDERS & BUDDY SAUNDERS
LONE STAR COMICS/MYCOMICSHOP.COM
BUDDY SAUNDERS

As I write this in early December 2023, Lone Star Comics/MyComicShop sales are up over last year, but when we account for inflation, our actual year-to-year growth was marginal.

The recent price bubble in the comic book market is self-correcting, as are the effects of Covid. Were it not for inflation, the outlook for hobby and industry would be more positive.

We sell both new and back issue comics.

The effect of inflation on new comic sales is readily apparent. As cover prices increase, readers, already hit by higher prices across much of the economy, are more selective and are buying fewer comics. Thus, it is in new comic sales, both preorders and new in stock on our website, that we've seen sales decline, 0.5% preorder sub, and 13% new stock.

We've also seen a decline in consignment sales, 3.8%, a category where heretofore growth has been double digit year-to-year. We think that many who paid a premium during the market bubble are hesitant to consign and sell at a loss. Likewise, those who already have their comics listed with us at fixed price are reluctant to drop their prices to accommodate current market. Confirming this is that never before have we had more comics consigned with us at fixed price, yet actual sales are down.

Back issue sales, primarily comics and graphic novels, but with pulps and vintage paper a growing category, are by far our largest segment. Sales in this category remain solid, with growth of 3.7% in the last year. This is good news because this category is the largest and the most profitable segment we have.

Gone are the days when Buddy Saunders was Lone Star Comics' only buyer. Our Seller Services Dept. has four full time people, not counting Conan and me, along with our many buying partners and pickers scattered from one end of the country to the other. 40+ full-time graders and other personnel process the comic collections and dealer stock comics that arrive at our loading docks— averaging more than one hundred long boxes per week, the larger lots arriving by the tractor-trailer load. Never a day passes that we are not buying.

As for me, I am currently spending much of my time buying on eBay and on other sites, and working with our programmers to further improve our database, especially with regard to non-comic vintage paper. In addition to having virtually every comic that ever existed in our database, we can now say the same for pulp magazines and for Big Little Books, as well as many other categories such as spicy titles from the 1920s and '30s, and men's magazines from the 1950s and '60s. At this time our database contains 248,585 issues, many thousands of which have comprehensive creator, character, and content information, with more content added weekly.

Looking to the future, we are confident that despite inflation, the market for comics as entertainment and investment will remain strong as more people discover what we true believers already know and love—the marvelous world of comics!

CONAN SAUNDERS

The biggest story in the comic market the past four years has been a macroeconomic one, first with Covid-era changes in leisure spending behavior and stimulus payments joining forces to push comic prices rapidly to new highs, and then a decline after prices peaked and gave up much if not all their gains. Most of the decline that started late summer 2022 concluded by spring 2023. It looks to me like prices have largely been steady since then—some books dropping slightly, some beginning to move back up, but the overall trend being stability.

I'd like to use my space here to document the changes we've seen from 2019 to 2023 across segments of the vintage market: Golden Age, Silver Age, Bronze Age, 1980s, and Vintage Paper.

All percentage changes in the following paragraphs are relative to the baseline year 2019; they are not year to year changes. I'm providing all numbers as a percentage of the base year 2019 to make it easier to see the overall trend for this four year period relative to the same starting year.

Golden Age: Golden Age average sale price - up 40% in 2020, up 39% in 2021, up 36% in 2022, and up 30% in 2023. Prices rose for Golden Age during the Covid years, but didn't go up as sharply as Silver, and have declined less than Silver in 2023.

Golden Age total sales - up 60% in 2020, up 78% in 2021, up 89% in 2022, and up 112% in 2023. Our overall sales have grown significantly each year, with sales in 2023 more than double our sales in the base year 2019. This reflects both the resilience of the Golden Age market in general, and for us specifically a stronger and stronger presence in Golden Age as we have been buying Golden Age heavily and had more and more Golden Age books consigned with us as our market has grown.

Of particular excitement for us as I write in December 2023 is the Oxford Collection, a group of 52 comics spanning the earliest portion of the Golden Age from 1936 to 1942 and consisting almost entirely of scarce #1 issues. This collection is being auctioned in our 2024 January Prime Auction on behalf of the estate of Mike Van Houten.

Silver Age: Silver Age average sale price - up 15% in 2020, up 56% in 2021, up 77% in 2022, up 63% in 2023. Big jumps in 2021 and 2022, partial retreat in 2023.

Silver Age total sales - up 16% in 2020, up 65% in 2021, up 59% in 2022, up 57% in 2023. Sharp increase in 2021, downturn in second-half of 2022, and 2023 doing a great job coming in just a tad below 2022 despite lower prices for many Silver Age keys than when 2022 opened.

Bronze Age: Bronze Age average sale price - up 6% in 2020, up 31% in 2021, up 42% in 2022, up 63% in 2023.

Interestingly, our average sale price (ASP) for Bronze books has continued climbing in 2023, not falling like Silver did. There are certainly Bronze Age keys that have seen their prices drop in 2023, I'm not disputing that, but looking at an average of all our sales of Bronze Age books, 2023 ASP is up from 2022 not down.

Bronze Age total sales - up 16% in 2020, up 55% in 2021, up 49% in 2022, and up 54% in 2023. Again we see strength in the Bronze Age in our total sales numbers.

1980s Comics: 1980s books average sale price: up 18% in 2020, up 59% in 2021, up 77% in 2022, up 106% in 2023. We see here the same pattern we saw with Bronze Age: the ASP rose in 2022 and then again in 2023, bucking the trend seen in Silver Age books. Average sale price in 2023 was a little more than double ASP in 2019.

1980s books total sales - up 34% in 2020, up 103% in 2021, up 100% in 2022, up 89% in 2023. Total sales were flat in 2022 vs 2021, and down a bit in 2023, though still nearly double where they were in 2019.

Vintage Paper: Lastly, Vintage Paper. Vintage Paper is our term for pulp magazines, digests, Big Little Books, men's interest and humor magazines, and other periodicals that aren't comic books but are of interest to many collectors of vintage comic books. Reminder, all percentage comparisons shown here are relative to the baseline year 2019 unless otherwise specified.

Vintage Paper average sale price - up 3% in 2020, up 10% in 2021, up 77% in 2022, and up 239% in 2023.

Vintage Paper total sales - up 79% in 2020, up 117% in 2021, up 140% in 2022, and up 828% in 2023.

This data shows two clear trends: as of 2023 we've been selling significantly many more higher end vintage paper items, especially pulps magazines, which has pushed the average sale price strongly up. And, you can see that we've enjoyed a huge increase in sales from the vintage paper segment in 2023. We have invested heavily in pulps and other vintage categories over the previous few years, and you can see that investment leading to a lot of sales in 2023.

Pulp grading has seemingly been just around the corner at CGC for a couple years now, but with recent announcements made November 2023 by CGC at the Collectors Summit in Dallas, it seems CGC grading of pulps is finally here. I know quite a few pulp enthusiasts who are excited about the further recognition and exposure that CGC grading will bring to the pulp market.

Thanks for reading! I hope 2024 is a good year for your health, your collection, and your families. We at Lone Star Comics and MyComicShop feel blessed to be part of this community of collectors and fans.

ALIKA SEKI, P.E.
MAUI COMICS & COLLECTIBLES

Aloha from Maui! As many of you know, the Lahaina and Kula fires of August 8th have destroyed so much of Maui. The impact of these disasters has been felt island wide. The pain that was caused by the initial tragedy is only compounded by the housing crisis that is only beginning to take shape. Businesses all over Maui are trying their best to get by while also being there to support our ohana that has lost so much. The global outpouring of support has been so incredible. We are often asked of good local organizations to donate to, and we always recommend Maui Rapid Response. We watched Maui Rapid Response grow from a small, motivated group of folks caring for and helping the most vulnerable people during the pandemic, to a support network providing the most basic needs of thousands of locals impacted by the fires. If you want to help the people of Maui with your donations, I can recommend them without reservation. As soon as the fires happened, our dear friend Frank Cho donated art that was auctioned by the new website Nerdcrawler. Frank and his manager Steve Morger used their connections in the comic industry to get donations from Art Adams and Dan Brereton towards the cause, and Eric Powell and Steve Lavigne gave generously. In total Frank Cho and friends ended up raising over $12,000 all of which was donated to the Maui Rapid Response non-profit.

There was initially some internal debate whether we should even proceed with the Maui Comic Con in 2023. After some discussion we realized that the event would serve as a much-needed respite from the unrelenting challenges facing the people of Lahaina. We decided that our free-to-the-public, family-friendly event would be a good way to foster joy in the community. Maui Comic Con happened on December 9 & 10, 2023 at the University of Hawaii, Maui College campus. Special guests included Frank Cho, Gail Simone, Rick Leonardi, Ryan Ottley, Trina Robbins, Steve Leialoha, Willie Ito and Peter Shinkoda. The convention featured over 40 local artists from across the islands, but emphasis should be put on those who were from Lahaina and Kula and exhibited with the convention. The Maui Strong comic anthology also announced its crowdfunding launch via Zoop with many of the contributors to the project appearing in artists alley. We say all of this to highlight the good that comics can do in any community – the true value of the medium.

I was also able to make a trip to Japan in November of 2023 with Ed Piskor of the popular comics YouTube channel Cartoonist Kayfabe that he co-hosts with fellow comic creator and aficionado Jim Rugg. Ed Piskor goes on an annual trip he affectionately dubs "Manga Quest" and had been throwing the invite out there and I was finally able to go. This was my first time to Japan and we spent quite a bit of time in various Mandarake locations (Shibuya, Asakusa, and Nakano Broadway) as well as the well-curated private showroom of Shawn the Japan Book Hunter. It was a crash course in manga, and I walked away with some new favorites; *Maruo*, *Hino* and *Gataro* among them. Seeing such a healthy and vibrant print media culture gives me hope for our market's future. There are a lot of grim forecasts and hot takes filled with doom and gloom, but one thing you can't deny is that people love comics and there's a comic for everyone.

It has been 10 years since the passing of my mentor Bruce Ellsworth III (senior advisor to the *Guide*) in 2013. Not a day goes by that I don't use some part of the education Bruce gave me in comics, whether in appreciation of the medium or pursuit of new collections. His respect for the lower grade reader books has served me well in maintaining a healthy stock of older, collectible books. We are still relying on the tried-and-true Marvel Silver Age books in low to mid grades. It's been a very slow year for our store, even without the lull in tourism that happened in August it was shaping up to be a slow year. Notable sales for our store include:

- *Amazing Spider-Man* #194 CGC 9.8 OW/WP first app Black Cat for $2,000
- *Detective Comics* #400 CGC 5.0 OW pages first app Man-Bat for $300
- *Amazing Spider-Man* #361 CGC 9.6 WP first app Carnage for $180
- *Brave and the Bold* #25 CGC 5.0 OW pages first app Suicide Squad for $1,000
- *Vampirella* #1 approximately Fine+ first app Vampirella for $1,000

Since I am always watching the trends on all things TMNT it is worth noting that the wave of record high sales of *Teenage Mutant Ninja Turtles* has crashed hard. *TMNT* #1 first printing in CGC 9.2 is closer to a $20,000 book or less, half of what it promised to fetch in 2022. While some of the gains for other Mirage books, such as the City at War arc (Mirage volume 1, issues #50-62) others have been all but lost and the books are back to being affordable. I would return to my advice from a couple of years ago to take this time to complete any collections for any of the die-hard TMNT fans out there.

Mahalo for checking out our report! If you would like to support the local people of Lahaina and Kula check out Maui Rapid Response on IG and Facebook and through their website, mauirapidresponse.org. If you plan on visiting our store let us know via social media on IG: @maui_comics, and FB: Maui Comics & Collectibles. If you are interested in attending the Maui Comic Con or even being a sponsor/vendor please visit MauiComicCon.com or contact us via social media on IG: @mauicomiccon, and FB: MAUI Comic Con. A hui hou!

TODD SHEFFER
HAKE'S AUCTIONS

Hake's Auctions enjoyed another great year of record results in 2023, with comics and collectibles continuing to be a strong investment. Sales and prices were still strong in all major categories such as comic books, comic art, action figures, sports and other pop culture collectibles.

Comic book sales show values still rising for key books from the Golden, Silver and Bronze Age, while Modern Age comics and limited run variants are still seeing amazing prices with the search for the next key high grade book. Certified comics show no slowing down as collectors try to purchase high grade examples. Some of the lower grade keys and newer "hot" books have calmed down slightly as prices find a new normal.

The comic art market keeps getting attention as record-breaking prices are paid at auction for covers and key pages from legends and hot new artists. Many new to market pieces are bringing top prices. Look for interest in comic art to continue to build with every high dollar sale result, sending collectors to auction to add new pieces to their collections.

Vintage Star Wars action figures continue to bring record-breaking prices. Disney+ will continue airing new Star Wars series and supporting the franchise while bringing in new collectors to the vintage market. Star Wars action figures are still going strong and we look for this interest to continue as even more collections come to market thanks to record prices.

Classic toys and collectibles from the 1980s and 1990s are seeing a steady increase in demand, with the generations that played with Masters of the Universe, G.I. Joe, Transformers and Teenage Mutant Ninja Turtles realizing the investment potential of their childhood toys. Growth continues in this sector as collectors look to reconnect to those childhood memories.

And just like certified comics, third party graded toys and action figures have seen another year of growth as well, with high grade examples of popular characters resulting in bidding wars that have frequently set new price benchmarks this year. These third party graders have seen sometimes overwhelming demand for their services, no doubt brought on in part from continued impressive prices for graded toys at auction.

Golden Age: Early DC and Timely superhero titles have a continued following with film and TV features attracting new collectors and driving already avid collectors to seek out the early appearances of key characters. EC and other pre-Code Horror have been running strong with that trend looking to continue. Pedigrees such as Mile High and others bring top dollar when they come to market. Uncertified issues also command high prices with scarce titles and issues getting scooped up by savvy collectors when they come up for sale.

Silver Age: Marvel continues to be the desired choice in Silver Age. *Amazing Fantasy* #15 and *Amazing Spider-Man* #1 show no signs of slowing down, with increases in value across all grades this past year. Spider-Man leads the pack as the hottest character, with early issues being highly sought after by collectors, especially those with first appearances of key villains. First appearances of all major Marvel characters continue to be in high demand as well. Look for more of

this as Hollywood and various streaming platforms ramp up production for 2024.

Bronze/Copper/Modern Age: TV and movies continue to drive these newer issues forward as well with Disney+, Amazon Prime, Netflix and others pulling material from comics. First appearances of characters such as Wolverine, Ghost Rider, Moon Knight and more modern characters like Harley Quinn, Deadpool, Cable, Miles Morales and others keep increasing with each new film project announced. Variant covers for these newer books keep bringing record-breaking prices as well.

Notable 2023 Comic Sales at Hakes.com: *Amazing Spider-Man* #1 CGC 9.6 $520,380 (World Record Auction Price, at this time), *Amazing Fantasy* #15 CGC 7.5 $170,844, *Amazing Spider-Man* #14 CGC 9.4 $38,615, *Amazing Spider-Man* #1 CGC 6.5 $32,969, *Teenage Mutant Ninja Turtles* #1 CGC 9.2 Signature Series $31,152, *X-Men* #1 CGC 7.0 $27,418, *Amazing Fantasy* #15 CGC 2.5 $24,255, *Amazing Fantasy* #15 CGC 2.0 $21,240, *Fantastic Four* #1 CGC 5.0 $19,973, *Gobbledygook* #1 CGC 5.5 $16,225.

Notable 2023 Comic Art Sales at Hakes.com: *Action Comics* #588 cover art by John Byrne $35,695, *Green Lantern* #80 page art by Neal Adams $25,057, *Amazing Spider-Man vs The Prodigy* complete story pages art by Ross Andru $19,210, *Kid Colt Outlaw* #72 complete story pages art by Jack Keller $18,204, *Super-Team Family* #15 cover art by Jose Luis Garcia Lopez $17,653, *Action Comics* #353 splash page art by Al Plastino $17,501, *Detective Comics* #585 cover art by Jerry Bingham $14,927, *Brave and the Bold* #179 cover art by Ross Andru $14,162, *Action Comics* #866 page art by Gary Frank $11,034, *Titans/Legion of Superheroes: Universe Ablaze* #4 cover art by Dan Jurgens $10,010, *Amazing Spider-Man* #36 complete story color guides art by Stan Goldberg $16,550.

Notable 2023 Pop Culture Collectible Sales at Hake's: *Star Wars* Boba Fett (Rocket-Firing L-Slot Prototype-no rocket) AFA 75+ $99,297, *Star Wars: The Empire Strikes Back* TolToys Vinyl Cape Jawa AFA 50 $49,324, *Star Wars* Toy Center Display AFA 90 $42,690, *Star Wars* Luke Skywalker (Double Telescoping Lightsaber) AFA 85 $38,940, *Star Wars* Early Bird Kit AFA 85 $25,571, 1936 Wolverine Gum Card PSA Graded Set $64,906, Captain Marvel Play Cape $28,556, Transformers Series 1 Optimus Prime (Trademark Logo) AFA 85 $34,462, Transformers Series 1 Optimus Prime (Error Box) AFA 80 $20,190, Masters Of The Universe - Eternia Playset AFA 70 $13,369, G.I. Joe U.S.S. Flagg AFA 60 $11,105, Teenage Mutant Ninja Turtles Undercover Leonardo AFA 80Y $5,062.

Marc Sims
Big B Comics - Barrie

2023 was a challenging year to be a retailer in the comic book industry. The market correction on Silver/Bronze/Copper that began midway through 2022 only accelerated in 2023. I've adjusted prices down by as much as 50% on big chunks of my inventory. New comic sales are in free fall, and people, forced to choose between collecting and putting food on the table, have left the hobby in droves. The bubble has officially and resoundingly burst.

Now, it's not all doom and gloom. Comics have been through boom and bust cycles before and savvy collectors and retailers have in the past prospered in these down times. If you have the cash, opportunities exist right now to buy in at great prices. I'd take an *Amazing Fantasy* #15 in mid grade at today's prices as a solid long term bet every day of the week. Importantly, my experience is that most people are buying less not because they don't want to buy – they simply can't afford to buy. The demand side of the equation is being tamped down by monetary policy (The Fed raising interest rates) that was designed to do exactly this: weaken demand and get inflation under control. The supply side in vintage comics remains unchanged. We continue to deal with old and fragile goods that they're not making any more of. If anything, the soft market means more inventory stays in private collections as people delay the decision to sell, hoping for a better market down the line. People still love comics and comic characters. We continue to be a society filled with collectors of "stuff". To me, this leaves a market with healthy fundamentals that is primed to roar right back once money starts flowing again. That might not be until 2025 when interest rates are projected to come down enough to get our wallets a bit fatter again, but I do think it is inevitable that we will see a growing vintage comic market again in the near future.

Of course if all you collect is Golden Age or Original Comic Art, you already know you can pretty much disregard everything you've just read. Golden Age comics, while not entirely immune to the downward pressures in the market, have performed exceedingly well all year. The difference in scarcity between 1942 and 1962 (never mind 1982) simply cannot be overstated and demand is impossible to meet. I have customers coming in to the shop or emailing me regularly asking about PCH, Timely, Baker, L.B. Cole, etc. I wish I could satisfy every one of them but it's tough!

At the shop we've made the choice to pivot ever so slightly away from being a luxury brand to more of a value brand in 2024. Of course I love old comics way too much to move away from stocking quality back issues. I'm just going to focus my energies more on pricing and making floor space for the reams of $2-4 comics I have in storage rather than busting my hump trying to always have Silver Age Marvel #1s in stock. $10,000 comics in the showcase are nice and all, but that's not getting feet through the door when times are tough. If anything, it's attracting the wrong kind of interest. Pro tip to new customers coming in to the shop for the first time: don't ask the clerk "What's your most expensive comic?". It immediately marks you as a potential B&E suspect and I can assure you there is not a single retailer who enjoys getting that question. Theft is rampant at stores and conventions right now. Every week I feel like I'm seeing another retailer posting a photo of a smashed glass door and grainy video of thieves looting their store in under 90 seconds flat. When we moved into our new bigger and better store this year, I spent about $30,000 turning it in to Fort Knox. It's not pleasant to think about, but all of us, collectors and dealers alike, have to figure out ways to avoid being the victim now. You don't have to go full crazy like I did, but you also can't just hope for the best.

Frank Simmons
Coast to Coast Comics

Greetings and Salutations Comic Galaxy. This year was an extraordinary year in so many ways, some very positive, while unfortunately world turmoil still affects our much-loved comic hobby. The great news is that prices on keys of all areas of the market seem to be holding well, Gold, Silver, Bronze, and even Modern.

The fact that prices haven't seen a reduction is telling. Demand continues to exceed supply. Those betting that comics are a great investment hedge against inflation have been rewarded handsomely in my opinion.

Our exposure to large ticket sales were less than prior years by choice. Coast to Coast focused on developing "core" strength by selling runs of titles and keys under $5K.

Larger volume sales have distinct advantages for a comic dealer. For example, we did sell a few San Francisco Timelys. What a great and original Pedigree. Coast to Coast did it "with a little help from our friends."

Our friends at ComicLink bring only the very best in service and true character. We feel privileged to have benefited firsthand from the kind of values, hard work and long-term dedication Josh Nathanson and his entire team have delivered. Thank you, gentleman at ComicLink.

This year original art was hot, and prices were mind-boggling and even record setting! 2024 looks bright indeed, tons of available material, demand and supply more suited to fuel sales again as in 2023, and no extreme price drops on major keys! A couple of sleepers I would like to mention here, *Captain America* comics with Jim Steranko or Jack Kirby covers from the late 1960s are still cheap and great for long term enjoyment and may even possibly appreciate in value too.

Be blessed in all you do in 2024 and enjoy collecting for the great hobby it is! Best from Coast To Coast Comics.

Lauren Sisselman
Comics Journalist

A Celebration of Ramona Fradon: When Ramona Fradon broke into comics, it was reason to celebrate. Prior to Fradon, women were seldom involved in the likes of the blossoming industry. Fradon herself came from a family of artists in their own ways. Her father, Peter Dom, was a graphic designer who worked with large luxury brands such as Elizabeth Arden. Other family members of hers were also in the arts, so to a young Fradon it likely made sense to follow in their footsteps, even if she wasn't so sure about her place in the arts.

According to *The Comics Journal,* Fradon didn't grow up reading the traditional comic books from her childhood. Like a large majority of people she did read the cartoon strips in newspapers, such as *The Phantom* and *Flash Gordon* – two franchises that would eventually have a successful comic book legacy as well. With a knowledge on pulp era cartoon heroes, it's easy to see where her influence came from. Fradon is most well known for her work on DC heroes, most notably Aquaman.

Her art and contributions for Aquaman are arguably what defined the character in the 1950s. The hero resembled what a typical Hollywood leading man would look like. Bulging muscles, a beautiful coifed blond hairdo, and a friendly smile. Fradon also helped co-create Aquaman's mother, Atlanna, who first appeared in *Adventure Comics* #260. The character was most famously portrayed by Nicole Kidman in 2018's *Aquaman,* alongside Jason Momoa as the titular hero.

Yet despite his wholesome '50s image, the character inevitably changed. Per an interview with *Vulture* in 2018, "When I was drawing him back in the '50s, he was nice and wholesome, with a nice haircut and pink cheeks. Very handsome. I had a crush on him. And you can see what happened to him! It got more and more violent, and then he lost his hand, then he had a beard and he looked psychotic." She laughs. "You know what? I don't get it."

To Fradon, the changing tone of comics was out of her depth of field. Even after a brief hiatus after having her daughter, Fradon was welcomed back to DC to help create the character Metamorpho in 1964. Fradon's Aquaman look is what I associate with the character, thanks in part to the cartoon show *Superfriends.* Despite growing up in the 1990s and being surrounded by Modern Age comics, Aquaman was still a wholesome, friendly hero in my mind.

Over the decades she continued to contribute to comics up until her retirement in early 2024. In one unique twist, Fradon created a few Mermaidman stories for *SpongeBob Comics,* which ran from 2011 until 2018. Fradon was also a convention regular, and could be regularly seen sketching out fun and unusual commissions for fans of all generations. Her work inspired generations of women to jump into the world of comics, myself included. She helped pave a road

that many of us are still on, and many more will join in the future. Her warm smile and subdued passion will be missed, and there will never be another like Ramona Fradon.

TONY STARKS
COMICS IN A FLASH!

One more market report that starts with "what a crazy year." The last 15 months (give or take a few) have seen a significant pullback in prices paid for books/titles most commonly bought and sold. I do not want to single out particular issues because right now I'm speaking in generalities. Examples like *Captain America* #100, *Fantastic Four* #52, *Savage She-Hulk* #1, *Uncanny X-Men* #266, *New Mutants* #98 and similar have, after doubling or tripling in price in 2020-2022, are now back to about the price they would have been with a "normal" increase in value of say 5% a year. Some, like the ones I mentioned, are close to their 2019 values.

A lot of dealers are commenting on social media about sales being really slow. Yet prices do not seem to be dropping past that floor of 2019/early 2020. Basically these books are in a hangover from the drunken excesses of the pandemic highs. Now might well be a buying opportunity for many of these books.

The state of the market also depends on what one is selling or trying to purchase. Silver/Bronze/Copper and Modern super hero from Marvel and DC are the most widely collected books - so end up most affecting our opinions of "the comic market". But if one collects or sells Crime, Good Girl Art, Pre-Code Horror and Romance then it is "what downturn?" The problem for buyers and sellers being these genres are much less likely to be in seller's inventories.

Pre-Code Horror? On Fire. Romance? Napalm. Crime comics? Where there is smoke….. Better Archie comics (that is double entendre or sexy covers) have been highly desirable for years now. Good Girl art, Frazetta Dells, 1960s Gold Key first issues and books mentioned in *Seduction of the Innocent.* You would never know the market is slow if you are looking to buy or sell this material.

This is challenging for me to report on, because except for Gold Keys I've never collected or sold a lot of the above mentioned books. Though I admit to warming up to Romance. They are just so….inappropriate LOL. But I submit to the grading companies thousands of books a year for other people. The last couple of years have seen a large increase in these genres.

Demand for Romance is way up. Yes, lots of love for Matt Baker covers/art. But it's not just that. The Fox and St. John Giants are 3x *Guide* as they are very hard to find, even in low grade. ACG, St. John, Atlas/Timely, ECs and DC Romance are in high demand. Even Charlton has some high demand titles. There are books that are just "run" books in the *Overstreet Guide* that are selling for many times the *Guide* price. What are collectors going for? The '60s psychedelic/peace covers are highly sought after, men being violent with women, bikini covers, women being bad girls. So a few examples: *Falling In Love* #99 VG/FN $200 (*Guide* $10). Not a romance, but a similar '60s cover is *Josie* #37 (Make Love Not War) CGC 7.5 @ $175. Pre-Code Horror also, with *Secret Diary of Eerie* (a Giant) nn CGC 3.0 @ $6,500.

So if you run across old Romance or Pre-Code Horror or Crime at *Guide* prices, maybe you should buy them. Probably some bargains in there. If you look at the cover and go "Wow, that is really great/gruesome/inappropriate" then for sure grab it.

Now for illustrative sales by us: We sell a lot of books in the dollar boxes. We sell a lot of stuff that is $25 or less. It adds up over a year. And there are of course some bigger sales: *Amazing Spider-Man* #116 VG @ $14; #118 VF @ $16. *Fantastic Four* #54 VF @ $40. *Iron Man* #1 VF/NM with amateur color touch $800; #100 VF @$30. *Iron Man & Sub-Mariner* #1 CGC 8.0 $375. *Looney Tunes and Merry Melodies* #91 VG @ $125 (first Wile E. Coyote). *Marvel Feature* #1 FN @ $100 (Defenders). *Robin Hood* #7 VG @ $40. *Shadowman* #1 NM @ $20, #43 NM @ $10. *All-New Collectors' Edition* C-56 (Superman Vs. Muhammad Ali) VF+ @ $140. *Thor* #200 VF+ @ $30, #216, #220, #224 NM @ $25 each, and *X-Men* #95 GD @ $15, #98 VF/NM @ $150.

So MAYBE – after three wild years – we might be seeing a return to a "normal" market again. Super heroes sure - but there's solid interest in the many other genres and publishers in our hobby.

WEST STEPHAN
DIRECTOR OF CBCS/SENIOR GRADER

Hello to all the fellow comic book collectors and dealers! 2023 was another successful year for CBCS, however, it ended having taken its toll on the vast majority of collectibles! With an economic downturn and a potential recession looming, everyone is more selective as to what they are purchasing. Bargain hunters are on the prowl looking to stretch every single dollar! As history has repeatedly shown in the comic hobby, these downward turns are typically short-lived as collectors and investors realize putting money into the hobby is still a solid investment compared to other revenue streams, and the money returns to our hobby with a vengeance!

CBCS had another banner year! We rolled through the Covid backlog with a lot of diligent work from our team! Our careful and selective process of adding new graders into the company in 2021 and 2022 really paid dividends and we now have a turn-around time, in all categories, second to none.

We introduced a new CBCS label, and the response has been overwhelmingly positive! After 10 months of focus groups, design work, computer programming and printer upgrades we are extremely excited by the response to our new label by the collecting community.

Early in the year we offered a new service for grading Dungeons & Dragons, Advanced D&D and other gaming books! If the RPG (Role Playing Game) items can fit in our magazine holder, we will grade them. We also grade RPG books still in the original shrinkwrap. The grade of the module will be the numerical grade you always see on a CBCS magazine, but we also give a letter grade to the shrinkwrap itself. Those letter grades are as follows; A+, A, A-, B+, B, B-, C+, C, C- & D. A+ is a perfectly wrapped module with no handling tears, wear or corners poking through the shrinkwrap. The lowest grade is a D, which as you can imaging would be in pretty rough shape! We have already graded several "9.8 Shrinkwrap: A+" modules!

In late 2023 we launched Manga grading! We are now grading Tankobon-size (maximum size of 5.9" wide by 8.19" tall by .85" deep) Manga comics! We're proud to be the first and only company to offer Manga grading. Many of you already know that Manga outsells American comic books by a huge factor. With certification you can expect Manga collecting to explode just like it when comic book certification began decades ago. We also hope to have the much larger Zasshi-size holders as well in early to mid-2024. One thing we wanted to do for Manga collectors is allow them to choose what label design they want encapsulated with each Manga issue submitted. You have 6 different styles to choose from.

Finally, we launched our much-anticipated Magazine tier. It took longer than expected, but we are happy it has taken off. CBCS customers have really taken to this service as there are a lot of magazine collectors. We grade all the comic magazines that fit into the holder, as well as pop culture magazines and *Playboy*. Keep in mind many of the 1970s issues are too thick to encapsule. We do offer a Raw Grade service that would fit thicker magazines. In fact, we can also Raw Grade Treasury-sized comics as well as all comic books from the Platinum Age through to current comics printed today.

2023 was a decent year for movies and TV series. My favorites were *Loki* Season 2, the *Blue Beetle* movie and *Guardians of the Galaxy 3*. I'm really looking forward to *What if?* Season 2. By the time you read this it will be out, hope it's as great as Season 1 was! I have not seen *The Marvels* movie yet, but it's on my list!

There were a lot of stand-out CBCS sales in 2023, including *Marvel Comics* #1 October Copy CBCS 2.5 (Restored) for $144,000, *Fantastic Four* #48 CBCS 9.4 for $13,200, *Venom Lethal Protector* #1 Black Error CBCS 9.8 for $7200, *Detective Comics* #12 CBCS 3.0 for $4800, *Playboy* #1 CBCS 4.0 (Signed by Hugh Hefner) for $5040 and an unsigned CBCS 2.5 copy for $2040, *Eerie* #1 Ashcan Edition CBCS 9.2 for $2280, *Tales to Astonish* #35, CBCS 9.4 for $20,400, *Cinderella Love* #29 CBCS 5.0 for $7800, *Scooby Doo… Where Are You!* #1 CBCS 4.0 for $1440 and *Wonderworld Comics* #32 CBCS 2.0 for $2880.

I am hopeful for a spectacular year in 2024. I think once we settle in it's going to be a fantastic journey for all of us. Thank you to Bob Overstreet, Mark Huesman, and JC Vaughn for all you do for the hobby!

AL STOLTZ
BASEMENT COMICS /
BASEMENT COMICS PRESSING

FIFTY YEARS OF BUYING *OVERSTREET GUIDES*!!

I bought my first *Overstreet Guide* in 1974 and it sported a fantastic Don Newton JSA cover. Before that I used Robert Bell paper catalogs as a pricing guide of sorts as I was buying and selling comics I got at the flea markets near my house. *Overstreet* completely blew my mind and was filled with so many titles of books I had no idea even existed. I spent hours just looking at each entry and was hoping I had a chance to own these books at some point in my life. Here almost fifty years later I am still buying *Overstreet Guides* and pouring through the info to learn something new. It's funny that two books changed the course of my life and lead me to being a comic seller for the last thirty one years, *Overstreet Guide* and *All in Color for A Dime*. Both shaped my desire and passion for comic books and related items, and I still have both original copies I bought and read to death in my personal collection.

The end of the year is coming quickly and I have finally sat down long enough to type another *Overstreet* report. The years are clocking by alarmingly fast. What a strange year for selling comics and comic-related material it has been as reflected in our show sales and online sales. Post-Covid speculation on lots of books we saw as artificially inflated by new and uneducated buyers have quickly leapt back to the lower levels of value. Some crazy Byrne-era *Fantastic Four* that we pressed and slabbed and got the magic 9.8 on was priced post-Covid from just over $500.00 to a paltry $54.99....after sitting at the huge price it did sell at the newly adjusted price after a little while. We repriced over a thousand graded books and maybe only a handful were priced more than sticker price. The rest were massively cut in price and sold to those I am guessing thought that the crash could reverse itself one day and they will profit from the investment. Even Marvel Sliver and Bronze Age books that were dependable lost 25-30% value in the decline and many of the non-keys still are sliding down to pre-Covid pump pricing. All of the genres took a hit on books that should have never attained such lofty prices BUT record prices are being paid still for high grade Keys and books in the runs of the Mighty Marvel Silver Age! Modern keys that used to be cheap are running way up now like *Crow* #1, *Turtles* #1, *Albedo* #2 and others. Books from the 1980s and 1990s are, and I hate to say it, OLD! It's 30 to 40 years old now and the buyers and lovers of that medium are aging and have disposable income to spend on their perceived Golden Age or Silver Age books from their past.

I just looked at two Marvel collections of Bronze and Silver Age Marvels before typing this report and didn't buy either one of them. Why didn't I buy the collections? Sellers at this point still haven't or don't want to realize that the bubble has burst a bit and these books are lower than they were a few years ago and continue to drop in mid to lower grades steadily. I made offers based on books that would actually sell quickly and the sellers were stunned at my offers. I just refuse to overpay for Silver and Bronze that seem to keep sinking in value, but instead I've switched to buying and posting more esoteric and Golden Age comics into our eBay store. I am getting older and I guess I am just settling into the niche that I will stay in until I retire from this business. Always hoping that eventually sellers will understand that purchases that they made during pandemic may have now tumbled a good bit and we are buying based on current market values.

Now a quick mentioning of a serious problem that is happening way too frequently in the hobby now - theft of comics in a larger scale. I see Facebook posts or get e-mails constantly warning of a store broken into or a robbery at a show during and after hours. The bad side of comic books becoming very valuable and that fact getting known by the public at large is that bad people or desperate people start to target comics and sell them out in the world and try to get away with it. A dealer just before writing this report had graded books stolen after hours at a large show by an employee of the building. Stores being broken into by professional thieves in the Virginia area that still have not been caught yet. Storage units being emptied by those who somehow found out where they were. Teams of skilled shoplifters working shows and stealing books of all values and I assume selling online or in different parts of the country. At shows we get hyper-vigilant and watch hands and bags and anyone that we allow to step behind the booth to look at better items. I have alarms and cameras at my office and home! I still see dealers doing huge shows alone and it just invites disaster as far as dollars walking away from the booth. I think 2024 is the time to step up and try to cover all the bases and at least make theft tougher for these thieves.

eBay and Etsy sales were really up and down, and oddly the last few months have been phenomenal! A few of the summer months were slow and who can really tell why people stop spending, and we read all the chat boards for the two selling platforms we participate on. As usual we sell a wide variety of items including a large animation collection we acquired along with a load of trade paperbacks and better hardcovers we had squirreled away and finally had a chance to get them listed. We have a large amount of Marvel and DC posters from 1980s-1990s that will get listed perhaps before the end of the year. We post plenty of comics and graded books but I think having a diversified inventory online is the best way to go. We also have kept a large rotation of items for auction on eBay and that seems to generate a steady flow of visitors to the main page on eBay. Online sales always seem to be changing and evolving so I spend hours looking around at what is selling and try to head the business ship in that direction if it looks like a good trend to follow. One can only hope that the economy stays at least at this level or starts to grow in 2024 so we can see a good growth rate for all products.

Shows that we did set up at in 2023 were very decent for us but the number of shows we set up a year has greatly diminished over the years. I'm just not interested in being a road warrior any longer. I'll just try to strategically target the few that I can expend energy on to see a good return on the investment of time and money. Little Giants Old Time Show in New Hampshire was our first stop and is a fantastic one day show that featured almost exclusively old comics and related items. Want to get the comic collecting juices going early in the year? Stop by this show in April and get ready to spend like crazy. Heroes Con in Charlotte in June is a monster of a show with a ton of comic sellers and artists and creators! It's one of my favorite shows to do since it's a fun comic show and food in that area is fantastic, and travelling to this show will not disappoint any potential comic addict. Terrific Con at the Mohegan Sun Casino is a fun weekend show and how bad can the experience be staying at a great resort with top notch food everywhere. Yes, great food as I got older is a must when doing shows.

Baltimore Comic Con was in September and as usual a great comic show for selling at and buying! I love this show because its only thirty five minutes from my house and I can go home everyday after the event. And yes, I can get great food on the way home and avoid dealing with any crazy times in Baltimore city. Maryland Toy show was autumn's last big show, and this show is run very very well. Two large buildings full of stuff for sale and it brought in the crowds the whole day. If I can put together more toy and related material by next Fall I'll beg my way back into this show and try it again. My local show, Clandestine Convention, that happens 5-6 times a year is run by Fred Edison and has been happening for over thirty years. Want to have fun at a small old time show? Then come to Maryland and experience Fred's Clandestine show!

Basement Comics Pressing is still buzzing along but has experienced a slowdown since the game of pressing anything and getting it graded to sell has dissipated. We are doing far more books of greater value and that sell immediately once graded. Still Cold Press only and have pressed over 100,000 books from simple start up to present these last eight years. Our turn around times are way down and this service is still very important to this hobby, and I can see us or someone doing it as long as grading comics or just making them look prettier for sale raw.

Where is our not so little hobby going in the future? No one can guess and I sure had no idea in 1974 when I bought my first *Overstreet* that fifty years later prices for comics could be greater than the price of cars or homes. Will the love of nostalgia or profit keep the progress moving along? Let's all hope so!

DOUG SULIPA
DOUG SULIPA'S COMIC WORLD

2023 was a year of market correction. Back issue prices jumped too fast in the hysteria of 2020-2021, they started to drop off in 2022, and in 2023 we saw prices fall even on the top keys like *Hulk* #181 and *Amazing Fantasy* #15. By the end of the year, prices leveled off and the market was stabilizing and getting back to normal.

Marvel and DC have made far too many changes to their characters, and there is too much political correctness, in both the comics and the cinematic universes, that they have alienated fans from the traditional characters we all fell in love with over the last 40-80 years. Most of the TV shows and movies based on comics have lost money over the last few years. Special effects and huge boring action sequences above storyline, gimmicks above interesting characters, and unrecognizable versions of beloved characters dilute and destroy the enjoyment. Time to reverse the downward trend, before the Era of comic movies comes to an end. My vote goes for getting back to a well-written intense fast paced story, grounded on Earth, with the characters we know and love, one great hero or team vs. one great villain or arch-enemy, and no money-grab gimmicks.

Four sample suggestions for the industry: 1-Doctor Doom with diplomatic immunity in Latveria, in a *What If* scenario, nearly succeeds in taking legitimate technological and financial control of the world, to become the benevolent Dictator of Earth, and the Fantastic Four stops him, only to discover they made a huge mistake, causing an unforeseen apocalyptic world. 2-Jonah Hex in the classic *Weird Western* style, dreamlike John Wick or Bruce Lee inspired "ten against one" action scenes. 3-*Elfquest*, Wendy Pini's masterpiece, done right by Pixar or DreamWorks, as a mature CGI movie trilogy or TV series. 4-*Uncle Scrooge* and *Donald Duck Adventures* in a series of annual 90-120 minute movies, based on Carl Barks masterpiece storylines, with the vision to treat them like the Disney animated classics of legend.

Marvel and DC superhero comics still dominate the marketplace, but in general are more common than other genres, so when there is a downturn, they are usually the most affected. Values for Uncommon to Scarce other genre comics from other publishers are rarely affected as they are saved by fans who cherish just finding any reasonable copy for their collections. Those genres include: Action, Adventure, Adult, Anthropomorphics, Archie, Cartoons, Children, Crime, Fantasy, Funny Animals, History, Horror, Hot-Rod, Hot-Rod & Car Cartoon mags, Humor, Jungle, Licensed Characters, Love/Romance, Manga, Martial Arts, Movie, Mythology, Mystery, Newspaper Comic Strip, Parody/Spoof, Pirates, Pop Music Stars, Radio, Rock, Sci-Fi, Soap Opera, Sports, Sword & Sorcery, Teen, TV, Underground, War, Western. For example Adult and Anthropomorphics comics, mostly with cover prices in the $1.50 to $3.00 range, many think would only bring cover price, often had low print runs, and FN or better copies typically bring $8 to $25 and up range, especially issue #1s.

The strongest trend of the year is the rise in demand for Horror comics. Charlton Horror comics of the 1968-1984 era are very under-valued in the *Guide*. Most 8.0 examples bring 9.2 prices, and there are very few CGC copies in the market. In particular, fans have finally discovered that Tom Sutton is an overlooked master of horror in his Charlton era. Demand for Sutton Charlton comics was about four times higher than Ditko comics of the same period, yet the Ditko issues often are twice the value in the *Guide*. Sutton issue prices need to be raised to be at least on par with the Ditko issues. Some of the Sutton classic cover and story issues need a 200% price bump. Some examples are *Ghost Manor* V2 #17, 18, 23, *Ghostly Haunts* #38, 40, 41, 49, *Ghostly Tales* #106, 110, 113, 127, *Haunted* #10, 15,1 7, *Haunted Love* #1, 6, 11, *Many Ghosts of Doctor Graves* #42, 45; and *Scary Tales* #2, 29. Classic covers sell for 300-1000% *Guide*, such as *Fightin' Marines* #117 (Nazi Hitman Swastika-c), *Many Ghosts of Dr. Graves* #54 (Byrne-c), *Phantom* #74 (Flag-c), and Love comics with psychedelic covers. Most of the VF or better copies of these comics have been absorbed into collections, with only Fine or lower grades available in the current marketplace. Fans have begun to notice Enrique Nieto, especially his psychedelic art. It is in high demand, often at 200-1000% of low *Guide* values.

Charlton had a lot of great painted covers in the 1970s, in a period when most other publishers stopped making them. Seek out the forgotten great Charlton art by John Byrne, Mike Zeck, Wayne Howard, Sanho Kim and others.

DC Horror issues of the 1968-1974 era are very under-valued in the *Guide*. In very high demand are Berni Wrightson and Neal Adams art (and especially cover) issues like *Dark Mansion* #1-4, *House of Mystery* #174-200, *House of Secrets* #81-100, *Sinister House* #1-4, *Unexpected* #104-128, *Weird War* #1-30, and *Witching Hour* #1-20. Most 8.0 examples bring 9.2 prices with very few CGC copies in the market. Those CGC copies bring 200-600% *Guide*. The 1975-1983 issues are much requested in VF or better, getting harder to find in higher grades. Nick Cardy and Mike Kaluta issues are also in higher demand.

All of the Marvel Horror comics are up in demand. The 1970s Marvel Horror magazines are in very high demand. Raw copies bring 150-250% *Guide*, while CGC copies bring 200-500% *Guide*. The Marvel supernatural characters of the 1970s (Death, Dracula, Frankenstein, Ghost Rider, Mummy, Scarecrow, Werewolf) are in constant demand, especially in VF or better. First issues bring 150-300% *Guide*, while issues #2-10s bring 125-150% *Guide*. Marvel Horror reprint comics (*Chamber of Chills*,

Vault of Evil, *Where Monsters Dwell*, etc.) are back up demand, especially in VF or better. Raw copies bring 125-150% *Guide,* while CGC copies bring 200-500% *Guide*.

Warren magazines *Creepy*, *Eerie* and *Vampirella* are in constant demand, especially in VF or better, bringing 120-150% *Guide*. The magazines by Skywald, Eerie Publications, Globe, Hamilton, Major, Modern Day, Stanley, Tempest Pub and World Famous, and are in low supply and have high demand, bringing 135-200% *Guide*. Nice Horror covers are popular for all publishers, and getting scarcer due to higher demand. Some are beginning to bring premiums, and high grade copies are a good long term investment. The popular genres within Horror include Greytone, Skulls, Skeletons, Grim Reaper, Zombie & Living Dead, Hitler, Nazi, WWII, Death Camps, Gothic, GGA, Bondage, UFO, Werewolves, Vampires, Halloween, Witches, Rock 'N' Roll, Satan, Gargoyles, Graveyards & Coffins, Ghosts, Apes, Robots, Tanks, Insects, Teddy Bears, Chess themed, Clowns, Mummy, Bigfoot, Voodoo, Dinosaurs, and Mermaids.

Archie Comics has some risqué sexual innuendo covers which continue to be highly collected. Many bring 200-2000% of *Guide*, for example: *Archie* #53(11/51), #78(1-2/56), #321(1/83), #455(1/97), #511(8/01), *Archie... Archie Andews Digest* #111, *Archie Giant* #551, *Betty & Me* #16, 37, 55, *Betty & Veronica* #65 (7/93), *Veronica* #23, and *Life with Archie* #27 (5/64), and its imitator from Dell, *Thirteen* #22 (4/67). Also in high demand are covers with: Cheerleaders, Girls in Bikinis & Swimsuits, Good Girl Art, Dan DeCarlo art, TV, Movie, Personality & Character parodies (*A-Team*, Donkey Kong, Hulk Hogan, Madonna, Pac-Man, Punk Rock, *Star Wars*) and Love Triangle covers (Archie, Betty & Veronica.) The circa-1960 Archie Horror and Sci-Fi cover issues have HUGE demand as compared to other issues of the period. Most sell for 200-1000% *Guide*. Some examples: *Life with Archie* #41(1st Godzilla and Mothra in comics; VG = $99); *Jughead* #79 (Creature From Black Lagoon app.) GD/VG $199; *Pep Comics* #155 (Catwoman-c) VG $199.

Love and Romance comics are up in demand from all years and all publishers. Guys want them because they are loaded with GGA and images of girls. Under-valued Pre-Code Love comics bring 125-150% *Guide* in any grade. Better covers and content Key issues can bring 200-400% Guide. Key content includes Good Girl Art, Spanking Panels, Swimsuit, Lingerie cover and panels, politically incorrect words and actions. 2023 saw many collectors buying up vintage DC Love comics, with 1950s-1960s High Grade beginning at VG/FN 5.0, and 1970s issues in FN/VF or better being tough to find.

VF copies often bring 200-600% Guide on eBay. *My Love* and *Our Love Story*, along with *Millie the Model* and *Chili* from Marvel are difficult sets to complete and are steady sellers at 125-150% *Guide*. We have seen increased demand for Charlton Love comics. There are a lot of interesting forgotten stories and art, with high interest in the better covers (most notably from the 1970s.)

We sold about 1,500 CGC comics in 2023, down from 2020-2022, but still a pretty good year. We sold about double our regular number of Silver Age Marvel and DC Comics, but the Bronze/Modern and Movie TV Titles were slower. We adjusted prices to current levels and they picked up again. Non-Marvel/DC comics TV and movie related comics performed quite well this year.

Notable CGC Sales: We sold *Winnie the Pooh* #1(Gold Key 1977)(6 copies in CGC 9.8 in the $849, $999, and $1,099 range; 2 copies in CGC 9.6 for $649 each); *X-Men* #130 (9.4 $295-349; 9.2 $195-240; 9.0 $149- $179; 8.0 $125-$140); we sold 12 CGC copies in various grades, and our last 6 Raw copies in 18 days due to the Taylor Swift/Dazzler rumor (and 10 *Dazzler* #1 in CGC 9.8 for $199 to $249 each within a month); *Peter The Little Pest* #1 CGC 9.6 $895; *Iron Man* #1 CGC 9.0 $2599; *Faust* #1 CGC 9.8 $995; *Strange Tales* #169 CGC 9.6 $4,995; *Beep Beep Road Runner* #1 (1966; 7.0 $399); *Darkwing Duck* #1(1991; 6 copies in 9.8 $295-$339); *Cerebus The Aardvark* #1 CGC 6.0 $2,995; *Rampaging Hulk* (all CGC 9.8; #3 $399, #6 $399, #7 $419); *Teenage Mutant Ninja Turtles* #8 (Cerebus crossover issue; set of 44 different 2023 Remastered Edition cover variants of the 1986 comic, 43 in CGC 9.8 and one in 9.2 = $6,000 for the lot); *Secrets of Haunted House* (both Wrightson-c) #5 CGC 9.6 $749 and #44 CGC 9.6 $399; *House of Mystery* (both Wrightson-c)#236 (9.4 $599; 9.2 $399; 9.0 $275) and #231 (9.4 $399; 8.5 $149); *Weird Mystery Tales* #21 Wrightson-c (9.4 $249; #23 9.6 $229); *Weird War Tales* #41 9.6 $249; *Super Mario* comics (22 assorted in the $125 to $499 each range); *Legend of Zelda* comics (10 in the $99 to $299 range); *Western Prairies* #61(1950; Canada Edition of Whip Wilson; 7.0 $300); *Friday Foster* #1 (1972 Dell Pam Grier Blaxploitation Film 1st Black Woman Title; 6.0 $239; 5.0 wp $199; 5.0 oww $189); 12 copies of *Toxic Avenger* #1 (1991; 9.8 $199-$239; 9.6 $89-99); *Godzilla* #1 (1977; 10 copies in CGC 9.6 $199 each range); *Silver Surfer* (1968-1970; #1 6.0 $1000; #3 8.0 $1,499; #4 3.5 $495; #14 8.5 $335; 15 others in varied grades); *Beneath the Planet of Apes* 1970 movie classic 9.0 $299; *Girls' Love Stories* #7 6.5 $170 and #37 6.5 $139; *Heart Throbs* #89 classic-c 7.5 $125 and #89 6.5 $99 each(2 copies); *Life with Archie* #7 Classic love triangle-c 4.0 $179 and #12 Dinosaur Sci-Fi Horror 6.0 $139; *Li'l Kids* (Calvin, African-American kids 1973 Marvel scarce) #10 (9.2 $299; #11 9.4 $279, #12 6.0 $179); *Barbie* #1(1991; 9 copies CGC 9.8 = $199-299 range); *Captain Canuck* #1(1975; 9 copies of CGC 9.8 @ $199 each) and *Space Ghost* #1(1967; 6.0 $459; 2.0 $239).

MICHAEL TIERNEY COLLECTOR'S EDITION & THE COMIC BOOK STORE

One of the negatives about being a business owner is that when your customers experience financial difficulties, they think nothing of making their problems into your problems. Operating in a rural state where the average per capital income is only greater than the U.S. territory of Puerto Rico, my stores were always hard hit by adverse economic circumstances. Since I switched from multiple brick-and-mortar locations to mail order, this has not been nearly as much a problem. Still, throughout 2023 a lot of customers experienced financial difficulties, and this was reflected in my previously recession-proof back issue sales.

I've never seen a tax return season without a significant sales bump, until 2023. The sales lull that began before the 2022 election continued well into the next year. There was a mini-surge around Independence Day in 2023, but overall this was the weakest year for back issue sales I've ever seen in my 40-plus years as a comics retailer.

There was some good news, as Marvel's sales of new comics saw a strong upswing when they shipped a full line of ongoing titles mostly on time. Reliability is nothing but a good thing, and increases in their cover prices had no discernible effect. Many fans widened the scope of their reading. Previously, this kind of stability would have translated well into back issue sales, but not this year.

DC on the other hand, was still running a skeleton crew of ongoing comics, and ignored the lessons of the past when they did yet another relaunch with the Dawn of the DC Universe. It was a perfect example of going back to the well too often, and what worked in the 1980s registered as a flatline on this year's sales seismograph. People buying titles before mostly maintained their subscriptions, but there was no interest from new readers.

My biggest sales were not actual comics, but comic-related material, with a DC Comics light up sign, that had hung on the wall of one of my stores from 1989 until I closed that location during the 2020 pandemic, selling for $250.

A complete set of six *Tarzan Super Scope Story Teller Books*, illustrated with rewritten scenes from the Sunday newspaper comics, which included the original cassette tapes sealed in shrink wrap by a secondary seller that did not include the original illustrated boxes, sold for $90.

The release of my *Robert E. Howard Art Chronology* was far and away my biggest seller of the year. The format for this 1600 page, four volume set matched my 2018 *Edgar Rice Burroughs Art Chronology*, and likewise included two volumes devoted to all related comics published in the US and UK. The standard hardcover sets sold briskly for $350 each, while my 10 copy signed and numbered Leather Edition sets sold for $500 each.

So there were people with money to spend. But most of activity on my eBay store came from bargain hunters making ridiculously low offers that were 80 or 90% below the asking price, which indicates that they must have had some success with desperate retailers, given the record number of offers I declined. Another disturbing new eBay trend was a phenomenal number of people who won auctions and then never paid—but would ask why their items never shipped. I had to auction one book four times before the winning bidder actually paid.

These were my notable comic sales for the year:

Battle #65 with a Jack Kirby cover sold in VG for $50.

A NM copy of the *Secret Codebook: Fox Box*, featuring Sonic and TMNT, went for $23 in NM. This was a bonus item from when I did a lot of local television advertising on the Fox Channel.

Sensational She-Hulk #52, featuring an early Adam Hughes cover sold in NM for $25.

Steadily sold a couple dozen *Spider-Man 2099* #1 in Mint for $15 each during the lead up to the animated movie, *Spider-Man: Across the Spider-Verse*, the second installment in the trilogy. Sales stopped when it was released.

TMNT Universe #1 from IDW, with a 1:25 Kevin Eastman variant cover sold in NM for $40

Finally sold the last two copies of my *Wolverine* (v2) #88 overstock. When it was initially solicited I bumped my orders because of Deadpool's appearance, but did not sell a single extra copy. That worked out well in the long run when I sold that stack of Mint, uncirculated copies for $80 each over the last few years.

Sold a pair of *Wolverine* (2023) #37 retailer bonus editions with virgin Greg Capullo covers in NM/Mint for $50 each.

TED VANLIEW
SUPERWORLD COMICS

Hi everyone! Well, it's been a topsy turvy year. We knew that the market couldn't sustain the pandemic era craziness, and things have been gradually settling into a more 'normal' rhythm.

Prices on books had gotten quite inflated, and had to start coming down, which they started to do early in the year. Modern books took the biggest hit, predictably, since they're the most common. '70's and Silver Age books have settled down in price quite a bit as well. Interestingly, Golden Age and Atomic Age books have held their value best, presumably because they're by far the scarcest issues. Possibly, many buyers have been looking to branch out, and the challenge of finding these amazing items is very exciting, especially when one or more is located!

Eventually, prices will start rising again on good stuff, as they always have. We anticipate more of a gradual climb, which is normal and definitely a welcome pattern. There are always the exceptions, where a book gets red hot for whatever reason, and the price spikes. The question is always whether it will sustain or whether it's just a speculator bubble. Will it be *Iron Man* #55 or *Moon Knight* #1? LOL

Golden Age: This has been a surprising growth area! Golden Age books have shown great strength and demand across the board. DCs are mostly great, led by *Batman*, *Detective*, *Wonder Woman*, but any classic cover is an immediate goner. Also, there are some titles that seldom turn up, such as *Green Lantern*. Secondary titles, such as *Leading* and *Comic Cavalcade* are quite popular as well. We especially love when we acquire Timelys, cause they pretty much get snapped up, esp. the War era issues and ones with exciting covers. There are many, many other publishers, some successful at the time, some not so much. Many of their books, whether they be from long run titles or short runs, are extremely popular: Fox, Hillman, Dell, Novelty, Harvey, Better/Nedor, Prize Pubs, and so many others. It's a true treasure hunt, and so much fun! While many are pricey, there are still plenty of bargains hiding in plain sight.

Atomic Age: This includes most of the great Horror, Crime, and Science Fiction books, among others. Avon, Ziff-Davis, Gilmore, EC, Aragon, Atlas, and many others were publishing really compelling books. Again, while some are pricey, there are tons of bargains in this category. Inevitably, a lot of good issues get overlooked in the shadows of the well known great issues. I'm partial to the Science Fiction stuff, with greats such as Wood, Williamson, Kubert, LB Cole, and others doing some of their finest work, but the Horror and Crime books are speckled with great covers and art as well. Of course, DC continued to publish their top titles, plus some great Mystery, Sci Fi, and Horror stuff. Atlas made a short lived attempt to revive their great heroes Captain America, Human Torch, and Sub-Mariner. These are not easy to get, and are underrated. Early Romita and Burgos art, and some of Bill Everett's most interesting work. *Venus* contains some Everett work that's positively psychedelic! Archie titles are quite scarce, and still underrated as well.

Silver Age: Some really great books have come down in price, and we think there are some issues that should definitely be picked up, as they've actually come down more than they should. Opportunities abound! Marvels always rule, and deservedly so, as they revolutionized the telling of stories in the format. Plus, nobody else had the King and Sturdy Steve!

It's shocking how cheap many DCs can be had. For example, a VF copy of *Atom* #12 is only @ $75. That's nothing, and should go for a lot more. Since I'm a broken record, I'll repeat my assertion that nicer condition DCs are 10 times harder to find than Marvels, especially pre-'65 or so. For example, *Hawkman*'s great stuff - Murphy Anderson in top form, but they are still cheap. Grumble. . .

There are other Silver Age sleepers, such as the Tower line - *Thunder Agents*, *Noman*, *Dynamo*, and more, and *Magnus Robot Fighter* and *Doctor Solar* from Gold Key. *Magnus* features the great Russ Manning's art, and will be a revelation for those of you who are unfamiliar. Many publishers jumped on the Superhero bandwagon in the mid-'60s, and while most of them aren't up to Marvel standards, they're still a lot of fun! Archies and Harvey titles are quite entertaining, and don't get the credit they're due.

Bronze Age: Most Bronze Age books are still readily available, as distribution and circulation was larger than in the '60s, esp. for Marvel, who took over as the preeminent publisher by 1972. There are so many titles to choose from. Both Marvel and DC introduced a plethora of major and good minor characters during this era. I'm still excited by the mentality of many of the writers and artists who were inspired by E.R. Burroughs, R.E.H., Lovecraft, Moorcroft, and other Fantasy and Horror masters. Their enthusiasm was transmitted to my generation, and we're glad it was! By the mid-'70s, a lot of people started saving everything, thinking the books'd have good value down the road. Due to this phenomenon (in all collectables), the books are much easier to locate now. Some have indeed accrued value, while others not so much. It's still so exciting to acquire high grade copies from any era though. It continues to amaze me that comics, which were 'throwaway' items, have come through the years in such superior condition.

Copper and Modern: We don't handle a lot of books from the '80s on to the present, but there are an increasing number of worthwhile books, and definitely some surprises, and occasional lightning in a bottle, such as *TMNT*. Many '80s & '90s series are coming of age, like *Transformers*, *G.I. Joe*, *Wolverine*, *Punisher*, and many others, which is nice to see. Regarding later books, one needs to keep abreast of what's getting 'hot', as there are lots of unlikely candidates, movie and TV tie ins, and other factors. Sometimes a new unheralded title just catches fire.

Well, that's all the drivel for this time out. Happy Collecting!

Some Noteable sales: *All Select* #8 VF $5,500, *Adventure Comics* #247 VG/FN $4,500, *Amazing Fantasy* #15 CGC 4.0 $39,000, *Amazing Spider-Man* #1 CGC 4.5 $13,500, #5 CGC 9.0 $9,500, 14 CGC 7.5 $6,000, *Avengers* #9 VF/NM $4,300, *Batman* #16 VG+ $4,800, #181 VF $4,900, *Brave and the Bold* #28 CGC 4.5 $3,600, *Contact* #12 VG/FN $4,500, *Daredevil* #1 FN $6,000, *Fantastic Four* #1 CGC 2.5 $17,000, #5 VG $7,500, *Giant-Size X-Men* #1 CGC 8.5 $4,500, *Hero for Hire* #1 CGC 9.4 $4,200, *Hulk* #1 CGC 3.0 $18,000, #6 VF $4,200, *Journey into Mystery* #83 CGC 4.5 $13,000, *Marvel Premiere* #15 CGC 9.8 $4,900, *Planet Comics* #31 VF+ $3,000, *Silver Surfer* #1 VF+ $3,200, *Strange Tales* #89 CGC 8.0 $8,800, #110 CGC 6.5 $6,500, *Tales of Suspense* #1 CGC 7.0 $6,600, #39 CGC 6.5 $20,000, *Weird Mysteries* #7 CGC 8.0 $5,000, *Wonderworld Comics* #32 CGC 2.0 $4,500, *X-Men* #1 GD/VG $7,600, and #4 FN/VF $3,300.

There you have it! May the Seven Suns of Cinnibus light your path.

FRANK VERZYL
LONG ISLAND COMICS

I'm writing this on Christmas Eve 2023 after noticing that Diamond Comics has sent out their annual solicitations for the May 2024 "Free Comic Book Day" titles, a huge selection of full-sized comic books, priced to dealers at a quarter apiece, designed to be given out in comic shops across America as "freebies". This will be the annual event's 22nd year (it was started in 2002), designed to attract thousands of interested new readers into the hobby. It is completely inexplicable why this farce continues to be promoted, as every year that passes, more and more readers continue to abandon the hobby.

Every year, the number of readers continues to dwindle

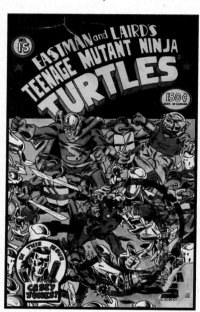

as more comics shops go belly-up with a disturbing regularity. The only reason the shops are still in operation is the ever-increasing cover prices of the new releases (some new comics are actually being priced at $5 to $10 apiece) and the shameful practice of luring the more obsessive-compulsive collectors to purchase six to ten different variant covers of the same issue! Eventually the needs of the real world intrude, and the readers quit collecting altogether as each one reaches his breaking point.

The comic book industry cannot be fixed with an annual batch of freebies handed out to a throng of mostly non-collectors who simply show up once a year to get something for free. Most of the attendees just grab up the free stuff, trampling all over the stock items on the low-lying shelves and just in general damaging everything in the store. The retailer won't see any of these people again until next year's event, especially since the free comics being distributed do nothing to resolve the problems that have been affecting the new comics industry for the past few decades. Each year, the market will continue to lose another layer of interested readers, yet the Big Two (Marvel and DC) feel they are doing their part to correct the problem with their annual flush of insipid giveaways. Wrong!

Having owned and operated Long Island Comics for 46 years, I have seen this once profitable market shrink with an alarming regularity, and one wonders how low the various print runs can go before they are cancelled altogether. Five years ago, if someone had told me the new comics would cost between $5 to $10 apiece, I would've told them they were crazy, and yet it is now common to see the books priced that high. (No one asks how, if Marvel and DC can produce FCBD issues for a quarter apiece, they have to price their monthly issues so expensively.) Just during the past year, I have seen dramatic resistance to the recent price increases on the part of the fans, with many of my reserve customers quitting the hobby altogether.

The ridiculous number of unnecessary variant covers is also dissuading many customers from collecting, since compulsive people tend to want to collect all of the covers so that their collections are complete, a task that is basically impossible to accomplish at this point (some comics having as many as twenty different variant covers on each issue). This is sheer greed on the part of the publishers, a practice that unfortunately has become a necessity nowadays since the publishers have to make up for their constantly decreasing readership. But how long can this bizarre practice continue before the bottom falls out?

Why not just fix the problem?

Another factor chasing potential readers away is the flooding of the market with dozens of unnecessary (and unwanted) spinoffs of the various superhero titles (15 different Batman-related titles per month, 9 different Spider-Man-related titles, ad nauseum). Characters like Wolverine may appear in four or five different magazines each month, involved in totally unrelated adventures all supposedly happening at the same time! Then throw in the readers' inability to mentally handle dozens of alternate universes all occurring at once, different versions of the same characters existing in various multiverses, not to mention the totally unwanted introduction of political and "woke" elements into the storylines, allowing the writers to force their bizarre political views into what was once a much simpler and kinder art form.

Reading a new comic book today has become way "too much work" for the average reader who doesn't have time to research the various characters on wikipedia before settling down to enjoy what really should be a relatively simple form of entertainment. In years past, the reader could pick up any comic off the newsstand and jump right into the story without reading a page or two of small text explaining the confusing events of "what went before". The writers filled the reader in as he went along with a few well-crafted word balloons and perhaps a brief footnote if needed. Today's storylines are so convoluted and involved, the casual reader cannot find a "jumping on point" to save his life. The individual comics are not even self-contained works any more, but rather just an endless stream of chapters that will later be collected into a (perhaps) more intelligible trade paperback version. But each and every issue should be a story in itself, and should contain enough entertainment value in and of itself to continue to bring the reader back month after month.

Even the covers of the new comics signify nothing. They may be flashy and colorful with their computerized animation, but today's cover illustrations do nothing to rope the reader in, to intrigue him or her to purchase the issue. Each cover features another empty pose (Punisher holding a pistol on one cover, Punisher holding a machine gun on another,

all of the characters grimacing angrily and looking more than a bit psychotic). Why would a parent feel a magazine with a grimacing psychotic on the cover would make good wholesome entertainment for his or her child? The covers all seem to be interchangeable, since none of them reflect an actual scene or situation from the story inside. Why would these assembly-line covers make a potential reader even want to buy the issue?

The cover should show a suspenseful scene from the story, an image that can actually be found inside the magazine. The old Silver Age comics were prime examples of this type of sensationalism. A typical 1960s cover might show Lois Lane transforming into a werewolf, with a word balloon saying "Help me, Superman! I can't stop the transformation!" and show Superman staring at her, thinking "Great Scott! How can I stop Lois from becoming a savage beast?" Now any casual reader looking at that cover has a reason to buy it, first to learn why Lois is becoming a monster and secondly to find out how Superman saves her. He or she now has two immediate reasons to buy the magazine, while a cover just showing Lois in an action pose doesn't trigger a purchase.

Another recent practice that is repelling many potential readers is the publishers' habit of restarting series over with a number one issue every year or two. This makes it almost impossible for the readers to keep their comics in chronological order. Some titles are already up to Volumes 8 or 9 (as with Iron Man and Hulk), and the constant renumberings weaken the value of the run. Every time a title reaches number ten or so, they restart it with a number one. Why? The buying public no longer even notices the appearance of a new Number One issue; it has long ago lost its ability to excite anyone.

Also, why has the comic book industry abandoned most of its female readers? In the 1970s, fully half of the readership was female. The endless array of superhero (male fantasy) comics have driven most of them away. Maybe this is a good time for the publishers to add some other genres to their line, such as Westerns, War comics, Romance and Horror titles? The return of women readers to the hobby might just be the thing that saves it for all of us.

The point is, Marvel and DC should stop the pretense that they are doing something constructive by sponsoring the giving away of their worthless Free Comic Book Day pamphlets and really get to work trying to fix the industry before there is nothing left to fix. The worst thing that ever happened to our industry is when the 7-11s and stationary stores stopped selling new comics in the mid '90s. The industry is no longer capable of reaching its full potential audience simply by distributing the new releases through a few thousand comic book shops. We are losing a whole generation of younger readers who cannot travel to comics shops that are located miles away from their homes. Millions of potential readers are being denied access to the industry's new products.

John Verzyl II & Rose Verzyl
Comic Heaven

Salutations, comic collectors! There are many changes coming over the horizon, so be warned! Now more than ever is the time to hunker down.

If you had told me a few years ago that the Marvel Age of Cinema would be over in one phase, I would have laughed in your face. Now, living at a point in time where no one cares is quite jarring to me. It is bewildering that a reputation that was painstakingly crafted in ten years was so easy to wipe away in less than five. There is no point in crying over spilt milk. The powers at play are going to continue making the same mistakes they have been, and that is perfectly fine. This is supposed to be a comic-collecting community, not a movie-about-comic-watching community.

Because of a series of baffling decisions, the looming threat of comic book values being untied from the movies has come to fruition. While this affects the vast majority of comic collectors, none of them will be hit harder than those who primarily collect Silver and Bronze Age Marvel. As far as high price tags and annual increases go, no other publisher or genre has fetched the consistently high numbers of these popular Marvel comics with prices influenced by movies.

Books that had aspiring potential like *Marvel Spotlight* #5 (GPAnalysis 9.2 2023 average down to $8,853 from 2022's $13,789), *Tomb of Dracula* #10 (GPAnalysis 9.2 2023 average down to $2,959 from 2022's $4,474), and *Werewolf by Night* #32 (GPAnalysis 9.2 2023 average down to $3,188 from 2022's $7,040) all find themselves to be the biggest losers in a sea of general fan apathy. These books and numerous others have been left out to dry after the destruction of the speculatory movie formula: buying a book before the eventual movie comes out, having said movie be announced, and then selling (or holding) at a profit. Something that a lot of us are aware of or participated in over the last decade.

And I think the erasure of this simple formula will have far-reaching consequences for those on the outer rim of the comic-collecting community. With this thought in mind, I would like to share with you a theory I have been developing called "The Spheres of Collecting". This is a tool you can use to gauge how widespread knowledge of your investment is. The more awareness your item has, the more collecting circles or "spheres" would be interested in purchasing it.

There are three circles: an inner circle of collectors, a middle circle of investors, and an outer circle of fans who are interested in joining the community. When you think of the inner circle, think of people you might know who attend every comic convention and scan every box looking for a deal. These are people who are highly specialized in the hobby and have connections to vendors that allow them to get expensive books at a reasonable price. When it comes to the middle circle, think of those with high-power jobs like a lawyer or a banker who have access to enough money to buy serious books with the potential to go up in value. If you were to look through their collection, you would mostly find high-value keys and no-brainer books that they are not particularly attached to. Finally, there is the outer circle, regular people with normal lives and normal jobs who are fans of the movies and want to collect the books. These are people you would most likely find on social media voicing their opinions on a new project and/or branching out from a different collecting hobby such as Funko Pops or trading cards.

This outer circle is extremely interesting. Most of the people who fall in this category I feel are a reflection of society as a whole. These are fans on the outside looking in at all the fun we are having with our comics. And them joining the community means that we have new blood and new opportunities to buy and sell more cool stuff. However, because there are no warning signs or instruction manuals for collecting comics, these people are usually the least prepared and informed with their purchases.

Imagine being a fan of Moon Knight at the beginning of 2021. Without GPAnalysis or *The Overstreet Comic Book Price Guide*, you look up *Werewolf by Night #32* on eBay. The first thing you quickly notice is that the price of the book is tied to the grade. Some people have 9.0s and 7.5s available for a price equivalent to the down payment on a car. Then, you see a really nice 5.0 at $900 (January 2021 sales include: $877, $750, and $900). You click on sold listings/completed listings and see the price is not too terrible. The only issue is that you barely have a few hundred dollars in the bank. So, with no other option, you decide to work harder and budget. You pick up more shifts, eat less, and even help your friend move his apartment for some spare change. After four months of hard work, you finally have enough money to comfortably spend the $900.

However, as April rolls around, the book has been going up as well. A sale on March 22nd for $1,350 has raised the price for all similar listings. Even the copy you wanted was raised to $1500, far above your savings. You have never gone into credit card debt before, but the fear of this being your last shot before it goes up even further overtakes you. After haggling back and forth with the seller, he agrees to sell the book for $1,350 (April 7th). However, with taxes and interest payments, you actually pay almost $1,560. Several months later, you check on the sales after paying off the worrisome debt. To your surprise, it went up even further (the next four sales in 2021 are $1,750, $1,875, $2,000, and $1,774), and one of the sales was $2,000! In 2021, you feel like a winner.

In 2023, you have lost. You would be lucky if you got 600 bucks for your 5.0 (at the time of writing, the last five sales are $600, $619, $565, $619, and $663). You watched the *Moon Knight* show, and it was fine. But everyone else felt the same, and no one cares for Moon Knight anymore. Even worse, you tricked yourself into thinking you are good at buying trendy comics. Now, all of your items are barely worth a third of their peak. Disappointed, you go to a local comic convention and sell everything, leaving the past behind you.

As a community, we still have a chance to stop this. People are cashing out of the hobby because it appears that there is no hope left. But there is hope. Tell them about the Golden Age, Horror, or even Silver Age DC. Let them know that Marvel keys are simply the beginning, the gateway to establishing a more unique collecting style. They may have lost now, but I believe holding their items for a few years is still a viable alternative instead of cutting their loses. As we venture out into a new world, comics will now have to stand on their own merit instead of movie tie-in potential. *Batman* #1 is now going to be expensive because it is *Batman* #1, not because in the coming year Joaquin Phoenix is going to waltz with Lady Gaga. Even if the last 4.5 (a CBCS with tape in Heritage) sold for under $300,000, it's still a great sale for $180,000 (November 16) because that is still above what it is worth the entire time. *Overstreet Guide* lists it at $164,925 in a 4.5, a number made with math and sales data, unburdened by multipliers and speculation. Honestly, now more than ever, *The Overstreet Comic Book Price Guide* is an essential tool in assessing the value of any comic, not just the Golden Age. While it might be difficult to find a vendor who is selling things at *Overstreet Guide* prices, it makes collecting in these tumultuous times less risky by sticking to its sage advice.

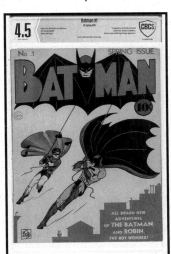

In closing, just because the movie industry is failing does not mean that the comics must as well. Now more than ever is the time to band together and give good deals. I fear that not showing love to your fellow collector will lead to the degradation of the outer layer of collectors, and strip us of our positive perception in the public eye. If you have books similar to the ones I described above, just hold them. You have already lost the money on them, the worst that can happen in five years is that they are still in the gutter. Comic-collecting is as much an investment as it is for entertainment. Instead of worrying about the price of your items tomorrow, relish in the fact that you own them today. Buy cautiously and stay safe in these trying times. Thank you for your time and happy hunting!

LON WEBB
DARK ADVENTURE COMICS

In 2022 we began to see the initial pumping of the brakes in the rather surreal, record-setting values race of the previous several years which encompassed virtually all comics across the board (in some cases, regardless of their inherent collectability). It was a predictable beginning to a return to coherence and sanity, possibly because a majority of collectors were finally just priced out of an almost out-of-control market dominated by an insular clique of deep-pocketed investors and large auction houses.

As we all rolled into 2023, the heady largesse of this and the pandemic stimulus was replaced by a practicality and common-sense pervading most all markets. The long breath taken last year was slowly exhaled through the first half of this year and cautious, regular breathing ensued. The markets did not crash, thankfully. They may have been mercilessly cranked, shilled, driven to a dangerous exuberance with no kiss, but there were many happy endings...just enough to avoid going over the cliff, but not enough to defer course correction, and to ignite and incite introspection.

By year's end, and at the time of this writing, we are deep into a complex weave of market corrections. If one looks at the hobby's history, this is not a bad thing. It's needed for the overall health of it all. Personally, I've had a slowdown and a decidedly sideways series of turns, but we're ending with a lot of wins for a lot of reasons. Primarily, our fourth quarter sales are up considerably from a year ago with projections for continued growth...all within a severe market correction that will be indefinitely ongoing.

I love the thrill-ride of an extended explosion in valuation and sales, but also love riding out an extended market correction. Both are finite and both ruled by supply and demand, but one is dictated by a small percentage of deep-pocketed investors and the other by a large percentage of real hobbyists. Speculators float through both sides but are tied to those percentage buyers. Dealers serve and are served by everyone, always at the front lines, always in the learning curves...which I find are the most interesting places to be. Especially as the only fact in this whole hobby (and basically in life) is that something is only worth what someone else is willing to pay for it at any given moment or circumstance. And it is now a buyer's market.

Buyers in the hobby generally fall into a handful of categories, with certain ones carrying the day based on the exuberance of whatever bulls and bears are active. Top-end collectors and investors are still very much at play out there, though bridled somewhat. The mid-tier hobbyists are a bit sluggish and exercising a pick and choose hand. Lower tier buyers and bargain hunters are always active, but now are moving into the forefront after having little offerings come their way for a long while.

Currently, buying decisions among all categories are slow and methodical and well-thought-out before any trigger is pulled, if at all. Market corrections always bring a hesitancy and hush down over the majority of the market as a whole. If it is not hot or key or imminently flippable, well, it sits for a bit, and even the sure thing appears a tad stodgy. Price points begin to start settling back into the area of reality rather than bullish flush.

An *X-Men* #1 that sold for $60k can't even get a hammer of $30k six months later. An *Incredible Hulk* #1 sale that sets a record price is applauded, but also is roundly acknowledged as selling cheap. Store and convention stocks begin to tout ever lowering discounts on *Guide* pricing. Collections bought at a premium last year are leaving money on the table this year. Yet, this is a good thing. When the rubber band has reached its pull limit and snaps back, it will settle for a time and await the next slow pull.

It is far from doom and gloom, as eventually the stalled machinery within the markets will begin another upward move once the price points in supply meet the fuel of demand. A great many buyers have simply been priced out of their own market. It is obvious that the top-end of the comics market will forever be ruled by deep-pockets, yet even that has its limits. It is also obvious that the other 80% of the market will not and cannot be made so, regardless of how big a movement is made towards that happening by the deep-pocketed investors, dealers and auction houses. Big money gets the news stories, but hobbyist money runs the hobby. What we are seeing is that at play during this correction.

As the year has progressed, I've seen the supply and availability of books steadily increase. High-end and top-tiered batches offered are now being accompanied by large general collections coming out and into play in the markets. Overall availability of even key books has overcome the supply chain issues from the pandemic and slow turnarounds in third-party-grading. Buyers that were priced out on these are now having a selection to choose from, plus a great many other items at price points that jog the wallets.

We are seeing a lot of variety buying. Many collectors are opting to pick up clean and solid lower grades of key or needed books rather than that upgrade or slabbed copy because of the pricing spreads on them, which are cheap. That affordability allows them to offer and pay above *Guide* for these, raw or graded. Low-tier buyers are also spreading their small wealth around on needed issues, in most cases regardless of grade, but absolutely with regards to pricing. As a result, our sales are increasing across the board on books that sat lonely in boxes during that several year high-end rush.

So, what is true is that even in a stalled and correcting market, when sales are overall down on several market segments, that our sales are increasing and up on all other segments. This is healthy. We are also purchasing more in-depth inventory than we have in years, and it is inventory that is beginning to move again. I love market corrections because they allow true buying and selling to begin anew and wane and crest and put books in our hands to put into the hands of others.

High-end and keys are also moving well, though not as frenzied as in the recent past. That end of the market is always vibrant, always perky. The perennial books in the hobby are the columns of it and bear the weight of the collective. These are '50s Horror, Timely issues (just about all of them), Atlas, key Super-hero in any age, '60s Marvels, and the list goes on.

We are seeing renewed activity in '60s-'80s DCs, '70s Marvels, '50s Charlton, Dell sci-fi, '50s and '60s Harvey, high grade giants and annuals of all types. '70s DC Horror cannot be kept in stock. Graded books of course, are still topping the sales lists, but we are selling far more quantity in raw material. A great many of our customers actually read their books. I've noted that many have actively created in their collections a separate stash of cherished books that are graded, while still maintaining the balance of their collection as predominantly raw books for enjoyment.

Much of this year has been about the fallout and blowback among most general collectors of this last valuation surge that lasted far longer than anyone could have expected. I suspect that auspices of this have carried over into the new comics market and are affecting sales there, especially with variant burn out. Couple that with the backlash in battle-lines being drawn there from the clashing left and the right point of view expressed on and off the page, and the major publishers are plainly firing and misfiring in reaction to it, creating buyer jeopardy at a precarious time among its ever-dwindling core base of readers.

The fact that that core base can no longer support major comic publishing for much longer is troubling. The number of comics published from all sources overall is growing, but the venues for distribution and end-sales are vanishing and the result is continually reducing sales from that degraded and aging core base. The unavailability of comic books to purchase for any new reader and any desire to do so is culturally criminal and is and has been problematic for years. The clock is ticking for any solution for any of this.

Currently, there also exists an acceptance strain showing in the public with comics movies and TV shows and their over-saturation. Character-driven appearances and key book valuations tied into those are also suffering a downside. There hasn't been so much a new generation of comic book readers as graphic novel readers and non-comic, comic-related-merchandise buying (a big distinction, and one that heralds the future...mark my words). Instead, a large, new collector/investor segment was created and fed by that movie/TV interest and third-party-grading and that segment is now in trouble as it cools.

1990s readers have also created their own market segment independent of the norm, and in spite of the massive availability of those it appears to be growing rather than shrinking, simply because of slabbing. Numerically graded encapsulation has engineered and promoted itself to begin to have more ephemeral meaning and value than what is encapsulated to begin with. The condition of the slab is even graded now. There is a lot going on outside of the same-old, but with enough characteristics of it to throw a flag down on all of this.

As a whole, the markets are vanishing, growing, and evolving as the readers continue to age in our now media-driven culture that still clings to its past nostalgia. Overall, the market's entirety is correcting after a substantial growth spurt that covered all of this multi-generational nostalgia. Where it is going and how it is evolving, and most importantly, where and how the markets will continue to grow are the questions to ponder from here forward. Especially, as the modern comic book format itself seeks survival in a time of growth, yet of diminishing sales...much like in this current market correction. Especially, as the concept of valuation becomes a venue all in itself.

Especially now, as the future philosophy seems to be no books, but mint empty slabs for sale?

HARLEY YEE
HARLEY YEE COMICS

After a couple of amazing years, 2023 struck at the notion that books always go up. In the long term, most will, but in 2023 they did not. Continuing the trend of the last few months of 2022, the market in Silver, Bronze, Copper and Modern is in correction territory. As I repriced these books upwards multiple times in 2021 and most of 2022, I have been forced to reprice these books down in 2022. Books in these years are not rare and the market has begun to realize this.

Fortunately the Golden Age books have held their prices better than the others. These books are rarer and I still see new collectors going straight into Golden Age. With many collectors also moving into Golden Age, this market should see growth in 2024. Especially strong are Golden Age DC books, which I think have been a little overlooked the last few years. EC comics have also been on the rise with the great artwork, edgy stories and classic covers in many titles.

The Silver, Bronze, Copper and Modern books should start to stabilize at the new lower prices. This should start to move to upwards as the general economy does rise. You can't stop buying, you just can't.

I will be doing a few less shows overall in 2024. However, I will be going to more collector shows, which in 2023 were the Berkeley Comic Show, Cal Comic Con, Little Giant, Scottsdale Comic and Art, Collector Summit, Short Box Con, Torpedo Con and Bedrock City Con.

Thanks to everyone who stopped by at one of the shows or ordered a book from me, and I hope to hear from you in 2024.

VINCENT ZURZOLO
& PETER BARBELLA
METROPOLIS COLLECTIBLES /
COMICCONNECT.COM
VINCENT ZURZOLO

Many of us collect for the sake of the simple love of comics. For those people, fluctuations in the market pricing may not matter as much. They'll keep buying and enjoying their comic books regardless of the peaks and valleys of the market. However, there are many collections where building an investment portfolio is at the forefront. From long, mid, and short-term holders to flippers, there are many different types with different goals. Regardless of your investing strategy, it must be noted that the market at large has been in flux for the last year.

With that being said, I would like to share one of the most important lessons I've learned in my 38 years in the comic book market: You shouldn't miss out on a great opportunity. This is a market filled with both downward pricing corrections and certain types of books immune to market fluctuations. There are signs to note, lessons to be learned, and opportunities everywhere.

In some cases, it will take an iron will to hold as prices may continue to fluctuate. In other cases, you will see your choices bear fruit very quickly. 2023 was (and I believe 2024 will be) a great time to make moves, take shots, and pick up pieces for your collection/portfolio with an eye on the future.

Silver, Bronze, and Modern Age Comics: In general terms, we have seen downward corrections on prices ranging from 25-50% in value from the heights of the pandemic years. *X-Men* #1 5.0 went from $30,000 to $16,000. *Incredible Hulk* #181 9.8 went from sky high prices of $135,000 down to $75,000. *Teenage Mutant Ninja Turtles* #1 9.8 dropped from $250,000 to $150,000. *Ultimate Fallout* #4 Variant Cover 9.8 dropped from a high of $42,000 down to $15,000. The bad news for those who bought during the pandemic is the prices have dropped. The good news for those who haven't is that the dust is settling. While I don't have a crystal ball, I do believe that now is the time to buy and hold. I believe the comic market is resilient and will come back. It will take some time, but I believe it will happen. But not all is doom and gloom. It is also important to note, there have been many strong prices in 2023 for comics from these time periods as well. An *X-Men* #1 9.0 sold for $125,000 showing stability in the market. *X-Men* #6 9.6 sold for $20,550. *Avengers* #1 5.5 sold for $11,750. A *Wizard* magazine #1 9.8 Newsstand File Copy signed by Todd McFarlane sold for $22,000.

Golden Age Comics: In general terms, we have seen stability and oftentimes increases in prices for comics from the 1930s-'50s. Blue chip titles like *Action*, *Detective*, *Captain America*, and *Marvel Mystery* have done very well, along with many categories such as Pre-Code Horror, Sci-Fi, and Romance. The basic economic principle of low supply and high demand is the reason for this. *Action Comics* #1 3.0 $1,600,000 was a great sale. $400,000 for an extensively restored *Detective* #27 9.0 was quite strong. A pre-Robin *Detective* #37 8.0 hit $53,000. $50,000 for a *Sensation* #1 5.5 was a solid sale. *Wonder Woman* #2 9.6 broke $65,000. *Famous Funnies* #213 7.0 hit $15,000. A stunning 9.4 copy of *Planet Comics* #33 sold for $18,500. Exceptions apply here as well, with downward sales on low grade copies of *Batman* #1 and *Superman* #1.

There is no broad stroke, steadfast rule to apply. To make informed decisions—well, you must inform yourself. Keep updated on sales in the market. Talk to dealers and watch auctions. Keep notes on not only what something sold for, but how the book looked. All these things will help you to better analyze what is happening, to see trends, and to make smart decisions.

2023 was an important year for me as I launched my first comic book, *The Addiction*, with my partner David Quinn. This was a childhood dream come true. We co-created and co-wrote the comics and put together a fantastic team to draw, color, and letter the book. Interior art by Claudia Balboni and cover art by Artgerm, David Mack, Alitha Martinez, and Andres Labrada helped make our premiere at New York Comic Con a smash hit. Excited comic fans stood in a line that stretched over forty feet at one point.

We launched as a print comic book, but also in a digital format on Veve where we sold out our 7,500 "drop" in 1 hour. Comics are synonymous with dreams for me. As a child, I dreamt of having superpowers. I dreamt of buying and selling comics. I dreamt of creating comic books. As of this point, I've accomplished two out of three. (I'm still working on the superpowers.)

But seriously, my point in sharing this is to first say follow your dreams to make them a reality. Secondly, the new comic market—although it is going through a tough time—has passionate fans and buyers, and remains strong in many ways. The future success for the new comic market will be dependent on creators making hit comics. That may sound obvious, but it is the truth.

In closing, I thank you for reading this market report and for supporting Metropolis, ComicConnect, and *The Addiction* as buyers, sellers, consignors, fans, and friends. Each day you help me to make my dreams come true, and I am truly grateful.

PETER BARBELLA

The comics market continued to change in 2023, but buyers and sellers found opportunities to thrive as collectors built portfolios and hot new trends emerged for investors.

Golden Age, of course, remains strong, and Pre-Code Horror is on fire. Golden Age keys and classic covers (especially World War II covers) continue to dominate the market. As higher-grade copies continue to be out of most collectors' resources, collectors are searching out single pages, covers, coverless and incomplete copies of GA keys. Timelys stayed at the front of the pack as second-tier publishers like MLJ, Better, Nedor and Fox gained traction.

EC, Avon, Harvey, and Charlton are all in high demand in all grades. Mid to low-grade comics which sold for $100-$200 just five years ago have skyrocketed to over $1,000. As far as Pre-Code Horror goes, the cover is king! Hangings, decapitations, blood & gore & torture, and, of course eye injuries—the more gruesome and ridiculous and macabre the cover, the better! Covers by Johnny Craig, Lou Morales, Lee Elias, Bernard Bailey, and L.B. Cole continue to draw (excuse the pun) premiums. Classic covers like *Black Cat Mystery* #50, *Crime SuspenStories* #22, *Chamber of Chills* #19 and *Tomb of Terror* #15 head (again, excuse the pun) everyone's want lists and continue to set records. Classic Sci-Fi covers aren't far behind.

Silver and Bronze Age (especially Marvel high-grade keys) continue to restabilize after the Covid boom of 2021-2022. DC keys are on a steady rise as they did not experience the same Covid price spikes as their Marvel counterparts.

International comics have arrived (once again, no pun intended) and are now the next big thing. Foreign editions of classic key and early Silver Age comics, as well as non-canon stories, are becoming highly collectible, especially those published contemporaneously or close to the original publishing date. These editions appeal to collectors for a variety of reasons:

• Cost-effective alternatives to the pricier original editions.

• Original or reworked covers or non-canonical stories never seen in the US. Some Golden Age foreign editions contain material from multiple publishers and original covers can feature characters never seen together in the U.S. (for example Timely and DC characters sharing the same cover!!).

• Completionists search these out. We had one collector looking to obtain an issue of a particular character in as many languages as possible.

For the last decade-plus, movies and TV shows (particularly those produced by Marvel Studios) have dominated the pop culture landscape and have been a driving force behind escalating back issue prices. Speculators looking to cash in on the short term—as well as long time collectors looking to secure a blue-chip key issue—followed trending titles as superhero films garnered critical and box office success. Not so much this year. Most productions fell flat, with some of the blockbusters outright flopping and failing to generate any heat to the back issue market. Maybe viewer fatigue has set in, or maybe a new approach is required. However, the future of comic book movies and series remains extremely fertile as there are hundreds of great stories and characters still to be utilized.

Event Auction 53 saw a record price realized for *Crime SuspenStories* #22. One of the most desirable EC comics, the Johnny Craig cover is the (dis-)embodiment of 1950s Pre-Code Horror. This Bill Gaines File Copy graded 9.4 sold for $90,112 eclipsing the previous high sale of $72,000 for a 9.0 copy earlier in the year. Other PCH issues hitting new highs included *Tomb of Terror* #12 7.5 ($9200) and *Vault of Horror* #12 9.0 ($27,200). Classic covers are a must-have! One of the most recognizable Golden Age covers, Fred Ray's *Superman* #14 depicting the Man of Steel with an American eagle in front of the stars & stripes shield, sold for $19,500 (highest price paid for an 8.0). Proving the scarcity of true Golden Age keys and collectors' desire to possess these in any grade available, a conserved NG copy of *Action Comics* #1 missing both the cover and centerfold sold for over $125,000.

Event Auction 53 March 2023 Highlights:
• *Captain America Comics* #1 CGC 7.0 - $300,150
• *Batman* #1 CGC 2.5 - $215,000
• *Whiz Comics* #1 CGC 5.5 - $188,600
• *Action Comics* #1 CGC 0.3 NG Conserved - $126,500
• *Fantastic Four* #5 CBCS 9.4 - $126,500
• *Amazing Fantasy* #15 CGC 6.5 - $91,355
• *Crime SuspenStories* #22 CGC 9.4 - $90,112
• *Mad* #1 CGC 9.8 - $81,000
• *Superman* #1 CGC 6.5 Restored (A-4) - $78,775
• *Venus* #19 CGC 8.5 - $76,000

Unicorn alert! For the first time in over 10 years, a CGC-graded Mint 9.9 copy of *Iron Man* #1 came to market and shattered the previous record selling for $106,000. L.B. Cole covers continue to command premiums as *Suspense Comics* #11 9.8 from the Promise Collection sold for $147,000.

Modern Age standards such as *New Mutants* #98 (9.9-$40,250) and *Ultimate Fallout* #4 (Variant Edition 9.8 Stan Lee Signature Series-$43,000) continued their march to new heights.

Event Auction 54 June 2023 Highlights:
• *Journey Into Mystery* #83 CGC 9.4 - $350,400
• *Superman* #1 GCC 2.0 - $245,000
• *Batman* #1 CGC 2.0 - $176,000
• *Suspense Comics* #11 CGC 9.8 - $147,000
• *Incredible Hulk* #1 CGC 8.0 - $111,157
• *Iron Man* #1 CGC 9.0 - $106,000
• *Amazing Fantasy* #15 CGC 6.0 - $78,000
• *Journey Into Mystery* #83 CGC 8.5 - $62,888
• *Amazing Spider-Man* #1 CGC 8.0 - $52,000
• *Amazing Fantasy* #15 CGC 5.0 - $50,500

Event Auction #55 saw comics featured from the Bobby Blue Collection (an original owner collection consisting of over 700 Golden Age issues) as well as newly discovered Jerry Siegel letters (where Siegel writes to various DC executives about his lack of compensation and general dissatisfaction—incredibly historical). Some near-impossible-to-find Atlas comics from the 1950s hit the auction block with unprecedented results: *Journey into Mystery* #1 7.5 Double Cover from the Bobby Blue Collection ($28,750) and *Black Knight* #1 8.0 ($33,350).

Event Auction 55 September 2023 Highlights:
• *Teenage Mutant Ninja Turtles* #1 CGC 9.8 - $155,250
• *Superman* #1 GCC 1.5 - $132,250
• *Fantastic Four* #48 CGC 9.8 Stan Lee Signature Series - $105,800
• *Pep Comics* #22 CGC 3.0 - $69,575
• *Batman* #1 CGC 2.5 Restored (C-1) - $69,000
• *Hero for Hire* #1 CGC 9.8 - $64,401
• *Sensation Comics* #1 CGC 6.0 - $58,000
• *Mask Comics* #1 CGC 7.5 - $54,625
• *Sgt. Fury* #1 CGC 9.0 - $53,155
• *Dynamic Comics* #8 CGC 4.5 - $45138

Famous Funnies #1 5.5 set a record selling for $25,000 shattering the previous sale of a 5.5 copy in 2015 for $6,900 and the highest price paid for any copy. LB Cole collectors could not contain themselves as *Blue Bolt* #112 (classic "The Beast from Below" cover) hit new heights selling for $17,277.

Event Auction 56 December 2023 Highlights:
• *Incredible Hulk* #1 CGC 7.7 - $65,888
• *Amazing Fantasy* #15 CGC 5.0 - $57,500
• *Incredible Hulk* #181 CGC 9.8 - $$56,925
• *Sensation Comics* #1 CGC 6.0 - $56,350
• *Fantastic Four* #11 CGC 9.4 - $50,555
• *Batman* #3 CGC 9.0 - $39,100
• *Amazing Spider-Man* #14 CGC 9.6 - $38,000
• *Fantastic Four* #1 CGC 6.5 Stan Lee Signature Series - $36,070
• *Amazing Spider-Man* #13 CGC 9.6 - $36,004
• *Tales of Suspense* #39 CGC 8.0 - $30,333

THE WAR REPORT

by Matt Ballesteros & the War Correspondents
(Andy Greenham, Mick Rabin and Brian "Shep" Sheppard)

We are proud to present the 15th edition of the War Report, an independent assessment of the war comic market segment researched and developed by avid enthusiasts of the niche. This reoccurring dispatch has covered the war segment of the comic book hobby for over 15 years now. It was originally created and is currently maintained for our own edification and, hopefully, for your enjoyment. Thanks to all our returning readers and supporters, your comments and encouragement have been tank fuel for us.

Preamble aside, this year we will dispense with the typical introductory formalities and get to the main objectives. However, before doing so I wanted to address, whether you noticed or not, that we skipped a year of reporting (as we did not submit a dispatch for the 2023 year). There were several factors influencing that decision, amongst them, our busy careers outside the comic hobby, and *Overstreet* wanting us to eventually focus on potentially publishing an individual and comprehensive war compendium. Lastly, we also took advantage of the fact that the war comic niche moves at a more methodical pace, thus surmising that skipping a year here and there would not be overly impactful. We will keep a keen eye on that as market and interest fluctuates and be reporting accordingly.

PLAN OF ATTACK

The above addressed, unless there are multiple actions to report on, we may be succinct in our field reports moving forward and hope to do so here with this War Report. Either way, we will always be at the ready in the event we need to broaden or embellish on any communique. This year we will have our focal point on one significant field report and follow suit with our typical "War Comic Ranking." We hope you enjoy both and, as always, we welcome your feedback.

FIELD INTELLIGENCE

Unbeknownst to our readers, while the War Correspondents were working diligently on returning from the battlefront with war comic intelligence these past few years, at the same time we had a special agent working on a highly classified operation. And now, after spending some time underground, we are delighted to report that Agent "Shep" Sheppard has returned from behind the front lines with what we believe to be some of the most important and profound intelligence to be uncovered during our war comic reporting campaign. You, of course, will ultimately be the judge of the information provided, but if recognized and ultimately sanctioned, it will definitively affect portions of our war comic crusade moving forward, and perhaps impact the broader comic book theater of operations as well.

We present the following dossier for your examination and consideration.

WAR SECRET UNCOVERED

OUR ARMY AT WAR #196

HAS A PIVOTAL BOOK OF THE BRONZE AGE BEEN HIDING IN PLAIN SIGHT?

by Brian "Shep" Sheppard

Several years ago, I was working on a project to do reviews of every DC war comic from the Bronze Age to the late 1980s. Doing hundreds of individual reviews, however, wasn't the real challenge – it turned out that the most difficult part of the process was determining what DC's first war comic of the Bronze Age was.

I thought it would be as simple as googling 'first Bronze Age comic' and then just picking the war book from that month. But I was struck to find that, unlike other ages in comic fandom, there was little consensus as to what that first comic was. Sadly, there was no obvious Bronze Age counterpart to *Action Comics* #1 or *Showcase* #4 to truly demark a shift away from one age towards the next.

According to Wikipedia's (I know, I know...) take on the origins of the Bronze Age, "a number of events at the beginning of the 1970s, taken together, can be seen as a shift away from the tone of comics in the previous decade". The key word in that phrase is 'tone'. And the tonal shift we're talking about was one that moved away from the fanciful-yet-wholesome vibe of the 1950s to mid-1960s Silver Age books, towards something that was often darker, more real, and more relevant to what was going on in the culture at that time.

So, using that general criteria for the DC war books, when

162

did that change in tone happen? Thankfully, that proved much easier to identify. Moreover, I learned that tonal change did not happen by accident. And I believe the key to this change rested with two people: Carmine Infantino and Joe Kubert.

During my research many years ago, I had an opportunity to interview Joe Kubert about his role in revitalizing DC's war books during the late 1960s and early 1970s. Kubert recounted that when Infantino became Editorial Director in 1966/67, Infantino asked him to take over editing the war books from previous Editor Bob Kanigher. Kubert said yes – but only if he could do them his way, to which Infantino agreed. Kubert revealed to me that he wanted none of the stories in DC's lineup war line up to glorify war in any way. Instead, he wanted to tell stories that were more real, genuine, and reflected men who didn't want to go to war but did so because there was an important job to be done.

During my interview with Kubert, he did not reference the war in Viet Nam directly, nor did he share any political views about that war, for or against. But it's relevant that Kubert was undertaking this editorial shift in early 1968 as America's involvement in Viet Nam was reaching its height. I mentioned to Joe that I felt that after 1967, the war books took on a much more realistic, human feel. And I specifically I asked him if was this a reflection of changes in the popular culture and if so, was it planned or was it just a natural evolution?

Kubert's reply was unequivocal. He said that the changes were not a natural evolution, but were planned. He felt that if I was going to be editing the books, he wanted them to take a specific direction that he had in mind. And that's why the changes took place.

With Kubert taking the reins of the war lineup, we now had a Senior Editor deciding to use comics to make a statement about war, at a time when the country happened to be involved in a very divisive military conflict overseas. This new direction quickly became evident not only in the storytelling that would be found in DC's war lineup, but also in other editorial decisions like the later inclusion of the 'Make War No More' bullet at the end of the war tales. (It's worth noting, too, that Kubert was very clear that this change in direction was not meant in any way to denigrate the work that had been done on the war lineup under previous Editor Bob Kanigher. In fact, Kubert wanted Kanigher to keep writing the war lineup, which he did to a large degree.)

Kubert's first issue at the editorial helm was *Our Army at War* #194 and it feels entirely like its recent predecessors, with typical shoot 'em up action. Issue #195 followed in the same vein.

But with *Our Army at War* #196 (August 1968) the direction that Joe Kubert wanted DC's war lineup to take became plainly evident, and some 55 years since its publication it remains stunning. The cover that greeted comic buyers in the spring of 1968 is unlike any DC war comic they would have seen before. Instead of seeing Rock flinging a grenade into a Nazi tank or rushing a machine gun position single-handed, we saw Sgt. Rock with his head in his hand, reaching out in desperation and screaming "Stop the war! I want to get out!" All set against an almost psychedelic, Op-Art background that shows the madness of war swirling around.

On the main story inside, across 12 evocative pages, Rock basically has a nervous breakdown as he questions why there is even war to begin with. The fact that Kubert drew the cover and wrote and drew the main story is just another indicator that he was now firmly taking over and taking things in a new direction with his titles. This was Joe Kubert laying down his marker on what DC's war books would now be like and you can tell that something clearly different is going on. The Sgt. Rock lead story in *Our Army at War* #196 is raw, emotional, and incredibly human – in a way few mainstream comics of the Silver Age ever were.

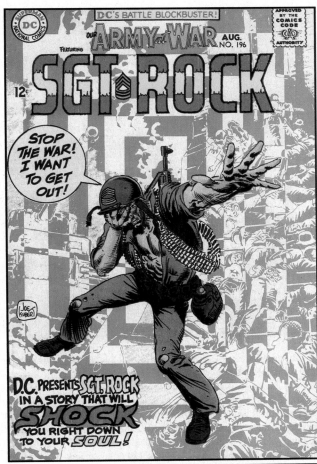

Our Army at War #196

<hr/>

After this issue, all the war books started following the course that Joe Kubert set with that *Our Army at War* #196. Within a couple of years, *Star Spangled War Stories* would have the mysterious, disfigured Unknown Soldier. *Our Fighting Forces* would get The Losers, a group of anti-heroes if ever there was one. In *G.I. Combat*, the crew of the Haunted Tank thought their commander was genuinely cracking up, because he talked to ghosts. Later, Kubert and Kanigher would give us *Blitzkrieg*, with war stories as seen through the enemy's eyes. And it all began with *Our Army at War* #196.

So, was *Our Army at War* #196 just one of several comics that heralded this new age of comics, one of the "number of events" that the Wikipedia article defines as beginning the Bronze Age? Or was it the starting gun that marks the true beginning of the incredible wave of creativity and tonally-different, more relevant storytelling that we saw in comics from the late 1960s to the mid-1970s?

CONTINUED ON 2ND PAGE FOLLOWING.

Many may disagree with me, but I'm in the latter camp. *Our Army at War* #196 ticks all the boxes of a genuine milestone. It is a single issue that shows a major change in tone towards something with more gravity, a change that reflected the culture of its time. It marked a deliberate shift undertaken by a new Editor, with the oversight and approval of a new Editorial Director. And this shift was not short-lived, but instead informed the entire war comics genre for years to come. It's also worth noting that this change did not happen on a marginal title; by the late 1960s Sgt. Rock was a very successful and important character in the DC pantheon, and *Our Army at War* was a strong, consistent seller. All these facts point to one conclusion: without a doubt, *Our Army at War* #196 is not a Silver Age Book; it's a Bronze Age book – the first Bronze Age book of its genre.

It also happens to be a book that predates *Conan the Barbarian* #1, *Green Lantern* #76, *House of Secrets* #92, and Jack Kirby's Fourth World books by a couple of years – comics that most fans now point to as foundational to this new era. Which makes one wonder: did *Our Army at War* #196 begin the Bronze Age of comics?

165

Here is the 15th edition of the war comic ranking. Each comic book's position in the ranks was based on criteria such as who was on the creative team, key storylines, art, first appearances, popularity, market value, scarcity, etc.

The Campaign to Rank War Comics

For new readers, here's how we developed our ranking system:

We went through the *OPG* and other third-party resource material to record every instance of a title or issue that was either a war comic, or that had war subject matter, until we had a list that reached well beyond 1000th line listings.

We then determined what truly constituted a "war comic," by narrowing the field by characterizing war comics as "stories centered on the military involved in armed conflicts." We eliminated many candidates by employing the notion that "Any war story blended with a superhero is, by definition, a 'fantasy' story and not a war story. We then created the sub-classification **War Battle Tales** over other themes, such as, war battle tales, war adventure, cold war, war propaganda, etc.—a refined list that still boasts over 700 listings.

Reporting has been primarily on our two age classifications: the Golden Age and the Atom/Silver/Bronze Age. Each year the War Correspondents and I vote anonymously on the ranking of the top war comics in existence. We judiciously update this "ranking" on a yearly basis, are careful not to make any brash changes, and attempt to ferret out which comics need more attention, or conversely, which received too much. We hope over the years this has been a valuable tool for fellow War Comic collectors.

Since we skipped a 2023 offering, this time the War Ranking will reflect two years' worth of deliberation, evolution, and progression. So, for you long time readers, you may see a couple noteworthy variances or additions.

Without further ado, here is 2024's War Comic Ranking:

TOP 50 ATOM / SILVER / BRONZE AGE WAR COMICS OF 2024

ISSUE	2024 RANK	2022 RANK	CHANGE	MERIT
Our Army at War #83	1	1		1st true app. of Sgt. Rock (Kanigher/Kubert Master Sgt.)
Sgt. Fury #1	2	2		1st app. of Sgt. Fury
G.I. Combat #87	3	3		1st app. of Haunted Tank
Two-Fisted Tales #18	4	6	+2	1st issue to start EC War run
Our Army at War #82	5	4	-1	Sgt. Rock prototype (Non Kanigher/Kubert 4th grade rate Sgt.)
Star Spangled War Stories #84	6	7	+1	1st app. of Mademoiselle Marie
Our Army at War #81	7	5	-2	Sgt. Rock prototype (Non Kanigher/Kubert "Sgt. Rocky")
G.I. Combat #68	8	8		Sgt. Rock prototype (Kanigher/Kubert "The Rock" story)
Frontline Combat #1	9	10	1	1st issue of EC all war title
Our Army at War #1	10	9	-1	1st issue of Big Five war title
Star Spangled War Stories #90	11	12	+1	1st Dinosaur "War That Time Forgot" issue
Our Army at War #90	12	10	-2	How Sgt. Rock got his stripes
Our Army at War #88	13	15	+2	1st Sgt. Rock cover (Kubert)
G.I. Combat #44	14	13	-1	1st DC issue of Big Five war title, early washtone
Our Army at War #85	15	18	+3	1st app. of Ice Cream Soldier and 2nd Kubert Sgt. Rock
Our Army at War #84	16	14	-2	2nd app. of Sgt Rock
G.I. Combat #1	17	22	+5	1st issue of Quality Comics title
Star Spangled War Stories #131	18	17	-1	1st issue of Big Five war title
Our Army at War #112	19	20	+1	Classic roster ("Brady Bunch") cover
Our Army at War #151	20	21	+1	1st app. of Enemy Ace
Our Fighting Forces #1	21	16	-5	1st issue of Big Five war title
All American Men of War #67	22	22		1st app. of Gunner & Sarge (predates OAAW #83)
Blazing Combat #1	23	25	+2	1st issue of Warren war magazine
All American Men of War #127	24	19	-5	1st issue of Big Five war title
Foxhole #1	25	33	+8	1st ish Mainline title (classic Kirby cover)
Our Army at War #196	26	28	+1	1st Bronze Age war comic (classic 1968 Kubert art & key story)
Battle #1	27	27		1st issue of Atlas war title
Combat #1	28	31	+3	1st issue of Atlas war title (black cover)
Our Fighting Forces #45	29	24	-5	Gunner & Sarge run begins (predates OAAW #83)
G.I. Combat #91	30	29	-1	1st Haunted Tank cover (washtone)

Issue	2024 Rank	2022 Rank	Change	Merit
War Comics #11	31	39	+8	Classic flamethrower cover
Star Spangled War Stories #151	32	30	-2	1st solo app. of Unknown Soldier
Our Army at War #91	33	26	-7	1st all Sgt. Rock issue
Our Army at War #168	34	34		1st app. of the Unknown Soldier
Our Army at War #100	35	32	-3	Scarce Kubert (black cover)
Two-Fisted Tales Annual #1	36	37	+1	Early 132 pg. EC war annual
Sgt. Fury #13	37	40	+3	2nd Silver Age solo app. of Captain America
G.I. Combat #75	38	35	-3	1st in "Perty Thirty" washtone run
Foxhole #4	39	na	na	Simon & Kirby war classic (last Mainline issue)
All American Men of War #28	40	36	-4	1st Sgt. Rock prototype (Kubert art)
Fightin' Marines 15 (#1)	41	41		1st issue of St. John war title (Baker art)
G.I. Combat #80	42	38	-4	Classic washtone cover
War Adventures #12	43	na	na	Classic cover
All American Men of War #89	44	41	-3	Historic issue influenced several Lichtenstein paintings
Our Army at War #95	45	44	-1	1st app. of Bulldozer
Our Army at War #128	46	43	-3	Training & origin of Sgt. Rock
G.I. Combat #69	47	45	-2	1st in Grandenetti washtone trifecta
Our Fighting Forces #49	48	49	+1	1st app. of Pooch
All American Men of War #82	49	46	-3	1st app. of Johnny Cloud
War Comics #26	50	na	na	Classic Heath cover

Honorable Mention: Battlefront #26 (Atlas), Sgt Rock #302 (DC), G.I. Combat #83 (DC)

Our Army at War #83

Two-Fisted Tales #18

G.I. Combat #44

Sgt. Fury #13

TOP 15 GOLDEN AGE WAR COMICS OF 2024

ISSUE	2024 RANK	2022 RANK	CHANGE	MERIT
Real Life #3	1	2	+1	Hitler Cover (early 1942 WWII)
Wings #1	2	1	-1	1st issue in long running air war title
War Comics #1	3	3		1st comic completely devoted
Contact Comics #1	4	5	+1	1st issue of air battles title
Don Winslow #1 (1937)	5	4	-1	Very early war adventure title to war content
Don Winslow #1 (1939)	6	6		Rare Four Color issue (#2)
US Marines #2	7	9	+2	Classic Cover (Bailey art)
Real Life Comics #1	8	7	-1	1st issue of adventure title
Rangers Comics #8	9	8	-1	US Rangers begin
Rangers Comics #26	10	10		Classic cover
Don Winslow of the Navy #1 ('43)	11	11		1st comic of 73 issue series (Captain Marvel on cover)
Wings Comics #2	12	12		2nd issue of key air war title
Bill Barnes Comics #1	13	13		1st issue of Air Ace title
Remember Pearl Harbor (nn)	14	13	-1	1942 illustrated story of the battle
American Library nn (#1)	15	15		"Thirty Seconds Over Tokyo" (movie)

Honorable Mention: American Library nn (#2), Guadalcanal Diary (David McKay)

Real Life Comics #3

Rangers Comics #8

TOP 15 ATLAS WAR COMICS OF 2024

ISSUE	2024 RANK	2022 RANK	CHANGE	MERIT
War Comics #11	1	3	+2	Classic flamethrower cover
Battle #1	2	1	-1	1st issue of Atlas war title
War Adventures #12	3	4	+1	Classic cover
Combat #1	4	2	-2	1st issue of Atlas War title (black cover)
Battlefront #15	5	5		Violent Heath cover
Battlefront #26	6	7	+1	Classic Heath minesweeper cover
War Action #1	7	6	-1	1st issue of Atlas War title
War Comics #1	8	7	-1	1st issue of Atlas War title
War Comics #26	9	10	+1	Classic Heath cover
Battlefield #6	10	9	-1	Heath flamethrower cover
Navy Action #2	11	12	+1	Heath cover
Navy Combat #8	12	11	-1	Classic Everett cover
Battle #37	13	13		Heath cover
Navy Action #1	14	14		Russ Heath cover kicks off series
Battle #38	15	15		Heath cover

War Comics #11

Battlefront #26

Fightin' Marines #15 (#1)

Soldier and Marine #1

TOP 5 CHARLTON WAR COMICS OF 2024

ISSUE	2024 RANK	2022 RANK	CHANGE	MERIT
Fightin' Marines #15 (#1)	1	1		1st issue in St. John war title (Baker art)
Attack #54	2	2		1st issue in short war title (100 pgs)
Soldier and Marine #11	3	4	+1	1st ish in short war title (Bob Powell art)
US Air Force #1	4	3	-1	1st issue of Charlton war title
Fightin' Navy #74	5	5		1st issue of Charlton war title (formerly Don Winslow)

Over and Out

Thanks for reading the War Report. A big thank you to those supporters who have stuck by our side and shared excellent thoughts and comments over the years. We so appreciate you. We also salute the squad behind this publication: Bob Overstreet, J.C. Vaughn, Amanda Sheriff, Yolanda Ramirez and Mark Huesman.

Thanks to the troops

As always, I am grateful and humbled by the contributions and sacrifices made by the War Correspondents, Andy, Mick, and Shep. Thanks squad, it's an honor to serve with you.

OVERSTREET

THE WAR REPORT:
The Mission Ahead

The War Report has been a vital part of <u>The Overstreet Comic Book Price Guide</u> for more than a decade now. It has served as an excellent example of how experts in one niche of our hobby can come together to increase awareness of their specialty, and in turn see its appeal to the broader comic book audience increase significantly.

This fall, we'll turn our attention to <u>The Overstreet Comic Book Price Guide To War Comics</u>, a specialty publication set for next April. Much like <u>The Overstreet Comic Book Price Guide To Lost Universes</u>.

It will spotlight the histories of the major titles, showcase some key original art, and illuminate the collecting habits of some of the masters of this historic area of collecting.

We hope you'll join us!

- The Overstreet Team

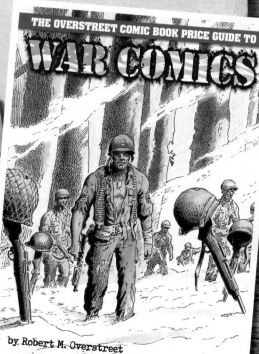

THE OVERSTREET COMIC BOOK PRICE GUIDE TO

WAR COMICS

by Robert M. Overstreet

Not Actual Cover Art

Every comic listed is pictured!
Key series spotlights!
Collector profiles!
Key original art!
Behind-the-scenes info!

KEY SALES FROM 2023-2024

The following lists of sales were reported to Gemstone during the year and represent only a small portion of the total amount of important books that have sold. For other sales information, please see the Overstreet Market Report starting on page 85.

GOLDEN AGE SALES

Action Comics #50 FN/VF $3,736
Air Ace Vol. 2 #2 CGC 3.0 $2,200
All-American Comics #18 CBCS 7.5 $5,640
All Star Comics #3 CGC 4.0 $19,200
America's Best Comics #4 CGC 5.0 $588
Batman #1 CGC 2.5 $156,000
Batman #2 CGC 0.5 $2,000
Batman #6 CGC 2.0 $1,500
Batman #13 CGC 3.5 $1,800
Batman #73 CGC 6.5 $2,885
Black Cat Comics #8 CGC 8.5 $1,200
Blue Bolt Weird Tales #115 CGC 3.0 $1,500
Captain America Comics #1 CGC 9.2 $750,000
Captain America Comics #1 CGC 3.0 $156,000
Captain America Comics #13 CGC 1.5 $4,200
Captain America Comics #38 CGC 8.0 $8,400
Chamber of Chills #19 CBCS 5.0 $18,000
Crime SuspenStories #17 CGC 5.0 $1,200
Detective Comics #27 CGC 3.0 $600,000
Detective Comics #31 CGC 2.5 $90,000
Detective Comics #118 CGC 9.2 $6,900
Exciting Comics #28 CGC 5.0 $6,211
Haunted Thrills #6 CGC 9.2 $50,400
Haunt of Fear #17 CGC 9.6 $12,000
   (Gaines File Copy)
Jo-Jo Comics #25 CGC 4.5 $2,400
Jungle Stories #1 CGC 5.0 $1,500
Kid Komics #5 CGC 7.5 $2,200
Leading Comics #1 CGC 8.5 $9,000

Marvel Mystery Comics #26 CGC 8.0 $11,400
Marvel Mystery Comics #64 CGC 4.0 $1,600
Marvel Tales #116 CGC 6.0 $2,000
Mask Comics #2 CGC 4.5 $20,400
Mystery Men Comics #2 CGC 6.5 $11,400
Pep Comics #39 CGC 6.0 $5,400
Phantom Lady #17 CGC 3.5 $28,800
Phantom Lady #22 CGC 1.8 $1,500
Punch Comics #12 CGC 5.5 $60,000
Science Comics #1 CGC 3.0 $5,280
Sensation Comics #1 CGC 9.6 $420,000
Shadow Comics #1 CGC 8.0 $10,200
Spotlight Comics #2 CGC 6.0 $1,000
Sub-Mariner Comics #17 CGC 7.5 $2,424
Sun Girl #1 CGC 7.5 $2,880
Superman #1 CGC 5.0 $504,000
Superman #2 CGC 3.5 $15,600
   (Williamsport Pedigree)
Tales From the Crypt #23 CBCS 9.6 $4,560
   (Gaines File Copy)
Tip Top Comics #186 CGC 7.0 $2,700
Torchy #1 CGC 5.0 $1,200
USA Comics #10 CGC 5.5 $4,520
Weird Science #12 CGC 5.0 $1,500
Wonder Comics #13 CGC 9.2 $6,300
Wonder Woman #1 CGC 8.0 $108,000
Wonder Woman #53 FN/VF $605
Zip Comics #14 CGC 9.6 $26,400
   (Mile High Pedigree)

SILVER AGE SALES

Action Comics #252 CGC 7.5 $8,400
Action Comics #252 CGC 3.0 $1,400
Amazing Fantasy #15 CGC 7.5 $162,000
Amazing Spider-Man #6 CGC 5.0 $2,000
Amazing Spider-Man #33 CGC 9.0 $1,500

Amazing Spider-Man #34 VF $399
Aquaman #1 CGC 9.4 $9,000
Avengers #1 CGC 9.6 $432,000
Avengers #4 CGC 7.5 $4,300
Batman Annual #1 CGC 9.6 $26,400

Brave and the Bold #28 CGC 4.0 $4,700

Captain Atom #83 CGC 9.6 $3,240

Daredevil #1 CGC 9.8 $360,000

Detective Comics #359 CGC 9.2 $8,400

Fantastic Four #48 CGC 9.8 $63,000

House of Secrets #92 CGC 4.5 $1,300

Incredible Hulk #6 CGC 7.0 $3,200

Incredible Hulk Annual #1 CGC 9.8 $13,200

Justice League of America #1 CGC 9.6 $348,000

Mystery in Space #36 CGC 9.4 $5,520

Our Army at War #81 CGC 8.5 $5,280

Secret Origins #1 CGC 9.6 $7,800

Showcase #20 CGC 9.4, $26,400

Showcase #34 CGC 9.0 $8,400

Silver Surfer #4 CGC 9.6 $12,600

Star Trek #1 CGC 9.4 $12,000

Strange Tales #110 CGC 3.0 $3,500

Sub-Mariner #1 CGC 9.8 $9,300

Superman Annual #1 CGC 9.2 $15,600

Tales of Suspense #39 CGC 9.8 $840,000

Tales to Astonish #27 CGC 7.5 $9,900

Uncle Scrooge #15 CGC 9.6 $4,080

Yellow Claw #1 CGC 9.2, $33,600

BRONZE AGE SALES

Amazing Spider-Man #100 CGC 9.8 $3,840

Amazing Spider-Man #121 CGC 9.8 $5,280

Amazing Spider-Man #129 CGC 9.4 $3,840

Batman #232 CGC 9.8 $15,000

Demon #1 CGC 9.0 $174

Detective Comics #411 CGC 9.4 $3,120

Doctor Strange #1 CGC 8.5 $119

Fantastic Four #112 CGC 8.5 $480

Giant-Size X-Men #1 CGC 9.8 $22,200

Green Lantern #76 CGC 9.6 $13,800

House of Secrets #92 CBCS 9.8 $58,800

Incredible Hulk #181 CGC 9.8 $72,000

Iron Man #55 CGC 8.5 $1,100 (Double cover)

Marvel Feature #1 CGC 9.6 $1,800

Marvel Premiere #15 CGC 9.8 $4,080

Marvel Spotlight #5 CGC 9.0 $4,080

Shazam! #1 CGC 9.9 $6,600

Star Wars #1 (30¢-c) CGC 9.8 $$4,440

Starnge Tales #179 CGC 8.0 $49

Superman #233 CGC 9.6 $5,520

Tomb of Dracula #10 CGC 9.6 $7,800

Werewolf By Night #32 CGC 9.8 $26,400

Wonder Woman #191 CGC 9.6 $960

Wonder Woman #204 CGC 8.5 $288

X-Men #94 CGC 9.8 $37,200

X-Men #94 CGC 8.5 $2,500

X-Men #99 CGC 9.6 $780

X-Men #100 CGC 9.8 $5,880

MODERN AGE SALES

Albedo #2 CGC 9.8 $55,200

Aliens #1 CGC 9.8 $6,600

Amazing Spider-Man #252 CGC 9.6 $396

Batman Adventures #12 CGC 9.8 $$2,880

Batman: The Killing Joke CGC 10 $28,800

Danger Girl #1 CGC 9.9 $2,880

Daredevil #168 CGC 9.8 $3,600

Macross #1 CGC 9.8 $1,140

New Mutants #87 CGC 9.2 $129

New Mutants #98 CGC 9.4 $336

Raphael #1 CGC 9.2 $384

Saga of the Swamp Thing #37 CGC 9.2 $288

Sandman #1 CGC 9.6, $204

Spawn #1 CGC 9.9 $4,800

Superman (Bradman promo) CGC 9.6 $3960

Teenage Mutant Ninja Turtles #1 CGC 9.8 $126,000

Teenage Mutant Ninja Turtles #3 CGC 9.6 $264,000

Ultimate Fallout #4 (Variant) CBCS 9.8 $9,900

Venom: Lethal Protector #1 (Black-c) CGC 9.6 $4,560

Walking Dead #1 CGC 9.9 $16,800

Web of Spider-Man #1 CGC 9.6 $154

Wolverine #1 CGC 9.9 $15,600

Wolverine Origins #10 Retailer Incentive) CGC 9.4 $204

X-Men #266 CGC 9.6 $204

TOP COMICS

The following tables denote the rate of appreciation of the top Golden Age, Platinum Age, Silver Age and Bronze Age comics, as well as selected genres over the past year. The retail value for a Near Mint- copy of each comic (or VF where a Near Mint- copy is not known to exist) in 2024 is compared to its Near Mint- value in 2023. The rate of return for 2024 over 2023 is given. The place in rank is given for each comic by year, with its corresponding value in highest known grade. These tables can be very useful in forecasting trends in the market place. For instance, the investor might want to know which book is yielding the best dividend from one year to the next, or one might just be interested in seeing how the popularity of books changes from year to year. For instance, *Flash Comics* #1 was in 15th place in 2023 and has increased to 13th place in 2024. Premium books are also included in these tables and are denoted with an asterisk(*).

The following tables are meant as a guide to the investor. However, it should be pointed out that trends may change at anytime and that some books can meet market resistance with a slowdown in price increases, while others can develop into real comers from a presently dormant state. In the long run, if the investor sticks to the books that are appreciating steadily each year, he shouldn't go very far wrong.

TOP 100 GOLDEN AGE COMICS

TITLE/ISSUE#	2024 RANK	2024 NM- PRICE	2023 RANK	2023 NM- PRICE	$ INCR.	% INCR.
Action Comics #1	1	$7,000,000	1	$6,600,000	$400,000	6%
Detective Comics #27	2	$4,800,000	2	$4,500,000	$300,000	7%
Superman #1	3	$3,000,000	3	$2,700,000	$300,000	11%
Marvel Comics #1	4	$1,400,000	4	$1,200,000	$200,000	17%
Batman #1	5	$1,300,000	5	$1,100,000	$200,000	18%
All-American Comics #16	6	$1,000,000	6	$975,000	$25,000	3%
Captain America Comics #1	7	$750,000	7	$715,000	$35,000	5%
Action Comics #7	8	$650,000	8	$630,000	$20,000	3%
Detective Comics #31	9	$525,000	9	$490,000	$35,000	7%
Whiz Comics #2 (#1)	10	$475,000	10	$450,000	$25,000	6%
Pep Comics #22	11	$455,000	11	$440,000	$15,000	3%
Action Comics #10	12	$420,000	12	$415,000	$5,000	1%
Flash Comics #1	13	$400,000	15	$375,000	$25,000	7%
Detective Comics #29	14	$395,000	13	$385,000	$10,000	3%
All Star Comics #8	15	$390,000	13	$385,000	$5,000	1%
More Fun Comics #52	16	$320,000	16	$300,000	$20,000	7%
Action Comics #2	17	$305,000	17	$290,000	$15,000	5%
Detective Comics #33	18	$290,000	18	$275,000	$15,000	5%
Wonder Woman #1	19	$265,000	19	$250,000	$15,000	6%
Sensation Comics #1	20	$250,000	20	$240,000	$10,000	4%
Action Comics #13	21	$240,000	23	$225,000	$15,000	7%
Detective Comics #35	21	$240,000	21	$235,000	$5,000	2%
Archie Comics #1	23	$235,000	22	$232,000	$3,000	1%
Detective Comics #38	24	$230,000	24	$220,000	$10,000	5%
Adventure Comics #40	25	$215,000	25	$205,000	$10,000	5%
Sub-Mariner Comics #1	26	$190,000	27	$175,000	$15,000	9%
Suspense Comics #3	26	$190,000	27	$175,000	$15,000	9%
More Fun Comics #73	28	$180,000	26	$176,000	$4,000	2%
Action Comics #3	29	$175,000	29	$172,000	$3,000	2%
Detective Comics #1	30	VF $165,000	30	VF $150,000	$15,000	10%
All Star Comics #3	31	$155,000	30	$150,000	$5,000	3%
Detective Comics #28	32	$150,000	32	$140,000	$10,000	7%
Captain Marvel Adventures #1	33	$140,000	33	$135,000	$5,000	4%
Detective Comics #36	34	$130,000	34	$125,000	$5,000	4%
Marvel Mystery Comics #9	35	$125,000	35	$119,000	$6,000	5%
Fantastic Comics #3	36	$120,000	36	$110,000	$10,000	9%
Marvel Mystery Comics #2	37	$118,000	36	$110,000	$8,000	7%
Marvel Mystery Comics #5	38	$100,000	38	$98,000	$2,000	2%
Superman #2	38	$100,000	39	$96,000	$4,000	4%
Green Lantern #1	40	$98,000	40	$95,000	$3,000	3%

TITLE/ISSUE#	2024 RANK	2024 NM- PRICE	2023 RANK	2023 NM- PRICE	$ INCR.	% INCR.
Action Comics #23	41	$95,000	42	$90,000	$5,000	6%
More Fun Comics #53	42	$94,000	41	$92,000	$2,000	2%
Marvel Mystery Comics #4	43	$90,000	44	$82,000	$8,000	10%
Detective Comics #37	44	$87,000	43	$85,000	$2,000	2%
Captain America Comics #3	45	$86,000	44	$82,000	$4,000	5%
Human Torch #2 (#1)	46	$82,000	46	$80,000	$2,000	3%
Action Comics #4	47	$80,000	48	$77,000	$3,000	4%
Action Comics #5	47	$80,000	48	$77,000	$3,000	4%
Captain America Comics #2	47	$80,000	50	$75,000	$5,000	7%
Action Comics #6	50	$79,000	47	$78,000	$1,000	1%
Action Comics #12	51	$75,000	51	$70,000	$5,000	7%
Amazing Man Comics #22	51	$75,000	63	$60,000	$15,000	25%
Detective Comics #40	51	$75,000	80	$50,000	$25,000	50%
Marvel Mystery Comics #3	51	$75,000	51	$70,000	$5,000	7%
Adventure Comics #48	55	$72,000	51	$70,000	$2,000	3%
All-American Comics #19	55	$72,000	51	$70,000	$2,000	3%
Batman #2	57	$70,000	55	$68,000	$2,000	3%
Captain America Comics #74	57	$70,000	60	$64,000	$6,000	9%
Mask Comics #1	57	$70,000	63	$60,000	$10,000	17%
More Fun Comics #54	57	$70,000	56	$65,000	$5,000	8%
More Fun Comics #55	57	$70,000	56	$65,000	$5,000	8%
Punch Comics #12	57	$70,000	63	$60,000	$10,000	17%
Wonder Comics #1	57	$70,000	56	$65,000	$5,000	8%
Motion Picture Funn. Wkly #1	64	$65,800	56	$65,000	$800	1%
Action Comics #15	64	$65,000	61	$62,000	$3,000	5%
All-American Comics #61	64	$65,000	63	$60,000	$5,000	8%
Daring Mystery Comics #1	64	$65,000	63	$60,000	$5,000	8%
Terrific Comics #5	64	$65,000	63	$60,000	$5,000	8%
Silver Streak Comics #6	69	$64,000	71	$58,000	$6,000	10%
Action Comics #8	70	$63,000	63	$60,000	$3,000	5%
Action Comics #9	70	$63,000	63	$60,000	$3,000	5%
New Fun Comics #1	70	VF $63,000	61	VF $62,000	$1,000	2%
All-Select Comics #1	73	$60,000	75	$55,000	$5,000	9%
Detective Comics #140	73	$60,000	71	$58,000	$2,000	3%
Phantom Lady #17	73	$60,000	73	$56,000	$4,000	7%
Red Raven Comics #1	73	$60,000	75	$55,000	$5,000	9%
Detective Comics #69	77	$58,000	75	$55,000	$3,000	5%
Detective Comics #168	77	$58,000	75	$55,000	$3,000	5%
Walt Disney's Comics & Stories #1	77	$58,000	73	$56,000	$2,000	4%
Four Color Ser. 1 (Donald Duck) #4	80	$54,000	79	$52,000	$2,000	4%
Detective Comics #225	81	$52,000	80	$50,000	$2,000	4%
Marvel Mystery Comics #46	81	$52,000	83	$48,000	$4,000	8%
Marvel Mystery Comics 132 pg.	81	VF $52,000	80	VF $50,000	$2,000	4%
Detective Comics #30	84	$50,000	85	$47,000	$3,000	6%
Marvel Mystery Comics #44	84	$50,000	88	$45,000	$5,000	11%
Superman #3	84	$50,000	83	$48,000	$2,000	4%
Mystic Comics #1	87	$49,000	85	$47,000	$2,000	4%
Amazing Man Comics #5	88	$48,000	87	$46,000	$2,000	4%
Detective Comics #66	89	$47,000	88	$45,000	$2,000	4%
Famous Funnies-Series 1 #1	90	VF $46,000	88	VF $45,000	$1,000	2%
Batman #11	91	$45,000	96	$40,000	$5,000	13%
Mystery Men Comics #1	91	$45,000	96	$40,000	$5,000	13%
Planet Comics #1	91	$45,000	96	$40,000	$5,000	13%
Detective Comics #2	94	VF $44,000	91	VF $43,000	$1,000	2%
Double Action Comics #2	94	$44,000	91	$43,000	$1,000	2%
Marvel Mystery Comics #8	94	$44,000	94	$42,000	$2,000	5%
Captain America Comics 132 pg.	97	VF $43,500	93	VF $42,750	$750	2%
All Winners Comics #1	98	$42,000	95	$41,000	$1,000	2%
Pep Comics #34	98	$42,000	100	$38,000	$4,000	11%
Action Comics #17	100	$40,000	100	$38,000	$2,000	5%
Chamber of Chills #19	100	$40,000	96	$40,000	$0	0%
Exciting Comics #9	100	$40,000	112	$35,000	$5,000	14%
Marvel Family #1	100	$40,000	114	$35,000	$5,000	14%

TOP 50 SILVER AGE COMICS

TITLE/ISSUE#	2024 RANK	2024 NM- PRICE	2023 RANK	2023 NM- PRICE	$ INCR.	% INCR.
Amazing Fantasy #15	1	$700,000	1	$650,000	$50,000	8%
Incredible Hulk #1	2	$430,000	2	$400,000	$30,000	8%
Fantastic Four #1	3	$350,000	3	$300,000	$50,000	17%
X-Men #1	4	$190,000	4	$185,000	$5,000	3%
Showcase #4	5	$185,000	5	$182,000	$3,000	2%
Amazing Spider-Man #1	6	$130,000	6	$120,000	$10,000	8%
Journey Into Mystery #83	7	$125,000	6	$120,000	$5,000	4%
Brave and the Bold #28	8	$95,000	8	$94,000	$1,000	1%
Tales of Suspense #39	9	$92,000	9	$88,000	$4,000	5%
Fantastic Four #5	10	$82,000	10	$80,000	$2,000	3%
Showcase #22	11	$70,000	11	$65,000	$5,000	8%
Tales to Astonish #27	12	$65,000	12	$60,000	$5,000	8%
Avengers #1	13	$62,000	12	$60,000	$2,000	3%
Adventure Comics #247	14	$42,000	14	$40,000	$2,000	5%
Flash #105	15	$38,000	15	$37,000	$1,000	3%
Action Comics #242	16	$36,000	16	$35,000	$1,000	3%
Action Comics #252	16	$36,000	17	$34,000	$2,000	6%
Sgt. Fury #1	18	$35,000	19	$31,000	$4,000	13%
Our Army at War #83	19	$33,000	19	$31,000	$2,000	6%
Justice League of America #1	20	$32,500	18	$32,500	$0	0%
Strange Tales #110	21	$31,000	19	$31,000	$0	0%
Amazing Spider-Man #2	22	$30,000	23	$28,000	$2,000	7%
Daredevil #1	22	$30,000	22	$29,000	$1,000	3%
Tales to Astonish #13	24	$29,000	23	$28,000	$1,000	4%
Amazing Spider-Man #3	25	$27,000	25	$26,000	$1,000	4%
Showcase #8	26	$26,500	25	$26,000	$500	2%
Journey Into Mystery #85	27	$26,000	25	$26,000	$0	0%
Batman #121	28	$24,000	32	$19,000	$5,000	26%
Fantastic Four #4	28	$24,000	28	$22,000	$2,000	9%
Incredible Hulk #2	28	$24,000	28	$22,000	$2,000	9%
Fantastic Four #3	31	$22,000	30	$20,000	$2,000	10%
Fantastic Four #2	32	$21,000	30	$20,000	$1,000	5%
Green Lantern #1	33	$19,500	32	$19,000	$500	3%
Amazing Spider-Man #4	34	$19,000	34	$18,000	$1,000	6%
Tales to Astonish #35	34	$19,000	34	$18,000	$1,000	6%
Showcase #17	36	$17,500	36	$17,000	$500	3%
Amazing Spider-Man #14	37	$17,000	37	$16,000	$1,000	6%
Superman's G.F. Lois Lane #1	38	$16,500	37	$16,000	$500	3%
Fantastic Four #12	39	$16,000	37	$16,000	$0	0%
Showcase #9	40	$15,000	40	$15,000	$0	0%
Journey Into Mystery #84	41	$14,000	45	$12,000	$2,000	17%
Showcase #6	41	$14,000	41	$13,500	$500	4%
Showcase #13	43	$13,500	42	$13,000	$500	4%
Showcase #14	43	$13,500	42	$13,000	$500	4%
Richie Rich #1	45	$13,000	45	$12,000	$1,000	8%
Avengers #4	46	$12,200	44	$12,200	$0	0%
Fantastic Four #48	47	$12,000	45	$12,000	$0	0%
Flash #106	47	$12,000	49	$11,000	$1,000	9%
Amazing Spider-Man #5	49	$11,000	51	$10,500	$500	5%
Fantastic Four #6	49	$11,000	52	$10,000	$1,000	10%
Fantastic Four #52	49	$11,000	48	$11,000	$0	0%
Our Army at War #81	49	$11,000	50	$11,000	$0	0%
Strange Tales #89	49	$11,000	53	$10,000	$1,000	10%

TOP 25 BRONZE AGE COMICS

TITLE/ISSUE#	2024 RANK	2024 NM- PRICE	2023 RANK	2023 NM- PRICE	$ INCR.	% INCR.
Star Wars #1 (35¢ price variant)	1	$16,000	1	$15,000	$1,000	7%
Incredible Hulk #181	2	$12,000	2	$12,000	$0	0%
Marvel Spotlight #5	3	$9,000	4	$9,000	$0	0%
Cerebus #1	4	$7,500	5	$7,000	$500	7%
House of Secrets #92	5	$6,800	6	$6,700	$100	1%
Giant-Size X-Men #1	6	$6,000	3	$10,000	-$4,000	-40%
Scooby Doo (1970) #1	7	$5,500	7	$5,400	$100	2%
Iron Fist #14 (35¢ price variant)	8	$5,000	9	$4,700	$300	6%
Werewolf By Night #32	8	$5,000	8	$5,000	$0	0%
Amazing Spider-Man #129	10	$4,000	10	$4,000	$0	0%
Tomb of Dracula #10	10	$4,000	10	$4,000	$0	0%
X-Men #94	12	$2,800	12	$2,800	$0	0%
Green Lantern #76	13	$2,700	13	$2,700	$0	0%
Incredible Hulk #180	14	$2,500	14	$2,500	$0	0%
Batman #227	15	$2,400	21	$1,900	$500	26%
Star Wars #2 (35¢ price variant)	16	$2,300	15	$2,200	$100	5%
Star Wars #3 (35¢ price variant)	17	$2,200	16	$2,100	$100	5%
Star Wars #4 (35¢ price variant)	17	$2,200	16	$2,100	$100	5%
Amazing Spider-Man #101	19	$2,000	18	$2,000	$0	0%
Hero For Hire #1	19	$2,000	18	$2,000	$0	0%
Iron Man #55	19	$2,000	18	$2,000	$0	0%
Batman #251	22	$1,700	22	$1,650	$50	3%
DC 100 Page Super Spectacular #5	23	$1,550	23	$1,450	$100	7%
Batman #232	24	$1,300	24	$1,300	$0	0%
Detective Comics #400	25	$1,100	26	$1,050	$50	5%
Detective Comics #411	25	$1,100	27	$1,050	$50	5%

TOP 25 COPPER AGE COMICS

TITLE/ISSUE#	2024 RANK	2024 NM- PRICE	2023 RANK	2023 NM- PRICE	$ INCR.	% INCR.
Gobbledygook #1	1	$36,000	1	$34,000	$2,000	6%
Teenage Mutant Ninja Turtles #1	2	$23,000	2	$22,000	$1,000	5%
Gobbledygook #2	3	$12,000	3	$10,000	$2,000	20%
Albedo #2	4	$8,500	4	$8,200	$300	4%
Crow, The #1	5	$1,050	6	$1,050	$0	0%
Miracleman Gold #1	6	$1,000	7	$1,000	$0	0%
Miracleman Blue #1	7	$850	8	$850	$0	0%
Primer #2	8	$775	5	$1,200	-$425	-35%
Sandman #8	9	$675	9	$650	$25	4%
Amazing Spider-Man #300	10	$600	9	$650	-$50	-8%
Teenage Mutant Ninja Turtles #2	10	$600	11	$600	$0	0%
Vampirella #113	12	$575	12	$575	$0	0%
Amazing Spider-Man #238	13	$425	13	$500	-$75	-15%
Caliber Presents #1	13	$425	14	$425	$0	0%
Spider-Man Platinum #1	15	$410	16	$390	$20	5%
Evil Ernie #1	16	$400	17	$375	$25	7%
New Mutants #98	17	$375	17	$375	$0	0%
Swamp Thing #37	18	$340	15	$400	-$60	-15%
Spider-Man #1 (Gold 2nd UPC)	19	$310	19	$290	$20	7%
Grendel #1	20	$265	21	$265	$0	0%
Batman #423	21	$250	22	$250	$0	0%
Eightball #1	21	$250	22	$250	$0	0%
Cry For Dawn #1	23	$240	24	$240	$0	0%
Amazing Spider-Man #252	24	$225	20	$275	-$50	-18%
Teenage Mutant Ninja Turtles #3	25	$225	25	$225	$0	0%

TOP 20 MODERN AGE COMICS

TITLE/ISSUE#	2024 RANK	2024 NM- PRICE	2023 RANK	2023 NM- PRICE	$ INCR.	% INCR.
Bone #1	1	$3,600	1	$3,600	$0	0%
Venom: Lethal Protector #1 (black-c)	2	$2,900	2	$2,800	$100	4%
Walking Dead #1	3	$1,250	3	$1,250	$0	0%
Hero Trade: A Brief Case #1	4	$1,000	4	$1,000	$0	0%
Invincible #1	4	$1,000	4	$1,000	$0	0%
Batman Adventures #12	6	$725	7	$725	$0	0%
Marvel Collectible Classics: Spider-Man #1	7	$650	9	$650	$0	0%
Star Wars: The Clone Wars #1	7	$650	6	$800	-$150	-19%
Spawn #1 (B&W edition)	9	$600	10	$600	$0	0%
Captain Marvel #17 (2012, 2nd printing)	10	$500	8	$700	-$200	-29%
Ultimate Fallout #4	10	$500	11	$500	$0	0%
Goon, The #1	12	$475	12	$475	$0	0%
Ult. Spider-Man (3rd series) #1 var-c (city)	13	$400	14	$400	$0	0%
Ult. Spider-Man (3rd) #1 var-c (unmasked)	13	$400	14	$400	$0	0%
Walking Dead #2	15	$380	17	$380	$0	0%
Spawn #174	16	$365	18	$365	$0	0%
Incredible Hulk #377 (3rd printing)	17	$350	19	$350	$0	0%
Strangers in Paradise #1	18	$325	20	$325	$0	0%
Bone #2	19	$300	21	$300	$0	0%
Harley Quinn #1 ('14, Hughes var-c)	19	$300	21	$300	$0	0%

TOP 10 PLATINUM AGE COMICS

TITLE/ISSUE#	2024 RANK	2024 PRICE	2023 RANK	2023 PRICE	$ INCR.	% INCR.
Yellow Kid in McFadden Flats	1	FN $20,000	1	FN $18,000	$2,000	11%
Little Sammy Sneeze	2	FN $8,700	2	FN $8,700	$0	0%
Mickey Mouse Book (1st printing)	3	VF $6,400	3	VF $6,300	$100	2%
Little Nemo 1906	4	FN $5,200	4	FN $5,100	$100	2%
Yellow Kid #1	5	FN $5,000	6	FN $4,500	$500	11%
Sam and His Laugh	6	VF $4,900	5	VF $4,800	$100	2%
Pore Li'l Mose	7	FN $4,500	6	FN $4,500	$0	0%
Little Nemo 1909	8	FN $4,100	8	FN $4,000	$100	3%
Dreams of the Rarebit Fiend	9	VF $3,750	9	VF $3,600	$15	4%
Happy Hooligan Book 1	10	VF $3,600	9	VF $3,600	$100	0%

TOP 10 CRIME COMICS

TITLE/ISSUE#	2024 RANK	2024 NM- PRICE	2023 RANK	2023 NM- PRICE	$ INCR.	% INCR.
Fight Against Crime #24	1	$38,000	1	$35,000	$3,000	9%
Crime Does Not Pay #24	2	$30,000	3	$25,000	$5,000	20%
Crime SuspenStories #22	2	$30,000	2	$26,000	$4,000	15%
Crime Does Not Pay #22	4	$15,500	4	$15,000	$500	3%
Crime SuspenStories #20	5	$15,000	5	$11,500	$3,500	30%
Crime Does Not Pay #33	6	$9,000	6	$8,000	$1,000	13%
Gangsters Can't Win #2	7	$5,800	8	$5,400	$400	7%
Crime Does Not Pay #23	8	$5,700	7	$5,600	$100	2%
Crime Reporter #2	9	$5,500	9	$5,000	$500	10%
True Crime Comics #2	10	$4,900	10	$4,700	$200	4%

TOP 10 HORROR COMICS

TITLE/ISSUE#	2024 RANK	2024 NM- PRICE	2023 RANK	2023 NM- PRICE	$ INCR.	% INCR.
Chamber of Chills #19	1	$40,000	1	$40,000	$0	0%
Journey into Mystery #1	2	$26,000	2	$24,000	$2,000	8%
Eerie #1	3	$22,000	3	$19,000	$3,000	16%
Tales of Terror Annual #1	4	VF $20,000	5	VF $17,500	$2,500	14%
Tales to Astonish #1	4	$20,000	3	$19,000	$1,000	5%
Strange Tales #1	6	$18,500	6	$17,000	$1,500	9%
Vault of Horror #12	7	$17,500	7	$16,500	$1,000	6%
Amazing Ghost Stories #14	8	$15,000	10	$10,000	$5,000	50%
Chamber of Chills #23	8	$15,000	8	$12,000	$3,000	25%
Crime Patrol #15	8	$15,000	8	$12,000	$3,000	25%

TOP 10 ROMANCE COMICS

TITLE/ISSUE#	2024 RANK	2024 NM- PRICE	2023 RANK	2023 NM- PRICE	$ INCR.	% INCR.
Giant Comics Edition #12	1	$25,000	1	$22,000	$3,000	14%
Daring Love #1	2	$8,400	2	$7,700	$700	9%
Giant Comics Edition #15	3	$4,800	3	$4,500	$300	7%
Negro Romance #1	4	$4,400	4	$4,100	$300	7%
Negro Romances #4	5	$4,100	5	$3,800	$300	8%
Intimate Confessions #1	6	$3,700	6	$3,600	$100	3%
Giant Comics Edition #13	7	$3,600	7	$3,400	$200	6%
Moon, A Girl... Romance #12	7	$3,600	7	$3,400	$200	6%
Negro Romance #2	7	$3,600	7	$3,400	$200	6%
Negro Romance #3	7	$3,600	7	$3,400	$200	6%

TOP 10 SCI-FI COMICS

TITLE/ISSUE#	2024 RANK	2024 NM- PRICE	2023 RANK	2023 NM- PRICE	$ INCR.	% INCR.
Showcase #17 (Adam Strange)	1	$17,500	1	$17,000	$500	3%
Mystery In Space #1	2	$8,600	2	$8,400	$200	2%
Weird Science-Fantasy Annual 1952	3	$7,500	3	$7,000	$500	7%
Weird Science #12 (#1)	4	$5,900	4	$5,800	$100	2%
Strange Adventures #1	5	$5,400	5	$5,300	$100	2%
Showcase #15 (Space Ranger)	6	$5,300	6	$5,200	$100	2%
Journey Into Unknown Worlds #36	7	$4,800	7	$4,800	$0	0%
Mystery in Space #53	8	$4,600	8	$4,600	$0	0%
Weird Fantasy #13 (#1)	8	$4,600	8	$4,600	$0	2%
Fawcett Movie #15 (Man From Planet X)	10	$4,100	10	$4,000	$100	3%

TOP 10 WESTERN COMICS

TITLE/ISSUE#	2024 RANK	2024 NM- PRICE	2023 RANK	2023 NM- PRICE	$ INCR.	% INCR.
Gene Autry Comics #1	1	$6,200	1	$6,000	$200	3%
*Lone Ranger Ice Cream 1939 2nd	2	VF $4,800	2	VF $4,700	$100	2%
Roy Rogers Four Color #38	3	$4,500	3	$4,500	$0	0%
Western Picture Stories #1	3	$4,500	4	$4,200	$300	7%
*Lone Ranger Ice Cream 1939	4	VF $4,350	4	VF $4,200	$150	4%
John Wayne Adventure Comics #1	6	$4,100	6	$4,100	$0	0%
Red Ryder Comics #1	6	$4,100	6	$4,100	$0	0%
*Tom Mix Ralston #1	8	$3,500	8	$3,500	$0	0%
Hopalong Cassidy #1	9	$3,100	9	$3,000	$100	3%
*Red Ryder Victory Patrol '42	10	$1,500	10	$1,500	$0	0%

GRADING DEFINITIONS

When grading a comic book, common sense must be employed. The overall eye appeal and beauty of the comic book must be taken into account along with its technical flaws to arrive at the appropriate grade.

10.0 GEM MINT (GM): This is an exceptional example of a given book - the best ever seen. The slightest bindery defects and/or printing flaws may be seen only upon very close inspection. The overall look is "as if it has never been handled or released for purchase." Only the slightest bindery or printing defects are allowed, and these would be imperceptible on first viewing. No bindery tears. Cover is flat with no surface wear. Inks are bright with high reflectivity. Well centered and firmly secured to interior pages. Corners are cut square and sharp. No creases. No dates or stamped markings allowed. No soiling, staining or other discoloration. Spine is tight and flat. No spine roll or split allowed. Staples must be original, centered and clean with no rust. No staple tears or stress lines. Paper is white, supple and fresh. No hint of acidity in the odor of the newsprint. No interior autographs or owner signatures. Centerfold is firmly secure. No interior tears.

9.9 MINT (MT): Near perfect in every way. Only subtle bindery or printing defects are allowed. No bindery tears. Cover is flat with no surface wear. Inks are bright with high reflectivity. Generally well centered and firmly secured to interior pages. Corners are cut square and sharp. No creases. Small, inconspicuous, lightly penciled, stamped or inked arrival dates are acceptable as long as they are in an unobtrusive location. No soiling, staining or other discoloration. Spine is tight and flat. No spine roll or split allowed. Staples must be original, generally centered and clean with no rust. No staple tears or stress lines. Paper is white, supple and fresh. No hint of acidity in the odor of the newsprint. Centerfold is firmly secure. No interior tears.

9.8 NEAR MINT/MINT (NM/MT): Nearly perfect in every way with only minor imperfections that keep it from the next higher grade. Only subtle bindery or printing defects are allowed. No bindery tears. Cover is flat with no surface wear. Inks are bright with high reflectivity. Generally well centered and firmly secured to interior pages. Corners are cut square and sharp. No creases. Small, inconspicuous, lightly penciled, stamped or inked arrival dates are acceptable as long as they are in an unobtrusive location. No soiling, staining or other discoloration. Spine is tight and flat. No spine roll or split allowed. Staples must be original, generally centered and clean with no rust. No staple tears or stress lines. Paper is off-white to white, supple and fresh. No hint of acidity in the odor of the newsprint. Centerfold is firmly secure. Only the slightest interior tears are allowed.

9.6 NEAR MINT+ (NM+): Nearly perfect with a minor additional virtue or virtues that raise it from Near Mint. The overall look is "as if it was just purchased and read once or twice." Only subtle bindery or printing defects are allowed. No bindery tears are allowed, although on Golden Age books bindery tears of up to 1/8" have been noted. Cover is flat with no surface wear. Inks are bright with high reflectivity. Well centered and firmly secured to interior pages. One corner may be almost imperceptibly blunted, but still almost sharp and cut square. Almost imperceptible indentations are permissible, but no creases, bends, or color break. Small, inconspicuous, lightly penciled, stamped or inked arrival dates are acceptable as long as they are in an unobtrusive location. No soiling, staining or other discoloration. Spine is tight and flat. No spine roll or split allowed. Staples must be original, generally centered, with only the slightest discoloration. No staple tears, stress lines, or rust migration. Paper is off-white, supple and fresh. No hint of acidity in the odor of the newsprint. Centerfold is firmly secure. Only the slightest interior tears are allowed.

9.4 NEAR MINT (NM): Nearly perfect with only minor imperfections that keep it from the next higher grade. Minor feathering that does not distract from the overall beauty of an otherwise higher grade copy is acceptable for this grade. The overall look is "as if it was just purchased and read once or twice." Subtle bindery defects are allowed. Bindery tears must be less than 1/16" on Silver Age and later books, although on Golden Age books bindery tears of up to 1/4" have been noted. Cover is flat with no surface wear. Inks are bright with high reflectivity. Generally well centered and secured to interior pages. Corners are cut square and sharp with ever-so-slight blunting permitted. A 1/16" bend is permitted with no color break. No creases. Small, inconspicuous, lightly penciled, stamped or inked arrival dates are acceptable as long as they are in an unobtrusive location. No soiling, staining or other discoloration apart from slight foxing. Spine is tight and flat. No spine roll or split allowed. Staples are generally centered; may have slight discoloration. No staple tears are allowed; almost no stress lines. No rust migration. In rare cases, a comic was not stapled at the bindery and therefore has a missing staple; this is not considered a defect. Any staple can be replaced on books up to Fine, but only vintage staples can be used on books from Very Fine to Near Mint. Mint books must have original staples. Paper is cream to off-white, supple and fresh. No hint of acidity in the odor of the newsprint. Centerfold is secure. Slight interior tears are allowed.

9.2 NEAR MINT– (NM–): Nearly perfect with only

a minor additional defect or defects that keep it from Near Mint. A limited number of minor bindery defects are allowed. A light, barely noticeable water stain or minor foxing that does not distract from the beauty of the book is acceptable for this grade. Cover is flat with no surface wear. Inks are bright with only the slightest dimming of reflectivity. Generally well centered and secured to interior pages. Corners are cut square and sharp with ever-so-slight blunting permitted. A 1/16"-1/8" bend is permitted with no color break. No creases. Small, inconspicuous, lightly penciled, stamped or inked arrival dates are acceptable as long as they are in an unobtrusive location. No soiling, staining or other discoloration apart from slight foxing. Spine is tight and flat. No spine roll or split allowed. Staples may show some discoloration. No staple tears are allowed; almost no stress lines. No rust migration. In rare cases, a comic was not stapled at the bindery and therefore has a missing staple; this is not considered a defect. Any staple can be replaced on books up to Fine, but only vintage staples can be used on books from Very Fine to Near Mint. Mint books must have original staples. Paper is cream to off-white, supple and fresh. No hint of acidity in the odor of the newsprint. Centerfold is secure. Slight interior tears are allowed.

9.0 VERY FINE/NEAR MINT (VF/NM): Nearly perfect with outstanding eye appeal. A limited number of bindery defects are allowed. Almost flat cover with almost imperceptible wear. Inks are bright with slightly diminished reflectivity. An 1/8" bend is allowed if color is not broken. Corners are cut square and sharp with ever-so-slight blunting permitted but no creases. Several lightly penciled, stamped or inked arrival dates are acceptable. No obvious soiling, staining or other discoloration, except for very minor foxing. Spine is tight and flat. No spine roll or split allowed. Staples may show some discoloration. Only the slightest staple tears are allowed. A very minor accumulation of stress lines may be present if they are nearly imperceptible. No rust migration. In rare cases, a comic was not stapled at the bindery and therefore has a missing staple; this is not considered a defect. Any staple can be replaced on books up to Fine, but only vintage staples can be used on books from Very Fine to Near Mint. Mint books must have original staples. Paper is cream to off-white and supple. No hint of acidity in the odor of the newsprint. Centerfold is secure. Very minor interior tears may be present.

8.5 VERY FINE+ (VF+): Fits the criteria for Very Fine but with an additional virtue or small accumulation of virtues that improves the book's appearance by a perceptible amount.

8.0 VERY FINE (VF): An excellent copy with outstanding eye appeal. Sharp, bright and clean with supple pages. A comic book in this grade has the appearance of having been carefully handled. A limited accumulation of minor bindery defects is allowed. Cover is relatively flat with minimal surface wear beginning to show, possibly including some minute

wear at corners. Inks are generally bright with moderate to high reflectivity. A 1/4" crease is acceptable if color is not broken. Stamped or inked arrival dates may be present. No obvious soiling, staining or other discoloration, except for minor foxing. Spine is almost flat with no roll. Possible minor color break allowed. Staples may show some discoloration. Very slight staple tears and a few almost very minor to minor stress lines may be present. No rust migration. In rare cases, a comic was not stapled at the bindery and therefore has a missing staple; this is not considered a defect. Any staple can be replaced on books up to Fine, but only vintage staples can be used on books from Very Fine to Near Mint. Mint books must have original staples. Paper is tan to cream and supple. No hint of acidity in the odor of the newsprint. Centerfold is mostly secure. Minor interior tears at the margin may be present.

7.5 VERY FINE- (VF-): Fits the criteria for Very Fine but with an additional defect or small accumulation of defects that detracts from the book's appearance by a perceptible amount.

7.0 FINE/VERY FINE (FN/VF): An above-average copy that shows minor wear but is still relatively flat and clean with outstanding eye appeal. A small accumulation of minor bindery defects is allowed. Minor cover wear beginning to show with interior yellowing or tanning allowed, possibly including minor creases. Corners may be blunted or abraded. Inks are generally bright with a moderate reduction in reflectivity. Stamped or inked arrival dates may be present. No obvious soiling, staining or other discoloration, except for minor foxing. The slightest spine roll may be present, as well as a possible moderate color break. Staples may show some discoloration. Slight staple tears and a slight accumulation of light stress lines may be present. Slight rust migration. In rare cases, a comic was not stapled at the bindery and therefore has a missing staple; this is not considered a defect. Any staple can be replaced on books up to Fine, but only vintage staples can be used on books from Very Fine to Near Mint. Mint books must have original staples. Paper is tan to cream, but not brown. No hint of acidity in the odor of the newsprint. Centerfold is mostly secure. Minor interior tears at the margin may be present.

6.5 FINE+ (FN+): Fits the criteria for Fine but with an additional virtue or small accumulation of virtues that improves the book's appearance by a perceptible amount.

6.0 FINE (FN): An above-average copy that shows minor wear but is still relatively flat and clean with no significant creasing or other serious defects. Eye appeal is somewhat reduced because of slight surface wear and the accumulation of small defects, especially on the spine and edges. A FINE condition comic book appears to have been read a few times and has been handled with moderate care. Some accumulation of minor bindery defects is allowed. Minor cover wear apparent, with minor to moderate creases. Inks show a major reduction in reflectivity. Blunted or abraded corners are more common, as is minor staining, soiling, discoloration, and/or foxing. Stamped or inked arrival dates may be present. A minor spine roll is allowed. There can also be a 1/4" spine split or severe color break. Staples show minor discoloration. Minor staple tears and an accumulation of stress lines may be present, as well as minor rust migration. In rare cases, a comic was not stapled at the bindery and therefore has a missing staple; this is not considered a defect. Any staple can be replaced on books up to Fine, but only vintage staples can be used on books from Very Fine to Near Mint. Mint books must have original staples. Paper is brown to tan and fairly supple with no signs of brittleness. No hint of acidity in the odor of the newsprint. Minor interior tears at the margin may be present. Centerfold may be loose but not detached.

5.5 FINE– (FN–): Fits the criteria for Fine but with an additional defect or small accumulation of defects that detracts from the book's appearance by a perceptible amount.

5.0 VERY GOOD/FINE (VG/FN): An above-average but well-used comic book. A comic in this grade shows some moderate wear; eye appeal is somewhat reduced because of the accumulation of defects. Still a desirable copy that has been handled with some care. An accumulation of bindery defects is allowed. Minor to moderate cover wear apparent, with minor to moderate creases and/or dimples. Inks have major to extreme reduction in reflectivity. Blunted or abraded corners are increasingly common, as is minor to moderate staining, discoloration, and/or foxing. Stamped or inked arrival dates may be present. A minor to moderate spine roll is allowed. A spine split of up to 1/2" may be present. Staples show minor discoloration. A slight accumulation of minor staple tears and an accumulation of minor stress lines may also be present, as well as minor rust migration. In rare cases, a comic was not stapled at the bindery and therefore has a missing staple; this is not considered a defect. Any staple can be replaced on books up to Fine, but only vintage staples can be used on books from Very Fine to Near Mint. Mint books must have original staples. Paper is brown to tan with no signs of brittleness. May have the faintest trace of an acidic odor. Centerfold may be loose but not detached. Minor tears may also be present.

4.5 VERY GOOD+ (VG+): Fits the criteria for Very Good but with an additional virtue or small accumulation of virtues that improves the book's appearance by a perceptible amount.

4.0 VERY GOOD (VG): The average used comic book. A comic in this grade shows some significant moderate wear, but still has not accumulated enough total defects to reduce eye appeal to the point that it is not a desirable copy. Cover shows moderate to significant wear, and may be loose but not completely detached. Moderate to extreme reduction in reflectivity. Can have an accumulation of creases or dimples. Cor-

ners may be blunted or abraded. Store stamps, name stamps, arrival dates, initials, etc. have no effect on this grade. Some discoloration, fading, foxing, and even minor soiling is allowed. As much as a 1/4" triangle can be missing out of the corner or edge; a missing 1/8" square is also acceptable. Only minor unobtrusive tape and other amateur repair allowed on otherwise high grade copies. Moderate spine roll may be present and/or a 1" spine split. Staples discolored. Minor to moderate staple tears and stress lines may be present, as well as some rust migration. Paper is brown but not brittle. A minor acidic odor can be detectable. Minor to moderate tears may be present. Centerfold may be loose or detached at one staple.

3.5 VERY GOOD– (VG–): Fits the criteria for Very Good but with an additional defect or small accumulation of defects that detracts from the book's appearance by a perceptible amount.

3.0 GOOD/VERY GOOD (GD/VG): A used comic book showing some substantial wear. Cover shows significant wear, and may be loose or even detached at one staple. Cover reflectivity is very low. Can have a book-length crease and/or dimples. Corners may be blunted or even rounded. Discoloration, fading, foxing, and even minor to moderate soiling is allowed. A triangle from 1/4" to 1/2" can be missing out of the corner or edge; a missing 1/8" to 1/4" square is also acceptable. Tape and other amateur repair may be present. Moderate spine roll likely. May have a spine split of anywhere from 1" to 1-1/2". Staples may be rusted or replaced. Minor to moderate staple tears and moderate stress lines may be present, as well as some rust migration. Paper is brown but not brittle. Centerfold may be loose or detached at one staple. Minor to moderate interior tears may be present.

2.5 GOOD+ (GD+): Fits the criteria for Good but with an additional virtue or small accumulation of virtues that improves the book's appearance by a perceptible amount.

2.0 GOOD (GD): Shows substantial wear; often considered a "reading copy." Cover shows significant wear and may even be detached. Cover reflectivity is low and in some cases completely absent. Book-length creases and dimples may be present. Rounded corners are more common. Moderate soiling, staining, discoloration and foxing may be present. The largest piece allowed missing from the front or back cover is usually a 1/2" triangle or a 1/4" square, although some Silver Age books such as 1960s Marvels have had the price corner box clipped from the top left front cover and may be considered Good if they would otherwise have graded higher. Tape and other forms of amateur repair are common in Silver Age and older books. Spine roll is likely. May have up to a 2" spine split. Staples may be degraded, replaced or missing. Moderate staple tears and stress lines may be present, as well as rust migration. Paper is brown but not brittle. Centerfold may be loose or detached. Moderate interior tears may be present.

1.8 GOOD– (GD–): Fits the criteria for Good but with an

additional defect or small accumulation of defects that detracts from the book's appearance by a perceptible amount.

1.5 FAIR/GOOD (FR/GD): A comic showing substantial to heavy wear. A copy in this grade still has all pages and covers, although there may be pieces missing up to and including missing coupons and/or Marvel Value Stamps that do not impact the story. Books in this grade are commonly creased, scuffed, abraded, soiled, and possibly unattractive, but still generally readable. Cover shows considerable wear and may be detached. Nearly no reflectivity to no reflectivity remaining. Store stamp, name stamp, arrival date and initials are permitted. Book-length creases, tears and folds may be present. Rounded corners are increasingly common. Soiling, staining, discoloration and foxing is generally present. Up to 1/10 of the back cover may be missing. Tape and other forms of amateur repair are increasingly common in Silver Age and older books. Spine roll is common. May have a spine split between 2" and 2/3 the length of the book. Staples may be degraded, replaced or missing. Staple tears and stress lines are common, as well as rust migration. Paper is brown and may show brittleness around the edges. Acidic odor may be present. Centerfold may be loose or detached. Interior tears are common.

1.0 FAIR (FR): A copy in this grade shows heavy wear. Some collectors consider this the lowest collectible grade because comic books in lesser condition are usually incomplete and/or brittle. Comics in this grade are usually soiled, faded, ragged and possibly unattractive. This is the last grade in which a comic remains generally readable. Cover may be detached, and inks have lost all reflectivity. Creases, tears and/or folds are prevalent. Corners are commonly rounded or absent. Soiling and staining is present. Books in this condition generally have all pages and most of the covers, although there may be up to 1/4 of the front cover missing or no back cover, but not both. Tape and other forms of amateur repair are more common. Spine roll is more common; spine split can extend up to 2/3 the length of the book. Staples may be

missing or show rust and discoloration. An accumulation of staple tears and stress lines may be present, as well as rust migration. Paper is brown and may show brittleness around the edges but not in the central portion of the pages. Acidic odor may be present. Accumulation of interior tears. Chunks may be missing. The centerfold may be missing if readability is generally preserved (although there may be difficulty). Coupons may be cut.

0.5 POOR (PR): Most comic books in this grade have been sufficiently degraded to the point where there is little or no collector value; they are easily identified by a complete absence of eye appeal. Comics in this grade are brittle almost to the point of turning to dust with a touch, and are usually incomplete. Extreme cover fading may render the cover almost indiscernible. May have extremely severe stains, mildew or heavy cover abrasion to the point that some cover inks are indistinct/absent. Covers may be detached with large chunks missing. Can have extremely ragged edges and extensive creasing. Corners are rounded or virtually absent. Covers may have been defaced with paints, varnishes, glues, oil, indelible markers or dyes, and may have suffered heavy water damage. Can also have extensive amateur repairs such as laminated covers. Extreme spine roll present; can have extremely ragged spines or a complete, book-length split. Staples can be missing or show extreme rust and discoloration. Extensive staple tears and stress lines may be present, as well as extreme rust migration. Paper exhibits moderate to severe brittleness (where the comic book literally falls apart when examined). Extreme acidic odor may be present. Extensive interior tears. Multiple pages, including the centerfold, may be missing that affect readability. Coupons may be cut.

0.3 INCOMPLETE (INC): Books that are coverless, but are otherwise complete, or covers missing their interiors.

0.1 INCOMPLETE (INC): Coverless copies that have incomplete interiors, wraps or single pages will receive a grade of .1 as will just front covers or just back covers.

PUBLISHERS' CODES

The following abbreviations are used with cover reproductions throughout the book for copyright purposes:

ABC-America's Best Comics	DC-DC Comics, Inc.	FH-Fiction House Magazines	MS-Mirage Studios	TC-Tower Comics
AC-AC Comics	DELL-Dell Publishing Co.	FOX-Fox Feature Syndicate	NOVP-Novelty Press	TM-Trojan Magazines
ACE-Ace Periodicals	DH-Dark Horse	GIL-Gilberton	NYNS-New York News Syndicate	TMP-Todd McFarlane Prods.
ACG-American Comics Group	DIS-Disney Enterprises, Inc.	GK-Gold Key	PG-Premier Group	TOBY-Toby Press
AJAX-Ajax-Farrell	DMP-David McKay Publishing	GP-Great Publications	PINE-Pines	TOPS-Tops Comics
ACP-Archie Comic Publications	DYN-Dynamite Entertainment	HARV-Harvey Publications	PMI-Parents' Magazine Institute	UFS-United Features Syndicate
BP-Better Publications	DS-D. S. Publishing Co.	H-B-Hanna-Barbera	PRIZE-Prize Publications	VAL-Valiant
C & L-Cupples & Leon	EAS-Eastern Color Printing Co.	HILL-Hillman Periodicals	QUA-Quality Comics Group	VITL-Vital Publications
CC-Charlton Comics	EC-E. C. Comics	HOKE-Holyoke Publishing Co.	REAL-Realistic Comics	WB-Warner Brothers.
CEN-Centaur Publications	ECL-Eclipse Comics	IM-Image Comics	RH-Rural Home	WEST-Western Publishing Co.
CCG-Columbia Comics Group	ENWIL-Enwil Associates	KING-King Features Syndicate	S & S-Street and Smith Publishers	WHIT-Whitman Publishing Co.
CG-Catechetical Guild	EP-Elliott Publications	LEV-Lev Gleason Publications	SKY-Skywald Publications	WHW-William H. Wise
CHES-Harry 'A' Chesler	ERB-Edgar Rice Burroughs	MAL-Malibu Comics	STAR-Star Publications	WMG-William M. Gaines (E. C.)
CM-Comics Magazine	FAW-Fawcett Publications	MAR-Marvel Characters, Inc.	STD-Standard Comics	WP-Warren Publishing Co.
CN-Cartoon Network	FC-First Comics	ME-Magazine Enterprises	STJ-St. John Publishing Co.	YM-Youthful Magazines
CPI-Conan Properties Inc.	FF-Famous Funnies	MLJ-MLJ Magazines	SUPR-Superior Comics	Z-D-Ziff-Davis Publishing Co.

OVERSTREET ADVISORS

Even before the first edition of *The Overstreet Comic Book Price Guide* was printed, author Robert M. Overstreet solicited pricing data, historical notations, and general information from a variety of sources. What was initially an informal group offering input quickly became an organized field of comic book collectors, dealers and historians whose opinions are actively solicited in advance of each edition of this book. Some of these Overstreet Advisors are specialists who deal in particular niches within the comic book world, while others are generalists who are interested in commenting on the broader marketplace. Each advisor provides information from their respective areas of interest and expertise, spanning the history of American comics.

While some choose to offer pricing and historical information in the form of annotated sales catalogs, auction catalogs, or documented private sales, assistance from others comes in the form of the market reports such as those beginning on page 93 in this book. In addition to those who have served as Overstreet Advisors almost since *The Guide*'s inception, each year new contributors are sought.

With that in mind, we are pleased to present our newest Overstreet Advisors:

THE CLASS OF 2024

PETER BARBELLA
Metropolis Collectibles
New York, NY

TOM RAUPP
POP Culture Playground
Ormond Beach, FL

185

METROPOLIS
COLLECTIBLES
www.metropoliscomics.com

CA$H FOR COMICS

Action #1.....................$4 MILLION	Detective #38................$250,000	New Fun #6........................$55,000
Action #7......................$500,000	Detective #168................$80,000	Pep Comics #22...............$325,000
Action #242....................$40,000	Detective #225................$80,000	Phantom Lady #17............$85,000
Adventure #40...............$150,000	Donald Duck #9................$28,000	Sensation Comics #1........$325,000
Adventure #48.................$80,000	Fantastic Comics #3........$150,000	Showcase #4....................$825,000
Adventure #210...............$50,000	Fantastic Four #1............$750,000	Showcase #22.................$150,000
All-American #16.............$600,000	Fantastic Four #5.............$65,000	Star Wars #1 (35c)...........$21,000
All-American #19..............$70,000	Flash Comics #1........$1.3 MILLION	Superboy #1.....................$30,000
All-Star #3....................$220,000	Green Lantern #1 (GA).......$60,000	Superman #1.............$3 MILLION
Amazing Fantasy #15.......$800,000	Green Lantern #1 (SA).......$28,000	Superman #14...................$90,000
Amazing Spider-Man #1....$175,000	House of Secrets #92...........$7,000	Suspense Comics #3.........$150,000
Amazing Spider-Man #129....$4,500	Human Torch #2 (#1).......$145,000	Tales of Suspense #39.......$115,000
Avengers #1....................$90,000	Incredible Hulk #1...........$650,000	Tales to Astonish #27.........$48,000
Avengers #4....................$25,000	Incredible Hulk #181.........$10,000	Target Comics V1 #7.........$15,000
Batman #1................$1.3 MILLION	Journey into Myst. #83.......$240,000	Teenage Mutant Ninja Turtles #1...$20,000
Batman Adventures #12..........$700	Justice League #1..............$90,000	Walt Disney C&S #1...........$55,000
Black Cat Mystery #50........$60,000	Marvel Comics #1......$1.8 MILLION	Whiz #2 (#1)...................$800,000
Brave & the Bold #28.........$250,000	Marvel Spotlight #5.............$6,000	Wonder Woman #1............$150,000
Captain America #1.........$850,000	More Fun #52................$250,000	X-Men #1.......................$175,000
Detective #1..................$350,000	More Fun #54.................$60,000	X-Men Giant-Size #1...........$5,000
Detective #27..........$3.5 MILLION	More Fun #55.................$55,000	Young Allies #1..................$30,000

Action Comics............#1-400	Classic Comics............#1-169	Jungle Comics............#1-163	Strange Tales............#1-145
Adventure Comics......#32-400	Comic Cavalcade..........#1-63	Justice League............#1-110	Sub-Mariner................#1-42
Advs. Into Weird Worlds..#1-30	Daredevil Comics.........#1-60	Mad.........................#1-50	Superboy...................#1-110
All-American Comics....#1-102	Daring Mystery.............#1-8	Marvel Mystery............#1-92	Superman.................#1-250
All-Flash Quarterly........#1-32	Detective Comics.........#1-450	Military Comics.............#1-43	Suspense Comics.........#1-11
All-Select.................#1-11	Donald Duck 4-Colors.....#4-up	More Fun Comics.........#7-127	Tales From The Crypt....#20-46
All-Star Comics............#1-57	Exciting Comics...........#1-69	Mystery in Space..........#1-75	Tales of Suspense........#1-80
All-Winners................#1-21	Fantastic Four...........#1-200	Mystic Comics.............#1-up	Tales to Astonish..........#1-80
Amazing Man.............#5-26	Fight Comics..............#1-86	National Comics............#1-75	Terrific Comics............#1-6
Amaz. Mystery Funnies.......all	Flash....................#105-150	New Adventure.........#12-31	Thing.......................#1-17
Amazing Spider-Man....#1-328	Flash Comics..............#1-104	New Comics...............#1-11	USA Comics...............#1-17
Avengers.................#1-200	Funny Pages..............#6-42	New Fun Comics...........#1-6	Weird Comics..............#1-20
Batman...................#1-300	Green Lantern (GA).......#1-38	Our Army at War........#1-200	Weird Mysteries...........#1-12
Blackhawk..............#9-130	Green Lantern (SA).......#1-90	Our Fighting Forces......#1-180	Weird Tales From The Future.#1-8
Boy Commandos..........#1-32	Hit Comics................#1-65	Planet Comics.............#1-73	Whiz Comics...............#1-155
Brave & the Bold.........#1-100	Human Torch........#2 (#1)-38	Rangers Comics...........#1-69	Wings Comics.............#1-124
Captain America..........#1-78	Incredible Hulk............#1-6	Reform School Girl............NN	Wonder Woman...........#1-20
Captain Marvel Advs.....#1-150	Jimmy Olsen............#1-150	Sensation Comics........#1-116	Wonderworld.............#3-33
Catman....................#1-32	Journey into Mystery....#1-125	Showcase................#1-100	World's Finest.............#1-200
Challengers................#1-25	Jumbo Comics............#1-167	Star-Spangled Comics...#1-130	X-Men.....................#1-30

JUST THE FACTS

FACT 1: ABSOLUTELY NO OTHER COMIC DEALER BUYS MORE 1930'S - 1980'S COMICS THAN METROPOLIS.

Although the pages of the price guide are filled with other dealers offering to pay "top dollar," the simple truth is that Metropolis spends more money on more quality comic book collections year in and year out than any other dealers in the country. We have the funds and the expertise to back up our word. The fact is that we have spent nearly $8 million dollars on vintage comic books, comic art, video games, VHS, pulps, toys, memorabilia and movie posters over the last year. If you have comic books to sell, please call us at toll-free 1-800-229-6387. A generous finder's fee will be given if you know of any collections that we purchase. All calls will be strictly confidential.

FACT 2: ABSOLUTELY NO OTHER COMIC DEALER SELLS MORE 1930'S - 1980'S COMICS THAN METROPOLIS.

We simply have the best stock of Golden and Silver Age comic books in the world. Tens of thousands of collectors familiar with our strict grading standards and excellent service can attest to this. Chances are, if you want it, we have it!

Discover Your Local Comic Shop
Where Stories Come to Life!

Are you a fan of thrilling adventures, epic battles, and unforgettable characters?

Your local comic shop is the ultimate destination for all things comics and collectibles!

Find Your Local Comic Shop Today

Visit comicshoplocator.com to find the comic shop neares to you and dive into a world of endless adventures.

Nationwide Vintage Comic Dealers

Graham Crackers Comics
Jamie Graham - President/CEO/Co-owner
GrahamCrackers.com - Co-owner
GrahamCrackers@AOL.com
JamieGraham@AOL.com
1271 Rickert Dr. #135, Naperville, IL 60540

PHILADELPHIA COMIC-CON!
Derek Woywood - Promoter
Philadelphiacomic-con.com
dwoywood@yahoo.com
PO Box 313, Clementon, NJ 08021
PH: (856) 217-5737

We buy and sell comics **Nationwide.**

Terry's Old School Comics
Terry O'Neill - owner
TerrysComics.com
Terry@TerrysComics.com
P.O. Box 2065, Orange, CA. 92859
P.O. Box 1186, Kelso, WA 98626
P: 714-288-8993 / C: 360-846-3714

CalComicCon
CalComicCon.com
Info@CalComicCon.com

THE SELLER'S GUIDE

Yes, here are the pages you're looking for. These percentages will help you determine the sale value of your collection. If you do not find your title, call with any questions. We have purchased many of the major well known collections. We are serious about buying your comics and paying you the most for them.

If you have comics or related items for sale call or send your list for a quote. No collection is too large or small. Immediate funds available of 500K and beyond.

These are some of the high prices we will pay. Percentages stated will be paid for any grade unless otherwise noted. All percentages based on this Overstreet *Guide*.

—*JAMES PAYETTE*

We are paying 100% of Guide for the following:

All-Select	1-up	Marvel Mystery	11-up
All Winners	6-up	Pep	22-45
America's Best	1-up	Prize	2-50
Black Terror	1-25	Reform School Girl	1
Captain Aero	3-25	Speed	10-30
Captain America	11-up	Startling	2-up
Cat-Man	1-up	Sub-Mariner	3-32
Dynamic	2-15	Thrilling	2-52
Exciting	3-50	U.S.A.	6-up
Human Torch	6-35	Wonder (Nedor)	1-up

We are paying 75% of Guide for the following:

Action 1-15	Daredevil (2nd) 1	Journey into Mystery 83
Adventure 247	Detective 2-26	Keen Detective Funnies all
All New 2-13	Detective Eye all	Marvel Mystery 1-10
All Winners 1-5	Detective Picture Stories all	Mystery Men all
Amazing Man all	Fantastic Four 1-2	Showcase 4
Amazing Mystery Funnies all	Four Favorites 3-27	Superman 1
Amazing Spider-Man 1-2	Funny Pages all	Superman's Pal 1
Andy Devine	Funny Picture Stories all	Tim McCoy all
Arrow all	Hangman all	Wonder (Fox)
Captain America 1-10	Jumbo 1-10	Young Allies all

BUYING & SELLING GOLDEN & SILVER AGE COMICS SINCE 1975

I BUY OLD COMICS
1930 to 1975

Any Title
Any Condition
Any Size Collection

Paducah, KY

Can Easily Travel to:
Atlanta
Chicago
Cincinnati
Dallas
Little Rock
Louisvillle
Memphis
St. Louis

I want your comics:
Superhero
Western
Horror
Humor
Romance

Leroy Harper
PO BOX 212
WEST PADUCAH, KY 42086

PHONE 270-748-9364
EMAIL LHCOMICS@hotmail.com

Over 20 years of experience

213

214

Why Choose CBCS?

- CBCS Cases are Tamper-Evident, with Built-In Security Features

- Slab Only, Witnessed Signature Only services allow for preservation of your comic books without grading

- CBCS Cases banish Newton Rings to the Phantom Zone

- Raw Grade Program offering grading insights without encapsulation

- All-inclusive color label for unrestored, restored & conserved books

- Verified Signature Program – like no other in the industry

- We have a grade for every magazine – we don't put 'No Grade' on our labels

- No processing fee to submit an order

- No minimum order amount needed to grade

COMIC HEAVEN

JOHN VERZYL II AND SISTER ROSE
"HARD AT WORK"

In 1979, John Verzyl Sr., with his wife Nanette, opened "COMIC HEAVEN", a retail store devoted entirely to the buying and selling of rare comic books. John had started collecting comics in 1965, and within ten years, he had amassed thousands of Golden and Silver Age collectibles. Over the years, he had come to be recognized as an authority in the field of comic books, and served as a special advisor to *The Overstreet Comic Book Price Guide* for 30 years. Thousands of his "near mint" pedigree comics were photographed for Ernst Gerber's *Photo-Journal Guide to Comic Books*. The first annual **Comic Heaven Auction** was held in 1987 and ran continuously for 24 years.

Sadly, John Verzyl passed away in 2018. His untimely death was a shock and a great loss to everyone who knew him. But his children, John II and Rose, having had a love of the hobby instilled in them since childhood by their dad, will continue to operate the business. We will continue to set up our huge retail displays at the annual San Diego Comic-Con, the August Chicago Comic Con, and the New York City Comic Con in October, and will continue to wow our wonderful customers with super-rare collectibles. We will also be updating and using our website, **ComicHeaven.net**, in new and exciting ways, with periodic updates of newly acquired stock items and news about our upcoming convention appearances.

www.ComicHeaven.net

Comic Heaven LLC
John II, Rose & Nanette Verzyl
P.O. Box 900, Big Sandy, TX 75755
www.ComicHeaven.net
(903) 539-8875

COMIC
BUY

Sell us your Golden, Silver and Bronze Age comics.

No collection is too large or too small.

We will travel anywhere in the USA to buy collections we want.
In previous years, we've traveled over **30,000** miles to buy comic books.

We are especially looking to buy:

- **Silver Age Marvels and DCs**
- **Golden Age Timelys and DCs**
- **Fox/ MLJ/ Nedor/ EC**
- **"Mile High" copies (Edgar Church Collection)**
- **Baseball cards, Movie posters and Original art**

223

THESE DIDN'T HAPPEN
WITHOUT YOUR HELP.

The Overstreet Comic Book Price Guide doesn't happen by magic.
A network of advisors – made up of experienced dealers, collectors and
comics historians – gives us input for every edition we publish.
If you spot an error or omission in this edition or any of our publications,
let us know!

Write to us at
Gemstone Publishing Inc.,
10150 York Rd., Suite 300,
Hunt Valley, MD 21030.
Or e-mail **feedback@gemstonepub.com**.

We want your help!

BIG LITTLE BOOKS

INTRODUCTION

In 1932, at the depths of the Great Depression, comic books were not selling despite their successes in the previous two decades. Desperate publishers had already reduced prices to 25¢, but this was still too much for many people to spend on entertainment.

Comic books quickly evolved into two newer formats, the comics magazine and the Big Little Book. Both types retailed for 10¢.

Big Little Books began by reprinting the art (and adapting the stories) from newspaper comics. As their success grew and publishers began commissioning original material, movie adaptations and other entertainment-derived stories became commonplace.

GRADING

Before a Big Little Book's value can be assessed, its condition or state of preservation must be determined. A book in **Near Mint** condition will bring many times the price of the same book in **Poor** condition. Many variables influence the grading of a Big Little Book and all must be considered in the final evaluation. Due to the way they are constructed, damage occurs with very little use - usually to the spine, book edges and binding. More important defects that affect grading are: Split spines, pages missing, page browning or brittleness, writing, crayoning, loose pages, color fading, chunks missing, and rolling or out of square. The following grading guide is given to aid the novice:

9.4 Near Mint: The overall look is as if it was just purchased and maybe opened once; only subtle defects are allowed; paper is cream to off-white, supple and fresh; cover is flat with no surface wear or creases; inks and colors are bright; small penciled or inked arrival dates are acceptable; very slight blunting of corners at top and bottom of spine are common; outside corners are cut square and sharp. Books in this grade could bring prices of guide and a half or more.

9.0 Very Fine/Near Mint: Limited number of defects; full cover gloss with only very slight wear on book corners and edges; very minor foxing; very minor tears allowed, binding still square and tight with no pages missing; paper quality still fresh from cream to off-white. Dates, stamps or initials allowed on cover or inside.

8.0 Very Fine: Most of the cover gloss retained with minor wear appearing at corners and around edges; spine tight with no pages missing; cream/tan paper allowed if still supple; up to 1/4" bend allowed on covers with no color break; cover relatively flat; minor tears allowed.

6.0 Fine: Slight wear beginning to show; cover gloss reduced but still clean, pages tan/brown but still supple (not brittle); up to 1/4" split or color break allowed; minor discoloration and/or foxing allowed.

4.0 Very Good: Obviously a read copy with original printing luster almost gone; some fading and discoloration, but not soiled; some signs of wear such as corner splits and spine rolling; paper can be brown but not brittle; a few pages can be loose but not missing; no chunks missing; blunted corners acceptable.

2.0 Good: An average used copy complete with only minor pieces missing from the spine, which may be partially split; slightly soiled or marked with spine rolling; color flaking and wear around edges, but perfectly sound and legible; could have minor tape repairs but otherwise complete.

1.0 Fair: Very heavily read and soiled with small chunks missing from cover; most or all of spine could be missing; multiple splits in spine and loose pages, but still sound and legible, bringing 50 to 70 percent of good price.

0.5 Poor: Damaged, heavily weathered, soiled or otherwise unsuited for collecting purposes.

IMPORTANT

Most BLBs on the market today will fall in the **Good** to **Fine** grade category. When **Very Fine** to **Near Mint** BLBs are offered for sale, they usually bring premium prices.

A WORD ON PRICING

The prices are given for **Good**, **Fine**, **Very Fine** and **Near Mint-** condition. A book in **Fair** would be 50-70% of the **Good** price. **Very Good** would be halfway between the **Good** and the **Fine** price. The prices listed were averaged from convention sales, dealers' lists, adzines, auctions, and by special contact with dealers and collectors from coast to coast. The prices and the spreads were determined from sales of copies in available condition or the highest grade known. Since most available copies are in the **Good** to **Fine** range, neither dealers nor collectors should let the **Very Fine** or **Near Mint-** column influence the prices they are willing to charge or pay for books in less than perfect condition.

The prices listed reflect spread ranges from 6 to 16 times, depending on the price level. We feel this spread accurately reflects the current market, especially when you condider the scarcity of books in **Very Fine** to **Near Mint-** condition. When one or both end sheets are missing, the book's value would drop about a half grade.

Books with movie scenes are of double importance due to the high crossover demand by movie collectors.

Abbreviations: a-art; c-cover; nn-no number; p-pages; r-reprint.

Publisher Codes: BRP-Blue Ribbon Press; **ERB-**Edgar Rice Burroughs; **EVW-**Engel van Wiseman; **FAW-**Fawcett Publishing Co.; **Gold-**Goldsmith Publishing Co.; **Lynn-**Lynn Publishing Co.; **McKay-**David McKay Co.; **Whit-**Whitman Publishing Co.; **World-**World Syndicate Publishing Co.

Terminology: *All Pictures Comics-*no text, all drawings; *Fast-Action-*A special series of Dell books highly collected; *Flip Pictures-*upper right corner of interior pages contain drawings that are put into motion when rifled; *Movie Scenes-*book illustrated with scenes from the movie. *Soft Cover-*A thin single sheet of cardboard used in binding most of the giveaway versions.

"Big Little Book" and "Better Little Book" are registered trademarks of Whitman Publishing Co. "Little Big Book" is a registered trademark of the Saalfield Publishing Co.

"Pop-Up" is a registered trademark of Blue Ribbon Press. "Little Big Book" is a registered trademark of the Saalfield Co.

Top 20 Big Little Books and related size books*

Issue#	Rank	Title	Price
731	1	Mickey Mouse the Mail Pilot	
		(variant version of Mickey Mouse #717)	
		(A VG copy sold at auction for $7,170)	
nn	2	Mickey Mouse and Minnie Mouse	
		at Macy's	$5,300
nn	3	Mickey Mouse and Minnie March	
		to Macy's	$4,200
717	4	Mickey Mouse (skinny Mickey on-c)	
			$3,900
725	5	Big Little Mother Goose HC	$2,600
W-707	6	Dick Tracy The Detective	$2,550
717	7	Mickey Mouse (reg. Mickey on-c)	$2,300
nn	8	Mickey Mouse Silly Symphonies	$2,000
nn	9	Mickey Mouse the Mail Pilot	
		(Great Big Midget Book)	$1,900
nn	10	Mickey Mouse and the Magic Carpet	$1,850
nn	10	Mickey Mouse	
		(Great Big Midget Book)	$1,850
725	12	Big Little Mother Goose SC	$1,800
721	13	Big Little Paint Book (336 pg.)	$1,750
nn	14	Mickey Mouse Sails For Treasure Island	
		(Great Big Midget Book)	$1,650
721	15	Big Little Paint Book (320 pg.)	$1,450
4063	16	Popeye Thimble Theater Starring...	
		(2nd printing)	$1,300
1126	17	Laughing Dragon of Oz	$1,275
4063	18	Popeye Thimble Theater Starring...	
		(1st printing)	$1,100
nn	19	Buck Rogers	$1,000
nn	20	Buck Rogers in the City of	
		Floating Globes	$975
731	20	Mickey Mouse the Mail Pilot (SC)	$975

*Includes only the various sized BLBs; no premiums, giveaways or other divergent forms are included.

1177 - Ace Drummond © WHIT

1485 - Andy Panda's Vacation © Walter Lantz

1497 - Bambi's Children © DIS

	GD	FN	VF	VF/NM
1175-0- Abbie an' Slats, 1940, Saalfield, 400 pgs.	10	25	64	100
1182- Abbie an' Slats-and Becky, 1940, Saalfield, 400 pgs.	10	25	64	100
nn- ABC's To Draw and Color, The, 1930s, Whitman, 4" x 5 1/4" x 1 1/12" deep, cardboard box contains 320 double-sided sheets to color and a box of crayons	25	63	175	300
1177- Ace Drummond, 1935, Whitman, 432 pgs.	11	28	68	110
Admiral Byrd (See Paramount Newsreel ...)				
nn- Adventures of Charlie McCarthy and Edgar Bergen, The, 1938, Dell, 194 pgs., Fast-Action Story, soft-c	21	53	145	230
1422- Adventures of Huckleberry Finn, The, 1939, Whitman, 432 pgs., Henry E. Vallely-a	10	25	64	100
1648- Adventures of Jim Bowie (TV Series), 1958, Whitman, 280 pgs.	4	10	24	35
1056- Adventures of Krazy Kat and Ignatz Mouse in Koko Land, 1934, Saalfield, 160 pgs., oblong size, hard-c, Herriman-c/a	48	120	336	625
1306- Adventures of Krazy Kat and Ignatz Mouse in Koko Land, 1934, Saalfield, 164 pgs., oblong size, soft-c, Herriman-c/a	56	140	392	725
1082- Adventures of Pete the Tramp, The, 1935, Saalfield, hard-c, by C. D. Russell	10	25	60	95
1312- Adventures of Pete the Tramp, The, 1935, Saalfield, soft-c, by C. D. Russell	10	25	60	95
1053- Adventures of Tim Tyler, 1934, Saalfield, hard-c, oblong size, by Lyman Young	18	45	128	200
1303- Adventures of Tim Tyler, 1934, Saalfield, soft-c, oblong size, by Lyman Young	18	45	128	200
1058- Adventures of Tom Sawyer, The, 1934, Saalfield, 160 pgs., hard-c, Park Sumner-a	10	25	60	95
1308- Adventures of Tom Sawyer, The, 1934, Saalfield, 160 pgs., soft-c, Park Sumner-a	10	25	60	95
1448- Air Fighters of America, 1941, Whitman, 432 pgs., flip picture	11	28	68	110
Alexander Smart, ESQ. (See Top Line Comics)				
759- Alice in Wonderland, 1933, Whitman, 160 pgs., hard-c, photo-c, movie scenes	42	105	294	500
1481- Allen Pike of the Parachute Squad U.S.A., 1941, Whitman, 432 pgs.	12	30	72	115
763- Alley Oop and Dinny, 1935, Whitman, 384 pgs., V. T. Hamlin-a	16	40	112	175
1473- Alley Oop and Dinny in the Jungles of Moo, 1938, Whitman, 432 pgs., V. T. Hamlin-a	16	40	112	175
nn- Alley Oop and the Missing King of Moo, 1938, Whitman, 36 pgs., 2 1/2" x 3 1/2", Penny Book	10	25	60	95
nn- Alley Oop in the Kingdom of Foo, 1938, Whitman, 68 pgs., 3 1/4" x 3 1/2", Pan-Am premium	18	45	128	200
nn- Alley Oop Taming a Dinosaur, 1938, Whitman, 68 pgs., 3 1/2" x 3 3/4", Pan-Am premium	18	45	128	200
nn- "Alley Oop the Invasion of Moo," 1935, Whitman, 260 pgs., Cocomalt premium, soft-c; V. T. Hamlin-a	12	30	76	125
Andy Burnette (See Walt Disney's...)				
Andy Panda (Also see Walter Lantz ...)				
531- Andy Panda, 1943, Whitman, 3 3/4x8 3/4", Tall Comic Book, All Pictures Comics	17	43	119	185
1425- Andy Panda and Tiny Tom, 1944, Whitman, All Pictures Comics	12	30	76	125
1431- Andy Panda and the Mad Dog Mystery, 1947, Whitman, 288 pgs., by Walter Lantz	12	30	76	125
1441- Andy Panda in the City of Ice, 1948, Whitman, All Picture Comics, by Walter Lantz	12	30	76	125
1459- Andy Panda and the Pirate Ghosts, 1949, Whitman, 288 pgs., by Walter Lantz	12	30	76	125
1485- Andy Panda's Vacation, 1946, Whitman, All Pictures Comics, by Walter Lantz	12	30	76	125
15- Andy Panda (The Adventures of), 1942, Dell, Fast-Action Story	17	43	119	185
707-10- Andy Panda and Presto the Pup, 1949, Whitman	12	30	76	125
1130- Apple Mary and Dennie Foil the Swindlers, 1936, Whitman, 432 pgs. (Forerunner to Mary Worth)	11	28	68	110

	GD	FN	VF	VF/NM
1403- Apple Mary and Dennie's Lucky Apples, 1939, Whitman, 432 pgs.	11	28	68	110
2017- (#17)-Aquaman-Scourge of the Sea, 1968, Whitman, 260 pgs., 39 cents, hard-c, color illos	3	8	22	32
1192- Arizona Kid on the Bandit Trail, The, 1936, Whitman, 432 pgs.	10	25	64	100
1469- Bambi (Walt Disney's), 1942, Whitman, 432 pgs.	21	53	145	230
1497- Bambi's Children (Disney), 1943, Whitman, 432 pgs., Disney Studios-a	21	53	145	230
1138- Bandits at Bay, 1938, Saalfield, 400 pgs.	9	23	56	90
1459- Barney Baxter in the Air with the Eagle Squadron, 1938, Whitman, 432 pgs.	10	25	60	95
1083- Barney Google, 1935, Saalfield, hard-c	15	38	100	160
1313- Barney Google, 1935, Saalfield, soft-c	15	38	100	160
2031-(#31)- Batman and Robin in the Cheetah Caper, 1969, Whitman, 258 pgs.	4	10	24	35
5771- Batman and Robin in the Cheetah Caper, 1974, Whitman, 258 pgs., 49 cents	1	3	10	14
5771-1- Batman and Robin in the Cheetah Caper, 1974, Whitman, 258 pgs., 69 cents	1	3	10	14
5771-2- Batman and Robin in the Cheetah Caper, 1975?, Whitman, 258 pgs.	1	3	10	14
nn- Beauty and the Beast, nd (1930s), np (Whitman), 36 pgs., 3" x 3 1/2" Penny Book	5	12	30	45
Beep Beep The Road Runner (See Road Runner)				
760- Believe It or Not!, 1933, Whitman, 160 pgs., by Ripley (c. 1931)	10	25	64	100
Betty Bear's Lesson (See Wee Little Books)				
1119- Betty Boop in Snow White, 1934, Whitman, 240 pgs., hard-c; adapted from Max Fleischer Paramount Talkartoon	50	125	350	650
1119- Betty Boop in Snow White, 1934, Whitman, 240 pgs., soft-c; same contents as hard-c (Scarce)	63	159	444	825
1158- Betty Boop in "Miss Gullivers Travels," 1935, Whitman, 288 pgs., hard-c (Scarce)	60	150	420	775
2070- Big Big Paint Book, 1936, Whitman, 432 pgs., 8 1/2" x 11 3/8", B&W pages to color	19	48	136	215
1432- Big Chief Wahoo and the Lost Pioneers, 1942, Whitman, 432 pgs., Elmer Woggon-a	12	30	72	115
1443- Big Chief Wahoo and the Great Gusto, 1938, Whitman, 432 pgs., Elmer Woggon-a	12	30	72	115
1483- Big Chief Wahoo and the Magic Lamp, 1940, Whitman, 432 pgs., flip pictures, Woggon-c/a	12	30	72	115
725- Big Little Mother Goose, The, 1934, Whitman, 580 pgs. (Rare) Hardcover	173	433	1470	2600
725- Big Little Mother Goose, The, 1934, Whitman, 580 pgs. (Rare) Softcover	123	308	925	1800
1005- Big Little Nickel Book, 1935, Whitman, 144 pgs., Blackie Bear stories and Donna the Donkey	9	23	54	85
1006- Big Little Nickel Book, 1935, Whitman, 144 pgs., Blackie Bear stories, folk tales in primer style	9	23	54	85
1007- Big Little Nickel Book, 1935, Whitman, 144 pgs., Peter Rabbit, etc.	9	23	54	85
1008- Big Little Nickel Book, 1935, Whitman, 144 pgs., Wee Wee Woman, etc.	9	23	54	85
721- Big Little Paint Book, The, 1933, Whitman, 320 pgs., 3 3/4" x 8 1/2", for crayoning; first printing has green page ends; second printing has purple page ends (both are rare)	104	260	728	1450
721- Big Little Paint Book, The, 1933, Whitman, 336 pgs., 3 3/4" x 8 1/2", for crayoning; first printing has green page ends; second printing has purple page ends (both are rare)	121	303	900	1750
1178- Billy of Bar-Zero, 1940, Saalfield, 400 pgs.	10	25	64	100
773- Billy the Kid, 1935, Whitman, 432 pgs., Hal Arbo-a	11	28	68	110
1159- Billy the Kid on Tall Butte, 1939, Saalfield, 400 pgs.	10	25	64	100
1174- Billy the Kid's Pledge, 1940, Saalfield, 400 pgs.	10	25	64	100
nn- Billy the Kid, Western Outlaw, 1935, Whitman, 260 pgs., Cocomalt premium, Hal Arbo-a, soft-c	13	33	92	145
1057- Black Beauty, 1934, Saalfield, hard-c	8	20	50	80
1307- Black Beauty, 1934, Saalfield, soft-c	8	20	50	80

	GD	FN	VF	VF/NM

1414- Black Silver and His Pirate Crew, 1937, Whitman, 300 pgs. — 11, 28, 68, 110

1447- Blaze Brandon with the Foreign Legion, 1938, Whitman, 432 pgs. — 11, 28, 68, 110

1410- Blondie and Dagwood in Hot Water, 1946, Whitman, 352 pgs., by Chic Young — 10, 25, 60, 95

1415- Blondie and Baby Dumpling, 1937, Whitman, 432 pgs., by Chic Young — 10, 25, 64, 100

1419- Oh, Blondie the Bumsteads Carry On, 1941, Whitman, 432 pgs., flip pictures, by Chic Young — 10, 25, 64, 100

1423- Blondie Who's Boss?, 1942, Whitman, 432 pgs., flip pictures, by Chic Young — 10, 25, 64, 100

1429- Blondie with Baby Dumpling and Daisy, 1939, Whitman, 432 pgs., by Chic Young — 10, 25, 64, 100

1430- Blondie Count Cookie in Too!, 1947, Whitman, 288 pgs., by Chic Young — 10, 25, 60, 95

1438- Blondie and Dagwood Everybody's Happy, 1948, Whitman, 288 pgs., by Chic Young — 10, 25, 60, 95

1450- Blondie No Dull Moments, 1948, Whitman, 288 pgs., by Chic Young — 10, 25, 60, 95

1463- Blondie Fun For All, 1949, Whitman, 288 pgs., by Chic Young — 10, 25, 60, 95

1466- Blondie or Life Among the Bumsteads, 1944, Whitman, 352 pgs., by Chic Young — 10, 25, 64, 100

1476- Blondie and Bouncing Baby Dumpling, 1940, Whitman, 432 pgs., by Chic Young — 10, 25, 64, 100

1487- Blondie Baby Dumpling and All!, 1941, Whitman, 432 pgs., flip pictures, by Chic Young — 10, 25, 64, 100

1490- Blondie Papa Knows Best, 1945, Whitman, 352 pgs., by Chic Young — 10, 25, 60, 95

1491- Blondie-Cookie and Daisy's Pups, 1943, Whitman, 1st printing, 432 pgs. — 10, 25, 64, 100

1491- Blondie-Cookie and Daisy's Pups, 1943, Whitman, 2nd printing with different back-c & 352 pgs. — 9, 23, 56, 90

703-10- Blondie and Dagwood Some Fun!, 1949, Whitman, by Chic Young — 8, 20, 48, 75

21- Blondie and Dagwood, 1936, Lynn, by Chic Young — 15, 38, 100, 160

1108- Bobby Benson on the H-Bar-O Ranch, 1934, Whitman, 300 pgs., based on radio serial — 12, 30, 72, 115

Bobby Thatcher and the Samarang Emerald (See Top-Line Comics)

1432- Bob Stone the Young Detective, 1937, Whitman, 240 pgs., movie scenes — 12, 30, 74, 120

2002- (#2)-Bonanza-The Bubble Gum Kid, 1967, Whitman, 260 pgs., 39 cents, hard-c, color illos — 3, 8, 21, 30

1139- Border Eagle, The, 1938, Saalfield, 400 pgs. — 8, 20, 48, 75

1153- Boss of the Chisholm Trail, 1939, Saalfield, 400 pgs. — 8, 20, 48, 75

1425- Brad Turner in Transatlantic Flight, 1939, Whitman, 432 pgs. — 10, 25, 60, 95

1058- Brave Little Tailor, The (Disney), 1939, Whitman, 5" x 5 1/2", 68 pgs., hard-c (Mickey Mouse) — 12, 30, 76, 125

1427- Brenda Starr and the Masked Impostor, 1943, Whitman, 352 pgs., Dale Messick-a — 12, 30, 74, 120

1426- Brer Rabbit (Walt Disney's ...), 1947, Whitman, All Picture Comics, from "Song Of The South" movie — 21, 53, 147, 240

704-10- Brer Rabbit, 1949, Whitman — 18, 45, 126, 195

1059- Brick Bradford in the City Beneath the Sea, 1934, Saalfield, hard-c, by William Ritt & Clarence Gray — 15, 38, 105, 165

1309- Brick Bradford in the City Beneath the Sea, 1934, Saalfield, soft-c, by Ritt & Gray — 15, 38, 105, 165

1468- Brick Bradford with Brocco the Modern Buccaneer, 1938, Whitman, 432 pgs., by Wm. Ritt & Clarence Gray — 10, 25, 64, 100

1133- Bringing Up Father, 1936, Whitman, 432 pgs. by George McManus — 12, 30, 76, 125

1100- Broadway Bill, 1935, Saalfield, photo-c, 4 1/2" x 5 1/4", movie scenes (Columbia Pictures, horse racing) — 11, 28, 68, 110

1580- Broadway Bill, 1935, Saalfield, soft-c, photo-c, movie scenes — 11, 28, 68, 110

1181- Broncho Bill, 1940, Saalfield, 400 pgs. — 10, 25, 64, 100

nn- Broncho Bill, 1935, Whitman, 148 pgs., 3 1/2" x 4", Tarzan Ice Cream cup lid premium — 22, 55, 154, 260

nn- Broncho Bill in Suicide Canyon (See Top-Line Comics)

1417- Bronc Peeler the Lone Cowboy, 1937, Whitman, 432 pgs., by Fred Harman, forerunner of Red Ryder (also see Red Death on the Range) — 10, 25, 60, 95

nn- Brownies' Merry Adventures, The, 1993, Barefoot Books, 202 pgs., reprints from Palmer Cox's late 1800s books — 3, 8, 20, 28

1470- Buccaneer, The, 1938, Whitman, 240 pgs., photo-c, movie scenes — 12, 30, 76, 125

1646- Buccaneers, The (TV Series), 1958, Whitman, 4 1/2" x 5 1/4", 280 pgs., Russ Manning-a — 3, 8, 21, 30

1104- Buck Jones in the Fighting Code, 1934, Whitman, 160 pgs., hard-c, movie scenes — 13, 33, 92, 145

1116- Buck Jones in Ride 'Em Cowboy (Universal Presents), 1935, Whitman, 240 pgs., photo-c, movie scenes — 13, 33, 92, 145

1174- Buck Jones in the Roaring West (Universal Presents), 1935, Whitman, 240 pgs., movie scenes — 13, 33, 92, 145

1188- Buck Jones in the Fighting Rangers (Universal Presents), 1936, Whitman, 240 pgs., photo-c, movie scenes — 13, 33, 85, 135

1404- Buck Jones and the Two-Gun Kid, 1937, Whitman, 432 pgs. — 10, 25, 60, 95

1451- Buck Jones and the Killers of Crooked Butte, 1940, Whitman, 432 pgs. — 10, 25, 60, 95

1461- Buck Jones and the Rock Creek Cattle War, 1938, Whitman, 432 pgs. — 10, 25, 60, 95

1486- Buck Jones and the Rough Riders in Forbidden Trails, 1943, Whitman, flip pictures, based on movie; Tim McCoy app. — 12, 30, 72, 115

3- Buck Jones in the Red Rider, 1934, EVW, 160 pgs., movie scenes — 21, 53, 145, 230

8- Buck Jones Cowboy Masquerade, 1938, Whitman, 132 pgs., soft-c, 3 3/4" x 3 1/2", Buddy Book premium — 22, 55, 154, 260

15- Buck Jones in Rocky Rhodes, 1935, EVW, 160 pgs., photo-c, movie scenes — 30, 75, 210, 360

4069- Buck Jones and the Night Riders, 1937, Whitman, 7" x 9", 320 pgs., Big Big Book — 33, 83, 235, 400

nn- Buck Jones on the Six-Gun Trail, 1939, Whitman, 36 pgs., 2 1/2" x 3 1/2", Penny Book — 10, 25, 60, 95

nn- Buck Jones Big Thrill Chewing Gum, 1934, Whitman, 8 pgs., 2 1/2" x 3 1/2" (6 diff.) each... — 14, 35, 95, 150

742- Buck Rogers in the 25th Century A.D., 1933, Whitman, 320 pgs., Dick Calkins-a — 42, 105, 294, 500

nn- Buck Rogers in the 25th Century A.D., 1933, Whitman, 204 pgs., Cocomalt premium, Calkins-a — 28, 70, 196, 340

765- Buck Rogers in the City Below the Sea, 1934, Whitman, 320 pgs., Dick Calkins-a — 31, 78, 217, 375

765- Buck Rogers in the City Below the Sea, 1934, Whitman, 324 pgs., soft-c, Dick Calkins-c/a (Rare) — 52, 130, 364, 675

1143- Buck Rogers on the Moons of Saturn, 1934, Whitman, 320 pgs., Dick Calkins-a — 31, 78, 217, 375

nn- Buck Rogers on the Moons of Saturn, 1934, Whitman, 324 pgs., premium w/no ads, soft 3-color-c, Dick Calkins-a — 42, 105, 295, 525

1169- Buck Rogers and the Depth Men of Jupiter, 1935, Whitman, 432 pgs., Calkins-a — 31, 78, 217, 375

1178- Buck Rogers and the Doom Comet, 1935, Whitman, 432 pgs., Calkins-a — 31, 78, 217, 375

1197- Buck Rogers and the Planetoid Plot, 1936, Whitman, 432 pgs., Calkins-a — 31, 78, 217, 375

1409- Buck Rogers Vs. the Fiend of Space, 1940, Whitman, 432 pgs., Calkins-a — 33, 83, 235, 400

1437- Buck Rogers in the War with the Planet Venus, 1938, Whitman, 432 pgs., Calkins-a — 31, 78, 217, 375

1474- Buck Rogers and the Overturned World, 1941, Whitman, 432 pgs., flip pictures, Calkins-a — 31, 78, 217, 375

1490- Buck Rogers and the Super-Dwarf of Space, 1943, Whitman, 11 Pictures Comics, Calkins-a — 31, 78, 217, 375

4057- Buck Rogers, The Adventures of, 1934, Whitman, 7" x 9 1/2", 320 pgs., Big Big Book, "The Story of Buck Rogers on the Planet Eros," Calkins-c/a — 65, 163, 455, 850

nn- Buck Rogers, 1935, Whitman, 4" x 3 1/2", Tarzan Ice Cream cup premium (Rare) — 73, 184, 515, 1000

nn- Buck Rogers in the City of Floating Globes, 1935, Whitman, 258 pgs., Cocomalt premium, soft-c, Dick Calkins-a — 73, 184, 514, 975

nn- Buck Rogers Big Thrill Chewing Gum, 1934, Whitman, 8 pgs., 2 1/2" x 3 " (6 diff.) each... — 19, 48, 136, 215

1135- Buckskin and Bullets, 1938, Saalfield, 400 pgs. — 8, 20, 50, 80

Buffalo Bill (See Wild West Adventures of ...)

nn- Buffalo Bill, 1934, World Syndicate, All pictures, by J. Carroll Mansfield — 10, 25, 60, 95

713- Buffalo Bill and the Pony Express, 1934, Whitman, hard-c, 384 pgs., Hal Arbo-a — 12, 30, 72, 115

nn- Buffalo Bill and the Pony Express, 1934, Whitman, soft-c, 384 pgs., Hal Arbo-a; three-color premium (Rare) — 37, 93, 260, 450

1194- Buffalo Bill Plays a Lone Hand, 1936, Whitman, 432 pgs., Hal Arbo-a — 10, 25, 60, 95

530- Bugs Bunny, 1943, Whitman, All Pictures Comics, Tall Comic Book, 3 1/4" x 8 1/4", reprints/Looney Tunes 1 & 5 — 16, 40, 112, 175

1403- Bugs Bunny and the Pirate Loot, 1947, Whitman, All Pictures Comics — 11, 28, 66, 105

1435- Bugs Bunny, 1944, Whitman, All Pictures Comics — 11, 28, 68, 110

1440- Bugs Bunny in Risky Business, 1948, Whitman, All Pictures & Comics — 11, 28, 66, 105

1455- Bugs Bunny and Klondike Gold, 1948, Whitman, 288 pgs. — 11, 28, 66, 105

1465- Bugs Bunny The Masked Marvel, 1949, Whitman, 288 pgs. — 11, 28, 66, 105

1496- Bugs Bunny and His Pals, 1945, Whitman, All Pictures Comics; r/Four Color Comics #33 — 11, 28, 66, 105

13- Bugs Bunny and the Secret of Storm Island, 1942, Dell, 194 pgs., Fast-Action Story — 28, 70, 196, 340

1427 - Brenda Starr and the Masked Imposter © WHIT

1496 - Bugs Bunny and His Pals © WB

Chicken Licken © WHIT

	GD	FN	VF	VF/NM
706-10- Bugs Bunny and the Giant Brothers, 1949, Whitman	10	25	60	95
2007- (#7)-Bugs Bunny-Double Trouble on Diamond Island, 1967, Whitman, 260 pgs., 39 cents, hard-c, color illos	3	8	23	34
2029-(#29)- Bugs Bunny, Accidental Adventure, 1969, Whitman, 256 pgs., hard-c, color illus.	2	3	17	24
2952- Bugs Bunny's Mistake, 1949, Whitman, 3 1/4" x 4", 24 pgs., Tiny Tales, full color (5 cents) (1030-5 on back-c)	10	25	60	95
5757-2- Bugs Bunny in Double Trouble on Diamond Island,1967, (1980-reprints #2007), Whitman, 260 pgs., soft-c, 79 cents, B&W	1	3	10	14
5758- Bugs Bunny, Accidental Adventure, 1973, Whitman, 256 pgs., soft-c, B&W illos.	1	3	10	14
5758-1- Bugs Bunny, Accidental Adventure, 1973, Whitman, 256 pgs., soft-c, B&W illus.	1	3	10	14
5772- Bugs Bunny the Last Crusader, 1975, Whitman, 49 cents, flip-it book	1	3	10	14
5772-2- Bugs Bunny the Last Crusader, 1975, Whitman, $1.00, flip-it book	1	3	5	6
1169- Bullet Benton, 1939, Saalfield, 400 pgs.	10	25	64	100
nn- Bulletman and the Return of Mr. Murder, 1941, Fawcett, 196 pgs., Dime Action Book	42	105	294	500
1142- Bullets Across the Border (A Billy The Kid story), 1938, Saalfield, 400 pgs.	10	25	60	95
Bunky (See Top-Line Comics)				
837- Bunty (Punch and Judy), 1935, Whitman, 28 pgs., Magic-Action with 3 pop-ups	13	33	90	140
1091- Burn 'Em Up Barnes, 1935, Saalfield, hard-c, movie scenes	10	25	60	95
1321- Burn 'Em Up Barnes, 1935, Saalfield, soft-c, movie scenes	10	25	60	95
1415- Buz Sawyer and Bomber 13,1946, Whitman, 352 pgs., Roy Crane-a	10	25	60	95
1412- Calling W-1-X-Y-Z, Jimmy Kean and the Radio Spies, 1939, Whitman, 300 pgs.	11	28	66	105
Call of the Wild (See Jack London's...)				
1107- Camels are Coming, 1935, Saalfield, movie scenes	10	25	60	95
1587- Camels are Coming, 1935, Saalfield, movie scenes	10	25	60	95
nn- Captain and the Kids, Boys Vill Be Boys, The, 1938, 68 pgs., Pan-Am Oil premium, soft-c	12	30	76	125
1128- Captain Easy Soldier of Fortune, 1934, Whitman, 432 pgs., Roy Crane-a	12	30	76	125
nn- Captain Easy Soldier of Fortune, 1934, Whitman, 436 pgs., Premium, no ads, soft 3-color-c, Roy Crane-a	21	53	145	230
1474- Captain Easy Behind Enemy Lines, 1943, Whitman, 352 pgs., Roy Crane-a	11	28	68	110
nn- Captain Easy and Wash Tubbs, 1935, Whitman, 260 pgs., Cocomalt premium, Roy Crane-a	11	28	68	110
1444- Captain Frank Hawks Air Ace and the League of Twelve, 1938, Whitman, 432 pgs.	11	28	68	110
nn- Captain Marvel, 1941, Fawcett, 196 pgs., Dime Action Book	52	130	364	675
1402- Captain Midnight and Sheik Jomak Khan, 1946, Whitman, 352 pgs.	17	43	123	190
1452- Captain Midnight and the Moon Woman, 1943, Whitman, 352 pgs.	20	50	143	225
1458- Captain Midnight Vs. The Terror of the Orient, 1942, Whitman, 432 pgs., flip pictures, Hess-a	20	50	143	225
1488- Captain Midnight and the Secret Squadron, 1941, Whitman, 432 pgs.	20	50	143	225
Captain Robb of.. (See Dirigible ZR90 ...)				
nn- Cauliflower Catnip Pearls of Peril, 1981, Teacup Tales, 290 pgs., Joe Wehrle Jr.-s/a; deliberately printed on aged-looking paper to look like an old BLB	3	8	20	28
20- Ceiling Zero, 1936, Lynn, 128 pgs., 7 1/2" x 5", hard-c, James Cagney, Pat O'Brien photos on-c, movie scenes, Warner Bros. Pictures	11	28	66	105
1093- Chandu the Magician, 1935, Saalfield, 5" x 5 1/4", 160 pgs., hard-c,				

	GD	FN	VF	VF/NM
Bela Lugosi photo-c, movie scenes	16	40	112	175
1323- Chandu the Magician, 1935, Saalfield, 5" x 5 1/4", 160 pgs., soft-c, Bela Lugosi photo-c	17	43	119	185
Charlie Chan (See Inspector ...)				
1459- Charlie Chan Solves a New Mystery (See Inspector..), 1940, Whitman, 432 pgs., Alfred Andriola-a	13	33	92	145
1478- Charlie Chan of the Honolulu Police, Inspector, 1939, Whitman, 432 pgs., Andriola-a	13	33	92	145
Charlie McCarthy (See Story Of ...)				
734- Chester Gump at Silver Creek Ranch, 1933, Whitman, 320 pgs., Sidney Smith-a	12	30	74	120
nn- Chester Gump at Silver Creek Ranch, 1933, Whitman, 204 pgs., Cocomalt premium, soft-c, Sidney Smith-a	13	33	85	135
nn- Chester Gump at Silver Creek Ranch, 1933, Whitman, 52 pgs., 4" x 5 1/2", premium-no ads, soft-c, Sidney Smith-a	17	43	119	185
766- Chester Gump Finds the Hidden Treasure, 1934, Whitman, 320 pgs., Sidney Smith-a	11	28	68	110
nn- Chester Gump Finds the Hidden Treasure, 1934, Whitman, 52 pgs., 3 1/2" x 5 3/4", premium-no ads, soft-c, Sidney Smith-a	17	43	119	185
nn- Chester Gump Finds the Hidden Treasure, 1934, Whitman, 52 pgs., 4" x 5 1/2", premium-no ads, Sidney Smith-a	17	43	119	185
1146- Chester Gump in the City Of Gold, 1935, Whitman, 432 pgs., Sidney Smith-a	12	30	72	115
nn- Chester Gump in the City Of Gold, 1935, Whitman, 436 pgs., premium-no ads, 3-color, soft-c, Sidney Smith-a	22	55	154	260
1402- Chester Gump in the Pole to Pole Flight, 1937, Whitman, 432 pgs.	11	28	68	110
5- Chester Gump and His Friends, 1934, Whitman, 132 pgs., 3 1/2" x 3 1/2", soft-c, Tarzan Ice Cream cup lid premium	22	55	154	260
nn- Chester Gump at the North Pole, 1938, Whitman, 68 pgs. soft-c, 3 3/4" x 3 1/2", Pan-Am giveaway	22	55	154	260
nn- Chicken Greedy, nd(1930s), np (Whitman), 36 pgs., 3" x 2 1/2", Penny Book	4	10	27	40
nn- Chicken Licken, nd (1930s), np (Whitman), 36 pgs., 3" x 2 1/2", Penny Book	4	10	27	40
1101- Chief of the Rangers, 1935, Saalfield, hard-c, Tom Mix photo-c, movie scenes from "The Miracle Rider"	13	33	90	140
1581- Chief of the Rangers, 1935, Saalfield, soft-c, Tom Mix photo-c, movie scenes	13	33	90	140
Child's Garden of Verses (See Wee Little Books)				
L14- Chip Collins' Adventures on Bat Island, 1935, Lynn, 192 pgs.	12	30	76	125
2025- Chitty Chitty Bang Bang, 1968, Whitman, movie photos	3	8	21	30
Chubby Little Books, 1935, Whitman, 3" x 2 1/2", 200 pgs.				
W803- Golden Hours Story Book, The	3	8	22	32
W803- Story Hours Story Book, The	3	8	22	32
W804- Gay Book of Little Stories, The	3	8	22	32
W804- Glad Book of Little Stories, The	3	8	22	32
W804- Joy Book of Little Stories, The	3	8	22	32
W804- Sunny Book of Little Stories, The	3	8	22	32
1453- Chuck Malloy Railroad Detective on the Streamliner,1938, Whitman, 300 pgs.	6	15	36	55
Cinderella (See Walt Disney's...)				
Clyde Beatty (See The Steel Arena)				
1410- Clyde Beatty Daredevil Lion and Tiger Tamer, 1939, Whitman, 300 pgs.	12	30	76	125
1480- Coach Bernie Bierman's Brick Barton and the Winning Eleven, 1938, 300 pgs.	10	25	60	95
1446- Convoy Patrol (A Thrilling U.S. Navy Story), 1942, Whitman, 432 pgs., flip pictures	10	25	60	95
1127- Corley of the Wilderness Trail, 1937, Saalfield, hard-c	10	25	60	95
1607- Corley of the Wilderness Trail, 1937, Saalfield, soft-c	10	25	60	95
1- Count of Monte Cristo, 1934, EVW, 160 pgs., (Five Star Library),				

	GD	FN	VF	VF/NM

movie scenes, hard-c (Rare) 19 48 136 215
1457- **Cowboy Lingo Boys' Book of Western Facts**, 1938,
Whitman, 300 pgs., Fred Harman-a 6 15 40 60
1171- **Cowboy Malloy**, 1940, Saalfield, 400 pgs. 5 12 30 45
1106- **Cowboy Millionaire**, 1935, Saalfield, movie scenes with
George O'Brien, photo-c, hard-c 12 30 72 115
1586- **Cowboy Millionaire**, 1935, Saalfield, movie scenes with
George O'Brien, photo-c, soft-c 12 30 72 115
724- **Cowboy Stories**, 1933, Whitman, 300 pgs., Hal Arbo-a
10 25 64 100
nn- **Cowboy Stories**, 1933, Whitman, 52 pgs., soft-c, premium-no ads,
4" x 5 1/2" Hal Arbo-a 12 30 72 115
1161- **Crimson Cloak, The**, 1939, Saalfield, 400 pgs.
10 25 60 95
L19- **Curley Harper at Lakespur**, 1935, Lynn, 192 pgs.
10 25 60 95
5785-2- **Daffy Duck in Twice the Trouble**, 1980, Whitman, 260 pgs.,
79 cents soft-c 1 3 5 6
2018-(#18)- **Daktari-Night of Terror**, 1968, Whitman, 260 pgs., 39 cents,
hard-c, color illos 3 8 20 28
1010- **Dan Dunn And The Gangsters' Frame-Up**, 1937, Whitman,
7 1/4" x 5 1/2", 64 pgs., Nickel Book 26 65 185 315
1116- **Dan Dunn "Crime Never Pays,"** 1934, Whitman, 320 pgs.,
by Norman Marsh 8 20 50 80
1125- **Dan Dunn on the Trail of the Counterfeiters**, 1936,
Whitman, 432 pgs., by Norman Marsh 8 20 50 80
1171- **Dan Dunn and the Crime Master**, 1937, Whitman, 432 pgs.,
by Norman Marsh 8 20 50 80
1417- **Dan Dunn and the Underworld Gorillas**, 1941, Whitman,
All Pictures Comics, flip pictures, by Norman Marsh 8 20 50 80
1454- **Dan Dunn on the Trail of Wu Fang**, 1938, Whitman, 432 pgs.,
by Norman Marsh 10 25 64 100
1481- **Dan Dunn and the Border Smugglers**, 1938, Whitman, 432 pgs.,
by Norman Marsh 6 15 40 60
1492- **Dan Dunn and the Dope Ring**, 1940, Whitman, 432 pgs.,
by Norman Marsh 6 15 40 60
nn- **Dan Dunn and the Bank Hold-Up**, 1938, Whitman, 36 pgs.,
2 1/2" x 3 1/2", Penny Book 9 23 54 85
nn- **Dan Dunn and the Zeppelin Of Doom**, 1938, Dell, 196 pgs.,
Fast-Action Story, soft-c 18 45 128 200
nn- **Dan Dunn Meets Chang Loo**, 1938, Whitman, 66 pgs., Pan-Am
premium, by Norman Marsh 23 58 165 280
nn- **Dan Dunn Plays a Lone Hand**, 1938, Whitman, 36 pgs.,
2 1/2" x 3 1/2", Penny Book 9 23 54 85
3 3/4" x 3 1/2", Buddy Book 24 61 171 290
6- **Dan Dunn Secret Operative 48 and the Counterfeiter Ring**, 1938,
Whitman, 132 pgs., soft-c, 3 3/4" x 3 1/2", Buddy Book premium
24 61 171 290
9- **Dan Dunn's Mysterious Ruse**, 1936, Whitman, 132 pgs., soft-c,
3 1/2" x 3 1/2", Tarzan Ice Cream cup lid premium 24 61 171 290
1177- **Danger Trail North**, 1940, Saalfield, 400 pgs. 10 25 60 95
1151- **Danger Trails in Africa**, 1935, Whitman, 432 pgs. 10 30 80 130
nn- **Daniel Boone**, 1934, World Syndicate, High Lights of History Series,
hard-c, All in Pictures 10 25 60 95
1160- **Dan of the Lazy L**, 1939, Saalfield, 400 pgs. 10 25 60 95
1148- **David Copperfield**, 1934, Whitman, hard-c, 160 pgs., photo-c,
movie scenes (W. C. Fields) 13 33 90 140
nn- **David Copperfield**, 1934, Whitman, soft-c, 164 pgs., movie scenes
13 33 90 140
1151- **Death by Short Wave**, 1938, Saalfield 11 28 68 110
1156- **Denny the Ace Detective**, 1938, Saalfield, 400 pgs.
11 28 66 105
1431- **Desert Eagle and the Hidden Fortress, The**, 1941, Whitman,
432 pgs., flip pictures 11 28 68 110
1458- **Desert Eagle Rides Again, The**, 1939, Whitman, 300 pgs.
11 28 68 110
1136- **Desert Justice**, 1938, Saalfield, 400 pgs. 10 25 64 100
1484- **Detective Higgins of the Racket Squad**, 1938, Whitman,
432 pgs. 10 25 64 100
1124- **Dickie Moore in the Little Red School House**, 1936, Whitman,
240 pgs., photo-c, movie scenes (Chesterfield Motion Picts. Corp)
12 30 80 130
W-707- **Dick Tracy the Detective, The Adventures of**, 1933, Whitman,
320 pgs. (The 1st Big Little Book), by Chester Gould
(Scarce) 170 425 1360 2550
nn- **Dick Tracy Detective, The Adventures of**, 1933, Whitman,
52 pgs., 4" x 5 1/2", premium-no ads, soft-c, by Chester Gould
82 205 575 1150
nn- **Dick Tracy Detective, The Adventures of**, 1933, Whitman,
52 pgs., 4" x 5 1/2", inside back-c & back-c ads for Sundial Shoes,
soft-c, by Chester Gould 86 215 600 1200
710- **Dick Tracy and Dick Tracy, Jr.** (The Advs. of ...), 1933, Whitman,
320 pgs., by Chester Gould 60 150 420 775
nn- **Dick Tracy and Dick Tracy, Jr.** (The Advs. of ...), 1933, Whitman,
52 pgs., premium-no ads, soft-c, 4" x 5 1/2", by Chester Gould
60 150 420 775

nn- **Dick Tracy the Detective and Dick Tracy, Jr.**, 1933, Whitman,
52 pgs., premium-no ads, 3 1/2"x 5 1/4", soft-c, by Chester Gould
60 150 420 775
723- **Dick Tracy Out West**, 1933, Whitman, 300 pgs., by Chester Gould
37 93 260 450
749- **Dick Tracy from Colorado to Nova Scotia**, 1933, Whitman,
320 pgs., by Chester Gould 26 65 180 310
nn- **Dick Tracy from Colorado to Nova Scotia**, 1933, Whitman, 204 pgs.,
premium-no ads, soft-c, by Chester Gould 28 70 192 335
1105- **Dick Tracy and the Stolen Bonds**, 1934, Whitman, 320 pgs.,
by Chester Gould 17 43 119 185
1112- **Dick Tracy and the Racketeer Gang**, 1936, Whitman,
432 pgs., by Chester Gould 14 35 95 150
1137- **Dick Tracy Solves the Penfield Mystery**, 1934, Whitman,
320 pgs., by Chester Gould 16 40 116 180
nn- **Dick Tracy Solves the Penfield Mystery**, 1934, Whitman, 324 pgs.,
premium-no ads, 3-color, soft-c, by Chester Gould 41 103 287 490
1163- **Dick Tracy and the Boris Arson Gang**, 1935, Whitman,
432 pgs., by Chester Gould 15 38 108 170
1170- **Dick Tracy on the Trail of Larceny Lu**, 1935, Whitman,
432 pgs., by Chester Gould 15 38 100 160
1185- **Dick Tracy in Chains of Crime**, 1936, Whitman, 432 pgs.,
by Chester Gould 15 38 100 160
1412- **Dick Tracy and Yogee Yamma**, 1946, Whitman, 352 pgs.,
by Chester Gould 14 35 95 150
1420- **Dick Tracy and the Hotel Murders**, 1937, Whitman, 432 pgs.,
by Chester Gould 15 38 100 160
1434- **Dick Tracy and the Phantom Ship**, 1940, Whitman, 432 pgs.,
by Chester Gould 15 38 100 160
1436- **Dick Tracy and the Mad Killer**, 1947, Whitman, 288 pgs., by
Chester Gould 13 33 85 135
1439- **Dick Tracy and His G-Men**, 1941, Whitman, 432 pgs., flip pictures,
by Chester Gould 15 38 100 160
1445- **Dick Tracy and the Bicycle Gang**, 1948, Whitman, 288 pgs.,
by Chester Gould 13 33 85 135
1446- **Detective Dick Tracy and the Spider Gang**, 1937, Whitman, 240 pgs.,
scenes from "Adventures of Dick Tracy" serial 19 48 136 215
1449- **Dick Tracy Special F.B.I. Operative**, 1943, Whitman, 432 pgs.,
by Chester Gould 15 38 100 160
1454- **Dick Tracy on the High Seas**, 1939, Whitman, 432 pgs.,
by Chester Gould 15 38 100 160
1460- **Dick Tracy and the Tiger Lilly Gang**, 1949, Whitman,
288 pgs., by Chester Gould 13 33 85 135
1478- **Dick Tracy on Voodoo Island**, 1944, Whitman, 352 pgs.,
by Chester Gould 13 33 85 135
1479- **Detective Dick Tracy Vs. Crooks in Disguise**, 1939, Whitman,
432 pgs., flip pictures, by Chester Gould 14 35 100 160
1482- **Dick Tracy and the Wreath Kidnapping Case**, 1945,
Whitman, 352 pgs. 13 33 95 150
1488- **Dick Tracy the Super-Detective**, 1939, Whitman, 432 pgs.,
by Chester Gould 15 38 100 160
1491- **Dick Tracy the Man with No Face**, 1938, Whitman, 432 pgs.
15 38 100 160
1495- **Dick Tracy Returns**, 1939, Whitman, 432 pgs., based on Republic
Motion Picture serial, Chester Gould-a 15 38 100 160
2001- (#1)- **Dick Tracy-Encounters Facey**, 1967, Whitman, 260 pgs.,
39 cents, hard-c, color illos 3 8 21 30
3912- **Dick Tracy Big Little Book Picture Puzzles**, 1938, Whitman,
7 1/2" x 10 1/4" box with 2 jigsaw puzzles 50 125 350 650
Variant set, same cover w/2 puzzles showing Dick Tracy & Jr. in crime
lab & Dick Tracy patting down a gangster 50 125 350 650
4055- **Dick Tracy, The Adventures of**, 1934, Whitman, 7" x 9 1/2", 320 pgs.,
Big Big Book, by Chester Gould 56 140 392 725
4071- **Dick Tracy and the Mystery of the Purple Cross**, 1938,
7" x 9 1/2", 320 pgs., Big Big Book, by Chester Gould
(Scarce) 52 130 364 675
nn- **Dick Tracy and the Invisible Man**, 1939, Whitman,
3 1/4" x 3 3/4", 132 pgs., stapled, soft-c, Quaker Oats premium;
NBC radio play script, Chester Gould-a 41 103 287 490
Vol. 2- **Dick Tracy's Ghost Ship**, 1939, Whitman, 3 1/2" x 3 1/2", 132 pgs.,
soft-c, stapled, Quaker Oats premium; NBC radio play script episode
from actual radio show; Gould-a 39 98 276 475
3- **Dick Tracy Meets a New Gang**, 1934, Whitman, 3" x 3 1/2", 132 pgs.,
soft-c, Tarzan Ice Cream cup lid premium 37 93 260 450
11- **Dick Tracy in Smashing the Famon Racket**, 1938, Whitman,
3 3/4" x 3 1/2", Buddy Book-ice cream premium, by Chester Gould
36 90 252 430
nn- **Dick Tracy Gets His Man**, 1938, Whitman, 36 pgs., 2 1/2" x 3 1/2",
Penny Book 8 20 50 80
nn- **Dick Tracy the Detective**, 1938, Whitman, 36 pgs., 2 1/2" x 3 1/2",
Penny Book 8 20 50 80
9- **Dick Tracy and the Frozen Bullet Murders**, 1941, Dell, 196 pgs.,
Fast-Action Story, soft-c, by Gould 37 93 260 450
6833- **Dick Tracy Detective and Federal Agent**, 1936, Dell, 244 pgs.,
Cartoon Story Books, hard-c, by Gould 40 100 284 485
nn- **Dick Tracy Detective and Federal Agent**, 1936, Dell, 244 pgs.,

1177 - Danger Trail North © Saalfied

1488 - Dick Tracy The Super-Detective © Tribune

1457 - Donald Duck in Volcano Valley © DIS

	GD	FN	VF	VF/NM
Fast-Action Story, soft-c, by Gould	34	85	238	410
nn- **Dick Tracy and the Blackmailers**, 1939, Dell, 196 pgs., Fast-Action Story, soft-c, by Gould	34	85	238	410
nn- **Dick Tracy and the Chain of Evidence, Detective**, 1938, Dell, 196 pgs., Fast-Action Story, soft-c, by Chester Gould	34	85	238	410
nn- **Dick Tracy and the Crook Without a Face**, 1938, Whitman, 68 pgs., 3 1/4" x 3 1/2", Pan-Am giveaway, Gould-c/a	29	73	203	350
nn- **Dick Tracy and the Maroon Mask Gang**, 1938, Dell, 196 pgs., Fast-Action Story, soft-c	34	85	238	410
nn- **Dick Tracy Cross-Country Race**, 1934, Whitman, 8 pgs., 2 1/2" x 3", Big Thrill chewing gum premium (6 diff.)	13	33	85	135
nn- **Dick Whittington and his Cat**, nd(1930s), np(Whitman), 36 pgs., Penny Book	3	8	20	28
Dinglehoofer und His Dog Adolph (See Top-Line Comics)				
Dinky (See Jackie Cooper in ...)				
1464- **Dirigible ZR90 and the Disappearing Zeppelin** (Captain Robb of ...), 1941, Whitman, 300 pgs., Al Lewin-a	15	38	100	160
1167- **Dixie Dugan Among the Cowboys**, 1939, Saalfield, 400 pgs.	10	25	60	95
1188- **Dixie Dugan and Cuddles**, 1940, Saalfield, 400 pgs., by Striebel & McEvoy	10	25	60	95
Doctor Doom (See Foreign Spies... & International Spy...)				
Dog of Flanders, A (See Frankie Thomas in ...)				
1114- **Dog Stars of Hollywood**, 1936, Saalfield, photo-c, photo-illos	11	28	68	110
1594- **Dog Stars of Hollywood**, 1936, Saalfield, photo-c, soft-c, photo-illos	11	28	68	110
nn- **Dolls and Dresses Big Little Set**, 1930s, Whitman, box contains 20 dolls on paper, 128 sheets of clothing to color & cut out, includes crayons	37	93	260	450
Donald Duck (See Silly Symphony... & Walt Disney's ...)				
800- **Donald Duck in Bringing Up the Boys**, 1948, Whitman, hard-c, Story Hour series	10	25	60	95
1404- **Donald Duck (Says Such a Life)** (Disney), 1939, Whitman, 432 pgs., Taliaferro-a	20	50	143	225
1411- **Donald Duck and Ghost Morgan's Treasure** (Disney), 1946, Whitman, All Pictures Comics, Barks-a; reprints FC #9	25	63	175	300
1422- **Donald Duck Sees Stars** (Disney), 1941, Whitman, 432 pgs., flip pictures, Taliaferro-a	19	48	135	210
1424- **Donald Duck Says Such Luck** (Disney), 1941, Whitman, 432 pgs., flip pictures, Taliaferro-a	19	48	133	210
1430- **Donald Duck Headed For Trouble** (Disney), 1942, Whitman, 432 pgs., flip pictures, Taliaferro-a	18	45	126	195
1432- **Donald Duck and the Green Serpent** (Disney), 1947, Whitman, All Pictures Comics, Barks-a; reprints FC #108	20	50	140	220
1434- **Donald Duck Forgets To Duck** (Disney), 1939, Whitman, 432 pgs., Taliaferro-a	20	50	143	225
1438- **Donald Duck Off the Beam** (Disney), 1943, Whitman, 352 pgs., flip pictures, Taliaferro-a	18	45	126	195
1438- **Donald Duck Off the Beam** (Disney), 1943, Whitman, 432 pgs., flip pictures, Taliaferro-a	18	45	126	195
1449- **Donald Duck Lays Down the Law**, 1948, Whitman, 288 pgs., Barks-a	19	48	133	210
1457- **Donald Duck in Volcano Valley** (Disney), 1949, Whitman, 288 pgs., Barks-a	19	48	133	210
1462- **Donald Duck Gets Fed Up** (Disney), 1940, Whitman, 432 pgs.,Taliaferro-a	19	48	133	210
1478- **Donald Duck-Hunting For Trouble** (Disney), 1938, Whitman, 432 pgs., Taliaferro-a	20	50	143	225
1484- **Donald Duck is Here Again!**, 1944, Whitman, All Pictures Comics, Taliaferro-a	18	45	126	195
1486- **Donald Duck Up in the Air** (Disney), 1945, Whitman, 352 pgs., Barks-a	21	53	145	230
705-10- **Donald Duck and the Mystery of the Double X**, (Disney), 1949, Whitman, Barks-a	12	30	76	125
2033-(#33)- **Donald Duck, Luck of the Ducks**, 1969, Whitman, 256 pgs., hard-c, 39 cents, color illos.	3	8	19	26
2009-(#9)-**Donald Duck-The Fabulous Diamond Fountain**, (Walt Disney), 1967, Whitman, 260 pgs., 39 cents, hard-c, color illos	4	10	24	35

	GD	FN	VF	VF/NM
5756- **Donald Duck-The Fabulous Diamond Fountain**, (Walt Disney), 1973, Whitman, 260 pgs., 79 cents, soft-c, color illos	2	3	17	24
5756-1- **Donald Duck-The Fabulous Diamond Fountain**, (Walt Disney), 1973, Whitman, 260 pgs., 79 cents, soft-c, color illos	2	3	17	24
5756-2- **Donald Duck-The Fabulous Diamond Fountain**, (Walt Disney), 1973, Whitman, 260 pgs., 79 cents, soft-c, color illos	2	3	17	24
5760- **Donald Duck in Volcano Valley** (Disney), 1973, Whitman, 39 cents, flip-it book	2	3	17	24
5760-2- **Donald Duck in Volcano Valley** (Disney), 1973, Whitman, 79 cents, flip-it book	2	3	12	16
5764- **Donald Duck, Luck of the Ducks**, 1969, Whitman, 256 pgs., soft-c, 49 cents, color illos.	2	3	17	24
5773- **Donald Duck - The Lost Jungle City**, 1975, Whitman, 49 cents, flip-it book; 6 printings through 1980	2	3	12	16
nn- **Donald Duck and the Ducklings**, 1938, Dell, 194 pgs., Fast-Action Story, soft-c, Taliaferro-a	39	98	276	475
nn- **Donald Duck Out of Luck** (Disney), 1940, Dell, 196 pgs., Fast-Action Story, has Four Color #4 on back-c, Taliaferro-a	37	93	260	450
8- **Donald Duck Takes It on the Chin** (Disney), 1941, Dell, 196 pgs., Fast-Action Story, soft-c, Taliaferro-a	36	90	252	430
L13- **Donnie and the Pirates**, 1935, Lynn, 192 pgs.	10	25	60	95
1438- **Don O'Dare Finds War**, 1940, Whitman, 432 pgs.	10	25	60	95
1107- **Don Winslow, U.S.N.**, 1935, Whitman, 432 pgs.	14	35	95	150
nn- **Don Winslow, U.S.N.**, 1935, Whitman, 436 pgs., premium-no ads, 3-color, soft-c	16	40	116	180
1408- **Don Winslow and the Giant Girl Spy**, 1946, Whitman, 352 pgs.	10	25	64	100
1418- **Don Winslow Navy Intelligence Ace**, 1942, Whitman, 432 pgs., flip pictures	13	33	90	140
1419- **Don Winslow of the Navy Vs. the Scorpion Gang**, 1938, Whitman, 432 pgs.	13	33	90	140
1453- **Don Winslow of the Navy and the Secret Enemy Base**, 1943, Whitman, 352 pgs.	13	33	90	140
1489- **Don Winslow of the Navy and the Great War Plot**, 1940, Whitman, 432 pgs.	13	33	90	140
nn- **Don Winslow U.S. Navy and the Missing Admiral**, 1938, Whitman, 36 pgs., 2 1/2" x 3 1/2", Penny Book	6	15	36	55
1137- **Doomed To Die**, 1938, Saalfield, 400 pgs.	11	28	68	110
1140- **Down Cartridge Creek**, 1938, Saalfield, 400 pgs.	11	28	68	110
1416- **Draftie of the U.S. Army**, 1943, Whitman, All Pictures Comics	11	28	68	110
1100B- **Dreams** (Your dreams & what they mean), 1938, Whitman, 36 pgs., 2 1/2" x 3 1/2", Penny Book	4	10	24	35
24- **Dumb Dora and Bing Brown**, 1936, Lynn	12	30	72	115
1400- **Dumbo, of the Circus - Only His Ears Grew!** (Disney), 1941, Whitman, 432 pgs., based on Disney movie	21	53	147	240
10- **Dumbo the Flying Elephant** (Disney), 1944, Dell, 194 pgs., Fast-Action Story, soft-c	33	83	235	400
nn- **East O' the Sun and West O' the Moon**, nd (1930s), np (Whitman), 36 pgs., " x 2 1/2", Penny Book	3	8	21	30
774- **Eddie Cantor in An Hour with You**, 1934, Whitman, 154 pgs., 4 1/4" x 5 1/4", photo-c, movie scenes	12	30	80	130
nn- **Eddie Cantor in Laughland**, 1934, Goldsmith, 132 pgs., soft-c, photo-c, Vallely-a	12	30	80	130
1106- **Ella Cinders and the Mysterious House**, 1934, Whitman, 432 pgs.	13	33	85	135
nn- **Ella Cinders and the Mysterious House**, 1934, Whitman, 52 pgs., premium-no ads, soft-c, 3 1/2" x 5 3/4"	15	38	108	170
nn- **Ella Cinders and the Mysterious House**, 1934, Whitman, 52 pgs., Lemix Korlix desserts ad by Perkins Products Co. on back-c, soft-c, 3 1/2" x 5 3/4"	18	45	128	200
nn- **Ella Cinders**, 1935, Whitman, 148 pgs., 3 1/4" x 4", Tarzan Ice Cream cup lid premium	23	58		280
nn- **Ella Cinders Plays Duchess**, 1938, Whitman, 68 pgs., 3 3/4" x 3 1/2", Pan-Am Oil premium	17	43	119	185
nn- **Ella Cinders Solves a Mystery**, 1938, Whitman, 68 pgs., Pan-Am Oil				

	GD	FN	VF	VF/NM
premium, soft-c	17	43	119	185

11- Ella Cinders' Exciting Experience, 1934, Whitman, 3 1/2" x 3 1/2",
132 pgs., Tarzan Ice Cream cup lid giveaway — 23, 58, 165, 280
1406- Ellery Queen the Adventure of the Last Man Club,
1940, Whitman, 432 pgs. — 12, 30, 80, 130
1472- Ellery Queen the Master Detective, 1942, Whitman, 432 pgs.,
flip pictures — 12, 30, 80, 130
1081- Elmer and his Dog Spot, 1935, Saalfield, hard-c — 8, 20, 50, 80
1311- Elmer and his Dog Spot, 1935, Saalfield, soft-c — 8, 20, 50, 80
722- Erik Noble and the Forty-Niners, 1934, Whitman, 384 pgs. — 8, 20, 50, 80
nn- Erik Noble and the Forty-Niners, 1934, Whitman, 386 pgs.,
3-color, soft-c (Rare) — 33, 83, 235, 400
684- Famous Comics (in open box), 1934, Whitman, 48 pgs., 3 3/4" x 8 1/2",
(3 books in set): Book 1 - Katzenjammer Kids, Barney Google, & Little Jimmy
Book 2 - Polly and Her Pals, Little Jimmy, & Katzenjammer Kids
Book 3 - Little Annie Rooney, Katzenjammer Kids, & Polly and Her Pals
Complete set — 48, 120, 336, 625
2019-(#19)- Fantastic Four in the House of Horrors, 1968, Whitman,
256 pgs., hard-c, color illos. — 3, 8, 21, 30
5775- Fantastic Four in the House of Horrors, 1976, Whitman,
256 pgs., soft-c, B&W illos. — 2, 3, 15, 20
5775-1- Fantastic Four in the House of Horrors, 1976, Whitman,
256 pgs., soft-c, B&W illos. — 2, 3, 15, 20
1058- Farmyard Symphony, The (Disney), 1939, 5" X 5 1/2",
68 pgs., hard-c — 12, 30, 72, 115
1129- Felix the Cat, 1936, Whitman, 432 pgs., Messmer-a — 24, 60, 168, 285
1439- Felix the Cat, 1943, Whitman, All Pictures Comics,
Messmer-a — 21, 53, 149, 250
1465- Felix the Cat, 1945, Whitman, All Pictures Comics,
Messmer-a — 16, 40, 112, 175
nn- Felix (Flip book), 1967, World Retrospective of Animation Cinema,
188 pgs., 2 1/2" x 4" by Otto Messmer — 3, 8, 21, 30
nn- Fighting Cowboy of Nugget Gulch, The, 1939, Whitman,
2 1/2" x 3 1/2", Penny Book — 3, 8, 21, 30
1401- Fighting Heroes Battle for Freedom, 1943, Whitman, All Pictures
Comics, from "Heroes of Democracy" strip, by Stookie Allen — 8, 20, 50, 80
6- Fighting President, The, 1934, EVW (Five Star Library), 160 pgs.,
photo-c, photo ill., F. D. Roosevelt — 11, 28, 68, 110
nn- Fire Chief Ed Wynn and "His Old Fire Horse," 1934, Goldsmith,
132 pgs., H. Vallely-a, photo, soft-c — 10, 25, 60, 95
1464- Flame Boy and the Indians' Secret, 1938, Whitman, 300 pgs.,
Sekakuku-a (Hopi Indian) — 8, 20, 50, 80
22- Flaming Guns, 1935, EVW, with Tom Mix, movie scenes
Hardcover — 42, 105, 294, 500
Softcover — 44, 110, 308, 550
1110- Flash Gordon on the Planet Mongo, 1934, Whitman,
320 pgs., by Alex Raymond — 41, 103, 287, 490
1166- Flash Gordon and the Monsters of Mongo, 1935, Whitman,
432 pgs., by Alex Raymond — 39, 98, 273, 470
nn- Flash Gordon and the Monsters of Mongo, 1935, Whitman, 436 pgs.,
premium-no ads, 3-color, soft-c, by Raymond — 62, 155, 434, 800
1171- Flash Gordon and the Tournaments of Mongo, 1935, Whitman,
432 pgs., by Alex Raymond — 37, 93, 260, 450
1190- Flash Gordon and the Witch Queen of Mongo, 1936,
Whitman, 432 pgs., by Alex Raymond — 37, 93, 260, 450
1407- Flash Gordon in the Water World of Mongo, 1937,
Whitman, 432 pgs., by Alex Raymond — 32, 80, 224, 385
1423- Flash Gordon and the Perils of Mongo, 1940, Whitman,
432 pgs., by Alex Raymond — 29, 73, 203, 350
1424- Flash Gordon in the Jungles of Mongo, 1947, Whitman,
352 pgs., by Alex Raymond — 22, 55, 155, 265
1443- Flash Gordon in the Ice World of Mongo, 1942, Whitman,
432 pgs., flip pictures, by Alex Raymond — 30, 75, 210, 360
1447- Flash Gordon and the Fiery Desert of Mongo, 1948,
Whitman, 288 pgs., Raymond-a — 22, 55, 154, 260
1469- Flash Gordon and the Power Men of Mongo, 1943,
Whitman, 352 pgs., by Alex Raymond — 31, 78, 217, 375
1479- Flash Gordon and the Red Sword Invaders, 1945,
Whitman, 352 pgs., by Alex Raymond — 29, 73, 203, 350
1484- Flash Gordon and the Tyrant of Mongo, 1941, Whitman,
432 pgs., flip pictures, by Alex Raymond — 31, 78, 217, 375
1492- Flash Gordon in the Forest Kingdom of Mongo, 1938,
Whitman, 432 pgs., by Alex Raymond — 41, 103, 287, 490
12- Flash Gordon and the Ape Men of Mor, 1942, Dell, 196 pgs.,
Fast-Action Story, by Alex Raymond — 37, 93, 260, 450
6833- Flash Gordon Vs. the Emperor of Mongo, 1936, Dell, 244 pgs.,
Cartoon Story Books, Raymond-c/a — 44, 110, 308, 550
nn- Flash Gordon Vs. the Emperor of Mongo, 1936, Dell, 244 pgs.,
Fast-Action Story, soft-c, Alex Raymond-c/a — 37, 93, 260, 450
1467- Flint Roper and the Six-Gun Showdown, 1941, Whitman,
300 pgs. — 10, 25, 60, 95
2014-(#14)- Flintstones-The Case of the Many Missing Things, 1968, Whitman,
260 pgs., 39 cents, hard-c, color illos — 3, 8, 22, 32

nn- Flintstones: A Friend From the Past, 1977, Modern Promotions,
244 pgs., 49 cents, soft-c, flip pictures — 2, 3, 12, 15
nn- Flintstones: It's About Time, 1977, Modern Promotions,
244 pgs., 49 cents, soft-c, flip pictures — 2, 3, 12, 15
nn- Flintstones: Pebbles & Bamm-Bamm Meet Santa Claus, 1977,
Modern Promotions, 244 pgs., 49 cents, soft-c, flip pictures — 2, 3, 12, 15
nn- Flintstones: The Great Balloon Race, 1977, Modern Promotions,
244 pgs., 49 cents, soft-c, flip pictures — 2, 3, 12, 15
nn- Flintstones: The Mystery of the Many Missing Things, 1977,
Modern Promotions, 244 pgs., 49 cents, soft-c, flip pictures — 2, 3, 12, 15
2003-(#3)- Flipper-Killer Whale Trouble, 1967, Whitman, 260 pgs.,
hard-c, 39 cents, color illos — 2, 3, 15, 20
2032-(#32)- Flipper, Deep-Sea Photographer, 1969, Whitman, 256 pgs.,
hard-c, color illos. — 2, 3, 15, 20
1108- Flying the Sky Clipper with Winsie Atkins, 1936,
Whitman, 432 pgs. — 10, 25, 60, 95
1460- Foreign Spies Doctor Doom and the Ghost Submarine,
1939, Whitman, 432 pgs., Al McWilliams-a — 12, 30, 74, 120
1100B- Fortune Teller, 1938, Whitman, 36 pgs., 2 1/2" x 3 1/2", Penny Book — 2, 3, 16, 22
1175- Frank Buck Presents Ted Towers Animal Master,
1935, Whitman, 432 pgs. — 11, 28, 68, 110
2015-(#15)-Frankenstein, Jr. - The Menace of the Heartless Monster, 1968,
Whitman, 260 pgs., 39 cents, hard-c, color illos. — 3, 8, 20, 28
16- Frankie Thomas in A Dog of Flanders, 1935, EVW,
movie scenes — 11, 28, 68, 110
1121- Frank Merriwell at Yale, 1935, 432 pgs. — 10, 25, 60, 95
Freckles and His Friends in the North Woods (See Top-Line Comics)
nn- Freckles and His Friends Stage a Play, 1938, Whitman,
36 pgs., 2 1/2" x 3 1/2", Penny Book — 10, 25, 60, 95
1164- Freckles and the Lost Diamond Mine, 1937, Whitman,
432 pgs., Merrill Blosser-a — 11, 28, 68, 110
nn- Freckles and the Mystery Ship, 1935, Whitman, 66 pgs.,
Pan-Am premium — 12, 30, 72, 115
1100B- Fun, Puzzles, Riddles, 1938, Whitman, 36 pgs., 2 1/2" x 3 1/2",
Penny Book — 2, 3, 16, 22
1433- Gang Busters Step In, 1939, Whitman, 432 pgs., Henry E. Vallely-a — 11, 28, 68, 110
1437- Gang Busters Smash Through, 1942, Whitman, 432 pgs. — 11, 28, 68, 110
1451- Gang Busters in Action!, 1938, Whitman, 432 pgs. — 11, 28, 68, 110
nn- Gang Busters and Guns of the Law, 1940, Dell, 4" x 5", 194 pgs.,
Fast-Action Story, soft-c — 28, 70, 196, 340
nn- Gang Busters and the Radio Clues, 1938, Whitman, 36 pgs.,
2 1/2" x 3 1/2", Penny Book — 8, 20, 48, 75
1409- Gene Autry and Raiders of the Range, 1946, Whitman,
352 pgs. — 12, 30, 76, 125
1425- Gene Autry and the Mystery of Paint Rock Canyon,
1947, Whitman, 288 pgs. — 12, 30, 76, 125
1428- Gene Autry Special Ranger, 1941, Whitman, 432 pgs., Erwin Hess-a — 15, 38, 105, 165
1433- Gene Autry in Public Cowboy No. 1, 1938, Whitman, 240 pgs.,
photo-c, movie scenes (1st Autry BLB) — 28, 70, 196, 340
1434- Gene Autry and the Gun-Smoke Reckoning, 1943,
Whitman, 352 pgs. — 15, 38, 100, 160
1439- Gene Autry and the Land Grab Mystery, 1948, Whitman,
290 pgs. — 12, 30, 74, 120
1456- Gene Autry in Special Ranger Rule, 1945, Whitman,
352 pgs., Henry E. Vallely-a — 15, 38, 100, 160
1461- Gene Autry and the Red Bandit's Ghost, 1949, Whitman,
288 pgs. — 12, 30, 72, 115
1483- Gene Autry in Law of the Range, 1939, Whitman, 432 pgs. — 15, 38, 100, 160
1493- Gene Autry and the Hawk of the Hills, 1942, Whitman,
428 pgs., flip pictures, Vallely-a — 15, 38, 100, 160
1494- Gene Autry Cowboy Detective, 1940, Whitman, 432 pgs.,
Erwin Hess-a — 15, 38, 100, 160
700-10- Gene Autry and the Bandits of Silver Tip, 1949,
Whitman — 12, 30, 72, 115
714-10- Gene Autry and the Range War, 1950, Whitman — 12, 30, 72, 115
nn- Gene Autry in Gun-Smoke, 1938, Dell, 196 pgs., Fast-Action story,
soft-c — 27, 68, 189, 325
2035-(#35)- Gentle Ben, Mystery of the Everglades, 1969, Whitman, 256 pgs.,
hard-c, color illos. — 2, 3, 15, 20
1176- Gentleman Joe Palooka, 1940, Saalfield, 400 pgs. — 10, 25, 60, 95
George O'Brien (See The Cowboy Millionaire)
1101- George O'Brien and the Arizona Badman, 1936?,
Whitman — 10, 25, 60, 95
1418- George O'Brien in Gun Law, 1938, Whitman, 240 pgs., photo-c,
movie scenes, RKO Radio Pictures — 10, 25, 60, 95
1457- George O'Brien and the Hooded Riders, 1940, Whitman,
432 pgs., Erwin Hess-a — 8, 20, 50, 80

1479 - Flash Gordon and the Red Sword Invaders © KFS

2021 - Goofy in Giant Trouble © DIS

1403 - Invisible Scarlet O'Neil © WHIT

	GD	FN	VF	VF/NM
nn- George O'Brien and the Arizona Bad Man, 1939, Whitman, 36 pgs., 2 1/2" x 3 1/2", Penny Book	8	20	50	80
1462- Ghost Avenger, 1943, Whitman, 432 pgs., flip pictures, Henry Vallely-a	10	25	60	95
nn- Ghost Gun Gang Meet Their Match, The, 1939. Whitman, 2 1/2" x 3 1/2", Penny Book	8	20	50	80
nn- Gingerbread Boy, The, nd(1930s), np(Whitman), 36 pgs., Penny Book	2	3	15	20
1118- G-Man on the Crime Trail, 1936, Whitman, 432 pgs.	12	30	74	120
1147- G-Man Vs. the Red X, 1936, Whitman, 432 pgs.	13	33	90	140
1162- G-Man Allen, 1939, Saalfield, 400 pgs.	12	30	74	120
1173- G-Man in Action, A, 1940, Saalfield, 400 pgs., J.R. White-a	12	30	74	120
1434- G-Man and the Radio Bank Robberies, 1937, Whitman, 432 pgs.	13	33	90	140
1469- G-Man and the Gun Runners, The, 1940, Whitman, 432 pgs.	13	33	90	140
1470- G-Man vs. the Fifth Column, 1941, Whitman, 432 pgs., flip pictures	13	33	90	140
1493- G-Man Breaking the Gambling Ring, 1938, Whitman, 432 pgs., James Gary-a	13	33	90	140
nn- G-Man on Lightning Island, 1936, Dell, 244 pgs., Fast-Action Story, soft-c, Henry E. Vallely-a	24	60	168	285
nn- G-Man, Underworld Chief, 1938, Whitman, Buddy Book premium,	27	68	189	325
6833- G-Man on Lightning Island, 1936, Dell, 244 pgs., Cartoon Story Book, hard-c, Henry E. Vallely-a	18	45	128	200
4- G-Men Foil the Kidnappers, 1936, Whitman, 132 pgs., 3 1/2" x 3 1/2", soft-c, Tarzan Ice Cream cup lid premium	23	58	165	280
1157- G-Men on the Trail, 1938, Saalfield, 400 pgs.	10	25	64	100
1168- G Men on the Job, 1935, Whitman, 432 pgs.	12	30	76	125
nn- G-Men on the Job Again, 1938, Whitman, 36 pgs., 2 1/2" x 3 1/2", Penny Book	10	25	64	100
nn- G-Men and Kidnap Justice, 1938, Whitman, 68 pgs., Pan-Am premium, soft-c	12	30	76	125
nn- G-Men and the Missing Clues, 1938, Whitman, 36 pgs., 2 1/2"x 3 1/2", Penny Book	10	25	64	100
1097- Go Into Your Dance, 1935, Saalfield, 160 pgs.. photo-c, movie scenes with Al Jolson & Ruby Keeler	12	30	80	130
1577- Go Into Your Dance, 1935, Saalfield, 160 pgs., photo-c, movie scenes, soft-c	12	30	80	130
2021- Goofy in Giant Trouble (Walt Disney's ...), 1968, Whitman, hard-c, 260 pgs., 39 cents, color illos.	2	3	15	20
5751- Goofy in Giant Trouble (Walt Disney's ...), 1968, Whitman, soft-c, 260 pgs., 39 cents, color illos.	2	3	15	20
5751-2- Goofy in Giant Trouble, 1968 (1980-reprint of '67 version), Whitman, soft-c, 260 pgs., 79 cents, B&W	1	3	6	10
8- Great Expectations, 1934, EVW, (Five Star Library), 160 pgs., photo-c, movie scenes	14	35	95	150
1453- Green Hornet Strikes!, The, 1940, Whitman, 432 pgs., Robert Weisman-a	35	88	248	425
1480- Green Hornet Cracks Down, The, 1942, Whitman, 432 pgs., flip pictures, Henry Vallely-a	33	83	235	400
1496- Green Hornet Returns, The, 1941, Whitman, 432 pgs., flip pictures	35	88	248	425
5778- Grimm's Ghost Stories, 1976, Whitman, 256 pgs., Laura French-s adapted from fairy tales; blue spine & back-c	1	3	10	14
5778-1- Grimm's Ghost Stories, 1976, Whitman, 256 pgs., reprint of #5778; yellow spine & back-c	1	3	10	14
1172- Gullivers' Travels, 1939, Saalfield, 320 pgs., adapted from Paramount Pict. Cartoons (Rare) Hardcover	25	63	175	300
(Scarce) Softcover	28	70	196	340
nn- Gumps In Radio Land, The (Andy Gump and the Chest of Gold), 1937, Lehn & Fink Prod. Corp., 100 pgs., 3 1/4" x 5 1/2", Pebeco Tooth Paste giveaway, by Gus Edson	20	50	140	220
nn- Gunmen of Rustlers' Gulch, The, 1939, Whitman, 36 pgs., 2 1/2" x 3 1/2", Penny Book	6	15	40	60
1426- Guns in the Roaring West, 1937, Whitman, 300 pgs.	6	15	40	60
1647- Gunsmoke (TV Series), 1958, Whitman, 280 pgs., 4 1/2" x 5 3/4"	4	10	27	40
1101- Hairbreath Harry in Department QT, 1935, Whitman, 384 pgs., by J. M. Alexander	9	23	56	90
1413- Hal Hardy in the Lost Land of Giants, 1938, Whitman, 300 pgs., "The World 1,000,000 Years Ago"	22	55	154	260
1159- Hall of Fame of the Air, 1936, Whitman, 432 pgs., by Capt. Eddie Rickenbacker	9	23	54	85
nn- Hansel and Grethel, The Story of, nd (1930s), no publ., 36 pgs., Penny Book	3	8	21	30
1145- Hap Lee's Selection of Movie Gags, 1935, Whitman, 160 pgs., photos of stars	12	30	80	130
Happy Prince, The (See Wee Little Books)				
1111- Hard Rock Harrigan-A Story of Boulder Dam, 1935, Saalfield, hard-c, photo-c, photo illos.	10	25	64	100
1591- Hard Rock Harrigan-A Story of Boulder Dam, 1935, Saalfield, soft-c, photo-c, photo illos.	10	25	64	100
1418- Harold Teen Swinging at the Sugar Bowl, 1939, Whitman, 432 pgs., by Carl Ed	10	25	64	100
nn- Hercules - The Legendary Journeys, 1998, Chronicle Books, 310 pgs., based on TV series, 1-color (brown) illos	1	3	6	10
1100B- Hobbies, 1938, Whitman, 36 pgs., 2 1/2" x 3 1/2", Penny Book	3	8	18	25
1125- Hockey Spare, The, 1937, Saalfield, hard-c	6	15	36	55
1605- Hockey Spare, The, 1937, Saalfield, soft-c	6	15	36	55
728- Homeless Homer, 1934, Whitman, by Dee Dobbin, for young kids	3	8	22	32
17- Hoosier Schoolmaster, The, 1935, EVW, movie scenes	12	30	80	130
715- Houdini's Big Little Book of Magic, 1927 (1933), 300 pgs.	17	43	119	185
nn- Houdini's Big Little Book of Magic, 1927 (1933), 196 pgs., American Oil Co. premium, soft-c	17	43	119	185
nn- Houdini's Big Little Book of Magic, 1927 (1933), 204 pgs., Cocomalt premium, soft-c	17	43	119	185
Huckleberry Finn (See The Adventures of...)				
nn- Huckleberry Hound Newspaper Reporter, 1977, Modern Promotions, 244 pgs., 49 cents, soft-c, flip pictures	1	3	10	14
1644- Hugh O'Brian TV's Wyatt Earp (TV Series), 1958, Whitman, 280 pgs.	3	8	22	32
5782-2- Incredible Hulk Lost in Time, 1980, 260 pgs., 79¢-c, soft-c, B&W	1	3	8	12
1424- Inspector Charlie Chan Villainy on the High Seas, 1942, Whitman, 432 pgs., flip pictures	15	38	100	160
1186- Inspector Wade of Scotland Yard, 1940, Saalfield, 400 pgs.	10	25	60	95
1194- Inspector Wade and The Feathered Serpent, 1939, Saalfield, 400 pgs.	10	25	60	95
1448- Inspector Wade Solves the Mystery of the Red Aces, 1937, Whitman, 432 pgs.	10	25	60	95
1148- International Spy Doctor Doom Faces Death at Dawn, 1937, Whitman, 432 pgs., Arbo-a	12	30	74	120
1155- In the Name of the Law, 1937, Whitman, 432 pgs., Henry E. Vallely-a	10	25	60	95
2012-(#12)-Invaders, The-Alien Missile Threat (TV Series), 1967, Whitman, 260 pgs., hard-c, 39 cents, color illos.	3	8	20	28
1403- Invisible Scarlet O'Neil, 1942, Whitman, All Pictures Comics, flip pictures	13	33	90	140
1406- Invisible Scarlet O'Neil Versus the King of the Slums, 1946, Whitman, 352 pgs.	11	28	68	110
1098- It Happened One Night, 1935, Saalfield, 160 pgs., Little Big Book, Clark Gable, Claudette Colbert photo-c, movie scenes from Academy Award winner	15	38	100	160
1578- It Happened One Night, 1935, Saalfield, 160 pgs., soft-c	15	38	100	160
Jack and Jill (See Wee Little Books)				
1432- Jack Armstrong and the Mystery of the Iron Key, 1939, Whitman, 432 pgs., Henry E. Vallely-a	13	33	90	140
1435- Jack Armstrong and the Ivory Treasure, 1937, Whitman, 432 pgs., Henry Vallely-a	13	33	90	140

	GD	FN	VF	VF/NM

Jackie Cooper (See Story Of..)

1084- Jackie Cooper in Peck's Bad Boy, 1934, Saalfield, 160 pgs., hard, photo-c, movie scenes — 15 / 38 / 100 / 160

1314- Jackie Cooper in Peck's Bad Boy, 1934, Saalfield, 160 pgs., soft, photo-c, movie scenes — 15 / 38 / 100 / 160

1402- Jackie Cooper in "Gangster's Boy," 1939, Whitman, 240 pgs., photo-c, movie scenes — 15 / 38 / 100 / 160

13- Jackie Cooper in Dinky, 1935, EVW, 160 pgs., movie scenes — 15 / 38 / 100 / 160

nn- Jack King of the Secret Service and the Counterfeiters, 1939, Whitman, 36 pgs., 2 1/2" x 3 1/2", Penny Book, by John G. Gray — 10 / 25 / 64 / 100

L11- Jack London's Call of the Wild, 1935, Lynn, 20th Cent. Pic., movie scenes with Clark Gable — 12 / 30 / 74 / 120

nn- Jack Pearl as Detective Baron Munchausen, 1934, Goldsmith, 132 pgs., soft-c — 12 / 30 / 80 / 130

1102- Jack Swift and His Rocket Ship, 1934, Whitman, 320 pgs. — 16 / 40 / 112 / 175

1498- Jane Arden the Vanished Princess, Whitman, 300 pgs. — 10 / 25 / 60 / 95

1179- Jane Withers in This is the Life (20th Century-Fox Presents...), 1935, Whitman, 240 pgs., photo-c, movie scenes — 12 / 30 / 80 / 130

1463- Jane Withers in Keep Smiling, 1938, Whitman, 240 pgs., photo-c, movie scenes — 12 / 30 / 80 / 130

Jaragu of the Jungle (See Rex Beach's ...)

1447- Jerry Parker Police Reporter and the Candid Camera Clue, 1941, Whitman, 300 pgs. — 10 / 25 / 60 / 95

Jim Bowie (See Adventures of ...)

nn- Jim Brant of the Highway Patrol and the Mysterious Accident, 1939, Whitman, 36 pgs., 2 1/2" x 3 1/2", Penny Book — 9 / 23 / 54 / 85

1466- Jim Craig State Trooper and the Kidnapped Governor, 1938, Whitman, 432 pgs. — 10 / 25 / 60 / 95

nn- Jim Doyle Private Detective and the Train Hold-Up, 1939, Whitman, 36 pgs., 2 1/2" x 3 1/2", Penny Book — 10 / 25 / 64 / 100

1180- Jim Hardy Ace Reporter, 1940, Saalfield, 400 pgs., Dick Moores-a — 10 / 25 / 64 / 100

1143- Jimmy Allen in the Air Mail Robbery, 1936, Whitman, 432 pgs. — 10 / 25 / 64 / 100

27- Jimmy Allen in The Sky Parade, 1936, Lynn, 130 pgs., 5 x 7 1/2", Paramount Pictures, movie scenes — 12 / 30 / 74 / 120

L15- Jimmy and the Tiger, 1935, Lynn, 192 pgs. — 10 / 25 / 64 / 100

1428- Jim Starr of the Border Patrol, 1937, Whitman, 432 pgs. — 10 / 25 / 64 / 100

Joan of Arc (See Wee Little Books)

1105- Joe Louis the Brown Bomber, 1936, Whitman, 240 pgs., photo-c, photo-illos. — 22 / 55 / 154 / 260

Joe Palooka (See Gentleman ...)

1123- Joe Palooka the Heavyweight Boxing Champ, 1934, Whitman, 320 pgs., Ham Fisher-a — 17 / 43 / 123 / 190

1168- Joe Palooka's Great Adventure, 1939, Saalfield — 15 / 38 / 100 / 160

nn- Joe Penner's Duck Farm, 1935, Goldsmith, Henry Vallely-a — 11 / 28 / 68 / 110

1402- John Carter of Mars, 1940, Whitman, 432 pgs., John Coleman Burroughs-a — 52 / 130 / 364 / 675

nn- John Carter of Mars, 1940, Dell, 194 pgs., Fast-Action Story, soft-c — 63 / 159 / 444 / 825

1164- Johnny Forty Five, 1938, Saalfield, 400 pgs. — 9 / 23 / 56 / 90

John Wayne (See Westward Ho!)

1100B- Jokes (A book of laughs galore), 1938, Whitman, 36 pgs., 2 1/2" x 3 1/2", Penny Book, laughing guy-c — 2 / 3 / 15 / 20

1100B- Jokes (A book of side-splitting funny stories), 1938, Whitman, 36 pgs., 2 1/2" x 3 1/2", Penny Book, clowns on-c — 2 / 3 / 15 / 20

2026-(#26)- Journey to the Center of the Earth, The Fiery Foe, 1968, Whitman — 3 / 8 / 21 / 30

Jungle Jim (See Top-Line Comics)

1138- Jungle Jim, 1936, Whitman, 432 pgs., Alex Raymond-a — 22 / 55 / 154 / 260

1139- Jungle Jim and the Vampire Woman, 1937, Whitman, 432 pgs., Alex Raymond-a — 22 / 55 / 154 / 260

1442- Junior G-Men, 1937, Whitman, 432 pgs., Henry E. Vallely-a — 11 / 28 / 68 / 110

nn- Junior G-Men Solve a Crime, 1939, Whitman, 36 pgs., 2 1/2" x 3 1/2", Penny Book — 11 / 28 / 68 / 110

1422- Junior Nebb on the Diamond Bar Ranch, 1938, Whitman, 300 pgs., by Sol Hess — 11 / 28 / 68 / 110

1470- Junior Nebb Joins the Circus, 1939, Whitman, 300 pgs. by Sol Hess — 11 / 28 / 68 / 110

nn- Junior Nebb Elephant Trainer, 1939, Whitman, 68 pgs., Pan-Am Oil premium, soft-c — 13 / 33 / 85 / 135

1052- "Just Kids" (Adventures of ...), 1934, Saalfield, oblong size, by Ad Carter — 17 / 43 / 123 / 190

1094- Just Kids and the Mysterious Stranger, 1935, Saalfield, 160 pgs., by Ad Carter — 13 / 33 / 85 / 135

1184- Just Kids and Deep-Sea Dan, 1940, Saalfield, 400 pgs., by Ad Carter — 12 / 30 / 72 / 115

1302- Just Kids, The Adventures of, 1934, Saalfield, oblong size, soft-c, by Ad Carter — 18 / 45 / 128 / 200

1324- Just Kids and the Mysterious Stranger, 1935, Saalfield, 160 pgs., soft-c, by Ad Carter — 13 / 33 / 85 / 135

1401- Just Kids, 1937, Whitman, 432 pgs., by Ad Carter — 13 / 33 / 85 / 135

1055- Katzenjammer Kids in the Mountains, 1934, Saalfield, hard-c, oblong, H. H. Knerr-a — 16 / 40 / 112 / 175

1305- Katzenjammer Kids in the Mountains, 1934, Saalfield, soft-c, oblong, H. H. Knerr-a — 16 / 40 / 112 / 175

14- Katzenjammer Kids, The, 1942, Dell, 194 pgs., Fast-Action Story, H. H. Knerr-a — 17 / 43 / 123 / 190

1411- Kay Darcy and the Mystery Hideout, 1937, Whitman, 300 pgs., Charles Mueller-a — 12 / 30 / 80 / 130

1180- Kayo in the Land of Sunshine (With Moon Mullins), 1937, Whitman, 432 pgs., by Willard — 13 / 33 / 90 / 140

1415- Kayo and Moon Mullins and the One Man Gang, 1939, Whitman, 432 pgs., by Frank Willard — 11 / 28 / 68 / 110

7- Kayo and Moon Mullins 'Way Down South, 1938, Whitman, 132 pgs., 3 1/2" x 3 1/2", Buddy Book — 20 / 50 / 140 / 220

1105- Kazan in Revenge of the North (James Oliver Curwood's...), 1937, Whitman, 432 pgs., Henry E. Vallely-a — 10 / 25 / 60 / 95

1471- Kazan, King of the Pack (James Oliver Curwood's...), 1940, Whitman, 432 pgs. — 9 / 23 / 54 / 85

1420- Keep 'Em Flying! U.S.A. for America's Defense, 1943, Whitman, 432 pgs., Henry E. Vallely-a, flip pictures — 10 / 25 / 60 / 95

1133- Kelly King at Yale Hall, 1937, Saalfield — 9 / 23 / 54 / 85

Ken Maynard (See Strawberry Roan & Western Frontier)

5- Ken Maynard in "Wheels of Destiny," 1934, EVW, 160 pgs., movie scenes (scarce) — 18 / 45 / 128 / 200

776- Ken Maynard in "Gun Justice," 1934, Whitman, 160 pgs., hard-c, movie scenes (Universal Pic.) — 13 / 33 / 90 / 140

776- Ken Maynard in "Gun Justice," 1934, Whitman, 160 pgs., soft-c, movie scenes (Universal Pic.) — 13 / 33 / 90 / 140

1430- Ken Maynard in Western Justice, 1938, Whitman, 432 pgs., Irwin Myers-a — 11 / 28 / 68 / 110

1442- Ken Maynard and the Gun Wolves of the Gila, 1939, Whitman, 432 pgs. — 11 / 28 / 68 / 110

nn- Ken Maynard in Six-Gun Law, 1938, Whitman, 36 pgs., 2 1/2" x 3 1/2", Penny Book — 9 / 23 / 54 / 85

1134- King of Crime, 1938, Saalfield, 400 pgs. — 10 / 25 / 60 / 95

King of the Royal Mounted (See Zane Grey)

nn- Kit Carson, 1933, World Syndicate, by J. Carroll Mansfield, High Lights Of History Series, hard-c — 10 / 25 / 60 / 95

nn- Kit Carson, 1933, World Syndicate, same as hard-c above but with a black cloth-c — 10 / 25 / 60 / 95

1105- Kit Carson and the Mystery Riders, 1935, Saalfield, hard-c, Johnny Mack Brown photo-c, movie scenes — 13 / 33 / 85 / 135

1585- Kit Carson and the Mystery Riders, 1935, Saalfield, soft-c, Johnny Mack Brown photo-c, movie scenes — 13 / 33 / 85 / 135

Krazy Kat (See Adventures of...)

2004- (#4)-Lassie-Adventure in Alaska (TV Series), 1967, Whitman, hard-c, 260 pgs., 39 cents, color illos — 3 / 8 / 20 / 29

5754- Lassie-Adventure in Alaska (TV Series), 1973, Whitman, soft-c, 260 pgs., 49 cents, color illos — 2 / 3 / 12 / 16

2027- Lassie and the Shabby Sheik (TV Series), 1968, Whitman, hard-c, 260 pgs., 39 cents — 3 / 8 / 19 / 26

5762- Lassie and the Shabby Sheik (TV Series), 1972, Whitman, soft-c, 260 pgs., 39 cents — 2 / 3 / 12 / 16

5769- Lassie, Old One-Eye (TV Series), 1975, Whitman, soft-c, 260 pgs., 49 cents, three printings — 2 / 3 / 10 / 15

1132- Last Days of Pompeii, The, 1935, Whitman, 5 1/4" x 6 1/4", 260 pgs., movie scenes — 14 / 35 / 95 / 150

1128- Last Man Out (Baseball), 1937, Saalfield, hard-c — 10 / 25 / 64 / 100

L30- Last of the Mohicans, The, 1936, Lynn, 192 pgs., movie scenes with Randolph Scott, United Artists Pictures — 13 / 33 / 90 / 140

1126- Laughing Dragon of Oz, The, 1934, Whitman 432 pgs., by Frank Baum (scarce) — 90 / 225 / 630 / 1275

1086- Laurel and Hardy, 1934, Saalfield, 160 pgs., hard-c, photo-c, movie scenes — 20 / 50 / 140 / 220

1316- Laurel and Hardy, 1934, Saalfield, 160 pgs. soft-c, photo-c, movie scenes — 20 / 50 / 140 / 220

1092- Law of the Wild, The, 1935, Saalfield, 160 pgs., photo-c, movie scenes of Rex, The Wild Horse & Rin-Tin-Tin Jr. — 11 / 28 / 68 / 110

1322- Law of the Wild, The, 1935, Saalfield, 160 pgs., photo-c, movie scenes, soft-c — 11 / 28 / 68 / 110

1100B- Learn to be a Ventriloquist, 1938, Whitman, 36 pgs. 2 1/2" x 3 1/2", Penny Book — 2 / 3 / 15 / 20

1149- Lee Brady Range Detective, 1938, Saalfield, 400 pgs. — 10 / 25 / 60 / 95

L10- Les Miserables (Victor Hugo's ...), 1935, Lynn, 192 pgs., by — 14 / 35 / 100 / 160

1441- Lightning Jim U.S. Marshal Brings Law to the West, 1940, Whitman, 432 pgs., based on radio program — 10 / 25 / 64 / 100

nn- Lightning Jim Whipple U.S. Marshal in Indian Territory, 1939, Whitman, 36 pgs., 2 1/2" x 3 1/2", Penny Book — 8 / 20 / 48 / 75

653- Lions and Tigers (With Clyde Beatty), 1934, Whitman, 160 pgs.,

1180 - Jim Hardy Ace Reporter © Saalfield

1128 - Last Man Out © Saalfield

1186 - Little Orphan Annie and the $1,000,000 Formula © WHIT

	GD	FN	VF	VF/NM
photo-c movie scenes	12	30	80	130
1187- Li'l Abner and the Ratfields, 1940, Saalfield, 400 pgs., by Al Capp	14	35	95	150
1193- Li'l Abner and Sadie Hawkins Day, 1940, Saalfield, 400 pgs., by Al Capp	14	35	95	150
1198- Li'l Abner in New York, 1936, Whitman, 432 pgs., by Al Capp	15	38	100	160
1401- Li'l Abner Among the Millionaires, 1939, Whitman, 432 pgs., by Al Capp	15	38	100	160
1054- Little Annie Rooney, 1934, Saalfield, oblong - 4" x 8", All Pictures Comics, hard-c	14	35	98	155
1304- Little Annie Rooney, 1934, Saalfield, oblong - 4" x 8", All Pictures, soft-c	14	35	98	155
1117- Little Annie Rooney and the Orphan House, 1936, Whitman, 432 pgs.	11	28	68	110
1406- Little Annie Rooney on the Highway to Adventure, 1938, Whitman, 432 pgs.	11	28	68	110
1149- Little Big Shot (With Sybil Jason), 1935, Whitman, 240 pgs., photo-c, movie scenes	12	30	80	130
nn- Little Black Sambo, nd (1930s), np (Whitman), 36 pgs., 3" x 2 1/2", Penny Book	14	35	98	155
Little Bo-Peep (See Wee Little Books)				
Little Colonel, The (See Shirley Temple)				
1148- Little Green Door, The, 1938, Saalfield, 400 pgs.	9	23	56	90
1112- Little Hollywood Stars, 1935, Saalfield, movie scenes (Little Rascals, etc.), hard-c	12	30	80	130
1592- Little Hollywood Stars, 1935, Saalfield, movie scenes, soft-c	12	30	80	130
1087- Little Jimmy's Gold Hunt, 1935, Saalfield, 160 pgs., hard-c, Little Big Book, by Swinnerton	15	38	108	170
1317- Little Jimmy's Gold Hunt, 1935, Saalfield, 160 pgs., 4 1/4" x 5 3/4", soft-c, by Swinnerton	15	38	108	170
Little Joe and the City Gangsters (See Top-Line Comics)				
Little Joe Otter's Slide (See Wee Little Books)				
1118- Little Lord Fauntleroy, 1936, Saalfield, movie scenes, photo-c, 4 1/2" x 5 1/4", starring Mickey Rooney & Freddie Bartholomew, hard-c	10	25	60	95
1598- Little Lord Fauntleroy, 1936, Saalfield, photo-c, movie scenes, soft-c	10	25	60	95
1192- Little Mary Mixup and the Grocery Robberies, 1940, Saalfield	10	25	60	95
8- Little Mary Mixup Wins A Prize, 1936, Whitman, 132 pgs., 3 1/2" x 3 1/2", soft-c, Tarzan Ice Cream cup lid premium	23	58	163	275
1150- Little Men, 1934, Whitman, 4 3/4" x 5 1/4", movie scenes (Mascot Prod.), photo-c, hard-c	10	25	64	100
9- Little Minister, The,-Katharine Hepburn, 1935, 160 pgs., 4 1/4" x 5 1/2", EVW (Five Star Library), movie scenes (RKO)	14	35	98	155
1120- Little Miss Muffet, 1936, Whitman, 432 pgs., by Fanny Y. Cory	11	28	68	110
708- Little Orphan Annie, 1933, Whitman, 320 pgs., by Harold Gray, the 2nd Big Little Book	40	100	280	480
nn- Little Orphan Annie, 1928('33), Whitman, 52 pgs., 4" x 5 1/2", premium-no ads, soft-c, by Harold Gray	27	68	189	325
716- Little Orphan Annie and Sandy, 1933, Whitman, 320 pgs., by Harold Gray	23	58	163	275
716- Little Orphan Annie and Sandy, 1933, Whitman, 300 pgs., by Harold Gray	18	45	128	200
nn- Little Orphan Annie and Sandy, 1933, Whitman, 52 pgs., premium, no ads, 4" x 5 1/2", soft-c by Harold Gray	27	68	189	325
748- Little Orphan Annie and Chizzler, 1933, Whitman, 320 pgs., by Harold Gray	14	35	98	155
1010- Little Orphan Annie and the Big Town Gunmen, 1937, 7 1/4" x 5 1/2", 64 pgs., Nickel Book	12	30	80	130
nn- Little Orphan Annie with the Circus, 1934, Whitman, 320 pgs., same cover as L.O.A. 708 but with blue background, Ovaltine giveaway stamp inside front-c, by Harold Gray	31	78	217	375
1103- Little Orphan Annie with the Circus, 1934, Whitman, 320 pgs.	14	35	98	155
1140- Little Orphan Annie and the Big Train Robbery,				
1934, Whitman, 300 pgs., by Gray	14	35	98	155
1140- Little Orphan Annie and the Big Train Robbery, 1934, Whitman, 300 pgs., premium-no ads, soft-c, by Harold Gray	21	53	149	250
1154- Little Orphan Annie and the Ghost Gang, 1935, Whitman, 432 pgs. by Harold Gray	14	35	98	155
nn- Little Orphan Annie and the Ghost Gang, 1935, Whitman, 436 pgs., premium-no ads, 3-color, soft-c, by Harold Gray	21	53	149	250
1162- Little Orphan Annie and Punjab the Wizard, 1935, Whitman, 432 pgs., by Harold Gray	14	35	98	155
1186- Little Orphan Annie and the $1,000,000 Formula, 1936, Whitman, 432 pgs., by Gray	13	33	90	140
1414- Little Orphan Annie and the Ancient Treasure of Am, 1939, Whitman, 432 pgs., by Gray	12	30	80	130
1416- Little Orphan Annie in the Movies, 1937, Whitman, 432 pgs., by Harold Gray	12	30	80	130
1417- Little Orphan Annie and the Secret of the Well, 1947, Whitman, 352 pgs., by Gray	11	28	68	110
1435- Little Orphan Annie and the Gooneyville Mystery, 1947, Whitman, 288 pgs., by Gray	12	30	72	115
1446- Little Orphan Annie in the Thieves' Den, 1949, Whitman, 288 pgs., by Harold Gray	12	30	72	115
1449- Little Orphan Annie and the Mysterious Shoemaker, 1938, Whitman, 432 pgs., by Harold Gray	12	30	80	130
1457- Little Orphan Annie and Her Junior Commandos, 1943, Whitman, 352 pgs., by H. Gray	10	25	60	95
1461- Little Orphan Annie and the Underground Hide-Out, 1945, Whitman, 352 pgs., by Gray	10	25	60	95
1468- Little Orphan Annie and the Ancient Treasure of Am, 1949 (Misdated 1939), 288 pgs., by Gray	10	25	60	95
1482- Little Orphan Annie and the Haunted Mansion, 1941, Whitman, 432 pgs., flip pictures, by Harold Gray	12	30	80	130
3048- Little Orphan Annie and Her Big Little Kit, 1937, Whitman, 384 pgs., 4 1/2" x 6 1/2" box, includes miniature box of 4 crayons-red, yellow, blue and green	62	155	434	800
4054- Little Orphan Annie, The Story of, 1934, Whitman, 7" x 9 1/2" 320 pgs., Big Big Book, Harold Gray-c/a	27	68	189	325
nn- Little Orphan Annie Gets into Trouble, 1938, Whitman, 36 pgs., 2 1/2" x 3 1/2", Penny Book	9	23	56	90
nn- Little Orphan Annie in Hollywood, 1937, Whitman, 3 1/2" x 3 1/4", Pan-Am premium, soft-c	21	53	149	250
nn- Little Orphan Annie in Rags to Riches, 1939, Dell, 194 pgs., Fast-Action Story, soft-c	21	53	149	250
nn- Little Orphan Annie Saves Sandy, 1938, Whitman, 36 pgs., 2 1/2" x 3 1/2", Penny Book	10	25	60	95
nn- Little Orphan Annie Under the Big Top, 1938, Dell, 194 pgs., Fast-Action Story, soft-c	21	53	149	250
nn- Little Orphan Annie Wee Little Books (In open box)				
nn, 1934, Whitman, 44 pgs., by H. Gray				
L.O.A. And Daddy Warbucks	9	23	54	85
L.O.A. And Her Dog Sandy	9	23	54	85
L.O.A. And The Lucky Knife	9	23	54	85
L.O.A. And The Pinch-Pennys	9	23	54	85
L.O.A. At Happy Home	9	23	54	85
L.O.A. Finds Mickey	9	23	54	85
Complete set with box	54	135	378	700
nn- Little Polly Flinders, The Story of, nd (1930s), no publ., 36 pgs., 2 1/2" x 3", Penny Book	2	3	15	20
nn- Little Red Hen, The, nd(1930s), np(Whitman), 36 pgs., Penny Book	2	3	15	20
nn- Little Red Riding Hood, nd(1930s), np(Whitman), 36 pgs., 3" x 2 1/2", Penny Book	2	3	15	20
nn- Little Red Riding Hood and the Big Bad Wolf (Disney), 1934, McKay, 36 pgs., stiff-c, Disney Studio-a				
Sized (7 3/4" x 10")	23	58	160	270
Different version (6 1/4" x 8 1/2") blue spine	15	38	108	170
757- Little Women, 1934, Whitman, 4 3/4" x 5 1/4", 160 pgs., photo-c, movie scenes, starring Katharine Hepburn	15	38	100	160
Littlest Rebel, The (See Shirley Temple)				
1181- Lone Ranger and his Horse Silver, 1935, Whitman, 432 pgs., Hal Arbo-a	18	45	128	200

	GD	FN	VF	VF/NM

1196- Lone Ranger and the Vanishing Herd, 1936, Whitman,
432 pgs.   15   38   100   160

1407- Lone Ranger and Dead Men's Mine, The, 1939, Whitman,
432 pgs.   13   33   90   140

1421- Lone Ranger on the Barbary Coast, The, 1944, Whitman,
352 pgs., Henry Vallely-a   12   30   74   120

1428- Lone Ranger and the Secret Weapon, The, 1943,
Whitman,   12   30   74   120

1431- Lone Ranger and the Secret Killer, The, 1937, Whitman
432 pgs., H. Anderson-a   15   38   108   170

1450- Lone Ranger and the Black Shirt Highwayman, The,
1939, Whitman, 432 pgs.   13   33   90   140

1465- Lone Ranger and the Menace of Murder Valley, The, 1938,
Whitman, 432 pgs., Robert Wiseman-a   12   30   80   130

1468- Lone Ranger Follows Through, The, 1941, Whitman,
432 pgs., H.E. Vallely-a   12   30   80   130

1477- Lone Ranger and the Great Western Span, The,
1942, Whitman, 424 pgs., H. E. Vallely-a   12   30   74   120

1489- Lone Ranger and the Red Renegades, The, 1939,
Whitman, 432 pgs.   15   38   100   160

1498- Lone Ranger and the Silver Bullets, 1946, Whitman,
352.pgs., Henry E. Vallely-a   12   30   74   120

712-10- Lone Ranger and the Secret of Somber Cavern, The,
1950, Whitman   9   23   56   90

2013- (#13)-Lone Ranger Outwits Crazy Cougar, The, 1968, Whitman,
260 pgs., 39 cents, hard-c, color illos   3   8   20   28

5774- Lone Ranger Outwits Crazy Cougar, The, 1976, Whitman,
260 pgs., 49 cents, soft-c, color illos   2   3   16   22

5774-1- Lone Ranger Outwits Crazy Cougar, The, 1979, Whitman,
260 pgs., 69 cents, soft-c, color illos   2   3   16   22

nn- Lone Ranger and the Lost Valley, The, 1938, Dell,
196 pgs., Fast-Action Story, soft-c   23   58   165   280

1405- Lone Star Martin of the Texas Rangers, 1939, Whitman,
432 pgs.   12   30   80   130

19- Lost City, The, 1935, EVW, movie scenes   13   33   85   135

1103- Lost Jungle, The (With Clyde Beatty), 1936, Saalfield,
movie scenes, hard-c   12   30   80   130

1583- Lost Jungle, The (With Clyde Beatty), 1936, Saalfield,
movie scenes, soft -c   11   28   68   110

753- Lost Patrol, The, 1934, Whitman, 160 pgs., photo-c, movie
scenes with Boris Karloff   12   30   74   120

nn- Lost World, The - Jurassic Park 2, 1997, Chronicle Books,
312 pgs., adapts movie, 1-color (green) illos   2   3   15   20

1189- Mac of the Marines in Africa, 1936, Whitman, 432 pgs.
  10   25   64   100

1400- Mac of the Marines in China, 1938, Whitman, 432 pgs.
  10   25   64   100

1100B- Magic Tricks (With explanations), 1938, Whitman, 36 pgs.,
2 1/2" x 3 1/2", Penny Book, rabbit in hat-c   2   3   15   20

1100B- Magic Tricks (How to do them), 1938, Whitman, 36 pgs.,
2 1/2" x 3 1/2", Penny Book, genie-c   2   3   15   20

Major Hoople (See Our Boarding House)

2022-(#22)- Major Matt Mason, Moon Mission, 1968, Whitman, 256 pgs.,
hard-c, color illos.   3   8   20   28

1167- Mandrake the Magician, 1935, Whitman, 432 pgs., by Lee Falk &
Phil Davis   16   40   116   180

1418- Mandrake the Magician and the Flame Pearls, 1946, Whitman,
352 pgs., by lee Falk & Phil Davis   13   33   90   140

1431- Mandrake the Magician and the Midnight Monster, 1939, Whitman,
432 pgs., by Lee Falk & Phil Davis   15   38   100   160

1454- Mandrake the Magician Mighty Solver of Mysteries, 1941, Whitman,
432 pgs., by Lee Falk & Phil Davis, flip pictures   15   38   100   160

2011-(#11)- Man From U.N.C.L.E., The-The Calcutta Affair (TV Series), 1967,
Whitman, 260 pgs., 39¢, hard-c, color illos   3   8   20   28

1429- Marge's Little Lulu Alvin and Tubby, 1947, Whitman, All Pictures
Comics, Stanley-a   25   63   175   300

1438- Mary Lee and the Mystery of the Indian Beads,
1937, Whitman, 300 pgs.   10   25   60   95

1165- Masked Man of the Mesa, The, 1939, Saalfield, 400 pgs.
  9   23   56   90

nn- Mask of Zorro, The, 1998, Chronicle Books, 312 pgs.,
adapts movie, 1-color (yellow-green) illos   1   3   6   10

1436- Maximo the Amazing Superman, 1940, Whitman, 432 pgs.,
Henry E. Vallely-a   13   33   92   145

1444- Maximo the Amazing Superman and the Crystals of Doom,
1941, Whitman,432 pgs., Henry E. Vallely-a   13   33   92   145

1445- Maximo the Amazing Superman and the Supermachine,
1941, Whitman, 432 pgs.   13   33   92   145

755- Men of the Mounted, 1934, Whitman, 320 pgs.   13   33   85   135

nn- Men of the Mounted, 1933, Whitman, 52 pgs., 3 1/2" x 5 3/4",
premium-no ads; other versions with Poll Parrot & Perkins ad; soft-c
  15   38   100   160

nn- Men of the Mounted, 1934, Whitman, Cocomalt premium,
soft-c, by Ted McCall   10   25   60   95

1475- Men With Wings, 1938, Whitman, 240 pgs., photo-c, movie scenes
(Paramount Pics.)   13   33   85   135

1170- Mickey Finn, 1940, Saalfield, 400 pgs., by Frank Leonard
  13   33   95   150

717- Mickey Mouse (Disney), (1st printing) 1933, Whitman, 320 pgs.,
Gottfredson-a, skinny Mickey on cover   250   625   2125   3900

717- Mickey Mouse (Disney), (2nd printing)1933, Whitman, 320 pgs.,
Gottfredson-a, regular Mickey on cover   153   383   1224   2300

nn- Mickey Mouse (Disney), 1933, Dean & Son, Great Big Midget Book,
320 pgs.   125   312   950   1850

731- Mickey Mouse the Mail Pilot (Disney), 1933, Whitman,
(This is the same book as the 1st Mickey Mouse BLB #717(2nd printing)
but with "The Mail Pilot" printed on the front. Lower left of back cover
has a small box printed over the existing "No. 717." "No. 731" is printed
next to it.) (Sold at auction in 2014 in VG+ condition for $7170, and in
FR/GD condition for $2,500)

726- Mickey Mouse in Blaggard Castle (Disney), 1934,
Whitman, 320 pgs., Gottfredson-a   35   88   248   425

731- Mickey Mouse the Mail Pilot (Disney), 1933, Whitman,
300 pgs., Gottfredson-a   33   83   235   400

731- Mickey Mouse the Mail Pilot (Disney), 1933, Whitman,
300 pgs., soft cover; Gottfredson-a (Rare)   73   183   511   975

nn- Mickey Mouse the Mail Pilot (Disney), 1933, Whitman, 292 pgs.,
American Oil Co. premium, soft-c, Gottfredson-a;
another version 3 1/2" x 4 3/4"   35   88   248   425

nn- Mickey Mouse the Mail Pilot (Disney), 1933, Dean & Son,
Great Big Midget Book, 320 pgs.   127   318   1016   1900

750- Mickey Mouse Sails for Treasure Island (Disney),
1933, Whitman, 320 pgs., Gottfredson-a   33   83   235   400

nn- Mickey Mouse Sails for Treasure Island (Disney), 1935, Whitman,
196 pgs., premium-no ads, soft-c, Gottfredson-a (Scarce)
  37   93   260   450

nn- Mickey Mouse Sails for Treasure Island (Disney), 1935, Whitman,
196 pgs., Kolynos Dental Cream premium (Scarce)
  37   93   260   450

nn- Mickey Mouse Sails for Treasure Island (Disney), 1933, Dean & Son,
Great Big Midget Book, 320 pgs.   118   295   826   1650

756- Mickey Mouse Presents a Walt Disney Silly Symphony (Disney),
1934, Whitman, 240 pgs., Bucky Bug app.   29   73   203   350

801- Mickey Mouse's Summer Vacation, 1948, Whitman,
hard-c, Story Hour series   13   33   85   135

1058- Mickey Mouse Box, The (Disney), 1939, Whitman, 10" x 11 1/2" x 1",
(set includes 6 books from the 1058 series, all 5" x 5 1/2", 68 pgs.
The six books are: The Brave Little Tailor, Mother Pluto, The Ugly
Ducklings, The Practical Pig, Timid Elmer, and The Farmyard Symphony
(a VF set sold for $5175 in Nov., 2014)

1111- Mickey Mouse Presents Walt Disney's Silly Symphonies Stories,
1936, Whitman, 432 pgs., Donald Duck app.   29   73   203   350

1128- Mickey Mouse and Pluto the Racer (Disney), 1936,
Whitman, 432 pgs., Gottfredson-a   27   68   189   325

1139- Mickey Mouse the Detective (Disney), 1934, Whitman,
300 pgs., Gottfredson-a   30   75   210   365

1139- Mickey Mouse the Detective (Disney), 1934, Whitman, 304 pgs.,
premium-no ads, soft-c, Gottfredson-a (Scarce)   48   120   335   625

1153- Mickey Mouse and the Bat Bandit (Disney), 1935,
Whitman, 432 pgs., Gottfredson-a   27   68   189   325

nn- Mickey Mouse and the Bat Bandit (Disney), 1935, Whitman, 436 pgs.,
premium-no ads, 3-color, soft-c, Gottfredson-a (Scarce)
  48   120   335   625

1160- Mickey Mouse and Bobo the Elephant (Disney),
1935, Whitman, 432 pgs., Gottfredson-a   27   68   189   325

1187- Mickey Mouse and the Sacred Jewel (Disney), 1936,
Whitman, 432 pgs., Gottfredson-a   27   68   189   325

1401- Mickey Mouse in the Treasure Hunt (Disney), 1941, Whitman,
430 pgs., flip pictures of Pluto, Gottfredson-a   23   58   165   280

1409- Mickey Mouse Runs His Own Newspaper (Disney),
1937, Whitman, 432 pgs., Gottfredson-a   24   61   170   290

1413- Mickey Mouse and the 'Lectro Box (Disney), 1946,
Whitman, 352 pgs., Gottfredson-a   16   40   112   175

1417- Mickey Mouse on Sky Island (Disney), 1941, Whitman, 432 pgs.,
flip pictures, Gottfredson-a; considered by Gottfredson to be his best
Mickey story   22   55   154   260

1428- Mickey Mouse in the Foreign Legion (Disney), 1940, Whitman,
432 pgs., Gottfredson-a   22   55   154   260

1429- Mickey Mouse and the Magic Lamp (Disney), 1942, Whitman,
432 pgs., flip pictures   22   55   154   260

1433- Mickey Mouse and the Lazy Daisy Mystery (Disney),
1947, Whitman, 288 pgs.   16   40   112   175

1444- Mickey Mouse in the World of Tomorrow (Disney),
1948, Whitman, 288 pgs., Gottfredson-a   24   60   168   285

1451- Mickey Mouse and the Desert Palace (Disney), 1948,
Whitman, 288 pgs.   16   40   112   175

1463- Mickey Mouse and the Pirate Submarine (Disney),
1939, Whitman, 432 pgs., Gottfredson-a   23   58   163   275

1464- Mickey Mouse and the Stolen Jewels (Disney), 1949,
Whitman, 288 pgs.   20   50   143   225

1471- Mickey Mouse and the Dude Ranch Bandit (Disney),

1103 - The Lost Jungle © Saalfield

717 - Mickey Mouse © DIS

1400 - Nancy and Sluggo © WHIT

	GD	FN	VF	VF/NM
1943, Whitman, 432 pgs., flip pictures	21	53	150	255
1475- Mickey Mouse and the 7 Ghosts (Disney), 1940, Whitman, 432 pgs., Gottfredson-a	23	58	163	275
1476- Mickey Mouse in the Race for Riches (Disney), 1938, Whitman, 432 pgs., Gottfredson-a	23	58	163	275
1483- Mickey Mouse Bell Boy Detective (Disney), 1945, Whitman, 352 pgs.	20	50	143	225
1499- Mickey Mouse on the Cave-Man Island (Disney), 1944, Whitman, 352 pgs.	20	50	143	225
2004- Mickey Mouse With This Big Big Color Set, Here Comes (Disney), 1936, Whitman, (Very Rare), 224 pgs., 12" x 8 1/4" box, with red, yellow and blue crayons, contains 224 loose pages to color, reprinted from early Mickey Mouse related movie and strip reprints. Attached to center of lid is a 5" tall separate die-cut cardboard Mickey Mouse figure (a VF/NM set sold for $1701 in July 2014)	239	598	2030	3700
2020-(#20)- Mickey Mouse, Adventure in Outer Space, 1968, Whitman, 256 pgs.,hard-c, color illos.	3	8	20	28
3059- Mickey Mouse Big Little Set (Disney), 1936, Whitman, 8 1/4" x 8 1/2", with crayons, box contains a 4" x 5 1/4" soft-c book with 160 pgs. of Mickey to color, reprinted from early Mickey Mouse BLBs, (Rare) (a copy in NM sold for $1897 in Nov, 2011, a VF copy sold for $1147 in 2013)				
5750- Mickey Mouse, Adventure in Outer Space, 1973, Whitman, 256 pgs.,soft-c, 39 cents, color illos.	2	3	10	15
3049- Mickey Mouse and His Big Little Kit (Disney), 1937, Whitman, 384 pgs., 4 1/2" x 6 1/2" box, includes miniature box of 4 crayons-red, yellow, blue and green (a copy in VF/NM sold for $335 in 2015)				
3061- Mickey Mouse to Draw and Color (The Big Little Set), nd (early 1930s), Whitman, with crayons; box contains 320 loose pages to color, reprinted from early Mickey Mouse BLBs	121	303	900	1750
4062- Mickey Mouse, The Story Of, 1935, Whitman, 7" x 9 1/2", 320 pgs., Big Big Book, Gottfredson-a	86	215	600	1200
4062- Mickey Mouse and the Smugglers, The Story Of, 1935, Whitman, (Scarce), 7" x 9 1/2", 320 pgs., Big Big Book, same contents as above version; Gottfredson-a	86	215	600	1200
708-10- Mickey Mouse on the Haunted Island (Disney), 1950, Whitman, Gottfredson-a	12	30	80	130
nn- Mickey Mouse and Minnie at Macy's, 1934 Whitman, 148 pgs., 3 1/4" x 3 1/2", soft-c, R. H. Macy & Co. Christmas giveaway (Rare, less than 20 known copies)	330	825	2970	5300
nn- Mickey Mouse and Minnie March to Macy's, 1935, Whitman, 148 pgs., 3 1/2" x 3 1/2", soft-c, R. H. Macy & Co. Christmas giveaway (scarce)	271	678	2300	4200
nn- Mickey Mouse and the Magic Carpet, 1935, Whitman, 148 pgs., 3 1/2"x 4", soft-c, giveaway, Gottfredson-a, Donald Duck app.	128	320	960	1850
nn- Mickey Mouse Silly Symphonies, 1934, Dean & Son, Ltd (England), 48 pgs., with 4 pop-ups, Babes In The Woods, King Neptune				
With dust jacket	133	333	1064	2000
Without dust jacket	93	233	650	1300
nn- Mickey Mouse the Sheriff of Nugget Gulch (Disney) 1938, Dell, 196 pgs., Fast-Action Story, soft-c, Gottfredson-a	35	88	248	425
nn- Mickey Mouse Waddle Book, 1934, BRP, 20 pgs., 7 1/2" x 10", forerunner of the Blue Ribbon Pop-Up books; with 4 removable articulated cardboard characters Book Only	75	188	525	1050
(A complete copy in VG/FN w/VF dustjacket sold for $5676 in 2010)				
(A complete copy in VF with dustjacket ramp & band sold for $573 in 2014)				
nn- Mickey Mouse with Goofy and Mickey's Nephews, 1938, Dell, Fast-Action Story, Gottfredson-a	37	93	260	450
16- Mickey Mouse and Pluto (Disney), 1942, Dell, 196 pgs., Fast-Action story	35	88	248	425
512- Mickey Mouse Wee Little Books (In open box), nn, 1934, Whitman, 44 pgs., small size, soft-c				
Mickey Mouse and Tanglefoot	13	33	90	140
Mickey Mouse at the Carnival	13	33	90	140
Mickey Mouse Will Not Quit!	13	33	90	140
Mickey Mouse Wins the Race!	13	33	90	140
Mickey Mouse's Misfortune	13	33	90	140
Mickey Mouse's Uphill Fight	13	33	90	140
Complete set with box	86	215	600	1200
1493- Mickey Rooney and Judy Garland and How They Got into the				

	GD	FN	VF	VF/NM
Movies, 1941, Whitman, 432 pgs., photo-c	13	33	85	135
1427- Mickey Rooney Himself, 1939, Whitman, 240 pgs., photo-c, movie scenes, life story	12	30	74	120
532- Mickey's Dog Pluto (Disney), 1943, Whitman, All Picture Comics, A Tall Comic Book , 3 3/4" x 8 3/4"	20	50	140	220
284- Midget Jumbo Coloring Book, 1935, Saalfield	42	105	294	500
2113- Midget Jumbo Coloring Book, 1935, Saalfield, 240 pgs.	42	105	294	500
21- Midsummer Night's Dream, 1935, EVW, movie scenes	13	33	92	145
nn- Minute-Man (Mystery of the Spy Ring), 1941, Fawcett, Dime Action Book	35	88	248	425
710- Moby Dick the Great White Whale, The Story of, 1934, Whitman, 160 pgs., photo-c, movie scenes from "The Sea Beast"	12	30	80	130
746- Moon Mullins and Kayo (Kayo and Moon Mullins-inside), 1933, Whitman, 320 pgs., Frank Willard-c/a	12	30	74	120
nn- Moon Mullins and Kayo, 1933, Whitman, Cocomalt premium, soft-c, by Willard	12	30	74	120
1134- Moon Mullins and the Plushbottom Twins, 1935, Whitman, 432 pgs., Willard-c/a	12	30	74	120
nn- Moon Mullins and the Plushbottom Twins, 1935, Whitman, 436 pgs., premium-no ads, 3-color, soft-c, by Willard	17	43	123	190
1058- Mother Pluto (Disney), 1939, Whitman, 68 pgs., hard-c	13	33	95	150
1100B- Movie Jokes (From the talkies), 1938, Whitman, 36 pgs., 2 1/2" x 3 1/2", Penny Book	2	3	12	16
1408- Mr. District Attorney on the Job, 1941, Whitman, 432 pgs., flip pictures	10	25	64	100
nn- Musicians of Bremen, The, nd (1930s), np (Whitman), 36 pgs., 3" x 2 1/2", Penny Book	2	3	12	16
1113- Mutt and Jeff, 1936, Whitman, 300 pgs., by Bud Fisher	25	63	175	300
1116- My Life and Times (By Shirley Temple), 1936, Saalfield, Little Big Book, hard-c, photo-c/illos	13	33	85	135
1596- My Life and Times (By Shirley Temple), 1936, Saalfield, Little Big Book, soft-c, photo-c/illos	13	33	85	135
1497- Myra North Special Nurse and Foreign Spies, 1938, Whitman, 432 pgs.	12	30	76	125
1400- Nancy and Sluggo, 1946, Whitman, All Pictures Comics, Ernie Bushmiller-a	12	30	74	120
1487- Nancy Has Fun, 1946, Whitman, All Pictures Comics	12	30	74	120
1150- Napoleon and Uncle Elby, 1938, Saalfield, 400 pgs., by Clifford McBride	11	28	68	110
1166- Napoleon Uncle Elby And Little Mary, 1939, Saalfield, 400 pgs., by Clifford McBride	11	28	68	110
1179- Ned Brant Adventure Bound, 1940, Saalfield, 400 pgs.	10	25	60	95
1146- Nevada Rides The Danger Trail, 1938, Saalfield, 400 pgs., J.R. White-a	10	25	60	95
1147- Nevada Whalen, Avenger, 1938, Saalfield, 400 pgs.	10	25	60	95
Nicodemus O'Malley (See Top-Line Comics)				
1115- Og Son of Fire, 1936, Whitman, 432 pgs.	13	33	85	135
1419- Oh, Blondie the Bumsteads (See Blondie)				
11- Oliver Twist, 1935, EVW (Five Star Library), movie scenes, starring Dickie Moore (Monogram Pictures)	12	30	80	130
718- Once Upon a Time, 1933, Whitman, 364 pgs., soft-c	12	30	80	130
712- 100 Fairy Tales for Children, The, 1933, Whitman, 288 pgs., Circle Library	10	25	60	95
1099- One Night of Love, 1935, Saalfield, 160 pgs., hard-c, photo-c, movie scenes, Columbia Pictures, starring Grace Moore	14	35	95	150
1579- One Night of Love, 1935, Sat, 160 pgs., soft-c, photo-c, movie scenes, Columbia Pictures, starring Grace Moore	14	35	95	150
1155- $1000 Reward, 1938, Saalfield, 400 pgs.	10	25	60	95
Orphan Annie (See Little Orphan ...)				
L17- O'Shaughnessy's Boy, 1935, Lynn, 192 pgs., movie scenes,				

	GD	FN	VF	VF/NM

w/Wallace Beery & Jackie Cooper (Metro-Goldwyn-Mayer)
12 30 72 115
1109- **Oswald the Lucky Rabbit**, 1934, Whitman, 288 pgs.
16 40 112 175
1403- **Oswald Rabbit Plays G-Man**, 1937, Whitman, 240 pgs., movie scenes by Walter Lantz
18 45 128 200
1190- **Our Boarding House, Major Hoople and his Horse**, 1940, Saalfield, 400 pgs.
11 28 68 110
1085- **Our Gang**, 1934, Saalfield, 160 pgs., photo-c, movie scenes, hard-c
15 38 100 160
1315- **Our Gang**, 1934, Saalfield, 160 pgs., photo-c, movie scenes, soft-c
15 38 100 160
1451- **"Our Gang" on the March**, 1942, Whitman, 432 pgs., flip pictures
15 38 100 160
1456- **Our Gang Adventures**, 1948, Whitman, 288 pgs. 12 30 80 130
nn- **Paramount Newsreel Men with Admiral Byrd in Little America**, 1934, Whitman, 96 pgs., 6 1/4" x 6 1/4", photo-c, photo ill.
14 35 98 155
nn- **Patch**, nd (1930s), np (Whitman), 36 pgs., 3" x 2 1/2", Penny Book
2 3 14 18
1445- **Pat Nelson Ace of Test Pilots**, 1937, Whitman, 432 pgs.
10 25 60 95
1411- **Peggy Brown and the Mystery Basket**, 1941, Whitman, 432 pgs., flip pictures, Henry E. Vallely-a
10 25 64 100
1423- **Peggy Brown and the Secret Treasure**, 1947, Whitman, 288 pgs., Henry E. Vallely-a
10 25 64 100
1427- **Peggy Brown and the Runaway Auto Trailer**, 1937, Whitman, 300 pgs., Henry E. Vallely-a
10 25 64 100
1463- **Peggy Brown and the Jewel of Fire**, 1943, Whitman, 352 pgs., Henry E. Vallely-a
10 25 64 100
1491- **Peggy Brown in the Big Haunted House**, 1940, Whitman, 432 pgs., Vallely-a
10 25 64 100
1143- **Peril Afloat**, 1938, Saalfield, 400 pgs. 10 25 64 100
1199- **Perry Winkle and the Rinkeydinks**, 1937, Whitman, 432 pgs., by Martin Branner
14 35 95 150
1487- **Perry Winkle and the Rinkeydinks get a Horse**, 1938, Whitman, 432 pgs., by Martin Branner
14 35 95 150
Peter Pan (See Wee Little Books)
nn- **Peter Rabbit**, nd(1930s), np(Whitman), 36 pgs., Penny Book, 3" x 2 1/2"
5 12 30 45
Peter Rabbit's Carrots (See Wee Little Books)
1100- **Phantom, The**, 1936, Whitman, 432 pgs., by Lee Falk & Ray Moore
31 78 217 375
1416- **Phantom and the Girl of Mystery, The**, 1947, Whitman, 352 pgs. by Falk & Moore
13 33 90 140
1421- **Phantom and Desert Justice, The**, 1941, Whitman, 432 pgs., flip pictures, by Falk & Moore
15 38 108 170
1468- **Phantom and the Sky Pirates, The**, 1945, Whitman, 352 pgs., by Falk & Moore
14 35 95 150
1474- **Phantom and the Sign of the Skull, The**, 1939, Whitman, 432 pgs., by Falk & Moore
17 43 119 185
1489- **Phantom, Return of the...**, 1942, Whitman, 432 pgs., flip pictures, by Falk & Moore
15 38 108 170
1130- **Phil Burton, Sleuth** (Scout Book), 1937, Saalfield, hard-c
5 12 30 45
Pied Piper of Hamlin (See Wee Little Books)
1466- **Pilot Pete Dive Bomber**, 1941, Whitman, 432 pgs., flip pictures
10 25 60 95
5776- **Pink Panther Adventures in Z-Land, The**, 1976, Whitman, 260 pgs., soft-c, 49 cents, B&W
1 3 6 10
5776-2- **Pink Panther Adventures in Z-Land, The**, 1980, Whitman, 260 pgs., soft-c, 79 cents, B&W
1 3 6 10
5783-2- **Pink Panther at Castle Kreep, The**, 1980, Whitman, 260 pgs., soft-c, 79 cents, B&W
1 3 6 10
Pinocchio and Jiminy Cricket (See Walt Disney's ...)
nn- **Pioneers of the Wild West** (Blue-c), 1933, World Syndicate, High Lights of History Series
5 12 34 50
With dustjacket
18 45 128 200
nn- **Pioneers of the Wild West** (Red-c), 1933, World Syndicate, High Lights of History Series
5 12 34 50
1123- **Plainsman, The**, 1936, Whitman, 240 pgs., photo-c, movie scenes with Gary Cooper (Paramount Pics.)
14 35 95 150
Pluto (See Mickey's Dog ... & Walt Disney's ...)
2114- **Pocket Coloring Book**, 1935, Saalfield 25 63 175 300
1060- **Polly and Her Pals on the Farm**, 1934, Saalfield, 164 pgs., hard-c, by Cliff Sterrett
12 30 76 125
1310- **Polly and Her Pals on the Farm**, 1934, Saalfield, soft-c
12 30 76 125
1051- **Popeye, Adventures of...**, 1934, Saalfield, oblong-size, E.C. Segar-a, hard-c
42 105 295 525
1088- **Popeye in Puddleburg**, 1934, Saalfield, 160 pgs., hard-c, E. C. Segar-a
18 45 128 200
1113- **Popeye Starring in Choose Your Weppins**, 1936, Saalfield, 160 pgs., hard-c, Segar-a
35 88 248 425
1117- **Popeye's Ark**, 1936, Saalfield, 4 1/2" x 5 1/2", hard-c, Segar-a
18 45 128 200

1163- **Popeye Sees the Sea**, 1936, Whitman, 432 pgs., Segar-a
20 50 140 220
1301- **Popeye, Adventures of...**, 1934, Saalfield, oblong-size, Segar-a
42 105 295 525
1318- **Popeye in Puddleburg**, 1934, Saalfield, 160 pgs., soft-c, Segar-a
19 48 133 210
1405- **Popeye and the Jeep**, 1937, Whitman, 432 pgs., Segar-a
20 50 140 220
1406- **Popeye the Super-Fighter**, 1939, Whitman, All Pictures Comics, flip pictures, Segar-a
18 45 128 200
1422- **Popeye the Sailor Man**, 1947, Whitman, All Pictures Comics
12 30 80 130
1450- **Popeye in Quest of His Poopdeck Pappy**, 1937, Whitman, 432 pgs., Segar-c/a
15 38 100 160
1458- **Popeye and Queen Olive Oyl**, 1949, Whitman, 288 pgs., Sagendorf-a
13 33 85 135
1459- **Popeye and the Quest for the Rainbird**, 1943, Whitman, Winner & Zaboly-a
14 35 95 150
1480- **Popeye the Spinach Eater**, 1945, Whitman, All Pictures Comics
12 30 80 130
1485- **Popeye in a Sock for Susan's Sake**, 1940, Whitman, 432 pgs., flip pictures
14 35 95 150
1497- **Popeye and Caster Oyl the Detective**, 1941, Whitman, 432 pgs. flip pictures, Segar-a
16 40 112 175
1499- **Popeye and the Deep Sea Mystery**, 1939, Whitman, 432 pgs., Segar-c/a
16 40 116 180
1593- **Popeye Starring in Choose Your Weppins**, 1936, Saalfield, 160 pgs., soft-c, Segar-a
16 40 116 180
1597- **Popeye's Ark**, 1936, Saalfield, 4 1/2" x 5 1/2", soft-c, Segar-a
16 40 116 180
2008-(#8)- **Popeye-Ghost Ship to Treasure Island**, 1967, Whitman, 260 pgs., 39 cents, hard-c, color illos
3 8 20 28
5755- **Popeye-Ghost Ship to Treasure Island**, 1973, Whitman; 260 pgs., soft-c, color illos
2 3 10 15
2034-(#34)- **Popeye, Danger Ahoy!**, 1969, Whitman, 256 pgs., hard-c, color illos.
3 8 18 25
5768- **Popeye, Danger Ahoy!**, 1975, Whitman, 256 pgs., soft-c, color illos.
2 3 10 15
4063- **Popeye, Thimble Theatre Starring**, 1935, Whitman, 7" x 9 1/2", 320 pgs., Big Big Book, Segar-c/a; (Cactus cover w/yellow logo)
79 198 550 1100
4063- **Popeye, Thimble Theatre Starring**, 1935, Whitman, 7" x 9 1/2", 320 pgs., Big Big Book, Segar-c/a; (Big Balloon-c with red logo), (2nd printing w/same contents as above)
93 233 650 1300
5761- **Popeye and Queen Olive Oyl**, 1973, 260 pgs., B&W soft-c
3 8 20 28
5761-2- **Popeye and Queen Olive Oyl**, 1973 (1980-reprint of 1973 version), 260 pgs., 79 cents, B&W, soft-c
2 3 10 15
103- **"Pop-Up" Buck Rogers in the Dangerous Mission** (with Pop-Up picture), 1934, BRP, 62 pgs., The Midget Pop-Up Book w/Pop-Up in center of book, Calkins-a
118 295 826 1650
206- **"Pop-Up" Buck Rogers - Strange Adventures in the Spider Ship, The**, 1935, BRP, 24 pgs., 8" x 9", 3 Pop-Ups, hard-c, by Dick Calkins
118 295 826 1650
nn- **"Pop-Up" Cinderella**, 1933, BRP, 7 1/2" x 9 3/4", 4 Pop-Ups, hard-c
With dustjacket
65 163 455 850
Without dustjacket
56 140 392 725
207- **"Pop-Up" Dick Tracy-Capture of Boris Arson**, 1935, BRP, 24 pgs., 8" x 9", 3 Pop-Ups, hard-c, by Gould
63 159 438 825
210- **"Pop-Up" Flash Gordon Tournament of Death, The**, 1935, BRP, 24 pgs., 8" x 9", 3 Pop-Ups, hard-c, by Alex Raymond
119 298 850 1700
202- **"Pop-Up" Goldilocks and the Three Bears, The**, 1934, BRP, 24 pgs., 8" x 9", 3 Pop-Ups, hard-c
35 88 248 425
nn- **"Pop-Up" Jack and the Beanstalk**, 1933, BRP, hard-c (50 cents), 1 Pop-Up
35 88 248 425
nn- **"Pop-Up" Jack the Giant Killer**, 1933, BRP, hard-c (50 cents), 1 Pop-Up
35 88 248 425
nn- **"Pop-Up" Jack the Giant Killer**, 1933, BRP, 4 Pop-Ups, hard-c
With dustjacket
62 155 434 800
Without dust jacket
54 135 378 700
105- **"Pop-Up" Little Black Sambo**, (with Pop-Up picture), 1934, BRP, 62 pgs., The Midget Pop-Up Book, one Pop-Up in center of book
52 130 364 675
208- **"Pop-Up" Little Orphan Annie and Jumbo the Circus Elephant**, 1935, BRP, 24 pgs., 8" x 9 1/2", 3 Pop-Ups, hard-c, by H. Gray
62 155 434 800
nn- **"Pop-Up" Little Red Ridinghood**, 1933, BRP, hard-c (50 cents), 1 Pop-Up
42 105 294 500
nn- **"Pop-Up" Mickey Mouse, The**, 1933, BRP, 34 pgs., 6 1/2" x 9", 3 Pop-Ups, hard-c, Gottfredson-a (75 cents)
52 130 364 675
nn- **"Pop-Up" Mickey Mouse in King Arthur's Court, The**, 1933, BRP, 56 pgs., 7 1/2" x 9 1/4", 4 Pop-Ups, hard-c, Gottfredson-a
With dust jacket
128 320 973 1850
Without dustjacket
96 241 672 1350
101- **"Pop-Up" Mickey Mouse in "Ye Olden Days"** (with Pop-Up picture),

	GD	FN	VF	VF/NM
1934, 62 pgs., BRP, The Midget Pop-Up Book, one Pop-Up in center of book, Gottfredson-a	110	275	770	1550
nn- "Pop-Up" Minnie Mouse, The, 1933, BRP, 36 pgs., 6 1/2" x 9", 3 Pop-Ups, hard-c (75 cents), Gottfredson-a	52	130	364	675
203- "Pop-Up" Mother Goose, The, 1934, BRP, 24 pgs., 8" x 9 1/4", 3 Pop-Ups, hard-c	42	105	290	500
nn- "Pop-Up" Mother Goose Rhymes, The, 1933, BRP, 96 pgs., 7 1/2" x 9 1/4", 4 Pop-Ups, hard-c				
With dustjacket	46	115	322	600
Without dustjacket	42	105	290	500
209- "Pop-Up" New Adventures of Tarzan, 1935, BRP, 24 pgs., 8" x 9", 3 Pop-Ups, hard-c	107	268	749	1500
104- "Pop-Up" Peter Rabbit, The (with Pop-Up picture), 1934, BRP, 62 pgs., The Midget Pop-Up Book, one Pop-Up in center of book	50	125	350	650
nn- "Pop-Up" Pinocchio, 1933, BRP, 7 1/2" x 9 3/4", 4 Pop-Ups, hard-c				
With dustjacket	65	163	455	850
Without dust jacket	56	140	392	725
102- "Pop-Up" Popeye among the White Savages (with Pop-Up picture), 1934, BRP, 62 pgs., The Midget Pop-Up Book, one Pop-Up in center of book, E. C. Segar-a	62	155	434	800
205- "Pop-Up" Popeye with the Hag of the Seven Seas, The, 1935, BRP, 24 pgs., 8" x 9", 3 Pop-Ups, hard-c, Segar-a	68	170	476	875
201- "Pop-Up" Puss In Boots, The, 1934, BRP, 24 pgs., 3 Pop-Ups, hard-c	33	83	235	400
nn- "Pop-Up" Silly Symphonies, The (Mickey Mouse Presents His ...), 1933, BRP, 56 pgs., 9 3/4" x 7 1/2", 4 Pop-Ups, hard-c				
With dust jacket	100	250	700	1400
Without dust jacket	72	180	504	950
nn- "Pop-Up" Sleeping Beauty, 1933, BRP, hard-c, (50 cents), 1 Pop-up	42	105	295	525
212- "Pop-Up" Terry and the Pirates in Shipwrecked, The, 1935, BRP, 24 pgs., 8" x 9", 3 Pop-Ups, hard-c	72	180	504	950
211- "Pop-Up" Tim Tyler in the Jungle, The, 1935, BRP, 24 pgs., 8" x 9", 3 Pop-Ups, hard-c	42	105	294	500
1404- Porky Pig and His Gang, 1946, Whitman, All Pictures Comics, Barks-a, reprints Four Color #48	18	45	128	200
1408- Porky Pig and Petunia, 1942, Whitman, All Pictures Comics, flip pictures, reprints Four Color #16 & Famous Gang Book of Comics	12	30	80	130
1176- Powder Smoke Range, 1935, Whitman, 240 pgs., photo-c, movie scenes, Hoot Gibson, Harey Carey app. (RKO Radio Pict.)	11	28	68	110
1058- Practical Pig!, The (Disney), 1939, Whitman, 68 pgs., 5" x 5 1/2", hard-c	11	28	68	110
758- Prairie Bill and the Covered Wagon, 1934, Whitman, 384 pgs., Hal Arbo-a	10	25	60	95
nn- Prairie Bill and the Covered Wagon, 1934, Whitman, 390 pgs., premium-no ads, 3-color, soft-c, Hal Arbo-a	12	30	80	130
1440- Punch Davis of the U.S. Aircraft Carrier, 1945, Whitman, 352 pgs.	8	20	50	80
nn- Puss in Boots, nd(1930s), np(Whitman), 36 pgs., Penny Book	2	3	15	20
1100B- Puzzle Book, 1938, Whitman, 36 pgs., 2 1/2" x 3 1/2", Penny Book	2	3	16	22
1100B- Puzzles, 1938, Whitman, 36 pgs., 2 1/2" x 3 1/2", Penny Book	2	3	16	22
1100B- Quiz Book, The, 1938, Whitman, 36 pgs., 2 1/2" x 3 1/2", Penny Book	2	3	16	22
1142- Radio Patrol, 1935, Whitman, 432 pgs., by Eddie Sullivan & Charlie Schmidt (#1)	12	30	72	115
1173- Radio Patrol Trailing the Safeblowers, 1937, Whitman, 432 pgs.	9	23	56	90
1496- Radio Patrol Outwitting the Gang Chief, 1939, Whitman, 432 pgs.	9	23	56	90
1498- Radio Patrol and Big Dan's Mobsters, 1937, Whitman, 432 pgs.	9	23	56	90
nn- Raiders of the Lost Ark, 1998, Chronicle Books, 304 pgs., adapts movie, 1-color (green) illos	2	3	16	22
1441- Range Busters, The, 1942, Whitman, 432 pgs., Henry E.				

	GD	FN	VF	VF/NM
Vallely-a	10	25	60	95
1163- Ranger and the Cowboy, The, 1939, Saalfield, 400 pgs.	9	23	56	90
1154- Rangers on the Rio Grande, 1938, Saalfield, 400 pgs.	9	23	56	90
1447- Ray Land of the Tank Corps, U.S.A., 1942, Whitman, 432 pgs., flip pictures, Hess-a	10	25	60	95
1157- Red Barry Ace-Detective, 1935, Whitman, 432 pgs., by Will Gould	12	30	80	130
1426- Red Barry Undercover Man, 1939, Whitman, 432 pgs., by Will Gould	12	30	72	115
20- Red Davis, 1935, EVW, 160 pgs.	11	28	68	110
1449- Red Death on the Range, The, 1940, Whitman, 432 pgs., Fred Harman-a (Bronc Peeler)	12	30	72	115
nn- Red Falcon Adventures, The, 1937, Seal Right Ice Cream, 8 pgs., set of 50 books, circular in shape				
Issue #1	39	98	276	475
Issue #2-5	27	68	189	325
Issue #6-10	23	58	163	275
Issue #11-50	16	40	112	175
nn- Red Hen and the Fox, The, nd(1930s), np(Whitman), 36 pgs., 3" x 2 1/2", Penny Book	2	3	15	20
1145- Red-Hot Holsters, 1938, Saalfield, 400 pgs.	9	23	56	90
1400- Red Ryder and Little Beaver on Hoofs of Thunder, 1939, Whitman, 432 pgs., Harman-c/a	13	33	85	135
1414- Red Ryder and the Squaw-Tooth Rustlers, 1946, Whitman, 352 pgs., Fred Harman-a	12	30	72	115
1427- Red Ryder and the Code of the West, 1941, Whitman, 432 pgs., flip pictures, by Harman	12	30	76	125
1440- Red Ryder the Fighting Westerner, 1940, Whitman, Harman-a	12	30	76	125
1443- Red Ryder and the Rimrock Killer, 1948, Whitman, 288 pgs., Harman-a	11	28	68	110
1450- Red Ryder and Western Border Guns, 1942, Whitman, 432 pgs., flip pictures, by Harman	12	30	76	125
1454- Red Ryder and the Secret Canyon, 1948, Whitman, 288 pgs., Harman-a	11	28	68	110
1466- Red Ryder and Circus Luck, 1947, Whitman, 288 pgs., by Fred Harman	11	28	68	110
1473- Red Ryder in War on the Range, 1945, Whitman, 352 pgs., by Fred Harman	12	30	72	115
1475- Red Ryder and the Outlaw of Painted Valley, 1943, Whitman, 352 pgs., by Harman	11	28	68	110
702-10- Red Ryder Acting Sheriff, 1949, Whitman, by Fred Hannan	10	25	64	100
nn- Red Ryder Brings Law to Devil's Hole, 1939, Dell, 196 pgs., Fast-Action Story, Harman-c/a	21	53	149	250
nn- Red Ryder and the Highway Robbers, 1938, Whitman, 36 pgs., 2 1/2" x 3 1/2", Penny Book	10	25	64	100
754- Reg'lar Fellers, 1933, Whitman, 320 pgs., by Gene Byrnes	11	28	68	110
nn- Reg'lar Fellers, 1933, Whitman, 202 pgs., Cocomalt premium, by Gene Byrnes	11	28	68	110
1424- Rex Beach's Jaragu of the Jungle, 1937, Whitman, 432 pgs.	8	20	50	80
12- Rex, King of Wild Horses in "Stampede," 1935, EVW, 160 pgs., movie scenes, Columbia Pictures	9	23	56	90
1100B- Riddles for Fun, 1938, Whitman, 36 pgs., 2 1/2" x 3 1/2", Penny Book	3	8	18	25
1100B- Riddles to Guess, 1938, Whitman, 36 pgs., 2 1/2" x 3 1/2", Penny Book	3	8	18	25
1425- Riders of Lone Trails, 1937, Whitman, 300 pgs.	10	25	60	95
1141- Rio Raiders (A Billy The Kid Story), 1938, Saalfield, 400 pgs.	10	25	60	95
2023-(#23)- The Road Runner, The Super Beep Catcher, 1968, Whitman, 256 pgs., hard-c, color illos.	1	3	8	12
5759- The Road Runner, The Super Beep Catcher, 1973, Whitman, 256 pgs., soft-c, 39 cents, B&W illos., and flip pictures	1	3	8	12
5767-2- Road Runner, The Lost Road Runner Mine, The,				

	GD	FN	VF	VF/NM
1974 (1980), 260 pgs., 79 cents, B&W, soft-c	1	3	8	12
5784- The Road Runner and the Unidentified Coyote, 1974, Whitman, 260 pgs., soft-c, flip pictures	1	3	8	12
5784-2- The Road Runner and the Unidentified Coyote, 1980, Whitman, 260 pgs., soft-c, flip pictures	1	3	8	12
nn- Road To Perdition, 2002, Dreamworks, screenplay from movie, hard-c (Dreamworks and 20th Century Fox)	1	3	6	9
Robin Hood (See Wee Little Books)				
10- Robin Hood, 1935, EVW, 160 pgs., movie scenes w/Douglas Fairbanks (United Artists), hard-c	13	33	85	135
719- Robinson Crusoe (The Story of...), nd (1933), Whitman, 364 pgs., soft-c	11	28	68	110
1421- Roy Rogers and the Dwarf-Cattle Ranch, 1947, Whitman, 352 pgs., Henry E. Vallely-a	11	28	68	110
1437- Roy Rogers and the Deadly Treasure, 1947, Whitman, 288 pgs.	11	28	68	110
1448- Roy Rogers and the Mystery of the Howling Mesa, 1948, Whitman, 288 pgs.	11	28	68	110
1452- Roy Rogers in Robbers' Roost, 1948, Whitman, 288 pgs.	11	28	68	110
1460- Roy Rogers Robinhood of the Range, 1942, Whitman, 432 pgs., Hess-a (1st)	13	33	85	135
1462- Roy Rogers and the Mystery of the Lazy M, 1949, Whitman	10	25	60	95
1476- Roy Rogers King of the Cowboys, 1943, Whitman, 352 pgs., Irwin Myers-a, based on movie	15	38	105	165
1494- Roy Rogers at Crossed Feathers Ranch, 1945, Whitman, 320 pgs., Erwin Hess-a , 3 1/4" x 5 1/2"	11	28	68	110
701-10- Roy Rogers and the Snowbound Outlaws, 1949, 3 1/4" x 5 1/2"	9	23	56	90
715-10- Roy Rogers Range Detective, 1950, Whitman, 2 1/2" x 5"	9	23	56	90
nn- Sandy Gregg Federal Agent on Special Assignment, 1939, Whitman, 36 pgs., 2 1/2" x 3 1/2", Penny Book	9	23	54	85
Sappo (See Top-Line Comics)				
1122- Scrappy, 1934, Whitman, 288 pgs.	12	30	72	115
L12- Scrappy (The Adventures of...), 1935, Lynn, 192 pgs., movie scenes	12	30	72	115
1191- Secret Agent K-7,1940, Saalfield, 400 pgs., based on radio show	10	25	60	95
1144- Secret Agent X-9, 1936, Whitman, 432 pgs., Charles Flanders-a	15	38	108	170
1472- Secret Agent X-9 and the Mad Assassin, 1938, Whitman, 432 pgs., Charles Flanders-a	15	38	108	170
1161- Sequoia, 1935, Whitman, 160 pgs., photo-c, movie scenes	12	30	72	115
1430- Shadow and the Living Death, The, 1940, Whitman, 432 pgs., Erwin Hess-a	42	105	294	500
1443- Shadow and the Master of Evil, The, 1941, Whitman, 432 pgs., flip pictures, Hess-a	42	105	294	500
1495- Shadow and the Ghost Makers, The, 1942, Whitman, 432 pgs., John Coleman Burroughs-c	42	105	294	500
2024- Shazzan, The Glass Princess, 1968, Whitman, Hanna-Barbera	2	3	15	20
Shirley Temple (See My Life and Times & Story of..)				
1095- Shirley Temple and Lionel Barrymore Starring In "The Little Colonel," 1935, Saalfield, photo hard-c, movie scenes	19	48	133	210
1115- Shirley Temple in "The Littlest Rebel," 1935, Saalfield, photo-c, movie scenes, hard-c	19	48	133	210
1575- Shirley Temple and Lionel Barrymore Starring In "The Little Colonel," 1935, Saalfield, photo soft-c, movie scenes	19	48	133	210
1595- Shirley Temple in "The Littlest Rebel," 1935, Saalfield, photo-c, movie scenes, soft-c	19	48	133	210
1195- Shooting Sheriffs of the Wild West, 1936, Whitman, 432 pgs.	6	15	40	60
1169- Silly Symphony Featuring Donald Duck (Disney), 1937, Whitman, 432 pgs., Taliaferro-a	27	68	189	325
1441- Silly Symphony Featuring Donald Duck and His (MIS) Adventures (Disney), 1937, Whitman, 432 pgs., Taliaferro-a	27	68	189	325
1155- Silver Streak, The, 1935, Whitman, 160 pgs., photo-c, movie scenes (RKO Radio Pict.)	12	30	74	120
Simple Simon (See Wee Little Books)				
1649- Sir Lancelot (TV Series), 1958, Whitman, 280 pgs.	4	10	24	35
1112- Skeezix in Africa, 1934, Whitman, 300 pgs., Frank King-a	9	23	56	90
1408- Skeezix at the Military Academy, 1938, Whitman, 432 pgs., Frank King-a	9	23	54	85
1414- Skeezix Goes to War, 1944, Whitman, 352 pgs., Frank King-a	9	23	54	85
1419- Skeezix on His Own in the Big City, 1941, Whitman, All Pictures Comics, flip pictures, Frank King-a	8	20	48	75
761- Skippy, 1934, Whitman, 320 pgs., by Percy Crosby	8	20	48	75
4056- Skippy, The Story of, 1934, Whitman, 320 pgs., 7" x 9 1/2", Big Big Book, Percy Crosby-a	20	50	140	220

	GD	FN	VF	VF/NM
nn- Skippy, The Story of, 1934, Whitman, Phillips Dental Magnesia premium, soft-c, by Percy Crosby	8	20	48	75
1127- Skyroads (Hurricane Hawk's name not on cover), 1936, Whitman, 432 pgs., by Lt. Dick Calkins, Russell Keaton-a	10	25	64	100
1439- Skyroads with Clipper Williams of the Flying Legion, 1938, Whitman, 432 pgs., by Lt. Dick Calkins, Keaton-a	10	25	64	100
1127- Skyroads with Hurricane Hawk, 1936, Whitman, 432 pgs., by Lt. Dick Calkins, Russell Keaton-a	9	23	56	90
Smilin' Jack and his Flivver Plane (See Top-Line Comics)				
1152- Smilin' Jack and the Stratosphere Ascent, 1937, Whitman, 432 pgs., Zack Mosley-a	13	33	85	135
1412- Smilin' Jack Flying High with "Downwind," 1942, Whitman, 432 pgs., Zack Mosley-a	12	30	80	130
1416- Smilin' Jack in Wings over the Pacific, 1939, Whitman, 432 pgs., Zack Mosley-a	12	30	80	130
1419- Smilin' Jack and the Jungle Pipe Line, 1947, Whitman, 352 pgs., Zack Mosley-a	12	30	74	120
1445- Smilin' Jack and the Escape from Death Rock, 1943, Whitman, 352 pgs., Mosley-a	12	30	74	120
1464- Smilin' Jack and the Coral Princess, 1945, Whitman, 352 pgs., Zack Mosley-a	12	30	74	120
1473- Smilin' Jack Speed Pilot, 1941, Whitman, 432 pgs., Zack Mosley-a	12	30	80	130
2- Smilin' Jack and his Stratosphere Plane, 1938, Whitman, 132 pgs., Buddy Book, soft-c, Zack Mosley-a	27	68	189	325
nn- Smilin' Jack Grounded on a Tropical Shore, 1938, Whitman, 36 pgs., 2 1/2" x 3 1/2", Penny Book	10	25	60	95
11- Smilin' Jack and the Border Bandits, 1941, Dell, 196 pgs., Fast-Action Story, soft-c, Zack Mosley-a	24	60	168	285
745- Smitty Golden Gloves Tournament, 1934, Whitman, 320 pgs., Walter Berndt-a	12	30	74	120
nn- Smitty Golden Gloves Tournament, 1934, Whitman, 204 pgs., Cocomalt premium, soft-c, Walter Berndt-a	13	33	85	135
1404- Smitty and Herby Lost Among the Indians, 1941, Whitman, All Pictures Comics	10	25	60	95
1477- Smitty in Going Native, 1938, Whitman, 300 pgs., Walter Berndt-a	11	28	68	110
2- Smitty and Herby, 1936, Whitman, 132 pgs., 3 1/2" x 3 1/2", soft-c, Tarzan Ice Cream cup lid premium	24	60	168	285
9- Smitty's Brother Herby and the Police Horse, 1938, Whitman, 132 pgs., 3 1/4" x 3 1/2", Buddy Book-ice cream premium, by Walter Berndt	24	60	168	285
1010- Smokey Stover Firefighter of Foo, 1937, Whitman, 7 1/4" x 5 1/2", 64 pgs., Nickel Book, Bill Holman-a	13	33	85	135
1413- Smokey Stover, 1942, Whitman, All Pictures Comics, flip pictures, Bill Holman-a	13	33	85	135
1421- Smokey Stover the Foo Fighter, 1938, Whitman, 432 pgs., Bill Holman-a	13	33	85	135
1481- Smokey Stover the Foolish Foo Fighter, 1942, Whitman, All Pictures Comics	13	33	85	135
1- Smokey Stover the Fireman of Foo, 1938, Whitman, 3 3/4" x 3 1/2", 132 pgs., Buddy Book-ice cream premium, by Bill Holman	21	53	149	250
1100A- Smokey Stover, 1938, Whitman, 36 pgs., 2 1/2" x 3 1/2", Penny Book	10	25	64	100
nn- Smokey Stover and the Fire Chief of Foo, 1938, Whitman, 36 pgs., 2 1/2" x 3 1/2", Penny Book, yellow shirt on-c	10	25	64	100
nn- Smokey Stover and the Fire Chief of Foo, 1938, Whitman, 36 pgs., Penny Book, green shirt on-c	10	25	64	100
1460- Snow White and the Seven Dwarfs (The Story of Walt Disney's ...), 1938, Whitman, 288 pgs.	20	50	143	225
1136- Sombrero Pete, 1936, Whitman, 432 pgs.	10	25	60	95
1152- Son of Mystery, 1939, Saalfield, 400 pgs.	10	25	60	95
1191- SOS Coast Guard, 1936, Whitman, 432 pgs., Henry E. Vallely-a	10	25	64	100
2016-(#16)-Space Ghost-The Sorceress of Cyba-3 (TV Cartoon), 1968, Whitman, 260 pgs., 39¢-c, hard-c, color illos	10	25	60	95
1455- Speed Douglas and the Mole Gang-The Great Sabotage Plot, 1941, Whitman, 432 pgs., flip pictures	10	25	60	95
5779- Spider-Man Zaps Mr. Zodiac, 1976, 260 pgs., soft-c, B&W	2	3	11	15
5779-2- Spider-Man Zaps Mr. Zodiac, 1980, 260 pgs., 79¢-c, soft-c, B&W	1	3	6	8
1467- Spike Kelly of the Commandos, 1943, Whitman, 352 pgs.	10	25	60	95
1144- Spook Riders on the Overland, 1938, Saalfield, 400 pgs.	10	25	60	95
768- Spy, The, 1936, Whitman, 300 pgs.	12	30	80	130
nn- Spy Smasher and the Red Death, 1941, Fawcett, 4" x 5 1/2", Dime Action Book	44	110	308	550
1120- Stan Kent Freshman Fullback, 1936, Saalfield, 148 pgs., hard-c	6	15	36	55
1132- Stan Kent, Captain, 1937, Saalfield	6	15	36	55
1600- Stan Kent Freshman Fullback, 1936, Saalfield, 148 pgs., soft-c	6	15	36	55

1460 - Skeezix on His Own in the Big City © WHIT

5779 - Spider-Man Zaps Mr. Zodiac © MAR

L16 - Tale of Two Cities © Lynn

	GD	FN	VF	VF/NM
1123- Stan Kent Varsity Man, 1936, Saalfield, 160 pgs., hard-c				
	6	15	36	55
1603- Stan Kent Varsity Man, 1936, Saalfield, 160 pgs., soft-c				
	6	15	36	55
nn- Star Wars - A New Hope, 1997, Chronicle Books, 320 pgs.,				
adapts movie, 1-color (blue) illos	2	3	15	20
nn- Star Wars - Empire Strikes Back, The, 1997, Chronicle Books,				
296 pgs., adapts movie, 1-color (blue) illos	2	3	15	20
nn- Star Wars - Episode 1 - The Phantom Menace, 1999, Chronicle Books,				
344 pgs., adapts movie, 1-color (blue) illos	1	3	6	10
nn- Star Wars - Episode 2 - Attack of the Clones, 2002, Chronicle Books,				
340 pgs., adapts movie, 1-color (blue) illos	1	3	6	10
nn- Star Wars - Return of the Jedi, 1997, Chronicle Books,				
312 pgs., adapts movie, 1-color (blue) illos	2	3	15	20
1104- Steel Arena, The (With Clyde Beatty), 1936, Saalfield, hard-c, movie				
scenes adapted from "The Lost Jungle"	12	30	72	115
1584- Steel Arena, The (With Clyde Beatty), 1936, Saalfield,				
soft-c, movie scenes	12	30	72	115
1426- Steve Hunter of the U.S. Coast Guard Under Secret Orders,				
1942, Whitman, 432 pgs.	10	25	60	95
1456- Story of Charlie McCarthy and Edgar Bergen, The,				
1938, Whitman, 288 pgs.	10	25	60	95
Story of Daniel, The (See Wee Little Books)				
Story of David, The (See Wee Little Books)				
1110- Story of Freddie Bartholomew, The, 1935, Saalfield, 4 1/2" x 5 1/4",				
hard-c, movie scenes (MGM)	10	25	60	95
1590- Story of Freddie Bartholomew, The, 1935, Saalfield, 4 1/2" x 5 1/4",				
soft-c, movie scenes (MGM)	10	25	60	95
Story of Gideon, The (See Wee Little Books)				
W714- Story of Jackie Cooper, The, 1933, Whitman, 240 pgs., photo-c,				
movie scenes, "Skippy" & "Sooky" movie	12	30	74	120
Story of Joseph, The (See Wee Little Books)				
Story of Moses, The (See Wee Little Books)				
Story of Ruth and Naomi (See Wee Little Books)				
1089- Story of Shirley Temple, The, 1934, Saalfield, 160 pgs., hard-c,				
photo-c, movie scenes	12	30	72	115
1319- Story of Shirley Temple, The, 1934, Saalfield, 160 pgs., soft-c,				
photo-c, movie scenes	12	30	72	115
1090- Strawberry-Roan, 1934, Saalfield, 160 pgs., hard-c, Ken Maynard				
photo-c, movie scenes	12	30	72	115
1320- Strawberry-Roan, 1934, Saalfield, 160 pgs., soft-c, Ken Maynard				
photo-c, movie scenes	12	30	72	115
Streaky and the Football Signals (See Top-Line Comics)				
5780-2- Superman in the Phantom Zone Connection, 1980, 260 pgs.,				
79¢-c, soft-c, B&W	1	3	8	12
582- "Swap It" Book, The, 1949, Samuel Lowe Co., 260 pgs., 3 1/2" x 4 1/2"				
1. Little Tex in the Midst of Trouble	4	10	24	35
2. Little Tex's Escape	4	10	24	35
3. Little Tex Comes to the XY Ranch	4	10	24	35
4. Get Them Cowboy	4	10	24	35
5. The Mail Must Go Through! A Story of the Pony Express				
	4	10	24	35
6. Nevada Jones, Trouble Shooter	4	10	24	35
7. Danny Meets the Cowboys	4	10	24	35
8. Flint Adams and the Stage Coach	4	10	24	35
9. Bud Shinners and the Oregon Trail	4	10	24	35
10. The Outlaws' Last Ride	4	10	24	35
Sybil Jason (See Little Big Shot)				
747- Tailspin Tommy in the Famous Pay-Roll Mystery, 1933, Whitman,				
hard-c, 320 pgs., Hal Forrest-a (# 1)	12	30	74	120
747- Tailspin Tommy in the Famous Pay-Roll Mystery, 1933, Whitman,				
soft-c, 320 pgs., Hal Forrest-a (# 1)	12	30	74	120
nn- Tailspin Tommy the Pay-Roll Mystery, 1934, Whitman, 52 pgs.,				
3 1/2" x 5 1/4", premium-no ads, soft-c; another version with				
Perkins ad, Hal Forrest-a	16	40	112	175
1110- Tailspin Tommy and the Island in the Sky, 1936,				
Whitman, 432 pgs., Hal Forrest-a	11	28	68	110
1124- Tailspin Tommy the Dirigible Flight to the North Pole,				
1934, Whitman, 432 pgs., H. Forrest-a	12	30	74	120
nn- Tailspin Tommy the Dirigible Flight to the North Pole,				
1934, Whitman, 436 pgs., 3-color, soft-c, premium-no ads,				
Hal Forrest-a	20	50	140	220
1172- Tailspin Tommy Hunting for Pirate Gold, 1935, Whitman,				
432 pgs., Hal Forrest-a	11	28	68	110
1183- Tailspin Tommy Air Racer, 1940, Saalfield, 400 pgs., hard-c				
	11	28	68	110
1184- Tailspin Tommy in the Great Air Mystery, 1936, Whitman,				
240 pgs., photo-c, movie scenes	12	30	74	120
1410- Tailspin Tommy the Weasel and His "Skywaymen," 1941, Whitman,				
All Pictures Comics, flip pictures	10	25	64	100
1413- Tailspin Tommy and the Lost Transport, 1940, Whitman,				
432 pgs., Hal Forrest-a	10	25	64	100
1423- Tailspin Tommy and the Hooded Flyer, 1937, Whitman,				
432 pgs., Hal Forrest-a	11	28	68	110
1494- Tailspin Tommy and the Sky Bandits, 1938, Whitman				
432 pgs., Hal Forrest-a	11	28	68	110
nn- Tailspin Tommy and the Airliner Mystery, 1938, Dell, 196 pgs.,				
Fast-Action Story, soft-c, Hal Forrest-a	26	65	185	315
nn- Tailspin Tommy in Flying Aces, 1938, Dell, 196 pgs.,				
Fast-Action Story, soft-c, Hal Forrest-a	26	65	185	315
nn- Tailspin Tommy in Wings Over the Arctic, 1934, Whitman,				
Cocomalt premium, Forrest-a	11	28	68	110
nn- Tailspin Tommy Big Thrill Chewing Gum, 1934,				
Whitman, 8 pgs., 2 1/2" x 3 " (6 diff.) each..	11	28	68	110
3- Tailspin Tommy on the Mountain of Human Sacrifice,				
1938, Whitman, soft-c, Buddy Book	33	83	235	400
7- Tailspin Tommy's Perilous Adventure, 1934, Whitman, 132 pgs.,				
3 1/2" x 3 1/2" soft-c, Tarzan Ice Cream cup premium				
	21	53	149	250
nn- Tailspin Tommy, 1935, Whitman, 148 pgs., 3 1/2" x 4",				
Tarzan Ice Cream cup premium	23	58	163	275
L16- Tale of Two Cities, A, 1935, Lynn, movie scenes	12	30	74	120
744- Tarzan of the Apes, 1933, Whitman, 320 pgs., by Edgar Rice				
Burroughs (1st)	29	73	203	350
nn- Tarzan of the Apes, 1935, Whitman, 52 pgs., 3 1/2" x 5 1/4", soft-c,				
stapled, premium, no ad; another version with a Perkins ad; reprints				
panels from Hal Foster's newspaper adaptation	40	100	280	480
769- Tarzan the Fearless, 1934, Whitman, 240 pgs., Buster Crabbe				
photo-c, movie scenes, ERB	21	53	149	250
770- Tarzan Twins, The, 1934, Whitman, 432 pgs., ERB				
	50	125	350	650
770- Tarzan Twins, The, 1935, Whitman, 432 pgs., ERB				
	40	100	280	480
nn- Tarzan Twins, The, 1935, Whitman, 52 pgs., 3 1/2" x 5 3/4",				
premium-with & without ads, soft-c, ERB	42	105	290	500
nn- Tarzan Twins, The, 1935, Whitman, 436 pgs., 3-color, soft-c,				
premium-no ads, ERB	42	105	295	525
778- Tarzan of the Screen (The Story of Johnny Weissmuller), 1934,				
Whitman, 240 pgs., photo-c, movie scenes	21	53	149	250
1102- Tarzan, The Return of, 1936, Whitman, 432 pgs., Edgar Rice				
Burroughs	15	38	108	170
1180- Tarzan, The New Adventures of, 1935, Whitman, 160 pgs.,				
Herman Brix photo-c, movie scenes, ERB	16	40	116	180
1182- Tarzan Escapes, 1936, Whitman, 240 pgs., Johnny Weissmuller				
photo-c, movie scenes, ERB	21	53	149	250
1407- Tarzan Lord of the Jungle, 1946, Whitman, 352 pgs., ERB				
	11	28	68	110
1410- Tarzan, The Beasts of, 1937, Whitman, 432 pgs., Edgar Rice				
Burroughs	15	38	100	160
1442- Tarzan and the Lost Empire, 1948, Whitman, 288 pgs., ERB				
	11	28	68	110
1444- Tarzan and the Ant Men, 1945, Whitman, 352 pgs., ERB				
	11	28	68	110
1448- Tarzan and the Golden Lion, 1943, Whitman, 432 pgs., ERB				
	14	35	95	150
1452- Tarzan the Untamed, 1941, Whitman, 432 pgs., flip pictures,				
ERB	14	35	95	150
1453- Tarzan the Terrible, 1942, Whitman, 432 pgs., flip pictures,				

	GD	FN	VF	VF/NM
ERB	14	35	95	150
1467- Tarzan in the Land of the Giant Apes, 1949, Whitman, ERB	11	28	68	110
1477- Tarzan, The Son of, 1939, Whitman, 432 pgs., ERB	14	35	95	150
1488- Tarzan's Revenge, 1938, Whitman, 432 pgs., ERB	14	35	95	150
1495- Tarzan and the Jewels of Opar, 1940, Whitman, 432 pgs.	14	35	95	150
4056- Tarzan and the Tarzan Twins with Jad-Bal-Ja the Golden Lion, 1936, Whitman, 7" x 9 1/2", 320 pgs., Big Big Book	42	105	290	500
709-10- Tarzan and the Journey of Terror, 1950, Whitman, 2 1/2" x 5", ERB, Marsh-a	7	18	45	70
2005- (#5)-Tarzan: The Mark of the Red Hyena, 1967, Whitman, 260 pgs., 39 cents, hard-c, color illos	3	8	20	28
nn- Tarzan, 1935, Whitman, 148 pgs., soft-c, 3 1/2" x 4", Tarzan Ice Cream cup premium, ERB (scarce)	52	130	364	675
nn- Tarzan and a Daring Rescue, 1938, Whitman, 68 pgs., Pan-Am premium, soft-c, ERB (blank back-c version also exists)	37	93	260	450
nn- Tarzan and his Jungle Friends, 1936, Whitman, 132 pgs., soft-c, 3 1/2" x 3 1/2", Tarzan Ice Cream cup premium, ERB (scarce)	52	130	364	675
nn- Tarzan in the Golden City, 1938, Whitman, 68 pgs., Pan-Am premium, soft-c, 3 1/2" x 3 3/4", ERB	37	93	260	450
nn- Tarzan The Avenger, 1939, Dell, 194 pgs., Fast-Action Story, ERB, soft-c	25	63	175	300
nn- Tarzan with the Tarzan Twins in the Jungle, 1938, Dell, 194 pgs., Fast-Action Story, ERB	25	63	175	300
1100B- Tell Your Fortune, 1938, Whitman, 36 pgs., 2 1/2" x 3 1/2", Penny Book	3	8	21	30
nn- Terminator 2: Judgment Day, 1998, Chronicle Books, 310 pgs., adapts movie, 1-color (blue-gray) illos	3	6	8	10
1156- Terry and the Pirates, 1935, Whitman, 432 pgs., Milton Caniff-a (#1)	14	35	95	150
nn- Terry and the Pirates, 1935, Whitman, 52 pgs., 3 1/2" x 5 1/4", soft-c, premium, Milton Caniff-a; 3 versions: No ad, Sears ad & Perkins ad	25	63	175	300
1412- Terry and the Pirates Shipwrecked on a Desert Island, 1938, Whitman, 432 pgs., Milton Caniff-a	12	30	72	115
1420- Terry and War in the Jungle, 1946, Whitman, 352 pgs., Milton Caniff-a	11	28	68	110
1436- Terry and the Pirates The Plantation Mystery, 1942, Whitman, 432 pgs., flip pictures, Milton Caniff-a	12	30	72	115
1446- Terry and the Pirates and the Giant's Vengeance, 1939, Whitman, 432 pgs., Caniff-a	12	30	72	115
1499- Terry and the Pirates in the Mountain Stronghold, 1941, Whitman, 432 pgs., Caniff-a	12	30	72	115
4073- Terry and the Pirates, The Adventures of, 1938, Whitman, 7" x 9 1/2", 320 pgs., Big Big Book, Milton Caniff-a	25	63	175	300
4- Terry and the Pirates Ashore in Singapore, 1938, Whitman, 132 pgs., 3 1/2" x 3 3/4", soft-c, Buddy Book premium	21	53	149	250
10- Terry and the Pirates Meet Again, 1936, Whitman, 132 pgs., 3 1/2" x 3 1/2", soft-c, Tarzan Ice Cream cup lid premium	25	63	175	300
nn- Terry and the Pirates, Adventures of, 1938, 36 pgs., 2 1/2" x 3 1/2", Penny Book, Caniff-a	7	18	45	70
nn- Terry and the Pirates and the Island Rescue, 1938, Whitman, 68 pgs., 3 1/4" x 3 1/2", Pan-Am premium	20	50	140	220
nn- Terry and the Pirates on Their Travels, 1938, 36 pgs., 2 1/2" x 3 1/2", Penny Book, Caniff-a	7	18	45	70
nn- Terry and the Pirates and the Mystery Ship, 1938, Dell, 194 pgs., Fast-Action Story, soft-c	25	63	175	300
1492- Terry Lee Flight Officer U.S.A., 1944, Whitman, 352 pgs., Milton Caniff-a	12	30	72	115
7- Texas Bad Man, The (Tom Mix), 1934, EVW, 160 pgs., (Five Star Library), movie scenes	16	40	112	175
1429- Texas Kid, The, 1937, Whitman, 432 pgs.	6	15	40	60
1135- Texas Ranger, The, 1936, Whitman, 432 pgs., Hal Arbo-a	6	15	40	60
nn- Texas Ranger, The, 1935, Whitman, 260 pgs., Cocomalt premium, soft-c, Hal Arbo-a	12	30	72	115
nn- Texas Ranger and the Rustler Gang, The, 1936, Whitman, Pan-Am giveaway	21	53	145	230
nn- Texas Ranger in the West, The, 1938, Whitman, 36 pgs., 2 1/2" x 3 1/2", Penny Book	6	15	40	60
nn- Texas Ranger to the Rescue, The, 1938, Whitman, 36 pgs., 2 1/2" x 3 1/2", Penny Book	6	15	40	60
12- Texas Ranger in Rustler Strategy, The, 1936, Whitman, 132 pgs., 3 1/2" x 3 1/2", soft-c, Tarzan Ice Cream cup lid premium	21	53	145	230
Tex Thorne (See Zane Grey)				
Thimble Theatre (See Popeye)				
26- 13 Hours By Air, 1936, Lynn, 128 pgs., 5" x 7 1/2", photo-c,				

	GD	FN	VF	VF/NM
movie scenes (Paramount Pictures)	12	30	74	120
nn- Three Bears, The, nd (1930s), np (Whitman), 36 pgs., 3" x 2 1/2", Penny Book	2	3	16	22
1129- Three Finger Joe (Baseball), 1937, Saalfield, Robert A. Graef-a	7	18	45	70
nn- Three Little Pigs, The, nd (1930s), np (Whitman), 36 pgs., 3" x 2 1/2", Penny Book	2	3	16	22
1131- Three Musketeers, 1935, Whitman, 182 pgs., 5 1/4" x 6 1/4", photo-c, movie scenes	13	33	90	140
1409- Thumper and the Seven Dwarfs (Disney), 1944, Whitman, All Pictures Comics	24	60	173	295
1108- Tiger Lady, The (The life of Mabel Stark, animal trainer), 1935, Saalfield, photo-c, movie scenes, hard-c	9	23	56	90
1588- Tiger Lady, The, 1935, Saalfield, photo-c, movie scenes, soft-c	9	23	56	90
1442- Tillie the Toiler and the Wild Man of Desert Island, 1941, Whitman, 432 pgs., Russ Westover-a	11	28	66	105
1058- "Timid Elmer" (Disney), 1939, Whitman, 5" x 5 1/2", 68 pgs., hard-c	11	28	66	105
1152- Tim McCoy in the Prescott Kid, 1935, Whitman, 160 pgs., hard-c, photo-c, movie scenes	16	40	116	180
1193- Tim McCoy in the Westerner, 1936, Whitman, 240 pgs., photo-c, movie scenes	12	30	76	125
1436- Tim McCoy on the Tomahawk Trail, 1937, Whitman, 432 pgs., Robert Weisman-a	11	28	68	110
1490- Tim McCoy and the Sandy Gulch Stampede, 1939, Whitman, 424 pgs.	10	25	60	95
2- Tim McCoy in Beyond the Law, 1934, EVW, Five Star Library, photo-c, movie scenes (Columbia Pict.) Hardcover	12	30	76	125
(Rare) Softcover	22	55	154	260
10- Tim McCoy in Fighting the Redskins, 1938, Whitman, 130 pgs., Buddy Book, soft-c	21	53	149	250
14- Tim McCoy in Speedwings, 1935, EVW, Five Star Library, 160 pgs., photo-c, movie scenes (Columbia Pictures)	14	35	95	150
nn- Tim the Builder, nd (1930s), np (Whitman), 36 pgs., 3" x 2 1/2", Penny Book	2	3	16	22
Tim Tyler (Also see Adventures of ...)				
1140- Tim Tyler's Luck Adventures in the Ivory Patrol, 1937, Whitman, 432 pgs., by Lyman Young	9	23	56	90
1479- Tim Tyler's Luck and the Plot of the Exiled King, 1939, Whitman, 432 pgs., by Lyman Young	9	23	56	90
767- Tiny Tim, The Adventures of, 1935, Whitman, 384 pgs., by Stanley Link	12	30	74	120
1172- Tiny Tim and the Mechanical Men, 1937, Whitman, 432 pgs., by Stanley Link	11	28	68	110
1472- Tiny Tim in the Big, Big World, 1945, Whitman, 352 pgs., by Stanley Link	11	28	68	110
2006- (#6)-Tom and Jerry Meet Mr. Fingers, 1967, Whitman, 39¢-c, 260 pgs., hard-c, color illos.	3	8	20	28
5752- Tom and Jerry Meet Mr. Fingers, 1973, Whitman, 39¢-c, 260 pgs., soft-c, color illos., 5 printings	2	3	10	15
2030-(#30)- Tom and Jerry, The Astro-Nots, 1969, Whitman, 256 pgs., hard-c, color illos.	2	3	15	20
5765- Tom and Jerry, The Astro-Nots, 1974, Whitman, 256 pgs., soft-c, color illos.	2	3	10	15
5787-2- Tom and Jerry Under the Big Top, 1980, Whitman, 79¢-c, 260 pgs., soft-c, B&W	2	3	10	15
723- Tom Beatty Ace of the Service, 1934, Whitman, 256 pgs., George Taylor-a	12	30	72	115
nn- Tom Beatty Ace of the Service, 1934, Whitman, 260 pgs., soft-c	12	30	72	115
1165- Tom Beatty Ace of the Service Scores Again, 1937, Whitman, 432 pgs., Weisman-a	11	28	66	105
1420- Tom Beatty Ace of the Service and the Big Brain Gang, 1939, Whitman, 432 pgs.	11	28	66	105
nn- Tom Beatty Ace Detective and the Gorgon Gang, 1938?, Whitman, 36 pgs., 2 1/2" x 3 1/2", Penny Book	10	25	60	95
nn- Tom Beatty Ace of the Service and the Kidnapers, 1938?, Whitman, 36 pgs., 2 1/2" x 3 1/2", Penny Book	10	25	60	95
1102- Tom Mason on Top, 1935, Saalfield, 160 pgs., Tom Mix photo-c, from Mascot serial "The Miracle Rider," movie scenes, hard-c	14	35	95	150
1582- Tom Mason on Top, 1935, Saalfield, 160 pgs., Tom Mix photo-c, movie scenes, soft-c	14	35	95	150
Tom Mix (See Chief of the Rangers, Flaming Guns & Texas Bad Man)				
762- Tom Mix and Tony Jr. in "Terror Trail," 1934, Whitman, 160 pgs., movie scenes	14	35	95	150
1144- Tom Mix in the Fighting Cowboy, 1935, Whitman, 432 pgs., Hal Arbo-a	12	30	72	115
nn- Tom Mix in the Fighting Cowboy, 1935, Whitman, 436 pgs., premium-no ads, 3 color, soft-c, Hal Arbo-a	18	45	128	200
1166- Tom Mix in the Range War, 1937, Whitman, 432 pgs., Hal Arbo-a	10	25	60	95
1173- Tom Mix Plays a Lone Hand, 1935, Whitman, 288 pgs., hard-c, Hal Arbo-a	10	25	60	95

709-10 - Tarzan and the Journey of Terror © ERB

1108 - The Tiger Lady © Saalfield

845 - Walt Disney's Minnie Mouse and the Antique Chair © DIS

	GD	FN	VF	VF/NM
1183- Tom Mix and the Stranger from the South, 1936, Whitman, 432 pgs.	10	25	60	95
1462- Tom Mix and the Hoard of Montezuma, 1937, Whitman, H. E. Vallely-a	10	25	60	95
1482- Tom Mix and His Circus on the Barbary Coast, 1940, Whitman, 432 pgs., James Gary-a	10	25	60	95
3047- Tom Mix and His Big Little Kit, 1937, Whitman, 384 pgs., 4 1/2" x 6 1/2" box, includes miniature box of 4 crayons- red, yellow, blue and green	46	115	322	600
4068- Tom Mix and the Scourge of Paradise Valley, 1937, Whitman, 7" x 9 1/2", 320 pgs., Big Big Book, Vallely-a	21	53	145	230
6833- Tom Mix in the Riding Avenger, 1936, Dell, 244 pgs., Cartoon Story Book, hard-c	14	35	95	150
nn- Tom Mix Rides to the Rescue, 1939, 36 pgs., 2 1/2" x 3", Penny Book	7	18	42	65
nn- Tom Mix Avenges the Dry Gulched Range King, 1939, Dell, 196 pgs., Fast-Action Story, soft-c	15	38	100	160
nn- Tom Mix in the Riding Avenger, 1936, Dell, 244 pgs., Fast-Action Story	15	38	100	160
nn- Tom Mix the Trail of the Terrible 6, 1935, Ralston Purina Co., 84 pgs., 3" x 3 1/2", premium	13	33	90	140
4- Tom Mix and Tony in the Rider of Death Valley, 1934, EVW, Five Star Library, 160 pgs., movie scenes (Universal Pictures), hard-c	12	30	80	130
4- Tom Mix and Tony in the Rider of Death Valley, 1934, EVW, Five Star Library, 160 pgs., movie scenes (Universal Pictures), soft-c (Rare)	25	63	175	300
7- Tom Mix in the Texas Bad Man, 1934, EVW, Five Star Library, 160 pgs., movie scenes, hard-c	13	33	90	140
7- Tom Mix in the Texas Bad Man, 1934, EVW, Five Star Library, 160 pgs., movie scenes; soft-c (Rare)	25	63	175	300
10- Tom Mix in the Tepee Ranch Mystery, 1938, Whitman, 132 pgs., Buddy Book, soft-c	16	40	112	175
1126- Tommy of Troop Six (Scout Book), 1937, Saalfield, hard-c	7	18	42	65
1606- Tommy of Troop Six (Scout Book), 1937, Saalfield, soft-c	7	18	42	65
Tom Sawyer (See Adventures of ...)				
1437- Tom Swift and His Magnetic Silencer, 1941, Whitman, 432 pgs., flip pictures	21	53	149	250
1485- Tom Swift and His Giant Telescope, 1939, Whitman, 432 pgs., James Gary-a	16	40	116	180
540- Top-Line Comics (In Open Box), 1935, Whitman, 164 pgs., 3 1/2" x 3 1/2", 3 books in set, all soft-c:				
Bobby Thatcher and the Samarang Emerald	12	30	76	125
Broncho Bill in Suicide Canyon	12	30	76	125
Freckles and His Friends in the North Woods	12	30	76	125
Complete set with box	37	93	260	450
541- Top-Line Comics (In Open Box), 1935, Whitman, 164 pgs., 3 1/2" x 3 1/2", 3 books in set; all soft-c:				
Little Joe and the City Gangsters	12	30	76	125
Smilin' Jack and His Flivver Plane	12	30	76	125
Streaky and the Football Signals	12	30	76	125
Complete set with box	37	93	260	450
542- Top-Line Comics (In Open Box), 1935, Whitman, 164 pgs., 3 1/2" x 3 1/2", 3 books in set; all soft-c:				
Dinglehoofer Und His Dog Adolph by Knerr	12	30	76	125
Jungle Jim by Alex Raymond	14	35	95	150
Sappo by Segar	14	35	95	150
Complete set with box	42	105	290	500
543- Top-Line Comics (In Open Box), 1935, Whitman, 164 pgs., 3 1/2" x 3 1/2", 3 books in set; all soft-c:				
Alexander Smart, ESQ by Winner	12	30	76	125
Bunky by Billy de Beck	12	30	76	125
Nicodemus O'Malley by Carter	12	30	76	125
Complete set with box	37	93	260	450
1158- Tracked by a G-Man, 1939, Saalfield, 400 pgs.	8	20	48	75
25- Trail of the Lonesome Pine, The, 1936, Lynn, movie scenes	10	25	60	95
nn- Trail of the Terrible 6 (See Tom Mix ...)				
1185- Trail to Squaw Gulch, The, 1940, Saalfield, 400 pgs.	8	20	48	75
720- Treasure Island, 1933, Whitman, 362 pgs.	10	25	60	95
1141- Treasure Island, 1934, Whitman, 164 pgs., hard-c, 4 1/4" x 5 1/4", Jackie Cooper photo-c, movie scenes	10	25	60	95
1141- Treasure Island, 1934, Whitman, 164 pgs., soft-c, 4 1/4" x 5 1/4", Jackie Cooper photo-c, movie scenes	10	25	60	95
1018- Trick and Puzzle Book, 1939, Whitman, 100 pgs., soft-c	3	8	18	25
1100B- Tricks Easy to Do (Slight of hand & magic), 1938, Whitman, 36 pgs., 2 1/2" x 3 1/2", Penny Book	3	8	18	25
1100B- Tricks You Can Do, 1938, Whitman, 36 pgs., 2 1/2" x 3 1/2", Penny Book	3	8	18	25
5777- Tweety and Sylvester, The Magic Voice, 1976, Whitman, 260 pgs., soft-c, flip-it feature; 5 printings	1	3	8	12
1104- Two-Gun Montana, 1936, Whitman, 432 pgs., Henry E. Vallely-a	10	25	60	95
nn- Two-Gun Montana Shoots it Out, 1939, Whitman, 36 pgs., 2 1/2" x 3 1/2", Penny Book	10	25	60	95
1058- Ugly Duckling, The (Disney), 1939, Whitman, 68 pgs., 5" x 5 1/2", hard-c	12	30	80	130
nn- Ugly Duckling, The, nd (1930s), np (Whitman), 36 pgs., 3" x 2 1/2", Penny Book	3	8	20	28
Unc' Billy Gets Even (See Wee Little Books)				
1114- Uncle Don's Strange Adventures, 1935, Whitman, 300 pgs., radio star-Uncle Don Carney	10	25	64	100
722- Uncle Ray's Story of the United States, 1934, Whitman, 300 pgs.	10	25	64	100
1461- Uncle Sam's Sky Defenders, 1941, Whitman, 432 pgs., flip pictures	11	28	68	110
1405- Uncle Wiggily's Adventures, 1946, Whitman, All Pictures Comics	12	30	72	115
1411- Union Pacific, 1939, Whitman, 240 pgs., photo-c, movie scenes	11	28	66	105
With Union Pacific letter	22	55	154	260
1189- Up Dead Horse Canyon, 1940, Saalfield, 400 pgs.	7	18	42	65
1455- Vic Sands of the U.S. Flying Fortress Bomber Squadron, 1944, Whitman, 352 pgs.	11	28	66	105
nn- Visit to Santa Claus, 1938?, Whitman, Pan Am premium by Snow Plane; soft-c (Rare)	23	58	163	275
1645- Walt Disney's Andy Burnett on the Trail (TV Series), 1958, Whitman, 280 pgs.	3	8	20	28
803- Walt Disney's Bongo, 1948, Whitman, hard-c, Story Hour Series	9	23	56	90
711-10- Walt Disney's Cinderella and the Magic Wand, 1950, Whitman, 2 1/2" x 5", based on Disney movie	10	25	60	95
845- Walt Disney's Donald Duck and his Cat Troubles (Disney), 1948, Whitman, 100 pgs., 5" x 5 1/2", hard-c	12	30	72	115
845- Walt Disney's Donald Duck and the Boys, 1948, Whitman, 100 pgs., 5" x 5 1/2", hard-c, Barks-a	18	45	128	200
2952- Walt Disney's Donald Duck in the Great Kite Maker, 1949, Whitman, 24 pgs., 3 1/4" x 4", Tiny Tales, full color (5 cents)	10	25	60	95
804- Walt Disney's Mickey and the Beanstalk, 1948, Whitman, hard-c, Story Hour Series	12	30	72	115
845- Walt Disney's Mickey Mouse and the Boy Thursday, 194 pgs., Whitman, 5" x 5 1/2", 100 pgs.	12	30	72	115
845- Walt Disney's Mickey Mouse the Miracle Maker, 1948, Whitman, 5" x 5 1/2", 100 pgs.	12	30	72	115
2952- Walt Disney's Mickey Mouse and the Night Prowlers, Whitman, 1949, 24 pgs., 3 1/4" x 4", Tiny Tales, full color (5 ¢)	10	25	60	95
5770- Walt Disney's Mickey Mouse - Mystery at Disneyland, Whitman, 1975, 260 pgs., four printings	1	3	10	14
5781-2- Walt Disney's Mickey Mouse - Mystery at Dead Man's Cove, Whitman, 1980, 260 pgs., two printings	1	3	8	12
845- Walt Disney's Minnie Mouse and the Antique Chair, 1948, Whitman, 5" x 5 1/2", 100 pgs.	12	30	72	115
1435- Walt Disney's Pinocchio and Jiminy Cricket, 1940,				

	GD	FN	VF	VF/NM
Whitman, 432 pgs.	29	73	203	350
nn- **Walt Disney's Pinocchio and Jiminy Cricket**, Fast Action Story, 1940, Dell, 432 pgs.	37	93	260	450
845- **Walt Disney's Poor Pluto**, 1948, Whitman, 5" x 5 1/2", 100 pgs., hard-c	12	30	76	125
1467- **Walt Disney's Pluto the Pup** (Disney), 1938, Whitman, 432 pgs., Gottfredson-a	15	38	108	170
1066- **Walt Disney's Story of Clarabelle Cow** (Disney), 1938, Whitman, 100 pgs.	12	30	72	115
66- **Walt Disney's Story of Dippy the Goof** (Disney), 1938, Whitman, 100 pgs.	12	30	72	115
1066- **Walt Disney's Story of Donald Duck** (Disney), 1938, Whitman, 100 pgs., hard-c, Taliaferro-a	12	30	72	115
1066- **Walt Disney's Story of Goofy** (Disney), 1938, Whitman, 100 pgs., hard-c	12	30	76	125
1066- **Walt Disney's Story of Mickey Mouse** (Disney), 1938, Whitman, 100 pgs., hard-c, Gottfredson-a, Donald Duck app.	12	30	72	115
1066- **Walt Disney's Story of Minnie Mouse** (Disney), 1938, Whitman, 100 pgs., hard-c	12	30	72	115
1066- **Walt Disney's Story of Pluto the Pup**, (Disney), 1938, Whitman, 100 pgs., hard-c	12	30	76	125
2952- **Walter Lantz Presents Andy Panda's Rescue**, 1949, Whitman, Tiny Tales, full color (5 cents) (1030-5 on back-c)	11	28	66	105
751- **Wash Tubbs in Pandemonia**, 1934, Whitman, 320 pgs., Roy Crane-a	12	30	72	115
nn- **Wash Tubbs in Pandemonia**, 1934, Whitman, 52 pgs., 4" x 5 1/2", premium-no ads, soft-c, Roy Crane-a	18	45	128	200
1455- **Wash Tubbs and Captain Easy Hunting For Whales**, 1938, Whitman, 432 pgs., Roy Crane-a	12	30	76	125
6- **Wash Tubbs in Foreign Travel**, 1934, Whitman, soft-c, 3 1/2" x 3 1/2", Tarzan Ice Cream cup premium	21	53	149	250
513- **Wee Little Books** (In Open Box), 1934, Whitman, 44 pgs., small size, 6 books in set (children's classics) (Both Red box and Green box editions exist)				
Child's Garden of Verses	4	10	24	35
The Happy Prince (The Story of)	4	10	24	35
Joan of Arc (The Story of)	4	10	24	35
Peter Pan (The Story of)	4	10	24	35
Pied Piper Of Hamlin	4	10	24	35
Robin Hood (A Story of...)	4	10	24	35
Complete set with box	25	63	175	300
514- **Wee Little Books** (In Open Box), 1934, Whitman, 44 pgs., small size, 6 books in set				
Jack And Jill	4	10	24	35
Little Bo-Peep	4	10	24	35
Little Tommy Tucker	4	10	24	35
Mother Goose	4	10	24	35
Old King Cole	4	10	24	35
Simple Simon	4	10	24	35
Complete set with box	25	63	175	300
518- **Wee Little Books** (In Open Box), 1933, Whitman, 44 pgs., small size, 6 books in set, written by Thornton Burgess				
Betty Bear's Lesson-1930	4	10	24	35
Jimmy Skunk's Justice-1933	4	10	24	35
Little Joe Otter's Slide-1929	4	10	24	35
Peter Rabbit's Carrots-1933	4	10	24	35
Unc' Billy Gets Even-1930	4	10	24	35
Whitefoot's Secret-1933	4	10	24	35
Complete set with box	25	63	175	300
519- **Wee Little Books** (In Open Box) (Bible Stories), 1934, Whitman, 44 pgs., small size, 6 books in set, Helen Janes-a				
The Story of David	4	10	24	35
The Story of Gideon	4	10	24	35
The Story of Daniel	4	10	24	35
The Story of Joseph	4	10	24	35
The Story of Ruth and Naomi	4	10	24	35
The Story of Moses	4	10	24	35
Complete set with box	25	63	175	300
1471- **Wells Fargo**, 1938, Whitman, 240 pgs., photo-c, movie scenes	10	25	64	100
L18- **Western Frontier**, 1935, Lynn, 192 pgs., starring Ken Maynard, movie scenes	12	30	76	125
1121- **West Pointers on the Gridiron**, 1936, Saalfield, 148 pgs., hard-c, sports book	5	12	34	50
1601- **West Pointers on the Gridiron**, 1936, Saalfield, 148 pgs., soft-c, sports book	5	12	34	50
1124- **West Point Five, The**, 1937, Saalfield, 4 3/4" x 5 1/4", sports book, hard-c	5	12	34	50
1604- **West Point Five, The**, 1937, Saalfield, 4 1/4" x 5 1/4", sports book, soft-c	5	12	34	50
1164- **West Point of the Air**, 1935, Whitman, 160 pgs., photo-c, movie scenes	9	23	54	85
18- **Westward Ho!**, 1935, EVW, 160 pgs., movie scenes, star ring John Wayne (Scarce)	42	105	290	500

	GD	FN	VF	VF/NM
1109- **We Three**, 1935, Saalfield, 160 pgs., photo-c, movie scenes, by John Barrymore, hard-c	10	25	60	95
1589- **We Three**, 1935, Saalfield, 160 pgs., photo-c, movie scenes, by John Barrymore, soft-c	10	25	60	95
Whitefoot's Secret (See Wee Little Books)				
nn- **Who's Afraid of the Big Bad Wolf**, "Three Little Pigs" (Disney), 1933, McKay, 36 pgs., 6" x 8 1/2", stiff-c, Disney studio-a	21	53	149	250
nn- **Wild West Adventures of Buffalo Bill**, 1935, Whitman, 260 pgs., Cocomalt premium, soft-c, Hal Arbo-a	12	30	72	115
1096- **Will Rogers, The Story of**, 1935, Saalfield, photo-hard-c	7	18	45	70
1576- **Will Rogers, The Story of**, 1935, Saalfield, photo-soft-c	7	18	45	70
1458- **Wimpy the Hamburger Eater**, 1938, Whitman, 432 pgs., E.C. Segar-a	16	40	112	175
1433- **Windy Wayne and His Flying Wing**, 1942, Whitman, 432 pgs., flip pictures	10	25	60	95
1131- **Winged Four, The**, 1937, Saalfield, sports book, hard-c	10	25	60	95
1407- **Wings of the U.S.A.**, 1940, Whitman, 432 pgs., Thomas Hickey-a	10	25	60	95
nn- **Winning of the Old Northwest, The**, 1934, World Syndicate, High Lights of History Series, full color-c	10	25	60	95
nn- **Winning of the Old Northwest, The**, 1934, World Syndicate, High Lights of History Series; red & silver-c	10	25	60	95
1122- **Winning Point, The**, 1936, Saalfield, (Football), hard-c	5	12	30	45
1602- **Winning Point, The**, 1936, Saalfield, soft-c	5	12	30	45
nn- **Wizard of Oz Waddle Book**, 1934, BRP, 20 pgs., 7 1/2" x 10", forerunner of the Blue Ribbon Pop-Up books; with 6 removable articulated cardboard characters. Book only	42	105	295	525
Dust jacket only	48	120	336	625
Near Mint Complete - $12,500				
710-10- **Woody Woodpecker Big Game Hunter**, 1950, Whitman, by Walter Lantz	7	18	42	65
2010-(#10)- **Woody Woodpecker-The Meteor Menace**, 1967, Whitman, 260 pgs., 39¢-c, hard-c, color illos.	3	8	21	30
5753- **Woody Woodpecker-The Meteor Menace**, 1973, Whitman, 260 pgs., no price, soft-c, color illos.	1	3	6	9
2028- **Woody Woodpecker-The Sinister Signal**, 1969, Whitman	2	3	16	22
5763- **Woody Woodpecker-The Sinister Signal**, 1974, Whitman, 1st printing-no price; 2nd printing-39¢-c	1	3	5	6
23- **World of Monsters, The**, 1935, EVW, Five Star Library, movie scenes	15	38	100	160
779- **World War in Photographs, The**, 1934, Whitman, photo-c, photo illus.	10	25	60	95
Wyatt Earp (See Hugh O'Brian ...)				
nn- **Xena - Warrior Princess**, 1998, Chronicle Books, 310 pgs., based on TV series, 1-color (purple) illos	1	3	6	10
nn- **Yogi Bear Goes Country & Western**, 1977, Modern Promotions, 244 pgs., 49 cents, soft-c, flip pictures	1	3	10	14
nn- **Yogi Bear Saves Jellystone Park**, 1977, Modern Promotions, 244 pgs., 49 cents, soft-c, flip pictures	1	3	10	14
nn- **Zane Grey's Cowboys of the West**, 1935, Whitman, 148 pgs., 3 3/4" x 4", Tarzan Ice Cream Cup premium, soft-c, Arbo-a	21	53	149	250
Zane Grey's King of the Royal Mounted (See Men of the Mounted)				
1010- **Zane Grey's King of the Royal Mounted in Arctic Land**, 1937, Whitman, 7 1/4" x 5 1/2", 64 pgs., Nickel Book	10	25	64	100
1103- **Zane Grey's King of the Royal Mounted**, 1936, Whitman, 432 pgs.	10	25	60	95
nn- **Zane Grey's King of the Royal Mounted**, 1935, Whitman, 260 pgs., Cocomalt premium, soft-c	10	25	64	100
1179- **Zane Grey's King of the Royal Mounted and the Northern Treasure**, 1937, Whitman, 432 pgs.	10	25	60	95
1405- **Zane Grey's King of the Royal Mounted the Long Arm of the Law**, 1942, Whitman, All Pictures Comics	10	25	60	95
1452- **Zane Grey's King of the Royal Mounted Gets His Man**, 1938, Whitman, 432 pgs.	10	25	60	95
1486- **Zane Grey's King of the Royal Mounted and the Great Jewel Mystery**, 1939, Whitman, 432 pgs.	10	25	60	95
5- **Zane Grey's King of the Royal Mounted in the Far North**, 1938, Whitman, 132 pgs., Buddy Book, soft-c (Rare)	29	73	203	350
nn- **Zane Grey's King of the Royal Mounted in Law of the North**, 1939, Whitman, 36 pgs., 2 1/2" x 3 1/2", Penny Book	6	15	36	55
nn- **Zane Grey's King of the Royal Mounted Policing the Frozen North**, 1938, Dell, 196 pgs., Fast-Action Story, soft-c	14	35	95	150
1440- **Zane Grey's Tex Thorne Comes Out of the West**, 1937, Whitman, 432 pgs.	10	25	60	95
1465- **Zip Saunders King of the Speedway**, 1939, 432 pgs., Weisman-a	10	25	60	95

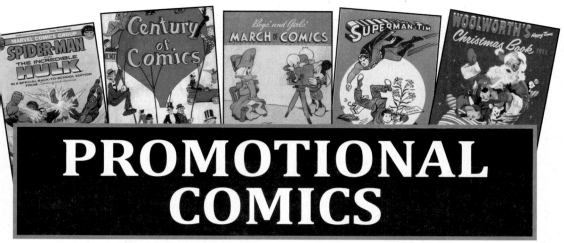

PROMOTIONAL COMICS

The Marketing of a Medium

By Carrie Wood

When it comes to four-letter words, most people probably rank "free" among some of their favorites. But of course, just because you didn't pay for something doesn't mean that there isn't a catch involved. Comic books have hardly been immune to this – a free comic usually meant that someone was trying to sell the reader something additional. And this practice of hiding a sales pitch behind some fun, colorful characters has been around in comics since the very beginning of the medium.

Even as early as the Platinum and Victorian Ages of comics, companies had realized the value of comic strips as promotional material. By the 1850s, free almanacs such as Hostetter's and Wright's were using comics as a way to help sell everything from shoe polish to patent medicine. These books are remarkably rare today, and it's difficult to compile an accurate or complete history (though you can read more about them in the Victorian Comics essay elsewhere in this book). By the end of the 1800s, the popularity of characters like the Yellow Kid and The Brownies heralded in a new age of comics-as-promos.

The very idea of funny pages within newspapers were, essentially, using comics as promotions to help sell more papers. The news publishers of the time started adding supplements to Sunday papers, and soon after, thanks to the key arrival of Buster Brown as a wildly popular character, comics were being nationally licensed for newspapers. And the sales-minded goal of using free comic strip pages to help driver readership? That worked remarkably well. The Yellow Kid, The Brownies, Buster Brown and others helped increase newspaper sales nationwide.

Some of the earliest characters that were used as successful tools in promotional comics were Palmer Cox's creation "The Brownies." The illustration shown here showcases them drinking and endorsing Seal Brand Coffee.

We can even attribute the debut of the comic book itself to promotions: in 1933, Harry Wildenberg managed to convince Procter & Gamble to sponsor the very first comic book, *Funnies on Parade*, as a premium item. *Funnies on Parade* was just a few pages long and contained reprints of various comic strips, and it was sent out for free to customers who mailed in coupons clipped from Procter & Gamble products. That book was such a success that it led to the creation of *Famous Funnies*, the first true "comic book" as we know it today.

A 1933 article in *Fortune* magazine recognized the incredible marketing power of the comic book, seemingly right away – but it wasn't such a fan of the idea, suggesting that businesses that engaged in such a thing were going against classic decorum and that using comics to sell products was somehow bringing those products "down to the level" of comics. In spite of that, it was clear from the get-go that businessfolk recognized what kind of promotional power comics held.

By the 1950s, promotional comics were being given away for more than just the sake of selling something inside; they were now being used to help educate children on a huge number of topics, from banking and mathematics to great moments in history. A few years later in the '70s, promotional comics were being included as a premium in just about everything, with major characters from DC and Marvel showing up to help save various company mascots in their time of need. By the '80s, comics were being included as premiums with action figures and video games – Atari especially took a liking to comics, leading to a regular newsstand comic series with the company's popular game characters.

In 2002, a whole holiday was created based around free promotional comics: Free Comic Book Day. Facilitated by Diamond Comic Distributors, the day (the first Saturday each May) features dozens of books given away at no charge to the

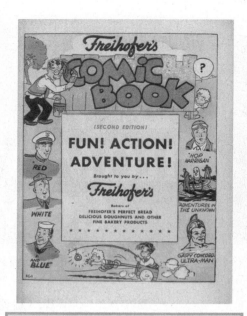

Every market and product has been on the promotional comic book bandwagon. Freihofer's Baking Company distributed a comic in the 1940s that featured reprinted pages from **All-American Comics**.

customer, from some of the most popular publishers in the business. These books are often used to promote upcoming or current releases from these publishers, and by giving readers a taste of the story, they hope that the customer will then come back and spend their money on the rest of the series. For the comic shops that host it, these promo books serve the purpose of simply getting people in the door – at which point they'll hopefully find something to spend some money on, thanks to the typical big FCBD sales weekends that shop owners host to play up the event. It's comics-as-advertising in its purest form: giving free comics away for the sake of selling more comics.

So much as a simple skim through this section will highlight the numerous purposes for which promotional comics have been created: from telling kids not to smoke (*Captain America Meets the Asthma Monster*), to trying to sway elections (*The Story of Harry Truman*), to showing the importance of environmentalism (*Our Spaceship Earth*), to explaining history (*Louisiana Purchase*), to recruiting for the armed forced (*Li'l Abner Joins the Navy*) and much more. There's also been the occasional oddball branded team-up that simply served to promote the brand, such as *The Craftsman Bolt-On System Saves the Justice League*, *The KFC Colonel Meets the DC Multiverse*, and *The X-Men at the Texas State Fair*.

Whether being used to educate, entertain or endorse, comics have proven themselves a powerful promotional tool. And as long as people still love the word "free," they'll keep picking them up – meaning that the industry will continue to produce promos.

The promotional title **March of Comics** was a prolific comic that ran for 36 years and 488 issues featuring a variety of subjects and characters. (#20 shown)

Adventures @ eBay #1 © eBay

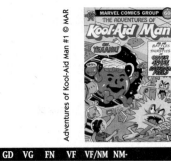
Adventures of Kool-Aid Man #1 © MAR

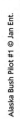
Alaska Bush Pilot #1 © Jan Ent.

	GD 2.0	VG 4.0	FN 6.0	VF 8.0	VF/NM 9.0	NM- 9.2

ACTION COMICS
DC Comics: 1947 - 1998 (Giveaway)

1 (1976) paper cover w/10¢ price, 16 pgs. in color; reprints complete Superman story from #1 ('38)	5	10	15	33	57	80
1 (1976) Safeguard Giveaway; paper cover w/"free", 16 pgs. in color; reprints complete Superman story from #1 ('38)	5	10	15	33	57	80
1 (1983) paper cover w/10¢ price, 16 pgs. in color; reprints complete Superman story from #1 ('38)	3	6	9	16	24	32
1 (1987 Nestle Quik; 1988, 50¢)	2	4	6	9	12	15
1 (1992)-Came w/Reign of Superman packs						5.00
1 (1998 U.S. Postal Service, $7.95) Reprints entire issue; extra outer half-cover contains First Day Issuance of 32¢ Superman stamp with Sept. 10, 1998 Cleveland, OH postmark	1	2	3	5	6	8
Theater (1947, 32 pgs., 5" x 7", nn)-Vigilante story based on Columbia Vigilante serial; no Superman-c or story	90	180	270	576	988	1400

ACTION ZONE
CBS Television: 1994 (Promotes CBS Saturday morning cartoons)

1-WildC.A.T.s, T.M.N.Turtles, Skeleton Warriors stories; Jim Lee-c	1	2	3	5	6	8

ADVENTURE COMICS
IGA: No date (early 1940s) (Paper-c, 32 pgs.)

Two diff. issues; Super-Mystery V2 #3-r from 1941; Jim Mooney-c	41	82	123	256	428	600

ADVENTURE IN DISNEYLAND
Walt Disney Productions (Dist. by Richfield Oil): May, 1955 (Giveaway, soft-c, 16 pgs)

nn	20	40	60	114	182	250

ADVENTURES @ EBAY
eBay: 2000 (6 3/4 x 4 1/2", 16 pgs.)

1-Judd Winick-a/Rucka & Van Meter-s; intro to eBay comic buying						5.00

ADVENTURES IN JET POWER
General Electric: 1950

nn	8	16	24	40	50	60

ADVENTURES OF BIG BOY (Also titled Adventures of the Big Boy)
Timely Comics/Webs Adv. Corp./Illus. Features: 1956 - Present (Giveaway) (East & West editions of early issues)

1-Everett-c/a	135	270	405	864	1482	2100
2-Everett-c/a	52	104	156	328	552	775
3-5: 4-Robot-c	21	42	63	126	206	285
6-10: 6-Sci/fic issue	10	20	30	67	141	215
11-20: 11,13-DeCarlo-a	6	12	18	41	76	110
21-30	4	8	12	27	44	60
31-50	3	6	9	17	26	35
51-100	2	4	6	9	13	16
101-150	2	4	6	8	10	12
151-240: 239-Wizard of Oz parody-c	1	2	3	5	7	9
241-265,267-269,271-300:						6.00
266-Superman x-over	3	6	9	17	26	35
270-TV's Buck Rogers-c/s	3	6	9	14	20	25
301-400						4.00
401-500						3.00
1-(2nd series - '76-'84,Paragon Prod.) (...Shoney's Big Boy)	1	3	4	6	8	10
2-20						5.00
21-76						3.00
Summer, 1959 issue, large size	7	14	21	46	86	125

ADVENTURES OF G. I. JOE
1969 (3-1/4x7") (20 & 16 pgs.)

First Series: 1-Danger of the Depths. 2-Perilous Rescue. 3-Secret Mission to Spy Island. 4-Mysterious Explosion. 5-Fantastic Free Fall. 6-Eight Ropes of Danger. 7-Mouth of Doom. 8-Hidden Missile Discovery. 9-Space Walk Mystery. 10-Fight for Survival. 11-The Shark's Surprise.

Second Series: 2-Flying Space Adventure. 4-White Tiger Hunt. 7-Capture of the Pygmy Gorilla. 12-Secret of the Mummy's Tomb.

Third Series: Reprinted surviving titles of First Series. Fourth Series: 13-Adventure Team Headquarters. 14-Search For the Stolen Idol.

each....	3	6	9	18	28	38

ADVENTURES OF JELL-O MAN AND WOBBLY, THE
Welsh Publishing Group: 1991 ($1.25)

1						5.00

ADVENTURES OF KOOL-AID MAN
Marvel Comics: 1983 - No. 3, 1985 (Mail order giveaway)
Archie Comics: No. 4, 1987 - No. 9, 1989

1	3	6	9	14	20	25
2-9: 4-9-Dan DeCarlo-a/c	2	4	6	8	10	12

ADVENTURES OF MARGARET O'BRIEN, THE
Bambury Fashions (Clothes): 1947 (20 pgs. in color, slick-c, regular size) (Premium)

In "The Big City" movie adaptation (scarce)	24	48	72	142	234	325

ADVENTURES OF QUIK BUNNY
Nestle's Quik: 1984 (Giveaway, 32 pgs.)

nn-Spider-Man app.	2	4	6	11	16	20

ADVENTURES OF STUBBY, SANTA'S SMALLEST REINDEER, THE
W. T. Grant Co.: nd (early 1940s) (Giveaway, 12 pgs.)

nn	11	22	33	62	86	110

ADVENTURES OF VOTEMAN, THE
Foundation For Citizen Education Inc.: 1968

nn	4	8	12	27	44	60

ADVENTURES WITH SANTA CLAUS
Promotional Publ. Co. (Murphy's Store): No date (early 50's)
(9-3/4x 6-3/4", 24 pgs., giveaway, paper-c)

nn-Contains 8 pgs. ads	8	16	24	44	57	70
16 pg. version	9	18	27	47	61	75

AIR POWER (CBS TV & the U.S. Air Force Presents)
Prudential Insurance Co.: 1956 (5-1/4x7-1/4", 32 pgs., giveaway, soft-c)

nn-Toth-a? Based on 'You Are There' TV program by Walter Cronkite	12	24	36	67	94	120

ALASKA BUSH PILOT
Jan Enterprises: 1959 (Paper cover, 10¢)

1-Promotes Bush Pilot Club (A 9.0 copy sold for $77 in Sept. 2022)						
NOTE: A CGC certified 9.9 Mint sold for $632.50 in 2005.						

ALICE IN BLUNDERLAND
Industrial Services: 1952 (Paper cover, 16 pgs. in color)

nn-Facts about government waste and inefficiency	19	38	57	111	176	240

ALICE IN WONDERLAND
Western Printing Company/Whitman Publ. Co.: 1965; 1969; 1982

Meets Santa (1950s), nd, 16 pgs.	9	18	27	50	65	80
Rexall Giveaway(1965, 16 pgs., 5x7-1/4) Western Printing (TV, Hanna-Barbera)	4	8	12	23	37	50
Wonder Bakery Giveaway(1969, 16 pgs, color, nn, nd) (Continental Baking Company)	3	6	9	19	30	40

ALL ABOARD, MR. LINCOLN
Assoc. of American Railroads: Jan, 1959 (16 pgs.)

nn-Abraham Lincoln and the Railroads	7	14	21	35	43	50

ALL NEW COMICS
Harvey Comics: Oct, 1993 (Giveaway, no cover price, 16 pgs.)(Hanna-Barbera)

1-Flintstones, Scooby Doo, Jetsons, Yogi Bear & Wacky Races previews for upcoming Harvey's new Hanna-Barbera line-up	1	3	4	6	8	10
NOTE: Material previewed in Harvey giveaway was eventually published by Archie.						

ALL STAR SUPERMAN SPECIAL EDITION (Sears promotion for the 2013 Man of Steel movie)
DC Comics: Jun, 2013 (Giveaway, no cover price, some copies bagged with Sears insert)

1-Reprints 1st issue; regular Quitely cover and Sears exclusive cover by Camuncoli						7.00

AMAZING SPIDER-MAN, THE
Marvel Comics Group

Acme & Dingo Children's Boots (1980)-Spider-Woman app.	3	6	9	19	30	40
Adventures in Reading Starring... (1990,1991) Bogdanove & Romita-c/a						6.00
Aim Toothpaste Giveaway (36 pgs., reg. size)-1 pg. origin recap; Green Goblin-c/story	3	6	9	15	22	28
Aim Toothpaste Giveaway (16 pgs., reg. size)-Dr. Octopus app.	3	6	9	14	19	24
All Detergent Giveaway (1979, 36 pgs.), nn-Origin-r	3	6	9	16	23	30
Amazing Fantasy #15 (8/02) reprint included in Spider-Man DVD Collector's Gift Set						12
Amazing Fantasy #15 (2006) News America Marketing newspaper giveaway	1	2	3	5	8	10
Amazing Spider-Man nn (#1) (1990, 6-1/8x9", 28 pgs.)-Shan-Lon giveaway; reprints Amazing Spider-Man #319 w/McFarlane-c/a	2	4	6	8	10	12
Amazing Spider-Man nn (#2) (1990, 6-1/8x9", 28 pgs.)-Shan-Lon giveaway; retells origin of Spider-Man from Annual #1; Bagley-a/Saviuk-c	2	4	6	8	10	12
Amazing Spider-Man nn (#3) (1990, 6-1/8x9", 28 pgs.)-Shan-Lon giveaway; reprints Amazing Spider-Man #303 w/McFarlane-c/a	2	4	6	8	10	12
Amazing Spider-Man #1 Reprint (1990, 4-1/4x6-1/4", 28 pgs.)-Packaged with the book "Start Collecting Comic Books" from Running Press						5.00
Amazing Spider-Man #3 Reprint (2004)-Best Buy/Sony giveaway						4.00
Amazing Spider-Man #50 (Sony Pictures Edition) (8/04)-mini-comic included in Spider-Man 2						

	GD 2.0	VG 4.0	FN 6.0	VF 8.0	VF/NM 9.0	NM- 9.2

movie DVD Collector's Gift Set; r/#50 & various ASM covers with Dr. Octopus — 4.00

Amazing Spider-Man #129 (Lion Gate Films) (6/04)-promotional comic given away at movie theaters on opening night for The Punisher — 4.00

...& Power Pack (1984, nn)(Nat'l Committee for Prevention of Child Abuse) (two versions, mail offer & store giveaway)-Mooney-a; Byrne-c

	GD 2.0	VG 4.0	FN 6.0	VF 8.0	VF/NM 9.0	NM- 9.2
Mail offer	2	4	6	10	14	18
Store giveaway	1	3	4	6	8	10

...& The Hulk (Special Edition)(6/8/80; 20 pgs.)-Supplement to Chicago Tribune

	3	6	9	16	23	30

...& The Incredible Hulk (1981, 1982; 36 pgs.)-Sanger Harris or May D&F supplement to Dallas Times, Dallas Herald, Denver Post, Kansas City Star, Tulsa World; Foley's supplement to Houston Chronicle (1982, 16 pgs.)- "Great Rodeo Robbery"; The Jones Store-giveaway (1983, 16 pgs.)

	3	7	11	17	25	34

...and the New Mutants Featuring Skids nn (1990, National Committee for Prevention of Child Abuse/K-Mart giveaway)-Williams-c(i)

	2	4	6	8	10	12

...Battles Ignorance (1992)(Sylvan Learning Systems) giveaway; Mad Thinker app. Kupperberg-a

	2	4	6	8	11	14

...Captain America, The Incredible Hulk, & Spider-Woman (1981) (7-11 Stores giveaway; 36 pgs.)

	3	6	9	15	21	26

...Christmas in Dallas (1983) (Supplement to Dallas Times Herald) giveaway

	3	6	9	15	21	26

...Danger in Dallas (1983) (Supplement to Dallas Times Herald) giveaway

	3	6	9	15	21	26

...Danger in Denver (1983) (Supplement to Denver Post) giveaway for May D&F stores

	3	6	9	15	21	26

...Fire-Star, and Ice-Man at the Dallas Ballet Nutcracker (1983; supplement to Dallas Times Herald)-Mooney-p

	3	6	9	15	21	26

Giveaway-Esquire Magazine (2/69)-Miniature-Still attached (scarce)

	15	30	45	105	233	360

Giveaway-Eye Magazine (2/69)-Miniature-Still attached

	10	20	30	69	147	225

...: Riot at Robotworld (1991; 16 pgs.)(National Action Council for Minorities in Engineering, Inc.) giveaway; Saviuk-c

	1	2	3	5	6	8

...; Storm & Powerman (1982; 20 pgs.)(American Cancer Society) giveaway; also a 1991 2nd printing and a 1994 printing

	2	4	6	8	10	12

...Vs. The Hulk (Special Edition; 1979, 20 pgs.)(Supplement to Columbus Dispatch)

	3	6	9	17	26	35

...Vs. The Prodigy (Giveaway, 16 pgs. in color (1976, 5x6-1/2")-Sex education; (1 million printed; 35-50¢)

	2	4	6	10	14	18

Spidey & The Mini-Marvels Halloween 2003 Ashcan (12/03, 8 1/2"x 5 1/2") Giarusso-s/a; Venom and Green Goblin app. — 3.00

AMERICA MENACED!
Vital Publications: 1950 (Paper-c)

	GD 2.0	VG 4.0	FN 6.0	VF 8.0	VF/NM 9.0	NM- 9.2
nn-Anti-communism	43	86	129	271	461	650

AMERICAN COMICS
Theatre Giveaways (Liberty Theatre, Grand Rapids, Mich. known): 1940's

Many possible combinations. "Golden Age" superhero comics with new cover added and given away at theaters. Following known: Superman #59, Capt. Marvel #20, 21, Capt. Marvel Jr. #5, Action #33, Classics Comics #8, Whiz #39. Value would vary with book and should be 70-80 percent of the original.

AMERICA UNDER SOCIALISM
National Research Bureau: 1950 (Paper-c)

nn-Anti-communism; 16 pages — (a CGC 9.2 copy sold for $2520 in Nov. 2020)

ANDY HARDY COMICS
Western Printing Co.:

...& the New Automatic Gas Clothes Dryer (1952, 5x7-1/4", 16 pgs.) Bendix Giveaway (soft-c)

	7	14	21	35	43	50

ANIMANIACS EMERGENCY WORLD
DC Comics: 1995

	GD 2.0	VG 4.0	FN 6.0	VF 8.0	VF/NM 9.0	NM- 9.2
nn-American Red Cross	1	2	3	5	6	8

APACHE HUNTER
Creative Pictorials: 1954 (18 pgs. in color) (promo copy) (saddle stitched)

	GD 2.0	VG 4.0	FN 6.0	VF 8.0	VF/NM 9.0	NM- 9.2
nn-Severin, Heath stories	16	32	48	92	144	195

AQUATEERS MEET THE SUPER FRIENDS
DC Comics: 1979

	GD 2.0	VG 4.0	FN 6.0	VF 8.0	VF/NM 9.0	NM- 9.2
nn	2	4	6	11	16	20

ARCHIE AND HIS GANG (Zeta Beta Tau Presents...)
Archie Publications: Dec. 1950 (St. Louis National Convention giveaway)

nn-Contains new cover stapled over Archie Comics #47 (11-12/50) on inside; produced for Zeta Beta Tau

	36	72	108	211	343	475

ARCHIE COMICS (Also see Sabrina)
Archie Publications

... And Friends and the Shield (10/02, 8 1/2"x 5 1/2") Diamond Comic Dist. — 4.00
... And Friends - A Halloween Tale (10/98, 8 1/2"x 5 1/2") Diamond Comic Dist.; Sabrina and Sonic app.; Dan DeCarlo-a — 6.00
... And Friends - A Timely Tale (10/01, 8 1/2"x 5 1/2") Diamond Comic Dist. — 4.00
... And Friends Monster Bash 2003 (8 1/2"x 5 1/2") Diamond Comic Dist. Halloween — 4.00

...And His Friends Help Raise Literacy Awareness In Mississippi nn (3/94)

...And His Friends Vs. The Household Toxic Wastes nn (1993, 16 pgs.) produced for the San Diego Regional Household Hazardous Materials Program

	1	3	4	6	8	10

...And His Pals in the Peer Helping Program nn (2/91, 7"x4 1/2") produced by the FBI

	1	3	4	6	8	10

...And the History of Electronics nn (5/90, 36 pgs.)-Radio Shack giveaway; Bender-c/a

	1	3	4	6	8	10

Fairmont Potato Chips Giveaway-Mini comics 1970 (6 issues-nn-s,.6 7/8" x 2 1/4", 8 pgs. each)

	3	6	9	21	33	45

Fairmont Potato Chips Giveaway-Mini comics 1971 (4 issues-nn-s,.6 7/8" x 5", 8 pgs. each)

	3	6	9	21	33	45

Little Archie, The House That Wouldn't Move ('07, 8-1/2"x 5-3/8") Halloween mini-comic — 4.00
...'s Ham Radio Adventure (1997) Morse code instruction; Goldberg-a

	GD 2.0	VG 4.0	FN 6.0	VF 8.0	VF/NM 9.0	NM- 9.2
	1	3	4	6	8	10

...'s Weird Mysteries (9/99, 8 1/2" x 5 1/2") Diamond Comic Dist. Halloween giveaway — 4.00
Tales From Riverdale (2006, 8 1/2" x 5 1/2") Diamond Comic Dist. Halloween giveaway — 4.00
...: The Dawn of Time ('10, 8-1/2" x 5-3/8" Halloween mini-comic — 4.00
...: The Mystery of the Museum Sleep-In ('08, 8-1/2" x 5-3/8" Halloween mini-comic) — 4.00
... Your Official Store Club Magazine nn (10/48, 9-1/2x6-1/2, 16 pgs.)- "Wolf Whistle" Archie on front-c; B. R. Baker Co. ad on back-c (a CGC 7.5 copy sold for $1912 in Feb. 2013)

ARCHIE SHOE-STORE GIVEAWAY
Archie Publications: 1944-50 (12-15 pgs. of games, puzzles, stories like Superman-Tim books, no nos. - came out monthly)

	GD 2.0	VG 4.0	FN 6.0	VF 8.0	VF/NM 9.0	NM- 9.2
(1944-47)-issues	36	72	108	211	343	475
2/48-Peggy Lee photo-c	30	60	90	177	289	400
3/48-Marylee Robb photo-c	22	44	66	132	216	300
4/48-Gloria De Haven photo-c	30	60	90	177	289	400
5/48, 6/48, 7/48	22	44	66	132	216	300
8/48-Story on Shirley Temple	30	60	90	177	289	400
10/48-Wolf whistle-c	103	206	309	659	1130	1600
5/49-Kathleen Hughes photo-c	22	44	66	130	213	295
6/49, 7/49, 9/49	20	40	60	117	189	260
8/49-Archie photo-c from radio show	36	72	108	211	343	475
10/49-Gloria Mann photo-c from radio show	26	52	78	154	252	350
11/49, 12/49, 2/50, 3/50	22	44	66	130	213	295

ARCHIE'S JOKE BOOK MAGAZINE (See Joke Book ...)
Archie Publications

Drug Store Giveaway (No. 39 w/new-c)

	10	20	30	56	76	95

ARCHIE'S TEN ISSUE COLLECTOR'S SET (Title inside of cover only)
Archie Publications: June, 1997 - No. 10, June, 1997 ($1.50, 20 pgs.)

1-10: 1,7-Archie. 2,8-Betty & Veronica. 3,9-Veronica. 4-Betty. 5-World of Archie. 6-Jughead. 10-Archie and Friends each..... — 5.00

ASTRO COMICS
American Airlines (Harvey): 1968 - 1979 (Giveaway)(Reprints of Harvey comics)

1968-Richie Rich, Hot Stuff, Casper, Wendy on-c only; Spooky and Nightmare app. inside

	4	8	12	23	37	50

1970-Casper, Spooky, Hot Stuff, Stumbo the Giant, Little Audrey, Little Lotta, & Richie Rich reprints. Five different versions

	3	6	9	17	26	35

1973,1975,1976: 1973-Three different versions

	2	4	6	11	16	20

1977-r/Richie Rich & Casper #20. 1978-r/Richie Rich & Casper #25. 1979-r/Richie Rich & Casper #30 (scarce)

	2	4	6	9	13	16

ATARI FORCE (Given away with Atari games)
DC Comics: 1982 - No. 5, 1983

	GD 2.0	VG 4.0	FN 6.0	VF 8.0	VF/NM 9.0	NM- 9.2
1-3 (1982, 5x7", 52 pgs.)	2	4	6	10	14	18
4,5 (1982-1983, 52 pgs.)(scarcer)	3	6	9	14	20	25

AURORA COMIC SCENES INSTRUCTION BOOKLET (Included with superhero model kits)
Aurora Plastics Co.: 1974 (6-1/4x9-3/4", 8 pgs., slick paper)

	GD 2.0	VG 4.0	FN 6.0	VF 8.0	VF/NM 9.0	NM- 9.2
181-140-Tarzan; Neal Adams-a	3	6	9	18	27	38
182-140-Spider-Man.	4	8	12	23	37	50

183-140-Tonto(Gil Kane art). 184-140-Hulk. 185-140-Superman. 186-140-Superboy. 187-140-Batman. 188-140-The Lone Ranger(1974-by Gil Kane). 192-140-Captain America(1975). 193-140-Robin

	3	6	9	16	23	30

BACK TO THE FUTURE
Harvey Comics

Special nn (1991, 20 pgs.)-Brunner-c; given away at Universal Studios in Florida

	3	6	9	15	22	28

BALTIMORE COLTS
American Visuals Corp.: 1950 (Giveaway)

	GD 2.0	VG 4.0	FN 6.0	VF 8.0	VF/NM 9.0	NM- 9.2
nn-Eisner-a	53	106	159	334	567	800

BAMBI (Disney)
K. K. Publications (Giveaways): 1941, 1942

1941-Horlick's Malted Milk & various toy stores; text & pictures; most copies mailed out with store stickers on-c

	47	94	141	296	498	700

1942-Same as 4-Color #12, but no price (Same as '41 issue?) (Scarce)

	100	200	300	640	1095	1550

BATMAN
DC Comics: 1966 - Present

Act II Popcorn mini-comic(1998)

	GD 2.0	VG 4.0	FN 6.0	VF 8.0	VF/NM 9.0	NM- 9.2
	1	3	4	6	8	10

Batman #121 Toys R Us edition (1997) r/1st Mr. Freeze

	3	6	9	14	19	24

Batman #279 Mini-comic with Monogram Model kit (1995)

	1	3	4	6	8	10

	GD 2.0	VG 4.0	FN 6.0	VF 8.0	VF/NM 9.0	NM- 9.2
Batman #362 Mervyn's edition (1989)	2	4	6	11	16	20
Batman #608 New York Post edition (2002)	2	4	6	8	10	12

Batman Adventures #25 Best Western edition (1997) — 6.00
Batman and Other DC Classics 1 (1989, giveaway)-DC Comics/Diamond Comic Distributors; Batman origin-r/Batman #47, Camelot 3000-r, Justice League-r('87), New Teen Titans-r — 5.00
Batman and Robin movie preview (1997, 8 pgs.) Kellogg's Cereal promo — 5.00

	GD 2.0	VG 4.0	FN 6.0	VF 8.0	VF/NM 9.0	NM- 9.2
Batman Beyond Six Flags edition	2	4	6	11	16	20
Batman: Canadian Multiculturalism Custom (1992)	1	2	3	5	6	8
Batman Claritan edition (1999)	2	4	6	11	16	20

Kellogg's Poptarts comics (1966, Set of 6, 16 pgs.); All were folded and placed in Poptarts boxes. Infantino art on Catwoman and Joker issues.
"The Man in the Iron Mask", "The Penguin's Fowl Play", "The Joker's Happy Victims", "The Catwoman's Catnapping Caper", "The Mad Hatter's Hat Crimes", "The Case of the Batman II"

	each.....	6	12	18	37	66	95

Mask of the Phantasm (1993) Mini-comic released w/video

	2	4	6	8	11	14

Onstar - Auto Show Special Edition (OnStar Corp., 2001, 8 pgs.) Riddler app. — 4.00
Pizza Hut giveaway (12/77)-exact-r of #122,123; Joker app.

	2	4	6	13	18	22

Prell Shampoo giveaway (1966, 16 pgs.)- "The Joker's Practical Jokes"

Archie - Fairmont Potato Chips mini-comics © ACP

Batman and Robin Movie Preview © DC

Blue Bird Comics - Freddy #3 © CC

	GD 2.0	VG 4.0	FN 6.0	VF 8.0	VF/NM 9.0	NM- 9.2
(6-7/8x3-3/8")	12	24	36	80	173	265
Revell in pack (1995)						6.00
...: The 10-Cent Adventure (3/02, 10¢) intro. to the "Bruce Wayne: Murderer" x-over; Rucka-s/ Burchett & Janson-a/Dave Johnson-c; these are alternate copies with special outer half-covers (at least 10 different) promoting comics, toys and games shops						4.00

BATMAN RECORD COMIC
National Periodical Publications: 1966 (one-shot)

1-With record (still sealed)	15	30	45	103	227	350
Comic only	10	20	30	69	147	225

BEETLE BAILEY
Charlton Comics: 1969-1970 (Giveaways)

Armed Forces ('69)-same as regular issue (#68)	2	4	6	10	14	18
Armed Forces ('70)	2	4	6	10	14	18
Bold Detergent ('69)-same as regular issue (#67)	2	4	6	10	14	18
Cerebral Palsy Assn. V2#71('69) - V2#73(#1,1/70)						3.00
Red Cross (1969, 5x7", 16 pgs., paper-c)	2	4	6	10	14	18

BELLAIRE BICYCLE CO.
Bellaire Bicycle Co.: 1940 (promotional comic)(64 pgs.)

nn-Contains Wonderworld #12 w/new-c. Contents can vary w/diff. 1940's books	55	110	165	352	601	850

BEST WESTERN GIVEAWAY
DC Comics: 1999

nn-Best Western hotels						4.00

BETTER LIFE FOR YOU, A
Harvey Publications Inc.: (16 pgs., paper cover)

nn-Better living through higher productivity	3	6	9	15	22	28

BEWARE THE BOOBY TRAP
Malcolm Alter: 1970 (5" x 7")

nn-Deals with drug abuse	5	10	15	34	60	85

B-FORCE (Milwaukee Brewers and Wisconsin Dental Asso.)
Dark Horse Comics: 2001 (School and stadium giveaway)

nn-Brewers players combat the evils of smokeless tobacco						4.00

BIG BOY (see Adventures of...)

BIG JIM'S P.A.C.K.
Mattel, Inc. (Marvel Comics): No date (1975) (16 pgs.)

nn-Giveaway with Big Jim doll; Buscema/Sinnott-c/a	4	8	12	27	44	60

"BILL AND TED'S EXCELLENT ADVENTURE" MOVIE ADAPTATION
DC Comics: 1989 (No cover price)

nn-Torres-a	1	3	4	6	8	10

BIONICLE (LEGO robot toys)
DC Comics: Jun, 2001 - No. 27, Nov, 2005 ($2.25/$3.25, 16 pgs, available to LEGO club members)

1	2	4	6	9	12	15
2-5						6.00
6-13						4.00
14-27						3.00
The Legend of Bionicle (McDonald's Mini-comic, 4-1/4 x 7")						4.00
Special Edition #0 (Six Heroes...One Destiny) '03 San Diego Comic Con; Ashley Wood-c	1	3	4	6	8	10

BLACK GOLD
Esso Service Station (Giveaway): 1945? (8 pgs. in color)

nn-Reprints from True Comics	7	14	21	37	46	55

BLADE SINS OF THE FATHER
Marvel Comics: Aug, 1996 (24 pgs. with paper cover)

1-Theatrical preview; possibly limited to 2000 copies				(Value will be based on sale)		

BLAZING FOREST, THE (See Forest Fire and Smokey Bear)
Western Printing: 1962 (20 pgs., 5x7", slick-c)

nn-Smokey The Bear fire prevention	3	6	9	14	20	26

BLESSED PIUS X
Catechetical Guild (Giveaway): No date (Text/comics, 32 pgs., paper-c)

nn	14	28	42	76	108	140

BLIND JUSTICE (Also see Batman: Blind Justice)
DC Comics/Diamond Comic Distributors: 1989 (Giveaway, squarebound)

nn-Contains Detective #598-600 by Batman movie writer Sam Hamm, w/covers; published same time as originals?	1	2	3	5	6	8

BLONDIE COMICS
Harvey Publications: 1950-1964

1950 Giveaway	10	20	30	58	79	100
1962,1964 Giveaway	3	6	9	18	28	38

	GD 2.0	VG 4.0	FN 6.0	VF 8.0	VF/NM 9.0	NM- 9.2
N. Y. State Dept. of Mental Hygiene Giveaway-(1950) Regular size; 16 pgs.; no #	5	10	15	33	57	80
N. Y. State Dept. of Mental Hygiene Giveaway-(1956) Regular size; 16 pgs.; no #	3	6	9	24	33	45
N. Y. State Dept. of Mental Hygiene Giveaway-(1961) Regular size; 16 pgs.; no #	3	6	9	16	24	32

BLOOD IS THE HARVEST
Catechetical Guild: 1950 (32 pgs., paper-c)

(Scarce)-Anti-communism (35 known copies)	275	550	925	1746	2923	4300
Black & white version (5 known copies), saddle stitched	142	284	426	909	1555	2200
Untrimmed version (only one known copy); estimated value - $5000						

NOTE: In 1979 nine copies of the color version surfaced from the old Guild's files plus the five black & white copies.

BLUE BIRD CHILDREN'S MAGAZINE, THE
Graphic Information Service: V1#2, 1957 - No. 10 1958 (16 pgs., soft-c, regular size)

V1#2-10: Pat, Pete & Blue Bird app.	2	4	6	11	16	20

BLUE BIRD COMICS
Various Shoe Stores: 1947 - 1950 (Giveaway, 36 pgs.)
Charlton Comics: 1959 - 1964 (Giveaway)

nn-(1947-50, not Charlton)(36 pgs.)-Several issues; Human Torch, Sub-Mariner app. in some	22	44	66	132	216	300
1959-(Charlton) Lil Genius, Wild Bill Hickok, Black Fury, Masked Raider, Timmy The Timid Ghost, Freddy (All #1)	3	6	9	15	22	28
1959-(Charlton, same 6 titles; all #2-5) except (#5) Masked Raider #21	3	6	9	14	20	25
1959-(#5) Masked Raider #21	3	6	9	16	23	30
1960-(6 titles, all #6-9) Black Fury, Masked Raider, Freddy, Timmy the Timid Ghost, Li'l Genius, Six Gun Heroes	3	6	9	14	19	24
1961-(All #10's) Black Fury, Masked Raider, Freddy, Timmy the Timid Ghost, Li'l Genius, Six Gun Heroes (Charlton)	2	4	6	13	18	22
1961-(All #11-13) Lil Genius, Wyatt Earp, Black Fury, Timmy the Timid Ghost, Atomic Mouse, Freddy	2	4	6	13	18	22
1962-(All #14) Lil Genius, Wyatt Earp, Black Fury, Timmy the Timid Ghost, Atomic Mouse, Freddy	2	4	6	13	18	22
1962-(6 titles, all #15) Lil Genius, Six Gun Heroes, Black Fury, Timmy the Timid Ghost, Texas Rangers, Freddy	2	4	6	13	18	22
1962-(7 titles, all #16) Lil Genius, Six Gun Heroes, Black Fury, Timmy the Timid Ghost, Texas Rangers, Wyatt Earp, Atomic Mouse	2	4	6	13	18	22
1963-(All #17) My Little Margie, Lil Genius, Timmy the Timid Ghost, Texas Rangers (Charlton)	2	4	6	13	16	16
1964-(All #18) Mysteries of Unexplored Worlds, Teenage Hotrodders, War Heroes, Wyatt Earp (Charlton)	2	4	6	13	16	16

NOTE: Reprints comics of regular issue, with Blue Bird shoe promo on back cover, with upper front cover imprint of various shoe retailers. Printed from 1959 to 1962, with issues 1 thru 16. The 8 different front cover imprints for issues 1 thru 16 are, 1) Blue Bird Shoes, 2) Schiff's Shoes, 3) Big Shoe Store, 4) E.D. Edwards Shoe Store, 5) R & S Shoe store, 6) Federal Shoe Store, 7) Kirby's Shoes, 8) Gallenkamps.

BOB & BETTY & SANTA'S WISHING WHISTLE (Also see A Christmas Carol, Merry Christmas From Sears Toyland, and Santa's Christmas Comic Variety Show)
Sears Roebuck & Co.: 1941 (Christmas giveaway, 12 pgs., oblong)

nn	27	54	81	160	263	365

BOBBY BENSON'S B-BAR-B RIDERS (Radio)
Magazine Enterprises/AC Comics

...in the Tunnel of Gold-(1936, 5-1/4x8"; 100 pgs.) Radio giveaway by Hecker-H.O. Company (H.O. Oats); contains 22 color pgs. of comics, rest in novel form	14	28	42	76	108	140
...And The Lost Herd-same as above	14	28	42	76	108	140

BOBBY GETS HEP
Bell Telephone: 1946

nn-Bell Telephone Systems giveaway	8	16	24	44	57	70

BOBBY SHELBY COMICS
Shelby Cycle Co./Harvey Publications: 1949

nn	7	14	21	37	46	55

BOY SCOUT ADVENTURE
Boy Scouts of America: 1954 (16 pgs., paper cover)

nn	6	12	18	28	34	40

BOYS' RANCH
Harvey Publications: 1951

Shoe Store Giveaway #5,6 (Identical to regular issues except Simon & Kirby centerfold replaced with ad)	14	28	42	80	115	150

BOZO THE CLOWN (TV)
Dell Publishing Co.: 1961

Giveaway-1961, 16 pgs., 3-1/2x7-1/4", Apsco Products	5	10	15	31	53	75

	GD 2.0	VG 4.0	FN 6.0	VF 8.0	VF/NM 9.0	NM- 9.2

BRER RABBIT IN "ICE CREAM FOR THE PARTY"
American Dairy Association: 1955 (5x7-1/4", 16 pgs., soft-c) (Walt Disney) (Premium)

	GD 2.0	VG 4.0	FN 6.0	VF 8.0	VF/NM 9.0	NM- 9.2
nn-(Scarce)	43	86	129	271	461	650

BUCK ROGERS (In the 25th Century)
Kelloggs Corn Flakes Giveaway: 1933 (6x8", 36 pgs)

370A-By Phil Nowlan & Dick Calkins; 1st Buck Rogers radio premium & 1st app. in comics (tells origin) (Reissued in 1995)	80	160	240	600	-	-
with envelope	105	210	315	775	-	-

BUGS BUNNY (Puffed Rice Giveaway)
Quaker Cereals: 1949 (32 pgs. each, 3-1/8x6-7/8)

A1-Traps the Counterfeiters, A2-Aboard Mystery Submarine, A3- Rocket to the Moon, A4-Lion Tamer, A5-Rescues the Beautiful Princess, B1-Buried Treasure, B2-Outwits the Smugglers, B3-Joins the Marines, B4-Meets the Dwarf Ghost, B5-Finds Aladdin's Lamp, C1-Lost in the Frozen North, C2-Secret Agent, C3-Captured by Cannibals, C4-Fights the Man from Mars, C5-And the Haunted Cave

each….	8	16	24	44	57	70
Mailing Envelope (has illo of Bugs on front)(Each envelope designates what set it contains, A,B or C on front)	8	16	24	44	57	70

BUGS BUNNY (3-D)
Cheerios Giveaway: 1953 (Pocket size) (15 titles)

each….	10	20	30	58	79	100
Mailing Envelope (has Bugs drawn on front)	10	20	30	58	79	100

BUGS BUNNY
DC Comics: May, 1997 ($4.95, 24 pgs., comic-sized)

1-Numbered ed. of 100,000; "1st Day of Issue" stamp cancellation on-c						6.00

BUGS BUNNY POSTAL COMIC
DC Comics: 1997 (64 pgs., 7.5" x 5")

nn -Mail Fan; Daffy Duck app.						4.50

BULLETMAN
Fawcett Publications

Well Known Comics (1942)-Paper-c, glued binding; printed in red (Bestmaid/Samuel Lowe giveaway)	18	36	54	105	165	225

BULLS-EYE (Cody of The Pony Express No. 8 on)
Charlton: 1955 (Great Scott Shoe Store giveaway)

Reprints #2 with new cover	20	40	60	118	192	265

BUSTER BROWN COMICS (Radio)(Also see My Dog Tige in Promotional sec.)
Brown Shoe Co.: 1945 - No. 43, 1959 (No. 5: paper-c)

nn, nn (#1,scarce)-Featuring Smilin' Ed McConnell & the Buster Brown gang "Midnight" the cat, "Squeaky" the mouse & "Froggy" the Gremlin; covers mention diff. shoe stores.

Contains adventure stories	71	142	213	454	777	1100
2	22	44	66	128	209	290
3,5-10	14	28	42	80	115	150
4 (Rare)-Low print run due to paper shortage	20	40	60	115	188	260
11-20	9	18	27	52	69	85
21-24,26-28	7	14	21	35	43	50
25,33-37,40,41-Crandall-a in all	10	20	30	58	79	100
29-32-"Interplanetary Police Vs. the Space Siren" by Crandall (pencils only #29)	11	22	33	62	86	110
38,39,42,43	7	14	21	35	43	50

BUSTER BROWN COMICS (Radio)
Brown Shoe Co: 1950s

…Goes to Mars (2/58-Western Printing), slick-c, 20 pgs., reg. size	15	30	45	83	124	165
…In "Buster Makes the Team!" (1959-Custom Comics)	9	18	27	47	61	75
…In The Jet Age ('50s), slick-c, 20 pgs., 5x7-1/4"	11	22	33	60	83	105
…Of the Safety Patrol ('60-Custom Comics)	3	6	9	19	30	40
…Out of This World ('59-Custom Comics)	7	14	21	37	46	55
…Safety Coloring Book ('58, 16 pgs.)-Slick paper	7	14	21	37	46	55

CALL FROM CHRIST
Catechetical Educational Society: 1952 (Giveaway, 36 pgs.)

nn	7	14	21	37	46	55

CANCELLED COMIC CAVALCADE
DC Comics, Inc.: Summer, 1978 - No. 2, Fall, 1978 (8-1/2x11", B&W)
(Xeroxed-copies on one side only w/blue cover and taped spine)(Only 35 sets produced)

1-(412 pgs.) Contains xeroxed copies of art for: Black Lightning #12, cover to #13; Claw #13,14; The Deserter #1; Doorway to Nightmare #6; Firestorm #6; The Green Team #2,3.

2-(532 pgs.) Contains xeroxed copies of art for: Kamandi #60 (including Omac), #61; Prez #5; Shade #9 (including The Odd Man); Showcase #105 (Deadman), 106 (The Creeper); Secret Society of Super Villains #16 & 17; The Vixen #1; and covers to Army at War #2, Battle Classics #3, Demand Classics #1 & 2, Dynamic Classics #3, Mr. Miracle #26, Ragman #6, Weird Mystery #25 & 26, & Western Classics #1 & 2.

(A FN set of Number 1 & 2 was sold in 2005 for $3680; a VG set sold in 2007 for $2629)

NOTE: In June, 1978, DC cancelled several of their titles. For copyright purposes, the unpublished original art for these titles was xeroxed, bound in the above books, published and distributed. Only 35 copies were made. Beware of bootleg copies.

CAP'N CRUNCH COMICS (See Quaker Oats)
Quaker Oats Co.: 1963; 1965 (16 pgs.; miniature giveaways; 2-1/2x6-1/2")

(1963 titles)- "The Picture Pirates", "The Fountain of Youth", "I'm Dreaming of a Wide Isthmus".
(1965 titles)- "Bewitched, Betwitched, & Betweaked", "Seadog Meets the Witch Doctor", "A Witch in Time"

	5	10	15	33	57	80

CAPTAIN ACTION (Toy)
National Periodical Publications

…& Action Boy ('67)-Ideal Toy Co. giveaway (1st app. Captain Action)	12	24	36	79	170	260

CAPTAIN AMERICA
Marvel Comics Group

…& The Campbell Kids (1980, 36pg. giveaway, Campbell's Soup/U.S. Dept. of Energy)	2	4	6	11	16	20

	GD 2.0	VG 4.0	FN 6.0	VF 8.0	VF/NM 9.0	NM- 9.2
…Goes To War Against Drugs(1990, no #, giveaway)-Distributed to direct sales shops; 2nd printing exists	2	4	6	9	12	15
…Meets The Asthma Monster (1987, no #, giveaway, Your Physician and Glaxo, Inc.)	2	4	6	8	10	12
Return of The Asthma Monster Vol. 1 #2 (1992, giveaway, Your Physician & Allen & Hanbury's)	2	4	6	8	10	12
…Vs. Asthma Monster (1990, no #, giveaway, Your Physician & Allen & Hanbury's)	2	4	6	8	10	12

CAPTAIN AMERICA COMICS
Timely/Marvel Comics: 1954

Shoestore Giveaway #77	206	412	618	1318	2259	3200

CAPTAIN ATOM
Nationwide Publishers

…- Secret of the Columbian Jungle (16 pgs. in color, paper-c, 3-3/4x5-1/8")- Fireside Marshmallow giveaway	6	12	18	31	38	45

CAPTAIN BEN DIX
Bendix Aviation Corporation: 1943 (Small size)

nn	10	20	30	58	79	100

CAPTAIN BEN DIX IN ACTION WITH THE INVISIBLE CREW
Bendix Aviation Corp.: 1940s (nd), (20 pgs, 8-1/4"x11", heavy paper)

nn-WWII bomber-c; Japanese app.	9	18	27	50	65	80

CAPTAIN BEN DIX IN SECRETS OF THE INVISIBLE CREW
Bendix Aviation Corp.: 1940s (nd), (32 pgs, soft-c)

nn	9	18	27	50	65	80

CAPTAIN FORTUNE PRESENTS
Vital Publications: 1955 - 1959 (Giveaway, 3-1/4x6-7/8", 16 pgs.)

"Davy Crockett in Episodes of the Creek War", "Davy Crockett at the Alamo", "In Sherwood Forest Tells Strange Tales of Robin Hood" ('57), "Meets Bolivar the Liberator" ('59), "Tells How Buffalo Bill Fights the Dog Soldiers" ('57), "Young Davy Crockett"

	4	8	12	17	21	24

CAPTAIN GALLANT (…of the Foreign Legion) (TV)
Charlton Comics

Heinz Foods Premium (#1?)(1955; regular size)-U.S. Pictorial; contains Buster Crabbe photos; Don Heck-a	2	4	6	9	12	15
Mailing Envelope						25.00

CAPTAIN JOLLY ADVENTURES
Johnston and Cushing: 1950's, nd (Post Corn Fetti cereal giveaway) (5-1/4" x 4-1/2)

1-3: 1-Captain Jolly Advs. 2-Captain Jolly and His Pirate Crew in Off To Treasure Island. 3-C.J. & His Pirate Crew in The Terror Of The Deep

	4	7	10	14	17	20

CAPTAIN MARVEL ADVENTURES
Fawcett Publications

Bond Bread Giveaways-(24 pg.; pocket size-7-1/4x3-1/2"; paper cover): "…& the Stolen City" ('48), "The Boy Who Never Heard of Capt. Marvel", "Meets the Weatherman" (1950)

(reprint) each……	27	54	81	160	283	365
…Well Known Comics (1944; 12 pgs.; 8-1/2x10-1/2")-printed in red & in blue; soft-c; glued binding - (Bestmaid/Samuel Lowe Co. giveaway)	20	40	60	117	189	260

CAPTAIN MARVEL ADVENTURES (Also see Flash and Funny Stuff)
Fawcett Publications (Wheaties Giveaway): 1945 (6x8", full color, paper-c)

nn- "Captain Marvel & the Threads of Life" plus 2 other stories (32 pgs.)	65	130	325	650	-	-

NOTE: All copies were taped at each corner to a box of Wheaties and are never found in Fine or Mint condition. Prices listed for each grade include tape. File copy stamped "June 21, 1947".

CAPTAIN MARVEL AND THE LTS. OF SAFETY
Ebasco Services/Fawcett Publications: 1950 - 1951 (3 issues - no No.'s)

nn (#1) "Danger Flies a Kite" ('50, scarce)	41	82	123	256	428	600
nn (#2)"Danger Takes to Climbing" ('50),	29	58	87	172	281	390
nn (#3)"Danger Smashes Street Lights" ('51)	29	58	87	172	281	390

CAPTAIN MARVEL, JR.
Fawcett Publications: (1944; 12 pgs.; 8-1/2x10-1/2")

…Well Known Comics (Printed in blue; paper-c, glued binding)-Bestmaid/Samuel Lowe Co. giveaway	15	30	45	90	140	190

CARDINAL MINDSZENTY (The Truth Behind the Trial of…)
Catechetical Guild Education Society: 1949 (24 pgs., paper cover)

nn-Anti-communism	16	32	48	94	147	200
Press Proof-(Very Rare)-(Full color, 7-1/2x11-3/4", untrimmed) Only two known copies						500.00
Preview Copy (B&W, stapled), 18 pgs.; contains first 13 pgs. of Cardinal Mindszenty and was sent out as an advance promotion. Only one known copy						500.00 - 600.00

NOTE: Regular edition also printed in French. There was also a movie released in 1949 called "Guilty of Treason" which is a fact-based account of the trial and imprisonment of Cardinal Mindszenty by the Communist regime in Hungary.

CARNIVAL OF COMICS
Fleet-Air Shoes: 1954 (Giveaway)

nn-Contains a comic bound with new cover; several combinations possible; Charlton's Eh! known	6	12	18	31	38	45

CARTOON NETWORK
DC Comics: 1997 (Giveaway)

nn-reprints Cow and Chicken, Scooby-Doo, & Flintstones stories	1	3	4	6	8	10

CARVEL COMICS (Amazing Advs. of Capt. Carvel)
Carvel Corp. (Ice Cream): 1975 - No. 5, 1976 (25¢; #3-5: 35¢) (#4,5: 3-1/4x5")

1	3	6	9	14	20	25
2,3	2	4	6	9	12	15
4,5(1976)-Baseball theme	2	4	6	10	14	18

CASE OF THE WASTED WATER, THE
Rheem Water Heating: 1972? (Giveaway)

Captain Jolly Comics #2 © Post

Centipede #1 © DC

Christmas at the Rotunda 1958 © Ford

	GD 2.0	VG 4.0	FN 6.0	VF 8.0	VF/NM 9.0	NM- 9.2
nn-Neal Adams-a	4	8	12	28	47	65

CASPER SPECIAL
Target Stores (Harvey): nd (Dec, 1990) (Giveaway with $1.00 cover)

Three issues-Given away with Casper video						6.00

CASPER, THE FRIENDLY GHOST (Paramount Picture Star…)(2nd Series)
Harvey Publications
American Dental Association (Giveaways):

	GD	VG	FN	VF	VF/NM	NM-
…'s Dental Health Activity Book-1977	2	4	6	8	11	14
…Presents Space Age Dentistry-1972	2	4	6	9	13	16
…, His Den, & Their Dentist Fight the Tooth Demons-1974	2	4	6	9	13	16
Casper Rides the School Bus (1960, 7x3.5", 16 pgs.)	2	4	6	9	13	16

CELEBRATE THE CENTURY SUPERHEROES STAMP ALBUM
DC Comics: 1998 - No. 5, 2000 (32 pgs.)

1-5: Historical stories hosted by DC heroes						5.00

CENTIPEDE
DC Comics: 1983

	GD	VG	FN	VF	VF/NM	NM-
1-Based on Atari video game	2	4	6	13	18	22

CENTURY OF COMICS
Eastern Color Printing Co.: 1933 (100 pgs.)
Bought by Wheatena, Malt-O-Milk, John Wanamaker, Kinney Shoe Stores, & others to be used as premiums and radio giveaways. No publisher listed.

	GD	VG	FN	VF	VF/NM	NM-
nn-Mutt & Jeff, Joe Palooka, etc. reprints	2050	4100	6150	15,500	–	–

CHEERIOS PREMIUMS (Disney)
Walt Disney Productions: 1947 (16 titles, pocket size, 32 pgs.)

	GD	VG	FN	VF	VF/NM	NM-
Mailing Envelope for each set "W,X,Y & Z" (has Mickey illo on front)(each envelope designates the set it contains on the front)	9	18	27	50	65	80

Set "W"

	GD	VG	FN	VF	VF/NM	NM-
W1-Donald Duck & the Pirates	9	18	27	52	69	85
W2-Bucky Bug & the Cannibal King	6	12	18	27	33	38
W3-Pluto Joins the F.B.I.	6	12	18	27	33	38
W4-Mickey Mouse & the Haunted House	6	12	18	29	36	42

Set "X"

	GD	VG	FN	VF	VF/NM	NM-
X1-Donald Duck, Counter Spy	9	18	27	50	65	80
X2-Goofy Lost in the Desert	6	12	18	27	33	38
X3-Br'er Rabbit Outwits Br'er Fox	6	12	18	27	33	38
X4-Mickey Mouse at the Rodeo	6	12	18	31	38	45

Set "Y"

	GD	VG	FN	VF	VF/NM	NM-
Y1-Donald Duck's Atom Bomb by Carl Barks. Disney has banned reprinting this book	71	142	213	454	777	1100
Y2-Br'er Rabbit's Secret	6	12	18	27	33	38
Y3-Dumbo & the Circus Mystery	6	12	18	27	33	38
Y4-Mickey Mouse Meets the Wizard	6	12	18	33	41	48

Set "Z"

	GD	VG	FN	VF	VF/NM	NM-
Z1-Donald Duck Pilots a Jet Plane (not by Barks)	9	18	27	47	61	75
Z2-Pluto Turns Sleuth Hound	5	10	15	25	31	36
Z3-The Seven Dwarfs & the Enchanted Mtn.	6	12	18	33	41	48
Z4-Mickey Mouse's Secret Room	6	12	18	33	41	48

CHEERIOS 3-D GIVEAWAYS (Disney)
Walt Disney Productions: 1954 (24 titles, pocket size) (Glasses came in envelopes)

	GD	VG	FN	VF	VF/NM	NM-
Glasses only…	4	7	10	14	17	20
Mailing Envelope (no art on front)	6	12	18	27	33	38

(Set 1)

	GD	VG	FN	VF	VF/NM	NM-
1-Donald Duck & Uncle Scrooge, the Firefighters	7	14	21	35	43	50
2-Mickey Mouse & Goofy, Pirate Plunder	7	14	21	35	43	50
3-Donald Duck's Nephews, the Fabulous Inventors	7	14	21	37	46	55
4-Mickey Mouse, Secret of the Ming Vase	6	12	18	29	36	42
5-Donald Duck with Huey, Dewey, & Louie; …the Seafarers (title on 2nd page)	7	14	21	35	43	50
6-Mickey Mouse, Moaning Mountain	6	12	18	29	36	42
7-Donald Duck, Apache Gold	7	14	21	35	43	50
8-Mickey Mouse, Flight to Nowhere	6	12	18	29	36	42

(Set 2)

	GD	VG	FN	VF	VF/NM	NM-
1-Donald Duck, Treasure of Timbuktu	7	14	21	35	43	50
2-Mickey Mouse & Pluto, Operation China	6	12	18	29	36	42
3-Donald Duck and the Magic Cows	7	14	21	35	43	50
4-Mickey Mouse & Goofy, Kid Kokonut	6	12	18	29	36	42
5-Donald Duck, Mystery Ship	7	14	21	35	43	50
6-Mickey Mouse, Phantom Sheriff	6	12	18	29	36	42
7-Donald Duck, Circus Adventures	7	14	21	35	43	50
8-Mickey Mouse, Arctic Explorers	6	12	18	29	36	42

(Set 3)

	GD	VG	FN	VF	VF/NM	NM-
1-Donald Duck & Witch Hazel	7	14	21	35	43	50
2-Mickey Mouse in Darkest Africa	6	12	18	29	36	42
3-Donald Duck & Uncle Scrooge, Timber Trouble	7	14	21	35	43	50

	GD	VG	FN	VF	VF/NM	NM-
4-Mickey Mouse, Rajah's Rescue	6	12	18	29	36	42
5-Donald Duck in Robot Reporter	7	14	21	35	43	50
6-Mickey Mouse, Slumbering Sleuth	6	12	18	29	36	42
7-Donald Duck in the Foreign Legion	7	14	21	35	43	50
8-Mickey Mouse, Airwalking Wonder	6	12	18	29	36	42

CHESTY AND COPTIE (Disney)
Los Angeles Community Chest: 1946 (Giveaway, 4pgs.)

nn-(One known copy) by Floyd Gottfredson   (a GD copy sold for $371.65 on 2/12/17)

CHESTY AND HIS HELPERS (Disney)
Los Angeles War Chest: 1943 (Giveaway, 12 pgs., 5-1/2x7-1/4")

	GD	VG	FN	VF	VF/NM	NM-
nn-Chesty & Coptie	54	108	162	343	574	825

CHOCOLATE THE FLAVOR OF FRIENDSHIP AROUND THE WORLD
The Nestle Company: 1955

	GD	VG	FN	VF	VF/NM	NM-
nn	7	14	21	35	43	50

CHRISTMAS ADVENTURE, THE
S. Rose (H. L. Green Giveaway): 1963 (16 pgs.)

	GD	VG	FN	VF	VF/NM	NM-
nn	2	4	6	11	16	20

CHRISTMAS ADVENTURES WITH ELMER THE ELF
1949 (paper-c)

	GD	VG	FN	VF	VF/NM	NM-
nn	5	10	15	24	30	35

CHRISTMAS AT THE ROTUNDA (Titled Ford Rotunda Christmas Book 1957 on)
Ford Motor Co. (Western Printing): 1954 - 1961 (Given away every Christmas at one location)

	GD	VG	FN	VF	VF/NM	NM-
1954-56 issues (nn's)	9	18	27	50	65	80
1957-61 issues (nn's)	8	16	24	44	57	70

CHRISTMAS CAROL, A
Sears Roebuck & Co.: No date (1942-43) (Giveaway, 32 pgs., 8-1/4x10-3/4", paper cover)

	GD	VG	FN	VF	VF/NM	NM-
nn-Comics & coloring book	50	50	75	150	245	340

CHRISTMAS CAROL, A (Also see Bob & Santa's Wishing Whistle, Merry Christmas From Sears Toyland, and Santa's Christmas Comic Variety Show)
Sears Roebuck & Co.: 1940s? (Christmas giveaway, 20 pgs.)

	GD	VG	FN	VF	VF/NM	NM-
nn-Comic book & animated coloring book	24	48	72	140	230	320

CHRISTMAS CAROLS
Hot Shoppes Giveaway: 1959? (16 pgs.)

	GD	VG	FN	VF	VF/NM	NM-
nn	5	10	15	22	26	30

CHRISTMAS COLORING FUN
H. Burnside: 1964 (20 pgs., slick-c, B&W)

	GD	VG	FN	VF	VF/NM	NM-
nn	2	4	6	11	16	20

CHRISTMAS DREAM, A
Promotional Publishing Co.: 1950 (Kinney Shoe Store Giveaway, 16 pgs.)

	GD	VG	FN	VF	VF/NM	NM-
nn	6	12	18	28	34	40

CHRISTMAS DREAM, A
J. J. Newberry Co.: 1952? (Giveaway, paper cover, 16 pgs.)

	GD	VG	FN	VF	VF/NM	NM-
nn	5	10	15	23	28	32

CHRISTMAS DREAM, A
Promotional Publ. Co.: 1952 (16 pgs., paper cover)

	GD	VG	FN	VF	VF/NM	NM-
nn	5	10	15	23	28	32

CHRISTMAS FUN AROUND THE WORLD
No publisher: No date (early 50's) (16 pgs., paper cover)

	GD	VG	FN	VF	VF/NM	NM-
nn	6	12	18	28	34	40

CHRISTMAS FUN BOOK
G. C. Murphy Co.: 1950 (Giveaway, paper cover)

	GD	VG	FN	VF	VF/NM	NM-
nn-Contains paper dolls	7	14	21	37	46	55

CHRISTMAS IS COMING!
No publisher: No date (early 50's?) (Store giveaway, 16 pgs.)

	GD	VG	FN	VF	VF/NM	NM-
nn-Santa cover	6	12	18	32	39	46

CHRISTMAS JOURNEY THROUGH SPACE
Promotional Publishing Co.: 1960

	GD	VG	FN	VF	VF/NM	NM-
nn-Reprints 1954 issue Jolly Christmas Book with new slick cover	3	6	9	16	23	30

CHRISTMAS ON THE MOON
W. T. Grant Co.: 1958 (Giveaway, 20 pgs., slick cover)

	GD	VG	FN	VF	VF/NM	NM-
nn	10	20	30	54	72	90

CHRISTMAS PLAY BOOK
Gould-Stoner Co.: 1946 (Giveaway, 16 pgs., paper cover)

	GD	VG	FN	VF	VF/NM	NM-
nn	11	22	33	62	86	110

CHRISTMAS ROUNDUP

	GD 2.0	VG 4.0	FN 6.0	VF 8.0	VF/NM 9.0	NM- 9.2

Promotional Publishing Co.: 1960

nn-Marv Levy-c/a	2	4	6	9	13	16

CHRISTMAS STORY CUT-OUT BOOK, THE
Catechetical Guild: No. 393, 1951 (15¢, 36 pgs.)

393-Half text & half comics	9	18	27	47	61	75

CHRISTMAS USA (Through 300 Years) (Also see Uncle Sam's…)
Promotional Publ. Co.: 1956 (Giveaway)

nn-Marv Levy-c/a	4	8	12	17	21	24

CHRISTMAS WITH SNOW WHITE AND THE SEVEN DWARFS
Kobackers Giftstore of Buffalo, N.Y.: 1953 (16 pgs., paper-c)

nn	9	18	27	52	69	85

CHRISTOPHERS, THE
Catechetical Guild: 1951 (Giveaway, 36 pgs.) (Some copies have 15¢ sticker)

nn-Stalin as Satan in Hell; Hitler & Lincoln app.	29	58	87	172	281	390

CHUCKY JACK'S A-COMIN'
Great Smoky Mountains Historical Assn., Gatlinburg, TN: 1956 (Reg. size)

nn-Life of John Sevier, founder of Tennessee	8	16	24	42	54	65

CINDERELLA IN "FAIREST OF THE FAIR" (Walt Disney)
American Dairy Association (Premium): 1955 (5x7-1/4", 16 pgs., soft-c)

nn	12	24	36	67	94	120

CINEMA COMICS HERALD
Paramount Pictures/Universal/RKO/20th Century Fox/Republic:
1941 - 1943 (4-pg. movie "trailers", paper-c, 7-1/2x10-1/2")(Giveaway)

"Mr. Bug Goes to Town" (1941)	20	40	60	114	182	250
"Bedtime Story"	14	28	42	81	118	155
"Lady For A Night", John Wayne, Joan Blondell ('42)	22	44	66	130	213	295
"Reap The Wild Wind" (1942)	15	30	45	84	127	170
"Thunder Birds" (1942)	14	28	42	81	118	155
"They All Kissed the Bride"	15	30	45	83	124	165
"Arabian Nights" (nd)	15	30	45	84	127	170
"Bombardie" (1943)	14	28	42	81	118	155
"Crash Dive" (1943)-Tyrone Power	15	30	45	84	127	170

NOTE: The 1941-42 issues contain line art with color photos. 1943 issues are line art.

CLASSICS GIVEAWAYS (Classic Comics reprints)

12/41—Walter Theatre Enterprises (Huntington, WV) giveaway containing #2 (orig.)

w/new generic-c (only 1 known copy)	116	232	348	742	1271	1800

1942—Double Comics containing CC#1 (orig.) (diff. cover) (not actually a giveaway)

(very rare) (also see Double Comics) (only one known copy)	187	374	561	1197	2049	2900

12/42—Saks 34th St. Giveaway containing CC#7 (orig.) (diff. cover)

(very rare; only 6 known copies)	371	742	1113	2600	4550	6500

2/43—American Comics containing CC#8 (orig.) (Liberty Theatre giveaway) (different cover)

(only one known copy) (see American Comics)	142	284	426	909	1555	2200

12/44—Robin Hood Flour Co. Giveaway - #7-CC(R) (diff. cover) (rare)

(edition probably 5 [22])	290	580	870	1856	3178	4500

NOTE: How are editions determined without CC covers? 1942 is dated 1942, and CC#1-first reprint did not come out until 5/43. 12/42 and 2/43 are determined by blue note at bottom of first text page only in original edition. 12/44 is estimated from page width each subsequent reprint edition had progressively slightly smaller page width.

1951—Shelter Thru the Ages (C.I. Educational Series) (actually Giveaway by the Ruberoid Co.) (16 pgs.) (contains original artwork by H. C. Kiefer) (there are 5 diff. back cover ad variations: "Ranch" house ad, "Igloo" ad, "Doll House" ad, "Tree House" ad & blank)

(scarce)	77	154	231	493	847	1200

1952—George Daynor Biography Giveaway (CC logo) (partly comic book/pictures/newspaper articles) (story of man who built Palace Depression out of junkyard swamp in NJ) (64 pgs.)

(very rare; only 3 known copies, one missing back-c)	400	800	1200	2800	4900	7000

1953—Westinghouse/Dreams of a Man (C.I. Educational Series) (Westinghousebio./ Westinghouse Co. giveaway) (contains original artwork by H. C. Kiefer) (16 pgs.) (also French/Spanish/Italian versions) (scarce)

	57	114	171	362	619	875

NOTE: Reproductions of 1951, 1952, and 1953 exist with color photocopy covers and black & white photocopy interior ("W.C.N. Reprint")

	3	5	7	10	12	14

1951-53—Coward Shoe Giveaways (all editions very rare); 2 variations of back-c ad exist: With back-c photo ad: 5 (87), 12 (89), 22 (85), 32 (85), 49 (85), 69 (87), 72 (no HRN), 80 (0), 91 (0), 92 (0), 96 (0), 98 (0), 100 (0), 101 (0), 103-105 (all Os)

	34	68	102	199	325	450

With back-c cartoon ad: 106-109 (all 0s), 110 (111), 112 (0)

	34	68	102	204	332	460

1956—Ben Franklin 5-10 Store Giveaway (#65-PC with back cover ad)

(scarce)	26	52	78	154	252	350

1956—Ben Franklin Insurance Co. Giveaway (#65-PC with diff. back cover ad)

(very rare)	52	104	156	328	552	775

11/56—Sealtest Co. Edition - #4 (135) (identical to regular edition except for Sealtest logo printed, not stamped, on front cover) (only two copies known to exist)

	32	64	96	188	307	425

1958—Get-Well Giveaway containing #15-CI (new cartoon-type cover) (Pressman Pharmacy) (only one copy known to exist)

	32	64	96	188	307	425

1967-68—Twin Circle Giveaway Editions - all HRN 166, with back cover ad for National Catholic Press.

2(R68), 4(R67), 10(R68), 13(R68)	3	6	9	21	33	45
48(R67), 128(R68), 535(576-R68)	4	8	12	23	37	50
16(R68), 68(R67)	5	10	15	30	50	70

12/69—Christmas Giveaway ("A Christmas Adventure") (reprints Picture Parade #4-1953, new cover) (4 ad variations)

Stacey's Dept. Store	4	8	12	25	40	55
Anne & Hope Store	5	10	15	33	57	80
Gibson's Dept. Store (rare)	5	10	15	33	57	80
"Merry Christmas" & blank ad space	4	8	12	25	40	55

CLEAR THE TRACK!
Association of American Railroads: 1954 (paper-c, 16 pgs.)

nn	6	12	18	31	38	45

CLIFF MERRITT SETS THE RECORD STRAIGHT

Brotherhood of Railroad Trainsmen: Giveaway (2 different issues)

…and the Very Candid Candidate by Al Williamson	4	8	12	28	47	65
…Sets the Record Straight by Al Williamson (2 different-c: one by Williamson, the other by McWilliams)	4	8	12	28	47	65

CLYDE BEATTY COMICS (Also see Crackajack Funnies)
Commodore Productions & Artists, Inc.

…African Jungle Book('56)-Richfield Oil Co. 16 pg. giveaway, soft-c	12	24	36	69	97	125

C-M-O COMICS
Chicago Mail Order Co.(Centaur): 1942 - No. 2, 1942 (68 pgs., full color)

1-Invisible Terror, Super Ann, & Plymo the Rubber Man app. (all Centaur costume heroes)	181	362	543	1158	1979	2800
2-Invisible Terror, Super Ann app.	106	212	318	682	1166	1650

COCOMALT BIG BOOK OF COMICS
Harry 'A' Chesler (Cocomalt Premium): 1938 (Reg. size, full color, 52 pgs.)

1-(Scarce)-Biro-c/a; Little Nemo by Winsor McCay Jr., Dan Hastings; Jack Cole, Guardineer, Gustavson, Bob Wood-a	239	478	717	1530	2615	3700

COLONEL OF TWO WORLDS, THE
DC Comics: 2015 (Kentucky Fried Chicken promotion, no price)

1-Flash, Green Lantern and Colonel Sanders vs. the evil Colonel of Earth-3; Derenick-a					4.00	

COMIC BOOK (Also see Comics From Weatherbird)
American Juniors Shoe: Giveaway

Contains a comic rebound with new cover. Several combinations possible. Contents determine price.

COMIC BOOK CONFIDENTIAL
Sphinx Productions: 1988 (Giveaway, 16 pgs.)

1-Tie-in to a documentary about comic creators; creator biographies; Chester Brown-c	1	2	3	5	6	8

COMIC BOOK MAGAZINE
Chicago Tribune & other newspapers: 1940 - 1943 (Similar to Spirit sections) (7-3/4x10-3/4"; full color; 16-24 pgs. ea.)

1940 issues	9	18	27	50	65	80
1941, 1942 issues	8	16	24	42	54	65
1943 issues	8	16	24	40	50	60

NOTE: Published weekly. Texas Slim, Kit Carson, Spooky, Josie, Nuts & Jolts, Lew Loyal, Brenda Starr, Daniel Boone, Captain Storm, Rocky, Smokey Stover, Tiny Tim, Little Joe, Fu Manchu appear among others. Early issues had photo stories with pictures from the movies; later issues had comic art.

COMIC BOOKS (Series 1)
Metropolitan Printing Co. (Giveaway): 1950 (16 pgs.; 5-1/4x8-1/2"; full color; bound at top; paper cover)

1-Boots and Saddles; intro The Masked Marshal	8	16	24	42	54	65
1-The Green Jet; Green Lama by Raboy	24	48	72	142	234	325
1-My Pal Dizzy (Teen-age)	6	12	18	31	38	45
1-New World; origin Atomaster (costumed hero)	12	24	36	67	94	120
1-Talullah (Teen-age)	6	12	18	31	38	45

COMIC CAVALCADE
All-American/National Periodical Publications

Giveaway (1944, 8 pgs., paper-c, in color)-One Hundred Years of Co-operation- r/Comic Cavalcade #9	47	94	141	296	498	700
Giveaway (1945, 16 pgs., paper-c, in color)-Movie "Tomorrow The World" (Nazi theme); r/Comic Cavalcade #10	65	130	195	416	708	1000
Giveaway (c. 1944-45; 8 pgs, paper-c, in color)-The Twain Shall Meet-r/Comic Cavalcade #8	47	94	141	296	498	700

COMIC SELECTIONS (Shoe store giveaway)
Parents' Magazine Press: 1944-46 (Reprints from Calling All Girls, True Comics, True Aviation, & Real Heroes) (All contain WWII-c/s)

1	7	14	21	35	43	50
2-6	5	10	15	24	30	35

COMICS FROM WEATHER BIRD (Also see Comic Book, Edward's Shoes, Free Comics to You & Weather Bird)
Weather Bird Shoes: 1954 - 1957 (Giveaway)

Contains a comic bound with new cover. Many combinations possible. Contents would determine price. Some issues do not contain complete comics, but only parts of comics. Value equals 40 to 60 percent of contents.

COMICS READING LIBRARIES (Educational Series)
King Features (Charlton Publ.): 1973, 1977, 1979 (36 pgs. in color) (Giveaways)

R-01-Tiger, Quincy	2	4	6	9	13	16
R-02-Beetle Bailey, Blondie & Popeye	2	4	6	11	16	20
R-03-Blondie, Beetle Bailey	2	4	6	8	11	14
R-04-Tim Tyler's Luck, Felix the Cat	3	6	9	16	23	30
R-05-Quincy, Henry	2	4	6	8	11	14
R-06-The Phantom, Mandrake	3	6	9	18	27	36
1977 reprint(R-04)	2	4	6	9	13	16
R-07-Popeye, Little King	2	4	6	13	18	22
R-08-Prince Valiant (Foster), Flash Gordon	3	6	9	19	30	40
1977 reprint	2	4	6	11	16	20
R-09-Hagar the Horrible, Boner's Ark	2	4	6	10	14	18
R-10-Redeye, Tiger	2	4	6	8	11	14
R-11-Blondie, Hi & Lois	2	4	6	8	11	14
R-12-Popeye-Swee'pea, Brutus	2	4	6	13	18	22
R-13-Beetle Bailey, Little King	2	4	6	8	11	14
R-14-Quincy-Hamlet	2	4	6	8	11	14
R-15-The Phantom, The Genius	3	6	9	14	20	25
R-16-Flash Gordon, Mandrake	3	6	9	21	33	45
1977 reprint	2	4	6	10	14	18
Other 1977 editions…	2	4	6	8	10	12
1979 editions (68 pgs.)	2	4	6	8	10	12

NOTE: Above giveaways available with purchase of $45.00 in merchandise. Used as a reading skills aid for small children.

COMMANDMENTS OF GOD
Catechetical Guild: 1954, 1958

300-Same contents in both editions; diff-c	5	10	15	24	29	34

Clear the Track! © AAR

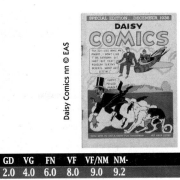

Daisy Comics nn © EAS

Detective Comics #373 WB Home Video © DC

	GD 2.0	VG 4.0	FN 6.0	VF 8.0	VF/NM 9.0	NM- 9.2

COMPLIMENTARY COMICS
Sales Promotion Publ.: No date (1950's) (Giveaway)

	GD 2.0	VG 4.0	FN 6.0	VF 8.0	VF/NM 9.0	NM- 9.2
1-Strongman by Powell, 3 stories	8	16	24	44	57	70

COPPER - THE OLDEST AND NEWEST METAL
Commercial Comics: 1959

nn	3	6	9	14	20	25

CRACKAJACK FUNNIES (Giveaway)
Malto-Meal: 1937 (Full size, soft-c, full color, 32 pgs.)(Before No. 1?)

nn-Features Dan Dunn, G-Man, Speed Bolton, Buck Jones, The Nebbs, Clyde Beatty, Freckles, Major Hoople, Wash Tubbs	103	206	309	659	1130	1600

CRAFTSMAN BOLT-ON SYSTEMS SAVE THE JUSTICE LEAGUE
DC Comics: 2012 (Giveaway promo for Craftsman Bolt-On Tool System)
1-Christian Duce-a/c; New-52 Justice League, The Key and Royal Flush Gang app.   4.00

CRISIS AT THE CARSONS
Pictorial Media: 1958 (Reg. size)

nn	6	12	18	31	38	45

CROSLEY'S HOUSE OF FUN (Also see Tee and Vee Crosley…)
Crosley Div. AVCO Mfg. Corp.: 1950 (Giveaway, paper cover, 32 pgs.)

nn-Strips revolve around Crosley appliances	6	12	18	28	34	40

DAGWOOD SPLITS THE ATOM (Also see Topix V8#4)
King Features Syndicate: 1949 (Science comic with King Features characters) (Giveaway)

nn-Half comic, half text; Popeye, Olive Oyl, Henry, Mandrake, Little King, Katzenjammer Kids app.	8	16	24	44	57	70

DAISY COMICS (Daisy Air Rifles)
Eastern Color Printing Co.: Dec, 1936 (5-1/4x7-1/2")

nn-Joe Palooka, Buck Rogers (2 pgs. from Famous Funnies No. 18, 1st full cover app.), Napoleon Flying to Fame, Butty & Fally	41	82	123	256	428	600

DAISY LOW OF THE GIRL SCOUTS
Girl Scouts of America: 1954, 1965 (16 pgs., paper-c)

1954-Story of Juliette Gordon Low	6	12	18	28	34	40
1965	2	4	6	9	13	16

DAN CURTIS GIVEAWAYS
Western Publishing Co.:1974 (3x6", 24 pgs., reprints)

1-Dark Shadows	2	4	6	11	16	20
2,6-Star Trek	2	4	6	11	16	20
3,4,7-9: 3-The Twilight Zone. 4-Ripley's Believe it or Not! 7-The Occult Files of Dr. Spektor. 8-Dagar the Invincible. 9-Grimm's Ghost Stories		4	6	8	11	14
5-Turok, Son of Stone (partial-r/Turok #78)	2	4	6	10	14	18

DANNY AND THE DEMOXICYCLE
Virginia Highway Safety Division: 1970s (Reg. size, slick-c)

nn	3	6	9	19	30	40

DANNY KAYE'S BAND FUN BOOK
H & A Selmer: 1959 (Giveaway)

nn	7	14	21	37	46	55

DAREDEVIL
Marvel Comics Group: 1993
…Vs. Vapora 1 (Engineering Show Giveaway, 16 pg.) - Intro Vapora   6.00

DAVY CROCKETT (TV)
Dell Publishing Co.

…Christmas Book (no date, 16 pgs., paper-c)-Sears giveaway	6	12	18	31	38	45
…Safety Trails (1955, 16pgs, 3-1/4x7")-Cities Service giveaway	8	16	24	40	50	60

DAVY CROCKETT
Charlton Comics

Hunting With… nn ('55, 16 pgs.)-Ben Franklin Store giveaway (Publ.-S. Rose)	5	10	15	24	30	35

DAVY CROCKETT
Walt Disney Prod.: (1955, 16 pgs., 5x7-1/4", slick, photo-c)

…In the Raid at Piney Creek-American Motors giveaway	8	16	24	40	50	60

DC SAMPLER
DC Comics: nn (#1) 1983 - No. 3, 1984 (36 pgs.; 6 1/2" x 10", giveaway)

nn(#1) -3: nn-Wraparound-c, previews upcoming issues. 3-Kirby-a	1	2	3	4	5	7

DC SPOTLIGHT
DC Comics: 1985 (50th anniversary special) (giveaway)
1-Includes profiles on Batman: The Dark Knight & Watchmen

	GD 2.0	VG 4.0	FN 6.0	VF 8.0	VF/NM 9.0	NM- 9.2
	4	8	12	18	22	25

DENNIS THE MENACE
Hallden (Fawcett)

…& Dirt ('59)-Soil Conservation giveaway; r-# 36; Wiseman-c/a	3	6	9	17	26	35
…& Dirt ('68)-reprints '59 edition	2	4	6	10	14	18
…Away We Go('70)-Caladryl giveaway	2	4	6	9	12	15
…Coping with Family Stress-giveaway	2	4	6	9	12	15
…Takes a Poke at Poison('61)-Food & Drug Admin. giveaway; Wiseman-c/a	2	4	6	10	14	18
…Takes a Poke at Poison-Revised 1/66, 11/70	1	2	3	5	6	8
…Takes a Poke at Poison-Revised 1972, 1974, 1977, 1981	1	2	3	4	5	7

DESERT DAWN
E.C./American Museum of Natural History: 1935 (paper-c)
nn-Johnny Jackrabbit stars. Seven known copies: A CGC 2.5 copy (brittle) sold for $2034 in 2022. A CGC 6.5 copy sold for $3720 in Sept. 2022. Another CGC 6.5 sold for $1800 in Nov. 2022.

DETECTIVE COMICS (Also see other Batman titles)
National Periodical Publications/DC Comics

27 (1984)-Oreo Cookies giveaway (32 pgs., paper-c) r-/Det. #27,#38 & Batman #1 (1st Joker)	6	12	18	38	69	100
38 (1995) Blockbuster Video edition; reprints 1st Robin app.		4	5	7	8	10
38 (1997) Toys R Us edition	2	4	5	7	8	10
359 (1997) Toys R Us edition; reprints 1st Batgirl app.	2	4	5	7	8	10
373 (1997, 6 1/4" x 4") Warner Brothers Home Video	2	4	5	7	8	10

DICK TRACY GIVEAWAYS
1939 - 1958; 1990

Buster Brown Shoes Giveaway (1939, 36 pgs. in color); 1938-39-r by Gould	28	56	84	165	270	375
Gillmore Giveaway (See Superbook)						
…Hatful of Fun (No date, 1950-52, 32pgs.- 8-1/2x10")-Dick Tracy hat promotion; Dick Tracy games, magic tricks. Miller Bros. premium	19	38	57	111	176	240
Motorola Giveaway (1953)-Reprints Harvey Comics Library #2; "The Case of the Sparkle Plenty TV Mystery"	8	16	24	40	50	60
Original Dick Tracy by Chester Gould, The (Aug, 1990, 16 pgs., 5-1/2x8-1/2")- Gladstone Publ.; Bread Giveaway	1	3	4	6	8	10
Popped Wheat Giveaway (1947, 16 pgs. in color)-1940-r; Sig Feuchtwanger Publ.; Gould-a	6	12	18	31	38	45
…Presents the Family Fun Book; Tip Top Bread Giveaway, no date or number (1940, Fawcett Publ., 16 pgs. in color)-Spy Smasher, Ibis, Lance O'Casey app.	36	72	108	211	343	475
Same as above but without app. of heroes & Dick Tracy on cover only	15	30	45	86	133	180
Service Station Giveaway (1958, 16 pgs. in color)(regular size, slick cover)- Harvey Info. Press	7	14	21	35	43	50
Shoe Store Giveaway (Weatherbird and Triangle Stores)(1939, 16 pgs.)-Gould-a	16	32	48	94	147	200

DICK TRACY SHEDS LIGHT ON THE MOLE
Western Printing Co.: 1949 (16 pgs.) (Ray-O-Vac Flashlights giveaway)

nn-Not by Gould	10	20	30	58	79	100

DICK WINGATE OF THE U.S. NAVY
Superior Publ./Toby Press: 1951; 1953 (no month)

nn-U.S. Navy giveaway	8	16	24	40	50	60
1(1953, Toby)-Reprints nn issue? (same-c)	6	12	18	31	38	60

DIG 'EM
Kellogg's Sugar Smacks Giveaway: 1973 (2-3/8x6", 16 pgs.)

nn-4 different issues	1	3	4	6	8	10

DISNEY MAGAZINE
Procter and Gamble giveaway: nn (#1), Sept, 1976 - nn (#4), Jan, 1977

nn-All have an original Mickey story in color, 12-13 pgs. ea. and info/articles on Disney movies, cartoons. All have partial photo covers of a movie star with 1-2 pg. story. Covers: 1-Bob Hope, 2-Debbie Reynolds, 3-Groucho Marx, 4-Rock Hudson.	2	4	6	10	14	18

DOC CARTER VD COMICS
Health Publications Institute, Raleigh, N. C. (Giveaway): 1949 (16 pgs. in color) (Paper-c)

nn	36	72	108	211	343	475

DONALD AND MICKEY MERRY CHRISTMAS (Formerly Famous Gang Book Of Comics)
K. K. Publ./Firestone Tire & Rubber Co.: 1943 - 1949 (Giveaway, 20 pgs.)
Put out each Christmas; 1943 issue titled "Firestone Presents Comics" (Disney)

1943-Donald Duck-r/WDC&S #32 by Carl Barks	97	194	291	621	1061	1500
1944-Donald Duck-r/WDC&S #35 by Barks	93	186	279	591	1021	1450

1945- "Donald Duck's Best Christmas", 8 pgs. Carl Barks; intro. & 1st app.

	GD 2.0	VG 4.0	FN 6.0	VF 8.0	VF/NM 9.0	NM- 9.2

Grandma Duck in comic books — 123 246 369 787 1344 1900

1946-Donald Duck in "Santa's Stormy Visit", 8 pgs. Carl Barks
— 76 152 228 486 831 1175

1947-Donald Duck in "Three Good Little Ducks", 8 pgs. Carl Barks
— 76 152 228 486 831 1175

1948-Donald Duck in "Toyland", 8 pgs. Carl Barks
— 76 152 228 486 831 1175

1949-Donald Duck in "New Toys", 8 pgs. Barks
— 69 138 207 442 759 1075

DONALD DUCK
K. K. Publications: 1944 (Christmas giveaway, paper-c, 16 pgs.)(2 versions)

nn-Kelly cover reprint — 135 270 405 864 1482 2100

DONALD DUCK AND THE RED FEATHER
Red Feather Giveaway: 1948 (8-1/2x11", 4 pgs., B&W)

nn — 24 48 72 142 234 325

DONALD DUCK IN "THE LITTERBUG"
Keep America Beautiful: 1963 (5x7-1/4", 16 pgs., soft-c) (Disney giveaway)

nn — 5 10 15 33 57 80

DONALD DUCK "PLOTTING PICNICKERS" (See Frito-Lay Giveaway)

DONALD DUCK'S SURPRISE PARTY
Walt Disney Productions: 1948 (16 pgs.) (Giveaway for Icy Frost Twins Ice Cream Bars)

nn-(Rare)-Kelly-c/a — 239 478 717 1530 2615 3700

DON FORTUNE MAGAZINE
Fawcett Publications: 1940s (Mini-comic)

1-3 (Rare)   (A set of 3 in 9.0 sold for $116 in 2016)

DOT AND DASH AND THE LUCKY JINGLE PIGGIE
Sears Roebuck Co.: 1942 (Christmas giveaway, 12 pgs.)

nn-Contains a war stamp album and a punch out Jingle Piggie bank
— 14 28 42 80 115 150

DOUBLE TALK (Also see Two-Faces)
Feature Publications: No date (1961) (32 pgs., full color, slick-c)
Christian Anti-Communism Crusade (Giveaway)

nn-Sickle with blood-c — 30 60 90 177 289 400

DRUMMER BOY AT GETTYSBURG
Eastern National Park & Monument Association: 1976

nn-Fred Ray-a — 3 6 9 15 22 28

DUMBO (Walt Disney's..., The Flying Elephant)
Weatherbird Shoes/Ernest Kern Co.(Detroit)/ Wieboldt's (Chicago): 1941
(K.K. Publ. Giveaway)

nn-16 pgs., 9x10" (Rare) — 50 100 150 315 533 950

nn-52 pgs., 5-1/2x8-1/2", slick cover in color; B&W interior; half text, half
reprints 4-Color No. 17 (Dept. store) — 26 52 78 154 252 350

DUMBO WEEKLY
Walt Disney Prod.: 1942 (Premium supplied by Diamond D-X Gas Stations)(4 pgs. each)

1 — 37 74 111 222 361 500

2-16 — 15 30 45 83 124 165

Binder only (linen-like stock) — 190
NOTE: A cover and binder came separate at gas stations. Came with membership card.

EAT RIGHT TO WORK AND WIN
Swift & Company: 1942 (16 pgs.) (Giveaway)

Blondie, Henry, Flash Gordon by Alex Raymond, Toots & Casper, Thimble Theatre(Popeye), Tillie the Toiler,
The Phantom, The Little King, & Bringing up Father - original strips just for this book -(in daily strip form which shows
what foods we should eat and why) — 34 68 102 199 325 450

EDWARD'S SHOES GIVEAWAY
Edward's Shoe Store: 1954 (Has clown on cover)

Contains comic with new cover. Many combinations possible. Contents determines price, 50-60 percent of original.
(Similar to Comics From Weatherbird & Free Comics to You)

EE-YI-EE-YI-OH!
Consumer Power Co.: 1972 (Paper-c)

nn - A barnyard fable about ecology — 2 4 6 9 12 15

ELSIE THE COW
D. S. Publishing Co.

Borden's cheese comic picture bk ("40, giveaway) — 22 44 66 132 216 300

Borden Milk Giveaway-(16 pgs., nn) (3 ishs, "A Trip Through Space" and 2 others, 1957)
— 15 30 45 94 147 200

Elsie's Fun Book(1950; Borden Milk) — 15 30 45 94 147 200

Everyday Birthday Fun With... (1957; 20 pgs.)(100th Anniversary); Kubert-a
— 15 30 45 94 147 200

ESCAPE FROM FEAR
Planned Parenthood of America: 1956, 1962, 1969 (Giveaway, 8 pgs., color) (On birth control)

1956 edition — 14 28 42 78 112 145

1962 edition — 5 10 15 30 50 70

1969 edition — 3 6 9 21 33 45

EVEL KNIEVEL
Marvel Comics Group (Ideal Toy Corp.): 1974 (Giveaway, 20 pgs.)

nn-Contains photo on inside back-c — 6 12 18 41 76 110

FAIR PLAY
Anti-Defamation League, NY: 1950s (soft-c, regular size)

nn-Anti-racism/anti-discrimination   (A copy sold for $480 in Aug. 2018)

FAMOUS COMICS (Also see Favorite Comics)
Zain-Eppy/United Features Syndicate: No date; Mid 1930's (24 pgs., paper-c)

nn-Reprinted from 1933 & 1934 newspaper strips in color; Joe Palooka, Hairbreadth Harry,
Napoleon, The Nebbs, etc. (Many different versions known)
— 97 194 291 621 1061 1500

FAMOUS FAIRY TALES
K. K. Publ. Co.: 1942; 1943 (32 pgs.); 1944 (16 pgs.) (Giveaway, soft-c)

1942-Kelly-a — 42 84 126 265 445 625

1943-r-/Fairy Tale Parade No. 2,3; Kelly-a — 29 58 87 172 281 390

1944-Kelly-a — 27 54 81 160 263 365

FAMOUS FUNNIES - A CARNIVAL OF COMICS
Eastern Color: 1933

36 pgs., no date given, no publisher, no number; contains strip reprints of The Bungle Family, Dixie Dugan,
Hairbreadth Harry, Joe Palooka, Keeping Up With the Jones, Mutt & Jeff, Reg'lar Fellers, S'Matter Pop, Strange As It
Seems, and others. This book was sold by M. C. Gaines to Wheatena, Malt-O-Milk, John Wanamaker, Kinney Shoe
Stores, & others to be given away as premiums and radio giveaways (1933). Originally came with a mailing envelope.
— 676 1352 2028 4935 8718 12,500

FAMOUS GANG BOOK OF COMICS (Becomes Donald & Mickey Merry Christmas 1943 on)
Firestone Tire & Rubber Co.: Dec, 1942 (Christmas giveaway, 32 pgs., paper-c)

nn-(Rare)-Porky Pig, Bugs Bunny, Mary Jane & Sniffles, Elmer Fudd; r/Looney Tunes
— 135 270 405 864 1482 2100

FANTASTIC FOUR
Marvel Comics

nn (1981, 32 pgs.) Young Model Builders Club — 2 4 6 9 13 16

Vol. 3 #60 Baltimore Comic Book Show (10/02, newspaper supplement) 200,000 copies were
distributed to Baltimore Sun home subscribers to promote Baltimore Comic Con — 4.00

FATHER OF CHARITY
Catechetical Guild Giveaway: No date (32 pgs.; paper cover)

nn — 6 12 18 27 33 38

FAVORITE COMICS (Also see Famous Comics)
Grocery Store Giveaway (Diff. Corp.) (detergent): 1934 (36 pgs.)

Book 1-The Nebbs, Strange As It Seems, Napoleon, Joe Palooka, Dixie Dugan,
S'Matter Pop, Hairbreadth Harry, etc. reprints — 375 750 1125 1700 — —

Book 2,3 — 255 510 765 1150 — —

FAWCETT MINIATURES (See Mighty Midget)
Fawcett Publications: 1946 (3-3/4x5", 12-24 pgs.) (Wheaties giveaways)

Captain Marvel "And the Horn of Plenty"; Bulletman story
— 14 28 42 76 108 140

Captain Marvel "& the Raiders From Space"; Golden Arrow story
— 14 28 42 76 108 140

Captain Marvel Jr. "The Case of the Poison Press!" Bulletman story
— 14 28 42 76 108 140

Delecta of the Planets; C. C. Beck art; B&W inside; 12 pgs.; 3 printing
variations (coloring) exist — 20 40 60 114 182 250

FEARLESS FOSDICK
Capp Enterprises Inc.: 1951

...& The Case of The Red Feather — 8 16 24 44 57 70

FIFTY WHO MADE DC GREAT
DC Comics: 1985 (Reg. size, slick-c)

nn — 2 4 6 8 10 12

FIGHT FOR FREEDOM
National Assoc. of Mfgrs./General Comics: 1949, 1951 (Giveaway, 16 pgs.)

nn-Dan Barry-c/a; used in POP, pg. 102 — 8 16 24 44 57 70

FIRE AND BLAST
National Fire Protection Assoc.: 1952 (Giveaway, 16 pgs., paper-c)

nn-Mart Baily A-Bomb-c; about fire prevention — 20 40 60 114 182 250

FIRE CHIEF AND THE SAFE OL' FIREFLY, THE
National Board of Fire Underwriters: 1952 (16 pgs.) (Safety brochure given away at schools)
(produced by American Visuals Corp.)(Eisner)

nn-(Rare) Eisner-c/a — 43 86 129 271 461 650

FLASH, THE
DC Comics

nn-(1990) Brochure for CBS TV series — 5.00

The Flash Comes to a Standstill (1981, General Foods giveaway, 8 pages, 3-1/2 x 6-3/4",
oblong) — 3 6 9 14 20 25

FLASH COMICS (Also see Captain Marvel and Funny Stuff)
National Periodical Publications: 1946 (6-1/2x8-1/4", 32 pgs.)(Wheaties Giveaway)

nn-Johnny Thunder, Ghost Patrol, The Flash & Kubert Hawkman app.; Irwin Hasen-c/a
— 100 200 700 1000 — —
NOTE: All known copies were taped to Wheaties boxes and are never found in mint condition. Copies with light
tape residue bring the listed prices in all grades

FLASH GORDON
Dell Publishing Co.: 1943 (20 pgs.)

Macy's Giveaway-(Rare); not by Raymond; Japanese war cover
— 68 136 204 435 743 1050

FLASH GORDON
Harvey Comics: 1951 (16 pgs. in color, regular size, paper-c) (Gordon Bread giveaway)

1,2: 1-r/strips 10/24/37 - 2/6/38. 2-r/strips 7/14/40 - 10/6/40; Reprints by Raymond
each.... — 3 6 9 18 28 34
NOTE: Most copies have brittle edges.

FLINTSTONES FUN BOOK, THE
Denny's giveaway: 1990

1-20 — 1 3 4 6 8 10

FLOOD RELIEF
Malibu Comics (Ultraverse): Jan, 1994 (36 pgs.)(Ordered thru mail w/$5.00 to Red Cross)

1-Hardcase, Prime & Prototype app. — 6.00

FOREST FIRE (Also see The Blazing Forest and Smokey Bear)
American Forestry Assn.(Commerical Comics): 1949 (dated-1950) (16 pgs., paper-c)

nn-Intro/1st app. Smokey The Forest Fire Preventing Bear; created by Rudy Wendelein;
Wendelein/Sparling-a; 'Carter Oil Co.' on back-c of original
— 22 44 66 132 216 300

FOREST RANGER HANDBOOK

Double Talk © Feature

Flood Relief #1 © Malibu

Funnies on Parade © EAS

	GD 2.0	VG 4.0	FN 6.0	VF 8.0	VF/NM 9.0	NM- 9.2

Wrather Corp.: 1967 (5x7", 20 pgs., slick-c)
nn-With Corey Stuart & Lassie photo-c ... 2 / 4 / 6 / 13 / 18 / 22

FORGOTTEN STORY BEHIND NORTH BEACH, THE
Catechetical Guild: No date (8 pgs., paper-c)
nn ... 6 / 12 / 18 / 27 / 33 / 38

FORK IN THE ROAD
U.S. Army Recruiting Service: 1961 (16 pgs., paper-c)
nn ... 2 / 4 / 6 / 11 / 16 / 20

48 FAMOUS AMERICANS
J. C. Penney Co. (Cpr. Edwin H. Stroh): 1947 (Giveaway) (Half-size in color)
nn - Simon & Kirby-a; war cover ... 15 / 30 / 45 / 85 / 130 / 175

FOXHOLE ON YOUR LAWN
No Publisher: No date (Early 1950s)
nn-Charles Biro art ... 5 / 10 / 15 / 23 / 28 / 32

FRANKIE LUER'S SPACE ADVENTURES
Luer Packing Co.: 1955 (5x7", 36 pgs., slick-c)
nn - With Davey Rocket ... 5 / 10 / 15 / 23 / 28 / 32

FREDDY
Charlton Comics
Schiff's Shoes Presents... #1 (1959)-Giveaway ... 5 / 10 / 14 / 20 / 24 / 28

FREE COMIC BOOK DAY EDITIONS (Now listed in the regular section)

FREE COMICS TO YOU FROM... (name of shoe store) (Has clown on cover & another with a rabbit) (Like comics from Weather Bird & Edward's Shoes)
Shoe Store Giveaway: Circa 1956, 1960-61
Contains a comic bound with new cover - several combinations possible; some Harvey titles known. Contents determine price.

FREEDOM TRAIN
Street & Smith Publications: 1948 (Giveaway)
nn-Powell-c w/mailer; patriotic cover ... 20 / 40 / 60 / 114 / 182 / 250

FREIHOFER'S COMIC BOOK
All-American Comics: 1940s (7 1/2 x 10 1/4")(Freihofer's Donuts promotional)
2nd edition-(Scarce) Cover features All-American Comics characters Ultra-Man, Hop Harrigan, Red, White and Blue, Scribbly and others (A CGC 3.0 copy sold for $1200 in 2018)

FRIENDLY GHOST, CASPER, THE
Harvey Comics: 1967 (16 pgs.)
American Dental Assoc. giveaway-Small size ... 3 / 6 / 9 / 17 / 25 / 32

FRITO-LAY GIVEAWAY
Frito-Lay: 1962 (3-1/4x7", soft-c, 16 pgs.) (Disney)
nn-Donald Duck "Plotting Picnickers" ... 5 / 10 / 15 / 31 / 53 / 75
nn-Ludwig Von Drake "Fish Stampede" ... 3 / 6 / 9 / 21 / 33 / 45
nn- Mickey Mouse & Goofy "Bicep Bungle" ... 4 / 8 / 12 / 23 / 37 / 50

FROM GOODWILL INDUSTRIES, A GOOD LIFE
Goodwill Industries: 1950s (regular size)
1 ... 8 / 16 / 24 / 44 / 57 / 70

FRONTIER DAYS
Robin Hood Shoe Store (Brown Shoe): 1956 (Giveaway)
1 ... 4 / 8 / 12 / 17 / 21 / 24

FRONTIERS OF FREEDOM
Institute of Life Insurance: 1950 (Giveaway, paper cover)
nn-Dan Barry-a ... 9 / 18 / 27 / 50 / 65 / 80

FUNNIES ON PARADE (Premium)(See Toy World Funnies)
Eastern Color Printing Co.: 1933 (36 pgs., slick cover)
No date or publisher listed
nn-Contains Sunday page reprints of Mutt & Jeff, Joe Palooka, Hairbreadth Harry, Reg'lar Fellers, Skippy, & others (10,000 print run). This book was printed for Proctor & Gamble to be given away & came out before Famous Funnies or Century of Comics. ... 1325 / 2650 / 3975 / 10,070 / 18,285 / 26,500

FUNNY PICTURE STORIES
Comics Magazine Co./Centaur Publications: 1930s (Giveaway, 16-20 pgs., slick-c)
Promotes diff. laundries; has box on cover where "your Laundry Name" is printed ... 63 / 116 / 189 / 403 / 689 / 975

FUNNY STUFF (Also see Captain Marvel & Flash Comics)
National Periodical Publications (Wheaties Giveaway): 1946 (6-1/2x8-1/4")
nn-(Scarce)-Dodo & the Frog, Three Mousekeeters, etc.; came taped to Wheaties box; never found in better than fine ... 48 / 96 / 144 / 480 / — / —

FUTURE COP: L.A.P.D. (Electronic Arts video game)
DC Comics (WildStorm): 1998

	GD 2.0	VG 4.0	FN 6.0	VF 8.0	VF/NM 9.0	NM- 9.2

nn-Ron Lim-a/Dave Johnson-c ... 4.00

GABBY HAYES WESTERN (Movie star)
Fawcett Publications
Quaker Oats Giveaway nn's(#1-5, 1951, 2-1/2x7") (Kagran Corp.)-...In Tracks of Guilt, ...In the Fence Post Mystery, ...In the Accidental Sherlock, ...In the Frame-Up, ...In the Double Cross Brand known ... 10 / 20 / 30 / 54 / 72 / 90
Mailing Envelope (has illo of Gabby on front) ... 10 / 20 / 30 / 54 / 72 / 90

GARY GIBSON COMICS (Donut club membership)
National Dunking Association: 1950 (Included in donut box with pin and card)
1-Western soft-c, 16 pgs.; folded into the box ... 7 / 14 / 21 / 37 / 46 / 55

GENE AUTRY COMICS
Dell Publishing Co.
...Adventure Comics And Play-Fun Book ('47)-32 pgs., 8x6-1/2"; games, comics, magic (Pillsbury premium) ... 20 / 40 / 60 / 120 / 196 / 270
Quaker Oats Giveaway(1950)-2-1/2x6-3/4"; 5 different versions; "Death Card Gang", "Phantoms of the Cave", "Riddle of Laughing Mtn.", "Secret of Lost Valley", "Bond of the Broken Arrow" (came in wrapper) each... ... 10 / 20 / 30 / 58 / 79 / 100
Mailing Envelope (has illo. of Gene on front) ... 10 / 20 / 30 / 58 / 79 / 100
3-D Giveaway(1953)-Pocket-size; 5 different ... 10 / 20 / 30 / 58 / 79 / 100
Mailing Envelope (no art on front) ... 8 / 16 / 24 / 44 / 57 / 70

GENE AUTRY TIM (Formerly Tim) (Becomes Tim in Space)
Tim Stores: 1950 (Half-size) (B&W Giveaway)
nn-Several issues (All Scarce) ... 19 / 38 / 57 / 109 / 172 / 235

GENERAL FOODS SUPER-HEROES
DC Comics: 1979, 1980
1-4 (1979), 1-4 (1980) each... ... 12.00

G. I. COMICS (Also see Jeep & Overseas Comics)
Giveaways: 1945 - No. 73?, 1946 (Distributed to U. S. Armed Forces)
1-73-Contains Prince Valiant by Foster, Blondie, Smilin' Jack, Mickey Finn, Terry & the Pirates, Donald Duck, Alley Oop, Moon Mullins & Capt. Easy strip reprints (at least 73 issues known to exist) ... 9 / 18 / 27 / 47 / 61 / 75

GODZILLA VS. MEGALON
Cinema Shares Int.: 1976 (4 pgs. on newsprint) (Movie theater giveaway)
nn-1st. comic app. Godzilla in U.S. ... 8 / 16 / 24 / 51 / 96 / 140

GOLDEN ARROW
Fawcett Publications
...Well Known Comics (1944; 12 pgs.; 8-1/2x10-1/2"; paper-c; glued binding)- Bestmaid/ Samuel Lowe giveaway; printed in green ... 15 / 30 / 45 / 85 / 130 / 175

GOLDILOCKS & THE THREE BEARS
K. K. Publications: 1943 (Giveaway)
nn ... 14 / 28 / 42 / 78 / 112 / 145

GREAT PEOPLE OF GENESIS, THE
David C. Cook Publ. Co.: No date (Religious giveaway, 64 pgs.)
nn-Reprint/Sunday Pix Weekly ... 5 / 10 / 15 / 24 / 30 / 35

GREAT SACRAMENT, THE
Catechetical Guild: 1953 (Giveaway, 36 pgs.)
nn ... 5 / 10 / 15 / 22 / 26 / 30

GREEN JET COMICS, THE (See Comic Books, Series 1)

GRENADA
Commercial Comics Co.: 1983 (Giveaway produced by the CIA)
1-Air dropped over Grenada during 1983 invasion ... 5 / 10 / 15 / 31 / 53 / 75

GRIT (YOU'VE GOT TO HAVE...)
GRIT Publishing Co.: 1959
nn-GRIT newspaper sales recruitment comic; Schaffenberger-a. Later version has altered artwork ... 5 / 10 / 15 / 22 / 26 / 30

GROWING UP WITH JUDY
1952
nn-General Electric giveaway ... 5 / 10 / 15 / 23 / 28 / 32

GULF FUNNY WEEKLY (Gulf Comic Weekly No. 1-4)(See Standard Oil Comics)
Gulf Oil Company (Giveaway): 1933 - No. 422, 5/23/41 (in full color; 4 pgs.; tabloid size to 2/3/39; 2/10/39 on, regular comic book size)(early issues undated)
1 ... 87 / 174 / 261 / 553 / 952 / 1350
2-5 ... 40 / 80 / 120 / 246 / 411 / 575
6-30 ... 24 / 48 / 72 / 142 / 234 / 325
31-100 ... 15 / 30 / 45 / 90 / 140 / 190
101-196 ... 13 / 26 / 39 / 72 / 101 / 130
197-Wings Winfair begins(1/29/37); by Fred Meagher beginning in 1938 ... 28 / 56 / 84 / 165 / 270 / 375
198-300 (Last tabloid size) ... 15 / 30 / 45 / 90 / 140 / 190

	GD 2.0	VG 4.0	FN 6.0	VF 8.0	VF/NM 9.0	NM- 9.2

301-350 (Regular size) — 10 | 20 | 30 | 56 | 76 | 95
351-422 — 8 | 16 | 24 | 44 | 57 | 70

GULLIVER'S TRAVELS
Macy's Department Store: 1939, small size
nn-Christmas giveaway — 15 | 30 | 45 | 84 | 127 | 170

GUN THAT WON THE WEST, THE
Winchester-Western Division & Olin Mathieson Chemical Corp.: 1956 (Giveaway, 24 pgs.)
nn-Painted-c — 9 | 18 | 27 | 47 | 61 | 75

HAPPINESS AND HEALING FOR YOU (Also see Oral Roberts'...)
Commercial Comics: 1955 (36 pgs., slick cover) (Oral Roberts Giveaway)
nn — 13 | 26 | 39 | 74 | 105 | 135
NOTE: The success of this book prompted Oral Roberts to go into the publishing business himself to produce his own material.

HAPPI TIME FUN BOOK
Sears, Roebuck & Co.: 1940s - 1950s (32 pgs., soft-c)
nn-Comics, games, puzzles, & magic tricks cut -outs — 6 | 12 | 18 | | 34 | 40

HAPPY CHAMP, THE (The Story of Joker Osborn)
Western Publ.: 1965
nn-About water-skiing — 3 | 6 | 9 | 19 | 30 | 40

HAPPY TOOTH
DC Comics: 1996
1 — 4.00

HARLEM YOUTH REPORT (Also see All-Negro Comics and Negro Romances)
Custom Comics, Inc.: 1964 (Giveaway)(No issues #1-4)
5-"Youth in the Ghetto" and "The Blueprint For Change"; distr. in Harlem only; has map of central Harlem on back-c; hypo-c (scarce) — 161 | 322 | 483 | 1030 | 1765 | 2500

HAVE MORE FUN BY PLAYING SAFE
Commercial Comics: 1965 (Sheriff's Youth Foundation, 16 pages, paper-c)
nn — 3 | 6 | 9 | 19 | 30 | 40

HAWKMAN - THE SKY'S THE LIMIT
DC Comics: 1981 (General Foods giveaway, 8 pages, 3-1/2 x 6-3/4", oblong)
nn — 2 | 4 | 6 | 11 | 16 | 20

HAWTHORN-MELODY FARMS DAIRY COMICS
Everybody's Publishing Co.: No date (1950's) (Giveaway)
nn-Cheerie Chick, Tuffy Turtle, Robin Koo Koo, Donald & Longhorn Legends — 3 | 6 | 9 | 16 | 23 | 30

H–BOMB AND YOU
Commercial Comics: (? date) (small size, slick-c)
nn - H–Bomb explosion-c — 43 | 86 | 129 | 271 | 461 | 650

HENRY ALDRICH COMICS (TV)
Dell Publishing Co.: 1951 (16 pgs., soft-c)
Giveaway - Capehart radio — 4 | 8 | 12 | 24 | 47 | 65

HERE IS SANTA CLAUS
Goldsmith Publ. Co. (Kann's in Washington, D.C.): 1930s (16 pgs., 8 in color) (stiff paper covers)
nn — 15 | 30 | 45 | 90 | 140 | 190

HERE'S HOW AMERICA'S CARTOONISTS HELP TO SELL U.S. SAVINGS BONDS
Harvey Comics: 1950? (16 pgs., giveaway, paper cover)
Contains: Joe Palooka, Donald Duck, Archie, Kerry Drake, Red Ryder, Blondie & Steve Canyon — 22 | 44 | 66 | 132 | 216 | 300

HISTORY OF GAS
American Gas Assoc.: Mar, 1947 (Giveaway, 16 pgs., soft-c)
nn-Miss Flame narrates — 11 | 22 | 33 | 62 | 86 | 110

HOME DEPOT, SAFETY HEROES
Marvel Comics: Oct, 2005 (Giveaway)
nn-Spider-Man and the Fantastic Four on the cover; Olliffe-a/c; Roseman-s — 1 | 2 | 3 | 5 | 6 | 8

HONEYBEE BIRDWHISTLE AND HER PET PEPI (Introducing...)
Newspaper Enterprise Assoc.: 1969 (Giveaway, 24 pgs., B&W, slick cover)
nn-Contains Freckles newspaper strips with a short biography of Henry Fornhals (artist) & Fred Fox (writer) of the strip — 4 | 8 | 12 | 28 | 47 | 65

HOODS UP
Fram Corp.: 1953 (15¢, distributed to service station owners, 16 pgs.)
1-(Very Rare; only 2 known); Eisner-c/a in all (a CGC 9.0 copy sold for $1840 in 2006)
2-6-(Very Rare; only 1 known of #3, 2 known of #2,4) (a CGC 8.0 copy of #4 sold for $500 in 2012) — 58 | 116 | 174 | 371 | 636 | 900
NOTE: Convertible Connie gives tips for service stations, selling Fram oil filters.

HOOKED (Anti-drug comic distributed at NYC methadone clinics)
U.S. Dept. of Health: 1966 (giveaway, oblong)
nn-Distributed between May and July, 1966 — 6 | 12 | 18 | 42 | 79 | 115

HOPALONG CASSIDY
Fawcett Publications
Grape Nuts Flakes giveaway (1950,9x6") — 14 | 28 | 42 | 80 | 115 | 150
...& the Mad Barber (1951 Bond Bread giveaway)-7x5"; used in SOTI, pgs. 308,309 — 20 | 40 | 60 | 114 | 182 | 250
...Meets the Brend Brothers Bandits (1951 Bond Bread giveaway, color, paper-c, 16 pgs., 3-1/2x7")- Fawcett Publ. — 9 | 18 | 27 | 50 | 65 | 80
...Strange Legacy (1951 Bond Bread giveaway) — 9 | 18 | 27 | 50 | 65 | 80
White Tower Giveaway (1946, 16pgs., paper-c) — 10 | 20 | 30 | 54 | 72 | 90

HOPPY THE MARVEL BUNNY (WELL KNOWN COMICS)
Fawcett Publications: 1944 (8-1/2x10-1/2", paper-c)
Bestmaid/Samuel Lowe (printed in red or blue) — 14 | 28 | 42 | 80 | 115 | 150

HOT STUFF, THE LITTLE DEVIL

Harvey Publications (Illustrated Humor):1963
Shoestore Giveaway — 3 | 6 | 9 | 21 | 33 | 45

HOW KIDS ENJOY NEW YORK
American Airlines: 1966 (Giveaway, 40 pgs., 4x9")
nn-Includes 8 color pages by Bob Kane featuring a tour of New York and his studio (a FN+ copy sold for $250 in 2004, and a VF copy sold for $800 in 2018)

HOW STALIN HOPES WE WILL DESTROY AMERICA
Joe Lowe Co. (Pictorial Media): 1951 (Giveaway, 16 pgs.)
nn — 43 | 86 | 129 | 271 | 461 | 650

HURRICANE KIDS, THE (Also See Magic Morro, The Owl, Popular Comics #45)
R.S. Callender: 1941 (Giveaway, 7-1/2x5-1/4", soft-c)
nn-Will Ely-a. — 10 | 20 | 30 | 54 | 72 | 90

IF THE DEVIL WOULD TALK
Roman Catholic Catechetical Guild/Impact Publ.: 1950; 1958 (32 pgs.; paper cover; in full color)
nn-(Scarce)-About secularism (20-30 copies known to exist); very low distribution — 135 | 270 | 405 | 864 | 1482 | 2100
1958 Edition-(Impact Publ.); art & script changed to meet church criticism of earlier edition; 80 plus copies known to exist — 37 | 74 | 111 | 222 | 361 | 500
Black & White version of nn edition; small size; only 4 known copies exist — 42 | 84 | 126 | 265 | 445 | 625
NOTE: The original edition of this book was printed and killed by the Guild's board of directors. It is believed that a very limited number of copies were distributed. The 1958 version was a complete bomb with very limited, if any, circulation. In 1979, 11 original, 4 1958 reprints, and 4 B&W's surfaced from the Guild's old files in St. Paul, Minnesota.

IKE'S STORY
Sponsored Comics, Inc.: 1952 (soft-c)
nn-Dwight D. Eisenhower campaign (A 9.6 sold for $288 in 2018)

IN LOVE WITH JESUS
Catechetical Educational Society: 1952 (Giveaway, 36 pgs.)
nn — 8 | 16 | 24 | 40 | 50 | 60

INTERSTATE THEATRES' FUN CLUB COMICS
Interstate Theatres: Mid 1940's (10¢ on cover) (B&W cover) (Premium)
Cover features MLJ characters looking at a copy of Top-Notch Comics, but contains an early Detective Comic on inside; many combinations — 41 | 82 | 123 | 256 | 428 | 600

IN THE GOOD HANDS OF THE ROCKEFELLER TEAM
Country Art Studios: No date (paper cover, 8 pgs.)
nn-Joe Simon-a — 10 | 20 | 30 | 54 | 72 | 90

IRON GIANT
DC Comics: 1999 (4 pages, theater giveaway)
1-Previews movie — 2 | 4 | 6 | 9 | 12 | 15

IRON HORSE GOES TO WAR, THE
Association of American Railroads: 1960 (Giveaway, 16 pgs.)
nn-Civil War & railroads — 3 | 6 | 9 | 19 | 30 | 40

IS THIS TOMORROW?
Catechetical Guild: 1947 (One Shot) (3 editions) (52 pgs.)
1-Theme of communists taking over the USA; (no price on cover) Used in POP, pg. 102 — 50 | 100 | 150 | 315 | 533 | 750
1-(10¢ on cover)(Red price on yellow circle) — 50 | 100 | 150 | 315 | 533 | 750
1-(10¢ on cover)(Yellow price on red circle) — 50 | 100 | 150 | 315 | 533 | 750
1-(10¢ on cover)(Yellow price on black circle) — 50 | 100 | 150 | 315 | 533 | 750
1-Has blank circle with no price on cover — 50 | 100 | 150 | 315 | 533 | 750
Black & White advance copy titled "Confidential" (52 pgs.)-Contains script and art edited out of the color edition, including one page of extreme violence showing mob nailing a Cardinal to a door; (only two known copies). A VF+ sold in 2/08 for $3346. A NM 9.2 sold in 11/16 for $2629.
NOTE: The original color version first sold for 10 cents. Since sales were good, it was later printed as a giveaway. Approximately four million in total were printed. The two black and white copies listed plus two other versions as well as a full color untrimmed version surfaced in 1979 from the Guild's old files in St. Paul, Minnesota.

IT'S FUN TO STAY ALIVE
National Automobile Dealers Association: 1948 (Giveaway, 16 pgs., heavy stock paper)
Featuring: Bugs Bunny, The Berrys, Dixie Dugan, Elmer, Henry, Tim Tyler, Bruce Gentry, Abbie & Slats, Joe Jinks, The Toodles, & Cokey; all art copyright 1946-48 drawn especially for this book — 15 | 30 | 45 | 92 | 144 | 195

IT'S TIME FOR REASON - NOT TREASON
Liberty Lobby: 1967 (Reg. size, soft-c) (Anti-communist)
nn — 8 | 16 | 24 | 55 | 105 | 155

JACK AND CHUCK LEARN THE HARD WAY
Commercia Comics/Wagner Electric Co.: 1950s (Reg. size, soft-c)
nn-Automotive giveaway — 10 | 20 | 30 | 54 | 72 | 90

JACK & JILL VISIT TOYTOWN WITH ELMER THE ELF
Butler Brothers (Toytown Stores): 1949 (Giveaway, 16 pgs., paper cover)
nn — 6 | 12 | 18 | 28 | 34 | 40

JACK ARMSTRONG (Radio)(See True Comics)
Parents' Institute: 1949
12-Premium version (distr. in Chicago only); Free printed on upper right-c; no price (Rare) — 18 | 36 | 54 | 107 | 169 | 230

JACKIE JOYNER KERSEE IN HIGH HURDLES (Kellogg's Tony's Sports Comics)
DC Comics: 1992 (Sports Illustrated)
nn — 5.00

JACKPOT OF FUN COMIC BOOK
DCA Food Ind.: 1957, giveaway (paper cover, regular size)
nn-Features Howdy Doody — 14 | 28 | 42 | 76 | 108 | 140

JEDLICKA SHOES
DC Comics: 1961 (Funny animal-c)
nn-Contains Superman #142 — 9 | 18 | 27 | 60 | 120 | 180

JEEP COMICS

Hoods Up #1 © AVC

Kasco Komics #1 © Kasco

Kite Fun Book 1954 - Donald Duck © DIS

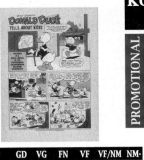

	GD 2.0	VG 4.0	FN 6.0	VF 8.0	VF/NM 9.0	NM- 9.2

R. B. Leffingwell & Co.: 1945 - 1946 (16 pgs.)(King Features Syndicate)

1-(Giveaways)-Strip reprints in all issues; Tarzan, Flash Gordon, Blondie, The Nebbs, Little
Iodine, Red Ryder, Don Winslow, The Phantom, Johnny Hazard, Katzenjammer Kids;
distr. to U.S. Armed Forces from 1945-1946 . . . 21 . . 42 . . 63 . . 122 . . 199 . . 275
2-5 . . . . 15 . . 30 . . 45 . . 88 . . 137 . . 185
6-46 . . . . 7 . . 14 . . 21 . . 35 . . 43 . . 50

JINGLE BELLS CHRISTMAS BOOK
Montgomery Ward (Giveaway): 1971 (20 pgs., B&W inside, slick-c)
nn . . . . 1 . . . 3 . . . 4 . . . 6 . . . 8 . . . 10

JOAN OF ARC
Catechetical Guild (Topix) (Giveaway): No date (28 pgs., blank back-c)
nn-Ingrid Bergman photo-c; Addison Burbank-a . . . 14 . . 28 . . 42 . . 80 . . 115 . . 150
NOTE: Unpublished version exists which came from the Guild's files.

JOE PALOOKA (2nd Series)
Harvey Publications
...Body Building Instruction Book (1958 B&M Sports Toy giveaway, 16 pgs., 5-1/4x7")-Origin
. . . . 8 . . 16 . . 24 . . 44 . . 57 . . 70
...Fights His Way Back (1945 Giveaway, 24 pgs.) Family Comics
. . . . 13 . . 26 . . 39 . . 72 . . 101 . . 130
...in Hi There! (1949 Red Cross giveaway, 12 pgs., 4-3/4x6")
. . . . 8 . . 16 . . 24 . . 42 . . 54 . . 65
...in It's All in the Family (1945 Red Cross giveaway, 16 pgs., regular size)
. . . . 8 . . 16 . . 24 . . 44 . . 57 . . 70

JOE THE GENIE OF STEEL (Also see "Return of...")
U.S. Steel Corp., Pittsburgh, PA: 1950 (16 pgs, reg size)
nn-Joe Magarac, the Paul Bunyan of steel . . . 9 . . 18 . . 27 . . 50 . . 66 . . 80

JOHNNY GETS THE WORD
Dept. of Health of New York City: 1963 (small size)
nn - Prevention of venereal diseases . . . . 6 . . 12 . . 18 . . 37 . . 66 . . 95
NOTE: A CGC 9.6 copy sold in 2016 for $263.

JOHNNY JINGLE'S LUCKY DAY
American Dairy Assoc.: 1956 (16 pgs.; 7-1/4x5-1/8") (Giveaway) (Disney)
nn . . . . 6 . . 12 . . 18 . . 28 . . 34 . . 40

JOHNSON MAKES THE TEAM
B.F. Goodrich: 1950 (Reg. size) (Football giveaway)
nn . . . . 7 . . 14 . . 21 . . 35 . . 43 . . 50

JO-JOY (The Adventures of...)
W. T. Grant Dept. Stores: 1945 - 1953 (Christmas gift comic, 16 pgs., 7-1/16x10-1/4")
1945-53 issues . . . . 8 . . 16 . . 24 . . 44 . . 57 . . 70

JOLLY CHRISTMAS BOOK (See Christmas Journey Through Space)
Promotional Publ. Co.: 1951; 1954; 1955 (36 pgs.; 24 pgs.)
1951-(Woolworth giveaway)-slightly oversized; no slick cover; Marv Levy-c/a
. . . . 8 . . 16 . . 24 . . 44 . . 57 . . 70
1954-(Hot Shoppes giveaway)-regular size-reprints 1951 issue; slick cover added; 24 pgs.;
no ads . . . . 8 . . 16 . . 24 . . 40 . . 50 . . 60
1955-(J. M. McDonald Co. giveaway)-reg. size . . . 7 . . 14 . . 21 . . 37 . . 46 . . 55

JOURNEY OF DISCOVERY WITH MARK STEEL (See Mark Steel)

JUMPING JACKS PRESENTS THE WHIZ KIDS
Jumping Jacks Stores giveaway: 1978 (In 3-D) with glasses (4 pgs.)
nn . . . . 2 . . . 4 . . . 6 . . . 8 . . . 10 . . . 12

JUNGLE BOOK FUN BOOK, THE (Disney)
Baskin Robbins: 1978
nn-Ice Cream giveaway . . . . 2 . . . 4 . . . 6 . . . 9 . . . 12 . . . 15

JUSTICE LEAGUE OF AMERICA
DC Comics: 1999 (included in Justice League of America Monopoly game)
nn - Reprints 1st app. in Brave and the Bold #28 . . . . 4.00

KASCO KOMICS
Kasko Grainfeed (Giveaway): 1945; No. 2, 1949 (Regular size, paper-c)
1(1945)-Similar to Katy Keene; Bill Woggon-a; 28 pgs.; 6-7/8x9-7/8")
. . . . 26 . . 52 . . 78 . . 154 . . 252 . . 350
2(1949)-Woggon-c/a . . . . 15 . . 30 . . 45 . . 94 . . 147 . . 200

KATY AND KEN VISIT SANTA WITH MISTER WISH
S. S. Kresge Co.: 1948 (Giveaway, 16 pgs., paper-c)
nn . . . . 8 . . 13 . . 24 . . 40 . . 50 . . 60

KELLOGG'S CINNAMON MINI-BUNS SUPER-HEROES
DC Comics: 1993 (4 1/4" x 2 3/4")
4 editions: Flash, Justice League America, Superman, Wonder Woman and the Star Riders
each..... . . . . 6.00

KERRY DRAKE DETECTIVE CASES

Publisher's Syndicate
...in the Case of the Sleeping City-(1951)-16 pg. giveaway for armed forces; paper cover
. . . . 8 . . 16 . . 24 . . 44 . . 57 . . 70

KEY COMICS
Key Clothing Co./Peterson Clothing: 1951 - 1956 (32 pgs.) (Giveaway)
Contains a comic from different publishers bound with new cover. Cover changed each year. Many combinations
possible. Distributed in Nebraska, Iowa, & Kansas. Contents would determine price, 40-60 percent of original.

KING JAMES "THE KING OF BASKETBALL"
DC Comics: 2004 (Promo comic for LeBron James and Powerade Flava23 sports drink)
nn - Ten different covers by various artists; 4 covers for retail, 4 for mail-in, 1 for military
commissaries, and 1 general market; Damion Scott-a/Gary Phillips-s
. . . . 1 . . . 3 . . . 4 . . . 6 . . . 8 . . . 10

KIRBY'S SHOES COMICS
Kirby's Shoes: 1959 - 1961 (8 pgs., soft-c, several different editions)
nn-(1959) Features Kirby the Golden Bear . . . 7 . . 14 . . 21 . . 35 . . 43 . . 50
nn-(1960,1961) Features Kirby the Golden Bear . . 4 . . . 8 . . 12 . . 17 . . 21 . . 24

KITE FUN BOOK
**Pacific, Gas & Electric/Sou. California Edison/Florida Power & Light/ Missouri Public
Service Co.:** 1952 - 1998 (16 pgs, 5x7-1/4, soft-c)
1952-Having Fun With Kites (P.G.&E.) . . . . . . 12 . . 24 . . 36 . . 69 . . 97 . . 125
1953-Pinocchio Learns About Kites (Disney) . . 43 . . 86 . . 129 . . 271 . . 461 . . 650
1954-Donald Duck Tells About Kites-Fla. Power, S.C.E. & version with label issues
-Barks pencils-8 pgs.: inks-7 pgs. (Rare) . . 219 . . 438 . . 637 . . 1402 . . 2401 . . 3400
1954-Donald Duck Tells About Kites-P.G.&E. issue -7th page redrawn changing middle 3
panels to show P.G.&E. in story line; (All Barks-a) Scarce
. . . . 194 . . 388 . . 582 . . 1242 . . 2121 . . 3000
1955-Brer Rabbit in "A Kite Tail" (Disney) . . 25 . . 50 . . 75 . . 150 . . 245 . . 340
1956-Woody Woodpecker (Lantz) . . . . 12 . . 24 . . 36 . . 67 . . 94 . . 120
1957-Ruff and Reddy (exist?)
1958-Tom And Jerry (M.G.M.) . . . . 9 . . 18 . . 27 . . 52 . . 69 . . 85
1959-Bugs Bunny (Warner Bros.) . . . . 4 . . . 8 . . 12 . . 27 . . 44 . . 60
1960-Porky Pig (Warner Bros.) . . . . 4 . . . 8 . . 12 . . 28 . . 47 . . 65
1960-Bugs Bunny (Warner Bros.) . . . . 4 . . . 8 . . 12 . . 28 . . 47 . . 65
1961-Huckleberry Hound (Hanna-Barbera) . . 5 . . 10 . . 15 . . 31 . . 53 . . 75
1962-Yogi Bear (Hanna-Barbera) . . . . 4 . . . 8 . . 12 . . 25 . . 40 . . 55
1963-Rocky and Bullwinkle (TV)(Jay Ward) . . 5 . . 10 . . 15 . . 35 . . 63 . . 90
1963-Top Cat (TV)(Hanna-Barbera) . . . . 3 . . . 6 . . . 9 . . 19 . . 30 . . 40
1964-Magilla Gorilla (TV)(Hanna-Barbera) . . . 3 . . . 6 . . . 9 . . 17 . . 26 . . 35
1965-Jinks, Pixie and Dixie (TV)(Hanna-Barbera) . . 3 . . . 6 . . . 9 . . 15 . . 22 . . 28
1965-Tweety and Sylvester (Warner); S.C.E. version with Reddy Kilowatt app.
. . . . 2 . . . 4 . . . 6 . . . 9 . . 13 . . 16
1966-Secret Squirrel (Hanna-Barbera); S.C.E. version with Reddy Kilowatt app.
. . . . 5 . . 10 . . 15 . . 30 . . 50 . . 70
1967-Beep! Beep! The Road Runner (TV)(Warner) . . 2 . . . 4 . . . 6 . . 11 . . 16 . . 20
1968-Bugs Bunny (Warner Bros.) . . . . 2 . . . 4 . . . 6 . . 13 . . 18 . . 22
1969-Dastardly and Muttley (TV)(Hanna-Barbera) . . 3 . . . 6 . . . 9 . . 19 . . 30 . . 40
1970-Rocky and Bullwinkle (TV)(Jay Ward) . . 4 . . . 8 . . 12 . . 27 . . 44 . . 60
1971-Beep! Beep! The Road Runner (TV)(Warner) . . 2 . . . 4 . . . 6 . . 11 . . 16 . . 20
1972-The Pink Panther (TV) . . . . 2 . . . 4 . . . 6 . . 10 . . 14 . . 18
1973-Lassie (TV) . . . . 3 . . . 6 . . . 9 . . 15 . . 22 . . 28
1974-Underdog (TV) . . . . 2 . . . 4 . . . 6 . . 11 . . 16 . . 20
1975-Ben Franklin . . . . 2 . . . 4 . . . 6 . . . 8 . . 10 . . 12
1976-The Brady Bunch (TV) . . . . 3 . . . 6 . . . 9 . . 16 . . 23 . . 30
1977-Ben Franklin (exist?) . . . . 2 . . . 4 . . . 6 . . . 8 . . 10 . . 12
1977-Popeye . . . . 2 . . . 4 . . . 6 . . . 9 . . 13 . . 16
1978-Happy Days (TV) . . . . 2 . . . 4 . . . 6 . . 11 . . 16 . . 20
1979-Eight is Enough (TV) . . . . 2 . . . 4 . . . 6 . . . 9 . . 13 . . 16
1980-The Waltons (TV, released in 1981) . . . 2 . . . 4 . . . 6 . . . 9 . . 13 . . 16
1982-Tweety and Sylvester . . . . 2 . . . 4 . . . 6 . . . 8 . . 11 . . 14
1984-Smokey Bear . . . . 1 . . . 3 . . . 4 . . . 6 . . . 8 . . 10
1986-Road Runner . . . . 1 . . . 2 . . . 3 . . . 5 . . . 6 . . . 8
1997-Thomas Edison 4.00
1998-Edison Field (Anaheim Stadium) 4.00

KNOWING'S NOT ENOUGH
Commercial Comics: 1956 (Reg. size, paper-c) (United States Steel safety giveaway)
nn . . . . 7 . . 14 . . 21 . . 37 . . 46 . . 55

KNOW YOUR MASS
Catechetical Guild: No. 303, 1958 (35¢, 100 Pg. Giant) (Square binding)
303-In color . . . . 7 . . 14 . . 21 . . 35 . . 43 . . 50

KOLYNOS PRESENTS THE WHITE GUARD
Whitehall Pharmacal Co.: 1949 (paper cover, 8 pgs.)
nn . . . . 6 . . 12 . . 18 . . 31 . . 38 . . 45

KOLYNOS PRESENTS THE WICKED WITCH
Whitehall Pharmacal Co.: 1951 (paper cover, 8 pgs.)

	GD 2.0	VG 4.0	FN 6.0	VF 8.0	VF/NM 9.0	NM- 9.2

nn-Anti-tooth decay — 5 / 10 / 14 / 20 / 24 / 28

K. O. PUNCH, THE (Also see Lucky Fights It Through & Sidewalk Romance)
E. C. Comics: 1952 (VD Educational giveaway)

	GD 2.0	VG 4.0	FN 6.0	VF 8.0	VF/NM 9.0	NM- 9.2
nn-Feldstein-splash; Kamen-a	459	918	1377	3350	5925	8500

KOREA MY HOME (Also see Yalta to Korea)
Johnstone and Cushing: nd (1950s, slick-c, regular size)

	GD 2.0	VG 4.0	FN 6.0	VF 8.0	VF/NM 9.0	NM- 9.2
nn-Anti-communist; Korean War	32	64	96	188	307	425

KRIM-KO KOMICS
Krim-ko Chocolate Drink: 5/18/35 - No. 6, 6/22/35; 1936 - 1939 (weekly)

	GD 2.0	VG 4.0	FN 6.0	VF 8.0	VF/NM 9.0	NM- 9.2
1-(16 pgs., soft-c, Dairy giveaways)-Tom, Mary & Sparky Advs. by Russell Keaton, Jim Hawkins by Dick Moores, Mystery Island! by Rick Yager begin	15	30	45	88	137	185
2-6 (6/22/35)	12	24	36	67	94	120
Lola, Secret Agent; 184 issues, 4 pg. giveaways - all original stories each….	9	18	27	50	65	80

LABOR IS A PARTNER
Catechetical Guild Educational Society: 1949 (32 pgs., paper-c)

	GD 2.0	VG 4.0	FN 6.0	VF 8.0	VF/NM 9.0	NM- 9.2
nn-Anti-communism	52	104	156	328	552	775

Confidential Preview-(8-1/2x11", B&W, saddle stitched)-only one known copy; text varies from color version, advertises next book on secularism (If the Devil Would Talk)
(A VF- copy sold for $2629 in 11/2016 and a VG/FN copy sold for $454 in 1/2017)

LADIES - WOULDN'T IT BE BETTER TO KNOW
American Cancer Society: 1969 (Reg. size)

	GD 2.0	VG 4.0	FN 6.0	VF 8.0	VF/NM 9.0	NM- 9.2
nn	4	8	12	22	35	48

LADY AND THE TRAMP IN "BUTTER LATE THAN NEVER"
American Dairy Assoc. (Premium): 1955 (16 pgs., 5x7-1/4", soft-c) (Disney)

	GD 2.0	VG 4.0	FN 6.0	VF 8.0	VF/NM 9.0	NM- 9.2
nn	9	18	27	52	69	85

LASSIE (TV)
Dell Publ. Co

	GD 2.0	VG 4.0	FN 6.0	VF 8.0	VF/NM 9.0	NM- 9.2
The Adventures of… nn-(Red Heart Dog Food giveaway, 1949)-16 pgs, soft-c; 1st app. Lassie in comics	41	82	123	256	428	600

LIFE OF THE BLESSED VIRGIN
Catechetical Guild: 1950 (68pgs.) (square binding)

	GD 2.0	VG 4.0	FN 6.0	VF 8.0	VF/NM 9.0	NM- 9.2
nn-Contains "The Woman of the Promise" & "Mother of Us All" rebound	11	22	33	64	90	115

LIGHTNING RACERS
DC Comics: 1989

	GD 2.0	VG 4.0	FN 6.0	VF 8.0	VF/NM 9.0	NM- 9.2
1						4.50

LI'L ABNER (Al Capp's) (Also see Natural Disasters!)
Harvey Publ./Toby Press

	GD 2.0	VG 4.0	FN 6.0	VF 8.0	VF/NM 9.0	NM- 9.2
…& the Creatures from Drop-Outer Space-nn (Job Corps giveaway; 36 pgs., in color) (entire book by Frank Frazetta)	26	52	78	154	252	350
…Joins the Navy (1950) (Toby Press Premium)	11	22	33	64	90	115
Al Capp by Li'l Abner (Circa 1946, nd, giveaway) Al Capp bio and his life as an amputee	11	22	33	64	90	115

LITTLE ALONZO
Macy's Dept. Store: 1938 (B&W, 5-1/2x8-1/2") (Christmas giveaway)

	GD 2.0	VG 4.0	FN 6.0	VF 8.0	VF/NM 9.0	NM- 9.2
nn-By Ferdinand the Bull's Munro Leaf	11	22	33	62	86	110

LITTLE ARCHIE (See Archie Comics)

LITTLE DOT
Harvey Publications

	GD 2.0	VG 4.0	FN 6.0	VF 8.0	VF/NM 9.0	NM- 9.2
Shoe store giveaway 2	4	8	12	28	47	65

LITTLE FIR TREE, THE
W. T. Grant Co.: nd (1942) (8-1/2x11") (12 pgs. with cover, color & B&W, heavy paper) (Christmas giveaway)

	GD 2.0	VG 4.0	FN 6.0	VF 8.0	VF/NM 9.0	NM- 9.2
nn-Story by Hans Christian Anderson; 8 pg. Kelly-r/Santa Claus Funnies (not signed); X-Mas-c	97	194	291	621	1061	1500

LITTLE KLINKER
Little Klinker Ventures: Nov. 1960 (20 pgs.) (slick cover) (Montgomery Ward Giveaway)

	GD 2.0	VG 4.0	FN 6.0	VF 8.0	VF/NM 9.0	NM- 9.2
nn - Christmas; Santa-c	3	6	9	14	20	25

LITTLE MISS SUNBEAM COMICS
Magazine Enterprises/Quality Bakers of America

	GD 2.0	VG 4.0	FN 6.0	VF 8.0	VF/NM 9.0	NM- 9.2
Bread Giveaway 1-4 (Quality Bakers, 1949-50)-14 pgs. each	8	16	24	44	57	70
Bread Giveaway (1957,61; 16pgs, reg. size)	6	12	18	31	38	45

LITTLE ORPHAN ANNIE
David McKay Publ./Dell Publishing Co.

Junior Commandos Giveaway (same-c as 4-Color #18, K.K. Publ.) (Big Shoe Store); same back cover as '47 Popped Wheat giveaway; 16 pgs; flag-c;

	GD 2.0	VG 4.0	FN 6.0	VF 8.0	VF/NM 9.0	NM- 9.2
r/strips 9/7/42-10/10/42	26	52	78	154	252	350
Popped Wheat Giveaway ('47)-16 pgs. full color; reprints strips from 5/3/40 to 6/20/40	5	10	15	22	26	30
Quaker Sparkies Giveaway (1940)	18	36	54	103	162	220
Quaker Sparkies Giveaway (1941, full color, 20 pgs.); "LOA and the Rescue"; r/strips 4/13/39-6/21/39 & 7/6/39-7/17/39. "LOA and the Kidnappers"; r/strips 11/28/38-1/28/39	15	30	45	94	147	200
Quaker Sparkies Giveaway (1942, full color, 20 pgs.); "LOA and Mr. Gudge"; r/strips 2/13/38-3/21/38 & 4/18/37-5/30/37. "LOA and the Great Am"	15	30	45	88	137	185

LITTLE TREE THAT WASN'T WANTED, THE
W. T. Grant Co. (Giveaway): 1960, (Color, 28 pgs.)

	GD 2.0	VG 4.0	FN 6.0	VF 8.0	VF/NM 9.0	NM- 9.2
nn-Christmas story, puzzles and games	4	8	12	23	37	50

LONE RANGER, THE
Dell Publishing Co.

Cheerios Giveaways (1954, 16 pgs., 2-1/2x7", soft-c) #1- "The Lone Ranger, His Mask & How He Met Tonto". #2- "The Lone Ranger & the Story of Silver"

	GD 2.0	VG 4.0	FN 6.0	VF 8.0	VF/NM 9.0	NM- 9.2
each….	12	24	36	69	97	125

Doll Giveaways (Gabriel Ind.)(1973, 3-1/4x5")- "The Story of The Lone Ranger," "The Carson City Bank Robbery" & "The Apache Buffalo Hunt"

	GD 2.0	VG 4.0	FN 6.0	VF 8.0	VF/NM 9.0	NM- 9.2
	2	4	6	12	16	20

How the Lone Ranger Captured Silver Book(1936)-Silvercup Bread giveaway

	GD 2.0	VG 4.0	FN 6.0	VF 8.0	VF/NM 9.0	NM- 9.2
	55	110	165	352	601	850

…In Milk for Big Mike (1955, Dairy Association giveaway), soft-c; 5x7-1/4", 16 pgs.

	GD 2.0	VG 4.0	FN 6.0	VF 8.0	VF/NM 9.0	NM- 9.2
	10	20	30	58	79	100

Legend of The Lone Ranger (1969, 16 pgs., giveaway)-Origin The Lone Ranger

	GD 2.0	VG 4.0	FN 6.0	VF 8.0	VF/NM 9.0	NM- 9.2
	4	8	12	21	33	45

Merita Bread giveaway (1954, 16 pgs., 5x7-1/4")- "How to Be a Lone Ranger Health & Safety Scout"

	GD 2.0	VG 4.0	FN 6.0	VF 8.0	VF/NM 9.0	NM- 9.2
	14	28	42	80	115	150

Merita Bread giveaway (1955, 16 pgs., 5x7-1/4")- "Official Lone Ranger and Tonto Coloring Book"

	GD 2.0	VG 4.0	FN 6.0	VF 8.0	VF/NM 9.0	NM- 9.2
	12	24	36	69	97	125

Merita Bread giveaway (1956, 16 pgs., 5x7-1/4")- "Tells the Story of Branding"

	GD 2.0	VG 4.0	FN 6.0	VF 8.0	VF/NM 9.0	NM- 9.2
	12	24	36	69	97	125

LONE RANGER COMICS, THE
Lone Ranger, Inc.: Book 1, 1939(inside) (shows 1938 on-c) (52 pgs. in color; regular size) (Ice cream mail order)

Book 1-(Scarce)-The first western comic devoted to a single character; not by Vallely

	GD 2.0	VG 4.0	FN 6.0	VF 8.0	VF/NM 9.0	NM- 9.2
	620	1240	1860	4350	–	–

2nd version w/large full color promo poster pasted over centerfold & a smaller poster pasted over back cover; includes new additional premiums not originally offered (Rare) (A CGC 7.0 copy sold in Nov. 2021 for $2,850)

	GD 2.0	VG 4.0	FN 6.0	VF 8.0	VF/NM 9.0	NM- 9.2
	685	1370	2055	4800	–	–

LOONEY TUNES
DC Comics: 1991, 1998

Claritin promotional issue (1998); Colgate mini-comic (1998) — 3.00
Tyson's 1-10 (1991) — 4.00

LUCKY FIGHTS IT THROUGH (Also see The K. O. Punch & Sidewalk Romance)
Educational Comics: 1949 (Giveaway, 16 pgs. in color, paper-c)

	GD 2.0	VG 4.0	FN 6.0	VF 8.0	VF/NM 9.0	NM- 9.2
nn-(Very Rare)-1st Kurtzman work for E.C.; V.D. prevention	194	388	582	1242	2121	3000
nn-Reprint in color (1977)						9.00

NOTE: Subtitled "The Story of That Ignorant, Ignorant Cowboy". Prepared for Communications Materials Center, Columbia University.

LUDWIG VON DRAKE (See Frito-Lay Giveaway)

MACO TOYS COMIC
Maco Toys/Charlton Comics: 1959 (Giveaway, 36 pgs.)

	GD 2.0	VG 4.0	FN 6.0	VF 8.0	VF/NM 9.0	NM- 9.2
1-All military stories featuring Maco Toys	5	10	15	25	31	36

MAD MAGAZINE
DC Comics: 1997, 1999, 2008

Special Edition (1997, Tang giveaway) — 6.00
Stocking Stuffer (1999) — 6.00
San Diego Comic-Con Edition (2008) Watchmen parody with Fabry-a; Aragonés cartoons

	GD 2.0	VG 4.0	FN 6.0	VF 8.0	VF/NM 9.0	NM- 9.2
	1	3	4	6	8	10

MAGAZINELAND USA
DC Comics: 1977

	GD 2.0	VG 4.0	FN 6.0	VF 8.0	VF/NM 9.0	NM- 9.2
nn-Kubert-c/a	4	8	12	23	37	50

MAGIC MORRO (Also see Super Comics #21, The Owl, & The Hurricane Kids)
K. K. Publications: 1941 (7-1/2 x 5-1/4", giveaway, soft-c)

	GD 2.0	VG 4.0	FN 6.0	VF 8.0	VF/NM 9.0	NM- 9.2
nn-Ken Ernst-a.	10	20	30	58	79	100

MAGIC OF CHRISTMAS AT NEWBERRYS, THE
E. S. London: 1967 (Giveaway) (B&W, slick-c, 20 pgs.)

	GD 2.0	VG 4.0	FN 6.0	VF 8.0	VF/NM 9.0	NM- 9.2
nn	2	4	6	8	10	12

MAGIC SHOE ADVENTURE BOOK
Western Publications: 1962 - No. 3, 1963 (Shoe store giveaway, Reg. size)

	GD 2.0	VG 4.0	FN 6.0	VF 8.0	VF/NM 9.0	NM- 9.2
nn-(1962)	5	10	15	34	60	85
1 (1963)-And the Flaming Threat	4	8	12	28	47	65
2 (1963)-And the Winning Run	4	8	12	28	47	65
3 (1963)-And the Missing Masterpiece Mystery	4	8	12	28	47	65

MAJOR INAPAK THE SPACE ACE
Magazine Enterprises (Inapac Foods): 1951 (20 pgs.) (Giveaway)

	GD 2.0	VG 4.0	FN 6.0	VF 8.0	VF/NM 9.0	NM- 9.2
1-Bob Powell-c/a	2	4	6	11	16	20

NOTE: Many warehouse copies surfaced in 1973.

MAMMY YOKUM & THE GREAT DOGPATCH MYSTERY
Toby Press: 1951 (Giveaway)

	GD 2.0	VG 4.0	FN 6.0	VF 8.0	VF/NM 9.0	NM- 9.2
nn-Li'l Abner	17	34	51	103	162	220
nn-Reprint (1956)	5	10	15	24	30	35

MAN NAMED STEVENSON, A
Democratic National Committee: 1952 (20 pgs., 5 1/4 x 7")

	GD 2.0	VG 4.0	FN 6.0	VF 8.0	VF/NM 9.0	NM- 9.2
nn	10	20	30	54	72	90

MAN OF PEACE, POPE PIUS XII
Catechetical Guild: 1950 (See Pope Pius XII… & To V2#8)

	GD 2.0	VG 4.0	FN 6.0	VF 8.0	VF/NM 9.0	NM- 9.2
nn-All Powell-a	8	16	24	40	50	60

MAN OF STEEL BEST WESTERN
DC Comics: 1997 (Best Western hotels promo)

3-Reprints Superman's first post-Crisis meeting with Batman — 6.00

MAN WHO RUNS INTERFERENCE
General Comics, Inc./Institute of Life Insurance: 1946 (Paper-c)

	GD 2.0	VG 4.0	FN 6.0	VF 8.0	VF/NM 9.0	NM- 9.2
nn-Football premium	7	14	21	37	46	55

MAN WHO WOULDN'T QUIT, THE
Harvey Publications Inc.: 1952 (16 pgs., paper cover)

	GD 2.0	VG 4.0	FN 6.0	VF 8.0	VF/NM 9.0	NM- 9.2
nn-The value of voting	5	10	15	25	31	36

Labor is a Partner © CG

Magic Morro © K.K. Pub.

March of Comics #54 © G. Autry

MARCH OF COMICS (Boys' and Girls'...#3-353)

K. K. Publications/Western Publishing Co.: 1946 - No. 488, April, 1982 (#1-4 are not numbered) (K.K. Giveaway) (Founded by Sig Feuchtwanger)

Early issues were full size, 32 pages, and were printed with and without an extra cover of slick stock, just for the advertiser. The binding was stapled if the slick cover was added; otherwise, the pages were glued together at the spine. Most 1948 - 1951 issues were full size, 24 pages, with pulp covers. Starting in 1952 they were half-size (with a few exceptions) and 32 pages with slick covers. 1959 and later issues had only 16 pages plus covers. 1952 -1959 issues read oblong; 1960 and later issues read upright. All have new stories except where noted.

	GD 2.0	VG 4.0	FN 6.0	VF 8.0	VF/NM 9.0	NM- 9.2
nn (#1, 1946)-Goldilocks; Kelly back-c (16 pgs., stapled)	57	114	171	362	619	875
nn (#2, 1946)-How Santa Got His Red Suit; Kelly-a (11 pgs., r/4-Color #61 from 1944) (16pgs., stapled)	36	72	108	211	343	475
nn (#3, 1947)-Our Gang (Walt Kelly)	37	74	111	222	361	500
nn (#4)-Donald Duck by Carl Barks, "Maharajah Donald", 28 pgs.; Kelly-c (Disney)	838	1676	2514	6117	10,809	15,500
5-Andy Panda (Walter Lantz)	20	40	60	114	182	250
6-Popular Fairy Tales; Kelly-c; Noonan-a(2)	20	40	60	115	185	255
7-Oswald the Rabbit	21	42	63	124	202	280
8-Mickey Mouse, 32 pgs. (Disney)	45	90	135	284	480	675
9(nn)-The Story of the Gloomy Bunny	14	28	42	78	112	145
10-Out of Santa's Bag	12	24	36	69	97	125
11-Fun With Santa Claus	11	22	33	62	86	110
12-Santa's Toys	11	22	33	62	86	110
13-Santa's Surprise	11	22	33	62	86	110
14-Santa's Candy Kitchen	11	22	33	62	86	110
15-Hip-It-Ty Hop & the Big Bass Viol	10	20	30	56	76	95
16-Woody Woodpecker (1947)(Walter Lantz)	14	28	42	78	112	145
17-Roy Rogers (1948)	20	40	60	120	195	270
18-Popular Fairy Tales	12	24	36	67	94	120
19-Uncle Wiggily	10	20	30	58	79	100
20-Donald Duck by Carl Barks, "Darkest Africa", 22 pgs.; Kelly-c (Disney)	272	544	816	1727	3014	4300
21-Tom and Jerry	11	22	33	62	86	110
22-Andy Panda (Lantz)	12	24	36	67	94	120
23-Raggedy Ann & Andy; Kerr-a	13	26	39	72	101	130
24-Felix the Cat, 1932 daily strip reprints by Otto Messmer	17	34	51	98	154	210
25-Gene Autry	17	34	51	100	158	215
26-Our Gang; Walt Kelly	16	32	48	96	151	205
27-Mickey Mouse; r/in M. M. #240 (Disney)	29	58	87	172	281	390
28-Gene Autry	17	34	51	98	154	210
29-Easter Bonnet Shop	9	18	27	47	61	75
30-Here Comes Santa	8	16	24	44	57	70
31-Santa's Busy Corner	8	16	24	44	57	70
32-No book produced						
33-A Christmas Carol (12/48)	9	18	27	50	65	80
34-Woody Woodpecker	11	22	33	62	86	110
35-Roy Rogers (1948)	19	38	57	112	179	245
36-Felix the Cat(1949); by Messmer; '34 strip-r	14	28	42	82	121	160
37-Popeye	14	28	42	78	112	145
38-Oswald the Rabbit	8	16	24	44	57	70
39-Gene Autry	16	32	48	94	147	200
40-Andy and Woody	8	16	24	44	57	70
41-Donald Duck by Carl Barks, "Race to the South Seas", 22 pgs.; Kelly-c	252	504	756	1613	2757	3900
42-Porky Pig	9	18	27	47	61	75
43-Henry	8	16	24	42	54	65
44-Bugs Bunny	9	18	27	52	69	85
45-Mickey Mouse (Disney)	22	44	66	128	209	290
46-Tom and Jerry	9	18	27	52	69	85
47-Roy Rogers	15	30	45	90	140	190
48-Greetings from Santa	6	12	18	31	38	45
49-Santa Is Here	6	12	18	31	38	45
50-Santa Claus' Workshop (1949)	6	12	18	31	38	45
51-Felix the Cat (1950) by Messmer	14	28	42	80	115	150
52-Popeye	11	22	33	62	86	110
53-Oswald the Rabbit	8	16	24	44	50	60
54-Gene Autry	15	30	45	84	127	170
55-Andy and Woody	8	16	24	44	50	60
56-Donald Duck; not by Barks; Barks art on back-c (Disney)	21	42	63	122	199	275
57-Porky Pig	8	16	24	40	50	60
58-Henry	7	14	21	35	43	50
59-Bugs Bunny	9	18	27	47	61	75
60-Mickey Mouse (Disney)	21	42	63	126	206	285
61-Tom and Jerry	8	16	24	40	50	60
62-Roy Rogers	15	30	45	90	140	190
63-Welcome Santa (1/2-size, oblong)	6	12	18	31	38	45
64(nn)-Santa's Helpers (1/2-size, oblong)	6	12	18	31	38	45
65(nn)-Jingle Bells (1950) (1/2-size, oblong)	6	12	18	31	38	45
66-Popeye (1951)	14	28	42	76	108	140
67-Oswald the Rabbit	7	14	21	35	43	50
68-Roy Rogers	14	28	42	80	115	150
69-Donald Duck; Barks-a on back-c (Disney)	21	42	63	122	199	275
70-Tom and Jerry	8	16	24	40	50	60
71-Porky Pig	8	16	24	42	54	65
72-Krazy Kat	9	18	27	47	61	75
73-Roy Rogers	14	28	42	82	121	160
74-Mickey Mouse (1951)(Disney)	20	40	60	115	190	250
75-Bugs Bunny	9	18	27	47	61	75
76-Andy and Woody	8	16	24	40	50	60
77-Roy Rogers	14	28	42	82	121	160
78-Gene Autry (1951); last regular size issue	14	28	42	80	115	150

Note: All pre #79 issues came with or without a slick protective wrap-around cover over the regular cover which advertised Poll Parrot Shoes, Sears, etc. This outer cover protects the inside pages making them in nicer condition. Issues with the outer cover are worth 15-25% more

	GD 2.0	VG 4.0	FN 6.0	VF 8.0	VF/NM 9.0	NM- 9.2
79-Andy Panda (1952, 5x7" size)	7	14	21	35	43	50
80-Popeye	8	16	24	40	50	60
81-Woody Woodpecker	6	12	18	29	36	42
82-Tarzan; Lex Barker photo-c	15	30	45	88	137	185
83-Bugs Bunny	7	14	21	37	46	55
84-Henry	6	12	18	29	36	42
85-Woody Woodpecker	6	12	18	29	36	42
86-Roy Rogers	11	22	33	62	86	110
87-Krazy Kat	8	16	24	44	57	70
88-Tom and Jerry	6	12	18	31	38	45
89-Porky Pig	6	12	18	29	36	42
90-Gene Autry	11	22	33	62	86	110
91-Roy Rogers & Santa	11	22	33	62	86	110
92-Christmas with Santa	5	10	15	24	30	35
93-Woody Woodpecker (1953)	5	10	15	23	28	32
94-Indian Chief	10	20	30	54	72	90
95-Oswald the Rabbit	5	10	15	23	28	32
96-Popeye	10	20	30	54	72	90
97-Bugs Bunny	7	14	21	35	43	50
98-Tarzan; Lex Barker photo-c	15	30	45	85	130	175
99-Porky Pig	5	10	15	23	28	32
100-Roy Rogers	10	20	30	58	79	100
101-Henry	5	10	15	22	26	30
102-Tom Corbett (TV)('53, early app.); painted-c	12	24	36	67	94	120
103-Tom and Jerry	5	10	15	23	28	32
104-Gene Autry	10	20	30	56	76	95
105-Roy Rogers	10	20	30	56	76	95
106-Santa's Helpers	5	10	15	24	30	35
107-Santa's Christmas Book - not published						
108-Fun with Santa (1953)	5	10	15	24	30	35
109-Woody Woodpecker (1954)	5	10	15	24	30	35
110-Indian Chief	6	12	18	31	38	45
111-Oswald the Rabbit	5	10	15	22	26	30
112-Henry	4	9	13	18	22	26
113-Porky Pig	5	10	15	22	26	30
114-Tarzan; Russ Manning-a	14	28	42	82	121	160
115-Bugs Bunny	6	12	18	27	33	38
116-Roy Rogers	10	20	30	56	76	95
117-Popeye	10	20	30	54	72	90
118-Flash Gordon; painted-c	14	28	42	76	108	140
119-Tom and Jerry	5	10	15	22	26	30
120-Gene Autry	10	20	30	58	76	95
121-Roy Rogers	10	20	30	58	76	95
122-Santa's Surprise (1954)	5	10	15	22	26	30
123-Santa's Christmas Book	5	10	15	22	26	30
124-Woody Woodpecker (1955)	4	9	13	18	22	26
125-Tarzan; Lex Barker photo-c	14	28	42	78	112	145
126-Oswald the Rabbit	4	9	13	18	22	26
127-Indian Chief	4	9	13	18	22	26
128-Tom and Jerry	4	8	12	17	21	24
129-Henry	4	9	13	18	22	26
130-Porky Pig	10	20	30	56	76	95
131-Roy Rogers	10	20	30	56	76	95
132-Bugs Bunny	5	10	15	23	28	32
133-Flash Gordon; painted-c	14	28	42	76	108	140
134-Popeye	8	16	24	42	54	65
135-Gene Autry	10	20	30	56	76	95
136-Roy Rogers	10	20	30	56	76	95
137-Gifts from Santa	4	7	10	14	17	20
138-Fun at Christmas (1955)	4	7	10	14	17	20
139-Woody Woodpecker (1956)	4	9	13	18	22	26
140-Indian Chief	7	14	21	35	43	50
141-Oswald the Rabbit	4	9	13	18	22	26
142-Flash Gordon	14	28	42	76	108	140
143-Porky Pig	4	9	13	18	22	26

	GD 2.0	VG 4.0	FN 6.0	VF 8.0	VF/NM 9.0	NM- 9.2
144-Tarzan; Russ Manning-a; painted-c	13	26	39	72	101	130
145-Tom and Jerry	4	9	13	18	22	26
146-Roy Rogers; photo-c	10	20	30	56	76	95
147-Henry	4	8	11	16	19	22
148-Popeye	8	16	24	42	54	65
149-Bugs Bunny	5	10	15	22	26	30
150-Gene Autry	10	20	30	56	76	95
151-Roy Rogers	10	20	30	56	76	95
152-The Night Before Christmas	4	9	13	18	22	26
153-Merry Christmas (1956)	4	9	13	18	22	26
154-Tom and Jerry (1957)	4	9	13	18	22	26
155-Tarzan; photo-c	12	24	36	69	97	125
156-Oswald the Rabbit	4	9	13	18	22	26
157-Popeye	7	14	21	35	43	50
158-Woody Woodpecker	4	9	13	18	22	26
159-Indian Chief	7	14	21	35	43	50
160-Bugs Bunny	5	10	15	22	26	30
161-Roy Rogers	9	18	27	52	69	85
162-Henry	4	8	11	16	19	22
163-Rin Tin Tin (TV)	8	16	24	42	54	65
164-Porky Pig	4	9	13	18	22	26
165-The Lone Ranger	9	18	27	50	65	80
166-Santa and His Reindeer	4	7	10	14	17	20
167-Roy Rogers and Santa	9	18	27	52	69	85
168-Santa Claus' Workshop (1957, full size)	4	8	11	16	19	22
169-Popeye (1958)	7	14	21	35	43	50
170-Indian Chief	7	14	21	35	43	50
171-Oswald the Rabbit	4	8	12	17	21	24
172-Tarzan	11	22	33	60	83	105
173-Tom and Jerry	4	8	12	17	21	24
174-The Lone Ranger	9	18	27	50	65	80
175-Porky Pig	4	8	12	17	21	24
176-Roy Rogers	9	18	27	47	61	75
177-Woody Woodpecker	4	8	12	17	21	24
178-Henry	4	8	11	16	19	22
179-Bugs Bunny	4	8	12	17	21	24
180-Rin Tin Tin (TV)	7	14	21	37	46	55
181-Happy Holiday	4	7	9	14	16	18
182-Happi Tim	4	7	9	14	16	18
183-Welcome Santa (1958, full size)	4	7	9	14	16	18
184-Woody Woodpecker (1959)	4	8	11	16	19	22
185-Tarzan; photo-c	10	20	30	58	79	100
186-Oswald the Rabbit	4	8	11	16	19	22
187-Indian Chief	6	12	18	28	34	40
188-Bugs Bunny	4	8	11	16	19	22
189-Henry	4	7	10	14	17	20
190-Tom and Jerry	4	8	11	16	19	22
191-Roy Rogers	8	16	24	44	57	70
192-Porky Pig	4	8	11	16	19	22
193-The Lone Ranger	9	18	27	47	61	75
194-Popeye	6	12	18	31	38	45
195-Rin Tin Tin (TV)	7	14	21	35	43	50
196-Sears Special - not published						
197-Santa Is Coming	4	7	10	14	17	20
198-Santa's Helpers (1959)	4	7	10	14	17	20
199-Huckleberry Hound (TV)(1960, early app.)	8	16	24	42	54	65
200-Fury (TV)	6	12	18	28	34	40
201-Bugs Bunny	4	8	11	16	19	22
202-Space Explorer	8	16	24	42	54	65
203-Woody Woodpecker	4	7	10	14	17	20
204-Tarzan	9	18	27	52	69	80
205-Mighty Mouse	6	12	18	33	41	48
206-Roy Rogers; photo-c	8	16	24	42	54	65
207-Tom and Jerry	4	7	10	14	17	20
208-The Lone Ranger; Clayton Moore photo-c	10	20	30	54	72	90
209-Porky Pig	4	7	10	14	17	20
210-Lassie (TV)	6	12	18	33	41	48
211-Sears Special - not published						
212-Christmas Eve	4	7	10	14	17	20
213-Here Comes Santa (1960)	4	7	10	14	17	20
214-Huckleberry Hound (TV)(1961)	7	14	21	35	43	50
215-Hi Yo Silver	8	16	24	40	50	60
216-Rocky & His Friends (TV)(1961); predates Rocky and His Fiendish Friends #1 (see Four Color #1128)	9	18	27	52	69	85
217-Lassie (TV)	6	12	18	31	38	45
218-Porky Pig	4	7	10	14	17	20
219-Journey to the Sun	5	10	15	24	30	35
220-Bugs Bunny	4	8	11	16	19	22
221-Roy and Dale; photo-c	8	16	24	42	54	65
222-Woody Woodpecker	4	7	10	14	17	20
223-Tarzan	9	18	27	50	65	80
224-Tom and Jerry	4	7	10	14	17	20
225-The Lone Ranger	8	16	24	40	50	60
226-Christmas Treasury (1961)	4	7	10	14	17	20
227-Letters to Santa (1961)	4	7	10	14	17	20
228-Sears Special - not published?						
229-The Flintstones (TV)(1962); early app.; predates 1st Flintstones Gold Key issue (#7)	11	22	33	62	86	110
230-Lassie (TV)	6	12	18	27	33	38
231-Bugs Bunny	4	8	11	16	19	22
232-The Three Stooges	10	20	30	54	72	90
233-Bullwinkle (TV) (1962, very early app.)	9	18	27	52	69	85
234-Smokey the Bear	5	10	15	23	28	32
235-Huckleberry Hound (TV)	7	14	21	35	43	50
236-Roy and Dale	7	14	21	35	43	50
237-Mighty Mouse	6	12	18	27	33	38
238-The Lone Ranger	8	16	24	40	50	60

	GD 2.0	VG 4.0	FN 6.0	VF 8.0	VF/NM 9.0	NM- 9.2
239-Woody Woodpecker	4	7	10	14	17	20
240-Tarzan	8	16	24	44	57	70
241-Santa Claus Around the World	4	7	9	14	16	18
242-Santa's Toyland (1962)	4	7	9	14	16	18
243-The Flintstones (TV)(1963)	9	18	27	50	65	80
244-Mister Ed (TV); early app.; photo-c	7	14	21	35	43	50
245-Bugs Bunny	4	8	11	16	19	22
246-Popeye	6	12	18	27	33	38
247-Mighty Mouse	6	12	18	27	33	38
248-The Three Stooges	10	20	30	54	72	90
249-Woody Woodpecker	4	7	10	14	17	20
250-Roy and Dale	7	14	21	35	43	50
251-Little Lulu & Witch Hazel	11	22	33	64	90	115
252-Tarzan; painted-c	8	16	24	42	54	65
253-Yogi Bear (TV)	8	16	24	40	50	60
254-Lassie (TV)	6	12	18	27	33	38
255-Santa's Christmas List	4	7	10	14	17	20
256-Christmas Party (1963)	4	7	10	14	17	20
257-Mighty Mouse	6	12	18	27	33	38
258-The Sword in the Stone (Disney)	8	16	24	44	57	70
259-Bugs Bunny	4	8	11	16	19	22
260-Mister Ed (TV)	6	12	18	31	38	45
261-Woody Woodpecker	4	7	10	14	17	20
262-Tarzan	8	16	24	40	50	60
263-Donald Duck; not by Barks (Disney)	9	18	27	52	69	85
264-Popeye	6	12	18	27	33	38
265-Yogi Bear (TV)	6	12	18	31	38	45
266-Lassie (TV)	5	10	15	23	28	32
267-Little Lulu; Irving Tripp-a	10	20	30	56	76	95
268-The Three Stooges	9	18	27	47	61	75
269-A Jolly Christmas	3	6	8	12	14	16
270-Santa's Little Helpers	3	6	8	12	14	16
271-The Flintstones (TV)(1965)	9	18	27	47	61	75
272-Tarzan	8	16	24	40	50	60
273-Bugs Bunny	4	8	11	16	19	22
274-Popeye	6	12	18	27	33	38
275-Little Lulu; Irving Tripp-a	9	18	27	50	65	80
276-The Jetsons (TV)	14	28	42	76	108	140
277-Daffy Duck	4	8	11	16	19	22
278-Lassie (TV)	5	10	15	23	28	32
279-Yogi Bear (TV)	6	12	18	31	38	45
280-The Three Stooges; photo-c	9	18	27	47	61	75
281-Tom and Jerry	4	7	9	14	16	18
282-Mister Ed (TV)	6	12	18	31	38	45
283-Santa's Visit	4	7	9	14	16	18
284-Christmas Parade (1965)	4	7	9	14	16	18
285-Astro Boy (TV); 2nd app. Astro Boy	36	72	108	211	343	475
286-Tarzan	7	14	21	37	46	55
287-Bugs Bunny	4	8	11	16	19	22
288-Daffy Duck	4	7	10	14	17	20
289-The Flintstones (TV)	8	16	24	44	57	70
290-Mister Ed (TV); photo-c	5	10	15	24	30	35
291-Yogi Bear (TV)	6	12	18	27	33	38
292-The Three Stooges; photo-c	9	18	27	47	61	75
293-Little Lulu; Irving Tripp-a	8	16	24	42	54	65
294-Popeye	5	10	15	24	30	35
295-Tom and Jerry	4	7	9	14	16	18
296-Lassie (TV); photo-c	5	10	15	22	26	30
297-Christmas Bells	3	6	8	12	14	16
298-Santa's Sleigh (1966)	3	6	8	12	14	16
299-The Flintstones (TV)(1967)	8	16	24	44	57	70
300-Tarzan	7	14	21	37	46	55
301-Bugs Bunny	4	7	10	14	17	20
302-Laurel and Hardy (TV); photo-c	6	12	18	28	34	40
303-Daffy Duck	3	6	8	12	14	16
304-The Three Stooges; photo-c	7	14	21	35	43	50
305-Tom and Jerry	3	6	8	12	14	16
306-Daniel Boone (TV); Fess Parker photo-c	7	14	21	35	43	50
307-Little Lulu; Irving Tripp-a	7	14	21	37	46	55
308-Lassie (TV); photo-c	5	10	15	22	26	30
309-Yogi Bear (TV)	5	10	15	24	30	35
310-The Lone Ranger; Clayton Moore photo-c	10	20	30	54	72	90
311-Santa's Show	4	7	9	14	16	18
312-Christmas Album (1967)	4	7	9	14	16	18
313-Daffy Duck (1968)	3	6	8	12	14	16
314-Laurel and Hardy (TV)	6	12	18	27	33	38
315-Bugs Bunny	4	7	10	14	17	20
316-The Three Stooges	8	16	24	40	50	60
317-The Flintstones (TV)	8	16	24	42	54	65
318-Tarzan	7	14	21	35	43	50
319-Yogi Bear (TV)	5	10	15	24	30	35
320-Space Family Robinson (TV); Spiegle-a	14	28	42	76	108	140
321-Tom and Jerry	3	6	8	12	14	16
322-The Lone Ranger	7	14	21	37	46	55
323-Little Lulu; not by Stanley	5	10	15	24	30	35
324-Lassie (TV); photo-c	5	10	15	22	26	30
325-Fun with Santa	3	6	8	12	14	16
326-Christmas Story (1968)	4	7	9	14	16	18
327-The Flintstones (TV)(1969)	8	16	24	42	54	65
328-Space Family Robinson (TV); Spiegle-a	13	26	39	74	105	135
329-Bugs Bunny	4	7	10	14	17	20
330-The Jetsons (TV)	10	20	30	56	76	95
331-Daffy Duck	3	6	8	12	14	16
332-Tarzan	6	12	18	28	34	40
333-Tom and Jerry	3	6	8	12	14	16
334-Lassie (TV)	4	9	13	18	22	26
335-Little Lulu	5	10	15	24	30	35

March of Comics #206 © Roy Rogers

March of Comics #438 © Leonardo TTV

Martin Luther King and The Montgomery Story #1 © F.R.

	GD 2.0	VG 4.0	FN 6.0	VF 8.0	VF/NM 9.0	NM- 9.2
336-The Three Stooges	8	16	24	40	50	60
337-Yogi Bear (TV)	5	10	15	24	30	35
338-The Lone Ranger	7	14	21	37	46	55
339-(Was not published)						
340-Here Comes Santa (1969)	3	6	8	12	14	16
341-The Flintstones (TV)	8	16	24	42	54	65
342-Tarzan	3	6	9	19	30	40
343-Bugs Bunny	2	4	6	10	14	18
344-Yogi Bear (TV)	3	6	9	16	23	30
345-Tom and Jerry	2	4	6	9	13	16
346-Lassie (TV)	3	6	9	15	21	26
347-Daffy Duck	2	4	6	9	13	16
348-The Jetsons (TV)	6	12	18	37	66	95
349-Little Lulu; not by Stanley	3	6	9	16	23	30
350-The Lone Ranger	3	6	9	17	26	35
351-Beep-Beep, the Road Runner (TV)	2	4	6	11	16	20
352-Space Family Robinson (TV); Spiegle-a	7	14	21	44	82	120
353-Beep-Beep, the Road Runner (1971)	2	4	6	11	16	20
354-Tarzan (1971)	3	6	9	17	26	35
355-Little Lulu; not by Stanley	3	6	9	16	23	30
356-Scooby Doo, Where Are You? (TV)	7	14	21	49	92	135
357-Daffy Duck & Porky Pig	2	4	6	8	11	14
358-Lassie (TV)	3	6	9	14	19	24
359-Baby Snoots	2	4	6	10	14	18
360-H. R. Pufnstuf (TV); photo-c	6	12	18	40	73	105
361-Tom and Jerry	2	4	6	8	11	14
362-Smokey Bear (TV)	2	4	6	8	11	14
363-Bugs Bunny & Yosemite Sam	2	4	6	9	13	16
364-The Banana Splits (TV); photo-c	5	10	15	33	57	80
365-Tom and Jerry (1972)	2	4	6	8	11	14
366-Tarzan	3	6	9	17	26	35
367-Bugs Bunny & Porky Pig	2	4	6	9	13	16
368-Scooby Doo (TV)(4/72)	6	12	18	38	69	100
369-Little Lulu; not by Stanley	3	6	9	14	19	24
370-Lassie (TV); photo-c	3	6	9	14	19	24
371-Baby Snoots	2	4	6	9	13	16
372-Smokey the Bear (TV)	2	4	6	8	11	14
373-The Three Stooges	4	8	12	23	37	50
374-Wacky Witch	2	4	6	8	11	14
375-Beep-Beep & Daffy Duck (TV)	2	4	6	8	11	14
376-The Pink Panther (1972) (TV)	2	4	6	10	14	18
377-Baby Snoots (1973)	2	4	6	9	13	16
378-Turok, Son of Stone; new-a	7	14	21	46	86	125
379-Heckle & Jeckle New Terrytoons (TV)	2	4	6	8	11	14
380-Bugs Bunny & Yosemite Sam	2	4	6	8	11	14
381-Lassie (TV)	2	4	6	11	16	20
382-Scooby Doo, Where Are You? (TV)	5	10	15	35	63	90
383-Smokey the Bear (TV)	2	4	6	8	11	14
384-Pink Panther (TV)	2	4	6	8	11	14
385-Little Lulu	2	4	6	13	18	22
386-Wacky Witch	2	4	6	8	11	14
387-Beep-Beep & Daffy Duck (TV)	2	4	6	8	11	14
388-Tom and Jerry (1973)	2	4	6	13	18	22
389-Little Lulu; not by Stanley	2	4	6	8	11	14
390-Pink Panther (TV)	2	4	6	8	10	12
391-Scooby Doo (TV)	4	8	12	28	47	65
392-Bugs Bunny & Yosemite Sam	2	4	6	8	10	12
393-New Terrytoons (Heckle & Jeckle) (TV)	2	4	6	8	10	12
394-Lassie (TV)	2	4	6	9	13	16
395-Woodsy Owl	2	4	6	8	10	12
396-Baby Snoots	2	4	6	8	11	14
397-Beep-Beep & Daffy Duck (TV)	2	4	6	8	10	12
398-Wacky Witch	2	4	6	8	10	12
399-Turok, Son of Stone; new-a	6	12	18	42	79	115
400-Tom and Jerry	2	4	6	8	10	12
401-Baby Snoots (1975) (r/#371)	2	4	6	8	11	14
402-Daffy Duck (r/#313)	1	3	4	6	8	10
403-Bugs Bunny (r/#343)	2	4	6	8	10	12
404-Space Family Robinson (TV)(r/#328)	6	12	18	37	66	95
405-Cracky	1	3	4	6	8	10
406-Little Lulu (r/#355)(r/#362)	2	4	6	10	14	18
407-Smokey the Bear (TV)(r/#362)	2	4	6	8	10	12
408-Turok, Son of Stone; c-r/Turok #20 w/changes; new-a	6	12	18	38	69	100
409-Pink Panther (TV)	1	3	4	6	8	10
410-Wacky Witch	1	2	3	5	6	8
411-Lassie (TV)(r/#324)	2	4	6	9	13	16
412-New Terrytoons (1975) (TV)	1	2	3	5	6	8
413-Daffy Duck (1976)(r/#331)	1	2	3	5	6	8
414-Space Family Robinson (r/#328)	5	10	15	35	63	90
415-Bugs Bunny (r/#329)	1	2	3	5	6	8

	GD 2.0	VG 4.0	FN 6.0	VF 8.0	VF/NM 9.0	NM- 9.2
416-Beep-Beep, the Road Runner (r/#353)(TV)	1	2	3	5	6	8
417-Little Lulu (r/#323)	2	4	6	10	14	18
418-Pink Panther (r/#384) (TV)	1	2	3	5	6	8
419-Baby Snoots (r/#377)	1	3	4	6	8	10
420-Woody Woodpecker	1	2	3	5	6	8
421-Tweety & Sylvester	1	2	3	5	6	8
422-Wacky Witch (r/#386)	1	2	3	5	6	8
423-Little Monsters	1	3	4	6	8	10
424-Cracky (12/76)	1	2	3	5	6	8
425-Daffy Duck	1	2	3	5	6	8
426-Underdog (TV)	3	6	9	21	33	45
427-Little Lulu (r/#335)	2	4	6	8	11	14
428-Bugs Bunny	1	2	3	5	6	8
429-The Pink Panther (TV)	1	2	3	5	6	8
430-Beep-Beep, the Road Runner (TV)	1	2	3	5	6	8
431-Baby Snoots	1	2	3	5	6	8
432-Lassie (TV)	2	4	6	8	10	12
433-437: 433-Tweety & Sylvester. 434-Wacky Witch. 435-New Terrytoons (TV). 436-Wacky Advs. of Cracky. 437-Daffy Duck	1	3	4	6		8
438-Underdog (TV)	3	6	9	19	30	40
439-Little Lulu (r/#349)	2	4	6	8	11	14
440-442,444-446: 440-Bugs Bunny. 441-The Pink Panther (TV). 442-Beep-Beep, the Road Runner (TV). 444-Tom and Jerry. 445-Tweety and Sylvester. 446-Wacky Witch		1	2	3	5	6	8
443-Baby Snoots	1	2	3	5	6	8
447-Mighty Mouse	2	4	6	8	10	12
448-455,457,458: 448-Cracky. 449-Pink Panther. 450-Baby Snoots. 451-Tom and Jerry. 452-Bugs Bunny. 453-Popeye. 454-Woody Woodpecker. 455-Beep-Beep, the Road Runner (TV). 457-Tweety & Sylvester. 458-Wacky Witch	1	2	3	5	6	8
456-Little Lulu (r/#369)	2	4	6	8	10	12
459-Mighty Mouse	2	4	6	8	10	12
460-466: 460-Daffy Duck. 461-The Pink Panther (TV). 462-Baby Snoots. 463-Tom and Jerry. 464-Bugs Bunny. 465-Popeye. 466-Woody Woodpecker	1	2	3	5	6	8
467-Underdog (TV)	3	6	9	17	26	35
468-Little Lulu (r/#385)	1	2	3	5	6	8
469-Tweety & Sylvester	1	2	3	5	6	8
470-Wacky Witch	1	2	3	5	6	8
471-Mighty Mouse	1	3	4	6	8	10
472-474,476-478: 472-Heckle & Jeckle(12/80). 473-Pink Panther(1/81)(TV). 474-Baby Snoots. 476-Bugs Bunny. 477-Popeye. 478-Woody Woodpecker	1	2	3	5	6	8
475-Little Lulu (r/#323)	1	3	4	6	8	10
479-Underdog (TV)	3	6	9	16	23	30
480-482: 480-Tom and Jerry. 481-Tweety and Sylvester. 482-Wacky Witch	1	2	3	4	5	8
483-Mighty Mouse	1	3	4	6	8	10
484-487: 484-Heckle & Jeckle. 485-Baby Snoots. 486-The Pink Panther (TV). 487-Bugs Bunny	1	2	3	4	5	8
488-Little Lulu (4/82) (r/#335) (Last issue)	2	4	6	10	14	18

MARCH TO MARKET, THE
Pictorial Media/Swift & Co.: 1948, 1950 (Giveaway)

	GD 2.0	VG 4.0	FN 6.0	VF 8.0	VF/NM 9.0	NM- 9.2
nn-The story of meat	5	10	15	22	26	30

MARGARET O'BRIEN (See The Adventures of...)

MARK STEEL
American Iron & Steel Institute: 1967, 1968, 1972 (Giveaway) (24 pgs.)

	GD 2.0	VG 4.0	FN 6.0	VF 8.0	VF/NM 9.0	NM- 9.2
1967,1968- "Journey of Discovery with..."; Neal Adams art	4	8	12	25	40	55
1972- "...Fights Pollution"; N. Adams-a	2	4	6	11	16	20

MARTIN LUTHER KING AND THE MONTGOMERY STORY
Fellowship Reconciliation: 1957 (Giveaway, 16 pgs.) (A Spanish edition also exists)

nn-In color with paper-c (a CGC 8.0 copy sold for $185 in 2017, a VF+ copy sold for $675 in 2019, a CGC 8.5 copy sold for $799 in May 2021, and a CGC 5.0 copy sold for $650 in April 2022)

MARTIN LUTHER KING AND THE MONTGOMERY STORY
Top Shelf/Fellowship Reconciliation: 2011, 2013 ($5.00, newsprint-c, 16 pgs.)

nn-(2011) Reprint of the 1957 giveaway published by Fellowship Reconciliation; stapled						15.00
nn-(2013) Reprint has glued binding unlike the stapled 2011 version						10.00

MARVEL COLLECTOR'S EDITION: X-MEN
Marvel Comics: 1993 (3-3/4x6-1/2")

1-4-Pizza Hut giveaways						6.00

MARVEL COMICS PRESENTS
Marvel Comics: 1987, 1988 (4 1/4 x 6 1/4, 20 pgs.)
...Mini Comic Giveaway

	GD 2.0	VG 4.0	FN 6.0	VF 8.0	VF/NM 9.0	NM- 9.2
nn-(1988) Alf	1	3	4	6	8	10
nn-(1987) Captain America r/ #250	1	3	4	6	8	10
nn-(1987) Care Bears (Star Comics...)	1	3	4	6	8	10
nn-(1988) Flintstone Kids	1	3	4	6	8	10

	GD 2.0	VG 4.0	FN 6.0	VF 8.0	VF/NM 9.0	NM- 9.2
nn-(1987) Heathcliffe (Star Comics...)	1	3	4	6	8	10
nn-(1987) Spider-Man-r/Spect. Spider-Man #21	1	3	4	6	8	10
nn-(1988) Spider-Man-r/Amazing Spider-Man #1	1	3	4	6	8	10
nn-(1988) X-Men-reprints X-Men #53; B. Smith-a	1	3	4	6	8	10

MARVEL GUIDE TO COLLECTING COMICS, THE
Marvel Comics: 1982 (16 pgs., newsprint pages and cover)

1-Simonson-c	2	4	6	8	10	12

MARVEL MINI-BOOKS
Marvel Comics Group: 1966 (50 pgs., B&W; 5/8x7/8") (6 different issues)
(Smallest comics ever published) (Marvel Mania Giveaways)

Millie the Model, Sgt. Fury, Thor each...	3	6	9	21	33	45
Captain America, Spider-Man, Hulk each...	4	8	12	23	37	50

NOTE: *Each came from gum machines in six different color covers, usually one color: Pink, yellow, green, etc.*

MARVEL SUPER-HERO ISLAND ADVENTURES
Marvel Comics: 1999 (Sold at the park polybagged with Captain America V3 #19, one other comic, 5 trading cards and a cloisonné pin)

1-Promotes Universal Studios Islands of Adventures theme park	1	2	3	5	6	8

MARY'S GREATEST APOSTLE (St. Louis Grignion de Montfort)
Catechetical Guild (Topix) (Giveaway): No date (16 pgs.; paper cover)

nn	5	10	15	25	31	36

MASK (Made for Kenner Toys)
DC Comics: 1985

1	4	8	12	23	37	50
2,3	2	4	6	8	10	12

MASKED PILOT, THE (See Popular Comics #43)
R.S. Callender: 1939 (7-1/2x5-1/4", 16 pgs., premium, non-slick-c)

nn-Bob Jenney-a	11	22	33	62	86	110

MASTERS OF THE UNIVERSE (He-Man)
DC Comics: 1982 (giveaways with action figures, at least 35 different issues, unnumbered)

nn	3	6	9	14	20	26

MATRIX, THE (1999 movie)
Warner Brothers: 1999 (Recalled by Warner Bros. over questionable content)

nn-Paul Chadwick-s/a (16 pgs.); Geof Darrow-c	5	10	15	31	53	75

McCRORY'S CHRISTMAS BOOK
Western Printing Co: 1955 (36 pgs., slick-c) (McCrory Stores Corp. giveaway)

nn-Painted-c	6	12	18	31	38	45

McCRORY'S TOYLAND BRINGS YOU SANTA'S PRIVATE EYES
Promotional Publ. Co.: 1956 (16 pgs.) (Giveaway)

nn-Has 9 pg. story plus 7 pgs. toy ads	5	10	15	22	26	30

McCRORY'S WONDERFUL CHRISTMAS
Promotional Publ. Co.: 1954 (20 pgs., slick-c) (Giveaway)

nn	6	12	18	31	38	45

McDONALDS COMMANDRONS
DC Comics: 1985

nn-Four editions	1	2	3	5	6	8

MEDAL FOR BOWZER, A (Giveaway)
American Visuals Corp.: 1966 (8 pgs.)

nn-Eisner-c/script; Bowzer (a dog) survives untried pneumonia cure and earns his medal; (medical experimentation on animals)	21	42	63	147	324	500

MEET HIYA A FRIEND OF SANTA CLAUS
Julian J. Proskauer/Sundial Shoe Stores, etc.: 1949 (18 pgs.?, paper-c)(Giveaway)

nn	8	16	24	40	50	60

MEET THE NEW POST-GAZETTE SUNDAY FUNNIES
Pittsburgh Post Gazette: 3/12/49 (7-1/4x10-1/4", 16 pgs., paper-c)
Commercial Comics (insert in newspaper) (Rare)
Dick Tracy by Gould, Gasoline Alley, Terry & the Pirates, Brenda Starr, Buck Rogers by Yager, The Gumps, Peter Rabbit by Fago, Superman, Funnyman by Siegel & Shuster, The Saint, Archie, & others done especially for this book. A fine copy sold at auction in 1985 for $276.00.

	260	520	780	1700	-	-

MEN OF COURAGE
Catechetical Guild: 1949

Bound Topix comics-V7#2,4,6,8,10,16,18,20	7	14	21	37	46	55

MEN WHO MOVE THE NATION
Publisher unknown: (Giveaway) (B&W)

nn-Neal Adams-a	7	14	21	35	43	50

MERRY CHRISTMAS, A
K. K. Publications (Child Life Shoes): 1948 (Giveaway)

nn-Santa cover	9	18	27	47	61	75

MERRY CHRISTMAS
K. K. Publications (Blue Bird Shoes Giveaway): 1956 (7-1/4x5-1/4")

nn-Santa cover	5	10	14	20	24	28

MERRY CHRISTMAS FROM MICKEY MOUSE
K. K. Publications: 1939 (16 pgs.) (Color & B&W) (Shoe store giveaway)

nn-Donald Duck & Pluto app.; text with art (Rare); c-reprint/Mickey Mouse Mag. V3#3 (12/37)(Rare)	271	542	813	1734	2967	4200

MERRY CHRISTMAS FROM SEARS TOYLAND (See Santa's Christmas Comic, Bob & Betty & Santa's Wishing Whistle, and A Christmas Carol)
Sears Roebuck Giveaway: 1939 (16 pgs.) (Color)(Die-cut)

nn-Dick Tracy, Little Orphan Annie, The Gumps, Terry & the Pirates	116	232	348	742	1271	1800

MICKEY MOUSE (Also see Frito-Lay Giveaway)
Dell Publ. Co

...& Goofy Explore Business(1978)	2	4	6	8	10	12
...& Goofy Explore Energy(1976-1978, 36 pgs.); Exxon giveaway in color; regular size	2	4	6	8	10	12
...& Goofy Explore Energy Conservation(1976-1978)-Exxon	2	4	6	8	10	12
...& Goofy Explore The Universe of Energy(1985, 20 pgs.); Exxon giveaway in color; regular size	1	2	3	5	7	9
The Perils of Mickey nn (1993, 5-1/4x7-1/4", 16 pgs.)-Nabisco giveaway w/ games, Nabisco coupons & 6 pgs. of stories; Phantom Blot app.					6.00	

MICKEY MOUSE MAGAZINE
Walt Disney Productions: V1#1, Jan, 1933 - V1#9, Sept, 1933 (5-1/4x7-1/4")
No. 1-3 published by Kamen-Blair (Kay Kamen) Inc.
(Scarce)-Distributed by dairies and leading stores through their local theatres.
First few issues had 5¢ listed on cover, later ones had no price.

V1#1	460	920	1840	5500	-	-
2	225	450	900	1800	-	-
3,4	170	340	680	1375	-	-
5-9	119	238	476	950	-	-

NOTE: *A rare V1#1 Hardbound copy with a glassine dust jacket sold in July 2017 for $13,145.*

MICKEY MOUSE MAGAZINE (Digest size)
Walt Disney Productions: V1#1, 11/33 - V2#12, 10/35 (Mills giveaways issued by different dairies)

V1#1	177	354	531	1150	1950	-
2-12: 2-X-mas issue	61	122	183	390	670	950
V2#1 (11/34) Donald Duck in sailor suit pg. 6 (cameo)	45	90	135	284	480	675
V2#2-4,6-12: 2-X-mas issue. 4-St. Valentine-c	42	84	126	265	445	625
V2#5 (3/35) 1st app. Donald Duck in sailor outfit on-c	116	232	348	742	1271	1800

MICKEY MOUSE MAGAZINE
K.K. Publications: V4#1, Oct, 1938 (Giveaway)

V4#1	50	100	150	315	533	750

MIGHTY ATOM, THE
Whitman

Giveaway (1959, '63, Whitman)-Evans-a	3	6	9	16	23	30
Giveaway ('64r, '65r, '66r, '67r, '68r)-Evans-r?	2	4	6	10	14	18
Giveaway ('73r, '76r)	2	4	6	8	11	14

MILES THE MONSTER (Initially sold only at the Dover Speedway track)
Dover International Speedway, Inc.: 2006 ($3.00)

1,2-Allan Gross & Mark Wheatley-s/Wheatley-a					4.00	

MILITARY COURTESY
Harvey Publications: 1950 (16 pgs.)

nn-Regulations and saluting instructions	6	12	18	28	34	40

MINUTE MAN
Sovereign Service Station giveaway: No date (16 pgs., B&W, paper-c blue & red)

nn-American history	5	10	15	22	26	30

MINUTE MAN ANSWERS THE CALL, THE
By M. C. Gaines: 1942,1943,1944,1945 (4 pgs.) (Giveaway inserted in Jr. JSA Membership Kit)

nn-Sheldon Moldoff-a	25	50	75	150	245	340

MIRACLE ON BROADWAY
Broadway Comics: Dec, 1995 (Giveaway)

1-Ernie Colon-c/a; Jim Shooter & Co. story; 1st known digitally printed comic book; 1st app. Spire & Knights on Broadway (1150 print run)	6	12	18	38	69	100

NOTE: *Miracle on Broadway was a limited edition comic given to 1100 VIPs in the entertainment industry for the 1995 Holiday Season.*

MISS SUNBEAM (See Little Miss Sunbeam)

MR. BUG GOES TO TOWN (See Cinema Comics Herald)
K.K. Publications: 1941 (Giveaway, 52 pgs.)

nn-Cartoon movie (scarce)	71	142	213	454	777	1100

MR. PEANUT, THE PERSONAL STORY OF
Planters Nut & Chocolate Co.: 1956

nn	4	8	12	23	37	50

MOTHER OF US ALL
Catechetical Guild Giveaway: 1950? (32 pgs.)

nn	5	10	15	24	30	35

MOTION PICTURE FUNNIES WEEKLY (Amazing Man #5 on?)
First Funnies, Inc.: 1939 (Giveaway)(B&W, 36 pgs.) No month given; last panel in Sub-Mariner story dated 4/39 (Also see Colossus, Green Giant & Invaders No. 20)

1-Origin & 1st printed app. Sub-Mariner by Bill Everett (8 pgs.); Fred Schwab-c; reprinted in Marvel Mystery #1 with color added over the craft tint which was used to shade the black & white version; Spy Ring, American Ace (reprinted in Marvel Mystery #3) app. (Rare)-only eight known copies, one near mint with white pages, the rest with brown pages.	9400	18,800	28,200	47,000	65,800	-
Covers only to #2-4 (set)						1000

NOTE: *Eight copies (plus one coverless) were discovered in 1974 in the estate of the deceased publisher. Covers only to issues No. 2-4 were also found which evidently were printed in advance along with #1. #1 was to be distributed only through motion picture movie houses. However, it is believed that only advanced copies were sent out and the motion picture houses not going for the idea. Possible distribution at local theaters in Boston suspected. The "pay" copy (graded at 9.0) was discovered after 1974, bringing the total known to nine. The last panel of Sub-Mariner contains a rectangular box with "Continued Next Week" printed in it. When reprinted in Marvel Mystery, the box was left in with lettering added.*

MY DOG TIGE (Buster Brown's Dog)
Buster Brown Shoes: 1957 (Giveaway)

nn	5	10	15	24	30	35

MY GREATEST THRILLS IN BASEBALL
Mission of California: 1957 (16 pg. Giveaway)

nn-By Mickey Mantle	57	114	171	362	619	875

MYSTERIOUS ADVENTURES WITH SANTA CLAUS
Lansburgh's: 1948 (paper cover)

Miles the Monster #1 © Dover Int. Speedway

New Avengers (#1) © MAR

Pius XII Man of Peace © CG

	GD 2.0	VG 4.0	FN 6.0	VF 8.0	VF/NM 9.0	NM- 9.2
nn	15	30	45	84	127	170

NAKED FORCE!
Commercial Comics: 1958 (Small size)

nn	4	9	13	18	22	26

NATURAL DISASTERS!
Graphic Information Service/ Civil Defense: 1956 (16 pgs., soft-c)

nn-Al Capp Li'l Abner-c; Li'l Abner cameo (1 panel); narrated by Mr. Civil Defense	11	22	33	60	83	105

NAVY: HISTORY & TRADITION
Stokes Walesby Co./Dept. of Navy: 1958 - 1961 (nn) (Giveaway)
1772-1778, 1778-1782, 1782-1817, 1817-1865, 1865-1936, 1940-1945:

1772-1778-16 pg. in color	5	10	15	22	26	30
1861: Naval Actions of the Civil War: 1865-36 pg. in color; flag-c	5	10	15	22	26	30

NEW ADVENTURE OF WALT DISNEY'S SNOW WHITE AND THE SEVEN DWARFS, A
(See Snow White Bendix Giveaway)

NEW ADVENTURES OF PETER PAN (Disney)
Western Publishing Co.: 1953 (5x7-1/4", 36 pgs.) (Admiral giveaway)

nn	14	28	42	82	121	160

NEW AVENGERS... (Giveaway for U.S Military personnel)
Marvel Comics: 2005 - Present (Distributed by Army & Air Force Exchange Service)

... Guest Starring the Fantastic Four (4/05) Bendis-s/Jurgens-a/c	5.00
...: Pot of Gold (AAFES 110th Anniversary Issue) (10/05) Jenkins-s/Nolan-a/c	5.00
(#3) ...: Avengers & X-Men Time Trouble (4/06) Kirkman-s	5.00
(#4) ...: Letters Home (12/06) Capt. America, Punisher, Silver Surfer, Ghost Rider on-c	5.00
5-The Spirit of America (10/05) Captain America app.	5.00
6-Fireline (8/08) Spider-Man, Iron Man & Hulk app. Richards-a/Dave Ross-c	5.00
7-An Army of One (2009) Frank Cho pin-up on back-c	5.00
8-The Promise (12/09) Captain America (Bucky) app.	5.00

NEW FRONTIERS
Harvey Information Press (United States Steel Corp.): 1958 (16 pgs., paper-c)

nn-History of barbed wire	5	10	14	20	24	28

NEW TEEN TITANS, THE
DC Comics: Nov. 1983

nn(11/83-Keebler Co. Giveaway)-In cooperation with "The President's Drug Awareness Campaign"; came in Presidential envelope w/letter from White House (Nancy Reagan)	1	2	3	4	5	6
nn-(re-issue of above on Mando paper for direct sales market); American Soft Drink Industry version; I.B.M. Corp. version						5.00

NEW USES FOR GOOD EARTH
Mined Land Conservation: 1960 (paper-c)

nn	3	6	9	19	30	40

NOLAN RYAN IN THE WINNING PITCH (Kellogg's Tony's Sports Comics)
DC Comics: 1992 (Sports Illustrated)

nn	6.00

OLD GLORY COMICS
Chesapeake & Ohio Railway: 1944 (Giveaway)

nn-Capt. Fearless reprint	9	18	27	52	69	85

ON THE AIR
NBC Network Comic: 1947 (Giveaway, paper-c, regular size)

nn-(Rare)	21	42	63	122	199	275

OPERATION SURVIVAL!
Graphic Information Service/ Civil Defense: 1957 (16 pgs., soft-c)

nn-Al Capp Li'l Abner-c; Li'l Abner cameo (1 panel); narrated by Mr. Civil Defense	10	20	30	58	79	100

OUT OF THE PAST A CLUE TO THE FUTURE
E. C. Comics (Public Affairs Comm.): 1946? (16 pgs.) (paper cover)

nn-Based on public affairs pamphlet "What Foreign Trade Means to You"	30	60	90	177	289	400

OUTSTANDING AMERICAN WAR HEROES
The Parents' Institute: 1944 (16 pgs., paper-c)

nn-Reprints from True Comics	6	12	18	31	38	45

OVERSEAS COMICS (Also see G.I. Comics & Jeep Comics)
Giveaway (Distributed to U.S. Armed Forces): 1944 - No. 105?, 1946
(7-1/4x10-1/4"; 16 pgs. in color)

23-105-Bringing Up Father (by McManus), Popeye, Joe Palooka, Dick Tracy, Superman, Gasoline Alley, Buz Sawyer, Li'l Abner, Blondie, Terry and the Pirates, Out Our Way	9	18	27	47	61	75

OWL, THE (See Crackajack Funnies #25 & Popular Comics #72)(Also see The Hurricane Kids & Magic Morro)
Western Pub. Co./R.S. Callender: 1940 (Giveaway)(7-1/2x5-1/4")(Soft-c, color)

	GD 2.0	VG 4.0	FN 6.0	VF 8.0	VF/NM 9.0	NM- 9.2
nn-Frank Thomas-a	18	36	54	105	165	225

OXYDOL-DREFT
Toby Press:1950 (Set of 6 pocket-size giveaways; distributed through the mail as a set) (Scarce)

1-3: 1-Li'l Abner. 2-Daisy Mae. 3-Shmoo	9	18	27	52	69	85
4-John Wayne; Williamson/Frazetta-c from John Wayne #3	14	28	42	76	108	140
5-Archie	13	26	39	72	101	130
6-Terrytoons Mighty Mouse	9	18	27	52	69	85
Mailing Envelope (has All Capp's Shmoo on front)	9	18	27	52	69	85

OZZIE SMITH IN THE KID WHO COULD (Kellogg's Tony's Sports Comics)
DC Comics: 1992 (Sports Illustrated)

nn-Ozzie Smith app.	5.00

PADRE OF THE POOR
Catechetical Guild: nd (Giveaway) (16 pgs., paper-c)

nn	6	12	18	28	34	40

PAUL TERRY'S HOW TO DRAW FUNNY CARTOONS
Terrytoons, Inc. (Giveaway): 1940's (14 pgs.) (Black & White)

nn-Heckle & Jeckle, Mighty Mouse, etc.	13	26	39	72	101	130

PERKY AND PAM
Kay Kamen: Late 1940's (soft-c)

nn-Christmas themes	(a VF copy sold for $320 in 2019)

PETER PAN (See New Adventures of Peter Pan)

PETER PENNY AND HIS MAGIC DOLLAR
American Bankers Association, N. Y. (Giveaway): 1947 (16 pgs.; paper-c; regular size)

nn-(Scarce)-Used in SOTI, pg. 310, 311	41	82	123	256	428	600
Diff. version (7-1/4x11")-redrawn, 16 pgs., paper-c	15	30	45	85	130	175

PETER WHEAT (The Adventures of…)
Bakers Associates Giveaway: 1948 - 1957? (16 pgs. in color) (paper covers)

nn(No.1)-States on last page, end of 1st Adventure of…; Kelly-a	28	56	84	165	270	375
nn(4 issues)-Kelly-a	15	30	45	86	133	180
6-10-All Kelly-a	10	20	30	54	72	90
11-20-All Kelly-a	9	18	27	50	65	80
21-35-All Kelly-a	8	16	24	40	50	60
36-66	6	12	18	28	34	40
…Artist's Workbook ('54, digest size)	6	12	18	28	34	40
…Four-In-One Fun Pack (Vol. 2, '54), oblong, comics w/puzzles	8	16	24	40	50	60
…Fun Book ('52, 32 pgs., paper-c, B&W & color, 8-1/2x10-3/4")-Contains cut-outs, puzzles, games, magic & pages to color	9	18	27	50	65	80

NOTE: Al Hubbard art #36; written by Del Connell.

PETER WHEAT NEWS
Bakers Associates: 1948 - No. 63, 1953 (4 pgs. in color)

Vol. 1-All have 2 pgs. Peter Wheat by Kelly	23	46	69	138	227	315
2-10	14	28	42	76	108	140
11-20	8	16	24	40	50	60
21-30	6	12	18	28	34	40
31-63	4	7	10	14	17	20

NOTE: Early issues have no date & Kelly art.

PINOCCHIO
Cocomalt/Montgomery Ward Co.: 1940 (10 pgs.; giveaway; linen-like paper)

nn-Cocomalt edition	47	94	141	296	498	700
nn-store edition	39	78	117	240	395	550

PIUS XII MAN OF PEACE
Catechetical Guild: No date (12 pgs.; 5-1/2x8-1/2") (B&W)

nn-Catechetical Guild Giveaway	7	14	21	37	46	55

PLOT TO STEAL THE WORLD, THE
Work & Unity Group: 1948, 16pgs., paper-c

nn-Anti communism	30	60	90	177	289	400

POCAHONTAS
Pocahontas Fuel Company (Coal): 1941 - No. 2, 1942

nn(#1), 2-Feat. life story of Indian princess Pocahontas & facts about Pocahontas coal, Pocahontas, VA.	22	44	66	132	216	300

POLL PARROT
Poll Parrot Shoe Store/International Shoe
K. K. Publications (Giveaway): 1950 - No. 4, 1951; No. 2, 1959 - No. 16, 1962

1 ('50)-Howdy Doody; small size	18	36	54	107	169	230
2-4('51)-Howdy Doody	15	30	45	88	137	185
2('59)-16('62): 2-The Secret of Crumbley Castle. 5-Bandit Busters. 6-Fortune Finders. 7-The Make-Believe Mummy. 8-Mixed Up Mission('60). 10-The Frightful Flight. 11-Showdown at Sunup. 12-Maniac at Mubu Island. 13-…and the Runaway Genie. 14-Bully for You. 15-Trapped In Tall Timber. 16-…& the Rajah's Ruby('62)	2	4	6	11	16	20

Grade columns throughout: **GD 2.0 | VG 4.0 | FN 6.0 | VF 8.0 | VF/NM 9.0 | NM- 9.2**

POPEYE
Whitman

Issue	GD 2.0	VG 4.0	FN 6.0	VF 8.0	VF/NM 9.0	NM- 9.2
Bold Detergent giveaway (Same as regular issue #94)	2	4	6	9	13	16
Quaker Cereal premium (1989, 16pp, small size,4 diff.)(Popeye & the Time Machine, --On Safari, --& Big Foot, --vs. Bluto)	2	4	6	8	10	12

POPEYE
Charlton (King Features) (Giveaway): 1972 - 1974 (36 pgs. in color)

Issue	GD 2.0	VG 4.0	FN 6.0	VF 8.0	VF/NM 9.0	NM- 9.2
E-1 to E-15 (Educational comics)	2	4	6	9	13	16
nn-Popeye Gettin' Better Grades-4 pgs. used as intro. to above giveaways (in color)	2	4	6	9	13	16

POPSICLE PETE FUN BOOK (See All-American Comics #6)
Joe Lowe Corp.: 1947, 1948

Issue	GD 2.0	VG 4.0	FN 6.0	VF 8.0	VF/NM 9.0	NM- 9.2
nn-36 pgs. in color; Sammy 'n' Claras, The King Who Couldn't Sleep & Popsicle Pete stories, games, cut-outs	12	24	36	67	94	120
Adventure Book ('48)-Has Classics ad with checklist to HRN #343 (Great Expectations #43)	10	20	30	56	76	95

PORKY'S BOOK OF TRICKS
K. K. Publications (Giveaway): 1942 (8-1/2x5-1/2", 48 pgs.)

Issue	GD 2.0	VG 4.0	FN 6.0	VF 8.0	VF/NM 9.0	NM- 9.2
nn-7 pg. comic story, text stories, plus games & puzzles	57	114	171	362	619	875

POST GAZETTE (See Meet the New...)

PUNISHER: COUNTDOWN (Movie)
Marvel Comics: 2004 (7 1/4" X 4 3/4" mini-comic packaged with Punisher DVD)

Issue	GD 2.0	VG 4.0	FN 6.0	VF 8.0	VF/NM 9.0	NM- 9.2
nn-Prequel to 2004 movie; Ennis-s/Dillon-a	2	4	6	8	10	12

PURE OIL COMICS (Also see Salerno Carnival of Comics, 24 Pages of Comics, & Vicks Comics)
Pure Oil Giveaway: Late 1930's (24 pgs., regular size, paper-c)

Issue	GD 2.0	VG 4.0	FN 6.0	VF 8.0	VF/NM 9.0	NM- 9.2
nn-Contains 1-2 pg. strips; i.e.; Hairbreadth Harry, Skyroads, Buck Rogers by Calkins & Yager, Olly of the Movies, Napoleon, S'Matter Pop, etc. Also a 16 pg. 1938 giveaway with Buck Rogers	39	78	117	231	378	525

QUAKER OATS (Also see Cap'n Crunch)
Quaker Oats Co.: 1965 (Giveaway) (2-1/2x5-1/2") (16 pgs.)

Issue	GD 2.0	VG 4.0	FN 6.0	VF 8.0	VF/NM 9.0	NM- 9.2
"Plenty of Glutton", starring Quake & Quisp;	3	6	9	15	22	28
"Lava Come-Back", "Kite Tale"	2	4	6	9	12	15

RAILROADS DELIVER THE GOODS!
Assoc. of American Railroads: Dec, 1954; Sept, 1957 (16 pgs., paper-c)

Issue	GD 2.0	VG 4.0	FN 6.0	VF 8.0	VF/NM 9.0	NM- 9.2
nn-The story of railway freight	6	12	18	31	38	45

RAILS ACROSS AMERICA!
Assoc. of American Railroads: nd (Early 1960s) (16 pgs.)

Issue	GD 2.0	VG 4.0	FN 6.0	VF 8.0	VF/NM 9.0	NM- 9.2
nn	6	12	18	28	34	40

READY THEN, READY NOW
Western Publications: 1966 (National Guard military giveaway, regular size)

Issue	GD 2.0	VG 4.0	FN 6.0	VF 8.0	VF/NM 9.0	NM- 9.2
nn	5	10	15	34	60	85

REAL FUN OF DRIVING!!, THE
Chrysler Corp.: 1965, 1966, 1967 (Regular size, 16 pgs.)

Issue	GD 2.0	VG 4.0	FN 6.0	VF 8.0	VF/NM 9.0	NM- 9.2
nn-Schaffenberger-a (12 pgs.)	1	3	4	6	8	10

REAL HIT
Fox Feature Publications: 1944 (Savings Bond premium)

Issue	GD 2.0	VG 4.0	FN 6.0	VF 8.0	VF/NM 9.0	NM- 9.2
1-Blue Beetle-r; Blue Beetle on-c	22	44	66	132	216	300

NOTE: Two versions exist, with and without covers. The coverless version has the title, No. 1 and price printed at top of splash page.

RED BALL COMIC BOOK
Parents' Magazine Institute: 1947 (Red Ball Shoes giveaway)

Issue	GD 2.0	VG 4.0	FN 6.0	VF 8.0	VF/NM 9.0	NM- 9.2
nn-Reprints from True Comics	5	10	15	22	26	30

REDDY GOOSE
International Shoe Co. (Western Printing): No number, 1958?; No. 2, Jan, 1959 - No. 16, July, 1962 (Giveaway)

Issue	GD 2.0	VG 4.0	FN 6.0	VF 8.0	VF/NM 9.0	NM- 9.2
nn (#1)	4	8	12	23	37	50
2-16	3	6	9	14	20	25

REDDY KILOWATT (5¢) (Also see Story of Edison)
Educational Comics (E. C.): 1946 - No. 2, 1947; 1956 - 1965 (no month) (16 pgs., paper-c)

Issue	GD 2.0	VG 4.0	FN 6.0	VF 8.0	VF/NM 9.0	NM- 9.2
nn-A Visit With Reddy (1948-1954?)	11	22	33	62	86	110
nn-Reddy Made Magic (1946, 5¢)	14	28	42	82	121	160
nn-Reddy Made Magic (1958)	11	22	33	62	86	110
2-Edison, the Man Who Changed the World (3/4" smaller than #1) (1947, 5¢)	14	28	42	82	121	160
...Comic Book 2 (1954)- "Light's Diamond Jubilee"	11	22	33	64	90	115
...Comic Book 2 (1956, 16 pgs.)- "Wizard of Light"	11	22	33	60	83	105
...Comic Book 2 (1958, 16 pgs.)- "Wizard of Light"	10	20	30	54	72	90
...Comic Book 2 (1965, 16 pgs.)- "Wizard of Light"	5	10	15	30	50	70
...Comic Book 3 (1956, 8 pgs.)- "The Space Kite"; Orlando story; regular size	11	22	33	60	83	105
...Comic Book 3 (1960, 8 pgs.)- "The Space Kite"; Orlando story; regular size	5	10	15	34	60	85

NOTE: Several copies surfaced in 1979.

REDDY MADE MAGIC
Educational Comics (E. C.): 1956, 1958 (16 pgs., paper-c)

Issue	GD 2.0	VG 4.0	FN 6.0	VF 8.0	VF/NM 9.0	NM- 9.2
1-Reddy Kilowatt-r (splash panel changed)	12	24	36	69	97	125
1 (1958 edition)	7	14	21	37	46	55

RED ICEBERG, THE
Impact Publ. (Catechetical Guild): 1960 (10¢, 16 pgs., Communist propaganda)

Issue	GD 2.0	VG 4.0	FN 6.0	VF 8.0	VF/NM 9.0	NM- 9.2
nn-(Rare)- "We The People" back-c	40	80	120	296	673	1050
2nd version- "Impact Press" back-c	32	64	96	230	515	800
3rd version- "Explains comic" back-c	32	64	96	230	515	800
4th version- "Impact Press w/World Wide Secret Heart Program ad"	32	64	96	230	515	800
5th version- "Chicago Inter-Student Catholic Action" back-c	32	64	96	230	515	800

NOTE: This book was the Guild's last anti-communist propaganda book and had very limited circulation. 3 - 4 copies surfaced in 1979 from the defunct publisher's files. Other copies turn up.

RED RYDER COMICS
Dell Publ. Co.

Issue	GD 2.0	VG 4.0	FN 6.0	VF 8.0	VF/NM 9.0	NM- 9.2
Buster Brown Shoes Giveaway (1941, color, soft-c, 32 pgs.)	22	44	66	128	209	290
Red Ryder Super Book of Comics (1944, paper-c, 32 pgs.; blank back-c) Magic Morro app.	22	44	66	128	209	290
Red Ryder Victory Patrol-nn(1942, 32 pgs.)(Langendorf bread; includes cut-out membership card and certificate, order blank and "Slide-Up" decoder, and a Super Book of Comics in color (same content as Super Book #4 w/diff. cover (Pan-Am)) (Rare)	97	194	291	621	1061	1500
Red Ryder Victory Patrol-nn(1943, 32 pgs.)(Langendorf bread; includes cut-out "Rodeomatic" radio decoder, order coupon for "Magic V-Badge", cut-out membership card and certificate and a full color Super Book of Comics comic book) (Rare)	65	130	195	416	708	1000
Red Ryder Victory Patrol-nn(1944, 32 pgs.)-r-/#43,44; comic has a paper-c & is stapled inside a triple cardboard fold-out-c; contains membership card, decoder, map of R.R. home range, etc. Herky app. (Langendorf Bread giveaway; sub-titled 'Super Book of Comics') (Rare)	65	130	195	416	708	1000
Wells Lamont Corp. giveaway (1950)-16 pgs. in color; regular size; paper-c; 1941-r	15	30	45	83	124	165

RETURN OF JOE THE GENIE OF STEEL (Also see Joe The Genie of Steel)
U. S. Steel Corp., Pittsburgh, PA/Commercial Comics: 1951 (U. S. Steel Corp. giveaway)

Issue	GD 2.0	VG 4.0	FN 6.0	VF 8.0	VF/NM 9.0	NM- 9.2
nn-Joe Magarac, the Paul Bunyan of steel	5	10	15	33	57	80

REX MORGAN M.D. TALKS ABOUT YOUR UNBORN CHILD
(No publisher) Fetal Alcohol, Tobacco & Firearms giveaway, 1980 (Reg. size, paper-c)

Issue	GD 2.0	VG 4.0	FN 6.0	VF 8.0	VF/NM 9.0	NM- 9.2
nn	3	6	9	21	33	45

RICHIE RICH, CASPER & WENDY NATIONAL LEAGUE
Harvey Publications: June, 1976 (52 pgs.) (newsstand edition also exists)

Issue	GD 2.0	VG 4.0	FN 6.0	VF 8.0	VF/NM 9.0	NM- 9.2
1 (Released-3/76 w/ 6/76 date)	3	6	9	17	26	35
1 (6/76)-2nd version w/San Francisco Giants & KTVU 2 logos; has "Compliments of Giants and Straw Hat Pizza" on-c	3	6	9	17	26	35
1-Variants for other 11 NL teams, similar to Giants version but with different ad on inside front-c	3	6	9	17	26	35

RIDE THE HIGH IRON!
Assoc. of American Railroads: Jan, 1957 (16 pgs.)

Issue	GD 2.0	VG 4.0	FN 6.0	VF 8.0	VF/NM 9.0	NM- 9.2
nn-The Story of modern passenger trains	5	10	15	24	30	35

RIPLEY'S BELIEVE IT OR NOT!
Harvey Publications

Issue	GD 2.0	VG 4.0	FN 6.0	VF 8.0	VF/NM 9.0	NM- 9.2
J. C. Penney giveaway (1948)	11	22	33	62	86	110

ROBIN HOOD (New Adventures of...)
Walt Disney Productions: 1952 (Flour giveaways, 5x7-1/4", 36 pgs.)

Issue	GD 2.0	VG 4.0	FN 6.0	VF 8.0	VF/NM 9.0	NM- 9.2
"New Adventures of Robin Hood", "Ghosts of Waylea Castle", & "The Miller's Ransom" each....	4	8	12	18	22	25

ROBIN HOOD'S FRONTIER DAYS (...Western Tales, Adventures of... #1)
Shoe Store Giveaway (Robin Hood Stores): 1956 (20 pgs., slick-c)(7 issues?)

Issue	GD 2.0	VG 4.0	FN 6.0	VF 8.0	VF/NM 9.0	NM- 9.2
nn	7	14	21	35	43	50
nn-Issues with Crandall-a	8	16	24	44	57	70

ROCKETS AND RANGE RIDERS
Richfield Oil Corp.: May, 1957 (Giveaway, 16 pgs., soft-c)

Issue	GD 2.0	VG 4.0	FN 6.0	VF 8.0	VF/NM 9.0	NM- 9.2
nn-Toth-a	22	44	66	132	216	300

ROMANCE OF MONEY, THE
Natamsa Publishing Co.: 1937,1947 (4-7/8" x 6-1/4")

Issue	GD 2.0	VG 4.0	FN 6.0	VF 8.0	VF/NM 9.0	NM- 9.2
1937 ed. -(Scarce) 24 pgs with blue logo and artwork; distributed by the National Savings Bank, Albany, NY. Art by H.T. Elmo, a pseudonym for Jacob Kurtzberg (Jack Kirby). Believed to be Kirby's first published comic book work	290	580	870	1750	-	-
1947 ed. -(Scarce) 16 pgs with red logo and artwork	150	300	450	900	-	-

ROUND THE WORLD GIFT
National War Fund (Giveaway): No date (mid 1940's) (4 pgs.)

Issue	GD 2.0	VG 4.0	FN 6.0	VF 8.0	VF/NM 9.0	NM- 9.2
	14	28	42	82	121	160

ROY ROGERS COMICS
Dell Publishing Co.

Issue	GD 2.0	VG 4.0	FN 6.0	VF 8.0	VF/NM 9.0	NM- 9.2
...& the Man From Dodge City (Dodge giveaway, 16 pgs., 1954)-Frontier, Inc. (5x7-1/4")	13	26	39	74	105	135
Official Roy Rogers Riders Club Comics (1952; 16 pgs., reg. size, paper-c)	15	30	45	90	140	190

RUDOLPH, THE RED-NOSED REINDEER
Montgomery Ward: 1939 (2,400,000 copies printed); Dec, 1951 (Giveaway)

Issue	GD 2.0	VG 4.0	FN 6.0	VF 8.0	VF/NM 9.0	NM- 9.2
Paper cover-1st app. in print; written by Robert May; ill. by Denver Gillen	34	68	102	199	325	450
Hardcover version	24	48	72	142	234	325
1951 Edition (Has 1939 date)-36 pgs., slick-c printed in red & brown; pulp interior printed in four mixed-ink colors: red, green, blue & brown	14	28	42	80	115	150
1951 Edition with red-spiral promotional booklet printed on high quality stock, 8-1/2"x11", in red & brown, 25 pages composed of 4 fold outs, single sheets and the Rudolph comic book inserted (rare)	53	106	159	334	567	800

SABRINA THE TEENAGE WITCH AND HER BOOK OF MAGIC
Archie Comic Publications: 1970 (small size giveaway)

2 (A graded 9.4 copy sold for $121 in 2014 and a graded 7.5 copy sold for $31 in 2018)

SAD CASE OF WAITING ROOM WILLIE, THE
American Visuals Corp. (For Baltimore Medical Society): (nd, 1950?) (14 pgs. in color; paper covers; regular size)

Issue	GD 2.0	VG 4.0	FN 6.0	VF 8.0	VF/NM 9.0	NM- 9.2
nn-By Will Eisner (Rare)	54	108	162	343	574	825

SAD SACK COMICS
Harvey Publications: 1957-1962

Red Ryder Victory Patrol 1943 © Dell

Salute to the Boy Scouts © AAR

Santa's Stories © K.K. Pub.

	GD 2.0	VG 4.0	FN 6.0	VF 8.0	VF/NM 9.0	NM- 9.2
Armed Forces Complimentary copies, HD #1 (1957)	5	10	15	34	60	85
2-40 (1957-1962)	3	6	9	16	24	32

SALERNO CARNIVAL OF COMICS (Also see Pure Oil Comics, 24 Pages of Comics, & Vicks Comics)
Salerno Cookie Co.: Late 1930s (Giveaway, 16 pgs, paper-c)

nn-Color reprints of Calkins' Buck Rogers & Skyroads, plus other strips from Famous Funnies	55	110	165	352	601	850

SALUTE TO THE BOY SCOUTS
Association of American Railroads: 1960 (16 pgs., paper-c, regular size)

nn-History of scouting and the railroad	3	6	9	16	23	30

SANTA AND POLLYANNA PLAY THE GLAD GAME
Western Publ.: Aug, 1960 (16 pgs.) (Disney giveaway)

nn	3	6	9	14	20	25

SANTA & THE BUCCANEERS
Promotional Publ. Co.: 1959 (Giveaway, paper-c)

nn-Reprints 1952 Santa & the Pirates	2	4	6	13	18	22

SANTA & THE CHRISTMAS CHICKADEE
Murphy's: 1974 (Giveaway, 20 pgs.)

nn	2	4	6	9	12	15

SANTA & THE PIRATES
Promotional Publ. Co.: 1952 (Giveaway)

nn-Marv Levy-c/a	5	10	15	24	30	35

SANTA CLAUS FUNNIES (Also see The Little Fir Tree)
W. T. Grant Co./Whitman Publishing: nd; 1940 (Giveaway, 8x10"; 12 pgs., color & B&W, heavy paper)

nn-(2 versions- no date and 1940)	47	94	141	296	498	700

SANTA IS HERE!
Western Publ. (Giveaway): 1949 (oblong, slick-c)

nn	7	14	21	35	43	50

SANTA ON THE JOLLY ROGER
Promotional Publ. Co. (Giveaway): 1965

nn-Marv Levy-c/a	2	4	6	9	12	15

SANTA! SANTA!
R. Jackson: 1974 (20 pgs.) (Montgomery Ward giveaway)

nn	2	4	6	8	10	12

SANTA'S BUNDLE OF FUN
Gimbels: 1969 (Giveaway, B&W, 20 pgs.)

nn-Coloring book & games	2	4	6	9	12	15

SANTA'S CHRISTMAS COMIC VARIETY SHOW (See Merry Christmas From Sears Toyland, Bob & Betty & Santa's Wishing Whistle, and A Christmas Carol)
Sears Roebuck & Co.: 1943 (24 pgs.)

Contains puzzles & new comics of Dick Tracy, Little Orphan Annie, Moon Mullins, Terry & the Pirates, etc.	55	110	165	352	601	850

SANTA'S CHRISTMAS TIME STORIES
Premium Sales, Inc.: nd (Late 1940s) (16 pgs., paper-c) (Giveaway)

nn	8	16	24	40	50	60

SANTA'S CIRCUS
Promotional Publ. Co.: 1964 (Giveaway, half-size)

nn-Marv Levy-c/a	2	4	6	10	14	18

SANTA'S FUN BOOK
Promotional Publ. Co.: 1951, 1952 (Regular size, 16 pgs., paper-c) (Murphy's giveaway)

nn	7	14	21	35	43	50

SANTA'S GIFT BOOK
No Publisher: No date (16 pgs.)

nn-Puzzles, games only	5	10	15	22	26	30

SANTA'S NEW STORY BOOK
Wallace Hamilton Campbell: 1949 (16 pgs., paper-c) (Giveaway)

nn	8	16	24	40	50	60

SANTA'S REAL STORY BOOK
Wallace Hamilton Campbell/W. W. Orris: 1948, 1952 (Giveaway, 16 pgs.)

nn	8	16	24	40	50	60

SANTA'S RIDE
W. T. Grant Co.: 1959 (Giveaway)

nn	5	10	15	22	26	30

SANTA'S RODEO
Promotional Publ. Co.: 1964 (Giveaway, half-size)

nn-Marv Levy-a	2	4	6	10	14	18

SANTA'S SECRET CAVE
W. T. Grant Co.: 1960 (Giveaway, half-size)

nn	2	4	6	11	16	20

SANTA'S SECRETS
Sam B. Anson Christmas giveaway: 1951, 1952? (16 pgs., paper-c)

nn-Has games, stories & pictures to color	5	10	15	24	30	35

SANTA'S STORIES
K. K. Publications (Klines Dept. Store): 1953 (Regular size, paper-c)

nn-Kelly-a	18	36	54	105	165	225
nn-Another version (1953, glossy-c, half-size, 7-1/4x5-1/4")-Kelly-a	17	34	51	98	154	210

SANTA'S SURPRISE
K. K. Publications: 1947 (Giveaway, 36 pgs., slick-c)

nn	9	18	27	50	65	80

SANTA'S TOYTOWN FUN BOOK
Promotional Publ. Co.: 1953 (Giveaway)

nn-Marv Levy-c	5	10	15	22	26	30

SANTA TAKES A TRIP TO MARS
Bradshaw-Diehl Co., Huntington, W.VA.: 1950s (nd) (Giveaway, 16 pgs.)

nn	4	8	12	28	47	65

SCHWINN BIKE THRILLS
Schwinn Bicycle Co.: 1959 (Reg. size)

nn	8	16	24	44	57	70

SCIENCE FAIR STORY OF ELECTRONICS
Radio Shack/Tandy Corp.: 1975 - 1987 (Giveaway)

11 different issues (approx. 1 per year) each....						5.00

SECRETS BEHIND THE COMICS
Famous Enterprises, Inc.: 1947 (Small size; advertised in Timely comics)

nn - By Stan Lee; profile of Syd Shores (w/4 pgs. of his Blonde Phantom), Mike Sekowsky, Basil Wolverton, Al Jaffee & Martin Goodman; description of Captain America's creation with images	148	296	444	947	1624	2300

SEEING WASHINGTON
Commercial Comics: 1957 (also sold at 25¢)(Slick-c, reg. size)

nn	6	12	18	31	38	45

SERGEANT PRESTON OF THE YUKON
Quaker Cereals: 1956 (4 comic booklets) (Soft-c, 16 pgs., 7x2-1/2" & 5x2-1/2") Giveaways
"How He Found Yukon King", "The Case That Made Him A Sergeant", "How Yukon King Saved Him From The Wolves", "How He Became A Mountie"

each…	9	18	27	52	69	85

SHAZAM! (Visits Portland Oregon in 1943)
DC Comics: 1989 (69¢ cover)

nn-Promotes Super-Heroes exhibit at Oregon Museum of Science and Industry; reprints Golden Age Captain Marvel story	3	6	9	16	23	30

SHERIFF OF COCHISE, THE (TV)
Mobil: 1957 (16 pgs.) Giveaway

nn-Schaffenberger-a	5	10	15	22	26	30

SIDEWALK ROMANCE (Also see The K. O. Punch & Lucky Fights It Through)
Health Publications: 1950

nn-VD educational giveaway	53	106	159	334	567	800

SILLY PUTTY MAN
DC Comics: 1978

1	3	6	9	14	19	24

SKATING SKILLS
Custom Comics, Inc./Chicago Roller Skates: 1957 (36 & 12 pgs.; 5x7", two versions) (10¢)

nn-Resembles old ACG cover plus interior art	4	8	12	17	21	24

SKIPPY'S OWN BOOK OF COMICS (See Popular Comics)
No publisher listed: 1934 (Giveaway, 52 pgs., strip reprints)

nn-(Scarce)-By Percy Crosby	360	720	1080	2520	4410	6300

Published by Max C. Gaines for Phillip's Dental Magnesia to be advertised on the Skippy Radio Show and given away with the purchase of a tube of Phillip's Tooth Paste. This is the first four-color comic book of reprints about one character.

SKY KING "RUNAWAY TRAIN" (TV)
National Biscuit Co.: 1964 (Regular size, 16 pgs.)

nn	6	12	18	37	66	95

SLAM BANG COMICS
Post Cereal Giveaway: No. 9, No date (Early 1940s)

9-Dynamic Man, Echo, Mr. E, Yankee Boy app.	13	26	39	72	101	130

SMILIN' JACK
Dell Publishing Co.

	GD 2.0	VG 4.0	FN 6.0	VF 8.0	VF/NM 9.0	NM- 9.2

Popped Wheat Giveaway (1947)-1938 strip reprints; 16 pgs. in full color

| | 5 | 10 | 14 | 20 | 24 | 28 |

Shoe Store Giveaway-1938 strip reprints; 16 pgs.

| | 6 | 12 | 18 | 31 | 38 | 45 |

Sparked Wheat Giveaway (1942)-16 pgs. in full color

| | 6 | 12 | 18 | 31 | 38 | 45 |

SMOKEY BEAR (See Forest Fire for 1st app.)
Dell Publ. Co.: 1959,1960
True Story of..., The -U.S. Forest Service giveaway-Publ. by Western Printing Co.; reprints
1st 16 pgs. of Four Color #932. Inside front-c differs slightly in 1959 & 1960 editions

| | 6 | 12 | 18 | 31 | 38 | 45 |

1964,1969 reprints

| | 2 | 4 | 6 | 11 | 16 | 20 |

SMOKEY STOVER
Dell Publishing Co.
General Motors giveaway (1953)

| | 9 | 18 | 27 | 52 | 69 | 85 |

National Fire Protection giveaway(1953 & 1954)-16 pgs., paper-c

| | 9 | 18 | 27 | 52 | 69 | 85 |

SNOW FOR CHRISTMAS
W. T. Grant Co.: 1957 (16 pgs.) (Giveaway)
nn

| | 5 | 10 | 15 | 22 | 26 | 30 |

SNOW WHITE AND THE SEVEN DWARFS
Bendix Washing Machines: 1952 (32 pgs., 5x7-1/4", soft-c) (Disney)
nn

| | 14 | 28 | 42 | 82 | 121 | 160 |

SNOW WHITE AND THE SEVEN DWARFS
Promotional Publ. Co.: 1957 (Small size)
nn

| | 8 | 16 | 24 | 40 | 50 | 60 |

SNOW WHITE AND THE SEVEN DWARFS
Western Printing Co.: 1958 (16 pgs, 5x7-1/4", soft-c) (Disney premium)
nn- "Mystery of the Missing Magic"

| | 7 | 14 | 21 | 37 | 46 | 55 |

SNOW WHITE AND THE 7 DWARFS IN "MILKY WAY"
American Dairy Assoc.: 1955 (16 pgs., soft-c, 5x7-1/4") (Disney premium)
nn

| | 8 | 16 | 24 | 42 | 54 | 65 |

SOLDIER OF GOD
Conventual Franciscans of Marytown: 1982 ($1.00)
nn-Story of Father Maximilian Kobe, priest in WWII Poland; Ray Chatton-a

| | | | | | | 9.00 |

SPACE GHOST COAST TO COAST
Cartoon Network: Apr, 1994 (giveaway to Turner Broadcasting employees)
1-(8 pgs.); origin of Space Ghost

| | 2 | 4 | 6 | 11 | 16 | 20 |

SPACE PATROL (TV)
Ziff-Davis Publishing Co. (Approved Comics)
...'s Special Mission (8 pgs., B&W, Giveaway)

| | 50 | 100 | 150 | 315 | 533 | 750 |

SPARKY
Fire Protection Association: 1961 (Reg. size, paper-c)
nn

| | 3 | 6 | 9 | 18 | 27 | 36 |

SPECIAL AGENT
Assoc. of American Railroads: Oct, 1959 (16 pgs.)
nn-The Story of the railroad police

| | 6 | 12 | 18 | 29 | 36 | 42 |

SPECIAL DELIVERY
Post Hall Synd.: 1951 (32 pgs.; B&W) (Giveaway)
nn-Origin of Pogo, Swamp, etc.; 2 pg. biog. on Walt Kelly (One copy sold in 1980 for $150.00)

SPECIAL EDITION (U. S. Navy Giveaways)
National Periodical Publs.: 1944 - 1945 (Reg. comic format with wording simplified, 52 pgs.)

1-Action (1944)-Reprints Action #80	103	206	309	659	1130	1600
2-Action (1944)-Reprints Action #81	97	194	291	621	1061	1500
3-Superman (1944)-Reprints Superman #33	97	194	291	621	1061	1500
4-Detective (1944)-Reprints Detective #97	97	194	291	621	1061	1500
5-Superman (1945)-Reprints Superman #34	97	194	291	621	1061	1500
6-Action (1945)-Reprints Action #84	97	194	291	621	1061	1500

NOTE: *Wayne Boring* c-1, 2, 6. *Dick Sprang* c-4.

SPIDER-MAN (See Amazing Spider-Man, The)

SPIRIT, THE (Weekly Comic Book)(Distributed through various newspapers & other sources)
Will Eisner: 6/2/40 - 10/5/52 (16 pgs.; 8 pgs.) (no cover) (in color)
NOTE: *Eisner* script, pencils/inks for the most part from 6/2/40-4/26/42; a few stories assisted by Jack Cole, Fine, Powell and Kotsky.

6/2/40(#1)-Origin/1st app. The Spirit; reprinted in Police #11; Lady Luck (Brenda Banks)
(1st app.) by Chuck Mazoujian & Mr. Mystic (1st app.) by S. R. (Bob) Powell begin
(rare)

| | 595 | 1190 | 1785 | 4350 | 7675 | 11,000 |

6/9/40(#2)

| | 103 | 206 | 309 | 659 | 1130 | 1600 |

6/16/40(#3)-Black Queen app. in Spirit

| | 48 | 96 | 144 | 302 | 514 | 725 |

6/23/40(#4)-Mr. Mystic receives magical necklace

| | 37 | 74 | 111 | 222 | 361 | 500 |

6/30/40(#5)

| | 37 | 74 | 111 | 222 | 361 | 500 |

7/7/40(#6)-1st app. Spirit carplane; Black Queen app. in Spirit

| | 39 | 78 | 117 | 231 | 378 | 525 |

7/14/40(#7)-8/4/40(#10): 7/21/40-Spirit becomes fugitive wanted for murder

| | 31 | 62 | 93 | 186 | 303 | 420 |

8/11/40-9/22/40: 9/15/40-Racist-c

| | 29 | 58 | 87 | 172 | 281 | 390 |

9/29/40-Ellen drops engagement with Homer Creep

| | 24 | 48 | 72 | 142 | 234 | 325 |

10/6/40-10/31/40

| | 24 | 48 | 72 | 142 | 234 | 325 |

11/10/40-The Black Queen app.

| | 25 | 50 | 75 | 150 | 245 | 340 |

11/17/40, 11/24/40

| | 24 | 48 | 72 | 142 | 234 | 325 |

12/1/40-Ellen spanking by Spirit on cover & inside; Eisner-1st 3 pgs., J. Cole rest

| | 41 | 82 | 123 | 256 | 428 | 600 |

12/8/40-3/9/41

| | 34 | 51 | 103 | 162 | 220 | |

3/16/41-Intro. & 1st app. Silk Satin

| | 23 | 46 | 69 | 138 | 227 | 315 |

3/23/41-6/1/41: 5/11/41-Last Lady Luck by Mazoujian. 5/18/41-Lady Luck by
Nick Viscardi begins, ends 2/22/42

| | 17 | 34 | 51 | 103 | 162 | 220 |

6/8/41-2nd app. Satin; Spirit learns Satin is also a British agent

| | 21 | 42 | 63 | 122 | 199 | 275 |

6/15/41-1st app. Twilight

| | 19 | 38 | 57 | 112 | 179 | 245 |

6/22/41-Hitler app. in Spirit

| | 20 | 40 | 60 | 114 | 182 | 250 |

6/29/41-1/25/42,2/8/42

| | 15 | 30 | 45 | 84 | 127 | 170 |

2/1/42-1st app. Duchess

| | 18 | 36 | 54 | 105 | 165 | 225 |

2/15/42-4/26/42-Lady Luck by Klaus Nordling begins 3/1/42

| | 15 | 30 | 45 | 94 | 147 | 200 |

5/3/42-8/16/42-Eisner/Fine/Quality staff assists on Spirit

| | 13 | 26 | 39 | 74 | 105 | 135 |

8/23/42-Satin cover splash; Spirit by Eisner/Fine although signed by Fine

| | 19 | 38 | 57 | 111 | 176 | 240 |

8/30/42,9/27/42-10/11/42,10/25/42-11/8/42-Eisner/Fine/Quality staff assists
on Spirit

| | 13 | 26 | 39 | 72 | 101 | 130 |

9/6/42-9/20/42,10/18/42-Fine/Belfi art on Spirit; scripts by Manly Wade Wellman

| | 10 | 20 | 30 | 54 | 72 | 90 |

11/15/42-12/6/42,12/20/42,12/27/42,1/17/43-4/18/43,5/9/43-8/8/43-Wellman/
Woolfolk scripts, Fine pencils, Quality staff inks

| | 10 | 20 | 30 | 54 | 72 | 90 |

12/13/42,1/3/43,1/10/43,4/25/43,5/2/43-Eisner scripts/layouts; Fine pencils,
Quality staff inks

| | 10 | 20 | 30 | 58 | 79 | 100 |

8/15/43-Eisner script/layout; pencils/inks by Quality staff; Jack Cole-a

| | 9 | 18 | 27 | 47 | 61 | 75 |

8/22/43-12/12/43-Wellman/Woolfolk scripts, Fine pencils, Quality staff inks;
Mr. Mystic by Guardineer-10/10/43-10/24/43

| | 9 | 18 | 27 | 47 | 61 | 75 |

12/19/43-8/13/44-Wellman/Woolfolk/Jack Cole scripts; Cole, Fine & Robin King-a;
Last Mr. Mystic-5/14/44

| | 8 | 16 | 24 | 44 | 57 | 70 |

8/20/44-12/16/45-Wellman/Woolfolk scripts; Fine art with unknown staff assists

| | 8 | 16 | 24 | 44 | 57 | 70 |

NOTE: *Scripts/layouts by Eisner, Eisner/Nordling, Eisner/Mercer or Spranger/Eisner; inks by Eisner or Eisner/Spranger in issues 12/23/45-2/2/47.*

12/23/45-1/6/46: 12/23/45-Christmas-c

| | 10 | 20 | 30 | 54 | 72 | 90 |

1/13/46-Origin Spirit retold

| | 14 | 28 | 42 | 80 | 115 | 150 |

1/20/46-1st postwar Satin app.

| | 13 | 26 | 39 | 74 | 105 | 135 |

1/27/46-3/10/46: 3/3/46-Last Lady Luck by Nordling

| | 10 | 20 | 30 | 56 | 76 | 95 |

3/17/46-Intro. & 1st app. Nylon

| | 12 | 24 | 36 | 69 | 97 | 125 |

3/24/46,3/31/46,4/14/46

| | 10 | 20 | 30 | 54 | 72 | 90 |

4/7/46-2nd app. Nylon

| | 10 | 20 | 30 | 58 | 79 | 100 |

4/21/46-Intro. & 1st app. Mr. Carrion & His Pet Buzzard Julia

| | 14 | 28 | 42 | 80 | 115 | 150 |

4/28/46-5/12/46,5/26/46-6/30/46: Lady Luck by Fred Schwab in issues
5/5/46-11/3/46

| | 10 | 20 | 30 | 54 | 72 | 90 |

5/19/46-2nd app. Mr. Carrion

| | 10 | 20 | 30 | 58 | 79 | 100 |

7/7/46-Intro. & 1st app. Dulcet Tone & Skinny

| | 12 | 24 | 36 | 69 | 97 | 125 |

7/14/46-9/29/46

| | 10 | 20 | 30 | 54 | 72 | 90 |

10/6/46-Intro. & 1st app. P'Gell

| | 14 | 28 | 42 | 78 | 112 | 145 |

10/13/46-11/3/46,11/16/46-11/24/46

| | 10 | 20 | 30 | 54 | 72 | 90 |

11/10/46-2nd app. P'Gell

| | 12 | 24 | 36 | 67 | 94 | 120 |

12/1/46-3rd app. P'Gell

| | 10 | 20 | 30 | 56 | 76 | 95 |

12/8/46-2/2/47

| | 9 | 18 | 27 | 52 | 69 | 85 |

NOTE: *Scripts, pencils/inks by Eisner except where noted in issues 2/9/47-12/19/48.*

2/9/47-7/6/47: 6/8/47-Eisner self satire

| | 9 | 18 | 27 | 52 | 69 | 85 |

7/13/47- "Hansel & Gretel" fairy tales

| | 12 | 24 | 36 | 69 | 97 | 125 |

7/20/47-Li'L Abner, Daddy Warbucks, Dick Tracy, Fearless Fosdick parody; A-Bomb blast-c

| | 14 | 28 | 42 | 80 | 115 | 150 |

7/27/47-9/14/47

| | 9 | 18 | 27 | 52 | 69 | 85 |

9/21/47-Pearl Harbor flashback

| | 13 | 26 | 39 | 74 | 105 | 135 |

9/28/47-1st mention of Flying Saucers in comics - three months after 1st sighting in Idaho
on 6/25/47

| | 22 | 44 | 66 | 128 | 209 | 290 |

10/5/47- "Cinderella" fairy tales

| | 13 | 26 | 39 | 74 | 105 | 135 |

10/12/47-11/30/47

| | 9 | 18 | 27 | 52 | 69 | 85 |

12/7/47-Intro. & 1st app. Powder Pouf

| | 14 | 28 | 42 | 82 | 121 | 160 |

12/14/47-12/28/47

| | 9 | 18 | 27 | 52 | 69 | 85 |

1/4/48-2nd app. Powder Pouf

| | 10 | 20 | 30 | 58 | 79 | 100 |

1/11/48-1st app. Sparrow Fallon; Powder Pouf app.

| | 10 | 20 | 30 | 56 | 76 | 95 |

1/18/48-He-Man ad cover; satire issue

| | 10 | 20 | 30 | 56 | 76 | 95 |

1/25/48-Intro. & 1st app. Castanet

| | 14 | 28 | 42 | 76 | 108 | 140 |

2/1/48-2nd app. Castanet

| | 10 | 20 | 30 | 54 | 72 | 90 |

2/8/48-3/7/48

| | 9 | 18 | 27 | 52 | 69 | 85 |

3/14/48-Only app. Kretchma

| | 10 | 20 | 30 | 54 | 72 | 90 |

3/21/48,3/28/48,4/11/48-4/25/48

| | 9 | 18 | 27 | 52 | 69 | 85 |

4/4/48-Only app. Wild Rice

| | 10 | 20 | 30 | 54 | 72 | 90 |

5/2/48-2nd app. Sparrow

| | 9 | 18 | 27 | 52 | 69 | 85 |

5/9/48-6/27/48,7/11/48,7/18/48: 6/13/48-TV issue

| | 9 | 18 | 27 | 52 | 69 | 85 |

7/4/48-Spirit by Andre Le Blanc

| | 8 | 16 | 24 | 44 | 57 | 70 |

7/25/48-Ambrose Bierce's "The Thing" adaptation classic by Eisner/Grandenetti

| | 19 | 38 | 57 | 111 | 176 | 240 |

8/1/48-8/15/48,8/29/48-9/12/48

| | 9 | 18 | 27 | 52 | 69 | 85 |

8/22/48-Poe's "Fall of the House of Usher" classic by Eisner/Grandenetti

| | 17 | 34 | 51 | 105 | 165 | 225 |

9/19/48-Only app. Lorelei

| | 10 | 20 | 30 | 56 | 76 | 95 |

9/26/48-10/31/48

| | 9 | 18 | 27 | 52 | 69 | 85 |

11/7/48-Only app. Plaster of Paris

| | 12 | 24 | 36 | 69 | 97 | 125 |

11/14/48-12/19/48

| | 9 | 18 | 27 | 52 | 69 | 85 |

NOTE: *Scripts by Eisner or Feiffer or Eisner/Feiffer or Nordling. Art by Eisner with backgrounds by Eisner, Grandenetti, Le Blanc, Stallman, Nordling, Dixon and/or others in issues 12/26/48-4/1/51 except where noted.*

12/26/48-Reprints some covers of 1948 with flashbacks

| | 9 | 18 | 27 | 52 | 69 | 85 |

1/2/49-1/16/49

| | 9 | 18 | 27 | 52 | 69 | 85 |

1/23/49,1/30/49-1st & 2nd app. Thorne

| | 10 | 20 | 30 | 56 | 76 | 95 |

2/6/49-8/14/49

| | 9 | 18 | 27 | 52 | 69 | 85 |

8/21/49,8/28/49-1st & 2nd app. Monica Veto

| | 10 | 20 | 30 | 56 | 76 | 95 |

9/4/49,9/11/49

| | 9 | 18 | 27 | 52 | 69 | 85 |

9/18/49-Love comic cover; has gag love comic ads on inside

| | 10 | 20 | 30 | 56 | 76 | 95 |

9/25/49-Only app. Ice

| | 10 | 20 | 30 | 54 | 72 | 90 |

10/2/49,10/9/49-Autumn News appears & dies in 10/9 issue

| | 10 | 20 | 30 | 54 | 72 | 90 |

10/16/49-11/27/49,12/18/49,12/25/49

| | 9 | 18 | 27 | 52 | 69 | 85 |

12/4/49,12/11/49-1st & 2nd app. Flaxen

| | 10 | 20 | 30 | 54 | 72 | 90 |

1/1/50-Flashbacks to all of the Spirit girls-Thorne, Ellen, Satin, & Monica

| | 15 | 30 | 45 | 83 | 124 | 165 |

PROMOTIONAL

Special Edition #3 © DC

The Spirit 8/03/52 © Will Eisner

Strange As It Seems © McN

	GD 2.0	VG 4.0	FN 6.0	VF 8.0	VF/NM 9.0	NM- 9.2
1/8/50-Intro. & 1st app. Sand Saref	15	30	45	92	144	195
1/15/50-2nd app. Sand Saref	14	28	42	76	108	140
1/22/50-2/5/50	9	18	27	52	69	85
2/12/50-Roller Derby issue	10	20	30	56	76	95
2/19/50-Half Dead Mr. Lox - Classic horror	14	28	42	76	108	140
2/26/50-4/23/50,5/14/50,5/28/50,7/23/50-9/3/50	9	18	27	52	69	85
4/30/50-Script/art by Le Blanc with Eisner framing	8	16	24	42	54	65
5/7/50,6/4/50-7/16/50-Abe Kanegson-a	8	16	24	42	54	65
5/21/50-Script by Feiffer/Eisner, art by Blaisdell, Eisner framing	8	16	24	42	54	65
9/10/50-P'Gell returns	10	20	30	56	76	95
9/17/50-1/7/51	8	16	24	42	54	65
1/14/51-Life Magazine cover; brief biography of Comm. Dolan, Sand Saref, Silk Satin, P'Gell, Sammy & Willum, Darling O'Shea, & Mr. Carrion & His Pet Buzzard Julia, with pin-ups by Eisner	14	28	42	78	112	145
1/21/51,2/4/51-4/1/51	9	18	27	52	69	85
1/28/51- "The Meanest Man in the World" by Eisner	14	28	42	78	112	145
4/8/51-7/29/51,8/12/51-Last Eisner issue	10	20	30	54	72	90
8/5/51,8/19/51-7/20/52-Not Eisner	8	16	24	42	54	65
7/27/52-(Rare)-Denny Colt in Outer Space by Wally Wood; 7 pg. S/F story of E.C. vintage	61	122	183	390	670	950
8/3/52-(Rare)- "Mission…The Moon" by Wood	61	122	183	390	670	950
8/10/52-(Rare)- "A DP On The Moon" by Wood	61	122	183	390	670	950
8/17/52-(Rare)- "Heart" by Wood/Eisner	61	122	183	390	670	950
8/24/52-(Rare)- "Rescue" by Wood	61	122	183	390	670	950
8/31/52-(Rare)- "The Last Man" by Wood	61	122	183	390	670	950
9/7/52-(Rare)- "The Man in The Moon" by Wood	61	122	183	390	670	950
9/14/52-(Rare)-Eisner/Wenzel-a	40	80	120	246	411	575
9/21/52-(Rare)- "Denny Colt, Alias The Spirit/Space Report" by Eisner/Wenzel	40	80	120	246	411	575
9/28/52-(Rare)- "Return From The Moon" by Wood	54	108	162	343	574	825
10/5/52-(Rare)- "The Last Story" by Eisner	37	74	111	222	361	500

Large Tabloid pages from 1946 on (Eisner) - Price 200 percent over listed prices.
NOTE: Spirit sections came out in both large and small format. Some newspapers went to the 8-pg. format months before others. Some printed the pages so they cannot be folded into a small comic book section; these are worth less. (Also see Three Comics & Spiritman).

SPY SMASHER
Fawcett Publications

	GD 2.0	VG 4.0	FN 6.0	VF 8.0	VF/NM 9.0	NM- 9.2
Well Known Comics (1944, 12 pgs., 8-1/2x10-1/2"), paper-c, glued binding, printed in green; Bestmaid/Samuel Lowe giveaway	18	36	54	105	165	225

STANDARD OIL COMICS (Also see Gulf Funny Weekly)
Standard Oil Co.: 1932-1934 (Giveaway, tabloid size, 4 pgs. in color)

	GD 2.0	VG 4.0	FN 6.0	VF 8.0	VF/NM 9.0	NM- 9.2
nn (Dec. 1932)	71	142	213	454	777	1100
1-Series has original art	55	110	165	352	601	850
2-5	23	46	69	136	223	310
6-14: 14-Fred Opper strip, 1 pg.	15	30	45	88	137	185
1A (Jan 1933)	55	110	165	352	601	850
2A-14A (1933)	39	78	117	231	378	525
1B (1934)	42	84	126	265	445	625
2B-7B (1934)	39	78	117	231	318	525

NOTE: Series A contains Frederick Opper's Si & Mirandi; Series B contains Goofus: He's From The Big City; McVittle by Walter O'Ehrle; interior strips include Pesty And His Pop & Smiling Slim by Sid Hicks.

STARS AND STRIPES
Centaur Publications: Oct. 1942 (regular size)
5 - World's Greatest Parade of Comics and Fun Promotional Cover Edition (Atlas Theater)
(A certified CGC 2.5 copy sold for $460 in 2019)

STAR TEAM
Marvel Comics Group: 1977 (6-1/2x5", 20 pgs.) (Ideal Toy Giveaway)

	GD 2.0	VG 4.0	FN 6.0	VF 8.0	VF/NM 9.0	NM- 9.2
nn	3	6	9	16	23	30

STEVE CANYON COMICS
Harvey Publications

	GD 2.0	VG 4.0	FN 6.0	VF 8.0	VF/NM 9.0	NM- 9.2
Dept. Store giveaway #3(6/48, 36pp)	10	20	30	58	79	100
…'s Secret Mission (1951, 16 pgs., Armed Forces giveaway); Caniff-a	9	18	27	52	69	85
Strictly for the Smart Birds (1951, 16 pgs.)-Information Comics Div. (Harvey) Premium	8	16	24	44	57	70

STORIES OF CHRISTMAS
K. K. Publications: 1942 (Giveaway, 32 pgs., paper cover)

	GD 2.0	VG 4.0	FN 6.0	VF 8.0	VF/NM 9.0	NM- 9.2
nn-Adaptation of "A Christmas Carol"; Kelly story "The Fir Tree"; Infinity-c	55	110	165	352	601	850

STORY HOUR SERIES (Disney)
Whitman Publ. Co.: 1948, 1949; 1951-1953 (36 pgs., paper-c) (4-3/4x6-1/2")
Given away with subscription to Walt Disney's Comics & Stories

	GD 2.0	VG 4.0	FN 6.0	VF 8.0	VF/NM 9.0	NM- 9.2
nn(1948)-Mickey Mouse and the Boy Thursday	13	26	39	74	105	135
nn(1948)-Mickey Mouse the Miracle Master	13	26	39	74	105	135
nn(1948)-Minnie Mouse and Antique Chair	13	26	39	74	105	135
nn(1949)-The Three Orphan Kittens(B&W & color)	9	18	27	47	61	75
nn(1949)-Danny-The Little Black Lamb	9	18	27	47	61	75
800(1948)-Donald Duck in "Bringing Up the Boys"	16	32	48	92	144	195
1953 edition	11	22	33	64	90	115
801(1948)-Mickey Mouse's Summer Vacation	10	20	30	56	76	95
1951, 1952 editions	7	14	21	35	43	50
802(1948)-Bugs Bunny's Adventures	9	18	27	50	65	80
803(1948)-Bongo	8	16	24	40	50	60
804(1948)-Mickey and the Beanstalk	9	18	27	47	61	75
805-15(1949)-Andy Panda and His Friends	8	16	24	40	50	60
806-15(1949)-Tom and Jerry	8	16	24	44	57	70
808-15(1949)-Johnny Appleseed	8	16	24	40	50	60

1948, 1949 Hard Cover Edition of each….30% - 40% more.

STOP AND GO, THE SAFETY TWINS
J.C. Penney: No date (early 1950s) (giveaway)

	GD 2.0	VG 4.0	FN 6.0	VF 8.0	VF/NM 9.0	NM- 9.2
nn	5	10	15	24	30	35

STORY OF CHECKS THE
Federal Reserve Bank: 1979 (Reg. size)

	GD 2.0	VG 4.0	FN 6.0	VF 8.0	VF/NM 9.0	NM- 9.2
nn	1	3	4	6	8	10

STORY OF CHECKS AND ELECTRONIC PAYMENTS
Federal Reserve Bank: 1983 (Reg size)

	GD 2.0	VG 4.0	FN 6.0	VF 8.0	VF/NM 9.0	NM- 9.2
nn	1	2	3	5	6	8

STORY OF CONSUMER CREDIT
Federal Reserve Bank: 1980 (Reg. size)

	GD 2.0	VG 4.0	FN 6.0	VF 8.0	VF/NM 9.0	NM- 9.2
nn	1	2	3	5	6	8

STORY OF EDISON, THE
Educational Comics: 1956 (16 pgs.) (Reddy Killowatt)

	GD 2.0	VG 4.0	FN 6.0	VF 8.0	VF/NM 9.0	NM- 9.2
nn-Reprint of Reddy Kilowatt #2(1947)	8	16	24	40	50	60

STORY OF FOREIGN TRADE AND EXCHANGE
Federal Reserve Bank: 1985 (Reg. size)

	GD 2.0	VG 4.0	FN 6.0	VF 8.0	VF/NM 9.0	NM- 9.2
nn	1	2	3	5	6	8

STORY OF HARRY S. TRUMAN, THE
Democratic National Committee: 1948 (Giveaway, regular size, soft-c, 16 pg.)

	GD 2.0	VG 4.0	FN 6.0	VF 8.0	VF/NM 9.0	NM- 9.2
nn-Gives biography on career of Truman; used in SOTI, pg. 311	15	30	45	88	137	185

STORY OF INFLATION, THE
Federal Reserve Bank: 1980s (Reg size)

	GD 2.0	VG 4.0	FN 6.0	VF 8.0	VF/NM 9.0	NM- 9.2
nn	1	3	4	6	8	10

STORY OF MONEY
William C. Popper: 1962, 1965

	GD 2.0	VG 4.0	FN 6.0	VF 8.0	VF/NM 9.0	NM- 9.2
nn-Soft-c	3	6	9	16	23	30

STORY OF MONEY
Federal Reserve Bank: 1984 (Reg. size)

	GD 2.0	VG 4.0	FN 6.0	VF 8.0	VF/NM 9.0	NM- 9.2
nn	1	3	4	6	8	10

STORY OF THE BALLET, THE
Selva and Sons, Inc.: 1954 (16 pgs., paper cover)

	GD 2.0	VG 4.0	FN 6.0	VF 8.0	VF/NM 9.0	NM- 9.2
nn	5	10	15	22	26	30

STRANGE AS IT SEEMS
McNaught Syndicate: 1936 (B&W, 5" x 7", 24 pgs.)

	GD 2.0	VG 4.0	FN 6.0	VF 8.0	VF/NM 9.0	NM- 9.2
nn-Ex-Lax giveaway	11	22	33	62	86	110

STRIKES AND THE PUBLIC
Socialist Labor Party: no date
nn-Calling worker class to organize against capitalist class (a FN/VF copy sold for $216 in 2018)

SUGAR BEAR
Post Cereal Giveaway: No date, circa 1975? (2 1/2" x 4 1/2", 16 pgs.)

	GD 2.0	VG 4.0	FN 6.0	VF 8.0	VF/NM 9.0	NM- 9.2
"The Almost Take Over of the Post Office", "The Race Across the Atlantic", "The Zoo Goes Wild" each…	1	3	4	6	8	10

SUNDAY WORLD'S EASTER EGG FULL OF EASTER MEAT FOR LITTLE PEOPLE
Supplement to the New York World: 3/27/1898 (soft-c, 16pg, 4"x8" approx., opens at top, color & B&W)(Giveaway)(shaped like an Easter egg)

	GD 2.0	VG 4.0	FN 6.0	VF 8.0	VF/NM 9.0	NM- 9.2
nn-By R.F. Outcault	22	44	66	128	209	290

SUPER BOOK OF COMICS
Western Publ. Co.: nd (1942-1943?) (Soft-c, 32 pgs.) (Pan-Am/Gilmore Oil/Kelloggs premiums)

	GD 2.0	VG 4.0	FN 6.0	VF 8.0	VF/NM 9.0	NM- 9.2
nn-Dick Tracy (Gilmore)-Magic Morro app. (2 versions: Dick Tracy Jr. on cover and a filing cabinet cover)	41	82	123	256	428	600
1-Dick Tracy & The Smuggling Ring; Stratosphere Jim app. (Rare) (Pan-Am)	36	72	108	211	343	475
1-Smilin' Jack, Magic Morro (Pan-Am)	15	30	45	85	130	175
2-Smilin' Jack, Stratosphere Jim (Pan-Am)	15	30	45	83	124	165
2-Smitty, Magic Morro (Pan-Am)	15	30	45	83	124	165
3-Captain Midnight, Magic Morro (Pan-Am)	24	48	72	142	234	325
3-Moon Mullins?	14	28	42	78	112	145

	GD 2.0	VG 4.0	FN 6.0	VF 8.0	VF/NM 9.0	NM- 9.2

4-Red Ryder, Magic Morro (Pan-Am). Same content as Red Ryder Victory
  Patrol comic w/diff. cover — 15 30 45 88 137 185
4-Smitty, Stratosphere Jim (Pan-Am) — 14 28 42 78 112 145
5-Don Winslow, Magic Morro (Gilmore) — 15 30 45 88 137 185
5-Don Winslow, Stratosphere Jim (Pan-Am) — 15 30 45 88 137 185
5-Terry & the Pirates — 17 34 51 103 162 220
6-Don Winslow, Stratosphere Jim (Pan-Am)-McWilliams-a
   — 15 30 45 88 137 185
6-King of the Royal Mounted, Magic Morro (Pan-Am) 15 30 45 88 137 185
7-Dick Tracy, Magic Morro (Pan-Am) — 20 40 60 115 185 255
7-Little Orphan Annie — 12 24 36 67 94 120
8-Dick Tracy, Stratosphere Jim (Pan-Am) — 17 34 51 100 158 215
8-Dan Dunn, Magic Morro (Pan-Am) — 12 24 36 67 94 120
9-Terry & the Pirates, Magic Morro (Pan-Am) 17 34 51 100 158 215
10-Red Ryder, Magic Morro (Pan-Am) — 15 30 45 86 133 180

SUPER-BOOK OF COMICS
Western Publishing Co.: (Omar Bread & Hancock Oil Co. giveaways) 1944 - No. 30, 1947 (Omar); 1947 - 1948 (Hancock) (16 pgs.)
NOTE: The Hancock issues are all exact reprints of the earlier Omar issues. The issue numbers were removed in some of the reprints.

1-Dick Tracy (Omar, 1944) — 18 36 54 105 165 225
1-Dick Tracy (Hancock, 1947) — 14 28 42 82 121 160
2-Bugs Bunny (Omar, 1944) — 8 16 24 40 50 60
2-Bugs Bunny (Hancock, 1947) — 6 12 18 32 39 46
3-Terry & the Pirates (Omar, 1944) — 11 22 33 60 83 105
3-Terry & the Pirates (Hancock, 1947) — 10 20 30 54 72 90
4-Andy Panda (Omar, 1944) — 8 16 24 40 50 60
4-Andy Panda (Hancock, 1947) — 6 12 18 32 39 46
5-Smokey Stover (Omar, 1945) — 6 12 18 32 39 46
5-Smokey Stover (Hancock, 1947) — 5 10 15 24 30 35
6-Porky Pig (Omar, 1945) — 8 16 24 40 50 60
6-Porky Pig (Hancock, 1947) — 6 12 18 32 39 46
7-Smilin' Jack (Omar, 1945) — 8 16 24 40 50 60
7-Smilin' Jack (Hancock, 1947) — 6 12 18 32 39 46
8-Oswald the Rabbit (Omar, 1945) — 6 12 18 32 39 46
8-Oswald the Rabbit (Hancock, 1947) — 5 10 15 24 30 35
9-Alley Oop (Omar, 1945) — 11 22 33 64 90 115
9-Alley Oop (Hancock, 1947) — 11 22 33 60 83 105
10-Elmer Fudd (Omar, 1945) — 6 12 18 32 39 46
10-Elmer Fudd (Hancock, 1947) — 5 10 15 24 30 35
11-Little Orphan Annie (Omar, 1945) — 8 16 24 42 53 64
11-Little Orphan Annie (Hancock, 1947) — 7 14 21 36 45 54
12-Woody Woodpecker (Omar, 1945) — 6 12 18 32 39 46
12-Woody Woodpecker (Hancock, 1947) — 5 10 15 24 30 35
13-Dick Tracy (Omar, 1945) — 11 22 33 64 90 115
13-Dick Tracy (Hancock, 1947) — 11 22 33 60 83 105
14-Bugs Bunny (Omar, 1945) — 6 12 18 32 39 46
14-Bugs Bunny (Hancock, 1947) — 5 10 15 24 30 35
15-Andy Panda (Omar, 1945) — 6 12 18 28 34 40
15-Andy Panda (Hancock, 1947) — 5 10 15 24 30 35
16-Terry & the Pirates (Omar, 1945) — 11 22 33 60 83 105
16-Terry & the Pirates (Hancock, 1947) — 9 18 27 47 61 75
17-Smokey Stover (Omar, 1946) — 6 12 18 32 39 46
17-Smokey Stover (Hancock, 1948?) — 5 10 15 24 30 35
18-Porky Pig (Omar, 1946) — 6 12 18 28 34 40
18-Porky Pig (Hancock, 1948?) — 5 10 15 24 30 35
19-Smilin' Jack (Omar, 1946) — 6 12 18 32 39 46
nn-Smilin' Jack (Hancock, 1948) — 5 10 15 24 30 35
20-Oswald the Rabbit (Omar, 1946) — 6 12 18 28 34 40
nn-Oswald the Rabbit (Hancock, 1948) — 5 10 15 24 30 35
21-Gasoline Alley (Omar, 1946) — 8 16 24 42 53 64
nn-Gasoline Alley (Hancock, 1948) — 7 14 21 36 45 54
22-Elmer Fudd (Omar, 1946) — 6 12 18 28 34 40
nn-Elmer Fudd (Hancock, 1948) — 5 10 15 24 30 35
23-Little Orphan Annie (Omar, 1946) — 8 16 24 40 50 60
nn-Little Orphan Annie (Hancock, 1948) — 6 12 18 32 39 46
24-Woody Woodpecker (Omar, 1946) — 6 12 18 28 34 40
nn-Woody Woodpecker (Hancock, 1948) — 5 10 15 24 30 35
25-Dick Tracy (Omar, 1946) — 11 22 33 60 83 105
nn-Dick Tracy (Hancock, 1948) — 9 18 27 50 65 80
26-Bugs Bunny (Omar, 1946)) — 6 12 18 28 34 40
nn-Bugs Bunny (Hancock, 1948) — 5 10 15 24 30 35
27-Andy Panda (Omar, 1946) — 6 12 18 28 34 40
27-Andy Panda (Hancock, 1948) — 5 10 15 24 30 35
28-Terry & the Pirates (Omar, 1946) — 11 22 33 60 83 105
28-Terry & the Pirates (Hancock, 1948) — 9 18 27 47 61 75
29-Smokey Stover (Omar, 1947) — 6 12 18 28 34 40
29-Smokey Stover (Hancock, 1948) — 5 10 15 24 30 35
30-Porky Pig (Omar, 1947) — 6 12 18 28 34 40
30-Porky Pig (Hancock, 1948) — 5 10 15 24 30 35
nn-Bugs Bunny (Hancock, 1948)-Does not match any Omar book
   — 6 12 18 28 34 40

SUPER CIRCUS (TV)
Cross Publishing Co.
1-(1951, Weather Bird Shoes giveaway) — 10 20 30 54 72 90

SUPER FRIENDS
DC Comics: 1981 (Giveaway, no ads, no code or price)
...Special 1 -r/Super Friends #19 & 36 — 3 6 9 14 20 25

SUPERGEAR COMICS
Jacobs Corp.: 1976 (Giveaway, 4 pgs. in color, slick paper)
nn-(Rare)-Superman, Lois Lane; Steve Lombard app. (500 copies printed, over half destroyed?)
   — 21 42 63 147 324 500

SUPERGIRL
DC Comics: 1984, 1986 (Giveaway, Baxter paper)

nn-(American Honda/U.S. Dept. Transportation) Torres-c/a
   — 2 4 6 10 14 18

SUPER HEROES PUZZLES AND GAMES
General Mills Giveaway (Marvel Comics Group): 1979 (32 pgs., regular size)
nn-Four 2-pg. origin stories of Spider-Man, Captain America, The Hulk, & Spider-Woman
   — 3 6 9 15 22 28

SUPERMAN
National Periodical Publ./DC Comics
72-Giveaway(9-10/51)-(Rare)-Price blackened out; came with banner wrapped around book;
  without banner — 90 180 270 576 988 1400
72-Giveaway with banner — 135 270 405 864 1482 2100
Bradman birthday custom (1988)(extremely limited distribution) - a CGC 9.6 copy sold for
  $2600, a NM copy sold for $1125, and a FN/VF copy sold for $800 in 2011-2012, plus
  a CGC 9.0 sold for $421 in 12/12 and a CGC 9.6 copy sold for $1314 in 8/15
... For the Animals (2000, Doris Day Animal Foundation, 36 pgs.) polybagged with Gotham
  Adventures #22, Hourman #12, Impulse #58, Looney Tunes #62, Stars and S.T.R.I.P.E.
  #8 and Superman Adventures #41 — 4.00
Kelloggs Giveaway-(2/3 normal size, 1954)-r-two stories/Superman #55
   — 36 72 108 211 343 475
Kenner: Man of Steel (Doomsday is Coming) (1995, 16 pgs.) packaged with set
  of Superman and Doomsday action figures — 5.00
...Meets the Quik Bunny (1987, Nestles Quik premium, 36 pgs.)
   — 1 2 3 5 7 9
Pizza Hut Premiums (12/77)-Exact reprints of 1950s comics except for paid ads
  (set of 6 exist?); Vol. 1-r/#97 (#113-r also known) 2 4 6 9 12 15
Radio Shack Giveaway-36 pgs. (7/80) "The Computers That Saved Metropolis", Starlin/
  Giordano-a; advertising insert in Action #509, New Advs. of Superboy #7, Legion of
  Super-Heroes #265, & House of Mystery #282. (All comics were 68 pgs.) Cover of inserts
  printed on newsprint. Giveaway contains 4 extra pgs. of Radio Shack advertising that
  inserts do not have — 1 2 3 5 7 9
Radio Shack Giveaway-(7/81) "Victory by Computer" 1 2 3 5 7 9
Radio Shack Giveaway-(7/82) "Computer Masters of Metropolis"
   — 1 2 3 5 7 9

SUPERMAN ADVENTURES, THE (TV)
DC Comics: 1996 (Based on animated series)
1-(1996) Preview issue distributed at Warner Bros. stores
   — 1 2 3 5 6 8
Titus Game Edition (1998) — 4.00

SUPERMAN AND THE GREAT CLEVELAND FIRE
National Periodical Publ.: 1948 (Giveaway, 4 pgs., no cover) (Hospital Fund)
nn-In full color — 97 194 291 621 1061 1500

SUPERMAN AT THE GILBERT HALL OF SCIENCE
National Periodical Publ.: 1948 (Giveaway) (Gilbert Chemistry Sets / A.C. Gilbert Co.)
nn-(8 1/2" x 5 1/2") — 41 82 123 256 428 600

SUPERMAN (Miniature)
National Periodical Publ.: 1942; 1955 - 1956 (3 issues, no #'s, 32 pgs.)
The pages are numbered in the 1st issue: 1-32; 2nd: 1A-32A, and 3rd: 1B-32B
No date-Py-Co-Pay Tooth Powder giveaway (8 pgs.) circa 1942)(The Adventures of...)
  Japanese air battle — 40 80 120 246 411 575
1-The Superman Time Capsule (Kellogg's Sugar Smacks)(1955)
   — 22 44 66 132 216 300
1A-Duel in Space (1955) — 21 42 63 124 202 280
1B-The Super Show of Metropolis (also #1-32, no B)(1955)
   — 21 42 63 124 202 280
NOTE: Numbering variations exist. Each title could have any combination-#1, 1A, or 1B.

SUPERMAN RECORD COMIC
National Periodical Publications: 1966 (Golden Records)
(With record)-Record reads origin of Superman from comic; came with iron-on patch, decoder,
  membership card & button; comic-r/Superman #125,146
   — 12 24 36 82 179 275
Comic only — 6 12 18 38 69 100

SUPERMAN'S BUDDY (Costume Comic)
National Periodical Publs.: 1954 (4 pgs., slick paper-c; one-shot) (Came in box w/costume)
1-With box & costume — 142 284 426 909 1555 2200
  Comic only — 60 120 180 381 653 925
1-(1958 edition)-Printed in 2 colors — 18 36 54 109 172 235

SUPERMAN'S CHRISTMAS ADVENTURE
National Periodical Publications: 1940, 1944 (Giveaway, 16 pgs.) Distributed by Nehi drinks,
Bailey Store, Ivey-Keith Co., Kennedy's Boys Shop, Macy's Store, Boston Store
1(1940)-Burnley-a; F. Ray-c/r from Superman #6 (Scarce)-Superman saves Santa Claus.
  Santa makes real Superman Toys offered in 1940. 1st merchandising story; versions with
  Royal Crown Cola ad on front-c & Boston Store ad on front-c; cover art on each has the
  same layout but different art — 595 1190 1785 4350 7675 11,000
nn(1944) w/Santa Claus & X-mas tree-c — 129 258 387 826 1413 2000
nn(1944) w/Candy cane & Superman-c — 129 258 387 826 1413 2000
nn(1944) w/1940-c (Santa over chimney); Superman image (from Superman #6) on back-c
   — 129 258 387 826 1413 2000

SUPERMAN-TIM (Becomes Tim)
Superman-Tim Stores/National Periodical Publ.: Aug, 1942 - May, 1950 (Half size)
(B&W Giveaway w/2 color covers) (Publ. monthly 2/43 on)(All have Superman illos)
8/42 (#1)- 2 pg. Superman story — 161 322 483 1030 1765 2500
9/42 (#2) Superman/Uncle Sam flag-c — 63 126 189 403 689 975
12/42-Christmas-c — 52 104 156 328 552 775
1/43 — 50 100 150 315 533 750
2/43, 3/43-Classic flag-c — 47 94 141 296 498 700
4/43, 5/43, 6/43, 8/43 — 40 80 120 246 411 575
7/43-Classic Superman bomb-c — 45 90 135 284 480 675
9/43, 10/43, 11/43, 12/43 — 33 66 99 194 317 440
1/44-12/44 — 27 54 81 162 266 370
1/45-5/45, 8/45, 10-12/45 (X-mas-c), 1/46-8/46 25 50 75 150 245 340

Super-Book of Comics #13 © KFS

Swordquest #2 © DC

Time of Decision © HARV

	GD 2.0	VG 4.0	FN 6.0	VF 8.0	VF/NM 9.0	NM- 9.2
6/45-Classic Superman-c	27	54	81	158	259	360
7/45-Classic Superman flag-c	27	54	81	162	266	370
9/45-1st stamp album issue	52	104	156	328	552	775
9/46-2nd stamp album issue	45	90	135	284	480	675
10/46-1st Superman story	34	68	102	199	325	450
11/46, 12/46, 1/47-8/47 issues-Superman story in each; 2/47-Infinity-c. All 36 pgs.	32	64	96	188	307	425
9/47-Stamp album issue & Superman story	42	84	126	265	445	625
10/47, 11/47, 12/47-Superman stories (24 pgs.)	31	62	93	182	296	410
1/48-7/48,10/48, 11/48, 12/48, 2/49, 4/49-11/49	25	50	75	150	245	340
8/48-Contains full page ad for Superman-Tim watch giveaway	25	50	75	150	245	340
9/48-Stamp album issue	34	68	102	199	325	450
1/49-Full page Superman bank cut-out	25	50	75	150	245	340
3/49-Full page Superman boxing game cut-out	25	50	75	150	245	340
12/49-3/50, 5/50-Superman stories	27	54	81	160	263	365
4/50-Superman story, baseball stories; photo-c without giveaway	33	66	99	194	317	440

NOTE: All issues have Superman illustrations throughout. The page count varies depending on whether a Superman-Tim comic story is inserted. If it is, the page count is either 36 or 24 pages. Otherwise all issues are 16 pages. Each issue has a special place for inserting a full color Superman stamp. The stamp album issues had spaces for the stamps given away the past year. The books were mailed as a subscription premium. The stamps were given away free only when you made a purchase) only when you physically came into the store.

SUPER SEAMAN SLOPPY
Allied Pristine Union Council, Buffalo, NY: 1940s, 8pg., reg. size (Soft-c)

	GD	VG	FN	VF	VF/NM	NM-
nn	37	74	111	222	361	500

SURVEY
Marvel Comics Group: 1948 (Readership survey for advertisers, reg. size)

nn-Harvey Kurtzman-c/a	119	238	357	762	1306	1850

SWAMP FOX, THE
Walt Disney Productions: 1960 (14 pgs, small size) (Canada Dry Premiums)
Titles: (A)-Tory Masquerade, (B)-Turnabout Tactics, (C)-Rindau Rampage; each came in paper sleeve, books 1,2 & 3;

Set with sleeves	5	10	15	33	57	80
Comic only	3	6	9	14	20	25

SWORDQUEST
DC Comics/Atari Pub.: 1982, 52pg., 5"x7" (Giveaway with video games)
1,2-Roy Thomas & Gerry Conway-s; George Pérez & Dick Giordano-c/a in all

	2	4	6	10	14	18
3-Low print	3	6	9	15	22	28

SYNDICATE FEATURES (Sci/fi)
Harry A. Chesler Syndicate: V1#3, 11/15/37; V1#5, 12/15/37 (Tabloid size, 3 colors, 4 pgs.) (Editors premium) (Came folded)

V1#3,5-Dan Hastings daily strips-Guardiner-a	174	348	522	1114	1907	2700

TAKING A CHANCE
American Cancer Society: no date (late 1970s) (giveaway)

nn-Anti-smoking	3	6	9	15	22	28

TASTEE-FREEZ COMICS (Also see Harvey Hits and Richie Rich)
Harvey Comics: 1957 (10¢, 36 pgs.)(6 different issues given away)

1-Little Dot on cover; Richie Rich "Ride 'Em Cowboy" story published one year prior to being printed in Harvey Hits #9.	8	16	24	54	102	150
2,4,5: 2-Rags Rabbit. 4-Sad Sack. 5-Mazie	2	4	6	8	10	12
3-Casper	2	4	6	11	16	20
6-Dick Tracy	2	4	6	11	16	20
nn-Brings You Space Facts and Fun Book	1	2	3	5	6	8

TAYLOR'S CHRISTMAS TABLOID
Dept. Store Giveaway: Mid 1930s, Cleveland, Ohio (Tabloid size; in color)
nn-(Very Rare)-Among the earliest pro work of Siegel & Shuster; one full color page called "The Battle in the Stratosphere", with a pre-Superman look; Shuster art throughout.
(Only 1 known copy)

TAZ'S 40TH BIRTHDAY BLOWOUT
DC Comics: 1994 (K-Mart giveaway, 16 pgs.)
nn-Six pg. story, games and puzzles ... 5.00

TEE AND VEE CROSLEY IN TELEVISION LAND COMICS (Also see Crosley's House of Fun)
Crosley Division, Avco Mfg. Corp.: 1951 (52 pgs.; 8x11"; paper cover; in color) (Giveaway)

Many stories, puzzles, cut-outs, games, etc.	9	18	27	47	61	75

TEEN-AGE BOOBY TRAP
Commercial Comics: 1970 (Small size)

nn	3	6	9	17	26	35

TENNESSEE JED (Radio)
Fox Syndicate? (Wm. C. Popper & Co.): nd (1945) (16 pgs.; paper-c; reg. size; giveaway)

nn	24	48	72	142	234	325

TENNIS (...For Speed, Stamina, Strength; Skill)
Tennis Educational Foundation: 1956 (16 pgs.; soft cover; 10¢)

	GD 2.0	VG 4.0	FN 6.0	VF 8.0	VF/NM 9.0	NM- 9.2
Book 1-Endorsed by Gene Tunney, Ralph Kiner, etc. showing how tennis has helped them	6	12	18	31	38	45

TERRY AND THE PIRATES
Dell Publishing Co.: 1939 - 1953 (By Milton Caniff)

Buster Brown Shoes giveaway(1938)-32 pgs.; in color	22	44	66	130	213	295
Canada Dry Premiums-Books #1-3(1953, 36 pgs.; 2x5")-Harvey; #1-Hot Shot Charlie Flies Again; 2-In Forced Landing; 3-Dragon Lady in Distress)	15	30	45	84	127	170
Gambles Giveaway (1938, 16 pgs.)	11	22	33	60	83	105
Gillmore Giveaway (1938, 24 pgs.)	11	22	33	60	83	105
Popped Wheat Giveaway(1938)-Strip reprints in full color; Caniff-a	4	7	10	14	17	20
Shoe Store giveaway (Weatherbird & Poll-Parrot)(1938, 16 pgs., soft-c)(2-diff.)	11	22	33	62	86	110
Sparked Wheat Giveaway(1942, 16 pgs.)-In color	11	22	33	62	86	110

TERRY AND THE PIRATES
Libby's Radio Premium: 1941 (16 pgs.; reg. size)(shipped folded in the mail)

"Adventure of the Ruby of Genghis Khan" - Each pg. is a puzzle that must be completed to read the story	430	860	1290	2800	-	-

THAT THE WORLD MAY BELIEVE
Catechetical Guild Giveaway: No date (16 pgs.) (Graymoor Friars distr.)

nn	5	10	15	22	26	30

THREAT TO FREEDOM
1965 (Small size)

nn - Anti-communism pamphlet; hammer & sickle-c	10	20	30	68	144	220

3-D COLOR CLASSICS (Wendy's Kid's Club)
Wendy's Int'l Inc.: 1995 (5 1/2" x 8", comes with 3-D glasses)

The Elephant's Child, Gulliver's Travels, Peter Pan, The Time Machine, 20,000 Leagues Under the Sea: Neal Adams-a in all each....	1	2	3	5	6	8

350 YEARS OF AMERICAN DAIRY FOODS
American Dairy Assoc.: 1957 (5x7", 16 pgs.)

nn-History of milk	4	8	12	18	22	25

THUMPER (Disney)
Grosset & Dunlap: 1942 (50¢, 32pgs., hardcover book, 7"x8-1/2" w/dust jacket)

nn-Given away (along with a copy of Bambi) for a $2.00, 2-year subscription to WDC&S in 1942. (Xmas offer). Book only	20	40	60	114	182	250
Dust jacket only	12	24	36	67	94	120

TILLY AND TED-TINKERTOTLAND
W. T. Grant Co.: 1945 (Giveaway, 20 pgs.)

nn-Christmas comic	12	24	36	67	94	120

TIM (Formerly Superman-Tim; becomes Gene Autry-Tim)
Tim Stores: June, 1950 - Oct, 1950 (B&W, half-size)

4 issues: 6/50, 9/50, 10/50 known	19	38	57	111	176	240

TIM AND SALLY'S ADVENTURES AT MARINELAND
Marineland Restaurant & Bar, Marineland, CA: 1957 (5x7", 16 pgs., soft-c)

nn-copyright Oceanarium, Inc.	2	4	6	11	16	20

TIME OF DECISION
Harvey Publications Inc.: Early 1950s (16 pgs., paper cover)

nn-ROTC recruitment		12	18	31	38	45

TIM IN SPACE (Formerly Gene Autry Tim; becomes Tim Tomorrow)
Tim Stores: 1950 (1/2 size giveaway) (B&W)

nn	15	30	45	90	140	190

TIM TOMORROW (Formerly Tim In Space)
Tim Stores: 8/51, 9/51, 10/51, Christmas, 1951 (5x7-3/4")

nn-Prof. Fumble & Captain Kit Comet in all	15	30	45	85	133	180

TIM TYLER'S LUCK
Standard Comics (King Feat. Syndicate): 1950s (Reg. size, slick-c)

nn-Felix the Cat app.	5	10	15	25	31	36

TOM MIX (...Commandos Comics #10-12)
Ralston-Purina Co.: Sept, 1940 - No. 12, Nov, 1942 (36 pgs.); 1983 (one-shot)
Given away for two Ralston box-tops; 1983 came in cereal box

1-Origin (life) Tom Mix; Fred Meagher-a	226	452	678	1448	2473	3500
2	50	100	150	315	533	750
3-9	39	78	117	240	395	550
10-12: 10-Origin Tom Mix Commando Unit; Speed O'Dare begins; Japanese sub-c. 12-Sci/fi-c	33	66	99	194	317	440
1983- "Taking of Grizzly Grebb", Toth-a; 16 pg. miniature	2	4	6	9	12	15

TOM SAWYER COMICS
Giveaway: 1951? (Paper cover)

	GD 2.0	VG 4.0	FN 6.0	VF 8.0	VF/NM 9.0	NM- 9.2

nn-Contains a coverless Hopalong Cassidy from 1951; other combinations known
| | 6 | 12 | 18 | 27 | 33 | 38 |

TOO MUCH, TOO LITTLE
Federal Reserve Bank: 1989 (Reg. size)
| 9-13 | 1 | 3 | 4 | 6 | 8 | 10 |

TOP-NOTCH COMICS
MLJ Magazines/Rex Theater: 1940s (theater giveaway, sepia-c)
1-Black Hood-c; content & covers can vary
| | 65 | 130 | 195 | 415 | 708 | 1000 |

TOWN THAT FORGOT SANTA, THE
W. T. Grant Co.: 1961 (Giveaway, 24 pgs.)
| nn | 3 | 6 | 9 | 16 | 23 | 30 |

TOY LAND FUNNIES (See Funnies On Parade)
Eastern Color Printing Co.: 1934 (32 pgs., Hecht Co. store giveaway)
nn-Reprints Buck Rogers Sunday pages #199-201 from Famous Funnies #5.
A rare variation of Funnies On Parade; same format, similar contents, same cover except
for large Santa placed in center (value will be based on sale)

TOY WORLD FUNNIES (See Funnies On Parade)
Eastern Color Printing Co.: 1933 (36 pgs., slick cover, Golden Eagle and Wanamaker giveaway)
nn-Contains contents from Funnies On Parade/Century Of Comics. A rare variation of
Funnies On Parade; same format, similar contents, same cover except for large Santa
placed in center. A GD/VG 3.0 copy sold for $5258 in May 2016.

TRAPPED
Harvey Publications (Columbia Univ. Press): 1951 (Giveaway, soft-c, 16 pgs)
nn-Drug education comic (30,000 printed?) distributed to schools.; mentioned
in *SOTI*, pgs. 256,350
| | 12 | 24 | 36 | 69 | 97 | 125 |

NOTE: Many copies surfaced in 1979 causing a setback in price; beware of trimmed edges, because many copies have a trimmed edge.

TRIPLE-A BASEBALL HEROES
Marvel Comics: 2007 (Minor league baseball stadium giveaway)
1-Special John Watson painted-c for Memphis, Durham and Buffalo; generic cover with
team logos for each of the other 27 teams; Spider-Man, Iron Man, FF app. 4.00

TRIP TO OUTER SPACE WITH SANTA
Sales Promotions, Inc/Peoria Dry Goods: 1950s (paper-c)
nn-Comics, games & puzzles
| | 6 | 12 | 18 | 33 | 41 | 50 |

TRIP WITH SANTA ON CHRISTMAS EVE, A
Rockford Dry Goods Co.: No date (Early 1950s) (Giveaway, 16 pgs., paper-c)
| nn | 6 | 12 | 18 | 27 | 33 | 38 |

TRUTH BEHIND THE TRIAL OF CARDINAL MINDSZENTY, THE (See Cardinal Mindszenty)

TURNING WHEELS
Studebaker: 1954 (paper-c)
nn-The Studebaker story (A CGC 9.6 sold in 2018 for $1016 & a CGC 9.6 sold in 2019 for $156)

24 PAGES OF COMICS (No title) (Also see Pure Oil Comics, Salerno Carnival of Comics, & Vicks Comics)
Giveaway by various outlets including Sears: Late 1930s
nn-Contains strip reprints-Buck Rogers, Napoleon, Sky Roads, War on Crime
| | 39 | 78 | 117 | 231 | 378 | 525 |

TWO FACES OF COMMUNISM (Also see Double Talk)
Christian Anti-Communism Crusade, Houston, Texas: 1961 (Giveaway, paper-c, 36 pgs.)
| nn | 37 | 74 | 111 | 222 | 361 | 500 |

2001, A SPACE ODYSSEY (Movie)
Marvel Comics Group
Howard Johnson giveaway (1968, 8pp); 6 pg. movie adaptation, 2 pg. games, puzzles;
McWilliams-a
| | 2 | 4 | 6 | 11 | 16 | 20 |

UNCLE SAM'S CHRISTMAS STORY
Promotional Publ. Co.: 1958 (Giveaway)
nn-Reprints 1956 Christmas USA
| | 3 | 6 | 9 | 16 | 23 | 30 |

UNCLE WIGGILY COMICS
Herberger's Clothing Store: 1942 (32 pgs., paper cover)
nn-Comic panels with 6 pages of puzzles
| | 16 | 32 | 48 | 94 | 147 | 200 |

UNKEPT PROMISE
Legion of Truth: 1949 (Giveaway, 24 pgs.)
nn-Anti-alcohol
| | 13 | 26 | 39 | 74 | 105 | 135 |

UNTOLD LEGEND OF THE BATMAN, THE
DC Comics: 1989 (28 pgs., 6X9", limited series of cereal premiums)
| 1-1st & 2nd printings known; Byrne-a | 2 | 4 | 6 | 9 | 13 | 16 |
| 2,3: 1st & 2nd printings known | 1 | 3 | 4 | 6 | 8 | 10 |

UNTOUCHABLES, THE (TV)
Leaf Brands, Inc.
Topps Bubblegum premiums produced by Leaf Brands, Inc.-2-1/2x4-1/2", 8 pgs. (3 diff. issues)
"The Organization, Jamaica Ginger, The Otto Frick Story (drug), 3000 Suspects, The
Antidote, Mexican Stakeout, Little Egypt, Purple Gang, Bugs Moran Story, & Lily Dallas
Story"
| | 3 | 6 | 9 | 18 | 27 | 36 |

VICKS COMICS (See Pure Oil Comics, Salerno Carnival of Comics & 24 Pages of Comics)
Eastern Color Printing Co. (Vicks Chemical Co.): nd (circa 1938) (Giveaway, 68 pgs. in color)
nn-Famous Funnies-r (before #40); contains 5 pgs. Buck Rogers (4 pgs. from F.F. #15, & 1 pg.
from #16) Joe Palooka, Napoleon, etc. app.
| | 74 | 148 | 222 | 470 | 810 | 1150 |

nn-16 loose, untrimmed page giveaway; paper-c; r/Famous Funnies #14; Buck Rogers,
Joe Palooka app. Has either "Vicks Comics" printed on cover or only a local store name
as the logo.
| | 30 | 60 | 90 | 177 | 289 | 400 |

WALT DISNEY'S COMICS & STORIES
K.K. Publications: 1942-1963 known (7-1/3"x10-1/4", 4 pgs. in color, slick paper)
(folded horizontally once or twice as mailers) (Xmas subscription offer)

1942 mailer-r/Kelly cover to WDC&S 25; 2-year subscription + two Grosset & Dunlap
hardcover books (32-pages each), of Bambi and of Thumper, offered for $2.00; came in an
illustrated C&S envelope with an enclosed postage paid envelope
(Rare)
Mailer only	30	60	90	177	289	400
with envelopes	33	66	99	194	317	440
1947,1948 mailer	20	40	60	120	195	270

1949 mailer-A rare Barks item: Same WDC&S cover as 1942 mailer, but with art changed so
that nephew is handing teacher Donald a comic book rather than an apple, as originally
drawn by Kelly. The tiny, 7/8"x1-1/4" cover shown was a rejected cover by Barks that was
intended for C&S 110, but was redrawn by Kelly for C&S 111. The original art has been lost
and this is its only app. (Rare)
| | 42 | 84 | 126 | 265 | 445 | 625 |

1950 mailer-P.1 r/Kelly cover to Dell Xmas Parade 1 (without title); p.2 r/Kelly cover to C&S 101
(w/o title), but with the art altered to show Donald reading C&S 122 (by Kelly); hardcover
book, "Donald Duck in Bringing Up the Boys" given with a $1.00 one-year subscription; P.4
r/full Kelly Xmas cover to C&S 99 (Rare)
| | 20 | 40 | 60 | 114 | 182 | 250 |

| 1952 mailer-P1 r/cover WDC&S #88 | 16 | 32 | 48 | 94 | 147 | 200 |

1953 mailer-P.1 r/cover Dell Xmas Parade 4 (w/o title); insides offer "Donald Duck Full Speed
Ahead," a 28-page, color, 5-5/8"x6-5/8" book, not the Story Hour series; P.4 r/Barks
C&S 148 cover (Rare)
| | 16 | 32 | 48 | 94 | 147 | 200 |

1963 mailer-Pgs. 1,2 & 4 r/GK Xmas art; P.3 r/a 1963 C&S (Scarce)
| | 7 | 14 | 21 | 48 | 89 | 130 |

NOTE: It is essentially a different mailer was printed each Xmas for at least twenty years.

WALT DISNEY'S COMICS & STORIES
Walt Disney Productions: 1943 (36 pgs.) (Dept. store Xmas giveaway)
nn-X-Mas-c with Donald & the Boys; Donald Duck by Jack Hannah; Thumper
by Ken Hultgren
| | 84 | 168 | 252 | 538 | 919 | 1300 |

WARLORD
DC Comics: (Remco Toy giveaway, 2-3/4x4")
| nn | | | | | | 5.00 |

WATCH OUT FOR BIG TALK
General Comics: 1950
nn-Dan Barry-a; about crooked politicians
| | 13 | 26 | 39 | 72 | 101 | 130 |

WEATHER-BIRD (See Comics From..., Dick Tracy, Free Comics to You..., Super Circus & Terry and the Pirates)
International Shoe Co./Western Printing Co.: 1958 - No. 16, July, 1962 (Shoe store giveaway)
| 1 | 4 | 8 | 12 | 25 | 40 | 55 |
| 2-16 | 3 | 6 | 9 | 14 | 19 | 24 |

NOTE: The numbers are located in the lower bottom panel, pg. 1. All feature a character called Weather-Bird.

WEATHER BIRD COMICS (See Comics From Weather Bird)
Weather Bird Shoes: 1955 - 1958 (Giveaway)
nn-Contains a comic bound with new cover. Several combinations possible; contents
determine price (40 - 60 percent of contents).

WEEKLY COMIC MAGAZINE
Fox Publications: May 12, 1940 (16 pgs.) (Others exist w/o super-heroes)
(1st Version)-8 pg. Blue Beetle story, 7 pg. Patty O'Day story; two copies known to exist.
(a VF copy sold in 5/07 for $1553)
(2nd Version)-7 two-pg. adventures of Blue Beetle, Patty O'Day, Yarko, Dr. Fung, Green Mask,
Spark Stevens, & Rex Dexter (two known copies, a FN sold in 2007 for $1912, other is GD)
(3rd version)-Captain Valor (only one known copy, in VG+; it sold in 2005 for $480)
Discovered with business papers, letters and exploitation material promoting *Weekly Comic Magazine* for use by
newspapers in the same manner of *The Spirit* weeklies. Interesting note: these are dated three weeks before the first
Spirit comic. Letters indicate that samples may have been sent to a few newspapers. These sections were actually
15-1/2x22" pages which will fold down to an approximate 8x10" comic booklet. Other various comic sections were
found with the above, but were more like the Sunday comic sections in format.

WE HIT THE JACKPOT
General Comics, Inc./American Affairs: 1947 (Promotional comic)(Paper-c)
| nn | 8 | 16 | 24 | 42 | 54 | 65 |

WHAT DO YOU KNOW ABOUT THIS COMICS SEAL OF APPROVAL?
No publisher listed (DC Comics giveaway): nd (1955) (4 pgs., slick paper-c)
| nn-(Rare) | 300 | 600 | 900 | 2010 | 3505 | 5000 |

WHAT IF THEY CALL ME "CHICKEN"?
Kiwanis International: 1970 (giveaway)
nn-Educational anti-marijuana comic
| | 4 | 8 | 12 | 27 | 44 | 60 |

WHAT'S BEHIND THESE HEADLINES
William C. Popper Co.: 1948 (16 pgs.)
nn-Comic insert "The Plot to Steal the World"
| | 9 | 18 | 27 | 47 | 61 | 75 |

WHAT'S IN IT FOR YOU?
Harvey Publications Inc.: Early 1950s (16 pgs., paper cover)
nn-National Guard recruitment
| | 5 | 10 | 14 | 20 | 24 | 28 |

WHEATIES (Premiums)
Walt Disney Productions: 1950 & 1951 (32 titles, pocket-size, 32 pgs.)
Mailing Envelope (no art on front)(Designates sets A,B,C or D on front)
| | 7 | 14 | 21 | 37 | 46 | 55 |

(Set A-1 to A-8, 1950)
A-1-Mickey Mouse & the Disappearing Island, A-5-Mickey Mouse, Roving Reporter
| each... | 6 | 12 | 18 | 31 | 38 | 45 |

A-2-Grandma Duck, Homespun Detective, A-6-Li'l Bad Wolf, Forest Ranger,
A-7-Goofy, Tightrope Acrobat, A-8-Pluto & the Bogus Money
| each... | 6 | 12 | 18 | 28 | 34 | 40 |

A-3-Donald Duck & the Haunted Jewels, A-4-Donald Duck & the Giant Ape
| each... | 8 | 16 | 24 | 44 | 57 | 70 |

(Set B-1 to B-8, 1950)
B-1-Mickey Mouse & the Pharoah's Curse, B-4-Mickey Mouse & the Mystery
Sea Monster each...
| | 7 | 14 | 21 | 35 | 43 | 50 |

B-2-Pluto, Canine Cowpoke, B-5-Li'l Bad Wolf in the Hollow Tree Hideout,
B-7-Goofy & the Gangsters each...
| | 6 | 12 | 18 | 28 | 34 | 40 |

B-3-Donald Duck & the Buccaneers, B-6-Donald Duck, Trail Blazer, B-8 Donald Duck,
Klondike Kid each...
| | 8 | 16 | 24 | 44 | 57 | 70 |

(Set C-1 to C-8, 1951)

Unkept Promise © LoT

Wolverine #145 Nabisco © MAR

Wonder Book of Rubber © BFG

	GD 2.0	VG 4.0	FN 6.0	VF 8.0	VF/NM 9.0	NM- 9.2

C-1-Donald Duck & the Inca Idol, C-5-Donald Duck in the Lost Lakes,
C-8-Donald Duck Deep-Sea Diver each... 8 16 24 44 57 70
C-2-Mickey Mouse & the Magic Mountain, C-6-Mickey Mouse & the Stagecoach Bandits
each... 7 14 21 35 45 50
C-3-Li'l Bad Wolf, Fire Fighter, C-4-Gus & Jaq Save the Ship, C-7-Goofy, Big Game Hunter
each... 6 12 18 28 34 40
(Set D-1 to D-8, 1951)
D-1-Donald Duck in Indian Country, D-5-Donald Duck, Mighty Mystic
each... 8 16 24 44 57 70
D-2-Mickey Mouse and the Abandoned Mine, D-6-Mickey Mouse & the Medicine Man
each... 7 14 21 35 43 50
D-3-Pluto & the Mysterious Package, D-4-Bre'r Rabbit's Sunken Treasure,
D-7-Li'l Bad Wolf and the Secret of the Woods, D-8-Minnie Mouse, Girl Explorer
each... 6 12 18 28 34 40
NOTE: Some copies lack the Wheaties ad.

WHEEL OF PROGRESS, THE
Assoc. of American Railroads: Oct, 1957 (16 pgs.)
nn-Bill Bunce 6 12 18 29 36 42

WHIZ COMICS (Formerly Flash Comics & Thrill Comics #1)
Fawcett Publications
Wheaties Giveaway(1946, Miniature, 6-1/2x8-1/4", 32 pgs.); all copies were taped at each
corner to a box of Wheaties and are never found in very fine or mint condition;
"Capt. Marvel & the Water Thieves", plus Golden Arrow, Ibis, Crime Smasher stories
83 166 415 - - -

WILD KINGDOM (TV) (Mutual of Omaha's...)
Western Printing Co.: 1965, 1966 (Giveaway, regular size, slick-c, 16 pgs.)
nn-Front & back-c are different on 1966 edition 2 4 6 9 12 15

WISCO/KLARER COMIC BOOK (Miniature)
Marvel Comics/Vital Publ./Fawcett Publ.: 1948 - 1964 (3-1/2x6-3/4", 24 pgs.)
Given away by Wisco "99" Service Stations, Carnation Malted Milk, Klarer Health Wieners, Fleers Dubble Bubble
Gum, Rodeo All-Meat Wieners, Perfect Potato Chips, & others; see ad in Tom Mix #21

Blackstone & the Gold Medal Mystery (1948) 8 16 24 40 50 60
Blackstone "Solves the Sealed Vault Mystery" (1950) 8 16 24 40 50 60
Blaze Carson in "The Sheriff Shoots It Out" (1950) 8 16 24 40 50 60
Captain Marvel & Billy's Big Game (r/Capt. Marvel Adv. #76) 26 52 78 154 252 350
(Prices vary widely on this book)
China Boy in "A Trip to the Zoo" #10 (1948) 4 8 12 18 22 25
Indoors-Outdoors Game Book 4 8 12 18 22 25
Jim Solar Space Sheriff in "Battle for Mars", "Between Two Worlds", "Conquers Outer Space",
"The Creatures on the Comet", "Defeats the Moon Missile Men", "Encounter Creatures on
Comet", "Meet the Jupiter Jumpers", "Meets the Man From Mars", "On Traffic Duty",
"Outlaws of the Spaceways", "Pirates of the Planet X", "Protects Space Lanes", "Raiders
From the Sun", "Ring Around Saturn", "Robots of Rhea", "The Sky Ruby", "Spacetts of
the Sky", "Spidermen of Venus", "Trouble on Mercury"
6 12 18 29 36 42
Johnny Starboard & the Underseas Pirates (1948) 4 8 12 18 22 25
Kid Colt in "He Lived by His Guns" (1950) 8 16 24 40 50 60
Little Aspirin as the "Crook Catcher" #2 (1950) 3 6 9 11 13 15
Little Aspirin in "Naughty But Nice" #6 (1950) 3 6 9 11 13 15
Return of the Black Phantom (not M.E. character)(Roy Dare)(1948)
6 12 18 28 34 40
Secrets of Magic 4 7 9 14 16 18
Slim Morgan "Brings Justice to Mesa City" #3 4 7 9 14 16 18
Super Rabbit(1950)-Cuts Red Tape, Stops Crime Wave!
8 16 24 44 57 70
Tex Farnum, Frontiersman (1948) 4 8 12 18 22 25
Tex Taylor in "Draw or Die, Cowpoke!" (1950) 6 12 18 28 34 40
Tex Taylor in "An Exciting Adventure at the Gold Mine" (1950)
6 12 18 27 33 38
Wacky Quacky in "All-Aboard" 3 5 7 10 12 14
When School Is Out 3 5 7 10 12 14
Willie in a "Comic-Comic Book Fall" #1 4 7 9 14 16 18
Wonder Duck "An Adventure at the Rodeo of the Fearless Quacker!" (1950)
8 16 24 44 57 70
Rare uncut version of three; includes Capt. Marvel, Tex Farnum, Black Phantom
(A VG copy sold in Sept. 2015 for $147)
Rare uncut version of three; includes China Boy, Blackstone, Johnny Starboard
& the Underseas Pirates (A FN/VF copy sold in Sept. 2015 for $137)
Rare uncut version of three; all Jim Solar (A VG copy sold in Sept. 2015 for $79)
Rare uncut version of three; includes Willie in a "Comic-Comic Book Fall", Little Aspirin #2,
Slim Morgan Brings Justice to Mesa City (a VF/FN copy sold for $54 in Nov. 2007)

WIZARD OF OZ
MGM: 1967 (small size)
"Dorothy and Friends Visit Oz", "Dorothy Meets the Wizard", "The Tin Woodsman Saves
Dorothy" each... 3 6 9 14 19 24

WOLVERINE
Marvel Comics

	GD 2.0	VG 4.0	FN 6.0	VF 8.0	VF/NM 9.0	NM- 9.2

145-(1999 Nabisco mail-in offer) Sienkiewicz-c 32 64 96 230 515 800
...Son of Canada (4/01, ed. of 65,000) Spider-Man & The Hulk app.; Lim-a
2 4 6 8 10 12

WOMAN OF THE PROMISE, THE
Catechetical Guild: 1950 (General Distr.) (Paper cover, 32 pgs.)
nn 6 12 18 28 34 40

WONDER BOOK OF RUBBER
B.F. Goodrich: 1947 (Promo giveaway)
nn 5 10 15 24 30 35

WONDERFUL WORLD OF DUCKS (See Golden Picture Story Book)
Colgate Palmolive Co.: 1975
1-Mostly-r 1 3 4 6 8 10

WONDER WOMAN
DC Comics: 1977
Pizza Hut Giveaways (12/77)-Reprints #60,62 3 6 9 14 20 25
... - The Minotaur (1981, General Foods giveaway, 8 pages, 3-1/2 x 6-3/4",
oblong) 3 6 9 14 20 26

WONDER WORKER OF PERU
Catechetical Guild: No date (5x7", 16 pgs., B&W, giveaway)
nn 6 12 18 28 34 40

WOODY WOODPECKER
Dell Publishing Co.
Clover Stamp-Newspaper Boy Contest('56)-9 pg. story-(Giveaway)
8 16 24 40 50 60
In Chevrolet Wonderland(1954-Giveaway)(Western Publ.)-20 pgs., full story line;
Chilly Willy app. 19 38 57 111 176 240
...Meets Scotty MacTape(1953-Scotch Tape giveaway)-16 pgs., full size
18 36 54 105 165 225

WOOLWORTH'S CHRISTMAS STORY BOOK (See Jolly Christmas Book)
Promotional Publ. Co.(Western Printing Co.): 1952 - 1954 (16 pgs., paper-c)
nn: 1952 issue-Marv Levy c/a 9 18 27 47 61 75

WOOLWORTH'S HAPPY TIME CHRISTMAS BOOK
F. W. Woolworth Co. (Western Printing Co.): 1952 (Christmas giveaway)
nn-36 pgs. 8 16 24 44 57 70

WORLD'S FINEST COMICS
National Periodical Publ./DC Comics
Giveaway (c. 1944-45, 8 pgs., in color, paper-c)-Johnny Everyman-r/World's Finest
25 50 75 150 245 340
Giveaway (c. 1949, 8 pgs., in color, paper-c)- "Make Way For Youth" r/World's Finest;
based on film of same name 22 44 66 128 209 290
#176, #179- Best Western reprint edition (1997) 1 2 3 5 6 8

WORLD'S GREATEST SUPER HEROES
DC Comics (Nutra Comics) (Child Vitamins, Inc.): 1977 (Giveaway, 3-3/4x3-3/4", 24 pgs.)
nn-Batman & Robin app.; health tips 3 6 9 14 20 25

WYOMING THE COWBOY STATE
1954 (Giveaway, slick-c)
nn 5 10 15 24 30 35

XMAS FUNNIES
Kinney Shoes: No date (Giveaway, paper cover, 36 pgs.?)
Contains 1933 color strip-r; Mutt & Jeff, etc. 36 72 108 214 347 480

X-MEN THE MOVIE
Marvel Comics/Toys R' Us: 2000
Special Movie Prequel Edition 2 4 6 8 10 12

X2 PRESENTS THE ULTIMATE X-MEN #2
Marvel Comics/New York Post: July, 2003
Reprint distributed inside issue of the New York Post 4.00

YALTA TO KOREA (Also see Korea My Home)
M. Phillip Corp. (Republican National Committee): 1952 (Giveaway, paper-c)
nn-(8 pgs.)-Anti-communist propaganda book 22 44 66 132 216 300

YOGI BEAR (TV)
Dell Publishing Co.
Giveaway ('84, '86)-City of Los Angeles, "Creative First Aid" & "Earthquake Preparedness
for Children" 1 2 3 4 5 7

YOUR TRIP TO NEWSPAPERLAND
Philadelphia Evening Bulletin (Printed by Harvey Press): June, 1955 (14x11-1/2", 12 pgs.)
nn-Joe Palooka takes kids on newspaper tour 6 12 18 31 38 45

YOUR VOTE IS VITAL!
Harvey Publications Inc.: 1952 (5" x 7", 16 pgs., paper cover)
nn-The importance of voting 6 12 18 28 34 40

The American Comic Book: 1500s-1828

For the last few years, we have featured a tremendous article by noted historian and collector Eric C. Caren on the foundations of what we now call "The Pioneer Age" of comics. We look forward to a new article on this significant topic in a future edition of *The Overstreet Comic Book Price Guide*.

In the meantime, should you need it, Caren's article may be found in the 35th through 39th editions.

That said, even with the space constraints in this edition of the *Guide*, we could not possibly exclude reference to these incredible, formative works.

Why are these illustrations and sequences of illustrations important to the comic books of today?

German broadsheet, dated 1569.

Quite frankly, because we can see in them the very building blocks of the comic art form.

The Murder of King Henry III (1589).

The shooting of the Italian Concini (1617).

Over the course of just a few hundred years, we the evolution of narration, word balloons, panel-to-panel progression of story, and so much more. If these stories aren't developed first, how would be every have reached the point that that *The Adventures of Mr. Obadiah Oldbuck* could have come along in 1842?

As the investigation of comic book history has blown away the notion that comic books were a 20 century invention, it hasn't been easy to convince some, even with the clear, linear progression of the artful melding of illustration and words.

"Want to avoid an argument in social discourse? Steer clear of politics and religion. In the latter category, the most controversial subject is human evolution. Collectors can become just as squeamish when you start messing with the evolution of a particular collectible," Eric Caren wrote in his article. "In most cases, the origin of a particular comic character will be universally agreed upon, but try tackling the origin of printed comics and you are asking for trouble."

"The Bubblers Medley" (1720).

"Join, or Die" from the
Pennsylvania Gazette, May 9, 1754.

"Amusement for John Bull…" from
The European Magazine (1783).

But the evidence is there for any who choose to look. Before the original comics of the Golden Age, there were comic strip reprints collected in comic book form. The practice dated back decades earlier, of course, but coalesced into the current form when the realities of the Great Depression spawned the modern incarnation of the comic book and its immediate cousin, the Big Little Book.

Everything that came later, though, did so because the acceptance of the visual language had already been worked out. Before Spider-Man and the Hulk, before Superman and Batman, before the Yellow Kid, Little Nemo, and the Brownies, cartoonists and editorial illustrators were working out how to tell a story or simply convey their ideas in this new artform.

Without this sort of work, without these pioneers, we simply wouldn't be where we are today.

Cartoons satirizing Napoleon
on the front page of the **Connecticut Mirror**,
dated January 7, 1811.

Another Napoleon cartoon,
this time dubbing him
"The Corsican Munchausen,"
from the **London Strand**,
December 4, 1813.

"A Consultation at the Medical Board" from
The Pasquin or General Satirist (1821).

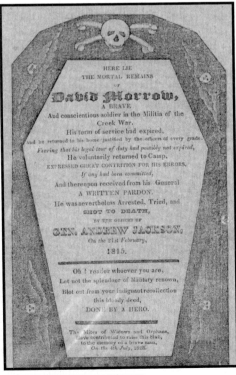

Above left, the front page of **The New Hampshire Journal**, *dated October 20, 1828, with multiple tombstone "panels." To the right is a detail of the bottom right tombstone.*

THE
VICTORIAN AGE

Comic Strips and Books: 1646-1900

By Carrie Wood

Comics were appearing in publications long before caped heroes graced the newsstands around the country. The Victorian and Platinum Ages of comics pre-date the Golden Age arrival of superheroes by decades, though these eras are notable for far more than just the publication dates. We'll delve into the Platinum Age in the following section, and here we'll be focusing on Victorian comics, which began in the 1840s and ran through the end of the century, overlapping with the Platinum Age for a few years.

In terms of subject matter, the commonly-held attitudes and beliefs of 19th century America can be found throughout these cartoons – for better or for worse, by today's standards. And when it comes to the layout of the comics themselves, there's several things worth noting. For instance, word balloons in the Victorian Age were almost never used, and on the rare occasions they were found they were almost completely inconsequential. Typical comics of this time were single-panel illustrations, with narration or dialogue found beneath the panels rather than within the art itself.

There's a wealth of information to discuss about the Victorian Age, and especially with regards to pricing these historical comics, but we found it prudent to hit some of the most important events here before moving into this year's pricing section:

- The Victorian Age began in different countries at different times, depending entirely on when the first sequential comic art was published. Many European countries had a significant head start on the U.S. in this regard.

- America had non-sequential comic art in the years before the Victorian Age began, with woodcut prints occurring as early as the mid-1600s. The 1800s also introduced the States to memorable cartoon artwork, with one of the best-remembered being Benjamin Franklin's "Join or Die" piece, published in 1754; it represented the American Colonies at the time as severed snake parts. These early political cartoons helped introduce an initial baseline for comic art in publications around the country.

- In America, the Victorian Age began proper with the publication of *The Adventures of Mr. Obadiah Oldbuck* in 1842. This story was an unlicensed copy of the original work, *Histoire de M. Vieux Bois*, by Rodolphe Topffer, who had not granted permission of any sort to the periodical that published it (*Brother Jonathan Extra*).

- Topffer was a novelist, artist and teacher from Switzerland who began working on what he referred to

The earliest-known sequential comic book published in America, **The Adventures of Mr. Obadiah Oldbuck**, from September 1842.

The Strange and Wonderful Adventures of Bachelor Butterfly
by Rodolphe Töpffer (New York, 1846), America's 3rd comic book.

as "picture novels" or "graphic literature" by the late 1820s. By the time his work found its way to Paris, they were a significant success. The demand for his work quickly outmatched the supply available, leading to the widespread piracy of his comics; in a world that didn't yet have any sort of international copyright law, this was perfectly legal at the time.

- *Brother Jonathan* began in 1839, with the newspaper being created to exploit a loophole in the postage rates, as magazines were held to a higher postage rate than newspapers. Despite being printed in newspaper format, it didn't contain any news, and instead focused on fictional stories, most of which were pirated from European works. Later that year, the publisher introduced *Brother Jonathan Extra*, a book-sized publication that reprinted novels. The publication of *Obadiah Oldbuck* in this format, which was reformatted from the European original, closely resembled a modern American comic book.

- George Cruikshank was another British cartoonist popular during this era. He was known for his caricature work during his early working years, and he later moved into providing illustrations for books such as *Grimms' Fairy Tales* and for his friend, novelist Charles Dickens. Cruikshank produced numerous cartoons over the course of his career, many of which saw international success.

George Cruikshank's **The Bottle** from 1847, popular enough to be reprinted numerous times into the 20th century.

- Thanks to the success of *Obadiah Oldbuck* in the U.S., it was followed up with printings of Cruikshank's *The Bachelor's Own Book*, which became the second known sequential comic book in the U.S.

- Cruikshank's *The Bottle* debuted in London in 1847 and told the story of a man with alcoholism and how it ruined his family and his life. It was reprinted in a British-American co-publication later that year. Both printings were in a large folio format. This was followed up with a smaller printing the following year, included in the volume *Temperance Tales; Or, Six Nights with the Washing-tonians*. *The Bottle* would see reprintings again and again by numerous publishers well into the 20th century.

- It was during this era that the humor magazine first made its debut, largely in part to the success of published comics in other periodicals. These included *Punch*, a British comic weekly which debuted in 1841. It was a huge success in both England and in the U.S., with thousands of copies being exported to the States with every issue.

- With the success of *Punch*, American businessmen quickly tried to seize upon the market for humorous content, founding the various short-lived publications of *Yankee Doodle, Judy, The John-Donkey* and *The Elephant* – none of which lasted more than a year, though all of which helped the comics market grow.

Journey to the Gold Diggins By Jeremiah Saddlebags, June 1849, so far the earliest known sequential comic book by American creators, J.A. and D.F. Read, shown with a pair of sample pages.

- The earliest-known American-created comic book appeared in 1849: *Journey to the Gold Diggins by Jeremiah Saddlebags*, created by cartoonists James and Donald Read. The brothers had worked for *Yankee Doodle* before creating this work, which told of the California gold rush (a wildly popular subject matter for cartoonists of the era).

- Following the international success of *Punch* were collections that reprinted cartoons from the popular magazine, including *Merry Pictures by the Comic Hands* (1859) and others for decades to come. Newspapers would also reprint cartoons from *Punch*, which later would often be replaced by new original American cartoon work.

- *Harper's Monthly* began publishing comics shortly after it began publication in late 1850. The periodical began by reprinting *Punch* cartoons at the end of every issue, later moving into reprints from the British publication *Town Talk* before hiring Frank Bellew to create original comics.

- Bellew provided a huge number of sequential cartoon work during this era, and his work could be found in nearly every American comic or humor publication for decades. His work included contributions to *The Lantern, New York Picayune, The Comic Monthly, Wild Oats,*

Punchinello, Momus, and plenty more. His work would go on to influence further generations of comic creators.

- Thomas Nast is another artist of note from this era, known more for his political cartoons than for his sequential comic artwork. Nast's work could be found in *Harper's Weekly*, where he worked from 1862-1886. His work helped to popularize the double-page folio-sized cartoon, a size which he practically invented on his own.

- The German humor magazine *Puck* launched first in 1871, founded by Joseph Keppler. An English-language version of the magazine launched the following year, though both were shut down by the end of 1872. Keppler relaunched *Puck* in 1876, this time to much greater success; it featured lithographed cartoons, and in color, and on top of that was being published on an ambitious weekly schedule. By 1880, *Puck* was a massive success, becoming the benchmark by which all other humor magazines were measured against.

- In 1881, *Judge* debuted, seeking to be the rival to *Puck*. This periodical was founded by former *Puck* artist James A. Wales, and it struggled financially for several years up until the point where politicians realized the power of these cartoons to influence the public. This led the Republican party at the time to help finance W.J. Arkell's purchase of the publication in 1886.

- *Life* arrived in 1883, becoming the third pillar of the comic scene during this era. Though it was priced the same as *Puck* and *Judge*, it was smaller in size and printed in black and white – though that didn't stop it from gaining a significant audience. Its earliest artists included Palmer Cox and Charles Dana Gibson. While *Puck* and *Judge* both altered their content as the world entered the 20th century, *Life* stayed almost exactly the same and maintained its audience better for it.

- On top of magazines, numerous almanacs and other publications rose around this time to start publishing comic art. We also started seeing promotional comics enter the scene during this era – you can learn more about those in our Promotional Comics section of this book.

Puck (January 27, 1885 shown) and *Judge* (June 7, 1890 shown) were the top two humor magazine titles of the late 19th century.

The Strange and Wonderful Adventures
of Bachelor Butterfly by Rodolphe Töpffer
1870s © Dick & Fitzgerald, NYC

Barker's "Komic" Picture Souvenir, 3rd Edition
1894 © Barker, Moore & Klein Medicine Co.

FR 1.0 GD 2.0 FN 6.0

COLLECTOR'S NOTE: Most of the books listed in this section were published well over a century before organized comics fandom began archiving and helping to preserve these fragile popular culture artifacts. With some of these comics now over 160 years old, they almost never surface in Fine+ or better shape. Be happy when you simply find a copy.

This year has seen price growth in quite a few comic books in this era. Since this section began growing almost a decade now, comic books from Wilson, Brother Jonathan, Huestis & Cozans, Garrett, Dick & Fitzgerald, Frank Leslie, Street & Smith and others continue to be recognized by the more savvy in this fine hobby as legitimate comic book collectors' items. We had been more concerned with simply establishing what is known to exist. For the most part, that work is now a *fait accompli* in this section compiled, revised, and expanded by Robert Beerbohm with special thanks this year to Terrance Keegan plus acknowledgment to Bill Blackbeard, Chris Brown, Alfredo Castelli, Darrell Coons, Leonardo De Sá, Scott Deschaine, Joe Evans, Ron Friggle, Tom Gordon III, Michel Kempeneers, Andy Konkykru, Don Kurtz, Richard Olson, Robert Quesinberry, Joseph Rainone, Steve Rowe, Randy Scott, John Snyder, Art Spiegelman, Steve Thompson, Richard Samuel West, Doug Wheeler and Richard Wright. Special kudos to long-time collector and scholar Gabriel Laderman.

The prices given for Fair, Good and Fine categories are for strictly graded editions. If you need help grading your item, we refer you to the grading section in this book or contact the authors of this essay. Items marked Scarce, Rare or Very Rare we are still trying to figure out how many copies might still be in existence. We welcome additions and corrections from any interested collectors and scholars at feedback@gemstonepub.com.

For ease ascertaining the contents of each item of this listing and the Platinum index list, we offer the following list of categories found immediately following most of the titles:
E - EUROPEAN ORIGINAL COMICS MATERIAL; Printed in Europe or reprinted in USA
G - GRAPHIC NOVEL (LONGER FORMAT COMIC TELLING A SINGLE STORY)
H - "HOW TO DRAW CARTOONS" BOOKS
I - ILLUSTRATED BOOKS NOTABLE FOR THE ARTIST, BUT NOT A COMIC.
M - MAGAZINE / PERIODICAL COMICS MATERIAL REPRINTS
N - NEWSPAPER COMICS MATERIAL REPRINTS
O - ORIGINAL COMIC MATERIAL NOT REPRINTED FROM ANOTHER SOURCE
P - PROMOTIONAL COMIC, EITHER GIVEN AWAY FOR FREE, OR A PREMIUM GIVEN IN
  CONJUNCTION WITH THE PURCHASE OF A PRODUCT.
S - SINGLE PANEL / NON-SEQUENTIAL CARTOONS

Measurements are in inches. The first dimension given is Height and the second is Width. Some original British editions are included in this section, so as to better explain and differentiate their American counterparts.

ACROBATIC ANIMALS
R.H. Russell: 1899 (9x11-7/8", 72 pgs, B&W, hard-c)

nn (Scarce)	125.00	250.00	750.00

NOTE: *Animal strips by Gustave Verbeck, presented 1 panel per page.*

ALMY'S SANTA CLAUS (P,E)
Edward C. Almy & Co., Providence, R.I.: nd (1880's) (5-3/4x4-5/8", 20 pgs, B&W, paper-c)

nn - (Rare)	23.00	46.00	140.00

NOTE: *Department store Christmas giveaway containing an abbreviated 28-panel reprinting of George Cruikshank's **The Tooth-ache**. Santa Claus cover.*

AMERICAN COMIC ALMANAC, THE (OLD AMERICAN COMIC ALMANAC 1839-1846)
Charles Ellms: 1831-1846 (5x8, 52 pgs, B&W)

1-First American comic almanac ever printed	617.00	1234.00	3700.00
2-16	105.00	210.00	625.00

NOTE:#1 from 1831 is the First American Comic Almanac

AMERICAN PUNCH
American Punch Publishing Co: Jan 1879-March 1881, J.A. Cummings Engraving Co (last 3 issues) (Quarto Monthly)

Most issues	32.00	64.00	190.00

THE AMERICAN WIT
Richardson & Collins, NY: 1867-68 (18-1/2x13. 8 pgs, B&W)

2/3 Frank Bellew single panels	79.00	158.00	475.00

AMERICAN WIT AND HUMOR
Harper & Bros, NY: 1859 (

nn - numerous McLenan sequential comic strips	146.00	292.00	875.00

ATTWOOD'S PICTURES - AN ARTIST'S HISTORY OF THE LAST TEN YEARS OF THE NINETEENTH CENTURY (M,S)
Life Publishing Company, New York: 1900 (11-1/4x9-1/8", 156 pgs, B&W, gilted blue hard-c)

nn - By Attwood	37.00	74.00	220.00

NOTE: *Reprints monthly calendar cartoons which appeared in LIFE, for 1887 through 1899.*

BACHELOR BUTTERFLY, THE VERITABLE HISTORY OF MR. (E,G)
D. Bogue, London: 1845 (5-1/2x10-1/4", 74 pgs, B&W, gilted hardcover)

nn - By Rodolphe Töpffer (Scarce)	533.00	1066.00	3200.00
nn - Hand colored edition (Very Rare)		(no known sales)	

NOTE: *This is the British Edition, translated from the re-engraved by Cham serialization found in L'Illustration - a periodical from Paris publisher Dubochet. Predates the first French collected edition. Third Töpffer comic book published in English. The first story page is numbered Page 3. Page 17 shows Bachelor Butterfly being swallowed by a whale.*

BACHELOR BUTTERFLY, THE STRANGE ADVENTURES OF (E,G)
Wilson & Co., New York: 1846 (5-3/8x10-1/8", 68 pgs, B&W, soft-c)

nn - By Rodolphe Töpffer	567.00	1134.00	3400.00
nn - At least one hand colored copy exists (Very Rare)		(no known sales)	

NOTE: *2nd Töpffer comic book published in the U.S., 3rd earliest known sequential comic book in the USA. Reprinted from the British D. Bogue 1845 edition, itself from the earlier French language Histoire de Mr. Cryptogame. Released the same year as the French Dubochet edition. Two variations known, the earlier*

printing with Page number 17 placed on the inside (left) bottom corner in error, with slightly later printings corrected to place page number 17 on the outside (right) bottom corner of that page. Another first printing indicator is pages 17 and 20 are printed on the wrong side of the page. For both printings: the first story page is numbered 2. Page 17 shows Bachelor Butterfly already in the whale. In most panels with 3 lines of text, the third line is indented further than the second, which is in turn indented further than the first.

BACHELOR BUTTERFLY, THE STRANGE ADVENTURES
Brother Jonathan Press, NY: 1854 (5-1/2x10-5/8", 68 pgs, paper-c, B&W) (Very Rare)

nn - By Rodolphe Töpffer	233.00	466.00	1400.00

BACHELOR BUTTERFLY,THE STRANGE & WONDERFUL ADVENTURES OF
Dick & Fitzgerald, New York: 1870s-1888 (various printings 30 Cent cover price, 68 pgs, B&W, paper cover) (all versions Rare) (E,G)

nn - Black print on blue cover (5-1/2x10-1/2"); string bound	104.00	208.00	625.00
nn - Black print on green cover (5-1/2x10-1/2"); string bound	83.00	166.00	500.00

NOTE: *Reprints the earlier Wilson & Co. edition. Page 2 is the first story page. Page 17 shows Bachelor Butterfly already in the whale. In most panels with 3 lines of text, the second and third lines are equally indented in from the first. Unknown which cover (blue or green) is earlier.*

BACHELOR'S OWN BOOK. BEING THE PROGRESS OF MR. LAMBKIN, (GENT.) IN THE PURSUIT OF PLEASURE AND AMUSEMENT (E,O,G)
(See also PROGRESS OF MR. LAMBKIN)
D. Bogue, London: August 1, 1844 (5x8-1/4", 28 pgs printed one side only, cardboard cover & interior) (all versions Rare)

nn - First printing hand colored	200.00	400.00	1200.00
nn - First printing black & white	183.00	366.00	1100.00

NOTE: *First printing has misspellings in the title. "PURSUIT" is spelled "PERSUIT", and "AMUSEMENT" is spelled "AMUSEMEMT".*

nn - Second printing hand colored	154.00	308.00	925.00
nn - Second printing black & white	150.00	300.00	900.00

NOTE: *Second printing. The misspelling of "PURSUIT" has been corrected, but "AMUSEMEMT" error is still present.*

nn - Third printing hand colored No misspellings	150.00	300.00	900.00
nn - Third printing black & white	150.00	300.00	900.00

NOTE: *By George Cruikshank. This is the British Edition. Issued both in black & white, and professionally hand-colored editions. Hand-colored editions have survived in higher quantities than uncolored. Originally made with thin paper sheets covering the plates.*

BACHELOR'S OWN BOOK, OR, THE PROGRESS OF MR. LAMBKIN, (GENT.), IN THE PURSUIT OF PLEASURE AND AMUSEMENT, AND ALSO IN SEARCH OF HEALTH AND HAPPINESS, THE (E,O,G)
David Bryce & Son: Glasgow: 1884 (one shilling; 7-5/8 x5-7/8", 62 pgs printed one side only, illustrated hardcover, page edges guilt

nn - Reprints the 1844 edition with altered title	25.00	50.00	150.00
nn - soft cover edition exists	12.00	24.00	75.00

BACHELOR'S OWN BOOK. BEIN-G TWENTY-FOUR PASSAGES IN THE LIFE OF MR. LAMBKIN, GENT. (E,G)
Burgess, Stringer & Co., New York on cover; Carey & Hart, Philadelphia on title page: 1845 (31-1/4 cents, 7-1/2x4-5/8", 28 pgs, B&W, paper cover)

nn - By George Cruikshank (Very Rare)		(no known sales)	

NOTE: *This is the second known sequential comic book story published in America. Reprints the earlier British edition. Pages printed on one side only. New cover art by an unknown artist.*

BAD BOY'S FIRST READER (O,S)
G.W. Carleton & Co.: 1881 (5-3/4 x 4-1/8", 44 pgs, B&W, paper cover)

nn - By Frank Bellew (Senior)	45.00	90.00	270.00

NOTE: *Parody of a children's ABC primer, one cartoon illustration plus text per page. Includes one panel of Boss Tweed. Frank Bellew is considered the "Father of the American Sequential Comics."*

BALL OF YARN OR, QUEER, QUIANT & QUIZZICAL STORIES, UNRAVELED WITH NEARLY 200 COMIC ENGRAVINGS OF FREAKS, FOLLIES & FOIBLES OF QUEER FOLKS BY THAT PRINCE OF COMICS, ELTON, THE (M)
Philip. J. Cozans, 116 Nassau St, NY: early 1850s (7-1/4x3-1/2", 76 pgs, yellow-wraps)

nn - sequential comic strips plus singles		(no known sales)	

NOTE: *Mose Keyser-r, Jones, Smith & Robinson Goes To A Ball-r; The Adventures of Mr Goliah Starvemouse-r are all sequential comic strips printed in a number of sources*

BARKER'S ILLUSTRATED ALMANAC (O,P,S)
Barker, Moore & Mein Medicine Co: 1878-1932+ (36 pgs, B&W, color paper-cr)

1878-1879 (Rare)	65.00	130.00	390.00

NOTE: *Not known yet what the cover art is.*

1880 Farmer Plowing Field-c	37.00	74.00	220.00
1881-1883 (Scarce,7-3/4x6-1/8") 4-mast ships & lighthouse-c	27.00	54.00	160.00
1884-1889 (8x6-1/4") Horse & Rider jumping picket fence-c	27.00	54.00	160.00
1890-1897 (8-1/8x6-1/4")	27.00	54.00	160.00
1898-1899 (7-3/8x5-7/8")	27.00	54.00	160.00
1900+: see the Platinum Age Comics section (7x5-7/8")			

NOTE: *Barker's Almanacs were actually issued in November of the year preceding the year which appears on the almanac. For example, the 1878 dated almanac was issued November 1877. They were given away to retailers of Barker's farm animal medicinal products, in turn be given away to customers. Each Barker's Almanac contains 10 full page cartoons. These frequently included racist stereotypes of blacks. Each cartoon contained advertisements for Barker's products. It is unknown whether the cartoons appeared only in the almanacs, or if they also ran as newspaper ads or flyers. Originally issued with a metal hook attached in the upper left hand corner, which could be used to hang the almanac.*

BARKER'S "KOMIC" PICTURE SOUVENIR (P,S)
Barker, Moore & Mein Medicine Co: nd (1892-94) (color cardboard cover, B&W interior) (all unnumbered editions Very Rare)

nn - (1892) (1st edition, 6-7/8x10-1/2, 150 pgs) wraparound cover showing people headed towards Chicago for the 1893 World's Fair	200.00	400.00	1200.00
nn - (1893) (2nd edition, ??? pgs) same cover as 1st edition	167.00	334.00	1000.00

nn - (1894) (3rd edition, 180 pgs, 6-3/4x10-3/8")   167.00   334.00   1000.00
NOTE: New cover art showing crowd of people laughing with a copy of Barker's Almanac. The crowd picture is flanked on both sides by picture of a tall thin person.

nn - (1894) (4th edition, 124 pgs, 6-3/8x9-3/8") same-c as 3rd edition   133.00   266.00   800.00
NOTE: Essentially same-c as 3rd edition, except flanking picture on left edge is now gone. The 2nd through 4th editions state their printing on the first interior page, in the paragraph beneath the picture of the Barker's Building. These have been confirmed as premium comic books, predating the Buster Brown premiums. They reprint advertising cartoons from Barker's Illustrated Almanac. For the 50 page booklets by this same name, numbered as "Part"s, see the PLATINUM AGE SECTION. All "Editions in Parts", without exception, were published after 1900.

BEAU OGLEBY, THE COMICAL ADVENTURES OF (E,G)
Tilt & Bogue: nd (c1843) (5-7/8x9-1/8", 72 pgs, printed one side only, green gilted hard-c, B&W)

nn - By Rodolphe Töpffer (Rare)   333.00   666.00   2000.00
nn - Hand coloured edition (Very Rare)   (no known sales)
NOTE: British Edition; no known American Edition. 2nd Töpffer comic book published in English. Translated from Paris publisher Aubert's unauthorized redrawn 1839 bootleg edition of Töpffer's Histoire de Mr. Jabot. The back most interior page is an advertisement for Obadiah Oldbuck, showing its comic book cover

BEE, THE
Bee Publishing Co: May 16 1898-Aug 2 1898 (Chromolithographic Weekly)

most issues   33.00   66.00   200.00
8 June Yellow Kid Hearst cover issue   142.00   284.00   850.00

BEFORE AND AFTER. A LOCOFOCO CHRISTMAS PRESENT. (O, C)
D.C. Johnston, Boston: 1837 (4-3/4x3", 1 page, hand colored cardboard)

nn - (Very Rare) by David Claypoole Johnston   (sold at auction for $400 in GD)
NOTE: Pull-tab cartoon envelope, parodying the 1836 New York City mayoral election, picturing the candidate of the Locofoco Party smiling "Before the N.York election", then, when the tab is pulled, picturing him with an angry sneer "After the N.York election".

BILLY GOAT AND OTHER COMICALITIES, THE (M)
Charles Scribner's Sons: 1898 (6-3/4x8-1/2", 116 pgs., B&W, Hardcover)

nn - By E. W. Kemble   100.00   200.00   600.00

BLACKBERRIES, THE (N.S) (see Coontown's 400)
R. H. Russell: 1897 (9"x12", 76 pgs, hard-c, every other page in color, every other page in one color sepia tone)

nn - By E. W. Kemble   350.00   700.00   2100.00
NOTE: Tastefully done comics about Black Americana during the USA's Jim Crow days.

BOOK OF BUBBLES, YE (S)
Endicott & Co., New York: March 1864 (6-1/4 x 9-7/8",160 pgs, guilt-illus. hard-c, B&W

nn - By unknown   108.00   216.00   650.00
NOTE: Subtitle: A contribution to the New York Fair in aid of the Sanitary Commission; 68 single-sided pages of B&W cartoons, each with an accompanying limerick. A few are sequential.

BOOK OF DRAWINGS BY FRED RICHARDSON (N.S)
Lakeside Press, Chicago: 1899 (13-5/8x10-1/2", 116 pgs, B&W, hard-c)

nn -   58.00   116.00   350.00
NOTE: Reprinted from the Chicago Daily News. Mostly single panel. Includes one Yellow Kid parody, some Spanish-American War cartoons.

BOTTLE, THE (E,O) (see also THE DRUNKARD'S CHILDREN, and TEA GARDEN TO TEA POT, and TEMPERANCE TALES; OR, SIX NIGHTS WITH THE WASHINGTONIANS)
D. Bogue, London, with others in later editions: nd (1846) (16-1/2x11-1/2", 16 pgs, printed one side only, paper cover)

D. Bogue, London (nd; 1846): first edition:
nn - Black & white (Scarce)   200.00   400.00   1200.00
nn - Hand colored (Rare)   (no known sales)

D. Bogue, London, and Wiley and Putnam, New York (nd; 1847) : second edition, misspells American publisher "Putnam" as "Putman":
nn - Black & white (Scarce)   125.00   250.00   750.00
nn - Hand colored (Rare)   (no known sales)

D. Bogue, London, and Wiley and Putnam, New York (nd; 1847) : third edition has "Putnam" spelled correctly.
nn - Black & white (Scarce)   125.00   250.00   750.00
nn - Hand colored (Rare)   (no known sales)

D. Bogue, London, Wiley and Putnam, New York, and J. Sands, Sydney, New South Wales: (nd; 1847) : fourth edition with no misspellings
nn - Black & white (Scarce)   125.00   250.00   750.00
nn - Hand colored (Rare)   (no known sales)
NOTE: By George Cruikshank. Temperance/anti-alcohol story. All editions are in precisely identical format. The only difference is to be found on the cover, where it lists who published it. Cover is text only - no cover art.

BOTTLE, THE HISTORY OF THE
J.C. Becket, 22 Grea St James St, Montreal, Canada: 1851 (9-1/8x6", B&W)

nn - From Engravings by Cruikshank   129.00   258.00   775.00
NOTE: As published in The Canada Temperance Advocate.

BOTTLE, THE (E)
W. Tweedie, London: nd (1862) (11-1/2x17-1/3", 16 pgs, printed one side only, paper cover)

nn - Black & white; By George Cruikshank (Scarce)   67.00   134.00   400.00
nn - Hand colored (Scarce)   (no known sales)

BOTTLE, THE (E)
Geo. Gebbie, Philadelphia: nd (c.1871) (11-3/8x17-1/8", 42 pgs, tinted interior, hard-c)

nn - By George Cruikshank   67.00   134.00   400.00
NOTE: New cover art (cover not by Cruikshank).

BOTTLE, THE (E)
National Temperance, London: nd (1881) (11-1/2x16-1/2", 16 pgs, printed one side only, paper-c, color)

nn - By George Cruikshank   67.00   134.00   400.00
NOTE: See Platinum Age section for 1900s printings.

BOTTLE, THE (E)
Marques, Pittsburgh, PA: 1884/85 (6x8", 8 plates, full color, illustrated envelope)

nn - art not by Cruickshank; New Art   42.00   84.00   250.00
NOTE: Says Presented by J.M. Gusky, Dealer in Boots and Shoes

BROAD GRINS OF THE LAUGHING PHILOSOPHER
Dick & Fitzgerald,NY: 1870s

nn - (4) panel sequential strip   30.00   60.00   180.00

BROTHER JONATHAN
Wilson & Co/Benj H Day, 48 Beekman, NYC: 1839-???

July 4 1846 - ads for Obadiah & Butterfly   48.00   96.00   290.00
July 4 1856 catalog list - front cover comic strip   71.00   142.00   425.00
Xmas/New Years 1856   55.00   110.00   330.00
average large size issues   22.00   44.00   130.00
NOTE: has full page advert for Fredinand Flipper comic book116

BULL CALF, THE (P,M)
Various: nd (c1890's) (3-7/8x4-1/8", 16 pgs, B&W, paper-c)

nn - By A.B. Frost Creme Oatmeal Toilet Soap   33.00   66.00   200.00
nn - By A.B. Frost Thompson & Taylor Spice Co, Chicago   33.00   66.00   200.00
NOTE: Reprints the popular strip story by Frost, with the art modified to place a sign for Creme Oatmeal Soap within each panel. The back cover advertises the specific merchant who gave this booklet away - multiple variations exist.

BULL CALF AND OTHER TALES, THE (M)
Charles Scribner's Sons: 1892 (120 pgs., 6-3/4x8-7/8", B&W, illus. hard cover)

nn - By Arthur Burdett Frost   50.00   100.00   300.00
NOTE: Blue, grey, tan hard covers known to exist.

BULL CALF, THE STORY OF THE MAN OF HUMANITY AND THE (P,M)
C.H. Fargo & Co.: 1890 (5-1/4x6-1/4", 24 pgs, B&W, color paper-c)

nn - By A.B. Frost   33.00   66.00   200.00
NOTE: Fargo shoe company giveaway; pages alternate between shoe advertisements and the strip story.

BUSHEL OF MERRY THOUGHTS, A (see Mischief Book, The) (E)
Sampson Low Son & Marsten: 1868 (68 pgs, handcolored hardcover, B&W)

nn - (6-1/4 x 9-7/8", 138 pgs) red binding, publisher's name on title page only;
   has hand colored interior by publisher   167.00   334.00   1000.00
nn - (6-1/2 x 10", 134 pgs) green binding, publisher's name on cover & title page;
   has hand colored interior by publisher   167.00   334.00   1000.00
NOTE: Cover plus story title pages designed by Leighton Brothers, based on Busch art. Translated by Harry Rogers (who is credited instead of Busch). This is a British publication, notable as the earliest known English language anthology collection of Wilhelm Busch comic strips. Page 13 of second story missing from all editions (panel dropped). Unknown which of the two editions was published first. A modern reprint, by Dover in 1971.

BUTTON BURSTER, THE (M) (says on cover "ten cents hard cash")
M.J. Ivers & Co., 86 Nassau St., New York: 1873 (11x8-1/8", soft paper, B&W)

By various cartoonists (Very Rare)   110.00   220.00   660.00
NOTE: Reprints from various 1873 issues of Wild Oats; has (5) different sequential comic strips: (3) by Livingston Hopkins, (1) by Thomas Worth, other one creator presently unknown; Bellew, Sr. single panel cartoons.

BUZZ A BUZZ OR THE BEES (E)
Griffith & Farran, London: September 1872 (8-1/2x5-1/2", 168 pgs, printed one side only, orange, black & white hardcover, B&W interior)

nn - By Wilhelm Busch (Scarce)   54.00   108.00   325.00
NOTE: Earliest published by Phillipson & Golder, Chester; text written by English to accompany Busch art.

BUZZ A BUZZ OR THE BEES (E)
Henry Holt & Company, New York: 1873 (9x6", 96 pgs, gilted hardcover, hand colored)

nn - By Wilhelm Busch (Scarce)   54.00   108.00   325.00
NOTE: Completely different translation than the Griffith & Farran version. Also, contains 28 additional illustrations by Park Benjamin. The lower page count is because the Henry Holt edition prints on both sides of each page, and the Griffith & Farran edition prints one side only.

CALENDAR FOR THE MONTH; YE PICTORIAL LYSTE OF YE MATTERS OF INTEREST FOR SUMMER READING (P,M)
S.E. Bridgman & Company, Northampton, Mass: nd (c. late 1880's-1890's) (5-5/8x7-1/4", 64 pgs, paper-c, B&W)

nn - (Very Rare) T.S. Sullivant-c/a   83.00   166.00   500.00
NOTE: Book seller's catalog, with every other page reprinting cartoons and strips (from Life??). Art by: Chips Bellew, Gibson, Howarth, Kemble, Sullivant, Townsend, Woolf.

CARICATURE AND OTHER COMIC ART
Harper & Brothers, NY: 1877 (9-5/16x7-1/8", 360 pgs, B&W, green hard-c)

nn - By James Parton (over 200 illustrations)   54.00   108.00   325.00
NOTE: This is the earliest known serious history of comics & related genre from around the world produced by an American. Parton was a cousin of Thomas Nast's wife Sarah. A large portion of this book was first serialized in Harper's Monthly in 1875.

CARPET BAG, THE
Snow & Wilder, later Wilder & Pickard, Boston: March 21 1851-March 26 1853

Each average issue   17.00   34.00   100.00
Samuel "Mark Twain" Clemmons issues (first app in print)   583.00   1166.00   3500.00
NOTE: Many issues contain cartoons by DC Johnston, Frank Bellew, others; literature includes Artemus Ward's Miss Partington who had a mischevious little Katzenjammer Kids-like brat. Carpet Bag was not considered derogatory pre-Civil War.

CARROT-POMADE (O,G)
James G. Gregory, Publisher, New York: 1864 (9x6-7/8", 36 pgs, B&W)

nn - By Augustus Hoppin   55.00   110.00   330.00
NOTE: The story of a quack remedy for baldness, sequentially told in the format parodying ABC primers. Has protective tissue pages (not part of page count).

CARTOONS BY HOMER C. DAVENPORT (M,N,S)
De Witt Publishing House: 1898 (16-1/8x12", 102 pgs, hard-c, B&W)

nn   80.00   160.00   480.00
NOTE: Reprinted from Harper's Weekly and the New York Journal. Includes cartoons about the Spanish-American War. Title page reads "Davenport's Cartoons".

CARTOONS BY WILL E. CHAPIN (P,N,S)
The Times-Mirror Printing and Binding House, Los Angeles: 1899 (15-1/4x12", 98 pgs, hard-c, B&W)

nn - scarce   79.00   158.00   475.00
NOTE: Premium item for subscribing to the Los-Angeles Times-Mirror newspaper, from which these cartoons were reprinted. Includes cartoons about the Spanish-American War.

CARTOONS OF OUR WAR WITH SPAIN (N,S)
Frederick A. Stokes Company: 1898 (11-1/2x10", 72 pgs, hardcover, B&W)

nn - By Charles Nelan (r-New York Herald)   40.00   80.00   240.00
nn - 2nd printing noted on copy right page   24.00   48.00   145.00

CARTOONS OF THE WAR OF 1898 (E,M,N,S)
Belford, Middlebrook & Co., Chicago: 1898 (7x10-3/8",190 pgs, B&W, hard-c)

nn   37.00   74.00   225.00
NOTE: Reprints single panel editorial cartoons on the Spanish-American War, from American, Spanish, Latino, and European newspapers and magazines, at rate of 2 to 6 cartoons per page. Art by Bart, Berryman, Bowman,

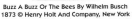

Buzz A Buzz Or The Bees By Wilhelm Busch
1873 © Henry Holt And Company, New York

Centennial Fun (Keppler cover)
July 1876 © Frank Leslie

Comic Monthly v3 #11
April 1862 © J.C.Haney, NY

Bradley, Chapin, Gillam, Nelan, Tenniel, others.

CENTENNIAL FUN (O,S) (Rare)
Frank Leslie, Philadelphia: (July) 1876 (25c, 11x8", 32 pgs, paper cover, B&W)
nn - By Joseph Keppler-c/a;Thomas Worth-a   130.00   260.00   780.00
NOTE: Issued for the 1876 Centennial Exposition in Philadelphia. Exists with black & white, and orange, black & white covers. One copy of the latter had an embossed newsstand label from Partland, Maine, implying that the orange cover version, at least, was distributed and sold outside of Philadelphia.

CHAMPAIGNE
Frank Leslie: June-Dec 1871
1-7 scarce   67.00   134.00   400.00

CHIC
Chic Publishing Co: 1880-81 (Chromolithographic Weekly)
1-38 Frank Leslie, Charles Kendrick, CW Weldon   54.00   108.00   325.00

CHILDREN'S CHRISTMAS BOOK, THE
The New York Sunday World: 1897 (10-1/4x8-3/4", 16 pgs, full color)
Dec 12, 1897 - By George Luks, G.H. Grant, Will Crawford, others) (Rare)
     58.00   116.00   350.00

CHIP'S DOGS (M)
R.H. Russell and Son Publishers: 1895 hardcover, B&W
nn - By Frank P. W. "Chip" Bellew   20.00   40.00   120.00
   Early printing 80 pgs, 8-7/8x11-7/8"; dark green border of hardcover surrounds all four sides of pasted on cover image; pages arranged in error -- see NOTE below.   (more scarce)
nn - By Frank P. W. "Chip" Bellew   10.00   20.00   60.00
   Later printing 72 pgs, 8-7/8x11-3/4";green border only on the binding side (one side) of the cover image.
NOTE: Both are strip reprints from LIFE . The difference in page count is due to more blank pages in the first printing -- all printings have the same comics contents, but with the pages in the first printing arranged differently. This is noticeable particularly in the 2-page strip "Getting a Pointer", which appears on the 2nd & 3rd to last pages of the later printings, but in the early printing the first half of this strip is near the middle of the book, while the last half appears on the 2nd to last story page.

CHIP'S OLD WOOD CUTS (M,S)
R.H. Russell & Son: 1895 (8-7/8x11-3/4", 72 pgs, hardcover, B&W)
nn - By Frank P. W. ("Chip") Bellew   28.00   56.00   170.00
nn - 1897 reprint   13.00   26.00   80.00

CHIP'S UN-NATURAL HISTORY (O,S)
Frederick A. Stokes & Brother: 1888 (7x5-1/4", 64 pgs, hardcover, B&W)
nn - By Frank P. W. ("Chip") Bellew   12.00   24.00   70.00
NOTE: Title page lists publisher as "Successors to White, Stokes & Allen."

CLOWN, OR THE BANQUET OF WIT, THE (E,M,O)
Fisher & Brother, Philadelphia, Baltimore, New York, Boston: nd (c.1851)
(7-3/8x4-1/2", 88 pgs, paper cover, B&W)
nn - (Very Rare; 3 known copies)   483.00   966.00   2900.00
NOTE: Earliest known multi-artist anthology of sequential comics; contains multiple sequential comics, plus numerous single panel cartoons. A mixture of reprinted and original material, involving both European and American artists. "Jones, Smith, and Robinson Goes to a Ball" by Richard Doyle (1st app. of Doyle's "Foreign Tour" in America, reprinted from PUNCH, August 24, 1850); "Moses Keyser The Bowery Bully's Trip to the Californian Gold Mines", by John H. Manning; "The Adventures of Mr. Gulp" (by the Read brothers?); more comics by artists unknown; cartoons by George Cruikshank, Grandville, Blum.

COLD CUTS AND PICKLED EELS' FEET; DONE BROWN BY JOHN BROWN
P.J. Cozans, New York: nd (c1855-60) (B&W)
nn - (Very Rare)   67.00   134.00   400.00
NOTE: Mostly a children's book. But, pages 87 to 110, and 111 to 122, contain narrative sequential stories.

COLLEGE SCENES (O,G)
N. Hayward, Boston: 1850 (5x6-3/4", 72 pgs, printed one side only, B&W lithography)
nn - (Rare) by Nathan Hayward   129.00   258.00   775.00
NOTE: This is the 2nd such production for an American University; the first issued at Yale circa 1845, decent funny art of story about life of a Harvard student from his entrance thru graduation entirely in caricature. Has art on back cover as well.

COLLEGE CUTS Chosen From The Columbia Spectator 1880-81-82 (S)
White & Stokes, NY: 1882 (8x9-5/8", 92 pgs, B&W)
By F. Benedict Herzog, H. McVickar, W. Bard McVickar, others 21.00   42.00   125.00
nn - 2nd edition reprint (1888) (8-1/4x10-3/8)   8.00   16.00   50.00

COMICAL COONS (M)
R.H. Russell: 1898 (8-7/8 x 11-7/8", 68 pgs, hardcover, B&W)
nn - By E. W. Kemble   317.00   634.00   1900.00
NOTE: Black Americana collection of 2-panel stories.

COMICAL ALMANAC
Anton Bicker, Cinncinati, OH: 1885 (9x6, 260 pgs, B&W, illustrated-c)
nn - two (12) page unsigned Busch comic strips   50.00   100.00   300.00

COMIC ALMANAC, THE
John Berger. Baltimore: 1854-? (7-1/2x6-1/4, 36 pgs, B&W)
nn -   50.00   100.00   300.00

COMIC ANNUAL, AMERICAN (O,I)
Richardson, Lord, & Holbrook, Boston: 1831 (6-7/8x4-3/8", 268 pgs, B&W, hard-c)
nn - (Scarce)   125.00   250.00   750.00
NOTE: Mostly text; front & back cover illustrations, 13 full page, and scattered smaller illustrations by David Claypoole Johnston; edited by Henry J. Finn.

COMIC HISTORY OF THE UNITED STATES, (I)
Carleton & Co., NY: 1876 (6-7/8x5-1/8", 336 pgs, hardcover, B&W)

nn - By Livingston Hopkins.   20.00   40.00   120.00
2nd printing: Cassell, Petter, Galpin & Co.: 1880 (6-7/8x5-1/8", 336 pgs, hardcover, B&W)
nn - By Livingston Hopkins.   17.00   34.00   100.00
NOTE: Text with many B&W illustrations; some are multi-panel comics. Not to beconfused with Bill Nye's Comic History Of The U.S. which contains Frederick Opper illustrations.

COMIC MONTHLY, THE
J.C. Haney, N.Y.: March 1859-1880 (16 x 11-1/2", 30 pgs average, B&W)
Certain average issues with sequential comics   43.00   86.00   260.00
11 (Jan 1860) Bellew-c   23.00   46.00   140.00
v2#2 (Apr 1860) Bellew-c   23.00   46.00   140.00
v2#3 (May 1860) Bellew-c   23.00   46.00   140.00
v2#4 (June 1860) Bellew-c   43.00   86.00   260.00
v2#5 (July 1860) Bellew-c; (12) panel Explaining American Politics To An Intelligent Foreigner; (10) panel The Art of Stump Speaking; (15) panel Mr. Dibbs Goes to Pike's Peak and Comes Back Again   92.00   184.00   550.00
v2#7 (Sept 1860) Comic Strip Cover; (24) panel double page spread The Prince of Wales In America   43.00   86.00   260.00
v2#8 (18) panel The Three Young Friends Sillouette Strip 23.00   46.00   140.00
v2#9 (Nov 1860) (9) panel sequential   23.00   46.00   140.00
v2#10 11 not indexed   23.00   46.00   140.00
v2#12 (Jan 1861) (12) panel double page spread   23.00   46.00   140.00

COMIC TOKEN FOR 1836, A COMPANION TO THE COMIC ALMANAC, THE
Charles Ellms, Boston: 1836 (8x5', 48 pgs, B&W)
nn -   43.00   86.00   260.00

COMIC WEEKLY, THE
???, NYC: 1881-???
issues with comic strips (Chips, etc)   46.00   92.00   275.00

COMIC WORLD
???: 1876-1879 (Quarto Monthly)
issues with comic strips   50.00   100.00   300.00

COMICS FROM SCRIBNER'S MAGAZINE (M)
Scribner's: nd (1891) (10 cents, 9-1/2x6-5/8", 24 pgs, paper cover, side stapled, B&W)
nn - (Rare) F.M.Howarth C&A   120.00   240.00   725.00
NOTE: Advertised in SCRIBNER'S MAGAZINE in the June 1891 issue, page 793, as available by mail order for 10 cents. Collects together comics material which ran in the back pages of Scribner's Magazine. Art by Attwood, "Chip" Bellew, Dües, Frost, Gibson, Zim.

COMUS OFFERING CONTAINING HUMOROUS SCRAPS OF DIVERTING COMICALITIES, THE (O, S)
B. Franklin Edmands, 25 Court St, Boston: c1830-31 (8-7/8x10-3/4", 16 pgs, thin brown paper-c, blank on backs,
nn - (William F Straton, Engraver, 15 Water St, Boston)   (no known sales)
NOTE: All hand-colored single panel cartoons format definitely inspired by D.C. Johnston's Scraps with every panel character using well-defined word balloons. Might become a seminal step in the evolution of the American comic book. More research is needed.

CONTRASTS AND CONCEITS FOR CONTEMPLATION BY LUKE LIMNER (O)
Ackerman & Co, 96 Strand, London: c1848 (9-3/4x6-1/4, 48 pgs, B&W)
nn - By John Leighton   46.00   92.00   275.00

COONTOWN'S 400 (M) (see **Blackberries**) (M)
The Life (Magazine) Inc.: 1899 (10-15/16x8-7/8, 68 pgs, cloth light-brown hard-c, B&W
nn - By E.W. Kemble (scarce)   350.00   700.00   2100.00
NOTE: Tastefully drawn depictions of Black Americana over one hundred years ago during Jim Crow days.

CROSSING THE ATLANTIC (O,G)
James R. Osgood & Co., Boston: 1872 (10-7/8x16", 68 pgs, hardcover, B&W);
Houghton, Osgood & Co., Boston: 1880
1st printing - by Augustus Hoppin   33.00   66.00   200.00
2nd printing (1880; 66 pgs; 8-1/8x11-1/8")   25.00   50.00   150.00

C.R. PITT'S COMIC ALMANAC
C.R. Pitt: 1880 (7-1/2x4-5/8", 28 pgs)
nn - contains (8) panel sequential   36.00   72.00   215.00

CRUIKSHANK'S OMNIBUS: A VEHICLE FOR FUN AND FROLIC (E,S)
E. Ferrett & Co., Philadelphia: 1845 (25 cents, 7-1/2" x 4-5/8", 96 pgs, B&W, paper-c)
nn - By George Cruikshank c/a (Very Rare)   142.00   284.00   850.00
NOTE: Mostly prose, with 10 plates of cartoons printed on one-side (about half the plates with multiple cartoons), plus illustrated cover, all by George Cruikshank. First (perhaps only) American printing of Cruikshank's Omnibus, which was published first in Britain. It is only a partial reprinting.

CYCLISTS' DICTIONARY (S)
Morgan & Wright, Chicago: 1894 (5 x3-3/4, 80 pgs, soft-c, B&W
nn - By Unknown   33.00   66.00   200.00

THE DAILY GRAPHIC
The Graphic Company, 39 Park Place, NY: 1873-Sept 23, 1889 (14x20-1/2, 8 pgs, B&W)
Average issues with comic strips   23.00   46.00   140.00
Average issues without comic strips   8.00   16.00   45.00

DAVY CROCKETT'S COMIC ALMANACK
???, Nashville, TN, then elsewhere: 1835-end (32 pages plus wraps) (Published by "the heirs of Col. Crockett")
1   467.00   934.00   2800.00
2-13 15 end   300.00   600.00   1800.00

	FR 1.0	GD 2.0	FN 6.0
	FR 1.0	GD 2.0	FN 6.0

14 contains (17) panel Crocket comic strip bio 1848   583.00   1166.00   3500.00

DAY'S DOINGS (was The Last Sensation) (Becomes New York Illustrated Times)
James Watts, NYC: #1 June 6 1868-early 1876 (11x16, 16 pgs, B&W)

average issue with comic strips	5.00	10.00	30.00
Paul Pry & Alley Sloper character issues	17.00	34.00	100.00
Aug 19 1871 - First Alley Sloper in America??	33.00	66.00	200.00

NOTE: James Watts was a shadow company for Frank Leslie; outright sold to Frank Leslie in 1873. There are a lot of issues with comic strips from 1868 up.

DAY'S SPORT - OR, HUNTING ADVENTURES OF S. WINKS WATTLES, A SHOPKEEPER, THOMAS TITT, A "LEGAL GENT," AND MAJOR NICHOLAS NOGGIN, A JOLLY GOOD FELLOW GENERALLY, A (O)
Brother Jonathan, NY: c1850s (5-7/8x8-1/4, 44 pgs)

nn - By Henry L. Stephens, Philadelphia (Very Rare)   (no known sales)

DEVIL'S COMICAL OLDMANICK WITH COMIC ENGRAVINGS OF THE PRINCIPAL EVENTS OF TEXAS, THE
Turner & Fisher, NY & Philadelphia: 1837 (7-7/8x5", 24 pgs)

nn- many single panel cartoons   100.00   200.00   600.00

DIE VEHME, ILLUSTRIRTES WOCHENBLATT FUR SCHERZ UND ERNEST (M,O)
Heinrich Binder, St. Louis: No.1 Aug 28, 1869 - No.?? Aug 20, 1870 (10 cents, 8 pgs, B&W, paper-c) (see also PUCK)

1-?? (Very Rare) by Joseph Keppler   71.00   142.00   425.00
NOTE: Joseph Keppler's first attempt at a weekly American humor periodical. Entirely in German. The title translates into: "The Star Chamber: An Illustrated Weekly Paper in Fun and Ernest".

DOMESTIC MANNERS OF THE AMERICANS
The Imprint Society, Barre, Mass: 1969 (9-3/4 x 7-1/4", 390 pgs, hard-c in slipcase, B&W)

nn -   12.00   24.00   70.00
NOTE: Reprints the 1832 edition of this book by Mrs. Trollope with an added insert. The 28-page insert is what is of primary interest to us -- it reproduces SCRAPS No. 4 (1833) by D.C. Johnston.

DRUNKARD'S CHILDREN, THE (see also THE BOTTLE) (E,O)
David Bogue, London; John Wiley and G.P. Putnam, New York; J. Sands, Sydney, New South Wales: July 1, 1848 (16x11", 16 pgs, printed on one side only, paper-c)

nn - Black & white edition (Scarce)	217.00	434.00	1300.00
nn - Hand colored edition (Rare)			

NOTE: Sequel story to THE BOTTLE, by George Cruikshank. Temperance/anti-alcohol story. British-American-Australian co-publication. Cover is text only - no cover art.

DRUNKARD'S PROGRESS, OR THE DIRECT ROAD TO POVERTY, WRETCHEDNESS & RUIN, THE
J. W. Barber, New Haven, Conn.: Sept 1826 (single sheet)

nn - By John Warner Barber (Very Rare)   (no known sales)
NOTE: Broadside designed and printed by Barber contains four large wood engravings showing "The Morning Dram" which is "The Beginning of Sorrow"; "The Grog Shop" with its "Bad Company"; "The Confirmed Drunkard" in a state of "Beastly Intoxication"; and the "Concluding Scene" with the family being drive off to the alms house. It is an interesting set of cuts, faintly reminiscent of Hogarth. Many modern reprints exist.

DUEL FOR LOVE, A (O,P)
E.C. DeWitt & Co., Chicago: nd (c1880's) (3-3/8" x 2-5/8", 12 pgs, B&W, paper-c)

nn - Art by F.M. Howarth (Rare)   25.00   50.00   150.00
NOTE: Advertising giveaway for DeWitt's Little Early Risers, featuring an 8-panel strip story, spread out 1 panel per page.

DURHAM WHIFFS (O, P)
Blackwells Durham Tobacco Co: Jan 8 1878 (9x6.5", 8 pgs, color-c, B&W)

v1 #1 w/Trade Card Insert   167.00   334.00   1000.00
NOTE: Sold in 2008 CGC 9.4 $1250

DYNALENE LAFLETS (P)
The Dynalene Company: nd (3 x 3-1/2", 16 pgs, B&W, paper cover)

nn - Dynalene Dyes promo (9) panel comic strip   17.00   34.00   100.00

ELEPHANT, THE
William H Graham, Tribune Building, NYC: Jan 22 1848-Feb 19 1848 (11x8.5", B&W)

1-5 Rare - single panel cartoons   117.00   234.00   700.00

ELTON'S COMIC ALL-MY-NACK (E,O,S)
Elton, Publisher, 18 Division & 98 Nassau St, NY: 1833-1852 (7-1/2x4-1/2", 36pgs, B&W

1-5 99% single panel cartoons	79.00	158.00	475.00
6 (1839)	79.00	158.00	475.00

NOTE: Two different covers & different interiors exist for this title and number

7-15 - 99% single panel cartoons	71.00	142.00	425.00
16 - contains 6 panel "A Tales of a Taylor" 1848-49	117.00	234.00	700.00

17 - contains "Moses Keyser, The Bowery Bully's Trip To the California Gold Mines" 1850
By John H. Manning, early comics creator, told in 15 panels   117.00   234.00   700.00
18-19 presently unknown contents   75.00   150.00   450.00
NOTE: Contains both original American, and pirated European, cartoons. All single panel material, except where noted. Almanacs are published near the end of the year prior to that for which they are printed -- like calendars today. Thus, the 1833 No. 1 issue was really published in the last months of 1832. #17 has Elton's Californian Comic-All-My-Nack on the cover.

ELTON'S COMIC ALMANAC (Publsiher change)
GW Cottrell & Co, Publishers & C Cornhill, Boston, Mass: 1853 (7-7/8x4-5/8,36pgs,B&W
20 - (2) sequential comic strips (9) panel "Jones, Smith and Robinson Goes To A Ball;
(21) panel "The Adventures of Mr. Gulp" Rare   250.00   500.00   1500.00
NOTE: Both strips appear in The Clown, Or The Banquet of Wit

ELTON'S FUNNY ALMANACK (title change to Almanac)
Elton Publisher and Engraver, New York: 1846 (8x6-1/2", 36 pgs)

1   54.00   108.00   325.00

ELTON'S FUNNY ALMANAC (#1 titled Almanack)
Elton & Co, New York: 1847-1853 (8x6-1/4, 36 pgs, B&W)

2 (1847) #3 (1848)   54.00   108.00   325.00
nn 1853 (8-1/8x4-7/8"; (5) panel comic strip "The Adventures of Mr. Goliah Starvemouse"

ELTON'S RIPSNORTER COMIC ALMANAC
Elton, 90 Nassau St, NY: 1850 (8x5, 24 pgs, B&W, paper-c)

nn - scarce   54.00   108.00   325.00

ENGLISH SOCIETY (S)
Harper & Brothers, Publishers, New York: 1897 (9-5/8x12-1/4", 206 pgs, B&W)

nn - by George Du Maurier   20.00   40.00   120.00

ENGLISH SOCIETY AT HOME (S)

James R. Osgood and Company: 1881 (10-7/8x8-5/8, 182 pgs, protective sheets on some pages - not included in pages count, hard-c, B&W)

nn - by George Du Maurier   20.00   40.00   120.00

ESQUIRE BROWN AND HIS MULE, STORY OF
A.C. Meyer, Baltimore, Maryland: 1880s (5x3/7/8", 28 pgs, B&W)

Booklet (9 panel story plus cough remedies catalog)	27.00	54.00	160.00
Fold-Out of Booklet (9 panel version)	27.00	54.00	160.00

"EVENTS OF THE WEEK" REPRINTED FROM THE CHICAGO TRIBUNE
Henry O. Shepard Co, Chicago: 1874 (5-3/8x15-7/8", 110 pg, B&W, hard-c)

First Series, Second Series - By HR Heaton   27.00   54.00   160.00

EVERYBODY'S COMICK ALMANACK
Turner & Fisher, NY & Philadelphia: 1837 (7-7/8x5", 36 pgs, B&W)

nn   42.00   84.00   250.00

EVOLUTION OF A DEMOCRAT - A DARWINIAN TALE, THE (O,G)
Paquet & Co., New York: 1888 (25 cents, 7-7/8x5-1/2", 100 pgs, printed one side only, orange paper cover, B&W) (Very Rare)

nn - Written by Henry Liddell, art by G. Roberty   267.00   534.00   1600.00
NOTE: Political parody about the rise of an Irishman through Tammany Hall. Grover Cleveland appears as linked with Tammany. Ireland becomes the next state in the USA.

FABLES FOR THE TIMES (S, I)
R.H. Russell & Son, New York: 1896 (9-1/8x12-1/8", 52 pgs, yellow hard-c)

nn - By H.W. Phillips and T.S. Sullivant Scarce   54.00   108.00   325.00

FERDINAND FLIPPER, ESQ., THE FORTUNES OF (O,G)
Brother Jonathan, Publisher, NY: nd (1851) (5-3/4 x 9-3/8", 84 pgs, B&W, printed both sides)

nn - By Various (Very Rare)   633.00   1266.00   3800.00
NOTE: Extended title: "...Commencing With A Period of Four Months And Anterior To His Birth Going Thru The Various Stages of His Infancy, Childhood, Verdant Years, Manhood, Middle Life, and Green and Ripe Old Age, And Ending A Short Time Subsequent to His Sudden Decease With His Final Exit, Funeral And Burial." Extremely unique comic book, put together by gathering 145 independent single illustrations and cartoons, by various artists, and stringing them together into a sequential story. The majority of panels are by Grandville. Also included are at least 19 signed Charles Martin, verdant from 1847 issues of Yankee Doodle, 5 panels from D.C. Johnston, plus other panels by F.O.C. Darley, T.H. Matheson, and others. The story also contains several panels of Gold Rush content . Printed by E.A. Alverds. The 1851 date is derived from an advertisement found in the Oct-Dec 1851 issue of the Brother Jonathan newspaper. It ispossible, however, that it actually came out even earlier.

FERDINAND FLIPPER, ESQ., THE FORTUNES OF (G)
Dick & Fitzgerald, New York: nd (1870's to 1888) (30 Cents, 84 pgs, B&W, paper cover)

nn - (Very Rare reprint - several editions possible)   367.00   734.00   2200.00

FINN'S COMIC ALMANAC
Marsh, Capen, & Lyon; Boston: 1835-??? (4.5x7.5, 36 pgs, B&W)

nn   71.00   142.00   425.00

FINN'S COMIC SKETCHBOOK (S)
Peabody & Co., 223 Broadway, NY: 1831 (10-1/2x16", 12 pgs, B&W)

nn - By Henry J. Finn (Very Rare)   (An incomplete copy sold for $1375 in Oct. 2014)
NOTE: Designs on copper plates; etched by J. Harris, NY; should have tissue paper in front of each plate.

50 GREAT CARTOONS (M,P,S)
Ram's Horn Press: 1895 (14x10-3/4, 112 pgs, hard-c)

nn - By Frank Beard   21.00   42.00   125.00
NOTE: Premium in return for a subscription to The Ram's Horn magazine.

FISHER'S COMIC ALMANAC
Ames Fisher and Brother, No 12 North Sixth St, Philadelphia , Charles Small in NYC, Also in Boston: 1841-1873 (4-1/2 x 7-1/4, 36 pgs, B&W)

1-7 (1841-1847)	92.00	184.00	550.00
12 reprints mermaid-c with word balloon (1868)	83.00	166.00	500.00

F*** A*** K*****, OUTLINES ILLUSTRATIVE OF THE JOURNAL OF** (O,S)
D.C. Johnston, Boston: 1835 (9-5/16 x 6", 12 pgs, printed one side only, blue paper cover, B&W interior) (see also SCRAPS)

nn - by David Claypoole Johnston (Scarce)   300.00   600.00   1800.00
NOTE: This is a series of 8 plates parodying passages from the Journal of Fanny (Frances) A. Kemble, a British woman who wrote a highly negative book about American Culture written from the U.S. Though remembered now for her campaign against slavery, she was prejudiced against and resenting American culture, thus inspiring Johnston's satire. Contains 4 protective sheets (not part of page count.)

FLYING DUTCHMAN; OR, THE WRATH OF HERR VONSTOPPELNOZE, THE (E)
Carleton Publishing, New York: 1862 (7-5/8x5-1/4", 84 pgs, printed on one side only, gilted hardcover, B&W)

nn - By Wilhelm Busch (Scarce)   29.00   58.00   175.00
nn - 1975 Scarce 100 copy-r 74 pgs Visual Studies Workshop 3.00   6.00   20.00
NOTE: This is the earliest known English language book publication of a Wilhelm Busch work. The story is plagiarized by American poet John G. Saxe, who is credited with the text, while the uncredited Busch cartoons are described merely as accompanying illustrations.

FLYING LEAVES (E)
E.R. Herrick & Company, New York: nd (c1889/1890's) (8-1/4" x 11-1/2", 76 pgs, B&W interior, orange, b&w hard-c)

nn- (Scarce)   43.00   86.00   260.00
NOTE: Reprints strips and single panel cartoons from 1888 Fliegende Blatter issues, translated into English. Various artists, including Bechstein, Adolf Hengeler, Lothar Meggendorfer, Emil Reinicke.

FOOLS PARADISE WITH THE MANY ADVENTURES THERE AS SEEN IN THE STRANGE SURPRISING PEEP SHOW OF PROFESSOR WOLLEY COBBLE, THE (E)
(see also THE COMICAL PEEP SHOW)
John Camden Hotten, London: Nov 1871 (1 crown, 9-7/8x7-3/8", 172 pgs, printed one side only, gilted green hardcover, hand colored interior)

nn - By Wilhelm Busch (Scarce)   367.00   734.00   2200.00
NOTE: Title on cover is: WALK IN! WALK IN!! JUST ABOUT TO BEGIN!!! the FOOLS PARADISE; below the above title page. Anthology of Wilhelm Busch comics, translated into English.

FOOLS PARADISE WITH THE MANY WONDERFUL SIGHTS AS SEEN IN THE STRANGE SURPRISING PEEP SHOW OF PROFESSOR WOLLEY COBBLE, FURTHER ADVENTURES IN (E)
Chatto & Windus, London: 1873 (10x7-3/8", 128 pgs, printed one side only, brown hardcover, hand colored interior)

nn - By Wilhelm Busch (Rare)   283.00   566.00   1700.00
NOTE: Sequel to the 1871 FOOLS PARADISE, containing a completely different set of Busch stories, translated into English.

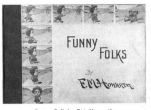

The Daily Graphic #158
Sept. 4, 1873 © The Graphic Company, NY

Durham Whiffs #1
1878 © Blackwells

Funny Folk by F.M. Howarth
1899© E.P. Dutton

FR 1.0 GD 2.0 FN 6.0

FR 1.0 GD 2.0 FN 6.0

FOOLS PARADISE MIRTH AND FUN FOR THE OLD & YOUNG (E)
Griffith & Farran, London: May 1883 (9-3/4x7-5/8", 78 pgs, color cover, color interior)

nn - By Wilhelm Busch (Rare)	92.00	184.00	550.00

NOTE: *Collection of selected stories reprinted from both the 1871 & 1873 FOOLS PARADISE.*

FOOLS PARADISE - MIRTH AND FUN FOR THE OLD & YOUNG (E)
E.P. Dutton and Co., NY: May 1883 (9-3/4x7-5/8", 78 pgs, color cover, color interior)

nn - By Wilhelm Busch (Rare)	83.00	166.00	500.00

NOTE: *Collection of selected stories reprinted from both the 1871 & 1873 FOOLS PARADISE.*

FOREIGN TOUR OF MESSRS. BROWN, JONES, AND ROBINSON, THE (see Messrs....,)

FRANK LESLIE'S BOYS AND GIRLS
Frank Leslie, NYC: Oct 13 1866-#905 Feb 9 1884

average issue with comic strip	13.00	26.00	75.00

FRANK LESLIE'S BUDGET OF FUN
Frank Leslie, Ross & Tousey, 121 Nassau St, NYC: Jan 1859-1878 (newspaper size)

1-5 no comic strips	50.00	100.00	300.00
6 June 1859 (9) panel "The Wonderful Hunting Tour of Mr Borridge After the Deer"	83.00	163.00	500.00
7-9 no comic strips	27.00	54.00	160.00
10 Sept 1859 sequential comic strip	48.00	96.00	290.00
11 (8) panel sequential "Apropos of the Great Eastern"	48.00	96.00	290.00
12-14	27.00	54.00	160.00
15 Feb 1860 (12) panel "The Ballet Girl" strip	48.00	96.00	290.00
16-18	27.00	54.00	160.00
19 June 1860 comic strip front cover	79.00	158.00	475.00

NOTE: *Cover is (11) panel "The Very Latest Fashionable Amusement..."; Back cover comic strip "Mr Jogg's Reasons For Preferring to Board to Keeping House" (7) panels using word balloons. Plus centerfold double page (18) panel spread "The New York May, Moving in General, and Mrs. Grundy's In Particular."*

20 24 25 no comic strips	27.00	54.00	160.00
21 (7/15/60) (8) panel Mr Septimus Verdilater Visits the Baltimore Convention"	48.00	96.00	290.00
22 (8/1/60) (3) panel	27.00	54.00	160.00
23 (8/15/60) (12) panel "Superb Scheme For Perfecting of Dramatic Entertainment"	48.00	96.00	290.00
25 (9/15/60) (9) panel sequential	27.00	54.00	160.00
27 AbrahamLincoln Word Balloon cover	50.00	100.00	300.00
28 Wilhelm Busch sequential strip-r begin	48.00	96.00	290.00
29, 31-51	27.00	54.00	160.00
30 (12/15/60) (3) panel sequential strip	27.00	54.00	160.00
31 (Jan 1861) (12) panel The Boarding School Miss	27.00	54.00	160.00
32 (Feb 1861) (10) panel Telegraphic Horrors; Or, Mr Buchanan Undergoing A Series of Electric Shocks	54.00	108.00	325.00
35 (4/1/61) Abraham Lincoln Word Balloon cover	54.00	108.00	325.00
43 44 no sequential comic strips	27.00	54.00	160.00
45 (Nov 1861) (6) panel sequential; (11) panel The Budget Army and Infantry Tactics; First Bellew here? - Many Bellew full pagers begin	48.00	96.00	290.00
48 (Feb 1862) Bellew-c; (2) panel Bellew strip plus singles	48.00	96.00	290.00
49 (Mar 1862) Bellew-c; (16) panel Wilhelm Busch "The Fly Or The Disturbed Dutchtman A Story without Words"	50.00	100.00	300.00
50 (April 1862) Bellew-c "Succession Bath" plus singles	27.00	54.00	160.00
51 (May 1862) Bellew-c; (25) panel Busch The Toothache (6) panel Definitions of the Day	48.00	96.00	290.00
52 (June 1862) Bellew-c; (9) panel A Cock & A Bull Expedition; (6) panel Bellew The First Campaign of the Home Guard	48.00	96.00	290.00

NOTE: *Johnny Bull & Louis Napolean with Brother Jonathan*

53-67 To Be Indexed in the Future	28.00	56.00	170.00
68 (11/18///63) (6) panel Bellew strip "Cuts On Cowards"	28.00	56.00	170.00

NOTE: *contains (1) panel William Newman 1817-1870, mentor to Thomas Nast*

71 (Feb 1864) Word Balloon Jefferson Davis-c	28.00	56.00	170.00
72 (Mar 1864) Word Balloon-c	28.00	56.00	170.00
73 (April 1864) Word Balloon-c in (6) panels	28.00	56.00	170.00
74 (May 1864) Newman Word Balloon-c	28.00	56.00	170.00
75 77 78 no sequentials	28.00	56.00	170.00
76 (July 1864) Newman Word Balloon-c	28.00	56.00	170.00
79 (Oct 1864) Word Balloon-c	28.00	56.00	170.00
80 (Nov 1864) Robt E Lee & Jeff Davis-c; no sequentials	28.00	56.00	170.00
81 (Dec 1864) Word Balloon "Abyss of War"-c	28.00	56.00	170.00
83 (2/18/65) Back-c (6) panel "Petroleum"	28.00	56.00	170.00
84 (Mar 1865) (6) panel sequential	28.00	56.00	170.00
85 (Apr 1865) Word Balloon-c	28.00	56.00	170.00
86 89 90 92 no sequentials	28.00	56.00	170.00
88 (7/6/65) (6) panel "Marriage"	28.00	56.00	170.00
91 (Oct 1865) (6) panel "Brief Confab At The Corner	28.00	56.00	170.00
93-98 yet to be indexed	28.00	56.00	170.00
99 (June 1866) (18) panel Mr Paul Peters Adventures While Trout-Fishing In The Adirondacks	48.00	96.00	290.00
100 (July 1866) (4) panel sequential comic strip	24.00	48.00	145.00
102 (Sept 1866) (6) panel sequential comic strip	24.00	48.00	145.00
103 (Oct 1866) (9) panel strip; (12) panel;l back cover Adventures of McTiffin At Long Branch	48.00	96.00	290.00
104 (Nov 1866) (4) panel "The Budget Rebuses; (2) panel Glut On Treason Market;back-c; (6) sequential strip	27.00	54.00	160.00
105 (12/18/66) Word Balloon-c; (20) panel sequential back-c	30.00	60.00	180.00

NOTE: *Artists include William Newman (1863-1868), William Henry Shelton, Joseph Keppler (1873-1876),*

James A. Wales (1876-1878), Frederick Burr Opper (1878)

FRANK LESLIE'S LADY'S MAGAZINE
Frank Leslie, NYC: Feb 1863-Dec 1882 (8.5x12", typically 152 pgs)

issues with comic strips	12.00	24.00	70.00

FRANK LESLIE'S PICTORIAL WEEKLY
Frank Leslie, Ross & Tousey, 121 Nassau St, NYC:

average issue (Very Rare)	42.00	84.00	250.00

FRANK TOUSEY'S NEW YORK COMIC MONTHLY
Frank Tousey, NYC: (no known sales)

FREAKS
???, Philadelphia: Jan 8, 1881-April? 1881 (Chromolithographic Weekly)

(Very Rare)	108.00	216.00	650.00

FREELANCE, THE
A.M. Soteldo Jr, Edito, 292 Broadway, NYC: 1874-75 (Folio Weekly)

(Rare)	19.00	38.00	115.00

FREE MASONRY EXPOSED
Winchell & Small, 113 Fulton, NY: 1871 (7-5/8x10-1/2", 36pgs, blue paper-c, B&W)

nn- Thomas Worth Scarce	100.00	200.00	600.00

NOTE: *Scathing satirical look at Free Masons thru many cartoons, their power waning by the 1870s*

FREETHINKERS' PICTORIAL TEXT-BOOK, THE (S,O)
The Truth Seeker Company, New York: 1890, 1896, 1898 (9x12, hard-c, B&W)

1 (1890 edition) - Scarce 382 pgs By Watson Heston	192.00	384.00	1150.00
1 (1896 edition) - Scarce 378 pgs By Watson Heston (1890-r)	104.00	208.00	625.00
2 (1898 edition) - Scarce 408 pgs By Watson Heston	104.00	208.00	625.00

NOTE: *Sought after by collectors of Freethought/Atheism material. There is also 200 copy Modern Reprint.*

FRITZ SPINDLE-SHANKS, THE RAVEN BLACK
Cosack & C o, Buffalo, NY: 1870/80s (4-3/8x2-3/4", color)

(10) card comic strip set by Wilhelm Busch	18.00	36.00	110.00

FUN BY RALL
Unknown: circa 1865 (11x7-7/8", 68 pgs, soft-c, B&W)

nn - By presently unknown (Very Rare)	83.00	166.00	500.00

NOTE: *Wraparound soft cover like modern comic book; yellow paper cover with red & black ink.*

FUN FOR THE FAMILY IN PICTURES
D. Lothrop and Company: 1886 (4 x 7", 48 pgs, Silver & Red stiff-c; interior pages have various single color inks)

nn - By unknown hand	42.00	84.00	250.00

NOTE: *Single panel cartoons and sequential stories.*

FUN FROM LIFE
Frederick A Stokes & Brother, New York: 1889 (9 1/8 by 7 1/8, 72 pages, hard-c)

nn - Mostly by Frank "Chips" Bellew Jr	42.00	84.00	250.00

NOTE: *Contains both single panel and many sequential comics reprints from Life.*

FUNNYEST OF AWL AND THE FUNNIEST SORT OF PHUN,
AT Bellew Or W. Jennings Demorest, 121 Nassau St, NY : 1865-67 (30 issues, 16x11 tabloid 16 pgs B&W Monthly, 1-8 © American News; 9-on © A.T. Bellews)

1 (April 1864) Bellew-c	40.00	80.00	240.00
4 (1865) Bellew-c	38.00	76.00	225.00
5 (1865) Busch (20) panel comic srtip The Toothache	67.00	134.00	400.00
7 (1865) Bellew-c	38.00	76.00	225.00
8 (1865) Special Petroleum oil issue - much cartoon art	83.00	166.00	500.00
9 (July 1865) Bellew Bullfrog-c; centerfold double page spread hanging many Confederates; (6) panel strip hanging Jeff Davis	83.00	166.00	500.00
10 (Aug 1865) Bellew-c (13) panel Busch strip with two ducks, a frog and a butcher who gets the ducks in the end	83.00	166.00	500.00
11 (Sept 1865) Bellew Bull Frog Anti-French-c	38.00	76.00	225.00
13 14 15 (12/65-1/66) Bellew-c no sequential comic strips	38.00	76.00	225.00
16 (March 1866) address change to 39 Park Ave	38.00	76.00	225.00
22 (Sept 1866) 133 Nassau St	38.00	76.00	225.00
34 (Oct 1867) 133 Nassau St (7) panel Baseball comic strip; Last Known Issue - were there more?	83.00	166.00	500.00

NOTE: *Radical Republican politics distributed by Great American News Company; owned by Frank Bellew's wife as a front for her husband. When the Civil War ended, the brutal anti-Confederate comic strips and jokes switched to frogs and began attacking France. Funny thing, history says without France's help in the 1700s, there just might not have been a United States.*

FUNNY ALMANAC
Elton & Co., NY: 1853 (8-1/8x4-7/8, 36 pgs)

nn - sequential comic strip	42.00	84.00	250.00

NOTE: *(5) panel strip "The Adventures of Mr. Goliah Starvemouse"*

FUNNY FELLOWS OWN BOOK, A COMPANION FOR THE LOVERS OF FROLIC AND GLEE, THE (M,N)
Philip. J. Cozans, 116 Nassau ST, NY: 1852 (4-1/2x7-1/2", 196 pgs, burnt orange paper-c)

nn - contains many sequential comic strips (Very Rare)	(no known sales)		

NOTE: *Collected from many different Comic Alamac(k)s including Mose Keyser (Calif Gold Rush); Jones, Smith and Robinson Goes To A Ball; Adventures of Mr. Gulp, Or the Effects of A Dinner Party; The Bowery Bully's Trip To The California Gold Mines plus lots more. This one is a sleeper so far.*

FUNNY FOLK (M)
E. P. Dutton: 1899 (12x16-1/2", 90 pgs,14 strips in color-rest in b&w, hard-c)

nn - By Franklin Morris Howarth	333.00	666.00	2000.00

nn - London: J.M. Dent, 1899 embossed-c; same interior 208.00 416.00 1250.00
NOTE: *Reprints many sequential strips & single panel cartoons from Puck. This is considered by many to be yet another "missing link" between Victorian & Platinum Age comic books. Most comic books 1900-1917 reprinting Sunday newspaper comic strips follow this size format, except using cardboard-c rather than hard-c.*

FUNNY SKETCHES...Also Embracing Comic Illustrations
Frank Harrison, New York: 1881 (6-5/8x5", 68 pgs, B&W, Color-c)
nn - contains (3) sequential comic strips; one strip is (6) pages long;
plus one (3) pages; one more (2) pager 58.00 116.00 350.00

GIBSON BOOK, THE (M,S)
Charles Scribner's Sons & R.H. Russell, New York: 1906 (11-3/8x17-5/8", gilted red hard-c, B&W)
Book I 33.00 66.00 200.00
NOTE: *Reprints in whole the books: Drawings, Pictures of People, London, Sketches and Cartoons, Education of Mr. Pipp, Americans. 414 pgs. 1907 2nd editions exist same value.*
Book II 33.00 66.00 200.00
NOTE: *Reprints in whole the books: A Widow and Her Friends, The Weaker Sex, Everyday People, Our Neighbors. 314 pgs 1907 second edition for both also exists. Same value.*

GIBSON'S PUBLISHED DRAWINGS, MR. (M,S) (see Plat index for later issues post 1900)
R.H. Russell, New York: No.1 1894 - No. 9 1904 (11x17-3/4", hard-c, B&W)
nn (No.1; 1894) Drawings 96 pgs 30.00 60.00 180.00
nn (No.2; 1896) Pictures of People 92 pgs 25.00 50.00 150.00
nn (No.3; 1898) Sketches and Cartoons 94 pgs 25.00 50.00 150.00
nn (No.4; 1899) The Education of Mr. Pipp 88 pgs 25.00 50.00 150.00
nn (No.5; 1900) Americans 25.00 50.00 150.00
NOTE: *By Charles Dana Gibson cartoons, reprinted from magazines, primarily LIFE. The Education of Mr. Pipp tells a story. Series continues how long after 1904? Each of these books originally came in a boxx and are worth more with the box.*

GIRL WHO WOULDN'T MIND GETTING MARRIED, THE (O)
Frederick Warne & Co., London & New York: nd (c1870's) (9-1/2x11-1/2", 28 pgs, printed 1 side, paper-c, B&W)
nn - By Harry Parkes 50.00 100.00 300.00
NOTE: *Published simultaneously with its companion volume, The Man Who Would Like to Marry.*

GOBLIN SNOB, THE (O)
DeWitt & Davenport, New York: nd (c1853-56) (24 x 17 cm, 96 pgs, B&W, color hard-c)
nn - (Rare) by H.L. Stephens 200.00 400.00 1200.00

GOLDEN ARGOSY
Frank A. Munsey, 81 Warren St, NYC: 1880s (10-1/2x12, 16 pgs, B&W)
Issues with full page comic strips by Chips and Bisbee 15.00 30.00 90.00

GOLDEN DAYS, THE
James Elverson, Publisher, NYC: March 6 1880-May 11 1907 weekly, 16 pgs
issues with comic strips 4.00 8.00 25.00
Horatio Alger issues 8.00 16.00 45.00
v10 #49-v11#1 1889 first Stratemeyer story 17.00 34.00 100.00

GOLDEN WEEKLY, THE
Frank Tousey, NYC: #1 Sept 25, 1889 - #145 Aug 18, 1892 (10-3/4x14-1/2, 16 pgs, B&W)
average issue with comic striips 12.00 24.00 70.00

GREAT LOCOFOCO JUGGERNAUT, THE (S)
publisher unknown: Fall/Winter 1837 (7-5/8x3-1/4, handbill single page)
nn - By David Claypoole Johnston (a GD copy sold for $1050 in 2018)
nn- Imprint Society: 1971 (reprint) 4.00 8.00 25.00

HALF A CENTURY OF ENGLISH HISTORY (S. M)
G.P. Putnam's Sons - The Knickerbocker Press, New York and London: 1884 (7-3/4 x 5-3/4", 316 pgs, illustrated hard-c)
nn - By Various 38.00 76.00 225.00
NOTE: *Subtitle: Pictorially Presented in a Series of Cartoons from the Collection of Mr. Punch. Comprising 150 plates by Doyle, Leech, Tenniel, and others, in which are portrayed the political careers of Peel, Palmerston, Russell, Cobden, Bright, Beaconsfield, Derby, Salisbury, Gladstone and other English statesmen.*

HAIL COLUMBIA! HISTORICAL, COMICAL, AND CENTENNIAL (O,S)
The Graphic Co., New York & Walter F. Brown: Providence, RI: 1876 (10x11-3/8", 60 pgs, red gilted hard-c, B&W)
nn - by Walter F. Brown (Scarce) 96.00 192.00 575.00

HANS HUCKEBEIN'S BATCH OF ODD STORIES ODDLY ILLUSTRATEDED
McLoughlin Bros., New York: 1880s (9-3/4x7-3/8, 36?? pg?
nn - By Wilhelm Busch (Rare) 54.00 108.00 325.00

HANS THE SWAPPER, THE STORY OF (O)
L. Pranc & Co., 159 Washington St, Boston: 1865 (33 inch long fold out in colors)
nn - Unique fold out comic book on one long piece of paper 60.00 120.00 360.00

HARPER'S NEW MONTHLY MAGAZINE
Harper & Brothers, Franklin Square, NY: 1850-1870s (6-3/4x10, 140 pgs, paper-c, B&W)
1850s issues with comic strips in back advert section 17.00 34.00 100.00

HEALTH GUYED (I)
Frederick A. Stokes Company: 1890 (5-3/8 x 8-3/8, 56 pgs, hardcover, B&W)
nn - By Frank P.W. ("Chip") Bellew (Junior) 33.00 66.00 200.00
NOTE: *Text & cartoon illustration parody of a health guide.*

HEATHEN CHINEE, THE (O)
Western News Co.: 1870 (5-1/32x7-1/4, B&W, paper)
nn - 10 sheets printed on one side came in envelope 77.00 154.00 460.00

HITS AT POLITICS (M,S)
R.H. Russell, New York: 1899 (15" x 12", 156 pgs, B&W, hard-c)
nn - W.A. Rogers c/a 58.00 116.00 350.00
NOTE: *Collection of W.A. Rogers cartoons, all reprinted from Harper's Weekly. Includes Spanish-American War cartoons.*

HOME CIRCLE, THE
Garrett & Co, NY: 1854-56 (26x19", 4 pgs, B&W)
1 (1/54) beautiful ad of Garrett Building 75.00 150.00 450.00
2/4 (4/66) Cover ad for Yale College Scraps 72.00 144.00 430.00
2/5 (5/55) First ad for Oscas Shanghai 50.00 100.00 300.00
2/6 (6/55) another ad for Oscas Snanghai 50.00 100.00 300.00
2/8 (#20) (8/55) Oscar Shanghai comic book cover repro 183.00 366.00 1100.00
3/1 (#25) (1/56) 183.00 366.00 1100.00

NOTE: *Garrett's 2nd comic book Courtship of Chavalier Slyfox-Wikoff*
3/8 (#32) (8/56) 33.00 66.00 200.00
NOTE: *First print ad for Foreign Tour of Messrs. Brown, Jones, and Robinson*
35 (11/56) first official Garrett, Dick & Fitzgerald issue 33.00 66.00 200.00
37 (1/57) 75.00 150.00 450.00
NOTE: *Front page comic strip repro ad for Messrs. Brown, Jones, and Robinson's Foreign Tour; Back cover full of short sequentials, singles panel*

HOME MADE HAPPY. A ROMANCE FOR MARRIED MEN IN SEVEN CHAPTERS (O,P)
Genuine Durham Smoking Tobacco & The Graphic Co.: nd (c1870's) (5-1/4 tall x 3-3/8" wide folded, unfolded, color cardboard)
nn - With all 8 panels attached (Scarce) 33.00 66.00 200.00
nn - Individual panels/cards 4.00 8.00 25.00
NOTE: *Consists of 8 attached cards, printed on one side, which unfold into a strip story of title card & 7 panels. Scrapbook hobbyists in the 19th Century tended to pull the panels apart to paste into their scrapbooks, making copies with all panels still attached scarce.*

HOME PICTURE BOOK FOR LITTLE CHILDREN (O,P)
Home Insurance Company, New York: July 1887 (8 x 6-1/8", 36 pgs, b&w, color paper-c)
nn (Scarce) 33.00 66.00 200.00
NOTE: *Contains an abbreviated 32-panel reprinting of "The Toothache" by George Cruikshank. Remainder of booklet does not contain comics. Some copies known to exist do not contain The Toothache - buyer beware!*

HOOD'S COMICALITIES. COMICAL PICTURES FROM HIS WORKS (E,S)
Porter & Coates: 1880 (8-1/2x10-3/8", 104 pgs, printed one side, hard-c, B&W)
nn 20.00 40.00 120.00
NOTE: *Reprints 4 cartoon illustrations per page from the British Hood's Comic Annuals, which were poetry books by Thomas Hood.*

HOOKEYBEAK THE RAVEN, AND OTHER TALES (see also JACK HUCKABACK, THE SCAPEGRACE RAVEN) (E)
George Routledge and Sons, London and New York: nd (1878) (7-1/4x5-5/8", 104 pgs, hardcover, B&W)
nn - By Wilhelm Busch (Rare) 92.00 184.00 550.00

HOW ADOLPHUS SLIM-JIM USED JACKSON'S BEST, AND WAS HAPPY. A LENGTHY TALE IN 7 ACTS. (O,P)
Jackson's Best Chewing Tobacco & Donaldson Brothers: nd (c1870's) (5-1/8 tall x 3-3/8" wide folded, 27" wide unfolded, color cardboard)
nn - With all 8 panels attached (Scarce) 40.00 80.00 240.00
nn - Individual panels/cards 5.00 10.00 30.00
NOTE: *Consists of 8 attached cards, printed on one side, which unfold into a strip story of title card & 7 panels. Scrapbook hobbyists in the 19th Century tended to pull the panels apart to paste into their scrapbooks, making copies with all panels still attached scarce.*

HOW DAYS' DURHAM STANDARD OF THE WORLD SMOKING TOBACCO MADE TWO PAIRS OF TWINS HAPPY (O,P)
J.R. Day & Bro. Standard Durham Smoking Tobacco, Durham, NC: nd (c late 1870's/ early 1880's) (3-5/8" x 5-1/2", folded, 21-3/4" tall unfolded, color cardboard)
nn- With all 6 panels attached (Scarce) 121.00 242.00 725.00
nn- Individual panels/cards 13.00 26.00 80.00
NOTE: *Highly sought by both Black Americana and Tobacciana collectors. Recurring mid-19th Century story about two African-American twin brothers who romance and marry a pair of African-American twin sisters. Although the text is racist at points, the art is not. Consists of 6 attached cards, printed on one side, which unfold downwards into a strip story of title card & 5 panels. Scrapbook hobbyists in the 19th Century tended to pull the panels apart and paste into their scrapbooks, making copies with all panels attached scarce. Note, there are numerous cartoon tellings of this same story, including several card series versions (with different art, and story variations, each time). But, the above is the only version which unfolds as a strip of attached cards. The cards from all the unattached versions are smaller sized, and thus distinguishable.*

HUGGINIANA; OR, HUGGINS' FANTASY, BEING A COLLECTION OF THE MOST ESTEEMED MODERN LITERARY PRODUCTIONS (I,S,P)
H.C. Southwick, New York: 1808 (296 pgs, printed one side, B&W, hard-c)
nn - (Very Rare) (no known sales)
NOTE: *The earliest known surviving collected promotional cartoons in America. This is a booklet containing 7 folded plus 1 full page flyer advertisements for barber John Richard Desborus Huggins, who hired American artists Elkanah Tisdale and William S. Leney to modify previously published illustrations into cartoons referring to his barber shop.*

HUMOROUS MASTERPIECES - PICTURES BY JOHN LEECH (E,M)
Frederick A. Stokes: nd (late 1900's - early 1910's) (5-5/8x3-7/8", 68 pgs, cardboard covers, B&W)
1- John Leech (single panel cartoon-r from Punch) 20.00 40.00 120.00
2- John Leech (single panel cartoon-r from Punch) 20.00 40.00 120.00

HUMOURIST, THE (E,I,S)
C.V. Nickerson and Lucas and Deaver, Baltimore: No.1 Jan 1829 - No.12 Dec 1829 (5-3/4x4-3/4", B&W text w/hand colored cartoon pg.)
Bound volume No.1-12 (Very Rare; copies in libraries 270 pgs) (no known sales)
NOTE: *Earliest known American published periodical to contain a cartoon every issue. Surviving individual issues currently unknown -- all information comes from 1 surviving bound volume. This issue is mostly text, with one full page hand-colored cartoon. Bound volume contains an additional hand-colored cartoons at front of each six month set (total of 14 cartoons in volume). Cartoons appear to be of British origin, possibly by George Cruikshank.*

HUMPTY DUMPTY, ADVENTURES OF... (I,P)
1877 (Promotional 4x3-1/2", 12 page chapbook from Gantz, Jones & Co, 10¢-c.)
nn-Promotes Gantz Sea Foam Baking Powder; early app. of a costumed character, dressed as Humpty Dumpty 21.00 42.00 125.00

HUSBAND AND WIFE, OR THE STORY OF A HAIR. (O,P)
Garland Stoves and Ranges, Michigan Stove Co.: 1883 (4-3/16 tall x 2-11/16" wide folded, 16" wide unfolded, color cardboard)
nn - With all 6 panels attached (Scarce) 25.00 50.00 150.00
nn - Individual panels/cards 5.00 10.00 30.00
NOTE: *Consists of 6 attached cards, printed on one side, which unfold into a strip story of title card & 5 panels. Scrapbook hobbyists in the 19th Century tended to pull the panels apart to paste into their scrapbooks, making copies with all panels still attached scarce.*

ICHABOD ACADEMICUS, THE COLLEGE EXPERIENCES OF (O,G)
William T. Peters, New Haven, CT: 1850 (5-1/2x9-3/4",108 pgs, B&W)
nn - By William T. Peters (Rare) 733.00 1466.00 4400.00
NOTE: *Pages are cut in two. Also, a copy showed up on eBay with misspelled Academicus. Has "n" instead of "m" - not known yet which printing is earliest version.*

ICHABOD ACADEMICUS, THE COLLEGE EXPERIENCES OF (O,G)
Dick & Fitzgerald, New York: nd (1870s-1888) (paper-c, B&W)
nn - By William T. Peters (Very Rare) 200.00 400.00 1200.00

The Story of Han's The Swapper Cover & First Two Panels
1865 © L. Pranc & Co, Boston

Humpty Dumpty, The Adventures of...
© Gantz, Jones and Co.

Imagerie d'Epinal
1888 © Mumoristic Publishing Co.

FR1.0 GD2.0 FN6.0　　　　　　　　　　　**FR1.0 GD2.0 FN6.0**

NOTE: *Pages are uniform in size.*

ILLUSTRATED SCRAP-BOOK OF HUMOR AND INTELLIGENCE (M)
John J. Dyer & Co.: nd (c1859-1860)

nn - Very Rare	183.00	366.00	1100.00

NOTE: *A "printed scrapbook" of images culled from some unidentified periodical. About half of it is illustrations that would have accompanied prose pieces. There are pages of single panel cartoons (multiple per page). And there are roughly 8 to 12 pages of sequential comics (all different stories, but appears to all be by the same presently unidentified artist).*

ILLUSTRATED WEEKLY, THE
Chars C Lucas & Co, 11 Dey St, NY: 1876 (15x18", 8pgs, 8¢ per issue)

2/8 (2/19/76) back-c all sequential comic strips	70.00	140.00	425.00
2/12 (3/18/76) full page of British-r sequentials	70.00	140.00	425.00
2/14 (4/1/76) April Fool Issue - (6) panel center; plus more	70.00	140.00	425.00
2/15 (4/8/76) (6) panel sequential	70.00	140.00	425.00
issues without comic strips	21.00	42.00	125.00

ILLUSTRATIONS OF THE POETS: FROM PASSAGES IN THE LIFE OF LITTLE BILLY VIDKINS (See A Day's Sport...)
S. Robinson, Philadelphia: May 1849 (14.7 cm x 11.3 cm, 32 pgs, B&W)

nn - by Henry Stephens (very rare)	(no known sales)

NOTE: *Predates Journey to the Gold Diggins By Jeremiah Saddlebags by a few months and is an original American proto-comic strip book. More research needs to be done. A later edition brought $800 in G/VG 2007*

IMAGERIE d'EPINAL (untrimmed individual sheets) (E)
Pellerin for Humoristic Publishing Co, Kansas City, Mo.: nd (1888) No.1-60
(15-7/8x31", single sheets, hand colored) (All are Rare)

1-14, 21, 22, 25-46, 49-60 - in the Album d'Images	14.00	28.00	85.00
15-20, 23,24, 47, 48 - not in the Album d'Images	23.00	46.00	140.00

NOTE: *Printed and hand colored in France expressly for the Humoristic Publishing Company. Printed on one side only. These are single sheets, sold separately. Reprints and translates the sheets from their original French.*

IMAGERIE d'EPINAL ALBUM d'IMAGES (E)
Pellerin for Humoristic Publishing Co., Kansas City. Mo: nd (1888)
(15-1/2x11-1/2",108 pgs plus full color hard-c, hand colored interior)

nn - Various French artists (Rare)	333.00	666.00	2000.00

NOTE: *Printed and hand colored in France expressly for the Humoristic Publishing Company. Printed on one side only. This is supposedly a collection of sixty broadsheets, originally sold separately. All copies known only have fifty of these sixty known sheets (slightly bigger, before binding, trimming the margins in the process, down to 15-1/4x11-3/8".). Three slightly different covers known to exist, with or without the indication in French "Textes en Anglais" ("Texts in English"), with or without the general title "Contes de FEes" ("Fairy Tales"). All known copies were collected with sheets 15-20, 23,24, 47, and the 48 missing.*

IN LAUGHLAND (M)
R.H. Russell, New York: 1899 (14-9/16x12", 72 pgs, hard-c)

nn - By Henry "Hy" Mayer (scarce)	117.00	234.00	700.00

NOTE: *Mostly strips plus single panel cartoon-r from various magazines. The majority are reprinted from Life, with the rest from: Truth, Dramatic Mirror, Black and White, Figaro Illustre, Le Rire, and Fliegende Blatter.*

IN THE "400" AND OUT (M,S) (see also THE TAILOR-MADE GIRL)
Keppler & Schwarzmann, New York: 1888 (8-1/4x12", 64 pgs, hardc, B&W)

nn - By C.J. Taylor	35.00	70.00	210.00

NOTE: *Cartoons reprinted from Puck. The "400" is a reference to New York City's aristocratic elite.*

IN VANITY FAIR (M,S)
R.H.Russell & Son, New York: 1896 (11-7/8x17-7/8", 80 pgs, hard-c, B&W)

nn - By A.B.Wenzell, r-LIFE and HARPER'S	38.00	76.00	225.00

JACK HUCKABACK, THE SCAPEGRAVE RAVEN (see also HOOKEYBEAK THE RAVEN) (E)
Stroefer & Kirchner, New York: nd (c1877) (9-3/8x6-3/8", 56 pgs, printed one side only, hand colored hardcover, B&W interior)

nn - By Wilhelm Busch (Rare)	83.00	166.00	500.00

NOTE: *The 1877 date is derived from a gift signature on one known copy. The publication date might in truth be earlier. There are also professionally hand colored copies known to exist which would be worth more.*

JEFF PETTICOATS
American News Company, NY: July 1865 (23 inches folded out; 6-1/4x8 folded., B&W)

nn - Very Rare Frank Bellew (6) panel sequential foldout (10c)	(no known sales)

NOTE: *printed also in FUNNYEST OF AWL AND THE FUNNIEST SORT OF PHUN #9 (July 1865) (6) panel strip featuring Jeff Davis; This sold hundreds of thousand of copies in its day*

JINGO (M,O)
Art Newspaper Co., Boston & New York: No.1 Sept 10, 1884 - No.11 Nov 19, 1884
(10 cents, 13-7/8" x 10-1/4",16 pgs, color front/back-c and center, remainder B&W, paper-c)

1-11(Rare)	48.00	96.00	285.00

NOTE: *Satirical Republican propaganda magazine, modeled after Puck and Judge, which was published during the last couple months of the 1884 Presidential Election campaign. The Republicans lost, Jingo ceased publication, and Republican backers soon after purchased Judge.*

JOHN-DONKEY, THE (O, S)
George Dexter, Burgess, Stringer & Co., NYC: 1848 (10x7.5",16 pgs,B&W, 6¢)

1 Jan 1 1848	71.00	142.00	425.00
2-end (last issue Aug 12 1848)	46.00	92.00	275.00

JOLLY JOKER
Frank Leslie, NY: 1862-1878 (B&W, 10¢)

20/6 (July 1877) (Bellew Opper cover & single panels	108.00	216.00	650.00

JOLLY JOKER, OR LAUGH ALL-ROUND
Dick & Fitzgerald: 1870s? (8-1/4x4-7/8", 148, B&W, illustrated green cover)

nn - cartoons on every page	75.00	150.00	450.00

JONATHAN'S WHITTLINGS OF THE WAR (O, S)
T.W. Strong, 98 Nassau St, NYC: April 1854-July 8 1854 (11.5x8.5", 16 pgs, B&W)

1 April 1854	70.00	140.00	420.00

NOTE: *Begins Frank Bellew's sequential comic strip "Mr. Hookemcumsnivey, A Russian Gentleman, Hears That His Country Is In A State of War"*

2-12 (July 8 1854) Many Bellew & Hopkins	70.00	140.00	420.00

JOURNAL CARRIER'S GREETING
???, Minn, Minn: 1897-98? (giveaway promo, 10-1/8x8-1/4, 36, B&W, paper-c)

nn - rare	32.00	64.00	190.00

JOURNEY TO THE GOLD DIGGINS BY JEREMIAH SADDLEBAGS (O,G)
Various publishers: 1849 (25 cents, 5-5/8 x 8-3/4", 68 pgs, green & black paper cover, B&W interior)

nn -- New York edition, Stringer & Townsend, Publishers (Very Rare) By J.A. and D.F. Read.	2467.00	4934.00	14,800.00
nn -- Cincinnati, Ohio edition, published by U.P. James (Very Rare) By J.A. and D.F. Read.	2467.00	4934.00	14,800.00
nn -- 1950 reprint, with introduction, published by William P. Wreden, Burlingame, California: 1950 (5-7/8 x 9", 92 pgs, hardcover, color interior) (390 copies printed) By J.A. and D.F. Read.	13.00	26.00	75.00

NOTE: *Earliest known original sequential comic book by an American creator; directly inspired by Töpffer's Obadiah Oldbuck and Bachelor Butterfly. The New York and Cincinnati editions were both published in 1849, one soon after the other. Antiquarian Book sources have traditionally cited that the Cincinnati edition preceded the New York, but without referencing any direct evidence. Conflicting with this, the Cincinnati edition lists the New York publishers' 1849 copyright, while the New York edition makes no reference to the Cincinnati publishers. Such would indicate that the New York edition was first. Both are very rare, and until resolved both will be regarded as published simultaneously. A New York copy with missing back cover, detached front cover, and G/VG interior sold for $2000 in 2000. Two copies sold at auction in 2006 for $11,500 and 12,000. (Prices vary widely).*

JUDGE (M,O)
Judge Publishing, New York: No.1 Oct 29, 1881 - No. 950, Dec ??, 1899
(10 cents, color front/back c and centerspread, remainder B&W, paper-c)

1 (Scarce)		(no known sales)	
2-26 (Volume 1; Scarce)	21.00	42.00	125.00
27-790,792-950	8.00	16.00	50.00
791 (12/12/1896; Vol.31) - classic satirical-c depicting Tammany Hall politicians as the Yellow Kid & Cox's Brownies	100.00	200.00	600.00

Bound Volumes (six month, 26 issue each):

Vol. 1 (Scarce)		(no known sales)	
Vol. 2-30,32-37	100.00	200.00	600.00
Vol. 31 - includes issue 791 YK/Brownies parody	117.00	234.00	700.00

NOTE: *Rival publication to Puck. Purchased by Republican Party backers, following their loss in the 1884 Presidential Election, to become a Republican propaganda satire magazine.*

JUDGE, GOOD THINGS FROM
Judge Publishing Co., NY: 1887 (13-3/4x10.5", 68 pgs, color paper-c)

1 first printing	33.00	66.00	200.00

NOTE: *Zimmerman, Hamilton, Victor, Woolf, Beard, Ehrhart, De Meza, Howarth, Smith, Alfred Mitchell*

JUDGE'S LIBRARY (M)
Judge's Publishing, New York: No.1, April 1890 - No. 141, Dec 1899 (10 cents, 11x8-1/8", 36 pgs, color paper-c, B&W)

1	19.00	38.00	115.00
2-141	15.00	30.00	90.00
151-??? (post-1900 issues; see Platinum Age section)			

NOTE: *Judge's Library was a monthly magazine reprinting cartoons & prose from Judge, with each issue's material organized around the same subject. The cover art was often original. All issues were kept in print for the duration of the series, so later issues are more scarce than earlier ones.*

JUDGE'S QUARTERLY (M)
Judge Publishing Company/Arkell Publishing Company, New York: No.1 April 1892 - 31 Oct 1899 (25c, 13-3/4x10-1/4", 64 pgs, color paper-c, B&W)

1-11 13-31 contents presently unknown to us	11.00	22.00	65.00
12 ZIM Sketches From Judge Jan 1895	75.00	150.00	450.00

NOTE: *Similar to Judge's Library, except larger in size, and issued quarterly. All reprint material, except for the cover art.*

JUDGE'S SERIALS (M,S)
Judge Publishing, New York: March 1888 (10x7.5", 36 pgs)

#3 - Eugene Zimmerman	42.00	84.00	250.00

NOTE: *A bit of sequential comic strips; mostly single panel cartoons. This series runs to at least #8.*

JUDY
Burgess, Stringer & Co., 17 Ann St, NYC: Nov 28 1846-Feb 20 47 (11x8.5",12 pgs,B&W)

1 Nov 28 1846	46.00	92.00	275.00
2-13	38.00	76.00	230.00

JUVENILE GEM, THE (see also THE ADVENTURES OF MR. TOM PLUMP, and OLD MOTHER MITTEN) (O,I)
Huestis & Cozans: nd (1850-1852) (6x3-7/8", 64 pgs, hand colored paper-c, B&W)
(all versions Very Rare)

nn - First printing(s) publisher's address is 104 Nassau Street (1850-1851)	
	(1 copy sold for $800.00 in Fair)
nn - 2nd printing(s) publisher's address is 116 Nassau Street (1851-1852) (no known sales)	
nn - 3rd printing(s) publisher's address is 107 Nassau Street (1852+) (no known sales)	

NOTE: *The JUVENILE GEM is a gathering of multiple booklets under a single, hand colored cover (none of the interior booklets have the covers which they were given when sold separately). The publisher appears to have gathered whichever printings of each booklet were available when copies of THE JUVENILE GEM was assembled, so that the booklets within, and the conglomerate cover, may be from a mixture of printings. Contains two sequential comic booklets: THE ADVENTURES OF MR. TOM PLUMP, and OLD MOTHER*

MITTEN AND HER FUNNY KITTEN, plus five heavily illustrated children's booklets - *The Pretty Primer*, *The Funny Book*, *The Picture Book*, *The Two Sisters*, and *Story Of The Little Drummer*. Six of these -- including the two comic books -- were reprinted in the 1960's by Americana Review as a set of individual booklets, and included in a folder collectively titled "Six Children's Books of the 1850's".

LANTERN, THE
Stringer & Townsend: 1852-1853 (11x8-3/8", 12 pgs, soft paper, 6 ¢)

1 Jan 10, 1852	32.00	64.00	190.00
2	22.00	44.00	130.00
3-First Frank Bellew cartoons onwards each issue	31.00	62.00	185.00
4-Bellew 's Mr Blobb begins 1/31/52	42.00	84.00	250.00

NOTE: *Bellew serial sequential comic strip "Mr Blobb In Search Of A Physician" becomes 2nd earliest known recurring character in American comic strips plus full page single panel Bellew cartoon "The Modern Frankenstein" take-off on Shelly's story.*

5-Hunsdale 2-panel "The Horrors of Slavery"; Mr Blobb	42.00	84.00	250.00
6-DF Read 15 panel "A Volley of Valentines"; Mr Blobb	38.00	76.00	230.00
7-8,10-Bellew's Mr Blobb continues	21.00	42.00	125.00
9-Four panel "The Perils of Leap Year" MrBlobb	38.00	76.00	230.00
11-no Mr Blobb	19.00	38.00	115.00
12-Bellew's Mr Blobb continues 3/27/52	38.00	76.00	230.00
13-Bellew (10) panel sequential "Stump Speaking Studied"	38.00	76.00	230.00
14-no comic strips	18.00	36.00	110.00
15-Bellew's Mr Blobb ends (5) panel 4/17/52	38.00	76.00	230.00
16-Bellew begins new comic strip serial, "Mr. Bulbear, A Stockbroker, After having Supped at Delmonicos, Has A Dream", Part One, (6) panels	38.00	76.00	230.00
17-Bellew's Mr Bulbear continues	21.00	42.00	125.00
18-Bellew (8) panel "Trials of a Witness"	38.00	76.00	230.00
19-Bellew's Mr Bulbear's Dream continues	21.00	42.00	125.00
20-23-No comic strips	19.00	38.00	115.00
24 Bellew "Trials of a Publisher" (6) panel	38.00	76.00	230.00
25 comic strip "Travels of Jonathan Verdant"recurring character	21.00	42.00	125.00
26-49 contents still to be indexed			
50 (12/18/52) (2) panel Impertinent Smile	21.00	42.00	125.00
58 (2/12/53) (6) panel Trip to California	21.00	42.00	125.00
66 (4/9/53) (3) panel sequential strip	21.00	42.00	125.00

LAST SENSATION, THE (Becomes Day's Doings)
James Watts, NYC: Dec 27 1867-May 30 1868 (11x16 folio-size, 16 pgs, B&W)

Issues with comic strips	36.00	72.00	215.00

LAUGH AND GROW FAT COMIC ALMANAC
Fisher & Brother, Philadelphia, New York & Boston: 1860-? (36 pgs)

nn	46.00	92.00	275.00

LEGEND OF SAM'L OF POSEN (O.S)
M.B. Curtis Company: 1884-85 (8x3-3/8", 44 pgs, Color-c, B&W interior)

nn - By M.B. Curtis	36.00	72.00	215.00

NOTE: *Cover blurb says: From Early Days in Fatherland to affluence And Success in the Land of His Adoption, America*

LESLIE'S YOUNG AMERICA (O. S.)
Leslie & Co, 98 Chamber St, NY: 1881-82 (11-1/2x8", 5¢, B&W)

1 (7/9/81) back cover (6) panel strip	108.00	216.00	650.00
2 (7/16/81) back cover (9) panel strip	43.00	86.00	260.00
3 (7/23/81) back cover (16) panel Busch strip	50.00	100.00	300.00
9 (9/3/81) sequentials; Hopkins singles	43.00	86.00	260.00
15 (10/15/81) Zim or Frost? (6) panel strip	43.00	86.00	260.00
19 (11/12/81) (9) panel back-c strip	43.00	86.00	260.00
24 (4) panel strip 25 (2) panel back-c strip	43.00	86.00	260.00
26 27 (6) panel back-c strip	43.00	86.00	260.00
29 31 (12) panel strip	43.00	86.00	260.00
32 (2/11/82) (8) panel strip	43.00	86.00	260.00
issues without comic strips or Jules Verne	21.00	42.00	125.00

NOTE: *Jules Verne stories begin with #1 and run thru at least #42*

LIFE (M,O) (continues with Vol.35 No. 894+ in the Platinum Age section)
J.A.Mitchell: Vol.1 No.1 Jan. 4, 1883 - Vol-1 No.26 June 29, 1883 (10-1/4x8", 16 pgs, B&W, paper cover); J.A. Mitchell: Vol. 2 No. 27, July 5, 1883 - Vol. 6 No.148, Oct 29, 1885 (10-1/4x8-1/4", 16 pgs., B&W, paper cover); Mitchell & Miller: Vol.6 No.149, Nov. 5, 1885 - Vol. 31, No. 796, March 17, 1898 (10-3/8x8-3/8", 16 pgs., B&W, paper cover); Life Publishing Company: Vol. 31 No. 797, March 24, 1898 - Vol. 34 No. 893, Dec 28, 1899 (10-3/8 x 8-1/2", 20 pgs., B&W, paper cover)

1-26 (Scarce) (no known individual sales, 1st 12-issues in a bound volume sold for $1554)			
27-799	5.00	10.00	30.00
800 (4/7/1898) parody Yellow Kid / Spanish-American War cover (not by Outcault)	58.00	116.00	350.00
801-893	4.00	8.00	25.00

NOTE: *All covers for issues 1 - 26 are identical, apart from issue number & date.*
Hard bound collected volumes:

V. 1 (No.1-26) (Scarce)	50.00	100.00	300.00
V. 2-34	30.00	60.00	180.00
V. 31 YK #800 parody-c not by RFO	54.00	108.00	325.00

NOTE: *Because the covers of all issues in Volume 1 are identical, it was common practice to remove the covers before binding the issues together. This is not true of later volumes, though, in all volumes it was common to drop the advertising pages which appeared at the rear of each issue. Information on many more individual issues will expand next Guide.*

LIFE AND ADVENTURES OF JEFF DAVIS (I)
J.C. Haney & Co., NY: 1865 (10 cents, 7-1/2" x 4", 36 pgs, B&W, paper-c)

nn - By McArone (Scarce)	150.00	300.00	900.00
nn - 1974 Reprint (350) copies 6-3/4x4-3/8	3.00	6.00	20.00
nn - 1997 Reprint (7th Fla. Sutler, Clearwater, 6-3/4x4-1/4")			5.00

NOTE: *Humorous telling of the capture of Confederate President Jeff Davis in women's clothing, from the publisher of Merryman's Monthly. It contains an ad page for that publication; the material is perhaps reprinted from it. J.C. Haney licensed it to local printers, and so various publishers are found -- all printings currently regarded as simultaneous. (The Geo. H. Hees printing, Oswego, NY, contains an ad for the upcoming October 1865 issue of Merryman's Monthly, thus placing that printing in September 1865.) Modern facsimile editions have been produced.*

LIFE IN PHILADELPHIA
W. Simpson, 66 Chestnut, Philadelphia; Siltart, No. 65 South Third St, Philadelphia: 1830 (7-3/4x6-7/8", 15 loose plates, hand colored copies exist, maybe B&W also)

nn - By Edward Williams Clay (1799-1857) (Very Rare)	(no known sales)		

NOTE: *First 13 plates etched; with many word balloons; scenes of exaggerated Black Americana in Philadelphia viewed one by one as broadsides. Had several publishers over the years. Was also eventually collected into a book of same name but only with the first 13 plates used; the last two not used in book. Collected book not yet viewed to share info.*

LIFE'S BOOK OF ANIMALS (M.S)
Doubleday & McClure Co.: 1898 (7-1/4x10-1/8", 88 pgs, color hardcover, B&W)

nn	21.00	42.00	125.00

NOTE: *Reprints funny animal single panel and strip cartoons reprinted from LIFE. Art by Blaisdell, Chip Bellew, Kemble, Hy Mayer, Sullivant, Woolf.*

LIFE'S COMEDY (M,S)
Charles Scribner's Sons: Series 1 1897 - Series 3 1898 (12x9-3/8", hardcover, B&W)

1 (142 pgs). 2, 3 (138 pgs)	50.00	100.00	300.00

NOTE: *Gibson a-1-3; c-3. Hy Mayer a-1-3. Rose O'Neill a-2-3. Stanlaws a-2-3. Sullivant a-1-2. Verbeek a-2. Wenzell a-1-3; c(painted)-2.*

LIFE, THE GOOD THINGS OF (M,S)
White, Stokes, & Allen, NY: 1884 - No.3 1886 ; Frederick A. Stokes, NY: No.4 1887; Frederick Stokes & Brother, NY: No.5 1888 - No.6 1889; Frederick A. Stokes Company, NY: No. 7 1890 - No.10 1893 (8-3/8x10-1/2", 74 pgs, gilted hardcover, B&W)

nn - 1884 (most common issue)	27.00	54.00	160.00
2 - 1885	27.00	54.00	160.00
3 - 1886 (76 pgs)	27.00	54.00	160.00
4 - 1887 (76 pgs)	27.00	54.00	160.00
5 - 1888	27.00	54.00	160.00
6 - 1889	27.00	54.00	160.00
7 - 1890	27.00	54.00	160.00
8 - 1891 (scarce)	53.00	106.00	320.00
9 - 1892	27.00	54.00	160.00
10 - 1893	27.00	54.00	160.00

NOTE: *Contains mostly single panel, and some sequential, comics reprinted from LIFE. Attwood a-1-4,10. Roswell Bacon a-5. Chip Bellew a-4-6. Frank Bellew a-4,6. Palmer Cox a-1-5. H. E. Dey a-5. C. D. Gibson a-4-10. F.M. Howarth a-5-6. Kemble a-1-3. Klapp a-5. Walt McDougall a-1-2. H. McVickar a-5; J. A. Mitchell a-5. Peter Newell a-4-5,7. J. Smith a-5. Albert E. Steiner a-5; T. S. Sullivant a-7-9. Wenzell a-8-10. Wilder a-3. Woolf a-3-6.)*

LIFE, THE SPICE OF (E,M,)
White and Allen: NY & London: 1888 (8-3/8x10-1/2",76 pgs, hard-c, B&W)

nn	42.00	84.00	250.00

NOTE: *Resembles THE GOOD THINGS OF LIFE in layout and format, and appears to be an attempt to compete with their former partner Frederick A. Stokes. However, the material is not from LIFE, but rather is reprinted and translated German sequential and single panel comics.*

LIFE'S PICTURE GALLERY (becomes LIFE'S PRINTS) (M,S,P)
Life Publishing Company, New York: nd (1898-1899) (paper cover, B&W) (all are scarce)

nn - (nd; 1898, 100 pgs, 5-1/4x8-1/2") Gibson-c of a woman with closed umbrella; 1st interior page announcing that after January 1, 1899 Gibson will draw exclusively for LIFE; the word "SPECIMEN" is printed in red, diagonally, across every print;

a-Gibson, Rose O'Neill, Sullivant	25.00	50.00	150.00

nn - (nd; 1899, 128 pgs, 4-7/8x7-3/8") Gibson-c of a woman golfer; 1st interior page announcing that Gibson & Hanna, Jr. draw exclusively for LIFE; the word "SPECIMEN" is printed in red, horizontally, across every print. Includes prints from Gibson's *THE EDUCATION OF MR. PIPP*

a-Gibson, Sullivant	25.00	50.00	150.00

NOTE: *Catalog of prints reprinted from LIFE covers & centerspreads. The first catalog was given away free to anyone requesting it, but after many people got the catalog without ordering anything, subsequent catalogs were sold at 10 cents.*

LIGHT AND SHADE
William Drey Doppel Soap: 1892 (3-3/4x5-3/8", 20 pgs, B&W, color cover)

nn - By J.C.	40.00	80.00	240.00

NOTE: *Contains (8) panel comic strip of black boy whose skin turns white using this soap.*

LITTLE SICK BEAR, THE
Edwin W. Joy Co, San Francisco, CA: 1897 (6-1/4x5", 20 pgs, B&W, Scarce)

nn - By James Swinnerton one long sequential comic strip	150.00	300.00	900.00

LONDON OUT OF TOWN, OR THE ADVENTURES OF THE BROWNS AT THE SEA SIDE BY LUKE LIMNER, ESQ. (O)
David Bogue, 86 Fleet St, London: c1847 (5-1/2x4-1/4, 32 pgs, yellow paper hard-c, B&W)

nn - By John Leighton	120.00	240.00	725.00

NOTE: *one long sequential comic strip multiple-panel per page story; each page crammed with panels inspired by the Töpffer comic books Bogue began several years earlier.*

LORGNETTE, THE (S)
George J Coombes, New York: 1886 (6-1/2x8-3/4", 38 pgs, hard-c, B&W

nn - By J.K. Bangs	33.00	66.00	200.00

LOVING BALLAD OF LORD BATEMAN, THE (E,I)
G.W. Carleton & Co., Publishers, Madison Square, NY: 1871 (9x5-7/8",16 pgs, soft-c, 6¢)

nn - By George Cruikshank	33.00	66.00	200.00

MADISON'S EXPOSITION OF THE AWFUL & TERRIFYING CEREMONIES OF THE ODD FELLOWS
T.E. Peterson & Brothers, 306 Chestnut St, Phila: 1870s? (5-3/4x9-1/4, 68 pgs, B&W)

nn - single panel cartoons	38.00	76.00	225.00

MANNERS AND CUSTOMS OF YE HARVARD STUDENTE (M,S)
Houghton Mifflin & Co., Boston & Moses King, Cambridge: 1877 (7-7/8x11", 72 pgs, printed one side, hardc, B&W)

nn - by F.G. Attwood	83.00	166.00	500.00

NOTE: *Collection of cartoons originally serialized in the Harvard Lampoon. Attwood later became a major cartoonist for Life.*

MAN WHO WOULD LIKE TO MARRY, THE (O)
Frederick Warne & Co., London & New York: nd (c 1880's) (9-1/2x11-1/2", 28 pgs, printed 1 side, paper-c, B&W)

nn - By Harry Parkes	54.00	108.00	325.00

NOTE: *Published simultaneously with its companion volume, The Girl Who Wouldn't Mind Getting Married.*

MAX AND MAURICE: A JUVENILE HISTORY IN SEVEN TRICKS (E)
(see also Teasing Tom and Naughty Ned)
Roberts Brothers, Boston: 1871 first edition (8-1/8 x 5-1/2", 76 pgs, hard & soft-c B&W)

nn - By Wilhelm Busch (green or brown cloth hardbound)	217.00	434.00	1300.00
nn - exactly the same, but soft paper cover	117.00	234.00	700.00

NOTE: *Page count includes 56 pgs of art, two blank endpapers at the front (one colored), 8 pgs of ads at the back, two blank endpapers at the end (one colored), and the covers. Green or brown illustrated hardcover. The*

Merryman's Monthly v3#5 with Bellew strip
May 1865 © J. C. Haney & Co., New York

The Mischief Book by Wilhelm Busch
color cover art variation
1880 © R. Worthington, New York

FR 1.0 GD 2.0 FN 6.0

name of the author is given on the title page as "William Busch." We assume this to be the 1st edition. Back side of title page states: Entered according to Act of Congress, in the year 1870, by Roberts Brothers, In the office of the Librarian of Congress at Washington.

nn - By Wilhelm Busch (1872 edition)	217.00	434.00	1300.00
nn - 1875 reprint	75.00	150.00	450.00
nn - 1882 reprint (76 pgs, hand colored- c/a, 75¢)	67.00	134.00	400.00
nn- 1889 reprint with new art on cover printed in full color	67.00	134.00	400.00

NOTE: Each of the above contains 56 pages of art and text in a transitional format between a regular children's book and a comic book (the page count difference is ad pages in back). Seminal inspiration for William Randolph Hearst to acquire as a "new comic" (following the wild success of Outcault's Yellow Kid) to license M&M from Busch and hire Rudolph Dirks in late 1897 to create a New York American newspaper incarnation. In Hearst's English language newspapers it was called The Katzenjammer Kids and in his German language NYC newspaper it was titled Max & Moritz, Busch's original title. At least 50 other reprints versions are reputed to exist printed thru 1900. Various others are still sorting out the edition confusion.

MAX AND MAURICE: A JUVENILE HISTORY IN SEVEN TRICKS (E)
(see also Teasing Tom and Naughty Ned)
Little, Brown, and Company, Boston: 1898-1902 (8-1/8 x 5-3/4", 72 pgs, hardcover, black ink on orange paper) (various early reprints)

nn - 1898 , 1899 By Wilhelm Busch	55.00	110.00	330.00
nn - 1902 (64 pages, B&W)	17.00	34.00	100.00

MERRY MAPLE LEAVES Or A Summer In The Country (S)
E.P. Dutton And Company, New York: 1872 (9-3/8x7-3/8", 90 and 86 pgs pgs, hard-c)

nn - By Abner Perk	28.00	56.00	170.00

NOTE: Each drawing contained in a maple leaf motif by Livingston Hopkins and others.

MERRYMAN'S MONTHLY A COMIC MAGAZINE FOR THE FAMILY (M,O,E)
J.C. Haney & Co, NY: 1863-1875 (10-7/8x7-13/16", 30 pgs average, B&W)

Certain issues with sequential comics	79.00	158.00	475.00

NOTE: Sequential strips by Frank Bellew Sr, Wilhelm Busch found so far; others?

MERRYTHOUGHT, OR LAUGHTER FROM YEAR TO YEAR, THE
Fisher & Brother, Phila, Baltimore: early 1850s (4-1/2x7", B&W)

nn - many singles, some sequential (Very Rare)	(no known sales)

NOTE: See Vict article for back cover pic which is earliest known use of the term Comic Book

MESSRS BROWN JONES AND ROBINSON, THE AMERICAN TOUR OF (O,G)
D. Appleton & Co., New York: 1872 (11-5/8x9-1/2", 158 pgs, printed one side only, B&W, green gilted hard-c)

nn - By Toby	100.00	200.00	600.00

NOTE: Original American graphic novel sequel to Richard Doyle's Foreign Tour of Brown, Jones, and Robinson, with the same characters visiting New York, Canada, and Cuba. Protective sheets between each page (not part of page count).

MESSRS. BROWN, JONES, AND ROBINSON, THE FOREIGN TOUR OF
(see also THE CLOWN, OR THE BANQUET OF WIT) (E,M,O,G)
Bradbury & Evans, London: 1854 (11-5/8x9-1/2", 196 pgs, gilted hard-c, B&W)

nn - By Richard Doyle	45.00	90.00	270.00
nn - Bradbury & Evans 1900 reprint	17.00	34.00	100.00

NOTE: Protective sheets between each page (not part of page count). Expanded and redrawn sequential comics story from the serialized episodes originally published in PUNCH. Also comes in a 174 pg 8-3/4x11" version.

MESSRS. BROWN, JONES, AND ROBINSON, THE FOREIGN TOUR OF (E,M,G)
D. Appleton & Co., New York: 1860 & 1877 (11-5/8x9-1/2", 196 pgs, gilted hard-c, B&W)

nn - (1860 printing) by Richard Doyle	37.00	74.00	220.00
nn - (1871 printing) by Richard Doyle	25.00	50.00	150.00
nn - (1877 printing) by Richard Doyle	25.00	50.00	150.00

NOTE: Protective sheets between each page (not part of page count). Reprints the Bradbury & Evans edition.

MESSRS. BROWN, JONES, AND ROBINSON, THE LAUGHABLE ADVENTURES OF (E,M,G)
Garrett, Dick & Fitzgerald, NY: nd (1856 or 1857) (5-3/4x9-1/4", 100 pgs, printed one side only, paper-c, B&W)

nn - (Very Rare) by Richard Doyle c/a	242.00	434.00	1450.00

NOTE: 1st American reprinting of the "Foreign Tour"; reformatted into a small oblong format. Links the earlier Garrett & Co. to the later Dick & Fitzgerald. Back cover reprints full size the Garrett & Co. version cover for Oscar Shanghai. Interior front cover reprints full size the Garrett & Co. version cover for Slyfox-Wikof. Issued without a title page.

MESSRS. BROWN, JONES, AND ROBINSON, THE LAUGHABLE ADVEN. OF (E,M,G)
Dick & Fitzgerald, NY: nd (late 1870's - 1888) (5-3/4x9-1/4", 100 pgs, printed one side only, green paper-c, B&W)

nn - (Scarce) by Richard Doyle	83.00	166.00	500.00

NOTE: Reprints the Garrett, Dick & Fitzgerald printing, with the following changes: Takes what had been page 12 in the Garrett, D&F printing (art by M.H. Henry), and makes it a title page, which is numbered page 1. The first story page, "Go to the Races", is numbered 2 (whereas it is numbered 1 in the Garrett, Dick & Fitzgerald version). Numbering stays ahead of the G,D&F edition by 1 page up through page 12, after which the page numbering becomes consistent.

MINNEAPOLIS JOURNAL CARTOONS (N,S)
Minneapolis Journal: nn 1894 - No.2 1895 (7-3/4" x 10-7/8", 76 pgs, B&W, paper-c)

nn (1894) (Rare)	37.00	74.00	220.00
Second Series (1895) (Rare)	37.00	74.00	220.00
nn- "War Cartoons" Jan 1899 (9x8", 160 pgs, paperback, punched & string bound) (Scarce)	32.00	64.00	190.00

NOTE: Reprints single panel cartoons from the prior year, by Charles "Bart" L. Bartholomew.

MINNEAPOLIS TRIBUNE CARTOON BOOK FOR 1901
Roland C. Bowman: 1901

nn	(a FR/GD copy sold in 2010 for $134)

MISCHIEF BOOK, THE (E)

FR 1.0 GD 2.0 FN 6.0

R. Worthington, New York: 1880 (7-1/8 x 10-3/4", 176 pgs, hard-c, B&W)

nn - Green cloth binding; green on brown cover; cover art by R. Lewis based on Busch art by Wilhelm Busch	167.00	334.00	1000.00
nn - Blue cloth binding; hand colored cover; completely different cover art based on Busch art by Wilhelm Busch	167.00	334.00	1000.00

NOTE: Translated by Abby Langdon Alger. American published anthology collection of Wilhelm Busch comic strips. Includes two of the strips found in the British "Bushel of Merry-Thoughts" collection, translated better, and with the dropped panel restored. Unknown which cover version was first.

MISSES BROWN, JONES AND ROBINSON, THE FOREIGN TOUR OF THE (E,O,G)
Bickers & Sons, London: nd (c1850's) (12-1/4" x 9-7/8", 108 pgs, printed on one side, B&W, hard-c)

nn- "by Miss Brown" (Rare)	73.00	146.00	440.00

NOTE: A female take on Doyle's Foreign Tour, by an unknown woman artist, using the pseudonym "Miss Brown."

MISS MILLY MILLEFLEUR'S CAREER (S)
Sheldon & Co., NY: 1869 (10-3/4x9-7/8", 74 pgs, purple hard-c)

nn - Artist unknown (Rare)	57.00	114.00	340.00

MR PODGER AT COUP'S GREATEST SHOW ON EARTH HIS HAPS AND MISHAPS, THE ADVENTURES OF (O,S)
W.C. Coup, New York: 1884 (5-5/8x4-1/4", 20 pgs, color-c, B&W)

nn - Circus Themes; Similar to Barker's Comic Almanacs	21.00	42.00	125.00

MR. TOODLES' GREAT ELEPHANT HUNT (See Peter Piper in Bengal)
Brother Jonathan, NYC: 1850s (4-1/4x7-7/8", page count presently unknown)

nn - catalog contains comic strip (Very Rare)	(no known sales)

MR. TOODLES' TERRIFIC ELEPHANT HUNT
Dick & Fitzgerald, NYC: 1860s (5-3/4x9-1/4", 32 pgs, paper-c, B&W) (Very Rare)

nn - catalog reprint contains 28 panel comic strip	117.00	234.00	700.00

MRS GRUNDY
Mrs Grundy Publishing Co, NYC: July 8 1865-Sept 30 1865 (weekly)

1-13 Thomas Nast, Hoppin, Stephens,	42.00	84.00	250.00

MUSEUM OF WONDERS, A (O,I)
Routledge & Sons: 1894 (13x10", 64 pgs, color-c, color thru out)

nn - By Frederick Opper	100.00	200.00	600.00

MY FRIEND WRIGGLES, A (Laughter) Moving Panorama, of His Fortunes And Misfortunes, Illustrated With Over 200 Engravings, of Most Comic Catastrophes And Side-Splitting Merriment) (O,G)
Stearn & Co, 202 Williams St, NY: 1850s (5-7/8x9-3/4", 100 pgs, B&W)

nn - By S. P. Avery (also the engraver) (Very Rare)	200.00	400.00	1200.00

MY SKETCHBOOK (E,S)
Dana Estes & Charles E. Lauriat, Boston; J. Sabins & Sons, New York: circa 1880s (9-3/8x12", brown hard-c)

nn - By George Cruikshank	27.00	54.00	160.00

NOTE: Reprints British editions 1834-36; extensive usage of word balloons.

NASBY'S LIFE OF ANDY JONSON (O, M)
Jesse Haney Co., Publishers No. 119 Nassau St, NY: 1866 (4-1/2x7-1/2, 48 pgs, B&W)

nn - President Andrew Johnson satire	100.00	200.00	600.00

NOTE: Book further reads: With a True Pictorial History of His STumping Tour Out West By Petroleum V. Nasby, A Dimmicrat of Thirty Years Standing, And Who Allus Tuk His Licker Straight. Front of book has long sequential comic strip satire on President Andrew Johnson, misspelling his name on the cover on purpose.

NAST'S ILLUSTRATED ALMANAC
Harper & Brothers, Franklin Square, NYC: 1872-1874 (8x5.5", 80 pgs, B&W, 35¢)

nn	48.00	96.00	290.00

NAST'S WEEKLY (O,S)
???: 1892-93 (Quarto Weekly)

all issues scarce	33.00	66.00	200.00

NATIONAL COMIC ALMANAC
An Association of Gentlemen, Boston: 1836 (8.25x4.75", 34 pgs, B&W)

nn	50.00	100.00	300.00

NEW AMERICAN COMIC ALL-IMAKE (ELTON'S BASKET OF COMICAL SCRAPS), THE
Elton, Publisher, New York: 1839 (7-1/2x4-5/8, 24 pgs)

1	71.00	142.00	425.00

NEW BOOK OF NONSENSE, THE: A Contribution To The Great Central Fair In Aid Of the Sanitary Commission (O,S)
Ashmead & Evans, No. 724 Chestnut St, Philadelphia: June 1864 (red hard-c)

nn - Artists unknown (Scarce)	58.00	116.00	350.00

NEW YORK ILLUSTRATED NEWS
Frank Leslie, NYC: 10/14/76-June 1884

average issues with comic strips	19.00	38.00	115.00

NEW YORK PICAYUNE (see PHUN FOTOCRAFT)
Woodward & Hutchings: 1850-1855 newspaper-size weekly; 1856-1857 Folio Monthly 16x10.5; 1857-1858 Quarto Weekly; 1858-1860 Quarto Weekly

Average Issue With Comic Strips	40.00	80.00	240.00
Issues with Full Front Page Comic Strip	71.00	142.00	425.00

NOTE: Many issues contain Frank Bellew sequential comic strips & single panel cartoons. Later issues published by Woodward, Levison & Robert Gun (1853-1857) ; Levison & Thompson (1857-1860)

NICK-NAX
Levison & Haney, NY: 1857-1858? (11x7-3/4", 32 pgs, B&W, paper-c)
v2 #10 Feb 1858 has many single panel cartoons   45.00   90.00   270.00

99 "WOOLFS" FROM TRUTH (see Sketches of Lowly Life in a Great City, Truth)
Truth Company, NY: 1896 (9x5-1/2", 72 pgs, varnished paper-like cloth hard-c, 25 cents)
nn - By Michael Angelo Woolf   (Rare)   117.00   234.00   700.00
NOTE: Woolf's cartoons are regarded as a primary influence on R.F. Outcault in the later development of The Yellow Kid newspaper strip. Copy sold in 2002 on eBay for $800.00.

NONSENSE OR, THE TREASURE BOX OF UNCONSIDERED TRIFLES
Fisher & Brother, 12 North Sixth St, Phila, PA, 64 Baltimore St, Baltimore, MD: early 1850s (4-1/2x7", 128 pgs, B&W)
nn - much Davy Crocket sequential story-telling comic strips   258.00   516.00   1550.00

OBADIAH OLDBUCK, THE ADVENTURES OF MR. (E,G)
Tilt & Bogue, London: nd (1840-41) (5-15/16x9-3/16", 176 pgs,B&W, gilted hard-c)
nn - By Rodolphe Töpffer   583.00   1166.00   3500.00
nn - Hand coloured edition   (Very Rare)   (no known sales)
NOTE: This is the British edition, translating the unauthorized redrawn 1839 edition from Parisian publisher Aubert, adapted from Töpffer's "Les Amours de Mr. Vieux Bois" (aka "Histoire de Mr. Vieux Bois"), originally published in French in Switzerland, in 1837 (2nd ed. 1839). Early 19th century books are often found rebound, with original cover and/or title page gone. To distinguish editions having no cover or title page: the British oblong editions (published by Tilt & Bogue) use Roman Numerals to number pages. American oblong shaped editions use Arabic Numerals. British are printed on one side only. This is the earliest known English language sequential comic book. Has a new title page with art by Robert Cruikshank.

OBADIAH OLDBUCK, THE ADVENTURES OF MR. (E,G)
Wilson and Company, New York: September 14, 1842 (11-3/4x9", 44 pgs, B&W, yellow paper-c on bookstand editions, hemp paper interior)
Brother Jonathan Extra No. IX - Rare bookstand edition   2667.00   5334.00   16,000.00
Brother Jonathan Extra No. IX Very Rare subscriber/mailorder
   2833.00   5666.00   17,000.00
NOTE: By Rodolphe Töpffer. Earliest known sequential American comic book, reprinting the 1841 British edition. Pages are numbered via Roman numerals. States "BROTHER JONATHAN EXTRA - ADVENTURES OF MR. OBADIAH OLDBUCK." at the top of each page. Prints 2 to 3 tiers of panels on both sides of each page. Copies could be had for ten cents according to adverts in Brother Jonathan. By Rodolphe Töpffer with cover masthead design by David Claypool Johnston, and cover art beneath the masthead reprinting Robert Cruik-shank's title page art from the Tilt & Bogue edition. A special, additional cover was added for copies sold on stands (it was not issued with mail order or subscriber copies). Only 1 known copy possesses (partially) this very thin outer yellow cover. A decent (subscriber) copy sold on eBay in later October 2002 for over $3500.00. In 2005, a GD/VG for $20,000; and a VG for $20,000. An apparent GD copy sold in auction in 2007 for $9560. A FR/GD copy sold in 2008 for $4182.50. A bound edition sold in 2010 for $2270.50. A copy in GD (restored) sold in 2012 for $5377. A poor condition copy sold in 2014 for $4780. A Fair condition copy sold for $3107 in 2018. (Prices vary widely.)

OBADIAH OLDBUCK, THE ADVENTURES OF MR. (E,G)
Wilson & Co, New York: nd (1849) (5-11/16x8-3/8", 84 pgs, B&W,paper-c)
nn - by Rodolphe Töpffer; title page by Robert Cruikshank (Very Rare)
   767.00   1534.00   4600.00
NOTE: 2nd Wilson & Co printing, reformatted into a small oblong format, with nine panels edited out, and text modified to smooth out this removal. Results in four less printed tiers/strips. Pages are numbered via Arabic numerals. Every panel on Pages 11, 14, 19, 21, 24, 34, 35 has one line of text. Reformatted to conform with British first edition.

OBADIAH OLDBUCK, THE ADVENTURES OF MR. (E,G)
Wilson & Co, 162 Nassau, NY: nd (early-1850s) (5-11/16x8-3/8", 84 pgs, B&W, yellow-c)
nn - 3rd USA Printing by Rodolphe Töpffer; title page by Robert Cruikshank (Very Rare)
Says By Timothy Crayon, an obvious pseudonym   767.00   1534.00   4600.00
NOTE: Front cover banner the giant is holding says "Done With Drawings By Timothy Crayon, Gypsographer, 188 Comic Etchings On Antimony" Title page changes address to No. 15 Spruce-Street. (Late 162 Nassau Street.)

OBADIAH OLDBUCK, THE ADVENTURES OF MR.. (E,G)
Brother Jonathan Offices: ND (mid-1850s) (5-11/16x8-3/8", 84 pages, B&W, oblong)
nn - 4th printing; Originally by Rodolphe Töpffer (Very Rare) 767.00   1534.00   4600.00
NOTE: Cover States: "New York: Published at the Brother Jonathan Office". Front cover banner the giant is holding says "Done With Drawings By Timothy Crayon, Gypsographer, 188 Comic Designs On Antimony."

OBADIAH OLDBUCK, THE ADVENTURES OF MR. (E,G)
Dick & Fitzgerald, New York: nd (various printings; est. 1870s to 1888)
(Thirty Cents, 84 pgs, B&W, paper-c) (all versions scarce)
nn - Black print on green cover(5-11/16x8-15/16"); string bound 217.00   434.00   1300.00
nn - Black print on blue cover; same format as green-c   217.00   434.00   1300.00
nn - Black print on white cover(5-13/16x9-3/16"); staple bound beneath cover);
this is a later printing than the blue or green-c   217.00   434.00   1300.00
NOTE: Reprints the abbreviated 1849 Wilson & Co. 2nd printing. Pages are numbered via Arabic numerals. Many of the panels on Pages 11, 14, 19, 21, 24, 34, 35 take two lines of text in the same words found in the Wilson & Co version, which used only one text line for the same panels. Unknown whether the blue or green cover is earlier. White cover version has "thirty cents" line blackened out on the two copies known to exist. Robert Cruikshank's title page has been made the cover in the D&F editions.

OLD FOGY'S COMIC ALMANAC
Philip J. Cozans, NY: 1858 (4-7/8x7-1/4, 48 pgs)
nn - sequential comic strip told one panel per page   50.00   100.00   300.00
NOTE: Contains (12) panel "Fourth of July in New York" sequential

OLD MOTHER MITTEN AND HER FUNNY KITTEN (see also **The Juvenile Gem**) (O)
Huestis & Cozans: nd(1850-1852) (6x3-7/8"12pgs, hand colored paper-c, B&W)
nn - first printing(s) publisher's address is 104 Nassau Street (1850-1851)
(Very Rare)   (no known sales)
NOTE: A hand colored outer cover is highly rare, with only 1 recorded copy possessing it. Front cover image and text is repeated precisely on page 3 (albeit b&w), and only interior pages are numbered, together leading owners of coverless copies to believe they have the cover. The true back cover has ads for the publisher. Cover was issued only with copies which were sold separately - books which were bound together as part of THE JUVENILE GEM never had such covers.

OLD MOTHER MITTEN AND HER FUNNY KITTEN (see JUVENILE GEM) (O)
Philip J. Cozans: nd (1850-1852) (6x3-7/8",12 pgs, hand colored paper-c, B&W)
nn - Second printing(s) publisher's address is 116 Nassau Street (1851-1852)
(Very Rare)   (no known sales)
nn - Third printing(s) publisher's address is 107 Nassau Street (1852+)
(Very Rare)   (no known sales)

OLD MOTHER MITTEN AND HER FUNNY KITTEN
Americana Review, Scotia, NY: nd (1960's) (6-1/4x4-1/8", 8 pgs, side-stapled, cardboard, B&W)
nn - Modern reprint   4.00   8.00   25.00
NOTE: Issued within a folder titled SIX CHILDREN'S BOOKS OF THE 1850'S. States "Reprinted by American Review" at bottom of front cover. Reprints the 104 Nassau Street address.

ON THE NILE (O,G)
James R. Osgood & Co., Boston: 1874 ; **Houghton, Osgood & Co., Boston:** 1880 (112 pgs, gilted green hardcover, B&W)
1st printing (1874; 10-3/4x16") - by Augustus Hoppin   38.00   76.00   225.00
2nd printing (1880; smaller sized)   22.00   44.00   130.00

OSCAR SHANGHAI, THE EXTRAORDINARY AND MIRTH-PROVKING ADVENTURES BY SEA & LAND OF (O, G)
Garrett & Co., Publishers, No. 18 Ann Street, New York: May 1855 (5-3/4x9-1/4", 100 pgs, printed one side only, paper-c, 25¢, B&W)
nn - Samuel Avery-c; interior by ALC Very Rare   700.00   1400.00   4200.00
NOTE: Not much is known of this first edition as the data comes from a recently rediscovered Brother Jonathan catalog issued circa 1853-55. No original known yet to exist.

OSCAR SHANGHAI, THE WONDERFUL AND AMUSING DOINGS BY SEA AND LAND OF (G)
Dick & Fitzgerald, 10 Ann St, NY: nd (1870s-1880) (25¢, 5-3/4x9-1/4", 100 pgs, printed one side only, green paper c, B&W)
nn - Cover by Samuel Avery; interior by ALC (Rare)   242.00   486.00   1450.00
NOTE: Exact reprint of Garrett & Co original.

OUR ARTIST IN CUBA (O)
Carleton, New York: 1865 (6-5/8x4-3/8", 120 pgs, printed one side only, gilted hard-c, B&W)
nn - By Geo. W. Carleton   38.00   76.00   225.00

OUR ARTIST IN CUBA, PERU, SPAIN, AND ALGIERS (O)
Carleton: 1877 (6-1/2x5-1/8", 156 pgs, hard-c, B&W)
nn - By Geo. W. Carleton   38.00   76.00   225.00
nn - By Geo. W. Carleton (wraps paper cover) (Rare)   38.00   76.00   225.00
NOTE: Reprints OUR ARTIST IN CUBA and OUR ARTIST IN PERU, then adds new section on Spain and Algiers.

OUR ARTIST IN PERU (O)
Carleton, New York: 1866 (7-3/4x5-7/8", 68 pgs, gilted hardcover, B&W)
nn - By Geo. W. Carleton   28.00   56.00   170.00
NOTE: Contains advertisement for the upcoming books OUR ARTIST IN ITALY and OUR ARTIST IN FRANCE, but no such publications have been found to date.

PARSON SOURBALL'S EUROPEAN TOUR (O)
Duff and Ashmead: 1867 (6x7-1/2", 76 pgs, blue embossed title hard-c)
nn - By Horace Cope   75.00   150.00   450.00
NOTE: see REV. MR. SOURBALL'S EUROPEAN TOUR, THE for the soft paper cover version

PEN AND INK SKETCHES OF YALE NOTABLES (O,S)
Soule, Thomas and Winsor, St. Louis: 1872 (12-1/4x9-3/4", B&W)
By Squills   22.00   44.00   130.00
NOTE: Printed by Steamlith Press, The R.P. Studley Company, St Louis.

PETER PIPER IN BENGAL
Bengamin H Day,Publisher, Brother Jonathan Cheap Book Establishment, 48 Beekman, NY: 1953-55 (6-5/8x4-1/4, 36 pgs, yellow paper-c, B&W, 3 cents - two dollars per hundred) (Very Rare)
nn - By John Tenniel - 32 panel comic strip Punch-r   433.00   866.00   2600.00
NOTE: Actually also a catalog of inexpensive books, prints, maps and half a dozen comic books for sale on separate pages from publishers Day and Garrett - see full story of this brand new find in the Victorian Era essay. A complete copy with split spine sold in November 2002 for $750.00. Published date most likely 1855.

THE PHILADELPHIA COMIC ALMANAC (S)
G. Strong, 44 Strawberry St, NYC: 1835 (8-1/2x5", 36 pgs)
nn -   113.00   226.00   675.00
NOTE: 77 engravings full of recurring cartoon characters but not sequential; early use of recurring characters.

PHIL MAY'S SKETCH BOOK (E,S,M)
R.H. Russell, New York: 1899 (14-5/8x10", 64 pgs, brown hard-c, B&W)
nn - By Phil May   27.00   54.00   160.00
NOTE: American reprint of the British edition.

PHUNNY PHELLOW, THE
Oakie, Dayton & Jones: Oct 1859-1876; **Street & Smith** 1876: (Folio Monthly)
average issue with Thomas Nast   50.00   100.00   300.00

PHUN FOTOCRAFT, KEWREUS KONSEETS KOMICALLY ILLUSTRATED BY A KWEER FELLER (N) (see **NEW YORK PICAYUNE**)
The New York Picayune, NY: 1850s (104 pgs)
nn - Mostly Frank Bellew, some John Leach   250.00   500.00   1500.00
NOTE: Many sequential comic strips as well as single cartoons all collected from The New York Picayune. Ross & Tousey, Agents, 121 Nassau St, NY. The Picayune ran many sequential comic strips in its decade.

PICTORIAL HISTORY OF SENATOR SLIM'S VOYAGE TO EUROPE
Dr. Herrick & Brother, Chemists, Albany, NY: 1860 (3-1/4x4-3/4", 32 pgs, B&W)
nn - By John McLenan Very Rare   104.00   208.00   625.00

PICTURES OF ENGLISH SOCIETY (Parchment-Paper Series, No.4) (M,S,E)
D. Appleton & Co., New York: 1884 (5-5/8x4-3/8", 108 pgs, paper-c, B&W)
4 - By George du Maurier; Punch-r   23.00   46.00   135.00
NOTE: Every other page is a full page cartoon, with the opposite page containing the cartoon's caption.

PICTURES OF LIFE AND CHARACTER (M,S,E)
Bradbury and Evans, London: No.1 1855 - No.5 c1864 (12-1/2x18", 100 pgs, illustrated hard-c, B&W)
nn (No.1) (1855)   32.00   64.00   190.00
2 (1858), 3 (1860)   32.00   64.00   190.00
4 (nd; c1862)   5 (nd; c1864)   32.00   64.00   190.00
nn (nd (late 1860's)   28.00   56.00   170.00
NOTE: 2-1/2x18-1/4", 494 pgs, green gilted-c) reprints 1-5 in one book
1-3 John Leech's... (nd; 12-3/8x10", ? pgs, red gilted-c).   20.00   40.00   120.00
NOTE: Reprints John Leech cartoons from Punch. note that the Volume Number is mentioned only on the last page of these versions.

PICTURES OF LIFE AND CHARACTER (E,M,S)
G.P. Putnam's Sons: 1880's (8-5/8x6-1/4", 218 pgs, hardcover, color-cr, B&W)
nn - John Leech (single panel Punch cartoon-r)   33.00   66.00   200.00
NOTE: Leech reprints which extend back to the 1850s.

PICTURES OF LIFE AND CHARACTER (Parchment-Paper Series) (E,M,S)
(see also **Humerous Masterpieces**)
D. Appleton & Co., NY: 1884 (30¢, 5-3/4 x 4-1/2", 104 pgs, paper-c, B&W)
nn - John Leech (single panel Punch cartoon-r)   28.00   56.00   170.00
NOTE: An advertisement in the back refers to a cloth-bound edition for 50 cents.

The Wonderful and Amusing Doings by Sea & Land of
Oscar Shanghai
1870s © Dick & Fitzgerald, New York

The Adventures of Obadiah Oldbuck
© Brother Jonathan Offices, NY

FR1.0 GD2.0 FN6.0

PIPPIN AMONG THE WIDE-AWAKES (O,S)
Werill & Chapin, 113 Nassau St, NYC, NY): 1860 (6x4-1/2", 36 pgs, 6 cents)

nn - Artist unknown (Very Rare)	79.00	158.00	475.00

PLISH AND PLUM (E.G)
Roberts Brothers, Boston: 1883 (8-1/8x5-3/4", 80 pgs, hardcover, B&W)

nn - By Wilhelm Busch	38.00	76.00	230.00
nn - Reprint (Roberts Brothers, 1895)	33.00	66.00	200.00
nn - Reprint (Little, Brown & Co., 1899)	33.00	66.00	200.00

NOTE: *The adventures of two dogs.*

POUNDS OF FUN
Frank Tousey, 34 North Moore St, NY: 1881 (6-1/2x9-1/2", 68pgs, B&W)

nn - Bellew, Worth, Woolf, Chips	38.00	76.00	220.00

PRESIDENTS MESSAGE, THE
G.P. Putnam's Sons, NY: 1887 (5-3/4x7-5/8, 44 pgs)

nn - (19) Thomas Nast single panel full page cartoons	38.00	76.00	230.00

PROTECT THE U.S. FROM JOHN BULL - PROTECTION PICTURES FROM JUDGE
Judge Publishing, New York: 1888 ((10 cents, 6-7/8x10-3/8", 36 pgs, paper-c, B&W)

nn - (Scarce)	27.00	54.00	160.00

NOTE: *Reprints both cartoons and commentary from Puck, concerning the issue of tariffs which were then being debated in Congress. Art by Gillam, Hamilton, Victor.*

PUCK (German language edition, St. Louis) (M,O) (see also Die Vehme)
Publisher unknown, St. Louis: No.1, March 18, 1871 - No. ??, Aug. 24, 1872 (B&W, paper-c)

1-?? (Very Rare) by Joseph Keppler		(no known sales)

NOTE: *Joseph Keppler's second attempt at a weekly humor periodical, following Die Vehme one year earlier. This was his first attempt to launch using the title Puck. This German language version ran for a full year before being joined by an English language version.*

PUCK (English language edition, St. Louis) (M,O)
Publisher unknown, St. Louis: No.1, March ?? 1872 - No. ??, Aug. 24, 1872 (B&W, paper c)

1-?? (Very Rare) by Joseph Keppler		(no known sales)

NOTE: *Same material as in the German language edition, but in English.*

PUCK, ILLUSTRIRTES HUMORISTISCHES WOCHENBLATT (German language edition, NYC) (M,O)
Keppler & Schwarzmann, New York: No.1 Sept (27) 1876 - 1164 Dec ?? 1899 (10 cents, color front/back-c and centerspread, remainder B&W, paper-c)

1-26 (Volume 1; Rare) by Joseph Keppler - these issues precede the English language			
version, and contain cartoons not found in them. Includes cartoons on the controversial			
Tilden-Hayes 1876 Presidential Election debacle.			(no known sales)
27-52 (Volume 2; Rare) by Joseph Keppler - contains some cartoon material not found in			
the English language editions. Particularly in the earlier issues.			(no known sales)
53-1164	12.00	24.00	70.00

Bound Volumes (six month, 26 issue run each):

Vol. 1 (Rare)			(no known sales)
Vol. 2-4 (Rare)			(no known sales)
Vol. 5-47	52.00	104.00	310.00

NOTE: *Joseph Keppler's second, and successful, attempt to launch Puck. In German. The first six months precede the launch of the English language edition. Soon after (but not immediately after) the launch of the English edition, both editions began sharing the same cartoons, but, their prose material always remained different. The German language edition ceased publication at the end of 1899, while the English language edition continued into the early 20th Century. First American periodical to feature printed color every issue.*

PUCK (English language edition, NYC) (M,O)
Keppler & Schwarzmann, New York: No.1 March (14) 1877 - 1190 Dec ?? 1899 (10 cents, color front/back-c and centerspread, remainder B&W, paper-c)

1 (Rare) by Joseph Keppler			(no known sales)
2-26 (Rare) by Joseph Keppler			(no known sales)
27-1190	12.00	24.00	70.00

(see Platinum Age section for year 1900+ issues)

Bound volumes (six month, 26 issue run each):

Vol. 1 (Rare)		(one set sold on eBay for $2300.00)
Vol. 2 (Scarce)		(one set sold on eBay for $1500.00)
Vol. 3-6 (pre-1880 issues)	145.00	290.00	870.00
Vol. 7-46	108.00	216.00	650.00

NOTE: *The English language editions began six months after the German editions, and so the English edition numbering is always one volume number, and 26 issue numbers, behind its parallel German language edition. Pre-1880 & post-1900 issues are more scarce than 1880's & 1890's.*

PUCK (miniature) (M,P,I)
Keppler & Schwarzmann, New York: nd (c1895) (7x5-1/8", 12 pgs, color front & back paper-c, B&W interior)

nn - Scarce	22.00	44.00	130.00

NOTE: *C.J.Taylor-c; F.M.Howarth-a; F.Opper-a; giveaway item promoting Puck's various publications. Mostly text, with art reprinted from Puck.*

PUCK, CARTOONS FROM (M,S)
Keppler & Schwarzmann, New York: 1893 (14-1/4x11-1/2", 244 pgs, hard-c, mostly B&W)

nn - by Joseph Keppler (Signed and Numbered)	92.00	184.00	550.00

NOTE: *Reprints Keppler cartoons from 1877 to 1893, mostly in B&W, though a few in color, with a text opposite each cartoon explaining the situation then being satirized. Issued only in an edition of 300 numbered issues, signed by Keppler. Only 114 of the pages are cartoons.*

PUCK'S LIBRARY (M)
Keppler & Schwarzmann, New York: No.1, July, 1887 - No. 174, Dec, 1899 (10 cents, 11-1/2x8-1/4", 36 pgs, color paper-c, B&W)

1- "The National Game" (Baseball)	55.00	110.00	330.00

2-149	12.00	24.00	70.00

NOTE: *Puck's Library was a monthly magazine reprinting cartoons & prose from Puck, with each issue's material organized around the same subject. The cover art was often original. All issues were kept in print for the duration of the series, so later issues are more scarce than earlier ones.*

PUCK, PICKINGS FROM (M)
Keppler & Schwarzmann, New York: No.1, Sept, 1891 - No. 34, Dec, 1899
(25 cents, 13-1/4x10-1/4", 68 pgs, color paper-c, B&W)

1-34 Scarce	22.00	44.00	130.00

NOTE: *Similar to Puck's Library, except larger in size, and issued quarterly. All reprint material, except for the cover art. There also exist variations with "RAILROAD EDITION 30 CENTS" printed on the cover in place of the standard 25 cent price.*

PUCK PROOFS (M,P,S)
Keppler & Schwarzmann, New York: nd (1906-1909) (74 pgs, paper cover; B&W)
(all are Scarce)

nn - (c.1906, no price, 4-1/8x5-1/4") B&W painted -c of couple kissing over a chess board;			
1905 & 1906-r	23.00	46.00	140.00
nn- (c.1909, 10 cents, 4-3/8x5-3/8") plain green paper-c; 76 pgs 1905-1909-r			
	23.00	46.00	140.00

NOTE: *Catalog of prints available from Puck, reprinting mostly cover & centerspread art from Puck. There likely exist more as yet unreported Puck Proofs catalogs. Art by Rose O'Neill.*

PUCK'S OPPER BOOK (M)
Keppler & Schwarzmann, New York: 1888 (11-3/4x13-7/8", color paper-c, 68 pgs, interior B&W, 30¢)

nn - (Very Rare) by F. Opper	146.00	292.00	875.00

NOTE: *Puck's first book collecting work by a single artist.; mostly sequential comic strips.*

PUCK'S PRINTING BOOK FOR CHILDREN (S,O,I)
Keppler & Schwarzmann, Pubs, NY: 1891 (10-3/8x7-7/8", 52 pgs, color-c, B&W and color)

nn - Frederick B Opper (Very Rare)		(no known sales)

NOTE: *Left side printed in color; Right side B&W to be colored in.*

PUCK, THE TARIFF ?, CARTOONS AND COMMENTS FROM (M,S)
Keppler & Schwarzmann, New York: 1888 (10 cents, 6-7/8x10-3/8", 36 pgs, paper-c, B&W)

nn - (Scarce)	40.00	80.00	240.00

NOTE: *Reprints both cartoons and commentary from Puck, concerning the issue of tariffs which were then being debated in Congress. Art by Gillam, Keppler, Opper, Taylor.*

PUCK, WORLD'S FAIR
Keppler & Schwarzmann, PUCK BUILDING, World's Fair Grounds, Chicago: No.1 May 1, 1893 - No.26 Oct 30, 1893 (10 cents, 11-1/4x8-3/4, 14 pgs, paper-c, color front/back/center pages, rest B&W)(All issues Scarce to Rare)

1-26	29.00	58.00	175.00
1-26 bound volume:	433.00	866.00	2600.00

NOTE: *Art by Joseph Keppler, F. Opper, F.M. Howarth, C.J. Taylor, W.A. Rogers. This was a separate, parallel run of Puck, published during the 1893 Chicago World's Fair from within the fairgrounds, and containing all new and different material than the regular weekly Puck. Smaller sized and priced the same, this originally sold poorly, and had not as wide distribution as Puck, and so consequently issues are much more rare than regular Puck issues from the same period. Not to be confused with the larger sized regular Puck issues from 1893 which sometimes also contained World's Fair related material, and sometimes had the words "World's Fair" appear on the cover. Can also be distinguished by the fact that Puck's issue numbering was in the 800's in 1893, while these are issue number 1 through 26.*

PUNCHINELLO
Punchinello Publishing Co, NYC: April 2-Dec 24 1870 (weekly)

1-39 Henry L. Stephens, Frank Bellew, Bowlend	19.00	38.00	115.00

NOTE: *Funded by the Tweed Ring, mild politics attacking Grant Admin & other NYC newspapers. Bound copies exist.*

QUIDDITIES OF AN ALASKAN TRIP (O,G)
G.A. Steel & Co., Portland, OR: 1873 (6-3/4x10-1/2", 80 pgs, gilted hard-c, Red-c and Blue-c exist, B&W) (A nice copy sold for $87 in 2018)

nn - By William H. Bell (Scarce)	300.00	600.00	1800.00

NOTE: *Highly sought Western Americana collectors. Parody of a trip from Washington DC to Alaska, by a member of the team which went to survey Alaska, purchase commonly known from as "Seward's Folly".*

"RAG TAGS" AND THEIR ADVENTURES, THE (N,S)
A. M. Robertson, San Francisco: 1899 (10-1/4x13-7/8, 84 pgs, color hard-c, B&W inside)

nn - By Arthur M. Lewis (SF Chronicle newspaper-r) (Scarce)	52.00	104.00	310.00

RAYS OF LIGHT (O,P)
Morse Bros., Canton, Mass.: No.1 1886 (7-1/8x5-1/8", 8 pgs, color paper-c, B&W)

1- (Rare)	33.00	66.00	200.00

NOTE: *Giveaway pamphlet in guise of an educational publication, consisting entirely of a sequential story in which a teacher instructs her classroom of young girls in the use of Rising Sun Stove Polish. Color front & back covers.*

RELIC OF THE ITALIAN REVOLUTION OF 1849, A
Gabici's Music Stores, New Orleans: 1849 (10-1/8x12-3/4", 144 pgs, hardcover)

nn - By G. Daelli (Scarce)	75.00	150.00	450.00

NOTE: *From the title page: "Album of fifty line engravings, executed on copper, by the most eminent artists at Rome in 1849; secreted from the papal police after the 'Restoration of Order,' And just imported into America."*

REMARKS ON THE JACOBINIAD (I,S)
E.W. Weld & W. Greenough, Boston: 1795-98 (8-1/4x5-1/8", 72 pgs, a number of B&W plates with text)

nn - Written by Rev. James Sylvester Gardner, artist unknown (Rare)		(no known sales)

NOTE: *Early comics-type characters. Not sequential comics, but uses word balloons. Satire directed against "The Jacobin Club," supporters of the French Revolution and Radical Republicans. Gardner came to America from England in 1783, was minister of Trinity Church, Boston. There appears to be some reprints of this done as late as 1798.*

REV. MR. SOURBALL'S EUROPEAN TOUR, THE RECREATION OF A CITY, THE
Duffield Ashmead, Philadelphia: 1867 (7-5/8x6-1/4", 72 pgs, turquoise blue soft wrappers)
By Horace Cope (Rare)   38.00   75.00   225.00
NOTE: see PARSON SOURBALL'S EUROPEAN TOUR for the hard cover version.

RHYMES OF NONSENSE TRUTH & FICTION (S)
G.W. Carleton & Co, Publishers, NY: 1874 (10x7-3/4", 44 pgs, hard-c, B&W) (Very Rare)
nn - By Chaucer Jones and Michael Angelo Raphael Smith   96.00   192.00   575.00
NOTE: Creator names obviously pseudonyms; looks like weak A.B. Frost.

ROMANCE OF A HAMMOCK, THE - AS RECITED BY MR. GUS WILLIAMS IN "ONE OF THE FINEST" (O,P)
Unknown: 1880s (5-1/2x3-5/8" folded, 7 attached cardboard cards which fold out into a strip, color)
nn - By presently unknown Scarce   67.00   134.00   400.00
NOTE: 12-panel story, which one begins reading on one side of the folded-out strip, then flip to the other side to continue -- unlike the vast majority of folded strips, which are printed on only one side. This was a promotional handout, for a play titled "One of the Finest". The story pictured comes from a poem read in the play by then famous New York stage actor Gus Williams, who is pictured on the "cover"/title card."

SAD TALE OF THE COURTSHIP OF CHEVALIER SLYFOX-WIKOF, SHOWING HIS HEART-RENDING ASTOUNDING & MOST WONDERFUL LOVE ADVENTURES WITH FANNY ELSSLER AND MISS GAMBOL, THE (O,G)
Garrett & Co., NY: Jan 1856 (25 ¢, 5-3/4x9-1/4", 100 pages, paper-c, B&W)
nn - By T.C. Bond ?? (Very Rare)   433.00   866.00   2600.00
NOTE: No surviving copies reported -- known via ads in Home Circle published by Garrett. Cover art by John McLenan and Samuel Avery. Graphic novel parodying the real-life romance between European actress/dancer Fanny Elssler and American aristocrat Henry Wikoff. The entire graphic novel is reprinted in the 1976 book "Fanny Elssler in America."

SAD TALE OF THE COURTSHIP OF CHEVALIER SLYFOX-WIKOF, SHOWING HIS HEART-RENDING ASTOUNDING & MOST WONDERFUL LOVE ADVENTURES WITH FANNY ELSSLER AND MISS GUMBEL, THE (G) (25 cents printed on cover)
Dick And Fitzgerald, NY: 1870s-1888 (5-3/4x9-1/4", ??? pages, soft paper-c, B&W)
nn - By T.C. Bond ?? (Very Rare)   233.00   466.00   1400.00
NOTE: Reprint of Garrett original printing before G,D&F partnership begins.

SALT RIVER GUIDE FOR DISAPPOINTED POLITICIANS
Winchell, Small & Co., 113 Fulton St, NY: 1870s (16 pgs, 10¢)
nn - single panel cartoons from Wild Oats (Rare)   54.00   108.00   325.00

SAM SLICK'S COMIC ALMANAC
Philip J. Cozans, NYC: 1857 (7.5x4.5, 48 pgs, B&W)
nn - By T.C. Bond ?? (Very Rare)   73.00   146.00   440.00
NOTE: Contains reprint of "Moses Keyser the Bowery Bully's Trip to the California Gold Mines" from Elton's Comic Almanac #17 1850.

SCRAPS (O,S) (see also F****** A*** K*****)
D.C. Johnston, Boston: 1828 - No.8 1840; New Series No.1 1849 (12 pgs, printed one side only, paper-c, B&W)
1 - 1828 (9-1/4 x 11-3/4") (Very Rare)   (no known sales)
2 - 1830 (9-3/4 x 12-3/4") (Very Rare)   (no known sales)
3 - 1832 (10-7/8 x 13-1/8") (Very Rare)   (no known sales)
4 - 1833 (11 x 13-5/8") (Very Rare)   (no known sales)
5- 1834 (10-3/8 x 13-3/8") (Very Rare)   (no known sales)
6 - 1835 (10-3/8 x 13-1/4") red lettering in title SCRAPS (Very Rare)
                                              217.00   434.00   1300.00
6 - 1835 (10-3/8 x 13-1/4") no red lettering in title (Rare)
                                              183.00   366.00   1100.00
7 - 1837 (10-3/4 x 13-7/8") 1st Edition (Very Rare) 150.00 300.00 900.00
7 - 1837 (10-3/4 x 13-3/4") 2nd Edition (so stated) 63.00 125.00 375.00
NOTE: 20 pgs. of text (double-sided), 4 pgs. of art (single-sided), plus the covers. There are no protective sheets between the art pages.
8 - 1840 (10-1/2 x 13-7/8") (Rare)   150.00   300.00   900.00
New Series 1- 1849 (10-7/8 x 13-3/4")   83.00   166.00   500.00
NOTE: By David Claypoole Johnston. All issues consist of four one-sided sheets with 9 to 12 single panel cartoons per sheet. The other pages are blank or text. With #1-5 the size of the pages can vary up to an inch. Contains 4 protective sheets (not part of page count) Only 1 3 4 and the 1849 New Series Number 1 has cover art along with 4 art pgs. (single sided) with 4 protective sheets and no text pages.New Series Number 1, as well as #6 with no red lettering and the second printing of issue 7, have survived in higher numbers due to a 1940s warehouse discovery.

THE SETTLEMENT OF RHODE ISLAND (O)
The Graphic Co. Photo-Lith 39 & 41, Park Place, New York: 1874 (11-3/8x10, 40 pgs, gilted blue hard-c
nn - Charles T. Miller & Walter F. Brown   50.00   100.00   300.00
NOTE: This is also the Same Walter F. Brown that did "Hail Columbia".

SHAKESPEARE WOULD RIDE THE BICYCLE IF ALIVE TODAY. "THE REASON WHY" (O,P,S)
Cleveland Bicycles H.A. Lozier & Co., Toledo, OH: 1896 (5-1/2x4",16 pgs, paper-c, color)
nn - By F. Opper (Rare)   63.00   126.00   375.00
NOTE: Original cartoons of Shakespearian characters riding bicycles; also popular amongst collectors of bicycle ephemera.

SHAKINGS - ETCHINGS FROM THE NAVAL ACADEMY BY A MEMBER OF THE CLASS OF '67 (O,S)
Lee & Shepard, Boston: 1867 (7-7/8x10", 132 pages, blue hard-c)
By: Park Benjamin   29.00   58.00   175.00
NOTE: Park Benjamin later became editor of Harper's Bazaar magazine.

SHOO FLY PICTORIAL (S)
John Stetson, Chestnut sT Theatre, Phila, PA: June 1870 (15-1/2x11-1/2", 8 pgs, B&W)
1   58.00   116.00   350.00

SHYS AT SHAKSPEARE
J.P. and T.C.P., Philadelphia: 1869 (9-1/4x6", 52 pgs)
nn - Artist unknown   54.00   108.00   325.00

SKETCHES OF LOWLY LIFE IN A GREAT CITY (M,S) (See 99 "Woolfs" From Truth)
G. P. Puntam's Sons: 1899 (8-5/8x11-1/4", 200 pgs, hard-c, B&W)
(reprints from Life and Judge of Woolf's cartoons of NYC slum children)
nn - By Michael Angelo Woolf   71.00   142.00   425.00
NOTE: Woolf's cartoons are regarded as a primary influence on R.F. Outcault in the later development of The Yellow Kid newspaper strip.

SNAP (O,S)
Valentine & Townsend, Tribune Bldg, NYC: March 13,1885 (17x11, 8 pgs, B&W)
1-Contains a sequential comic strip   33.00   66.00   200.00

SOCIETY PICTURES (M,S,E)
Charles H. Sergel Company, Chicago: 1895 (5-1/4x7-3/4", 168 pgs, printed 1 side, paper-c, B&W)
nn - By George du Maurier; reprints from Punch.   21.00   42.00   125.00

SOLDIERS AND SAILORS HALF DIME TALES OF THE LATE REBELLION
Soldiers & Sailors Publishing Co: 1868 (5-1/4x7-7/8", 32 pgs)
v1#1-#16 v2#1-#10   10.00   20.00   60.00
v2 #11 contains (2) page comic strip   17.00   34.00   100.00
NOTE: Changes to Soldiers & Sailors Half Dime Magazine with v2 #1.

SOUVENIR CONTAINING CARTOONS ISSUED BY THE PRESS BUREAU OF THE OHIO STATE REPUBLICAN EXECUTIVE COMMITTEE, A (S)
Ohio State Republican Executive Committee, Columbus, OH: 1899 (10-3/8x13-1/2, 248 pgs, Hard-c, B&W)
nn - By William L. Bloomer (Scarce)   79.00   158.00   475.00

SOUVENIR OF SOHMER CARTOONS FROM PUCK, JUDGE, AND FRANK LESLIE'S (M,S,P)
Sohmer Piano Co.: nd(c.1893) (6x4-3/4", 16 pgs, paper-c, B&W)
nn   20.00   40.00   120.00
NOTE: Reprints painted "cartoon" Sohmer Piano advertisements which appeared in the above publications. Artists include Keppler, Gillam, others.

SPORTING NEW YORKER, THE
Ornum & Co, Beekman ST, NYC: 1870s
issues with sequential comic strips (Rare)   38.00   76.00   225.00

STORY OF THE MAN OF HUMANITY AND THE BULL CALF, THE
(see Bull Calf, The Story of The Man Of Humanity And The)
NOTE: Reprints of two of A. B. Frost's mostfamous sequential comic strips.

STREET & SMITH'S LITERARY ALBUM
Street & Smith, NY: #1 Dec 23 1865-#225 Apr 9 1870 (11-3/4x16-3/4", 16 pgs, B&W)
1 (23 Dec 1865)   17.00   34.00   100.00
2-129 131-225 (issues with short sequential strips)   17.00   34.00   100.00
130 (Steam Man satire parody)   58.00   116.00   350.00

STUFF AND NONSENSE (Harper's Monthly strip-r) (M)
Charles Scribner's Sons: 1884 (10-1/4x7-3/4", 100 pgs, hardcover, B&W)
nn - By Arthur Burdett Frost   71.00   142.00   425.00
nn - By A.B. Frost (1888 reprint, 104 pgs)   36.00   72.00   215.00
NOTE: Earliest known anthology devoted to collecting the comic strips of a single American artist. 1888 2nd printing has a different cover and is layed out somewhat differently inside with a new title page, 3 added pages of cartoons, and a couple more illustrations. For more Frost, the 2nd is worth checking ng out also.

STUMPING IT (LAUGHING SERIES BRICKTOP STORIES #8) (O,S)
Collin & Small, NY: 1876 (6-5/8x9-1/4", 68 pgs, perfect bound, B&W)
nn - Thomas Worth art abounds (some sequentials)   142.00   425.00
NOTE: Mainly single panel cartoons w/text; however, some sequential comic strips inside worth picking up

SUMMER SCHOOL OF PHILOSOPHY AT MT. DESERT, THE
Henry Holt Co.: 1881 (10-3/8x8-5/8", 60 pgs, illus. gilt hard-c, B&W)
nn - By J. A. Mitchell   44.00   88.00   265.00
NOTE: J.A.Mitchell went on to found LIFE two years later in 1883. Also, the long-running mascot for LIFE was Cupid - which you see multitudes of Cupids flying around in this story.

SURE WATER CURE, THE
Carey Grey & Hart, Phila, PA: c1841-43 (8-/2x5, 32 pgs, B&W
nn - proto-comic-strip Very Rare   150.00   300.00   900.00

TAILOR-MADE GIRL, HER FRIENDS, HER FASHIONS, AND HER FOLLIES, THE
(see also IN THE "400" AND OUT) (M)
Charles Scribner's Sons, New York: 1888 (8-3/8x10-1/2", 68 pgs, hard-c, B&W)
nn - Art by C.J. Taylor   25.00   50.00   150.00
NOTE: Format is a full page cartoon on every other page, with a script style vignette, written by Philip H. Welch, on every page opposite the art.

TALL STUDENT, THE
Roberts Brothers, Boston: 1873 (7x5", 48 pgs, printed one side only, gilted hard-c, B&W)
nn - By Wilhelm Busch (Scarce)

TARIFF ?, CARTOONS AND COMMENTS FROM PUCK, THE (see Puck, The Tariff....)

TEASING TOM AND NAUGHTY NED WITH A SPOOL OF CLARK'S COTTON, THE ADVENTURES OF (O,P)
Clark's O.N.T. Spool Cotton: 1879 (4-1/4x3", 12 pgs, B&W, paper-c)
nn   18.00   36.00   110.00
NOTE: Knock-off of the "First Trick" in Wilhelm Busch's Max and Maurice, modified to involve Clark's Spool Cotton in the story, with similar but new art by an artist identified as "HB". The back cover advertises the specific merchant who gave this booklet away -- multiple variations of back cover suspected.

TEMPERANCE TALES; OR, SIX NIGHTS WITH THE WASHINGTONIANS, VOL I & II
W.A. Leary & Co., Philadelphia: 1848 (50¢, 6-1/8x4", 328 pgs, B&W, hard-c)
nn   108.00   216.00   650.00
NOTE: Mostly text. This edition gathers Volume I & II together. The first 8 pages reprint George Cruikshank's THE BOTTLE, re-drawn & re-engraved by Phil A. Pilliner. Later editions of this book do not include THE BOTTLE reprint and are therefore of little interest to comics collectors.

TEXAS SIFTINGS
Texas Siftings Publishing Co, Austin, Texas (1881-1887), NYC (1887-1897): 1881-1885 newspaper-size weekly; 1886-1897 folio weekly (15x10-3/4", 16 pgs, B&W 10¢
1881-1885 issues   23.00   46.00   140.00
v6#1 (5/8/86) (8) panel strip Afterwhich He Emigrated;
    (16) panel The Tenor's Triumph Veni Vidi Vici   17.00   34.00   100.00
v6#2 (5/16/86) (5) panel sewuential   17.00   34.00   100.00
v6#3 no sequentials   17.00   34.00   100.00
v6#4 (5/29/86) Worth-c (4) panel Worth strip; (2) panel   17.00   34.00   100.00
v6#5 no sequentials   17.00   34.00   100.00
v6#6 (6/12/86) Comic Strip Cover (11) panels The Rise of a Great Artist
    (5) panel sequential   34.00   68.00   205.00
v6#7 (6/19/86) Worth-c (2) panel Wiorth;
    (10) panel Ha! Ha! The Honest Youth & the Lordly Villain   18.00   36.00   110.00
v6#8 (6/26/86) Worth-c; (15) panel The Kangaroo Hunter   18.00   36.00   110.00
v6#9 (7/3/86) Worth-c; Bellew (2) panel How Wives Get What They Want
                                               17.00   34.00   100.00
v6#10 ((7/10/86) Baseball-c; (3) panel;

Rays of Light
1886 © Morse Bros., Canton, Mass.

Shakespeare Would Ride The Bicycle If Alive Today
1896 © Cleveland Bicycles, Toledo, OH.

Wreck-Elections Of Busy Life
Kellogg & Buckeley © 1864?

	FR 1.0	GD 2.0	FN 6.0
(5) panel A Story Without Words from Fliegende Blätter	17.00	34.00	100.00
v6 #11 12 13 Worth-c no sequentials	17.00	34.00	100.00
v6#14 (8/7/86) Wiorth-c; (7) panel Mrs Cleveland Presents The President With A New Rocking Chair	17.00	34.00	100.00
v6#15 (8/14/86) Worth-c; (6) panel Worth strip	17.00	34.00	100.00
v6#16 (8/21/86) Worth-c Asleep At Post USA/Mexico Border (6) panel sequential	17.00	34.00	100.00
v6#17 no sequrntials	17.00	34.00	100.00
v6#18 (9/4/86) Worth-c; (3) panel from Fliegende	17.00	34.00	100.00
v6#19 (9/11/86) Worth Anarchist & Uncle Sam-c; (5) panel Duel of the Dudes	17.00	34.00	100.00
v6#20 (9/18/86) Worth-c (6) panel sequential	17.00	34.00	100.00
v6#21 (9/25/86) Worth-c; Verbeck single panel; (9) panel	17.00	34.00	100.00
v6#22 (10/2/86) Verbeck-c plus interiors	17.00	34.00	100.00
v6#23 (10/9/86) Worth-c Geronimo & Devil cover; Verbeck and Chips singles	17.00	34.00	100.00
v6#24 (10/16/86) Worth-c Verbeck strip "Evolution"	17.00	34.00	100.00
v6#25 no sequential strips	17.00	34.00	100.00
v6#26 (10/30/86) Worth-c; (6) panel Verbeck "A Warning To Smokers"	17.00	34.00	100.00

NOTE: Many Thomas Worth sequential comic strips. Frank Bellew and Dan McCarthy appear. Wilhelm Busch-r from German Fliegende Blaetter. Later issues in 1890s comics become sporadic

THAT COMIC PRIMER (S)
G.W. Carleton & Co., Publishers: 1877 (6-5/8x5", 52 pgs, paper soft-c, B&W)

nn - By Frank Bellew	50.00	100.00	300.00

NOTE: Premium for the United States Life Insurance Company, New York.

TIGER, THE LEFTENANT AND THE BOSUN, THE
Prudential Insurance Home Office, 878 & 880 Broad St, Newark, NJ: 1889 (4.5x3.25", 12 pgs) (Scarce)

nn - 8 panel sequential story in color	40.00	80.00	240.00

TOM PLUMP, THE ADVENTURES OF MR. (see also The Juvenile Gem) (O)
Huestis & Cozans, New York: nd (c1850-1851) (6x3-7/8", 12 pgs, hand colored paper-c, B&W)

nn- First printing(s) publisher's address is 104 Nassau Street (1850-1851) (Very Rare)	567.00	1134.00	3400.00

NOTE: California Gold Rush story. The hand colored outer cover is highly rare, with only 1 recorded copy possessing it. The front cover image and text is repeated precisely on page 3 (albeit b&w), and only interior pages are numbered, together leading owners of coverless copies to believe they have the cover. The true back cover contains ads for the publisher. The cover was issued only with copies which were sold separately - booklets which were bound together as part of THE JUVENILE GEM had no such covers.

TOM PLUMP, THE ADVENTURES OF MR. (see also The Juvenile Gem) (O)
Philip J. Cozans: nd (1851-1852) (6x3-7/8", 12 pgs,hand colored paper-c, B&W)

nn- Second printing(s) publisher's address is 116 Nassau Street (1851-1852) (Very Rare)	300.00	600.00	1800.00
nn- Third printing(s) publisher's address is 107 Nassau Street (1852+) (Very Rare)	300.00	600.00	1800.00

TOM PLUMP, THE ADVENTURES OF MR.
Americana Review, Scotia, NY: nd(1960's) (6-1/4x4-1/8", 8 pgs, side-stapled, cardboard-c, B&W)

nn - Modern reprint	8.00	16.00	50.00

NOTE: Issued within a folder titled SIX CHILDREN'S BOOKS OF THE 1850'S. States "Reprinted by American Review" at bottom of front cover. Reprints the 104 Nassau Street address.)

nn - Modern rep. (Scarce 1980s) (5-1/2x4-1/4", 8 pgs,side-stapled)	3.00	6.00	20.00

NOTE: Photocopy reprint by a comix zine publisher, from an Americana Review copy; vailable by mail order

TOOTH-ACHE, THE (E,O)
D. Bogue, London: 1849 (5-1/4x3-3/4)

nn - By Cruikshank, B&W (Very Rare)	275.00	550.00	1650.00
nn - By Cruikshank, hand colored (Rare)		(no known sales)	

NOTE: Scripted by Horace Mayhew, art by George Cruikshank. This is the British edition. Price 1/6 b&w, 3 hand colored. In British editions, the panels are not numbered. Publisher's name appears on cover. Booklet's "pages" unfold into a single, long, strip.

J.L. Smith, Philadelphia, PA: nd (1849) (5-1/8"x 3-3/4" folded, 86-7/8" wide unfolded, 26 pgs, cardboard-c, color, 15¢)

nn - By Cruikshank, hand colored (Very Rare)	317.00	634.00	1900.00

NOTE: Reprints the D. Bogue edition. In American editions, the panels are numbered (43 panels, not counting front & back cover). Publisher's name stamped on inside front cover, plus printed along left-hand side of first interior page. Page 1 is pasted to inside back cover, and unfolds from there. Front cover not attached to back cover by design. Booklet's "pages" unfold into a single, long, strip (made from four individual strips pasted together on the blank back side). There is a fairly common1974 British Arts Council reprint.

TRAMP, THE: His Tricks, Tallies, and Tell-Tales, with His Signs, Countersigns, Grips, Passwords and Villainies Exposed (O,S)
Dick & Fitzgerald, New York: 1878 (11-3/8x8, 36 pgs, paper-c, B&W, 25¢) (Rare)

1 Frank Bellew	142.00	284.00	850.00

NOTE: Edited by Frank Bellew, A Bee And A Chip (Bellew's daughter and son Frank).

TRUTH (See Platinum Age section for 1900-1906 issues)
TRUTH
Truth Company, NY: 1886-1906? (13-11/16x10-5/16", 16 pgs, process color-c & centerfolds, rest B&W)

1886-1887 issues	18.00	36.00	110.00
1888-1895 issues non Outcault issues	14.00	28.00	85.00
Mar 10 1894 - precursor Yellow Kid RFO	79.00	158.00	475.00
#372 June 2 1894 - first app Yellow Kid RFO	233.00	466.00	1400.00
June 23 1894 - precursor Yellow Kid R. F. Outcault	79.00	158.00	475.00
July 14 1894 -2nd app Yellow Kid RFO	142.00	284.00	850.00

	FR 1.0	GD 2.0	FN 6.0
Sept 15 1894 - (2) 3rd app YK RFO plus YK precursor	142.00	284.00	850.00
Feb 9 1895 - 4th app Yellow Kid RFO	142.00	284.00	850.00
1896-1899 issues	10.00	20.00	60.00

NOTE: This magazine contains the earliest known appearances of The Yellow Kid by Richard Felton Outcault. Feb 9 1895 issue's YK cartoon was reprinted one week later in the New York World Feb 17 1895 edition. We are still sorting out further Outcault appearances. Truth also contained full color sequential strips by Hy Mayer on the back plus Woolf, Verbeek, etc.

TRUTH, SELECTIONS FROM
Truth Company, NY: 1894-Spr 1897 (13-11/16x10-1/4, color-c, quarterly)

1-4	19.00	38.00	115.00
5-Outcault's early Yellow Kid	92.00	184.00	550.00
6-13	15.00	30.00	90.00

NOTE: #5 reprints all early Outcault Yellow Kid appearances

TURNER'S COMIC ALMANAC
Charles Strong, 298 Pearl St, NYC: ???-1843 (7.25x4.5", 36 pgs, B&W)

nn	48.00	96.00	290.00

TURNER'S COMICK ALMA-NACK
Turner & Fisher, NYC: 1839-?? (7.25x4.5", 36 pgs, B&W)

nn	48.00	96.00	285.00

TWO HUNDRED SKETCHES, HUMOROUS AND GROTESQUE, BY GUSTAVE DORE (E)
Frederick Warne & Co, London: 1867 (13-3/4x11-3/8, 94 pgs, hard-c, B&W)

nn - (1867) by Gustave Dore	108.00	216.00	650.00
nn - (Second Edition; 1871)- by Gustave Dore	46.00	92.00	275.00
nn - (Third Edition; 1870's- by Gustave Dore	43.00	86.00	260.00
nn - (Fourth Edition; 1870's- by Gustave Dore	43.00	86.00	260.00

NOTE: Contains sequential comics stories, single panel cartoons, and sketches. Reprints and translates material which originally appeared in the French publications "Le Journal pour Rire", circa 1848-49. Although dated 1867, it was likely published & available for the 1866 Christmas Season, as has been confirmed for the American edition. Printed by Dalziel. The American & first British editions were printed simultaneously, the American edition is not a reprint of the British.

TWO HUNDRED SKETCHES, HUMOROUS AND GROTESQUE, BY GUSTAVE DORE (E)
Roberts Brothers, Boston: 1867 (13-3/4x11-3/8", 96 pgs, hard-c, B&W)

nn - By Gustave Dore	121.00	242.00	725.00

NOTE: Although dated 1867, it was published & available for the 1866 Christmas Season. Printed by Dalziel in England, and imported to the USA expressly for a USA publisher.

UNCLE JOSH'S TRUNK-FUL OF FUN
Dick & Fitzgerald, 18 Ann St, NY: 1870s (5-3/4x9", 68 pgs, B&W & Red-c, B&W inside)

nn - Rare	38.00	76.00	230.00

NOTE: Many single panel cartoons; (2) pages of early boxing sequential strip

UNCLE SAM'S COMIC ALMANAC
M.J. Meyers, NY: 1879 (11x8", 32 pgs)

nn	36.00	72.00	215.00

UNDER THE GASLIGHT
Gaslight Publishing Co (Frank Tousey): Oct 13 1878-Apr 12 1879 (Folio, 16pgs)

1-27	33.00	66.00	200.00

UNITED STATES COMIC ALMANAC
King & Baird, Philadelphia: 1851-?? (7.5x4.5", 36 pgs, B&W)

nn	48.00	96.00	290.00

UPS AND DOWNS ON LAND AND WATER (O.G)
James R. Osgood & Co., Boston: 1871 ; **Houghton, Osgood & Co., Boston:** 1880 (108 pgs, gilted hard-c, B&W)

1st printing (1871; 10-3/4x16") - By Augustus Hoppin	36.00	72.00	215.00
2nd printing (1880; smaller sized)	22.00	44.00	130.00

NOTE: Exists as blue or orange hard covers.

VANITY FAIR
William A. Stephens (for Thompson & Camac): Dec 29 1859-July 4 1863 Quarto Weekly

Average issues with comic strips	20.00	40.00	120.00

VERDICT, THE
Verdict Publishing Co: Dec 19 1898-Nov 12 1900 (Chromolithographic Weekly)

Average issues	45.00	90.00	270.00

NOTE: Artists included George B. Luks, Horace Taylor, MIRS. Striking anti-Republican weekly full o fsome of the most savage political cartoons of the era. The last brilliant burst of energy for the political cartoon weekly

VERY VERY FUNNY (M,S)
Dick & Fitzgerald, New York: nd(c1880's) (10¢, 7-1/2x5", 68 pgs, paper-c, B&W)

nn - (Rare)	63.00	125.00	375.00

NOTE: Unauthorized reprints of prose and cartoons extracted from Puck, Texas Siftings, and other publications. Includes art by Chips Bellew, Bisbee, Graetz, Opper, Wales, Zim.

VIM
H. Wimmel, NYC: June 22-Aug 24 1898 (Chromolithographic Weekly)

average issue	36.00	72.00	215.00
Yellow Kid by Leon Barritt issues	71.00	142.00	425.00

WAR IN THE MIDST OF AMERICA. FROM A NEW POINT OF VIEW. (E,O,G)
Ackermann & Co., London: 1864 (4-3/8" x 5-7/8", folded, 36 feet wide unfolded, 80 pgs, hard-c, B&W)

nn- by Charles Dryden (rare)	367.00	734.00	2200.00

NOTE: British graphic novel about the American Civil War, with a pro-Confederate bent. Adventures of a British artist who decides to visually summarize the American Civil War for his countrymen, from newspaper accounts. Reaching current events, he finds he can not finish the story until the War ends, and so he travels to America, to end it. Book unfolds into a single long strip (binding was issued split, to enable the unfolding).

WASP, THE ILLUSTRATED SAN FRANCISCO
F. Korbel & Bros and Numerous Others: August 5 1876-April 25 1941 (Chromolithographic Weekly)

average 1800s issues with comic strips	35.00	70.00	210.00

WHAT I KNOW OF FARMING: Founded On The Experience of Horace Greeley (S)
The American News Company, New York: 1871 (7-1/4x4-1/2", paper-c, B&W)

nn - By Joseph Hull (Scarce)	32.00	64.00	190.00

NOTE: Pay & Cox, Printers & Engravers, NY; political tract regarding Presidential elections.

WILD FIRE
Wild Fire Co, NYC: Nov 30 1877-at least#16 Mar 1878 (Folio, 16 pgs)

1-16	21.00	42.00	125.00

WILD OATS, An Illustrated Weekly Journal of Fun, Satire, Burlesque, and Nits at Persons and Events of the Day (O)
Winchell & Small, 113 Fulton St /48 Ann St, NYC: Feb 1870-1881 (16-1/4x11", generally 16 pages, B&W, began as monthly, then bi-weekly, then weekly) All loose issues Very Rare (See *The Overstreet Price Guide #35* 2005 for a detailed index of single issue contents)

1-25 Very Rare - contents to be indexed in a future edition	50.00	100.00	300.00
26-28 30 32 35 36 39 40 41 43-46 1872 (sequential strips)	44.00	88.00	265.00
29 33 37 42 no sequential strips	30.00	60.00	180.00
31 34 38 47 Hopkins sequential comic strips	42.00	84.00	250.00
48 (1/16/73) Worth 13 panel sequential; first Woolf-c	42.00	84.00	250.00
49 51 53 54 60 62 61 64 65 66 67 69 1873 sequential strips	42.00	84.00	250.00
50 52 56 59 63 71 no sequential strips	30.00	60.00	180.00
51 (Worth 18 panel double page spread, Woolf 9 panel	42.00	84.00	250.00
55 Hopkins 22 panel double page spread; Bellew-c	54.00	108.00	325.00
57 Intense unknown 6 panel "Two Relics of Barbarism, or A Few Contrasted Pictures, Showing the origin of the North American Indian	42.00	84.00	250.00
58 (6/5/73) unknown 19 panel double pager "The Terrible Adventures of Messrs Buster & Stumps, About Exterminating the Indians" reads across both pages like Popeye #2095 (1933); Woolf-c	79.00	158.00	475.00
68 (10/16/73) unknown 9 panel "Adv of New Jersey Mosquito" looks like Winsor McCay type style: early inspiration for McCay's animated cartoon? 42.00		84.00	250.00
70 unknown 6 panel; Hopkins 6 panel "Hopkins novel: A Tale of True Love, with all the variations"; Bellew-c	38.00	76.00	230.00
72 (12/11/73) Worth 11 panel; Wales President Grant war-c	38.00	76.00	230.00
73 74 75 Hopkins sequential comic strip	52.00	104.00	310.00
76 77 sequential strips	38.00	76.00	230.00
78 Bellew 5 panel double pager	38.00	76.00	230.00
79-105 (March 1874-Dec 1874) contents presently unknown	38.00	76.00	230.00
106 107 111 no sequentials;Bellew-c #106 110;Wales-c #107	38.00	76.00	230.00
108 (1/20/75) Wales 12 panel double pg spread; Bellew-c	38.00	76.00	230.00
109 (1/27/75) unknown 6 panel; Wales-c	38.00	76.00	230.00
111 Busch 13 panel "The Conundrum of the Day - Is Lager Beer Intoxicating?"; Bellew-c	38.00	76.00	230.00
112 116 sequential comic strips	38.00	76.00	230.00
113 114 115 no sequentials Worth-c #114	30.00	60.00	180.00
117 intense Wales 6 panel "One of the Oppresions of the Civil Rights Laws" Bellew-c	58.00	116.00	350.00
118-137 (3/31/75-8/4/75) no sequential comic strips	30.00	60.00	180.00
138 (8/18/75) Bellew Sr & Bellew "Chips" Jr singles appear	38.00	76.00	225.00
139-143 145-147 154-157 159 no sequentials	30.00	60.00	180.00
144 (9/29/75) Hopkins 8 panel sequential; Wales-c	38.00	76.00	230.00
148 (10/27/75) Opper's first cover; many Opper singles	53.00	106.00	320.00
149 150 151 152 153 all Opper-c and much interior work	38.00	76.00	230.00
158 (1/5/76) Palmer Cox 1rst comic strip 24 panel double page spread "The Adv of Mr & Mrs Sprowl And Their Christmas Turkey - A Crashing Chasing Tearful Tragedy But Happily Ending Well"; Opper-c	75.00	150.00	450.00
159 160 162 165 167 169-173 no sequentials	30.00	60.00	180.00
161 163 164 166 168 179 182 Palmer Cox sequential strips	75.00	150.00	450.00
174 (4/26/76) Cox 24 panel double pager "The Tramp's Progress; A Story of the West And the Union Pacific Railroad"	75.00	150.00	450.00
175-178 183-189 no sequentials	30.00	60.00	180.00
180 (6/7/76) Beard & Opper jam; Woolf, Bellew singles	38.00	76.00	230.00
181 more Mann two panel jobs; Opper-c	38.00	76.00	230.00
190 Bellew 9 panel "Rodger's Patent Mosquito Armour"	53.00	106.00	320.00
191-end contents to be indexed in the near future	30.00	60.00	180.00

NOTE: There are very few known ouse issues. All loose issues are Very Rare. Prices vary widely on this magazine. Issues with sequential comic strips would be in higher demand than issues with no comic strips. We present this index from the Library of Congress and New York Historical Society bound sets. We would love to hear from any one who turns up loose copies. This scarce humor bi-weekly contains easily a couple hundred original first-time published sequential comic strips found in most issues plus innumerable single panel cartoons in every issue

WOMAN IN SEARCH OF HER RIGHTS, THE ADVENTURES OF (G)
Lee & Shepard, Boston And New York: early 1870s (8-3/8x13", 40 pgs, hard-c)

By Florence Claxton (Very Rare)	383.00	766.00	2300.00

NOTE: Earliest known original comic book sequential story by a woman; contains "nearly 100 original drawings by the author, which have been reproduced in fac-simile by the photogype process of engraving." Tinted two color lithography; orange tint printed first, then printed 2nd time with black ink; early women's sufferage.

WORLD OVER, THE (I)
G. W. Dillingham Company, New York: 1897 (192 pgs, hard-c)

nn - By Joe Kerr; 80 illustrations by R.F. Outcault (Rare)	225.00	450.00	1350.00

NOTE: soft cover editions also exist

WRECK-ELECTIONS OF BUSY LIFE (S)
Kellogg & Bulkeley: 1867 (9-1/4x11-3/4", ??? pages, soft-c)

nn - By J. Bowker (Rare)	75.00	150.00	450.00

NOTE: Says "Sold by American News Company, New York" on cover.

WYMAN'S COMIC ALMANAC FOR THE TIMES
T.W. Strong, NY: 1854 (8x5", 24 pgs)

nn -	37.00	74.00	220.00

YANKEE DOODLE
W.H. Graham, Tribune Building, NYC: Oct 10 1846-Oct 2 1847 (Quarto weekly)

average issue	45.00	90.00	270.00

YANKEE NOTIONS, OR WHITTLINGS OF JONATHAN'S JACK-KNIFE
T.W. Strong, 98 Nassau St, NYC: Jan. 1852-1875 (11x8, 32 pgs, paper-c, 12.5¢, monthly)

1 Brother Jonathan character single panel cartoons	46.00	92.00	275.00

NOTE: Begins continuing character sequential comic strip, "The Adventures of Jeremiah Oldpot" in "A Bird in the Hand Is Worth Two in The Bush"

2-4	23.00	46.00	140.00
5 British X-Over	23.00	46.00	140.00

NOTE: Single panel of John Bull & Brother Jonathan exchanging civilities (issues of Punch & Yankee Notions)

6 end of Jeremiah Oldpot continued strip	23.00	46.00	140.00
v2#1 begin "Hoosier Bragg" sequential strip - six issue serial	22.00	44.00	130.00
v2#2 Feb 1853 two pg 12 panel sequential "Mr Vanity's Exploits, Arising Out Of A Valentine"	33.00	66.00	200.00
v2#3-v2#5 continues Hoosier Bragg	22.00	44.00	130.00
v2#6 June 1853 Lion Eats Hoosier Bragg, end of story	22.00	44.00	130.00
v3#1 begins referring to its cartoons as "Comic Art"	33.00	66.00	200.00
v4#1-V4#6 v5#1-v5#2 no sequential comic strips	17.00	34.00	100.00
v5#3 two sequential comic strips	35.00	70.00	210.00

NOTE: Mr Take-A-Drop And The Maine Law (5) panels and The First Segar (7) panels (about smoking tobacco)

v5#4 April 1856 begin Billy Vidkins	35.00	70.00	210.00

NOTE: Begins reprinting "From Passages in the Life of Little Billy Vidkins, first issued as a stand alone proto-comic book in 1849 Illustrations of the Poets

v5#5 The McBargem Guards (9) panel sequential; Vidkins	22.00	44.00	130.00
v5#6 v5 #9 no comics	17.00	34.00	100.00
v5#7 Billy Vidkins continues	22.00	44.00	130.00
v5#8 end of Vidkins By HL Stephens, Esq.	22.00	44.00	130.00
v5#10 (6) panel "How We Learn To Ride"; Timber is hero	22.00	44.00	130.00
v5#11 (7) panel "How Mr. Green Sparrowgrass Voted-A Warning For the Benefit of Quiet Citizens About To Excercize the Elective Franchise" plus Pt Two "How We Learn to Ride"	33.00	66.00	200.00
v5#12 (6) panel "How Mr Pipp Got Struck"; "The Eclipse" featuring Mr Phips; Pt 3 "How We Learn to Ride"	22.00	44.00	130.00
v6#1 (Jan 1857) (12) panel "A Tale of An Umbrella; (4) panel begins a serial "The Man Who Bought The Elephant; (8) panel How Our Young New Yorkers Celebrate New Years Day	22.00	44.00	130.00
v6#2 (Feb 1857) Pt 2 (4) panels The Man Who Bought the Elephant; (7) panel A Game of All Fours	22.00	44.00	130.00
v6#3 (Mar 1857) Pt 3 (4) panels The Man Who Bought the Elephant ending; (4) panel Ye Great Crinoline Monopoly	22.00	44.00	130.00
v6#4 no comic strips	22.00	44.00	130.00
v6#5 (May 1850) (3) panel A Short Trip to Mr Bumps, And How It Ended; (2) panel How Mr Trembles Was Garrotted	22.00	44.00	130.00
v6#6 no comic strips	22.00	44.00	130.00
v6#7 (July 1857) (5) panel Alma Mater; (3) panel Three Tableaux In The Life of A Broadway Swell	22.00	44.00	130.00
v6 #8 9 no comic strips	22.00	44.00	130.00
v6#10 (Oct 1857) (3) panel Adv of Mr Near-Sight	22.00	44.00	130.00
v6#11 (Nov 1857) (11) panel Mrs Champignon's Dinner Party And the Way She Arranged Her Guests; (4) panel A Stroll in August	22.00	44.00	130.00
v6#12 (Dec 1857) (8) panel strip; (12) panel Young Fitz At A Blow Out in the Fifth Ave	22.00	44.00	130.00
v10#1 (Jan 1860) comic strip Bibbs at Central Park Skating Pond using word balloons	22.00	44.00	130.00

YE TRUE ACCOUNTE OF YE VISIT TO SPRINGFIELDE BY YE CONSTABEL HIS SPECIAL REPORTER
Frank Leslie: 1861 (5-1/8 x 5-1/4 or 93 inches when folded out, paper-c, B&W)

nn - Very Rare fold-out of 18 comic strip panels plus covers (a FN copy sold in 2010 for $101.85)			

NOTE: 8 panels contain word balloons (Very Rare - only one copy known to exist). First printed in Frank Leslie's Budget of Fun Jan 1 1861 issue. Abraham Lincoln Biography.

YE VERACIOUS CHRONICLE OF GRUFF & POMPEY IN 7 TABLEAUX. (O,P)
Jackson's Best Chewing Tobacco & Donaldson Brothers: nd (c1870's) (5-1/8 tall x 3-3/8" wide folded, 27" wide unfolded, color cardboard)

nn - With all 8 panels attached (Scarce)	38.00	76.00	230.00
nn - Individual panels/cards	5.00	10.00	30.00

NOTE: Black Americana interest. Consists of 8 attached cards, printed on one side, which unfold into a strip story of title card & 7 panels. Scrapbook hobbyists in the 19th Century tended to pull the panels apart and paste into their scrapbooks, making copies with all panels attached scarce.

YOUNG AMERICA (continues as Yankee Doodle)
T.W. Strong, NYC: 1856

1-30 John McLennon	44.00	88.00	265.00

YOUNG AMERICA'S COMIC ALMANAC
T.W. Strong, NY: 1857 (7-1/2x5", 24 pgs)

nn	44.00	88.00	265.00

THE YOUNG MEN OF AMERICA (becomes Golden Weekly) (S)
Frank Tousey, NYC: 1887-88 (14x10-1/4", 16 pgs, B&W)

527 (10/13/87) Bellew strip "Story of A Black Eye"	19.00	38.00	115.00
530 (11/3/87) Thomas Worth (6) panel strip	21.00	42.00	125.00
531 (11/10/87) Thomas Worth(3) panel strip			
537 (12/22/87) H.E. Patterson (3) panel strip			
544 (2/9/88) Carans' Ache (6) panel strip-r	19.00	38.00	115.00
555 (4/26/88) Thomas Worth (6) panel strip			
556 (5/3/88) Thomas Worth (6) panel strip; Kit Carson-c	60.00	120.00	360.00
569 (8/21/88) Frank Bellew (2) panel strip			
570 (8/9/88) Kemble (2) panel strip			
571 (8/16/88) Kemble (2) panel strip; first Davy Crockett	60.00	120.00	360.00
Issues with just single panel cartoons	8.00	16.00	50.00

ZIM'S QUARTERLY (M)
(13-13/16x10-1/8", 60 pgs, color-c; mostly B&W, some interior color)

1 - Eugene Zimmerman	88.00	176.00	525.00

NOTE: Approx. half sequential comic strips, other half single panel cartoons.

Any additions or corrections to this section are always welcome, very much encouraged and can be sent to **feedback@gemstonepub.com** to be processed for next year's Guide.

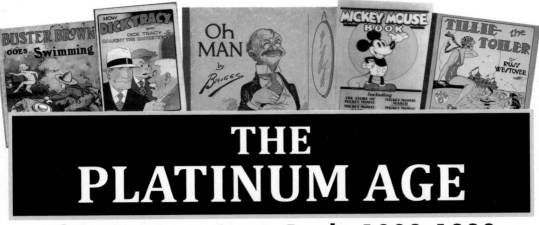

THE PLATINUM AGE

The American Comic Book: 1883-1938

The comic book ages tend to overlap a bit with one another – DC's Silver Age started with *Showcase* #4, but Marvel's didn't begin until *Fantastic Four* #1, for instance – so it's not surprising that the Platinum Age and Victorian Age tend to overlap a bit, with the Victorian Age in some ways running through the end of the 19th century. The Platinum Age of comics is marked by the introduction of several important elements, including three distinct and important features: the rise of licensed character merchandise, panel formats, and the evolution of the speech balloon.

The Platinum Age of Comics began with Palmer Cox's creation of *The Brownies* in 1883. Cox introduced a significant change to the medium with his work, and all at once rather than slowly and incrementally – he produced his art specifically with children in mind, and then merchandised his characters extensively. *The Brownies* became the first North American comic characters to be internationally merchandised. Their first standalone book, *The Brownies: Their Book*, debuted in 1887.

By the mid-1890s, newspaper publishers had caught on to the idea that comic characters could help sell more papers, having seen what they did to boost circulation of various magazines. The idea of a Sunday "comic supplement" was born at this time.

Throughout the Platinum Age, there are numerous important landmarks: James Swinnerton's *The Little Bears* (later *Little Bears*

& Tykes), debuted in 1892, Richard F. Outcault's *Hogan's Alley* first appeared in 1894 in the *New York World* and The Yellow Kid first appeared in 1895 and had his first word balloon on October 25, 1896.

By the early 1900s, many other characters and strips were enjoying successful collections in volume format. Strips like *The Blackberries*, *Opper's Folks in Funnyville*, *Vaudevilles and Other Things*, *Mutt & Jeff*, *Bringing Up Father*, *The Katzenjammer Kids* and many others had circulations significantly higher than the early superheroes.

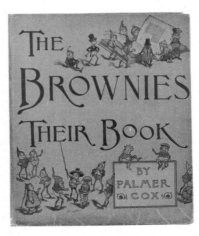

The Brownies' first book in 1887 set a precedent for the Platinum Age, collecting and reprinting previously published material.

IN MEMORIAM
RICHARD OLSON, PH.D. • ROBERT BEERBOHM

Richard Olson and Robert Beerbohm each contributed mightily to *The Overstreet Comic Book Price Guide*, particularly to the Platinum Age section, over the years. While both have passed, their contributions to our understanding of this foundational era of comic books will continue to impact scholars, readers, and dealers for years to come.

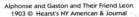

Alphonse and Gaston and Their Friend Leon
1903 © Hearst's NY American & Journal

American-Journal-Examiner Joke Book Spec.
Supplement #2. 1911 © N.Y. American

At The Bottom Of The Ladder
1926 © J.P. Lippincott Company

	GD 2.0	FN 6.0	VF 8.0

COLLECTOR'S NOTE: The books listed in this section were published many decades before organized comics fandom began archiving and helping to preserve these fragile popular culture artifacts. Consequently, copies of most all of these comics do not often surface in Fine+ or better shape. eBay has proven after more than a decade that many items once considered rare actually are not, though they almost always are in higher grades. For items marked scarce, we are trying to ascertain how many copies might still be in existence. Your input is always welcome.

Most Platinum Age comic books are in the Fair to VG range. If you want to collect these only in high grade, your collection will be extremely small. The prices given for Good, Fine and Very Fine categories are for strictly graded editions. If you need help grading your item, we refer you to the grading section in the front of this price guide or contact the authors of the Platinum essay. Most measurements are in inches. A few measurements are in centimeters. The first dimension given is Height and the second is Width.

For ease of ascertaining the contents of each item of this listing, there is a code letter or two following most titles we have been adding in over the years to aid you. A helpful list of categories pertaining to these codes can be found at the beginning of the Victorian Age pricing sections. This section created, revised, and expanded by Robert Beerbohm and Richard Olson with able assistance from Ray Agricola, Jon Berk, Bill Blackbeard, Roy Bonario, Ray Bottorff Jr., Chris Brown, Alfredo Castelli, Darrell Coons, Sol Davidson, Leonardo De Sá, Scott Deschaine, Mitchell Duval, Joe Evans, Tom Gordon III, Bruce Hamilton, Andy Konkykru, Don Kurtz, Gabriel Laderman, Bruce Mason, Donald Puff, Robert Quesinberry, Steve Rowe, Randy Scott, John Snyder, Art Spiegelman, Steve Thompson, Joan Crosby Tibbets, Richard Samuel West, Doug Wheeler, Richard Wright and Craig Yoe.

ADVENTURES OF EVA, PORA AND TED (M)
Evaporated Milk Association: 1932 (5x15", 16 pgs, B&W)

nn - By Steve	19.00	57.00	115.00

NOTE: Appears to have had green, blue or white paper cover versions.

ADVENTURES OF HAWKSHAW (N) (See Hawkshaw The Detective)
The Saalfield Publishing Co.: 1917 (9-3/4x13-1/2", 48 pgs., color & two-tone)

nn - By Gus Mager (only 24 pgs. of strips, reverse of each pg. is blank)	65.00	195.00	390.00
nn - 1927 Reprints 1917 issue	43.00	129.00	260.00

NOTE: Started Feb 23, 1913-Sept 4, 1922, then begins again Dec 13, 1931-Feb 11, 1952.

ADVENTURES OF SLIM AND SPUD, THE (M)
Prairie Farmer Publ. Co.: 1924 (3-3/4x 9-3/4", 104 pgs., B&W strip reprints)

nn	31.00	93.00	185.00

NOTE: Illustrated mailing envelope exists postmarked out of Chicago, add 50%.

ADVENTURES OF WILLIE WINTERS, THE (O,P)
Kelloggs Toasted Corn Flake Co.: 1912 (6-7/8x9-1/2", 20 pgs, full color)

nn - By Byron Williams & Dearborn Melvill	62.00	186.00	370.00

ADVENTURES OF WILLIE GREEN, THE (N) (see The Willie Green Comics)
Frank M. Acton Co.: 1915 (50¢, 52 pgs, 8-1/2X16", B&W, soft-c)

Book 1 - By Harris Brown; strip-r	62.00	186.00	370.00

A. E. F. IN CARTOONS BY WALLY, THE (N)
Don Sowers & Co.: 1933 (12x10-1/8", 88 pgs, hardcover B&W)

nn - By Wally Wallgren (WW One Stars & Stripes-r)	46.00	138.00	275.00

AFTER THE TOWN GOES DRY (I)
The Howell Publishing Co, Chicago: 1919 (48 pgs, 6-1/2x4", hardbound two color-c)

nn - By Henry C. Taylor; illus by Frank King	28.00	84.00	165.00

AIN'T IT A GRAND & GLORIOUS FEELING? (N) (Also see Mr. & Mrs.)
Whitman Publishing Co.: 1922 (9x9-3/4", 52 pgs., stiff cardboard-c)

nn - 1921 daily strip-r; B&W, color-c; Briggs-a	43.00	129.00	255.00
nn - -(9x9-1/2", 28pgs., stiff cardboard-c)-Sunday strip-r in color (inside front-c says "More of the Married Life of Mr. & Mrs".)	43.00	129.00	255.00

NOTE: Strip started in 1917; This is the 2nd Whitman comic book, after Brigg's MR. & MRS.

ALL THE FUNNY FOLKS (I)
World Press Today, Inc.: 1926 (11-1/2x8-1/2", 112 pgs., color, hard-c)

nn-Barney Google, Spark Plug, Jiggs & Maggie, Tillie The Toiler, Happy Hooligan, Hans & Fritz, Toots & Casper, etc.	129.00	387.00	775.00
With Dust Jacket By Louis Biedermann	283.00	849.00	1700.00

NOTE: Booklength race horse story masterfully enveloping all major King Features characters.

ALPHONSE AND GASTON AND THEIR FRIEND LEON
Hearst's New York American & Journal: 1902,1903 (10x15-1/4", Sunday strip reprints in color)

nn - (1902) - By Frederick Opper (scarce)	750.00	2250.00	–
nn - (1903) - By Frederick Opper (scarce) (72 pages)	640.00	1920.00	–

NOTE: Strip ran Sept 22, 1901 to at least July 17, 1904.

ALWAYS BELITTLIN' (see Skippy; That Rookie From the 13th Squad; Between Shots)
Henry Holt & Co.: 1927 (6x8", hard-c with DJ)

nn -By Percy Crosby (text with cartoons)	58.00	174.00	350.00

ALWAYS BELITTLIN' (I) (see Skippy; That Rookie From the 13th Squad; Between Shots)
Percy Crosby, Publisher: 1933 (14 1/4 x 11", 72 pgs, hard-c, B&W)

nn - By Percy Crosby	57.00	171.00	340.00

NOTE: Self-published; primarily political cartoons with text pages denouncing prohibition's gang warfare effects and cuts in the national defense budget as Crosby saw war looming in Europe and with Japan.

AMERICAN-JOURNAL-EXAMINER JOKE BOOK SPECIAL SUPPLEMENT (O)
New York American: 1911-12 (12 x 9 3/4", 16 pgs) (known issues) (Very Rare)

1 Tom Powers Joke Book(12/10/11)	108.00	325.00	–
2 Mutt & Jeff Joke Book (Bud Fisher 12/17/11)	133.00	400.00	–
3 TAD's Joke Book (Thomas Dorgan 12/24/11)	103.00	310.00	–
4 F. Opper's Joke Book (Frederick Burr Opper 12/31/11) (contains Happy Hooligan)	125.00	375.00	–
5 not known to exist			
6 Swinnerton's Joke Book (Jimmy Swinnerton 01/14/12) (contains Mr. Jack)	137.00	410.00	–
7 The Monkey's Joke Book (Gus Mager 01/21/12) (contains Sherlocko the Monk)	120.00	360.00	–
8 Joys And Glooms Joke Book (T. E. Powers 01/28/12)	103.00	310.00	–
9 The Dingbat Family's Joke Book (George Herriman 02/04/12) (contains early Krazy Kat & Ignatz)	275.00	825.00	–
10 Valentine Joke Book, A (Opper, Howarth, Mager, T. E. Powers 02/11/12)	105.00	315.00	–
11 Little Hatchet Joke Book (T. E. Powers 02/18/12)	105.00	315.00	–
12 Jungle Joke Book (Dirks, McCay 02/25/12)	137.00	410.00	–
13 The Hayseeds Joke Book (03/03/12)	103.00	310.00	–
14 Married Life Joke Book (T.E. Powers 03/10/12)	103.00	310.00	–

NOTE: These were insert newspaper supplements similar to Eisner's later Spirit sections. A Valentine Joke Book recently surfaced from Hearst's Boston Sunday American proving that other cities besides New York City had these special supplements. Each issue also contains work by other cartoonists besides the cover featured creator and those already listed above such as Sidney Smith, Winsor McCay, Hy Mayer, Grace Weiderseim (later Drayton), others.

AMERICA'S BLACK & WHITE BOOK 100 Pictured Reasons Why We Are At War (N,S)
Cupples & Leon: 1917 (10 3/4 x 8", 216 pgs)

nn - W. A. Rogers (New York Herald-r)	40.00	120.00	240.00

AMONG THE FOLKS IN HISTORY
Rand McNally Print Guild: 1928 (192 pgs, 8-1/2x9-1/2", hard-c, B&W)

nn - By Gaar Williams	27.00	81.00	160.00

AMONG THE FOLKS IN HISTORY
The Book and Print Guild: 1935 (200 pgs, 8-1/2x9-1/2:,

nn - By Gaar Williams	25.00	75.00	150.00

NOTE: Both the above are evidently different editions and contain largely full-page, single panel cartoons similar to Briggs' work of that sort. 8 or 10 pages are broken into panels, usually with a "this is how it was in the old days, this is how it is today theme."

ANGELIC ANGELINA (N)
Cupples & Leon Company: 1909 (11-1/2x17", 56 pgs., 2 colors)

nn - By Munson Paddock	71.00	213.00	425.00

NOTE: Strip ran March 22, 1908-Feb 7, 1909.

ANDY GUMP, HIS LIFE STORY (I)
The Reilly & Lee Co, Chicago: 1924 (192 pgs, hardbound)

nn - By Sidney Smith (over 100 illustrations)	41.00	123.00	245.00

ANIMAL CIRCUS, THE (from Puggery Wee)
Rand McNally + Company: 1908 (48 pgs, 11x8-1/2", color-c, 3-color insides)

nn - By unknown	29.00	87.00	175.00

NOTE: Illustrated verse, many pages with multiple illustrations.

ANIMAL SERIALS
T. Y. Crowell: 1906 (9x6-7/8", 214 pgs, hard-c, B&W)

nn - By E Warde Blaisdell	27.00	81.00	160.00

NOTE: Multi-page comic strip stories. Reprints of Sunday strip "Bunny Bright He's All-Right".

A NOBODY'S SCRAP BOOK
Frederik A. Stokes Company, New York: 1900 (11" x 8-5/8", hard-c, color)

nn- (Scarce)	71.00	213.00	425.00

NOTE: Designed in England, printed in Holland, on English paper -- which likely explains the mispelling of Frederick Stokes' name. Highly fragile paper. Strips and cartoons, all by the same unidentified artist, "A Nobody", almost certainly reprinted from somewhere, as they are very professional.

AT THE BOTTOM OF THE LADDER (M)
J.P. Lippincott Company: 1926 (11x8-1/4", 296 pgs, hardcover, B&W)

nn - By Camillus Kessler	47.00	141.00	280.00

NOTE: Hilarious single panel cartoons showing first jobs of then important "captains of industry."

AUTO FUN, PICTURES AND COMMENTS FROM "LIFE"
Thomas Y. Crowell & Co.: 1905 (152 pgs, 9x7", hard-c, B&W)

nn -By various	71.00	213.00	425.00

NOTE: The cover just has "Auto Fun" but the title page also has the subheading listed here. This is similar to other reprint books of Life cartoons printed in the guide. Largely single panel cartoons but also several sequential. One or more cartoons by Kemble, Levering, Dirks, Sullivant. Sequential cartoons by Kemble, Levering, Sullivant, and the highpoint, a 2 pg 6 panel piece by Winsor McCay.

BANANA OIL (N) (see also HE DONE HER WRONG)
MS Publ. Co.: 1924 (9-7/8x10", 52 pgs., B&W)

nn - Milt Gross comic strips; not reprints	200.00	600.00	1200.00

BARKER'S ILLUSTRATED ALMANAC (O,P,S) (See Barkers in Victorian Era section)
Barker, Moore & Mein Medicine Co: 1900-1932+ (36 pgs, B&W, color paper-c)

1900-1932+ (7x5-7/8")	27.00	81.00	160.00

BARKER'S "KOMIC" PICTURE SOUVENIR (P,S) (see Barker's in Victorian)
Barker, Moore & Mein Medicine Co: nd (Parts 1-3, 1901-1903; Parts 1-4, 1906+) (color cardboard-c, B&W interior, 50 pages)

Parts 1-3 (Rare, earliest printing, nd (1901))	167.00	500.00	1000.00

NOTE: Same cover as in 4th edition in Victorian Age Section, except has "Part 1", "Part 2", or "Part 3" printed in the blank space beneath the crate on which central figure is sitting. States "Edition in 3 Parts" on the first interior page, beneath the picture of the Barker's Building.

Parts 1-3 (nd, c1901-1903)	125.00	375.00	750.00

NOTE: New cover art on all Parts. States "Edition in 3 Parts" on the first interior page.

Parts 1-4 (c1906+)	100.00	300.00	600.00

NOTE: States "Edition in 4 Parts" on the first interior page. Various printings known. These have been confirmed as premium comic books, predating the Buster Brown premiums. These represent advertising cartoons from Barker's Illustrated Almanac. For the 50 page booklets by this same name, numbered as "Part"s, without exception, were published after 1900. Some editions are found to have 54 pages.

BARNEY GOOGLE AND SPARK PLUG (N) (See Comic Monthly)
Cuples & Leon Co.: 1923 - No.6, 1928 (9-7/8x9-3/4"; 52 pgs., B&W, daily-r)

1 (nn)-By Billy DeBeck	113.00	339.00	675.00
2-4 (#5 & #6 do not exist)	58.00	174.00	350.00

NOTE: Started June 17, 1919 as newspaper strip; Spark Plug introduced July 17, 1922; strip still running making it one of the oldest still in existence.

BART'S CARTOONS FOR 1902 FROM THE MINNEAPOLIS JOURNAL (N,S)
Minneapolis Journal: 1903 (11x9", 102 pgs, paperback, B&W)

nn - By Charles L. Bartholomew	30.00	90.00	175.00

BELIEVE IT OR NOT! by Ripley (N,S)
Simon & Schuster: 1929 (8x 5-1/4", 68 pgs, red, B&W cover, B&W interior)

nn - By Robert Ripley (strip-r text & art)	50.00	150.00	300.00

NOTE: 1929 was the first printing of many reprintings . Strip began Dec 19, 1918 and is still running.

BEN WEBSTER
Standard Printing Company: 1928-1931 (13-3/4x4-7/16", 768 pgs, soft-c)

1 - "Bound to Win"	52.00	156.00	310.00
2 - "...in old Mexico	52.00	156.00	310.00
3 - "...At Wilderness Lake	52.00	156.00	310.00
4 - "...in the Oil Fields	52.00	156.00	310.00

NOTE: Self Published by Edwin Alger, also contains fan's letter pages.

BIG SMOKER
W.T. Blackwell & Co.: 1908 (16 pgs, 5-1/2x3-1/2", color-c & interior)

nn - By unknown	21.00	63.00	125.00

NOTE: Stated reprint of 1878 version. no known copies yet of original printing.

BILLY BOUNCE (I)
Donohue & Co.: 1906 (288 pgs, hardbound)

nn - By W.W. Denslow & Dudley Bragdon	217.00	651.00	1300.00

NOTE: Billy Bounce was created in 1901 as a comic strip by W. W. Denslow (strip ran from 1901 NOV 11 to 1905 DEC 3), but the series is best remembered by the C. W. Kahles version (from 1902 SEP 28). Denslow resumed his character in the above illustrated book.

BILLY HON'S FAMOUS CARTOON BOOK (H)
Wasley Publishing Co.: 1927 (7-1/2x10", 68 pgs, softbound wraparound)

nn - By Billy Hon	19.00	57.00	115.00

BILLY THE BOY ARTIST'S BOOK OF FUNNY PICTURES
C.M.Clark Publishing Co.: 1910 (9x12", hardcover-c, Boston Globe strip-r)

nn - By Ed Payne	125.00	375.00	750.00

NOTE: This long lived strip ran in The Boston Globe from Nov 5 1899-Jan 7 1955; one of the longer run strips.

BILLY THE BOY ARTIST'S PAINTING BOOK OF FUNNY PICTURES
(known to exist; more data required)

	—	—	—

BIRD CENTER CARTOONS: A Chronicle of Social Happenings (N,S)
A. C. McClurg & Co.: 1904 (12-3/8x9-1/2", 216 pgs, hardcover, B&W, single panels)

nn - By John McCutcheon	42.00	126.00	250.00

NOTE: Strip began in The Chicago Tribune in 1903. Satirical cartoons and text concerning a mythical town.

BLASTS FROM THE RAM'S HORN
The Rams Horn Company: 1902 (330 pgs, 7x9", B&W)

nn - By various	27.00	81.00	160.00

NOTE: Cartoons reprinted from what was, apparently, a religious newspaper. Many cartoons by Frank Beard. Mostly single panel but occasionally sequential. Allegorical cartoons similar to the Christian Cartoons book. This book mixes cartoons and text sort of like the Caricature books. One or more cartoons on every page.

BOBBY THATCHER & TREASURE CAVE (N)
Altemus Co.: 1932 (9x7", 86 pgs., B&W, hard-c)

nn - Reprints; Storm-a	71.00	213.00	425.00
w/dust jacket			550.00

BOBBY THATCHER'S ROMANCE (N)
The Bell Syndicate/Henry Altemus Co.: 1931 (8-3/4x7", color cover, B&W)

nn - By Storm	79.00	237.00	475.00
w/dust jacket			550.00

BOOK OF CARTOONS, A (M,S)
Edward T. Miller: 1903 (12-1/4x9-1/4", 120 pgs, hardcover, B&W)

nn - By Harry J. Westerman (Ohio State Journal-r)	24.00	72.00	145.00

BOOK OF DRAWINGS BY A.B. FROST, A (M,S)
P.F. Collier & Son: 1904 (15-3/8 x 11", 96 pgs, B&W)

nn - A.B. Frost	54.00	162.00	325.00

NOTE: Pages alternate verses by Wallace Irwin and full-page plated by A.B.Frost. 39 plates.

BOTTLE, THE (E) (See Victorian Age section for earlier editions)
Gowans & Gray, London & Glasgow: June 1905 (3-3/4x6", 72 pgs, printed one side only, paper cover, B&W)

nn - 1st printing (June 1905)	29.00	87.00	175.00
nn - 2nd printing (March 1906)	20.00	60.00	120.00
nn - 3rd printing (January 1911)	20.00	60.00	120.00

NOTE: By George Cruikshank. Reprints both THE BOTTLE and THE DRUNKARD'S CHILDREN. Cover is text only - no cover art.

BOTTLE, THE (E)
Frederick A. Stokes: nd (c1906) (3-3/4x6", 72 pgs, printed one side only, paper-c, B&W)

nn- by George Cruikshank	20.00	60.00	120.00

NOTE: Reprint of the Gowans & Gray edition. Reprints both THE BOTTLE and THE DRUNKARD'S CHILDREN. Cover is text only - no cover art.

BOYS AND FOLKS (N).
George H. Dornan Company: 1917 (10-1/4 x 8-1/4", 232 pgs. (single-sided), B&W strip-r.

nn - By Webster	28.00	84.00	165.00

NOTE: Four sections: Life's Darkest Moments, Mostly About Folks, The Thrill That Comes Once in a Lifetime,

and Our Boyhood Ambitions. Most are single-panel cartoons, but there are some sequential comic strips.

BOY'S & GIRLS' BIG PAINTING BOOK OF INTERESTING COMIC PICTURES (N)
M. A. Donohue & Co.: 1914-16 (9x15, 70 pgs)

nn - By Carl "Bunny" Schultze (Foxy Grandpa-r)	110.00	330.00	—
#2 (1914)	110.00	330.00	—
#337 (1914) (sez "Big Painting & Drawing Book")	110.00	330.00	—
nn - (1916) (sez "Big Painting Book")(9-1/4x15")	110.00	330.00	—

NOTE: Are all Foxy Grandpa items.

BRAIN LEAKS: Dialogues of Mutt & Flea (N)
O. K. Printing Co. (Rochester Evening Times): 1911 (76 pgs, 6-5/8x4-5/8, hard-c, B&W)

nn - By Leo Edward O'Melia; newspaper strip-r	35.00	105.00	210.00

BRAINY BOWERS AND DROWSY DUGGAN (N)
Star Publishing: 1905 (7-1/4 x 4-9/16", 98 pgs., blue, brown & white color cover, B&W interior, 25¢) (daily strip-r 1902-04 Chicago Daily News)

#74 - By R. W. Taylor (Scarce)	667.00	2000.00	

NOTE: Part of a series of Atlantic Library Heart Series. Strip begins in 1901 and runs thru 1915. Taylor also created Yen the Janitor for the New York World.

BRAIN BOWERS AND DROWSY DUGAN (N)
Max Stein Pub. House, Chicago: 1905 (6-3/16x4-3/8", 64 pgs, B&W)

nn - By R.W. Taylor (Scarce)	700.00	2100.00	

NOTE: A coverless copy of this surfaced on eBay in 2002 selling for $700.00.;

BRAINY BOWERS AND DROWSY DUGGAN GETTING ON IN THE WORLD WITH NO VISIBLE MEANS OF SUPPORT (STORIES TOLD IN PICTURES TO MAKE THEIR TELLING SHORT) (N)
Max Stein/Star Publishing: 1905 (7-3/8x5 1/8", 164 pgs, slick black, red & tan color cover, interior newsprint) (daily strip-r 1902-04 Chicago Daily News)

nn - By R. W. Taylor (Scarce)	667.00	2000.00	
nn - Possible hard cover edition also?			

NOTE: These Brainy Bowers editions are the earliest known daily newspaper strip reprint books.

BRINGING UP FATHER (N)
Star Co. (King Features): 1917 (5-1/2x16-1/2", 100 pgs., B&W, cardboard-c)

nn - (Scarcer)-Daily strip- by George McManus	200.00	600.00	1200.00

BRINGING UP FATHER (N)
Cuples & Leon Co.: 1919 - No. 26, 1934 (10x10", 52 pgs., B&W, stiff cardboard-c) (No. 22 is 9-1/4x9-1/2")

1-Daily strip-r by George McManus in all	68.00	204.00	410.00
2-10	51.00	153.00	305.00
11-20	68.00	204.00	410.00
21-26 (Scarcer)	102.00	306.00	610.00
The Big Book 1 (1926)-Thick book (hardcover, 142 pgs.)	183.00	549.00	1100.00
w/dust jacket (rare)	267.00	801.00	1600.00
The Big Book 2 (1929)	142.00	426.00	850.00
w/dust jacket (rare)	250.00	750.00	1500.00

NOTE: The Big Books contain 3 regular issues rebound. Strip began Jan 2 1913-May 28 2000.

BRINGING UP FATHER, THE TROUBLE OF (N)
Embee Publ. Co.: 1921 (9-3/4x15-3/4", 46 pgs, Sunday-r in color)

nn - (Rare)	121.00	363.00	725.00

NOTE: Ties with Mutt & Jeff (EmBee) and Jimmie Dugan And The Reg'lar Fellers (C&L) as the last of the oblong size era. This was self published by George McManus.

BRINGING UP FATHER (N) (see SAGARA'S ENGLISH CARTOONS)
Publisher unknown (actually, unreadable), Tokyo: October 1924 (9-7/8" x 7-1/2", 90 pgs, color hard-c, B&W)

nn- (Scarce) by George McManus C&A		(no known sales)	

NOTE: Published in Tokyo, Japan, with all strips in both English and Japanese, to facilitate learning English. Introduction by George McManus. Scarce in USA.

BRONX BALLADS (I)
Simon & Schuster, NY: 1927 (9-1/2x7-1/4", hard-c with dust jacket, B&W)

nn - By Robert Simon and Harry Hershfield	54.00	162.00	325.00

BROWNIES, THE (not sequential comic strips)
The Century Co.: 1887 - 1914 (all came with dust jackets; add $100-150 to value if original dust jacket is included and intact)

Book 1 - The Brownies: Their Book (1887)	250.00	750.00	1500.00
Book 2 - Another Brownies Book (1890)	208.00	624.00	1250.00
Book 3 - The Brownies at Home (1893)	150.00	450.00	900.00
Book 4 - The Brownies Around the World (1894)	121.00	363.00	725.00
Book 5 - The Brownies Through the Union (1895)	121.00	363.00	725.00
Book 6 - The Brownies Abroad (1899)	121.00	363.00	725.00
Book 7 - The Brownies in the Philippines (1904)	121.00	363.00	725.00
Book 8 - The Brownies' Latest Adventures (1910)	121.00	363.00	725.00
Book 9 - The Brownies Many More Nights (1914)	121.00	363.00	725.00
...Raid on Kleinmaier Bros. (c. 1910, 16 pages) Kleinmaier Bros. Clothing, Marion, Ohio		(no known sales)	

BROWN CLOWN OF BROWNIE TOWN (N)
The Century Co.: 1908 (6-7/8 x 9-3/8", 112 pgs, color hardcover & interior)

nn - By Palmer Cox (rare; 1907 newspaper comic strip-r)	208.00	624.00	1250.00

NOTE: The Brownies created 1883 in St Nicholas Magazine.

BUDDY TUCKER & HIS FRIENDS (N) (Also see Buster Brown Nuggets)
Cuples & Leon Co.: 1906 (11-5/8 x17", 58 pgs, color) (Scarce)

nn - 1905 Sunday strip-r by R. F. Outcault	517.00	1551.00	3100.00

NOTE: Strip began Apr 30, 1905 thru at least Oct 1905.

BUFFALO BILL'S PICTURE STORIES
Street & Smith Publications: 1909 (Soft cardboard cover)

nn - Very rare	79.00	237.00	475.00

BUGHOUSE FABLES (N) (see also Comic Monthly)
Embee Distributing Co. (King Features): 1921 (10c, 4x4-1/2", 48 pgs.)

1-By Barney Google (Billy DeBeck)	71.00	213.00	425.00

BUG MOVIES (O) (Also see Clancy The Cop & Deadwood Gulch)
Dell Publishing Co.: 1931 (9-13/16x9-7/8", 52 pgs., B&W)

nn - Original material; Stookie Allen-a	108.00	324.00	650.00

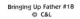

Bringing Up Father #18
© C&L

Brownie Clown of Brownie Town
© The Century Co.

Buster Brown's Amusing Capers
1908 © Cupples & Leon

GD2.0 FN6.0 VF8.0

BULL
Bull Publishing Company, New York: No.1, March, 1916 - No.12, Feb, 1917
(10 cents, 10-3/4x8-3/4", 24 pgs, color paper-c, B&W)

1-12 (Very Rare)	–	–	–

NOTE: *Pro-German, Anti-British cartoon/humor monthly, whose goal was to keep the U.S. neutral and out of World War I. We know of no copies which have sold in the past few years.*

BUNNY'S BLUE BOOK (see also Foxy Grandpa) (N)
Frederick A. Stokes Co.: 1911 (10x15, 60¢)

nn - By Carl "Bunny" Schultze strip-r	133.00	400.00	–

BUNNY'S RED BOOK (see also Foxy Grandpa) (N)
Frederick A. Stokes Co.: 1912 (10-1/4x15-3/4", 64 pgs.)

nn - By Carl "Bunny" Schultze strip-r	133.00	400.00	–

BUNNY'S GREEN BOOK (see also Foxy Grandpa) (N)
Frederick A. Stokes Co.: 1913 (10x15")

nn - By Carl "Bunny" Schultze	133.00	400.00	–

BUSTER BROWN (C) (Also see Brown's Blue Ribbon Book of Jokes and Jingles & Buddy Tucker & His Friends)
Frederick A. Stokes Co.: 1903 - 1916 (Daily strip-r in color)

1903...& His Resolutions (11-1/4x16", 66 pgs.) by R.F. Outcault (Rare)-1st nationally distributed comic. Distr. through Sears & Roebuck	1100.00	3300.00	–
1904...His Dog Tige & Their Troubles (11-1/4x16-1/4", 66 pgs.)(Rare)	567.00	1700.00	–
1905...Pranks (11-1/4x16-3/8", 66 pgs.)	483.00	1450.00	–
1906...Antics (11x16-3/8", 66 pgs.)	483.00	1450.00	–
1906...And Company (11x16-1/2", 66 pgs.)	333.00	1000.00	–
1906...Mary Jane & Tige (11-1/4x16, 66 pgs.)	333.00	1000.00	–

NOTE: *Yellow Kid pictured on two pages.*

1908 Collection of Brown Comics	275.00	825.00	–
1909 Outcault's Real Buster and The Only Mary Jane (11x16, 66 pgs, Stokes)	275.00	825.00	–
1910...Up to Date (10-1/8x15-3/4", 66 pgs.)	167.00	501.00	1000.00
1911...Fun And Nonsense (10-1/8x15-3/4", 66 pgs.)	183.00	549.00	1100.00
1912...The Fun Maker (10-1/8x15-3/4", 66 pgs.) -Yellow Kid (4 pgs.)	183.00	549.00	1100.00
1913...At Home (10-1/8x15-3/4", 56 pgs.)	167.00	501.00	1000.00
1914...And Tige Here Again (10x16, 62 pgs, Stokes)	142.00	426.00	850.00
1915...And His Chum Tige (10x16, Stokes)	142.00	426.00	850.00
1916...The Little Rogue (11-3/8x16-3/4", 62 pgs.)	162.00	567.00	1000.00
1917...And the Cat (5-1/2x 6-1/2, 26 pgs, Stokes)	113.00	339.00	675.00
1917...Disturbs the Family (5-1/2x 6 1/2, 26 pgs, Stokes	113.00	339.00	675.00

NOTE: *Story featuring statue of "the Chinese Yellow Kid"*

1917...The Real Buster Brown (5-1/2x 6 -/2, 26 pgs, Stokes	113.00	339.00	675.00

Frederick A. Stokes Co. Hard Cover Series (I)

...Abroad (1904, 10-1/4x8", 86 pgs., B&W, hard-c)-R. F. Outcault-a (Rare)	142.00	426.00	850.00
...Abroad (1904, B&W, 67 pgs.)-R. F. Outcault-a	142.00	426.00	850.00

NOTE: *Buster Brown Abroad is not an actual comic book, but prose with illustrations.*

..."Tige" His Story 1905 (10x8", 63 pgs., B&W) (63 illos.) nn-By RF Outcault	167.00	500.00	–
...My Resolutions 1906 (10x8", B&W, 68 pgs.)-R.F. Outcault-a (Rare)	217.00	650.00	1300.00
...Autobiography 1907 (10x8", B&W, 71 pgs.) (16 color plates & 36 B&W illos)	68.00	204.00	410.00
...And Mary Jane's Painting Book 1907 (10x13-1/4", 60 pgs, both card & hardcover versions exist			
nn-RFO (first printing blank on top of cover)	72.00	216.00	430.00
First Series- this is a reprint if it says First Series	72.00	216.00	430.00
Volume Two - By RFO	72.00	216.00	430.00
... My Resolutions by Buster Brown (1907, 68 pgs, small size, cardboard covers) scarce	46.00	138.00	275.00

NOTE: *Not actual comic book per se, but a compilation of the Resolutions panels found at the end of Outcault's Buster Brown newspaper strips.*

BUSTER BROWN (N)
Cupples & Leon Co./N. Y. Herald Co.: 1906 - 1917 (11x17", color, strip-r)
NOTE: *Early issues by R. F. Outcault; most C&L editions are not by Outcault.*

1906...His Dog Tige And Their Jolly Times (11-3/8x16-5/8", 68 pgs.)	333.00	1000.00	2000.00
1906...His Dog & Their Jolly Times (11x16, 46 pgs.)	200.00	600.00	1200.00
1907...Latest Frolics (11-3/8x16-5/8", 66 pgs, r/'05-06 strips)183.00		550.00	1100.00
1908...Amusing Capers (58 pgs)	126.00	378.00	760.00
1909...The Busy Body (11-3/8x16-5/8", 62 pgs.)	126.00	378.00	760.00
1910...On His Travels (11x16", 58 pgs.)	126.00	378.00	760.00
1911...Happy Days (11-3/8x16-5/8", 58 pgs.)	126.00	378.00	760.00
1912...In Foreign Lands (10x16", 58 pgs.)	126.00	378.00	760.00
1913...And His Pets (11x16", 58 pgs.) STOKES????	126.00	378.00	760.00
1913...And His Pets (26 pg partial reprint)	–	–	–
1914...Funny Tricks (11-3/8x16-5/8", 58 pgs.)	126.00	378.00	760.00
1916...At Play (10x16, 58 pgs)	126.00	378.00	760.00

BUSTER BROWN NUGGETS (N)

GD2.0 FN6.0 VF8.0

Cupples & Leon Co./N.Y.Herald Co.: 1907 (1905, 7-1/2x6-1/2", 36 pgs., color, strip-r, hard-c)(By R. F. Outcault) (NOTE: books are all unnumbered)

Buster Brown Goes Fishing, Goes Swimming, Plays Indian, Goes Shooting, Plays Cowboy, On Uncle Jack's Farm, Tige And the Bull, And Uncle Buster	60.00	180.00	360.00
Buddy Tucker Meets Alice in Wonderland	75.00	225.00	450.00
Buddy Tucker Visits The House That Jack Built	60.00	180.00	360.00

BUSTER BROWN MUSLIN SERIES (N)
Saalfield: 1907 (also contain copyright Cupples & Leon)

...Goes Fishing, Plays Indian, And the Donkey (1907, 6-7/8x6-1/8", 24 pgs., color)-r/1905 Sunday comics page by Outcault (Rare)	58.00	174.00	350.00
...Plays Cowboy (1907, 6-3/4x6", 10 pgs., color)-r/1905 Sunday comics page by Outcault (Rare)	55.00	165.00	330.00

NOTE: *These are muslin versions of the C&L BB Nugget series. Muslin books are all cloth books, made to be washable so are not easily stained/destroyed by very young children. The Muslin contain one strip each (the title strip), to the more common NUGGET's three strips.*

BUSTER BROWN PREMIUMS (Advertising premium booklets)
Various Publishers: 1904 - 1912 (3x5" to 5x7"; sizes vary)

American Fruit Product Company, Rochester, NY
Buster Brown Duffy's 1842 Cider (1904, 7x5". 12 pgs, C.E. Sherin Co, NYC)

nn - By R. F. Outcault (scarce)	108.00	325.00	650.00

The Brown Shoe Company, St. Louis, USA
Set of five books (5x7", 16 pgs., color)

Brown's Blue Ribbon Book of Jokes and Jingles Book 1 (nn, 1904)-By R.F. Outcault; Buster Brown & Tige, Little Tommy Tucker, Jack & Jill, Little Boy Blue, Dainty Jane; The Yellow Kid app. on back-c (1st BB comic book premium)	350.00	1050.00	2100.00
Buster Brown's Blue Ribbon Book of Jokes and Jingles Book 2 (1905)- Original color art by Outcault	208.00	625.00	1250.00
Buster's Book of Jokes & Jingles Book 3 (1909) not by R.F. Outcault	158.00	474.00	950.00

NOTE: *Reprinted from the Blue Ribbon post cards with advert jingles added.*

Buster's Book of Instructive Jokes and Jingles Book 4 (1910)-Original color art not by R.F. Outcault	190.00	570.00	1150.00
...Book of Travels nn (1912, 3x5")-Original color art not signed by Outcault	125.00	375.00	750.00

NOTE: *Estimated 5 or 6 known copies exist of books #1-4.*

The Buster Brown Bread Company

"Buster Brown" Bread Book of Rhymes, The (1904, 4x6", 12 pgs., half color, half B&W)- Original color art not signed by RFO	200.00	600.00	1200.00

Buster Brown's Hosiery Mills

"Buster Brown's Latest" nn (1909, 7x5-1/4". 20 pgs, color paper cover and color interior By R.F. Outcault (a GD+ copy sold for $150)			
"How Buster Brown Got The Pie" nn (nd, 7x5-1/4". 16 pgs, color paper cover and color interior By R.F. Outcault	104.00	312.00	625.00
"The Autobiography of Buster Brown" nn (nd,9x6-1/8", 36 pgs, text story & art by R.F. Outcault	104.00	312.00	625.00

NOTE: *Similar to, but a distinctly different item than "Buster Brown's Autobiography."*

The Buster Brown Stocking Company
Buster Brown Drawing Book, The nn (nd, 5x6", 20 pgs.)-B&W reproductions of 1903 R.F. Outcault art to trace

	75.00	225.00	450.00

NOTE: *Reprints a comic strip from Burr McIntosh Magazine, which includes Buster, Yellow Kid, and Pore Li'l Mose (only known story involving all three.)*

Buster Brown Stocking Magazine nn (Jan. 1906, 7-3/4x5-3/8", 36 pgs.) R.F. Outcault	50.00	150.00	300.00

NOTE: *This was actually a store bought item selling for 5 cents per copy.*

Collins Baking Company

Buster Brown Drawing Book nn (1904, 5x3", 12 pgs.)-Original B&W art to trace, not signed by R.F. Outcault	68.00	204.00	410.00

C. H. Morton, St. Albans, VT

Merry Antics of Buster Brown, Buddy Tucker & Tige nn (nd, 3-1/2x5-1/2", 12 pgs.) -Original B&W art by R.F. Outcault	92.00	276.00	550.00

Ivan Frank & Company

Buster Brown nn (1904, 3x5", 12 pgs.)-B&W repros of R. F. Outcault Sunday pages (First premium to actually reproduce Sunday comic pages – may be first premium comic strip-r book?)	167.00	500.00	1000.00
Buster Brown's Pranks (1904, 3-1/2x5-1/8", 12 pgs.)-reprints intro of Buddy Tucker into the BB newspaper strip before he was spun off into his own short lived newspaper strip	142.00	426.00	850.00

Kaufmann & Strauss

Buster Brown Drawing Book (1906, 28 pages, 5x3-1/2") Color Cover, B+W original story signed by Outcault, tracing paper inserted as alternate pages. Back cover imprinted for Nox' Em All Shoes	58.00	174.00	350.00

Pond's Extract

Buster Brown's Experiences With Pond's Extract nn (1904, 6-3/4x4-1/2", 28 pgs.) Original color art by R.F. Outcault (may be the first BB premium comic book with original art)	125.00	375.00	750.00

C. A. Cross & Co.

Red Cross Drawing Book nn (1906, 4-7/8x3-1/2", color paper -c, B&W interior, 12 pgs.)	57.00	171.00	340.00

NOTE: *This is Red Cross coffee; not the health organization.*

Ringen Stove Company

Quick Meal Steel Ranges nn (nd, 5x3", 16 pgs.)-Original B&W art not signed by R.F. Outcault	75.00	225.00	450.00

Steinwender Stoffregen Coffee Co.
"Buster Brown Coffee" (1905, 4-7/8x3", color paper cover, B&W interior, 12 print ed pages, plus 1 tracing paper page above each interior image (total of 8 sheets) (Very Rare)

| | 108.00 | 324.00 | 650.00 |

NOTE: Part of a BB drawing contest. If instructions had been followed, more copies would have ended up destroyed.

U. S. Playing Card Company
Buster Brown - My Own Playing Cards (1906, 2-1/2x1-3/4", full color)

| nn - By R. F. Outcault | 46.00 | 138.00 | 275.00 |

NOTE: Series of full color panels tell stories, average about 5 cards per story.

Publisher Unknown
The Drawing Book nn (1906, 3-9/16x5", 8 pgs.)-Original B&W art to trace

| not by R.F. Outcault | 58.00 | 174.00 | 350.00 |

BUTLER BOOK A Series of Clever Cartoons of Yale Undergraduate Life
Yale Record: June 16, 1913 (10-3/4 x 17", 34 pgs, paper cover B&W)

| nn - By Alban Bernard Butler | 27.00 | 81.00 | 160.00 |

NOTE: Cartoons and strips reprinted from The Yale Record student newspaper.

BUTTONS & FATTY IN THE FUNNIES
Whitman Publishing Co.: nd 1927 (10-1/4x15-1/2", 28pg., color)

| W936 - Signed "M.E.B.", probably M.E. Brady; strips in color copyright The Brooklyn Daily Eagle; (very rare) | 83.00 | 249.00 | 500.00 |

BY BRIGGS (M,N,P) (see also OLD GOLD THE SMOOTHER AND BETTER CIGARETTE)
Old Gold Cigarettes: nd (c1920's) (11" x 9-11/16", 44 pgs, cardboard-c, B&W)

| nn- (Scarce) | 40.00 | 120.00 | 240.00 |

NOTE: Collection reprinting strip cartoons by Clare Briggs, advertising Old Gold Cigarettes. These strips originally appeared in various magazines, play program booklets, newspapers, etc. Some of the strips involve regular Briggs type series. Contains all of the strips in the smaller, color "OLD GOLD" giveaways, plus more.

CAMION CARTOONS
Marshall Jones Company: 1919 (7-1/2x5", 136 pgs, B&W)

| nn - By Kirkland H. Day (W.W.One occupation) | 25.00 | 75.00 | 150.00 |

CANYON COUNTRY KIDDIES (M)
Doubleday, Page & Co: 1923 (8x10-1/4", 88 pgs, hard-c, B&W)

| nn - By James Swinnerton | 42.00 | 126.00 | 250.00 |

CARLO (H)
Doubleday, Page & Co.: 1913 (8 x 9-5/8, 120 pgs, hardcover, B&W)

| nn - By A.B. Frost | 52.00 | 156.00 | 310.00 |

NOTE: Original sequential strips about a dog. Became short lived newspaper comic strip in 1914. Originally published with a dust jacket which increases value 50%.

CARTOON BOOK, THE
Bureau of Publicity, War Loan Organization, Treasury Department, Washington, D.C.: 1918 (6-1/2x4-7/8", 48 pgs, paper cover, B&W)

| nn - By various artists | 42.00 | 126.00 | 250.00 |

NOTE: U.S. government issued booklet of WW I propaganda cartoons by 46 artists promoting the third sale of Liberty Loan bonds. The artists include: Berryman, Clare Briggs, Cesare, J. N. "Ding" Darling, Rube Goldberg, Kemble, McCutcheon, George McManus, F. Opper, T. E. Powers, Ripley, Satterfield, H. T. Webster, Gaar Williams.

CARTOON CATALOGUE (S)
The Lockwood Art School, Kalamazoo, Mich.: 1919 (11-5/8x9, 52 pgs, B&W)

| nn - Edited by Mr. Lockwood | 23.00 | 69.00 | 140.00 |

NOTE: Jammed with 100s of single panel cartoons and some sequential comics; Mr Lockwood began the very first commercial cartoon school back in 1892. Clare Briggs was one of his students.

CARTOON COMICS
Lasco Publications, Detroit, Mich: #1, April 1930 - #2, May 1930 (8-3/6x5-1/5")

| 1, 2 - By Lu Harris | 20.00 | 60.00 | 120.00 |

NOTE: Contains recurring characters Hollywood Horace, Campus Charlie, Pair-A-Dice Alley and Jocko Monkey. Not much is presently known about the creator(s) or publisher.

CARTOON HISTORY OF ROOSEVELT'S CAREER, A
The Review of Reviews Company: 1910 (276 pgs, 8-1/4x11",

| nn - By various | 71.00 | 213.00 | 425.00 |

NOTE: Reprints editorial cartoons about Teddy Roosevelt from U.S. and international newspapers and cartoons from the humor magaines (Puck, Judge, etc.) A few cartoonists whose work is included are Dalrymple, Opper, McDougall, McCutcheon, Remington, Rogers, Kemble. Mostly single panel but 10 or so are sequential strips.

CARTOON HUMOR
Collegian Press: 1938 (102 pgs, squarebound, B&W)

| nn | 24.00 | 72.00 | 145.00 |

NOTE: Contains cartoons & strips by Otto Soglow, Syd Hoff, Peter Arno, Abner Dean, others.

CARTOONIST'S PHILOSOPHY, A
Percy Crosby: 1931, HC, 252 pgs, 5-1/2x7-1/2", hard-c, celluloid dust wrapper

| nn - By Percy Crosby (10 plates, 6 are of Skippy) | 25.00 | 75.00 | 150.00 |

NOTE: Crosby's partial autobiography regarding his return to France in 1929, and portrayals of Normandy, the "cliff dwellers" on Normandy cliffs (destroyed in WWII), his visit to London, comments on art, philosophy, several poems, and political dialogue. His description of his Cockney driver, " Harold" is amusing. Also describes his experience visiting Chicago to speak out against Capone, his concerns over the evils of Prohibition, and the economy prior to the 1929 crash. This book reveals he was aware of the dangers of his outspoken views, and is prophetic, re: his later years as political prisoner. Also reveals his religious beliefs.

CARTOONS BY BRADLEY: CARTOONIST OF THE CHICAGO DAILY NEWS
Rand McNally & Company: 1917 (11-1/4x8-3/4", 112 pgs, hardcover, B&W)

| nn - By Luther D. Bradley (editorial) | 21.00 | 63.00 | 125.00 |

CARTOONS BY FONTAINE FOX (Toonerville Trolley) (S)
Harper & Brothers Publishers: nd early '20s (9x7-7/8",102 pgs., hard-c, B&W)

| Second Book- By Fontaine Fox (Toonerville-r) | 93.00 | 279.00 | 560.00 |

CARTOONS BY HALLADAY (N,S)
Providence Journal Co., Rhode Island: Dec 1914 (116 pgs, 10-1/2x 7-3/4", hard-c, B&W)

| nn- (Scarce) | 46.00 | 138.00 | 275.00 |

NOTE: Cartoons on Rhode Island politics, plus some Teddy Roosevelt & WW I cartoons.

CARTOONS BY McCUTCHEON (S)
A. C. McClurg & Co.: 1903 (12-3/8x9-3/4", 212 pgs., hardcover, B&W)

| nn - By John McCutcheon | 23.00 | 69.00 | 140.00 |

CARTOONS BY W. A. IRELAND (S)
The Columbus-Evening Dispatch: 1907 (13-3/4 x 10-1/2", 66 pgs, hardcover)

| nn - By W. A. Ireland (strip-r) | 25.00 | 75.00 | 150.00 |

CARTOONS MAGAZINE (I,N,S)
H. H. Windsor, Publisher: Jan 1912-June 1921; July 1921-1923; 1923-1924; 1924-1927 (1912-July 1913 issues 12x9-1/4", 68-76 pgs; 1913-1921 issues 10x7", average 112 to 188 pgs, color covers)

1912-Jan-Dec	29.00	87.00	175.00
1913-1917	29.00	87.00	175.00
1917-(Apr) "How Comickers Regard Their Characters"	31.00	93.00	185.00
1917-(June) "A Genius of the Comic Page" - long article on George Herriman, Krazy Kat, etc with lots of Herriman art; "Cartoonists and Their Cars"	129.00	387.00	775.00
1918-1919	28.00	84.00	170.00
1920-June 1921	28.00	84.00	170.00
July 1921-1923 titled Wayside Tales & Cartoons Magazine	28.00	84.00	170.00
1923-1924 becomes Cartoons Magazine again	28.00	84.00	170.00
1924-1927 becomes Cartoons & Movie Magazine	28.00	84.00	170.00

NOTE: Many issues contain a wealth of historical background on then current cartoonists of the day with an international slant; each issue profusely illustrated with many cartoons. We are unsure if this magazine continued after 1927.

CARTOONS BY J. N. DARLING (S,N - some sequential strips)
The Register & Tribune Co., Des Moines, Iowa: 1909?-1920 (12x8-7/8",B&W)

Book 1	31.00	93.00	185.00
Book 2 Education of Alonzo Applegate (1910)	23.00	69.00	140.00
2nd printing	23.00	69.00	140.00
Book 3 Cartoons From The Files (1911)	23.00	69.00	140.00
Book 4	23.00	69.00	140.00
Book 5 In Peace And War (1916)	23.00	69.00	140.00
Book 6 Aces & Kings War Cartoons (Dec 1, 1918)	23.00	69.00	140.00
Book 7 The Jazz Era (Dec 1920)	23.00	69.00	140.00
Book 8 Our Own Outlines of History (1922)	23.00	69.00	140.00

NOTE: Some of the most inspired hard hitting cartoons ever printed. Are there more?

CARTOONS THAT MADE PRINCE HENRY FAMOUS, THE (N,S)
The Chicago Record-Herald: Feb/March 1902 (12-1/8" x 9", 32 pgs, paper-c, B&W)

| nn- (Scarce) by McCutcheon | 21.00 | 63.00 | 125.00 |

NOTE: Cartoons about the visit of the British Prince Henry to the U.S.

CAVALRY CARTOONS (O)
R. Montalboddi: nd (c1918) (14-1/4" x 11", 30 pgs, printed on one side, olive & black construction paper-c, B&W interior)

| nn - By R.Montalboddi | 19.00 | 57.00 | 115.00 |

NOTE: Comics about the U.S.Cavalry during World War I, by a soldier who was in the 1st Cavalry.

CAWS AND EFFECT
L.D. Gallison Pub., NY: nd (7 two-sided panels, 4-5/8 x 3", B&W)

| nn - By Edgar Ape O. | (a GVG copy sold for $111.55 in 2010) |

CHARLIE CHAPLIN (N)
Essanay/M. A. Donohue & Co.: 1917 (9x16", B&W, large size soft-c)

Series 1, #315-Comic Capers (9-3/4x15-3/4")-20 pgs. by Segar;			
Series 1, #316-In the Movies	217.00	650.00	1300.00
#317-Up in the Air (20 pgs), #318-In the Army	250.00	750.00	1500.00
Funny Stunts-(12-1/2x16-3/8",16 color pgs)	250.00	750.00	1500.00

NOTE: All contain pre-Thimble Theatre Segar art. The thin paper used makes high grade copies very scarce.

CHASING THE BLUES
Doubleday Page: 1912 (7-1/2x10", 108 pgs., B&W, hard-c)

| nn - By Rube Goldberg | 200.00 | 600.00 | 1200.00 |

NOTE: Contains a dozen Foolish Questions, baseball, a few Goldberg poems and lots of sequential strips.

CHRISTIAN CARTOONS (N,S)
The Sunday School Times Company: 1922 (7-1/4 x 6-1/8,104 pgs, brown hard-c, B&W)

| nn - E.J. Pace | 19.00 | 57.00 | 115.00 |

NOTE: Religious cartoons reprinted from The Sunday School Times.

CLANCY THE COP (O)
Dell Publishing Co.: 1930 - No. 2, 1931 (10x10", 52 pgs., B&W, cardboard-c) (Also see Bug Movies & Deadwood Gulch)

| 1, 2-By VEP Victor Pazimino (original material; not reprints) | 100.00 | 300.00 | 600.00 |

CLIFFORD McBRIDE'S IMMORTAL NAPOLEON & UNCLE ELBY (N)
The Castle Press: 1932 (12x17") soft-c cartoon book)

| nn - Intro. by Don Herod | 43.00 | 129.00 | 260.00 |

COLLECTED DRAWINGS OF BRUCE BAIRNSFATHER, THE
W. Colston Leigh: 1931 (11-1/4x8-1/4 ", 168 pages, hardcover, B&W)

| nn - By Bruce Bairnsfather | 38.00 | 114.00 | 225.00 |

COMICAL PEEP SHOW
McLoughlin Bros.: 1902 (36 pgs, B&W)

| nn | 32.00 | 96.00 | 190.00 |

NOTE: Comic stories of Wilhelm Busch redrawn; two versions with green or gold front cover logos; back covers different.

COMIC ANIMALS (I)
Charles E. Graham & Co.: 1903 (9-3/4x7-1/4", 90 pgs, color cover)

| nn - By Walt McDougall (not comic strips) | 54.00 | 162.00 | 325.00 |

COMIC CUTS (O)
H. L. Baker Co., Inc.: 5/19/34-7/28/34 (Tabloid size 10-1/2x15-1/2", 24 pgs., 5¢) (full color, not reprints; published weekly; created for news stand sales)

| V1#1 - V1#7(6/30/34), V1#8(7/14/34), V1#9(7/28/34)-Idle Jack strips | 200.00 | 600.00 | 1200.00 |

NOTE: According to a 1958 Lloyd Jacquet interview, this short-lived comics mag was the direct inspiration for Major Malcolm Wheeler-Nicholson's New Fun Comics and then Famous Funnies.

COMIC MONTHLY (N)
Embee Dist. Co.: Jan, 1922 - No. 12, Dec, 1922 (10¢, 8-1/2"x9", 28 pgs., 2-color covers) (1st monthly newsstand comic publication) (Reprints 1921 B&W dailies)

1-Polly & Her Pals by Cliff Sterrett	450.00	1350.00	2700.00
2-Mike & Ike by Rube Goldberg	200.00	600.00	1200.00
3-S'Matter, Pop?	200.00	600.00	1200.00
4-Barney Google by Billy DeBeck	200.00	600.00	1200.00
5-Tillie the Toiler by Russ Westover	200.00	600.00	1200.00
6-Indoor Sports by Tad Dorgan	200.00	600.00	1200.00

NOTE: #6 contains more Judge Rummy than Indoor Sports.

Charlie Chaplin in the Army by Segar
1917 © Essaney

Comic Painting and Crayoning Book
1917 © Saalfield

How Dick Tracy and Dick Tracy, Jr.
Caught the Racketeers by Chester Gould
1933 © Cupples & Leon

	GD 2.0	FN 6.0	VF 8.0
7-Little Jimmy by James Swinnerton	200.00	600.00	1200.00
8-Toots and Casper b y Jimmy Murphy	200.00	600.00	1200.00
9-New Bughouse Fables by Barney Google	200.00	600.00	1200.00
10-Foolish Questions by Rube Goldberg	200.00	600.00	1200.00
11-Barney Google & Spark Plug by Billy DeBeck	200.00	600.00	1200.00
12-Polly & Her Pals by Cliff Sterrett	200.00	600.00	1200.00

NOTE: This series was published by George McManus (Bringing Up Father) as Em & Rudolph Block, Jr., son of Hearst's cartoon editor for many years, as "Bee." One would have thought this series would have done very well considering the tremendous amount of talent assembled. All issues are extremely hard to find these days and rarely show up in any type of higher grade.

COMIC PAINTING AND CRAYONING BOOK (H)
Saalfield Publ. Co.: 1917 (13-1/2x10", 32 pgs.) (No price on-c)

nn - Tidy Teddy by F. M. Follett, Clarence the Cop, Mr. & Mrs. Butt-In; regular comic stories			
to read or color	60.00	180.00	360.00

COMPLETE TRIBUNE PRIMER, THE (I)
Mutual Book Company: 1901 (7 1/4 x 5", 152 pgs, red hard-c)

nn - By Frederick Opper; has 75 Opper cartoons	29.00	87.00	175.00

COURTSHIP OF TAGS, THE (N)
McCormick Press: pre-1910 (9x4", 88 pgs, red & B&W-c, B&W interior)

nn - By O. E. Wertz (strip-r Wichita Daily Beacon)	29.00	87.00	175.00

DAFFYDILS (N)
Cupples & Leon: 1911 (5-3/4x7-7/8", 52 pgs., B&W, hard-c)

nn - By "Tad" Dorgan	60.00	180.00	360.00

NOTE: Also exists in self-published TAD edition: The T.A. Dorgan Company; unknown which is first printing.

DAN DUNN SECRET OPERATIVE 48 (Also See Detective Dan) (N)
Whitman Publishing: 1937 ((5 1/2 x 7 1/4", 68pgs., color cardboard-c, B&W)

1010 And The Gangsters' Frame-Up	60.00	180.00	360.00

NOTE: There are two versions of the book the later printing has a 5 cent cover price. Dick Tracy look-alike character by Norman Marsh.

DANGERS OF DOLLY DIMPLE, THE (N)
Penn Tobacco Co.: nd (1930's) (9-3/8x7-7/8", 28 pgs, red cardboard-c, B&W)

nn - (Rare) by Walter Enright	31.00	93.00	185.00

NOTE: Reprints newspaper comic strip advertisements, in which every episode, Dolly Dimple's life is saved by Penn's Smoking Tobacco. - how very un-P.C. by today's standards.

DEADWOOD GULCH (O) (See The Funnies 1929)(also see Bug Movies & Clancy The Cop)
Dell Publishing: 1931 (10x10", 52 pgs., B&W, color covers, B&W interior)

nn - By Charles "Boody" Rogers (original material)	104.00	312.00	625.00

DESTINY A Novel In Pictures (O)
Farrar & Rinehart: 1930 (8x7", 424 pgs., B&W, hard-c with dust jacket)

nn - By Otto Nuckel (original graphic novel)	67.00	201.00	400.00

DICK TRACY & DICK TRACY JR. CAUGHT THE RACKETEERS, HOW
Cupples & Leon Co.: 1933 (8-1/2x7", 88 pgs., hard-c) (See Treasure Box of Famous Comics) (N)

2-(Numbered on pg. 84)-Continuation of Stooge Viller book (daily strip reprints			
from 8/3/33 thru 11/8/33)(Rarer than #1)	130.00	390.00	775.00
With dust jacket…	200.00	600.00	1200.00

DICK TRACY & DICK TRACY JR. AND HOW THEY CAPTURED "STOOGE" VILLER (N)
Cupples & Leon Co.: 1933 (8-1/2x7", 100 pgs., hard-c, one-shot)
Reprints 1932 & 1933 Dick Tracy daily strips

nn(No.1)-1st app. of "Stooge" Viller	129.00	387.00	775.00
With dust jacket…	200.00	600.00	1200.00

DIMPLES By Grace Drayton (N) (See Dolly Dimples)
Hearst's International Library Co.: 1915 (6 1/4 x 5 1/4, 12 pgs) (5 known)

nn-Puppy and Pussy; nn-She Goes For a Walk; nn-She Had A Sneeze; nn-She Has a			
Naughty Play Husband; nn-Wait Till Fido Comes Home	29.00	87.00	175.00

DOINGS OF THE DOO DADS, THE (N)
Detroit News (Universal Feat. & Specialty Co.): 1922 (50¢, 7-3/4x7-3/4", 34 pgs, B&W, red & white-c, square binding)

nn-Reprints 1921 newspaper strip "Text & Pictures" given away as prize in the			
Detroit News Doo Dads contest; by Arch Dale	60.00	180.00	360.00

DOINGS OF THE VAN-LOONS, THE (N) (from same company as Mutt & Jeff #1-#5)
Ball Publications: 1912 (5-3/4X15-1/2", 68pg., B&W, hard-c)

nn - By Fred I. Leipziger (scarce)	100.00	300.00	600.00

DOING THE GRAND CANYON
Fred Harvey: 1922 (7 x 4-3/4", 24 pgs, B&W, paper cover)

nn - John McCutcheon	19.00	57.00	115.00

NOTE: Text & 8 cartoons about visiting the Grand Canyon.

DOLLY DIMPLES & BOBBY BOUNCE (See Dimples)
Cupples & Leon Co.: 1933 (8-3/4x7", color hardcover, B&W)

nn - Grace Drayton-a	29.00	87.00	175.00

DOO DADS, THE (Sleepy Sam and Tiny the Elephant)
Universal Feature * Specialty Co: 1922 (5-1/4x14", 36 pgs.,B&W, R&W-c,square binding)

nn - By Arch Dale	48.00	144.00	290.00

DRAWINGS BY HOWARD CHANDLER CHRISTIE (S, M)
Moffat, Yard & Company, NY: 1905 (11-7/8x16-1/2", 68 pgs, hard-c, B&W)

	GD 2.0	FN 6.0	VF 8.0
nn - Howard C. Christie	28.00	84.00	165.00

NOTE: Reprints1898-1905 from Hapter & Bros, Ch. Scribners Sons, Leslie's, MacMillians, McLurg, Russell.

DREAMS OF THE RAREBIT FIEND (N)
Frederick A. Stokes Co.:1905 (10-1/4x7-1/2", 68 pgs, thin paper cover all B&W)
newspaper reprints from the New York Evening Telegram printed on yellow paper

nn-By Winsor "Silas" McCay (Very Rare) (Five copies known to exist)			
Estimated value…	1250.00	3750.00	—

NOTE: A G/VG copy sold for $2,045 in May 2004. This item usually turns up with fragile paper.

DRISCOLL'S BOOK OF PIRATES (O)
David McKay Publ.: 1934 (9x7", 124 pgs, B&W, hardcover)

nn - By Montford Amory ("Pieces of Eight strip-r)	29.00	87.00	175.00

DUCKY DADDLES
Frederick A. Stokes Co.: July 1911 (15x10")

nn - By Grace Weiderseim (later Drayton) strip-r	63.00	189.00	375.00

DUMBUNNIES AND THEIR FRIENDS IN RABBITBORO, THE (O)
Albertine Randall Wheelan: 1931 (8-3/4x7-1/8", 82 pgs, color hardcover, B&W)

nn - By Albertine Randall Wheelan (self-pub)	42.00	126.00	250.00

EDISON - INSPIRATION TO YOUTH (N)(Also see Life of Thomas---)
Thomas A. Edison, Incorporated: 1939 (9-1/2 x 6-1/2, paper cover, B&W)

nn - Photo-c	50.00	150.00	310.00

NOTE: Reprints strip material found in the 1928 Life of Thomas A. Edison in Word and Picture.

'ERBIE AND 'IS PLAYMATES
Democratic National Committee: 1932 (8x9-1/2, 16 pgs, B&W)

nn - By Frederick Opper (Rare)	70.00	210.00	415.00

NOTE: Anti-Hoover/Pro-Roosevelt political comics.

EXPANSION BEING BART'S BEST CARTOONS FOR 1899
Minneapolis Journal: 1900 (10-1/4x8-1/4", 124 pgs, paperback, B&W)

v2#1 - By Charles L. Bartholomew	24.00	70.00	140.00

FAMOUS COMICS (N)
King Features Synd. (Whitman Pub. Co.): 1934 (100 pgs., daily newspaper-r)
(3-1/2x8-1/2"; paper cover)(came in an illustrated box)

684 (#1) - Little Jimmy, Katz Kids & Barney Google	50.00	150.00	300.00
684 (#2) - Polly, Little Jimmy, Katzenjammer Kids	50.00	150.00	300.00
684 (#3) - Little Annie Rooney, Polly and Her Pals, Katzenjammer Kids	50.00	150.00	300.00
Box price…	75.00	225.00	450.00

FAMOUS COMICS CARTOON BOOKS (N)
Whitman Publishing Co.: 1934 (8x7-1/4", 72 pgs, B&W hard-c, daily strip-r)

1200-The Captain & the Kids; Dirks reprints credited to Bernard			
Dibble	38.00	114.00	225.00
1202-Captain Easy & Wash Tubbs by Roy Crane; 2 slightly different			
versions of cover exist	43.00	129.00	260.00
1203-Ella Cinders By Conselman & Plumb	38.00	114.00	225.00
1204-Freckles & His Friends	36.00	108.00	215.00

NOTE: Called Famous Funnies Cartoon Books inside back area sales advertisement.

FANTASIES IN HA-HA (M)
Meyer Bros & Co.: 1900 (14 x 11-7/8", 64 pgs, color cover hardcover, B&W)

nn - By Hy Mayer	58.00	174.00	350.00

FELIX (N)
Henry Altemus Company: 1931 (6-1/2"x8-1/4", 52 pgs., color, hard-c w/dust jacket)

1-3-Sunday strip reprints of Felix the Cat by Otto Messmer. Book No. 2 r/1931 Sunday panels mostly two to a page in a continuity format oddly arranged so each tier of panels reads across two pages, then drops to the next tier. (Books 1 & 3 have not been documented.)(Rare)

Each	183.00	550.00	1100.00
With dust jacket	267.00	800.00	1600.00

FELIX THE CAT BOOK (N)
McLoughlin Bros.: 1927 (8"x15-3/4", 52 pgs, half in color-half in B&W)

nn - Reprints 23 Sunday strips by Otto Messmer from 1926 & 1927, every other one in			
color, two pages per strip. (Rare)	333.00	1000.00	2000.00
260-Reissued (1931), reformatted to 9-1/2"x10-1/4" (same color plates, but one strip per			
every three pages), retitled ("Book" dropped from title) and abridged (only eight strips			
repeated from first issue, 28 pgs.).(Rare)	117.00	350.00	700.00

F. FOX'S FUNNY FOLK (see Toonerville Trolley; Cartoons by Fontaine Fox) (C)
George H. Doran Company: 1917 (10-1/4x8-1/4", 228 pgs, red, B&W cover, B&W interior, hardcover; dust jacket?)

nn - By Fontaine Fox (Toonerville Trolley strip-r)	130.00	390.00	775.00

52 CAREY CARTOONS (O,S)
Carey Cartoon Service, NY: 1915 (25 cents, 6-3/4" x 10-1/2", 118 pgs, printed on one side, color cardboard-c, B&W)

nn - (1915) War	—	—	—

NOTE: The Carey Cartoon Service supplied a weekly, hand-colored single panel cartoon broadsheet, on current news events, starting in 1906 or 1907, for window display in Carey Fountain Pen chain stores. These broadsheets were 22-1/2" x 33" in size. Starting circa 1915, Carey Fountain Pens began offering subscriptions for the broadsheets to other merchants, for window display in their stores as well. This collects, in B&W, the cartoons for 1915. An "Edition Deluxe" was also advertised, with all cartoons hand colored. It is currently unknown whether a reprint collection was only issued in 1915, or if other editions exist.

52 LETTERS TO SALESMEN
Steven-Davis Company: 1926 - 1927

nn - (Rare)	23.00	69.00	140.00

NOTE: *52 motivational letters to salesmen, with page of comics for each week, bound into embossed leather binder.*

FOLKS IN FUNNYVILLE (S)
R.H. Russell: 1900 (12"x9-1/4", 48 pgs.)(cardboard-c)

nn - By Frederick Opper	383.00	1150.00

NOTE: *Reprinted from Hearst's NY Journal American Humorist supplements.*

FOOLISH QUESTIONS (S)
Small, Maynard & Co.: 1909 (6-7/8 x 5-1/2", 174 pgs, hardcover, B&W)

nn - By Rube Goldberg (first Goldberg item)	90.00	270.00	550.00

NOTE: *Comic strip began Oct 23, 1908 running thru 1941. Also drawn by George Frink in 1909.*

FOOLISH QUESTIONS THAT ARE ASKED BY ALL
Levi Strauss & Co./Small, Maynard & Co.: 1909 (5-1/2x5-3/4", 24 pgs, paper-c, B&W)

nn - (Rare) by Rube Goldberg	60.00	180.00	360.00

FOOLISH QUESTIONS (Boxed card set) (S)
Wallie Dorr Co., N.Y.: 1919 (5-1/4x3-3/4")(box & card backs are red)

nn - Boxed set w/52 B&W comics on cards; each a single panel gag complete set w/box	85.00	255.00	510.00

NOTE: *There are two diff sets put out simultaneously with the first set, by the same company. One set continues/picks up the numbering of the cards from the other set.*

FOOLISH QUESTIONS (S)
EmBee Distributing Co.: 1921 (10¢, 4x5 1/2; 52 pgs, 3 color covers; B&W)

1-By Rube Goldberg	50.00	150.00	305.00

FOXY GRANDPA
Foxy Grandpa Company, 33 Wall St, NY: 1900 (9x15", 84 pgs, full color, cardboard-c)

nn - By Carl Schultze (By Permission of New York Herald)	433.00	1300.00	—

NOTE: *This seminal comic strip began Jan 7, 1900 and was collected later that same year.*

FOXY GRANDPA (Also see The Funnies, 1st series) (N)
N. Y. Herald/Frederick A. Stokes Co/M. A. Donahue & Co./Bunny Publ.
(L. R. Hammersly Co.): 1901 - 1916 (Strip-r in color, hard-c)

1901- 9x15" in color-N. Y. Herald	367.00	1100.00	—
1902- "Latest Larks of...", 32 pgs., 9-1/2x15-1/2"	197.00	590.00	—
1902- "The Many Advs. of...", 9"x12", 148 pgs., Hammersly Co.	213.00	640.00	—
1903- "Latest Advs.", 9x15", 24 pgs., Hammersly Co.	197.00	590.00	—
1903- "...'s New Advs.", 11x15", 66 pgs., Stokes	197.00	590.00	—
1904- "Up to Date", 10x15", 66 pgs., Stokes	157.00	470.00	940.00
1904- "The Many Adventures of...", 9x15, 144pgs, Donohue	157.00	470.00	940.00
1905- "& Flip-Flaps", 9-1/2x15-1/2", 52 pgs.	157.00	470.00	940.00
1905- "The Latest Advs. of...", 9x15", 28, 52 & 68 pgs, M.A. Donohue Co.; re-issue of 1902 issue	120.00	360.00	720.00
1905- "Latest Larks of...", 9-1/2x15-1/2", 52 pgs., Donahue; re-issue of 1902 issue with more pages added	120.00	360.00	720.00
1905- "Latest Larks of...", 9-1/2x15-1/2", 24 pgs. edition, Donahue; re-issue of 1902 issue	120.00	360.00	720.00
1905- "Merry Pranks of...", 9-1/2x15-1/2", 28, 52 & 62 pgs., Donahue	120.00	360.00	720.00
1905-"...Surprises",10x15", color, 64 pg.Stokes, 60¢	120.00	360.00	720.00
1906- "Frolics", 10x15", 30 pgs., Stokes	120.00	360.00	720.00
1907?-"...& His Boys", 10x15", 64 color pgs, Stokes	120.00	360.00	720.00
1907- "Triumphs", 10x15", 62 pgs., Stokes	120.00	360.00	720.00
1908-"...Mother Goose", Stokes	120.00	360.00	720.00
1909- "...& Little Brother", 10x15, 58 pgs, Stokes	120.00	360.00	720.00
1911- "Latest Tricks", 11x15", 64 pgs. Stokes	120.00	360.00	720.00
1914-(9-1/2x15-1/2", 24 pgs.)-6 color cartoons/page, Bunny Publ. Co.	105.00	315.00	625.00
1915 - ...Always Jolly (10x16, Stokes)	105.00	315.00	625.00
1916- "Merry Book", (10x15", 64 pgs, Stokes)	105.00	315.00	625.00
1917-"...Adventures (5 1/2 x 6 1/2, 26 pgs, Stokes)	80.00	240.00	480.00
1917-"...Frolics (5 1/2 x 6 1/2, 26 pgs, Stokes)	80.00	240.00	480.00
1917-"...Triumphs (5 1/2 x 6 1/2, 26 pgs, Stokes)	80.00	240.00	480.00

FOXY GRANDPA, FUNNY TRICKS OF (The Stump Books)
M.A. Donahue Co, Chicago: approx 1903 (1-7/8x6-3/8", 44 pgs, blue hardcover)

nn - By Carl Schultze	63.00	189.00	375.00

NOTE: *One of a series of ten "stump" books; the only comics one.*

FOXY GRANDPA'S MOTHER GOOSE (M)
Stokes: October 1903 (10-11/16x8-1/2", 86 pgs, hard-c)

nn - By Carl Schultze (not comics - illustrated book)	63.00	189.00	375.00

FOXY GRANDPA SPARKLETS SERIES (N)
M. A. Donahue & Co.: 1908 (7-3/4x6-1/2"; 24 pgs., color)

"... Rides the Goat", "...& His Boys", "...Playing Ball", "...Fun on the Farm", "...Fancy Shooting", "...Show His Boys Up-To-Date Sports", "...Plays Santa Claus" each....	100.00	300.00	600.00
900- "Playing Ball"; Bunny illos; 8 pgs., linen like pgs., no date	75.00	225.00	450.00

FOXY GRANDPA VISITS RICHMOND (O,P)
Dietz Printing Co., Richmond, VA / Hotel Rueger: nd (c1920's) (5-7/8" x 4-1/2", 16 pgs, paper-c, B&W)

nn - (Scarce) By Bunny	48.00	144.00	285.00

NOTE: *Promotional comic given away to its guests by the Hotel Rueger, about Foxy Grandpa visiting and enjoying the Hotel. Originally came in an envelope, with the words "Foxy Grandpa Visits Richmond -- and Rueger's" printed on it.*

FOXY GRANDPA VISITS WASHINGTON, D.C. (P)
Dietz Printing Co., Richmond, VA / Hamilton Hotel: nd (c1920's) (5-7/8" x 4-1/2", 16 pgs, paper-c, B&W)

nn - (Scarce) By Bunny	38.00	114.00	225.00

NOTE: *Mostly reprints "... Visits Richmond", changing all references to Hotel Rueger, to Hamilton Hotel instead. Also, changes depictions of a waiter and a cook from black to white, plus incompletely erases the cover art on a book Foxy Grandpa falls asleep with (the latter is how we know that the Richmond version was first).*

FRAGMENTS FROM FRANCE (S)

G. P. Putnam & Sons: 1917 (9x6-1/4", 168 pgs, hardcover, $1.75)

nn - By Bruce Bairnsfather	29.00	87.00	175.00

NOTE: *WW1 trench warfare cartoons; color dust jacket.*

FUNNIES, THE (H) (See Clancy the Cop, Deadwood Gulch, Bug Movies)
Dell Publishing Co.: 1929 - No. 36, 10/18/30 (10¢; 5¢ No. 22 on) (16 pgs.)
Full tabloid size in color; not reprints; published every Saturday

1-My Big Brudder, Jonathan, Jazzbo & Jim, Foxy Grandpa, Sniffy, Jimmy Jams & other strips begin; first four-color comic newsstand publication; also contains magic, puzzles & stories	317.00	951.00	1900.00
2-21 (1930, 10¢)	113.00	339.00	675.00
22(nn-7/12/30-5¢)	113.00	339.00	675.00
23(nn-7/19/30-5¢), 24(nn-7/26/30-5¢), 25(nn-8/2/30), 26(nn-8/9/30), 27(nn-8/16/30), 28(nn-8/23/30), 29(nn-8/30/30), 30(nn-9/6/30), 31(nn-9/13/30), 32(nn-9/20/30), 33(nn-9/27/30), 34(nn-10/4/30), 35(nn-10/11/30), 36(nn, no date-10/18/30) each....	108.00	324.00	650.00

GASOLINE ALLEY (Also see Popular Comics & Super Comics)
Reilly & Lee Publishers: 1929 (8-3/4x7", B&W daily strip-r, hard-c)

nn - By King (96 pgs.)	104.00	312.00	625.00
with scarce Dust Wrapper	183.00	550.00	1100.00

NOTE: *Of all the Frank King reprint books, this is the only one to reprint actual complete newspaper strips - all others are illustrated prose text stories.*

GIBSON'S PUBLISHED DRAWINGS, MR. (M,S) (see Victorian index for earlier issues)
R.H. Russell, New York: 1894 - No. 9 1904 (11x17-3/4", hard-c, B&W)

nn (No.6; 1901) A Widow and her Friends (90 pgs.)	20.00	60.00	120.00
nn (No.7; 1902) The Social Ladder (88 pgs.)	20.00	60.00	120.00
8 - 1903 The Weaker Sex (88 pgs.)	20.00	60.00	120.00
9 - 1904 Everyday People (88 pgs.)	20.00	60.00	120.00

NOTE: *By Charles Dana Gibson cartoons, reprinted from magazines, primarily LIFE. The Education of Mr. Pipp tells a story. Series continues how long after 1904?*

GIGGLES
Pratt Food Co., Philadelphia, PA: 1908-09? (12x9", 8 pgs, color, 5 cents-c)

1-8; By Walt McDougall (#8 dated March 1909)	65.00	195.00

NOTE: *Appears to be monthly; almost tabloid size; yearly subscriptions was 25 cents.*

GOD'S MAN (H)
Jonathan Cape and Harrison Smith Inc.: 1929 (8-1/4x6", 298 pgs, B&W hardcover w/dust jacket) (original graphic novel in wood cuts)

nn - By Lynd Ward	63.00	189.00	375.00

GOLD DUST TWINS
N. K. Fairbank Co.: 1904 (4-5/8x6-3/4", 18 pgs, color and B&W)

nn - By E. W. Kemble (Rare)	54.00	162.00	325.00

NOTE: *Promo comic for Gold DustWashing Powder; includes page of watercolor paints.*

GOLF
Volland Co.: 1916 (9x12-3/4", 132 pgs, hard-c, B&W)

nn - By Clair Briggs	75.00	225.00	450.00

GUMPS, THE (N)
Landfield-Kupfer: No. 1, 1918 - No. 6, 1921; (B&W Daily strip-r)

Book No. 1 (1918)(scarce)-cardboard-c, 5-1/4x13-1/3", 64 pgs., daily strip-r by Sidney Smith	85.00	255.00	510.00
Book No. 2 (1918)-(scarce); 5-1/4x13-1/3"; paper cover; 36 pgs. daily strip reprints by Sidney Smith	85.00	255.00	510.00
Book No. 3	118.00	354.00	710.00
Book No. 4 (1918) 5-3/8x13-7/8", 20 pgs. Color card-c	118.00	354.00	710.00
Book No. 5 10-1/4x13-1/2", 20 pgs. Color paper-c	118.00	354.00	710.00
Book No. 6 (Rare, 20 pgs, 8x13-3/8, strip-r 1920-21)	127.00	380.00	760.00

GUMPS, ANDY AND MIN, THE (N)
Landfield-Kupfer Printing Co., Chicago/Morrison Hotel: nd (1920s) (Giveaway, 5-1/2"x14", 20 pgs., B&W, soft-c)

nn - Strip-r by Sidney Smith; art & logo embossed on cover w/hotel restaurant menu on back-c or a hotel promo ad; 4 different contents of issues known	54.00	162.00	325.00

GUMPS, THE (N)
Cupples & Leon: 1924-1930 (10x10, 52 pgs, B&W)

1 - By Sidney Smith	63.00	190.00	375.00
2-7	42.00	126.00	250.00

THE GUMPS (P)
Cupples & Leon Company: 1924 (9 x 7-1/2", 28 pgs, paper cover)

nn (1924)	43.00	129.00	260.00

NOTE: *Promotional comic for Sunshine Andy Gump Biscuits. Daily strip-r from 1922-24.*

GUMP'S CARTOON BOOK, THE (N)
The National Arts Company: 1931 (13-7/8x10", 36 pgs, color covers, B&W)

nn - By Sidney Smith	68.00	204.00	410.00

GUMPS PAINTING BOOK, THE (N)
The National Arts Company: 1931 (11 x 15 1/4", 20 pgs, half in full color)

nn - By Sidney Smith	68.00	204.00	410.00

HALT FRIENDS! (see also HELLO BUDDY)
???: 1918? (4-3/8x5-3/4", 36 pgs, color-c, B&W, no cover price listed)

nn - Unknown	22.00	66.00	130.00

NOTE: *Says on front cover: "Comics of War Facts of Service Sold on its merits by Unemployed or Disabled Ex-Service Men. Credentials Shown On Request. Price - Pay What You Please." These are very common; contents vary widely.*

HAMBONE'S MEDITATIONS
Jahl & Co.: 1917, no date (1920) (6-1/8 x 7-1/2, 108 pgs, paper cover, B&W)

nn - (1917, 68 pgs.) By J. P. Alley	(a copy in GD sold in 2010 for $278)		
nn - (nd, 108 pgs.) By J. P. Alley	63.00	189.00	375.00

NOTE: *Reprint of racist single panel newspaper series, 2 cartoons per page.*

HAN OLA OG PER (N)
Anundsen Publishing Co, Decorah, Iowa: 1927 (10-3/8 x 15-3/4", 54 pgs, paper-c, B&W)

nn - American origin Norwegian language strips-r	40.00	120.00	240.00

NOTE: *1940s and modern reprints exist.*

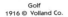

Golf
1916 © Volland Co.

The Gumps Book No. 6
1920 © Cupples & Leon

Happy Hooligan New Edition 1903
© Frederick A. Stokes

GD 2.0   FN 6.0   VF 8.0

HANS UND FRITZ (N)
The Saalfield Publishing Co.: 1917, 1927-29 (10x13-1/2", 28 pgs., B&W)

nn - By R. Dirks (1917, r-1916 strips)	105.00	315.00	625.00
nn - By R. Dirks (1923 edition- reprint of 1917 edition)	54.00	162.00	325.00
nn - By R. Dirks (1926 edition- reprint of 1917 edition)	54.00	162.00	325.00
The Funny Larks Of... By R. Dirks (©1917 outside cover; ©1916 inside indicia)	105.00	315.00	625.00
The Funny Larks Of... (1927) reprints 1917 edition of 1916 strips Halloween-c	54.00	162.00	325.00
The Funny Larks Of... 2 (1929)	54.00	162.00	325.00
193 - By R. Dirks; contains 1916 Sunday strip reprints of Katzenjammer Kids & Hawkshaw the Detective - reprint of 1917 nn edition (1929) this edition is not rare	54.00	162.00	325.00

HAPPY DAYS (S)
Coward-McCann Inc.: 1929 (12-1/2x9-5/8", 110 pgs, hardcover B&W)

nn - By Alban Butler (WW 1 cartoons)	23.00	69.00	140.00

HAPPY HOOLIGAN (See Alphonse...) (N)
Hearst's New York American & Journal: 1902,1903

Book 1-(1902)-"And His Brother Gloomy Gus", By Fred Opper; has 1901-02-r; (yellow & black)(86 pgs.)(10x15-1/4")	600.00	1800.00	3600.00
New Edition, 1903 -10x15" 82 pgs. in color	500.00	1500.00	—

NOTE: Strip ran March 26, 1900-Aug 14, 1932 and is widely recognized as setting the format standard for all newspaper comic strips which came after it. Opper (1857-1937) was going blind towards the end.

HAPPY HOOLIGAN (N) (By Fredrick Opper)
Frederick A. Stokes Co.: 1906-08 (10-1/4x15-3/4", cardboard color-c)

1906 - :Travels of...), 68 pgs,10-1/4x15-3/4", 1905-r	317.00	950.00	—
1907 - "--Home Again", 68 pgs., 10x15-3/4", 60¢; full color-c	317.00	950.00	—
1908 - "Handy--", 68 pgs, color	317.00	950.00	—

HAPPY HOOLIGAN, THE STORY OF (G)
McLoughlin Bros.: No. 281, 1932 (12x9-1/2", 20 pgs., soft-c)

281-Three-color text, pictures on heavy paper	82.00	246.00	490.00

NOTE: An homage to Opper's creation on its 30th Anniversary in 1932.

HAROLD HARDHIKE'S REJUVENATION
O'Sullivan Rubber: 1917 (6-1/4x3-1/2, 16 pgs, B&W)

nn	38.00	114.00	225.00

NOTE: Comic book to promote rubber shoe heels.

HAROLD TEEN (N)
Cupples & Leon Co.: 1929 (9-7/8x9-7/8", 52 pgs, cardboard covers)

1 - By Carl Ed	88.00	264.00	530.00
nn - (1931, 8-11/16x6-7/8", 96 pgs, hardcover w/dj)	50.00	150.00	300.00

NOTE: Title 2nd book: HAROLD TEEN AND HIS OLD SIDE-KICK– POP JENKINS, (Adv. of...). Precursor for Archie Andrews & comic strip began May 4, 1919 running into 1959.

HAROLD TEEN PAINT AND COLOR BOOK (N)
McLoughlin Bros Inc.: 1932 (13x9-3/4, 28 pgs, B&W and color)

#2054	36.00	108.00	215.00

HAWKSHAW THE DETECTIVE (See Advs. of..., Hans Und Fritz & Okay) (N)
The Saalfield Publishing Co.: 1917 (10-1/2x13-1/2", 24 pgs., B&W)

nn - By Gus Mager (Sunday strip-r)	63.00	189.00	375.00
nn - By Gus Mager (1923 reprint of 1917 edition)	31.00	93.00	185.00
nn - By Gus Mager (1926 reprint of 1917 edition)	31.00	93.00	185.00

NOTE: Runs Feb 23, 1913-Sept 4, 1922, starts again from Dec 13, 1931-Feb 11, 1952; Sherlock Holmes spoof.

HEALTH IN PICTURES
American Public Health Association, NYC: 1930 (6-1/2" x 5-3/16", 76 pgs, green & black paper-c, B&W interior)

nn - By various	22.00	66.00	130.00

NOTE: Collection of strips and cartoons put out by the Public Health Association, on topics ranging from boating and food safety, to small pox and typhoid prevention.

HE DONE HER WRONG (O) (see also BANANA OIL)
Doubleday, Doran & Company: 1930 (8-1/4x 7-1/4", 276pgs, hard-c with dust jacket, B&W interiors)

nn - By Milt Gross	71.00	213.00	425.00

NOTE: A seminal original-material wordless graphic novel, not reprints. Several modern reprints.

HENRY (N)
David McKay Co.: 1935 (25¢, soft-c with dust jacket)

Book 1 - By Carl Anderson	79.00	237.00	475.00

NOTE: Strip began March 19 1932; this book ties with Popeye (David McKay) and Little Annie Rooney (David McKay) as the last of the 10x10" Platinum Age comic books.

HENRY (M)
Greenberg Publishers Inc.: 1935 (11-1/4x 8-5/8", 72 pgs, red & blue color hard-c, dust jacket, B&W interiors) (strip-r from Saturday Evening Post)

nn - By Carl Anderson	75.00	225.00	450.00

HIGH KICKING KELLYS, THE (M)
Vaudeville News Corporation, NY: 1926 (5x11", B&W, two color soft-c)

nn - By Jack H. Ward (scarce)	54.00	162.00	325.00

HIGHLIGHTS OF HISTORY (N)

World Syndicate Publishing Co.: 1933-34 (4-1/2x4", 288 pgs)

nn - 5 different unnumbered issues; daily strip-r	20.00	60.00	120.00

NOTE: Titles include Buffalo Bill, Daniel Boone, Kit Carson, Pioneers of the Old West, Winning of the Old Northwest. There are line drawing color covers and embossed hardcover versions. It is unknown which came out first.

HOMER HOLCOMB AND MAY (N)
no publisher listed: 1920s (4 x 9-1/2", 40 pgs, paper cover, B&W)

nn - By Doc Bird Finch (strip-r)	15.00	45.00	90.00

HOME, SWEET HOME (N)
M.S. Publishing Co.: 1925 (10-1/4x10")

nn - By Tuthill	39.00	117.00	235.00

HOW THEY DRAW PROHIBITION (S)
Association Against Prohibition: 1930 (10x9", 100 pgs.)

nn - Single panel and multi-panel comics (rare)	108.00	324.00	650.00

NOTE: Contains art by J.N. "Ding" Darling, James Flagg, Rollin Kirby, Winsor McCay, T.E. Powers, H.T. Webster, others. Also comes with a loose sheet listing all the newspapers where the cartoons originally appeared.

HOW TO BE A CARTOONIST (H)
Saalfield Pub. Co: 1936 (10-3/8x12-1/2", 16 pgs, color-c, B&W)

nn - By Chas. H. Kuhn	22.00	66.00	130.00

HOW TO DRAW: A PRACTICAL BOOK OF INSTRUCTION (H)
Harper & Brothers: 1904 (9-1/4x12-3/8", 128 pgs, hardcover, B&W)

nn - Edited by Leon Barritt	67.00	201.00	400.00

NOTE: Strips reprinted include: "Buster Brown" by Outcault, "Foxy Grandpa" by Bunny, "Happy Hooligan" by Opper, "Katzenjammer Kids" by Dirks, "Lady Bountiful" by Gene Carr, "Mr. Jack" by Swinnerton, "Panhandle Pete" by George McManus, "Mr E.Z. Mark" by F.M. Howarth others; non-character strips by Hy Mayer, Winsor McCay, T.E. Powers, others; single panel cartoons by Davenport, Frost, McDougall, Nast, W.A. Rogers, Sullivant, others.

HOW TO DRAW CARTOONS (H)
Garden City Publishing Co.: 1926, 1937 (10 1/4 x 7 1/2, 150 pgs)

1926 first edition By Clare Briggs	30.00	90.00	180.00
1937 2nd edition By Clare Briggs	21.00	63.00	125.00

NOTE: Seminal "how to" break into the comics syndicates with art by Briggs, Fisher, Goldberg, King, Webster, Opper, Tad, Hershfield, McCay, Ding, others. Came with Dust Jacket -add 50%.

HOW TO DRAW FUNNY PICTURES: A Complete Course in Cartooning (H)
Frederick J. Drake & Co., Chicago: 1936 (10-3/8x6-7/8", 168 pgs, hardcover, B&W)

nn - By E.C. Matthews (200 illus by Eugene Zimmerman)	21.00	63.00	125.00

HY MAYER (M)
Puck Publishing: 1915 (13-1/2 x 20-3/4", 52 pgs, hardcover cover, color & B&W interiors)

nn - By Hy Mayer(strip reprints from Puck)	58.00	174.00	350.00

HYSTERICAL HISTORY OF THE CIVILIAN CONSERVATION CORPS
Peerless Engraving: 1934 (10-3/4x7-1/2", 104 pgs, soft-c, B&W)

nn - By various	29.00	87.00	175.00

NOTE: Comics about CCC life, includes two color insert postcards in back.

INDOOR SPORTS (N,S)
National Specials Co., New York: nd circa 1912 (25 cents, 6 x 9", 68 pgs, B&W)

nn - Tad	48.00	144.00	290.00

NOTE: Cartoons reprinted from Hearst papers.

IT HAPPENS IN THE BEST FAMILIES (N)
Powers Photo Engraving Co.: 1920 (52 pgs.)(9-1/2x10-3/4")

nn - By Briggs; B&W Sunday strips-r	42.00	126.00	250.00
Special Railroad Edition (30¢)-r/strips from 1914-1920	39.00	117.00	235.00

JIMMIE DUGAN AND THE REG'LAR FELLERS (N)
Cupples & Leon: 1921, 46 pgs. (11"x16")

nn - By Gene Byrne	88.00	264.00	525.00

NOTE: Ties with EmBee's Mutt & Jeff and Trouble of Bringing Up Father as the last of this size.

JIMMY (N) (see Little Jimmy Picture & Story Book)
N. Y. American & Journal: 1905 (10x15", 84 pgs., color)

nn - By Jimmy Swinnerton (scarce)	367.00	1100.00	2200.00

NOTE: James Swinnerton was one of the original first pioneers of the American newspaper comic strip.

JIMMY AND HIS SCRAPES (N)
Frederick A. Stokes: 1906, (10-1/4x15-1/4", 66 pgs, cardboard-c, color)

nn - By Jimmy Swinnerton (scarce)	333.00	1000.00	2000.00

JOE PALOOKA (N)
Cupples & Leon Co.: 1933 (9-13/16x10", 52 pgs., B&W daily strip-r)

nn - By Ham Fisher (scarce)	192.00	576.00	1150.00

JOHN, JONATHAN AND MR. OPPER BY F. OPPER (S,I,N)
Grant, Richards, 48 Leicester Square, W.C.: 1903 (9-5/8x8-3/8", 108 pgs, hard-c B&W)

nn - Opper (Scarce)	77.00	231.00	460.00

NOTE: British precursor-type companion to Willie And His Poppa reprints from Hearst's NY American & Journal Opper cartoons interfacing Uncle Sam precursor Brother Jonathan, John Bull. Uses name Happy Hooligan in one cartoon, has John Bull smoking opium in another.

JOLLY POLLY'S BOOK OF ENGLISH AND ETIQUETTE (S)
Jos. J. Frisch: 1931 (60 cents, 8 x 5-1/8, 88 pgs, paper-c, B&W)

nn - By Jos. J. Frisch	21.00	63.00	125.00

NOTE: Reprint of single panel newspaper series, 4 per page, of English and etiquette lessons taught by a flapper.

JOYS AND GLOOMS (N)
Reilly & Britton Co.: 1912 (11x8", 72 pgs, hard-c, B&W interior)

nn - By T. E. Powers (newspaper strip-r)	60.00	180.00	360.00

JUDGE - yet to be indexed

JUDGE'S LIBRARY - yet to be indexed

JUST KIDS COMICS FOR CRAYON COLORING
King Features. NYC: 1928 (11x8-1/2, 16 pgs., soft-c)

nn - By Ad Carter	40.00	120.00	240.00

NOTE: Porous better grade paper; top pics printed in color; lower in b&w to color.

JUST KIDS, THE STORY OF (I)
McLoughlin Bros.: 1932 (12x9-1/2, 20 pgs., paper-c)

283-Three-color text, pictures on heavy paper	50.00	150.00	300.00

KAPTIN KIDDO AND PUPPO (N)
Frederick A. Stokes Co.: 1910-1913 (11x16-1/2", 62 pgs)

1910-By Grace Wiederseim (later Drayton)	53.00	159.00	315.00
1910-Turr-ble Tales of... By Grace Wiederseim (Edward Stern & Co., 11x16-1/2", 64 pgs.)	44.00	132.00	265.00
1913- ...'Speriences By Grace Drayton	44.00	132.00	265.00

NOTE: Strip ran approx. 1909-1912.

KATZENJAMMER KIDS, THE (Also see Hans Und Fritz)
New York American & Journal: 1902,1903 (10x15-1/4", 86 pgs., color)
(By Rudolph Dirks; strip first appeared in 1897) © W.R. Hearst
NOTE: All KK books 1902-1905 all have the same exact title page with a 1902 copyright by W.R. Hearst; almost always look instead on the front cover.

1902 (Rare) (red & black); has 1901-02 strips	967.00	2900.00	–
1903- A New Edition (Rare), 86 pgs	767.00	2300.00	–
1904- 10x15", 84 pgs	300.00	900.00	–
1905?-The Cruise of the, 10x15", 60¢, in color	300.00	900.00	–
1905-A Series of Comic Pictures, 10x15", 84 pgs. in color, possible reprint of 1904 edition	267.00	800.00	–
1905-Tricks of... (10x15", 66 pgs, Stokes)	267.00	800.00	–
1906-Stokes (10x16", 32 pgs. in color)	267.00	800.00	–
1907- The Cruise of the, 10x15", 62 pgs 1905-r?	267.00	800.00	–
1910-The Komical...(10x15)	133.00	400.00	800.00
1921-Embee Dist. Co., 10x16", 20 pgs. in color	133.00	400.00	800.00

KATZENJAMMER KIDS MAGIC DRAWING AND COLORING BOOK (N)
Sam L Gabriel Sons And Company: 1931 (8 1/2 x 12", 36 pages, stiff-c)

838-By Knerr	63.00	189.00	380.00

KEEPING UP WITH THE JONESES (N)
Cupples & Leon Co.: 1920 - No. 2, 1921 (9-1/4x9-1/4",52 pgs.,B&W daily strip-r)

1,2-By Pop Momand	58.00	174.00	350.00

KID KARTOONS (N,S)
The Century Co.: 1922 (232 pgs, printed 1 side, 9-3/4 x 7-3/4", hard-c, B&W)

nn - By Gene Carr (Metropolitan Movies strip-r)	48.00	144.00	290.00

KING OF THE ROYAL MOUNTED (Also See Dan Dunn) (N)
Whitman Publishing: 1937 (5 1/2 x 7 1/4", 68 pgs., color cardboard-c, B&W)

1010	46.00	138.00	275.00

LADY BOUNTIFUL (N)
Saalfield Publ. Co./Press Publ. Co.: 1917 (13-3/8x10", 36 pgs, color cardboard-c, B&W interiors)

nn - By Gene Carr / 2 panels per page	54.00	162.00	325.00
1935 - 2nd printing (13-1/8x10",28 pgs color-c, B&W)	35.00	105.00	210.00

LAUGHS YOU MIGHT HAVE HAD From The Comic Pages of Six Week Day Issues of the Post-Dispatch (N)
St. Louis Post-Dispatch: 1921 (9 x 10 1/2", 28 pgs, B&W, red ink cover)

nn - Various comic strips	48.00	144.00	290.00

LIFE, DOGS FROM (N)
Doubleday, Page & Company: nn 1920 - No.2 1926 (130 pgs, 11-1/4 x 9", color painted-c, hard-c, B&W)

nn (No.1)	133.00	400.00	–
Second Litter	110.00	330.00	–

NOTE: Reprints strips & cartoons featuring dogs, from Life Magazine. Edited by Thomas L. Masson. Highly sought by collectors of dog ephemera. Art in both books is mostly by Robert L. Dickey. Other art: Carl Anderson-1,2; Barbes-1; Chip Bellew-1; Larry Campbell-1,2; Percy Crosby-1,2; Edwina-2; Frueh-2; R.B. Fuller-1; Gibson-2; Don Herold-2; Gus Mager-2; Orr-1; J.R. Shaver-1,2; T.S. Sullivant-2; Russ Westover-1,2; Crawford Young-1.

LIFE OF DAVY CROCKETT IN PICTURE AND STORY, THE
Cupples & Leon: 1935 (8-3/4x7", 64 pgs, B&W hard-c, dust jacket)

nn - By C. Richard Schaare	40.00	120.00	240.00

LIFE OF THOMAS A. EDISON IN WORD AND PICTURE, THE (N)(Also see Edison...)
Thomas A. Edison Industries: 1928 (10x8", 56 pgs, paper cover, B&W)

nn - Photo-c	67.00	201.00	400.00

NOTE: Reprints newspaper strip which ran August to November 1927.

LIFE'S LITTLE JOKES (S)
M.S. Publ. Co.: No date (1924)(10-1/16x10", 52 pgs., B&W)

nn - By Rube Goldberg	93.00	279.00	560.00

LIFE, MINIATURE (see also LIFE (miniature reprint of issue No. 1)) (M,P,S)
Life Publishing Co.: No. 1 - No. 4 1913, 1916, 1919 (5-3/4x4-5/8", 20 pgs, color paper-c)

1- 3 (1913) 4 (1916) 5 (1919)	36.00	108.00	215.00

NOTE: Giveaway item from Life, to promote subscriptions. All reprint material. No.2: James Montgomery Flagg-c;-a-Chip Bellew, Gus Dirks, Gibson, F.M.Howarth, Art Young.

LIFE'S PRINTS (was LIFE'S PICTURE GALLERY - See Victorian Age section) (M,S,P)
Life Publishing Company, New York: nd c1907) (7x4-1/2", 132 pgs, paper cover, B&W)

nn - (nd; c1907) unillustrated black construction paper cover; reprints art from 1895-1907; art by J.M.Flagg, A.B.Frost, Gibson (Scarce)	–	–	–
nn - (nd; c1908) b&w cardboard painted cover by Gibson, showing angel raising a champagne glass; reprints art from 1901-1908; art by J.M.Flagg, A.B.Frost, Gibson, Walt Kuhn, Art Young (Scarce)	–	–	–

NOTE: Catalog of prints reprinted from LIFE covers & centerspreads. There are likely more as yet unreported

catalogs.

LIFE, THE COMEDY OF LIFE
Life Publishing Company: 1907 (130 pgs, 11-3/4x9-1/4",embossed printed cloth covered board-c, B+W)

nn - By various	23.00	69.00	140.00

NOTE: Single cartoons and some sequential cartoons. Artists include Charles Dana Gibson, Harrison Cady, E.W. Kemble, James Montgomery Flagg.

LILY OF THE ALLEY IN THE FUNNIES
Whitman Publishing Co.: No date (1927) (10-1/4x15-1/2"; 28 pgs., color)

W936 - By T. Burke (Rare)	75.00	225.00	450.00

LITTLE ANNIE ROONEY (N)
David McKay Co.: 1935 (25¢, soft-c)

Book 1	60.00	180.00	360.00

NOTE: Ties with Henry & Popeye (David McKay) as the last of the 10x10" size Plat comic books.

LITTLE ANNIE ROONEY WISHING BOOK (G) (See Happy Hooligan, Story of #281)
McLoughlin Bros.: 1932 (12x9-1/2", 16 pgs., soft-c, 3-color text, heavier paper)

282 - By Darrell McClure	49.00	147.00	295.00

LITTLE BIRD TOLD ME, A (E)
Life Publishing Co.: 1905? (96 pgs, hardbound)

nn - By Walt Kuhn (Life-r)	49.00	147.00	295.00

LITTLE FOLKS PAINTING BOOK (N)
The National Arts Company: 1931 (10-7/8 x 15-1/4", 20 pgs, half in full color)

nn - By "Tack" Knight (strip-r)	49.00	147.00	295.00

LITTLE JIMMY PICTURE AND STORY BOOK (I) (see Jimmy)
McLaughlin Bros., Inc.: 1932 (13-1/4 x 9-3/4", 20 pgs, cardstock color cover)

284 Text by Marion Kincaird; illus by Swinnerton	83.00	249.00	475.00

LITTLE JOHNNY & THE TEDDY BEARS (Judge-r) (M) (see Teddy Bear Books)
Reilly & Britton Co.: 1907 (10x14"; 68 pgs, green, red, black interior color)

nn - By J. R. Bray-a/Robert D. Towne-s	100.00	300.00	600.00

LITTLE JOURNEY TO THE HOME OF BRIGGS THE SKY-ROCKET, THE
Lockhart Art School: 1917 (10-3/4x7-7/8", 20 pgs, B&W) (I)

nn - About Clare Briggs (bio & lots of early art)	50.00	150.00	300.00

LITTLE KING, THE (see New Yorker Cartoon Albums for 1st appearance) (M)
Farrar & Reinhart, Inc: 1933 (10-1/4 x 8-3/4, 80 pgs, hardcover w/dust jacket)

nn - By Otto Soglow (-r The New Yorker)	97.00	291.00	580.00

NOTE: Copies with dust jacket are worth 30% more. Also exists in a 12x8-size edition.

LITTLE LULU BY MARGE (N)
Rand McNally & Company, Chicago: 1936 (6-9/16x6", 68 pgs, yellow hard-c, B&W)

nn - By Marjorie Henderson Buell	54.00	162.00	325.00

NOTE: Reprints reprinting single panel Little Lulu cartoons which began with Saturday Evening Post Feb. 23, 1935. This book was reprinted several times as late as 1940.

LITTLE NAPOLEON
No publisher listed: 1924 , 50 pages, 10" by 10", Color cardstock-c, B&W

nn - By Bud Counihan (Cupples &Leon format)	50.00	150.00	300.00

LITTLE NEMO (...in Slumberland) (N) (see also Little Sammy Sneeze, Dreams...Rarebit F)
Doffield & Co.(1906)/Cupples & Leon Co.(1909): 1906, 1909 (Sunday strip-r in color, cardboard covers)

1906-11x16-1/2" by Winsor McCay; 30 pgs. (scarce)	1733.00	5200.00	–
1909-10x14" by Winsor McCay (scarce)	1367.00	4100.00	–

LITTLE ORPHAN ANNIE (See Treasure Box of Famous Comics) (N)
Cupples & Leon Co.: 1926 - 1934 (8-3/4x7", 100 pgs., B&W daily strip-r, hard-c)

1 (1926)-Little Orphan Annie (softback see Treasure Box)	71.00	213.00	425.00
2 (1927)-In the Circus (softback see Wonder Box...)	45.00	135.00	270.00
3 (1928)-The Haunted House (softback see Wonder Box...)	45.00	135.00	270.00
4 (1929)-Bucking the World	45.00	135.00	270.00
5 (1930)-Never Say Die	38.00	114.00	230.00
6 (1931)-Shipwrecked	38.00	114.00	230.00
7 (1932)-A Willing Helper	32.00	96.00	190.00
8 (1933)-In Cosmic City	32.00	96.00	190.00
9 (1934)-Uncle Dan (not rare)	32.00	96.00	190.00

NOTE: Each book reprints dailies from the previous year. Each hardcover came with a dust jacket. Books with out dust jackets are worth 50% less. Many copies of #9 Uncle Dan have been turning up on eBay recently.

LITTLE ORPHAN ANNIE RUMMY CARDS
Whitman Publishing Co., Racine: 1935 (box: 5 x 6 1/2" Cards: 3 1/2 x 2 1/4")

nn-Harold Gray	22.00	66.00	130.00

NOTE: 36 cards, including 1 instruction card, 5 character cards and 30 cards forming 5 sequential stories (6 cards each).

LITTLE SAMMY SNEEZE (N) (see also Little Nemo, Dreams of A Rarebit Fiend)
New York Herald Co.: Dec 1905 (11x16-1/2", 72 pgs., color)

nn - By Winsor McCay (Very Rare)	2900.00	8700.00	–

NOTE: Rarely found in fine to mint condition.

LIVE AND LET LIVE
Travelers Insurance Co.: 1936 (5-3/4x7/3/4", 16 pgs. color and B&W)

nn - Bill Holman, Carl Anderson, etc	22.00	66.00	130.00

LULU AND LEANDER (N) (see also Funny Folk, 1899, in Victorian section)
New York American & Journal: 1904 (76 pgs); **William A Stokes & Co:** 1906

nn - By F.M. Howarth	317.00	951.00	1900.00
nn - The Trials of...(1906, 10x16", 68 pgs. in color)	317.00	951.00	1900.00

NOTE: F. M. Howarth helped pioneer the American comic strip in the pages of PUCK magazine in the early 1890s before the Yellow Kid.

MADMAN'S DRUM (O)
Jonathan Cape and Harrison Smith Inc.: 1930 (8-1/4x6", 274 pgs, B&W hardcover w/dust jacket) (original graphic novel in wood cuts)

nn - By Lynd Ward	63.00	189.00	375.00

MAMA'S ANGEL CHILD IN TOYLAND (I)
Rand McNally, Chicago: 1915 (128 pgs, hardbound with dust jacket)

nn - By M.T. "Penny" Ross & Marie C, Sadler	44.00	132.00	265.00

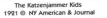

The Katzenjammer Kids
1921 © NY American & Journal

Mickey Mouse Book
1930 © DIS

Mr. & Mrs.
1922 © WHIT

MU

PLATINUM AGE

GD 2.0 FN 6.0 VF 8.0

NOTE: *Mamma's Angel Child published as a comic strip by the "Chicago Tribune" 1908 Mar 1 to 1920 Oct 17.This novel dedicated to Esther Starring Richartz, "the original Mamma's Angel Kid."*

MAUD (N) (see also *Happy Hooligan*)
Frederick A. Stokes Co.: 1906 - 1908? (10x15-1/2", cardboard-c)

1906-By Fred Opper (Scarce), 66 pgs. in color	467.00	1400.00	–
1907-The Matchless, 10x15" 70 pgs in color	367.00	1100.00	–
1908-The Mirthful Mule, 10x15", 64 pgs in color	367.00	1100.00	–

NOTE: *First run of strip began July 24, 1904 to at least Oct 6, 1907, spun out of Happy Hooligan.*

MEMORIAL EDITION The Drawings of Clare Briggs (S)
Wm H. Wise & Company: 1930 (7-1/2x8-3/4", 284 pgs, pebbled false black leather, B&W) (posthumous boxed set of 7 books by Clare Briggs)
nn - The Days of Real Sport; nn-Golf; nn-Real Folks at Home; nn-Ain't it a Grand and Glorious Feeling?; nn-That Guiltiest Feeling; nn-Somebody's Always Taking the Joy Out of Life; nn-When a Feller Needs a Friend

Each book....	28.00	84.00	165.00

NOTE: *Also exists in a whitish cream colored paper back edition; first edition unknown presently.*

MENACE CARTOONS (M, S)
Menace Publishing Company, Aurora, Missouri: 1914 (10-3/8x8", 80 pgs, cardboard-c, B&W)

nn - (Rare)	125.00	375.00	750.00

NOTE: *Reprints anti-Catholic cartoons from K.K.K. related publication The Menace.*

MEN OF DARING (N)
Cupples & Leon Co.: 1933 (8-3/4x7", 100 pgs)

nn - By Stookie Allen, intro by Lowell Thomas	37.00	111.00	220.00

MICKEY MOUSE BOOK
Bibo & Lang: 1930-1931 (12x9", stapled-c, 20 pgs., 4 printings)
nn - First Disney licensed publication (a magazine, not a book–see first book, Adventures of Mickey Mouse). Contains story of how Mickey met Walt and got his name; games, cartoons & song "Mickey Mouse (You Cute Little Feller)," written by Irving Bibo; Minnie, Clarabelle Cow, Horace Horsecollar & caricature of Walt shaking hands with Mickey. The changes made with the 2nd printing have been verified by billing affidavits in the Walt Disney Archives and include:Two Win Smith Mickey strips of 4/15/30 and 4/17/30 added to page 8 & back-c; "Printed in U.S.A." added to front cover; Bobette Bibo's age of 11 years added to title page; faulty type on the word "tail" corrected top of page 3; the word "start" added to bottom of page 7, removing the words "start 1 2 3 4" from the top of page 7; music and lyrics were rewritten on pages 12-14. A green ink border was added beginning with 2nd printing and some covers have inking variations. Art by Albert Barbelle, drawn in an Ub Iwerks style. Total circulation : 97,938 copies varying from 21,000 to 26,000 per printing.

1st printing. Contains the song lyrics **censored** in later printings, "When little Minnie's pursued by a big bad villain we feel so bad then we're glad when you up and kill him." Attached to the Nov. 15, 1930 issue of the Official Bulletin of the Mickey Mouse Club notes: "Attached to this Bulletin is a new Mickey Mouse Book that has just been published." This is thought to be the reason why a slightly disproportionate larger number of copies of the first printing still exist

	800.00	2400.00	6400.00

1st printing (variant) All white-c and has advertising on inside front & back-cvrs. All other examples have blank inside cvrs. Has word "kill" in the song. One of the ads is for a Mickey Mouse Club. A Fine copy sold on 12/24/17 for $2375.
2nd printing with a theater/advertising. Christmas greeting added to inside front cover
(1 copy known with Dec. 27, 1930 date)

2nd-4th printings	600.00	1800.00	3600.00

NOTE: *Theater/advertising copies do not qualify as separate printings. Most copies are missing pages 9 & 10 which had a puzzle to be cut out. Puzzle (pages 9 and 10) cut out or missing, subtract 60% to 75%.*

MICKEY MOUSE COLORING BOOK (S)
Saalfield Publishing Company:1931 (15-1/4x10-3/4", 32 pgs, color soft cover, half printed in full color interior, rest B&W)

871 - By Ub Iwerks & Floyd Gottfredson (rare-1?)	450.00	1350.00	2700.00

NOTE: *Contains reprints of the earliest MM daily strip ever, including the "missing" speck the chicken is after found only on the original daily strip art by Iwerks plus other very early MM art. There were several other Saalfield Mickey Mouse coloring books manufactured around the same time.*

MICKEY MOUSE, THE ADVENTURES OF (I)
David McKay Co., Inc.: Book I, 1931 - Book II, 1932 (5-1/2"x8-1/2", 32 pgs.)
Book I-First Disney book, by strict definition (1st printing-50,000 copies)(see Mickey Mouse Book by Bibo & Lang). Illustrated text refers to Clarabelle Cow as "Carolyn" and Horace Horsecollar as "Henry". The name "Donald Duck" appears with a non-costumed generic duck on back cover & inside, not in the context of the character that later debuted in the Wise Little Hen.

Hardback w/characters on back-c	217.00	651.00	1300.00
Softcover w/characters on back-c	150.00	450.00	900.00
Version without characters on back-c	150.00	450.00	900.00

Book II-Less common than Book I. Character development brought into conformity with the Mickey Mouse cartoon shorts and syndicated strips. Captain Church Mouse, Tanglefoot, Peg-Leg Pete and Pluto appear with Mickey & Minnie

	146.00	438.00	875.00

MICKEY MOUSE COMIC (N)
David McKay Co.: 1931 - No. 4, 1934 (10"x9-3/4", 52 pgs., card board-c) (Later reprints exist)
1 (1931)-Reprints Floyd Gottfredson daily strips in black & white from 1930 & 1931, including the famous two week sequence in which Mickey tries to commit suicide

	450.00	1350.00	2700.00

2 (1932)-1st app. of Pluto reprinted from 7/8/31 daily. All pgs. from 1931

	242.00	726.00	1450.00

3 (1933)-Reprints 1932 & 1933 Sunday pages in color, one strip per page, including the

"Lair of Wolf Barker" continuity pencilled by Gottfredson and inked by Al Taliaferro & Ted Thwaites. First app. Mickey's nephews, Morty & Ferdie, one identified by name of Mortimer Fieldmouse, not to be confused with Uncle Mortimer Mouse who is introduced in the Wolf Barker story

	333.00	1000.00	2000.00

4 (1934)-1931 dailies, include the only known reprint of the infamous strip of 2/4/31 where the villainous Kat Nipp snips off the end of Mickey's tail with a pair of scissors

	208.00	624.00	1250.00

MICKEY MOUSE (N)
Whitman Publishing Co.: 1933-34 (10x8-3/4", 34 pgs, cardboard-c)
948-1932 & 1933 Sunday strips in color, printed from the same plates as Mickey Mouse Book #3 by David McKay, but only pages 5-17 & 32-48 (including all of the "Wolf Barker" continuity)

	250.00	750.00	1500.00

NOTE: *Some copies bound with back cover upside down. Variance doesn't affect value. Same art appears on front and back covers of all copies. Height of Whitman reissue trimmed 1/2 inch.*

MILITARY WILLIE (N)
J. I. Austen Co.: 1907 (7x9-1/2", 12 pgs., every other page in color, stapled)

nn - By F. R. Morgan	67.00	201.00	400.00

MINNEAPOLIS TRIBUNE CARTOON BOOK (S)
Minneapolis Tribune: 1899-1903 (11-3/8x9-3/8", B&W, paper cover)

nn (#1) (1899)	42.00	126.00	250.00
nn (#2) (1900)	42.00	126.00	250.00
nn (#3) (1901) (published Jan 01, 1901)	42.00	126.00	250.00
nn (#4) (1902) (114 pgs)	42.00	126.00	250.00
nn (#5) (1903) (9x10-3/4",110 pgs, B&W; color-c)	42.00	126.00	250.00

NOTE: *All by Roland C. Bowman (editorial-r).*

MINUTE BIOGRAPHIES: INTIMATE GLIMPSES INTO THE LIVES OF 150 FAMOUS MEN AND WOMEN
Grossett & Dunlap: 1931, 1933 (10-1/4x7-3/4", 168 pgs, hardcover, B&W)

nn - By Nisenson (art) & Parker(text)	28.00	84.00	170.00
More.... (1933)	28.00	84.00	170.00

MISCHIEVOUS MONKS OF CROCODILE ISLE, THE (N)
J. I. Austen Co., Chicago: 1908 (8-1/2x11-1/2", 12 pgs., 4 pgs. in color)

nn - By F. R. Morgan; reads longwise	113.00	339.00	675.00

MR. & MRS. (Also see Ain't It A Grand and Glorious Feeling?) (N)
Whitman Publishing Co.: 1922 (9x9-1/2", 52 & 28 pgs., cardboard-c)

nn - By Briggs (B&W, 52 pgs.)	44.00	132.00	265.00
nn - 28 pgs.-(9x9-1/2")-Sunday strips-r in color	50.00	150.00	300.00

NOTE: *The earliest presently-known Whitman comic books*

MR. BLOCK (N)
Industrial Workers of the World (IWW): 1913, 1919

nn - By Ernest Riebe (C)	58.00	175.00	–
...And The Profiteers (original material) (H)	58.00	175.00	–

NOTE: *Mr Block was a daily strip published from 1912 NOV 7 to 1913 SEP ? by the socialist newspaper "Industrial Worker"; Mr Block was a "square" (you'd say he has head was in fact a block) who enthusiastically supported the same system that exploited him. The noted Joe Hill wrote a song about him (Mr Block,1913, on the air of "It loooks me like a big time tonight") for the "Industrial Worker Songbook".*

MR. TWEE-DEEDLE (N)
Cupples & Leon: 1913, 1917 (11-3/8 x 16-3/4" color strips-r from NY Herald)

nn - By John B. Gruelle (later of Raggedy Ann fame)	367.00	1100.00	2200.00
nn - "Further Adventures of..." By Gruelle	367.00	1100.00	2200.00

NOTE: *Strip ran Feb 5, 1911-March 10, 1918.*

MONKEY SHINES OF MARSELEEN AND SOME OF HIS ADVENTURES (C)
McLaughlin Bros. New York: 1906 (10 x 12-3/8", 36 pgs, full color hardcover)

nn - By Norman E. Jennett strip-r NY Evening Telegram	96.00	288.00	575.00

NOTE: *Strip began in 1906 until at least March 13, 1910.*

MONKEY SHINES OF MARSELEEN (N)
Cupples & Leon Co.: 1909 (11-1/2 x 17", 58 pgs. in two colors)

nn - By Norman E. Jennett (strip-r New York Herald)	96.00	288.00	575.00

MOON MULLINS (N)
Cupples & Leon Co.: 1927 - 1933 (52 pgs., B&W daily strip-r)

Series 1 ('27)-By Willard	92.00	267.00	550.00
Series 2 ('28), Series 3 ('29), Series 4 ('30)	50.00	150.00	300.00
Series 5 ('31), 6 ('32), 7 ('33)	50.00	150.00	300.00
Big Book 1 ('30)-B&W (scarce)	120.00	360.00	725.00
w/dust jacket (rare)	183.00	550.00	1100.00

MOVING PICTURE FUNNIES
Saml Gabriel Sons & Company: 1918 (5-1/4 x 10-1/4", 52 pgs, B&W, illustrated hard-c)

nn	21.00	63.00	125.00

NOTE: *823 Comical illustrations that show a different scene when folded.*

MUTT & JEFF (...Cartoon, The) (N)
Ball Publications: 1911 - No. 5, 1916 (5-3/4 x 15-1/2", 72 pgs, B&W, hard-c)

1 (1910)(50¢) very common	100.00	300.00	600.00
2,3: 2 (1911)-Opium den panels; Jeff smokes opium (pipe dreams).	92.00	276.00	550.00
3 (1912) both very common	54.00	162.00	325.00
2-(1911) Reprint of 1911 edition with black ink cover	54.00	162.00	325.00
4 (1915) (50¢) (Scarce)	121.00	363.00	725.00
5 (1916) (Rare) -Photos of Fisher, 1st pg. (68 pages)	183.00	549.00	1100.00

	GD 2.0	FN 6.0	VF 8.0

5-Scarce 84 page reprint edition 150.00 450.00 900.00
NOTE: Mutt & Jeff first appeared in newspapers in 1907. Cover variations exist showing Mutt & Jeff reading various newspapers; i.e., The Oregon Journal, The American, and The Detroit News. Reprinting of each issue began soon after publication. No. 4 and 5 may not have been reprinted. Values listed include the reprints. Mutt & Jeff was the first successful American daily newspaper comic strip and as such remains one of the seminal strips of all time.

MUTT & JEFF (N)
Cupples & Leon Co.: No. 6, 1919 - No. 22, 1934? (9-1/2x9-1/2", 52 pgs., B&W dailies, stiff-c)
6, 7 - By Bud Fisher (very common) 38.00 114.00 225.00
8-10 .... 54.00 162.00 325.00
11-18 (Somewhat Scarcer) (#19-#22 do not exist) 71.00 213.00 425.00
nn (1920) (Advs. of...) 11x16"; 44 pgs.; full color reprints of 1919 Sunday strips
.... 108.00 324.00 650.00
Big Book nn (1926, 144 pgs., hardcovers) 125.00 375.00 750.00
w/dust jacket 217.00 650.00 1300.00
Big Book 1 (1928) - Thick book (hardcovers) 117.00 350.00 700.00
w/dust jacket (rare) 208.00 624.00 1250.00
Big Book 2 (1929) - Thick book (hardcovers) 125.00 375.00 750.00
w/dust jacket (rare) 208.00 624.00 1250.00
NOTE: The Big Books contain three previous issues rebound.

MUTT & JEFF (N)
Embee Publ. Co.: 1921 (9x15", color cardboard-c & interior)
nn - Sunday strips in color (Rare)- BY Bud Fisher 183.00 550.00 1100.00
NOTE: Ties with The Trouble of Bringing Up Father (EmBee) and Jimmie Dugan & The Reg'lar Fellers (C&L) as the last of this size.

MYSTERIOUS STRANGER AND OTHER CARTOONS, THE
McClure, Phillips & Co.: 1905 (12-3/8x9-3/4", 338 pgs, hardcover, B&W)
nn - By John McCutcheon 46.00 138.00 275.00

MY WAR - Szeged (Szuts)
Wm. Morrow Co.: 1932 (7x10-1/2", 210 pgs, hard-c, B&W)
nn - (All story panels, no words - powerful) 47.00 141.00 280.00

NAUGHTY ADVENTURES OF VIVACIOUS MR. JACK, THE
New York American & Journal: 1904 (15x10", color strips)
nn - By James Swinnerton; (Very Rare - 3 known copies) 467.00 1401.00 2800.00

NEBBS, THE (N)
Cupples & Leon Co.: 1928 (52 pgs., B&W daily strip-r)
nn - By Sol Hess; Carlson-a 50.00 150.00 300.00

NERVY NAT'S ADVENTURES (E)
Leslie-Judge Co.: 1911 (90 pgs, 85¢, 1903 strip reprints from **Judge**)
nn - By James Montgomery Flagg 80.00 240.00 480.00

THE NEWLYWEDS AND THEIR BABY (N)
Saalfield Publ. Co.: 1907 (13x10", 52 pgs., hardcover)
...& Their Baby' by McManus; daily strips 50% color 400.00 1200.00
NOTE: Strip ran Apr 10, 1904 thru Jan 14, 1906 and then May 19, 1907-Dec 5, 1916; was a huge success with Baby Snookums long before McManus invented Bringing Up Father; Snookums brought back as a topper strip over BUF Nov 19, 1944-Dec 30, 1956.

THE NEWLYWEDS AND THEIR BABY'S COMIC PICTURES FOR PAINTING AND CRAYONING (N)
Saalfield Publishin Company: 1916 (10-1/4x14-3/4", 52 pgs. Cardboard-c)
nn - 44 B&W pages, covers, and one color wrap glued to B&W title page.
Color wrap: color title pg. & 3 pgs of color strips 92.00 276.00 550.00
nn - (1917, 10x14", 20 pgs, oblong, cardboard-c) partial reprint of 1916 edition 47.00 140.00 280.00

THE NEWLYWEDS AND THEIR BABY (N)
Saalfield Publishing Company: 1917 (10-1/8x13-9/16 ", 52 pgs, full color cardstock-c, some pages full color, others two color (orange, blue))
nn 75.00 225.00 450.00

NEW YORKER CARTOON ALBUM, THE (M)
Doubleday, Doran & Company Inc.: (1928-1931); **Harper & Brothers:** (1931-1933); **Random House** (1935-1937), 12x9", various pg counts, hardcovers w/dust jackets
1928: nn-114 pgs Arno, Held, Soglow, Williams, etc 22.00 66.00 130.00
1928: SECOND-114 pgs Arno, Bairnsfather, Gross, Held, Soglow, Williams 13.00 39.00 80.00
1930: THIRD-172 pgs Arno, Bairnsfather, Held, Soglow, Art Young 13.00 39.00 80.00
1931: FOURTH-154 pgs Arno, Held, Soglow, Steig, Thurber, Williams, Art Young, "Little King" by Soglow begins 13.00 39.00 80.00
1932: FIFTH-156 pgs Arno, Bairnsfather, Held, Hoff, Soglow, Steig, Thurber, Williams 13.00 39.00 80.00
1933: SIXTH-156 pgs same as above 13.00 39.00 80.00
1935: SEVENTH-164 pgs 13.00 39.00 80.00
1937: 168 pgs; Charles Addams plus same as above but no Little King, two page "Gone With The Wind" parody strip 16.00 48.00 95.00
NOTE: Some sequential strips but mostly single panel cartoons.

NIPPY'S POP (N)
The Saalfield Publishing Co.: 1917 (10-1/2x13-1/2", 36 pgs., B&W, Sunday strip-r)
nn - Charles M Payne (better known as S'Matter Pop) 54.00 162.00 325.00

OH, MAN (A Bully Collection of Those Inimitable Humor Cartoons) (S)
P.F. Volland & Co.: 1919 (8-1/2x13", 136 pgs.)
nn - By Briggs 50.00 150.00 300.00
NOTE: Originally came in illustrated box with Briggs art (box is Rare - worth 50% more with box).

OH SKIN-NAY! (S)
P.F. Volland & Co.: 1913 (8-1/2x13", 136 pgs.)
nn - The Days Of Real Sport by Briggs 52.00 156.00 310.00
NOTE: Originally came in illustrated box with Briggs art (box is Rare - worth 50% more with box).

OLD GOLD THE SMOOTHER AND BETTER CIGARETTE...NOT A COUGH IN A CARLOAD (M,N,P) (see also BY BRIGGS)
Old Gold Cigarettes: nd (c1920's) (16 pgs, paper-c, color) (both Scarce)
nn- (4-1/4" x 3-7/8") cover strip is "Oh, Man!"; also contains: "Real Folks at Home", "Ain't It a Grand and Glorious Feelin?", "It Happens in the Best Regulated Families", and "Mr. and Mrs." .... (no known sales)

1440- (5-9/16" x 5-1/4") cover strip is "Frank and Ernest"; also contains: "That Guiltiest Feeling", "Real Folks at Home", "Oh, Man!", "When a Feller Needs a Friend". .... (no known sales)
NOTE: Collection reprinting strip cartoons by Clare Briggs, advertising Old Gold Cigarettes. These strips originally appeared in various magazines, play program booklets, newspapers, etc. Some of the strips involve regular Briggs strip series. The two booklets contain a completely different set of comics.

ON AND OFF MOUNT ARARAT (also see **Tigers**) (N)
Hearst's New York American & Journal: 1902, 86pgs. 10x15-1/4"
nn - Rare Noah's Ark satire by Jimmy Swinnerton (rare) .... 600.00 1800.00 –

ON THE LINKS
Associated Feature Service: Dec, 1926 (9x10", 48 pgs.)
nn - Daily strip-r by Robert Hunter 46.00 138.00 275.00

ONE HUNDRED WAR CARTOONS (S)
Idaho Daily Statesman: 1918 (7-3/4x10", 102 pgs, paperback, B&W)
nn - By Villeneuve (WW I cartoons) 28.00 84.00 165.00

OUR ANTEDILUVIAN ANCESTORS (N,S)
New York Evening Journal, NY: 1903 (11-3/8x8-7/8", hardcover)
nn - By F Opper 79.00 237.00 475.00
NOTE: There is a simultaneously published British edition, identical size and contents, from C. Arthur Pearson Ltd, London. A collection of single panel cartoons about cavemen. Similar to an earlier British cartoon book "Prehistoric Peeps from Punch", by E.T. Reed.

OUTBURSTS OF EVERETT TRUE, THE (N)
Saalfield Publ. Co.(Werner Co.): 1907 (92 pgs, 9-7/16x5-1/4')
1907 (2-4 panel strips-r)-By Condo & Raper 125.00 375.00 750.00
1921-Full color-c; reprints 56 of 88 cartoons from 1907 ed. (10x10", 32 pgs B&W) 63.00 189.00 375.00

OVER THERE COMEDY FROM FRANCE
Observer House Printing: nd (WW I era) (6x14", 60 pgs, paper cover)
nn - Artist(s) unknown 23.00 69.00 140.00

OWN YOUR OWN HOME (I)
Bobbs-Merrill Company, Indianapolis: 1919 (7-7/16x5-1/4")
nn - By Fontaine Fox ....

PECKS BAD BOY (N)
Charles C. Thompson Co, Chicago (by Walt McDougal): 1906-1908 (strip-r)
The Adventures of... (1906) 11-1/2x16-1/4", 68 pgs 146.00 438.00 875.00
...& His Country Cousin Cynthia (1907) 12x16-1/2", 34 pgs In color 146.00 438.00 875.00
Advs. of...And His Country Cousins (1907) 5-1/2x10 1/2", 18 pgs In color 71.00 213.00 425.00
Advs. of...And His Country Cousins (1907) 11-1/2x16-1/4", 36 pgs 71.00 213.00 425.00
...& Their Advs With The Teddy Bear (1907) 5-1/2x10-1/2", 18 pgs in color 71.00 213.00 425.00
...& Their Balloon Trip To the Country (1907) 5-1/2x 10-1/2, 18 pgs 71.00 213.00 425.00
...With the Teddy Bear Show (1907) 5-1/2x 10-1/2 .... 71.00 213.00 425.00
...With The Billy Whiskers Goats (1907) 5-1/2 x 10-1/2, 18 pgs in color 71.00 213.00 425.00
...& His Chums (1908) - 11x16-3/8", 36 pgs. Stanton & Van Vliet Co 146.00 438.00 875.00
...& His Chums (1908)-Hardcover; full color;16 pgs. 125.00 375.00 750.00
Advs. of...in Pictures (1908) (11x17, 36 pgs)-In color; Stanton & Van V. Liet Co. 142.00 426.00 850.00

PERCY & FERDIE (N)
Cupples & Leon Co.: 1921 (10x10", 52 pgs., B&W dailies, cardboard-c)
nn - By H. A. MacGill (Rare) 92.00 276.00 550.00

PETER RABBIT (N)
John H. Eggers Co. The House of Little Books Publishers: 1922 - 1923
B1-B4-(Rare)-(Set of 4 books which came in a cardboard box)-Each book reprints half of a Sunday page per page and contains 8 B&W and 2 color pages; by Harrison Cady (9-1/4x6-1/4", paper-c) each... .... 60.00 180.00 360.00
Box only 77.00 231.00 460.00

PHILATELIC CARTOONS (M)
Essex Publishing Company, Lynn, Mass.: 1916 (8-11/16" x 5-7/8", 40 pgs, light blue construction paper-c, B&W interior)
nn - By Leroy S. Bartlett 48.00 144.00 290.00
NOTE: Comics reprinted from The New England Philatelist.

PICTORIAL HISTORY OF THE DEPARTMENT OF COMMERCE UNDER HERBERT HOOVER (see Picture Life of a Great American) (O)
Hoover-Curtis Campaign Committee of New York State: no date, 1928 (3-1/4 x 5-1/4, 32 pgs, paper cover, B&W)
nn - By Satterfield (scarce) 50.00 150.00 300.00
NOTE: 1928 Presidential Campaign giveaway. Original material, contents completely different from Picture Life of a Great American.

PICTURE LIFE OF A GREAT AMERICAN (see Pictorial History of the Department of Commerce under Herbert Hoover) (O)
Hoover-Curtis Campaign Committee of New York State: no date, 1928 (paper cover, B&W)
nn - (8-3/4 x 7, 20 pgs) Text cover, 2 page text introduction, 18 pgs of comics (scarcer first print) 46.00 138.00 275.00
nn - (9 x 6-3/4,24 pgs) Illustrated cover,5 page text introduction, 18 pgs of comics (scarce) 46.00 138.00 275.00
NOTE: 1928 Presidential Campaign giveaway. Unknown which above version was published first. Both contain the same original comics material by Satterfield.

PINK LAFFIN (I)
Whitman Publishing Co.: 1922 (9x12")(Strip-r; some of these actually text joke books)
...the Lighter Side of Life, ...He Tells 'Em, ...and His Family, ...Knockouts; Ray Gleason-a (All rare) each... .... 29.00 87.00 175.00

POLLY (AND HER PALS) - (N)
Newspaper Feature Service: 1916 (3x2-1/2", color)
Altogether: Three Rahs and a Tiger! by Cliff Sterrett 28.00 84.00 170.00

Oh Skin-nay!
1913 @ Volland & Co.

Secret Agent X-9 Book 2
1934 © David McKay

Winnie Winkle No. 2
1931 © Cupples & Leon

GD 2.0 FN 6.0 VF 8.0

	GD	FN	VF
There Is A Limit To Pa's Patience by Cliff Sterrett	28.00	84.00	170.00
Pa's Lil Book Has Some Uncut Pages by Sterrett	28.00	84.00	170.00

NOTE: Single newsprint sheet printed in full color on both sides, unfolds to show 12 panel story.

POPEYE PAINT BOOK (N)
McLaughlin Bros, Inc., Springfield, Mass.: 1932 (9-7/8x13", 28 pgs, color-c)

	GD	FN	VF
2052 - By E. C. Segar	117.00	351.00	700.00

NOTE: Contains a full color panel above and the exact same art in below panel in B&W which one was to color in; strip-r panels.

POPEYE CARTOON BOOK (N)
The Saalfield Co.: 1934 (8-1/2x13", 40 pgs, cardboard-c)

	GD	FN	VF
2095-(scarce)-1933 strip reprints in color by Segar. Each page contains a vertical half of a Sunday strip, so the continuity reads row by row completely across each double page spread. If each page is read by itself, the continuity makes no sense. Each double page spread reprints one complete Sunday page from 1933	400.00	1200.00	2400.00
12 Page Version	133.00	400.00	1000.00

POPEYE (See Thimble Theatre for earlier Popeye-r from Sonnett) (N)
David McKay Publications: 1935 (25¢, 52 pgs, B&W) (By Segar)

	GD	FN	VF
1-Daily strip reprints- "The Gold Mine Thieves"	183.00	549.00	1100.00
2-Daily strip-r (scarce)	183.00	549.00	1100.00

NOTE: Ties with Henry & Little Annie Rooney (David McKay) as the last of the 10x10" size books.

PORE LI'L MOSE (N)
New York Herald Publ. by Grand Union Tea
Cupples & Leon Co.: 1902 (10-1/2x15", 78 pgs., color)

	GD	FN	VF
nn - By R. F. Outcault; Earliest known C&L comic book (scarce in high grade - very high demand)	1500.00	4500.00	—

NOTE: Black Americana one page newspaper strips; falls in between Yellow Kid & Buster Brown. Complete copies have become scarce. Some have cut this book apart thinking that reselling individual pages will bring them more money.

PRETTY PICTURES (M)
Farrar & Rinehart: 1931 (12 x 8-7/8", 104 pgs, color hardcover w/dust jacket, B&W; reprints from New Yorker, Judge, Life, Collier's Weekly)

	GD	FN	VF
nn - By Otto Soglow (contains "The Little King")	46.00	138.00	275.00

QUAINT OLD NEW ENGLAND (S)
Triton Syndicate: 1936 (5-1/4x6-1/4", 100 pgs, soft-c squarebound, B&W)

	GD	FN	VF
nn - By Jack Withycomb	40.00	120.00	240.00

NOTE: Comics about weird doings in Old New England.

RED CARTOONS (S)
Daily Worker Publishing Company: 1926 (12 x 9", 68 pgs, cardboard cover, B&W)

	GD	FN	VF
nn - By Various (scarce)	48.00	144.00	290.00

NOTE: Reprint of American Communist Party editorial cartoons, from The Daily Worker, The Workers Monthly, and the Liberator. Art by Fred Ellis, William Gropper, Clive Weed, Art Young.

REG'LAR FELLERS (See All-American Comics, Jimmie Dugan & The..., Popular Comics & Treasure Box of Famous Comics) (N)
Cupples & Leon Co./MS Publishing Co.: 1921-1929

	GD	FN	VF
1 (1921)-52 pgs. B&W dailies (Cupples & Leon, 10x10")	58.00	174.00	350.00
1925, 48 pgs. B&W dailies (MS Publ.)	50.00	150.00	300.00
Hardcover (1929, 8-3/4x7-1/2"; 96 pgs.)-B&W-r	75.00	225.00	450.00

REG'LAR FELLERS STORY PAINT BOOK
Whitman, Racine, Wisc.: 1932 (8-3/4x12-1/8", 132 pgs, red soft-c)

	GD	FN	VF
By Gene Byrnes	29.00	87.00	175.00

ROGER BEAN, R. G. (Regular Guy) (N)
The Indiana News Co, Distributers.: 1915 - No. 2, 1915 (5-3/8x17", 68 pgs., B&W, hardcovers) **#3-#5 published by Chas. B. Jackson:** 1916-1919
(No. 1 2 4 & 5 bound on side, No. 3 bound at top)

	GD	FN	VF
1-By Chas B. Jackson (1915)(Scarce)	63.00	189.00	375.00
2- 5-5/8x17-1/8", 66 pgs (says 1913 inside - an obvious printing error) (red or green binding)	60.00	180.00	360.00
3-Along the Firing Line... (1916; 68 pgs, 6x17")	60.00	180.00	360.00
3-Along the Firing Line side-bound versions	60.00	180.00	360.00
4-Into the Trenches and Out Again with... (1917, 68 pgs)	60.00	180.00	360.00
5 ...And The Reconstruction Period (1919, 5-3/8x15-1/2", 84 pgs) (Scarce) (has $1 printed on cover)	60.00	180.00	360.00
Baby Grand Editions 1-5 (10x10", cardboard-c)	60.00	180.00	360.00

NOTE: No. 1 & 2 of the Twin Baby Grands (nd) 8-1/4x10-7/8", 52 pgs. #3 & #4 9x10-7/8" Cardboard cover. B&W strip reprints. Cover also says "Politics Pickles People Police."

	GD	FN	VF
nn - 9x11, 68 pgs	60.00	180.00	360.00

NOTE: Has picture of Chic Jackson and a posthumous dedication from his three children. strip-r 1931-32

ROGER BEAN PHILOSOPHER
Schnull & Co: 1917 (5-1/2x17", 36 pgs., B&W, brown & black paper-c, square binding)

	GD	FN	VF
nn - By Chic Jackson	(no known sales)		

ROOKIE FROM THE 13TH SQUAD, THAT (N) (also Between Shots; Always Belittlin'; Skippy)
Harper & Brothers Publishers: Feb. 1918 (8x9-1/4", 72 pgs, hardcover, B&W)

	GD	FN	VF
nn - By Lieut. P(ercy) L. Crosby	63.00	189.00	380.00

NOTE: Strip began in 1917 at an Army base during basic training.

ROUND THE WORLD WITH THE DOO-DADS (see Doings of the Doo-Dads, Doo Dads)
Universal Feature And Specialty Co, Chicago: 1922 (12x10-1/2", 52 pgs, B&W, red & light blue-c, square binding)

	GD	FN	VF
nn - By Arch Dale newspaper strip-r	58.00	174.00	350.00

GD 2.0 FN 6.0 VF 8.0

NOTE: Intermixed single panel and sequential comic strips with scenes from Scotland, Ireland, England, Holland, Italy, Spain, Egypt, Africa, and Lions & Elephants along the Nile River, China, Australia & back home.

RUBAIYKT OF THE EGG
The John C Winston Co, Philadelphia: 1905 (7x5/12", 64 pgs, purple-c, B&W)

	GD	FN	VF
nn - By Clare Victor Dwiggins	32.00	96.00	190.00

NOTE: Book is printed & cut into the shape of an egg.

RULING CLAWSS, THE (N,S)
The Daily Worker: 1935 (192 pgs, 10-1/4 x 7-3/8", hard-c, B&W)

	GD	FN	VF
nn - By Redfield	92.00	275.00	—

NOTE: Reprints cartoons from the American Communist Party newspaper The Daily Worker.

SAGARA'S ENGLISH CARTOONS AND CARTOON STORIES (N)
Bunkosha, Tokyo: nd (c1925) (6-5/8" x 4-1/4", 272 pgs, hard-c, B&W)

	GD	FN	VF
nn- (Scarce)	—	—	—

NOTE: Published in Tokyo, Japan, with all strips in both English and Japanese, to facilitate learning English. Majority of book is Bringing Up Father by George McManus. Also contains Japanese strip Father Takes it Easy, by T. Sagara, reprinted from the Kokusai News Agency.

SAM AND HIS LAUGH (N)
Frederick A. Stokes: 1906 (10x15", cardboard-c, Sunday strip-r in color)

	GD	FN	VF
nn - By Jimmy Swinnerton (Extremely Rare)	817.00	2451.00	4900.00

NOTE: Strip ran July 24, 1904-Dec 26 1906; its ethnic humor might be considered racist by today's standards.

SCHOOL DAYS (N)
Harper & Bros.: 1919 (9x8", 104 pgs.)

	GD	FN	VF
nn - By Clare Victor Dwiggins	50.00	150.00	300.00

SEAMAN SI - A Book of Cartoons About the Funniest "Gob" in the Navy (N)
Pierce Publishing Co.: 1916 (4x8-1/2, 200 pgs, hardcover, B&W); 1918 (4-1/8x8-1/4, 104 pgs, hardcover, B&W)

	GD	FN	VF
nn - By Perce Pearce (1916)	54.00	162.00	325.00
nn - 1918 - (Reilly & Britton Co.)	35.00	105.00	210.00

NOTE: There exists two different covers for the 1918 reprints. The earlier edition was self published by the artist. The newspaper strip is sometimes also known as "The American Sailor."

SECRET AGENT X-9 (N)
David McKay Pbll.: 1934 (Book 1: 84 pgs; Book 2: 124 pgs.) (8x7-1/2")

	GD	FN	VF
Book 1-Contains reprints of the first 13 weeks of the strip by Dashiell Hammett & Alex Raymond, complete except for 2 dailies	113.00	339.00	675.00
Book 2-Contains reprints immediately following contents of Book 1, for 20 weeks by Dashiell Hammett & Alex Raymond; complete except for two dailies. Last 5 strips misdated from 6/34, continuity correct	113.00	339.00	675.00

SILK HAT HARRY'S DIVORCE SUIT (N)
M. A. Donoghue & Co.: 1912 (5-3/4x15-1/2", oblong, B&W)

	GD	FN	VF
nn - Newspaper-r by Tad (Thomas A. Dorgan)	71.00	213.00	425.00

SINBAD A DOG'S LIFE (M)
Coward - McCann, Inc.: 1930 (11x 8-3/4", 104 pgs., single-sided, illustrated hard-c, B&W)

	GD	FN	VF
nn - By Edwina	23.00	69.00	135.00
Sinbad...Again (1932, 10-15/16x 8-9/16", 104 pgs.)	23.00	69.00	135.00

NOTE: Wordless comic strips from LIFE.

SIS HOPKINS OWN BOOK AND MAGAZINE OF FUN
Leslie-Judge Co.: 1899-July 1911 (36 pgs, color-c, B&W) (merged into Judge's Library, later titled Film Fun)

	GD	FN	VF
Any issue - By various	36.00	108.00	215.00

NOTE: Zim, Flagg, Young, Newell, Adams, etc.

SKEEZIX (Also see Gasoline Alley & Little Skeezix Books listed below) (I)
Reilly & Lee Co.: 1925 - 1928 (Strip-r, soft covers) (pictures & text)

	GD	FN	VF
...and Uncle Walt (1924)-Origin	40.00	120.00	240.00
...and Pal (1925), ...at the Circus (1926)	27.00	81.00	160.00
...& Uncle Walt (1927) (does this actually exist? reprint? never seen one yet)			
...Out West (1928)	36.00	108.00	215.00
Hardback Editions...	42.00	126.00	250.00

SKEEZIX BOOKS, LITTLE (Also see Skeezix, Gasoline Alley) (G)
Reilly & Lee Co.: No date (1928, 1929) (Boxed set of three Skeezix books)

	GD	FN	VF
nn - Box with 3 issues of Skeezix. Skeezix & Pal, Skeezix at the Circus, Skeezix & Uncle Walt known. 1928 Set	63.00	189.00	375.00
nn - Box with 4 issues of (3) above Skeezix plus "Out West"	92.00	276.00	550.00

SKEEZIX COLOR BOOK (N)
McLaughlin Bros. Inc, Springfield, Mass: 1929 (9-1/2x10-1/4", 28 pgs, one third in full color, rest in B&W)

	GD	FN	VF
2023 - By Frank King; strip-r to color	31.00	93.00	185.00

SKIPPY (see also Life Presents Skippy, Always Belittlin', That Rookie From 13th Squad)
No publisher listed: Circa 1920s (10x8", 16 pgs., color/B&W cartoons)

	GD	FN	VF
nn - By Percy Crosby	28.00	84.00	165.00

SKIPPY, LIFE PRESENTS (M)
Life Publishing Company & Henry Holt, NY: nd 1924 (134 pgs, 10-13/16x8-3/4", color hard-c, B&W)

	GD	FN	VF
nn - By Percy L Crosby	96.00	288.00	575.00

NOTE: Many sequential & single panel reprints from Skippy's earliest appearances in Life Magazine.

SKIPPY
Greenberg, Publisher, Inc, NY: 1925. (11-14x8-5/8, 72 pgs, hard-c, B&W and color

	GD 2.0	FN 6.0	VF 8.0			GD 2.0	FN 6.0	VF 8.0

nn - By Percy L. Crosby   48.00 144.00 285.00
NOTE: *Some but not all of these comics were also in Life Presents Skippy; issued with dust wrapper.*

SKIPPY AND OTHER HUMOR
Greenberg: Publisher, NY: 1929 (11-1/4x8-1/2",72 pgs,tan hard-c, B&W and color)
nn - By Percy L. Crosby   28.00 84.00 170.00
NOTE: *Came with a dust jacket.*

SKIPPY (I)
Grossett & Dunlap: 1929 (7-3/8x6, 370 pgs, hardcover text with some art)
nn - By Percy Crosby (issued with a dust jacket)   35.00 105.00 210.00
NOTE: *This is worth very little without the dust wrapper; very common without the dust jacket.*

SKIPPY
Greenberg Press: 1930 (soft cover, ca. 16 pp.,
nn - By Percy Crosby (scarce)   51.00 153.00 305.00
NOTE: *Reprints from LIFE cartoons, color, b/w. Crosby told Greenberg to withdraw from the market as it cheapened the hard cover prior editions. Greenberg then stopped publishing per agreement, and sent Crosby all the copper & zinc bookplates, which were in Crosby estate until 1996.*

SKIPPY CRAYON AND COLORING BOOK (I)
McLoughlin Bros, Inc., Springfield, MA: 1931 (13x9-3/4", 28 pgs, color-c, color & B&W)
2050 - By Percy Crosby   34.00 102.00 205.00
NOTE: *This item says on the front cover: "Licensed by Percy Crosby" because he owned his creation. About half the pages have one panel pre-printed in full color with same one b&w below for person to copy the colors.*

SKIPPY RAMBLES (I)
G.P. Putnam's Sons: 1932 (7 1/8 x 5 1/8, 202 pgs)
nn - By Percy Crosby   32.00 96.00 190.00
NOTE: *Issued with a dustjacket. Has Skippy plates by Crosby every 4 or 5 pages.*

SKUDDABUD STARRY STORY SERIES - FOLK FROM THE FUTURE (O,G)
no publisher listed: 1931 (9" x 11-7/8", 48 pgs, cardboard-c, B&W)
Book One (Rare) "Parachuting" (a VG/FN copy sold for $268 in 2010) 30.00   90.00 180.00
NOTE: *By Columba Krebs. Top half of each page is a continuing strip story, while bottom half are different stories, in prose, about the same characters -- a race of aliens who have migrated to Earth, from their dying world.*

S'MATTER POP? (N)
Saalfield Publ. Co.: 1917 (10x14", 44 pgs., B&W, cardboard-c,)
nn - By Charlie Payne, in full color; pages printed on one side 50.00   150.00 300.00

S'MATTER POP? (N) (25 ¢ cover price)
E.I. Company, New York: 1927 (8-15/16x7-1/8", 52 pgs, yellow soft-c perfect bound
nn - By C.M. Payne (scarce)   28.00 84.00 165.00
NOTE: *First comic book published by Hugo Gernsback, noted for inventing Amazing Stories among other memorable science fiction pulps. The World Science Fiction Convention award, The Hugo, is named for him.*

SMITTY (See Treasure Box of Famous Comics) (N)
Cupples & Leon Co.: 1928 - 1933 (9x7", 96 pgs., B&W strip-r, hardcover)
1928-(96 pgs. 7x8-3/4") By Walter Berndt   58.00 174.00 350.00
1929-At the Ball Game (Babe Ruth on cover)   92.00 276.00 550.00
1930-The Flying Office Boy, 1931-The Jockey, 1932-In the North Woods
  each...   51.00 153.00 305.00
1933-At Military School   51.00 153.00 305.00
NOTE: *Each hardbound was published with a dust jacket; worth 50% more with dust jacket. The 1929 edition is very popular with baseball collectors. Strip debuted Nov 27, 1922.*

SMOKEY STOVER (See Dan Dunn & King of the Royal Mounted) (N)
Whitman Publishing: 1937 (5 1/2 x 7 1/4", 68pgs., color cardboard-c, B&W)
1010   51.00 153.00 305.00

SOCIAL COMEDY (M)
Life Publishing Company: 1902 (11-3/4 x 9-1/2", 128 pgs, B&W, illustrated hardcover)
nn - Artists include C.D. Gibson & Kemble.   29.00 87.00 175.00
NOTE: *Reprints cartoons and a few sequential comics from LIFE. Came in unmarked slipcase.*

SOCIAL HELL, THE (O)
Rich Hill: 1902
nn - By Ryan Walker   29.00 87.00 175.00
NOTE: *"The conditions of workers and the corruption of a political system beholden to corporate interests have been a major focus of human rights concerns since the 19th century. This early graphic novel depicts the social evils of unreformed capitalism. Ryan Walker was a syndicate cartoonist for many mainstream newspapers as well as for the communist Daily Worker." This description comes from http://www.lib.uconn.edu/DoddCenter/ascexh3.html, where you can find also a reproduction of the cover. I add that Ryan Walker was the editor of "The Saint Louis Republic" comic section since its inception in 1897; the supplement published "Alma and Oliver", George McManus's first series.*

SPORT AND THE KID (see The Umbrella Man) (N)
Lowman & Hanford Co.: 1913 (6-1/4x6-5/8",114 pgs, hardcover, B&W&orange)
nn - By J.R. "Dok" Hager   28.00 84.00 170.00

STORY OF CONNECTICUT (N)
The Hartford Times: Vol.1 1935 - Vol.3 1936 (10-1/2" x 7-3/8",304 pgs,color hard-c, B&W)
Vol.1 - 3   27.00 81.00 160.00
NOTE: *Collects a newspaper strip on Connecticut State history, which ran in the Hartford Times. Strip is in a similar format to "Texas History Movies". Also published in a plain, blue hardcover.*

STORY OF JAPAN IN CHINA, THE (N,S)
Trans-Pacific News Service, NYC: Vol. 3, No.1 March 10, 1938 (9" x 6", 36 pgs, construction paper-c, B&W)
Vol.3 No.1   27.00 81.00 160.00
NOTE: *Part of the "China Reference Series" of booklets, detailing the Japanese occupation and brutalization of China. Consists entirely of cartoons. The other booklets in the series have no cartoons. Art by: Ding, Fitzpatrick, Herblock, Herman, Rollin Kirby, Knox, Low, Manning, Orr, Shoemaker, Talburt.*

STRANGE AS IT SEEMS (S)
Blue-Star Publishing Co.: 1932 (64 pgs., B&W, square binding)
1-Newspaper-r (Published with & without No. 1 and price on cover.) 40.00   120.00 240.00
Ex-Lax giveaway (1936, B&W, 24 pgs., 5x7") - McNaught Synd.   23.00 69.00 135.00

SULLIVAN'S ABC ZOO (N)
The Old Wine Press: 1946 (11-3/4x9-3/8", hardcover)
nn - By T.S. Sullivant (Rare)   58.00 174.00 350.00
NOTE: *Reprints Mitchell & Miller material 1895-1898 and Life Publishing 1898-1926.*

TAILSPIN TOMMY STORY & PICTURE BOOK (N)
McLoughlin Bros.: No. 266, 1931 (nd) (10x10-1/2", color strip-r)
266 - By Forrest   53.00 159.00 315.00

TAILSPIN TOMMY (Also see Famous Feature Stories & The Funnies)(N)
Cupples & Leon Co.: 1932 (100 pgs., hard-c) (B&W 1930 strip reprints)
nn - (Scarce)- by Hal Forrest & Glenn Chaffin   65.00 195.00 390.00

TALES OF DEMON DICK AND BUNKER BILL (N)
Whitman Publishing Co.: 1934 (5-1/4x10-1/2", 80 pgs, color hardcover, B&W)
793 - By Spencer   63.00 189.00 375.00

TARZAN BOOK (The Illustrated…) (N)
Grosset & Dunlap: 1929 (9x7", 80 pgs.)
1(Rare)-Contains 1st B&W Tarzan newspaper comics from 1929. By Hal Foster
  Cloth reinforced spine & dust jacket (50¢) - Foster-c
    With dust jacket…   133.00 400.00 800.00
    Without dust jacket…   65.00 195.00 390.00
2nd Printing(1934, 25¢, 76 pgs.)-4 Foster pgs. dropped; paper spine, circle in lower right
  cover with 25¢ price. The 25c is barely visible on some copies
    46.00 138.00 275.00
1967-House of Greystoke reprint-7x10", using the complete 300 illustrations/text from the
  1929 edition minus the original indicia, foreword, etc. Initial version bound in gold paper
  & sold for $5.00. Officially titled Burroughs Bibliophile #2. A very few additional copies
  were bound in heavier blue paper.   Gold binding…   8.00 24.00 45.00
      Blue binding…   8.00 24.00 45.00

TARZAN OF THE APES TO COLOR (N)
Saalfield Publishing Co.: No. 988, 1933 (15-1/4x10-3/4", 24 pgs) (Coloring book)
988-(Very Rare)-Contains 1929 daily reprints with some new art by Hal Foster. Two panels
  blown up large on each page with one at the top of opposing pages on every other
  double-page spread. Believed to be the only time these panels appeared in color. Most
  color panels are reproduced a second time in B&W to be colored
    300.00 900.00 2400.00

TARZAN OF THE APES The Big Little Cartoon Book (N)
Whitman Publishing Company: 1933 (4-1/2x3 5/8", 320 pgs, color-c, B&W)
744 - By Hal Foster (comic strips on every page)   29.00 187.00 350.00

TECK HASKINS AT OHIO STATE (S)
Lea-Mar Press: 1908 (7-1/4x5-3/8", 84 pgs, B&W hardcover)
nn - By W.A. Ireland; football cartoons-r from Columbus Ohio Evening Dispatch
    33.00 100.00 200.00
NOTE: *Small blue & white patch of cover art pasted atop a color cloth quilt patter; pasted patch can easily peel off some copies.*

TECK 1909 (S)
Lea-Mar Press: 1909 (8-5/8 x 8-1/8", 124 pgs., B&W hardcover, 25¢)
nn - By W.A. Ireland; Ohio State University baseball cartoons-r
  from Columbus Evening Dispatch   31.00 93.00 185.00

TEDDY BEAR BOOKS, THE (M) (see also LITTLE JOHNNY AND THE TEDDY BEARS)
Reilly & Britton Co., Chicago: 1907 (7-1/16" x 5-3/8", 24 pgs, hard-c, color
The Teddy Bears Come to Life, The Teddy Bears at the Circus, The Teddy Bears in a
  Smashup, The Teddy Bears on a Lark, The Teddy Bears on a Toboggan, The Teddy
  Bears at School, The Teddy Bears Go Fishing, The Teddy Bears in Hot Water
    32.00 96.00 190.00
NOTE: *Books are all unnumbered. C & A by J.R. Bray; s-Robert D. Towne. Reprints "Little Johnny & the Teddy Bears" strips, from Judge Magazine. Similar in format to the Buster Brown Nuggets series. All eight books debuted simultaneously.*

TEDDY BEARS IN FUN AND FROLIC (M) (see also LITTLE JOHNNY & THE TEDDY BEARS)
Reilly & Britton Co., Chicago: 1908 (8-3/4" x 8-3/4", 50 pgs, cardboard-c, color)
nn - (Rare) by J.R. Bray-a; Robert D. Towne-s   121.00 363.00 725.00
NOTE: *Reprints "Little Johnny & the Teddy Bears" strips, from Judge Magazine. Unknown if there were any other "Teddy Bear" titles published in this format.*

TEENIE WEENIES, THE
Reilly & Britton, Chicago: 1916 (16-3/8x10-1/2", 52 pgs, cardboard-c, full color)
nn - By Wm. Donahey (Chicago Tribune-r)   163.00 489.00 975.00

TERROR OF THE TINY TADS (see also UPSIDE DOWNS OF LITTLE LADY LOVEKINS AND OLD MAN MUFFAROO)
Cupples & Leon: 1909 (11x17, 26 Sunday strips in Black & Red, Stiff cardboard-c)
nn - By Gustave Verbeek (Very Rare)   (no known sales)

TEXAS HISTORY MOVIES (N)
Various editions, 1928 to 1986 (B&W)
Book I -1928 Southwest Press (7-1/4 x 5-3/8, 56 pgs, cardboard cover)
  for the Magnolia Petroleum Company   60.00 180.00 360.00
nn - 1928 Southwest Press (12-3/8 x 9-1/4, 232 pgs, HC)   79.00 237.00 475.00
nn - 1935 Magnolia Petroleum Company (6 x 9, 132 pgs, paper cover)
    32.00 96.00 190.00
NOTE: *Exists with either Wagon Train or Texas Flag & Lafitte/pirate covers.*
nn - 1943 Magnolia Petroleum Company (132 pgs, paper-c)   23.00 69.00 140.00
nn - 1963 Graphic Ideas Inc (11 x 8-1/2, softcover)   14.00 42.00 85.00
NOTE: *Reprints daily newspaper strips from the Dallas News, on Texas history. 1935 editions onward distributed within the Texas Public School System. Prior to that they appear to be giveaway comic books for the Magnolia Petroleum Company. There are many more editions than the ones pointed out above.*

THAT ROOKIE FROM THE 13TH SQUAD (N)
Harper & Brothers Publ.: 1918 (B&W)
1-By Lieut. Percy Crosby   29.00 87.00 175.00

THAT SON-IN-LAW OF PA'S! (N)
Newspaper Feature Service: 1914 (2-1/2 x 3", color)
nn - Imprinted on back for THE LESTER SHOE STORE.   15.00 45.00 90.00
NOTE: *Single sheet printed in full color on both sides, unfolds to show 12 panel story.*

THIMBLE THEATRE STARRING POPEYE (See also Popeye)
Sonnet Publishing Co.: 1931 - No. 2, 1932 (25¢, B&W, 52 pgs.)(Rare)
1-Daily strip serial-r in both by Segar   206.00 618.00 1650.00
2   159.00 477.00 1275.00
NOTE: *The very first Popeye reprint book. The first Thimble Theatre Sunday page appeared Dec 19, 1919. Popeye first entered Thimble Theatre on Jan 17, 1929.*

THREE FUN MAKERS, THE (N)
Stokes and Company: 1908 (10x15", 64 pgs., color) (1904-06 Sunday strip-r)
nn - Maud, Katzenjammer Kids, Happy Hooligan   767.00 2300.00 —

NOTE: *This is the first comic book to compile more than one newspaper strip together.*

TIGERS (Also see On and Off Mount Ararat) (N)
Hearst's New York American & Journal: 1902, 86 pgs. 10x15-1/4"

nn - Funny animal strip-r by Jimmy Swinnerton	617.00	1850.00	–

NOTE: *The strip began as The Journal Tigers in The New York Journal Dec 12, 1897–Sept 28 1903*

TILLIE THE TOILER (N)
Cupples & Leon Co.: 1925 - No. 8, 1933 (52 pgs., B&W, daily strip-r)

nn (#1) By Russ Westover	83.00	249.00	500.00
2-8	63.00	189.00	375.00

NOTE: *First newspaper strip appearance was in January, 1921.*

TILLIE THE TOILER MAGIC DRAWING AND COLORING BOOK
Sam L Gabriel Sons And Company: 1931 (8-1/2 x 12", 36 pages, stiff-c)

838-By Russ Westover	48.00	144.00	290.00

TIMID SOUL, THE (N)
Simon & Schuster: 1931 (12-1/4x9", 136 pgs, B&W hardcover, dust jacket?)

nn - By H. T. Webster (newspaper strip-r)	47.00	141.00	280.00

TIM McCOY, POLICE CAR 17 (O)
Whitman Publishing Co.: 1934 (14-3/4x11", 32 pgs, stiff color covers)

674-1933 original material	83.00	249.00	500.00

NOTE: *Historically important as first movie adaptation in comic books.*

TOAST BOOK
John C. Winston Co: 1905 (7-1/4 x 6,104 pgs, skull-shaped book, feltcover, B&W)

nn - By Clare Dwiggins	55.00	165.00	330.00

NOTE: *Cartoon illustrations accompanying toasts/poems, most involving alcohol.*

TOM SAWYER & HUCK FINN (N)
Stoll & Edwards Co.:1925 (10x10-3/4", 52 pgs, stiff covers)

nn - By "Dwig" Dwiggins; 1923, 1924-r color Sunday strips	60.00	180.00	360.00

NOTE: *By Permission of the Estate of Samuel L. Clemons and the Mark Twain Company.*

TOONERVILLE TROLLEY AND OTHER CARTOONS (N) (See Cartoons by Fontaine Fox)
Cupples & Leon Co.: 1921 (10 x10", 52 pgs., B&W, daily strip-r)

1 - By Fontaine Fox	104.00	312.00	625.00

TRAINING FOR THE TRENCHES (M)
Palmer Publishing Company: 1917 (5-3/8 x 7", 20 pgs., paper-c, 10¢)

nn - By Lieut. Alban B. Butler, Jr.	30.00	90.00	180.00

NOTE: *Subtitle: "A book of humorous cartoons on a serious subject." Single-panels about military training.*

TREASURE BOX OF FAMOUS COMICS (N) (see Wonder Chest of Famous Comics)
Cupples & Leon Co.: 1934 (8-1/2 x 6-7/8", 36 pgs, soft covers) (Boxed set of 5 books)

Little Orphan Annie (1926)	31.00	93.00	185.00
Reg'lar Fellers (1928)	28.00	84.00	165.00
Smitty (1928)	28.00	84.00	165.00
Harold Teen (1931)	28.00	84.00	165.00
How Dick Tracy & Dick Tracy Jr. Caught The Racketeers (1933)	42.00	126.00	250.00
Softcover set of five books in box	283.00	849.00	1700.00
Box only	71.00	213.00	425.00

NOTE: *Dates shown are copyright dates; all books actually came out in 1934 or later. The softcovers are abbreviated versions of the hardcover editions listed under each character.*

T.R. IN CARTOONS (N)
A.C. McClurg & Co., Chicago: June 13, 1910 (10-5/8" x 8", 104? pgs, paper-c, B&W)

nn - By McCutcheon about Teddy Roosevelt	-	-	–

TRUTH (See Victorian section for earlier issues including the first Yellow Kid appearances)
Truth Company, NY: 1886-1906? (13-11/16x10-5/16", 16 pgs, process color-c & centerfolds, rest B&W)

1900-1906 issues	22.00	66.00	130.00

TRUTH SAVE IT FROM ABUSE & OVERWORK BEING THE EPISODE OF THE HIRED HAND & MRS. STIX PLASTER, CONCERTIST (N)
Radio Truth Society of WBAP: no date, 1924 (6-3/8 x 4-7/8, 40 pgs, paper cover, B&W)

nn - By V.T. Hamlin (Very Rare)	125.00	375.00	750.00

NOTE: *Radio station WBAP giveaway reprints strips from the Ft. Worth Texas Star-Telegram set at local radio station. 1st collected work by V.T. Hamlin, pre-Alley Oop.*

TWENTY FIVE YEARS AGO (see At The Bottom Of The Ladder) (M,S)
Coward-McCann: 1931 (5-3/4x8-1/4, 328 pgs, hardcover, B&W)

nn - By Camillus Kessler	40.00	120.00	240.00

NOTE: *Multi-image panel cartoons showing historical events for dates during the year.*

UMBRELLA MAN, THE (N) (See Sport And The Kid)
Lowman & Hanford Co.: 1911 (8-7/8x5-7/8",112 pgs, hard-c, B&W & orange)

nn - By J.R. "Dok" Hager (Seattle Times-r)	25.00	75.00	150.00

UNCLE REMUS AND BRER RABBIT (N)
Frederick A. Stokes Co.: 1907 (64 pgs, hardbound, color)

nn - By Joel C Harris & J.M. Conde	67.00	200.00	400.00

UPSIDE DOWNS OF LITTLE LADY LOVEKINS AND OLD MAN MUFFAROO
New York Herald: 1905 (?) (N)

nn - By Gustav Verbeck; (Also see Terror Of The Tiny Tads)	142.00	426.00	850.00

VAUDEVILLES AND OTHER THINGS (N)
Isaac H. Blandiard Co.: 1900 (13x10-1/2", 22 pgs., color) plus two reprints

nn - By Bunny (Scarce)	317.00	950.00	–
nn - 2nd print "By the Creator of Foxy Grandpa" on-c but only has copyright info of 1900 (10-1/2x15 1/2, 28 pgs, color)	283.00	850.00	–
nn - 3rd print "By the creator of Foxy Grandpa" on-c; has both 1900 and 1901 copyright info (11x13")	208.00	625.00	–

WALLY - HIS CARTOONS OF THE A.E.F. (N)
Stars & Stripes: 1917 (96 and 108 pgs, B&W)

nn - By Abian A "Wally" Wallgren (7x18; 96 pgs)	21.00	63.00	125.00
nn - another edition (7x17-1/2)	21.00	63.00	125.00

NOTE: *World War One cartoons reprints from Stars & Stripes; sold to U.S. servicemen with profits to go to French War Orphans Fund. various editions from 1917-1920; there might be more than what we list here.*

WAR CARTOONS (S)
Dallas News: 1918 (11x9", 112 pgs, hardcover, B&W)

nn - By John Knott (WWOne cartoons)	28.00	84.00	170.00

WAR CARTOONS FROM THE CHICAGO DAILY NEWS (N,S)
Chicago Daily News: 1914 (10 cents, 7-3/4x10-3/4", 68 pgs, paper-c, B&W)

nn - By L.D. Bradley	27.00	81.00	160.00

WEBER & FIELD'S FUNNYISMS (S,M,O)
Arkell Comoany, NY: 1904 (10-7/8x8", 112 pgs, color-c, B&W)

1 - By various (only issue?)	29.00	87.00	175.00

NOTE: *Contains some sequential & many single panel strips by Outcault, George Luks, CA David, Houston, L Smith, Hy Mayer, Verbeck, Woolf, Sydney Adams, Frank "Chip" Bellew, Eugene "ZIM" Zimmerman, Phil May, FT Richards, Billy Marriner, Grosvenor and many others.*

WE'RE NOT HEROES (O,S)
E.C. Wells and J.W. Moss: 1933 (8-11/16" x 5-7/8", 52 pgs, B&W interior)

nn - By Eddie Wells; red & black paper-c	14.00	42.00	85.00

NOTE: *Amateurish cartoons about World War I vets in the Walter Reed Veteran's Hospital.*

WHEN A FELLER NEEDS A FRIEND (S)
P. F. Volland & Co.: 1914 (11-11/16x8-7/8)

nn - By Clare Briggs	33.00	100.00	200.00

NOTE: *Originally came in box with Briggs art (box is Rare); also numerous more modern reprints*

WILD PILGRIMAGE (O)
Harrison Smith & Robert Haas: 1932 (9-7/8x7", 210 pgs, B&W hardcover w/dust jacket)
(original wordless graphic novel in woodcuts)

nn - By Lynd Ward	54.00	162.00	325.00

WILLIE AND HIS PAPA AND THE REST OF THE FAMILY (I)
Grossett & Dunlap: 1901 (9-1/2x8", 200 pgs, hardcover from N.Y. Evening Journal by Permission of W. R. Hearst) (pictures & text)

nn - By Frederick Opper	71.00	213.00	425.00

NOTE: *Political satire series of single panel cartoons, involving whiny child Willie (President William McKinley), his rambunctious and uncontrollable cousin Teddy (Vice President Roosevelt), and Willie's Papa (trusts/monopolies) and their Maid (Senator) Hanna.*

WILLIE GREEN COMICS, THE (N) (see Adventures of Willie Green)
Frank M. Acton Co./Harris Brown: 1915 (8x15, 36 pgs); 1921 (6x10-1/8", 52 pgs, color paper cover, B&W interior, 25¢)

Book No. 1 By Harris Brown	62.00	186.00	370.00
Book 2 (#2 sold via mail order directly from the artist)(very rare)	71.00	213.00	425.00

NOTE: *Book No. 1 possible reprint of Adv. of Willie Green; definitely two different editions.*

WILLIE WESTINGHOUSE EDISON SMITH THE BOY INVENTOR (N)
William A. Stokes Co.: 1906 (10x16", 36 pgs. in color)

nn - By Frank Crane (Scarce)	250.00	750.00	1500.00

NOTE: *Comic strip began May 27, 1900 and ran thru 1914. Parody of inventors Westinghouse and Edison.*

WINNIE WINKLE (N)Strip began as a daily Sept 20, 1920.
Cupples & Leon Co.: 1930 - No. 4, 1933 (52 pgs., B&W daily strip-r)

1	63.00	189.00	375.00
2-4	63.00	189.00	375.00

WISDOM OF CHING CHOW, THE (see also The Gumps)
R. J. Jefferson Printing Co.: 1928 (4x3", 100 pgs, red & B&W cardboard cover) (newspaper strip-r The Chicago Tribune)

nn - By Sidney Smith (scarce)	32.00	96.00	190.00

WONDER CHEST OF FAMOUS COMICS (N) see Treasure Box of Famous Comics
Cupples & Leon Co.: 1935? 8-1/2x(6-7/8", 36 pgs, soft covers) (Boxed set of 5 books)

Little Orphan Annie #2 (1927) (Haunted House)	26.00	78.00	155.00
Little Orphan Annie #3 (1928) (in the Circus)	26.00	78.00	155.00
Smitty #2 (1929) (Babe Ruth app.)	26.00	78.00	155.00
Dolly Dimples and Bobby Bounce (1933) by Grace Drayton	26.00	78.00	155.00
How Dick Tracy & Dick Tracy Jr. Caught The Racketeers (1933)	38.00	114.00	225.00
Softcover set of five books in box	163.00	489.00	1300.00
Box only	67.00	200.00	400.00

NOTE: *Dates shown are original copyright dates of the first printings; all actually came out in 1934 or later. Extremely abbreviated versions of the hardcover editions listed under each character. It is suspected this came out the Christmas season following Treasure Chest of Famous Comics. which contains earlier editions.*

WORLD OF TROUBLE, A (S)
Minneapolis Journal: 1901 (10x8-3/4", 100 pgs, 40 pgs full color)

v3#1 - By Charles L. Bartholomew (editorial-r)	33.00	100.00	200.00

WRIGLEY'S "MOTHER GOOSE" (N)
Wm. Wrigley Jr. Company, Chicago: 1915 (6" x 4", 28 pgs, full color)

nn - Promotional comics for Wrigley's gum. Intro Wrigley's "Spearmen	29.00	87.00	175.00
Book No. 2	29.00	87.00	175.00

YELLOW KID, THE (Magazine)(I) (becomes **The Yellow Book** #10 on)
Howard, Ainslee & Co., N.Y.: Mar. 20, 1897 - #11, Sept, 1897
(5¢, B&W w/color covers, 52p., stapled) (not a comic book)

1-R.F. Outcault Yellow kid on-c only #1-6. The same Yellow Kid color ad app. on back-c			
#1-6 (advertising the New York Sunday Journal)	1667.00	5000.00	–
2-6 (#2 4/3/97, #5 5/22/97, #6, 6/5/97)	1133.00	3400.00	–
7-9 (Yellow Kid not on-c)	317.00	950.00	–
10,11	308.00	925.00	–

NOTE: *Richard Outcault's Yellow Kid from the Hearst New York American represents the very first successful newspaper comic strip in America. Listed here due to historical importance. A set of #1-9 sold in 2015 for $20,315.*

YELLOW KID IN McFADDEN'S FLATS, THE (N)
G. W. Dillingham Co., New York: 1897 (50¢, 7-1/2x5-1/2", 196 pgs., B&W, squarebound)

nn - The first "comic" book featuring The Yellow Kid; E. W. Townsend narrative w/R.F. Outcault Sunday comic page art-r & some original drawings			
(Prices vary widely. Rare.)	7200.00	20,000.00	–

NOTE: *A Fair condition copy sold for $2,901 in August 2004.; restored app VF sold for $10,500 in 2005. A copy in Fine+ (spine intact) and loose back cover sold for $17,000 in 2006. An apparent FN+ copy sold for $6,572.50 in 2011. An apparent VF/NM copy sold for $4,182 in 2012.*

YESTERDAYS (S)
The Reilly & Lee Co.: 1930 (8-3/4 x 7-1/2", 128 pgs, illustrated hard-c with dust jacket)

nn - Text and cartoons about Victorian times by Frank Wing	20.00	60.00	120.00

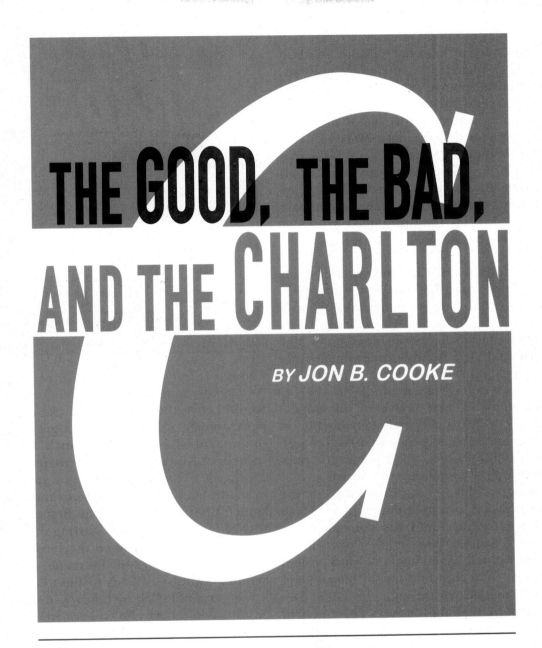

THE GOOD, THE BAD, AND THE CHARLTON

BY JON B. COOKE

If you were too young to experience the comic book line of Charlton, you still likely know of their "Action Heroes" legacy in the forms of Peacemaker and Blue Beetle, or you may have encountered the connection those 1960s' creations have with Alan Moore and Dave Gibbons' *Watchmen*, which was adapted as a movie and HBO series. Comic fans of a certain age and older are all too familiar with the Derby, Connecticut-based "all-in-one" publishing house and can attest to some truths in the outfit's 1950s-era tagline that was adorned the top of every comic book page for a period, "Charlton Comics Give You More." The slogan begs the question, "Charlton give us more… what, exactly?"

A cynic could find much to criticize with the Charlton line, but despite an abundance of hacked-out material, spotty distribution, poorly printed and badly edited issues, incoherent numbering, and absurd concepts, the historian within recognizes that the back story of Charlton is more fascinating – by far – than that of any other American comics publisher. It's a tale that, through the years, reflects the times in which the company existed. (Plus they produced a number of great comics!)

The founder of Charlton, which would produce some 6,300 issues of about 324 titles (plus 13 or so magazines of mostly comics) in its history spanning 1941–1991, started his publishing career as a criminal. The shady, under-the-counter origins of DC and other early comics houses don't hold a candle to the beginnings of one Giovanni Santangelo [1899–1979], a recent Italian immigrant who served a sentence in 1940 for selling 10,000 copies of his song lyric publications – containing the words to the day's popular songs, printed without the permission of copyright holders. From the early '30s until his comeuppance, which landed him in the New Haven County Jail, Santangelo – now called John – had sold millions of illegal song lyric magazines through the Great Depression, making him very rich. As luck would have it, he shared a cellblock with fellow prisoner (and dime novel enthusiast) Edward Levy, convicted lawyer previously embroiled in a kickback scheme, a scandal that rocked a nearby city, and given a light sentence for ratting out fellow city hall officials. Upon their release, they formed Charlton Publishing, naming their new business after their respective two oldest sons, both named Charles.

Though Charlton's *Hit Parader* and (by 1950) *Song Hits* song lyric mags would prove the mainstay for the company, which occupied an ever-growing printing plant on the Naugatuck River shoreline, Santangelo was perhaps encouraged by New England newspaper magnate Sherman Bowles to cautiously launch Charlton Comics. The first effort was *Yellowjacket Comics*, starring the titular superhero nicknamed the "Scourge of Sinners," who (despite his name) commanded swarms of bees to fight crime. It was soon followed by *Courage Comics* (curiously a job produced anonymously for their former jail warden), and then *Zoo Comics*, a funny animal title.

Producing about 50 separate ho-hum issues during the decade, Charlton's commitment to comics was lackluster in the 1940s, though the outfit did surreptitiously form a sub-imprint, Catholic Publications, publishing 30 issues of *Catholic Comics*. But it wouldn't be until 1952 (as sales of song lyric mags were

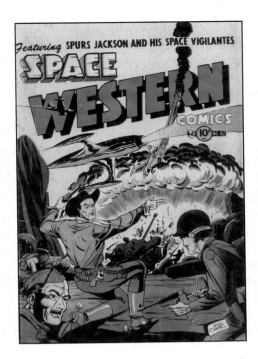

in temporary decline) when their outfit sparked with the arrival of editor/funny animal artist Al Fago, who infused enthusiasm into the line. It had been the comics packaging firm of Lloyd Jacquet, previously known as Funnies, Incorporated, who had serviced Charlton in its earliest years, but it took the reign of Fago – and the important addition of wife, Blanche – to bring Charlton into the '50s and distinguish itself. Soon it was delving into numerous genres: hot rods, crime, science fiction, and horror, along with tried-and-true Western and romance comics.

While never achieving the overall quality of EC Comics or slickness of DC, Charlton produced its share of unforgettable (if not stellar) titles in the '50s. There was the wild hybrid whose title says it all: *Space Western*, starring Spurs Jackson and His Space Vigilantes fighting flying saucers. *The Thing!* is still reputed to be one of the most horrific of the pre-Code horror anthologies, enough to

have a single issue cited twice in *Seduction of the Innocent,* helping to make it a must-have classic title for collectors of such dreadful artifacts. Then there was *Za Za the Mystic* (about a fake spiritualist/crimefighter) and also the ridiculous quasi-superheroes, *Nature Boy* and *Mr. Muscles.* Far less short-lived was the emergence during that time of two major talents from Charlton, Steve Ditko (future co-creator of Spider-Man and much more) and Dick Giordano (eventually executive editor of DC and superb artist in his own right).

Despite Hurricane Diane devastating the plant under an epic 18 feet of water in 1955, Charlton surfaced from the disaster to become the anonymous publisher of Harvey Kurtzman's *Humbug,* the satirical genius' *MAD* magazine successor. Santangelo's magazine division published the first national magazine devoted to African-American music, *Rhythm & Blues.* As the company – which was known for an idea arriving through the front door and leaving out the back as a fully finished product loaded onto trucks to be distributed – closed out the decade as the third largest comic publisher in the U.S.

The '60s began with the debut of Captain Atom, born of a nuclear explosion to become a fantastically powered Cold War superhero and fighter of commies. Though the creation of writer Joe Gill and artist Ditko wouldn't catch on with the initial *Space Adventures* appearances (and the less said about successor Mercury Man, the better), it took a new editor – as the Fagos had acrimoniously departed long before – to lead the first true Charlton Comics universe, the "Action Heroes" line of Dick Giordano. (Beforehand, the previous editor had tepidly stepped into the superhero field, then quite hot stuff at DC and Marvel, by resurrecting *Blue Beetle*, which had briefly been absentmindedly revived in the '50s, and launching a (short-lived) Thor-wannabe, *Son of Vulcan*.)

If the good captain was the line's "Superman," Blue Beetle, the third version of a character that first appeared in 1939, was Charlton's "Spider-Man" (by way, if you will, of Batman), and why not? The actual co-creator of Marvel's web-slinging superstar had returned to the company fold after quitting the House of Ideas to draw and often write Captain Atom and a new Blue Beetle. He also originated one of the most unique characters in comics history, The Question, a fascinating byproduct of the artist's preoccupation with Ayn Rand's objectivist philosophy.

Other dynamite Action Heroes titles included *Peter Cannon, Thunderbolt*, an outstanding series written and drawn by Pete Morisi; *Judo Maste*r, a martial arts/

costumed crimefighter created by artist Frank McLaughlin; Giordano and Pat Masulli's *Sarge Steel*, a tough private eye with a literal steel fist; and the wacky and wild *Peacemaker* series, about a character sporting the tagline, "A man who loves peace so much he's willing to fight for it," written by Gill and drawn by Pat Boyette. There were also great back-up series, among them (to name only a few), the Marvel Comics-inspired "Sentinels," drawn by late arriving comics artist Sam Grainger; "Nightshade," a Captain Atom spinoff and Charlton's only female hero with her own strip; and "Wander," an extraterrestrial wandering the Old West (the latter two drawn by ex-ad man Jim Aparo).

Though unappreciated until many years later, Charlton during this time was also home to some innovative, even revolutionary concepts. Among them was writer Dennis O'Neil's extraordinary dystopian science fiction saga, "Children of Doom," which appeared unheralded in *Charlton Premiere*. And there was the multi-chapter tale of a US serviceman trapped behind enemy lines, "The Lonely War of Capt. Willy Schultz," by teenage scribe Will Franz and artist Sam Glanzman. The continuing and thinly veiled anti-war epic appeared in *Fightin' Army* that foretold the coming age of graphic novels.

An unprecedented level of fan enthusiasm invigorated the Giordano-era books with the help of an entirely new generation of comic book writers, including O'Neil, Roy Thomas, Gary Friedrich, and Steve Skeates. Among the burgeoning artists to receive their first professional assignments were Aparo and Pat Boyette (though both were mature and successful in other careers), with veterans Glanzman and Rocke Mastroserio, among others, producing exemplary work. But, unexpectedly, management abruptly canceled the "Action Heroes" titles in mid-1967 and Giordano quit to join DC Comics, and Charlton was again in the doldrums.

By the early 1970s, the company, which also boasted a robust and profitable magazine publishing empire and a vast periodical distribution business, focused extensively on licensed animated properties. They included Popeye and The Flintstones, as well as some (arguably) more sophisticated TV and comic strip fare, such as The Partridge Family and The Phantom. Particularly notable was their growing line of quasi-horror titles, almost all hosted by whimsical, mildly spooky characters, interspersed with an occasionally somber presence of Dr. Graves or Baron Wulf. The best of these genre titles was *Midnight Tales*, a showcase for (and creation of) writer/artist Wayne Howard, the Wally Wood protégé, who produced gag-infused covers and humorously macabre stories regularly featuring the father/daughter team of Professor Coffin ("the Midnight Philosopher") and Arachne.

The ascent of George Wildman, longtime cartoonist of *Popeye* comics, to top editorial position (where he perched for 15 years, longer than any other Charlton comics editor) would jolt the line. He hired another one-time Wally Wood assistant, Nicola Cuti, as his assistant editor, whose connection to comics fandom benefited much of their output. Wildman made use of his previous years of advertising experience and rebranded the line with a clever new logo (that added the word "bullseye" to the company's legacy). He also connected directly with the fandom by attending comic book conventions and authorizing a company fanzine.

Debuting in 1974, The Charlton Portfolio was a slickly produced publication that included articles, pin-ups, and an entire, previously unpublished Blue Beetle story by comics legend Ditko (who, incidentally, had returned to the fold after a brief foray at DC in the late '60s). It was a handsome – albeit financially disastrous – effort headed by future comics pro Bob Layton, whose fanzines had caught the attention of Wildman and Cuti. This led to a five-issue run of *Charlton Bullseye*, an ambitious and energetic fanzine that lasted a little over a year and included a beautiful Question story written by Michael Uslan and drawn by comics genius Alex Toth.

Bullseye was but one aspect of the next great age of Charlton, which occurred roughly between 1973–1976, starting when Cuti persuaded his boss to allow the creation of a new company superhero. Effervescently drawn by cartoonist newcomer Joe Staton and written by Cuti, *E-Man* was an exceptional series injected with charm and whimsy, a humor-filled adventure title in the spirit of Plastic Man and the original Captain Marvel. The "E=MC²" character, along with comely partner Nova, would survive multiple publishers over the decades, always drawn by Staton and mostly written, until his passing, by Cuti.

E-Man spearheaded a new push by Wildman and company, an attempt to puncture the sales dominance of the superhero dominated DC and Marvel. Charlton also introduced *Yang*, a series inspired by the *Kung Fu* TV show and part of the then-popular martial arts craze, written by Joe Gill and drawn with panache by

Warren Sattler. Other titles included *The House of Yang*, a *Yang* spinoff drawn by innovative South Korean artist San-ho Kim; and *Vengeance Squad,* a crime comic book spotlighting the work of Pat Morisi. Latecomer *Doomsday + 1*, a post-apocalyptic science fiction series written by Gill, was drawn by perhaps Charlton's greatest artistic find of the decade, John Byrne (whose "Rog 2000" strips for Layton's fanzines had first attracted Wildman and Cuti's attention). While Byrne would, of course, move on to stardom as X-Men and Superman artist, the outstanding creator's work for the Derby outfit was no less enthusiastic.

As the E-Man-led revitalization campaign failed to catch fire in an ever-diminishing newsstand marketplace, Charlton zeroed in on some live-action TV properties it had been offered. This included a new science fiction series hoping to replicate *Star Trek*'s success, *Space: 1999*, as well as a medical-action series, *Emergency*, and adventure show *The Six-Million Dollar Man*. Given its presence in the consumer magazine field, Charlton decided to simultaneously produce color comics and black-and-white comics magazines. Despite the efforts of Neal Adams and his Continuity Studios, Gray Morrow and his group of Spanish artists, as well as artists Jack Sparling and Joe Staton, the two-pronged effort failed. (A far more successful – at least initially – magazine-related effort was Santangelo's deal with Larry Flynt to distribute the first issues of *Hustler* magazine. That eventually led to a lawsuit between the parties that socked the Derby publisher with a $3.7 million fine!)

Amid paper shortages and national recession, Charlton found itself struggling, and by 1977, it ceased publishing comics completely. Quite quickly though, a deal with jobber Modern Promotions to reprint 60 comics (under a "Modern Comics" emblem) had presses starting up again that year and the comics division limped along publishing reprints for the remainder of its days. (Within a few years, John Santangelo was deceased.)

The final hurrah was to be a new *Charlton Bullseye*, edited by Bill Pearson, Wildman's assistant editor – and former Wood assist – who'd arrived in the wake of Cuti's departure. This version was a color title showcasing creator-owned material, assignments remunerating artists and writers with printed copies in lieu of actual money. Highlights included Marty Greim's "Thunderbunny" and Arn Saba's "Neil, the Dancing Horse."

Charlton closed its comics division by 1986 (despite a last-minute push by Ditko to keep it alive for the direct market) and gave up the ghost completely in 1991. It did produce innumerable magazines over its 40-year history, periodicals scarcely mentioned here and many oth-

er notable comics that have been overlooked in this essay. There's much more to say about its comics, whether the unauthorized and excellent four-issue run of *Jungle Tales of Tarzan* [1964–1965], "Thane of Bagarth" strip by Skeates and Aparo backing-up the equally entertaining Hercules [1966–1969] series by Gill, O'Neil, and Glanzman, and many others. Why, one could write a book on it!

About Jon B. Cooke

Once editor of Comic Book Artist, *the five-time Eisner Award-winning magazine, Jon B. Cooke is an Overstreet Advisor and is currently editor of* Comic Book Creator, *published by TwoMorrows Publishing. He literally wrote the Eisner-nominated book on the subject of Charlton,* The Charlton Companion *[TwoMorrows, 2022]. He is also author of* The Book of Weirdo *[Last Gasp, 2019] and the forthcoming history,* Mind Candy: The Outrageous Saga of Last Gasp of San Francisco *[due Fall 2024], and is co-writer of* The Pacific Comics Companion *[2023, TwoMorrows], among other projects.*

	GD 2.0	VG 4.0	FN 6.0	VF 8.0	VF/NM 9.0	NM- 9.2

The correct title listing for each comic book can be determined by consulting the indicia (publication data) on the beginning interior pages of the comic. The official title is determined by those words of the title in capital letters only, and not by what is on the cover. Titles are listed in this book as if they were one word, ignoring spaces, hyphens, and apostrophes, to make finding titles easier. Exceptions are made in rare cases. Comic books listed should be assumed to be in color unless noted "B&W".

PRICING IN THIS GUIDE: Prices for **GD 2.0** (Good), **VG 4.0** (Very Good), **FN 6.0** (Fine), **VF 8.0** (Very Fine), **VF/NM 9.0** (Very Fine/Near Mint), and **NM– 9.2** (Near Mint–) are listed in whole U.S. dollars except for prices below $7 which show dollars and cents. **The minimum price listed is $3.00**, the cover price for current new comics. Many books listed at this price can be found in $1.00 boxes at conventions and dealers stores.

A-1 (See A-One)

A&A: THE ADVENTURES OF ARCHER & ARMSTRONG
Valiant Entertainment: Mar, 2016 - No. 12, Feb, 2017 ($3.99)

1-12: 1-Rafer Roberts-s/David Lafuente-a. 5-Faith app. 5-12-Norton-a						4.00
10-Cat cosplay photo variant-c						4.00

AARDVARK COMICS (Reprints from Cerebus in Hell)(Also see Batvark)
Aardvark-Vanaheim: Sept, 2017 ($4.00, B&W)

1-Cerebus figures placed over original Gustave Doré artwork of Hell; Action #1-c swipe						6.00

ABADAZAD
CrossGen (Code 6): Mar, 2004 - No. 3, May, 2004 ($2.95)

1-3-Ploog-a/c; DeMatteis-s						4.00
1-2nd printing with new cover						4.00

ABATTOIR
Radical Comics: Oct, 2010 - No. 6, Aug, 2011 ($3.99/$3.50, limited series)

1-($3.99) Cansino-a/Levin & Peteri-s						6.00
2-6-($3.50)						4.00

ABBIE AN' SLATS (...With Becky No. 1-4) (See Comics On Parade, Fight for Love, Giant Comics Edition 2, Giant Comics Editions #1, Sparkler Comics, Tip Topper, Treasury of Comics, & United Comics)
United Features Syndicate: 1940; March, 1948 - No. 4, Aug, 1948 (Reprints)

	GD 2.0	VG 4.0	FN 6.0	VF 8.0	VF/NM 9.0	NM- 9.2
Single Series 25 ('40)	43	86	129	271	461	650
Single Series 28	37	74	111	222	361	500
1 (1948)	20	40	60	114	182	250
2-4: 3-r/Sparkler #68-72	12	24	36	69	97	125

ABBOTT
BOOM! Studios: Jan, 2018 - No. 5, May, 2018 ($3.99, limited series)

	GD 2.0	VG 4.0	FN 6.0	VF 8.0	VF/NM 9.0	NM- 9.2
1-Saladin Ahmed-s/Sami Kivelä; red regular-c	2	4	6	9	12	15
1-Yellow-c by Micaela Dawn	2	4	6	11	16	20
1-Blue-c by Tula Lotay	3	6	9	14	20	25
1-Second printing with purple-c by Tag Tenfold	1	2	3	5	6	8
2	1	3	4	6	8	10
3-5						4.00

ABBOTT AND COSTELLO (...Comics)(See Giant Comics Editions #1 & Treasury of Comics)
St. John Publishing Co.: Feb, 1948 - No. 40, Sept, 1956 (Mort Drucker-a in most issues)

	GD 2.0	VG 4.0	FN 6.0	VF 8.0	VF/NM 9.0	NM- 9.2
1	103	206	309	659	1130	1600
2	61	122	183	390	670	950
3-9 (#8, 8/49; #9, 2/50)	37	74	111	222	361	500
10-Son of Sinbad story by Kubert (new)	41	82	123	256	428	600
11,13-20 (#11, 10/50; #13, 8/51; #15, 12/52)	26	52	78	154	252	350
12-Movie issue	27	54	81	160	263	365
21-30: 28-r/#8. 29,30-Painted-c	19	38	57	112	179	245
31-40: 33,36,38-Reprints	15	30	45	90	140	190
3-D #1 (11/53, 25¢)-Infinity-c	37	74	111	218	354	490

ABBOTT AND COSTELLO (TV)
Charlton Comics: Feb, 1968 - No. 22, Aug, 1971 (Hanna-Barbera)

	GD 2.0	VG 4.0	FN 6.0	VF 8.0	VF/NM 9.0	NM- 9.2
1	9	18	27	59	117	175
2	5	10	15	33	57	80
3-10	4	8	12	27	44	60
11-22	4	8	12	23	37	50

ABBOTT: 1973
BOOM! Studios: Jan, 2021 - No. 5, May, 2021 ($3.99, limited series)

1-5-Saladin Ahmed-s/Sami Kivelä						4.00

ABBOTT: 1979
BOOM! Studios: Oct, 2023 - Present ($4.99, limited series)

1-4-Saladin Ahmed-s/Sami Kivelä						5.00

ABC (See America's Best TV Comics)

ABC: A-Z (one-shots)
America's Best Comics: Nov, 2005 - July, 2006 ($3.99, one-shots)

... Greyshirt and Cobweb (1/06) character bios; Veitch-s/a; Gebbie-a; Dodson-c						6.00
... Terra Obscura and Splash Brannigan (3/06) character bios; Barta-a; Dodson-c						6.00
... Tom Strong and Jack B. Quick (11/05) character bios; Sprouse-a; Nowlan-a; Dodson-c						4.00
... Top Ten and Teams (7/06) character bios; Ha & Cannon-a; Veitch-a; Dodson-c						4.00

ABE SAPIEN... (Hellboy character)
Dark Horse Comics: Apr, 2013 - No. 36, Aug, 2016 ($3.50/$3.99)

	GD 2.0	VG 4.0	FN 6.0	VF 8.0	VF/NM 9.0	NM- 9.2
1-Subtitled "Dark and Terrible"; Mignola & Allie-s/Fiumara-a/c						
	1	3	4	6	8	10
2-33: 2-"Dark and Terrible". 8-Oeming-a. 23-Hellboy app.; Nowlan-a						4.00
34-36-($3.99)						4.00
...: Drums of the Dead (3/98, $2.95) 1-Thompson-a. Hellboy back-up; Mignola-s/a/c						
	1	2	3	5	6	8
...: The Abyssal Plain (6/10 - No. 2, 7/10, $3.50) 1,2-Mignola & Arcudi-s/Snejbjerg-a						5.00
...: The Devil Does Not Jest (9/11 - No. 2, 10/11, $3.50) Mignola & Arcudi-s. 1-Two covers by Johnson & Francavilla						6.00
...: The Drowning (2/08 - No. 5, 6/08, $2.99) 1-5-Mignola-s/c; Alexander-a						4.00
...: The Haunted Boy (10/09, $3.50) 1-Mignola & Arcudi-a/Reynolds-a/Johnson-c						4.00

ABIGAIL AND THE SNOWMAN
Boom Entertainment (KaBOOM!): Dec, 2014 - No. 4, Mar, 2015 ($3.99, limited series)

	GD 2.0	VG 4.0	FN 6.0	VF 8.0	VF/NM 9.0	NM- 9.2
1-Roger Langridge-s/a; covers by Langridge & Liew	1	2	3	5	6	8
2-4						4.00

A. BIZARRO
DC Comics: Jul, 1999 - No. 4, Oct, 1999 ($2.50, limited series)

1-4-Gerber-s/Bright-a						4.00

ABOMINATIONS (See Hulk)
Marvel Comics: Dec, 1996 - No. 3, Feb, 1997 ($1.50, limited series)

1-3-Future Hulk storyline						4.00

ABRAHAM LINCOLN LIFE STORY (See Dell Giants)

ABRAHAM STONE
Marvel Comics (Epic): July, 1995 - No. 2, Aug, 1995 ($6.95, limited series)

1,2-Joe Kubert-s/a						7.00

ABSENT-MINDED PROFESSOR, THE (see Shaggy Dog & The... under Movie Comics)

ABSOLUTE CARNAGE
Marvel Comics: Oct, 2019 - No. 5, Jan, 2020 ($7.99/$4.99, limited series)

	GD 2.0	VG 4.0	FN 6.0	VF 8.0	VF/NM 9.0	NM- 9.2
1-($7.99) Donny Cates/Ryan Stegman-a; Venom, Carnage Spider-Man app.						
	2	4	6	9	12	15
2-5-($4.99) 2-Miles Morales & The Grendel Symbiote app. 3-Hulk app. 5-Knull freed						6.00
.... Avengers 1 (12/19, $4.99) Captain America, Hawkeye, The Thing, Wolverine app.						5.00
.... Captain Marvel 1 (1/20, $4.99) Carnage possesses the Flerkin Chewie						5.00
.... Immortal Hulk 1 (12/19, $4.99) Ewing/Andrade-a; Betty Ross & Venom app.						5.00
.... Separation Anxiety 1 (10/19, $4.99) The Life Foundation symbiotes app.						6.00
.... Symbiote of Vengeance 1 (11/19, $4.99) Ghost Rider vs. Carnage						5.00
.... Symbiote Spider-Man 1 (11/19, $4.99) Peter Parker app.; White Rabbit app.						5.00
.... Weapon Plus 1 (1/20, $4.99) Raffaele-a; Weapon Plus vs. Carnage						5.00

ABSOLUTE CARNAGE: LETHAL PROTECTORS
Marvel Comics: Oct, 2019 - No. 3, Dec, 2019 ($3.99, limited series)

1-Iron Fist, Misty Knight, Cloak & Dagger, Firestar & Morbius						6.00
2,3						4.00

ABSOLUTE CARNAGE: MILES MORALES
Marvel Comics: Oct, 2019 - No. 3, Dec, 2019 ($3.99, limited series)

1-Scorpion & Silver Sable app.; Ahmed-s/Vicentini-a						6.00
2,3						4.00

ABSOLUTE CARNAGE: SCREAM
Marvel Comics: Oct, 2019 - No. 3, Dec, 2019 ($3.99, limited series)

1-3-Bunn-s/Sandoval-a; Andi Benton app.						4.00

ABSOLUTE CARNAGE VS. DEADPOOL
Marvel Comics: Oct, 2019 - No. 3, Dec, 2019 ($3.99, limited series)

1-Tieri-s/Ferreira-a; Spider-Man app.						6.00
2,3						4.00

ABSOLUTE VERTIGO
DC Comics (Vertigo): Winter, 1995 (99¢, mature)

	GD 2.0	VG 4.0	FN 6.0	VF 8.0	VF/NM 9.0	NM- 9.2
nn-1st app. Preacher. Previews upcoming titles including Jonah Hex: Riders of the Worm, The Invisibles (King Mob), The Eaters, Ghostdancing & Preacher						
	2	4	6	10	14	18

ABSOLUTION
AWA Studios: Jul, 2022 - No. 5, Nov, 2022 ($3.99, limited series)

1-5-Peter Milligan-s/Mike Deodato Jr.-a. 1-Frank Cho-c						4.00

ABYSS, THE (Movie)
Dark Horse Comics: June, 1989 - No. 2, July, 1989 ($2.25, limited series)

1,2-Adaptation of film; Kaluta & Moebius-a						5.00

ACCELERATE
DC Comics (Vertigo): Aug, 2000 - No. 4, Nov, 2000 ($2.95)

1-4-Pander Bros.-a/Kadrey-s						3.00

ACCLAIM ADVENTURE ZONE
Acclaim Books: 1997 ($4.50, digest size)

	GD 2.0	VG 4.0	FN 6.0	VF 8.0	VF/NM 9.0	NM- 9.2
... Ninjak The Boss	3	6	9	21	33	45
... Turok Dinosaur Rodeo, ... Turok Extinction	2	4	6	9	12	15

ACCUSED, THE (Civil War II tie-in)
Marvel Comics: Oct, 2016 ($4.99, one-shot)

1-The trial of Hawkeye; Matt Murdock app.; Guggenheim-s/Bachs & Brown-a/Mack-c						5.00

ACE COMICS
David McKay Publications: Apr, 1937 - No. 151, Oct-Nov, 1949 (All contain some newspaper strip reprints)

	GD 2.0	VG 4.0	FN 6.0	VF 8.0	VF/NM 9.0	NM- 9.2
1-Jungle Jim by Alex Raymond, Blondie, Ripley's Believe It Or Not, Krazy Kat begin (1st app. of each)	394	788	1182	2502	4701	6900
2	123	246	369	787	1344	1900
3-5	76	152	228	486	831	1175
6-10	58	116	174	371	636	900
11-The Phantom begins (1st app., 2/38) (in brown costume)	595	1190	1785	4350	7675	11,000
12-20	45	90	135	284	480	675
21-25,27-30	40	80	120	246	411	575
26-Origin & 1st app. Prince Valiant (5/39); begins series?	219	438	657	1402	2401	3400
31-40: 37-Krazy Kat ends	25	50	75	150	245	340
41-60	17	34	51	98	154	210
61-64,66-76-(7/43; last 68 pgs.)	15	30	45	84	127	170
65-(8/42)-Flag-c	26	52	78	154	252	350
77-84 (3/44; all 60 pgs.)	14	28	42	76	108	140
85-99 (52 pgs.)	12	24	36	67	94	120
100 (7/45; last 52 pgs.)	14	28	42	76	108	140
101-134: 128-(11/47)-Brick Bradford begins. 134-Last Prince Valiant (all 36 pgs.)	11	22	33	62	86	110

ABC: A-Z Tom Strong & Jack B. Quick #1 © ABC

Abe Sapien #23 © Mike Mignola

Action Comics #25 © DC

	GD 2.0	VG 4.0	FN 6.0	VF 8.0	VF/NM 9.0	NM- 9.2
135-151: 135-(6/48)-Lone Ranger begins	10	20	30	56	76	95

ACE KELLY (See Tops Comics & Tops In Humor)

ACE KING (See Adventures of Detective...)

ACES
Acme Press (Eclipse): Apr, 1988 - No. 5, Dec, 1988 ($2.95, B&W, magazine)

1,2	1	2	3	5	6	8
3-5						4.00

ACES HIGH
E.C. Comics: Mar-Apr, 1955 - No. 5, Nov-Dec, 1955

1-Not approved by code	43	86	129	271	461	650
2	24	48	72	144	237	330
3-5	22	44	66	132	216	300

NOTE: All have stories by **Davis**, **Evans**, **Krigstein**, and **Wood**. Evans c-1-5.

ACES HIGH
Gemstone Publishing: Apr, 1999 - No. 5, Aug, 1999 ($2.50)

1-Reprints E.C. issue	1	3	4	6	8	10
2-5-Reprints E.C. issues						6.00
Annual 1 ($13.50) r/#1-5						14.00

ACID CHIMP VS. BUSINESS DOG (Characters from My Bad and Billionaire Island)
AHOY Comics: 2024 ($3.99, one-shot)

1-Ingman-s/Krause-s; Russell-s/Pugh-a						4.00

ACME NOVELTY LIBRARY, THE
Fantagraphics Books: Winter 1993-94 - Present (quarterly, various sizes)

1-Introduces Jimmy Corrigan; Chris Ware-s/a in all	3	6	9	17	26	35
1-2nd and later printings	1	3	4	6	8	10
2,3: 2-Quimby	2	4	6	10	14	18
4-Sparky's Best Comics & Stories	3	6	9	14	20	25
5-12: Jimmy Corrigan in all	2	4	6	9	12	15
13,15-($10.95-c)	2	4	6	11	16	20
14-($12.95-c) Concludes Jimmy Corrigan saga						22.00
16,19-($15.95, hardcover) Rusty Brown						22.00
17-($16.95, hardcover) Rusty Brown						22.00
18-($17.95, hardcover)						22.00
Jimmy Corrigan, The Smartest Kid on Earth (2000, Pantheon Books, Hardcover, $27.50, 380 pgs.) Collects Jimmy Corrigan stories; folded dust jacket						28.00
Jimmy Corrigan, The Smartest Kid on Earth (2003, Softcover, $17.95)						18.00

NOTE: Multiple printings exist for most issues.

ACROSS THE UNIVERSE: THE DC UNIVERSE STORIES OF ALAN MOORE (Also see DC Universe: The Stories of Alan Moore)
DC Comics: 2003 ($19.95, TPB)

nn-Reprints selected Moore stories from '85-'87; Superman, Batman, Swamp Thing app.						20.00

ACTION ADVENTURE (War) (Formerly Real Adventure)
Gillmor Magazines: V1#2, June, 1955 - No. 4, Oct, 1955

V1#2-4	9	18	27	52	69	85

ACTION COMICS (...Weekly #601-642) (Also see The Comics Magazine #1, More Fun #14-17 & Special Edition) (Also see Promotional Comics section)
National Periodical Publ./Detective Comics/DC Comics: 6/38 - No. 583, 9/86; No. 584, 1/87 - No. 904, Oct, 2011

1-Origin & 1st app. Superman by Siegel & Shuster, Marco Polo, Tex Thomson, Pep Morgan, Chuck Dawson & Scoop Scanlon; 1st app. Zatara & Lois Lane; Superman story missing 4 pgs. which were included when reprinted in Superman #1; Clark Kent works for Daily Star; story continued in #2

368,000	736,000	1,288,000	2,575,000	4,788,000	7,000,000

1-Reprint, Oversize 13-1/2x10". **WARNING:** for its size. DC published it in 1974 with a second cover titling it as a Famous First Edition. There have been many reported cases of the outer cover being removed and the interior sold as the original edition. The reprint with the new outer cover removed is practically worthless. See Famous First Edition for value.

2-O'Mealia non-Superman covers thru #6	16,500	33,000	49,500	123,800	214,400	305,000
3 (Scarce)-Superman apps. in costume in only one panel		9450	18,900	28,350	70,900	122,950	175,000
4,5	4325	8650	12,975	32,400	56,200	80,000
6-1st Jimmy Olsen (called office boy)	4250	8500	12,750	31,900	55,450	79,000

7-1st time the name Superman is printed on a comic cover; 2nd Superman cover

52,000	104,000	156,000	312,000	481,000	650,000
8,9	3400	6800	10,200	25,500	44,250	63,000

10-3rd Superman cover by Shuster; splash panel used as cover art for Superman #1

33,600	67,200	100,800	201,600	310,800	420,000

11,14: 1st X-Ray Vision? 14-Clip Carson begins, ends #41; Zatara-c

	1725	3450	5175	12,900	22,450	32,000

12-Has 1 panel Batman ad for Det. #27 (5/39); Zatara sci-fi cover

13-Shuster Superman-c; last Scoop Scanlon; centerspread has a 2-page ad for Superman #1

4050	8100	12,150	30,400	52,700	75,000
20,000	40,000	60,000	120,000	180,000	240,000

15-Guardineer Superman-c; has ad mentioning Detective Comics and Batman; full page ad for New York World's Fair 1939 with 25¢-c

3500	7000	10,500	26,250	45,625	65,000

16-Has full page ad and 1 panel ad for New York World's Fair 1939 25¢ cover edition

975	1950	2925	7300	12,650	18,000

17-Superman cover; last Marco Polo; full page ad for New York World's Fair 1939 with 15¢-c

2160	4320	6480	16,200	28,000	40,000

18-Origin 3 Aces; has a 1 panel ad for New York World's Fair 1939 at the end of the Superman story (ad also in #16,17,19)

950	1900	2850	7100	12,300	17,500
19-Superman covers begin	2050	4100	6150	15,400	26,700	38,000

20-The 'S' left off Superman's chest; Clark Kent works at 'Daily Star'

2050	4100	6150	15,400	26,700	38,000
21-Has 2 ads for More Fun #52 (1st Spectre)	1000	2000	3000	7600	13,800	20,000
22	838	1676	2514	6117	10,809	15,500

23-1st app. Luthor (w/red hair) & Black Pirate; Black Pirate by Moldoff; 1st mention of The Daily Planet (4/40)-Has 1 panel ad for Spectre in More Fun

5900	11,800	17,700	41,300	68,150	95,000

24,25: 24-Kent at Daily Planet. 25-Last app. Gargantua T. Potts, Tex Thomson's sidekick

595	1190	1785	4350	7675	11,000
26,28,30	486	972	1458	3550	6275	9000
27-(8/40) 1st Lois Lane-c	595	1190	1785	4350	7675	11,000
29-2nd Lois Lane-c	595	1190	1785	4350	7675	11,000
31,32: 32-Intro/1st app. Krypto Ray Gun in Superman story by Burnley			354	708	1062	2478	4339	6200

33-Origin Mr. America; Superman by Burnley; has half page ad for All Star Comics #3

383	766	1149	2681	4691	6700

34,35,38,39

337	674	1011	2359	4130	5900

36,40: 36-Classic robot-c. 40-(9/41)-Intro/1st app. Star Spangled Kid & Stripesy; Jerry Siegel photo

400	800	1200	2800	4900	7000
37-Origin Congo Bill	343	686	1029	2400	4200	6000

41,43-46,48-50: 44-Fat Man's i.d. revealed to Mr. America. 45-1st app. Stuff (Vigilante's Asian sidekick)

300	600	900	2070	3635	5200

42-1st app./origin Vigilante; Bob Daley becomes Fat Man; origin Mr. America's magic flying carpet; The Queen Bee & Luthor app; Black Pirate ends; not in #41

314	628	942	2198	3849	5500
47-1st Luthor cover in comics (4/42)	443	886	1329	3234	5717	8200
51-1st app. The Prankster	300	600	900	2070	3635	5200

52-Fat Man & Mr. America become the Ameri-commandos; origin Vigilante retold; classic Superman and back-ups-c

411	822	1233	2877	5039	7200
53-56: 56-Last Fat Man	290	580	870	1856	3178	4500
57-3rd Lois Lane-c in Action (2/43)	271	542	813	1734	2967	4200
58-"Slap a Jap"-c	541	1082	1623	3950	6975	10,000
59-Nazi tank-c	300	600	900	2010	3505	5000
60-First app. Lois Lane as Super-woman	300	600	900	2070	3635	5200
61-Historic Atomic Radiation-c (6/43)	331	662	993	2317	4059	5800
62-Japan war-c	290	580	870	1856	3178	4500
63-Japan war-c; last 3 Aces	400	800	1200	2800	4900	7000
64-Intro Toyman	239	478	717	1530	2615	3700
65-70: 66-69-Kubert-i on Vigilante	190	380	570	1207	2079	2950
71-79: 74-Last Mr. America	152	304	456	965	1658	2350
80-2nd app. & 1st Mr. Mxyztplk-c (1/45)	187	374	561	1197	2049	2900
81-88,90: 83-Intro Hocus & Pocus	138	276	414	876	1513	2150
89-Classic rainbow cover	174	348	522	1114	1907	2700
91-99: 93-X-Mas-c. 99-1st small logo (8/46)	116	232	348	742	1271	1800
100	168	336	504	1075	1838	2600
101-Nuclear explosion-c (10/46)	300	600	900	1920	3310	4700
102-Mxyztplk-c	116	232	348	742	1271	1800
103,104,106,107,109-116,118-120	110	220	330	704	1202	1700
105,117-Christmas covers	119	238	357	762	1306	1850
108-Classic molten metal-c	168	336	504	1075	1838	2600
121,122,124-126,128-140: 135,136,138-Zatara by Kubert		103	206	309	659	1130	1600

123-(8/48) Superman flies (See Superman #30 for 1st time he flies, not leaps)

148	296	444	947	1624	2300

127-Vigilante by Kubert; Tommy Tomorrow begins (12/48, see Real Fact #6)

110	220	330	704	1202	1700
141-150,152-155,157,159-161: 161- Last 52 pgs.	97	194	291	621	1061	1500
151-Luthor/Mr. Mxyztplk/Prankster team-up	142	284	426	909	1555	2200
156-Lois as Super Woman	129	258	387	826	1413	2000
158-Origin Superman retold	155	310	465	992	1696	2400
162-180: 168,176-Used in **POP**, pg. 90. 173-Robot-c	93	186	279	591	1021	1450
181-201: 191-Intro. Janu in Congo Bill. 198-Last Vigilante. 201-Last pre-code issue		87	174	261	553	952	1350

	GD 2.0	VG 4.0	FN 6.0	VF 8.0	VF/NM 9.0	NM- 9.2
202-220,232: 212-(1/56)-Includes 1956 Superman calendar that is part of story. 232-1st Curt Swan-c in Action	68	136	204	435	743	1050
221-231,233-240: 221-1st S.A. issue. 224-1st Golden Gorilla story. 228-(5/57)-Kongorilla in Congo Bill story (Congorilla try-out)	58	116	174	371	636	900
241-Batman x-over	77	154	231	493	847	1200
242-Origin & 1st app. Brainiac (7/58); 1st mention of Shrunken City of Kandor	900	1800	3600	10,800	23,400	36,000
243-251: 248-Origin/1st app. Congorilla; Congo Bill renamed Congorilla. 251-Last Tommy Tomorrow	50	100	150	315	533	750
252-Origin & 1st app. Supergirl (5/59); 1st app. Metallo	900	1800	3600	10,800	23,400	36,000
253-2nd app. Supergirl	100	200	300	635	1093	1550
254-1st meeting of Bizarro & Superman-c/story; 3rd app. Supergirl	97	194	291	621	1061	1500
255-1st Bizarro Lois Lane-c/story & both Bizarros leave Earth to make Bizarro World; 4th app. Supergirl	65	130	195	416	708	1000
256-260: 259-Red Kryptonite used	40	80	120	244	402	575
261-1st X-Kryptonite which gave Streaky his powers; last Congorilla in Action; origin & 1st app. Streaky The Super Cat	47	94	141	296	498	700
262,264-266,268-270	36	72	108	211	343	475
263-Origin Bizarro World (continues in #264)	47	94	141	296	498	700
267(8/60)-3rd app. Chameleon Boy, Colossal Boy, & Invisible Kid, 1st app of Supergirl as Superwoman.	78	156	228	486	831	1175
271-275,277-282: 274-Lois Lane as Superwoman. 280-Brief origin of Supergirl & Brainiac retold; Brainiac-c. 282-Last 10¢ issue	29	58	87	172	281	390
276(5/61)-6th Legion app; 1st app. Brainiac 5, Phantom Girl, Triplicate Girl, Bouncing Boy, Sun Boy, & Shrinking Violet; Supergirl joins Legion	109	206	309	659	1130	1600
283(12/61)-Legion of Super-Villains app. 1st 12¢	15	30	45	103	227	350
284(1/62)-Mon-El app.	16	32	48	110	243	375
285(2/62)-12th Legion app; Brainiac 5 cameo; Supergirl's existence revealed to world; JFK & Jackie, LBJ & Khrushchev cameos	36	72	108	259	580	900
286-287,289-292,294-299: 286(3/62)-Legion of Super Villains app. 293(4/62)-15th Legion app. (cameo). 289(6/62)-16th Legion app. (Adult); Lightning Man & Saturn Woman's marriage 1st revealed. 290(7/62)-Legion app. (cameo); Phantom Girl app. 1st Supergirl emergency squad. 291-1st meeting Supergirl & Mr. Mxyzptlk. 292-2nd app. Superhorse (see Adv.#293). 297-General Zod, Phantom Zone villains & Mon-El app. 298-General Zod app.; Legion cameo	12	24	36	84	185	285
288-Mon-El app.; r-origin Supergirl	13	26	39	86	188	290
293-Origin Comet (Superhorse)	16	32	48	108	239	370
300-(5/63)	16	32	48	110	243	375
301-303,305,307,308,310-312,315-320: 307-Saturn Girl app. 317-Death of Nor-Kan of Kandor. 319-Shrinking Violet app.	10	20	30	64	132	200
304,306,313: 304-Origin/1st app. Black Flame (9/63). 306-Brainiac 5, Mon-El app. 313-Batman app.	10	20	30	67	141	215
309-(2/64)-Legion app.; Batman & Robin-c & cameo; JFK app. (he died 11/22/63; on stands last week of Dec, 1963)	15	30	45	103	227	350
314-Retells origin Supergirl; J.L.A. x-over	10	20	30	69	147	225
321-333,335-339: 336-Origin Akvar (Flamebird)	8	16	24	56	108	160
334-Giant G-20; origin Supergirl, Streaky, Superhorse & Legion (all-r)	10	20	30	70	150	230
340-Origin, 1st app. of the Parasite; 2 pg. pin-up	26	52	78	182	404	625
341,344,350,358: 341-Batman app. in Supergirl back-up story. 344-Batman x-over. 350-Batman, Green Arrow & Green Lantern app. in Supergirl back-up story. 358-Superboy meets Supergirl	7	14	21	48	89	130
342,343,345,346,348,349,351-357,359: 342-UFO story. 345-Allen Funt/Candid Camera story.	7	14	21	46	86	125
347,360-Giant Supergirl G-33,G-45; 347-Origin Comet-r plus Bizarro story. 360-Legion app.-r; r/origin Supergirl	9	18	27	59	117	175
361-2nd app. Parasite	8	16	24	54	102	150
362-364,367-372,374-378: 362-366-Leper/Death story. 370-New facts about Superman's origin. 376-Last Supergirl in Action; last 12¢ issue (thru #392)	6	12	18	37	66	95
365,366: 365-JLA & Legion app. 366-JLA app.	6	12	18	42	79	115
373-Giant Supergirl G-57; Legion-r	8	16	24	56	108	160
379,380,382-399,401: 388-Sgt. Rock app., last Legion in Action; Saturn Girl gets new costume. 393-401-All Superman issues. 395-Bonus "Secrets of Superman's Fortress" 2-page spread	4	8	12	27	44	60
381-Superman as Dictator of Earth-c/s	5	10	15	34	60	85
400	4	8	12	27	44	60
402-Last 15¢ issue; Superman vs. Supergirl duel	4	8	12	27	44	60
403-413: All 52 pg. issues. 411-Origin Eclipso-(r). 413-Metamorpho begins, ends #418	4	8	12	25	40	55
414-418,420-424: 421-Intro Capt. Strong; Green Arrow begins. 422,423-Origin Human Target	3	6	9	14	19	24
419-Intro. Human Target	7	14	21	44	82	120
425-Neal Adams-a(p); The Atom begins	3	6	9	21	33	45
426-431,433-436,438,439	2	4	6	9	13	16
432-1st Bronze Age Toyman app. (2/74)	3	6	9	21	33	45
437,443-(100 pg. Giants)	6	12	18	37	66	95
440-1st Grell-a on Green Arrow	3	6	9	16	23	30
441,442,444-448: 441-Grell-a on Green Arrow continues	2	4	6	9	13	16
449-(68 pgs.)	3	6	9	15	22	28
450-465,467-470,474-483,486,489-499: 454-Last Atom. 456-Grell Jaws-c. 458-Last Green Arrow		2	4	6	8	10
466,487,488: 466-Batman, Flash app. 487,488-(44 pgs.). 487-Origin & 1st app. Microwave Man; origin Atom retold	2	4	6	8	10	12
471-(5/77) 1st app. Faora Hu-Ul	3	6	9	19	30	40
472,473-Faora app. 473-Faora, General Zod app.	3	6	9	15	22	28
481-483,486-492,495-499,501-505,507,508-Whitman variants (low print run; none bear issue # on cover)	3	6	9	14	20	26
484-Earth II Superman & Lois Lane wed; 40th anniversary issue(6/78)	3	6	9	19	30	40
484-Variant includes 3-D Superman punchout doll in cello. pack; 4 different inserts; (Canadian promo?)	7	14	21	44	82	120
485-Classic Neal Adams Superman-c	3	6	9	14	20	25
485-Whitman variant	4	8	12	28	47	65
500-($1.00, 68 pgs.)-Infinity-c; Superman life story retold; shows Legion statues in museum	3	6	9	16	23	30
501-520,522-543,545,547-551: 511-514-Airwave II solo stories. 513-The Atom begins. 517-Aquaman begins; ends #541. 528-530-Three-part Brainiac storyline. 532,536-New Teen Titans cameo. 535,536-Omega Men app. 551-Starfire becomes Red-Star	1	3	4	6	8	10
521-1st app. The Vixen	5	10	15	35	63	90
537-Includes Masters of the Universe preview	3	6	9	14	20	25
544-(6/83, Mando paper, 68 pgs.)-45th Anniversary issue; origins new Luthor & Brainiac; Omega Men app.; Shuster-a (pin-up); article by Siegel	3	6	9	14	20	25
546-J.L.A., New Teen Titans app.	2	4	6	8	11	14
552,553-Animal Man, Cave Carson, Congorilla, Sea Devils-c/app.; Dolphin, Immortal Man, Rip Hunter, Suicide Squad app (2/84 & 3/84)	1	3	4	6	8	10
554-582: 577-Intro. Caitiff, the First Vampire	1	2	3	5	6	8
583-(9/86) Alan Moore scripts; last Earth 1 Superman story (cont'd from Superman #423)	3	6	9	17	26	35
584-(1/87) Byrne-a begins; New Teen Titans app.	1	3	4	6	8	10
585-599: 586-Legends x-over. 595-1st app. Silver Banshee. 596-Millennium x-over; Spectre app. 598-1st Checkmate	1	2	3	5	6	8
600-($2.50, 84 pgs., 5/88)	2	4	6	9	12	15
601-608,610-642: (#601-642 are weekly issues) ($1.50, 52 pgs.) 601-Re-intro The Secret Six; death of Katma Tui. 611-614-Catwoman stories (new costume in #611). 613-618-Nightwing stories	1	2	3	5	6	8
609-Black Canary-c by Bolland	2	4	6	8	10	12
643-Superman & monthly issues begin again; Perez-c/a/scripts begin; swipes cover to Action #1	1	3	4	6	8	10
644,646-649,651-661,663-666,668-671,673,675-682: 654-Part 3 of Batman storyline. 655-Free extra 8 pgs. 660-Death of Lex Luthor. 661-Begin $1.00-c. 675-Deathstroke cameo. 679-Last $1.00 issue						6.00
645-1st app. Maxima	2	4	6	11	16	20
650,667: 650-($1.50, 52 pgs.)-Lobo cameo (last panel). 667-($1.75, 52 pgs.)	1	2	3	5	6	8
662-Clark Kent reveals i.d. to Lois Lane; story cont'd in Superman #53		2	4	6	8	10
672-Sonic the Hedgehog mini-comic insert		3	6	9	12	15
674-Supergirl logo & c/story (reintro)	1	3	4	6	8	10
683-1st Jackal; Doomsday cameo	3	6	9	15	22	28
683-685-2nd & 3rd printings						4.00
684,685: 684-Doomsday battle issue. 685-Funeral for a Friend issue; Supergirl app.	2	4	6	11	16	20
686-Funeral for a Friend issue; Supergirl app.						5.00
687-($1.95)-Collector's Ed.w/die-cut-c						5.00
687-($1.50)-Newsstand Edition with mini-poster						4.00
688-699,701-703-($1.50): 688-Guy Gardner-c/story. 697-Bizarro-c/story. 703-(9/94)-Zero Hour						4.00
695-($2.50)-Collector's Edition w/embossed foil-c						6.00
700-($2.95, 68 pgs.)-Fall of Metropolis Pt 1, Guice-a; Pete Ross marries Lana Lang and Smallville flashbacks with Curt Swan art & Murphy Anderson inks						6.00
700-Platinum						20.00
700-Gold						25.00
704(11/94)-719,721-731: 710-Begin $1.95-c. 714-Joker app. 719-Batman-c/app. 721-Mr. Mxyzptlk app. 723-Dave Johnson-c. 727-Final Night x-over.						4.00
720-Lois breaks off engagement w/Clark						5.00
720-2nd print.						4.00
732,734,749,751-764,767,767: 732-New powers. 733-New costume, Ray app. 738-Immonen-a(p) begins. 741-Legion app. 744-Millennium Giants x-over. 745-747-70's-style Superman vs. Prankster. 753-JLA-c/app. 757-Hawkman-c. 760-1st Encantadora. 761-Wonder Woman app. 766-Batman-c/app.						4.00
750-($2.95)						5.00
765-Super Harley-c/app.	2	4	6	9	13	16
768,769,771-774: 768-Begin $2.25-c; Marvel Family-c/app. 771-Nightwing-c/app. 772,773-Ra's al Ghul app. 774-Martian Manhunter-c/app.						4.00
770-($3.50) Conclusion of Emperor Joker x-over	1	2	3	5	6	8
775-($3.75) Bradstreet-c; intro. The Elite	3	6	9	16	23	30
775-(2nd printing)	2	4	6	8	10	12
776-799: 776-Farewell to Krypton; Rivoche-c. 780-782-Our Worlds at War x-over. 781-Hippolyta and Major Lane killed. 782-War ends. 784-Joker: Last Laugh; Batman & Green Lantern app. 793-Return to Krypton. 795-The Elite app. 798-Van Fleet-c						4.00
800-($4.03, $3.95) Struzan painted-c; guest artists include Ross, Jim Lee, Jurgens, Sale	2	4	6	8	10	12
801-811: 801-Raney-a. 809-The Creeper app. 811-Mr. Majestic app.						3.00
812-Godfall part 1; Turner-c; Caldwell-a(p)						3.00
812-2nd printing; B&W sketch-c by Turner						3.00
813-Godfall pt. 4; Turner-c; Caldwell-a(p)						4.00
814-824,826-830,833,834,836: 814-Reis-a/Art Adams-c; Darkseid app.; begin $2.50-c. 815,816-Teen Titans-c/app. 820-Doomsday app. 826-Capt. Marvel app. 827-Byrne-c/a begin. 831-Villains United tie-in. 836-Infinite Crisis; revised origin						3.00
825-($2.99, 40 pgs.) Doomsday app.						4.00
829-Omac Project x-over Sacrifice pt. 2						5.00
829-(2nd printing) red tone cover						4.00
835-1st Livewire app. in regular DCU	3	6	9	14	19	24
837-843-One Year Later; powers return after Infinite Crisis; Johns & Busiek-s						3.00
844-Donner & Johns-s/Adam Kubert-a/c begin; brown-toned cover						6.00
844-Andy Kubert variant-c						6.00
844-2nd printing with red-toned Adam Kubert cover						3.00
845-849,851-857: 845-Bizarro-c/app.; re-intro. General Zod, Ursa & Non. 846-Jax-Ur app. 847-849-No Kubert-a. 855-857-Bizarro app.; Powell-a/c						4.00
850-($3.99) Supergirl and LSH app., origin re-told; Guedes-a/c						4.00
858-($3.50) Supergirl and Brainiac app.; origin re-told; Johns-s/Frank-a/c						5.00
858-Variant-c (Superman & giant Brainiac robot) by Frank						5.00
858-Second printing with regular cover with red background instead of yellow						3.00
858-Special Edition (7/10, $1.00) r/#858 with "What's Next?" cover logo						3.00
859-868,870-878: 859-863-Legion of Super-Heroes app.; var-c on each (859-Andy Kubert. 860-Lightle. 861-Grell. 862-Giffen. 863-Frank) 864-Batman and Lightning Lad app. 866-Brainiac returns. 870-Pa Kent dies. 871-New Krypton; Ross-c						3.00

Action Comics #472 © DC

Action Comics #1045 © DC

A.D.: After Death Book 1
© Snyder & 171 Studios

	GD	VG	FN	VF	VF/NM	NM-
	2.0	4.0	6.0	8.0	9.0	9.2

869-Initial printing recalled because of beer bottles on cover
| 9 | 18 | 27 | 61 | 123 | 185 |
869-"Soda Pop" cover edition 6.00
879-896: 879-($3.99) Back-up Capt. Atom feature begins. 890-Luthor stories begin.
893-Comics debut of Chloe Sullivan (Smallville TV show) in regular DCU.
894-Death (from Sandman) app. 896-Secret Six app. 4.00
897-899, 901-903-($2.99) 897-Joker app. 898-Larfleeze app. 899-Brainiac app. 3.00
900 (6/11, $5.99, 96 pgs.) Conclusion of Luthor Black Ring saga; Doomsday app.; bonus short stories by various; Superman renounces U.S. citizenship 6.00
904-(10/11) Last issue of first volume; Doomsday app.; Rocafort-c 4.00
904-Variant-c by Ordway | 1 | 3 | 4 | 6 | 8 | 10 |
#0-(10/94) Zero Hour tie-in; released between #703 & #704 .... 3.00
#1,000,000 (11/98) Gene Ha-c; 853rd Century x-over 3.00
Annual 1 ('87, $2.95) Art Adams-c/a(p); Batman app. | 1 | 3 | 4 | 6 | 8 | 10 |
Annual 2-6 ('89-'94, $2.95)-2-Pérez-c/a(i). 3-Armageddon 2001. 4-Eclipso vs. Shazam.
5-Bloodlines; 1st app. Loose Cannon. 6-Elseworlds story 5.00
Annual 7,9 ('95, '97, $3.95) 7-Year One story. 9-Pulp Heroes story 5.00
Annual 8 (1996, $2.95) Legends of the Dead Earth story 5.00
Annual 10 ('07, $3.99) Short stories by Johns & Donner and various incl. A. Adams, J. Kubert, Wight, Morales; origin of Phantom Zone, Mon-El; Metallo app.: Adam & Joe Kubert-c 6.00
Annual 11 (7/08, $4.99) Conclusion to General Zod story continued from #851; Kubert-a 5.00
Annual 12 (8/09, $4.99) Origin of Nightwing and Flamebird 5.00
Annual 13 (2/11, $4.99) 1st meeting of Luthor and Darkseid; Ra's al Ghul app. 5.00
NOTE:*Super* girl's origin in 262, 280, 285, 291, 305, 309. **N. Adams**-c356, 358, 359, 361-364, 366, 367, 370-374, 377-379i, 398-400, 402, 404,405, 419p, 466, 468, 469, 473i, 485. **Aparo** a-642. **Austin** c/a-682i. **Baily** a-24, 25. **Boring** a-164, 194, 211, 223, 233, 241, 250, 261, 266-268, 344, 348, 352, 356, 357. **Burnley** a-28-33; c-487, 53-55, 58, 59?, 60-63, 65, 66p, 67p, 70p, 71p, 79p, 82p, 84-86p, 90-92p, 93p?, 94p, 107p, 108p. **Byrne** a-584-598p, 599i, 600p; c-584-591, 596-600. **Ditko** a-560, 563, 565, 577, 579; c-539, 560, 563, 565, 577, 579. **Grell** a-440-442, 444-446, 450-452, 456-458; c-456. **Guardineer** a-24, 25; c-8, 11, 12, 14-16, 18, 25. **Guice** a(p)-676-681, 683-698, 700; c-684-698. **Giffen** a-560, 563, 565. **Infantino** a-642. **Kaluta** c-673. **Bob Kane's** Clip Carson-14-41. **Gil Kane** a-443r, 493r, 539-541, 544-546, 551-554, 601-605, 642; c-535p, 540, 541, 544p, 545-546, 551-554, 580, 627. **Kirby** c-638. **Meskin** a-42-121(most). **Mignola** a-600, Annual 2; c-614. **Moldoff** a-23-25, 443r. **Mooney** a-667p. **Mortimer** c-153, 154, 159-172, 174, 178-181, 184, 186-189, 191-193, 196, 200, 206. **Orlando** a-617p; c-621. **Perez** a-600i, 643-652p, Annual 2p; c-529p, 602, 643-651, Annual 2p. **Quesada** c-Annual 4p. **Fred Ray** c-34, 36-46, 50-52. **Siegel & Shuster** a-1-27. **Simon** a-509; c-631. **Leonard Starr** a-597i(part). **Staton** a-525p, 526p, 531p, 535p, 536p. **Swan/Moldoff** c-281, 286, 287, 293, 298, 334. **Thibert** c-676, 677p, 678-681, 684. **Toth** a-406, 407, 413, 431; c-616. **Tuska** a-486p, 550. **Williamson** a-568i. **Zeck** c-Annual 5

ACTION COMICS (2nd series)(DC New 52)(Numbering reverts to original V1 #957 after #52)
DC Comics: Nov, 2011 - No. 52, Jul, 2016 ($3.99)

1-Grant Morrison-s/Rags Morales-a/c; re-introduces Superman
| 2 | 4 | 6 | 8 | 11 | 14 |
1-Variant-c by Jim Lee of Superman in new armor costume
| 2 | 4 | 6 | 11 | 16 | 20 |
1-(2nd - 5th printings) 4.00
2-8,10-12: 2-Morales & Brent Anderson-a; behind the scenes sketch art and commentary. 3-Gene Ha & Morales-a. 4-Re-intro. Steel. 5-Flashback to Krypton; Andy Kubert-a. 6-Legion of Super-Heroes app.; Andy Kubert-a. 7-Gets the new costume; intro. Steel 4.00
2-8,10-12-Variant covers. 2-Van Sciver. 3-Ha. 4-Choi. 5,6-Morales. 8-Frank 5.00
9-1st Calvin Ellis as Superman | 2 | 4 | 6 | 11 | 16 | 20 |
13-17,19-23: 13-Re-intro of Krypto. 14-Neil deGrasse Tyson app. 15-Legion app. 4.00
18-($4.99) Last Morrison-s; Mxyzptlk, The Legion and the Wanderers app. 5.00
23.1, 23.2, 23.3, 23.4 (11/13, $2.99, regular covers 3.00
23.1 (11/13, $3.99, 3-D cover) "Cyborg Superman #1" on cover; Zor-El & Brainiac app. 5.00
23.2 (11/13, $3.99, 3-D cover) "Zod #1" on cover; origin of Zod on Krypton; Faora app. 5.00
23.3 (11/13, $3.99, 3-D cover) "Lex Luthor #1" on cover; Kuder-c 5.00
23.4 (11/13, $3.99, 3-D cover) "Metallo #1" on cover; Fisch-s/Pugh-a 5.00
24-49,51,52: 25-Zero Year. 30-Doomsday app. 31-35-Doomed x-over. 40-Bizarro app.
51-Supergirl app. 52-Wonder Woman, Batman and pre-Flashpoint Superman app. 5.00
50-($4.99) Vandal Savage and the Justice League app. 5.00
#0 (11/12, $3.99) Flashback to Lois' 1st Superman sighting; Oliver-a; 4.00
Annual 1 (12/12, $4.99) Superman vs. K-Man; Fisch-s/Hamner-a; Atomic Skull app. 5.00
Annual 2 (12/13, $4.99) Rocafort & Jurgens-a; H'El & Faora app.; back-up Mad sampler 5.00
Annual 3 (9/14, $4.99) Superman Doomed x-over; Brainiac app. 5.00
...: Futures End 1 (11/14, $2.99, regular-c) Five years later; Alixe-a 3.00
...: Futures End 1 (11/14, $3.99, 3-D cover) 4.00

ACTION COMICS (Numbering reverts to original V1 #957 after #52 from 2011-2016 series)
DC Comics: No. 957, Aug, 2016 - Present ($2.99/$3.99/$4.99)

957-Jurgens-a/Zircher-a; the pre-52 Superman vs. Lex Luthor & Doomsday (DC Universe rebirth) | 1 | 2 | 3 | 5 | 6 | 8 |
958-974: 960-962-Wonder Woman app. 973-Superwoman & Steel app. 3.00
975-($3.99) Superman Reborn pt. 2; back-up by Mxyzptlk; Dini-s/Churchill-a. 6.00
976-986,992-999: 976-Superman Reborn pt. 4. 977,978-Origin revised. 979-Cyborg Superman returns. 984-Intro Ursa and Zod. 992-998-Booster Gold app. 3.00
987-991-($2.99) The Oz Effect regular covers; Jor-El returns 3.00
987-991-($3.99) The Oz Effect lenticular covers 4.00
1000-(6/18, $7.99) Short stories and pin-ups by various incl. Jurgens, Swan, Coipel, Ordway,

Gleason, García-López; intro. Rogol Zaar; Bendis-s/Jim Lee-a; 9 covers 8.00
1001-1028: 1001-Intro. Red Cloud; Gleason-a. 1004-1006-Sook-a. 1007-1011-Leviathan Rising; Epting-a. 1012-1016-Kudranski-a; Red Cloud and Thorn app. 1015-1016-Batman & Naomi app. 1017-1027-Romita, Jr.-a. 1017-1021-Legion of Doom app. 1020-1022-Young Justice app. 1028-Last Bendis-s 4.00
1029-1049-($4.99) P.K. Johnson-s begins. 1029-1034-Back-up with Midnighter; Cloonan-s. 1035-Superman & The Authority go to Warworld. 1037-1042-Martian Manhunter back-up 5.00
1050-(2/23, $5.99) Superman's secret ID restored; art by various 6.00
1051-1063: 1051-1056-Metallo app.; 1051-1053-Back-up Power Girl story 5.00
2021 Annual 1 (9/21, $5.99) Tales of the House of El; Kara & future Supermen 6.00
2022 Annual 1 (7/22, $5.99) Mongul's secret origin; flashback to Clark's youth 6.00
2023 Annual 1 (2/24, $5.99) The Demon and Bloodwynd app. 6.00
...: Presents: Doomsday Special 1 (10/23, $5.99) Watters-s/Barrows & Ferreira-a 6.00
...: Special 1 (7/18, $4.99) Jurgens/Conrad-a; Russell-s/Thompson-a; Landis/Manapul-a 5.00

ACTION COMICS
DC Comics: (no date)

1-Ashcan comic, not distributed to newsstands, only for in-house use. Cover art is the rejected art to Detective Comics #2 and interior from Detective Comics #1.
A CGC certified 9.0 copy sold for $17,825 in 2002, $29,000 in 2008, and $50,000 in 2010.
A CGC certified 9.2 copy sold for $204,000 in April 2021.

ACTION COMICS 1 (FACSIMILE EDITION)
DC Comics: 2022 ($6.99)

1-Reprints the entire 1938 Action Comics #1 with original ads
| 1 | 3 | 4 | 6 | 8 | 10 |

ACTION FORCE (Also see G.I. Joe European Missions)
Marvel Comics Ltd. (British): Mar, 1987 - No. 50, 1988 ($1.00, weekly, magazine)

1,3: British G.I. Joe series. 3-w/poster insert | 3 | 6 | 9 | 14 | 20 | 25 |
2,4 | 2 | 4 | 6 | 8 | 10 | 12 |
5-10 | 1 | 2 | 3 | 5 | 6 | 8 |
11-50 .... 5.00
...Special 1 (7/87) Summer holiday special; Snake Eyes-c/app. | 2 | 4 | 6 | 9 | 12 | 15 |
...Special 2 (10/87) Winter special 6.00

ACTION FUNNIES
DC Comics: 1937/1938

nn - Ashcan comic, not distributed to newsstands, only for in house use. Cover art is Action Comics #3 and interior from Detective Comics #10. The Mallette/Brown copy in VG+ condition sold for $15,000 in 2005. A VF+ copy sold for $10,157.50 in 2012.
A CGC certified 8.5 copy sold for $57,600 in April 2022.

ACTION GIRL
Slave Labor Graphics: Oct, 1994 - No. 19 ($2.50/$2.75/$2.95, B&W)

1-19: 4-Begin $2.75-c. 19-Begin $2.95-c 5.00
1-6 ($2.75, 2nd printings): All read 2nd Print in indicia. 1-(2/96). 2-(10/95). 3-(2/96). 4-(7/96).
5-(2/97). 6-(9/97) 3.00
1-4 ($2.75, 3rd printings): All read 3rd Print in indicia. 3.00

ACTION MAN (Based on the Hasbro G.I. Joe-type action figure)
IDW Publishing: Jun, 2016 - No. 4, Sept, 2016 ($3.99, limited series)

1-4-John Barber-s/Paolo Villanelli-a 4.00
...: Revolution (10/16, $3.99) Tie-in to Hasbro toy titles x-over; Barber-s/Villanelli-a 4.00

ACTION PHILOSOPHERS!
Dark Horse Comics: Oct, 2014 ($1.00, one-shot)

1-Van Lente-s/Dunlavey-a 4.00

ACTION PLANET COMICS
Action Planet: 1996 - No. 3, Sept, 1997 ($3.95, B&W, 44 pgs.)

1-3: 1-Intro Monster Man by Mike Manley & other stories 4.00
Giant Size Action Planet Halloween Special (1998, $5.95, oversized) 6.00

ACTUAL CONFESSIONS (Formerly Love Adventures)
Atlas Comics (MPI): No. 13, Oct, 1952 - No. 14, Dec, 1952

13,14 | 15 | 30 | 45 | 88 | 137 | 185 |

ACTUAL ROMANCES (Becomes True Secrets #3 on?)
Marvel Comics (IPS): Oct, 1949 - No. 2, Jan, 1950 (52 pgs.)

1-Photo-c | 22 | 44 | 66 | 132 | 216 | 300 |
2-Photo-c | 15 | 30 | 45 | 86 | 137 | 185 |

A.D.: AFTER DEATH
Image Comics: Book 1, Nov, 2016 - Book 3, May, 2017 ($5.99, limited series, square-bound 8"x11")

1-3-Scott Snyder-s/Jeff Lemire-a 6.00

ADAM AND EVE

	GD 2.0	VG 4.0	FN 6.0	VF 8.0	VF/NM 9.0	NM- 9.2

Spire Christian Comics (Fleming H. Revell Co.): 1975,1978 (35¢/39¢/49¢)

nn-By Al Hartley (1975 edition)	3	6	9	14	20	25
nn (1978 edition)	2	4	6	10	14	18

ADAM: LEGEND OF THE BLUE MARVEL
Marvel Comics: Jan, 2009 - No. 5, May, 2009 ($3.99, limited series)

1-First app. Blue Marvel (Adam Brashear); Grevioux-s/Broome-a; Avengers app.

	12	24	36	82	179	275
2	5	10	15	31	53	75
3,5	3	6	9	21	33	45
4-Namor app.	4	8	12	27	44	60

ADAM STRANGE (Also see Green Lantern #132, Mystery In Space #53 & Showcase #17)
DC Comics: 1990 - No. 3, 1990 ($3.95, 52 pgs, limited series, squarebound)

Book One - Three: Andy & Adam Kubert-c/a						5.00
...: The Man of Two Worlds (2003, $19.95, TPB) r/#1-3; sketch pages by Andy Kubert						20.00

ADAM STRANGE (Leads into the Rann/Thanagar War mini-series)
DC Comics: Nov, 2004 - No. 8, June, 2005 ($2.95, limited series)

1-8-Andy Diggle-s/Pascal Ferry-a/c. 1-Superman app.						3.00
... Planet Heist TPB (2005, $19.99) r/series; sketch pages						20.00
... Special (11/08, $3.50) Takes place during Rann/Thanagar Holy War series; Starlin-s						4.00

ADAM STRANGE / FUTURE QUEST SPECIAL
DC Comics: May, 2017 ($4.99, one-shot)

1-Adam Strange meets Jonny Quest and team; back-up Top Cat story; Batman app. ... 5.00

ADAM-12 (TV)
Gold Key: Dec, 1973 - No. 10, Feb, 1976 (Photo-c)

1		6	12	18	42	79	115
2-10		4	8	12	23	37	50

ADAM WARLOCK: STRANGE TALES
Marvel Comics: Jun, 2023 ($3.99, one-shot)

No. 178 Facsimile Edition - Reprints issue with original 1975 ads ... 4.00

ADDAMS FAMILY (TV cartoon)
Gold Key: Oct, 1974 - No. 3, Apr, 1975 (Hanna-Barbera)

1	14	28	42	96	211	325
2,3	6	12	18	36	69	100

ADDAMS FAMILY
IDW Publishing: Oct, 2019; Jul, 2023 ($4.99, one-shot)

...: The Bodies Issue - Zöe Quinn-s/Philip Murphy-a	1	3	4	6	8	10
...: The Bodies Issue (Second printing)						5.00

ADDAMS FAMILY: CHARLATAN'S WEB
IDW Publishing: Dec, 2023 - No. 2, Feb, 2024 ($5.99, limited series)

1,2-Leah Williams & Chynna Clugston Flores-s/Juan Samu & Francine Delgado-a ... 6.00

ADDICTION, THE
ZQ Studios: Oct, 2023 - No. 3 ($4.99, limited series)

1-Vincent Zurzolo & David Quinn-s/Claudia Balboni-a						5.00
... Premiere (10/23) New York Comic-Con edition; Artgerm-c						35.00
... Premiere (10/23) New York Comic-Con edition; David Mack-c						20.00

ADLAI STEVENSON
Dell Publishing Co.: Dec, 1966

12-007-612-Life story; photo-c	3	6	9	21	33	45

ADOLESCENT RADIOACTIVE BLACK BELT HAMSTERS (See Clint)
Comic Castle/Eclipse Comics: 1986 - No. 9, Jan, 1988 ($1.50, B&W)

1	2	4	6	8	11	14
1-In 3-D (7/86), 2-4 in 3-D ($2.50)						6.00
2-4						6.00
5-9						4.00
1-9 (Second printings)						4.00
Massacre The Japanese Invasion #1 (8/89, $2.00)						4.00

ADOLESCENT RADIOACTIVE BLACK BELT HAMSTERS
Dynamite Entertainment: 2008 - No. 4, 2008 ($3.50, limited series)

1-4-Tom Nguyen-a/Keith Champagne-s; 2 covers by Nguyen and Oeming ... 4.00

ADRENALYNN (See The Tenth)
Image Comics: Aug, 1999 - No. 4, Feb, 2000 ($2.50)

1-4-Tony Daniel-s/Marty Egeland-a; origin of Adrenalynn ... 3.00

ADULT TALES OF TERROR ILLUSTRATED (See Terror Illustrated)

ADVANCED DUNGEONS & DRAGONS (Also see TSR Worlds)
DC Comics: Dec, 1988 - No. 36, Dec, 1991 (Newsstand #1 is Holiday, 1988-89) ($1.25-$1.75)

1-Based on TSR role playing game	3	6	9	16	23	30
2	1	2	3	5	6	8
3-36: 25-$1.75-c begins						4.00
Annual 1 (1990, $3.95, 68 pgs.)						5.00

ADVENTURE BOUND
Dell Publishing Co.: Aug, 1949

Four Color 239	6	12	18	41	76	110

ADVENTURE COMICS (Formerly New Adventure)(...Presents Dial H For Hero #479-490)
National Periodical Publications/DC Comics: No. 32, 11/38 - No. 490, 2/82; No. 491, 9/82 - No. 503, 9/83

32-Anchors Aweigh (ends #52); Barry O'Neil (ends #60, not in #33), Captain Desmo (ends #47), Dale Daring (ends #47), Federal Men (ends #70), The Golden Dragon (ends #36), Rusty & His Pals (ends #52) by Bob Kane, Todd Hunter (ends #38) and Tom Brent (ends #46) begin

	620	1240	1860	3350	5025	6700
33-35,38	435	870	1305	2350	3525	4700
36 (scarce)	760	1520	2280	4100	6150	8200
37-Cover used on Double Action #2	740	1480	2220	4000	6000	8000
39(6/39)- Jack Wood begins, ends #42; early mention of Marijuana in comics	600	1200	1800	3250	4875	6500
40-(Rare, 7/39, on stands 6/10/39)-The Sandman begins by Bert Christman (who died in						

WWII); believed to be 1st conceived story (see N.Y. World's Fair for 1st published app.); Socko Strong begins, ends #54

	8600	17,200	25,800	63,600	139,300	215,000
41-O'Mealia shark-c	757	1514	2271	5526	9763	14,000
42,44-Sandman-c by Flessel. 44-Opium story	1000	2000	3000	7600	13,800	20,000
43,45: 45-Full page ad for Flash Comics #1	497	994	1491	3628	6414	9200
46-Sandman cover by Flessel	919	1938	2757	6709	11,855	17,000
47-Sandman cover by Flessel; Steve Conrad Adventurer begins, ends #76	757	1514	2271	5526	9763	14,000
48-1st app. The Hourman by Bernard Baily; Baily-c (Hourman c-48,50,52-59)	3050	6100	9150	22,700	47,350	72,000
49	320	640	960	2240	3920	5600
50-2nd Hourman-c; Cotton Carver by Jack Lehti begins, ends #64	337	674	1011	2359	4130	5900
51,60-Sandman-c: 51-Sandman-c by Flessel.	432	864	1296	3154	5577	8000
52-59: 53-1st app. Jimmy "Minuteman" Martin & the Minutemen of America in Hourman; ends #78. 58-Paul Kirk Manhunter begins (1st app.), ends #72	290	580	870	1856	3178	4500
61-1st app. Starman by Jack Burnley (4/41); Starman c-61-72; Starman by Burnley in #61-80	1750	3500	5250	13,100	25,550	38,000
62-65,67,68,70: 67-Origin & 1st app. The Mist; classic Burnley-c. 70-Last Federal Men	284	568	852	1818	3109	4400
66-Origin/1st app. Shining Knight (9/41)	335	670	1005	864	1482	5200
69-1st app. Sandy the Golden Boy (Sandman's sidekick) by Paul Norris (in a Bob Kane style); Sandman dons new costume	300	600	900	2010	3505	5000
71-Jimmy Martin becomes costumed aide to the Hourman; 1st app. Hourman's Miracle Ray machine	284	568	852	1818	3109	4400
72-1st Simon & Kirby Sandman (3/42, 1st DC work)	1000	2000	3000	7300	13,400	19,500
73-Origin Manhunter by Simon & Kirby; begin new series; Manhunter-c (scarce)	1275	2550	3825	9550	18,275	27,000
74-78,80: 74-Thorndyke replaces Jimmy, Hourman's assistant; new Sandman-c begin by S&K. 75-Thor app. by Kirby; 1st Kirby Thor (see Tales of the Unexpected #16). 77-Origin Genius Jones; Mist story. 80-Last S&K Manhunter & Burnley Starman	200	400	600	1280	2190	3100
79-Classic Manhunter-c	331	662	993	2317	4059	5800
81-90: 83-Last Hourman. 84-Mike Gibbs begins, ends #102	129	258	387	826	1413	2000
91-Last Simon & Kirby Sandman	135	270	405	864	1482	2100
92-99,101,102: 92-Last Manhunter. 101-Shining Knight origin retold. 102-Last Starman, Sandman, & Genius Jones; most-S&K-c (Genius Jones cont'd in More Fun #108)	103	206	309	659	1130	1600
100-S&K-c	135	270	405	864	1482	2100
103-Aquaman, Green Arrow, Johnny Quick & Superboy all move over from More Fun Comics #107; 8th app. Superboy; Superboy-c begin; 1st small logo (4/46)	320	640	960	2240	3920	5600
104-Needle in a haystack-c	135	270	405	864	1482	2100
105-110	93	186	279	591	1021	1450
111,112,114-120	84	168	252	538	919	1300
113-X-Mas-c	145	290	435	921	1586	2250
121,122-126,128-130: 128-1st meeting Superboy & Lois Lane	77	154	231	493	847	1200
127-Brief origin Shining Knight retold	81	162	243	518	884	1250
131-141,143-149: 132-Shining Knight 1st return to King Arthur time; inside app Sir Butch	68	136	204	435	743	1050
142-Origin Shining Knight & Johnny Quick retold	87	174	261	563	952	1350
150,151,153,155,157,159,161,163-All have 6 pg. Shining Knight stories by Frank Frazetta. 159-Origin Johnny Quick. 161-1st Lana Lang app. in this title	81	162	243	518	884	1250
152,154,156,158,160,162,164-166: 166-Last Shining Knight. 168-Last 52 pg. issue	58	116	174	371	636	900
170-180	54	108	162	343	574	825
181-199: 189-B&W and color illo in POP	53	106	159	334	567	800
200 (5/54)	68	136	204	435	743	1050
201-208: 207-Last Johnny Quick (not in 205)	50	100	150	315	533	750
209-Last pre-code issue; origin Speedy	55	110	165	352	601	850
210-1st app. Krypto (Superdog) & story (3/55)	890	1780	3560	8000	14,000	20,000
211-213,215-219	48	96	144	302	514	725
214-2nd app. Krypto	119	238	357	762	1306	1850
220-Krypto-c/sty	58	116	174	371	636	900
221-228,230-246: 237-1st Intergalactic Vigilante Squadron (6/57). 239-Krypto-c	39	78	117	240	395	550
229-1st S.A. issue; Green Arrow & Aquaman app.	81	162	243	518	884	1250
247(4/58)-1st Legion of Super Heroes app.; 1st app. Cosmic Boy, Saturn Girl & Lightning Boy (later Lightning Lad in #267) (origin)	1325	2650	5300	13,250	27,625	42,000
248-252,254,255-Green Arrow in all: 255-Intro. Red Kryptonite in Superboy (used in #252 but with no effect)	37	74	111	222	361	500
253-1st meeting of Superboy & Robin; Green Arrow by Kirby in #250-255 (also see World's Finest #96-99)	43	86	129	271	461	650
256-Origin Green Arrow by Kirby	80	160	240	520	1135	1750
257-259: 258-Green Arrow x-over in Superboy	30	60	90	177	289	400
260-1st Silver Age origin Aquaman (5/59)	125	250	375	1000	2000	3000
261-265,268,270: 262-Origin Speedy in Green Arrow. 270-Congorilla begins, ends #281,283	35	70	105	138	227	315
266-(11/59)-Origin & 1st app. Aquagirl (tryout, not same as later character)	39	78	117	240	378	525
267(12/59)-2nd Legion of Super Heroes; Lightning Boy now called Lightning Lad; new costumes for Legion	100	200	300	630	1865	3100
269-Intro. Aqualad (2/60); last Green Arrow (not in #206)	81	162	243	518	884	1250
271-Origin Luthor retold	57	114	171	362	619	875
272-274,277-280: 279-Intro White Kryptonite in Superboy. 280-1st meeting Superboy & Lori Lemaris	21	42	63	126	206	285
275-Origin Superman-Batman team retold (see World's Finest #94)	36	72	108	211	343	475
276-(9/60) Robinson Crusoe-like story	24	48	72	142	234	325
281,284,287-289: 281-Last Congorilla. 284-Last Aquaman in Adv.; Mooney-a. 287,288-Intro Dev-Em, the Knave from Krypton. 287-1st Bizarro Perry White & Jimmy Olsen						

Adam Strange Special #1 © DC

Adventure Comics #111 © DC

Adventure Comics (2009 series) #12 © DC

	GD 2.0	VG 4.0	FN 6.0	VF 8.0	VF/NM 9.0	NM- 9.2

288-Bizarro-c. 289-Legion cameo (statues) 20 40 60 117 189 260
282-(3/61) 5th Legion app; intro/origin Star Boy 47 94 141 296 498 700
283-Intro. The Phantom Zone; 1st app. of General Zod (cameo in 2 panels)
135 270 405 864 1482 2100
285-1st Tales of the Bizarro World-c/story (ends #299) in Adv. (see Action #255)
32 64 96 188 307 425
286-1st Bizarro Mxyzptlk; Bizarro-c 27 54 81 158 259 360
290(11/61)-9th Legion app; origin Sunboy in Legion (last 10¢ issue)
37 74 111 222 361 500
291,292,295-298: 291-1st 12¢ ish, (12/61). 292-1st Bizarro Lana Lang & Lucy Lane.
295-Bizarro-c; 1st Bizarro Titano 11 22 33 73 157 240
293(2/62)-13th Legion app; Mon-El app.; Legion of Super Pets 1st app./origin; 1st Superhorse;
2nd app. General Zod; 1st Bizarro Luthor & Kandor
48 96 144 302 514 725
294-1st Bizarro Marilyn Monroe, Pres. Kennedy 14 28 42 96 211 325
299-1st Gold Kryptonite (8/62) 12 24 36 79 170 260
300-Tales of the Legion of Super-Heroes series begins (9/62); Mon-El leaves Phantom Zone
(temporarily), joins Legion 62 124 186 500 1250 2000
301-Origin Bouncing Boy 18 36 54 124 275 425
302-305: 303-1st app. Matter-Eater Lad. 304-Death of Lightning Lad in Legion
14 28 42 96 211 325
306-310: 306-Intro. Legion of Substitute Heroes. 307-1st app. Element Lad in Legion.
308-1st app. Lightning Lass in Legion. 309-1st app. Legion of Super-Monsters
13 26 39 87 191 295
311-320: 312-Lightning Lad back in Legion. 315-Last new Superboy story; Colossal Boy app.
316-Origins & powers of Legion given. 317-Intro. Dream Girl in Legion; Lightning Lass
becomes Light Lass; Hall of Fame series begins. 320-Dev-Em 2nd app.
10 20 30 69 147 225
321-Intro. Time Trapper 10 20 30 66 138 210
322-330: 327-Intro/1st app. Lone Wolf in Legion. 329-Intro The Bizarro Legionnaires; intro.
Legion flight rings 9 18 27 59 117 175
331-340: 337-Chlorophyll Kid & Night Girl app. 340-Intro Computo in Legion
9 18 27 59 117 175
341-Triplicate Girl becomes Duo Damsel 8 16 24 54 102 150
342-345,347-351: 345-Last Hall of Fame; returns in 356,371. 348-Origin Sunboy; intro Dr.
Regulus in Legion. 349-Intro Universo & Rond Vidar. 351-1st app. White Witch
7 14 21 48 89 130
346-1st app. Karate Kid, Princess Projectra, Ferro Lad, & Nemesis Kid.
27 54 81 194 435 675
352,354-360: 354,355-Superman meets the Adult Legion. 355-Insect Queen joins Legion (4/67)
7 14 21 44 82 120
353-Death of Ferro Lad in Legion 11 22 33 76 163 250
361-364,366,368-370: 369-Intro Mordru in Legion
6 12 18 41 76 110
365,367: 365-Intro Shadow Lass (memorial in Shadow Woman app. in #354's Adult Legion-s);
lists origins & powers of L.S.H. 367-New Legion headquarters
8 16 24 54 102 150
371,372: 371-Intro. Chemical King (mentioned in #354's Adult Legion-s). 372-Timber Wolf &
Chemical King join 8 16 24 51 96 140
373,374,376-380: 373-Intro. Tornado Twins (Barry Allen Flash descendants). 374-Article on
comics fandom. 380-Last Legion in Adventure; last 12¢-c
6 12 18 37 66 95
375-Intro Quantum Queen & The Wanderers 6 12 18 41 76 110
381-Supergirl begins; 1st full length Supergirl story & her 1st solo book (6/69)
14 28 42 98 217 335
382-389 5 10 15 34 60 85
390-Giant Supergirl G-69 7 14 21 46 86 125
391-396,398 4 8 12 25 40 55
397-1st app. new Supergirl 5 10 15 35 63 90
399-Unpubbed G.A. Black Canary story 5 10 15 30 50 70
400-New costume for Supergirl (12/70) 6 12 18 42 79 115
401,402,404-408-(15¢-c) 3 6 9 18 28 38
403-68 pg. Giant G-81; Legion-r/#304,305,308,312 6 12 18 41 76 110
409-411,413-415,417-420-(52 pgs.): 413-Hawkman by Kubert r/B&B #44; G.A. Robotman-
r/Det. #178; Zatanna by Morrow. 414-r/2nd Animal Man/Str. Advs. #184. 415-Animal Man-
r/Str. Adv.#190 (origin recap). 417-Morrow Vigilante; Frazetta Shining Knight-r/Adv. #161;
origin The Enchantress; no Zatanna. 418-Prev. unpub. Dr. Mid-Nite story from 1948; no
Zatanna. 420-Animal Man-r/Str. Adv. #195 3 6 9 19 30 40
412-(52 pgs.) Reprints origin & 1st app. of Animal Man from Strange Adventures #180
6 12 18 39 65 95
416-Also listed as DC 100 Pg. Super Spectacular #10; Golden Age-r; r/1st app. Black Canary
from Flash #86; no Zatanna 11 22 33 75 160 245
421,425: 421 Demon spawn story; Zatanna app. 425-New look, content change to adventure;
Kaluta-c; Toth-a, origin Capt. Fear 3 6 9 17 26 35
422-424: 424-Last Supergirl in Adventure 3 6 9 14 20 25
426-1st Adventurers Club 2 4 6 10 14 18

427-Monster-c by Luis Domínguez; last Vigilante 3 6 9 14 20 25
428-Origin/1st app. Black Orchid (c/story, 6-7/73) 11 22 33 76 163 250
429,430-Black Orchid-c/stories 4 8 12 27 44 60
431-Spectre by Aparo begins, ends #440. 6 12 18 39 69 100
432-439-Spectre app. 433-437-Cover title is Weird Adventure Comics. 436-Last 20¢ issue
3 6 9 21 33 45
440-New Spectre origin 4 8 12 25 40 55
441-458: 441-452-Aquaman. 443-Fisherman app. 445-447-The Creeper app. 446-Flag-c.
449-451-Martian Manhunter app. 450-Weather Wizard app. in Aquaman story.
453-458-Superboy begins. 453-Intro. Mighty Girl. 457,458-Eclipso app.
2 4 6 9 12 14
459,460 (68 pgs.): 459-New Gods/Darkseid storyline concludes from New Gods #19 (#459 is
dated 9-10/78) without missing a month. 459-Flash (ends #466), Deadman (ends #466),
Wonder Woman (ends #464), Green Lantern (ends #460). 460-Aquaman (ends #478)
3 6 9 16 24 32
461-($1.00, 68 pgs.) Justice Society begins; ends 466 4 8 12 27 44 60
462-($1.00, 68 pgs.) Death Earth II Batman 5 10 15 35 63 90
463-466 ($1.00 size, 68 pgs.) 2 4 6 11 16 20
467-Starman by Ditko & Plastic Man begins; 1st app. Prince Gavyn (Starman)
2 4 6 11 16 20
468-490: 470-Origin Starman. 479-Dial 'H' For Hero begins, ends #490. 478-Last Starman &
Plastic Man. 480-490: Dial 'H' For Hero 2 4 6 10 12 14
491-503: 491-100pg. Digest size begins; r/Legion of Super Heroes/Adv. #247, 267; Spectre,
Aquaman, Superboy, S&K Sandman, Black Canary & new Shazam by Newton begin.
492,495,496,499-S&K Sandman-r/Adventure in all. 493-Challengers of the Unknown begins
by Tuska w/brief origin. 493-495,497-499-G.A. Captain Marvel-r. 494-499-Spectre-r/Spectre
1-3, 5-7. 496-Capt. Marvel Jr. new-s, Cockrum-a. 498-Mary Marvel new-s; Plastic Man-r
begin; origin Bouncing Boy-r/ #301. 500-Legion-r (Digest size, 148 pgs.)
2 4 6 10 14 18
501-503: G.A.-r 2 4 6 10 14 18
... 80 Page Giant (10/98, $4.95) Wonder Woman, Shazam, Superboy, Supergirl, Green Arrow,
Legion, Bizarro World stories 2 4 6 8 10 12
...No 260 (Facsimile Edition) (2/24, $3.99) Reprints #260 with original ads 4.00
NOTE: Bizarro covers-285, 286, 288, 294, 295, 329. Vigilante app.-420, 426, 427. N. Adams a(r)-495(-498(: c-365-
369, 371-373, 375-379, 381-383. Aparo a-431-433, 434i, 435, 436, 437i, 438i, 449-452, 503r; c-431-452. Austin
a-449i 451i. Bernard Baily c-48, 50, 52-59. Bolland c-475. Burnley c-61-72, 116-120p. Chaykin a-438. Ditko
a-467-478p; c-467p. Creig Flessel c-32, 33, 40, 42, 44, 46, 47, 51, 60. Giffen c-491p-494p, 500p. Grell a-435-437,
440. Guardineer c-34, 35, 45. Infantino a-416r. Kaluta c-425. Bob Kane a-38. G. Kane a-414r, 425; c-496-499,
537. Kirby a-250-256. Kubert a-81,125,127. Moldoff a-49r. Morrow a-413-415, 417, 425,
502r; 503r. Netzer/Nasser a-449-451. Newton a-459-461, 464-466, 491p, 492p. Paul Norris a-69. Orlando a-457p,
458p. Perez a-484-486, 490p. Simon/Kirby a-503r; c-73-97, 100-102. Starlin c-471. Staton a-445-447i, 456-458p,
459, 460, 461p-465p, 466,467p-478p, 502p(r); c-458, 461(back). Toth a-419, 425, 431, 495p-497p. Tuska
a-494p.

ADVENTURE COMICS (Also see All Star Comics 1999 crossover titles)
DC Comics: May, 1999 ($1.99, one-shot)
1-Golden Age Starman and the Atom; Snejbjerg-a 4.00

ADVENTURE COMICS (See Final Crisis: Legion of Three Worlds)
DC Comics: No. 0, Apr, 2009 - No. 12, Aug, 2010; No. 516, Sept, 2010 - No. 529, Oct, 2011
($1.00/$3.99)
0-($1.00) R/Adventure Comics #247; new Luthor & Braniac back-up-s; Lopresti-c 3.00
1-7-($3.99) Superboy begins; Johns-s/Manapul-a; Legion back-up-s. 5-7-Blackest Night 4.00
1-12-Variant 7-panel covers by various numbered with original #504-#515 5.00
8-12: 8-11-New Krypton x-over. 11-Mon-El leaves 21st century. 12-Legion; Levitz-s 4.00
516-521: 516-9/10, resumes original numbering) flashback to Legion formation; Atom
back-ups. 521-Adult Legion resumes; Mon-El joins Green Lanterns 4.00
522-529-($2.99) Legion Academy. 523-527-Jimenez-a/c 3.00

ADVENTURE COMICS SPECIAL (See New Krypton issues in 2009 Superman titles)
DC Comics: Jan, 2009 ($2.99, one-shot)
... Featuring the Guardian - James Robinson-s/Pere Pèrez-a; origin re-told; intro. Gwen 3.00

ADVENTURE INTO MYSTERY
Atlas Comics (BFP No. 1/OPI No. 2-8): May, 1956 - No. 8, July, 1957
1-Powell s/f-a; Forte-a; Everett-c 97 194 291 621 1061 1500
2-Flying Saucer story 41 82 123 256 428 600
3,6-Everett-c 39 78 117 231 378 525
4,5,7: 4-Williamson-a, 4 pgs; Powell-a. 5-Everett-c/a, Orlando-a. 7-Torres-a;
Everett-c 39 78 117 240 395 550
8-Moreira, Sale, Torres, Woodbridge-a, Severin-a 41 82 123 256 428 600

ADVENTURE IS MY CAREER
U.S. Coast Guard Academy/Street & Smith: 1945 (44 pgs.)
nn-Simon, Milt Gross-a 26 52 78 154 252 350

ADVENTUREMAN
Image Comics: Jun, 2020 - Present ($3.99, limited series)
1-9-Matt Fraction-s/Terry Dodson-a 4.00

	GD 2.0	VG 4.0	FN 6.0	VF 8.0	VF/NM 9.0	NM- 9.2

ADVENTUREMAN GHOST LIGHTS
Image Comics: Jan, 2024 - No. 2, Mar, 2024 ($3.99, limited series)

	GD	VG	FN	VF	VF/NM	NM-
1,2-Matt Fraction-s/Terry Dodson-a						4.00

ADVENTURERS, THE
Aircel Comics/Adventure Publ.: Aug, 1986 - No. 10, 1987 ($1.50, B&W)
V2#1, 1987 - V2#9, 1988; V3#1, Oct, 1989 - V3#6, 1990

	GD	VG	FN	VF	VF/NM	NM-
1-Peter Hsu-a	1	3	4	6	8	10
1-Cover variant, limited ed.	2	4	6	10	14	18
1-2nd print (1986); 1st app. Elf Warrior						3.00
2,3,0 (#4, 12/86)-Origin, 5-10, Book II, reg. & Limited Ed. #1						4.00
Book II, #2,3,0,4-9						3.00
Book III, #1 (10/89, $2.25)-Reg. & limited-c, Book III, #2-6						3.00

ADVENTURES (No. 2 Spectacular... on cover)
St. John Publishing Co.: Nov, 1949 - No. 2, Feb, 1950 (No. 1 ...in Romance on cover)
(Slightly larger size)

	GD	VG	FN	VF	VF/NM	NM-
1(Scarce)-Bolle, Starr-a(2)	43	86	129	271	461	650
2(Scarce)-Slave Girl; China Bombshell app.; Bolle, L. Starr-a	54	108	162	343	574	825

ADVENTURES FOR BOYS
Bailey Enterprises: Dec, 1954

	GD	VG	FN	VF	VF/NM	NM-
nn-Comics, text, & photos	9	18	27	50	65	90

ADVENTURES IN PARADISE (TV)
Dell Publishing Co.: Feb-Apr, 1962

	GD	VG	FN	VF	VF/NM	NM-
Four Color 1301	6	12	18	38	69	100

ADVENTURES IN ROMANCE (See Adventures)

ADVENTURES IN SCIENCE (See Classics Illustrated Special Issue)

ADVENTURES IN THE DC UNIVERSE
DC Comics: Apr, 1997 - No. 19, Oct. 1998 ($1.75/$1.95/$1.99)

	GD	VG	FN	VF	VF/NM	NM-
1-Animated style in all: JLA-c/app						5.00
2-11,13-17,19: 2-Flash app. 3-Wonder Woman. 4-Green Lantern. 6-Aquaman. 7-Shazam Family. 8-Blue Beetle & Booster Gold. 9-Flash. 10-Legion. 11-Green Lantern & Wonder Woman. 13-Impulse & Martian Manhunter. 14-Superboy/Flash race						3.50
12,18-JLA-c/app						3.50
Annual 1(1997, $3.95)-Dr. Fate, Impulse, Rose & Thorn, Superboy, Mister Miracle app.						4.50

ADVENTURES IN THE RIFLE BRIGADE
DC Comics (Vertigo): Oct, 2000 - No. 3, Dec, 2000 ($2.50, limited series)

	GD	VG	FN	VF	VF/NM	NM-
1-3-Ennis-s/Ezquerra-a/Bolland-c						3.00
TPB (2004, $14.95) r/series and Operation Bollock series						15.00

ADVENTURES IN THE RIFLE BRIGADE: OPERATION BOLLOCK
DC Comics (Vertigo): Oct, 2001 - No. 3, Jan, 2002 ($2.50, limited series)

	GD	VG	FN	VF	VF/NM	NM-
1-3-Ennis-s/Ezquerra-a/Fabry-c						3.00

ADVENTURES IN 3-D (With glasses)
Harvey Publications: Nov, 1953 - No. 2, Jan, 1954 (25c)

	GD	VG	FN	VF	VF/NM	NM-
1-Nostrand, Powell-a, 2-Powell-a	14	28	42	80	115	150

ADVENTURES INTO DARKNESS (See Seduction of the Innocent 3-D)
Better-Standard Publications/Visual Editions: No. 5, Aug, 1952- No. 14, 1954

	GD	VG	FN	VF	VF/NM	NM-
5-Katz-c/a-Toth(p)	142	284	426	909	1555	2200
6-Tuska, Katz-a; skeleton cover	181	362	543	1158	1979	2800
7-Classic horror-c; Katz-c/a	258	516	774	1651	2826	4000
8,9-Toth-a(p)	110	220	330	704	1202	1700
10-Jack Katz-a; skeleton cover	77	154	141	296	498	1200
11,12-Classic horror-c: 11-Jack Katz-a. 12-Toth-a; lingerie panel	161	322	483	1030	1765	2500
13-Toth-a(p); Cannibalism story cited by T. E. Murphy articles	258	516	774	1651	2826	4000
14-Skeleton cover	161	322	483	1030	1765	2500

NOTE: Fawcette a-13. Moreira a-5. Sekowsky a-10, 11, 13(2).

ADVENTURES INTO TERROR (Formerly Joker Comics)
Marvel/Atlas Comics (CDS): No. 43, Nov, 1950 - No. 31, May, 1954

	GD	VG	FN	VF	VF/NM	NM-
43(#1)	123	246	369	787	1344	1900
44(#2, 2/51)-Sol Brodsky-c	110	220	330	704	1202	1700
3(4/51), 4	55	110	165	352	601	850
5-Wolverton-c panel/Mystic #6; Rico-c panel also; Atom Bomb story	68	122	192	470	670	950
6,8: 8-Wolverton text illo r-/Marvel Tales #104; prototype of Spider-Man villain The Lizard	53	106	159	334	567	800
7-Wolverton-a "Where Monsters Dwell", 6 pgs.; Tuska-c; Maneely-c panels	81	162	243	518	884	1250
9,10,12-Krigstein-a. 9-Decapitation panels	48	96	144	302	514	725
11,13-20	42	84	126	265	445	625
21-24,26-31	42	84	123	256	428	600
25-Matt Fox-a	47	94	141	296	498	700

NOTE: Ayers a-21. Colan a-3, 5, 14, 21, 24, 25, 28, 29; c-27. Colletta a-30. Everett c-13, 21, 25. Fass a-28, 29. Forte a-28. Heath a-43, 44, 4-6, 22, 24, 26; c-43, 9, 11. Lazarus a-7. Maneely a-7(3 pg.), 10, 11, 21, 22 c-15, 29. Don Rico a-4, 5(3 pg.). Sekowsky a-43, 3, 4. Sinnott a-8, 9, 11, 24, 28. Tuska a-14; c-7.

ADVENTURES INTO THE UNKNOWN
American Comics Group: Fall, 1948 - No. 174, Aug, 1967 (No. 1-33: 52 pgs.)
(1st continuous series Supernatural comic; see Eerie #1)

	GD	VG	FN	VF	VF/NM	NM-
1-Guardineer-a; adapt. of 'Castle of Otranto' by Horace Walpole	595	1190	1785	4350	7675	11,000
2-Skull Island-c	290	580	870	1856	3178	4500
3-Feldstein-a (9 pgs)	142	284	426	909	1555	2200
4,5: 5- 'Spirit Of Frankenstein' series begins, ends #12 (except #11)	74	148	222	470	810	1150
6-10	41	82	123	256	428	600
11-14,16,18-20: 13-Starr-a	37	74	111	218	354	490
15-Hitler app.	42	84	126	265	445	625
17-Story similar to movie 'The Thing'	43	86	129	271	461	650
21-26,28-30	30	60	90	177	289	400
27-Williamson/Krenkel-a (8 pgs.)	58	116	174	371	636	900
31-37,39-50	24	48	72	142	234	325
38-Atom bomb panels; Devil-c	36	72	108	211	343	475
51-(1/54)-(3-D effect-c/story)-Only white cover	71	142	213	454	777	1100
52-58: (3-D effect-c/stories with black covers). 52-E.C. swipe/Haunt Of Fear #14	61	122	183	390	670	950
59-3-D effect story only; new logo	39	78	117	240	395	550
60-Woodesque-a by Landau	19	38	57	112	179	240
61-Last pre-code issue (1-2/55)	19	38	57	112	179	240
62-70	9	18	27	58	114	170
71-90: 80-Hydrogen bomb panel	7	14	21	44	82	120
91,96(#95 on inside),107,116-All have Williamson-a	7	14	21	48	89	130
92-95,97-99,101-106,108-115,117-128: 109-113,118-Whitney painted-c. 128-Williamson/Krenkel/Torres-a(r)/Forbidden Worlds #63; last 10c issue	6	12	18	37	66	95
100	7	14	21	44	82	120
129-153,157: 153,157-Magic Agent app.	4	8	12	28	47	65
154-Nemesis series begins (origin), ends #170	5	10	15	35	63	90
155,156,158-167,170-174: 174-Flying saucer-c	4	8	12	27	44	60
168-Ditko-a(p)	5	10	15	31	53	75
169-Nemesis battles Hitler	5	10	15	33	57	80
Nemesis Archives: Vol. One (Dark Horse Books), 9/08, $59.95) r/#154-170; creator bios						60.00

NOTE: "Spirit of Frankenstein" series in 5, 6, 8-10, 12, 16. Buscema a-100, 106, 108-110, 158r, 165; Cameron a-34. Craig a-152, 160. Goode a-45, 47, 60. Landau a-51, 59-63. Lazarus a-34, 48, 51, 52, 56, 58, 79, 87; c-31-56, 58. Reinman a-102, 111, 112, 115-118, 124, 130, 137, 141, 145, 164. Whitney c-12-30, 57, 59-on (most.) Torres/Williamson a-116.

ADVENTURES INTO WEIRD WORLDS
Marvel/Atlas Comics (ACI): Jan, 1952 - No. 30, June, 1954

	GD	VG	FN	VF	VF/NM	NM-
1-Atom bomb panels	148	296	444	947	1624	2300
2-Sci/fic stories (2); one by Maneely	57	114	171	362	619	875
3-10: Tongue ripped out. 10-Krigstein, Everett-a	50	100	150	315	533	750
11-20	43	86	129	271	461	650
21-Hitler in Hell story	58	116	174	371	636	900
22-26: 24-Man holds hypo & splits in two-c	42	84	126	265	445	625
27-Matt Fox end of world story; severed head-c	74	148	222	470	810	1150
28-Atom bomb story; decapitation panels	50	100	150	315	533	750
29,30	43	86	129	271	461	650

NOTE: Ayers a-8, 26. Everett a-4, 5; c-6, 8, 10-13, 18, 19, 22, 24, 25; a-4, 25. Fass a-7. Forte a-21, 24. Al Hartley a-2. Heath a-1, 4, 17, 22; c-7, 9, 20. Maneely a-2, 3, 11, 20, 22. Reinman a-24, 28. Rico a-13. Robinson a-23. Sinnott a-25, 30. Tuska a-1, 2, 12, 15. Whitney a-7. Wildey a-28. Bondage c-22.

ADVENTURES IN WONDERLAND (Also see Uncle Charlies Fables)
Lev Gleason Publications: April, 1955 - No. 5, Feb, 1956 (Jr. Readers Guild)

	GD	VG	FN	VF	VF/NM	NM-
1-Maurer-a	15	30	45	84	127	170
2-4	9	18	27	50	65	80
5-Christmas issue	9	18	27	52	69	85

ADVENTURES OF ALAN LADD, THE
National Periodical Publ.: Oct-Nov, 1949 - No. 9, Feb-Mar, 1951 (All 52 pgs.)

	GD	VG	FN	VF	VF/NM	NM-
1-Photo-c	90	180	270	576	988	1400
2-Photo-c	41	82	123	256	428	600
3-6: Last photo-c	36	72	108	211	343	475
7-9	30	60	90	177	289	400

NOTE: Dan Barry a-1. Moreira a-3-7.

ADVENTURES OF ALICE (Also see Alice in Wonderland) (Becomes Alice at Monkey Island #3)
Civil Service Publ./Pentagon Publishing Co.: 1945

	GD	VG	FN	VF	VF/NM	NM-
1	19	38	57	111	176	240
2-Through the Magic Looking Glass	15	30	45	84	127	170

ADVENTURES OF BARON MUNCHAUSEN, THE
Now Comics: July, 1989 - No. 4, Oct, 1989 ($1.75, limited series)

	GD	VG	FN	VF	VF/NM	NM-
1-4: Movie adaptation						5.00

ADVENTURES OF BARRY WEEN, BOY GENIUS, THE
Image Comics: Mar, 1999 - No. 3, May, 1999 ($2.95, B&W, limited series)

	GD	VG	FN	VF	VF/NM	NM-
1-3-Judd Winick-s/a						3.00
...: Secret Origin Files (Oni, 7/04, Free Comic Book Day giveaway) - Winick-s/a						3.00
TPB (Oni Press, 11/99, $8.95) r/#1-3						9.00

ADVENTURES OF BARRY WEEN, BOY GENIUS 2.0, THE
Oni Press: Feb, 2000 - No. 3, Apr, 2000 ($2.95, B&W)

	GD	VG	FN	VF	VF/NM	NM-
1-3-Judd Winick-s/a						3.00
TPB (2000, $8.95)						9.00

ADVENTURES OF BARRY WEEN, BOY GENIUS 3, THE : MONKEY TALES
Oni Press: Feb, 2001 - No. 6, Feb, 2002 ($2.95, B&W, limited series)

	GD	VG	FN	VF	VF/NM	NM-
1-6-Judd Winick-s/a						3.00
TPB (2001, $8.95) r/#1-3; intro. by Peter David						9.00
...4 TPB (5/02, $8.95) r/#4-6						9.00

ADVENTURES OF BAYOU BILLY, THE (Based on video game)
Archie Comics: Sept, 1989 - No. 5, June, 1990 ($1.00)

	GD	VG	FN	VF	VF/NM	NM-
1-5: Esposito-c/a(i). 5-Kelley Jones-c						4.00

ADVENTURES OF BOB HOPE, THE (Also see True Comics #59)
National Per. Publ.: Feb-Mar, 1950 - No. 109, Feb-Mar, 1968 (#1-10: 52pgs.)

	GD	VG	FN	VF	VF/NM	NM-
1-Photo-c	258	516	774	1651	2826	4000
2-Photo-c	92	184	276	584	1005	1425
3,4-Photo-c	57	114	171	362	619	875
5-10: 9-Horror-c	41	82	123	256	428	600
11-20	29	58	87	170	278	385
21-31 (2-3/55; last precode)	20	40	60	117	189	260
32-40	9	18	27	61	123	185
41-50	8	16	24	54	102	150
51-70	7	14	21	46	86	125
71-93	5	10	15	35	63	90
94-Aquaman cameo	6	12	18	42	79	115
95-1st app. Super-Hip & 1st monster issue (11/65)	9	18	27	60	120	180
96-105: Super-Hip and monster stories in all. 103-Batman, Robin, Ringo Starr cameos						

Adventures into Terror #14 © MAR

Adventures into Weird Worlds #16 © MAR

Adventures of Mighty Mouse #12 © STJ

	GD 2.0	VG 4.0	FN 6.0	VF 8.0	VF/NM 9.0	NM- 9.2
	6	12	18	38	69	100
106-109-All monster-c/stories by N. Adams-c/a	8	16	24	55	105	155

NOTE: Buzzy in #34. Kitty Karr of Hollywood in #15, 17-20, 23, 28. Liz in #26, 109. Miss Beverly Hills of Hollywood in #7, 8, 10, 13, 14. Miss Melody Lane of Broadway in #15. Rusty in #23, 25. Tommy in #24. No 2nd feature in #2-4, 6, 8, 11, 12, 28-108.

ADVENTURES OF CAPTAIN AMERICA
Marvel Comics: Sept, 1991 - No. 4, Jan, 1992 ($4.95, 52 pgs., squarebound, limited series)

1-4: 1-Origin in WW2; embossed-c; Nicieza scripts; Maguire-c/a(p) begins, ends #3.						
2-4-Austin-a(i). 3,4-Red Skull app.						5.00

ADVENTURES OF CYCLOPS AND PHOENIX (Also See Askani'son & The Further Adventures of Cyclops And Phoenix)
Marvel Comics: May, 1994 - No. 4, Aug, 1994 ($2.95, limited series)

1-4-Characters from X-Men; origin of Cable						4.00
Trade paperback ($14.95)-reprints #1-4						15.00

ADVENTURES OF DEAN MARTIN AND JERRY LEWIS, THE
(The Adventures of Jerry Lewis #41 on) (See Movie Love #12)
National Periodical Publications: July-Aug, 1952 - No. 40, Oct, 1957

1	200	400	600	1280	2190	3100
2-Three pg. origin on how they became a team	60	120	180	381	653	925
3-10: 3- I Love Lucy text featurette	36	72	108	211	343	475
11-19: Last precode (2/55)	22	44	66	132	216	300
20-30	17	34	51	98	154	210
31-40	15	30	45	83	124	165

ADVENTURES OF DETECTIVE ACE KING, THE (Also see Bob Scully-- & Detective Dan)
Humor Publ. Corp.: No date (1933) (36 pgs., 9-1/2x12") (10¢, B&W, one-shot) (paper-c)

Book 1-Along with Bob Scully & Detective Dan, the first comic w/original art & the first of a single theme.; Not reprints; Ace King by Martin Nadle (The American Sherlock Holmes). A Dick Tracy look-alike	825	1650	2475	6600	-	-

ADVENTURES OF EVIL AND MALICE, THE
Image Comics: June, 1999 - No. 3, Nov, 1999 ($3.50/$3.95, limited series)

1-3-Jimmie Robinson-s/a. 3-($3.95-c)						4.00

ADVENTURES OF FELIX THE CAT, THE
Harvey Comics: May, 1992 ($1.25)

1-Messmer-r						6.00

ADVENTURES OF FORD FAIRLANE, THE
DC Comics: May, 1990 - No. 4, Aug, 1990 ($1.50, limited series, mature)

1-4: Andrew Dice Clay movie tie-in; Don Heck inks						4.00

ADVENTURES OF HOMER COBB, THE
Say/Bart Prod. : Sept, 1947 (Oversized) (Published in the U.S., but printed in Canada)

1-(Scarce)-Feldstein-c/a	58	116	174	371	636	900

ADVENTURES OF HOMER GHOST (See Homer The Happy Ghost)
Atlas Comics: June, 1957 - No. 2, Aug, 1957

V1#1,2: 2-Robot-c	21	42	63	122	199	275

ADVENTURES OF JERRY LEWIS, THE (Adventures of Dean Martin & Jerry Lewis No. 1-40) (See Super DC Giant)
National Periodical Publ.: No. 41, Nov, 1957 - No. 124, May-June, 1971

41	9	18	27	62	126	190
42-60	7	14	21	49	92	135
61-67,69-73,75-80	6	12	18	41	76	110
68,74-Photo-c (movie)	9	18	27	60	120	180
81,82,85-87,90,91,94,96,98,99	5	10	15	34	60	85
83,84,88: 83-1st Monsters-c/s. 84-Jerry as a Super-hero-c/s. 88-1st Witch, Miss Kraft	6	12	18	42	79	115
89-Bob Hope app.; Wizard of Oz & Alfred E. Neuman in MAD parody	8	16	24	56	108	160
92-Superman cameo	8	16	24	56	108	160
93-Beatles parody as babies	7	14	21	44	82	120
95-1st Uncle Hal Wack-A-Boy Camp-c/s	8	16	24	41	76	110
97-Batman/Robin/Joker-c/story; Riddler & Penguin app; Dick Sprang-c.	10	20	30	67	141	210
100	6	12	18	42	79	115
101,103,104-Neal Adams-c/a	8	16	24	54	102	150
102-Beatles app.; Neal Adams-c/a	9	18	27	61	123	185
105-Superman x-over	7	14	21	44	82	120
106-111,113-116	4	8	12	28	47	65
112,117: 112-Flash x-over. 117-W. Woman x-over	7	14	21	44	82	120
118-124	4	8	12	27	44	60

NOTE: Monster-c/s-90,93,96,98,101. Wack-A-Buy Camp-c/s-96,99,102,107,108.

ADVENTURES OF JO-JOY, THE (See Jo-Joy)

	GD 2.0	VG 4.0	FN 6.0	VF 8.0	VF/NM 9.0	NM- 9.2

ADVENTURES OF LASSIE, THE (See Lassie)

ADVENTURES OF LUTHER ARKWRIGHT, THE
Valkyrie Press/Dark Horse Comics: Oct, 1987 - No. 9, Jan, 1989 ($2.00, B&W) V2, #1, Mar, 1990 - V2#9, 1990 ($1.95, B&W)

1-Alan Moore intro.	1	2	3	5	6	8
2-9, V2#1-9 (Dark Horse): r-1st series; new-c						4.00
TPB (1997, $14.95) r/#1-9 w/Michael Moorcock intro.						15.00

ADVENTURES OF MIGHTY MOUSE (Mighty Mouse Adventures No. 1)
St. John Publishing Co.: No. 2, Jan, 1952 - No. 18, May, 1955

2	33	66	99	194	317	440
3-5	18	36	54	103	162	220
6-18	14	28	42	80	115	150

ADVENTURES OF MIGHTY MOUSE (2nd Series) (Becomes Mighty Mouse #161 on)
(Two No. 144's; formerly Paul Terry's Comics; No. 129-137 have nn's)
St. John/Pines/Dell/Gold Key: No. 126, Aug, 1955 - No. 160, Oct, 1963

126(8/55), 127(10/55), 128(11/55)-St. John	10	20	30	56	76	95
nn(129, 4/56)-144(8/59)-Pines	5	10	15	30	50	70
144(10-12/59)-155(7-9/62) Dell	4	8	12	27	44	60
156(10/62)-160(10/63) Gold Key	4	8	12	27	44	60

NOTE: Early issues titled "Paul Terry's Adventures of ...."

ADVENTURES OF MIGHTY MOUSE (Formerly Mighty Mouse)
Gold Key: No. 166, Mar, 1979 - No. 172, Jan, 1980

166-172	1	3	4	6	8	10

ADVS. OF MR. FROG & MISS MOUSE (See Dell Junior Treasury No. 4)

ADVENTURES OF OZZIE & HARRIET, THE (See Ozzie & Harriet)

ADVENTURES OF PATORUZU
Green Publishing Co.: Aug, 1946 - Winter, 1946

nn's-Contains Animal Crackers reprints	9	18	27	47	61	75

ADVENTURES OF PINKY LEE, THE (TV)
Atlas Comics: July, 1955 - No. 5, Dec, 1955

1	32	64	96	188	307	425
2-5	20	40	60	114	182	250

ADVENTURES OF PIPSQUEAK, THE (Formerly Pat the Brat)
Archie Publications (Radio Comics): No. 34, Sept, 1959 - No. 39, July, 1960

34	4	8	12	28	47	65
35-39	4	8	12	23	37	50

ADVENTURES OF QUAKE & QUISP, THE (See Quaker Oats "Plenty of Glutton")

ADVENTURES OF REX THE WONDER DOG, THE (Rex...No. 1)
National Periodical Publ.: Jan-Feb, 1952 - No. 45, May-June, 1959; No. 46, Nov-Dec, 1959

1-(Scarce)-Toth-c/a	300	600	900	2010	3505	5000
2-(Scarce)-Toth-c/a	97	194	291	621	1061	1500
3-(Scarce)-Toth-a	71	142	213	454	777	1100
4,5	54	108	162	343	574	825
6-10	45	90	135	284	480	675
11-Atom bomb-c/story; dinosaur-c/sty	55	110	165	352	601	850
12-19: 19-Last precode (1-2/55)	36	72	108	211	343	475
20-46	25	50	75	150	245	340

NOTE: Infantino, Gil Kane art in 5-19 (most)

ADVENTURES OF ROBIN HOOD, THE (Formerly Robin Hood)
Magazine Enterprises (Sussex Publ. Co.): No. 6, Jun, 1957 - No. 8, Nov, 1957 (Based on Richard Greene TV Show)

6-8-Richard Greene photo-c. 6,7-Powell-a	15	30	45	88	137	185

ADVENTURES OF ROBIN HOOD, THE
Gold Key: Mar, 1974 - No. 7, Jan, 1975 (Disney cartoon) (36 pgs.)

1(90291-403)-Part-r of $1.50 editions	3	6	9	16	23	30
2-7: 1-7 are part-r	2	4	6	10	14	18

ADVENTURES OF SNAKE PLISSKEN
Marvel Comics: Jan, 2997 ($2.50, one-shot)

1-Based on Escape From L.A. movie; Brereton-c	2	4	6	11	16	20

ADVENTURES OF SPAWN, THE
Image Comics (Todd McFarlane Prods.): Jan, 2007; Nov, 2008 ($5.99)

1,2-Printed adaptation of the Spawn.com web comic; Khary Randolph-a	2	4	6	11	16	20

ADVENTURES OF SPIDER-MAN, THE (Based on animated TV series)
Marvel Comics: Apr, 1996 - No. 12, Mar, 1997 (99¢)

	GD 2.0	VG 4.0	FN 6.0	VF 8.0	VF/NM 9.0	NM- 9.2

1-Punisher app. — 2 4 6 8 10 12
2-12: 2-Venom cameo. 3-X-Men. 6-Fantastic Four — 4.00

ADVENTURES OF SUPERBOY, THE (See Superboy, 2nd Series)

ADVENTURES OF SUPERGIRL (Based on the TV series)
DC Comics: Early Jul, 2016 - No. 6, Sept, 2016 ($2.99)(Printing of stories first appearing online)

1-Rampage app.; Bengal-a/Staggs-c — 1 3 4 6 8 10
2-6 — 5.00

ADVENTURES OF SUPERMAN (Formerly Superman)
DC Comics: No. 424, Jan, 1987 - No. 499, Feb, 1993; No. 500, Early June, 1993 - No. 649, Apr, 2006 (This title's numbering continues with Superman #650, May, 2006)

424-Ordway-c/a; Wolfman-s begin following Byrne's Superman revamp; 1st Cat Grant — 2 4 6 8 10 12
425-435,437-462: 426-Legends x-over. 432-1st app. Jose Delgado who becomes Gangbuster in #434. 437-Millennium x-over. 438-New Brainiac app 440-Batman app. 449-Invasion — 4.00
436-Byrne scripts begin; Millennium x-over — 5.00
463-Superman/Flash race; cover swipe/Superman #199 — 2 4 6 8 11 14
464-Lobo-c & app. (pre-dates Lobo #1) — 1 3 4 6 8 10
465-1st app. Hank Henshaw (later becomes Cyborg Superman) — 2 4 6 8 11 14
466-479,481-495: 467-Part 2 of Batman story. 473-Hal Jordan, Guy Gardner x-over. — 4.00
477-Legion app. 491-Last $1.00-c. 495-Forever People-c/story; Darkseid app. — 4.00
480,496,497: 480-($1.75, 52 pgs.). 496-Doomsday cameo. 497-Doomsday battle issue — 4.00
496,497-2nd printings — 4.00
498,499-Funeral for a Friend; Supergirl app. — 5.00
498-2nd & 3rd printings — 3.00
500-($2.95, 68 pgs.)-Collector's edition w/card — 2 4 6 8 10 12
500-($2.50, 68 pgs.)-Regular edition w/different-c — 6.00
500-Platinum edition — 85.00
501-($1.95)-Collector's edition with die-cut-c — 5.00
501-($1.50)-Regular edition w/mini-poster & diff.-c — 4.00
502-516: 502-Supergirl-c/story. 508-Challengers of the Unknown app. 510-Bizarro-c/story. — 3.00
516-(9/94)-Zero Hour tie-in w/page #0 for next issue — 5.00
505-($2.50)-Holo-grafx foil-c edition — 5.00
517-523: 517-(11/94) — 4.00
524-549,551-580: 524-Begin $1.95-c. 527-Return of Alpha Centurion (Zero Hour). 533-Impulse-c/app. 535-Luthor-c/app. 536-Brainiac app. 537-Parasite app. 540-Final Night x-over. 541-Superboy-c/app.; Lois & Clark honeymoon. 545-New powers. 546-New costume. 555-Red & Blue Supermen battle. 557-Millennium Giants x-over. 558-560: Superman Silver Age-style story; Krypto app. 561-Begin $1.99-c. 565-JLA app. — 3.00
550-($3.50)-Double sized — 4.00
581-588: 581-Begin $2.25-c. 583-Emperor Joker. 588-Casey-s — 3.00
589-595: 589-Return to Krypton; Rivoche-c. 591-Wolfman-s. 593-595-Our Worlds at War x-over. 593-New Suicide Squad formed. 594-Doomsday-c/app. — 3.00
596-Aftermath of "War" x-over has panel showing damaged World Trade Center buildings; issue went on sale the day after the Sept. 11 attack — 6.00
597-599,601-624: 597-Joker: Last Laugh. 604,605-Ultraman, Owlman, Superwoman app. 606-Return to Krypton. 612-616,619-623-Nowlan-c. 624-Mr. Majestic app. — 3.00
600-($3.95) Wieringo-a; painted-c by Adel; pin-ups by various — 4.00
625,626-Godfall parts 2,5; Turner-c; Caldwell-a(p) — 4.00
627-641,643-648: 627-Begin $2.50-c, Rucka-s/Clark-a/Ha-c begin. 628-Wagner-c. 631-Bagged with Super Captain CD; Lois shot. 634-Mxyzptlk visits DC offices. 639-Capt. Marvel & Eclipso app. 641-OMAC app. 643-Sacrifice aftermath; Batman & Wonder Woman app. — 3.00
642-OMAC Project x-over Sacrifice pt. 3; JLA app. — 5.00
642-(2nd printing) red tone cover — 3.00
649-Last issue; Infinite Crisis x-over, Superman vs. Earth-2 Superman — 4.00
#0-(10/94) Zero Hour tie-in; released between #516 & #517 — 3.00
#1,000,000 (11/98) Gene Ha-c; 853rd Century x-over — 5.00
Annual 1 (1987, $1.25, 52 pgs.)-Starlin-c & scripts — 4.00
Annual 2,3 (1990, 1991, $2.00, 68 pgs.): 2-Byrne-a/(a)(i); Legion '90 (Lobo) app. —
3-Armageddon 2001 x-over — 5.00
Annual 4-6 ('92-'94, $2.50, 68 pgs.): 4-Guy Gardner/Lobo-c/story; Eclipso storyline; Quesada-c(p). 5-Bloodlines storyline. 6-Elseworlds sty. — 4.00
Annual 7,9('95, '97, $3.95)-7-Year One story. 9-Pulp Heroes sty — 4.00
Annual 8 (1996, $2.95)-Legends of the Dead Earth story — 4.00
NOTE: *Erik Larsen a-431.*

ADVENTURES OF SUPERMAN
DC Comics: Jul, 2013 - No. 17, Nov, 2014 ($3.99)

1-17-Short story anthology by various. 1-Lemire-s/a. 4-Timm-c. 6-Mongul app. 14-Joker app.; Sugar & Spike app.; Hester-a — 4.00

ADVENTURES OF SUPERMAN: JON KENT (Follows Superman: Son of Kal-El series)
DC Comics: May, 2023 - No. 6, Oct, 2023 ($3.99)

1-6: 1-Taylor-s/Henry-a; Val-Zod and Ultraman app. 2-6-Injustice Superman app. — 4.00

ADVENTURES OF THE DOVER BOYS
Archie Comics (Close-up): September, 1950 - No. 2, 1950 (No month given)

1,2 — 14 28 42 76 108 140

ADVENTURES OF THE FLY (The Fly #1-6; Fly Man No. 32-39; See The Double Life of Private Strong, The Fly, Laugh Comics & Mighty Crusaders)
Archie Publications/Radio Comics: Aug, 1959 - No. 30, Oct, 1964; No. 31, May, 1965

1-Shield app.; origin The Fly; S&K-c/a — 61 122 183 488 1094 1700
2-Williamson, S&K-a — 30 60 90 216 483 750
3-Origin retold; Davis, Powell-a — 28 56 84 202 451 700
4-Neal Adams-a(p)(1 panel); S&K-c; Powell-a; 2 pg. Shield story — 42 84 126 311 706 1100
5,6,9,10: 10-Black Hood app. — 13 26 39 86 188 290
7,8: 7-1st S.A. app. Black Hood (7/60). 8-1st S.A. app. Shield (9/60) — 18 36 54 124 275 425
9-1st app. Cat Girl; Shield app. — 15 30 45 103 227 350
11-13,15-20: 13-1st app. Fly Girl w/o costume. 16-Last 10¢ issue. 20-Origin Fly Girl retold — 9 18 27 58 114 170
14-Origin & 1st app. Fly Girl in costume — 10 20 30 64 132 200
21-30: 23-Jaguar cameo. 27-29-Black Hood 1 pg. strips. 30-Comet x-over (1st S.A. app.) in Fly Girl — 7 14 21 48 89 130

31-Black Hood, Shield, Comet app. — 7 14 21 49 92 135
Vol. 1 TPB ('04, $12.95) r/#1-4 & Double Life of Private Strong #1,2; foreward by Joe Simon — 13.00
NOTE: *Simon c-2-4. Tuska a-1. Cover title to #31 is Flyman; Advs. of the Fly inside.*

ADVENTURES OF THE JAGUAR, THE (See Blue Ribbon Comics, Laugh Comics & Mighty Crusaders)
Archie Publications (Radio Comics): Sept, 1961 - No. 15, Nov, 1963

1-Origin Jaguar (1st app?) by J. Rosenberger — 27 54 81 189 420 650
2,3: 3-Last 10¢ issue — 12 24 36 81 176 270
4-6-Catgirl app. (#4's-c is same as splash pg.) — 9 18 27 59 117 175
7-Catgirl app. — 7 14 21 49 92 135
8-10 — 6 12 18 42 79 115
11-15: 13,14-Catgirl, Black Hood app. in both — 6 12 18 42 79 115

ADVENTURES OF THE MASK (TV cartoon)
Dark Horse Comics: Jan, 1996 - No. 12, Dec, 1996 ($2.50)

1-Based on animated series — 2 4 6 9 12 15
2 — 1 2 3 5 6 8
3-12 — 5.00

ADVENTURES OF THE NEW MEN (Formerly Newmen #1-21)
Maximum Press: No. 22, Nov, 1996; No. 23, March, 1997 ($2.50)

22,23-Sprouse-c/a — 3.00

ADVENTURES OF THE OUTSIDERS, THE (Formerly Batman & The Outsiders; also see The Outsiders)
DC Comics: No. 33, May, 1986 - No. 46, June, 1987

33-46: 39-45-r/Outsiders #1-7 by Aparo — 4.00

ADVENTURES OF THE SUPER MARIO BROTHERS (See Super Mario Bros.)
Valiant: Feb, 1991 - No. 9, Oct, 1991 ($1.50)

V2#1 — 9 18 27 59 117 175
2-9 — 3 6 9 14 19 24

ADVENTURES OF THE SUPER SONS (Jon Kent and Damian Wayne)
DC Comics: Oct, 2018 - No. 12, Sept, 2019 ($3.99)

1-12: 1-Intro Rex Luthor and Joker Jr.; Tomasi-s/Barberi-a. 6-Tommy Tomorrow app. — 4.00

ADVENTURES OF THE THING, THE (Also see The Thing)
Marvel Comics: Apr, 1992 - No. 4, July, 1992, ($1.25, limited series)

1-4: 1-r/Marvel Two-In-One #50 by Byrne; Kieth-c. 2-4-r/Marvel Two-In-One #80,51 & 77; 2-Ghost Rider-c/story; Quesada-a. 3-Miller-r/Quesada-c; new Perez-a (4 pgs.) — 4.00

ADVENTURES OF THE X-MEN, THE (Based on animated TV series)
Marvel Comics: Apr, 1996 - No. 12, Mar, 1997 (99¢)

1-Wolverine/Hulk battle — 2 4 6 8 10 12
2-12: 3-Spider-Man-c. 5,6-Magneto-c/app. — 4.00

ADVENTURES OF TINKER BELL (See Tinker Bell, 4-Color No. 896 & 982)

ADVENTURES OF TOM SAWYER (See Dell Junior Treasury No. 10)

ADVENTURES OF YOUNG DR. MASTERS, THE
Archie Comics (Radio Comics): Aug, 1964 - No. 2, Nov, 1964

1 — 4 8 12 28 47 65
2 — 3 6 9 17 26 35

ADVENTURES ON OTHER WORLDS (See Showcase #17 & 18)

ADVENTURES ON THE PLANET OF THE APES (Also see Planet of the Apes)
Marvel Comics Group: Oct, 1975 - No. 11, Dec, 1976

1-Planet of the Apes magazine-r in color; Starlin-c; adapts movie thru #6 — 6 12 18 42 79 115
2-5: 5-(25¢-c edition) — 3 6 9 19 30 40
5-7-(30¢-c variants, limited distribution) — 7 14 21 44 82 120
6-10: 6,7-(25¢-c edition). 7-Adapts 2nd movie (thru #11) — 3 6 9 16 23 30
11-Last issue; concludes 2nd movie adaptation — 4 8 12 23 37 50
NOTE: *Alcala a-6-11r. Buckler c-2p. Nasser c-7. Ploog a-1-9. Starlin c-6. Tuska a-1-5r.*

ADVENTURES WITH THE DC SUPER HEROES (Interior also inserted into some DC issues)
DC Comics/Geppi's Entertainment Museum: 2007 Free Comic Book Day giveaway

"The Batman and Cal Ripken, Jr. Hall of Fame Edition "A Rare Catch" " in indicia — 1 3 4 6 8 10

ADVENTURE TIME (With Finn & Jake) (Based on the Cartoon Network animated series)
Boom Entertainment (KaBOOM!): Feb, 2012 - No. 75, Apr, 2018 ($3.99)

1-Cover A — 36.00
1-Covers B & C; interlocking image — 30.00
1-Cover D variant by Jeffrey Brown — 35.00
1-Cover E wraparound — 50.00
1-Second & third printings — 5.00
2-Four covers — 15.00
3-24,26-49,51-74-Multiple covers on all — 4.00
25-($4.99) Art by Dustin Nguyen, Jess Fink, Jeffrey Brown & others; multiple covers — 8.00
50-($4.99) Hastings-s/McGinty-a; multiple covers — 5.00
75-($4.99) Last issue; multiple covers — 5.00
2013 Annual #1 (5/13, $4.99) Three covers; s/a by Langridge, Nguyen & others — 5.00
2013 Spoooktacular (10/13, $4.99) Halloween-themed; s/a by Fraser Irving & others — 8.00
2013 Summer Special (7/13, $4.99) Multiple covers — 5.00
2014 Annual #1 (4/14, $4.99) Three covers; stories printed sideways — 8.00
2014 Winter Special (1/14, $4.99) Multiple covers — 8.00
2015 Spoooktacular (10/15, $4.99) a Marceline story; s/a by Hanna K — 8.00
2016 Spoooktacular (9/16, $4.99) Short stories by various; 2 covers by Bartel & McClaren — 8.00
2017 Spoooktacular (10/17, $4.99) Short stories by various; 2 covers — 8.00
... BMO Bonanza 1 (3/18, $7.99) Short stories by various — 15.00
... Cover Showcase (12/12, $3.99) Gallery of variant covers for #1-9; Paul Pope-c — 4.00
... Free Comic Book Day Edition (5/12) Giveaway flip book with Peanuts — 5.00
... with Fionna and Cake 2018 Free Comic Book Day Special (5/18) Giveaway — 4.00

ADVENTURE TIME: BANANA GUARD ACADEMY (Cartoon Network)
Boom Entertainment (KaBOOM!): Jul, 2014 - No. 6, Dec, 2014 ($3.99, limited series)

1-6-Multiple covers on all; Mad Rupert-a — 4.00

Adventures of Superman (2013 series) #4 © DC

Adventure Time #36 © CN

Agents of Atlas (2009 series) #1 © MAR

	GD 2.0	VG 4.0	FN 6.0	VF 8.0	VF/NM 9.0	NM- 9.2

ADVENTURE TIME: BEGINNING OF THE END (Cartoon Network)
Boom Entertainment (KaBOOM!): May, 2018 - No. 3, Jul, 2018 ($3.99, limited series)

1-3-Multiple covers on all; Ted Anderson-s/Marina Julia-a						4.00

ADVENTURE TIME: CANDY CAPERS (Cartoon Network)
Boom Entertainment (KaBOOM!): Jul, 2013 - No. 6, Dec, 2013 ($3.99, limited series)

1-6-Multiple covers on all; McGinty-a						4.00

ADVENTURE TIME COMICS (Cartoon Network)
Boom Entertainment (KaBOOM!): Jul, 2016 - No. 25, Jul, 2018 ($3.99)

1-24-Short stories by various. 1-Baltazar, Cook, Millionaire, Leyh-s/a						4.00
25-($4.99) Sonny Liew-s/a; Morgan Beem-s/a						5.00

ADVENTURE TIME: ICE KING (Cartoon Network)
Boom Entertainment (KaBOOM!): Jan, 2016 - No. 6, Jun, 2016 ($3.99, limited series)

1-6-Multiple covers on all; Naujokaitis-s/Andrewson-a						4.00

ADVENTURE TIME: MARCELINE AND THE SCREAM QUEENS (Cartoon Network)
Boom Entertainment (KaBOOM!): Jul, 2012 - No. 6, Dec, 2012 ($3.99, limited series)

	GD	VG	FN	VF	VF/NM	NM-
1-Multiple covers on all	1	3	4	6	8	10
2-6						4.00

ADVENTURE TIME: MARCELINE GONE ADRIFT (Cartoon Network)
Boom Entertainment (KaBOOM!): Jan, 2015 - No. 6, Jun, 2015 ($3.99, limited series)

1-6-Multiple covers on all; Meredith Gran-s/Carey Pietsch-a						4.00

ADVENTURE TIME: MARCY & SIMON (Cartoon Network)
Boom Entertainment (KaBOOM!): Jan, 2019 - No. 6, Jun, 2019 ($3.99, limited series)

1-6-Multiple covers on all; Olivia Olson-s/Slimm Fabert; former Ice King apology tour						4.00

ADVENTURE TIME/ REGULAR SHOW (Cartoon Network)
Boom Entertainment (KaBOOM!): Aug, 2017 - No. 6, Jan, 2018 ($3.99, limited series)

1-6-McCreery-s/Di Meo-a; multiple covers on each						4.00

ADVENTURE TIME: SEASON 11 (Cartoon Network)
Boom Entertainment (KaBOOM!): Oct, 2018 - No. 6, Mar, 2019 ($3.99)

1-6-Follows the television finale; Ted Anderson-s/Marina Julia-a						4.00

ADVENTURE TIME: THE FLIP SIDE (Cartoon Network)
Boom Entertainment (KaBOOM!): Jan, 2014 - No. 6, Jun, 2014 ($3.99, limited series)

1-6-Multiple covers on all; Tobin & Coover-s; Wook Jin Clark-a						4.00

ADVENTURE TIME WITH FIONNA & CAKE (Cartoon Network)
Boom Entertainment (KaBOOM!): Jan, 2013 - No. 6, Jun, 2013 ($3.99, limited series)

1-6-Multiple covers on all						4.00

ADVENTURE TIME WITH FIONNA & CAKE CARD WARS (Cartoon Network)
Boom Entertainment (KaBOOM!): Jul, 2015 - No. 6, Dec, 2015 ($3.99, limited series)

1-6-Multiple covers on all; Jen Wang-s/Britt Wilson-a. 1-Polybagged with a game card						4.00

AEON FLUX (Based on the 2005 movie which was based on the MTV animated series)
Dark Horse Comics: Oct, 2005 - No. 4, Jan, 2006 ($2.99, limited series)

	GD	VG	FN	VF	VF/NM	NM-
1-Timothy Green II-a/Mike Kennedy-s	2	4	6	9	12	15
2-4						4.00
TPB (5/06, $12.95) r/series; cover gallery						16.00

AERO (See War of the Realms: New Agents of Atlas #4)
Marvel Comics: Sept, 2019 - No. 12, Dec, 2020 ($3.99)

1-Liefen-s/Kang-a; Shanghai-based heroine; origin back-up by Pak-s/Mhan-a						6.00
2-10						4.00

A-FORCE (Secret Wars tie-in)
Marvel Comics: Jul, 2015 - No. 5, Dec, 2015 ($3.99, limited series)

	GD	VG	FN	VF	VF/NM	NM-
1-All-Female Avengers team; Bennett & Willow Wilson-s/Molina-a; intro. Singularity						
	2	4	6	9	12	15
2-5						4.00

A-FORCE (Follows Secret Wars)
Marvel Comics: Mar, 2016 - No. 10, Dec, 2016 ($3.99)

1-10: 1-Medusa, She-Hulk, Dazzler, Nico, Capt. Marvel, Singularity team; Wilson-s/Molina-a. 5-7-Thompson-s/Caldwell-a. 8-10-Civil War II tie-in						4.00

AFRICA
Magazine Enterprises: 1955

	GD	VG	FN	VF	VF/NM	NM-
1(A-1 #137)-Cave Girl, Thun'da; Powell-c/a(4)	41	82	123	256	428	600

AFRICAN LION (Disney movie)
Dell Publishing Co.: Nov, 1955

	GD	VG	FN	VF	VF/NM	NM-
Four Color 665	5	10	15	35	63	90

AFTER DARK

Sterling Comics: No. 6, May, 1955 - No. 8, Sept, 1955

	GD	VG	FN	VF	VF/NM	NM-
6-8-Sekowsky-a in all	14	28	42	76	108	140

AFTER DARK (Co-created by Wesley Snipes)
Radical Comics: No. 0, Jun, 2010 - No. 3 ($1.00/$4.99, limited series)

0-($1.00) Milligan-s/Nentrup & Mattina-a						3.00
1-3-($4.99) Milligan-s/Manco-a						5.00

AFTERDARK
AfterShock Comics: Oct, 2021 ($6.99, oversized 8-1/2" x 10-7/8", one shot)

1-Horror anthology by various incl. Starlin, Bunn, Kudranski, Tieri, Pruett, Eisma						7.00

AFTERLIFE WITH ARCHIE
Archie Comic Publications: Sept, 2013 - Present ($2.99/$3.99)

1-Aguirre-Sacasa-s/Francavilla-a; zombies in Riverdale; Sabrina app.; 4 covers						28.00
1-Second printing; new cover by Francavilla						6.00
2-Covers by Francavilla & Seeley; back-up short story r/Chilling Advs. in Sorcery						14.00
3-6: 3,4-Covers by Francavilla & Seeley on each; back-up r/Chilling Advs. in Sorcery.						
5,6-Pepoy variant-c. 6-Back-up preview of Chilling Advs. of Sabrina #1						8.00
7-10-($3.99) 7-Covers by Francavilla & Pepoy; back-up r/Chilling Advs. in Sorcery						6.00
... Halloween ComicFest Edition 1 (2014, giveaway) Grey-toned reprint of #1						4.00
... Halloween ComicFest Edition 1 (2016, giveaway) Grey-toned reprint of #7						4.00

AFTER REALM QUARTERLY, THE
Image Comics: Feb, 2020 - Present ($5.99, quarterly)

1-3-Michael Avon Oeming-s/a; intro/origin of Oona Lightfoot						6.00

AFTERSHOCK GENESIS
AfterShock Comics: May, 2016 ($1.00, one-shot)

1-Short stories by various and previews of upcoming AfterShock titles						3.00

AFTERSHOCK TRIPLE PLAY
AfterShock Comics: Dec, 2021 ($4.99, one-shot)

1-Stories from Animosity, Dark Ark & We Live; gatefold front-c						5.00

AFTER THE CAPE
Image Comics (Shadowline): Mar, 2007 - No. 3, May, 2007 ($2.99, B&W, limited series)

1-3-Jim Valentino-s/Marco Rudy-a						3.00
... Volume One TPB (9/07, $12.99) r/series; scripts, sketch pages, character profiles						13.00
...II (11/07 - No. 3, 1/08, $2.99) 1-3-Jim Valentino-s/Sergio Carrera-a						3.00

AGENCY, THE
Image Comics (Top Cow): August, 2001 - No. 6, Mar, 2002 ($2.50/$2.95/$4.95)

1-5: 1-Jenkins-s/Hotz-a; three covers by Hotz, Turner, Silvestri. 3-5-($2.95)						3.00
6-($4.95) Flip-c preview of Jeremiah TV series						5.00
Preview (2001, 16 pgs.) B&W pages, cover previews, sketch pages						3.00

AGENT CARTER: S.H.I.E.L.D. 50TH ANNIVERSARY
Marvel Comics: Nov, 2015 ($3.99, one-shot)

1-Kathryn Immonen-s/Rich Ellis-a; set in 1966; Sif, Dum Dum and Nick Fury app.						4.00

AGENT 47: BIRTH OF THE HITMAN (Based on the Io-Anteractive video game)
Dynamite Entertainment: 2017 - No. 6, 2018 ($3.99)

1-6: 1-Sebela-s/Lau-a; multiple covers on each						4.00

AGENT LIBERTY SPECIAL (See Superman, 2nd Series)
DC Comics: 1992 ($2.00, 52 pgs, one-shot)

1-1st solo adventure; Guice-c/a(i)						4.00

AGENTS, THE
Image Comics: Apr, 2003 - No. 6, Sept, 2003 ($2.95, B&W)

	GD	VG	FN	VF	VF/NM	NM-
1-5-Ben Dunn-c/a in all						3.00
6-Five pg. preview of The Walking Dead #1	3	6	9	19	30	40

AGENTS OF ATLAS
Marvel Comics: Oct, 2006 - No. 6, Mar, 2007 ($2.99, limited series)

1-Golden Age heroes Marvel Boy & Venus app.; Kirk-a						6.00
2-6						3.00
... MGC 1 (7/10, $1.00) r/#1 with "Marvel's Greatest Comics" logo on cover						3.00
HC (2007, $24.99, dustjacket) r/#1-6, What If? #9, agents' debuts in '40s-'50s Atlas comics, creator interviews, character design art						25.00

AGENTS OF ATLAS (Dark Reign)
Marvel Comics: Jun, 2009 - No. 11, Nov, 2009 ($3.99)

1-11: 1-Pagulayan-a; 2 covers by Art Adams and McGuinness; back-up with Wolverine app. 5-New Avengers app. 8-Hulk app.						4.00

AGENTS OF ATLAS (Continues in Atlantis Attacks #1)(Also see Future Fight Firsts)
Marvel Comics: Oct, 2019 - No. 5, Feb, 2020 ($4.99/$3.99)

1-($4.99) Team of Shang-Chi, Brawn, Silk, Jimmy Woo, Luna Snow, Aero & others						5.00

	GD	VG	FN	VF	VF/NM	NM-		GD	VG	FN	VF	VF/NM	NM-
	2.0	4.0	6.0	8.0	9.0	9.2		2.0	4.0	6.0	8.0	9.0	9.2

2-5-($3.99) Greg Pak-s/Nico Leon-a. 5-Namor app. — 4.00

AGENTS OF LAW (Also see Comics' Greatest World)
Dark Horse Comics: Mar, 1995 - No. 6, Sept, 1995 ($2.50)
1-6: 5-Predator app. 6-Predator app.; death of Law — 3.00

AGENTS OF S.H.I.E.L.D. (Characters from the TV series)
Marvel Comics: Mar, 2016 - No. 10, Dec, 2016 ($3.99)
1-10: 1-Guggenheim-s/Peralta-a; Tony Stark app. 3,4-Standoff tie-in. 5-Spider-Man app.
7-10-Civil War II tie-in. 9,10-Elektra app. — 4.00

AGENT X (Continued from Deadpool)
Marvel Comics: Sept. 2002 - No. 15, Dec, 2003 ($2.99/$2.25)
1-($2.99) Simone-s/Udon Studios-a; Taskmaster app. — 5.00
2-9-($2.25) 2-Punisher app. — 3.00
10-14-($2.99) 10,11-Evan Dorkin-s. 12-Hotz-a — 3.00

| 15-Final issue | 1 | 2 | 3 | 5 | 6 | 8 |

AGE OF APOCALYPSE (See Uncanny X-Force)
Marvel Comics: May, 2012 - No. 14, Jun, 2013 ($2.99)
1-Lapham-s/De La Torre-a/Ramos-c — 6.00
2-14: 13-Leads into X-Termination x-over — 3.00

AGE OF APOCALYPSE (Secret Wars tie-in)
Marvel Comics: Sept, 2015 - No. 5, Dec, 2015 ($4.99/$3.99, limited series)
1-($4.99) Nicieza-s/Sandoval-a; alternate X-Men vs. Apocalypse — 5.00
2-5-($3.99) Covers #1-5 form one image; Blink, Sabretooth & Magneto app. — 4.00

AGE OF APOCALYPSE: THE CHOSEN
Marvel Comics: April, 1995 ($2.50, one-shot)
1-Wraparound-c — 5.00

AGE OF BRONZE
Image Comics: Nov, 1998 - Present ($2.95/$3.50, B&W)
1-6-Eric Shanower-c/s/a — 3.50
7-33-($3.50) — 3.50
...Behind the Scenes (5/02, $3.50) background info and creative process — 3.50
Image Firsts: Age of Bronze #1 (4/10, $1.00) r/#1 with "Image Firsts" cover logo — 3.00
...Special (6/99, $2.95) Story of Agamemnon and Menelaus — 3.50
A Thousand Ships (7/01, $19.95, TPB) r/#1-9 — 20.00
Sacrifice (9/04, $19.95, TPB) r/#10-19 — 20.00

AGE OF CONAN: BELIT
Marvel Comics: May, 2019 - No. 5, Sept, 2019 ($3.99, limited series)
1-5-Tini Howard-s/Kate Niemczyk-a/Sana Takeda-c; back-up serialized text story — 4.00

AGE OF CONAN: VALERIA
Marvel Comics: Oct, 2019 - No. 5, Feb, 2020 ($3.99, limited series)
1-5-Meredith Finch-s/Aneke-a; origin from childhood; back-up serialized text story — 4.00

AGE OF HEROES, THE
Halloween Comics/Image Comics #3 on: 1996 - No. 5, 1999 ($2.95, B&W)
1-5: James Hudnall scripts; John Ridgway-c/a — 3.00
...Special ($4.95) r/#1,2 — 5.00
...Special 2 ($6.95) r/#3,4 — 7.00
...Wex 1 ('98, $2.95) Hudnall-s/Angel Fernandez-a — 3.00

AGE OF HEROES (The Heroic Age)
Marvel Comics: Jul, 2010 - No. 4, Oct, 2010 ($3.99, limited series)
1-4-Short stories of Avengers members by various. 4-Jae Lee-c — 4.00

AGE OF INNOCENCE: THE REBIRTH OF IRON MAN
Marvel Comics: Feb, 1996 ($2.50, one-shot)
1-New origin of Tony Stark — 4.00

AGE OF REPTILES
Dark Horse Comics: Nov, 1993 - No. 4, Feb, 1994 ($2.50, limited series)
1-4-Delgado-c/a/scripts in all — 4.00
... Ancient Egyptians 1-4 (6/15 - No. 4, 9/15, $3.99) Delgado-c/a/scripts; wraparound-c — 4.00
... The Hunt 1-5 (5/96 - No. 5, 9/96, $2.95) Delgado-c/a/scripts in all — 4.00
... The Journey 1-4 (11/09 - No. 4, 7/10, $3.50) Delgado-c/a/scripts in all; wraparound-c — 3.50

AGE OF THE SENTRY, THE
Marvel Comics: Nov, 2008 - No. 6, Mar, 2010 ($2.99, limited series)
1-6-Silver Age style stories. 1-Origin retold; Bullock-c. 3-Coover-a — 3.00

AGE OF ULTRON
Marvel Comics: May, 2013 - No. 10, Aug, 2013 ($3.99, limited series)
1-Wraparound cardstock foil-c; Hitch-a/c — 6.00
2-9: 2-5-Hitch-a/c. 6-Peterson & Pacheco-a, Hank Pym killed — 4.00
10-Polybagged; Angela joins the Marvel Universe | 1 | 3 | 4 | 6 | 8 | 10 |
10AU (8/13, $3.99) Waid-s/Araljio-a/Pichelli-c; Hank Pym's origin re-told | | 9 | 14 | 20 | 25 |

AGE OF ULTRON VS. MARVEL ZOMBIES (Secret Wars tie-in)
Marvel Comics: Aug, 2015 - No. 4, Nov, 2015 ($3.99, limited series)
1-4-James Robinson-s/Steve Pugh-a; Vision, Wonder Man & Jim Hammond app. — 4.00

AGE OF X (X-Men titles crossover)
Marvel Comics: ($3.99, limited series)
... Alpha 1 (3/11, $3.99) Short stories by various; covers by Bachalo & Coipel — 6.00
...: Universe 1,2 (5/11 - No. 2, 6/11, $3.99) Pham-c; Bianchi-c; Avengers & Spider-Man app. | | 1 | 3 | 4 | 6 | 8 | 10 |

AGE OF X-MAN
Marvel Comics: Mar, 2019 - Sept, 2019 ($4.99/$3.99, limited series)
... Alpha 1 (3/19, $4.99) Rosanas-a; world where everyone is a mutant — 5.00
...: Apocalypse and the X-Tracts 1-5 (5/19 - No. 5, 9/19 $3.99) Seeley-s/Espin-a — 4.00
...: Nextgen 1-5 (4/19 - No. 5, 8/19, $3.99) 1-4-To-a; Bachalo-c. 5-Werneck-a — 4.00
...: Omega 1 (9/19, $4.99) Conclusion; leads into House of X #1; Buonfantino-a — 5.00
...: Prisoner X 1-5 (5/19 - No. 5, 9/19, $3.99) Peralta-a; Bishop, Polaris, Beast, Gabby app. — 4.00
...: The Amazing Nightcrawler 1-5 (4/19 - No. 5, 8/19, $3.99) Frigeri-a — 4.00
...: The Marvelous X-Men 1-5 (4/19 - No. 5, 8/19, $3.99) Failla-a/Noto-c; X-Man app. — 4.00

...: X-Tremists 1-5 (4/19 - No. 5, 8/19, $3.99) Jeanty-a/Rahzzah-c — 4.00

AGGIE MACK
Four Star Comics Corp./Superior Comics Ltd.: Jan, 1948 - No. 8, Aug, 1949

1-Feldstein-a, "Johnny Prep"	53	106	159	334	567	800
2,3-Kamen-c	32	64	96	188	307	425
4-Feldstein "Johnny Prep"; Kamen-c	39	78	117	240	395	550
5-8-Kamen-c/a. 7-Burt Lancaster app. on-c	34	68	102	199	325	450

AGGIE MACK
Dell Publishing Co.: Apr - Jun, 1962

| Four Color 1335 | 6 | 12 | 18 | 37 | 66 | 95 |

AIR
DC Comics (Vertigo): Oct, 2008 - No. 24, Oct, 2010 ($2.99)
1-6,8-24-G. Willow Wilson-s/M.K. Perker-a — 3.00
7-($1.00) Includes story re-cap — 3.00
... A History of the Future TPB (2011, $14.99) r/#18-24 — 15.00
... Flying Machine TPB (2009, $12.99) r/#6-10; Wilson intro. — 13.00
... Letters From Lost Countries TPB (2009, $9.99) r/#1-5; character sketch pages — 10.00
... Pure Land TPB (2010, $14.99) r/#11-17 — 15.00

AIR ACE (Formerly Bill Barnes No. 1-12)
Street & Smith Publications: V2#1, Jan, 1944 - V3#8(No. 20), Feb-Mar, 1947

V2#1-Nazi concentration camp-c	110	220	330	704	1202	1700
V2#2-Classic Japanese WWII-c	432	864	1296	3154	5577	8000
V2#3-WWII-c	36	72	108	211	343	475
V2#4-6,8-12	20	40	60	120	195	270
V2#7-Sci-fi-c; Powell-a	28	56	84	165	270	375
V3#1-Incinerated Japanese soldier on cover	25	50	75	150	245	340
V3#2-6: 2-Atomic explosion on-c	17	34	51	98	154	210
V3#7-Powell bondage-c/a; all atomic issue	65	130	195	416	708	1000
V3#8 (V5#8 on-c)-Powell-c/a	18	36	54	105	165	225

AIRBOY (Also see Airmaidens, Skywolf, Target: Airboy & Valkyrie)
Eclipse Comics: July, 1986 - No. 50, Oct, 1989 (#1-8, 50¢, 20 pgs., bi-weekly; #9-on, 36 pgs.; #34-on monthly)

1		1	3	4	6	8	10
2-4: 2-1st Marisa; Skywolf gets new costume. 3-The Heap begins						5.00
5-Valkyrie returns; Dave Stevens-c		3	6	9	17	26	35
6-49: 9-Begin $1.25-c; Skywolf begins. 11-Origin of G.A. Airboy & his plane Birdie. 28-Mr. Monster vs. The Heap. 33-Begin $1.75-c. 38-40-The Heap by Infantino. 41-r/1st app. Valkyrie from Air Fighters. 42-Begin $1.95-c. 46,47-part-r/Air Fighters. 48-Black Angel-r/A.F.						4.00
50 ($4.95, 52 pgs.)-Kubert-c						5.00
51-(It's Alive Press, Jul, 2019, $9.99) Chuck Dixon-s/Brent McKee-a; The Heap back-up						10.00
52-(It's Alive Press, Aug, 2022, $9.99) Chuck Dixon-s/Stipe Kalajzic-a; bonus pin-ups						10.00

NOTE: *Evans* c-21. *Gulacy* c-7, 20. *Spiegle* a-34, 35, 37. *Ken Steacy* painted c-17, 33.

AIRBOY
Image Comics: Jun, 2015 - No. 4, Nov, 2015 ($2.99, limited series, mature)
1-4: 1-Airboy meets writer James Robinson and artist Greg Hinkle. 3,4-Valkyrie app. — 3.00

AIRBOY COMICS (Air Fighters Comics No. 1-22)
Hillman Periodicals: V2#11, Dec, 1945 - V10#4, May, 1953 (No V3#3)

V2#11	71	142	213	454	777	1100
12-Valkyrie-c/app.	81	162	243	518	884	1250
V3#1,2(no #3)	45	90	135	284	480	675
4-The Heap app. in Skywolf	42	84	126	265	445	625
5,7,8,10,11	37	74	111	222	361	500
6-Valkyrie-c/app.	45	90	135	284	480	675
9-Origin The Heap	43	86	129	271	461	650
12-Skywolf & Airboy x-over; Valkyrie-c/app.	45	90	135	284	480	675
V4#1-Iron Lady app.	37	74	111	222	361	500
2,3,12: 2-Rackman begins	30	60	90	177	289	400
4-Simon & Kirby-c	36	72	108	211	343	475
5-7,9,11-All S&K-a	34	68	102	199	325	450
8-Classic bondage/torture-c; S&K-a	290	580	870	1856	3178	4500
10-Valkyrie-c/app.	43	86	129	271	461	650
V5#1-4,6-11: 4-Infantino Heap. 10-Origin The Heap	22	44	66	132	216	300
5-Skull-c	32	64	96	188	307	425
12-Kristein-a(p)	24	48	72	140	230	320
V6#1-3,5-12: 6,8-The Heap	21	42	63	124	202	280
4-Origin retold	25	50	75	150	245	340
V7#1-12: 7,8,10-Origin The Heap. 12-(1/51)	21	42	63	122	199	275
V8#1-3,5-12: 5-UFO-c (6/51)	20	40	60	118	192	265
4-Krigstein-a	21	42	63	122	199	275
V9#1,3,4,6-12: 7-One pg. Frazetta ad	18	36	54	105	165	225
2-Valkyrie app.	19	38	57	112	179	245
5(#100)	19	38	57	109	172	235
V10#1-4	17	34	51	98	154	210

NOTE: *Barry* a-V2#3, 7. *Bolle* a-V4#12. *McWilliams* a-V3#7, 9. *Powell* a-V7#2, 3, V8#1, 6. *Starr* a-V5#1, 12. *Dick Wood* a-V4#12. Bondage-c-V5#8.

AIRBOY MEETS THE PROWLER
Eclipse Comics: Aug, 1987 ($1.95, one-shot)
1-John Snyder, III-c/a — 5.00

AIRBOY-MR. MONSTER SPECIAL
Eclipse Comics: Aug, 1987 ($1.75, one-shot)
1 — 5.00

AIRBOY VERSUS THE AIR MAIDENS
Eclipse Comics: July, 1988 ($1.95)
1 — 5.00

AIR FIGHTERS CLASSICS
Eclipse Comics: Nov, 1987 - No. 6, May, 1989 ($3.95, 68 pgs., B&W)
1-6: Reprints G.A. Air Fighters #2-7. 1-Origin Airboy — 4.00

AIR FIGHTERS COMICS (Airboy Comics #23 (V2#11) on)
Hillman Periodicals: Nov, 1941; No. 2, Nov, 1942 - V2#10, Fall, 1945

Age of Ultron #1 © MAR

Air Ace V3 #2 © S&S

Alan Scott: The Green Lantern #1 © DC

	GD 2.0	VG 4.0	FN 6.0	VF 8.0	VF/NM 9.0	NM- 9.2

V1#1-(Produced by Funnies, Inc.); No Airboy; Black Commander only app.

	232	464	696	1485	2543	3600

2(11/42)-(Produced by Quality artists & Biro for Hillman); Origin & 1st app. Airboy & Iron Ace; Black Angel (1st app.), Flying Dutchman & Skywolf (1st app.) begin; Fuje-a; Biro-c/a

	530	1060	1590	3869	6835	9800

3-Origin/1st app. The Heap; origin Skywolf; 2nd Airboy app./c

	232	464	696	1485	2543	3600
4-Japan war-c	184	368	552	1168	2009	2850
5-Japanese octopus War-c	200	400	600	1280	2190	3100
6-Japanese soldiers as rats-c	239	478	717	1530	2615	3700
7-Classic Nazi swastika-c	219	438	657	1402	2401	3400
8-12: 8,10,11-War covers	93	186	279	591	1021	1450

V2#1-Classic Nazi War-c

	116	232	348	742	1271	1800

2-Skywolf by Giunta; Flying Dutchman by Fuje; 1st meeting Valkyrie & Airboy (she worked for the Nazis in beginning); 1st app. Valkyrie (11/43); Valkyrie-c

	300	600	900	2010	3505	5000
3,4,6,8,9	68	136	204	435	743	1050
5-Flag-c; Fuje-a	84	168	252	538	919	1300
7-Valkyrie app.	110	220	330	704	1202	1700
10-Origin The Heap & Skywolf	77	154	231	493	847	1200

NOTE: Fuje a-V1#2, 5, 7, V2#2, 3, 5, 7-9. Giunta a-V2#2, 3, 7.

AIRFIGHTERS MEET SGT. STRIKE SPECIAL, THE
Eclipse Comics: Jan, 1988 ($1.95, one-shot, stiff-c)

1-Airboy, Valkyrie, Skywolf app.						4.00

AIR FORCES (See American Air Forces)

AIRMAIDENS SPECIAL
Eclipse Comics: August, 1987 ($1.75, one-shot, Baxter paper)

1-Marisa becomes La Lupina (origin)						5.00

AIR RAIDERS
Marvel Comics (Star Comics)/Marvel #3 on: Nov, 1987- No. 5, Mar, 1988 ($1.00)

1,5: Kelley Jones-a in all						5.00
2-4: 2-Thunderhammer app.						4.00

AIRTIGHT GARAGE, THE (Also see Elsewhere Prince)
Marvel Comics (Epic Comics): July, 1993 - No. 4, Oct, 1993 ($2.50, lim. series, Baxter paper)

1-Moebius-c/a/scripts in all	2	4	6	10	14	18
2,3	2	4	6	9	12	15
4	3	6	9	14	20	25

AIR WAR STORIES
Dell Publishing Co.: Sept-Nov, 1964 - No. 8, Aug, 1966

1-Painted-c; Glanzman-c/a begins	5	10	15	31	53	75
2-8: 2,3-Painted-c	3	6	9	21	33	45

A.K.A. GOLDFISH
Caliber Comics: 1994 - 1995 (B&W, $3.50/$3.95)

...:Ace; ...:Jack; ...:Queen; ...:Joker; ...:King -Brian Michael Bendis-s/a						4.00
TPB (1996, $17.95)						20.00
Goldfish: The Definitive Collection (Image, 2001, $19.95) r/series plus promo art and new prose story; intro. by Matt Wagner						20.00
10th Anniversary HC (Image, 2002, $49.95)						50.00

AKIKO
Sirius: Mar, 1996 - No. 52, Feb, 2004 ($2.50/$2.95, B&W)

1-Crilley-c/a/scripts in all						6.00
2						4.00
3-49,51,52: 25-($2.95, 32 pgs.)-w/Asala back-up pages. 40-Begin $2.95-c						3.00
50-($3.50)						3.50
Flights of Fancy TPB (5/02, $12.95) r/various features, pin-ups and gags						13.00
TPB Volume 1,4 ('97, 2/00, $14.95) 1-r/#1-7. 4-r/#19-25						15.00
TPB Volume 2,3 ('98, '99, $11.95) 2-r/#8-13. 3- r/#14-18						12.00
TPB Volume 5 (12/01, $12.95) r/#26-31						13.00
TPB Volume 6,7 (6/03, 4/04, $14.95) 6-r/#32-38. 7-r/#40-47						15.00

AKIKO ON THE PLANET SMOO
Sirius: Dec, 1995 ($3.95, B&W)

V1#1-($3.95)-Crilley-c/a/scripts; gatefold-c						5.00
Ashcan ('95, mail offer)						3.00
Hardcover V1#1 (12/95, $19.95, B&W, 40 pgs.)						20.00
The Color Edition(2/00,$4.95)						5.00

AKIRA
Marvel Comics (Epic): Sept, 1988 - No. 38, Dec, 1995 ($3.50/$3.95/$6.95, deluxe, 68 pgs.)

1-1st English translation of Katsuhiro Otomo's manga	5	10	15	31	53	75
1,2-2nd printings (1989, $3.95)	1	2	3	5	6	8

	GD 2.0	VG 4.0	FN 6.0	VF 8.0	VF/NM 9.0	NM- 9.2
2	3	6	9	16	24	32
3-5	2	4	6	11	16	20
6-16	2	4	6	8	10	12
17-19: 17-$3.95-c begins	1	3	4	6	8	10
20-33 (Lower print run)	3	6	9	16	23	30
34,35: 34-(1994)-$6.95-c begins. 35-(1995)	3	6	9	19	30	40
36-Miyako's Last Stand	4	8	12	28	47	65
37-Texeira back-up, Gibbons, Williams pin-ups	6	12	18	41	76	110
38-Moebius, Allred, Pratt, Toth, Romita, Van Fleet, O'Neill, Madureira pin-ups; last Otomo issue	11	22	33	76	163	250

ALADDIN & HIS WONDERFUL LAMP (See Dell Jr Treasury #2)

ALAN LADD (See The Adventures of...)

ALAN MOORE'S AWESOME UNIVERSE HANDBOOK (Also see Across the Universe:...)
Awesome Entertainment: Apr, 1999 ($2.95, B&W)

1-Alan Moore-text/ Alex Ross-sketch pages and 2 covers						5.00

ALAN MOORE...
DC Comics (WildStorm): TPB

...'s Complete WildC.A.T.S. (2007, $29.99) r/#21-34,50; ...Homecoming & ...Gang War						30.00
...: Wild Worlds (2007, $24.99) r/various WildStorm one-shots and limited series						25.00

ALAN SCOTT: THE GREEN LANTERN
DC Comics: Dec, 2023 - No. 6 ($3.99, limited series)

1-5-Origin expanded; set in 1936 and 1941; Sheridan-s/Tormey-a. 3-The Spectre app.						
4-Origin of the Crimson Flame						4.00

ALARMING ADVENTURES
Harvey Publications: Oct, 1962 - No. 3, Feb, 1963

1-Crandall/Williamson-a	9	18	27	59	117	175
2-Williamson/Crandall-a	5	10	15	35	63	90
3-Torres-a	5	10	15	33	57	80

NOTE: Bailey a-1, 3. Crandall a-1p, 2i. Powell a-2(2). Severin c-1-3. Torres a-2? Tuska a-1. Williamson a-1i, 2p.

ALARMING TALES
Harvey Publications (Western Tales): Sept, 1957 - No. 6, Nov, 1958

1-Kirby-c/a(4); Kamandi prototype story by Kirby	39	78	117	240	395	550
2-Kirby-a(4)	25	50	75	150	245	340
3,4-Kirby-a. 4-Powell, Wildey-a	20	40	60	117	189	260
5-Kirby/Williamson-a; Wildey-a; Severin-c	20	40	60	118	192	265
6-Williamson-a?; Severin-c	16	32	48	94	147	200

ALBATROSS EXPLODING FUNNYBOOKS
Albatross Funnybooks: 2022 - Present ($5.99)

1-Anthology series with The Goon, La Diabla, Hillbilly, Lester and more; Eric Powell-s/a/c						6.00

ALBEDO
Thoughts And Images: Summer, 1983 - No. 14, Spring, 1989 (B&W)
Antarctic Press: (Vol. 2) Jan, 1991 - No. 10 ($2.50)

0-Yellow cover; 50 copies	18	36	54	124	275	425
0-White cover, 450 copies	10	20	30	66	138	210
0-Blue, 1st printing, 500 copies	9	18	27	60	120	180
0-Blue, 2nd printing, 1000 copies	5	10	15	31	53	75
0-3rd & 4th printing	3	6	9	14	20	26
1-Dark red, 1st printing - low print run	29	58	87	209	467	725
1-Bright red, later printings - low print run	9	18	27	57	111	165
2-(11/84) 1st app. Usagi Yojimbo by Stan Sakai; 2000 copies - no 2nd printing	567	1134	1700	3970	6235	8500
3	9	18	27	60	120	180
4-Usagi Yojimbo-c	10	20	30	64	132	200
5-14	1	2	3	5	6	8
(Vol. 2) 1	2	4	6	8	10	12
2-10, Color Special	1	2	3	5	6	8

ALBEDO ANTHROPOMORPHICS
Antarctic Press: (Vol. 3) Spring, 1994 - No. 4, Jan, 1996 ($2.95, color); (Vol. 4) Dec, 1999 - No. 2, Jan, 1999 ($2.95/$2.99, B&W)

V3#1-Steve Gallacci-c/a	2	4	6	11	16	20
V3#2-4-Steve Gallacci-c/a. V4#1,2	2	4	6	8	10	12

ALBERTO (See The Crusaders)

ALBERT THE ALLIGATOR & POGO POSSUM (See Pogo Possum)

ALBION (Inspired by 1960s IPC British comics characters)
DC Comics (WildStorm): Aug, 2005 - No. 6, Nov, 2006 ($2.99, limited series)

1-6-Alan Moore, Leah Moore & John Reppion-s/Shane Oakley-a; Dave Gibbons-c						3.00
TPB (2007, $19.99) r/series; intro by Neil Gaiman; reprints from 1960s British comics						20.00

ALBUM OF CRIME (See Fox Giants)

	GD 2.0	VG 4.0	FN 6.0	VF 8.0	VF/NM 9.0	NM- 9.2

ALBUM OF LOVE (See Fox Giants)

AL CAPONE, VAMPIRE (Also see Vampire, PA)
American Mythology Productions: Oct, 2023 - No. 4, Jan, 2024 ($4.99)

1-4-J.C. Vaughn-s/Brendon & Brian Fraim-a; multiple covers on each						5.00
1-3 (Crowdfunded Editions, 7/22 - No. 3, 10/23, $20.00) Bonus stories and interviews						20.00

AL CAPP'S DOGPATCH (Also see Mammy Yokum)
Toby Press: No. 71, June, 1949 - No. 4, Dec, 1949

71(#1)-Reprints from Tip Top #112-114	19	38	57	111	176	240
2-4- 4-Reprints from Li'l Abner #73	15	30	45	83	124	165

AL CAPP'S SHMOO (Also see Oxydol-Dreft & Washable Jones & Shmoo)
Toby Press: July, 1949 - No. 5, Apr, 1950 (None by Al Capp)

1-1st app. Super-Shmoo	32	64	96	188	307	425
2-5- 3-Sci-fi trip to moon. 4-X-Mas-c	21	42	63	126	206	285

AL CAPP'S WOLF GAL
Toby Press: 1951 - No. 2, 1952

1-Edited-r from Li'l Abner #63	41	82	123	256	428	600
2-Edited-r from Li'l Abner #64	26	52	78	154	252	350

ALEISTER ARCANE
IDW Publishing: Apr, 2004 - No. 3, June, 2004 ($3.99, limited series)

1-3-Steve Niles-s/Breehn Burns-a						4.00
TPB (10/04, $17.99) r/series; sketch pages						18.00

ALEXANDER THE GREAT (Movie)
Dell Publishing Co.: No. 688, May, 1956

Four Color 688-Buscema-a; photo-c	7	14	21	46	86	125

ALEX + ADA
Image Comics: Nov, 2013 - No. 15, Jun, 2015 ($2.99/$3.99)

1-14-Jonathan Luna-a/c; Sarah Vaughn & Luna-s						3.00
15-($3.99) Conclusion						4.00

ALF (TV) (See Star Comics Digest)
Marvel Comics: Mar, 1988 - No. 50, Feb, 1992 ($1.00)

1-Photo-c	3	6	9	16	23	30
1-2nd printing						5.00
2-5	2	4	6	8	10	12
6-19: 6-Photo-c						6.00
20-22: 20-Conan parody. 21-Marx Brothers. 22-X-Men parody	1	3	4	6	8	10
23-30: 24-Rhonda-c/app. 29-3-D cover						4.00
31-43,46,47,49						4.00
44-X-Men parody	2	4	6	10	14	18
45-Wolverine, Punisher, Capt. America-c	1	3	4	6	8	10
48-(12/91) Risqué Alf with seal cover	11	22	33	73	157	240
50-($1.75, 52 pgs.)-Final issue; photo-c	2	4	6	9	12	15
Annual 1-3: 1-Rocky & Bullwinkle app. 2-Sienkiewicz-c. 3-TMNT parody	1	2	3	5	6	8
Comics Digest 1,2: 1-(1988)-Reprints Alf #1,2	2	4	6	8	10	12
Holiday Special 1,2 ('88, Wint. '89, 68 pgs.): 2-X-Men parody-c						10.00
Spring Special 1 (Spr/89, $1.75, 68 pgs.) Invisible Man parody						10.00
TPB (1990, 68 pgs.) r/#1-3; photo-c						10.00

ALFRED HARVEY'S BLACK CAT
Lorne-Harvey Productions: 1995 ($3.50, B&W/color)

1-Origin by Mark Evanier & Murphy Anderson; contains history of Alfred Harvey & Harvey Publications; 5 pg. B&W Sad Sack story; Hildebrandts-c						6.00

ALGIE (LITTLE...)
Timor Publ. Co.: Dec, 1953 - No. 3, 1954

1-Teenage	10	20	30	58	79	100
1-Algie #1 cover w/Secret Mysteries #19 inside	12	24	36	69	97	125
2	7	14	21	37	46	55
3-Good Girl-a	11	22	33	76	163	250
Accepted Reprint #2(2nd)	4	7	10	14	17	20
Super Reprint #15	2	4	6	10	14	18

ALIAS:
Now Comics: July, 1990 - No. 5, Nov, 1990 ($1.75)

1-5: 1-Sienkiewicz-c						4.00

ALIAS (Also see Jessica Jones apps. in New Avengers and The Pulse)
Marvel Comics (MAX Comics): Nov, 2001 - No. 28, Jan, 2004 ($2.99)

1-Bendis-s/Gaydos-a/Mack-c; intro Jessica Jones; Luke Cage app.	14	21	46	86	125
2-4	1	2	3	5	6	8
5-23: 7,8-Sienkiewicz-a (2 pgs.) 16-21-Spider-Woman app. 22,23-Jessica's origin						5.00
24-Killgrave The Purple Man app.; Avengers app.	2	4	6	9	12	15
25-27-The Purple Man app.; Avengers app. 25,26-Flashback-a by Bagley.						
26-Flashback-a by Rick Mays	1	3	4	6	8	10
28-Last issue; Purple Man app.	2	4	6	9	12	15
...MGC 1 (6/10, $1.00) r/#1 with "Marvel's Greatest Comics" logo on cover						3.00
HC (2002, $29.99) r/#1-9; intro. by Jeph Loeb						30.00
Omnibus (2006, $69.99, hardcover with dustjacket) r/#1-28 and What If Jessica Jones Had Joined the Avengers?; original pitch, script and sketch pages						70.00
Vol. 1: TPB (2003, $19.99) r/#1-9						20.00
Vol. 2: Come Home TPB (2003, $13.99) r/#11-15						14.00
Vol. 3: The Underneath TPB (2003, $16.99) r/#10,16-21						17.00

ALICE (New Adventures in Wonderland)
Ziff-Davis Publ. Co.: No. 10, 7-8/51 - No. 11(#2), 11-12/51

10-Painted-c; Berg-a	39	78	117	231	378	525
11-(#2 on inside) Dave Berg-a	22	44	66	128	209	290

ALICE AT MONKEY ISLAND (Formerly The Adventures of Alice)
Pentagon Publ. Co. (Civil Service): No. 3, 1946

3	14	28	42	80	115	150

ALICE COOPER (Also see Last Temptation)
Dynamite Entertainment: 2014 - No. 6, 2015 ($3.99)

1-6: 1-5-Joe Harris-s/Eman Casallos-a/David Mack-c. 6-Jerwa-s/Tenorio-a						5.00

ALICE COOPER (Volume 2)
Dynamite Entertainment: 2023 - No. 5, 2024 ($4.99)

1-5-Rodney Barnes-s/Edu Menna-a; Lucifer app.						5.00

ALICE COOPER VS. CHAOS!
Dynamite Entertainment: 2015 - No. 6, 2016 ($3.99, limited series)

1-Chastity, Purgatori, Evil Ernie, Lady Demon & The Queen of Sorrows app.	1	3	4	6	8	10
2-6						4.00

ALICE EVER AFTER
BOOM! Studios: Apr, 2022 - No. 5, Aug, 2022 ($3.99, limited series)

1-5-Panosian-s/Spalletta & Panosian-a; adult Alice returning to Wonderland						4.00

ALICE IN WONDERLAND (Disney; see Advs. of Alice, Dell Jr. Treasury #1, The Dreamery, Movie Comics, Walt Disney Showcase #22, and World's Greatest Stories)
Dell Publishing Co.: No. 24, 1940; No. 331, 1951; No. 341, July, 1951

Single Series 24 (#1)(1940)	74	148	222	470	810	1150
Four Color 331, 341-"Unbirthday Party w/..."	19	38	57	131	291	450
1-(Whitman, 3/84, pre-pack only)-r/4-Color #331	4	8	12	25	40	55

ALICE NEVER AFTER (Sequel to Alice Ever After)
BOOM! Studios: Jul, 2023 - No. 5, Nov, 2023 ($3.99, limited series)

1-5-Panosian-s/Spalletta & Panosian-a; adult Alice in Wonderland						4.00

ALIEN (Based on the creatures from the 1979 movie)
Marvel Comics: May, 2021 - No. 12, Jul, 2022 ($3.99)

1-12-P.K. Johnson-s/Salvador Larroca-a						4.00
Annual 1 (9/22, $4.99) P.K. Johnson-s/Salvador Larroca-a						5.00

ALIEN (Based on the creatures from the 1979 movie)
Marvel Comics: Nov, 2022 - No. 6, Apr, 2023 ($3.99)

1-6-P.K. Johnson-s/Julius Ohta-a						4.00

ALIEN (Based on the creatures from the 1979 movie)
Marvel Comics: Jun, 2023 - No. 5, Oct, 2023 ($4.99)

1-5-Declan Shalvey-s/Andrea Broccardo-a						5.00
Annual 1 (12/23, $5.99) Declan Shalvey-s/Danny Earls-a						6.00

ALIEN (Based on the creatures from the 1979 movie)
Marvel Comics: Jan, 2024 - No. 4, Apr, 2024 ($5.99/$4.99)

1-($5.99)-Declan Shalvey-s/Andrea Broccardo-a						6.00
2-4-($4.99)						5.00

ALIENATED
BOOM! Studios: Feb, 2020 - No. 6, Sept, 2020 ($3.99, limited series)

1-6-Spurrier-s/Wildgoose-a						4.00

ALIEN: BLACK, WHITE & BLOOD (From the 1979 movie)
Marvel Comics: Apr, 2024 - Present ($5.99/$4.99, B&W&red&green)

1-($5.99)-Short story anthology						6.00

ALIEN ENCOUNTERS (Replaces Alien Worlds)
Eclipse Comics: June, 1985 - No. 14, Aug, 1987 ($1.75, Baxter paper, mature)

1-7,9,10: Nudity, strong language in all. 9-Snyder-a						4.00
8-Marilyn Monroe on cover	2	4	6	8	10	12
11-14-Low print run						5.00

ALIEN LEGION (See Epic & Marvel Graphic Novel #25)
Marvel Comics (Epic Comics): Apr, 1984 - No. 20, Sept, 1987

nn-With bound-in trading card; Austin-i	2	4	6	8	10	12
2-20: $1.50-c. 7,8-Portacio-i						4.00

ALIEN LEGION (2nd Series)
Marvel Comics (Epic): Aug, 1987(indicia)(10/87 on-c) - No. 18, Aug, 1990

V2#1-18-Stroman-a in all. 7-18-Farmer-i						4.00
...: Force Nomad TPB (Checker Book Pub. Group, 2001, $24.95) r/#1-11						25.00
...: Piecemaker TPB (Checker Book Pub. Group, 2002, $19.95) r/#12-18						20.00

ALIEN LEGION: (Series of titles; all Marvel/Epic Comics)
--BINARY DEEP, 1993 ($3.50, one-shot, 52 pgs.), nn-With bound-in trading card

						4.00

--JUGGER GRIMROD, 8/92 ($5.95, one-shot, 52 pgs.) Book 1

						6.00

--ONE PLANET AT A TIME, 5/93 - Book 3, 7/93 ($4.95, squarebound, 52 pgs.)

Book 1-3: Hoang Nguyen-a						5.00

--ON THE EDGE (The... #2 & 3), 11/90 - No. 3, 1/91 ($4.50, 52 pgs.)

1-3-Stroman & Farmer-a						4.50

--TENANTS OF HELL, '91 - No. 2, '91 ($4.50, squarebound, 52 pgs.)

Book 1,2-Stroman-c/a(p)						4.50

ALIEN LEGION: UNCIVIL WAR
Titan Comics: Jul, 2014 - No. 4, Oct, 2014 ($3.99)

1-4-Dixon-s/Stroman-a						4.00

ALIEN LIFE (Cerebus in Hell)
Aardvark-Vanaheim: May, 2022 ($4.00, B&W)

1-Cerebus figures with Gustave Doré artwork of Hell; Alf #48-c swipe						4.00

ALIEN NATION (Movie)
DC Comics: Dec, 1988 ($2.50; 68 pgs.)

1-Adaptation of film; painted-c						4.00

ALIEN PIG FARM 3000
Image Comics (RAW Studios): Apr, 2007 - No. 4, July, 2007 ($2.99, limited series)

1-4-Steve Niles, Thomas Jane & Todd Farmer-s/Don Marquez-a						4.00

ALIEN RESURRECTION (Movie)
Dark Horse Comics: Oct, 1997 - No. 2, Nov, 1997 ($2.50; limited series)

1,2-Adaptation of film; Dave McKean-c						5.00

Al Capone, Vampire #1
© Vaughn & Solof & Fraim & Fraim

Alice Cooper #1 © Nightmare Inc.

Aliens: Dead Orbit #1 © 20Fox

	GD 2.0	VG 4.0	FN 6.0	VF 8.0	VF/NM 9.0	NM- 9.2
ALIENS, THE (Captain Johner and...)(Also see Magnus Robot Fighter...)						
Gold Key: Sept-Dec, 1967; No. 2, May, 1982						
1-Reprints from Magnus #1,3,4,6-10; Russ Manning-a in all	4	8	12	25	40	55
2-(Whitman) Same contents as #1	2	4	6	8	10	12
ALIENS (Movie) (See Alien: The Illustrated..., Dark Horse Comics & Dark Horse Presents #24)						
Dark Horse Comics: May, 1988 - No. 6, July, 1989 ($1.95, B&W, limited series)						
1-Based on movie sequel; 1st app. Aliens in comics	7	14	21	49	92	135
1-2nd printing	2	4	6	8	10	12
1-3rd - 6th printings; 4th w/new inside front-c						4.00
2	3	6	9	16	23	30
2-2nd & 3rd printing, 3-6-2nd printings						4.00
3	2	4	6	10	14	18
4,5	1	2	3	5	6	8
6-Last issue	2	4	6	8	10	12
Mini Comic #1 (2/89, 4x6")-Was included with Aliens Portfolio						6.00
Collection 1 ($10.95,)-r/#1-6 plus Dark Horse Presents #24 plus new-a						15.00
Collection 1-2nd printing (1991, $11.95)-On higher quality paper than 1st print; Dorman painted-c						12.00
Hardcover ('90, $24.95, B&W)-r/1-6, DHP #24						30.00
... Omnibus Vol. 1 (7/07, $24.95, 9x6")-r/1st & 2nd series and Aliens: Earth War						50.00
... Omnibus Vol. 2 (12/07, $24.95, 9x6") r/Genocide, Harvest and Colonial Marines series						40.00
... Omnibus Vol. 3 (3/08, $24.95, 9x6") r/Rogue, Salvation and Sacrifice, Labyrinth series						40.00
... Omnibus Vol. 4 (8/08, $24.95, 9x6") r/Music of the Spears, Stronghold, Berserker, Mondo Pest and Mondo Heat series and one-shots						40.00
... Omnibus Vol. 5 (11/08, $24.95, 9x6") r/Alchemy, Survival, Havoc series and various						40.00
... Omnibus Vol. 6 (2/09, $24.95, 9x6") r/Apocalypse GN, Xenogenesis & one-shots						100.00
... Outbreak (3rd printing, 8/96, $17.95)-Bolton-c						18.00
Platinum Edition - (See Dark Horse Presents: Aliens Platinum Edition)						-
ALIENS						
Dark Horse Comics: V2#1, Aug, 1989 - No. 4, 1990 ($2.25, limited series)						
V2#1-Painted art by Denis Beauvais	2	4	5	7	8	10
1-2nd printing (1990), 2-4						3.00
...: Nightmare Asylum TPB (12/96, $16.95) r/series; Bolton-c	3	6	9	16	23	30
ALIENS						
Dark Horse Comics: May, 2009 - No. 4, Nov, 2009 ($3.50, limited series)						
1-Howard-c	2	4	6	9	12	15
2-4-John Arcudi-s/Zach Howard-a. 2-Howard-c. 3,4-Swanland-c						5.00
ALIENS: (Series of titles, all Dark Horse)						
--ALCHEMY, 10/97 - No. 3, 11/97 ($2.95),1-3-Corben-c/a, Arcudi-s	1	2	3	5	6	8
--APOCALYPSE - THE DESTROYING ANGELS, 1/99 - No. 4, 4/99 ($2.95)						
1-4-Doug Wheatly-a/Schultz-s						6.00
--BERSERKERS, 1/95 - No. 4, 4/95 ($2.50) 1-4						6.00
--COLONIAL MARINES, 1/93 - No. 10, 7/94 ($2.50) 1-10						5.00
--DEAD ORBIT, 4/17 - No. 4, 12/17 ($3.99) 1-4-James Stokoe-s/a	1	3	4	6	8	10
--DEFIANCE, 4/16 - No. 12, 6/17 ($3.99) 1-Brian Wood-s/Tristan Jones-a	2	4	5	7	8	10
2-12: 2-Brian Wood-s/Tristan Jones-a						5.00
--DUST TO DUST, 4/18 - No. 4, 1/19 ($3.99) 1-4-Gabriel Hardman-s/a						6.00
--EARTH ANGEL, 8/94 ($2.95) 1-Byrne-a/story; wraparound-c						6.00
--EARTH WAR, 6/90 - No. 4, 10/90 ($2.50) 1-All have Sam Kieth-a & Bolton painted-c						6.00
1-2nd printing, 3,4						4.00
2						5.00
--GENOCIDE, 11/91 - No. 4, 2/92 ($2.50) 1-4-Suydam painted-c. 4-Wraparound-c, poster						4.00
--GLASS CORRIDOR, 6/98 ($2.95) 1-David Lloyd-s/a						10.00
--HARVEST (See Aliens: Hive)						
--HAVOC, 6/97 - No. 2, 7/97 ($2.95) 1,2: Schultz-s, Kent Williams-c, 40 artists including Art Adams, Kelley Jones, Duncan Fregedo, Kevin Nowlan						6.00
--HIVE, 2/92 - No. 4,5/92 ($2.50) 1-4: Kelley Jones-c/a in all						4.00
...Harvest TPB ('98, $16.95) r/series; Bolton-c						17.00
--KIDNAPPED, 12/97 - No. 3, 2/98 ($2.50) 1-3						6.00
--LABYRINTH, 9/93 - No. 4, 1/94 ($2.50) 1-4: 1-Painted-c						5.00
--LIFE AND DEATH, 9/16 - No. 4, 12/16 ($3.99) 1-4-Abnett-s/Moritat-a						4.00
--LOVESICK, 12/96 ($2.95) 1						8.00

	GD 2.0	VG 4.0	FN 6.0	VF 8.0	VF/NM 9.0	NM- 9.2
--MONDO HEAT, 2/96 ($2.50) nn-Sequel to Mondo Pest						8.00
--MONDO PEST, 4/95 ($2.95, 44 pgs.) nn-r/Dark Horse Comics #22-24						5.00
--MUSIC OF THE SPEARS, 1/94 - No. 4, 4/94 ($2.50) 1-4						5.00
--NEWT'S TALE, 6/92 - No. 2, 7/92 ($4.95) 1,2-Bolton-c						8.00
--PIG, 3/97 ($2.95)1	1	3	4	6	8	10
--PREDATOR: THE DEADLIEST OF THE SPECIES, 7/93 - No. 12,8/95 ($2.50)						
1-Bolton painted-c; Guice-a(p)						6.00
1-Embossed foil platinum edition	2	4	6	9	12	15
2-12: Bolton painted-c. 2,3-Guice-a(p)						4.00
--PURGE, 8/97 ($2.95) nn-Hester-a	1	3	4	6	8	10
--RESCUE, 7/19 - No. 4, 10/19 ($3.99) 1-4-Brian Wood-s/Kieran McKeown-a						5.00
--RESISTANCE, 1/19 - No. 4, 4/19 ($3.99) 1-4-Brian Wood-s/Robert Carey-a						6.00
--ROGUE, 4/93 - No. 4, 7/93 ($2.50) 1-4: Painted-c						4.00
--SACRIFICE, 5/93 ($4.95, 52 pgs.) nn-P. Milligan scripts; painted-c/a	1	3	4	6	8	10
--SALVATION, 11/93 ($4.95, 52 pgs.) nn-Mignola-c/a(p); Gibbons script	2	4	6	10	14	18
--SPECIAL, 6/97 ($2.50) 1	2	4	6	8	10	12
--STALKER, 6/98 ($2.50)1-David Wenzel-s/a	2	4	6	8	10	12
--STRONGHOLD, 5/94 - No. 4, 9/94 ($2.50) 1-4						5.00
--SURVIVAL, 2/98 - No. 3, 4/98 ($2.95) 1-3-Tony Harris-c						6.00
--TRIBES, 1992 ($24.95, hardcover graphic novel) Bissette text-s with Dorman painted-a						25.00
...softcover ($9.95)						10.00
ALIENS: AFTERMATH (Based on the creatures from the 1979 movie)						
Marvel Comics: Sept, 2021 ($4.99, one-shot)						
1-Benjamin Percy-s/Dave Wachter-a						4.00
ALIENS: FIRE AND STONE (Crossover with AvP, Predator, and Prometheus)						
Dark Horse Comics: Sept, 2014 - No. 4, Dec, 2014 ($3.50, limited series)						
1-4-Roberson-s/Reynolds-a						6.00
ALIENS/ VAMPIRELLA (See Vampirella/Aliens)						
ALIENS VS. PARKER (Not based on the Alien movie series)						
BOOM! Studios: Mar, 2013 - No. 4, May, 2013 ($3.99, limited series)						
1-4: 1-Paul Scheer & Nick Giovannetti-s; Bracchi-a/Noto-c						4.00
ALIENS VS. PREDATOR (See Dark Horse Presents #36)						
Dark Horse Comics: June, 1990 - No. 4, Dec, 1990 ($2.50, limited series)						
1-Painted-c	3	6	9	14	19	24
1-2nd printing						4.00
0-(7/90, $1.95, B&W)-r/Dark Horse Pres. #34-36	3	6	9	14	19	24
2,3	1	2	3	5	6	8
4-Dave Dorman painted-c						6.00
Annual (7/99, $4.95) Jae Lee-c	1	2	3	5	6	8
... : Booty (1/96, $2.50) painted-c	1	2	3	5	6	8
... Omnibus Vol. 1 (5/07, $24.95, 9x6") r/#1-4 & Annual; ...: War; ...: Eternal						50.00
... Omnibus Vol. 2 (10/07, $24.95, 9x6") r/...: Xenogenesis #1-4; ...: Deadliest of the Species; ...: Booty and stories from ... Annual						40.00
... : One For One (8/10, $1.00) r/#1 with red cover frame						6.00
... : Thrill of the Hunt (9/04, $6.95, digest-size TPB) Based on 2004 movie						7.00
... : Wraith 1 (7/98, $2.95) Jay Stephens-s						6.00
--VS. PREDATOR: DUEL, 3/95 - No. 2, 4/95 ($2.50) 1,2						6.00
--VS. PREDATOR: ETERNAL, 6/98 - No. 4, 9/98 ($2.50)1-4: Edginton-s/Maleev-a; Fabry-c						4.00
--VS. PREDATOR: THREE WORLD WAR, 1/10 - No. 6, 9/10 ($3.50) 1-6-Leonardi-a	1	3	4	6	8	10
--VS. PREDATOR VS. THE TERMINATOR, 4/00 - No. 4, 7/00 ($2.95)						
1-Ripley app.	2	4	6	11	16	20
2-4-Ripley app.	2	4	6	8	10	12
--VS. PREDATOR: WAR, No. 0, 5/95 - No. 4, 8/95 ($2.50) 0-4: Corben painted-c						6.00
--VS. PREDATOR: XENOGENESIS, 12/99 - No. 4, 3/00 ($2.95) 1-4: Watson-s/Mel Rubi-a						5.00
--XENOGENESIS, 8/99 - No. 4, 11/99 ($2.95) 1-4: T&M Bierbaum-s						5.00
ALIENS VS. ZOMBIES (Not based on the Alien movie series)						
Zenescope Entertainment: Jul, 2015 - No. 5, Dec, 2015 ($3.99, limited series)						
1-5: 1-Brusha-s/Riccardi-a; multiple covers on each						4.00
ALIEN TERROR (See 3-D Alien Terror)						
ALIEN: THE ILLUSTRATED STORY (Also see Aliens)						

	GD 2.0	VG 4.0	FN 6.0	VF 8.0	VF/NM 9.0	NM- 9.2

Heavy Metal Books: 1980 ($3.95, soft-c, 8x11")

	GD 2.0	VG 4.0	FN 6.0	VF 8.0	VF/NM 9.0	NM- 9.2
nn-Movie adaptation; Simonson-a	6	12	18	41	76	110

ALIEN: THE ORIGINAL SCREENPLAY
Dark Horse Comics: Aug, 2020 - No. 5, Dec, 2020 ($3.99, limited series)

	GD 2.0	VG 4.0	FN 6.0	VF 8.0	VF/NM 9.0	NM- 9.2
1-Adaptation of Dan O'Bannon's original 1976 screenplay; Seixas-s/Balbi-a	1	3	4	6	8	10
2-5						6.00

ALIEN³ (Movie)
Dark Horse Comics: June, 1992 - No. 3, July, 1992 ($2.50, limited series)

	NM- 9.2
1-3: Adapts 3rd movie; Suydam painted-c	5.00

ALIEN 3 (WILLIAM GIBSON'S...) (Movie)
Dark Horse Comics: Nov, 2018 - No. 5, Mar, 2019 ($3.99, limited series)

	NM- 9.2
1-5-Adapts William Gibson's unproduced screenplay for Alien 3; Johnnie Christmas-s/a	4.00

ALIEN VS. PREDATOR: FIRE AND STONE (Crossover with Aliens, Predator, and Prometheus)
Dark Horse Comics: Oct, 2014 - No. 4, Jan, 2015 ($3.50, limited series)

	GD 2.0	VG 4.0	FN 6.0	VF 8.0	VF/NM 9.0	NM- 9.2
1-4-Sebela-s/Olivetti-a	1	2	3	5	6	8

ALIEN VS. PREDATOR: LIFE AND DEATH (Crossover with Aliens, Predator, and Prometheus)
Dark Horse Comics: Dec, 2016 - No. 4, Mar, 2017 ($3.99, limited series)

	NM- 9.2
1-4-Abnett-s/Theis-a	5.00

ALIEN VS. PREDATOR: THICKER THAN BLOOD
Dark Horse Comics: Dec, 2019 - No. 4 ($3.99, limited series)

	NM- 9.2
1,2-Jeremy Barlow-s/Doug Wheatey-a	4.00

ALIEN WORLDS (Also see Eclipse Graphic Album #22)
Pacific Comics/Eclipse: Dec, 1982 - No. 9, Jan, 1985

	GD 2.0	VG 4.0	FN 6.0	VF 8.0	VF/NM 9.0	NM- 9.2
1,2,4: 2,4-Dave Stevens-c/a	2	4	6	9	12	15
3,5-7	1	2	3	5	6	8
8,9	2	4	6	8	11	14
3-D No. 1-Art Adams 1st published art	2	4	6	8	11	14

ALISON DARE, LITTLE MISS ADVENTURES (Also see Return of ...)
Oni Press: Sept, 2000 ($4.50, B&W, one-shot)

	NM- 9.2
1-J. Torres-s/J.Bone-c/a	6.00

ALISON DARE & THE HEART OF THE MAIDEN
Oni Press: Jan, 2002 - No. 2, Feb, 2002 ($2.95, B&W, limited series)

	NM- 9.2
1,2-J. Torres-s/J.Bone-c/a	3.00

ALISTER THE SLAYER
Midnight Press: Oct, 1995 ($2.50)

	NM- 9.2
1-Boris-c/a	4.00

ALL-AMERICAN COMICS (...Western #103-126, ...Men of War #127 on; also see The Big All-American Comic Book)
All-American/National Periodical Publ.: April, 1939 - No. 102, Oct, 1948

	GD 2.0	VG 4.0	FN 6.0	VF 8.0	VF/NM 9.0	NM- 9.2
1-Hop Harrigan (1st app.), Scribbly by Mayer (1st DC app.), Toonerville Folks, Ben Webster, Spot Savage, Mutt & Jeff, Red White & Blue (1st app.), Adventures in the Unknown, Tippie, Reg'lar Fellers, Skippy, Bobby Thatcher, Mystery Men of Mars, Daiseybelle, Wiley of West Point begin	730	1460	2190	5329	9415	13,500
2-Ripley's Believe It or Not begins, ends #24	252	504	756	1613	2757	3900
3-5: 5-The American Way begins, ends #10	219	438	657	1402	2401	3400
6,7: 6-Last Spot Savage; Popsicle Pete begins #26, 28. 7-Last Bobby Thatcher	168	336	504	1075	1838	2600
8-The Ultra Man begins & 1st-c app.	470	940	1410	3431	6066	8700
9,10: 10-X-Mas-c	161	322	483	1030	1765	2500
11,15: 11-Ultra Man-c. 15-Last Tippie & Reg'lar Fellars; Ultra Man-c	226	452	678	1446	2473	3500
12-14: 12-Last Toonerville Folks	148	296	444	947	1624	2300
16-(Rare)-Origin/1st app. Green Lantern by Sheldon Moldoff (c/a)(7/40) & begin series; appears in costume on-c & only one panel inside; created by Martin Nodell. Inspired in 1940 by a switchman's green lantern that would give trains the go ahead to proceed. G.L. cover pose swiped from last panel of a Jan, 1939 Flash Gordon Sunday page.	30,700	61,400	92,100	227,400	613,700	1,000,000
17-2nd Green Lantern	1540	3080	4620	11,550	24,275	37,000
18-N.Y. World's Fair-c/story (scarce); The Atom app. in one panel announcing debut in next issue	1400	2800	4200	10,500	22,250	34,000
19-Origin/1st app. The Atom (10/40); last Ultra Man	3100	6200	9300	23,250	47,625	72,000
20-Atom dons costume; Ma Hunkle becomes Red Tornado (1st app.)(1st DC costumed heroine, before Wonder Woman, 11/40); Rescue on Mars begins, ends #25; 1 pg. origin Green Lantern	784	1568	2352	5723	10,112	14,500
21-Last Wiley of West Point & Skippy; classic Moldoff-c	676	1352	2028	4935	8718	12,500
22,23: 23-Last Daiseybelle; 3 Idiots begin, end #82	389	778	1167	2723	4762	6800
24-Sisty & Dinky become the Cyclone Kids; Ben Webster ends; origin Dr. Mid-Nite & Sargon, The Sorcerer in text with app.	389	778	1167	2723	4762	6800
25-Origin & 1st story app. Dr. Mid-Nite by Stan Asch; Hop Harrigan becomes Guardian Angel; last Adventure in the Unknown (scarce)	1400	2800	4200	10,500	22,250	34,000
26-Origin/1st story app. Sargon, the Sorcerer. No appearing on-c.	423	846	1269	3000	5250	7500
27: #27-32 are misnumbered in indicia with correct No. appearing on-c. Intro. Doiby Dickles, Green Lantern's sidekick	405	810	1215	2835	4968	7100
28-Hop Harrigan gives up costumed i.d.	232	464	696	1485	2543	3600
29,30	226	452	678	1446	2473	3500
31-40: 35-Doiby learns Green Lantern's i.d.	187	374	561	1197	2049	2900
41-50: 50-Sargon ends	148	296	444	947	1624	2300
51-60: 59-Scribbly & the Red Tornado ends	126	252	378	806	1378	1950
61-Origin/1st app. Solomon Grundy (11/44)	3050	6100	9150	22,900	43,950	65,000
62-70: 70-Kubert Sargon; intro Sargon's helper, Maximillian O'Leary	113	226	339	718	1234	1750
71-88: 71-Last Red White & Blue. 72-Black Pirate begins (not in #74-82); last Atom. 73-Winky, Blinky & Noddy begins, ends #82. 79,83-Mutt & Jeff-c. 85-1st Crusher Crock (becomes Sportsmaster); Hasen "Derby" cover	87	174	261	553	952	1350
89-Origin & 1st app. Harlequin (Molly Mayne)	459	918	1377	3350	5925	8500

	GD 2.0	VG 4.0	FN 6.0	VF 8.0	VF/NM 9.0	NM- 9.2
90,92,96-99: 90-Origin/1st app. Icicle. 98-Sportsmaster-c. 99-Last Hop Harrigan	174	348	522	1114	1907	2700
91,93,94,95-Harlequin-c	239	478	717	1530	2615	3700
100-1st app. Johnny Thunder by Alex Toth (8/48); western theme begins (Scarce)	226	452	678	1446	2473	3500
101-Last Mutt & Jeff (Scarce)	155	310	465	992	1696	2400
102-Last Green Lantern, Black Pirate & Dr. Mid-Nite (Scarce)	271	542	813	1734	2967	4200
...No. 16 (Facsimile Edition) (12/23, $6.99) Reprints entire issue with original ads						7.00

NOTE: *No Atom in 47, 62-69.* **Kinstler** *Black Pirate-89.* **Stan Aschmeier** *a (Dr. Mid-Nite) 25-84; c-7.* **Mayer** *c-1, 2(part), 6, 10.* **Moldoff** *c-16-23.* **Nodell** *c-31.* **Paul Reinman** *a (Green Lantern)-53-55p, 56-84, 87; (Black Pirate)-83-88, 90; c-52, 55-76, 78, 80, 81, 87.* **Toth** *a-88, 92, 96, 98-102; c(p)-92, 96-102. Scribbly by* **Mayer** *in #1-59. Ultra Man by* **Mayer** *in #8-19.*

ALL AMERICAN COMICS
DC Comics: April 1939

nn - Ashcan comic, not distributed to newsstands, only for in house use. Cover art is Adventure Comics #33 and interior from Detective Comics #23. A CGC 7.5 copy sold for $7466 in December 2014 and for $15,000 in July 2017.

ALL-AMERICAN COMICS (Also see All Star Comics 1999 crossover titles)
DC Comics: May, 1999 ($1.99, one-shot)

	NM- 9.2
1-Golden Age Green Lantern and Johnny Thunder; Barreto-a	4.00

ALL-AMERICAN MEN OF WAR (Previously All-American Western)
National Periodical Publ.: No. 127, Aug-Sept, 1952 - No. 117, Sept-Oct, 1966

	GD 2.0	VG 4.0	FN 6.0	VF 8.0	VF/NM 9.0	NM- 9.2
127 (#1, 1952)	145	290	435	1196	2698	4200
128 (1952)	64	128	192	512	1156	1800
2(12-1/52-53)-5	55	110	165	444	997	1550
6-Devil Dog story; Ghost Squadron story	42	84	126	311	706	1100
7-10: 8-Sgt. Storm Cloud-s	42	84	126	311	706	1100
11-16,18: 18-Last precode; 1st Kubert-c (2/55)	36	72	108	266	596	925
17-1st Frogman-s in this title	38	76	114	285	641	1000
19,20,22-27	29	58	87	209	467	725
21-Easy Co. prototype	35	70	105	252	564	875
28 (12/55)-1st Sgt. Rock prototype; Kubert-a	68	136	204	544	1222	1900
29,30,32-Wood-a	29	58	87	209	467	725
31,33,34,36-38,40: 34-Gunner prototype-s. 36-Little Sure Shot prototype-s. 38-1st S.A. issue	27	54	81	189	400	650
35-Greytone-c	36	72	108	259	580	900
39 (11/56)-2nd Sgt. Rock prototype; 1st Easy Co.?	46	92	138	340	770	1200
41,43-47,49,50: 46-Tankbusters-c	23	46	69	161	356	550
42-Pre-Sgt. Rock Easy Co.-c/s	30	60	90	216	483	750
48-Easy Co.-c/s; Nick app.; Kubert-a	30	60	90	216	483	750
51-56,58-62,65,66: 61-Gunner-c/s	19	38	57	131	291	450
57(5/58),63,64-Pre-Sgt. Rock Easy Co.-c/s	25	50	75	175	388	600
67-1st Gunner & Sarge by Andru & Esposito	61	122	183	488	1094	1700
68,69: 68-2nd app. Gunner & Sarge. 69-1st Tank Killer-c/s	23	46	69	161	356	550
70	17	34	51	117	259	400
71-80: 71,72,76-Tank Killer-c/s. 74-Minute Commandos-c/s	13	26	39	89	195	300
81-Greytone-c	13	26	39	91	201	310
82-Johnny Cloud begins(1st app.), ends #117	36	72	108	259	580	900
83-2nd Johnny Cloud	18	36	54	128	284	440
84-88: 88-Last 10¢ issue	11	22	33	76	163	250
89-100: 89-Battle Aces of 3 Wars begins, ends #98. 89,90-Panels from these issues used by artist Roy Lichtenstein for famous paintings	9	18	27	60	120	180
101-111,113-116: 110,11-Greytone-c. 111,114,115-Johnny Cloud	7	14	21	44	82	120
112-Balloon Buster series begins, ends #114,116	7	14	21	48	89	130
117-Johnny Cloud-c & 3-part story	7	14	21	49	92	135

NOTE: *Frogman stories in 17, 38, 44, 45, 50, 51, 53, 55-58, 63, 65, 66, 72, 76, 77.* **Colan** *a-112.* **Drucker** *a-47, 58, 61, 63, 65, 69, 71, 74, 76.* **Grandenetti** *c(p)-127, 128, 2-17(most).* **Heath** *a-14, 27, 32, 38, 41, 43, 53, 55, 58, 62, 64, 71, 75, 76, 78, 95, 111-117; c-85, 91, 94-96, 100, 101, 110-112, others?* **Infantino** *a-8.* **Kirby** *a-29.* **Krigstein** *a-128('52), 2, 3.* **Kubert** *a-22, 24, 28, 38, 39, 41-43, 47-50, 52, 53, 55, 56, 69, 63-65, 69, 71-73, 76, 102, 103, 105, 106, 108, 114; c-41, 44, 52, 54, 55, 58, 64, 69, 76, 77, 79, 102-106, 108, 113-117, others? Tank Killer in 69, 71, 76 by Kubert?* **Russ Heath** *c-55, 57, 61, 62, 71, 72, 74-76, 80.* **J. Severin** *a-58.*

ALL AMERICAN MEN OF WAR
DC Comics: Aug/Sept. 1952

nn - Ashcan comic, not distributed to newsstands, only for in-house use. Cover art is All Star Western #58 and interior from Mr. District Attorney #21. A GD+ copy sold for $1195 in 2012.

ALL-AMERICAN SPORTS
Charlton Comics: Oct, 1967

	GD 2.0	VG 4.0	FN 6.0	VF 8.0	VF/NM 9.0	NM- 9.2
1	4	8	14	23	37	50

ALL-AMERICAN WESTERN (Formerly All-American Comics; Becomes All-American Men of War)
National Periodical Publ.: No. 103, Nov, 1948 - No. 126, June-July, 1952 (103-121: 52 pgs.)

	GD 2.0	VG 4.0	FN 6.0	VF 8.0	VF/NM 9.0	NM- 9.2
103-Johnny Thunder & his horse Black Lightning continues by Toth, ends #126; Foley of The Fighting 5th, Minstrel Maverick, & Overland Coach begin; Captain Tootsie by Beck; mentioned in Love and Death	68	136	204	435	743	1050
104-Kubert-a	41	82	123	256	428	600
105,107-Kubert-a	37	74	111	222	361	500
106,108-110,112: 112-Kurtzman's "Pot-Shot Pete" (1 pg.)	30	60	90	177	289	400
111,114-116-Kubert-a	32	64	96	188	307	425
113-Intro. Swift Deer, J. Thunder's new sidekick (4-5/50); classic Toth-c; Kubert-a	36	72	108	211	343	475
117-126: 121-Kubert-a; bondage-c	24	44	66	132	216	300

NOTE: *G. Kane c(p)-112, 119, 120, 123.* **Kubert** *a-103-105, 107, 111, 112(1 pg.), 113-116, 121.* **Toth** *a-103-125; c(p)-103-111,113-116, 121, 122, 124-126. Some copies of #125 have #12 on-c.*

ALL COMICS
Chicago Nite Life News: 1945

	GD 2.0	VG 4.0	FN 6.0	VF 8.0	VF/NM 9.0	NM- 9.2
1	21	42	63	122	199	275

ALLEGRA
Image Comics (WildStorm): Aug, 1996 - No. 4, Dec, 1996 ($2.50)

	NM- 9.2
1-4	4.00

All-American Men of War #67 © DC

All Flash #1 © DC

All Funny Comics #10 © DC

	GD 2.0	VG 4.0	FN 6.0	VF 8.0	VF/NM 9.0	NM- 9.2

ALL EIGHT EYES
Dark Horse Comics: Apr, 2023 - No. 4, Jul, 2023 ($3.99)

1-4-Steve Foxe-s/Piotr Kowalski-a						4.00

ALLEY CAT (Alley Baggett)
Image Comics: July, 1999 - No. 6, Mar, 2000 ($2.50/$2.95)

Preview Edition						6.00
Prelude						5.00
Prelude w/variant-c						6.00
1-Photo-c						3.00
1-Painted-c by Dorian						4.00
1-Another Universe Edition, 1-Wizard World Edition						7.00
2-4: 4-Twin towers on-c						3.00
5,6-($2.95)						3.00
Lingerie Edition (10/99, $4.95) Photos, pin-ups, cover gallery						5.00
...Vs. Lady Pendragon ('99, $3.00) Stinsman-c						3.00

ALLEY OOP (See The Comics, The Funnies, Red Ryder and Super Book #9)
Dell Publishing Co.: No. 3, 1942

Four Color 3 (#1)	57	114	171	456	1028	1600

ALLEY OOP
Argo Publ.: Nov, 1955 - No. 3, Mar, 1956 (Newspaper reprints)

1	21	42	63	122	199	275
2,3	14	28	42	82	121	160

ALLEY OOP
Dell Publishing Co.: 12-2/62-63 - No. 2, 9-11/63

1	6	12	18	41	76	110
2	5	10	15	34	60	85

ALLEY OOP
Standard Comics: No. 10, Sept, 1947 - No. 18, Oct, 1949

10	36	72	108	211	343	475
11-16	26	52	78	154	252	350
17,18-Schomburg-c	42	84	126	265	445	625

ALLEY OOP ADVENTURES
Antarctic Press: Aug, 1998 - No. 3, Dec, 1998 ($2.95)

1-3-Jack Bender-s/a						3.00

ALLEY OOP ADVENTURES (Alley Oop Quarterly in indicia)
Antarctic Press: Sept, 1999 - No. 3, Mar, 2000 ($2.50/$2.99, B&W)

1-3-Jack Bender-s/a						3.00

ALL-FAMOUS CRIME (2nd series - Formerly Law Against Crime #1-3; becomes All-Famous Police Cases #6 on)
Star Publications: No. 8, 5/51 - No. 10, 11/51; No. 4, 2/52 - No. 5, 5/52;

8 (#1-1st series)	39	78	117	240	395	550
9 (#2)-Used in SOTI, illo- "The wish to hurt or kill couples in lovers' lanes is a not uncommon perversion;" L.B. Cole-c/a(r)/Law-Crime #3	53	106	159	334	567	800
10 (#3)	32	64	96	188	307	425
4 (#4-2nd series)-Formerly Law-Crime	32	64	96	188	307	425
5 (#5) Becomes All-Famous Police Cases #6	30	60	90	177	289	400

NOTE: All have L.B. Cole covers.

ALL FAMOUS CRIME STORIES (See Fox Giants)

ALL-FAMOUS POLICE CASES (Formerly All Famous Crime #5)
Star Publications: No. 6, Feb, 1952 - No. 16, Sept, 1954

6	47	94	141	296	498	700
7-Matt Baker story	84	168	252	538	919	1300
8-Marijuana story	53	106	159	334	567	800
9-16	30	60	90	177	289	400

NOTE: L. B. Cole c-all; a-15, 1pg. Hollingsworth a-15.

ALL-FLASH (...Quarterly No. 1-5)
National Per. Publ./All-American: Summer, 1941 - No. 32, Dec-Jan, 1947-48

1-Origin The Flash retold by E. E. Hibbard; Hibbard c-1-10,12-14,16,31p.						
	1475	2950	4425	10,300	17,650	25,000
2-Origin recap	300	600	900	1856	3178	4500
3,4	174	348	522	1114	1907	2700
5-Winky, Blinky & Noddy begins (1st app.), ends #32						
	129	258	387	826	1413	2000
6-Has full page ad for Wonder Woman #1	123	246	369	787	1344	1900
7-10	116	232	348	742	1271	1800
11,13: 13-The King app.	106	212	318	673	1162	1650
12-Origin/1st The Thinker	135	270	405	864	1482	2100
14-Green Lantern cameo	119	238	357	762	1306	1850

15-20: 18-Mutt & Jeff begins, ends #22	90	180	270	576	988	1400
21-31	74	148	222	470	810	1150
32-Origin/1st app. The Fiddler; 1st Star Sapphire	314	628	942	2198	3849	5500
All-Flash Quarterly ashcan			(a CGC 7.0 copy sold for $8150 in 2012)			

NOTE: Book length stories in 2-13, 16. Bondage c-31, 32. Martin Nodell c-15, 17-28.

ALL FLASH (Leads into Flash [2nd series] #231)
DC Comics: Sept, 2007 ($2.99, one-shot)

1-Wally West hunts down Bart's killers; Waid-s; two covers by Middleton & Sienkiewicz						3.00

ALL FOR LOVE (Young Love V3#5-on)
Prize Publications: Apr-May, 1957 - V3#4, Dec-Jan, 1959-60

V1#1	13	26	39	89	195	300
2-6: 5-Orlando-c	7	14	21	46	86	125
V2#1-5(1/59), 5(3/59)	6	12	18	38	69	100
V3#1(5/59), 1(7/59)-4: 2-Powell-a	5	10	15	35	63	90

ALL FUNNY COMICS
Tilsam Publ./National Periodical Publications (Detective): Winter, 1943-44 - No. 23, May-June, 1948

1-Genius Jones (see Adventure #77 for debut), Buzzy (1st app., ends #4), Dover & Clover (see More Fun #93) begin; Bailey-a	68	136	204	435	743	1050
2	27	54	81	158	259	360
3-10	17	34	51	98	154	210
11-13,15,18,19-Genius Jones app.	15	30	45	88	137	185
14,17,20-23	12	24	36	69	97	125
16-DC Super Heroes app.	37	74	111	222	361	500

ALL GOOD
St. John Publishing Co.: Oct, 1949 (50¢, 260 pgs.)

nn-(8 St. John comics bound together)	129	258	387	826	1413	2000

NOTE: Also see Li'l Audrey Yearbook & Treasury of Comics.

ALL GOOD COMICS (See Fox Giants)
Fox Feature Syndicate: Spring, 1946 (36 pgs.)

1-Joy Family, Dick Transom, Rick Evans, One Round Hogan	32	64	96	188	307	425

ALL GREAT
William H. Wise & Co.: nd (1945?) (132 pgs.)

nn-Capt. Jack Terry, Joan Mason, Girl Reporter, Baron Doomsday; Torture scenes	53	106	159	334	567	800

ALL GREAT COMICS (See Fox Giants)
Fox Feature Syndicate: 1946 (36 pgs.)

1-Crazy House, Bertie Benson Boy Detective, Gussie the Gob	31	62	93	182	296	410

ALL GREAT COMICS (Formerly Phantom Lady #13? Dagar, Desert Hawk. No. 14 on)
Fox Feature Syndicate: No. 14, Oct, 1947 - No. 13, Dec, 1947 (Newspaper strip reprints)

14(#12)-Brenda Starr & Texas Slim-r (Scarce)	68	136	204	435	743	1050
13-Origin Dagar, Desert Hawk; Brenda Starr (all-r); Kamen-c; Dagar covers begin	142	284	426	909	1555	2200

ALL-GREAT CONFESSION MAGAZINE (See Fox Giants)

ALL-GREAT CONFESSIONS (See Fox Giants)

ALL GREAT CRIME STORIES (See Fox Giants)

ALL GREAT JUNGLE ADVENTURES (See Fox Giants)

ALL HALLOW'S EVE
Innovation Publishing: 1991 ($4.95, 52 pgs.)

1-Painted-c/a	1	3	4	6	8	10

ALL HERO COMICS
Fawcett Publications: Mar, 1943 (100 pgs., cardboard-c)

1-Capt. Marvel Jr., Capt. Midnight, Golden Arrow, Ibis the Invincible, Spy Smasher, Lance O'Casey; 1st Banshee O'Brien; Raboy-c	206	412	618	1318	2259	3200

ALL HUMOR COMICS
Quality Comics Group: Spring, 1946 - No. 17, December, 1949

1	28	56	84	165	270	375
2-Atomic Tot story; Gustavson-a	15	30	45	83	124	165
3-9: 9-Intro Kelly Poole who is cover feature #3 on. 5-1st app. Hickory?						
8-Gustavson-a	10	20	30	56	76	95
10-17	9	18	27	52	69	85

ALLIGATOR LOKI (Printing of Infinity Comics digital series from the Marvel Unlimited app)
Marvel Comics: Nov, 2023 ($5.99, one-shot)

1-Silent all-ages short humor stories; Thor & Loki app.; Alyssa Wong-s/Bob Quinn-a						6.00

ALL LOVE (...Romances No. 26)(Formerly Ernie Comics)

	GD	VG	FN	VF	VF/NM	NM-		GD	VG	FN	VF	VF/NM	NM-
	2.0	4.0	6.0	8.0	9.0	9.2		2.0	4.0	6.0	8.0	9.0	9.2

Ace Periodicals (Current Books): No. 26, May, 1949 - No. 32, May, 1950

	GD	VG	FN	VF	VF/NM	NM-
26 (No. 1)-Ernie, Lily Belle app.	17	34	51	98	154	210
27-L. B. Cole-a	19	38	57	111	176	240
28-32	14	28	42	80	115	150

ALL-NEGRO COMICS
All-Negro Comics: June, 1947 (15¢)

	GD	VG	FN	VF	VF/NM	NM-
1 (Rare)	3200	6400	9600	17,300	24,650	32,000

NOTE: Seldom found in fine or mint condition; many copies have brown pages.

ALL-NEW ALL-DIFFERENT AVENGERS (Follows Secret Wars event)
Marvel Comics: Jan, 2016 - No. 15, Dec, 2015 ($4.99/$3.99)

1-($4.99) Spider-Man (Miles), Ms. Marvel, Nova join; Waid-s/Adam Kubert & Asrar-a ... 5.00
2-15-($3.99) Main cover by Alex Ross. 2,3-Warbringer app.; Kubert-a. 4-6,9-10-Asrar-a.
7,8-Standoff tie-in; Adam Kubert-a. 9-Intro. new Wasp (Nadia). 13-15-Civil War II tie-in ... 4.00
Annual 1 (10/16, $4.99) Fan-fic short stories by various incl. Waid/Zdarsky & Allegri ... 5.00

ALL-NEW ALL-DIFFERENT MARVEL UNIVERSE
Marvel Comics: May, 2016 ($4.99, one-shot)

1-Handbook-style entries; profiles of major characters; Marquez-c ... 5.00

ALL-NEW ALL-DIFFERENT POINT ONE (Follows Secret Wars event)
Marvel Comics: Dec, 2015 ($5.99, one-shot)

1-Preludes to new titles: Carnage, Daredevil, All-New Inhumans, Agents of S.H.I.E.L.D.,
Rocket Raccoon & Groot, and Contest of Champions; Del Mundo-c ... 6.00

ALL-NEW ATOM, THE (See The Atom and DCU Brave New World)
DC Comics: Sept, 2006 - No. 25, Sept, 2008 ($2.99)

1-25: 1-18-Simone-s. 1-Intro Ryan Choi; Byrne-a thru #3. 4-11-Barrows-a. 12,13-Chronos
app. 14,15-Countdown x-over. 17,18-Wonder Woman app. ... 3.00
...: Future/Past TPB (2007, $14.99) r/#7-11 ... 15.00
...: My Life in Miniature TPB (2007, $14.99) r/#1-6 and app. in DCU Brave New World #1 ... 15.00
...: Small Wonder TPB (2008, $17.99) r/#17,18,21-25 ... 18.00
...: The Hunt For Ray Palmer TPB (2008, $14.99) r/#12-16 ... 15.00

ALL-NEW BATMAN: BRAVE & THE BOLD (See Batman: The Brave and the Bold)

ALL-NEW CAPTAIN AMERICA (See Captain America #25 - 2014 series)
Marvel Comics: Jan, 2015 - No. 6, Jun, 2015 ($3.99)

	GD	VG	FN	VF	VF/NM	NM-
1-Sam Wilson as Captain America, Ian as Nomad; Immonen-a		2	4	6	8	10	12
2-6							4.00
... Special 1 (7/15, $4.99) Loveness-s/Morgan-a; Inhumans & Spider-Man app.							5.00

ALL-NEW CAPTAIN AMERICA: FEAR HIM (Sam Wilson as Cap)
Marvel Comics: Jan, 2015 - No. 4, Apr, 2015 ($3.99, limited series)

1-4-Hopeless & Remender-s/Kudranski-a/Bianchi-c; The Scarecrow app. ... 4.00

ALL-NEW CLASSIC CAPTAIN CANUCK
Chapterhouse Comics: No. 0, Feb, 2016 - No. 4, Apr, 2017 ($4.99/$3.99)

0-($4.99) Short stories; Ed Brisson-s; art by various ... 5.00
1-4-($3.99) Brisson-s/Freeman-a; 2 covers on each ... 4.00

ALL-NEW COLLECTORS' EDITION (Formerly Limited Collectors' Edition: see for C-57, C-59)
DC Comics, Inc.: Jan, 1978 - Vol. 8, No. C-62, 1979 (No. 54-58: 76 pgs.)

	GD	VG	FN	VF	VF/NM	NM-
C-53-Rudolph the Red-Nosed Reindeer	5	10	15	35	63	90
C-54-Superman Vs. Wonder Woman	6	12	18	38	69	100
C-55-Superboy & the Legion of Super-Heroes; Wedding of Lightning Lad &						
Saturn Girl; Grell-c/a	4	8	12	28	47	65
C-56-Superman Vs. Muhammad Ali: Wraparound Neal Adams-c/a; Adams & O'Neil-s						
(see "Superman Vs. Muhammad Ali" for reprint)	12	24	36	83	182	280
C-56-Superman Vs. Muhammad Ali (Whitman variant)-low print						
	15	30	45	103	227	350

C-57, C-59-(See Limited Collectors' Edition)

	GD	VG	FN	VF	VF/NM	NM-
C-58-Superman Vs. Shazam; Buckler-c/a; Black Adam's 2nd Bronze Age app.						
	6	12	18	37	66	95
C-60-Rudolph's Summer Fun(8/78)	5	10	15	31	53	75

C-61-(See Famous First Edition-Superman #1)

	GD	VG	FN	VF	VF/NM	NM-
C-62-Superman the Movie (68 pgs.; 1979)-Photo-c from movie plus photos inside (also see						
DC Special Series #25 for Superman II)	4	8	12	23	37	50

ALL-NEW COMICS (...Short Story Comics No. 1-3)
Family Comics (Harvey Publications): Jan, 1943 - No. 14, Nov, 1946; No. 15, Mar-Apr, 1947
(10 x 13-1/2")

	GD	VG	FN	VF	VF/NM	NM-
1-Steve Case, Crime Rover, Johnny Rebel, Kayo Kane, The Echo, Night Hawk, Ray O'Light,						
Detective Shane begin (all 1st app.?); Red Blazer on cover only; Sultan-a; Nazi WWII-c						
	303	606	909	1924	3711	5300
2-Origin Scarlet Phantom by Kubert; Nazi WWII-c	181	362	543	1158	1979	2800
3-Nazi WWII-c	135	270	405	864	1482	2100
4-Sci-fi Nazi monsters bondage-c	300	600	900	2010	3505	5000
5-Classic Schomburg Japanese WWII-c showing Japanese using Human Suicide bombs						
falling on the Capitol building	290	580	870	1856	3178	4500
6-11: Schomburg on all. 9-11-Japanese WWII-c. 6-8 Nazi WWII-c. 6-The Boy Heroes						
& Red Blazer (text story) begin, end #12; Black Cat app.; intro. Sparky in Red Blazer.						
7-Kubert, Powell-a; Black Cat & Zebra app. 8,9-Shock Gibson app.; Kubert, Powell-a;						
Schomburg-c. 9-Black Cat app.; Kubert-a. 10-The Zebra app. (from Green Hornet Comics);						
Kubert-a(3). 11-Girl Commandos, Man In Black app.						
	187	374	561	1197	2049	2900
12-Kubert-a; Japanese WWII-c	103	206	309	659	1130	1600
13-Stuntman by Simon & Kirby; Green Hornet, Joe Palooka, Flying Fool app.;						
Green Hornet-c	58	116	174	371	636	900
14-The Green Hornet & The Man in Black Called Fate by Powell, Joe Flying Fool app.;						
Flying Fool app.; J. Palooka-c by Ham Fisher	47	94	141	296	498	700
15-(Rare)-Small size (5-1/2x8-1/2"; B&W; 32 pgs.). Distributed to mail subscribers only.						
Black Cat and Joe Palooka app.	200	400	600	1280	2190	3100

NOTE: Also see Boy Explorers No. 2, Flash Gordon No. 5, and Stuntman No. 3. **Powell** a-11. **Schomburg** c-5-11. Captain Red Blazer & Spark on c-5-11 (w/Boy Heroes #12).

ALL-NEW DOOP (X-Men)
Marvel Comics: Jun, 2014 - No. 5, Nov, 2014 ($3.99, limited series)

1-5-Milligan-s/Lafuente-a; Kitty Pryde and X-Men app. 3-5-The Anarchist app. ... 4.00

ALL-NEW EXECUTIVE ASSISTANT: IRIS (Volume 4) (Also see Executive Assistant: Iris)
Aspen MLT: Sept, 2013 - No. 5, Jun, 2014 ($1.00/$3.99)

1-($1.00) Buccellato-s/Qualano-a; multiple covers ... 3.00
2-5-($3.99) Multiple covers ... 4.00
...: Enemies Among Us 1 (12/16, $4.99) Wohl-s/Cafaro-a; Hernandez-s/Green-a; multiple-c 5.00

ALL NEW FATHOM (See Fathom)

ALL-NEW FIREFLY (Also see Firefly)
BOOM! Studios: Feb, 2022 - No. 10, Nov, 2022 ($4.99)

1-10: 1-4-Booher-s/Pérez-a. 5-10-Federici-a ... 5.00
...: Big Damn Finale 1 (12/22, $8.99) Polybagged with cardboard to conceal cover image 9.00

ALL-NEW GHOST RIDER (Also see the 2017 Ghost Rider series)
Marvel Comics: May, 2014 - No. 12, May, 2015 ($3.99)

1-Felipe Smith-s/Tradd Moore-a; origin of Robbie Reyes ... 5.00

		GD	VG	FN	VF	VF/NM	NM-
2		3	6	9	19	30	40
		1	3	4	6	8	10
3-12: 6-10-Damion Scott-a							5.00

ALL-NEW GUARDIANS OF THE GALAXY (Continues in Guardians of the Galaxy #146)
Marvel Comics: Jul, 2017 - No. 12, Dec, 2017 ($3.99)

1-12: 1-Grandmaster app.; Duggan-s/Kuder-a. 2,4-The Collector app. 3-Irving-a ... 4.00
Annual 1 (8/17, $4.99) Tie-in to Secret Empire; Beyruth-a; Yondu & Mantis app. ... 5.00

ALL-NEW HAWKEYE
Marvel Comics: May, 2015 - No. 5, Nov, 2015 ($3.99)

1-Jeff Lemire-s/Ramón Pérez-a/c; Kate Bishop app.; flashback to circus childhood ... 6.00
2-5 ... 5.00

ALL-NEW HAWKEYE
Marvel Comics: Jan, 2016 - No. 6, Jun, 2016 ($3.99)

1-Lemire-s/Pérez-a/c; Kate Bishop app.; flashforward 30 years; Mandarin app. ... 6.00
2-6: 2,3-Flashforward 30 years; Mandarin app. ... 4.00

ALL-NEW INHUMANS
Marvel Comics: Feb, 2016 - No. 11, Nov, 2016 ($3.99)

1-($4.99)-Asmus & Soule-s/Caselli-a; Crystal & Gorgon app. ... 5.00
2-11-($3.99) 2-4-The Commissar app. 5,6-Spider-Man app. ... 4.00

ALL-NEW INVADERS
Marvel Comics: Mar, 2014 - No. 15, Apr, 2015 ($3.99)

1-15: 1-Capt. America, Bucky, Namor & Jim Hammond team; Robinson-s/Pugh-a.
6,7-Original Sin tie-in ... 4.00

ALL-NEW MARVEL NOW! POINT ONE
Marvel Comics: Mar, 2014 ($5.99, one-shot preview of upcoming series)

1-Previews of Loki, Silver Surfer, Black Widow, Ms. Marvel, Avengers, All-New Invaders 6.00
... No. 1 Facsimile Edition (9/23, 7.99) Reprints issue with original promotional ads ... 8.00

ALL NEW MICHAEL TURNER'S FATHOM (See Fathom)

ALL NEW MICHAEL TURNER'S SOULFIRE (See Soulfire)

ALL-NEW OFFICIAL HANDBOOK OF THE MARVEL UNIVERSE A TO Z
Marvel Comics: 2006 - No. 12, 2006 ($3.99, limited series)

1-12-Profile pages of Marvel characters not covered in 2004-2005 Official Handbooks 4.00
...: Update 1-4 (2007, $3.99) Profile pages ... 4.00

ALL-NEW ULTIMATES
Marvel Comics: Jun, 2014 - No. 12, Mar, 2015 ($3.99)

1-12: Miles Morales Spider-Man, Spider-Woman, Cloak and Dagger, Kitty Pryde and
Bombshell team. 5,6-Crossbones app. ... 4.00

ALL-NEW WOLVERINE (Laura Kinney X-23 as Wolverine)
Marvel Comics: Jan, 2016 - No. 35, Jul, 2018 ($4.99/$3.99)

		GD	VG	FN	VF	VF/NM	NM-
1-($4.99) Tom Taylor-s/David Lopez-a; Angel app.		5	6	9	16	23	30
2-Intro. Gabby Kinney; Taskmaster app.		4	8	12	25	40	55
3-2nd app. Gabby Kinney; Taskmaster app.		1	3	5	6	8
4-27,29-35-($3.99) 4-Doctor Strange app. 5-Janet Van Dyne app. 7-Squirrel Girl app.							
8,9-Fin Fang Foom app. 10-12-Civil War II tie-in. 16-18-Gambit app. 19-21-Ironheart app.							
22-24-Guardians of the Galaxy app.; Yu-c. 25-30-Daken app. 31-Deadpool app.							
33-"Old Woman Laura"; future against Doom							4.00
28-1st Honey Badger; Daken app.							6.00
Annual 1 (10/16, $4.99) Gwen Stacy app.; Tom Taylor-s/Marcio Takara-a			1	2	3	5	6	8

ALL-NEW X-FACTOR
Marvel Comics: Mar, 2014 - No. 20, Mar, 2015 ($3.99)

1-20: 1-12-David-s/DiGiandomenico-a; Gambit, Polaris, Quicksilver, Danger app.
13,14-Mhan-a. 14-Scarlet Witch app. 15-17-Axis tie-in ... 4.00

ALL-NEW X-MEN
Marvel Comics: Jan, 2013 - No. 41, Aug, 2015 ($3.99)

1-Bendis-s; Immonen-a and wraparound-c; original X-Men time travel to present ... 6.00
2-24: 6-8-Marquez-a. 9-Avengers app. 8-Avengers app. 16,17-Battle of the Atom tie-in.
18-New uniforms. 22-24-Trial of Jean Grey; Guardians of the Galaxy app. ... 4.00
25-($4.99) Art by Marquez with pages by Timm, Mack, Young, Campbell & many others 5.00
26-41: 30-Pichelli-a. 31-36-X-Men in Ultimate universe; Miles Morales app. 38,39-Black
Vortex x-over; Ronan & Guardians of the Galaxy app.; Sorrentino-a. 40-Iceman revealed
as gay ... 4.00
Annual 1 (2/15, $4.99) Sorrentino-a: Eva Bell and Morgana Le Fey in the past ... 4.00
Special 1 (12/13, $4.99) Superior Spider-Man and the Hulk app. ... 5.00

ALL-NEW X-MEN
Marvel Comics: Feb, 2016 - No. 19, May, 2017 ($3.99)

1-8-Hopeless-s/Bagley-a; original X-Men, Wolverine (X-23), Kid Apocalypse app. ... 4.00
9-($4.99) Apocalypse Wars x-over; Beast & Kid Apocalypse in ancient Egypt ... 5.00
10-19: 10,11-Apocalypse Wars; young Apocalypse app. 17,18-Inhumans app. ... 4.00
Annual 1 (1/17, $4.99) Spotlight on Idie; Sina Grace-s/Cory Smith-a ... 5.00
#1.MU (4/17, $4.99) Monsters Unleashed tie-in; Barberi & Lim-a; Gambit app. ... 5.00

ALL NIGHTER
Image Comics: Jun, 2011 - No. 5, Oct, 2011 ($2.99, B&W, limited series)

All-New X-Men #1 © MAR

All Star Batman #1 © DC

All Star Comics #12 © DC

	GD 2.0	VG 4.0	FN 6.0	VF 8.0	VF/NM 9.0	NM- 9.2

1-5-David Haun-s/a/c ... 3.00

ALL-OUT AVENGERS (Story continues in Avengers Beyond #1)
Marvel Comics: Nov, 2022 - No. 5, Mar, 2023 ($3.99)
1-5-Derek Landy/Greg Land-a; Avengers, Spider-Man and Blade app. ... 4.00

ALL-OUT WAR
DC Comics: Sept-Oct, 1979 - No. 6, Aug, 1980 ($1.00, 68 pgs.)
1-The Viking Commando (origin), Force Three(origin), & Black Eagle Squadron begin
  2 4 6 13 18 22
2-6   2 4 6 8 10 12
NOTE: Ayers a(p)-1-6. Elias r-2. Evans a-1-6. Kubert c-16.

ALL PICTURE ADVENTURE MAGAZINE
St. John Publishing Co.: Oct, 1952 - No. 2, Nov, 1952 (100 pg. Giants, 25¢, squarebound)
1-War comics 65 130 195 416 708 1000
2-Horror-crime comics 84 168 252 538 919 1300
NOTE: Above books contain three St. John comics rebound; variations possible. *Baker* art known in both.

ALL PICTURE ALL TRUE LOVE STORY
St. John Publishing Co.: Oct., 1952 - No. 2, Nov., 1952 (100 pgs., 25¢)
1-Canteen Kate by Matt Baker 258 516 774 1651 2826 4000
2-Baker-c/a 90 180 270 576 988 1400

ALL-PICTURE COMEDY CARNIVAL
St. John Publishing Co.: October, 1952 (100 pgs., 25¢)(Contains 4 rebound comics)
1-Contents can vary; Baker-a 55 110 165 352 601 850

ALL REAL CONFESSION MAGAZINE (See Fox Giants)

ALL ROMANCES (Mr. Risk No. 7 on)
A. A. Wyn (Ace Periodicals): Aug, 1949 - No. 6, June, 1950
1 26 52 78 154 252 350
2 15 30 45 83 124 165
3-6 13 26 39 74 105 135

ALL-SELECT COMICS (Blonde Phantom No. 12 on)
Timely Comics (Daring Comics): Fall, 1943 - No. 11, Fall, 1946
1-Capt. America (by Rico #1), Human Torch, Sub-Mariner begin; Black Widow story (4 pgs.); Classic Schomburg-c 2850 5700 8550 18,800 39,400 60,000
2-Red Skull app. 1100 2200 3300 8350 15,175 22,000
3-The Whizzer begins 541 1082 1623 3950 6975 10,000
4,5-Last Sub-Mariner 432 864 1296 3154 5577 8000
6-9: 6-The Destroyer begins. 8-No Whizzer 314 628 942 2198 3849 5500
10-The Destroyer & Sub-Mariner app.; last Capt. America & Human Torch issue 326 652 978 2282 3991 5700
11-1st app. Blonde Phantom; Miss America app.; all Blonde Phantom-c by Shores 432 864 1296 3154 5577 8000
NOTE: *Schomburg* c-1-10. *Sekowsky* a-7. #7 & 8 show 1944 in indicia, but should be 1945.

ALL SELECT COMICS 70TH ANNIVERARY SPECIAL
Marvel Comics: Sept, 2009 ($3.99, one-shot)
1-New stories of Blonde Phantom and Marvex the Super Robot; r/Marvex G.A. app. ... 6.00

ALL SPORTS COMICS (Formerly Real Sports Comics; becomes All Time Sports Comics No. 4 on)
Hillman Periodicals: No. 2, Dec-Jan, 1948-49; No. 3, Feb-Mar, 1949
2-Krigstein-a(p), Powell, Starr-a 39 78 117 240 395 550
3-Mort Lawrence-a 26 52 78 154 240 350

ALL STAR BATMAN
DC Comics: Oct, 2016 - No. 14, Dec, 2017 ($4.99)
1-Snyder-s/Romita Jr.-a; Two-Face app.; back-up with Shalvey-a 1 3 4 6 8 10
1-Director's Cut ($5.99) r/#1 with B&W art and original script; variant cover gallery ... 10.00
2-5-Snyder-s/Romita Jr.-a; Two-Face app.; back-up with Shalvey-a ... 5.00
6-9-Back-up w/Francavilla-a. 6-Jock-a; Mr. Freeze app. 7-Lotay-a; Poison Ivy app ... 5.00
10-14-Albuquerque-a; back-up with Fiumara-a ... 5.00

ALL STAR BATMAN & ROBIN, THE BOY WONDER
DC Comics: Sept, 2005 - No. 10, Aug, 2008 ($2.99)
1-Two covers; retelling of Robin's origin; Frank Miller-s/Jim Lee-c/a 1 3 4 6 8 10
1-Diamond Retailer Summit Edition (9/05) sketch-c ... 65.00
2-10: 2-7-Two covers by Lee and Miller. 3-Black Canary app. 4-Six pg. Batcave gatefold. 10-Edition without profanity ... 3.00
8-10: 8,9-Variant cover by Neal Adams. 10-Variant-c by Quitely ... 5.00
10-Recalled edition with insufficiently covered profanity inside; Jim Lee-c ... 24.00
10-Recalled edition with variant Quitely-c ... 45.00
... Special Edition (2/06, $3.99) r/#1 with Lee pencil pages and Miller script; new Miller-c ... 4.00
Vol. 1 HC (2008, $24.99, dustjacket) r/#1-9; cover gallery, sketch pages; Schreck intro.

Vol. 1 SC (2009, $19.99) r/#1-9; cover gallery, sketch pages; Schreck intro. ... 20.00

ALL STAR COMICS
DC Comics: Spring 1940
1-Ashcan comic, not distributed to newsstands, only for in-house use. Cover art is Flash Comics #1 and interior from Detective Comics #37. A CGC certified 7.0 copy sold for $15,600 in 2002 and for $21,000 in May 2014.

ALL STAR COMICS (All Star Western No. 58 on)
National Periodical Publ./All-American/DC Comics: Sum, 1940 - No. 57, Febr-Mar, 1951; No. 58, Jan-Feb, 1976 - No. 74, Sept-Oct, 1978
1-The Flash (#1 by E.E. Hibbard), Hawkman (by Shelly), Hourman (by Bernard Baily), The Sandman (by Creig Flessel), The Spectre (by Baily), Biff Bronson, Red White & Blue (ends #2) begin; Ultra Man's only app. (#1-3 are quarterly; #4 begins bi-monthly issues) 1550 3100 4650 11,600 21,800 32,000
2-Green Lantern (by Martin Nodell), Johnny Thunder begin; Green Lantern figure swipe from the cover of All-American Comics #16; Flash figure swipe from cover of Flash Comics #8; Moldoff/Bailey/a-c (cut & paste-c.) 703 1406 2109 5132 9066 13,000
3-Origin & 1st app. The Justice Society of America (Win/40); Dr. Fate & The Atom begin, Red Tornado cameo 6750 13,500 20,250 54,000 104,500 155,000
3-Reprint, Oversize 13-1/2x10". **WARNING:** This comic is an exact reprint of the original except for its size. DC published in 1974 with a second cover titling it as a Famous First Edition. There have been many reported cases of the outer cover being removed and the interior sold as the original edition. The reprint with the new outer cover removed is practically worthless. See Famous First Edition for value.
4-1st adventure for J.S.A. 730 1460 2190 5329 9415 13,500
5-1st app. Shiera Sanders as Hawkgirl (1st costumed super-heroine, 6-7/41) 703 1406 2109 5132 9066 13,000
6-Johnny Thunder joins JSA 300 600 900 2040 3570 5100
7-First time ever Superman and Batman appear in a story together; Superman, Batman and Flash become honorary members; last Hourman; Doiby Dickles app. 432 864 1296 3154 5577 8000
8-Origin & 1st app. Wonder Woman (12-1/41-42)(added as 9 pgs. book is 76 pgs.; origin cont'd in Sensation #1; see W.W. #1 for more detailed origin); Dr. Fate dons new helmet; Hop Harrigan text stories & Starman begin; Shiera app.; Hop Harrigan JSA guest; Starman & Dr. Mid-Nite become members 22,500 45,000 67,500 180,000 285,000 390,000
9-11: 9-JSA's girlfriends cameo; Shiera app.; J. Edgar Hoover of FBI made associate member of JSA. 10-Flash, Green Lantern cameo; Sandman new costume. 11-Wonder Woman begins; Spectre cameo; Shiera app.; Moldoff Hawkman-c 314 628 942 2198 3849 5500
12-Wonder Woman becomes JSA Secretary 320 640 960 2240 3920 5600
13,15: Sandman w/Sandy in #14 & 15. 13-Hitler app. in book-length sci-fi story. 15-Origin & 1st app. Brain Wave; Shiera app. 277 554 831 1759 3030 4300
14-(12/42) Junior JSA Club begins; w/membership offer & premiums 290 580 870 1856 3178 4500
16-20: 19-Sandman w/Sandy. 20-Dr. Fate & Sandman cameo 258 516 774 1651 2826 4000
21-23: 21-Spectre & Atom cameo; Dr. Fate by Kubert; Dr. Fate, Sandman end. 22-Last Hop Harrigan; Flag-c. 23-Origin/1st app. Psycho Pirate; last Spectre & Starman 248 400 600 1280 2190 3100
24-Flash & Green Lantern cameo; Mr. Terrific only app.; Wildcat, JSA guest; Kubert Hawkman begins; Hitler-c 213 426 639 1363 2332 3300
25-27: 25-Flash & Green Lantern start again. 26-Robot-c. 27-Wildcat, JSA guest (#24-26: only All-American imprint) 181 362 543 1158 1979 2800
28-32 168 336 504 1075 1838 2600
33-Solomon Grundy & Doiby Dickles app; classic Solomon Grundy cover 443 886 1329 3234 5717 8200
34,35-Johnny Thunder cameo in both 155 310 465 992 1696 2400
36-Batman & Superman JSA guests 423 846 1269 3000 5250 7500
37-Johnny Thunder cameo; origin & 1st app. Injustice Society; last Kubert Hawkman 300 600 900 1920 3310 4700
38-Black Canary begins; JSA Death issue 265 530 795 1694 2897 4100
39,40: 39-Last Johnny Thunder 168 336 504 1075 1838 2600
41-Black Canary joins JSA; Injustice Society app. (2nd app.?) 194 388 582 1242 2121 3000
42-Atom & the Hawkman don new costumes 219 438 657 1402 2401 3400
43-49,51-56: 43-New logo; Robot-c. 55-Sci-Fi story. 56-Robot-c 148 296 444 947 1624 2300
50-Frazetta art, 3 pgs. 155 310 465 992 1696 2400
57-Kubert-a, 6 pgs. (Scarce); last app. G.A. Green Lantern, Flash & Dr. Mid-Nite 226 452 678 1485 2543 3500
V12 #58-(1976) JSA (Flash, Hawkman, Dr. Mid-Nite, Wildcat, Dr. Fate, Green Lantern, Robin & Star Spangled Kid) app.; intro. Power Girl 12 24 36 79 170 260
V12 #59,60: 59-Estrada & Wood-a 3 6 9 21 33 45
V12 #61-68: 62-65-Wood-c/a; Vandal Savage app. 66-Injustice Society app. 68-Psycho Pirate app. 3 6 9 21 33 45

	GD 2.0	VG 4.0	FN 6.0	VF 8.0	VF/NM 9.0	NM- 9.2

V12 #69-1st Earth-2 Huntress (Helena Wayne) — 6 12 18 42 79 115
V12 #70-73: 70-Full intro. of Huntress. 72-Thorn on c-3 — 33 45
V12 #74-(44 pgs.) Last issue, story continues in Adventure Comics #461 & 462 (death of Earth-2 Batman; Staton-c/a — 5 10 15 30 50 70
...No. 3 (Facsimile Edition) (1/24, $6.99) Reprints entire issue with original ads — 7.00
(See Justice Society Vol. 1 TPB for reprints of V12 revival)
NOTE: No Atom-27, 36; no Dr. Fate-13; no Flash-8, 9, 11-23; no Green Lantern-8, 9,11-23; Hawkman in 1-57 (only one to app. in all 57 issues); no Johnny Thunder-5, 36; no Wonder Woman-9, 10, 23. Book length stories in 4-9, 11-14, 18-22, 25, 26, 29, 30, 32-36, 40, 42, 43. Johnny Peril in #42-46, 48, 49, 51, 52,54-57. Baily a-1-10, 12, 13, 14i, 15-20. Burnley Starman-8-13; c-12, 13. Grell c-58. E.E. Hibbard c-3, 4, 6-10. Infantino c-40. Lampert/Baily/Flessel c-1, 2. Moldoff Hawkman-3-23; c-11. Mart Nodell c-25i, 26i, 27-32. Purcell c-5. Simon & Kirby Sandman 14-17, 19. Staton a-66-74p. c-74p. Toth a-37(2), 38(2), 40, 41. Wood a-58-63i, 64, 65; c-63i, 64, 65. Issues 1-7, 9-16 are 68 pgs.; #8 is 76 pgs.; #17-19 are 60 pgs.; #20-57 are 52 pgs.

ALL STAR COMICS (Also see crossover 1999 editions of Adventure, All-American, National, Sensation, Smash, Star Spangled and Thrilling Comics)
DC Comics: May, 1999 - No. 2, May, 1999 ($2.95, bookends for JSA x-over)
1,2-Justice Society in World War 2; Robinson-s/Johnson-c — 5.00
1-RRP Edition — 60.00
...80-Page Giant (9/99, $4.95) Phantom Lady app. — 1 2 3 6 8

ALL STAR INDEX, THE
Independent Comics Group (Eclipse): Feb, 1987 ($2.00, Baxter paper)
1 — 1 3 4 6 8 10

ALL-STAR SECTION EIGHT (Also see Sixpack and Dogwelder: Hard Travelin' Heroz)
DC Comics: Aug, 2015 - No. 6, Feb, 2016 ($2.99, limited series)
1-6-Ennis-s/McCrea-a/Conner-c. 1-Batman app. 4-Wonder Woman app. 6-Superman — 4.00

ALL-STAR SQUADRON (See Justice League of America #193)
DC Comics: Sept, 1981 - No. 67, Mar, 1987
1-Original Atom, Hawkman, Dr. Mid-Nite, Robotman (origin), Plastic Man, Johnny Quick, Liberty Belle, Shining Knight begin — 2 4 6 10 14 18
2-10: 3-Solomon Grundy app. 4,7-Spectre app. 8-Re-intro Steel, the Indestructable Man — 6.00
11-24,26-48,49: 12-Origin G.A. Hawkman retold. 15-JLA, JSA & Crime Syndicate app. 23-Origin/1st app. The Amazing Man. 24-Batman app. 26-Origin Infinity, Inc.(2nd app.); Robin app. 27-Dr. Fate vs. The Spectre. 30-35-Spectre app. 33-Origin Freedom Fighters of Earth-X. 36,37-Superman vs. Capt. Marvel; Ordway-c. 41-Origin Starman — 5.00
25-1st app. Nuklon (Atom Smasher) & Infinity, Inc. (Ordway-a/9/83) — 3 6 9 19 30 40
47-Origin Dr. Fate; McFarlane-a (1st full story)/part-c (7/85) — 3 6 9 21 33 45
50-Double size; Crisis x-over — 2 4 6 8 10 12
51-66: 51-56-Crisis x-over. 61-Origin Liberty Belle. 62-Origin The Shining Knight. 63-Origin Robotman. 65-Origin Johnny Quick. 66-Origin Tarantula
67-Last issue; retells first case of the Justice Society — 2 4 6 10 14 18
Annual 1-3: 1(11/82)-Retells origin of G.A. Atom, Guardian & Wildcat; Jerry Ordway's 1st pencils for DC. (1st work was inking Carmine Infantino in Mystery in Space #117). 2(11/83)-Infinity, Inc. app. 3(9/84) — 6.00
NOTE: Buckler a-1-5; c-1, 3-5, 51. Kubert c-2, 7-18. JLA app. in 4, 15. JSA app. in 4, 14, 15, 19, 27, 28.

ALL-STAR STORY OF THE DODGERS, THE
Stadium Communications: Apr, 1979 ($1.00)
1 — 2 4 6 10 14 18

ALL-STAR SUPERMAN (Also see Sears Special Edition in the Promotional Comics section)
DC Comics: Jan, 2006 - No. 12, Oct, 2008 ($2.99)
1-Grant Morrison-s/Frank Quitely-a/c — 1 3 4 6 8 10
1-Variant-c by Neal Adams — 25.00
1-Special Edition (2009, $1.00) r/#1 with "After Watchmen" cover logo frame — 3.00
2,4-12: 7,8-Bizarro app. — 3.00
3-Lois gets super powers — 1 2 3 5 6 8
Free Comic Book Day giveaway (6/08) reprints #1 — 4.00
Vol. 1 HC (2007, $19.99, dustjacket) r/#1-6; Bob Schreck intro. — 20.00
Vol. 1 SC (2008, $12.99) r/#1-6; Schreck intro. — 13.00
Vol. 2 HC (2009, $19.99, dustjacket) r/#7-12; Mark Waid intro. — 20.00
Vol. 2 SC (2009, $12.99) r/#7-12; Mark Waid intro. — 13.00

ALL STAR WESTERN (Formerly All Star Comics No. 1-57)
National Periodical Publ.: No. 58, Apr-May, 1951 - No. 119, June-July, 1961
58-Trigger Twins (ends #116), Strong Bow, The Roving Ranger & Don Caballero begin — 58 116 174 371 636 900
59,60: Last 52 pgs. — 34 68 102 199 325 450
61-66: 61-64-Toth-a — 28 56 84 165 270 375
67-Johnny Thunder begins; Gil Kane-a — 39 78 117 231 378 525
68-81: Last precode (3/55) — 19 38 57 111 176 240
82-98: 97-1st S.A. issue — 15 30 45 90 140 190
99-Frazetta-r/Jimmy Wakely #4 — 17 34 51 98 154 210
100 — 16 32 48 92 144 195
101-107,109-116,118,119: 103-Grey tone-c — 15 30 45 84 127 170
108-Origin J. Thunder; J. Thunder logo begins — 56 60 90 177 289 400
117-Origin Super Chief — 22 44 66 128 209 290
NOTE: Gil Kane c/p-58, 59, 61, 63, 64, 68, 69, 70-95(most), 97-199(most). Infantino art in most issues. Madame .44 app.-#117-119.

ALL-STAR WESTERN (Weird Western Tales No. 12 on)
National Periodical Publications: Aug-Sept, 1970 - No. 11, Apr-May, 1972
1-Pow-Wow Smith-r; Infantino-a — 6 12 18 42 79 115
2-Outlaw begins by Morrow; El Diablo by Morrow begins; has cameos by Williamson, Torres, Kane, Giordano & Phil Seuling — 6 12 18 38 69 100
3-Origin El Diablo — 5 10 15 31 53 75
4-6: 5-Last Outlaw issue. 6-Billy the Kid begins, ends #8 — 4 8 12 23 37 50
7-9-(52 pgs.) 9-Frazetta-a, 3pgs.(r) — 4 8 12 25 40 55
10-(52 pgs.) 2nd app. Jonah Hex begins (1st app., 2-3/72) — 40 80 120 296 673 1050
11-(52 pgs.) 2nd app. Jonah Hex; 1st cover — 13 26 39 76 163 250
NOTE: Neal Adams c-2-5; Aparo a-5. G. Kane a-3, 4, 6, 8. Kubert a-4r, 7-9r. Morrow a-2-4, 10, 11. No 7-11 have 52 pgs.

ALL STAR WESTERN (DC New 52)
DC Comics: Nov, 2011 - No. 34, Oct, 2014 ($3.99)
1-34: 1-Jonah Hex in 1880s Gotham City; Gray & Palmiotti-s/Moritat-a. 2,3-El Diablo back-up. 9-11-Court of Owls. 10-Bat Lash back-up; Garcia-López-a. 13-16-Tomahawk back-up. 19-21-Booster Gold app. 21-28-Hex in present day. 22-Batman app. 27-Superman app. 30,31-Madame .44 back-up; Garcia-López-a. 34-Darwyn Cooke-c/a — 4.00
#0 (11/12, $3.99) Jonah Hex's full origin; Gray & Palmiotti-s/Moritat-a — 4.00

ALL SURPRISE (Becomes Jeanie #13 on) (Funny animal)
Timely/Marvel (CPC): Fall, 1943 - No. 12, Winter, 1946-47
1-Super Rabbit, Gandy & Sourpuss begin — 77 154 231 493 847 1200
2 — 31 62 93 182 296 410
3-10,12 — 22 44 66 132 216 300
11-Kurtzman "Pigtales" art — 24 48 72 142 234 325

ALL TEEN (Formerly All Winners; All Winners & Teen Comics No. 21 on)
Marvel Comics (WFP): No. 20, January, 1947
20-Georgie, Mitzi, Patsy Walker, Willie app.; Syd Shores-c — 48 96 144 302 514 725

ALL-TIME SPORTS COMICS (Formerly All Sports Comics)
Hillman Per.: V2, No. 4, Apr-May, 1949 - V2, No. 7, Oct-Nov, 1949 (All 52 pgs.)
V2#4 — 30 60 90 177 289 400
5-7: 5-(V1#5 inside)-Powell-a; Ty Cobb sty. 7-Kristgein-p; Walter Johnson & Knute Rockne sty — 21 42 63 122 199 275

ALL TOP
William H. Wise Co.: 1944 (132 pgs.)
nn-Capt. V, Merciless the Sorceress, Red Robbins, One Round Hogan, Mike the M.P., Snooky, Pussy Katnip app. — 71 142 213 454 777 1050

ALL TOP COMICS (My Experience No. 19 on)
Fox Feature Synd./Green Publ./Norlen Mag.: 1945; No. 2, Sum, 1946 - No. 18, Jul, 1949; 1957 - 1959
1-Cosmo Cat & Flash Rabbit begin (1st app.) — 39 78 117 231 378 525
2 (#1-7 are funny animal) — 20 40 60 117 189 260
3-7: 7-Two diff. issues (7/47 & 9/47) — 15 30 45 90 140 190
8-Blue Beetle, Phantom Lady, & Rulah, Jungle Goddess begin (11/47); Kamen-c — 303 606 909 2121 3711 5300
9-Kamen-c — 181 362 543 1158 1979 2800
10-Classic Kamen bondage/torture/dwarf-c — 226 452 678 1446 2473 3500
11-13,15,17: 11,12-Rulah-c. 15-No Blue Beetle — 142 284 426 909 1555 2200
14-No Blue Beetle; used in SOTI, illo- "Corpses of colored people strung up by their wrists" — 219 438 657 1402 2401 3400
16-Classic Good Girl octopus-c — 486 972 1458 3550 6275 9000
18-Dagar, Jo-Jo app; no Phantom Lady or Blue Beetle — 126 252 378 806 1378 1950
6(1957-Green Publ.)-Patoruzu the Indian; Cosmo Cat on cover only. 6(1958-Literary Ent.)-Muggy Doo; Cosmo Cat on cover only. 6(1959-Norlen)-Atomic Mouse. 6(1959)-Little Eva. 6(Cornell)-Supermouse on-c — 7 14 21 35 45 50
NOTE: No Blue Beetle by Kamen-12,18.

ALL TRUE ALL PICTURE POLICE CASES
St. John Publishing Co.: Oct, 1952 - No. 2, Nov, 1952 (100 pgs.)
1-Three rebound St. John crime comics — 68 136 204 435 743 1050
2-Three comics rebound — 50 100 150 315 533 750
NOTE: Contents may vary.

ALL-TRUE CRIME (...Cases No. 26-35; formerly Official True Crime Cases)
Marvel/Atlas Comics: No. 26, Feb. 1948 - No. 52, Sept, 1952
(OFI #26,27/CFI #28,29/LCC #30-46/LMC #47-52)
26(#1)-Syd Shores-c — 50 100 150 315 533 750
27(#4)-Electric chair-c — 42 84 126 265 445 625
28-41,43-48,50-52: 35-37-Photo-c — 20 40 60 117 189 260
42,49-Krigstein-a. 49-Used in POP, Pg 79 — 21 42 63 112 199 275
NOTE: Colan a-46. Keller a-46. Robinson a-47, 50. Sale a-46. Shores c-26. Tuska a-48(3).

ALL-TRUE DETECTIVE CASES (Kit Carson No. 5 on)
Avon Periodicals: No. 2, Apr-May, 1954 - No. 4, Aug-Sept, 1954
2(#1)-Wood-a — 36 72 108 211 343 475
3-Kinstler-c — 20 40 60 118 192 265
4-r/Gangsters And Gun Molls #2; Kamen-a — 28 56 84 165 270 375
nn(100 pgs.)-7 pg. Kubert-a, Kinstler back-c — 58 116 174 371 636 900

ALL TRUE ROMANCE (...Illustrated No. 3)
Artful Publ. #1-3/Harwell(Comic Media) #4-20?/Ajax-Farrell(Excellent Publ.)
No. 22 on/Four Star Comic Corp.: 3/51 - No. 20, 12/54; No. 22, 3/55 - No. 30?, 7/57; No. (#31), 9/57; No. 4(#32), 11/57; No. 33, 2/58 - No. 34, 6/58
1 (3/51) — 34 68 102 199 325 450
2-(10/51; 11/51 on-c) — 18 36 54 107 169 230
3(12/51) - #5(5/52) — 16 32 48 92 144 195
6-Wood-a, 9 pgs. (exceptional) — 28 56 84 165 270 375
7,9,10 [two #7s: #7(11/52, 9/52 inside), #7(11/52, 11/52 inside)(no #8)]. 10-Hollingsworth-a — 15 30 45 88 137 185
11-13,15,19-(9/54),20(12/54) (no #21): 11,13-Heck-a — 14 28 42 82 121 160
14-Marijuana story — 15 30 45 90 130 175
22- Last precode issue (3/55) — 14 28 42 82 121 160
23-27,29,30(7/57): 29-Disbrow-a — 14 28 42 76 108 140
28 (9/6)-L. B. Cole, Disbrow-a — 16 32 48 94 147 200
3(#31, 9/57),4(#32, 11/57),33,34 (Farrell, '57-'58) — 12 24 36 69 97 125

ALL WESTERN WINNERS (Formerly All Winners; becomes Western Winners with No. 5; see Two-Gun Kid No. 5)
Marvel Comics(CDS): No. 2, Winter, 1948-49 - No. 4, April, 1949
2-Black Rider (origin/1st app.) & his horse Satan, Kid Colt & his horse Steel, & Two-Gun Kid & his horse Cyclone begin; Shores c-2-4 — 103 206 309 659 1130 1600
3-Anti-Wertham editorial — 48 96 144 302 514 725
4-Black Rider i.d. revealed; Heath, Shores-a — 47 94 141 296 498 700

ALL WINNERS COMICS (All Teen #20) (Also see Timely Presents: ...)
USA No. 1-7/WFP No. 10-19/YAI No. 21: Summer, 1941 - No. 19, Fall, 1946; No. 21, Winter, 1946-47; (No #20). No. 21 continued from Young Allies No. 20)
1-The Angel & Black Marvel only app.; Capt. America by Simon & Kirby, Human Torch &

All-Star Squadron #1 © DC

All Top Comics #1 © FOX

Alpha Flight (2023 series) #1 © MAR

	GD	VG	FN	VF	VF/NM	NM-
	2.0	4.0	6.0	8.0	9.0	9.2

Sub-Mariner begin (#1 was advertised as All Aces); 1st app. All-Winners Squad in text story
by Stan Lee ... 2100 4200 6300 14,900 28,450 42,000
2-The Destroyer & The Whizzer begin; Simon & Kirby Captain America
757 1514 2271 5526 9763 14,000
3 ... 649 1298 1947 4738 8369 12,000
4-Classic War-c by Al Avison ... 1000 2000 3000 7300 12,900 18,500
5 ... 427 854 1281 3117 5509 7900
6-The Black Avenger only app.; no Whizzer story; Hitler, Hirohito & Mussolini-c
975 1950 2919 7100 12,550 18,000
7-10 ... 420 840 1260 2940 5170 7400
11,13-15: 11-1st Atlas globe on-c (Winter, 1943-44; also see Human Torch #14).
14,15-No Human Torch ... 320 640 960 2240 3920 5600
12-Red Skull story; last Destroyer; no Whizzer story
568 1136 1704 4146 7323 10,500
16-18: 16-No Human Torch ... 290 580 870 1856 3178 4500
19-(Scarce)-1st story app. & origin All Winners Squad (Capt. America & Bucky, Human Torch
& Toro, Sub-Mariner, Whizzer, & Miss America; r-in Fantasy Masterpieces #10
1050 2100 3150 7650 16,075 24,500
21-(Scarce)-All Winners Squad; bondage-c ... 730 1460 2190 5330 11,415 17,500
NOTE: *Everett* Sub-Mariner-1, 3, 4; *Burgos* Torch-1, 3, 4. *Schomburg* c-1, 7-18. *Shores* c-19p, 21.
(2nd Series - August, 1948, Marvel Comics (CDS))
(Becomes All Western Winners with no. 2)
1-The Blonde Phantom, Capt. America, Human Torch, & Sub-Mariner app.
371 742 1113 2600 4550 6500

ALL WINNERS COMICS 70th ANNIVERARY SPECIAL
Marvel Comics: Oct, 2009 ($3.99, one-shot)
1-New story of All Winners Squad; r/G.A. Capt Anerica app. from All Winners #12 ... 5.00

ALL-WINNERS SQUAD: BAND OF HEROES
Marvel Comics: Aug, 2011 - No. 5, Dec, 2011 ($2.99, unfinished limited series of 8 issues)
1-5-WWII story of the Young Avenger and Captain Flame; Jenkins-s/DiGiandomenico-a ... 3.00

ALL YOUR COMICS (See Fox Giants)
Fox Feature Syndicate (R. W. Voight): Spring, 1946 (36 pgs.)
1-Red Robbins, Merciless the Sorceress app. ... 36 72 108 211 343 475

ALMANAC OF CRIME (See Fox Giants)

ALMOST AMERICAN
AfterShock Comics: Sept, 2021 - No. 5, Feb, 2022 ($4.99/$3.99, limited series)
1-($4.99) Ron Marz-s/Marco Castiello-a; husband-and-wife Russian spies ... 5.00
2-5-($3.99) ... 4.00

AL OF FBI (See Little Al of the FBI)

ALOHA, HAWAIIAN DICK (Also see Hawaiian Dick)
Image Comics: Apr, 2016 - No. 5, Aug, 2016 ($3.99, limited series)
1-5-B. Clay Moore-s. 1-4-Jacob Wyatt-a. 5-Paul Reinwand-a ... 4.00

ALONE IN THE DARK (Based on video game)
Image Comics: Feb, 2003 ($4.95)
1-Matt Haley-c/a; Jean-Marc & Randy Lofficier-s ... 5.00

ALPHA AND OMEGA
Spire Christian Comics (Fleming H. Revell): 1978 (49c)
nn ... 2 4 6 9 13 16

ALPHA: BIG TIME (See Amazing Spider-Man #692-694)
Marvel Comics: Apr, 2013 - No. 5, Aug, 2015 ($2.99)
1-5-Fialkov-s/Plati-a/Ramos-c. 1,3,5-Superior Peter Parker app. 4-Thor app. ... 3.00

ALPHA CENTURION (See Superman, 2nd Series & Zero Hour)
DC Comics: 1996 ($2.95, one-shot)
1 ... 3.00

ALPHA FLIGHT (See X-Men #120,121 & X-Men/Alpha Flight)
Marvel Comics: Aug, 1983 - No. 130, Mar, 1994 (#52-on are direct sales only)
1-(52 pgs.) Byrne-a begins (thru #28) -Wolverine & Nightcrawler cameo
3 6 9 16 23 30
2-11,13-28: 2-Vindicator becomes Guardian; origin Marrina & Alpha Flight. 3-Concludes
origin Alpha Flight. 6-Origin Shaman. 7-Origin Snowbird. 10,11-Origin Sasquatch.
13-Wolverine app. 16,17-Wolverine cameo. 17-X-Men x-over (mostly r-/X-Men #109).
19-Origin/1st app. Talisman. 20-New headquarters. 25-Return of Guardian. 28-Last Byrne
issue ... 6.00
12-(52 pgs.)-Death of Guardian ... 1 2 3 5 6 8
29-32,35-49: 39-47,49-Portacio-a(i) ... 4.00
33-1st app. Lady Deathstrike; Wolverine app. ... 3 6 9 15 22 28
34-2nd app. Lady Deathstrike; origin Wolverine ... 6.00
50-Double size; Portacio-a(i) ... 4.00

51-Jim Lee's 1st work at Marvel (10/87); Wolverine cameo; 1st Lee Wolverine; Portacio-a(i)
2 4 6 13 18 22
52,53-Wolverine app.; Lee-a on Wolverine; Portacio-a(i); 53-Lee/Portacio-a ... 4.00
54-73,76-86,91-99,101-105: 54,63,64-No Jim Lee-a. 54-Portacio-a(i). 55-62-Jim Lee-a(p).
71-Intro The Sorcerer (villain). 91-Dr. Doom app. 94-F.F. x-over. 99-Galactus, Avengers
app. 102-Intro Weapon Omega ... 3.00
74,75,87-90,100: 74-Wolverine, Spider-Man & The Avengers app. 75-Double size ($1.95,
52 pgs.). 87-90-Wolverine. 4 part story w/Jim Lee-c. 89-Original Guardian returns.
100-($2.00, 52 pgs.)-Avengers & Galactus app. ... 4.00
106-Northstar revealed to be gay ... 2 4 6 8 11 14
106-2nd printing (direct sale only) ... 3.00
107-109,112-119,121-129: 107-X-Factor x-over. 112-Infinity War x-overs. 115-1st Wyre
110,111: Infinity War x-overs, Wolverine app. 111-Thanos cameo ... 3.00
120-($2.25)-Polybagged w/Paranormal Registration Act poster ... 4.00
130-($2.25, 52 pgs.) ... 1 3 4 6 8 10
Annual 1,2 (9/86, 12/87) ... 4.00
...Classics Vol. 1 TPB (2007, $24.99) r/#1-8; character profile pages; Byrne interview ... 25.00
... No. 1 Facsimile Edition (7/19, $4.99) r/#1 with original 1983 ads and letter column ... 5.00
Special V2#1(6/92, $2.50, 52 pgs.)-Wolverine-c/story ... 4.00
NOTE: *Austin* c-1i, 2i, 53i. *Byrne* c-81, 82. *Guice* c-85, 91-99. *Jim Lee* a(p)-51, 53, 55-62, 64; c-53, 87-90. *Mignola*
a-29-31p. *Whilce Portacio* a(i)-39-47, 49-54.

ALPHA FLIGHT (2nd Series)
Marvel Comics: Aug, 1997 - No. 20, Mar, 1999 ($2.99/$1.99)
1-($2.99)-Wraparound cover ... 6.00
2,3: 2-Variant-c ... 4.00
4-11: 8,9-Wolverine-c/app. ... 3.00
12-($2.99) Death of Sasquatch; wraparound-c ... 4.00
13-15,18-20 ... 3.00
16-1st app. cameo Honey Lemon (Big Hero 6) ... 1 2 3 5 6 8
17-1st app. Big Hero 6 ... 2 4 6 10 14 18
.../Inhumans '98 Annual ($3.50) Raney-a ... 4.00

ALPHA FLIGHT (3rd Series)
Marvel Comics: May, 2004 - No. 12, April, 2005 ($2.99)
1-12: 6-Lobdell-s/Henry-c/a ... 3.00
... Vol. 1: You Gotta Be Kiddin' Me (2004, $14.99) r/#1-6 ... 15.00

ALPHA FLIGHT (4th Series)
Marvel Comics: No. 0.1, Jul, 2011 - No. 8, Mar, 2012 ($2.99)
0.1-Pak & Van Lente-s/Oliver & Green-a; Kara Killgrave app. ... 3.00
1-(8/11, $3.99) Fear Itself tie-in; Eaglesham-a/Jimenez-c; bonus design sketch pages ... 4.00
2-8-($2.99) Fear Itself tie-in. 2-Puck returns. 5-Taskmaster app. 7,8-Wolverine app. ... 3.00

ALPHA FLIGHT (5th Series)
Marvel Comics: Oct, 2023 - No. 5, Feb, 2024 ($3.99)
1-5-Brisson-s/Godlewski-a ... 4.00

ALPHA FLIGHT: IN THE BEGINNING
Marvel Comics: July, 1997 ($1.95, one-shot)
(-1)-Flashback w/Wolverine ... 4.00

ALPHA FLIGHT SPECIAL
Marvel Comics: July, 1991 - No. 4, Oct, 1991 ($1.50, limited series)
1-4: 1-3-r-A. Flight #97-99 w/covers. 4-r-A.Flight #100 ... 4.00

ALPHA FLIGHT: TRUE NORTH
Marvel Comics: Nov, 2019 ($4.99, one-shot)
1-Short stories by Canadian creators incl. Jim Zub, Dunbar, Brisson, MacKay, Hepburn ... 5.00

ALPHA KING (3 FLOYDS:...)
Image Comics: May, 2016 - No. 5, Nov, 2017 ($3.99)
1-5-Azzarello-s/Bisley-a/c ... 4.00

ALTERED IMAGE
Image Comics: Apr, 1998 - No. 3, Sept, 1998 ($2.50, limited series)
1-3-Spawn, Witchblade, Savage Dragon; Valentino-s/a ... 4.00

ALTERED STATES
Dynamite Entertainment: 2015 ($3.99, series of one-shots)
.... Doc Savage - Alternate reality Doc Savage in caveman past; Philip Tan-c ... 4.00
.... Red Sonja - Alternate reality Sonja in modern day New York City; Philip Tan-c ... 4.00
.... The Shadow - Alternate reality Shadow in sci-fi future; Philip Tan-c ... 4.00
.... Vampirella - Alternate reality Vampirella as a mortal on Drakulon; Collins-s ... 4.00

ALTER EGO
First Comics: May, 1986 - No. 4, Nov, 1986 (Mini-series)
1-4 ... 3.00

ALTERNATES, THE (Listed as: From The World Of Minor Threats: The Alternates)

	GD 2.0	VG 4.0	FN 6.0	VF 8.0	VF/NM 9.0	NM- 9.2

ALTER NATION
Image Comics: Feb, 2004 - No. 4, Jun, 2004 ($2.95, limited series)

1-4: 1-Two covers by Art Adams and Barberi; Barberi-a						3.00

ALTERS
AfterShock Comics: Sept, 2016 - No. 10, Feb, 2018 ($3.99)

1-10: 1-Paul Jenkins-s/Leila Leiz-a						4.00

ALVIN (TV) (See Four Color Comics No. 1042 or Three Chipmunks #1)
Dell Publishing Co.: Oct-Dec, 1962 - No. 28, Oct, 1973

12-021-212 (#1)	10	20	30	64	132	200
2	5	10	15	34	60	85
3-10	4	8	12	28	47	65
11-"Chipmunks sing the Beatles' Hits"	5	10	15	34	60	85
12-28	4	8	12	23	37	50
Alvin For President (10/64)	5	10	15	31	53	75
...& His Pals in Merry Christmas with Clyde Crashcup & Leonardo 1 (25¢ Giant) (02-120-402)-(12-2/64)	7	14	21	46	86	125
Reprinted in 1966 (12-023-604)	4	8	12	23	37	50

ALVIN & THE CHIPMUNKS
Harvey Comics: July, 1992 - No. 5, May, 1994

1-5: 1-Richie Rich app.						5.00

AMALGAM AGE OF COMICS, THE: THE DC COMICS COLLECTION
DC Comics: 1996 ($12.95, trade paperback)

nn-r/Amazon, Assassins, Doctor Strangefate, JLX, Legends of the Dark Claw, & Super Soldier	4	8	12	23	37	50

AMANDA AND GUNN
Image Comics: Apr, 1997 - No. 4, Oct, 1997 ($2.95, B&W, limited series)

1-4						3.00

AMAZING ADULT FANTASY (Formerly Amazing Adventures #1-6; becomes Amazing Fantasy #15) (See Amazing Fantasy for Omnibus HC reprint of #1-15)
Marvel Comics Group (AMI): No. 7, Dec, 1961 - No. 14, July, 1962

7-Ditko-c/a begins, ends #14	64	128	192	512	1156	1800
8-Last 10¢ issue	55	110	165	440	995	1550
9-13: 12-1st app. Mailbag. 13-Anti-communist story	54	108	162	432	966	1500
13-2nd printing (1994)	2	4	6	9	12	15
14-Prototype issue (Professor X)	69	138	207	552	1251	1950

AMAZING ADVENTURE FUNNIES (Fantoman No. 2 on)
Centaur Publications: June, 1940 - No. 2, Sept. 1940

1-The Fantom of the Fair by Gustavson (r/Amaz. Mystery Funnies V2#7,V2#8), The Arrow, Skyrocket Steele From the Year X by Everett (r/AMF #2); Burgos-a	343	686	1029	2400	4200	6000
2-Reprints; Published after Fantoman #2	174	348	522	1114	1907	2700

NOTE: *Burgos* a-1(2). *Everett* a-1(2), 2(3). *Gustavson* a-1(5), 2(3). *Pinajian* a-2.

AMAZING ADVENTURES (Also see Boy Cowboy & Science Comics)
Ziff-Davis Publ. Co.: 1950; No. 1, Nov, 1950 - No. 6, Fall, 1952 (Painted covers)

1950 (no month given) (Rare) Has the front & back cover plus Schomburg story used in Amazing Advs. #1 (Sent to subscribers of Z-D s/f magazines & ordered through mail for 10¢. Used to test market)	103	206	309	659	1130	1600
1-Wood, Schomburg, Anderson, Whitney-a	119	238	357	762	1306	1850
2,3,5: 2-Schomburg-a. 2,5-Anderson-a. 3,5-Starr-a	57	114	171	362	619	875
4-Classic-c; Anderson-a	343	686	1029	2400	4200	6000
6-Krigstein-a	55	110	165	352	601	850

AMAZING ADVENTURES (Becomes Amazing Adult Fantasy #7 on) (See Amazing Fantasy for Omnibus HC reprint of #1-15)
Atlas Comics (AMI)/Marvel Comics No. 3 on: June, 1961 - No. 6, Nov, 1961

1-Origin Dr. Droom (1st Marvel-Age Superhero who later becomes Doctor Druid) by Kirby; Kirby/Ditko-a (5 pgs.). Ditko & Kirby-a in all; Kirby monster-c/a c-6	152	304	456	1254	2827	4400
2	59	118	177	472	1061	1650
3-6: 6-Last Dr. Droom	54	108	162	432	966	1500

AMAZING ADVENTURES
Marvel Comics Group: Aug, 1970 - No. 39, Nov, 1976

1-Inhumans by Kirby(p) & Black Widow (1st app. in Tales of Suspense #52) double feature begins	9	18	27	57	111	165
2-4: 2-F.F. brief app. 4-Last Inhumans by Kirby	4	8	12	25	40	55
5-8: Adams-a(p); 8-Last Black Widow; last Inhumans	5	10	15	31	53	75
9,10: Magneto app. 10-Last Inhumans (origin-r by Kirby)	5	10	15	31	53	75
11-New Beast begins(1st app. in mutated form; origin in flashback); X-Men cameo in flashback (#11-17 are X-Men tie-ins)	24	48	72	168	372	575
12-17: 12-Beast battles Iron Man. 13-Brotherhood of Evil Mutants x-over from X-Men. 15-X-Men app. 16-Rutland Vermont - Bald Mountain Halloween x-over; Juggernaut app. 17-Last Beast (origin); X-Men app.	8	16	24	51	96	140
18-War of the Worlds begins (5/73); 1st app. Killraven; Neal Adams-a(p)	5	10	15	35	63	90
19-35,38,39: 19-Chaykin-a. 25-Buckler-a. 35-Giffen's first published story (art), along with Deadly Hands of Kung-Fu #22 (3/76)	2	4	6	8	10	12
36,37-(Regular 25¢ edition)(7-8/76)	2	4	6	8	10	12
36,37-(30¢ variants, limited distribution)	5	10	15	31	57	80

NOTE: *N. Adams* c-6-8. *Buscema* a-1p, 2p. *Colan* a-3-5p, 26p. *Ditko* a-24r. *Everett* a(i)3-5, 7-9. *Giffen* a-35i, 38p. *G. Kane* c-11, 25p, 29p. *Ploog* a-12i. *Russell* a-27-32, 34-37, 39; c-28, 30-32, 33i, 34, 35, 37, 39i. *Starlin* c-15p, 16, 17, 27. *Sutton* a-11-15p.

AMAZING ADVENTURES
Marvel Comics Group: Dec, 1979 - No. 14, Jan, 1981

V2#1-Reprints story/X-Men #1 & 38 (origins)	3	6	9	21	33	45
2-14: Early X-Men-r. 7,8-Origin Iceman	2	4	6	8	10	12

NOTE: *Byrne* c-6p, 9p. *Kirby* a-1-14r; c-7, 9. *Steranko* a-12r. *Tuska* a-7-9.

AMAZING ADVENTURES
Marvel Comics: July, 1988 ($4.95, squarebound, one-shot, 80 pgs.)

1-Anthology; Austin, Golden-a						5.00

AMAZING ADVENTURES OF CAPTAIN CARVEL AND HIS CARVEL CRUSADERS, THE
(See Carvel Comics in the Promotional Comics section)

AMAZING BATVARK (Cerebus in Hell)
Aardvark-Vanaheim: Feb, 2021 ($4.00, B&W)

1-Cerebus figures placed over Doré artwork of Hell; Amazing Spider-Man #50-c swipe						4.00

AMAZING CEREBUS (Reprints from Cerebus in Hell)(Also see Aardvark Comics)
Aardvark-Vanaheim: Feb, 2018 ($4.00, B&W)

1-Cerebus figures placed over original Doré artwork; Amazing Spider-Man #300-c swipe						4.00

AMAZING CHAN & THE CHAN CLAN, THE (TV)
Gold Key: May, 1973 - No. 4, Feb, 1974 (Hanna-Barbera)

1-Warren Tufts-a in all	4	8	12	28	47	65
2-4	3	6	9	17	26	35

AMAZING COMICS (Complete Comics No. 2)
Timely Comics (EPC): Fall, 1944

1-The Destroyer, The Whizzer, The Young Allies (by Sekowsky), Sergeant Dix; Schomburg-c	500	900	1350	3015	—	—

AMAZING DETECTIVE CASES (Formerly Suspense No. 2?)
Marvel/Atlas Comics (CCC): No. 3, Nov, 1950 - No. 14, Sept, 1952

3	40	80	120	246	411	575
4-6: 6-Jerry Robinson-a	23	46	69	136	223	310
7-10	20	40	60	120	195	270
11,12: 11-(3/52)-Horror format begins. 12-Krigstein-a	68	136	204	435	743	1050
13-(Scarce)-Everett-a; electrocution-c/story	77	154	231	493	847	1200
14	60	120	180	381	653	925

NOTE: *Colan* a-9. *Maneely* c-13. *Sekowsky* a-12. *Sinnott* a-13. *Tuska* a-10.

AMAZING FANTASY (Formerly Amazing Adult Fantasy #7-14)
Atlas Magazines/Marvel: #15, Aug, 1962 (Sept, 1962 shown in indicia) #16, Dec, 1995 - #18, Feb, 1996

15-Origin/1st app. of Spider-Man by Steve Ditko (11 pgs.); 1st app. Aunt May & Uncle Ben; Kirby/Ditko-c	14,900	29,800	59,600	171,300	435,650	700,000
16-18 ('95-'96, $3.95): Kurt Busiek scripts; painted-c/a by Paul Lee						5.00
Amazing Fantasy #15 Facsimile Edition (12/19, $3.99) r/#15 with original 1962 ads	3	6	9	19	30	40
Amazing Fantasy #15: Spider-Man! (8/12, $3.99) recolored rep. of #15 and ASM #1	2	4	6	11	16	20
Amazing Fantasy Omnibus HC ("Amazing Adult Fantasy" on-c) (2007, $75.00, dustjacket) r/Amazing Adventures #1-6, Amazing Adult Fantasy #7-14 and Amazing Fantasy #15 with letter pages; foreword by Bissette; cover gallery from '70s reprint titles						150.00

AMAZING FANTASY (Continues from #6 in Araña: The Heart of the Spider)
Marvel Comics: Aug - No. 20, June, 2006 ($2.99)

1-Intro. Anya Corazon; Avery-s/Brooks-c/a	3	6	9	16	23	30
2-6,8,9,11-14,16-20: 3,4-Roger Cruz-a. 13,14-Back-up Captain Universe stories.						3.00
16-20-Death's Head						
7-Intro. new Scorpion; Kirk-a	3	6	9	14	20	25
10-Intro. Vampire By Night	4	8	12	23	37	50
15-($3.99, 1/06) Spider-Man app.; intro 6 new characters incl. Amadeus Cho/Mastermind Excello seen in World War Hulk series; s/a by various	7	14	21	46	86	125
Death's Head 3.0: Unnatural Selection TPB (2006, $13.99) r/#16-20						14.00
Scorpion: Poison Tomorrow (2005, $7.99, digest) r/#7-13						8.00

AMAZING FANTASY
Marvel Comics: Sept, 2021 - No. 5, Jan, 2022 ($4.99, limited series)

1-5-Kaare Andrews-s/a; WWII Capt. America, Teenage Spidey, & Black Widow app.						5.00

AMAZING FANTASY 1000
Marvel Comics: Oct, 2022 ($7.99, square-bound, one-shot)

1-Short Spider-Man stories by various incl. Busiek, Cheung, Coipel, Dodson, Gaiman, Hickman, Janson, McNiven, Nauck & Slott						8.00

AMAZING GHOST STORIES (Formerly Nightmare)
St. John Publishing Co.: No. 14, Oct, 1954 - No. 16, Feb, 1955

14-Pit & the Pendulum story by Kinstler; Baker-a	811	1622	2433	5920	10,460	15,000
15-r/Weird Thrillers #5; Baker-c, Powell-a	129	258	387	826	1413	2000
16-Kubert reprints from Weird Thrillers #4; Baker-c; Roussos, Tuska-a; Kinstler-a (1 pg.)	84	168	252	538	919	1300

AMAZING HIGH ADVENTURE
Marvel Comics: 8/84; No. 2, 10/85; No. 3, 10/86 - No. 5, 1986 ($2.00)

1-5: Painted-c on all. 3,4-Baxter paper.						4.00

NOTE: *Bissette* a-4. *Severin* a-1, 3. *Sienkiewicz* a-1,2. *Paul Smith* a-2. *Williamson* a-2i.

AMAZING JOY BUZZARDS
Image Comics: 2005 - No. 4, 2005 ($2.95, B&W with pink spot color in #1)

1-4-Mark Andrew Smith-s/Dan Hipp-a. 1-Mahfood back-c. 2-Morse back-c						3.00
Vol. 1 TPB (2005, $11.95) r/#1-4; bonus art and character design sketches						12.00
TPB (2008, $19.99) r/#1-4 and Vol. 2 #1-5						20.00

AMAZING JOY BUZZARDS (Volume 2)
Image Comics: Oct, 2005 - No. 5, Aug, 2006 ($2.99, B&W)

1-5: 1-Mark Andrew Smith-s/Dan Hipp-a. 4-Mahfood-a; Crosland-a. 5-Holgate-a						3.00
Vol. 2 TPB (2006, $12.99) r/#1-4; bonus art, pin-ups and character sketches						13.00

AMAZING-MAN COMICS (Formerly Motion Picture Funnies Weekly?)
(Also see Stars And Stripes Comics, and Amazing Mystery Funnies nn)
Centaur Publications: No. 5, Sept, 1939 - No. 26, Jan, 1942

5(#1)(Rare)-Origin/1st app. A-Man the Amazing Man by Bill Everett; The Cat-Man by Tarpe Mills (also #8), Mighty Man by Filchock, Minimidget & sidekick Ritty, & The Iron Skull by Burgos begins	2340	4680	7020	18,700	33,350	48,000
6-Origin The Amazing Man retold; The Shark begins; Ivy Menace by Tarpe Mills app.	649	1298	1947	4738	8369	12,000
7-Magician From Mars begins; ends #11	366	732	1098	2562	4481	6400
8-Cat-Man dresses as woman	300	600	900	1950	3375	4800
9-Magician From Mars battles the 'Elemental Monster,' swiped into The Spectre in More Fun						

Amazing Fantasy (2021 series) #3 © MAR

Amazing Spider-Girl #1 © MAR

Amazing Spider-Man #11 © MAR

	GD	VG	FN	VF	VF/NM	NM-
	2.0	4.0	6.0	8.0	9.0	9.2

	GD	VG	FN	VF	VF/NM	NM-
	2.0	4.0	6.0	8.0	9.0	9.2

#54 & 55. Ties w/Marvel Mystery #4 for 1st Nazi War-c on a comic (2/40)

	354	708	1062	2478	4339	6200

10,11: 11-Zardi, the Eternal Man begins; ends #16; Amazing Man dons costume;
last Everett issue

	258	516	774	1651	2826	4000

12,13

	239	478	717	1530	2615	3700

14-Reef Kinkaid, Rocke Wayburn (ends #20), & Dr. Hypno (ends #21) begin;
no Zardi or Chuck Hardy

	213	426	639	1363	2332	3300

15,17-20: 15-Zardi returns; no Rocke Wayburn. 17-Dr. Hypno returns; no Zardi

	174	348	522	1114	1907	2700

16-Mighty Man's powers of super strength & ability to shrink & grow explained; Rocke Wayburn
returns; no Dr. Hypno; Al Avison (a character) begins, ends #18 (a tribute to the famed
artist)

	194	388	582	1242	2121	3000

21-Origin Dash Dartwell (drug-use story); origin & only app. T.N.T.

	219	438	657	1402	2401	3400

22-Dash Dartwell, the Human Meteor & The Voice app; last Iron Skull & The Shark;
Silver Streak app. (classic Nazi monster-c)

	3750	7500	11,250	28,500	51,700	75,000

23-Two Amazing Man stories; intro/origin Tommy the Amazing Kid; The Marksman only app.

	194	388	582	1242	2121	3000

24-King of Darkness, Nightshade, & Blue Lady begin; end #26; 1st app. Super-Ann

	206	412	618	1318	2259	3200

25 (Scarce) Meteor Martin by Wolverton

	1000	2000	3000	7600	13,800	20,000

26 (Scarce) Meteor Martin by Wolverton; Electric Ray app.

	1750	3500	5250	13,300	24,150	35,000

NOTE: *Everett* a-5-11; c-5-11. *Gilman* a-14-20. *Giunta/Mirando* a-7-10. *Sam Glanzman* a-14-16, 18-21, 23. *Louis
Glanzman* a-6, 9-11, 14-21; c-13-19, 21. *Robert Golden* a-9. *Gustavson* a-6; c-22, 23. *Lubbers* a-14-21. *Simon*
a-10. *Frank Thomas* a-6; 9-11, 14, 15, 17-21.

AMAZING MARY JANE (Mary Jane Watson)
Marvel Comics: Dec, 2019 - No. 6, May 2020 ($3.99)

1-6-Mary Jane & Mysterio filming a super-hero movie; Savage Six app.; Leah Williams-s

	1	2	3	5	6	8

AMAZING MYSTERIES (Formerly Sub-Mariner Comics No. 31)
Marvel Comics (CCC): No. 32, May, 1949 - No. 35, Jan, 1950 (1st Marvel Horror Comic)

32-The Witness app.

	258	516	774	1651	2826	4000

33-Horror format

	90	180	270	576	988	1400

34,35-Changes to Crime. 34,35-Photo-c

	36	72	108	211	343	475

AMAZING MYSTERY FUNNIES
Centaur Publications: Aug, 1938 - No. 24, Sept, 1940 (All 52 pgs.)

V1#1-Everett-c(1st); Dick Kent Adv. story; Skyrocket Steele in the Year X on cover only

	975	1950	2919	7100	12,550	18,000

2-Everett 1st-a (Skyrocket Steele)

	423	846	1269	3000	5250	7500

3

	290	580	870	1856	3178	4500

3(#4, 12/38)-nn on cover, #3 on inside; bondage-c

	300	600	900	2010	3505	5000

V2#1,3,4,6: 3-Air-Sub DX begins by Burgos. 4-Dan Hastings, Sand Hog begins (ends #5).

	245	490	735	1568	2684	3800

6-Last Skyrocket Steele

	649	1298	1947	4738	8369	12,000

2-Classic-c; drug use story

	1000	2000	3000	7600	13,800	20,000

5-Classic Everett-c

	486	972	1458	3550	6275	9000

7 (Scarce)-Intro. The Fantom of the Fair & begins; Everett, Gustavson, Burgos-a

	258	516	774	1651	2826	4000

8-Origin & 1st app. Speed Centaur

	194	388	582	1242	2121	3000

9-11: 11-Self portrait and biog. of Everett; Jon Linton begins; early Robot cover (11/39)

	300	600	900	1950	3375	4800

12 (Scarce)-1st Space Patrol; Wolverton-a (12/39); new costume Phantom of the Fair

	168	336	504	1075	1838	2600

V3#1(#17, 1/40)-Intro. Bullet; Tippy Taylor serial begins, ends #24
(continued in The Arrow #2)

18,20: 18-Fantom of the Fair by Gustavson

	161	322	483	1030	1765	2500

19,21-24: Space Patrol by Wolverton in all

	194	388	582	1242	2121	3000

NOTE: *Burgos* a-V2#3-9. *Eisner* a-V1#2, 3(2). *Everett* a-V1#2-4, V2#1, 3-6; c-V1#1-4,V2#3, 5, 18. *Filchock*
a-V2#9. *Flessel* a-V2#6. *Guardineer* a-V1#4, V2#4-6; *Gustavson* a-V2#4, 5, 9-12, V3#1, 18, 19; c-V2#7, 9, 12,
V3#1, 21, 22; *McWilliams* a-V2#9, 10. *TarpeMills* a-V2#2, 4-6, 9-12, V3#1. *Leo Morey*(Pulp artist) c-V2#10; text
illo-V2#11. *FrankThomas* a-6-V2#11. *Webster* a-V2#4.

AMAZING MYSTERY FUNNIES
Centaur Publications: 1942

nn (#23)-Cover from Amazing Man Comics #23 w/interior from Amazing Man Comics #25.
(2 known copies). A CGC 2.0 copy sold in March 2019 for $4,400.

AMAZING SAINTS
Logos International: 1974 (39¢)

nn-True story of Phil Saint

	2	4	6	9	13	16

AMAZING SCARLET SPIDER
Marvel Comics: Nov, 1995 - No. 2, Dec, 1995 ($1.95, limited series)

1,2: Replaces "Amazing Spider-Man" for two issues. 1-Venom/Carnage cameos.

2-Green Goblin & Joystick-c/app.

						5.00

AMAZING SCREW-ON HEAD, THE
Dark Horse Comics (Maverick): May, 2002 ($2.99, one-shot)

1-Mike Mignola-s/a/c

	1	3	4	6	8	10

AMAZING SPIDER-GIRL (Also see Spider-Girl and What If...? (2nd series) #105)
Marvel Comics: No. 0, 2006; No. 1, Dec, 2006 - No. 30, May, 2009 ($2.99)

0-($1.99) Recap of the Spider-Girl series and character profiles; A.F. #15 cover swipe

	2	4	6	10	14	18

1-Frenz & Buscema-a

	2	4	6	8	10	12

2-14,16-24,26-($2.99) Frenz & Buscema-a. 9-Carnage returns. 19-Has #17 on cover | | | | | | 6.00 |

15,25,30-($3.99) 15-10th Anniversary issue. 25-Three covers

	2	3	5	6	8

... **Vol. 1:** What Ever Happened to the Daughter of Spider-Man? TPB (2007, $14.99) r/#0-6 30.00
... **Vol. 2:** Comes the Carnage! TPB (2007, $13.99) r/#7-12 14.00
... **Vol. 3:** Mind Games TPB (2008, $13.99) r/#13-18 14.00

AMAZING SPIDER-MAN, THE (See All Detergent Comics, Amazing Fantasy, America's Best TV Comics,
Aurora, Deadly Foes of..., Fireside Book Series, Friendly Neighborhood..., Giant-Size..., Giant Size Super-Heroes
Featuring..., Marvel Age..., Marvel Collectors Item Classics, Marvel Fanfare, Marvel Graphic Novel, Marvel
Knoghts..., Marvel Spec. Ed., Marvel Tales, Marvel Team-Up, Marvel Treasury Ed., New Avengers, Nothing Can
Stop the Juggernaut, Official Marvel Index To..., Peter Parker..., Power Record Comics, Spectacular..., Spider-
Man, Spider-Man Digest, Spider-Man Saga, Spider-Man 2099, Spider-Man Vs. Wolverine, Spidey Super Stories,
Strange Tales Annual #2, Superior Spider-Man, Superman Vs. ..., Try-Out Winner Book, Ultimate Marvel Team-Up,
Ultimate Spider-Man, Web of Spider-Man & Within Our Reach)

AMAZING SPIDER-MAN, THE
Marvel Comics Group: March, 1963 - No. 441, Nov, 1998

1-Retells origin by Steve Ditko; 1st Fantastic Four x-over (ties with F.F. #12 as first Marvel
x-over); intro. John Jameson & The Chameleon; Spider-Man's 2nd app.; Kirby/Ditko-c;
Ditko-c/a #1-38

	2600	5200	10,400	15,600	39,000	84,500	130,000

1-Reprint from the Golden Record Comic set

	68	136	204	544	1222	1900

Sealed with record (1966)

	141	282	423	1142	2571	4000

2-1st app. the Vulture & the Terrible Tinkerer

	1200	2400	3600	8600	19,300	30,000

3-1st app. Doc Octopus; 1st full-length story; Human Torch cameo;
Spider-Man pin-up by Ditko

	1080	2160	3240	7780	17,390	27,000

4-Origin & 1st app. The Sandman (see Strange Tales #115 for 2nd app.); 1st monthly issue;
intro. Betty Brant & Liz Allen

	760	1520	2280	5470	12,235	19,000

5-Dr. Doom app.

	367	734	1100	3120	7060	11,000

6-1st app. Lizard

	317	634	951	2695	6098	9500

7-Vs. The Vulture

	193	386	579	1592	3596	5600

8-Fantastic Four app. in back-up story by Kirby & Ditko

	136	272	408	1088	2444	3800

9-Origin & 1st app. Electro (2/64)

	259	518	777	2137	4819	7500

10-1st app. Big Man & The Enforcers

	114	228	342	912	2056	3200

11-1st app. Bennett Brant

	176	352	528	1452	3276	5100

12-Doc Octopus unmasks Spider-Man-c/story

	102	204	306	816	1833	2850

13-1st app. Mysterio

	303	606	909	2500	5650	8800

14-(7/64)-1st app. The Green Goblin (c/story)(Norman Osborn); Hulk x-over

	680	1360	2040	4900	10,950	17,000

15-1st app. Kraven the Hunter; 1st mention of Mary Jane Watson (not shown)

	300	600	900	2475	5588	8700

16-Spider-Man battles Daredevil (1st x-over 9/64); still in old yellow costume

	125	250	375	1000	2250	3500

17-2nd app. Green Goblin (c/story); Human Torch x-over (also in #18 & #21)

	93	186	279	744	1672	2600

18-1st app. Ned Leeds who later becomes Hobgoblin; Fantastic Four cameo;
3rd app. Sandman

	64	128	192	512	1158	1800

19-Sandman app.

	48	96	144	374	862	1350

20-Origin & 1st app. The Scorpion

	148	296	444	1221	2761	4300

21-2nd app. The Beetle (see Strange Tales #123)

	50	100	150	400	900	1400

22-1st app. Princess Python

	46	92	138	359	805	1250

23-3rd app. The Green Goblin-c/story; Norman Osborn app.; Marvel Masterwork pin-up by
Ditko; fan letter by Jim Shooter

	55	110	165	440	995	1550

24

	44	88	132	326	738	1150

25-(6/65)-1st brief app. Mary Jane Watson (face not shown); 1st app. Spencer Smythe;
Norman Osborn app.

	48	96	144	384	867	1350

26-4th app. The Green Goblin-c/story; 1st app. Crime Master; dies in #27;
Norman Osborn app.

	46	92	138	368	834	1300

27-5th app. The Green Goblin-c/story; Norman Osborn app.

	46	92	138	359	805	1250

28-Origin & 1st app. Molten Man (9/65; scarcer in high grade)

	166	332	498	1370	3534	5500

29-Vs. Scorpion

	40	80	120	296	673	1050

30

	35	70	105	252	564	875

31-(12/65)-1st app. Gwen Stacy, Prof. Warren, and Harry Osborn who later becomes
2nd Green Goblin

	176	352	528	1452	3276	5100

	GD 2.0	VG 4.0	FN 6.0	VF 8.0	VF/NM 9.0	NM- 9.2
32-38: 34-4th app. Kraven the Hunter. 36-1st app. Looter. 37-Intro. Norman Osborn. 38-(7/66)-2nd brief app. Mary Jane Watson (face not shown); last Ditko issue	26	52	76	182	404	625
39-The Green Goblin-c/story; Green Goblin's identity revealed as Norman Osborn; Osborn learns Spider-Man's secret identity; Romita-a begins (8/66; see Daredevil #16 for 1st Romita-a on Spider-Man)	75	150	225	600	1350	2100
40-1st told origin The Green Goblin-c/story	68	136	204	544	1222	1900
41-1st app. Rhino	107	214	321	856	1928	3000
42-(11/66)-3rd app. Mary Jane Watson (cameo in last 2 panels); 1st time face is shown	36	72	108	266	596	925
43-45,47-49: 43-Origin of the Rhino. 44,45-2nd & 3rd app. The Lizard. 47-M.J. Watson & Peter Parker 1st date. 47-Green Goblin cameo; Harry & Norman Osborn app. 47,49-5th & 6th app. Kraven the Hunter. 48-1st new Vulture (Blackie Drago)	21	42	63	147	324	500
46-Intro/origin The Shocker	52	104	156	416	933	1450
50-1st app. Kingpin (7/67)	300	600	900	2550	5775	9000
51-2nd app. Kingpin; Joe Robertson 1-panel cameo	52	104	156	416	933	1450
52-58,60: 52-1st app. Joe Robertson & 3rd app. Kingpin. 56-1st app. Capt. George Stacy. 57,58-Ka-Zar app.	16	32	48	107	236	365
59-1st app. Brainwasher (alias Kingpin); 1st-c app. M. J. Watson	18	36	54	124	275	425
61-74: 61-1st Gwen Stacy cover app. 67-1st app. Randy Robertson. 69-Kingpin-c. 69,70-Kingpin app. 70-1st app. Vanessa Fisk (Kingpin's wife)(only seen in shadow). 73-1st app. Silvermane. 74-Last 12¢ issue	12	24	36	82	179	275
75-77,79-83,87-89,91,92,95,99: 79-The Prowler app. 83-1st app. Schemer; Vanessa Fisk app. (only previously seen in shadow in #70)	11	22	33	73	157	240
78-1st app. The Prowler	26	52	78	182	404	625
84,85,93: 84,85-Kingpin-c/story. 93-1st app. Arthur Stacy	11	22	33	73	157	240
86-Re-intro & origin Black Widow in new costume	22	44	66	154	340	525
90-Death of Capt. Stacy	17	34	51	117	259	400
94-Origin retold	14	28	42	93	204	315
96-98-Green Goblin app. (97,98-Green Goblin-c); drug books not approved by CCA	14	28	42	93	204	315
100-Anniversary issue (9/71); Green Goblin cameo (2 pgs.)	23	46	69	161	356	550
101-1st app. Morbius the Living Vampire; Lizard cameo; Stan Lee co-plots with Roy Thomas; last 15¢ issue (10/71)	71	142	213	568	1284	2000
101-Silver ink 2nd printing (9/92, $1.75)	4	8	12	27	44	60
101 Facsimile Edition 1 (4/21, $3.99) r/#101 with original 1971 ads and letter column	1	2	3	5	6	8
102-Origin & 2nd app. Morbius (25¢, 52 pgs.)	16	32	48	107	236	365
103-118: 103,104-Roy Thomas-s. 104,111-Kraven the Hunter-c/stories. 105-109-Stan Lee-s. 108-1st app. Sha-Shan. 109-Dr. Strange-c/story. 110-1st app. Gibbon; Conway-s begin. 113-1st app. Hammerhead. 116-Reprints story from Spectacular Spider-Man Mag. in color with some changes	8	16	24	54	102	150
119,120-Spider-Man vs. Hulk (4 & 5/73)	12	24	36	82	179	275
121-Death of Gwen Stacy (6/73) (killed by Green Goblin)(reprinted in Marvel Tales #98 & 192); Harry Osborn LSD overdose	38	76	114	281	628	975
122-Death of The Green Goblin-c/story (7/73) (reprinted in Marvel Tales #99 & 192)	28	56	84	202	451	700
123-Cage app.	9	18	27	62	126	190
124-1st app. Man-Wolf (9/73)	21	42	63	147	324	500
125-Man-Wolf origin	9	18	27	60	120	180
126-128: 126-1st mention of Harry Osborn becoming Green Goblin	6	12	18	42	79	115
129-1st app. The Punisher (2/74); 1st app. Jackal	400	800	1200	2000	3000	4000
130-133: 131-Last 20¢ issue	6	12	18	37	66	95
134-(7/74); 1st app. Tarantula; Harry Osborn discovers Spider-Man's ID; Punisher cameo	13	26	39	89	195	300
135-2nd full Punisher app. (8/74)	17	34	51	117	259	400
136-1st app. Harry Osborn in Green Goblin costume	10	20	30	67	141	215
137-Green Goblin-c/story (2nd Harry Osborn Goblin)	7	14	21	44	82	120
138-141: 139-1st app Grizzly. 140-1st app. Glory Grant	4	8	12	28	47	65
142-Mysterio app.; Gwen Stacy clone cameo	5	10	15	35	63	90
143-Gwen Stacy clone cameo; 1st app. Cyclone	7	14	21	44	82	120
144-147: 144-Full app. of Gwen Stacy clone. 145,146-Gwen Stacy clone storyline continues. 147-Spider-Man learns Gwen Stacy is clone	4	8	12	28	47	65
148-Jackal revealed	7	14	21	49	92	135
149-Spider-Man clone story begins, clone dies (?); origin of Jackal	13	26	39	89	195	300
150-Spider-Man decides he is not the clone	6	12	18	38	69	100
151-Spider-Man disposes of clone body; Len Wein-s begins; thru #180	6	12	18	38	69	100
152-155,157-160:(Regular 25¢ editions). 152-vs. the Shocker. 154-vs. Sandman. 157-159-Doc Octopus & Hammerhead app. 159-Last 25c issue(8/76). 160-Spider-Mobile destroyed	8	16	24	54	102	150
155-159-(30¢-c variants, limited distribution)	9	18	27	63	129	195
156-1st Mirage	5	10	15	33	57	80
161-Nightcrawler app. from X-Men; Punisher cameo; Wolverine & Colossus app.	5	10	15	35	63	90
162-Punisher, Nightcrawler app.; 1st Jigsaw	6	12	18	42	79	115
163-168: 163-164-vs. the Kingpin. 165-vs. Stegron. 166-Stegron & the Lizard app. 167-1st app. Will O' The Wisp. 168-Will O' The Wisp app.	3	6	9	21	33	45
169-170,172-173: 169-Clone story recapped; Stan Lee Cameo. 170-Dr. Faustus app. 172-1st Rocket Racer. 173-vs Molten Man	3	6	9	19	30	40
171-Nova app. x-over w/Nova #12	3	6	9	18	30	40
169-173-(35¢-c variants, limited dist.)(6-10/77)	21	42	63	147	324	500
174,175-Punisher app.	4	8	12	24	45	65
176-180-Green Goblin (Barton Hamilton) app.; Harry Osborn Green Goblin in #180 only. 177-180-Silvermane app.	3	6	9	21	33	45
181-186: 181-Origin retold; gives life history of Spidey; Punisher cameo in flashback (1 panel). 182-(7/78)-Peter's first proposal to Mary Jane, but she declines (in #183). 183-Rocket Racer & the Big Wheel app. 184-vs. the second White Dragon. 185-Peter graduates college	9	18	27	63	129	195
187,188: 187-Captain America app. 188-vs. Jigsaw	4	8	12	24	45	65
189,190-Byrne-a; Man-Wolf app.	4	8	12	23	37	50
191-193,196-199: 191-vs. the Spider-Slayer. 192-Death of Spencer Smythe. 193-Peter & Mary Jane break up; the Fly app. 196-Faked death of Aunt May. 197-vs. the Kingpin. 198,199-Mysterio app.	3	6	9	16	23	30
NOTE: Whitman 3-packs containing #192-194,196 exist.						
194-1st app. Black Cat	22	44	66	154	340	525
195-2nd app. Black Cat & origin Black Cat	5	10	15	31	53	75
200-Giant origin issue (1/80); death of the burglar (from Amazing Fantasy #15)	4	8	12	28	47	65
201-Punisher app.; classic bullseye-c	5	10	15	33	57	80
202-Punisher app.	4	8	12	23	37	50
203,204: 203-3rd Dazzler (4/80). 204-Black Cat app.; last Wolfman-s	3	6	9	15	33	45
205-208,211,213-219: 205-Black Cat app. 206-Byrne-a. 207-vs Mesmero. 211-Sub-Mariner app. 214,215-New Frightful Four app: Wizard, Trapster, Sandman & Llyra (Namor foe). 216-Madame Web app. 217-Sandman vs Hydro-Man. 219-Grey Gargoyle app.; Frank Miller-c	3	6	9	14	20	25
209-Kraven the Hunter app; 1st app. origin Calypso	3	6	9	21	33	45
210-1st app. Madame Web	10	20	30	64	132	200
212-1st app. & origin Hydro-Man	5	10	15	30	50	70
220-Moon Knight app.	4	8	12	23	37	50
221-224,226,227: 222-1st app. of the Whizzer as Speed Demon. 223-vs. The Red Ghost & the Super-Apes; Roger Stern-s begins. 224-Vulture app. 225-Foolkiller II-c/story	2	4	6	10	14	18
226,227-Black Cat returns	3	6	9	18	28	38
229,230: Classic 'Nothing can stop the Juggernaut' story	3	6	9	21	33	45
231-237: 231,232-Cobra & Mr Hyde app. 233-Tarantula app. 234-Free 16 pg. insert "Marvel Guide to Collecting Comics", Tarantula & Will O' The Wisp app. 235-Origin Will 'O The Wisp. 236-Tarantula dies. 237-Stilt-Man app.	2	4	6	10	14	18
238-(3/83)-1st app. Hobgoblin (Ned Leeds); came with skin 'Tattooz' decal.						
NOTE: The same decal appears in the more common Fantastic Four #252 which is being removed & placed in this issue as incentive to increase value. (No "Tattooz" were included in the Canadian edition)						
(Value with tattooz)	18	36	54	124	275	425
(Value without tattooz)	8	16	24	38	69	100
238 Facsimile Edition 1 (5/22, $3.99) r/#238 with original 1983 ads and letter column						6.00
239-2nd app. Hobgoblin; 1st battle w/Spidey	5	10	15	33	57	80
240-243,246-248: 240,241-Vulture app. (origin in #241). 242-Mary Jane Watson cameo (last panel). 243-Reintro Mary Jane after 4 year absence. 248-Classic 'The Kid Who Collects Spider-Man' story; Spider-Man tells origin & reveals identity to young boy with leukemia	2	4	6	10	14	18
244-3rd app. Hobgoblin (cameo)	3	6	9	16	23	30
245-1st app (10/83)-4th app. Hobgoblin (cameo); Lefty Donovan gains powers of Hobgoblin & battles Spider-Man	3	6	9	19	30	45
249-251: 249-1st Hobgoblin/Spider-Man battle. 249-Retells origin & death of 1st Green Goblin. 251-Last old costume	2	4	6	10	14	18
252-Spider-Man dons new black costume (5/84); ties with Marvel Team-Up #141 & Spectacular Spider-Man #90 for 1st new costume in regular title (See Marvel Super-Heroes Secret Wars #8 (12/84) for acquisition of costume); last Roger Stern-s	10	20	30	69	147	225
253-1st app. The Rose; Tom DeFalco-s begin	3	6	9	16	23	30
254,255: 254-Jack O' Lantern app. 255-1st app Black Fox	2	4	6	11	14	18
256,257: 256-1st app. Puma. 257-Hobgoblin cameo; 2nd app. Puma; M.J. Watson reveals she knows Spidey's i.d.	3	6	9	21	33	45
258-Spider-Man discovers black costume is an alien symbiote; Mister Fantastic, Human Torch, Hobgoblin app.	4	8	12	27	44	60
259-Full Hobgoblin app.; Spidey back to old costume; origin Mary Jane Watson	3	6	9	14	20	30
260,261-Hobgoblin app. 261-Painted-c by Vess	3	6	9	17	25	34
262-Spider-Man unmasked; photo-c	3	6	9	14	20	25
263,264,266-268: 266-Toad & Frogman app.; Peter David-s. 268-Secret Wars II x-over	2	4	6	8	11	14
265-1st app. Silver Sable (6/85)	4	8	12	28	47	65
265-Silver ink 2nd printing ($1.25)	4	8	12	16	21	26
269-274,277-280,282-283: 269-Spider-Man vs Firelord. 272-1st app. Slyde. 273-Secret Wars II x-over; Beyonder app. 274-Secret Wars II x-over; Zarathos app. (The Spirit of Vengeance). 277-Vess-c & back-up art. 278-Scourge app; death of the Wraith. 279-Jack O' Lantern-c/s. 280-1st Sinister Syndicate: Beetle, Boomerang, Hydro-Man, Rhino, Speed Demon.	2	4	6	10	14	18
282-X-Factor app.	2	4	6	10	14	18
270,276: 270-Avengers app. 276-Hobgoblin app.	2	4	6	10	14	18
275-($1.25, 52 pgs.)-Hobgoblin-c/story; origin-r by Ditko	3	6	9	17	26	35
281-Hobgoblin battles Jack O'Lantern	3	6	9	14	19	24
284,285: 284-Punisher cameo; Gang War Pt.1; Hobgoblin-c/story. 285-Punisher app.; minor Hobgoblin app.; last Tom DeFalco-s; Gang War Pt. 2	3	6	9	14	19	24
286-288: Gang War Parts 3-5. 286-Hobgoblin-c & app. (minor). 287-Hobgoblin app. (minor). 288-Full Hobgoblin app.; Gang War ends	2	4	6	8	11	14
289-(6/87, $1.25, 52 pgs.)-Hobgoblin's i.d. revealed as Ned Leeds; death of Ned Leeds; Macendale (Jack O'Lantern) becomes new Hobgoblin (1st app.)	3	6	9	19	30	40
290-292,295-297: 290-Peter proposes to Mary Jane; 1st David Michelinie-s. 291,292-Spider-Slayer app. 292-She accepts; leads into wedding in Amazing Spider-Man Annual #21. 295-'Mad Dog Ward' Pt. 2; x-over w/Web of Spider-Man #33 & Spectacular Spider-Man #133. 296-297-Doc Octopus app.	2	4	6	8	10	12
293,294-Part 2 & 5 of Kraven story from Web of Spider-Man. 293-Continued from Web of Spider-Man #31; continues into Spectacular Spider-Man #131. 294-Death of Kraven; continued from Web of Spider-Man #32; continues in Spectacular Spider-Man #132	3	6	9	17	26	35
298-Todd McFarlane-c/a begins (3/88); 1st brief app. Eddie Brock who becomes Venom; (last pg.)	6	12	18	38	69	100
299-1st brief app. Venom with costume	6	12	18	38	69	100
300-(5/88, $1.50, 52 pgs.)-25th Anniversary)-1st full Venom app.; last black costume	25	45	75	175	388	600
301-$1.00 issues begin. Classic McFarlane-c	6	12	18	42	79	115
302-305: 302-303-Silver Sable app. 304,305-Black Fox app. 304-1st bi-weekly issue	2	4	6	11	16	20

Amazing Spider-Man #176 © MAR

Amazing Spider-Man #313 © MAR

Amazing Spider-Man #410 © MAR

	GD 2.0	VG 4.0	FN 6.0	VF 8.0	VF/NM 9.0	NM- 9.2
306-Swipes-c from Action #1	4	8	12	27	44	60
307-311,313,314: 307-Chameleon app. 308-Taskmaster app. 309-1st app. Styx & Stone. 310-Killer Shrike app. 311-Inferno x-over; Mysterio app. 313-Lizard app.; origin retold.	2	4	6	11	16	20
314-Christmas-c						
312-Hobgoblin battles Green Goblin; Inferno x-over	3	6	9	19	30	40
315,317-Venom app.	4	8	12	23	37	50
316-Classic Venom-c	8	16	24	54	102	150
318-322: 318-Scorpion app. 319-Bi-weekly begins again; Scorpion, Rhino, Backlash app. 320-'Assassination Nation Plot' Pt.1 (ends in issue #325); Paladin & Silver Sable app. 321-Paladin & Silver Sable app. 322-Silver Sable app.; fan letters from Stan Lee and Charlie Novinskie	2	4	6	8	11	14
323,324: 323-Captain America app. 324-Sabretooth app.; McFarlane cover only	2	4	6	11	16	20
325-Captain America & Red Skull app.	3	6	9	16	23	30
326,327: 326-Acts of Vengeance x-over; vs Graviton. 327-Acts of Vengeance x-over; vs. Magneto; Cosmic storyline continues in Spectacular Spider-Man; Erik Larsen-a.	1	3	4	6	8	10
328-Acts of Vengeance; vs. the Hulk; last McFarlane issue	3	6	9	17	26	35
329-Acts of Vengeance x-over; vs. the Tri-Sentinel; Sebastian Shaw app.; Erik Larsen-a (continuous through issue #344)	3	6	9	15	22	28
330-333: 330,331-Punisher app. 331-Minor Venom app. 332,333-Venom-c/story	3	6	9	14	20	25
334-336,338-343: 334-339-Return of the Sinister Six. 341-Tarantula app; Spider-Man loses his cosmic powers. 342,343-Black Cat app.	1	3	4	6	8	10
337-Hobgoblin app.	3	6	9	14	20	25
344-(2/91) 1st app. Cletus Kasady (Carnage)	3	6	9	19	30	40
345-1st full app. Cletus Kasady; Venom cameo on last pg.; 1st Mark Bagley-a on Spider-Man	3	6	9	19	30	40
346,347-Venom app.	3	6	9	19	30	40
347 Facsimile Edition (3/20, $3.99) r/#347 with original 1991 ads and letter column						4.00
348,349,351-359: 348-Avengers app. 351-Bagley-a begins. 351,352-Nova of New Warriors app. 353-Darkhawk app.; brief Punisher app. 354-Punisher cameo & Nova, Night Thrasher (New Warriors), Darkhawk & Moon Knight app. 357,358-Punisher, Darkhawk, Moon Knight, Night Thrasher, Nova x-over. 358-3 part gatefold-c; last $1.00-c						6.00
350-($1.50, 52pgs.)-Origin retold; Spidey vs Dr. Doom; last Erik Larsen-a pin-ups; Uncle Ben app.	1	3	4	6	8	10
360-Carnage cameo	3	6	9	19	30	40
361-(4/92) Intro. Carnage (the Spawn of Venom); begin 3 part story; recap of Spidey's alien costume became Venom	7	14	21	46	86	125
361-($1.25)-2nd printing; silver-c	5	10	15	33	57	80
362,363-Carnage & Venom-c/story	3	6	9	16	23	30
362-2nd printing	2	4	6	11	14	18
364-366,373,376,377,381-387: 364-The Shocker app. (old villain). 366-Peter's parents-c/story; Red Skull, Viper & Taskmaster app. 367-Red Skull, Viper & Taskmaster app. 368-Invasion of the Spider-Slayers Pt.6 (through #373). 369-Harry Osborn back-up (Gr. Goblin II). Electro app. 370-Black Cat & Scorpion app. 373-Venom back-up. 376,377-Cardiac app. 381,382-Hulk app. 383-The Jury app. 383-385-vs The Jury. 384-Venom/Carnage app. 386-Vulture app. 387-Vulture is de-aged & gets new costume						4.00
365-(8/92) $3.95, 84 pgs.)-30th anniversary issue w/Spidey/Venom/Carnage pull-out poster; contains 5 pg. preview of Spider-Man 2099 (intro., Spider-Man 2099 appears on a pull-out poster in Web of Spider-Man #90 one month earlier); Spidey's origin retold; Lizard app.; reintro Peter's parents in Stan Lee 3 pg. text w/illo of costumes; story continues thru #370)	4	8	12	23	37	50
374-Venom-c/story	3	6	9	14	20	25
375-(3/93, $3.95, 68 pgs.)-Holo-grafx foil-c; vs. Venom; ties into Venom: Lethal Protector #1; intro. Ann Weying; Pat Olliffe-a.	4	8	12	23	37	50
378-380: Parts 3,7 and 11 of Maximum Carnage. 378-Continued from Web of Spider-Man #101; Venom vs Carnage; continued in Spider-Man #35. 379-Continued from Web of Spider-Man #102; Deathlok, Firestar, Black Cat & Morbius app.; continued in Spider-Man #36. 380-Continued from Web of Spider-Man #103; Captain America & Cloak and Dagger app.; continued in Spider-Man #37					3	5
388-($2.25, 68 pgs.)-Newsstand edition; Venom back-up & Cardiac & chance back-up; last David Michelinie-s (6-year run)						6.00
388-($2.95, 68 pgs.)-Collector's edition w/foil-c	1	2	3	5	6	8
389-1st print (3 cards) attached to the staples; harder to find in true high grade due to creases caused by the cards; Green Goblin app.						6.00
390-393,395,396: 390-393-Venom app. 390-393-vs. Shriek. 395-Puma app. 396-Daredevil & the Owl app.						4.00
390-($2.95)-Collector's edition polybagged w/16 pg. insert of new animated Spidey TV show plus animation cel	1	2	3	5	6	8
394-($2.95, 48 pgs.)-Deluxe edition; flip book w/Birth of a Spider-Man Pt.2; silver foil both-c; Power & Responsibility Pt.2; Judas Traveller, the Jackal and the Gwen Stacy Clone app. 1st app. Scrier	1	2	3	5	6	8
394-Newsstand edition ($1.50-c)	1	2	3	5	6	8

	GD 2.0	VG 4.0	FN 6.0	VF 8.0	VF/NM 9.0	NM- 9.2
397-($2.25)-Flip book w/Ultimate Spider-Man						6.00
398,399: 398-Web of Death Pt.3; continued from Spectacular Spider-Man #220; Doc Octopus & Kaine app.; continued in Spectacular Spider-Man #221. 399-Smoke and Mirrors Pt.2; continued from Web of Spider-Man #122; Jackal, Scarlet Spider, Gwen Stacy Clone app; continued in Spider-Man #56						6.00
400-($2.95)-Death of Aunt May; newsstand edition	3	6	9	19	30	40
400-($3.95)-Death of Aunt May; embossed grey overlay cover	3	6	9	15	22	28
400-Collector's Edition; white embossed-c; (10,000 print run)	5	10	15	34	60	85
401,402,405,406-409: 401-The Mark of Kaine Pt.2; continued from Web of Spider-Man #124; Scarlet Spider app; continues in Spider-Man #58. 402-Judas Traveller & Scrier app. 405-Exiled Pt.2; continued from Web of Spider-Man #128; Scarlet Spider app.; continues in Spider-Man #62. 406-1st full app. of the female Doc Octopus (Carolyn Trainer); continues in Spider-Man #63; Marvel Overpower card insert; harder to find in higher grades due to card indenting; last JM DeMatteis-s. 407-Human Torch, Sandman & Silver Sable app. Tom DeFalco-s (returns to Spider-Man; last-s in 1987). 408-Regular ed; Media Blizzard pt.2; Mysterio app; continued from Sensational Spider-Man #1; continues in Spider-Man #65. 409-The Return of Kaine Pt.3; continued from Spectacular Spider-Man #231; Kaine & Rhino app. Continued in Spider-Man #66						6.00
403-The Trial of Peter Parker Pt. 2; continued from Web of Spider-Man #126; Carnage app; continues in Spider-Man #60.	2	4	6	8	10	12
404-Maximum Clonage Pt.3; continued from Web of Spider-Man #127; Scarlet Spider, Jackal, Scrier & Kaine app; continued in Spider-Man #61						6.00
408-($2.95)-Polybagged version with TV theme song cassette; scarce in high grade due to damage caused by the cassette indenting the actual comic	7	14	21	46	86	125
408-Direct edition (without cassette & out of polybag)	4	8	12	23	37	50
408-Newsstand edition; variant cover	5	10	15	31	53	75
410-Web of Carnage Pt.2; continued from Sensational Spider-Man #3; Carnage app; continues in Spider-Man #67	3	6	9	21	33	45
411,412,414,417-424: 411-Blood Brothers Pt.2; continued from Sensational Spider-Man #4; Gaunt app; continued in Spider-Man #68. 412-Blood Brothers Pt.6; continued from Sensational Spider-Man #5; vs Gaunt. 414-The Rose app. 417-Death of Scrier. 418-Revelations Pt.3; continued from Spectacular Spider-Man #240; Norman Osborn returns; 'death' of Peter and Mary Jane's baby (May Parker); continued in Spider-Man #75. 419-1st minor app. of the Black Tarantula. 420-X-Man app. 422,423-Electro app. 424-Elektra app.						6.00
413-Contains a free packet of Island Twists Kool-Aid and Spider-Man For Kids magazine subscriber card; harder to find in true high grade	1	3	4	6	8	10
415-Onslaught Impact 2; Green Goblin (Phil Urich) app. vs. Mark IV Sentinels; last Mark Bagley-a (5 year run)	1	3	4	6	8	10
416-Epilogue to Onslaught; harder to find in high grade due to Marvel Overpower card insert	2	4	6	9	13	16
425-($2.99)-48 pgs., wraparound-c; X-Man app.	2	4	6	8	10	12
426,428,429,432,435-438,440: 426-Female Dr. Octopus app. 428-Dr. Octopus app. 429-Absorbing Man app. 432-Spider-Hunt Pt.2; continued from Sensational Spider-Man #25; Black Tarantula & Norman Osborn app. 433-Mr. Hyde app. 435-Identity Crisis; Black Tarantula & Kaine app. 436-Black Tarantula app. 437-Plantman app. 438-Daredevil app. 440-Gathering of Five Pt.2; continued from Sensational Spider-Man #32; John Byrne-s; Molten Man & Norman Osborn app; continued in Spider-Man #96						6.00
427-Return of Dr. Octopus; double-gatefold-c	1	3	4	6	8	10
430-Carnage & Silver Surfer app.	4	8	12	23	37	50
431-Cosmic-Carnage vs Silver Surfer; Galactus cameo	4	8	12	28	47	65
432-Variant yellow-c 'Wanted Dead or Alive'	2	4	6	11	16	20
434-Identity Crisis; Black Tarantula app.	2	4	6	10	14	18
434-Variant 'Amazing Ricochet #1'-c	2	4	6	10	14	18
439-Alternate future story; Avengers app; last Tom DeFalco-s	2	4	6	8	11	14
441-The Final Chapter Pt.1; John Byrne-s; Norman Osborn app; last issue (Dec. 1998); story continues in Spider-Man #97	2	4	6	8	11	14
#500-up (See Amazing Spider-Man Vol. 2; series resumed original numbering after Vol. 2 #58)						
# (-1) Flashback issue (7/97, $1.95-c)						5.00
Annual 1 (1964, 72 pgs.) Origin Spider-Man; 1st app. Sinister Six (Dr. Octopus, Electro, Kraven the Hunter, Mysterio, Sandman, Vulture) (new 41 pg. story); plus gallery of Spidey foes; early X-Men app.	400	800	1200	3400	7700	12,000
Annual #1 Facsimile Edition 1 (6/22, $7.99) rep. entire issue with original 1964 ads						8.00
Annual 2 (1965, 25¢, 72 pgs.) Reprints from #1,2,5 plus new Doctor Strange story	44	88	132	326	738	1150
Special 3 (11/66, 25¢, 72 pgs.) New Avengers story & Hulk x-over; Doctor Octopus-r from #11,12; Romita-a	22	44	66	154	340	525
Special 4 (11/67, 25¢, 68 pgs.) Spidey battles Human Torch (new 41 pg. story)	14	28	42	93	204	315
Special 5 (11/68, 25¢, 68 pgs.) New 40 pg. Red Skull story; 1st app. Peter Parker's parents;						

	GD 2.0	VG 4.0	FN 6.0	VF 8.0	VF/NM 9.0	NM- 9.2
last annual with new-a	12	24	36	84	185	285
Special 5-2nd printing (1994)	2	4	6	9	13	16
Special 6 (11/69, 25¢, 68 pgs.) Reprints 41 pg. Sinister Six story from Annual #1 plus 2 Kirby/Ditko stories (r)	16	32	48	110	243	375
Special 7 (12/70, 25¢, 68 pgs.) All-r(#1,2) new Vulture-c	6	12	18	38	69	100
Special 8 (12/71) All-r	6	12	18	38	69	100
King Size 9 ('73) Reprints Spectacular Spider-Man (mag.) #2; 40 pg. Green Goblin-c/story (re-edited from #58 pg.)	4	8	12	41	76	110
Annual 10 (1976) Origin Human Fly (vs. Spidey); new-a begins	8	12	18	27	44	60
Annual 11-13 ('77-'79): 12-Spidey vs. Hulk-r/#119,120. 13-New Byrne/Austin-a; Dr. Octopus x-over/Spectacular S-M Ann. #1	3	6	9	16	23	30
Annual 14 (1980) Miller-c/a(p); Doctor Strange and Doctor Doom app.	4	8	12	18	27	36
Annual 15 (1981) Miller-c/a(p); Punisher and Doctor Octopus app.; 4 bonus pin-ups (Man-Wolf, The Jackal, Punisher and Tarantula)	3	6	9	19	30	40
Annual 16 (1982)-Origin/1st app. new Captain Marvel (female heroine Monica Rambeau)	5	10	15	33	57	80
Annual 17-20: 17 ('83)-Kingpin app. 18 ('84)-Scorpion app.; JJJ weds. 19 ('85). 20 ('86)-Origin Iron Man of 2020	2	4	6	8	11	14
Annual 21 (1987) Special wedding issue; newsstand & direct sale versions exist & are worth same	4	8	12	25	40	55
Annual 22 (1988, $1.75, 68 pgs.) 1st app. Speedball; Evolutionary War x-over; Daredevil app.		4	6	16	24	32
Annual 23 (1989, $2.00, 68 pgs.) Atlantis Attacks; origin Spider-Man retold; She-Hulk app.; Byrne-c; Liefeld-a(p), 23 pgs.	2	4	6	9	12	15
Annual 24 (1990, $2.00, 68 pgs.) -Ant-Man app.	1	2	3	5	6	8
Annual 25 (1991, $2.25, 68 pgs.) 3 pg. origin recap; Iron Man app.; 1st Venom solo story; Ditko-a (6 pgs.)	1	3	4	6	8	10
Annual 26 (1992, $2.25, 68 pgs.) New Warriors-c/story; Venom solo story cont'd in Spectacular Spider-Man Annual #12	2	4	6	9	13	16
Annual 27 ('93, $2.95, 68 pgs.) Bagged w/card; 1st app. Annex						6.00
Annual 28 ('94, $2.95, 68 pgs.) Carnage-c/story	2	4	6	8	11	14
'96 Special-($2.95, 64 pgs.)-"Blast From The Past"						6.00
'97 Special-($2.99)-Wraparound-c, Sundown app.						6.00
...: Carnage (6/93, $6.95)-r/ASM #344,345,359-363	2	4	6	8	11	14
Marvel Graphic Novel - Parallel Lives (3/89, $8.95)	2	4	6	8	11	14
...: Parallel Lives 1 (2012, $4.99) r/1989 GN						6.00
Marvel Graphic Novel - Spirits of the Earth (1990, $18.95, HC)		2	4	6	10	15	19
...: No. 1 Facsimile Edition (12/22, $3.99) Reprints #1 with original 1963 ads	1	3	4	6	8	10
...: No. 121 Facsimile Edition (8/23, $3.99) Reprints #121 with original 1973 ads						5.00
...: No. 122 Facsimile Edition (8/23, $3.99) Reprints #122 with original 1973 ads						4.00
...: No. 252 Facsimile Edition 1 (6/19, $4.99) Reprints #252 with original 1984 ads						5.00
...: No. 252 Facsimile Edition (3/24, $4.99) Reprints #252 with original 1984 ads						5.00
...: No. 253 Facsimile Edition (4/24, $4.99) Reprints #253 with original 1984 ads						5.00
...: No. 300 Facsimile Edition (10/23, $6.99) Reprints #300 with original 1988 ads						7.00
Super Special 1 (4/95, $3.95)-Flip Book	3	6	9	14	20	25
...: Skating on Thin Ice 1 (1990, $1.25, Canadian)-McFarlane-c; anti-drug issue; Electro app.						6.00
...: Skating on Thin Ice (2/93, $1.50, American)	2	4	6	8	10	12
...: Double Trouble 2 (1990, $1.25, Canadian)	1	2	3	5		6
...: Double Trouble 2 (2/93, $1.50, American)	1	3	4	6	8	10
...: Hit and Run 3 (1990, $1.25, Canadian)-Ghost Rider-c/story	1	2	3	5	7	9
...: Hit and Run 3 (2/93, $1.50, American)						6.00
...: Chaos in Calgary 4 (Canadian; part of 5 part series)-Turbine,Night Rider, Frightful app.	2	4	6	8	11	14
...: Chaos in Calgary 4 (2/93, $1.50, American)						5.00
...: Deadball 5 (1993, $1.60, Canadian)-Green Goblin-c/story; features Montreal Expos	2	4	6	11	16	20

Note: Prices listed above are for English Canadian editions. French editions are worth double.

...: Soul of the Hunter nn (8/92, $5.95, 52 pgs.)-Zeck-c/a(p)

	GD 2.0	VG 4.0	FN 6.0	VF 8.0	VF/NM 9.0	NM- 9.2
...: Venom 3D No. 1 (10/19, $7.99) Reprints ASM #300 in 3D; bagged with glasses						25.00
Wizard #1 Ace Edition (13.99) r/#1 w/ new Ramos acetate-c						18.00
Wizard #129 Ace Edition (13.99) r/#129 w/ new Ramos acetate-c						25.00

NOTE: Austin a(i)-248, 335, 337, Annual 12. Bagley a(p)-72, 73, 76-81, 84, 85. Byrne a-189p, 190p, 206p, Annual 3r, 6r, 7r, 13p; c-189p, 268, 296, Annual 12. Ditko a-1-38, Annual 1, Special 3; 2, 24(2); c-1, 2-38, Annual 1. Guice c/a-Annual 18i. Gil Kane c(p)-89-105, 120-124, 150, Annual 10, 12i, 24p; c-90p, 96, 99, 101-105p, 129p, 131p, 132p, 137-140p, 143p, 148p, 149p, 151p, 153p, 160p, 161p, Annual 10p. 24. Kirby a-8. Erik Larsen a-324, 327, 329-350; c-327, 329-350, 354i, Annual 25. McFarlane a-298p, 299p, 300-303, 304-323p, 325p, 328; c-298-325, 328. Miller c-218, 219. Mooney a-65i, 67-82i, 84-88i, 173i, 178i, 189i, 190i, 192i, 193i, 196-202i, 207i, 211-219i, 221i, 222i, 226i, 227i, 229-233i, Annual 11i, 17i. Nasser c-228p. Nebres a-Annual 24i. Russell c-357i. Simonson c-222, 337i. Starlin a-113i, 114i, 187p. Williamson a-365i.

AMAZING SPIDER-MAN (Volume 2) (Some issues reprinted in "Spider-Man, Best Of" hardcovers)
Marvel Comics: Jan, 1999 - No. 700, Feb, 2013 (1/$1.99/$2.25)

	GD 2.0	VG 4.0	FN 6.0	VF 8.0	VF/NM 9.0	NM- 9.2
1-($2.99)-Byrne-a; Avengers, Fantastic Four & Green Goblin app.	2	4	6	8	10	12
1-Sunburst variant-c	3	6	9	14	19	24
1-($6.95) Dynamic Forces variant-c by the Romitas	3	6	9	14	20	26
1-Marvel Matrix sketch variant-c	3	6	9	19	30	40
2-($1.99) Two covers -by Byrne & Andy Kubert	1	2	3	5	6	8
3,4,6-11: 4-Fantastic Four app.						4.00
5-1st Maddie Franklin as Spider-Woman	3	6	9	14	19	24
12-($2.99) Sinister Six return (cont. in Peter Parker #12)						5.00
13-17: 13-Mary Jane's plane explodes						4.00
18-Begin $2.25-c; Green Goblin app.	2	4	6	10	14	18
19-Venom-c	2	4	6	11	16	20
20-($2.99, 100 pgs.) Super Spider-Slayer issue; new story and reprints	2	4	6	11	16	20
21-24,26-28: 24-Maximum Security						4.00
25-($2.99) Regular cover; Peter Parker becomes the Green Goblin						6.00
25-($3.99) Holo-foil enhanced cover	2	4	6	11	16	20
29-Peter is reunited with Mary Jane	2	4	6	8	10	12
30-Straczynski-s/Campbell-c begin; intro. Ezekiel	3	6	9	17	26	35
31-35: Battles Morlun						5.00
36-Black cover; aftermath of the Sept. 11 tragedy in New York						
37-49: 39-'Nuff Said issue 42-Dr. Strange app. 43-45-Doctor Octopus app. 46-48-Cho-c	4	8	12	28	47	65
50-Peter and MJ reunite; Captain America & Dr. Doom app.; Campbell-c						4.00
	2	4	6	8		10
51-58: 51,52-Campbell-c. 55,56-Avery scripts. 57,58-Avengers, FF, Cyclops app.						8

(After #58 [Nov, 2003] numbering reverts back to original Vol. 1 with #500, Dec, 2003)

	GD 2.0	VG 4.0	FN 6.0	VF 8.0	VF/NM 9.0	NM- 9.2
500-($3.50) J. Scott Campbell-c; Romita Jr. & Sr.-a; Uncle Ben app.			6	11	16	20
501-524: 501-Harris-c. 503-504-Loki app. 506-508-Ezekiel app. 509-514-Sins Past; intro. Gabriel and Sarah Osborn; Deodato-a. 519-Moves into Avengers HQ. 521-Begin $2.50-c. 524-Harris-c						4.00
525,526-Evolve or Die x-over. 525-David-s. 526-Hudlin-s; Spider-Man loses eye						5.00
525-528-2nd printings with variant-c. 525-Ben Reilly costume. 526-Six-Armed Spidey. 527-Spider-Man 2099. 528-Spider-Ham						6.00
527,528: Evolve or Die pt. 9,12						4.00
529-Debut of red and gold costume (Iron Spider); Garney-a						28.00
529-2nd printing	1	2	3	5	6	8
529-3rd printing with Wieringo-c						8.00
530,531-Titanium Man app.; Kirkham-a. 531-Begin $2.99-c						10.00
532-538-Civil War tie-in. 538-Aunt May shot						6.00
539,540-Back in Black. 539-Peter wears the black costume						
	1	3	4	6	8	10
541-543-Back in Black						4.00
544-($3.99) "One More Day" pt. 1; Quesada-a/Straczynski-s						12.00
545-($3.99) "One More Day" pt. 4; Quesada-a/Straczynski-s, Peter & MJ's marriage un-done; r/wedding from ASM Annual #21; 2 covers by Quesada and Djurdjevic						12.00
546-($3.99) Brand New Day begins; McNiven-a; Deodato, Winslade, Land, Romita Jr.-a; 1st app. Mr. Negative						25.00
546-Variant-c by Bryan Hitch						30.00
546-Second printing with new McNiven-c of Peter Parker						12.00
546-MGC (7/10, $1.00) r/#546 with "Marvel's Greatest Comics" logo on cover						3.00
547-549,551-564,566,567: 547,548-McNiven-a. 549-551-Larroca-a. 555-557-Bachalo-a. 559-Intro. Screwball. 560,561-MJ app. 566,567-Spidey in Daredevil costume						3.00
550-Intro. Menace (Lily Hollister)						12.00
565-Intro Ana Kravinoff						25.00
568-($3.99) Romita Jr.-a begins; two covers by Romita Jr. and Alex Ross						12.00
568-Variant-c by John Romita Sr.						28.00
568-2nd printing with Romita Jr. Anti-Venom costume cover						6.00
569-Debut of Anti-Venom; Norman Osborn and Thunderbolts app.; Romita Jr.-c						50.00
569-Variant Venom-c by Granov						55.00
569-2nd printing with Romita Jr.-c						200.00
570-572-Two covers on each						10.00
573-($3.99) New Ways to Die conclusion; Spidey meets Stephen Colbert back-up; Ollife-a; two covers by Romita Jr. and Maguire						6.00
573-Variant cover with Stephen Colbert; cover swipe of AF #15 by Quesada						25.00
574-582: 577-Punisher app.						3.00
583-($3.99) Spidey meets Obama back-up story; regular Romita Sr. "Cougars" cover						4.00
583-($3.99) Obama variant-c with Spidey on left; Spidey meets Obama back-up story						70.00
583-($3.99) Second printing Obama variant-c with Spidey on right and yellow bkgrd						10.00
583-($3.99) 3rd-5th printings Obama variant-c: 3rd-Blue bkgrd w/flag. 4th-White bkgrd w/flag. 5th-Lincoln Memorial bkgrd						5.00
584-587, 589-599: 585-Menace ID revealed. 590,591-Fantastic Four app. 594-Aunt May engaged. 595-599-American Son; Osborn Avengers app. app.						3.00
588-($3.99) Conclusion to "Character Assassination"; Romita Jr.-a						4.00
600-(9/09, $4.99) Aunt May's wedding; Romita Jr.-a; Doc Octopus, FF app.; Mary Jane cameo; back-up story by Stan Lee; back-up with Doran-a; 2 covers by Romita Jr. & Ross						18.00
600-Variant covers by Romita Sr. and Quesada						20.00
601-Mary Jane cover by Campbell; back-up w/Quesada-a						110.00
602-1st new Slyde						15.00
603,604,608-610,613-616,618-621,623-627: 612-The Gauntlet begins; Waid-s. 615,616-Sandman app. 621-Black Cat app. 624-Peter Parker fired. 626-Gaydos-a						3.00
605,612,617,622,628-($3.99): 605-Mayhew-a. 613-Rhino back-up story. 617-New Rhino. 622-Bianchi-c; Morbius app. 628-Captain Universe app.						4.00
606-Black Cat app.; Campbell-c	4	8	12	28	47	65
607 Black Cat app.; Campbell-c	6	12	18	38	69	100
611-Deadpool-c/app.						25.00
629-633-($3.99)-Bachalo-a; Lizard app.						3.00
634-636,638-641-($3.99) 634-637-Grim Hunt; Kaine app. 635-Kraven returns.						4.00
638-641-"One Moment in Time" wedding flashback/retcon; Quesada-s						4.00
637-1st Araña(Anya Corazon) as Spider-Girl						50.00
638-641-Variant covers by Quesada						15.00
642-646-($2.99) Waid-s/Azaceta-a; interlocking covers by Djurdjevic						4.00
647-($4.99) Short stories by various; Djurdjevic-c; cover gallery of Brand New Day issues						5.00
648-650,652,653,655-691-($3.99) 648-Big Time begins; Ramos-a; Hobgoblin app. 655-Martin-a. 657-660-Fantastic Four app. 666-673-Spider Island. 667-672-Ramos-a; Avengers app. 677-X-over w/Daredevil #8. 682-687-Avengers app.						4.00
651-Hobgoblin & Black Cat app.						12.00
651-Tron variant-c by Mark Brooks						100.00
654-Flash Thompson becomes Venom; Marla Jameson killed						40.00
654.1-(4/11, $2.99) Flash Thompson as Venom; Ramos-a						20.00
679.1-(4/12, $2.99) Morbius the Living Vampire app.						15.00
692-($5.99) Debut of Alpha; Ramos-a; back-up short stories						10.00
693-697: 694-Cover swipe of Superman vs. Spider-Man						4.00
698, 699, 699.1: 698-Doctor Octopus brain switch revealed. 699.1-Morbius origin						4.00
700-($7.99) Collage cover; Leads into Superior Spider-Man #1; back-up short stories						40.00
700-Variant skyline-c by Marcos						55.00
700-Second printing cover with Doctor Octopus on an ASM #300 swipe						15.00
700.1 - 700.5 (2/14, weekly limited series, $3.99) 700.1-Janson-a/Ferry-a						5.00
1999, 2000 Annual (6/99, '00, $3.50) 1999-Buscema-a						5.00
2001 Annual ($2.99) Follows Peter Parker: S-M #29; last Mackie-s						6.00
Annual 1 (2008, $3.99) McKone-a; secret of Jackpot revealed; death of Jackpot						5.00
Annual 36 (9/09, $3.99) Debut of Raptor; Olliffe-a						4.00
Annual 37 (7/10, $3.99) Untold 1st meeting with Captain America; back-up w/Olliffe-a						4.00
Annual 38 (6/11, $3.99) Deadpool & Hulk app.; Garbett-a/McNiven-c						4.00
Annual 39 (7/12, $3.99) Avengers app.; Garbett-a/c						4.00

Amazing Spider-Man #546 © MAR

Amazing Spider-Man #672 © MAR

Amazing Spider-Man (2022 series) #6 © MAR

	GD 2.0	VG 4.0	FN 6.0	VF 8.0	VF/NM 9.0	NM- 9.2		GD 2.0	VG 4.0	FN 6.0	VF 8.0	VF/NM 9.0	NM- 9.2

...: Big Time 1 (8/11, $5.99) r/#648-650 — 6.00
Collected Edition #30-32 ($3.95) reprints #30-32 w/cover #30 — 20.00
... 500 Covers HC (2004, $49.99) reprints covers for #1-500 & Annuals; yearly re-caps — 50.00
...: Ends of the Earth (7/12, $3.99) Silas-a/Fiumara-c; Big Hero Six app. — 4.00
...: Family Business HC (2014, $24.99) Kingpin app.; Waid & Robinson-s/Dell'Otto-a — 25.00
Free Comic Book Day 2011 (Spider-Man) 1-Ramos-c/a; Spider-Woman & Shang-Chi app. — 10.00
.../Ghost Rider: Motorstorm 1 ('11, $2.99) r/#558-560 — 8.00
... Hooky 1 (2012, $4.99) r/Marvel Graphic Novel #22 (1986) with Wrightson-a — 20.00
... Infested 1 (11/11, $3.99) Spider Island tie-in; short stories by various; Ramos-c — 6.00
... Omnibus HC (2007, $99.99, dustjacket) r/Amazing Fantasy #15, Amazing Spider-Man #1-38, Annual #1,2, Strange Tales Annual #2 & Fantastic Four Annual #1; letter pages, bonus art, intro. by Stan Lee; bios, essays, Marvel Tales cover gallery — 200.00
Spider-Man: Brand New Day - Extra!! #1 (9/08, $3.99) short stories; Bachalo,Olliffe-a — 4.00
Spider-Man: Brand New Day Yearbook #1 (2008, $4.99) plot synopses; profile pages — 5.00
... Spidey Sunday Spectacuar (7/11, $3.99) collects back-ups from ASM #634-645 — 6.00
...: Swing Shift (2007 FCBD Edition) Jimenez-c/a; Slott-s — 15.00
... Swing Shift Director's Cut (2008, $3.99) story from 2007 FCBD; Brand New Day info — 10.00
The Many Loves of the Amazing Spider-Man (7/10, $3.99) short stories of Black Cat, Gwen & Carlie, and Mary Jane; s/a by various — 8.00
...: The Short Halloween (7/09, $3.99) Bill Hader & Seth Meyers-s/Maguire-a — 7.00
...: You're Hired 1 (5/11, $3.99) r/story from New York Daily News insert — 4.00
...Vol. 1: Coming Home (2001, $15.95)¹ r/#30-35; J. Scott Campbell-c — 16.00
...Vol. 2: Revelations (2002, $8.99) r/#36-39; Kaare Andrews-c — 9.00
...Vol. 3: Until the Stars Turn Cold (2002, $12.99) r/#40-45; Romita Jr.-c — 13.00
...Vol. 4: The Life and Death of Spiders (2003, $11.99) r/#46-50; Campbell-c — 12.00
...Vol. 5: Unintended Consequences (2003, $12.99) r/#51-56; Dodson-c — 13.00
...Vol. 6: Happy Birthday (2003, $12.99) r/#57,58,500-502 — 13.00
...Vol. 7: The Book of Ezekiel (2004, $12.99) r/#503-508; Romita Jr.-c — 13.00
...Vol. 8: Sins Past (2005, $12.99) r/#509-514; cover sketch gallery — 13.00
...Vol. 9: Skin Deep (2005, $9.99) r/#515-518 — 10.00
...Vol. 10: New Avengers (2005, $14.99) r/#519-524 — 15.00
Brand New Day #1-3 (11/08-1/09, $3.99) reprints #546-551 — 4.00
Civil War: Amazing Spider-Man TPB (2007, $17.99) r/#532-538; variant covers — 18.00

AMAZING SPIDER-MAN (Follows Superior Spider-Man)(Also see Spider-Verse Team-Up)
Marvel Comics: Jun, 2014 - No. 20.1 , Oct, 2015 ($3.99)(there was no #19 or 20)

1-($5.99) 1st app. Cindy Moon (cameo, becomes Silk in #4); Slott-s/Ramos-a; bonus shorts with Electro, Black Cat, Spider-Man 2099, Kaine; bonus r/Inhuman #1; Ramos-c — 12.00
1-Variant-c by J. Scott Campbell — 15.00
2,3-Cindy Moon app. 2-Avengers app. 3-Black Cat app. — 5.00
4-1st app. Silk (Cindy Moon); Original Sin tie-in — 110.00
5-8: 5-6,Silk, Black Cat app. 7,8-Ms. Marvel app.; back-up Spider-Verse; Morlun app. — 4.00
9-($4.99) Spider-Verse part 1; Variant Spider-Men & Spider-Gwen app.; Coipel-a — 30.00
10-15-Spider-Verse; Superior Spider-Man returns. 13,14-Uncle Ben app.; Camuncoli-a — 4.00
16-18-Ghost Rider.; Ramos-a; back-up with Black Cat — 4.00
16.1, 17.1, 18.1, 19.1, 20.1-($3.99) Spiral parts 1-5; Conway-s/Barberi-a — 4.00
Annual 1 (11/14, $4.99) Sean Ryan-s/Peterson-a/c; Nitz-s/Salas-a — 5.00
Special 1 (5/15, $4.99) Crossover with Inhumans and All-New Captain America specials — 4.00
#1.1-1.5 (Learning to Crawl) 1-Ramos-c/a (7/14-11/14, $3.99) Re-tells early career; Alex Ross-c — 4.00

AMAZING SPIDER-MAN (Follows Secret Wars)
Marvel Comics: Dec, 2015 - No. 32, Nov, 2017; No. 789, Dec, 2017 - No. 801, Aug, 2018 ($5.99/$3.99)

1-($5.99) Slott-s/Camuncoli-a; main-c by Alex Ross; back-up previews of Spider-titles — 8.00
2-18-($3.99) 3,5-Human Torch app. 6-8-Cloak & Dagger app. 13-15-Iron Man app. — 4.00
15-Mary Jane in the Iron Spider suit. 17-New female Electro — 5.00
19-($4.99) Clone Conspiracy tie-in; Kingpin & Rhino app. — 4.00
20-24: Clone Conspiracy tie-ins. 20-Doctor Octopus gets his body back. 21-Kaine returns — 4.00
25-($9.99) Osborn Identity begins; Silver Sable returns; debut of The Superior Octopus — 10.00
26-32: 26-28,32-Norman Osborn app.. 29-31-Secret Empire tie-ins — 4.00
[Title switches to legacy numbering after #32 (11/17)]
789-799,801: 789-791-"Fall of Parker"; Immonen-a. 792,793-Venom Inc. x-over. 795-Osborn merges with Carnage; Loki app. — 4.00
800-(7/18, $9.99, 80 pages) Spider-Man vs. Red Goblin; death of Flash Thompson; art by Immonen, Ramos, Bradshaw, Camuncoli, Martin — 12.00
#1.1-1.6 (Amazing Grace) (2/16-9/16, $3.99) The Santerians app.; Bianchi-a — 4.00
Annual 1 (1/17, $4.99) Short stories by various incl. Wayne Brady, Ramos, Gage, Asmus — 5.00
Annual 42 (4/18, $4.99) Dan Slott-s/Cory Smith-a — 5.00

AMAZING SPIDER-MAN
Marvel Comics: Sept, 2018 - No. 93, May, 2022 ($5.99/$3.99)

1-($5.99) Spencer-s/Ottley-a; Mysterio app. — 8.00
2-15-($3.99) 2-Taskmaster app. 6-10-Ramos-a. 8-10-Black Cat app. 14,15-Bachalo-a. — 4.00
16,17-($4.99) Kraven & Arcade app. — 5.00
18-24: 18-23-Hunted. 18,20,22-Ramos-a. 22-Kraven dies. 23-Ottley-a. 24-Mysterio app. — 4.00
16HU-($3.99) Hunted story arc; Coello-a; Black Cat, Taskmaster, Black Ant app. — 4.00
18HU,19HU,20HU-($3.99) Hunted; 18-The Gibbon. 19-The Lizard; Bachalo-a. 20-Vulture — 4.00
25-($7.99) Mysterio and Electro app.; art by Ottley, Ramos, Gleason, Walker — 8.00
26-44,46-48: 30,31-Absolute Carnage tie-in. 32-36-Spider-Man 2099. 41-Lethal Legion returns. 46-48-Sins Rising. 47,48-Norman Osborn app. — 4.00
45-($4.99) Sins Rising begins; Spencer-s/Bagley-a; The Sin-Eater app. — 5.00
49-($9.99) 850th issue celebration; Spidey vs. Green Goblin; back-up stories by various — 10.00
50-($5.99) Last Remains; Dr. Strange app.; Kindred revealed as Harry Osborn — 6.00
51-54,57-62,64-66: 51-54-Last Remains. 58,59-Mr. Negative app. 61-New costume — 4.00
53.LR,54.LR-($3.99) Last Remains; Order of the Web vs. Kindred — 4.00
55-Last Remains ends — 24.00
56-($4.99) Last Remains Post Mortem; Norman Osborn, Kingpin app.; Bagley-a — 5.00
63,67-($4.99) 63-King's Ransom pt. 1. 67-Chameleon Conspiracy pt. 1 — 5.00
68-73,76-92: 71-73-Sinister War. 77,78-Pichelli-a; Morbius app. 81-Miles app. — 4.00
74-(11/21, $9.99) End of the Kindred saga; Mephisto app.; back-up with Ben Reilly — 10.00
75-($5.99) Beyond pt. 1; Wells-s/Gleason-a; Ben Reilly back as Spider-Man — 6.00
80.BEY-($4.99) Aunt May meets with Otto Octavius; Fiorelli-a — 5.00
88.BEY-($4.99) The Slingers app.; Hobie Brown as The Hornet — 5.00
92.BEY-($4.99) Morbius & Monica Rambeau app. — 6.00
93-($5.99) Peter Parker vs. Ben Reilly — 5.00
Annual 1 (11/18, $4.99) Flashback to early days with the black costume (Venom) — 5.00
Annual 2 (9/21, $4.99) Infinite Destinies tie-in; Star app.; Pacheco-s/Carlini-a — 5.00
...: Full Circle 1 (12/19, $9.99) Seven creative teams with successive chapters of 1 story; Hickman, Duggan, Zdarsky & others-s/Bachalo, Allred, Bagley & others-a — 10.00
...: Going Big 1 (11/19, $4.99) Conway-s/Bagley-a; Macchio-s/Nauck-a; Larsen-s/a — 5.00
...: Sins Rising Prelude 1 (9/20, $4.99) Spencer-s/Sanna-a; story of the Sin-Eater — 5.00
...: The Sins of Norman Osborn 1 (11/20, $4.99) Spencer-s/Vicentini-a; leads into #49 — 5.00

AMAZING SPIDER-MAN
Marvel Comics: Jun, 2022 - Present ($5.99/$3.99/$4.99)

1-($5.99) Zeb Wells-s/John Romita Jr.-a; Tombstone app. — 6.00
2-5,7-13-($3.99) 5-Black Cat app. 7,8-Vulture app. 8-1st Spider-Glider. 9-Wolverine app. — 4.00
6-($9.99) Legacy issue #900; The Sinister Seven app.; McGuinness-a — 10.00
14-($4.99) Dark Web begins; Ben Reilly & Madelyne Pryor app. — 5.00
15-24,27-30,32-34: 15-18-Dark Web; McGuinness-a. 19,20-Black Cat app. — 4.00
25-($6.99) "Death" of Ms. Marvel; Fantastic Four app. (see Fallen Friend #1) — 7.00
26-($4.99) "Death" of Ms. Marvel; Fantastic Four app. (see Fallen Friend #1) — 5.00
31-($9.99) 925th Legacy issue; Wedding of Randy Robertson & Janice Lincoln; back-up stories by various; Ms Marvel app.; Mary Jane gets her Jackpot costume — 10.00
35-38,40-44-($4.99) 35-Gleason-a. 36-McGuinness-a; Rek-rap app.40-44-Gang War — 5.00
39-($3.99) Start of Gang War; Miles, She-Hulk Elektra, Spider-Woman app. — 6.00
Annual 1 (10/23, $4.99) Hallows' Eve app.; Schultz-s/Shaw-a — 5.00
...: Gang War First Strike 1 (1/24, $5.99) Wells-s/Vazquez-a; Miles app. — 6.00

AMAZING SPIDER-MAN & SILK: THE SPIDER(FLY) EFFECT
Marvel Comics: May, 2016 - No. 4, Aug, 2016 ($3.99)

	1	2	3	5	6	8
1-4: 1-Robbie Thompson/Todd Nauck-a; time-travelling Peter & Silk meet Ben Parker	1	2		3	5	6	8

AMAZING SPIDER-MAN EXTRA! (Continued from Spider-Man: Brand New Day - Extra!! #1)
Marvel Comics: No. 2, Mar, 2009 - No. 3, May, 2009 ($3.99)

2,3: 2-Anti-Venom app.; Bachalo-a. 3-Ana Kraven app.; Jimenez-a — 4.00

AMAZING SPIDER-MAN FAMILY (Also see Spider-Man Family)
Marvel Comics: Oct, 2008 - No. 8, Sept, 2009 ($4.99, anthology)

1-8-New tales and reprints. 1-Includes r/ASM #300; Granov-c. 2-Deodato-c. 5-Spider-Girl new story. 6-Origin of Venom — 5.00

AMAZING SPIDER-MAN PRESENTS: AMERICAN SON
Marvel Comics: Jul, 2010 - No. 4, Oct, 2010 ($3.99, limited series)

1-4-Reed-s/Briones-a/Djurdjevic-c; Gabriel Stacy app. — 4.00

AMAZING SPIDER-MAN PRESENTS: ANTI-VENOM - NEW WAYS TO LIVE
Marvel Comics: Nov, 2009 - No. 3, Feb, 2010 ($3.99, limited series)

1-3-Wells-s/Siqueira-a; Punisher app. — 4.00

AMAZING SPIDER-MAN PRESENTS: JACKPOT
Marvel Comics: Mar, 2010 - No. 3, Jun, 2010 ($3.99, limited series)

1-3-Guggenheim-s/Melo-a; Boomerang and White Rabbit app. — 4.00

AMAZING SPIDER-MAN: RENEW YOUR VOWS (Secret Wars tie-in)
Marvel Comics: Aug, 2015 - No. 5, Nov, 2015 ($3.99, limited series)

1-5-Adam Kubert-a; wife Mary Jane and daughter Annie app. 1-Venom app. — 4.00

AMAZING SPIDER-MAN: RENEW YOUR VOWS (Series) (Leads into Spider-Girls #1)
Marvel Comics: Jan, 2017 - No. 23, Nov, 2018 ($4.99/$3.99)

1-($4.99) Conway-s/Stegman-a; Mole Man app.; back-up Holden-s/a; Leth-s/Sauvage-a — 5.00
2-23-($3.99) 6,7-X-Men & Magneto app. 8,9-Venom app. 13-Jumps to 8 years later — 4.00

AMAZING SPIDER-MAN: THE DAILY BUGLE

	GD 2.0	VG 4.0	FN 6.0	VF 8.0	VF/NM 9.0	NM- 9.2

Marvel Comics: Mar, 2020 - No. 5 ($3.99, limited series)

1,2-Mat Johnson-s/Mack Chater-a — 4.00

AMAZING SPIDER-MAN: THE MOVIE
Marvel Comics: Aug, 2012 - No. 2, Aug, 2012 ($3.99, limited series)

1,2-Partial adaptation of the 2012 movie; Neil Edwards-a; photo covers — 4.00

AMAZING SPIDER-MAN: THE MOVIE ADAPTATION
Marvel Comics: Mar, 2014 - No. 2, Apr, 2014 ($2.99, limited series)

1,2-Adaptation of the 2012 movie; Wellington Alves-a; photo covers — 3.00

AMAZING SPIDER-MAN: VENOM INC. (Crossover with ASM #792,793 & Venom #159,160)
Marvel Comics: 2018 ($4.99, bookends of crossover story)

... Alpha 1 (2/18, $4.99) Part 1 of x-over; Stegman-a; Eddie Brock & Anti-Venom app. — 5.00
... Omega 1 (3/18, $4.99) Concluding Part 6 of x-over; Stegman-a — 5.00

AMAZING SPIDER-MAN: WAKANDA FOREVER (Crossover with Wakanda Forever title)
Marvel Comics: 2018 ($4.99, one-shot)

1-Spider-Man teams with Dora Milaje; Nnedi Okorafor-s/Rafael Albuquerque-a — 5.00

AMAZING WILLIE MAYS, THE
Famous Funnies Publ.: No date (Sept, 1954)

nn — 90 | 180 | 270 | 576 | 988 | 1400

AMAZING WORLD OF DC COMICS
DC Comics: Jul, 1974 - No. 17, 1978 ($1.50, B&W, mail-order DC Pro-zine)

	GD 2.0	VG 4.0	FN 6.0	VF 8.0	VF/NM 9.0	NM- 9.2
1-Kubert interview; unpublished Kirby-a; Infantino-c	8	16	24	51	96	140
2-4: 3-Julie Schwartz profile. 4-Batman; Robinson-c	5	10	15	35	63	90
5-Sheldon Mayer	5	10	15	31	53	75

6,8,13: 6-Joe Orlando; EC-r; Wrightson pin-up. 8-Infantino; Batman-r from Pop Tart giveaway. 13-Humor; Aragonés-c; Wood/Ditko-a; photos from serials of Superman, Batman, Captain Marvel — 4 | 8 | 12 | 25 | 40 | 55

7,10-12: 7-Superman; r/1955 Pep comic giveaway. 10-Behind the scenes at DC; Showcase article. 11-Super-Villains; unpubl. Secret Society of S.V. story.

12-Legion; Grell-c/interview — 4 | 8 | 12 | 27 | 44 | 60

9-Legion of Super-Heroes; lengthy bios and history; Cockrum-c — 7 | 14 | 21 | 46 | 86 | 125

	GD 2.0	VG 4.0	FN 6.0	VF 8.0	VF/NM 9.0	NM- 9.2
14-Justice League	4	8	12	27	44	60
15-Wonder Woman; Nasser-c	5	10	15	33	57	80
16-Golden Age heroes	5	10	15	30	50	70
17-Shazam; G.A.; '70s, TV and Fawcett heroes	4	8	12	27	44	60
Special 1 (Digest size)	3	6	9	21	33	45

AMAZING WORLD OF GUMBALL, THE (Based on the Cartoon Network series)
Boom Entertainment (kaBOOM!): Jun, 2014 - No. 8, Mar, 2015 ($3.99)

1-8-Multiple covers on each — 4.00
... 2015 Grab Bag Special (9/15, $4.99) Short stories and pin-ups by various; 3 covers — 5.00
... 2015 Special (1/15, $4.99) Short stories by various; 3 covers — 5.00
... 2016 Grab Bag Special (8/16, $4.99) Short stories and pin-ups by various — 5.00
... 2017 Grab Bag Special (8/17, $7.99) Short stories and pin-ups by various — 8.00
... 2018 Grab Bag Special (8/18, $7.99) Short stories by various; Aguirre-c — 8.00
... Spring Break Smash 1 (2/19, $7.99) Short stories by various — 8.00

AMAZING WORLD OF SUPERMAN (See Superman)

AMAZING X-MEN
Marvel Comics: Mar, 1995 - No. 4, July, 1995 ($1.95, limited series)

1-Age of Apocalypse; Andy Kubert-c/a — 6.00
2-4 — 4.00

AMAZING X-MEN
Marvel Comics: Jan, 2014 - No. 19, Jun, 2015 ($3.99)

1-19: 1-Nightcrawler returns; Aaron-s/McGuinness-a; wraparound-c. 7-Firestar, Iceman and Spider-Man app. 8-12-World War Wendigo. 19-Colossus vs. the Juggernaut — 4.00
Annual 1 (8/14, $4.99) Larroca-a/c; back-up w/Juan Doe-a — 5.00

AMAZON, THE
Comico: Mar, 1989 - No. 3, May, 1989 ($1.95, limited series)

1-3: Ecological theme; Steven Seagle-s/Tim Sale-a — 5.00
1-3-(Dark Horse, 3/09 - No. 3, 5/09, $3.50) recolored reprint with creator interviews — 3.50

AMAZON (Also see Marvel Versus DC #3 & DC Versus Marvel #4)
DC Comics (Amalgam): Apr, 1996 ($1.95, one-shot)

1-John Byrne-c/a/scripts — 6.00

AMAZON ATTACK 3-D
The 3-D Zone: Sept, 1990 ($3.95, 28 pgs.)

1-Chaykin-a — 1 | 3 | 4 | 6 | 8 | 10

AMAZONS ATTACK (See Wonder Woman #8 - 2006 series)
DC Comics: Jun, 2007 - No. 6, Late Oct, 2007 ($2.99, limited series)

1-6-Queen Hippolyta and Amazons attack Wash., DC; Pfeifer-s/Woods-a — 3.00

AMAZONS ATTACK (Dawn of DC)
DC Comics: Dec, 2023 - No. 6 ($3.99, limited series)

1-5-Queen Nubia, Yara, Mary Marvel as fugitives; Campbell-s/Georgiev-a — 4.00

AMAZON WOMAN (1st Series)
FantaCo: Summer, 1994 - No. 2, Fall, 1994 ($2.95, B&W, limited series, mature)

1,2: Tom Simonton-c/a/scripts — 3 | 6 | 9 | 14 | 19 | 24

AMAZON WOMAN (2nd Series)
FantaCo: Feb, 1996 - No. 4, May, 1996 ($2.95, B&W, limited series, mature)

	GD 2.0	VG 4.0	FN 6.0	VF 8.0	VF/NM 9.0	NM- 9.2
1-4: Tom Simonton-a/scripts	2	4	6	11	16	20
...: Invaders of Terror ('96, $5.95) Simonton-a/s	2	4	6	8	12	15

AMBASSADORS, THE (Also see Big Game)
Image Comics: Mar, 2023 - No. 6, Jun, 2023 ($3.99/$5.99, limited series)

1-5-($3.99) Mark Millar-s. 1-Quitely-a; intro Choon-He; bonus script and B&W art pages. 2-Kerschl-a. 3-Charest-a. 4-Coipel-a. 5-Buffagni-a — 4.00
6-($5.99) Scalera-a — 6.00

AMBER BLAKE
IDW Publishing: Feb, 2019 - No. 4, May, 2019 ($3.99, oversized 8-3/8" x 11", limited series)

1-4:-Jade Lagardére-s/Butch Guice-a; 2 covers on each — 4.00

AMBUSH BUG (Also see Son of...)
DC Comics: June, 1985 - No. 4, Sept, 1985 (75¢, limited series)

1-4: Giffen-c/a in all — 5.00
Nothing Special 1 (9/92, $2.50, 68 pg.)-Giffen-c/a — 5.00
Stocking Stuffer (2/86, $1.25)-Giffen-c/a — 5.00

AMBUSH BUG: YEAR NONE
DC Comics: Sept, 2008 - No. 5, Jan, 2009; No. 7, Dec, 2009 ($2.99, limited series, no #6)

1-5,7-Giffen-s/a; Jonni DC app. 4-Conner-c. 7-Baltazar & Franco-a; Giffen-a — 3.00

AME-COMI GIRLS (Based on the Anime-styled statue series)
DC Comics: Oct, 2012 - No. 5, Apr, 2013 ($3.99, printed version of digital-first series)

	GD 2.0	VG 4.0	FN 6.0	VF 8.0	VF/NM 9.0	NM- 9.2
1-Wonder Woman; Conner-c/a	2	4	6	8	10	12
1-Variant-c by Dustin Nguyen	5	10	15	35	63	90
2-5: 2-Batgirl. 3-Duela Dent; Naifeh-a						4.00

AME-COMI GIRLS (Based on the Anime-styled statue series)
DC Comics: May, 2013 - No. 8, Dec, 2013 ($3.99)

1-8: 1-Palmiotti & Gray-s/Francisco-a; story continues from earlier series — 4.00

AMERICA (From Young Avengers and The Ultimates)
Marvel Comics: May, 2017 - No. 12, Apr, 2018 ($3.99)

1-12: 1-Gabby Rivera-s/Joe Quinones-a; Captain Marvel & Spectrum app. 2-Moon Girl app. 3-Storm & the X-Men app. — 4.00

AMERICA AT WAR - THE BEST OF DC WAR COMICS (See Fireside Book Series)

AMERICA CHAVEZ: MADE IN THE USA (From Young Avengers and The Ultimates)
Marvel Comics: May, 2021 - No. 5, Oct, 2021 ($3.99)

1-5-Kalinda Vasquez-s/Carlos Gómez-a. 1-Kate Bishop & Spider-Man app. — 4.00

AMERICA IN ACTION
Dell (Imp. Publ. Co.)/ Mayflower House Publ.: 1942; Winter, 1945 (36 pgs.)

	GD 2.0	VG 4.0	FN 6.0	VF 8.0	VF/NM 9.0	NM- 9.2
1942-Dell-(68 pg.)		22	44	66	128	209	290
1-(1945)-Has 3 adaptations from American history; Kiefer, Schrotter & Webb-a	16	32	48	92	144	195

AMERICAN, THE
Dark Horse Comics: July, 1987 - No. 8, 1989 ($1.50/$1.75, B&W)

1-8: ($1.50) — 4.00
Collection ($5.95, B&W)-Reprints — 6.00
Special 1 (1990, $2.25, B&W) — 4.00

AMERICAN AIR FORCES, THE, (See A-1 Comics)
William H. Wise(Flying Cadet Publ. Co/Hasan(No.1)/Life's Romances/ Magazine Ent. No. 5 on): Sept-Oct, 1944-No. 4, 1945; No. 5, 1951-No. 12, 1954

1-Article by Zack Mosley, creator of Smilin' Jack; German war-c

	GD 2.0	VG 4.0	FN 6.0	VF 8.0	VF/NM 9.0	NM- 9.2
		54	108	162	343	574	825
2-Classic-Japan war-c	168	336	504	1075	1838	2600
3-Japan war-c	34	68	102	199	325	450
4-Japan war-c	23	46	69	136	223	310

NOTE: All part comic, part magazine. Art by Whitney, Chas. Quinlan, H. C. Kiefer, and Tony Diprata.

	GD 2.0	VG 4.0	FN 6.0	VF 8.0	VF/NM 9.0	NM- 9.2
5(A-1 45)(Formerly Jet Powers), 6(A-1 54), 7(A-1 58), 8(A-1 65), 9(A-1 67), 10(A-1 74), 11(A-1 79), 12(A-1 91)	12	24	36	69	97	125

NOTE: Powell c/a-5-12.

AMERICAN CARNAGE
DC Comics (Vertigo): Jan, 2019 - No. 9, Sept, 2019 ($3.99)

1-9: 1-Bryan Hill-s/Leandro Fernandez-a — 4.00

AMERICAN CENTURY
DC Comics (Vertigo): May, 2001 - No. 27, Oct, 2003 ($2.50/$2.75)

1-Chaykin-s/painted-c; Tischman-s; Laming-a — 4.00
2-27: 5-New story arc begins. 10-16,22-27-Orbik-c. 17-21-Silke-c. 18-$2.75-c begins — 3.00
Hollywood Babylon (2002, $12.95, TPB) r/#5-9; w/sketch-to-art pages — 13.00
Scars & Stripes (2001, $8.95, TPB) r/#1-4; Tischman intro. — 9.00

AMERICAN DREAM (From the M2 Avengers)
Marvel Comics: Jul, 2008 - No. 5, Sept, 2008 ($2.99, limited series)

1-5-DeFalco-s/Nauck-a — 3.00

AMERICAN FLAGG! (See First Comics Graphic Novel 3,9,12,21 & Howard Chaykin's..)
First Comics: Oct, 1983 - No. 50, Mar, 1988

1,21-27: 1-Chaykin-c/a begins. 21-27-Alan Moore scripts — 5.00
2-20,28-49: 31-Origin Bob Violence — 4.00
50-Last issue — 5.00
Special 1 (11/86)-Introduces Chaykin's Time2 — 5.00
...: Hard Times TPB (6/85, $11.95) r/#1-7; intro. by Michael Moorcock; bonus materials — 12.00
...: Definitive Collection Volume 1 HC (2008, $49.99) r/#1-14 and material from the...: Hard Times TPB; intro by Michael Chabon; afterword by Jim Lee — 50.00

AMERICAN FREAK: A TALE OF THE UN-MEN
DC Comics (Vertigo): Feb, 1994 - No. 5, Jun, 1994 ($1.95, mini-series, mature)

1-5 — 4.00

AMERICAN GODS (Based on the Neil Gaiman novel)
Dark Horse Comics: Mar, 2017 - No. 9, Nov, 2017 ($3.99)

1-9: 1-Gaiman & Russell-s/Scott Hampton-a. 3-Simonson-a (4 pgs.). 4-Doran-a (9 pgs.) — 4.00

AMERICAN GODS: MY AINSEL (Based on the Neil Gaiman novel)
Dark Horse Comics: Mar, 2018 - No. 9, Dec, 2018 ($3.99)

1-9: 1-Gaiman & Russell-s/Scott Hampton-a. 5-Buckingham-a — 4.00

AMERICAN GODS: THE MOMENT OF THE STORM (Based on the Neil Gaiman novel)
Dark Horse Comics: Apr, 2019 - No. 9, Jan, 2020 ($3.99)

1-9-Gaiman & Russell-s/Scott Hampton-a — 4.00

AMERICAN GRAPHICS
Henry Stewart: No. 1, 1954; No. 2, 1957 (25¢)

	GD 2.0	VG 4.0	FN 6.0	VF 8.0	VF/NM 9.0	NM- 9.2
1-The Maid of the Mist, The Last of the Eries (Indian Legends of Niagara) (sold at Niagara Falls)	16	32	48	94	147	200
2-Victory at Niagara & Laura Secord (Heroine of the War of 1812)						

Amazing World of Comics #2 © DC

America (2017 series) #1 © MAR

American Monster #4 © Brian Azzarello

AM

	GD	VG	FN	VF	VF/NM	NM-
	2.0	4.0	6.0	8.0	9.0	9.2
	9	18	27	50	65	80

AMERICAN INDIAN, THE (See Picture Progress)

AMERICAN JESUS: REVELATION (Also see Chosen)
Image Comics: Oct, 2022 - No. 3, Jan, 2023 ($3.99, limited series)

1-3-Mark Millar-s/Peter Gross-a						4.00

AMERICAN JESUS: THE NEW MESSIAH (Also see Chosen)
Image Comics: Dec, 2019 - No. 3, Feb, 2020 ($3.99, limited series)

1-3-Mark Millar-s/Peter Gross-a						4.00

AMERICAN LIBRARY
David McKay Publ.: 1943 - No. 6, 1944 (15¢, 68 pgs., B&W, text & pictures)

	GD	VG	FN	VF	VF/NM	NM-
nn (#1)-Thirty Seconds Over Tokyo (movie)	52	104	156	328	552	775
nn (#2)-Guadalcanal Diary; painted-c (only 10¢)	36	72	108	211	343	475
3-6: 3-Look to the Mountain. 4-Case of the Crooked Candle (Perry Mason).						
5-Duel in the Sun. 6-Wingate's Raiders	18	36	54	105	165	225

AMERICAN: LOST IN AMERICA, THE
Dark Horse Comics: July, 1992 - No. 4, Oct, 1992 ($2.50, limited series)

1-4: 1-Dorman painted-c. 2-Phillips painted-c. 3-Mignola-c. 4-Jim Lee-c						4.00

AMERICAN MONSTER
AfterShock Comics: Jan, 2016 - No. 6, May, 2017 ($3.99)

1-6-Brian Azzarello-s/Juan Doe-a						4.00

AMERICAN MYTHOLOGY ARCHIVES: LAUREL AND HARDY
American Mythology Prods.: 2020 ($3.99)

1-Reprints Laurel and Hardy #1 (1972)						4.00

AMERICAN MYTHOLOGY ARCHIVES PRESENTS ZORRO
American Mythology Prods.: 2019 ($3.99)

1-Reprints Four Color #882; art by Alex Toth						4.00

AMERICAN MYTHOLOGY DARK: WEREWOLVES VS DINOSAURS
American Mythology Prods.: 2016 - No. 2, 2017 ($3.99)

1,2-Chris Scalf & Eric Dobson-s/a; 3 covers						4.00

AMERICAN PSYCHO (Based on the movie)
Sumerian Comics: 2023 - Present ($4.99, limited series)

1-3-Calero-s/Kowalski-a						5.00

AMERICAN RONIN
AWA Inc.: Oct, 2020 - No. 5 ($3.99, limited series)

1-4-Peter Milligan-s/Aco-a						4.00

AMERICAN SPLENDOR: (Series of titles)
Dark Horse Comics: Aug, 1996 - Apr, 2001 (B&W, all one-shots)

--COMIC-CON COMICS (8/96) 1-H. Pekar script. --MUSIC COMICS (11/97) nn-H. Pekar-s/						
Sacco-a; r/Village Voice jazz strips. --ODDS AND ENDS (12/97) 1-Pekar-s. --ON THE JOB						
(5/97) 1-Pekar-s. --A STEP OUT OF THE NEST (8/94) 1-Pekar-s. --TERMINAL (9/99)						
1-Pekar-s. --TRANSATLANTIC (7/98) 1-"American Splendour" on cover; Pekar-s						4.00
--A PORTRAIT OF THE AUTHOR IN HIS DECLINING YEARS (4/01, $3.99) 1-Photo-c.						
--BEDTIME STORIES (6/00, $3.95)						4.00

AMERICAN SPLENDOR
DC Comics: Nov, 2006 - No. 4, Feb, 2007 ($2.99, B&W)

1-4-Pekar-s/art by Haspiel and various. 1-Fabry-c						3.00
...: Another Day TPB (2007, $14.99) r/#1-4						15.00

AMERICAN SPLENDOR (Volume 2)
DC Comics (Vertigo): Jun, 2008 - No. 4, Sept, 2008 ($2.99, B&W)

1-4-Pekar-s/art by Haspiel and various. 1-Bond-c. 3-Cooke-c						3.00
...: Another Dollar TPB (2009, $14.99) r/#1-4						15.00

AMERICAN SPLENDOR: UNSUNG HERO
Dark Horse Comics: Aug, 2002 - No. 3, Oct, 2002 (B&W, $3.99, limited series)

1-3-Pekar script/Collier-a; biography of Robert McNeill						4.00
TPB (8/03, $11.95) r/#1-3						12.00

AMERICAN SPLENDOR: WINDFALL
Dark Horse Comics: Sept, 1995 - No. 2, Oct,1995 ($3.95, B&W, limited series)

1,2-Pekar script						4.00

AMERICAN TAIL: FIEVEL GOES WEST, AN
Marvel Comics: Early Jan, 1992 - No. 3, Early Feb, 1992 ($1.00, limited series)

1-3-Adapts Universal animated movie; Wildman-a						4.00
1-($2.95-c, 69 pgs.) Deluxe squarebound edition						5.00

AMERICAN VAMPIRE
DC Comics (Vertigo): May, 2010 - No. 34, Feb, 2013 ($3.99/$2.99)

	GD	VG	FN	VF	VF/NM	NM-
	2.0	4.0	6.0	8.0	9.0	9.2

1-Snyder-s/Albuquerque-a; back-up story by Stephen King						
	2	4	6	8	10	12
1-5-Variant-c: 1-Jim Lee. 2-Berni Wrightson. 3-Andy Kubert. 5-Paul Pope						
	2	4	6	9	13	16
2-10: 2-9-Snyder-s/Albuquerque-a. 2-5-Back-up story by Stephen King continues						5.00
11-34-($2.99) 11-Santolouco-a. 12-Zezelj-a. 19-21-Bernet-a						3.00
... Anthology 1 (10/13, $7.99) Short stories by various; Albuquerque-c						8.00
...: The Long Road to Hell 1 (8/13, $6.99) Snyder-s/Albuquerque-a						7.00
HC (2010, $24.99, d.j.) r/#1-5; intro. by Stephen King; script pages and sketch art						25.00
...Volume Two HC (2011, $24.99, d.j.) r/#6-11; cover design art						25.00

AMERICAN VAMPIRE: LORD OF NIGHTMARES
DC Comics (Vertigo): Aug, 2012 - No. 5, Dec, 2012 ($2.99, limited series)

1-5-Set in 1954 England; Snyder-s/Nguyen-a/c. 2-Origin of Dracula						3.00

AMERICAN VAMPIRE: 1976
DC Comics (Vertigo): Dec, 2020 - No. 10, Oct, 2021 ($3.99/$4.99, limited series)

1-9-($3.99) Snyder-s/Albuquerque-a/c						4.00
10-($4.99)						5.00

AMERICAN VAMPIRE: SECOND CYCLE
DC Comics (Vertigo): May, 2014 - No. 11, Jan, 2016 ($3.99/$2.99, limited series)

1,8-10-($3.99) Snyder-s/Albuquerque-a/c						4.00
2-7-($2.99) 5-Bergara-a						3.00
11-($4.99) Snyder-s/Albuquerque-a/c						5.00

AMERICAN VAMPIRE: SURVIVAL OF THE FITTEST
DC Comics (Vertigo): Aug, 2011 - No. 5, Dec, 2011 ($2.99, limited series)

1-5-Set during WWII; Snyder-s/Murphy-a/c						3.00

AMERICAN VIRGIN
DC Comics (Vertigo): May, 2006 - No. 23, Mar, 2008 ($2.99)

1-23-Steven Seagle-s/Becky Cloonan-a in most. 1-3-Quitely-c. 4-14-Middleton-c						3.00
...: Head (2006, $9.99, TPB) r/#1-4; interviews with the creators and page development						10.00
...: Going Down (2007, $14.99, TPB) r/#5-9						15.00
...: Wet (2007, $12.99, TPB) r/#10-14						13.00
...: Around the World (Vol. 4) (2008, $17.99, TPB) r/#15-23						18.00

AMERICAN WAY, THE
DC Comics (WildStorm): Apr, 2006 - No. 8, Nov, 2006 ($2.99, limited series)

1-8-John Ridley-s/Georges Jeanty-a						3.00

AMERICAN WAY, THE: THOSE ABOVE AND THOSE BELOW
DC Comics (Vertigo): Sept, 2017 - No. 6, Apr, 2018 ($3.99, limited series)

1-6-John Ridley-s/Georges Jeanty-a/c; sequel set in 1972						4.00

AMERICA'S BEST COMICS
Nedor/Better/Standard Publications: Feb, 1942; No. 2, Sept, 1942 - No. 31, July, 1949
(New logo with #9)

	GD	VG	FN	VF	VF/NM	NM-
1-The Woman in Red, Black Terror, Captain Future, Doc Strange, The Liberator,						
& Don Davis, Secret Ace begin	420	840	1260	2940	5170	7400
2-Origin The American Eagle; The Woman in Red ends						
	206	412	618	1318	2259	3200
3-Pyroman begins (11/42, 1st app.); also see Startling Comics #18, 12/42)						
	187	374	561	1197	2049	2900
4-6: 5-Last Capt. Future (not in #4); Lone Eagle app. 6-American Crusader app.						
	148	296	444	947	1624	2300
7-Hitler, Mussolini & Hirohito-c	423	846	1269	3000	5250	7500
8-Last Liberator	206	412	618	1318	2259	3200
9-The Fighting Yank begins; The Ghost app.	155	310	465	992	1696	2400
10-Flag-c	258	516	774	1651	2826	4000
11-Hirohito & Tojo-c. (10/44)	226	452	678	1446	2473	3500
12	129	258	387	826	1413	2000
13-Japanese WWII-c	194	388	582	1242	2121	3000
14-17: 14-American Eagle ends; Doc Strange vs. Hitler story						
	90	180	270	576	988	1400
18-Classic-c	155	310	465	992	1696	2400
19-21: 21-Infinity-c	77	154	231	493	847	1200
22-Capt. Future app.	68	136	204	435	743	1050
23-Miss Masque begins; last Doc Strange	142	284	426	909	1555	2200
24-Miss Masque bondage-c	123	246	369	787	1344	1900
25-Last Fighting Yank; Sea Eagle app.	129	258	387	826	1413	2000
26-Miss Masque motorcycle-c; The Phantom Detective & The Silver Knight app.; Frazetta						
text illo & some panels in Miss Masque	155	310	465	992	1696	2400
27-31: 27,28-Commando Cubs. 27-Doc Strange. 28-Tuska Black Terror. 29-Last Pyroman						
	68	136	204	435	743	1050

NOTE: *American Eagle not in 3, 8, 9, 13. Fighting Yank not in 10, 12. Liberator not in 2, 6, 7. Pyroman not in 9, 11, 14-16, 23, 25-27.* **Schomburg** (*Xela*) *c-5, 7-31. Bondage c-18, 24.*

	GD	VG	FN	VF	VF/NM	NM-
	2.0	4.0	6.0	8.0	9.0	9.2

AMERICA'S BEST COMICS
America's Best Comics: 1999 - 2008

... Preview (1999, Wizard magazine supplement) - Previews Trong Strong, Top Ten,
  Promethea, Tomorrow Stories — 4.00
... Primer (2008, $4.99, TPB) r/Tom Strong #1, Tom Strong's Terrific Tales, Top Ten #1,
  Promethea #1, Tomorrow Stories #1,6 — 5.00
... Sketchbook (2002, $5.95, square-bound)-Design sketches by Sprouse, Ross, Adams,
  Nowlan, Ha and others — 6.00
Special 1 (2/01, $6.95)-Short stories of Alan Moore's characters; art by various; Ross-c — 7.00
TPB (2004, $17.95) Reprints short stories and sketch pages from ABC titles — 18.00

AMERICA'S BEST TV COMICS (TV)
American Broadcasting Co. (Prod. by Marvel Comics): 1967 (25¢, 68 pgs.)

1-Spider-Man, Fantastic Four (by Kirby/Ayers), Casper, King Kong, George of the Jungle,
  Journey to the Center of the Earth stories (promotes new TV cartoon show)

	10	20	30	69	147	225

AMERICA'S BIGGEST COMICS BOOK
William H. Wise: 1944 (196 pgs., one-shot)

1-The Grim Reaper, The Silver Knight, Zudo, the Jungle Boy, Commando Cubs,
  Thunderhoof app.

	61	122	183	390	670	950

AMERICA'S FUNNIEST COMICS
William H. Wise: 1944 - No. 2, 1944 (15¢, 80 pgs.)

nn(#1), 2-Funny Animal	28	56	84	168	274	380

AMERICA'S GOT POWERS
Image Comics: Apr, 2012 - No. 7, Oct, 2013 ($2.99, limited series)

1-7-Jonathan Ross-s/Bryan Hitch-a/c. 1-Wraparound-c — 3.00

AMERICA'S GREATEST COMICS
Fawcett Publications: May?, 1941 - No. 8, Summer, 1943 (15¢, 100 pgs., soft cardboard-c)

1-Bulletman, Spy Smasher, Capt. Marvel, Minute Man & Mr. Scarlet begin; Classic Mac
  Raboy-c. 1st time that Fawcett's major super-heroes appear together as a group on a
  cover. Fawcett's 1st squarebound comic

	371	742	1113	2600	4550	6500
2	161	322	483	1030	1765	2500
3	123	246	369	787	1344	1900
4,5: 4-Commando Yank begins; Golden Arrow, Ibis the Invincible & Spy Smasher cameo in Captain Marvel	84	168	252	538	919	1300
6,7: 7-Balbo the Boy Magician app.; Captain Marvel, Bulletman cameo in Mr. Scarlet	74	148	222	470	810	1150
8-Capt. Marvel Jr. & Golden Arrow app.; Spy Smasher x-over in Capt. Midnight; no Minute Man or Commando Yank	77	154	231	493	847	1200

AMERICA'S SWEETHEART SUNNY (See Sunny, ...)

AMERICA VS. THE JUSTICE SOCIETY
DC Comics: Jan, 1985 - No. 4, Apr, 1985 ($1.00, limited series)

1-Double size; Alcala-a(i) in all	2	4	6	8	10	12
2-4: 3,4-Spectre cameo	1	2	3	5	7	9

AMERICOMICS
Americomics: April, 1983 - No. 6, Mar, 1984 ($2.00, Baxter paper/slick paper)

1-Intro/origin The Shade; Intro. The Slayer, Captain Freedom and The Liberty Corps; Perez-c — 6.00
1,2-2nd printings ($2.00) — 4.00
2-6: 2-Messenger app. & 1st app. Tara on Jungle Island. 3-New & old Blue Beetle battle.
  4-Origin Dragonfly & Shade. 5-Origin Commando D. 6-Origin the Scarlet Scorpion — 4.00

Special 1 (8/83, $2.00)-Sentinels of Justice (Blue Beetle, Captain Atom, Nightshade & The Question)	1	2	3	5	6	8

AMETHYST
DC Comics: Jan, 1985 - No. 16, Aug, 1986 (75¢)

1-16: 8-Fire Jade's i.d. revealed — 4.00
Special 1 (10/86, $1.25) — 5.00
1-4 (11/87 - 2/88)(Limited series) — 4.00

AMETHYST (Princess of Gemworld)(Also see Young Justice)
DC Comics (Wonder Comics): Apr, 2020 - No. 6, Feb, 2021 ($3.99)

1-6: 1-Amy Reeder-s/a; origin re-told in flashback — 4.00

AMETHYST, PRINCESS OF GEMWORLD (See Legion of Super-Heroes #298)
DC Comics: May, 1983 - No. 12, Apr, 1984 (Maxi-series)

1-(60¢)	2	4	6	8	10	12
1,2-(35¢): tested in Austin & Kansas City	6	12	18	40	73	105
2-12, Annual 1(9/84): 5-11-Pérez-c(p)						4.00

NOTE: *Issues #1 & 2 also have Canadian variants with a 75¢ cover price.*

AMORY WARS (Based on the Coheed and Cambria album The Second Stage Turbine Blade)
Image Comics: Jun, 2007 - No. 5, Jan, 2008 ($2.99, limited series)

1-5: 1-Claudio Sanchez-s/Gus Vasquez-a — 3.00

AMORY WARS II
Image Comics: Jun, 2008 - No. 5, Oct, 2008 ($2.99, limited series)

1-5-Claudio Sanchez-s/Gabriel Guzman-a — 3.00

AMORY WARS: GOOD APOLLO, I'M BURNING STAR IV
BOOM! Studios: Apr, 2017 - No. 12, Oct, 2018 ($3.99)

1-12: 1-Claudio Sanchez-s/Chris Burnham-a. 1-Four covers — 4.00

AMORY WARS IN KEEPING SECRETS OF SILENT EARTH: 3
BOOM! Studios: May, 2010 - No. 12, Jun, 2011 ($3.99)

1-12: 1-Claudio Sanchez & Peter David-s/Chris Burnham-a. 1-Four covers — 4.00

AMY RACECAR COLOR SPECIAL (See Stray Bullets)
El Capitán Books: July, 1997; Oct, 1999 ($2.95/$3.50)

1,2-David Lapham-a/scripts. 2-($3.50) — 3.50

ANALOG
Image Comics: Apr, 2018 - No. 10, Mar, 2020 ($3.99)

1-10-Gerry Duggan-s/David O'Sullivan-a — 4.00

ANARCHO DICTATOR OF DEATH (See Comics Novel)

ANARKY (See Batman titles)
DC Comics: May, 1997 - No. 4, Aug, 1997 ($2.50, limited series)

1 — 3.50
2-4 — 3.00

ANARKY (See Batman titles)
DC Comics: May, 1999 - No. 8, Dec, 1999 ($2.50)

1-8: 1-JLA app.; Grant-s/Breyfogle-a. 3-Green Lantern app. 7-Day of Judgment;
  Haunted Tank app. 8-Joker-c/app. — 3.00

ANCHORS ANDREWS (The Saltwater Daffy)
St. John Publishing Co.: Jan, 1953 - No. 4, July, 1953 (Anchors the Saltwater... No. 4)

1-Canteen Kate by Matt Baker (9 pgs.)	36	72	108	211	343	475
2-4	14	28	42	80	115	150

ANCIENT ENEMIES
Frank Miller Presents: 2022 - No. 6, 2023 ($7.99/$5.99, limited series)

1-($7.99) DiDio-s/Beyruth-a — 8.00
2-6-($5.99) DiDio-s/Beyruth-a — 6.00
...: First Responder 1 ('23, $3.99) Origin/spotlight on Sonny Palmer; DiDio-s — 4.00
...: The Djinni 1 ('23, $3.99) Origin story; DiDio & Van Hook-s — 4.00
...: The Greater Good 1 ('23, $3.99) Origin story; DiDio-s/Calafiore-a — 4.00
...: The Wraith and Son 1 ('23, $3.99) Origin story; DiDio-s/Calafiore-a — 4.00

ANDY & WOODY (See March of Comics No. 40, 55, 76)

ANDY BURNETT (TV, Disney)
Dell Publishing Co.: Dec, 1957

Four Color 865-Photo-c	9	18	27	57	111	165

ANDY COMICS (Formerly Scream Comics; becomes Ernie Comics)
Current Publications (Ace Magazines): No. 20, June, 1948-No. 21, Aug, 1948

20,21: Archie-type comic	30	60	90	177	289	400

ANDY DEVINE WESTERN
Fawcett Publications: Dec, 1950 - No. 2, 1951

1-Photo-c	47	94	141	296	498	700
2-Photo-c	32	64	96	192	314	435

ANDY GRIFFITH SHOW, THE (TV)(1st show aired 10/3/60)
Dell Publishing Co.: #1252, Jan-Mar, 1962; #1341, Apr-Jun, 1962

Four Color 1252(#1)	42	84	126	311	706	1100
Four Color 1341-Photo-c	36	72	108	266	596	925

ANDY HARDY COMICS (See Movie Comics #3 by Fiction House)
Dell Publishing Co.: April, 1952 - No. 6, Sept-Nov, 1954

Four Color 389(#1)	8	16	24	54	102	150
Four Color 447,480,515, #5,#6	5	10	15	31	53	75

ANDY PANDA (Also see Crackajack Funnies #39, The Funnies, New Funnies & Walter Lantz...)
Dell Publishing Co.: 1943 - No. 56, Nov-Jan, 1961-62 (Walter Lantz)

Four Color 25(#1, 1943)	46	92	138	340	770	1200
Four Color 54(1944)	25	50	75	175	388	600
Four Color 85(1945)	15	30	45	103	227	350
Four Color 130(1946),154,198	10	20	30	70	150	230
Four Color 216,240,258,280,297	8	16	24	55	105	155
Four Color 326,345,358	6	12	18	41	76	110
Four Color 383,409	5	10	15	35	63	90
16(11-1/52-53) - 30	4	8	12	28	47	65
31-56	4	8	12	23	37	50

(See March of Comics #5, 22, 79, & Super Book #4, 15, 27.)

A-NEXT (See Avengers)
Marvel Comics: Oct, 1998 - No. 12, Sept, 1999 ($1.99)

1-Next generation of Avengers; Frenz-a						5.00
2,3,5,6,8-11: 2-Two covers. 3-Defenders app.						3.00
4-1st app. American Dream	1	3	4	6	8	10
7-1st app. of Hope Pym	2	4	6	9	12	15
12-1st full app. of Hope Pym	1	3	4	6	8	10
Spider-Girl Presents Avengers Next Vol. 1: Second Coming (2006, $7.99, digest) r/#1-6						
	2	4	6	8	12	15

ANGEL
Dell Publishing Co.: Aug, 1954 - No. 16, Nov-Jan, 1958-59

Four Color 576(#1, 8/54)	5	10	15	34	60	85
2(5-7/55) - 16	3	6	9	17	26	35

ANGEL (TV) (Also see Buffy the Vampire Slayer)
Dark Horse Comics: Nov, 1999 - No. 17, Apr, 2001 ($2.95/$2.99)

1-17: 1-3,5-7,10-14-Zanier-a. 1-4,7,10-Matsuda & photo-c. 16-Buffy-c/app. — 3.00
...: Earthly Possessions TPB (4/01, $9.95) r/#5-7, photo-c — 10.00
...: Surrogates TPB (12/00, $9.95) r/#1-3; photo-c — 10.00

ANGEL (Buffy the Vampire Slayer)
Dark Horse Comics: Sept, 2001 - No. 4, May, 2002 ($2.99, limited series)

1-4-Joss Whedon & Matthews-s/Rubi-a; photo-c and Rubi-c on each — 3.00

ANGEL (Buffy the Vampire Slayer) (Previously titled Angel: After the Fall)
IDW Publishing: No. 18, Feb, 2009 - No. 44, Apr, 2011 ($3.99)

18-44: Multiple covers on all. 25-Juliet Landau-s — 4.00

ANGEL (one-shots) (Buffy the Vampire Slayer)
IDW Publishing: ($3.99/$7.49)

...: Connor (8/06, $3.99) Jay Faerber-s/Bob Gill-a; 4 covers + 1 retailer cover — 4.00
...: Doyle (7/06, $3.99) Jeff Mariotte-s/David Messina-a; 4 covers + 1 retailer cover — 4.00
...: Gunn (5/06, $3.99) Dan Jolley-s/Mark Pennington-a; 4 covers + 2 retailer covers — 4.00
...: Illyria (5/06, $3.99) Peter David-s/Nicola Scott-a; 4 covers + 2 retailer covers — 4.00
...: Masks (10/06, $7.49) short stories of Angel, Illyria, Cordilia & Lindsay; puppet Angel app. — 8.00
...: 100-Page Spectacular (4/11, $7.99) reprints of 4 issues; Runge-c — 8.00
... Special · Lorne (3/10, $7.99) John Byrne-s/a; The Groosalugg app. — 8.00
Team Angel 100-Page Spectacular (4/11, $7.99) reprints; Runge-c — 8.00
...: Vs. Frankenstein (10/09, $3.99) John Byrne-s/a/c — 4.00

America's Greatest Comics #2 © MAR

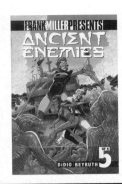

Ancient Enemies #5 © FMP

Angel & Faith #14 © 20Fox

	GD 2.0	VG 4.0	FN 6.0	VF 8.0	VF/NM 9.0	NM- 9.2

...: Vs. Frankenstein II (10/10, $3.99) John Byrne-s/a/c — 4.00
...: Wesley (6/06, $3.99) Scott Tipton-s/Mike Norton-a; 4 covers + 1 retailer cover — 4.00
Spotlight TPB (12/06, $19.99) r/Connor, Doyle, Gunn, Illyria & Wesley one-shots — 20.00
... Yearbook (5/11, $7.99) short stories by various; 3 covers — 8.00

ANGEL (Buffy the Vampire Slayer)(Title changes to Angel + Spike with #9)
BOOM! Studios: No. 0, Apr, 2019 - No. 8, Jan, 2020 ($3.99)

0-Bryan Edward Hill-s/Gleb Melnikov-a; Angel in Los Angeles; origin re-told — 4.00
1-8: 1-(5/19). 3-Intro. Fred. 4-Intro. Gunn. 5-8-Hellmouth tie-ins with Buffy — 4.00

ANGEL (Buffy the Vampire Slayer)
BOOM! Studios: Jan, 2022 - Present ($3.99)

1-8-Cantwell-s/Bayliss-a — 4.00

ANGELA
Image Comics (Todd McFarlane Prod.): Dec, 1994 - No. 3, Feb, 1995 ($2.95, lim. series)

1-Gaiman scripts & Capullo-c/a in all; Spawn app. 1 3 4 6 8 10
2 — 5.00
3 — 4.00
Special Edition (1995)-Pirate Spawn-c 2 4 6 11 16 20
Special Edition (1995)-Angela-c 2 4 6 11 16 20
TPB ($9.95, 1995) reprints #1-3 & Special Ed. w/additional pin-ups — 10.00

ANGELA: ASGARD'S ASSASSIN (The Image Comics character in the Marvel Universe)
Marvel Comics: Feb, 2015 - No. 6, Jul, 2015 ($3.99)

1-6: 1-Gillen-s/Jimenez-a; multiple covers. 4-6-Guardians of the Galaxy app. — 4.00

ANGEL: AFTER THE FALL (Buffy the Vampire Slayer) (Follows the last TV episode)
IDW Publishing: Nov, 2007 - No. 17, Dec, 2009 ($3.99)(Continues as Angel with #18)

1-Whedon & Lynch-s; multiple covers — 5.00
2-17: Multiple covers on all — 4.00

ANGELA/GLORY: RAGE OF ANGELS (See Glory/Angela: Rage of Angels)
Image Comics (Todd McFarlane Productions): Mar, 1996 ($2.50, one-shot)

1-Liefeld-c/Cruz-a(p); Darkchylde preview flip book — 4.00
1-Variant-c — 4.00

ANGEL: A HOLE IN THE WORLD (Adaptation of the 2-part TV episode)
IDW Publishing: Dec, 2009 - No. 5, Apr, 2010 ($3.99, limited series)

1-5-Fred becomes Illyria; Casagrande-a/c — 4.00

ANGEL & FAITH (Follows Buffy the Vampire Slayer Season Eight)
Dark Horse Comics: Aug, 2011 - No. 25, Aug, 2013 ($2.99)

1-Gage-s/Isaacs-a; two covers by Morris & Chen — 3.00
2-25-Two covers by Morris & Isaacs. 5-Harmony & Clem app.; Noto-a. 7-Drusilla app.
11-14-Willow & Connor app. 20-Spike app.; Archie style-c — 3.00

ANGEL & FAITH SEASON 10 (Buffy the Vampire Slayer)
Dark Horse Comics: Apr, 2014 - No. 25, Apr, 2016 ($3.50/$3.99)

1-15-Two covers on each. 1-Gischler-s/Conrad-a. 5-Santacruz-a. 6-10-Amy app.
10-Fred returns — 3.50
16-25-($3.99) 17-Drusilla returns — 4.00

ANGEL AND THE APE (Meet Angel No. 7) (See Limited Collector's Edition C-34 & Showcase #77)
National Periodical Publications: Nov-Dec, 1968 - No. 6, Sept-Oct, 1969

1-(11-12/68)-Not Wood-a 6 12 18 42 79 115
2-5-Wood inks in all. 4-Last 12¢ issue 4 8 12 27 44 60
6-Wood inks 5 10 15 30 50 70

ANGEL AND THE APE (2nd Series)
DC Comics: Mar, 1991 - No. 4, June, 1991 ($1.00, limited series)

1-4 — 5.00

ANGEL AND THE APE (3rd Series)
DC Comics (Vertigo): Oct, 2001 - No. 4, Jan 2002 ($2.95, limited series)

1-4-Chaykin & Tischman-s/Bond-a/Art Adams-c — 3.00

ANGELA: QUEEN OF HEL (The Image Comics character in the Marvel Universe)
Marvel Comics: Dec, 2015 - No. 7, Jun, 2016 ($3.99)

1-5: 1-Bennett-s/Jacinto & Hans-a. 4,5-Hela app. 6,7-Thor (Jane) app. — 4.00

ANGEL: AULD LANG SYNE (Buffy the Vampire Slayer)
IDW Publishing: Nov, 2006 - No. 5, Mar, 2007 ($3.99, limited series)

1-5: 1-Three covers plus photo-c; Tipton-s/Messina-a — 4.00

ANGEL: BARBARY COAST (Buffy the Vampire Slayer)
IDW Publishing: Apr, 2010 - No. 3, Jun, 2010 ($3.99, limited series)

1-3-Angel in 1906 San Francisco; Tischman/Urru-a; 2 covers on each — 4.00

ANGEL: BLOOD & TRENCHES (Buffy the Vampire Slayer)
IDW Publishing: Mar, 2009 - No. 4, June, 2009 ($3.99, B&W&Red, limited series)

1-4-Angel in World War II Europe; John Byrne-s/a/c — 4.00

ANGEL: ILLYRIA: HAUNTED (Buffy the Vampire Slayer)
IDW Publishing: Nov, 2010 - No. 4, Feb, 2011 ($3.99, limited series)

1-4-Tipton & Huehner-s/Casagrande-a; 2 covers — 4.00

ANGEL LOVE
DC Comics: Aug, 1986 - No. 8, Mar, 1987 (75¢, limited series)

1-8, Special 1 (1987, $1.25, 52 pgs.) — 4.00

ANGEL: NOT FADE AWAY (Buffy the Vampire Slayer)
IDW Publishing: May, 2009 - No. 3, July, 2009 ($3.99, limited series)

1-3-Adaptation of TV show's final episodes; Mooney-a — 4.00

ANGEL OF LIGHT, THE (See The Crusaders)

ANGEL: OLD FRIENDS (Buffy the Vampire Slayer)
IDW Publishing: Nov, 2005 - No. 5, Mar, 2006 ($3.99)

1-5: Four covers plus photo-c on each; Mariotte-s/Messina-a; Gunn, Spike and Illyria app. 4.00
... Cover Gallery (6/06, $3.99) gallery of variant covers for the series — 4.00
... Cover Gallery (12/06, $3.99) gallery of variant covers; preview of Angel: Auld Lang Syne 4.00
TPB (2006, $19.99) r/series; gallery of Messina covers — 20.00

ANGEL: ONLY HUMAN (Buffy the Vampire Slayer)
IDW Publishing: Aug, 2009 - No. 5, Dec, 2009 ($3.99, limited series)

1-5-Lobdell-s/Messina-a; covers by Messina and Dave Dorman — 4.00

ANGEL + SPIKE (Buffy the Vampire Slayer)(Title changed from Angel after #8)
BOOM! Studios: No. 9, Feb, 2020 - No. 16, Nov, 2020 ($3.99)

9-16: 9-12-Hill-s/Melnikov-a. 13-Kowalski-a. 14-16-Sherman-a — 4.00

ANGEL: REVELATIONS (X-Men character)
Marvel Comics: July, 2008 - No. 5, Nov, 2008 ($3.99, limited series)

1-5-Origin from childhood re-told; Adam Pollina-a/Aguirre-Sacasa-s — 4.00

ANGEL SEASON 11 (Buffy the Vampire Slayer)
Dark Horse Comics: Jan, 2017 - No. 12, Dec, 2017 ($3.99)

1-12: 1-4-Bechko-s/Borges-a; Fred & Illyria app. — 4.00

ANGEL: SMILE TIME (Buffy the Vampire Slayer)
IDW Publishing: Dec, 2008 - No. 3, Apr, 2009 ($3.99, limited series)

1-3-Adaptation of TV episode; Messina-a; Messina and photo covers for each — 4.00

ANGEL: THE CURSE (Buffy the Vampire Slayer)
IDW Publishing: June, 2005 - No. 5, Oct, 2005 ($3.99, limited series)

1-5-Four covers on each; Mariotte-s/Messina-a — 4.00
TPB (1/06, $19.99) r/#1-5; cover gallery of Messina covers — 20.00

ANGELTOWN
DC Comics (Vertigo): Jan, 2005 - No. 5, May, 2005 ($2.95, limited series)

1-5-Gary Phillips-s/Shawn Martinbrough-a — 3.00

ANGELUS
Image Comics (Top Cow): Dec, 2007; Dec, 2009 - Nov, 2010 ($2.99)

... Pilot Season 1-(12/07) Sejic-a/c; Edington-s; origin re-told — 3.00
1-6-Marz-s/Sejic-a; multiple covers on each — 3.00

ANGRY BIRDS COMICS (Based on the Rovio videogame)(Also see Super Angry Birds)
IDW Publishing: Jun, 2014 - No. 12, Jun, 2015 ($3.99)

1-12-Short stories by Jeff Parker, Paul Tobin and various; wraparound-c on most — 4.00
Volume 2 (1/16 - 12/16, $3.99) 1-12-Wraparound-c on all — 4.00
...: Holiday Special (12/14, $5.99) Terence in charge of the North Pole — 6.00
... Quarterly: Furious Fowl (8/17, $5.99) Short stories by various — 6.00
... Quarterly: Monsters and Mistletoe (12/17, $5.99) Short stories by various — 6.00

ANGRY BIRDS: FLIGHT SCHOOL (Based on the Rovio videogame)
IDW Publishing: Feb, 2017 - No. 3, Jun, 2017 ($3.99)

1-3-Short stories by various — 4.00

ANGRY BIRDS GAME PLAY (Based on the Rovio videogame)
IDW Publishing: Jan, 2017 - No. 3, May, 2017 ($3.99)

1-3-Short stories by various; wraparound-c — 4.00

ANGRY BIRDS TRANSFORMERS (Based on the Rovio videogame)
IDW Publishing: Nov, 2014 - No. 4, Feb, 2015 ($3.99, limited series)

1-4-Barber-s; the Eggspark lands on Piggy Island — 4.00

ANGRY CHRIST COMIX (See Cry For Dawn)

ANIMA
DC Comics: Mar, 1994 - No. 15, July, 1995 ($1.75/$1.95/$2.25)

1-7,0,8-15: 7-(9/94)-Begin $1.95-c; Zero Hour tie-in. 0-(10/94) released between #7 & #8 3.00

	GD 2.0	VG 4.0	FN 6.0	VF 8.0	VF/NM 9.0	NM- 9.2

ANIMAL ADVENTURES
Timor Publications/Accepted Publ. (reprints): Dec, 1953 - No. 3, May?, 1954

	GD	VG	FN	VF	VF/NM	NM-
1-Funny animal	12	24	36	69	97	125
2,3: 2-Featuring Soopermutt (2/54)	8	16	24	44	57	70
1-3 (reprints, nd)	4	7	10	13	17	20

ANIMAL ANTICS
DC Comics: Feb, 1946

nn - Ashcan comic, not distributed to newsstands, only for in-house use. Cover art is Star Spangled Comics #49 and interior is Boy Commandos #12; a NM cover sold for $1000 in 2012, and FN/VF copy sold for $1553.50 in 2012.

ANIMAL ANTICS (Movietown... No. 24 on)
National Periodical Publ: Mar-Apr, 1946 - No. 23, Nov-Dec, 1949 (All 52 pgs.?)

	GD	VG	FN	VF	VF/NM	NM-
1-Raccoon Kids begins by Otto Feuer; many-c by Grossman; Seaman Sy Wheeler by Kelly in some issues; Grossman-a in most issues	61	122	183	390	670	950
2	26	52	78	154	252	350
3-10: 10-Post-c/a	18	36	54	103	162	220
11-23: 14,15,18,19-Post-a	14	28	42	76	108	140

ANIMAL COMICS
Dell Publishing Co.: Dec-Jan, 1941-42 - No. 30, Dec-Jan, 1947-48

	GD	VG	FN	VF	VF/NM	NM-
1-1st Pogo app. by Walt Kelly (Dan Noonan art in most issues)	161	322	483	1030	1765	2500
2-Uncle Wiggily begins	65	130	195	416	708	1000
3,5	28	56	84	202	451	700
4,6,7-No Pogo	17	34	51	119	265	410
8-10	21	42	63	147	324	500
11-15	13	26	39	86	188	290
16-20	10	20	30	64	132	200
21-30: 24-30- "Jigger" by John Stanley	9	18	27	58	114	170

NOTE: Dan Noonan a-18-30. Gollub art in most later issues; c-29, 30. Kelly c-7-26, part #27-30.

ANIMAL CRACKERS (Also see Adventures of Patoruzu)
Green Publ. Co./Norlen/Fox Feat.(Hero Books): 1946; No. 31, July, 1950; No. 9, 1959

	GD	VG	FN	VF	VF/NM	NM-
1-Super Cat begins (1st app.)	24	48	72	142	234	325
2	14	28	42	76	108	140
31(Fox)-Formerly My Love Secret	10	20	30	54	72	90
9(1959-Norlen)-Infinity-c	6	12	18	28	34	40
nn, nd ('50s), no publ.; infinity-c	8	16	24	40	50	60

ANIMAL FABLES
E. C. Comics (Fables Publ. Co.): July-Aug, 1946 - No. 7, Nov-Dec, 1947

	GD	VG	FN	VF	VF/NM	NM-
1-Freddy Firefly (clone of Human Torch), Korky Kangaroo, Petey Pig, Danny Demon begin	81	162	243	518	884	1250
2-Aesop Fables begin	45	90	135	284	480	675
3-6	40	80	120	246	411	575
7-Origin Moon Girl	103	206	309	659	1130	1600

ANIMAL FAIR (Fawcett's...)
Fawcett Publications: Mar, 1946 - No. 11, Feb, 1947

	GD	VG	FN	VF	VF/NM	NM-
1-Hoppy the Marvel Bunny-c	36	72	108	211	343	475
2	17	34	51	98	154	210
3-6	14	28	42	82	121	160
7-11	11	22	33	62	86	110

ANIMAL FUN
Premier Magazines: 1953 (25¢, came w/glasses)

	GD	VG	FN	VF	VF/NM	NM-
1-(3-D)-Ziggy Pig, Silly Seal, Billy & Buggy Bear	45	90	135	284	480	675

ANIMAL MAN (See Action Comics #552, 553, DC Comics Presents #77, 78, Last Days of Animal Man, Secret Origins #39, Strange Adventures #180 & Wonder Woman #267, 268)
DC Comics (Vertigo imprint #57 on): Sept, 1988 - No. 89, Nov, 1995 ($1.25/$1.50/$1.75/$1.95/$2.25, mature)

	1	2	3	4	5	7
1-Grant Morrison scripts begin, ends #26	2	4	6	10	14	18

	1	2	3	4	5	7
2-4,6-10: 2-Superman cameo. 9-Manhunter-c/story. 10-Psycho Pirate app.	2	4	6	11	16	20
5-Crafty Coyote	2	4	6	11	16	20

11-49,51-55,57-89: 23,24-Psycho Pirate app. 24-Arkham Asylum story; Bizarro Superman app. 25-Inferior Five app. 26-Morrison apps. in story; part photo-c (of Morrison?) ... 4.00
50-($2.95, 52 pgs.)-Last issue w/Veitch scripts ... 5.00
56-($3.50, 68 pgs.) ... 5.00
Annual 1 (1993, $3.95, 68 pgs.)-Bolland-c; Children's Crusade Pt. 3 ... 6.00
...: Deus Ex Machina TPB (2003, $19.95) r/#18-26; Morrison-s; new Bolland-c ... 20.00
...: Origin of the Species TPB (2002, $19.95) r/#10-17 & Secret Origins #39 ... 20.00
NOTE: Bolland c-1-63. 71-Sutton-a(i)

ANIMAL MAN (DC New 52)
DC Comics: Nov, 2011 - No. 29, May, 2014 ($2.99)

1-Jeff Lemire s/Travel Foreman-a/c; 1st printing with yellow cover background ... 8.00
1-Second printing (red cover background), Third printing (grey cover background) ... 3.00
2-29: 2-4 Foreman-a. 5-Huat-a. 10 Justice League Dark app. 13-17-Rotworld ... 3.00
#0 (11/12, $2.99) Lemire-s/Pugh-a/c; Buddy Baker's origin re-told ... 3.00
Annual 1 (7/12, $4.99) Swamp Thing app.; Lemire-s/Green-a ... 5.00
Annual 2 (9/13, $4.99) Lemire-s/Foreman-a ... 5.00

ANIMAL MYSTIC (See Dark One...)
Cry For Dawn/Sirius: 1993 - No. 4, 1995 ($2.95?/$3.50, B&W)

	1	2	3	5	6	8
1	1	2	3	5	6	8
1-Alternate	2	4	6	10	14	18
1-2nd printing						4.00
2						4.00
2,3-2nd prints (Sirius)						3.50
3,4: 4-Color poster insert, Linsner-s						4.00
TPB ($14.95) r/series						15.00

ANIMAL MYSTIC WATER WARS
Sirius: 1996 - No. 6, Oct, 1998 ($2.95, limited series)

1-6-Dark One-c/a/scripts ... 4.00

ANIMAL POUND

BOOM! Studios: Dec, 2023 - Present ($4.99, limited series)

1,2-Tom King-s/Peter Gross-a ... 5.00
No. 1 Ashcan (11/23, $2.99) B&W preview of #1; essay by Tom King; bonus sketch art ... 3.00

111ANIMAL WORLD, THE (Movie)
Dell Publishing Co.: No. 713, Aug, 1956

	GD	VG	FN	VF	VF/NM	NM-
Four Color 713	5	10	15	34	60	85

ANIMANIACS (TV)
DC Comics: May, 1995 - No. 59, Apr, 2000 ($1.50/$1.75/$1.95/$1.99)

	GD	VG	FN	VF	VF/NM	NM-
1	3	6	9	14	19	24
2-10	1	3	4	6	8	10
11-20: 13-Manga issue. 19-X-Files parody; Miran Kim-c; Adlard-a (4 pgs.)						6.00
21-59: 26-E.C. parody-c. 34-Xena parody. 43-Pinky & the Brain take over						4.00
A Christmas Special (12/94, $1.50, "1" on-c)	3	6	9	14	19	24

ANIMATED COMICS
E. C. Comics: No date given (Summer, 1947?)

	GD	VG	FN	VF	VF/NM	NM-
1 (Rare) Funny Animal	123	246	369	767	1344	1900

ANIMATED FUNNY COMIC TUNES (See Funny Tunes)

ANIMATED MOVIE-TUNES (Movie Tunes No. 3)
Margood Publishing Corp. (Timely): Fall, 1945 - No. 2, Sum, 1946

	GD	VG	FN	VF	VF/NM	NM-
1,2-Super Rabbit, Ziggy Pig & Silly Seal	47	94	141	296	498	700

ANIMAX
Marvel Comics (Star Comics): Dec, 1986 - No. 4, June, 1987

1-4: Based on toys; Simonson-a ... 4.00

ANIMOSITY (Also see World of Animosity one-shot)
AfterShock Comics: Aug, 2016 - Present ($3.99)

1-Marguerite Bennett-s/Rafael de Latorre-a; 2 covers ... 15.00
2 ... 8.00
3-28: 17-Savarese-a. 19-28-Thomasi-a ... 4.00
... Tales 1 (5/19, Free Comic Book Day giveaway) Bennett-s/Thomasi-a ... 3.00

ANIMOSITY: EVOLUTION
AfterShock Comics: Oct, 2017 - No. 10, Jan, 2019 ($3.99, limited series)

1-10-Bennett-s/Gapstur-a; San Francisco one month after the awakening ... 4.00

ANIMOSITY: THE RISE
AfterShock Comics: Jan, 2017 - No. 3, Sept, 2017 ($3.99, limited series)

1-3-Bennett-s/Juan Doe-a; the early days after the animals awoke ... 4.00

ANITA BLAKE (Circus of the Damned - The Charmer on cover)
Marvel Comics: July, 2010 - No. 5, Dec, 2010 ($3.99, limited series)

1-5-Laurell K. Hamilton & Jess Ruffner-s/Ron Lim-a/ Brett Booth-c ... 4.00
... - The Ingenue 1-5 (3/11 - No. 5, 10/11, $3.99) Hamilton & Ruffner-s/Lim-a/Booth-c ... 4.00
... - The Scoundrel 1-4 (11/11 - No. 5, 5/12, $3.99) Hamilton & Ruffner-s/Lim-a/Booth-c ... 4.00

ANITA BLAKE: VAMPIRE HUNTER GUILTY PLEASURES
Marvel Comics (Dabel Brothers): Dec, 2006 - No. 12, Aug, 2008 ($2.99)

1-Laurell K. Hamilton/Brett Booth-a; blue cover ... 6.00
1-Variant-c by Greg Horn ... 20.00
1-Sketch cover ... 25.00
1-2nd printing with red cover ... 3.00
2-Two covers ... 5.00
3-12 ... 3.00
...: Handbook (2007, $3.99) profile pages of characters; glossary ... 4.00
... Volume One HC (6/07, $19.99, dust jacket) r/#1-6; cover gallery ... 20.00

ANITA BLAKE: VAMPIRE HUNTER THE FIRST DEATH, (LAURELL K. HAMILTON'S...)
Marvel Comics (Dabel Brothers): July, 2007 - No. 2, Dec, 2007 ($3.99)

1,2-Laurell K. Hamilton & Jonathon Green-s/Wellington Alves-a. 2-Marvel Zombie var-c ... 4.00
... HC (2008, $19.99, dust jacket) r/#1,2 & Guilty Pleasures Handbook ... 20.00

ANITA BLAKE, VAMPIRE HUNTER: THE LAUGHING CORPSE
Marvel Comics: Dec, 2008 - No. 5, Apr, 2009 ($3.99)

... - Book One (12/08 - No. 5, 4/09) 1-5-Laurell K. Hamilton-s/Ron Lim-a/c ... 4.00
... - Necromancer 1-5 (6/09 - No. 5, 11/09, $3.99) Lim-a/c ... 4.00
Anita Blake (Executioner on-c) #11-15 (12/09 - No. 15, 5/10) numbering continued; Lim-a ... 4.00

ANNE RICE'S INTERVIEW WITH THE VAMPIRE
Innovation Books: 1991 - No. 12, Jan, 1994 ($2.50, limited series)

	GD	VG	FN	VF	VF/NM	NM-
1-Adapts novel; Moeller-a	1	2	3	5	6	8
2-12-Continues adaptation						4.00

ANNE RICE'S THE MASTER OF RAMPLING GATE
Innovation Books: 1991 ($6.95, one-shot)

1-Bolton painted-c; Colleen Doran painted-a ... 7.00

ANNE RICE'S THE MUMMY OR RAMSES THE DAMNED
Millennium Publications: Oct, 1990 - No. 12, Feb, 1992 ($2.50, limited series)

	GD	VG	FN	VF	VF/NM	NM-
1-Adapts novel; Mooney-p in all	1	3	4	6	8	10
2-12-Continues adaptation						4.00

ANNE RICE'S THE WITCHING HOUR
Millennium Publ./Comico: 1992 - No. 13, Jan, 1993 ($2.50, limited series)

1-13 ... 4.00

ANNETTE (Disney, TV)
Dell Publishing Co.: No. 905, May, 1958; No. 1100, May, 1960
(Mickey Mouse Club)

	GD	VG	FN	VF	VF/NM	NM-
Four Color 905-Annette Funicello photo-c	24	48	72	168	372	575
Four Color 1100-...'s Life Story (Movie); A. Funicello photo-c	18	36	54	125	276	430

ANNEX (See Amazing Spider-Man Annual #27 for 1st app.)
Marvel Comics: Aug, 1994 - No. 4, Nov, 1994 ($1.75)

1-4: 1,4-Spider-Man app. ... 3.00

ANNIE
Marvel Comics Group: Oct, 1982 - No. 2, Nov, 1982 (60¢)

Animal Man (2011 series) #7 © DC

Animosity #13 © M. Bennett

Ant-Man (2015 series) #4 © MAR

	GD 2.0	VG 4.0	FN 6.0	VF 8.0	VF/NM 9.0	NM- 9.2

	GD 2.0	VG 4.0	FN 6.0	VF 8.0	VF/NM 9.0	NM- 9.2
1,2-Movie adaptation						5.00
Treasury Edition ($2.50, tabloid size)	3	6	9	17	26	35

ANNIE OAKLEY (See Tessie The Typist #19, Two-Gun Kid & Wild Western)
Marvel/Atlas Comics(MPI No. 1-4/CDS No. 5 on): Spring, 1948 - No. 4, 11/48; No. 5, 6/55 - No. 11, 6/56

	GD 2.0	VG 4.0	FN 6.0	VF 8.0	VF/NM 9.0	NM- 9.2
1 (1st Series, 1948)-Hedy Devine app.	90	180	270	576	988	1400
2 (7/48, 52 pgs.)-Kurtzman-a, "Hey Look", 1 pg; Intro. Lana; Hedy Devine app; Captain Tootsie by Beck	43	86	129	271	461	650
3,4	37	74	111	222	361	500
5 (2nd Series, 1955)-Reinman-a; Maneely-c	25	50	75	150	245	340
6-9: 6,8-Woodbridge-a. 9-Williamson-a (4 pgs.)	19	38	57	112	179	240
10,11: 11-Severin-c	19	38	57	112	179	240

ANNIE OAKLEY AND TAGG (TV)
Dell Publishing Co./Gold Key: 1953 - No. 18, Jan-Mar, 1959; July, 1965 (Gail Davis photo-c #3 on)

	GD 2.0	VG 4.0	FN 6.0	VF 8.0	VF/NM 9.0	NM- 9.2
Four Color 438 (#1)	13	26	39	89	195	300
Four Color 481,575 (#2,3)	9	18	27	59	117	175
4(7-9/55)-10	7	14	21	46	86	125
11-18(1-3/59)	6	12	18	38	69	100
1(7/65-Gold Key)-Photo-c (c-r/#6)	4	8	12	27	44	60

NOTE: **Manning** a-13. Photo back c-4, 9, 11.

ANNIHILATION
Marvel Comics: May, 2006 - No. 6, Mar, 2007 ($3.99/$2.99, limited x-over series)

Prologue (5/06, $3.99, one-shot) Nova, Thanos and Silver Surfer app.						4.00
1-6: 1-(10/06) Giffen-s/DiVito-a; Annihilus app.						3.00
...: Heralds of Galactus 1,2 (4/07-5/07, $3.99) 2-Silver Surfer app.						4.00
...: Nova 1-4 (6/06-9/06, $2.99) Abnett & Lanning-s/Walker-a/Dell'Otto-c. 2,3-Quasar app.						3.00
...: Ronan 1-4 (6/06-9/06, $2.99) Furman-s/Lucas-a/Dell'Otto-c						3.00
...: Saga (2007, $1.99) re-cap of the series; DiVito-c						3.00
...: Silver Surfer 1-4 (6/06-9/06, $2.99) Giffen-s/Arlem-a/Dell'Otto-c						3.00
...: Super-Skrull 1-4 (6/06-9/06, $2.99) Grillo-Marxuach-s/Titus-a/Dell'Otto-c						3.00
...: The Nova Corps Files (2006, $3.99) profile pages of characters and alien races						4.00
Annihilation Book 1 HC (2007, $29.99, dustjacket) r/Drax the Destroyer #1-4, Annihilation Prologue and Annihilation: Nova #1-4; sketch and layout pages						30.00
Annihilation Book 1 SC (2007, $24.99) same content as HC						25.00
Annihilation Book 2 HC (2007, $29.99, dustjacket) r/Annihilation: Silver Surfer #1-4, ...: Super Skrull #1-4 and ...: Ronan #1-4; sketch and layout pages						30.00
Annihilation Book 2 SC (2007, $24.99) same content as HC						25.00
Annihilation Book 3 HC (2007, $29.99, dustjacket) r/Annihilation #1-6, Annihilation: Heralds of Galactus #1,2 and Annihilation: Nova Corps Files; sketch pages						30.00
Annihilation Book 3 SC (2007, $24.99) same content as HC						25.00

ANNIHILATION: CONQUEST (Also see Nova 2007 series)
Marvel Comics: Jan, 2008 - No. 6, Jun, 2008 ($3.99/$2.99, limited x-over series)

Prologue (8/07, $3.99, one-shot) the new Quasar, Moondragon app.; Perkins-a		2	4	6	8	11	14
1-5-Raney-a; Ultron app. 3-Moondragon dies						5.00
6-($3.99) Guardians of the Galaxy team forms	4	8	12	25	40	55
...: Quasar 1-4 (9/07-No. 4, 12/07, $2.99) Gage-s/Lilly-a. 1-Super-Adaptoid app.						3.00
...: Starlord 1-4 (9/07-No. 4, 12/07, $2.99) Giffen-s/Green-a						6.00
...: Wraith 1-4 (9/07-No. 4, 12/07, $2.99) Hotz-a/Grillo-Marxuach-s						3.00
Annihilation: Conquest Book 1 HC (2008, $29.99, dustjacket) r/Prologue; ...Quasar #1-4, ...Star-Lord #1-4; Annihilation Saga; design pages						30.00

ANNIHILATION – SCOURGE
Marvel Comics: Jan, 2020 - Feb, 2020 ($4.99, limited series)

Alpha (1/20, $4.99) Annihilus, Blastaar, Nova, and The Sentry app.						5.00
Omega (2/20, $4.99) Conclusion of series; Lockjaw, Beta Ray Bill, Fantastic Four app.						5.00
...: Beta Ray Bill 1 (2/20, $4.99) Lockjaw and The Sentry app.						5.00
...: Fantastic Four 1 (2/20, $4.99) Gage-s/Olortegui-a						5.00
...: Nova 1 (2/20, $4.99) Rosenberg-s/Roberson-a; Richard Rider app.						5.00
...: Silver Surfer 1 (2/20, $4.99) Abnett-s/Davidson-a; Surfer merges with Bob Reynolds						5.00

ANNIHILATOR
Legendary Comics: Sept, 2014 - No. 6, Jun, 2015 ($3.99)

1-6-Grant Morrison-s/Frazer Irving-a/c						4.00

ANNIHILATORS
Marvel Comics: May, 2011 - No. 4, Aug, 2011 ($4.99, limited series)

1-4: Quasar, Silver Surfer, Beta-Ray Bill, Ronan, Gladiator app.; Huat-a						5.00

ANNIHILATORS: EARTHFALL
Marvel Comics: Nov, 2011 - No. 4, Feb, 2012 ($3.99, limited series)

1-4-Avengers app.; Abnett & Lanning-s/Huat-a/Christopher-c						4.00

ANNO DRACULA: 1895 SEVEN DAYS IN MAYHEM (Based on the Kim Newman novels)
Titan Comics: Apr, 2017 - No. 5, Sept, 2017 ($3.99, limited series)

1-5-Kim Newman-s/Paul McCaffrey-a; multiple covers on each						4.00

ANOTHER WORLD (See Strange Stories From...)

ANSWER!, THE
Dark Horse Comics: Jan, 2013 - No. 4 ($3.99, limited series)

1-3-Dennis Hopeless-s/Mike Norton-a						4.00

ANT
Image Comics: Aug, 2005 - No. 11, Feb, 2007; No. 12, Jun, 2021 ($2.99)

1-11: 1-Mario Gully-s/a. 2-Savage Dragon & Spawn app. 3-Spawn-c/app.						3.00
12-(6/21, $3.99) Series finished by Erik Larsen-s/a; covers by Larsen & Gully						4.00
Vol. 1: Reality Bites TPB (2006, $12.99) r/#1-4; sketch and concept art						13.00

ANT
Image Comics: Oct, 2021 - Present ($3.99)

1-6: 1-Erik Larsen-s/a/c; bonus sketch and concept art. 3,5,6-Spawn app.						4.00

ANTARCTICA
Image Comics (Top Cow): Jul, 2023 - Present ($3.99)

1-8-Simon Birks-s/Willi Roberts-a						4.00

ANTHEM (Based on the Electronic Arts videogame)
Dark Horse Comics: Feb, 2019 - No. 3, May, 2019 ($3.99, limited series)

1-3-Freed-s/Francisco-a						4.00

ANTHRO (See Showcase #74)
National Periodical Publications: July-Aug, 1968 - No. 6, July-Aug, 1969

	GD 2.0	VG 4.0	FN 6.0	VF 8.0	VF/NM 9.0	NM- 9.2
1-(7-8/68)-Howie Post-a in all	5	10	15	34	60	85
2-5: 5-Last 12¢ issue	3	6	9	21	33	45
6-Wood-c/a (inks)	4	8	12	27	44	60

ANTI-HITLER COMICS
New England Comics Press: Summer, 1992 ($2.75, B&W, one-shot)

	GD 2.0	VG 4.0	FN 6.0	VF 8.0	VF/NM 9.0	NM- 9.2
1-Reprints Hitler as Devil stories from wartime comics	1	3	4	6	8	10

ANT-MAN (See Irredeemable Ant-Man, The)

ANT-MAN (Also see Astonishing Ant-Man)
Marvel Comics: Mar, 2015 - No. 5, Jul, 2015 ($3.99)

1-($4.99) Scott Lang as Ant-Man; Spencer-s/Rosanas-a; main-c by Brooks						5.00
2-5-($3.99) 2,3-Taskmaster app. 4-Darren Cross returns						4.00
Annual 1 (9/15, $4.99) Giant-Man & Egghead app.; intro. Raz Malhotra						5.00
...: Larger Than Life 1 (8/15, $3.99) movie Hank Pym story; r/Tales to Astonish #27 & #35						4.00
...: Last Days 1 (10/15, $3.99) Secret Wars tie-in; Spencer-s; Miss Patriot app.						4.00

ANT-MAN
Marvel Comics: Apr, 2020 - No. 5, Oct, 2020 ($3.99, limited series)

1-5-Wells-s/Burnett-a; Scott Lang & Stinger (Cassie). 3-Spider-Man & Black Cat app.						4.00

ANT-MAN
Marvel Comics: Sept, 2022 - No. 4, Dec, 2022 ($3.99, limited series)

1-4-Al Ewing-s/Tom Reilly-a. 2-Eric O'Grady app. 3-Scott Lang & Cassie app. 4-Intro/origin Zayn Asghar, the future Ant-Man; Ultron app.						4.00

ANT-MAN & THE WASP
Marvel Comics: Aug, 2018 - No. 5, Nov, 2018 ($3.99, limited series)

1-5-Waid-s/Garrón-a; Scott Lang & Nadia Van Dyne						4.00
...: Living Legends 1 (8/18, $3.99) Macchio-s/Di Vito-a; Scott Lang & Janet Van Dyne						4.00

ANT-MAN & WASP
Marvel Comics: Jan, 2011 - No. 3, Mar, 2011 ($3.99, limited series)

1-3-Tim Seeley-s/a; Espin-c; Tigra app.						5.00

ANT-MAN'S BIG CHRISTMAS
Marvel Comics: Feb, 2000 ($5.95, square-bound, one-shot)

1-Bob Gale-s/Phil Winslade-a; Avengers app.						6.00

ANT-MAN: SEASON ONE
Marvel Comics: 2012 ($24.99, hardcover graphic novel)

HC - Origin story; DeFalco-s/Domingues-a/Tedesco painted-c						25.00

ANTONY AND CLEOPATRA (See Ideal, a Classical Comic)

ANYTHING GOES
Fantagraphics Books: Oct, 1986 - No. 6, 1987 ($2.00, #1-5 color & B&W/#6 B&W, lim. series)

1-6: 1-Flaming Carrot app. (1st in color?) G. Kane-c. 2-6: 2-Miller-c(p); Alan Moore scripts; Kirby-a; early Sam Kieth-a (2 pgs). 3-Capt. Jack, Cerebus app.; Cerebus-c by N. Adams. 4-Perez-c. 5-3rd color Teenage Mutant Ninja Turtles app.						4.00

	GD	VG	FN	VF	VF/NM	NM-		GD	VG	FN	VF	VF/NM	NM-
	2.0	4.0	6.0	8.0	9.0	9.2		2.0	4.0	6.0	8.0	9.0	9.2

A-1
Marvel Comics (Epic Comics): 1992 - No. 4, 1993 ($5.95, limited series, mature)
1-4: 1-Fabry-c/a, Russell-, S. Hampton-a. 3-Bisley-c; Kent Williams-a.
4-McKean-a; Dorman-s/a   1   2   3   4   5   7

A-1 COMICS (A-1 appears on covers No. 1-17 only)(See individual title listings for #11-139)
(1st two issues not numbered.)
Life's Romances Publ.-No. 1/Compix/Magazine Ent.: 1944 - No. 139, Sept-Oct, 1955 (No #2)
nn-(1944) (See Kerry Drake Detective Cases)
1-Dotty Dripple (1 pg.), Mr. Ex, Bush Berry, Rocky, Lew Loyal (20 pgs.)
| | | 25 | 50 | 75 | 150 | 245 | 340 |
3-8,10: Texas Slim & Dirty Dalton, The Corsair, Teddy Rich, Dotty Dripple, Inca Dinca, Tommy Tinker, Little Mexico & Tugboat Tim, The Masquerader & others. 7-Corsair-c/s. 8-Intro Rodeo Ryan
| | | 15 | 30 | 45 | 83 | 124 | 165 |
9-All Texas Slim
| | | 15 | 30 | 45 | 84 | 127 | 170 |

(See Individual Alphabetical listings for prices)
11-Teena; Ogden Whitney-c
12,15-Teena
13-Guns of Fact & Fiction (1948). Used in SOTI, pg. 19; Ingels & Johnny Craig-a
14-Tim Holt Western Adventures #1
16-Vacation Comics; The Pixies, Tom Tom, Flying Fredd, & Koko & Kola
17-Tim Holt #2; photo-c; last issue to carry A-1 on cover (9-10/48)
18,20-Jimmy Durante; photo covers on both
19-Tim Holt #3; photo-c
21-Joan of Arc (1949)-Movie adaptation; Ingrid Bergman photo-covers & interior photos; Whitney-a
22-Dick Powell (1949)-Photo-c
23-Cowboys and Indians #6; Doc Holiday-c/story
24-Trail Colt #1-Frazetta-r in-Manhunt #13; Ingels-c; L. B. Cole-a
25-Fibber McGee & Molly (1949) (Radio)
26-Trail Colt #2-Ingels-a
27-Ghost Rider #1(1950)-Origin
28-Christmas-(Koko & Kola #6) ("50)
29-Ghost Rider #2-Frazetta-c (1950)
30-Jet Powers #1-Powell-a
31-Ghost Rider #3-Frazetta-c & origin ('51)
32-Jet Powers #2
33-Muggsy Mouse #1('51)
34-Ghost Rider #4-Frazetta-c (1951)
35-Jet Powers #3-Williamson/Evans-a
36-Muggsy Mouse #2; Racist-c
37-Ghost Rider #5-Frazetta-c (1951)
38-Jet Powers #4-Williamson/Wood-a
39-Muggsy Mouse #3
40-Dogface Dooley #1('51)
41-Cowboys 'N' Indians #7 (1951)
42-Best of the West #1-Powell-a
43-Dogface Dooley #2
44-Ghost Rider #6
45-American Air Forces #5-Powell-c/a
46-Best of the West #2
47-Thun'da, King of the Congo #1-Frazetta-c/a('52)
48-Cowboys 'N' Indians #8
49-Dogface Dooley #3
50-Danger Is Their Business #11 ('52)-Powell-a
51-Ghost Rider #7 ('52)
52-Best of the West #3
53-Dogface Dooley #4
54-American Air Forces #6(8/52)-Powell-a
55-U.S. Marines #5-Powell-a
56-Thun'da #2-Powell-c/a
57-Ghost Rider #8
58-American Air Forces #7-Powell-a
59-Best of the West #4
60-The U.S. Marines #6-Powell-a
61-Space Ace #5('53)-Guardineer-a
62-Starr Flagg, Undercover Girl #5 (#1) reprinted from A-1 #24
63-Manhunt #13-Frazetta
64-Dogface Dooley #5
65-American Air Forces #8-Powell-a
66-Best of the West #5
67-American Air Forces #9-Powell-a
68-U.S. Marines #7-Powell-a
69-Ghost Rider #9(10/52)
70-Best of the West #6
71-Ghost Rider #10(12/52)-Vs. Frankenstein
72-U.S. Marines #8-Powell-a(3)
74-American Air Forces #10-Powell-a
73-Thun'da #3-Powell-c/a
76-Best of the West #7
75-Ghost Rider #11(3/52)
78-Thun'da #4-Powell-c/a
77-Manhunt #14
80-Ghost Rider #12(6/52)-One-eyed Devil-c
79-American Air Forces #11-Powell-a
81-Best of the West #8
83-Thun'da #5-Powell-c/a
82-Cave Girl #11(1953)-Powell-c/a; origin (#1)
84-Ghost Rider #13(7-8/53)
85-Best of the West #9
86-Thun'da #6-Powell-c/a
87-Best of the West #10(9-10/53)
88-Bobby Benson's B-Bar-B Riders #20
89-Home Run #3-Powell-a; Stan Musial photo-c
90-Red Hawk #11(1953)-Powell-a
91-American Air Forces #12-Powell-a
92-Dream Book of Romance #5-Photo-c; Guardineer-a
93-Great Western #8('54)-Origin The Ghost Rider; Powell-a
94-White Indian #11-Frazetta-a(r); Powell-c
95-Muggsy Mouse #4
96-Cave Girl #12, with Thun'da; Powell-c/a
97-Best of the West #11
98-Undercover Girl #6-Powell-c
99-Muggsy Mouse #5
100-Badmen of the West #1-Meskin-a(?)
101-White Indian #12-Frazetta-a(r)
101-Dream Book of Romance #6 (4-6/54)-Marlon Brando photo-c; Powell, Bolle, Guardineer-a
103-Best of the West #12-Powell-a
104-White Indian #13-Frazetta-a(r) ('54)
105-Great Western #9-Ghost Rider app.; Powell-a, 6 pgs.; Bolle-c
106-Dream Book of Love #1 (6-7/54)-Powell, Bolle-a; Montgomery Clift, Donna Reed photo-c
107-Hot Dog #2
108-Red Fox #15 (1954)-L.B. Cole-c/a; Powell-a
109-Dream Book of Romance #7 (7-8/54)-Powell-a; movie photo-c
110-Dream Book of Romance #8 (10/54)-Movie photo-c
111-I'm a Cop #1 ('54); drug mention story; Powell-a
112-Ghost Rider #14 ('54)
113-Great Western #10; Powell-a
114-Dream Book of Love #2- Guardineer, Bolle-a; Piper Laurie, Victor Mature photo-c
115-Hot Dog #3
116-Cave Girl #13-Powell-c/a
117-White Indian #14
118-Undercover Girl #7-Powell-c
119-Straight Arrow's Fury #1 (origin); Fred Meagher-c/a
120-Badmen of the West #2
121-Mysteries of Scotland Yard #1; reprinted from Manhunt (5 stories)
122-Black Phantom #1 (11/54)
124-Dream Book of Romance #8 (10-11/54)
123-Dream Book of Love #3 (10-11/54)-Movie photo-c
125-Cave Girl #14
126-I'm a Cop #2-Powell-a
127-Great Western #11('54)-Powell-a
128-I'm a Cop #3-Powell-a
129-The Avenger #1('55)-Powell-c
130-Strongman #1-Powell-a (2-3/55)
131-The Avenger #2('55)-Powell-c
132-Strongman #2
133-The Avenger #3-Powell-c/a
134-Strongman #3
135-White Indian #15
136-Hot Dog #4
137-Africa #1-Powell-c/a(4)
138-The Avenger #4-Powell-c/a
139-Strongman #4-Powell-a
NOTE: Bolle a-110. Photo-c-17-22, 89, 92, 101, 106, 109, 110, 114, 123, 124.

APACHE
Fiction House Magazines: 1951
| | 1 | | 27 | 54 | 81 | 158 | 259 | 360 |
| I.W. Reprint No. 1-r/#1 above | | 4 | 8 | 12 | 22 | 35 | 48 |

APACHE DELIVERY SERVICE
Dark Horse Comics: Jan, 2022 - No. 4, Apr, 2022 ($3.99, limited series)
1-4-Matt Kindt-s/Tyler Jenkins-a   4.00

APACHE KID (Formerly Reno Browne; Western Gunfighters #20 on)
(Also see Two-Gun Western & Wild Western)
Marvel/Atlas Comics(MPC No. 53-10/CPS No. 11 on): No. 53, 12/50 - No. 10, 1/52; No. 11, 12/54 - No. 19, 4/56
53(#1)-Apache Kid & his horse Nightwind (origin), Red Hawkins by Syd Shores begins
| | | 45 | 90 | 135 | 284 | 480 | 675 |
2(2/51)
| | | 21 | 42 | 63 | 124 | 202 | 280 |
3-5
| | | 15 | 30 | 45 | 90 | 140 | 190 |
6-10 (1951-52): 7-Russ Heath-a
| | | 14 | 28 | 42 | 82 | 121 | 160 |
11-19 (1954-56)
| | | 13 | 26 | 39 | 72 | 101 | 130 |
NOTE: Heath a-7, c-11, 13. Maneely a-53; c-53(#1), 12, 14-16. Powell a-14. Severin c-17.

APACHE MASSACRE (See Chief Victorio's...)

APACHE SKIES
Marvel Comics: Sept, 2002 - No. 4, Dec, 2002 ($2.99, limited series)
1-4-Apache Kid app.; Ostrander-s/Manco-c/a   3.00
TPB (2003, $12.99) r/#1-4   13.00

APACHE TRAIL
Steinway/America's Best: Sept, 1957 - No. 4, June, 1958
| | 1 | | 15 | 30 | 45 | 84 | 127 | 170 |
| 2-4: 2-Tuska-a | | 9 | 18 | 27 | 52 | 69 | 85 |

APE (Magazine)
Dell Publishing Co.: 1961 (52 pgs., B&W)
1-Comics and humor   5   10   15   31   53   75

APEX LEGENDS: OVERTIME (Based on the EA videogame)
Dark Horse Comics: Jun, 2021 - No. 4, Sept, 2022 ($3.99, limited series)
1-4-Jesse Stern-s/Neil Edwards-a   4.00

APHRODITE IX
Image Comics (Top Cow): Sept, 2000 - No. 4, Mar, 2002 ($2.50)
1-3: 1-Four covers by Finch, Turner, Silvestri, Benitez   4.00
1-Tower Record Ed.; Finch-c   3.00
1-DF Chrome ($14.99)   15.00
4-($4.95) Double-sized issue; Finch-c   5.00
Convention Preview   10.00
...: Time Out of Mind TPB (6/04, $14.99) r/#1-4, & #0; cover gallery   15.00
Wizard #0 (4/00, bagged w/Tomb Raider magazine) Preview & sketchbook   5.00
#0-(6/01, $2.95) r/Wizard #0 with cover gallery   3.00

APHRODITE IX (Volume 2)
Image Comics (Top Cow): May, 2013 - No. 11, Jun, 2014 ($2.99/$3.99)
1-Free Comic Book Day giveaway; Hawkins-s/Sejic-a   3.00
2-10-($2.99) Hawkins-s/Sejic-a   3.00
11-($3.99) Leads into Aphrodite IX Cyber Force #1   4.00
...: Ares #1 (9/18, $3.99) Glaser-s/Kaepen-a; Marsh-s/Renna-a   4.00
... Cyber Force #1 (7/14, $5.99) Hawkins-s/Sejic-a; leads into IXth Generation #1   6.00
... Hidden Files 1 (1/14, $2.99) Character profiles; Sejic-a   3.00

APHRODITE V
Image Comics (Top Cow): Jul, 2018 - No. 4, Oct, 2018 ($3.99)
1-4-Bryan Hill-s/Jeff Spokes-a. 1-Origin re-told   4.00

A+X (Avengers Plus X-Men)
Marvel Comics: Dec, 2012 - No. 18, May, 2014 ($3.99)
1-18: 1-Hulk & Wolverine team-up; Keown-c. 2-Black Widow/Rogue; Bachalo-c/a. 14-Superior Spider-Man app.   4.00
1-Variant baby-c by Skottie Young   5.00

APOCALYPSE NERD
Dark Horse Comics: January, 2005 - No. 6, Oct, 2007 ($2.99, B&W)
1-6-Peter Bagge-s/a   3.00

APOLLO IX (See Aphrodite IX)
Image Comics (Top Cow): Aug, 2015 ($3.99, one-shot)
1-Ashley Robinson-s/Fernando Argosino-a; 2 covers   4.00

APPARITION
Caliber Comics: 1995 ($3.95, 52 pgs., B&W)
1 ($3.95)   4.00
V2#1-6 ($2.95)   3.00
Visitations   4.00

APPLESEED
Eclipse Comics: Sept, 1988 - Book 4, Vol. 4, Aug, 1991 ($2.50/$2.75/$3.50, 52/68 pgs, B&W)
Book One, Vol. 1-5: -5(1/89), Book Two, Vol. 1(2/89) -5(7/89): Art Adams-c, Book Three, Vol. 1-(8/89) -4 ($2.75), Book Three, Vol. 5 ($3.50), Book Four, Vol. 1 (1/91) - 4 (8/91) ($3.50, 68 pgs.)
| | | 1 | 3 | 4 | 6 | | 10 |

APPLESEED DATABOOK
Dark Horse Comics: Apr, 1994 - No. 2, May, 1994 ($3.50, B&W, limited series)
1,2: -Flip book format   1   3   4   6   8   10

APPROVED COMICS (Also see Blue Ribbon Comics)
St. John Publishing Co. (Most have no c-price): March, 1954 - No. 12, Aug, 1954 (Painted-c on #1-5,7,8,10)
1-The Hawk #5-r
| | | 14 | 28 | 42 | 82 | 121 | 160 |
2-Invisible Boy (3/54)-Origin; Saunders-c
| | | 21 | 42 | 63 | 124 | 202 | 280 |

A+X #13 © MAR

Aquaman #6 © DC

Aquaman (2016 series) #25 © DC

	GD 2.0	VG 4.0	FN 6.0	VF 8.0	VF/NM 9.0	NM- 9.2
3-Wild Boy of the Congo #11-r (4/54)	13	26	39	74	105	135
4,5: 4-Kid Cowboy-r. 5-Fly Boy-r	13	26	39	74	105	135
6-Daring Adv.-r (5/54); Krigstein-a(2); Baker-c	65	130	195	416	708	1000
7-The Hawk #6-r	14	28	42	80	115	150
8-Crime on the Run (6/54); Powell-a; Saunders-c	14	28	42	76	108	140
9-Western Bandit Trails #3-r, with new-c; Baker-c/a	45	90	135	284	480	675
10-Dinky Duck (Terrytoons)	9	18	27	47	61	75
11-Fightin' Marines #3-r (8/54); Canteen Kate app; Baker-c/a	58	116	174	371	636	900
12-Northwest Mounties #4-r(8/54); new Baker-c	55	110	165	352	601	850

AQUAMAN (See Adventure Comics #260, Brave & the Bold, DC Comics Presents #5, DC Special #28, DC Special Series #1, DC Super Stars #7, Detective Comics, JLA, Justice League of America, More Fun #73, Showcase #30-33, Super DC Giant, Super Friends, and World's Finest Comics)

AQUAMAN (1st Series)
National Periodical Publications/DC Comics: Jan-Feb, 1962 - No. 56, Mar-Apr, 1971; No. 57, Aug-Sept, 1977 - No. 63, Aug-Sept, 1978

	GD 2.0	VG 4.0	FN 6.0	VF 8.0	VF/NM 9.0	NM- 9.2
1-(1-2/62)-Intro. Quisp	234	468	702	1931	5569	7500
2	38	76	114	281	628	975
3-5	22	44	66	154	340	525
6-10	15	30	45	100	220	340
11-1st app. Mera	114	228	342	912	2056	3200
12-17,19,20	12	24	36	79	170	260
18-Aquaman weds Mera; JLA cameo	14	28	42	122	271	420
21-28,30,32: 23-Birth of Aquababy. 26-Huntress app.(3-4/66). 30-Batman & Superman-c & cameo	8	16	24	55	105	155
29-1st app. Ocean Master, Aquaman's step-brother	44	88	132	326	738	1150
33-1st app. Aqua-Girl (see Adventure #266)	16	32	48	112	249	385
34,36-40: 40-Jim Aparo's 1st DC work (8/68)	7	14	21	46	86	125
35-1st app. Black Manta	71	142	213	568	1284	2000
41,43-46,47,49: 45-Last 12¢-c	6	12	18	38	69	100
42-Black Manta-c	13	26	39	91	201	310
48-Origin reprinted	7	14	21	46	86	125
50-52-Deadman by Neal Adams	8	16	24	56	108	160
53-56('71): 56-1st app. Crusader; last 15¢-c	4	8	12	23	37	50
57-('77) Black Manta-c	3	6	9	17	26	35
58-63: 58-Origin retold	2	4	6	10	14	18
...: Death of a Prince TPB (2011, $29.99) r/#58-63 and Adventure #435,441-455						30.00

NOTE: *Aparo* a-40-45, 46p, 47-59; c-58-63. *Nick Cardy* c-1-40. *Newton* a-60-63.

AQUAMAN (1st Series)
DC Comics: Feb, 1986 - No. 4, May, 1986 (75¢, limited series)

	GD 2.0	VG 4.0	FN 6.0	VF 8.0	VF/NM 9.0	NM- 9.2
1-New costume; 1st app. Nuada of Thierna Na Oge	2	4	6	9	12	15
2-4: 3-Retelling of Aquaman & Ocean Master's origins.						5.00
Special 1 (1988, $1.50, 52 pgs.)						5.00

NOTE: *Craig Hamilton* c/a-1-4p. *Russell* c-2-4i.

AQUAMAN (2nd limited series)
DC Comics: June, 1989 - No. 5, Oct, 1989 ($1.00, limited series)

1-Giffen plots/breakdowns; Swan-a(p) in all	6.00
2-5	4.00
Special 1 (Legend of..., $2.00, 1989, 52 pgs.)-Giffen plots/breakdowns; Swan-a(p)	4.00

AQUAMAN (2nd Series)
DC Comics: Dec, 1991 - No. 13, Dec, 1992 ($1.00/$1.25)

1	5.00
2-5	3.00
6-13: 6-Begin $1.25-c. 9-Sea Devils app.	3.00

AQUAMAN (3rd Series)(Also see Atlantis Chronicles)
DC Comics: Aug, 1994 - No. 75, Jan, 2001 ($1.50/$1.75/$1.95/$1.99/$2.50)

1-(8/94)-Peter David scripts begin; reintro Dolphin	6.00
2-(9/94)-Aquaman loses hand; continues in Aquaman #0	6.50
3-8: 3-(11/94)-Superboy-c/app. 4-Lobo app. 6-Deep Six app.	3.50
9-69: 9-Begin $1.75-c. 10-Green Lantern app. 11-Reintro Mera. 15-Re-intro Kordax. 16-vs. JLA. 18-Reintro Ocean Master & Atlan (Aquaman's father). 19-Reintro Garth (Aqualad). 23-1st app. Deep Blue (Neptune Perkins & Tsunami's daughter). 24-Neptune Perkins, Nuada, Tsunami, Arion, Power Girl, & The Sea Devils app. 26-Final Night. 28-Martian Manhunter-c/app. 29-Black Manta-c/app. 32-Swamp Thing-c/app. 37-Genesis x-over. 41-Maxima-c/app. 43-Millennium Giants x-over; Superman-c/app. 44-G.A. Flash & Sentinel app. 50-Larsen-a begins. 53-Superman app. 60-Tempest marries Dolphin; Teen Titans app. 63-Kaluta covers begin. 66-JLA app.	3.00
70-75: 70-Begin $2.50-c. 71-73-Warlord-c/app. 75-Final issue	3.00
#0-(10/94)-Aquaman replaces lost hand with hook; released between #2 & #3	6.50
#1,000,000 (11/98) 853rd Century x-over	3.00
Annual 1 (1995, $3.50)-Year One story	4.00
Annual 2 (1996, $2.95)-Legends of the Dead Earth story	4.00

Annual 3 (1997, $3.95)-Pulp Heroes story	4.00
Annual 4,5 ('98, ''99, $2.95)-4-Ghosts; Wrightson-c. 5-JLApe	4.00
...Secret Files 1 (12/98, $4.95) Origin-s and pin-ups	5.00

NOTE: *Art Adams*-c, Annual 5. *Mignola* c-6. *Simonson* c-15.

AQUAMAN (4th Series)(Titled Aquaman: Sword of Atlantis #40-on) (Also see JLA #69-75)
DC Comics: Feb, 2003 - No. 57, Dec, 2007 ($2.50/$2.99)

1-Veitch-s/Guichet-a/Maleev-c	4.00
2-14: 2-Martian Manhunter app. 8-11-Black Manta app.	3.00
15-39: 15-San Diego flooded; Pfeifer-s/Davis-c begin. 23,24-Sea Devils app. 33-Mera returns. 39-Black Manta app.	3.00
40-Sword of Atlantis; One Year Later begins ($2.99-c) Guice-a ; two covers	4.00
41-49,51-57: 41-Two covers. 42-Sea Devils app. 44-Ocean Master app.	3.00
50-($3.99) Tempest app.; McManus-a	4.00
...Secret Files 2003 (5/03, $4.95) background on Aquaman's new powers; pin-ups	5.00
...: Once and Future TPB (2006, $12.99) r/#40-45	13.00
...: The Waterbearer TPB (2003, $12.95) r/#1-4, stories from Aquaman Secret Files and JLA/JSA Secret Files #1; JG Jones-c	13.00

AQUAMAN (DC New 52)
DC Comics: Nov, 2011 - No. 52, Jul, 2016 ($2.99/$3.99)

	1	2	3	5	6	8
1-Geoff Johns-s/Ivan Reis-a/c	1	2	3	5	6	8
2-23,24,26-40: 7-13-Black Manta app. 14-17-Throne of Atlantis. 15,16-Justice League app. 24-Story of Atlan. 26-Pelletier-a. 31-Swamp Thing app. 37-Grodd app.						3.00
23.1, 23.2 (11/13, $2.99, regular covers)						3.00
23.1 (11/13, $3.99, 3-D cover) "Black Manta #1" on cover; Crime Syndicate app.						5.00
23.2 (11/13, $3.99, 3-D cover) "Ocean Master #1" on cover; Crime Syndicate app.						5.00
25-($3.99) "Death of a King" finale; last Johns-s						4.00
41-49,51,52: 41-($3.99-c begin)						5.00
50-($3.99) Booth-a						5.00
#0 (11/12, $2.99) Aquaman & Vulko's return to Atlantis; Johns-s/Reis-a/c						3.00
Annual 1 (12/13, $4.99) The Others app.; Pelletier-c/Ostrander-s						5.00
Annual 2 (9/14, $4.99) Wonder Woman app.; Parker-s/Guichet-a						5.00
...: Futures End 1 (11/14, $2.99, regular-c) Five years later; Jurgens-s						3.00
...: Futures End 1 (11/14, $3.99, 3-D cover)						4.00

AQUAMAN (DC Rebirth) (Also see Mera: Queen of Atlantis)
DC Comics: Aug, 2016 - No. 66, Feb, 2021 ($2.99/$3.99)

1-24: 1-Abnett-s/Walker-a; Black Manta app. 5,6-Superman app. 14,15-Black Manta app.	3.00
25-49-($3.99) 25-Sejic-a; leads into Justice League #24. 34-Kelley Jones-a. 39-X-over with Suicide Squad #45,46. 41,42-Drowned Earth. 43-DeConnick-a begins	4.00
50-($4.99) Black Manta returns; Wonder Woman app.	5.00
51-66: 51-54-Year of The Villain tie-ins; Black Manta app. 54-Acetate-c. 57-Princess Andy born. 57-61-Ocean Master app. 62,63-Black Manta app. 66-Endless Winter pt. 4	4.00
Annual 1 (1/18, $4.99) Fiumara-a; future Aquaman & Mera with son Tom	5.00
Annual 2 (12/19, $4.99) Year of the Villain tie-in; Aqualad app.; Ibáñez-a	5.00
... and the Lost Kingdom Special 1 (12/23, $6.99) Tie-in/prelude to the 2013 movie	7.00
.../ Jabberjaw Special 1 (7/18, $4.99) Abnett-s/Pelletier-a; back-up Capt. Caveman story	5.00
.../ Justice League: Drowned Earth Special 1 (1/19, $4.99) Leads into #43; Manapul-a	5.00
...: Rebirth (8/16, $2.99) Abnett-s/Eaton & Jiménez-a; Black Manta app.	3.00

AQUAMAN: ANDROMEDA
DC Comics (Black Label): Aug, 2022 - No. 3, Dec, 2022 ($6.99, oversized 8-1/2" x 10-3/4")

1-3-Ram V-s/Christian Ward-a; Black Manta app.	7.00

AQUAMAN & THE FLASH: VOIDSONG
DC Comics: Aug, 2022 - No. 3, Oct, 2022 ($6.99, squarebound, limited series)

1-3-Kelly & Lanzing-s/Georgiev-a	7.00

AQUAMAN AND THE OTHERS (DC New 52)
DC Comics: Jun, 2014 - No. 11, May, 2015 ($2.99)

1-11: 1-Jurgens-s/Medina-a	3.00
...: Futures End 1 (11/14, $2.99, regular-c) Five years later; Cont'd from Aquaman: FE #1	3.00
...: Futures End 1 (11/14, $3.99, 3-D cover)	4.00

AQUAMAN 80TH ANNIVERSARY 100-PAGE SUPER SPECTACULAR
DC Comics: Oct, 2021 ($9.99, squarebound, one-shot)

1-Short stories & pin-ups by various; Black Manta & Aqualad app.; multiple covers	10.00

AQUAMAN GIANT
DC Comics: 2019 - No. 4, 2020 ($4.99, 100 pgs., squarebound, Mass Market & Direct Market editions exist for each issue, with different covers)

1-4-Two new stories and reprints in each. 1-Black Manta app. 2-Sea Devils app.	5.00

AQUAMAN / GREEN ARROW - DEEP TARGET
DC Comics: Dec, 2021 - No. 7, Jun, 2022 ($3.99, limited series)

1-7-Thomas-s/Cliquet-a; Arthur Curry & Oliver Queen switch lives	4.00

AQUAMAN: THE BECOMING (Leads into Aquamen #1)

	GD	VG	FN	VF	VF/NM	NM-
	2.0	4.0	6.0	8.0	9.0	9.2

DC Comics: Nov, 2021 - No. 6, Apr, 2022 ($3.99, limited series)
1-6-Spotlight on Aqualad Jackson Hyde. 3-Intro. Delilah ... 4.00

AQUAMAN: TIME & TIDE (3rd limited series) (Also see Atlantis Chronicles)
DC Comics: Dec, 1993 - No. 4, Mar, 1994 ($1.50, limited series)
1-4: Peter David scripts; origin retold. ... 4.00
Trade paperback ($9.95) ... 10.00

AQUAMEN (Follows Aquaman: The Becoming)
DC Comics: Feb, 2022 - No. 6, Sept, 2022 ($3.99, limited series)
1-6-Aquaman, Aqualad Jackson Hyde and Black Manta app. 3,4-Batwoman app. ... 4.00

AQUANAUTS (TV)
Dell Publishing Co.: May - July, 1961

	GD	VG	FN	VF	VF/NM	NM-
Four Color 1197-Photo-c	8	16	24	55	105	155

ARABIAN NIGHTS (See Cinema Comics Herald)

ARACHNOPHOBIA (Movie)
Hollywood Comics (Disney Comics): 1990 ($5.95, 68 pg. graphic novel)
nn-Adaptation of film; Spiegle-a ... 6.00
Comic edition ($2.95, 68 pgs.) ... 4.00

ARAK/SON OF THUNDER (See Warlord #48)
DC Comics: Sept, 1981 - No. 50, Nov, 1985
1,24,50: 1-1st app. Angelica, Princess of White Cathay. 24,50-(52 pgs.) ... 4.00
2-23,25-49: 3-Intro Valda. 12-Origin Valda. 20-Origin Angelica ... 3.00
Annual 1(10/84) ... 4.00

ARAÑA THE HEART OF THE SPIDER (See Amazing Fantasy (2004) #1-6)
Marvel Comics: March, 2005 - No. 12, Feb, 2006 ($2.99)
1-12: 1-Avery-s/Cruz-a. 5-Spider-Man-c/app. ... 3.00
Vol. 1: Heart of the Spider (2005, $7.99, digest) r/Amazing Fantasy (2004) #1-6 ... 8.00
Vol. 2: In the Beginning (2005, $7.99, digest) r/#1-6 ... 8.00
Vol. 3: Night of the Hunter (2006, $7.99, digest) r/#7-12 ... 8.00

A.R.C.
Image Comics: Mar, 2023 ($4.99, one-shot)
1-Hawkins, Cady and Feinstein-s/Rojo-a ... 5.00

ARCADIA
BOOM! Studios: May, 2015 - No. 8, Feb, 2016 ($3.99)
1-8-Paknadel-s/Pfeiffer-a ... 3.00

ARCANA (Also see Books of Magic limited & ongoing series and Mister E)
DC Comics (Vertigo): 1994 ($3.95, 68 pgs., annual)
1-Bolton painted-c; Children's Crusade/Tim Hunter story ... 4.00

ARCANUM
Image Comics (Top Cow Productions): Apr, 1997 - No. 8, Feb, 1998 ($2.50)
1/2 Gold Edition ... 12.00
1-Brandon Peterson-s/a(p), 1-Variant-c, 4-American Ent. Ed. ... 4.00
2-8 ... 3.00
3-Variant-c ... 4.00
....: Millennium's End TPB (2005, $16.99) r/#1-8 & #1/2; cover gallery and sketch pages ... 17.00

ARCHANGEL (See Uncanny X-Men, X-Factor & X-Men)
Marvel Comics: Feb, 1996 ($2.50, B&W, one-shot)
1-Milligan story ... 4.00

ARCHANGEL 8
AWA Studios: Mar, 2020 - No. 5, Sept, 2020 ($3.99, limited series)
1-5-Michael Moreci-s/C.P. Smith-a ... 4.00

ARCHARD'S AGENTS (See Ruse)
CrossGeneration Comics: Jan, 2003; Nov, 2003; Apr, 2004 ($2.95)
1-Dixon-s/Perkins-a ... 3.00
...: The Case of the Puzzled Pugilist (11/03) Dixon-s/Perkins-a ... 3.00
Vol. 3 - Deadly Dare (4/04) Dixon-s/McNiven-a; preview of Lady Death: The Wild Hunt ... 3.00

ARCHENEMIES
Dark Horse Comics: Apr, 2006 - No. 4, July, 2006 ($2.99, limited series)
1-4-Melbourne-s/Guichet-a ... 3.00

ARCHER & ARMSTRONG
Valiant: July (June inside), 1992 - No. 26, Oct, 1994 ($2.50)

	GD	VG	FN	VF	VF/NM	NM-
0-(7/92)-B. Smith-c/a; Reese-i assists	2	4	6	8	10	12
0-(with Gold Valiant Logo)	6	12	18	41	76	110

1,2: 1-(8/92)-Origin & 1st app. Archer; Miller-c; B. Smith/Layton-a. 2-2nd app. Turok (c/story); Smith/Layton-a; Simonson-c ... 5.00
3-7: 3,4-Smith-c&a(p) & scripts ... 4.00
8-($4.50, 52 pgs.)-Combined with Eternal Warrior #8; B. Smith-c/a & scripts; 1st app. Ivar the Time Walker ... 5.00
9-26: 10-2nd app. Ivar. 10,11-B. Smith-c. 21,22-Shadowman app. 22-w/bound-in trading card. 25-Eternal Warrior app. 26-Flip book w/Eternal Warrior #26 ... 3.00
...: First Impressions HC (2008, $24.95) recolored reprints #0-6; new "Formation of the Sect" story by Jim Shooter and Sal Velutto; Shooter commentary; new cover by Golden ... 25.00

ARCHER & ARMSTRONG
Valiant Entertainment: Aug, 2012 - No. 25, Oct, 2014 ($3.99)
1-24: 1-Van Lente-s/Henry-a; two covers; origin. 5-8-Eternal Warrior app. ... 4.00
1,4-8-Pullbox variants: 1-Clayton Henry. 4-Juan Doe. 7,8-Emanuela Lupacchino ... 4.00
1-Variant-c by David Aja ... 10.00
1-Variant-c by Neal Adams ... 28.00
25-($4.99) Van Lente-s/Henry-a; back-up short stories by various; cover gallery ... 5.00
#0-(5/13, $3.99) Van Lente-s/Henry-a ... 4.00
...Archer #0-(2/14, $3.99) Van Lente-s/Pere Pérez-a; childhood origin ... 4.00
...: The One Percent #1 (11/14, $3.99) Fawkes-s/Eisma-a/Juan Doe-c ... 4.00

ARCHER & ARMSTRONG FOREVER
Valiant Entertainment: May, 2022 - Present ($3.99)
1-4: 1-Steve Foxe-s/Marcio Fiorito-a ... 4.00

ARCHIE (See Archie Comics) (Also see Afterlife With..., Christmas & Archie, Everything's..., Explorers of the

---

Unknown, Jackpot, Life With..., Little..., Oxydol-Dreft, Pep, Riverdale High, Teenage Mutant Ninja Turtles Adventures & To Riverdale and Back Again)

ARCHIE
Archie Comic Publs.: Sept, 2015 - No. 32, Sept, 2018; No. 699, Nov, 2018 - Present ($3.99)
1-32-Mark Waid-s; multiple covers on all; back-up classic reprints. 1-3-Fiona Staples-a. 4-Annie Wu-a. 5-10-Veronica Fish-a. 13-Re-intro. Cheryl Blossom; back-up r/1st app. from B&V #320. 13-17-Eisma-a. 18-22-Pete Woods-a. 23-32-Audrey Mok-a ... 4.00
699-(11/18, $1.00) Recaps of events from #1-32; preview of #700; Sauvage-c ... 5.00
700-711 700-704-($3.99) Spencer-s/Sauvage-a; Sabrina app. 705-709-"Archie and Sabrina" on cover. 710-713-"Archie and Katy Keene" on cover ... 4.00
... Collector's Edition (2/16, $9.99) r/#1-3 with creator intros and variant cover gallery ... 10.00
FCBD Edition (2016, giveaway) #1; Staples-c; back-up Jughead story ... 4.00

ARCHIE ALL CANADIAN DIGEST
Archie Publications: Aug, 1996 ($1.75, 96 pgs.)

1		2	4	6	8	10	12

ARCHIE AMERICANA SERIES, BEST OF THE FORTIES
Archie Publications: 1991, 2002 ($10.95, trade paperback)
Vol. 1,2-r/early strips from 1940s 1-Intro. by Steven King. 2-Intro. by Paul Castiglia ... 12.00

ARCHIE AMERICANA SERIES, BEST OF THE FIFTIES
Archie Publications: 1991 ($8.95, trade paperback)
Vol. 2-r/strips from 1950's ... 12.00
2nd printing (1998, $9.95) ... 12.00
Book 2 (2003, $10.95) ... 12.00

ARCHIE AMERICANA SERIES, BEST OF THE SIXTIES
Archie Publications: 1995 ($9.95, trade paperback)
Vol. 3-r/strips from 1960s; intro. by Frankie Avalon ... 12.00

ARCHIE AMERICANA SERIES, BEST OF THE SEVENTIES
Archie Publications: 1997, 2008 ($9.95/$10.95, trade paperback)
Vol. 4 (1997, $9.95)-r/strips from 1970s ... 12.00
Vol. 8 Book 2 (2008, $10.95)-r/other strips from 1970s ... 12.00

ARCHIE AMERICANA SERIES, BEST OF THE EIGHTIES
Archie Publications: 2001 ($10.95, trade paperback)
Vol. 5-r/strips from 1980s; foreward by Steve Geppi ... 12.00

ARCHIE AMERICANA SERIES, BEST OF THE '90S
Archie Publications: 2008 ($11.95, trade paperback)
Vol. 9-r/strips from 1990s; new Lindsey cover ... 12.00

ARCHIE AND BIG ETHEL
Spire Christian Comics (Fleming H. Revell Co.): 1982 (69¢)

nn-(Low print run)		3	6	9	14	19	24

ARCHIE & FRIENDS
Archie Comics: Dec, 1992 - No. 159, Feb, 2012 ($1.25-$2.99)
1 ... 6.00
2,4,10-14,17,18,20-Sabrina app. 20-Archie's Band-c ... 4.00
3,5-9,16 ... 3.00
15-Babewatch-s with Sabrina app. ... 6.00
19-Josie and the Pussycats app.; E.T. parody-c/s ... 5.00
21-46 ... 3.00
47-All Josie and the Pussycats issue; movie and actress profiles/photos ... 4.00
48-142: 48-56,58,60,96-Josie and the Pussycats-c/s. 79-Cheryl Blossom returns. 100-The Veronicas-c/app. 101-Katy Keene begins. 129-Begin $2.50. 130,131-Josie and the Pussycats. 137-Cosmo, Super Duck, Pat the Brat and other old characters app. ... 3.00
143-159: 143-Begin $2.99-c. 146-Archie Babies-s. 145-Jersey Shore spoof. 146,147-Twilite. 154-Little Archie ... 3.00

ARCHIE & FRIENDS (Classic-style reprints with new lead story)
Archie Publications: Apr, 2019 - Present ($2.99, quarterly)
...: Music #1; ...: Beach Party #1 (#2), ...: Back to School #1 (#3), ...: Travel #1 (#4), ...: Winter Wonderland #1 (#5), ...: Geeks and Games #1 (#6), ... Endless Summer #1 (#7), ...: Fall Festival #1 (#8), ...: Guide to Dating #1 (#9), ...: Superheroes #1 (#10), ...: Summer Vacation (#11), ...: Christmas Calamity #1 (#12), ...: Summer Lovin' #1 (#13), ...: Thrills and Chills #1 (#14), ...: All-Action #1 (#15), (#16)(Hot Summer Movies) ... 3.00

ARCHIE & FRIENDS DOUBLE DIGEST MAGAZINE
Archie Comics: Feb, 2011 - No. 33, Jan, 2014 ($3.99, digest-size)
1-32: 1-Staton-a. 7-13-SuperTeens app. ... 4.00
33-($5.99, 320 pages) Double Double Digest ... 6.00

ARCHIE AND ME (See Archie Giant Series Mag. #578, 591, 603, 616, 626)
Archie Publications: Oct, 1964 - No. 2, Aug, 1965 - No. 161, Feb, 1987

	GD	VG	FN	VF	VF/NM	NM-
1	24	48	72	168	372	575
2-(8/65)	10	20	30	67	141	215
3-5: 3-(12/65)	6	12	18	41	76	110
6-10: 6-(8/66)	5	10	15	30	50	70
11-20: 11-(4/68)	3	6	9	21	33	45
21(6/68)-26,28-30: 21-UFO story. 26-X-Mas-c	3	6	9	16	24	32
27-Groovyman & Knowman superhero-s; UFO-sty	3	6	9	19	30	40
31-42: 37-Japan Expo '70-c/s	3	6	9	14	19	24
43-48,50-63-(All Giants): 43-(8/71) Mummy-s. 44-Mermaid-s. 62-Elvis cameo-c.						
63-(2/74)	3	6	9	15	22	28
49-(Giant) Josie & the Pussycats-c/app.	4	8	12	22	35	48
64-66,68-99-(Regular size): 85-Bicentennial-s. 98-Collectors Comics						
	2	4	6	8	10	12
67-Sabrina app.(8/74)	2	4	6	10	14	18
100-(4/78)	2	4	6	8	11	14
101-120: 107-UFO-s	1	2	3	5	6	8
121(8/80)-159: 134-Riverdale 2001						6.00
160,161: 160-Origin Mr. Weatherbee; Caveman Archie gang story. 161-Last issue						
	1	3	4	6	8	10

ARCHIE & ME COMICS DIGEST
Archie Comics: Dec, 2017 - No. 23, Jan, 2020 ($6.99/$7.99, digest-size)
1-20-Reprints include Archie Babies in early issues ... 7.00
21-23-($7.99) ... 8.00

Archer & Armstrong (2014 series) #23 © VAL

Archie (2015 series) #25 © ACP

Archie Comics #23 © ACP

	GD	VG	FN	VF	VF/NM	NM-
	2.0	4.0	6.0	8.0	9.0	9.2

ARCHIE AND MR. WEATHERBEE
Spire Christian Comics (Fleming H. Revell Co.): 1980 (59¢)

nn - (Low print run)	3	6	9	14	19	24

ARCHIE...ARCHIE ANDREWS, WHERE ARE YOU? (...Comics Digest #9, 10;
...Comics Digest Mag. No. 11 on)
Archie Publications: Feb, 1977 - No. 114, May, 1998 (Digest size, 160-128 pgs., quarterly)

1	3	6	9	19	30	40
2,3,5,7-9-N. Adams-a; 8-r-/origin The Fly by S&K. 9-Steel Sterling-r						
	2	4	6	10	14	18
4,6,10 ($1.00/$1.50)	2	4	6	8	11	14
11-20: 17-Katy Keene story	2	4	6	8	9	10
21-50,100	1	2	3	5	6	8
51-70						4.00
71-99,101-114: 113-Begin $1.95-c						3.00

ARCHIE AS PUREHEART THE POWERFUL (Also see Archie Giant Series #142, Jughead as
Captain Hero, Life With Archie & Little Archie)
Archie Publications (Radio Comics): Sept, 1966 - No. 6, Nov, 1967

1-Super hero parody	13	26	39	86	188	290
2	8	16	24	51	96	140
3-6	6	12	18	42	79	115

NOTE: Evilheart cameos in all. Title: Archie As Pureheart the Powerful #1-3; ...As Capt. Pureheart-#4-6.

ARCHIE AT RIVERDALE HIGH (See Archie Giant Series Magazine #573, 586, 604 &
Riverdale High)
Archie Publications: Aug, 1972 - No. 113, Feb, 1987

1	9	18	27	59	117	175
2	5	10	15	21	53	75
3-5	3	6	9	16	23	30
6-10	2	4	6	11	16	20
11-30	2	4	6	8	10	12
31(12/75)-46,48-50(12/77)	1	3	4	6	8	10
47-Archie in drag-s; Betty mud wrestling-s	2	4	6	11	16	20
51-80,100 (12/84)	1	2	3	5	6	8
81(8/81)-88, 91,93-95,98						6.00
89,90-Early Cheryl Blossom app. 90-Archies Band app.						
	3	6	9	15	22	28
92,96,97,99-Cheryl Blossom app. 96-Anti-smoking issue						
	2	4	6	13	18	22
101,102,104-109,111,112: 102-Ghost-c						6.00
103-Archie dates Cheryl Blossom-s	2	4	6	13	18	22
110,113: 110-Godzilla-s. 113-Last issue	1	2	3	5	6	8

ARCHIE CHRISTMAS SPECTACULAR
Archie Comics: Feb, 2018; Feb, 2019; Feb, 2020; Feb, 2021; Jan, 2022; Jan, 2023; Jan, 2024
($2.99)

1, nn (2019), nn (2020), nn (2021); 1 (2022), 1 (2023), 1 (2024)-New story with reprints						4.00

ARCHIE COMICS (See Pep Comics #22 [12/41] for Archie's debut) (1st Teen-age comic;
Radio show first aired 6/2/45 by NBC)
MLJ Magazines No. 1-19/Archie Publ. No. 20 on: Winter, 1942-43 - No. 19, 3-4/46; No. 20,
5-6/46 - No. 666, Jul, 2015

1 (Scarce)-Jughead, Veronica app.; 1st app. Mrs. Andrews						
	15,150	30,300	53,025	106,000	170,500	235,000
2 (Scarce)	2050	4100	6150	15,400	25,700	35,000
3 (60 pgs.)(scarce)	1000	2000	3000	7500	13,500	19,500
4-Article about Archie radio series	595	1190	1785	4350	7675	11,000
5-Halloween-c	497	994	1491	3628	6414	9200
6-Christmas-c	383	766	1149	2681	4691	6700
7-1st definitive love triangle story	411	822	1233	2877	5039	7200
8-10: 9-1st Miss Grundy cover	326	652	978	2282	3991	5700
11-15: 15-Dotty & Ditto by Woggon	187	374	561	1197	2049	2900
16-20: 15,17,18-Dotty & Ditto by Woggon. 16,19-Woggon-a. 18-Halloween pumpkin-c.						
	155	310	465	992	1696	2400
21-30: 23-Betty & Veronica by Woggon. 25-Woggon-a. 30-Coach Piffle app., a Coach Kleats						
prototype. 34-Pre-Dilton try-out (named Dilbert)	97	194	291	621	1061	1500
31-40	58	116	174	371	636	900
41-49	48	96	144	302	514	725
50-Classic Montana Betty headlight-c (5-6/51)	514	1028	1542	3750	6625	9500
51-60	20	40	60	140	310	480
61-70 (1954): 65-70, Katy Keene app.	17	34	51	117	259	400
71-80: 72-74-Katy Keene app.	14	28	42	94	207	320
81-93,95-99	10	20	30	64	132	200
94-1st Coach Kleats in this title (see Pep #24)	13	26	39	90	198	300
100	17	34	51	117	259	400
101-Headlight-c	10	20	30	69	147	225

102-122,126,128-130 (1962)	7	14	21	44	82	120
123-125,127-Horror/SF covers. 123-UFO-c/s	12	24	36	83	182	280
131,132,134-157,159,160: 137-1st Caveman Archie gang story. 159-James Bond on cover						
	5	10	15	30	50	70
133 (12/62)-1st app. Cricket O'Dell	7	14	21	46	86	125
158-Archie in drag story	7	14	21	46	86	125
161(2/66)-184,186-188,190-195,197-199: 168-Superhero gag-c. 176,178-Twiggy-c						
	3	6	9	19	30	40
183-Caveman Archie gang story						
185-1st "The Archies" Band story	4	8	12	28	47	65
189 (3/69)-Archie's band meets Don Kirshner who developed the Monkees						
	4	8	12	23	37	50
196 (12/69)-Early Cricket O'Dell app.	4	8	12	23	37	50
200 (6/70)	3	6	9	21	33	45
201-230(11/73): 213-Sabrina/Josie-c cameos. 229-Lost Child issue						
	3	6	9	14	19	24
231-260(3/77): 253-Tarzan parody	2	4	6	8	11	14
261-270,272-282, 284-299	1	3	4	6	8	10
271-Pearl necklace cover	15	30	45	103	227	350
283(8/79)-Cover/story plugs "International Children's Appeal" which was a fraudulent charity,						
according to TV's 20/20 news program broadcast July 20, 1979						
	2	4	6	8	10	12
300(1/81)-Anniversary issue	2	4	6	8	11	14
301-321,323-325,327-335,337-350: 323-Cheryl Blossom pin-up. 325-Cheryl Blossom app.						6.00
322-E.T. story	1	2	3	5	6	8
326-Early Cheryl Blossom story	4	8	12	11	16	20
336-Michael Jackson/Boy George parody	2	4	6	10	14	18
351-399: 356-Calgary Olympics Special. 393-Infinity-c; 1st comic book printed on recycled						
paper						5.00
400 (6/92)-Shows 1st meeting of Little Archie and Veronica						6.00
401-428						4.00
429-Love Showdown part 1						5.00
430-599: 467- "A Storm Over Uniforms" x-over parts 3,4. 538-Comic-Con issue						3.00
600-602: 600-10/09) Archie proposes to Veronica. 601-Marries Veronica. 602-Twins born						4.00
603-605: 603-(1/10) Archie proposes to Betty. 604-Marries Betty. 605-Twins born						4.00
606-615,618-626: 609-Begin $2.99-c. 610-613-Man From RIVERDALE. 625-70th Anniversary.						
626-Michael Strahan app.						3.00
616,617-Obama & Palin app.; two covers on each						4.00
627-630-Archie Meets KISS; 2 covers on each by Parent & Francavilla						4.00
631-658: 632-634-Archie marries Valerie from the Pussycats. 635-Jill Thompson var-c.						
636-Gender swap. 641-644-Crossover with Glee; 2 covers. 648-Simonson var-c.						
655-Cosmo the Merry Martian app. 656-Intro. Harper Lodge						3.00
650-Variant "Battle of the Bands" cover by Fiona Staples						5.00
659-665-($3.99) Two covers on each. 664-Game of Thrones parody. 665-Harper app.						4.00
666-Last issue; 6 interlocking covers with vintage title logos (Archie Comics, Blue Ribbon						
Comics, Top-Notch Comics, Pep Comics, Zip Comics, and Jackpot Comics)						4.00
Annual 1 ('50)-116 pgs. (Scarce)	325	650	975	2100	4400	6700
Annual 2 ('51)	124	248	372	790	1595	2400
Annual 3 ('52)	71	142	213	450	875	1300
Annual 4,5 (1953-54)	60	120	180	380	690	1000
Annual 6-10 (1955-59): 8,9-(100 pgs.). 10-(84 pgs.) Elvis record on-c						
	20	40	60	138	307	475
Annual 11-15 (1960-65): 12,13-(84 pgs.). 14,15-(68 pgs.)						
	11	22	33	73	157	240
Annual 16-20 (1966-70)(all 68 pgs.): 20-Archie's band-c						
	7	14	21	46	86	125
Annual 21,22,24-26 (1971-75): 21,22-(68 pgs.). 22-Archie's band-s.						
24-26-(52 pgs.). 25-Cavemen-s	4	8	12	25	40	55
Annual 23-Archie's band-c/s; Josie/Sabrina-c	5	10	15	31	53	75
Annual Digest 27 ('75)	4	8	12	25	40	55
...28-30	3	6	9	14	20	25
...31-34	2	4	6	9	13	16
...35-40 (...Magazine #35 on)	1	3	4	6	8	10
...41-65 ('94)						5.00
...66-69						3.00
...All-Star Specials (Winter '75, $1.25)-6 remaindered Archie comics rebound in each; titles:						
"The World of Giant Comics", "Giant Grab Bag of Comics", "Triple Giant Comics" &						
"Giant Spec. Comics	6	12	18	38	67	100

NOTE: Archies Band-s-185, 188-192, 197, 198, 201, 204, 205, 208, 209, 215, 329, 330; Band-c-191, 330. Cavemen
Archie Gang-s-183, 192, 197, 208, 210, 220, 223, 282, 333, 335, 338, 340. Al Fagly c-17-35. Bob Montana c-38,
41-50, 58, Annual 1-4. Bill Woggon c-53, 54.

ARCHIE COMICS DIGEST (...Magazine No. 37-95)
Archie Publications: Aug, 1973 - No. 267, Nov, 2010 (Digest-size, 160-128 pgs.)

1-1st Archie digest	11	22	33	76	163	250
2	5	10	15	35	63	90
3-5	4	8	12	23	37	50

	GD 2.0	VG 4.0	FN 6.0	VF 8.0	VF/NM 9.0	NM- 9.2

	GD 2.0	VG 4.0	FN 6.0	VF 8.0	VF/NM 9.0	NM- 9.2
6-10	3	6	9	16	23	30
11-33: 32,33-The Fly-r by S&K	2	4	6	10	14	18
34-60	1	3	4	6	8	10
61-80,100	1	2	3	5	6	8
81-99						5.00
101-140: 36-Katy Keene story						4.00
141-165						3.00
166-235,237-267: 194-Begin $2.39-c. 225-Begin $2.49-c						3.00
236-65th Anniversary issue, r/1st app. in Pep #22 and entire Archie Comics #1 (1942)						5.00

NOTE: **Neal Adams** a-1, 2, 4, 5, 19-21, 24, 25, 27, 29, 31, 33. X-mas c-88, 94, 100, 106.

ARCHIE COMICS DIGEST (Continues from Archie's Double Digest #252)
Archie Publications: No. 253, Sept, 2014 - Present ($4.99-$9.99, digest-size)

	NM- 9.2
253,254,257-259,261,262,264,267,269,270,272,273,275,277,279,281-($4.99)	5.00
255,260,266,274,276,282,283,285-300-($6.99) Titled Archie Jumbo Comics Digest	7.00
256,263,265,268,271,278,280,284-($5.99): 256,263,268,278-Titled Archie Comics Annual	6.00
302-325-($7.99)	8.00
326-336-($8.99)	9.00
337-348-($9.99)	10.00

ARCHIE COMICS (Free Comic Book Day editions) (Also see Pep Comics)
Archie Publications: 2003 - Present

	NM- 9.2
Free Comic Book Day Edition 1,2: 1-(7/03). 2-(9/04)	3.00
Little Archie "The Legend of the Lost Lagoon" FCBD Edition (5/07) Bolling-s/a	3.00
Past, Present & Future Fun! (8/21) FCBD giveaway; 80th Anniversary celebration	3.00
Presents the Mighty Archie Art Players ('09) Free Comic Book Day giveaway	3.00
's 65th Anniversary Bash ('06) Free Comic Book Day giveaway	3.00
's Summer Splash FCBD Edition (5/10) Parent-a; Cheryl Blossom app.	3.00

ARCHIE COMICS PRESENTS: THE LOVE SHOWDOWN COLLECTION
Archie Publications: 1994 ($4.95, squarebound)

	GD 2.0	VG 4.0	FN 6.0	VF 8.0	VF/NM 9.0	NM- 9.2
nn-r/Archie #429, Betty #19, Betty & Veronica #82, & Veronica #39	1	3	4	6	8	10

ARCHIE COMICS SUPER SPECIAL
Archie Publications: Dec, 2012 - No. 7, Jan, 2017 ($9.99, squarebound magazine-sized, quarterly)

	NM- 9.2
1-7: 1-Christmas themed. 2-Valentine's themed	10.00

ARCHIE DIGEST (Free Comic Book Day edition)
Archie Comic Publications: June/July 2014 (digest-size giveaway)

	NM- 9.2
1-Reprints; Parent-c	3.00

ARCHIE DOUBLE DIGEST (See Archie's Double Digest Quarterly Magazine)

ARCHIE 80TH ANNIVERSARY: EVERYTHING'S ARCHIE
Archie Comic Publications: Aug, 2021 (one-shot)

	NM- 9.2
1-New story & reprints; includes r/Betty #46 (from 1997, Betty in 2021 AD with virtual school classes over video monitors)	4.00

ARCHIE 80TH ANNIVERSARY JUMBO COMICS DIGEST
Archie Comic Publications: Mar, 2021 - No. 5, Jan, 2022 ($7.99, digest-size)

	NM- 9.2
1-5: 1-Reprints from all eras including Archie's debut in Pep Comics #22	8.00

ARCHIE GETS A JOB
Spire Christian Comics (Fleming H. Revell Co.): 1977

	GD 2.0	VG 4.0	FN 6.0	VF 8.0	VF/NM 9.0	NM- 9.2
nn	3	6	9	14	20	26

ARCHIE GIANT SERIES MAGAZINE
Archie Publications: 1954 - No. 632, July, 1992 (No #36-135, no #252-451)
(#1 not code approved) (#1-233 are Giants; #12-184 are 68 pgs.,#185-194,197-233 are 52 pgs.; #195,196 are 84 pgs.; #234-up are 36 pgs.)

	GD 2.0	VG 4.0	FN 6.0	VF 8.0	VF/NM 9.0	NM- 9.2
1-Archie's Christmas Stocking	200	400	600	1280	2190	3100
2-Archie's Christmas Stocking ('55)	97	194	291	621	1061	1500
3-6-Archie's Christmas Stocking ('56- '59)	60	120	180	381	653	925
7-10: 7-Katy Keene Holiday Fun (9/60); Bill Woggon-c. 8-Betty & Veronica Summer Fun (10/60); baseball story w/Babe Ruth & Lou Gehrig. 9-The World of Jughead (12/60); Neal Adams-a. 10-Archie's Christmas Stocking(1/61)	41	82	123	256	428	600
11,13,16,18: 11-Betty & Veronica Spectacular (6/61). 13-Betty & Veronica Summer Fun (10/61). 16-Betty & Veronica Spectacular (6/62). 18-Betty & Veronica Summer Fun (10/62)	60	90	177	289	400	
12,14,15,17,19,20: 12-Katy Keene Holiday Fun (9/61). 14-The World of Jughead (12/61); Vampire-s. 15-Archie's Christmas Stocking (1/62). 17-Archie's Jokes (8/62); Katy Keene app. 19-The World of Jughead (12/62). 20-Archie's Christmas Stocking (1/63)	20	40	60	114	195	270
21,23,28: 21-Betty & Veronica Spectacular (6/63). 23-Betty & Veronica Summer Fun (10/63). 28-Betty & Veronica Summer Fun (9/64)	10	20	30	66	138	210
22,24,25,27,29,30: 22-Archie's Jokes (9/63). 24-The World of Jughead (12/63). 25-Archie's Christmas Stocking (1/64). 27-Archie's Jokes (8/64). 29-Around the World with Archie (10/64); Doris Day-s. 30-The World of Jughead (12/64)	8	16	24	56	108	160
26-Betty & Veronica Spectacular (6/64); all pin-ups; DeCarlo-c/a	10	20	30	67	141	215
31,33-35: 31-Archie's Christmas Stocking (1/65). 33-Archie's Jokes (8/65). 34-Betty & Veronica Summer Fun (9/65). 35-Around the World with Archie (10/65).	6	12	18	41	76	110
32-Betty & Veronica Spectacular (6/65); all pin-ups; DeCarlo-c/a	9	18	27	60	120	180

36-135-Do not exist

	GD 2.0	VG 4.0	FN 6.0	VF 8.0	VF/NM 9.0	NM- 9.2
136-141: 136-The World of Jughead (12/65). 137-Archie's Christmas Stocking (1/66). 138-Betty & Veronica Spect. (6/66). 139-Archie's Jokes (6/66). 140-Betty & Veronica Summer Fun (8/66). 141-Around the World with Archie (9/66)	6	12	18	41	76	110
142-Archie's Super-Hero Special (10/66)-Origin Capt. Pureheart, Capt. Hero, and Evilheart	9	18	27	51	111	165
143-The World of Jughead (12/66); Capt. Hero-c/s; Man From R.I.V.E.R.D.A.L.E., Pureheart, Superteen app.	6	12	18	41	76	110
144-160: 144-Archie's Christmas Stocking (1/67). 145-Betty & Veronica Spectacular (6/67). 146-Archie's Jokes (6/67). 147-Betty & Veronica Summer Fun (8/67) 148-World of Archie (9/67). 149-World of Jughead (10/67). 150-Archie's Christmas Stocking (1/68). 151-World of Archie (2/68). 152-World of Jughead (2/68). 153-Betty & Veronica Spectacular (6/68). 154-Archie Jokes (6/68). 155-Betty & Veronica Summer Fun (8/68). 156-World of Archie (10/68). 157-World of Jughead (12/68). Archie's Christmas Stocking (1/69).						

	GD 2.0	VG 4.0	FN 6.0	VF 8.0	VF/NM 9.0	NM- 9.2
159-Betty & Veronica Christmas Spectacular (1/69). 160-World of Archie (2/69); Frankenstein-s	each	4	8	12	25	40	55
161-World of Jughead (2/69); Super-Jughead-s; 11 pg. early Cricket O'Dell-s	4	8	12	27	44	60
162-183: 162-Betty & Veronica Spectacular (6/69). 163-Archie's Jokes(8/69). 164-Betty & Veronica Summer Fun (9/69). 165-World of Archie (9/69). 166-World of Jughead (9/69). 167-Archie's Christmas Stocking (1/70). 168-Betty & Veronica Christmas Spect. (1/70). 169-Archie's Christmas Love-In (1/70). 170-Jughead's Eat-Out Comic Book Mag. (12/69). 171-World of Archie (2/70). 172-World of Jughead (2/70). 173-Betty & Veronica Spectacular (6/70). 174-Archie's Jokes (8/70). 175-Betty & Veronica Summer Fun (9/70). 176-Li'l Jinx Giant Laugh-Out (8/70). 177-World of Archie (9/70). 178-World of Jughead (9/70). 179-Archie's Christmas Stocking(1/71). 180-Betty & Veronica Christmas Spect. (1/71). 181-Archie's Christmas Love-In (1/71). 182-World of Archie (2/71). 183-World of Jughead (2/71)-Last squarebound	each	3	6	9	19	30	40
184-189,193,194,197-199 (52 pgs.): 184-Betty & Veronica Spectacular (6/71). 185-Li'l Jinx Giant Laugh-Out (6/71). 186-Archie's Jokes (8/71). 187-Betty & Veronica Summer Fun (9/71). 188-World of Archie (9/71). 189-World of Jughead (9/71). 193-World of Archie (3/72).194-World of Jughead (4/72). 197-Betty & Veronica Spectacular (6/72). 198-Archie's Jokes (8/72). 199-Betty & Veronica Summer Fun (9/72)	each	3	6	9	16	23	30
190-Archie's Christmas Stocking (12/71); Sabrina-c	5	10	15	31	53	75
191-Betty & Veronica Christmas Spect.(2/72); Sabrina app.	5	10	15	31	53	75
192-Archie's Christmas Love-In (1/72); Archie Band-c/s	3	6	9	21	33	45
195-(84 pgs.)-Li'l Jinx Christmas Bag (1/72)	4	8	12	23	37	50
196-(84 pgs.)-Sabrina's Christmas Magic (1/72)	7	14	21	44	82	120
200-(52 pgs.)-World of Archie (10/72)	3	6	9	21	33	45
201-206,208-219,221-230,232,233 (All 52 pgs.): 201-Betty & Veronica Spectacular (10/72). 202-World of Jughead (11/72). 203-Archie's Christmas Stocking (12/72). 204-Betty & Veronica Christmas Spectacular (2/73). 205-Archie's Christmas Love-In (1/73). 206-Li'l Jinx Christmas Bag (12/72). 208-World of Archie (3/73). 209-World of Jughead (4/73). 210-Betty & Veronica Spectacular (6/73). 211-Archie's Jokes (8/73). 212-Betty & Veronica Summer Fun (9/73). 213-World of Archie (10/73). 214-Betty & Veronica Spectacular (10/73). 215-World of Jughead (11/73). 216-Archie's Christmas Stocking (12/73). 217-Betty & Veronica Christmas Spectacular (2/74). 218-Archie's Christmas Love-In (1/74). 219-Li'l Jinx Christmas Bag (12/73). 221-Betty & Veronica Spectacular (Advertised as World of Archie) (6/74). 222-Archie's Jokes (advertised as World of Archie) (8/74). 223-Li'l Jinx (8/74). 224-Betty & Veronica Summer Fun (9/74). 225-World of Archie (9/74). 226-Betty & Veronica Spectacular (10/74). 227-World of Jughead (10/74). 228-Archie's Christmas Stocking (12/74). 229-Betty & Veronica Christmas Spectacular (2/74). 230-Archie's Christmas Love-In (1/75). 232-World of Archie (3/75). 233-World of Jughead (4/75)	each	3	6	9	14	19	24
207,220,231,243: Sabrina's Christmas Magic. 207-(12/72). 220-(12/73). 231-(1/75). 243-(1/76)	each	3	6	9	18	27	36
234-242,244-251 (36 pgs.): 234-Betty & Veronica Spectacular (6/75). 235-Archie's Jokes (8/75). 236-Betty & Veronica Summer Fun (9/75). 237-World of Archie (9/75). 238-Betty & Veronica Spectacular (10/75). 239-World of Jughead (10/75). 240-Archie's Christmas Stocking (12/75). 241-Betty & Veronica Christmas Spectacular (2/75). 242-Archie's Christmas Love-In (1/76). 244-World of Archie (3/76). 245-World of Jughead (4/76). 246-Betty & Veronica Spectacular (6/76). 247-Archie's Jokes (8/76). 248-Betty & Veronica Summer Fun (9/76). 249-World of Archie (9/76). 250-Betty & Veronica Spectacular (10/76). 251-World of Jughead	each	2	4	6	10	14	18

252-451-Do not exist

	GD 2.0	VG 4.0	FN 6.0	VF 8.0	VF/NM 9.0	NM- 9.2
452-454,456-466,468-478, 480-490,492-499: 452-Archie's Christmas Stocking (12/76). 453-Betty & Veronica Christmas Spectacular (12/76). 454-Archie's Christmas Love-In (1/77). 456-World of Archie (3/77). 457-World of Jughead (4/77). 458-Betty & Veronica Spectacular (6/77). 459-Archie's Jokes (8/77)-Shows B#76 in error. 460-Betty & Veronica Summer Fun (9/77). 461-World of Archie (9/77). 462-Betty & Veronica Spectacular (10/77). 463-World of Jughead (10/77). 464-Archie's Christmas Stocking (12/77). 465-Betty & Veronica Christmas Spectacular (12/77). 466-Archie's Christmas Love-In (1/78). 468-World of Archie (2/78). 469-World of Jughead (2/78). 470-Betty & Veronica Summer Fun (9/78). 471-Archie's Jokes (8/78). 472-Betty & Veronica Summer Fun (9/78). 473-World of Archie (9/78). 474-Betty & Veronica Spectacular (10/78). 475-World of Jughead (10/78). 476-Archie's Christmas Stocking (12/78). 477-Betty & Veronica Christmas Spectacular (12/78). 478-Archie's Christmas Love-In (1/79). 480-The World of Archie (3/79). 481-World of Jughead (4/79). 482-Betty & Veronica Spectacular (6/79). 483-Archie's Jokes (8/79). 484-Betty & Veronica Summer Fun(9/79). 485-The World of Archie (9/79). 486-Betty & Veronica Spectacular (10/79). 487-The World of Jughead (10/79). 488-Archie's Christmas Stocking (12/79). 489-Betty & Veronica Spectacular (1/80). 490-Archie's Christmas Love-In (1/80). 492-The World of Archie (2/80). 493-The World of Jughead (4/80). 494-Betty & Veronica Spectacular (6/80). 495-Archie's Jokes (8/80). 496-Betty & Veronica Summer Fun (9/80). 497-The World of Archie (9/80). 498-Betty & Veronica Spectacular (10/80). 499-The World of Jughead (10/80)	each	2	4	6	8	10	12
455,467,479,491,503-Sabrina's Christmas Magic: 455-(1/77). 467-(1/78). 479-(1/79) Dracula/Werewolf-s. 491-(1/80), 503(1/81)	2	4	6	13	18	22
500-Archie's Christmas Stocking (12/80)	2	4	6	8	11	14
501-514,516-527,529-532,534-539,541-543,545-550: 501-Betty & Veronica Christmas Spectacular (12/80). 502-Archie's Christmas Love-In (1/81). 504-The World of Archie (3/81). 505-The World of Jughead (4/81). 506-Betty & Veronica Spectacular (6/81). 507-Archie's Jokes (8/81). 508-Betty & Veronica Summer Fun (9/81). 509-The World of Archie (9/81). 510-Betty & Veronica Spectacular (9/81). 511-The World of Jughead (10/81). 512-Archie's Christmas Stocking (12/81). 513-Betty & Veronica Christmas Spectacular (12/81). 514-Archie's Christmas Love-in (1/82). 516-The World of Archie(3/82). 517-The World of Jughead (4/82). 518-Betty & Veronica Spectacular (6/82). 519-Archie's Jokes (8/82). 520-Betty & Veronica Summer Fun (9/82). 521-The World of Archie (9/82). 522-Betty & Veronica Spectacular (10/82). 523-The World of Jughead (10/82).524-Archie's Christmas Stocking (1/83). 525-Betty & Veronica Christmas Spectacular (1/83). 526-Betty and Veronica Spectacular (5/83). 527-Little Archie (8/83). 529-Betty and Veronica Summer Fun (8/83). 530-Betty and Veronica Spectacular (9/83). 531-The World of Jughead (9/83). 532-The World of Archie (10/83). 534-Little Archie (1/84). 535-Archie's Christmas Stocking (1/84). 537-Betty and Veronica Spectacular (6/84). 538-Little Archie (8/84). 539-Betty and Veronica Summer Fun (8/84). 541-Betty and Veronica Spectacular (9/84). 542-The World of Jughead (9/84). 543-The World of Archie (10/84). 545-Little Archie (12/84). 546-Archie's Christmas Stocking (12/84). 547-Betty and Veronica Christmas Spectacular (12/84). 548-Betty and Veronica Spectacular (6/85). 549-Little Archie. 550-Betty and Veronica Summer Fun						

Archie Giant Series Magazine #175 © ACP

Archie Halloween Spectacular 2020 © ACP

Archie Meets Batman '66 #5 © ACP & DC

	GD 2.0	VG 4.0	FN 6.0	VF 8.0	VF/NM 9.0	NM- 9.2

	GD 2.0	VG 4.0	FN 6.0	VF 8.0	VF/NM 9.0	NM- 9.2
each...	1	2	3	5	7	9

515,528,533,540,544: 515-Sabrina's Christmas Magic (1/82). 528-Josie and the Pussycats (8/83). 533-Sabrina; Space Pirates by Frank Bolling (10/83). 540-Josie and the Pussycats (8/84). 544-Sabrina the Teen-Age Witch (10/84).

	GD 2.0	VG 4.0	FN 6.0	VF 8.0	VF/NM 9.0	NM- 9.2
	2	4	6	11	16	20
551,562,571,584,597-Josie and the Pussycats	2	4	6	9	12	15

552-561,563-570,572-583,585-596,598-600: 552-Betty & Veronica Spectacular. 553-The World of Jughead. 554-The World of Archie. 555-Betty's Diary. 556-Little Archie (1/86). 557-Archie's Christmas Stocking (1/86). 558-Betty & Veronica Spectacular (1/86). 559-Betty & Veronica Spectacular. 560-Little Archie. 561-Betty & Veronica Summer Fun. 563-Betty & Veronica Spectacular. 564-World of Jughead. 565-World of Archie. 566-Little Archie. 567-Archie's Christmas Stocking. 568-Betty & Veronica Christmas Spectacular. 569-Betty & Veronica Spring Spectacular. 570-Little Archie. 571-Dracula-c/s. 572-Betty & Veronica Summer Fun. 573-Archie At Riverdale High. 574-World of Archie. 575-Betty & Veronica Spectacular. 576-Pep. 577-World of Jughead. 578-Archie And Me. 579-Archie's Christmas Spectacular. 580-Betty and Veronica Christmas Spectacular. 581-Little Archie Christmas Special. 582-Betty & Veronica Spring Spectacular. 583-Little Archie. 585-Betty & Veronica Summer Fun. 586-Archie At Riverdale High. 587-The World of Archie (10/88); 1st app. Explorers of the Unknown. 588-Betty & Veronica Spectacular. 589-Pep (10/88). 590-The World of Jughead. 591-Archie & Me. 592-Archie's Christmas Stocking. 593-Betty & Veronica Christmas Spectacular. 594-Little Archie. 595-Betty & Veronica Spring Spectacular. 596-Little Archie. 598-Betty & Veronica Summer Fun. 599-The World of Archie (10/89); 2nd app. Explorers of the Unknown. 600-Betty and Veronica Spectacular

each....						6.00

601,602,604-609,611-629: 601-Pep. 602-The World of Jughead. 604-Archie at Riverdale High. 605-Archie's Christmas Stocking. 606-Betty and Veronica Christmas Spectacular. 607-Little Archie. 608-Betty and Veronica Spectacular. 609-Little Archie. 611-Betty and Veronica Summer Fun. 612-The World of Archie. 613-Betty and Veronica Spectacular. 614-Pep (10/90). 615-Veronica's Summer Space. 616-Archie and Me. 617-Archie's Christmas Stocking. 618-Betty & Veronica Christmas Spectacular. 619-Little Archie. 620-Betty and Veronica Spectacular. 621-Betty and Veronica Summer Fun. 622-Josie & the Pussycats; not published. 623-Betty and Veronica Spectacular. 624-Pep Comics. 625-Veronica's Summer Special. 626-Archie and Me. 627-World of Archie. 628-Archie's Pals 'n' Gals Holiday Special. 629-Betty & Veronica Christmas Spectacular.

	GD 2.0	VG 4.0	FN 6.0	VF 8.0	VF/NM 9.0	NM- 9.2
each....						4.00
603-Archie and Me; Titanic app.						5.00
610-Josie and the Pussycats	1	3	4	6	8	10
630-631: 630-Archie's Christmas Stocking. 631-Archie's Pals 'n' Gals						4.00
632-Last issue; Betty & Veronica Spectacular	1	3	4	6	8	10

NOTE: Archies Band-c-173,180,192; s-189,192. Archie Cavemen-165,225,232,244,249. Little Sabrina-527,534, 538,545,556,566. UFO-s-178,487,594.

ARCHIE HALLOWEEN SPECTACULAR
Archie Comic Publs: Dec, 2017 - Nov, 2023 ($2.99/$3.99, annual)

	GD 2.0	VG 4.0	FN 6.0	VF 8.0	VF/NM 9.0	NM- 9.2
1-Halloween-themed reprints; Shultz-c	1	2	3	5	6	8
nn (12/18) Parent-c; nn (12/19) Parent-c; Sabrina app.; nn (12/20); nn (12/21); nn (11/22)						3.00
nn (11/23, 3.99) New story and Halloween-themed reprints Sabrina app.						4.00

ARCHIE JUMBO COMICS DIGEST (See Archie Comic Digest)
ARCHIE – LOVE & HEARTBREAK SPECIAL
Archie Comic Publications: Apr, 2022 ($3.99, one-shot)

1-Short romantic stories by various incl. Pitilli, Grace, Cooke, Sterle, Zanfardino						4.00

ARCHIE MEETS BATMAN '66
Archie Comic Publications: Sept, 2018 - No. 6, Mar, 2019 ($3.99, limited series)

1-Parker & Moreci-s/Parent-a; multiple covers; Poison Ivy, Bookworm, Siren app.						
	1	3	4	6	8	10
2-6-Joker, Riddler, Penguin & Catwoman app. 6-Super Teens app.						5.00

ARCHIE MEETS RAMONES
Archie Comic Publications: 2016 ($4.99, one-shot)

1-Segura & Rosenberg-s/Lagace-a; multiple covers; The Archies go to 1976; Sabrina app.						
	2	4	6	11	16	20

ARCHIE MEETS RIVERDALE
Archie Comic Publications: Jul, 2022 ($3.99, one-shot)

1-The Archie comics gang meet their TV counterparts; Kibblesmith-s						4.00

ARCHIE MEETS THE B-52s
Archie Comic Publications: Apr, 2020 ($3.99, one-shot)

1-Set in the '80s with the original line-up; Segura & Rosenberg-s/Parent-a; multiple covers						4.00

ARCHIE MEETS THE PUNISHER (Same contents as The Punisher Meets Archie)
Marvel Comics & Archie Comics Publ.: Aug, 1994 ($2.95, 52 pgs., one-shot)

1-Batton Lash story, John Buscema-a on Punisher, Stan Goldberg-a on Archie						
	3	6	9	14	19	24

ARCHIE MILESTONES JUMBO COMICS DIGEST

Archie Comics: Apr, 2019 - Present ($6.99/$7.99/$8.99, digest-size)

1-5-($6.99)						7.00
6-12-($7.99)						8.00
13-17-($8.99) 16-Best of the 2000s. 17-Best of the 1980s						9.00
18-23-($9.99) 18-Jughead Guide to Life. 21-Time Police						10.00

ARCHIE 1941
Archie Comic Publications: Nov, 2018 - No. 5, Mar, 2019 ($3.99, limited series)

1-5-Set in 1941 during WWII; Augustyn & Waid-s/Krause-a						4.00

ARCHIE 1955
Archie Comic Publications: Nov, 2019 - No. 5, Apr, 2020 ($3.99, limited series)

1-5-Set in 1955 at the dawn of Rock 'n' Roll; Augustyn & Waid-s/Grummett-a						4.00

ARCHIES, THE
Archie Comic Publications: Jul, 2017; Nov, 2017 - No. 7, Jul, 2018 ($4.99/$3.99)

1-7-($3.99) Segura & Rosenberg-s/Eisma-a. 3-Chvrches app. 4-The Monkees app. 6-Blondie app. 7-Josie and the Pussycats app.						4.00
... Anniversary Spectacular 1 (5/22, $2.99) New silent story; r/Life With Archie #80						3.00
..., One-Shot (7/17, $4.99) Segura & Rosenberg-s/Eisma-a; Archie forms the band						5.00

ARCHIE'S ACTIVITY COMICS DIGEST MAGAZINE
Archie Enterprises: 1985 - No. 4 (Annual, 128 pgs., digest size)

	GD 2.0	VG 4.0	FN 6.0	VF 8.0	VF/NM 9.0	NM- 9.2
1 (Most copies are marked)	2	4	6	9	13	16
2-4	1	2	3	5	7	9

ARCHIE'S CAR
Spire Christian Comics (Fleming H. Revell co.): 1979 (49¢)

nn	3	6	9	14	19	24

ARCHIE'S CHRISTMAS LOVE-IN (See Archie Giant Series Mag. No. 169, 181,192, 205, 218, 230, 242, 454, 466, 478, 490, 502, 514)

ARCHIE'S CHRISTMAS STOCKING (See Archie Giant Series Mag. No. 1-6,10, 15, 20, 25, 31, 137, 144, 150, 158, 167, 179, 190, 203, 216, 228, 240, 452, 464, 476, 488, 500, 512, 524, 535, 546, 557, 567, 579, 592, 605, 617, 630)

ARCHIE'S CHRISTMAS STOCKING
Archie Comics: 1993 - No. 7, 1999 ($2.00-$2.29, 52 pgs.)(Bound-in calendar poster in all)

1-Dan DeCarlo-c/a	2	4	6	8	10	12
2-5						5.00
6,7: 6-(1998, $2.25). 7-(1999, $2.29)						5.00

ARCHIE'S CIRCUS
Barbour Christian Comics: 1990 (69¢)

nn	2	4	6	10	14	18

ARCHIE'S CLASSIC CHRISTMAS STORIES
Archie Comics: 2002 ($10.95, TPB)

Volume 1 - Reprints stories from 1955-1964 Archie's Christmas Stocking issues						12.00

ARCHIE'S CLEAN SLATE
Spire Christian Comics (Fleming H. Revell Co.): 1973 (35¢/49¢)

1-(35¢-c edition)(Some issues have nn)	3	6	9	14	19	24
1-(49¢-c edition)	2	4	6	10	14	18

ARCHIE'S DATE BOOK
Spire Christian comics (Fleming H. Revell Co.): 1981

nn-(Low print)	2	4	6	13	18	22

ARCHIE'S DOUBLE DIGEST QUARTERLY MAGAZINE
Archie Comics: 1981 - No. 252, Aug, 2014 ($1.95-$3.99, 256 pgs.) (Archie's Double Digest Magazine No. 10 on)(Title becomes Archie's Comics Digest #253 on)

1	3	6	9	17	26	35
2-10; 6-Katy Keene story.	2	4	6	10	14	18
11-30: 29-Pureheart story	2	4	6	8	10	12
31-50	1	2	3	4	5	7
51-70,100						5.00
71-99,101-237,239-251: 123-Begin $3.29-c. 170-Begin $3.69. 197-Begin $3.99-c						4.00
238-Titled Archie Double Double Digest (4/13, $5.99, 320 pages)						6.00
252-($4.99) Title changes to Archie's Comics Digest with #253						5.00

ARCHIE'S FAMILY ALBUM
Spire Christian Comics (Fleming H. Revell Co.): 1978 (39¢/49¢, 36 pgs.)

nn	2	4	6	13	18	22
nn (49¢-c edition)	2	4	6	9	13	16

ARCHIE'S FESTIVAL
Spire Christian Comics (Fleming H. Revell Co.): 1980 (49¢)

nn	2	4	6	13	18	22

ARCHIE'S FUNHOUSE DOUBLE DIGEST

	GD	VG	FN	VF	VF/NM	NM-
	2.0	4.0	6.0	8.0	9.0	9.2

Archie Comics: Feb, 2014 - No. 28, Nov, 2017 ($3.99-$7.99, digest-size)

	GD 2.0	VG 4.0	FN 6.0	VF 8.0	VF/NM 9.0	NM- 9.2
1-5						4.00
6,19,21: 6,19-Titled Archie's Funhouse Double Double Digest ($5.99, 320 pgs.)						6.00
7-10,12-14,16,18,25,28-($4.99) Title becomes Archie's Funhouse Comics Digest						5.00
11-($7.99) Titled Archie's Funhouse Jumbo Comics Digest						8.00
15,17,20,22-($6.99) Archie's Funhouse Jumbo Comics Digest						7.00
23,24,26,27-($5.99) 23-Titled Archie's Funhouse Christmas Annual Double Digest						6.00

ARCHIE'S GIRLS, BETTY AND VERONICA (Becomes Betty & Veronica)(Also see Veronica)
Archie Publications (Close-Up): 1950 - No. 347, Apr, 1987

	GD 2.0	VG 4.0	FN 6.0	VF 8.0	VF/NM 9.0	NM- 9.2
1	366	732	1098	2562	4481	6400
2	155	310	465	992	1696	2400
3-5: 3-Betty's 1st ponytail. 4-Dan DeCarlo's 1st Archie work	97	194	291	621	1061	1500
6-9	65	130	195	416	708	1000
10-Katy Keene app. (2 pgs.)	77	154	231	493	847	1200
11-20: 11,13,14,17-19-Katy Keene app. 17-Last pre-code issue (3/55). 20-Debbie's Diary (2 pgs.)	47	94	141	296	498	700
21-30: 27,30-Katy Keene app. 29-Tarzan	37	74	111	237	361	500
31-43,45-50: 41-Marilyn Monroe and Brigitte Bardot mentioned. 45-Fabian 1 pg. photo & bio. 46-Bobby Darin 1 pg. photo & bio	21	42	63	126	206	285
44-Elvis Presley 1 pg. photo & bio	24	48	72	144	237	330
51-55,57-74: 67-Jackie Kennedy homage. 73-Sci-fi-c	9	18	27	57	111	165
56-Elvis and Bobby Darin records parody	10	20	30	66	138	210
75-Betty & Veronica sell souls to Devil	27	54	81	189	420	650
76-99: 82-Bobby Rydell 1 pg. illustrated bio; Elvis mentioned on-c. 83-Rick Nelson illo/text page. 84-Connie Francis 1 pg. illustrated bio	6	12	18	38	69	100
100	6	12	18	42	79	115
101-104, 106-117,120 (12/65): 113-Monsters-s	4	8	12	28	47	65
105-Beatles wig parody (5 pg. story)(9/64)	5	10	15	34	60	85
118-(10/65) 1st app./origin Superteen (also see Betty & Me #3)	6	12	18	42	79	115
119-2nd app./last Superteen story	5	10	15	33	57	80
121,122,124-126,128-140 (8/67): 135,140-Mod-c. 136-Slave Girl-s	3	6	9	19	30	40
123-"Jingo"-Ringo parody-c	4	8	12	23	37	50
127-Beatles Fan Club-s	5	10	15	31	53	75
141-156,158-163,165-180 (12/70)	3	6	9	15	22	28
157,164-Archies Band	3	6	9	18	28	38
181-193,195-199	2	4	6	11	16	20
194-Sabrina-c/s	4	8	12	23	37	50
200-(8/72)	3	6	9	14	19	24
201-205,207,209,211-215,217-240	2	4	6	8	10	12
206,208,210, 216: 206,208,216-Sabrina c/app. 206-Josie-c. 210-Sabrina app.	3	6	9	15	22	28
241 (1/76)-270 (6/78)	1	3	4	6	8	10
271-299: 281-UFO-s	1	2	3	5	7	9
300 (12/80)-Anniversary issue	2	4	6	9	10	12
301-309	1	2	3	4	5	7
310-John Travolta parody story	1	3	4	6	8	10
311-319						6.00
320 (10/82)-Intro. of Cheryl Blossom on cover and inside story (she also appears, but not on the cover, in Jughead #325 with same 10/82 publication date)	20	40	60	138	307	475
321-Cheryl Blossom app.	7	14	21	44	82	120
322-Cheryl Blossom app.; Cheryl meets Archie for the 1st time	8	16	24	54	102	150
323,326,329,330,331,333-338: 333-Monsters-s						6.00
324,325-Crickett O'Dell app.	2	4	6	9	12	15
327,328-Cheryl Blossom app.	4	8	12	22	35	48
332,339: 332-Superhero costume party. 339-(12/85) Betty dressed as Madonna.	2	4	6	10	14	18
340-346 Low print	1	3	4	6	8	10
347 (4/87) Last issue; low print	2	4	6	8	10	12
Annual 1 (1953)	148	296	444	947	1624	2300
Annual 2 (1954)	60	120	180	381	653	925
Annual 3-5 (1955-1957)	43	86	129	271	461	650
Annual 6-8 (1958-1960)	30	60	90	177	289	400

ARCHIE'S HOLIDAY FUN DIGEST
Archie Comics: Feb, 1997 - No. 12, Dec, 2007 ($1.75/$1.95/$1.99/$2.19/$2.39/$2.49, annual)

	GD 2.0	VG 4.0	FN 6.0	VF 8.0	VF/NM 9.0	NM- 9.2
1-12-Christmas stories						4.00

ARCHIE'S HOLIDAY MAGIC SPECIAL
Archie Comic Publications: Feb, 2022 ($3.99, one-shot)

	GD 2.0	VG 4.0	FN 6.0	VF 8.0	VF/NM 9.0	NM- 9.2
1-Short Christmas/Hanukkah stories by various incl. Ostow, Lusky, Schoening, Torres						4.00

ARCHIE SHOWCASE DIGEST
Archie Comics: Sept, 2020 - Present ($7.99/$8.99/$9.99, digest)

	GD 2.0	VG 4.0	FN 6.0	VF 8.0	VF/NM 9.0	NM- 9.2
1-6-Reprints from all eras. 2-Jughead spotlight. 3-Love Showdown						8.00
7-11-($8.99) 9,11-Christmas-c. 10-Sabrina						9.00
12-17-($9.99) 14,16-Christmas-c. 17-Valentine's Day						10.00

ARCHIE'S JOKEBOOK COMICS DIGEST ANNUAL (See Jokebook...)

ARCHIE'S JOKE BOOK MAGAZINE (See Joke Book ...)
Archie Publ: 1953 - No. 3, Sum, 1954; No. 15, Fall, 1954 - No. 288, 11/82 (subtitled...Laugh-In #127-140; ...Laugh-Out #141-194)

	GD 2.0	VG 4.0	FN 6.0	VF 8.0	VF/NM 9.0	NM- 9.2
1953-One Shot (#1)	164	328	492	1053	1802	2550
2	61	122	183	390	670	950
3 (no #4-14)	47	94	141	296	498	700
15-20: 15-Formerly Archie's Rival Reggie #14; last pre-code issue (Fall/54).						
15-17-Katy Keene app.	27	54	81	162	266	370
21-30	16	32	48	98	154	210
31-43: 42-Bio of Ed "Kookie" Byrnes. 43-story about guitarist Duane Eddy	14	28	42	80	115	150
44-1st pro comic work by Neal Adams, 4 pgs.	37	74	111	222	361	500
45-47-N. Adams-a in all, 2-6 pgs.	22	44	66	128	209	290
48-Four pgs. N. Adams-a	22	44	66	128	209	290

	GD 2.0	VG 4.0	FN 6.0	VF 8.0	VF/NM 9.0	NM- 9.2
49,50	6	12	18	57	66	95
51-56,60 (1962)	4	8	12	28	47	65
57-Elvis mentioned; Marilyn Monroe cameo	6	12	18	58	69	100
58,59-Horror/Sci-fi-c	9	18	27	62	126	190
61-80 (8/64): 66-(12¢ cover). 76-Robot-c	3	6	9	19	30	40
66-(15¢ cover variant)	4	8	12	28	47	65
81-89,91,92,94-99	3	6	9	15	22	28
90,93: 90-Beatles gag. 93-Beatles cameo	3	6	9	17	26	35
100 (5/66)	3	6	9	15	22	28
101,103-117,119-123,127,129,131-140 (9/69): 105-Superhero gag-c. 108-110-Archies Archers Band-s. 116-Beatles/Monkees/Bob Dylan cameos (posters)	3	6	9	14	19	24
102 (7/66) Archie Band prototype-c; Elvis parody panel, Rolling Stones mention	3	6	9	18	28	38
118,124,125,126,128,130: 118-Archie Band-c; Veronica & Groovers band-s. 124-Archies Band-c/app. 125-Beatles cameo (poster). 126,130-Monkees cameo. 128-Veronica/Archies Band app.	3	6	9	16	24	32
141-173,175-181,183-199	2	4	6	9	13	16
174-Sabrina-c. 182-Sabrina cameo	2	4	6	10	14	18
200 (9/74)	2	4	6	10	14	18
201-230 (3/77)	1	3	4	6	8	10
231-239,241-287						6.00
240-Elvis record-c	2	4	6	8	10	12
288-Last issue	1	3	4	6	8	10

NOTE: Archies Band-c-118,124,147,172; 1 pg.-s-127,128,138,140,143,147,167; 2 pg.-s-124,131, 155. Sabrina app.-247,248,252-259,261,262,264,266-270,274,277,284-286.
(See Archie Giant Series Mag. No. 17, 22, 27, 33, 139, 146, 154, 163, 174, 186, 198, 211, 222, 235, 247, 459, 471, 483, 495, 519)

ARCHIE'S JOKES (See Archie Giant Series Mag. No. 17, 22, 27, 33, 139, 146, 154, 163, 174, 186, 198, 211, 222, 235, 247, 459, 471, 483, 495, 519)

ARCHIE'S LOVE SCENE
Spire Christian Comics (Fleming H. Revell Co.): 1973 (35¢/39¢/49¢/no price)

	GD 2.0	VG 4.0	FN 6.0	VF 8.0	VF/NM 9.0	NM- 9.2
1-(35¢ Edition)	3	6	9	16	23	30
1-(39¢/49¢ Edition/no price) (Some copies have nn)	2	4	6	11	16	20

ARCHIE'S LOVE SHOWDOWN SPECIAL
Archie Publications: 1994 ($2.00, one-shot)

	GD 2.0	VG 4.0	FN 6.0	VF 8.0	VF/NM 9.0	NM- 9.2
1-Concludes x-over from Archie #429, Betty #19, B&V #82, Veronica #39	2	4	6	8	10	12

ARCHIE'S MADHOUSE (Madhouse Ma-ad No. 67 on)
Archie Publications: Sept, 1959 - No. 66, Feb, 1969

	GD 2.0	VG 4.0	FN 6.0	VF 8.0	VF/NM 9.0	NM- 9.2
1-Archie begins	52	104	156	411	931	1450
2	16	32	48	110	243	375
3-5	10	20	30	68	144	220
6-10	7	14	21	46	86	125
11-17 (Last w/regular characters)	6	12	18	35	63	90
18-21,23,29: 18-New format begins. 19-1st app. Witch Hilda. 23-No Sabrina.						
22-Flying saucer-c	5	10	15	34	60	85
22-1st app. Sabrina, the Teen-age Witch and Salem the cat (10/62)	276	552	828	2277	5139	8000
24-2nd app. Sabrina and Salem; 1st app. Witch Hazel in a Sabrina story	81	162	243	648	1460	2400
25,26,28-Sabrina app. 25-1st app. Captain Sprocket (4/63); 3rd app. Sabrina; sci-fi/horror-c	14	28	42	97	214	330
27-Sabrina-c; no story	10	20	30	67	141	215
30-33,36,37-Sabrina app. 37-Witch Hilda now called Aunt Hilda	9	18	27	59	117	175
34,38-40: No Sabrina. 34-Bordered-c begin.	4	8	12	28	47	65
35-Beatles cameo. No Sabrina	5	10	15	31	53	75
41-44,46,47,51,54,56,57,60-62,64,66: No Sabrina. 43-Mighty Crusaders cameo. 44-Swipes Mad #4 (Super-Duperman) in "Bird Monsters From Outer Space"	4	8	12	23	37	50
45,48-50,52,53,55,58,59,63,65-Sabrina stories. 45-1st app. Rosalind. 65-1st app. Aunt Zelda	6	12	18	42	79	115
Annual 1 (1962-63) no Sabrina	13	26	39	89	195	300
Annual 2 (1964) no Sabrina	6	12	18	42	79	115
Annual 3 (1965)-r/1st app. Sabrina from #22	13	26	39	89	195	300
Annual 4,5('66-68)(Becomes Madhouse Ma-ad Annual #7 on) no Sabrina	5	10	15	31	53	75
Annual 6 (1969)-Sabrina the Teen-age Witch-sty	8	16	24	52	99	145

NOTE: Cover title to #61-65 is "Madhouse" and to #66 is "Madhouse Ma-ad Jokes". Sci-Fi/Horror covers 6, 8, 11, 13, 15-26, 29, 35, 36, 38, 42, 43, 48, 51, 58, 60.

ARCHIE'S MECHANICS
Archie Publications: Sept, 1954 - No. 3, 1955

	GD 2.0	VG 4.0	FN 6.0	VF 8.0	VF/NM 9.0	NM- 9.2
1-(15¢; 52 pgs.)	123	246	369	787	1344	1900
2-(10¢)-Last pre-code issue	68	136	204	435	743	1050
3-(10¢)	57	114	171	362	619	875

ARCHIE'S MYSTERIES (Continued from Archie's Weird Mysteries)
Archie Comics: No. 25, Feb, 2003 - No. 34, June, 2004 ($2.19)

	GD 2.0	VG 4.0	FN 6.0	VF 8.0	VF/NM 9.0	NM- 9.2
25-34- Archie and gang as "Teen Scene Investigators"						4.00

ARCHIE'S ONE WAY
Spire Christian Comics (Fleming H. Revell Co.): 1972 (35¢/39¢/49¢, 36 pgs.)

	GD 2.0	VG 4.0	FN 6.0	VF 8.0	VF/NM 9.0	NM- 9.2
nn-(35¢ Edition)	3	6	9	16	23	30
nn-(39¢, 49¢, no price editions)	3	6	9	14	19	24

ARCHIE'S PAL, JUGHEAD (Jughead No. 126 on)
Archie Publications: 1949 - No. 125, Oct, 1965

	GD 2.0	VG 4.0	FN 6.0	VF 8.0	VF/NM 9.0	NM- 9.2
1 (1949)-1st app. Moose (see Pep #33)	314	628	942	2198	3849	5500
2 (1950)	119	238	357	762	1306	1850
3-5	63	126	189	403	689	975
6-10: 7-Suzie app.	42	84	126	265	445	625
11-20: 20-Jughead as Sherlock Holmes parody	45	90	135	285	485	675
21-30: 23-25,28-30-Katy Keene app. 23-Early Dilton-s. 28-Debbie's Diary app.	16	32	48	115	179	245
31-50: 49-Archies Rock 'N' Rollers band-c	8	16	24	54	102	150
51-57,59-70: 59- Bio of Will Hutchins of TV's Sugarfoot. 68-Early Archie Gang Cavemen-s	6	12	18	38	69	100

Archie's Girls, Betty and Veronica #11 © ACP

Archie Showcase Digest #5 © ACP

Archie's Super-Teens #1 © ACP

	GD 2.0	VG 4.0	FN 6.0	VF 8.0	VF/NM 9.0	NM- 9.2
58-Neal Adams-a	7	14	21	44	82	120
71-76,83,89-99: 72-Jughead dates Betty & Veronica. 83 (4/62) 1st mention of Secret Society of Jughead Hating Girls. 95-2nd app. Cricket O'Dell	5	10	15	30	50	70
77,78,80-82,85,86,88-Horror/Sci-Fi-c. 86(7/62) 1st app. The Brain	9	18	27	57	111	165
79-Creature From the Black Lagoon-c; 1st app. Big Ethel	52	104	156	411	931	1450
84-2nd app. Big Ethel	11	22	33	73	157	240
87-3rd app. of Big Ethel; UGAJ (United Girls Against Jughead)-s	5	10	15	35	63	90
100	8	16	24	51	96	140
101-Return of Big Ethel	5	10	15	30	50	70
102-125	4	8	12	23	37	50
Annual 1 (1953, 25¢)	113	226	339	718	1234	1750
Annual 2 (1954, 25¢)-Last pre-code issue	58	116	174	371	636	900
Annual 3-5 (1955-57, 25¢)	37	74	111	218	354	490
Annual 6-8 (1958-60, 25¢)	23	46	69	138	227	315

ARCHIE'S PAL JUGHEAD COMICS (Formerly Jughead #1-45)
Archie Comic Publ.: No. 46, June, 1993 - No. 214, Sept, 2012 ($1.25-$2.99)

	GD 2.0	VG 4.0	FN 6.0	VF 8.0	VF/NM 9.0	NM- 9.2
46-214: 100-"A Storm Over Uniforms" x-over part 1,2. 166-Three Geeks cameo. 200-Tom Root-s; Sabrina cameo. 201-Begin $2.99-c						4.00

ARCHIE'S PALS 'N' GALS (Also see Archie Giant Series Magazine #628)
Archie Publ.: 1952-53 - No. 6, 1957-58; No. 7, 1958 - No. 224, Spring, 1991
(...All News Stories on-c #49-59)

	GD 2.0	VG 4.0	FN 6.0	VF 8.0	VF/NM 9.0	NM- 9.2
1-(116 pgs., 25¢)	129	258	387	826	1413	2000
2(Annual)('54, 25¢)	55	110	165	352	601	850
3-5(Annual, '55-57, 25¢): 3-Last pre-code issue	40	80	120	246	411	575
6-10('58-'60)	25	50	75	150	245	340
11,13,14,16,17,20-(84 pgs.): 17-B&V paper dolls	14	28	42	82	121	160
12,15-(84 pgs.) Neal Adams-a. 12-Harry Belafonte 2 pg. photos & bio.	16	32	48	94	147	200
18-(84 pgs.) Horror/Sci-Fi-c	16	38	57	111	176	240
19-Marilyn Monroe app.	20	40	60	117	189	260
21,22,24-28,30 (68 pgs.)	7	14	21	44	82	120
23-(Wint./62) 6 pg. Josie-s with Pepper and Melody (1st app.) by DeCarlo; Betty in towel pin-up	71	142	213	568	1284	2000
29-Beatles satire (68 pgs.)	10	20	30	64	132	200
31(Wint. 64/65)-39 -(68 pgs.)	5	10	15	34	60	85
40-Early Superteen-s; with Pureheart	7	14	21	44	82	120
41(8/67)-43,45-50(2/69) (68 pgs.)	4	8	12	25	40	55
44-Archies Band-s; WEB cameo	4	8	12	28	47	65
51(4/69),52,55-64(6/71): 62-Last squarebound	3	6	9	18	28	38
53-Archies Band-c/s	3	6	9	21	33	45
54-Satan meets Veronica-s	5	10	15	34	60	85
65(8/70),67-70,73,74,76-81,83(6/74) (52 pgs.)	3	6	9	21	33	45
66,82-Sabrina-s	3	6	9	21	33	45
71,72-Two part gag story (8/72,9/72)	3	6	9	21	33	45
75-Archies Band-s	3	6	9	16	24	32
84-99	2	4	6	8	10	12
100 (12/75)	2	4	6	9	13	16
101-130(3/79): 125,126-Riverdale 2001-s	1	2	3	5	6	8
131-160,162-170 (7/84)						6.00
161 (11/82) 3rd app.1st solo Cheryl Blossom-s and pin-up; 2nd Jason Blossom	6	12	18	42	79	115
171-173,175,177-197,199: 197-G. Colan-a						5.00
174,176,198: 174-New Archies Band-s. 176-Cyndi Lauper-s. 198-Archie gang on strike at Archie Ent. offices						6.00
200(9/88)-Illiteracy-s						6.00
201,203-223: Later issues $1.00 cover						4.00
202-Explains end of Archie's jalopy; Dezerland-c/s; James Dean cameo						6.00
224-Last issue						6.00

NOTE: *Archies Band-c-45,47,49,53,56; s-44,53,75,174. UFO-s-50,63,209,220.*

ARCHIE'S PALS 'N' GALS DOUBLE DIGEST MAGAZINE
Archie Comic Publications: Nov, 1992 - No. 146, Dec, 2010 ($2.50-$3.99)

	GD 2.0	VG 4.0	FN 6.0	VF 8.0	VF/NM 9.0	NM- 9.2
1-Capt. Hero story; Pureheart story	2	4	6	9	11	14
2-10: 2-Superduck story; Little Jinx in all. 4-Begin $2.75-c	1	2	3	4	5	7
11-29						4.00
30-146: 40-Begin $2.99-c. 48-Begin $3.19-c. 56-Begin $3.29-c. 72-Begin $3.59-c. 100-Story uses screen captures from classic animated series. 102-Begin $3.69-c. 125-128-"New Look" art; Moose and Midge break up. 130-Begin $3.99-c. 133-Reggie spotlight, also reprints early apps.						4.00

ARCHIE'S PARABLES
Spire Christian Comics (Fleming H. Revell Co.): 1973,1975 (39/49¢, 36 pgs.)

	GD 2.0	VG 4.0	FN 6.0	VF 8.0	VF/NM 9.0	NM- 9.2
nn-By Al Hartley; 39¢ Edition	3	6	9	14	20	25
49¢, no price editions	2	4	6	10	14	18

ARCHIE'S R/C RACERS (Radio controlled cars)
Archie Comics: Sept, 1989 - No. 10, Mar, 1991 (95¢/$1)

	GD 2.0	VG 4.0	FN 6.0	VF 8.0	VF/NM 9.0	NM- 9.2
1	1	2	3	5	6	8
2,5-7,10: 5-Elvis parody. 7-Supervillain-c/s. 10-UFO-c/s						5.00
3,4,8,9						4.00

ARCHIE'S RIVAL REGGIE (Reggie & Archie's Joke Book #15 on)
Archie Publications: 1949 - No. 14, July, 1954

	GD 2.0	VG 4.0	FN 6.0	VF 8.0	VF/NM 9.0	NM- 9.2
1-Reggie 1st app. in Jackpot Comics #5	142	284	426	909	1555	2200
2	58	116	174	371	636	900
3-5	41	82	123	256	428	600
6-10	29	58	87	172	281	390
11-14: Katy Keene in No. 10-14, 1-2 pgs.	22	44	66	132	216	300

ARCHIE'S RIVERDALE HIGH (See Riverdale High)

ARCHIE'S ROLLER COASTER
Spire Christian Comics (Fleming H. Revell Co.): 1981 (69¢)

	GD 2.0	VG 4.0	FN 6.0	VF 8.0	VF/NM 9.0	NM- 9.2
nn-(Low print)	2	4	6	13	18	22

ARCHIE'S SOMETHING ELSE
Spire Christian Comics (Fleming H. Revell Co.): 1975 (39/49¢, 36 pgs.)

	GD 2.0	VG 4.0	FN 6.0	VF 8.0	VF/NM 9.0	NM- 9.2
nn-(39¢-c) Hell's Angels Biker on motorcycle-c	3	6	9	14	19	24
nn-(49¢-c)	2	4	6	10	14	18
Barbour Christian Comics Edition ('86, no price listed)	2	3	4	6	8	10

ARCHIE'S SONSHINE
Spire Christian Comics (Fleming H. Revell Co.): 1973, 1974 (39/49¢, 36 pgs.)

	GD 2.0	VG 4.0	FN 6.0	VF 8.0	VF/NM 9.0	NM- 9.2
39¢ Edition	3	6	9	14	19	24
49¢, no price editions	2	4	6	9	13	16

ARCHIE'S SPORTS SCENE
Spire Christian Comics (Fleming H. Revell Co.): 1983 (no cover price)

	GD 2.0	VG 4.0	FN 6.0	VF 8.0	VF/NM 9.0	NM- 9.2
nn-(Low print)	2	4	6	13	18	22

ARCHIE'S SPRING BREAK
Archie Comics: 1996 - No. 5, 2000 ($2.00/$2.49, 48 pgs., annual)

	GD 2.0	VG 4.0	FN 6.0	VF 8.0	VF/NM 9.0	NM- 9.2
1-5: 1,2-Dan DeCarlo-c						4.00

ARCHIE'S STORY & GAME COMICS DIGEST MAGAZINE
Archie Enterprises: Nov, 1986 - No. 39, Jan, 1998 ($1.25-$1.95, 128 pgs., digest-size)

	GD 2.0	VG 4.0	FN 6.0	VF 8.0	VF/NM 9.0	NM- 9.2
1: Marked-up copies are common	2	4	6	11	16	20
2-10	2	4	6	8	10	12
11-20	1	2	3	4	5	7
21-39: 39-($1.95)						4.00

ARCHIE'S SUPER HERO SPECIAL (See Archie Giant Series Mag. No. 142)

ARCHIE'S SUPER HERO SPECIAL (...Comics Digest Mag. 2)
Archie Publications (Red Circle): Jan, 1979 - No. 2, Aug, 1979 (95¢, 148 pgs.)

	GD 2.0	VG 4.0	FN 6.0	VF 8.0	VF/NM 9.0	NM- 9.2
1-Simon & Kirby r-/Double Life of Pvt. Strong #1,2; Black Hood, The Fly, Jaguar, The Web app.	3	6	9	16	23	30
2-Contains contents to the never published Black Hood #1; origin Black Hood; N. Adams, Wood, Channing, McWilliams, Morrow, S&K-a(r); N. Adams-c. The Shield, The Fly, Jaguar, Hangman, Steel Sterling, The Web, The Fox-r	3	6	9	15	22	28

ARCHIE'S SUPER TEENS
Archie Comic Publications, Inc.: 1994 - No. 4, 1996 ($2.00, 52 pgs.)

	GD 2.0	VG 4.0	FN 6.0	VF 8.0	VF/NM 9.0	NM- 9.2
1-Staton/Esposito-c/a; pull-out poster	2	4	6	8	10	12
2-4: 2-Fred Hembeck script; Bret Blevins/Terry Austin-a						4.00

ARCHIE'S SUPER TEENS VERSUS CRUSADERS
Archie Publications: Aug, 2018 - No. 2, Sept, 2018 ($3.99, limited series)

	GD 2.0	VG 4.0	FN 6.0	VF 8.0	VF/NM 9.0	NM- 9.2
1,2-Black Hood, Steel Sterling, The Fox, The Web, The Comet, and The Shield app.						4.00

ARCHIE'S TV LAUGH-OUT ("...Starring Sabrina" on-c #1-50)
Archie Publications: Dec, 1969 - No. 105, Feb, 1986 (#1-7: 68 pgs.)

	GD 2.0	VG 4.0	FN 6.0	VF 8.0	VF/NM 9.0	NM- 9.2
1-Sabrina begins, thru #105. 1st app. Ambrose Spellman (Sabrina's cousin) and Harvey Kinkle (Sabrina's boyfriend). 1st app. of the Archie gang (Archie, Jughead, Reggie, Betty and Veronica) in a Sabrina story as Sabrina now attends Riverdale High	13	26	39	89	195	300
2 (68 pgs.)	7	14	21	46	86	125
3-6 (68 pgs.)	5	10	15	31	53	70
7-Josie begins, thru #105; Archie's & Josie's Bands cover logos begin	8	16	24	52	99	145

	GD 2.0	VG 4.0	FN 6.0	VF 8.0	VF/NM 9.0	NM- 9.2

8-23 (52 pgs.): 10-1st Josie on-c. 12-1st Josie and Pussycats on-c. 14-Beatles cameo on poster — 8, 12, 27, 44, 60

24-40: 37,39,40-Bicentennial-c — 3, 6, 9, 14, 20, 25

41,47,56: 41-Alexandra rejoins J&P band. 47-Fonz cameo; voodoo-s. 56-Fonz parody; B&V with Farrah hair-c — 3, 6, 9, 15, 22, 28

42-46,48-55,57-60 — 2, 4, 6, 9, 12, 15

61-68,70-80: 63-UFOs-s. 79-Mummy-s — 1, 3, 4, 6, 8, 10

69-Sherlock Holmes parody — 1, 3, 4, 6, 8, 10

81-90,94,95,97-99: 84 Voodoo-s — 1, 2, 3, 5, 6, 8

91-Early Cheryl Blossom-s; Sabrina/Archies Band-c — 3, 6, 9, 21, 33, 45

92-A-Team parody — 1, 3, 4, 6, 8, 10

93-(2/84) Archie in drag-c; Hill Street Blues-s; Groucho Marx parody; cameo parody app. of Batman, Spider-Man, Wonder Woman and others — 2, 4, 6, 9, 12, 15

96-MASH parody-s; Jughead in drag; Archies Band-c — 1, 3, 4, 6, 8, 10

100-(4/85) Michael Jackson parody-c/s; J&P band and Archie band on-c — 2, 4, 6, 10, 14, 18

101-104-Lower print run. 104-Miami Vice parody-c — 1, 2, 3, 5, 7, 9

105-Wrestling/Hulk Hogan parody-c; J&P band on-c — 1, 2, 4, 6, 9, 12

NOTE: *Dan DeCarlo a 78-up(most). c-89-up(most). Archies Band-s 2,7,9-11,15,20,25,37,64,65,67,68,70,73, 76,78,79,83,84,86,90,96,100,101; Archies Band-c 2,17,20,91,94,96,99-103. Josie-s 12,21,26,35,52,78,80,90. Josie-c 10,91,94. Josie and the Pussycats (as a band in costume)-s 7,9,10,37,38,41,42,66,84,99-101,105. Josie/Pussycats member Valerie &/or Melody-s 17,20,22,25,27-29,31,33,36,39,40,43-51,53-65,67-77,79,81- 83,85-89,92-94,102-104. Josie w/Pussycats band-c 12,14,17,18,22,24. Sabrina-s 1-9,11-86,88-106. Sabrina-c 1-18,21,23,27,49,91,94.*

ARCHIE'S VACATION SPECIAL
Archie Publications: Winter, 1994 - No. 8, 2000 ($2.00/$2.25/$2.29/$2.49, annual)

1 — 5.00
2-8: 8-(2000, $2.49) — 4.00

ARCHIE'S VALENTINE'S SPECTACULAR
Archie Comic Publications: Mar, 2022; Mar, 2023; Mar, 2024 ($2.99, one-shots)

1-(2022) New romantic story by Rotante/Galvan-a; reprints by various incl. Parent — 3.00
1-(2023) New story introducing Cassie Cloud — 3.00
1-(2024) New stories and reprints; Sabrina app. — 3.00

ARCHIE'S WEIRD MYSTERIES (Continues as Archie's Mysteries from #25 to #34)
Archie Comics: Feb, 2000 - No. 24, Dec, 2002 ($1.79/$1.99)

1 — 1, 3, 4, 6, 8, 10
2-24: 3-Mighty Crusaders app. 14-Super Teens-c/app.; Mighty Crusaders app. — 5.00

ARCHIE'S WORLD
Spire Christian Comics (Fleming H. Revell Co.): 1973, 1976 (39/49¢)

39¢ Edition — 3, 6, 9, 14, 19, 24
49¢ Edition, no price editions — 2, 4, 6, 9, 13, 16

ARCHIE: THE MARRIED LIFE – 10TH ANNIVERSARY
Archie Comics: Sept, 2019 - No. 6, Mar, 2020 ($3.99, limited series)

1-6-Sequel to future stories in Archie #600-605; Uslan-s/Parent-a; multiple covers — 4.00

ARCHIE 3000
Archie Comics: May, 1989 - No. 16, July, 1991 (75¢/95¢/$1.00)

1,16: 16-Aliens-c/s — 5.00
2-15: 6-Begin $1.00-c; X-Mas-c — 4.00

ARCHIE VS. PREDATOR
Dark Horse Comics: Apr, 2015 - No. 4, Jul, 2015 ($3.99, limited series)

1-4-The Archie gang hunted by the Predator; de Campi-s/Ruiz-a; 3 covers on each — 4.00

ARCHIE VS. PREDATOR II
Archie Comics: Sept, 2019 - No. 5, Mar, 2020 ($3.99, limited series)

1-5-Multiverse Archie gangs; de Campi-s/Hack-a; 3 covers on each — 4.00

ARCHIE VS. SHARKNADO
Archie Comics: 2015 ($4.99, one-shot)

1-Based on the Sharknado movie series; Ferrante-s/Parent-a; 3 covers — 5.00

ARCHIE VS. THE WORLD
Archie Comics: Mar, 2023 ($3.99, one-shot)

1-The Archie gang in a post-apocalyptic world; Sitterson-s/Dougherty-a — 4.00

ARCOMICS PREMIERE
Arcomics: July, 1993 ($2.95)

1-1st lenticular-c on a comic (flicker-c) — 4.00

AREA 52
Image Comics: Jan, 2001 - No. 4, June, 2001 ($2.95)

1-4-Haberlin-s/Henry-a — 3.00

ARES
Marvel Comics: Mar, 2006 - No. 5, July, 2006 ($2.99, limited series)

1-5-Oeming-s/Foreman-a — 3.00
...: God of War TPB (2006, $13.99) r/series — 14.00

ARES IX: THE DARKNESS
Image Comics (Top Cow): Dec, 2018 ($3.99, one-shot)

1-Hodgson-s/Valyogos-a; Crapo-s/Whitaker-a; The Darkness app. — 4.00

ARE YOU AFRAID OF DARKSEID?
DC Comics: Dec, 2021 ($9.99, squarebound, one-shot)

1-Campfire-style ghost stories; Teen Titans, Darkseid, Harley Quinn, Batman app. — 10.00

ARGUS (See Flash, 2nd Series) (Also see Showcase '95 #1,2)
DC Comics: Apr, 1995 - No. 6, Oct, 1995 ($1.50, limited series)

1-6: 4-Begin $1.75-c — 3.00

ARIA
Image Comics (Avalon Studios): Jan, 1999 - No. 4, Nov, 1999 ($2.50)

Preview (11/98, $2.95) — 5.00
1-Anacleto-c/a — 1, 2, 3, 5, 6, 8
1-Variant-c by Michael Turner — 1, 2, 3, 5, 6, 8
1-($10.00) Alternate-c by Turner — 1, 3, 4, 6, 8, 10
1,2-(Blanc & Noir) Black and white printing of pencil art — 3.00
1-(Blanc & Noir) DF Edition — 5.00

2-4: 2,4-Anacleto-c/a. 3-Martinez-a — 3.00
4-($6.95) Glow in the Dark-c — 1, 3, 4, 6, 8, 10

Aria Angela 1 (2/00, $2.95) Anacleto-a; 4 covers by Anacleto, JG Jones, Portacio and Quesada — 3.00
Aria Angela Blanc & Noir 1 (4/00, $2.95) Anacleto-c — 3.00
Aria Angela European Ashcan — 10.00
Aria Angela 2 (10/00, $2.95) Anacleto-a/c — 3.00
...: A Midwinter's Dream 1 (1/02, $4.95, 7"x7") text-s w/Anacleto panels — 5.00
...: Heavenly Creatures (2/21, $6.99) Reprints Aria Angela issues with Angela replaced — 7.00
...: The Enchanted Collection (5/04, $16.95) r/Summer's Spell & The Uses of Enchantment — 17.00

ARIA: SUMMER'S SPELL
Image Comics (Avalon Studios): Mar, 2002 - No. 2, Jun, 2002 ($2.95)

1,2-Anacleto-c/Holguin-s/Pajarillo & Medina-a — 3.00

ARIA: THE SOUL MARKET
Image Comics (Avalon Studios): Mar, 2001 - No. 6, Dec, 2001 ($2.95)

1-6-Anacleto-c/Holguin-s — 3.00
HC (2002, $26.95, 8.25" x 12.25") oversized r/#1-6 — 27.00
SC (2004, $16.95, 8.25" x 12.25") oversized r/#1-6 — 17.00

ARIA: THE USES OF ENCHANTMENT
Image Comics (Avalon Studios): Feb, 2003 - No. 4, Sept, 2003 ($2.95)

1-4-Anacleto-c/Holguin-s/Medina-a — 3.00

ARIANE AND BLUEBEARD (See Night Music #8)

ARIEL & SEBASTIAN (See Cartoon Tales & The Little Mermaid)

ARION, LORD OF ATLANTIS (Also see Crisis on Infinite Earths & Warlord #55)
DC Comics: Nov, 1982 - No. 35, Sept, 1985

1-Story cont'd from Warlord #62 — 4.00
2-35 — 3.00
... Special #1 (11/85) — 4.00

ARION THE IMMORTAL (Also see Arion, Lord of Atlantis & Showcase '95 #7)
DC Comics: July, 1992 - No. 6, Dec, 1992 ($1.50, limited series)

1-6: 4-Gustovich-a(i) — 3.00

ARISTOCATS (See Movie Comics & Walt Disney Showcase No. 16)

ARISTOKITTENS, THE (...Meet Jiminy Cricket No. 1)(Disney)
Gold Key: Oct, 1971 - No. 9, Oct, 1975

1 — 3, 6, 9, 19, 30, 40
2-5,7-9 — 3, 6, 9, 14, 19, 24
6-(52 pgs.) — 3, 6, 9, 15, 22, 28

ARIZONA KID, THE (Also see The Comics & Wild Western)
Marvel/Atlas Comics(CSI): Mar, 1951 - No. 6, Jan, 1952

1 — 31, 62, 93, 184, 300, 415
2-4: 2-Heath-a(3) — 15, 30, 45, 88, 137, 185
5,6 — 14, 28, 42, 78, 112, 145

NOTE: *Heath a-1-3; c-1-3. Maneely c-4-6. Morisi a-4-6. Sinnott a-6.*

ARK, THE (See The Crusaders)

ARKAGA
Image Comics: Sept, 1997 ($2.95, one-shot)

1-Jorgensen-s/a — 3.00

ARKANIUM
Dreamwave Productions: Sept, 2002 - No. 5 ($2.95)

1-5: 1-Gatefold wraparound-c — 3.00

ARKHAM ASYLUM: LIVING HELL
DC Comics: July, 2003 - No. 6, Dec, 2003 ($2.50, limited series)

1-6-Ryan Sook-a; Batman app. 3-Batgirl-c/app. — 4.00

ARKHAM ASYLUM: MADNESS
DC Comics: 2010 ($19.99, HC graphic novel, dustjacket)

HC-Sam Kieth-s/a/c; Joker, Two-Face, Harley and Ivy app. — 20.00
SC-(2011, $14.99) Sam Kieth-s/a/c; Joker, Two-Face, Harley and Ivy app. — 15.00

ARKHAM CITY: THE ORDER OF THE WORLD
DC Comics: Dec, 2021 - No. 6, May, 2022 ($3.99, limited series)

1-6-Watters-s/Dani-a; Ten-Eyed Man, Mad Hatter, Ratcatcher & Azrael app. — 4.00

ARKHAM MANOR (Follows events in Batman Eternal #30)
DC Comics: Dec, 2014 - No. 6, May, 2015 ($2.99)

1-6-Arkham Asylum re-opens in Wayne Manor; Duggan-s/Crystal-a — 3.00
...: Endgame 1 (6/15, $2.99) Tieri-s/Albuquerque-c; tie-in with other Batman titles — 3.00

ARKHAM REBORN
DC Comics: Dec, 2009 - No. 3, Feb, 2010 ($2.99, limited series)

1-3-David Hine-s/Jeremy Haun-a — 3.00
Batman: Arkham Reborn TPB (2010, $12.99) r/#1-3, Detective Comics #864,865 and Batman: Battle For the Cowl: Arkham Asylum #1 — 16.00

ARMAGEDDON
Chaos! Comics: Oct, 1999 - No. 4, Jan, 2000 ($2.95, limited series)

Preview — 2, 4, 6, 11, 16, 20
1-4-Lady Death, Evil Ernie, Purgatori app. — 4.00

ARMAGEDDON: ALIEN AGENDA
DC Comics: Nov, 1991 - No. 4, Feb, 1992 ($1.00, limited series)

1-4 — 3.00

ARMAGEDDON FACTOR, THE
AC Comics: 1987 - No. 2, 1987; No. 3, 1990 ($1.95)

1,2: Sentinels of Justice, Dragonfly, Femforce — 4.00
3-($3.95, color)-Almost all AC characters app. — 5.00

ARMAGEDDON: INFERNO
DC Comics: Apr, 1992 - No. 4, July, 1992 ($1.00, limited series)

1-4: Many DC heroes app. 3-A. Adams/Austin-a — 4.00

Archie vs. Predator #1 © ACP & 20Fox

Armor Wars #5 © MAR

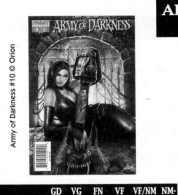

Army of Darkness #10 © Orion

	GD 2.0	VG 4.0	FN 6.0	VF 8.0	VF/NM 9.0	NM- 9.2

ARMAGEDDON 2001
DC Comics: May, 1991 - No. 2, Oct, 1991 ($2.00, squarebound, 68 pgs.)

1-Features many DC heroes; intro Waverider						5.00
1-2nd & 3rd printings; 3rd has silver ink-c						4.00
2						4.00

ARMED & DANGEROUS
Acclaim Comics (Armada): Apr, 1996 - No.4, July, 1996 ($2.95, B&W)

1-4-Bob Hall-c/a & scripts						3.00
Special 1 (8/96, $2.95, B&W)-Hall-c/a & scripts.						3.00

ARMED & DANGEROUS HELL'S SLAUGHTERHOUSE
Acclaim Comics (Armada): Oct, 1996 - No. 4, Jan, 1997 ($2.95, B&W)

1-4: Hall-c/a/scripts.						3.00

ARMOR (AND THE SILVER STREAK) (Revengers Featuring... in indicia for #1-3)
Continuity Comics: Sept, 1985 - No.13, Apr, 1992 ($2.00)

1-Intro/origin Armor & the Silver Streak; Neal Adams-c/a (Newstand Ed.; red logo)						4.00
1-Direct Edition (silver logo)						5.00
2-12: 7-Origin Armor; Nebres-i						4.00
13-Direct Edition (green background)						5.00
13-Newstand Edition (purple background)	1	3	4	6	8	10

ARMORCLADS
Valiant Entertainment: Mar, 2022 - No. 5, Jul, 2022 ($3.99, limited series)

1-5-O'Connor & Buccellato-s/Garcia-a						4.00

ARMOR (DEATHWATCH 2000)
Continuity Comics: Apr, 1993 - No. 6, Nov, 1993 ($2.50)

1-6: 1-3-Deathwatch 2000 x-over						3.00

ARMOR HUNTERS
Valiant Entertainment: Jun, 2014 - No. 4, Sept, 2014 ($3.99)

1-4-Venditti-s/Braithwaite-a; X-O vs. the Hunters. 2-4-Bloodshot app. 4-Ninjak app.						4.00
...: Aftermath 1 (10/14, $3.99) Venditti-s/Cafu-a; leads into Unity #0						4.00

ARMOR HUNTERS: BLOODSHOT
Valiant Entertainment: Jul, 2014 - No. 3, Sept, 2014 ($3.99, limited series)

1-3-Joe Harris-s/Hairsine-a; Malgam app.						4.00

ARMOR HUNTERS: HARBINGER
Valiant Entertainment: Jul, 2014 - No. 3, Sept, 2014 ($3.99, limited series)

1-3-Dysart-s/Gill-a						4.00

ARMORINES (See X-O Manowar #25 for 16 pg. bound-in Armorines #0)
Valiant: June, 1994 - No. 12, June, 1995 ($2.25)

0-Stand-alone edition with cardstock-c						34.00
0-Gold						28.00
1						4.00
2-11: 7-Wraparound-c						3.00
12-Byrne-c/swipe (X-Men, 1st Series #138)						5.00

ARMORINES (Volume 2)
Acclaim Comics: Oct, 1999 - No. 4, Mar, 2000 ($3.95/$2.50, limited series)

1-($3.95) Calafiore & P. Palmiotti-a						6.00
2,3-($2.50)						4.00
4-Low print run		4	8	12	27	44	60

ARMOR WARS (Secret Wars tie-in)
Marvel Comics: Aug, 2015 - No. 5, Nov, 2015 ($3.99, limited series)

1-5-Tony Stark and other armor-clad citizens of Technopolis; Robinson-s/Takara-a						4.00

ARMOR X
Image Comics: March, 2005 - No. 4, June, 2005 ($2.95, limited series)

1-Keith Champagne-s/Andy Smith-a; flip covers on #2-4						3.00

ARMSTRONG AND THE VAULT OF SPIRITS (Archer and Armstrong)
Valiant Entertainment: Feb, 2018 ($3.99, one-shot)

1-Van Lente-s/Cafu & Robertson-a; Archer, Faith, Quantum & Woody, Ivar app.						4.00

ARMY AND NAVY COMICS (Supersnipe No. 6 on)
Street & Smith Publications: May, 1941 - No. 5, July, 1942

1-Cap Fury & Nick Carter	74	148	222	470	810	1150
2-Cap Fury & Nick Carter	40	80	120	246	411	575
3,4: 4-Jack Farr-c/a	33	66	99	194	317	440
5-Supersnipe app.; see Shadow V2#3 for 1st app.; Story of Douglas MacArthur; George Marcoux-c/a	65	130	195	416	708	1000

ARMY @ LOVE
DC Comics (Vertigo): May, 2007 - No. 12, Apr, 2008;

V2 #1, Oct, 2008 - No. 6, Mar, 2009 ($2.99)

1-12-Rick Veitch-s/a(p); Gary Erskine-a(i)						3.00
(Vol. 2) 1-6-Veitch-s/a(p); Erskine-a(i)						3.00
...: Generation Pwned TPB (2008, $12.99) r/#6-12						13.00
...: The Hot Zone Club TPB (2007, $9.99) r/#1-5; intro. by Peter Kuper						10.00

ARMY ATTACK
Charlton Comics: July, 1964 - No. 4, Feb, 1965; V2#38, July, 1965 - No. 47, Feb, 1967

V1#1	5	10	15	33	57	80
2-4(2/65)	3	6	9	21	33	45
V2#38(7/65)-47 (formerly U.S. Air Force #1-37)	3	6	9	16	24	32

NOTE: *Glanzman* a-1-3. *Montes/Bache* a-44.

ARMY AT WAR (Also see Our Army at War & Cancelled Comic Cavalcade)
DC Comics: Oct-Nov, 1978

1-Kubert-c; all new story and art	3	6	9	16	24	32

ARMY OF DARKNESS
Dark Horse Comics: Nov, 1992 - No. 2, Dec, 1992; No. 3, Oct, 1993 ($2.50, limited series)

1-Bolton painted-c/a in all	3	6	9	20	31	42
2,3	2	4	6	11	16	20
... Movie Adaptation TPB (2006, $14.99) r/#1-3; intro. by Busiek; Bruce Campbell interview 15.00						

ARMY OF DARKNESS (Also see Marvel Zombies vs. Army of Darkness)
Dynamite Entertainment: 2005 - No. 13, 2007 ($2.99)

1-4 (Vs. Re-Animator):1,2-Four covers; Greene-a/Kuhoric-s. 3,4-Three covers						4.00
5-13: 5-7-Kuhoric-s/Sharpe-a; four covers. 8-11-Ash Vs. Dracula. 12,13-Death of Ash						4.00

ARMY OF DARKNESS: ... (Also see Death to the Army of Darkness)
Dynamite Entertainment: 2007 - No. 27, 2010 ($3.50/$3.99)

... From the Ashes 1-4-Kuhoric-s/Blanco-a; covers by Blanco & Suydam						4.00
5-8-(The Long Road Home); two covers on each						4.00
9-25: 9-12-(Home Sweet Hell), 13-King For A Day. 14-17-Hellbillies and Deadnecks						4.00
26,27-($3.99) Raicht-s/Cohn-a/c						4.00
#1992.1 (2014, $7.99, squarebound) Short stories by Kuhoric, Niles and others						8.00
...: Ash's Christmas Horror Special (2008, $4.99) Kuhoric-s/Simons-a; 2 covers						5.00
...: Convention Invasion (2014, $7.99, squarebound) Moreci-s/Peeples-a						8.00
... Election Special 1 (2016, $5.99) Serrano-s/Galindo-a						6.00
... Halloween Special One-Shot (2018, $4.99) art by Marron & Lofti; Blackbeard app.						5.00
.../ Reanimator One Shot (2013, $4.99) Rahner-s/Valiente-a						5.00

ARMY OF DARKNESS VOLUME 3
Dynamite Entertainment: 2012 - No. 13, 2013 ($3.99)

1-13: 1-Female Ash; Michaels-a						4.00

ARMY OF DARKNESS VOLUME 4
Dynamite Entertainment: 2014 - No. 5, 2015 ($3.99)

1-5-Ash in space; Bunn-s/Watts-a; multiple covers						4.00

ARMY OF DARKNESS: ASHES 2 ASHES (Movie)
Devil's Due Publ.: July, 2004 - No. 4, 2004 ($2.99, limited series)

1-4-Four covers for each; Nick Bradshaw-a						4.00
1-Director's Cut (12/04, $4.99) r/#1, cover gallery, script and sketch pages						5.00
TPB (2005, $14.99) r/series; cover gallery; Bradshaw interview and sketch pages						15.00

ARMY OF DARKNESS: ASH GETS HITCHED
Dynamite Entertainment: 2014 - No. 4, 2014 ($3.99, limited series)

1-4-Ash in medieval times; Niles-s/Tenorio-a; multiple covers						4.00

ARMY OF DARKNESS: ASH SAVES OBAMA
Dynamite Entertainment: 2009 - No. 4, 2009 ($3.50, limited series)

1-4-Serrano-s/Padilla-a; covers by Parrillo and Nauck. 4-Obama app.						6.00

ARMY OF DARKNESS/BUBBA HO-TEP
Dynamite Entertainment/IDW: 2019 - No. 4, 2019 ($3.99, limited series)

1-4-Ash meets Elvis; Duvall-s/Federici-a; multiple covers						4.00

ARMY OF DARKNESS: FOREVER
Dynamite Entertainment: 2023 - Present ($3.99, limited series)

1-5-Tony Fleecs-s/Justin Greenwood-a						4.00

ARMY OF DARKNESS FURIOUS ROAD
Dynamite Entertainment: 2016 - No. 6, 2016 ($3.99, limited series)

1-6-Nancy Collins-s/Kewber Baal-a. 1-Multiple covers						4.00

ARMY OF DARKNESS: 1979
Dynamite Entertainment: 2021 - No. 5, 2022 ($3.99, limited series)

1-5-Rodney Barnes-s/Tom Garcia & Ed Mennu-a; multiple covers on all; Ash in 1979 NY						4.00

ARMY OF DARKNESS: SHOP TILL YOU DROP DEAD (Movie)

	GD	VG	FN	VF	VF/NM	NM-
	2.0	4.0	6.0	8.0	9.0	9.2

Devil's Due Publ.: Jan, 2005 - No. 4, July, 2005 ($2.99, limited series)
1-4:1-Five covers; Bradshaw-a/Kuhoric-s. 2-4: Two covers. 3-Greene-a ... 4.00

ARMY OF DARKNESS VS. HACK/SLASH
Dynamite Entertainment: 2013 - No. 6, 2014 ($3.99, limited series)
1-6-Tim Seeley-s/Daniel Leister-a; multiple covers on each ... 4.00

ARMY OF DARKNESS VS. REANIMATOR: NECRONOMICON RISING
Dynamite Entertainment: 2022 - No. 5, 2022 ($3.99, limited series)
1-5-Burnham-s/Cassallos-a; multiple covers on each ... 4.00

ARMY OF DARKNESS / XENA
Dynamite Entertainment: 2008 - No. 4, 2008 ($3.50, limited series)
1-4-Layman-s/Montenegro-a; two covers on each ... 4.00

ARMY OF DARKNESS XENA: WARRIOR PRINCESS FOREVER... AND A DAY
Dynamite Entertainment: 2016 - No. 6, 2017 ($3.99, limited series)
1-6-Lobdell-s. 1-Multiple covers. 1,2-Fernandez-a. 3-6-Galindo-a ... 4.00

ARMY SURPLUS KOMIKZ FEATURING CUTEY BUNNY
Army Surplus Komikz/Eclipse Comics: 1982 - No. 5, 1985 ($1.50, B&W)
1-Cutey Bunny begins ... 2 ... 4 ... 6 ... 10 ... 14 ... 18
2-5: 5-(Eclipse)-JLA/X-Men/Batman parody ... 5.00

ARMY WAR HEROES (Also see Iron Corporal)
Charlton Comics: Dec, 1963 - No. 38, June, 1970
1 ... 8 ... 16 ... 24 ... 55 ... 105 ... 155
2-10 ... 4 ... 8 ... 12 ... 25 ... 40 ... 55
11-21,23-30: 24-Intro. Archer & Corp. Jack series ... 3 ... 6 ... 9 ... 16 ... 23 ... 30
22-Origin/1st app. Iron Corporal series by Glanzman ... 5 ... 10 ... 15 ... 31 ... 53 ... 75
31-38 ... 2 ... 4 ... 6 ... 10 ... 14 ... 18
Modern Comics Reprint 36 ('78) ... 5.00
NOTE: *Montes/Bache* a-1, 16, 17, 21, 23-25, 27-30.

AROUND THE BLOCK WITH DUNC & LOO (See Dunc and Loo)

AROUND THE WORLD IN 80 DAYS (Movie) (See A Golden Picture Classic)
Dell Publishing Co.: Feb, 1957
Four Color 784-Photo-c ... 7 ... 14 ... 21 ... 46 ... 86 ... 125

AROUND THE WORLD UNDER THE SEA (See Movie Classics)

AROUND THE WORLD WITH ARCHIE (See Archie Giant Series Mag. #29, 35, 141)

AROUND THE WORLD WITH HUCKLEBERRY & HIS FRIENDS (See Dell Giant No. 44)

ARRGH! (Satire)
Marvel Comics Group: Dec, 1974 - No. 5, Sept, 1975 (25¢)
1-Dracula story; Sekowsky-a(p) ... 3 ... 6 ... 9 ... 20 ... 31 ... 42
2-5: 2-Frankenstein. 3-Mummy. 4-Nightstalker(TV); Dracula-c/app., Hunchback. 5-Invisible Man, Dracula ... 3 ... 6 ... 9 ... 14 ... 20 ... 25
NOTE *Alcala* a-2; c-3. *Everett* a-1r, 2r. *Grandenetti* a-4. *Maneely* a-4r. *Sutton* a-1-3.

ARROW (See Protectors)
Malibu Comics: Oct, 1992 ($1.95, one-shot)
1-Moder-a(p) ... 4.00

ARROW (Based on the 2012 television series)
DC Comics: Jan, 2013 - No. 12, Dec, 2013 ($3.99, printings of digital-first stories)
1-Photo-c; origin retold; Grell-a ... 1 ... 2 ... 3 ... 5 ... 6 ... 8
1-Special Edition (2012, giveaway) Grell-c; back-up preview of Green Arrow #0 ... 4.00
2-12: 8-12-Photo-c ... 4.00

ARROW SEASON 2.5 (Follows the second season of the 2012 television series)
DC Comics: Dec, 2014 - No. 12, Nov, 2015 ($2.99, printings of digital-first stories)
1-12-Photo-c on most. 1-5-Brother Blood app. 5,6-Suicide Squad app. ... 3.00

ARROW, THE (See Funny Pages)
Centaur Publications: Oct, 1940 - No. 2, Nov, 1940; No. 3, Oct, 1941
1-The Arrow begins(r/Funny Pages) ... 429 ... 858 ... 1287 ... 3132 ... 5516 ... 7900
2,3: 2-Tippy Taylor serial continues from Amazing Mystery Funnies #24. 3-Origin Dash Dartwell, the Human Meteor; origin The Rainbow-r; bondage-c ... 300 ... 600 ... 900 ... 1980 ... 3440 ... 4900
NOTE: *Gustavson* a-1, 2; c-3.

ARROWHEAD (See Black Rider and Wild Western)
Atlas Comics (CPS): April, 1954 - No. 4, Nov, 1954
1-Arrowhead & his horse Eagle begin ... 28 ... 56 ... 84 ... 165 ... 270 ... 375
2-4: 4-Forte-a ... 16 ... 32 ... 48 ... 94 ... 147 ... 200
NOTE: *Heath* c-3. *Jack Katz* a-3. *Maneely* c-2. *Pakula* a-1-4; c-1. *Sinnott* a-1-4.

ARROWSMITH (Also see Astro City/Arrowsmith flip book)
DC Comics (Cliffhanger): Sept, 2003 - No. 6, May, 2004 ($2.95)
1-6-Pacheco-a/Busiek-s ... 3.00
...: So Smart in Their Fine Uniforms TPB (2004, $14.95) r/#1-6 ... 15.00

ARROWSMITH: BEHIND ENEMY LINES
Image Comics: Jan, 2022 - No. 6, Jun, 2022 ($3.99)
1-6-Pacheco-a/Busiek-s ... 4.00

ARSENAL (Teen Titans' Speedy)
DC Comics: Oct, 1998 - No. 4, Jan, 1999 ($2.50, limited series)
1-4: Grayson-s. 1-Black Canary app. 2-Green Arrow app. ... 4.00

ARSENAL SPECIAL (See New Titans, Showcase '94 #7 & Showcase '95 #8)
DC Comics: 1996 ($2.95, one-shot)
1 ... 4.00

ARTBABE
Fantagraphics Books: May, 1996 - Apr, 1999 ($2.50/$2.95/$3.50, B&W)
V1 #5, V2 #1-3 ... 4.00
#4-($3.50) ... 5.00

ART BRUT
Image Comics: Dec, 2022 - No. 4, Mar, 2023 ($3.99, limited series)
1-4-Prince-s/Morazzo-a ... 4.00

ARTEMIS & THE ASSASSIN
AfterShock Comics: Mar, 2020 - No. 5, Sept, 2020 ($4.99/$3.99)
1-($4.99) Stephanie Phillips-s/Meghan Hetrick & Francesca Fantini-a ... 5.00
2-5-($3.99) 3-5-Fantini-a ... 4.00

ARTEMIS IX (See Aphrodite IX)
Image Comics (Top Cow): Aug, 2015 ($3.99, one-shot)
1-Dan Wickline-s/Johnny Desjardins-a; 2 covers ... 4.00

ARTEMIS: REQUIEM (Also see Wonder Woman, 2nd Series #90)
DC Comics: June, 1996 - No. 6, Nov, 1996 ($1.75, limited series)
1-6: Messner-Loebs scripts & Benes-c/a in all. 1,2-Wonder Woman app. ... 3.00

ARTEMIS: WANTED (Wonder Woman)
DC Comics: Sept, 2022 ($5.99, one-shot)
1-Ayala-s/Patridge-a; Donna Troy and Cassie Sandsmark app. ... 6.00

ARTIFACT ONE
Aspen MLT: No. 0, Aug, 2018 - No. 4, Mar, 2019 ($3.99)
0-($1.50) Krul & Hernandez-s/Moranelli-a ... 3.00
1-4: 1-(10/18, $3.99) Krul & Hernandez-s/Moranelli-a; bonus Aspen Mascots story ... 4.00

ARTIFACTS
Image Comics (Top Cow): Jul, 2010 - No. 40, Nov, 2014 ($3.99, intended as a limited series)
0-(5/10, free) Free Comic Book Day edition; Sejic-a ... 3.00
1-39: 1-6-Marz-s/Broussard-a. 1-Multiple covers; back-up origin of Witchblade. 7,8-Portacio-a. 9-12-Haun-a. 10-Wraparound-c by Sejic. 13-Keown-a. 14-25-Sejic-a ... 4.00
40-($5.99) Steve Foxe-s/Adalor Alvarez-a/Sejic-c; back-up stories ... 6.00
... Lost Tales 1 (5/15, $3.99) Short stories app by Talent Hunt runners-up ... 4.00
...Origins (1/12, $3.99) Two-page spread origins of the 13 artifacts; wraparound-c ... 4.00

ART OF HOMAGE STUDIOS, THE
Image Comics: 1993 ($4.95, one-shot)
1-Short stories and pin-ups by Jim Lee, Silvestri, Williams, Portacio & Chiodo ... 5.00

ART OF ZEN INTERGALACTIC NINJA, THE
Entity Comics: 1994 - No. 2, 1994 ($2.95)
1,2 ... 5.00

ART OPS
DC Comics (Vertigo): Dec, 2015 - No. 12, Dec, 2016 ($3.99)
1-12: Shaun Simon-s/Mike Allred-c. 1-5,8,9,12-Mike Allred-a. 6,7-Eduardo Risso-a ... 4.00

ARZACH (See Moebius...)
Dark Horse Comics: 1996 ($6.95, one-shot)
nn-Moebius-c/a/scripts ... 6 ... 12 ... 18 ... 38 ... 69 ... 100

ASCENCIA
Wake Entertainment: Jan, 2021 - Present ($3.99/$4.99)
1-11-John Dolmayan-s/Tony Parker-a ... 4.00
12-21 ($4.99) 13-Frank Cho-c ... 5.00

ASCENDER (Also see Descender)
Image Comics: Apr, 2019 - Aug, 2021 ($3.99)
1-18-Lemire-s/Nguyen-a/c in all. 4-Telsa app. ... 4.00

ASCENSION
Image Comics (Top Cow Productions): Oct, 1997 - No. 22, Mar, 2000 ($2.50)
Preview ... 6.00
Preview Gold Edition ... 1 ... 3 ... 4 ... 6 ... 8 ... 10
Preview San Diego Edition ... 2 ... 4 ... 6 ... 8 ... 11 ... 14
0 ... 4.00
1/2 ... 6.00
1-David Finch-s/a(p)/Batt-s/a(i) ... 4.00
1-Variant-c w/Image logo at lower right ... 6.00
2-22 ... 3.00
... Collected Edition 1,2 (1998 - No. 2, $4.95, squarebound) 1-r/#1,2. 2-r/#3,4 ... 5.00
Fan Club Edition ... 5.00

ASGARDIANS OF THE GALAXY
Marvel Comics: Nov, 2018 - No. 10, Aug, 2019 ($3.99)
1-10-Angela, Valkyrie, Skurge, Thunderstrike, Throg (Thor Frog), The Destroyer team ... 4.00

ASH
Event Comics: Nov, 1994 - No. 6, Dec, 1995; No. 0, May, 1996 ($2.50/$3.00)
0-Present & Future (Both 5/96, $3.00, foil logo-c)-w/pin-ups ... 3.00
0-Blue Foil logo-c (Present and Future) (1000 each) ... 4.00
0-Silver Prism logo-c (Present and Future) (500 each) ... 10.00
0-Red Prism logo-c (Present and Future) (250 each) ... 20.00
0-Gold Hologram logo-c (Present and Future) (1000 each) ... 8.00
1-Quesada-p/story; Palmiotti-i/story: Barry Windsor-Smith pin-up ... 2 ... 4 ... 6 ... 8 ... 10 ... 12
2-Mignola Hellboy pin-up ... 1 ... 2 ... 3 ... 4 ... 5 ... 7
3,4: 3-Big Guy pin-up by Geoff Darrow. 4-Jim Lee pin-up ... 4.00
4-Fahrenheit Gold ... 7.00
4-6-Fahrenheit Red (5,6-1000) ... 8.00
4-6-Fahrenheit White ... 12.00
5, 6-Double-c w/Hildebrandt Bros.-a, Quesada & Palmiotti. 6-Texeira-c ... 3.00
5,6-Fahrenheit Gold (2000) ... 4.00
6-Fahrenheit White (500)-Texeira-c ... 12.00
Volume 1 (1996, $14.95, TPB)-r/#1-5, intro by James Robinson ... 15.00
Wizard Mini-Comic (1996, magazine supplement) ... 3.00
Wizard #1/2 (1997, mail order) ... 4.00

ASH AND THE ARMY OF DARKNESS (Leads into Army of Darkness: Ash Gets Hitched)
Dynamite Entertainment: 2013 - No. 8, 2014 ($3.99)
1-8: 5-Niles-s/Calero-a. 1-Three covers. 2-8-Two covers. 6-8-Tenorio-a ... 4.00

ASH & THORN
AHOY Comics: 2020 - No. 5, 2020 ($3.99)
1-5-Mariah McCourt-s/ Soo Lee-a/ Jill Thompson-c ... 4.00

ASH: CINDER & SMOKE

Arrow #1 © DC

Ascender #12 © 171 Studios & D. Nguyen

Assassin's Creed #1 © Ubisoft

	GD 2.0	VG 4.0	FN 6.0	VF 8.0	VF/NM 9.0	NM- 9.2

Event Comics: May, 1997 - No. 6, Oct, 1997 ($2.95, limited series)
1-6: Ramos-a/Waid, Augustyn-s in all. 2-6-variant covers by Ramos and Quesada — 3.00

ASH: FILES
Event Comics: Mar, 1997 ($2.95, one-shot)
1-Comics w/text — 3.00

ASH: FIRE AND CROSSFIRE
Event Comics: Jan, 1999 - No. 5 ($2.95, limited series)
1,2-Robinson-s/Quesada & Palmiotti-c/a — 3.00

ASH: FIRE WITHIN, THE
Event Comics: Sept, 1996 - No. 2, Jan, 1997 ($2.95, unfinished limited series)
1,2: Quesada & Palmiotti-c/s/a — 3.00

ASH/ 22 BRIDES
Event Comics: Dec, 1996 - No. 2, Apr, 1997 ($2.95, limited series)
1,2: Nicieza-s/Ramos-c/a — 3.00

ASH VS. THE ARMY OF DARKNESS
Dynamite Entertainment: No. 0, 2017 - No. 5, 2017 ($3.99)
0-5: 0-Sims & Bowers-s/Vargas-a; multiple covers on each — 4.00

ASKANI'SON (See Adventures of Cyclops & Phoenix limited series)
Marvel Comics: Jan, 1996 - No. 4, May, 1996 ($2.95, limited series)
1-4: Story cont'd from Advs. of Cyclops & Phoenix; Lobdell/Loeb story; Gene Ha-c/a(p) — 4.00
TPB (1997, $12.99) r/#1-4; Gene Ha painted-c — 13.00

ASPEN (MICHAEL TURNER PRESENTS:...) (Also see Fathom)
Aspen MLT, Inc.: July, 2003 - No. 3, Aug, 2003 ($2.99)
1-Fathom story; Turner-a/Johns-s; interviews w/Turner & Johns; two covers by Turner — 3.00
2,3:2-Fathom story; Turner-a/Johns-s; two covers by Turner; pin-ups and interviews — 3.00
... Presents: The Adventures of the Aspen Universe (10/16, free) coloring book; Oum-a — 3.00
... Seasons: Fall 2005 (12/05, $2.99) short stories by various; Turner-c — 3.00
... Seasons: Spring 2005 (4/05, $2.99) short stories by various; Turner-c — 3.00
... Seasons: Summer 2006 (10/06, $2.99) short stories by various; Turner-c — 3.00
... Seasons: Winter 2009 (3/09, $2.99) short stories by various; Benitez-c — 3.00
... Showcase: Aspen Matthews 1 (7/08, $2.99) Caldwell-a — 3.00
... Showcase: Kiani 1 (10/09, $2.99) Scott Clark-a; covers by Clark and Caldwell — 3.00
... Sketchbook 1 (2003, $2.99) sketch pages by Michael Turner and Talent Caldwell — 3.00
... Splash: 2006 Swimsuit Spectacular 1 (3/06, $2.99) pin-up pages by various; Turner-c — 3.00
... Splash: 2007 Swimsuit Spectacular 1 (8/07, $2.99) pin-up pages by various; Turner-c — 3.00
... Splash: 2008 Swimsuit Spectacular 1 (7/08, $2.99) pin-up pages by various; Turner-c — 3.00
... Splash: 2010 Swimsuit Spectacular 1 (8/10, $2.99) pin-up pages by various; 2 covers — 3.00
... Splash: 2018 Swimsuit Spectacular 1 (7/18, $3.99) pin-up pages by various; 2 covers — 4.00
...: The Year Ahead 2019 1 (2/19, 25c) Previews, summaries of TPBs, creator profiles — 3.00
... Universe Sourcebook 1 (7/16, $5.99) Character profiles for Fathom, Soulfire, Iris — 6.00

ASPEN SHOWCASE
Aspen MLT: Oct, 2008 ($2.99)
...: Benoist 1 (10/08) - Krul-s/Gunnell-a; two covers by Gunnell & Manapul — 3.00
...: Ember 1 (2/09) - Randy Green-a; two covers by Gunnell & Green — 3.00

ASPEN UNIVERSE: DECIMATION
Aspen MLT: No. 0, May, 2017; No. 1, Oct, 2017 - No. 4, Jan, 2018 (free/$3.99)
0-(5/17, free) Prelude to Aspen crossover series; Hernandez-s/Renna & Bazaldua-a — 3.00
1-4-($3.99) Hernandez-s/Renna-a — 4.00

ASPEN UNIVERSE: REVELATIONS
Aspen MLT: Jul, 2016 - No. 5, Dec, 2016 ($3.99)
1-5-Fathom & Soulfire crossover; Fialkov & Krul-s/Gunderson-a; multiple covers — 4.00

ASPEN VISIONS
Aspen MLT: Jan, 2019 - Mar, 2019 ($3.99)
...: Executive Assistant: Iris: The Midst of Chaos 1 (1/19) - Northcott-s/Tran-a; 4 covers — 4.00
...: Fathom: Spinning Our Fate 1 (2/19) - Northcott-s/Sta Maria-a; 4 covers — 4.00
...: Soulfire: The Heart of Eternity 1 (3/19) - Northcott-s/Cafaro-a; 4 covers — 4.00

ASSASSINISTAS
IDW Publishing (Black Crown): Dec, 2017 - No. 6, May, 2018 ($3.99)
1-6-Tini Howard-s/Gilbert Hernandez-a — 4.00

ASSASSIN NATION
Image Comics (Skybound): Mar, 2019 - No. 5, Jul, 2019 ($3.99, limited series)
1-5-Kyle Starks-s/Erica Henderson-a/c — 4.00

ASSASSINS
DC Comics (Amalgam): Apr, 1996 ($1.95)
1-McDaniel-a; Daredevil/Ravager hybrid with Catwoman/Elektra hybrid — 4.00

ASSASSIN'S APPRENTICE (Adaptation of Robin Hobb's fantasy novel)
Dark Horse Comics: Dec, 2022 - No. 6, May, 2023 ($3.99, limited series)
1-6-Robin Hobb & Jody Houser-s/Ryan Kelly-a — 4.00

ASSASSIN'S APPRENTICE II (Adaptation of Robin Hobb's fantasy novel)
Dark Horse Comics: Dec, 2023 - Present ($3.99, limited series)
1-3-Robin Hobb & Jody Houser-s/Ryan Kelly-a — 4.00

ASSASSIN'S CREED (Based on the Ubisoft Entertainment videogame)
Titan Comics: Nov, 2015 - No. 14, Feb, 2017 ($3.99/$4.99)
1-Trial By Fire; Del Col & McCreery-s/Edwards-a; multiple-c — 6.00
2-12: 2-5-Trial By Fire. 6-11-Setting Sun — 4.00
13,14-($4.99) Homecoming — 5.00
... Free Comic Book Day (5/16, giveaway) Alves-a; Great Wall back-up w/Calero-a — 3.00

ASSASSIN'S CREED: AWAKENING (Based on the Ubisoft Entertainment videogame)
Titan Comics: Dec, 2016 - No. 6, May, 2017 ($4.99, B&W manga style, reads right to left)
1-6-Takashi Yano-s/Kenji Oiwa-a — 5.00

ASSASSIN'S CREED: CONSPIRACIES (Based on the Ubisoft Entertainment videogame)
Titan Comics: Sept, 2018 - No. 2, Oct, 2018 ($5.99, limited series)
1,2: 1-Dorison-s/Hostache-a. 2-Pion-a — 6.00

ASSASSIN'S CREED: LOCUS (Based on the Ubisoft Entertainment videogame)
Titan Comics: Oct, 2016 - No. 4, Jan, 2017 ($3.99, limited series)
1-4-Edginton-s/Wijngaard-a — 4.00

ASSASSIN'S CREED: ORIGINS (Based on the Ubisoft Entertainment videogame)
Titan Comics: Mar, 2018 - No. 4, Jul, 2018 ($3.99, limited series)
1-4-Del Col-s/Kaiowa-a. 1-Four covers. 2-4-Two covers — 4.00

ASSASSIN'S CREED: REFLECTIONS (Based on the Ubisoft Entertainment videogame)
Titan Comics: Apr, 2017 - No. 4, Aug, 2017 ($3.99, limited series)
1-4-Edginton-s/Favoccia-a — 4.00

ASSASSIN'S CREED: THE FALL (Based on the Ubisoft Entertainment videogame)
DC Comics: Jan, 2011 - No. 3, Mar, 2011 ($3.99, limited series)
1-3-Cam Stewart & Karl Kerschl-s/a — 4.00

ASSASSIN'S CREED: UPRISING (Based on the Ubisoft Entertainment videogame)
Titan Comics: Feb, 2017 - No. 8, Nov, 2017 ($3.99)

	GD 2.0	VG 4.0	FN 6.0	VF 8.0	VF/NM 9.0	NM- 9.2
1-Paknadel & Watters-s/Holder-a; multiple covers	1	2	3	5	6	8
2-8-Paknadel & Watters-s/Holder-a; multiple covers						5.00

ASSASSIN'S CREED VALHALLA: FORGOTTEN MYTHS (Ubisoft Entertainment videogame)
Dark Horse Comics: Mar, 2022 - No. 3, May, 2022 ($3.99)
1-3-Alexander Freed-s/Martin Túnica-a — 4.00

ASSASSIN'S CREED VALHALLA: SONG OF GLORY (Ubisoft Entertainment videogame)
Dark Horse Comics: Oct, 2020 - No. 3, Dec, 2020 ($3.99)
1-3-Cavan Scott-s/Martín Túnica-a — 4.00

ASSIGNMENT, THE (Adapts screenplay of 2017 movie The Assignment)
Titan Comics (Hard Case Crime): Feb, 2017 - No. 3, Apr, 2017 ($5.99)
1-3-Walter Hill & Denis Hamill-s/Jef-a; English version of French comic — 6.00

ASSAULT ON NEW OLYMPUS PROLOGUE
Marvel Comics: Jan, 2010 ($3.99, one-shot)
1-Spider-Man, Hercules, Amadeus Cho app.; Granov-c; leads into Inc. Hercules #138 — 4.00

ASTONISHING (Formerly Marvel Boy No. 1, 2)
Marvel/Atlas Comics(20CC): No. 3, Apr, 1951 - No. 63, Aug, 1957

	GD 2.0	VG 4.0	FN 6.0	VF 8.0	VF/NM 9.0	NM- 9.2
3-Marvel Boy continues; 3-5-Marvel Boy-c	232	464	696	1485	2543	3600
4-Classic skeletons-c; 4-Stan Lee app.	245	490	735	1568	2684	3800
5,6-Last Marvel Boy	161	322	483	1030	1765	2500
7-10: 7-Maneely s/f story. 10-Sinnott s/f story	65	130	195	416	708	1000
11,12,15,17,20	55	110	165	352	601	850
13,14,16,18,19-Krigstein-a. 18-Jack The Ripper sty	57	114	171	362	619	875
21,22,24	45	90	135	284	480	675
23-E.C. swipe "The Hole In The Wall" from Vault Of Horror #16	55	110	165	352	601	850
25,29: 25-Crandall-a. 29-Decapitation-c	45	90	135	284	480	675
26-28	42	84	126	265	445	625
30-Tentacled eyeball-c/story; classic-c	649	1298	1947	4738	8369	12,000
31-Classic story: man develops atomic powers after exposure to A-bomb; four A-bomb panels	77	154	231	493	847	1200
32-37-Last pre-code issues	39	78	117	231	378	525
38-43,46,48-52,56,58,59,61	30	60	90	177	289	400

44,45,47,53-55,57,60: 44-Crandall swipe/Weird Fantasy #22. 45,47-Krigstein-a. 53-Ditko-a.

	GD	VG	FN	VF	VF/NM	NM-
	2.0	4.0	6.0	8.0	9.0	9.2

54-Torres-a, 55-Crandall, Torres-a. 57-Williamson/Krenkel-a (4 pgs.).

	GD	VG	FN	VF	VF/NM	NM-
60-Williamson/Mayo-a (4 pgs.).	34	68	102	199	325	450
62,63: 62-Torres, Powell-a. 63-Woodbridge-a	34	68	102	199	325	450

NOTE: *Ayers* a-16, 49. *Berg* a-36, 53, 56. *Cameron* a-50. *Gene Colan* a-12, 20, 29. *Ditko* a-53. *Drucker* a-41, 62. *Everett* a-3-6(3), 6, 10, 12, 37, 47, 48, 58; c-3-5, 13,15, 16, 18, 29, 47, 49, 51, 53-55, 57, 59-63. *Fass* a-11, 34. *Forte* a-26, 48, 53, 58, 60. *Fuje* a-11. *Heath* a-8, 29; c-8, 9, 19, 22, 25, 26. *Kirby* a-56. *Lawrence* a-28, 37, 38, 42. *Maneely* a-7(2), 19; c-7, 31, 33, 34, 56. *Moldoff* a-33. *Morisi* a-10. *Morrow* a-52, 61. *Orlando* a-47, 58, 61. *Pakula* a-10. *Powell* a-43, 44, 48. *Ravielli* a-26, 28. *Reinman* a-32, 34, 38. *Robinson* a-20. *J. Romita* a-13, 24, 43, 57,61. *Roussos* a-55. *Sale* a-28, 38, 59; c-32. *Sekowsky* a-13. *Severin* c-46. *Shores* a-16, 60. *Sinnott* a-15, 30, 31. *Whitney* a-33. *Ed Win* a-20. *Canadian reprints exist.*

ASTONISHING ANT-MAN (Scott Lang)
Marvel Comics: Dec, 2015 - No. 13, Dec, 2016 ($3.99)

1-12: 1-Spencer-s/Rosanas-a; Cassie Lang app. 2,3-Capt. America (Sam Wilson) app.	4.00
13-($4.99) Spencer-s/Schoonover & Rosanas-a; Yellowjacket app.	5.00

ASTONISHING ICEMAN
Marvel Comics: Oct, 2023 - No. 5, Feb, 2024 ($3.99)

1-5-Orlando-s/Carratu-a. 4-Spider-Man app.	4.00

ASTONISHING SPIDER-MAN AND WOLVERINE
Marvel Comics: Jul, 2010 - No. 6, Jul. 2011 ($3.99, limited series)

1-6-Adam Kubert-a/Jason Aaron-s. 1-Bonus pin-up gallery; wraparound-c	4.00
1-Director's Cut (10/10, $4.99) r/#1 with full script & B&W art	5.00
....Another Fine Mess (6/11, $4.99) r/#1-3; wraparound-c	5.00

ASTONISHING TALES (See Ka-Zar)
Marvel Comics Group: Aug, 1970 - No. 36, July, 1976 (#1-7: 15¢; #8: 25¢)

	GD	VG	FN	VF	VF/NM	NM-
1-Ka-Zar (by Kirby(p) #1,2; by B. Smith #3-6) & Dr. Doom (by Wood #1-4; by Tuska #5,6; by Colan #7,8; 1st Marvel villain solo series) double feature begins; Kraven the Hunter-c/story; Nixon cameo	6	12	18	38	69	100
2-Kraven the Hunter-c/story; Kirby, Wood-a	4	8	12	25	40	55
3-5: B. Smith-p; Wood-a/#3,4. 5-Red Skull app.	4	8	12	27	44	60
6-1st app. Bobbi Morse (later becomes Mockingbird); Doctor Doom vs. Black Panther-c/sty;	10	20	30	69	147	225
7-Last 15¢ issue; Black Panther app.	3	6	9	20	31	42
8-(25¢, 52 pgs.)-Last Dr. Doom of series	4	8	12	28	47	65
9-All Ka-Zar issues begin; Lorna-r/Lorna #14	3	6	9	14	19	24
10-B. Smith/Sal Buscema-a.	3	6	9	15	22	28
11-Origin Ka-Zar & Zabu; death of Ka-Zar's father	3	6	9	15	22	28
12-2nd app.Man-Thing; by Neal Adams (see Savage Tales #1 for 1st app.)						
	11	22	33	73	157	240
13-3rd app.Man-Thing	7	14	21	46	86	125
14-20: 14-Jann of the Jungle-r (1950s); reprints censored Ka-Zar-s from Savage Tales #1. 17-S.H.I.E.L.D. begins. 19-Starlin-a(p). 20-Last Ka-Zar (continues into 1974 Ka-Zar series); Nick Fury & S.H.I.E.L.D.-a.	4	8	10		8	12
21-(12/73)-It! the Living Colossus begins, ends #24 (see Supernatural Thrillers #1)						
	4	8	12	27	44	60
22	3	6	9	18	28	38
23,24-It! the Living Colossus vs. Fin Fang Foom	4	8	12	28	47	65
25-1st app. Deathlok the Demolisher; full length stories begin, end #36; Perez's 1st work, 2 pgs. (8/74)	12	24	36	82	179	275
26-Deathlok app.	4	8	12	27	44	60
27,28,30	3	6	9	15	22	28
29-Reprints origin/1st app. Guardians of the Galaxy from Marvel Super-Heroes #18 plus-c w/4 pgs. omitted; no Deathlok story	4	8	12	27	44	60
31,32,34: 31-Watcher-r/Silver Surfer #3	2	4	6	11	16	20
33-1st Hellinger	4	8	12	25	40	55
35,36-Regular 25¢ edition)(5,7/76)	2	4	6	11	16	20
35,36-(30¢-c, low distribution)	8	16	24	31	96	140

NOTE: *Buckler* a-13i, 16p, 25, 26p, 27p, 28, 29p-36p; c-13, 25p, 26-30, 32-35p, 36. *John Buscema* a-9, 12p-14p, 16p; c-4-6p, 12p. *Colan* a-7p, 8p. *Ditko* a-21r. *Everett* a-6i. *G. Kane* a-11p, 15p; c-9, 10p, 11p, 14, 15p, 21p. *McWilliams* a-30i. *Starlin* a-19p; c-16p. *Sutton & Trimpe* a-8. *Tuska* a-5p, 6p, 8p. *Wood* a-1-4. *Wrightson* c-31i.

ASTONISHING TALES (Anthology)
Marvel Comics: Apr, 2009 - No. 6, Sept, 2009 ($3.99, limited series)

1-6-Wolverine, Punisher, Iron Man and Iron Man 2020 app. 1-Wraparound-c	4.00

ASTONISHING THOR
Marvel Comics: Jan, 2011 - No. 5, Sept, 2011 ($3.99, limited series)

1-5: 1-Robert Rodi-s/Mike Choi-a/Esad Ribic-c	4.00

ASTONISHING X-MEN
Marvel Comics: Mar, 1995 - No. 4, July, 1995 ($1.95, limited series)

1-Age of Apocalypse; Magneto-c	6.00
2-4	3.00

ASTONISHING X-MEN
Marvel Comics: Sept, 1999 - No. 3, Nov, 1999 ($2.50, limited series)

1-New team, Cable & X-Man app.; Peterson-a	6.00
2,3	3.00
TPB (11/00, $15.95) r/#1-3, X-Men #92 & #95, Uncanny X-Men #375	16.00

ASTONISHING X-MEN (See Giant-Size Astonishing X-Men for story folllowing #24)
Marvel Comics: July, 2004 - No. 68, Dec, 2013 ($2.99/$3.99)

	GD	VG	FN	VF	VF/NM	NM-
1-Whedon-s/Cassaday-c/a; team of Cyclops, Beast, Wolverine, Emma Frost & Kitty Pryde						8.00
1-Director's Cut (2004, $3.99) different Cassaday partial sketch-c; cover gallery, sketch pages and script excerpt						6.00
1-Variant-c by Cassaday						12.00
1-Variant-c by Dell'Otto						10.00
2,5-X-Men battle Ord (in #2-6)						3.00
3-1st app. (cameo) Abigail Brand	3	6	9	14	19	24
4-Colossus returns	2	4	6	8	10	12
4-Variant Colossus cover by Cassaday	2	4	6	9	12	15
6-1st full app. Abigail Brand	3	6	9	16	24	32
7-24: 7-Fantastic Four app. 9,10-X-Men vs. the Danger Room						3.00
7,9,10-12,19-24-Second printing variant covers						3.00
25-35: 25-Ellis-s/Bianchi-a begins; Bianchi wraparound-c. 31-Jimenez-a begins						3.00
36-68-($3.99): 36-Pearson wraparound-c; Way-s/Pearson-a. 44-47-McKone-a.						
51-Northstar wedding; wraparound-c. 60-X-Termination tie-in						4.00
Annual 1 (1/13, $4.99) Gage-s/Baldeon-a; bonus r/Alpha Flight #106						4.00
.../Amazing Spider-Man: The Gauntlet Sketchbook ('09, giveaway) flip book preview						3.00

...: Ghost Boxes 1,2 (12/08-1/09, $3.99) Ellis-s/Davis & Granov-a; full Ellis script	4.00
... Saga (2006, $3.99) reprints highlights from #1-12; sketch pages and cover gallery	4.00
... Sketchbook Special ('08, $2.99) Costume sketches & blueprints by Bianchi & Larroca	3.00
...Vol. 1 HC (2006, $29.99, dust jacket) r/#1-12; interviews, sketch pages and covers	30.00
...Vol. 1: Gifted (2004, $14.99) r/#1-6; variant cover gallery	15.00
...Vol. 2: Dangerous (2005, $14.99) r/#7-12; variant cover gallery	15.00
...Vol. 3: Torn (2007, $14.99) r/#13-18; variant & sketch cover gallery	15.00

ASTONISHING X-MEN
Marvel Comics: Sept, 2017 - No. 17, Jan, 2019 ($4.99/$3.99)

1-($4.99) Soule-s/Cheung-a; Old Man Logan, Rogue, Bishop, Gambit, Psylocke app.	5.00
2-17-($3.99) 2-Deodato-a; Mystique app. 3-McGuinness-a. 4-Pacheco-a. 7-Xavier returns; Noto-a. 13,14-Havok & Banshee return; Land-a	4.00
Annual 1 (10/18, $4.99) Rosenberg-s/Foreman-a; Xavier & Lucifer app.	5.00

ASTONISHING X-MEN: XENOGENESIS
Marvel Comics: July, 2010 - No. 5, Apr, 2011 ($3.99, limited series)

1-5-Warren Ellis-s/Kaare Andrews-a/c. 1-Wraparound-c; script	4.00
1-Director's Cut (2010, $4.99) r/#1 with full script & B&W art; cover sketches	5.00

ASTOUNDING SPACE THRILLS: THE COMIC BOOK
Image Comics: Apr, 2000 - No. 4, Dec, 2000 ($2.95, limited series)

1-4-Steve Conley-s/a. 2,3-Flip book w/Crater Kid	3.00
Galaxy-Sized Astounding Space Thrills 1 (10/01, $4.95)	5.00

ASTOUNDING WOLF-MAN
Image Comics: Jun, 2007 - No. 25, Nov, 2010 ($2.99)

1-Free Comic Boy Day issue; Kirkman-s/Howard-a; origin story	3.00
2-24: 11-Invincible x-over from Invincible #57	3.00
25-($4.99) Wraparound-c; Wolfcorps app.	5.00
Vol. 1 TPB (2008, $14.99) r/#1-7; sketch pages; Kirkman intro.	15.00

ASTRA
CPM Manga: 2001 - No. 8 ($2.95, B&W, limited series)

1-8: Created by Jerry Robinson; Tanaka-a. 1-Balent variant-c	3.00
TPB (2002, $15.95) r/#1-8; JH Williams III-c from #3	16.00

ASTRO BOY (TV) (See March of Comics #285 & The Original...)
Gold Key: August, 1965 (12¢)

	GD	VG	FN	VF	VF/NM	NM-
1(10151-508) 1st app. Astro Boy in comics	38	76	114	285	641	1000

ASTRO BOY THE MOVIE (Based on the 2009 CGI movie)
IDW Publishing: 2009 ($3.99, limited series)

...Official Movie Adaptation 1-4 (8/09 - No. 4, 9/09, $3.99) EJ Su-a	4.00
...Official Movie Prequel 1-4 (5/09 - No. 4, 8/09) Jourdan-a/c; Ashley Wood var-c on each	4.00

ASTRO CITY (Also see Kurt Busiek's Astro City)
DC Comics (WildStorm Productions): Dec, 2004 - Dec, 2009 (one-shots)

...#1 Special Edition (8/10, $1.00) reprints first issue with "What's Next?" cover logo	4.00
... Astra Special 1,2 (11/09, 12/09, $3.99) Busiek-s/Anderson-a/Ross-c	4.00
... A Visitor's Guide (12/04, $5.95) short story, city guide and pin-ups by various; Ross-c	6.00
... Beautie (4/08, $3.99) Busiek-s/Anderson-a/Ross-c; origin	4.00
... Samaritan (9/06, $3.99) Busiek-s/Anderson-a/Ross-c; origin of Infidel	4.00
... Shining Stars HC (2011, $24.99, d.j.) r/: Astra Special 1,2, ...: Beautie, ...: Samaritan, and ...: Silver Agent 1,2; bonus design art and Ross cover sketch art	25.00
...: Silver Agent 1,2 (8/9/10, $3.99) Busiek-s/Anderson-a/Ross-c	4.00

ASTRO CITY (Also see Kurt Busiek's Astro City)
DC Comics (Vertigo): Aug, 2013 - No. 52, Aug, 2018 ($3.99)

1-52-Busiek-s/Ross-c; Anderson-a in most. 12-Nolan-a. 17-Grummett-a. 22,25-Merino-a. 35,36-Ron Randall-a; Jack-In-The Box app. 39,40-Carnero-a. 47-Origin G-Dog	4.00

ASTRO CITY / ARROWSMITH (Flip book)
DC Comics (WildStorm Productions): Jun, 2004 ($2.95, one-shot flip book)

1-Intro. Black Badge; Ross-c; Arrowsmith a/c by Pacheco	5.00

ASTRO CITY: DARK AGE
DC Comics (WildStorm Productions): Aug, 2005 - No. 4, Dec, 2005 ($2.95, limited series)

Book One 1-4-Busiek-s/Anderson-a/Ross-c; Silver Agent and The Blue Knight app.	3.00
Book Two #1-4 (1/07-11/07, $2.99) Busiek-s/Anderson-a/Ross-c	3.00
Book Three #1-4 (7/09-10/09, $3.99) Busiek-s/Anderson-a/Ross-c	4.00
Book Four #1-4 (3/10-6/10, $3.99) Busiek-s/Anderson-a/Ross-c	4.00
... 1: Brothers and Other Strangers HC (2008, $29.99, d.j.) r/Book One #1-4, Book Two #1-4 and story from Astro City/Arrowsmith #1; Marc Guggenheim intro.; new Ross-c	30.00
... 1: Brothers and Other Strangers SC (2009, $19.99) same contents as HC	20.00
... 2: Brothers in Arms HC ('10, $29.99, d.j.) r/Book Three #1-4, Book Four #1-4, Ross-c	30.00

ASTRO CITY: LOCAL HEROES
DC Comics (WildStorm Productions): Apr, 2003 - No. 5, Feb, 2004 ($2.95, limited series)

1-5-Busiek-s/Anderson-a/Ross-c	3.00
HC (2005, $24.95) r/series; Kurt Busiek's Astro City V2 #21,22; stories from Astro City/ Arrowsmith #1; and 9-11, The World's Finest... Vol. 2; Alex Ross sketch pages	25.00
SC (2005, $17.99) same contents as HC	18.00

ASTRO CITY: THAT WAS THEN... SPECIAL
Image Comics: Mar, 2022 ($7.99, one-shot)

1-Spotlight on the Jayhawks; Busiek-s/Anderson-a/Ross-c	4.00

ASTRO HUSTLE
Dark Horse Comics: Mar, 2019 - No. 2, Apr, 2019 ($3.99, unfinished limited series of 4 issues)

1,2-Jai Nitz-s/Tom Reilly-a	4.00

ASTRONAUTS IN TROUBLE
Image Comics: Jun, 2015 - No. 11 ($2.99, B&W, reprints of earlier Astronauts in Trouble)

1-11-Larry Young-s. 1-3-Reprints the Space: 1959 series; Charlie Adlard-a. 4-9-Reprints the Live From the Moon series. 4-6-Matt Smith-a. 7-11-Adlard-a	3.00

ASYLUM
Millennium Publications: 1993 ($2.50)

1-3: 1-Bolton-c/a; Russell 2-pg. illos	4.00

ASYLUM
Maximum Press: Dec, 1995 - No. 11, Jan, 1997 ($2.95/$2.99, anthology)

Astonishing X-Men (2017 series) #1 © MAR

Astro City (2013 series) #10 © Juke Box

Atlas United #1 © Nemesis Group

	GD 2.0	VG 4.0	FN 6.0	VF 8.0	VF/NM 9.0	NM- 9.2

(#1-6 are flip books)
1-11: 1-Warchild by Art Adams, Beanworld, Avengelyne, Battlestar Galactica. 2-Intro Mike
Deodato's Deathkiss. 4-1st app.Christian; painted Battlestar Galactica story begins.
6-Intro Bionix (Six Million Dollar Man & the Bionic Woman). 7-Begin $2.99-c. 8-B&W-c.
9- Foot Soldiers & Kid Supreme. 10-Lady Supreme by Terry Moore-c/app. ... 4.00

ATARI FORCE (Also see Promotional comics section)
DC Comics: Jan, 1984 - No. 20, Aug, 1985 (Mando paper)
1-(1/84)-Intro Tempest, Packrat, Babe, Morphea, & Dart; García-López-a

		2	4	6	8	10	12

2-20 ... 5.00
Special 1 (4/86) ... 6.00
NOTE: *Byrne* c-Special 1i. *Giffen* a-12p, 13i. *Rogers* a-18p, Special 1p.

A-TEAM, THE (TV) (Also see Marvel Graphic Novel)
Marvel Comics Group: Mar, 1984 - No. 3, May, 1984 (limited series)

1-Marie Severin-a/John Romita-c	3	6	9	17	26	35
2,3: 2-Mooney-a. 3-Kupperberg-s/a	2	4	6	9	12	15
1,2-(Whitman bagged set) w/75¢-c	3	6	9	19	30	40
3-(Whitman, no bag) w/75¢-c	3	6	9	16	23	30

A-TEAM: SHOTGUN WEDDING (Based on the 2010 movie)
IDW Publishing: Mar, 2010 - No. 4, 2010 ($3.99, limited series)
1-4-Co-plotted by Joe Carnahan; Stephen Mooney-a; Snyder III-c ... 4.00

A-TEAM: WAR STORIES (Based on the 2010 movie)
IDW Publishing: Mar, 2010 - Apr, 2010 ($3.99, series of one-shots)
...: B.A. (3/10) Dixon & Burnham-s/Maloney-a/Gaydos & photo-c ... 4.00
...: Face (4/10) Dixon & Burnham-s/Muriel-a/Gaydos & photo-c ... 4.00
...: Hannibal (3/10) Dixon & Burnham-s/Petrus-a/Gaydos & photo-c ... 4.00
...: Murdock (4/10) Dixon & Burnham-s/Vilanova-a/Gaydos & photo-c ... 4.00

ATHENA INC. THE MANHUNTER PROJECT
Image Comics: Dec, 2001; Apr, 2002 - No. 6 ($2.95/$4.95/$5.95)
...The Beginning (12/01, $5.95) Anacleto-c/a; Haberlin-s ... 6.00
1-5: 1-(4/02, $2.95) two covers by Anacleto ... 3.00
6-($4.95) ... 5.00
...: Agents Roster #1 (11/02, $5.95, 8 1/2 x 11") bios and sketch pages by Anacleto ... 6.00
Vol. 1 TPB (4/03, $19.95) r/#1-6 & Agents Roster; cover gallery ... 20.00

ATHENA
Dynamite Entertainment: 2009 - No. 4, 2010 ($3.50)
1-4-Murray-a/Neves-a; multiple covers on each. 1-Obama flip cover ... 3.50

ATHENA IX (See Aphrodite IX)
Image Comics (Top Cow): Jul, 2015 ($3.99, one-shot)
1-Ryan Cady-s/Phillip Sevy; 3 covers ... 4.00

ATLANTIS ATTACKS (Continued from Agents of Atlas 2019-2020 series)
Marvel Comics: Jan, 2020 - No. 5, Feb, 2020 ($3.99, limited series)
1-5-Greg Pak-s/Ario Anindito-a; the current and the original Agents of Atlas app. ... 4.00

ATLANTIS CHRONICLES, THE (Also see Aquaman, 3rd Series & Aquaman: Time & Tide)
DC Comics: Mar, 1990 - No 7, Sept, 1990 ($2.95, limited series, 52 pgs.)
1-7: 1-Peter David scripts. 7-True origin of Aquaman; nudity panels ... 4.00

ATLANTIS, THE LOST CONTINENT
Dell Publishing Co.: May, 1961

Four Color 1188-Movie, photo-c	9	18	27	62	126	190

ATLAS (See 1st Issue Special)
ATLAS
Dark Horse Comics: Feb, 1994 - No. 4, 1994 ($2.50, limited series)
1-4 ... 4.00

ATLAS (Agents of Atlas)(The Heroic Age)
Marvel Comics: Jul, 2010 - No. 5, Oct, 2010 ($3.99/$2.99)
1-($3.99) Parker-s/Hardman-a/Dodson-c; 3-D Man app.; profile page ... 4.00
2-5-($2.99) 2,3,5-Pagulayan-a. 4-Jae Lee-c ... 3.00

ATLAS UNIFIED
Atlas Comics: No. 0, Oct, 2011 - No. 2, Feb, 2012 ($2.99, unfinished limited series)
0 Prelude: Midnight (10/11) Phoenix, Kromag, Sgt. Hawk app.; bonus sketch pages ... 3.00
1,2: 1-Three covers; Peyer-s/Salgado-a; x-over of Grim Ghost, Wulf, Phoenix & others ... 3.00

ATMOSPHERICS
Avatar Press: June, 2002 ($5.95, B&W, one-shot graphic novel)
1-Warren Ellis-s/Ken Meyer Jr.-painted-a/c ... 6.00

ATOM, THE (See Action #425, All-American #19, Brave & the Bold, D.C. Special Series #1, Detective Comics,

---

Flash Comics #80, Hawkman, Identity Crisis, JLA, Power Of The Atom, Showcase #34 -36, Super Friends, Sword
of The Atom, Teen Titans & World's Finest)

ATOM, THE (...& the Hawkman No. 39 on)
National Periodical Publ.: June-July, 1962 - No. 38, Aug-Sept, 1968

	GD 2.0	VG 4.0	FN 6.0	VF 8.0	VF/NM 9.0	NM- 9.2
1-(6-7/62)-Intro Plant-Master; 1st app. Maya	118	236	354	944	2122	3300
2	31	62	93	223	499	775
3-1st Time Pool story; 1st app. Chronos (origin)	26	52	78	182	404	625
4,5: 4-Snapper Carr x-over	15	30	45	103	227	350
6,9,10	11	22	33	76	163	250
7-Hawkman x-over (6-7/63; 1st Atom & Hawkman team-up); 1st app. Hawkman since Brave & the Bold tryouts	23	46	69	161	356	550
8-Justice League, Dr. Light app.	13	26	39	91	201	310
11-15: 13-Chronos-c/story	9	18	27	60	120	180
16-18,20	7	14	21	46	86	125
19-Zatanna x-over; 2nd app.	18	38	57	131	291	450
21-28,30: 26-Two-page pin-up. 28-Chronos-c/story	6	12	18	41	76	110
29-1st solo Golden Age Atom x-over in S.A.	12	24	36	81	176	270
31-35,37,38: 31-Hawkman x-over. 37-Intro. Major Mynah; Hawkman cameo	5	10	15	35	63	90
36-G.A. Atom x-over	7	14	21	48	89	130

NOTE: *Anderson* a-1-11i; c-inks-1-25, 31-35, 37. *Sid Greene* a-8i-37i. *Gil Kane* a-1p-37p; c-1p-28p, 29, 33p,
34; c-26i. *George Roussos* a-38i. *Mike Sekowsky* a-38p. Time Pool stories also in 6, 9,12, 17, 21, 27, 35.

ATOM, THE (See All New Atom and Tangent Comics/ The Atom)

ATOM AGE (See Classics Illustrated Special Issue)

ATOM-AGE COMBAT
St. John Publishing Co.: June, 1952 - No. 5, Apr, 1953; Feb, 1958

1-Buck Vinson in all	65	130	195	416	708	1000
2-Flying saucer story	40	80	120	246	411	575
3,5: 3-Mayo-a (6 pgs.). 5-Flying saucer-c/story	36	72	108	211	343	475
4 (Scarce)	40	80	120	246	411	575
1(2/58-St. John)	32	64	96	188	307	425

ATOM-AGE COMBAT
Fago Magazines: No. 2, Jan, 1959 - No. 3, Mar, 1959

2-A-Bomb explosion-c;	39	78	117	236	388	540
3	28	56	84	165	270	375

ATOMAN
Spark Publications: Feb, 1946 - No. 2, April, 1946

1-Origin & 1st app. Atoman; Robinson/Meskin-a; Kidcrusaders, Wild Bill Hickok, Marvin the Great app.	97	194	291	621	1061	1500
2-Robinson/Meskin-a; Robinson c-1,2	53	106	159	334	567	800

ATOM & HAWKMAN, THE (Formerly The Atom)
National Periodical Publ: No. 39, Oct-Nov, 1968 - No. 45, Oct-Nov, 1969; No. 46, Mar, 2010

39-43: 40-41-Kubert/Anderson-a. 43-(7/69)-Last 12¢ issue; 1st S.A. app. Gentleman Ghost	5	10	15	35	63	90
44,45: 44-(9/69)-1st 15¢-c; origin Gentleman Ghost	5	10	15	35	63	90
46-(3/10, $2.99) Blackest Night crossover one-shot; Geoff Johns-s/Ryan Sook-a/c						3.00

NOTE: *M. Anderson* a-39, 40i, 41i, 43, 44. *Sid Greene* a-40i-45i. *Kubert* a-40p, 41p; c-39-45.

ATOM ANT (TV) (See Golden Comics Digest #2) (Hanna-Barbera)
Gold Key: January, 1966 (12¢)

1-(10170-601)-1st app. Atom Ant, Precious Pup, and Hillbilly Bears	17	34	51	114	252	390

ATOM ANT & SECRET SQUIRREL (See Hanna-Barbera Presents)

ATOMIC AGE
Marvel Comics (Epic Comics): Nov, 1990 - No. 4, Feb, 1991 ($4.50, limited series,
squarebound, 52 pgs.)
1-4: Williamson-a(i); sci-fi story set in 1957 ... 4.50

ATOMIC ATTACK (True War Stories; formerly Attack, first series)
Youthful Magazines: No. 5, Jan, 1953 - No. 8, Oct, 1953 (1st story is sci/fi in all issues)

5-Atomic bomb-c; science fiction stories in all	58	116	174	371	636	900
6-8	37	74	111	222	361	500

ATOMIC BOMB
Jay Burtis Publications: 1945 (36 pgs.)

1-Superheroes Airmale & Stampy (scarce)	87	174	261	553	952	1350

ATOMIC BUNNY (Formerly Atomic Rabbit)
Charlton Comics: No. 12, Aug, 1958 - No. 19, Dec, 1959

12	14	28	42	80	115	150
13-19	9	18	27	47	61	75

ATOMIC COMICS

	GD 2.0	VG 4.0	FN 6.0	VF 8.0	VF/NM 9.0	NM- 9.2

Daniels Publications (Canadian): Jan, 1946 (Reprints, one-shot)
1-Rocketman, Yankee Boy, Master Key app. — 53 106 159 334 567 800

ATOMIC COMICS
Green Publishing Co.: Jan, 1946 - No. 4, July-Aug, 1946 (#1-4 were printed w/o cover gloss)
1-Radio Squad by Siegel & Shuster; Barry O'Neal app.; Fang Gow cover-r/ Detective Comics (Classic-c) — 103 206 309 659 1130 1600
2-Inspector Dayton; Kid Kane by Matt Baker; Lucky Wings, Congo King, Prop Powers (only app.) begin; atomic monster-c — 71 142 213 454 777 1100
3,4: 3-Zero Ghost Detective app.; Baker-a(2) each; 4-Baker-c — 50 100 150 315 533 750

ATOMIC KNIGHTS (See Strange Adventures #117)
DC Comics: 2010 ($39.99, HC with dustjacket)
HC-Reprints the original 1960-64 run from debut in Strange Adventures #117 to S.A. #160; new intro. by Murphy Anderson — 40.00

ATOMIC MOUSE (TV, Movies) (See Blue Bird, Funny Animals, Giant Comics Edition & Wotalife Comics)
Capitol Stories/Charlton Comics: 3/53 - No. 52, 2/63; No. 1, 12/84; V2#10, 9/85 - No. 12, 1/86
1-Origin & 1st app.; Al Fago-c/a in most — 43 86 129 271 461 650
2 — 16 32 48 94 147 200
3-10: 5-Timmy The Timid Ghost app.; see Zoo Funnies — 11 22 33 62 86 110
11-13,16-25 — 8 16 24 40 50 60
14,15-Hoppy The Marvel Bunny app. — 9 18 27 50 65 80
26-(68 pgs.) — 12 24 36 67 94 120
27-40: 36,37-Atom The Cat app. — 6 12 18 29 36 42
41-52 — 5 10 15 22 26 30
1 (1984)-Low print run; rep/#7-c w/diff. stories — 2 4 6 8 10 12
V2#10 (9/85) -12(1/86)-Low print run — 1 3 4 6 8 10

ATOMIC RABBIT (Atomic Bunny #12 on; see Giant Comics #3 & Wotalife)
Charlton Comics: Aug, 1955 - No. 11, Mar, 1958
1-Origin & 1st app.; Al Fago-c/a in all? — 37 74 111 222 361 500
2 — 15 30 45 86 133 180
3-10 — 10 20 30 58 79 100
11-(68 pgs.) — 14 28 42 82 121 160

ATOMICS, THE
AAA Pop Comics: Jan, 2000 - No. 15, Nov, 2001 ($2.95)
1-11-Mike Allred-s/a; 1-Madman-c/app. — 3.00
12-15-($3.50): 13-15-Savage Dragon-c/app. 15-Afterword by Alex Ross; colored reprint of 1st Frank Einstein story — 3.50
...King-Size Giant Spectacular: Jigsaw (2000, $10.00) r/#1-4 — 10.00
...King-Size Giant Spectacular: Lessons in Light, Lava, & Lasers (2000, $8.95) r/#5-8 — 9.00
...King-Size Giant Spectacular: Running with the Dragon ('02, $8.95) r/#13-15 and r/1st Frank Einstein app. in color — 9.00
...King-Size Giant Spectacular: Worlds Within Worlds ('01, $8.95) r/#9-12 — 9.00
Madman and the Atomics, Vol. 1 TPB (2007, $24.99) r/#1-15, cover gallery, pin-ups, afterword by Alex Ross — 25.00
...: Spaced Out & Grounded in Snap City TPB (10/03, $12.95) r/one-shots - It Girl, Mr. Gum, Spaceman and Crash Metro & the Star Squad; sketch pages — 13.00

ATOMIC SPY CASES
Avon Periodicals: Mar-Apr, 1950 (Painted-c)
1-No Wood-a; A-bomb blast panels; Fass-a — 58 116 174 371 636 900

ATOMIC THUNDERBOLT, THE
Regor Company: Feb, 1946 (one-shot) (scarce)
1-Intro. Atomic Thunderbolt & Mr. Murdo — 116 232 348 742 1271 1800

ATOMIC TOYBOX
Image Comics: Dec, 1999 ($2.95)
1- Aaron Lopresti-c/s/a — 4.00

ATOMIC WAR!
Ace Periodicals (Junior Books): Nov, 1952 - No. 4, Apr, 1953
1-Atomic bomb-c — 258 516 774 1651 2826 4000
2,3: Atomic bomb-c — 81 162 243 518 884 1250
4-Used in POP, pg. 96 & illo. — 93 186 279 591 1021 1450

ATOMIKA
Speakeasy Comics/Mercury Comics: Mar, 2005 - No. 12, Jun, 2011 ($2.99)
1-12: 1-Alex Ross-c/Sal Abbinanti-a/Dabb-s. 3-Fabry-c. 4-Four covers; Romita back-c — 3.00
... God is Red TPB (5/06, $19.99) r/#1-6; cover gallery; Dabb foreword — 20.00

ATOMIK ANGELS
Crusade Comics: May, 1996 - No. 4, Nov. 1996 ($2.50)
1-4: 1-Freefall from Gen 13 app. — 4.00
1-Variant-c — 5.00
Intrep-Edition (2/96, B&W, giveaway at launch party)-Previews Atomik Angels #1; includes Billy Tucci interview. — 6.00

ATOM SPECIAL (See Atom & Justice League of America)
DC Comics: 1993/1995 ($2.50/$2.95)(68pgs.)
1,2: 1-Dillon-c/a. 2-McDonnell-a/Bolland-c/Peyer-s — 4.00

ATOM THE CAT (Formerly Tom Cat; see Giant Comics #3)
Charlton Comics: No. 9, Oct, 1957 - No. 17, Aug, 1959
9 — 10 20 30 58 79 100
10,13-17 — 7 14 21 37 46 55
11,12: 11(64 pgs)-Atomic Mouse app. 12(100 pgs.) — 13 26 39 74 105 135

ATTACK
Youthful Mag./Trojan No. 5 on: May, 1952 - No. 4, Nov, 1952; No. 5, Jan, 1953 - No. 5, Sept, 1953
1-(1st series)-Extreme violence — 60 120 180 381 653 925
2,3-Both Harrison-c/a; bondage, whipping — 34 68 102 199 325 450
4-Krenkel-a (7 pgs.); Harrison-a (becomes Atomic Attack #5 on) — 53 106 159 334 567 800

5-(#1, Trojan, 2nd series) — 30 60 90 177 289 400
6-8 (#2-4), 5 — 16 32 48 94 147 200

ATTACK
Charlton Comics: No. 54, 1958 - No. 60, Nov, 1959
54 (25¢, 100 pgs.) — 15 30 45 83 124 165
55-60 — 9 18 27 50 65 80

ATTACK!
Charlton Comics: 1962 - No. 15, 3/75; No. 16, 8/79 - No. 48, 10/84
nn(#1)-('62) Special Edition — 8 16 24 54 102 150
2('63), 3(Fall, '64) — 4 8 12 44 60
V4#3(10/66), 4(10/67)-(Formerly Special War Series #2; becomes Attack At Sea V4#5): 3-Tokyo Rose story — 3 6 9 21 33 45
1(9/71)-D-Day story — 3 6 9 17 25 34
2-5: 2-Hitler app. 4-American Eagle app. — 2 4 6 9 12 15
6-15(3/75): 8-Nixon app. — 1 3 4 6 8 10
16(8/79) - 40 — 5.00
41-47 Low print run — 7.00
48(10/84)-Wood-r; S&K-c (low print) — 1 3 4 6 8 10
Modern Comics 13('78)-r — 5.00
NOTE: Sutton a-9,10,13.

ATTACK!
Spire Christian Comics (Fleming H. Revell Co.): 1975 (39¢/49¢, 36 pgs.)
nn — 3 6 9 14 19 24

ATTACK AT SEA (Formerly Attack!, 1967)
Charlton Comics: V4#5, Oct, 1968 (one-shot)
V4#5 — 3 6 9 21 33 45

ATTACK ON PLANET MARS (See Strange Worlds #18)
Avon Periodicals: 1951
nn-Infantino, Fawcette, Kubert & Wood-a; adaptation of Tarrano the Conqueror by Ray Cummings — 123 246 369 787 1344 1900

ATTRACTIVE COUSINS (Cerebus)
Aardvark-Vanaheim: Aug, 2020 ($4.00, B&W)
1-Cerebus figures with original Gustave Doré artwork; Supergirl Action #252-c swipe — 4.00

AUDREY & MELVIN (Formerly Little...)(See Little Audrey & Melvin)
Harvey Publications: No. 62, Sept, 1974
62 — 2 4 6 10 14 18

AUGIE DOGGIE (TV) (See Hanna-Barbera Band Wagon, Quick-Draw McGraw, Spotlight #2, Top Cat & Whitman Comic Books)
Gold Key: October, 1963 (12¢)
1-Hanna-Barbera character — 16 32 48 107 236 365

AUNTIE AGATHA'S HOME FOR WAYWARD RABBITS
Image Comics: Nov, 2018 - No. 6, Apr, 2019 ($3.99, limited series)
1-6-Keith Giffen-s/Benjamin Roman-a — 4.00

AUTHENTIC POLICE CASES
St. John Publishing Co.: 2/48 - No. 6, 11/48; No. 7, 5/50 - No. 38, 3/55
1-Hale the Magician by Tuska begins — 81 162 243 518 884 1250
2-Lady Satan, Johnny Rebel app. — 55 110 165 352 601 850
3-Veiled Avenger app.; blood drainage story plus 2 Lucky Coyne stories; used in SOTI, illo. from Red Seal #16 — 90 180 270 576 988 1400
4,5: 4-Masked Black Jack app. 5-Late 1930s Jack Cole-a(r); transvestism story — 52 104 156 328 552 775
6-Matt Baker-a; used in SOTI, illo- "An invitation to learning", r-in Fugitives from Justice #3; Jack Cole-a; also used by the N.Y. Legis. Comm. — 314 628 942 2198 3849 5500
7,8,10-14: 7-Jack Cole-a; 12-Matt Baker-a begins #8, nude #?; Vic Flint in #10-14. — 52 104 156 328 552 775
10-12-Baker-a(2 each) — 65 130 195 416 708 1000
9-No Vic Flint — 57 114 171 362 619 875
15-Drug-c/story; Vic Flint app.; Baker-c — 142 284 426 909 1555 2200
16,17,19,22-Baker-c — 61 122 183 390 670 950
18,20,21,23: Baker-a(i) — 47 94 141 296 498 700
24-28 (All 100 pgs.): 26-Transvestism — 77 154 231 493 847 1200
29,31,32-Baker-c — 55 110 165 352 601 850
30 — 36 72 108 211 343 475
33-38: 33-Baker-c. 34-Baker-c/a; drug story; r/#9. 35-Baker-c/a(2); r/#10. 36-r/#11; Vic Flint strip-r; Baker-c/a(2) unsigned. 37-Baker-c; r/#17. 38- Baker-c/a; r/#18 — 53 106 159 334 567 800
NOTE: Matt Baker c-6-16, 17, 19, 22, 27, 29, 31-38; a-13, 16. Bondage c-1, 3.

AUTHORITY, THE (See Stormwatch and Jenny Sparks: The Secret History of...)
DC Comics (WildStorm): May, 1999 - No. 29, Jul, 2002 ($2.50)
1-Wraparound-c; Warren Ellis-s/Bryan Hitch and Paul Neary-a — 3 6 9 21 33 45
1-Special Edition (7/10, $1.00) r/#1 with "What's Next?" logo on cover — 4.00
2-4 — 5.00
5-12: 12-Death of Jenny Sparks; last Ellis-s — 6.00
13-Mark Millar-s/Frank Quitely-c/a begins — 6.00
14-16-Authority vs. Marvel-esque villains — 4.00
17-29: 17,18-Weston-a. 19,20,22-Quitely-a. 21-McCrea-a. 23-26-Peyer-s/Nguyen-a; new Authority. 25,26-Jenny Sparks app. 27,28-Millar-s/Art Adams-a/c — 4.00
Annual 2000 ($3.50) Devil's Night x-over; Hamner-a/Bermejo-c — 4.00
Absolute Authority Slipcased Hardcover (2002, $49.95) oversized r/#1-12 plus script pages by Ellis and Hitch — 60.00
...: Earth Inferno and Other Stories TPB (2002, $14.95) r/#17-20, Annual 2000, and Wildstorm Summer Special; new Quitely-c — 15.00
... Human on the Inside HC (2004, $24.95, dust jacket) Ridley-s/Oliver-a/c — 25.00
... Human on the Inside SC (2004, $17.99) Ridley-s/Oliver-a/c — 18.00
... Kev (10/02, $4.95) Ennis-s/Fabry-c/a — 5.00
...: Relentless TPB (2000, $17.95) r/#1-8 — 18.00
...: Scorched Earth (2/03, $4.95) Robbie Morrison-s/Frazer Irving/Ashley Wood-a — 5.00
...: Transfer of Power TPB (2002, $17.95) r/#22-29 — 18.00
... Under New Management TPB (2000, $17.95) r/#9-16; new Quitely-c — 18.00

AUTHORITY, THE (See previews in Sleeper, Stormwatch: Team Achilles and Wildcats Version 3.0)

Attack! #22 © CC

The Authority #3 © DC

Avatar: The Next Shadow #1 © 20th Century

	GD 2.0	VG 4.0	FN 6.0	VF 8.0	VF/NM 9.0	NM- 9.2

DC Comics (WildStorm): Jul, 2003 - No. 14, Oct, 2004 ($2.95)

1-14: 1-Robbie Morrison-s/Dwayne Turner-a. 5-Huat-a. 14-Portacio-a						3.00
#0 (10/03, $2.95) r/preview back-up-s listed above; Turner sketch pages						3.00
...: Fractured Worlds TPB (2005, $17.95) r/#6-14; cover gallery						18.00
...: Harsh Realities TPB (2004, $14.95) r/#0-5; cover gallery						15.00
.../Lobo: Jingle Hell (2/04, $4.95) Bisley-c/a; Giffen & Grant-s						5.00
.../Lobo: Spring Break Massacre (8/05, $4.99) Bisley-c/a; Giffen & Grant-s						5.00

AUTHORITY, THE (Volume 4) (The Lost Year)
DC Comics (WildStorm): Dec, 2006 - No. 2, May 2007; No. 3, Jan, 2010 - No. 12, Oct, 2010 ($2.99)

1,2-Grant Morrison-s/Gene Ha-a/c						3.00
1-Variant cover by Art Adams						5.00
3-12: 3-(1/10) Morrison & Giffen-s/Robertson-a. 3-12-Ha-c. 12-Ordway-a						3.00
...Reader: The Lost Year (1/10, $2.99) r/#1,2						3.00
... Book One (2010, $17.99) r/#1-7; cover sketch art						18.00

AUTHORITY, THE, THE (Volume 5) (World's End)
DC Comics (WildStorm): Oct, 2008 - No. 29, Jan, 2011 ($2.99)

1-29: 1-5-Simon Coleby-a/c; Lynch back-up story w/Hairsine-a/Gage-s. 21-Simonson-c						3.00
...: Rule Britannia TPB (2010, $19.99) r/#8-17						20.00
...: World's End TPB (2009, $17.99) r/#1-7						18.00

AUTHORITY, THE: MORE KEV
DC Comics (WildStorm): Jul, 2004 - No. 4, Dec, 2004 ($2.95, limited series)

1-4-Garth Ennis-s/Glenn Fabry-c/a						3.00
...: Kev TPB (2005, $14.99) r/Authority: Kev one-shot and Authority: More Kev series						15.00

AUTHORITY, THE: PRIME
DC Comics (WildStorm): Dec, 2007 - No. 6, May, 2008 ($2.99, limited series)

1-6-Gage-s/Robertson-c/a; Bendix app.						3.00
TPB (2008, $17.99) r/#1-6						18.00

AUTHORITY, THE: REVOLUTION
DC Comics (WildStorm): Dec, 2004 - No. 12, Dec, 2005 ($2.95/$2.99)

1-12-Brubaker-s/Nguyen-a. 5-Henry Bendix returns. 7-Jenny Sparks app.						3.00
...: Book One TPB (2005, $14.99) r/#1-6; cover gallery and Nguyen sketch pages						15.00
...: Book Two TPB (2006, $14.99) r/#7-12; cover gallery and Nguyen sketch pages						15.00

AUTHORITY, THE: THE MAGNIFICENT KEV
DC Comics (WildStorm): Nov, 2005 - No. 5, Feb, 2006 ($2.99, limited series)

1-5-Garth Ennis-s/Carlos Ezquerra-a/Glenn Fabry-c						3.00
TPB (2006, $14.99) r/#1-5						15.00

AUTOMATIC KAFKA
DC Comics (WildStorm): Sept, 2002 - No. 9, Jul, 2003 ($2.95)

1-9-Ashley Wood-c/a; Joe Casey-s						3.00

AUTUMN ADVENTURES (Walt Disney's...)
Disney Comics: Autumn, 1990; No. 2, Autumn, 1991 ($2.95, 68 pgs.)

1-Donald Duck-r(2) by Barks, Pluto-r, & new-a						4.00
2-D. Duck-r by Barks; new Super Goof story						4.00

AUTUMNLANDS: TOOTH & CLAW (Titled Tooth & Claw for issue #1, Autumnlands for #7-14)
Image Comics: Nov, 2014 - No. 14, Jan, 2017 ($2.99)

1-14: 1-Busiek-s/Dewey-a. 2-Variant-c by Alex Ross						3.00

AVANT-GUARDS, THE
BOOM! Studios (Boom! Box): Jan, 2019 - No. 8, Sept, 2019 ($3.99)

1-8-Carly Usdin-s/Noah Hayes-a						4.00

AVATAARS: COVENANT OF THE SHIELD
Marvel Comics: Sept, 2000 - No. 3, Nov, 2000 ($2.99, limited series)

1-3-Kaminski-s/Oscar Jimenez-a						3.00

AVATAR
DC Comics: Feb, 1991 - No. 3, Apr, 1991 ($5.95, limited series, 100 pgs.)

1-3: Based on TSR's Forgotten Realms						6.00

AVATAR: ADAPT OR DIE (Characters from the James Cameron movie)
Dark Horse Comics: May, 2022 - No. 6, Oct, 2022 ($3.99, limited series)

1-6-Corinna Bechko-s/Beni R. Lobel-a; Grace app.						4.00

AVATAR: FRONTIERS OF PANDORA (Characters from the James Cameron movies)
Dark Horse Comics: Feb, 2024 - No. 6 ($3.99, limited series)

1-Ray Fawkes-s/Gabriel Guzman-a						4.00

AVATAR: THE NEXT SHADOW (Based on the James Cameron movie)
Dark Horse Comics: Jan, 2021 - No. 4, Apr, 2021 ($3.99, limited series)

1-4-Takes place 2 weeks after the movie; Jeremy Barlow-s/Josh Hood-a						4.00

AVATAR: TSU'TEY'S PATH (Based on the James Cameron movie)
Dark Horse Comics: Jan, 2019 - No. 6, Aug, 2019 ($3.99, limited series)

1-6-Sherri L. Smith-s/Jan Duursema-a						4.00

AVENGELYNE
Maximum Press: May, 1995 - No. 3, July, 1995 ($2.50/$3.50, limited series)

	GD	VG	FN	VF	VF/NM	NM-
1/2		1	3	4	6	8	10
1/2 Platinum						18.00
1-Newstand ($2.50)-Photo-c; poster insert						6.00
1-Direct Market ($3.50)-Chromium-c; poster		1	2	3	5	6	8
1-Glossy edition		2	4	6	12	16	20
1-Gold						12.00
2-3: 2-Polybagged w/card						4.00
3-Variant-c; Deodato pin-up						5.00
...Bible (10/96, $3.50)						4.00
.../Glory (9/95, $3.95) 2 covers						4.00
.../Glory Swimsuit Special (6/96, $2.95) photo and illos. covers						4.00
.../Glory: The Godyssey (9/96, $2.99) 2 covers (1 photo)						4.00
...Revelation One (Avatar, 1/01, $3.50) 3 covers by Haley, Rio, Shaw; Shaw-a						5.00
.../Shi (Avatar, 11/01, $3.50) Eight covers; Waller-a		1	2	3	6	8	10
...Swimsuit (8/95, $2.95)-Pin-ups/photos. 3-Variant-c exist (2 photo, 1 Liefeld-a)						4.00
...Swimsuit (1/96, $3.50, 2nd printing)-photo-c						4.00
Trade paperback (12/95, $9.95)						10.00
.../Warrior Nun Areala 1 (11/96, $2.99) also see Warrior Nun/Avengelyne						4.00

AVENGELYNE
Maximum Press: V2#1, Apr, 1996 - No. 14, Apr, 1997 ($2.95/$2.50)

V2#1-Four covers exist (2 photo-c).						4.00
V2#2-Three covers exist (1 photo-c); flip book w/Darkchylde						5.00
V2#0, 3-14: 0-(10/96).3-Flip book w/Priest preview. 5-Flip book w/Blindside						3.00

AVENGELYNE (Volume 3)
Awesome Comics: Mar, 1999 ($2.50)

1-Fraga & Liefeld-a						5.00

AVENGELYNE (4th series)
Image Comics: Jul, 2011 - No. 8, May, 2012 ($2.99)

1-8-Liefeld & Poulson-s/Gieni-a. 1-Three covers by Liefeld, Gieni, and Benitez						3.00

AVENGELYNE: ARMAGEDDON
Maximum Press: Dec, 1996 - No. 3, Feb, 1997 ($2.99, limited series)

1-3-Scott Clark-a(p)						4.00

AVENGELYNE: DEADLY SINS
Maximum Press: Feb, 1996 - No. 2, Mar, 1996 ($2.95, limited series)

1,2: 1-Two-c exist (1 photo, 1 Liefeld-a). 2-Liefeld-c; Pop Mhan-a(p)						4.00

AVENGELYNE/POWER
Maximum Press: Nov, 1995 - No.3, Jan, 1996 ($2.95, limited series)

1-3: 1,2-Liefeld-c. 3-Three variant-c. exist (1 photo-c)						4.00

AVENGELYNE · PROPHET
Maximum Press: May, 1996; No. 2, Feb. 1997 ($2.95, unfinished lim. series)

1,2-Liefeld-c/a(p)						4.00

AVENGER, THE (See A-1 Comics)
Magazine Enterprises: Feb-Mar, 1955 - No. 4, Aug-Sept, 1955

	GD	VG	FN	VF	VF/NM	NM-
1(A-1 #129)-Origin	65	130	195	416	708	1000
2(A-1 #131), 3(A-1 #133) Robot-c, 4(A-1 #138)	61	122	183	390	670	950
IW Reprint #9('64)-Reprints #1 (new cover)	4	8	12	27	44	60
NOTE: *Powell* a-2-4; c-1-4.

AVENGER, THE (Pulp Hero from Justice Inc.)
Dynamite Entertainment: 2014 ($7.99)

... Special 2014: The Television Killers - Rahner-s/Menna-a/Hack-c						8.00

AVENGERS, THE (TV)(Also see Steed and Mrs. Peel)
Gold Key: Nov, 1968 ("John Steed & Emma Peel" cover title) (15¢)

	GD	VG	FN	VF	VF/NM	NM-
1-Photo-c	11	22	33	73	157	240
1-(Variant with photo back-c)	18	38	54	124	275	425

AVENGERS, THE (See Essential..., Giant-Size..., JLA/..., Kree/Skrull War Starring..., Marvel Graphic Novel #27, Marvel Super Action, Marvel Super Heroes('66), Marvel Treasury Ed., Marvel Triple Action, New Avengers, Solo Avengers, Tales Of Suspense #49, West Coast Avengers & X-Men Vs....)

AVENGERS, THE (The Mighty Avengers on cover only #63-69)
Marvel Comics Group: Sept, 1963 - No. 402, Sept, 1996

	GD	VG	FN	VF	VF/NM	NM-
1-Origin & 1st app. The Avengers (Thor, Iron Man, Hulk, Ant-Man, Wasp); Loki app.	1375	2750	5500	13,750	37,875	62,000
2-Hulk leaves Avengers	148	296	444	1221	2761	4300

	GD 2.0	VG 4.0	FN 6.0	VF 8.0	VF/NM 9.0	NM- 9.2

3-2nd Sub-Mariner x-over outside the F.F. (see Strange Tales #107 for 1st); Sub-Mariner & Hulk team-up & battle Avengers; Spider-Man cameo (1/64)
118 · 236 · 354 · 944 · 2122 · 3300

4-Revival of Captain America who joins the Avengers; 1st Silver Age app. of Captain America & Bucky (3/64)
500 · 1000 · 1500 · 3500 · 7850 · 12,500

4-Reprint from the Golden Record Comic set With Record (1966)
25 · 50 · 75 · 175 · 388 · 600

5-Hulk app.
33 · 66 · 99 · 238 · 532 · 825

6-1st app. original Zemo & his Masters of Evil
68 · 136 · 204 · 544 · 1222 · 1900

7-Rick Jones app. in Bucky costume
64 · 128 · 192 · 512 · 1156 · 1800

8-Intro Kang
172 · 344 · 516 · 1419 · 3210 · 5000

9-Intro Wonder Man who dies in same story
125 · 250 · 375 · 1000 · 2250 · 3500

10-Intro/1st app. Immortus; early Hercules app. (11/64)
50 · 100 · 150 · 400 · 900 · 1400

11-Spider-Man-c & x-over (12/64)
44 · 88 · 132 · 326 · 738 · 1150

12,13
47 · 94 · 141 · 296 · 498 · 700

14,15: 15-Death of original Zemo
37 · 74 · 111 · 222 · 361 · 500

16-New Avengers line-up (Hawkeye, Quicksilver, Scarlet Witch join; Thor, Iron Man, Giant-Man, Wasp leave)
50 · 100 · 150 · 400 · 900 · 1400

17,18: 17-Minor Hulk app.
15 · 30 · 45 · 103 · 227 · 350

19-1st app. Swordsman; origin Hawkeye (8/65)
32 · 64 · 96 · 230 · 515 · 800

20-22: Wood inks. 20-Intro. Power Man (Erik Josten) (2)
12 · 24 · 36 · 80 · 173 · 265

23-Romita Sr. inks (1st Silver Age Marvel work); Avengers vs. Kang; 1st app. Princess Ravonna
58 · 116 · 174 · 371 · 636 · 900

24,26,27,29,30: 24-Avengers vs. Kang
10 · 20 · 30 · 69 · 147 · 225

25-Dr. Doom-c/story
30 · 60 · 90 · 216 · 483 · 750

28-(5/66) First app. of The Collector; Giant-Man becomes Goliath
29 · 58 · 87 · 209 · 467 · 725

31-40: 32-1st Sons of the Serpent. 34-Last full Stan Lee plot/script. 35-1st Roy Thomas script w/Stan Lee plot. 38-40-Hercules app. 40-Sub-Mariner app.
15 · 30 · 45 · 103 · 159 · 175

41-46,50: 43-1st app. Red Guardian (dies in #44). 45-Hercules joins. 46-Ant-Man returns (re-intro, 11/67)
8 · 16 · 24 · 55 · 105 · 155

47-Magneto-c/story. Dane Whitman who becomes the new Black Knight in #48
23 · 46 · 69 · 164 · 362 · 550

48-(1/68) Origin/1st app. new Black Knight (Dane Whitman)
46 · 92 · 138 · 368 · 834 · 1300

49-Magneto-c/story
8 · 16 · 24 · 56 · 108 · 160

51-The Collector app.
8 · 16 · 24 · 56 · 108 · 160

52-Black Panther joins; 1st app. The Grim Reaper
16 · 32 · 48 · 107 · 236 · 365

53-X-Men app.
13 · 26 · 39 · 89 · 195 · 300

54-1st Ultron app. (1 panel); new Masters of Evil
12 · 24 · 36 · 84 · 185 · 285

55-1st full app. Ultron (8/68) (1 panel reveal in #54)
16 · 32 · 48 · 111 · 246 · 380

56-Zemo app; story explains how Capt. America was imprisoned in ice during WWII, only to be rescued in Avengers #4
10 · 20 · 30 · 69 · 147 · 225

57-1st app. S.A. Vision (10/68); death of Ultron-5
66 · 132 · 198 · 528 · 1189 · 1850

57 Facsimile Edition (1/21, $3.99) Reprints #57 with original ads and letter column
1 · 2 · 3 · 5 · 6 · 8

58-Origin The Vision
12 · 24 · 36 · 84 · 185 · 285

59-Intro. Yellowjacket
14 · 28 · 42 · 96 · 211 · 325

60,61,63-65: 60-Wasp & Yellowjacket wed. 61-Dr. Strange app. 63-Goliath becomes Yellowjacket; Hawkeye becomes the new Goliath. 65-Last 12¢ issue
8 · 16 · 24 · 54 · 102 · 150

62-1st Man-Ape
21 · 42 · 63 · 147 · 324 · 500

66-B. Smith-a; vs. Ultron-6; 1st mention of adamantium metal
10 · 20 · 30 · 64 · 132 · 200

67-Ultron-6 cvr/sty; B. Smith-a
10 · 20 · 30 · 68 · 144 · 220

68-Buscema-a
8 · 16 · 24 · 52 · 99 · 145

69-1st brief app. Squadron Sinister (Dr. Spectrum, Hyperion, Nighthawk)
27 · 54 · 81 · 189 · 420 · 650

70-1st full app. Nighthawk
17 · 34 · 51 · 117 · 259 · 400

71-1st app. The Invaders (12/69); Black Knight joins
19 · 38 · 57 · 131 · 291 · 450

72-79,81,82,84,86,90-91: 72-1st Zodiac; Captain Marvel & Nick Fury app. 73,74-Sons of the Serpent. 75-1st app. Arkon. 78-1st app. Lethal Legion (Man-Ape, Living Laser, Power Man, Grim Reaper, Swordsman). 82-Daredevil app. 86-2nd Squadron Supreme app.
7 · 14 · 21 · 46 · 86 · 125

80-1st app. Red Wolf
12 · 24 · 36 · 84 · 185 · 285

83-Intro. The Liberators (Wasp, Valkyrie, Scarlet Witch, Medusa & the Black Widow)
15 · 30 · 45 · 103 · 227 · 350

85-1st app. Squadron Supreme (American Eagle, Dr. Spectrum, Hawkeye (Wyatt McDonald), Hyperion, Lady Lark, Nighthawk (Kyle Richmond), Tom Thumb, Whizzer)
15 · 30 · 45 · 103 · 227 · 350

87-Origin The Black Panther
15 · 30 · 45 · 100 · 220 · 340

88-Written by Harlan Ellison; Hulk app.
7 · 14 · 21 · 46 · 86 · 125

88-2nd printing (1994)
2 · 4 · 6 · 9 · 13 · 16

89-Classic Captain Marvel execution-c; beginning of Kree/Skrull War (runs through issue #97)
9 · 18 · 27 · 57 · 111 · 165

92-Last 15¢ issue; Neal Adams-c
9 · 18 · 27 · 59 · 117 · 175

93-(52 pgs.)-Neal Adams-c/a
18 · 36 · 54 · 128 · 284 · 440

94-96-Neal Adams-c/a
9 · 18 · 27 · 59 · 117 · 175

97-G.A. Capt. America, Sub-Mariner, Human Torch, Patriot, Vision, Blazing Skull, Fin, Angel, and new Capt. Marvel x-over
8 · 16 · 24 · 56 · 108 · 160

98,99: 98-Goliath becomes Hawkeye; Smith-c/a(i). 99-Smith-c, Smith/Sutton-a
7 · 15 · 35 · 63 · 90

100-(6/72)-Smith-c/a; featuring everyone who was an Avenger
11 · 22 · 33 · 73 · 157 · 240

101-Harlan Ellison scripts
5 · 10 · 15 · 31 · 53 · 75

102-106,108,109
4 · 8 · 12 · 27 · 44 · 60

107-Starlin-a(p)
5 · 10 · 15 · 30 · 50 · 70

110,111-X-Men and Magneto app.
6 · 12 · 18 · 42 · 79 · 115

112-1st app. Mantis
13 · 26 · 39 · 89 · 195 · 300

113-115,119-124,126,128-130: 114-Swordsman returns; joins Avengers, first Mantis-c. 115-Prologue to Avengers/Defenders War. 119-Rutland, Vermont Halloween issue. 120-123-vs. Zodiac. 123,124-Mantis origin. 124-1st Star-Stalker. 126-Klaw & Solarr app. 129-Kang app; story continues in Giant-Size Avengers #2
4 · 8 · 12 · 23 · 37 · 50

116-118-Avengers/Defenders War; x-over w/Defenders #8-11. 116-Silver Surfer vs Vision.

117-Captain America vs. Sub-Mariner. 118-Avengers & Defenders vs. Loki & Dormammu
6 · 12 · 18 · 38 · 69 · 100

125-Thanos-c & brief app.; story continues in Captain Marvel #33
8 · 16 · 24 · 55 · 105 · 155

127-Ultron-7 app; story continues in Fantastic Four #150
4 · 8 · 12 · 24 · 44 · 60

131-133,136-140: 131,132-Vs. Kang. 131-1st Legion of the Unliving. 132-Continues in Giant-Size Avengers #3. 133-Origin of the Kree. 136-Ploog-r/Amazing Advs. #12. 137-Moondragon joins; Beast app; becomes provisional member; officially joins in #151; Wasp & Yellowjacket return
3 · 6 · 9 · 19 · 30 · 40

134,135-Origin of the Vision revised (also see Avengers Forever mini-series). 135-Continues in Giant-Size Avengers #4
4 · 8 · 12 · 28 · 47 · 65

141-143: 141-Squadron Supreme app; Pérez-a(p) begins. 142,143-Marvel Western heroes app. (Kid Colt, Rawhide Kid, Two-Gun Kid, Ringo Kid, Night Rider). 143-Vs. Kang (last 1970s app.)
3 · 6 · 9 · 17 · 25 · 34

144-Origin & 1st app. Hellcat (Patsy Walker)
8 · 16 · 24 · 55 · 105 · 155

145,146: Published out of sequence; Tony Isabella-s; originally intended to be in Giant-Size Avengers #5
3 · 6 · 9 · 15 · 22 · 28

146-149-(30¢-c variants, limited distribution)
7 · 14 · 21 · 48 · 89 · 130

147-149-(Reg. 25¢ editions)(5-7/76) Squadron Supreme app.
3 · 6 · 9 · 14 · 20 · 25

150-Kirby-a(r) pgs. 7-18 (from issue #16); pgs. 1-6 feature new-a by Pérez; new line-up: Capt. America, Iron Man, Scarlet Witch, Wasp, Yellowjacket, Vision & The Beast
3 · 6 · 9 · 17 · 31 · 42

150-(30¢-c variant, limited distribution)
7 · 14 · 21 · 48 · 89 · 130

151-Wonder Man returns w/new costume; Champions app.; The Collector app.
3 · 6 · 9 · 17 · 26 · 35

152-154,157,159,160,163: 152-1st app Black Talon. 154-vs. Attuma; continues in Super-Villain Team-up #9. 160-Grimm Reaper app. 163-Vs. The Champions
3 · 6 · 9 · 11 · 16 · 20

155,156-Dr. Doom app.
3 · 6 · 9 · 14 · 20 · 25

158-1st app. Graviton; Wonder Man vs. Vision; Jim Shooter plots begin
4 · 8 · 12 · 25 · 40 · 55

160-164-(35¢-c variants, limited dist.)(6-10/77)
10 · 20 · 30 · 66 · 138 · 210

161,162-Ultron-8 app; Henry Pym appears as Ant-Man. 162-1st app. Jocasta
3 · 6 · 9 · 17 · 26 · 35

164,165-Byrne-a; vs. Lethal Legion
3 · 6 · 9 · 16 · 23 · 30

166-Byrne-a; vs. Count Nefaria
3 · 6 · 9 · 16 · 23 · 30

167,168-Guardians of the Galaxy app.
3 · 6 · 9 · 15 · 21 · 27

169,172,178-180: 172-Hawkeye rejoins
2 · 4 · 6 · 9 · 12 · 15

170,171-Ultron & Jocasta app. 170-Minor Guardians of the Galaxy app.
3 · 6 · 9 · 15 · 22 · 28

173-177-Korvac Saga issues; 173-175-The Collector app. 173,177-Guardians of the Galaxy app. 174-Thanos cameo. 176-Starhawk app.
2 · 4 · 6 · 9 · 13 · 16

181-(3/79) Byrne-a/Pérez-c; new line-up: Capt. America, Scarlet Witch, Iron Man, Wasp, Vision, Beast & The Falcon; debut of Scott Lang who becomes Ant-Man in Marvel Premiere #47 (4/79)
6 · 12 · 18 · 38 · 69 · 100

182-184,187-191-Byrne-a: 183-Ms. Marvel joins. 184-vs. Absorbing Man. 187-vs. Mordred the Mystic. 188-Intro. The Elements of Doom. 189-Deathbird app. 190,191-vs. Grey Gargoyle
2 · 4 · 6 · 9 · 13 · 16

185-Origin Quicksilver & Scarlet Witch
3 · 6 · 9 · 17 · 26 · 35

186-1st app. of Chthon in Avengers (1st app. was in Marvel Chillers #1 (1975))
5 · 10 · 15 · 34 · 60 · 85

192-194,197-199: 197-199-vs Red Ronin
2 · 4 · 6 · 8 · 10 · 12

195-1st Taskmaster cameo
4 · 8 · 12 · 27 · 44 · 60

196-1st full Taskmaster app.
9 · 18 · 27 · 59 · 117 · 175

200-(10/80, 52 pgs.)-Ms. Marvel leaves; 1st actual app. of Marcus Immortus
3 · 6 · 9 · 16 · 24 · 32

201,203-210,212: 204,205-vs. Yellow Claw
1 · 3 · 4 · 6 · 8 · 10

202-Ultron app.
3 · 6 · 9 · 15 · 22 · 28

211-New line-up: Capt. America, Iron Man, Tigra, Thor, Wasp & Yellowjacket; Angel, Beast, Dazzler app.
2 · 4 · 6 · 8 · 11 · 14

213,215,216,239,240,250: 213-Controversial Yellowjacket slapping Wasp issue; Yellowjacket leaves. 215,216-Silver Surfer app. 216-Tigra leaves. 239-(1/84) Avengers app. on David Letterman show. 240-Spider-Woman revived. 250-($1.00, 52 pgs.) West Coast Avengers app. vs. Maelstrom
2 · 4 · 6 · 8 · 10 · 12

214-Ghost Rider app.
2 · 4 · 6 · 9 · 13 · 16

217-218,222,224-226,228-235,238: 217-Yellowjacket & Wasp return. 222-1st app. Egghead's Masters of Evil. 225,226-Black Knight app. 229-Death of Egghead. 230-Yellowjacket quits. 231-Iron Man leaves. 232-Starfox (Eros) joins. 233-Byrne-a. 234-Origin Quicksilver & Scarlet Witch. 238-Origin Blackout
2 · 4 · 6 · 8 · 10

219,220-Drax the Destroyer app. 220-Moondragon vs. Drax
2 · 4 · 6 · 8 · 11 · 14

221-Hawkeye & She-Hulk join; Spider-Man, Spider-Woman, Dazzler app.
3 · 6 · 9 · 21 · 33 · 45

223-Taskmaster app.
3 · 6 · 9 · 18 · 28 · 38

227-Captain Marvel (Monica Rambeau) joins; Roger Stern plots begin
3 · 6 · 9 · 14 · 20 · 25

236,237-Spider-Man tries to join the Avengers
3 · 6 · 9 · 12 · 15

241-249,251-256,258,262: 242-Dr. Strange app. 243-Vision becomes chairman. 244,245-vs. Dire Wraiths. 246-248-Eternals app. 249-x-over with Thor #350. 252-vs. the Blood Brothers. 253-Vision vs. Quasimodo. 254-West Coast Avengers app. 255-John Buscema & Tom Palmer return as artists; 1st app Nebula's pirate crew. 256-Terminus app. 258-x-over with Amazing Spider-Man #269-270; Spider-Man & Firelord app. 258-260-Nebula app. 260-261-Secret Wars II X-over; Beyonder app. 262-Hercules vs. Sub-Mariner
1 · 2 · 3 · 5 · 6 · 8

257-1st app. Nebula (from the Guardians of the Galaxy movie)
4 · 8 · 12 · 27 · 44 · 60

263-(1/86) Return of Jean Grey, leading into X-Factor #1(story continues in FF #286)
1 · 4 · 8 · 11 · 14

264-265,268,269: 264-1st new Yellowjacket (Rita Demara) 266-Secret Wars II x-over; vs. The Beyonder. 268,269-Kang app.
6.00

266-Secret Wars II epilogue; Silver Surfer & Molecule Man app.
1 · 2 · 3 · 5 · 6 · 8

267-Council of Kangs
4 · 8 · 12 · 23 · 37 · 50

270-277-Baron Zemo and the new Masters of Evil app. 272-Alpha Flight app. 274-277-Siege of Avengers Mansion. 274-Hercules injured. 275-Jarvis severely beaten. 276-Thor returns.

Avengers #58 © MAR

Avengers #201 © MAR

Avengers V2 #6 © MAR

	GD	VG	FN	VF	VF/NM	NM-		GD	VG	FN	VF	VF/NM	NM-
	2.0	4.0	6.0	8.0	9.0	9.2		2.0	4.0	6.0	8.0	9.0	9.2

277-Capt. America vs. Baron Zemo — 1 2 3 5 6 8

278-283: 279-Capt. Marvel (Monica Rambeau) becomes Avengers leader; Dr. Druid joins. 280-Jarvis flashback issue. 281-283-Olympian Gods app. 282-Sub-Mariner rejoins — 6.00

284,285-vs. the Olympian Gods. 285 Avengers vs. Zeus; Hercules recovers — 1 2 3 5 6 8

286-299: 286-Fixer app. Awesome Android & Super Adaptoid app. 287-Mentallo app. 288-1st app. 'Heavy Metal' (TESS-One, Intergalactic Sentry #459, Machine Man, Super-Adaptoid). 290-West Coast Avengers app. 291-$1.00 issues begin. 292-1st app. the Leviathan (Marrina). 293-Death of Marrina. 294-Capt. Marvel (Monica Rambeau) leaves. 295-vs. the Cross-Time Kangs. 297-Dr. Druid leaves; Thor, Black Knight & She-Hulk resign. 298-Inferno x-over. 299-Inferno x-over; New Mutants app. — 6.00

300-(2/89, $1.75, 68 pgs., squarebound) New line-up; the Captain (Steve Rogers), Thor, Invisible Woman, Mr. Fantastic & Gilgamesh (formerly the Forgotten one) Inferno x-over; Simonson-a — 1 3 4 6 8 10

301-304,306-313,319-325,327,330-343: 301-Firelord app. 1st app. Super-Nova. 302-Re-intro Quasar; Firelord app. 303-vs. Super-Nova. Quasar, Firelord & West Coast Avengers app.; Mr. Fantastic & Invisible Woman leave. 308-310-Eternals app. 311-313-Acts of Vengeance x-over. 312-Freedom Force app. 320-324-Alpha Flight app. 327-2nd app. Rage. 332,333-Dr. Doom app. 334-Intro. Thane Ector & the Brethren; Inhumans & Quicksilver app. 335-339-vs. the Brethren. 341,342-New Warriors & Sons of the Serpent app. 343-Intro. the Gatherers; Bob Harras scripts begin (end #395); last $1.00-c — 5.00

305,314-318: 305-Byrne scripts begin; most current & non-active Avengers app. 314-318-Spider-Man x-over.

326-1st app. Rage (11/90) — 2 4 6 8 10 12

328,329: 328-Origin Rage. 329-New line-up (Capt. America, Quasar, Sersi, She-Hulk, Thor, Vision, Black Widow) Spider-Man becomes a reserve member; Rage & Sandman become probationary members — 6.00

344-346, 348-349,351-359: 344-1st app. Proctor, leader of the Gatherers. 345,346-Operation Galactic Storm x-overs. 345-Pt.5-Deathbird app. 346-Pt.12-Intro. Starforce (super-powered Kree warriors) 349-Thor vs. Hercules. 351-Starjammers app. 352-354-Grimm Reaper app. — 5.00

347-Double-sized issue ($1.75, 39 pgs.) Operation Galactic Storm conclusion (Pt.19) end of the Kree/Shi'ar War; 'death' of the Supreme Intelligence — 6.00

350-($2.50, 68 pgs.) Double gatefold-c showing-c to #1; r/#53 w/cover in flip book format; vs. The Starjammers — 1 2 3 5 6 8

360-($2.95, 68 pgs.) Embossed all-foil-c; 30th ann. — 1 3 4 6 8 10

361,362,364,365,367: 361-Galactic Storm aftermath. 364-365-vs. Galen-Kor of the Kree — 5.00

363-($3.95)-All silver foil-c; vs. Proctor & the Gatherers; 1st cameo app. Deathcry (unnamed) — 6.00

366-($3.95, 68 pgs)-Embossed all gold foil-c; Deadpool app. in back-up story — 6.00

368,376-378: 368-Bloodties pt.1; Avengers/X-Men x-over — 6.00

369-($2.95)-Foil embossed-c; Bloodties pt.5; X-Men/Avengers vs. Exodus — 6.00

370-373: 370-371-Ghaur the Deviant app. 372-373-vs. Proctor & the Gatherers — 5.00

374-Bound-in trading card sheet; origin of Proctor as an alternate-Earth Black Knight revealed (scarcer in NM due to the card insert) — 6.00

375-($2.00, 52 pgs.)-Regular ed.; Thunderstrike returns; leads into Malibu Comic's Black September; end of the Gatherers saga (since #343); death of Proctor; Black Knight & Sersi leave; last Epting-a — 5.00

375-($2.50, 52 pgs.)-Collectors ed. — 6.00

379-382-Regular editions: 379-Galen Kor & Kree Lunatic Legion app. 380-382-High Evolutionary app. 380-1st Mike Deodato-a. 381-Exodus app. — 5.00

379-382-Marvel Double Feature editions ($2.50, 45 pgs.)-All have Giant-Man stories in a flip-book format — 6.00

383-385: 383-Fantastic Force app. 384-Hercules stripped of immortality & banished from Olympus. 385-Red Skull app. — 6.00

386-389, 398-399: 386-Red Skull app.; 'Taking of AIM' prelude; continues in Capt. America #440. 387-Taking of AIM Pt.2; Red Skull app.; re-intro Modok; continues in Capt. America #441. 388-Taking of AIM Pt.4; Red Skull & Modok app. — 1 3 4 6 8 10

390-393: 390-'The Crossing' prelude; leads into Avengers: the Crossing 1. 391,392-The Crossing. 391-Overpower game card insert; scarcer in NM. 392-393-The Crossing — 1 2 3 5 6 8

394,397: 394-The Crossing; 1st new Wasp; story cont. in Avengers Timeslide #1; 397-x-over w/Hulk #440-441 — 1 2 3 5 7 9

395-The Crossing/Timeslide; 'death' of Tony Stark; Bob Harras co-plot only, last work on Avengers — 1 3 4 6 8 10

396-First Sign Pt.4; vs. the Zodiac — 1 2 3 5 6 8

400-(Double-size, 32 pgs.)-Mark Waid scripts; Loki app. — 1 2 3 5 7 9

401,402: 401-Onslaught Impact #1; Magneto app. 402-Onslaught Impact #2; vs. Onslaught & Holocaust; last issue; continues in X-Men #56 — 1 3 4 6 8 10

#500-503 (See Avengers Vol. 3; series resumed original numbering after Vol. 3 #84)

Special 1 (9/67, 25¢, 68 pgs.)-New-a; original & new Avengers team-up — 14 28 42 96 211 325

Special 2 (9/68, 25¢, 68 pgs.)-New-a; original vs. new Avengers — 14 28 42 96 211 325

Special 3 (9/69, 25¢, 68 pgs.)-r/Avengers #4 plus 13 Capt. America stories by Kirby (art); origin Red Skull — 7 14 21 44 82 120

Special 4 (1/71, 25¢, 68 pgs.)-Kirby-r/Avengers #5,6 — 8 12 28 47 65

Special 5 (1/72, 52 pgs.)-All-reprint issue; Kirby-r Avengers #8/Heck-r w/Spider-Man from issue #1 — 5 10 15 31 53 75

Annual 6 (11/76) Pérez-a; Kirby-c; vs. Nuklo — 3 6 9 17 26 35

Annual 7 (11/77)-Starlin-c/a; Warlock dies; Thanos app.; x-over w/Marvel Two-in-one Ann #2 — 7 14 21 46 86 125

Annual 8 (1978)-Dr. Strange, Ms. Marvel app. vs. Hyperion, Dr. Spectrum & Whizzer — 2 4 6 11 16 20

Annual 9 (1979)-Newton-a(p); Intro. Arsenal — 2 4 6 10 14 18

Annual 10 (1981)-Golden-a; X-Men cameo; 1st app. Rogue & Madelyne Pryor — 8 16 24 54 102 150

Annual 11-13: 11 (1982)-Vs. The Defenders. 12 ('83)-Inhumans app. 13 ('84)-Ditko/Byrne-a — 1 3 4 6 8 10

Annual 14-15,17-18: 14 ('85)-x-over w/Fantastic Four Ann. #19; vs. the Skrulls. 15 ('86)-vs. Freedom Force; x-over w/Avengers West Coast Ann. #1. 17('88)-Evolutionary War x-over. 18('89)-Atlantis Attacks — 6.00

Annual 16 (1987)-x-over w/Avengers West Coast Ann. #2; Silver Surfer app. vs. the Grandmaster and Legion of the Unliving (including Drax, Captain Marvel & Green Goblin) — 1 2 3 5 6 8

Annual 19-22: 19 ('90)-Terminus Factor Pt.5 (conclusion) continued from Avengers West Coast Ann. #5. 20 ('91)-Subterranean Saga Pt.1; cont. in Hulk Ann. #17. 21 ('92)-Citizen Kang pt.4; vs. Terminatrix. 22 ('93)-Bagged w/card; 1st app. Bloodwraith — 5.00

Annual 23 (1994)-Buscema-a; Roy Thomas-s; vs. Loki & Pluto; x-over w/Thor Ann. #195.00

Avengers 1: The Coming of the Avengers! (2012, $3.99) recolored reprint/#1 — 1 2 3 4 5 7

...: Galactic Storm Vol. 1 ('06, $29.99, TPB) r/Kree-Shi'ar war from Avengers #345-346, Capt. America #398-399, Avengers West Coast #80-81, Quasar #32-33, Wonder Man #7-8, Iron Man #278 and Thor #445; new Epting-c — 30.00

...: Galactic Storm Vol. 2 ('06, $29.99, TPB) r/Kree-Shi'ar war from Avengers #347, Capt. America #400-401, Avengers West Coast #82, Quasar #34-36, Wonder Man #9, Iron Man #279, Thor #446 and What If #55-56 — 30.00

...: Kang - Time and Time Again ('05, $19.99, TPB) r/Avengers #69-71 & 267-269, Thor #140 and Incredible Hulk #135 — 20.00

...Kree-Skrull War ('00, $24.95, TPB) new Neal Adams-c — 25.00

...: Legends Vol. 3. George Perez ('03, $16.99)-r/#161,162,194-196,201, Ann. #6 & 8 — 17.00

Marvel Double Feature...Avengers/Giant-Man #379 ($2.50, 52 pgs.)-Same as Avengers #379 w/Giant-Man flip book — 4.00

Marvel Graphic Novel - Deathtrap: The Vault (1991, $9.95) Venom-c/app. — 2 4 6 11 16 20

No. 1 Facsimile Edition (7/23, $3.99) Reprints the 1963 issue #1 with original ads — 4.00

No. 8 Facsimile Edition (5/23, $3.99) Reprints the debut of Kang with original ads — 4.00

No. 9 Facsimile Edition (5/23, $3.99) Reprints the debut of Wonder Man with original ads — 4.00

The Korvac Saga TPB (2003, $19.95)-r/#167,168,170-177; Perez-c — 20.00

The Serpent Crown TPB (2005, $15.99)-r/#141-144,147-149; Hellcat app. — 16.00

The Yesterday Quest ($6.95)-r/#181,182,185-187 — 1 2 3 4 5 7

Under Siege ('98, $16.95, TPB) r/#270,271,273-277 — 17.00

...: Vision and the Scarlet Witch TPB (2005, $15.99) r/wedding from Giant-Size Avengers #4 and "Vision and the Scarlet Witch" mini-series #1-4 — 16.00

...: Visionaries ('99, $16.95)-r/early George Perez art — 17.00

NOTE: Austin c(i)-157, 167, 168, 170-177, 181, 183-188, 198-201, Annual 8. John Buscema a-41-44p, 46p, 47p, 49, 50, 51-62p, 74-77, 79-85, 87-91, 97, 105p, 121p, 124p,125p, 152, 153p, 255-279p, 281-302p; c-41-46, 68-71, 73-91, 97-99, 178, 256-259p, 261-279p. Byrne a-164-166p, 181-191p, 233p, Annual 13; 14p; c-186-190p, 233p, 260, 305p; scripts-305-312. Colan a(p)-63-65, 111, 206-208, 210, 211; c(p)-65, 206-208, 210,211. Ditko a-Annual 13. Guice a-Annual 12p. Don Heck a-9-15, 17-40, 157. Kane c-37p, 159p. Kane/Everett c-97. Kirby a-1-8p, Special 3r; 4r(p); c-1-30, 148, 151-158; layouts-14-16. Ron Lim c(p)-335-341. Miller c-196. Mooney a-86i, 179p, 180p. Nebres a-178i; c-179i. Newton a-204p, Annual 9p; 8; c(p)-160-162, 164-166, 170-174. Perez a(p)-141, 143, 144, 148, 150, 154, 155, 160, 161, 162, 167-168, 170, 171, 194-196, 198-202, Annual 6, 8; c(p)-167-168, 170-174, 181, 183-185, 191, 192, 194-201, 379-382, Annual 8. Starlin c-121, 135. Staton a-127-134i. Tuska a-47i, 48i, 51i, 53i, 54i, 106p, 107p, 135p, 137-140p, 163p. Guardians of the Galaxy app. in #167, 168, 170, 173, 175, 181.

AVENGERS, THE (Volume Two)
Marvel Comics: V2#1, Nov. 1996 - No. 13, Nov. 1997 ($2.95/$1.95/$1.99) (Produced by Extreme Studios)

1-($2.95)-Heroes Reborn begins; intro new team (Captain America, Swordsman, Scarlet Witch, Vision, Thor, Hellcat & Hawkeye); 1st app. Avengers Island; Loki & Enchantress app.; Rob Liefeld-s & plot; Chap Yaep-p; Jim Valentino scripts; variant-c exists — 1 2 3 5 7

1-($2.95)-Variant-c — 1 3 4 6 8 10

2-13: 2,3-Jeph Loeb scripts begin, Kang app. 4-Hulk-c/app. 5-Thor/Hulk battle; 2 covers. 10,11,13-"World War 3"-pt. 2, x-over w/Image characters. 12-($2.99) "Heroes Reunited"-pt. 2 — 4.00

Heroes Reborn: Avengers (2006, $29.99, TPB) r/#1-13; pin-up and cover gallery — 30.00

AVENGERS, THE (Volume Three)(See New Avengers for next series)
Marvel Comics: Feb. 1998 - No. 84, Aug, 2004; No. 500, Sept, 2004 - No. 503, Dec, 2004

($2.99/$1.99/$2.25)

1-($2.99, 48 pgs.) Busiek-s/Pérez-a/wraparound-c; Avengers reassemble after
Heroes Return; many Avengers app. vs. Morgan Le Fey ... 6.00

1-Variant Heroes Return sunburst cover   1   2   3   5   6   8

1-Dynamic Forces Ltd Edition (1500 copies); sunburst-c signed by Perez
4   8   12   25   40   55

1-Rough Cut-Features original script and pencil pages ... 4.00

2-($1.99) Pérez-c; vs. Morgan Le Fey, alternate painted-c by Lago ... 4.00

3,4: 3-Wonder Man-c/app. & "dies". 4-Final roster chosen; Captain America, Thor, Hawkeye,
Iron Man, Scarlet Witch, Vision, Warbird (formally Ms. Marvel: Carol Danvers) ... 3.00

5-6,8-11; 5-6: Squadron Supreme-c/app.: Hyperion, Dr. Spectrum, Power Princess, Whizzer,
Haywire, Lady Lark, Shape & Moonglow. 8-1st app; Triathlon & Silverclaw; vs. Moses
Magnum. 9-1st mention of the Triune Understanding. 10-Grimm Reaper & Ultron app;
return of the Legion of the Unliving: Captain Mar-Vell, Dr. Druid, Mockingbird, Swordsman,
Wonder Man & Thunderstrike. 11-Legion of the Unliving app; Hellcat, Spider-Man,
Daredevil & Fantastic Four guest app; Wonder Man returns to life ... 3.00

7-Live Kree or Die pt. 4; continued from Quicksilver #10; Warbird leaves; vs. Kree Lunatic
Legion ... 4.00

12-($2.99, 38 pgs.) Thunderbolts app; Firebird and Justice (of the New Warriors) join the
Avengers. ... 4.00

12-Alternate-c of Avengers w/white background; no logo
3   6   9   16   23   30

12-Dynamic Forces alternate-c; ltd. to 5000 copies   2   4   6   8   10   12

12-Dynamic Forces alternate-c; ltd. to 1500 copies; signed by Pérez, Vey and Smith
3   9   15   22   28

13-18,23,26: 13-New Warriors app.; 1st app. Lord Templar; 1st (shadowed) app. Jonathan
Tremont – leader of the Triune Understanding. 14-Beast app. vs. Lord Templar; 1st app.
Pagan. 15-1st full app. of Jonathan Tremont; Pagan and Lord Templar, the Wrecking Crew
and Ultron app. 16-18-Ordway-s/a; vs. the Doomsday Man in #17; vs. the Wrecking Crew
in #18. 23-Vision & Scarlet Witch history retold. 26-Immonen-a; Lord Templar & Taskmaster
app. ... 3.00

16-Variant-c w/purple background ... 5.00

19,20: Ultron Unlimited pt. 1-2; Black Panther app.; Giant-Man (Henry Pym app. in #20-22)
1   2   3   5   8

21,22-Ultron Unlimited pt. 3-4; vs. Ultron; Black Panther app. ... 6.00

24-Continued from Juggernaut; the Eighth Day #1; vs. the Exemplars ... 4.00

25-Vs. the Exemplars; Spider-Man, New Warriors, Juggernaut and Quicksilver app. ... 5.00

27-($2.99, 100 pgs. 'Monster') New line up - Justice, Firestar & Thor leave, Triathlon &
She-Hulk join, Wonder Man becomes a reserve member; Ant-Man app.; reprints issues
(all Vol.1) #101,150,151; Annual #19; Note: Due to the 100 pages, this issue often suffers
from tears around the staples. ... 6.00

28-32: 28-30-vs. Kulan Gath. 31-Vision rejoins; vs. Grimm Reaper. 32-Life story & secret
origin of Madame Masque revealed ... 3.00

33-Thunderbolts x-over w/Thunderbolts #44; Madame Masque & Count Nefaria app.
2   4   6   9   12   15

34-($2.99, 38 pgs.) Last Perez-a; continued from Thunderbolts #44; vs. Count Nefaria;
Black Widow app ... 6.00

35-37: 35-Maximum Security x-over; Romita Jr.-a; 36-37; vs. Bloodwraith; Epting-a ... 4.00

38-Davis-a begins (35-39); new line up - Captain America, Goliath (Henry Pym), Thor,
Quicksilver, Wasp, Iron Man, Vision, Scarlet Witch, Triathlon, Wonder Man & Warbird
(Carol Danvers) ... 4.00

39,40: Hulk app. ... 5.00

41-47,49: 41-Vs. Scarlet Centurion; Kang app. 42-44-Kang, Scarlet Centurion & the Presence
app. 43-Jack of Hearts joins; last Davis-a. 45-Origin of the Scarlet Centurion; Kang is the
Master of the World (from Alpha Flight issues) app. 46-Vs. Kang and his army; Scarlet
Centurion & the Master of the World app. 47-Origin of Scarlet Centurion continued with
flashback to issue #200 w/Ms. Marvel (Carol Danvers); 1st full app of the Triple Evil
(ancient cosmic menace). 49-'Nuff Said story; Kang attacks Washington DC ... 3.00

48-($3.50, 100 pgs.) vs. Kang and his legions; Scarlet Centurion app.; death of Master of the
World; Triple Evil app. ... r/#98-100 ... 4.00

50-($3.50); vs. the Triple Evil (destroyed); Lord Pagan & Templar app. (both die); Jonathan
Tremont & the Triune Understanding revealed as villains; 3-D Man app. ... 5.00

51,52: 51-Kang app. as ruler of the Earth; Wonder Man and Scarlet Witch app.; features
2 pg. tribute to the late John Buscema who passed away on January 10th 2002.
52-Avengers vs. Kang; Scarlet Centurion & the Presence app. ... 4.00

53-Avengers vs. Kang; death of Jonathan Tremont. ... 6.00

54-56: 54-Conclusion of the Kang war w/Kang defeated; death of Scarlet Centurion.
55-Kang war aftermath; Thor leaves. 56-Beast app; last Busiek issue ... 4.00

57-62,65-84: 57-Geoff Johns-s begins; 'World Trust' pt. 1; ends with pt. 4 in issue #60.
64-Solo Falcon story; vs Scarecrow. 65-70-Red Zone pt. 1-6; vs. the Red Skull. Wasp
and Yellowjacket (Henry Pym) app.; Plantman and Whirlwind. 71-74; Search for
She-Hulk pt. 1-4; Hulk app. in #73-74. 77-Last Johns issue. 78-81; Chuck Austen-s begin;
Lionheart of Avalon pt. 1-5; special 50-c issue. 79-81; Captain Britain (Brian Braddock)
app. 82-84-Once an Invader pt. 1-4; intro. New invaders team: Blazing Skull, Spitfire,
US Agent & Union Jack; Namor app. in #83-84 ... 4.00

63-Standoff pt. 3; continued from Thor (Vol. 2) #58; Thor vs. Iron Man; Dr. Doom app.
2   4   6   9   12   15

(After #84 [Aug, 2004], numbering reverted back to original Vol. #500, Sept, 2004)

500-($3.50) "Avengers Disassembled" begins; Bendis-s/Finch-a; Ant-Man (Scott Lang)
and Jack of Hearts killed, Vision destroyed by the Scarlet Witch
1   2   3   5   6   8

500-Director's Cut ($4.99) Cassaday foil variant-c plus interviews and galleries
2   4   6   8   10   12

501, 502-($2.25): 501-Numerous Avengers and ex-team members app. 502-Hawkeye killed
... 5.00

503-($3.50) "Avengers Disassembled" ends; reprint pages from Avengers V1#16; Dr. Strange
and Magneto app; story continues in Avengers Finale #1 ... 4.00

#11/2 (12/99, $2.50) Timm-c/a; Stern-s; 1963-style issue ... 3.00

.../ Squadron Supreme '98 Annual ($2.99) ... 4.00

1999, 2000 Annual (7/99, '00, $3.50) 1999-Manco-a. 2000-Breyfogle-a. ... 4.00

2001 Annual ($2.99) Reis-a; back-ups art by Churchill ... 4.00

...: Above and Beyond TPB ('05, $24.99) r/#36-40,56, Annual 2001, & Avengers: The Ultron
Imperative; Alan Davis-c ... 25.00

... Assemble HC ('04, $29.95, oversized) r/#1-11 & '98 Annual; Busiek intro.; Pérez pencil art
and Busiek script from Avengers #1 ... 30.00

... Assemble Vol. 2 HC ('05, $29.95, oversized) r/#12-22, #0 & Ann. 1999; Ordway intro. ... 30.00

... Assemble Vol. 3 HC ('06, $34.99, oversized) r/#23-34, #1 1/2 & Thunderbolts #42-44 ... 35.00

... Assemble Vol. 4 HC ('07, $34.99, oversized) r/#35-40, Avengers 2000, Avengers 2001,
Avengers: The Ultron Imperative, Maximum Security #1-3 & ...Dangerous Planet ... 35.00

... Assemble Vol. 5 HC ('07, $39.99, oversized) r/#41-56 and Avengers 2001 ... 40.00

...: Clear and Present Dangers TPB ('01, $19.95) r/#8-15 ... 20.00

.... Defenders War HC ('07, $19.99) r/#115-118 & Defenders #8-11; Englehart intro. ... 20.00

... Disassembled HC ('06, $24.99) r/#500-503 & Avengers Finale; Director's Cut extras ... 25.00

... Disassembled TPB ('05, $15.99) r/#500-503 & Avengers Finale; Director's Cut extras ... 16.00

...Finale 1 (1/05, $3.50) Epilogue to Avengers Disassembled; Neal Adams-c; art by various
incl. Perez, Maleev, Oeming, Powell, Mayhew, Mack, McNiven, Cheung, Frank ... 4.00

Free Comic Book Day (5/09, giveaway) New Avengers 1st battle vs. Dark Avengers ... 4.00

... Living Legends TPB ('04, $19.99) r/#23-30; last Busiek/Pérez arc ... 18.00

...Supreme Justice TPB (4/01, $17.95) r/Squadron Supreme appearances in Avengers #5-7,
'98 Annual, Iron Man #7, Capt. America #8, Quicksilver #10; Pérez-c ... 18.00

The Kang Dynasty TPB ('02, $29.99) r/#41-55 & 2001 Annual ... 30.00

The Morgan Conquest TPB ('00, $14.95) r/#1-4 ... 15.00

.../Thunderbolts Vol. 1: The Nefaria Protocols (2004, $19.99) r/#31-34, 42-44 ... 20.00

Ultron Unleashed TPB (8/99, $3.50) reprints early app. ... 4.00

Ultron Unlimited TPB (4/01, $14.95) r/#19-22 & #0 prelude ... 15.00

Wizard #0-Ultron Unlimited prelude ... 4.00

Vol. 1: World Trust TPB ('03, $14.99) r/#57-62 & Marvel Double-Shot #2 ... 15.00

Vol. 2: Red Zone TPB ('04, $14.99) r/#64-70 ... 15.00

Vol. 3: The Search For She-Hulk TPB ('04, $12.99) r/#71-76 ... 13.00

Vol. 4: The Lionheart of Avalon TPB ('04, $11.99) r/#77-81 ... 12.00

Vol. 5: Once an Invader TPB ('04, $14.99) r/#82-84, V1 #71; Invaders #0 & Ann #1 ('77) ... 15.00

AVENGERS (The Heroic Age)

Marvel Comics: July, 2010 - No. 34, Jan, 2013 ($3.99)

1-New team assembled; Bendis-s/Romita Jr.-a; Kang app.; back-up text Avengers history ... 6.00

1-Variant-c by Land ... 8.00

1-Variant covers by Djurdjevic and John Romita Sr. ... 12.00

1-3-Second printings ... 4.00

2,3: 2-Wonder Man app. ... 5.00

4-12: 4-6-Ultron app. 7-Red Hulk app. 12-Red Hulk joins ... 4.00

12.1 -(6/11, $2.99) Hitch & Neary-c/a; The Wizard & The Intelligencia app.; Ultron returns ... 3.00

13-24: 13-17-Fear Itself tie-ins. 13,15-Bachalo-a. 17-New Avengers app. 18-20-Acuña-a.
19-Vision returns, Storm joins ... 4.00

24.1 -(5/12, $2.99) Peterson-a; Magneto, She-Hulk app. ... 3.00

25-33: 25-30-Avengers vs. X-Men tie-ins; Simonson-a. 31-34-Janet Van Dyne app. ... 4.00

34-($4.99) Art by Peterson, Mayhew & Dodson; Deodato, Simonson, Yu, Cheung, Coipel
art pages; Bendis afterword ... 5.00

... Annual 1 (3/12, $4.99) Bendis-s/Dell'Otto-c/a; Wonder Man app. ... 5.00

...: Assemble 1 (7/10, $3.99) Handbook-style profiles of Avengers, enemies, allies ... 4.00

...: Infinity Quest 1 (8/11, $4.99) r/#7-9 with variant covers ... 5.00

...: Roll Call 1 (2012, $4.99) Updated handbook-style profiles of Avengers & enemies ... 5.00

...: Spotlight (7/10, $3.99) Creator interviews, previews, history of the team; trivia ... 4.00

AVENGERS (Marvel NOW!)

Marvel Comics: Feb, 2013 - No. 44, Jun, 2015 ($3.99)

1-13: 1-Hickman-s/Opeña-a/Weaver-c. 4-6-Adam Kubert-a ... 5.00

14-23: 14-17-Prelude to Infinity. 18-23-Infinity tie-ins ... 4.00

24-($4.99) Rogue Planet; Ribic-a; Iron Man 3030 app. ... 5.00

25-28-Hickman-s/Larroca-a. 27-Includes reprint of All-New Invaders #1 ... 4.00

29-($4.99) Original Sin tie-in; Yu-a/Cho-c ... 5.00

30-34-Original Sin tie-in; Hickman-s/Yu-a ... 4.00

34.1 (11/14), 34.2 (1/15), 35 ($4.99) 34.1-Spotlight on Hyperion; Keown-a. 34.2-Spotlight
on Starbrand; Bengal-a. 35-Cheung, Medina-a ... 5.00

36-39,41-43: 37,39,41-Deodato-a. 39-Leads into New Avengers #28 ... 4.00

40-($4.99) Thanos-c/app.; Caselli-a ... 5.00

44-($4.99) Follows New Avengers #33; Thanos app.; leads into Secret Wars #1 ... 5.00

Annual (2/14, $4.99) Christmas-themed; Lafuente-a ... 5.00

...: Endless Wartime HC (2013, $24.99, OGN) Ellis-s/McKone-a; intro by Clark Gregg ... 25.00

...: No More Bullying (3/15, $1.99) Short stories; Avengers, Spider-Man, GOTG app. ... 3.00

...: Now! Handbook 1 (2/15, $4.99) Updated version with new characters from 2014 ... 5.00

...: The Enemy Within (7/13, $2.99) DeConnick-s/Hepburn-a; Captain Marvel tie-in ... 3.00

...: Vs 1 (7/15, $5.99) Printing of 4 digital-first stories; Raney-c ... 6.00

100th Anniversary Special: Avengers 1 (9/14, $3.99) James Stokoe-s/a ... 4.00

AVENGERS (After Secret Wars)

Marvel Comics: No. 0, Dec, 2015 ($5.99)

0-Short story preludes for the various Avengers 2016 titles; Deadpool app. ... 6.00

AVENGERS (Follows events of Civil War II)

Marvel Comics: Jan, 2017 - No. 11, Nov, 2017; No. 672, Dec, 2017 - No. 690, Jun, 2018
($4.99/$3.99)

1-($4.99) Spider-Man, Capt. America (Sam), Thor (Jane), Wasp, Vision, Hercules team ... 5.00

2-11-($3.99) 2-6-Kang app.; Waid-s/del Mundo-a. 7,8-Infamous Iron Man app.; Noto-a. ... 4.00

9,10-Secret Empire tie-ins ... 4.00

[Title switches to legacy numbering after #11 (11/17)]

672-674,676-683,685-688,690: 672-674-The Champions app. 676-690-No Surrender.
681-Origin of Voyager. 682-Hulk returns ... 4.00

675-($4.99) No Surrender Part 1; "return" of Voyager; lenticular wraparound-c by Brooks ... 5.00

684-($4.99) No Surrender Part 10; re-cap of Hulk origin and many deaths ... 5.00

689-($4.99) No Surrender Part 15; Larraz-a ... 5.00

#1.MU (3/17, $4.99) Monsters Unleashed tie-in; Zub-s/Izaakse-a ... 5.00

...: Shards of Infinity 1 (6/18, $3.99) Macchio-s/Di Vito-a; Black Panther app. ... 4.00

AVENGERS

Marvel Comics: Jul, 2018 - No. 66, May, 2023 ($4.99/$3.99)

1-($4.99) Aaron-s/McGuinness-a; Avengers re-form vs. the Celestials ... 5.00

2-9-($3.99) Loki app. 7-Origin of prehistoric Ghost Rider; Pichelli-a. 9-Namor app. ... 4.00

10-($5.99) 700th issue; Namor and The Winter Guard app.; McGuinness-a ... 6.00

11-30,32-49,51-66: 11-Phil Coulson app. 12-Blade joins. 15-17-Marquez-a. 16-Johnny Blaze
app. 18-20-War of the Realms tie-ins; McGuinness-a. 18,21-Squadron Supreme app.
22,23-Hellstrom app. 23-25-Cosmic Ghost Rider app. 32-Mephisto & Dracula app.
39,41-44-Enter The Phoenix. 39-Keown-a. 40-Doom app. 46-49-World War She-Hulk.
60-AXE Judgment Day tie-in.; Russell-s/Land-a ... 4.00

31-($4.99) "The Temptation of Anthony Stark"; Aaron-s; art by various ... 5.00

50-($9.99) 750th issue; Doctor Doom & Galactus app.; McGuinness, Pacheco, Kuder-a ... 10.00

Annual 1-(10/21, $4.99) MacKay-s/Foreman-a.; Infinite Fury tie-in ... 5.00

Avengers (2017 series) #10 © MAR

Avengers Academy #31 © MAR

Avengers Inc. #1 © MAR

	GD	VG	FN	VF	VF/NM	NM-
	2.0	4.0	6.0	8.0	9.0	9.2

... & Moon Girl 1 (10/22, $4.99) Shuri & Captain Marvel app. 5.00
... Assemble Alpha 1 (1/23, $5.99) Aaron-s/Hitch-a; leads into Avengers #63 (2023) and
    Avengers Forever #12 6.00
...: Curse of the Man-Thing 1 (5/21, $4.99) Orlando-s/Mobili-a (Also see Spider-Man: Curse
    of the Man-Thing and X-Men: Curse of the Man-Thing) 5.00
...: Edge of Infinity 1 (6/19, $3.99) Macchio-s/Di Vito-a; M.O.D.O.K. app. 4.00
...: End Times 1 (4/23, $7.99) Reprints Avengers (2010) #31-34; return of Janet Van Dyne 8.00
...: Halloween Special 1 (12/18, $4.99) Short stories by various; Geoff Shaw-c 5.00
...: Loki Unleashed 1 (11/19, $4.99) Takes place after Avengers #277; Stern-s/Lim-a 5.00
...: Marvels Snapshots 1 (1/21, $4.99) Barbara Kesel-s/Staz Johnson-a 5.00
... 1,000,000 BC #1 (10/22, $4.99) Aaron-s/Walker-a; Phoenix Force app. 5.00

AVENGERS (Flashback to new team roster from Avengers #16 [1965])
Marvel Comics: No. 1.1, Jan, 2017 - No. 5.1, May, 2017 ($3.99)
    1.1, 2.1, 3.1, 4.1, 5.1- Hawkeye, Quicksilver and Scarlet Witch join team; Waid-s/Kitson-a 4.00

AVENGERS (Marvel Action all ages)(Title changes to Marvel Action: Avengers with #6)
IDW Publishing: Dec, 2018 - No. 5, Apr, 2019 ($3.99)
    1-5-Iron Man, Captain America, Thor, Hawkeye, Black Widow, Black Panther & Hulk app. 4.00

AVENGERS
Marvel Comics: Jul, 2023 - Present ($4.99/$3.99)
    1,6-($4.99) 1-MacKay-s/Villa-a; Captain Marvel assembles the new line-up 5.00
    2-10-($3.99) 2-Kang app. 4.00
    Annual 1 (11/23, $4.99) Tie-in to "Contest of Chaos;" Agatha Harkness app. 5.00

AVENGERS ACADEMY (The Heroic Age)(Also see Avengers Arena)
Marvel Comics: Aug, 2010 - No. 39, Jan, 2013 ($3.99/$2.99)
    1-($3.99) Gage-s/McKone-a/c; Intro. team of Veil, Hazmat, Striker, Mettle, Finesse, Reptil 4.00
    1-Variant-c by Djurdjevic 8.00
    2-14,14.1 -($2.99) 3,4-Juggernaut app. 5-Molina-a. 7-Absorbing Man app.; Raney-a. 3.00
    15-39: 15-20-Fear Itself tie-in. 22-Magneto app. 27,28-Runaways app. 29-33-Tie in to
    Avengers vs. X-Men event 3.00
... Giant Size 1 (7/11, $7.99) Young Allies and Arcade app.; Tobin-s/Baldeon-a 8.00

AVENGERS: AGE OF ULTRON POINT ONE (Free Comic Book Day)
Marvel Comics: 2012 (Free giveaway)
    #0.1 - Reprints Avengers 12.1 (6/11); Bendis-s/Hitch & Neary-c/a 4.00

AVENGERS: A.I. (Follows Age of Ultron series)
Marvel Comics: Sept, 2013 - No. 12, Jun, 2014 ($2.99)
    1-12- Humphries-s/Araújo-a; Hank Pym, Vision app. 7-Daredevil app. 3.00

AVENGERS AND POWER PACK ASSEMBLE!
Marvel Comics: June, 2006 - No. 4, Sept, 2006 ($2.99, limited series)
    1-4-GuriHiru-a/Sumerak-s. 1-Capt. America app. 2-Iron Man. 3-Spider-Man, Kang app. 3.00
    TPB (2006, $6.99, digest-size) r/#1-4 7.00

AVENGERS AND THE INFINITY GAUNTLET
Marvel Comics: Oct, 2010 - No. 4, Jan, 2011 ($2.99, limited series)
    1-4: 1-Clevinger-s/Churilla-a; Dr. Doom and Thanos app. 1-Ramos-c. 2-Lim-c 3.00

AVENGERS & X-MEN: AXIS
Marvel Comics: Dec, 2014 - No. 9, Feb, 2015 ($4.99/$3.99, limited series)
    1-($4.99) Remender-s/Adam Kubert-a; Red Skull as Red Onslaught 5.00
    2-8-($3.99): 2,7-Kubert-a. 3,4,8-Yu-a. 3-Adult Apocalypse app. 5,6-Dodson-a 4.00
    9-($4.99) Cheung, Dodson, Yu & Kubert-a 5.00

AVENGERS ARENA
Marvel Comics: Feb, 2013 - No. 18, Jan, 2014 ($2.99)
    1-18: 1-Avengers Academy members & Runaways in Arcade's Murder World; Walker-a 3.00

AVENGERS ASSEMBLE (Also see Marvel Universe Avengers Assemble)
Marvel Comics: May, 2012 - No. 25, May, 2014 ($3.99)
    1-25: 1-Bendis-s/Bagley-a/c; movie roster in regular Marvel universe. 3-Thanos returns.
    4-8-Guardians of the Galaxy app. 9-DeConnick-s begin. 13,14-Age of Ultron tie-in.
    18-20-Infinity tie-in. 21-23-Inhumanity 4.00
    Annual 1 (3/13, $4.99) Gage-s/Coker-a; spotlight on The Vision 5.00

AVENGERS ASSEMBLE OMEGA (Takes place after Avengers Forever #15)
Marvel Comics: Jun, 2023 ($7.99, one-shot)
    1-Jason Aaron-s/Aaron Kuder-a 8.00

AVENGERS: BACK TO BASICS
Marvel Comics: 2018 ($14.99, squarebound, printing of original digital comics)
    nn-Peter David-s/Brian Level & Juanan Ramírez-a; Ms. Marvel & Kang app. 15.00

AVENGERS: BEYOND
Marvel Comics: May, 2023 - No. 5, Sept, 2023 ($3.99, limited series)
    1-5-Derek Landy-s/Greg Land-a; The Beyonder and the Black Order app. 4.00

AVENGERS: CELESTIAL QUEST
Marvel Comics: Nov, 2001 - No. 8, June, 2002 ($2.50/$3.50, limited series)
    1-7-Englehart-s/Santamaría-a; Thanos app. 3.00
    8-($3.50) 4.00

AVENGERS: CLASSIC
Marvel Comics: Aug, 2007 - No. 12, Juy, 2008 ($3.99/$2.99)
    1,12-($3.99) 1-Reprints Avengers #1 ('63) with new stories about that era; Art Adams-c 4.00
    2-11-($2.99) R/#2-11 with back-up w/art by Oeming and others 3.00

AVENGERS COLLECTOR'S EDITION, THE
Marvel Comics: 1993 (Ordered through mail w/candy wrapper, 20 pgs.)
    1-Contains 4 bound-in trading cards 5.00

AVENGERS: EARTH'S MIGHTIEST HEROES
Marvel Comics: Jan, 2005 - No. 8, Apr, 2005 ($3.50, limited series)
    1-8-Retells origin; Casey-s/Kolins-a 4.00
    HC (2005, $24.99, 7 1/2" x 11" with dustjacket) r/#1-8 25.00

AVENGERS: EARTH'S MIGHTIEST HEROES (Based on the Disney animated series)
Marvel Comics: Jan, 2011 - No. 4, Apr, 2011 ($3.99)
    1-4-Yost-s/Wegener-a. 1-Hero profile pages. 2-Villain profile pages 4.00

AVENGERS EARTH'S MIGHTIEST HEROES (Titled Marvel Universe... for #1)
Marvel Comics: Jun, 2012 - No. 17, Oct, 2013 ($2.99)
    1-17-All ages title. 13-FF & Dr. Doom app. 17-Ant-Man, Luke Cage & Iron Fist app. 4.00

AVENGERS: EARTH'S MIGHTIEST HEROES II
Marvel Comics: Jan, 2007 - No. 8, May, 2007 ($3.99, limited series)
    1-8-Retells time when the Vision joined; Casey-s/Rosado-a. 6-Hank & Janet's wedding 4.00
    HC (2007, $24.99, 7 1/2" x 11" with dustjacket) r/#1-8; cover sketches 25.00

AVENGERS FAIRY TALES
Marvel Comics: May, 2008 - No. 4, Dec, 2008 ($2.99, limited series)
    1-4: 1-Peter Pan-style tale; Cebulski-a/Lemos-a. 2-The Vision. 3-Miyazawa-a 3.00

AVENGERS FOREVER
Marvel Comics: Dec, 1998 - No. 12, Feb, 2000 ($2.99)
    1-Busiek-s/Pacheco-a in all 5.00
    2-12- Four covers. 6-Two covers. 8-Vision origin revised. 12-Rick Jones becomes
    Capt. Marvel 4.00
    TPB (1/01, $24.95) r/#1-12; Busiek intro.; new Pacheco-c 25.00

AVENGERS FOREVER (See Avengers Assemble Omega for story conclusion)
Marvel Comics: No. 15, May, 2018 - No. 15, May, 2023 ($4.99/$3.99)
    1-($4.99) Aaron-s/Kuder-a; Ant-Man Tony Stark and multiversal Avengers vs. Black Skull 5.00
    2-15-($3.99) 2,3-Deathlok and Ghost Rider app. 9-Carol Corps 4.00

AVENGERS INC.
Marvel Comics: Nov, 2023 - No. 5, Mar, 2024 ($4.99/$3.99)
    1-($4.99) Ewing-s/Kirk-a; a Janet Van Dyne investigation 5.00
    2-5-($3.99) 2-The Vision app. 4.00

AVENGERS INFINITY
Marvel Comics: Sept, 2000 - No. 4, Dec, 2000 ($2.99, limited series)
    1-4-Stern-s/Chen-a 4.00

AVENGERS/ INVADERS
Marvel Comics: Jul, 2008 - No. 12, Aug, 2009 ($2.99, limited series)
    1-Invaders journey to the present; Alex Ross-s/Sadowski-a; Thunderbolts app. 3.00
    2-12: 2-New Avengers app.; Perkins variant-c. 3-12-Variant-c on each 3.00
    ... Sketchbook (2008, giveaway) Ross and Sadowski sketch art; Krueger commentary 3.00

AVENGERS/ JLA (See JLA/Avengers for #1 & #3)
DC Comics: No. 2, 2003; No. 4, 2003 ($5.95, limited series)

		GD	VG	FN	VF	VF/NM	NM-
2-Busiek-s/Pérez-a; wraparound-c; Krona, Galactus app.		3	6	9	14	20	25
4-Busiek-s/Pérez-a; wraparound-c		3	6	9	21	33	45

AVENGERS LOG, THE
Marvel Comics: Feb, 1994 ($1.95)
    1-Gives history of all members; Pérez-c 6.00

AVENGERS MECH STRIKE
Marvel Comics: Apr, 2021 - No. 5, Sept, 2021 ($3.99, limited series)
    1-5-Avengers with new giant robots vs. giant monsters; Jed MacKay-s/Carlos Magno-a 4.00

AVENGERS: MILLENNIUM
Marvel Comics: Jun, 2015 - No. 4, Jun, 2015 ($3.99, weekly limited series)
    1-4-Di Giandomenico-a; Scarlet Witch & Quicksilver app. 1-Yu-c. 2-4-Deodato-c. 4.00

	GD	VG	FN	VF	VF/NM	NM-
	2.0	4.0	6.0	8.0	9.0	9.2

AVENGERS NEXT (See A-Next and Spider-Girl)
Marvel Comics: Jan, 2007 - No. 5, Mar, 2007 ($2.99, limited series)

1-5-Lim-a/Wieringo-c; Spider-Girl app. 1-Avengers vs. zombies. 2-Thena app. 3.00
.... - Rebirth TPB (2007, $13.99) r/#1-5 .... 14.00

AVENGERS 1959
Marvel Comics: Dec, 2011 - No. 5, Mar, 2012 ($2.99, limited series)

1-5-Chaykin-s/a/c; Nick Fury, Kraven, Namora, Sabretooth, Dominic Fortune app. 3.00

AVENGERS NO ROAD HOME
Marvel Comics: Apr, 2019 - No. 10, Jun, 2019 ($4.99/$3.99, weekly limited series)

1-($4.99) Waid, Ewing & Zub-s/Medina-a; intro Nyx; Rocket Raccoon & Hercules app. 5.00
2-5,7,9-($3.99) 2-Nightmare app. 4-Izaakse-a. 5-Conan cameo on last page. 7-9-Conan app. 7,9-Medina-a. 8-Barberi-a 4.00
6-($4.99) Conan the Barbarian and Scarlet Witch team-up; Izaakse-a. 5.00
10-($4.99) Izaakse-a; Conan goes to the Savage Land 5.00

AVENGERS OF THE WASTELANDS
Marvel Comics: Mar, 2020 - No. 5, Nov, 2020 ($3.99, limited series)

1-5-Brisson-s/Scharf-a; set in the future during Old Man Logan & Dead Man Logan series 4.00

AVENGERS: OPERATION HYDRA
Marvel Comics: Jun, 2015 ($3.99, one-shot)

1-Movie team; Pilgrim-s/Di Vito-a; bonus reprint of Avengers #16 (1965) 4.00

AVENGERS ORIGINS (Series of one-shots)
Marvel Comics: Jan, 2012 ($3.99)

...: Ant-Man & The Wasp 1 (1/12) Aguirre-Sacasa-s/Hans-a/Djurdjevic-c; origin of both 4.00
...: Luke Cage 1 (1/12) Glass & Benson-s/Talajic-a/Djurdjevic-c; 4.00
...: Scarlet Witch & Quicksilver 1 (1/12) McKeever-s/Pierfederici-a/Djurdjevic-c 4.00
...: Thor 1 (1/12) K. Immonen-s/Barrionuevo-a/Djurdjevic-c 4.00
...: Vision 1 (1/12) Higgins & Siegel-s/Perger-a/Djurdjevic-c; Ultron-5 app. 4.00

AVENGERS PRIME (The Heroic Age)
Marvel Comics: Aug, 2010 - No. 5, Mar, 2011 ($3.99, limited series)

1-5-Thor, Iron Man & Steve Rogers; Bendis-s/Davis-a; Enchantress app. 4.00
1-Variant-c by Djurdjevic 8.00

AVENGERS: RAGE OF ULTRON
Marvel Comics: 2015 ($24.99, hardcover graphic novel)

HC - Remender-s/Opeña-a; intro by Busiek 25.00
... — Marvel Tales 1 (5/23, $7.99) Reprints the graphic novel; intro by Ralph Macchio 8.00

AVENGERS: SEASON ONE
Marvel Comics: 2013 ($24.99, hardcover graphic novel)

HC - Origin story; Peter David-a/Tedesco painted-c; bonus script outline 25.00

AVENGERS: SOLO
Marvel Comics: Dec, 2011 - No. 5, Apr, 2012 ($3.99, limited series)

1-5-Hawkeye; back-up Avengers Academy 4.00

AVENGERS SPOTLIGHT (Formerly Solo Avengers #1-20)
Marvel Comics: No. 21, Aug, 1989 - No. 40, Jan, 1991 (75¢/$1.00)

21-Byrne-c/a 5.00
22-40: 26-Acts of Vengeance story. 31-34-U.S. Agent series. 36-Heck-i. 37-Mortimer-i. 40-The Black Knight app. 4.00

AVENGERS STANDOFF (Crossover with Avengers titles and other Marvel titles)
Marvel Comics: Apr, 2016 - Jun, 2016 ($4.99)

...: Assault on Pleasant Hill Alpha 1 (5/16) Part 2 of crossover; Spencer-s/Saiz-a 5.00
...: Assault on Pleasant Hill Omega 1 (6/16) Part 3 of crossover; Spencer-s/Acuña-a; new Quasar debut; Red Skull app. 5.00
...: Welcome to Pleasant Hill 1 (4/16) Part 1 of crossover; Spencer-s/Bagley-a/Acuña-c 5.00

AVENGERS STRIKEFILE
Marvel Comics: Jan, 1994 ($1.75, one-shot)

1 .... 4.00

AVENGERS: TECH-ON
Marvel Comics: Oct, 2021 - No. 6, Mar, 2022 ($3.99, limited series)

1-6-Power-drained Avengers & Spider-Man with mech-suits; Jim Zub-s/Jeffrey Cruz-a 4.00

AVENGERS: THE CHILDREN'S CRUSADE
Marvel Comics: Sept, 2010 - No. 9, May, 2012 ($3.99, limited series)

1-9-Young Avengers search for Scarlet Witch; Heinberg-s/Cheung-a. 6-9-X-Men app. 4.00
1-4-Variant-c. 1-Jelena Djurdjevic. 2-Travis Charest. 3,4-Art Adams 6.00
... - Young Avengers 1 (3/11, $3.99) Takes place between #4&5; Alan Davis-a/c 4.00

AVENGERS: THE CROSSING
Marvel Comics: July, 1995 ($4.95, one-shot)

1-Deodato-c/a; 1st app. Thor's new costume	1	2	3	5	6	8

AVENGERS: THE INITIATIVE (See Civil War and related titles)
Marvel Comics: Jun, 2007 - No. 35, Jun, 2010 ($2.99)

1-Caselli-a/Slott-s/Cheung-c; War Machine app. 4.00
2-35: 4,5-World War Hulk. 6-Uy-a. 14-19-Secret Invasion; 3-D Man app. 16-Skrull Kill Krew returns. 20-Tigra pregnancy revealed. 21-25-Ramos-a. 32-35-Siege 3.00
Annual 1 (1/08, $3.99) Secret Invasion tie-in; Cheung-c 4.00
... Featuring Reptil (5/09, $3.99) Gage-s/Uy-a 4.00
... Special 1 (1/09, $3.99) Slott & Gage-s/Uy-a 4.00
...: Vol. 1 - Basic Training HC (2007, $19.99, d.j.) r/#1-6 .... 20.00
...: Vol. 1 - Basic Training SC (2008, $14.99) r/#1-6 .... 15.00

AVENGERS: THE ORIGIN
Marvel Comics: Jan, 2010 - No. 5, Oct, 2010 ($3.99, limited series)

1-5-Casey-s/Noto-a/c; team origin (pre-Capt. America) re-told; Loki app. 4.00

AVENGERS: THE TERMINATRIX OBJECTIVE
Marvel Comics: Sept, 1993 - No. 4, Dec, 1993 ($1.25, limited series)

1 ($2.50)-Holo-grafx foil-c	1	3		6	8	10
2-4-Old vs. current Avengers						4.00

AVENGERS: THE ULTRON IMPERATIVE

Marvel Comics: Nov, 2001 ($5.99, one-shot)

1-Follow-up to the Ultron Unlimited ending in Avengers #42; BWS-c 6.00

AVENGERS, THOR & CAPTAIN AMERICA: OFFICIAL INDEX TO THE MARVEL UNIVERSE
Marvel Comics: Jun, 2010 - No. 15, 2011 ($3.99)

1-15-Each issue has chronological synopses, creator credits, character lists for 30-40 issues of Avengers, Captain America and Journey Into Mystery starting with debuts 4.00

AVENGERS/THUNDERBOLTS
Marvel Comics: May, 2004 - No. 6, Sept, 2004 ($2.99, limited series)

1-6-Busiek & Nicieza-s/Kitson-c. 1,2-Kitson-a. 3-6-Grummett-a 3.00
Vol. 2: Best Intentions (2004, $14.99) r/#1-6 .... 15.00

AVENGERS: TIMESLIDE
Marvel Comics: Feb, 1996 ($4.95, one-shot)

1-Foil-c 5.00

AVENGERS: TWILIGHT
Marvel Comics: Mar, 2024 - Present ($5.99/$4.99, limited series)

1-($5.99) Zdarsky-s/Acuña-a; set in the future with elderly Steve Rogers 6.00
2,3-($4.99) Captain America returns; Luke Cage, Kamala Khan app. 5.00

AVENGERS TWO: WONDER MAN & BEAST
Marvel Comics: May, 2000 - No. 3, July, 2000 ($2.99, limited series)

1-3: Stern-s/Bagley-a 3.00
... - Marvel Tales 1 (3/23, $7.99) Reprints series; intro. by Ralph Macchio 8.00

AVENGERS/ULTRAFORCE (See Ultraforce/Avengers)
Marvel Comics: Oct, 1995 ($3.95, one-shot)

1-Wraparound foil-c by Pérez 4.00

AVENGERS: ULTRON FOREVER
Marvel Comics: Jun, 2015 ($4.99)(Continues in New Avengers: Ultron Forever)

1-Part 1 of 3-part crossover with New Avengers and Uncanny Avengers; Ewing-s/ Alan Davis-a; team-up of past, present and future Avengers vs. Ultron 5.00

AVENGERS UNDERCOVER (Follows Avengers Arena series)
Marvel Comics: May, 2014 - No. 10, Nov, 2014 ($2.99)

1-10: Hopeless-s in all; Masters of Evil app. 1,2,4,5,7,Kev Walker-a. 3,6,9-Green-a 3.00

AVENGERS UNITED THEY STAND
Marvel Comics: Nov, 1999 - No. 7, June, 2000 ($2.99/$1.99)

1-Based on the animated series 5.00
2-6-($1.99) 2-Avengers battle Hydra. 6-The Collector app. 4.00
7-($2.99) Devil Dinosaur-c/app.; The Collector app.; r/Avengers Action Figure Comic 5.00

AVENGERS UNIVERSE
Marvel Comics: Jun, 2000 - No. 3, Oct, 2000 ($3.99)

1-3-Reprints recent stories 4.00

AVENGERS UNPLUGGED
Marvel Comics: Oct, 1995 - No. 6, Aug, 1996 (99¢, bi-monthly)

1-4,6 .... 4.00

5-Monica Rambeau becomes Photon	3	6	9	14	19	24

AVENGERS VS. ATLAS (Leads into Atlas #1)
Marvel Comics: Mar, 2010 - No. 4, Jun, 2010 ($3.99, limited series)

1-4-Hardman-a; Ramos-c. 1-Back-up w/Miyazawa-a. 2-4-Original Avengers app. 4.00

AVENGERS VS INFINITY
Marvel Comics: Jan, 2016 ($5.99, one-shot)

1-Short stories with The Wrecker, Doctor Doom, Bossman & Dracula; Alves & Lim-a 6.00

AVENGERS VS. PET AVENGERS
Marvel Comics: Dec, 2010 - No. 4, Mar, 2011 ($2.99, limited series)

1-4-Eliopoulos-s/Guara-a; Fin Fang Foom app. 3.00

AVENGERS VS. X-MEN (Also see AVX: VS and AVX: Consequences)
Marvel Comics: No. 0, May, 2012 - No. 12, Dec, 2012 ($3.99/$4.99, bi-weekly limited series)

0-Bendis & Aaron-s; Frank Cho-a/c; Scarlet Witch and Hope featured 4.00
1-11: 1-5-Romita Jr.-a. 6,7,11-Coipel-a. 8-10-Adam Kubert-a. 11-Hulk app. 4.00
12-($4.99) Adam Kubert-a; Cyclops as Dark Phoenix 5.00

AVENGERS: WAR ACROSS TIME
Marvel Comics: Mar, 2023 - No. 5, Jul, 2023 ($5.99/$3.99, limited series)

1-($5.99) Paul Levitz-s/Alan Davis-a; takes place after Avengers #11 (1964); Kang app. 6.00
2-5-($3.99) Sindri, forger of Mjolnir app. 4.00

AVENGERS WEST COAST (Formerly West Coast Avengers)
Marvel Comics: No. 48, Sept, 1989 - No. 102, June, 1994 ($1.00/$1.25)

48,49: 48-Byrne-c/a & scripts continue thru #57 .... 4.00
50-Re-intro original Human Torch 5.00
51-69,71-74,76-83,85,86,89-99: 54-Cover swipe/F.F. #1. 78-Last $1.00-c. 79-Dr. Strange x-over. 93-95-Darkhawk app. 4.00
70,75,84,87,88: 70-Spider-Woman app. 75 (52 pgs.)-Fantastic Four x-over. 84-Origin Spider-Woman retold; Spider-Man app. (also in #85,86). 87,88-Wolverine-c/story 5.00
100-($3.95, 68 pgs.)-Embossed all red foil-c 5.00
101,102: 101-X-Men x-over 5.00
Annual 5-8 ('90-'93, 68 pgs.)-5,6-West Coast Avengers in indicia. 7-Darkhawk app. 8-Polybagged w/card 4.00
...: Darker Than Scarlet TPB (2008, $24.99) r/#51-57,60-62; Byrne-s/a 25.00
...: Vision Quest TPB (2005, $24.99) r/#42-50; Byrne-s/a 25.00

AVENGERS WORLD
Marvel Comics: Mar, 2014 - No. 21, Jul, 2015 ($3.99)

1-21: 1-Hickman & Spencer-s/Caselli-a. 6-Neal Adams-c. 15,16-Doctor Doom app. 16-Cassie Lang brought back to life. 21-Leads into Secret Wars #1 .... 4.00

AVENGERS: X-SANCTION
Marvel Comics: Feb, 2012 - No. 4, May, 2012 ($3.99, limited series)

1-4-Loeb-s/McGuinness-a/c; Cable battles the Avengers. 3,4-Wolverine & Spidey app. 4.00

AVENGING SPIDER-MAN (Spider-Man and Avengers member team-ups)
Marvel Comics: Jan, 2012 - No. 22, Aug, 2013 ($3.99)

Avengers Prime #3 © MAR

Avenging Spider-Man #16 © MAR

Azrael #22 © DC

	GD	VG	FN	VF	VF/NM	NM-
	2.0	4.0	6.0	8.0	9.0	9.2

1-Madureira-a/Wells-s; Madureira-c; Red Hulk & Avengers app.

	1	2	3	5	6	8

1-Variant-c by Ramos   2   4   6   8   10   12
1-Variant-c by J. Scott Campbell   2   4   6   8   10   12
2-8,11-15: 2,3-Madureira-a/Wells-s; Madureira-c. 2,3-Red Hulk & Avengers app. 4-Hawkeye.
   5-Captain America app.; Yu-a. 11-Dillon-a. 12,13-Deadpool app. 14,15-Devil Dinosaur 4.00
9-(9/12) Carol Danvers (Ms. Marvel) takes the name Captain Marvel

	5	10	15	33	57	80

10-Carol Danvers app.   1   3   4   6   8   10
15.1 (2/13, $2.99) Follows Amazing Spider-Man #700; 1st Superior Spider-Man   5.00
16-22-Superior Spider-Man. 16-Wolverine & X-Men app. 18-Thor app. 22-Punisher app.   4.00
Annual 1 (12/12, $4.99) Spider-Man (Peter Parker) and The Thing; Zircher-c   5.00

AVIATION ADVENTURES AND MODEL BUILDING (True Aviation Advs. …No. 15)
Parents' Magazine Institute: No. 16, Dec, 1946 - No. 17, Feb, 1947
16,17-Half comics and half pictures   9   18   27   52   69   85

AVIATION CADETS
Street & Smith Publications: 1943
nn   22   44   66   132   216   300

A-V IN 3-D
Aardvark-Vanaheim: Dec, 1984 ($2.00, 28 pgs. w/glasses)
1-Cerebus, Flaming Carrot, Normalman & Ms. Tree   4.00

AVX: CONSEQUENCES (Aftermath of Avengers Vs. X-Men series)
Marvel Comics: Dec, 2012 - No. 5, Jan, 2013 ($3.99, weekly limited series)
1-5-Cyclops in prison; Gillen-s/art by various   4.00

AVX: VS (Tie-in to Avengers Vs. X-Men series)
Marvel Comics: Jun, 2012 - No. 6, Nov, 2012 ($3.99, limited series)
1-6-Spotlight on the individual fights from Avengers Vs. X-Men #2; art by various   4.00

AWAKEN SKIES
Aspen MLT: No. 0, Jun, 2018 ($1.50, one-shot)
0-($1.50) Mastromauro-s/Lorenzana-a; two covers   3.00

AWESOME ADVENTURES
Awesome Entertainment: Aug, 1999 ($2.50)
1-Alan Moore-s/ Steve Skroce-a; Youngblood story   4.00

AWESOME HOLIDAY SPECIAL
Awesome Entertainment: Dec, 1997 ($2.50, one-shot)
1-Flip book w/covers of Fighting American & Coven. Holiday stories also featuring Kaboom   4.00
   and Shaft by regular creators.
1-Gold Edition   5.00

AWFUL OSCAR (Formerly & becomes Oscar Comics with No. 13)
Marvel Comics: No. 11, June, 1949 - No. 12, Aug, 1949
11,12   18   36   54   105   165   225

AW YEAH COMICS: ACTION CAT & ADVENTURE BUG
Dark Horse Graphics: Mar, 2016 - No. 4, Jun, 2016 ($2.99, limited series)
1-4-Art Baltazar & Franco-s/a   3.00

AXA
Eclipse Comics: Apr, 1987 - No. 2, Aug, 1987 ($1.75)
1,2   6.00

AXCEND
Image Comics: Oct, 2015 - No. 5, Jul, 2016 ($3.50/$3.99)
1-3-Shane Davis-s/a   3.50
4,5-($3.99)   4.00

A.X.E.: AVENGERS (Tie-in to A.X.E.: Judgment Day)
Marvel Comics: Dec, 2022 ($3.99, one-shot)
1-Gillen-s/Vicentini-a; Iron Man, Wolverine, Jean Grey & Mr. Sinister app.   4.00

AXE COP: BAD GUY EARTH
Dark Horse Comics: Mar, 2011 - No. 3, May, 2011 ($3.50, limited series)
1-3-Malachai Nicolle-s/Ethan Nicolle-a   3.50

AXE COP: PRESIDENT OF THE WORLD
Dark Horse Comics: Jul, 2012 - No. 3, Sept, 2012 ($3.50, limited series)
1-3-Malachai Nicolle-s/Ethan Nicolle-a   3.50

AXE COP: THE AMERICAN CHOPPERS
Dark Horse Comics: May, 2014 - No. 3, Jul, 2014 ($3.99, limited series)
1-3-Malachai Nicolle-s/Ethan Nicolle-a. 3-Origin of Axe Cop   4.00

A.X.E.: DEATH TO THE MUTANTS (Tie-in to A.X.E.: Judgment Day)

Marvel Comics: Oct, 2022 - No. 3, Dec, 2022 ($3.99, limited series)
1-3-Gillen-s/Vilanova-a; Eternals' Druig vs. the Mutants   4.00

A.X.E.: ETERNALS (Tie-in to A.X.E.: Judgment Day)
Marvel Comics: Dec, 2022 ($3.99, one-shot)
1-Gillen-s/Ferry-a; Iron Man, Wolverine, Jean Grey & Mr. Sinister app.   4.00

A.X.E.: EVE OF JUDGMENT (Tie-in to A.X.E.: Judgment Day)
Marvel Comics: Sept, 2022 ($3.99, one-shot)
1-Gillen-s/Ferry-a; prelude to A.X.E.: Judgment Day series; Uranos app.   4.00

A.X.E.: IRON FIST (Tie-in to A.X.E.: Judgment Day)
Marvel Comics: Dec, 2022 ($3.99, one-shot)
1-Alyssa Wong-s/Michael Yg & Marika Cresta-a; Iron Fist (Lin Lie) & Loki app.   4.00

A.X.E.: JUDGMENT DAY (Avengers, X-Men, Eternals)
Marvel Comics: Sept, 2022 - No. 6, Dec, 2022 ($5.99/$4.99, limited series)
1,6-($5.99)-Gillen-s/Schiti-a; Eternals launch war on the mutants   6.00
2-5-($4.99)-Gillen-s/Schiti-a. 2-Intro. The Progenitor. 3,4-Starfox app.   5.00
...: Omega 1 (1/23, $4.99) Gillen-s/Vilanova-a; follows #6   5.00

AXEL PRESSBUTTON (No. 5; see Laser Eraser &...)
Eclipse Comics: Nov, 1984 - No. 6, July, 1985 ($1.50/$1.75, Baxter paper)
1-6: Reprints Warrior (British mag.). 1-Bolland-c; origin Laser Eraser & Pressbutton   4.00

A.X.E.: STARFOX (Tie-in to A.X.E.: Judgment Day)
Marvel Comics: Dec, 2022 ($3.99, one-shot)
1-Gillen-s/Di Nicuolo-a; Mentor, Sui-San & Zuras app.   4.00

A.X.E.: X-MEN (Tie-in to A.X.E.: Judgment Day)
Marvel Comics: Dec, 2022 ($3.99, one-shot)
1-Gillen-s/Mobili-a; Sersi, Iron Man, Wolverine, Jean Grey & Mr. Sinister app.   4.00

AXIS ALPHA
Axis Comics: Feb, 1994 ($2.50, one-shot)
V1-Previews Axis titles including, Tribe, Dethgrip, B.E.A.S.T.I.E.S. & more; Pitt app.   4.00
   in Tribe story.

AXIS: CARNAGE (Tie-in to Avengers & X-Men Axis series)
Marvel Comics: Dec, 2014 - No. 3, Feb, 2015 ($3.99, limited series)
1-3-Spears-s/Peralta-a; Carnage as a hero; Sin-Eater app.   4.00

AXIS: HOBGOBLIN (Tie-in to Avengers & X-Men Axis series)
Marvel Comics: Dec, 2014 - No. 3, Feb, 2015 ($3.99, limited series)
1-3-Shinick-s/Rodriguez-a; Hobgoblin as a hero; Goblin King app.   4.00

AXIS: RESOLUTIONS (Tie-in to Avengers & X-Men Axis series)
Marvel Comics: Dec, 2014 - No. 4, Feb, 2015 ($3.99, limited series)
1-4-Two stories per issue; s/a by various. 1-Lashley-s/a. 4-Chaykin-s/a   4.00

AZ
Comico: 1983 - No. 2, 1983 ($1.50, limited series)
1,2-Phil Lasorda-s/a   4.00

AZRAEL (...Agent of the Bat #47 on)(Also see Batman: Sword of Azrael)
DC Comics: Feb, 1995 - No. 100, May, 2003 ($1.95/$2.25/$2.50/$2.95)
1-Dennis O'Neil scripts begin   1   2   3   5   6   8
2,3   4.00
4-46,48-62: 5,6-Ras Al Ghul app. 13-Nightwing-c/app. 15-Contagion Pt. 5 (Pt. 4 on-c).
   16-Contagion Pt. 10. 22-Batman-c/app. 23,27-Batman app. 27,28-Joker app. 35-Hitman
   app. 36-39-Batman, Bane app. 50-New costume. 53-Joker-c/app. 56,57,60-New
   Batgirl app.   3.00
47-($3.95) Flip book with Batman: Shadow of the Bat #80   4.00
63-74,76-92: 63-Huntress-app. 73-Azrael returns to old costume. 67-Begin $2.50-c.
   70-79-Harris-a. 83-Joker x-over. 91-Bruce Wayne: Fugitive pt. 15   3.00
75-($3.95) New costume; Harris-c   4.00
93-100: 93-Begin $2.95-c. 95,96-Two-Face app. 100-Last issue; Zeck-c   3.00
#1,000,000 (11/98) Giarrano-a   3.00
Annual 1 (1995, $3.95)-Year One story   4.00
Annual 2 (1996, $2.95)-Legends of the Dead Earth story   4.00
Annual 3 (1997, $3.95)-Pulp Heroes story; Orbik-c   4.00
.../Ash (1997, $4.95) O'Neil-s/Quesada, Palmiotti-a   5.00
Plus (12/96, $2.95)-Question-c/app.   4.00

AZRAEL
DC Comics: Dec, 2009 - No. 18, May, 2011 ($2.99)
1-18: 1-9-Nicieza-s/Bachs-a. 1-Covers by Jock & Irving. 2,3-Jock-c. 5-Ragman app.   3.00
...: Angel in the Dark TPB (2010, $17.99) r/#1-6; cover gallery   18.00

AZRAEL: DEATH'S DARK KNIGHT

	GD 2.0	VG 4.0	FN 6.0	VF 8.0	VF/NM 9.0	NM- 9.2

DC Comics: May, 2009 - No. 3, Jul, 2009 ($2.99, limited series)

1-Battle For the Cowl tie-in; Nicieza-s/Irving-a/March-c						3.00
TPB (2010, $14.99) r/#1-3, Batman Annual #27 and Detective Annual #11						15.00

AZTEC ACE
Eclipse Comics: Mar, 1984 - No. 15, Sept, 1985 ($2.25/$1.50/$1.75, Baxter paper)

1-$2.25-c (52 pgs.)						5.00
2-15: 2-Begin 36 pgs.						4.00

NOTE: *N. Redondo a-1l-8i, 10i. c-6-8i.*

AZTEK: THE ULTIMATE MAN
DC Comics: Aug, 1996 - No. 10, May 1997 ($1.75)

1-1st app. Aztek & Synth; Grant Morrison & Mark Millar scripts in all						6.00
2-9: 2-Green Lantern app. 3-1st app. Death-Doll. 4-Intro The Lizard King. 5-Origin. 6-Joker app.; Batman cameo. 7-Batman app. 8-Author app. 9-vs. Parasite-c/app.						4.00
10-Joins the JLA; JLA-c/app.	2	4	6	8		10
JLA Presents: Aztek the Ultimate Man TPB (2008, $19.99) r/#1-10						20.00

NOTE: *Breyfogle c-5p. N. Steven Harris a-1-5p. Porter c-1p. Wieringo c-2p.*

BABE (...Darling of the Hills, later issues)(See Big Shot and Sparky Watts)
Prize/Headline/Feature: June-July, 1948 - No. 11, Apr-May, 1950

1-Boody Rogers-a	71	142	213	454	777	1100
2-Boody Rogers-a	42	84	126	265	445	625
3-11-All by Boody Rogers	34	68	102	199	325	450

BABE
Dark Horse Comics (Legend): July, 1994 - No. 4, Jan, 1994 ($2.50, lim. series)

1-4: John Byrne-c/a/scripts; ProtoTykes back-up story						4.00

BABE RUTH SPORTS COMICS (Becomes Rags Rabbit #11 on?)
Harvey Publications: April, 1949 - No. 11, Feb, 1951

1-Powell-a	45	90	135	284	480	675
2-Powell-a	30	60	90	177	289	400
3-11- Powell-a in most	24	48	72	142	234	325

NOTE: *Baseball c-2,4, 9. Basketball c-1, 6. Football c-5. Yogi Berra c/story-8. Joe DiMaggio c/story-3. Bob Feller c/story-4. Stan Musial c-9.*

BABES IN TOYLAND (Disney, Movie) (See Golden Pix Story Book ST-3)
Dell Publishing Co.: No. 1282, Feb-Apr, 1962

Four Color 1282-Annette Funicello photo-c	13	26	39	86	188	290

BABES OF BROADWAY
Broadway Comics: May, 1996 ($2.95, one-shot)

1-Pin-ups of Broadway Comics' female characters; Alan Davis, Michael Kaluta, J.G. Jones, Alan Weiss, Guy Davis & others-a; Giordano-c.						5.00

BABE 2
Dark Horse Comics (Legend): Mar, 1995 - No. 2, May, 1995 ($2.50, lim. series)

1,2: John Byrne-c/a/scripts						4.00

BABY HUEY
Harvey Comics: No. 1, Oct, 1991 - No. 9, June, 1994 ($1.00/$1.25/$1.50, quarterly)

1 ($1.00): 1-Cover says "Big Baby Huey"						6.00
2-9 ($1.25-$1.50)						4.00

BABY HUEY AND PAPA (See Paramount Animated...)
Harvey Publications: May, 1962 - No. 33, Jan, 1968 (Also see Casper The Friendly Ghost)

1	13	26	39	86	188	290
2	7	14	21	49	92	135
3-5	5	10	15	33	57	80
6-10	3	6	9	20	31	42
11-20	3	6	9	15	22	28
21-33	2	4	6	13	18	22

BABY HUEY DIGEST
Harvey Publications: June, 1992 (Digest-size, one-shot)

1-Reprints	1	3	4	6	8	10

BABY HUEY DUCKLAND
Harvey Publications: Nov, 1962 - No. 15, Nov, 1966 (25¢ Giants, 68 pgs.)

1	10	20	30	66	138	210
2-5	5	10	15	34	60	85
6-15	3	6	9	21	33	45

BABY HUEY, THE BABY GIANT (Also see Big Baby Huey, Casper, Harvey Hits #22, Harvey Comics Hits #60, & Paramount Animated Comics)
Harvey Publ: 9/56 - #97, 10/71; #98, 10/72; #99, 10/80; #100, 10/90; #101, 11/90

1-Infinity-c	54	108	162	432	966	1500
2	21	42	63	147	324	500
3-Baby Huey takes anti-pep pills	13	26	39	89	195	300
4,5	9	18	27	61	123	185
6-10	6	12	18	40	73	105
11-20	5	10	15	31	53	75
21-40	4	8	12	23	37	50
41-60	3	6	9	16	23	30
61-79 (12/67)	2	4	6	13	18	22
80(12/68) - 95-All 68 pg. Giants	3	6	9	16	24	32
96,97-Both 52 pg. Giants	3	6	9	14	19	24
98-Regular size	2	4	6	9	12	15
99-Regular size	1	3	5			7
100,101 ($1.00)						4.00

BABYLON 5 (TV)
DC Comics: Jan, 1995 - No. 11, Dec, 1995 ($1.95/$2.50)

1	2	4	6	9	13	16
2-5	1	2	3	5	7	9
6-11: 7-Begin $2.50-c	1	2	3	4	5	7
... The Price of Peace (1998, $9.95, TPB) r/#1-4,11						10.00

BABYLON 5: IN VALEN'S NAME
DC Comics: Mar, 1998 - No. 3, May, 1998 ($2.50, limited series)

1-3						5.00

BABY SNOOTS (Also see March of Comics #359,371,396,401,419,431,443,450,462,474,485)
Gold Key: Aug, 1970 - No. 22, Nov, 1975

1	3	6	9	19	30	50
2-11	2	4	6	11	16	20
12-22: 22-Titled Snoots, the Forgetful Elefink	2	4	6	8	10	12

BABYTEETH
AfterShock Comics: Jun, 2017 - No. 20, Sept, 2021 ($3.99)

1-Donny Cates-s/Garry Brown-a	1	3	4	6	8	10
2-20						4.00
... #1: Halloween Edition (10/17, giveaway) r/#1 in B&W; Elizabeth Torque-c						3.00

BABY YODA CEREBUS
Aardvark-Vanaheim: May, 2021 ($4.00, B&W)

1-Yoda-type character placed over original Gustave Doré background art						4.00

BACCHUS (Also see Eddie Campbell's ...)
Harrier Comics (New Wave): 1988 - No. 2, Aug, 1988 ($1.95, B&W)

1,2: Eddie Campbell-c/a/scripts.	1	2	3		6	8

BACHELOR FATHER (TV)
Dell Publishing Co.: No. 1332, 4-6/62 - No. 2, Sept.-Nov., 1962

Four Color 1332 (#1), 2-Written by Stanley	7	14	21	49	92	135

BACHELOR'S DIARY
Avon Periodicals: 1949 (15¢)

1(Scarce)-King Features panel cartoons & text-r; pin-up, girl wrestling photos; similar to Sideshow	155	310	465	992	1696	2400

BACKLASH (Also see The Kindred)
Image Comics (WildStorm Prod.): Nov,1994 - No. 32, May, 1997 ($1.95/$2.50)

1-Double-c; variant-double-c						6.00
2-24,26-32: 5-Intro Mindscape; 2 pinups. 8-Wildstorm Rising Pt 8 (newsstand & Direct Market versions. 19-Fire From Heaven Pt 2. 20-Fire From Heaven Pt 10. 31-WildC.A.T.S app.						4.00
25-($3.95)-Double-size						5.00
...& Taboo's African Holiday (9/99, $5.95) Booth-s/a(p)						6.00

BACKLASH/SPIDER-MAN
Image Comics (WildStorm Productions): Aug, 1996 - No. 2, Sept, 1996 ($2.50, lim. series)

1,2: Pike (villain from WildC.A.T.S) & Venom app.						5.00

BACKPACK MARVELS (B&W backpack-sized reprint collections)
Marvel Comics: Nov, 2000 ($6.95, B&W, digest-size)

Avengers 1 -r/Avengers #181-189; profile pages						10.00
Spider-Man 1-r/ASM #234-240						10.00
X-Men 1-r/Uncanny X-Men #167-173						10.00
X-Men 2-r/Uncanny X-Men #174-179; new painted-c by Greg Horn						10.00

BACKSTAGERS, THE
Boom Entertainment (BOOM! Box): Aug, 2016 - No. 8, Mar, 2017 ($3.99)

1-8: 1-James Tynion IV-s/Rian Sygh-a/Veronica Fish-c						4.00
...: Halloween Intermission 1 (10/18, $7.99) Short stories by Tynion, Sygh and others						8.00
...: Valentine's Intermission 1 (2/18, $7.99) Short stories by Tynion, Sygh and others						8.00

BACK TO THE FUTURE (Movie, TV cartoon)
Harvey Comics: Nov, 1991 - No. 4, June, 1992 ($1.25)

1-Gil Kane-c; based on animated cartoon	3	6	9	16	23	30
2-Gil Kane-c	1	3	4	6	8	10
3						6.00
4-Last issue	2	4	6	11	16	20

BACK TO THE FUTURE (Movie, TV cartoon)
IDW Publishing: Oct, 2015 - No. 25, Oct, 2017 ($3.99)

1-Story by Bob Gale; multiple covers; Doc & Marty's first meeting						
2-24-Multiple covers. 3-Archie variant-c						4.00
25-($4.99)						5.00

BACK TO THE FUTURE: BIFF TO THE FUTURE
IDW Publishing: Jan, 2017 - No. 6, Jun, 2017 ($3.99, limited series)

1-5-Biff's rise to power with the sports almanac; Gale & Fridolfs-s/Alan Robinson-a						4.00

BACK TO THE FUTURE: CITIZEN BROWN (Based on the Telltale Games video game)
IDW Publishing: May, 2016 - No. 5, Sept, 2016 ($4.99, limited series)

1-5-Erik Burnham-s/Alan Robinson-a; multiple covers on all						5.00

BACK TO THE FUTURE: FORWARD TO THE FUTURE
Harvey Comics: Oct, 1992 - No. 3, Feb, 1993 ($1.50, limited series)

1	2	4	6	9	12	15
2,3						5.00

BACK TO THE FUTURE: TALES FROM THE TIME TRAIN
IDW Publishing: Dec, 2017 - No. 6, May, 2018 ($3.99, limited series)

1-6-Doc Brown, Clara and their kids; Gale & Barber-s/Levens-a. 2-6-1939 World's Fair						4.00

BACKWAYS
AfterShock Comics: Dec, 2107 - No. 5, May, 2018 ($3.99)

1-5-Justin Jordan-s/Eleonora Carlini-a						4.00

BAD ASS
Dynamite Entertainment: 2014 - No. 4. 2014 ($3.99)

1-4-Hanna-s/Bessadi-a						4.00

BAD BLOOD
Dark Horse Comics: Jan, 2014 - No. 5, May, 2014 ($3.99, limited series)

1-5-Vampire story; Jonathan Maberry-s/Tyler Crook-a						4.00

BAD BOY
Oni Press: Dec, 1997 ($4.95, one-shot)

1-Frank Miller-s/Simon Bisley-a/painted-c						5.00

BAD COMPANY
Quality Comics/Fleetway Quality #15 on: Aug, 1988 - No. 19?, 1990 ($1.50/$1.75, high quality paper)

Babes of Broadway #1 © Broadway

Badger #23 © FC

Baltimore: The Play #1 © Mignola & Golden

	GD 2.0	VG 4.0	FN 6.0	VF 8.0	VF/NM 9.0	NM- 9.2

	GD 2.0	VG 4.0	FN 6.0	VF 8.0	VF/NM 9.0	NM- 9.2
1-19: 5,6-Guice-c						4.00

BADGE OF JUSTICE (Formerly Crime And Justice #21)
Charlton Comics: No. 22, Jan, 1955; No. 2, Apr, 1955 - No. 4, Oct, 1955

	GD 2.0	VG 4.0	FN 6.0	VF 8.0	VF/NM 9.0	NM- 9.2
22(#1)-Giordano-c	15	30	45	86	133	180
2-4	11	22	33	62	86	110

BADGER, THE
Capital Comics(#1-4)/First Comics: Dec, 1983 - No. 70, Apr, 1991; V2#1, Spring, 1991

	GD 2.0	VG 4.0	FN 6.0	VF 8.0	VF/NM 9.0	NM- 9.2
1	2	4	6	9	12	15
2-49,51-70: 52-54-Tim Vigil-c/a						4.00
50-($3.95, 52 pgs.)						5.00
V2#1 (Spring, 1991, $4.95) Badger Bedlam on cover (unofficial #71)						5.00

BADGER, THE
Image Comics: V3#78, May, 1997 - V3#88, Mar, 1988 ($2.95, B&W)

78-Cover lists #1, Baron-s	4.00
79/#2, 80/#3, 81(indicia lists #80)/#4,82-88/#5-11	4.00

BADGER, THE
Devil's Due/1First Comics: 2016 - No. 5, 2016 ($3.99)

1-5: 1-Mike Baron-s/Jim Fern-a/Val Mayerik-c; origin story. 2-5-Putin app.	4.00

BADGER GOES BERSERK
First Comics: Sept, 1989 - No. 4, Dec, 1989 ($1.95, lim. series, Baxter paper)

1-4: 2-Paul Chadwick-c/a(2pgs.)	4.00

BADGER: SHATTERED MIRROR
Dark Horse Comics: July, 1994 - No. Oct, 1994 ($2.50, limited series)

1-4	4.00

BADGER: ZEN POP FUNNY-ANIMAL VERSION
Dark Horse Comics: July, 1994 - No. 2, Aug, 1994 ($2.50, limited series)

1,2	4.00

BAD GIRLS
DC Comics: Oct, 2003 - No. 5, Feb, 2004 ($2.50, limited series)

1-5-Steve Vance-s/Jennifer Graves-a/Darwyn Cooke-c	3.00
TPB (2009, $14.99) r/#1-5; Graves sketch pages	15.00

BAD IDEA CRASS PROMOTIONAL MODULE
Bad Idea: Jan, 2021 (giveaway)

1-Previews Eniac & Tankers series	5.00

BAD IDEAS
Image Comics: Apr, 2004 - No. 2, July, 2004 ($5.95, B&W, limited series)

1,2-Chinsang-s/Mahfood & Crosland-a	6.00
..., Vol. 1: Collected! (2005, $12.99) r/#1,2	13.00

BAD KITTY ONE SHOT (CHAOS!...)
Dynamite Entertainment: 2014 ($5.99)

1-Spence-s/Rafael-a/c; origin	6.00

BADLANDS
Vortex Comics: May, 1990 ($3.00, glossy stock, mature)

1-Chaykin-c	4.00

BADLANDS
Dark Horse Comics: July, 1991 - No. 6, Dec, 1991 ($2.25, B&W, limited series)

1-6: 1-John F. Kennedy-c; reprints Vortex Comics issue	4.00

BAD LUCK CHUCK
Dark Horse Comics: Mar, 2019 - No. 4, Jun, 2019 ($3.99, limited series)

1-4-Lela Gwenn-s/Matthew Dow Smith-a	4.00

BADMEN OF THE WEST (Giant) (132 pgs., painted-c)
Avon Periodicals: 1951

1-Contains rebound copies of Jesse James, King of the Bad Men of Deadwood, Badmen of Tombstone; other combinations possible.

	GD 2.0	VG 4.0	FN 6.0	VF 8.0	VF/NM 9.0	NM- 9.2
Issues with Kubert-a...	61	122	183	390	670	950

BADMEN OF THE WEST! (See A-1 Comics)
Magazine Enterprises: 1953 - No. 3, 1954

	GD 2.0	VG 4.0	FN 6.0	VF 8.0	VF/NM 9.0	NM- 9.2
1 (A-1 100)-Meskin-a/c	28	56	84	168	274	380
2 (A-1 120), 3: 2-Larsen-a	18	36	54	105	165	225

BADMEN OF TOMBSTONE
Avon Periodicals: 1950

	GD 2.0	VG 4.0	FN 6.0	VF 8.0	VF/NM 9.0	NM- 9.2
nn	20	40	60	115	190	260

BAD MOTHER

AWA Studios: Aug, 2020 - No. 5, Dec, 2020 ($3.99, limited series)

1-5-Christa Faust-s/Mike Deodato Jr.-a	4.00

BAD PLANET
Image Comics (Raw Studios): Dec, 2005 - No. 6, Nov, 2008 ($2.99)

1-6: 1-Thomas Jane & Steve Niles-s/Larosa & Bradstreet-a/c. 2-Wrightson-c. 3-"3-D" pgs.	3.00

BAD RECEPTION
AfterShock Comics: Aug, 2019 - No. 5, Jul, 2020 ($3.99, limited series)

1-5-Juan Doe-s/a	4.00

BADROCK (Also see Youngblood)
Image Comics (Extreme Studios): Mar, 1995 - No. 2, Jan, 1996 ($1.75/$2.50)

1-Variant-c (3)	5.00
2-Liefeld-c/a & story; Savage Dragon app, flipbook w/Grifter/Badrock #2; variant-c exist	4.00
Annual 1(1995,$2.95)-Arthur Adams-c	5.00
Annual 1 Commemorative ($9.95)-3,000 printed	10.00
.../Wolverine (6/96, $4.95, squarebound)-Sauron app; pin-ups; variant-c exists	5.00
.../Wolverine (6/96)-Special Comicon Edition	5.00

BADROCK AND COMPANY (Also see Youngblood)
Image Comics (Extreme Studios): Sept, 1994 - No.6, Feb, 1995 ($2.50)

1-6 : 6-Indicia reads "October 1994"; story cont'd in Shadowhawk #17	4.00

BAFFLING MYSTERIES (Formerly Indian Braves No. 1-4; Heroes of the Wild Frontier No. 26-on)
Periodical House (Ace Magazines): No. 5, Nov, 1951 - No. 26, Oct, 1955

	GD 2.0	VG 4.0	FN 6.0	VF 8.0	VF/NM 9.0	NM- 9.2
5	60	120	180	381	653	925
6,9-19,21-24: 10-E.C. Crypt Keeper swipe on-c. 24-Last pre-code issue	42	84	126	265	445	625
7,8-Classic-c: 8-Woodish-a by Cameron	194	388	562	1242	2121	3000
20-Classic bondage-c	58	116	174	371	636	900
25-Reprints; surrealistic-c	39	78	117	231	378	525
26-Reprints	34	68	102	199	325	450

NOTE: *Cameron* a-8, 10, 16-18, 20-22. *Colan* a-5, 11, 25r/5. *Sekowsky* a-5, 6, 22. Bondage c-20, 23. Reprints in 18(1), 19(1), 24(3).

BAKER STREET PECULIARS, THE
Boom Entertainment (kaboom!): Mar, 2016 - No. 4, Jun, 2016 ($3.99, limited series)

1-4-Roger Langridge-s/Andy Hirsch-a	4.00

BALBO (See Master Comics #33 & Mighty Midget Comics)

BALDER THE BRAVE (Character from Thor)
Marvel Comics Group: Nov, 1985 - No. 4, 1986 (Limited series)

1-4: Walt Simonson-c/s; Sal Buscema-a	4.00

BALLAD OF HALO JONES, THE
Quality Comics: Sept, 1987 - No. 12, Aug, 1988 ($1.25/$1.50)

1-12: Alan Moore scripts in all	4.00

BALL AND CHAIN
DC Comics (Homage): Nov, 1999 - No. 4, Feb, 2000 ($2.50, limited series)

1-4-Lobdell-s/Garza-a	5.00

BALLISTIC (Also See Cyberforce)
Image Comics (Top Cow Productions): Sept, 1995 - No. 3, Dec, 1995 ($2.50, limited series)

1-3: Wetworks app, Turner-c/a	4.00
... Action (5/96, $2.95) Pin-ups of Top Cow characters participating in outdoor sports	4.00
... Imagery (1/96, $2.50, anthology) Cyberforce app.	4.00
.../ Wolverine (2/97, $2.95) Devil's Reign pt. 4; Witchblade cameo (1 page)	5.00

BALOO & LITTLE BRITCHES (Disney)
Gold Key: Apr, 1968

	GD 2.0	VG 4.0	FN 6.0	VF 8.0	VF/NM 9.0	NM- 9.2
1-From the Jungle Book	5	10	15	31	53	75

BALTIMORE: ... (One-shots)
Dark Horse Comics: ($3.50)

... The Inquisitor (6/13) Mignola & Golden-s; Stenbeck-a/c	3.50
... The Play (11/12) Mignola & Golden-s; Stenbeck-a/c	3.50
... The Widow and the Tank (2/13) Mignola & Golden-s; Stenbeck-a/c	3.50

BALTIMORE: CHAPEL OF BONES
Dark Horse Comics: Jan, 2014 - No. 2, Feb, 2014 ($3.50, limited series)

1,2-Mignola & Golden-s; Stenbeck-a/c	3.50

BALTIMORE: EMPTY GRAVES
Dark Horse Comics: Apr, 2016 - No. 5, Aug, 2016 ($3.99, limited series)

1-5-Mignola & Golden-s; Bergting-a; Stenbeck-c	4.00

BALTIMORE: DR. LESKOVAR'S REMEDY
Dark Horse Comics: Jun, 2012 - No. 2, Jul, 2012 ($3.50, limited series)

	GD 2.0	VG 4.0	FN 6.0	VF 8.0	VF/NM 9.0	NM- 9.2

1,2-Mignola & Golden-s; Stenbeck-a/c ... 3.50

BALTIMORE: THE CULT OF THE RED KING
Dark Horse Comics: May, 2015 - No. 5, Sept, 2015 ($3.99, limited series)
1-5-Mignola & Golden-s; Bergting-a; Stenbeck-c ... 4.00

BALTIMORE: THE CURSE BELLS
Dark Horse Comics: Aug, 2011 - No. 5, Dec, 2011 ($3.50, limited series)
1-5-Mignola-s/c; Stenbeck-a. 1-Variant-c by Francavilla ... 3.50

BALTIMORE: THE INFERNAL TRAIN
Dark Horse Comics: Sept, 2013 - No. 3, Nov, 2013 ($3.50, limited series)
1-3-Mignola & Golden-s; Stenbeck-a/c ... 3.50

BALTIMORE: THE PLAGUE SHIPS
Dark Horse Comics: Aug, 2010 - No. 5, Dec, 2010 ($3.50, limited series)
1-5-Mignola-s/c; Stenbeck-a; Lord Baltimore hunting vampires in 1916 Europe ... 3.50

BALTIMORE: THE RED KINGDOM
Dark Horse Comics: Feb, 2017 - No. 5, Jun, 2017 ($3.99, limited series)
1-5-Mignola & Golden-s; Bergting-a; Stenbeck-c ... 4.00

BALTIMORE: THE WITCH OF HARJU
Dark Horse Comics: Jul, 2014 - No. 3, Sept, 2014 ($3.50, limited series)
1-3-Mignola & Golden-s; Bergting-a; Stenbeck-c ... 3.50

BALTIMORE: THE WOLF AND THE APOSTLE
Dark Horse Comics: Oct, 2014 - No. 2, Nov, 2014 ($3.50, limited series)
1,2-Mignola & Golden-s; Stenbeck-a/c ... 3.50

BAMBI (Disney) (See Movie Classics, Movie Comics, and Walt Disney Showcase No. 31)
Dell Publishing Co.: No. 12, 1942; No. 30, 1943; No. 186, Apr, 1948; 1984

	GD 2.0	VG 4.0	FN 6.0	VF 8.0	VF/NM 9.0	NM- 9.2
Four Color 12-Walt Disney's...	54	108	162	432	956	1500
Four Color 30-Bambi's Children (1943)	44	88	132	326	738	1150
Four Color 186-Walt Disney's...; reprinted as Movie Classic Bambi #3 (1956)	17	34	51	117	259	400
1-(Whitman, 1984; 60¢)-r/Four Color #186 (3-pack)	2	4	6	11	16	20

BAMBI (Disney)
Grosset & Dunlap: 1942 (50¢, 7"x8-1/2", 32 pg, hard-c w/dust jacket)
nn-Given away w/a copy of Thumper for a $2.00, 2-yr. subscription to WDC&S in 1942 (Xmas offer).

	GD 2.0	VG 4.0	FN 6.0	VF 8.0	VF/NM 9.0	NM- 9.2
Book only	24	48	72	140	230	320
w/dust jacket	40	80	120	244	402	560

BAMM BAMM & PEBBLES FLINTSTONE (TV)
Gold Key: Oct, 1964 (Hanna-Barbera)

	GD 2.0	VG 4.0	FN 6.0	VF 8.0	VF/NM 9.0	NM- 9.2
1	9	18	27	58	114	170

BANANA SPLITS, THE (TV) (See Golden Comics Digest & March of Comics No. 364)
Gold Key: June, 1969 - No. 8, Oct, 1971 (Hanna-Barbera)

	GD 2.0	VG 4.0	FN 6.0	VF 8.0	VF/NM 9.0	NM- 9.2
1-Photo-c on all	10	20	30	69	147	225
2-8	6	12	18	37	66	95

B&V FRIENDS FOREVER (See Betty and Veronica Friends Forever)

BAND WAGON (See Hanna-Barbera Band Wagon)

BANE: CONQUEST
DC Comics: Jul, 2017 - No. 12, Aug, 2018 ($3.99, limited series)
1-12: 1-Chuck Dixon-s/Graham Nolan-a; covers by Nolan and Kelley Jones. 4,5-Catwoman app. 6-12-Kobra app. ... 4.00

BANG!
Dark Horse Comics: Feb, 2020 - No. 5, Nov, 2020 ($3.99, limited series)
1-5-Matt Kindt-s/Wilfredo Torres-a ... 4.00

BANG! TANGO
DC Comics (Vertigo): Apr, 2009 - No. 6, Sept, 2009 ($2.99, limited series)
1-6-Kelly-s/Sibar-a/Chaykin-c ... 3.00

BANG-UP COMICS
Progressive Publishers: Dec, 1941 - No. 3, June, 1942

	GD 2.0	VG 4.0	FN 6.0	VF 8.0	VF/NM 9.0	NM- 9.2
1-Nazi WWII-c; Cosmo Mann & Lady Fairplay begin; Buzz Balmer by Rick Yager in all (origin #1)	142	284	426	909	1555	2200
2-Nazi zeppelin WWII-c	97	194	291	621	1061	1500
3-Japanese WWII-c	77	154	231	493	847	1200

BANISHED KNIGHTS (See Warlands)
Image Comics: Dec, 2001 - No. 4, June, 2002 ($2.95)
1-4-Two covers (Alvin Lee, Pat Lee) ... 3.00

BANNER COMICS (Becomes Captain Courageous No. 6)
Ace Magazines: 3, Sept, 1941 - No. 5, Jan, 1942

	GD 2.0	VG 4.0	FN 6.0	VF 8.0	VF/NM 9.0	NM- 9.2
3-Captain Courageous (1st app.) & Lone Warrior & Sidekick Dicky begin; Nazi WWII-c by Jim Mooney	300	600	900	1950	3375	4800
4,5: 4-Flag-c	232	464	696	1485	2543	3600

BARACK OBAMA (See Presidential Material: Barack Obama, Amazing Spider-Man #583, Savage Dragon #137)

BARACK THE BARBARIAN
Devil's Due Publishing: Jun, 2009 - No. 4, Oct, 2009 ($3.50/$3.99, limited series)
...Quest For The Treasure of Stimuli 1-3-($3.50) Conan spoof with Barack Obama; Hama-s 3.50
...Quest For The Treasure of Stimuli 4-($3.99) ... 4.00
...: The Red of Red Sarah 1 ($5.99, B&W) Sarah Palin satire; Hama-s ... 6.00

BARBALIEN: RED PLANET (From Black Hammer)
Dark Horse Comics: Nov, 2020 - No. 5, Mar, 2021 ($3.99, limited series)
1-5-Lemire-s/Brombal-s/Walta-a ... 4.00

BARBARELLA (Volume 1)
Dynamite Entertainment: 2017 - No. 12, 2018 ($3.99)
1-12-Mike Carey-s/Kenan Yarar-a in most; multiple covers on each. 4-Fornés-a 4.00
... Holiday Special One Shot (2018, $5.99) Niklaus von Claus app.; J-M Lofficier-s 6.00

BARBARELLA (Volume 2)
Dynamite Entertainment: 2021 - No. 10, 2022 ($3.99)

	GD 2.0	VG 4.0	FN 6.0	VF 8.0	VF/NM 9.0	NM- 9.2

1-10: 1-Sarah Hoyt-s/Madibek Musabekov-a; multiple covers on each ... 4.00

BARBARELLA / DEJAH THORIS
Dynamite Entertainment: 2019 - No. 4, 2019 ($3.99, limited series)
1-4-Leah Williams-s/Germán García-a; multiple covers on each ... 4.00

BARBARELLA: THE CENTER CANNOT HOLD
Dynamite Entertainment: 2023 - No. 5, 2023 ($3.99, limited series)
1-5-Sarah Hoyt-s/Riccardo Bogani-a; multiple covers ... 4.00

BARBARIANS, THE
Atlas Comics/Seaboard Periodicals: June, 1975

	GD 2.0	VG 4.0	FN 6.0	VF 8.0	VF/NM 9.0	NM- 9.2
1-Origin, only app. Andrax; Iron Jaw app.; Marcos-a	3	6	9	16	24	32

BARBIE
Marvel Comics: Jan, 1991 - No. 63, Mar, 1996 ($1.00/$1.25/$1.50)

	GD 2.0	VG 4.0	FN 6.0	VF 8.0	VF/NM 9.0	NM- 9.2
1-Polybagged w/doorknob hanger; Romita-c	3	6	9	14	19	24
2-49,51-62	1	2	3	5	7	9
50,63: 50-(Giant). 63-Last issue	2	4	6	8	10	12
... And Baby Sister Kelly (1995, 99¢-c, part of a Marvel 4-pack) scarce	3	6	9	14	20	25

BARBIE & KEN
Dell Publishing Co.: May-July, 1962 - No. 5, Nov-Jan, 1963-64

	GD 2.0	VG 4.0	FN 6.0	VF 8.0	VF/NM 9.0	NM- 9.2
01-053-207(#1)-Based on Mattel toy dolls	44	88	132	326	738	1150
2-4	26	52	78	182	404	625
5 (Last issue)	27	54	81	189	420	650

BARBIE FASHION
Marvel Comics: Jan, 1991 - No. 53, May, 1995 ($1.00/$1.25/$1.50)

	GD 2.0	VG 4.0	FN 6.0	VF 8.0	VF/NM 9.0	NM- 9.2
1-Polybagged w/Barbie Pink Card	2	4	6	11	16	20
2-49,51,52: 4-Contains preview to Sweet XVI	1	2	3	5	7	9
50,53: 50-(Giant). 53-Last issue	2	4	6	8	10	12

BARB WIRE (See Comics' Greatest World)
Dark Horse Comics: Apr, 1994 - No. 9, Feb, 1995 ($2.00/$2.50)
1-9: 1-Foil logo ... 4.00
Trade paperback (1996, $8.95)-r/#2,3,5,6 w/Pamela Anderson bio 9.00

BARB WIRE (Volume 2)
Dark Horse Comics: Jul, 2015 - No. 8, Feb, 2016 ($3.99)
1-8-Adam Hughes-c on all. 1-Warner-s/Olliffe-a; two covers by Hughes 4.00

BARB WIRE: ACE OF SPADES
Dark Horse Comics: May, 1996 - No. 4, Sept, 1996 ($2.95, limited series)
1-Chris Warner-c/a(p)/scripts; Tim Bradstreet-c/a(i) in all 6.00
2-4 4.00

BARB WIRE COMICS MAGAZINE SPECIAL
Dark Horse Comics: May, 1996 ($3.50, B&W, magazine, one-shot)

	GD 2.0	VG 4.0	FN 6.0	VF 8.0	VF/NM 9.0	NM- 9.2
nn-Adaptation of film; photo-c; poster insert.	2	4	6	8	10	12

BARB WIRE MOVIE SPECIAL
Dark Horse Comics: May, 1996 ($3.95, one-shot)

	GD 2.0	VG 4.0	FN 6.0	VF 8.0	VF/NM 9.0	NM- 9.2
nn-Adaptation of film; photo-c; 1st app. new look	1	3	4	6	8	10

BARKER, THE (Also see National Comics #42)
Quality Comics Group/Comic Magazine: Autumn, 1946 - No. 15, Dec, 1949

	GD 2.0	VG 4.0	FN 6.0	VF 8.0	VF/NM 9.0	NM- 9.2
1	37	74	111	222	361	500
2	18	36	54	107	169	230
3-10	14	28	42	76	108	140
11-14	10	20	30	56	76	95
15-Jack Cole-a(p)	11	22	33	64	90	115

NOTE: *Jack Cole a-in some issues.*

BARNABY
Civil Service Publications Inc.: 1945 (25¢,102 pgs., digest size)

	GD 2.0	VG 4.0	FN 6.0	VF 8.0	VF/NM 9.0	NM- 9.2
V1#1-r/Crocket Johnson strips from 1942	8	16	24	40	50	60

BARNEY AND BETTY RUBBLE (TV) (Flintstones' Neighbors)
Charlton Comics: Jan, 1973 - No. 23, Dec, 1976 (Hanna-Barbera)

	GD 2.0	VG 4.0	FN 6.0	VF 8.0	VF/NM 9.0	NM- 9.2
1	5	10	15	33	57	80
2-11: 11(2/75)-1st Mike Zeck-a (illos)	3	6	9	14	20	25
12-23: 17-Columbo parody	2	4	6	10	14	18
Digest Annual (1972, B&W, 100 pgs.) (scarce)	4	8	12	28	47	65

BARNEY BAXTER (Also see Magic Comics)
David McKay/Dell Publishing Co./Argo: 1938 - No. 2, 1956

	GD 2.0	VG 4.0	FN 6.0	VF 8.0	VF/NM 9.0	NM- 9.2
Feature Books 15(McKay-1938)	52	104	156	328	552	775
Four Color 20(1942)	29	58	87	209	467	725
1,2 (1956-Argo)	10	20	30	54	72	90

BARNEY BEAR ...
Spire Christian Comics (Fleming H. Revell Co.): 1977-1982
...Home Plate nn-(1979, 49¢), ...In Toyland nn-(1982, 49¢),...Lost and Found nn-(1979, 49¢), Out of The Woods nn-(1980, 49¢), Sunday School Picnic nn-(1981, 69¢), The Swamp Gang!-(1977, 39¢)

	GD 2.0	VG 4.0	FN 6.0	VF 8.0	VF/NM 9.0	NM- 9.2
	2	4	6	9	13	16

BARNEY GOOGLE & SNUFFY SMITH
Dell Publishing Co./Gold Key: 1941 - 1943; April, 1964

	GD 2.0	VG 4.0	FN 6.0	VF 8.0	VF/NM 9.0	NM- 9.2
Four Color 19(1941)	61	122	183	390	670	950
Four Color 40(1944)	21	42	63	147	324	500
Large Feature Comic 11(1943)	44	88	123	256	428	600
1(10113-404)-Gold Key (4/64)	4	8	12	27	44	60

BARNEY GOOGLE & SNUFFY SMITH
Toby Press: June, 1951 - No. 4, Feb, 1952 (Reprints)

	GD 2.0	VG 4.0	FN 6.0	VF 8.0	VF/NM 9.0	NM- 9.2
1	15	30	45	88	137	185
2,3	9	18	27	52	69	85
4-Kurtzman-a "Pot Shot Pete", 5 pgs.; reprints John Wayne #5	14	28	42	78	112	145

BARNEY GOOGLE AND SNUFFY SMITH
Charlton Comics: Mar, 1970 - No. 6, Jan, 1971

Bane: Conquest #8 © DC

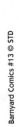
Barnyard Comics #13 © STD

Basilisk #1 © Bunn & Scharf

	GD 2.0	VG 4.0	FN 6.0	VF 8.0	VF/NM 9.0	NM- 9.2
1	3	6	9	18	27	36
2-6	2	4	6	11	16	20

BARNSTORMERS (Printing of digital series first appearing on comiXology Originals)
Dark Horse Comics: Jul, 2023 - No. 3, Sept, 2023 ($4.99, limited series)

1-3-Scott Snyder-s/Tula Lotay-a						5.00

BARNUM!
DC Comics (Vertigo): 2003; 2005 ($29.95, $19.95)

Hardcover (2003, $29.95, with dust jacket)-Chaykin & Tischman-s/Henrichon-a						30.00
Softcover (2005, $19.95)-Chaykin & Tischman-s/Henrichon-a						20.00

BARNYARD COMICS (Dizzy Duck No. 32 on)
Nedor/Polo Mag./Standard(Animated Cartoons): Jun, 1944 - No. 31, Sept, 1950; No. 10, 1957

	GD	VG	FN	VF	VF/NM	NM-
1 (nn, 52 pgs.)-Funny animal	30	60	90	177	289	400
2 (52 pgs.)	16	32	48	94	147	200
3-5	13	26	39	74	105	135
6-12,16	11	22	33	62	86	110
13-15,17,21,23,26,27,29-All contain Frazetta text illos	12	24	36	69	97	125
18-20,22,24,25-All contain Frazetta & text illos	15	30	45	85	130	175
28,30,31	10	20	30	54	72	90
10 (1957)(Exist?)	4	8	12	17	21	24

BARRIER
Image Comics: May, 2018 - No. 5, May, 2018 ($4.99/$3.99, limited series, printed sideways)

1,5-($4.99) Brian K. Vaughan-s/Marcos Martin-a						5.00
2-4-($3.99)						4.00

BARRY M. GOLDWATER
Dell Publishing Co.: Mar, 1965 (Complete life story)

	GD	VG	FN	VF	VF/NM	NM-
12-055-503-Photo-c	5	10	15	30	50	70

BARRY WINDSOR-SMITH: STORYTELLER
Dark Horse Comics: Oct, 1996 - No. 9, July, 1997 ($4.95, oversize)

1-9: 1-Intro Young Gods, Paradox Man & the Freebooters; Barry Smith-c/a/scripts						5.00
Preview						4.00

BAR SINISTER (Also see Shaman's Tears)
Acclaim Comics (Windjammer): Jun, 1995 - No. 4, Sept, 1995 ($2.50, lim. series)

1-4: Mike Grell-c/a/scripts						4.00

BARTMAN (Also see Simpsons Comics & Radioactive Man)
Bongo Comics: 1993 - No. 6, 1994 ($1.95/$2.25)

	GD	VG	FN	VF	VF/NM	NM-
1-($2.95)-Foil-c; bound-in jumbo Bartman poster	3	6	9	16	23	30
1-($1.95) Regular cover	2	4	6	9	13	16
2-6: 3-w/trading card						6.00
...: Spectacularly Super Secret Saga (2018, $7.99) Adult Bartman 20 years in the future						15.00

BART SIMPSON (See Simpsons Comics Presents Bart Simpson)

BASEBALL COMICS
Will Eisner Productions: Spring, 1949 (Reprinted later as a Spirit section)

	GD	VG	FN	VF	VF/NM	NM-
1-Will Eisner-c/a	77	154	231	493	847	1200

BASEBALL COMICS
Kitchen Sink Press: 1991 ($3.95, coated stock)

1-r/1949 ish. by Eisner; contains trading cards						6.00

BASEBALL HEROES
Fawcett Publications: 1952 (one-shot)

	GD	VG	FN	VF	VF/NM	NM-
nn (Scarce)-Babe Ruth photo-c; baseball's Hall of Fame biographies	90	180	270	576	988	1400

BASEBALL'S GREATEST HEROES
Magnum Comics: Dec, 1991 - No. 2, May, 1992 ($1.75)

	GD	VG	FN	VF	VF/NM	NM-
1-Mickey Mantle #1; photo-c; Sinnott-a(p)	1	3	4	6	8	10
2-Brooks Robinson #1; photo-c; Sinnott-a(i)						6.00

BASEBALL THRILLS
Ziff-Davis Publ. Co.: No. 10, Sum, 1951 - No. 3, Sum, 1952 (Saunders painted-c No.1,2)

	GD	VG	FN	VF	VF/NM	NM-
10(#1)-Bob Feller, Musial, Newcombe & Boudreau stories	47	94	141	296	498	700
2-Powell-a(2)(Late Sum, '51); Feller, Berra & Mathewson stories	34	68	102	199	325	450
3-Kinstler-c/a; Joe DiMaggio story	34	68	102	199	325	450

BASEBALL THRILLS 3-D
The 3-D Zone: May, 1990 ($2.95, w/glasses)

1-New L.B. Cole-c; life stories of Ty Cobb & Ted Williams						

	GD 2.0	VG 4.0	FN 6.0	VF 8.0	VF/NM 9.0	NM- 9.2
1	3	4	6	8	10	

BASICALLY STRANGE (Magazine)
John C. Comics (Archie Comics Group): Dec, 1982 ($1.95, B&W)

	GD	VG	FN	VF	VF/NM	NM-
1-(21,000 printed; all but 1,000 destroyed; pages out of sequence)						
1-Wood, Toth-a; Corben-c; reprints & new art	3	6	9	17	25	34
	2	4	6	13	18	22

BASIC HISTORY OF AMERICA ILLUSTRATED
Pendulum Press: 1976 (B&W) (Soft-c $1.50; Hard-c $4.50)

07-1999-America Becomes a World Power 1890-1920. 07-2251-The Industrial Era 1865-1915. 07-226x-Before the Civil War 1830-1860. 07-2278-Americans Move Westward 1800-1850. 07-2286-The Civil War 1850-1876; Redondo-a. 07-2294-The Fight for Freedom 1750-1783. 07-2308-The New World 1500-1750. 07-2316-Problems of the New Nation 1800-1830. 07-2324-Roaring Twenties and the Great Depression 1920-1940. 07-2332-The United States Emerges 1783-1800. 07-2340-America Today 1945-1976. 07-2359-World War II 1940-1945

	GD	VG	FN	VF	VF/NM	NM-
Softcover editions each	1	2	3	4	5	7
Hardcover editions each						14.00

BASIC INSTINCT
Sumerian Comics: 2023 - Present ($4.99)

1-4-Sam Freeman-s/Vanesa Del Rey-a						5.00

BASIL (...the Royal Cat)
St. John Publishing Co.: Jan, 1953 - No. 4, Sept, 1953

	GD	VG	FN	VF	VF/NM	NM-
1-Funny animal	9	18	27	50	65	80
2-Hitler Mouse app.	10	20	30	54	72	90
3,4	6	12	18	31	38	45
I.W. Reprint	2	4	6	9	12	15

BASILISK
BOOM! Studios: Jun, 2021 - No. 12, Oct, 2022 ($3.99)

1-12-Cullen Bunn-s/Jonas Scharf-a						4.00

BASIL WOLVERTON'S FANTASTIC FABLES
Dark Horse Comics: Oct, 1993 - No. 2, Dec, 1993 ($2.50, B&W, limited series)

	GD	VG	FN	VF	VF/NM	NM-
1-Wolverton-c/a(r)	1	3	4	6	8	10
2-Wolverton-c/a(r)						6.00

BASIL WOLVERTON'S GATEWAY TO HORROR
Dark Horse Comics: June, 1988 ($1.75, B&W, one-shot)

	GD	VG	FN	VF	VF/NM	NM-
1-Wolverton-r	1	3	4	6	8	10

BASIL WOLVERTON'S PLANET OF TERROR
Dark Horse Comics: Oct, 1987 ($1.75, B&W, one-shot)

	GD	VG	FN	VF	VF/NM	NM-
1-Wolverton-r; Alan Moore-c	1	3	4	6	8	10

BASKETFUL OF HEADS (Also see Refrigerator Full of Heads)
DC Comics (Hill House Comics): Dec, 2019 - No. 7, Jun. 2020 ($3.99, limited series)

1-7-Joe Hill-s/Leomacs-a; based on serial Sea Dogs in each; Murakami-c						4.00
1-($4.99) Variant cardstock-c by Josh Middleton						5.00

BASTARD SAMURAI
Image Comics: Apr, 2002 - No. 3, Aug, 2002 ($2.95)

1-3-Oeming & Gunter-s; Shannon-a/Oeming-i						3.00
TPB (2003, $12.95) r/#1-3; plus sketch pages and pin-ups						13.00

BATGIRL (See Batman: No Man's Land series)
DC Comics: Apr, 2000 - No. 73, Apr, 2006 ($2.50)

	GD	VG	FN	VF	VF/NM	NM-
1-Scott & Campanella-a	2	4	6	10	14	18
1-(2nd printing)						4.00
2-10: 8-Lady Shiva app.						5.00
11-24: 12-"Officer Down" x-over. 15-Joker-c/app. 24-Bruce Wayne: Murderer pt. 2.						4.00
25-($3.25) Batgirl vs Lady Shiva						4.50
26-29: 27- Bruce Wayne: Fugitive pt. 5; Noto-a. 29-B.W.:F. pt. 13						4.00
30-49,51-73: 30-32-Connor Hawke app. 39-Intro. Black Wind. 41-Superboy-c/app. 53-Robin (Spoiler) app. 54-Bagged w/back serial Sea Dogs in each; Murakami-c. 63,64-Deathstroke app. 67-Birds of Prey app. 70-1st app. Lazara (Nora Fries). 73-Lady Shiva origin; Sale-c						4.00
50-($3.25) Batgirl vs Batman						5.00
Annual 1 ('00, $3.50) Planet DC; intro. Aruna						5.00
...: A Knight Alone (2001, $12.95, TPB) r/#7-11,13,14						13.00
...: Death Wish (2003, $14.95, TPB) r/#17-20,22,23,25 & Secret Files and Origins #1						15.00
...: Destruction's Daughter (2006, $19.99, TPB) r/#65-73						25.00
...: Fists of Fury (2004, $14.95, TPB) r/#15,16,21,26-28						15.00
...: Kicking Assassins (2005, $14.99, TPB) r/#60-64						18.00
...: Secret Files and Origins (8/02, $4.95) origin-s Noto-a; profile pages and pin-ups						5.00
...: Silent Running (2001, $12.95, TPB) r/#1-6						18.00

BATGIRL (Cassandra Cain)
DC Comics: Sept, 2008 - No. 6, Feb, 2009 ($2.99)

	GD 2.0	VG 4.0	FN 6.0	VF 8.0	VF/NM 9.0	NM- 9.2

1-6-Beechen-s/Calafiore-a 4.00

BATGIRL (Spoiler/Stephanie Brown)(Batman: Reborn)
DC Comics: Oct., 2009 - No. 24, Oct. 2011 ($2.99)
1-Garbett-a/Noto-c ... 2 ... 4 ... 6 ... 9 ... 12 ... 15
1-Variant-c by Hamner ... 3 ... 6 ... 9 ... 14 ... 20 ... 25
2-24: 2-7-Garbett-a/Noto-c. 3-New costume. 8-Caldwell-a. 9-14-Lau-a. 14-Supergirl-c. 4.00
...: Batgirl Rising TPB (2010, $17.99) r/#1-7 .... 30.00
...: The Flood TPB (2011, $14.99) r/#9-14 .... 30.00

BATGIRL (Barbara Gordon)(DC New 52)(See Secret Origins #10)
DC Comics: Nov, 2011 - No. 52, Jul, 2016 ($2.99)
1-Barbara Gordon back in costume; Simone-s/Syaf-a/Hughes-c 20.00
1-Second & Third printings 5.00
2-12: 2-6-Hughes-c. 3-Nightwing app. 7-12-Syaf-a. 9-Night of the Owls. 12-Batwoman app. 4.00
13-Die-cut cover; Death of the Family tie-in; Batwoman app. 10.00
13-24: 14-16-Death of the Family tie-in; Joker app. 20,21-Intro. The Ventriloquist 3.00
25-($3.99) Zero Year tie-in; Bennett-a/Pasarin-a 4.00
26-34: 27-Gothtopia tie-in. 28,29-Strix app. 31-34-Simone-s. 31-Ragdoll app. 3.00
35-49,51,52: 35-New costume; Tarr-a/Stewart-c. 37-Bagger Type app. 41,42-Batman (Gordon) & Livewire app. 45-Dick Grayson app. 48,49-Black Canary app. 3.00
50-($4.99) Black Canary, Spoiler & Bluebird app.; Tarr-a 5.00
#0 (11/12, $2.99) Batgirl origin updated; Simone-s/Benes-a 3.00
Annual 1 (12/12, $4.99) Catwoman and the Talons app.; Simone-s/Wijaya-a/Benes-c 5.00
Annual 2 (6/14, $4.99) Future app.; Simone-s/Gill-a/Benes-c 5.00
Annual 3 (9/15, $4.99) Dick Grayson, Spoiler & Batwoman app. 5.00
...: Endgame 1 (5/15, $2.99) Tie-in with other Endgame stories in Batman titles 3.00
...: Futures End 1 (11/14, $2.99, regular-c) Five years later; Bane app.; Simone-s 3.00
...: Futures End 1 (11/14, $3.99, 3-D cover) 4.00

BATGIRL (DC Rebirth)
DC Comics: Sept, 2016 - No. 50, Dec, 2020 ($2.99/$3.99)
1-9: 1-Hope Larson-s/Rafael Albuquerque-a. 6-Poison Ivy app. 9-Penguin app. 3.00
10-24-($3.99): 10,11-Penguin app. 13-Catwoman app. 18-Harley Quinn app. 4.00
25-($4.99) Short stories by various; art by Derenick, Panosian, Pelletier, Lupacchino 5.00
26-49: 26-New costume. 30-34-Jason Bard app. 34-36-Terrible Trio app. 37-41-Year of the Villain tie-ins; new Oracle app. 41-Acetate-c. 47,48-Joker War tie-ins 4.00
50-($5.99) Intro. Ryan Wilder (1 pg.); Lupacchino-a; back-up w/Sauvage-a 6.00
Annual 1 (5/17, $4.99) Supergirl app. (story cont'd in Supergirl #9); Larson-s; Bengal-a 5.00
Annual 2 (10/18, $4.99) Casagrande-a; brother James Gordon app. 5.00

BATGIRL ADVENTURES (See Batman Adventures, The)
DC Comics: Feb, 1998 ($2.95, one-shot) (Based on animated series)
1-Harley Quinn and Poison Ivy app.; Timm-c ... 5 ... 10 ... 15 ... 31 ... 53 ... 75

BATGIRL AND THE BIRDS OF PREY (DC Rebirth)
DC Comics: Aug, 2016 - No. 22, Jul, 2018 ($2.99/$3.99)
1-8: 1-Julie & Shawna Benson-s/Claire Roe-a. 3-8-Antonio-a. 8-Nightwing app. 3.00
9-22-($3.99) 10-Nightwing & Green Arrow app. 12-17-Catwoman & Poison Ivy app. 4.00
...: Rebirth 1 (9/16, $2.99) Batgirl, Black Canary & Huntress team up; Claire Roe-a 3.00

BATGIRLS (Stephanie Brown and Cassandra Cain)
DC Comics: Feb, 2022 - No. 19, Aug, 2023 ($3.99)
1-19: 1-Cloonan & Conrad-s/Corona-a; vs. the Saints (Tarsus, Valentine & Assisi) 4.00
2022 Annual (1/23, $5.99) Rodriguez-a; Steph and Cass switch bodies; continues in #13 .... 6.00

BATGIRL SPECIAL
DC Comics: 1988 ($1.50, one-shot, 52 pgs)
1-Kitson-a/Mignola-c ... 2 ... 4 ... 6 ... 11 ... 16 ... 20

BATGIRL: YEAR ONE
DC Comics: Feb, 2003 - No. 9, Oct, 2003 ($2.95, limited series)
1-Barbara Gordon becomes Batgirl; Killer Moth app.; Beatty & Dixon-s ... 2 ... 4 ... 6 ... 8 ... 10 ... 12
2-9 .... 4.00
TPB (2003, $17.95) r/#1-9 .... 25.00

BAT LASH (See DC Special Series #16, Showcase #76, Weird Western Tales)
National Periodical Publications: Oct-Nov, 1968 - No. 7, Oct-Nov, 1969 (12¢/15¢)
1-(10-11/68, 12¢-c)-2nd app. Bat Lash; classic Nick Cardy-c/a in all ... 7 ... 14 ... 21 ... 49 ... 92 ... 135
2-7: 6,7-(15¢-c) ... 4 ... 8 ... 12 ... 28 ... 47 ... 65

BAT LASH
DC Comics: Feb, 2008 - No. 6, Jul, 2008 ($2.99, limited series)
1-6-Aragonés & Brandvold-s/John Severin-a. 1-Two covers by Severin and Simonson 3.00

BATMAN (See All Star Batman & Robin, Anarky, Aurora [in Promo. Comics section], Azrael, The Best of DC #2, Blind Justice, The Brave & the Bold, Cosmic Odyssey, DC 100-Page Super Spec. #14,20, DC Special, DC Special Series, Detective Comics, Dynamic Classics, 80-Page Giants, Gotham By Gaslight, Gotham Nights, Greatest Batman Stories Ever Told, Greatest Joker Stories Ever Told, Heroes Against Hunger, JLA, The Joker, Justice League of America, Justice League Int., Legends of the Dark Knight, Limited Coll. Ed., Man-Bat, Nightwing, Power Record Comics, Real Fact #5, Robin, Saga of Ra's al Ghul, Shadow of the..., Star Spangled, Super Friends, 3-D Batman, Untold Legend of..., Wanted... & World's Finest Comics)

BATMAN
National Per. Publ./Detective Comics/DC Comics: Spring, 1940 - No. 713, Oct, 2011 (#1-5 were quarterly)
1-Origin The Batman reprinted (2 pgs.) from Detective Comics #33 w/splash from #34 by Bob Kane; 1st app. Joker (2 stories intended for 2 separate issues of Detective which would have been 1st & 2nd app.); splash pg. to 2nd Joker story is similar to cover of Detective #40 (story intended for #40); 1st app. The Cat (Catwoman)(1st villainess in comics); has Batman story (w/Hugo Strange) without Robin originally planned for Detective #38; mentions location (Manhattan) where Batman lives (see Detective #31). This book was created entirely from the inventory of Detective Comics; 1st Batman/Robin pin-up on back-c; has text piece & photo of Bob Kane
86,500 ... 173,000 ... 259,500 ... 588,200 ... 944,100 ... 1,300,000
1-Reprint, oversize 13-1/2x10". **WARNING:** This comic is an exact duplicate reprint of the original except for its size. DC published in 1974 with a second cover titling it as a Famous First Edition. There have been many recorded cases of the outer cover being removed and the interior sold as the original edition. The reprint with the new outer cover removed is practically worthless. See Famous First Edition for value.

2-2nd app. The Joker; 2nd app. Catwoman (out of costume) in Joker story; 1st time called Catwoman (NOTE: A 15¢-c for Canadian distr. exists.)
3575 ... 7150 ... 10,725 ... 25,400 ... 47,700 ... 70,000
3-3rd app Catwoman (1st in costume & 1st costumed villainess); 1st Puppet Master app.; classic Kane & Robinson-c
1750 ... 3500 ... 5250 ... 13,100 ... 25,550 ... 38,000
4-4th app. The Joker (see Det. #45 for 3rd); 1st mention of Gotham City in a Batman comic (on newspaper)(Win/40)
1750 ... 3500 ... 5250 ... 13,100 ... 25,550 ... 38,000
5-1st app. the Batmobile with its bat-head front
1000 ... 2000 ... 3000 ... 7500 ... 13,500 ... 19,500
6,7: 7-Bullseye-c; Joker app.
892 ... 1784 ... 2676 ... 6512 ... 11,506 ... 16,500
8-Infinity-c by Fred Ray; Joker app.
838 ... 1676 ... 2514 ... 6117 ... 10,809 ... 15,500
9-1st Batman Christmas story; Burnley-c
811 ... 1622 ... 2433 ... 5920 ... 10,460 ... 15,000
10-Catwoman story (gets new costume)
649 ... 1298 ... 1947 ... 4738 ... 8369 ... 12,000
11-Classic Joker-c by Ray/Robinson (3rd Joker-c, 6-7/42); Joker & Penguin app.
2250 ... 4500 ... 6750 ... 17,100 ... 31,050 ... 45,000
12,15: 12-Joker app. 15-New costume Catwoman
486 ... 972 ... 1458 ... 3550 ... 6275 ... 9000
13-Jerry Siegel (Superman's co-creator) appears in a Batman story; Batman parachuting on black-c
465 ... 930 ... 1395 ... 3395 ... 5998 ... 8600
14-2nd Penguin-c; Penguin app. (12-1/42-43)
432 ... 864 ... 1296 ... 3154 ... 5577 ... 8000
16-Intro/origin Alfred (4-5/43); cover is a reverse of #9 cover by Burnley; 1st small logo
1350 ... 2700 ... 4050 ... 10,300 ... 18,650 ... 27,000
17-Classic war-c; Penguin app.
432 ... 864 ... 1296 ... 3154 ... 5577 ... 8000
18-Hitler, Hirohito, Mussolini-c
757 ... 1514 ... 2271 ... 5526 ... 9763 ... 14,000
19-Joker app.
295 ... 590 ... 885 ... 1888 ... 3244 ... 4600
20-1st Batmobile (12-1/43-44); Joker app.
541 ... 1082 ... 1623 ... 3950 ... 6975 ... 10,000
21,24,26,28-30: 21-1st skinny Alfred in Batman (3/44). 21,30-Penguin app. 28-Joker story
226 ... 452 ... 678 ... 1446 ... 2473 ... 3500
22-1st Alfred solo-c/story (Alfred solo stories in 22-32,36); Catwoman & The Cavalier app.
300 ... 600 ... 900 ... 2040 ... 3570 ... 5100
23-Joker-c/story; classic black-c
919 ... 1838 ... 2757 ... 6709 ... 11,855 ... 17,000
25-Only Joker/Penguin team-up; 1st team-up between two major villains
497 ... 994 ... 1491 ... 3628 ... 6414 ... 9200
27-Classic Burnley Christmas-c; Penguin app.
284 ... 568 ... 852 ... 1818 ... 3109 ... 4400
31,34-36,39: 35-Catwoman story (in new costume w/o cat head mask). 36-Penguin app.
168 ... 336 ... 504 ... 1075 ... 1838 ... 2600
32-Origin Robin retold; Joker app.
219 ... 438 ... 657 ... 1402 ... 2401 ... 3400
33-Christmas-c
200 ... 400 ... 600 ... 1280 ... 2190 ... 3100
37-Joker spotlight on black-c
595 ... 1190 ... 1785 ... 4350 ... 7675 ... 11,000
38-Penguin-c/story
343 ... 686 ... 1029 ... 2400 ... 4200 ... 6000
40-Joker-c/story
389 ... 778 ... 1167 ... 2723 ... 4762 ... 6800
41-1st Sci-fi cover/story in Batman; Penguin app.(6-7/47)
168 ... 336 ... 504 ... 1075 ... 1838 ... 2600
42-2nd Catwoman-c (1st in Batman)(8-9/47); Catwoman story also.
514 ... 1028 ... 1542 ... 3750 ... 6625 ... 9500
43-Penguin-c/story
314 ... 628 ... 942 ... 2198 ... 3849 ... 5500
44-Classic Joker-c
919 ... 1838 ... 2757 ... 6709 ... 11,855 ... 17,000
45-Christmas-c/story; Catwoman story
181 ... 362 ... 543 ... 1158 ... 1979 ... 2800
46-Joker app.
295 ... 590 ... 885 ... 1888 ... 3244 ... 4600
47-1st detailed origin The Batman (6-7/48); 1st Bat-signal-c this title (see Detective #108); Batman tracks down his parent's killer and reveals i.d. to him
1050 ... 2100 ... 3150 ... 8000 ... 14,500 ... 21,000
48-1000 Secrets of the Batcave; r-in #203; Penguin story
349 ... 698 ... 1047 ... 2443 ... 4272 ... 6100
49-Joker-c/story; 1st app. Mad Hatter; 1st app. Vicki Vale
595 ... 1190 ... 1785 ... 4350 ... 7675 ... 11,000
50-Two-Face impostor app.
354 ... 708 ... 1062 ... 2478 ... 4339 ... 6200
51-Pee-Wee, the Talking Penguin
206 ... 412 ... 618 ... 1318 ... 2259 ... 3200
52-Joker-c/story
568 ... 1136 ... 1704 ... 4146 ... 7323 ... 10,500
53-Joker story
194 ... 388 ... 582 ... 1242 ... 2121 ... 3000
54,56,57,60: 57-Centerfold is a 1950 calendar; Joker app.
142 ... 284 ... 426 ... 909 ... 1555 ... 2200
55-Joker-c/stories
459 ... 918 ... 1377 ... 3360 ... 5925 ... 8500
58,61: 58-Penguin-c. 61-Origin Batplane II
226 ... 452 ... 678 ... 1446 ... 2473 ... 3500
59-1st app. Deadshot; Batman in the future-c/sty
541 ... 1082 ... 1623 ... 3950 ... 6975 ... 10,000
62-Origin Catwoman; Catwoman-c
454 ... 908 ... 1362 ... 3344 ... 5857 ... 8400
63-1st app. Killer Moth; Joker story; flying saucer story(2-3/51)
371 ... 742 ... 1113 ... 2600 ... 4550 ... 6500
64,70-72,74-77,79: 70-Robot-c. 72-Last 52 pg. issue. 74-Used in POP, Pg. 90. 75-Gorilla-c. 76-Penguin story. 79-Vicki Vale in "The Bride of Batman"
119 ... 238 ... 357 ... 762 ... 1306 ... 1850
65,69-Catwoman-c/stories
389 ... 778 ... 1167 ... 2723 ... 4762 ... 6800
66,73-Catwoman-c/stories. 66-Pre-2nd Batman & Robin team try-out. 73-Vicki Vale story
423 ... 846 ... 1269 ... 3000 ... 5250 ... 7500
67-Joker story
155 ... 310 ... 465 ... 992 ... 1696 ... 2400
68,81-Two-Face-c/stories
295 ... 590 ... 885 ... 1888 ... 3244 ... 4600
78-(8-9/53)-Roh Kar, The Man Hunter from Mars story-the 1st lawman of Mars to come to Earth (green skinned)
271 ... 542 ... 813 ... 1734 ... 2967 ... 4200
80-Joker stories
155 ... 310 ... 465 ... 992 ... 1696 ... 2400
82,83,87-89: 89-Last pre-code issue
106 ... 212 ... 318 ... 673 ... 1162 ... 1650
84-Catwoman-c/story; Two-Face story
303 ... 606 ... 909 ... 2121 ... 3711 ... 5300
85,86-Joker story. 86-Intro Batmarine (Batman's submarine)
116 ... 232 ... 348 ... 742 ... 1271 ... 1800
90,91,93-96,98,99: 99-(4/56)-Last G.A. Penguin app.
93 ... 186 ... 279 ... 591 ... 1021 ... 1450
92-1st app. Bat-Hound-c/story
331 ... 662 ... 993 ... 2317 ... 4059 ... 5800
97-2nd app. Bat-Hound-c/story; Joker story
226 ... 452 ... 678 ... 1446 ... 2473 ... 3500
100-(6/56)
371 ... 742 ... 1113 ... 2600 ... 4550 ... 6500
101-(8/56)-Clark Kent x-over who protects Batman's i.d. (3rd story)
100 ... 200 ... 300 ... 635 ... 1093 ... 1550
102-104,106-109: 103-1st S.A. issue; 3rd Bat-Hound-c/story
84 ... 168 ... 252 ... 538 ... 919 ... 1300
105-1st Batwoman in Batman (2nd anywhere)
174 ... 348 ... 522 ... 1114 ... 1907 ... 2700
110-Joker story
90 ... 180 ... 270 ... 576 ... 988 ... 1400
111-120: 112-1st app. Signalman (super villain). 113-1st app. Fatman; Batman meets his counterpart on Planet X w/a chest plate similar to S.A. Batman's design (yellow oval w/black design inside)
74 ... 148 ... 232 ... 470 ... 810 ... 1150
121-Origin/1st app. of Mr. Zero (Mr. Freeze)
1200 ... 2400 ... 3600 ... 9100 ... 16,550 ... 24,000
122,124-126,128,130: 122,126-Batwoman-c/story. 125-2nd app. Signal Man.

Batgirl (2016 series) #27 © DC

Batman #121 © DC

Batman #408 © DC

	GD 2.0	VG 4.0	FN 6.0	VF 8.0	VF/NM 9.0	NM- 9.2
128-Batwoman cameo. 130-Lex Luthor app.	61	122	183	390	670	950
123,127: 123-Joker story; Bat-Hound-c/app. 127-(10/59)-Batman vs. Thor the Thunder God c/story; Joker story; Superman cameo	61	122	183	390	670	950
129-Origin Robin retold; bondage-c; Batwoman-c/story (reprinted in Batman Family #8)	81	162	243	518	884	1250
131-135,137,138,141-143: 131-Intro 2nd Batman & Robin series (see #66; also in #135,145,154,159,163). 133-1st app. Bat-Mite in Batman (3rd app. anywhere). 134-Origin The Dummy (not Vigilante's villain). 141-2nd app. original Bat-Girl. 143-(10/61)-Last 10¢ issue	52	104	156	328	552	775
136-Joker-c/story	71	142	213	454	777	1100
139-Intro 1st original Bat-Girl; only app. Signalman as the Blue Bowman	226	452	678	1446	2473	3500
140-Joker story, Batwoman-c/s; Superman cameo	52	104	156	328	552	775
144-(12/61)-1st 12¢ issue; Joker story	53	106	159	334	567	800
145,148-Joker-c/stories	77	154	231	493	847	1200
146,147,149,150	45	90	135	284	480	675
151-154,156-158,160-162,164-168,170: 152-Joker story. 156-Ant-Man/Robin team-up(6/63). 164-New Batmobile(6/64) new look & Mystery Analysts series begins	37	74	111	222	361	500
155-1st S.A. app. The Penguin (5/63)	271	542	813	1734	2967	4200
159,163-Joker-c/stories. 159-Bat-Girl app. 163-Last Bat-Girl app. until Teen Titans #50	52	104	156	328	552	775
169-2nd SA Penguin app.	48	96	144	302	514	725
171-1st Riddler app.(5/65) since Dec. 1948	258	516	774	1651	2826	4000
172-175,177,178,180,184	13	26	39	86	188	290
176-(80-Pg. Giant G-17)-Joker-c/story; Penguin in strip-r; Catwoman reprint	17	34	51	117	259	400
179-2nd app. Silver Age Riddler	32	64	96	230	515	800
181-Poison Ivy; Batman & Robin poster insert	300	600	900	2550	5775	9000
182,187-(80 Pg. Giants G-24, G-30)-Joker-c/stories	13	26	39	89	195	300
183-2nd app. Poison Ivy	19	38	57	131	291	450
185-(80 Pg. Giant G-27)	13	26	39	89	195	300
186-Joker-c/story	19	38	57	131	291	450
188,191,192,194-196,199	10	20	30	68	144	220
189-1st S.A. app. Scarecrow; retells origin of G.A. Scarecrow from World's Finest #3 (1st app.)	68	136	204	544	1222	1900
190-Penguin-c/app.	19	38	57	131	291	450
193-(80 Pg. Giant G-37)	11	22	33	75	160	245
197-4th S.A. Catwoman app. cont'd from Det. #369; 1st new Batgirl app. in Batman (5th anywhere)	19	38	57	131	291	450
198-(80-Pg. Giant G-43); Joker-c/story-r/World's Finest #61; Catwoman-r/Det. #211; Penguin-r; origin-r/#47	12	24	36	82	179	275
200-(3/68)-Scarecrow app.; Joker, Penguin, Killer Moth cameos; retells origin of Batman & Robin; 1st Neal Adams work this title (cover only)	14	28	42	93	204	315
201-Joker story	9	18	27	59	117	175
202,204-207,209-212: 210-Catwoman-c/app. 212-Last 12¢ issue	8	16	24	54	102	150
203-(80 Pg. Giant G-49); r/#48, 61, & Det. 185; Batcave Blueprints	11	22	33	73	157	240
208-(80 Pg. Giant G-55); New origin Batman by Gil Kane plus 3 G.A. Batman reprints w/Catwoman, Vicki Vale & Batwoman	10	20	30	64	132	200
213-(80 Pg. Giant G-61); 30th anniversary issue (7-8/69); origin Alfred r/Batman #16), Joker(r/Det. #168), Clayface; new origin Robin with new facts	10	20	30	66	138	210
214-217: 216-Alfred given a new last name- "Pennyworth" (see Detective #96)	7	14	21	48	89	130
218-(68 pg. Giant G-67)	9	18	27	63	129	195
219-Neal Adams-a	10	20	30	69	147	225
220,221,224-226,229-231	6	12	18	38	69	100
222-Beatles take-off; art lesson by Joe Kubert	25	50	75	175	388	600
223,228,233,228-(68 pg. Giants G-73,G-79). 233-G-85-(68 pgs. "64 pgs." on-c)	8	16	24	51	96	140
227-Neal Adams cover swipe of Detective #31	86	172	258	688	1544	2400
232-(6/71) Adams-a. Intro/1st app. Ra's al Ghul; origin Batman & Robin retold; last 15¢ issue (see Detective #411 (5/71) for Talia's debut)	81	162	243	518	834	1300
234-(9/71)-1st modern app. of Harvey Dent/Two-Face with origin re-told in brief; (see World's Finest #173 for Batman as Two-Face; only S.A. mention of character); N. Adams-a; 52 pg. issues begin, end #242	36	72	108	259	580	900
235-Ra's al Ghul & Talia app.	17	34	51	117	259	400
236,239-242: 239-XMas-c. 241-Reprint/#5	7	14	21	44	82	120
237-N. Adams-c/a. 1st Rutland Vermont - Bald Mountain Halloween x-over. 1st app. The Reaper; Holocaust reference; Wrightson/Ellison plots; G.A. Batman-r/Detective #37	20	40	60	138	307	475
238-Also listed as DC 100 Page Super Spectacular #8; Batman, Legion, Aquaman-r; G.A. Atom, Sargon (r/Sensation #57), Plastic Man (r/Police #14) stories; Doom Patrol origin-r;						

	GD 2.0	VG 4.0	FN 6.0	VF 8.0	VF/NM 9.0	NM- 9.2
N. Adams wraparound-c	18	36	54	124	275	425
243,245-Neal Adams-a	12	24	36	79	170	260
244-Ra's al Ghul app.; Neal Adams-a	22	44	66	154	340	525
246-250,252,253: 246-Scarecrow app. 253-Shadow-c & app.	6	12	18	38	69	100
251-(9/73)-N. Adams-c/a; Joker-c/story	61	122	183	488	1094	1700
254,256,257,259,261-All 100 pg. editions; part-r: 254-(2/74)-Man-Bat-c/app. 256-Catwoman app. 257-Joker & Penguin app. 259-Shadow-c/app.	8	16	24	52	99	145
255-(100 pgs.)-N. Adams-c/a; tells of Bruce Wayne's father who wore bat costume & fought crime (r/Det. #235); r/story Batman #22	9	18	27	59	117	175
258-First mention of Arkham (Hospital, renamed Arkham Asylum in #260)	10	20	30	68	144	220
260-(100 pgs.) Joker-c/story; 2nd Arkham Asylum (see #258 for 1st mention)	9	18	27	60	120	180
262 (68 pgs.)	6	12	18	40	73	105
263,264,266-285,287-290,292,293,295-299: 266-Catwoman back to old costume	3	6	9	17	26	35
265-Wrightson-a(i)	3	6	9	18	28	38
286,291,294: 294-Joker-c/stories	4	8	12	23	37	50
300-Double-size	5	10	15	33	57	80
301-(7/78)-306,308-310,312,314,315,317-320,325-331,333-352: 304-(44 pgs.). 306-3rd app. Black Spider. 310-1st modern app. The Gentleman Ghost in Batman; Kubert-c. 312,314-Two-Face-c/stories. 318-Intro Firebug. 319-2nd modern age app. of The Gentleman Ghost; Kubert-c. 331-1st app./death original Electrocutioner. 344-Poison Ivy app. 345-1st app. new Dr. Death. 345,346,351-Catwoman back-ups. 346-Two-Face-c/app.	3	6	9	11	16	20
306-308,311-320,323,324,326-(Whitman variants; low print run; none show issue # on cover)	3	6	9	17	25	34
307-1st app. Lucius Fox (1/79)	5	10	15	31	53	75
311,316,322-324: 311-Batgirl-c/story; Batgirl reteams w/Batman. 316-Robin returns. 322-324-Catwoman (Selina Kyle) app. 322,323-Cat-Man cameos (1st in Batman, 1 panel each). 323-1st meeting Catwoman & Cat-Man. 324-1st full app. Cat-Man this title	4	8	12	23	37	50
313-1st app. Timothy Fox (7/79)(see Future State: The Next Batman); Two-Face app.; 2nd app. Calendar Man	8	16	24	51	96	140
321-Joker-c/story	6	12	18	38	69	100
332-Catwoman's 1st solo	3	6	9	21	33	45
353-Joker-c/story; preview of Masters of the Universe	4	8	12	23	37	50
354-356,360,362-365,369,370: 362-Riddler-c/story with origin retold in brief	2	4	6	9	13	16
357-1st app. Jason Todd (3/83); see Det. #524; brief app. Croc (see Detective #523 (2/83) for earlier cameo)	9	18	27	58	114	170
358-Early Croc app.	3	6	9	19	30	40
359-Joker-c/story	3	6	9	18	27	50
361-Debut of Harvey Bullock (7/83)(see Detective #441,('74) for a similar Lt. Bullock, no first name given, appeared in 3 panels)	3	6	9	17	26	35
366-Jason Todd 1st in Robin costume; Joker-c/story	5	10	15	31	53	75
367-Jason in red & green costume (not as Robin)	2	4	6	10	14	18
368-1st new Robin in costume (Jason Todd)	4	8	12	25	40	55
371,372,375-385,388-399,401-403: 371-Cat-Man-c/story; brief origin Cat-Man (cont'd in Det. #538). 390-391-Catwoman app. 398-Catwoman & Two-Face app. 401-2nd app. Magpie (see Man of Steel #3 for 1st). 403-Joker-c/story	2	4	6	8	10	12
373-Scarecrow-c	3	6	9	14	19	24
374-Elongated Man app.	2	4	6	11	16	20

NOTE: Issues 397-399, 401-403, 408-416, 421-425, 430-432 all have 2nd printings in 1989; some with up to 8 printings. Some are not identified as reprints but have newer ads copyrighted after cover dates. All reprints have different back-c ads. These are scarcer than 1st prints and have same value to variant collectors.

	GD 2.0	VG 4.0	FN 6.0	VF 8.0	VF/NM 9.0	NM- 9.2
386-Intro Black Mask (villain)	5	10	15	35	63	90
387-Intro Black Mask continues	3	6	9	18		22
400 ($1.50, 68pgs.)-Dark Knight special; intro by Stephen King; Art Adams/Austin-a	4	8	12	23	37	50
404-Miller scripts begin (end 407); Year 1; 1st modern app. Catwoman (2/87)	4	8	12	23	37	50
405-407: 407-Year 1 ends (See Detective Comics #575-578 for Year 2)	3	6	9	14	20	25
408-410: New Origin Jason Todd (Robin)	3	6	9	14	18	22
411-416,421,422,424,425: 411-Two-face app. 412-Origin/1st app. Mime. 414-Starlin scripts begin, end #429. 416-Nightwing-c/story	1	3	4	6	8	10
417-420: "Ten Nights of the Beast" storyline	11	22	33	76	163	250
423-McFarlane-c	2	4	6	11	14	18
426-($1.50, 52 pgs.)- "A Death In The Family" storyline begins, ends #429	4	8	12	22	35	48
427- "A Death In The Family" part 2. (Direct Sales version has inside back-c page for phone poll; newsstand version has an ad on inside back-c and UPC code on front-c)	3	6	9	19	30	40

	GD 2.0	VG 4.0	FN 6.0	VF 8.0	VF/NM 9.0	NM- 9.2
428-Death of Robin (Jason Todd)	4	8	12	25	40	55
429-Joker-c/story; Superman app.	3	6	9	17	26	35
430-435: 433-435-Many Deaths of the Batman story by John Byrne-c/scripts						8
436-Year 3 begins (ends #439); origin original Robin retold by Nightwing (Dick Grayson); 1st app. Timothy Drake 4/87	3	6	9	16	23	30
436-441: 436-2nd printing. 437-Origin Robin cont. 440,441: "A Lonely Place of Dying" Parts 1 & 3	1	2	3	5	6	8
442-1st app. Timothy Drake in Robin costume	2	4	6	11	16	20
443-456,458,459,462-464: 445-447-Batman goes to Russia. 448,449-The Penguin Affair Pts 1 & 3. 450-Origin Joker. 450,451-Joker-c/stories. 452-454-Dark Knight Dark City storyline; Riddler app. 455-Alan Grant scripts begin, ends #466, 470. 464-Last solo Batman story; free 16 pg. preview of Impact Comics line						6.00
457-Timothy Drake officially becomes Robin & dons new costume	3	6	9	16	23	30
457-Direct sale edition (has #000 in indicia)	3	6	9	17	26	35
460,461,465-487: 460,461-Two part Catwoman story. 465-Robin returns to action with Batman. 470-War of the Gods x-over. 475-1st app. Renee Montoya. 475,476-Return of Scarface. 476-Last $1.00-c. 477,478-Photo-c						6.00
488-Cont'd from Detective #4; Azrael-c & app.	1	3	4	6	8	10
489-Bane-c/story; 1st app. Azrael in Bat-costume	2	4	6	10	14	18
490-Riddler-c/story; Azrael & Bane app.	2	4	6	8	10	12
491,492: 491-Knightfall lead-in; Joker-c/story; Azrael & Bane app.; Kelley Jones-c begin. 492-Knightfall part 1; Bane app.	1	3	4	6	8	10
492-Platinum edition (promo copy)	3	6	9	14	19	24
493-496: 493-Knightfall Pt. 3. 494-Knightfall Pt. 5; Joker-c & app. 495-Knightfall Pt. 7; brief Bane & Joker apps. 496-Knightfall Pt. 9, Joker-c/story; Bane cameo	1	2	3	5	6	8
497-(Late 7/93)-Knightfall Pt. 11; Bane breaks Batman's back; B&W outer-c; Aparo-a(p); Giordano-a(i)	3	6	9	14	19	24
497-499: 497-2nd printing. 497-Newsstand edition w/o outer cover. 498-Knightfall part 15; Bane & Catwoman-c & app. (see Showcase 93 #7 & 8) 499-Knightfall Pt. 17; Bane app.						6.00
500-($2.50, 68 pgs.)-Knightfall Pt. 19; Azrael in new Bat-costume; Bane-c/story	1	3	6	9	12	15
500-($3.95, 68 pgs.)-Collector's Edition w/die-cut double-c w/foil by Joe Quesada & 2 bound-in post cards	2	4	6	11	16	20
501-508,510,511: 501-Begin $1.50-c. 501-508-Knightquest. 503,504-Catwoman app. 507-Ballistic app.; Jim Balent(a(p). 510-KnightsEnd Pt. 7. 511-(9/94)-Zero Hour; Batgirl-c/story						5.00
509-($2.50, 52 pgs.)-KnightsEnd Pt. 1	1	2	3	5	6	8
512-514,516-518: 512-(11/94)-Dick Grayson assumes Batman role						5.00
515-Special Ed.($2.50)-Kelley Jones-a begins; all black embossed-c; Troika Pt. 1	1	3	4	6	8	
515-Regular Edition						5.00
519-534,536-549: 519-Begin $1.95-c. 521-Return of Alfred. 522-Swamp Thing app. 525-Mr. Freeze app. 527,528-Two Face app. 529-Contagion Pt. 6. 530-532-Deadman app. 533-Legacy prelude. 534-Legacy Pt. 5. 536-Final Night x-over; Man-Bat-c/app. 540,541-Spectre-c/app. 544-546-Joker & The Demon; 548,549-Penguin-c/app.						5.00
530-532 ($2.50)-Enhanced edition; glow-in-the-dark-c.						6.00
535-(10/96, $2.95)-1st app. The Ogre	1	3	4	6	8	10
535-(10/96, $3.95)-1st app. The Ogre; variant, cardboard, foldout-c						5.00
550-($3.50)-Collector's Ed.; includes 4 collector cards; intro. Chase, return of Clayface; Kelley Jones-c	1	2	3	5	6	8
550-($2.95)-Standard Ed.; Williams & Gray-c						6.00
551-562: 551,552-Ragman c/app. 553-Cataclysm pt.3. 554-Cataclysm pt. 12.						5.00
563-No Man's Land; Joker-c by Campbell; Gale-s	2	4	6	8	11	14
564-566,568,569,571-574: 569-New Batgirl-c/app.						5.00
567-1st Cassandra Cain	4	8	12	27	44	60
570-Joker and Harley Quinn story	3	6	9	16	23	30
575-579: 575-New look Batman begins; McDaniel-a						
580-599: 580-Begin $2.25-c. 587-Gordon shot. 591,592-Deadshot-c/app. 599-Bruce Wayne: Murderer pt. 7						5.00
600-($3.95) Bruce Wayne: Fugitive pt. 1; back-up homage stories in '50s, 60's, & 70s styles; by Aragonés, Gaudiano, Shanower and others	1	2	3	5	6	8
600-(2nd printing)						5.00
601-604, 606,607: 601,603-Bruce Wayne: Fugitive pt.3,13. 606,607-Deadshot-c/app.						5.00
605-($2.95) Conclusion to Bruce Wayne: Fugitive x-over; Noto-c						5.00
608-(12/02) Hush begins; Jim Lee-a/c & Jeph Loeb-s begin; Poison Ivy & Catwoman app.	3	6	9	16	23	30
608-2nd printing; has different cover with Batman standing on gargoyle						160.00
608-Special Edition; has different cover; 200 printed; used for promotional purposes (a CGC certified 9.2 copy sold for $700, and a CGC certified 9.8 copy sold for $2,100)						
608-Special Edition (9/09, $1.00) printing has new "After Watchmen" logo cover frame						8.00
609-Huntress app.	3	6	9	15	22	28
610,611: 610-Killer Croc-c/app.; Batman & Catwoman kiss						
612-Batman vs. Superman; 1st printing with full color cover	2	4	6		10	12
612-2nd printing with B&W sketch cover						26.00
613-Harley Quinn & Joker-c/app.	2	4	6	11	14	18
614-Joker-c/app.	2	4	6	8	10	12
615-617: 615-Reveals ID to Catwoman. 616-Ra's al Ghul app. 617-Scarecrow app.						8.00
618-Batman vs. "Jason Todd"						6.00
619-Newsstand cover; Hush story concludes; Riddler app.						6.00
619-Two variant tri-fold covers; one Heroes group, one Villains group						6.00
619-2nd printing with Riddler chess cover						6.00
620-Broken City pt. 1; Azzarello-s/Risso-a; Killer Croc app.						6.00
621-633: 621-625-Azzarello-s/Risso-a/c. 626-630-Winick-s/Nguyen-a/Wagner-c; Penguin & Scarecrow app. 631-633-War Games. 633-Conclusion to War Games x-over						5.00
634,636,637-Winick-s/Nguyen-a/Wagner-c; Red Hood app. 637-Amazo app.						6.00
635-1st app. Red Hood (later revealed as Jason Todd in #638)	7	14	21	48	89	130
638-Red Hood unmasked as Jason Todd; Nguyen-a	2	4	6	10	14	18
639-650: 640-Superman app. 641-Begin $2.50-c. 643,644-War Crimes; Joker app.						6.00
650-Infinite Crisis; Joker and Jason Todd app.						5.00
651-654-One Year Later; Bianchi-c						6.00
655-Begin Grant Morrison-s/Andy Kubert-a; Kubert-c w/red background	4	8	12	23	37	50
655-Variant cover by Adam Kubert, brown-toned image	6	12	18	41	76	110
656-Intro. Damian, son of Talia and Batman (see Batman: Son of the Demon)	3	6	9	16	24	32
657-Damian in Robin costume	2	4	6	8	11	14
658-665: 659-662-Mandrake-a. 663-Van Fleet-a. 664-Bane app.						5.00
666-Future story of adult Damian; Andy Kubert-a	3	6	9	19	30	40
667-675: 667-669-Williams III-a. 670,671-Resurrection of Ra's al Ghul; Daniel-a. 671-2nd printing						5.00
676-Batman R.I.P. begins; Morrison-s/Daniel-a/Alex Ross-c						10.00
676-Variant-c by Tony Daniel						14.00
676-Second (red-tinted Daniel-c) & third (B&W Daniel-c) printings						4.00
677-685: Batman R.I.P.; Alex Ross-c. 678-Bat-Mite app. 681-($3.99) Batman R.I.P. conclusion. 682-685-Last Rites						5.00
677-Variant-c with Red Hood by Tony Daniel						14.00
677-Second printing with B&W-red-tinted Daniel-c						5.00
686-($3.99) Gaiman-s/Andy Kubert-a; continues in Detective #853; Kubert sketch pgs.; covers by Kubert and Ross; 2nd & 3rd printings exist						6.00
687-($3.99) Batman: Reborn begins; Dick Grayson becomes Batman; Winick-s/Benes-a						6.00
688-699: 688-691-Bagley-a. 692-697,699-Tony Daniel-a/c. 692-Catwoman app.						5.00
700-(8/10, $4.99) Morrison-s; art by Daniel, Quitely, Finch & Andy Kubert; Finch-c						16.00
700-Variant-c by Mignola						60.00
701-712: 701,702-Morrison-s; R.I.P story. 704-Batman Inc. begins; Daniel-s/a						5.00
713-(10/11) Last issue of first volume; Nicieza-s; Robin flashbacks						12.00
#0 (10/94)-Zero Hour issue released between #511 & #512; origin retold						5.00
#1,000,000 (11/98) 853rd Century x-over						5.00
Annual 1 (8-10/61)-Swan-c	62	124	186	496	1123	1750
Annual 2	27	54	81	194	435	675
Annual 3 (Summer, '62)-Joker-c/story	27	54	81	189	420	650
Annual 4,5	15	30	45	100	220	340
Annual 6 (80 pgs., 25¢)	12	24	36	84	185	285
Annual 7 (7/64, 25¢, 80 pgs.)	12	24	36	82	179	275
Annual V5#8 (1982)-Painted-c	2	4	6	8	11	14
Annual 9,10,12; 9(7/85). 10(1986). 12(1988, $1.50)	1	3	4	6	8	10
Annual 11 (1987, $1.25)-Penguin-c/story; Moore-s	2	4	6	8	11	14
Annual 13 (1989, $1.75, 68 pgs.)-Gives history of Bruce Wayne, Dick Grayson, Jason Todd, Alfred, Comm. Gordon, Barbara Gordon (Batgirl) & Vicki Vale; Morrow-i						6.00
Annual 14-17 ('90-'93, 48 pgs.)-14-Origin Two-Face. 15-Armageddon 2001 x-over; Joker app. 15 (2nd printing). 16-Joker-c/s; Kieth-c. 17 (1993, $2.50, 68 pgs.)-Azrael in Bat-costume; intro Ballistic						5.00
Annual 18 (1994, $2.95)						5.00
Annual 19 (1995, $3.95)-Year One story; retells Scarecrow's origin						5.00
Annual 20 (1996, $2.95)-Legends of the Dead Earth story; Giarrano-a						5.00
Annual 21 (1997, $3.95)-Pulp Heroes story						5.00
Annual 22,23 ('98, '99, $2.95)-22-Ghosts; Wrightson-c. 23-JLApe; Art Adams-a						5.00
Annual 24 ('00, $3.50) Planet DC; intro. The Boggart; Aparo-a						5.00
Annual 25 ('06, $4.99) Infinite Crisis-revised story of Jason Todd; unused Aparo page						12.00
Annual 26 ('07, $3.99) Origin of Ra's al Ghul; Damian app.						5.00
Annual 27 ('09, $4.99) Nguyen-a/c Alien app.; Calafiore-a; back-up story w/Kelley Jones-a						5.00
Annual 28 (2/11, $4.99) The Question, Nightrunner and Veil app.; Lau-a						5.00
... No. 1 (Facsimile Edition)(11/23, $6.99) Reprints entire issue with original ads						7.00
... No. 5 (Facsimile Edition) (2/24, $6.99) Reprints entire issue with original ads						7.00
... No. 181 (Facsimile Edition)(2019, $3.99) Reprints Poison Ivy debut with original ads						6.00
... No. 181 (Facsimile Edition) (2/24, $3.99) Reprints Poison Ivy debut with original ads						5.00
... No. 232 (Facsimile Edition) (2019, $3.99) Reprints Ra's al Ghul debut with original ads						10.00
... No. 251 (Facsimile Edition)(2019, $3.99) Reprints Joker issue with original ads						25.00
... No. 357 (Facsimile Edition) (2023, $3.99) Reprints Jason Todd debut with original ads						5.00
... No. 404 (Facsimile Edition) (2/24, $3.99) R/Batman Year One pt. 1 with original ads						4.00
... No. 405 (Facsimile Edition) (2/24, $3.99) R/Batman Year One pt. 2 with original ads						4.00
... No. 406 (Facsimile Edition) (2/24, $3.99) R/Batman Year One pt. 3 with original ads						4.00
... No. 407 (Facsimile Edition) (2/24, $3.99) R/Batman Year One pt. 4 with original ads						4.00
... No. 428: Robin Lives (2/24, $4.99) R/Batman #428 (alternate version) with original ads						4.00
... No. 608 (Facsimile Edition) Batman Day Special Edition (11/23, $9.99) Facsimile of #608; chrome-c						10.00

NOTE: **Art Adams** a-400p; **Neal Adams** c-200, 203, 210, 217, 219-222, 224-227, 229, 230, 232, 234, 236-241, 243-246, 251, 255, Annual 14. **Aparo** a-414-420, 426-435, 440-448, 450, 451, 480-483, 486-491, 494-500; c-414-416, 481, 482, 463i, 486, 487i. **Bolland** a-400; c-445-447. **Burnley** a-10, 12-18, 20, 22, 25, 27; c-9, 15, 16, 27, 28p, 40p, 42p. **Byrne** c-401, 433-435, 533-535, Annual 11. **Travis Charest** c-488-490p. **Colan** a-340, 343-345p, 348-351p, 373p, 383p; c-343p, 345p, 350p. **J. Cole** a-238r. **Cowan** a-Annual 10p. **Golden** a-295p, 303p, 484, 485. **Alan Grant** scripts-455-466, 470, 474-476, 479, 480, Annual 16(part). **Grell** c-287, 288p, 289p, 290; c-287-290. **Infantino/Anderson** c-167, 173, 175, 181, 186, 191, 192, 194, 195, 198. **Infantino/Giella** c-190. **Kelley Jones** a-513-519, 521-525, 527; c-491-499, 500(newsstand), 501-510, 513. **Kaluta** c-242, 248, 253, Annual 12. **G. Kane/Anderson** c-178-180. **Rod Kane** a-1, 2, 5; c-1-5, 7, 17. **G. Kane** a(p)-254, 255, 259, 261, 353i. **Kubert** a-238r, 400; c-310, 319p, 327, 328, 344. **McFarlane** c-423. **Mignola** c-426-429, 452-454, Annual 18. **Moldoff** c-101-140. **Moldoff/Giella** a-164-175, 177-181, 183, 184, 186. **Moldoff/Greene** a-169, 172-174, 177-179, 181, 184. **Mooney** a-255r. **Morrow** a-Annual 13i. **Newton** a-305, 306, 328p, 331p, 332p, 337p, 338p, 346p, 352-357p, 360-372p, 374-378p; c-374p, 378p. **Nino** a-Annual 14. **Novick** c-201, 202. **Perez** a-400; c-436-442. **Fred Ray** c-8, 10; w/Robinson-11. **Robinson/Roussos** a-12-17, 20, 22, 24, 25, 27, 28, 31, 33, 37. **Robinson** a-12, 14, 18, 22-32,34, 36, 37, 255r, 260r, 261r; c-6, 10, 12-14, 18, 21, 24, 26, 30, 37, 39. **Simonson** a-300, 312, 321, 366, 413i. **P. Smith** a-Annual 9. **Dick Sprang** c-19, 20, 22, 23, 25, 29, 31-36, 38, 51, 55, 66, 73, 76. **Starlin** c/a-402. **Staton** a-334. **Sutton** a-400. **Wrightson** a-265i, 400; c-320r. Bat-Hound app. in 92, 97, 103, 123, 125, 133, 156, 158. Bat-Mite app. in 133, 136, 144, 146, 158, 161. Batwoman app. in 105, 116, 122, 125, 128, 129, 131, 133, 139, 140, 141, 144, 145, 150, 151, 153, 154, 157, 159, 162, 163. **Zeck** c-417-420. Catwoman back-ups in 332, 345, 346, 348-351. Joker app. in 1, 2, 4, 5, 7-9, 11-13, 19, 20, 23, 25, 28, 32 & many more. Robin solo back-up stories in 337-339, 341-343.

BATMAN (DC New 52)
DC Comics: Nov. 2011 - No. 52, Jul. 2016 ($2.99/$3.99)

	GD 2.0	VG 4.0	FN 6.0	VF 8.0	VF/NM 9.0	NM- 9.2
1-Snyder-s/Capullo-a/c	4	8	12	23	37	50
1-Variant-c by Van Sciver	3	6	9	21	33	45
1-2nd-5th printings	3	6	9	14	20	25
2-4		3	6	9	12	15
2-5-Variant covers. 2-Jim Lee. 3-Ivan Reis. 4-Mike Choi, 5-Burnham. 6-Gary Frank	2	4	6	8	12	15
5-7-Court of Owls. 7-Debut Harper Row	2	4	6	9	12	15
5-7 Combo Pack ($3.99) polybagged with digital download code						6.00
8-11: 8-Begin $3.99-c. 8,9-Night of the Owls. 11-Court of the Owls finale						6.00
12-Story of Harper Row; Cloonan-a						5.00
13-Death of the Family; Joker and Harley Quinn app.; die-cut-c						5.00

Batman #686 © DC
Batman (2011 series) #38 © DC

Batman (2016 series) #118 © DC

	GD 2.0	VG 4.0	FN 6.0	VF 8.0	VF/NM 9.0	NM- 9.2

```
                                                    2    4    6    8    11   14
14-20: 14-17-Death of the Family. 17-Death of the Family conclusion. 18-Andy Kubert-a   5.00
21-Zero Year begins; 1st app. Duke Thomas (unnamed)
                                                    1    3    4    6    8    10
22,23                                               5.00
23.1, 23.2, 23.3, 23.4 (11/13, $2.99, regular covers)   4.00
23.1 (11/13, $3.99, 3-D cover) "Joker #1" on cover; Andy Kubert-s/Andy Clarke-a   12.00
23.2 (11/13, $3.99, 3-D cover) "Riddler #1" on cover; Jeremy Haun-a   8.00
23.3 (11/13, $3.99, 3-D cover) "Penguin #1" on cover; Tieri-s/Duce-a/Fabok-c   8.00
23.4 (11/13, $3.99, 3-D cover) "Bane #1" on cover; Nolan-a/March-c   8.00
24-(12/13, $6.99) Batman vs. Red Hood at Ace Chemicals re-told; Dark City begins   10.00
24-New York Comic Con variant with Detective #27 cover swipe
                                                    3    6    9    15   22   28
25,29,33-($4.99) 25-All black cover: Doctor Death app. 33-Zero Year finale   6.00
26-28,30-32,34: 28-Nguyen-a; Harper Row as Bluebird; Stephanie Brown returns   4.00
35-($4.99) Endgame pt. 1; Justice League app.; back-up with Kelley Jones   5.00
36-39-Endgame; Joker app.; (back-up stories in each; 37-McCrea-a, 38-Kieth-a, 39-Nguyen)
   39-Alfred attacked   4.00
40-($4.99) Endgame conclusion   5.00
41-43,45-49,51,52: 41-Gordon dons the robot suit. 49-Paquette-a. 52-Tynion-s   4.00
44-($4.99) Snyder & Azzarello-s/Jock-a   5.00
50-($5.99) Bruce Wayne back as Batman; new costume   6.00
#0 (11/12, $3.99) Flashbacks; Red Hood gang app.   5.00
Annual 1 (7/12, $4.99) Origin of Mr. Freeze; Snyder-s/Fabok-c
                                                    2    4    6    9    12   15
Annual 2 (9/13, $4.99) Origin of the Anchoress; Jock-a   6.00
Annual 3 (2/15, $4.99) Joker app.; Tynion-s/Antonio-a/Albuquerque-c   5.00
Annual 4 (11/15, $4.99) Joker app.; Tynion-s/Antonio-a/Murphy-c   5.00
... Endgame 40 Director's Cut 1 (1/16, $5.99) Pencil art and original script for #40   6.00
...: Futures End 1 (11/14, $2.99, regular-c) Five years later; Fawkes-s; Bizarro app.   3.00
...: Futures End 1 (11/14, $3.99, 3-D cover)   4.00
... Zero Year Director's Cut (9/13, $5.99) Reprints Batman #21 original pencil art pages with
   word balloons; Scott Snyder's script   6.00
```

BATMAN (DC Rebirth)
DC Comics: Aug, 2016 - Present ($2.99/$3.99/$4.99)

```
1-King/Finch-a/c; intro. Gotham and Gotham Girl   1    2    3    5    6    8
1-Director's Cut (1/17, $9.99) r/#1 in pencil-a; original script; variant cover gallery   6.00
2-20: 2-Hugo Strange app. 3-Psycho Pirate returns. 5-Justice League app. 7,8-Night of the
   Monster Men x-overs; Batwoman & Nightwing app. 9-13-I Am Suicide; Bane app.   3.00
21,22-The Button x-over with Flash #21,22; Eobard Thawne & Flashpoint Batman app.   3.00
23,24: 23-Swamp Thing app. 24-Batman proposes to Catwoman   3.00
25-($3.99) War of Jokes and Riddles part 1; Joker & Riddler app.   4.00
26-35,38-49: 26-32-War of Jokes and Riddles. 27-Kite Man app. 33-35,39,40,44-Joëlle
   Jones-a. 42-Justice League app. 45-47-Booster Gold app.   3.00
36,37-Superman & Lois app.; Clay Mann-a   3.00
50-(4/18, $4.99) The Wedding; art by Janin with pages by Adams, Miller, Kubert, Sale,
   Conner, Garcia-Lopez, Finch, Jim Lee, Capullo, Cloonan, Fabok and others   5.00
51-74: 51-53-Weeks-a; trial of Mr. Freeze. 54-Wagner-a. 55-Nightwing shot. 64,65-X-over
   with Flash #64,65; tie-in to Heroes in Crisis. 67-Weeks-a. 68-Conner-a   4.00
75-($4.99) City of Bane part 1; Gotham Girl app.; Daniel-a   4.00
76-84-City of Bane. 77-Alfred killed by Bane. 80,81-Romita Jr.-a. 82-Acetate-c   4.00
85-($4.99) City of Bane conclusion   5.00
86-88,90,91,93,94: 86-Tynion IV-s begin; Deathstroke & Cheshire app.; 1st app. the
   Nightclimber. 91,93-Harley Quinn app. 93,94-Joker and Punchline app.   4.00
89-1st app. Punchline in cameo; intro. The Designer   4    8    12   25   40   55
92-1st full app. Punchline in title; Joker & Harley app.   1    2    3    5    6    8
95-99-Joker War: War-1st app. Clownhunter   4.00
100-(Early 12/20, $6.99) Conclusion to Joker War; intro. The Ghost-Maker   7.00
101-105: 101-Grifter app. 102-105-The Ghost-Maker & Clownhunter app.   4.00
106-124,126-134-($4.99) 106-Back-up Robin story. 107-109-Backup Ghost-Maker.
   108-Debut of Miracle Molly. 112-117-Fear State. 118-Williamson-s begins   5.00
125-(9/22, $5.99) Zdarsky-s/Jimenez-a begins; intro Failsafe; back-up Catwoman story   6.00
135-(9/22, $6.99) Legacy 900th issue; multiverse Batmen app.   7.00
136-145: 137,138-Gotham War tie-ins; Vandal Savage app. 142-144-Joker Year One   5.00
Annual 1 (1/17, $4.99) Short stories by various incl. Adams, Dini, Snyder, Finch; Finch-c   5.00
Annual 2 (1/18, $4.99) King-s/Weeks & Lark-a; Batman & Catwoman's early encounters   5.00
Annual 3 (2/19, $4.99) Taylor-s/Schmidt-a; spotlight on Alfred   5.00
Annual 4 (2/20, $4.99) King-s/Fornes & Norton-a; Alfred's diary of Batman's exploits   5.00
2021 Annual 1 (1/22, $5.99) Ghost-Maker saga concludes; Tynion IV-s/Ortiz-a   6.00
2022 Annual 1 (7/22, $5.99) Ghost-Maker takes over Batman Inc.; Brisson-s/Timms-a   6.00
...: Rebirth 1 (8/16, $2.99) King & Snyder-s/Janin-a; Duke Thomas & Calendar Man app.   3.00
```

BATMAN (Hardcover books and trade paperbacks)
...: ABSOLUTION (2002, $24.95)-Hard-c.; DeMatteis/Ashmore painted-a   25.00

```
...: ABSOLUTION (2003, $17.95)-Soft-c.; DeMatteis-s/Ashmore painted-a   18.00
...: A LONELY PLACE OF DYING (1990, $3.95, 132 pgs.)-r/Batman #440-442 & New Titans
   #60,61; Perez-c   18.00
...: ANARKY TPB (1999, $12.95) r/early appearances   18.00
...AND DRACULA: RED RAIN nn (1991, $24.95)-Hard-c; Elseworlds storyline   35.00
...AND DRACULA: RED RAIN nn (1992, $9.95)-SC   12.00
...AND SON HC (2007, $24.99, dustjacket) r/Batman #655-658,663-666   25.00
...AND SON SC (2008, $14.99) r/Batman #655-658,663-666   15.00
...ANNUALS (See DC Comics Classics Library for reprints of early Annuals)
ARKHAM ASYLUM Hard-c; Morrison-s/McKean-a (1989, $24.95)   30.00
ARKHAM ASYLUM Soft-c ($14.95)   20.00
ARKHAM ASYLUM 15TH ANNIVERSARY EDITION Hard-c (2004, $29.95) reprint with
   Morrison's script and annotations, original page layouts; Karen Berger afterword   30.00
ARKHAM ASYLUM 15TH ANNIVERSARY EDITION Soft-c (2005, $17.99)   18.00
... AS THE CROW FLIES-(2004, $12.95) r/#626-630; Nguyen sketch pages   13.00
BIRTH OF THE DEMON Hard-c (1992, $24.95)-Origin of Ra's al Ghul   40.00
BIRTH OF THE DEMON Soft-c (1993, $12.95)   20.00
BLIND JUSTICE nn (1992, $7.50)-r/Det. #598-600   12.00
BLOODSTORM (1994, $24.95,HC) Kelley Jones-c/a   28.00
BRIDE OF THE DEMON Hard-c (1990. $.95)   25.00
BRIDE OF THE DEMON Soft-c ($12.95)   15.00
...: BROKEN CITY HC (2003, $24.95) r/#620-625; new Johnson-c; intro by Schreck   25.00
...: BROKEN CITY SC-(2004, $14.99) r/#620-625; new Johnson-c; intro by Schreck   15.00
...: BRUCE WAYNE: FUGITIVE Vol. 1 ('02, $12.95)-r/ story arc   15.00
...: BRUCE WAYNE: FUGITIVE Vol. 2 ('03, $12.95)-r/ story arc   15.00
...: BRUCE WAYNE: FUGITIVE Vol. 3 ('03, $12.95)-r/ story arc   15.00
...: BRUCE WAYNE-MURDERER? ('02, $19.95)-r/ story arc   25.00
...: BRUCE WAYNE - THE ROAD HOME HC ('11, $24.99) r/Bruce Wayne: The Road Home
   one-shots   25.00
...: CATACLYSM ('99, $17.95)-r/ story arc   30.00
...: CHILD OF DREAMS (2003, $24.95, B&W, HC) Reprint of Japanese manga with Kia
   Asamiya-s/a/c; English adaptation by Max Allan Collins; Asamiya interview   25.00
...: CHILD OF DREAMS (2003, $19.95, B&W, SC)   20.00
...CHRONICLES VOL. 1 (2005, $14.99)-r/apps. in Detective Comics #27-38; Batman #1   15.00
...CHRONICLES VOL. 2 (2006, $14.99)-r/apps. in Detective Comics #39-45 and NY World's
   Fair 1940; Batman #2,3   15.00
...CHRONICLES VOL. 3 (2007, $14.99)-r/apps. in Detective Comics #46-50 and World's Best
   Comics #1; Batman #4,5   15.00
...CHRONICLES VOL. 4 (2007, $14.99)-r/apps. in Detective Comics #51-56 and World's
   Finest Comics #2,3; Batman #6,7   15.00
...CHRONICLES VOL. 5 (2008, $14.99)-r/apps. in Detective Comics #57-61 and World's
   Finest Comics #4; Batman #8,9   15.00
...CHRONICLES VOL. 6 (2008, $14.99)-r/apps. in Detective Comics #62-65 and World's
   Finest Comics #5,6; Batman #10,11   15.00
...CHRONICLES VOL. 7 (2009, $14.99)-r/apps. in Detective Comics #66-70 and World's
   Finest Comics #7; Batman #12,13   15.00
...CHRONICLES VOL. 8 (2009, $14.99)-r/apps. in Detective Comics #71-74 and World's
   Finest Comics #8; Batman #14,15   15.00
...CHRONICLES VOL. 9 (2010, $14.99)-r/apps. in Detective Comics #75-77 and World's
   Finest Comics #10; Batman #16,17   15.00
...CHRONICLES VOL. 10 (2010, $14.99)-r/apps. in Detective Comics #78-81 and World's
   Finest Comics #11; Batman #18,19   15.00
...: CITY OF CRIME (2006, $19.99) r/Detective Comics #800-808,811-814; Lapham-s   20.00
...: COLLECTED LEGENDS OF THE DARK KNIGHT nn (1994, $12.95)-r/Legends of the
   Dark Knight #32-34,38,42,43   18.00
...: CRIMSON MIST (1999, $24.95,HC)-Vampire Batman Elseworlds story
   Doug Moench/Kelley Jones-c/a   50.00
...: CRIMSON MIST (2001, $14.95,SC)   20.00
...: DARK JOKER-THE WILD (1993, $24.95,HC)-Elseworlds story; Moench-s/Jones-c/a   25.00
...: DARK JOKER-THE WILD (1993, $9.95,SC)   12.00
...DARK KNIGHT DYNASTY nn (1997, $24.95)-Hard-c.; 3 Elseworlds stories; Barr-s/
   S. Hampton painted-a, Gary Frank, McDaniel-a(p)   28.00
...DARK KNIGHT DYNASTY Softcover (2000, $14.95) Hampton-c   15.00
...: DEADMAN: DEATH AND GLORY nn (1996, $24.95)-Hard-c.; Robinson-s/ Estes-c/a   32.00
...: DEADMAN: DEATH AND GLORY ($12.95)-SC   18.00
DEATH AND THE CITY (2007, $14.99, TPB)-r/Detective #827-834   15.00
DEATH BY DESIGN (2012, $24.99, HC)-Chip Kidd-s/Dave Taylor-s   25.00
DEATH IN THE FAMILY (1988, $3.95, trade paperback)-r/Batman #426-429 by Aparo   20.00
DEATH IN THE FAMILY: (2nd -5th printings)   9.00
...: DETECTIVE (2007, $14.99) r/Detective Comics #821-826   15.00
...: DETECTIVE #27 HC (2003, $19.95)-Elseworlds; Uslan-s/Snejbjerg-a   20.00
...: DETECTIVE #27 SC (2004, $12.95)-Elseworlds; Uslan-s/Snejbjerg-a   13.00
DIGITAL JUSTICE nn (1990, $24.95, Hard-c.)-Computer generated art   25.00
...: EARTH ONE HC (2012, $22.99)-Updated re-imagining of Batman's origin & debut;
   Geoff Johns-s/Gary Frank-a   23.00
```

	GD	VG	FN	VF	VF/NM	NM-
	2.0	4.0	6.0	8.0	9.0	9.2

... : EGO AND OTHER TALES HC (2007, $24.99)-r/Batman: Ego, Catwoman: Selina's Big
Score, and stories from Batman Black and White and Solo; Darwyn Cooke-s/a 25.00
... : EGO AND OTHER TALES SC (2008, $17.99) same contents as HC 18.00
... :EVOLUTION (2001, $12.95, SC)-r/Detective Comics #743-750 13.00
... FACES (1995, $9.95, TPB) r/Legends of the Dark Knight #28-30 13.00
... FACES (2008, $12.99, TPB) Second printing 13.00
... FACE THE FACE (2006, $14.99, TPB)-r/Batman #651-654, Detective #817-820 15.00
... FALSE FACES HC (2008, $19.99)-r/Batman #588-590, Wonder Woman #160,161;
Batman: Gotham City Secret Files #1 and Detective #787; Brian K. Vaughn intro. 20.00
... : FALSE FACES SC (2008, $14.99)-r/Batman #588-590, Wonder Woman #160,161;
Batman: Gotham City Secret Files #1 and Detective #787; Brian K. Vaughn intro. 15.00
... FORTUNATE SON HC (1999, $24.95) Gene Ha-a 25.00
... FORTUNATE SON SC (2000, $14.95) Gene Ha-a 15.00
FOUR OF A KIND TPB (1998, $14.95)-r/1995 Year One Annuals featuring Poison Ivy, Riddler,
Scarecrow, & Man-Bat 35.00
... GOING SANE (2008, $14.95, TPB) r/Legends of the Dark Knight #65-68,200 15.00
... GOTHAM BY GASLIGHT (2006, $12.99, TPB) r/Gotham By Gaslight & Master of the
Future one-shots; Elseworlds Batman vs. Jack the Ripper 13.00
... GOTHIC (1992, $12.95, TPB)-r/Legends of the Dark Knight #6-10 20.00
... GOTHIC (2007, $14.99, TPB)-r/Legends of the Dark Knight #6-10 15.00
... HARVEST BREED-(2000, $24.95) George Pratt-s/painted-a 25.00
... HARVEST BREED-(2003, $17.95) George Pratt-s/painted-a 18.00
... HAUNTED KNIGHT-(1997, $12.95) r/ Halloween specials 18.00
... HEART OF HUSH HC-(2009, $19.99) r/#Detective #846-850; pin-ups 20.00
... HEART OF HUSH SC-(2010, $14.99) r/#Detective #846-850; pin-ups 15.00
... HONG KONG HC (2003, $24.95) Doug Moench-s/Tony Wong-a 25.00
... HONG KONG SC (2004, $17.95) Doug Moench-s/Tony Wong-a 18.00
... HUSH DOUBLE FEATURE-(2003, $3.95) r/#608,609(1st 2 Jim Lee-a issues) 6.00
... HUSH SC-(2009, $24.99) r/#608-619; Wizard 0; variant cover gallery; Loeb intro 25.00
... HUSH UNWRAPPED-(2011, $39.99, HC) r/#608-619's original Jin Lee pencil art 40.00
... HUSH VOLUME 1 HC-(2003, $19.95) r/#608-612; & new 2 pg. origin w/Lee-a 20.00
... HUSH VOLUME 1 SC-(2004, $12.95) r/#608-612; includes CD of DC GN art 13.00
... HUSH VOLUME 2 HC-(2003, $19.95) r/#613-619; Lee intro & sketchpages 20.00
... HUSH VOLUME 2 SC-(2004, $12.95) r/#613-619; Lee intro & sketchpages 13.00
... ILLUSTRATED BY NEAL ADAMS VOLUME 1 HC-(2003, $49.95) r/Batman, Brave and the
Bold, and Detective Comics stories and covers 50.00
... ILLUSTRATED BY NEAL ADAMS VOLUME 2 HC-(2004, $49.95) r/Adams' Batman art from
1969-71; intro. by Dick Giordano 50.00
... ILLUSTRATED BY NEAL ADAMS VOLUME 3 HC-(2004, $49.95) r/Adams' Batman art from
1971-74; covers, pin-ups and design art; intro. by Denny O'Neil 50.00
... IMPOSTERS TPB (2011, $14.99) r/Detective Comics #867-870 15.00
... INTERNATIONAL TPB (2010, $17.99) R/Batman: Scottish Connection, Batman in
Barcelona: Dragon's Knight and Batman: Legends of the DK #52,53; Jim Lee-c 18.00
... IN THE FORTIES TPB ($19.95) Intro. by Bill Schelly 20.00
... IN THE FIFTIES TPB ($19.95) Intro. by Michael Uslan 20.00
... IN THE SIXTIES TPB ($19.95) Intro. by Adam West 20.00
... IN THE SEVENTIES TPB ($19.95) Intro. by Dennis O'Neil 20.00
... IN THE EIGHTIES TPB ($19.95) Intro. by John Wells 20.00
... / JUDGE DREDD FILES (2004, $14.95) reprints cross-overs 15.00
... KING TUT'S TOMB TPB (2010, $14.99) r/Batman Confidential #26-28, Batman #353 and
Brave and the Bold #164,171 15.00
... LEGACY-(1996, $17.95) reprints Legacy 30.00
... LIFE AFTER DEATH HC-(2010, $19.99, dustjacket) r/#Batman #692-699 20.00
... LONG SHADOWS HC-(2010, $19.99, dustjacket) r/#Batman #687-691 20.00
... LONG SHADOWS SC-(2011, $14.99, TPB) r/#Batman #687-691 15.00
... LOVERS & MADMEN-(See Batman Confidential)
... MAD LOVE AND OTHER STORIES HC (2009, $19.99) r/Batman Adventures: Mad Love,
Batman Advs. Holiday Special and other Dini/Timm collaborations; commentary 20.00
... : THE MANY DEATHS OF THE BATMAN (1992, $3.95, 84 pgs.)-r/Batman #433-435
w/new Byrne-c 12.00
... MONSTERS (2009, $19.99, TPB)-r/Legends of the Dark Knight #71-73,83,84,89,90 20.00
... THE MOVIES (1997, $19.95)-r/movie adaptations of Batman, Batman Returns,
Batman Forever, Batman and Robin 30.00
... NINE LIVES HC (2002, $24.95, sideways format) Motter-s/Lark-a 25.00
... NINE LIVES SC (2003, $17.95, sideways format) Motter-s/Lark-a 18.00
... OFFICER DOWN (2001, $12.95)-r/Commissioner shot x-over; Talon-c 13.00
... / PLANETARY DELUXE HC (2011, $22.99)-r/Planetary/Batman: Night on Earth; script 23.00
... PREY (1992, $12.95) Gulacy/Austin-a 24.00
... PRIVATE CASEBOOK HC (2008, $19.99)-r/Detective Comics #840-845 and story from
DC Infinite Halloween Special #1 20.00
... PRODIGAL (1997, $14.95) Gulacy/Austin-a 30.00
... R.I.P.: THE DELUXE EDITION HC (2009, $24.99)-r/Batman #676-683 and story from
DC Universe #0 25.00
... R.I.P. SC (2010, $14.99)-r/Batman #676-683 and story from DC Universe #0 15.00
... SCARECROW TALES (2005, $19.99, TPB) r/Scarecrow stories & pin-ups from World's
Finest #3 to present 20.00
... SECRETS OF THE BATCAVE (2007, $17.99, TPB) r/Batcave stories 18.00
... SHAMAN (1993, $12.95)-r/Legends/D.K. #1-5 55.00
... SNOW (2007, $14.99, TPB)-r/Legends of the Dark Knight #192-196; Fisher-a 15.00
... SON OF THE DEMON Hard-c (9/87, $14.95) (see Batman #655-658) 35.00
... SON OF THE DEMON limited signed & numbered Hard-c (1,700) 60.00
... SON OF THE DEMON Soft-c w/new-c ($8.95) 12.00
... SON OF THE DEMON Soft-c (1989, $9.95, 2nd printing - 5th printing) 10.00
... STRANGE APPARITIONS ($12.95) r/'77-'78 Englehart/Rogers stories from
Detective #469-479; also Simonson-a 30.00
TALES OF THE DEMON (1991, $17.95, 212 pgs.)-Intro by Sam Hamm; reprints by Neal
Adams(3) & Golden; contains Saga of Ra's al Ghul #1 20.00
TALES OF THE MULTIVERSE: BATMAN - VAMPIRE (2007, $19.99) r/Batman & Dracula: Red
Rain, Batman: Bloodstorm and Batman: Crimson Mist; Van Lustbader foreword 20.00
... TEN NIGHTS OF THE BEAST (1994, $5.95)-r/Batman #417-420 18.00
... TERROR (2003, $12.95, TPB)-r/Legends of the Dark Knight #137-141; Gulacy-c 13.00
... THE BLACK GLOVE (2009, $17.99, TPB) r/Batman #667-669,672-675 18.00
... THE CHALICE (HC, '99, $24.95) Van Fleet painted-a 25.00
... THE CHALICE (SC, '00, $14.95) Van Fleet painted-a 15.00
... THE GREATEST STORIES EVER TOLD (2005, $19.99, TPB) Les Daniels intro. 20.00
... THE GREATEST STORIES EVER TOLD VOLUME TWO (2007, $19.99, TPB) 20.00
... THE JOKER'S LAST LAUGH ('08, $17.99) r/Joker's Last Laugh series #1-6 18.00

... THE LAST ANGEL (1994, $12.95, TPB) Lustbader-s 15.00
... THE RESURRECTION OF RA'S AL GHUL (2008, $29.99, HC w/DJ) r/x-over 30.00
... THE RESURRECTION OF RA'S AL GHUL (2009, $19.99, SC) r/x-over 20.00
... THE RING, THE ARROW AND THE BAT (2003, $19.99) r/Legends of the DCU #7-9
& Batman: Legends of the Dark Knight #127-131; Green Lantern & Green Arrow app. 20.00
... THE STRANGE DEATHS OF BATMAN ('09, $19.99) r/Batman #291-294, Det. #347,
World's Finest #184,269, Brave & the #115, Nightwing #52; Aparo-a 20.00
... THE WORLD ('21, $24.99) New stories set around the world by non-American creators
incl. Bermejo, Kowalski, Mauro, Valdés, Jaekwang Park, Qiu Kun 25.00
... THE WRATH ('09, $17.99) r/Batman Special #1 and Batman Confidential #13-16 18.00
... THRILLKILLER (1998, $12.95, TPB)-r/series & Thrillkiller '62 20.00
... TIME AND THE BATMAN HC ('11, $19.99)-r/Batman #700-703; cover gallery 20.00
... TWO-FACE AND SCARECROW YEAR ONE (2009, $19.99, TPB)-r/Year One: Batman
Scarecrow #1,2 and Two Face: Year One #1,2 20.00
... UNDER THE COWL (2010, $17.99, TPB)-r/app. Dick Grayson, Tim Drake, Damian Wayne,
Jean Paul Valley and Terry McGinnis as Batman 18.00
... UNDER THE HOOD (2005, $9.99, TPB)-r/Batman #635-641 10.00
... UNDER THE HOOD Vol. 2 (2006, $9.99, TPB)-r/Batman #645-650 & Annual #25 10.00
... UNDER THE RED HOOD (2011, $29.99, TPB)-r/Batman #635-641,645-650, Ann. #25 30.00
... VENOM (1993, $9.95, TPB)-r/Legends of the Dark Knight #16-20; embossed-c 25.00
... VS. TWO-FACE (2008, $19.99, TPB) r/initial (Det. #80) & classic battles; Bianchi-c 20.00
... WAR CRIMES (2006, $12.99, TPB) r/x-over; James Jean-c 13.00
... WAR DRUMS (2004, $17.95) r/Detective #790-796 & Robin #126-128 18.00
... WAR GAMES ACT 1,2,3 (2005, $14.95/$14.99, TPB) r/x-over; James Jean-c; each.. 15.00
... WHATEVER HAPPENED TO THE CAPED CRUSADER? HC-(2009, $24.99, d.j.) r/Batman
#686, Detective #853 and other Gaiman Batman stories; Gaiman intro.; Andy Kubert
sketch pages; new Kubert cover 25.00
... WHATEVER HAPPENED TO THE CAPED CRUSADER? SC-(2010, $14.99) 15.00
YEAR ONE Hard-c (1988, $12.95) r/Batman #404-407 20.00
YEAR ONE (1988, $9.95, TPB)-r/Batman #404-407 by Miller; intro by Miller 15.00
YEAR ONE (TPB, 2nd & 3rd printings) 10.00
YEAR ONE Deluxe HC (2005, $19.99, die-cut d.j.) new intro. by Miller and developmental
material from Mazzucchelli; script pages and sketches 20.00
YEAR ONE (Deluxe) SC (2007, $14.99) r/story plus bonus material from 2005 HC 15.00
YEAR TWO (1990, $9.95, TPB)-r/Det. 575-578 by McFarlane; wraparound-c 15.00

BATMAN (one-shots)
... ABDUCTION, THE (1998, $5.95) 10.00
... ALLIES SECRET FILES AND ORIGINS 2005 (8/05, $4.99) stories/pin-ups by various 5.00
... & ROBIN (1997, $5.95)-Movie adaptation 6.00
... : ARKHAM ASYLUM - TALES OF MADNESS (5/98, $2.95) Cataclysm x-over pt. 16 8.00
... : BANE (1997, $4.95)-Dixon-s/Burchett-a; Stelfreeze-c; cover art interlocks
w/Batman:(Batgirl, Mr. Freeze, Poison Ivy) 10.00
... : BATGIRL (1997, $4.95)-Puckett-s/Haley,Kesel-a; Stelfreeze-c; cover art interlocks
w/Batman:(Bane, Mr. Freeze, Poison Ivy) 10.00
... : BATGIRL (6/98, $1.95)-Girlfrenzy; Balent-a 6.00
... : BLACKGATE (1/97, $3.95) Dixon-s 6.00
... : BLACKGATE - ISLE OF MEN (4/98, $2.95) Cataclysm x-over pt. 8; Moench-s/Aparo-a 4.00
... BOOK OF SHADOWS, THE (1999, $5.95) 8.00
... BROTHERHOOD OF THE BAT (1995, $5.95)-Elseworlds-s 8.00
... BULLOCK'S LAW (8/99, $4.95) Dixon-s 5.00
... /CAPTAIN AMERICA (1996, $5.95, DC/Marvel) Elseworlds story; Byrne-c/s/a 15.00
... : CASTLE OF THE BAT (1994, $5.95)-Elseworlds story 8.00
... : CATWOMAN DEFIANT nn (1992, $4.95, prestige format)-Milligan scripts; cover art
interlocks w/Batman: (Penguin Triumphant; special foil logo 10.00
... /CATWOMAN: FOLLOW THE MONEY (1/11, $4.99) Chaykin-c/s/a 8.00
... /DANGER GIRL (2/05, $4.95)-Leinil Yu-a/c; Joker, Harley Quinn & Catwoman app. 8.00
... /DAREDEVIL (2000, $5.95)-Barreto-a 12.00
... : DARK ALLEGIANCES (1996, $5.95)-Elseworlds story, Chaykin-c/a 8.00
... : DARK KNIGHT GALLERY (1/96, $3.50)-Pin-ups by Pratt, Balent, & others 8.00
... :DAY OF JUDGMENT (11/99, $3.95) 5.00
... : DAY SPECIAL EDITION 1 (10/17, giveaway) r/Batman #16 (2017) with Harley Quinn
framing pages by Palmiotti & Conner; Blevins-a 3.00
... :DEAR DETECTIVE (2022, $7.99)-Lee Bermejo's Batman covers reprinted w/new story 8.00
... :DEATH OF INNOCENTS (12/96, $3.95)-O'Neil-s/ Staton-a(p) 8.00
... :DEMON (1996, $4.95)-Alan Grant scripts 8.00
... :DEMON: A TRAGEDY (2000, $5.95)-Grant-s/Murray painted-a 12.00
... :D.O.A. (1999, $6.95)-Bob Hall-s/a 7.00
... :DOC SAVAGE SPECIAL (2010, $4.99)-Azzarello-s/Noto-a/covers by JG Jones & Morales;
preview of First Wave line (Batman, Doc Savage, The Spirit, Blackhawks) 5.00
... :DREAMLAND (2000, $5.95)-Grant-s/Breyfogle-a 6.00
... : EGO (2000, $6.95)-Darwyn Cooke-s/a 7.00
... : 80-PAGE GIANT (8/98, $4.95) Stelfreeze-c 6.00
... : 80-PAGE GIANT 2 (2/10, $5.99) Andy Kubert-c; Catwoman, Poison Ivy app. 6.00
... : 80-PAGE GIANT 2 (10/99, $4.95) Luck of the Draw 6.00
... : 80-PAGE GIANT 3 (7/00, $5.95) Calendar Man 6.00
... : 80-PAGE GIANT 2011 (11/11, $5.99) Nguyen-c; short stories of villains by various 6.00
... : 80-PAGE GIANT 2011 (10/11, $5.99) Nguyen-c; art by Naifeh & others 6.00
... :ELMER FUDD SPECIAL 1 (8/17, $4.99) Tom King-s/Lee Weeks-a; cartoony back-up
with Bugs Bunny; King-s/Vaughns-a 18.00
... /ELMER FUDD SPECIAL 1 (10/17, $4.99) 2nd printing; brighter red bkgd on cover 8.00
... : FAZE CLAN 1 (5/22, $3.99) Trujillo-s/Eaton-a; real life gamer group app. 4.00
... : FOREVER (1995, $5.95, direct market) 8.00
... : FOREVER (1995, $3.95, newsstand) 6.00
FULL CIRCLE nn (1991, $5.95, 68 pgs.)-Sequel to Batman: Year Two 10.00
... GALLERY, The 1 (1992, $2.95)-Pin-ups by Miller, N. Adams & others 5.00
... GOLDEN STREETS OF GOTHAM (2003, $6.95) Elseworlds in early 1900s 14.00
... GOTHAM BY GASLIGHT (1989, $3.95) Elseworlds; Mignola-a/Augustyn-s 14.00
GOTHAM CITY SECRET FILES 1 (4/00, $4.95) Batgirl app. 6.00
... GOTHAM NOIR (2001, $6.95)-Elseworlds; Brubaker-s/Phillips-c/a 28.00
... /GREEN ARROW: THE POISON TOMORROW nn (1992, $5.95, square-bound, 68 pgs.)
Netzer-c/a 8.00
... HALLOWEEN COMIC FEST SPECIAL EDITION 1 (11/17, giveaway) r/Batman #7 ('16) 3.00
... HIDDEN TREASURES 1 (12/10, $4.99) unpubl. story Wrightson-a; r/Swamp Thing #7 5.00
HOLY TERROR nn (1991, $4.95, 52 pgs.)-Elseworlds story 8.00
... :HOUDINI: THE DEVIL'S WORKSHOP (1993, $5.95) 10.00
... :HUNTRESS/SPOILER - BLUNT TRAUMA (5/98, $2.95) Cataclysm pt. 13;
Dixon-s/Barreto & Sienkiewicz-a 4.00

Batman R.I.P. HC © DC

Batman: Penguin Triumphant #1 © DC

Batman Adventures #28 © DC

	GD	VG	FN	VF	VF/NM	NM-
	2.0	4.0	6.0	8.0	9.0	9.2

...: I, JOKER nn (1998, $4.95)-Elseworlds story; Bob Hall-s/a						8.00
... IN BARCELONA: DRAGON'S KNIGHT 1 (7/09, $3.99) Waid-s/Olmos-a/Jim Lee-c						4.00
... IN DARKEST KNIGHT nn (1994, $4.95, 52 pgs.)-Elseworlds story; Batman						
w/Green Lantern's ring.						10.00
...JOKER'S APPRENTICE (5/99, $3.95) Von Eeden-a						5.00
...JOKER'S DAUGHTER (4/14, $4.99) Bennett-s/Hetrick-a/Jeanty-c						5.00
.../ JOKER: SWITCH (2003, $6.95)-Bolton-a/Grayson-s						7.00
...JUDGE DREDD: JUDGEMENT ON GOTHAM nn (1991, $5.95, 68 pgs.) Simon Bisley-c/a;						
Grant/Wagner scripts						8.00
...JUDGE DREDD: JUDGEMENT ON GOTHAM nn (2nd printing)						6.00
...JUDGE DREDD: THE ULTIMATE RIDDLE (1995, $4.95)						6.00
...JUDGE DREDD: VENDETTA IN GOTHAM (1993, $5.95)						7.00
...KNIGHTGALLERY (1995, $3.50)-Elseworlds sketchbook.						4.00
... – KNIGHTWATCH BATMAN DAY SPECIAL EDITION 1 (11/21, giveaway) Torres-s						3.00
...LEGENDS OF GOTHAM (3/23, $5.99) Katana, Red Hood & Black Lightning app.						6.00
...LOBO (2000, $5.95)-Elseworlds; Joker app.; Bisley-a						6.00
...: MASK OF THE PHANTASM (1994, $2.95)-Movie adapt.						15.00
...: MASK OF THE PHANTASM (1994, $4.95)-Movie adapt.						20.00
...: MASQUE (1997, $6.95)-Elseworlds; Grell-c/s-a						7.00
...: MASTER OF THE FUTURE nn (1991, $5.95, 68 pgs.)-Elseworlds; sequel to Gotham By						
Gaslight; Barreto-a; embossed-c						6.00
...MITEFALL (1995, $4.95)-Alan Grant script, Kevin O'Neill-a						6.00
...: MR. FREEZE (1997, $4.95)-Dini-s/Buckingham-a; Stelfreeze-c; cover art interlocks						
w/Batman:(Bane, Batgirl, Poison Ivy)						10.00
.../NIGHTWING: BLOODBORNE (2002, $5.95) Cypress-a; McKeever-c						6.00
...NOEL (2011, $22.99, HC graphic novel with dustjacket) Lee Bermejo-s/a; Jim Lee intro.;						
Catwoman, Superman & The Joker app.; bonus sketch & layout art pages						23.00
...NOSFERATU (1999, $5.95) McKeever-a						15.00
...: OF ARKHAM (2000, $5.95)-Elseworlds; Grant-s/Alcatena-a						6.00
...: OUR WORLDS AT WAR (8/01, $2.95)-Jae Lee-c						3.00
...PENGUIN TRIUMPHANT nn (1992, $4.95)-Bolland-c						5.00
...PENNYWORTH R.I.P. 1 (4/20, $4.99) Short story reminiscences after Alfred's death						5.00
...•PHANTOM STRANGER nn (1997, $4.95) nn-Grant-s/Ransom-a						6.00
...: PLUS (2/97, $2.95) Arsenal-c/app.						4.00
...: POISON IVY (1997, $4.95)-J.F. Moore-s/Apthorp-a; Stelfreeze-c; cover art interlocks						
w/Batman:(Bane, Batgirl, Mr. Freeze)						6.00
...: POISON IVY: CAST SHADOWS (2004, $6.95) Van Fleet-c/a; Nocenti-s						7.00
.../PUNISHER: LAKE OF FIRE (1994, $4.95, DC/Marvel)						8.00
...: REIGN OF TERROR ('99, $4.95) Elseworlds						4.00
...RETURNS MOVIE SPECIAL (1992, $3.95)						6.00
...RETURNS MOVIE PRESTIGE (1992, $5.95, squarebound)-Dorman painted-c						6.00
...RIDDLER-THE RIDDLE FACTORY (1995, $4.95)-Wagner script						6.00
...: ROOM FULL OF STRANGERS (2004, $5.95) Scott Morse-s/c-a						6.00
...SCARECROW 3-D (12/98, $3.95) w/glasses						6.00
.../ SCARFACE: A PSYCHODRAMA (2001, $5.95)-Adlard-a/Sienkiewicz-c						6.00
...: SCAR OF THE BAT nn (1996, $4.95)-Elseworlds; Max Allan Collins script; Barreto-a						6.00
...SCOTTISH CONNECTION (1998, $5.95) Quitely-a						5.00
...: SEDUCTION OF THE GUN (1992, $2.50, 68 pgs.)						
.../SPAWN: WAR DEVIL nn (1994, $4.95, 52 pgs.)	1	3	4	6	8	10
...: SPECIAL 1 (4/84)-Mike W. Barr story; Golden-c/a	2	4	6	11	16	20
...: SPECIAL (FCBD) 1 (10/21)-Preview of Fear State storyline & I Am Batman #0						3.00
.../SPIDER-MAN (1997, $4.95) Dematteis-s/Nolan & Kesel-a						
		2	4	6	11	16	20
...: THE ABDUCTION ('98, $5.95)						10.00
...: THE AUDIO ADVENTURES SPECIAL (12/21, $9.99) Short stories by various; 3 covers						10.00
...: THE BLUE, THE GREY, & THE BAT (1992, $5.95)-Weiss/Lopez-a						
		1	2	3	5	6	8
...: THE HILL (5/00, $5.95)-Priest/Martinbrough-a						3.00
...: THE JOKER WAR ZONE (11/20, $5.99)-Short stories by various incl. Coipel, Stokoe						6.00
...: THE KILLING JOKE (1988, deluxe 52 pgs., mature readers)-Bolland-c/a; Alan Moore						
scripts; Joker cripples Barbara Gordon	5	10	15	34	60	85
...: THE KILLING JOKE (2nd thru 14th printing)					10	20	25
...: THE KILLING JOKE : THE DELUXE EDITION (2008, $17.99, HC) re-colored version along						
with Bolland-s/a from Batman Black and White #4; sketch pages; Tim Sale intro.						18.00
...: THE MAN WHO LAUGHS (2005, $6.95)-Retells 1st meeting with the Joker; Mahnke-a						
		2	4	6	9	12	15
...: THE OFFICIAL COMIC ADAPTATION OF THE WARNER BROS. MOTION PICTURE						
(1989, $2.50, regular format, 68 pgs.)-Ordway-a		2	4	6	9	12	15
...: THE OFFICIAL COMIC ADAPTATION OF THE WARNER BROS. MOTION PICTURE						
(1989, $4.95, prestige format, 68 pgs.)-same interiors but different-c						
		2	4	6	9	12	15
...: THE ORDER OF BEASTS (2004, $5.95)-Elseworlds; Eddie Campbell-a						6.00
...: THE SMILE KILLER (8/20, $5.99)-Epilogue to Joker: Killer Smile series; Sorrentino-a						6.00
...: THE SPIRIT (1/07, $4.99)-Loeb-s/Cooke-a; P'Gell & Commissioner Dolan app.						5.00
...: THE 10-CENT ADVENTURE (3/02, 10¢) intro. to the "Bruce Wayne: Murderer" x-over;						

Rucka-s/Burchett & Janson-a/Dave Johnson-c						3.00
NOTE: (Also see Promotional Comics section for alternate copies with special outer half-covers promoting local comic shops)						
...: THE 12-CENT ADVENTURE (10/04, 12¢) intro. to the "War Games" x-over;						
Grayson-s/Bachs-a; Catwoman & Spoiler app.						3.00
...: THE WORLD BATMAN DAY SPECIAL EDITION 1 (11/21, giveaway) r/from GN						3.00
...: TWO-FACE-CRIME AND PUNISHMENT-(1995, $4.95)-McDaniel-a						6.00
...: TWO FACES (1998, $4.95) Elseworlds						6.00
...Vs. THE INCREDIBLE HULK (1995, $3.95)-r/DC Special Series #27						25.00
...: VILLAINS SECRET FILES (1998, $4.95) Origin-s						8.00
... VILLAINS SECRET FILES AND ORIGINS 2005 (7/05, $4.99) Clayface origin w/ Mignola-a;						
Black Mask story, pin-up of villains by various; Barrionuevo-c						6.00
BATMAN ADVENTURES, THE (Based on animated series)(See DC Classics for reprints)						
DC Comics: Oct, 1992 - No. 36, Oct, 1995 ($1.25/$1.50)						
1-Penguin-c/story	3	6	9	17	26	35
1 ($1.95, Silver Edition)-2nd printing	1	2	3	5	6	8
2,4-6,8-11,13-15,17-19: 2-Catwoman-c/story. 5-Scarecrow-c/story. 10-Riddler-c/story.						
11-Man-Bat-c/story. 18-Batgirl-c/story. 19-Scarecrow-c/story						5.00
3-Joker-c/story	3	6	9	14	19	24
7-Special edition polybagged with Man-Bat trading card						
	1	3	4	6	8	10
12-(9/93) 1st Harley Quinn app. in comics; 1st animated-version Batgirl app. in title						
	75	150	225	340	533	725
16-Joker-c/story; begin $1.50-c	3	6	9	19	30	40
20-24,26,27,29-32: 26-Batgirl app.						5.00
25-($2.50, 52 pgs.)-Superman app.	2	4	6	9	13	16
28-Joker & Harley Quinn-c; 2nd app. Harley Quinn	3	6	9	17	26	35
33-36: 33-Begin $1.75-c						5.00
Annual 1 ('94) 3rd app. Harley Quinn	3	6	9	21	33	45
Annual 2 ('95) Demon-c/story; Ra's al Ghul app.						6.00
...: Dangerous Dames & Demons (2003, $14.95, TPB) r/Annual 1,2, Mad Love & Adventures						
in the DC Universe #3; Bruce Timm painted-c						30.00
Holiday Special 1 (1995, $2.95) Harley Quinn app.	5	10	15	34	60	85
The Collected Adventures Vol. 1,2 ('93, '95, $5.95)						15.00
TPB ('98, $7.95) r/#1-6; painted wraparound-c						10.00
BATMAN ADVENTURES (Based on animated series)						
DC Comics: Jun, 2003 - No. 17, Oct, 2004 ($2.25)						
1-Timm-c	3	6	9	15	22	28
1-Free Comic Book Day edition (6/03) Timm-c						4.00
1-Halloween Fest Special Edition (12/15) Timm-c						4.00
2,4-9,11-15,17: 4-Ra's al Ghul app. 6-8-Phantasm app. 14-Grey Ghost app.						4.00
3-Joker & Harley Quinn-c/app.	3	6	9	19	30	40
10-Catwoman-c/app.	3	6	9	18	27	36
16-Joker & Harley Quinn-c/app.	5	10	15	35	63	90
Batman/Scooby-Doo Halloween Fest 1 (12/12, giveaway flipbook with Scooby-Doo) r/#1						6.00
Vol. 1: Rogues Gallery (2004, $6.95, digest size) r/#1-4 & Batman: Gotham Advs. #50						
	3	6	9	16	23	30
Vol. 2: Shadows & Masks (2004, $6.95, digest) r/#5-9	1	3	4	6	8	10
BATMAN ADVENTURES, THE: MAD LOVE						
DC Comics: Feb, 1994 ($3.95/$4.95)						
1-Origin of Harley Quinn; Dini-s/Timm-c/a	6	12	18	38	69	100
1-($4.95, Prestige format) new Timm painted-c	7	14	21	44	82	120
BATMAN ADVENTURES, THE: THE LOST YEARS (TV)						
DC Comics: Jan, 1998 - No. 5, May, 1998 ($1.95) (Based on animated series)						
1-Leads into Fall '97's new animated episodes	2	4	6	8	10	12
2-5: 4-Tim Drake becomes Robin. 5-Dick becomes Nightwing						
		1	2	3	5	6	8
TPB-(1999, $9.95) r/series						25.00
BATMAN/ALIENS						
DC Comics/Dark Horse: Mar, 1997 - No. 2, Apr, 1997 ($4.95, limited series)						
1,2: Wrightson-c/a.	2	4	6	8	10	12
TPB-(1997, $14.95) w/prequel from DHP #101,102						25.00
BATMAN/ALIENS II						
DC Comics/Dark Horse: 2003 - No. 3, 2003 ($5.95, limited series)						
1-3-Edginton-s/Staz Johnson-a	1	3	4	6	8	10
TPB-(2003, $14.95) r/#1-3						20.00
BATMAN AND... (See Batman and Robin [2011 series] #19-on)						
BATMAN AND ROBIN (See Batman R.I.P. and Batman: Battle For The Cowl series)						
DC Comics: Aug, 2009 - No. 26, Oct, 2011 ($2.99)						
1-Grant Morrison-s/Frank Quitely-a/c; Dick Grayson & Damian Wayne team						8.00

	GD	VG	FN	VF	VF/NM	NM-
	2.0	4.0	6.0	8.0	9.0	9.2

1-Variant cover by J.G. Jones
1-Second thru Fourth printings - recolored Quitely covers — 20.00
2-16-Quitely-c. 2-Three printings. 4-6-Tan-a. 7-9-Stewart-a; Batwoman & Squire app. — 3.00
13-15-Joker app.; Irving-a. 16-Bruce Wayne returns; Batman Inc. announced
2-Variant-c by Adam Kubert — 10.00
17-26: 17-McDaniel-a/March-c. 21,22-Gleason-a. 23-25-Red Hood app. — 3.00
... #1 Special Edition (6/10, $1.00) r/#1 with "What's Next?" cover logo — 3.00
...: Batman and Robin Must Die - The Deluxe Edition HC (2011, $24.99) r/#13-16; cover and costume design sketch art — 25.00
...: Batman Reborn - The Deluxe Edition HC (2010, $24.99) r/#1-6; design sketch art — 25.00
...: Batman Reborn SC (2011, $14.99) r/#1-6; cover and character design sketch art — 15.00
...: Batman vs. Robin - The Deluxe Edition HC (2010, $24.99) r/#7-12; cover sketch art — 25.00

BATMAN AND ROBIN (DC New 52)(Cover title changes each issue from #19-32)
DC Comics: Nov, 2011 - No. 40, May, 2015 ($2.99)
1-Bruce and Damian Wayne in costume; Tomasi-s/Gleason-a — 4.00
2-14: 5,6-Ducard flashback. 9-Night of the Owls — 3.00
15-Death of the Family tie-in; die-cut Joker cover — 5.00
16-18: 16-Death of the Family tie-in. 18-Requiem — 3.00
19-23: 19-Red Robin. 20-Red Hood. 21-Batgirl. 22-Catwoman. 23-Nightwing — 3.00
23.1, 23.2, 23.3, 23.4 (11/13, $2.99, regular covers) — 3.00
23.1 (11/13, $3.99, 3-D cover) "Two Face #1" on cover; March-a; Scarecrow app. — 6.00
23.2 (11/13, $3.99, 3-D cover) "Court of Owls #1" on cover; history of the Owls — 5.00
23.3 (11/13, $3.99, 3-D cover) "Ra's al Ghul #1" on cover; history of Ra's retold — 5.00
23.4 (11/13, $3.99, 3-D cover) "Killer Croc #1" on cover; Croc's origin — 5.00
24-40: 24-28-Two-Face. 25-Matches Malone app. 29-Aquaman. 30-Wonder Woman. 31-Frankenstein. 32-Ra's al Ghul. 33-38-Title back to Batman and Robin. 37-Darkseid app.; Damian returns; cont'd in Robin Rises: Alpha. 39,40-Justice League app. — 3.00
#0 (11/12, $2.99) Damian's childhood training with Talia; Tomasi-s/Gleason-a. — 3.00
Annual 1 (3/13, $4.99) Damian in the Batman #666 costume; Andy Kubert-c — 5.00
Annual 2 (3/14, $4.99) Mahnke-a; flashback to Dick Grayson's first week as Robin — 5.00
Annual 3 (6/15, $4.99) Ryp-a/Syaf-c — 5.00
...: Futures End 1 (11/14, $2.99, regular-c) Five years later; Nguyen-a; 1st app. Duke Thomas as future Robin — 3.00
...: Futures End 1 (11/14, $3.99, 3-D cover) — 4.00

BATMAN AND ROBIN (Dawn of DC)
DC Comics: Nov, 2023 - Present ($4.99)
1-7: 1-Williamson-s/Di Meo-a — 5.00
2024 Annual 1 (3/24, $5.99) Bloodsport app.; Williamson-s/Porter-a — 6.00

BATMAN AND ROBIN ADVENTURES (TV)
DC Comics: Nov, 1995 - No. 25, Dec, 1997 ($1.75) (Based on animated series)

1-Dini-s	2	4	6	8	13	18

2-4,6,7,9-15,17,19,20,22,23: 2-4-Dini script. 4-Penguin-c/app. 9-Batgirl & Talia-c/app. 10-Ra's al Ghul-c/app. 11-Man-Bat app. 12-Bane-c/app. 13-Scarecrow-c/app. 15-Deadman-c/app. — 5.00

5-Joker-c/story	1	3	4	6	8	10
8-Poison Ivy & Harley Quinn-c/app.	3	6	9	14	20	25
16,24: 16-Catwoman-c/app. 24-Poison Ivy app.	2	4	6	8	11	14
18-Joker-c/app.	3	6	9	15	22	28
21-Batgirl-c	3	6	9	21	33	45
25-($2.95, 48 pgs.)	1	2	3	5	6	8
Annual 1 (11/96) Phantasm-c/app.	2	4	6	9	12	15
Annual 2 (11/97) Zatara & Zatanna-c/app.	2	4	6	8	10	12
...: Sub-Zero(1998, $3.95) Adaptation of animated video						
	2	4	6	9	12	15

BATMAN AND ROBIN AND HOWARD
DC Comics: May, 2024 - No. 4 ($3.99, limited series)
1-All ages story; Jeffrey Brown-s/a — 4.00

BATMAN & ROBIN ETERNAL (Sequel to Batman Eternal)
DC Comics: Dec, 2015 - No. 26, May, 2016 ($3.99/$2.99, weekly series)
1-($3.99) Tynion IV & Snyder-s/Daniel-a; Cassandra Cain app. — 4.00
2-25-($2.99) Dick Grayson, Red Hood, Red Robin, Bluebird, Spoiler app. 6-1st app. Mother. 9,10,15,16,24,25-Azrael app. 23-25-Midnighter app. — 3.00
26-($3.99) Conclusion; Tony Daniel-a — 4.00

BATMAN & SCOOBY-DOO MYSTERIES, THE
DC Comics: Jun, 2021 - No. 12, May, 2022 ($2.99, limited series)

1-Mystery of Batman's original purple gloves	1	2	3	5	6	8

2-12: 4-Black Mask app. 8-Joker & Harley app. 10-The Question (Renee) app. — 3.00

BATMAN & SCOOBY-DOO MYSTERIES, THE
DC Comics: Dec, 2022 - No. 12, Nov, 2023 ($2.99, limited series)
1-12: 1-Batmen of All Nations app. 2-Poison Ivy app. 5-Batwoman app. — 3.00

BATMAN & SCOOBY-DOO MYSTERIES, THE
DC Comics: Feb, 2024 - Present ($2.99, limited series)
1-3: 1-Nightwing app. 2-Solomon Grundy app. — 3.00

BATMAN AND SUPERMAN ADVENTURES: WORLD'S FINEST
DC Comics: 1997 ($6.95, square-bound, one-shot) (Based on animated series)
1-Adaptation of animated crossover episode; Dini-s/Timm-c; Harley Quinn on cover

		3	6	9	14	20	25

BATMAN AND SUPERMAN: WORLD'S FINEST
DC Comics: Apr, 1999 - No. 10, Jan, 2000 ($4.95/$1.99, limited series)

1-($4.95, squarebound) Taylor-a	1	3	4	6	8	10

2-9-($1.99) 5-Batgirl app. 8-Catwoman-c/app. — 4.00
10-($4.95, squarebound) Taylor-a — 6.00
TPB (2003, $19.95) r/#1-10 — 20.00

BATMAN & THE JOKER: THE DEADLY DUO
DC Comics: Jan, 2023 - No. 7, Jul, 2023 ($4.99/$5.99, limited series)
1-6-Marc Silvestri-s/a; Harley Quinn app. — 5.00
1 Batman Day Special Edition (11/23, giveaway) r/#1 — 3.00
7-($5.99) — 6.00
...: Unplugged 1 (2/24, $4.99) r/#1&2, just B&W inked art pages, no text — 5.00

BATMAN AND THE OUTSIDERS (The Adventures of the Outsiders #33 on) (Also see Brave & The Bold #200 & The Outsiders) (Replaces The Brave and the Bold)
DC Comics: Aug, 1983 - No. 32, Apr, 1986 (Mando paper #5 on)
1-Batman, Halo, Geo-Force, Katana, Metamorpho & Black Lightning begin

	3	6	9	15	22	28

2-32: 5-New Teen Titans x-over. 9-Halo begins. 11,12-Origin Katana. 18-More info on Metamorpho's origin. 28-31-Lookers origin. 32-Team disbands — 4.00
Annual 1,2 (9/84, 9/85): 2-Metamorpho & Sapphire Stagg wed — 6.00
NOTE: Aparo a-1-9, 11-13p, 16-20; c-1-4, 5i, 6-21, Annual 1, 2. B. Kane a-3r. Layton a-19i, 20i. Lopez a-3p. Miller c-Annual 1. Perez c-5p. B. Willingham a-14p.

BATMAN AND THE OUTSIDERS (Continues as The Outsiders for #15-39)
DC Comics: Dec, 2007 - No. 14, Feb, 2009; No. 40, Jul, 2011 ($2.99)
1-14: 1-Batman, Catwoman, Martian Manhunter, Katana, Metamorpho, Thunder & Grace begin. 4-Batgirl joins. 11-13-Batman R.I.P. — 3.00
40 (7/11) Final issue; Didio-s/Tan-a; history of the team — 3.00
... Special (3/09, $3.99) Alfred assembles a new team; Andy Kubert-a; two covers — 4.00
...: The Chrysalis TPB (2008, $14.99) r/#1-5 — 15.00
...: The Snare TPB (2008, $14.99) r/#6-10 — 15.00

BATMAN & THE OUTSIDERS
DC Comics: Jul, 2019 - No. 17, Dec, 2020 ($3.99)
1-17: 1-Batman, Black Lightning, Katana, The Signal and Orphan team; Hill-s/Soy-a — 4.00
Annual 1 (12/19, $4.99) Max Raynor-a; spotlight on Katana — 5.00

BATMAN & THE SIGNAL
DC Comics: Mar, 2018 - No. 3, Jun, 2018 ($3.99)
1-3-Batman and Duke Thomas; Hamner-a — 4.00

BATMAN: ARKHAM CITY (Prequel to the video game)
DC Comics: Early Jul, 2011 - No. 5, Oct, 2011 ($2.99, limited series)
1-5-Dini-s/D'Anda-a; Joker app. — 3.00
...: End Game (1/13, $6.99) Story bridges Arkham City and Arkham Unhinged series — 7.00

BATMAN: ARKHAM KNIGHT (Prequel to the Arkham video game trilogy finale)
DC Comics: May, 2015 - No. 12, Feb, 2016 ($3.99)
1-Tomasi-s/Bogdanovic/Panosian-c; 1st comic app. of Arkham Knight — 6.00
2-12: 2-Harley Quinn cover — 4.00
Annual 1 (11/15, $4.99) Tomasi-s/Segovia-a; Firefly app. — 5.00
...: Robin 1 (1/16, $2.99) Tomasi-s/Rocha-a — 3.00

BATMAN: ARKHAM KNIGHT: GENESIS
DC Comics: Oct, 2015 - No. 6, 2016 ($2.99, limited series)
1-4: 1-Tomasi-s/Borges-a/Sejic-c; Jason Todd's origin. 4-Harley Quinn cover — 3.00

BATMAN: ARKHAM UNHINGED (Based on the Batman: Arkham City video game)
DC Comics: Jun, 2012 - No. 20, Jan, 2014 ($2.99)
1-20: 1-Wilkins-c; Catwoman, Two-Face & Hugo Strange app. — 3.00

BATMAN: BANE OF THE DEMON
DC Comics: Mar, 1998 - No. 4, June, 1998 ($1.95, limited series)
1-4-Dixon-s/Nolan-a; prelude to Legacy x-over — 5.00

BATMAN: BATTLE FOR THE COWL (Follows Batman R.I.P. storyline)
DC Comics: May, 2009 - No. 3, Jul, 2009 ($3.99, limited series)
1-3-Tony Daniel-s/a/c; 2 covers on each — 4.00
.... Arkham Asylum (6/09, $2.99) Hine-s/Haun-a/Ladronn-c — 3.00
.... Commissioner Gordon (5/09, $2.99) Mandrake-a/Ladronn-c; Mr. Freeze app. — 3.00
.... Man-Bat (6/09, $2.99) Harris-s/Calafiore-a/Ladronn-c; Dr. Phosphorus app. — 3.00
.... The Network (7/09, $2.99) Nicieza-s/Calafiore & Kramer-a/Ladronn-c — 3.00
.... The Underground (6/09, $2.99) Yost-s/Raimondi-a/Ladronn-c; Harley Quinn app. — 3.00
Companion SC (2009, $14.99) r/ five one-shots — 15.00
HC (2009, $19.99) r/#1-3 & Gotham Gazette: Batman Dead & Gotham Gazette: Batman Alive; gallery of variant covers and sketch art — 20.00
SC (2010, $14.99) same contents as HC — 15.00

BATMAN BEYOND (Based on animated series)
DC Comics: Mar, 1999 - No. 6, Aug, 1999 ($1.99, limited series)

1-Adaptation of pilot episode; Timm-c	13	26	39	89	195	300
2-Adaptation of pilot episode cont.; Timm-c	4	8	12	27	44	60
3	3	6	9	21	33	45
4,5: 4-Darwyn Cooke-c; The Demon app.	2	4	6	9	13	16
6-1st app. Blight	4	8	12	23	37	50

...No. 1 (Facsimile Edition) (3/24, $3.99) r/#1 with original ads — 4.00
TPB (1999, $9.95) r/#1-6 — 15.00

BATMAN BEYOND (Based on animated series)(Continuing series)
DC Comics: Nov, 1999 - No. 24, Oct, 2001 ($1.99)

1-Rousseau-a; Batman vs. Batman	3	6	9	14	20	25
2	2	4	6	9	12	15

3,5-24: 14-Demon-c/app. 21,22-Justice League Unlimited-c/app. — 6.00

4-1st app. Melanie Walker/Ten (Royal Flush Gang)	4	8	12	25	40	55

...: Return of the Joker (2/01, $2.95) adaptation of video release

	4	8	12	27	44	60

BATMAN BEYOND (Animated series)(See Superman/Batman Annual #4)
DC Comics: Aug, 2010 - No. 6, Jan, 2011 ($2.99, limited series)

1-Benjamin-c; Nguyen-c; return of Hush	2	4	6	9	12	15
1-Variant-c by J.H. Williams III	2	4	6	10	15	20
2-6						4.00

...: Hush Beyond TPB (2011, $14.99) r/#1-6 — 15.00

BATMAN BEYOND
DC Comics: Mar, 2011 - No. 8, Oct, 2011 ($2.99)
1-8: 1-3-Justice League app.; Beechen-s/Benjamin-a/Nguyen-c. 8-Inque app. — 4.00
1-Variant-c by Darwyn Cooke — 5.00

BATMAN BEYOND (Tim Drake as Batman)
DC Comics: Aug, 2015 - No. 16, Nov. 2016 ($2.99)
1-16: 1-Jurgens-s/Chang-a. 4-Inque app. 5-New suit. 7,16-Stephen Thompson-a. 10-Tuftan app. 11-Superman's son app. 12-Tan-a. 16-Terry McGinnis back as Batman — 3.00

Batman and Robin (2011 series) #16 © DC

Batman Beyond Unlimited #5 © DC

Batman Confidential #22 © DC

	GD	VG	FN	VF	VF/NM	NM-
	2.0	4.0	6.0	8.0	9.0	9.2

BATMAN BEYOND (DC Rebirth)
DC Comics: Dec, 2016 - No. 50, Feb, 2021 ($2.99/$3.99)

1-6: 1-3,6-Dan Jurgens-s/Bernard Chang-a. 4,5-Pete Woods-a						3.00
7-24,26-50-($3.99) 8-11,44-47-Damian app. 22-24-New Scarecrow. 26-30-Joker app.						
36-Flash app. 37-Intro. new Batwoman. 40-Batwoman ID revealed; Dick Grayson app.						
48,49-Booster Gold app. 50-Wonder Woman & Inque app.						4.00
25-($4.99) Jurgens-s/Hamner-a; Joker app.						5.00
...: Rebirth 1 (11/16, $2.99) Terry McGinnis in the suit; Jurgens-s/Sook-a						3.00

BATMAN BEYOND: NEO-GOTHIC
DC Comics: Sept, 2023 - No. 6, Feb, 2024 ($4.99, limited series)

1-6-Kelly & Lanzing-s/Dunbar-a; The Court of Owls app.						5.00

BATMAN BEYOND: NEO-YEAR
DC Comics: Jun, 2022 - No. 6, Nov, 2022 ($3.99, limited series)

1-6-Kelly & Lanzing-s/Dunbar-a; The Sword of Gotham app.						4.00

BATMAN: BEYOND THE WHITE KNIGHT
DC Comics: May, 2022 - No. 8, Apr, 2023 ($4.99, limited series)

1-8-Sean Murphy-s/a; intro Terry McGinnis with the Batman Beyond suit						5.00
1-Second printing (7/22) Variant-c with Terry McGinnis in the Batman Beyond suit						5.00
... Showcase Edition (7/22, $5.99) Reprints #1 & 2						6.00

BATMAN BEYOND UNIVERSE
DC Comics: Oct, 2013 - No. 16, Jan, 2015 ($3.99)

1-12: 1-Superman & the JLB app.; Sean Murphy-c. 8-12-Wonder Woman app. 9-12-Justice Lords app. 13,14-Phantasm returns. 15-Royal Flush Gang app.						4.00

BATMAN BEYOND UNLIMITED
DC Comics: Apr, 2012 - No. 18, Sept, 2013 ($3.99)

1-18: 1-Beechen-s/Breyfogle-a; Superman & Justice League back-ups; Nguyen-c. 17-Metal Men return; Marvel Family app. 18-New Batgirl						4.00

BATMAN: BLACK & WHITE
DC Comics: June, 1996 - No. 4, Sept, 1996 ($2.95, B&W, limited series)

1-Stories by McKeever, Timm, Kubert, Chaykin, Goodwin; Jim Lee-c; Allred inside front-c; Moebius inside back-c			3	4	6	8	10
2-4: 2-Stories by Simonson, Corben, Bisley & Gaiman; Miller-c. 3-Stories by M. Wagner, Janson, Sienkiewicz, O'Neil & Kristiansen; B. Smith-c; Russell inside front-c; Silvestri inside back-c. 4-Stories by Bolland, Goodwin & Gianni, Strnad & Nowlan, O'Neil & Stelfreeze; Toth-c; pin-ups by Neal Adams & Alex Ross						4.00
Hardcover ('97, $39.95) r/series w/new art & cover plate						40.00
Softcover ('00, $19.95) r/series						20.00
Volume 2 HC ('02, $39.95, 7 3/4"x12") r/B&W stories from Batman: Gotham Knights #1-16; stories and art by various incl. Ross, Buscema, Byrne, Ellison, Sale; Mignola-c						40.00
Volume 2 SC ('03, $19.95, 7 3/4"x12") same contents as HC						20.00
Volume 2 SC ('08, $19.99, reg. size) same contents as HC						20.00
Volume 3 HC ('07, $24.99, reg. size) r/B&W back-ups from Batman: Gotham Knights #17-49; stories and art by various incl. Davis, DeCarlo, Morse, Schwartz, Thompson, Miller-c						25.00

BATMAN: BLACK & WHITE
DC Comics: Nov, 2013 - No. 6, Apr, 2014 ($4.99, B&W, limited series)

1-6-Short story anthology by various. 1-Silvestri-c; Neal Adams-a. 2-Steranko-c; Nino-a. 3-Bermejo-s/a. 4-Conner-c; Allred-s/a. 6-Mahnke-c; Hughes, Cloonan, Chiang-a						5.00

BATMAN: BLACK & WHITE
DC Comics: Jan, 2021 - No. 6, Jul, 2021 ($5.99, B&W, limited series)

1-6-Short story anthology by various. 1-Dini-s/Kubert-a; JH Williams III-s/a. 2-King-s/Gerads-a. 3-Future State Batman by Ridley-s/Coipel-a; Bengal-s/a. 6-Snyder-s/Romita Jr.-a						6.00

BATMAN: BOOK OF THE DEAD
DC Comics: Jun, 1999 - No. 2, July, 1999 ($4.95, limited series, prestige format)

1,2-Elseworlds; Kitson-a						8.00

BATMAN CACOPHONY
DC Comics: Jan, 2009 - No. 3, Mar, 2009 ($3.99, limited series)

1-3-Kevin Smith-s/Walt Flanagan-a; Joker and Onomatoaoeoia app.; Adam Kubert-c						4.00
1-3-Variant-c by Sienkiewicz						15.00
HC (2009, $19.99, d.j.) r/#1-3; Kevin Smith intro.; script for #3, cover gallery						20.00
SC (2010, $14.99) r/#1-3; Kevin Smith intro.; script for #3, cover gallery						15.00

BATMAN/CATWOMAN
DC Comics (Black Label): Feb, 2021 - No. 12, Aug, 2022 ($4.99)

1-12: 1-King-s/Mann-a; Andrea Beaumont and The Joker app. 3-Intro. Helena Wayne. 5-Harley Quinn app. 7-9-Liam Sharp-a						5.00
... Special 1 (3/22, $9.99) Tom King/John Paul Leon & others-a; tributes to J.P. Leon						10.00

BATMAN: CATWOMAN DEFIANT (See Batman one-shots)

BATMAN/CATWOMAN: THE GOTHAM WAR
DC Comics: Oct, 2023 - Dec, 2023 (series of one-shots within Batman & Catwoman crossover)

... Battle Lines (11/23, $5.99) Howard & Zdarsky-s; leads into Batman #137, Catwoman #57						6.00
... Prelude 1 Batman Day Special Edition 11/23, free giveaway) Previews pages from Batman #137, Catwoman #57, Red Hood #1						3.00
... Red Hood 1,2 ($3.99, 11/23,12/23) Rosenberg-s/Cizmesija-a						4.00
... Scorched Earth 1 (12/23, $5.99) Conclusion of the crossover						6.00

BATMAN/CATWOMAN: TRAIL OF THE GUN
DC Comics: 2004 - No. 2, 2004 ($5.95, limited series, prestige format)

1,2-Elseworlds; Van Sciver-a/Nocenti-s						8.00

BATMAN CHRONICLES, THE (See the Batman TPB listings for the Golden Age reprint series that shares this title)
DC Comics: Summer, 1995 - No. 23, Winter, 2001 ($2.95, quarterly)

1-3,5-19: 1-Dixon/Grant/Moench script. 3-Bolland-c. 5-Oracle Year One story, Richard Dragon app., Chaykin-c. 6-Kaluta-c; Ra's al Ghul story. 7-Superman-c/app.11-Paul Pope-s/a. 12-Cataclysm pt. 10. 18-No Man's Land						5.00
4-Hitman story by Ennis, Contagion tie-in; Balent-c	2	4	6	9	12	15
20,22,23: 20-Catwoman and Relative Heroes-c/app.						4.00
21-Brian Michael Bendis-s (1st for DC)/Gaydos-a; Giordano-a; Pander Bros.-a/c						6.00
...Gallery (3/97, $3.50) Pin-ups						4.00
...Gauntlet, The (1997, $4.95, one-shot)						6.00

BATMAN: CITY OF LIGHT
DC Comics: Dec, 2003 - No. 8, July, 2004 ($2.95, limited series)

1-8-Pander Brothers-a/s; Paniccia-s						3.00

BATMAN: CITY OF MADNESS
DC Comics (Black Label): Dec, 2023 - No. 3, Apr, 2024 ($6.99, squarebound, oversized, limited series)

1-Christian Ward-s/a/c; Court of Owls app.						7.00

BATMAN CONFIDENTIAL
DC Comics: Feb, 2007 - No. 54, May, 2011 ($2.99)

1-49,51-54: 1-6-Diggle-s/Portacio-a/c. 7-12-Cowan-a; Joker's origin. 13-16-Morales-a. 17-21-Batgirl vs. Catwoman; Maguire-a. 22-25-McDaniel-a; Joker app. 26-28-King Tut app.; Garcia-Lopez-a. 40-43-Kieth-s/a. 44-48-Mandrake-a/c						3.00
50-($4.99) Bingham-a; back-up Silver Age-style JLA story						5.00
...: Dead to Rights SC (2010, $14.99) r/#22-25,29,30						15.00
...: Lovers and Madmen HC (2008, $24.99, dustjacket) r/#7-12; Brad Meltzer intro.						25.00
...: Lovers and Madmen SC (2009, $14.99) r/#7-12; Brad Meltzer intro.						15.00
...: Rules of Engagement HC (2007, $24.99, dustjacket) r/#1-6						25.00
...: The Bat and the Beast SC (2010, $12.99) r/#31-35						13.00
...: The Cat and the Bat SC (2009, $12.99) r/#17-21						13.00
...: Vs. the Undead SC (2010, $14.99) r/#44-48						15.00

BATMAN: CREATURE OF THE NIGHT
DC Comics: Jan, 2018 - No. 4, Jan, 2020 ($5.99, squarebound, limited series)

1-4-Kurt Busiek-s/John Paul Leon-a; story of Bruce Wainwright						6.00

BATMAN: CURSE OF THE WHITE KNIGHT (Sequel to Batman: White Knight series)
DC Comics (Black Label): Sept, 2019 - No. 8, May, 2020 ($4.99, limited series)

1-8-Sean Murphy-s/a; flashbacks to 1685 Edmond Wayne in Gotham; Azrael returns						6.00

BATMAN: DAMNED
DC Comics (Black Label): Nov, 2018 - No. 3, Aug, 2019 ($6.99, squarebound, oversized, limited series)

1-Azzarello-s/Bermejo-a/c; Constantine & Deadman app.; nudity	3	6	9	21	33	45
1-Variant cover by Jim Lee	4	8	12	23	37	50
2,3-Harley Quinn, Constantine & Deadman app.; covers by Bermejo & Lee			3	4	6	8	10

BATMAN: DARK DETECTIVE
DC Comics: Early July, 2005 - No. 6, Late September, 2005 ($2.99, limited series)

1-Englehart-s/Rogers & Austin-a; Silver St. Cloud and The Joker app.; Joker-c		1	3	4	6	8	10
2-6						4.00

BATMAN: DARK KNIGHT OF THE ROUND TABLE
DC Comics: 1999 - No. 2, 1999 ($4.95, limited series, prestige format)

1,2-Elseworlds; Giordano-a						7.00

BATMAN: DARK VICTORY
DC Comics: 1999 - No. 13, 2000 ($4.95/$2.95, limited series)

Wizard #0 Preview						4.00
1-($4.95) Loeb-s/Sale-c/a						6.00
2-12-($2.95)						3.00

	GD	VG	FN	VF	VF/NM	NM-
	2.0	4.0	6.0	8.0	9.0	9.2

13-($4.95) 5.00
Hardcover (2001, $29.95) with dust jacket; r/#0,1-13 ...... 30.00
Softcover (2002, $19.95) r/#0,1-13 .... 20.00

BATMAN: DEATH AND THE MAIDENS
DC Comics: Oct, 2003 - No. 9, Aug, 2004 ($2.95, limited series)
1-Ra's al Ghul app.; Rucka-s/Janson-a 4.00
2-9: 9-Ra's al Ghul dies 3.00
TPB (2004, $19.95) r/#1-9 & Detective #783 .... 20.00

BATMAN/ DEATHBLOW: AFTER THE FIRE
DC Comics/WildStorm: 2002 - No. 3, 2002 ($5.95, limited series)
1-3-Azzarello-s/Bermejo & Bradstreet-a 6.00
TPB (2003, $12.95) r/#1-3; plus concept art 13.00

BATMAN: DEATH MASK
DC Comics/CMX: Jun, 2008 - No. 4, Sept, 2008 ($2.99, B&W, lim. series, right-to-left manga style)
1-4-Yoshinori Natsume-s/a 3.00
TPB (2008, $9.99, digest size) r/#1-4; interview with Yoshinori Natsume .. 10.00

BATMAN/ DYLAN DOG
DC Comics: May, 2024 - Present ($4.99, limited series)
1-Recchioni-s/Cavenago-a; Joker and Catwoman app. 5.00

BATMAN: '89 (Based on the 1989 Michael Keaton movie)
DC Comics: Oct, 2021 - No. 6, Sept, 2022 ($3.99, limited series)
1-6-Hamm-s/Quinones-a; Harvey Dent app. 1-Intro. Drake Winston. 2-Selina Kyle app. .. 4.00

BATMAN: '89 ECHOES (Based on the 1989 Michael Keaton movie)
DC Comics: Jan, 2024 - No. 6, ($3.99, limited series)
1,2-Hamm-s/Quinones-a; intro. Harleen Quinzel 4.00

BATMAN ETERNAL (Also see Arkham Manor series)
DC Comics: Jun, 2014 - No. 52, Jun, 2015 ($2.99, weekly series)
1-Snyder-s/Fabok-a; Professor Pyg & Jason Bard app. 5.00
2-51: 2-Carmine Falcone returns. 3-Stephanie Brown app. 6,14-17,26,29,30,37-Joker's Daughter app. 20-Spoiler dons costume. 30-Arkham Asylum destroyed.
41-Bluebird in costume 3.00
52-($3.99) Jae Lee-c; art by various 4.00

BATMAN: EUROPA
DC Comics: Jan, 2016 - No. 4, Apr, 2016 ($4.99, limited series)
1-4: 1-Joker app.; Casali & Azzarello-s/Camuncoli & Jim Lee-a. 2-Camuncoli-a .. 5.00
... Director's Cut 1 (8/16, $5.99) r/#1 with Jim Lee's pencil art; bonus original script .. 6.00

BATMAN FAMILY, THE
National Periodical Pub./DC Comics: Sept-Oct, 1975 - No. 20, Oct-Nov, 1978
(#1-4, 17-on: 68 pgs.) (Combined with Detective Comics with No. 481)
1-Origin/2nd app. Batgirl-Robin team-up (The Dynamite Duo); reprints plus one new story begins; N. Adams-a(r); r/1st app. Man-Bat from Det. #400

| | 5 | 10 | 15 | 34 | 60 | 85 |

2-5: 2-r/Det. #369. 3-Batgirl & Robin learn each's i.d.; r/Batwoman app. from Batman #105.
4-r/1st Fatman app. from Batman #113. 5-r/1st Bat-Hound app. from Batman #92

| | 3 | 6 | 9 | 16 | 23 | 30 |

6-(7-8/76) Joker's daughter on cover (1st app.) ....

| | 7 | 14 | 21 | 46 | 86 | 125 |

7,8,14-16: 8-r/Batwoman app.14-Batwoman app. 15-3rd app. Killer Moth. 16-Bat-Girl cameo (last app. in costume until New Teen Titans #47)

| | 2 | 4 | 6 | 13 | 18 | 22 |

9-Joker's daughter-c/app.

| | 6 | 12 | 18 | 38 | 69 | 100 |

10-1st revival Batwoman; Cavalier app.; Killer Moth app.

| | 3 | 6 | 9 | 20 | 31 | 42 |

11-13,17-20: 11-13-Rogers-a(p): 11-New stories begin; Man-Bat begins. 13-Batwoman cameo.
17-($1.00 size)-Batman, Huntress begin; Batwoman & Catwoman 1st meet.
18-20: Huntress by Staton in all. 20-Origin Ragman retold

| | 3 | 6 | 9 | 17 | 26 | 35 |

NOTE: Aparo a-17; c-11-16. Austin a-12i. Chaykin a-14p. Michael Golden a-15-17,18-20p. Grell a-1; c-17. Gil Kane a-17, 19. Newton a-13. Robinson a-1r, 3i(r); 9r. Russell a-18i, 19i. Starlin a-17; c-18, 20.

BATMAN: FAMILY
DC Comics: Dec, 2002 - No. 8, Feb, 2003 ($2.95/$2.25, weekly limited series)
1,8-($2.95): 1-John Francis Moore-s/Hoberg & Gaudiano-a .. 5.00
2-7-($.25): 3-Orpheus & Black Canary app. 3.00

BATMAN: FEAR STATE
DC Comics: Alpha, Oct, 2021 - Omega, Jan, 2022 ($4.99, bookends of crossover event)
...: Alpha 1 - Tynion IV-s/Federici-a; Scarecrow app. 5.00
...: Omega 1 - Tynion IV-s/Federici, Duce, Benjamin, March & Hairsine-a .. 5.00

BAT-MAN, THE : FIRST KNIGHT
DC Comics (Black Label): May, 2024 - No. 3, ($6.99, squarebound, oversized, limited series)
1-Set in the 1939 purple glove era; Jurgens-s/Perkins-a ... 7.00

BATMAN / FORTNITE: FOUNDATION (Based on the videogame)
DC Comics: Dec, 2021 ($4.99, one-shot, bagged with a Fortnite code)
1-Batman, Justice League, Lex Luthor and The Batman Who Laughs app.; Hixson-a .. 5.00

BATMAN / FORTNITE: ZERO POINT (Based on the videogame)
DC Comics: Jun, 2021 - No. 6, Sept, 2021 ($4.99, limited series, bagged with a Fortnite code)
1-6: Batman and Catwoman in the land of Fortnite 5.00
... Batman Day Special Edition (11/21, free giveaway, not bagged) r/#1 .. 3.00

BATMAN: FORTRESS
DC Comics: Jul, 2022 - No. 8, Mar, 2023 ($3.99, limited series)
1-8-Gary Whitta-s/Darick Robertson-a 4.00

BATMAN: GARGOYLE OF GOTHAM
DC Comics: Nov, 2023 - No. 4 ($6.99, squarebound, limited series)
1,2-Rafael Grampá-s/a 7.00
... Noir Edition 1,2 ($6.99) B&W inked art with minimal red spot color .. 7.00

BATMAN: GATES OF GOTHAM
DC Comics: Jul, 2011 - No. 5, Late Oct, 2011 ($2.99, limited series)
1-5-Flashbacks to 1880s Gotham City; Snyder-s/Higgins-a .. 4.00

BATMAN: GCPD

DC Comics: Aug, 1996 - No. 4, Nov, 1996 ($2.25, limited series)
1-4: Features Jim Gordon; Aparo/Sienkiewicz-a 4.00

BATMAN GIANT (See reprint of new stories in Batman Universe)
DC Comics: 2018 - No. 14, 2019 ($4.99, 100 pgs., squarebound, Walmart exclusive)
1-New story Palmiotti-s/Zircher-a; reprints from Batman #608 (Hush), Nightwing ('11), and Harley Quinn ('14) in all .. 10.00
2,3,5-14: 2-Palmiotti-s/Zircher-a plus reprints. 3-Bendis-s/Derrington-a begins plus reprints.
8-Green Lantern & Jonah Hex app. in new story; Batgirl reprints replace Harley Quinn .. 5.00
4-Debut of Ginny Hex (Young Justice) in new story; Bendis-s/Derrington-a .. 8.00

BATMAN GIANT
DC Comics: 2019 - No. 5, 2020 ($4.99, 100 pgs., squarebound, Mass Market & Direct Market editions exist for each issue, with different covers)
1-5-Two new stories and reprints in each. 1-Batwoman vs. Lord Death Man .. 5.00

BATMAN: GORDON OF GOTHAM
DC Comics: June, 1998 - No. 4, Sept, 1998 ($1.95, limited series)
1-4: Gordon's early days in Chicago 4.00

BATMAN: GORDON'S LAW
DC Comics: Dec, 1996 - No. 4, Mar, 1997 ($1.95, limited series)
1-4: Dixon-s/Janson-c/a 4.00

BATMAN: GOTHAM ADVENTURES (Based on Kids WB Batman animated series)
DC Comics: June, 1998 - No. 60, May, 2003 ($2.95/$1.95/$1.99/$2.25)

1-($2.95)	3	6	9	14	19	24
2-($1.95) Two-Face-c/app.						5.00
3-($1.95) Grey Ghost app.	3	6	9	16	23	30
4-9,11-13,15-28: 4-Begin $1.99-c. 5-Deadman-c. 13-MAD #1 cover swipe						4.00
10,14-Harley Quinn c/app.	2	4	6	13	18	22
29,43-Harley Quinn c/app.	2	4	6	13	18	22
30,32-42,44,46-52,54-59: 50-Catwoman-c/app. 58-Creeper-c/app.						4.00
31-Joker-c/app.	1	2	3	5	6	8
45-Harley Quinn c/app.	3	6	9	16	24	35
53-Poison Ivy-c/app.; Harley Quinn cameo	2	4	6	12	13	15
60-Joker-c/app.	3	6	9	15	22	28
TPB (2000, $9.95) r/#1-6						24.00

BATMAN: GOTHAM AFTER MIDNIGHT
DC Comics: July, 2008 - No. 12, Jun, 2009 ($2.99, limited series)
1-12-Steve Niles-s/Kelley Jones-a/c. 1-Scarecrow app. 5,6-Man-Bat app. .. 4.00
TPB (2009, $19.99) r/#1-12; John Carpenter intro.; Jones sketch pages .. 20.00

BATMAN: GOTHAM COUNTY LINE
DC Comics: 2005 - No. 3, 2005 ($5.99, square-bound, limited series)
1-3-Steve Niles-s/Scott Hampton-a. 2,3-Deadman app. 6.00
TPB (2006, $17.99) r/#1-3 .... 18.00

BATMAN: GOTHAM KNIGHTS
DC Comics: Mar, 2000 - No. 74, Apr, 2006 ($2.50/$2.75)
1-Grayson-s; B&W back-up by Warren Ellis & Jim Lee 6.00
2-10-Grayson-s; B&W back-ups by various. 6-Killing Joke flashback .. 3.00
11-($3.25) Bolland-c; Kyle Baker back-up story 4.00
12-24: 13-Officer Down x-over; Ellison back-up-s. 15-Colan back-up. 20-Superman-c/app. .. 3.50
25,26-Bruce Wayne: Murderer pt. 4,10 .... 3.50
27-31: 28,30,31-Bruce Wayne: Fugitive pt. 7,14,17 .... 3.00
32-49: 32-Begin $2.75-c; Kaluta-a back-up. 33,34-Bane-c/app. 35-Mahfood-a back-up.
38-Bolton-a back-up. 43-Jason Todd & Batgirl app. 44-Jason Todd flashback .. 3.00
50-54-Hush returns-Barrionuevo-a/Bermejo-c. 53,54-Green Arrow app. .. 4.00
55-($3.75) Batman vs. Hush; Joker & Riddler app. 5.00
56-74: 56-58-War Games; Jae Lee-c. 60-65-Hush app. 66-Villains United tie-in; Talia app. .. 3.00
BATMAN: Hush Returns TPB (2006, $12.99) r/#50-55,66; cover gallery .. 13.00

BATMAN: GOTHAM KNIGHTS – GILDED CITY (Based on the Gotham Knights videogame)
DC Comics: Dec, 2022 - No. 6, Mar, 2023 ($4.99, limited series)
1-5-Narcisse-s/Abel-a; prequel series to the video game: Gotham Knights .. 5.00

BATMAN: GOTHAM NIGHTS II (First series listed under Gotham Nights)
DC Comics: Mar, 1995 - No. 4, June, 1995 ($1.95, limited series)
1-4 .... 4.00

BATMAN/GRENDEL (1st limited series)
DC Comics: 1993 - No. 2, 1993 ($4.95, limited series, squarebound; 52 pgs.)
1,2: Batman vs. Hunter Rose. 1-Devil's Riddle; Matt Wagner-c/a/scripts. 2-Devil's Masque; Matt Wagner-c/a/scripts .. 7.00

BATMAN/GRENDEL (2nd limited series)
DC Comics: June, 1996 - No. 2, July, 1996 ($4.95, limited series, squarebound)
1,2: Batman vs. Grendel Prime. 1-Devil's Bones. 2-Devil's Dance; Wagner-c/a/s .. 6.00

BATMAN: HARLEY & IVY
DC Comics: Jun, 2004 - No. 3, Aug, 2004 ($2.50, limited series)

| 1-Paul Dini-s/Bruce Timm-c/a in all | 4 | 8 | 12 | 22 | 35 | 48 |
| 2,3 | 3 | 6 | 9 | 14 | 20 | 26 |

TPB (2007, $14.99) r/series; newly colored story from Batman: Gotham Knights #14 and Harley and Ivy: Love on the Lam story .. 20.00

BATMAN: HARLEY QUINN
DC Comics: 1999 ($5.95, prestige format)

| 1-Intro. of Harley Quinn into regular DC continuity; Dini-s/Alex Ross-c | 8 | 16 | 24 | 56 | 108 | 160 |
| 1-(2nd printing) | 5 | 10 | 15 | 30 | 50 | 70 |

BATMAN: HAUNTED GOTHAM
DC Comics: No. 1 - No. 4, 2000 ($4.95, limited series, squarebound)
1-4-Doug Moench-s/Kelley Jones-c/a 6.00
TPB (2009, $19.99) r/#1-4 .... 20.00

BATMAN/HELLBOY/STARMAN
DC Comics/Dark Horse: Jan, 1999 - No. 2, Feb, 1999 ($2.50, limited series)

| 1,2: Robinson-s/Mignola-a. 2-Harris-c | 1 | 2 | 3 | 5 | 6 | 8 |

Batman: Harley & Ivy #2 © DC

Batman: Kings of Fear #5 © DC

Batman: Li'l Gotham #6 © DC

	GD	VG	FN	VF	VF/NM	NM-
	2.0	4.0	6.0	8.0	9.0	9.2

BATMAN: HOLLYWOOD KNIGHT
DC Comics: Apr, 2001 - No. 3, Jun, 2001 ($2.50, limited series)

1-3-Elseworlds Batman as a 1940's movie star; Giordano-a/Layton-s ... 3.00

BATMAN/ HUNTRESS: CRY FOR BLOOD
DC Comics: June, 2000 - No. 6, Nov, 2000 ($2.50, limited series)

1-6: Rucka-s/Burchett-a; The Question app. ... 3.00
TPB (2002, $12.95) r/#1-6 ... 13.00

BATMAN, INC.
DC Comics: Jan, 2011 - No. 8, Aug, 2011 ($3.99/$2.99)

1-3-Morrison-s/Paquette-a; covers by Paquette & Williams ... 4.00
4-8-($2.99) 4-Burnham-a, original Batwoman (Kathy Kane) app. ... 3.00
...: Leviathan Strikes (2/12, $6.99) Morrison-s/Burnham & Stewart-a; cover gallery ... 7.00

BATMAN INCORPORATED
DC Comics: Jul, 2012 - No. 13, Sept, 2013 ($2.99)

1-7-Morrison-s/Burnham-a/c. 2-Origin of Talia. 3-Matches Malone returns ... 3.00
1-Variant-c by Quitely ... 5.00
8-Death of Damian ... 5.00
9-13: 9,10,12,13-Morrison-s/Burnham-a/c ... 3.00
#0 (11/12, $2.99) Frazer Irving-a; the start of Batman Incorporated ... 3.00
... Special 1 (10/13, $4.99) Short stories about international Batmen; s/a by various ... 5.00

BATMAN INCORPORATED
DC Comics: Dec, 2022 - No. 12, Nov, 2023 ($3.99)

1-12: 1-Brisson-s/Timms-a; Ghost-Maker leads the team. 6,7-Bandini-a. 8-11-Joker app. ... 4.00

BATMAN: JEKYLL & HYDE
DC Comics: June, 2005 - No. 6, Nov, 2005 ($2.99, limited series)

1-6-Paul Jenkins-s; Two-Face app. 1-3-Jae Lee-a. 4-6-Sean Phillips-a ... 3.00
TPB (2008, $14.99) r/#1-6 ... 15.00

BATMAN: JOKER TIME (...: It's Joker Time! on cover)
DC Comics: 2000 - No. 3 ($4.95, limited series, squarebound)

1-3-Bob Hall-s/a ... 6.00

BATMAN: JOURNEY INTO KNGHT
DC Comics: Oct, 2005 - No. 12, Nov, 2006 ($2.50/$2.99, limited series)

1-9-Andrew Helfer-s/Tan Eng Huat-a/Pat Lee-c ... 3.00
10-12-($2.99) Joker app. ... 3.00

BATMAN/ JUDGE DREDD "DIE LAUGHING"
DC Comics: 1998 - No. 2, 1999 ($4.95, limited series, squarebound)

1,2: 1-Fabry-c/a. 2-Jim Murray-c/a		1		3	4		6	8	10

BATMAN: KILLING TIME
DC Comics: May, 2022 - No. 6, Oct, 2022 ($4.99, limited series)

1-6-Tom King-s/David Marquez-a. 1-Intro The Help ... 5.00

BATMAN: KINGS OF FEAR
DC Comics: Oct, 2018 - No. 6, Mar, 2019 ($3.99, limited series)

1-6-Scott Peterson-s/Kelley Jones-a; Scarecrow app. ... 4.00

BATMAN: KNIGHTGALLERY (See Batman one-shots)

BATMAN – KNIGHTWATCH
DC Comics: Nov, 2022 - No. 5, Mar, 2023 ($2.99, printing of the digital-first series)

1-5: 1-Clayface & Mr. Freeze app. 2-Penguin & Joker app. 3-Man-Bat & Firefly app. ... 3.00

BATMAN: LAST KNIGHT ON EARTH
DC Comics: Jul, 2019 - No. 3, Feb, 2020 ($5.99, limited series, squarebound)

1-3-Snyder-s/Capullo-a ... 6.00

BATMAN: LEAGUE OF BATMEN
DC Comics: 2001 - No. 2, 2001 ($5.95, limited series, squarebound)

1,2-Elseworlds; Moench-s/Bright & Tanghal-a/Van Fleet-c ... 6.00

BATMAN: LEGENDS OF THE DARK KNIGHT (Legends of the Dark...#1-36)
DC Comics: Nov, 1989 - No. 214, Mar, 2007 ($1.50/$1.75/$1.95/$1.99/$2.25/$2.50/$2.99)

1- "Shaman" begins, ends #5; outer cover has four different color variations, all worth same; O'Neil-s/Hannigan-a		1	2		3		5	6	8
2-10: 6-10- "Gothic" by Grant Morrison (scripts)									4.00
11-15: 11-15-Gulacy/Austin-a. 13-Catwoman app.									4.00
16-Intro drug Bane uses; begin Venom story									6.00
17-20									5.00
21-49,51-63: 38-Bat-Mite-c/story. 46-49-Catwoman app. w/Heath-c/a. 51-Ragman app.; Joe Kubert-c. 59,60,61-Knightquest x-over. 62,63-KnightsEnd Pt. 4 & 10									3.00
50-($3.95, 68 pgs.)-Bolland embossed gold foil-c; Joker-a/story; pin-ups by Chaykin, Simonson, Williamson, Kaluta, Russell, others		2		4	6		13	18	22

64-99: 64-(9/94)-Begin $1.95-c. 71-73-James Robinson-s,Watkiss-c/a-s. 74,75-McKeever-c/a/s. 76-78-Scott Hampton-c/a/s. 81-Card insert. 83,84-Ellis-s. 85-Robinson-s. 91-93-Ennis-s. 94-Michael T. Gilbert-s/a. ... 3.00
100-($3.95) Alex Ross painted-c; gallery by various ... 5.00
101-115: 101-Ezquerra-a. 102-104-Robinson-s ... 3.00
116-No Man's Land stories begin; Huntress-c ... 4.00
117-119,121-126: 122-Harris-c ... 3.00

120-ID of new Batgirl revealed		2		4	6		9	13	16

127-131: Return to Legends stories; Green Arrow app. ... 3.00
132-199, 201-204: 135-136 ($2.25-c) Archie Goodwin-s/Rogers-a. 137-141-Gulacy-a. 142-145-Joker and Ra's al Ghul app. 146-148-Kitson-a. 158-Begin $2.50-c

169-171-Tony Harris-c/a. 182-184-War Games. 182-Bagged with Sky Captain CD									3.00
200-($4.99) Joker-c/app.		1		2	3		5	6	8

205-214: 205-Begin $2.99-c. 207,208-Olivetti-a. 214-Deadshot app. ... 3.00
#0-(10/94)-Zero Hour; Quesada/Palmiotti-c; released between #64 & #65 ... 3.00
Annual 1-7 ('91-'97, $3.50-$3.95, 68 pgs.): 1-Joker app. 2-Netzer-c/a. 3-New Batman (Azrael) app. 4-Elseworlds story. 5-Year One; Man-Bat app. 6-Legend of the Dead Earth story.

7-Pulp Heroes story									4.00
... Halloween Special 1 (12/93, $6.95, 84 pgs.)-Embossed and foil stamped-c		2		4	6		8	10	12

... Halloween Special Edition 1 (12/14, giveaway) Sale-a/c ... 3.00
Batman Madness-...Halloween Special (1994, $4.95) ... 6.00
Batman Ghosts-...Halloween Special (1995, $4.95) ... 6.00
NOTE: Aparo a-Annual 1. Chaykin scripts-24-26. Giffen a-Annual 1. Golden c-Annual 1. Alan Grant scripts-38, 52, 53. Gil Kane a-24-26. Mignola a-54; c-54, 62. Morrow a-Annual 3i. Quesada a-Annual 3. James Robinson scripts- 71-73. Russell c/a-42, 43. Sears a-21, 23; c-21, 23. Zeck a-69; 70; c-69, 70.

BATMAN-LEGENDS OF THE DARK KNIGHT: JAZZ
DC Comics: Apr, 1995 - No. 3, June, 1995 ($2.50, limited series)

1-3 ... 4.00

BATMAN: LI'L GOTHAM
DC Comics: Jun, 2013 - No. 12, May, 2014 ($2.99, printings of stories that 1st appeared online)

1-12-Dustin Nguyen-a/c; Nguyen & Fridolfs-s; holiday themed short stories ... 3.00
Halloween Comic Fest 2013 (12/13, no cover price) Halloween giveaway; r/#1 ... 3.00

BATMAN/LOBO
DC Comics: Oct, 2007 - No. 2, Nov, 2007 ($5.99, squarebound, limited series)

1,2-Sam Kieth-s/a		1		3	4		6	8	10

BATMAN: LOST (Tie-in to Dark Nights: Metal series)
DC Comics: Jan, 2018 ($4.99, one-shot)

1-Snyder, Tynion IV & Williamson-s/Mahnke, Paquette & Jimenez-a; Coipel foil-c ... 5.00

BATMAN: MANBAT
DC Comics: Oct, 1995 - No. 3, Dec, 1995 ($4.95, limited series)

1-3-Elseworlds-Delano-script; Bolton-a ... 6.00
TPB-(1997, $14.95) r/#1-3 ... 15.00

BATMAN: MITEFALL (See Batman one-shots)

BATMAN MINIATURE (See Batman Kellogg's)

BATMAN: NEVERMORE
DC Comics: June, 2003 - No. 5, Oct, 2003 ($2.50, limited series)

1-5-Elseworlds Batman & Edgar Allan Poe; Wrightson-c/Guy Davis-a/Len Wein-s ... 4.00

BATMAN: NO MAN'S LAND (Also see 1999 Batman titles)
DC Comics: (one shots)

nn (3/99, $2.95) Alex Ross-c; Bob Gale-s; begins year-long story arc ... 4.00
Collector's Ed. (3/99, $3.95) Ross lenticular-c ... 6.00
#0 (: Ground Zero on cover) (12/99, $4.95) Orbik-c ... 6.00
...: Gallery (7/99, $3.95) Jim Lee-c ... 4.00
...: Secret Files (12/99, $4.95) Maleev-c ... 6.00
TPB ('99, $12.95) r/early No Man's Land stories; new Batgirl early app. ... 13.00
No Law and a New Order TPB(1999, $5.95) Ross-c ... 8.00
Volume 2 ('00, $12.95) r/later No Man's Land stories; Batgirl (Huntress) app.; Deodato-c ... 13.00
Volume 3-5 ('00-'01 $12.95) 3-Intro. new Batgirl. 4-('00). 5-('01) Land-c ... 13.00

BATMAN: ODYSSEY
DC Comics: Sept, 2010 - No. 6, Feb, 2011 ($3.99, limited series)

1-6-Neal Adams-s/a/c. 1-Man-Bat app.; bonus sketch pages. 5,6-Joker app. ... 4.00
1-6-Variant B&W-version cover ... 5.00
Vol. 2 (12/11 - No. 7, 6/12) 1-7-Neal Adams-a/c ... 4.00

BATMAN: OFF-WORLD
DC Comics: Jan, 2024 - Present ($3.99, limited series)

1-3-Jason Aaron-s/Doug Mahnke-a ... 4.00

BATMAN – ONE BAD DAY
DC Comics: Oct, 2022 - May, 2023 ($7.99, series of one-shots)

	GD 2.0	VG 4.0	FN 6.0	VF 8.0	VF/NM 9.0	NM- 9.2

...: Bane 1 (3/23) Williamson-s/Porter-a ... 8.00
...: Catwoman 1 (2/23) G. Willow Wilson-s/Jamie McKelvie-a ... 8.00
...: Clayface 1 (4/23) Kelly & Lanzing-s/Xermánico-a ... 8.00
...: Mr. Freeze 1 (1/23) Duggan-s/Scalera-a ... 8.00
...: Penguin 1 (12/22) Ridley-s/Camuncoli-a; Penguin vs. The Umbrella Man ... 8.00
...: Ra's al Ghul 1 (5/23) Tom Taylor-s/Ivan Reis-a ... 8.00
...: The Riddler 1 (10/22) Tom King-s/Mitch Gerads-a; childhood flashback ... 8.00
...: Two-Face 1 (11/22) Mariko Tamaki-s/Javier Fernandez-a ... 8.00

BATMAN: ONE DARK KNIGHT
DC Comics (Black Label): Feb, 2022 - No. 3, Sept, 2022 ($6.99, oversized 8-1/2" x 10-3/4", lim. series)
1-3-Jock-s/a/c ... 7.00

BATMAN: ORPHANS
DC Comics: Early Feb, 2011 - No. 2, Late Feb, 2011 ($3.99, limited series)
1,2-Berganza-s/Barberi-a/c ... 4.00

BATMAN: ORPHEUS RISING
DC Comics: Oct, 2001 - No. 5, Feb, 2002 ($2.50, limited series)
1-5-Intro. Orpheus; Simmons-s/Turner & Miki-a ... 3.00

BATMAN: OUTLAWS
DC Comics: 2000 - No. 3, 2000 ($4.95, limited series)
1-3-Moench-s/Gulacy-a ... 5.00

BATMAN: PENGUIN TRIUMPHANT (See Batman one-shots)

BATMAN/PREDATOR III: BLOOD TIES
DC Comics/Dark Horse Comics: Nov, 1997 - No. 4, Feb, 1998 ($1.95, lim. series)

1-4: Dixon-s/Damaggio-c/a	1	2	3	5	6	8

TPB-(1998, $7.95) r/#1-4 ... 25.00

BATMAN: PRELUDE TO THE WEDDING
DC Comics: Jul, 2018 - Aug, 2018 ($3.99, series of one-shots)
...: Batgirl vs. Riddler 1 (8/18) Tim Seeley-s/Minkyu Jung-a ... 4.00
...: Harley Quinn vs. Joker 1 (8/18) Tim Seeley-s/Sami Basri-a; leads into Batman #48 ... 4.00
...: Nightwing vs. Hush 1 (8/18) Tim Seeley-s/Travis Moore-a; Superman app. ... 4.00
...: Red Hood vs. Anarky 1 (8/18) Tim Seeley-s/Javier Fernandez-a; Joker app. ... 4.00
...: Robin vs. Ra's al Ghul 1 (7/18) Tim Seeley-s/Brad Walker-a; Selina Kyle app. ... 4.00

BATMAN/RA'S AL GHUL (See Year One:...)

BATMAN: REPTILIAN
DC Comics: Aug, 2021 - No. 6, Dec, 2021 ($4.99, limited series)
1-6-Garth Ennis-s/Liam Sharp-a; Killer Croc app. ... 5.00

BATMAN RETURNS MOVIE SPECIAL (See Batman one-shots)

BATMAN: RIDDLER-THE RIDDLE FACTORY (See Batman one-shots)

BATMAN: RUN, RIDDLER, RUN
DC Comics: 1992 - Book 3, 1992 ($4.95, limited series)
Book 1-3: Mark Badger-a & plot ... 6.00

BATMAN - SANTA CLAUS: SILENT KNIGHT
DC Comics: Feb, 2024 - No. 4, Feb, 2024 ($3.99, weekly limited series)
1-4: 1-Jeff Parker-s/Michele Bandini-a; Zatanna & the Bat-Family app. vs. Krampus ... 4.00

BATMAN SCARECROW (See Year One:...)

BATMAN SCOOBY-DOO MYSTERIES, THE (See The Batman & Scooby-Doo Mysteries)

BATMAN: SECRET FILES
DC Comics: Oct, 1997; Dec, 2018; Sept, 2019; Jun, 2020; 2021 ($4.95/$4.99)
1-New origin-s and profiles ... 6.00
1-(12/18, $4.99) Short stories by various; Detective Chimp app. ... 5.00
2-(9/19, $4.99) Short stories by various; Joker, Riddler, Bane, Hugo Strange app. ... 5.00
3-(6/20, $4.99) Short stories; Deathstroke, Cheshire, Merlyn, Mr. Teeth & Gunsmith ... 5.00
...: Clownhunter 1 (10/21, $4.99) Punchline & Red Hood app.; Brisson-s/Kämpe-a ... 5.00
...: Huntress 1 (9/21, $4.99) Tamaki-s/Lapham-a ... 5.00
...: Miracle Molly 1 (11/21, $4.99) Tynion IV-s/Dani-a ... 5.00
...: Peacekeeper-01 1 (12/21, $4.99) "Fear State" tie-in; Tynion IV & Brisson-s/Hixson-a ... 5.00
...: The Gardener 1 (12/21, $4.99) "Fear State" tie-in; Poison Ivy app.; Ward-a ... 5.00
...: The Signal 1 (9/21, $4.99) Patrick-s/Duce-a ... 5.00

BATMAN: SECRETS
DC Comics: May, 2006 - No. 5, Sept, 2006 ($2.99, limited series)
1-5-Sam Kieth-s/a/c; Joker app. ... 3.00
TPB (2007, $12.99) r/series ... 13.00

BATMAN'S GRAVE, THE
DC Comics: Dec, 2019 - No. 12, Feb, 2021 ($3.99, limited series)
1-12-Warren Ellis-s/Bryan Hitch-a ... 4.00

BATMAN / SHADOW (Pulp hero)
DC Comics: June, 2017 - No. 6, Nov, 2017 ($3.99, limited series)
1-6: Snyder & Orlando-s/Rossmo-a; Lamont Cranston in current Gotham City ... 4.00

BATMAN: SHADOW OF THE BAT
DC Comics: June, 1992 - No. 94, 2000 ($1.50/$1.75/$1.95/$1.99)
1-The Last Arkham-c/story begins; 1st app. Victor Zsasz; Alan Grant scripts in all

	2	4	6	10	14	18

1-($2.50)-Deluxe edition polybagged w/poster, pop-up & book mark

	2	4	6	10	14	18

2-7: 4-The Last Arkham ends. 7-Last $1.50-c ... 5.00
8-28: 14,15-Staton-a(p). 16-18-Knightfall tie-ins. 19-28-Knightquest tie-ins w/Azrael as Batman. 25-Silver ink-c; anniversary issue
29-($2.95, 52 pgs.)-KnightsEnd Pt. 2 ... 5.00
30-72: 30-KnightsEnd Pt. 8. 31-(9/94)-Begin $1.95-c; Zero Hour. 32-(11/94). 33-Robin-a. 35-Troika-Pt.2. 43,44-Cat-Man & Catwoman-c. 48-Contagion Pt. 1; card insert. 49-Contagion Pt.7. 56,57,58-Poison Ivy-c/app. 62-Two-Face app. 69,70-Fate app. ... 4.00
35-($2.95)-Variant embossed-c ... 4.00
73,74,76-78: Cataclysm x-over pts. 1,9. 76-78-Orbik-c ... 4.00
75-($2.95) Mr. Freeze & Clayface app.; Orbik-c ... 4.00
79,81,82: 79-Begin $1.99-c; Orbik-c ... 4.00

80-($3.95) Flip book with Azrael #47 ... 5.00
83-No Man's Land; intro. new Batgirl (Huntress)

	2	4	6	11	16	20

84,85-No Man's Land ... 5.00
86-92,94: 87-Deodato-a. 90-Harris-c. 92-Superman app. 94-No Man's Land ends ... 4.00
93-Joker and Harley app. ... 5.00
#0 (10/94) Zero Hour tie-in; released between #31 & #32 ... 4.00
#1,000,000 (11/98) 853rd Century x-over; Orbik-c ... 4.00
Annual 1-5 ('93-'97 $2.95-$3.95, 68 pgs.): 3-Year One story; Poison Ivy app. 4-Legends of the Dead Earth story; Starman cameo. 5-Pulp Heroes story; Poison Ivy app. ... 4.00

BATMAN: SINS OF THE FATHER (Based on the Batman: The Telltale Series video game)
DC Comics: Apr, 2018 - No. 6, Sept, 2018 ($2.99, printing of digital first stories)
1-6-Gage-s/Ienco-a; Deadshot app. ... 3.00

BATMAN '66 (Characters and likenesses based on the 1966 television series)
DC Comics: Sept, 2013 - No. 30, Feb, 2016 ($3.99/$2.99, printings of stories that first appeared online)
1-Jeff Parker-s/Jonathan Case-a/Mike Allred-c; Riddler & Catwoman app.

	2	4	6	9	12	15
1-Variant-c by Jonathan Case	2	4	6	10	14	18
1-San Diego Comic-Con variant action figure photo-c	3	6	9	17	26	35

			1	2	3	4
2-4: 2-Penguin & Mr. Freeze app.; Templeton-a. 3-Joker app.						

			1	2	3	4

5-12: 5,10,11-Batgirl app. 8-King Tut app. 11,20-Joker app. ... 4.00
13-24,27-30: 14-Selfie variant-c. 16,20-Egghead app. 18,21,27,29-Batgirl app. 21-Lord Death Man app. 22-Oeming-a. 27-Bane app. 30-Allred-a ... 3.00
25,26: 25-1st app. The Harlequin; back-up Mad Men spoof with Batgirl. 26-Poison Ivy app.
... Meets the Legion of Super-Heroes 1 (9/17, $3.99) Lee Allred-s/Mike Allred-a/c ... 4.00
... The Lost Episode 1 (1/15, $9.99) Harlan Ellison 1960s script adapted by Len Wein; García-López-a; Two-Face app.; covers by García-López & Ross; original pencil art ... 10.00

BATMAN '66 MEETS STEED AND MRS. PEEL (TV's The Avengers)
DC Comics: Sept, 2016 - No. 6, Feb, 2017 ($3.99, printings of stories that first appeared online)
1-6-Edginton-s/Dow Smith-a/Allred-c. 1,2-Catwoman app. 3-6-Mr. Freeze app. ... 3.00

BATMAN '66 MEETS THE GREEN HORNET
DC Comics: Aug, 2014 - No. 6, Jan, 2015 ($2.99, printings of stories that first appeared online)
1-6-Kevin Smith & Ralph Garman-s/Ty Templeton-a/Alex Ross-c ... 3.00

BATMAN '66 MEETS THE MAN FROM U.N.C.L.E.
DC Comics: Feb, 2016 - No. 6, Jul, 2016 ($3.99, limited series)
1-6-Jeff Parker-s/David Haun-a/Allred-c. 1-Olga and Penguin app. ... 3.00

BATMAN '66 MEETS WONDER WOMAN '77
DC Comics: Mar, 2017 - No. 6, Aug, 2017 ($3.99, limited series)
1-6-Parker & Andreyko-s/Haun-a; Ra's al Ghul & Talia app. 5,6-Robin as Nightwing ... 6.00

BATMAN: SON OF THE DEMON (Also see Batman #655-658 and Batman Hardcovers)
DC Comics: 2006 ($5.99, reprints the 1987 HC in comic book format)
nn-Talia has Batman's son; Mike W. Barr-s/Jerry Bingham-a; new Andy Kubert-c ... 6.00

BATMAN/SPAWN
DC Comics: Feb, 2023 ($6.99, squarebound one-shot)
1-McFarlane-s/Capullo-a; the Court of Owls and the Joker app. ... 7.00
... Unplugged 1 (4/23, $6.99) B&W inked pages with no text ... 7.00

BATMAN-SPAWN: WAR DEVIL (See Batman one-shots)

BATMAN SPECTACULAR (See DC Special Series No. 15)

BATMAN: STREETS OF GOTHAM (Follows Batman: Battle For The Cowl series)
DC Comics: Aug, 2009 - No. 21, May, 2011 ($3.99/$2.99)
1-18: 1-Dini-s/Nguyen-a; back-up Manhunter feature; Jeanty-a. 10,11-Zsasz app. ... 4.00
19-21-(2/99) 19-Joker app. ... 3.00
...- Hush Money HC (2010, $19.99) r/#1-4, Detective #852 and Batman #685 ... 20.00
...- Hush Money SC (2011, $14.99) r/#1-4, Detective #852 and Batman #685 ... 15.00
...- Leviathan HC (2010, $19.99) r/#5-11 ... 20.00
...- The House of Hush HC (2011, $22.99) r/#12-14,16-21 ... 23.00

BATMAN STRIKES!, THE (Based on the 2004 animated series)
DC Comics: Nov, 2004 - No. 50, Dec, 2008 ($2.25)

1-Penguin app.	1	2	3	5	6	8

1-Free Comic Book Day edition (6/05) Penguin app. ... 3.00
2,4-27,29-31,33,34,36-38,40,42,44,46,48-50: 2-Man-Bat app. 4-Bane app. 9-Joker app. 11-Penguin app. 18-Batgirl debut. 29-Robin debuts. 33-Cal Ripken 8-pg. insert. 44-Superman app. ... 3.00
3-($2.95) Joker-c/app.; Catwoman & Wonder Woman-r from Advs. in the DCU ... 4.00
28,32-Joker-c/app. 32-Cal Ripken 8-pg. insert. ... 5.00

35-Harley Quinn & Poison Ivy-c/app.	2	4	6	10	14	18

39,47-Black Mask-c/app. ... 6.00

41-Harley Quinn & Poison Ivy-c/app.	2	4	6	11	16	20
43-Harley Quinn-c/app.	2	4	6	10	14	18
45-Harley Quinn, Poison Ivy, Catwoman-c/app.	2	4	6	11	16	20

Jam Packed Action (2005, $7.99, digest) adaptations of two TV episodes ... 8.00
... Vol. 1: Crime Time (2005, $6.99, digest) r/#1-5 ... 7.00
... Vol. 2: In Darkest Knight (2005, $6.99, digest) r/#6-10 ... 7.00

BATMAN/ SUPERMAN
DC Comics: Aug, 2013 - No. 32, Jul, 2016 ($3.99)
1-4-Greg Pak-s/Jae Lee-a/c; Catwoman & Wonder Woman app. ... 4.00
3.1 (11/13, $2.99, regular cover) ... 3.00
3.1 (11/13, $3.99, 3-D cover) "Doomsday #1" on cover; Booth-a; Zod app. ... 6.00
5-7-Booth-a; reads sideways; Maguire app. ... 4.00
8,9-First Contact x-over with Worlds' Finest #20,21; Power Girl & Huntress app.; Lee-a ... 4.00
10-31: 11-Doomed tie-in. 13-Jae Lee-a. 13-15-Catwoman app. 17-Lobo app. 21-Batman (Gordon in robot suit). 23,24-Aquaman app. 25-27-Vandal Savage app. ... 4.00
32-The Great Ten app.; 1st app. Chinese Super-Man (Kong Kenan) ... 5.00
Annual 1 (5/14, $5.99) Supergirl, Krypto, Cyborg, Batgirl, Red Hood app.; Jae Lee-c ... 5.00
Annual 2 (5/15, $4.99) Killer Croc, Cheshire & Bane app.; Syaf-c ... 6.00
...: Futures End 1 (11/14, $2.99, regular-c) Five years later; Pak-s ... 3.00
...: Futures End 1 (11/14, $3.99, 3-D cover) ... 4.00

Batman '66 #8 © DC

Batman/Superman: World's Finest #18 © DC

Batman: The Dark Knight #19 © DC

	GD	VG	FN	VF	VF/NM	NM-
	2.0	4.0	6.0	8.0	9.0	9.2

BATMAN/ SUPERMAN
DC Comics: Oct, 2019 - No. 22, Nov, 2021 ($3.99)

1-22: 1-5-The Batman Who Laughs app.; Williamson-s/Marquez-a. 4-Acetate-c. 7,8-General
Zod & Ra's al Ghul app. 9-11-Ultra-Humanite app. 15-Solomon Grundy app. ... 4.00
Annual 1 (11/20, $4.99) Bat-Mite and Mr. Mxyzptlk app.; Eaglesham & Melnikov-a ... 5.00
2021 Annual 1 (10/21, $5.99) Yang-s/Francavilla & Pelletier-a ... 6.00
...: The Authority Special 1 (1/22, $5.99) P.K. Johnson-s/Hairsine, Beredo, Templesmith-a ... 6.00

BATMAN/ SUPERMAN/WONDER WOMAN: TRINITY
DC Comics: 2003 - No. 3, 2003 ($6.95, limited series, squarebound)

1-3-Matt Wagner-s/a/c. 1-Ra's al Ghul & Bizarro app. ... 7.00
HC (2004, $24.95, with dust-jacket) r/series; intro. by Brad Meltzer ... 30.00
SC (2004, $17.99) r/series; intro. by Brad Meltzer ... 18.00

BATMAN/ SUPERMAN: WORLD'S FINEST
DC Comics: May, 2022 - Present ($3.99)

1-24: 1-5-Waid-s/Mora-a; Doom Patrol app. 6,18,19-Travis Moore-a. 7-Intro Boy Thunder.
9-11-Joker and The Key app. 20-22-Kingdom Come; Gog & Magog app. ... 4.00
2024 Annual 1 (3/24, $4.99) Bumblebee, Metamorpho, Challengers of the Unknown app. ... 5.00

BATMAN: SWORD OF AZRAEL (Also see Azrael & Batman #488,489)
DC Comics: Oct, 1992 - No. 4, Jan, 1993 ($1.75, limited series)

		3	6	9	14	19	24
1-Wraparound gatefold-c; Quesada-c/a(p) in all; 1st app. Azrael		1	2	3	5	6	8
2-4: 4-Cont'd in Batman #488							

Silver Edition 1-4 (1993, $1.95)-Reprints #1-4 ... 3.00
Trade Paperback (1993, $9.95)-Reprints #1-4 ... 12.00
Trade Paperback Gold Edition ... 18.00

BATMAN/ TARZAN: CLAWS OF THE CAT-WOMAN
Dark Horse Comics/DC Comics: Sept, 1999 - No. 4, Dec, 1999 ($2.95, limited series)

1-4: Marz-s/Kordey-a ... 4.00

BATMAN/ TEENAGE MUTANT NINJA TURTLES
DC Comics: Feb, 2016 - No. 6, Jul, 2016 ($3.99, limited series)

1-6-Tynion IV-s/Williams II-a; Penguin, Croc & Shredder app. ... 5.00
... Director's Cut 1 (11/16, $5.99) r/#1 in B&W and pencil-a; original script ... 6.00

BATMAN/ TEENAGE MUTANT NINJA TURTLES II
DC Comics: Feb, 2018 - No. 6, Jun, 2018 ($3.99, limited series)

1-6-Tynion IV-s/Williams II-a; Bane app. ... 4.00

BATMAN/ TEENAGE MUTANT NINJA TURTLES III
DC Comics: Jul, 2019 - No. 6, Dec, 2019 ($3.99, limited series)

1-6-Tynion IV-s/Williams II-a; Crisis in a Half Shell; Anti-Monitor and Krang app. ... 4.00

BATMAN/ TEENAGE MUTANT NINJA TURTLES ADVENTURES
IDW Publishing: Nov, 2016 - No. 6, Apr, 2017 ($3.99, limited series)

1-6-Manning-s/Sommariva-a; Clayface, Joker and Harley Quinn app.; multiple covers ... 4.00
... Director's Cut 1 (2/17, $4.99) r/#1 in B&W and pencil-a; original script ... 5.00

BATMAN: TENSES
DC Comics: 2003 - No. 2, 2003 ($6.95, limited series)

1,2-Joe Casey-s/Cully Hamner-a; Bruce Wayne's first year back in Gotham ... 7.00

BATMAN: THE ADVENTURES CONTINUE (Set in Batman: The Animated Series continuity)
DC Comics: Jun, 2020 - No. 8, Mar, 2021 ($3.99, printing of digital first stories)

1-7-Dini & Burnett-s/Templeton-a. 2,3-Deathstroke app. 4-Azrael app. 5,6-Red Hood app.;
Jason Todd origin as Robin. 6-Joker & Harley Quinn app. ... 4.00
8-($4.99) Harley Quinn, Poison Ivy, Scarface and Joker app. ... 5.00

BATMAN: THE ADVENTURES CONTINUE SEASON TWO (Batman: The Animated Series)
DC Comics: Aug, 2021 - No. 7, Feb, 2022 ($3.99, printing of digital first stories)

1-7: 1,2-Dini & Burnett-s/Templeton-a. 3,5-7-Burchett-a ... 4.00

BATMAN: THE ADVENTURES CONTINUE SEASON THREE (Batman: The Animated Series)
DC Comics: Mar, 2023 - No. 8, Dec, 2023 ($3.99, printing of digital first stories)

1-8: 1-Dini & Burnett-s/Gibson-a. 2-Altieri-a. 3-Templeton-a; Task Force X app. ... 4.00

BATMAN: THE ANKH
DC Comics: 2002 - No. 2, 2002 ($5.95, limited series)

1,2-Dixon-s/Van Fleet-a ... 6.00

BATMAN: THE AUDIO ADVENTURES
DC Comics: Nov, 2022 - No. 7, Sept, 2023 ($3.99, limited series)

1-7: Killer Croc app. ... 4.00

BATMAN: THE BRAVE AND THE BOLD (Based on the 2008 animated series)
DC Comics: Mar, 2009 - No. 22, Dec, 2010 ($2.50/$2.99)

1-18: 1-Power Girl app. 4-Sugar & Spike cameo. 7-Doom Patrol app. 9-Catman app. ... 3.00

19-22-($2.99) Cyborg Superman and the Green Lantern Corps app. 22-Aquaman app. ... 3.00
TPB (2009, $12.99) r/#1-6 ... 13.00
...: Emerald Knight TPB (2011, $12.99) r/#13,14,16,18,19,21 ... 13.00
...: The Fearsome Fangs Strike Again TPB (2010, $12.99) r/#7-12 ... 13.00

BATMAN: THE BRAVE AND THE BOLD (Titled "All New Batman: Brave & the Bold" for #1-13)
DC Comics: Jan, 2011 - No. 16, Apr, 2012 ($2.99)

1-16: 1-Superman. 4-Wonder Woman app. 8-Aquaman app. 9-Hawkman app. ... 3.00

BATMAN: THE BRAVE AND THE BOLD
DC Comics: Jul, 2023 - Present ($7.99, square-bound)

1-10-Serialized short stories by various. 1,2-Joker app. 4-Kelley Jones-a ... 8.00

BATMAN: THE CULT
DC Comics: 1988 - No. 4, Nov, 1988 ($3.50, deluxe limited series)

			1	3	4	6	8	10
1-Wrightson-a/painted-c in all			1	3	4	6	8	10
2-4								6.00

Trade Paperback (1991, $14.95)-New Wrightson-c; Starlin intro. ... 25.00
Trade Paperback (2009, $19.99) ... 20.00

BATMAN: THE DARK KNIGHT
DC Comics: Jan, 2011 - No. 5, Oct, 2011 ($3.99/$2.99)

1-David Finch-s/a; Penguin & Killer Croc app.; covers by Finch and Clarke ... 4.00
2-5-($2.99) Demon app. ... 3.00

BATMAN: THE DARK KNIGHT (DC New 52)
DC Comics: Nov, 2011 - No. 29, May, 2014 ($2.99)

1-29: 1-Jenkins & Finch-s/Finch-a/c; White Rabbit debut. 3-Flash app. 5,6-Superman app.
6,7-Bane app. 9-Night of the Owls. 22-25-Maleev-a. 28-Van Sciver-a/c ... 3.00
23.1, 23.2, 23.3, 23.4 (11/13, $2.99, regular covers) ... 3.00
23.1 (11/13, $3.99, 3-D cover) "Ventriloquist #1" on cover; Simone-s/Santacruz-a ... 6.00
23.2 (11/13, $3.99, 3-D cover) "Mr. Freeze #1" on cover; Gray & Palmiotti-s ... 5.00
23.3 (11/13, $3.99, 3-D cover) "Clayface#1" on cover; Richards-a ... 5.00
23.4 (11/13, $3.99, 3-D cover) "Joker's Daughter #1" on cover; origin story; Jeanty-a ... 12.00
#0 (11/12, $2.99) Hurwitz-s/Suayan & Ryp-a; flashback to aftermath of parents' murder ... 3.00
Annual 1 (7/13, $4.99) Hurwitz-s/Kudranski-a/Maleev-c; Scarecrow, Penguin Mad Hatter ... 5.00

BATMAN: THE DARK KNIGHT RETURNS (Also see Dark Knight Strikes Again)
DC Comics: Mar, 1986 - No. 4, 1986 ($2.95, squarebound, limited series)

		9	18	27	57	111	165
1-Miller story & c/a(p); set in the future		9	18	27	57	111	165
1,2-2nd & 3rd printings, 3-2nd printing		3	6	9	19	30	40
2-Carrie Kelley becomes 1st female Robin		5	10	15	31	53	75
3-Death of Joker; Superman app.		3	6	9	20	31	42
4-Death of Alfred; Superman app.		3	6	9	20	31	42

Hardcover, signed & numbered edition ($40.00)(4000 copies) ... 300.00
Hardcover, trade edition ... 70.00

		2	4	6	11	16	20
Softcover, trade edition (1st printing only)		2	4	6	11	16	20
Softcover, trade edition (2nd thru 8th printings)		2	4	6	8	10	12

10th Anniv. Slipcase set ('96, $100.00): Signed & numbered hard-c edition (10,000 copies),
sketchbook, copy of script for #1, 2 color prints ... 150.00
10th Anniv. Hardcover ('96, $45.00) ... 50.00
10th Anniv. Softcover ('97, $14.95) ... 25.00
Hardcover 2nd printing ('02, $24.95) with 3 1/4" tall partial dustjacket ... 25.00
NOTE: The #2 second printings can be identified by matching the grey background colors on the inside front cover
and facing page. The inside front cover of the second printing has a dark grey background which does not match
the lighter grey of the facing page. On the true 1st printings, the backgrounds are both light grey. All other issues
are clearly marked.

BATMAN: THE DARK PRINCE CHARMING
DC Comics: Jan, 2018 - No. 2, Jun, 2018 ($12.99, HC, limited series)

1,2-Enrico Marini-s/a; Joker & Harley Quinn app. ... 13.00

BATMAN: THE DAWNBREAKER (Tie-in to Dark Nights: Metal series)
DC Comics: Dec, 2017 ($3.99, one-shot)

1-Humphries-s/Van Sciver-a; Fabok foil-c; Wayne as Dark Multiverse Green Lantern ... 4.00

BATMAN: THE DETECTIVE
DC Comics: Jun, 2021 - No. 6, Jan, 2022 ($3.99, limited series)

1-6-Tom Taylor-s/Andy Kubert-a; Knight and Squire app. ... 4.00

BATMAN: THE DOOM THAT CAME TO GOTHAM
DC Comics: 2000 - No. 3, 2001 ($4.95, limited series)

1-3-Elseworlds; Mignola-c/s; Nixey-a; Etrigan app. ... 6.00

BATMAN: THE DEVASTATOR (Tie-in to Dark Nights: Metal series)
DC Comics: Jan, 2018 ($3.99, one-shot)

1-Tieri-s/Daniel-a; Fabok foil-c; Bruce Wayne as Dark Multiverse Doomsday ... 4.00

BATMAN: THE DROWNED (Tie-in to Dark Nights: Metal series)
DC Comics: Dec, 2017 ($3.99, one-shot)

	GD 2.0	VG 4.0	FN 6.0	VF 8.0	VF/NM 9.0	NM- 9.2

1-Abnett-s/Tan-a; Fabok foil-c; female Bryce Wayne as Dark Multiverse Aquawoman 4.00

BATMAN: THE IMPOSTER
DC Comics (Black Label): Dec, 2021 - No. 3, Feb, 2022 ($5.99, limited series)
1-3-Mattson Tomlin-s/Andrea Sorrentino-a 6.00

BATMAN: THE KILLING JOKE (See Batman one-shots)

BATMAN: THE KNIGHT
DC Comics: Mar, 2022 - No. 10, Dec, 2022 ($4.99, limited series)
1-10-Zdarsky-s/Di Giandomenico-a; flashbacks to his training days. 7-Zatanna app. 5.00
...: Compendium Edition 1 (7/22, $7.99) Reprints #1-3 8.00

BATMAN: THE LONG HALLOWEEN
DC Comics: Oct, 1996 - No. 13, Oct, 1997 ($2.95/$4.95, limited series)

1-($4.95)-Loeb-s/Sale-c/a in all	4	8	12	28	47	65
2,4,5 ($2.95): 2-Solomon Grundy-c/app.	2	4	6	8	11	14
3-Joker-c/app., Catwoman, Poison Ivy app.	3	6	9	14	20	25
6,8-10: 6-Poison Ivy-c	1	2	3	5	6	8
7-Riddler-c/app.	2	4	6	11	16	20
11,12	1	2	3	5	6	8
13-($4.95, 48 pgs.)-Killer revelations	2	4	6	10	14	18

Special 1 (12/21, $7.99) Loeb-s/Sale-a; continuation of story; Calendar Man app. 8.00
Special Edition (Halloween Comic Fest 2013) (12/13, free giveaway) r/#1 5.00
Absolute Batman: The Long Halloween (2007, $75.00, oversized HC) r/series; interviews with the creators; Sale sketch pages; action figure line; unpubbed 4-page sequence 130.00
HC-($29.95) r/series 65.00
SC-($19.95) 20.00

BATMAN: THE MAD MONK ("Batman & the Mad Monk" on cover)
DC Comics: Oct, 2006 - No. 6, Mar, 2007 ($3.50, limited series)
1-6-Matt Wagner-s/a/c. 1-Catwoman app. 3.50
TPB (2007, $14.99) r/#1-6 15.00

BATMAN / THE MAXX: ARKHAM DREAMS
IDW Publishing/DC Comics: Sept, 2018 - No. 5 ($4.99, limited series)
1-3-Sam Kieth-s/a; 3 covers on each. 2-Joker app. 5.00
... The Lost Year Compendium (9/20, $7.99) Reprints #1-3; thumbnail previews of #4 8.00

BATMAN: THE MERCILESS (Tie-in to Dark Nights: Metal series)
DC Comics: Dec, 2017 ($3.99, one-shot)
1-Tomasi-s/Manapul-a; Fabok foil-c; Bruce Wayne as Dark Multiverse God of War 4.00

BATMAN: THE MONSTER MEN ("Batman & the Monster Men" on cover)
DC Comics: Jan, 2006 - No. 6, June, 2006 ($2.99, limited series)
1-6-Matt Wagner-s/a/c 3.00
TPB (2006, $14.99) r/#1-6 15.00

BATMAN: THE MURDER MACHINE (Tie-in to Dark Nights: Metal series)
DC Comics: Nov, 2017 ($3.99, one-shot)
1-Tieri-s/Federici-a; Fabok foil-c; Bruce Wayne as Dark Multiverse Cyborg 4.00

BATMAN: THE OFFICIAL COMIC ADAPTATION OF THE WARNER BROS. MOTION PICTURE
(See Batman one-shots)

BATMAN: THE RED DEATH (Tie-in to Dark Nights: Metal series)
DC Comics: Nov, 2017 ($3.99, one-shot)
1-Williamson-s/Di Giandomenico-a; Fabok foil-c; Bruce Wayne as Dark Multiverse Flash 4.00

BATMAN: THE RETURN
DC Comics: Jan, 2011 ($4.99, one-shot)
1-Morrison-s/Finch-a; covers by Finch & Ha; costume design sketch art; script pages 5.00

BATMAN: THE RETURN OF BRUCE WAYNE (Follows Batman's "death" in Final Crisis #6)
DC Comics: Early Jul, 2010 - No. 6, Dec, 2010 ($3.99, limited series)
1-6-Bruce Wayne's time travels; Morrison-s/Andy Kubert-c. 1-Sprouse-a. 4-Jeanty-a 4.00
1-Second & third printings; 4.00
1-6-Variant covers: 1-Sprouse. 2-Irving. 3-Paquette. 4-Jeanty. 5-Sook. 6-Garbett 8.00
... - The Deluxe Edition HC (2011, $29.99) r/#1-6; sketch pages 30.00

BATMAN: THE ULTIMATE EVIL
DC Comics: 1995 ($5.95, limited series, prestige format)
1,2-Barrett, Jr. adaptation of Vachss novel. 6.00

BATMAN: THE WIDENING GYRE
DC Comics: Oct, 2009 - No. 6, Sept, 2010 ($3.99/$2.99/$4.99, limited series)
1-($3.99) Kevin Smith-s/Walt Flanagan-a; debut Baphomet; Demon app.; Sienkiewicz-c 4.00
1-5-Variant covers by Gene Ha 8.00
2-5-($2.99) 2-Silver St. Cloud returns. 5-Catwoman app. 3.00
6-($4.99) Joker, Deadshot & Catwoman app. 5.00
6-Variant cover by Gene Ha 10.00
HC (2010, $19.99, dj) r/#1-6; variant covers; afterword by Kevin Smith 20.00

BATMAN 3-D (Also see 3-D Batman)
DC Comics: 1990 ($9.95, w/glasses, 8-1/8x10-3/4")

nn-Byrne-a/scripts; Riddler, Joker, Penguin & Two-Face app. plus r/1953 3-D Batman; pin-ups by many artists	2	4	6	9	13	16

BATMAN: THREE JOKERS
DC Comics (Black Label): Oct, 2020 - No. 3, Dec, 2020 ($6.99, limited series)

1-3-Johns-s/Fabok-a. 1-Red Hood & Batgirl app. 2,3-Joe Chill app.	1	2	3	4	5	7

BATMAN: TOYMAN
DC Comics: Nov, 1998 - No. 4, Feb, 1999 ($2.25, limited series)
1-4-Hama-s 3.00

BATMAN: TURNING POINTS
DC Comics: Jan, 2001 - No. 5, Jan, 2001 ($2.50, weekly limited series)
1-5: 2-Giella-a. 3-Kubert-c/Giordano-a. 4-Chaykin-c/Brent Anderson-a. 5-Pope-c/a 3.00
TPB (2007, $14.99) r/#1-5 15.00

BATMAN: TWO-FACE-CRIME AND PUNISHMENT (See Batman one-shots)

BATMAN: TWO-FACE STRIKES TWICE

DC Comics: 1993 - No. 2, 1993 ($4.95, 52 pgs.)
1,2-Flip book format w/Staton-a (G.A. side) 6.00

BATMAN UNIVERSE (Reprints serialized story from Walmart exclusive Batman Giant)
DC Comics: Sept, 2019 - No. 6, Feb, 2020 ($4.99, limited series)
1-6: 1-Ginny Hex debut. 2-Green Arrow & Vandal Savage app. 3,4,6-Jonah Hex app. 5.00

BATMAN UNSEEN
DC Comics: Early Dec, 2009 - No. 5, Feb, 2010 ($2.99, limited series)
1-5-Doug Moench-s/Kelley Jones-a/c. Black Mask app. 3.00
SC (2010, $14.99) r/#1-5 15.00

BATMAN: URBAN LEGENDS
DC Comics: May, 2021 - No. 23, Mar, 2023 ($7.99, squarebound, anthology)
1-23: 1-Short stories with Red Hood, The Outsiders, Harley & Ivy, Grifter.
11-16-Ace the Bat-Hound; Russell-s 8.00

BATMAN: VENGEANCE OF BANE (Also see Batman #491)
DC Comics: Jan, 1993; 1995 ($2.50, 68 pgs.)

... Special 1 - Origin & 1st app. Bane; Dixon-s/Nolan & Barreto-a/Fabry-c	6	12	18	41	76	110
... Special 1 (2nd printing)	2	4	6	9	17	26	35
.... II nn (1995, $3.95)-sequel; Dixon-s/Nolan & Barreto-a/Fabry-c	2	4	6	11	16	20

...1 (Facsimile Edition) 2023, $6.99) Reprints issue with original ads 7.00

BATMAN VS. BIGBY! A WOLF IN GOTHAM
DC Comics (Black Label): Nov, 2021 - No. 6, Apr, 2022 ($3.99, limited series)
1-6-Willingham-s/Level-a; Batman hunts Bigby Wolf from Fables 4.00

BATMAN VERSUS PREDATOR
DC Comics/Dark Horse Comics: 1991 - No. 3, 1992 ($4.95/$1.95, limited series)
(1st DC/Dark Horse x-over)

1 (Prestige format, $4.95)-1 & 3 contain 8 Batman/Predator trading cards; Andy & Adam Kubert-a; Suydam painted-c	2	4	6	9	12	15
1-3 (Regular format, $1.95)-No trading cards						4.00
2,3-(Prestige)-2-Extra pin-ups inside; Suydam-c						6.00
TPB (1993, $5.95, 132 pgs.)-r/#1-3 w/new introductions & forward plus new wraparound-c by Dave Gibbons	3	6	9	14	20	25

BATMAN VERSUS PREDATOR II: BLOODMATCH
DC Comics: Late 1994 - No. 4, 1995 ($2.50, limited series)

1-4-Huntress app.; Moench scripts; Gulacy-a						4.00
TPB (1995, $6.95)-r/#1-4	1	3	4	6	8	10

BATMAN VS. RA'S AL GHUL
DC Comics: Nov, 2019 - No. 6, Jun, 2021 ($3.99, limited series)
1-6-Neal Adams-s/a; Deadman app. 4.00

BATMAN VS. ROBIN (Leads into Lazarus Planet mini-series)
DC Comics: Nov, 2022 - No. 5, Apr, 2023 ($5.99, limited series)
1-5: 1-Waid-s/Asrar-a; Damian attacks; Alfred & Zatanna app. 5-Lazarus Planet epilogue 6.00

BATMAN VS. THE INCREDIBLE HULK (See DC Special Series No. 27)

BATMAN: WAR ON CRIME
DC Comics: Nov, 1999 ($9.95, treasury size, one-shot)
nn-Painted art by Alex Ross; story by Alex Ross and Paul Dini 30.00

BATMAN: WHITE KNIGHT
DC Comics: Dec, 2017 - No. 8, Jul, 2018 ($3.99, limited series)
1-7-Sean Murphy-s/a; Joker is cured. 2-7-Harley Quinn app. 4.00
8-($4.99) Murphy-s/a 5.00
... Presents Von Freeze (Black Label, 1/20, $5.99) Murphy-s/Janson-a; Fries flashback 6.00

BATMAN: WHITE KNIGHT PRESENTS: GENERATION JOKER
DC Comics (Black Label): Jul, 2023 - No. 6, May, 2024 ($4.99, limited series)
1-6-Katana Collins & Clay McCormack-s/Mirka Andolfo-a 5.00

BATMAN: WHITE KNIGHT PRESENTS HARLEY QUINN
DC Comics (Black Label): Dec, 2020 - No. 6, May, 2021 ($4.99, limited series)
1-6-Katana Collins & Sean Murphy-s/Matteo Scalera-a 5.00

BATMAN: WHITE KNIGHT PRESENTS: RED HOOD
DC Comics (Black Label): Sept, 2022 - No. 2 ($4.99, limited series)
1-2-Clay McCormack & Sean Murphy-s/Simone Di Meo-a 5.00

BATMAN WHO LAUGHS, THE (See Dark Nights: Metal)
DC Comics: Feb, 2019 - No. 7, Sept, 2019 ($4.99, limited series)
1-7-Snyder-s/Jock-a; Joker and The Grim Knight app. 5.00
...: The Grim Knight 1 (5/19, $4.99) origin of the Grim Knight; Risso-a 5.00

BATMAN/WILDCAT
DC Comics: Apr, 1997 - No. 3, June, 1997 ($2.25, mini-series)
1-3: Dixon/Smith-s: 1-Killer Croc app. 4.00

BATMAN: YEAR 100
DC Comics: 2006 - No. 4, 2006 ($5.99, squarebound, limited series)
1-4-Paul Pope-s/a/c 6.00
TPB (2007, $19.99) r/series 20.00

BAT MASTERSON (TV) (Also see Tim Holt #28)
Dell Publishing Co.: Aug-Oct, 1959; Feb-Apr, 1960 - No. 9, Nov-Jan, 1961-62

Four Color 1013 (#1) (8-10/59)	11	22	33	72	154	235
2-9: Gene Barry photo-c on all. 2,3,6-Two different back-c exist; variants have a comic strip on the back-c	6	12	18	40	73	105

BAT-MITE
DC Comics: Aug, 2015 - No. 6, Jan, 2016 ($2.99, limited series)
1-Jurgens-s/Howell-a; Batman app. 5.00
2-6: 4-Booster Gold app. 5-Inferior Five app. 3.00

BATS (See Tales Calculated to Drive You Bats)

BATS, CATS & CADILLACS

Batman: Urban Legends #23 © DC

Battle #38 © MAR

Battle Cry #1 © Stanmore

	GD 2.0	VG 4.0	FN 6.0	VF 8.0	VF/NM 9.0	NM- 9.2

Now Comics: Oct, 1990 - No. 2, Nov, 1990 ($1.75)
1,2: 1-Gustovich-a(i); Snyder-c — — — — — 4.00

BAT-THING
DC Comics (Amalgam): June, 1997 ($1.95, one-shot)
1-Hama-s/Damaggio & Sienkiewicz-a — — — — — 5.00

BATTLE
Marvel/Atlas Comics(FPI #1-62/ Male #63 on): Mar, 1951 - No. 70, Jun, 1960

1	87	174	261	553	952	1350
2	40	80	120	246	411	575
3-10: 4-1st Buck Pvt. O'Toole. 10-Pakula-a	33	66	99	194	317	440
11-20: 11-Check-a. 17-Classic Hitler story	28	56	84	165	270	375
21,23-Krigstein-a	29	58	87	172	281	390
22,24-36: 32-Tuska-a. 36-Everett-a	24	48	72	140	230	320
37-Kubert-a (Last precode, 2/55)	25	50	75	150	245	340
38-40,42-48	22	44	66	128	209	290
41,49: 41-Kubert/Moskowitz-a. 49-Davis-a	24	48	72	140	230	320
50-54,56-58: 56-Colan-a; Ayers-a	21	42	63	126	206	285
55-Williamson-a (5 pgs.)	24	48	72	140	230	320
59-Torres-a	22	44	66	128	209	290
60-62: 60,62-Combat Kelly app. 61-Combat Casey app.	24	48	72	140	230	320
63-Ditko-a	36	72	108	211	343	475
64-66-Kirby-a. 66-Davis-a; has story of Fidel Castro in pre-Communism days (an admiring profile)	33	66	99	194	317	440
67,68: 67-Williamson/Crandall-a (4 pgs.); Kirby, Davis-a. 68-Kirby/Williamson-a (4 pgs.); Kirby/Ditko-a	37	74	111	218	354	490
69,70: 69-Kirby-a. 70-Kirby/Ditko-a	33	66	99	194	317	440

NOTE: Andru a-37. Berg a-38, 14, 60-62. Colan a-19, 33, 43, 55. Everett a-36, 50, 70; c-56, 57. Heath a-6, 9, 13, 31, 69; c-6, 9, 12, 26, 35, 37. Kirby c-64-69. Maneely a-4-7, 31, 61; c-4, 22, 27, 33, 43, 48, 59, 61. Orlando a-47. Powell a-5, 12, 26. Robinson a-4, 8-10, 14, 26, 32, 48. Romita a-14, 26. Severin a-28, 32-34, 66-69; c-36, 50, 55. Sinnott a-33, 37, 63, 66. Whitney s-10. Woodbridge a-52, 55.

BATTLE ACTION
Atlas Comics (NPI): Feb, 1952 - No. 12, 5/53; No. 13, 10/54 - No. 30, 8/57

1-Pakula-a	58	116	174	371	636	900
2	32	64	96	188	307	425
3,4,6,7,9,10: 6-Robinson-c/a. 7-Partial nudity	21	42	63	122	199	275
5-Used in POP, pg. 93,94	22	44	66	132	216	300
8-Krigstein-a	24	48	72	142	234	325
11-15 (Last precode, 2/55)	20	40	60	118	192	265
16-30: 20-Romita-a. 22-Pakula-a. 27,30-Torres-a	19	38	57	112	179	245

NOTE: Battle Brady app. 5-7, 10-12. Berg a-3. Check a-11. Everett a-7; c-13, 25. Heath a-3, 8, 18; c-3,15, 18, 21. Maneely a-1; c-5. Reinman a-1, 2, 20. Robinson a-6, 7; c-6. Shores a-7(2); 12, 20; c-11. Sinnott a-3, 27. Woodbridge a-28, 30.

BATTLE ATTACK
Stanmor Publications: Oct, 1952 - No. 8, Dec, 1955

1	20	40	60	114	182	255
2	13	26	39	74	105	135
3-8: 3-Hollingsworth-a	11	22	33	60	83	105

BATTLEAXES
DC Comics (Vertigo): May, 2000 - No. 4, Aug, 2000 ($2.50, limited series)
1-4: Terry LaBan-s/Alex Horley-a — — — — — 3.00

BATTLE BEASTS
Blackthorne Publishing: Feb, 1988 - No. 4, 1988 ($1.50/$1.75, B&W/color)
1-4: 1-3-(B&W)-Based on Hasbro toys. 4-Color — — — — — 4.00

BATTLE BEASTS
IDW Publishing: Jul, 2012 - No. 4. Oct, 2012 ($3.99, limited series)
1-4-Curnow-s/Schiti-a; 2 covers on each — — — — — 4.00

BATTLE BRADY (Formerly Men in Action No. 1-9; see 3-D Action)
Atlas Comics (IPC): No. 10, Jan, 1953 - No. 14, June, 1953

10: 10-12-Syd Shores-c	39	78	117	231	378	525
11-Used in POP, pg. 95 plus B&W & color illos	26	52	78	154	252	350
12-14	20	40	60	118	192	265

BATTLE CHASERS
Image Comics (Cliffhanger): Apr, 1998 - No. 4, Dec, 1998;
DC Comics (Cliffhanger): No. 5, May, 1999 - No. 8, May, 2001 ($2.50)
Image Comics: No. 9, Sept, 2001; No. 10, Jun, 2023 - Present ($3.50/$3.99)

Prelude (2/98)	2		4	6	8	10	12
Prelude Gold Ed.	3	6	9	14	19	24
1-Madureira & Sharrieff-s/Madureira(p)/Charest-c	2	4	6	11	16	20
1-American Ent. Ed. w/"racy" cover	2	4	6	9	12	15

	GD 2.0	VG 4.0	FN 6.0	VF 8.0	VF/NM 9.0	NM- 9.2
1-Gold Edition	4	8	12	27	44	60
1-Chromium cover	4	8	12	27	44	60
1-2nd printing						4.00
2						6.00
2-Dynamic Forces BattleChrome cover	2	4	6	9	12	15
3-Red Monika cover by Madureira						4.00
4-8: 4-Four covers. 6-Back-up by Adam Warren-s/a. 7-Three covers (Madureira, Ramos, Campbell)						4.00
9-(9/01, $3.50, Image) Flip cover/story by Adam Warren						4.00
10-12-(2003, $3.99, Image) Joe Madureira/Ludd Lullabi-a; story resumes						4.00
...A Gathering of Heroes HC ('99, $24.95) r/#1-5, Prelude, Frank Frazetta Fantasy Ill.; cover gallery						25.00
...A Gathering of Heroes SC ('99, $14.95)						15.00
...Collected Edition 1,2 (11/98, 5/99, $5.95) 1-r/#1,2. 2-r/#3,4						6.00

BATTLE CLASSICS (See Cancelled Comic Cavalcade)
DC Comics: Sept-Oct, 1978 (44 pgs.)
1-Kubert-r; new Kubert-c — 2 — 4 — 6 — 8 — 10 — 12

BATTLE CRY
Stanmor Publications: 1952 (May) - No. 20, Sept, 1955

1-Russian soldier flame broiled on cover	303	606	909	2121	3711	5300
2-(7/52)	16	32	48	94	147	200
3,5-10: 8-Pvt. Ike begins, ends #13,17	14	28	42	81	118	155
4-Classic E.C. swipe	34	68	102	199	325	450
11-20	14	28	42	76	108	140

NOTE: Hollingsworth a-9; c-20.

BATTLEFIELD (War Adventures on the...)
Atlas Comics (ACI): April, 1952 - No. 11, May, 1953

1-Pakula, Reinman-a	53	106	159	334	567	800
2-5: 2-Heath, Maneely, Pakula, Reinman-a	26	52	78	154	252	350
6-11	21	42	63	122	199	275

NOTE: Colan a-11. Everett a-8. Heath a-1, 2, 5p,7; c-2, 8, 9, 11. Ravielli a-11.

BATTLEFIELD ACTION (Formerly Foreign Intrigues)
Charlton Comics: No. 16, Nov, 1957 - No. 62, 2-3/66; No. 63, 7/80 - No. 89, 11/84

V2#16	10	20	30	58	79	100
17,20-30: 29-D-Day story	7	14	21	35	43	50
18,19-Check-a (2 stories in #18)	4	8	12	25	40	55
31-34,36-62(1966): 40-Panel from this issue used by artist Roy Lichtenstein for famous painting. 55,61-Hitler app.	3	6	9	19	30	40
35-Hitler-c	5	10	15	33	57	80
63-80(1983-84)						5.00
81-83,85-89 (Low print run)	1	2	3	4	5	7
84-Kirby reprints; 3 stories	1	3	4	6	8	10

NOTE: Montes/Bache a-43, 55, 62. Glanzman a-87r.

BATTLEFIELDS
Dynamite Entertainment: 2008 - No. 9, 2010 ($3.50, limited series then numbered issues)
...: Dear Billy 1-3 ('09 - No. 3, '09, $3.50) Ennis-s/Snejbjerg-a/Cassaday-c.1-Leach var-c — 3.50
...: Happy Valley 1-3 ('09 - No. 3, '09, $3.50) Ennis-s/Holden-a/Leach-c — 3.50
...: The Night Witches 1-3 ('08 - No. 3, '09, $3.50) Ennis-s/Braun-a/Cassaday-c; Russian female pilots in WW2. 1-Leach var-c — 3.50
...: The Tankies 1-3 ('09 - No. 3, '09, $3.50) Ennis-s/Ezquerra-a/Cassaday-c. 1-Leach var-c — 3.50
4-9: 4-6-Ezquerra/Leach-c. 7-9-Sequel to "The Night Witches"; Braun-a — 3.50

BATTLEFIELDS (Volume 2)
Dynamite Entertainment: 2012 - No. 6, 2013 ($3.99, limited series)
1-6: 1-3-Ennis-s/Ezquerra-a/Leach-c. 4-6-Braun-a — 4.00

BATTLE FIRE
Aragon Magazine/Stanmor Publications: Apr, 1955 - No. 7, 1955

1	20	40	60	117	189	260
2-(6/55)	13	26	39	74	105	135
3-7	11	22	33	62	86	110

BATTLE FOR A THREE DIMENSIONAL WORLD
3D Cosmic Publications: May, 1983 (20 pgs., slick paper w/stiff-c, $3.00)
nn-Kirby c/a in 3-D; shows history of 3-D — 2 — 4 — 6 — 9 — 13 — 16

BATTLEFORCE
Blackthorne Publishing: Nov, 1987 - No. 2, 1988 ($1.75, color/B&W)
1-Based on game; In color — 1 — 3 — 4 — 6 — 8 — 10
2-B&W — — — — — 4.00

BATTLE FOR INDEPENDENTS, THE (Also See Cyblade/Shi & Shi/Cyblade: The Battle For Independents)
Image Comics (Top Cow Productions)/Crusade Comics: 1995 ($29.95)

	GD	VG	FN	VF	VF/NM	NM-		GD	VG	FN	VF	VF/NM	NM-
	2.0	4.0	6.0	8.0	9.0	9.2		2.0	4.0	6.0	8.0	9.0	9.2

nn-Boxed set of all editions of Shi/Cyblade & Cyblade/Shi plus new variant

| | 3 | 6 | 9 | 19 | 30 | 40 |

BATTLE FOR THE PLANET OF THE APES (See Power Record Comics)

BATTLEFRONT
Atlas Comics (PPI): June, 1952 - No. 48, Aug, 1957

1-Heath-c	61	122	183	390	670	950
2-Robinson-a(4)	34	68	102	199	325	450
3-5-Robinson-a	27	54	81	160	263	365
6-10: Combat Kelly in No. 6-10. 6-Romita-a	23	46	69	136	223	310
11-22,24-28: 14,16-Battle Brady app. 22-Teddy Roosevelt & His Rough Riders						
story. 28-Last pre-code (2/55)	21	42	63	126	206	285
23,43-Check-a	22	44	66	128	209	290
29-39,41,44-47	20	40	60	118	192	265
40,42-Williamson-a	21	42	63	126	203	285
48-Crandall-a	21	42	63	122	199	275

NOTE: **Ayers** a-18, 19, 25, 32, 35. **Berg** a-44. **Colan** a-21, 22, 24, 25, 33, 35, 38, 40, 42, 43, 45. **Drucker** a-28, 29. **Everett** a-44. **Heath** c-23, 26, 27, 29, 32. **Maneely** a-21-23, 26; c-2, 7, 13, 22, 24, 25, 34, 35, 41. **Morisi** a-42. **Morrow** a-41. **Orlando** a-17. **Powell** a-19, 21, 25, 29, 32, 41. **Robinson** a-1-3, 4&5(4); c-4, 5. **Robert Sale** a-19, 24. **Severin** a-32; c-40, 42, 45. **Sinnott** a-26, 45, 48. **Woodbridge** a-45, 46.

BATTLEFRONT
Standard Comics: No. 5, June, 1952

5-Toth-a	21	42	63	124	202	280

BATTLE GODS: WARRIORS OF THE CHAAK
Dark Horse Comics: Apr, 2000 - No. 4, July, 2000 ($2.95)

1-4-Francisco Ruiz Velasco-s/a						3.00

BATTLE GROUND
Atlas Comics (OMC): Sept, 1954 - No. 20, Sept, 1957

1	47	94	141	296	498	700
2-Jack Katz-a (11/54)	26	52	78	154	252	350
3,4: 3-Jack Katz-a. 4-Last precode (3/55)	21	42	63	126	206	285
5-8,10 (3/56)	20	40	60	115	185	255
9,11,13,18: 9-Krigstein-a. 11,13,18-Williamson-a in each						
	21	42	63	122	199	275
12,15-17,19,20	19	38	57	109	172	235
14-Kirby-a	24	48	72	142	234	325

NOTE: **Ayers** a-4, 6, 13, 16. **Colan** a-3, 11, 13. **Drucker** a-7, 12, 13, 20. **Heath** c-2, 3, 5, 7, 13. **Maneely** a-3, 14, 19; c-1, 6, 18, 19. **Orlando** a-17. **Pakula** a-6, 11. **Reinman** a-2. **Severin** a-4, 5, 12, 19. c-20. **Sinnott** a-7, 16. **Tuska** a-11.

BATTLE HEROES
Stanley Publications: Sept, 1966 - No. 2, Nov, 1966 (25¢, squarebound giants)

1	5	10	15	30	50	70
2	3	6	9	21	33	45

BATTLE HYMN
Image Comics: Jan, 2005 - No. 5, Oct, 2005 ($2.95/$2.99, limited series)

1-5-WW2 super team; B. Clay Moore-s/Jeremy Haun-a; flip cover on #1-4						3.00

BATTLE OF THE BULGE (See Movie Classics)

BATTLE OF THE PLANETS (Based on syndicated cartoon by Sandy Frank)
Gold Key/Whitman No. 6 on: 6/79 - No. 10, 12/80

1: Mortimer-a-1-4,7-10	10	20	30	64	132	200
2-6,10	4	8	12	25	40	55
7-Low print run	8	16	24	55	105	155
8,9-Low print run: 8(11/80). 9-(3-pack only?)	6	12	18	38	69	100

BATTLE OF THE PLANETS (Also see Thundercats/...)
Image Comics (Top Cow): Aug, 2002 - No. 12, Sept, 2003 ($2.95/$2.99)

1-($2.95) Alex Ross-c & art director; Tortosa-a(p); re-intro. G-Force						6.00
1-($5.95) Holofoil-c by Ross	1	3	4	6	8	10
2-11-($2.99) Ross-c on all						3.00
12-($4.99)						5.00
#1/2 (7/03, $2.99) Ross-c; Alex Ross sketch pages						3.00
... Battle Book 1 (5/03, $4.99) background info on characters, equipment, stories						5.00
... : Jason 1 (7/03, $4.99) Ross-c; Erwin David-a; preview of Tomb Raider: Epiphany						5.00
... : Mark 1 (5/03, $4.99) Ross-c; Erwin David-a; preview of BotP: Jason						5.00
.../Thundercats 1 (Image/WildStorm, 5/03, $4.99) 2 covers by Ross & Campbell						5.00
.../Witchblade 1 (2/03, $5.95) Ross-c; Christina and Jo Chen-a						6.00
Vol. 1: Trial By Fire (2003, $7.99) r/#1-3						8.00
Vol. 2: Blood Red Sky (9/03, $16.95) r/#4-9						17.00
Vol. 3: Destroy All Monsters (11/03, $19.95) r/#10-12, ...: Jason, ...: Mark, .../Witchblade						20.00
Vol. 1: Digest (1/04, $9.99, 7-3/8x5", B&W) r/#1-9 & ...: Mark						10.00
Vol. 2: Digest (8/04, $9.99, B&W) r/#10-12, ...: Jason, ...: Manga #1-3, .../Witchblade						10.00

BATTLE OF THE PLANETS: MANGA
Image Comics (Top Cow): Nov, 2003 - No. 3, Jan, 2004 ($2.99, B&W)

1-3-Edwin David-a/David Wohl-a; previews for Wanted & Tomb Raider #35						3.00

BATTLE OF THE PLANETS: PRINCESS
Image Comics (Top Cow): Nov, 2004 - No. 6, May, 2005 ($2.99, B&W, limited series)

1-6-Tortosa/Wohl-s. 1-Ross-c. 2-Tortosa-c						3.00

BATTLE POPE
Image Comics: June, 2005 - No. 14, Apr, 2007 ($2.99/$3.50, reprints 2000 B&W series in color)

1-5-Kirkman-s/Moore-a						3.50
6-10,12-14-($3.50) 14-Wedding						3.50
11-($4.99) Christmas issue						5.00
... Vol. 1: Genesis TPB (2006, $12.95) r/#1-4; sketch pages						13.00
... Vol. 2: Mayhem TPB (2006, $12.95) r/#5-8; sketch pages						13.00
... Vol. 3: Pillow Talk TPB (2007, $12.99) r/#9-11; sketch pages						13.00

BATTLEPUG
Image Comics: Sept, 2019 - No. 5, Jan, 2020 ($3.99)

1-5-Mike Norton-s/a						4.00

BATTLER BRITTON (British comics character who debuted in 1956)
DC Comics (WildStorm): Sept, 2006 - No. 5, Jan, 2007 ($2.99, limited series)

1-5-WWII fighter pilots; Garth Ennis-s/Colin Wilson-a						3.00
TPB (2007, $19.99) r/#1-5; background of the character's British origins in the 1950s						20.00

BATTLE REPORT
Ajax/Farrell Publications: Aug, 1952 - No. 6, June, 1953

1	20	40	60	117	189	260
2-6	13	26	39	74	105	135

BATTLE SCARS
Marvel Comics: Jan, 2012 - No. 6, Jun, 2012 ($2.99, limited series)

1-Intro. Marcus Johnson and Cheese (later ID'd as Phil Coulson in #6); Eaton-a/Pagulayan-c	2	4	6	9	12	15
2-5: 4-Deadpool app. 5-Nick Fury app.						4.00
6-Marcus Johnson becomes Nick Fury Jr.; resembles movie version; Cheese joins SHIELD						
and is ID'd as Agent Coulson	2	4	6	9	12	15

BATTLE SQUADRON
Stanmor Publications: April, 1955 - No. 5, Dec, 1955

1	18	36	54	105	165	225
2-5: 3-Iwo Jima & flag-c	12	24	36	69	97	125

BATTLESTAR GALACTICA (TV) (Also see Marvel Comics Super Special #8)
Marvel Comics: Mar, 1979 - No. 23, Jan, 1981

1: 1-5 adapt TV episodes	3	6	9	17	26	35
2-23: 1-3-Partial-r	2	4	6	8	10	12

NOTE: **Austin** c-9i, 10i. **Golden** c-18. **Simonson** a(p)-4, 5, 11-13, 15-20, 22, 23; c(p)-4, 5,11-17, 19, 20, 22, 23.

BATTLESTAR GALACTICA (TV) (Also see Asylum)
Maximum Press: July, 1995 - No. 4, Nov, 1995 ($2.50, limited series)

1-4: Continuation of 1978 TV series						4.00
Trade paperback (12/95, $12.95)-reprints series						13.00

BATTLESTAR GALACTICA (1978 TV series)
Realm Press: Dec, 1997 - No. 5, July, 1998 ($2.99)

1-5-Chris Scalf-s/painted-a/c						4.00
...Search For Sanctuary (9/98, $2.99) Scalf & Kuhoric-s						4.00
...Search For Sanctuary Special (4/00, $3.99) Kuhoric/Scalf & Scott-a						4.00

BATTLESTAR GALACTICA (2003-2009 TV series)
Dynamite Entertainment: No. 0, 2006 - No. 12, 2007 (25¢/$2.99)

0-(25¢-c) Two covers; Pak-s/Raynor-a						3.00
1-($2.99) Covers by Turner, Tan, Raynor & photo-c; Pak-s/Raynor-a						3.00
2-12-Four covers on each						3.00
... Pegasus (2007, $4.99) story of Battlestar Pegasus & Admiral Cain; 2 covers						5.00
... Volume 1 HC (2007, $19.99) r/#0-4; cover gallery; Raynor sketch pages; commentary						20.00
... Volume 1 TPB (2007, $14.99) r/#0-4; cover gallery; commentary						15.00
... Volume 2 HC (2007, $19.99) r/#5-8; cover gallery; Raynor sketch pages						20.00
... Volume 2 TPB (2007, $14.99) r/#5-8; cover gallery; Raynor sketch pages						15.00

BATTLESTAR GALACTICA, (Classic...) (1978 TV series characters)
Dynamite Entertainment: 2006 - No. 5, 2006 ($2.99)

1-5: 1-Two covers by Dorman & Caldwell; Rafael-a. 2-Two covers						3.00

BATTLESTAR GALACTICA, (Classic...) (Volume 2) (1978 TV series characters)
Dynamite Entertainment: 2013 - No. 12, 2014 ($3.99)

1-12: 1-5-Two covers by Alex Ross & Chris Eliopoulos on each; Abnett & Lanning-s						4.00

BATTLESTAR GALACTICA, (Classic...) (Volume 3) (1978 TV series characters)
Dynamite Entertainment: 2016 - No. 5, 2016 ($3.99)

1-5: 1-Cullen Bunn-s/Alex Sanchez-a; multiple covers						4.00

BATTLESTAR GALACTICA, (Classic...) (Volume 4) (1978 TV series characters)
Dynamite Entertainment: No. 0, 2018 - No. 5, 2019 ($3.99)

0-(35¢, listed as #1 in indicia) John Jackson Miller-s/Daniel HDR-a; multiple covers						3.00
1-5-Multiple covers on each						4.00

BATTLESTAR GALACTICA: APOLLO'S JOURNEY (1978 TV series)
Maximum Press: Apr, 1996 - No. 3, June, 1996 ($2.95, limited series)

1-3: Richard Hatch scripts						4.00

BATTLESTAR GALACTICA: BSG VS. BSG (1978 characters meet 2003 characters)
Dynamite Entertainment: 2018 - No. 6, 2018 ($3.99, limited series)

1-6-Peter David-s; multiple covers. 1-Johnny DesJardins-a. 4-6-Edu Menna-a						4.00

BATTLESTAR GALACTICA: CYLON APOCALYPSE (1978 TV series)
Dynamite Entertainment: 2007 - No. 4, 2007 ($2.99)

1-4-Carlos Rafael-a; 4 covers on each						3.00
TPB (2007, $14.99) r/series with cover gallery						15.00

BATTLESTAR GALACTICA: CYLON WAR (2003-2009 TV series)
Dynamite Entertainment: 2009 - No. 4, 2010 ($3.99, limited series)

1-3-First cylon war 40 years before the Caprica attack; Raynor-a; 2 covers						4.00

BATTLESTAR GALACTICA 1880, STEAMPUNK... (1978 TV series characters)
(Title changes from "(Classic) Battlestar Galactica Vol. 2" after #1)
Dynamite Entertainment: 2014 - No. 4, 2014 ($3.99)

1-4-Tony Lee-s/Aneke-a; multiple covers						4.00

BATTLESTAR GALACTICA: GHOSTS (2003-2009 TV series)
Dynamite Entertainment: 2008 - No. 4, 2009 ($4.99, 40 pgs., limited series)

1-4-Intro. of the Ghost Squadron; Jerwa-s/Lau-a/Calero-c						5.00

BATTLESTAR GALACTICA: GODS AND MONSTERS (2003-2009 TV series)
Dynamite Entertainment: 2016 - No. 5, 2017 ($3.99, limited series)

1-5-Karl Kesel-s/Alec Morgan & Dan Schkade-a						4.00

BATTLESTAR GALACTICA: JOURNEY'S END (1978 TV series)
Maximum Press: Aug, 1996 - No. 4, Nov, 1996 ($2.99, limited series)

1-4-Continuation of the T.V. series						4.00

BATTLESTAR GALACTICA: ORIGINS (2003-2009 TV series)
Dynamite Entertainment: 2007 - No. 11, 2008 ($3.50)

1-11: 1-4-Baltar's origin; multiple covers. 5-8-Adama's origin. 9-11-Starbuck & Helo						3.50

BATTLESTAR GALACTICA: SEASON III
Realm Press: June/July, 1999 - No. 3, Sept, 1999 ($2.99)

Battle Scars #6 © MAR

Battlestar Galactica: Origins #1 © Universal

Batwoman (2016 series) #18 © DC

	GD 2.0	VG 4.0	FN 6.0	VF 8.0	VF/NM 9.0	NM- 9.2

1-3: 1-Kuhoric-s/Scalf & Scott-a; two covers by Scalf & Jae Lee. 2,3-Two covers — 4.00
Gallery (4/00, $3.99) short story and pin-ups — 4.00
1999 Tour Book (5/99, $2.99) — 4.00
1999 Tour Book Convention Edition (6.99) — 7.00
...Special: Centurion Prime (12/99, $3.99) Kuhoric-s — 4.00

BATTLESTAR GALACTICA: SEASON ZERO (2003-2009 TV series)
Dynamite Entertainment: 2007 - No. 12, 2008 ($2.99)
1-12-Set 2 years before the Cylon attack; multiple covers — 3.00
.../The Lone Ranger 2007 Free Comic Book Day Edition; flip book with Cassaday
   Lone Ranger-c — 3.00

BATTLESTAR GALACTICA: SIX (2003-2009 TV series)
Dynamite Entertainment: No. 1, 2014 - No. 5, 2015 ($3.99, limited series)
1-5: 1-J.T. Krul-s/Igor Lima-a; multiple covers. 3-5-Rodolfo-a. 5-Baltar app. — 4.00

BATTLESTAR GALACTICA: SPECIAL EDITION (TV)
Maximum Press: Jan, 1997 ($2.99, one-shot)
1-Fully painted; Scalf-c/s/a; r/Asylum — 4.00

BATTLESTAR GALACTICA: STARBUCK (TV)
Maximum Press: Dec, 1995 - No. 3, Mar, 1996 ($2.50, limited series)
1-3 — 4.00

BATTLESTAR GALACTICA: STARBUCK, (Classic...) (1978 TV series characters)
Dynamite Entertainment: 2013 - No. 4, 2014 ($3.99, limited series)
1-4-Tony Lee-s/Eman Casallos-a. 1-Childhood flashback — 4.00

BATTLESTAR GALACTICA: THE COMPENDIUM (TV)
Maximum Press: Feb, 1997 ($2.99, one-shot)
1 — 4.00

BATTLESTAR GALACTICA: THE DEATH OF APOLLO, (Classic...) (1978 TV series)
Dynamite Entertainment: 2014 - No. 6, 2015 ($3.99, limited series)
1-6-Dan Abnett-s/Dietrich Smith-a; multiple covers on each — 4.00

BATTLESTAR GALACTICA: THE ENEMY WITHIN (TV)
Maximum Press: Nov, 1995 - No. 3, Feb, 1996 ($2.50, limited series)
1-3: 3-Indicia reads Feb, 1995 in error. — 4.00

BATTLESTAR GALACTICA: THE FINAL FIVE (2003 series)
Dynamite Entertainment: 2009 - No. 4, 2009 ($3.99, limited series)
1-4-Raynor-a; 2 covers on each — 4.00

BATTLESTAR GALACTICA: TWILIGHT COMMAND (2003 series)
Dynamite Entertainment: 2019 - No. 5, 2019 ($3.99, limited series)
1-5-Moreci-s/Tamura-a; 2 covers; takes place during season 3 of the 2003 series — 4.00

BATTLESTAR GALACTICA ZAREK (2003 series)
Dynamite Entertainment: 2007 - No. 4, 2007 ($3.50, limited series)
1-4-Origin story of political activist Tom Zarek; 2 covers on each — 3.50

BATTLE STORIES (See XMas Comics)
Fawcett Publications: Jan, 1952 - No. 11, Sept, 1953

	2.0	4.0	6.0	8.0	9.0	9.2
1-Evans-a (Korean War)	22	44	66	132	216	300
2	14	28	42	82	121	160
3-11	12	24	36	67	94	120

BATTLE STORIES
Super Comics: 1963 - 1964
Reprints #10-13,15-18: 10-r/U.S Tank Commandos #? 11-r/? 11, 12,17-r/Monty Hall #?;
13-Kintsler-a (1pg).15-r/American Air Forces #7 by Powell; Bolle-r. 18-U.S. Fighting Air

	2.0	4.0	6.0	8.0	9.0	9.2
Force #?	2	4	6	11	16	20

BATTLETECH (See Blackthorne 3-D Series #41 for 3-D issue)
Blackthorne Publishing: Oct, 1987 - No. 6, 1988 ($1.75/$2.00)

	2.0	4.0	6.0	8.0	9.0	9.2
1-Based on game; full color	1	3	4	6	8	10
2-6: 2-Begin B&W						4.00
Annual 1 ($4.50, B&W)						5.00

BATTLETECH
Malibu Comics: Feb, 1995 ($2.95)
0 — 5.00

BATTLETECH FALLOUT
Malibu Comics: Dec, 1994 - No. 4, Mar, 1995 ($2.95)
1-4-Two edi. exist #1; normal logo — 4.00
1-Gold version w/foil logo stamped "Gold Limited Edition — 10.00
1-Full-c holographic limited edition — 15.00

BATTLETIDE (Death's Head II & Killpower...)

Marvel Comics UK, Ltd.: Dec, 1992 - No. 4, Mar, 1993 ($1.75, mini-series)
1-4: Wolverine, Psylocke, Dark Angel app. — 4.00

BATTLETIDE II (Death's Head II & Killpower...)
Marvel Comics UK, Ltd.: Aug, 1993 - No. 4, Nov, 1993 ($1.75, mini-series)
1-($2.95)-Foil embossed logo — 5.00
2-4: 2-Hulk-c/story — 4.00

BATVARK (Reprints from Cerebus in Hell)
Aardvark-Vanaheim: Aug, 2017 ($4.00, B&W)
1-Cerebus figures placed over original Gustave Doré artwork of Hell; Batman #1-c swipe — 4.00
... A Poet in the Family (4/22, $4.00) Batman #428-c swipe — 4.00
... Penis (9/20, $4.00) Homage to Batman: Damned; Michelangelo's David app. — 4.00
... XXXXX (1/21, $4.00) 2nd printing — 4.00

BATWING (DC New 52)
DC Comics: Nov, 2011 - No. 34, Oct, 2014 ($2.99)
1-24: 1-3,5-Judd Winick-s/Ben Oliver-a. 4-Origin; Chriscross-a. 9-Night of the Owls — 3.00
25-($3.99) Zero Year tie-in; Luke Fox's first meeting with Batman; Conner-c — 4.00
26-34: 26,27-Darwyn Cooke-c — 3.00
#0 (11/12, $2.99) origin of David Zavimbe; Winick-s/To-a. — 3.00
...: Futures End 1 (11/14, $2.99, regular-c) Five years later; Panosian-c — 3.00
...: Futures End 1 (11/14, $3.99, 3-D cover) — 4.00

BATWOMAN (See 52 #9 & 11 for debut and Detective Comics #854-860)
DC Comics: No. 0, Jan, 2011; No. 1, Nov, 2011 - No. 40, May, 2015 ($2.99)
0-(1/11) Williams III-s; art by Williams III and Reeder; Williams III-c — 3.00
0-(1/11)-Variant-c by Reeder — 5.00
1-New DC 52; Williams III-a; Williams III & Blackman-s; Bette Kane app. — 5.00
2-24: 2-Cameron Chase returns. 6-8-Reeder-a/c. 9-11,15,18-20,22,23-McCarthy-a.
   12-17-Wonder Woman app. 21-Francavilla-a; Killer Croc app. — 3.00
25-($3.99) Zero Year tie-in; Maggie Sawyer & Bruce Wayne app. — 4.00
26-40: 26-31-Wolf Spider. 35-Etrigan, Clayface, Ragman & Alice app. — 3.00
#0 (11/12, $2.99) Flashback to Kate's training; Williams III-a — 3.00
Annual 1 (6/14, $4.99) Continued from #24; Batman app.; McCarthy & Moritat-a — 5.00
Annual 2 (6/15, $4.99) Continued from #40; Jeanty-c/a — 5.00
... Elegy The Deluxe Edition HC (2010, $24.99, d.j.) r/Detective #854-860; gallery of variant
   covers, sketch art and script pages; intro. by Rachel Maddow — 25.00
... Elegy SC (2011, $17.99) same contents as Deluxe HC — 18.00
...: Futures End 1 (11/14, $2.99, regular-c) Five years later; Red Alice app. — 3.00
...: Futures End 1 (11/14, $3.99, 3-D cover) — 4.00

BATWOMAN (DC Rebirth)
DC Comics: May, 2017 - No. 18, Oct, 2018 ($2.99/$3.99)
1-18: 1-($3.99) M. Bennett & Tynion IV-s/Epting-a; covers by Epting & JG Jones. 6-Arlem-a
   8-10-Scarecrow app. 13-Alice returns — 4.00
...: Rebirth 1 (4/17, $2.99) Bennett & Tynion-s/Epting-a; origin re-capped — 3.00

BATWOMAN/SUPERGIRL: WORLD'S FINEST GIANT
DC Comics: 2019 - Present, 100 pgs., squarebound, Mass Market & Direct Market
editions exist for each issue, with different covers)
1-Three new stories plus reprints; Alice app.; Joëlle Jones-c — 5.00

BAY CITY JIVE
DC Comics (WildStorm): Jul, 2001 - No. 3, Sept, 2001 ($2.95, limited series)
1-3: Intro Sugah Rollins in 1970s San Francisco; Layman-s/Johnson-a — 3.00

BAYWATCH COMIC STORIES (TV) (Magazine)
Acclaim Comics (Armada): May, 1996 - No. 4, 1997 ($4.95) (Photo-c on all)

	2.0	4.0	6.0	8.0	9.0	9.2
1-Photo comics based on TV show	3	6	9	16	23	30
2-4	2	4	6	9	12	15

BEACH BLANKET BINGO (See Movie Classics)

BEAGLE BOYS, THE (Walt Disney)(See The Phantom Blot)
Gold Key: 11/64; No. 2, 11/65; No. 3, 8/66 - No. 47, 2/79 (See WDC&S #134)

	2.0	4.0	6.0	8.0	9.0	9.2
1	6	12	18	38	69	100
2-5	3	6	9	17	26	35
6-10	3	6	9	15	22	28
11-20: 11,14,19-r	2	4	6	11	16	20
21-30: 27-r	2	4	6	8	11	14
31-47	1	3	4	6	8	10

BEAGLE BOYS VERSUS UNCLE SCROOGE
Gold Key: Mar, 1979 - No. 12, Feb, 1980

	2.0	4.0	6.0	8.0	9.0	9.2
1	2	4	6	9	13	16
2-12: 9-r	1	2	3	5	6	8

BEANBAGS

	GD 2.0	VG 4.0	FN 6.0	VF 8.0	VF/NM 9.0	NM- 9.2

Ziff-Davis Publ. Co. (Approved Comics): Winter, 1951 - No. 2, Spring, 1952

1,2	18	36	54	105	165	225

BEANIE THE MEANIE
Fago Publications: No. 3, May, 1959

3	8	16	24	40	50	60

BEANY AND CECIL (TV) (Bob Clampett's...)
Dell Publishing Co.: Jan, 1952 - 1955; July-Sept, 1962 - No. 5, July-Sept, 1963

Four Color 368	26	52	78	182	404	625
Four Color 414,448,477,530,570,635(1/55)	14	28	42	96	211	325
01-057-209 (#1)	12	24	36	84	185	285
2-5	9	18	27	63	129	195

BEAR COUNTRY (Disney)
Dell Publishing Co.: No. 758, Dec, 1956

Four Color 758-Movie	5	10	15	34	60	85

BEAST (See X-Men)
Marvel Comics: May, 1997 - No. 3, 1997 ($2.50, mini-series)

1-3-Giffen-s/Nocon-a						4.00

BEAST BOY (See Titans)
DC Comics: Jan, 2000 - No. 4, Apr, 2000 ($2.95, mini-series)

1-4-Justiano-c/a; Raab & Johns-s						4.00

BEASTS OF BURDEN (See Dark Horse Book of Hauntings, ...Monsters, ...The Dead, ...Witchcraft)
Dark Horse Comics: Sept, 2009 - No. 4, Dec, 2009 ($2.99, limited series)

1-4-Evan Dorkin-s/Jill Thompson-a/c						3.00
...: Hunters & Gatherers (3/14, $3.50) Evan Dorkin-s/Jill Thompson-a/c						3.50
...: Neighborhood Watch (8/12, $3.50) Evan Dorkin-s/Jill Thompson-a/c						3.50
...: What the Cat Dragged In (5/16, $3.99) Evan Dorkin & Sarah Dyer-s/Jill Thompson-a/c						4.00
Volume 1: Animal Rites HC (6/10, $19.99) r/#1-4 & short stories from Dark Horse Books						20.00

BEASTS OF BURDEN: OCCUPIED TERRITORY
Dark Horse Comics: Apr, 2021 - No. 4, Jul, 2021 ($3.99, limited series)

1-4-Evan Dorkin & Sarah Dyer-s/Benjamin Dewey-a/c						4.00

BEASTS OF BURDEN: THE PRESENCE OF OTHERS
Dark Horse Comics: May, 2019 - No. 2, Jun, 2019 ($3.99, limited series)

1,2-Evan Dorkin-s/Jill Thompson-a/c						4.00

BEASTS OF BURDEN: WISE DOGS AND ELDRITCH MEN
Dark Horse Comics: Aug, 2018 - No. 4, Dec, 2018 ($3.99, limited series)

1-4-Evan Dorkin-s/Benjamin Dewey-a/c						4.00

BEATLES, THE (See Girls' Romances #109, Go-Go, Heart Throbs #101, Herbie #5, Howard the Duck Mag. #4, Laugh #166, Marvel Comics Super Special #4, My Little Margie #54, Not Brand Echh, Strange Tales #130, Summer Love, Superman's Pal Jimmy Olsen #79, Teen Confessions #37, Tippy's Friends & Tippy Teen)

BEATLES, THE (Life Story)
Dell Publishing Co.: Sept-Nov, 1964 (35¢)

1-(Scarce)-Stories with color photo pin-ups; Paul S. Newman-s/Joe Sinnott-a; photo-c	52	104	156	411	931	1450

BEATLES EXPERIENCE, THE
Revolutionary Comics: Mar, 1991 - No. 8, 1991 ($2.50, B&W, limited series)

1-8: 1-Gold logo						5.00

BEATLES YELLOW SUBMARINE (See Movie Comics under Yellow...)

BEAUTIFUL KILLER
Black Bull Comics: Sept., 2002 - No. 3, Jan, 2003 ($2.99, limited series)

...Limited Preview edition preview pgs. & creator interviews						5.00
1-Noto-a/Palmiotti-s; Hughes-c; intro Brigit Cole						3.00
2,3: 2-Noto-a 3-Noto-c						3.00
TPB (5/03, $9.99) r/#1-3; cover gallery and Adam Hughes sketch pages						10.00

BEAUTIFUL PEOPLE
Slave Labor Graphics: Apr, 1994 ($4.95, 8-1/2x11", one-shot)

nn						5.00

BEAUTIFUL STORIES FOR UGLY CHILDREN
DC Comics (Piranha Press): 1989 - No. 30, 1991 ($2.00/$2.50, B&W, mature)

Vol. 1	2	4	6	11	16	20
2-8	1	2	3	5	6	8
9-20: 12-$2.50-c begins						5.00
21-25						5.00
26-29-(Lower print run)	1	3	4	6	8	10
30-(Lower print run)	3	6	9	14	19	24
A Cotton Candy Autopsy ($12.95, B&W)-Reprints 1st two volumes						20.00

BEAUTY, THE (Also see Pilot Season: The Beauty)
Image Comics: Aug, 2015 - Sept, 2021 ($3.50/$3.99)

1-6-Jeremy Haun & Jason Hurley-s/Haun-a. 1-Three covers; reprints Pilot Season issue						4.00
7-29-($3.99) 7-Huddleston-a. 8-10-Weldele-a. 12-Haun-a. 13-29-Nachlik-a						4.00
... All Good Things (9/21, $4.99) Conclusion of the series						5.00

BEAUTY AND THE BEAST, THE
Marvel Comics Group: Jan, 1985 - No. 4, Apr, 1985 (limited series)

1-4: Dazzler & the Beast from X-Men; Sienkiewicz-c on all						5.00

BEAUTY AND THE BEAST (Graphic novel)(Also see Cartoon Tales & Disney's New Adventures of...)
Disney Comics: 1992

nn-($4.95, prestige edition)-Adapts animated film						7.00
nn-($2.50, newsstand edition)						4.00

BEAUTY AND THE BEAST
Disney Comics: Sept., 1992 - No. 2, 1992 ($1.50)

1,2						4.00

BEAUTY AND THE BEAST: PORTRAIT OF LOVE (TV)
First Comics: May, 1989 - No. 2, Mar, 1990 ($5.95, 60 pgs., squarebound)

1,2: 1-Based on TV show, Wendy Pini-a/scripts. 2-...: Night of Beauty; by Wendy Pini						6.00

BEAVER VALLEY (Movie)(Disney)
Dell Publishing Co.: No. 625, Apr, 1955

Four Color 625	6	12	18	37	66	95

BEAVIS AND BUTTHEAD (MTV's...)(TV cartoon)
Marvel Comics: Mar, 1994 - No. 28, June, 1996 ($1.95)

1-Silver ink-c. 1, 2-Punisher & Devil Dinosaur app.	3	6	9	14	19	24
1-2nd printing						4.00
2,3: 2-Wolverine app. 3-Man-Thing, Spider-Man, Venom, Carnage, Mary Jane & Stan Lee cameos; John Romita, Sr. art (2 pgs.)	1	2	3	5	6	8
4-28: 5-War Machine, Thor, Loki, Hulk, Captain America & Rhino cameos. 6-Psylocke, Polaris, Daredevil & Bullseye app. 7-Ghost Rider & Sub-Mariner app. 8-Quasar & Eon app. 9-Prowler & Nightwatch app. 11-Black Widow app. 12-Thunderstrike & Bloodaxe app. 13-Night Thrasher app. 14-Spider-Man 2099 app. 15-Warlock app. 16-X-Factor app. 25-Juggernaut app.						5.00

BECK & CAUL INVESTIGATIONS
Gauntlet Comics (Caliber): Jan, 1994 - No. 5, 1995? ($2.95, B&W)

1-5						3.00
Special 1 ($4.95)						5.00

BEDKNOBS AND BROOMSTICKS (See Walt Disney Showcase No. 6 & 50)

BEDLAM!
Eclipse Comics: Sept, 1985 - No. 2, Sept, 1985 (B&W-r in color)

1,2: Bissette-a						4.00

BEDTIME STORIES FOR IMPRESSIONABLE CHILDREN
Moonstone Books/American Mythology: Nov, 2010; Feb, 2017 ($3.99, B&W)

1-(11/10) Short story anthology; Vaughn, Kuhoric & Tinnell-s; 3 covers						4.00
1-(2/17) Short story anthology; Vaughn, Shooter & Nelms-s; 4 covers						4.00

BEDTIME STORY (See Cinema Comics Herald)

BEE AND PUPPYCAT
Boom Entertainment (KaBOOM!): May, 2014 - No. 11, Apr, 2016 ($3.99)

1-11: Multiple covers on each. 1,2-Natasha Allegri-s/a						4.00

BEELZELVIS
Slave Labor Graphics: Feb, 1994 ($2.95, B&W, one-shot)

1						4.00

BEEP BEEP, THE ROAD RUNNER (TV) (See Dell Giant Comics Bugs Bunny Vacation Funnies #8 for 1st app.) (Also see Daffy & Kite Fun Book)
Dell Publishing Co./Gold Key No. 1-88/Whitman No. 89 on: July, 1958 - No. 14, Aug-Oct, 1962; Oct, 1966 - No. 105, 1984

Four Color 918 (#1, 7/58)	15	30	45	103	227	350
Four Color 1008,1046 (11-1/59-60)	8	16	24	54	102	150
4(2-4/60)-14(Dell)	7	14	21	46	86	125
1(10/66, Gold Key)	7	14	21	46	86	125
2-5	4	8	12	27	44	60
6-14	3	6	9	19	30	40
15-18,20-40	3	6	9	16	23	30
19-With pull-out poster	4	8	12	25	40	55
41-50	3	6	9	14	19	24
51-70	2	4	6	9	13	16
71-88	2	3	4	6	8	10
89,90,94-101: 100(3/82), 101(4/82)	2	4	6	8	10	12
91(8/80), 92(9/80), 93 (3-pack?) (low printing)	8	16	24	51	96	140
102-105 (All #90189 on-c; nd or date code; pre-pack) 102(6/83), 103(7/83), 104(5/84), 105(6/84)	3	6	9	19	30	40
#63-2970 (Now Age Books/Pendulum Pub. Comic Digest, 1971, 75¢, 100 pages, B&W) collection of one-page gags	4	8	12	27	44	60

NOTE: See March of Comics #351, 353, 375, 387, 397, 416, 430, 442, 455. #5, 8-10, 35, 53, 59-62, 68-r; 96-102, 104 are 1/3-r.

BEETLE BAILEY (See Giant Comic Album, Sarge Snorkel; also Comics Reading Libraries in the Promotional Comics section)
Dell Publishing Co./Gold Key #39-53/King #54-66/Charlton #67-119/Gold Key #120-131/ Whitman #132: #459, 5/53 - #38, 5/57-62; #39, 11/62 - #53, 5/66; #54, 8/66 - #65, 12/67;#67, 2/69 - #119, 11/76; #120, 4/78 - #132, 4/80

Four Color 469 (#1)-By Mort Walker	13	26	39	89	195	300
Four Color 521,552,622	7	14	21	49	92	135
5(2-4/56)-10(5-7/57)	5	10	15	35	63	90
11-20(4-5/59)	4	8	12	28	47	65
21-38(5-7/62)	3	6	9	20	31	42
39-53(5/66)	3	6	9	17	26	35
54-65	3	6	9	16	23	30
66 (only exists as U.S. published complimentary copies given away overseas)						
	3	6	9	16	23	30
67-69: 69-Last 12¢ issue	3	6	9	14	20	25
70-99	2	4	6	9	13	16
100	2	4	6	11	16	20
101-111,114-119	1	3	4	6	8	10
112,113-Byrne illos. (4 each)	2	4	6	9	12	18
120-132	1	2	3	4	5	7

BEETLE BAILEY
Harvey Comics: V2#1, Sept, 1992 - V2#9, Aug, 1994 ($1.25/$1.50)

V2#1						5.00
2-9-($1.50)						3.50
Big Book 1(11/92),2(5/93)(Both $1.95, 52 pgs.)						4.00
Giant Size V2#1(10/92),2(3/93)(Both $2.25,68 pgs.)						4.00

BEETLEJUICE (TV)
Harvey Comics: Oct, 1991 ($1.25)

1	4	8	12	28	47	65

BEETLEJUICE CRIMEBUSTERS ON THE HAUNT
Harvey Comics: Sept, 1992 - No. 3, Jan, 1993 ($1.50, limited series)

1-3	3	6	9	14	20	25

BEE 29, THE BOMBARDIER

Bee and Puppycat #5 © Frederator

Beetle Bailey #14 © DELL

Before Watchmen: Ozymandias #4 © DC

	GD 2.0	VG 4.0	FN 6.0	VF 8.0	VF/NM 9.0	NM- 9.2

Neal Publications: Feb, 1945

	GD 2.0	VG 4.0	FN 6.0	VF 8.0	VF/NM 9.0	NM- 9.2
1-(Funny animal)	41	82	123	256	428	600

BEFORE THE FANTASTIC FOUR: BEN GRIMM AND LOGAN
Marvel Comics: July, 2000 - No. 3, Sept, 2000 ($2.99, limited series)

1-3-The Thing and Wolverine app.; Hama-s						3.00

BEFORE THE FANTASTIC FOUR: REED RICHARDS
Marvel Comics: Sept, 2000 - No. 3, Dec, 2000 ($2.99, limited series)

1-3-Peter David-s/Duncan Fegredo-c/a						3.00

BEFORE THE FANTASTIC FOUR: THE STORMS
Marvel Comics: Dec, 2000 - No. 3, Feb, 2001 ($2.99, limited series)

1-3-Adlard-a						3.00

BEFORE WATCHMEN: COMEDIAN (Prequel to 1986 Watchmen series)
DC Comics: Aug, 2012 - No. 6, Jun, 2013 ($3.99, limited series)

1-6-Brian Azzarello-s/J.G. Jones-a/c; The Comedian during the Vietnam War; back-up Crimson Corsair serial in #1-4; Higgins-a						5.00
1-Variant-c by Jim Lee						60.00
1-6-Variant covers. 1-Risso. 2-Bradstreet. 3-Leon. 4-Stelfreeze. 5-Frank. 6-Albuquerque						10.00

BEFORE WATCHMEN: DOLLAR BILL (Prequel to 1986 Watchmen series)
DC Comics: Mar, 2013 ($3.99, one-shot)

1-Len Wein-s/Steve Rude-a/c; origin and demise of Dollar Bill						5.00
1-Variant-c by Jim Lee						60.00
1-Variant-c by Darwyn Cooke						10.00

BEFORE WATCHMEN: DR. MANHATTAN (Prequel to 1986 Watchmen series)
DC Comics: Oct, 2012 - No. 4, Apr, 2013 ($3.99, limited series)

1-4-Straczynski-s/Hughes-a/c; back-up Crimson Corsair serial in #1-3; Higgins-a						5.00
1-Variant-c by Jim Lee						60.00
1-4-Variant covers. 1-Pope. 2-Russell. 3-Neal Adams. 4-Sienkiewicz						10.00

BEFORE WATCHMEN: MINUTEMEN (Prequel to 1986 Watchmen series)
DC Comics: Aug, 2012 - No. 6, Mar, 2013 ($3.99, limited series)

1-6-Darwyn Cooke-a/c; The team flashback to 1939; back-up Crimson Corsair serial in #1-5; Higgins-a						5.00
1-Variant-c by Jim Lee						40.00
1-6-Variant covers. 1-Golden. 2-Garcia-Lopez-c. 3-Chiang. 4-Rude. 6-Cloonan						10.00

BEFORE WATCHMEN: MOLOCH (Prequel to 1986 Watchmen series)
DC Comics: Jan, 2013 - No. 2, Feb, 2013 ($3.99, limited series)

1,2-Straczynski-s/Risso-a/c; origin; back-up Crimson Corsair serial in both; Higgins-a						5.00
1-Variant-c by Jim Lee						40.00
1,2-Variant covers. 1-Matt Wagner. 2-Olly Moss						10.00

BEFORE WATCHMEN: NITE OWL (Prequel to 1986 Watchmen series)
DC Comics: Aug, 2012 - No. 4, Feb, 2013 ($3.99, limited series)

1-4-Straczynski-s/Andy Kubert-a/c; Joe Kubert-a(i) in #1-3; back-up Crimson Corsair serial in #1-3; Higgins-a						5.00
1-Variant-c by Jim Lee						50.00
1-4-Variant covers. 1-Nowlan. 2-Finch. 3-Samnee. 4-Van Sciver						10.00

BEFORE WATCHMEN: OZYMANDIAS (Prequel to 1986 Watchmen series)
DC Comics: Sept, 2012 - No. 6, Apr, 2013 ($3.99, limited series)

1-6-Len Wein-s/Jae Lee-a/c; origin of master plan; back-up Crimson Corsair serial in #1-4; Higgins-a						4.00
1-Variant-c by Jim Lee						50.00
1-6-Variant covers. 1-Jimenez. 2-Noto. 3-Carnevale. 4-Kaluta. 5-Thompson. 6-Sook						8.00

BEFORE WATCHMEN: RORSCHACH (Prequel to 1986 Watchmen series)
DC Comics: Oct, 2012 - No. 4, Apr, 2013 ($3.99, limited series)

1-4-Azzarello-s/Bermejo-a/c; back-up Crimson Corsair serial in #1-3; Higgins-a						5.00
1-Variant-c by Jim Lee						75.00
1-4-Variant covers. 1-Steranko. 2-Jock. 3-Kidd. 4-Reis						10.00

BEFORE WATCHMEN: SILK SPECTRE (Prequel to 1986 Watchmen series)
DC Comics: Aug, 2012 - No. 4, Jan, 2013 ($3.99, limited series)

1-4-Cooke & Conner-s/Conner-a/c; back-up Crimson Corsair serial in all; Higgins-a						5.00
1-Variant-c by Jim Lee						60.00
1-4-Variant covers. 1-Dave Johnson. 2-Middleton. 3-Allred. 4-Timm						10.00

BEHIND PRISON BARS
Realistic Comics (Avon): 1952

	GD 2.0	VG 4.0	FN 6.0	VF 8.0	VF/NM 9.0	NM- 9.2
1-Kinstler-c	57	114	171	362	619	875

BEHOLD THE HANDMAID
George Pflaum: 1954 (Religious) (25¢ with a 20¢ sticker price)

	GD 2.0	VG 4.0	FN 6.0	VF 8.0	VF/NM 9.0	NM- 9.2
nn	7	14	21	37	46	55

BELIEVE IT OR NOT (See Ripley's...)

BÊLIT & VALERIA: SWORDS VS. SORCERY (From The Cimmerian)
Ablaze Publishing: 2022 - No. 5, 2022 ($3.99)

1-5-Robert E. Howard characters; Bemis-s/Buchemi-a						4.00

BEN AND ME (Disney)
Dell Publishing Co.: No. 539, Mar, 1954

	GD 2.0	VG 4.0	FN 6.0	VF 8.0	VF/NM 9.0	NM- 9.2
Four Color 539	5	10	15	33	57	80

BEN BOWIE AND HIS MOUNTAIN MEN
Dell Publishing Co.: 1952 - No. 17, Nov-Jan, 1958-59

	GD 2.0	VG 4.0	FN 6.0	VF 8.0	VF/NM 9.0	NM- 9.2
Four Color 443 (#1)	9	18	27	63	129	195
Four Color 513,557,599,626,657	5	10	15	34	60	85
7(5-7/56)-11: 11-Intro/origin Yellow Hair	4	8	12	25	40	55
12-17	4	8	12	23	37	50

BEN CASEY (TV)
Dell Publishing Co.: June-July, 1962 - No. 10, June-Aug, 1965 (Photo-c)

	GD 2.0	VG 4.0	FN 6.0	VF 8.0	VF/NM 9.0	NM- 9.2
12-063-207 (#1)	5	10	15	35	63	90
2(10/62),3,5-10	4	8	12	23	37	50
4-Marijuana & heroin use story	5	10	15	30	50	70

BEN CASEY FILM STORIES (TV)
Gold Key: Nov, 1962 (25¢) (Photo-c)

	GD 2.0	VG 4.0	FN 6.0	VF 8.0	VF/NM 9.0	NM- 9.2
30009-211-All photos	6	12	18	38	69	100

BENEATH THE PLANET OF THE APES (See Movie Comics & Power Record Comics)

BEN FRANKLIN (See Kite Fun Book)

BEN HUR
Dell Publishing Co.: No. 1052, Nov, 1959

	GD 2.0	VG 4.0	FN 6.0	VF 8.0	VF/NM 9.0	NM- 9.2
Four Color 1052-Movie, Manning-a	10	20	30	66	138	210

BEN ISRAEL
Logos International: 1974 (39¢)

	GD 2.0	VG 4.0	FN 6.0	VF 8.0	VF/NM 9.0	NM- 9.2
nn-Christian religious	2	4	6	10	14	18

BEN REILLY: SCARLET SPIDER
Marvel Comics: Jun, 2017 - No. 25, Dec, 2018 ($3.99)

1-25: 1-Peter David-s/Mark Bagley-a. 6,7-Sliney-a. 7-Death app. 8-10-The Hornet app. 15-17-Damnation tie-in; Mephisto app. 23,25-Mephisto app.						4.00

BEN REILLY: SPIDER-MAN
Marvel Comics: Mar, 2022 - No. 5, Jul, 2022 ($3.99, limited series)

1-5-DeMatteis-s/Baldeón-a. 1,2,5-Scorpion app.						4.00

BEN 10 (Cartoon Network)
IDW Publishing: Nov, 2013 - No. 4, Feb, 2014 ($3.99, limited series)

1-4: Henderson-s/Purcell-a; multiple covers on each						4.00

BEOWULF (Also see First Comics Graphic Novel #1)
National Periodical Publications: Apr-May, 1975 - No. 6, Feb-Mar, 1976

	GD 2.0	VG 4.0	FN 6.0	VF 8.0	VF/NM 9.0	NM- 9.2
1	2	4	6	11	16	20
2,3,5,6: 5-Flying saucer-c/story	1	2	3	5	6	8
4-Dracula-c/s	1	3	4	6	8	10

BeQUEST, THE
AfterShock Comics: Mar, 2021 - No. 4, Jun, 2021 ($4.99, limited series)

1-4-Tim Seeley-s/Freddie Williams II-a						5.00

BERMUDA
IDW Publishing: Jul, 2021 - No. 4, Oct, 2021 ($4.99, limited series)

1-4-John Layman-s/Nick Bradshaw-a; multiple covers on each						5.00

BERNI WRIGHTSON, MASTER OF THE MACABRE
Pacific Comics/Eclipse Comics No. 5: July, 1983 - No. 5, Nov, 1984 ($1.50, Baxter paper)

1-5: Wrightson-c/a(r). 4-Jeff Jones-r (11 pgs.)						6.00

BERRYS, THE (Also see Funny World)
Argo Publ.: May, 1956

	GD 2.0	VG 4.0	FN 6.0	VF 8.0	VF/NM 9.0	NM- 9.2
1-Reprints daily & Sunday strips & daily Animal Antics by Ed Nofziger						
	8	16	24	40	50	60

BERZERKER (Milo Ventimiglia Presents...)
Image Comics (Top Cow): No. 0, Dec, 2009 - No. 6, Jun, 2010 ($2.99/$3.99)

0-3-Jeremy Haun-a/Rick Loverd-s/Dale Keown-c. 0-Creator interviews						3.00
4-6-($3.99) Covers by Haun & Keown						4.00

BERZERKERS (See Youngblood V1#2)

	GD	VG	FN	VF	VF/NM	NM-
	2.0	4.0	6.0	8.0	9.0	9.2

Image Comics (Extreme Studios): Aug, 1995 - No. 3, Oct, 1995 ($2.50, limited series)

1-3: Beau Smith scripts, Fraga-a — — — — — 4.00

BERZERKER UNBOUND
Dark Horse Comics: Aug, 2019 - No. 4, Nov, 2019 ($3.99, limited series)

1-4 Jeff Lemire-s/Mike Deodato-a/c. 1-Mignola var-c. 2-Sorrentino var-c. 3-Nguyen var-c 4.00

BEST ARCHIE COMIC EVER!, THE
Archie Comic Publications: Aug, 2022 ($3.99, one-shot)

1-Three short stories by various; Pureheart the Powerful app. — — — — — 4.00

BEST COMICS
Better Publications: Nov, 1939 - No. 4, Feb, 1940(10-11/16" wide x 8" tall, reads sideways)

	2.0	4.0	6.0	8.0	9.0	9.2
1-(Scarce)-Red Mask begins (1st app., 1st African American superhero in comics) & c/s-all	476	952	1428	3475	6138	8800
2-4: 3-Racist-c. 4-Cannibalism story	271	542	813	1734	2967	4200

BEST FROM BOY'S LIFE, THE
Gilberton Company: Oct, 1957 - No. 5, Oct, 1958 (35¢)

	2.0	4.0	6.0	8.0	9.0	9.2
1-Space Conquerors & Kam of the Ancient Ones begin, end #5; Bob Cousy photo/story	14	28	42	82	121	160
2,3,5	8	16	24	42	54	65
4-L.B. Cole-a	9	18	27	47	61	75

BEST LOVE (Formerly Sub-Mariner Comics No. 32)
Marvel Comics (MPI): No. 33, Aug, 1949 - No. 36, April, 1950 (Photo-c 33-36)

	2.0	4.0	6.0	8.0	9.0	9.2
33-Kubert-a	21	42	63	122	199	275
34 (10/49)	15	30	45	83	124	165
35,36-Everett-a	15	30	45	88	137	185

BEST OF ARCHIE, THE
Perigee Books: 1980 ($7.95, softcover TPB)

nn-Intro by Michael Uslan & Jeffrey Mendel — 5 — 15 35 63 90

BEST OF BUGS BUNNY, THE
Gold Key: Oct, 1966 - No. 2, Oct, 1968

1,2-Giants 4 8 12 27 44 60

BEST OF DC, THE (Blue Ribbon Digest) (See Limited Coll. Ed. C-52)
DC Comics: Sept-Oct, 1979 - No. 71, Apr, 1986 (100-148 pgs; mostly reprints)

	2.0	4.0	6.0	8.0	9.0	9.2
1-Superman, w/"Death of Superman"-r	3	6	9	14	20	25
2,5-9: 2-Batman 40th Ann. Special. 5-Best of 1979. 6,8-Superman. 7-Superboy. 9-Batman, Creeper app.	2	4	6	8	10	12
3-Superfriends	2	4	6	9	12	15
4-Rudolph the Red Nosed Reindeer	2	4	6	9	13	16
10-Secret Origins of Super Villains; 1st ever Penguin origin-s	3	6	9	16	23	30
11-16,18-20: 11-The Year's Best Stories. 12-Superman Time and Space Stories.13-Best of DC Comics Presents. 14-New origin stories of Batman villains. 15-Superboy. 16-Superman Anniv. 18-Teen Titans new-s., Adams, Kane-a; Perez-c. 19-Superman. 20-World's Finest	1	2	3	5	7	9
17-Supergirl	2	4	6	8	10	12
21,22: 21-Justice Society. 22-Christmas; unpublished Sandman story w/Kirby-a	2	4	6	10	14	18
23-27: 23-(148 pgs.)-Best of 1981. 24 Legion, new story and 16 pgs. new costumes. 25-Superman. 26-Brave & Bold. 27-Superman vs. Luthor	2	4	6	9	12	15
28,29: 28-Binky, Sugar & Spike app. 29-Sugar & Spike, 3 new stories; new Stanley & his Monster story	2	4	6	9	13	16
30,32-36,38,40: 30-Detective Comics. 32-Superman. 33-Secret origins of Legion Heroes and Villains. 34-Metal Men; has #497 on-c from Adv. Comics. 35-The Year's Best Comics Stories (148 pgs.). 36-Superman vs. Kryptonite. 38-Superman vs. Krypton. 40-World of Krypton	2	4	6	9	12	15
31-JLA	2	4	6	9	12	15
34-Corrected version with "#34" on cover	2	4	6	10	14	18
37,39: 37-"Funny Stuff", Mayer-a. 39-Binky	2	4	6	10	14	18
41,43,45,47,49,53,55,58,60,63,65,68,70: 41-Sugar & Spike new stories with Mayer-a. 43,49,55-Funny Stuff. 45,53,70-Binky. 47,65,68-Sugar & Spike. 58-Super Jrs. Holiday Special; Sugar & Spike. 60-Plop!; Wood-c(r) & Aragonés-r (5/85). 63-Plop!; Wrightson-a(r)	3	6	9	14	19	24
42,44,46,48,50-52,54,56,57,59,61,62,64,66,67,69,71: 42,56-Superman vs. Aliens. 44,57,67-Superboy & LSH. 46-Jimmy Olsen. 48-Superman Team-ups. 50-Year's best Superman. 51-Batman Family. 52 Best of 1984. 54,56,59-Superman. 61-(148 pgs.)Year's best. 62-Best of Batman 1985. 69-Year's best Team stories. 71-Year's best	2	4	6	10	14	18

NOTE: **N. Adams** a-2r, 14r, 18r, 26, 51. **Aparo** a-9, 14, 28, 30; c-9, 14, 26. **Austin** a-51i. **Buckler** a-40p; c-16, 22. **Giffen** a-50, 52; c-33p. **Grell** a-33p. **Grossman** a-37. **Heath** a-26. **Infantino** a-10r; 18. **Kaluta** a-40r. **G. Kane** a-10r, 18r; c-40, 44. **Kubert** a-10r, 21, 26. **Layton** a-21. **S. Mayer** c-29, 37, 41, 43, 47; a-28, 29, 37, 41, 43, 47, 58, 65, 68. **Moldoff** c-64p. **Morrow** a-40; c-40. **W. Mortimer** a-39p. **Newton** a-5, 51. **Perez** a-24, 50p; c-18, 21, 23. **Rogers** a-14, 51p. **Simonson** a-17r. **Spiegle** a-52. **Staton** a-5, 21. **Staton** a-5, 21. **Tuska** a-24. **Wolverton** a-60r. **Wood** a-60, 63; c-60, 63. **Wrightson** a-60r. New art in #14, 18, 24.

BEST OF DENNIS THE MENACE, THE
Hallden/Fawcett Publications: Summer, 1959 - No. 5, Spring, 1961 (100 pgs.)

	2.0	4.0	6.0	8.0	9.0	9.2
1-All reprints; Wiseman-a	6	12	18	42	79	115
2-5: 2-Christmas-c	5	10	15	34	50	65

BEST OF DONALD DUCK, THE
Gold Key: Nov, 1965 (12¢, 36 pgs.)(Lists 2nd printing in indicia)

1-Reprints Four Color #223 by Barks 7 14 21 49 92 135

BEST OF DONALD DUCK & UNCLE SCROOGE, THE
Gold Key: Nov, 1964 - No. 2, Sept, 1967 (25¢ Giants)

	2.0	4.0	6.0	8.0	9.0	9.2
1(30022-411)('64)-Reprints 4-Color #189 & 408 by Carl Barks; cover of F.C. #189 redrawn by Barks	8	16	24	54	102	150
2(30022-709)('67)-Reprints 4-Color #256 & "Seven Cities of Cibola" & U.S. #8 by Barks	7	14	21	44	82	120

BEST OF HORROR AND SCIENCE FICTION COMICS
Bruce Webster: 1987 ($2.00)

1-Wolverton, Frazetta, Powell, Ditko-r 2 4 6 8 10 12

BEST OF JOSIE AND THE PUSSYCATS
Archie Comics: 2001 ($10.95, TPB)

1-Reprints 1st app. and noteworthy stories — — — — — 12.00

BEST OF MARMADUKE, THE
Charlton Comics: 1960

1-Brad Anderson's strip reprints 3 6 9 21 33 45

BEST OF MS. TREE, THE
Pyramid Comics: 1987 - No. 4, 1988 ($2.00, B&W, limited series)

1-4 — — — — — 4.00

BEST OF THE BRAVE AND THE BOLD, THE (See Super DC Giant)
DC Comics: Oct, 1988 - No. 6, Jan, 1989 ($2.50, limited series)

1-6: Neal Adams-r, Kubert-r & Heath-r in all — — — — — 4.00

BEST OF THE SPIRIT, THE
DC Comics: 2005 ($14.99, TPB)

nn-Reprints 1st app. and noteworthy stories; intro by Neil Gaiman; Eisner bio. — — — — — 15.00

BEST OF THE WEST (See A-1 Comics)
Magazine Enterprises: 1951 - No. 12, April-June, 1954

	2.0	4.0	6.0	8.0	9.0	9.2
1(A-1 42)-Ghost Rider, Durango Kid, Straight Arrow, Bobby Benson begin	53	106	159	334	567	800
2(A-1 46)	25	50	75	150	245	340
3(A-1 52), 4(A-1 59), 5(A-1 66)	20	40	60	118	192	265
6(A-1 70), 7(A-1 76), 8(A-1 81), 9(A-1 85), 10(A-1 87), 11(A-1 97), 12(A-1 103)	16	32	48	94	147	200

NOTE: **Bolle** a-9. **Borth** a-12. **Guardineer** a-5, 12. **Powell** a-1, 12.

BEST OF UNCLE SCROOGE & DONALD DUCK, THE
Gold Key: Nov, 1966 (25¢)

1(30030-611)-Reprints part 4-Color #159 & 456 & Uncle Scrooge #6,7 by Carl Barks 7 14 21 44 82 120

BEST OF WALT DISNEY COMICS, THE
Western Publishing Co.: 1974 ($1.50, 52 pgs.) (Walt Disney) (8-1/2x11" cardboard covers; 32,000 printed of each)

	2.0	4.0	6.0	8.0	9.0	9.2
96170-Reprints 1st two stories less 1 pg. each from 4-Color #62	6	12	18	37	66	95
96171-Reprints Mickey Mouse and the Bat Bandit of Inferno Gulch from 1934 (strips) by Gottfredson	6	12	18	37	66	95
96172-r/Uncle Scrooge #386 & two other stories	6	12	18	37	66	95
96173-Reprints "Ghost of the Grotto" (from 4-Color #159) & "Christmas on Bear Mountain" (from 4-Color #178)	6	12	18	37	66	95

BEST ROMANCE
Standard Comics (Visual Editions): No. 5, Feb-Mar, 1952 - No. 7, Aug, 1952

	2.0	4.0	6.0	8.0	9.0	9.2
5-Toth-a; photo-c	21	42	63	122	199	275
6,7-Photo-c	14	28	42	81	118	155

BEST SELLER COMICS (See Tailspin Tommy)

BEST WESTERN (Formerly Terry Toons? or Miss America Magazine)
Marvel Comics (IPC): V7#24(#57)?; Western Outlaws & Sheriffs No. 60 on)
No. 58, June, 1949 - No. 59, Aug, 1949

58,59-Black Rider, Kid Colt, Two-Gun Kid app.; both have Syd Shores-c 36 72 108 211 343 475

BETA RAY BILL (Thor)
Marvel Comics: May, 2021 - No. 5, Sept, 2021 ($4.99/$3.99, limited series)

	2.0	4.0	6.0	8.0	9.0	9.2
1-($4.99)-Daniel Warren Johnson-s/a; Fin Fang Foom app.; Walt Simonson interview						5.00
2-5-($3.99) 2,3-Skurge & Pip app. 4,5-Surtur app.						4.00

BETA RAY BILL: GODHUNTER
Marvel Comics: Aug, 2009 - No. 3, Oct, 2009 ($3.99, limited series)

1-3-Kano-a; Thor and Galactus app.; reprints form Thor #337-339. 2,3-Silver Surfer app. 4.00

BETRAYAL OF THE PLANET OF THE APES (Set 20 years before the first movie)
BOOM! Studios: Nov, 2011 - No. 4, Feb, 2012 ($3.99, limited series)

1-4-Dr. Zaius app.; Bechko-s/Hardman-a. 1-Three covers. 2-Two covers 4.00

BETROTHED
AfterShock Comics: Mar, 2018 - No. 5, Jul, 2018 ($3.99, limited series)

1-5-Sean Lewis-s/Steve Uy-a — — — — — 4.00

BETSY BRADDOCK: CAPTAIN BRITAIN
Marvel Comics: Apr, 2023 - No. 5, Aug, 2023 ($3.99, limited series)

1-5-Morgan LeFay & Rachel Summers app.; Howard-s/Georgiev-a — — — — — 4.00

BETTIE PAGE
Dynamite Entertainment: 2017 - No. 8, 2018 ($3.99)

	2.0	4.0	6.0	8.0	9.0	9.2
1-Bettie Page in 1951 Hollywood; Avallone-s/Worley-a; multiple covers	2	4	6	8	10	12
2-8-Multiple covers on each						6.00
... Halloween Special One-Shot (2018, $4.99) Avallone-s; art by Ohta & Ruiz						10.00
... Halloween Special One-Shot (2019, $4.99) Avallone-s; art by Martinez & Ruiz						10.00

BETTIE PAGE AND THE ALIEN AGENDA, VOLUME 6
Dynamite Entertainment: 2022 - No. 5, 2022 ($3.99)

1-5-Bettie Page alien-hunting in Egypt in 1950s; Ani-Mia-s; multiple covers on each 4.00

BETTIE PAGE AND THE CURSE OF THE BANSHEE, VOLUME 5
Dynamite Entertainment: 2021 - No. 5, 2021 ($3.99)

1-5-Bettie Page monster-hunting in Ireland in 1954; multiple covers on each 4.00

BETTIE PAGE COMICS
Dark Horse Comics: Mar, 1996 ($3.95)

1-Dave Stevens-c; Blevins & Heath-a; Jaime Hernandez pin-up 3 6 9 19 30 40

BETTIE PAGE COMICS: QUEEN OF THE NILE
Dark Horse Comics: Dec, 1999 - No. 3, Apr, 2000 ($2.95, limited series)

1-Silke-s/a; Stevens-c 3 6 9 15 22 28

Best of Bugs Bunny #1 © WB

Bettie Page V3 #4 © Bettie Page LLC

Betty and Veronica #6 © ACP

	GD 2.0	VG 4.0	FN 6.0	VF 8.0	VF/NM 9.0	NM- 9.2
2,3-Silke-s/a; Stevens-c	2	4	6	11	16	20
BETTIE PAGE COMICS: SPICY ADVENTURE						
Dark Horse Comics: Jan, 1997 ($2.95, one-shot, mature)						
nn-Silke-c/s/a	2	4	6	8	10	12
BETTIE PAGE UNBOUND						
Dynamite Entertainment: 2019 - No. 10, 2020 ($3.99)						
1-10-Multiple covers on each: 1-Bettie as Red Sonja. 2-Bettie as Vampirella						4.00
BETTIE PAGE: VOLUME 2						
Dynamite Entertainment: 2018 - No. 5, 2019 ($3.99)						
1-5-Bettie Page in 1952 England. 1-4-Avallone-s/Ohta-a; multiple covers on each						5.00
BETTIE PAGE: VOLUME 3						
Dynamite Entertainment: 2020 - No. 5, 2020 ($3.99)						
1-5-Bettie Page shooting a movie in the Caribbean; multiple covers on each						4.00
BETTIE PAGE, VOLUME 6						
Dynamite Entertainment: 2023 - No. 4, 2023 ($3.99)						
1-4-Andolfo & Blengino-s/Ferrari-a; multiple covers on each						4.00
BETTY (See Pep Comics #22 for 1st app.)						
Archie Comics: Sept, 1992 - No. 195, Jan, 2012 ($1.25-$2.99)						
1	2	4	6	8	10	12
2-7,9-18,20-24: 20-1st Super Sleuther-s						5.00
8-Risqué bikini-c	5	10	15	35	63	90
19-Love Showdown part 2						6.00
25-Pin-up page of Betty as Marilyn Monroe, Madonna, Lady Di						6.00
26-45,47-50						3.00
46-(2/97) "High School 2021 A.D." shows future with virtual classes over computer monitors						4.00
51-53,55-195: 57- "A Storm Over Uniforms" x-over part 5,6. 186-Begin $2.99-c						3.00
54-Bondage-c	1	3	4	6	8	10
BETTY AND HER STEADY (Going Steady with Betty No. 1)						
Avon Periodicals: No. 2, Mar-Apr, 1950						
2	16	32	48	92	144	195
BETTY AND ME						
Archie Publications: Aug, 1965 - No. 200, Aug, 1992						
1	25	50	75	175	388	600
2,3: 3-Origin Superteen	9	18	27	59	117	175
4-8: Superteen in new costume #4-7; dons new helmet in #5, ends #8.	5	10	15	34	60	85
9,10: Girl from R.I.V.E.R.D.A.L.E. 9-UFO-s	4	8	12	27	44	60
11-15,17-20(4/69)	3	6	9	21	33	45
16-Classic cover; w/risqué cover dialogue	54	108	162	432	966	1500
21,24-35: 33-Paper doll page	3	6	9	16	23	30
22-Archies Band-s	3	6	9	16	24	32
23-I Dream of Jeannie parody	3	6	9	19	30	40
36(8/71),37,41-55 (52 pgs.): 42-Betty as vamp-s	4	8	12	25	40	55
38-Sabrina app.	3	6	9	19	30	40
39-Josie and Sabrina cover cameos	3	6	9	17	26	35
40-Archie & Betty share a cabin						
56(4/71)-80(12/76): 79 Betty Cooper mysteries thru #86. 79-81-Drago the Vampire-s	2	4	6	9	13	16
81-99: 83-Harem-c. 84-Jekyll & Hyde-c/s	2	4	6	8	10	12
100(3/79)	2	4	6	9	12	15
101,118: 101-Elvis mentioned. 118-Tarzan mentioned 1	2	3	5	7		9
102-117,119-130(9/82): 103,104-Space-s. 124-DeCarlo-c begins						7.00
131-135,137,138,140,142-147,149-154,156-158: 135-Jason Blossom app. 137-Space-s. 138-Tarzan parody						5.00
136-Classic-c; Cheryl Blossom cameo	5	10	15	34	60	85
139,141,148: 139-Katy Keene collecting-s; Archie in drag-s. 141-Tarzan parody-s. 148-Cyndi Lauper parody-s						6.00
155,159,160(8/87): 155-Archie in drag-s. 159-Superhero gag-c. 160-Wheel of Fortune parody						6.00
161-169,171-199						4.00
170,200: 170-New Archie Superhero-s						6.00
BETTY AND VERONICA (Also see Archie's Girls...)						
Archie Enterprises: June, 1987 - No. 278, Dec, 2015 (75c-$3.99)						
1	3	6	9	16	23	30
2,3,7-10						6.00
4,5,13,14,16,24,27,33-all bikini covers	1	3	4	6	8	10
6-Bubble bath-c	2	4	6	9	12	15
11,12,15,17-21,23,25,26,28-30						4.00
22-Swimsuit headlights-c	3	6	9	14	20	25

	GD 2.0	VG 4.0	FN 6.0	VF 8.0	VF/NM 9.0	NM- 9.2
31,32,34-53,56-58,60-62,64,65,67,70-78,81						3.00
54,55,65-Bikini-c	2	4	6	11	16	20
59-Halloween-c	1	3	4	6	8	10
63-Headlights-c	2	4	6	8	10	12
66,68,69,79,80,93,103,104,115,116,176-178,190,205,248-Bikini covers	2	4	6	9	12	15
82-Love Showdown part 3						5.00
83-92,94-102,105-114,117,119-126,129-139,141-175,179-189,191-204,206-247,249-260, 263-266,268,270,271: 242-Begin $2.50-c. 247-Begin $2.99-c. 264-271-Two covers						3.00
118,140: 118-Bikini Halloween-c. 140-Bikini-c	2	4	6	11	16	20
127,128-Bikini-c	3	6	9	17	26	35
261-1st Veronica as Vampironica	6	12	18	38	69	100
262-Veronica as Vampironica contines	5	10	15	33	57	80
267-Mermaid variant-c by Fiona Staples	2	4	6	11	16	20
269-Angel & Devil-c	2	4	6	11	16	20
272-274,276-278-($3.99): 272-274,276,277-Two covers. 278-Last issue; 6 covers						4.00
275-($4.99) Five covers by Adam Hughes, Ramona Fradon & others						5.00
... Free Comic Book Day Edition #1 (6/05) Katy Keene-c/app.; Cheryl Blossom app.						3.00
BETTY AND VERONICA (Volume 3)						
Archie Comic Publications: Sept, 2016 - No. 3, Aug, 2017 ($3.99, limited series)						
1-3-Adam Hughes-s/a; multiple covers on each; back-up classic pin-ups						4.00
... No. 1: FCBD Edition (5/17, giveaway) r/#1; bonus Riverdale TV show character guide						3.00
BETTY AND VERONICA (Volume 4)						
Archie Comic Publications: Feb, 2019 - No. 5, Jul, 2019 ($3.99, limited series)						
1-5-Rotante/Lanz-a; Senior year in high school						4.00
BETTY & VERONICA ANNUAL DIGEST (...Digest Magazine #1-4, 44 on; ...Comics Digest Mag. #5-43)(Continues as Betty & Veronica Friends Double Digest #209-on)						
Archie Publications: Nov, 1980 - No. 208, Nov, 2010 ($1.00-$2.69, digest size)						
1	3	6	9	16	23	30
2-10: 2(11/81-Katy Keene story), 3(8/82)	2	4	6	9	13	16
11-30	1	3	4	6	8	10
31-50	1	2	3	4	5	7
51-70						4.00
71-191: 110-Begin $2.19-c. 135-Begin $2.39-c. 165-Begin $2.49. 185-Includes reprint of Archie's Girls B&V #1 (1950) and new story where 1950 & 2008 B&V meet						3.00
192-208: 192-Begin $2.69-c						3.00
BETTY & VERONICA ANNUAL DIGEST MAGAZINE						
Archie Comics: Sept, 1989 - No. 16, Aug, 1997 ($1.50/$1.75/$1.79, 128 pgs.)						
1	1	2	3	5	7	9
2-10: 9-Neon ink logo						5.00
11-16: Begin $1.79-c						3.00
BETTY & VERONICA CHRISTMAS SPECTACULAR (See Archie Giant Series Magazine #159, 168, 180, 191, 204, 217, 229, 241, 453, 465, 477, 489, 501, 513, 525, 536, 547, 558, 568, 580, 593, 606, 618)						
BETTY & VERONICA DOUBLE DIGEST MAGAZINE						
Archie Enterprises: 1987 - Present ($2.25-$9.99, digest size, 256 pgs.)(...Digest #12 on)						
1	2	4	6	8	10	12
2-10	1	2	3	4	5	7
11-25: 5,17-Xmas-c. 16-Capt. Hero story						5.00
26-50						4.00
51-150: 87-Begin $3.19-c. 95-Begin $3.29-c. 114-Begin $3.59-c. 142-Begin $3.69-c						4.00
151-211,213-222: 151-(7/07)-Realistic style Betty & Veronica debuts (thru #154). 160-Cheryl Blossom spotlight. 170-173-Realistic style						4.00
212,223,237,240-($5.99) Titled Betty & Veronica Double Digest						6.00
224-($5.99) Titled Betty & Veronica Comics Annual (192 pgs.)						6.00
225,228,238,242,247,250,255,257,260-275-($6.99) Titled Betty & Veronica Jumbo Comics Digest (320 pgs.)						7.00
226,227,229-232,234-236,239,241,243,245,246,249,251,254,256-($4.99) Titled Betty & Veronica Comics Digest or Comics Double Digest						5.00
244,248,252,253,258-($5.99) 244,253-Titled Betty & Veronica Summer Ann.						6.00
276-299-($7.99): 287-Halloween-c						8.00
300-309-($8.99)						9.00
310-323-($9.99)						10.00
Betty & Veronica: in Bad Boy Trouble Vol.1 TPB (2007, $7.49) r/new style from #151-154						8.00
BETTY & VERONICA FRIENDS DOUBLE DIGEST (Continues from B&V Digest Mag. #208)						
Archie Publications: No. 209, Jan, 2011 - No. 286, Jan, 2021 ($3.99-$7.99, digest size)						
209-236,238: 209-Cheryl Blossom app.						4.00
237,246-Titled Betty & Veronica Friends Double Digest ($5.99, 320 pages)						6.00
239-($4.99) Double Digest						5.00
240,245,250,252,254,256,257-273-($6.99) 257-Winter Annual						7.00
241-244,248-($4.99) Titled Betty & Veronica Friends Comics Digest. 244-Pussycats app.						5.00
247,249,251,253,255-($5.99) 247-Easter Annual. 251-Halloween Annual						6.00

	GD 2.0	VG 4.0	FN 6.0	VF 8.0	VF/NM 9.0	NM- 9.2

274-286-($7.99) ... 8.00

BETTY & VERONICA FRIENDS FOREVER
Archie Publications: Jun, 2018 - Present ($2.99/$3.99, quarterly)
1-Classic-style stories; Parent-a ... 3.00
1-(#2) Travel Tales on cover, 1-(#3) Storybook Tales, 1-(#4) Go To Work, 1-(#5) Pets,
1-(#6) Return to Storybook Land, 1-(#7) Supernatural Stories, 1-(#8) What If...?,
1-(#9) It's All Relative. 1-(#10) Danger Zone. 1-(#11) Good Citizens. 1-(#12) Winterfest
1-(#13) Spring Break. 1-(#14) Summer Fun. 1-(#15) Halloween Spooktacular
1-(#16) Power-Ups. 1-(#17) Summer Surf Party. 1-(#18) Christmas Party. 1-(#19) Rock and
Roll; intro. Jola Kitt. 1-(#20) Game On.
1-($3.99)(#21) Beach Party ... 4.00

BETTY & VERONICA JUMBO COMICS DIGEST (See Betty & Veronica Double Digest Magazine)

BETTY & VERONICA SPECTACULAR (See Archie Giant Series Mag. #11, 16, 21, 26, 32, 138, 145, 153, 162, 173, 184, 197, 201, 210, 214, 221, 226, 234, 238, 246, 250, 458, 462, 470, 482, 486, 494, 498, 506, 510, 518, 522, 526, 530, 537, 552, 559, 563, 569, 575, 582, 588, 600, 608, 613, 620, 623, and Betty & Veronica)

BETTY AND VERONICA SPECTACULAR
Archie Comics: Oct, 1992 - No. 90, Sept, 2009 ($1.25/$1.50/$1.75/$1.99/$2.19/$2.25/$2.50)
1-Dan DeCarlo-c/a ... 5.00
2-90: 48-Cheryl Blossom leaves Riverdale. 64-Cheryl Blossom returns ... 3.00

BETTY & VERONICA SPRING SPECTACULAR (See Archie Giant Series Magazine #569, 582, 595)

BETTY & VERONICA SUMMER FUN (See Archie Giant Series Mag. #8, 13, 18, 23, 28, 34, 140, 147, 155, 164, 175, 187, 199, 212, 224, 238, 460, 484, 496, 508, 520, 529, 539, 550, 561, 572, 585, 598, 611, 621)
Archie Comics: 1994 - No. 6, 1999 ($2.00/$2.25/$2.29, annual)
1-($2.00, 52 pgs. plus poster) ... 4.00
2-6: 5-($2.25-c). 6-($2.29-c) ... 3.00
Vol. 1 (2003, $10.95) reprints stories from Archie Giant Series editions ... 12.00

BETTY & VERONICA: VIXENS
Archie Comics Publications: Jan, 2018 - No. 10, Nov, 2018 ($3.99)
1-10: 1-Betty & Veronica form a biker gang; Cabrera-a; South Side Serpents app. ... 4.00

BETTY BOOP (Volume 1)
Dynamite Entertainment: 2016 - No. 4, 2017 ($3.99)
1-4-Langridge-s/Lagacé-a; Koko app.; multiple covers on each ... 4.00

BETTY BOOP'S BIG BREAK
First Publishing: 1990 ($5.95, 52 pgs.)
nn-By Joshua Quagmire; 60th anniversary ish. ... 6.00

BETTY PAGE 3-D COMICS
The 3-D Zone: 1991 ($3.95, "7-1/2x10-1/4", 28 pgs., no glasses)
1-Photo inside covers; back-c nudity ... 2 | 4 | 6 | 11 | 16 | 20

BETTY'S DIARY (See Archie Giant Series Magazine No. 555)
Archie Enterprises: April, 1986 - No. 40, Apr, 1991 (#1:65¢; 75¢/95¢)
1 ... 2 | 4 | 6 | 8 | 10 | 12
2-10 ... 5.00
11-40 ... 4.00

BETTY'S DIGEST
Archie Enterprises: Nov, 1996 - No. 2 ($1.75/$1.79)
1,2 ... 4.00

BEVERLY HILLBILLIES (TV)
Dell Publishing Co.: 4-6/63 - No. 18, 8/67; No. 19, 10/69; No. 20, 10/70; No. 21, Oct, 1971

	GD 2.0	VG 4.0	FN 6.0	VF 8.0	VF/NM 9.0	NM- 9.2
1-Photo-c	18	36	54	124	275	425
2-Photo-c	8	16	24	55	105	155
3-9: All have photo covers	6	12	18	40	73	105
10: No photo cover	5	10	15	30	50	70
11-21: All have photo covers. 18-Last 12¢ issue. 19-21-Reprint #1-3 (covers and insides)	5	10	15	33	57	80

NOTE: #1-9, 11-21 are photo covers.

BEWARE (Formerly Fantastic; Chilling Tales No. 13 on)
Youthful Magazines: No. 10, June, 1952 - No. 12, Oct, 1952

	GD 2.0	VG 4.0	FN 6.0	VF 8.0	VF/NM 9.0	NM- 9.2
10-E.A. Poe's Pit & the Pendulum adaptation by Wildey; Harrison/Bache-a; atom bomb and shrunken head-c	129	258	387	826	1413	2000
11-Harrison-a; Ambrose Bierce adapt.	110	220	330	704	1202	1700
12-Used in SOTI, pg. 388; Harrison-a	110	220	330	704	1202	1700

BEWARE
Trojan Magazines/Merit Publ. No. ?: No. 13, 1/53 - No. 16, 7/53; No. 5, 9/53 - No. 15, 5/55

	GD 2.0	VG 4.0	FN 6.0	VF 8.0	VF/NM 9.0	NM- 9.2
13(#1)-Harrison-a	110	220	330	704	1202	1700
14(#2, 3/53)-Krenkel/Harrison-c; dismemberment, severed head panels; Good Girl-a	187	374	561	1197	2049	2900
15,16(#3, 5/53; #4, 7/53)-Harrison-a	58	116	174	371	636	900
5,9,12,13(1/55)	55	110	165	352	601	850
6-Ill. in SOTI: "Children are first shocked and then desensitized by all this brutality." Corpse on cover swipe/V.O.H. #26; girl on cover swipe/Advs. Into Darkness #10	300	600	900	2010	3505	5000
7,8-Check-a	77	154	231	493	847	1200
10-Frazetta/Check-c; Disbrow, Check-a	432	864	1296	3154	5577	8000
11-Disbrow-a; heart torn out, blood drainage story	155	310	465	992	1696	2400
14,15: 14-Myron Fass-c. 15-Harrison-a	55	110	165	352	601	850

NOTE: Fass a-5, 6, 8; c-6, 11, 14. Forte a-8. Hollingsworth a-15(#3), 16(#4), 9; c-16(#4), 8, 9. Kiefer a-16(#4), 5, 6, 10.

BEWARE (Becomes Tomb of Darkness No. 9 on)
Marvel Comics Group: Mar, 1973 - No. 8, May, 1974 (All reprints)

	GD 2.0	VG 4.0	FN 6.0	VF 8.0	VF/NM 9.0	NM- 9.2
1-Everett-c; Kirby & Sinnott-r ('54)	6	12	18	37	66	95
2-8: 2-Forte, Colan-r. 6-Tuska-a. 7-Torres-r/Mystical Tales #7	4	8	12	23	37	50

NOTE: Infantino a-4r. Gil Kane c-4. Wildey a-7r.

BEWARE TERROR TALES
Fawcett Publications: May, 1952 - No. 8, July, 1953

	GD 2.0	VG 4.0	FN 6.0	VF 8.0	VF/NM 9.0	NM- 9.2
1-E.C. art swipe/Haunt of Fear #5 & Vault of Horror #26	90	180	270	576	988	1400
2	58	116	174	371	636	900
3-5,7	47	94	141	296	498	700
6-Classic skeleton-c	129	258	387	826	1413	2000
8-Tothish-a; people being cooked-c	181	362	543	1158	1979	2800

NOTE: Andru a-2. Bernard Bailey a-1; c-1-5. Powell a-1, 2, 8. Sekowsky a-2.

BEWARE THE BATMAN (Based on the Cartoon Network series)
DC Comics: Dec, 2013 - No. 6, May, 2014 ($2.99)
1-6: 1-Anarky app. 4-Man-Bat app. 6-Killer Croc app. ... 3.00

BEWARE THE CREEPER (See Adventure, Best of the Brave & the Bold, Brave & the Bold, 1st Issue Special, Flash #318-323, Showcase #73, World's Finest Comics #249)
National Periodical Publications: May-June, 1968 - No. 6, Mar-Apr, 1969 (All 12¢ issues)

	GD 2.0	VG 4.0	FN 6.0	VF 8.0	VF/NM 9.0	NM- 9.2
1-(5-6/68)-Classic Ditko-c; Ditko-a in all	9	18	27	57	111	165
2-6: 2-5-Ditko-a. 2-Intro. Proteus. 6-Gil Kane-c	5	10	15	33	57	80

BEWARE THE CREEPER
DC Comics (Vertigo): Jun, 2003 - No. 5, Oct, 2003 ($2.95, limited series)
1-5-Female vigilante in 1920s Paris; Jason Hall-s/Cliff Chiang-a ... 3.00

BEWARE THE EYE OF ODIN
Image Comics: Jun, 2022 - No. 4, Sept, 2022 ($4.99)
1-4-Doug Wagner-s/Tim Odland-a ... 5.00

BEWARE THE PLANET OF THE APES
Marvel Comics: Mar, 2024 - Present ($4.99/$3.99)
1-($4.99) Takes place prior to Taylor's arrival; Nova app.; Guggenheim-s/Lopez-a ... 5.00
2-($3.99) Includes panels from Adventures on the Planet of the Apes (1975) ... 4.00

BEWITCHED (TV)
Dell Publishing Co.: 4-6/65 - No. 11, 10/67; No. 12, 10/68 - No. 13, 1/69; No. 14, 10/69

	GD 2.0	VG 4.0	FN 6.0	VF 8.0	VF/NM 9.0	NM- 9.2
1-Photo-c	17	34	51	114	252	390
2-No photo-c	8	16	24	56	108	160
3-13-All have photo-c. 12-Rep. #1. 13-Last 12¢-c	7	14	21	46	86	125
14-No photo-c; reprints #2	5	10	15	35	63	90

BEYOND!
Marvel Comics: Sept, 2006 - No. 6, Feb, 2007 ($2.99, limited series)
1-6-McDuffie-s/Kolins-a; Spider-Man, Venom, Gravity, Wasp app. 6-Gravity dies ... 3.00

BEYOND, THE
Ace Magazines: Nov, 1950 - No. 30, Jan, 1955

	GD 2.0	VG 4.0	FN 6.0	VF 8.0	VF/NM 9.0	NM- 9.2
1-Bakerish-a(p)	181	362	543	1158	1979	2800
2-Bakerish-a(p)	54	108	162	343	574	825
3-10: 10-Woodish-a by Cameron	40	80	120	246	411	575
11-20: 18-Used in POP, pgs. 81,82	36	72	108	211	343	475
21-26,28-30	32	64	96	188	307	425
27-Used in SOTI, pg. 111	181	362	543	1158	1979	2800

NOTE: Cameron a-10, 11p, 12p, 15, 16, 21-27, 30; c-20. Colan a-6, 13, 17. Sekowsky a-2, 3, 5, 7, 11, 14, 27r. No. 1 was to appear as Challenge of the Unknown No. 7.

BEYONDERS
AfterShock Comics: Aug, 2018 - No. 5, Mar, 2019 ($3.99, limited series)
1-5-Paul Jenkins-s/Wesley St. Claire-a ... 4.00

BEYOND THE BREACH
AfterShock Comics: Jul, 2021 - Present ($4.99/$3.99)
1-($4.99) Ed Brisson-s/Damian Couceiro-a ... 5.00
2-5-($3.99) ... 4.00

BEYOND THE FRINGE (Based on the TV series Fringe)
DC Comics: May, 2012 ($3.99, one-shot)
1-Joshua Jackson-s/Jorge Jimenez/Drew Johnson-c ... 4.00

BEYOND THE GRAVE
Charlton Comics: July, 1975 - No. 6, June, 1976; No. 7, Jan, 1983 - No. 17, Oct, 1984

	GD 2.0	VG 4.0	FN 6.0	VF 8.0	VF/NM 9.0	NM- 9.2
1-Ditko-a (6 pgs.); Sutton painted-c	5	10	15	31	53	75
2-6: 2-5-Ditko-a; Ditko c-2,3,6	3	6	9	17	26	35
7-17: ('83-'84) Reprints. 8,11,16-Ditko-a. 11-Staton-a. 13-Aparo-r(r). 15-Sutton-a (low print run). 16-Palais-a	2	3	6	8	10	

Modern Comics Reprint 2('78) ... 6.00
NOTE: Howard a-4. Kim a-1. Larson a-4, 6.

BIBLE, THE: EDEN
IDW Publishing: 2003 ($21.99, hardcover graphic novel)
HC-Scott Hampton painted-a; adaptation of Genesis by Dave Elliot and Keith Giffen ... 22.00

BIBLE TALES FOR YOUNG FOLK (...Young People No. 3-5)
Atlas Comics (OMC): Aug, 1953 - No. 5, Mar, 1954

	GD 2.0	VG 4.0	FN 6.0	VF 8.0	VF/NM 9.0	NM- 9.2
1	32	64	96	188	307	425
2-Everett, Krigstein, Maneely-a; Robinson-c	19	38	57	109	172	235
3-5: 4,5-Robinson-a	16	32	48	92	144	195

BIG (Movie)
Hit Comics (Dark Horse Comics): Mar, 1989 ($2.00)
1-Adaptation of film; Paul Chadwick-c ... 4.00

BIG ALL-AMERICAN COMIC BOOK, THE (See All-American Comics)
All-American/National Per. Publ.: 1944 (132 pgs., one-shot) (Early DC Annual)

	GD 2.0	VG 4.0	FN 6.0	VF 8.0	VF/NM 9.0	NM- 9.2
1-Wonder Woman, Green Lantern, Flash, The Atom, Wildcat, Scribbly, The Whip, Ghost Patrol, Hawkman by Kubert (1st on Hawkman), Hop Harrigan, Johnny Thunder, Little Boy Blue, Mr. Terrific, Mutt & Jeff app.; Sargon on cover only; cover by Kubert/Hibbard/Mayer and others	750	1500	2250	5500	10,250	15,000

BIG BABY HUEY (See Baby Huey)

BIG BANG COMICS (Becomes Big Bang #4)
Caliber Press: Spring, 1994 - No. 4, Feb, 1995; No. 0, May, 1995 ($1.95, lim. series)
1-4-($1.95-c) ... 4.00
0-(5/95, $2.95) Alex Ross-c; color and B&W pages ... 3.00
Your Big Book of Big Bang Comics TPB ('98, $11.00) r/#0-2 ... 11.00

BIG BANG COMICS (Volume 2)
Image Comics (Highbrow Ent.): V2#1, May, 1996 - No. 35, Jan, 2001 ($1.95-$3.95)
1-23,26: 1-Mighty Man app. 2-4-S.A. Shadowhawk app. 5-Begin $2.95-c. 6-Curt Swan/Murphy

Bewitched #4 © Screen Gems

Big All-American Comic Book #1 © DC

Big Game #1 © Netflix

	GD 2.0	VG 4.0	FN 6.0	VF 8.0	VF/NM 9.0	NM- 9.2

Anderson-c. 7-Begin B&W. 12-Savage Dragon-c/app. 16,17,21-Shadow Lady — 3.00
24,25,27-35-($3.95): 35-Big Bang vs. Alan Moore's "1963" characters — 4.00
...Presents the Ultiman Family (2/05, $3.50) — 3.50
...Round Table of America (2/04, $3.95) Don Thomas-a — 4.00
...Summer Special (8/03, $4.95) World's Nastiest Nazis app. — 5.00

BIG BANG PRESENTS (Volume 3)
Big Bang Comics: July, 2006 - No. 5 ($2.95/$3.95, B&W)
1,2: 1-Protoplasman (Plastic Man homage) — 3.00
3-5-($3.95) 3-Origin of Protoplasman. 4-Flip book — 4.00

BIG BANG UNIVERSE
AC Comics: 2015 ($9.95, B&W)
1-Four new stories; Ultiman, Knight Watchman, Galahad & Whiz Kids app. — 10.00

BIG BLACK KISS
Vortex Comics: Sep, 1989 - No, 3, Nov, 1989 ($3.75, B&W, lim. series, mature)
1-3-Chaykin-s/a — 5.00

BIG BLOWN BABY (Also see Dark Horse Presents)
Dark Horse Comics: Aug, 1996 - No. 4, Nov, 1996 ($2.95, lim. series, mature)
1-Bill Wray-c/a/scriptsin all — 1 3 4 6 8 10
2-4: Bill Wray-c/a/scripts — 5.00

BIG BOOK OF ..., THE
DC Comics (Paradox Press): 1994 - 1999 (B&W)($12.95 - $14.95)
nn-...BAD,1998 ($14.95),...CONSPIRACIES, 1995 ($12.95), ...DEATH,1994 ($12.95),
...FREAKS, 1996 ($14.95), ...GRIMM, 1999 ($14.95), ...HOAXES, 1996 ($14.95),
...LITTLE CRIMINALS, 1996 ($14.95),...LOSERS,1997 ($14.95), ...MARTYRS, 1997
($14.95),...SCANDAL,1997 ($14.95), ...THE WEIRD WILD WEST,1998 ($14.95),
...THUGS, 1997 ($14.95),...UNEXPLAINED, 1997 ($14.95), ...URBAN LEGENDS, 1994
($12.95),...VICE, 1994 ($14.95), ...WEIRDOS, 1995 ($12.95) — cover price

BIG BOOK OF FUN COMICS (See New Book of Comics)
National Periodical Publications: Spring, 1936 (Large size, 52 pgs.)
(1st comic book annual & DC annual)
1 (Very rare)-r/New Fun #1-5 — 2750 5500 8250 18,000 - -

BIG BOOK ROMANCES
Fawcett Publications: Feb, 1950 (no date given) (148 pgs.)
1-Contains remaindered Fawcett romance comics - several combinations possible
— 93 186 279 591 1021 1450

BIG CHIEF WAHOO
Eastern Color Printing/George Dougherty (distr. by Fawcett): July, 1942 - No. 7, Wint., 1943/44?(no year given)(Quarterly)
1-Newspaper-r (on sale 6/15/42) — 50 100 150 315 533 750
2-Steve Roper app. — 24 48 72 144 237 330
3-5: 4-Chief is holding a Katy Keene comic in one panel — 19 38 57 112 179 245
6-7 — 15 30 45 84 127 170
NOTE: Kerry Drake in some issues.

BIG CIRCUS, THE (Movie)
Dell Publishing Co.: No. 1036, Sept-Nov, 1959
Four Color 1036-Photo-c — 6 12 18 40 73 105

BIG CON JOB, THE (PALMIOTTI & BRADY'S...)
BOOM! Studios: Mar, 2015 - No. 4, Jun, 2015 ($3.99, limited series)
1-4-Palmiotti & Brady-s/Stanton-a/Conner-c — 4.00

BIG COUNTRY, THE (Movie)
Dell Publishing Co.: No. 946, Oct, 1958
Four Color 946-Photo-c — 6 12 18 42 79 115

BIG DADDY DANGER
DC Comics: Oct, 2002 - No. 9, June, 2003 ($2.95, limited series)
1-9-Adam Pollina-s/c/a — 3.00

BIG DADDY ROTH (Magazine)
Millar Publications: Oct-Nov, 1964 - No. 4, Apr-May, 1965 (35c)
1-Toth-a; Batman & Robin parody — 22 44 66 154 340 525
2-4-Toth-a — 13 26 39 89 195 300

BIGFOOT
IDW Publishing: Feb, 2005 - No. 4, May, 2005 ($3.99, limited series)
1-4-Steve Niles & Rob Zombie-s/Richard Corben-a/c — 4.00

BIG GAME
Image Comics: Jul, 2023 - No. 5 ($4.99, limited series)

1-4-Mark Millar-s/Pepe Larraz; Wesley Gibson (Wanted) hunting the Millarverse heroes — 5.00
5-($7.99) Hit-Girl app. — 8.00

BIG GIRLS
Image Comics: Aug, 2020 - No. 6, Jan, 2021 ($3.99)
1-6-Jason Howard-s/a — 4.00

BIGG TIME
DC Comics (Vertigo): 2002 ($14.95, B&W, graphic novel)
nn-Ty Templeton-s/c/a — 15.00

BIG GUY AND RUSTY THE BOY ROBOT, THE (Also See Madman Comics #6,7 & Martha Washington Stranded In Space)
Dark Horse (Legend): July, 1995 - No. 2, Aug, 1995 ($4.95, oversize, limited series)
1-Frank Miller scripts & Geoff Darrow-c/a — 2 4 6 9 12 15
2 — 1 3 4 6 8 10

BIG HERO ADVENTURES (See Jigsaw)

BIG HERO 6 (Also see Sunfire & Big Hero Six)
Marvel Comics: Nov, 2008 - No. 5, Mar, 2009 ($3.99, limited series)
1-Claremont-s/Nakayama-a; 1-Character design pages & Handbook entries — 3 6 9 21 33 45
2-5 — 1 3 4 6 8 10
...: Brave New Heroes 1 (11/12, $8.99) r/#1-5 — 2 4 6 11 16 20

BIG HERO 6: THE SERIES (Based on the Disney Channel animated series)
IDW Publishing: Nov, 2019 - Present ($3.99)
1-Blumenreich & Caramagna-s/Baldari-a; two covers — 4.00

BIG JON & SPARKIE (Radio) (Formerly Sparkie, Radio Pixie)
Ziff-Davis Publ. Co.: No. 4, Sept-Oct, 1952 (Painted-c)
4-Based on children's radio program — 22 44 66 128 209 290

BIG LAND, THE (Movie)
Dell Publishing Co.: No. 812, July, 1957
Four Color 812-Alan Ladd photo-c — 8 16 24 52 99 145

BIG LIE, THE
Image Comics: Sept, 2011 ($3.99, one-shot)
1-Revisits the 9-11 attacks; Rick Veitch-s/a(p); Thomas Yeates-c — 4.00

BIG MAN PLANS
Image Comics: Mar, 2015 - No. 4 ($3.50, limited series)
1-4-Eric Powell & Tim Wiesch-s/Powell-a/c — 3.50

BIG MOOSE (Character from Archie Comics)
Archie Comics Publications: Jun, 2017 ($4.99, limited series)
..., One Shot - short stories by various; art by Cory Smith, Pitilli & Jampole — 4.00

BIG RED (See Movie Comics)

BIG SHOT COMICS
Columbia Comics Group: May, 1940 - No. 104, Aug, 1949
1-Intro. Skyman; The Face (1st app.; Tony Trent), The Cloak (Spy Master), Marvelo, Monarch of Magicians; Joe Palooka, Charlie Chan, Tom Kerry, Dixie Dugan, Rocky Ryan begin; Charlie Chan moves over from Feature Comics #31 (4/40) — 300 600 900 1980 3440 4900
2 — 106 212 318 673 1162 1650
3-The Cloak called Spy Chief; Skyman-c — 100 200 300 635 1093 1550
4,5 — 65 130 195 416 708 1000
6-10: 8-Christmas-c — 52 104 156 328 552 775
11-13 — 48 96 144 302 514 725
14-Origin & 1st app. Sparky Watts (6/41) — 54 108 162 343 574 825
15-Origin The Cloak — 63 126 189 403 689 975
16-20 — 40 80 120 246 411 575
21-23,27,30: 30-X-Mas-c, WWII-c — 36 72 108 211 343 475
24-Classic Tojo-c — 161 322 483 1030 1765 2500
25-Hitler-c — 123 246 369 787 1344 1900
26,29-Japanese WWII-c. 29-Intro. Capt. Yank; Bo (a dog) newspaper strip-r by Frank Beck begin, ends #104. — 47 94 141 296 498 700
28-Hitler, Tojo & Mussolini-c — 155 310 465 992 1696 2400
31,33-40 — 26 52 78 152 249 340
32-Vic Jordan newspaper strip reprints begin, ends #52; Hitler, Tojo & Mussolini-c — 129 258 387 826 1413 2000
41,42,44,45,47-50: 42-No Skyman. 50-Origin The Face retold — 22 44 66 128 209 290
43-Hitler-c — 123 246 369 787 1344 1900
46-Hitler, Tojo-c (6/44) — 123 246 369 787 1344 1900
51-Tojo Japanese war-c — 50 100 150 315 533 750

	GD 2.0	VG 4.0	FN 6.0	VF 8.0	VF/NM 9.0	NM- 9.2
52-56,58-60:	19	38	57	111	176	240
57-Hitler, Tojo Halloween mask-c	50	100	150	315	533	750
61-70: 63 on-Tony Trent, the Face	15	30	45	85	130	175

71-80: 73-The Face cameo. 74-(2/47)-Mickey Finn begins. 74,80-The Face app. in Tony Trent.

78-Last Charlie Chan strip-r	14	28	42	80	115	150

81-90: 85-Tony Trent marries Babs Walsh. 86-Valentines-c

	12	24	36	67	94	120

91-99,101-104: 69-94-Skyman in Outer Space. 96-Christmas-c

	11	22	33	60	83	105
100	14	28	42	80	115	150

NOTE: **Mart Bailey** art on "The Face" No. 1-104. **Guardineer** art-a5. Sparky Watts by **Boody Rogers**-No. 14-42, 77-104, (by others No. 43-76). Others than Tony Trent wear "The Face" mask in No. 46-63, 93. Skyman by **Ogden Whitney**-No. 1, 2, 4, 12-37, 49, 70-101. Skyman covers-No. 1, 3, 7-12, 14, 16, 20, 27, 89, 95, 100.

BIG SMASH BARGAIN COMICS
No publisher listed: 1950 - No. 6, 1951 (25¢, 160pgs., Canadian reprints)

1-6: Contains 4 comics from various companies bundled with new cover (scarce)						
	50	100	150	315	533	750

BIG TEX
Toby Press: June, 1953

1-Contains (3) John Wayne stories-r with name changed to Big Tex

	15	30	45	88	137	185

BIG-3
Fox Feature Syndicate: Fall, 1940 - No. 7, Jan, 1942

1-Blue Beetle, The Flame, & Samson begin	300	600	900	2070	3635	5200
2	135	270	405	864	1482	2100
3-5	106	212	318	673	1162	1650
6-Last Samson	81	162	243	518	884	1250
7-WWII Nazi-c; V-Man app.	116	232	348	742	1271	1800

BIG THUNDER MOUNTAIN RAILROAD (Disney Studios)
Marvel Comics: May, 2015 - No. 5, Oct, 2015 ($3.99, limited series)

1-5: 1-Dennis Hopeless-s/Tigh Walker-a/Pasqual Ferry-c. 3-Ruiz-a						4.00

BIG TOP COMICS, THE (TV's Great Circus Show)
Toby Press: 1951 - No. 2, 1951 (No month)

1	14	28	42	81	118	155
2	11	22	33	62	86	110

BIG TOWN (Radio/TV) (Also see Movie Comics, 1946)
National Periodical Publ: Jan, 1951 - No. 50, Mar-Apr, 1958 (No. 1-9: 52pgs.)

1-Dan Barry-a begins	74	148	222	470	810	1150
2	39	78	117	231	378	525
3-10	24	48	72	142	234	325
11-20	19	38	57	111	176	240
21-31: Last pre-code (1-2/55)	14	28	42	80	115	150
32-50: 46-Grey tone cover	11	22	33	60	83	105

BIG TROUBLE IN LITTLE CHINA (Based on the 1986 Kurt Russell movie)
BOOM! Studios: Jun, 2014 - No. 25, Jun, 2016 ($3.99)

1-12-Continuing advs. of Jack Burton; John Carpenter & Eric Powell-s; Brian Churilla-a; multiple covers by Powell and others on each						4.00
13-24: 13-16-Van Lente-s/Eisma-a. 17-20-McDaid-a. 21-24-Santos-a						4.00
25-($4.99) Van Lente-s/Santos-a						5.00

BIG TROUBLE IN LITTLE CHINA / ESCAPE FROM NEW YORK (Based on the movies)
BOOM! Studios: Oct, 2016 - No. 6, Mar, 2017 ($3.99)

1-6-Jack Burton meets Snake Plisskin; Greg Pak-s/Daniel Bayliss-a						4.00

BIG TROUBLE IN LITTLE CHINA: OLD MAN JACK (Based on the movie)
BOOM! Studios: Sept, 2017 - No. 12, Aug, 2018 ($3.99)

1-12-Old Jack Burton battles Lo Pan; Carpenter & Burch-s/Corona-a; multiple covers						4.00

BIG VALLEY, THE (TV)
Dell Publishing Co.: June, 1966 - No. 5, Oct, 1967; No. 6, Oct, 1969

1: Photo-c #1-5	5	10	15	33	57	80
2-6: 6-Reprints #1	3	6	9	21	33	45

BIKER MICE FROM MARS (TV)
Marvel Comics: Nov, 1993 - No. 3, Jan, 1994 ($1.50, limited series)

1-3: 1-Intro Vinnie, Modo & Throttle. 2-Origin						5.00

BILL & TED... (Movie)
OPUS: Sept, 2020 - No. 4, Dec, 2020 ($3.99, limited series)

...Present: Death (10/22, $6.66) Burnham-s/Manfredi-a; Beethoven app.						7.00
...'s Day of the Dead (11/22, $6.99) Montezuma, Freda Khalo, Death app.						7.00
...'s Excellent Holiday Special (12/22, $6.99) Christmas-themed						7.00

BILL & TED ARE DOOMED (Movie)
Dark Horse Comics: Sept, 2020 - No. 4, Dec, 2020 ($3.99, limited series)

1-4-Evan Dorkin-s/Roger Langridge-a; set in the year 2000 after the 2nd movie						4.00

BILL & TED GO TO HELL (Movie)
BOOM! Studios: Feb, 2016 - No. 4, May, 2016 ($3.99, limited series)

1-4-Joines-s/Bachan-a						4.00

BILL & TED ROLL THE DICE (Prequel to Bill & Ted's Bogus Journey)
OPUS: Jun, 2022 - No. 4, Sept, 2022 ($4.99, limited series)

1-4-Dungeons & Dragons themed adventure set before the 2nd movie						5.00

BILL & TED SAVE THE UNIVERSE (Movie)
BOOM! Studios: Jun, 2017 - No. 5, Oct, 2017 ($3.99, limited series)

1-5-Joines-s/Bachan-a						4.00

BILL & TED'S BOGUS JOURNEY
Marvel Comics: Sept, 1991 ($2.95, squarebound, 84 pgs.)

1-Adapts movie sequel						6.00

BILL & TED'S EXCELLENT COMIC BOOK (Movie)
Marvel Comics: Dec, 1991 - No. 12, 1992 ($1.00/$1.25)

1-12: 3-Begin $1.25-c						4.00

BILL & TED'S MOST TRIUMPHANT RETURN (Movie)
BOOM! Studios: Mar, 2015 - No. 6, Aug, 2015 ($3.99, limited series)

1-6: 1-Follows the end of the second movie; Lynch-s/Gaylord-a/Guillory-c						4.00

BILL BARNES COMICS (...America's Air Ace Comics No. 2 on) (Becomes Air Ace V2#1 on; also see Shadow Comics)
Street & Smith Publications: Oct, 1940(No. month given) - No. 12, Oct, 1943

1-23 pgs.-comics; Rocket Rooney begins	123	246	369	787	1344	1900
2-Barnes as The Phantom Flyer app.; Tuska-a	63	126	189	403	689	975
3-5-War covers	50	100	150	315	533	750
6,8,10,12-War covers	43	86	129	271	461	650
7-(1942) Story about dropping atomic bomb on Japan	314	628	942	2198	3849	5500
9-Classic WWII cover	90	180	270	576	988	1400
11-Japanese WWII Gremlin cover	55	110	165	352	601	850

BILL BATTLE, THE ONE MAN ARMY (Also see Master Comics 133)
Fawcett Publications: Oct, 1952 - No. 4, Apr, 1953 (All photo-c)

1	18	36	54	105	165	225
2	11	22	33	64	90	115
3,4	10	20	30	56	76	95

BILL BLACK'S FUN COMICS
Paragon #1-3/Americomics #4: Dec, 1982 - No. 4, Mar, 1983 ($1.75/$2.00, Baxter paper) (1st AC comic)

1-(B&W fanzine; 7x8-1/2"; low print) Intro. Capt. Paragon, Phantom Lady & Commando D						
		3	6	9	16	23	30
2-4: 2,3-(B&W fanzines; 8-1/2x11"). 3-Kirby-a. 4-($2.00, color)-Origin Nightfall (formerly Phantom Lady); Nightveil app.; Kirby-a	2	4	6	8	11	14

BILL BOYD WESTERN (Movie star; see Hopalong Cassidy & Western Hero)
Fawcett Publ: Feb, 1950 - No. 23, June, 1952 (1-3,7,11,14-on: 36 pgs.)

1-Bill Boyd & his horse Midnite begin; photo front/back-c	32	64	96	188	307	425
2-Painted-c	16	32	48	94	147	200
3-Photo-c begin, end #23; last photo back-c	14	28	42	80	115	150
4-6(52 pgs.)	12	24	36	69	97	125
7,11(36 pgs.)	10	20	30	56	76	95
8-10,12,13(52 pgs.)	10	20	30	58	79	100
14-22	9	18	27	52	69	85
23-Last issue	10	20	30	56	76	95

BILL BUMLIN (See Treasury of Comics No. 3)

BILL ELLIOTT (See Wild Bill Elliott)

BILLI 99
Dark Horse Comics: Sept, 1991 - No. 4, 1991 ($3.50, B&W, lim. series, 52 pgs.)

1-4: Tim Sale-c/a						4.00

BILLIONAIRE ISLAND
AHOY Comics: 2020 - No. 6, 2020 ($3.99, limited series)

1-6-Mark Russell-s/Steve Pugh-a						4.00

BILLIONAIRE ISLAND: CULT OF DOGS
AHOY Comics: 2022 - No. 6, 2023 ($3.99, limited series)

1-6-Mark Russell-s/Steve Pugh-a						4.00

BILL STERN'S SPORTS BOOK
Ziff-Davis Publ. Co.(Approved Comics): Spring-Sum, 1951 - V2#2, Win, 1952

V1#10-(1951) Whitney painted-c	22	44	66	128	209	290
2-(Sum/52: reg. size)	17	34	51	100	158	215
V2#2-(1952, 96 pgs.)-Krigstein, Kinstler-a	26	52	78	154	252	350

BILL THE BULL: ONE SHOT, ONE BOURBON, ONE BEER
Boneyard Press: Dec, 1994 ($2.95, B&W, mature)

1						4.00

BILLY AND BUGGY BEAR (See Animal Fun)
I.W. Enterprises/Super: 1964

I.W. Reprint #1, #7('58)-All Surprise Comics #?(Same issue-r for both)

	2	4	6	13	18	22
Super Reprint #10(1964)	2	4	6	10	14	18

BILLY BATSON AND THE MAGIC OF SHAZAM! (Follows Shazam: The Monster Society of Evil mini-series)
DC Comics: Sept, 2008 - No. 21, Dec, 2010 ($2.25/$2.50, all ages title)

1-17: 1-4-Mike Kunkel-s/a/c; Theo (Black) Adam app. 5-DeStefano-a. 13-16-Black Adam						4.00
1-Variant B&W sketch cover						4.00
18-21 ($2.99) 21-Justice League cameo						4.00
TPB (2010, $12.99) r/#1-6; cover and character sketches						13.00
...: Mr. Mind Over Matter TPB (2011, $12.99) r/#7-12						13.00

BILLY BUCKSKIN WESTERN (2-Gun Western No. 4)
Atlas Comics (IMC No. 1/MgPC No. 2,3): Nov, 1955 - No. 3, Mar, 1956

1-Mort Drucker-a; Maneely-c/a	21	42	63	122	199	275
2-Mort Drucker-a	12	24	36	69	97	125
3-Williamson, Drucker-a	14	28	42	80	115	150

BILLY BUNNY (Black Cobra No. 6 on)
Excellent Publications: Feb-Mar, 1954 - No. 5, Oct-Nov, 1954

1	11	22	33	64	90	115
2	8	16	24	40	50	60
3-5	6	12	18	31	38	45

BILLY BUNNY'S CHRISTMAS FROLICS
Farrell Publications: 1952 (25¢ Giant, 100 pgs.)

	25	50	75	150	245	340

BILLY MAKE BELIEVE
United Features Syndicate: No. 14, 1939

Single Series 14	34	68	102	199	325	450

BILLY NGUYEN, PRIVATE EYE

Bill & Ted Go To Hell #4 © CLC

Billionaire Island #1 © Mark Russell

Bionic Woman #1 © Universal Studios

	GD	VG	FN	VF	VF/NM	NM-
	2.0	4.0	6.0	8.0	9.0	9.2

Caliber Press: V2#1, 1990 ($2.50)
V2#1 .... 4.00

BILLY THE KID (Formerly The Masked Raider; also see Doc Savage Comics & Return of the Outlaw)
Charlton Publ. Co.: No. 9, Nov, 1957 - No. 121, Dec, 1976; No. 122, Sept 1977 - No. 123, Oct, 1977; No. 124, Feb, 1978 - No. 153, Mar, 1983

9	12	24	36	69	97	125
10,12,14,17-19: 12-2 pg Check-sty	8	16	24	42	54	65
11-(68 pgs.)-Origin & 1st app. The Ghost Train	9	18	27	52	69	85
13-Williamson/Torres-a	9	18	27	47	61	75
15-Origin; 2 pgs. Williamson-a	9	18	27	47	61	75
16-Williamson-a, 2 pgs.	8	16	24	44	57	70
20-26-Severin-a(3-4 each)	9	18	27	47	61	75
27-30: 30-Masked Rider app.	3	6	9	20	31	42
31-40	3	6	9	15	22	28
41-60	2	4	6	13	18	22
61-65	2	4	6	10	14	18
66-Bounty Hunter series begins.	3	6	9	14	20	25
67-80: Bounty Hunter series; not in #79,82,84-86	2	4	6	10	14	18
81-84,86-90: 87-Last Bounty Hunter. 88-1st app. Mr. Young of the Boothill Gazette	2	4	6	8	10	12
85-Early Kaluta-a (4 pgs.)	2	4	6	9	13	16
91-123: 110-Mr. Young of Boothill app. 111-Origin The Ghost Train. 117-Gunsmith & Co., The Cheyenne Kid app.	1	2	3	5	6	8
Modern Comics 109 (1977 reprint)						6.00
124(2/78)-153						5.00

NOTE: *Boyette* a-88-110. *Kim* a-73. *Morsi* a-12,14. *Sattler* a-118-123. *Severin* a-(r)-121-129, 134; c-23, 25. *Sutton* a-111.

BILLY THE KID ADVENTURE MAGAZINE
Toby Press: Oct, 1950 - No. 29, 1955

1-Williamson/Frazetta-a (2 pgs) r/from John Wayne Adventure Comics #2; photo-c	35	70	105	208	339	470
2-Photo-c	14	28	42	80	115	150
3-Williamson/Frazetta "The Claws of Death", 4 pgs. plus Williamson art	37	74	111	222	361	500
4,5,7,8,10: 4,7-Photo-c	9	18	27	52	69	85
6-Frazetta assist on "Nightmare"; photo-c	16	32	48	92	144	195
9-Farnham Pot-Shot Pete; photo-c	11	22	33	64	90	115
11,12,15-20: 11-Photo-c	8	16	24	42	54	65
13-Kurtzman-r/John Wayne #12 (Genius)	9	18	27	47	61	75
14-Williamson/Frazetta; r-of #1 (2 pgs.)	11	22	33	62	86	110
21,23-29	7	14	21	37	46	55
22-Williamson/Frazetta-r(1pg.)/#1; photo-c	9	18	27	47	61	75

BILLY THE KID AND OSCAR (Also see Fawcett's Funny Animals)
Fawcett Publications: Winter, 1945 - No. 3, Fall, 1946 (Funny animal)

1	18	36	54	105	165	225
2,3	12	24	36	69	97	125

BILLY THE KID'S OLD TIMEY ODDITIES
Dark Horse Comics: Apr, 2005 - No. 4, July, 2005 ($2.99, limited series)
1-4-Eric Powell-s/c; Kyle Hotz-a 4.00
TPB (2005, $13.95) r/series 14.00
... and the Ghostly Fiend of London (9/10 - No. 4, 12/10, $3.99) 1-4-Powell-s/c; Kyle Hotz-a;
Goon back-up; Powell-s/a 4.00
... and the Orm of Loch Ness (10/12 - No. 4, 1/13, $3.50) 1-4-Powell-s/Hotz-a/c ... 4.00

BILLY WEST (Bill West No. 9,10)
Standard Comics (Visual Editions): 1949-No. 9, Feb, 1951; No. 10, Feb, 1952

1	22	44	66	132	216	300
2	15	30	45	83	124	165
3-6,9,10	12	24	36	69	97	125
7,8-Schomburg-c	14	28	42	82	121	160

NOTE: *Celardo* a-1-6, 9; c-1-3. *Moreira* a-3. *Roussos* a-2.

BING CROSBY (See Feature Films)

BINGO (...Comics) (H. C. Blackerby)
Howard Publ.: 1945 (Reprints National material)
1-L.B. Cole opium-c; blank back-c 48 96 144 302 514 725

BINGO, THE MONKEY DOODLE BOY
St. John Publishing Co.: Aug, 1951; Oct, 1953

1(8/51)-By Eric Peters	14	28	42	80	115	150
1(10/53)	10	20	30	56	76	95

BINKY (Formerly Leave It to...)
National Periodical Publ./DC Comics: No. 72, 4-5/70 - No. 81, 10-11/71; No. 82, Summer/77

72-76	5	10	15	30	50	70
77-79: (68 pgs.). 77-Bobby Sherman 1pg. story w/photo. 78-1 pg. sty on Barry Williams of Brady Bunch. 79-Osmonds 1pg. story	6	12	18	38	69	100
80,81 (52 pgs.)-Sweat Pain story	5	10	15	34	60	85
82 (1977, one-shot)	5	10	15	30	50	70

BINKY'S BUDDIES
National Periodical Publications: Jan-Feb, 1969 - No. 12, Nov-Dec, 1970

1	9	18	27	61	123	185
2-12: 3-Last 12¢ issue	5	10	15	31	53	75

BIONIC MAN (TV)
Dynamite Entertainment: 2011 - No. 26, 2013 ($3.99)
1-26: 1-Kevin Smith & Phil Hester-s; Lau-a; multiple covers. 12-15-Bigfoot app. ... 4.00
Annual 1 (2013, $4.99) The Venus Probe; Beatty-s/Mayhew-c 5.00

BIONIC MAN VS. THE BIONIC WOMAN (TV)
Dynamite Entertainment: 2013 - No. 5, 2013 ($3.99, limited series)
1-5-Champagne-s/Luis-a; 3 covers on each 4.00

BIONIC WOMAN, THE (TV)
Charlton Publications: Oct, 1977 - No. 5, June, 1978

1	6	12	18	38	69	100
2-5	4	8	12	23	37	50

BIONIC WOMAN, THE (TV)
Dynamite Entertainment: 2013 - No. 10, 2013 ($3.99)
1-10: 1-Tobin-s/Renaud-c/Carvalho-a; origin re-told 4.00

BIONIC WOMAN, THE: SEASON FOUR (TV)
Dynamite Entertainment: 2014 - No. 4, 2014 ($3.99, limited series)
1-4-Jerwa-s/Cabrera-a. 1-Reg & photo-c 4.00

BIRDS OF PREY (Also see Black Canary/Oracle: Birds of Prey)
DC Comics: Jan, 1999 - No. 127, Apr, 2009 ($1.99/$2.50/$2.99)

1-Dixon-s/Land-c/a	2	4	6	10	14	18
2-4						6.00
5-7,9-15: 15-Guice-a begins.						4.00
8-Nightwing-c/app.; Barbara & Dick's circus date	4	8	12	27	44	60
16-38: 23-Grodd-c/app. 26-Bane app. 32-Noto-c begin						3.00
39,40-Bruce Wayne: Murderer pt. 5,12						3.50
41-Bruce Wayne: Fugitive pt. 2						4.00
42-46: 42-Fabry-a. 45-Deathstroke-c/app.						3.00
47-74,77-91: 47-49-Terry Moore-s/Conner & Palmiotti-a; Noto-c. 50-Gilbert Hernandez-s begin. 52,54-Metamorpho app. 56-Simone-s/Benes-a begin. 65,67,68,70-Land-c. 86-Timm-a (7 pgs.)						3.00
75-($2.95) Pearson-c; back-up story of Lady Blackhawk						4.00
76-Debut of Black Alice (from Day of Vengeance)	2	4	6	9	12	15
92-99,101-127: 92-One Year Later. 94-Begin $2.99-c; Prometheus app. 96,97-Black Alice app. 98,99-New Batgirl app. 99-Black Canary leaves the team. 104-107-Secret Six app.						3.00
100-($3.99) new team recruited; Black Canary origin re-told						4.00
TPB (1999, $17.95) r/ previous series and one-shots						18.00
...: Batgirl 1 (2/98, $2.95) Dixon-s/Frank-c						5.00
...: Batgirl/Catwoman 1 ('03, $5.95) Robertson-a; cont'd in BOP: Catwoman/Oracle 1						6.00
...: Between Dark & Dawn TPB (2006, $14.99) r/#69-75						18.00
...: Blood and Circuits TPB (2007, $17.99) r/#96-103						18.00
...: Catwoman/Oracle 1 ('03, $5.95) Cont'd from BOP: Batgirl/Catwoman 1; David Ross-a						6.00
...: Club Kids TPB (2008, $17.99) r/#109-112,118						18.00
...: Dead of Winter TPB (2008, $17.99) r/#104-108						18.00
...: Metropolis or Dust TPB (2008, $17.99) r/#113-117						18.00
...: Of Like Minds TPB (2004, $14.95) r/#55-61						15.00
...: Old Friends, New Enemies TPB (2003, $17.95) r/#1-6, ...: Batgirl, ...: Wolves						18.00
...: Perfect Pitch TPB (2007, $17.99) r/#86-90,92-95						18.00
...: Platinum Flats TPB (2009, $17.99) r/#119-124						18.00
...: Revolution 1 (1997, $2.95) Frank-c/Dixon-s						5.00
...: Secret Files 2003 (8/03, $4.95) Short stories, pin-ups and profile pages; Noto-c						5.00
...: Sensei and Student TPB (2005, $17.95) r/#62-68						18.00
...: The Battle Within TPB (2007, $17.99) r/#76-85						18.00
...: The Ravens 1 (6/98, $1.95)-Dixon-s; Girlfrenzy issue						4.00
...: Wolves 1 (10/97, $2.95) Dixon-s/Giordano & Faucher-a						5.00

BIRDS OF PREY (Brightest Day)
DC Comics: Jul, 2010 - No. 15, Oct, 2011 ($2.99)
1-Simone-s/Benes-a/c; Hawk and Dove join team, Penguin app. 4.00
1-Variant cover by Chiang 6.00
2-15: 2-4-Penguin app. 7-10-"Death of Oracle." 11-Catman app. 14,15-Tucci-a .. 3.00
... End Run HC (2011, $22.99, d.j.) r/#1-6 .... 23.00

	GD 2.0	VG 4.0	FN 6.0	VF 8.0	VF/NM 9.0	NM- 9.2

BIRDS OF PREY (DC New 52)
DC Comics: Nov, 2011 - No. 34, Oct, 2014 ($2.99)
1-24: 1-Swierczynski-s/Saiz-a; intro. Starling. 2-Katana & Poison Ivy join. 9-Night of the Owls. 16-Strix joins. 18-20-Mr. Freeze app. ... 3.00
25-($3.99) Zero Year tie-in; flashback to Dinah's childhood; John Lynch app. ... 4.00
26-34: 26-Birds vs. Basilisk. 28-Gothtopia tie-in; Ra's al Ghul app. 32-34-Suicide Squad ... 3.00
#0 (11/12, $2.99) Black Canary and Batgirl first meeting; Molenaar-a/Lau-c ... 3.00
...: Futures End 1 (11/14, $2.99, regular-c) Five years later; The Red League ... 3.00
...: Futures End 1 (11/14, $3.99, 3-D cover) ... 4.00

BIRDS OF PREY (Dawn of DC)
DC Comics: Nov, 2023 - Present ($3.99)
1-7: 1-Thompson-s/Romero-a; team of Black Canary, Harley, Barda, Cassie & Zealot ... 4.00
...: Uncovered 1 (2/24, $5.99) Gallery of recent variant cover images; Nakayama-c ... 6.00

BIRDS OF PREY GIANT
DC Comics: 2019 ($4.99, 100 pgs., squarebound, Mass Market & Direct Market editions exist for each issue, with different covers)
1-Three new stories plus reprints; Harley Quinn app.; Lupacchino-c ... 5.00

BIRDS OF PREY: MANHUNT
DC Comics: Sept, 1996 - No. 4, Dec, 1996 ($1.95, limited series)
1-Features Black Canary, Oracle, Huntress, & Catwoman; Chuck Dixon scripts; Gary Frank-c on all.   1   2   3   5   6   8
2-4 ... 6.00
NOTE: *Gary Frank c-1-4. Matt Haley a-1-4p. Wade Von Grawbadger a-1i.*

BIRTH CAUL, THE
Eddie Campbell Comics: 1999 ($5.95, B&W, one-shot)
1-Alan Moore-s/Eddie Campbell-a ... 6.00

BIRTH OF THE DEFIANT UNIVERSE, THE
Defiant: May, 1993
nn-Contains promotional artwork & text; limited edition of 1000 copies signed & numbered by Jim Shooter   6   12   18   41   76   110
Regular unsigned issue   5   10   15   31   53   75

BIRTHRIGHT
Image Comics (Skybound): Oct, 2014 - No. 50, Jun, 2021 ($2.99/$3.99)
1-25-Joshua Williamson-s/Andrei Bressan-a ... 3.00
26-50-($3.99) 27-Regular & Walking Dead tribute covers. 45-Bonus preview of Stillwater ... 4.00

BISHOP (See Uncanny X-Men & X-Men)
Marvel Comics: Dec, 1994 - No.4, Mar, 1995 ($2.95, limited series)
1-4: Foil-c; Shard & Mountjoy in all. 1-Storm app. ... 4.00

BISHOP THE LAST X-MAN
Marvel Comics: Oct, 1999 - No. 16, Jan, 2001 ($2.99/$1.99/$2.25)
1-($2.99)-Jeanty-a ... 5.00
2-8-($1.99): 2-Two covers ... 4.00
9-11,13-16: 9-Begin $2.25-c. 15-Maximum Security x-over; Xavier app. ... 4.00
12-($2.99) ... 5.00

BISHOP: WAR COLLEGE
Marvel Comics: Apr, 2023 - No. 5, Aug, 2023 ($4.99, limited series)
1-($4.99) Holtham-s/Hill-a; Armor & Surge app. ... 5.00
2-5-($3.99) ... 4.00

BISHOP: XAVIER SECURITY ENFORCER
Marvel Comics: Jan, 1998 - No.3, Mar, 1998 ($2.50, limited series)
1-3: Ostrander-s ... 4.00

BITCH PLANET
Image Comics: Dec, 2014 - No. 9, Apr, 2017 ($3.50/$3.99)
1-DeConnick-s/De Landro-a/c ... 5.00
2-9: 3-Origin of Penny Rolle. 5-Begin $3.99-c. 6-Meiko flashback ... 4.00

BITCH PLANET: TRIPLE FEATURE
Image Comics: Jun, 2017 - No. 5, Oct, 2017 ($3.99)
1-5-Short story anthology by various; De Landro-c. 5-Charretier-a ... 4.00

BITE CLUB
DC Comics (Vertigo): Jun, 2004 - No. 6, Nov, 2004 ($2.95, limited series)
1-6-Chaykin-s/Tischman-a/Quitely-c ... 3.00
TPB Digest (2005, $9.99) r/#1-6; cover gallery ... 10.00
The Complete Bite Club TPB (2007, $19.99) r/#1-6 and ...: Vampire Crime Unit #1-5 ... 20.00

BITE CLUB: VAMPIRE CRIME UNIT
DC Comics (Vertigo): Jun, 2006 - No. 5, Oct, 2006 ($2.99, limited series)
1-5: 1-Chaykin & Tischman-s/Hahn-a/Quitely-c. 4-Chaykin-c ... 3.00

BITTER ROOT
Image Comics: Nov, 2018 - Present ($3.99)
1-15-David F. Walker & Chuck Brown-s/Sanford Greene-a ... 4.00
... Red Summer Special 1 (7/19, $5.99) Short stories by various; Greene-c ... 6.00

BIZARRE ADVENTURES (Formerly Marvel Preview)
Marvel Comics Group: No. 25, 3/81 - No. 34, 2/83 (#25-33: Magazine-$1.50)
25-Lethal Ladies   3   6   9   18   28   38
26-King Kull; Bolton-c/a   2   4   6   11   16   20
27,28: 27-Phoenix, Iceman & Nightcrawler app. 28-The Unlikely Heroes; Elektra by Miller; Neal Adams-a   2   4   6   14   20   25
29,30,32,33: 29-Stephen King's Lawnmower Man. 30-Tomorrow; 1st app. Silhouette. 32-Gods; Thor-c/s. 33-Horror; Dracula app.; photo-c   2   3   4   6   8   10
31-After The Violence Stops; new Hangman story; Miller-a   2   4   6   8   12   15
34 ($2.00, Baxter paper, comic size)-Son of Santa; Christmas special; Howard the Duck by Paul Smith   3   6   9   13   16
NOTE: *Alcala a-27i. Austin a-25i, 28i. Bolton a-26, 32. J. Buscema a-27p, 29, 30p; c-26. Byrne a-31 (2 pg.). Golden a-25p, 28p. Perez a-27p. Rogers a-25p. Simonson a-29; c-29. Paul Smith a-34.*

BIZARRO

DC Comics: Aug, 2015 - No. 6, Jan, 2016 ($2.99, limited series)
1-6-Corson-s/Duarte-a; Jimmy Olsen app. 4-Zatanna app. 6-Superman app. ... 3.00

BIZARRO COMICS!
DC Comics: 2001 ($29.95, hardcover, one-shot)
HC-Short stories of DC heroes by various alternative cartoonists including Dorkin, Pope, Haspiel, Kidd, Kochalka, Millionaire, Stephens, Wray; includes "Superman's Babysitter" by Kyle Baker from Elseworlds 80-Page Giant recalled by DC; Groening-c ... 30.00
Softcover (2003, $19.95) ... 20.00

BIZARRO WORLD
DC Comics: 2005 ($29.95, hardcover, one-shot)
HC-Short stories by various alternative cartoonists including Bagge, Baker, Dorkin, Dunn, Kupperman, Morse, Oswalt, Pekar, Simpson, Stewart; Jaime Hernandez-a ... 30.00
Softcover (2006, $19.99) ... 20.00

BLACK ADAM (See 52 and Countdown)
DC Comics: Oct, 2007 - No. 6, Mar, 2008 ($2.99, limited series)
1-Mahnke-a/c; Isis returns; Felix Faust app.   1   3   4   6   8   10
1-Variant-c by Alex Ross   5   10   15   33   57   80
2-6 ... 5.00
....: Endless Winter Special (2/21, $3.99) Part 8 of crossover event; Frost King app. ... 5.00
..: The Dark Age TPB (2008, $17.99) r/#1-6; Alex Ross-c ... 18.00
....: Year of the Villain 1 (12/19, $4.99) Jenkins-s/Miranda-a; battles King Shazam ... 5.00

BLACK ADAM
DC Comics: Aug, 2022 - No. 12, Aug, 2023 ($3.99)
1-12: 1-Intro. Malik White. 2-Debut of White Adam. 6-Batman app. ... 4.00

BLACK ADAM – THE JUSTICE SOCIETY FILES (From the 2022 movie)
DC Comics: Sept, 2022 - Dec, 2022 ($5.99, series of one-shots)
..: Atom Smasher 1 (11/22) Early adventures; Cavan Scott-s/Travis Mercer-a ... 6.00
...: Cyclone 1 (10/22) Maxine Hunkel's invite to the JSA; Hawkman app.; Scott-s/Sanapo-a ... 6.00
..: Dr. Fate 1 (12/22) Prelude to the movie; Scott-s/Merino-a ... 6.00
...: Hawkman 1 (9/22) Gentleman Ghost app.; Scott-s/Eaton-a ... 6.00

BLACK AND WHITE (See Large Feature Comic, Series I)

BLACK & WHITE (Also see Codename: Black & White)
Image Comics (Extreme): Oct, 1994 - No. 3, Jan, 1995 ($1.95, limited series)
1-3: Thibert-c/story ... 4.00

BLACK & WHITE MAGIC
Innovation Publishing: 1991 ($2.95, 98 pgs., B&W w/30 pgs. color, squarebound)
1-Contains rebound comics w/covers removed; contents may vary ... 4.00

BLACK AXE
Marvel Comics (UK): Apr, 1993 - No. 7, Oct, 1993 ($1.75)
1-4: 1-Romita Jr.-c. 2-Sunfire-c/s ... 4.00
5-7: 5-Janson-c; Black Panther app. 6,7-Black Panther-c/s ... 4.00

BLACK BADGE
BOOM! Studios: Aug, 2018 - No. 12, Jul, 2019 ($3.99)
1-12-Matt Kindt-s/Tyler Jenkins-a ... 4.00

BLACKBALL COMICS
Blackball Comics: Mar, 1994 ($3.00)
1-Trencher-c/story by Giffen; John Pain by O'Neill ... 4.00

BLACK BAT, THE
Dynamite Entertainment: 2013 - No. 12, 2014 ($3.99)
1-12-Buccellato-s/Cliquet-a; multiple covers on each ... 4.00

BLACKBEARD'S GHOST (See Movie Comics)

BLACK BEAUTY (See Son of Black Beauty)
Dell Publishing Co.: No. 440, Dec, 1952
Four Color 440   6   12   18   35   69   100

BLACK BEETLE, THE
Dark Horse Comics: Jan, 2013 - No. 4, Jun, 2013 ($3.99)
1-4-Francavilla-s/a/c ... 4.00

BLACKBIRD
Image Comics: Oct, 2018 - No. 6, Mar, 2019 ($3.99)
1-6-Sam Humphries-s/Jen Bartel-a ... 4.00

BLACK BOLT (The Inhumans)
Marvel Comics: Jul, 2017 - No. 12, Jun, 2018 ($3.99)
1-12: 1-6-Saladin Ahmed-s/Christian Ward-a; Absorbing Man app. 7-Irving-a ... 4.00

BLACK BOLT: SOMETHING INHUMAN THIS WAY COMES
Marvel Comics: Sept, 2018 ($7.99, one-shot)
1-Reprints Black Bolt app. in Amazing Adventures #5-10 & Avengers #95 ... 8.00

BLACKBURNE COVENANT, THE
Dark Horse Comics: Apr, 2003 - No. 4, July, 2003 ($2.99, limited series)
1-4-Nicieza-s/Raffaele-a ... 3.00
TPB (2003, $12.95) r/#1-4 ... 13.00

BLACK CANARY (See All Star Comics #38, Flash Comics #86, Justice League of America #75 & World's Finest #244)
DC Comics: Nov, 1991 - No. 4, Feb, 1992 ($1.75)
1-4 ... 4.00

BLACK CANARY
DC Comics: Jan, 1993 - No. 12, Dec, 1993 ($1.75)
1-Sarah Byam-s/Trevor Von Eeden-a/c ... 6.00
2-7 ... 4.00
8-12: 8-The Ray-c/story. 9,10-Huntress-c/story ... 4.00

BLACK CANARY (Follows Oliver Queen's marriage proposal in Green Arrow #75)
DC Comics: Early Sept, 2007 - No. 4, Late Oct, 2007 ($2.99, bi-weekly limited series)
1-4-Bedard-s/Siqueira-a ... 3.00
... Wedding Planner 1 (11/07, $2.99) Roux-c/Ferguson & Norrie-a ... 3.00

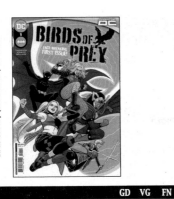
Birds of Prey (2023 series) #1 © DC

Black Badge #1 © Kindt & Jenkins

Black Cat (2021 series) #1 © MAR

	GD	VG	FN	VF	VF/NM	NM-
	2.0	4.0	6.0	8.0	9.0	9.2

BLACK CANARY
DC Comics: Aug, 2015 - No. 12, Aug, 2016 ($2.99)
1-12: 1-Fletcher-s/Annie Wu-a/c. 4,5-Guerra-a. 8-Vixen app. 9-Moritat-a. 10-Batgirl app. 3.00

BLACK CANARY AND ZATANNA; BLOODSPELL
DC Comics: 2014 ($22.99, hardcover graphic novel, dustjacket)
HC-Paul Dini-s/Joe Quinones-a; includes script and sketch art 23.00

BLACK CANARY/ORACLE: BIRDS OF PREY (Also see Showcase '96 #3)
DC Comics: 1996 ($3.95, one-shot)
1-Chuck Dixon scripts & Gary Frank-c/a. 2 4 6 13 18 22

BLACK CAT (From Spider-Man)
Marvel Comics: Aug, 2019 - No. 12, Oct, 2020 ($4.99/$3.99)
1-($4.99)-MacKay-s/Foreman-a; back-up story with The Black Fox & Dracula 5.00
2-12-($3.99) 4,5-Johnny Storm app. 9,10-Wolverine app. 11,12-Iron Man app. 4.00
Annual 1 (1/20, $4.99) MacKay-s; "Wedding" of Spider-Man & Black Cat 5.00

BLACK CAT (From Spider-Man)(Story concludes in Giant-Size Black Cat: Infinity Score)
Marvel Comics: Feb, 2021 - No. 10, Nov, 2021 ($3.99)
1-10: 1-3-"King In Black" tie-ins; MacKay-s/Villa-a. 10-Nighthawk app. 4.00
Annual 1 (8/21, $4.99) MacKay-s/Vazquez-a; Infinite Destinies; The White Fox app. 5.00

BLACK CAT (AMAZING SPIDER-MAN PRESENTS...)
Marvel Comics: Aug, 2010 - No. 4, Dec, 2010 ($3.99, limited series)
1-4-Van Meter-s/Pulido-a/Conner-c; Spider-Man & Ana Kraven app. 5.00

BLACK CAT COMICS (...Western #16-19; ...Mystery #30 on)
(See All-New #7,9, The Original Black Cat, Pocket & Speed Comics)
Harvey Publications (Home Comics): June-July, 1946 - No. 29, June, 1951
1-Kubert-a; Joe Simon c-1,2	116	232	348	742	1271	1800
2-Kubert-a	50	100	150	315	533	750
3,4: 4-The Red Demons begin (The Demon #4 & 5)	40	80	120	246	411	575
5,6,7: 5,6-The Scarlet Arrow app. in ea. by Powell; S&K-a in both. 6-Origin Red Demon.
7-Vagabond Prince by S&K plus 1 more story	45	90	135	284	480	675
8-S&K-a; Kerry Drake begins, ends #13	50	100	150	315	533	750
9-Origin Stuntman (r/Stuntman #1)	44	96	144	302	514	725
10-20: 14,15,17-Mary Worth app. plus Invisible Scarlet O'Neil-#15,20,24
	33	66	99	194	317	440
21-26	25	50	75	150	245	340
27,28: 27-Used in SOTI, pg. 193; X-Mas-c; 2 pg. John Wayne story. 28-Intro.
Kit, Black Cat's new sidekick	30	60	90	177	289	400
29-Black Cat bondage-c; Black Cat stories	65	130	195	416	708	1000

BLACK CAT MYSTERY (Formerly Black Cat; ...Western Mystery #54; ...Western #55,56;
...Mystery #57; ...Mystic #58-62; Black Cat #63-65)
Harvey Publications: No. 30, Aug, 1951 - No. 65, Apr, 1963
30-Black Cat on cover and first page only	48	96	144	302	514	725
31,32,34,37,38,40	39	78	117	231	378	525
33-Used in POP, #28; electrocution-c	77	154	231	493	847	1200
35-Atomic disaster cover/story	65	130	195	416	708	1000
36,39-Used in SOTI: #36-Pgs. 270,271; #39-Pgs. 386-388
	68	136	204	435	743	1050
41-43	37	74	111	222	361	500
44-Eyes, ears, tongue cut out; Nostrand-a	129	258	387	826	1413	2000
45-Classic "Colorama" by Powell; Nostrand-a	161	322	483	1030	1765	2500
46-49,51-Nostrand-a in all. 51-Story has blank panel covering censored art (post-Code)
	39	78	117	240	395	550
50-Check-a; classic Warren Kremer-c showing a man's face & hands burning away
	1250	2500	3750	9500	17,250	25,000
52,53 (r/#34 & 35)	25	50	75	150	245	340
54-Two Black Cat stories (2/55, last pre-code)	28	56	84	168	274	380
55,56-Black Cat app.	24	48	72	142	234	325
57(7/56)-Kirby-c	25	50	75	150	245	340
58-60-Kirby-a(4). 58,59-Kirby-c. 60,61-Simon-c	29	58	87	172	281	390
61-Nostrand-a; "Colorama" r/#45	28	56	84	165	270	375
62 (3/58)-E.C. story swipe	24	48	72	142	234	325
63-65: Giants(10/62,1/63, 4/63); Reprints; Black Cat plus 63-origin Black Kitten.
65-1 pg. Powell-a	28	56	84	165	270	375
NOTE: Kremer a-37, 39, 43; c-36, 37, 47. Meskin a-51. Palais a-30, 31(2), 32(2), 33-35, 37-40. Powell a-32-35, 36(2), 40, 41, 43-53, 57. Simon c-63-65. Sparling a-44. Bondage c-32, 34, 43.

BLACK CLOUD
Image Comics: Apr, 2017 - No. 10, Jun, 2018 ($3.99)
1-10: 1-Latour & Brandon-s/Hinkle-a 4.00

BLACK COBRA (Bride's Diary No. 4 on) (See Captain Flight #8)

Ajax/Farrell Publications(Excellent Publ.): No. 1, 10-11/54; No. 6(No. 2), 12-1/54-55;
No. 3, 2-3/55
1-Re-intro Black Cobra & The Cobra Kid (costumed heroes)
	52	104	156	328	552	775
6(#2)-Formerly Billy Bunny	30	60	90	177	289	400
3-(Pre-code)-Torpedoman app.	27	54	81	158	259	360

BLACK CONDOR (Also see Crack Comics, Freedom Fighters & Showcase '94 #10,11)
DC Comics: June, 1992 - No. 12, May, 1993 ($1.25)
1-8-Heath-c 4.00
9-12: 9,10,12-Heath-c. 9,10-The Ray app. 12-Batman-c/app. 4.00

BLACK CROSS SPECIAL (See Dark Horse Presents)
Dark Horse Comics: Jan, 1988 ($1.75, B&W, one-shot)(Reprints & new-a)
1-1st printing 4.00
1-(2nd printing) has 2 pgs. new-a 4.00
...: Dirty Work 1 (4/97, $2.95) Chris Warner-c/s/a 4.00

BLACK CROWN QUARTERLY
IDW Publishing: Oct, 2017 - No. 3, Apr, 2018 ($6.99, quarterly)
1-3-Short story anthology with creator interviews and series previews 7.00

BLACK DIAMOND
Americomics: May, 1983 - No. 5, 1984 (no month)($2.00-$1.75, Baxter paper)
1-3-Movie adapt.; 1-Colt back-up begins 5.00
4,5 4.00
NOTE: Bill Black a-1; c-1. Gulacy c-2-5. Sybil Danning photo back-c-1.

BLACK DIAMOND WESTERN (Formerly Desperado No. 1-8)
Lev Gleason Publ.: No. 9, Mar, 1949 - No. 60, Feb, 1956 (No. 9-28: 52 pgs.)
9-Black Diamond & his horse Reliapon begin; origin & 1st app. Black Diamond
	22	44	66	132	216	300
10	12	24	36	69	97	125
11-15	10	20	30	54	72	90
16-28(11/49-11/51)-Wolverton's Bingbang Buster	14	28	42	76	108	140
29-40: 31-One pg. Frazetta anti-drug ad	9	18	27	47	61	75
41-50,53-59	8	16	24	40	50	60
51-3-D effect-c/story	15	30	45	85	130	175
52-3-D effect story	14	28	42	81	118	155
60-Last issue	8	16	24	44	57	70
NOTE: Biro c-9-35? Cooper a-12. Myron Foss a-54-58; c-54-56, 58. Guardineer a-9, 12, 15, 18. Jack Keller a-12. Kida a-9. Maurer a-10. Ed Moore a-16. Morisi a-55. William Overgard a-9-23. Tuska a-10, 48. Bill Walton a-57.

BLACK DRAGON, THE
Marvel Comics (Epic Comics): May, 1985 - No. 6, Oct, 1985 (Baxter paper, mature)
1-6: 1-Chris Claremont story & John Bolton painted-c/a in all 4.00
TPB (Dark Horse, 4/96, $17.95, B&W, trade paperback) r/#1-6; intro by Anne McCaffrey 18.00

BLACK DYNAMITE (Based on the Michael Jai White film)
IDW Publishing: Dec, 2013 - No. 4, Aug, 2014 ($3.99)
1-4: 1-Ash-s/Wimberly-a; multiple covers. 2,3-Ferreira-a 4.00

BLACKEST NIGHT (2009 Green Lantern & DC crossover) (Leads into Brightest Day series)
DC Comics: No. 0, Jun, 2009 - No. 8, May, 2010 ($3.99, limited series)
0-Free Comic Book Day edition; Johns-s/Reis-a; profile pages of different corps 3.00
1-8: 1-($3.99) Black Lantern Corps arises; Johns-s/Reis-c/a; Hawkman & Hawkgirl killed.
| | | | | | | 5.00 |
4-Nekron rises. 7-Black heroes return 10.00
1-Variant cover by Van Sciver 4.00
1-3,5: 2nd-4th printings 4.00
2-8: 2-Cascioli variant-c. 3-Van Sciver variant-c. 4-7-Migliari variant-c. 8-Mahnke var-c. 8.00
...: Director's Cut (6/10, $5.99) Commentary with story panels; cover gallery, script pgs. 6.00
HC (2010, $29.99, d.j.) r/#0-8 & Blackest Night Director's Cut; variant cover gallery 30.00
SC (2011, $19.99) r/#0-8 & Blackest Night Director's Cut; variant cover gallery 20.00
...: Black Lantern Corps Vol. 1 HC (2010, $24.99, d.j.) r/BN: Batman, BN: Superman, and
   BN: Titans series; cover gallery and character sketch designs 25.00
...: Black Lantern Corps Vol. 1 SC (2011, $19.99) same contents as HC edition 20.00
...: Black Lantern Corps Vol. 2 HC (2010, $24.99, d.j.) r/BN: The Flash, BN: JSA, and
   BN: Wonder Woman series; cover gallery and character sketch designs 25.00
...: Rise of the Black Lanterns HC (2010, $24.99) r/one-shots Atom and Hawkman #46,
   Catwoman #83, Phantom Stranger #42, Power of Shazam #48, The Question #37, Starman
   #81, Weird Western Tales #71, Green Arrow #30 & Adventure Comics #7; sketch art 25.00
...: Rise of the Black Lanterns SC (2011, $19.99) same contents as HC edition 20.00

BLACKEST NIGHT: BATMAN (2009 Green Lantern & DC crossover)
DC Comics: Oct, 2009 - No. 3, Dec, 2009 ($2.99, limited series)
1-3: 1-Bat-parents rise as Black Lanterns; Deadman app.; Syaf-a/Andy Kubert-c; 2 printings.
| | | | | | | 3.00 |
3-Flying Graysons return 3.00
1-3-Variant-c by Sienkiewicz 5.00

	GD	VG	FN	VF	VF/NM	NM-
	2.0	4.0	6.0	8.0	9.0	9.2

BLACKEST NIGHT: JSA (2009 Green Lantern & DC crossover)
DC Comics: Feb, 2010 - No. 3, Apr, 2010 ($2.99, limited series)
1-3-Original Sandman, Dr. Midnite and Mr. Terrific rise; Barrows-a/c — 3.00
1-3-Variant-c by Gene Ha — 5.00

BLACKEST NIGHT: SUPERMAN (2009 Green Lantern & DC crossover)
DC Comics: Oct, 2009 - No. 3, Dec, 2009 ($2.99, limited series)
1-3-Earth-2 Superman and Lois become Black Lanterns; Barrows-a/c; 2 printings — 3.00
1-3-Variant-c by Shane Davis — 5.00

BLACKEST NIGHT: TALES OF THE CORPS (2009 Green Lantern & DC crossover)
DC Comics: Sept, 2009 - No. 3, Sept, 2009 ($3.99, weekly limited series)
1-3-Short stories by various; interlocking cover images. 3-Commentary on B.N. #0 — 4.00
HC (2010, $24.99) r/#1-3 & Adventure Comics #4,5 & Green Lantern #49; sketch art — 25.00
SC (2011, $19.99) r/#1-3 & Adventure Comics #4,5 & Green Lantern #49; sketch art — 20.00

BLACKEST NIGHT: THE FLASH (2009 Green Lantern & DC crossover)
DC Comics: Feb, 2010 - No. 3, Apr, 2010 ($2.99, limited series)
1-3-Rogues vs. Dead Rogues; Johns-s/Kolins-a — 3.00
1-3-Variant-c by Manapul — 5.00

BLACKEST NIGHT: TITANS (2009 Green Lantern & DC crossover)
DC Comics: Oct, 2009 - No. 3, Nov, 2009 ($2.99, limited series)
1-3-Terra and the original Hawk return; Benes-a/c — 3.00
1-3-Variant-c by Brian Haberlin — 5.00

BLACKEST NIGHT: WONDER WOMAN (2009 Green Lantern & DC crossover)
DC Comics: Feb, 2010 - No. 3, Apr, 2010 ($2.99, limited series)
1-3-Maxwell Lord returns; Rucka-s/Scott-a/Horn-c. 2,3-Mera app.; Star Sapphire — 3.00
1-3-Variant-c by Ryan Sook — 5.00

BLACK-EYED KIDS
AfterShock Comics: Apr, 2016 - No. 15, Dec, 2017 ($3.99)
1-15: 1-($1.99) Joe Pruett-s/Szymon Kudranski-a/Francesco Francavilla-c. 2-15-($3.99) — 4.00

BLACK FLAG (See Asylum #5)
Maximum Press: Jan, 1995 - No.4, 1995; No. 0, July, 1995 ($2.50, B&W) (No. 0 in color)
Preview Edition (6/94, $1.95, B&W)-Fraga/McFarlane-c. — 4.00
0-4: 0-(7/95)-Liefeld/Fraga-c. 1-(1/95). — 4.00
1-Variant cover — 5.00
2,4-Variant covers — 4.00
NOTE: Fraga a-0-4, Preview Edition; c-1-4. Liefeld/Fraga c-0. McFarlane/Fraga c-Preview Edition.

BLACK FURY (Becomes Wild West No. 58) (See Blue Bird)
Charlton Comics Group: May, 1955 - No. 57, Mar-Apr, 1966 (Horse stories)

	GD	VG	FN	VF	VF/NM	NM-
1	13	26	39	72	101	130
2	7	14	21	37	46	55
3-10	6	12	18	28	34	40
11-15,19,20	4	8	10	18	22	25
16-18-Ditko-a	12	24	36	67	94	120
21-30	4	7	10	14	17	20
31-57	3	6	8	12	14	16

BLACK GOLIATH (See Avengers #32-35,41,54 and Civil War #4)
Marvel Comics Group: Feb, 1976 - No. 5, Nov, 1976

	GD	VG	FN	VF	VF/NM	NM-
1-Tuska(p) thru #3	5	10	15	31	53	75
2-5: 2-4-(Regular 25¢ editions). 4-Kirby/Buckler-a	2	4	6	11	16	20
2-4-(30¢-c variants, limited distribution)(4,6,8/76)	6	12	18	40	73	105

BLACK HAMMER
Dark Horse Comics: Jul, 2016 - No. 13, Sept, 2017 ($3.99)

	GD	VG	FN	VF	VF/NM	NM-
1-13: 1-Lemire-s/Ormston-a; covers by Ormston & Lemire	3	6	9	17	25	34
2	2	4	6	9	12	15

3-13: 3-8,10,11,13-Lemire-s/Ormston-a; covers by Ormston & Lemire. 9,12-Rubin-a — 6.00
...: Cthu-Louise (12/18, $3.99) Lemire-s/Lenox-a; cover by Lenox & Jill Thompson — 4.00
... Director's Cut (1/19, $4.99) r/#1 in original B&W ink with original script

... Giant-Sized Annual (1/17, $5.99) Short stories by various incl. Nguyen, Allred, Kindt

	GD	VG	FN	VF	VF/NM	NM-
		3	6	13	18	22
	2	4	6	8	10	12

BLACK HAMMER: AGE OF DOOM
Dark Horse Comics: Apr, 2018 - No. 12, Sept, 2019 ($3.99)

	GD	VG	FN	VF	VF/NM	NM-
1-Lemire-s/Ormston-a	1	2	3	5	6	8

2-12: 2-5,8-12-Lemire/Ormston-a. 6,7-Tammaso-a — 4.00

BLACK HAMMER '45
Dark Horse Comics: Mar, 2019 - No. 4, Jun, 2019 ($3.99, limited series)
1-4-Fawkes/Kindt-a; flashbacks to the Black Hammer Squadron in WWII — 4.00

BLACK HAMMER / JUSTICE LEAGUE: HAMMER OF JUSTICE!
Dark Horse Comics: Jul, 2019 - No. 5, Nov, 2019 ($3.99, limited series)
1-5-Lemire-s/Walsh-a; Justice League switches places with the Black Hammer crew — 4.00

BLACK HAMMER REBORN
Dark Horse Comics: Jun, 2021 - No. 12, May, 2022 ($3.99, limited series)
1-12: 1-The daughter of the original Black Hammer. 3,4,7,8,12-Colonel Weird app. — 4.00

BLACK HAMMER THE END
Dark Horse Comics: Aug, 2023 - No. 6, Mar, 2024 ($3.99, limited series)
1-5-Jeff Lemire-s/Malachi Ward-a — 4.00

BLACK HAMMER: VISIONS
Dark Horse Comics: Feb, 2021 - No. 8, Sept, 2021 ($3.99, limited series)
1-8: 1-Spotlight on Golden Gail; Patton Oswalt-s/Dean Kotz-a. 2-Johns-s. 3-Zdarsky-s — 4.00

BLACKHAWK (Formerly Uncle Sam #1-8; see Military Comics & Modern Comics)
Comic Magazines(Quality)No. 9-107(12/56); National Periodical Publications No. 108 (1/57) -250; DC Comics No. 251 on: No. 9, Winter, 1944 - No. 243, 10-11/68; No. 244, 2/76 - No. 250, 2/77; No. 251, 10/82 - No. 273, 11/84

	GD	VG	FN	VF	VF/NM	NM-
9 (1944)	290	580	870	1856	3178	4500
10 (1946)	116	232	348	742	1271	1800
11-15: 14-Ward-a; 13,14-Fear app.	84	168	252	538	919	1300
16-19	68	136	204	435	743	1050
20-Classic Crandall bondage-c; Ward Blackhawk	135	270	405	864	1482	2100
21-30 (1950)	52	104	156	328	552	775
31-40: 31-Chop Chop by Jack Cole	41	82	123	250	418	585
41-49,51-60: 42-Robot-c	36	72	108	216	351	485
50-1st Killer Shark; origin in text	41	82	123	256	428	600
61,62: 61-Used in POP, pg. 91. 62-Used in POP, pg 92 & color illo	36	72	108	211	343	475
63-70,72-80: 65-H-Bomb explosion panel. 66-B&W & color illos POP, pg. 92 H-Bomb-c. 67-Hitler-s. 70-Return of Killer Shark; atomic explosion panel. 75-Intro. Blackie the Hawk	31	62	93	186	303	420
71-Origin retold; flying saucer-c; A-Bomb panels	39	78	117	240	395	550
81-86: Last precode (3/55)	27	54	81	162	266	370
87-92,94-99,101-107: 91-Robot-c. 105-1st S.A.	22	44	66	132	216	300
93-Origin in text	23	46	69	136	223	310
100	31	62	93	186	303	420
108-1st DC issue (1/57); re-intro. Blackie, the Hawk, their mascot; not in #115	46	92	136	340	770	1200
109-117: 117-(10/57)-Mr. Freeze app.	15	30	45	100	220	340
118-(11/57)-Frazetta-r/Jimmy Wakely #4 (3 pgs.)	17	34	51	117	259	400
119-130 (11/58): 120-Robot-c	12	24	36	79	170	260
131,132,134-140 (9/59)	10	20	30	66	138	210
133-Intro. Lady Blackhawk	148	296	444	947	1624	2300
141-Cat-Man returns-c/s	21	42	63	124	202	280
142-150,152-163,165,166: 143-Kurtzman-r/Jimmy Wakely #4. 150-(7/60)-King Condor returns.	31	62	93	186	303	420
166-Last 10¢ issue		16	24	54	102	150
151-Lady Blackhawk receives & loses super powers	19	36	54	105	165	225
164-Origin retold	9	18	27	60	120	180
167-180	6	12	18	37	66	95
181-190	5	10	15	31	53	75
191-196,199: 196-Combat Diary series begins	4	8	12	27	44	60
197,198,200: 197-New look for Blackhawks. 198-Origin retold	4	8	12	28	47	65
201,202,204-210	3	6	9	21	33	45
203-Origin Chop Chop (12/64)	4	8	12	27	44	60
211-227,229-243(1968): 230-Blackhawks become superheroes; JLA cameo	3	6	9	17	26	35
242-Return to old costumes	5	10	15	30	50	70
228-Batman, Green Lantern, Superman, The Flash cameos	1	2	3	5	6	8

244 ('76) - 250: 250-Chuck dies — 5.00
251-273: 251-Origin retold; Black Knights return. 252-Intro Domino. 253-Part origin Hendrickson. 258-Blackhawk's Island destroyed. 259-Part origin Chop-Chop.
265-273 (75¢ cover price) — 5.00
NOTE: Chaykin a-260; c-257-260, 262. Crandall a-10, 11, 13, 16?, 18-20, 22-26, 30-33, 35p, 36(2), 37, 38?, 39-44, 46-50, 52-58, 60, 63, 64, 66, 67; c-14-20, 22-63(most except #28-33, 36, 37, 39). Evans a-244, 245,246i, 248-250i. G. Kane c-263, 264. Kubert c-242, 245. Newton a-266p. Severin a-257 Spiegle a-261-267, 269-273; c-265-272. Toth a-260p. Ward a-16-27(Chop Chop, 8pgs. ea.); pencilled stories no. 17-63(approx.). Wildey a-268. Chop Chop solo stories in #10-95?

BLACKHAWK
DC Comics: Mar, 1988 - No. 3, May, 1988 ($2.95, limited series, mature)
1-3-Chaykin painted-c/a/scripts — 4.00

BLACKHAWK (Also see Action Comics #601)
DC Comics: Mar, 1989 - No. 16, Aug, 1990 ($1.50, mature)
1 — 5.00
2-6,8-16: 16-Crandall-c swipe — 4.00
7-($2.50, 52 pgs.)-Story-r/Military #1 — 5.00
Annual 1 (1989, $2.95, 68 pgs.)-Recaps origin of Blackhawk, Lady Blackhawk, and others — 5.00
Special 1 (1992, $3.50, 68 pgs.)-Mature readers — 5.00

BLACKHAWK INDIAN TOMAHAWK WAR, THE
Avon Periodicals: 1951 (Also see Fighting Indians of the Wild West)

	GD	VG	FN	VF	VF/NM	NM-
nn-Kinstler-c; Kit West story	24	48	72	142	234	325

BLACKHAWKS (DC New 52)
DC Comics: Nov, 2011 - No. 8, Jun, 2012 ($2.99)
1-8: 1-Costa-s/Nolan & Lashley-a — 3.00

BLACK HOLE (See Walt Disney Showcase #54) (Disney, movie)
Whitman Publishing Co.: Mar, 1980 - No. 4, Sept, 1980

	GD	VG	FN	VF	VF/NM	NM-
11295(#1) (1979, Golden, $1.50-c, 52 pgs., graphic novel; 8 1/2x11") Photo-c; Spiegle-a.	3	6	9	15	22	28
1-3: 1,2-Movie adaptation. 2,3-Spiegle-a. 3-McWilliams-a; photo-c.	2	4	6	10	14	18
3-New stories	2	4	6	10	14	18
4-Sold only in pre-packs; new story; Spiegle-a	34	68	102	245	548	850

BLACK HOOD, THE (See Blue Ribbon, Flyman & Mighty Comics)
Red Circle Comics (Archie): June, 1983 - No. 3, Oct, 1983 (Mandell paper)

	GD	VG	FN	VF	VF/NM	NM-
1-Morrow, McWilliams, Wildey-a; Toth-c	1	2	3	5	6	8

2,3: The Fox by Toth-c/a; Boyette-a. 3-Morrow-a; Toth wraparound-c — 4.00
NOTE: Also see Archie's Super-Hero Special Digest #2

BLACK HOOD
DC Comics (Impact Comics): Dec, 1991 - No. 12, Dec, 1992 ($1.00)
1 — 5.00
2-12: 11-Intro The Fox. 12-Origin Black Hood — 4.00
Annual 1 (1992, $2.50, 68 pgs.)-w/Trading card — 4.00

BLACK HOOD, THE
Archie Comic Publications (Dark Circle Comics): Apr, 2015 - No. 11, Aug, 2016 ($3.99)
1-11: 1-Origin retold; Swierczynski-s/Gaydos-a; five covers. 6-Chaykin-a. 8-Hack-a — 4.00

BLACK HOOD, THE (Volume 2)
Archie Comic Publications (Dark Circle Comics): Dec, 2016 - No. 5, Aug, 2017 ($3.99)
1-5-Swierczynski-s/Greg Scott-a — 4.00

BLACK HOOD COMICS (Formerly Hangman #2-8; Laugh Comics #20 on; also see Black Swan, Jackpot, Roly Poly & Top-Notch #9)
MLJ Magazines: No. 9, Wint., 1943-44 - No. 19, Sum., 1946 (on radio in 1943)

	GD	VG	FN	VF	VF/NM	NM-
9-The Hangman & The Boy Buddies cont'd	187	374	561	1197	2049	2900

Black Hammer #8 © 171 Studios & Ormston

Blackhawk #42 © QUA

Black Magick #3 © Rucka & Scott

	GD 2.0	VG 4.0	FN 6.0	VF 8.0	VF/NM 9.0	NM- 9.2
10-Hangman & Dusty, the Boy Detective app.	129	258	387	826	1413	2000
11-Dusty app.; no Hangman	93	186	279	591	1021	1450
12,13,15-18: 17-Hal Foster swipe from Prince Valiant; 1st issue with "An Archie Magazine" on-c	77	154	231	493	847	1200
14-Kinstler blood-c	155	310	465	992	1696	2400
19-I.D. exposed; last issue	103	206	309	659	1130	1600

NOTE: *Hangman by Fuje in 9, 10. Kinstler a-15, c-14-16.*

BLACK JACK (Rocky Lane's...; formerly Jim Bowie)
Charlton Comics: No. 20, Nov. 1957 - No. 30, Nov. 1959

20	10	20	30	58	79	100
21,27,29,30	7	14	21	35	43	50
22,23: 22-(68 pgs.). 23-Williamson/Torres-a	8	16	24	42	54	65
24-26,28-Ditko-a	11	22	33	60	83	105

BLACK KNIGHT, THE
Toby Press: May, 1953; 1963

1-Bondage-c	300	600	900	2010	3505	5000
Super Reprint No. 11 (1963)-Reprints 1953 issue	3	6	9	19	30	40

BLACK KNIGHT, THE
Atlas Comics (MgPC): May, 1955 - No. 5, April, 1956

1-Origin Crusader; Maneely-c/a	1000	2000	3000	7600	13,800	20,000
2-Maneely-c/a(4)	245	490	735	1568	2684	3800
3-5: 4-Maneely-c/a. 5-Maneely-c, Shores-a	219	438	657	1402	2401	3400
...No. 1 Facsimile Edition (4/21, $3.99) Reprints #1 with original ads						8.00

BLACK KNIGHT (See The Avengers #48, Marvel Super Heroes & Tales To Astonish #52)
Marvel Comics: June, 1990 - No. 4, Sept. 1990 ($1.50, limited series)

1-Original Black Knight returns	3	6	9	17	26	35
2-4: 3,4-Dr. Strange app.						5.00
... (MDCU) 1 (01/10, $3.99) Origin re-told; Frenz-a; originally from Marvel Digital Comics						4.00

NOTE: *Buckler c-1-4p*

BLACK KNIGHT (See Weirdworld and Secret Wars 2015 series)
Marvel Comics: Jan, 2016 - No. 5, May, 2016 ($3.99)

1-Tieri-s/Pizzari-a	1	3	4	6	8	10
2-5-Uncanny Avengers app.						4.00

BLACK KNIGHT: CURSE OF THE EBONY BLADE (Dane Whitman)
Marvel Comics: May, 2021 - No. 5, Sept. 2021 ($3.99, limited series)

1-5-Spurrier-s/Dávila-a. 1-Avengers app. 2-5-Mordred app.						4.00

BLACK KNIGHT: EXODUS
Marvel Comics: Dec, 1996 ($2.50, one-shot)

1-Raab-s; Apocalypse-c/app.						5.00

BLACK LAMB, THE
DC Comics (Helix): Nov, 1996 - No, 6, Apr, 1997 ($2.50, limited series)

1-6: Tim Truman-c/a/scripts						4.00

BLACK LAUGHTER
Black Laughter Publ.: Nov, 1972 (35¢)

V1#1-African American humor; James Dixon-s/a; 1st app. of Mr. Habeus Corpus
(a CGC 8.5 copy sold for $1400 in 6/2021, and a CGC 7.5 sold for $750 in 12/2021)

BLACKLIGHT (From ShadowHawk)
Image Comics: June, 2005 - No. 2, Jul, 2005 ($2.99)

1,2-Toledo & Deering-a/Wherle-s						3.00

BLACK LIGHTNING (See The Brave & The Bold, Cancelled Comic Cavalcade, DC Comics Presents #16, Detective Comics #490 and World's Finest #257)
National Periodical Publ./DC Comics: Apr, 1977 - No. 11, Sept-Oct, 1978

1-Origin Black Lightning; 1st app. Tobias Whale	7	14	21	46	86	125
2,3,6-10: 2-Talia and Merlyn app.	2	4	6	9	13	16
4,5-Superman-c/s. 4-Intro Cyclotronic Man	2	4	6	13	18	22
11-The Ray new solo story	2	4	6	11	16	20

NOTE: *Buckler c-1-3p, 6-11p. #11 is 44 pgs.*

BLACK LIGHTNING (2nd Series)
DC Comics: Feb, 1995 - No. 13, Feb, 1996 ($1.95/$2.25)

1-Tony Isabella scripts begin, ends #8	1	3	4	6	8	10
2-1st app. Painkiller	1	3	4	6	8	10
3-13: 6-Begin $2.25-c. 13-Batman-c/app.						3.00

BLACK LIGHTNING: COLD DEAD HANDS
DC Comics: Jan, 2018 - No. 6, Jun, 2018 ($3.99, limited series)

1-6-Tony Isabella-s/Clayton Henry-a; Tobias Whale app.						4.00

BLACK LIGHTNING / HONG KONG PHOOEY SPECIAL
DC Comics: Jul, 2018 ($3.99, one-shot)

1-Cowan & Sienkiewicz-a/Hill-s; takes place in 1976; Funky Phantom back-up story   4.00

BLACK LIGHTNING: YEAR ONE
DC Comics: Mar, 2009 - No. 6, May, 2009 ($2.99, bi-weekly limited series)

1-6-Van Meter-s/Hamner-a. 1-Two printings (white and yellow cover title logos)						3.00
TPB (2009, $17.99) r/#1-6						18.00

BLACK LIST, THE (Based on the TV show)
Titan Comics: Aug, 2015 - No. 10, Jul, 2016 ($3.99)

1-10-Art & photo-c for each: 1-Nicole Phillips-s/Beni Lobel-a.   4.00

BLACK MAGIC (...Magazine) (Becomes Cool Cat V8#6 on)
Crestwood Publ. V1#1-4,V6#1-V7#5/Headline V1#5-V5#3,V7#6-V8#5: 10-11/50 - V4#1, 6-7/53: V4#2, 9-10/53 - V5#3, 11-12/54; V6#1, 9-10/57 - V7#2, 11-12/58: V7#3, 7-8/60 - V8#5, 11-12/61 (V1#1-5, 52pgs.; V1#6-V3#3, 44pgs.)

V1#1-S&K-a, 10 pgs.; Meskin-a(2)	187	374	561	1197	2049	2900
2-S&K-a, 17 pgs.; Meskin-a	81	162	243	518	884	1250
3-6(8-9/51)-S&K, Roussos, Meskin-a	68	136	204	435	743	1050
V2#1(10-11/51),4,5,7(#13),9(#15),12(#18)-S&K-a	45	90	135	284	488	675
2,3,6,8,10,11(#17)	37	74	111	222	361	500
V3#1(#19, 12/52) - 6(#24, 5/53)-S&K-a	39	78	117	231	378	525
V4#1(#25, 6-7/53), 2(#26, 9-10/53)-S&K(a3-4)	39	78	117	240	395	550
3(#27, 11-12/53)-S&K-a; Ditko-a (2nd published-a); also see Captain 3-D, Daring Love #1, Strange Fantasy #9, & Fantastic Fears #5 (Fant. Fears was 1st drawn, but not 1st publ.)	77	154	231	493	847	1200
4(#28)-Eyes ripped out/story-S&K, Ditko-a	55	110	165	352	601	850
5(#29, 3-4/54)-S&K, Ditko-a	40	80	120	246	411	560
6(#30, 5-6/54)-S&K, Powell?-a	34	68	102	199	325	450
V5#1(#31, 7-8/54 - 3(#33, 11-12/54)-S&K, Ditko-a	22	44	66	132	216	300
V6#1(#34, 9-10/57), 2(#35, 11-12/57)	14	28	42	81	118	155
3(1-2/58) - 6(7-8/58)	14	28	42	78	112	145
V7#1(#19, 12/52) - 3(7-8/60), S&K-a	11	22	33	64	90	115
5(11-12/60)-Hitler-c; Torres-a	25	50	75	150	245	340
6(1-2/61)-Powell-a(2)	11	22	33	64	90	115
V8#1(3-4/61)-Powell-c/a	11	22	33	64	90	115
2(5-6/61)-E.C. story swipe/W.F. #22; Ditko, Powell-a	14	28	42	76	108	140
3(7-8/61)-E.C. story swipe/W.F. #22; Powell-a(2)	14	28	42	76	108	140
4(9-10/61)-Powell-a(5)	11	22	33	64	90	115
5-E.C. story swipe/W.S.F. #28; Powell-a(3)	12	24	36	69	97	125

NOTE: *Bernard Baily a-V4#6?, V5#3(2). Grandenetti a-V2#3. 11. Kirby c-V1#1-6, V2#1-12, V3#1-6, V4#1, 2, 4-6, V5#1-3. McWilliams a-V1#1(2), 2, 3, 4(2), 5(2), 6, V2#1, 2, 3(2), 4(3), 5, 6(2), 7-9, 11, 12. Meskin a-V1#1(2), 2, 3, 4(2). 2. Orlando a-V6#1, 4, V7#2; c-V6/1-6. Powell a-V5#17. Roussos a-V1#3-5, 6(2), V2#3(2), 4, 5(2), 6, 8, 9, 10(2), 11, 12p, V3#1(2), 2), 5, V5#2. Simon a-V2#12, V3#2, V7#5? c-V4#3?, V7#3?, 4, 5?, 6?, V8#1-5. Simon & Kirby a-V1#1, 2(2), 3-6, V2#1, 4, 5, 7, 9, 12, V3#1-6, V4#1(3), 2(4), 3(2), 4(2), 5, 6, V5#1-3; c-V2#1. Leonard Starr a-V1#1. Tuska a-V6#3, 4. Woodbridge a-V7#4.*

BLACK MAGIC
National Periodical Publications: Oct-Nov, 1973 - No. 9, Apr-May, 1975

1-S&K reprints	3	6	9	19	30	40
2-8-S&K reprints	2	4	6	11	16	20
9-S&K reprints	3	6	9	14	19	24

BLACK MAGICK
Image Comics: Oct, 2015 - Present ($3.99)

1-16-Greg Rucka-s/Nicola Scott-a   4.00

BLACKMAIL TERROR (See Harvey Comics Library)

BLACK MANTA
DC Comics: Nov, 2021 - No. 6, Apr, 2022 ($3.99, limited series)

1-6: 1-Black Manta vs. Capt. Demo. 2,3-Gentleman Ghost app.   4.00

BLACK MARKET
BOOM! Studios: Jul, 2014 - No. 4, Oct, 2014 ($3.99, limited series)

1-4-Barbiere-s/Santos-a   4.00

BLACK MASK
DC Comics: 1993 - No. 3, 1994 ($4.95, limited series, 52 pgs.)

1-3   5.00

BLACK MASK: YEAR OF THE VILLAIN
DC Comics: Oct, 2019 ($4.99, one-shot)

1-Tom Taylor-s/Cully Hamner-a; Apex Lex Luthor & Batwoman app.   5.00

BLACK MONDAY MURDERS, THE
Image Comics: Aug, 2016 - No. 8, Feb, 2018 ($4.99/$3.99, limited series)

1-4-Jonathan Hickman-s/Tomm Coker-a						5.00
5-8-($3.99)						4.00

BLACK OPS

	GD 2.0	VG 4.0	FN 6.0	VF 8.0	VF/NM 9.0	NM- 9.2

Image Comics (WildStorm): Jan, 1996 - No. 5, May, 1996 ($2.50, lim. series)

1-5						4.00

BLACK ORCHID (See Adventure Comics #428 & Phantom Stranger)
DC Comics: Holiday, 1988-89 - No. 3, 1989 ($3.50, lim. series, prestige format)

Book 1,3: Gaiman scripts & McKean painted-a in all						6.00
Book 2-Arkham Asylum story; Batman app.	1	2	3	5	6	8
TPB (1991, $19.95) r/#1-3; new McKean-c						20.00

BLACK ORCHID
DC Comics: Sept, 1993 - No. 22, June, 1995 ($1.95/$2.25)

1-22: Dave McKean-a all issues						4.00
1-Platinum Edition						12.00
Annual 1 (1993, $3.95, 68 pgs.)-Children's Crusade						5.00

BLACK ORDER (The Warmasters of Thanos)
Marvel Comics: Jan, 2019 - No. 5, May, 2019 ($3.99, limited series)

1-5: 1-Landy-s/Tan-a. 3-5-Nova app. 5-Magno-a						4.00

BLACKOUT
Dark Horse Comics: Mar, 2014 - No. 4, Jul, 2014 ($2.99, limited series)

1-4-Barbiere-s/Lorimer-a; King Tiger back-up by Stradley-s/Doug Wheatley-a						3.00

BLACKOUTS (See Broadway Hollywood...)

BLACK PANTHER, THE (Also see Avengers #52, Fantastic Four #52, Jungle Action, Marvel Premiere #51-53 and Rise of the Black Panther)
Marvel Comics Group: Jan, 1977 - No. 15, May, 1979

	GD 2.0	VG 4.0	FN 6.0	VF 8.0	VF/NM 9.0	NM- 9.2
1-Jack Kirby-s/a thru #12	10	20	30	64	132	200
2	4	8	12	27	44	60
3-5: 4,5-(Regular 30¢ editions).	4	8	12	23	37	50
4,5-(35¢-c variants, limited dist.)(7,9/77)	11	22	33	73	157	240
6-13: 8-Origin	3	6	9	19	30	40
14,15-Avengers x-over. 14-Origin	3	6	9	20	31	42
...By Jack Kirby Vol. 1 TPB (2005, $19.99) r/#1-7; unused covers and sketch pages						20.00
...By Jack Kirby Vol. 2 TPB (2006, $19.99) r/#8-12 by Kirby and #13 non-Kirby						20.00
NOTE: *J. Buscema c*-15p. *Layton c*-13i.						

BLACK PANTHER
Marvel Comics Group: July, 1988 - No. 4, Oct, 1988 ($1.25)

1-Gillis-s/Cowan & Delarosa-a	2	4	6	11	16	20
2-4	1	2	3	5	6	8

BLACK PANTHER (Marvel Knights)
Marvel Comics: Nov, 1998 - No. 62, Sept, 2003 ($2.50)

1-Texeira-a/c; Priest-s	3	6	9	19	30	40
1-($6.95) DF edition w/Quesada & Palmiotti-a	3	6	9	19	30	40
2,3: 2-Two covers by Texeira and Timm. 3-Fantastic Four app.						
	1	2	3	5	6	8
4-1st White Wolf	2	4	6	11	16	20
5-22,24-35,37-40: 5-Evans-a. 6-8-Jusko-a. 8-Avengers-c/app. 15-Hulk app. 22-Moon Knight app. 25-Maximum Security x-over. 26-Storm-c/app. 28-Magneto & Sub-Mariner-c/app. 29-WWII flashback meeting w/Captain America. 35-Defenders-c/app. 37-Luke Cage and Falcon-c/app.						3.00
23-Deadpool & the Avengers app.	3	6	9	15	22	28
36-($3.50, 100 pgs.) 35th Anniversary issue incl. r/1st app. in FF #52						4.00
41-56: 41-44-Wolverine app. 47-Thor app. 48,49-Magneto app.						3.00
57-62: 57-Begin $2.99-c. 59-Falcon app.						3.00
...: The Client (6/01, $14.95, TPB) r/#1-5						15.00
... 2099 #1 (11/04, $2.99) Kirkman-s/Hotz-a/Pat Lee-c						3.00

BLACK PANTHER (Marvel Knights)
Marvel Comics: Apr, 2005 - No. 41, Nov, 2008 ($2.99)

1-Reginald Hudlin-s/John Romita Jr. & Klaus Janson-a; covers by Romita & Ribic						
	2	4	6	10	14	18
2-1st app. Shuri	5	10	15	33	57	80
3-7,9-15,17-20: 7-House of M; Hairsine-a. 10-14-Luke Cage app. 12,13-Blade app. 17-Linsner-c. 19-Doctor Doom app.						3.00
8-Cho-c; X-Men app.						5.00
8-2nd printing variant-c						4.00
16-($3.99) Wedding of T'Challa and Storm; wraparound Cho-c; Hudlin-s/Eaton-a						4.00
21-Civil War x-over; Namor app.						8.00
21-2nd printing with new cover and Civil War logo						3.00
22-25-Civil War: 23-25-Turner-a.						4.00
26-41: 26-30-T'Challa and Storm join the Fantastic Four. 27-30-Marvel Zombies app. 28-30-Suydam-c. 39-41-Secret Invasion						3.00
Annual 1 (4/08, $3.99) Hudlin-s/Stroman & Lashley-a; alternate future; Uatu app.						4.00
...: Bad Mutha TPB (2006, $10.99) r/#10-13						11.00
...: Civil War TPB (2007, $17.99) r/#19-25						18.00
...: Four the Hard Way TPB (2007, $13.99) r/#26-30; page layouts and character designs						14.00
...: Little Green Men TPB (2008, $10.99) r/#31-34						11.00
...: The Bride TPB (2006, $14.99) r/#14-18; interview with the dress designer						15.00
...: Who Is The Black Panther HC (2006, $21.99) r/#1-6; Hudlin afterword; cover gallery						22.00
...: Who Is The Black Panther SC (2006, $14.99) r/#1-6; Hudlin afterword; cover gallery						15.00

BLACK PANTHER
Marvel Comics: Apr, 2009 - No. 12, Mar, 2010 ($3.99/$2.99)

1-($3.99) Hudlin/Lashley-a; covers by Campbell & Lashley; Dr. Doom & Shuri app.						
	5	10	15	33	57	80
2-12-($2.99) 2-6-Campbell-a. 6-Shuri becomes female Black Panther						4.00

BLACK PANTHER
Marvel Comics: Jun, 2016 - No. 18, Nov, 2017; No. 166, Dec, 2017 - No. 172, Jun, 2018 ($4.99/$3.99)

1-($4.99) Ta-Nehisi Coates-s/Brian Stelfreeze-a; bonus Stelfreeze interview & art						
	1	3	4	6	8	10
2,4-18-($3.99) 2,4,9,12-Stelfreeze-a. 5-8,10-12,16-18-Sprouse-a. 13-17-Ororo app.						4.00
3-1st Midnight Angels; Stelfreeze-a	1	3	4	6	8	10
[Title switches to legacy numbering after #18 (11/17)]						
166-172: 166-Klaw app.; Coates-s/Kirk-a						4.00
Annual 1 (4/18, $4.99) Stories by Priest, Perkins, McGregor, Acuña, Hudlin & Lashley						5.00

BLACK PANTHER
Marvel Comics: Jul, 2018 - No. 25, Jul, 2021 ($4.99/$3.99)

1-($4.99) Ta-Nehisi Coates-s/Daniel Acuña-a; Intergalactic Empire of Wakanda						5.00
2-24-($3.99) 2-Intro Emperor N'Jadaka. 6,12-Jen Bartel-a. 7-11-Walker-a. 14-17-Acuña-a						4.00
25-($5.99) Coates-s/Acuña & Stelfreeze-a						6.00

BLACK PANTHER (All ages title)
IDW Publishing (Marvel): Jan, 2019 - No. 6, Jun, 2019 ($3.99, limited series)

1-6: 1-3-Kyle Baker-s; Shuri app. 4-6-Vita Ayala-s						4.00

BLACK PANTHER
Marvel Comics: Jan, 2022 - No. 15, May, 2023 ($4.99/$3.99)

1-($4.99) John Ridley-s/Juann Cabal-a; Avengers app.						5.00
2,4-15-($3.99) Shuri app. 7,8-Ororo app. 9-15-Avengers app. 13-15-Namor app.						4.00
3-($5.99) Legacy 200th issue; X-Men app.; back up by Juni Ba-s/a; intro. Tosin Oduye						6.00
...: Unconquered 1 (1/23, $3.99) Bryan Hill-s/Alberto Foche-a						4.00

BLACK PANTHER
Marvel Comics: Aug, 2023 - Present ($4.99/$3.99)

1-($4.99) Eve Ewing-s/Chris Allen-a; intro Beisa						5.00
2-9-($3.99) 2-4-Deathlok app.						4.00

BLACK PANTHER AND THE AGENTS OF WAKANDA
Marvel Comics: Nov, 2019 - Present ($3.99)

1-8: 1-Team with Janet Van Dyne, Okoye, Gorilla-Man, and Broo. 5,6-Deadpool app.						4.00

BLACK PANTHER AND THE CREW
Marvel Comics: Jun, 2017 - No. 6, Oct, 2017 ($3.99)

1-6-Storm, Luke Cage, Misty Knight & Manifold app.; Ta-Nehisi Coates-s/Butch Guice-a						4.00

BLACK PANTHER/CAPTAIN AMERICA: FLAGS OF OUR FATHERS
Marvel Comics: Jan, 2010 - No. 4, Sept, 2010 ($3.99, limited series)

1-4-Hudlin-s/Cowan-a; WW2 story; Howling Commandos & Red Skull app.						4.00

BLACK PANTHER LEGENDS
Marvel Comics: Dec, 2021 - No. 4, Jun, 2022 ($3.99, limited series)

1-4-T'Challa's childhood revisited; Onyebuchi-s/Fiadzigbey-a. 2-Ororo app.						4.00

BLACK PANTHER: PANTHER'S PREY
Marvel Comics: May, 1991 - No. 4, Oct, 1991 ($4.95, squarebound, lim. series, 52 pgs.)

1-4: McGregor-s/Turner-a						6.00

BLACK PANTHER: THE MAN WITHOUT FEAR (Continues from Daredevil #512)
Marvel Comics: No. 513, Feb, 2011 - No. 523, Nov, 2011 ($2.99)

513-523: 513-Shadowland aftermath; Liss-s/Francavilla-a/Bianchi-c. 521-523-Fear Itself						3.00
513-Variant-c by Francavilla						5.00

BLACK PANTHER: THE MOST DANGEROUS MAN ALIVE
Marvel Comics: No. 523.1, Nov, 2011 - No. 529, Apr, 2012 ($2.99)

523.1, 524-529: 523.1-Palo-a/Zircher-c. 524-Spider Island tie-in; Lady Bullseye app.						4.00

BLACK PANTHER: THE SOUND AND THE FURY
Marvel Comics: Apr, 2018 ($3.99, one-shot)

1-Klaw app.; Macchio-s/Di Vito-a; reprint of Fantastic Four #53 (origin/1st app. Klaw)						4.00

BLACK PANTHER VS. DEADPOOL
Marvel Comics: Dec, 2018 - No. 5, Apr, 2019 ($3.99, limited series)

1-5: 1-Kibblesmith-s/Ortiz-a; Willie Lumpkin app.						4.00

BLACK PANTHER: WORLD OF WAKANDA
Marvel Comics: Jan, 2017 - No. 6, Jun, 2017 ($4.99/$3.99, limited series)

1-($4.99) Roxanne Gay-s/Alitha E. Martinez-a; spotlight on The Dora Milaje						
	1	3	4	6	8	10
2-6-($3.99) 6-Rembert Browne-s/Joe Bennett-a; White Tiger app.						4.00

BLACK PEARL, THE
Dark Horse Comics: Sept, 1996 - No. 5, Jan, 1997 ($2.95, limited series)

1-Mark Hamill scripts in all	1	2	3	5	6	8
2-5						3.00

BLACK PHANTOM (See Tim Holt #25, 38)
Magazine Enterprises: Nov, 1954 (one-shot) (Female-outlaw)

1 (A-1 #122)-The Ghost Rider story plus 3 Black Phantom stories; Headlight-c/a						
	87	174	261	553	952	1350

BLACK PHANTOM
AC Comics: 1989 - No. 3, 1990 ($2.50, B&W; #2 color)(Reprints & new-a)

1-3: 1-Ayers-r, Bolle-r/B.P. #1-3-Redmask-r						6.00

BLACK PHANTOM, RETURN OF THE (See Wisco)

BLACK RACER AND SHILO NORMAN SPECIAL, THE (Jack Kirby 100th Birthday tribute)
DC Comics: Oct, 2017 ($4.99, one-shot)

1-Black Racer origin; Hudlin-s/Cowan-a; reprint pages from New Gods #5,7,8						5.00

BLACK RIDER (Western Winners #1-7; Western Tales of Black Rider #28-31; Gunsmoke Western #32 on)(See All Western Winners, Best Western, Kid Colt, Outlaw Kid, Rex Hart, Two-Gun Kid, Two-Gun Western, Western Gunfighters, Western Winners, & Wild Western)
Marvel/Atlas Comics(CDS No. 8-17/CPS No. 19 on): No. 8, 3/50 - No. 18, 1/52; No. 19, 11/53 - No. 27, 3/55

8 (#1)-Black Rider & his horse Satan begin; 36 pgs; Stan Lee photo-c as Black Rider	89	178	267	712	1606	2500
9-52 pgs. begin, end #14	34	68	102	199	325	450
10-Origin Black Rider	37	74	111	222	361	500
11-14: Last 52pgs.	22	44	66	132	216	300
15-19: 19-Two-Gun Kid app.	20	40	60	117	189	260
20-Classic-c; Two-Gun Kid app.	28	56	84	165	270	375
21-27: 21-23-Two-Gun Kid app. 24,25-Arrowhead app. 26-Kid Colt app. 27-Last issue; last precode. Kid Colt app. The Spider (a villain) burns to death						
	19	38	57	111	176	240
NOTE: *Ayers c*-22. *Jack Keller a*-15, 26, 27. *Maneely a*-14; c-9, 16, 17, 24, 25, 27. *Syd Shores a*-19, 21, 22, 23(3), 24(3), 25-27; c-19, 21, 23. *Sinnott a*-24, 25. *Tuska a*-12, 19-21.						

BLACK RIDER RIDES AGAIN!, THE

Black Panther (2006 series) #18 © MAR

Black Terror #9 © BP

Black Widow (2010 series) #4 © MAR

	GD 2.0	VG 4.0	FN 6.0	VF 8.0	VF/NM 9.0	NM- 9.2

Atlas Comics (CPS): Sept, 1957

| 1-Kirby-a(3); Powell-a; Severin-c | 42 | 84 | 126 | 265 | 445 | 625 |

BLACK ROAD
Image Comics: Apr, 2016 - No. 10, May, 2017 ($3.99)

| 1-10-Brian Wood-s/Garry Brown-a | | | | | | 4.00 |

BLACK SCIENCE
Image Comics: Nov, 2013 - No. 43, Sept, 2019 ($3.50/$3.99)

1-Remender-s/Scalera-a; multiple covers	2	4	6	8	10	12
2						6.00
3-33: 11,16,21-33,35-43-$3.99-c						4.00
34-($4.99)						5.00

BLACK SEPTEMBER (Also see Avengers/Ultraforce, Ultraforce (1st series) #10 & Ultraforce/Avengers)
Malibu Comics (Ultraverse): 1995 ($1.50, one-shot)

| Infinity-Intro to the new Ultraverse; variant-c exists. | | | | | | 4.00 |

BLACK'S MYTH
AHOY Comics: 2021 - No. 5, 2021 ($3.99, B&W, limited series)

| 1-5-Palicki-s/Cavalcanti-a | | | | | | 4.00 |

BLACKSTONE (See Super Magician Comics & Wisco Giveaways)

BLACKSTONE, MASTER MAGICIAN COMICS
Vital Publ./Street & Smith Publ.: Mar-Apr, 1946 - No. 3, July-Aug, 1946

| 1 | 43 | 86 | 129 | 271 | 461 | 650 |
| 2,3 | 28 | 56 | 84 | 165 | 270 | 375 |

BLACKSTONE, THE MAGICIAN (...Detective on cover only #3 & 4)
Marvel Comics (CnPC): No. 2, May, 1948 - No. 4, Sept, 1948 (No #1?) (Cont'd from E.C. #1?)

| 2-The Blonde Phantom begins, ends #4 | 119 | 238 | 357 | 762 | 1306 | 1850 |
| 3,4: 3-Blonde Phantom by Sekowsky | 65 | 130 | 195 | 416 | 708 | 1000 |

BLACKSTONE, THE MAGICIAN DETECTIVE FIGHTS CRIME
E. C. Comics: Fall, 1947

| 1-1st app. Happy Houlihans | 90 | 180 | 270 | 576 | 988 | 1400 |

BLACK SUN (X-Men Black Sun on cover)
Marvel Comics: Nov, 2000 - No. 5, Nov, 2000 ($2.99, weekly limited series)

| 1-(...: X-Men), 2-(...: Storm), 3-(...: Banshee and Sunfire), 4-(...: Colossus and Nightcrawler), 5-(...: Wolverine and Thunderbird); Claremont-s in all; Evans interlocking painted covers; Magik returns | | | | | | 4.00 |

BLACK SUN (WildStorm)
DC Comics: Nov, 2002 - No. 6, Jun, 2003 ($2.95, limited series)

| 1-6-Andreyko-s/Scott-a | | | | | | 3.00 |

BLACK SWAN COMICS
MLJ Magazines (Pershing Square Publ. Co.): 1945

| 1-The Black Hood reprints from Black Hood No. 14; Bill Woggon-a; Suzie app. Caribbean Pirates-c | 30 | 60 | 90 | 177 | 289 | 400 |

BLACK TAPE
Artists, Writers, & Artisans, Inc.: Feb, 2023 - No. 4, May, 2023 ($3.99, limited series)

| 1-4-Panosian-s/Talajic-a | | | | | | 4.00 |

BLACK TARANTULA (See Feature Presentations No. 5)

BLACK TERROR (See America's Best Comics & Exciting Comics)
Better Publications/Standard: Winter, 1942-43 - No. 27, June, 1949

1-Black Terror, Crime Crusader begin; Japanese WWII-c	459	918	1377	3350	3925	8500
2	245	490	735	1568	2684	3800
3-Nazi WWII-c	232	464	696	1485	2543	3600
4,5-Nazi & Japanese WWII-c	187	374	561	1197	2049	2900
6-8: 6,8-Classic Nazi WWII-c. 7-Classic Japanese WWII-c; The Ghost app.	219	438	657	1402	2401	3400
9,10-Nazi & Japanese WWII-c	168	336	504	1075	1838	2600
11,13-19	84	168	252	538	919	1300
12-Japanese WWII-c	116	232	348	742	1271	1800
20-Classic-c; The Scarab app.	155	310	465	992	1696	2400
21-Miss Masque app.	103	206	309	659	1130	1600
22-Part Frazetta-a on one Black Terror story	116	232	348	742	1271	1800
23,25-27	71	142	213	454	777	1100
24-Frazetta-a (1/4 pg.)	129	258	387	826	1413	2000

NOTE: **Schomburg (Xela)** c-2-27; bondage c-2, 17, 24. Meskin a-27. Moreira a-27. Robinson/Meskin a-23, 24(3), 25, 26. Roussos/Mayo a-24. Tuska a-26, 27.

BLACK TERROR, THE (Also see Total Eclipse)

Eclipse Comics: Oct, 1989 - No. 3, June, 1990 ($4.95, 52 pgs., squarebound, limited series)

| 1-3: Beau Smith & Chuck Dixon scripts; Dan Brereton painted-c/a | | | | | | 5.00 |

BLACK TERROR (Also see Project Superpowers)
Dynamite Entertainment: 2008 - No. 14, 2011 ($3.50/$3.99)

| 1-14-Golden Age hero. 1-Alex Ross-c/Mike Lilly-a; various variant-c exist | | | | | | 4.00 |

BLACK TERROR VOLUME 2
Dynamite Entertainment: 2019 - No. 5, 2020 ($3.99, limited series)

| 1-5: 1-Set in 1974; Bemis-s/Gaudio-a. 2-5-Coleman-a; multiple covers for each | | | | | | 4.00 |

BLACKTHORNE 3-D SERIES
Blackthorne Publishing Co.: May, 1985 - No. 80, 1989 ($2.25/$2.50)

1-Sheena in 3-D #1. D. Stevens-c/retouched-a	3	6	9	16	23	30
2-10: 2-MerlinRealm in 3-D #1. 3-3-D Heroes #1. Goldyn in 3-D #1. 5-Bizarre 3-D Zone #1. 6-Salimba in 3-D #1. 7-Twisted Tales in 3-D #1. 8-Dick Tracy in 3-D #1.						
9-Salimba in 3-D #2. 10-Gumby in 3-D #1	1	2	3	5	6	8
11-19: 11-Betty Boop in 3-D #1. 12-Hamster Vice in 3-D #1. 13-Little Nemo in 3-D #1. 14-Gumby in 3-D #3. 15-Hamster Vice #6 in 3-D. 16-Laffin' Gas #6 in 3-D. 17-Gumby in 3-D #3. 18-Bullwinkle and Rocky in 3-D. 19-The Flintstones in 3-D #1						
	1	2	3	5	6	8
20(#1),26(#2),35(#3),39(#4),52(#5),62,71(#6)-G.I. Joe in 3-D. 62-G.I. Joe Annual						
	2	4	6	8	11	14
21-24,28: 21-Gumby in 3-D #4. 22-The Flintstones in 3-D #2. 23-Laurel & Hardy in 3-D #1. 24-Bozo the Clown in 3-D. 28-Gumby in 3-D #5						6.00
25,29,37-The Transformers in 3-D	2	4	6	11	16	20
27,40-Bravestarr in 3-D #1 & #2	3	6	9	14	20	25
30-Star Wars in 3-D #1	3	6	9	17	26	35
31-34,36,38: 31-The California Raisins in 3-D #1. 32-Richie Rich & Casper in 3-D #1. 33-Gumby in 3-D #6. 34-Laurel & Hardy in 3-D #2. 36-The Flintstones in 3-D #3. 38-Gumby in 3-D #7	1	2	3	5	6	8
41-46,49,50: 41-Battletech in 3-D #1. 42-The Flintstones in 3-D #4. 43-Underdog in 3-D #1. 44-The California Raisins in 3-D #2. 45-Red Heat in 3-D #1 (movie adapt.). 46-The California Raisins in 3-D #3. 49-Rambo in 3-D #1. 49-Sad Sack in 3-D #1. 50-Bullwinkle For President in 3-D #1	1	2	3	5	6	8
47,48-Star Wars in 3-D #2,3	3	6	9	14	19	24
51,53-60: 51-Kull in 3-D #1. 53-Red Sonja in 3-D #1. 54-Bozo in 3-D #2. 55-Waxwork in 3-D #1 (movie adapt.). 57-Casper in 3-D #1. 58-Baby Huey in 3-D #1. 59-Little Dot in 3-D #1. 60-Solomon Kane in 3-D #1						
61,63-70,72-74,76-80: 61-Werewolf in 3-D #1. 63-The California Raisins in 3-D #4. 64-To Die For in 3-D #1. 65-Capt. Holo in 3-D #1. 66-Playful Little Audrey in 3-D #2. 67-Kull in 3-D #2. 69-The California Raisins in 3-D #5. 70-Wendy in 3-D #1. 72-Sports Hall of Shame #1. 74-The Noid in 3-D #1. 80-The Noid in 3-D #2	1	2	3	4	5	7
75-Moonwalker in 3-D #1 (Michael Jackson movie adapt.)						
	5	10	15	30	50	70

BLACK VORTEX (See Guardians of the Galaxy & X-Men: The Black Vortex)

BLACK WIDOW (Marvel Knights) (Also see Marvel Graphic Novel)
Marvel Comics: May, 1999 - No. 3, Aug, 1999 ($2.99, limited series)

1-(June on-c) Devin Grayson-s/J.G. Jones-c/a; intro. Yelena Belova; Daredevil app.						
	3	6	9	19	30	40
1-Variant-c by J.G. Jones	5	10	15	30	50	70
2,3						5.00
...Web of Intrigue (6/99, $3.50) r/origin & early appearances						
	1	2	3	5	6	7
TPB (7/01, $15.95) r/Vol. 1 & 2; Jones-c						16.00

BLACK WIDOW (Marvel Knights) (Volume 2)
Marvel Comics: Jan, 2001 - No. 3, May, 2001 ($2.99, limited series)

| 1-3-Grayson & Rucka-s/Scott Hampton-c/a; Daredevil app. | | | | | | 4.00 |

BLACK WIDOW (Marvel Knights)
Marvel Comics: Nov, 2004 - No. 6, Apr, 2005 ($2.99, limited series)

| 1-6-Sienkiewicz-a/Land-c | | | | | | 4.00 |

BLACK WIDOW (Continues in Widowmaker #1)
Marvel Comics: Jun, 2010 - No. 8, Jan, 2011 ($3.99/$2.99)

1-($3.99) Liu-s/Acuña-a; Wolverine app.; back-up history text						
	1	2	3	5	6	8
1-Variant photo-c of Scarlett Johansson from Iron Man 2 movie						
	10	20	30	64	132	200
2-8-($2.99) 2-5-Acuña-a. 2,3-Elektra app.						3.00

BLACK WIDOW (All-New Marvel Now!)
Marvel Comics: Mar, 2014 - No. 20, Sept, 2015 ($3.99)

| 1-20: 1-Edmonson-s/Noto-a/c. 7-Daredevil app. 8-Winter Soldier app. 11-X-23 app. | | | | | | 4.00 |

BLACK WIDOW

	GD 2.0	VG 4.0	FN 6.0	VF 8.0	VF/NM 9.0	NM- 9.2

Marvel Comics: May, 2016 - No. 12, May, 2017 ($3.99)

1-12: 1-Waid-s/Samnee-s&a. 6-Iron Man app. 9,10-Winter Soldier app. ... 4.00

BLACK WIDOW
Marvel Comics: Mar, 2019 - No. 5, Jul, 2019 ($3.99, limited series)

1-5: 1-Jen & Sylvia Soska-s/Flaviano-a; Captain America app. 2,3-Madame Masque app. 4.00

BLACK WIDOW
Marvel Comics: Jun, 2020 - No. 15, May, 2022 ($3.99)

1-15: 1-Kelly Thompson-s/Elena Casagrande; Yelena Belova & Arcade app. 4.00
....: Widow's Sting 1 (12/20, $3.99) Macchio-s/Buonfantino-a 4.00

BLACK WIDOW & THE MARVEL GIRLS
Marvel Comics: Feb, 2010 - No. 4, Apr, 2010 ($2.99, limited series)

1-Enchantress app.; Tobin-s	1	3	4	6	8	10
2-4-Tobin-s. 2-Avengers app. 4-Storm app.; Miyazawa-a						4.00

BLACK WIDOW: DEADLY ORIGIN
Marvel Comics: Jan, 2010 - No. 4, Apr, 2010 ($3.99, limited series)

1-Wolverine and Bucky app.; origin retold	1	3	4	6	8	10
2-4-Granov-c. 3-Daredevil app.						4.00

BLACK WIDOW: PALE LITTLE SPIDER (Marvel Knights) (Volume 3)
Marvel Comics: Jun, 2002 - No. 3, Aug, 2002 ($2.99, limited series)

1-Rucka-s/Kordey-a/Horn-c	1	3	4	6	8	10
2,3						4.00

BLACK WIDOW 2 (THE THINGS THEY SAY ABOUT HER) (Marvel Knights)
Marvel Comics: Nov, 2005 - No. 6, Apr, 2006 ($2.99, limited series)

1-6-Phillips & Sienkiewicz-a/Morgan-s; Daredevil app. 4.00
TPB (2006, $15.99) r/#1-6 16.00

BLACKWOOD
Dark Horse Comics: May, 2018 - No. 4, Aug, 2018 ($3.99, limited series)

1-4-Evan Dorkin-s/Veronica Fish-a 4.00

BLACKWOOD: THE MOURNING AFTER
Dark Horse Comics: Feb, 2020 - No. 4, Sept, 2020 ($3.99, limited series)

1-4-Evan Dorkin-s/Veronica Fish-a 4.00

BLACKWULF
Marvel Comics: June, 1994 - No. 10, Mar, 1995 ($1.50)

1-($2.50)-Embossed-c; Angel Medina-a 5.00
2-10 4.00

BLADE (The Vampire Hunter)
Marvel Comics

1-(3/98, $3.50) Colan-a(p)/Christopher Golden-s 6.00
... Black & White TPB (2004, $19.99, B&W) reprints from magazines Vampire Tales #8,9; Marvel Preview #3,6; Crescent City Blues #1 and Marvel Shadow and Light #1 16.00
San Diego Con Promo (6/97) Wesley Snipes photo-c 4.00
...Sins of the Father (10/98, $5.99) Sears-a; movie adaption 6.00
Blade 2: Movie Adaptation (5/02, $5.95) Ponticelli-a/Bradstreet-c 6.00

BLADE (The Vampire Hunter)
Marvel Comics: Nov, 1998 - No. 3, Jan, 1999 ($3.50/$2.99)

1-($3.50) Contains Movie insider pages; McKean-a	2	4	6	10	14	18
2,3-($2.99): 2-Two covers	1	3	4	6	8	10

BLADE (Volume 2)
Marvel Comics (MAX): May, 2002 -No. 6, Oct, 2002 ($2.99)

1-6-Bradstreet-c/Hinz-s. 1-5-Pugh-a. 6-Homs-a 3.00

BLADE
Marvel Comics: Nov, 2006 - No. 12, Oct, 2007 ($2.99)

1-12: 1-Chaykin-a/Guggenheim-s; origin retold; Spider-Man app. 2-Dr. Doom-c/app. 5-Civil War tie-in; Wolverine app. 6-Blade loses a hand. 10-Spider-Man app. 3.00
...: Sins of the Father TPB (2007, $14.99) r/#7-12; afterword by Guggenheim 15.00
...: Undead Again TPB (2007, $14.99) r/#1-6; letters pages from #1&2 15.00

BLADE (The Vampire Hunter)
Marvel Comics: Sept, 2023 - Present ($4.99/$3.99)

1-($4.99) Bryan Hill-s/Elena Casagrande-a 5.00
2-8-($3.99) 6-Dracula app. 7-Hulk app. 4.00

BLADE OF THE IMMORTAL (Manga)
Dark Horse Comics: June, 1996 - No. 131, Nov, 2007 ($2.95/$2.99/$3.95, B&W)

1-Hiroaki Samura-s/a in all	2	4	6	8	11	14
2-5: 2-#1 on cover in error						6.00
6-10						5.00
11,19,20,34-($3.95, 48 pgs.): 34-Food one-shot						4.00
12-18,21-33,35-41,43-105,107-131: 12-20-Dreamsong. 21-28-On Silent Wings. 29-33-Dark Shadow. 35-42-Heart of Darkness. 43-57-The Gathering						3.00
42-($3.50) Ends Heart of Darkness						3.50
106-($3.99)						4.00

BLADE RUNNER (Movie)
Marvel Comics Group: Oct, 1982 - No. 2, Nov, 1982

1-r/Marvel Super Special #22; Williamson-c/a	3	6	9	21	33	45
2-Williamson-a	3	6	9	15	22	28

BLADE RUNNER
Titan Comics: 2021 (Free giveaway)

... Free Comic Book Day Issue (2021) Previews the Blad Runner Origins and 2029 series 3.00

BLADE RUNNER: BLACK LOTUS
Titan Comics: Sept, 2022 - No. 4, Dec, 2022 ($3.99)

1-4-Nancy A. Collins-s/Enid Balam-a; multiple covers on each 4.00

BLADE RUNNER ORIGINS
Titan Comics: Mar, 2021 - No. 12, Jul, 2022 ($3.99)

1-12-Story of the first Blade Runner. 1-Dagnino-a; multiple covers 4.00

BLADE RUNNER 2019

Titan Comics: Aug, 2019 - No. 12, Dec, 2020 ($3.99)

1-12: 1-Green & Johnson-s/Guinaldo-a; multiple covers on each. 5-Jumps to 2026 4.00

BLADE RUNNER 2029
Titan Comics: Jan, 2021 - No. 12, Mar, 2022 ($3.99)

1-12: 1-Mike Johnson-s/Andres Guinaldo-a; multiple covers on each 4.00

BLADE RUNNER 2039
Titan Comics: Jan, 2023 - Present ($3.99)

1-10: 1-Mike Johnson and Mellow Brown-s/Andres Guinaldo-a; multiple covers on each 4.00

BLADE: THE VAMPIRE-HUNTER
Marvel Comics: July, 1994 - No. 10, Apr, 1995 ($1.95)

1-($2.95)-Foil-c; Dracula returns; Wheatley-c/a	4	8	12	25	40	55
2-Dracula-c/app.	2	4	6	8	10	12
3-10: 3,10-Dracula-c/app. 8-Morbius app.						4.00

BLADE: VAMPIRE-HUNTER
Marvel Comics: Dec, 1999 - No. 6, May, 2000 ($3.50/$2.50)

1-($3.50)-Bart Sears-s; Sears and Smith-a	3	6	9	14	20	25
2-6-($2.50): 2-Regular & Wesley Snipes photo-c						5.00

BLADE: VAMPIRE NATION
Marvel Comics: Jan, 2023 ($4.99, one-shot)

1-Russell-s/Wachter-a; Dracula app. 5.00

BLAIR WITCH CHRONICLES, THE
Oni Press: Mar, 2000 - No. 4, July, 2000 ($2.95, B&W, limited series)

1-4-Van Meter-s.1-Guy Davis-a. 2-Mireault-a 4.00
1-DF Alternate-c by John Estes 5.00
TPB (9/00, $15.95) r/#1-4 & Blair Witch Project one-shot 16.00

BLAIR WITCH: DARK TESTAMENTS
Image Comics: Oct, 2000 ($2.95, one-shot)

1-Edington-s/Adlard-a; story of murderer Rustin Parr	1	2	3	5	6	8

BLAIR WITCH PROJECT, THE (Movie companion, not adaptation)
Oni Press: July, 1999 ($2.95, B&W, one-shot)

1-(1st printing) History of the Blair Witch, art by Edwards, Mireault, and Davis; Van Meter-s; only the stick figure is red on the cover	2	4	6	9	12	15
1-(2nd printing) Stick figure and title lettering are red on cover						6.00
1-(3rd printing) Stick figure, title, and creator credits are red on cover						5.00
DF Glow in the Dark variant-c ($10.00)						10.00

BLASFAMOUS
DSTLRY: Feb, 2024 - Present ($8.99, oversized 10-7/8 x 8-1/2")

1-Mirka Andolfo-s/a 9.00

BLAST (Satire Magazine)
G & D Publications: Feb, 1971 - No. 2, May, 1971

1-Wrightson & Kaluta-a/Everette-c	8	16	24	51	96	140
2-Kaluta-c/a	5	10	15	35	63	90

BLAST CORPS
Dark Horse Comics: Oct, 1998 ($2.50, one-shot, based on Nintendo game)

1-Reprints from Nintendo Power magazine; Mahn-a 4.00

BLASTERS SPECIAL
DC Comics: 1989 ($2.00, one-shot)

1-Peter David scripts; Invasion spin-off 4.00

BLAST-OFF (Three Rocketeers)
Harvey Publications (Fun Day Funnies): Oct, 1965 (12¢)

1-Kirby/Williamson-a(2); Williamson/Crandall-a; Williamson/Torres/Krenkel-a; Kirby/Simon-c						
	7	14	21	44	82	120

BLAZE
Marvel Comics: Aug, 1994 - No. 12, July, 1995 ($1.95)

1-($2.95)-Foil embossed-c 5.00
2-12: 2-Man-Thing-c/story. 11,12-Punisher app. 4.00

BLAZE CARSON (Rex Hart #6 on)(See Kid Colt, Tex Taylor, Wild Western, Wisco)
Marvel Comics (USA): Sept, 1948 - No. 5, June, 1949

1-Tex Taylor app.; Shores-c	39	78	117	231	378	525
2,4,5: 2-Tex Morgan app.; Shores-c. 4-Two-Gun Kid app. 5-Tex Taylor app.						
	24	48	72	142	234	325
3-Used by N.Y. State Legis. Comm. (injury to eye splash); Tex Morgan app.						
	25	50	75	150	245	340

BLAZE: LEGACY OF BLOOD (See Ghost Rider & Ghost Rider/Blaze)
Marvel Comics (Midnight Sons imprint): Dec, 1993 - No. 4, Mar, 1994 ($1.75, limited series)

1-4 4.00

BLAZE OF GLORY
Marvel Comics: Feb, 2000 - No. 4, Mar, 2000 ($2.99, limited series)

1-4-Ostrander-s/Manco-a; Two-Gun Kid, Rawhide Kid, Red Wolf and Ghost Rider app. 4.00
TPB (7/02, $9.99) r/#1-4 10.00

BLAZE THE WONDER COLLIE (Formerly Molly Manton's Romances #1?)
Marvel Comics(SePI): No. 2, Oct, 1949 - No. 3, Feb, 1950 (Both have photo-c)

2(#1), 3-(Scarce)	34	68	102	199	325	450

BLAZING BATTLE TALES
Seaboard Periodicals (Atlas): July, 1975

1-Intro. Sgt. Hawk & the Sky Demon; Severin, McWilliams, Sparling-a; Nazi-c by Thorne						
	3	6	9	16	23	30

BLAZING COMBAT (Magazine)
Warren Publishing Co: Oct, 1965 - No. 4, July, 1966 (35¢, B&W)

1-Frazetta painted-c on all	50	100	150	400	900	1400
2	10	20	30	69	147	225
3,4: 4-Frazetta half pg. ad	10	20	30	64	132	200
nn-Anthology (reprints from No. 1-4) (low print)	10	20	30	64	132	200

Blade (2023 series) #1 © MAR

Blaze Carson #1 © MAR

Blondie Comics #155 © HARV

	GD	VG	FN	VF	VF/NM	NM-		GD	VG	FN	VF	VF/NM	NM-
	2.0	4.0	6.0	8.0	9.0	9.2		2.0	4.0	6.0	8.0	9.0	9.2

NOTE: **Adkins** a-4. **Colan** a-3,4,nn. **Crandall** a-all. **Evans** a-1,4. **Heath** a-4,nn. **Morrow** a-1-3,nn. **Orlando** a-1-3,nn. **J. Severin** a-all. **Torres** a-1-4. **Toth** a-all. **Williamson** a-2. and **Wood** a-3,4,nn.

BLAZING COMBAT: WORLD WAR I AND WORLD WAR II
Apple Press: Mar, 1994 ($3.75, B&W)

1,2: 1-r/Colan, Toth, Goodwin, Severin, Wood-a. 2-r/Crandall, Evans, Severin, Torres, Williamson-a						6.00

BLAZING COMICS (Also see Blue Circle Comics and Red Circle Comics)
Enwil Associates/Rural Home: 6/44 - #3, 9/44; #4, 2/45; #5, 3/45; #5(V2#2), 3/55 - #6(V2#3), 1955?

	GD	VG	FN	VF	VF/NM	NM-
1-The Green Turtle, Red Hawk, Black Buccaneer begin; origin Jun-Gal; classic Japanese WWII splash	90	180	270	576	988	1400
2-5: 2-Japanese WWII-c. 3-Briefer-a. 5-(V2#2 inside)	53	06	159	334	567	800
5(3/55, V2#2-inside)-Black Buccaneer-c, 6(V2#3-inside, 1955)-Indian/Japanese-c; cover is from Apr. 1945	30	60	90	177	289	400

NOTE: No. 5 & 6 contain remaindered comics rebound and the contents can vary. Cloak & Daggar, Will Rogers, Superman 64, Star Spangled 130, Kaanga known. Value would be half of contents.

BLAZING SIXGUNS
Avon Periodicals: Dec, 1952

1-Kinstler-c/a; Larsen/Alascia-a(2), Tuska?-a; Jesse James, Kit Carson, Wild Bill Hickok app.	47	94	141	296	498	700

BLAZING SIXGUNS
I.W./Super Comics: 1964

I.W. Reprint #1,8,9: 1-r/Wild Bill Hickok #26, Western True Crime #? & Blazing Sixguns #1 by Avon; Kinstler-c. 8-r/Blazing Western #?; Kinstler-c. 9-r/Blazing Western #1; Ditko-r; Kinstler-c reprinted from Dalton Boys #1

	3	6	9	14	20	25
Super Reprint #10,11,15-17: 10,11-r/The Rider #2,1. 15-r/Silver Kid Western #?. 16-r/Buffalo Bill #?; Wildey-r; Severin-a. 17(1964)-r/Western True Crime #?	3	6	9	14	20	25
12-Reprints Bullseye #3; S&K-a	4	8	12	23	37	50
18-r/Straight Arrow #? by Powell; Severin-c	3	6	9	14	20	25

BLAZING SIX-GUNS (Also see Sundance Kid)
Skywald Comics: Feb, 1971 - No. 2, Apr, 1971 (52 pgs.)

1-The Red Mask (3-D effect in story, not true 3-D), Sundance Kid begin (new-s), Avon's Geronimo reprint by Kinstler; Wyatt Earp app.	3	6	9	14	20	25
2-Wild Bill Hickok, Jesse James, Kit Carson-r plus M.E. Red Mask-r (3-D effect)	2	4	6	10	14	18

BLAZING WEST (The Hooded Horseman #21 on)(52 pgs.)
American Comics Group (B&I Publ./Michel Publ.): Fall, 1948 - No. 20, Nov-Dec, 1951

1-Origin & 1st app. Injun Jones, Tenderfoot & Buffalo Belle; Texas Tim & Ranger begins, ends #13	28	56	84	165	270	375
2,3 (1-2/49)	15	30	45	84	127	170
4-Origin & 1st app. Little Lobo; Starr-a (3-4/49)	14	28	42	82	121	160
5-10: 5-Starr-a	11	22	33	64	90	115
11-13	10	20	30	58	79	100
14(11-12/50)-Origin/1st app. The Hooded Horseman	17	34	51	98	154	210
15-20: 15,16,18,19-Starr-a	11	22	33	62	86	110

BLAZING WESTERN
Timor Publications: Jan, 1954 - No. 5, Sept, 1954

1-Ditko-a (1st Western-a?); text story by Bruce Hamilton	25	50	75	150	245	340
2-4	12	24	36	67	94	120
5-Disbrow-a; L.B. Cole-c	12	24	36	69	97	125

BLINDSIDE
Image Comics (Extreme Studios): Aug, 1996 ($2.50)

1-Variant-c exists						4.00

BLINK (See X-Men Age of Apocalypse storyline)
Marvel Comics: March, 2001 - No. 4, June, 2001 ($2.99, limited series)

1-4-Adam Kubert-c/Lobdell-s/Winick-script; leads into Exiles #1						3.00

BLIP
Marvel Comics Group: Feb, 1983 - 1983 (Video game mag. in comic format)

1-1st app. Donkey Kong & Mario Bros. in comics, 6pgs. comics; photo-c	10	20	30	69	147	225
2-Spider-Man photo-c; 6pgs. Spider-Man comics w/Green Goblin	4	8	12	25	40	55
3,4,6	2	4	6	9	12	15
5-E.T., Indiana Jones; Rocky-c	3	6	9	16	23	30
7-6pgs. Hulk comics; Pac-Man & Donkey Kong Jr. Hints	3	6	9	14	20	25

BLISS
Image Comics: Jul, 2020 - No. 8, Jun, 2021 ($3.99)

1-8-Sean Lewis-s/Caitlin Yarsky-a						4.00

BLISS ALLEY
Image Comics: July, 1997 - No. 2, Sept, 1997 ($2.95, B&W)

1,2-Messner-Loebs-s/a						4.00

BLITZKRIEG
National Periodical Publications: Jan-Feb, 1976 - No. 5, Sept-Oct, 1976

1-Kubert-c on all	5	10	15	33	57	80
2-5	3	6	9	17	25	34

BLOCKBUSTERS OF THE MARVEL UNIVERSE
Marvel Comics: March, 2011 ($4.99, one-shot)

1-Handbook-style summaries of Marvel crossover events like Civil War & Heroes Reborn						5.00

BLONDE PHANTOM (Formerly All-Select #1-11; Lovers #23 on)(Also see Blackstone, Marvel Mystery, Millie The Model #2, Sub-Mariner Comics #25 & Sun Girl)
Marvel Comics (MPC): No. 12, Winter, 1946-47 - No. 22, Mar, 1949

12-Miss America begins, ends #14	300	600	900	2010	3505	5000
13-Sub-Mariner begins (not in #16)	181	362	543	1158	1979	2800
14,15: 15-Kurtzman's "Hey Look"	168	336	504	1075	1838	2600
16-Captain America with Bucky story by Rico(p), 6 pgs.; Kurtzman's "Hey Look" (1 pg.)	206	412	618	1318	2259	3200
17-22: 22-Anti Wertham editorial	142	284	426	909	1555	2200

NOTE: Shores c-12-18.

BLONDIE (See Ace Comics, Comics Reading Libraries (Promotional Comics section), Dagwood, Daisy & Her Pups, Eat Right to Work…, King & Magic Comics)
David McKay Publications: 1942 - 1946

Feature Books 12 (Rare)	116	232	348	742	1271	1800
Feature Books 27-29,31,34(1940)	25	50	75	150	245	340
Feature Books 36,38,40,42,43,45,47	22	44	66	132	216	300
…1944 (Hard-c, 1938, B&W, 128 pgs.)-1944 daily strip-r	19	38	57	111	176	240

BLONDIE & DAGWOOD FAMILY
Harvey Publ. (King Features Synd.): Oct, 1963 - No. 4, Dec, 1965 (68 pgs.)

1	5	10	15	30	50	70
2-4	3	6	9	19	30	40

BLONDIE COMICS (…Monthly No. 16-141)
David McKay #1-15/Harvey #16-163/King #164-175/Charlton #177 on:
Spring, 1947 - No. 163, Nov, 1965; No. 164, Aug, 1966 - No. 175, Dec, 1967; No. 177, Feb, 1969 - No. 222, Nov, 1976

1	55	110	165	352	601	850
2	24	48	72	142	234	325
3-5	18	36	54	105	165	225
6-10	15	30	45	85	130	175
11-15	11	22	33	60	83	105
16-(3/50; 1st Harvey issue)	12	24	36	67	94	120
17-20: 20-(3/51)-Becomes Daisy & Her Pups #21 & Chamber of Chills #21	5	10	15	34	60	85
21-30	5	10	15	31	53	75
31-50	4	8	12	27	44	60
51-80	4	8	12	23	37	50
81-99	3	6	9	21	33	45
100	4	8	12	25	40	55
101-124,126-130	3	6	9	17	26	35
125 (80 pgs.)	4	8	12	27	44	60
131-136,138,139	3	6	9	16	24	32
137,140-(80 pgs.)	4	8	12	25	40	55
141-147,149-154,156,160,164-167	3	6	9	16	23	30
148,155,157-159,161-163 are 68 pgs.	3	6	9	21	33	45
168-175	2	4	6	11	16	20
177-199 (no #176)-Moon landing-c/s	2	4	6	9	13	16
200-Anniversary issue; highlights of the Bumsteads	2	4	6	10	14	18
201-210,213-222	2	4	6	8	10	12
211,212-1st & 2nd app. Super Dagwood	2	4	6	9	13	16
Blondie, Dagwood & Daisy by Chic Young #1(Harvey, 1953, 100 pg. squarebound giant) new stories; Popeye (1 pg.) and Felix (1pg.) app.	11	22	33	64	90	115

BLOOD
Marvel Comics (Epic Comics): Feb, 1988 - No. 4, Apr, 1988 ($3.25, mature)

1-4: DeMatteis scripts & Kent Williams-c/a						5.00

BLOOD AND GLORY (Punisher & Captain America)

	GD	VG	FN	VF	VF/NM	NM-
	2.0	4.0	6.0	8.0	9.0	9.2

Marvel Comics: Oct, 1992 - No. 3, Dec, 1992 ($5.95, limited series)

1-3: 1-Embossed wraparound-c by Janson; Chichester & Clarke-s ... 6.00

BLOOD & ROSES: FUTURE PAST TENSE (Bob Hickey's...)
Sky Comics: Dec, 1993 ($2.25)

1-Silver ink logo ... 4.00

BLOOD & ROSES: SEARCH FOR THE TIME-STONE (Bob Hickey's...)
Sky Comics: Apr, 1994 ($2.50)

1 ... 4.00

BLOOD AND SHADOWS
DC Comics (Vertigo): 1996 - Book 4, 1996 ($5.95, squarebound, mature)

Books 1-4: Joe R. Lansdale scripts; Mark A. Nelson-c/a. ... 6.00

BLOOD AND WATER
DC Comics (Vertigo): May, 2003 - No. 5, Sept, 2003 ($2.95, limited series)

1-5-Judd Winick-s/Tomm Coker-a/Brian Bolland-c ... 3.00
TPB (2009, $14.99) r/#1-5 ... 15.00

BLOOD: A TALE
DC Comics (Vertigo): Nov, 1996 - No. 4, Feb, 1997 ($2.95, limited series)

1-4: Reprints Epic series w/new-c; DeMatteis scripts; Kent Williams-c/a. ... 4.00
TPB (2004, $19.95) r/#1-4 ... 20.00

BLOODBATH
DC Comics: Early Dec, 1993 - No. 2, Late Dec, 1993 ($3.50, 68 pgs.)

1-Neon ink-c; Superman app.; new Batman-c /app. ... 4.00

2-Hitman 2nd app.	1	2	3	4	5	7

BLOOD BLISTER
AfterShock Comics: Jan, 2017 - No. 2, Apr, 2017 ($3.99)

1,2-Phil Hester-s/Tony Harris-a ... 4.00

BLOODBORNE (Based on the Sony computer game)
Titan Comics: Mar, 2018 - No. 16, Nov, 2019 ($3.99)

1-16-Ales Kot-s/Piotr Kowalski-a ... 4.00

BLOOD COMMANDMENT
Image Comics: Nov, 2023 - No. 4, Feb, 2024 ($3.99, limited series)

1-4-Szymon Kudranski-s/a ... 4.00

BLOODHOUND
DC Comics: Sept, 2004 - No. 10, June, 2005 ($2.95)

1-10: 1-Jolley-s/Kirk-a/Johnson-c. 5-Firestorm app. (cont. from Firestorm #7) ... 3.00

BLOODHOUND: CROWBAR MEDICINE
Dark Horse Comics: Oct, 2013 - No. 5, Mar, 2014 ($3.99)

1-5-Jolley-s/Kirk-a/c ... 4.00

BLOOD LEGACY
Image Comics (Top Cow): May, 2000 - No. 4, Nov, 2000; Apr, 2003 ($2.50/$4.99)

...: The Story of Ryan 1-4-Kerri Hawkins-s. 1-Andy Park-a(p); 3 covers ... 3.00
...: The Young Ones 1 (4/03, $4.99, one-shot) Basaldua-c/a ... 5.00
Preview Special ('00, $4.95) B&W flip-book w/The Magdalena Preview ... 5.00

BLOODLINE: DAUGHTER OF BLADE
Marvel Comics: Apr, 2023 - No. 5, Aug, 2023 ($3.99, limited series)

1-5-Danny Lore-s/Karen S. Darboe-a ... 4.00

BLOODLINES
DC Comics: Jun, 2016 - No. 6, Nov, 2016 ($2.99, limited series)

1-6: 1-Krul-s/Bivens-a ... 3.00

BLOODLINES: A TALE FROM THE HEART OF AFRICA (See Tales From the Heart of Africa)
Marvel Comics (Epic Comics): 1992 ($5.95, 52 pgs.)

1-Story cont'd from Tales From... ... 6.00

BLOOD OF DRACULA
Apple Comics: Nov, 1987 - No. 20?, 1990 ($1.75/$1.95, B&W)($2.25 #14,16 on)

1-3,5-14,20: 1-10-Chadwick-c ... 4.00

4,16-19-Lost Frankenstein pgs. by Wrightson	1	2	3	4	5	7

15-Contains stereo flexidisc ($3.75) ... 5.00

BLOOD OF THE DEMON (Etrigan the Demon)
DC Comics: May, 2005 - No. 17, Sept, 2006 ($2.50/$2.99)

1-14-Byrne(a)(p) & plot/Pfeifer-script. 3,4-Batman app. 13-One Year Later ... 3.00
15-17-($2.99) ... 3.00

BLOOD OF THE INNOCENT (See Warp Graphics Annual)
WaRP Graphics: 1/7/86 - No. 4, 1/28/86 (Weekly mini-series, mature)

1-4 ... 4.00

BLOODPACK
DC Comics: Mar, 1995 - No. 4, June, 1995 ($1.50, limited series)

1-4 ... 4.00

BLOODPOOL
Image Comics (Extreme): Aug, 1995 - No. 4, Nov, 1995 ($2.50, limited series)

1-4: Jo Duffy scripts in all ... 4.00
Special (3/96, $2.50)-Jo Duffy scripts ... 4.00
Trade Paperback (1996, $12.95)-r/#1-4 ... 13.00

BLOOD QUEEN, THE
Dynamite Entertainment: 2014 - No. 6, 2014 ($3.99, limited series)

1-6-Brownfield-s/Casas-a/Anacleto-c; variant covers on each ... 4.00
Annual 2014 ($7.99) Prequel stories to the series ... 8.00

BLOOD QUEEN VS. DRACULA
Dynamite Entertainment: 2015 - No. 4, 2015 ($3.99, limited series)

1-4-Brownfield-s/Baal-a/Anacleto-c; variant covers on each ... 4.00

BLOOD RED DRAGON (Stan Lee and Yoshiki...)
Image Comics: No. 0, Aug, 2011 - No. 3, Nov, 2011 ($3.99)

0-3-Goff-s/Soriano-a ... 4.00

BLOODSCENT
Comico: Oct, 1988 ($2.00, one-shot, Baxter paper)

1-Colan-p ... 4.00

BLOODSEED
Marvel Comics (Frontier Comics): Oct, 1993 - No. 2, Nov, 1993 ($1.95)

1,2: Sharp/Cam Smith-a ... 4.00

BLOODSHOT (See Eternal Warrior #4 & Rai #0)
Valiant/Acclaim Comics (Valiant): Feb, 1993 - No. 51, Aug, 1996 ($2.25/$2.50)

0-(3/94, $3.50)-Wraparound chromium-c by Quesada(p); origin ... 5.00
0-Gold variant; no cover price ... 40.00
Note: There is a "Platinum variant"; press run error of Gold ed. (25 copies exist)
(A CGC certified 9.4 copy sold for $1690 in 2017 and a 9.0 for $1200 in 2020)
1-($3.50)-Chromium embossed-c by B. Smith w/poster

	2	4	6	8	10	12

2-5,8-14: 3-$2.25-c begins; cont'd in Hard Corps #5. 4-Eternal Warrior-c/story. 5-Rai & Eternal Warrior app. 14-(3/94)-Reese-c(i) ... 4.00
6,7: 6-1st app. Ninjak (out of costume). 7-Ninjak in costume

	2	4	6	8	10	12

15(4/94)-50: 16-w/bound-in trading card ... 3.00

51-Bloodshot dies?	4	8	12	25	40	55

Yearbook 1 (1994, $3.95) ... 4.00
Special 1 (3/94, $5.95)-Zeck-a(p); Last Stand

	2	4	6	8	10	12

...: Blood of the Machine HC (2012, $24.99) r/#1-8; new 8 pg. story; intro. by VanHook ... 25.00

BLOODSHOT (Volume Two)
Acclaim Comics (Valiant): July, 1997 - No. 16, Oct, 1998 ($2.50)

1,2,4-14: 1-Two covers. 5-Copycat-c. X-O Manowar-c/app. ... 3.00

3-1st Chainsaw	2	4	6	8	10	12

15,16 ... 6.00

BLOODSHOT (Re-titled Bloodshot and H.A.R.D.Corps for #14-23)
Valiant Entertainment: July, 2012 - No. 25, Nov, 2014 ($3.99)

1-13: 1-Sweirczynski-s/Garcia & Lozzi-a. 10-13-Harbinger Wars tie-ins ... 4.00
1-9-Pullbox variants ... 4.00

1-Variant-c by David Aja	2	4	6	9	12	15
1-Variant-c by Esad Ribic	2	4	6	11	16	20

14-24: 14-23-Bloodshot and H.A.R.D.Corps ... 4.00
25-($4.99) Milligan-s/Larosa-a; back-up Chaykin-s/a; short features by various ... 5.00
#0 (8/13) Kindt-s/ChrisCross-a; covers by Lupacchino & Bullock ... 4.00
Bloodshot and H.A.R.D.Corps #0 (2/14, $3.99) History of Project Rising Spirit ... 4.00
Bloodshot's Day Off 1 (7/17, $3.99) Rahal-s/Evans-a; Viet Man app. ... 4.00

BLOODSHOT
Valiant Entertainment: Sept, 2019 - No. 12, Mar, 2021 ($3.99)

1-12: 1-Tim Seeley-s/Brett Booth-a; multiple covers on each ... 4.00
#0 (2/20, $3.99) Tim Seeley-s/Marc Laming-a; Bloodshot in Siberia; leads into issue #7 ... 4.00

BLOODSHOT REBORN
Valiant Entertainment: Apr, 2015 - No. 18, Oct, 2016 ($3.99)

1-18: 1-4-Lemire-s/Suayan-a. 1-1st app. Bloodsquirt. 6-9-Guice-a. 10-13-Set 30 years later. 14-1st app. Deathmate ... 4.00
#0 (3/17, $3.99) Lemire-s/Guedes-a ... 4.00
Annual 2016 #1 (3/16, $5.99) Short stories by various incl. Kano, Lemire, Bennett ... 6.00
...: Bloodshot Island - Director's Cut 1 (6/16, $4.99) r/#1 in B&W; original script ... 5.00

BLOODSHOT RISING SPIRIT
Valiant Entertainment: Nov, 2018 - No. 8, Jun, 2019 ($3.99)

1-8: 1-Grevioux-s/Lashley-a; Bloodshot prototype; bonus Livewire #12 preview ... 4.00

BLOODSHOT SALVATION
Valiant Entertainment: Sept, 2017 - No. 12, Aug, 2018 ($3.99)

1-12: 1-Lemire-s/LaRosa-a; bonus Ninjak #1 preview ... 4.00

BLOODSHOT UNLEASHED
Valiant Entertainment: Sept, 2022 - No. 4, Dec, 2022 ($3.99, limited series)

1-4: 1-Deniz Camp-s/Jon Davis-Hunt-a. 4-Zawadzki-a ... 4.00

BLOODSHOT U.S.A.
Valiant Entertainment: Oct, 2016 - No. 4, Jan, 2017 ($3.99, limited series)

1-4-Lemire-s/Braithwaite-a; Ninjak and Deathmate app. ... 4.00

BLOOD STAINED TEETH
Image Comics: Apr, 2022 - Present ($3.99)

1-10-Christian Ward-s/Patric Reynolds-a ... 4.00

BLOODSTONE
Marvel Comics: Dec, 2001 - No. 4, Mar, 2002 ($2.99)

1-Intro. Elsa Bloodstone; Abnett & Lanning-s/Lopez-a

	8	16	24	51	96	140
2,3	2	4	6	8	10	12
4-Last issue	3	6	9	19	30	40

BLOODSTRIKE (See Supreme V2#3) (Issue #25 published between #10 & #11)
Image Comics (Extreme Studios): 1993 - No. 22, May, 1995; No. 25, May, 1994 ($1.95/$2.50)

1-22, 25: Liefeld layouts in early issues. 1-Blood Brothers prelude. 2-1st app. Lethal. 5-1st app. Noble. 9-Black and White part 6 by Art Thibert; Liefeld pin-up. 9,10-Have coupon #3 & 7 for Extreme Prejudice #0. 10-(4/94). 11-(7/94). 16-Platt-c; Prophet app. 17-19-polybagged w/card. 25-(5/94)-Liefeld/Fraga-c ... 4.00
#0-(6/18, $3.99) Brutalists part 1; origin of the team; Michel Fiffe-s/a ... 4.00
#23,24-(6/18, $3.99) Brutalists parts 2&3; retroactively fills story gap between #22&25 ... 4.00
...: #1 Remastered Edition (11/17, $3.99) Two covers by Fraga & Liefeld ... 4.00
NOTE: *Giffen* story/layouts 4-6. *Jae Lee c*-7. *Rob Liefeld* layouts 1-3. *Art Thibert* c-6i.

BLOODSTRIKE
Image Comics: No. 26, Mar, 2012 - No. 33, Dec, 2012 ($2.99/$3.99)

26-29: 26-Two covers by Seeley & Liefeld; Seeley-s/Gaston-a ... 3.00
30-33-($3.99) 32,33-Suprema app. ... 4.00

BLOODSTRIKE (Volume 2)

Blood of the Demon #16 © DC

Bloodshot (2019 series) #11 © VAL

Blue Beetle (2006 series) #1 © DC

	GD 2.0	VG 4.0	FN 6.0	VF 8.0	VF/NM 9.0	NM- 9.2

Image Comics: Jul, 2015 - No. 2, Sept, 2015 ($2.99/$3.99)
1-($3.99) Liefeld-s/a — 4.00
2-(9/15, $2.99) Liefeld-s/a — 3.00

BLOODSTRIKE ASSASSIN
Image Comics (Extreme Studios): June, 1995 - No. 3, Aug, 1995; No. 0, Oct, 1995 ($2.50, limited series)
0-3: 3-(8/95)-Quesada-c. 0-(10/95)-Battlestone app. — 4.00

BLOOD SWORD, THE
Jademan Comics: Aug, 1988 - No. 53, Dec, 1992 ($1.50/$1.95, 68 pgs.)
1-53-Kung Fu stories in all — 4.00

BLOOD SWORD DYNASTY
Jademan Comics: 1989 - No. 41, Jan, 1993 ($1.25, 36 pgs.)
1-Ties into Blood Sword — 5.00
2-41: Ties into Blood Sword — 4.00

BLOOD SYNDICATE
DC Comics (Milestone): Apr, 1993 - No. 35, Feb, 1996 ($1.50-$3.50)

	GD	VG	FN	VF	VF/NM	NM-
1-($2.95)-Collector's Edition; polybagged with poster, trading card, & acid-free backing board (direct sale only)	1	3	4	6	8	10

1-9,11-24,26,27,29,33: 8-Intro Kwai. 15-Byrne-c. 16-Worlds Collide Pt. 6; Superman-c/app.
17-Worlds Collide Pt. 13. 29-(99c); Long Hot Summer x-over — 4.00

	GD	VG	FN	VF	VF/NM	NM-
10-Shadow War, Milestone's 1st x-over, continues from Xombi #0; Simonson-c	1	2	3	5	6	8
25-($2.95, 52 pgs.)						5.00
28,30-32: 30-Long Hot Summer x-over						4.00
34	3	6	9	16	23	30
35-Kwai disappears; last issue	4	8	12	27	44	60

BLOOD SYNDICATE: SEASON ONE
DC Comics (Milestone): Jul, 2022 - No. 6, Jan, 2023 ($3.99, limited series)
1-6: 1-4-Geoffrey Thorne-s/Chriscross-a — 4.00

BLOODWULF
Image Comics (Extreme): Feb, 1995 - No. 4, May, 1995 ($2.50, limited series)
1-4: 1-Liefeld-c w/4 different captions & alternate-c. — 4.00
Summer Special (8/95, $2.50)-Jeff Johnson-c/a; Supreme app; story takes place between Legend of Supreme #3 & Supreme #23. — 4.00

BLOODY MARY
DC Comics (Helix): Oct, 1996 - No. 4, Jan, 1997 ($2.25, limited series)
1-4: Garth Ennis scripts; Ezquerra-c/a in all — 4.00
TPB (2005, $19.99) r/#1-4 and Bloody Mary: Lady Liberty #1-4 — 20.00

BLOODY MARY: LADY LIBERTY
DC Comics (Helix): Sept, 1997 - No. 4, Dec, 1997 ($2.50, limited series)
1-4: Garth Ennis scripts; Ezquerra-c/a in all — 4.00

BLOSSOMS: 666 (Archie Comics' Cheryl & Jason Blossom Satanic Horror)
Archie Comic Publications: Mar, 2019 - No. 5, Sept, 2019 ($3.99, limited series)
1-5-Cullen Bunn-s/Laura Braga-a; multiple covers. 2-Intro. Julian Blossom — 4.00

BLUE
Image Comics (Action Toys): Aug, 1999 - No. 2, Apr, 2000 ($2.50)
1,2-Aronowitz-s/Struzan-c — 4.00

BLUE & GOLD (Blue Beetle and Booster Gold)
DC Comics: Sept, 2021 - No. 8, Jun, 2022 ($3.99, limited series)
1-8: 1-Jurgens-s/Sook-a. 1,2-Justice League app. 4-Flashback pages with Maguire-a — 4.00

BLUEBEARD
Slave Labor Graphics: Nov, 1993 - No. 3, Mar, 1994 ($2.95, B&W, lim. series)
1-3: James Robinson scripts. 2-(12/93) — 4.00
Trade paperback (6/94, $9.95) — 13.00
Trade paperback (2nd printing, 7/96, $12.95)-New-c — 13.00

BLUE BEETLE, THE (Also see All Top, Big-3, Mystery Men & Weekly Comic Magazine)
Fox Publ. No. 1-11, 31-60; Holyoke 12-30: Winter, 1939-40 - No. 57, 7/48; No. 58, 4/50 - No. 60, 8/50

	GD	VG	FN	VF	VF/NM	NM-
1-Reprints from Mystery Men #1-5; Blue Beetle origin; Yarko the Great-r/from Wonder Comics /Wonderworld #2-5 all by Eisner; Master Magician app.; (Blue Beetle in 4 different costumes)	1000	2000	3000	7600	13,800	20,000
2-K-51-r by Powell/Wonderworld #8,9	300	600	900	1980	3440	4900
3-Simon-c	232	464	696	1485	2543	3600
4-Marijuana drug mention story	181	362	543	1158	1979	2800
5-Zanzibar The Magician by Tuska	129	258	387	826	1413	2000
6-Dynamite Thor begins (1st); origin Blue Beetle	123	246	369	787	1344	1900

	GD	VG	FN	VF	VF/NM	NM-
7,8-Dynamo app. in both. 8-Last Thor	119	238	357	762	1306	1850
9-12: 9,10-The Blackbird & The Gorilla app. 10-Bondage/hypo-c. 11(2/42)-Bondage-c; The Gladiator app. 12(6/42)-The Black Fury app.	103	206	309	659	1130	1600
13-V-Man begins (1st app.), ends #19; Kubert-a; centerfold spread	142	284	426	909	1555	2200
14,15-Kubert-a in both. 14-Intro. side-kick (c/text only), Sparky (called Spunky #17-19); BB vs. The Red Robe (Red Skull swipe)	100	200	300	635	1093	1550
16-18: 17-Brodsky-c	74	148	222	470	810	1150
19-Kubert-a	81	162	243	518	884	1250
20-Origin/1st app. Tiger Squadron; Arabian Nights begin	87	174	261	553	952	1350
21-26: 24-Intro. & only app. The Halo. 26-General Patton story & photo	61	122	183	390	670	950
27-Tamaa, Jungle Prince app.	58	116	174	371	636	900
28-30(2/44): 29-WWII Nazi bondage-c(1/44)	53	106	159	334	567	800
31(6/44), 33,34,36-40: 34-38-"The Threat from Saturn" serial. 40-Shows #20 in indicia	42	84	126	265	445	625
32-Hitler-c	155	310	465	992	1696	2400
35-Extreme violence	53	106	159	334	567	800
41-45 (#43 exist?)	41	82	123	256	428	600
46-The Puppeteer app.	55	110	165	352	601	850
47-Kamen & Baker-a begin	226	452	678	1446	2473	3500
48-50	155	310	465	992	1696	2400
51,53	135	270	405	864	1482	2100
52-Kamen bondage-c; true crime stories begin	290	580	870	1856	3178	4500
54-Used in SOTI. Illo. "Children call these 'headlights' comics"; classic-c	1000	2000	3000	7600	13,800	20,000
55-57: 56-Used in SOTI, pg. 145. 57(7/48)-Last Kamen issue; becomes Western Killers-c	129	258	387	826	1413	2000
58(4/50)-60-No Kamen-a	39	78	117	240	395	550

NOTE: *Kamen* a-47-51, 53, 55-57; c-47, 49-52. *Powell* a-4(2). *Bondage*-c 9-12, 46, 52. *Headlight*-c 46, 48, 57.

BLUE BEETLE (Formerly The Thing; becomes Mr. Muscles No. 22 on) (See Charlton Bullseye & Space Adventures)
Charlton Comics: No. 18, Feb, 1955 - No. 21, Aug, 1955

	GD	VG	FN	VF	VF/NM	NM-
18,19-(Pre-1944)-r. 18-Last pre-code issue. 19-Bouncer, Rocket Kelly-r	50	100	150	315	533	750
20-Joan Mason by Kamen	52	104	156	328	552	775
21-New material	41	82	123	256	428	600

BLUE BEETLE (Unusual Tales #1-49; Ghostly Tales #55 on)(See Captain Atom #83 & Charlton Bullseye)
Charlton Comics: V2#1, June, 1964 - V2#5, Mar-Apr, 1965; V3#50, July, 1965 - V3#54, Feb-Mar, 1966; #1, June, 1967 - #5, Nov, 1968

	GD	VG	FN	VF	VF/NM	NM-
V2#1-Origin/1st S.A. app. Dan Garrett-Blue Beetle	32	64	96	230	515	800
2-5: 5-Weiss illo; 1st published-a?	8	16	24	55	105	155
V3#50-54-Formerly Unusual Tales	8	16	24	51	96	140
1(1967)-Question series begins by Ditko	30	60	90	216	483	750
2-Origin Ted Kord-Blue Beetle (see Capt. Atom #83 for 1st Ted Kord Blue Beetle); Dan Garrett x-over	11	22	33	73	157	240
3-5 (All Ditko-c/a in 1-5)	7	14	21	44	82	120
1 (Modern Comics-1977)-Reprints	4	8	12	27	44	60
3 (Modern Comics-1977)-Reprints	2	4	6	10	14	18

NOTE: *#6 only appeared in the fanzine 'The Charlton Portfolio'.*

BLUE BEETLE (Also see Americomics, Crisis On Infinite Earths, Justice League & Showcase '94 #2-4)
DC Comics: June, 1986 - No. 24, May, 1988

	GD	VG	FN	VF	VF/NM	NM-
1-Origin retold; intro. Firefist.	3	6	9	16	23	30
2-10,15-19,21-24: 2-Origin Firefist. 5-7-The Question app. 21-Millennium tie-in						4.00
11-14,20: 11-14-New Teen Titans app. 20-Justice League app.; Millennium tie-in						4.00

BLUE BEETLE (See Infinite Crisis, Teen Titans, and Booster Gold #21)
DC Comics: May, 2006 - No. 36, Apr, 2009 ($2.99)

	GD	VG	FN	VF	VF/NM	NM-
1-Hamner-a/Giffen & Rogers-s; Guy Gardner app.	1	2	3	5	6	8
1-2nd & 3rd printings						3.00
1-Special Edition (9/23, $3.99) Reprints #1						4.00

2-36: 2-Intro Peacemaker. 4-Oracle app. 5-Phantom Stranger app. 16-Eclipso app. 18,33-Teen Titans app. 20-Sinestro Corps. 21-Spectre app. 26-Spanish issue — 3.00
...: Black and Blue TPB (2010, $17.99) r/#27,28,35,36 & Booster Gold #21-25,28,29 — 18.00
...: Boundaries TPB (2009, $14.99) r/#29-34 — 15.00
...: End Game TPB (2008, $14.99) r/#20-26; English script for #26 — 15.00
...: Reach For the Stars TPB (2008, $14.99) r/#13-19 — 15.00
...: Road Trip TPB (2007, $12.99) r/#7-12 — 13.00
...: Shellshocked TPB (2006, $12.99) r/#1-6 — 13.00

BLUE BEETLE (DC New 52) (Also see Threshold)
DC Comics: Nov, 2011 - No. 16, Mar, 2013 ($2.99)

	GD 2.0	VG 4.0	FN 6.0	VF 8.0	VF/NM 9.0	NM- 9.2

1-16: 1-Bedard-s/Ig Guara-a; new origin. 9-Green Lantern (Kyle) app. 11-Booster Gold 3.00
#0 (11/12, $2.99) Origin of the scarab 3.00

BLUE BEETLE (DC Rebirth)
DC Comics: Nov, 2016 - No. 18, Apr, 2018 ($2.99/$3.99)
1-7-Giffen-s/Kolins-a. 4-7-Doctor Fate app. 3.00
8-18-($3.99) 8-11-Doctor Fate, Arion and OMAC app. 12-Batman app. 4.00
...: Rebirth 1 (10/16, $2.99) Giffen-s/Kolins-a; Ted Kord & Doctor Fate app. 3.00

BLUE BEETLE (Dawn of DC)
DC Comics: Nov, 2023 - Present ($3.99)
1-7: 1-Trujillo-s/Gutierrez-a; Ted Kord app. 4.00

BLUE BEETLE: GRADUATION DAY (Jaime Reyes)
DC Comics: Jan, 2023 - No. 6, Jun, 2023 ($3.99)
1-6-Trujillo-s/Gutierrez-a; intro. Dynastes. 2-4-Ted Kord app. 3-Starfire app. 4.00

BLUEBERRY (See Lt. Blueberry & Marshal Blueberry)
Marvel Comics (Epic Comics): 1989 - No. 5, 1990 ($12.95/$14.95, graphic novel)

	GD 2.0	VG 4.0	FN 6.0	VF 8.0	VF/NM 9.0	NM- 9.2
1-($12.95) Moebius-a	5	10	15	31	53	75
2-5: 2-($14.95). 3,4,5-($12.95)-Moebius-a in all	3	6	9	19	30	40

BLUE BOLT
Funnies, Inc. No. 1/Novelty Press/Premium Group of Comics: June, 1940 - No. 101 (V10#2), Sept-Oct, 1949

	GD 2.0	VG 4.0	FN 6.0	VF 8.0	VF/NM 9.0	NM- 9.2
V1#1-Origin Blue Bolt by Joe Simon, Sub-Zero Man, White Rider & Super Horse, Dick Cole, Wonder Boy & Sgt. Spook (1st app. of each)	423	846	1269	3088	5444	7800
2-Simon & Kirby's 1st art & 1st super-hero (Blue Bolt)	300	600	900	2010	3505	5000
3-1 pg. Space Hawk by Wolverton; 2nd S&K-a on Blue Bolt (same cover date as Red Raven #1); Simon-c	284	568	852	1818	3109	4400
4-S&K-a; classic Everett shark-c	290	580	870	1856	3178	4500
5-S&K-a; Everett-a begins on Sub-Zero; 1st time S&K names app. in a comic	226	452	678	1446	2473	3500
6,8-10-S&K-a	187	374	561	1197	2049	2900
7-Classic S&K-c/a (scarce)	271	542	813	1734	2967	4200
11-Classic Everett Giant Robot-c (scarce)	232	464	696	1485	2543	3600
12-Nazi submarine-c	206	412	618	1318	2259	3200
V2#1-Origin Dick Cole & The Twister; Twister x-over in Dick Cole, Sub-Zero, Blue Bolt; origin Simba Karno who battles Dick Cole thru V2#5 & becomes main supporting character V2#6 on; battle-c	61	122	183	390	670	950
2-Origin The Twister retold in text	48	96	144	302	514	725
3-5: 5-Intro. Freezum	39	78	117	240	395	550
6-Origin Sgt. Spook retold	40	80	120	246	411	575
7-12: 7-Lois Blake becomes Blue Bolt's costume aide; last Twister. 12-Text-sty by Mickey Spillane	32	64	96	188	307	425
V3#1-3	26	52	78	154	252	350
4-12: 4-Blue Bolt abandons costume	22	44	66	128	209	290
V4#1-Hitler, Tojo, Mussolini-c	155	310	465	992	1696	2400
V4#2-Liberty Bell-c	22	44	66	128	209	290
V4#3-12: 3-Shows V4#3 inside (9-10/43). 5-Infinity-c. 8-Last Sub-Zero	18	36	54	107	169	230
V5#1-8, V6#1-3,5,7,9,10, V7#1-12	15	30	45	90	140	190
V6#4-Racist cover	53	106	159	334	567	800
V6#6-Cross-dressing, hooded-c	58	116	164	362	619	900
V6#8-Girl fight-c	22	44	66	132	216	300
V8#1-6,8-12, V9#1-4,7,8, V10#1(#100),V10#2(#101)-Last Dick Cole, Blue Bolt	14	28	42	81	118	155
V8#7,V9#6,9-L. B. Cole-a	28	56	84	165	270	375
V9#5-Classic fish in the face-c	53	106	159	334	567	800

NOTE: **Everett** c-V1#4, 11, V2#1, 2. **Gustavson** a-V1#1-12, V2#1-7. **Kiefer** c-V3#1. **Rico** a-V6#10, V7#4. Blue Bolt not in V9#8.

BLUE BOLT (Becomes Ghostly Weird Stories #120 on; continuation of Novelty Blue Bolt) (...Weird Tales of Terror #111,112,...Weird Tales #113-119)
Star Publications: No. 102, Nov-Dec, 1949 - No. 119, May-June, 1953

	GD 2.0	VG 4.0	FN 6.0	VF 8.0	VF/NM 9.0	NM- 9.2
102-The Chameleon, & Target app.	55	110	165	352	601	850
103,104-The Chameleon app. 104-Last Target	47	94	141	296	498	700
105-Origin Blue Bolt (from #1) retold by Simon; Chameleon & Target app.; opium den story	865	1730	2595	6315	11,158	16,000
106-Blue Bolt by S&K begins; Spacehawk reprints from Target by Wolverton begin, ends #110; Sub-Zero begins; ends #109	258	516	774	1651	2824	4000
107-110: 108-Last S&K Blue Bolt reprint. 109-Wolverton-c(r)/inside Spacehawk splash.						
110-Target app.	103	206	309	659	1130	1600
111,112: 111-Red Rocket & The Mask-r; last Blue Bolt; 1pg. L. B. Cole-a; classic-c						
112-Last Torpedo Man app.	290	580	870	1856	3178	4500
113-Wolverton's Spacehawk-r/Target V3#7	206	412	618	1318	2259	3200
114,116: 116-Jungle Jo-r	168	336	504	1075	1838	2600
115-Classic-c; Sgt. Spook app.	423	846	1269	3000	5250	7500
117-Jo-Jo & Blue Bolt-r; Hollingsworth-a	187	374	561	1197	2049	2900
118-"White Spirit" by Wood	174	348	522	1114	1907	2700
119-Disbrow/Cole-c; Jungle Jo-r	206	412	618	1318	2259	3200
Accepted Reprint #103(1957?, nd)	17	34	51	100	158	215

NOTE: **L. B. Cole** c-102-108, 110 on. **Disbrow** a-112(2), 113(3), 114(2), 115(2), 116-118. **Hollingsworth** a-117. **Palais** a-112r. Sci/Fi c-105-110. Horror c-111.

BLUE BOOK
Dark Horse Comics: Feb, 2023 - No. 5, Jun, 2023 ($4.99, B&W& blue)
1-5-Tynion IV-s/Oeming-a; retells 1961 UFO encounter by Betty & Barney Hill 5.00

BLUE BOOK: 1947
Dark Horse Comics: Feb, 2024 - Present ($4.99, B&W& blue)
1-Tynion IV-s/Oeming-a; retells 1947 UFO encounter by Kenneth Arnold 5.00

BLUE BULLETEER, THE (Also see Femforce Special)
AC Comics: 1989 ($2.25, B&W, one-shot)
1-Origin by Bill Black; Bill Ward-a 4.00

BLUE BULLETEER (Also see Femforce Special)
AC Comics: 1996 ($5.95, B&W, one-shot)
1-Photo-c 6.00

BLUE CIRCLE COMICS (Also see Red Circle Comics, Blazing Comics & Roly Poly Comic Book)
Enwil Associates/Rural Home: June, 1944 - No. 6, Apr, 1945

	GD 2.0	VG 4.0	FN 6.0	VF 8.0	VF/NM 9.0	NM- 9.2
1-The Blue Circle begins (1st app.); origin & 1st app. Steel Fist	50	100	150	315	533	750
2	28	56	84	168	274	380
3-Hitler parody-c	300	600	900	2010	3505	5000
4-6: 5-Last Steel Fist.	24	48	72	144	237	330
6-(Dated 4/45, Vol. 2#3 inside)-Leftover covers to #6 were later restapled over early 1950's coverless comics; variations of the coverless comics exist. Colossal Features known.	55	110	165	352	601	850

BLUE DEVIL (See Fury of Firestorm #24, Underworld Unleashed, Starman (2nd) #38, Infinite Crisis and Shadowpact)
DC Comics: June, 1984 - No. 31, Dec, 1986 (75¢/$1.25)
1 .... 5.00
2-16,19-31: 4-Origin Nebiros. 7-Gil Kane-a. 8-Giffen-a 4.00
17,18-Crisis x-over 5.00
Annual 1 (11/85)-Team-ups w/Black Orchid, Creeper, Demon, Madame Xanadu, Man-Bat & Phantom Stranger 5.00

BLUE MONDAY: ... (one-shots)
Oni Press: Feb, 2002 - Dec, 2008 (B&W, Chynna Clugston-Major-s/a/c in all)
Dead Man's Party (10/02, $2.95) Dan Brereton painted back-c 3.00
Inbetween Days (9/03, $9.95, 8" x 5-1/2") r/Dead Man's Party, Lovecats, & Nobody's Fool 10.00
Lovecats (2/02, $2.95) Valentine's Day themed 3.00
Nobody's Fool (2/03, $2.95) April Fool's Day themed 3.00
Thieves Like Us (12/08, $3.50) Part 1 of an unfinished 5-part series 3.50

BLUE MONDAY: ABSOLUTE BEGINNERS
Oni Press: Feb, 2001 - No. 4, Sept, 2001 ($2.95, B&W, limited series)
1-4-Chynna Clugston-Major-s/a/c 3.00
TPB (12/01, $11.95, 8" x 6") r/series 12.00

BLUE MONDAY: PAINTED MOON
Oni Press: Feb, 2004 - No. 4, Mar, 2005 ($2.99, B&W, limited series)
1-4-Chynna Clugston-Major-s/a/c 3.00
TPB (4/05, $11.95, digest-sized) r/series; sketch pages 12.00

BLUE MONDAY: THE KIDS ARE ALRIGHT
Oni Press: Feb, 2000 - No. 3, May, 2000 ($2.95, B&W, limited series)
1-3-Chynna Clugston-Major-s/a/c. 1-Variant-c by Warren. 2-Dorkin-c 3.00
3-Variant cover by J. Scott Campbell 4.00
TPB (12/00, $10.95, digest-sized) r/#1-3 & earlier short stories 11.00

BLUE PHANTOM, THE
Dell Publishing Co.: June-Aug, 1962

	GD 2.0	VG 4.0	FN 6.0	VF 8.0	VF/NM 9.0	NM- 9.2
1(01-066-208)-by Fred Fredericks	4	8	12	23	37	50

BLUE RIBBON COMICS (...Mystery Comics No. 9-18)
MLJ Magazines: Nov, 1939 - No. 22, Mar, 1942 (18 MLJ series)

	GD 2.0	VG 4.0	FN 6.0	VF 8.0	VF/NM 9.0	NM- 9.2
1-Dan Hastings, Richy the Amazing Boy, Rang-A-Tang the Wonder Dog begin (1st app. of each); Little Nemo app. (not by W. McCay); Jack Cole-a(3) (1st MLJ comic)	300	600	900	2070	3635	5200
2-Bob Phantom, Silver Fox (both in #3), Rang-A-Tang Club & Cpl. Collins begin (1st app. of each); Jack Cole-a	245	490	735	1568	2684	3800
3-J. Cole-a	110	220	330	704	1202	1700
4-Doc Strong, The Green Falcon, & Hercules begin (1st app. each); origin & 1st app. The Fox & Ty-Gor, Son of the Tiger	123	246	369	787	1344	1900
5-8: 8-Last Hercules; 6,7-Biro, Meskin-a. 7-Fox app on-c	97	194	291	621	1061	1500
9-(Scarce)-Origin & 1st app. Mr. Justice (2/41)	411	822	1233	5039	5039	7200
10-13: 12-Last Doc Strong. 13-Inferno, the Flame Breather begins, ends #19; Devil-c	174	348	522	1114	1907	2700
14,15,18: 15-Last Green Falcon	161	322	483	1030	1765	2500
16-Origin & 1st app. Captain Flag (9/41)	258	516	774	1651	2826	4000
17-Bondage-c	290	580	870	1856	3178	4500
19,20,22: 20-Last Ty-Gor. 22-Origin Mr. Justice retold	135	270	405	864	1482	2100
21-Classic Black Hood-c	541	1082	1623	3950	6975	10,000

NOTE: **Biro** c-3-5, a-2 (Cpl. Collins & Scoop Cody). **S. Cooper** c-9-17. 20-22 contain "Tales From the Witch's Cauldron" (same strip as "Stories of the Black Witch" in Zip Comics). **Meskin** a-c. **McWilliams** a-8. Captain Flag c-16-18 (w/ Mr. Justice), 19-22.

BLUE RIBBON COMICS (Becomes Teen-Age Diary Secrets #4)
(Also see Approved Comics, Blue Ribbon Comics and Heckle & Jeckle)
Blue Ribbon (St. John): Feb, 1949 - No. 6, Aug, 1949

	GD 2.0	VG 4.0	FN 6.0	VF 8.0	VF/NM 9.0	NM- 9.2
1-Heckle & Jeckle (Terrytoons)	20	40	60	117	189	260
2(4/49)-Diary Secrets; Baker-c	90	180	270	576	988	1400
3-Heckle & Jeckle (Terrytoons)	14	28	42	78	112	145
4(6/49)-Diary Secrets; Baker c/a(2)	129	258	387	826	1413	2000
5(8/49)-Teen-Age Diary Secrets; Oversize; photo-c; Baker-a(2)- Continues as Teen-Age Diary Secrets	123	246	369	787	1344	1900
6-Dinky Duck(8/49)(Terrytoons)	9	18	27	52	69	85

BLUE RIBBON COMICS
Red Circle Prod./Archie Ent. No. 5 on: Nov, 1983 - No. 14, Dec, 1984

	GD 2.0	VG 4.0	FN 6.0	VF 8.0	VF/NM 9.0	NM- 9.2
1-S&K-r/Advs. of the Fly #1,2; Williamson/Torres-r/Fly #2; Ditko-c	1	2	3	6	8	10
2-7,9,10: 3-Origin Steel Sterling. 5-S&K Shield-r; new Kirby-c. 6,7-The Fox app.	1	2	3	5	6	8
8-Toth centerspread; Black Hood app.; Neal Adams-a(r)	1	2	3	6	8	10
11,13,14: 11-Black Hood. 13-Thunder Bunny. 14-Web & Jaguar	1	2	3	4	6	8
12-Thunder Agents; Noman new Ditko-a	1	3	4	6	8	10

NOTE: **N. Adams** a(r)-8. **Buckler** a-4i. **Nino** a-2i. **McWilliams** a-8. **Morrow** a-8.

BLUE STREAK (See Holyoke One-Shot No. 8)

BLUNTMAN AND CHRONIC TPB (Also see Jay and Silent Bob, Clerks, and Oni Double Feature)
Image Comics: Dec, 2001 ($14.95, TPB)

Blueberry #1 © MAR

Bob's Burgers #1 © 20Fox

Bob Steele Western #7 © FAW

	GD 2.0	VG 4.0	FN 6.0	VF 8.0	VF/NM 9.0	NM- 9.2

nn-Tie-in for "Jay & Silent Bob Strike Back" movie; new Kevin Smith-s/Michael Oeming-a; r/app. from Oni Double Feature #12 in color; Ben Affleck & Jason Lee afterwords 15.00

BLYTHE (Marge's)
Dell Publishing Co.: No. 1072, Jan-Mar, 1960

Four Color 1072	5	10	15	34	60	85

B-MAN (See Double-Dare Adventures)

BO (Tom Cat #4 on) (Also see Big Shot #29 & Dixie Dugan)
Charlton Comics Group: June, 1955 - No. 3, Oct, 1955 (A dog)

1-3: Newspaper reprints by Frank Beck; Noodnik the Eskimo app.	8	16	24	44	57	70

BOATNIKS, THE (See Walt Disney Showcase No. 1)

BOB BURDEN'S ORIGINAL MYSTERYMEN PRESENTS
Dark Horse Comics: 1999 - No. 4 ($2.95/$3.50)

1-3-Bob Burden-s/Sadowski-a(p)						3.50
4-($3.50) All Villain issue						3.50

BOBBY BENSON'S B-BAR-B RIDERS (Radio) (See Best of The West, The Lemonade Kid & Model Fun)
Magazine Enterprises/AC Comics: May-June, 1950 - No. 20, May-June, 1953

1-The Lemonade Kid begins; Powell-a (Scarce)	47	94	141	296	498	700
2	19	38	57	111	176	240
3-5: 4,5-Lemonade Kid-c (#4-Spider-c)	14	28	42	81	118	155
6-8,10	14	28	42	78	112	145
9,11,13-Frazetta-c; Ghost Rider in #13-15 by Ayers-a. 13-Ghost Rider-c	45	90	135	284	480	675
12,17-20: 20-(A-1 #88)	13	26	39	72	101	130
14-Decapitation/Bondage-c & story; classic horror-c	58	116	174	371	636	900
15-Ghost Rider-c	32	64	96	188	307	425
16-Photo-c	15	30	45	83	124	165
1 (1990, $2.75, B&W)-Reprints; photo-c & inside covers						5.00

NOTE: Ayers a-13-15, 20. Powell a-1-12(4 ea.), 13(3), 14-16(Red Hawk only); c-1-8,1 0, 12. Lemonade Kid in most 1-13.

BOBBY COMICS
Universal Phoenix Features: May, 1946

1-By S. M. Iger	17	34	51	100	158	215

BOBBY SHERMAN (TV)
Charlton Comics: Feb, 1972 - No. 7, Oct, 1972

1-Based on TV show "Getting Together"	5	10	15	33	57	80
2-7: Photo-c on all. 7-Bobby Sherman for President	4	8	12	23	37	50

BOB COLT (See XMas Comics)
Fawcett Publications: Nov, 1950 - No. 10, May, 1952

1-Bob Colt, his horse Buckskin & sidekick Pablo begin; photo front/back-c begin	27	54	81	162	266	370
2	14	28	42	82	121	160
3-5	13	26	39	72	101	130
6-Flying Saucer story	11	22	33	62	86	110
7-10: 9-Last photo back-c	9	18	27	52	69	85

BOB HOPE (See Adventures of... & Calling All Boys #12)

BOB MARLEY, TALE OF THE TUFF GONG (Music star)
Marvel Comics: Aug, 1994 - No, 3, Nov, 1994 ($5.95, limited series)

1-3						6.00

BOB PHANTOM
Archie Comic Publications: Jan, 2023 ($3.99, one-shot)

1-Re-imagining of the 1939 hero; James III-s/Richard Ortiz & Juan Bobillo-a						4.00

BOB POWELL'S TIMELESS TALES
Eclipse Comics: March, 1989 ($2.00, B&W)

1-Powell-r/Black Cat #5 (Scarlet Arrow), 9 & Race for the Moon #1						4.00

BOB'S BURGERS (TV)
Dynamite Entertainment: 2014 - No. 5, 2014 ($3.99)

1-Short stories by various; multiple covers	3	6	9	15	22	28
2-5-Short stories by various						6.00

BOB'S BURGERS (Volume 2)(TV)
Dynamite Entertainment: 2015 - No. 16, 2016 ($3.99)

1-Short stories by various; multiple covers	2	4	6	8	10	12
2-16-Short stories by various; multiple covers on all						4.00
... Free Comic Book Day 2015 (giveaway) Reprints various short stories from Vol. 1						3.00
... Free Comic Book Day 2016 (giveaway) Reprints various short stories						3.00

... Free Comic Book Day 2018 (giveaway) Reprints various short stories 3.00
... Free Comic Book Day 2019 (giveaway) Reprints various short stories 3.00

BOB SCULLY, THE TWO-FISTED HICK DETECTIVE (Also see Advs. of Detective Ace King and Detective Dan)
Humor Publ. Co.: No date (1933) (36 pgs., 9-1/2x11", B&W, paper-c; 10¢-c)

nn-By Howard Dell; not reprints; along with Advs. of Detective Ace King and Detective Dan, the first comic w/original art & the first of a single theme; has a blue 2-tone cover	725	1450	2175	5800	--	--

BOB SON OF BATTLE
Dell Publishing Co.: No. 729, Nov, 1956

Four Color 729	5	10	15	30	50	70

BOB STEELE WESTERN (Movie star)
Fawcett Publications/AC Comics: Dec, 1950 - No. 10, June, 1952; 1990

1-Bob Steele & his horse Bullet begin; photo front/back-c begin	37	74	111	222	361	500
2	19	38	57	109	172	235
3-5: 4-Last photo back-c	14	28	42	82	121	160
6-10: 10-Last photo-c	13	26	39	72	101	130
1 (1990, $2.75, B&W)-Bob Steele & Rocky Lane reprints; photo-c & inside covers						4.00

BOB SWIFT (Boy Sportsman)
Fawcett Publications: May, 1951 - No. 5, Jan, 1952

1	12	24	36	67	94	120
2-5: Saunders painted-c #1-5	7	14	21	35	43	50

BOB, THE GALACTIC BUM
DC Comics: Feb, 1995 - No. 4, June, 1995 ($1.95, limited series)

1-4: 1-Lobo app.						4.00

BODIES
DC Comics (Vertigo): Sept, 2014 - No. 8, Apr, 2015 ($3.99, limited series)

1-8-Spencer-s; art by Hetrick, Ormston, Lotay & Winslade						4.00

BODY BAGS
Dark Horse Comics (Blanc Noir): Sept, 1996 - No. 4, Jan, 1997 ($2.95, mini-series, mature)
(1st Blanc Noir series)

1,2-Jason Pearson-c/a/scripts in all. 1-Intro Clownface & Panda						5.00
3,4						4.00
Body Bags 1 (Image Comics, 7/05, $5.99) r/#1&2						6.00
Body Bags 2 (Image Comics, 8/05, $5.99) r/#3&4						6.00
...: 3 The Hard Way (Image, 2/06, $5.99) new story & r/Dark Horse Presents Annual 1997 and Dark Horse Maverick 2000; Pearson-c						6.00
...: One Shot (Image, 11/08, $5.99) wraparound-c; Pearson-c/a/s						6.00

BODYCOUNT (Also see Casey Jones & Raphael)
Image Comics (Highbrow Entertainment): Mar, 1996 - No. 4, July, 1996 ($2.50, lim. series)

1-4: Kevin Eastman-a(p)/scripts; Simon Bisley-c/a(i); Turtles app.	3	6	9	14	20	25
2-4	1	3	4	6	8	10

BODY DOUBLES (See Resurrection Man)
DC Comics: Oct, 1999 - No. 4, Jan, 2000 ($2.50, limited series)

1-4-Lanning & Abnett-s. 2-Black Canary app. 4-Wonder Woman app.						4.00
... (Villains) (2/98, $1.95, one-shot) 1-Pearson-c; Deadshot app.						4.00

BOFFO LAFFS
Paragraphics: 1986 - No. 5 ($2.50/$1.95)

1-($2.50) First comic cover with hologram						5.00
2-Classic horror back-c	2	4	6	9	12	15
3-5						4.00

BOLD ADVENTURE
Pacific Comics: Nov, 1983 - No. 3, June, 1984 ($1.50)

1-Time Force, Anaconda, & The Weirdling begin						4.00
2,3: 2-Soldiers of Fortune begins. 3-Spitfire						4.00

NOTE: Kaluta c-3. Nebres a-1-3. Nino a-2, 3. Severin a-3.

BOLD STORIES (Also see Candid Tales & It Rhymes With Lust)
Kirby Publishing Co.: Mar, 1950 - July, 1950 (Digest size, 144 pgs.)

March issue (Very Rare) - Contains "The Ogre of Paris" by Wood	300	600	900	1920	3310	4700
May issue (Very Rare) - Contains "The Cobra's Kiss" by Graham Ingels (21 pgs.)	245	490	735	1568	2684	3800
July issue (Very Rare) - Contains "The Ogre of Paris" by Wood	245	490	735	1568	2684	3800

BOLERO

	GD	VG	FN	VF	VF/NM	NM-		GD	VG	FN	VF	VF/NM	NM-
	2.0	4.0	6.0	8.0	9.0	9.2		2.0	4.0	6.0	8.0	9.0	9.2

Image Comics: Jan, 2022 - No. 5, May, 2022 ($5.99, limited series, squarebound)

1-5-Wyatt Kennedy-s/Luana Vecchio-a ... 6.00

BOLT AND STAR FORCE SIX
Americomics: 1984 ($1.75)

1-Origin Bolt & Star Force Six ... 4.00
Special 1 (1984, $2.00, 62pgs., B&W) ... 5.00

BOMBARDIER (See Bee 29, the Bombardier & Cinema Comics Herald)

BOMBAST
Topps Comics: 1993 ($2.95, one-shot) (Created by Jack Kirby)

1-Polybagged w/Kirbychrome trading card; Savage Dragon app.; Kirby-c;
has coupon for Amberchrome Secret City Saga #0 ... 4.00

BOMBA THE JUNGLE BOY (TV)
National Periodical Publ.: Sept-Oct, 1967 - No. 7, Sept-Oct, 1968 (12¢)

| 1-Intro. Bomba; Infantino/Anderson-c | 5 | 10 | 15 | 35 | 63 | 90 |
| 2-7 | 3 | 6 | 9 | 19 | 30 | 40 |

BOMBER COMICS
Elliot Publ. Co./Melverne Herald/Farrell/Sunrise Times: Mar, 1944 - No. 4, Winter, 1944-45

1-Wonder Boy, & Kismet, Man of Fate begin	116	232	348	742	1271	1800
2-Hitler-c and 8 pg. story	258	516	774	1651	2826	4000
3: 2-4-Have Classics Comics ad to HRN 20	65	130	195	416	708	1000
4-Hitler, Tojo & Mussolini-c; Sensation Comics #13-c/swipe; has Classics Comics ad to HRN 20.	206	412	618	1318	2259	3200

BOMB QUEEN
Image Comics (Shadowline): Feb, 2006 - No. 4, May, 2006 ($3.50, mature)

1-Jimmie Robinson-s/a in all	3	6	9	16	26	35
2-4	1	2	3	5	6	8
...-vs. Blacklight One Shot #1 (8/06, $3.50) Robinson-a; Shadowhawk app.						5.00
..., Vol. 1: WMD: Woman of Mass Destruction TPB (7/06, $12.99) r/#1-4; bonus art						13.00

BOMB QUEEN II
Image Comics (Shadowline): Oct, 2006 - No. 3, Dec, 2006 ($3.50, mature)

1-Jimmie Robinson-s/a; intro. The Four Queens	2	4	6	11	16	20
2,3						6.00
..., Vol. 2: Dirty Bomb - Queen of Hearts TPB (7/07, $14.99) r/#1-3 & Blacklight One Shot; bonus art; Robinson interview						15.00

BOMB QUEEN III THE GOOD, THE BAD & THE LOVELY
Image Comics (Shadowline): Mar, 2007 - No. 4, Jun, 2007 ($3.50, mature)

1-4-Jimmie Robinson-a/Jim Valentino-s; Blacklight & Rebound app. 1-Linsner-c ... 4.00

BOMB QUEEN IV SUICIDE BOMBER
Image Comics (Shadowline): Aug, 2007 - No. 4, Dec, 2007 ($3.50, mature)

1-4-Jim Robinson-s/a. 3-She-Spawn app. ... 4.00

BOMB QUEEN (Volumes 5-8)
Image Comics (Shadowline): May, 2008 - Present ($3.50/$3.99, mature)

Vol. 5 #1-6 (5/08 - No. 6, 3/09) Jimmie Robinson-s/a ... 4.00
Vol. 6 #1-4 (9/09 - No. 4, 1/11, $3.50) Obama satire ... 3.50
Vol. 7 #1-4 (12/11 - No. 4, 5/12, $3.50) Bomb Queen returns in 2112 ... 3.50
Vol. 8 #1-4 (8/20 - No. 4, 2/20, $3.99) Donald Trump satire ... 4.00
... Presents: All Girl Comics (5/09, $3.50) Dee Rail, Blacklight, Rebound, Tempest app. ... 3.50
... Presents: All Girl Special (7/11, $3.50) President Palin app. ... 3.50
... vs. Hack/Slash (2/11, $3.50) Cassie and Vlad app.; Robinson-s/a ... 3.50

BOMBSHELLS: UNITED (Continued from DC Comics: Bombshell series)
DC Comics: Nov, 2017 - No. 19, Early Aug, 2018 ($2.99)

1-19: 1-Bennett-s/Sauvage-a/Dodson-c; intro. Dawnstar & Clayface. 9,17-Siya Oum-a ... 3.00

BONANZA (TV)
Dell/Gold Key: June-Aug, 1960 - No. 37, Aug, 1970 (All Photo-c)

Four Color 1110 (6-8/60)	32	64	96	230	515	800
Four Color 1221,1283, & #01070-207, 01070-210	15	30	45	100	220	340
1(12/62-Gold Key)	16	32	48	110	243	375
2	9	18	27	58	114	170
3-10	7	14	21	44	82	120
11-20	5	10	15	34	60	85
21-37: 29-Reprints	5	10	15	30	50	70

BONE
Cartoon Books #1-20, 28 on/Image Comics #21-27: Jul, 1991 - No. 55, Jun, 2004 ($2.95, B&W)

1-Jeff Smith-c/a in all	129	258	387	1032	2316	3600
1-2nd printing	3	6	9	19	30	40
1-3rd thru 5th printings						6.00
2-1st printing	13	26	39	89	195	300
2-2nd & 3rd printings	1	2	3	5	6	8
3-1st printing	7	14	21	49	92	135
3-2nd thru 4th printings						4.00
4,5	5	10	15	35	63	90
6-10	3	6	9	14	20	25
11-20	1	2	3	5	6	8
13 1/2 (1/95, Wizard)	2	4	6	9	12	15
13 1/2 (Gold)	2	4	6	11	16	20
21-37: 21-1st Image issue						5.00
38-($4.95) Three covers by Miller, Ross, Smith	1	2	3	4	5	7
39-55-($2.95)						4.00
1-27-($2.95): 1-Image reprints begin w/new-c. 2-Allred pin-up.						3.00
nn (2008, 8-1/2" x 5-3/8" Halloween mini-comic giveaway)						3.00
... Holiday Special (1993, giveaway)						5.00
... Reader -($9.95) Behind the scenes info						10.00
... Sourcebook-San Diego Edition						4.00
...10th Anniversary Edition (8/01, $5.95) r/#1 in color; came with figure						6.00
Complete Bone Adventures Vol 1,2 ('93, '94, $12.95) r/#1-6 & #7-12)						15.00
...: One Volume Edition (2004, $39.95, 1300 pgs.)						40.00
...: One Volume Limited Edition HC (2004, signed by Jeff Smith, numbered edition of 2000)	21	42	63	147	324	500

Volume 1-($19.95, hard-c)-"Out From Boneville"						20.00
Volume 1-($12.95, soft-c)						13.00
Volume 2,5-($22.95, hard-c) "The Great Cow Race" & "Rock Jaw"						23.00
Volume 2-($14.95, soft-c)						15.00
Volume 3,4-($24.95, hard-c) "Eyes of the Storm" & "The Dragonslayer"						25.00
Volume 3,4,7-($16.95, soft-c)						17.00
Volume 5-($15.95, soft-c)-"Old Man's Cave"						16.00
Volume 7-($24.95, hard-c)-"Ghost Circles"						25.00
Volume 8-($23.95, hard-c)-"Treasure Hunters"						24.00

NOTE: Printings not listed sell for cover price.

BONE ORCHARD: TENEMENT
Image Comics: Jun, 2023 - Present ($3.99)

1-9-Lemire-s/Sorrentino-a ... 4.00

BONE ORCHARD: TEN THOUSAND BLACK FEATHERS
Image Comics: Sept, 2022 - No. 5, Jan, 2023 ($3.99)

1-5-Lemire-s/Sorrentino-a ... 4.00

BONE ORCHARD: THE PASSAGEWAY
Image Comics: Jun, 2022 ($17.99, hardcover)

HC-Lemire-s/Sorrentino-a ... 18.00

BONE PARISH
BOOM! Studios: Jul, 2018 - No. 12, Aug, 2019 ($3.99)

1-12-Cullen Bunn-s/Jonas Scharf-a ... 4.00

BONGO (See Story Hour Series)

BONGO & LUMPJAW (Disney, see Walt Disney Showcase #3)
Dell Publishing Co.: No. 706, June, 1956; No. 886, Mar, 1958

| Four Color 706 (#1) | 6 | 12 | 18 | 41 | 76 | 110 |
| Four Color 886 | 5 | 10 | 15 | 31 | 53 | 75 |

BONGO COMICS ...
Bongo Comics: 2005 - Present (Free Comic Book Day giveaways)

Gimme Gimme Giveaway! (2005) - Short stories from Simpsons Comics, Futurama Comics and Radioactive Man ... 3.00
Free-For-All! (2006, 2007, 2008, 2009, 2010, 2011, 2013-2018) - Short stories ... 3.00
Free-For-All! 2012 - Flip book with SpongeBob Comics ... 3.00

BONGO COMICS PRESENTS RADIOACTIVE MAN (See Radioactive Man)

BON VOYAGE (See Movie Classics)

BOOF
Image Comics (Todd McFarlane Prod.): July, 1994 - No. 6, Dec, 1994 ($1.95)

1-6 ... 4.00

BOOF AND THE BRUISE CREW
Image Comics (Todd McFarlane Prod.): July, 1994 - No. 6, Dec, 1994 ($1.95)

1-6 ... 4.00

BOOK AND RECORD SET (See Power Record Comics)

BOOK OF ALL COMICS
William H. Wise: 1945 (196 pgs.)(Inside f/c has Green Publ. blacked out)

| nn-Green Mask, Puppeteer & The Bouncer | 84 | 168 | 252 | 538 | 919 | 1300 |

BOOK OF ANTS, THE
Artisan Entertainment: 1998 ($2.95, B&W)

1-Based on the movie Pi; Aronofsky-s ... 5.00

BOOK OF BALLADS AND SAGAS, THE
Green Man Press: Oct, 1995 - No. 4 ($2.95/$3.50/$3.25, B&W)

1-4: 1-Vess-c/a; Gaiman story. ... 4.00

BOOK OF BUTCHER (From Something is Killing the Children and House of Slaughter)
BOOM! Studios: Dec, 2023 ($9.99, squarebound, one-shot)

1-Tynion IV-s/Dell'edera-a ... 10.00

BOOK OF COMICS, THE
William H. Wise: No date (1944) (25¢, 132 pgs.)

| nn-Captain V app.; WWII-c | 68 | 136 | 204 | 435 | 743 | 1050 |

BOOK OF DEATH
Valiant Entertainment: Jul, 2015 - No. 4, Oct, 2015 ($3.99, limited series)

1-4-Venditti-s/Gill & Braithwaite-a; multiple covers in each. 4-Flip book with preview for Wrath of the Eternal Warrior series ... 4.00
...: Fall of Bloodshot (7/15, $3.99) Lemire-s/Braithwaite-a; Armstrong app. ... 4.00
...: Fall of Harbinger (9/15, $3.99) Dysart-s/Kano-a; future deaths of the team ... 4.00
...: Fall of Ninjak (8/15, $3.99) Kindt-s/Hairsine-a ... 4.00
...: Fall of X-O Manowar (10/15, $3.99) Venditti-s/Henry-a; future death of Aric ... 4.00

BOOK OF FATE, THE (See Fate)
DC Comics: Feb, 1997 - No. 12, Jan, 1998 ($2.25/$2.50)

1-12: 4-Two-Face-c/app. 6-Convergence. 11-Sentinel app. ... 4.00

BOOK OF LOST SOULS, THE
Marvel Comics (Icon): Dec, 2005 - No. 6, June, 2006 ($2.99)

1-6-Colleen Doran-a/c; J. Michael Straczynski-s ... 3.00
... Vol. 1: Introductions All Around (2006, $16.99, TPB) r/series ... 17.00

BOOK OF LOVE (See Fox Giants)

BOOK OF NIGHT, THE
Dark Horse Comics: July, 1987 - No. 3, 1987 ($1.75, B&W)

1-3: Reprints from Epic Illustrated; Vess-a ... 4.00
TPB-r/#1-3 ... 15.00
Hardcover-Black-c with red crest ... 120.00
Hardcover w/slipcase (1991) signed and numbered ... 60.00

BOOK OF SHADOWS
Valiant Entertainment: Jul, 2022 - No. 4, Feb, 2023 ($3.99)

1-4-Cullen Bunn-s/Vicente Cifuentes-a; Shadowman, Eternal Warrior, Punk Mambo app. 4.00

BOOK OF SLAUGHTER (From Something is Killing the Children and House of Slaughter)

Bombshells United #17 © DC

Book of Shadows #2 © VAL

Booster Gold (2007 series) #4 © DC

	GD 2.0	VG 4.0	FN 6.0	VF 8.0	VF/NM 9.0	NM- 9.2

BOOM! Studios: Dec, 2022 ($9.99, squarebound, one-shot)

1-Tynion IV-s/Dell'edera-a; bonus guidebook of the Order of St. George
  10.00

BOOK OF THE DEAD
Marvel Comics: Dec, 1993 - No. 4, Mar, 1994 ($1.75, limited series, 52 pgs.)

1-Ploog Frankenstein & Morrow Man-Thing begin; Wrightson-r/Chamber of Darkness #7
| 2 | 4 | 6 | 9 | 12 | 15 |

2-4: 2-Morrow new painted-c; Chaykin/Morrow Man-Thing; Krigstein-r/Uncanny Tales #54; r/Fear #10. 3-r/Astonishing Tales #10 & Starlin Man-Thing. 3,4-Painted-c
| 1 | 2 | 3 | 5 | 6 | 8 |

BOOKS OF DOOM (Dr. Doom from Fantastic Four)
Marvel Comics: Jan, 2006 - No. 6, June, 2006 ($2.99, limited series)

1-6-Life story/origin of Dr. Doom; Brubaker-s/Raimondi-a/Rivera-c
  3.00
Fantastic Four: Books of Doom HC (2006, $19.99) r/#1-6
  20.00
Fantastic Four: Books of Doom SC (2007, $14.99) r/#1-6
  15.00

BOOKS OF FAERIE, THE
DC Comics (Vertigo): Mar, 1997 - No. 3, May, 1997 ($2.50, limited series)

1-3-Gross-a
  4.00
TPB (1998, $14.95) r/#1-3 & Arcana Annual #1
  15.00

BOOKS OF FAERIE, THE : AUBERON'S TALE
DC Comics (Vertigo): Aug, 1998 - No. 3, Oct, 1998 ($2.50, limited series)

1-3-Gross-a
  4.00

BOOKS OF FAERIE, THE : MOLLY'S STORY
DC Comics (Vertigo): Sept, 1999 - No. 4, Dec, 1999 ($2.50, limited series)

1-4-Ney Rieber-s/Mejia-a
  4.00

BOOKS OF MAGIC
DC Comics: 1990 - No. 4, 1991 ($3.95, 52 pgs., limited series, mature)

1-Bolton painted-c/a; Phantom Stranger app.; Gaiman scripts in all
| 2 | 4 | 6 | 9 | 12 | 15 |

2,3: 2-John Constantine, Dr. Fate, Spectre, Deadman app. 3-Dr. Occult app.; minor Sandman app.
| 1 | 2 | 3 | 4 | 5 | 7 |

4-Early Death-c/app. (early 1991)
| 1 | 2 | 3 | 5 | 6 | 8 |

Trade paperback-($19.95)-Reprints limited series
  20.00

BOOKS OF MAGIC (Also see Hunter: The Age of Magic and Names of Magic)
DC Comics (Vertigo): May, 1994 - No. 75, Aug, 2000 ($1.95/$2.50, mature)

1-Charles Vess-c
| 2 | 4 | 6 | 9 | 12 | 15 |

1-Platinum
| 2 | 4 | 6 | 13 | 18 | 22 |

2-4: 4-Death app.
| 1 | 2 | 3 | 4 | 5 | 7 |

5-14: Charles Vess-c
  4.00
15-75: 15-$2.50-c begins. 22-Kaluta-c. 25-Death-c/app; Bachalo-c. 51-Peter Gross-s/a begins. 55-Medley-a
  3.00
Annual 1-3 (2/97, 2/98, '99, $3.95)
  5.00
Bindings (1995, $12.95, TPB)-r/#1-4
  13.00
Death After Death (2001, $19.95, TPB)-r/#42-50
  20.00
Girl in the Box (1999, $14.95, TPB)-r/#51-13
  15.00
Reckonings (1997, $12.95, TPB)-r/#14-20
  13.00
Summonings (1996, $17.50, TPB)-r/#5-13, Vertigo Rave #1
  17.50
The Burning Girl (2000, $17.95, TPB)-r/#33-41
  18.00
Transformations (1998, $12.95, TPB)-r/#21-25
  13.00

BOOKS OF MAGIC (The Sandman Universe)
DC Comics (Vertigo for #1-13, Black Label #14-on): Dec, 2018 - No. 23, Nov, 2020 ($3.99)

1-23: 1-Howard-s/Fowler-a; Tim Hunter's story continues from 1990 series; Dr. Rose app. 19-Barnett-s begins
  4.00

BOOKS OF MAGICK, THE : LIFE DURING WARTIME (See Books of Magic)
DC Comics (Vertigo): Sept, 2004 - No. 15, Dec, 2005 ($2.50/$2.75)

1-15: 1-Spencer-s/Ormston-a/Quitely-c; Constantine app. 2-Bagged with Sky Captain CD 6-Fegredo-a. 7-Constantine & Zatanna-a
  3.00
... Book One TPB (2005, $9.95) r/#1-5
  10.00

BOOM! STUDIOS...
BOOM! Studios

... Free Comic Book Day 2019 No. 1 (5/19) Short stories of Buffy, Angel, Firefly
  3.00
... Ten Year Celebration 2015 Free Comic Book Day Special (5/15, giveaway) short stories of Adventure Time, Peanuts, Garfield, Lumberjanes, Regular Show & others
  3.00
... Summer Blast (5/16, FCBD giveaway) Mouse Guard, Labyrinth, Adventure Time
  3.00
... 2017 Summer Blast (5/17) FCBD giveaway; Mouse Guard, Brave Chef Brianna
  3.00

BOONDOCK SAINTS (Based on the movie)
12-Gauge Comics: May, 2010 - No. 2, Jun, 2010 ($3.99, limited series)

...: In Nomine Patris 1,2-Troy Duffy-s/Guus Floor-a
  4.00

...: In Nomine Patris Vol. 2 (10/10 - No. 2, 11/10): 1,2-Duffy-s/Floor-a
  4.00
...: In Nomine Patris Vol. 3 (3/11 - No. 2, 4/11): 1,2-Duffy-s/Floor-a
  4.00

BOOSTER GOLD (See Justice League #4)
DC Comics: Feb, 1986 - No. 25, Feb, 1988 (75¢)

1-Dan Jurgens-s/a(p); 1st app. of Booster Gold
| 5 | 10 | 15 | 31 | 53 | 75 |

2-25: 4-Rose & Thorn app. 6-Origin. 6,7,23-Superman app. 8,9-LSH app. 22-JLI app. 24,25-Millennium tie-ins
  5.00
NOTE: *Austin c-22i. Byrne c-23i.*

BOOSTER GOLD (See DC's weekly series 52)
DC Comics: Oct, 2007 - No. 47, Oct, 2011 ($3.50/$2.99/$3.99)

1-Geoff Johns-s/Dan Jurgens-a(p); covers by Jurgens and Art Adams; Rip Hunter app.
  5.00
2-4,6-20: 3-Jonah Hex app. 8-Superman app.
  3.00
5-Joker and Batgirl app.; Killing Joke-style-c.
  6.00
21-29-($3.99) 21-Blue Beetle back-ups begin. 22-New Teen Titans app. 23-Photo-c. 26,27-Blackest Night; Ted Kord rises. 29-Cyborg Superman app.
  4.00
30-47-($2.99): 32-34-Giffen & DeMatteis-s. 32-Emerald Empress app. 40-Origin retold. 43-Legion of S.H. app. 44,45-Flashpoint tie-in; Doomsday app.
  3.00
#0-(4/08) Blue Beetle (Ted Cord) returns; takes place between #6&7
  3.00
#1,000,000-(9/08) Michelle Carter returns; takes place between #10&11
  3.00
... Futures End 1 (11/14, $2.99, regular-c) Jurgens-s; Kamandi, LSH, Captain Atom app.
  3.00
... Futures End 1 (11/14, $3.99, 3-D cover)
  4.00
.../ The Flintstones Special 1 (5/17, $4.99) Russell-s/Leonardi-a; Jetsons back-up
  5.00

BOOTS AND HER BUDDIES
Standard Comics/Visual Editions/Argo (NEA Service):
No. 5, 9/48 - No. 9, 9/49; 12/55 - No. 3, 1956

5-Strip-r
| 41 | 82 | 123 | 256 | 428 | 600 |
6,8
| 16 | 32 | 48 | 94 | 147 | 200 |
7-(Scarce)
| 21 | 42 | 63 | 122 | 199 | 275 |
9-(Scarce)-Frazetta-a (2 pgs.)
| 55 | 110 | 165 | 352 | 601 | 850 |
1-3-(Argo-1955-56)-Reprints
| 8 | 16 | 24 | 42 | 54 | 65 |

BOOTS & SADDLES (TV)
Dell Publ. Co.: No. 919, July, 1958; No. 1029, Sept, 1959; No. 1116, Aug, 1960

Four Color 919 (#1)-Photo-c
| 7 | 14 | 21 | 48 | 89 | 130 |
Four Color 1029, 1116-Photo-c
| 5 | 10 | 15 | 34 | 60 | 85 |

BORDERLANDS: ... (Based on the video game)
IDW Publishing: Jul, 2014 - No. 8, Feb, 2015 ($3.99)

1-8: 1-4-The Fall of Fyrestone. 5-8-Tannis and the Vault
  4.00

BORDERLANDS: ORIGINS (Based on the video game)
IDW Publishing: Nov, 2012 - No. 4, Feb, 2013 ($3.99, limited series)

1-4: 1-Spotlight on Roland. 2-Lilith. 3-Mordecai. 4-Brick
  4.00

BORDER PATROL
P. L. Publishing Co.: May-June, 1951 - No. 3, Sept-Oct, 1951

1
| 20 | 40 | 60 | 117 | 189 | 260 |
2,3
| 13 | 26 | 39 | 74 | 105 | 135 |

BORDER TOWN
DC Comics (Vertigo): Dec, 2018 - No. 4, Feb, 2019 ($3.99, unfinished series)

1-4-Esquivel-s/Villalobos-a
  4.00

BORDER WORLDS (Also see Megaton Man)
Kitchen Sink Press: Feb - No. 7, 1987; V2#1, 1990 - No. 4, 1990 ($1.95-$2.00, B&W, mature)

1-7, V2#1-4: Donald Simpson-c/a/scripts
  4.00

BOREALIS
Dark Horse Comics: Dec, 2023 - No. 3, Feb, 2024 ($3.99, limited series)

1-3-Mark Verheiden & Aaron Douglas-s/Cliff Richards-a
  4.00

BORIS KARLOFF TALES OF MYSTERY (TV) (...Thriller No. 1,2)
Gold Key: No. 3, Apr, 1963 - No. 97, Feb, 1980

3-5-(Two #5's, 10/63,11/63): 5-(10/63)-11 pgs. Toth-a.
| 6 | 12 | 18 | 37 | 66 | 95 |
6-8,10: 10-Orlando-a
| 4 | 8 | 12 | 28 | 47 | 65 |
9-Wood-a
| 5 | 10 | 15 | 31 | 53 | 75 |
11-Williamson-a, 8 pgs.; Orlando-a, 5 pgs.
| 5 | 10 | 15 | 30 | 50 | 70 |
12-Torres, McWilliams-a; Orlando-a(2)
| 4 | 8 | 12 | 23 | 37 | 50 |
13,14,16-20
| 3 | 6 | 9 | 18 | 28 | 38 |
15-Crandall
| 3 | 6 | 9 | 19 | 30 | 40 |
21-Jeff Jones-a(3 pgs.) "The Screaming Skull"
| 3 | 6 | 9 | 19 | 30 | 40 |
22-First 15¢ issue
| 3 | 6 | 9 | 16 | 23 | 30 |
23-30: 23-Reprint; photo-c
| 3 | 6 | 9 | 15 | 22 | 28 |
31-50: 36-Weiss-a
| 3 | 6 | 9 | 14 | 19 | 24 |
51-74: 74-Origin & 1st app. Taurus
| 2 | 4 | 6 | 10 | 14 | 18 |

	GD 2.0	VG 4.0	FN 6.0	VF 8.0	VF/NM 9.0	NM- 9.2

	GD 2.0	VG 4.0	FN 6.0	VF 8.0	VF/NM 9.0	NM- 9.2
75-79,87-97: 90-r/Torres, McWilliams-a/#12; Morrow-c2		4	6	9	12	15
80-86-(52 pgs.)		5	6	10	14	18
Story Digest 1(7/70-Gold Key)-All text/illos.; 148 pg.		5	10	15	31	53	75

(See Mystery Comics Digest No. 2, 5, 8, 11, 14, 17, 20, 23, 26)
NOTE: *Boîle* a-51-54, 56, 58, 59. *McWilliams*-a-12, 14, 18, 19, 72, 80, 81, 93. *Orlando* a-11-15, 21. Reprints: 78, 81-86, 88, 90, 92, 95, 97.

BORIS KARLOFF THRILLER (TV) (Becomes Boris Karloff Tales…)
Gold Key: Oct., 1962 - No. 2, Jan, 1963 (84 pgs.)

	GD	VG	FN	VF	VF/NM	NM-
1-Photo-c	11	22	33	77	166	255
2	6	12	18	42	79	115

BORIS THE BEAR
Dark Horse Comics/Nicotat Comics #13 on: Aug, 1986 - No. 34, 1990 ($1.50/$1.75/$1.95, B&W)

	GD	VG	FN	VF	VF/NM	NM-
1	1	2	3	5	6	8
1 (2nd printing),2,3,4A,4B,5-12, 14-34						4.00
8,13: 8-(44 pgs.). 13-1st Nicotat Comics issue						4.00
Annual 1 (1988, $2.50)						5.00

BORIS THE BEAR INSTANT COLOR CLASSICS
Dark Horse Comics: July, 1987 - No. 3, 1987 ($1.75/$1.95)

1-3						4.00

BORN
Marvel Comics: 2003 - No. 4, 2003 ($3.50, limited series)

1-4-Frank Castle (the Punisher) in 1971 Vietnam; Ennis-s/Robertson-a						4.00
HC (2004, $17.99) oversized reprint of series; proposal, layout pages						18.00
Punisher: Born SC (2004, $13.99) r/series; proposal, layout pages						14.00

BORN AGAIN
Spire Christian Comics (Fleming H. Revell Co.): 1978 (39¢)

	GD	VG	FN	VF	VF/NM	NM-
nn-Watergate, Nixon, etc.	3	6	9	19	30	40

BOUNCE, THE
Image Comics: May, 2013 - No. 12, May, 2014 ($2.99)

1-12-Casey-s/Messina-a						3.00

BOUNCER, THE (Formerly Green Mask #9)
Fox Feature Syndicate: 1944 - No. 14, Jan, 1945

	GD	VG	FN	VF	VF/NM	NM-
nn(1944, #10?)	39	78	117	240	395	550
11 (9/44)-Origin; Rocket Kelly, One Round Hogan app.	29	58	87	172	281	390
12-14: 14-Reprints no # issue	22	44	66	132	216	300

BOUNTY
Dark Horse Comics: Jul, 2016 - No. 5, Dec, 2016 ($3.99, limited series)

1-5-Kurtis Wiebe-s/Mindy Lee-a						4.00

BOUNTY GUNS (See Luke Short's…, Four Color 739)

BOX OFFICE POISON
Antarctic Press: 1996 - No. 21, Sept, 2000 ($2.95, B&W)

	GD	VG	FN	VF	VF/NM	NM-
1-Alex Robinson-s/a in all	1	2	3	5	6	8
2-5						4.00
6-21, …Kolor Karnival 1 (5/99, $2.99)						3.00
…Super Special 0 (5/97, $4.95)						5.00
Sherman's March: Collected BOP Vol. 1 (9/98, $14.95) r/#0-4						15.00
TPB (2002, $29.95, 608 pgs.) r/entire series						30.00

BOX OFFICE POISON COLOR COMICS
IDW Publishing: Jan, 2017 - No. 5, May, 2017 ($3.99)

1-5-Colored reprints of 1996 series; Alex Robinson-s/a in all; bonus commentary						4.00

BOY AND THE PIRATES, THE (Movie)
Dell Publishing Co.: No. 1117, Aug, 1960

	GD	VG	FN	VF	VF/NM	NM-
Four Color 1117-Photo-c	6	12	18	37	66	95

BOY COMICS (Captain Battle No. 1 & 2; Boy Illustories No. 43-108) (Stories by Charles Biro)
(Also see Squeeks)
Lev Gleason Publ. (Comic House): No. 3, Apr, 1942 - No. 119, Mar, 1956

	GD	VG	FN	VF	VF/NM	NM-
3 (No.1)-1st app. & origin Crimebuster (ends #110); Young Robin Hood (ends # 32), Yankee Longago (ends #28), Hero of the Month (ends #31); Case 1001-1005, 1006-1009 (ends #10); Swoop Storm begins (ends #32); Pepper Casey only app.; 1st app. Iron Jaw; Crimebuster's pet monkey Squeeks begins	349	698	1047	2443	4272	6100
4-Hitler, Tojo Mussolini-c; Iron Jaw app. Little Wise Guys (prototype of later version) begins, ends #5	343	686	1029	2400	4200	6000
5-Japanese war-c	168	336	504	1075	1838	2600
6-Origin Iron Jaw; origin & death of Iron Jaw's son killed by his father; Hitler app.; Little Dynamite begins, ends #39; 1st Iron Jaw-c	343	686	1029	2400	4200	6000
7-Flag & Hitler, Tojo, Mussolini-c; Dickey Dean app.	271	542	813	1734	2967	4200
8-Death of Iron Jaw; Iron Jaw-c & spash pg.	116	232	348	742	1271	1800
9-Iron Jaw classic-c (does not appear in story)	331	662	993	2317	4059	5800
10-Return of Iron Jaw; classic Biro Iron Jaw/Nazi-c	541	1082	1623	3950	6975	10,000
11-Iron Jaw sty/classic/c	258	516	774	1651	2826	4000
12-Classic Japanese WWII bondage torture interrogation-c	155	310	465	992	1696	2400
13-Nazi firing squad-c	142	284	426	909	1555	2200
14-Iron Jaw-c	103	206	309	659	1130	1600
15-Death of Iron Jaw, killed by The Rodent	135	270	405	864	1482	2100
16,18,20 (2/45)	55	110	165	352	601	850
17-(8/44)-Flag-c; The Moth app.	68	136	204	435	743	1050
19-One of the greatest all-time stories	58	116	174	371	636	900
21-24: 24-Concentration camp story	39	78	117	231	378	525
25-Devil-c; hanging story (52 pgs.)	43	86	129	271	461	650
26-Bondage, torture/c/story (68 pgs.)	50	100	150	315	533	750
27-29,31,32-(All 68 pgs.). 28-Yankee Longago ends. 32-Swoop Storm & Young Robin Hood end	37	74	111	222	361	500
30-(10/46, 68 pgs.)-Origin Crimebuster retold from #3 w/Iron Jaw; Nazi work camp story	43	86	129	271	461	650
33-40: 34-Crimebuster story (2); suicide-c/story	25	50	75	150	245	340
41-50-41-Daredevil illus. text story	20	40	60	117	189	260

	GD 2.0	VG 4.0	FN 6.0	VF 8.0	VF/NM 9.0	NM- 9.2
51-59: 57(9/50)-Dilly Duncan begins, ends #71	18	36	54	103	162	220
60-(12/50)-Iron Jaw returns c/sty	20	40	60	117	189	260
61-Origin Crimebuster & Iron Jaw retold c/sty	20	40	60	120	195	270
62-(2/51)-Death of Iron Jaw explained w/Iron Jaw-c	20	40	60	117	189	260
63-67,69-72: 63-McWilliams-a	14	28	42	80	115	150
68,73-Iron Jaw c/sty; 73-Frazetta 1 pg. ad	14	28	42	83	121	130
74,78,81-Iron Jaw c/sty (2-3)	13	26	39	72	101	130
75-77,84	12	24	36	69	97	125
79,80-Iron Jaw sty: 80(8/52)-1st app. Rocky X of the Rocketeers; becomes "Rocky" #101; Iron Jaw, Sniffer & the Deadly Dozen in #80-118	12	24	36	69	97	125
82-Iron Jaw-c (apps. in one panel)	12	24	36	67	94	120
83,85-88-Iron Jaw c/sty. 87-The Deadly Dozen begins; becomes Iron Jaw #88 (4/53)	12	24	36	69	97	125
89(5/53)-92-The Claw serial app. in Rocky X (also see Silver Streak & Daredevil); on-c. 89-"Iron Jaw" becomes "Sniffrer & Iron Jaw" (ends #118); Iron Jaw c/story in all	14	28	42	76	108	140
93-Claw cameo & last app.; Woodesque-a on Rocky X by Sid Check; Iron Jaw c/sty	13	26	39	72	101	130
94-97-Iron Jaw-c/sty in all	11	22	33	64	90	115
98,100:(4/54): 98-Rocky X by Sid Check	12	24	36	67	94	120
99,101-107,109,111,119: 101-Rocky X becomes spy strip. 106-Robin Hood app. 111-Crimebuster becomes Chuck Chandler, ends #119	10	20	30	56	76	95
108-(2/55)-Kubert & Ditko-c (Crimebuster, 8 pgs.)	12	24	36	67	94	120
110,112-118-Kubert-a	11	22	33	62	86	110

(See Giant Boy Book of Comics)
NOTE: *Boy Movies* in 3-5,40,41. *Iron Jaw app.* 3,4,6,8,10,11,13-15; returns-60,62, 68, 69, 72-79, 81-118; c-60-62, 73, 74, 78, 81-83, 85-97. *Biro* c-all. *Jack Alderman* a-26. *Dan Barry* a-31,32, 35-38. *Al Borth* a- 51. *Dick Briefer* a-3-28, 124. *Sid Check*-a-93, 98. *Ditko*-a-108. *Bob Fujitani (Fuje)* a-55, 18pgs. *Jerry Gandenetti* a-52. *R. W. Hall* a-19-22. *Hubbell* a-30, 106, 108, 110, 111. *Joe Kubert* a-108, 110, 112-118. *Kenneth Landau* a-92. *George Mandel* a-3-30. *Norman Maurer* a-4-9, 11-13, 31, 32, 35, 41, 43, 46, 51, 57, 61, 73, 74, 78-83. *Bob Montana* a-4, 16, 19. *Pete Morisi* a-111. *William Overgard* a-68, 71, 74, 86, 88. *Palais* a-14, 16, 17, 19, 20, 25, 26. among others. *Tuska* a-30. *Bob Wood* a-8-13.

BOY COMMANDOS (See Detective #64 & World's Finest Comics #8)
National Periodical Publications: Winter, 1942-43 - No. 36, Nov-Dec, 1949

	GD	VG	FN	VF	VF/NM	NM-
1-Origin Liberty Belle; The Sandman & The Newsboy Legion x-over in Boy Commandos; S&K-a, 48 pgs.; S&K cameo? (classic WWII-c)	400	1087	1200	2800	4900	7000
2-Last Liberty Belle; Hitler-c; S&K-a, 46 pgs.; WWII-c	265	530	795	1694	2897	4100
3-S&K-a, 45 pgs.; WWII-c	135	270	405	864	1482	2100
4-6: 6-S&K-a	87	174	261	553	952	1350
7-10: All WWII-c	55	110	165	352	601	850
11-13: All WWII-c. 11-Infinity-c	40	80	120	246	411	575
14,16,18-19-All have S&K-a. 18-2nd Crazy Quilt-c	34	68	102	204	332	460
15-1st app. Crazy Quilt, their arch nemesis	47	94	141	296	498	700
17,20-Sci/fi-c/stories	42	84	126	265	445	625
21,22,25: 22-3rd Crazy Quilt-c; Judy Canova x-over	27	54	81	162	266	370
23-S&K-c/a(all)	39	78	117	231	378	525
24-1st costumed superhero satire-c (11-12/47)	43	86	129	271	461	650
26-Flying Saucer story (3-4/48)-4th of this theme; see The Spirit 9/28/47(1st), Shadow Comics V7#10 (2nd, 1/48) & Captain Midnight #60 (3rd, 2/48)	39	78	117	231	378	525
27,28,30: 30-Cleveland Indians story	27	54	81	158	259	360
29-S&K story (1)	28	56	84	168	274	380
31-35: 32-Dale Evans app. on-c & in story. 33-Last Crazy Quilt-c. 34-Intro. Wolf, their mascot	24	48	72	140	230	320
36-Intro The Atomibile c/sci/story (Scarce)	45	90	135	284	480	675

The Boy Commandos by Joe Simon & Jack Kirby Volume One HC (2010, $49.99) reprints appl. in Detective #64-72, World's Finest #8,9 & Boy Commandos #1,2; Buhle intro. 50.00
NOTE: *Most issues signed by Simon & Kirby are not by them.* S&K c-1-9, 13, 14, 17, 21, 23, 24, 30-32. *Feller* c-30.

BOY COMMANDOS
National Per. Publ.: Sept-Oct, 1973 - No. 2, Nov-Dec, 1973 (G.A. S&K reprints)

	GD	VG	FN	VF	VF/NM	NM-
1,2: 1-Reprints story from Boy Commandos #1 plus-c & Detective #66 by S&K. 2-Infantino/Orlando-c	2	4	6	10	14	18

BOY COMMANDOS COMICS
DC Comics: Sept/Oct. 1942

1-Ashcan comic, not distributed to newsstands, only for in-house use. Cover art is the splash page from the Boy Commandos story in Detective Comics #68 interior is from an unidentified issue of Detective Comics (A FN- copy sold for $1912 in 2012)						
nn - (9-10/42) Ashcan comic, not distributed to newsstands, only for in-house use. Cover art is the splash page from the Boy Commandos story in Detective Comics #68 interior is from Detective Comics #68 (no known sales)						

BOY COWBOY (Also see Amazing Adventures & Science Comics)
Ziff-Davis Publ. Co.: 1950 (8 pgs. in color)

	GD	VG	FN	VF	VF/NM	NM-
nn-Sent to subscribers of Ziff-Davis mags. & ordered through mail for 10¢; used to test market for Kid Cowboy	39	78	117	231	378	525

BOY DETECTIVE
Avon Periodicals: May-June, 1951 - No. 4, May, 1952

	GD	VG	FN	VF	VF/NM	NM-
1	30	60	90	177	289	400
2-4: 3,4-Kinstler-c	19	38	57	112	179	240

BOY EXPLORERS COMICS (Terry and The Pirates No. 3 on)
Family Comics (Harvey Publ.): May-June, 1946 - No. 2, Sept-Oct, 1946

	GD	VG	FN	VF	VF/NM	NM-
1-Intro The Explorers, Duke of Broadway, Calamity Jane & Danny Dixon…Cadet; S&K-c/a, 24 pgs.	93	186	279	591	1021	1450
2-(Rare)-Small size (5-1/2x8-1/2"; B&W; 32 pgs.) Distributed to mail subscribers only; S&K-a	168	336	504	1075	1838	2600

(Also see All New No. 15, Flash Gordon No. 5, and Stuntman No. 3)

BOY ILLUSTORIES (See Boy Comics)

BOY LOVES GIRL (Boy Meets Girl No. 1-24)
Lev Gleason Publications: No. 25, July, 1952 - No. 57, June, 1956

	GD	VG	FN	VF	VF/NM	NM-
25(#1)	19	38	57	111	176	240
26,27,29-33: 30-33-Serial, 'Loves of My Life'	14	28	42	76	108	140
34-42: 39-Lingerie panels	13	26	39	74	105	135
28-Drug propaganda story	14	28	42	80	115	150

Boy Comics #24 © LEV

The Boys #3 © Spitfire & Robertson

B.P.R.D.: King of Fear #4 © Mike Mignola

	GD 2.0	VG 4.0	FN 6.0	VF 8.0	VF/NM 9.0	NM- 9.2
43-Toth-a	14	28	42	78	112	145
44-50: 47-Toth-a? 49-Roller Derby-c. 50-Last pre-code (2/55)						
	12	24	36	67	94	120
51-57: 57-Ann Brewster-a	10	20	30	58	79	100

BOY MEETS GIRL (Boy Loves Girl No. 25 on)
Lev Gleason Publications: Feb, 1950 - No. 24, June, 1952 (No. 1-17: 52 pgs.)

1-Guardineer-a	27	54	81	158	259	360
2	16	32	48	92	144	195
3-10	15	30	45	84	127	170
11-24	14	28	42	81	115	150

NOTE: *Briefer a-24. Fuje c-3,7. Painted-c 1-17. Photo-c 19-23, 23.*

BOYS, THE (Inspired the 2019 Amazon Prime TV series)
DC Comics (WildStorm)/Dynamite Ent. #7 on: Oct, 2006 - No. 72, 2012 ($2.99/$3.99)

1-Garth Ennis-s/Darick Robertson-a	6	12	18	42	79	115
2,3	3	6	9	21	33	45
4,5	3	6	9	14	20	25
6-20		3	4	6	8	10
21-50: 19-Origin of the Homelander. 23-Variant-c by Cassaday						
	1	2	3	5	6	8
51-64,66-71-($3.99) Russ Braun-a in most. 54,55-McCrea-a						5.00
65,72-($4.99): 65-End of the Homelander. 72-Last issue; bonus pin-ups; cover gallery						
	1	2	3	5	6	8
#1: Dynamite Edition (2009, $1.00) r/#1; flip book with Battlefields Night Witches						5.00
... Dynamite Edition 1-3 (2021 - Present, no price on-c) r/#1-3						4.00
... Volume 1: The Name of the Game TPB (2007, $14.99) r/#1-6; intro. by Simon Pegg						15.00
... Volume 2: Get Some TPB (2008, $19.99) r/#7-14						20.00
... Volume 3: Good For The Soul TPB (2008, $19.99) r/#15-22						20.00
... Volume 5: We Gotta Go Now TPB (2009, $19.99) r/#23-30; cover gallery						20.00
... Volume 5: Herogasm TPB (2009, $19.99) r/#Herogasm 1-6						20.00

BOYS, THE: BUTCHER, BAKER, CANDLESTICKMAKER
Dynamite Entertainment: 2011 - No. 6, 2011 ($3.99, mature)

1-6-Garth Ennis-s/Darick Robertson-a; Billy Butcher's early years						4.00

BOYS, THE: DEAR BECKY
Dynamite Entertainment: 2020 - No. 8, 2020 ($3.99, mature)

1-8-Garth Ennis-s/Russ Braun-a/Darick Robertson-c; set 12 years later, plus flashbacks						4.00

BOYS, THE: HEROGASM
Dynamite Entertainment: 2009 - No. 6, 2009 ($2.99, mature)

1-Garth Ennis-s/John McCrea-a	4	8	12	23	37	50
2-6						5.00

BOYS, THE: HIGHLAND LADDIE
Dynamite Entertainment: 2010 - No. 6, 2011 ($3.99, mature)

1-6-Garth Ennis-s/John McCrea-a						4.00

BOYS' AND GIRLS' MARCH OF COMICS (See March of Comics)

BOYS' RANCH (Also see Western Tales & Witches' Western Tales)
Harvey Publ.: Oct, 1950 - No. 6, Aug, 1951 (No.1-3, 52 pgs.; No. 4-6, 36 pgs.)

1-S&K-c/a(3)	65	130	195	416	708	1000
2-S&K-c/a(3)	41	82	123	256	428	600
3-S&K-c/a(2); Meskin-a	40	80	120	244	402	560
4-S&K-c/a, 5 pgs.	36	72	108	211	343	475
5,6-S&K-c, splashes & centerspread only; Meskin-a						
	21	42	63	122	199	275

BOZO (Larry Harmon's Bozo, the World's Most Famous Clown)
Innovation Publishing: 1992 ($6.95, 68 pgs.)

1-Reprints Four Color #285(#1)	1	2	3	4	5	7

BOZO THE CLOWN (TV) (Bozo No. 7 on)
Dell Publishing Co.: July, 1950 - No. 4, Oct-Dec, 1963

Four Color 285(#1)	19	38	57	131	291	450
2(7-9/51)-7(10-12/52)	10	20	30	67	141	215
Four Color 464,508,551,594(10/54)	9	18	27	61	123	185
1(nn, 5-7/62)	7	14	21	46	86	125
2 - 4 (1963)	6	12	18	38	69	95

BOZZ CHRONICLES, THE
Marvel Comics (Epic Comics): Dec, 1985 - No. 6, 1986 (Lim. series, mature)

1-6-Logan/Wolverine look alike in 19th century. 1,3,5-Blevins-a						4.00

B.P.R.D. (Bureau of Paranormal Research and Defense) (Also see Hellboy titles)
Dark Horse Comics: (one-shots)

... Dark Waters (7/03, $2.99) Guy Davis-c/a; Augustyn-a						3.00
... Night Train (9/03, $2.99) Johns & Kolins-s; Kolins & Stewart-a						3.00

	GD 2.0	VG 4.0	FN 6.0	VF 8.0	VF/NM 9.0	NM- 9.2
... The Ectoplasmic Man (6/08, $2.99) Stenbeck-a/Mignola-c; origin of Johann Kraus						3.00
... There's Something Under My Bed (11/03, $2.99) Pollina-a						3.00
... The Soul of Venice (5/03, $2.99) Oeming-a/c; Gunter & Oeming-s						3.00
... The Soul of Venice and Other Stories TPB (8/04, $17.95) r/one-shots & new story by Mignola and Cam Stewart; sketch pages by various						18.00
... War on Frogs (6/08,12/08, 6/09, 12/09, $2.99) 1-Trimpe-a/Mignola-c; Abe Sapien app. 2-Severin-a. 3-Moline-a. 4-Snejberg						3.00

B.P.R.D.: GARDEN OF SOULS
Dark Horse Comics: Mar, 2007 - No. 5, July, 2007 ($2.99, limited series)

1-5-Mignola & Arcudi-s/Guy Davis-a/Mignola-c						3.00

B.P.R.D.: HELL ON EARTH
Dark Horse Comics: (5 limited series)

... Exorcism (6/12 - No. 2, 7/12) 1,2-Mignola-s/Stewart-a/Kalvachev -c						3.50
... Gods (1/11 - No. 3, 3/11) 1-Mignola & Arcudi-s/Guy Davis-a; Ryan Sook-c						3.50
... Monsters (7/11 - No. 2, 8/11) 1,2-Mignola & Arcudi-s -1-Sook & Francavilla covers						3.50
... New World (8/10 - No. 5, 12/10) 1-5-Mignola & Arcudi-s/Guy Davis-a/c						3.50
... Russia (9/11 - No. 5, 1/12) 1-5-Mignola & Arcudi-s/Crook-a						3.50
... The Devil's Engine (5/12 - No. 3, 7/12) 1-3-Mignola & Arcudi-s/Crook-a/Fegredo-c						3.50
... The Long Death (2/12 - No. 3, 4/12) 1-3-Mignola & Arcudi-s/Harren-a/Fegredo-c						3.50
... The Pickens County Horror (3/12 - No. 2, 4/12) 1,2-Mignola & Allie-s/Latour-a						3.50
... The Transformation of J.H. O'Donnell (5/12) 1-Mignola & Allie-s/Fiumara-a						3.50
... The Return of the Master (8/12 - No. 5, 12/12) 1-5-Mignola & Arcudi-s/Crook-a; 3-5-Also numbered as #100-102 on cover and indicia						3.50
103-141: 103-(1/13). 103,104-The Abyss of Time. 105,106-A Cold Day in Hell						3.50
142-147-($3.99)						4.00

B.P.R.D.: HOLLOW EARTH (Mike Mignola's...)
Dark Horse Comics: Jan, 2002 - No. 3, June, 2002 ($2.99, limited series)

1-3-Mignola, Golden & Sniegoski-s/Sook-a/Mignola-c; Hellboy and Abe Sapien app.						5.00
... and Other Stories TPB (1/03, $17.95) r/#1-3, Hellboy; Box Full of Evil, Abe Sapien: Drums of the Dead, and Dark Horse Extra; plus sketch pages						18.00

B.P.R.D.: KILLING GROUND
Dark Horse Comics: Aug, 2007 - No. 5, Dec, 2007 ($2.99, limited series)

1-5-Mignola & Arcudi-s/Guy Davis-a/c						3.00

B.P.R.D.: KING OF FEAR
Dark Horse Comics: Jan, 2010 - No. 5, May, 2010 ($2.99, limited series)

1,2-Mignola & Arcudi-s/Guy Davis-a; Mignola-c						3.00

B.P.R.D.: 1946
Dark Horse Comics: Jan, 2008 - No. 5, May, 2008 ($2.99, limited series)

1-5-Mignola & Dysart-s/Azaceta-a; Mignola-c						3.00

B.P.R.D.: 1947
Dark Horse Comics: Jul, 2009 - No. 5, Nov, 2009 ($2.99, limited series)

1-5-Mignola & Dysart-s/Bá & Moon-a; Mignola-c						3.00

B.P.R.D.: 1948
Dark Horse Comics: Oct, 2012 - No. 5, Feb, 2013 ($3.50, limited series)

1-5-Mignola & Arcudi-s/Fiumara-a; Johnson-c						3.50

B.P.R.D.: PLAGUE OF FROGS
Dark Horse Comics: Mar, 2004 - No. 5, July, 2004 ($2.99, limited series)

1-5-Mignola-s/Guy Davis-c/a						3.00
TPB (1/05, $17.95) r/series; sketchbook pages & afterword by Davis & Mignola						18.00

B.P.R.D.: THE BLACK FLAME
Dark Horse Comics: Sept, 2005 - No. 6, Jan, 2006 ($2.99, limited series)

1-6-Mignola & Arcudi-s/Guy Davis-a/ Mignola-c						3.00
TPB (7/06, $17.95) r/series; sketchbook pages & afterword by Davis & Mignola						18.00

B.P.R.D.: THE BLACK GODDESS
Dark Horse Comics: Jan, 2009 - No. 5, May, 2009 ($2.99, limited series)

1-5-Mignola & Arcudi-s/Guy Davis-a/Nowlan-c						3.00

B.P.R.D.: THE DEAD
Dark Horse Comics: Nov, 2004 - No. 5, Mar, 2005 ($2.99, limited series)

1-5-Mignola-s/Guy Davis-c/a						3.00

B.P.R.D.: THE DEAD REMEMBERED
Dark Horse Comics: Apr, 2011 - No. 3, Jun, 2011 ($3.50, limited series)

1-3-Mignola-s; Moline-a; Jo Chen-c. 1-Variant-c by Moline						3.50

B.P.R.D.: THE DEVIL YOU KNOW
Dark Horse Comics: Jul, 2017 - No. 15, Apr, 2019 ($3.99, mature)

1-15: 1-Mignola & Allie-s/Laurence Campbell-a/Fegredo-c. 6-8-Fiumara-a						4.00

	GD 2.0	VG 4.0	FN 6.0	VF 8.0	VF/NM 9.0	NM- 9.2

B.P.R.D.: THE UNIVERSAL MACHINE
Dark Horse Comics: Apr, 2006 - No. 5, Aug, 2006 ($2.99, limited series)
1-5-Mignola & Arcudi-s/Guy Davis-a/Mignola-c. 5-Mignola-a (5 pgs.) — 3.00
TPB (1/07, $17.95) r/series; sketchbook pages by Davis; Mignola afterword — 18.00

B.P.R.D.: THE WARNING
Dark Horse Comics: July, 2008 - No. 5, Nov, 2008 ($2.99, limited series)
1-5-Mignola & Arcudi-s/Guy Davis-c/a — 3.00

B.P.R.D.: VAMPIRE
Dark Horse Comics: Mar, 2013 - No. 5, Jul, 2013 ($3.50, limited series)
1-5-Mignola-s/Bá & Moon-a; Moon-c — 3.50

BRADLEYS, THE (Also see Hate)
Fantagraphics Books: Apr, 1999 - No. 6, Jan, 2000 ($2.95, B&W, limited series)
1-6-Reprints Peter Bagge's-s/a — 3.00

BRADY BUNCH, THE (TV)(See Kite Fun Book and Binky #78)
Dell Publishing Co.: Feb, 1970 - No. 2, May, 1970 (photo-c)

	GD 2.0	VG 4.0	FN 6.0	VF 8.0	VF/NM 9.0	NM- 9.2
1	13	26	39	89	195	300
2	10	20	30	64	132	200

BRAIN, THE
Sussex Publ. Co./Magazine Enterprises: Sept, 1956 - No. 7, 1958

	GD 2.0	VG 4.0	FN 6.0	VF 8.0	VF/NM 9.0	NM- 9.2
1-Dan DeCarlo-a in all including reprints	15	30	45	85	130	175
2,3	9	18	27	52	69	85
4-7	7	14	21	35	50	70
I.W. Reprints #1-4,8-10('63),14: 2-Reprints Sussex #2 with new cover added	2	4	6	11	16	20
Super Reprint #17,18(nd)	2	4	6	11	16	20

BRAINBANX
DC Comics (Helix): Mar, 1997 - No. 6, Aug, 1997 ($2.50, series)
1-6: Elaine Lee-s/Temujin-a — 4.00

BRAIN BOY
Dell Publishing Co.: Apr-June, 1962 - No. 6, Sept-Nov, 1963 (Painted c-#1-6)

	GD 2.0	VG 4.0	FN 6.0	VF 8.0	VF/NM 9.0	NM- 9.2
Four Color 1330(#1)-Gil Kane-a; origin	10	20	30	69	147	225
2(7-9/62),3,6- 4-Origin retold	6	12	18	41	76	110

BRAIN BOY
Dark Horse Comics: Sept, 2013 - No. 3, Nov, 2013 ($2.99, series)
1-3-Van Lente/Silva-a/Olivetti-c — 3.00
#0-(12/13, $2.99) Reprints stories from Dark Horse Presents #23-25; Olivetti-c — 3.00

BRAIN BOY: THE MEN FROM G.E.S.T.A.L.T.
Dark Horse Comics: May, 2014 - No. 4, Aug, 2014 ($2.99, limited series)
1-4-Van Lente/Freddie Williams II-a/c — 3.00

BRAM STOKER'S DRACULA (Movie)(Also see Dracula: Vlad the Impaler)
Topps Comics: Oct, 1992 - No. 4, Jan, 1993 ($2.95, limited series, polybagged)
1-(1st & 2nd printing)-Adaptation of film begins; Mignola-c/a in all; 4 trading cards & poster; photo scenes of movie — 6.00
1-Crimson foil edition (limited to 500) — 24.00
2-4: 2-Bound-in poster & cards. 4 trading cards in both. 3-Contains coupon to win 1 of 500 crimson foil-c edition of #1. 4-Contains coupon to win 1 of 500 uncut sheets of all 16 trading cards — 4.00

BRAND ECHH (See Not Brand Echh)

BRAND OF EMPIRE (See Luke Short's... Four Color 771)

BRASS
Image Comics (WildStorm Productions): Aug, 1996 - No. 3, May, 1997 ($2.50, lim. series)
1-($4.50) Folio Ed.; oversized — 5.00
1-3: Wiesenfeld-s/Bennett-a. 3-Grunge & Roxy(Gen 13) cameo — 4.00

BRASS
DC Comics (WildStorm): Aug, 2000 - No. 6, Jan, 2001 ($2.50, series)
1-6-Arcudi-s — 3.00

BRATH
CrossGeneration Comics: Feb, 2003 - No. 14, June, 2004 ($2.95)
Prequel-Dixon-s/Di Vito-a — 3.00
1-14: 1-(3/03)-Dixon-s/Di Vito-a — 3.00
Vol. 1: Hammer of Vengeance (2003, $9.95) Digest-sized reprint of Prequel & #1-6 — 10.00

BRATS BIZARRE
Marvel Comics (Epic/Heavy Hitters): 1994 - No. 4, 1994 ($2.50, limited series)
1-4: All w/bound-in trading cards — 4.00

BRAVADOS, THE (See Wild Western Action)
Skywald Publ. Corp.: Aug, 1971 (52 pgs., one-shot)

	GD 2.0	VG 4.0	FN 6.0	VF 8.0	VF/NM 9.0	NM- 9.2
1-Red Mask, The Durango Kid, Billy Nevada-r; Bolle-a; 3-D effect story	3	6	9	16	23	30

BRAVE AND THE BOLD, THE (See Best Of... & Super DC Giant) (Replaced by Batman & the Outsiders)
National Periodical Publ./DC Comics: Aug-Sept, 1955 - No. 200, July, 1983

	GD 2.0	VG 4.0	FN 6.0	VF 8.0	VF/NM 9.0	NM- 9.2
1-Viking Prince by Kubert, Silent Knight, Golden Gladiator begin; part Kubert-c	400	800	1200	3400	7700	12,000
2	141	282	423	1163	2632	4100
3,4	82	164	246	656	1478	2300
5-Robin Hood begins (4-5/56, 1st DC app.), ends #15; see Robin Hood Tales #7	86	172	258	668	1544	2400
6-10: 6-Robin Hood by Kubert; last Golden Gladiator app.; Silent Knight; no Viking Prince. 8-1st S.A. issue	55	110	165	440	996	1550
11-22,24: 12,14-Robin Hood-c. 18,21-23-Grey tone-c. 22-Last Silent Knight. 24-Last Viking Prince by Kubert (2nd solo book)	46	92	138	340	770	1200
23-Viking Prince origin by Kubert; 1st B&B single theme issue & 1st Viking Prince solo book	54	108	162	432	966	1500
25-1st app. Suicide Squad (8-9/59)	314	628	942	2622	5961	9300
26-Suicide Squad	50	100	150	400	900	1400

	GD 2.0	VG 4.0	FN 6.0	VF 8.0	VF/NM 9.0	NM- 9.2
27-Suicide Squad	46	92	138	359	805	1250
28-(2-3/60)-Justice League 1st app.; battle Starro; 1st app. Snapper Carr	1450	2900	5800	18,600	56,800	95,000
28 (Facsimile Edition)(2020, $3.99) Reprints #28 with original ads and letter column						4.00
28 (Facsimile Edition)(2022, $3.99) Reprints #28 with original ads and letter column						4.00
29-Justice League (4-5/60)-2nd app. battle the Weapons Master; robot-c	255	510	765	2104	4752	7400
30-Justice League (6-7/60)-3rd app.; vs. Amazo	203	406	609	1675	3788	5900
31-1st app. Cave Carson (8-9/60); scarce in high grade; 1st try-out series	53	106	165	440	995	1550
32,33-Cave Carson	27	54	81	189	420	650
34-Origin/1st app. Silver-Age Hawkman, Hawkgirl & Byth (2-3/61); Gardner Fox story; Kubert-c/a ; 1st S.A. Hawkman tryout series; 2nd in #42-44; both series predate Hawkman #1 (4-5/64)	224	448	672	1848	4174	6500
35-Hawkman by Kubert (4-5/61)-2nd app.	42	84	126	311	706	1100
36-Hawkman by Kubert; origin & 1st app. Shadow Thief (6-7/61)-3rd app.	36	72	108	266	596	925
37-Suicide Squad (2nd tryout series)	30	60	90	216	483	750
38,39-Suicide Squad. 38-Last 10¢ issue	22	44	66	154	340	525
40,41-Cave Carson Inside Earth (2nd try-out series). 40-Kubert-a. 41-Meskin-a	14	28	42	96	211	325
42-Hawkman by Kubert (2nd tryout series); Hawkman earns helmet wings; Byth app.	22	44	66	154	340	525
43-Hawkman by Kubert; more detailed origin	24	48	72	168	372	575
44-Hawkman by Kubert; grey-tone-c	22	44	66	154	340	525
45-49-Strange Sports Stories by Infantino	9	18	27	61	123	185
50-The Green Arrow & Manhunter From Mars (10-11/63); 1st Manhunter x-over outside of Detective Comics (pre-dates House of Mystery #143); team-ups begin	21	42	63	147	324	500
51-Aquaman & Hawkman (12-1/63-64); pre-dates Hawkman #1	20	40	60	136	303	470
52-(2-3/64)-3 Battle Stars; Sgt. Rock, Haunted Tank, Johnny Cloud, & Mlle. Marie team-up for 1st time by Kubert (c/a)	25	50	75	175	388	600
53-Atom & The Flash by Toth	10	20	30	69	147	225
54-Kid Flash, Robin & Aqualad; 1st app./origin Teen Titans (6-7/64)	111	222	333	888	1994	3100
55-Metal Men & The Atom	9	18	27	61	123	185
56-The Flash & Manhunter From Mars	9	18	27	61	123	185
57-Origin & 1st app. Metamorpho (12-1/64-65)	32	64	96	230	515	800
58-2nd app. Metamorpho by Fradon	9	18	27	60	147	225
59-Batman & Green Lantern; 1st Batman team-up in Brave and the Bold	13	26	38	188	290	
60-Teen Titans (2nd app.)-1st app. new Wonder Girl (Donna Troy), who joins Titans (7-65)	68	136	204	544	1222	1900
61-Origin Starman & Black Canary by Anderson	13	26	39	89	195	300
62-Origin Starman & Black Canary cont'd. 62-1st S.A. app. Wildcat (10-11/65); 1st S.A. app. of G.A. Huntress (W.W. villain)	11	22	33	75	160	245
63-Supergirl & Wonder Woman	10	20	30	66	138	215
64-Batman Versus Eclipso (see H.O.S. #61)	8	16	24	51	96	140
65-Flash & Doom Patrol (4-5/66)	7	14	21	44	82	120
66-Metamorpho & Metal Men (6-7/66)	7	14	21	44	82	120
67-Batman & The Flash by Infantino; Batman team-ups begin, end #200 (8-9/66)	10	20	30	105	155	
68-Batman/Metamorpho/Joker/Riddler/Penguin-c/story; Batman as Bat-Hulk (Hulk parody)	8	16	56	108	160	
69-Batman & Green Lantern	6	12	18	38	69	100
70-Batman & Hawkman; Craig-a(p)	6	12	18	38	69	100
71-Batman & Green Arrow	6	12	18	38	69	100
72-Spectre & Flash (6-7/67); 4th app. The Spectre; predates Spectre #1	7	14	21	46	86	125
73-Aquaman & The Atom	6	12	18	38	69	100
74-Batman & Metal Men	6	12	18	38	69	100
75-Batman & The Spectre (12-1/67-68); 6th app. Spectre; came out between Spectre #1 & #2	7	14	21	48	89	130
76-Batman & Plastic Man (2-3/68); came out between Plastic Man #8 & #9	6	12	18	40	73	105
77-Batman & The Atom	6	12	18	37	66	95
78-Batman, Wonder Woman & Batgirl	8	16	24	56	108	160
79-Batman & Deadman by Neal Adams (8-9/68); early Deadman app.	11	22	33	72	154	235
80-Batman & Creeper (10-11/68); N. Adams-a; early app. The Creeper; came out between Creeper #3 & #4	8	16	24	52	99	145
81-Batman & Flash; N. Adams-a	9	18	27	57	111	165
82-Batman & Aquaman; N. Adams-a; origin Ocean Master retold (2-3/69)	9	18	27	59	117	175
83-Batman & Teen Titans; N. Adams-a (4-5/69)	8	16	24	55	105	155
84-Batman (G.A., 1st S.A. app.) & Sgt. Rock; N. Adams-a; last 12¢ issue (6-7/69)	9	18	27	57	111	165
85-Batman & Green Arrow; 1st new costume for Green Arrow by Neal Adams (8-9/69)	16	32	48	110	243	375
86-Batman & Deadman (10-11/69); N. Adams-a; story concludes from Strange Adventures #216 (1-2/69)	9	18	27	59	117	175
87-Batman & Wonder Woman	5	10	15	33	57	80
88-Batman & Wildcat	4	8	12	27	44	60
89-Batman & Phantom Stranger (4-5/70); early Phantom Stranger app. (came out between Phantom Stranger #6 & 7	4	8	12	27	44	60
90-Batman & Adam Strange	4	8	12	27	44	60
91-Batman & Black Canary (8-9/70)	4	8	12	27	44	60
92-Batman; intro the Bat Squad	4	8	12	27	44	60
93-Batman-House of Mystery; N. Adams-a	10	20	30	69	147	225
94-Batman-Teen Titans	4	8	12	27	47	65
95-Batman & Plastic Man	3	6	9	21	33	45
96-Batman & Sgt. Rock; last 15¢ issue	3	6	9	21	33	45
97-Batman & Wildcat; 52 pg. issues begin, end #102; reprints origin & 1st app. Deadman from Strange Advs. #205	3	6	9	21	33	45
98-Batman & Phantom Stranger; 1st Jim Aparo Batman-a?	3	6	9	21	33	45

Brain Boy #1 © DH

Brave and the Bold #83 © DC

Bravest Warriors #1 © Frederator

	GD 2.0	VG 4.0	FN 6.0	VF 8.0	VF/NM 9.0	NM- 9.2
99-Batman & Flash	3	6	9	21	33	45
100-(2-3/72, 25¢, 52 pgs.)-Batman-Green Lantern-Green Arrow-Black Canary-Robin;						
Deadman-r by Adams/Str. Advs. #210	6	12	18	40	73	105
101-Batman & Metamorpho; Kubert Viking Prince	3	6	9	20	31	42
102-Batman-Teen Titans; N. Adams-a(p)	5	10	15	31	53	75
103-107,109,110: Batman team-ups: 103-Metal Men. 104-Deadman. 105-Wonder Woman.						
106-Green Arrow. 107-Black Canary. 109-Demon. 110-Wildcat						
	3	6	9	16	23	30
108-Sgt. Rock	3	6	9	17	26	35
111-Batman/Joker-c/story	5	10	15	30	50	70
112-117: All 100 pgs.; Batman team-ups: 112-Mr. Miracle. 113-Metal Men; reprints origin/1st						
Hawkman from Brave and the Bold #34; r/origin Multi-Man/Challengers #14. 114-Aquaman.						
115-Atom; r/origin Viking Prince from #23; r/Dr. Fate/Hourman/Solomon Grundy/Green						
Lantern from Showcase #55. 116-Spectre. 117-Sgt. Rock; last 100 pg. issue						
	5	10	15	30	50	70
118-Batman/Wildcat/Joker-c/story	3	6	9	21	33	45
119,121-123,125-128,132-140: Batman team-ups: 119-Man-Bat. 121-Metal Men. 122-Swamp						
Thing. 123-Plastic Man/Metamorpho. 125-Flash. 126-Aquaman. 127-Wildcat.						
128-Mr. Miracle. 132-Kung-Fu Fighter. 133-Deadman. 134-Green Lantern. 135-Metal Men.						
136-Metal Men/Green Arrow. 137-Demon. 138-Mr. Miracle. 139-Hawkman.						
140-Wonder Woman	2	4	6	8	10	12
120-Kamandi (68 pgs.)	3	6	9	14	19	24
124-Sgt. Rock; Jim Aparo app. on cover & in story	2	4	6	10	14	18
129,130-Batman/Green Arrow/Atom parts 1 & 2; Joker & Two Face-c/stories						
	3	6	9	15	22	28
131-Batman & Wonder Woman vs. Catwoman-c/sty	3	6	9	14	20	25
141-Batman/Black Canary vs. Joker-c/story	3	6	9	15	22	28
142-160: Batman team-ups: 142-Aquaman. 143-Creeper; origin Human Target (44 pgs.).						
144-Green Arrow; origin Human Target part 2 (44 pgs.). 145-Phantom Stranger. 146-G.A.						
Batman/Unknown Soldier. 147-Supergirl. 148-Plastic Man; X-Mas-c. 149-Teen Titans.						
150-Anniversary issue; Superman. 151-Flash. 152-Atom. 153-Red Tornado.						
154-Metamorpho. 155-Green Lantern. 156-Dr. Fate. 157-Batman vs. Kamandi (ties into						
Kamandi #59). 158-Wonder Woman. 159-Ra's Al Ghul. 160-Supergirl						
	1	3	4	6	8	10
145(11/79)-147,150-159,165(8/80)-(Whitman variants; low print run;						
none show issue # on cover)	2	4	6	11	16	20
161-181,183-190,192-195,198,199: Batman team-ups: 161-Adam Strange. 162-G.A. Batman/						
Sgt. Rock. 163-Black Lightning. 164-Hawkman. 165-Man-Bat. 166-Black Canary; Nemesis						
(intro) back-up story begins, ends #192; Penguin-c/story. 167-G.A. Batman/Blackhawk/						
origin Nemesis. 168-Green Arrow. 169-Zatanna. 170-Nemesis. 171-Scalphunter.						
172-Firestorm. 173-Guardians of the Universe. 174-Green Lantern. 175-Lois Lane.						
176-Swamp Thing. 177-Elongated Man. 178-Creeper. 179-Legion. 180-Spectre. 181-Hawk						
& Dove. 183-Riddler. 184-Huntress & Earth II Batman. 185-Green Arrow. 186-Hawkman.						
187-Metal Men. 188,189-Rose & the Thorn. 190-Adam Strange. 192-Superboy vs. Mr. I.Q.						
194-Flash. 195-I...Vampire. 198-Karate Kid. 199-Batman vs. The Spectre					6.00	
182-G.A. Robin; G.A. Starman app.; 1st modern app. G.A. Batwoman						
	2	4	6	9	13	16
191-Batman/Joker-c/story; Nemesis app.	3	6	9	17	26	35
196-Ragman; origin Ragman retold.	1	2	3	5	6	8
197-Catwoman; Earth II Batman & Catwoman marry; 2nd modern app. of G.A. Batwoman;						
Scarecrow story in Golden Age style	3	6	9	18	27	36
200-Double-sized (64 pgs.); printed on Mando paper; Earth One & Earth Two Batman app. in						
separate stories; intro/1st app. Batman & The Outsiders; 1st app. Katana						
	4	8	12	23	37	50

NOTE: **Neal Adams**-a-79-86, 93, 100r, 102; c-75, 76, 79-86, 88-90, 93, 95, 99, 100r. **M. Anderson** a-115r; c-72i, 96i. **Andru/Esposito** c-25-27. **Aparo** a-98, 100-102, 104-125, 126i, 127-136, 138-145, 147, 148i, 149-152, 154, 155, 157, 158i, 161-170, 173-178, 180-182, 184, 186i-189i, 191i-193i, 195, 196 200i; c-105-109, 111-114, 116-118, 138-175, 177, 180-184, 186-200. **Austin** a-166i. **Bernard Baily** c-32, 33, 58. **Buckler** a-185, 186p; c-137, 178p, 185p, 186p. **Giordano** a-143, 144. **Infantino** a-67p, 72p, 98r, 115r, 172p, 183p, 190p, 194p; c-45-49, 67p, 69p, 70p, 72p, 96p, 98r. **Kaluta** c-176. **Kane** a-115r; c-59, 64. **Kubert** &/or **Heath** a-1-24; reprints-101, 113, 115, 117. **Kubert** a-99r; c-22-24, 34-36, 40, 42-44, 52. **Mooney** a-114r. **Mortimer** a-64, 69. **Newton** a-153p, 156p, 165p. **Irv Novick** a-1(part), 2-21. **Fred Ray** a-78r. **Roussos** a-50, 76i, 114r. **Staton** 148p, 52 pgs.-97, 100; 68 pgs.-120; 100 pgs.-112-117.

BRAVE AND THE BOLD, THE
DC Comics: Dec, 1991 - No. 6, June, 1992 ($1.75, limited series)

1-6-Green Arrow, The Butcher, The Question in all; Grell scripts in all						4.00

NOTE: Grell c-3, 4-6.

BRAVE AND THE BOLD, THE
DC Comics: Apr, 2007 - No. 35, Aug, 2010 ($2.99)

1-Batman & Green Lantern team-up; Roulette app.; Waid-s/Peréz-c/a; 2 covers — 5.00
2-32,34,35: 2-GL & Supergirl. 3-Batman & Blue Beetle vs. Fatal Five; Lobo app.
4-6-LSH app. 12-Megistus conclusion; Ordway-a. 14-Kolins-a. 16-Superman & Catwoman.
28-Blackhawks app. 29-Batman/Brother Power the Geek. 31-Atom/Joker — 3.00
33-Batgirl, Zatanna & W.W.; prelude to Killing Joke — 3 6 9 17 26 35
...: Demons and Dragons HC (2009, $24.99, dustjacket) r/#13-16; Brave & the Bold V1 #181,

Flash V3 #107 and Impulse #17; Mark Waid commentary — 25.00
...: Demons and Dragons SC (2010, $17.99) same contents as HC — 18.00
...: Milestone SC (2010, $17.99) r/#24-26 and Static #12, Hardware #16, Xombi #6 — 18.00
Team-up of the Brave and the Bold HC (2010, $24.99) r/#27-33 — 25.00
...: The Book of Destiny HC (2008, $24.99, dustjacket) r/#7-12; Ordway sketch pages — 25.00
...: The Book of Destiny SC (2009, $17.99) r/#7-12; Ordway sketch pages — 18.00
...: The Lords of Luck HC (2007, $24.99, dustjacket) r/#1-6 with Waid intro & annotations — 25.00
...: The Lords of Luck SC (2008, $17.99) r/#1-6 with Waid intro & annotations — 18.00
...: Without Sin SC (2009, $17.99) r/#17-22 — 18.00

BRAVE AND THE BOLD ANNUAL NO. 1 1969 ISSUE, THE
DC Comics: 2001 ($5.95, one-shot)
1-Reprints Silver Age team-ups in 1960s-style 80 pg. Giant format — 6.00

BRAVE AND THE BOLD: BATMAN AND WONDER WOMAN, THE
DC Comics: Apr, 2018 - No. 6, Sept, 2018 ($3.99, limited series)
1-6-Liam Sharp-s/a — 4.00

BRAVE AND THE BOLD SPECIAL, THE (See DC Special Series No. 8)

BRAVE EAGLE (TV)
Dell Publishing Co.: No. 705, June, 1956 - No. 929, July, 1958

	GD 2.0	VG 4.0	FN 6.0	VF 8.0	VF/NM 9.0	NM- 9.2
Four Color 705 (#1)-Photo-c	7	14	21	46	86	125
Four Color 770, 816, 879 (2/58), 929-All photo-c	5	10	15	33	57	80

BRAVE NEW WORLD (See DCU Brave New World)

BRAVE OLD WORLD (V2K)
DC Comics (Vertigo): Feb, 2000 - No. 4, May, 2000 ($2.50, mini-series)
1-4-Messner-Loeb-s/Guy Davis & Phil Hester-a — 3.00

BRAVE ONE, THE (Movie)
Dell Publishing Co.: No. 773, Mar, 1957

	GD 2.0	VG 4.0	FN 6.0	VF 8.0	VF/NM 9.0	NM- 9.2
Four Color 773-Photo-c	5	10	15	35	63	90

BRAVEST WARRIORS (Based on the animated web series)
BOOM! Entertainment (KaBOOM!): Oct, 2012 - No. 36, Sept, 2015 ($3.99)
1-36-Multiple covers on each — 4.00
2014 Annual (1/14, $4.99) Short stories featuring Catbug; multiple covers — 5.00
2014 Impossibear Special 1 (6/14, $4.99) Short stories; multiple covers — 5.00
... Paralyzed Horse Giant 1 (11/14, $4.99) Short stories; multiple covers — 5.00
...: Tales From the Holo John 1 (5/15, $4.99) Short stories; multiple covers — 5.00

BRAVURA
Malibu Comics (Bravura): 1995 (mail-in offer)
0-wraparound holographic-c; short stories and promo pin-ups of Chaykin's Power & Glory,
Gil Kane's & Steven Grant's Edge, Starlin's Breed, & Simonson's Star Slammers — 5.00
1 1/2 — 7.00

BREACH
DC Comics: Mar, 2005 - No. 11, Jan, 2006 ($2.95/$2.50)
1-11: 1-Marcos Martin-a/Bob Harras-s; origin. 4-JLA-c/app. — 3.00

BREAKDOWN
Devil's Due Publ.: Oct, 2004 - No. 6, Apr, 2005 ($2.95)
1-6: 1-Two covers by Dave Ross and Leinil Yu; Dixon-s/Ross-a — 3.00

BREAKFAST AFTER NOON
Oni Press: May, 2000 - No. 6, Jan, 2001 ($2.95, B&W, limited series)
1-6-Andi Watson-s/a — 3.00
TPB (2001, $19.95) r/series — 20.00

BREAKING INTO COMICS THE MARVEL WAY
Marvel Comics: May, 2010 - No. 2, May, 2010 ($3.99, limited series)
1,2-Short stories by various newcomer artists; artist profiles — 4.00

BREAKNECK BLVD.
MotioN Comics/Slave Labor Graphics Vol. 2: No. 0, Feb, 1994 - No. 2, Nov, 1994; Vol. 2#1,
Jul, 1995 - #6, Dec., 1996 ($2.50/$2.95, B&W)
0-2, V2#1-6: 0-Pérez/Giordano-c — 4.00

BREAK-THRU (Also see Exiles V1#4)
Malibu Comics (Ultraverse): Dec, 1993 - No. 2, Jan, 1994 ($2.50, 44 pgs.)
1,2-Pérez-c/a(p); has x-overs in Ultraverse titles — 5.00

BREATH OF BONES: A TALE OF THE GOLEM
Dark Horse Comics: Jun, 2013 - No. 3, Aug, 2013 ($3.99, B&W, limited series)
1-3-Niles-s/Wachter-a — 4.00

BREATHTAKER
DC Comics: 1990 - No. 4, 1990 ($4.95, 52 pgs., prestige format, mature)

	GD	VG	FN	VF	VF/NM	NM-		GD	VG	FN	VF	VF/NM	NM-
	2.0	4.0	6.0	8.0	9.0	9.2		2.0	4.0	6.0	8.0	9.0	9.2

Book 1-4: Mark Wheatley-painted-c/a & scripts; Marc Hempel-a ... 5.00
TPB (1994, $14.95) r/#1-4; intro by Neil Gaiman ... 15.00

'BREED
Malibu Comics (Bravura): Jan, 1994 - No. 6, 1994 ($2.50, limited series)

1-(48 pgs.)-Origin/1st app. of 'Breed by Starlin; contains Bravura stamps; spot varnish-c ... 5.00
2-6: 2-5-contains Bravura stamps. 6-Death of Rachel ... 4.00
....:Book of Genesis (1994, $12.95)-reprints #1-6 ... 13.00

'BREED II
Malibu Comics (Bravura): Nov, 1994 - No. 6, Apr, 1995 ($2.95, limited series)

1-6: Starlin-c/a/scripts in all. 1-Gold edition ... 4.00

'BREED III
Image Comics: May, 2011 - No. 7, Dec, 2011 ($2.99)

1-7: Starlin-c/a/scripts in all. ... 3.00

BREEZE LAWSON, SKY SHERIFF (See Sky Sheriff)

BRENDA LEE'S LIFE STORY
Dell Publishing Co.: July-Sept., 1962

01-078-209 ... 8 ... 16 ... 24 ... 54 ... 102 ... 150

BRENDA STARR (Also see All Great)
Four Star Comics Corp./Superior Comics Ltd.: No. 13, 9/47; No. 14, 3/48; V2#3, 6/48 - V2#12, 12/49

V1#13-By Dale Messick	135	270	405	864	1482	2100
14-Classic Kamen bondage-c	1000	2000	3000	7600	13,800	20,000
V2#3-Baker-a?	93	186	279	591	1021	1450
4-Used in SOTI, pg. 21; Kamen-c	148	296	444	947	1624	2300
5-10	81	162	243	518	884	1250
11,12 (Scarce)	84	168	252	538	919	1300

NOTE: Newspaper reprints plus original material through #6. All original #7 on.

BRENDA STARR (...Reporter)(Young Lovers No. 16 on?)
Charlton Comics: No. 13, June, 1955 - No. 15, Oct, 1955

13-15-Newspaper-r ... 37 ... 74 ... 111 ... 222 ... 361 ... 500

BRENDA STARR REPORTER
Dell Publishing Co.: Oct, 1963

1 ... 12 ... 24 ... 36 ... 79 ... 170 ... 260

BRER RABBIT (See Kite Fun Book, Walt Disney Showcase #28 and Wheaties)
Dell Publishing Co.: No. 129, 1946; No. 208, Jan, 1949; No. 693, 1956 (Disney)

Four Color 129 (#1)-Adapted from Disney movie "Song of the South"	36	72	108	259	580	900
Four Color 208 (1/49)	14	28	42	96	211	325
Four Color 693-Part-r #129	11	22	33	76	163	250

BRIAN PULIDO'S LADY DEATH... (See Lady Death)

BRIAR
BOOM! Studios: Sept, 2022 - No. 4 ($4.99/$3.99)

1-($4.99) A Sleeping Beauty pastiche; Cantwell-s/Garcia-a ... 5.00
2-4-($3.99) ... 4.00

BRICK BRADFORD (Also see Ace Comics & King Comics)
King Features Syndicate/Standard: No. 5, July, 1948 - No. 8, July, 1949 (Ritt & Grey reprints)

5	24	48	72	144	237	330
6-Robot-c (by Schomburg?).	300	600	900	2010	3505	5000
7-Schomburg-c. 8-Says #7 inside, #8 on-c	20	40	60	117	189	260

BRICKLEBERRY (Based on the animated series)
Dynamite Entertainment: 2016 - No. 4, 2016 ($3.99, limited series)

1-4-Waco O'Guin & Roger Black-s ... 4.00

BRIDE'S DIARY (Formerly Black Cobra No. 3)
Ajax/Farrell Publ.: No. 4, May, 1955 - No. 10, Aug, 1956

4 (#1)	15	30	45	85	130	175
5-8	11	22	33	64	90	115
9,10-Disbrow-a	13	26	39	74	105	135

BRIDES IN LOVE (Hollywood Romances & Summer Love No. 46 on)
Charlton Comics: Aug, 1956 - No. 45, Feb, 1965

1	18	36	54	105	165	225
2	10	20	30	58	79	100
3-6,8-10	5	10	15	31	53	75
7-(68 pgs.)	5	10	15	35	63	90
11-20	4	8	12	25	40	55
21-45	3	6	9	18	27	36

BRIDES OF HELHEIM
Oni Press: Oct, 2014 - No. 6, May, 2015 ($3.99)

1-6-Cullen Bunn-s/Joëlle Jones-a ... 4.00

BRIDES ROMANCES
Quality Comics Group: Nov, 1953 - No. 23, Dec, 1956

1	28	56	84	165	270	375
2	15	30	45	85	130	175
3-10: Last precode (3/55)	15	30	45	84	127	170
11-17,19-22: 15-Baker-a(p)?; Colan-a	14	28	42	80	115	150
18-Baker-a	17	34	51	98	154	210
23-Baker-c/a	30	60	90	177	289	400

BRIDE'S SECRETS
Ajax/Farrell(Excellent Publ.)/Four-Star: Apr-May, 1954 - No. 19, May, 1958

1	21	42	63	124	202	280
2	15	30	45	85	130	175
3-6: Last precode (3/55)	13	26	39	74	105	135
7-11,13-19: 18-Hollingsworth-a	12	24	36	69	97	125
12-Disbrow-a	14	28	42	80	115	150

BRIDE-TO-BE ROMANCES (See True...)

BRIGADE

Image Comics (Extreme Studios): Aug, 1992 - No. 4, 1993 ($1.95, lim. series)

1-Liefeld part plots/scripts in all, Liefeld-c(p); contains 2 Brigade trading cards ... 5.00
1-Gold foil stamped logo edition ... 8.00
2-Contains coupon for Image Comics #0 & 2 trading cards ... 4.00
2-With coupon missing ... 3.00
3,4: 3-Contains 2 trading cards; 1st Birds of Prey. 4-Flip book featuring Youngblood #5 ... 4.00

BRIGADE
Image Comics (Extreme): V2#1, May, 1993 - V2#22, July, 1995, V2#25, May, 1996 ($1.95/$2.50)

V2#1-22,25: 1-Gatefold-c; Liefeld co-plots; Blood Brothers part 1; Bloodstrike app. 2-(6/93, V2#1 on inside)-Foil merricote-c (newsstand ed. w/out foil-c exists). 3-Perez-c(i); Liefeld scripts. 8,9-Coupons #2 & 6 for Extreme Prejudice #0 bound-in. 11-(8/94, $2.50) WildC.A.T.S app. 16-Polybagged w/ trading card. 22-"Supreme Apocalypse" Pt. 4; w/ trading card ... 4.00
0-(9/93)-Liefeld scripts; 1st app. Warcry; Youngblood & Wildcats app.; ... 4.00
20-Variant-c. by Quesada & Palmiotti ... 4.00
Remastered Edition #1 (9/22, $3.99) #1's pages redrawn by modern artists; flipbook with Heirborne by Rob Liefeld-s/a ... 5.00
Sourcebook 1 (8/94, $2.95) ... 4.00
1-(Awesome Ent., 7/00, $2.99) Flip book w/Century preview ... 4.00
1-(6/10, $3.99) Liefeld-s/Mychaels-a; covers by Liefeld & Mychaels ... 4.00

BRIGAND, THE (See Fawcett Movie Comics No. 18)

BRIGGS LAND
Dark Horse Comics: Aug, 2016 - No. 6, Jan, 2017 ($3.99)

1-6-Brian Wood-s/Mack Chater-a/Tula Lotay-c ... 4.00

BRIGGS LAND: LONE WOLVES
Dark Horse Comics: Jun, 2017 - No. 6, Nov, 2017 ($3.99)

1-6: 1-Brian Wood-s/Mack Chater-a/Matthew Woodson-c. 4-Del Ray-a ... 4.00

BRIGHTEST DAY (Also see Blackest Night and Green Lantern)
DC Comics: No. 0, Jun, 2010 - No. 24, Late Jun, 2011 ($3.99/$2.99)

0-($3.99) Johns & Tomasi-s/Pasarin-a/Finch-c ... 4.00
0-Variant-c by Reis ... 8.00
1-23-($2.99) 1-Black Manta returns. 4-Intro. Jackson (new Aqualad) 16-Aqualad origin. 18-Hawkman & Hawkgirl killed. 20-Aquaman killed ... 3.00
1-23: Variant covers. 1-6,9-18,20-23-by Reis, 7,8 White Lantern by Sook. 19-by Frank ... 6.00
24-($4.99) Swamp Thing and John Constantine return to DC universe ... 5.00
24-($4.99) Variant cover by Reis ... 8.00
...: The Atom Special (9/10, $2.99) Lemire-s/Asrar-a/Frank-c ... 3.00
... Volume 1 HC (2010, $29.99) r/#0-7; cover gallery ... 30.00
... Volume 2 HC (2011, $29.99) r/#8-16; cover gallery ... 30.00

BRIGHTEST DAY AFTERMATH: THE SEARCH FOR SWAMP THING
DC Comics: Aug, 2011 - No. 3, Oct, 2011 ($2.99, limited series)

1-3-Vankin-s/Castiello-a; covers by Syaf & Jones; John Constantine & Zatanna app. ... 3.00

BRILLIANT
Marvel Comics (Icon): Jul, 2011 - No. 5, Mar, 2014 ($3.95, limited series)

1-5-Bendis-s/Bagley-a/c ... 4.00

BRILLIANT TRASH
AfterShock Comics: Nov, 2017 - No. 6, May, 2018 ($3.99)

1-6: 1-Tim Seeley-s/Priscilla Petraites-a. 6-Steve Kurth-a ... 4.00

BRING BACK THE BAD GUYS (Also see Fireside Book Series)
Marvel Comics: 1998 ($24.95, TPB)

1-Reprints stories of Marvel villains' secrets ... 25.00

BRING ON THE BAD GUYS (See Fireside Book Series)

BRING THE THUNDER
Dynamite Entertainment: 2010 - No. 4, 2011 ($3.99)

1-4-Alex Ross-c/Ross & Nitz-s/Tortosa-a ... 4.00

BRITANNIA
Valiant Entertainment: Sept, 2016 - No. 4, Dec, 2016 ($3.99, limited series)

1-4-Milligan-s/Ryp-a; set in 60-66 A.D.; Emperor Nero app. ... 4.00
... One Dollar Debut #1 (5/19, $1.00) r/#1 ... 3.00

BRITANNIA: LOST EAGLES OF ROME
Valiant Entertainment: Jul, 2018 - No. 4, Oct, 2018 ($3.99, limited series)

1-4-Milligan-a/Gill-a; Antonius Axia and Achillia in Egypt; multiple covers on each ... 4.00

BRITANNIA: WE WHO ARE ABOUT TO DIE
Valiant Entertainment: Apr, 2017 - No. 4, Jul, 2017 ($3.99, limited series)

1-4-Milligan-s/Ryp-a; further story of Antonius Axia; multiple covers on each ... 4.00

BRITISH PARANORMAL SOCIETY, THE : TIME OUT OF MIND (From Hellboy)
Dark Horse Comics: Apr, 2022 - No. 4, Oct, 2022 ($3.99, limited series)

1-4-Roberson-s/Mutti-a ... 4.00

BROADWAY HOLLYWOOD BLACKOUTS
Stanhall: Mar-Apr, 1954 - No. 3, July-Aug, 1954

| 1 | 37 | 74 | 111 | 222 | 361 | 500 |
| 2,3 | 23 | 46 | 69 | 136 | 223 | 310 |

BROADWAY ROMANCES
Quality Comics Group: January, 1950 - No. 5, Sept, 1950

1-Ward-c/a (9 pgs.); Gustavson-a	58	116	174	371	636	900
2-Ward-a (9 pgs.); photo-c	36	72	108	214	347	480
3-5: All-Photo-c	20	40	60	117	189	260

BROKEN ARROW (TV)
Dell Publishing Co.: No. 855, Oct, 1957 - No. 947, Nov, 1958

| Four Color 855 (#1)-Photo-c | 7 | 14 | 21 | 44 | 82 | 120 |
| Four Color 947-Photo-c | 5 | 10 | 15 | 33 | 57 | 80 |

BRINGING UP FATHER
Dell Publishing Co.: No. 9, 1942 - No. 37, 1944

| Large Feature Comic 9 | 41 | 82 | 123 | 256 | 428 | 600 |
| Four Color 37 | 21 | 42 | 63 | 147 | 324 | 500 |

Brickleberry #1 © 20Fox

Brightest Day #5 © DC

BRZRKR #5 © 74850 Inc.

	GD	VG	FN	VF	VF/NM	NM-
	2.0	4.0	6.0	8.0	9.0	9.2

BROKEN CROSS, THE (See The Crusaders)

BROKEN MOON
American Gothic Press: Sept, 2015 - No. 4, Jan, 2016 ($3.99, limited series)

1-4-Steve Niles-s/Nat Jones-a; covers by Jones & Sanjulian ... 4.00

BROKEN PIECES
Aspen MLT: No. 0, Sept, 2011; Oct, 2011 - No. 5, Dec, 2012 ($2.50/$3.50, limited series)

0-($2.50)-Roslan-s/Kaneshiro-a; three covers ... 3.00
1-5: 1-($3.50)-Roslan-s/Kaneshiro-a; three covers ... 3.50

BROKEN TRINITY
Image Comics (Top Cow): July, 2008 - No. 3, Nov, 2008 ($2.99, limited series)

1-3-Witchblade, Darkness & Angelus app.; Marz-s/Sejic & Hester-a; two covers ... 3.00
...: Aftermath 1 (4/09, $2.99) Marz & Hill-s/Lucas & Kirkham-a ... 3.00
...: Angelus 1 (12/08, $2.99) Marz-s/Stelfreeze-a; two covers ... 3.00
...: Pandora's Box 1-6 (2/10 - No. 6, 4/11 $3.99) Tommy Lee Edwards-c ... 4.00
...: The Darkness 1 (8/08, $2.99) Hester-s/Lucas-a; two covers ... 3.00
...: Witchblade 1 (12/08, $2.99) Marz-s/Blake-a; two covers ... 3.00

BRONCHO BILL (See Comics On Parade, Sparkler & Tip Top Comics)
United Features Syndicate/Standard(Visual Editions) No. 5-on: 1939 - 1940; No. 5, 1?/48 - No. 16, 8?/50

Single Series 2 ('39)	63	126	189	403	689	975
Single Series 19 ('40)(#2 on cvr)	47	94	141	296	498	700
5	18	36	54	107	169	230
6(4/48)-10(4/49)	12	24	36	67	94	120
11(6/49)-16	10	20	30	56	76	95

NOTE: *Schomburg* c-6, 7, 9-13, 15, 16.

BRONZE AGE BOOGIE
AHOY Comics: 2019 - No. 6, 2019 ($3.99, limited series)

1-6-Stuart Moore-s/Alberto Ponticelli-a ... 4.00

BROOKLYN ANIMAL CONTROL
IDW Publishing: Dec, 2015 ($7.99, square-bound, one-shot)

1-J.T. Petty-s/Stephen Thompson-a; werewolves in Brooklyn ... 8.00

BROOKS ROBINSON (See Baseball's Greatest Heroes #2)

BROTHER BILLY THE PAIN FROM PLAINS
Marvel Comics Group: 1979 (68pgs.)

1-B&W comics, satire, Jimmy Carter-c & x-over w/Brother Billy peanut jokes.
Joey Adams-a (scarce) ... 5 10 15 31 53 75

BROTHERHOOD, THE (Also see X-Men titles)
Marvel Comics: July, 2001 - No. 9, Mar, 2002 ($2.25)

1-Intro. Orwell & the Brotherhood; Ribic-a/X-s/Sienkiewicz-c ... 3.00
2-9: 2-Two covers (JG Jones & Sienkiewicz). 4-6-Fabry-a. 7-9-Phillips-c/a ... 3.00

BROTHER POWER, THE GEEK (See Saga of Swamp Thing Annual & Vertigo Visions)
National Periodical Publications: Sept-Oct, 1968 - No. 2, Nov-Dec, 1968

1-Origin; Simon-c(i?) ... 5 10 15 34 60 85
2 ... 3 6 9 19 30 40

BROTHERS DRACUL
AfterShock Comics: Apr, 2018 - No. 5, Aug, 2018 ($3.99, limited series)

1-5-Cullen Bunn-s/Mirko Colak-a ... 4.00

BROTHERS, HANG IN THERE, THE
Spire Christian Comics (Fleming H. Revell Co.): 1979 (49¢)

nn ... 2 4 6 13 18 22

BROTHERS IN ARMS (Based on the World War II military video game)
Dynamite Entertainment: 2008 - No. 4, 2008 ($3.99/$3.50)

1-($3.99) Fabbri & Sejic two covers by Fabbri & Sejic ... 4.00
2-4-($3.50) Two covers by Fabbri & Sejic on each ... 3.50

BROTHERS OF THE SPEAR (Also see Tarzan)
Gold Key/Whitman No. 18: June, 1972 - No. 17, Feb, 1976; No. 18, May, 1982

1 ... 5 10 15 31 53 75
2-Painted-c begin, end #17 ... 3 6 9 18 28 38
3-10 ... 3 6 9 15 22 28
11-18: 12-Line drawn-c. 13-17-Spiegle-a. 18(5/82)-r/#2; Leopard Girl-r ... 4 6 11 16 20

BROTHERS, THE CULT ESCAPE, THE
Spire Christian Comics (Fleming H. Revell Co.): 1980 (49¢)

nn ... 3 6 9 14 19 24

BROWNIES (See New Funnies)

Dell Publishing Co.: No. 192, July, 1948 - No. 605, Dec, 1954

Four Color 192(#1)-Kelly-a	15	30	45	103	227	350
Four Color 244(9/49), 293 (9/50)-Last Kelly c/a	11	22	33	73	157	240
Four Color 337(7-8/51), 365(12-1/51-52), 398(5/52)	6	12	18	41	76	110
Four Color 436(11/52), 482(7/53), 522(12/53), 605	6	12	18	37	66	95

BRUCE GENTRY
Better/Standard/Four Star Publ./Superior No. 3: Jan, 1948 - No. 8, Jul, 1949

1-Ray Bailey strip reprints begin, end #3; E.C. emblem appears as a monogram on stationery in story; negligee panels ... 87 174 261 553 952 1350
2,3: 2-Negligee panels ... 45 90 135 284 480 675
4-8 ... 32 64 96 188 307 425

NOTE: *Kamenish* a-2-7; c-1-8.

BRUCE JONES' OUTER EDGE
Innovation: 1993 ($2.50, B&W, one-shot)

1-Bruce Jones-c/a/script ... 4.00

BRUCE LEE (Also see Deadly Hands of Kung Fu)
Malibu Comics: July, 1994 - No. 6, Dec, 1994 ($2.95, 36 pgs.)

1-6: 1-(44 pgs.)-Mortal Kombat prev., 1st app. in comics. 2,6-(36 pgs.) ... 6.00

BRUCE WAYNE: AGENT OF S.H.I.E.L.D. (Also see Marvel Vs. DC #3 & DC Vs. Marvel #4)
Marvel Comics (Amalgam): Apr, 1996 ($1.95, one-shot)

1-Chuck Dixon scripts and Cary Nord-c/a. ... 4.00

BRUCE WAYNE: THE ROAD HOME (See Batman: The Return of Bruce Wayne)
(See Batman: Bruce Wayne - The Road Home HC for reprints)
DC Comics: Dec, 2010 ($2.99, series of one-shots with interlocking covers)

...: Batgirl 1 - Bryan Miller-s/Pere Pérez-a ... 5.00
...: Batman and Robin 1 - Nicieza-s/Richards-a; Vicki Vale app. ... 5.00
...: Catwoman 1 - Fridolfs-s/Nguyen-a; Harley & Ivy app. ... 5.00
...: Commissioner Gordon 1 - Beechen-s/Kudranski-a; Penguin app. ... 5.00
...: Oracle 1 - Andreyko-s/Padilla-a; Man-Bat & Manhunter app. ... 5.00
...: Outsiders 1 - Barr-s/Saltares-a ... 5.00
...: Ra's al Ghul 1 - Nicieza-s/McDaniel-a ... 5.00
...: Red Robin 1 - Nicieza-s/Bachs-a; Ra's al Ghul app. ... 5.00

BRUTAL NATURE
IDW Publishing: May, 2016 - No. 4, Aug, 2016 ($3.99, limited series)

1-4-Ariel Olivetti-a/Luciano Saracino-s ... 4.00

BRUTAL NATURE: CONCRETE FURY
IDW Publishing: Mar, 2017 - No. 5, Jul, 2017 ($3.99, limited series)

1-5-Ariel Olivetti-a/Luciano Saracino-s ... 4.00

BRUTE, THE
Seaboard Publ. (Atlas): Feb, 1975 - No. 3, July, 1975

1-Origin & 1st app; Sekowsky-a(p) ... 3 6 9 17 26 35
2-Sekowsky-a(p); Fleisher-s ... 2 4 6 11 16 20
3-Brunner/Starlin/Weiss-a(p) ... 2 4 6 13 18 22

BRUTE & BABE
Ominous Press: July, 1994 - No. 2, Aug, 1994

1-($3.95, 8 tablets plus-c)-"...It Begins..."; tablet format ... 5.00
2-($2.50, 36 pgs.)-"Mael's Rage", 2-(40 pgs.)-Stiff additional variant-c ... 4.00

BRUTE FORCE
Marvel Comics: Aug, 1990 - No. 4, Nov, 1990 ($1.00, limited series)

1-4: Animal super-heroes; Delbo & DeCarlo-a ... 4.00

BRZRKR
BOOM! Studios: Feb, 2021 - No. 12, Mar, 2023 ($4.99/$3.99, limited series)

1-($4.99) Keanu Reeves & Matt Kindt-s/Ron Garney-a ... 5.00
2-($3.99) Origin story ... 4.00
3-11-($3.99) 3-Origin story continues ... 4.00
12-($6.99) ... 7.00
...: Fallen Empire 1 (11/23, $9.99) Tomlin-s/Isaacs-a ... 10.00
...: Pen & Ink 1 (10/23, $6.99) Reprints #1 in B&W with Garney commentary on each page ... 7.00
...: Poetry 1 (7/23, $9.99) Steve Skroce-s/a; Unute in ancient Atlantis ... 10.00

B-SIDES (The Craptacular...)
Marvel Comics: Nov, 2002 - No. 3, Jan, 2003 ($2.99, limited series)

1-3-Kieth-c/Weldele-a. 2-Dorkin-a (1 pg.) 2-FF cameo. 3-FF app. ... 3.00

BUBBA HO-TEP AND THE COSMIC BLOODSUCKERS
IDW Publications: Mar, 2018 - No. 5, Jul, 2018 ($3.99, limited series)

1-5-Jabcuga-s/Galusha-a; Elvis Presley vs. vampires and voodoo; Nixon app. ... 4.00

BUBBLEGUM CRISIS: GRAND MAL

	GD 2.0	VG 4.0	FN 6.0	VF 8.0	VF/NM 9.0	NM- 9.2

Dark Horse Comics: Mar, 1994 - No. 4, June, 1994 ($2.50, limited series)

1-4-Japanese manga						5.00

BUBBLEGUN
Aspen MLT: Jun, 2013 - No. 5, Mar, 2014 ($1.00/$3.99)

| 1-($1.00) Roslan-s/Bowden-a; multiple covers | | | | | | 3.00 |
| 2-5-($3.99) Multiple covers on each | | | | | | 4.00 |

BUBBLEGUN (Volume 2)
Aspen MLT: May, 2017 - No. 5, Sept, 2017 ($3.99)

| 1-5-Roslan-s/Tovar-a; multiple covers | | | | | | 4.00 |

BUCCANEER
I. W. Enterprises: No date (1963)

| I.W. Reprint #1(r-/Quality #20), #8(r-/#23): Crandall-a in each | | | | | | |
| | 3 | 6 | 9 | 17 | 26 | 35 |

BUCCANEERS (Formerly Kid Eternity)
Quality Comics: No. 19, Jan, 1950 - No. 27, May, 1951 (No. 24-27: 52 pgs.)

19-Captain Daring, Black Roger, Eric Falcon & Spanish Main begin;						
Crandall-a	52	104	156	328	552-	775
20,23-Crandall-a	37	74	111	222	361	500
21-Crandall-c/a	41	82	123	256	428	600
22-Bondage-c	29	58	87	170	278	385
24-26: 24-Adam Peril, U.S.N. begins. 25-Origin & 1st app. Corsair Queen.						
26-Last Spanish Main	24	48	72	142	234	325
27-Crandall-c/a	37	74	111	222	361	500
Super Reprint #12 (1964)-Crandall-r/#21	3	6	9	16	23	30

BUCCANEERS, THE (TV)
Dell Publishing Co.: No. 800, 1957

| Four Color 800-Photo-c | 6 | 12 | 18 | 42 | 79 | 115 |

BUCKAROO BANZAI (Movie)
Marvel Comics Group: Dec, 1984 - No. 2, Feb, 1985

1-Movie adaptation; r/Marvel Super Special #33; Texiera-c/a						
	1	3	4	6	8	10
2-Adaptation continues						6.00

BUCKAROO BANZAI: RETURN OF THE SCREW
Moonstone: 2006 - No. 3, 2006 ($3.50, limited series)

| 1-3: 1-Three covers by Haley, Stribling, Beck; Thompson-a | | | | | | 3.50 |
| Preview (2006, 50¢) B&W preview; history of movie and spin-off projects | | | | | | 3.00 |

BUCK DUCK
Atlas Comics (ANC): June, 1953 - No. 4, Dec, 1953

| 1-Funny animal stories in all | 23 | 46 | 69 | 136 | 223 | 310 |
| 2-4: 2-Ed Win-a(5) | 14 | 28 | 42 | 82 | 121 | 160 |

BUCK JONES (Also see Crackajack Funnies, Famous Feature Stories, Master Comics #7 & Wow Comics #1, 1936)
Dell Publishing Co.: No. 299, Oct, 1950 - No. 850, Oct, 1957 (All Painted-c)

Four Color 299(#1)-Buck Jones & his horse Silver-B begin; painted back-c begins, ends #5						
	14	28	42	93	204	315
2(4-6/51)	7	14	21	49	92	135
3-8(10-12/52)	6	12	18	38	69	100
Four Color 460,500,546,589	6	12	18	42	79	115
Four Color 652,733,850	5	10	15	35	63	90

BUCK ROGERS (Also see Famous Funnies, Pure Oil Comics, Salerno Carnival of Comics, 24 Pages of Comics, & Vicks Comics)
Famous Funnies: Winter, 1940-41 - No. 6, Sept, 1943

NOTE: Buck Rogers first appeared in the pulp magazine Amazing Stories Vol. 3 #5 in Aug, 1928.

1-Sunday strip reprints by Rick Yager; begins with strip #190; Calkins-a						
	377	754	1131	2639	4620	6600
2 (7/41)-Calkins-c	161	322	483	1030	1765	2500
3 (2/41), 4 (7/42)	129	258	387	826	1413	2000
5,6: 5-Story continues from Famous Funnies No. 80; Buck Rogers, Sky Roads. 6-Reprints of 1939 dailies; contains B.R. story "Crater of Doom" (2 pgs.) by Calkins not-r from Famous Funnies	110	220	330	704	1202	1700

BUCK ROGERS
Toby Press: No. 100, Jan, 1951 - No. 9, May-June, 1951

| 100(#7)-All strip-r begin; Anderson, Chatton-a | 37 | 74 | 111 | 222 | 361 | 500 |
| 101(#8), 9-All Anderson(1947-49-r/dailies) | 28 | 56 | 84 | 168 | 274 | 380 |

BUCK ROGERS (...in the 25th Century No. 5 on) (TV)
Gold Key/Whitman No. 7 on: Oct, 1964; No. 2, July, 1979 - No. 16, May, 1982 (No #10; story was written but never released. #17 exists only as a press proof without covers and was never published)

1(10128-410, 12¢)-1st S.A. app. Buck Rogers & 1st new B. R. in comics since 1933 giveaway; painted-c; back-c pin-up	13	26	39	91	201	310
2(7/79)-6: 3,4,6-Movie adaptation; painted-c	2	4	6	11	16	20
7,11 (Whitman)	3	6	9	14	19	24
8,9 (prepack)(scarce)	5	10	15	35	63	90
12-16: 14(2/82), 15(3/82), 16(5/82)	2	4	6	8	10	12
Giant Movie Edition 11296(64pp, Whitman, $1.50), reprints GK #2-4 minus cover; tabloid size; photo-c (See Marvel Treasury)	3	6	9	17	26	35
Giant Movie Edition 02489(Western/Marvel, $1.50), reprints GK #2-4 minus cover						
	3	6	9	16	24	32

NOTE: **Bolle** a-2p,3p, Movie Ed.(p). **McWilliams** a-2i,3i, 5-11, Movie Ed.(i). Painted c-1-9,11-13.

BUCK ROGERS (Comics Module)
TSR, Inc.: 1990 - No. 10, 1991 ($2.95, 44 pgs.)

| 1-10 (1990): 1-Begin origin in 3 parts. 2-Indicia says #1. 2,3-Black Barney back-up story. 4-All Black Barney issue; B. B.-c. 5-Indicia says #6; Black Barney-c & lead story; Buck Rogers back-up story. 10-Flip book (72pgs.) | | | | | | |
| | | | | | | 4.00 |

BUCK ROGERS
Dynamite Entertainment: No. 0, 2009 - No. 12, 2010 (25¢/$3.50)

| 0-(25¢) Beatty-s/Rafael-a/Cassaday-c | | | | | | 3.00 |

| 1-12: 1-($3.50) Three covers by Cassaday, Ross and Wagner; origin re-told | | | | | | 3.50 |
| Annual 1 (2011, $4.99) Rafael-a; covers by Rafael & Sadowski | | | | | | 5.00 |

BUCK ROGERS
Hermes Press: 2013 - No. 4, 2013 ($3.99)

| 1-4-Howard Chaykin-s/a/c | | | | | | 4.00 |

BUCKSKIN (TV)
Dell Publishing Co.: No. 1011, July, 1959 - No. 1107, June-Aug, 1960

| Four Color 1011 (#1)-Photo-c | 7 | 14 | 21 | 44 | 82 | 120 |
| Four Color 1107-Photo-c | 6 | 12 | 18 | 40 | 73 | 105 |

BUCKY BARNES: THE WINTER SOLDIER (See Captain America titles)
Marvel Comics: Dec, 2014 - No. 11, Nov, 2015 ($3.99)

| 1-11: 1-Ales Kot-s/Marco Rudy-a; Daisy Johnson app. 2,8,9,10-Loki app. 4-7,9-Crossbones app. 7-Foss-a | | | | | | 4.00 |

BUCKY O'HARE (Funny Animal)
Continuity Comics: 1986 ($5.95, graphic novel)

| 1-Golden-c/a(r); r/serial-Echo of Futurepast #1-6 | 8 | 6 | 9 | 16 | 24 | 32 |
| Deluxe Hardcover ($40.00, 52 pg., 8 x 11") | | | | | | 45.00 |

BUCKY O'HARE
Continuity Comics: Jan, 1991 - No. 5, 1991 ($2.00)

1-Michael Golden-c/a	3	6	9	15	22	28
2	1	2	3	5	6	8
3-6						4.00

BUDDIES IN THE U.S. ARMY
Avon Periodicals: Nov, 1952 - No. 2, 1953

| 1-Lawrence-c | 50 | 100 | 150 | 315 | 533 | 750 |
| 2-Mort Lawrence-c/a | 19 | 38 | 57 | 111 | 176 | 240 |

BUFFALO BEE (TV)
Dell Publishing Co.: No. 957, Nov, 1958 - No. 1061, Dec-Feb, 1959-60

| Four Color 957 (#1) | 9 | 18 | 27 | 59 | 117 | 175 |
| Four Color 1002 (8-10/59), 1061 | 6 | 12 | 18 | 42 | 79 | 115 |

BUFFALO BILL (See Frontier Fighters, Super Western Comics & Western Action Thrillers)
Youthful Magazines: No. 2, Oct, 1950 - No. 9, Dec, 1951

| 2-Annie Oakley story | 16 | 32 | 48 | 94 | 147 | 200 |
| 3-9: 2-4-Walter Johnson-c/a. 9-Wildey-a | 12 | 24 | 36 | 67 | 94 | 120 |

BUFFALO BILL CODY (See Cody of the Pony Express)

BUFFALO BILL, JR. (TV) (See Western Roundup)
Dell/Gold Key: Jan, 1956 - No. 13, Aug-Oct, 1959; 1965 (All photo-c)

Four Color 673 (#1)	9	18	27	62	126	190
Four Color 742,766,798,828,856(11/57)	6	12	18	37	66	95
7(2-4/58)-13	5	10	15	31	53	75
1(6/65, Gold Key)-Photo-c(r/F.C. #798); photo-b/c	4	8	12	23	37	50

BUFFALO BILL PICTURE STORIES
Street & Smith Publications: June-July, 1949 - No. 2, Aug-Sept, 1949

| 1,2-Wildey, Powell-a in each | 15 | 30 | 45 | 90 | 140 | 190 |

BUFFY '97
BOOM! Studios: Jun, 2022 ($7.99, one-shot)

| 1-Lambert-s/Ignazzi-a | | | | | | 8.00 |

BUFFY: THE HIGH SCHOOL YEARS (Based on the TV series)
Dark Horse Comics

| ... - Glutton For Punishment (10/16, $10.99, 6" x 9") McDonald-s/Li-a | | | | | | 11.00 |
| ... - Parental Parasite (6/17, $10.99, 6" x 9") McDonald-s/Li-a | | | | | | 11.00 |

BUFFY THE LAST VAMPIRE SLAYER
BOOM! Studios: Dec, 2021 - No. 4, Mar, 2022 ($4.99, limited series)

| 1-4-Set 50 years in the future; Gilly-s/Jaro-a | | | | | | 5.00 |
| ... Special 1 (3/23, $4.99) Thessaly & Spike app.; Gilly-s/Jaro-a | | | | | | 5.00 |

BUFFY THE LAST VAMPIRE SLAYER
BOOM! Studios: Aug, 2023 - No. 5, Dec, 2023 ($4.99, limited series)

| 1-5-Set 50 years in the future; Gilly-s/Roig-a | | | | | | 5.00 |

BUFFY: THE LOST SUMMER
BOOM! Studios: May, 2023 ($7.99, one-shot)

| 1-Gilly-s/Knight-a | | | | | | 8.00 |

BUFFY THE VAMPIRE SLAYER (Based on the TV series)(Also see Angel and Faith, Spike, Tales of the Vampires and Willow)
Dark Horse Comics: 1998 - No. 63, Nov, 2003 ($2.95/$2.99)

1-Bennett-a/Watson-s; Art Adams-c	2	4	6	10	14	18
1-Variant photo-c	2	4	6	11	16	20
1-Gold foil logo Art Adams-c						18.00
1-Gold foil logo photo-c						20.00
2-4-Photo-c	1	3	4	6	8	10
5-15-Regular and photo-c. 4-7-Gomez-a. 5,8-Green-c						5.00
16-49: 29,30-Angel x-over. 43-45-Death of Buffy. 47-Lobdell-s begin. 48-Pike returns						3.00
50-($3.50) Scooby gang battles Adam; back-up story by Watson						4.00
51-63: 51-54-Viva Las Buffy; pre-Sunnydale Buffy & Pike in Vegas						3.00
Annual '99 ($4.95)-Two stories and pin-ups	1	2	3	4	5	7
...: A Stake to the Heart TPB (3/04, $12.95) r/#60-63						13.00
...: Chaos Bleeds (6/03, $2.99) Based on the video game; photo & Campbell-a						3.00
...: Creatures of Habit (3/02, $17.95) text with Horton & Paul Lee-a						18.00
...: Jonathan 1 (1/01, $2.99) two covers; Richards-a						3.00
...: Lost and Found 1 (3/02, $2.99) aftermath of Buffy's death; Richards-a						3.00
...: Lovers Walk (2/01, $2.99) short stories by various; Richards & photo-c						3.00
...: Note From the Underground (3/03, $12.95) r/#47-50						13.00
...: Omnibus Vol. 1 (7/07, $24.95, 9x6") r/Spike & Dru #3, Origin #1-3 and Buffy #51-59						25.00
...: Omnibus Vol. 2 (9/07, $24.95, 9x6") r/Buffy #60-63 and various one-shots & specials						25.00
...: Omnibus Vol. 3 (1/08, $24.95, 9x6") r/Buffy #1-8,12,16, Annual '99						25.00
...: Omnibus Vol. 4 (5/08, $24.95, 9x6") r/Buffy #9-11,13-15,17-20,50 and various						25.00
...: Omnibus Vol. 5 (9/08, $24.95, 9x6") r/Buffy #21-28 and various and specials						25.00

Bucky Barnes: The Winter Soldier #2 © MAR

Buffy the Vampire Slayer (2019 series) #4 © 20Fox

Bugaloos #4 © Krofft Prods.

	GD 2.0	VG 4.0	FN 6.0	VF 8.0	VF/NM 9.0	NM- 9.2

...: Omnibus Vol. 6 (2/09, $24.95, 9x6") r/Buffy #29-38 and various one-shots & specials   25.00
... One For One (9/10, $1.00) r/#1 with red cover frame   3.00
... Reunion (6/02, $3.50) Buffy & Angel's; Espenson-s; art by various   3.50
... Slayer Interrupted TPB (2003, $14.95) r/#56-59   15.00
... Tales of the Slayers (10/02, $3.50) art by Matsuda and Colan; art & photo-c   3.50
... The Death of Buffy TPB (8/02, $15.95) r/#43-46   16.00
... Viva Las Buffy TPB (7/03, $12.95) r/#51-54   13.00
Wizard #1/2   1 2 3 6 8 9

BUFFY THE VAMPIRE SLAYER ("Season Eight" of the TV series)
Dark Horse Comics: Mar, 2007 - No. 40, Jan, 2011 ($2.99)
1-Joss Whedon-s/Georges Jeanty-a/Jo Chen-c   6.00
1-Variant cover by Jeanty   6.00
1-RRP with B&W Jeanty cover (edition of 1000)   85.00
1-4: 1-2nd thru 5th printings. 3,4-2nd & 3rd printings   3.00
2-5-Jeanty-a; covers by Chen & Jeanty   4.00
6-13,16,19-Two covers by Chen & Jeanty. 6-9-Faith app.; Vaughan-s. 10,11-Whedon-s.
  12-15-Goddard-s; Dracula app. 16-19-Fray app.; Whedon-s/Moline-a   3.00
20-40: 20-28,31-40-Two covers by Chen and Jeanty. 20-Animation style flashback.
  21,26-30-Espenson-s. 30-Hughes-c. 31-Whedon-s. 32-35-Meltzer-s. 36-40-Whedon-s   3.00
...: Riley (8/10, $3.50) Espenson-s/Moline-a; Riley Finn and Sam; Angel app.   3.50
... Tales of the Vampires (6/09, $2.99) Cloonan-s/Lolos-a; covers by Chen & Bà/Moon   3.50
...: Willow (12/09, $3.50) Whedon-s/Moline-a; Willow meets the Snake Guide   3.50

BUFFY THE VAMPIRE SLAYER ("Season Nine" of the TV series)
Dark Horse Comics: Sept, 2011 - No. 25, Sept, 2013 ($2.99)
1-25: 1-Whedon-s/Jeanty-a; covers by Morris & Chen. 2-5-Chambliss-s; two covers by Morris
  & Jeanty. 5-Moline-a; Nikki flashback. 6,7-Two covers by Jeanty & Noto. 8-10-Richards-s.
  14-Espenson-s; intro. Billy. 16-19-Illyria app.   3.00
...: Buffyverse Sampler (1/13, $4.99) r/#1, Angel & Faith #1, Spike #1, Willow #1   5.00
FCBD (5/12, giveaway) Buffy vs. Alien; Jeanty-a; flip book with The Guild   3.00

BUFFY THE VAMPIRE SLAYER (SEASON TEN)
Dark Horse Comics: Mar, 2014 - No. 30, Aug, 2016 ($3.50/$3.99)
1-16: 1-Gage-s/Isaacs-a; covers by Morris & Isaacs. 2-5-Dracula app.
  3-5,7,12,13-Nicholas Brendon & Gage-s. 8-Corben-a (3 pgs)   3.50
17-30-($3.99) Nicholas Brendon & Gage-s. 19-Nicholas Brendon & Gage-s. 25-Levens-a   4.00

BUFFY THE VAMPIRE SLAYER SEASON ELEVEN
Dark Horse Comics: Nov, 2016 - No. 12, Oct, 2017 ($3.99)
1-12: 1-Gage-s/Isaacs-a; covers by Morris & Isaacs. 5,9-Jeanty-a   4.00

BUFFY THE VAMPIRE SLAYER SEASON 12
Dark Horse Comics: Jun, 2018 - No. 4, Sept, 2018 ($3.99)
1-4-Gage & Whedon-s/Jeanty-a; Melaka Fray, Angel, Illyria app.   4.00

BUFFY THE VAMPIRE SLAYER
Dark Horse Comics: Jan, 2019 - No. 34, Feb, 2022 ($3.99)
1-24: 1-Rebooted Buffy first meets the Scooby gang in high school; Bellaire-s/Mora-a.
  4-Xander attacked. 5-12-David López-a. 8-12-Hellmouth x-over with Angel #5-8.
  10-Intro. Kendra. 11-Intro. Anya. 19-Faith arrives   4.00
25-($4.99) Scoobies travel to the 1998 TV series reality   5.00
26-34   4.00
...: Chosen Ones 1 (8/19, $7.99) Short stories of previous slayers   8.00
...: Every Generation 1 (4/20, $7.99) Short stories of previous slayers; Andolfo-c   8.00
...: Faith 1 (2/21, $7.99) Lambert-s/Carlini-a; flashbacks to childhood and recruitment   8.00
...: Tea Time 1 (6/21, $7.99) Mirka Andolfo-s/Siya Oum-a; "What If" Giles was a vampire   8.00

BUFFY THE VAMPIRE SLAYER: ANGEL
Dark Horse Comics: May, 1999 - No. 3, July, 1999 ($2.95, limited series)
1-Gomez-a; Matsuda-c & photo-c for each   1 2 3 5 6 8
2,3   4.00

BUFFY THE VAMPIRE SLAYER: GILES
Dark Horse Comics: Oct, 2000 ($2.95, one-shot)
1-Eric Powell-a; Powell & photo-c   4.00

BUFFY THE VAMPIRE SLAYER: HAUNTED
Dark Horse Comics: Dec, 2001 - No. 4, Mar, 2002 ($2.99, limited series)
1-4-Faith and the Mayor app.; Espenson-s/Richards-a   4.00
TPB (9/02, $12.95) r/series; photo-c   13.00

BUFFY THE VAMPIRE SLAYER: OZ
Dark Horse Comics: July, 2001 - No. 3, Sept, 2001 ($2.99, limited series)
1-3-Totleben-a & photo-c; Golden-s   4.00

BUFFY THE VAMPIRE SLAYER: SPIKE AND DRU
Dark Horse Comics: Apr, 1999; No. 2, Oct, 1999; No. 3, Dec, 2000 ($2.95)
1-Photo-c   1 2 3 5 6 8

2,3: 2-Photo-c. 3-Two covers (photo & Sook)   4.00

BUFFY THE VAMPIRE SLAYER: THE ORIGIN (Adapts movie screenplay)
Dark Horse Comics: Jan, 1999 - No. 3, Mar, 1999 ($2.95, limited series)
1-3-Brereton-s/Bennett-a; reg & photo-c for each   4.00

BUFFY THE VAMPIRE SLAYER 25th ANNIVERSARY SPECIAL
BOOM! Studios: Mar, 2022 ($9.99, one-shot)
1-Short stories by various; Frany-c   10.00

BUFFY THE VAMPIRE SLAYER: WILLOW
BOOM! Studios: Jul, 2020 - No. 5, Nov, 2020 ($3.99, limited series)
1-5-Mariko Tamaki-s/Natacha Bustos-a   4.00

BUFFY THE VAMPIRE SLAYER: WILLOW & TARA
Dark Horse Comics: Apr, 2001 ($2.99, one-shot)
1-Terry Moore-a/Chris Golden & Amber Benson-s; Moore-c & photo-c   4.00
TPB (4/03, $9.95) r/#1 & W&T - Wilderness; photo-c   10.00

BUFFY THE VAMPIRE SLAYER: WILLOW & TARA - WILDERNESS
Dark Horse Comics: Jul, 2002 - No. 2, Sept, 2002 ($2.99, limited series)
1,2-Chris Golden & Amber Benson-s; Jothikaumar-c & photo-c   4.00

BUG
Marvel Comics: Mar, 1997 ($2.99, one-shot)
1-Micronauts character   2 4 6 9 12 15

BUGALOOS (Sid & Marty Krofft TV show)
Charlton Comics: Sept, 1971 - No. 4, Feb, 1972
1   5 10 15 35 63 90
2-4   3 6 9 21 33 45
NOTE: No. 3(1/72) went on sale late in 1972 (after No. 4) with the 1/73 issues.

BUGHOUSE (Satire)
Ajax/Farrell (Excellent Publ.): Mar-Apr, 1954 - No. 4, Sept-Oct, 1954
V1#1   37 74 111 222 361 500
2-4   19 38 57 111 176 240

BUGS BUNNY (See The Best of..., Camp Comics, Comic Album #2, 6, 10, 14, Dell Giant #28, 32, 46, Dynabrite, Golden Comics Digest #1, 3, 5, 6, 8, 10, 14, 15, 17, 21, 26, 30, 34, 39, 42, 47, Kite Fun Book, Large Feature Comic #8, Looney Tunes and Merry Melodies, March of Comics #44, 59, 75, 83, 97, 115, 132, 149, 160, 179, 188, 201, 220, 231, 245, 259, 273, 287, 301, 315, 329, 343, 363, 367, 380, 392, 403, 415, 428, 440, 452, 464, 476, 487, Porky Pig, Puffed Wheat, Story Hour Series #802, Super Book #14, 26 and Whitman Comic Books)

BUGS BUNNY (See Dell Giants for annuals)
Dell Publishing Co./Gold Key No. 86-218/Whitman No. 219 on: 1942 - No. 245, April, 1984

	GD 2.0	VG 4.0	FN 6.0	VF 8.0	VF/NM 9.0	NM- 9.2
Large Feature Comic 8(1942)-(Rarely found in fine-mint condition)	300	600	900	1980	3440	4900
Four Color 33 ('43) Bondage/torture-c	136	272	408	1088	2444	3800
Four Color 51	41	82	123	303	689	1075
Four Color 88-Sci-fi-c	26	52	78	182	404	625
Four Color 123('46),142,164	17	34	51	117	259	400
Four Color 187,200,217,233	12	24	36	84	185	285
Four Color 250-Used in SOTI, pg. 309	16	32	48	110	243	375
Four Color 266,274,281,289,298('50)	10	20	30	67	141	215
Four Color 307,317(#1),327(#2),338,347,355,366,376,393	9	18	27	59	117	175
Four Color 407,420,432(10/52)	8	16	24	54	102	150
Four Color 498(9/53),585(9/54),647(9/55)	6	12	18	41	76	110
Four Color 724(9/56),838(9/57),1064(12/59)	5	10	15	34	60	85
28(12-1/52-53)-30	4	8	12	28	47	65
31-50	4	8	12	23	37	50
51-85(7-9/62)	4	8	12	23	37	50
86(10/62)-88-Bugs Bunny's Showtime-(25¢, 80pgs.)	5	10	15	35	63	90
89-99	3	6	9	16	24	32
100	3	6	9	17	26	35
101-118: 108-1st Honey Bunny. 118-Last 12¢ issue	3	6	9	14	19	24
119-140	2	4	6	11	16	20
141-170	2	4	6	9	12	15
171-218: 218-Publ. by Whitman only?	2	4	6	8	10	12
219,220,225-237(5/82): 229-Swipe of Barks story/WDC&S #223. 233(2/82)	2	4	6	8	10	12
221(9/80),222(11/80)-Pre-pack? (Scarce)	4	8	12	28	47	65
223 (1/81, 50¢-c), 224 (3/81)-Low distr.	3	6	9	14	20	25
223 (1/81, 40¢-c) Cover price error variant	3	6	9	17	26	35
238-245 (#90070 on-c, nd, nd code; pre-pack): 238(5/83), 239(6/83), 240(7/83), 241(7/83), 242(8/83), 243(8/83), 244(3/84), 245(4/84)	3	6	9	15	22	28

NOTE: Reprints-100,102-104,110,115,123,143,144,147,167,173,175-177,179-185,187,190.
nn (Xerox Pub. Comic Digest, 1971, 100 pages, B&W)
  collection of one-page gags   4 8 12 23 37 50

	GD 2.0	VG 4.0	FN 6.0	VF 8.0	VF/NM 9.0	NM- 9.2

...Comic-Go-Round 11196-(224 pgs.)($1.95)(Golden Press, 1979)
4 · 8 · 12 · 25 · 40 · 55

...Winter Fun 1(12/67-Gold Key)-Giant
5 · 10 · 15 · 30 · 50 · 70

BUGS BUNNY
DC Comics: June, 1990 - No. 3, Aug, 1990 ($1.00, limited series)
1-3: Daffy Duck, Elmer Fudd, others app. — 5.00

BUGS BUNNY (...Monthly on-c)
DC Comics: 1993 - No. 3, 1994? ($1.95)
1-3-Bugs, Porky Pig, Daffy, Road Runner — 3.50

BUGS BUNNY (Digest-size reprint from Looney Tunes)
DC Comics: 2005 ($6.99, digest)
Vol. 1: What's Up Doc? - Reprints from Looney Tunes #37,41,43-45,48,52,55,57-59,63 — 7.00

BUGS BUNNY & PORKY PIG
Gold Key: Sept, 1965 (Paper-c, giant, 100 pgs.)
1(30025-509) — 6 · 12 · 18 · 38 · 69 · 100

BUGS BUNNY'S ALBUM (See Bugs Bunny, Four Color 498,585,647,724)
BUGS BUNNY LIFE STORY ALBUM (See Bugs Bunny, Four Color No. 838)
BUGS BUNNY MERRY CHRISTMAS (See Bugs Bunny, Four Color No. 1064)

BUG! THE ADVENTURES OF FORAGER (From New Gods)
DC Comics (Young Animal): Jul, 2017 - No. 6, Feb, 2018 ($3.99)
1-6-Lee Allred-s/Mike Allred-a/c. 1-Sandman, Brute & Glob app. 2-G.A. Sandman, Sandy, Blue Beetle and The Losers app. 3-Atlas app. 5-Omac app. — 4.00

BUILDING, THE
Kitchen Sink Press: 1987; 2000 (8 1/2" x 11" sepia toned graphic novel)
nn-Will Eisner-s/c/a — 15.00
nn-(DC Comics, 9/00, $9.95) reprints 1987 edition — 10.00

BULLET CROW, FOWL OF FORTUNE
Eclipse Comics: Mar, 1987 - No. 2, Apr, 1987 ($2.00, B&W, limited series)
1,2-The Comic Reader-r & new-a — 6.00

BULLETMAN (See Fawcett Miniatures, Master Comics, Mighty Midget Comics, Nickel Comics & XMas Comics)
Fawcett Publications: Sum, 1941 - #12, 2/12/43; #14, Spr, 1946 - #16, Fall, 1946 (No #13)

	2.0	4.0	6.0	8.0	9.0	9.2
1-Silver metallic-c	417	834	1251	2919	5110	7300
2-Raboy-c	187	374	561	1197	2049	2900
3,5-Raboy-c each	148	296	444	947	1624	2300
4	103	206	309	659	1130	1600
6,8,9	90	180	270	576	988	1400
7-Ghost Stories told by night watchman of cemetery begins; Eisnerish-a; hidden message "Chic Stone is a jerk".	100	200	300	550	1050	1550
10-Intro. Bulletdog	103	206	309	659	1130	1600
11,12,14-16 (nn 13): 12-Robot-c	65	130	195	416	708	1000

NOTE: *Mac Raboy* c-1-3, 5, 6, 10. "Bulletman the Flying Detective" on cover #8 on.

BULLET POINTS
Marvel Comics: Jan, 2007 - No. 5, May, 2007 ($2.99, limited series)
1-5: 1-Steve Rogers becomes Iron Man; Straczynski-s/Edwards-a. 4,5-Galactus app. — 3.00
TPB (2007, $13.99) r/#1-5; layout pages by Edwards — 14.00

BULLETPROOF MONK (Inspired the 2003 film)
Image Comics (Flypaper Press): 1998 - No. 3, 1999 ($2.95)
1-3-Oeming-a — 3.00
...: Tales of the BPM (3/03, $2.95) Flip book; 2 covers by Sale; art by Sale, Oeming, Dave Johnson; Seann William Scott afterword — 3.00
TPB (2002, $9.95) r/#1-3; foreword by John Woo — 10.00

BULLETS AND BRACELETS (Also see Marvel Versus DC #3 & DC Versus Marvel #4)
Marvel Comics (Amalgam): Apr, 1996 ($1.95)
1-John Ostrander script & Gary Frank-c/a — 4.00

BULLSEYE (Daredevil villain)
Marvel Comics: Apr, 2017 - No. 5, Aug, 2017 ($4.99/$3.99, limited series)
1-($4.99) Brisson-s/Sanna-a; back-up with Wolfman-s/Morgan-a — 5.00
2-5-($3.99) Brisson-s/Sanna-a — 4.00

BULLS-EYE (Cody of The Pony Express No. 8 on)
Mainline No. 1-5/Charlton No. 6,7: 7-8/54-No. 5, 3-4/55; No. 6, 6/55; No. 7, 8/55

	2.0	4.0	6.0	8.0	9.0	9.2
1-S&K-c, 2 pgs.-a	97	194	291	621	1061	1500
2-S&K-c/a	68	136	204	435	743	1050
3-5-S&K-c/a(2 each). 4-Last pre-code issue (1-2/55). 5-Censored issue with tomahawks removed in battle scene	55	110	165	352	601	850
6-S&K-c/a	50	100	150	315	533	750
7-S&K-c/a(3)	55	110	165	352	601	850

BULLS-EYE COMICS (Formerly Komik Pages #10; becomes Kayo #12)
Harry 'A' Chesler: No. 11, 1944
11-Origin K-9, Green Knight's sidekick, Lance; The Green Knight, Lady Satan, Yankee Doodle Jones app. — 541 · 1082 · 1623 · 3650 · 6975 · 10,000

BULLSEYE: GREATEST HITS (Daredevil villain)
Marvel Comics: Nov, 2004 - No. 5, Mar, 2005 ($2.99, limted series)
1-5-Origin of Bullseye; Steve Dillon-a/Deodato-c. 3-Punisher app. — 3.00
TPB (2005, $13.99) r/#1-5 — 14.00

BULLSEYE: PERFECT GAME (Daredevil villain)
Marvel Comics: Jan, 2011 - No. 2, Feb, 2011 ($3.99, limited series)
1,2-Huston-s/Martinbrough-a; Bullseye as baseball pitcher — 4.00

BULLWHIP GRIFFIN (See Movie Comics)

BULLWINKLE (...and Rocky No. 22 on; See March of Comics #233 and Rocky & Bullwinkle) (TV) (Jay Ward)
Dell/Gold Key: 3-5/62 - #11, 4/74; #12, 6/76 - #19, 3/78; #20, 4/79 - #25, 2/80

	2.0	4.0	6.0	8.0	9.0	9.2
Four Color 1270 (3-5/62)	16	32	48	112	249	385
01-090-209 (Dell, 7-9/62)	13	26	39	89	195	300
1(11/62, Gold Key)	12	24	36	82	179	275
2(2/63)	8	16	24	54	102	150
3(4/72)-11(4/74-Gold Key)	5	10	15	31	53	75
12-14: 12(6/76)-Reprints. 13(9/76), 14-New stories	3	6	9	17	26	35
15-25	2	4	6	11	16	20
Mother Moose Nursery Pomes 01-530-207 (5-7/62, Dell)	16	32	48	107	236	365

NOTE: Reprints: 6, 7, 20-24.

BULLWINKLE AND ROCKY (TV)
Charlton Comics: July, 1970 - No. 7, July, 1971
1-Has 1 pg. pin-up — 7 · 14 · 21 · 46 · 86 · 125
2-7: 3-Snidely Whiplash app. — 5 · 10 · 15 · 30 · 50 · 70

BULLWINKLE AND ROCKY
Star Comics/Marvel Comics No. 3 on: Nov, 1987 - No. 9, Mar, 1989
1-9: Boris & Natasha in all. 3,5,8-Dudley Do-Right app. 4-Reagan-c — 5.00
Marvel Moosterworks (1/92, $4.95) — 2 · 4 · 6 · 8 · 10 · 12

BULLY WARS
Image Comics: Sept, 2018 - No. 5, Jan, 2019 ($3.99, limited series)
1-5-Skottie Young-s/Aaron Conley-a — 4.00

BUMMER
Fantagraphics Books: June, 1995 ($3.50, B&W, mature)
1 — 3.50

BUNNY (Also see Harvey Pop Comics and Fruitman Special)
Harvey Publications: Dec, 1966 - No. 20, Dec, 1971; No. 21, Nov, 1976

	2.0	4.0	6.0	8.0	9.0	9.2
1-68 pg. Giants begin	7	14	21	49	92	135
2-10: 3-1st app. Fruitman. 6,8-10-Fruitman	4	8	12	28	47	65
11-18: 18-Last 68 pg. Giant	4	8	12	27	44	60
19-21-52 pg. Giants: 21-Fruitman app.	4	8	12	25	40	55

BUNNY MASK
AfterShock Comics: Jun, 2021 - No. 4, Sept, 2021 ($4.99, limited series)
1-4-Paul Tobin-s/Andrea Mutti-a — 5.00

BUNNY MASK VOL. 2 (... THE HOLLOW INSIDE on cover)
AfterShock Comics: May, 2022 - No. 4, Aug, 2022 ($4.99, limited series)
1-4-Paul Tobin-s/Andrea Mutti-a — 5.00

BURKE'S LAW (TV)
Dell Publ.: 1-3/64 - No. 2, 5-7/64; No. 3, 5-8/65 (All have Gene Barry photo-c)
1-Photo-c — 5 · 10 · 15 · 31 · 53 · 75
2,3-Photo-c — 4 · 8 · 12 · 23 · 37 · 50

BURNING FIELDS
BOOM! Studios: Jan, 2015 - No. 8, Sept, 2015 ($3.99, limited series)
1-6-Moreci & Daniel-s/Lorimer-a — 4.00

BURNING ROMANCES (See Fox Giants)

BURNOUTS
Image Comics: Sept, 2018 - No. 5, Jan, 2019 ($3.99)
1-5-Dennis Culver-s/Geoffo-a — 4.00

BUSTER BEAR
Quality Comics Group (Arnold Publ.): Dec, 1953 - No. 10, June, 1955

	2.0	4.0	6.0	8.0	9.0	9.2
1-Funny animal	15	30	45	83	124	165
2	8	16	24	42	54	65
3-10	7	14	21	35	43	50
I.W. Reprint #9,10 (Super on inside)	2	4	6	11	16	20

BUSTER BROWN COMICS (See Promotional Comics section)

BUSTER BUNNY
Standard Comics(Animated Cartoons)/Pines: Nov, 1949 - No. 16, Oct, 1953

	2.0	4.0	6.0	8.0	9.0	9.2
1-Frazetta 1 pg. text illo.	16	32	48	94	147	200
2	9	18	27	47	61	75
3-14,16	8	16	24	42	54	65
15-Racist-c	15	30	45	88	137	185

BUSTER CRABBE (TV)
Famous Funnies Publ.: Nov, 1951 - No. 12, 1953

	2.0	4.0	6.0	8.0	9.0	9.2
1-1st app.(?) Frazetta anti-drug ad; text story about Buster Crabbe & Billy the Kid	45	90	135	284	480	675
2-Williamson/Evans-c; text story about Wild Bill Hickok & Pecos Bill	40	80	120	246	411	575
3-Williamson/Evans-c/a	42	84	126	265	445	625
4-Frazetta-c/a, 1pg.; bondage-c	84	168	252	538	919	1300
5-Classic Frazetta sci-fi cover; Williamson/Krenkel/Orlando-a, 11pgs. (per Mr. Williamson)	219	438	657	1402	2401	3400
6,8	26	52	78	154	252	350
7-Frazetta one pg. ad	25	50	75	150	245	340
9-One pg. Frazetta Boy Scouts ad (1st?)	20	40	60	117	189	260
10-12	15	30	45	84	127	170

NOTE: Eastern Color sold 3 dozen each NM file copies of #s 9-12 a few years ago.

BUSTER CRABBE (The Amazing Adventures of...)(Movie star)
Lev Gleason Publications: Dec, 1953 - No. 4, June, 1954
1,4: 1-Photo-c. 4-Flash Gordon-c — 27 · 54 · 81 · 158 · 259 · 360
2,3-Toth-a — 23 · 46 · 69 · 136 · 223 · 310

BUTCH CASSIDY (TV)
Skywald Comics: June, 1971 - No. 3, Oct, 1971 (52 pgs.)
1-Pre-code reprints and new material; Red Mask reprint, retitled Maverick; Bolle-a; Sutton-a — 3 · 6 · 9 · 15 · 22 · 28
2,3: 2-Whip Wilson-r. 3-Dead Canyon Days reprint/Crack Western No. 63; Sundance Kid app.; Crandall-a — 2 · 4 · 6 · 10 · 14 · 18

BUTCH CASSIDY (...& the Wild Bunch)
Avon Periodicals: 1951
1-Kinstler-c/a — 28 · 56 · 84 · 168 · 274 · 380

Bullseye (2017 series) #4 © MAR

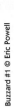

Buzzard #1 © Eric Powell

Cable (2008 series) #1 © MAR

	GD 2.0	VG 4.0	FN 6.0	VF 8.0	VF/NM 9.0	NM- 9.2

NOTE: *Reinman* story; Issue number on inside spine.

BUTCH CASSIDY (See Fun-In No. 11 & Western Adventure Comics)

BUTCHER, THE (Also see Brave and the Bold, 2nd Series)
DC Comics: May, 1990 - No. 5, Sept, 1990 ($1.50, mature)

1-5: 1-No indicia inside						4.00

BUTCHER KNIGHT
Image Comics (Top Cow): Jan, 2001 - No. 4, June, 2001 ($2.95, limited series)

Preview (B&W, 16 pgs.) Dwayne Turner-c/a						3.00
1-4-Dwayne Turner-c/a						3.00

BUTCHER OF PARIS, THE
Dark Horse Comics: Dec, 2019 - No. 5, Apr, 2020 ($3.99, limited series)

1-5-Serial killer in 1944 Paris; Stephanie Phillips-s/Dean Kotz-a						4.00

BUTTERFLY
Archaia: Sept, 2014 - No. 4, Dec, 2014 ($3.99, limited series)

1-4: Phil Noto-c on all. 1-Marguerite Bennett-s/Antonio Fuso-a. 3,4-Simeone-a						4.00

BUZ SAWYER (Sweeney No. 4 on)
Standard Comics: June, 1948 - No. 3, 1949

	GD	VG	FN	VF	VF/NM	NM-
1-Roy Crane-a	30	60	90	177	289	400
2-Intro his pal Sweeney	17	34	51	98	154	210
3	13	26	39	72	101	130

BUZ SAWYER'S PAL, ROSCOE SWEENEY (See Sweeney)

BUZZ, THE (Also see Spider-Girl)
Marvel Comics: July, 2000 - No. 3, Sept, 2000 ($2.99, limited series)

1-3-Buscema-a/DeFalco & Frenz-s						3.00

BUZZARD (See The Goon)
Dark Horse Comics: Jun, 2010 - No. 3, Aug, 2010 ($3.50, limited series)

1-3-Eric Powell-c; Buzzard story w/Powell-s/a; Billy The Kid back-up; Powell-s/Hotz-a						3.50

BUZZ BUZZ COMICS MAGAZINE
Horse Press: May, 1994 (B&W, over-sized magazine)

1-Paul Pope-c/a/scripts; Moebius-a						5.00

BUZZY (See All Funny Comics)
National Periodical Publications/Detective Comics: Winter, 1944-45 - No. 75, 1-2/57; No. 76, 10/57; No. 77, 10/58

	GD	VG	FN	VF	VF/NM	NM-
1 (52 pgs. begin); "America's favorite teenster"	45	90	135	284	480	675
2 (Spr, 1945)	24	48	72	142	234	325
3-5	19	38	57	111	176	240
6-10	15	30	45	86	133	180
11-20	14	28	42	78	112	145
21-30	13	26	39	72	101	130
31,35-38	11	22	33	64	90	115
32-34,39-Last 52 pgs. Scribbly story by Mayer in each (these four stories were done for Scribbly #14 which was delayed for a year)	12	24	36	69	97	125
40-77: 62-Last precode (2/55)	11	22	33	62	86	110

BUZZY THE CROW (See Harvey Comics Hits #60 & 62, Harvey Hits #18 & Paramount Animated Comics #1)

BY BIZARRE HANDS
Dark Horse Comics: Apr, 1994 - No. 3, June, 1994 ($2.50, B&W, mature)

1-3: Lansdale stories						4.00

BY NIGHT
Boom Entertainment (BOOM! Box): Jun, 2018 - No. 12, Jun, 2019 ($3.99)

1-12-John Allison-s/Christine Larsen-a						4.00

BYTE-SIZED
AWA, Inc.: Dec, 2020 - No. 4, Mar, 2021 ($3.99, limited series)

1-4-Cullen Bunn-s/Nelson Blake II-a						4.00

CABBOT: BLOODHUNTER (Also see Bloodstrike & Bloodstrike: Assassin)
Maximum Press: Jan, 1997 ($2.50, one-shot)

1-Rick Veitch-a/script; Platt-c; Thor, Chapel & Prophet cameos						4.00

CABLE (See Ghost Rider &...., & New Mutants #87) (Title becomes Soldier X)
Marvel Comics: May, 1993 - No. 107, Sept, 2002 ($3.50/$1.95/$1.50-$2.25)

	GD	VG	FN	VF	VF/NM	NM-
1-($3.50, 52 pgs.)-Gold foil & embossed-c; Thibert a-1-p; c-1-3						
	2	4	6	9	13	16
2,4-15: 4-Liefeld-a assist; last Thibert-a(p). 6-8-Reveals that Baby Nathan is Cable; gives background on Stryfe. 9-Omega Red-c/story. 11-Bound-in trading card sheet						4.00
3-1st Weasel; extra 16 pg. X-Men/Avengers ann. preview						
	1	2	3	6		8
16-Newsstand edition						3.00

16-Enhanced edition						5.00
17-20-($1.95)-Deluxe edition, 20-w/bound in '95 Fleer Ultra cards						4.00
17-20-($1.50)-Standard edition						3.00
21-24, 26-44, -1(7/97): 21-Begin $1.95-c; return from Age of Apocalypse. 24-Grizzly dies. 28-vs. Sugarman; Mr. Sinister app. 30-X-Man-c/app.; Exodus app. 31-vs. X-Man. 32-Post app. 33-Post-c/app; Mandarin app (flashback); includes "Onslaught Update". 34-Onslaught x-over; Hulk-c/app; Apocalypse app. (cont'd in Hulk #444). 35-Onslaught x-over; Apocalypse vs. Cable. 38-Weapon X-c/app; Psycho Man & Micronauts app. 40-Scott Clark-a(p). 41-Bishop-c/app.						3.00
25 ($3.95)-Foil gatefold-c						5.00
45-49,51-74: 45-Operation Zero Tolerance. 51-1st Casey-s. 54-Black Panther. 55-Domino-c/app. 62-Nick Fury-c/app.63-Stryfe-c/app. 67,68-Avengers-c/app. 71,73-Liefeld-a						3.00
50-($2.99) Double sized w/wraparound-c						4.00
75 -($2.99) Liefeld-c/a; Apocalypse: The Twelve x-over						4.00
76-79: 76-Apocalypse: The Twelve x-over						3.00
80-96: 80-Begin $2.25-c. 87-Mystique-c/app.						3.00
97-99,101-107: 97-Tischman/Kordey-a/c begin						3.00
100-($3.99) Dialogue-free 'Nuff Said back-up story						4.00
... Classic Vol. 1 TPB (2008, $29.99) r/#1-4, New Mutants #87, Cable: Blood & Metal #1,2						30.00
.../Machine Man '98 Annual ($2.99) Wraparound-c						4.00
.../X-Force '96 Annual ($2.95) Wraparound-c						4.00
...'99 Annual ($3.50) vs. X-Man; computer photo-c						4.00
...Second Genesis 1 (9/99, $3.99) r/New Mutants #99, 100 and X-Force #1; Liefeld-c						4.00
...: The End (2002, $14.99, TPB) r/#101-107						15.00

CABLE
Marvel Comics: May, 2008 - No. 25, Jun, 2009 ($2.99/$3.99)

	GD	VG	FN	VF	VF/NM	NM-
1-23: 1-10-Olivetti-c/a. 1-Liefeld var-c. 2-Finch var-c. 3-Romita Jr. var-c. 4-Bishop app.; Djurdjevic var-c. 5-Silvestri var-c. 6-Liefeld var-c. 13-15-Messiah War x-over; Deadpool app. 16,17-Gulacy-a						3.00
24-($3.99) Bishop app.						4.00
25-($3.99) Deadpool app.; Medina-a	1	2	3	5	6	8

CABLE
Marvel Comics: Jul, 2017 - No. 5, Nov, 2017; No. 150, Dec, 2017 - No. 159, Sept, 2018 ($3.99)

1-5: 1-Robinson-s/Pacheco-a. 4-Rasputin app.						4.00
[Title switches to legacy numbering after #5 (11/17)]						
150-159: 150-154-The Externals app.						4.00
... Deadpool Annual 1 (10/18, $4.99) David F. Walker-s; art by various						5.00

CABLE
Marvel Comics: May, 2020 - No. 12, Sept, 2021 ($4.99/$3.99)

1-($4.99) Duggan-s/Noto-a; young Cable on Krakoa; Wolverine app.						5.00
2-12-($3.99) 3-Space Knights and Deadpool app. 4-6-"X of Swords" tie-ins						4.00
... Reloaded 1 (10/21, $4.99) Ewing-s/Quinn-a; Rocket Raccoon app.						5.00

CABLE
Marvel Comics: Mar, 2024 - Present ($4.99/$3.99)

1-($4.99) Nicieza-s/Eaton-a						5.00
2-($3.99) Grey Gargoyle app.						4.00

CABLE AND X-FORCE (Marvel NOW!)
Marvel Comics: Feb, 2013 - No. 19, Mar, 2014 ($3.99)

1-19: 1-Hopeless-s/Larroca-a; Cable, Colossus, Domino, Forge & Dr. Nemesis team						4.00

CABLE - BLOOD AND METAL (Also see New Mutants #87 & X-Force #8)
Marvel Comics: Oct, 1992 - No. 2, Nov, 1992 ($2.50, limited series, 52 pgs.)

1-Fabian Nicieza scripts; John Romita, Jr.-c/a in both; Cable vs. Stryfe; 2nd app. of The Wild Pack (becomes The Six Pack); wraparound-c						6.00
2-Prelude to X-Cutioner's Song						5.00

CABLE/DEADPOOL ("Cable & Deadpool" on cover)
Marvel Comics: May, 2004 - No. 50, Apr, 2008 ($2.99)

	GD	VG	FN	VF	VF/NM	NM-
1-Nicieza-s/Liefeld-c	4	8	12	28	47	65
2,3	2	4	6	8	10	12
4-23,25-37: 7-9-X-Men app. 17-House of M. 21-Heroes For Hire app. 30,31-Civil War. 30-Great Lakes Avengers app. 33-Liefeld-c						5.00
24-Spider-Man app.	5	10	15	31	53	75
38-1st Bob, Agent of HYDRA	2	4	6	13	18	22
39-49: 43,44-Wolverine app.						
50-($3.99) Final issue; Spider-Man and the Avengers app.; 1st Venompool	8	12	23	37		50
Cable & Deadpool MCG 1 (7/11, $1.00) r/#1 with "Marvel's Greatest Comics" cover logo						5.00
... Vol. 1: If Looks Could Kill TPB (2004, $14.99) r/#1-6						15.00
... Vol. 2: The Burnt Offering TPB (2005, $14.99) r/#7-12						15.00
... Vol. 3: The Human Race TPB (2005, $14.99) r/#13-18						15.00
... Vol. 4: Bosom Buddies TPB (2006, $14.99) r/#19-24						15.00

	GD 2.0	VG 4.0	FN 6.0	VF 8.0	VF/NM 9.0	NM- 9.2

... Vol. 5: Living Legends TPB (2006, $13.99) r/#25-29 — 14.00
... Vol. 6: Paved With Good Intentions TPB (2007, $14.99) r/#30-35 — 15.00
... Vol. 7: Separation Anxiety TPB (2007, $17.99) r/#36-42; sketch pages — 18.00
Deadpool Vs. The Marvel Universe TPB (2008, $24.99) r/#43-50 — 25.00

CADET GRAY OF WEST POINT (See Dell Giants)

CADILLACS & DINOSAURS (TV)
Marvel Comics (Epic Comics): Nov, 1990 - No. 6, Apr, 1991 ($2.50, limited series)

	GD	VG	FN	VF	VF/NM	NM-
1-Reprints Xenozoic Tales in color w/new-c	1	3	4	6	8	10
2-6						5.00
...In 3-D #1 (7/92, $3.95, Kitchen Sink)-With glasses	1	3	4	6	8	10

CADILLACS AND DINOSAURS (TV)
Topps Comics: V2#1, Feb, 1994 - V2#9, 1995 ($2.50, limited series)

	GD	VG	FN	VF	VF/NM	NM-
V2#1-($2.95)-Collector's edition w/Stout-c & bound-in poster; Buckler-a; foil stamped logo; Giordano-a in all						6.00
V2#1-9: 1-Newsstand edition w/Giordano-c. 2,3-Collector's editions w/Stout-c & posters. 2,3-Newsstand ed. w/Giordano-c; w/o posters. 4-6-Collectors & Newsstand editions; Kieth-c. 7-9-Linsner-c						4.00

CAGE (Also see Hero for Hire, Power Man & Punisher)
Marvel Comics: Apr, 1992 - No. 20, Nov, 1993 ($1.25)

	GD	VG	FN	VF	VF/NM	NM-
1,3,10,12: 3-Punisher-c & minor app. 10-Rhino & Hulk-c/app. 12-(52 pgs.)-Iron Fist app.						4.00
2,4-9,11,13-20: 9-Rhino-c/story; Hulk cameo						4.00

CAGE (Volume 3)
Marvel Comics (MAX): Mar, 2002 - No. 5, Sept, 2002 ($2.99, mature)

	GD	VG	FN	VF	VF/NM	NM-
1-5-Corben-c/a; Azzarello-s						3.00
HC (2002, $19.99, with dustjacket) r/#1-5; intro. by Darius James; sketch pages						20.00
SC (2003, $13.99) r/#1-5; intro. by Darius James						14.00

CAGE! (Luke Cage)
Marvel Comics: Dec, 2016 - No. 4, Mar, 2017 ($3.99, limited series)

	GD	VG	FN	VF	VF/NM	NM-
1-4-Genndy Tartakovsky-s/a; set in 1977						4.00

CAGED HEAT 3000 (Movie)
Roger Corman's Cosmic Comics: Nov, 1995 - No. 3, Jan, 1996 ($2.50)

	GD	VG	FN	VF	VF/NM	NM-
1-3: Adaptation of film						4.00

CAGE HERO
Dynamite Entertainment: 2015 - No. 4, 2016 ($3.99, limited series)

	GD	VG	FN	VF	VF/NM	NM-
1-4-Kevin Eastman & Ian Parker-s/Renalto Rei-a						4.00

CAGES
Tundra Publ.: 1991 - No. 10, May, 1996 ($3.50/$3.95/$4.95, limited series)

	GD	VG	FN	VF	VF/NM	NM-
1-Dave McKean-c/a in all	2	4	6	8	10	12
2-Misprint exists	1	2	3	5	6	8
3-9: 5-$3.95-c begins						4.00
10-($4.95)						5.00

CAIN'S HUNDRED (TV)
Dell Publishing Co.: May-July, 1962 - No. 2, Sept-Nov, 1962

	GD	VG	FN	VF	VF/NM	NM-
nn (01-094-207)	4	8	12	25	40	55
2	3	6	9	16	23	30

CAIN/VAMPIRELLA FLIP BOOK
Harris Comics: Oct, 1994 ($6.95, one-shot, squarebound)

	GD	VG	FN	VF	VF/NM	NM-
nn-contains Cain #3 & #4; flip book is r/Vampirella story from 1993 Creepy Fearbook	1	3	4	6	8	10

CALAMITY KATE
Dark Horse Comics: Mar, 2019 - No. 4, Jun, 2019 ($3.99, limited series)

	GD	VG	FN	VF	VF/NM	NM-
1-4-Magdalene Visaggio-s/Corin Howell-a						4.00

CALIBER PRESENTS
Caliber Press: Jan, 1989 - No. 24, 1991 ($1.95/$2.50, B&W, 52 pgs.)

	GD	VG	FN	VF	VF/NM	NM-
1-Anthology; 1st app. The Crow; Tim Vigil-c/a	18	36	54	124	275	425
2-Deadworld story; Tim Vigil-a	2	4	6	11	16	20
3-24: 15-24 ($3.50, 68 pgs.)						4.00
...: Cinderella on Fire 1 (1994, $2.95, B&W, mature)						3.00

CALIBER SPOTLIGHT
Caliber Press: May, 1995 ($2.95, B&W)

	GD	VG	FN	VF	VF/NM	NM-
1-Kabuki app.						4.00

CALIFORNIA GIRLS
Eclipse Comics: June, 1987 - No. 8, May, 1988 ($2.00, 40 pgs, B&W)

	GD	VG	FN	VF	VF/NM	NM-
1-8: All contain color paper dolls						6.00

CALL, THE
Marvel Comics: June, 2003 - No. 4, Sept, 2003 ($2.25)

	GD	VG	FN	VF	VF/NM	NM-
1-4-Austen-s/Olliffe-a						3.00

CALLING ALL BOYS (Tex Granger No. 18 on)
Parents' Magazine Institute: Jan, 1946 - No. 17, May, 1948 (Photo c-1-5,7,8)

	GD	VG	FN	VF	VF/NM	NM-
1	22	44	66	132	216	300
2-Contains Roy Rogers article	14	28	42	76	108	140
3-7,9,11,14-17: 6-Painted-c. 11-Rin Tin Tin photo on-c; Tex Granger begins. 14-J. Edgar Hoover photo on-c. 15-Tex Granger-c begin	10	20	30	58	79	100
8-Milton Caniff story	14	28	42	76	108	140
10-Gary Cooper photo on-c	14	28	42	76	108	140
12-Bob Hope photo on-c	16	32	48	96	151	180
13-Bing Crosby photo on-c	15	30	45	86	133	180

CALLING ALL GIRLS
Parents' Magazine Institute: Sept, 1941 - No. 89, Sept, 1949 (Part magazine, part comic)

	GD	VG	FN	VF	VF/NM	NM-
1-Photo-c	34	68	102	204	332	460
2-Photo-c	17	34	51	98	154	210
3-Shirley Temple photo-c	22	44	66	132	216	300
4-10: 4,5,7,9-Photo-c. 9-Flag-c	14	28	42	81	118	155
11-Tina Thayer photo-c; Mickey Rooney photo-b/c; B&W photo inside of Gary Cooper as Lou Gehrig in "Pride of Yankees"	15	30	45	86	133	180

	GD	VG	FN	VF	VF/NM	NM-
12-20	12	24	36	67	94	120
21-39,41-43(10-11/45)-Last issue with comics	11	22	33	62	86	110
40-Liz Taylor photo-c	34	68	102	199	325	450
44-51(7/46)-Last comic book size issue	10	20	30	54	72	90
52-89	9	18	27	50	65	80

NOTE: *Jack Sparling* art in many issues; becomes a girls' magazine "Senior Prom" with #90.

CALLING ALL KIDS (Also see True Comics)
Parents' Magazine Institute: Dec-Jan, 1945-46 - No. 26, Aug, 1949

	GD	VG	FN	VF	VF/NM	NM-
1-Funny animal	22	44	66	132	216	300
2	14	28	42	76	108	140
3-10	10	20	30	56	76	95
11-26	9	18	27	52	69	85

CALL OF DUTY: BLACK OPS III (Based on the Activision video game)
Dark Horse Comics: Nov, 2015 - No. 6, Oct, 2016 ($3.99, limited series)

	GD	VG	FN	VF	VF/NM	NM-
1-Prequel to the game; Hama-s/Ferreira-a	1	2	3	5	6	8
2-6-Hama-s/Ferreira-a						4.00

CALL OF DUTY, THE : THE BROTHERHOOD
Marvel Comics: Aug, 2002 - No. 6, Jan, 2003 ($2.25)

	GD	VG	FN	VF	VF/NM	NM-
1-Exploits of NYC Fire Dept.; Finch-c/a; Austen & Bruce Jones-s						4.00
2-6-Austen-s						3.00
...Vol 1: The Brotherhood & The Wagon TPB (2002, $14.99) r/#1-6 & ...The Wagon #1-4						15.00

CALL OF DUTY, THE : THE PRECINCT
Marvel Comics: Sept, 2002 - No. 5, Jan, 2003 ($2.25, limited series)

	GD	VG	FN	VF	VF/NM	NM-
1-Exploits of NYC Police Dept.; Finch-c; Bruce Jones/Mandrake-a						3.00
2-4						3.00
...Vol 2: The Precinct TPB (2003, $9.99) r/#1-4						10.00

CALL OF DUTY, THE : THE WAGON
Marvel Comics: Oct, 2002 - No. 4, Jan, 2003 ($2.25, limited series)

	GD	VG	FN	VF	VF/NM	NM-
1-4-Exploits of NYC EMS Dept.; Finch-c; Austen/Zelzej-a						3.00

CALL OF DUTY: ZOMBIES (Based on the Activision video game)
Dark Horse Comics: Oct, 2016 - No. 6, Aug, 2017 ($3.99, limited series)

	GD	VG	FN	VF	VF/NM	NM-
1-Justin Jordan-s/Jonathan Wayshak-a/Bisley-c	3	6	9	19	30	40
2-6	1	3	4	6	8	10

CALL OF DUTY: ZOMBIES 2 (Based on the Activision video game)
Dark Horse Comics: Sept, 2018 - No. 3, Dec, 2018 ($3.99, limited series)

	GD	VG	FN	VF	VF/NM	NM-
1-Justin Jordan-s/Andres Ponce-a/E.M. Gist-c	1	2	3	5	6	8
2,3						4.00

CALVIN (See Li'l Kids)

CALVIN & THE COLONEL (TV)
Dell Publishing Co.: No. 1354, Apr-June, 1962 - No. 2, July-Sept, 1962

	GD	VG	FN	VF	VF/NM	NM-
Four Color 1354(#1) (The last Four Color issue)	10	20	30	64	132	200
2	5	10	15	35	63	90

CAMELOT 3000
DC Comics: Dec, 1982 - No. 11, July, 1984; No. 12, Apr, 1985 (Direct sales, maxi series, Mando paper)

	GD	VG	FN	VF	VF/NM	NM-
1-12: 1-Mike Barr scripts & Brian Bolland-c/a in all. 5-Intro Knights of New Camelot						5.00
TPB (1988, $12.95) r/#1-12						15.00
...: The Deluxe Edition (2008, $34.99, HC) r/#1-12; oversized & recolored; Barr intro.; design and promotional art; original proposal page						40.00

NOTE: *Austin* a-7i-12i. *Bolland* a-1-12p; c-1-12.

CAMERA COMICS
U.S. Camera Publishing Corp./ME: July, 1944 - No. 9, Summer, 1946

	GD	VG	FN	VF	VF/NM	NM-
nn (7/44)	45	90	135	284	480	675
nn (9/44)	34	68	102	204	332	460
1(10/44)-The Grey Comet (slightly smaller page size than subsequent issues); WWII-c	39	78	117	240	395	550
2-16 pgs. of photos with 32 pgs. of comics	26	52	78	154	252	350
3-Nazi WW II-c; photos	58	116	174	371	636	900
4-9: All 1/3 photos	21	42	63	124	202	280

CAMP CANDY (TV)
Marvel Comics: May, 1990 - No. 6, Oct, 1990 ($1.00, limited series)

	GD	VG	FN	VF	VF/NM	NM-
1-Post-c/a(p); featuring John Candy	1	3	4	6	8	10
2-6						6.00

CAMP COMICS
Dell Publishing Co.: Feb, 1942 - No. 3, April, 1942 (All have photo-c)(All issues are scarce)

	GD	VG	FN	VF	VF/NM	NM-
1- "Seaman Sy Wheeler" by Kelly, 7 pgs.; Bugs Bunny app.; Mark Twain adaptation	103	206	309	659	1130	1600
2-Kelly-a, 12 pgs.; Bugs Bunny app.; classic-c	97	194	291	621	1061	1500
3-(Scarce)-Dave Berg & Walt Kelly-a	71	142	213	454	777	1100

CAMP RUNAMUCK (TV)
Dell Publishing Co.: Apr, 1966

	GD	VG	FN	VF	VF/NM	NM-
1-Photo-c	3	6	9	21	33	45

CAMPUS LOVES
Quality Comics Group (Comic Magazines): Dec, 1949 - No. 5, Aug, 1950

	GD	VG	FN	VF	VF/NM	NM-
1-Ward-c/a (9 pgs.)	50	100	150	315	533	750
2-Ward-c/a	39	78	117	231	378	525
3-5	21	42	63	122	199	275

NOTE: *Gustavson* a-1-5. Photo c-3-5.

CAMPUS ROMANCE (...Romances on cover)
Avon Periodicals/Realistic: Sept-Oct, 1949 - No. 3, Feb-Mar, 1950

	GD	VG	FN	VF	VF/NM	NM-
1-Walter Johnson-a; c-/Avon paperback #348	55	110	165	352	601	850
2-Grandenetti-a; c-/Avon paperback #151	39	78	117	240	395	550
3-c-/Avon paperback #201	39	78	117	240	395	550
Realistic reprint	20	40	60	118	192	265

CANADA DRY PREMIUMS (See Swamp Fox, The & Terry & The Pirates in the Promotional Comics section)

CANADIAN VARK! (Reprints from Cerebus in Hell)

Call of Duty: Zombies 2 #2 © Activision

Canteen Kate #2 © STJ

Captain Action #4 © DC

	GD	VG	FN	VF	VF/NM	NM-
	2.0	4.0	6.0	8.0	9.0	9.2

Aardvark-Vanaheim: Dec, 2018 ($4.00, B&W)

1-Cerebus figures placed over original Doré artwork of Hell; American Flagg #1-c swipe 4.00

CANARY
Dark Horse Comics: Nov, 2023 - No. 3, Feb, 2024 ($5.99/$4.99, limited series)

1,3-($5.99) Western story; Scott Snyder-s/Dan Panosian-a 6.00
2-($4.99) 5.00

CANCELLED COMIC CAVALCADE (See the Promotional Comics section)

CANDID TALES (Also see Bold Stories & It Rhymes With Lust)
Kirby Publ. Co.: April, 1950; June, 1950 (Digest size) (144 pgs.) (Full color)

| nn-(Scarce) Contains Wood female pirate story, 15 pgs., and 14 pgs. in June issue; Powell-a | 314 | 628 | 942 | 2198 | 3849 | 5500 |

NOTE: Another version exists with Dr. Kilmore by Wood; no female pirate story.

CANDY (Teen-age)(Also see Police Comics #37)
Quality Comics Group (Comic Magazines): Autumn, 1947 - No. 64, Jul, 1956

1-Gustavson-a	34	68	102	199	325	450
2-Gustavson-a	20	40	60	115	185	255
3-10	14	28	42	81	118	155
11-30	12	24	36	67	94	120
31-64: 64-Ward-c(p)?	10	20	30	54	72	90
Super Reprint No. 2,10,12,16,17,18('63- '64):17-Candy #12	3	6	9	14	19	24

NOTE: Jack Cole 1-2 pg. art in many issues.

CANDY COMICS
William H. Wise & Co.: Fall, 1944 - No. 3, Spring, 1945

| 1-Two Scoop Scuttle stories by Wolverton | 48 | 96 | 144 | 302 | 514 | 725 |
| 2,3-Scoop Scuttle by Wolverton, 2-4 pgs. | 33 | 66 | 99 | 194 | 317 | 440 |

CANNON (See Heroes, Inc. Presents Cannon)

CANNIBAL
Image Comics: Oct, 2016 - No. 8, Oct, 2017 ($3.99)

1-8-Young & Buccellato-s/Bergara-a 4.00

CANNON: DAWN OF WAR (Michael Turner's...)
Aspen MLT, Inc.: Nov, 2004 ($2.99)

1-Turnbull-a; two covers by Turnbull and Turner 3.00

CANNONBALL COMICS
Rural Home Publishing Co.: Feb, 1945 - No. 2, Mar, 1945

| 1-The Crash Kid, Thunderbrand, The Captive Prince & Crime Crusader begin; skull-c | 295 | 590 | 885 | 1888 | 3244 | 4600 |
| 2-Devil-c | 232 | 464 | 696 | 1485 | 2543 | 3600 |

CANTEEN KATE (See All Picture All True Love Story & Fightin' Marines)
St. John Publishing Co.: June, 1952 - No. 3, Nov, 1955

1-Matt Baker-c/a	194	388	582	1242	2121	3000
2-Matt Baker-c/a	84	168	252	538	919	1300
3-(Rare)-Used in POP, pg. 75; Baker-c/a	103	206	309	659	1130	1600

CANTO
IDW Pubishing: Jun, 2019 - No. 6, Nov, 2019 ($3.99)

1-David M. Booher-s/Drew Zucker-a	4	8	12	28	47	65
2	2	4	6	9	12	15
3-6						6.00
... & The Clockwork Fairies (5/20, $3.99) Zucker-a	1	2	3	5	6	8

CANTO & THE CITY OF GIANTS
IDW Pubishing: Apr, 2019 - No. 3, Jun, 2021 ($3.99)

1-3-David M. Booher-s/Sebastian Piriz-a 4.00

CANTO II: THE HOLLOW MEN
IDW Pubishing: Aug, 2020 - No. 5, Jan, 2021 ($3.99)

| 1-David M. Booher-s/Drew Zucker-a | 1 | 3 | 4 | 6 | 8 | 10 |
| 2-5 | | | | | | 4.00 |

CANTO III: LIONHEARTED
IDW Pubishing: Jul, 2021 - No. 6, Jan, 2022 ($3.99)

1-6-David M. Booher-s/Drew Zucker-a 4.00

CANTO: TALES OF THE UNNAMED WORLD
IDW Pubishing: Jun, 2022 - No. 2, Jul, 2022 ($3.99)

1,2-David M. Booher-s/Drew Zucker-a 4.00

CAPE, THE
IDW Pubishing: Dec, 2010; Jul, 2011 - No. 4, Jan, 2012 ($3.99)

1-(12/10) Zach Howard-c/a; Jason Ciaramella-s 4.00

						4.00
1-4: 1-(7/11) Story continues from 12/10 issue						
...: Fallen (6/18 - No. 4, 12/18, $3.99) 1-4-Ciaramella-s; Zach Howard-a						4.00
...: Greatest Hits (6/18, $1.00) reprints #1 (12/10) and previews The Cape: Fallen series						3.00
...: Legacy Edition (6/11, $5.99) r/#1 (12/10) with Joe Hill's original short story						6.00
...: 1969 (7/12 - No. 4, 10/12, $3.99) 1-4-Ciaramella-s; origin in Vietnam						4.00

CAPER
DC Comics: Dec, 2003 - No. 12, Nov, 2004 ($2.95, limited series)

1-12: 1-4-Judd Winick-s/Farel Dalrymple-a. 5-8-John Severin-a. 9-12-Fowler-a 3.00

CAPES
Image Comics: Sept, 2003 - No. 3, Nov, 2003 ($3.50)

| 1-Robert Kirkman-s; 5 pg. preview of The Walking Dead #1 | 4 | 8 | 12 | 24 | 38 | 52 |
| 2,3-Robert Kirkman-s/Mark Englert-a/c | | | | | | 5.00 |

CAP'N QUICK & A FOOZLE (Also see Eclipse Mag. & Monthly)
Eclipse Comics: July, 1984 - No. 3, Nov, 1985 ($1.50, color, Baxter paper)

1-3-Rogers-c/a 4.00

CAPTAIN ACTION (Toy)
National Periodical Publications: Oct-Nov, 1968 - No. 5, June-July, 1969 (Based on Ideal toy)

1-Origin; Wally Wood-a; Superman-c app.	7	14	21	49	92	135
2,3,5-Gil Kane/Wally Wood-a	5	10	15	33	57	80
4- Gil Kane-c	4	8	12	28	47	65

CAPTAIN ACTION CAT: THE TIMESTREAM CATASTROPHE
Dynamite Entertainment: 2014 - No. 4, 2014 ($3.99, limited series)

1-4-Art Baltazar-s/a; Franco & Smits-s; all ages cat version of Capt. Action characters; Ghost, X, Captain Midnight, Skyman & The Occultist app. 4.00

CAPTAIN ACTION COMICS (Toy)
Moonstone: No. 0, 2008 - No. 5 (Based on the Ideal toy)

0-($1.99) Origin re-told; Sparacio-a; three covers; character history by Michael Eury						3.00
1-5: 1-($3.99) Sparacio-a; intro. by Jim Shooter						4.00
... Comics Special 1 (2010, $5.99) 3 covers by Barreto, Ordway & Spiegle						6.00
... Exclusive Special 1 (2011, no price) Gulacy-c; Barreto-a						4.00
...: First Mission, Last Day (2008, $3.99) origin story re-told; Nicieza-s/Procopio-a						4.00
... King Size Special 1 (2011, $6.99) 1-Covers by Byrne, Wheatley & M. Benes						7.00
... Season 2 (2010, $3.99) 1-3: -Covers by Allred & Texiera; Obama app.						4.00
... Winter Special (2011, $4.99) Green Hornet & Kato on-c & text story						5.00

CAPTAIN AERO COMICS (Samson No. 1-6; also see Veri Best Sure Fire & Veri Best Sure Shot Comics)
Holyoke Publishing Co.: V1#7(#1), Dec, 1941 - V2#4(#10), Jan, 1943; V3#9(#11), Sept, 1943 -V4#3(#17), Oct, 1944; #21, Dec, 1944 - #26, Aug, 1946 (No #18-20)

V1#7(#1)-Flag-Man & Solar, Master of Magic, Captain Aero, Cap Stone, Adventurer begin; Nazi WWII-c	239	478	717	1530	2615	3700
8,10: 8(#2)-Pals of Freedom app. 10(#4)-Origin The Gargoyle; Kubert-a	116	232	348	742	1271	1800
9(#3)-Hitler-sty; Catman back-c; Alias X begins; Pals of Freedom app.; Nazi WWII-c	148	296	444	947	1624	2300
11,12(#5,6)-Kubert-a; Miss Victory in #6	97	194	291	621	1061	1500
V2#1,2(#7,8)- 8-Origin The Red Cross; Miss Victory app.; Brodsky-c(i)	77	154	231	493	847	1200
3(#9)-Miss Victory app.	161	322	483	1030	1765	2500
4(#10)-Miss Victory app.; Japanese WWII-c	123	246	369	787	1344	1900
V3#9 - V3#12(#11-14): All Quinlan Japanese WWII-c. 9-Miss Victory app.	97	194	291	621	1061	1500
V3#13(#15),V4#2(#16): Schomburg Japanese WWII-c. 13-Miss Victory app.	119	238	357	762	1306	1850
V4#3(#17)-Miss Victory app.; L.B. Cole Japanese WWII-c	90	180	270	576	988	1400
21-24-L.B. Cole Japanese WWII covers. 22-Intro/origin Mighty Mite	77	154	231	493	847	1200
25-L.B. Cole Sci-fi-c	129	258	387	826	1413	2000
26-L.B. Cole Sci-fi-c; Palais-a(2) (scarce)	459	918	1377	3350	5925	8500

NOTE: L.B. Cole c-17, 21-26. Hollingsworth a-23. Infantino a-23, 26. Schomburg c-15, 16.

CAPTAIN AMERICA (See Adventures of..., All-Select, All Winners, Aurora, Avengers #4, Blood and Glory, Captain Britain 16-20, Giant-Size..., The Invaders, Marvel Double Feature, Marvel Fanfare, Marvel Mystery, Marvel Super-Action, Marvel Super Heroes V2#3, Marvel Team-Up, Marvel Treasury Special, Power Record Comics, Ultimates, USA Comics, Young Allies & Young Men)

CAPTAIN AMERICA (Formerly Tales of Suspense #1-99) (Captain America and the Falcon #134-223 & Steve Rogers: Captain America #444-454 appears on cover only)
Marvel Comics Group: No. 100, Apr, 1968 - No. 454, Aug, 1996

| 100-Flashback on Cap's revival with Avengers & Sub-Mariner; story continued from Tales of Suspense #99; Kirby-c/a begins | 100 | 200 | 300 | 700 | 1275 | 1850 |

	GD 2.0	VG 4.0	FN 6.0	VF 8.0	VF/NM 9.0	NM- 9.2

101-The Sleeper-c/story; Red Skull app. — 10 20 30 64 132 200
102-104: 102-Sleeper-c/s. 103,104-Red Skull-c/sty — 8 16 24 54 102 150
105,106,108 — 7 14 21 44 82 120
107-Red Skull & Hitler-c — 9 18 27 60 120 180
109-Origin Capt. America retold in detail — 18 36 54 122 271 420
109-2nd printing (1994) — 2 4 6 9 12 15
110-Rick Jones dons Bucky's costume & becomes Cap's partner; Hulk x-over; Steranko-a — 22 44 66 154 340 525
Classic Steranko-a
111-Classic Steranko-c/a; Death of Steve Rogers — 15 30 45 103 227 350
112-S.A. recovery retold; last Kirby-c/a — 8 16 24 54 102 150
113-Cap's funeral; Avengers app.; classic Steranko-a — 12 24 36 81 176 270
114-116,119,120: 114-Red Skull Cosmic Cube story. 115,116-Red Skull-c. 119-Cap vs. Red Skull; Cosmic Cube "destroyed"; Falcon app. — 5 10 15 34 60 85
117-1st app. The Falcon (9/69) — 68 136 204 544 1222 1900
117 Facsimile Edition (3/21, $3.99) Reprints #117 with original ads and letter column — 1 3 4 6 8 10
118-2nd app. The Falcon — 14 28 42 94 207 320
121-136,139,140: 121-Retells origin; Avengers app. 122-Cap vs. Scorpion. 124-Modok appears. 125-Mandarin app. 129-Red Skull app. 133-The Falcon becomes Cap's partner; origin Modok. 139,140-Grey Gargoyle app.; origin in #140 — 4 8 12 28 47 65
137,138-Spider-Man x-over — 5 10 15 34 60 85
141,142-Grey Gargoyle app. 141-Last Stan Lee issue. 142-Last 15¢ issue — 4 8 12 27 44 60
143-(52 pgs) Cap vs. Red Skull — 5 10 15 30 50 70
144-New costume Falcon — 4 8 12 27 44 60
145-152: 145-147-Cap vs. the Supreme Hydra. 146-1st Sal Buscema-a on title. 147-Supreme Hydra revealed to be Kingpin's son. 148-Red Skull app. 150-The Stranger app. 151,152- Cap vs. Mr. Hyde & The Scorpion. 152-1st app. Boss Morgan — 3 6 9 16 24 32
153-155: 153-1st brief app. Jack Monroe; return of 1950s Captain America. 154-1st full app. Jack Monroe (Nomad); 1950s Captain America and Avengers app. 155-Origin retold; origin Jack Monroe and the 1950s Captain America — 5 10 15 30 50 70
156-Cap vs. the 1950s Captain America; Jack Monroe app; classic Cap vs Cap cover — 4 8 12 23 37 50
157-162,165-167,177-179: 157-1st app. Viper. 159-Cap vs. Eel, Porcupine & Scarecrow. 160-1st app. Solarr. 161,162-Peggy Carter app. 164-1st Nightshade. 165-167-Cap vs. Yellow Claw. 177-Lucifer app. 178-1st time Peggy Carter meets Steve Rogers — 3 6 9 14 19 24
179-Hawkeye app. as the Golden Archer — 3 6 9 14 19 24
163-1st Serpent Squad: Viper, Eel and Cobra — 3 6 9 14 20 26
164-1st app. Nightshade; Queen of Werewolves — 3 6 9 16 24 32
168-1st Helmut Zemo (as the Phoenix) — 7 14 21 46 86 125
169-1st app. Quentin Harderman; Moonstone 1st app. (cameo) — 3 6 9 16 24 30
170-New Falcon costume with wings for flying; Moonstone 1st full app. & origin — 4 8 12 23 37 50
171-Black Panther & Iron Man app. — 4 8 12 28 47 65
172-175: X-Men x-over. 174-1st app. Number 1 — 3 6 9 19 30 40
176-Steve Rogers quits being Cap.; Avengers app. — 3 6 9 16 23 30
180-Intro/origin of Nomad (Steve Rogers) — 10 20 30 64 132 200
181-Intro/origin new Cap. — 3 6 9 21 33 45
182,184,185,187-191: 182,184,185-Red Skull app. 182-Frank Robbins-a. 189,190-Cap vs. Nightshade. 191-Iron Man app. — 2 4 6 10 14 18
183-Death of new Cap; Steve Rogers drops Nomad I.D.; returns to being Capt. America — 3 6 9 15 20 26
186-True origin The Falcon; Red Skull app. — 3 6 9 16 23 30
192-1st app. Dr. Karla Sofen (later becomes Moonstone) — 5 10 15 63 90
193-Kirby-c/a begins — 5 10 15 34 60 85
194-199-(Regular 25¢ edition)(4-7/76) — 3 6 9 14 19 24
196-199-(30¢-c variants, limited distribution) — 7 14 21 44 82 120
200-(Regular 25¢ edition)(8/76) — 3 6 9 15 22 28
200-(30¢-c variant, limited distribution) — 8 16 24 54 105 155
201-214-Kirby-c/a. 208-1st Arnim Zola. 209,210- Arnim Zola app. 210-212 –vs Red Skull — 2 4 6 10 14 18
210-214-(35¢-c variants, limited dist.)(6-10/77) — 11 22 33 72 154 235
215,216,218-229: 215-Origin retold. 216-r/Strange Tales #114. 218-Sal Buscema-a resumes. 226,227-Red Skull app. 228-Cap vs. Constrictor. 229-Marvel Man app. — 2 4 6 8 11 14
217-Intro. Marvel Boy (Wendell Vaughan); becomes Marvel Man in #218; later becomes Quasar (2/78) — 5 10 15 35 63 90
230-Battles Hulk-c/story cont'd in Inc. Hulk #232 — 3 6 9 16 23 30
231-234,236-240,242-246: 233-"Death" of Sharon Carter. 234-Daredevil app. 244,245-Miller-c — 1 3 4 6 8 10
235-(7/79) Daredevil x-over; Miller-a(p) — 2 4 6 9 12 15
241-Punisher app.; Miller-c — 6 12 18 37 66 95
241-2nd print — 2 4 6 8 10 12
247-252-Byrne-a — 2 4 6 8 10 12
253,255: 253-Byrne-a; Baron Blood app. 255-Origin retold; Miller-c — 3 6 9 14 19 24
254-Byrne-a; death of Baron Blood; intro new Union Jack — 3 6 9 16 23 30
256-262: 257-Hulk app. 258-Zeck-a begins. 259-Cap vs. Dr. Octopus. 261,262-Red Skull app. — 1 2 3 5 6 8
263-266: 263-Red Skull-c/story. 264-Original X-Men app. 265,266-Spider-Man app. — 1 3 4 6 8 10
267-280: 267-1st app. Everyman. 268-Defenders app. 269-1st Team America. 272-1st Vermin. 273,274-Baron Strucker. 275-1st Baron Zemo (formally the Phoenix). 276-278-Cap vs. Baron Zemo. 279-(3/83)-Contains Tattooz skin decals. 280-Scarecrow app. — 1 2 3 5 6 8
281-1950's Bucky returns. Spider-Woman and Viper app. — 1 3 4 6 8 10
282-Bucky becomes new Nomad (Jack Monroe) — 2 4 6 9 12 15
282-Silver ink 2nd print ($1.75) w/original date (6/83) — 5.00

283-289,291-300: 283-Cap vs. Viper. 284-Patriot (Jack Mace) app. 285-Death of Patriot. 286-288-Deathlok app. 293,294-Nomad app. 293-299-Red Skull and Baron Zemo app. 298-Origin Red Skull. 300- "Death" of Red Skull — 1 2 3 5 6 8
290-1st Mother Superior (Red Skull's daughter, later becomes Sin) — 3 6 9 14 19 24
301-322,324-331: 301-Avengers app. 305,306-Captain Britain app. 307-1st Madcap; 1st Mark Gruenwald's (begins 8-year run). 308-Secret Wars II x-over. 310-1st Serpent Society. 312-1st Flag Smasher. 313-Death of Modok. 314-Squadron Supreme x-over. 317-Hawkeye & Mockingbird app. 318-Scourge app; death of Blue Streak and Adder. 319-Scourge kills numerous villians. 320- "Death" of Scourge. 321-Cap vs. Flag Smasher; classic Zeck cover Cap with machine gun. 322-Cap vs. Flag Smasher. 325-Nomad app. 327-Cap vs Super-Patriot. 328,330-Demolition Man (D-Man) app. — 1 2 3 5 6 8
323-1st app. new Super-Patriot (see Nick Fury) — 4 8 12 27 44 60
332-Old Captain America resigns — 3 6 9 14 20 26
333-Super Patriot becomes new Captain America — 3 6 9 16 23 30
334-343,345-349: 334-Intro new Bucky; Freedom Force app. 337-Serpent Society app; Avengers #4 homage-c; Steve Rogers becomes 'the Captain'; becomes Captain America again in origin at #350. 339-Fall of the Mutants tie-in. 341-Cap vs Iron Man; x-over with Iron Man #228. 342-Cap vs. Viper and the Serpent Squad — 1 2 3 5 6 8
344-($1.50, 52 pgs.)-Ronald Reagan cameo as a snake man — 2 4 6 8 10
350-($1.75, 68 pgs.)-Return of Steve Rogers (original Cap) to original costume — 1 3 4 6 8 10
351,353,355-358,361-382,384-396: 351-Nick Fury app. 357-Bloodstone hunt Pt. 1 (of 6). 358-Baron Zemo app. 365,366-Acts of Vengeance x-overs. 367-Magneto vs Red Skull. 372-378-Streets of Poison. 374-Bullseye app. 375-Daredevil app. 376-Black Widow app. 377-Bullseye vs. Crossbones; Red Skull app. 379-Quasar app. 380-382-Serpent Society app. 386-U.S. Agent app. 387-392-Superia Stratagem. 387-389-Red Skull back-up stories. 394-Red Skull app. 395-Thor app. (Eric Masterson; also in #396-397); Red Skull app. 396-Red Skull and new (1st) Jack O Lantern app. — 1 2 3 5 6 8
352-1st Supreme Soviet Soldiers — 2 4 6 9 12 15
354-John Walker's 1st app. as U.S.Agent — 5 10 15 31 53 75
354 Facsimile Edition (3/21, $3.99) Reprints #354 with original ads and letter column — 4.00
359-Crossbones debut (cameo); Baron Zemo app. — 3 6 9 14 20 26
360-1st app. Crossbones; Baron Zemo app. — 3 6 9 19 30 40
383-($2.00, 68 pgs., squarebound)-50th anniversary issue; Red Skull story; Jim Lee-c(i) — 2 4 6 9 12 15
397-399,401-424: 397-New Jack O Lantern app. 398,399-Operation Galactic Storm x-overs. 401-Operation Galactic storm epilogue. 402-Begin 6 part Man-Wolf story w/Wolverine in #403-407. 405-410-New Jack O Lantern app. in back-up story. 406-Cable & Shatterstar cameo. 407-Capwolf vs. Cable-c/story. 408-Infinity War x-over; Falcon back-up story. 409-Red Skull & Crossbones app. 410-Crossbones app. 414-Black Panther app. 419-Red Skull app; x-over with Silver Sable #15. 423- Cap vs. Namor-c/story — 6.00
400-($2.25, 84 pgs.) Flip book format w/double gatefold-c; Operation Galactic Storm x-over; r/Avengers #4 plus-c contains cover pin-up — 1 3 4 6 8 10
425-($2.95, 52 pgs.)-Embossed Foil-c edition; Fighting Chance Pt. 1 — 2 4 6 8 10 12
425-($1.75, 52 pgs.)-non-embossed-c edition; Fighting Chance Pt. 1 — 2 4 6 8 10 12
426-439,442,443: 426-437-Fighting Chance Pt. 2-12. 427-Begins $1.50-c; bound-in trading card sheet. 438-Fighting Chance epilogue. 431-1st Free Spirit. 431-1st Americop. 438-Jack Flag. 438-Fighting Chance epilogue. 443-Last Gruenwald issue — 5.00
440,441,444,445: 440,441-Avengers x-overs; 'Taking A.I.M.' story. 444-Mark Waid-s (1st on Cap) & Ron Garney-c/a(p) begins, ends #454; Avengers app. 445-Operation rebirth Pt.1; vs. Red Skull; Sharon Carter returns — 6.00
446,447-Operation Rebirth; Red Skull app. 446-Hitler app. — 1 2 3 4 6 8
448-($2.95, double-sized issue) Waid script & Garney-c/a; Red Skull "dies" — 6.00
449-Thor app; story x-overs with Thor, Iron Man and Avengers titles — 6.00
450- "Man Without a Country" begins; Steve Rogers-c — 1 2 3 5 6 8
450-Captain America-c with white background — 1 3 4 6 8 10
451-453: 451-1st app. Cap's new costume. 453-Cap gets old costume back; Bill Clinton app. — 5.00
454-Last issue of the regular series (8/96) — 6.00
#600-up (See Captain America 2005 series, resumed original numbering after #50)
Special 1(1/71)-All reprint issue from Tales Of Suspense #63,69,70,71,75 — 7 14 21 49 92 135
Special 2(1/72, 52 pgs.)-All reprint issue from Tales Of Suspense #72-74 and Not Brand Ecch #5 — 5 10 15 31 53 75
Annual 3('76, 52 pgs.)-Kirby-c/a(new) — 3 6 9 17 26 35
Annual 4('77, 34 pgs.)-Magneto-c/story — 3 6 9 17 26 35
Annual 5-7: (52 pgs.)('81-'83) — 1 2 3 5 6 8
Annual 8(9/86)-Wolverine-c/story:Zeck-c — 8 16 24 47 87 65
Annual 9-13('90-'94, 68 pgs.)-9-Nomad back-up. 10-Origin retold (2 pgs.). 11-Falcon solo story. 12-Bagged w/card. 13-Red Skull-c/story — 6.00
...Ashcan Edition ('95, 75¢) — 4.00
... and the Falcon: Madbomb TPB (2004, $16.99) r/#193-200; Kirby-s/a — 17.00
... and the Falcon: Nomad TPB (2006, $24.99) r/#177-186; Cap becomes Nomad — 25.00
... and the Falcon: Secret Empire TPB (2005, $19.99) r/#169-176 — 20.00
... and the Falcon: The Swine TPB (2006, $29.99) r/#206-214 & Annual 3/4 — 30.00
... By Jack Kirby: Bicentennial Battles TPB (2005, $19.99) r/#201-205 & Marvel Treasury Special Featuring Captain America's Bicentennial Battles; Kirby-s/a — 20.00
...: Deathlok Lives! nn(10/93, $4.95)-r/#286-288 — 6.00
...Drug War 1-(1994, $2.00, 52 pgs.)-New Warriors app. — 4.00
...Man Without a Country(1998, $12.99, TPB)-r/#450-453 — 13.00
...Medusa Effect 1 (1994, $2.95, 68 pgs.)-Origin Baron Zemo — 4.00
...Operation Rebirth (1996, $9.95)-r/#445-448 — 10.00
...65th Anniversary Special (5/06, $3.99) WWII flashback with Bucky; Brubaker-s — 5.00
...Streets of Poison ($15.95)-r/#372-378 — 16.00
...: The Movie Special nn (5/92, $3.50, 52 pgs.)-Adapts movie; printed on coated stock; The Red Skull app. — 4.00

NOTE: *Austin* -c225i, 239i, 246i. *Buscema* a-115p, 217p; c-136p, 217, 297. *Byrne* c-223(part), 238, 239, 247p-254p, 290, 291, 313p; a-247-254p, 255, 313p. *Colan* a(p)-116-137, 256. *Annual* 5; c(p)-116-123, 126, 129. *Everett* a-136i, 137i; c-126i. *Garney* a(p)-444-454. *Gil Kane* a-145p; c-147p, 149p, 150p, 170p, 172-174, 180, 181p, 183-190p, 215, 216, 220, 221. *Kirby* a(p)-100-109, 112, 193-214, 216, Special 1, 2(layouts), Annual 3, 4; c-100-109, 112, 126p, 193-214. *Ron Lim* a(p)-366, 368-378, 380-386; c-366p, 368-378p, 379, 380-393p. *Miller*

Captain America #171 © MAR

Captain America V2 #1 © MAR

Captain America (2018 series) #4 © MAR

	GD	VG	FN	VF	VF/NM	NM-
	2.0	4.0	6.0	8.0	9.0	9.2

	GD	VG	FN	VF	VF/NM	NM-
	2.0	4.0	6.0	8.0	9.0	9.2

c-241p, 244p, 245p, 255p, Annual 5. **Mooney** a-149i. **Morrow** a-144. **Perez** c-243p, 246p. **Robbins** c(p)-183-187, 189-192, 225. **Roussos** a-140i, 168i. **Shores** a-102i, 107i, 109i. **Starlin/Sinnott** c-162. **Sutton** a-244i. **Tuska** a-112i, 215p, Special 2. **Waid** scripts-444-454. **Williamson** a-313i. **Wood** a-127i. **Zeck** a-263-289; c-300.

CAPTAIN AMERICA (Volume Two)
Marvel Comics: V2#1, Nov, 1996 - No. 13, Nov, 1997($2.95/$1.95/$1.99)
(Produced by Extreme Studios)

1-($2.95)-Heroes Reborn begins; Liefeld-c/a; Loeb scripts; reintro Nick Fury						
	2	4	6	8	10	12
1-($2.95)-(Variant-c)-Liefeld-c/a	1	3	4	6	8	10
1-(7/96, $2.95)-(Exclusive Comicon Ed.)-Liefeld-c/a	2	4	6	8	11	14
2-4,6-11,13: 6-Cable-c/app. 13-"World War 3"-pt. 4, x-over w/Image						4.00
5-1st cover app. of Rikki Barnes; two covers		1	3	4	6	10
12-($2.99) "Heroes Reunited"-pt. 4						3.00
Heroes Reborn: Captain America (2006, $29.99, TPB) r/#1-12 & Heroes Reborn #1/2						30.00

CAPTAIN AMERICA (Vol. Three) (Also see Capt. America: Sentinel of Liberty)
Marvel Comics: Jan, 1998 - No. 50, Feb, 2002 ($2.99/$1.99/$2.25)

1-($2.99) Mark Waid-s/Ron Garney-a	4.00
1-Variant cover	6.00
2-($1.99): 2-Two covers	3.00
3-11: 3-Returns to old shield. 4-Hawkeye app. 5-Thor-c/app. 7-Andy Kubert-c/a begin. 9-New shield	3.00
12-($2.99) Battles Nightmare; Red Skull back-up story	4.00
13-17,19-Red Skull returns	3.00
18-($2.99) Cap vs. Korvac in the Future	4.00
20-24,26-29: 20,21-Sgt. Fury back-up story painted by Evans	3.00
25-($2.99) Cap & Falcon vs. Hatemonger	4.00
30-49: 30-Begin $2.25-c. 32-Ordway-a. 33-Jurgens-s/a begins; U.S. Agent app. 36-Maximum Security x-over. 41,46-Red Skull app.	3.00
50-($5.95) Stories by various incl. Jurgens, Quitely, Immonen; Ha-c	6.00
...Citizen V '98 Annual ($3.50) Busiek & Kesel-s	4.00
1999 Annual ($3.50) Flag Smasher app.	4.00
2000 Annual ($3.50) Continued from #35 vs. Protocide; Jurgens-s	4.00
2001 Annual ($2.99) Golden Age flashback; Invaders app.	4.00
...: To Serve and Protect TPB (2002, $17.95) r/Vol. 3 #1-7	18.00

CAPTAIN AMERICA (Volume 4)
Marvel Comics: Jun, 2002 - No. 32, Dec, 2004 ($3.99/$2.99)

1-Ney Rieber-s/Cassaday-c/a	4.00
2-9-($2.99) 3-Cap reveals Steve Rogers ID. 7-9-Hairsine-a	3.00
10-32: 10-16-Jae Lee-a. 17-20-Gibbons-a/Weeks-a. 21-26-Bachalo-a. 26-Bucky flashback. 27,28-Eddie Campbell-a. 29-32-Red Skull app.	3.00
...Vol. 1: The New Deal HC (2003, $22.99) r/#1-6; foreward by Max Allan Collins	23.00
...Vol. 2: The Extremists TPB (2003, $13.99) r/#7-11; Cassaday-c	14.00
...Vol. 3: Ice TPB (2003, $12.99) r/#12-16; Jae Lee-a; Cassaday-c	13.00
...Vol. 4: Cap Lives TPB (2004, $12.99) r/#17-22 & Tales of Suspense #66	13.00
Avengers Disassembled: Captain America TPB (2004, $17.99) r/#29-32 and Captain America and the Falcon #5-7	18.00

CAPTAIN AMERICA
Marvel Comics: Jan, 2005 - No. 50, Jul, 2009; No. 600, Aug, 2009 - No. 619, Aug, 2011 ($2.99/$3.99)

1-Brubaker-s/Epting-c/a; Red Skull app.	3	6	9	16	23	30
2-5	1	2	3	5	6	8
6-1st full app. of the Winter Soldier; swastika-c	5	10	15	30	50	70
6-Retailer variant cover	6	12	18	42	79	115
7-24: 9-House of M. 11-Origin of the Winter Soldier. 13-Iron Man app. 24-Civil War						5.00
8-Variant Red Skull cover	2	4	6	8	10	12
25-($3.99) Captain America shot dead; handcuffed red glove cover by Epting						14.00
25-($3.99) Variant edition with running Cap cover by McGuinness						10.00
25-($3.99) 2nd printing with "The Death of The Dream" cover by Epting						5.00
25-Director's Cut-($4.99) w/script with Brubaker commentary; pencil pages, variant and un-used covers gallery; article on media hype						8.00
26-33-Bucky & Winter Soldier app.						3.00
34-(3/08) Bucky becomes the new Captain America; Alex Ross-c						12.00
34-Variant-c by Steve Epting						8.00
34-($3.99) Director's Cut; includes script; pencil art, costume designs, cover gallery						5.00
34-DF Edition with Alex Ross portrait cover; signed by Ross						40.00
35-49-Bucky as Captain America. 43-45-Batroc app. 46,47-Sub-Mariner app.						3.00
50-(7/09, $3.99) Various flashbacks; Captain America's life synopsis; Martin-a						4.00
(After #50, numbering reverts to original with #600, Aug, 2009)						
600-(8/09, $4.99) Covers by Ross and Epting; leads into Captain America: Reborn series; art by Guice, Chaykin, Ross, Eaglesham; commentary by Joe Simon; cover gallery						5.00
601-615,617-619-($3.99) 601-Gene Colan-a; 3 covers. 602-Nomad back-up feature begins.						
606-Baron Zemo returns. 611-615-Trial of Captain America						4.00
615.1 (5/11) Brubaker-s/Breitweiser-a/Acuña-c						3.00

616-(5/11, $4.99) 70th Anniversary Issue; short stories by Brubaker, Chaykin, Deodato, McGuinness, Grist and others, Charest-c	5.00
616-Variant-c by Epting	8.00
...: America's Avenger (8/11, $4.99) Handbook format profiles of friends and foes	5.00
... and Batroc (5/11, $3.99) Gillen-s/Arlem-a; Bucky vs. Batroc in Paris	4.00
... and Crossbones (5/11, $3.99) Harms-s/Shalvey-a/Tocchini-a	4.00
... and Falcon (5/11, $3.99) Williams-s/Isaacs-a/Tocchini-a	4.00
... and the First Thirteen (5/11, $3.99) Peggy Carter in WWII France 1943	4.00
... and the Secret Avengers (5/11, $3.99) DeConnick-s/Tocchini-a/c; Black Widow app.	4.00
... and Thor: Avengers 1 (9/11, $4.99) Movie version Cap; prequel to Thor movie; Lim-c	5.00
...: By Ed Brubaker Omnibus Vol. 1 HC (2007, $74.99, dustjacket) r/#1-25; Capt. America 65th Anniv. Spec. and Winter Soldier: Winter Kills; Brubaker intro.; bonus material	75.00
Civil War: Captain America TPB (2007, $11.99) r/#22-24 & Winter Soldier: Winter Kills	12.00
...: Fighting Avenger (6/11, $4.99) 1st WWII mission; Gurihiru-a; Kitson var-c	5.00
...MGC #1 (5/10, $1.00) r/#1 with "Marvel's Greatest Comics" cover logo	3.00
...: Rebirth 1 (8/11, $4.99) r/origin & Red Skull apps. from Tales of Suspense #63,65-68	5.00
...: Red Menace Vol. 1 SC (2006, $11.99) r/#15-17 and 65th Anniversary Special	12.00
...: Red Menace Vol. 2 SC (2006, $10.99) r/#18-21; Brubaker interview	11.00
...: Spotlight (7/11, $3.99) creator interviews; features on the movie and The Invaders	4.00
...: Theater of War: America First! (2/09, $4.99) 1950s era tale; Chaykin-s/a; reprints	5.00
...: Theater of War: America the Beautiful (3/09, $4.99) WW2 tale; Jenkins-s/Erskine-a	5.00
...: Theater of War: Operation Zero-Point (12/08, $3.99) WW2 tale; Breitweiser-a	4.00
...: The Death of Captain America Vol. 1 HC (2007, $19.99) r/#25-30; variant covers	20.00
...: The Death of Captain America Vol. 2 HC (2008, $19.99) r/#31-36; variant covers	20.00
...Vol. 1: Winter Soldier HC (2005, $21.99) r/#1-7; concept sketches	22.00
...Vol. 1: Winter Soldier SC (2006, $16.99) r/#1-7; concept sketches	17.00
...: Who Won't Wield the Shield (6/10, $3.99) Deadpool & Forbush Man app.	4.00
...: Winter Soldier Vol. 2 HC (2006, $19.99) r/#8,9,11-14	20.00
...: Winter Soldier Vol. 2 SC (2006, $14.99) r/#8,9,11-14	15.00

CAPTAIN AMERICA
Marvel Comics: Sept, 2011 - No. 19, Dec, 2012 ($3.99)

1-19: 1-5-Brubaker-s/McNiven-c/a. 1-Nick Fury & Baron Zemo app. 6-10-Davis-a/c						4.00
1-Variant-c by John Romita Sr.		1	3	4	6	8	10
1-Movie photo variant-c of Chris Evans in costume	4	8	12	23	37	50

CAPTAIN AMERICA (Marvel NOW!)
Marvel Comics: Jan, 2013 - No. 25, Dec, 2014 ($3.99)

1-10-Remender-s/Romita Jr.-a/c; Cap in Dimension Z; Arnim Zola app.; 1st app. Jet Black. 10-Sharon Carter supposedly killed						4.00
11-24: 11,12,14,15-Pacheco-a; Nuke returns. 16-Red Skull app.; Alixe-a. 21-Steve Rogers rapidly aged. 22-24-Pacheco-a; Avengers app. 23-Sharon Carter returns						4.00
25-($4.99) Sam Wilson becomes the new Captain America; Pacheco-a						
		3	6	9	17	25	34
...: Homecoming 1 (5/14, $3.99) Van Lente-s/Grummett-a; bonus rep of Capt. Am. #117						4.00
...: Peggy Carter, Agent of S.H.I.E.L.D. (2014, $7.99) r/notable appearances						8.00

CAPTAIN AMERICA (Secret Empire tie-in)(Follows Captain America: Sam Wilson #24)
Marvel Comics: No. 25, Oct, 2017 ($3.99)

25-Leads into Secret Empire #8; Black Panther, Namor app.; Spencer-s/Saiz-a	5.00

CAPTAIN AMERICA (Marvel Legacy)
Marvel Comics: No. 695, Jan, 2018 - No. 704, Aug, 2018 ($3.99)

695-699: 695-Follows Secret Empire; Waid-s/Samnee-a. 697-Kraven app.	4.00
700-(6/18, $5.99) Waid-s/Samnee-a; back-up story by Waid using unpublished Kirby art	6.00
701-704-Romero-a. 701-Hughes-a (4 pgs). 702-Chaykin-a (5 pgs). 703-Davis-a (5 pgs)	4.00

CAPTAIN AMERICA
Marvel Comics: Sept, 2018 - No. 30, Sept, 2021 ($4.99/$3.99)

1-($4.99) Ta-Nehisi Coates-s/Leinil Francis Yu-a; wraparound-c by Alex Ross	5.00
2-24,26-30-($3.99) 3-Black Panther app. 4,5-Taskmaster app. 7-12-Adam Kubert-a. 12-Daughters of Liberty regroup; back in time w/Steve Rogers uniform. 14-Sin app. 16-John Walker app. 22,23-Shuri app. 23-Sharon Carter de-aged. 24-Red Skull app. 26-Red Hulk app.	4.00
25-($4.99) Red Skull, Falcon, Winter Soldier app.; back-up with Michael Cho-a	5.00
Annual 1 (11/18, $4.99) Howard-s/Sprouse & Lim-a; takes place in 1940; Bucky app.	5.00
Annual 1 (8/21, $4.99) Duggan-s/Castiello-a; "Infinite Destinies" tie-in; Black Widow app.	5.00
...& The Invaders: Bahamas Triangle 1 (9/19, $4.99) Roy Thomas-s/Jerry Ordway-a	5.00
... Anniversary Tribute 1 (5/21, $6.99) Captain America Comics #1 and Avengers #4 re-drawn by modern artists, one page each; McNiven-c swipe of Avengers #4	7.00
... The End 1 (4/20, $4.99) Erik Larsen-s/a; M.O.D.O.K. app.	5.00

CAPTAIN AMERICA (Leads into Captain America: Sentinel of Liberty #1 and Captain America: Symbol of Truth #1)
Marvel Comics: No. 0, Jun, 2022 ($4.99, one-shot)

0-De Iulis-a; Steve Rogers & Sam Wilson as Captain America; Arnim Zola app.	5.00

CAPTAIN AMERICA (Leads into Captain America Finale)
Marvel Comics: No. 750, Sept, 2023 ($7.99, one-shot)

	GD 2.0	VG 4.0	FN 6.0	VF 8.0	VF/NM 9.0	NM- 9.2

750-Stories of Sam Wilson and Steve Rogers; short back-ups by various ... 8.00

CAPTAIN AMERICA
Marvel Comics: Nov, 2023 - Present ($5.99/$4.99)

1-($5.99) Straczynski-s/Saiz-a; flashbacks to 1936 ... 6.00
2-6-($4.99) 2-Spider-Man app. ... 5.00

CAPTAIN AMERICA AND ... (Numbering continues from Captain America #619)
Marvel Comics: No. 620, Sept, 2011 - No. 640, Feb, 2013 ($2.99)

... Bucky 620-628: 620-624-Brubaker & Andreyko-s/Samnee-a/McGuinness-c. 620-Bucky's
  early WWII days. 625-628-Francavilla-c/a ... 3.00
... Hawkeye 629-632: 629-(6/12) Bunn-s/Vitti-aDell'Otto-c ... 3.00
... Iron Man 633-635: 635-(8/12) Bunn-s/Kitson-a/Andrasofszky-c; Batroc-app. ... 3.00
... Namor 635.1 (10/12) World War III flashback; Will Conrad-a/Immonen-c ... 3.00
... Black Widow 636-640: 636-(11/12) Bunn-s/Francavilla-a/c ... 3.00

CAPTAIN AMERICA AND THE FALCON
Marvel Comics: May, 2004 - No. 14, June, 2005 ($2.99, limited series)

1-4-Priest-s/Sears-a ... 3.00
5-14: 5-8-Avengers Disassembled x-over. 6,7-Scarlet Witch app. 8-12-Modok app. ... 3.00
... Vol. 1: Two Americas (2005, $9.99) r/#1-4 ... 10.00
... Vol. 2: Brothers and Keepers (2005, $17.99) r/#8-14 ... 18.00

CAPTAIN AMERICA & THE KORVAC SAGA
Marvel Comics: Feb, 2011 - No. 4, May, 2011 ($2.99, limited series)

1-4-McCool-s/Rousseau-a/c. 4-Galactus app. ... 3.00

CAPTAIN AMERICA & THE MIGHTY AVENGERS (Sam Wilson as Captain America)
Marvel Comics: Jan, 2015 - No. 9, Aug, 2015 ($3.99)

1-9: 1-3-AXIS tie-ins; Luke Ross-a. 8,9-Secret Wars tie-in ... 4.00

CAPTAIN AMERICA & THE WINTER SOLDIER
Marvel Comics: Jan, 2023 $4.99, one-shot)

1-Origin of the Outer Circle; story continues in Captain America: Sentinel of Liberty #7 ... 5.00

CAPTAIN AMERICA/BLACK PANTHER (See Black Panther/Captain America: Flags of Our Fathers)

CAPTAIN AMERICA COLD WAR (Crossover event with Captain America: Symbol of Truth #12,13 and Captain America: Sentinel of Liberty #12,13)
Marvel Comics: Jun, 2023 - Aug, 2023 ($4.99, bookends for crossover)

Alpha (6/23) Part 1; White Wolf app.; Magno-a ... 5.00
Omega (8/23) Part 6; Magno-a; continues in Captain America #750 ... 5.00

CAPTAIN AMERICA COMICS
Timely/Marvel Comics (TCI 1-20/CmPS 21-68/MjMC 69-75/Atlas Comics (PrPI 76-78):
Mar, 1941 - No. 75, Feb, 1950; No. 76, 5/54 - No. 78, 9/54
(No. 74 & 75 titled Capt. America's Weird Tales)

1-Origin & 1st app. Captain America & Bucky by Simon & Kirby; Hurricane, Tuk the Caveboy begin by S&K; 1st app. Red Skull; Hitler-c (by Simon?); intro of the "Capt. America Sentinels of Liberty Club" (advertised on inside front-c.); indicia reads Vol. 2, Number 1	39,500	79,000	118,500	263,500	434,500	750,000
2-S&K Hurricane; Tuk by Avison (Kirby splash); classic Hitler-c; 1st app. Cap's round shield	3300	6600	9900	25,000	52,500	80,000
3-Classic Red Skull-c & app; Stan Lee's 1st text (1st work for Marvel)	3700	7400	11,100	28,000	57,000	86,000
4-Early use of full pg. panel in comic; back-c pin-up of Captain America and Bucky	1675	3350	5025	12,600	23,800	35,000
5-Classic Kirby Nazi/torture Wheel of Death/Red Skull-c	1500	3000	4500	11,400	20,700	30,000
6-Origin Father Time; Tuk the Caveboy ends	1200	2400	3600	9100	16,550	24,000
7-Red Skull app.; classic-c	1400	2800	4200	10,600	19,300	28,000
8-10-Last S&K issue; (S&K centerfold #6-10)	1050	2100	3150	8000	14,500	21,000
11-Last Hurricane, Headline Hunter; Al Avison Captain America begins, ends #20; Avison-c(p)	811	1622	2433	5927	10,460	15,000
12-The Imp begins, ends #16; last Father Time	757	1514	2271	5526	9763	14,000
13-Origin The Secret Stamp; classic "Remember Pearl Harbor"-c	1500	3000	4500	11,400	20,700	30,000
14-"Remember Pearl Harbor" Japanese bondage/torture-c	1000	2000	3000	7600	13,800	20,000
15	919	1838	2757	6709	11,855	17,000
16-Red Skull unmasks Cap; Red Skull-c	1200	2400	3600	9100	16,550	24,000
17-The Fighting Fool only app.	703	1406	2109	5132	9066	13,000
18-Classic-c	757	1514	2271	5526	9763	14,000
19-Human Torch begins #19	649	1298	1947	4738	8369	12,000
20-Sub-Mariner app.; no Human Torch	508	1060	1590	3869	6835	9800
21-23	508	1016	1524	3708	6554	9400
24-Classic Japanese torture with boiling tar and fingernail removal	865	1730	2595	6315	11,158	16,000
25-Cap drinks liquid opium	541	1082	1623	3950	6975	10,000
26-30: 27-Last Secret Stamp; Nazi WWII-c; last 68 pg. issue. 28-60 pg. issues begin.	508	1016	1524	3708	6554	9400
31-35,39,40: 34-Centerfold poster of Cap	470	940	1414	3431	6066	8700
36-Classic Hitler-c	1500	3000	4500	11,400	20,700	30,000
37-Red Skull app.	1500	3000	4500	11,400	20,700	30,000
38-Japanese bondage-c	514	1028	1542	3750	6625	9500
41-Last Japan War-c	423	846	1269	3000	5250	7500
42-45	314	628	942	2198	3849	5500
46-German Holocaust-c; classic	4100	8200	12,300	27,300	47,650	68,000
47-Last German War-c	389	778	1167	2723	4762	6800
48-58,60	290	580	870	1856	3178	4500
59-Origin retold	423	846	1269	3046	5323	7600
61-Red Skull-c/story	486	972	1458	3550	6275	9000
62,64,65: 65-Kurtzman's "Hey Look"	300	600	900	2010	3505	5000
63-Intro/origin Asbestos Lady	309	618	927	2163	3782	5400
66-Bucky is shot; Golden Girl teams up with Captain America & learns his i.d; origin Golden Girl	423	846	1269	3088	5444	7800
67-69: 67-Captain America/Golden Girl team-up; Mxyztplk swipe; last Toro in Human Torch. 68-Sub-Mariner/Namora, and Captain America/Golden Girl team-up. 69-Human Torch/ Sun Girl team-up.	389	778	1167	2723	4762	6800
70-73: 70-Sub-Mariner/Namora, and Captain America/Golden Girl team-up. 70-SciFi-c/story.						

71-Anti Wertham editorial; The Witness, Bucky app.	423	846	1269	3088	5444	7800
74-(Scarce)(10/49)-Titled "Captain America's Weird Tales"; Red Skull-c & app.; classic-c	4200	8400	12,600	28,000	49,000	70,000
75(2/50)-Titled "C.A.'s Weird Tales"; no C.A. app.; horror cover/stories	423	846	1269	3088	5444	7800
76-78(1954): Human Torch/Toro stories; all have communist-c/stories	300	600	900	2010	3505	5000
132-Pg. Issue (B&W-1942)(Canadian)-Very rare. Has blank inside-and back-c; contains Marvel Mystery #33 & Captain America #18 w/cover from Captain America #22; same contents as one version of the Marvel Mystery annuals	5800	11,600	17,400	43,500	--	--

NOTE: *Crandall* a-2i, 3i, 9i, 10i. *Kirby* c-1, 2, 5-8p. *Rico* c-69-71. *Romita* c-77, 78. *Schomburg* c-3, 4, 26-29, 31, 33, 37-39, 41, 42, 45-54, 58. *Sekowsky* c-55, 56. *Shores* c-1i, 2i, 5-7i, 11i, 20-25, 30, 32, 34, 35, 40, 57, 59-67. *S&K* c-9, 10. *Bondage* c-3, 7, 15, 16, 34, 38.

CAPTAIN AMERICA COMICS #1 70TH ANNIVERSARY EDITION
Marvel Comics: May, 2011 ($4.99, one-shot)

1-Recolored reprint of entire 1941 issue including Hurricane & Tuk stories; Ching-c		2	4	6	10	14	18

CAPTAIN AMERICA COMICS 70TH ANNIVERSARY SPECIAL
Marvel Comics: June, 2009 ($3.99, one-shot)

1-WWII flashback; Marcos Martin-a; Marcos-2 covers; r/Capt. America Comics #7		2	4	6	8	10	12

CAPTAIN AMERICA CORPS
Marvel Comics: Aug, 2011 - No. 5, Dec, 2011 ($2.99, limited series)

1-5-Stern-s/Briones-a/Jimenez-a; various versions of Captain America team-up ... 3.00

CAPTAIN AMERICA: DEAD MEN RUNNING
Marvel Comics: Mar, 2002 - No. 3, May, 2002 ($2.99, limited series)

1-3-Macan-s/Zezelj-a ... 3.00

CAPTAIN AMERICA FINALE (Continues story from Captain America #750)
Marvel Comics: Oct, 2023 ($4.99, one-shot)

1-Lanzing & Kelly-s/Carnero-a; Cap & Sharon vs. the Outer Circle ... 5.00

CAPTAIN AMERICA: FIRST VENGEANCE (Based on the 2011 movie version)
Marvel Comics: Jul, 2011 - No. 4, Aug, 2011 ($2.99, limited series)

1-4-Van Lente-s; art by Luke Ross & others. 2-Movie photo-c ... 3.00

CAPTAIN AMERICA: FOREVER ALLIES
Marvel Comics: Oct, 2010 - No. 4, Jan, 2011 ($3.99, limited series)

1-4-Stern-s/Dragotta-a; Bucky in present & WW2 flashbacks; Young Allies app. ... 4.00

CAPTAIN AMERICA: HAIL HYDRA
Marvel Comics: Mar, 2011 - No. 5, Jul, 2011 ($2.99, limited series)

1-5-Cap vs. Hydra; Granov-c. 1-WWII flashback. 2-Kirby-style art by Scioli. 4-Hotz-a ... 3.00

CAPTAIN AMERICA / IRON MAN
Marvel Comics: Jan, 2022 - No. 5, May, 2022 ($3.99)

1-5-Landy-s/Unzueta-a; main covers by Alex Ross ... 4.00

CAPTAIN AMERICA: LIVING LEGEND
Marvel Comics: Dec, 2013 - No. 4, Feb, 2014 ($3.99, limited series)

1-4: 1-Diggle-s/Granov-a/c. 2-4-Alessio-a ... 4.00

CAPTAIN AMERICA: MAN OUT OF TIME
Marvel Comics: Jan, 2011 - No. 5, May, 2011 ($3.99, limited series)

1-5-Waid-s/Molina-a/Hitch-c; Cap's unfreezing in modern times re-told ... 4.00

CAPTAIN AMERICA/NICK FURY: BLOOD TRUCE
Marvel Comics: Feb, 1995 ($5.95, one-shot, squarebound)

nn-Chaykin story ... 6.00

CAPTAIN AMERICA/NICK FURY: THE OTHERWORLD WAR
Marvel Comics: Oct, 2001 ($6.95, one-shot, squarebound)

nn-Manco-a; Bucky and Red Skull app. ... 7.00

CAPTAIN AMERICA: PATRIOT
Marvel Comics: Nov, 2010 - No. 4, Feb, 2011 ($3.99, limited series)

1-4-Kesel-s/Breitweiser-a. 1-WW2 story; Patriot & the Liberty Legion app. ... 4.00

CAPTAIN AMERICA: REBORN (Titled Reborn in #1-3)
Marvel Comics: Sept, 2009 - No. 6, Mar, 2010 ($3.99, limited series)

1-6-Steve Rogers returns from the dead; Brubaker-s/Hitch & Guice-a. 1-Covers by Hitch, Ross & Quesada. 2-Origin re-told. 4-Joe Kubert var-c ... 4.00
1-4-Variant-c by Cassaday. 2-Variant-c by Sale. 5-Finch var-c ... 10.00
... MGC #1 (5/11, $1.00) r/#1 with "Marvel's Greatest Comics" logo on cover ... 3.00
...: Who Will Wield the Shield? (2/10, $3.99) Aftermath of series; Guice & Luke Ross-a ... 4.00

CAPTAIN AMERICA: RED, WHITE & BLUE
Marvel Comics: Sept, 2002 ($29.99, one-shot, hardcover with dustjacket)

nn-Reprints from Lee & Kirby, Steranko, Miller and others; and new short stories and pin-ups by various incl. Ross, Dini, Timm, Waid, Dorkin, Sienkiewicz, Miller, Bruce Jones, Collins, Piers-Rayner, Pope, Deodato, Quitely, Nino; Stelfreeze-c ... 30.00
TPB (2007, $19.99) ... 20.00

CAPTAIN AMERICA: ROAD TO WAR
Marvel Comics: Jun, 2016 ($4.99, one-shot)

1-Prelude to Captain America: Civil War movie; bonus r/Tales of Suspense #58 ... 5.00

CAPTAIN AMERICA: SAM WILSON (Leads into Captain America #25 (Oct. 2017))
Marvel Comics: Dec, 2015 - No. 24, Sept, 2017 ($3.99)

1-6: 1-Spencer-s/Acuña-a; Misty Knight & D-Man app. 3-6-Sam as CapWolf ... 4.00
7-($5.99) 75th Anniversary issue; Steve Rogers regains his youth; Standoff tie-in; bonus short stories by Whedon & Cassaday, Tim Sale, and Rucka & Perkins ... 6.00
8-24: 8-Standoff tie-in; Baron Zemo app. 10-13-Civil War II tie-in. 11-13-U.S. Agent app. 22-24-Secret Empire tie-ins ... 4.00

CAPTAIN AMERICA, SENTINEL OF LIBERTY (See Fireside Book Series)

CAPTAIN AMERICA: SENTINEL OF LIBERTY
Marvel Comics: Sept, 1998 - No. 12, Aug, 1999 ($1.99)

Captain America Comics #74 © MAR

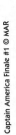

Captain America Finale #1 © MAR

Captain America Finale #1 © MAR

Captain Atom: Armageddon #7 © DC

	GD	VG	FN	VF	VF/NM	NM-
	2.0	4.0	6.0	8.0	9.0	9.2

	GD	VG	FN	VF	VF/NM	NM-
	2.0	4.0	6.0	8.0	9.0	9.2

1-Waid-s/Garney-a — 5.00
1-Rough Cut ($2.99) Features original script and pencil pages — 4.00
2-5- 2-Two-c; Invaders WW2 story — 3.00
6-($2.99) Iron Man-c/app. — 4.00
7-11- 8-Falcon-c/app. 9-Falcon poses as Cap — 3.00
12-($2.99) Final issue; Bucky-c/app. — 4.00

CAPTAIN AMERICA: SENTINEL OF LIBERTY (Steve Rogers as Captain America)
Marvel Comics: Aug, 2022 - No. 13, Aug, 2023 ($4.99/$3.99)
1-($4.99) Lanzing & Kelly-s/Carnero-a; Bucky and The Destroyer app. — 5.00
2-13-($3.99) 2-Peggy Carter returns. 12,13-"Cold War" parts 3 & 5 — 4.00

CAPTAIN AMERICA SPECIAL EDITION
Marvel Comics: Feb, 1984 - No. 2, Mar, 1984 ($2.00, Baxter paper)
1-Steranko-c/a(r) in both; r/capt. America #110,111 1 3 4 6 8 10
2-Reprints the scarce Our Love Story #5, and C.A. #113
1 3 4 6 8 10

CAPTAIN AMERICA: STEVE ROGERS (Also see Captain America: Sam Wilson)
Marvel Comics: Jul, 2016 - No. 19, Sept, 2017 ($4.99/$3.99)
1-Spencer-s/Saiz-a; childhood flashbacks to Hydra recruitment; Red Skull app. — 5.00
2-19-($3.99) 2-Kobik app. 4-6-Civil War II tie-in. 14,15-Red Skull app. 16-19-Secret Empire
tie-ins. 18-Namor app. 19-Leads into Captain America #25 (10/17) — 4.00

CAPTAIN AMERICA: SYMBOL OF TRUTH (Sam Wilson as Captain America)
Marvel Comics: Aug, 2022 - Present ($4.99/$3.99)
1-($4.99) Onyebuchi-s/Silva-a; Misty Knight and Crossbones app. — 5.00
2-14-($3.99) 2,3-Deadpool app. 4,5-Black Panther app. 12,13-"Cold War" parts 2 & 4 — 4.00

CAPTAIN AMERICA THEATER OF WAR
Marvel Comics: 2009 - 2010 ($3.99, series of one-shots)
...: A Brother in Arms (6/09) Jenkins-s/McCrea-a; WWII story — 4.00
...: Ghosts of My Country (12/09) Jenkins-s/Bonetti-a/Guice-c — 4.00
...: Prisoners of Duty (2/10) Higgins & Siegel-s/Padilla-a; WWII story — 4.00
...: To Soldier On (10/09) Jenkins-s/Blanco-a/Noto-c; Captain America in Iraq — 4.00

CAPTAIN AMERICA: THE CHOSEN
Marvel Comics: Nov, 2007 - No. 6, Mar, 2008 ($3.99, limited series)
1-6-Breitweiser-a/Morrell-s — 4.00

CAPTAIN AMERICA: THE CLASSIC YEARS
Marvel Comics: Jun, 1998 - No. 2 (trade paperbacks)
1-($19.95) Reprints Captain America Comics #1-5 — 25.00
2-($24.95) Reprints Captain America Comics #6-10 — 25.00

CAPTAIN AMERICA: THE FIRST AVENGER ADAPTATION (MARVEL'S...)
Marvel Comics: Jan, 2014 - No. 2, Feb, 2014 ($2.99, limited series)
1,2-Adaptation of the 2011 movie; Peter David-s/Wellinton Alves-a/photo-c — 3.00

CAPTAIN AMERICA: THE LEGEND
Marvel Comics: Sept, 1996 ($3.95, one-shot)
1-Tribute issue; wraparound-c — 5.00

CAPTAIN AMERICA: THE 1940S NEWSPAPER STRIP
Marvel Comics: Aug, 2010 - No. 3, Oct, 2010 ($3.99, limited series)
1-3-Karl Kesel-s/a; new feature set in WW2 formatted like 1940s newspaper comics — 4.00

CAPTAIN AMERICA: UNFORGIVEN (Takes place after X-Men: Unforgiven #1)
Marvel Comics: Jun, 2023 ($4.99, one-shot)
1-Tim Seeley-s/Sid Kotian-a — 5.00

CAPTAIN AMERICA: WHAT PRICE GLORY
Marvel Comics: May, 2003 - No. 4, May, 2003 ($2.99, weekly limited series)
1-4-Bruce Jones-s/Steve Rude & Mike Royer-a — 3.00

CAPTAIN AMERICA: WHITE
Marvel Comics: No. 0, Sept, 2008; No. 1, Nov, 2015 - No. 5, Feb, 2016 (limited series)
0-Bucky's origin retold; Loeb-s/Sale-a in all; interviews with creators; Sale sketch art — 3.00
1-($4.99) Flashback to 1941; Sgt. Fury and the Howling Commandos app. — 5.00
2-5-($3.99) 3-5-Red Skull app. — 4.00

CAPTAIN AMERICA: WINTER SOLDIER DIRECTOR'S CUT
Marvel Comics: Jun, 2014 ($4.99, one-shot)
1-Reprints Captain America (2005) #1; bonus Brubaker script & series proposal — 5.00

CAPTAIN AND THE KIDS, THE (See Famous Comics Cartoon Books)

CAPTAIN AND THE KIDS, THE (See Comics on Parade, Katzenjammer Kids, Okay Comics & Sparkler Comics)
United Features Syndicate/Dell Publ. Co.: 1938 -12/39; Sum, 1947 - No. 32, 1955; Four Color No. 881, Feb, 1958

Single Series 1(1938) 129 258 387 826 1413 2000
Single Series 1(Reprint)(12/39- "Reprint" on-c) 52 104 156 328 552 775
1(Summer, 1947-UFS)-Katzenjammer Kids 21 42 63 122 199 275
2 11 22 33 62 86 110
3-10 10 20 30 54 72 90
11-20 8 16 24 44 57 70
21-32 (1955) 8 16 24 40 50 60
50th Anniversary issue-(1948)-Contains a 2 pg. history of the strip, including an account of the
famous Supreme Court decision allowing both Pulitzer & Hearst to run the same strip
under different names 19 38 57 111 176 240
Special Summer issue, Fall issue (1948) 12 24 36 69 97 125
Four Color 881 (Dell) 5 10 15 30 50 70

CAPTAIN ATOM
Nationwide Publishers: 1950 - No. 7, 1951 (5¢, 5x7-1/4", 52 pgs.)
1-Science fiction 43 86 129 271 461 650
2-7 27 54 81 158 259 360

CAPTAIN ATOM (Formerly Strange Suspense Stories #77)(Also see Space Adventures and Thunderbolt)
Charlton Comics: V2#78, Dec, 1965 - V2#89, Dec, 1967
V2#78-Origin retold; Bache-a (3 pgs.) 8 16 24 56 108 160
79-81- 79-1st app. Dr. Spectro; 3 pg. Ditko cut & paste /Space Adventures #24.
6 12 18 38 69 100
82-Intro. Nightshade (9/66) 13 26 39 86 188 290
83-(11/66)-1st app. Ted Kord/Blue Beetle 46 92 138 368 834 1300
84-86- Ted Kord Blue Beetle in all. 84-1st app. new Captain Atom. 85-1st app. Punch and
Jewelee 5 10 15 35 63 90
87-89- Nightshade by Aparo in all 5 10 15 34 60 85
83-(Modern Comics-1977)-reprints 3 6 9 21 33 45
84,85-(Modern Comics-1977)-reprints 1 3 4 6 8 10
NOTE: Aparo a-87-89. Ditko c/a(p) 78-89. #90 only published in fanzine 'The Charlton Bullseye' #1, 2.

CAPTAIN ATOM (Also see Americomics & Crisis On Infinite Earths)
DC Comics: Mar, 1987 - No. 57, Sept, 1991 (Direct sales only #35 on)
1-(44 pgs.)-Origin/1st app. with new costume 1 2 3 5 6 8
2-49- 5-Firestorm x-over. 6-Intro. new Dr. Spectro. 11-Millennium tie-in. 14-Nightshade app.
16-Justice League app. 17-$1.00-c begins; Swamp Thing app. 20-Blue Beetle x-over.
24,25-Invasion tie-in. 4.00
50-($2.00, 52 pgs.) 5.00
51-57- 57-War of the Gods x-over 4.00
Annual 1,2 ('88, '89)-1-Intro Major Force 5.00

CAPTAIN ATOM (DC New 52)
DC Comics: Nov, 2011 - No. 12, Oct, 2012; No. 0, Nov, 2012 ($2.99)
1-12-J.T. Krul-s/Freddie Williams II-a. 3-Flash app. 3.00
#0 (11/12, $2.99) origin of Captain Atom re-told 3.00

CAPTAIN ATOM: ARMAGEDDON (Restarts the WildStorm Universe)
DC Comics (WildStorm): Dec, 2005 - No. 9, Aug, 2006 ($2.99, limited series)
1-9-Captain Atom appears in WildStorm Universe; Pfeifer-s/Camuncoli-a. 1-Lee-c 3.00
TPB (2007, $19.99) r/series 20.00

CAPTAIN BATTLE (Boy Comics #3 on) (See Silver Streak Comics)
New Friday Publ./Comic House: Summer, 1941 - No. 2, Fall, 1941
1-Origin Blackout by Rico; Captain Battle begins (1st appeared in Silver Streak #10, 5/41)
classic hooded villain background/torture-c 239 478 717 1530 2615 3700
2-Origin Doctor Horror & only app.; classic story "House of Giants"
113 226 339 718 1234 1750

CAPTAIN BATTLE (2nd Series)
Magazine Press/Picture Scoop No. 5: No. 3, Wint, 1942-43; No. 5, Sum, 1943 (No #4)
3-Origin Silver Streak-r/SS#3; origin Lance Hale-r/SS #2; Cloud Curtis, Presto Martin
1st app.-r/SS #7; Simon-a(r) (52 pgs., nd) 129 258 387 826 1413 2000
5-Origin Blackout-r/#1 (68 pgs.); Japanese WWII-c 116 232 348 742 1271 1800

CAPTAIN BATTLE, JR.
Comic House (Lev Gleason): Fall, 1943 - No. 2, Winter, 1943-44
1-Nazi WWII-c by Rico. Hitler/Claw sty; The Claw vs. The Ghost
177 354 531 1124 1937 2750
2-Wolverton's Scoop Scuttle; Don Rico-c/a; The Green Claw story is reprinted from
Silver Streak #6; Japanese WWII bondage/torture-c by Rico
113 226 339 718 1234 1750

CAPTAIN BEN DIX (See Promotional Comics section)

CAPTAIN BRITAIN (Also see Marvel Team-Up #65, 66)
Marvel Comics International: Oct. 13, 1976 - No. 39, July 6, 1977 (Weekly)
1-1st app & origin of Captain Britain (Brian Braddock); with Capt. Britain's face mask inside

	GD 2.0	VG 4.0	FN 6.0	VF 8.0	VF/NM 9.0	NM- 9.2

	GD 2.0	VG 4.0	FN 6.0	VF 8.0	VF/NM 9.0	NM- 9.2
Claremont-s/Trimpe-a	27	54	81	189	420	650
2-Origin, part II; Capt. Britain's Boomerang inside	6	12	18	42	79	115
3-7: 3-Vs. Bank Robbers. 4-7-Vs. Hurricane	2	4	6	11	16	20
8-(12/76) 1st app. Betsy Braddock, the sister of Capt. Britain (Brian Braddock) who later becomes Psylocke (X-Men); 1st app. Dr. Synne	27	54	81	189	420	650
9-11-Battles Dr. Synne. 9,10-Betsy Braddock app.	2	4	6	11	16	20
12-23,25-27: (low print run)-12,13-Vs. Dr. Synne. 14,15-Vs. Mastermind. 16-23,25,26-With Captain America. 17-Misprinted & color section reprinted in #18. 27-Origin retold	3	6	9	17	25	34
24-With Capt. Britain's Jet Plane inside	9	18	27	59	117	175
28-32,36-39: 28-32-Vs. Lord Hawk. 30-32-Inhumans app. 35-Dr. Doom app. 37-39-Vs. Highwayman & Manipulator	2	4	6	8	10	12
33-35-More on origin	2	4	6	8	11	14
Annual (1978, Hardback, 64 pgs.)-Reprints #1-7 with pin-ups of Marvel characters	3	6	9	17	26	35
Summer Special (1980, 52 pgs.)-Reprints	2	4	6	8	10	12

NOTE: No. 1, 2, & 24 are rarer in mint due to inserts. Distributed in Great Britain only. Nick Fury-r by Steranko in 1-20, 24-31, 35-37. Fantastic Four-r by J. Buscema in all. New Buscema-a in 24-30. Story from No. 39 continues in Super Spider-Man (British weekly) No. 231-247. Following cancellation of his series, new Captain Britain stories appeared in "Super Spider-Man" (British weekly) No. 231-247. Captain Britain stories which appear in Super-Spider-Man No 248-253 are reprints of Marvel Team-Up No. 65&66. Capt. Britain strips also appeared in Hulk Comic (weekly) 1, 3-30, 42-55, 57-60, in Marvel Superheroes (monthly) 377-388, in Daredevils (monthly) 1-11, Mighty World of Marvel (monthly) 7-16 & Captain Britain (monthly) 1-14. Issues 1-23 have B&W & color, paper-c, and are 32 pgs. Issues 24 on are all B&W w/glossy-c & are 36 pgs.

CAPTAIN BRITAIN AND MI: 13 (Also see Secret Invasion x-over titles)
Marvel Comics: Jul, 2008 - No. 15, Sept, 2009 ($2.99)

1-Skrull invasion; Black Knight app.; Kirk-a	1	3	4	6	8	10
1-2nd printing with Kirk variant-c; 3rd printing with B&W cover						3.00
2-15: 5-Blade app. 9,10-Dracula app.						3.00
... Annual 1 (8/09, $3.99) Land-c; Meggan in Hell; Dr. Doom cameo; Collins-a						4.00

CAPTAIN BRITAIN AND THE MIGHTY DEFENDERS (Secret Wars tie-in)
Marvel Comics: 2015 - No. 2, 2015 ($3.99, limited series)

1,2-Ho Yinsen, Faiza Hussain, White Tiger, She-Hulk app.; Al Ewing-s/Alan Davis-a						4.00

CAPTAIN CANUCK
Comely Comix (Canada)(All distr. in U. S.): Jul,1975 - No. 4, Jul, 1977; No. 4, Jul-Aug, 1979 - No. 14, Mar-Apr, 1981

1-1st app. Captain Canuck, C.I.S.O. & Bluefox; Richard Comely-c/a	5	9	19	30	40	
2,3(5-7/76)- 2- 1st app. Dr. Walker, Redcoat & Kebec. 3-1st app. Heather	1	3	4	6	8	10
4 (1st printing-2/77)-10x14-1/2". (5.00); B&W; 300 copies serially numbered and signed with one certificate of authenticity	10	20	30	67	121	215
4 (2nd printing-7/77)-11x17", B&W; only 15 copies printed; signed by creator Richard Comely, serially #'d and two certificates of authenticity inserted; orange cardboard covers (Very Rare)	14	28	42	93	204	315
4-14: 4(7-8/79)-1st app. Tom Evans & Mr. Gold; origin The Catman. 5-Origin Capt. Canuck's powers; 1st app. Earth Patrol & Chaos Corps. 5-7-Three-part neo-Nazi story set in 1994. 8-Jonn 'The Final Chapter'; 1st app. Mike & Saskia. 9-1st World Beyond. 11-1st 'Chariots of Fire' story. 12-A-bomb explosion panel	1	2	3	5	6	8
15-(8/04, $15.00) Limited edition of unpublished issue from 1981; serially #'d edition of 150; signed by creator Richard Comely	8	16	24	51	96	140
... Legacy 1 (9-10/06) Comely-s/a						4.00
... Legacy Special Edition ($7.95, 52 pgs., limited ed. of 1000) Comely-s/a						4.00
Special Collectors Pack (#1 & #2 polybagged)	2	4	6	8	10	12
Summer Special 1	2	4	6	9	13	16
Summer Special 1(7-9/80, 95¢, 64 pgs.) George Freeman-c/a; pin-ups by Gene Day, Tom Grummett, Dave Sim and others						6.00
Summer Special / Canada Day Edition #1 (2014, no cover price) 2 new stories, background on animated web series; regular-c shows a parade; variants exist						5.00

NOTE: 30,000 copies of No. 2 were destroyed in Winnipeg.

CAPTAIN CANUCK
Chapterhouse Comics: May, 2015 - No. 12, May, 2017 ($3.99)

1-Kalman Andrasofszky-s/a; 3 covers	1	3	4	6	8	10
2-12: 2-Andrasofszky-s/a. 3-12-Leonard Kirk-a						4.00
#0/FCBD Edition (5/15, giveaway) previews #1; origin re-told; character profiles						3.00
... Free Comic Book Day Issue 2019 (5/19) Intro. of a new Captain Canuck						3.00

CAPTAIN CANUCK (Season 5)
Chapterhouse Comics: Nov, 2020 - Present ($4.99)

1,2-Ho Che Anderson/Felipe Cunha-a						5.00

CAPTAIN CANUCK: UNHOLY WAR
Comely Comix: Oct, 2004 - No. 3, Jan, 2005; No. 4, Sept, 2007 ($2.50, limited series)

1-3-Riel Langlois-a/Drue Langlois-a: 1-1st app. David Semple (West Coast Capt. Canuck); Clair Sinclair as Bluefox						3.00
4-(Low print run) Black Mack the Lumberjack, Torchie, Splatter app.						6.00

CAPTAIN CANUCK YEAR ONE
Chapterhouse Comics: May, 2017; Nov, 2017 ($1.99)

1-($1.99) Baruchel & Andrasofszky-s; Marcus To-a; back-up Die Kitty Die story						3.00
#1/FCBD Edition (5/17, giveaway) back-up Die Kitty Die story						3.00

CAPTAIN CARROT AND HIS AMAZING ZOO CREW (Also see New Teen Titans & Oz-Wonderland War)
DC Comics: Mar, 1982 - No. 20, Nov, 1983

1-Superman app.	2	4	6	8	10	12
2-20: 3-Re-intro Dodo & The Frog. 9-Re-intro Three Mouseketeers, the Terrific Whatzit. 10,11-Pig Iron reverts back to Peter Porkchops. 20-Changeling app.						5.00

CAPTAIN CARROT AND THE FINAL ARK (DC Countdown tie-in)
DC Comics: Dec, 2007 - No. 3, Feb, 2008 ($2.99, limited series)

1-3-Bill Morrison-s/Scott Shaw!-a. 3-Batman, Red Arrow, Hawkgirl & Zatanna app.						3.00
TPB (2008, $19.99) r/#1-3; Captain Carrot and His Amazing Zoo Crew #1,14,15; New Teen Titans #16 and stories from Teen Titans (2003 series) #30,31; cover gallery						20.00

CAPTAIN CARTER (Multiverse super soldier Peggy Carter)
Marvel Comics: May, 2022 - No. 5, Oct, 2022 ($3.99)

1-5-Adventures in modern times; McKelvie/Cresta-a. 4,5-Tony Stark app.						4.00

CAPTAIN CARVEL AND HIS CARVEL CRUSADERS (See Carvel Comics in the Promotional section)

CAPTAIN CONFEDERACY
Marvel Comics (Epic Comics): Nov, 1991 - No. 4, Feb, 1992 ($1.95)

1-All new stories	1	2	3	5	6	8
2-4-All new stories						4.00

CAPTAIN COURAGEOUS COMICS (Banner #3-5; see Four Favorites #5)
Periodical House (Ace Magazines): No. 6, March, 1942

6-Origin & 1st app. The Sword; Lone Wonder, Capt. Courageous app.; Capt. moves to Four Favorites #5 in May	148	296	444	947	1624	2300

CAPT'N CRUNCH COMICS (See Cap'n...)

CAPTAIN DAVY JONES
Dell Publishing Co.: No. 598, Nov, 1954

Four Color 598	6	12	18	38	69	100

CAPTAIN EASY (See The Funnies & Red Ryder #3-32)
Hawley/Dell Publ./Standard(Visual Editions)/Argo: 1939 - No. 17, Sept, 1949; April, 1956

nn-Hawley(1939)-Contains reprints from The Funnies & 1938 Sunday strips by Roy Crane	116	232	348	742	1271	1800
Four Color 24 (1942)	65	130	195	416	708	1000
Four Color 111(6/46)	14	28	42	93	204	315
10(Standard-10/47)	18	36	54	105	165	225
11,12,14,15,17: 11-17 all contain 1930s & '40s strip-r	13	26	39	74	105	135
13,16: Schomburg-c	22	44	66	132	216	300
Argo 1(4/56)-Reprints	9	18	27	47	61	75

CAPTAIN EASY & WASH TUBBS (See Famous Comics Cartoon Books)

CAPTAIN ELECTRON
Brick Computer Science Institute: Aug, 1986 ($2.25)

1-Disbrow-a						4.00

CAPTAIN EO 3-D (Michael Jackson Disney theme parks movie)
Eclipse Comics: July, 1987 (Eclipse 3-D Special #18, $3.50, Baxter)

1-Adapts 3-D movie; Michael Jackson-c/app.	4	8	12	23	37	50
1-2-D limited edition	6	12	18	37	66	95
1-Large size (11x17", 8/87)-Sold only at Disney Theme parks ($6.95)	4	8	12	28	47	65

CAPTAIN FEARLESS COMICS (Also see Holyoke One-Shot #6, Old Glory Comics & Silver Streak #1)
Helnit Publishing Co. (Holyoke Publ. Co.): Aug, 1941 - No. 2, Sept, 1941

1-Origin Mr. Miracle, Alias X, Captain Fearless, Citizen Smith Son of the Unknown Soldier; Miss Victory (1st app.) begins (1st patriotic heroine? before Wonder Woman)	181	362	543	1158	1979	2800
2-Grit Grady, Captain Stone app.	65	130	195	416	708	1000

CAPTAIN FLAG (See Blue Ribbon Comics #16)

CAPTAIN FLASH
Sterling Comics: Nov, 1954 - No. 4, July, 1955

1-Origin; Sekowsky-a; Tomboy (female super hero) begins; only pre-code issue; atomic rocket-c	58	116	174	371	636	900
2-4: 4-Flying saucer invasion-c	37	74	111	222	361	500

CAPTAIN FLEET (Action Packed Tales of the Sea)
Ziff-Davis Publishing Co.: Fall, 1952

1-Painted-c	26	52	78	154	252	350

CAPTAIN FLIGHT COMICS
Four Star Publications: May, 1944 - No. 10, Dec, 1945; No. 11, Feb-Mar, 1947

nn-Captain Flight begins	97	194	291	621	1061	1500
2-4: 4-Rock Raymond begins, ends #7	57	114	171	362	619	875
5-Bondage, classic torture-c; Red Rocket begins; the Grenade app. (scarce)	309	618	927	2163	3782	5400
6-L. B. Cole-a, 8 pgs.	65	130	195	416	708	1000
7-10: 7-L. B. Cole covers begin, end #11. 7-9-Japanese WWII-c. 8-Yankee Girl begins; intro. Black Cobra & Cobra Kid & begins. 9-Torpedoman app.; last Yankee Girl; Kinstler-a. 10-Deep Sea Dawson, Zoom of the Jungle, Rock Raymond, Red Rocket, & Black Cobra app; bondage-c	135	270	405	864	1482	2100
11-Torpedoman, Blue Flame (Human Torch clone) app.; last Black Cobra, Red Rocket; classic L. B. Cole sci-fi robot-c (scarce)	703	1404	2109	5132	9066	13,000

CAPTAIN GALLANT (...of the Foreign Legion) (TV) (Texas Rangers in Action No. 5 on?)
Charlton Comics: 1955; No. 2, Jan, 1956 - No. 4, Sept, 1956

Non-Heinz version (#1)-Buster Crabbe photo on-c; full page Buster Crabbe photo inside front-c	9	18	27	47	61	75
(Heinz version is listed in the Promotional Comics section)						
2-4: Buster Crabbe in all. 2-Crabbe photo back-c	7	14	21	35	43	50

CAPTAIN GINGER
AHOY Comics: 2018 - Present ($3.99)

1-4: Space-faring cats; Stuart Moore-s/June Brigman-a; back-up text stories by various						4.00
... Season Two (2020 - Present) 1,2-Moore-s/Brigman-a						4.00
...: The Last Feeder 1,2-Moore-s/Brigman-a						4.00

CAPTAIN GLORY
Topps Comics: Apr, 1993 ($2.95) (Created by Jack Kirby)

1-Polybagged w/Kirbychrome trading card; Ditko-a & Kirby-c; has coupon for Amberchrome Secret City Saga #0						4.00

CAPTAIN HERO (See Jughead as...)

CAPTAIN HERO COMICS DIGEST MAGAZINE
Archie Publications: Sept, 1981

1-Reprints of Jughead as Super-Guy	2	4	6	10	14	18

CAPTAIN HOBBY COMICS
Export Publication Ent. Ltd. (Dist. in U.S. by Kable News Co.): Feb, 1948 (Canadian)

1	16	32	48	94	147	200

CAPT. HOLO IN 3-D (See Blackthorne 3-D Series #65)

Captain Canuck #2 © Richard Comely

Captain Easy #12 © Pines

Captain Marvel (2012 series) #1 © MAR

	GD 2.0	VG 4.0	FN 6.0	VF 8.0	VF/NM 9.0	NM- 9.2

	GD 2.0	VG 4.0	FN 6.0	VF 8.0	VF/NM 9.0	NM- 9.2
	2	4	6	9	13	16
44,45-(Regular 25¢ editions)(5,7/76)	2	4	6	8	10	12
44,45-(30¢-c variants, limited distribution)	5	10	15	30	50	70
51,52-(Regular 30¢ editions)(7,9/77)	2	4	6	8	10	12
51,52-(35¢-c variants, limited distribution)	8	16	24	54	102	150
57-Thanos appears in flashback	3	6	9	14	19	24
58-Thanos cameo; Drax app.	2	4	6	11	16	20

NOTE: *Alcala* a-35. *Austin* a-46i, 49-53i; c-52i. *Buscema* a-18p-21p. *Colan* a(p)-1-4; c(p)1-4, 8, 9. *Heck* a-5-10p, 16p. *Gil Kane* a-17-21p; c-17-24p, 37p, 53. *Starlin* a-36. *McWilliams* a-40i. #25-34 were reprinted in The Life of Captain Marvel.

CAPTAIN HOOK & PETER PAN (Movie)(Disney)
Dell Publishing Co.: No. 446, Jan, 1953

Four Color 446	10	20	30	69	147	225

CAPTAIN JET (Fantastic Fears No. 7 on)
Four Star Publ./Farrell/Comic Media: May, 1952 - No. 5, Jan, 1953

1-Bakerish-a	30	60	90	177	289	400
2	20	40	60	114	182	250
3-5,6(?)	14	28	42	82	121	160

CAPTAIN JOHNER & THE ALIENS
Valiant: May, 1995 - No. 2, May, 1995 ($2.95, shipped in same month)

1,2: Reprints Magnus Robot Fighter 4000 A.D. back-up stories; new Paul Smith-c						4.00

CAPTAIN JUSTICE (TV)
Marvel Comics: Mar, 1988 - No. 2, Apr, 1988 (limited series)

1,2-Based on the 1987 "Once a Hero" television series						4.00

CAPTAIN KANGAROO (TV)
Dell Publishing Co.: No. 721, Aug, 1956 - No. 872, Jan, 1958

Four Color 721 (#1)-Photo-c	13	26	39	91	201	310
Four Color 780, 872-Photo-c	12	24	36	79	170	260

CAPTAIN KID
AfterShock Comics: Jul, 2016 - No. 5, Mar, 2017 ($3.99)

1-5-Mark Waid & Tom Peyer-s/Wilfredo Torres-a						4.00

CAPTAIN KIDD (Formerly Dagar; My Secret Story #26 on)(Also see Comic Comics & Fantastic Comics)
Fox Feature Syndicate: No. 24, June, 1949 - No. 25, Aug, 1949

24,25: 24-Features Blackbeard the Pirate	20	40	60	117	189	260

CAPTAIN KRONOS - VAMPIRE HUNTER (Based on the 1974 Hammer film)
Titan Comics (Hammer Comics): Oct, 2017 - No. 4, Jan, 2018 ($3.99)

1-4-Abnett-s/Mandrake-a; multiple covers on each (art & photo)						4.00

CAPTAIN MARVEL (See All Hero, All-New Collectors' Ed., America's Greatest, Fawcett Miniature, Gift, JSA, Kingdom Come, Legends, Limited Collectors' Ed., Marvel Family, Master No. 21, Mighty Midget Comics, Power of Shazam!, Shazam!, Special Edition Comics, Whiz, Wisco (in Promotional Comics section), World's Finest #253 and XMas Comics)

CAPTAIN MARVEL (Becomes ...Presents the Terrible 5 No. 5)
M. F. Enterprises: April, 1966 - No. 4, Nov, 1966 (25¢ Giants)

nn-(#1 on pg. 5)-Origin; created by Carl Burgos	8	16	24	54	102	150
2-4: 3-(#3 on pg. 4)-Fights the Bat	5	10	15	35	63	90

CAPTAIN MARVEL (Marvel's Space-Born Super-Hero! Captain Marvel #1-6; see Giant-Size..., Life Of..., Marvel Graphic Novel #1 & Marvel Spotlight V2#1 & Marvel Super-Heroes #12)
Marvel Comics Group: May, 1968 - No. 19, Dec, 1969; No. 20, June, 1970 - No. 21, Aug, 1970; No. 22, Sept, 1972 - No. 62, May, 1979

1	23	46	69	161	356	550
2-Super Skrull-c/story	8	16	24	54	102	150
3-5: 4-Captain Marvel battles Sub-Mariner	6	12	18	38	69	100
6-11: 11-Capt. Marvel given great power by Zo the Ruler; Smith/Trimpe-c; Death of Una	4	8	12	25	40	55
12,13,15,19,20	3	6	9	17	26	35
14-Capt. Marvel vs. Iron Man; last 12¢ issue.	5	10	15	33	57	80
16-1st new Captain Marvel (cameo)	5	10	15	33	57	80
17-1st new Captain Marvel app.	11	22	33	73	157	240
18-Carol Danvers gets powers	11	22	33	75	160	245
21-Capt. Marvel battles Hulk; last 15¢ issue	6	12	18	40	73	105
22-24	3	6	9	17	26	35
25-Starlin-c/a begins; Starlin's 1st Thanos saga begins (3/73), ends #34; Thanos cameo (5 panels)	8	16	24	52	99	145
26-2nd app. Thanos (see Iron Man #55); 1st Thanos-c	10	20	30	67	141	215
27-2nd app. Eros (Starfox)(7/73); 3rd app. Thanos	12	24	36	83	182	280
28-Thanos-c/s (4th app.); Avengers app.	10	20	30	64	132	200
29,30-Thanos cameos. 29-C.M. gains more powers	5	10	15	34	60	85
31-Thanos app.; last 20¢ issue; Avengers app.	5	10	15	34	60	85
32-Thanos-c & app.; Avengers app.	5	10	15	35	63	90
33-Thanos-c & app.; Capt. Marvel battles Thanos; Thanos origin re-told	9	18	27	58	114	170
34-1st app. Nitro; C.M. contracts cancer which eventually kills him; last Starlin-c/a	5	10	15	31	53	75
35,37-40,42,46-48,50,53-56,59-62: 39-Origin Watcher. 42,59-62-Drax app.	2	4	6	8	10	12
36,41,43,49: 36-R-origin/1st app. Capt. Marvel from Marvel Super-Heroes #12. 41-Drax app.; Wrightson part inks; #43-c(i). 49-Starlin & Weiss-p assists						

CAPTAIN MARVEL
Marvel Comics: Nov, 1989 ($1.50, one-shot, 52 pgs.)

1-Monica Rambeau gains new powers; McDuffie-s	4	8	12	25	40	55

CAPTAIN MARVEL
Marvel Comics: Feb, 1994 ($1.75, 52 pgs.)

1-(Indicia reads Vol 2 #2)-Minor Captain America app.	1	3	4	6	8	10

CAPTAIN MARVEL
Marvel Comics: Dec, 1995 - No. 6, May, 1996 ($2.95/$1.95)

1 ($2.95)-Advs. of Mar-Vell's son begins; Fabian Nicieza scripts; foil-c		1	2	3	5	6	8
2-6: 2-Begin $1.95-c						4.00

CAPTAIN MARVEL (Vol. 3) (See Avengers Forever)
Marvel Comics: Jan, 2000 - No. 35, Oct, 2002 ($2.50)

1-Peter David-s in all; two covers		1	2	3	5	6	8
2-10: 2-Two covers; Hulk app. 9-Silver Surfer app.						3.00
11-35: 12-Maximum Security x-over. 17,18-Starlin-a. 27-30-Spider-Man 2099 app.						3.00
Wizard #0-Preview and history of Rick Jones						4.00
...: First Contact (8/01, $16.95, TPB) r/#0,1-6						17.00

CAPTAIN MARVEL (Vol. 4) (See Avengers Forever)
Marvel Comics: Nov, 2002 - No. 25, Sept, 2004 ($2.25/$2.99)

1-Peter David-s/Chriscross-a; 3 covers by Ross, Jusko & Chriscross						5.00
2-7: 2,3-Punisher app. 3-Alex Ross-c; new costume debuts. 4-Noto-c. 7-Thor app.						3.00
3-Sketchbook Edition-($3.50) includes Ross' concept design pages for new costume						4.00
8-15,18-25: 8-Begin $2.99-c; Thor app. 10-Spider-Man-c/app. 15-Neal Adams-c						3.00
16-1st Phyla-Vell (cameo)	3	6	9	17	26	35
17-2nd Phyla-Vell (full app.)	4	8	12	27	44	60
Vol. 1: Nothing To Lose (2003, $14.99, TPB) r/#1-6						15.00
Vol. 2: Coven (2003, $14.99, TPB) r/#7-12						15.00
Vol. 3: Crazy Like a Fox (2004, $14.99, TPB) r/#13-18						15.00
Vol. 4: Odyssey (2004, $16.99, TPB) r/#19-25						17.00

CAPTAIN MARVEL (Vol. 5) (See Secret Invasion x-over titles)
Marvel Comics: Jan, 2008 - No. 5, Jun, 2008 ($2.99)

1-5-Mar-Vell "from the past in the present"; McGuinness-c/Weeks-a						3.00
3,4-Skrull variant-c						4.00

CAPTAIN MARVEL
Marvel Comics: Sept, 2012 - No. 17, Jan, 2014 ($2.99)

1-Carol Danvers as Captain Marvel; DeConnick-s/Soy-a	3	6	9	16	24	32
2-5						6.00
6-13,15,16: 13-The Enemy Within. 15,16-Infinity tie-in						5.00
14-1st cameo of Kamala Khan (new Ms. Marvel); Andrade-a; The Enemy Within cont'd	5	10	15	35	63	90
17-($3.99) Cameo of Kamala Khan (new Ms. Marvel); Andrade-a	3	6	9	16	23	30
17-($3.99, 2nd printing) Kamala Khan (new Ms. Marvel) in costume on cover	21	42	63	147	324	500

CAPTAIN MARVEL
Marvel Comics: May, 2014 - No. 15, Jul, 2015 ($3.99)

1-Carol Danvers; DeConnick-s/Lopez-a	3	6	9	15	22	28
2,3-Guardians of the Galaxy app.						6.00
4-9,11-15: 7,8-Rocket Raccoon app. 14-Black Vortex x-over						4.00
10-($4.99) 100th issue! War Machine & Spider-Woman app.; Lopez & Takara-a						5.00

CAPTAIN MARVEL (Follows Secret Wars event)(Also see Mighty Captain Marvel)
Marvel Comics: Mar, 2016 - No. 10, Jan, 2017 ($3.99)

1-5-Carol Danvers; Fazekas & Butters-s/Anka-a; Aurora, Sasquatch & Puck app.						4.00
6-9-Civil War II tie-in						4.00
10-($4.99) Civil War II tie-in; Gage & Gage-s/Silas-a; Alpha Flight app.						5.00

CAPTAIN MARVEL (Follows Mighty Captain Marvel)
Marvel Comics: No. 125, Dec, 2017 - No. 129, Apr, 2018 ($3.99)

	GD	VG	FN	VF	VF/NM	NM-
	2.0	4.0	6.0	8.0	9.0	9.2

125-129-Carol Danvers; Stohl-s/Bandini-a; Alpha Flight app.   4.00

CAPTAIN MARVEL (Carol Danvers)(Also see Star series)
Marvel Comics: Mar, 2019 - No. 50, Aug, 2023 ($4.99/$3.99)

1-($4.99) Thompson-s/Carnero-a; Spider-Woman, Hazmat, Nuclear Man app.   5.00
2-29,31-49-($3.99) 2,3-Echo & She-Hulk app. 3-5-Rogue app. 6,7-War of The Realms tie-in.
   8-Debut of Star. 11-Star gets the Reality Stone. 12-16-The Last Avenger. 17-Wolverine app.
   18-21-Empyre tie-in; Carol as The Accuser; intro. Lauri-ell. 31-Miyazawa-a   4.00
30-($4.99) Enchantress & Ove app.; back-up with McKelvie-s/a; Ms. Marvel app.   5.00
50-($4.99) Cameos from Ms. Marvel, Jeff the Shark, She-Hulk, Spider-Woman   5.00
Annual 1 (6/22, $4.99) Starjammers app.; Gronbekk-s/Gomez-a   5.00
...: Braver & Mightier 1 (4/19, $3.99) Houser-s/Buonfantino-a   4.00
...: Marvels Snapshots 1 (4/21, $4.99) Mark Waid-s/Claire Roe-a; Kamala app.   5.00
...: The End 1 (3/20, $4.99) Carol's last adventure, set in 2051; Thompson-s/Carnero-a   5.00

CAPTAIN MARVEL (Carol Danvers)
Marvel Comics: Dec, 2023 - Present ($4.99/$3.99)

1-($4.99) Wong-s/Bazaldua-a; The Omen app.   5.00
2-5-($3.99) 3-Doctor Strange and Clea app.   4.00
...: Assault on Eden 1 (12/23, $4.99) Oliviera-s/Carlini-a; back-up Monica Rambeau story   5.00

CAPTAIN MARVEL ADVENTURES (See Special Edition Comics for pre #1)
Fawcett Publications: 1941 (March) - No. 150, Nov, 1953 (on stands 1/16/41)

	GD	VG	FN	VF	VF/NM	NM-
	2.0	4.0	6.0	8.0	9.0	9.2
nn(#1)-Captain Marvel & Sivana by Jack Kirby. The cover was printed on unstable paper stock and is rarely found in Fine or Mint condition; blank back inside-c						
	7800	15,600	31,200	62,400	101,200	140,000
2-(Advertised as #3, which was counting Special Edition Comics as the real #1); Tuska-a	497	994	1491	3628	6414	9200
3-Metallic silver-c	349	698	1047	2443	4272	6100
4-Three Lt. Marvels app.	252	504	756	1613	2757	3900
5-WWII-c	213	426	639	1363	2332	3300
6-10- 9-1st Otto Binder scripts on Capt. Marvel	148	296	444	947	1624	2300
11-15: 12-Capt. Marvel joins the Army. 13-Two pg. Capt. Marvel pin-up.						
15-Comix Cards on back-c begin, end #26	116	232	348	742	1271	1800
16,17: 17-Painted-c	110	220	330	704	1202	1700
18-Origin & 1st app. Mary Marvel & Marvel Family (12/11/42); classic painted-c;						
Mary Marvel by Marcus Swayze	1000	2000	3000	7600	13,800	20,000
19-Mary Marvel x-over; classic Christmas-c	116	232	348	742	1271	1800
20,21,23-Attached to the cover, each has a miniature comic just like the Mighty Midget Comics #11, except that each has a full color promo ad on the back cover. Most copies were circulated without the miniature comic. These issues with miniatures attached are very rare, and should not be mistaken for copies with the similar Mighty Midget glued in its place. The Mighty Midgets had blank back covers or had a small victory stamp seal. Only the Capt. Marvel, Captain Marvel Jr. and Golden Arrow No. 11 miniatures have been positively documented as having been affixed to these covers. Each miniature was only partially glued by its back cover to the Captain Marvel comic making it easy to see if it's the genuine miniature rather than a Mighty Midget.						
with comic attached....	481	962	1443	1513	5206	8900
20,23-Without miniature	81	162	243	518	884	1250
21-Without miniature; Hitler-c	300	600	900	2010	3505	5000
22-Mr. Mind serial begins; Mr. Mind first heard	123	246	369	787	1344	1900
24,25	81	162	243	518	884	1250
26-28,30: 26-Flag-c; subtle Mr. Mind 2-panel cameo. 27-1st full Mr. Mind app. (his voice was only heard over the radio before now) (9/43)	61	122	183	390	670	950
29-1st Mr. Mind-c (11/43)	81	162	243	518	884	1250
31-35: 35-Origin Radar (5/44, see Master #50)	55	110	165	352	601	850
36-40: 37-Mary Marvel x-over	52	104	156	328	552	775
41-46: 42-Christmas-c. 43-Capt. Marvel 1st meets Uncle Marvel; Mary Batson cameo.						
46-Mr. Mind serial ends	42	84	126	265	445	625
47-50	40	80	120	246	411	575
51-53,55-60: 51-63-Bi-weekly issues. 52-Origin & 1st app. Sivana Jr.; Capt. Marvel Jr. x-over						
	36	72	108	211	343	475
54-Special oversize 68 pg. issue	39	78	117	231	378	525
61-The Cult of the Curse serial begins	37	74	111	222	361	500
62-65-Serial cont.; Mary Marvel x-over in #65	34	68	102	204	332	460
66-Serial ends; Atomic War-c	43	86	129	271	461	650
67-77,79: 69-Billy Batson's Christmas; Uncle Marvel, Mary Marvel, Capt. Marvel Jr. x-over.						
71-Three Lt. Marvels app. 72-Empire State Building photo-c. 79-Origin Mr. Tawny						
	31	62	93	186	303	420
78-Origin Mr. Atom	37	74	111	218	354	490
80-Origin Capt. Marvel retold; origin scene-c	97	194	291	621	1061	1500
81-84,86-90: 81,90-Mr. Atom app. 82-Infinity-c. 82,86,88,90-Mr. Tawny app.						
	31	62	93	186	305	420
85-Freedom Train issue	35	70	105	208	339	470
91-99: 92-Mr. Tawny app. 96-Gets 1st name "Tawky"	30	60	90	177	289	400
100-Origin retold; silver metallic-c	57	114	171	362	619	875
101-115,117-120	30	60	90	177	289	400
116-Flying Saucer issue (1/51)	37	74	111	218	354	490
121-Origin retold	39	78	117	240	395	550
122-137,139,140	30	60	90	177	289	400
138-Flying Saucer issue (11/52)	39	78	117	231	378	525
141-Pre-code horror story "The Hideous Head-Hunter"						
	39	78	117	240	395	550
142-149: 142-used in **POP**, pgs. 92,96	34	68	102	204	332	460
150-(Low distribution)	71	142	213	454	777	1100

NOTE: **Swayze**-a-12, 14, 15, 18, 19, 40; c-12, 15, 19.

CAPTAIN MARVEL AND THE CAROL CORPS (Secret Wars tie-in)
Marvel Comics: Aug, 2015 - No. 4, Nov, 2015 ($3.99, limited series)

1-4: 1-Carol Danvers' squad; DeConnick & Thompson-s/Lopez-a. 4-Braga-a   4.00

CAPTAIN MARVEL AND THE GOOD HUMOR MAN (Movie)
Fawcett Publications: 1950

nn-Partial photo-c w/Jack Carson & the Captain Marvel Club Boys						
	61	122	183	390	670	950

CAPTAIN MARVEL COMIC STORY PAINT BOOK (See Comic Story...)

CAPTAIN MARVEL: DARK TEMPEST (Carol Danvers)
Marvel Comics: Sept, 2023 - No. 5, Jan, 2024 ($4.99/$3.99)

1-($4.99) Nocenti-s/Villanelli-a; Nitro returns   5.00
2-5-($3.99) Spider-Woman app. 3-Intro The Feral Five   4.00

CAPTAIN MARVEL, JR. (See Fawcett Miniatures, Marvel Family, Master Comics, Mighty Midget Comics, Shazam & Whiz Comics)

CAPTAIN MARVEL, JR.
Fawcett Publications: Nov, 1942 - No. 119, June, 1953 (No #34)

	GD	VG	FN	VF	VF/NM	NM-
	2.0	4.0	6.0	8.0	9.0	9.2
1-Origin Capt. Marvel Jr. retold (Whiz #25); Capt. Nazi app. Classic Raboy-c						
	757	1514	2271	5526	9763	14,000
2-Vs. Capt. Nazi; origin Capt. Nippon	239	478	717	1530	1615	3700
3-Infinity Pied Piper-c	135	270	405	864	1482	2100
4-Classic Raboy-c	245	490	735	1568	2684	3800
5-Vs. Capt. Nazi	116	232	348	742	1271	1800
6-8: 8-Vs. Capt. Nazi	93	186	288	591	1021	1450
9-Classic flag-c	119	238	357	762	1306	1850
10-Hitler-c	300	600	900	2070	3635	5200
11,12,15-Capt. Nazi app.	87	174	261	553	952	1350
13-Classic Hitler, Tojo and Mussolini football-c	300	600	900	2070	3635	5200
14,16-20: 14-Christmas-c. 16-Capt. Marvel & Sivana x-over. 17-Futuristic city-c; Raboy-c/a(3).						
19-Capt. Nazi & Capt. Nippon app.	61	122	183	390	670	950
21-30: 25-Flag-c	48	96	144	302	514	725
31-33,36-40: 37-Infinity-c	35	70	105	208	339	470
35-#34 on inside; cover shows origin of Sivana Jr. which is not on inside. Evidently the cover to #35 was printed out of sequence and bound with contents to #34						
	36	72	108	214	347	480
41-52,54-70: 42-Robot-c	31	62	93	182	296	410
53-Atomic Bomb-c/story	41	82	123	256	428	600
71-99,101-104: 87,93-Robot-c. 104-Used in **POP**, pg. 89						
	27	54	81	162	266	370
100	31	62	93	186	303	420
105-114,116-118: 116-Vampira, Queen of Terror app.						
	30	60	90	177	289	400
115-Classic injury to eye-c; Eyeball story w/injury-to-eye panels						
	200	400	600	1280	2190	3100
119-Electric chair-c (scarce)	93	186	288	591	1021	1450

NOTE: **Mac Raboy** c-1-28, 30-32, 57, 59 among others.

CAPTAIN MARVEL PRESENTS THE TERRIBLE FIVE
M. F. Enterprises: Aug, 1966; V2#5, Sept, 1967 (No #2-4) (25¢)

	GD	VG	FN	VF	VF/NM	NM-
	2.0	4.0	6.0	8.0	9.0	9.2
1	7	14	21	44	82	120
V2#5-(Formerly Captain Marvel)	5	10	15	30	50	70

CAPTAIN MARVEL'S FUN BOOK
Samuel Lowe Co.: 1944 (1/2" thick) (cardboard covers)(25¢)

nn-Puzzles, games, magic, etc.; infinity-c	53	106	159	334	567	800

CAPTAIN MARVEL SPECIAL EDITION (See Special Edition)

CAPTAIN MARVEL STORY BOOK
Fawcett Publications: Summer, 1946 - No. 4, Summer?, 1948

1-Half text	68	136	204	435	743	1050
2-4	48	96	144	302	514	725

CAPTAIN MARVEL THRILL BOOK (Large-Size)
Fawcett Publications: 1941 (B&W w/color-c)

1-Reprints from Whiz #8,10, & Special Edition #1 (Rare)						
	480	960	1440	4800	--	--

NOTE: Rarely found in Fine or Mint condition.

CAPTAIN MIDNIGHT (TV, radio, films) (See The Funnies, Popular Comics & Super Book of Comics)(Becomes Sweethearts No. 68 on)
Fawcett Publications: Sept, 1942 - No. 67, Fall, 1948 (#1-14: 68 pgs.)

	GD	VG	FN	VF	VF/NM	NM-
	2.0	4.0	6.0	8.0	9.0	9.2
1-Origin Captain Midnight, star of radio and movies; Captain Marvel cameo on cover						
	349	698	1047	2443	4272	6100
2-Smashes the Jap Juggernaut	168	336	504	1075	1838	2600
3-Classic Nazi war-c	158	316	474	1003	1727	2450
4,5: 4-Grapples the Gremlins	119	238	357	762	1306	1850
6-8: 7-WWII-c	71	142	213	454	777	1100
9-Raboy-c	84	168	252	538	919	1300
10-Raboy Flag-c/WWII-c	84	168	252	538	919	1300
11-20: 11,17,18-Raboy-c. 16 (1/44)	50	100	150	315	533	750
21-Classic WWII-c	68	136	204	435	743	1050
22,25-30: 22-War savings stamp-c	41	82	123	256	428	600
23-WWII Concentration Camp-c	60	120	180	381	653	925
24-Japan flag sunburst-c	68	136	204	435	743	1050
31-40	34	68	102	199	325	450
41-59,61-67: 50-Sci/fi theme begins?	27	54	81	158	259	360
60-Flying Saucer issue (2/48)-3rd of this theme; see The Spirit 9/28/47 (1st), Shadow Comics V7#10 (2nd, 1/48) & Boy Commandos #26 (4th, 3-4/48)						
	41	82	123	256	428	600

CAPTAIN MIDNIGHT
Dark Horse Comics: No. 0, Jun, 2013 - No. 24, Jun, 2015 ($2.99)

0-24: 0-Williamson-s/Ibáñez-a; WWII hero appears in modern times. 4,5-Skyman app.   3.00
One For One: Captain Midnight #1 (1/14, $1.00) r/#1   3.00

CAPTAIN NICE (TV)
Gold Key: Nov, 1967 (one-shot)

1(10211-711)-Photo-c	6	12	18	38	69	100

CAPTAIN N: THE GAME MASTER (TV)
Valiant Comics: 1990 - No. 5, 1990 ($1.95, thick stock, coated-c)

1	5	10	15	35	63	90
2-4: 3-Quesada-a (1st pro work). 4-Layton-c	2	4	6	8	10	12
5-Last issue; Layton-c	4	8	12	25	40	55

CAPTAIN PARAGON (See Bill Black's Fun Comics)
Americomics: Dec, 1983 - No. 4, 1985

1-Intro/1st app. Ms. Victory   5.00
2-4   4.00

CAPTAIN PARAGON AND THE SENTINELS OF JUSTICE
AC Comics: April, 1985 - No. 6, 1986 ($1.75)

1-6: 1-Capt. Paragon, Commando D., Nightveil, Scarlet Scorpion, Stardust & Atoman   4.00

Captain Marvel Adventures #3 © FAW

Captain Marvel, Jr. #4 © FAW

Carbon Grey #1 © H. Nguyen

	GD	VG	FN	VF	VF/NM	NM-
	2.0	4.0	6.0	8.0	9.0	9.2

CAPTAIN PLANET AND THE PLANETEERS (TV cartoon)
Marvel Comics: Oct, 1991 - No. 12, Oct, 1992 ($1.00/$1.25)

1-N. Adams painted-c	3	6	9	14	20	25
2-12: 3-Romita-c						6.00

CAPTAIN POWER AND THE SOLDIERS OF THE FUTURE (TV)
Continuity Comics: Aug, 1988 - No. 2, 1988 ($2.00)

1,2: 1-Neal Adams-c/layouts/inks; variant-c exists.						4.00

CAPTAIN PUREHEART (See Archie as…)

CAPTAIN ROCKET
P. L. Publ. (Canada): Nov, 1951

1-Harry Harrison-a	68	136	204	435	743	1050

CAPT. SAVAGE AND HIS LEATHERNECK RAIDERS (…And His Battlefield Raiders #9 on)
Marvel Comics Group (Animated Timely Features): Jan, 1968 - No. 19, Mar, 1970
(See Sgt. Fury No. 10)

1-Sgt. Fury & Howlers cameo	7	14	21	46	86	125
2,7,11: 2-Origin Hydra. 7-Pre-"Thing" Ben Grimm story. 11-Sgt. Fury app.						
	3	6	9	17	26	35
3-6,8-10,12-14: 4-Origin Hydra. 14-Last 12¢ issue	3	6	9	16	23	30
15-19	3	6	9	14	19	24

NOTE: **Ayres/Shores** a-1-8,11. **Ayres/Severin** a-9,10,17-19. **Heck/Shores** a-12-15.

CAPTAIN SCIENCE (Fantastic No. 8 on)
Youthful Magazines: Nov, 1950; No. 2, Feb, 1951 - No. 7, Dec, 1951

1-Wood-a; origin; 2 pg. text w/ photos of George Pal's "Destination Moon."						
	124	258	387	826	1413	2000
2-Flying saucer-c swipes Weird Science #13(#2)-c	103	206	309	659	1130	1600
3,7; 3-Bondage c-swipes/Wings #94	129	258	387	826	1413	2000
4,5-Wood/Orlando-c/a(2) each	116	232	348	742	1271	1800
6-Bondage c-swipes/Wings #91	168	336	504	1075	1838	2600

NOTE: **Fass** a-4. **Bondage** c-3, 6, 7.

CAPTAIN SILVER'S LOG OF SEA HOUND (See Sea Hound)

CAPTAIN SINBAD (Movie Adaptation) (See Fantastic Voyages of… & Movie Comics)

CAPTAIN STERNN: RUNNING OUT OF TIME
Kitchen Sink Press: Sept, 1993 - No. 5, 1994 ($4.95, limited series, coated stock, 52 pgs.)

1-5: Berni Wrightson-c/a/scripts						6.00
1-Gold ink variant						10.00

CAPTAIN STEVE SAVAGE (…& His Jet Fighters, No. 2-13)
Avon Periodicals: 1950 - No. 8, 1/53; No. 5, 9-10/54 - No. 13, 5-6/56

nn(1st series)-Harrison/Wood art, 22 pgs. (titled "…Over Korea")						
	54	108	162	343	574	825
1(4/51)-Reprints nn issue (Canadian)	27	54	81	158	259	360
2-Kamen-a	21	42	63	122	199	275
3-11 (#6, 11-12/54, last precode)	17	34	51	98	154	210
12-Wood-a (6 pgs.)	21	42	63	122	199	275
13-Check, Lawrence-a	17	34	51	100	158	215

NOTE: **Kinstler** c-2-5, 7-9, 11. **Lawrence** a-8. **Ravielli** a-5, 9.

5(9-10/54-2nd series)(Formerly Sensational Police Cases)						
	14	28	42	78	112	145
6-Reprints nn issue; Harrison/Wood-a	14	28	42	80	115	150
7-13: 9,10-Kinstler-c. 10-r/cover #2 (1st series). 13-r/cover #8 (1st series)						
	12	24	36	67	94	120

CAPTAIN STONE (See Holyoke One-Shot No. 10)

CAPT. STORM (Also see G. I. Combat #138)
National Periodical Publications: May-June, 1964 - No. 18, Mar-Apr, 1967

1-Origin	11	22	33	73	157	240
2-7,9,18: 3,6,13-Kubert-a. 4-Colan-a. 12-Kubert-c	7	14	21	44	82	120
8-Grey-tone-c	8	16	24	54	102	150

CAPTAIN 3-D (Super hero)
Harvey Publications: December, 1953 (25¢, came with 2 pairs of glasses)

1-Kirby/Ditko-a (Ditko's 3rd published work tied with Strange Fantasy #9, see also Daring Love #1 & Black Magic V4 #3); shows cover in 3-D on inside; Kirby/Meskin-a						
	14	28	42	78	112	145

NOTE: Half price without glasses.

CAPTAIN THUNDER AND BLUE BOLT
Hero Comics: Sept, 1987 - No. 10, 1988 ($1.95)

1-10: 1-Origin Blue Bolt. 3-Origin Capt. Thunder. 6-1st app. Wicket. 8-Champions x-over						4.00

CAPTAIN TOOTSIE & THE SECRET LEGION (Advs. of…)(Also see Monte Hale #30,39 & Real Western Hero)
Toby Press: Oct, 1950 - No. 2, Dec, 1950

1-Not Beck-a; both have sci/fi covers	43	86	129	271	461	650
2-The Rocketeer Patrol app.; not Beck-a	25	50	75	150	245	340

CAPTAIN TRIUMPH (See Crack Comics #27)

CAPTAIN UNIVERSE… (5-part x-over)
Marvel Comics: 2005; Jan, 2006

…/ Daredevil 1 (1/06, $2.99) Part 2; Faerber-s/Santacruz-a						3.00
…/ Hulk 1 (1/06, $2.99) Part 1; Faerber-s/Magno-a						3.00
…/ Invisible Woman 1 (1/06, $2.99) Part 4; Faerber-s/Raiz-a; Gladiator app.						3.00
…/ Silver Surfer 1 (1/06, $2.99) Part 5; Faerber-s/Magno-a						3.00
…/ X-23 1 (1/06, $2.99) Part 3; Faerber-s/Portella-a; Scorpion app.						3.00
…: Power Unimaginable TPB (2005, $19.99)-Reprints from Marvel Spotlight #9-11, Incredible Hulk Ann. #10, Marvel Fanfare #25, Web of Spider-Man Ann. #5&6, Marvel Comics Presents #148, Cosmic Power Unlimited #5						20.00
…: The Hero Who Could Be You 1 (7/13, $7.99) r/Marvel Spotlight #9-11 & early apps.						8.00
…: Universal Heroes TPB (2005, $13.99) reprints …/Hulk, …/Daredevil, …X-23 and back-up stories from Amazing Fantasy (2005) #13,14						14.00

CAPTAIN VENTURE & THE LAND BENEATH THE SEA (See Space Family Robinson)
Gold Key: Oct, 1968 - No. 2, Oct. 1969

1-r/Space Family Robinson serial; Spiegle-a	5	10	15	34	60	85
2-Spiegle-a	4	8	12	27	44	60

CAPTAIN VICTORY AND THE GALACTIC RANGERS (Also see Kirby: Genesis)
Pacific Comics: Nov, 1981 - No. 13, Jan, 1984 ($1.00, direct sales, 36-48 pgs.)
(Created by Jack Kirby)

1-1st app. Mr. Mind	1	2	3	5	6	8
2-13: 3-N. Adams-a						4.00
Special 1-(10/83)-Kirby c/a(p)						4.00

NOTE: **Conrad** a-10, 11. **Ditko** a-6. **Kirby** a-1-3p; c-1-13.

CAPTAIN VICTORY AND THE GALACTIC RANGERS
Jack Kirby Comics: July, 2000 - No. 2, Sept, 2000 ($2.95, B&W)

1,2-New Jeremy Kirby-s with reprinted Jack Kirby-a; Liefeld pin-up art						3.00

CAPTAIN VICTORY AND THE GALACTIC RANGERS
Dynamite Entertainment: 2014 - No. 6, 2015 ($3.99)

1-6-Joe Casey-s; art by various. 3-Dalrymple & Mahfood-a						4.00

CAPTAIN VIDEO (TV) (See XMas Comics)
Fawcett Publications: Feb, 1951 - No. 6, Dec, 1951 (No. 1,5,6-36 pgs.; 2-4, 52 pgs.)

1-George Evans-a(2); 1st TV hero comic	110	220	330	704	1202	1700
2-Used in SOTI, pg. 382	77	154	231	493	847	1200
3-6-All Evans-a except #5 mostly Evans	60	120	180	381	653	925

NOTE: Minor **Williamson** assists on most issues. Photo c-1, 5, 6; painted c-2-4.

CAPTAIN WILLIE SCHULTZ (Also see Fightin' Army)
Charlton Comics: No. 76, Oct, 1985 - No. 77, Jan, 1986

76,77-Low print run	1	2	3	5	6	8

CAPTAIN WIZARD COMICS (See Meteor, Red Band & Three Ring Comics)
Rural Home: 1946

1-Capt. Wizard dons new costume; Impossible Man, Race Wilkins app.						
	55	110	165	352	601	850

CAPTAIN WONDER
Image Comics: Feb, 2011 ($4.99, 3-D comic with glasses)

1-Haberlin-s/Tan-a; sketch pages, crossword puzzle, paper dolls						5.00

CAPTURE CREATURES
BOOM! Entertainment (kaboom!): Nov, 2014 - No. 4, May, 2015 ($3.99)

1-4-Frank Gibson-s/Becky Dreistadt-a; multiple covers on each						4.00

CAPWOLF & THE HOWLING COMMANDOS
Marvel Comics: Dec, 2023 - No. 4, Mar, 2024 ($4.99/$3.99)

1-($4.99) Phillips-s/Magno-a; Captain America as werewolf in France 1944						5.00
2-4-($3.99)						4.00

CARBON GREY
Image Comics: Mar, 2011 - No. 3, May, 2011 ($2.99, limited series)

1-3-Khari Evans, Kinsun Loh & Hoang Nguyen-a; Nguyen-c						3.00
… Origins 1,2 (11/11 - No. 2, 3/12, $3.99) 1-Pop Mhan-a						4.00
Vol. 2 (7/12 - No. 3, 2/13, $3.99) 1-3-Gardner-s/Evans & Nguyen-a						4.00
Vol. 3 (12/13 - No. 2, 1/14) 1,2-Gardner-s/Evans & Nguyen-a						4.00

CARE BEARS (TV, Movie)(See Star Comics Magazine)
Star Comics/Marvel Comics No. 15 on: Nov, 1985 - No. 20, Jan, 1989

1-Post-a begins	4	8	12	23	37	50
2-20: 11-$1.00-c begins. 13-Madballs app.	2	4	6	8	10	12

	GD 2.0	VG 4.0	FN 6.0	VF 8.0	VF/NM 9.0	NM- 9.2

CARE BEARS (TV, Movie)(Subtitled "Unlock the Magic" on cover)
IDW Publishing: Jul, 2019 - No. 3, Sept, 2019 ($3.99, limited series)

1-3-Garbowska-a						4.00

CAREER GIRL ROMANCES (Formerly Three Nurses)
Charlton Comics: June, 1964 - No. 78, Dec, 1973

V4#24-31	3	6	9	19	30	40
32-Elvis Presley, Herman's Hermits, Johnny Rivers line drawn-c	16	32	48	110	243	375
33-37,39-50: 39-Tiffany Sinn app.	3	6	9	16	23	30
38-(2/67) 1st app. Tiffany Sinn, C.I.A. Sweetheart, Undercover Agent (also see Secret Agent #10; Dominguel-a	3	6	9	19	30	40
51-78: 54-Jonnie Love anti-drup PSA. 67-Susan Dey pin-up. 70-David Cassidy pin-up	3	6	9	14	19	24

CAR 54, WHERE ARE YOU? (TV)
Dell Publishing Co.: Mar-May, 1962 - No. 7, Sept-Nov, 1963; 1964 - 1965 (All photo-c)

Four Color 1257(#1, 3-5/62)	9	18	27	59	117	175
2(6-8/62)-7	5	10	15	30	50	70
2,3(10-12/64), 4(1-3/65)-Reprints #2,3,&4 of 1st series	3	6	9	19	30	40

CARL BARKS LIBRARY OF WALT DISNEY'S GYRO GEARLOOSE COMICS AND FILLERS IN COLOR, THE
Gladstone: 1993 ($7.95, 8-1/2x11", limited series, 52 pgs.)

1-6: Carl Barks reprints	1	3	4	6	8	10

CARL BARKS LIBRARY OF WALT DISNEY'S COMICS AND STORIES IN COLOR, THE
Gladstone: Jan, 1992 - No. 51, Mar, 1996 ($8.95, 8-1/2x11", 60 pgs.)

1,2,6,8-51: 1-Barks Donald Duck-r/WDC&S #31-35; 2-r/#36,38-41; 5-r/#57-61; 8-r/#67-71; 9-r/#72-76; 10-r/#77-81; 11-r/#82-86; 12-r/#87-91; 13-r/#92-96; 14-r/#97-101; 15-r/#102-106; 16-r/#107-111; 17-r/#112,114,117,124,125; 18-r/#126-130; 19-r/#131,132(2),133,134; 20-r/#135-139; 21-r/#140-144; 22-r/#145-149; 23-r/#150-154; 24-r/#155-159; 25-r/#160-164; 26-r/#165-169; 27-r/#170-174,28-r/#175-179; 29-r/#180-184; 30-r/#185-189; 31-r/#190-194; 32-r/#195-199;33-r/#200-204; 34-r/#205-209; 35-r/#210-214; 36-r/#215-219; 37-r/#220-224; 38-r/#225-229; 39-r/#230-234; 40-r/#235-239; 41-r/#240-244; 42r/#245-249; 43-r/#250-254; 44-50: All contain one Heroes & Villains trading card each	2	4	6	9	12	15
3,4,7: 3-r/#42-46. 4-r/#47-51. 7-r/#62-66.	2	4	6	11	16	20
5-r/#52-56	3	6	9	16	23	30

CARL BARKS LIBRARY OF WALT DISNEY'S DONALD DUCK ADVENTURES IN COLOR, THE
Gladstone: Jan, 1994 - No. 25, Jan, 1996 ($7.95-$9.95, 44-68 pgs., 8-1/2"x11")
(all contain one Donald Duck trading card each)

1-5,7-25-Carl Barks-r: 1-r/FC #9; 2-r/FC #62; 3-r/FC #108; 5-r/FC #147 & #79(Mickey Mouse); 7-r/FC #159. 8-r/FC #178 & 189. 9-r/FC #199 & 203; 10-r/FC 223 & 238; 11-r/Christmas Parade #1 & 2; 12-r/FC #296; 13-r/FC #263; 14-r/MOC #20 & 41; 15-r/FC 275 & 282; 16-r/FC #291&300; 17-r/FC #308 & 318; 18-r/Vac. Parade #1 & Summer Fun #2; 19-r/FC #328 & 367	2	4	6	9	12	15
6-r/MOC #4, Cheerios "Atom Bomb", D.D. Tells About Kites	3	6	9	14	20	25

CARL BARKS LIBRARY OF WALT DISNEY'S DONALD DUCK CHRISTMAS STORIES IN COLOR, THE
Gladstone: 1992 ($7.95, 44pgs., one-shot)

nn-Reprints Firestone giveaways 1945-1949	2	4	6	10	14	18

CARL BARKS LIBRARY OF WALT DISNEY'S UNCLE SCROOGE COMICS ONE PAGERS IN COLOR, THE
Gladstone: 1992 - No. 2, 1993 ($8.95, limited series, 60 pgs., 8-1/2x11")

1-Carl Barks one pg. reprints	3	6	9	16	23	30
2-Carl Barks one pg. reprints	2	4	6	10	14	18

CARNAGE
Marvel Comics: Dec, 2010 - No. 5, Aug, 2011 ($3.99, limited series)

1-5-Spider-Man & Iron Man app.; Clayton Crain-a/c; Wells-s						4.00
....: It's a Wonderful Life (10/96, $1.95) David Quinn scripts						3.00
....: Mind Bomb (2/96, $2.95) Warren Ellis script; Kyle Hotz-a						4.00

CARNAGE
Marvel Comics: Jan, 2016 - No. 16, Mar, 2017 ($3.99)

1-16: 1-Conway-s/Perkins-a; Eddie Brock app. 3-Man-Wolf app. 4,5-Toxin app.						4.00

CARNAGE
Marvel Comics: May, 2022 - No. 14, Aug, 2023 ($4.99/$3.99)

1-($4.99) Ram V-s/Francesco Manna-a; Hydro-Man app.						5.00
2-14-($3.99) 3-The Spot app. 4-Spiderling app.						4.00
... Forever 1 (4/22, $4.99) Leads into Carnage #1; Johnson-s/Salazar-a; V-s/Larroca-a						5.00

CARNAGE
Marvel Comics: Jan, 2024 - Present ($5.99/$4.99)

1-($5.99) Torunn Gronbekk-s/Pere Pérez-a; Flash Thompson app.						6.00
2-4-($4.99)						5.00

CARNAGE: BLACK, WHITE & BLOOD
Marvel Comics: May, 2021 - No. 4, Sept, 2021 ($4.99, B&W&red, limited series)

1-4-Anthology of short stories by various. 1-Spider-Man app. 2-Cates-s. 4-Bennett-a						5.00

CARNAGE REIGNS
Marvel Comics: Jul, 2023 - Aug, 2023 ($7.99/$4.99, limited series)

Alpha 1 (7/23, $7.99) Spider-Man (Miles) & The Scorpion app.; 3 back-up stories						8.00
Omega 1 (8/23, $4.99) Spider-Man (Miles) & Iron Man app.; new Iron Spider suit						5.00

CARNAGE, U.S.A.
Marvel Comics: Feb, 2012 - No. 5, Jun, 2012 ($3.99, limited series)

1-4-Clayton Crain-a/c; Wells-s; Spider-Man & Avengers app. 3,4-Venom app.						4.00

CARNATION MALTED MILK GIVEAWAYS (See Wisco/Klarer in the Promotional Comics section)

CARNEYS, THE
Archie Comics: Summer, 1994 ($2.00, 52 pgs)

1-Bound-in pull-out poster						4.00

CARNIVAL COMICS (Formerly Kayo #12; becomes Red Seal Comics #14)
Harry 'A' Chesler/Pershing Square Publ. Co.: 1945

nn (#13)-Guardineer-a	25	50	75	150	245	340

CAROLINE KENNEDY
Charlton Comics: 1961 (one-shot)

nn-Interior photo covers of Kennedy family	12	24	36	81	176	270

CAROUSEL COMICS
F. E. Howard, Toronto: V1#8, April, 1948

V1#8	15	30	45	90	140	190

CARS (Based on the 2006 Pixar movie)
Boom Entertainment: No. 0, Nov, 2009 - No. 7, Jun, 2010 ($2.99)

0-7: 0,1-Three covers on each. 2-7-Two covers on each						3.00
....: Adventures of Tow Mater 1-4 (7/10 - No. 4, 10/10, $2.99) 1-Two covers						3.00
....: Radiator Springs 1-4 (7/09 - No. 4, 10/09, $2.99) Two covers on each						3.00
....: The Rookie 1-4 (3/09 - No. 4, 6/09, $2.99) Origin of Lightning McQueen						3.00

CARS 2 (Based on the 2011 Pixar movie)
Marvel Worldwide (Disney Comics): Aug, 2011 - No. 2, Aug, 2011 ($3.99)

1,2-Movie adaptation; car profile pages						4.00

CARS, WORLD OF (Free Comic Book Day giveaway)
BOOM Kids!: May, 2009

1-Based on the Disney/Pixar movie						3.00

CARSON OF VENUS (Also see Edgar Rice Burroughs'...)
American Mythology Prods.: 2020 - 2020 ($3.99, limited series)

....: Realm of the Dead 1-3 - Wolfer-s/Mescarcia-a						4.00
....: The Eye of Amtor 1-3 - Wolfer-s/Carratu-a						4.00

CARTOON CARTOONS (Anthology)
DC Comics: Mar, 2001 - No. 33, Oct, 2004 ($1.99/$2.25)

1-33-Short stories of Cartoon Network characters. 3,6,10,13,15-Space Ghost. 13-Begin $2.25-c. 17-Dexter's Laboratory begins						3.00

CARTOON KIDS
Atlas Comics (CPS): 1957 (no month)

1-Maneely-c/a; Dexter The Demon, Willie The Wise-Guy, Little Zelda app.	20	40	60	117	189	260

CARTOON NETWORK ACTION PACK (Anthology)
DC Comics: July, 2006 - No. 67, May, 2012 ($2.25/$2.50/$2.99)

1-31-Short stories of Cartoon Network characters. 1,4,6-Rowdruff Boys app.						3.00
32-67: 32-Begin $2.50-c. 50-Ben 10/Generator Rex team-up						3.00

CARTOON NETWORK BLOCK PARTY (Anthology)
DC Comics: Nov, 2004 - No. 59, Sept, 2009 ($2.25/$2.50)

1,2,4-51-Short stories of Cartoon Network characters						3.00
3-($2.95) Bonus pages						4.00
52-59: 52-Begin $2.50-c. 59-Last issue; Powerpuff Girls app.						3.00
Cartoon Network 2-in-1: Ben 10 Alien Force/The Secret Saturdays TPB (2010, $12.99) reprints stories from #26-42						13.00
Cartoon Network 2-in-1: Foster's Home For Imaginary Friends/Powerpuff Girls TPB (2010, $12.99) reprints stories from #19-21,23,25,26,28,30,32,34-38,41						13.00
... Vol. 1: Get Down! (2005, $6.99, digest) reprints from Dexter's Lab and Cartoon Cartoons						7.00
... Vol. 2: Read All About It! (2005, $6.99, digest) reprints						7.00
... Vol. 3: Can You Dig It?; ... Vol. 4: Blast Off! (2006, $6.99, digest) reprints						7.00

CARTOON NETWORK PRESENTS
DC Comics: Aug, 1997 - No. 24, Aug, 1999 ($1.75-$1.99, anthology)

1-Dexter's Lab	3	6	9	17	26	35
1-Platinum Edition	3	6	9	16	23	30
2-Space Ghost	1	3	4	6	8	10
3-10						4.00
11-24: 12-Bizarro World						3.00

CARTOON NETWORK PRESENTS SPACE GHOST
Archie Comics: Mar, 1997 ($1.50)

1-Scott Rosema-p	2	4	6	13	18	22

CARTOON NETWORK STARRING... (Anthology)
DC Comics: Sept, 1999 - No. 18, Feb, 2001 ($1.99)

1-Powerpuff Girls	4	8	12	28	47	65
2-Johnny Bravo	3	6	9	19	30	40
3-18: 8,11,14,17-Johnny Bravo. 12,15,18-Space Ghost						4.00

CARTOON TALES (Disney's...)
W.D. Publications (Disney): nd, nn (1992) ($2.95, 6-5/8x9-1/2", 52 pgs.)

nn-Ariel & Sebastian-Serpent Teen; Beauty and the Beast; A Tale of Enchantment; Darkwing Duck - Just Us Justice Ducks; 101 Dalmatians - Canine Classics; Tale Spin - Surprise in the Skies; Uncle Scrooge - Blast to the Past						4.00

CARVERS
Image Comics (Flypaper Press): 1998 - No. 3, 1999 ($2.95)

1-3-Pander Bros.-a/Fleming-s						4.00

CAR WARRIORS
Marvel Comics (Epic): June, 1991 - No. 4, Sept, 1991 ($2.25, lim. series)

1-4: 1-Says April in indicia						4.00

CASANOVA
Image Comics: June, 2006 - No. 14, May, 2008 ($1.99, B&W & olive green or blue)

1-14: 1-7-Matt Fraction-s/Gabriel Bá-a/c. 8-14-Fabio Moon-a						3.00
... Luxuria TPB (2008, $12.99) r/#1-7; sketch pages and cover gallery						13.00
1-4 (Marvel Comics, 10/10 - No. 4, 12/10, $3.99) Recolored reprints Image series #1-7						4.00
...: Acedia 1-8 (Image, 1/15 - No. 8, 3/17) Fraction-s/various; back-up by Chabon-s/Bá-a						4.00
...: Avaritia (III) 1-4 (Marvel, 11/11 - No. 4, 8/12, $4.99) new story; Fraction-s/Bá-a						5.00
...: Gula (Marvel, 1/11 - No. 4, 4/11) r/Image series #8-14. 4-New story pages						4.00

CASE FILES: SAM & TWITCH (Also see the Spawn titles)
Image Comics: May, 2003 - No. 25, July, 2006 ($2.50/$2.95, color #1-6/B&W #7-on)

Carnage (2016 series) #4 © MAR

Cartoon Network Block Party #59 © CN

Casper's Ghostland #16 © HARV

	GD 2.0	VG 4.0	FN 6.0	VF 8.0	VF/NM 9.0	NM- 9.2

1-25: 1-5-Scott Morse-a/Marc Andreyko-s. 7-13-Paul Lee-a. 13-Niles-s — 3.00

CASE OF THE SHOPLIFTER'S SHOE (See Perry Mason, Feature Book No.50)
CASE OF THE WINKING BUDDHA, THE
St. John Publ. Co.: 1950 (132 pgs.; 25¢; B&W; 5-1/2x7-5-1/2x8")

| nn-Charles Raab-a; reprinted in Authentic Police Cases No. 25 | 68 | 136 | 204 | 435 | 743 | 1050 |

CASEY BLUE
DC Comics (WildStorm): Jul, 2008 - No. 6, Dec, 2008 ($2.99, limited series)

1-6-B. Clay Moore-s/Carlos Barberi-a — 3.00
...: Beyond Tomorrow TPB (2009, $19.99) r/#1-6; Barberi sketch pages — 20.00

CASEY-CRIME PHOTOGRAPHER (Two-Gun Western No. 5 on)(Radio)
Marvel Comics (BFP): Aug, 1949 - No. 4, Feb, 1950

| 1-Photo-c; 52 pgs. | 41 | 82 | 123 | 256 | 428 | 600 |
| 2-4: Photo-c | 27 | 54 | 81 | 158 | 259 | 360 |

CASEY JONES (TV)
Dell Publishing Co.: No. 915, July, 1958

| Four Color 915-Alan Hale photo-c | 6 | 12 | 18 | 40 | 73 | 105 |

CASEY JONES & RAPHAEL (See Bodycount)
Mirage Studios: Oct, 1994 ($2.75, unfinished limited series)

| 1-Bisley-c: Eastman story & pencils | 2 | 4 | 6 | 9 | 12 | 15 |

CASEY JONES: NORTH BY DOWNEAST
Mirage Studios: May, 1994 - No. 2, July, 1994 ($2.75, limited series)

1,2-Rick Veitch script & pencils; Kevin Eastman story & inks — 4.00

CASPER... (One-shots)
American Mythology Prods.: 2018 - 2019 ($3.99)

.. & Hot Stuff #1 (2018) Wolfer-s/Shanower-a and Shand-s/Scherer-a; r/Devil Kids #87 — 4.00
.. & Wendy #1 (2018) Check-s/Scherer-a and Shand-s/Sosa-a; r/Casper and Wendy #1 — 4.00
Casper's Classic Christmas #1 (2019, $3.99) Christmas-themed reprints; Hot Stuff app. — 4.00
Casper's Haunted Halloween #1 (2019) Spooky, Nightmare and the Ghostly Trio reprints — 4.00
... Spotlight: The Ghostly Trio #1 (2020) Reprints from 1971-1990 — 4.00
Casper's Spooksville #1 (2019) New stories by various — 4.00

CASPER ADVENTURE DIGEST
Harvey Comics: V2#1, Oct, 1992 - V2#8, Apr, 1994 ($1.75/$1.95, digest-size)

V2#1: Casper, Richie Rich, Spooky, Wendy — 6.00
2-8 — 4.00

CASPER AND...
Harvey Comics: Nov, 1987 - No. 12, June, 1990 (75¢/$1.00, all reprints)

1-Ghostly Trio — 6.00
2-12: 2-Spooky; begin $1.00-c. 3-Wendy. 4-Nightmare. 5-Ghostly Trio. 6-Spooky. 7-Wendy.
8-Hot Stuff. 9-Baby Huey. 10-Wendy.11-Ghostly Trio. 12-Spooky — 4.00

CASPER AND FRIENDS
Harvey Comics: Oct, 1991 - No. 5, July, 1992 ($1.00/$1.25)

1-Nightmare, Ghostly Trio, Wendy, Spooky — 5.00
2-5 — 4.00

CASPER AND FRIENDS MAGAZINE: Mar, 1997 - No. 3, July, 1997 ($3.99)

1-3 — 4.00

CASPER AND NIGHTMARE (See Harvey Hits# 37, 45, 52, 56, 59, 62, 65, 68,71, 75)
CASPER AND NIGHTMARE (Nightmare & Casper No. 1-5)
Harvey Publications: No. 6, 11/64 - No. 44, 10/73; No. 45, 6/74 - No. 46, 8/74 (25¢)

6: 68 pg. Giants begin, ends #32	5	10	15	34	60	85
7-10	3	6	9	21	33	45
11-20	3	6	9	17	26	35
21-37: 33-37-(52 pg. Giants)	3	6	9	14	20	26
38-46	2	4	6	10	14	18

NOTE: Many issues contain reprints.

CASPER AND SPOOKY (See Harvey Hits No. 20)
Harvey Publications: Oct, 1972 - No. 7, Oct, 1973

| 1 | 3 | 6 | 9 | 21 | 33 | 45 |
| 2-7 | 2 | 4 | 6 | 10 | 14 | 18 |

CASPER AND THE GHOSTLY TRIO
Harvey Pub.: Nov, 1972 - No. 7, Nov, 1973; No. 8, Aug, 1990 - No. 10, Dec, 1990

1	3	6	9	21	33	45
2-7	2	4	6	10	14	18
8-10						6.00

CASPER AND WENDY

Harvey Publications: Sept, 1972 - No. 8, Nov, 1973

| 1: 52 pg. Giant | 3 | 6 | 9 | 21 | 33 | 45 |
| 2-8 | 2 | 4 | 6 | 10 | 14 | 18 |

CASPER BIG BOOK
Harvey Comics: V2#1, Aug, 1992 - No. 3, May, 1993 ($1.95, 52 pgs.)

V2#1-Spooky app. — 4.00
2,3 — 4.00

CASPER CAT (See Dopey Duck)
I. W. Enterprises/Super: 1958; 1963

| 1,7: 1-Wacky Duck #?.7-Reprint, Super No. 14('63) | 3 | 6 | 9 | 14 | 20 | 25 |

CASPER DIGEST (...Magazine #?; ...Halloween Digest #8, 10)
Harvey Publications: Oct, 1986 - No. 18, Jan, 1991 ($1.25/$1.75, digest-size)

| 1 | 1 | 3 | 4 | 6 | 8 | 10 |
| 2-18: 11-Valentine-c. 18-Halloween-c | | | | | | 6.00 |

CASPER DIGEST (...Magazine #? on)
Harvey Comics: V2#1, Sept, 1991 - V2#14, Nov, 1994 ($1.75/$1.95, digest-size)

V2#1 — 6.00
2-14 — 4.00

CASPER DIGEST STORIES
Harvey Publications: Feb, 1980 - No. 4, Nov, 1980 (95¢, 132 pgs., digest size)

| 1 | 2 | 4 | 6 | 9 | 13 | 16 |
| 2-4 | 1 | 2 | 3 | 5 | 7 | 9 |

CASPER DIGEST WINNERS
Harvey Publications: Apr, 1980 - No. 3, Sept, 1980 (95¢, 132 pgs., digest-size)

| 1 | 2 | 4 | 6 | 9 | 13 | 16 |
| 2,3 | 1 | 2 | 3 | 5 | 7 | 9 |

CASPER ENCHANTED TALES DIGEST
Harvey Comics: May, 1992 - No. 10, Oct, 1994 ($1.75, digest-size, 98 pgs.)

| 1-Casper, Spooky, Wendy stories | 4 | 8 | 12 | 27 | 44 | 60 |
| 2-10 | 1 | 3 | 4 | 6 | 8 | 10 |

CASPER GHOSTLAND
Harvey Comics: May, 1992 ($1.25)

| 1 | 1 | 3 | 4 | 6 | 8 | 10 |

CASPER GIANT SIZE
Harvey Comics: Oct, 1992 - No. 4, Nov, 1993 ($2.25, 68 pgs.)

V2#1-Casper, Wendy, Spooky stories — 5.00
2-4 — 4.00

CASPER HALLOWEEN TRICK OR TREAT
Harvey Publications: Jan, 1976 (52 pgs.)

| 1 | 3 | 6 | 9 | 17 | 26 | 35 |

CASPER IN SPACE (Formerly Casper Spaceship)
Harvey Publications: No. 6, June, 1973 - No. 8, Oct, 1973

| 6-8 | 2 | 4 | 6 | 11 | 16 | 20 |

CASPER'S CAPERS
American Mythology Prods.: 2018 - No. 6, 2019 ($3.99)

1-6-Classic reprints with digital recoloring. 1-Includes 1st apps. of Casper and Wendy — 4.00

CASPER'S GHOSTLAND
Harvey Publications: Winter, 1958-59 - No. 97, 12/77; No. 98, 12/79 (25¢)

1-84 pgs. begin, ends #10	21	42	63	147	324	500
2	9	18	27	63	129	195
3-10	7	14	21	44	82	120
11-20: 11-68 pgs. begin, ends #61. 13-X-Mas-c	5	10	15	35	63	90
21-40	4	8	12	28	47	65
41-61	3	6	9	16	24	32
62-77: 62-52 pgs. begin	2	4	6	9	13	16
78-98: 94-X-Mas-c	2	4	6	8	10	12

NOTE: Most issues contain reprints w/new stories.

CASPER'S GHOSTLAND
American Mythology Prods.: 2018 - No. 2, 2018 ($3.99)

1,2-New stories; art by Shanower & others; Wendy, Hot Stuff, Ghostly Trio app. — 4.00

CASPER SPACESHIP (Casper in Space No. 6 on)
Harvey Publications: Aug, 1972 - No. 5, April, 1973

| 1: 52 pg. Giant | 3 | 6 | 9 | 21 | 33 | 45 |
| 2-5 | 2 | 4 | 6 | 11 | 16 | 20 |

CASPER'S SCARE SCHOOL

	GD 2.0	VG 4.0	FN 6.0	VF 8.0	VF/NM 9.0	NM- 9.2

Ape Entertainment: 2011 - No. 2 ($3.99, limited series)
1,2-New short stories and classic reprints — 4.00

CASPER'S SPOOKSVILLE
American Mythology Prods.: 2020 - No. 4, 2020 ($3.99)
1-4-New stories & reprints; art by Shanower & others; Wendy, Hot Stuff, Spooky app. — 4.00
... FCBD Edition 1 (2019, giveaway) New stories & reprints; art by Shanower — 3.00

CASPER STRANGE GHOST STORIES
Harvey Publications: October, 1974 - No. 14, Jan, 1977 (All 52 pgs.)

	GD	VG	FN	VF	VF/NM	NM-
1	3	6	9	18	28	38
2-14	2	4	6	11	16	20

CASPER, THE FRIENDLY GHOST (See America's Best TV Comics, Famous TV Funday Funnies, The Friendly Ghost..., Nightmare &..., Richie Rich and..., Tastee-Freez, Treasury of Comics, Wendy the Good Little Witch & Wendy Witch World)

CASPER, THE FRIENDLY GHOST (Becomes Harvey Comics Hits No. 61 (No. 6), and then continued with Harvey issue No. 7)(1st Series)
St. John Publishing Co.: Sept, 1949 - No. 5, Aug, 1951
1(1949)-Origin & 1st app. Baby Huey & Herman the Mouse (1st comic app. of Casper and the 1st time the name Casper app. in any media, even films)

	GD	VG	FN	VF	VF/NM	NM-
	811	1622	2433	5920	10,460	15,000
2,3 (2/50 & 8/50)	168	336	504	1075	1838	2600
4,5 (3/51 & 8/51)	110	220	330	704	1202	1700

CASPER, THE FRIENDLY GHOST (Paramount Picture Star...)(2nd Series)
Harvey Publications (Family Comics): No. 7, Dec, 1952 - No. 70, July, 1958
Note: No. 6 is Harvey Comics Hits No. 61 (10/52)

	GD	VG	FN	VF	VF/NM	NM-
7-Baby Huey begins, ends #9	50	100	150	400	900	1400
8,9	25	50	75	175	388	600
10-Spooky begins (1st app., 6/53), ends #70?	46	92	138	359	805	1250
11,12: 2nd & 3rd app. Spooky	17	34	51	117	259	400
13-18: Alfred Harvey app. in story	13	26	39	91	201	310
19-1st app. Nightmare (4/54)	30	60	90	216	483	750
20-Wendy the Witch begins (1st app., 5/54)	64	128	192	512	1156	1800
21-30: 24-Infinity-c	10	20	30	69	147	225
31-40: 38-Early Wendy app. 39-1st app. Samson Honeybun. 40-1st app. Dr. Brainstorm	9	18	27	57	111	165
41-1st Wendy app. on-c	17	34	51	117	259	400
42-50: 43-2nd Wendy-c. 46-1st app. Spooky's girl Pearl.	7	14	21	48	89	130
51-70 (Continues as Friendly Ghost... 8/58) 58-Early app. Bat Balfrey. 63-2nd app. Something the Baby Ghost. 66-1st app. Wildcat Witch	6	12	18	37	60	95

Harvey Comics Classics Vol. 1 TPB (Dark Horse Books, 6/07, $19.95) Reprints Casper's earliest appearances in this little, Little Audrey, and The Friendly Ghost Casper, mostly B&W with some color stories; history, early concept drawings and animation art — 20.00
NOTE: Baby Huey app. 7-9, 11, 121, 14, 16, 20. Buzzy app. 14, 16, 20. Nightmare app. 19, 27, 36, 37, 42, 46, 51, 53, 56, 70. Spooky app. 10-70. Wendy app. 20, 29-31, 35, 37, 38, 41-49, 51, 52, 54-58, 61, 64, 68.

CASPER THE FRIENDLY GHOST (Formerly The Friendly Ghost...)(3rd Series)
Harvey Comics: No. 254, July, 1990 - No. 260, Jan, 1991 ($1.00)
254-260 — 4.00

CASPER THE FRIENDLY GHOST (4th Series)
Harvey Comics: Mar, 1991 - No. 28, Nov, 1994 ($1.00/$1.25/$1.50)
1-Casper becomes Mighty Ghost; Spooky & Wendy app. — 6.00
2-28: 7,8-Post-a. 11-28-($1.50) — 4.00

CASPER THE FRIENDLY GHOST (5th Series)
American Mythology Prods.: 2017 - Present ($3.99)
1,2-New stories and reprints; Hot Stuff, Spooky & Wendy app. — 4.00
... Presents Hot Stuff Sizzlers 1 (2020) Reprints Hot Stuff from 1958-62 — 4.00
... Presents Wendy & the Witch Widow 1 (2020) Reprints Casper from 1955-56 — 4.00

CASPER T.V. SHOWTIME
Harvey Comics: Jan, 1980 - No. 5, Oct, 1980

	GD	VG	FN	VF	VF/NM	NM-
1	2	4	6	9	13	16
2-5	1	2	3	5	7	9

CASSETTE BOOKS (Classics Illustrated)
Cassette Book Co./I.P.S. Publ.: 1984 (48 pgs, b&w comic with cassette tape)
NOTE: This series was illegal. The artwork was illegally obtained, and the Classics Illustrated copyright owner, Twin Circle Publ. sued to get an injunction to prevent the continued sale of these comics. Many C.I. collectors obtained copies before the 1987 injunction, but now they are already scarce. Here again the market is just developing, but sealed mint copies of com ic and tape should be worth at least $25.
1001 (CI#1-A2)New-PC   1002(CI#3-A2)CI-PC   1003(CI#13-A2)CI-PC
1004(CI#25)CI-LDC   1005(CI#10-A2)New-PC   1006(CI#64)CI-LDC

CASTILIAN (See Movie Classics)

CASTLE: A CALM BEFORE STORM (Based on the ABC TV series Castle)
Marvel Comics: Feb, 2013 - No. 5, Jul, 2013 ($3.99, limited series)
1-5-Peter David-s/Robert Atkins-a/Mico Suayan-c — 4.00

CASTLE FULL OF BLACKBIRDS (From the world of Hellboy)
Dark Horse Comics: Sept, 2022 - No. 4, Mar, 2023 ($3.99, limited series)
1-4-Mignola & Slatter-s/Burzo-a — 4.00

CASTLE: RICHARD CASTLE'S ... (Based on the ABC TV series Castle)
Marvel Comics: 2011, 2012 ($19.99, hardcover graphic novels with dustjacket)
Deadly Storm HC (2011) - An "adaptation" of the show's fictional Derrick Storm novel; Bendis & DeConnick-s — 20.00
Storm Season HC (2012) - Bendis & DeConnick-s/Lupacchino-a — 20.00

CASTLEVANIA: THE BELMONT LEGACY
IDW Publishing: March 2005 - No. 5, July, 2005 ($3.99, limited series)
1-5-Marc Andreyko-s/E.J. Su-a — 4.00

CASTLE WAITING
Olio: 1997 - No. 7, 1999 ($2.95, B&W)
Cartoon Books: Vol. 2, Aug, 2000 - No. 16 ($2.95/$3.95, B&W)
Fantagraphics Books: Vol. 3, 2006 - No. 18, 2012 ($5.95/$3.95, B&W)

	GD	VG	FN	VF	VF/NM	NM-
1-Linda Medley-s/a in all	1	2	3	5	6	8

						4.00
2						4.00
3-7						3.00

The Lucky Road TPB r/#1-7 — 17.00
Hiatus Issue (1999) Crilley-c; short stories and previews — 3.00
Vol. 2 #1-6,14-16 (#5&6 also have #12&13 on cover, for series numbering) — 3.00
Vol. 3 #1 ($5.95) r/#15,16 and new story — 6.00
Vol. 3 #2-18 ($3.95) — 4.00

CASUAL FLING
AWA Studios: Feb, 2021 - No. 4, May, 2021 ($3.99, limited series)
1-4-Jason Starr-s/Dalibor Talajic-a — 4.00

CASUAL HEROES
Image Comics (Motown Machineworks): Apr, 1996 ($2.25, unfinished lim. series)
1-Steve Rude-c — 4.00

CAT, T.H.E. (TV) (See T.H.E. Cat)

CAT, THE (See Movie Classics)

CAT, THE (Female hero)
Marvel Comics Group: Nov, 1972 - No. 4, June, 1973

	GD	VG	FN	VF	VF/NM	NM-
1-Origin & 1st app. The Cat (who later becomes Tigra); Mooney-a(i); Wood-c(i)/a(i)	14	28	42	96	211	325
2,3: 2-Marie Severin/Mooney-a. 3-Everett inks	4	8	12	23	37	50
4-Starlin/Weiss-a(p)	4	8	12	25	40	55

CATACLYSM
Marvel Comics: No. 0.1, Dec, 2013 ($3.99)
0.1-Fialkov-s; Galactus threatens the Ultimate Universe — 4.00

CATACLYSM: THE ULTIMATES LAST STAND (Leads into Survive #1)
Marvel Comics: Jan, 2014 - No. 5, Apr, 2014 ($3.99, limited series)
1-5-Galactus in the Ultimate Universe; Ultimates & Spider-Man app.; Bendis-s/Bagley-a — 4.00

CATACLYSM: ULTIMATES
Marvel Comics: Jan, 2014 - No. 3, Mar, 2014 ($3.99, limited series)
1-3-Ultimates vs. Galactus; Fialkov-s/Giandomenico-a — 4.00

CATACLYSM: ULTIMATE SPIDER-MAN
Marvel Comics: Jan, 2014 - No. 3, Mar, 2014 ($3.99, limited series)
1-3-Spider-Man vs. Galactus; Bendis-s/Marquez-a — 4.00

CATACLYSM: ULTIMATE X-MEN
Marvel Comics: Jan, 2014 - No. 3, Mar, 2014 ($3.99, limited series)
1-3-Fialkov-s/Martinez-a; Captain Marvel app. — 4.00

CATALYST: AGENTS OF CHANGE (Also see Comics' Greatest World)
Dark Horse Comics: Feb, 1994 - No. 7, Nov, 1994 ($2.00, limited series)
1-7: 1-Foil stamped logo — 4.00

CATALYST COMIX (From Comics' Greatest World)
Dark Horse Comics: Jul, 2013 - No. 9, Mar, 2014 ($2.99)
1-9-Amazing Grace, Frank Wells, and Agents of Change app.; Casey-s/Grampá-c — 3.00

CATECHISM IN PICTURES
Catechetical Guild: Jan, 1958

	GD	VG	FN	VF	VF/NM	NM-
311-Addison Burbank-a	8	16	24	44	57	70

CAT FROM OUTER SPACE (See Walt Disney Showcase #46)

CATHOLIC COMICS (See Heroes All Catholic...)
Catholic Publications: June, 1946 - V3#10, July, 1949

	GD	VG	FN	VF	VF/NM	NM-
1	36	72	108	211	343	475
2	20	40	60	114	182	250
3-13(7/47): 11-Hollingsworth-a	15	30	45	90	140	190
V2#1-10	13	26	39	72	101	130
V3#1-10: Reprints 10-part Treasure Island serial from Target V2#2-11 (see Key Comics #5)	13	26	39	74	105	135

NOTE: Orlando c-V2#10, V3#5, 6, 8.

CATHOLIC PICTORIAL
Catholic Guild: 1947

	GD	VG	FN	VF	VF/NM	NM-
1-Toth-a(2) (Rare)	43	86	129	271	461	650

CAT-MAN AND KITTEN (From Project Superpowers)
Dynamite Entertainment: 2022 ($4.99, one-shot)
Volume 1 - Set in 1948; Jeff Parker-s/Joseph Cooper-a — 4.00

CAT-MAN COMICS (Formerly Crash Comics No. 1-5)
Holyoke Publishing Co./Continental Magazines V2#12, 7/44 on:
5/41 - No. 17, 1/43; No. 7/43 - No. 22, 12/43; No. 23, 3/44 - No. 26, 11/44; No. 27, 4/45 - No. 30, 12/45; No. 31, 6/46 - No. 32, 8/46

	GD	VG	FN	VF	VF/NM	NM-
1(V1#6)-New costume used (see Crash Comics for 1st app.) by Charles Quinlan; Origin-The Deacon & Sidekick Mickey, Dr. Diamond & Rag-Man; The Black Widow app. Blaze Baylor begins	892	1784	2676	6512	11,506	16,500
2(V1#7)	295	590	885	1873	3237	4600
3(V1#8)-The Pied Piper begins; classic Hitler, Stalin & Mussolini-c	541	1082	1623	3950	6975	10,000
4(V1#9)	290	580	870	1856	3178	4500
5(V2#10, 12/41)-Origin/1st app. The Kitten, Cat-Man's sidekick (cover re-dated w/cat image printed over Nov. date). Most of The Kitten's cover image blocked with sidebar	320	640	960	1240	3920	5600
6(V2#11) Mad scientist-c	486	972	1458	3550	6275	9000
7(V2#12)	295	590	885	1873	3237	4600
8(V2#13,3/42)-Origin Little Leaders; Volton by Kubert begins (his 1st comic book work)	331	662	993	2317	4059	5800
9 (V2#14, 4/42)-Classic-c showing a laughing Kitten slaughtering Japanese soldiers with a machine gun	541	1082	1623	3950	6975	10,000
10 (V2#15, 5/42)-Origin Blackout; Phantom Falcon begins	271	542	813	1734	2967	4200
11 (V3#1, 6/42)-Kubert-a	258	516	774	1651	2826	4000
12 (V3#2),15,17(1/43): 12-Volton by Brodsky, not Kubert	252	504	756	1613	2757	3900

Cataclysm: Ultimate Comics X-Men #3 © MAR

Catholic Comics V2 #8 © CP

Catwoman (2011 series) #28 © DC

	GD 2.0	VG 4.0	FN 6.0	VF 8.0	VF/NM 9.0	NM- 9.2		GD 2.0	VG 4.0	FN 6.0	VF 8.0	VF/NM 9.0	NM- 9.2
13-(9/42)(scarce) Weed of Doom (marijuana)	1000	2000	3000	7600	13,800	20,000	...: Catwoman Dies TPB (2008, $14.99) r/#66-72; Hughes cover gallery						15.00
14-(10/42) World War II-c; Brodsky-a	300	600	900	1980	3440	4900	... Crime Pays TPB (2008, $14.99) r/#73-77						15.00
16 (V3#5, 12/42)-Hitler, Tojo, Mussolini, Goehring-c							...: Crooked Little Town TPB (2003, $14.95) r/#5-10 & Secret Files; Oeming-c						15.00
	960	1920	2880	5050	8775	12,500	...: It's Only a Movie TPB (2007, $14.99) r/#59-65						20.00
18 (V3#8, 7/43)-(scarce)	460	920	1380	2400	4200	6000	... Relentless TPB (2005, $19.95) r/#12-19 & Secret Files						20.00
19 (V2#6, 9/43)-Hitler, Tojo, Mussolini-c	1000	2000	3000	5250	9125	13,000	... Secret Files and Origins (10/02, $4.95) origin-s Oeming-a; profiles and pin-ups						5.00
20 (V2#7, 10/43)-Classic Hitler-c	2000	4000	6000	10,500	18,250	26,000	...Selina's Big Score HC (2002, $24.95) Cooke-s/a; pin-ups by various						25.00
21,22 (V2#8, V2#9)	258	516	774	1651	2826	4000	...Selina's Big Score SC (2003, $17.95) Cooke-s/a; pin-ups by various						18.00
23 (V2#10, 3/44) World War II-c	277	542	813	1734	2967	4200	... The Dark End of the Street TPB (2002, $12.95) r/#1-4 & Slam Bradley back-up stories						
nn(V3#3, 5/44) Rico-a; Schomburg Japanese WWII bondage-c (Rare)							from Detective Comics #759-762						13.00
	486	972	1458	3550	6275	9000	...: The Long Road Home TPB (2009, $17.99) r/#78-82						18.00
nn(V2#12, 7/44) L.B. Cole-a (4 pgs)	194	388	582	1242	2121	3000	...: The Replacements TPB (2007, $14.99) r/#53-58						15.00
nn(V3#1, 9/44)-Origin The Golden Archer; Leatherface app.							...: Wild Ride TPB (2005, $14.99) r/#20-24 & Secret Files #1						15.00
	194	388	582	1242	2121	3000	**CATWOMAN (DC New 52)**						
27-Origins Catman & Kitten retold; L. B. Cole Flag-c; Infantino-a							**DC Comics:** Nov, 2011 - No. 52, Jul, 2016 ($2.99)						
	300	600	900	2010	3505	5000	1-Winick-s/March-a; Batman app.	1	2	3	5	6	8
28-Dr. Macabre app.; L. B. Cole-c/a	649	1298	1947	4738	8369	12,000	2-12: 2-6-March-a. 7,8-Melo-a. 9-Night of the Owls						3.00
29-32-L. B. Cole-c; bondage-#30	300	600	900	1950	3375	4800	13-(12/12) Death of the Family tie-in; die-cut Joker mask-c						12.00
NOTE: *Fuje* a-11, 28(2), 29(3), 30. *Palais* a-11, 16, 27, 28, 29(2), 30(2), 32; c-25(7/44). *Rico* a-11(2), 23, 27, 28.							13-Second printing with chessboard-c						5.00
CAT TALES (3-D)							14-22: 14-Death of the Family tie-in; Joker app						3.00
Eternity Comics: Apr, 1989 ($2.95)							23,24: 23-(10/13) Debut of Joker's Daughter in final panel. 24-Joker's Daughter app.						5.00
1-Felix the Cat-r in 3-D						5.00	25,26,28,49: 25-Zero Year. 26-Joker's Daughter app. 28-Gothtopia. 35-40-Jae Lee-c						3.00
CATWOMAN (Also see Action Comics Weekly #611, Batman #404-407, Detective Comics,							27-($3.99) Gothtopia x-over with Detective Comics #27; Olliffe & Richards-a						4.00
& Superman's Girlfriend Lois Lane #70, 71)							50-($4.99) Harley Quinn, Poison Ivy app.; back-up origin of Black Mask's mask						5.00
DC Comics: Feb, 1989 - No. 4, May, 1989 ($1.50, limited series, mature)							51,52: Black Mask & the False Face Society app.; Middleton-a						3.00
1		2	4	6	10	14	18	#0 (11/12, $2.99) Origin re-told; Nocenti/Melo-a/March-c						3.00
2-4: 3-Batman cameo. 4-Batman app.	1	2	3	5	7	9	Annual 1 (7/13, $4.99) Nocenti-s/Duce-a; Penguin app.						5.00
Her Sister's Keeper (1991, $9.95, trade paperback)-r/#1-4							Annual 2 (2/15, $4.99) Olliffe & McCrea-a						5.00
	2	4	6	11	16	20	...: Election Night 1 (1/17, $4.99) Meredith Finch-s/Shane Davis-a; Prez app.						5.00
CATWOMAN (Also see Showcase '93, Showcase '95 #4, & Batman #404-407)							...: Futures End 1 (11/14, $4.99) Five years later; Olliffe-a/Dodson-c						3.00
DC Comics: Aug, 1993 - No. 94, Jul, 2001 ($1.50-$2.25)							...: Futures End 1 (11/14, $3.99, 3-D cover)						4.00
1-($1.95)-Embossed-c; Bane app.; Balent c-1-10; a-1-10p							**CATWOMAN (Follows Batman #50 [2018])**						
	1	2	3	5	6	8	**DC Comics:** Sept, 2018 - Present ($3.99)						
2-20: 3-Bane flashback cameo. 4-Brief Bane app. 6,7-Knightquest tie-ins; Batman (Azrael)							1-12: 1-Joëlle Jones-s/a; new costume. 7,8-Casagrande-a; Penguin app. 9-Timms-a						4.00
app. 8-1st app. Zephyr. 12-KnightsEnd pt. 6. 13-new Knights End Aftermath.							13-24,26-49: 13-17-Year of the Villain tie-ins. 15-Andolfo-a. 17-Acetate-c. 18-Zatanna app.						
14-(9/94)-Zero Hour						4.00	23,24-Sean Murphy-c. 35-37-"Fear State" tie-ins. 36,37,43,44-Harley Quinn app.						4.00
21-24, 26-30, 33-49: 21-$1.95-c begins. 28,29-Penguin cameo app. 36-Legacy pt. 2.							13-($4.99) Year of the Villain cardstock-c by Artgerm						5.00
38-40-Year Two; Batman, Joker, Penguin & Two-Face app. 46-Two-Face app.						3.00	25-($5.99) Joker War tie-in; Riddler and Penguin app.; 2 back-up stories; J.P. Leon-a						6.00
25,31,32: 25-($2.95)-Robin app. 31,32-Contagion pt. 4 (Reads pt. 5 on-c) & pt. 9.						4.00	50-($5.99) Punchline app.						6.00
50-($2.95, 48 pgs.)-New armored costume						4.00	51-63: 51-55-Eiko Hasigawa as Catwoman. 57,58-Gotham War parts 3,5						4.00
50-($2.95, 48 pgs.)-Collector's Ed. w/metallic ink-c						5.00	Annual 1 (7/19, $4.99) Casagrande & Petrus-a						5.00
51-77: 51-Huntress-c/app. 54-Grayson-s begins. 56-Cataclysm pt.6. 57-Poison Ivy-c/app.							2021 Annual 1 (8/21, $5.99) Ram V-s/Kyle Hotz-a; Azrael app.						6.00
63-65-Joker-c/app. 72-No Man's Land; Ostrander-s begins						3.00	.../Tweety & Sylvester 1 (10/18, $4.99) Simone-s/Miranda-a; Black Canary app.						5.00
78-82: 80-Catwoman goes to jail						3.00	Uncovered 1 (10/23, $5.99) Gallery of recent variant cover art						6.00
83,84,89-Harley Quinn-c/app. 83-Begin $2.25-c	2	4	6	8	10	12	**CATWOMAN 80TH ANNIVERSARY 100-PAGE SUPER SPECTACULAR**						
85-88,90-94						3.00	**DC Comics:** Jun, 2020 ($9.99, squarebound, one-shot)						
#0-(10/94)-Zero Hour tie-in; origin retold; released between #14 & #15						5.00	1-Short stories & pin-ups by various; birth of Helena by King-s/Janin-a; multiple covers						10.00
#1,000,000 (11/98) 853rd Century x-over						3.00	**CATWOMAN/ GUARDIAN OF GOTHAM**						
Annual 1 (1994, $2.95, 68 pgs.)-Elseworlds story; Batman app.; no Balent-a						4.00	**DC Comics:** 1999 - No. 2, 1999 ($5.95, limited series)						
Annual 2,4 ('95, '97, $3.95) 2-Year One story. 4-Pulp Heroes						4.00	1,2-Elseworlds; Moench-s/Balent-a		2	4	6	8	10	12
Annual 3 (1996, $2.95)-Legends of the Dead Earth story						4.00	**CATWOMAN: LONELY CITY**						
...Plus 1 (11/97, $2.95) Screamqueen (Scare Tactics) app.						4.00	**DC Comics (Black Label):** Dec, 2021 - No. 4, Dec, 2022 ($6.99, oversized 8-1/2" x 10-3/4",						
TPB ($9.95) r/#15-19, Balent-c						12.00	lim. series)						
CATWOMAN (Also see Detective Comics #759-762)							1-4-Cliff Chiang-s/a/c; world without Batman; Killer Croc, Poison Ivy, Etrigan app.						7.00
DC Comics: Jan, 2002 - No. 82, Oct, 2008; No. 83, Mar, 2010 ($2.50/$2.99)							**CATWOMAN: NINE LIVES OF A FELINE FATALE**						
1-Darwyn Cooke & Mike Allred-a; Ed Brubaker-s	2	4	6	9	13	16	**DC Comics:** 2004 ($14.95, TPB)						
2-4	1	3	4	6	8	10	nn-Reprints notable stories from Batman #1 to the present; pin-ups by various; Boiland-c						15.00
5-43: 5-9-Rader-a/Paul Pope-c. 10-Morse-c. 16-JG Jones-c. 22-Batman-c/app.							**CATWOMAN: THE MOVIE (2004 Halle Berry movie)**						
34-36-War Games. 43-Killer Croc app.						5.00	**DC Comics:** 2004 ($4.95/$9.95)						
44-Adam Hughes-c begin	2	4	6	8	10	12	1-($4.95) Movie adaptation; Jim Lee-c and sketch pages; Derenick-a						8.00
45-Headlights-c; Hush & Clayface app.	3	6	9	19	30	40	... & Other Cat Tales TPB (2004, $9.95)-r/Movie adaptation; Jim Lee sketch pages,						
46-Captain Cold app.	3	6	9	15	22	30	r/Catwoman #0, Catwoman (2nd series) #11 & 25; photo-c						10.00
47,49,52-57,59-68,71,73,75-79: 52-Catwoman kills Black Mask. 53-One Year Later;							**CATWOMAN/VAMPIRELLA: THE FURIES**						
Helena born. 55-Begin $2.99-c. 56-58-Wildcat app. 75-78-Salvation Run						5.00	**DC Comics/Harris Publ.:** Feb, 1997 ($4.95, squarebound, 46 pgs.) (1st DC/Harris x-over)						
48,69		1	2	3	5	6	8	nn-Reintro Pantha; Chuck Dixon scripts; Balent-c/a	2	4	6	10	14	18
50,58,72-Zatanna-c/app.		1	3	4	6	8	10	**CATWOMAN: WHEN IN ROME**						
51-Classic Selina Kyle mugshot-c	7	14	21	44	82	120	**DC Comics:** Nov, 2004 - No. 6, Aug, 2005 ($3.50, limited series)						
70-Classic-c; "Amazons Attack" tie-in	4	8	12	27	44	60	1-6-Jeph Loeb-s/Tim Sale-a/c; Riddler app.						3.50
74-Zatanna app.	4	8	12	27	44	60							
80-82		1	3	4	6	8	10							
83-(3/10, $2.99) Blackest Night one-shot; Harley Quinn & Black Mask app.; Adam Hughes-c													
	1	3	4	8	9	10							

	GD 2.0	VG 4.0	FN 6.0	VF 8.0	VF/NM 9.0	NM- 9.2

HC (2005, $19.99, dustjacket) r/series; intro by Mark Chiarello; sketch pages — — — — — 20.00
SC (2007, $12.99) r/series; intro by Mark Chiarello; sketch pages — — — — — 13.00

CATWOMAN/WILDCAT
DC Comics: Aug, 1998 - No. 4, Nov, 1998 ($2.50, limited series)
1-4-Chuck Dixon & Beau Smith-s; Stelfreeze-c — — — — — 4.00

CAUGHT
Atlas Comics (VPI): Aug, 1956 - No. 5, Apr, 1957

	GD 2.0	VG 4.0	FN 6.0	VF 8.0	VF/NM 9.0	NM- 9.2
1	39	78	117	240	395	550
2-4: 3-Maneely, Pakula, Torres-a. 4-Maneely-a	20	40	60	117	189	260
5-Crandall, Krigstein-a	20	40	60	120	195	270

NOTE: *Drucker* a-2. *Heck* a-4. *Severin* c-1, 2, 4, 5. *Shores* a-4.

CAVALIER COMICS
A. W. Nugent Publ. Co.: 1945; 1952 (Early DC reprints)

	GD 2.0	VG 4.0	FN 6.0	VF 8.0	VF/NM 9.0	NM- 9.2
2(1945)-Speed Saunders, Fang Gow	26	52	78	154	252	350
2(1952)	15	30	45	83	124	165

CAVALRY, THE : S.H.I.E.L.D. 50TH ANNIVERSARY
Marvel Comics: Nov, 2015 ($3.99, one-shot)
1-Agent Melinda May on a training mission; Luke Ross-a; Keown-c — — — — — 4.00

CAVE CARSON HAS A CYBERNETIC EYE
DC Comics (Young Animal): Dec, 2016 - No. 12, Nov, 2017 ($3.99)
1-12-Jonathan Rivera & Gerald Way-s/Michael Avon Oeming-a; back-up Tom Scioli-s/a in #1-6. 7-Superman-c/app. — — — — — 4.00
.../ Swamp Thing Special 1 (4/18, $4.99) Part 4 of Milk Wars crossover; Rivera-a/Foss-a — — — — — 5.00

CAVE CARSON HAS AN INTERSTELLAR EYE
DC Comics (Young Animal): May, 2018 - No. 6, Oct, 2018 ($3.99)
1-6-Jonathan Rivera-s/Michael Avon Oeming-a; back-up with Maybury-a in #1-5 — — — — — 4.00

CAVE GIRL (Also see Africa)
Magazine Enterprises: No. 11, 1953 - No. 14, 1954

	GD 2.0	VG 4.0	FN 6.0	VF 8.0	VF/NM 9.0	NM- 9.2
11(A-1 82)-Origin; all Cave Girl stories	71	142	213	454	777	1100
12(A-1 96), 13(A-1 116), 14(A-1 125)-Thunda by Powell in each	45	90	135	284	480	675

NOTE: *Powell* c/a in all.

CAVE GIRL
AC Comics: 1988 ($2.95, 44 pgs.) (16 pgs. of color, rest B&W)
1-Powell-r/Cave Girl #11; Nyoka photo back-c from movie; Powell/Bill Black-c; Special Limited Edition on-c — — — — — 4.00

CAVE KIDS (TV) (See Comic Album #16)
Gold Key: Feb, 1963 - No. 16, Mar, 1967 (Hanna-Barbera)

	GD 2.0	VG 4.0	FN 6.0	VF 8.0	VF/NM 9.0	NM- 9.2
1	6	12	18	41	76	110
2-5	4	8	12	23	37	50
6-16: 7,12-Pebbles & Bamm Bamm app. 16-1st Space Kidettes	3	6	9	19	30	40

CAVEWOMAN
Basement Comics: Jan, 1994 - No. 6, 1995 ($2.95)

	GD 2.0	VG 4.0	FN 6.0	VF 8.0	VF/NM 9.0	NM- 9.2
1	10	20	30	64	132	200
2	4	8	12	25	40	55
3-6	2	4	6	10	14	18

...: Meets Explorers ('97, $2.95) — — — — — 5.00
...: One-Shot Special (7/00, $2.95) Massey-s/a — — — — — 5.00

CBLDF (Comic Book Legal Defense Fund) (See Liberty Comics)

CELESTINE (See Violator Vs. Badrock #1)
Image Comics (Extreme): May, 1996 - No. 2, June, 1996 ($2.50, limited series)
1,2: Warren Ellis scripts — — — — — 4.00

CEMETERY BEACH
Image Comics: Sept, 2018 - No. 7, Mar, 2019 ($3.99)
1-7-Warren Ellis-s/Jason Howard-a — — — — — 4.00

CENTIPEDE (Based on Atari videogame)
Dynamite Entertainment: 2017 - No. 5, 2017 ($3.99)
1-5: 1-Bemis-s/Marron-a; covers by Marron, Francavilla & Schkade — — — — — 4.00

CENTURION OF ANCIENT ROME, THE
Zondervan Publishing House: 1958 (no month listed) (B&W, 36 pgs.)

	GD 2.0	VG 4.0	FN 6.0	VF 8.0	VF/NM 9.0	NM- 9.2
(Rare) All by Jay Disbrow	113	226	339	718	1234	1750

CENTURIONS (TV)
DC Comics: June, 1987 - No. 4, Sept, 1987 (75¢, limited series)
1-4 — — — — — 4.00

CENTURY: DISTANT SONS
Marvel Comics: Feb, 1996 ($2.95, one-shot)
1-Wraparound-c — — — — — 4.00

CENTURY OF COMICS (See Promotional Comics section)

CENTURY WEST
Image Comics: Sept, 2013 ($7.99, squarebound, graphic novel)
nn-Howard Chaykin-s/a/c — — — — — 8.00

CEREBUS BI-WEEKLY
Aardvark-Vanaheim: Dec. 2, 1988 - No. 27, Nov. 24, 1989 ($1.25, B&W)
Reprints Cerebus The Aardvark #1-27

	GD 2.0	VG 4.0	FN 6.0	VF 8.0	VF/NM 9.0	NM- 9.2
1-16, 18, 19, 21-27:						4.00
17-Hepcats app.	2	4	6	8	10	12
20-Milk & Cheese app.	2	4	6	10	12	15

CEREBUS: CHURCH & STATE
Aardvark-Vanaheim: Feb, 1991 - No. 30, Apr, 1992 ($2.00, B&W, bi-weekly)
1-30: r/Cerebus #51-80 — — — — — 4.00

CEREBUS: HIGH SOCIETY
Aardvark-Vanaheim: Feb, 1990 - No. 25, 1991 ($1.70, B&W)

1-25: r/Cerebus #26-50 — — — — — 4.00

CEREBUS IN HELL?
Aardvark-Vanaheim: No. 0, 2016; No. 1, Jan, 2017 - No. 4, Apr, 2017 ($4.00, B&W)
0-4-Sim & Atwal-s; Cerebus figures placed over original Gustave Doré artwork of Hell — — — — — 4.00
Cerberus In Hell 1 (12/18, $4.00) new pages and reprints; cover swipe of Cerebus #1 — — — — — 4.00
Cerebus The Vark Knight Returns 1 (12/17, $4.00) new pages and reprints — — — — — 4.00
...Presents #59: Defective Comics 1 (2/22, $8.00) Cover swipe of Detective Comics #27 — — — — — 8.00
The Death of Cerebus In Hell 1 (11/17, $4.00) new pages and reprints — — — — — 4.00
... 2021 1 (1/21, $4.00) Cerebus figures with Doré art; calendar pages with parody covers — — — — — 4.00

CEREBUS JAM
Aardvark-Vanaheim: Apr, 1985
1-Eisner, Austin, Dave Sim-a (Cerebus vs. Spirit) — — — — — 6.00

CEREBUS THE AARDVARK (See A-V in 3-D, Nucleus, Power Comics)
Aardvark-Vanaheim: Dec, 1977 - No. 300, March, 2004 ($1.70/$2.00/$2.25, B&W)

	GD 2.0	VG 4.0	FN 6.0	VF 8.0	VF/NM 9.0	NM- 9.2
0						5.00
0-Gold						20.00
1-1st app. Cerebus; 2000 print run; most copies poorly printed	259	518	777	2137	4819	7500

Note: There is a counterfeit version known to exist. It can be distinguished from the original in the following ways: inside cover is glossy instead of flat, black background on the front cover is blotted or spotty. Reports show that a counterfeit #2 also exists.

	GD 2.0	VG 4.0	FN 6.0	VF 8.0	VF/NM 9.0	NM- 9.2
2-Dave Sim art in all	23	46	69	161	356	550
3-Origin Red Sophia	15	30	45	100	220	340
4-Origin Elrod the Albino	11	22	33	76	163	250
5,6	9	18	27	59	117	175
7-10	6	12	18	37	66	95
11,12: 11-Origin The Cockroach	5	10	15	31	53	75
13-15: 14-Origin Lord Julius	4	8	12	28	47	65
16-20	3	6	9	21	33	45
21-Barry Smith letter in letter column	5	10	15	33	57	80
22-Low distribution; no cover price	4	8	12	25	40	55
23-30: 23-Preview of Wandering Star by Teri S. Wood. 26-High Society begins, ends #50	3	6	9	16	23	30
31-Origin Moonroach	3	6	9	16	24	32
32-40, 53-Intro. Wolveroach (brief app.)	2	4	6	8	10	12
41-50,52: 48-1st app. Joshua "Wolverine" MacAlistaire in back-up. 52-Church & State begins, ends #111; Cutey Bunny app.	1	2	3	5	7	9
51,54: 51-Cutey Bunny app. 54-1st full Wolveroach story	2	4	6	8	11	14
55,56-Wolveroach app.; Normalman back-ups by Valentino	1	3	4	6	8	10
57-100: 61,62: Flaming Carrot app. 65-Gerhard begins						5.00
101-160: 104-Flaming Carrot app. 112/113-Double issue. 114-Jaka's Story begins, ends #136. 139-Melmoth begins, ends #150. 151-Mothers & Daughters begins, ends #200						4.00
161-Bone app.	1	3	4	6	8	10
162-231: 175-($2.25, 44 pgs). 186-Strangers in Paradise cameo. 201-Guys storyline begins; Eddie Campbell's Bacchus app. 220-231-Rick's Story						3.00
232-265-Going Home						3.00
266-288,291-299-Latter Days: 267-Five-Bar Gate. 276-Spore (Spawn spoof)						3.00
289&290 ($4.50) Two issues combined						5.00
300-Final issue						3.00
Free Cerebus (Giveaway, 1991-92?, 36 pgs.)-All-r						5.00

CEREBUS THE DUCK
Aardvark-Vanaheim: Apr, 2021 ($4.00, B&W, one-shot)
1-Cerebus figures placed over original Gustave Doré artwork; Howard the Duck #1 c-swipe 4.00

CEREBUS THE EMILY
Aardvark-Vanaheim: Mar, 2022 ($4.00, B&W, one-shot)
1-Cerebus figures placed over original Gustave Doré artwork; Emily the Strange #4 c-swipe 4.00

CEREBUS WOMAN
Aardvark-Vanaheim: May, 2019 ($4.00, B&W, one-shot)
1-Cerebus figures placed over original Gustave Doré artwork; Wonder Woman #1 c-swipe 4.00

CHAIN GANG WAR
DC Comics: July, 1993 - No. 12, June, 1994 ($1.75)
1-($2.50)-Embossed silver foil-c, Dave Johnson-c/a — — — — — 5.00
2-4,6-12: 3-Deathstroke app. 4-Brief Deathstroke app. 6-New Batman (Azrael) cameo. 11-New Batman-c/story. 12-New Batman app. — — — — — 4.00
5-($2.50)-Foil-c; Deathstroke app; new Batman cameo (1 panel) — — — — — 5.00

CHAINS OF CHAOS
Harris Comics: Nov, 1994 - No. 3, Jan, 1995 ($2.95, limited series)
1-3-Re-Intro of The Rook w/ Vampirella — — — — — 5.00

CHALLENGE OF THE SUPER SONS (Jon Kent and Damian Wayne)
DC Comics: Jun, 2021 - No. 7, Dec, 2021 ($3.99, limited series)
1-7-Tomasi-s/Raynor-a; Justice League, Felix Faust & Vandal Savage app. — — — — — 4.00

CHALLENGE OF THE UNKNOWN (Formerly Love Experiences)
Ace Magazines: No. 6, Sept, 1950 (See Web Of Mystery No. 19)

	GD 2.0	VG 4.0	FN 6.0	VF 8.0	VF/NM 9.0	NM- 9.2
6- "Villa of the Vampire" used in N.Y. Joint Legislative Comm. Publ; Sekowsky-a	77	154	231	493	847	1200

CHALLENGER, THE
Interfaith Publications/T.C. Comics: 1945 - No. 4, Oct-Dec, 1946

	GD 2.0	VG 4.0	FN 6.0	VF 8.0	VF/NM 9.0	NM- 9.2
nn; nd; 32 pgs.; Origin the Challenger Club; Anti-Fascist with funny animal filler	676	1352	2028	4935	8718	12,500
2-Classic Pandora's Box demons-c; Kubert-a	116	232	348	742	1271	1800
3,4: Kubert-a; 4-Fuje-a	61	122	183	390	670	950

CHALLENGERS OF THE FANTASTIC
Marvel Comics (Amalgam): June 1997 ($1.95, one-shot)
1-Karl Kesel-s/Tom Grummett-a — — — — — 4.00

CHALLENGERS OF THE UNKNOWN (See Showcase #6, 7, 11, 12, Super DC Giant, and Super Team Family) (See Showcase Presents for B&W reprints)
National Per. Publ./DC Comics: 4-5/58 - No. 77, 12-1/70-71; No. 78, 2/73 - No. 80, 6-7/73; No.

Centipede #5 © Atari

Chamber of Chills #5 © MAR

The Champions #13 © MAR

	GD 2.0	VG 4.0	FN 6.0	VF 8.0	VF/NM 9.0	NM- 9.2
81, 6-7/77 - No. 87, 6-7/78						
1-(4-5/58)-Kirby/Stein-a(2); Kirby-c	241	482	723	1988	4494	7000
2-Kirby/Stein-a(2)	75	150	225	600	1350	2100
3-Kirby/Stein-a(2); Rocky returns from space with powers similar to the Fantastic Four (9/58)						
	71	142	213	568	1284	2000
4-8-Kirby/Wood-a plus cover to #8	46	92	138	340	770	1200
9,10	27	54	81	194	435	675
11-Grey tone-c	36	72	108	266	596	925
12-15: 14-Origin/1st app. Multi-Man (villain)	19	38	57	131	291	450
16-22: 18-Intro. Cosmo, the Challengers Spacepet. 22-Last 10¢ issue						
	13	26	39	86	188	290
23-30	9	18	27	60	120	180
31-Retells origin of the Challengers	9	18	27	61	123	185
32-40	7	14	21	44	82	120
41-47,49,50,52-60: 43-New look begins. 47-1st Sponge-Man. 49-Intro. Challenger Corps.						
55-Death of Red Ryan. 60-Red Ryan returns	5	10	15	33	57	80
48,51: 48-Doom Patrol app. 51-Sea Devils app.	5	10	15	34	60	85
61-68: 64,65-Kirby origin-r, parts 1 & 2. 66-New logo. 68-Last 12¢ issue.						
	4	8	12	25	40	55
69-73,75-80: 69-1st app. Corinna. 77-Last 15¢ issue	3	6	9	17	26	35
74-Deadman by Tuska/Adams; 1 pg. Wrightson-a	7	14	21	44	82	120
81,83-87: 81-(6-7/77). 83-87-Swamp Thing app. 84-87-Deadman app.						
	2	4	6	9	12	15
82-Swamp Thing begins (thru #87, c/s	3	6	9	14	19	24
NOTE: N. Adams c-67, 68, 70, 72, 74i, 81i. Buckler c-83-86p. Giffen a-83-87p. Kirby a-75-80r; c-75, 77, 78. Kubert c-64, 66, 69, 76, 79. Nasser c/a-81p, 82p. Tuska a-73. Wood r-76.						

CHALLENGERS OF THE UNKNOWN
DC Comics: Mar, 1991 - No. 8, Oct, 1991 ($1.75, limited series)

1-Jeph Loeb scripts & Tim Sale-a in all (1st work together); Bolland-c						5.00
2-8: 2-Superman app. 3-Dr. Fate app. 6-G. Kane-c(p). 7-Steranko-c/swipe for Art Adams						4.00
... Must Die! (2004, $19.95, TPB) r/series; intro by Bendis; Sale sketch pages						20.00
NOTE: Art Adams c-7. Hempel a-8. Gil Kane c-6p. Sale a-1-8; c-3, 8. Wagner c-4.						

CHALLENGERS OF THE UNKNOWN
DC Comics: Feb, 1997 - No. 18, July, 1998 ($2.25)

1-18: 1-Intro new team; Leon-c/a(p) begins. 4-Origin of new team. 11,12-Batman app.						
15-Millennium Giants x-over; Superman-c/app.						4.00

CHALLENGERS OF THE UNKNOWN
DC Comics: Aug, 2004 - No. 6, Jan, 2005 ($2.95, limited series)

1-6-Intro. new team; Howard Chaykin-s/a						3.00

CHALLENGE TO THE WORLD
Catechetical Guild: 1951 (10¢, 36 pgs.)

nn	7	14	21	37	46	55

CHAMBER (See Generation X and Uncanny X-Men)
Marvel Comics: Oct, 2002 - No. 4, Jan, 2003 ($2.99, limited series)

1-4-Bachalo-c/Vaughan-s/Ferguson-a. 1-Cyclops app.						3.00

CHAMBER OF CHILLS (Formerly Blondie Comics No. 20; ...of Clues No. 27 on)
Harvey Publications/Witches Tales: No. 21, June, 1951 - No. 26, Dec, 1954

	GD 2.0	VG 4.0	FN 6.0	VF 8.0	VF/NM 9.0	NM- 9.2
21 (#1)	194	388	582	1242	2121	3000
22,24 (#2,4)	61	122	183	390	670	950
23 (#3)-Excessive violence; eyes torn out	77	154	231	493	847	1200
5(2/52)-Decapitation, acid in face scene	52	104	156	328	552	775
6-Woman melted alive	57	114	171	362	619	875
7-Used in SOTI, pg. 389; decapitation/severed head panels						
	60	120	180	381	653	925
8-10: 8-Decapitation panels	47	94	141	296	498	700
11,12	42	84	126	265	445	625
13,15-17,22,24-Nostrand-a in all. 13-Decapitation panels						
	45	90	135	284	480	675
14-Spider-Man precursor (11/52)	60	120	180	381	653	925
18-Atom bomb panels	116	232	348	742	1271	1800
19-Classic-c; Nostrand-a	2250	4500	6750	17,100	31,050	40,000
20-Classic Nostrand-c	81	162	243	518	884	1250
21-Classic skull-c; decapitation panels	155	310	465	992	1696	2400
23-Classic-c of corpse kissing woman; Nostrand-a	811	1622	2433	5920	10,460	15,000
25,26	43	86	129	271	461	650
NOTE: About half the issues contain bondage, torture, sadism, perversion, gore, cannabalism, eyes ripped out, acid in face, etc. Elias c-4-11, 14-21, 26. Kremer a-12, 17. Palais a-21(1), 23. Nostrand/Powell a-13, 15, 16. Powell a-21, 23, 24('51), 5-8, 11, 13, 18-21, 23-25. Bondage-c-24('51). 7-25-r/#5; c/d-r/#9.						

CHAMBER OF CHILLS
Marvel Comics Group: Nov, 1972 - No. 25, Nov, 1976

	GD 2.0	VG 4.0	FN 6.0	VF 8.0	VF/NM 9.0	NM- 9.2
1-Harlan Ellison adaptation	6	12	18	37	66	95

	GD 2.0	VG 4.0	FN 6.0	VF 8.0	VF/NM 9.0	NM- 9.2
2-5: 2-1st app. John Jakes' Brak the Barbarian	3	6	9	17	26	35
6-25: 22,23-(Regular 25¢ editions)	3	6	9	16	23	30
22,23-(30¢-c variants, limited distribution)(5,7/76)	8	16	24	54	102	150
NOTE: Adkins a-1i, 2i. Brunner a-2-4; c-4. Chaykin a-4. Ditko r-14, 16, 19, 23, 24. Everett a-3i, 11i,21r. Heath a-1r. Gil Kane c-2p. Kirby r-11, 18, 19, 22. Powell a-13r. Russell a-1p, 2p. Shores a-5 . Williamson/Mayo a-13r. Robert E. Howard horror story adaptation-2, 3.						

CHAMBER OF CLUES (Formerly Chamber of Chills)
Harvey Publications: No. 27, Feb, 1955 - No. 28, April, 1955

27-Kerry Drake-r/#19; Powell-a; last pre-code	16	24	44	57	70
28-Kerry Drake	7	14	21	37	46	55

CHAMBER OF DARKNESS (Monsters on the Prowl #9 on)
Marvel Comics Group: Oct, 1969 - No. 8, Dec, 1970

	GD 2.0	VG 4.0	FN 6.0	VF 8.0	VF/NM 9.0	NM- 9.2
1-Buscema-a(p)	8	16	24	54	102	150
2,3: 2-Neal Adams scripts. 3-Smith, Buscema-a	5	10	15	30	50	70
4-A Conan-esque tryout by Smith (4/70); reprinted in Conan #16; Marie						
Severin/Everett-a	9	18	27	62	126	190
5,8: 5-H.P. Lovecraft adaptation. 8-Wrightson-c	4	8	12	27	44	60
6	4	8	12	23	37	50
7-Wrightson-c/a, 7pgs. (his 1st work at Marvel); Wrightson draws himself in						
1st & last panels; Kirby/Ditko-r; last 15¢-c	6	12	18	42	79	115
1-(1/72; 25¢ Special, 52 pgs.)	4	8	12	25	40	55
NOTE: Adkins/Everett a-8. Buscema a-Special 1r. Craig a-5. Ditko a-6-8r. Heck a-1, 2, 8, Special 1r. Kirby a(p)-4, 5, 7r. Kirby/Everett c-5. Severin/Everett c-6. Shores a-2, 3i, Special 1r. Sutton a-1, 2i, 4, 7, Special 1r. Wrightson c-7, 8.						

CHAMP COMICS (Formerly Champion No. 1-10)
Worth Publ. Co./Champ Publ./Family Comics(Harvey Publ.): No. 11, Oct, 1940 - No. 24, Dec, 1942; No. 25, April, 1944

	GD 2.0	VG 4.0	FN 6.0	VF 8.0	VF/NM 9.0	NM- 9.2
11-Human Meteor cont'd. from Champion	168	336	504	1075	1838	2600
12-17,20: 14,15-Crandall-c. 20-The Green Ghost app.; Japanese WWII-c						
	135	270	405	864	1482	2100
18,19-Simon-c. 19-The Wasp app.	168	336	504	1075	1838	2600
21-23,25: 22-The White Mask app. 23-Flag-c	110	220	330	704	1202	1700
24-Hitler, Tojo & Mussolini-c	300	600	900	2010	3505	5000

CHAMPION (See Gene Autry's...)

CHAMPION COMICS
Worth Publ. Co.: Oct, 1939 (ashcan)

nn-Ashcan comic, not distributed to newsstands, only for in house use. A FN/VF copy sold for $2,261.76 in 2010.

CHAMPION COMICS (Formerly Speed Comics #1?; Champ Comics No. 11 on)
Worth Publ. Co.(Harvey Publications): No. 2, Dec, 1939 - No. 10, Aug, 1940 (no No.1)

	GD 2.0	VG 4.0	FN 6.0	VF 8.0	VF/NM 9.0	NM- 9.2
2-The Champ, The Blazing Scarab, Neptina, Liberty Lads, Jungleman, Bill						
Handy, Swingtime Sweetie begin	155	310	465	992	1696	2400
3-Classic-c	135	270	405	864	1482	2100
4-7: 7-The Human Meteor begins?	103	206	309	659	1130	1600
8,10: 8-Minute-c. 10-Bondage-c by Kirby	314	628	942	2198	3849	5500
9-1st S&K-c (1st collaboration together)	377	754	1131	2639	4620	6600

CHAMPIONS, THE
Marvel Comics Group: Oct, 1975 - No. 17, Jan, 1978

	GD 2.0	VG 4.0	FN 6.0	VF 8.0	VF/NM 9.0	NM- 9.2
1-Origin & 1st app. The Champions (The Angel, Black Widow, Ghost Rider, Hercules,						
Iceman) Venus x-over	3	6	9	17	37	66	95
2-6,8-10: 2-3 vs. Pluto, Venus x-over. 5,6-(Regular 25¢ edition)(4-6/76). 5-1st Rampage.						
6-Kirby-a(3). 8-Champions vs. Darkstar, Griffin & Titanium Man; 1st Yuri Petrovitch as new						
Crimson Dynamo. 10-Champions vs. Crimson Dynamo & Titanium Man						
	2	4	6	13	18	22
5,6-(30¢-c variants, limited distribution)	5	10	15	33	57	80
7-(Regular 25¢ edition)(8/76) 1st Darkstar, Griffin & Titanium Man app.						
	5	10	15	31	53	75
7-(30¢-c variant, limited distribution)	8	16	24	51	96	140
11-15: 11-Byrne-a begins. 12-Stilt-Man, Black Goliath &						
The Stranger app. 13-Black Goliath & The Stranger app. 14,15-(Regular 30¢ edition).						
14-1st Swarm; Iceman dons new costume. 15-Origin Swarm						
	3	6	9	13	19	24
14,15-(35¢-c variant, limited distribution)	7	14	21	46	86	125
16-Continued from Super-Villain Team-Up #14; Magneto & Dr. Doom app; Hulk & Beast						
guest app.	3	6	9	13	18	25
17-Last issue; vs. The Brotherhood of Evil Mutants; Sentinels app.; Champions app. next in						
Spectacular Spider-Man #17	3	6	9	14	19	24
... Classic Vol. 1 TPB (2006, $19.99) r/#1-11; unused cover to #7						20.00
... Classic Vol. 2 TPB (2007, $19.99) r/#12-17, Iron Man Ann. #4, Avengers #163, Super-Villain						
Team-Up #14 and Peter Parker, The Spectacular Spider-Man #17-18						20.00
...: No Time For Losers (2016, $7.99) r/#1-3,14,15; art by Heck, Tuska & Byrne						8.00
NOTE: Buckler/Adkins c-3. Byrne a-11-15, 17. Kane/Adkins c-1. Kane/Layton c-11. Tuska a-3p, 4p, 6p, 7p.						

	GD	VG	FN	VF	VF/NM	NM-		GD	VG	FN	VF	VF/NM	NM-
	2.0	4.0	6.0	8.0	9.0	9.2		2.0	4.0	6.0	8.0	9.0	9.2

Ghost Rider c-1-4, 7, 8, 10, 14, 16, 17 (4, 10, 14 are more prominent).

CHAMPIONS (Game)
Eclipse Comics: June, 1986 - No. 6, Feb, 1987 (limited series)

1-6: 1-Intro Flare; based on game. 5-Origin Flare						4.00

CHAMPIONS (Also see The League of Champions)
Hero Comics: Sept, 1987 - No. 12, 1989 ($1.95)

1-12: 1-Intro The Marksman & The Rose. 4-Origin Malice						4.00
Annual 1(1988, $2.75, 52 pgs.)-Origin of Giant						5.00

CHAMPIONS
Marvel Comics: Dec, 2016 - No. 27, Feb, 2019 ($4.99/$3.99)

1-($4.99) Ms. Marvel, Spider-Man (Miles), Hulk (Amadeus), Nova, Viv Vision team						5.00
2-24,26,27-($3.99) 3-Young Cyclops joins. 5-Gwenpool app. 9-Intro. Red Locust. 10,11-Secret Empire tie-ins. 13-15-Avengers app. 21-Zub-s/Izzaakse-a begins. 22-New Ironheart armor. 23-Man-Thing app. 27-Champions in Weirdworld						4.00
25-($4.99) Champions go to Weirdworld; Man-Thing app.						5.00
#1.MU (4/17, $4.99) Monsters Unleashed tie-in; Whitely-s/Stein & Brandt-a						5.00
Annual 1 (2/19, $4.99) Spotlight on Snowguard; Marcus To-a						5.00

CHAMPIONS
Marvel Comics: Mar, 2019 - No. 10, Dec, 2019 ($3.99)

1-10: 1-Zub-s/Cummings-a; Mephisto app. 5,6-War of The Realms tie-in						4.00

CHAMPIONS (Takes place after Outlawed #1)
Marvel Comics: Dec, 2020 - No. 10, Dec, 2021 ($3.99)

1-10: 1-Eve L. Ewing-s/Simone Di Meo-a; Ms. Marvel, Nova, Spider-Man (Miles) app.						4.00

CHAMPION SPORTS
National Periodical Publications: Oct-Nov, 1973 - No. 3, Feb-Mar, 1974

	GD	VG	FN	VF	VF/NM	NM-
1	3	6	9	16	23	30
2,3	2	4	6	9	12	15

CHANNEL ZERO
Image Comics: Feb, 1998 - No. 5 ($2.95, B&W, limited series)

1-5, ...Dupe (1/99) -Brian Wood-s/a						4.00

CHAOS (See The Crusaders)

CHAOS!
Dynamite Entertainment: 2014 - No. 6, 2014 ($3.99, limited series)

1-6-Seeley-s/Andolfo-a; multiple covers on each. Purgatori, Evil Ernie, Chastity app.						4.00
... Holiday Special 2014 ($5.99) Short stories by various; Lupacchino-c						6.00
...: Smiley The Psychotic Button 1 (2015, $4.99) origin re-told; Andolfo-c						5.00

CHAOS! BIBLE
Chaos! Comics: Nov, 1995 ($3.30, one-shot)

1-Profiles of characters & creators						4.00

CHAOS! CHRONICLES
Chaos! Comics: Feb, 2000 ($3.50, one-shot)

1-Profiles of characters, checklist of Chaos! comics and products						3.50

CHAOS EFFECT, THE
Valiant: 1994

	GD	VG	FN	VF	VF/NM	NM-
Alpha (Giveaway w/trading card checklist)						4.00
Alpha-Red variant						5.00
Omega (11/94, $2.25); Epilogue Pt. 1, 2 (12/94, 1/95; $2.95)						4.00
Omega-Gold variant	1	3	4	6	8	10

CHAOS! GALLERY
Chaos! Comics: Aug, 1997 ($2.95, one-shot)

1-Pin-ups of characters						5.00

CHAOS! QUARTERLY
Chaos! Comics: Oct, 1995 -No. 3, May, 1996 ($4.95, quarterly)

1-3: 1-Anthology; Lady Death-c by Julie Bell. 2-Boris "Lady Demon"-c						5.00
1-Premiere Edition (7,500)						25.00

CHAOS WAR
Marvel Comics: Dec, 2010 - No. 4, Mr, 2011 ($3.99, limited series)

1-5-Hercules, Thor and others vs. Chaos King; Pham-a. 3-5-Galactus app.						4.00
... Alpha Flight 1 (1/11, $3.99) McCann-s/Brown-a						4.00
... Ares 1 (2/11, $3.99) Oeming-s/Segovia-a						4.00
... Chaos King 1 (1/11, $3.99) Kaluta-a/c; Monclair-s						4.00
... Dead Avengers 1-3 (1/11 - No. 3, 3/11, $3.99) Grummett-a; Capt. Marvel app.						4.00
... God Squad 1 (2/11, $3.99) Sumerak-s/Panosian-a						4.00
... Thor 1,2 (1/11 - No. 2, 2/11, $3.99) DeMatteis-s/Ching-a						4.00
...: X-Men 1,2 (2/11 - No. 2, 3/11, $3.99) Braithwaite-a; Thunderbird, Banshee app.						4.00

CHAPEL (Also see Youngblood & Youngblood Strikefile #1-3)
Image Comics (Extreme Studios): No. 1 Feb, 1995 - No. 2, May, 1995 ($2.50, limited series)

1,2						4.00

CHAPEL (Also see Youngblood & Youngblood Strikefile #1-3)
Image Comics (Extreme Studios): V2 #1, Aug, 1995 - No. 7, Apr, 1996 ($2.50)

V2#1-7: 4-Babewatch x-over. 5-vs. Spawn. 7-Shadowhawk c/app; Shadowhunt x-over						4.00
#1-Quesada & Palmiotti variant-c						4.00

CHAPEL (Also see Youngblood & Youngblood Strikefile #1-3)
Awesome Entertainment: Sept, 1997 ($2.99, one-shot)

1 (Reg. & alternate covers)						4.00

CHARIOT
Artists, Writers & Artisans, Inc.: Mar, 2021 - No. 5, Jul, 2021 ($3.99, limited series)

1-5-Bryan Edward Hill-s/Priscilla Petraites-a						4.00

CHARISMAGIC
Aspen MLT: No. 0, Mar, 2011 - No. 6, Jul, 2012 ($1.99/$2.99/$3.50)

0-($1.99) Khary Randolph-a/ Vince Hernandez-s; 3 covers						3.00
1-4-($2.99) 1-4-Four covers on each						3.00
5,6-($3.50) Multiple covers on each						3.50
... Primer 1 (2/18, 25¢) Character profiles and story histories						3.00

...: The Death Princess 1-3 (11/12 - No. 3, 7/13, $3.99) Hernandez-s/Emilio Lopez-a						4.00

CHARISMAGIC (Volume 2)
Aspen MLT: May, 2013 - No. 6, Nov, 2013 ($1.00/$3.99)

1-($1.00) Vincenzo Cucca-a/ Vince Hernandez-s; multiple covers						3.00
2-6-($3.99) Multiple covers on each						4.00

CHARISMAGIC (Volume 3)
Aspen MLT: Feb, 2018 - No. 5, Jun, 2018 ($3.99)

1-5-Joey Vazquez-a/ Vince Hernandez-s; multiple covers						4.00

CHARLEMAGNE (Also see War Dancer)
Defiant: Mar, 1994 - No. 5, July, 1994 ($2.50)

1-(3/94, $3.50, 52 pgs.)-Adam Pollina-a						5.00
2,3,5: Adam Pollina-c/a. 2-War Dancer app. 5-Pre-Schism issue.						4.00
4-($3.25, 52 pgs.)						5.00
#0 (Hero Illustrated giveaway)-Adam Pollina-c/a; 1st app. of Ngu						4.00

CHARLIE CHAN (See Big Shot Comics, Columbia Comics, Feature Comics & The New Advs. of...)

CHARLIE CHAN (The Adventures of...) (Zaza The Mystic No. 10 on) (TV)
Crestwood(Prize) No. 1-5; Charlton No. 6(6/55) on: 6-7/48 - No. 5, 2-3/49; No. 6, 6/55 - No. 9, 3/56

	GD	VG	FN	VF	VF/NM	NM-
1-S&K-c, 2 pgs.; Infantino-a	110	220	330	704	1202	1700
2-5-S&K-c: 3-S&K-c/a	55	110	165	352	601	850
6 (6/55-Charlton)-S&K-c	40	80	120	246	411	575
7-9	24	48	72	142	234	325

CHARLIE CHAN
Dell Publishing Co.: Oct-Dec, 1965 - No. 2, Mar, 1966

	GD	VG	FN	VF	VF/NM	NM-
1-Springer-a/c	5	10	15	31	53	75
2-Springer-a/c	3	6	9	21	33	45

CHARLIE McCARTHY (See Edgar Bergen Presents...)
Dell Publishing Co.: No. 171, Nov, 1947 - No. 571, July, 1954 (See True Comics #14)

	GD	VG	FN	VF	VF/NM	NM-
Four Color 171	28	56	84	202	451	700
Four Color 196-Part photo-c; photo back-c	17	34	51	119	265	410
1(3-5/49)-Part photo-c; photo back-c	13	26	39	91	201	310
2-9(7/52; #5,6-52 pgs.)	8	16	24	51	96	140
Four Color 445,478,527,571	7	14	21	44	82	120

CHARLIE'S ANGELS (Based on the 1970s TV series)
Dynamite Entertainment: 2018 - No. 5, 2018 ($3.99)

1-5-John Layman-s/Joe Eisma-a; multiple covers on each; Jimmy Carter app.						4.00

CHARLIE'S ANGELS VS. THE BIONIC WOMAN (Based on the 1970s TV series)
Dynamite Entertainment: 2019 - No. 4, 2019 ($3.99)

1-4-Cameron DeOrdio-s/Soo Lee-a; multiple covers on each						4.00

CHARLTON ACTION: FEATURING "STATIC" (Also see Eclipse Monthly)
Charlton Comics: No, 11, Oct, 1985 - No. 12, Dec, 1985

	GD	VG	FN	VF	VF/NM	NM-
11,12-Ditko-c/a; low print run	1	2	3	5	6	8

CHARLTON ARROW
Charlton Neo: 2017 ($7.99)

1-New E-Man and Nova by Cuti & Staton; Monster Hunter, Mr. Mixit						8.00

CHARLTON BULLSEYE
CPL/Gang Publications: 1975 - No. 5, 1976 ($1.50, B&W, bi-monthly, magazine format)

	GD	VG	FN	VF	VF/NM	NM-
1: 1 & 2 are last Capt. Atom by Ditko/Byrne intended for the never published Capt. Atom #90; Nightshade app.; Jeff Jones-a	5	10	15	31	53	75
2-Part 2 Capt. Atom story by Ditko/Byrne	3	6	9	21	33	45
3-Wrong Country by Sanho Kim	2	4	6	13	18	22
4-Doomsday + 1 by John Byrne	3	6	9	17	26	36
5-Doomsday + 1 by Byrne, The Question by Toth; Neal Adams back-c; Toth-c	5	10	15	34	60	85

CHARLTON BULLSEYE
Charlton Publications: June, 1981 - No. 10, Dec, 1982; Nov, 1986

	GD	VG	FN	VF	VF/NM	NM-
1-1st Blue Beetle app. since '74, 1st app. The Question since '75; 1st app. Rocket Rabbit; Neil The Horse shown on preview page	3	6	9	21	33	45
2-5: 2-Charlton debut of Neil The Horse; Rocket Rabbit app. 4-Vanguards						6.00
6-10: Low print run. 6-Origin & 1st app. Thunderbunny. 7-1st apps. of Captain Atom & Nightshade since '75. 9-1st app. Bludd	2	4	6	8	10	12

NOTE: *Material intended for issue #11-up was published in Scary Tales #37-up.*

CHARLTON CLASSICS
Charlton Comics: Apr, 1980 - No. 9, Aug, 1981

1-Hercules-r by Glanzman in all						6.00
2-9						5.00

CHARLTON CLASSICS LIBRARY (1776)
Charlton Comics: V10 No.1, Mar, 1973 (one-shot)

	GD	VG	FN	VF	VF/NM	NM-
1776 (title) - Adaptation of the film musical "1776"; given away at movie theatres; also a newsstand version	3	6	9	14	19	24

CHARLTON PREMIERE (Formerly Marine War Heroes)
Charlton Comics: V1#19, July, 1967; V2#1, Sept, 1967 - No. 4, May, 1968

	GD	VG	FN	VF	VF/NM	NM-
V1#19, V2#1,4: V1#19-Marine War Heroes. V2#1-Trio; intro. Shape, Tyro Team & Spookman. 4-Unlikely Tales; Aparo, Ditko-a	3	6	9	16	24	32
V2#2-Children of Doom; Boyette classic-a	3	6	9	21	33	45
V2#3-Sinistro Boy Fiend; Blue Beetle & Peacemaker x-over	3	6	9	19	30	40

CHARLTON SPORT LIBRARY - PROFESSIONAL FOOTBALL
Charlton Comics: Winter, 1969-70 (Jan. on cover) (68 pgs.)

	GD	VG	FN	VF	VF/NM	NM-
1	4	8	12	27	44	60

CHARMED (TV)
Zenescope Entertainment: No. 0, Jun, 2010 - No. 24, Oct, 2012 ($3.50)

0-24-Multiple covers on most						3.50

CHARMED SEASON 10 (TV)
Zenescope Entertainment: Oct, 2014 - No. 17, Mar, 2016 ($3.99)

1-17: 1-Shand-s/Feliz-a/Seidman-c						4.00

Chaos! Chronicles #1 © Chaos!

Chastity #1 © DYN

Chew #19 © John Layman

	GD	VG	FN	VF	VF/NM	NM-
	2.0	4.0	6.0	8.0	9.0	9.2

CHARMED (Volume 1) (TV)
Dynamite Entertainment: 2017 - No. 5, 2017 ($3.99)

1-5-Schultz-s/Sanapo-a; multiple covers on all ... 4.00

CHASE (See Batman #550 for 1st app.)(Also see Batwoman)
DC Comics: Feb, 1998 - No. 9, Oct, 1998; #1,000,000 Nov, 1998 ($2.50)

1-9: 1-Williams III & Gray-a. 1-Includes 4 Chase cards. 4-Teen Titans app. 7,8-Batman app.
9-GL Hal Jordan-c/app. ... 4.00
#1,000,000 (11/98) Final issue; 853rd Century x-over ... 4.00

CHASING DOGMA (See Jay and Silent Bob)

CHASSIS
Millenium Publications: 1996 - No. 3 ($2.95)

1-3: 1-Adam Hughes-c. 2-Conner var-c. ... 4.00

CHASSIS
Hurricane Entertainment: 1998 - No. 3 ($2.95)

0,1-3: 1-Adam Hughes-c. 0-Green var-c. ... 4.00

CHASSIS (Vol. 3)
Image Comics: Nov, 1999 - No. 4 ($2.95, limited series)

1-4: 1-Two covers by O'Neil and Green. 2-Busch var-c. ... 4.00
1-($6.95) DF Edition alternate-c by Wieringo ... 7.00

CHASTITY
Chaos! Comics: (one-shots)

#1/2 (1/01, $2.95) Batista-a ... 3.00
Heartbreaker (3/02, $2.99) Adrian-a/Molenaar-c ... 3.00
Love Bites (3/01, $2.99) Vale-a/Romano-c ... 3.00
Reign of Terror 1 (10/00, $2.95) Grant-s/Ross-a/Rio-c ... 3.00
Re-Imagined 1 (7/02, $2.99) Conner-c; Toledo-a ... 3.00

CHASTITY
Dynamite Entertainment: 2014 - No. 6, 2014 ($3.99, limited series)

1-6: 1-Andreyko-s/Acosta-a; origin retold. Multiple covers on each ... 4.00

CHASTITY (VOLUME 2)
Dynamite Entertainment: 2019 - No. 5, 2020 ($3.99, limited series)

1-5: 1-Leah Williams-s/Daniel Maine-a; multiple covers on each ... 4.00

CHASTITY: CRAZYTOWN
Chaos! Comics: Apr, 2002 - No. 3, June, 2002 ($2.99, limited series)

1-3-Nicieza-s/Batista-c/a ... 3.00

CHASTITY: LUST FOR LIFE
Chaos! Comics: May, 1999 - No. 3, July, 1999 ($2.95, limited series)

1-3-Nutman-s/Benes-c/a ... 4.00

CHASTITY: ROCKED
Chaos! Comics: Nov, 1998 - No. 4, Feb, 1999 ($2.95, limited series)

1-4-Nutman-s/Justiniano-c/a ... 4.00

CHASTITY: SHATTERED
Chaos! Comics: Jun, 2001 - No. 3, Sept, 2001 ($2.99, limited series)

1-3-Kaminski & Pulido-s/Batista-c/a ... 3.00

CHASTITY: THEATER OF PAIN
Chaos! Comics: Feb, 1997 - No. 3, June, 1997 ($2.95, limited series)

1-3-Pulido-s/Justiniano-c/a ... 4.00
TPB (1997, $9.95) r/#1-3 ... 10.00

CHECKMATE (TV)
Gold Key: Oct, 1962 - No. 2, Dec, 1962

1-Photo-c on both	5	10	15	34	60	85
2	5	10	15	31	53	75

CHECKMATE! (See Action Comics #598 and The OMAC Project)
DC Comics: Apr, 1988 - No. 33, Jan, 1991 ($1.25)

1-33: 13: New format begins ... 4.00
NOTE: *Gil Kane* c-2, 4, 7, 8, 10, 11, 15-19.

CHECKMATE (See Infinite Crisis and The OMAC Project)
DC Comics: Jun, 2006 - No. 31, Dec, 2008 ($2.99)

1-Rucka-s/Saiz-a/Bermejo-c; Alan Scott, Mr. Terrific, Sasha Bordeaux app. ... 4.00
1-2nd printing with B&W cover ... 3.00
2-31: 2,3-Kobra, King Faraday, Amanda Waller, Fire app. 4-The Great Ten app.
13-15-Outsiders app. 26-Chimera app. ... 3.00
...: A King's GameTPB (2007, $14.99) r/#1-7 ... 15.00
...: Chimera TPB (2009, $17.99) r/#26-31 ... 18.00
...: Fall of the Wall TPB (2008, $14.99) r/#16-22 ... 15.00
...: Pawn Breaks TPB (2007, $14.99) r/#8-12 ... 15.00

CHECKMATE
DC Comics: Aug, 2021 - No. 6, Jan, 2022 ($3.99, limited series)

1-6-Bendis-s/Maleev-a; Checkmate vs. Leviathan; Damian & Talia app. ... 4.00

CHERISH
Dynamite Entertainment: 2022 - No. 5, 2023 ($3.99, limited series)

1-5-Katana Collins-s/Gabriel Caitano-a ... 4.00

CHERYL BLOSSOM (See Archie's Girls, Betty and Veronica #320 for 1st app.)
Archie Publications: Sept, 1995 - No. 3, Nov, 1995 ($1.50, limited series)

1	3	6	9	14	20	26
2,3	1	3	4	6	8	10
Special 1-4 ('95, '96, $2.00)	1	3	4	6	8	10

CHERYL BLOSSOM (Cheryl's Summer Job)
Archie Publications: July, 1996 - No. 3, Sept, 1996 ($1.50, limited series)

1-3	1	3	4	6	8	10

CHERYL BLOSSOM (...Goes Hollywood)
Archie Publications: Dec, 1996 - No. 3, Feb, 1997 ($1.50, limited series)

1-3	1	3	4	6	8	10

CHERYL BLOSSOM
Archie Publications: Apr, 1997 - No. 37, Mar, 2001 $1.50/$1.75/$1.79/$1.99

1-Dan DeCarlo-c/a	2	4	6	9	12	15
2-10: 2-7-Dan DeCarlo-c/a	1	2	3	5	6	8
11-37: 32-Begin $1.99-c. 34-Sabrina app.						5.00

CHESTY SANCHEZ
Antarctic Press: Nov, 1995 - No. 2, Mar, 1996 ($2.95, B&W)

1,2	1	3	4	6	8	10
...Super Special (2/99, $5.99)	1	2	3	5	6	8

CHEVAL NOIR
Dark Horse Comics: 1989 - No. 50, Jan, 1994 ($3.50, B&W, 68 pgs.)

1 ($3.50) Dave Stevens-c	5	10	15	31	53	75
2-6,8,10 ($3.50): 6-Moebius poster insert	1	3	4	6	8	10
7-Dave Stevens-c	4	8	12	23	37	50
9,11,13,15,17,20,22 ($3.95)	1	3	4	6	8	10
12,18,19,21,23 ($3.95): 12-Geary-a; Mignola-c						6.00
14-($4.95, 76 pgs.)(7 pgs. color)	1	2	3	5	6	8
16-($3.75): 16-19-Contain trading cards						6.00
24-($3.75) Good girl art-c	2	4	6	9	12	15
25-($3.95)						6.00
26-($3.95) Moebius-a begins	2	4	6	9	12	15
27-48 ($3.95): 33-Snyder III-c						5.00
49,50-Low print run	2	4	6	11	16	20

NOTE: *Bolland* a-2, 6, 7, 13, 14. *Bolton* a-2, 4, 45; c-4, 20, 49. *Chadwick* c-13. *Dorman* painted c-16. *Geary* a-13, 14. *Kelley Jones* c-27. *Kaluta* a-6; c-6, 18. *Moebius* c-5, 9, 26. *Dave Stevens* c-1, 7. *Sutton* painted c-36.

CHEW (See Walking Dead #61 for preview)(Also see Chu)
Image Comics: Jun, 2009 - No. 60, Nov, 2016 ($2.99/$3.50/$3.99)

1-Layman-s/Guillory-a	8	16	24	56	108	160
1-(2nd-4th printings)	2	4	6	9	12	15
2-1st printing	3	6	9	19	30	40
2-5-(2nd & 3rd printings)						6.00
3-1st printing	2	4	6	10	14	18
4,5-1st printings	2	4	6	8	10	12
6-10	1	3	4	6	8	10
11-15: 15-Gatefold wraparound-c						5.00
16-24: 19-Neon green cover ink						5.00
25-44,46-49: 27-(6/12) Second Helping Edition						3.00
27-(5/11) Future issue released between #18 & #19						3.50
45,50-55-($3.50) 49-Poyo cover. 53-Flintstones cover						3.50
56-59-($3.99)						4.00
60-($5.99) Final issue; double cover with gatefold; set in the future						6.00
...: Demon Chicken Poyo One-Shot (4/16, $3.99) Layman-s/Guillory-a; pin-up gallery						4.00
.../ Revival One Shot (5/14, $4.99) Flip book: Layman-s/Guillory-a & Selley-s/Norton-a						5.00
...: Warrior Chicken Poyo (7/14, $3.50) Layman-s/Guillory-a; bonus pin-up gallery						3.50
Image Firsts: Chew #1 (4/10, $1.00) r/#1 with "Image Firsts" cover logo						5.00

CHEWBACCA (Star Wars)
Marvel Comics: Dec, 2015 - No. 5, Feb, 2016 ($3.99, limited series)

1-5-Duggan-s/Noto-a; takes place after Episode 4 Battle of Yavin ... 4.00

CHEYENNE (TV)
Dell Publishing Co.: No. 734, Oct, 1956 - No. 25, Dec-Jan, 1961-62

	GD 2.0	VG 4.0	FN 6.0	VF 8.0	VF/NM 9.0	NM- 9.2
Four Color 734(#1)-Clint Walker photo-c	13	26	39	89	195	300
Four Color 772,803: Clint Walker photo-c	8	16	24	54	102	150
4(8-10/57) - 20: 4-9,13-20-Clint Walker photo-c. 10-12-Ty Hardin photo-c						
	6	12	18	37	66	95
21-25-Clint Walker photo-c on all	6	12	18	38	69	100

CHEYENNE AUTUMN (See Movie Classics)

CHEYENNE KID (Formerly Wild Frontier No. 1-7)
Charlton Comics: No. 8, July, 1957 - No. 99, Nov, 1973

	GD 2.0	VG 4.0	FN 6.0	VF 8.0	VF/NM 9.0	NM- 9.2
8 (#1)	8	16	24	44	57	70
9,15-19	6	12	18	29	36	42
10-Williamson/Torres-a(3); Ditko-c	11	22	33	60	83	105
11-(68 pgs.)-Cheyenne Kid meets Geronimo	10	20	30	58	79	100
12-Williamson/Torres-a(2)	10	20	30	58	79	100
13-Williamson/Torres-a (5 pgs.)	8	16	24	44	57	70
14-Williamson-a (5 pgs.?)	8	16	24	42	54	65
20-22,24,25-Severin c/a(3) each	4	8	12	21	33	45
23,27-29	3	6	9	15	22	28
26,30-Severin-a	3	6	9	17	26	35
31-59	2	4	6	10	14	18
60-65	2	4	6	8	11	14
66-Wander by Aparo begins, ends #87	2	4	6	10	14	18
67-80	2	4	6	8	11	14
81-99: Apache Red begins #88, origin in #89	2	4	6	8	11	14
Modern Comics Reprint 87,89(1978)						5.00

CHIAROSCURO (THE PRIVATE LIVES OF LEONARDO DA VINCI)
DC Comics (Vertigo): July, 1995 - No. 10, Apr, 1996 ($2.50/$2.95, limited series, mature)

1-9: McGreal and Rawson-s/Truog & Kayanan-a						4.00
10-($2.95)						4.00
TPB (2005, $24.99) r/series; intro. by Alisa Kwitney, afterword by Pat McGreal						25.00

CHICAGO MAIL ORDER (See C-M-O Comics in the Promotional Comics section)

CHICKEN DEVIL
AfterShock Comics: Oct, 2021 - No. 4, Jan, 2022 ($4.99, limited series)

1-4-Brian Buccellato-s/Hayden Sherman-a						5.00
Vol. 2 (10/22 - No. 4, 6/23) 1-4						5.00

CHIEF, THE (Indian Chief No. 3 on)
Dell Publishing Co.: No. 290, Aug, 1950 - No. 2, Apr-June, 1951

	GD 2.0	VG 4.0	FN 6.0	VF 8.0	VF/NM 9.0	NM- 9.2
Four Color 290(#1)	9	18	27	60	120	180
2	6	12	18	38	69	100

CHIEF CRAZY HORSE (See Wild Bill Hickok #21)
Avon Periodicals: 1950 (Also see Fighting Indians of the Wild West!)

	GD 2.0	VG 4.0	FN 6.0	VF 8.0	VF/NM 9.0	NM- 9.2
nn-Fawcette-c	30	60	90	177	289	400

CHIEF VICTORIO'S APACHE MASSACRE (See Fight Indians of/Wild West!)
Avon Periodicals: 1951

	GD 2.0	VG 4.0	FN 6.0	VF 8.0	VF/NM 9.0	NM- 9.2
nn-Williamson/Frazetta-a (7 pgs.); Larsen-a; Kinstler-c	71	142	213	454	777	1100

CHILD IS BORN, A
Apostle Arts: Nov, 2011 ($5.99, one-shot)

nn-Story of the birth of Jesus; Billy Tucci-s/a; cover by Tucci & Sparacio						6.00
HC (7/12, $15.99) Includes bonus interview with Billy Tucci and sketch art						16.00

CHILDREN OF FIRE
Fantagor Press: Nov, 1987 - No. 3, 1988 ($2.00, limited series)

1-3: by Richard Corben						4.00

CHILDREN OF THE ATOM (X-Men)
Marvel Comics: May, 2021 - No. 6, Oct, 2021 ($4.99/$3.99, limited series)

1-($4.99)-New team of teen "mutants"; X-Men app.; Ayala-s/Chang-a						5.00
2-6-($3.99) 4,5-X-Men app.						4.00

CHILDREN OF THE PLAGUE
Dark Horse Comics: Sept, 2021 ($4.99, one-shot)

1-Robert Love-s/a						5.00

CHILDREN OF THE VAULT (Follows events from X-Men: Hellfire Gala #1)
Dark Horse Comics: Oct, 2023 -No. 4, Jan, 2024 ($4.99/$3.99, limited series)

1-($4.99) Deniz Camp-s/Luca Maresca-a; Cable & Bishop app.						5.00
2-4-($3.99)						4.00

CHILDREN OF THE VOYAGER (See Marvel Frontier Comics Unlimited)
Marvel Frontier Comics: Sept, 1993 - No. 4, Dec, 1993 ($1.95, limited series)

1-($2.95)-Embossed glow-in-the-dark-c; Paul Johnson-c/a						5.00
2-4						4.00

CHILDREN'S BIG BOOK
Dorene Publ. Co.: 1945 (25¢, stiff-c, 68 pgs.)

	GD 2.0	VG 4.0	FN 6.0	VF 8.0	VF/NM 9.0	NM- 9.2
nn-Comics & fairy tales; David Icove-a	19	38	57	111	176	240

CHILDREN'S CRUSADE, THE
DC Comics (Vertigo): Dec, 1993 - No. 2, Jan, 1994 ($3.95, limited series)

1,2-Gaiman scripts & Bachalo-a; framing issues for Children's Crusade x-over						4.00

CHILD'S PLAY: THE SERIES (Movie)
Innovation Publishing: May, 1991 - No. 5, Dec, 1991 ($2.50, 28pgs.)

	GD 2.0	VG 4.0	FN 6.0	VF 8.0	VF/NM 9.0	NM- 9.2
1	3	6	9	19	30	40
2,3	2	4	6	11	16	20
4,5-Low print run	2	4	6	9	12	15

CHILD'S PLAY 2 THE OFFICIAL MOVIE ADAPTATION (Movie)
Innovation Publishing: 1990 - No. 3, 1990 ($2.50, bi-weekly limited series)

	GD 2.0	VG 4.0	FN 6.0	VF 8.0	VF/NM 9.0	NM- 9.2
1-Adapts movie sequel	3	6	9	21	33	45
2,3	2	4	6	11	16	20

CHILI (Millie's Rival)
Marvel Comics Group: 5/69 - No. 17, 9/70; No. 18, 8/72 - No. 26, 12/73

	GD 2.0	VG 4.0	FN 6.0	VF 8.0	VF/NM 9.0	NM- 9.2
1	10	20	30	69	147	225
2,4,5	5	10	15	35	63	90
3-Millie & Chili visit Marvel and meet Stan Lee & Stan Goldberg (6 pgs.)						
	7	14	21	44	82	120
6-17	5	10	15	30	50	70
18-26	4	8	12	27	44	60
Special 1(12/71, 52 pgs.)	5	10	15	35	63	90

CHILLER
Marvel Comics (Epic): Nov, 1993 - No. 2, Dec, 1993 ($7.95, lim. series)

	GD 2.0	VG 4.0	FN 6.0	VF 8.0	VF/NM 9.0	NM- 9.2
1,2-(68 pgs.)	1	2	3	5	6	8

CHILLING ADVENTURES IN SORCERY (...as Told by Sabrina #1, 2)
(Red Circle Sorcery No. 6 on)
Archie Publications (Red Circle Prods.): 9/72 - No. 2, 10/72; No. 3, 10/73 - No. 5, 2/74

	GD 2.0	VG 4.0	FN 6.0	VF 8.0	VF/NM 9.0	NM- 9.2
1-Sabrina cameo as narrator	7	14	21	46	86	125
2-Sabrina cameo as narrator	4	8	12	23	37	50
3-5: Morrow-c/a, all. 4,5-Alcazar-a	3	6	9	14	19	24

CHILLING ADVENTURES IN SORCERY (Also see Return of ...)
Archie Comic Publications: Dec, 2021 ($3.99)

1-Anthology of short horror stories hosted by Madam Satan; art by Federici, Charm						4.00

CHILLING ADVENTURES OF SABRINA (Inspired the 2018 Netflix series)(See Madam Satan)
Archie Comic Publications: Dec, 2014 - No. 8, Aug, 2017; No. 9, Dec, 2021 - Present ($3.99, mature content)

1-9: 1-Aguirre-Sacasa-s/Hack-a; two covers; origin re-told, set in the 1960s						4.00
1-(12/18, $1.00) r/#1 with Netflix art cover						3.00
... - Halloween ComicFest Edition 1 (2015, free) r/#1 in B&W						3.00
... - Halloween ComicFest Edition #1 2017 (free) r/#7 in B&W						3.00
... - Monster-Sized One-Shot 1 (5/19, $7.99) r/#6-8; Francavilla-c						8.00

CHILLING ADVENTURES OF SALEM (From Sabrina the Teenage Witch)
Archie Comic Publications: Dec, 2022 ($3.99, one-shot)

1-Short horror stories with the Archie characters						4.00

CHILLING ADVENTURES PRESENTS...
Archie Comic Publications: Oct, 2022 - Sept, 2023 ($3.99, series of one-shots)

... Betty The Final Girl 1 (4/23) Short horror stories; Josie and the Pussycats app.						4.00
... Camp Pickens 1 (8/23) Haunted summer camp horror stories						4.00
... Jinx: A Cursed Life 1 (7/23) Jinx & Danni with a Jughead exorcism						4.00
.... Jinx Grim Fairy Tales 1 (10/22) Short horror stories						4.00
... Pop's Chock'lit Shoppe of Horrors 1 (5/23) Short horror stories						4.00
... Strange Science 1 (9/23) Jinx, Danni & Dilton with a time machine mishap						4.00
... The Cult of That Wilkin Boy 1 (6/23) Bingo Wilkin's deal with a demon; Bunn-s						4.00
.... Weirder Mysteries 1 (11/22) Crashed UFO sci-fi story; Bingo Wilkin app.						4.00

CHILLING TALES (Formerly Beware)
Youthful Magazines: No. 13, Dec, 1952 - No. 17, Oct, 1953

	GD 2.0	VG 4.0	FN 6.0	VF 8.0	VF/NM 9.0	NM- 9.2
13(No.1)-Harrison-a; Matt Fox-c/a	400	800	1200	2800	4900	7000
14-Harrison-a	161	322	483	1030	1765	2500
15-Matt Fox-c; Harrison-a	400	800	1200	2800	4900	7000
16-Poe adapt.- 'Metzengerstein'; Rudyard Kipling adapt.- 'Mark of the Beast,'						
by Kiefer; bondage-c	423	846	1269	3000	5250	7500
17-Matt Fox-c; Sir Walter Scott & Poe adapt.	258	516	774	1651	2826	4000

CHILLING TALES OF HORROR (Magazine)
Stanley Publications: V1#1, 6/69 - V1#7, 12/70; V2#2, 2/71 - V2#6, 10/71(50¢, B&W, 52 pgs.)

	GD 2.0	VG 4.0	FN 6.0	VF 8.0	VF/NM 9.0	NM- 9.2
V1#1	10	20	30	69	147	225
2-4,(no #5),6,7: 7-Cameron-a	7	14	21	44	89	130
V2#2-6: 2-Two different #2 issues exist (2/71 & 4/71). 2-(2/71) Spirit of Frankenstein						
-r/Adventures into the Unknown #16. 4-(8/71) different from other V2#4(6/71)						
	6	12	18	41	76	110
V2#4-(6/71) r/9 pg. Feldstein-a from Adventures into the Unknown #3						
	7	14	21	44	82	120

NOTE: *Two issues of V2#2 exist, Feb, 1971 and April, 1971. Two issues of V2#4 exist, Jun, 1971 and Aug, 1971.*

CHILLY WILLY (Also see New Funnies #211)
Dell Publ. Co.: No. 740, Oct, 1956 - No. 1281, Apr-June, 1962 (Walter Lantz)

	GD 2.0	VG 4.0	FN 6.0	VF 8.0	VF/NM 9.0	NM- 9.2
Four Color 740 (#1)	9	18	27	62	126	190
Four Color 852 (2/58),967 (2/59),1017 (9/59),1074 (2-4/60),1122 (8/60),						
1177 (4-6/61),1212 (7-9/61),1281	6	12	18	37	66	95

CHIMERA
CrossGeneration Comics: Mar, 2003 - No. 4, July, 2003 ($2.95, limited series)

1-4-Marz-s/Peterson-c/a						3.00
Vol. 1 TPB (2003, $15.95) r/#1-4 plus sketch pages, 3-D models, how-to guides						16.00

CHIMICHANGA
Albatross Exploding Funny Books: 2010 ($3.00, B&W)

1-3-Eric Powell-s/a/c						5.00

CHIMICHANGA: THE SORROW OF THE WORLD'S WORST FACE
Dark Horse Comics: Oct, 2016 - No. 4, Dec, 2017 ($3.99, limited series)

1-4-Eric Powell-s/Stephanie Buscema-a						4.00

CHINA BOY (See Wisco in the Promotional Comics section)

CHIN MUSIC
Image Comics: May, 2013 - No. 2, Aug, 2013 ($2.99)

1,2-Steve Niles-s/Tony Harris-a/c						3.00

CHIP 'N' DALE (Walt Disney)(See Walt Disney's C&S #204)
Dell Publishing Co/Gold Key/Whitman No. 65 on: Nov, 1953 - No. 30, June-Aug, 1962; Sept, 1967 - No. 83, July, 1984

	GD 2.0	VG 4.0	FN 6.0	VF 8.0	VF/NM 9.0	NM- 9.2
Four Color 517(#1)	12	24	36	79	170	260
Four Color 581,636	6	12	18	42	79	115
4(12/55-2/56)-10	5	10	15	33	57	80
11-30	4	8	12	28	47	65
1(Gold Key, 1967)-Reprints	3	6	9	19	30	40
2-10	2	4	6	13	18	22
11-20	2	4	6	9	12	15
21-40	2	4	6	8	10	12

Chilling Adventures of Sabrina #9 © ACP

Chip 'n' Dale #17 © DIS

Chrononauts #4 © MillarWorld & Murphy

	GD 2.0	VG 4.0	FN 6.0	VF 8.0	VF/NM 9.0	NM- 9.2

41-64,70-77: 75(2/82), 76(2-3/82), 77(3/82) — 1, 2, 3, 5, 7, 9
65,66 (Whitman) — 2, 4, 6, 8, 11, 14
67-69 (3-pack? 1980): 67(8/80), 68(10/80) (scarce) — 4, 8, 12, 28, 47, 65
78-83 (All #90214; 3-pack, nd, nd code): 78(4/83), 79(5/83), 80(7/83), 81(8/83), 82(5/84), 83(7/84) — 3, 6, 9, 15, 22, 28
NOTE: All Gold Key/Whitman issues have reprints except No. 32-35, 38-41, 45-47. No. 23-28, 30-42, 45-47, 49 have new covers.

CHIP 'N DALE RESCUE RANGERS
Disney Comics: June, 1990 - No. 19, Dec, 1991 ($1.50)
1-New stories; origin begins — 2, 4, 6, 8, 10, 12
2-19: 2-Origin continued — 4.00

CHIP 'N DALE RESCUE RANGERS
BOOM! Studios: Dec, 2010 - No. 8, Jul, 2011 ($3.99)
1-8: 1-Brill-s/Castellani-a; 3 covers — 4.00
... Free Comic Book Day Edition (5/11) Flip book with Darkwing Duck FCBD — 1, 2, 3, 5, 6, 8

CHITTY CHITTY BANG BANG (See Movie Comics)

C.H.I.X.
Image Comics (Studiosaurus): Jan, 1998 ($2.50)
1-Dodson, Haley, Lopresti, Randall, and Warren-s/c/a — 5.00
1-($5.00) "X-Ray Variant" cover — 6.00
C.H.I.X. That Time Forgot 1 (8/98, $2.95) — 4.00

CHOICE COMICS
Great Publications: Dec, 1941 - No. 3, Feb, 1942
1-Origin Secret Circle; Atlas the Mighty app.; Zomba, Jungle Fight, Kangaroo Man, & Fire Eater begin — 174, 348, 522, 1114, 1907, 2700
2 — 142, 284, 426, 909, 1555, 2200
3-Double feature; Features movie "The Lost City" (classic cover); continued from Great Comics #3 — 245, 490, 735, 1568, 2684, 3800

CHOLLY AND FLYTRAP (Arthur Suydam's...)(Also see New Adventures of...)
Image Comics: Nov, 2004 - No. 4, June, 2005 ($4.95/$5.95, limited series)
1-($4.95) Arthur Suydam-s/a/c — 6.00
2-4-($5.95) — 6.00

CHOO CHOO CHARLIE
Gold Key: Dec, 1969
1-John Stanley-a — 5, 10, 15, 35, 60, 90

CHOSEN
Dark Horse Comics: Jan, 2004 - No. 3, Aug, 2004 ($2.99, limited series)
1-Story of the second coming; Mark Millar-s/Peter Gross-a — 2, 4, 6, 9, 12, 15
2,3 — 5.00

CHRIS CLAREMONT ANNIVERSARY SPECIAL
Marvel Comics: Mar, 2021 ($4.99, one-shot)
1-Claremont-s; art by Sienkiewicz, Chen, Olortegui, and Booth; Dani Moonstar app. — 5.00

CHRISTIAN (See Asylum)
Maximum Press: Jan, 1996 ($2.99, one-shot)
1-Pop Mhan-a — 4.00

CHRISTIAN HEROES OF TODAY
David C. Cook: 1964 (36 pgs.)
nn — 3, 6, 9, 17, 26, 35

CHRISTMAS (Also see A-1 Comics)
Magazine Enterprises: No. 28, 1950
A-1 28 — 14, 28, 42, 76, 108, 140

CHRISTMAS ADVENTURE, A (See Classics Comics Giveaways, 12/69)

CHRISTMAS ALBUM (See March of Comics No. 312)

CHRISTMAS ANNUAL
Golden Special: 1975 ($1.95, 100 pgs., stiff-c)
nn-Reprints Mother Goose stories with Walt Kelly-a — 3, 6, 9, 21, 33, 45

CHRISTMAS & ARCHIE
Archie Comics: Jan, 1975 ($1.00, 68 pgs., 10-1/4x13-1/4" treasury-sized)
1-(scarce) — 6, 12, 18, 37, 66, 95

CHRISTMAS BELLS (See March of Comics No. 297)

CHRISTMAS CARNIVAL
Ziff-Davis Publ. Co./St. John Publ. Co. No. 2: 1952; 1955 (25¢, one-shot, 100 pgs.)
nn-(1952) — 41, 82, 123, 256, 428, 600

2-(1955) Reprints Ziff-Davis issue plus-c — 20, 40, 60, 114, 182, 250

CHRISTMAS CAROL, A (See March of Comics No. 33)
CHRISTMAS EVE, A (See March of Comics No. 212)
CHRISTMAS IN DISNEYLAND (See Dell Giants)
CHRISTMAS PARADE (See Dell Giant No. 26, Dell Giants, March of Comics No. 284, Walt Disney Christmas Parade & Walt Disney's...)
CHRISTMAS PARADE (Walt Disney's)
Gold Key: 1962 (no month listed) - No. 9, Jan, 1972 (#1,5: 80 pgs.; #2-4,7-9: 36 pgs.)
1 (30018-301)-Giant — 8, 16, 24, 56, 108, 160
2-6: 2-r/F.C. #367 by Barks. 3-r/F.C. #178 by Barks. 4-r/F.C. #203 by Barks. 5-r/Christmas Parade #1 (Dell) by Barks; giant. 6-r/Christmas Parade #2 (Dell) by Barks (64 pgs.); giant — 5, 10, 15, 35, 63, 90
7-Pull-out poster (half pull-out poster w/o poster) — 5, 10, 15, 30, 50, 70
8-r/F.C. #367 by Barks; pull-out poster — 5, 10, 15, 35, 63, 90
9 — 4, 8, 12, 25, 40, 55

CHRISTMAS PARTY (See March of Comics No. 256)
CHRISTMAS STORIES (See Little People No. 959, 1062)
CHRISTMAS STORY (See March of Comics No. 326 in the Promotional Comics section)
CHRISTMAS STORY, THE
Catechetical Guild: 1955 (15¢)
393-Addison Burbank-a — 9, 18, 27, 47, 61, 75

CHRISTMAS STORY BOOK (See Woolworth's Christmas Story Book)
CHRISTMAS TREASURY, A (See Dell Giants & March of Comics No. 227)
CHRISTMAS WITH ARCHIE
Spire Christian Comics (Fleming H. Revell Co.): 1973, 1974 (49¢, 52 pgs.)
nn-Low print run — 3, 6, 9, 17, 26, 35

CHRISTMAS WITH MOTHER GOOSE
Dell Publishing Co.: No. 90, Nov, 1945 - No. 253, Nov, 1949
Four Color 90 (#1)-Kelly-a — 16, 32, 48, 111, 246, 380
Four Color 126 ('46), 172 (11/47)-By Walt Kelly — 12, 24, 36, 82, 179, 275
Four Color 201 (10/48), 253-By Walt Kelly — 10, 20, 30, 66, 138, 210

CHRISTMAS WITH SANTA (See March of Comics No. 92)
CHRISTMAS WITH THE SUPER-HEROES (See Limited Collectors' Edition)
DC Comics: 1988; No. 2, 1989 ($2.95)
1,2: 1-(100 pgs.)-All reprints; N. Adams-r, Byrne-c; Batman, Superman, JLA, LSH Christmas stories; r-Miller's 1st Batman/DC Special Series #21. 2-(68 pgs.)-Superman by Chadwick; Batman, Wonder Woman, Deadman, Green Lantern, Flash app.; Morrow-a; Enemy Ace by Byrne; all new-a — 1, 3, 4, 7, 8, 10

CHROMA-TICK, THE (...Special Edition, #1,2) (Also see The Tick)
New England Comics Press: Feb, 1992 - No. 8, Nov, 1993 ($3.95/$3.50, 44 pgs.)
1,2-Includes serially numbered trading card set — 1, 3, 4, 6, 8, 10
3-8 ($3.50, 36 pgs.): 6-Bound-in card — 5.00

CHROME
Hot Comics: 1986 - No. 3, 1986 ($1.50, limited series)
1-3 — 4.00

CHROMIUM MAN, THE
Triumphant Comics: Aug, 1993 - No.10, May, 1994 ($2.50)
1-1st app. Mr. Death; all serially numbered — 4.00
2-10: 2-1st app. Prince Vandal. 3-1st app. Candi, Breaker & Coil. 4,5-Triumphant Unleashed x-over. 8,9-(3/94). 10-(5/94) — 4.00
0-(4/94)-Four color-c, 0-All pink-c & all blue-c; no cover price — 4.00

CHROMIUM MAN: VIOLENT PAST, THE
Triumphant Comics: Jan, 1994 - No. 2, Jan, 1994 ($2.50, limited series)
1,2-Serially numbered to 22,000 each — 4.00

CHRONICLES OF CONAN, THE (See Conan the Barbarian)
CHRONICLES OF CORUM, THE (Also see Corum...)
First Comics: Jan, 1987 - No. 12, Nov, 1988 ($1.75/$1.95, deluxe series)
1-12: Adapts Michael Moorcock's novel; Thomas-s; Mignola-a/c — 4.00

CHRONONAUTS
Image Comics: Mar, 2015 - No. 4, Jun, 2015 ($3.50/$5.99)
1-3-Mark Millar-s/Sean Murphy-a — 3.50
4-($5.99) — 6.00

CHRONONAUTS: FUTURE SHOCK
Image Comics: Oct, 2019 - No. 4, Oct, 2019 ($3.99/$5.99, all 4 issues released the same day)

	GD 2.0	VG 4.0	FN 6.0	VF 8.0	VF/NM 9.0	NM- 9.2

1-3-Mark Millar-s/Eric Canete-a/Pasqual Ferry-c ... 3.50
4-($5.99) ... 6.00

CHRONOS
DC Comics: Mar, 1998 - No. 11, Feb. 1999 ($2.50)

1-11-J.F. Moore-s/Guinan-a ... 4.00
#1,000,000 (11/98) 853rd Century x-over ... 4.00

CHU (Characters from Chew)
Image Comics: Jul, 2020 - Present ($3.99)

1-10-Layman-s/Boultwood-a; Tony Chu and Saffron Chu app. ... 4.00

CHUCK (Based on the NBC TV series)
DC Comics (WildStorm): Aug, 2008 - No. 6, Jan, 2009 ($2.99, limited series)

1-6-Jeremy Haun-a/Kristian Donaldson-c; Noto back-up-a ... 3.00
TPB (2009, $19.99) r/#1-6; photo-c ... 20.00

CHUCKLE, THE GIGGLY BOOK OF COMIC ANIMALS
R. B. Leffingwell Co.: 1945 (132 pgs., one-shot)

1-Funny animal	32	64	96	188	307	425

CHUCK NORRIS (TV)
Marvel Comics (Star Comics): Jan, 1987 - No. 4, July, 1987

1-Ditko-a	3	6	9	14	20	26
2,3; Ditko-a	1	3	4	6	8	10
4-No Ditko-a (low print run)	2	4	6	8	10	12

CHUCK WAGON (See Sheriff Bob Dixon's...)

CHUCKY (Based on the 1988 killer doll movie Child's Play)
Devil's Due Publishing: Apr, 2007 - No. 4, Nov, 2007 ($3.50/$5.50)

1-Pulido-s/Medors-a; art & photo covers	3	6	9	16	23	30
2,3	2	4	6	8	10	12
4-($5.50)	3	6	9	14	20	25

TPB (2007, $18.99) r/series; gallery of variant covers; 4 pages of script and sketch art ... 19.00

CHYNA (WWF Wrestling)
Chaos! Comics: Sept, 2000; July, 2001 ($2.95/$2.99, one-shots)

1-Grant-s/Barrows-a; photo-c	1	3	4	6	8	10
1-($9.95) Premium Edition; Cleavenger-c	2	4	6	9	12	15
II -(7/01, $2.99) Deodato-a; photo-c						4.00

CICERO'S CAT
Dell Publishing Co.: July-Aug, 1959 - No. 2, Sept-Oct, 1959

1-Cat from Mutt & Jeff	4	8	12	28	47	65
2	4	8	12	25	40	55

CIMARRON STRIP (TV)
Dell Publishing Co.: Jan, 1968

1-Stuart Whitman photo-c	4	8	12	23	37	50

CIMMERIAN: BEYOND THE BLACK RIVER
Ablaze Publishing: 2020 - No. 2, 2020 ($3.99)

1,2-Conan adaptation from 1935; Mathieu Gabella-s/Anthony Jean-a; text back-up ... 4.00

CIMMERIAN: HOUR OF THE DRAGON
Ablaze Publishing: 2022 - No. 4, 2022 ($3.99)

1-4-Conan adaptation from 1935,1936; Valentin Sécher-a; text back-up ... 4.00

CIMMERIAN: IRON SHADOWS IN THE MOON
Ablaze Publishing: 2020 - No. 3, 2020 ($3.99)

1-3-Conan adaptation from 1934; Virginie Augustin-s/a; text back-up ... 4.00

CIMMERIAN: QUEEN OF THE BLACK COAST
Ablaze Publishing: 2020 - No. 2, 2020 ($3.99)

1,2-Conan adaptation from Queen of the Black Coast; Morvan-s/Alary-a; text back-up ... 4.00

CIMMERIAN: THE MAN-EATERS OF ZAMBOULA
Ablaze Publishing: 2020 - No. 2, 2020 ($3.99)

1,2-Conan adaptation from 1935; Gess-s/a; text back-up ... 4.00

CIMMERIAN, THE: PEOPLE OF THE BLACK CIRCLE
Ablaze Publishing: 2020 - No. 3, 2020 ($3.99, limited series)

1-3-Conan adaptation; Yasmina app.; Runberg-s/Jae Kwang Park-a; text back-up ... 4.00

CIMMERIAN, THE: FROST-GIANT'S DAUGHTER
Ablaze Publishing: 2020 - No. 3, 2020 ($3.99, limited series)

1-3-Conan adaptation; Atali app.; Robin Recht-a; text back-up ... 4.00

CIMMERIAN, THE: RED NAILS
Ablaze Publishing: 2020 - No. 2, 2020 ($3.99)

1,2-Conan adaptation; Valeria app.; Hautiere-s/Vatine & Cassegrain-a; text back-up ... 4.00

CINDER AND ASHE
DC Comics: May, 1988 - No. 4, Aug, 1988 ($1.75, limited series)

1-4; Mature readers ... 4.00

CINDERELLA (Disney) (See Movie Comics)
Dell Publishing Co.: No. 272, Apr, 1950 - No. 786, Apr, 1957

Four Color 272	15	30	45	105	233	360
Four Color 786-Partial-r #272	9	18	27	58	114	170

CINDERELLA
Whitman Publishing Co.: Apr, 1982

nn-Reprints 4-Color #272	1	2	3	4	5	7

CINDERELLA: FABLES ARE FOREVER (See Fables)
DC Comics (Vertigo): Apr, 2011 - No. 6, Sept, 2011 ($2.99, limited series)

1-6-Roberson-s/McManus-a/Zullo-c; Dorothy Gale app. ... 3.00

CINDERELLA: FROM FABLETOWN WITH LOVE (See Fables)
DC Comics (Vertigo): Jan, 2010 - No. 6, Jun, 2010 ($2.99, limited series)

1-6- Roberson-s/McManus-a/Zullo-c ... 3.00
TPB (2010, $14.99) r/#1-6 ... 15.00

CINDERELLA LOVE

Ziff-Davis/St. John Publ. Co. No. 12 on: No. 10, 1950; No. 11, 4-5/51; No. 12, 9/51; No. 4, 10-11/51 - No. 11, Fall, 1952; No. 12, 10/53 - No. 15, 8/54; No. 25, 12/54 - No. 29, 10/55 (No #16-24)

10(#1)(1st Series, 1950)-Painted-c	33	66	99	194	317	440
11(#2, 4-5/51)-Crandall-a; Saunders painted-c	22	44	66	132	216	300
12(#3, 9/51)-Photo-c	19	38	57	111	176	240
4-8: 4,6,7-Photo-c	17	34	51	98	154	210
9-Kinstler-a; photo-c	18	36	54	105	165	225
10,11-Photo-c	17	34	51	109	158	215
12(St. John-10/53)-#13: 13-Painted-c.	17	34	51	98	154	210
14-Matt Baker-a	43	86	129	271	461	660
15(8/54)-Matt Baker-c	116	232	348	742	1271	1800
25(2nd Series)(Formerly Romantic Marriage) Classic Matt Baker-c	400	800	1200	2800	4900	7000
26-Matt Baker-c; last precode (2/55)	194	388	582	1242	2121	3000
27-29: Matt Baker-c	129	258	387	826	1413	2000

CINDY COMICS (Cindy Smith No. 39, 40; Crime Can't Win No. 41 on)(Formerly Krazy Komics) (See Junior Miss & Teen Comics)
Timely Comics: No. 27, Fall, 1947 - No. 40, July, 1950

27-Kurtzman-a, 3 pgs: Margie, Oscar begin	53	106	159	334	567	800
28-31-Kurtzman-a	36	72	108	211	343	475
32-36,38-40: 33-Georgie story; anti-Wertham editorial. 39-Louise Altson painted-c	30	60	90	177	289	400
37-Classic greytone-c	400	800	1200	2000	3000	4000

NOTE: *Kurtzman's "Hey Look"-#27(3), 29(2), 30(2), 31; "Giggles 'n' Grins"-28.*

CINNAMON: EL CICLO
DC Comics: Oct, 2003 - No. 5, Feb, 2004 ($2.50, limited series)

1-5-Van Meter-s/Chaykin-c/Paronzini-a ... 3.00

CIRCUS (...the Comic Riot)
Globe Syndicate: June, 1938 - No. 3, Aug, 1938

1-(Scarce)-Spacehawks (2 pgs.), & Disk Eyes by Wolverton (2 pgs.), Pewee Throttle by Cole (2nd comic book work; see Star Comics V1#11), Beau Gus, Ken Craig & The Lords of Crillon, Jack Hinton by Eisner, Van Bragger by Kane	508	1016	1524	3708	6554	9400
2,3-(Scarce)-Eisner, Cole, Wolverton, Bob Kane-a in each	300	600	900	2010	3505	5000

CIRCUS BOY (TV) (See Movie Classics)
Dell Publishing Co.: No. 759, Dec, 1956 - No. 813, July, 1957

Four Color 759 (#1)-The Monkees' Mickey Dolenz photo-c	13	26	39	87	191	295
Four Color 785 (4/57), 813-Mickey Dolenz photo-c	10	20	30	64	132	200

CIRCUS COMICS
Farm Women's Pub. Co./D. S. Publ.: Apr, 1945 - No. 2, Jun, 1945; Wint., 1948-49

1-Funny animal	22	44	66	132	216	300
2	14	28	42	76	108	140
1(1948)-D.S. Publ.; 2 pgs. Frazetta	30	60	90	177	289	400

CIRCUS OF FUN COMICS
A. W. Nugent Publ. Co.: 1945 - No. 3, Dec, 1947 (A book of games & puzzles)

1	18	36	54	103	162	220
2,3	10	20	30	56	76	95

CISCO KID, THE (TV)
Dell Publishing Co.: July, 1950 - No. 41, Oct-Dec, 1958

Four Color 292(#1)-Cisco Kid, his horse Diablo, & sidekick Pancho & his horse Loco begin; line drawn cover	23	46	69	156	348	540
2(1/51) Painted-c begin	10	20	30	64	132	200
3-5	9	18	27	59	117	175
6-10	8	16	24	51	96	140
11-20	7	14	21	44	82	120
21-36-Last painted-c	6	12	18	37	66	95
37-41: All photo-c	7	14	21	46	86	125

NOTE: *Buscema a-40. Ernest Nordli painted c-5-16, 20, 35.*

CISCO KID COMICS
Bernard Bailey/Swappers Quarterly: Winter, 1944 (one-shot)

1-Illustrated Stories of the Operas: Faust; Funnyman by Giunta; Cisco Kid (1st app.) & Superbaby begin; Giunta-c	50	100	150	315	533	750

CITIZEN JACK
Image Comics: Nov, 2015 - No. 6, May, 2016 ($3.99, limited series)

1-6-Sam Humphries-s/Tommy Patterson-a ... 4.00

CITIZEN SMITH (See Holyoke One-Shot No. 9)

CITIZEN V AND THE V-BATTALION (See Thunderbolts)
Marvel Comics: June, 2001 - No. 3, Aug, 2001 ($2.99, limited series)

1-3-Nicieza-s; Michael Ryan-c/a ... 3.00
...: The Everlasting 1-4 (3/02 - No. 4, 7/02) Nicieza-s/LaRosa-a(p) ... 3.00

CITY BOY
DC Comics: Jul, 2023 - No. 6, Jan, 2024 ($3.99)

1-6: 1-Greg Pak-s/Minkyu Jung-a. 3-Superman app. 4,6-Nightwing app. ... 4.00

CITY OF HEROES (Online game)
Dark Horse Comics/Blue King Studios: Sept, 2002; May, 2004 - No. 7 ($2.95)

1-(no cover price) Dakan-s/Zombo-a ... 3.00
1-7-($2.95) ... 3.00

CITY OF HEROES (Online game)
Image Comics: June, 2005 - No. 20, Aug, 2007 ($2.99)

1-20: 1-Waid-s; Pérez-c. 6-Flip-c with City of Villains. 7-9-Jurgens-s ... 3.00

CITY OF OTHERS
Dark Horse Comics: Apr, 2007 - No. 4, Aug, 2007 ($2.99, limited series)

1-4-Bernie Wrightson-a/c; Steve Niles & Wrightson-s ... 3.00
TPB (2/08, $14.95) r/#1-4; Wrightson sketch pages ... 15.00

Chuck #1 © WB

City Boy #1 © DC

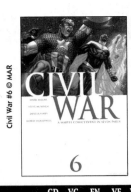

Civil War #6 © MAR

	GD 2.0	VG 4.0	FN 6.0	VF 8.0	VF/NM 9.0	NM- 9.2

CITY OF SILENCE
Image Comics: May, 2000 - No. 3, July, 2000 ($2.50)

1-3-Ellis-s/Erskine-a						3.00
TPB (6/04, $9.95) r/#1-3; pin-up gallery						10.00

CITY OF THE LIVING DEAD (See Fantastic Tales No. 1)
Avon Periodicals: 1952

nn-Hollingsworth-c/a	129	258	387	826	1413	2000

CITY OF TOMORROW
DC Comics (WildStorm): June, 2005 - No. 6, Nov, 2005 ($2.99, limited series)

1-6-Howard Chaykin-s/a						3.00
TPB (2006, $19.99) r/#1-6						20.00

CITY PEOPLE NOTEBOOK
Kitchen Sink Press: 1989 ($9.95, B&W, magazine sized)

nn-Will Eisner-s/a						15.00
nn-(DC Comics, 2000) Reprint						10.00

CITY SURGEON (Blake Harper…)
Gold Key: August, 1963

1(10075-308)-Painted-c	4	8	12	23	37	50

CIVIL WAR (Also see Amazing Spider-Man for TPB)
Marvel Comics: July, 2006 - No. 7, Jan, 2007 ($3.99/$2.99, limited series)

1-($3.99) Millar-s/McNiven-a & wraparound-c	3	6	9	14	19	24
1-Variant cover by Michael Turner	4	8	12	23	37	50
1-Aspen Comics Variant cover by Turner	3	6	9	19	30	40
1-Sketch Variant cover	3	6	9	16	23	30
1-Director's Cut (2006, $4.99) r/#1 plus promo art, variant covers, sketches and script						
	2	4	6	11	16	20
2-($2.99) Spider-Man unmasks	2	4	6	8	10	12
2-Turner variant cover	2	4	6	11	16	20
2-B&W sketch variant cover	3	6	9	16	23	30
2-2nd printing						5.00
3-7: 3-Thor returns. 4-Goliath killed	1	2	3	5	6	8
3-7-Turner variant covers	1	2	3	6	8	10
3-7-B&W sketch variant covers	3	6	9	14	20	25
TPB (2007, $24.99) r/#1-7; gallery of variant covers						25.00
…: Battle Damage Report (2007, $3.99) Post-Civil War character profiles; McGuinness-c						4.00
…: Choosing Sides (2007, $3.99) Colan-c; Howard the Duck app.; 2 covers by Yu & Colan						5.00
…: Companion TPB (2007, $13.99) r/Civil War Files, …:Battle Damage Report, Marvel Spotlight: Millar/McNiven, Marvel Spotlight: Civil War Aftermath and Daily Bugle CW						14.00
Daily Bugle Civil War Newspaper Special #1 (9/06, 50¢, newsprint) Daily Bugle "newspaper" overview of the crossover; Mayhew-a						3.00
…Files (2006, $3.99) profile pages of major Civil War characters; McNiven-c						4.00
…: Marvels Snapshots 1 (2/21, $4.99) Ahmed-s/Kelly-a; Alex Ross-c; Captain America app.						5.00
…: Marvels Snapshots TPB (2007, $11.99) r/Civil War: Choosing Sides, CW: The Return, She-Hulk #8, CW: The Initiative; She-Hulk sketch page; variant cover gallery						12.00
…: MGC #1 (6/10, $1.00) r/#1 with "Marvel's Greatest Comics" cover logo						3.00
…: The Confession (5/07, $2.99) Maleev-c/a; Bendis-s						3.00
…: The Initiative (4/07, $3.99) Silvestri-c/a; previews of post-Civil War series						5.00
…: The Return (3/07, $2.99) Captain Marvel returns; The Sentry app.; Raney-a						3.00
…:The Road to Civil War TPB (2007, $14.99) r/New Avengers: Illuminati, Fantastic Four #536 & 537, Amazing Spider-Man #529-531; Spider-Man costume sketches by Bachalo						15.00
… War Crimes (2/07, $3.99) Kingpin in prison; Tieri-s/Staz Johnson-a						4.00
… War Crimes TPB (2007, $17.99) r/Civil War: War Crimes one-shot and Underworld #1-5						18.00
… X-Men Universe TPB (2007, $13.99) r/Cable & Deadpool #30-32; X-Factor #8,9						14.00

CIVIL WAR (Secret Wars tie-in)
Marvel Comics: Sept, 2015 - No. 5, Dec, 2015 ($4.99/$3.99, limited series)

1-($4.99) Soule-s/Yu-a; Stark vs. Rogers on Battleworld						5.00
2-5-($3.99)						4.00

CIVIL WAR CHRONICLES (Reprints of Civil War and related Marvel issues)
Marvel Comics: Oct, 2007 - No. 12, Sept, 2008 ($4.99)

1-12: Reprints Civil War, Civil War: Frontline and x-over issues						5.00

CIVIL WAR: FRONTLINE (Tie-in to Civil War and related Marvel issues)
Marvel Comics: Aug, 2006 - No. 11, Apr, 2007 ($2.99, limited series)

1-Jenkins-s/Bachs-a/Watson-c; back-up stories by various						4.00
2-11: 3-Green Goblin app. 11-Aftermath of Civil War #7						3.00
… Book 1 TPB (2007, $14.99) r/#1-6						15.00
… Book 2 TPB (2007, $14.99) r/#7-11						15.00

CIVIL WAR: HOUSE OF M
Marvel Comics: Nov, 2008 - No. 5, Mar, 2009 ($2.99, limited series)

1-5-Gage-s/DiVito-a						3.00

CIVIL WAR MUSKET, THE (Kadets of America Handbook)
Custom Comics, Inc.: 1960 (25¢, half-size, 36 pgs.)

nn	3	6	9	15	22	28

CIVIL WAR II
Marvel Comics: No. 0, Jul, 2016 - No. 8, Feb, 2017 ($4.99/$5.99, limited series)

0-($4.99) Bendis-s/Coipel-a; intro. Ulysses						5.00
1-($5.99) Bendis-s/Marquez-a; Thanos kills War Machine						6.00
2-8-($4.99) 3-Banner killed. 4,5-Guardians of the Galaxy app. 7-Sorrentino-a (2 pgs.)						5.00
…: The Oath 1 (3/17, $4.99) Spencer-s; Capt. America named Director of SHIELD						5.00

CIVIL WAR II: AMAZING SPIDER-MAN
Marvel Comics: Aug, 2016 - No. 4, Nov, 2016 ($3.99, limited series)

1-4-Gage-s/Foreman-a; Ulysses app.; Clash returns						4.00

CIVIL WAR II: CHOOSING SIDES
Marvel Comics: Aug, 2016 - No. 6, Nov, 2016 ($4.99/$3.99, limited series)

1-($4.99) Short stories; Nick Fury, Night Thrasher & Damage Control app.						5.00
2-6-($3.99) Nick Fury story in all. 2-War Machine. 4-Punisher. 6-Jessica Jones						4.00

CIVIL WAR II: GODS OF WAR
Marvel Comics: Aug, 2016 - No. 4, Nov, 2016 ($3.99, limited series)

1-4-Abnett-s/Laiso-a/Anacleto-c. 1-Amadeus Cho app. 3-Avengers app.						4.00

CIVIL WAR II: KINGPIN
Marvel Comics: Sept, 2016 - No. 4, Dec, 2016 ($4.99/$3.99, limited series)

1-($4.99) Two stories; Rosenberg-s/Ortiz-a; Talajic-a; intro./origin Janus Jardeesh						5.00
2-4-($3.99) Rosenberg-s/Ortiz-a. 3-Punisher app.						4.00

CIVIL WAR II: ULYSSES
Marvel Comics: Oct, 2016 - No. 3, Dec, 2016 ($4.99, limited series)

1-3-Ewing-s/Kesel & Palo-a/Francavilla-c; Karnak and the Inhumans app.						4.00

CIVIL WAR II: X-MEN
Marvel Comics: Aug, 2016 - No. 4, Nov, 2016 ($3.99, limited series)

1-4-Bunn-s/Broccardo-a; Magneto app. 2-The Brood & Fantomex app. 4-Ulysses app.						4.00

CIVIL WAR: X-MEN (Tie-in to Civil War)
Marvel Comics: Sept, 2006 - No. 4, Dec, 2006 ($2.99, limited series)

1-4-Paquette-a/Hine-s; Bishop app.						3.00
1-Variant cover by Michael Turner						10.00
TPB (2007, $11.99) r/#1-4, profile pages of minor characters						12.00

CIVIL WAR: YOUNG AVENGERS & RUNAWAYS (Tie-in to Civil War)
Marvel Comics: Sept, 2006 - No. 4, Dec, 2006 ($2.99, limited series)

1-4-Caselli-a/Wells-s/Cheung-c						3.00
TPB (2007, $11.99) r/#1-4, profile pages of characters						12.00

CLAIRE VOYANT (Also see Keen Teens)
Leader Publ./Standard/Pentagon Publ.: 1946 - No. 4, 1947 (Sparling strip reprints)

nn	106	212	318	673	1162	1650
2-Kamen-c	84	168	252	538	919	1300
3-Kamen bridal-c; contents mentioned in Love and Death, a book by Gershom Legman(1949) referenced by Dr. Wertham in **SOTI**	129	258	387	826	1413	2000
4-Kamen bondage-c	110	220	330	704	1202	1700

CLANDESTINE (Also see Marvel Comics Presents & X-Men: ClanDestine)
Marvel Comics: Oct, 1994 - No. 12, Sept, 1995 ($2.95/$2.50)

1-($2.95)-Alan Davis-c/a(p)/scripts & Mark Farmer-c/a(i) begin, ends #8; Modok app.; Silver Surfer cameo; gold foil-c						5.00
2-12: 2-Wraparound-c. 2,3-Silver Surfer app. 5-Origin of ClanDestine. 6-Capt. America, Hulk, Spider-Man, Thing & Thor-c; Spider-Man cameo. 7-Spider-Man-c/app.; Punisher cameo. 8-Invaders & Dr. Strange app. 10-Captain Britain-c/app. 11-Sub-Mariner app.						4.00
Preview (10/94, $1.50)						4.00
… Classic HC (2008, $29.99, DJ) r/#1-8, Marvel Comics Presents #158, X-Men and Clandestine #1&2, sketch pages and cover gallery; Alan Davis afterword						30.00

CLANDESTINE
Marvel Comics: Apr, 2008 - No. 5, Aug, 2008 ($2.99, limited series)

1-5: 1-Alan Davis-c/a(p)/scripts & Mark Farmer-c/a(i) app. 2-5-Excalibur app.						3.00

CLARENCE (Based on the Cartoon Network series)
BOOM! Studios (kaboom): Jun, 2015 - No. 4, Sept, 2015 ($3.99)

1-4-Short stories by various; multiple covers on each						4.00
…: Quest 1 (6/16, $4.99) Cron-DeVico-s; art by Smigiel & Omac						5.00
…: Rest Stops 1 (12/15, $4.99) Short stories by various; two covers						5.00

CLANKILLERS
AfterShock Comics: Jul, 2018 - No. 5, Dec, 2018 ($3.99, limited series)

	GD	VG	FN	VF	VF/NM	NM-		GD	VG	FN	VF	VF/NM	NM-
	2.0	4.0	6.0	8.0	9.0	9.2		2.0	4.0	6.0	8.0	9.0	9.2

1-5-Sean Lewis-s/Antonio Fuso-a 4.00

CLANS OF BELARI
AfterShock Comics: Jul, 2021 - No. 4, Oct, 2021 ($4.99, limited series)

1-4-Peter & Rob Blackie-s/Daniel Maine-a 5.00

CLASH
DC Comics: 1991 - No. 3, 1991 ($4.95, limited series, 52 pgs.)

Book One - Three: Adam Kubert-c/a 5.00

CLASSIC BATTLESTAR GALACTICA (See Battlestar Galactica, Classic...)

CLASSIC COMICS/ILLUSTRATED - INTRODUCTION
by Dan Malan

Since the first publication of this special introduction to the **Classics** section, a number of revisions have been made to further clarify the listings. **Classics** reprint editions prior to 1963 had either incorrect dates or no dates listed. Those reprint editions should be identified only by the highest number on the reorder list (HRN). Past *Guides* listed what were calculated to be approximately correct dates, but many people found it confusing for the *Guide* to list a date not listed in the comic itself.

We have also attempted to clear up confusion about edition variations, such as color, printer, etc. Such variations are identified by letters. Editions are determined by three categories. Original edition variations are designated as Edition 1A, 1B, etc. All reprint editions prior to 1963 are identified by HRN only. All reprint editions from 9/63 on are identified by the correct date listed in the comic.

Information is also included on four reprintings of **Classics**. From 1968-1976, Twin Circle, the Catholic newspaper, serialized over 100 **Classics** titles. That list can be found under non-series items at the end of this section. In 1972, twelve **Classics** were reissued as **Now Age Books Illustrated**. They are listed under **Pendulum Illustrated Classics**. In 1982, 20 **Classics** were reissued, adapted for teaching English as a second language. They are listed under **Regents Illustrated Classics**. Then in 1984, six **Classics** were reissued with cassette tapes. See the listing under **Cassette Books**.

UNDERSTANDING CLASSICS ILLUSTRATED
by Dan Malan

Since **Classics Illustrated** is the most complicated comic book series, with all its reprint editions and variations, changes in covers and artwork, a variety of means of identifying editions, and the most extensive worldwide distribution of any comic-book series, this introductory section is provided to assist you in gaining expertise about this series.

THE HISTORY OF CLASSICS
The **Classics** series was the brain child of Albert L. Kanter, who saw in the new comic-book medium a means of introducing children to the great classics of literature. In October of 1941 his Gilberton Co. began the **Classic Comics** series with **The Three Musketeers**, with 64 pages of storyline. In those early years, the struggling series saw irregular schedules and numerous printers, not to mention variable art quality and literal story adaptations. With No.13 the page total was reduced to 56 (except for No. 33, originally scheduled to be No. 9), and with No. 15 the coming-next ad on the outside back cover moved inside. In 1945 the Jerry Iger Shop began producing all new CI titles, beginning with No. 23. In 1947 the search for a classier logo resulted in **Classics Illustrated**, beginning with No. 35. **Last Days of Pompeii**. With No. 45 the page total dropped again to 48, which was to become the standard.

Two new developments in 1951 had a profound effect upon the success of the series. One was the introduction of painted covers, instead of the old line drawn covers, beginning with No. 81, **The Odyssey**. The second was the switch to the major national distributor Curtis. They raised the cover price from 10 to 15 cents, making it the highest priced comic-book, but it did not slow the growth of the series, because they were marketed as books, not comics. Because of this higher quality image, **Classics** flourished during the fifties while other comic series were reeling from outside attacks. They diversified with their new **Juniors**, **Specials**, and **World Around Us** series.

Classics artwork can be divided into three distinct periods. The pre-Iger era (1941-44) was mentioned above for its variable art quality. The Iger era (1945-53) was a major improvement in art quality and adaptations. It came to be dominated by artists Henry Kiefer and Alex Blum, together accounting for some 50 titles. Their styles gave the first real personality to the series. The EC era (1954-62) resulted from the demise of the EC horror series, when many of their artists made the major switch to classical art.

But several factors brought the production of new CI titles to a complete halt in 1962. Gilberton lost its 2nd class mailing permit. External factors like television, cheap paperback books, and Cliff Notes were all eating away at their market. Production halted with No.167, **Faust**, even though many more titles were already in the works. Many of those found their way into foreign series, and are very desirable to collectors. In 1967, **Classics Illustrated** was sold to Patrick Frawley and his Catholic publication, Twin Circle. They issued two new titles in 1969 as part of an attempted revival, but succumbed to major distribution problems in 1971. In 1988, First Publishing acquired the rights to use the old CI series art, logo, and name from the Frawley Group, and released a short-lived series featuring contributions of modern creators. Acclaim Books and Twin Circles issued a series of **Classics** reprints from 1997-1998.

One of the unique aspects of the **Classics Illustrated** (CI) series was the proliferation of reprint variations. Some titles had as many as 25 editions. Reprinting began in 1943. Some **Classic Comics** (CC) reprints (r) had the logo format revised to a banner logo, and added a motto under the banner. In 1947 CC titles changed to the CI logo, but kept their line drawn covers (LDC). In 1948, Nos. 13, 18, 29 and 41 received second covers (LDC2), replacing covers considered too violent, and reprints of Nos. 13-44 had pages reduced to 48, except for No. 26, which had 48 pages to begin with.

Starting in the mid-1950s, 70 of the 80 LDC titles were reissued with new painted covers (PC). Thirty of them also received new interior artwork (A2). The new artwork was generally higher quality with larger art panels and more faithful but abbreviated storylines. Later on, there were 29 second painted covers (PC2), mostly by Twin Circle. Altogether there were 199 interior art variations (169 (O)s and 30 A2 editions) and 272 different covers (169 (O)s, four LDC2s, 70 new PCs of LDC (O)s, and 29 PC2s). It is mildly astounding to realize that there are nearly 1400 different editions in the U.S. CI series.

FOREIGN CLASSICS ILLUSTRATED
If U.S. Classics variations are mildly astounding, the veritable plethora of foreign CI variations will boggle your imagination. While we still anticipate additional discoveries, we presently know about series in 25 languages and 27 countries. There were 250 new CI titles in foreign series, and nearly 400 new foreign covers of U.S. titles. The 1400 U.S. CI editions pale in comparison to the 4000 plus foreign editions. The very nature of CI lent itself to flourishing as an international series. Worldwide, they published over one billion copies! The first foreign CI series consisted of six Canadian Classic Comic reprints in 1946.

The following chart shows when CI series first began in each country:
1946: Canada. 1947: Australia. 1948: Brazil/The Netherlands. 1950: Italy. 1951: Greece/ Japan/ Hong Kong(?)/England/Argentina/Mexico. 1952: West Germany. 1954: Norway. 1955: New Zealand/South Africa. 1956: Denmark/Sweden/Iceland. 1957: Finland/France. 1962: Singapore(?). 1964: India (8 languages). 1971: Ireland (Gaelic). 1973: Belgium(?) / Philippines(?) & Malaysia(?).

Significant among the early series were Brazil and Greece. In 1950, Brazil was the first country to begin doing its own new titles. They issued nearly 80 new CI titles by Brazilian authors. In Greece in 1951 they actually had debates in parliament about the effects of Classics Illustrated on Greek culture, leading to the inclusion of 88 new Greek History & Mythology titles in the CI series.

But by far the most important foreign CI development was the joint European series which began in 1956 in 10 countries simultaneously. By 1960, CI had the largest European distribution of any American publication, not just comics! So when all the problems came up with U.S. distribution, they literally moved the CI operation to Europe in 1962, and continued producing new titles in all four CI series. Many of them were adapted and drawn in the U.S., the most famous of which was the British CI #158A. Dr. No, drawn by Norman Nodel. Unfortunately, the British CI series ended in late 1963, which limited the European CI titles available in English to 15. Altogether there were 82 new CI art titles in the joint European series, which ran until 1976.

IDENTIFYING CLASSICS EDITIONS
HRN: This is the highest number on the reorder list. It should be listed in ( ) after the title number. It is crucial to understanding various CI editions.
ORIGINALS (O): This is the all-important First Edition. To determine (O)s,there is one primary rule and two secondary rules (with exceptions):
Rule No. 1: All (O)s and only (O)s have coming-next ads for the next number. Exceptions: No. 14(15) (reprint) has an ad on the last inside text page only. No. 14(0) also has a full-page outside back cover ad (also rule 2). Nos.55(75) and 57(75) have coming-next ads. (Rules 2 and 3 apply here). Nos. 168(0) and 169(0) do not have coming-next ads. No.168 was never reprinted; No. 169(0) has HRN (166). No. 169(169) is the only reprint.
Rule No. 2: On nos.1-80, all (O)s and only (O)s list 10c on the front cover. Exceptions: Reprint variations of Nos. 37(62), 39(71), and 46(62) list 10c on the front cover. (Rules 1 and 3 apply here.)
Rule No. 3: All (O)s have HRN close to that title No. Exceptions: Some reprints also have HRNs close to that title number: e.g. 5(61), 58(62), 60(62), 149(149), 152(149) 153(149), and title no. in the 160's. (Rules 1 and 2 apply here.)
DATES: Many reprint editions list either an incorrect date or no date. Since Gilberton apparently kept track of CI editions by HRN, they often left the (O) date on reprints. Often, someone with a CI collection for sale will swear that all their copies are originals. That is why we are so detailed in pointing out how to identify original editions. Except for original editions, which should have a coming-next ad, etc., all CI dates prior to 1963 are incorrect! So you want to go by HRN only if it is (165) or below, and go by listed date if it is 1963 or later. There are a few (167) editions with incorrect dates. They could be listed either as (167) or (62/3), which is meant to indicate that they were issued sometime between late 1962 and early 1963.
COVERS: A change from CC to LDC indicates a logo change, not a cover change; while a change from LDC to LDC2, LDC to PC, or from PC to PC2 does indicate a new cover. New PCs can be identified by HRN, and PC2s can be identified by HRN and date. Several covers had color changes, particularly from purple to blue.
Notes: If you see 15 cents in Canada on a front cover, it does not necessarily indicate a Canadian edition. Editions with an HRN between 44 and 75, with 15 cents on the cover are Canadian. Check the publisher's address. An HRN listing two numbers with a / between them indicates that there are two different reorder lists in the front and back covers. Official Twin Circle editions have a full-page back cover ad for their TC magazine, with no CI reorder list. Any CI with just a Twin Circle sticker on the front is not an official TC edition.

TIPS ON LISTING CLASSICS FOR SALE
It may be easy to just list Edition'17, but Classics collectors keep track of CI editions in terms of HRN and/or date, (O) or (r), CC or LDC, PC or PC2, A1 or A2, soft or stiff cover, etc. Try to help them out. For originals, just list (O), unless there are variations such as color (Nos. 10 and 61), printer (Nos. 18-22), HRN (Nos. 95, 108, 160), etc. For reprints, just list HRN if it's (165) or below. Above that, list HRN and date. Also, please list type of logo/cover/art for the convenience of buyers. They will appreciate it.

CLASSIC COMICS (Also see Best from Boys Life, Cassette Books, Famous Stories, Fast Fiction, Golden Picture Classics, King Classics, Marvel Classics Comics, Pendulum Illustrated Classics, Picture Parade, Picture Progress, Regents III. Classics, Spitfire, Stories by Famous Authors, Superior Stories, and World Around Us.)

CLASSIC COMICS (Classics Illustrated No. 35 on)
Elliot Publishing #1-3 (1941-1942)/**Gilberton Publications #4-167** (1942-1967) /**Twin Circle Pub.** (Frawley) **#168-169** (1968-1969):
10/41 - No. 34, 2/47; No. 35, 3/47 - No. 169, Spring 1969
(Reprint Editions of almost all titles 5/43 - Spring 1971)
(Painted Covers (0)s No. 81 on, and (r)s of most Nos. 1-80)

Abbreviations:
A–Art; C or c–Cover; CC–Classic Comics; CI–Classics Ill.; Ed–Edition; LDC–Line Drawn Cover; PC–Painted Cover; r–Reprint

1. The Three Musketeers

Ed	HRN	Date	Details	A	C	GD	VG	FN	VF	VF/NM	NM-
1	—	10/41	Date listed-1941; Elliot Pub; 68 pgs.	1	1	519	1038	1557	3789	6695	9600
2	10	–	10¢ price removed on all (r)s; Elliot Pub; CC-r	1	1	39	78	117	240	395	550
3	15	–	Long Isl. Ind. Ed.; CC-r	1	1	28	56	84	165	270	375
4	18/20	–	Sunrise Times Ed.; CC-r	1	1	19	38	57	109	172	235
5	21	–	Richmond Courier Ed.; CC-r	1	1	17	34	51	98	154	210
6	28	1946	CC-r	1	1	15	30	45	83	124	165
7	36	–	LDC-r	1	1	8	16	24	42	54	65
8	60	–	LDC-r	1	1	6	12	18	27	33	38
9	64	–	LDC-r	1	1	5	10	15	22	26	30
10	78	–	C-price 15¢;LDC-r	1	1	4	9	13	18	22	26
11	93	–	LDC-r	1	1	4	9	13	18	22	26
12	114	–	Last LDC-r	1	1	4	8	11	16	19	22

Classic Comics #1 © GIL

Classic Comics #3 © GIL

Classic Comics #5 © GIL

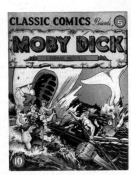

Ed	HRN	Date	Details	A	C	GD 2.0	VG 4.0	FN 6.0	VF 8.0	VF/NM 9.0	NM- 9.2
13	134	–	New-c; old-a; 64 pg. PC-r	1	2	3	6	9	18	28	38
14	143	–	Old-a; PC-r; 64 pg.	1	2	2	4	6	11	16	20
15	150	–	New-a; PC-r; Evans/Crandall-a	2	2	3	6	9	16	24	32
16	149	–	PC-r	2	2	2	4	6	8	11	14
17	167	–	PC-r	2	2	2	4	6	8	11	14
18	167	4/64	PC-r	2	2	2	4	6	8	11	14
19	167	1/65	PC-r	2	2	2	4	6	8	11	14
20	167	3/66	PC-r	2	2	2	4	6	8	11	14
21	166	11/67	PC-r	2	2	2	4	6	8	11	14
22	166	Spr/69	C-price 25¢; stiff-c; PC-r	2	2	2	4	6	8	11	14
23	169	Spr/71	C-r; stiff-c	2	2	2	4	6	8	11	14

2. Ivanhoe

Ed	HRN	Date	Details	A	C	2.0	4.0	6.0	8.0	9.0	9.2
1	(O)	12/41?	Date listed-1941; Elliot Pub; 68 pgs.	1	1	252	504	756	1613	2757	3900
2	10	–	Price & 'Presents' removed; Elliot Pub; CC-r			33	66	99	194	317	440
3	15	–	Long Isl. Ind. ed.; CC-r	1	1	21	42	63	124	202	280
4	18/20	–	Sunrise Times ed.; CC-r	1	1	18	36	54	103	162	225
5	21	–	Richmond Courier ed.; CC-r	1	1	16	32	48	94	147	200
6	28	1946	Last 'Comics'-r	1	1	15	30	45	83	124	165
7	36	–	1st LDC-r	1	1	9	18	27	47	61	75
8	60	–	LDC-r	1	1	6	12	18	27	33	38
9	64	–	LDC-r	1	1	5	10	15	22	26	30
10	78	–	C-price 15¢; LDC-r	1	1	4	9	13	18	22	26
11	89	–	LDC-r	1	1	4	8	12	17	21	24
12	106	–	LDC-r	1	1	4	7	10	14	17	20
13	121	–	Last LDC-r	1	1	4	7	10	14	17	20
14	136	–	New-c&a; PC-r	2	2	5	10	15	25	31	36
15	142	–	PC-r	2	2	2	4	6	9	13	16
16	153	–	PC-r	2	2	2	4	6	9	13	16
17	149	–	PC-r	2	2	2	4	6	9	13	16
18	167	–	PC-r	2	2	2	4	6	8	11	14
19	167	5/64	PC-r	2	2	2	4	6	8	11	14
20	167	1/65	PC-r	2	2	2	4	6	8	11	14
21	167	3/66	PC-r	2	2	2	4	6	8	11	14
22A	167	9/67	PC-r	2	2	2	4	6	8	11	14
22B	166	–	Center ad for Children's Digest & Young Miss; rare; PC-r	2	2	6	12	18	40	73	105
23	166	R/68	C-Price 25¢; PC-r	2	2	2	4	6	8	11	14
24	169	Win/69	Stiff-c	2	2	2	4	6	8	11	14
25	169	Win/71	PC-r; stiff-c	2	2	2	4	6	8	11	14

3. The Count of Monte Cristo

Ed	HRN	Date	Details	A	C	2.0	4.0	6.0	8.0	9.0	9.2
1	(O)	3/42	Elliot Pub; 68 pgs.			168	336	504	1075	1838	2600
2	10	–	Conray Prods; CC-r1			32	64	96	188	307	425
3	15	–	Long Isl. Ind. ed.; CC-r	1	1	24	48	72	142	234	325
4	18/20	–	Sunrise Times ed.; CC-r	1	1	20	40	60	117	189	260
5	20	–	Sunrise Times ed.; CC-r			18	36	54	103	162	220
6	21	–	Richmond Courier ed.; CC-r	1	1	17	34	51	98	154	210
7	28	1946	CC-r; new Banner logo	1	1	14	28	42	82	121	160
8	36	–	1st LDC-r	1	1	9	18	27	47	61	75
9	60	–	LDC-r	1	1	6	12	18	27	33	38
10	62	–	LDC-r	1	1	6	12	18	29	36	42
11	71	–	LDC-r	1	1	5	10	14	20	24	28
12	87	–	C-price 15¢; LDC-r	1	1	4	9	13	18	22	26
13	113	–	LDC-r	1	1	4	7	10	14	17	20
14	135	–	New-c&a; PC-r; Cameron-a	2	2	3	6	9	17	26	35
15	143	–	PC-r	2	2	2	4	6	8	13	16
16	153	–	PC-r	2	2	2	4	6	8	13	16
17	161	–	PC-r	2	2	2	4	6	8	13	16
18	167	–	PC-r	2	2	2	4	6	8	11	14
19	167	7/64	PC-r	2	2	2	4	6	8	11	14
20	167	7/65	PC-r	2	2	2	4	6	8	11	14
21	167	7/66	PC-r	2	2	2	4	6	8	11	14
22	166	R/68	C-price 25¢; PC-r	2	2	2	4	6	8	11	14
23	169	–	Win/69 Stiff-c; PC-r	2	2	2	4	6	8	11	14

4. The Last of the Mohicans

Ed	HRN	Date	Details	A	C	2.0	4.0	6.0	8.0	9.0	9.2
1	(O)	8/42	Date listed-1942; Gilberton #4(0) on; 68 pgs.	1	1	145	290	435	921	1586	2250
2	12	–	Elliot Pub; CC-r	1	1	27	54	81	158	259	360
3	15	–	Long Isl. Ind. ed.; CC-r	1	1	20	40	60	120	195	270
4	20	–	Long Isl. Ind. ed.; CC-r; banner logo	1	1	18	36	54	105	165	225
5	21	–	Queens Home News ed.; CC-r	1	1	16	32	48	94	147	200
6	28	1946	Last CC-r; new	1	1	15	30	45	83	124	165
7	36	–	1st LDC-r	1	1	9	18	27	47	61	75
8	60	–	LDC-r	1	1	6	12	18	27	33	38
9	64	–	LDC-r	1	1	5	10	14	20	24	28
10	78	–	C-price 15¢; LDC-r	1	1	4	9	13	18	22	26
11	89	–	LDC-r	1	1	4	8	12	17	21	24
12	117	–	Last LDC-r	1	1	4	7	10	14	17	20
13	135	–	New-c; PC-r	1	2	5	10	15	24	30	35
14	141	–	PC-r	1	2	4	7	9	14	16	18
15	150	–	New-a; PC-r; Severin, L.B. Cole-a	2	2	6	12	18	27	33	38
16	161	–	PC-r	2	2	2	4	6	8	11	14
17	167	–	PC-r	2	2	2	4	6	8	11	14
18	167	6/64	PC-r	2	2	2	4	6	8	11	14
19	167	8/65	PC-r	2	2	2	4	6	8	11	14
20	167	8/66	PC-r	2	2	2	4	6	8	11	14
21	166	R/67	C-price 25¢; PC-r	2	2	2	4	6	8	11	14
22	169	Spr/69	Stiff-c; PC-r	2	2	2	4	6	8	11	14

5. Moby Dick

Ed	HRN	Date	Details	A	C	2.0	4.0	6.0	8.0	9.0	9.2
1A	(O)	9/42	Date listed-1942; Gilberton; 68 pgs.	1	1	177	354	531	1124	1937	2750
1B			inside-c, rare free			271	542	813	1734	2967	4200
2	10	–	Conray Prods; Pg. 64 changed from 105 title list to letter from Editor; CC-r	1	1	30	60	90	177	289	400
3	15	–	Long Isl. Ind. ed.; Pg. 64 changed from Letter to the Editor to Ill. poem-Concord Hymn; CC-r	1	1	25	50	75	150	245	340
4	18/20	–	Sunrise Times ed.; CC-r	1	1	20	40	60	117	189	260
5	20	–	Sunrise Times ed.; CC-r	1	1	19	38	57	112	179	245
6	21	–	Sunrise Times ed.; CC-r	1	1	17	34	51	98	154	210
7	28	1946	CC-r; new banner logo	1	1	15	30	45	83	124	165
8	36	–	1st LDC-r	1	1	9	18	27	52	69	85
9	60	–	LDC-r	1	1	6	12	18	27	33	38
10	62	–	LDC-r	1	1	6	12	18	29	36	42
11	71	–	LDC-r	1	1	5	10	14	20	24	28
12	87	–	C-price 15¢; LDC-r	1	1	4	9	13	18	22	26
13	118	–	LDC-r	1	1	4	8	12	17	21	24
14	131	–	New c&a; PC-r	2	2	5	10	15	25	31	36
15	138	–	PC-r	2	2	2	4	6	9	12	16
16	148	–	PC-r	2	2	2	4	6	9	12	16
17	158	–	PC-r	2	2	2	4	6	8	12	16
18	167	–	PC-r	2	2	2	4	6	8	11	14

Ed	HRN	Date	Details	A	C	GD 2.0	VG 4.0	FN 6.0	VF 8.0	VF/NM 9.0	NM- 9.2
19	167	6/64	PC-r	2	2	2	4	6	8	11	14
20	167	7/65	PC-r	2	2	2	4	6	8	11	14
21	167	3/66	PC-r	2	2	2	4	6	8	11	14
22	166	9/67	PC-r	2	2	2	4	6	8	11	14
23	166	Win/69	New-c & c-price 25¢; Stiff-c; PC-r	2	3	3	6	9	16	23	30
24	169	Win/71	PC-r	2	3	3	6	9	14	19	24

6. A Tale of Two Cities

Ed	HRN	Date	Details	A	C	GD 2.0	VG 4.0	FN 6.0	VF 8.0	VF/NM 9.0	NM- 9.2
1	(O)	10/42	Date listed-1942; 68 pgs. Zeckerberg c/a	1	1	135	270	405	864	1482	2100
2	14	–	Elliot Pub; CC-r	1	1	25	50	75	150	245	340
3	18	–	Long Isl. Ind. ed.; CC-r	1	1	20	40	60	114	182	250
4	20	–	Sunrise Times ed.; CC-r	1	1	18	36	54	105	182	225
5	28	1946	Last CC-r; new banner logo	1	1	14	28	42	80	115	150
6	51	–	1st LDC-r	1	1	8	16	24	42	54	65
7	64	–	LDC-r	1	1	5	10	15	23	28	32
8	78	–	C-price 15¢; LDC-r	1	1	5	10	14	20	24	28
9	89	–	LDC-r	1	1	4	7	10	14	17	20
10	117	–	LDC-r	1	1	4	7	10	14	17	20
11	132	–	New-c&a; PC-r Joe Orlando-a	2	2	5	10	15	25	31	36
12	140	–	PC-r	2	2	2	4	6	8	11	14
13	147	–	PC-r	2	2	2	4	6	8	11	14
14	152	–	PC-r; very rare	2	2	17	34	51	98	154	210
15	153	–	PC-r	2	2	2	4	6	9	13	16
16	149	–	PC-r	2	2	2	4	6	9	13	16
17	167	–	PC-r	2	2	2	4	6	8	11	14
18	167	6/64	PC-r	2	2	2	4	6	8	11	14
19	167	8/65	PC-r	2	2	2	4	6	8	11	14
20	166	5/67	PC-r	2	2	2	4	6	8	11	14
21	166	Fall/68	New-c & 25¢; PC-r	2	3	3	6	9	16	24	32
22	169	Sum/70	Stiff-c; PC-r	2	3	2	4	6	13	18	22

7. Robin Hood

Ed	HRN	Date	Details	A	C	GD 2.0	VG 4.0	FN 6.0	VF 8.0	VF/NM 9.0	NM- 9.2
1	(O)	12/42	Date listed-1942; first Gift Box ad-bc; 68 pgs.	1	1	106	212	318	673	1162	1650
2	12	–	Elliot Pub; CC-r	1	1	24	48	72	140	230	320
3	18	–	Long Isl. Ind. ed.; CC-r	1	1	19	38	57	111	176	240
4	20	–	Nassau Bulletin ed.; CC-r	1	1	18	36	54	103	162	220
5	22	–	Queens Cty. Times ed.; CC-r	1	1	16	32	48	94	147	200
6	28	–	CC-r	1	1	14	28	42	81	118	155
7	51	–	LDC-r	1	1	8	16	24	42	54	65
8	64	–	LDC-r	1	1	5	10	15	24	30	35
9	78	–	LDC-r	1	1	4	9	13	18	22	26
10	97	–	LDC-r	1	1	4	8	12	17	21	24
11	106	–	LDC-r	1	1	4	7	10	14	17	20
12	121	–	LDC-r	1	1	4	7	10	14	17	20
13	129	–	New-c; PC-r	1	2	5	10	15	25	31	36
14	136	–	New-a; PC-r	1	2	5	10	15	24	29	34
15	143	–	PC-r	2	2	2	4	6	9	13	16
16	153	–	PC-r	2	2	2	4	6	9	13	16
17	164	–	PC-r	2	2	2	4	6	8	11	14
18	167	–	PC-r	2	2	2	4	6	8	11	14
19	167	6/64	PC-r	2	2	2	4	6	8	11	14
20	167	5/65	PC-r	2	2	2	4	6	8	11	14
21	167	7/66	PC-r	2	2	2	4	6	8	11	14
22	166	12/67	PC-r	2	2	2	4	6	8	11	14
23	169	Sum/69	Stiff-c; c-price 25¢; PC-r	2	2	2	4	6		11	14

8. Arabian Nights

Ed	HRN	Date	Details	A	C	GD 2.0	VG 4.0	FN 6.0	VF 8.0	VF/NM 9.0	NM- 9.2
1	(O)	2/43	Original; 68 pgs. Lilian Chestney-c/a	1	1	155	310	465	992	1696	2400
2	17	–	Long Isl. ed.; pg. 64 changed from Gift Box ad to Letter from British Medical Worker; CC-r	1	1	53	106	159	334	567	800
3	20	–	Nassau Bulletin; Pg. 64 changed from letter to article-Three Men Named Smith; CC-r	1	1	43	86	129	271	461	650
4A	28	1946	CC-r; new banner logo, slick-c	1	1	31	62	93	182	296	410
4B	28	1946	Same, but w/stiff-c	1	1	31	62	93	182	296	410
5	51	–	LDC-r	1	1	22	44	66	128	209	290
6	64	–	LDC-r	1	1	19	38	57	111	176	240
7	78	–	LDC-r	1	1	18	36	54	105	165	225
8	164	–	New-c&a; PC-r	2	2	15	30	45	90	140	190

9. Les Miserables

Ed	HRN	Date	Details	A	C	GD 2.0	VG 4.0	FN 6.0	VF 8.0	VF/NM 9.0	NM- 9.2
1A	(O)	3/43	Original; slick paper cover; 68 pgs.	1	1	106	212	318	673	1162	1650
1B	(O)	3/43	Original; rough, pulp type-c; 68 pgs.	1	1	126	252	378	806	1378	1950
2	14	–	Elliot Pub; CC-r	1	1	26	52	78	154	252	350
3	18	3/44	Nassau Bul. Pg.	1	1	22	44	66	128	209	290

Ed	HRN	Date	Details	A	C	GD 2.0	VG 4.0	FN 6.0	VF 8.0	VF/NM 9.0	NM- 9.2
			64 changed from Gift Box ad to Bill of Rights article; CC-r								
4	20	–	Richmond Courier ed.; CC-r	1	1	19	38	57	111	176	240
5	28	1946	Gilberton; pgs. 60-64 rearranged/illos added; CC-r	1	1	14	28	42	81	118	155
6	51	–	LDC-r	1	1	9	18	27	47	61	75
7	71	–	LDC-r	1	1	6	12	18	29	36	42
8	87	–	C-price 15¢; LDC-r	1	1	6	12	18	27	33	38
9	161	–	New-c&a; PC-r	2	2	7	14	21	37	46	55
10	167	9/63	PC-r	2	2	2	4	6	11	16	20
11	167	12/65	PC-r	2	2	2	4	6	11	16	20
12	166	R/1968	New-c & price 25¢; PC-r	2	3	3	6	9	17	26	35

10. Robinson Crusoe (Used in SOTI, pg. 142)

Ed	HRN	Date	Details	A	C	GD 2.0	VG 4.0	FN 6.0	VF 8.0	VF/NM 9.0	NM- 9.2
1A	(O)	4/43	Original; Violet-c; 68 pgs; Zuckerberg c/a	1	1	87	174	261	553	952	1350
1B	(O)	4/43	Original; blue-grey-c, 68 pgs.	1	1	97	194	291	621	1061	1500
2A	14	–	Elliot Pub; violet-c; 68 pgs; CC-r	1	1	30	60	90	177	289	400
2B	14	–	Elliot Pub; blue-grey-c; CC-r	1	1	26	52	78	154	252	350
3	18	–	Nassau Bul. Pg. 64 changed from Gift Box ad to Bill of Rights article; CC-r	1	1	19	38	57	111	176	240
4	20	–	Queens Home News ed.; CC-r	1	1	16	32	48	94	147	200
5	28	1946	Gilberton; pg. 64 changes from Bill of Rights to WWII article-One Leg Shot Away; last CC-r	1	1	14	28	42	80	115	150
6	51	–	LDC-r	1	1	8	16	24	42	54	65
7	64	–	LDC-r	1	1	6	12	18	27	33	38
8	78	–	C-price 15¢; LDC-r	1	1	5	10	14	20	24	28
9	97	–	LDC-r	1	1	4	9	13	18	22	26
10	114	–	LDC-r	1	1	4	7	10	14	17	20
11	130	–	New-c; PC-r	1	2	5	10	15	25	31	36
12	140	–	New-a; PC-r	2	2	5	10	15	24	29	34
13	153	–	PC-r	2	2	2	4	6	8	11	14
14	164	–	PC-r	2	2	2	4	6	8	11	14
15	167	–	PC-r	2	2	2	4	6	8	11	14
16	167	7/64	PC-r	2	2	2	4	6	10	14	18
17	167	5/65	PC-r	2	2	2	4	6	10	14	18
18	167	6/66	PC-r	2	2	2	4	6	8	11	14
19	167	Fall/68	C-price 25¢; PC-r	2	2	2	4	6	8	11	16
20	166	R/68	(No Twin Circle ad)	2	2	2	4	6	8	13	16
21	166	Sm/70	Stiff-c; PC-r	2	2	2	4	6	9	13	16

11. Don Quixote

Ed	HRN	Date	Details	A	C	GD 2.0	VG 4.0	FN 6.0	VF 8.0	VF/NM 9.0	NM- 9.2
1	10	5/43	First (O) with HRN list; 68 pgs.	1	1	89	178	267	565	970	1375
2	18	–	Nassau Bulletin ed.; CC-r	1	1	23	46	69	136	223	310
3	21	–	Queens Home News ed.; CC-r	1	1	19	38	57	111	176	240
4	28	–	CC-r	1	1	14	28	42	81	118	155
5	110	–	New-PC; PC-r	1	2	7	14	21	35	43	50
6	156	–	Pgs. reduced 68 to 52; PC-r	1	2	4	7	10	14	17	20
7	165	–	PC-r	1	2	2	4	6	9	13	16
8	167	1/64	PC-r	1	2	2	4	6	9	13	16
9	167	11/65	PC-r	1	2	2	4	6	9	13	16
10	166	R/1968	New-c & price 25¢; PC-r	1	3	3	6	9	18	27	36

12. Rip Van Winkle and the Headless Horseman

Ed	HRN	Date	Details	A	C	GD 2.0	VG 4.0	FN 6.0	VF 8.0	VF/NM 9.0	NM- 9.2
1	11	6/43	Original; 68 pgs.	1	1	92	184	276	584	1005	1425
2	15	–	Long Isl. Ind. ed.; CC-r	1	1	24	48	72	142	234	325
3	20	–	Long Isl. Ind. ed.;	1	1	20	40	60	114	182	250
4	22	–	Queens Cty. Times ed.; CC-r	1	1	16	32	48	94	147	200
5	28	–	CC-r	1	1	14	28	42	80	115	150
6	60	–	1st LDC-r	1	1	8	16	24	40	50	60
7	62	–	LDC-r	1	1	5	10	15	23	28	32
8	71	–	LDC-r	1	1	4	9	13	18	22	26
9	89	–	C-price 15¢; LDC-r	1	1	4	8	12	17	21	24
10	118	–	LDC-r	1	1	4	7	10	14	17	20
11	132	–	New-c; PC-r	1	2	5	10	15	25	31	36
12	150	–	New-a; PC-r	2	2	5	10	15	24	29	34
13	158	–	PC-r	2	2	2	4	6	8	13	16
14	167	–	PC-r	2	2	2	4	6	8	13	16
15	167	12/63	PC-r	2	2	2	4	6	8	11	14
16	167	4/65	PC-r	2	2	2	4	6	8	11	14
17	167	4/66	PC-r	2	2	2	4	6	8	11	14
18	166	R/1968	New-c&price 25¢; PC-r; stiff-c	2	3	3	6	9	14	20	26
19	169	Sm/70	Stiff-c; PC-r	2	3	2	4	6	10	14	18

13. Dr. Jekyll and Mr. Hyde (Used in SOTI, pg. 143)(1st horror comic?)

Ed	HRN	Date	Details	A	C

Classic Comics #8 © GIL

Classic Comics #13 © GIL

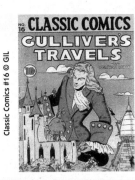

Classic Comics #16 © GIL

(Classic Comics #8 — Arabian Nights, continued)

Ed	HRN	Date	Details	A	C	GD 2.0	VG 4.0	FN 6.0	VF 8.0	VF/NM 9.0	NM- 9.2
1	12	8/43	Original 60 pgs.	1	1	155	310	465	992	1696	2400
2	15	–	Long Isl. Ind. ed.; CC-r	1	1	37	74	111	222	361	500
3	20	–	Long Isl. Ind. ed.; CC-r	1	1	27	54	81	158	259	360
4	28	–	No c-price; CC-r	1	1	20	40	60	117	189	260
5	60	–	New-c; Pgs. reduced from 60 to 52; H.C. Kiefer-c; LDC-r	1	2	9	18	27	52	69	85
6	62	–	LDC-r	1	2	6	12	18	28	34	40
7	71	–	LDC-r	1	2	5	10	15	23	28	32
8	87	–	Date returns (erroneous); LDC-r	1	2	5	10	15	22	26	30
9	112	–	New-c; PC-r; Cameron-a	2	3	7	14	21	35	43	50
10	153	–	PC-r	2	3	2	4	6	9	13	16
11	161	–	PC-r	2	3	2	4	6	9	13	16
12	167	–	PC-r	2	3	2	4	6	8	11	14
13	167	8/64	PC-r	2	3	2	4	6	8	11	14
14	167	11/65	PC-r	2	3	2	4	6	8	11	14
15	166	R/68	C-price 25¢; PC-r	2	3	2	4	6	8	11	14
16	169	Wn/69	PC-r; stiff-c	2	3	2	4	6	8	11	14

14. Westward Ho!

Ed	HRN	Date	Details	A	C	GD 2.0	VG 4.0	FN 6.0	VF 8.0	VF/NM 9.0	NM- 9.2
1	13	9/43	Original; last outside bc coming-next ad; 60 pgs.	1	1	194	388	582	1242	2121	3000
2	15	–	Long Isl. Ind. ed.; CC-r	1	1	58	116	174	371	636	900
3	21	–	Queens Home News; Pg. 56 changed from coming-next ad to Three Men Named Smith; CC-r	1	1	46	92	138	290	488	685
4	28	1946	Gilberton; Pg. 56 changed again to WWII article-Speaking for America; last CC-r	1	1	39	78	117	242	401	560
5	53	–	Pgs. reduced from 60 to 52; LDC-r	1	1	36	72	108	216	351	485

15. Uncle Tom's Cabin (Used in SOTI, pgs. 102, 103)

Ed	HRN	Date	Details	A	C	GD 2.0	VG 4.0	FN 6.0	VF 8.0	VF/NM 9.0	NM- 9.2
1	14	11/43	Original; Outside-bc ad: 2 Gift Boxes; 60 pgs.; color var. on-c; green tree trunk on left & brown trunk, root on left	1	1	87	174	261	553	952	1350
2	15	–	Long Isl. Ind. listed- bottom inside-fc; also Gilberton listed bottom-pg. 1; CC-r; no green tree trunk on cover	1	1	29	58	87	172	281	390
3	21	–	Nassau Bulletin ed.; CC-r has the normal fallen tree trunk & the green fallen tree trunk on cover	1	1	22	44	66	128	209	290
4	28	–	No c-price; CC-r	1	1	15	30	45	88	137	185
5	53	–	Pgs. reduced 60 to 52; LDC-r	1	1	9	18	27	47	61	75
6	71	–	LDC-r	1	1	6	12	18	33	41	48
7	89	–	C-price 15¢; LDC-r	1	1	6	12	18	28	34	40
8	117	–	New-c/lettering changes; PC-r	1	2	6	12	18	28	34	40
9	128	–	'Picture Progress' promo; PC-r	1	2	2	4	6	10	14	18
10	137	–	PC-r	1	2	2	4	6	9	13	16
11	146	–	PC-r	1	2	2	4	6	9	13	16
12	154	–	PC-r	1	2	2	4	6	9	13	16
13	161	–	PC-r	1	2	2	4	6	8	11	14
14	167	–	PC-r	1	2	2	4	6	8	11	14

(Classic Comics #13 — Dr. Jekyll and Mr. Hyde, continued)

Ed	HRN	Date	Details	A	C	GD 2.0	VG 4.0	FN 6.0	VF 8.0	VF/NM 9.0	NM- 9.2
15	167	6/64	PC-r	1	2	2	4	6	8	11	14
16	167	5/65	PC-r	1	2	2	4	6	8	11	14
17	166	5/67	PC-r	1	2	2	4	6	8	11	14
18	166	Wn/69	New-stiff-c; PC-r	1	3	3	6	9	15	22	28
19	169	Sm/70	PC-r; stiff-c	1	3	2	4	6	10	14	18

16. Gulliver's Travels

Ed	HRN	Date	Details	A	C	GD 2.0	VG 4.0	FN 6.0	VF 8.0	VF/NM 9.0	NM- 9.2
1	15	12/43	Original-Lilian Chestney c/a; 60 pgs.	1	1	84	168	252	538	919	1300
2	18/20	–	Price deleted; Queens Home News ed; CC-r	1	1	22	44	66	132	216	300
3	22	–	Queens Cty. Times ed.; CC-r	1	1	18	36	54	105	165	225
4	28	–	CC-r	1	1	14	28	42	80	115	150
5	60	–	Pgs. reduced to 48; LDC-r	1	1	6	12	18	31	38	45
6	62	–	LDC-r	1	1	5	10	15	23	28	32
7	78	–	C-price 15¢; LDC-r	1	1	5	10	14	20	24	28
8	89	–	LDC-r	1	1	4	8	12	17	21	24
9	155	–	New-c; PC-r	1	2	5	10	15	25	31	36
10	165	–	PC-r	1	2	2	4	6	8	11	14
11	167	5/64	PC-r	1	2	2	4	6	8	11	14
12	167	11/65	PC-r	1	2	2	4	6	8	11	14
13	166	R/1968	C-price 25¢; PC-r	1	2	2	4	6	8	11	14
14	169	Wn/69	PC-r; stiff-c	1	2	2	4	6	8	11	14

17. The Deerslayer

Ed	HRN	Date	Details	A	C	GD 2.0	VG 4.0	FN 6.0	VF 8.0	VF/NM 9.0	NM- 9.2
1	16	1/44	Original; Outside-bc ad: 3 Gift Boxes; 60 pgs.	1	1	68	136	204	435	743	1050
2A	18	–	Queens Cty Times (inside-fc); CC-r	1	1	24	48	72	140	230	320
2B	18	–	Gilberton (bottom-pg. 1); CC-r; Scarce	1	1	34	68	102	199	325	450
3	22	–	Queens Cty. Times ed.; CC-r	1	1	19	38	57	112	179	245
4	28	–	CC-r	1	1	14	28	42	81	118	155
5	60	–	Pgs.reduced to 52; LDC-r	1	1	7	14	21	37	46	55
6	64	–	LDC-r	1	1	5	10	15	22	26	30
7	85	–	C-price 15¢; LDC-r	1	1	4	8	12	17	21	24
8	118	–	LDC-r	1	1	4	7	10	14	17	20
9	132	–	Last LDC-r	1	1	4	7	10	14	17	20
10	167	11/66	New-c & price 25¢; PC-r	1	2	2	4	6	11	16	20
11	166	R/1968	PC-r	1	2	3	6	9	17	26	35
12	169	Spr/71	Stiff-c; letters from parents & educators; PC-r	1	2	2	4	6	10	14	18

18. The Hunchback of Notre Dame

Ed	HRN	Date	Details	A	C	GD 2.0	VG 4.0	FN 6.0	VF 8.0	VF/NM 9.0	NM- 9.2
1A	17	3/44	Orig.; Gilberton ed; 60 pgs.	1	1	110	220	330	704	1202	1700
1B	17	3/44	Orig.; Island Pub. Ed.; 60 pgs.	1	1	97	194	291	621	1061	1500
2	18/20	–	Queens Home News ed.; CC-r	1	1	30	60	90	177	289	400
3	22	–	Queens Cty. Times ed.; CC-r	1	1	24	48	72	142	234	325
4	28	–	CC-r	1	1	22	44	66	128	209	290
5	60	–	New-c; 8pgs. deleted; Kiefer-c; LDC-r	1	2	9	18	27	50	65	80
6	62	–	LDC-r	1	2	5	10	15	22	26	30
7	89	–	C-price 15¢; LDC-r	1	2	5	10	14	20	24	28
8A	89	–	H.C.Kiefer on bottom right-c; LDC-r	1	2	4	9	13	18	22	26
8B	89	–	Name omitted; LDC-r	1	2	5	10	15	24	30	35
9	118	–	LDC-r	1	2	4	8	12	17	21	24
10	140	–	New-c; PC-r	1	3	7	14	21	35	43	50
11	146	–	PC-r	1	3	5	10	15	22	26	30
12	158	–	New-c&a; PC-r; Evans/Crandall-a	2	4	5	10	15	25	31	36

Ed	HRN	Date	Details	A	C	GD 2.0	VG 4.0	FN 6.0	VF 8.0	VF/NM 9.0	NM- 9.2
13	165	–	PC-r	2	4	2	4	6	9	13	16
14	167	9/63	PC-r	2	4	2	4	6	9	13	16
15	167	10/64	PC-r	2	4	2	4	6	9	13	16
16	167	4/66	PC-r	2	4	2	4	6	8	11	14
17	166	R/1968	New price 25¢; PC-r	2	4	2	4	6	8	11	14
18	169	Sp/70	Stiff-c; PC-r	2	4	2	4	6	8	11	14

19. Huckleberry Finn

Ed	HRN	Date	Details	A	C	GD 2.0	VG 4.0	FN 6.0	VF 8.0	VF/NM 9.0	NM- 9.2
1A	18	4/44	Orig.; Gilberton ed.; 60 pgs.	1	1	57	114	171	362	619	875
1B	18	4/44	Orig.; Island Pub.; 60 pgs.	1	1	60	120	180	381	653	925
2	18	–	Nassau Bulletin ed.; fc-price 15¢-Canada; no coming-next ad; CC-r			24	48	72	140	230	320
3	22	–	Queens City Times ed.; CC-r	1	1	20	40	60	114	182	250
4	28	–	CC-r	1	1	14	28	42	82	121	160
5	60	–	Pgs. reduced to 48; LDC-r	1	1	6	12	18	31	38	45
6	62	–	LDC-r	1	1	5	10	15	23	28	32
7	78	–	LDC-r	1	1	4	9	13	18	22	26
8	89	–	LDC-r	1	1	4	8	12	17	21	24
9	117	–	LDC-r	1	1	4	7	10	14	17	20
10	131	–	New-c&a; PC-r	2	2	5	10	15	24	30	35
11	140	–	PC-r	2	2	2	4	6	9	13	16
12	150	–	PC-r	2	2	2	4	6	9	13	16
13	158	–	PC-r	2	2	2	4	6	9	13	16
14	165	–	PC-r (scarce)	2	2	3	6	9	14	19	24
15	167	–	PC-r	2	2	2	4	6	8	11	14
16	167	6/64	PC-r	2	2	2	4	6	8	11	14
17	167	6/65	PC-r	2	2	2	4	6	8	11	14
18	167	10/65	PC-r	2	2	2	4	6	8	11	14
19	166	9/67	PC-r	2	2	2	4	6	8	11	14
20	166	Win/69	C-price 25¢; PC-r; stiff-c	2	2	2	4	6	8	11	14
21	169	Sm/70	PC-r; stiff-c	2	2	2	4	6	8	11	14

20. The Corsican Brothers

Ed	HRN	Date	Details	A	C	GD 2.0	VG 4.0	FN 6.0	VF 8.0	VF/NM 9.0	NM- 9.2
1A	20	6/44	Orig.; Gilberton ed.;1 bc-ad: 4 Gift Boxes; 60 pgs.		1	51	102	153	321	546	770
1B	20	6/44	Orig.; Courier ed.; 60 pgs.	1	1	43	86	129	271	461	650
1C	20	6/44	Orig.; Long Island Ind. ed.; 60 pgs.	1	1	43	86	129	271	461	650
2	22	–	Queens Cty. Times ed.; white logo banner; CC-r			20	40	60	115	190	260
3	28	–	CC-r	1	1	19	38	57	109	172	235
4	60	–	CI logo; no price; 48 pgs.; LDC-r	1	1	15	30	45	90	140	190
5A	62	–	LDC-r; Classics Ill. logo at top of pgs.	1	1	15	30	45	83	124	165
5B	62	–	w/o logo at top of pg. (scarcer)	1	1	15	30	45	86	133	180
6	78	–	C-price 15¢; LDC-r	1	1	14	28	42	81	118	155
7	97	–	LDC-r	1	1	14	28	42	78	112	145

21. 3 Famous Mysteries ("The Sign of the 4", "The Murders in the Rue Morgue", "The Flayed Hand")

Ed	HRN	Date	Details	A	C	GD 2.0	VG 4.0	FN 6.0	VF 8.0	VF/NM 9.0	NM- 9.2
1A	21	7/44	Orig.; Gilberton ed.; 60 pgs.	1	1	113	226	339	718	1234	1750
1B	21	7/44	Orig. Island Pub. Co.; 60 pgs.	1	1	113	226	339	718	1234	1750
1C	21	7/44	Original; Courier Ed.; 60 pgs.	1	1	100	200	300	635	1093	1550
2	22	–	Nassau Bulletin ed.; CC-r			42	84	126	265	445	625
3	30	–	CC-r	1	1	32	64	96	188	307	425
4	62	–	LDC-r; 8 pgs. deleted; LDC-r	1	1	24	48	72	142	234	325
5	70	–	LDC-r	1	1	22	44	66	132	216	300
6	85	–	C-price 15¢; LDC-r	1	1	20	40	60	117	189	260
7	114	–	New-c; PC-r	1	2	20	40	60	117	189	260

22. The Pathfinder

Ed	HRN	Date	Details	A	C	GD 2.0	VG 4.0	FN 6.0	VF 8.0	VF/NM 9.0	NM- 9.2
1A	22	10/44	Orig.; No printer listed; ownership statement inside fc lists Gilberton & date; 60 pgs.	1	1	52	104	156	328	552	775
1B	22	10/44	Orig.; Island Pub. ed.; 60 pgs.	1	1	43	86	129	271	461	650
1C	22	10/44	Orig.; Queens Cty Times ed. 60 pgs.	1	1	43	86	129	271	461	650
2	30	–	C-price removed; CC-r	1	1	15	30	45	85	130	175
3	60	–	Pgs. reduced to 52; LDC-r	1	1	6	12	18	27	33	38
4	70	–	LDC-r	1	1	5	10	15	22	26	30
5	85	–	C-price 15¢; LDC-r	1	1	4	9	13	18	22	26
6	118	–	LDC-r	1	1	4	8	12	17	21	24
7	132	–	LDC-r	1	1	4	7	10	14	17	20
8	146	–	LDC-r	1	1	4	7	10	14	17	20
9	167	11/63	New-c; PC-r	1	2	4	8	12	23	37	50
10	167	12/65	PC-r	1	2	2	4	6	11	16	20
11	166	8/67	PC-r	1	2	2	4	6	11	16	20

23. Oliver Twist (1st Classic produced by the Iger Shop)

Ed	HRN	Date	Details	A	C	GD 2.0	VG 4.0	FN 6.0	VF 8.0	VF/NM 9.0	NM- 9.2
1	23	7/45	Original; 60 pgs.	1	1	53	106	159	334	567	800
2A	30		Printers Union logo on bottom left-fc same as 23(Orig.) (very rare); CC-r	1	1	32	64	96	188	307	425
2B	30		Union logo omitted; CC-r	1	1	15	30	45	84	127	170
3	60	–	Pgs. reduced to 48; LDC-r	1	1	6	12	18	29	36	42
4	62	–	LDC-r	1	1	5	10	15	23	28	32
5	71	–	LDC-r	1	1	5	10	14	20	24	28
6	85	–	C-price 15¢; LDC-r	1	1	4	9	13	18	22	26
7	94	–	LDC-r	1	1	4	7	10	14	17	20
8	118	–	LDC-r	1	1	4	7	10	14	17	20
9	136	–	New-PC, old-a; PC-r	1	2	5	10	15	24	30	35
10	150	–	Old-a; PC-r	1	2	4	7	10	14	17	20
11	164	–	Old-a; PC-r	1	2	4	8	11	16	19	22
12	164	–	New-a; PC-r; Evans/Crandall-a	2	2	4	8	12	23	37	50
13	167	–	PC-r	2	2	2	4	6	11	16	20
14	167	8/64	PC-r	2	2	2	4	6	8	11	14
15	167	12/65	PC-r	2	2	2	4	6	8	11	14
16	166	R/1968	New 25¢; PC-r	2	2	2	4	6	8	11	14
17	169	Win/69	Stiff-c; PC-r	2	2	2	4	6	8	11	14

24. A Connecticut Yankee in King Arthur's Court

Ed	HRN	Date	Details	A	C	GD 2.0	VG 4.0	FN 6.0	VF 8.0	VF/NM 9.0	NM- 9.2
1		9/45	Original	1	1	47	94	141	296	498	700
2	30	–	No price circle; CC-r	1	1	15	30	45	90	140	190
3	60	–	8 pgs. deleted; LDC-r	1	1	6	12	18	27	33	38
4	62	–	LDC-r	1	1	5	10	15	23	28	32
5	71	–	LDC-r	1	1	5	10	15	22	26	30
6	87	–	C-price 15¢; LDC-r	1	1	4	9	13	18	22	26
7	121	–	LDC-r	1	1	4	8	12	17	21	24
8	140	–	New-c&a; PC-r	2	2	5	10	15	25	31	36
9	153	–	PC-r	2	2	2	4	6	9	13	16
10	164	–	PC-r	2	2	2	4	6	8	11	14
11	167	–	PC-r	2	2	2	4	6	8	11	14
12	167	7/64	PC-r	2	2	2	4	6	8	11	14
13	167	6/66	PC-r	2	2	2	4	6	8	11	14
14	166	R/1968	C-price 25¢; PC-r	2	2	2	4	6	8	11	14
15	169	Spr/71	PC-r; stiff-c	2	2	2	4	6	8	11	14

25. Two Years Before the Mast

Ed	HRN	Date	Details	A	C	GD 2.0	VG 4.0	FN 6.0	VF 8.0	VF/NM 9.0	NM- 9.2
1		10/45	Original; Webb-Heames-a&c	1	1	45	90	135	284	480	675
2	30	–	Price circle blank; CC-r	1	1	15	30	45	86	133	180
3	60	–	8 pgs. deleted; LDC-r	1	1	6	12	18	27	33	38
4	62	–	LDC-r	1	1	5	10	15	23	28	32
5	71	–	LDC-r	1	1	4	9	13	18	22	26
6	85	–	C-price 15¢; LDC-r	1	1	4	7	10	14	17	20
7	114	–	LDC-r	1	1	4	7	10	14	17	20
8	156	–	3 pgs. replaced by fillers; new-c; PC-r	1	2	5	10	15	25	31	36
9	167	12/63	PC-r	1	2	2	4	6	8	11	14
10	167	12/65	PC-r	1	2	2	4	6	8	11	14
11	166	9/67	PC-r	1	2	2	4	6	8	11	14
12	169	Win/69	C-price 25¢; stiff-c PC-r	1	2	2	4	6	8	11	14

26. Frankenstein (2nd horror comic?)

Ed	HRN	Date	Details	A	C	GD 2.0	VG 4.0	FN 6.0	VF 8.0	VF/NM 9.0	NM- 9.2
1	26	12/45	Original; Webb/Brewster a&c; 52 pgs.	1	1	135	270	405	864	1482	2100
2A	30	–	Price circle blank; no indicia; CC-r	1	1	39	78	117	231	378	525
2B	30	–	With indicia; scarce; CC-r	1	1	40	80	120	246	411	575
3	60	–	LDC-r	1	1	20	40	60	114	182	250
4	62	–	LDC-r	1	1	18	36	54	103	162	220
5	71	–	LDC-r	1	1	9	18	27	50	65	80
6A	82	–	C-price 15¢; soft-c; LDC-r	1	1	8	16	24	44	57	70
6B	82	–	Stiff-c; LDC-r	1	1	9	18	27	50	65	80
7	117	–	LDC-r	1	1	5	10	15	24	30	35
8	146	–	New Saunders-c; PC-r	1	2	7	14	21	35	43	50
9	152	–	Scarce; PC-r	1	2	9	18	27	47	61	75
10	153	–	PC-r	1	2	2	4	6	11	16	20
11	160	–	PC-r	1	2	2	4	6	11	16	20
12	165	–	PC-r	1	2	2	4	6	10	14	18
13	167	–	PC-r	1	2	2	4	6	10	14	18
14	167	6/64	PC-r	1	2	2	4	6	10	14	18
15	167	6/65	PC-r	1	2	2	4	6	10	14	18
16	167	10/65	PC-r	1	2	2	4	6	10	14	18
18	169	Fall/69	C-price 25¢; stiff-c	1	2	2	4	6	10	14	18

Classic Comics #21 © GIL Classic Comics #28 © GIL Classic Comics #32 © GIL

Ed	HRN	Date	Details	A	C	GD 2.0	VG 4.0	FN 6.0	VF 8.0	VF/NM 9.0	NM- 9.2
			PC-r								
19	169	Spr/71	PC-r; stiff-c	1	2	2	4	6	10	14	18

27. The Adventures of Marco Polo

Ed	HRN	Date	Details	A	C	2.0	4.0	6.0	8.0	9.0	9.2
1	–	4/46	Original	1	1	47	94	141	296	498	700
2	30	–	Last 'Comics' reprint; CC-r	1	1	16	32	48	94	147	200
3	70	–	8 pgs. deleted; no c-price; LDC-r	1	1	5	10	15	24	30	35
4	87	–	C-price 15¢; LDC-r	1	1	4	9	13	18	22	26
5	117	–	LDC-r	1	1	4	7	10	14	17	20
6	154	–	New-c; PC-r	1	2	5	10	15	24	30	35
7	165	–	PC-r	1	2	2	4	6	8	11	14
8	167	4/64	PC-r	1	2	2	4	6	8	11	14
9	167	6/66	PC-r	1	2	2	4	6	8	11	14
10	167	Spr/69	New price 25¢; stiff-c; PC-r	1	2	2	4	6	8	11	14

28. Michael Strogoff

Ed	HRN	Date	Details	A	C	2.0	4.0	6.0	8.0	9.0	9.2
1	–	6/46	Original	1	1	42	84	126	265	445	625
2	51	–	8 pgs. cut; LDC-r	1	1	15	30	45	86	133	180
3	115	–	New-c; PC-r	1	2	6	12	18	31	38	45
4	155	–	PC-r	1	2	4	7	10	14	17	20
5	167	11/63	PC-r	1	2	2	4	6	9	13	16
6	167	7/66	PC-r	1	2	2	4	6	9	13	16
7	169	Sm/69	C-price 25¢; stiff-c PC-r	1	3	3	6	9	15	21	26

29. The Prince and the Pauper

Ed	HRN	Date	Details	A	C	2.0	4.0	6.0	8.0	9.0	9.2
1	–	7/46	Orig.; "Horror"-c	1	1	65	130	195	416	708	1000
2	60	–	8 pgs. cut; new-c by Kiefer; LDC-r	1	2	10	20	30	46	76	95
3	62	–	LDC-r	1	2	5	10	15	24	30	35
4	71	–	LDC-r	1	2	4	9	13	18	22	26
5	93	–	LDC-r	1	2	4	8	12	17	21	24
6	114	–	LDC-r	1	2	4	7	10	14	17	20
7	128	–	New-c; PC-r	1	3	5	10	15	24	30	35
8	138	–	PC-r	1	3	2	4	6	9	13	16
9	150	–	PC-r	1	3	2	4	6	9	13	16
10	164	–	PC-r	1	3	2	4	6	8	11	14
11	167	–	PC-r	1	3	2	4	6	8	11	14
12	167	7/64	PC-r	1	3	2	4	6	8	11	14
13	167	11/65	PC-r	1	3	2	4	6	8	11	14
14	166	R/68	C-price 25¢; PC-r	1	3	2	4	6	8	11	14
15	169	Sm/70	PC-r; stiff-c	1	3	2	4	6	8	11	14

30. The Moonstone

Ed	HRN	Date	Details	A	C	2.0	4.0	6.0	8.0	9.0	9.2
1	–	9/46	Original; Rico-c/a	1	1	42	84	126	265	445	625
2	60	–	LDC-r; 8pgs. cut	1	2	9	18	27	52	69	85
3	70	–	LDC-r	1	1	8	16	24	42	54	65
4	155	–	New L.B. Cole-c; PC-r	1	2	4	8	12	28	44	60
5	165	–	PC-r; L.B. Cole-c	1	2	3	6	9	16	23	30
6	167	1/64	PC-r; L.B. Cole-c	1	2	2	4	6	11	16	20
7	167	9/65	PC-r; L.B. Cole-c	1	2	2	4	6	9	14	18
8	166	R/1968	C-price 25¢; PC-r	1	2	2	4	6	9	13	16

31. The Black Arrow

Ed	HRN	Date	Details	A	C	2.0	4.0	6.0	8.0	9.0	9.2
1	30	10/46	Original	1	1	40	80	120	246	411	575
2	51	–	CI logo; LDC-r 8pgs. deleted	1	1	7	14	21	37	46	55
3	64	–	LDC-r	1	1	5	10	14	20	24	28
4	87	–	C-price 15¢; LDC-r	1	1	4	8	12	17	21	24
5	108	–	LDC-r	1	1	4	7	10	14	17	20
6	125	–	LDC-r	1	1	4	7	10	14	17	20
7	131	–	New-c; PC-r	1	2	6	12	18	28	34	40
8	140	–	PC-r	1	2	2	4	6	9	13	16
9	148	–	PC-r	1	2	2	4	6	8	11	14
10	161	–	PC-r	1	2	2	4	6	8	11	14
11	167	–	PC-r	1	2	2	4	6	8	11	14
12	167	7/64	PC-r	1	2	2	4	6	8	11	14
13	167	11/65	PC-r	1	2	2	4	6	8	11	14
14	166	R/1968	C-price 25¢; PC-r	1	2	2	4	6	8	11	14

32. Lorna Doone

Ed	HRN	Date	Details	A	C	GD 2.0	VG 4.0	FN 6.0	VF 8.0	VF/NM 9.0	NM- 9.2
1	–	12/46	Original; Matt Baker c&a	1	1	61	122	183	390	670	950
2	53/64	–	8 pgs. deleted; LDC-r	1	1	10	20	30	58	79	100
3	85	1951	C-price 15¢; LDC-r;1 Baker c&a	1	1	8	16	24	44	57	70
4	118	–	LDC-r	1	1	5	10	15	24	30	35
5	138	–	New-c; old-c becomes new title pg.; PC-r	1	2	7	14	21	35	43	50
6	150	–	PC-r	1	2	2	4	6	8	11	14
7	165	–	PC-r	1	2	2	4	6	8	11	14
8	167	1/64	PC-r	1	2	2	4	6	9	13	16
9	167	11/65	PC-r	1	2	2	4	6	9	13	16
10	166	R/1968	New-c; PC-r	1	3	3	6	9	16	24	32

33. The Adventures of Sherlock Holmes

Ed	HRN	Date	Details	A	C	2.0	4.0	6.0	8.0	9.0	9.2
1	33	1/47	Original; Kiefer-c; contains Study in Scarlet & Hound of the Baskervilles; 68 pgs.	1	1	139	278	417	883	1517	2150
2	53	–	"A Study in Scarlet" (17 pgs.) deleted; LDC-r	1	1	50	100	150	315	533	750
3	71	–	LDC-r	1	1	39	78	117	231	378	525
4A	89	–	C-price 15¢; LDC-r	1	1	30	60	90	117	289	400
4B	89	–	Kiefer's name omitted from-c	1	1	31	62	93	186	303	420

34. Mysterious Island (Last "Classic Comics" issue)

Ed	HRN	Date	Details	A	C	2.0	4.0	6.0	8.0	9.0	9.2
1	35	2/47	Original; Webb/Heames-c/a	1	1	41	82	123	256	428	600
2	60	–	8 pgs. deleted; LDC-r	1	1	7	14	21	37	46	55
3	62	–	LDC-r	1	1	5	10	15	23	28	32
4	71	–	LDC-r	1	1	6	12	18	31	38	45
5	78	–	C-price 15¢ in circle; LDC-r	1	1	5	10	14	20	24	28
6	92	–	LDC-r	1	1	4	9	13	18	22	26
7	117	–	LDC-r	1	1	4	7	10	14	17	20
8	140	–	New-c; PC-r	1	2	5	10	15	24	30	35
9	156	–	PC-r	1	2	2	4	6	9	13	16
10	167	10/63	PC-r	1	2	2	4	6	8	11	14
11	167	5/64	PC-r	1	2	2	4	6	8	11	14
12	167	6/66	PC-r	1	2	2	4	6	8	11	14
13	166	R/1968	C-price 25¢; PC-r	1	2	2	4	6	8	11	14

35. Last Days of Pompeii (First "Classics Illustrated")

Ed	HRN	Date	Details	A	C	2.0	4.0	6.0	8.0	9.0	9.2
1	35	3/47	Original; LDC; Kiefer-c/a	1	1	41	82	123	256	428	600
2	161	–	New c&a; 15¢; PC-r; Kirby/Ayers-a	2	2	5	10	15	31	53	75
3	167	1/64	PC-r	2	2	3	6	9	16	22	28
4	167	7/66	PC-r	2	2	3	6	9	16	22	28
5	169	Spr/70	New price 25¢; stiff-c; PC-r	2	2	3	6	9	16	22	28

36. Typee

Ed	HRN	Date	Details	A	C	2.0	4.0	6.0	8.0	9.0	9.2
1	36	4/47	Original	1	1	33	66	99	194	317	440
2	64	–	No c-price; 8 pg. ed.; LDC-r	1	1	8	16	24	42	54	65
3	155	–	New-c; PC-r	1	2	6	12	18	28	34	40
4	167	9/63	PC-r	1	2	2	4	6	9	13	16
5	167	7/65	PC-r	1	2	2	4	6	9	13	16
6	169	Sm/69	C-price 25¢; stiff-c; PC-r	1	2	2	4	6	9	13	16

37. The Pioneers

Ed	HRN	Date	Details	A	C	2.0	4.0	6.0	8.0	9.0	9.2
1	37	5/47	Original; Palais-c/a	1	1	31	62	93	182	296	410
2A	62	–	8 pgs. cut; LDC-r;	1	1	6	12	18	31	38	45

Ed	HRN	Date	Details	A	C	GD 2.0	VG 4.0	FN 6.0	VF 8.0	VF/NM 9.0	NM- 9.2
			price circle blank								
2B	62	—	10¢; LDC-r;	1	1	31	62	93	184	300	415
3	70	—	LDC-r	1	1	4	8	12	17	21	24
4	92	—	15¢; LDC-r	1	1	4	8	11	16	19	22
5	118	—	LDC-r	1	1	4	7	10	14	17	20
6	131	—	LDC-r	1	1	4	7	10	14	17	20
7	132	—	LDC-r	1	1	4	7	10	14	17	20
8	153	—	LDC-r	1	1	4	7	10	14	17	20
9	167	5/64	LDC-r	1	1	2	4	6	9	13	16
10	167	6/66	LDC-r	1	1	2	4	6	9	13	16
11	166	R/1968	New-c; 25¢; PC-r	1	2	3	6	9	18	27	36

38. Adventures of Cellini

Ed	HRN	Date	Details	A	C	GD 2.0	VG 4.0	FN 6.0	VF 8.0	VF/NM 9.0	NM- 9.2
1	—	6/47	Original; Froehlich c/a	1	1	32	64	96	192	314	435
2	164	—	New-c&a; PC-r	2	2	3	6	9	18	27	36
3	167	—	PC-r	2	2	2	4	6	10	14	18
4	167	7/66	PC-r	2	2	2	4	6	10	14	18
5	169	Spr/70	Stiff-c; new price 25¢; PC-r	2	2	2	4	6	11	16	20

39. Jane Eyre

Ed	HRN	Date	Details	A	C	GD 2.0	VG 4.0	FN 6.0	VF 8.0	VF/NM 9.0	NM- 9.2
1	—	7/47	Original	1	1	32	64	96	190	310	430
2	60	—	No c-price; 8 pgs. cut; LDC-r	1	1	7	14	21	35	43	50
3	62	—	LDC-r	1	1	5	10	15	24	30	35
4	71	—	LDC-r; c-price 10¢	1	1	5	10	15	22	26	30
5	92	—	C-price 15¢; LDC-r	1	1	4	9	13	18	22	26
6	118	—	LDC-r	1	1	4	8	12	17	21	24
7	142	—	New-c; old-a; PC-r	1	2	6	12	18	28	34	40
8	154	—	Old-a; PC-r	1	2	4	8	12	17	21	24
9	165	—	New-a; PC-r	2	2	3	6	9	17	26	35
10	167	12/63	PC-r	2	2	3	6	9	14	19	24
11	167	4/65	PC-r	2	2	2	4	6	13	18	22
12	167	8/66	PC-r	2	2	2	4	6	13	18	22
13	166	R/1968	New-c; PC-r	2	3	5	10	15	31	53	75

40. Mysteries ("The Pit and the Pendulum", "The Advs. of Hans Pfall" & "The Fall of the House of Usher")

Ed	HRN	Date	Details	A	C	GD 2.0	VG 4.0	FN 6.0	VF 8.0	VF/NM 9.0	NM- 9.2
1	40	8/47	Original; Kiefer-c/a, Froehlich, Griffiths-a	1	1	63	126	189	403	689	975
2	62	—	LDC-r; 8pgs. cut	1	1	26	52	78	154	252	350
3	75	—	LDC-r	1	1	20	40	60	115	185	255
4	92	—	C-price 15¢; LDC-r	1	1	17	34	51	100	158	215

41. Twenty Years After

Ed	HRN	Date	Details	A	C	GD 2.0	VG 4.0	FN 6.0	VF 8.0	VF/NM 9.0	NM- 9.2
1	—	9/47	Original; 'horror'-c	1	1	39	78	117	235	385	535
2	62	—	New-c; no c-price 8 pgs. cut; LDC-r; Kiefer-c	1	2	7	14	21	37	46	55
3	78	—	C-price 15¢; LDC-r	1	2	5	10	15	23	28	32
4	156	—	New-c; PC-r	1	3	5	10	15	24	30	35
5	167	12/63	PC-r	1	3	2	4	6	8	11	14
6	167	11/66	PC-r	1	3	2	4	6	8	11	14
7	169	Spr/70	New price 25¢; stiff-c; PC-r	1	3	2	4	6	8	11	14

42. Swiss Family Robinson

Ed	HRN	Date	Details	A	C	GD 2.0	VG 4.0	FN 6.0	VF 8.0	VF/NM 9.0	NM- 9.2
1	42	10/47	Orig.; Kiefer-c&a	1	1	32	64	96	188	307	425
2A	62	—	8 pgs. cut; outside bc: Gift Box ad; LDC-r	1	1	8	16	24	40	50	60
2B	62	—	8 pgs. cut; outside-bc: Reorder list; scarce; LDC-r	1	1	15	30	45	84	127	170
3	75	—	LDC-r	1	1	5	10	15	22	26	30
4	93	—	LDC-r	1	1	5	10	15	22	26	30
5	117	—	LDC-r	1	1	3	6	9	14	19	24
6	131	—	New-c; old-a; PC-r	1	2	3	6	9	15	21	26
7	137	—	Old-a; PC-r	1	2	2	4	6	10	14	18
8	141	—	Old-a; PC-r	1	2	2	4	6	10	14	18
9	152	—	New-a; PC-r	2	2	3	6	9	16	23	30
10	158	—	PC-r	2	2	2	4	6	8	11	14
11	165	—	PC-r	2	2	3	6	9	16	24	32
12	167	12/63	PC-r	2	2	2	4	6	8	11	14
13	167	4/65	PC-r	2	2	2	4	6	8	11	14
14	167	5/66	PC-r	2	2	2	4	6	8	11	14
15	166	11/67	PC-r	2	2	2	4	6	8	11	14
16	169	Spr/69	PC-r; stiff-c	2	2	2	4	6	8	11	14

43. Great Expectations (Used in SOTI, pg. 311)

Ed	HRN	Date	Details	A	C	GD 2.0	VG 4.0	FN 6.0	VF 8.0	VF/NM 9.0	NM- 9.2
1	43	11/47	Original; Kiefer-a/c	1	1	94	188	282	597	1025	1450
2	62	—	No c-price; 8 pgs. cut; LDC-r	1	1	58	116	174	371	636	900

44. Mysteries of Paris (Used in SOTI, pg. 323)

Ed	HRN	Date	Details	A	C	GD 2.0	VG 4.0	FN 6.0	VF 8.0	VF/NM 9.0	NM- 9.2
1A	44	12/47	Original; 56 pgs.; Kiefer-c/a	1	1	68	136	204	435	743	1050
1B	44	12/47	Orig.; printed on white/heavier paper; (rare)	1	1	77	154	231	493	847	1200
2A	62	—	8 pgs. cut; outside-bc: Gift Box ad; LDC-r	1	1	30	60	90	177	289	400
2B	62	—	8 pgs. cut; outside-bc: reorder list; LDC-r	1	1	30	60	90	177	289	400
3	78	—	C-price 15¢; LDC-r	1	1	25	50	75	147	241	335

45. Tom Brown's School Days

Ed	HRN	Date	Details	A	C	GD 2.0	VG 4.0	FN 6.0	VF 8.0	VF/NM 9.0	NM- 9.2
1	44	1/48	Original; 1st 48pg. issue	1	1	22	44	66	128	209	290
2	64	—	No c-price; LDC-r	1	1	8	16	24	42	54	65
3	161	—	New-c&a; PC-r	2	2	3	6	9	17	26	35
4	167	2/64	PC-r	2	2	2	4	6	9	13	16
5	167	8/66	PC-r	2	2	2	4	6	9	13	16
6	166	R/1968	C-price 25¢; PC-r	2	2	2	4	6	9	13	16

46. Kidnapped

Ed	HRN	Date	Details	A	C	GD 2.0	VG 4.0	FN 6.0	VF 8.0	VF/NM 9.0	NM- 9.2
1	47	4/48	Original; Webb-c/a	1	1	24	48	72	142	234	325
2A	62	—	Price circle blank; LDC-r	1	1	8	16	24	42	54	65
2B	62	—	C-price 10¢; rare; LDC-r	1	1	33	66	99	194	317	440
3	78	—	C-price 15¢; LDC-r	1	1	5	10	15	22	26	30
4	87	—	LDC-r	1	1	4	9	13	18	22	26
5	118	—	LDC-r	1	1	4	7	10	14	17	20
6	131	—	New-c; PC-r	1	2	5	10	15	23	28	32
7	140	—	PC-r	1	2	2	4	6	9	13	16
8	150	—	PC-r	1	2	2	4	6	9	13	16
9	164	—	Reduced pg.width; PC-r	1	2	2	4	6	8	11	14
10	167	—	PC-r	1	2	2	4	6	8	11	14
11	167	3/64	PC-r	1	2	2	4	6	8	11	14
12	167	6/65	PC-r	1	2	2	4	6	8	11	14
13	167	12/65	PC-r	1	2	2	4	6	8	11	14
14	166	9/67	PC-r	1	2	2	4	6	8	11	14
15	166	Win/69	New price 25¢; PC-r; stiff-c	1	2	2	4	6	8	11	14
16	169	Sm/70	PC-r; stiff-c	1	2	2	4	6	8	11	14

47. Twenty Thousand Leagues Under the Sea

Ed	HRN	Date	Details	A	C	GD 2.0	VG 4.0	FN 6.0	VF 8.0	VF/NM 9.0	NM- 9.2
1	47	5/48	Orig.; Kiefer-a&c	1	1	24	48	72	142	234	325
2	64	—	No c-price; LDC-r	1	1	7	14	21	35	43	50
3	78	—	C-price 15¢; LDC-r	1	1	4	9	13	18	22	26
4	94	—	LDC-r	1	1	4	8	12	17	21	24
5	118	—	LDC-r	1	1	4	7	10	14	17	20
6	128	—	New-c; PC-r	1	2	5	10	15	24	30	35
7	133	—	PC-r	1	2	2	4	6	10	14	18
8	140	—	PC-r	1	2	2	4	6	9	13	16
9	148	—	PC-r	1	2	2	4	6	9	13	16
10	156	—	PC-r	1	2	2	4	6	9	13	16
11	165	—	PC-r	1	2	2	4	6	9	13	16
12	167	—	PC-r	1	2	2	4	6	9	13	16
13	167	3/64	PC-r	1	2	2	4	6	9	13	16
14	167	8/65	PC-r	1	2	2	4	6	9	13	16
15	167	10/66	PC-r	1	2	2	4	6	9	13	16
16	166	R/1968	C-price 25¢; new-c; PC-r	1	3	3	6	9	15	22	28
17	169	Spr/70	Stiff-c; PC-r	1	3	2	4	6	13	18	22

48. David Copperfield

Ed	HRN	Date	Details	A	C	GD 2.0	VG 4.0	FN 6.0	VF 8.0	VF/NM 9.0	NM- 9.2
1	47	6/48	Original; Kiefer-c/a	1	1	22	44	66	132	216	300
2	64	—	Price circle replaced by motif of boy reading; LDC-r	1	1	7	14	21	35	43	50
3	87	—	C-price 15¢; LDC-r	1	2	5	10	14	20	24	28
4	121	—	New-c; PC-r	1	2	5	10	15	24	30	35
5	130	—	PC-r	1	2	2	4	6	9	13	16
6	140	—	PC-r	1	2	2	4	6	9	13	16
7	148	—	PC-r	1	2	2	4	6	9	13	16
8	156	—	PC-r	1	2	2	4	6	8	11	14
9	167	—	PC-r	1	2	2	4	6	8	11	14
10	167	4/64	PC-r	1	2	2	4	6	8	11	14
11	167	6/65	PC-r	1	2	2	4	6	8	11	14
12	167	5/67	PC-r	1	2	2	4	6	8	11	14
13	166	R/67	PC-r; C-price 25¢	1	2	2	4	6	10	14	18
14	166	Spr/69	C-price 25¢; stiff-c; PC-r	1	2	2	4	6	8	11	14
15	169	Win/69	Stiff-c; PC-r	1	2	2	4	6	8	11	14

49. Alice in Wonderland

Ed	HRN	Date	Details	A	C	GD 2.0	VG 4.0	FN 6.0	VF 8.0	VF/NM 9.0	NM- 9.2
1	47	7/48	Original; 1st Blum a & c	1	1	37	74	111	222	361	500
2	64	—	No c-price; LDC-r	1	2	9	18	27	50	65	80
3A	85	—	C-price 15¢; soft-c LDC-r	1	1	8	16	24	42	54	65
3B	85	—	Stiff-c; LDC-r	1	1	8	16	24	42	54	65
4	155	—	New PC, similar to orig.; PC-r	1	2	4	8	12	27	44	60
5	165	—	PC-r	1	2	3	6	9	18	28	38
6	167	3/64	PC-r	1	2	3	6	9	16	24	32
7	167	6/66	PC-r	1	2	4	8	12	28	47	65
8A	166	Fall/68	New-c; soft-c; 25¢ c-price; PC-r	1	3	4	8	12	27	44	60
8B	166	Fall/68	New-c; stiff-c; 25¢ c-price; PC-r	1	3	7	14	21	44	82	120

50. Adventures of Tom Sawyer (Used in SOTI, pg. 37)

Ed	HRN	Date	Details	A	C						

Classics Illustrated #42 © GIL

Classics Illustrated #50 © GIL

Classics Illustrated #57 © GIL

Ed	HRN	Date	Details	A	C	GD 2.0	VG 4.0	FN 6.0	VF 8.0	VF/NM 9.0	NM- 9.2
1A	51	8/48	Orig.; Aldo Rubano a&c	1	1	22	44	66	128	209	290
1B	51	9/48	Orig.; Rubano c&a	1	1	22	44	66	128	209	290
1C	51	9/48	Orig.; outside-bc: blue & yellow only; rare	1	1	28	56	84	168	274	380
2	64	–	No c-price; LDC-r	1	1	5	10	15	23	28	32
3	78	–	C-price 15¢; LDC-r	1	1	4	8	12	17	21	24
4	94	–	LDC-r	1	1	4	7	10	14	17	20
5	117	–	LDC-r	1	1	2	4	6	10	14	18
6	132	–	LDC-r	1	1	2	4	6	10	14	18
7	140	–	New-c; PC-r	1	2	3	6	9	17	26	35
8	150	–	PC-r	1	2	2	4	6	9	13	16
9	164	–	New-a; PC-r	2	2	3	6	9	17	26	35
10	167	–	PC-r	2	2	2	4	6	9	13	16
11	167	1/65	PC-r	2	2	2	4	6	8	11	14
12	167	5/66	PC-r	2	2	2	4	6	8	11	14
13	166	12/67	PC-r	2	2	2	4	6	8	11	14
14	169	Fall/69	C-price 25¢; stiff-c; PC-r	2	2	2	4	6	8	11	14
15	169	Win/71	PC-r	2	2	2	4	6	8	11	14

51. The Spy

Ed	HRN	Date	Details	A	C	GD 2.0	VG 4.0	FN 6.0	VF 8.0	VF/NM 9.0	NM- 9.2
1A	51	9/48	Original; inside-bc illo: Christmas Carol	1	1	22	44	66	128	209	290
1B	51	9/48	Original; inside-bc illo: Man in Iron Mask	1	1	22	44	66	128	209	290
1C	51	8/48	Original; outside-bc: full color	1	1	22	44	66	128	209	290
1D	51	8/48	Original; outside-bc: blue & yellow only; scarce	1	1	22	44	66	132	216	300
2	89	–	C-price 15¢; LDC-r	1	1	5	10	15	22	26	30
3	121	–	LDC-r	1	1	5	10	14	20	24	28
4	139	–	New-c; PC-r	1	2	3	6	9	19	30	40
5	156	–	PC-r	1	2	2	4	6	10	14	18
6	167	11/63	PC-r	1	2	2	4	6	9	13	16
7	167	7/66	PC-r	1	2	2	4	6	9	13	16
8A	166	Win/69	C-price 25¢; soft-c; scarce; PC-r	1	2	3	6	9	16	23	30
8B	166	Win/69	C-price 25¢; stiff-c; PC-r	1	2	2	4	6	9	13	16

52. The House of the Seven Gables

Ed	HRN	Date	Details	A	C	GD 2.0	VG 4.0	FN 6.0	VF 8.0	VF/NM 9.0	NM- 9.2
1	53	10/48	Orig.; Griffiths a&c	1	1	24	48	72	142	234	325
2	89	–	C-price 15¢; LDC-r	1	1	6	12	18	31	38	45
3	121	–	LDC-r	1	1	5	10	14	20	24	28
4	142	–	New-c&a; PC-r; Woodbridge-a	2	2	6	12	18	28	34	40
5	156	–	PC-r	2	2	2	4	6	9	13	16
6	165	–	PC-r	2	2	2	4	6	8	11	14
7	167	5/64	PC-r	2	2	2	4	6	9	13	16
8	167	3/66	PC-r	2	2	2	4	6	8	11	14
9	166	R/1968	C-price 25¢; PC-r	2	2	2	4	6	8	11	14
10	169	Spr/70	Stiff-c; PC-r	2	2	2	4	6	8	11	14

53. A Christmas Carol

Ed	HRN	Date	Details	A	C	GD 2.0	VG 4.0	FN 6.0	VF 8.0	VF/NM 9.0	NM- 9.2
1	53	11/48	Original & only ed; Kiefer-c/a	1	1	32	64	96	188	307	425

54. Man in the Iron Mask

Ed	HRN	Date	Details	A	C	GD 2.0	VG 4.0	FN 6.0	VF 8.0	VF/NM 9.0	NM- 9.2
1	55	12/48	Original; Froehlich-a, Kiefer-c	1	1	21	42	63	122	199	275
2	93	–	C-price 15¢; LDC-r	1	1	5	10	15	23	28	32
3A	111	–	(O) logo lettering; scarce; LDC-r	1	1	6	12	18	31	38	45
3B	111	–	New logo as PC; LDC-r	1	1	5	10	15	23	28	32
4	142	–	New-c&a; PC-r	2	2	5	10	15	24	30	35
5	154	–	PC-r	2	2	2	4	6	9	13	16
6	165	–	PC-r	2	2	2	4	6	8	11	14
7	167	5/64	PC-r	2	2	2	4	6	8	11	14
8	167	4/66	PC-r	2	2	2	4	6	8	11	14
9A	166	Win/69	C-price 25¢; soft-c; PC-r	2	2	3	6	9	15	21	26
9B	166	Win/69	Stiff-c	2	2	2	4	6	8	11	14

55. Silas Marner (Used in SOTI, pgs. 311, 312)

Ed	HRN	Date	Details	A	C	GD 2.0	VG 4.0	FN 6.0	VF 8.0	VF/NM 9.0	NM- 9.2
1	55	1/49	Original-Kiefer-c	1	1	21	42	63	122	199	275
2	75	–	Price circle blank; 'Coming Next' ad; LDC-r	1	1	6	12	18	31	38	45
3	97	–	LDC-r	1	1	3	6	9	14	19	24
4	121	–	New-c; PC-r	1	1	3	6	9	18	27	35
5	130	–	PC-r	1	2	2	4	6	9	13	16
6	140	–	PC-r	1	2	2	4	6	9	13	16
7	154	–	PC-r	1	2	2	4	6	9	13	16
8	165	–	PC-r	1	2	2	4	6	8	11	14
9	167	2/64	PC-r	1	2	2	4	6	8	11	14
10	167	6/65	PC-r	1	2	2	4	6	8	11	14
11	167	5/67	PC-r	1	2	2	4	6	8	11	14
12A	166	Win/69	C-price 25¢; soft-c; PC-r	1	2	3	6	9	15	21	26
12B	166	Win/69	C-price 25¢; stiff-c	1	2	2	4	6	8	11	14

56. The Toilers of the Sea

Ed	HRN	Date	Details	A	C	GD 2.0	VG 4.0	FN 6.0	VF 8.0	VF/NM 9.0	NM- 9.2
1	55	2/49	Original; A.M. Froehlich-c/a	1	1	27	54	81	158	259	360
2	165	–	New-c&a; PC-r; Angelo Torres-a	2	2	8	16	24	44	57	70
3	167	3/64	PC-r	2	2	3	6	9	16	23	30
4	167	10/66	PC-r	2	2	3	6	9	16	23	30

57. The Song of Hiawatha

Ed	HRN	Date	Details	A	C	GD 2.0	VG 4.0	FN 6.0	VF 8.0	VF/NM 9.0	NM- 9.2
1	55	3/49	Original; Alex Blum-c/a	1	1	20	40	60	117	189	260
2	75	–	No c-price w/15¢ sticker; 'Coming Next' ad; LDC-r	1	1	6	12	18	28	34	40
3	94	–	C-price 15¢; LDC-r	1	1	5	10	14	20	24	28
4	118	–	LDC-r	1	1	3	6	9	14	19	24
5	134	–	New-c; PC-r	1	2	3	6	9	17	26	35
6	139	–	PC-r	1	2	2	4	6	9	13	16
7	154	–	PC-r	1	2	2	4	6	9	13	16
8	167	–	Has orig.date; PC-r	1	2	2	4	6	8	11	14
9	167	9/64	PC-r	1	2	2	4	6	8	11	14
10	167	10/65	PC-r	1	2	2	4	6	8	11	14
11	166	F/1968	C-price 25¢; PC-r	1	2	2	4	6	8	11	14

58. The Prairie

Ed	HRN	Date	Details	A	C	GD 2.0	VG 4.0	FN 6.0	VF 8.0	VF/NM 9.0	NM- 9.2
1	60	4/49	Original; Palais c/a	1	1	19	38	57	111	176	240
2A	62	–	No c-price; no coming-next ad; LDC-r	1	1	9	18	27	50	65	80
2B	62	–	10¢ (rare)	1	1	20	40	60	120	195	270
3	78	–	C-price 15¢ in dbl. circle; LDC-r	1	1	5	10	15	22	26	30
4	114	–	LDC-r	1	1	4	8	12	17	21	24
5	131	–	LDC-r	1	1	4	7	10	14	17	20
6	132	–	LDC-r	1	1	4	7	10	14	17	20
7	146	–	New-c; PC-r	1	2	5	10	15	23	28	32
8	155	–	PC-r	1	2	2	4	6	9	13	16
9	167	5/64	PC-r	1	2	2	4	6	8	11	14
10	167	4/66	PC-r	1	2	2	4	6	8	11	14
11	169	Sm/69	New price 25¢; stiff-c; PC-r	1	2	2	4	6	8	11	14

59. Wuthering Heights

Ed	HRN	Date	Details	A	C	GD 2.0	VG 4.0	FN 6.0	VF 8.0	VF/NM 9.0	NM- 9.2
1	60	5/49	Original; Kiefer-c/a	1	1	20	40	60	117	189	260
2	85	–	C-price 15¢; LDC-r	1	1	7	14	21	35	43	50
3	156	–	New-c; PC-r	1	2	5	10	15	25	31	36
4	167	1/64	PC-r	1	2	2	4	6	9	13	16
5	167	10/66	PC-r	1	2	2	4	6	9	13	16
6	169	Sm/69	C-price 25¢;	1	2	2	4	6	9	13	16

				GD 2.0	VG 4.0	FN 6.0	VF 8.0	VF/NM 9.0	NM- 9.2

stiff-c; PC-r

60. Black Beauty

Ed	HRN	Date	Details	A	C	2.0	4.0	6.0	8.0	9.0	9.2
1	62	6/49	Original; Froehlich-c/a	1	1	18	36	54	103	162	220
2	62	—	No c-price; no coming-next ad; LDC-r (rare)	1	1	20	40	60	114	182	250
3	85	—	C-price 15¢; LDC-r	1	1	5	10	15	23	28	32
4	158	—	New L.B. Cole-c/a; PC-r	2	2	7	14	21	35	43	50
5	167	2/64	PC-r	2	2	2	4	6	11	16	20
6	167	3/66	PC-r	2	2	2	4	6	11	16	20
7	166	R/1968	New-c&price, 25¢; PC-r	2	3	5	10	15	30	50	70

61. The Woman in White

Ed	HRN	Date	Details	A	C	2.0	4.0	6.0	8.0	9.0	9.2
1A	62	7/49	Original; Blum-c/a fc-purple; bc: top illos light blue	1	1	21	42	63	126	206	285
1B	62	7/49	Original; Blum-c/a fc-pink; bc: top illos light violet	1	1	21	42	63	126	206	285
2	156	—	New-c; PC-r	1	2	6	12	18	28	34	40
3	167	1/64	PC-r	1	2	2	4	6	11	16	20
4	166	R/1968	C-price 25¢; PC-r	1	2	2	4	6	11	16	20

62. Western Stories ("The Luck of Roaring Camp" and "The Outcasts of Poker Flat")

Ed	HRN	Date	Details	A	C	2.0	4.0	6.0	8.0	9.0	9.2
1	62	8/49	Original; Kiefer-c/a	1	1	18	36	54	103	162	220
2	89	—	C-price 15¢; LDC-r	1	1	5	10	15	23	28	32
3	121	—	LDC-r	1	1	3	6	9	15	21	26
4	137	—	New-c; PC-r	1	2	3	6	9	17	26	35
5	152	—	PC-r	1	2	2	4	6	8	11	14
6	167	10/63	PC-r	1	2	2	4	6	8	11	14
7	167	6/64	PC-r	1	2	2	4	6	8	11	14
8	167	11/66	PC-r	1	2	2	4	6	8	11	14
9	166	R/1968	New-c&price 25¢; PC-r	1	3	3	6	9	16	24	32

63. The Man Without a Country

Ed	HRN	Date	Details	A	C	2.0	4.0	6.0	8.0	9.0	9.2
1	62	9/49	Original; Kiefer-c/a	1	1	20	40	60	120	195	270
2	78	—	C-price 15¢ in double circle; LDC-r	1	1	5	10	15	23	28	32
3	156	—	New-c, old-a; PC-r	1	2	6	12	18	28	34	40
4	165	—	New-a & text pgs.; PC-r; A. Torres-a	2	2	5	10	15	23	28	32
5	167	3/64	PC-r	2	2	2	4	6	8	11	14
6	167	8/66	PC-r	2	2	2	4	6	8	11	14
7	169	Sm/69	New price 25¢; stiff-c; PC-r	2	2	2	4	6	8	11	14

64. Treasure Island

Ed	HRN	Date	Details	A	C	2.0	4.0	6.0	8.0	9.0	9.2
1	62	10/49	Original; Blum-c/a	1	1	21	42	63	124	202	280
2A	82	—	C-price 15¢; soft-c LDC-r	1	1	5	10	15	22	26	30
2B	82	—	Stiff-c; LDC-r	1	1	5	10	15	23	28	32
3	117	—	LDC-r	1	1	3	6	9	15	21	26
4	131	—	New-c; PC-r	1	2	3	6	9	17	26	35
5	138	—	PC-r	1	2	2	4	6	9	13	16
6	146	—	PC-r	1	2	2	4	6	9	13	16
7	158	—	PC-r	1	2	2	4	6	9	13	16
8	165	—	PC-r	1	2	2	4	6	8	11	14
9	167	—	PC-r	1	2	2	4	6	8	11	14
10	167	6/64	PC-r	1	2	2	4	6	8	11	14
11	167	12/65	PC-r	1	2	2	4	6	8	11	14
12A	166	10/67	PC-r	1	2	2	4	6	8	11	14
12B	166	10/67	w/Grit ad stapled in book	1	2	10	20	30	66	138	210
13	169	Spr/69	New price 25¢; stiff-c; PC-r	1	2	2	4	6	9	13	16
14	—	1989	Long John Silver's Seafood Shoppes; $1.95, First/Berkley Publ.; Blum-r	1	2						5.00

65. Benjamin Franklin

Ed	HRN	Date	Details	A	C	2.0	4.0	6.0	8.0	9.0	9.2
1	64	11/49	Original; Kiefer-c; Iger Shop-a	1	1	20	40	60	114	182	250
2	131	—	New-c; PC-r	1	2	6	12	18	28	34	40
3	154	—	PC-r	1	2	2	4	6	9	13	16
4	167	2/64	PC-r	1	2	2	4	6	9	13	16
5	167	4/66	PC-r	1	2	2	4	6	9	13	16
6	169	Fall/69	New price 25¢; stiff-c; PC-r	1	2	2	4	6	9	13	16

66. The Cloister and the Hearth

Ed	HRN	Date	Details	A	C	2.0	4.0	6.0	8.0	9.0	9.2
1	67	12/49	Original & only ed; Kiefer-a & c	1	1	36	72	108	216	350	485

67. The Scottish Chiefs

Ed	HRN	Date	Details	A	C	2.0	4.0	6.0	8.0	9.0	9.2
1	67	1/50	Original; Blum-a&c	1	1	17	34	51	98	154	210
2	85	—	C-price 15¢; LDC-r	1	1	5	10	15	23	28	32
3	118	—	LDC-r	1	1	3	6	9	15	21	26
4	136	—	New-c; PC-r	1	2	3	6	9	18	27	36
5	154	—	PC-r	1	2	2	4	6	9	13	16
6	167	11/63	PC-r	1	2	2	4	6	11	16	20
7	167	8/65	PC-r	1	2	2	4	6	10	14	18

68. Julius Caesar (Used in SOTI, pgs. 36, 37)

Ed	HRN	Date	Details	A	C	2.0	4.0	6.0	8.0	9.0	9.2
1	70	2/50	Original; Kiefer-c/a	1	1	19	38	57	111	176	240
2	85	—	C-price 15¢; LDC-r	1	1	5	10	15	22	26	30
3	108	—	LDC-r	1	1	4	9	13	18	22	26
4	156	—	New L.B. Cole-c; PC-r	1	2	6	12	18	31	38	45
5	165	—	New-a by Evans, Crandall; PC-r	2	2	6	12	18	28	34	40
6	167	2/64	PC-r	2	2	2	4	6	8	11	14
7	167	10/65	Tarzan books inside cover; PC-r	2	2	2	4	6	8	11	14
8	166	R/1967	PC-r	2	2	2	4	6	8	11	14
9	169	Win/69	PC-r; stiff-c	2	2	2	4	6	8	11	14

69. Around the World in 80 Days

Ed	HRN	Date	Details	A	C	2.0	4.0	6.0	8.0	9.0	9.2
1	70	3/50	Original; Kiefer-c/a	1	1	19	38	57	111	176	240
2	87	—	C-price 15¢; LDC-r	1	1	5	10	15	22	26	30
3	125	—	LDC-r	1	1	4	9	13	18	22	26
4	136	—	New-c; PC-r	1	2	5	10	15	25	31	36
5	146	—	PC-r	1	2	2	4	6	9	13	16
6	152	—	PC-r	1	2	2	4	6	9	13	16
7	164	—	PC-r	1	2	2	4	6	8	11	14
8	167	—	PC-r	1	2	2	4	6	8	11	14
9	167	7/64	PC-r	1	2	2	4	6	8	11	14
10	167	11/65	PC-r	1	2	2	4	6	8	11	14
11	167	7/67	PC-r	1	2	2	4	6	8	11	14
12	169	Spr/69	C-price 25¢; stiff-c; PC-r	1	2	2	4	6	8	11	14

70. The Pilot

Ed	HRN	Date	Details	A	C	2.0	4.0	6.0	8.0	9.0	9.2
1	71	4/50	Original; Blum-c/a	1	1	16	32	48	92	144	195
2	92	—	C-price 15¢; LDC-r	1	1	5	10	15	23	28	32
3	125	—	LDC-r	1	1	4	9	13	18	22	26
4	156	—	New-c; PC-r	1	2	6	12	18	28	34	40
5	167	2/64	PC-r	1	2	2	4	6	11	16	20
6	167	5/66	PC-r	1	2	2	4	6	9	13	16

71. The Man Who Laughs

Ed	HRN	Date	Details	A	C	2.0	4.0	6.0	8.0	9.0	9.2
1	71	5/50	Original; Blum-c/a	1	1	24	48	72	142	234	325
2	165	—	New-c&a; PC-r	2	2	15	30	45	88	137	185
3	167	4/64	PC-r	2	2	13	26	39	74	105	135

72. The Oregon Trail

Ed	HRN	Date	Details	A	C	2.0	4.0	6.0	8.0	9.0	9.2
1	73	6/50	Original; Kiefer-c/a	1	1	15	30	45	84	127	170
2	89	—	C-price 15¢; LDC-r	1	1	5	10	15	23	28	32
3	121	—	LDC-r	1	1	4	9	13	18	22	26
4	131	—	New-c; PC-r	1	2	5	10	15	25	31	36
5	140	—	PC-r	1	2	2	4	6	9	13	16
6	150	—	PC-r	1	2	2	4	6	9	13	16
7	164	—	PC-r	1	2	2	4	6	8	11	14
8	167	—	PC-r	1	2	2	4	6	8	11	14
9	167	8/64	PC-r	1	2	2	4	6	8	11	14
10	167	10/65	PC-r	1	2	2	4	6	8	11	14
11	166	R/1968	C-price 25¢; PC-r	1	2	2	4	6	8	11	14

73. The Black Tulip

Ed	HRN	Date	Details	A	C	2.0	4.0	6.0	8.0	9.0	9.2
1	75	7/50	1st & only ed.; Alex Blum-c/a	1	1	40	80	120	244	402	560

74. Mr. Midshipman Easy

Ed	HRN	Date	Details	A	C	2.0	4.0	6.0	8.0	9.0	9.2
1	75	—	1st & only edition	1	1	38	76	114	228	369	510

75. The Lady of the Lake

Ed	HRN	Date	Details	A	C	2.0	4.0	6.0	8.0	9.0	9.2
1	75	9/50	Original; Kiefer-c/a	1	1	16	32	48	92	144	195
2	85	—	C-price 15¢; LDC-r	1	1	6	12	18	28	34	40
3	118	—	LDC-r	1	1	5	10	14	20	24	28
4	139	—	New-c; PC-r	1	2	5	10	15	25	31	36
5	154	—	PC-r	1	2	2	4	6	9	13	16
6	165	—	PC-r	1	2	2	4	6	8	11	14
7	167	4/64	PC-r	1	2	2	4	6	8	11	14
8	167	5/66	PC-r	1	2	2	4	6	8	11	14
9	169	Spr/69	New price 25¢; stiff-c; PC-r	1	2	2	4	6	8	11	14

76. The Prisoner of Zenda

Ed	HRN	Date	Details	A	C	2.0	4.0	6.0	8.0	9.0	9.2
1	75	10/50	Original; Kiefer-c/a	1	1	16	32	48	92	144	195
2	85	—	C-price 15¢; LDC-r	1	1	5	10	15	23	28	32
3	111	—	LDC-r	1	1	3	6	9	16	21	26
4	128	—	New-c; PC-r	1	2	3	6	9	17	26	35
5	152	—	PC-r	1	2	2	4	6	9	13	16
6	165	—	PC-r	1	2	2	4	6	8	11	14
7	167	4/64	PC-r	1	2	2	4	6	8	11	14
8	167	9/66	PC-r	1	2	2	4	6	8	11	14
9	169	Fall/69	New price 25¢; stiff-c; PC-r	1	2	2	4	6	8	11	14

77. The Iliad

Ed	HRN	Date	Details	A	C	2.0	4.0	6.0	8.0	9.0	9.2
1	78	11/50	Original; Blum-c/a	1	1	16	32	48	92	144	195
2	87	—	C-price 15¢; LDC-r	1	1	6	12	18	28	34	40

Classics Illustrated #63 © GIL

Classics Illustrated #69 © GIL

Classics Illustrated #83 © GIL

Ed	HRN	Date	Details	A	C	GD 2.0	VG 4.0	FN 6.0	VF 8.0	VF/NM 9.0	NM- 9.2
3	121	–	LDC-r	1	1	3	6	9	15	21	26
4	139	–	New-c; PC-r	1	2	3	6	9	16	24	32
5	150	–	PC-r	1	2	2	4	6	9	13	16
6	165	–	PC-r	1	2	2	4	6	8	11	14
7	167	10/63	PC-r	1	2	2	4	6	8	11	14
8	167	7/64	PC-r	1	2	2	4	6	8	11	14
9	167	5/66	PC-r	1	2	2	4	6	8	11	14
10	166	R/1968	C-price 25¢; PC-r	1	2	2	4	6	8	11	14

78. Joan of Arc

Ed	HRN	Date	Details	A	C	GD 2.0	VG 4.0	FN 6.0	VF 8.0	VF/NM 9.0	NM- 9.2
1	78	12/50	Original; Kiefer-c/a	1	1	16	32	48	92	144	195
2	87	–	C-price 15¢; LDC-r	1	1	5	10	15	23	28	32
3	113	–	LDC-r	1	1	3	6	9	15	21	26
4	128	–	New-c; PC-r	1	2	3	6	9	17	26	35
5	140	–	PC-r	1	2	2	4	6	9	13	16
6	150	–	PC-r	1	2	2	4	6	9	13	16
7	159	–	PC-r	1	2	2	4	6	8	11	14
8	167	–	PC-r	1	2	2	4	6	8	11	14
9	167	12/63	PC-r	1	2	2	4	6	8	11	14
10	167	6/65	PC-r	1	2	2	4	6	8	11	14
11	166	6/67	PC-r	1	2	2	4	6	8	11	14
12	166	Win/69	New-c&price, 25¢; PC-r; stiff-c	1	3	3	6	9	16	24	32

79. Cyrano de Bergerac

Ed	HRN	Date	Details	A	C	GD 2.0	VG 4.0	FN 6.0	VF 8.0	VF/NM 9.0	NM- 9.2
1	78	1/51	Orig.; movie promo inside front-c; Blum-c/a	1	1	15	30	45	88	137	185
2	85	–	C-price 15¢; LDC-r	1	1	5	10	15	23	28	32
3	118	–	LDC-r	1	1	3	6	9	17	23	28
4	133	–	New-c; PC-r	1	2	3	6	9	16	24	32
5	156	–	PC-r	1	2	2	4	6	11	16	20
6	167	8/64	PC-r	1	2	2	4	6	11	16	20

80. White Fang (Last line drawn cover)

Ed	HRN	Date	Details	A	C	GD 2.0	VG 4.0	FN 6.0	VF 8.0	VF/NM 9.0	NM- 9.2
1	79	2/51	Orig.; Blum-c/a	1	1	15	30	45	83	124	165
2	87	–	C-price 15¢; LDC-r	1	1	5	10	15	24	30	35
3	125	–	LDC-r	1	1	3	6	9	15	21	26
4	132	–	New-c; PC-r	1	2	3	6	9	16	24	32
5	140	–	PC-r	1	2	2	4	6	9	13	16
6	153	–	PC-r	1	2	2	4	6	9	13	16
7	167	–	PC-r	1	2	2	4	6	8	11	14
8	167	9/64	PC-r	1	2	2	4	6	8	11	14
9	167	7/65	PC-r	1	2	2	4	6	8	11	14
10	166	6/67	PC-r	1	2	2	4	6	8	11	14
11	169	Fall/69	New price 25¢; PC-r; stiff-c	1	2	2	4	6	8	11	14

81. The Odyssey (1st painted cover)

Ed	HRN	Date	Details	A	C	GD 2.0	VG 4.0	FN 6.0	VF 8.0	VF/NM 9.0	NM- 9.2
1	82	3/51	First 15¢ Original; Blum-c	1	1	15	30	45	88	137	185
2	167	8/64	PC-r	1	1	3	6	9	14	19	24
3	167	10/66	PC-r	1	1	3	6	9	14	19	24
4	169	Spr/69	New, stiff-c; PC-r	1	2	3	6	9	19	30	40

82. The Master of Ballantrae

Ed	HRN	Date	Details	A	C	GD 2.0	VG 4.0	FN 6.0	VF 8.0	VF/NM 9.0	NM- 9.2
1	82	4/51	Original; Blum-c	1	1	14	28	42	80	115	150
2	167	8/64	PC-r	1	1	3	6	9	15	22	28
3	166	Fall/68	New, stiff-c; PC-r	1	2	3	6	9	19	30	40

83. The Jungle Book

Ed	HRN	Date	Details	A	C	GD 2.0	VG 4.0	FN 6.0	VF 8.0	VF/NM 9.0	NM- 9.2
1	85	5/51	Original; Blum-c Bossert/Blum-a	1	1	15	30	45	86	137	185
2	110	–	PC-r	1	1	2	4	6	10	14	18
3	125	–	PC-r	1	1	2	4	6	9	13	16
4	134	–	PC-r	1	1	2	4	6	9	13	16
5	142	–	PC-r	1	1	2	4	6	9	13	16
6	150	–	PC-r	1	1	2	4	6	9	13	16
7	159	–	PC-r	1	1	2	4	6	8	11	14
8	167	–	PC-r	1	1	2	4	6	8	11	14
9	167	3/65	PC-r	1	1	2	4	6	8	11	14
10	167	11/65	PC-r	1	1	2	4	6	8	11	14
11	167	5/66	PC-r	1	1	2	4	6	8	11	14
12	166	R/1968	New c&a; stiff-c; PC-r	2	2	3	6	9	19	30	40

84. The Gold Bug and Other Stories ("The Gold Bug", "The Tell-Tale Heart", "The Cask of Amontillado")

Ed	HRN	Date	Details	A	C	GD 2.0	VG 4.0	FN 6.0	VF 8.0	VF/NM 9.0	NM- 9.2
1	85	6/51	Original; Blum-c/a Palais, Laverly-a	1	1	16	32	48	94	147	200
2	167	7/64	PC-r	1	1	11	22	33	64	90	115

85. The Sea Wolf

Ed	HRN	Date	Details	A	C	GD 2.0	VG 4.0	FN 6.0	VF 8.0	VF/NM 9.0	NM- 9.2
1	85	7/51	Original; Blum-c/a	1	1	14	28	42	76	108	140
2	121	–	PC-r	1	1	2	4	6	9	13	16
3	132	–	PC-r	1	1	2	4	6	9	13	16
4	141	–	PC-r	1	1	2	4	6	9	13	16
5	161	–	PC-r	1	1	2	4	6	8	11	14
6	167	2/64	PC-r	1	1	2	4	6	8	11	14
7	167	11/65	PC-r	1	1	2	4	6	8	11	14
8	169	Fall/69	New price 25¢; stiff-c; PC-r	1	1	2	4	6	8	11	14

86. Under Two Flags

Ed	HRN	Date	Details	A	C	GD 2.0	VG 4.0	FN 6.0	VF 8.0	VF/NM 9.0	NM- 9.2
1	87	8/51	Original; first delBourgo-a	1	1	14	28	42	80	115	150
2	117	–	PC-r	1	1	2	4	6	10	14	18
4	139	–	PC-r	1	1	2	4	6	9	13	16
5	158	–	PC-r	1	1	2	4	6	9	13	16
6	167	2/64	PC-r	1	1	2	4	6	8	11	14
6	167	8/66	PC-r	1	1	2	4	6	8	11	14
7	169	Sm/69	New price 25¢; stiff-c; PC-r	1	1	2	4	6	8	11	14

87. A Midsummer Nights Dream

Ed	HRN	Date	Details	A	C	GD 2.0	VG 4.0	FN 6.0	VF 8.0	VF/NM 9.0	NM- 9.2
1	87	9/51	Original; Blum c/a	1	1	14	28	42	78	112	145
2	161	–	PC-r	1	1	2	4	6	9	13	16
3	167	4/64	PC-r	1	1	2	4	6	8	11	14
4	167	5/66	PC-r	1	1	2	4	6	8	11	14
5	169	Sm/69	New price 25¢; stiff-c; PC-r	1	1	2	4	6	8	11	14

88. Men of Iron

Ed	HRN	Date	Details	A	C	GD 2.0	VG 4.0	FN 6.0	VF 8.0	VF/NM 9.0	NM- 9.2
1	89	10/51	Original	1	1	14	28	42	81	118	155
2	154	–	PC-r	1	1	2	4	6	9	13	16
3	167	1/64	PC-r	1	1	2	4	6	8	11	14
4	166	R/1968	C-price 25¢; PC-r	1	1	2	4	6	8	11	14

89. Crime and Punishment (Cover illo. in POP)

Ed	HRN	Date	Details	A	C	GD 2.0	VG 4.0	FN 6.0	VF 8.0	VF/NM 9.0	NM- 9.2
1	89	11/51	Original; Palais-a	1	1	15	30	45	85	130	175
2	152	–	PC-r	1	1	2	4	6	9	13	16
3	167	4/64	PC-r	1	1	2	4	6	8	11	14
4	167	5/66	PC-r	1	1	2	4	6	8	11	14
5	169	Fall/69	New price 25¢; stiff-c; PC-r	1	1	2	4	6	8	11	14

90. Green Mansions

Ed	HRN	Date	Details	A	C	GD 2.0	VG 4.0	FN 6.0	VF 8.0	VF/NM 9.0	NM- 9.2
1	89	12/51	Original; Blum-c/a	1	1	14	28	42	81	118	155
2	148	–	New L.B. Cole-c; PC-r	1	2	5	10	15	24	29	34
4	165	–	PC-r	1	2	2	4	6	8	11	14
5	167	4/64	PC-r	1	2	2	4	6	8	11	14
6	167	9/66	PC-r	1	2	2	4	6	8	11	14
6	169	Sm/69	New price 25¢; stiff-c; PC-r	1	2	2	4	6	8	11	14

91. The Call of the Wild

Ed	HRN	Date	Details	A	C	GD 2.0	VG 4.0	FN 6.0	VF 8.0	VF/NM 9.0	NM- 9.2
1	92	1/52	Orig.; delBourgo-a	1	1	15	30	45	83	124	165
2	112	–	PC-r	1	1	2	4	6	9	13	16
3	125	–	'Picture Progress' on back-c; PC-r	1	1	2	4	6	9	13	16
4	134	–	PC-r	1	1	2	4	6	9	13	16
5	143	–	PC-r	1	1	2	4	6	9	13	16
6	165	–	PC-r	1	1	2	4	6	8	11	14
7	167	–	PC-r	1	1	2	4	6	8	11	14

Ed	HRN	Date	Details	A	C	GD 2.0	VG 4.0	FN 6.0	VF 8.0	VF/NM 9.0	NM- 9.2
8	167	4/65	PC-r	1	1	2	4	6	8	11	14
9	167	3/66	PC-r	1	1	2	4	6	8	11	14
10	166	11/67	PC-r	1	1	2	4	6	8	11	14
11	169	Spr/70	New price 25¢; stiff-c; PC-r	1	1	2	4	6	8	11	14

92. The Courtship of Miles Standish

Ed	HRN	Date	Details	A	C	GD 2.0	VG 4.0	FN 6.0	VF 8.0	VF/NM 9.0	NM- 9.2
1	92	2/52	Original; Blum-c/a	1	1	14	28	42	81	118	155
2	165	–	New-c; PC-r	1	1	2	4	6	9	13	16
3	167	3/64	PC-r	1	1	2	4	6	9	13	16
4	166	5/67	PC-r	1	1	2	4	6	9	13	16
5	169	Win/69	New price 25¢; stiff-c; PC-r	1	1	2	4	6	9	13	16

93. Pudd'nhead Wilson

Ed	HRN	Date	Details	A	C	GD 2.0	VG 4.0	FN 6.0	VF 8.0	VF/NM 9.0	NM- 9.2
1	94	3/52	Orig.; Kiefer-c/a	1	1	14	28	42	81	118	155
2	165	–	New-c; PC-r	1	2	2	4	6	11	16	25
3	167	3/64	PC-r	1	2	2	4	6	9	13	16
4	166	R/1968	New price 25¢; soft-c; PC-r	1	2	2	4	6	9	13	16

94. David Balfour

Ed	HRN	Date	Details	A	C	GD 2.0	VG 4.0	FN 6.0	VF 8.0	VF/NM 9.0	NM- 9.2
1	94	4/52	Original; Palais-a	1	1	12	24	36	69	97	125
2	167	5/64	PC-r	1	1	2	4	6	11	16	20
3	166	R/1968	C-price 25¢; PC-r	1	1	2	4	6	13	18	22

95. All Quiet on the Western Front

Ed	HRN	Date	Details	A	C	GD 2.0	VG 4.0	FN 6.0	VF 8.0	VF/NM 9.0	NM- 9.2
1A	96	5/52	Orig.; del Bourgo-a	1	1	17	34	51	98	154	210
1B	99	5/52	Orig.; del Bourgo-a	1	1	14	28	42	82	121	160
2	167	10/64	PC-r	1	1	3	6	9	15	22	28
3	167	11/66	PC-r	1	1	3	6	9	15	22	28

96. Daniel Boone

Ed	HRN	Date	Details	A	C	GD 2.0	VG 4.0	FN 6.0	VF 8.0	VF/NM 9.0	NM- 9.2
1	97	6/52	Original; Blum-a	1	1	13	26	39	72	101	130
2	117	–	PC-r	1	1	2	4	6	9	13	16
3	128	–	PC-r	1	1	2	4	6	9	13	16
4	132	–	PC-r	1	1	2	4	6	9	13	16
5	134	–	"Story of Jesus" on back-c; PC-r	1	1	2	4	6	9	13	16
6	158	–	PC-r	1	1	2	4	6	9	13	16
7	167	1/64	PC-r	1	1	2	4	6	8	11	14
8	167	5/65	PC-r	1	1	2	4	6	8	11	14
9	167	11/66	PC-r	1	1	2	4	6	8	11	14
10	166	Win/69	New-c; price 25¢; PC-r; stiff-c	1	2	3	6	9	15	22	28

97. King Solomon's Mines

Ed	HRN	Date	Details	A	C	GD 2.0	VG 4.0	FN 6.0	VF 8.0	VF/NM 9.0	NM- 9.2
1	96	7/52	Orig.; Kiefer-a	1	1	14	28	42	80	115	150
2	118	–	PC-r	1	1	2	4	6	9	13	16
3	131	–	PC-r	1	1	2	4	6	9	13	16
4	141	–	PC-r	1	1	2	4	6	9	13	16
5	158	–	PC-r	1	1	2	4	6	9	13	16
6	167	2/64	PC-r	1	1	2	4	6	8	11	14
7	167	9/65	PC-r	1	1	2	4	6	8	11	14
8	169	Sm/69	New price 25¢; stiff-c; PC-r	1	1	2	4	6	8	11	14

98. The Red Badge of Courage

Ed	HRN	Date	Details	A	C	GD 2.0	VG 4.0	FN 6.0	VF 8.0	VF/NM 9.0	NM- 9.2
1	98	8/52	Original	1	1	14	28	42	80	115	150
2	118	–	PC-r	1	1	2	4	6	9	13	16
3	132	–	PC-r	1	1	2	4	6	9	13	16
4	142	–	PC-r	1	1	2	4	6	9	13	16
5	152	–	PC-r	1	1	2	4	6	9	13	16
6	161	–	PC-r	1	1	2	4	6	9	13	16
7	167	–	Has orig.date; PC-r	1	1	2	4	6	9	13	16
8	167	9/64	PC-r	1	1	2	4	6	9	13	16
9	167	10/65	PC-r	1	1	2	4	6	9	13	16
10	166	R/1968	New-c&price 25¢; PC-r; stiff-c	1	2	3	6	9	16	23	30

99. Hamlet (Used in POP, pg. 102)

Ed	HRN	Date	Details	A	C	GD 2.0	VG 4.0	FN 6.0	VF 8.0	VF/NM 9.0	NM- 9.2
1	98	9/52	Original; Blum-a	1	1	13	26	39	74	105	135
2	121	–	PC-r	1	1	2	4	6	9	13	16
3	141	–	PC-r	1	1	2	4	6	9	13	16
4	158	–	PC-r	1	1	2	4	6	9	13	16
5	167	–	Has orig.date; PC-r	1	1	2	4	6	8	11	14
6	167	7/65	PC-r	1	1	2	4	6	8	11	14
7	166	4/67	PC-r	1	1	2	4	6	8	11	14
8	169	Spr/69	New-c&price 25¢; PC-r; stiff-c	1	2	3	6	9	16	23	30

100. Mutiny on the Bounty

Ed	HRN	Date	Details	A	C	GD 2.0	VG 4.0	FN 6.0	VF 8.0	VF/NM 9.0	NM- 9.2
1	100	10/52	Original	1	1	11	22	33	62	86	110
2	117	–	PC-r	1	1	2	4	6	9	13	16
3	132	–	PC-r	1	1	2	4	6	9	13	16
4	142	–	PC-r	1	1	2	4	6	9	13	16
5	155	–	PC-r	1	1	2	4	6	9	13	16
6	167	–	Has orig. date;PC-r	1	1	2	4	6	9	13	16
7	167	5/64	PC-r	1	1	2	4	6	8	11	14
8	167	3/66	PC-r	1	1	2	4	6	8	11	14
9	169	Spr/70	PC-r; stiff-c	1	1	2	4	6	8	11	14

101. William Tell

Ed	HRN	Date	Details	A	C	GD 2.0	VG 4.0	FN 6.0	VF 8.0	VF/NM 9.0	NM- 9.2
1	101	11/52	Original; Kiefer-c	1	1	14	28	42	80	115	150

Ed	HRN	Date	Details	A	C	GD 2.0	VG 4.0	FN 6.0	VF 8.0	VF/NM 9.0	NM- 9.2
			delBourgo-a								
2	118	–	PC-r	1	1	2	4	6	9	13	16
3	141	–	PC-r	1	1	2	4	6	9	13	16
4	158	–	PC-r	1	1	2	4	6	9	13	16
5	167	–	Has orig.date; PC-r	1	1	2	4	6	8	11	14
6	167	11/64	PC-r	1	1	2	4	6	8	11	14
7	166	4/67	PC-r	1	1	2	4	6	8	11	14
8	169	Win/69	New price 25¢; stiff-c; PC-r	1	1	2	4	6	8	11	14

102. The White Company

Ed	HRN	Date	Details	A	C	GD 2.0	VG 4.0	FN 6.0	VF 8.0	VF/NM 9.0	NM- 9.2
1	101	12/52	Original; Blum-a	1	1	15	30	45	88	137	185
2	165	–	PC-r	1	1	3	6	9	16	23	30
3	167	4/64	PC-r	1	1	3	6	9	16	23	30

103. Men Against the Sea

Ed	HRN	Date	Details	A	C	GD 2.0	VG 4.0	FN 6.0	VF 8.0	VF/NM 9.0	NM- 9.2
1	104	1/53	Original; Kiefer-c; Palais-a	1	1	14	28	42	76	108	140
2	114	–	PC-r	1	1	4	8	11	16	19	22
3	131	–	New-c; PC-r	1	2	5	10	15	24	30	35
4	158	–	PC-r	1	1	4	7	10	14	17	20
5	149	–	White reorder list; came after HRN-158; PC-r	1	2	5	10	15	22	26	30
6	167	3/64	PC-r	1	2	2	4	6	9	13	16

104. Bring 'Em Back Alive

Ed	HRN	Date	Details	A	C	GD 2.0	VG 4.0	FN 6.0	VF 8.0	VF/NM 9.0	NM- 9.2
1	105	2/53	Original; Kiefer-c/a	1	1	14	28	42	76	108	140
2	118	–	PC-r	1	1	2	4	6	9	13	16
3	133	–	PC-r	1	1	2	4	6	9	13	16
4	150	–	PC-r	1	1	2	4	6	9	13	16
5	158	–	PC-r	1	1	2	4	6	9	13	16
6	167	10/63	PC-r	1	1	2	4	6	8	11	14
7	167	9/65	PC-r	1	1	2	4	6	8	11	14
8	169	Win/69	New price 25¢; stiff-c; PC-r	1	1	2	4	6	8	11	14

105. From the Earth to the Moon

Ed	HRN	Date	Details	A	C	GD 2.0	VG 4.0	FN 6.0	VF 8.0	VF/NM 9.0	NM- 9.2
1	106	3/53	Original; Blum-a	1	1	14	28	42	76	108	140
2	118	–	PC-r	1	1	2	4	6	9	13	16
3	132	–	PC-r	1	1	2	4	6	9	13	16
4	141	–	PC-r	1	1	2	4	6	9	13	16
5	146	–	PC-r	1	1	2	4	6	9	13	16
6	156	–	PC-r	1	1	2	4	6	9	13	16
7	167	–	Has orig. date; PC-r	1	1	2	4	6	8	11	14
8	167	5/64	PC-r	1	1	2	4	6	8	11	14
9	167	5/65	PC-r	1	1	2	4	6	8	11	14
10A	166	10/67	PC-r	1	1	2	4	6	8	11	14
10B	166	10/67	w/Grit ad stapled in book	1	1	9	18	27	59	117	175
11	169	Sm/69	New price 25¢; stiff-c; PC-r	1	1	2	4	6	8	11	14
12	169	Spr/71	PC-r	1	1	2	4	6	8	11	14

106. Buffalo Bill

Ed	HRN	Date	Details	A	C	GD 2.0	VG 4.0	FN 6.0	VF 8.0	VF/NM 9.0	NM- 9.2
1	107	4/53	Orig.; delBourgo-a	1	1	12	24	36	69	97	125
2	118	–	PC-r	1	1	2	4	6	9	13	16
3	132	–	PC-r	1	1	2	4	6	9	13	16
4	142	–	PC-r	1	1	2	4	6	9	13	16
5	161	–	PC-r	1	1	2	4	6	8	11	14
6	167	3/64	PC-r	1	1	2	4	6	8	11	14
7	167	7/67	PC-r	1	1	2	4	6	8	11	14
8	169	Fall/69	PC-r; stiff-c	1	1	2	4	6	8	11	14

107. King of the Khyber Rifles

Ed	HRN	Date	Details	A	C	GD 2.0	VG 4.0	FN 6.0	VF 8.0	VF/NM 9.0	NM- 9.2
1	108	5/53	Original; Ditko-a (earliest published; about 1/3 of book)	1	1	14	28	42	80	115	150
2	118	–	PC-r	1	1	2	4	6	9	13	16
3	146	–	PC-r	1	1	2	4	6	9	13	16
4	158	–	PC-r	1	1	2	4	6	9	13	16
5	167	–	Has orig.date; PC-r	1	1	2	4	6	8	11	14
6	167	10/66	PC-r	1	1	2	4	6	8	11	14

108. Knights of the Round Table

Ed	HRN	Date	Details	A	C	GD 2.0	VG 4.0	FN 6.0	VF 8.0	VF/NM 9.0	NM- 9.2
1A	108	6/53	Original; Blum-a	1	1	14	28	42	81	118	155
1B	109	6/53	Original; scarce	1	1	14	28	42	82	121	160
2	117	–	PC-r	1	1	2	4	6	9	13	16
3	165	–	PC-r	1	1	2	4	6	8	11	14
4	167	4/64	PC-r	1	1	2	4	6	8	11	14
5	166	4/67	PC-r	1	1	2	4	6	8	11	14
6	169	Sm/69	New price 25¢; stiff-c; PC-r	1	1	2	4	6	8	11	14

109. Pitcairn's Island

Ed	HRN	Date	Details	A	C	GD 2.0	VG 4.0	FN 6.0	VF 8.0	VF/NM 9.0	NM- 9.2
1	110	7/53	Original; Palais-a	1	1	14	28	42	78	112	145
2	165	–	PC-r	1	1	2	4	6	9	13	16
3	167	3/64	PC-r	1	1	2	4	6	9	13	16
4	166	6/67	PC-r	1	1	2	4	6	9	13	16

110. A Study in Scarlet

Ed	HRN	Date	Details	A	C	GD 2.0	VG 4.0	FN 6.0	VF 8.0	VF/NM 9.0	NM- 9.2
1	111	8/53	Original	1	1	15	30	45	90	140	190

Classics Illustrated #96 © GIL

Classics Illustrated #114 © GIL

Classics Illustrated #125 © GIL

						GD 2.0	VG 4.0	FN 6.0	VF 8.0	VF/NM 9.0	NM- 9.2
2	165	–	PC-r	1	1	12	24	36	67	94	120

111. The Talisman

Ed	HRN	Date	Details	A	C	GD 2.0	VG 4.0	FN 6.0	VF 8.0	VF/NM 9.0	NM- 9.2
1	112	9/53	Original; last H.C. Kiefer-a	1	1	13	26	39	74	105	135
2	165	–	PC-r	1	1	2	4	6	9	13	16
3	167	5/64	PC-r	1	1	2	4	6	9	13	16
4	166	Fall/68	C-price 25¢; PC-r	1	1	2	4	6	9	13	16

112. Adventures of Kit Carson

Ed	HRN	Date	Details	A	C	GD 2.0	VG 4.0	FN 6.0	VF 8.0	VF/NM 9.0	NM- 9.2
1	113	10/53	Original; Palais-a	1	1	11	22	33	62	86	110
2	129	–	PC-r	1	1	2	4	6	9	13	16
3	141	–	PC-r	1	1	2	4	6	9	13	16
4	152	–	PC-r	1	1	2	4	6	9	13	16
5	161	–	PC-r	1	1	2	4	6	8	11	14
6	167	–	PC-r	1	1	2	4	6	8	11	14
7	167	2/65	PC-r	1	1	2	4	6	8	11	14
8	167	5/66	PC-r	1	1	2	4	6	8	11	14
9	166	Win/69	New-c&price 25¢; PC-r; stiff-c	1	2	3	6	9	14	20	25

113. The Forty-Five Guardsmen

Ed	HRN	Date	Details	A	C	GD 2.0	VG 4.0	FN 6.0	VF 8.0	VF/NM 9.0	NM- 9.2
1	114	11/53	Orig.; delBourgo-a	1	1	14	28	42	82	121	160
2	166	7/67	PC-r	1	1	4	8	12	25	40	55

114. The Red Rover

Ed	HRN	Date	Details	A	C	GD 2.0	VG 4.0	FN 6.0	VF 8.0	VF/NM 9.0	NM- 9.2
1	115	12/53	Original	1	1	14	28	42	82	121	160
2	166	7/67	PC-r	1	1	4	8	12	25	40	55

115. How I Found Livingstone

Ed	HRN	Date	Details	A	C	GD 2.0	VG 4.0	FN 6.0	VF 8.0	VF/NM 9.0	NM- 9.2
1	116	1/54	Original	1	1	15	30	45	84	127	170
2	167	1/67	PC-r	1	1	4	8	12	27	44	60

116. The Bottle Imp

Ed	HRN	Date	Details	A	C	GD 2.0	VG 4.0	FN 6.0	VF 8.0	VF/NM 9.0	NM- 9.2
1	117	2/54	Orig.; Cameron-a	1	1	15	30	45	84	127	170
2	167	1/67	PC-r	1	1	4	8	12	27	44	60

117. Captains Courageous

Ed	HRN	Date	Details	A	C	GD 2.0	VG 4.0	FN 6.0	VF 8.0	VF/NM 9.0	NM- 9.2
1	118	3/54	Orig.; Costanza-a	1	1	14	28	42	81	118	155
2	167	2/67	PC-r	1	1	3	6	9	14	20	26
3	169	Fall/69	New price 25¢; stiff-c; PC-r	1	1	3	6	9	14	20	26

118. Rob Roy

Ed	HRN	Date	Details	A	C	GD 2.0	VG 4.0	FN 6.0	VF 8.0	VF/NM 9.0	NM- 9.2
1	119	4/54	Original; Rudy & Walter Palais-a	1	1	15	30	45	84	127	170
2	167	2/67	PC-r	1	1	4	8	12	27	44	60

119. Soldiers of Fortune

Ed	HRN	Date	Details	A	C	GD 2.0	VG 4.0	FN 6.0	VF 8.0	VF/NM 9.0	NM- 9.2
1	120	5/54	Schaffenberger-a	1	1	14	28	42	80	115	150
2	166	3/67	PC-r	1	1	3	6	9	14	20	26
3	169	Spr/70	New price 25¢; stiff-c; PC-r	1	1	3	6	9	14	20	26

120. The Hurricane

Ed	HRN	Date	Details	A	C	GD 2.0	VG 4.0	FN 6.0	VF 8.0	VF/NM 9.0	NM- 9.2
1	121	6/54	Orig.; Cameron-a	1	1	14	28	42	82	121	160
2	166	3/67	PC-r	1	1	4	8	12	22	34	50

121. Wild Bill Hickok

Ed	HRN	Date	Details	A	C	GD 2.0	VG 4.0	FN 6.0	VF 8.0	VF/NM 9.0	NM- 9.2
1	122	7/54	Original	1	1	12	24	36	67	94	120
2	132	–	PC-r	1	1	2	4	6	9	13	16
3	141	–	PC-r	1	1	2	4	6	9	13	16
4	154	–	PC-r	1	1	2	4	6	9	13	16
5	167	–	PC-r	1	1	2	4	6	8	11	14
6	167	8/64	PC-r	1	1	2	4	6	8	11	14
7	166	4/67	PC-r; stiff-c	1	1	2	4	6	8	11	14

122. The Mutineers

Ed	HRN	Date	Details	A	C	GD 2.0	VG 4.0	FN 6.0	VF 8.0	VF/NM 9.0	NM- 9.2
1	123	9/54	Original	1	1	12	24	36	69	97	125
2	136	–	PC-r	1	1	2	4	6	9	13	16
3	146	–	PC-r	1	1	2	4	6	9	13	16
4	158	–	PC-r	1	1	2	4	6	9	13	16
5	167	11/63	PC-r	1	1	2	4	6	8	11	14
6	167	3/65	PC-r	1	1	2	4	6	8	11	14
7	166	8/67	PC-r	1	1	2	4	6	8	11	14

123. Fang and Claw

Ed	HRN	Date	Details	A	C	GD 2.0	VG 4.0	FN 6.0	VF 8.0	VF/NM 9.0	NM- 9.2
1	124	11/54	Original	1	1	13	26	39	74	105	135
2	133	–	PC-r	1	1	2	4	6	9	13	16
3	143	–	PC-r	1	1	2	4	6	9	13	16
4	154	–	PC-r	1	1	2	4	6	9	13	16
5	167	–	Has orig.date; PC-r	1	1	2	4	6	8	11	14
6	167	9/65	PC-r	1	1	2	4	6	8	11	14

124. The War of the Worlds

Ed	HRN	Date	Details	A	C	GD 2.0	VG 4.0	FN 6.0	VF 8.0	VF/NM 9.0	NM- 9.2
1	125	1/55	Original; Cameron-c/a	1	1	15	30	45	90	140	190
2	131	–	PC-r	1	1	2	4	6	10	14	18
3	141	–	PC-r	1	1	2	4	6	10	14	18
4	148	–	PC-r	1	1	2	4	6	10	14	18
5	156	–	PC-r	1	1	2	4	6	10	14	18
6	165	–	PC-r	1	1	2	4	6	13	18	22
7	167	–	PC-r	1	1	2	4	6	9	13	16
8	167	11/64	PC-r	1	1	2	4	6	10	14	18
9	167	11/65	PC-r	1	1	2	4	6	9	13	16
10	166	R/1968	C-price 25¢; PC-r	1	1	2	4	6	9	13	16
11	169	Sm/70	PC-r; stiff-c	1	1	2	4	6	9	13	16

125. The Ox Bow Incident

Ed	HRN	Date	Details	A	C	GD 2.0	VG 4.0	FN 6.0	VF 8.0	VF/NM 9.0	NM- 9.2
1	–	3/55	Original; Picture Progress replaces reorder list	1	1	12	24	36	69	97	125
2	143	–	PC-r	1	1	2	4	6	9	13	16
3	152	–	PC-r	1	1	2	4	6	9	13	16
4	149	–	PC-r	1	1	2	4	6	9	13	16
5	167	–	PC-r	1	1	2	4	6	8	11	14
6	167	11/64	PC-r	1	1	2	4	6	8	11	14
7	166	4/67	PC-r	1	1	2	4	6	8	11	14
8	169	Win/69	New price 25¢; stiff-c; PC-r	1	1	2	4	6	8	11	14

126. The Downfall

Ed	HRN	Date	Details	A	C	GD 2.0	VG 4.0	FN 6.0	VF 8.0	VF/NM 9.0	NM- 9.2
1	–	5/55	Orig.; 'Picture Progress' replaces reorder list; Cameron-c/a	1	1	13	26	39	74	105	135
2	167	8/64	PC-r	1	1	2	4	6	13	18	22
3	166	R/1968	C-price 25¢; PC-r	1	1	2	4	6	13	18	22

127. The King of the Mountains

Ed	HRN	Date	Details	A	C	GD 2.0	VG 4.0	FN 6.0	VF 8.0	VF/NM 9.0	NM- 9.2
1	128	7/55	Original	1	1	13	26	39	74	105	135
2	167	6/64	PC-r	1	1	2	4	6	11	16	20
3	166	F/1968	C-price 25¢; PC-r	1	1	2	4	6	11	16	20

128. Macbeth (Used in POP, pg. 102)

Ed	HRN	Date	Details	A	C	GD 2.0	VG 4.0	FN 6.0	VF 8.0	VF/NM 9.0	NM- 9.2
1	128	9/55	Orig.; last Blum-a	1	1	13	26	39	74	105	135
2	143	–	PC-r	1	1	2	4	6	9	13	16
3	158	–	PC-r	1	1	2	4	6	9	13	16
4	167	–	PC-r	1	1	2	4	6	8	11	14
5	167	6/64	PC-r	1	1	2	4	6	8	11	14
6	166	4/67	PC-r	1	1	2	4	6	8	11	14
7	166	R/1968	R-Price 25¢; PC-r	1	1	2	4	6	8	11	14
8	169	Spr/70	Stiff-c; PC-r	1	1	2	4	6	8	11	14

129. Davy Crockett

Ed	HRN	Date	Details	A	C	GD 2.0	VG 4.0	FN 6.0	VF 8.0	VF/NM 9.0	NM- 9.2
1	129	11/55	Orig.; Cameron-a	1	1	15	30	45	85	130	175
2	167	9/66	PC-r	1	1	11	22	33	62	86	110

130. Caesar's Conquests

Ed	HRN	Date	Details	A	C	GD 2.0	VG 4.0	FN 6.0	VF 8.0	VF/NM 9.0	NM- 9.2
1	130	1/56	Original; Orlando-a	1	1	13	26	39	74	105	135
2	142	–	PC-r	1	1	2	4	6	9	13	16
3	152	–	PC-r	1	1	2	4	6	9	13	16

Ed	HRN	Date	Details	A	C	GD 2.0	VG 4.0	FN 6.0	VF 8.0	VF/NM 9.0	NM- 9.2
4	149	–	PC-r	1	1	2	4	6	9	13	16
5	167	–	PC-r	1	1	2	4	6	8	11	14
6	167	10/64	PC-r	1	1	2	4	6	8	11	14
7	167	4/66	PC-r	1	1	2	4	6	8	11	14

131. The Covered Wagon

Ed	HRN	Date	Details	A	C	GD 2.0	VG 4.0	FN 6.0	VF 8.0	VF/NM 9.0	NM- 9.2
1	131	3/56	Original	1	1	11	22	33	64	90	115
2	143	–	PC-r	1	1	2	4	6	9	13	16
3	152	–	PC-r	1	1	2	4	6	9	13	16
4	158	–	PC-r	1	1	2	4	6	8	13	16
5	167	–	PC-r	1	1	2	4	6	8	11	14
6	167	11/64	PC-r	1	1	2	4	6	8	11	14
7	167	4/66	PC-r	1	1	2	4	6	8	11	14
8	169	Win/69	New price 25¢; stiff-c; PC-r	1	1	2	4	6	8	11	14

132. The Dark Frigate

Ed	HRN	Date	Details	A	C	GD 2.0	VG 4.0	FN 6.0	VF 8.0	VF/NM 9.0	NM- 9.2
1	132	5/56	Original	1	1	13	26	39	74	105	135
2	150	–	PC-r	1	1	2	4	6	9	13	16
3	167	1/64	PC-r	1	1	2	4	6	9	13	16
4	166	5/67	PC-r	1	1	2	4	6	9	13	16

133. The Time Machine

Ed	HRN	Date	Details	A	C	GD 2.0	VG 4.0	FN 6.0	VF 8.0	VF/NM 9.0	NM- 9.2
1	132	7/56	Orig.; Cameron-a	1	1	8	16	24	52	99	145
2	142	–	PC-r	1	1	2	4	6	11	16	20
3	152	–	PC-r	1	1	2	4	6	11	16	20
4	158	–	PC-r	1	1	2	4	6	10	14	18
5	167	–	PC-r	1	1	2	4	6	10	14	18
6	167	6/64	PC-r	1	1	2	4	6	11	16	20
7	167	3/66	PC-r	1	1	2	4	6	10	13	18
8	166	12/67	PC-r	1	1	2	4	6	10	13	18
9	169	Win/71	New price 25¢; stiff-c; PC-r	1	1	2	4	6	10	13	18

134. Romeo and Juliet

Ed	HRN	Date	Details	A	C	GD 2.0	VG 4.0	FN 6.0	VF 8.0	VF/NM 9.0	NM- 9.2
1	134	9/56	Original; Evans-a	1	1	7	14	21	49	92	135
2	161	–	PC-r	1	1	2	4	6	9	13	16
3	167	9/63	PC-r	1	1	2	4	6	8	11	14
4	167	5/65	PC-r	1	1	2	4	6	8	11	14
5	166	6/67	PC-r	1	1	2	4	6	8	11	14
6	166	Win/69	New c&price 25¢; stiff-c; PC-r	1	2	3	6	9	18	27	36

135. Waterloo

Ed	HRN	Date	Details	A	C	GD 2.0	VG 4.0	FN 6.0	VF 8.0	VF/NM 9.0	NM- 9.2
1	135	11/56	Orig.; G. Ingels-a	1	1	7	14	21	46	86	125
2	153	–	PC-r	1	1	2	4	6	9	13	16
3	167	–	PC-r	1	1	2	4	6	8	11	14
4	167	9/64	PC-r	1	1	2	4	6	8	11	14
5	166	R/1968	C-price 25¢; PC-r	1	1	2	4	6	8	11	14

136. Lord Jim

Ed	HRN	Date	Details	A	C	GD 2.0	VG 4.0	FN 6.0	VF 8.0	VF/NM 9.0	NM- 9.2
1	136	1/57	Original; Evans-a	1	1	6	12	18	42	79	115
2	165	–	PC-r	1	1	2	4	6	8	11	14
3	167	3/64	PC-r	1	1	2	4	6	8	11	14
4	167	9/66	PC-r	1	1	2	4	6	8	11	14
5	169	Sm/69	New price 25 ¢; stiff-c; PC-r	1	1	2	4	6	8	11	14

137. The Little Savage

Ed	HRN	Date	Details	A	C	GD 2.0	VG 4.0	FN 6.0	VF 8.0	VF/NM 9.0	NM- 9.2
1	136	3/57	Original; Evans-a	1	1	6	12	18	42	79	115
2	148	–	PC-r	1	1	2	4	6	9	13	16
3	156	–	PC-r	1	1	2	4	6	9	13	16
4	167	–	PC-r	1	1	2	4	6	8	11	14
5	167	10/64	PC-r	1	1	2	4	6	8	11	14
6	166	8/67	PC-r	1	1	2	4	6	8	11	14
7	169	Spr/70	New price 25¢; stiff-c; PC-r	1	1	2	4	6	8	11	14

138. A Journey to the Center of the Earth

Ed	HRN	Date	Details	A	C	GD 2.0	VG 4.0	FN 6.0	VF 8.0	VF/NM 9.0	NM- 9.2
1	136	5/57	Original	1	1	8	16	24	56	108	160
2	146	–	PC-r	1	1	2	4	6	11	16	20
3	156	–	PC-r	1	1	2	4	6	11	16	20
4	158	–	PC-r	1	1	2	4	6	9	13	16
5	167	–	PC-r	1	1	2	4	6	8	11	14
6	167	6/64	PC-r	1	1	2	4	6	13	18	22
7	167	4/66	PC-r	1	1	2	4	6	13	18	22
8	166	R/68	C-price; PC-r	1	1	2	4	6	10	14	18

139. In the Reign of Terror

Ed	HRN	Date	Details	A	C	GD 2.0	VG 4.0	FN 6.0	VF 8.0	VF/NM 9.0	NM- 9.2
1	139	7/57	Original; Evans-a	1	1	6	12	18	42	79	115
2	154	–	PC-r	1	1	2	4	6	9	13	16
3	167	–	Has orig.date; PC-r	1	1	2	4	6	8	11	14
4	167	7/64	PC-r	1	1	2	4	6	8	11	14
5	166	R/1968	C-price 25¢; PC-r	1	1	2	4	6	8	11	14

140. On Jungle Trails

Ed	HRN	Date	Details	A	C	GD 2.0	VG 4.0	FN 6.0	VF 8.0	VF/NM 9.0	NM- 9.2
1	140	9/57	Original	1	1	6	12	18	40	73	105
2	150	–	PC-r	1	1	2	4	6	9	13	16
3	160	–	PC-r	1	1	2	4	6	8	11	14
4	167	9/63	PC-r	1	1	2	4	6	8	11	14
5	167	9/65	PC-r	1	1	2	4	6	8	11	14

141. Castle Dangerous

Ed	HRN	Date	Details	A	C	GD 2.0	VG 4.0	FN 6.0	VF 8.0	VF/NM 9.0	NM- 9.2
1	141	11/57	Original	1	1	7	14	21	44	82	120
2	152	–	PC-r	1	1	2	4	6	9	13	16
3	167	–	PC-r	1	1	2	4	6	9	13	16
4	166	7/67	PC-r	1	1	2	4	6	9	13	16

142. Abraham Lincoln

Ed	HRN	Date	Details	A	C	GD 2.0	VG 4.0	FN 6.0	VF 8.0	VF/NM 9.0	NM- 9.2
1	142	1/58	Original	1	1	6	12	18	42	79	115
2	154	–	PC-r	1	1	2	4	6	9	13	16
3	158	–	PC-r	1	1	2	4	6	9	13	16
4	167	10/63	PC-r	1	1	2	4	6	8	11	14
5	167	7/65	PC-r	1	1	2	4	6	8	11	14
6	166	11/67	PC-r	1	1	2	4	6	8	11	14
7	169	Fall/69	New price 25¢; stiff-c; PC-r	1	1	2	4	6	8	11	14

143. Kim

Ed	HRN	Date	Details	A	C	GD 2.0	VG 4.0	FN 6.0	VF 8.0	VF/NM 9.0	NM- 9.2
1	143	3/58	Original; Orlando-a	1	1	6	12	18	40	73	105
2	165	–	PC-r	1	1	2	4	6	8	11	14
3	167	11/63	PC-r	1	1	2	4	6	8	11	14
4	167	8/65	PC-r	1	1	2	4	6	8	11	14
5	169	Win/69	New price 25¢; stiff-c; PC-r	1	1	2	4	6	8	11	14

144. The First Men in the Moon

Ed	HRN	Date	Details	A	C	GD 2.0	VG 4.0	FN 6.0	VF 8.0	VF/NM 9.0	NM- 9.2
1	143	5/58	Original; Woodbridge/Williamson/Torres-a	1	1	9	18	27	57	111	165
2	152	–	(Rare)-PC-r	1	1	9	18	27	60	120	180
3	153	–	PC-r	1	1	2	4	6	9	13	16
4	161	–	PC-r	1	1	2	4	6	8	11	14
5	167	–	PC-r	1	1	2	4	6	8	11	14
6	167	12/65	PC-r	1	1	2	4	6	8	11	14
7	166	Fall/68	New-c&price 25¢; PC-r; stiff-c	1	2	3	6	9	16	23	30
8	169	Win/69	Stiff-c; PC-r	1	2	2	4	6	10	16	20

145. The Crisis

Ed	HRN	Date	Details	A	C	GD 2.0	VG 4.0	FN 6.0	VF 8.0	VF/NM 9.0	NM- 9.2
1	143	7/58	Original; Evans-a	1	1	7	14	21	46	86	125
2	156	–	PC-r	1	1	2	4	6	9	13	16
3	167	10/63	PC-r	1	1	2	4	6	8	11	14
4	167	3/65	PC-r	1	1	2	4	6	8	11	14
5	166	R/68	C-price 25¢; PC-r	1	1	2	4	6	8	11	14

146. With Fire and Sword

Ed	HRN	Date	Details	A	C	GD 2.0	VG 4.0	FN 6.0	VF 8.0	VF/NM 9.0	NM- 9.2
1	143	9/58	Original; Woodbridge-a	1	1	7	14	21	46	86	125
2	156	–	PC-r	1	1	2	4	6	10	14	18
3	167	11/64	PC-r	1	1	2	4	6	9	13	16
4	167	3/65	PC-r	1	1	2	4	6	9	13	16

147. Ben-Hur

Ed	HRN	Date	Details	A	C	GD 2.0	VG 4.0	FN 6.0	VF 8.0	VF/NM 9.0	NM- 9.2
1	147	11/58	Original; Orlando-a	1	1	8	16	24	54	102	150
2	152	–	Scarce; PC-r	1	1	8	16	24	52	99	145
3	153	–	PC-r	1	1	2	4	6	9	13	16
4	158	–	PC-r	1	1	2	4	6	9	13	16
5	167	–	Orig.date; but PC-r	1	1	2	4	6	8	11	14
6	167	2/65	PC-r	1	1	2	4	6	8	11	14
7	167	9/66	PC-r	1	1	2	4	6	8	11	14
8A	166	Fall/68	New-c&price 25¢; PC-r; soft-c	1	2	3	6	9	16	24	32
8B	166	Fall/68	New-c&price 25¢; PC-r; stiff-c; scarce	1	2	4	8	12	23	37	50

148. The Buccaneer

Ed	HRN	Date	Details	A	C	GD 2.0	VG 4.0	FN 6.0	VF 8.0	VF/NM 9.0	NM- 9.2
1	148	1/59	Orig.; Evans/Jenny-a; Saunders-c	1	1	6	12	18	42	79	115
2	568	–	Juniors list only	1	1	2	4	6	9	13	16
3	167	–	PC-r	1	1	2	4	6	8	11	14
4	167	9/65	PC-r	1	1	2	4	6	8	11	14
5	169	Sm/69	New price 25¢; PC-r; stiff-c	1	1	2	4	6	8	11	14

149. Off on a Comet

Ed	HRN	Date	Details	A	C	GD 2.0	VG 4.0	FN 6.0	VF 8.0	VF/NM 9.0	NM- 9.2
1	149	3/59	Orig.;G.McCann-a; blue reorder list	1	1	7	14	21	46	86	125
2	155	–	PC-r	1	1	2	4	6	9	13	16
3	149	–	PC-r; white reorder list; no coming-next ad	1	1	2	4	6	9	13	16
4	167	12/63	PC-r	1	1	2	4	6	8	11	14
5	167	2/65	PC-r	1	1	2	4	6	8	11	14
6	167	10/66	PC-r	1	1	2	4	6	8	11	14
7	166	Fall/68	New-c & price 25¢; PC-r	1	2	3	6	9	17	26	35

150. The Virginian

Ed	HRN	Date	Details	A	C	GD 2.0	VG 4.0	FN 6.0	VF 8.0	VF/NM 9.0	NM- 9.2
1	150	5/59	Original	1	1	7	14	21	44	82	120
2	164	–	PC-r	1	1	2	4	6	11	16	20
3	167	10/63	PC-r	1	1	3	6	9	15	21	26
4	167	12/65	PC-r	1	1	2	4	6	11	16	20

151. Won By the Sword

Ed	HRN	Date	Details	A	C	GD 2.0	VG 4.0	FN 6.0	VF 8.0	VF/NM 9.0	NM- 9.2
1	150	7/59	Original	1	1	6	12	18	42	79	115

Classics Illustrated #133 © GIL

Classics Illustrated #145 © GIL

Classics Illustrated #160 © GIL

#	HRN	Date	Details	A	C	GD 2.0	VG 4.0	FN 6.0	VF 8.0	VF/NM 9.0	NM- 9.2
2	164	–	PC-r	1	1	2	4	6	10	14	18
3	167	10/63	PC-r	1	1	2	4	6	10	14	18
4	166	7/67	PC-r	1	1	2	4	6	10	14	18

152. Wild Animals I Have Known

Ed	HRN	Date	Details	A	C	GD 2.0	VG 4.0	FN 6.0	VF 8.0	VF/NM 9.0	NM- 9.2
1	152	9/59	Orig.; L.B. Cole c/a	1	1	7	14	21	46	86	125
2A	149	–	PC-r; white reorder list; no coming-next ad; IBC: Jr. list #572	1	1	2	4	6	9	13	16
2B	149	–	PC-r; inside-bc: Jr. list to #555	1	1	2	4	6	9	13	16
2C	149	–	PC-r; inside-bc: has World Around Us ad; scarce	1	1	3	6	9	15	21	26
3	167	9/63	PC-r	1	1	2	4	6	8	11	14
4	167	8/65	PC-r	1	1	2	4	6	8	11	14
5	169	Fall/69	New price 25¢; stiff-c; PC-r	1	1	2	4	6	8	11	14

153. The Invisible Man

Ed	HRN	Date	Details	A	C	GD 2.0	VG 4.0	FN 6.0	VF 8.0	VF/NM 9.0	NM- 9.2
1	153	11/59	Original	1	1	9	18	27	61	123	185
2A	149	–	PC-r; white reorder ad; inside-bc: Jr. list to #572	1	1	3	6	9	16	23	30
2B	149	–	PC-r; inside-bc: Jr. list to #555	1	1	3	6	9	17	26	35
3	167	–	PC-r	1	1	2	4	6	9	13	16
4	167	2/65	PC-r	1	1	2	4	6	9	13	16
5	167	9/66	PC-r	1	1	2	4	6	9	13	16
6	166	Win/69	New price 25¢; PC-r; stiff-c	1	1	2	4	6	9	13	16
7	169	Spr/71	Stiff-c; letters spelling 'Invisible Man' are 'solid' not 'invisible;' PC-r	1	1	2	4	6	9	13	16

154. The Conspiracy of Pontiac

Ed	HRN	Date	Details	A	C	GD 2.0	VG 4.0	FN 6.0	VF 8.0	VF/NM 9.0	NM- 9.2
1	154	1/60	Original	1	1	7	14	21	41	82	120
2	167	11/63	PC-r	1	1	2	4	6	13	18	22
3	167	7/64	PC-r	1	1	2	4	6	13	18	22
4	166	12/67	PC-r	1	1	2	4	6	13	18	22

155. The Lion of the North

Ed	HRN	Date	Details	A	C	GD 2.0	VG 4.0	FN 6.0	VF 8.0	VF/NM 9.0	NM- 9.2
1	154	3/60	Original	1	1	6	12	18	42	79	115
2	167	1/64	PC-r	1	1	2	4	6	11	16	20
3	166	R/1967	C-price 25¢; PC-r	1	1	2	4	6	10	14	18

156. The Conquest of Mexico

Ed	HRN	Date	Details	A	C	GD 2.0	VG 4.0	FN 6.0	VF 8.0	VF/NM 9.0	NM- 9.2
1	156	5/60	Orig.; Bruno Premiani-c/a	1	1	6	12	18	42	79	115
2	167	1/64	PC-r	1	1	2	4	6	10	14	18
3	166	8/67	PC-r	1	1	2	4	6	10	14	18
4	169	Spr/70	New price 25¢; stiff-c; PC-r	1	1	2	4	6	9	13	16

157. Lives of the Hunted

Ed	HRN	Date	Details	A	C	GD 2.0	VG 4.0	FN 6.0	VF 8.0	VF/NM 9.0	NM- 9.2
1	156	7/60	Orig.; L.B. Cole-c	1	1	7	14	21	44	82	120
2	167	2/64	PC-r	1	1	2	4	6	13	18	22
3	166	10/67	PC-r	1	1	2	4	6	13	18	22

158. The Conspirators

Ed	HRN	Date	Details	A	C	GD 2.0	VG 4.0	FN 6.0	VF 8.0	VF/NM 9.0	NM- 9.2
1	156	9/60	Original	1	1	7	14	21	44	82	120
2	167	7/64	PC-r	1	1	2	4	6	13	18	22
3	166	10/67	PC-r	1	1	2	4	6	13	18	22

159. The Octopus

Ed	HRN	Date	Details	A	C	GD 2.0	VG 4.0	FN 6.0	VF 8.0	VF/NM 9.0	NM- 9.2
1	159	11/60	Orig.; Gray Morrow-a; L.B. Cole-c	1	1	8	16	24	54	102	150
2	167	2/64	PC-r	1	1	2	4	6	13	18	22
3	166	R/1967	C-price 25¢; PC-r	1	1	2	4	6	13	18	22

160. The Food of the Gods

Ed	HRN	Date	Details	A	C	GD 2.0	VG 4.0	FN 6.0	VF 8.0	VF/NM 9.0	NM- 9.2
1A	159	1/61	Original	1	1	8	16	24	55	105	155
1B	160	1/61	Original; same, except for HRN	1	1	8	16	24	52	99	145
2	167	1/64	PC-r	1	1	2	4	6	13	18	22
3	166	6/67	PC-r	1	1	2	4	6	13	18	22

161. Cleopatra

Ed	HRN	Date	Details	A	C	GD 2.0	VG 4.0	FN 6.0	VF 8.0	VF/NM 9.0	NM- 9.2
1	161	3/61	Original	1	1	8	16	24	56	108	160
2	167	1/64	PC-r	1	1	3	6	9	14	19	24
3	166	8/67	PC-r	1	1	3	6	9	14	19	24

162. Robur the Conqueror

Ed	HRN	Date	Details	A	C	GD 2.0	VG 4.0	FN 6.0	VF 8.0	VF/NM 9.0	NM- 9.2
1	162	5/61	Original	1	1	8	16	24	54	102	130
2	167	1/65	PC-r	1	1	3	6	9	14	19	24
3	166	8/67	PC-r	1	1	3	6	9	14	19	24

163. Master of the World

Ed	HRN	Date	Details	A	C	GD 2.0	VG 4.0	FN 6.0	VF 8.0	VF/NM 9.0	NM- 9.2
1	163	7/61	Original; Gray Morrow-a	1	1	7	14	21	44	82	120
2	167	1/65	PC-r	1	1	2	4	6	13	18	22
3	166	R/1968	C-price 25¢; PC-r	1	1	2	4	6	13	18	22

164. The Cossack Chief

Ed	HRN	Date	Details	A	C	GD 2.0	VG 4.0	FN 6.0	VF 8.0	VF/NM 9.0	NM- 9.2
1	164	(1961)	Orig.; nd(10/61?)	1	1	6	12	18	41	76	110
2	167	4/65	PC-r	1	1	2	4	6	13	18	22
3	166	Fall/68	C-price 25¢; PC-r	1	1	2	4	6	13	18	22

165. The Queen's Necklace

Ed	HRN	Date	Details	A	C	GD 2.0	VG 4.0	FN 6.0	VF 8.0	VF/NM 9.0	NM- 9.2
1	164	1/62	Original; Morrow-a	1	1	7	14	21	48	89	130
2	167	4/65	PC-r	1	1	2	4	6	13	18	22
3	166	Fall/68	C-price 25¢; PC-r	1	1	2	4	6	13	18	22

166. Tigers and Traitors

Ed	HRN	Date	Details	A	C	GD 2.0	VG 4.0	FN 6.0	VF 8.0	VF/NM 9.0	NM- 9.2
1	165	5/62	Original	1	1	9	18	27	59	117	175
2	167	2/64	PC-r	1	1	4	8	12	23	37	50
3	167	11/66	PC-r	1	1	4	8	12	23	37	50

167. Faust

Ed	HRN	Date	Details	A	C	GD 2.0	VG 4.0	FN 6.0	VF 8.0	VF/NM 9.0	NM- 9.2
1	165	8/62	Original	1	1	13	26	39	86	188	290
2	167	2/64	PC-r	1	1	6	12	18	37	66	95
3	166	6/67	PC-r	1	1	6	12	18	37	66	95

168. In Freedom's Cause

Ed	HRN	Date	Details	A	C	GD 2.0	VG 4.0	FN 6.0	VF 8.0	VF/NM 9.0	NM- 9.2
1	169	Win/69	Original; Evans/Crandall-a; stiff-c; 25¢; no coming-next ad;	1	1	14	28	42	96	211	325

169. Negro Americans The Early Years

Ed	HRN	Date	Details	A	C	GD 2.0	VG 4.0	FN 6.0	VF 8.0	VF/NM 9.0	NM- 9.2
1	166	Spr/69	Orig. & last issue; 25¢; Stiff-c; no coming-next ad; other sources indicate publication date of 5/69	1	1	14	28	42	96	211	325
2	169	Spr/69	Stiff-c	1	1	9	18	27	58	114	170

NOTE: Many other titles were prepared or planned but were only issued in British/European series.

CLASSIC POPEYE (See Popeye, Classic)

CLASSIC PUNISHER (Also see Punisher)
Marvel Comics: Dec, 1989 ($4.95, B&W, deluxe format, 68 pgs.)

1-Reprints Marvel Super Action #1 & Marvel Preview #2 plus new story   1   3   4   6   8   10

CLASSIC RED SONJA
Dynamite Entertainment: 2010 - No. 4, 2010 ($3.99)

1-4-Newly colored reprints of stories from Savage Sword of Conan magazine   4.00

CLASSICS ILLUSTRATED
First Publishing/Berkley Publishing: Feb, 1990 - No. 27, July, 1991 ($3.75/$3.95, 52 pgs.)

1-27: 1-Gahan Wilson-c/a. 4-Sienkiewicz painted-c/a. 6-Russell scripts/layouts. 7-Spiegle-a.

	GD 2.0	VG 4.0	FN 6.0	VF 8.0	VF/NM 9.0	NM- 9.2

9-Ploog-c/a. 16-Staton-a. 18-Gahan Wilson-c/a; 20-Geary-a. 26-Aesop's Fables (6/91). 26,27-Direct sale only ... 5.00

CLASSICS ILLUSTRATED
Acclaim Books/Twin Circle PublishingCo.: Feb, 1997 - Jan, 1998 ($4.99, digest-size) (Each book contains study notes)
A Christmas Carol-(12/97), A Connecticut Yankee in King Arthur's Court-(5/97), All Quiet on the Western Front-(1/98), A Midsummer's Night Dream-(4/97) Around the World in 80 Days-(1/98), A Tale of Two Cities-(2/97)Joe Orlando-r, Captains Courageous-(11/97), Crime and Punishment-(3/97), Dr. Jekyll and Mr. Hyde-(10/97), Don Quixote-(12/97), Frankenstein-(10/97), Great Expectations-(4/97), Hamlet-(3/97), Huckleberry Finn-(3/97), Jane Eyre-(2/97), Kidnapped-(1/98), Les Miserables-(5/97), Lord Jim-(9/97), Macbeth-(5/97), Moby Dick-(4/97), Oliver Twist-(5/97), Robinson Crusoe-(9/97), Romeo & Juliet-(2/97), Silas Marner-(11/97), The Call of the Wild-(9/97), The Count of Monte Cristo-(1/98), The House of the Seven Gables-(9/97), The Iliad-(9/97), The Invisible Man-(10/97), The Last of the Mohicans-(12/97), The Master of Ballantrae-(11/97), The Odyssey-(3/97), The Prince and the Pauper-(4/97), The Red Badge Of Courage-(9/97), Tom Sawyer-(2/97) Wuthering Heights-(11/97) ... 5.00
NOTE: *Stories reprinted from the original Gilberton Classic Comics and Classics Illustrated.*

CLASSICS ILLUSTRATED GIANTS
Gilberton Publications: Oct, 1949 (One-Shots - "OS")
These Giant Editions, all with new front and back covers, were advertised from 10/49 to 2/52. They were 50¢ on the newsstand and 60¢ by mail. They are actually four Classics in one volume. All the stories are reprints of the Classics Illustrated Series.
NOTE: There were also British hardback Adventure & Indian Giants in 1952, with the same covers but different contents: Adventure - 2, 7, 10; Indian - 17, 22, 37, 58. They are also rare.

	GD 2.0	VG 4.0	FN 6.0	VF 8.0	VF/NM 9.0	NM- 9.2
"An Illustrated Library of Great Adventure Stories" - reprints of No. 6,7,8,10 (Rare); Kiefer-c	165	330	495	1048	1799	2550
"An Illustrated Library of Exciting Mystery Stories" - reprints of No. 30,21,40, 13 (Rare); Blum-c	177	354	531	1124	1937	2750
"An Illustrated Library of Great Indian Stories" - reprints of No. 4,17,22,37 (Rare); Blum-c	168	336	504	1075	1838	2600

INTRODUCTION TO CLASSICS ILLUSTRATED JUNIOR

Collectors of Juniors can be put into one of two categories: those who want any copy of each title, and those who want all the originals. Those seeking every original and reprint edition are a limited group, primarily because Juniors have no changes in art or covers to spark interest, and because reprints are so low in value it is difficult to get dealers to look for specific reprint editions.

In recent years it has become apparent that most serious Classics collectors seek Junior originals. Those seeking reprints seek them for low cost. This has made the previous note about the comparative market value of reprints inadequate. Three particular reprint editions are worth even more. For the 535-Twin Circle edition, and two Giveaways. There are also reprint editions of 501 and 503 which have a full-page bc ad for the very rare Junior record. Those may sell as high as $10-$15 in mint. Original editions of 557 and 558 also have that ad.

There are no reprint editions of 577. The only edition, from 1969, is a 25 cent stiff-cover edition with no ad for the next issue. All other original editions have coming-next ad. But 577, like C.I. #168, was prepared in 1962 but not issued. Copies of 577 can be found in 1963 British/European series, which then continued with dozens of additional new Junior titles.

PRICES LISTED BELOW ARE FOR ORIGINAL EDITIONS, WHICH HAVE AN AD FOR THE NEXT ISSUE.
NOTE: *Non HRN 576 copies- many are written on or colored . Reprints with 576 HRN are worth about 1/3 original prices. All other HRN #'s are 1/2 original price*

CLASSICS ILLUSTRATED JUNIOR
Famous Authors Ltd. (Gilberton Publications): Oct, 1953 - Spring, 1971

	GD 2.0	VG 4.0	FN 6.0	VF 8.0	VF/NM 9.0	NM- 9.2
501-Snow White & the Seven Dwarfs; Alex Blum-a	12	24	36	69	97	125
502-The Ugly Duckling	9	18	27	47	61	75
503-Cinderella	8	16	24	41	57	70
504-512: 504-The Pied Piper. 505-The Sleeping Beauty. 506-The Three Little Pigs. 507-Jack & the Beanstalk. 508-Goldilocks & the Three Bears. 509-Beauty and the Beast. 510-Little Red Riding Hood. 511-Puss-N Boots. 512-Rumpelstiltskin	6	12	18	27	33	38
513-Pinocchio	7	14	21	37	46	55
514-The Steadfast Tin Soldier	8	16	24	44	57	70
515-Johnny Appleseed	6	12	18	27	33	38
516-Aladdin and His Lamp	6	12	18	29	36	42
517-519: 517-The Emperor's New Clothes. 518-The Golden Goose. 519-Paul Bunyan	6	12	18	27	33	38
520-Thumbelina	6	12	18	29	36	42
521-King of the Golden River	6	12	18	27	33	38
522,523,530: 522-The Nightingale. 523-The Gallant Tailor. 530-The Golden Bird	5	10	15	24	30	35
524-The Wild Swans	6	12	18	29	36	42
525,526: 525-The Little Mermaid. 526-The Frog Prince	6	12	18	29	36	42
527-The Golden-Haired Giant	6	12	18	27	33	38
528-The Penny Prince	6	12	18	27	33	38
529-The Magic Servants	6	12	18	27	33	38
531-Rapunzel	6	12	18	27	33	38
532-534: 532-The Dancing Princesses. 533-The Magic Fountain. 534-The Golden Touch	5	10	15	23	28	32
535-The Wizard of Oz	9	18	27	50	65	80
536-The Chimney Sweep	6	12	18	27	33	38
537-The Three Fairies	6	12	18	28	34	40
538-Silly Hans	5	10	15	23	28	32
539-The Enchanted Fish	6	12	18	31	38	45
540-The Tinder-Box	6	12	18	31	38	45
541-Snow White & Rose Red	5	10	15	24	30	35
542-The Donkey's Tale	5	10	15	24	30	35
543-The House in the Woods	6	12	18	27	33	38
544-The Golden Fleece	6	12	18	31	38	45
545-The Glass Mountain	5	10	15	24	30	35
546-The Elves & the Shoemaker	5	10	15	24	30	35
547-The Wishing Table	6	12	18	27	33	38
548-551: 548-The Magic Pitcher. 549-Simple Kate. 550-The Singing Donkey. 551-The Queen Bee	5	10	15	23	28	32
552-The Three Little Dwarfs	6	12	18	27	33	38
553,556: 553-King Thrushbeard. 556-The Elf Mound	5	10	15	23	28	32
554-The Enchanted Deer	6	12	18	27	36	42
555-The Three Golden Apples	5	10	15	24	30	35
557-Silly Willy	6	12	18	28	34	40
558-The Magic Dish; L.B. Cole-c; soft and stiff-c exist on original	7	14	21	35	43	50
559-The Japanese Lantern; 1 pg. Ingels-a; L.B. Cole-c	7	14	21	35	43	50
560-The Doll Princess; L.B. Cole-c	7	14	21	35	43	50
561-Hans Humdrum; L.B. Cole-c	6	12	18	29	36	42
562-The Enchanted Pony; L.B. Cole-c	7	14	21	35	43	50
563,565-568,570: 563-The Wishing Well; L.B. Cole-c. 565-The Silly Princess; L.B. Cole-c. 566-Clumsy Hans; L.B. Cole-c. 567-The Bearskin Soldier; L.B. Cole-c. 570-The Pearl Princess	6	12	18	27	33	38
564-The Salt Mountain; L.B.Cole-c. 568-The Happy Hedgehog; L.B. Cole-c.	6	12	18	28	34	40
569,573: 569-The Three Giants.573-The Crystal Ball	5	10	15	23	28	32
571,572: 571-How Fire Came to the Indians. 572-The Drummer Boy	6	12	18	29	36	42
574-Brightbody	5	10	15	24	30	35
575-The Fearless Prince	6	12	18	28	34	40
576-The Princess Who Saw Everything	7	14	21	35	43	50
577-The Runaway Dumpling	8	16	24	44	57	70

NOTE: *Prices are for original editions. Last reprint - Spring, 1971.* **Costanza & Schaffenberger** *art in many issues.*

CLASSICS ILLUSTRATED SPECIAL ISSUE
Gilberton Co.: (Came out semi-annually) Dec, 1955 - Jul, 1962 (35¢, 100 pgs.)

	GD 2.0	VG 4.0	FN 6.0	VF 8.0	VF/NM 9.0	NM- 9.2
129-The Story of Jesus (titled ...Special Edition) "Jesus on Mountain" cover	18	36	54	105	165	225
"Three Camels" cover (12/58)	19	38	57	109	172	235
"Mountain" cover (no date)-Has checklist on inside b/c to HRN #161 & different testimonial on back-c	14	28	42	76	108	140
"Mountain" cover (1968 re-issue; has white 50¢ circle)	10	20	30	56	76	95
132A-The Story of America (6/56); Cameron-a	12	24	36	67	94	120
135A-The Ten Commandments(12/56)	11	22	33	64	90	115
138A-Adventures in Science(6/57); HRN to 137	11	22	33	60	83	105
138A-(6/57)-2nd version w/HRN to 149	7	14	21	35	43	50
138A-(12/61)-3rd version w/HRN to 149	7	14	21	35	43	50
141A-The Rough Rider (Teddy Roosevelt)(12/57); Evans-a	11	22	33	62	86	110
144A-Blazing the Trails West(6/58)- 73 pgs. of Crandall/Evans plus Severin-a	11	22	33	64	90	115
147A-Crossing the Rockies(12/58)-Crandall/Evans-a	11	22	33	62	86	110
150A-Royal Canadian Police(6/59)-Ingels, Sid Check-a	11	22	33	62	86	110
153A-Men, Guns & Cattle(12/59)-Evans-a (26 pgs.); Kinstler-a	11	22	33	62	86	110
156A-The Atomic Age(6/60)-Crandall/Evans, Torres-a	11	22	33	62	86	110
159A-Rockets, Jets and Missiles(12/60)-Evans, Morrow-a	11	22	33	62	86	110
162A-War Between the States(6/61)-Kirby & Crandall/Evans-a; Ingels-a	17	34	51	100	158	215
165A-To the Stars(12/61)-Torres, Crandall/Evans, Kirby-a	14	28	42	76	108	140
166A-World War II('62)-Torres, Crandall/Evans, Kirby-a	11	30	45	85	130	175
167A-Prehistoric World(7/62)-Torres & Crandall/Evans-a; two versions exist (HRN to 165 & HRN to 167)	14	22	42	81	118	155
nn Special Issue-The United Nations (1964; 50¢; scarce); this is actually part of the European Special Series, which cont'd on after the U.S. series stopped issuing new titles in 1962. This English edition was prepared specifically for sale at the U.N. It was printed in Norway	50	100	150	315	533	750

NOTE: *There was another U.S. Special Issue prepared in 1962 with artwork by* **Torres** *entitled World War I. Unfortunately, it was never issued an any English-language edition. It was issued in 1964 in West Germany, The Netherlands, and some Scandanavian countries, with another edition in 1974 with a new cover.*

CLASSICS LIBRARY (See King Classics)

CLASSIC STAR WARS (Also see Star Wars)
Dark Horse Comics: Aug, 1992 - No. 20, June, 1994 ($2.50)

	GD 2.0	VG 4.0	FN 6.0	VF 8.0	VF/NM 9.0	NM- 9.2
1-Begin Star Wars strip-r by Williamson; Williamson redrew portions of the panels to fit comic book format	1	2	3	5	6	8
2-10: 8-Polybagged w/Star Wars Galaxy trading card. 8-M. Schultz-c						4.00
11-19: 13-Yeates-c. 17-M. Schultz-c. 19-Evans-c						3.00
20-($3.50, 52 pgs.)-Polybagged w/trading card						4.00
Escape To Hoth TPB ($16.95) r/#15-20						17.00
The Rebel Storm TPB - r/#8-14						17.00
Trade paperback ($29.95, slip-cased)-Reprints all movie adaptations						30.00

NOTE: *Williamson c-1-5,9,10,14,15,20.*

CLASSIC STAR WARS: (Title series). **Dark Horse Comics**
--A NEW HOPE, 6/94 - No. 2, 7/94 ($3.95)

	GD 2.0	VG 4.0	FN 6.0	VF 8.0	VF/NM 9.0	NM- 9.2
1,2: 1-r/Star Wars #1-3, 7-9 publ; 2-r/Star Wars #4-6, 10-12 publ. by Marvel Comics	1	2	3	5	6	8

--DEVILWORLDS, 8/96 - No. 2, 9/96 ($2.50) 1,2: r/Alan Moore-s

	GD 2.0	VG 4.0	FN 6.0	VF 8.0	VF/NM 9.0	NM- 9.2
	1	2	3	5	6	8

--HAN SOLO AT STARS' END, 3/97 - No. 3, 5/97 ($2.95)

	GD 2.0	VG 4.0	FN 6.0	VF 8.0	VF/NM 9.0	NM- 9.2
1-3: r/strips by Alfredo Alcala						4.00

--RETURN OF THE JEDI, 10/94 - No. 2, 11/94 ($3.50)

	GD 2.0	VG 4.0	FN 6.0	VF 8.0	VF/NM 9.0	NM- 9.2
1-r/1983-84 Marvel series; polybagged with w/trading card	2	4	6	11	16	20
2	1	2	3	5	6	8

--THE EARLY ADVENTURES, 8/94 - No. 9, 4/95 ($2.50) 1-8

	GD 2.0	VG 4.0	FN 6.0	VF 8.0	VF/NM 9.0	NM- 9.2
						4.00
9-Boba Fett-c	2	4	6	9	12	15

--THE EMPIRE STRIKES BACK, 8/94 - No. 2, 9/94 ($3.95)

	GD 2.0	VG 4.0	FN 6.0	VF 8.0	VF/NM 9.0	NM- 9.2
1-r/Star Wars #39-44 published by Marvel Comics						6.00

CLASSIC X-MEN (Becomes X-Men Classic #46 on)
Marvel Comics Group: Sept, 1986 - No. 45, Mar, 1990

Classics Illustrated Junior #507 © GIL

Claws #3 © MAR

Cloaked #3 © DH

	GD 2.0	VG 4.0	FN 6.0	VF 8.0	VF/NM 9.0	NM- 9.2
1-Begins-r of New X-Men	3	6	9	17	26	35
2-10: 10-Sabretooth app.						6.00
11-42,44,45: 11-1st origin of Magneto in back-up story. 17-Wolverine-c. 27-r/X-Men #121. 26-r/X-Men #120; Wolverine-c/app. 35-r/X-Men #129. 39-New Jim Lee back-up story (2nd-a on X-Men)						4.00
43-Byrne-c/a(r); ($1.75, double-size)						5.00

NOTE: *Art Adams* c(p)-1-10, 12-16, 18-23. *Austin* c-10,15-21,24-28i. *Bolton* back up stories in 1-28,30-35. *Williamson* c-12-14i.

CLAW (See Capt. Battle, Jr., Daredevil Comics & Silver Streak Comics)

CLAWS (See Wolverine & Black Cat: Claws 2 for sequel)
Marvel Comics: Oct, 2006 - No. 3, Dec, 2006 ($3.99, limited series)
| 1-3-Wolverine and Black Cat team-up; Linsner-a/c | | | | | | 4.00 |
| Wolverine & Black Cat: Claws HC (2007, $17.99, dustjacket) r/#1-3 & bonus Linsner art | | | | | | 18.00 |

CLAW THE UNCONQUERED (See Cancelled Comic Cavalcade)
National Periodical Publications/DC Comics: 5-6/75 - No. 9, 9-10/76; No. 10, 4-5/78 - No. 12, 8-9/78
| 1-1st app. Claw | 2 | 4 | 6 | 10 | 14 | 18 |
| 2-12: 3-Nudity panel. 9-Origin | 1 | 2 | 3 | 4 | 5 | 7 |

NOTE: *Giffen* a-8-12p. *Kubert* c-10-12. *Layton* a-9i, 12i.

CLAW THE UNCONQUERED (See Red Sonja/Claw: The Devil's Hands)
DC Comics: Aug, 2006 - No. 6, Jan, 2007 ($2.99)
| 1-6: 1,2-Chuck Dixon-s/Andy Smith; two covers by Smith & Van Sciver | | | | | | 3.00 |
| TPB (2007, $17.99) r/#1-6; cover gallery | | | | | | 18.00 |

CLAY CODY, GUNSLINGER
Pines Comics: Fall, 1957
| 1-Painted-c | 7 | 14 | 21 | 35 | 43 | 50 |

CLEAN FUN, STARRING "SHOOGAFOOTS JONES"
Specialty Book Co.: 1944 (10¢, B&W, oversized covers, 24 pgs.)
nn-Humorous situations involving Negroes in the Deep South						
White cover issue…	39	78	117	231	378	525
Dark grey cover issue…	36	72	108	211	343	475

CLEAN ROOM
DC Comics (Vertigo): Dec, 2015 - No. 18, Jun, 2017 ($3.99)
| 1-18: 1-Gail Simone-s/Jon Davis-Hunt-a/Jenny Frison-c | | | | | | 4.00 |

CLEAR (Printing of digital series first appearing on comiXology Originals)
Dark Horse Comics: Mar, 2023 - No. 3, May, 2023 ($4.99, limited series)
| 1-3-Scott Snyder-s/Francis Manapul-a | | | | | | 5.00 |

CLEMENTINA THE FLYING PIG (See Dell Jr. Treasury)

CLEOPATRA (See Ideal, a Classical Comic No. 1)

CLERKS: THE COMIC BOOK (Also see Tales From the Clerks and Oni Double Feature #1)
Oni Press: Feb, 1998 ($2.95, B&W, one-shot)
1-Kevin Smith-s	3	6	9	14	19	24
1-Second printing						6.00
…Holiday Special (12/98, $2.95) Smith-s	1	3	4	6	8	10
…The Lost Scene (12/99, $2.95) Smith-s/Hester-a	1	3	4	6	8	10

CLIFFHANGER (See Battle Chasers, Crimson, and Danger Girl)
WildStorm Prod./Wizard Press: 1997 (Wizard supplement)
| 0-Sketchbook preview of Cliffhanger titles | | | | | | 6.00 |

CLIMAX! (Mystery)
Gillmor Magazines: July, 1955 - No. 2, Sept, 1955
| 1 | 21 | 42 | 63 | 126 | 206 | 285 |
| 2 | 15 | 30 | 45 | 90 | 140 | 190 |

CLINT (Also see Adolescent Radioactive Black Belt Hamsters)
Eclipse Comics: Sept, 1986 - No. 2, Jan, 1987 ($1.50, B&W)
| 1,2 | | | | | | 4.00 |

CLINT & MAC (TV, Disney)
Dell Publishing Co.: No. 889, Mar, 1958
| Four Color 889-Alex Toth-a, photo-c | 10 | 20 | 30 | 67 | 141 | 215 |

CLIVE BARKER'S BOOK OF THE DAMNED: A HELLRAISER COMPANION
Marvel Comics (Epic): Oct, 1991 - No. 3, Nov, 1992 ($4.95, semi-annual, 52 pgs.)
| 1-Simon Bisley-a | 2 | 4 | 6 | 9 | 12 | 15 |
| 2,3: 2-(4/92). 3-(11/92)-McKean-a (1 pg.) | 1 | 3 | 4 | 6 | 8 | 10 |

CLIVE BARKER'S HELLRAISER (Also see Epic, Hellraiser Nightbreed –Jihad, Revelations, Son of Celluloid, Tapping the Vein & Weaveworld)
Marvel Comics (Epic Comics): 1989 - No. 20, 1993 ($4.50-6.95, mature, quarterly, 68 pgs.)

	GD 2.0	VG 4.0	FN 6.0	VF 8.0	VF/NM 9.0	NM- 9.2
Book 1: Based on Hellraiser & Hellbound movies	2	4	6	11	16	20
Book 2-4,10-16,18,19: Based on Hellraiser & Hellbound movies; Bolton-c/a; Spiegle & Wrightson-a (graphic album). 10-Foil-c. 12-Sam Kieth-a	1	3	4	6	8	10
Book 5-9 ($5.95): 7-Bolton-a. 8-Morrow-a	1	2	3	5	6	8
Book 17-Alex Ross-a, 34 pgs.	2	4	6	8	10	12
Book 20-By Gaiman/McKean	2	4	6	11	16	20
…Collected Best (Checker Books, '02, $21.95)-r/by various incl. Ross, Gaiman, Mignola						22.00
…Collected Best II ('03, $19.95)-r/by various incl. Bolton, L. Wachowski, Dorman						20.00
…Collected Best III ('04, $26.95)-r/by various incl. Bolton, L. Wachowski, Wrightson						27.00
…Dark Holiday Special ('92, $4.95)-Conrad-a	1	3	4	6	8	10
…Spring Slaughter 1 ('94, $6.95, 52 pgs.)-Painted-c	2	4	6	11	16	20
…Summer Special 1 ('92, $5.95, 68 pgs.)	1	3	4	6	8	10

CLIVE BARKER'S HELLRAISER
BOOM! Studios: Mar, 2011 - No. 20, Nov, 2012 ($3.99)
1-20: 1-Barker & Monfette-s/Manco-a; preview of Hellraiser Masterpieces; 3 covers						4.00
Annual 1 (3/12, $4.99) Hervás-a; three covers						5.00
2013 Annual (10/13, $4.99) Seifert-s/Hervás-a; Barker & Meares-s/Ordon-a						5.00
…: Bestiary 1-6 (8/14 - No. 6, 1/15, $3.99) short stories by various; multiple covers						4.00
…: Masterpieces 1-12 (11/11 - No. 12, 4/12, $3.99) reps from Marvel series. 1-Wrightson-a						4.00
…: The Dark Watch 1-12 (2/13 - No. 12, 1/14, $3.99) Tom Garcia-a; multiple covers						4.00
…: The Road Below 1-4 (10/12 - No. 4, 1/13, $3.99) Haemi Jang-a; multiple covers						4.00

CLIVE BARKER'S NEXT TESTAMENT
BOOM! Studios: 2013 - No. 12, Aug, 2014 ($3.99)
| 1-12: 1-Clive Barker & Mark Miller-s/Haemi Jang-a. 1-Four covers | | | | | | 4.00 |

CLIVE BARKER'S NIGHTBREED (Also see Epic)
Marvel Comics (Epic Comics): Apr, 1990 - No. 25, Mar, 1993 ($1.95/$2.25/$2.50, mature)
| 1-Adapts the horror movie | 1 | 3 | 4 | 6 | 8 | 10 |
| 2-25: 2-4-Adapt horror movie. 5-New stories; Guice-a(p) | | | | | | 4.00 |

CLIVE BARKER'S NIGHTBREED
BOOM! Studios: May, 2014 - No. 12, Apr, 2015 ($3.99)
| 1-12: 1-8-Andreyko-s/Kowalski-a. 9-11-Javier & Pramanik-a | | | | | | 4.00 |

CLIVE BARKER'S THE HARROWERS
Marvel Comics (Epic Comics): Dec, 1993 - No. 6, May, 1994 ($2.50)
| 1-($2.95)-Glow-in-the-dark-c; Colan-c/a in all | | | | | | 5.00 |
| 2-6 | | | | | | 4.00 |

NOTE: *Colan* a(p)-1-6; c-1-3, 4p, 5p. *Williamson* a(i)-2, 4, 5(part).

CLOAK AND DAGGER
Ziff-Davis Publishing Co.: Fall, 1952
| 1-Saunders painted-c | 45 | 90 | 135 | 284 | 480 | 675 |

CLOAK AND DAGGER (Also see Marvel Fanfare and Spectacular Spider-Man #64)
Marvel Comics Group: Oct, 1983 - No. 4, 1984 (Mini-series)
| 1-Mantlo-s/Leonardi-a/Austin-a(i) in all | 1 | 2 | 3 | 5 | 6 | 8 |
| 2-4: 4-Origin | | | | | | 5.00 |

CLOAK AND DAGGER (2nd Series)(Also see Marvel Graphic Novel #34 & Strange Tales)
Marvel Comics Group: July, 1985 - No. 11, Jan, 1987
1-Mantlo-s/Leonardi-a/Austin-a(i)	1	2	3	5	6	8
2-11: 7,8-Mignola-c. 9-Art Adams-p						4.00
…And Power Pack (1990, $7.95, 68 pgs.)						8.00

CLOAK AND DAGGER (3rd Series listed as Mutant Misadventures Of…)

CLOAK AND DAGGER
Marvel Comics: May, 2010 ($3.99, one-shot)
| 1-Stuart Moore-s/Mark Brooks-a; X-Men app. | | | | | | 6.00 |

CLOAK AND DAGGER: NEGATIVE EXPOSURE
Marvel Comics: 2019 ($19.99, squarebound TPB, printing of digital-first story)
| nn-Hopeless-s/Manna & Coleman-a; Mister Negative app.; bonus inked art pages | | | | | | 20.00 |

CLOAK AND DAGGER: SHADES OF GREY
Marvel Comics: 2018 ($19.99, squarebound TPB, printing of digital-first story)
| nn-Hopeless-s/Messina-a; bonus inked art pages | | | | | | 20.00 |

CLOAKED
Dark Horse Comics: Dec, 2021 - No. 4, Mar, 2022 ($3.99, limited series)
| 1-4-Mike Richardson-s/Jordi Armengol-a | | | | | | 4.00 |

CLOAKS
BOOM! Studios: Sept, 2014 - No. 4, Dec, 2014 ($3.99, limited series)
| 1-4-Monroe-s/Navarro-a | | | | | | 4.00 |

CLOBBERIN' TIME
Marvel Comics: Sept, 1995 ($1.95) (Based on card game)

	GD 2.0	VG 4.0	FN 6.0	VF 8.0	VF/NM 9.0	NM- 9.2

nn-Overpower game guide; Ben Grimm story — 4.00

CLOBBERIN' TIME
Marvel Comics: May, 2023 - No. 5, Sept, 2023 ($3.99, limited series)
1-5-Steve Skroce-s/a; The Thing, Hulk, Wolverine, Doctor Doom app. — 4.00

CLOCK, THE
Image Comics: Jan, 2020 - No. 2, Feb, 2020 ($3.99)
1,2-Matt Hawkins-s/Colleen Doran-a — 4.00

CLOCK MAKER, THE
Image Comics: Jan, 2003 - No. 4, May, 2003 ($2.50, comic unfolds to 10"x13" pages)
1-4-Krueger-s — 3.00
... Act Two (4/04, $4.95, standard format) Krueger-s/Matt Smith-c — 5.00

CLOCKWORK ANGELS (Based on Neil Peart's story and lyrics from Rush's album)
BOOM! Studios: Mar, 2014 - No. 6, Nov, 2014 ($3.99, limited series)
1-6-Kevin J. Anderson-s/Nick Robles-a; two covers on each — 4.00

CLONE CONSPIRACY, THE (Also see Amazing Spider-Man [2017] #18)
Marvel Comics: Dec, 2016 - No. 5, Apr, 2017 ($4.99/$3.99)
1-($4.99) Slott-s; Jim Cheung-a; Miles Warren, Gwen Stacy, Doc Ock & Rhino app. — 5.00
2-5-($3.99) Kaine app. 3-Ben Reilly returns — 4.00
...: Omega 1 (5/17, $4.99) Three short stories by various; aftermath of series — 5.00

CLONEZONE SPECIAL
Dark Horse Comics/First Comics: 1989 ($2.00, B&W)
1-Back-up series from Badger & Nexus — 4.00

CLOSE ENCOUNTERS (See Marvel Comics Super Special & Marvel Special Edition)

CLOSE SHAVES OF PAULINE PERIL, THE (TV cartoon)
Gold Key: June, 1970 - No. 4, March, 1971

1		5	10	15	31	53	75
2-4		3	6	9	19	30	40

CLOSET, THE
Image Comics: Jun, 2022 - No. 3, Aug, 2022 ($3.99, limited series)
1-3-James Tynion IV-s/Gavin Fullerton-a — 4.00

CLOUDBURST
Image Comics: June, 2004 ($7.95, squarebound)
1-Gray & Palmiotti-s/Shy & Gouveia-a — 8.00

CLOUDFALL
Image Comics: Nov, 2003 ($4.95, B&W, squarebound)
1-Kirkman-s/Su-a/o — 5.00

CLOWN COMICS (No. 1 titled Clown Comic Book)
Clown Comics/Home Comics/Harvey Publ.: 1945 - No. 3, Win, 1946

	GD 2.0	VG 4.0	FN 6.0	VF 8.0	VF/NM 9.0	NM- 9.2
nn (#1)	18	36	54	105	165	225
2,3	11	22	33	62	86	110

CLOWNS, THE (I Pagliacci)
Dark Horse Comics: 1998 ($2.95, B&W, one-shot)
1-Adaption of the opera; P. Craig Russell-script — 4.00

CLUBHOUSE RASCALS (#1 titled ...Presents?) (Also see Three Rascals)
Sussex Publ. Co. (Magazine Enterprises): June, 1956 - No. 2, Oct, 1956

	GD 2.0	VG 4.0	FN 6.0	VF 8.0	VF/NM 9.0	NM- 9.2
1-The Brain app. in both; DeCarlo-a	10	20	30	54	72	90
2	8	16	24	40	50	60

CLUB "16"
Famous Funnies: June, 1948 - No. 4, Dec, 1948

	GD 2.0	VG 4.0	FN 6.0	VF 8.0	VF/NM 9.0	NM- 9.2
1-Teen-age humor	37	74	111	222	361	500
2-4	20	40	60	114	182	250

CLUE (Based on the boardgame)
IDW Publishing: Jun, 2017 - No. 6, Nov, 2017 ($3.99)
1-6-Paul Allor-s/Nelson Daniel-a; multiple covers on each — 4.00

CLUE: CANDLESTICK (Based on the boardgame)
IDW Publishing: May, 2019 - No. 3, Jul, 2019 ($4.99, limited series)
1-3-Dash Shaw-s/a; multiple covers on each — 5.00

CLUE COMICS (Real Clue Crime V2#4 on)
Hillman Periodicals: Jan, 1943 - No. 15(V2#3), May, 1947

	GD 2.0	VG 4.0	FN 6.0	VF 8.0	VF/NM 9.0	NM- 9.2
1-Origin The Boy King, Nightmare, Micro-Face, Twilight, & Zippo	200	400	600	1280	2190	3100
2 (scarce)	103	206	309	659	1130	1600
3-5 (9/43)	53	106	159	334	567	800
6,8,9: 8-Palais-c/a(2)	39	78	117	240	395	550
7-Classic concentration camp torture-c (3/44)	148	296	444	947	1624	2300
10-Origin/1st app. The Gun Master & begin series; content changes to crime (10/46)	42	84	126	265	445	625
11 (12/46)	34	68	102	199	325	450
12-Origin Rackman; McWilliams-a, Guardineer-a(2)	41	82	123	256	428	600
V2#1-Nightmare new origin; Iron Lady app.; Simon & Kirby-a (3/47)	90	180	270	576	988	1400
V2#2-S&K-a(2)-Bondage/torture-c; man attacks & kills people with electric iron. Infantino-a	459	918	1377	3350	5925	8500
V2#3-S&K-a(3)	71	142	213	454	777	1100

CLUELESS: SENIOR YEAR (Movie)
Boom Entertainment (BOOM Box): Aug, 2017 ($14.99, SC, graphic novel)
nn-Sarah Kuhn & Amber Benson-s/Siobhan Keenan-a; sequel to the movie; bonus art — 15.00

CLUELESS SPRING SPECIAL (TV)
Marvel Comics: May, 1997 ($3.99, magazine sized, one-shot)
1-Photo-c from TV show — 4.00

CLUSTER
BOOM! Studios: Feb, 2015 - No. 8, Oct, 2015 ($3.99, limited series)
1-8-Ed Brisson-s/Damian Couceiro-a — 4.00

CLUTCHING HAND, THE
American Comics Group: July-Aug, 1954

	GD 2.0	VG 4.0	FN 6.0	VF 8.0	VF/NM 9.0	NM- 9.2
1-Gustavson, Moldoff-a	77	154	231	493	847	1200

CLYDE BEATTY COMICS (Also see Crackajack Funnies)
Commodore Productions & Artists, Inc.: October, 1953 (84 pgs.)

	GD 2.0	VG 4.0	FN 6.0	VF 8.0	VF/NM 9.0	NM- 9.2
1-Photo front/back-c; movie scenes and comics	28	56	84	165	270	375

CLYDE CRASHCUP (TV)
Dell Publishing Co.: Aug-Oct, 1963 - No. 5, Sept-Nov, 1964

	GD 2.0	VG 4.0	FN 6.0	VF 8.0	VF/NM 9.0	NM- 9.2
1-All written by John Stanley	7	14	21	44	82	120
2-5	4	8	12	27	44	60

COBB
IDW Publishing: May, 2006 - No. 3, July, 2007 ($3.99, B&W)
1-3-Beau Smith-s/Eduardo Barreto-a/c; regular and retailer incentive covers — 4.00

COBRA (G.I. Joe)
IDW Publishing: No. 10, Feb, 2012 - No. 21, Jan, 2013 ($3.99)
10-21 — 4.00
... Annual 2012: The Origin of Cobra Commander (1/12, $7.99) Dixon-s — 8.00

COBRA COMMANDER (G.I. Joe)
Image Comics (Skybound): Jan, 2024 - Present ($4.99/$3.99)
1-($4.99) Williamson-s/Milana-a — 5.00
2-($3.99) — 4.00

COBRA KAI: THE KARATE KID SAGA CONTINUES (Based on the Karate Kid movie)
IDW Publishing: Oct, 2019 - No. 3, Dec, 2019 ($3.99)
1-3-Johnny Lawrence's story before & during the movie; Kagan McLeod-a — 4.00

CODENAME: ACTION
Dynamite Entertainment: 2013 - No. 5, 2014 ($3.99, limited series)
1-5-Captain Action; Chris Roberson-s/Jonathan Lau-a; multiple covers on each — 4.00

CODE NAME: ASSASSIN (See 1st Issue Special)

CODENAME: BABOUSHKA
Image Comics: Oct, 2015 - No. 5, Mar, 2016 ($3.99, limited series)
1-5: 1-Antony Johnston-s/Shari Chankhamma-a — 4.00

CODENAME: DANGER
Lodestone Publishing: Aug, 1985 - No. 4, May, 1986 ($1.50)
1-4 — 4.00

CODENAME: FIREARM (Also see Firearm)
Malibu Comics (Ultraverse): June, 1995 - No. 5, Sept, 1995 ($2.95, bimonthly limited series)
0-5: 0-2-Alec Swan back-up story by James Robinson. 0-Pérez-c — 4.00

CODENAME: GENETIX
Marvel Comics UK: Jan, 1993 - No. 4, May, 1993 ($1.75, limited series)
1-4: Wolverine in all — 4.00

CODENAME: KNOCKOUT
DC Comics (Vertigo): No. 0, Jun, 2001 - No. 23, June, 2003 ($2.50/$2.75)
0-15: Rodi-s in all. 0-5-Small Jr. -a. 1-Two covers by Chiodo & Cho. 7,8,10,11,12-Paquette-a. 6,9,13,14-Conner-a — 3.00
16-23: 16-Begin $2.75-c. 23-Last issue; JG Jones-c — 3.00

CODENAME SPITFIRE (Formerly Spitfire And The Troubleshooters)
Marvel Comics Group: No. 10, July, 1987 - No. 13, Oct, 1987
10-13: 10-Rogers-c/a (low printing) — 4.00

CODENAME: STRYKE FORCE (Also See Cyberforce V1#4 & Cyberforce/Stryke Force: Opposing Forces)
Image Comics (Top Cow Productions): Jan, 1994 - No. 14, Sept, 1995 ($1.95-$2.25)
0,1-14: 1-12-Silvestri stories, Peterson-a. 4-Stormwatch app. 14-Story continues in Cyberforce/Stryke Force: Opposing Forces; Turner-a — 4.00
1-Gold, 1-Blue — 5.00

CODE OF HONOR
Marvel Comics: Feb, 1997 - No. 4, May, 1997 ($5.95, limited series)
1-4-Fully painted by various; Dixon-s — 6.00

CODY OF THE PONY EXPRESS (See Colossal Features Magazine)
Fox Feature Syndicate: Sept, 1950 (See Women Outlaws)(One shot)

	GD 2.0	VG 4.0	FN 6.0	VF 8.0	VF/NM 9.0	NM- 9.2
1-Painted-c	17	34	51	98	154	210

CODY OF THE PONY EXPRESS (Buffalo Bill...) (Outlaws of the West #11 on; Formerly Bullseye)
Charlton Comics: No. 8, Oct, 1955; No. 9, Jan, 1956; No. 10, June, 1956

	GD 2.0	VG 4.0	FN 6.0	VF 8.0	VF/NM 9.0	NM- 9.2
8-Bullseye on splash pg; not S&K-a	9	18	27	47	61	75
9,10: Buffalo Bill app. in all	6	12	18	32	39	46

CODY STARBUCK (1st app. in Star Reach #1)
Star Reach Productions: July, 1978

	GD 2.0	VG 4.0	FN 6.0	VF 8.0	VF/NM 9.0	NM- 9.2
nn-Howard Chaykin-c/a	3	6	9	14	20	25
2nd printing	2	4	6	8	10	12

NOTE: Both printings say First Printing. True first printing is on lower-grade paper, somewhat off-register, and snow in snow sequence has green tint.

CO-ED ROMANCES
P. L. Publishing Co.: November, 1951

	GD 2.0	VG 4.0	FN 6.0	VF 8.0	VF/NM 9.0	NM- 9.2
1	16	32	48	96	147	200

COFFEE WORLD
World Comics: Oct, 1995 ($1.50, B&W, anthology)
1-Shannon Wheeler's Too Much Coffee Man story — 4.00

COFFIN, THE
Oni Press: Sept, 2000 - No. 4, May, 2001 ($2.95, B&W, limited series)
1-4-Hester-s/Huddleston-a — 3.00

COFFIN BOUND
Image Comics: Aug, 2019 - No. 8, Nov, 2020 ($3.99/$4.99, limited series)

Clue Comics #2 © HILL

Codename: Action #1
© Captain Action Enterprises

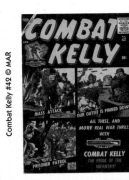

Combat Kelly #42 © MAR

	GD 2.0	VG 4.0	FN 6.0	VF 8.0	VF/NM 9.0	NM- 9.2

1-3,5,6,8-($3.99) Dan Watters-s/Dani-a ... 4.00
4,7-($4.99) 4-Bonus preview of Protector #1 ... 5.00

COFFIN HILL
DC Comics (Vertigo): Dec, 2013 - No. 20, Sept, 2015 ($2.99/$3.99)
1-18: 1-Caitlin Kittredge-s/Inaki Miranda-a; covers by Dave Johnson & Gene Ha ... 3.00
19,20-($3.99) Johnson-c ... 4.00

COJACARU THE SKINNER
Dark Horse Comics: Apr, 2021 - No. 2, May, 2021 ($3.99, limited series)
1,2-Mignola & Golden-s/Bergting-a ... 4.00

COLDER
Dark Horse Comics: Nov, 2012 - No. 5, Mar, 2013 ($3.99, limited series)
1-5-Tobin-s/Ferreyra-a/c ... 4.00

COLDER: THE BAD SEED
Dark Horse Comics: Oct, 2014 - No. 5, Feb, 2015 ($3.99, limited series)
1-5-Tobin-s/Ferreyra-a/c ... 4.00

COLDER: TOSS THE BONES
Dark Horse Comics: Sept, 2015 - No. 5, Jan, 2016 ($3.99, limited series)
1-5-Tobin-s/Ferreyra-a/c ... 4.00

COLD WAR
IDW Publishing: Oct, 2011 - No. 4, Jan, 2012 ($3.99, limited series)
1-4-John Byrne-s/a/c; two covers on each ... 4.00

COLD WAR
AfterShock Comics: Feb, 2018 - No. 5, Jun, 2018 ($3.99, limited series)
1-5-Sebela-a/Sherman-a ... 4.00

COLLAPSER
DC Comics (Young Animal): Sept, 2019 - No. 6, Feb, 2020 ($3.99, limited series)
1-6-Mikey Way & Shaun Simon-s/Ilias Kyriazis-a. 5-Superman #1 cover swipe ... 4.00

COLLECTORS DRACULA, THE
Millennium Publications: 1994 - No. 2, 1994 ($3.95, color/B&W, 52 pgs., limited series)
1,2-Bolton-a (7 pgs.) ... 5.00

COLLECTORS ITEM CLASSICS (See Marvel Collectors Item Classics)

COLLECTOR, THE : UNIT 731
Dark Horse Comics: Apr, 2022 - No. 4, Jul, 2022 ($3.99, limited series)
1-4-Will Conrad & Rod Monteiro-s/Conrad-a; set in a WWII Japanese POW camp ... 4.00

COLLIDER (See FBP: Federal Bureau Of Physics; title changed after issue #1)

COLONEL WEIRD: COSMAGOG (From Black Hammer)
Dark Horse Comics: Oct, 2020 - No. 4, Jan, 2021 ($3.99, limited series)
1-4-Jeff Lemire-s/Tyler Crook-a ... 4.00

COLONIZED, THE
IDW Publishing: Apr, 2013 - No. 4, Jul, 2013 ($3.99, limited series)
1-4-Aliens vs. Zombies; Dave Sim-c/Chris Ryall-s/Drew Moss-a ... 4.00

COLORS IN BLACK
Dark Horse Comics: Mar, 1995 - No. 4, June, 1995 ($2.95, limited series)
1-4 ... 4.00

COLOSSAL FEATURES MAGAZINE (Formerly I Loved) (See Cody of the Pony Express)
Fox Feature Syndicate: No. 33, 5/50 - No. 34, 7/50; No. 3, 9/50 (Based on Columbia serial)

	GD 2.0	VG 4.0	FN 6.0	VF 8.0	VF/NM 9.0	NM- 9.2
33,34: Cody of the Pony Express begins. 33-Painted-c. 34-Photo-c	21	42	63	124	202	280
3-Authentic criminal cases	74	148	222	470	810	1150

COLOSSAL SHOW, THE (TV cartoon)
Gold Key: Oct, 1969

	GD 2.0	VG 4.0	FN 6.0	VF 8.0	VF/NM 9.0	NM- 9.2
1	5	10	15	30	50	70

COLOSSUS (See X-Men)
Marvel Comics: Oct, 1997 ($2.99, 48 pgs., one-shot)
1-Raab-s/Hitch & Neary-a, wraparound-c ... 5.00

COLOSSUS COMICS (See Green Giant & Motion Picture Funnies Weekly)
Sun Publications (Funnies, Inc.?): March, 1940

	GD 2.0	VG 4.0	FN 6.0	VF 8.0	VF/NM 9.0	NM- 9.2
1-(Scarce)-Tulpa of Tsang(hero); Colossus app.	1050	2100	3150	8000	14,500	21,000

NOTE: Cover by artist that drew Colossus in Green Giant Comics.

COLOUR OF MAGIC, THE (Terry Pratchett's…)
Innovation Publishing: 1991 - No. 4, 1991 ($2.50, limited series)
1-4: Adapts 1st novel of the Discworld series ... 4.00

COLOUR YOUR OWN CEREBUS IN HELL?
Aardvark-Vanaheim: Oct, 2019 ($4.00, B&W)
1-Cerebus figures placed over original Gustave Doré artwork of Hell ... 4.00

COLT .45 (TV)
Dell Publishing Co.: No. 924, 8/58 - No. 1058, 11-1/59-60; No. 4, 2-4/60 - No. 9, 5-7/61

	GD 2.0	VG 4.0	FN 6.0	VF 8.0	VF/NM 9.0	NM- 9.2
Four Color 924(#1)-Wayde Preston photo-c on all	10	20	30	64	132	200
Four Color 1004,1058: 1004-Photo-b/c	8	16	24	51	96	140
4,5,7-9	7	14	21	48	89	130
6-Toth-a	8	16	24	51	96	140

COLUMBIA COMICS
William H. Wise Co.: 1943

	GD 2.0	VG 4.0	FN 6.0	VF 8.0	VF/NM 9.0	NM- 9.2
1-Joe Palooka, Charlie Chan, Capt. Yank, Sparky Watts, Dixie Dugan app.	39	78	117	231	378	525

COMANCHE
Dell Publishing Co.: No. 1350, Apr-Jun, 1962

	GD 2.0	VG 4.0	FN 6.0	VF 8.0	VF/NM 9.0	NM- 9.2
Four Color 1350-Disney movie; reprints FC #966 with title change from "Tonka" to "Comanche"; Sal Mineo photo-c	6	12	18	38	69	100

COMANCHEROS, THE
Dell Publishing Co.: No. 1300, Mar-May, 1962

	GD 2.0	VG 4.0	FN 6.0	VF 8.0	VF/NM 9.0	NM- 9.2
Four Color 1300-Movie, John Wayne photo-c	15	30	45	105	233	360

COMBAT
Atlas Comics (ANC): June, 1952 - No. 11, April, 1953

	GD 2.0	VG 4.0	FN 6.0	VF 8.0	VF/NM 9.0	NM- 9.2
1	54	108	162	343	574	825
2-Heath-c/a	31	62	93	182	296	410
3,5-9,11: 3-Romita-a. 6-Robinson-c; Romita-a	22	44	66	132	216	300
4-Krigstein-a	22	44	66	128	209	290
10-B&W and color illos. in POP; Sale-a, Forte-a	36	72	108	211	342	475

NOTE: Combat Casey in 7-11. Heath a-2, 3; c-1, 2, 5, 9. Maneely a-11; c-3, 10. Pakula a-1. Reinman a-1.

COMBAT
Dell Publishing Co.: Oct-Nov, 1961 - No. 40, Oct, 1973 (No #9)

	GD 2.0	VG 4.0	FN 6.0	VF 8.0	VF/NM 9.0	NM- 9.2
1-Painted-c (thru #17)	9	18	27	60	120	180
2,3,5	5	10	15	34	60	85
4-John F. Kennedy c/story (P.T. 109)	7	14	21	49	92	135
6,7,8(4-6/63), 8(7-9/63)	5	10	15	30	50	70
10-26: 26-Last 12¢ issue	4	8	12	25	40	55
27-40(reprints #1-14). 30-r/#4	3	6	9	16	24	32

COMBAT CASEY (Formerly War Combat)
Atlas Comics (SAI): No. 6, Jan, 1953 - No. 34, July, 1957

	GD 2.0	VG 4.0	FN 6.0	VF 8.0	VF/NM 9.0	NM- 9.2
6 (Indicia shows 1/52 in error)	39	78	117	240	395	550
7-R.Q. Sale-a	24	48	72	142	234	325
8-Used in POP, pg. 94	22	44	66	128	209	290
9,10,13-19-Violent art by R.Q. Sale; Battle Brady x-over #10	28	56	84	165	270	375
11,12,20-Last Precode (2/55)	19	38	57	109	172	235
21-34: 22,25-R.Q. Sale-a	18	36	54	103	162	220

NOTE: Everett a-6. Heath c-10, 17, 19, 23, 30. Maneely c-6, 8, 15. Powell a-29(5), 30(5), 34. Severin c-26, 33, 34.

COMBAT KELLY
Atlas Comics (SPI): Nov, 1951 - No. 44, Aug, 1957

	GD 2.0	VG 4.0	FN 6.0	VF 8.0	VF/NM 9.0	NM- 9.2
1-1st app. Combat Kelly; Heath-a	55	110	165	352	601	850
2	30	60	90	177	289	400
3-10	22	44	66	128	209	290
11-Used in POP, pgs. 94,95 plus color illo.	24	48	72	142	234	325
12-Color illo. in POP	20	40	60	120	195	270
13-16	20	40	60	114	182	250
17-Violent art by R. Q. Sale; Combat Casey app.	24	48	72	144	237	330
18-20,22-28: 18-Battle Brady app. 28-Last precode (1/55)	18	36	54	107	169	230
21-Transvestism-c	22	44	66	132	216	300
29-44: 38-Green Berets story (8/56)	18	36	54	103	162	220

NOTE: Berg a-8, 12-14, 15-17, 19-23, 25, 26, 28, 31-37, 39, 41-44; c-2. Colan a-42. Heath a-4, 18; c-31. Lawrence a-23. Maneely a-3-5(2), 6, 7(3), 8, 9(2), 11; c-4, 5, 7, 8, 10, 11, 25, 29, 39. R.Q. Sale a-17, 25. Severin c-41, 42. Whitney a-5.

COMBAT KELLY (…and the Deadly Dozen)
Marvel Comics Group: June, 1972 - No. 9, Oct, 1973

	GD 2.0	VG 4.0	FN 6.0	VF 8.0	VF/NM 9.0	NM- 9.2
1-Intro & origin new Combat Kelly; Ayers/Mooney-a; Severin-c (20¢)	5	10	15	35	63	90
2,5-8	3	6	9	14	20	25
3,4: 3-Origin. 4-Sgt. Fury-c/s	3	6	9	16	24	32
9-Death of the Deadly Dozen	4	8	12	27	44	60

	GD 2.0	VG 4.0	FN 6.0	VF 8.0	VF/NM 9.0	NM- 9.2

COMBAT ZONE: TRUE TALES OF GIS IN IRAQ
Marvel Comics: 2005 ($19.99, squarebound)
Vol. 1-Karl Zinsmeister scripts adapted from his non-fiction books; Dan Jurgens-a ... 20.00

COMBINED OPERATIONS (See The Story of the Commandos)
COMEBACK (See Zane Grey 4-Color 357)
COMEDY CARNIVAL
St. John Publishing Co.: no date (1950's) (100 pgs.)
nn-Contains rebound St. John comics   41 82 123 256 428 600

COMEDY COMICS (1st Series) (Daring Mystery #1-8) (Becomes Margie Comics #35 on)
Timely Comics (TCI 9,10): No. 9, April, 1942 - No. 34, Fall, 1946
9-(Scarce)-The Fin by Everett, Capt. Dash, Citizen V, & The Silver Scorpion app.;
Wolverton-a; 1st app. Comedy Kid; satire on Hitler & Stalin; The Fin, Citizen V & Silver
Scorpion cont. from Daring Mystery   314 628 942 2198 3849 5500
10-(Scarce)-Origin The Fourth Musketeer, Victory Boys; Monstro, the Mighty app.
    245 490 735 1568 2684 3800
11-Vagabond, Stuporman app.   77 154 231 493 847 1200
12,13   36 72 108 211 343 475
14-Origin/1st app. Super Rabbit (3/43) plus-c   123 246 369 787 1344 1900
15-19   32 64 96 188 307 425
20-Hitler parody-c   94 188 282 597 1024 1450
21-Tojo-c   71 142 213 454 777 1100
22-Hitler parody-c   194 388 582 1242 2121 3000
23-32   24 48 72 142 234 325
33-Kurtzman-a (5 pgs.)   24 48 72 144 237 330
34-Intro Margie; Wolverton-a (5 pgs.)   47 94 141 296 498 700

COMEDY COMICS (2nd Series)
Marvel Comics (ACI): May, 1948 - No. 10, Jan, 1950
1-Hedy, Tessie, Millie begin; Kurtzman's "Hey Look" (he draws himself)
    100 200 300 635 1093 1550
2   61 122 183 390 670 950
3,4-Kurtzman's "Hey Look": 3-(1 pg.) 4-(3 pgs)   90 180 270 576 988 1400
5-10   34 68 102 204 332 460

COMET, THE (See The Mighty Crusaders & Pep Comics #1)
Red Circle Comics (Archie): Oct, 1983 - No. 2, Dec, 1983
1-Re-intro & origin The Comet; The American Shield begins. Nino & Infantino art in both.
Hangman in both   6.00
2-Origin continues   5.00

COMET, THE
DC Comics (Impact Comics): July, 1991 - No. 18, Dec, 1992 ($1.00/$1.25)
1   5.00
2-18: 4-Black Hood app. 6-Re-intro Hangman. 8-Web x-over. 10-Contains Crusaders trading
card. 4-Origin. Netzer (Nasser) c(p)-11,14-17   4.00
Annual 1 (1992, $2.50, 68 pgs.)-Contains Impact trading card; Shield back-up story   5.00

COMET MAN, THE (Movie)
Marvel Comics Group: Feb, 1987 - No. 6, July, 1987 (limited series)
1-6: 3-Hulk app. 4-She-Hulk shower scene-c/s. Fantastic 4 app. 5-Fantastic 4 app.   4.00
NOTE: Kelley Jones a-1-6p.

COMIC ALBUM (Also see Disney Comic Album)
Dell Publishing Co.: Mar-May, 1958 - No. 18, June-Aug, 1962
1-Donald Duck   10 20 30 64 132 200
2-Bugs Bunny   5 10 15 31 53 75
3-Donald Duck   6 12 18 41 76 110
4-6,8-10: 4-Tom & Jerry. 5-Woody Woodpecker. 6,10-Bugs Bunny. 8-Tom & Jerry.
9-Woody Woodpecker   4 8 12 27 44 60
7,11,15: Popeye. 11-(9-11/60)   4 8 12 28 47 65
12-14: 12-Tom & Jerry. 13-Woody Woodpecker. 14-Bugs Bunny
    4 8 12 27 44 60
16-Flintstones (12-2/61-62)-3rd app. Early Cave Kids app.
    7 14 21 46 86 125
17-Space Mouse (3rd app.)   5 10 15 30 50 70
18-Three Stooges; photo-c   7 14 21 46 86 125

COMIC BOOK
Marvel Comics-#1/Dark Horse Comics-#2: 1995 ($5.95, oversize)
1-Spumco characters by John K.   1 2 3 4 5 7
2-(Dark Horse)   6.00

COMIC BOOK GUY: THE COMIC BOOK (BONGO COMICS PRESENTS...) (Simpsons)
Bongo Comics: 2010 - No. 5, 2010 ($3.99/$2.99, limited series)
1-($3.99) Four-layer cover w/classic swipes incl. FF#1; intro Graphic Novel Kid
    3 6 9 19 30 40
2-5-($2.99) 2-Stan Lee cameo. 3-Includes Little Lulu spoof. 4-Comic Book Guy origin
    1 2 3 5 6 8

COMIC CAPERS
Red Circle Mag./Marvel Comics: Fall, 1944 - No. 6, Fall, 1946
1-Super Rabbit, The Creeper, Silly Seal, Ziggy Pig, Sharpy Fox begin
    52 104 156 328 552 775
2   30 60 90 177 289 400
3-6: 4-(Summer 1945)   24 48 72 142 234 325

COMIC CAVALCADE
All-American/National Periodical Publications: Winter, 1942-43 - No. 63, June-July, 1954
(Contents change with No. 30, Dec-Jan, 1948-49 on)
1-The Flash, Green Lantern, Wonder Woman, Wildcat, The Black Pirate by Moldoff (also #2),
Ghost Patrol, and Red White & Blue begin; Scribbly app.; Minute Movie
    1050 2100 3150 8000 14,500 21,000
2-Mutt & Jeff begin; last Ghost Patrol & Black Pirate; Minute Movies
    290 580 870 1856 3178 4500
3-Hop Harrigan & Sargon, the Sorcerer begin; The King app.
    194 388 582 1242 2121 3000
4,5: 4-The Gay Ghost, The King, Scribbly, & Red Tornado app. 5-Christmas-c. 5-Prints ad for
Jr. JSA membership kit that includes "The Minute Man Answers The Call"
    187 374 561 1197 2049 2900
6-10: 7-Red Tornado & Black Pirate app.; last Scribbly. 9-Fat & Slat app.; X-Mas-c
    161 322 483 1030 1765 2500
11-Wonder Woman vs. The Cheetah   145 290 435 921 1586 2250
12,14: 12-Last Red White & Blue   123 246 369 787 1344 1900
13-Solomon Grundy app.; X-Mas-c   239 478 717 1530 2615 3700
15-Just a Story begins   123 246 369 787 1344 1900
16-20: 19-Christmas-c   113 226 339 718 1234 1750
21-23: 22-Johnny Peril begins. 23-Harry Lampert-c (Toth swipes)
    103 206 309 659 1130 1600
24-Solomon Grundy x-over in Green Lantern   142 284 426 909 1555 2200
25-28: 25-Black Canary app.; X-Mas-c. 26-28-Johnny Peril app. 28-Last Mutt & Jeff
    142 284 426 909 1555 2200
29-(10-11/48)-Last Flash, Wonder Woman, Green Lantern & Johnny Peril; Wonder Woman
invents "Thinking Machine"; 2nd computer in comics (after Flash Comics #52);
Leave It to Binky story (early app.)   135 270 405 864 1482 2100
30-(12-1/48-49)-The Fox & the Crow, Dodo & the Frog & Nutsy Squirrel begin
    48 96 144 302 514 725
31-35   25 50 75 150 245 340
36-49: 41-Last squarebound issue   19 38 57 111 176 240
50-62(Scarce)   22 44 66 132 216 300
63(Rare)   42 84 126 265 445 625
NOTE: *Grossman* a-30-63. *E.E. Hibbard* c-(Flash only)-1-4, 7-14, 16-19, 21. *Sheldon Mayer* a(2-3)-40-63. *Moulson* c(G.L.)-7, 15. *Nodell* c(G.L.)-3. *H.G. Peter* c/w (Woman only)-1, 3-21, 24. *Post* a-31, 36. *Purcell* c(G.L.)-2-5, 10. *Reinman* a(Green Lantern)-4-6, 8, 9, 13, 15-21; c(Gr. Lantern)-6, 8, 19. *Toth* a(Green Lantern)-26-28; c-27. Atom app.-22, 23.

COMIC COMICS
Fawcett Publications: Apr, 1946 - No. 10, Feb, 1947
1-Captain Kid; Nutty Comics #1 in indicia   20 40 60 120 195 270
2-10-Wolverton-a, 4 pgs. each. 5-Captain Kidd app. Mystic Moot by
Wolverton in #2-10?   18 36 54 105 165 225

COMIC LAND
Fact and Fiction Publ.: March, 1946
1-Sandusky & the Senator, Sam Stupor, Sleuth, Marvin the Great, Sir Passer, Phineas Gruff
app.; Irv Tirman & Perry Williams art   20 40 60 117 189 260

COMICO CHRISTMAS SPECIAL
Comico: Dec, 1988 ($2.50, 44 pgs.)
1-Rude/Williamson-a; Dave Stevens-c   2 4 6 10 14 18

COMICO COLLECTION (Also see Grendel)
Comico: 1987 ($9.95, slipcased collection)
nn-Contains exclusive Grendel: Devil's Vagary, 9 random Comico comics, a poster and
newsletter in black slipcase w/silver ink   25.00

COMICO PRIMER (See Primer)
COMIC PAGES (Formerly Funny Picture Stories)
Centaur Publications: V3#4, July, 1939 - V3#6, Dec, 1939
V3#4-Bob Wood-a   161 322 483 1030 1765 2500
5,6: 6-Schwab-a   142 284 426 909 1555 2200

COMICS (See All Good)
COMICS, THE
Dell Publ. Co.: Mar, 1937 - No. 11, Nov, 1938 (Newspaper strip-r; bi-monthly)
1-1st app. Tom Mix in comics; Wash Tubbs, Tom Beatty, Myra North, Arizona Kid,
Erik Noble & International Spy w/Doctor Doom begin
    200 400 600 1280 2190 3100
2   93 186 279 591 1021 1450
3-11: 3-Alley Oop begins   77 154 231 493 847 1200

COMICS AND STORIES (See Walt Disney's Comics and Stories)
COMICS & STORIES (Also see Wolf & Red)
Dark Horse Comics: Apr, 1996 - No. 4, July, 1996 ($2.95, lim. series) (Created by Tex Avery)
1-4: Wolf & Red app; reads Comics and Stories on-c. 1-Terry Moore-a. 2-Reed Waller-a   4.00

COMICS CALENDAR, THE (The 1946...)
True Comics Press (ordered through the mail): 1946 (25¢, 116 pgs.) (Stapled at top)
nn-(Rare) Has a "strip" story for every day of the year in color
    54 108 162 346 591 825

COMICS DIGEST (Pocket size)
Parents' Magazine Institute: Winter, 1942-43 (B&W, 100 pgs)
1-Reprints from True Comics (non-fiction World War II stories)
    15 30 45 83 124 165

COMICS EXPRESS
Eclipse Comics: Nov, 1989 - No. 2, Jan, 1990 ($2.95, B&W, 68pgs.)
1,2: Collection of strip-r; 2(12/89-c, 1/90 inside)   5.00

COMICS FOR KIDS
London Publ. Co./Timely: 1945 (no month); No. 2, Sum, 1945 (Funny animal)
1-Puffy Pig, Sharpy Fox   39 78 117 240 395 550
2-Puffy Pig, Sharpy Fox   28 56 84 165 270 375

COMICS' GREATEST WORLD
Dark Horse Comics: Jun, 1993 - V4#4, Sept, 1993 ($1.00, weekly, lim. series)
Arcadia (Wk 1): V1#1,2,4: 1-X: Frank Miller-c. 2-Pit Bulls. 4-Monster.   4.00
1-B&W Press Proof Edition (1500 copies)   1 3 4 6 8 10
1-Silver-c; distr. retailer bonus w/print & cards   1 2 3 5 6 8
3-Ghost, Dorman-c; Hughes-a   4.00
Retailer's Prem. Emb. Silver Foil Logo-r/V1#1-4   1 3 4 6 8 10
Golden City (Wk 2): V2#1-4: 1-Rebel; Ordway-c. 2-Mecha; Dave Johnson-a.
3-Titan; Walt Simonson-a; Perez-a.   4.00
1-Gold-c; distr. retailer bonus w/print & cards   6.00
Retailer's Prem. Embos. Gold Foil Logo-r/V2#1-4   1 2 3 5 6 8
Steel Harbor (Week 3): V3#1-Barb Wire; Dorman-c; Gulacy-a(p)   5.00
2-4: 2-The Machine. 3-Wolfgang. 4-Motorhead   4.00
1-Silver-c; distr. retailer bonus w/print & cards   1 3 4 6 8
Retailer's Prem. Emb. Red Foil Logo-r/V3#1-4.   1 3 4 6 8

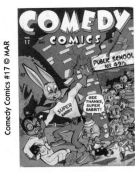

Comedy Comics #17 © MAR

Comic Cavalcade #14 © DC

Comics on Parade #23 © UFS

	GD	VG	FN	VF	VF/NM	NM-
	2.0	4.0	6.0	8.0	9.0	9.2

Vortex (Week 4): V4#1-4: 1-Division 13; Dorman-c. 2-Hero Zero; Art Adams-c.

3-King Tiger; Chadwick-a(p); Darrow-c. 4-Vortex; Miller-c.						4.00
1-Gold-c; distr. retailer bonus w/print & cards.						6.00
Retailer's Prem. Emb. Blue Foil Logo-r/V4#1-4.	1	2	3	5	6	8

COMICS' GREATEST WORLD: OUT OF THE VORTEX (See Out of The Vortex)

COMICS HITS (See Harvey Comics Hits)

COMICS MAGAZINE, THE (...Funny Pages #3)(Funny Pages #6 on)
Comics Magazine Co. (1st Comics Mag./Centaur Publ.): May, 1936 - No. 5, Sept, 1936 (Paper covers)

1-1st app. Dr. Mystic (a.k.a. Dr. Occult) by Siegel & Shuster (the 1st app. of a Superman prototype in comics). Dr. Mystic is not in costume but later appears in costume as a more pronounced prototype in More Fun #14-17. (1st episode of "The Koth and the Seven"; continues in More Fun #14; originally scheduled for publication at DC). 1 pg. Kelly-a; Sheldon Mayer-a		4325	8650	12,975	26,000	--	--
2-Federal Agent (a.k.a. Federal Men) by Siegel & Shuster; 1 pg. Kelly-a		470	940	1410	2820	3760	4700
3-5		410	820	1230	2460	3280	4100

COMICS NOVEL (Anarcho, Dictator of Death)
Fawcett Publications: 1947

1-All Radar; 51 pg anti-fascism story	48	96	144	302	514	725

COMICS ON PARADE (No. 30 on are a continuation of Single Series)
United Features Syndicate: Apr, 1938 - No. 104, Feb, 1955

1-Tarzan by Foster; Captain & the Kids, Little Mary Mixup, Abbie & Slats, Ella Cinders, Broncho Bill, Li'l Abner begin	405	810	1215	2835	4968	7100
2 (Tarzan & others app. on-c of #1-3,17)	155	310	465	992	1696	2400
3	123	246	369	787	1344	1900
4,5	84	168	252	538	919	1300
6-10	57	114	171	362	619	875
11-16,18-20	43	86	129	271	461	650
17-Tarzan-c	57	114	171	362	619	875
21-29: 22-Son of Tarzan begins. 22,24,28-Tailspin Tommy-c. 29-Last Tarzan issue	37	74	111	222	361	500
30-Li'l Abner	20	40	60	114	182	250
31-The Captain and the Kids	15	30	45	85	130	175
32-Nancy & Fritzi Ritz	14	28	42	78	112	145
33,36,39,42-Li'l Abner	16	32	48	94	147	200
34,37,40-The Captain & the Kids (10/41,6/42,3/43)	15	30	45	83	124	165
35,38-Nancy & Fritzi Ritz. 38-Infinity-c	14	28	42	76	108	140
41-Nancy & Fritzi Ritz	12	24	36	67	94	120
43-The Captain & the Kids	15	30	45	83	124	165
44 (3/44),47,50: Nancy & Fritzi Ritz	12	24	36	67	94	120
45-Li'l Abner	15	30	45	84	127	170
46,49-The Captain & the Kids	13	26	39	74	105	135
48-Li'l Abner (3/45)	15	30	45	84	127	170
51,54-Li'l Abner	14	28	42	76	108	140
52-The Captain & the Kids (3/46)	12	24	36	69	97	125
53,55,57-Nancy & Fritzi Ritz	11	22	33	62	86	110
56-The Captain & the Kids (r/Sparkler)	11	22	33	62	86	110
58-Li'l Abner; continues as Li'l Abner #61?	14	28	42	76	108	140
59-The Captain & the Kids	10	20	30	54	72	90
60-70-Nancy & Fritzi Ritz	9	18	27	47	61	75
71-99,101-104-Nancy & Sluggo: 71-76-Nancy only	8	16	24	42	54	65
100-Nancy & Sluggo	14	28	42	76	108	140
Special Issue, 7/46; Summer, 1948 - The Captain & the Kids app.	14	28	42	76	108	140

NOTE: Bound Volume (Very Rare) includes No. 1-12; bound by publisher in pictorial comic boards & distributed at the 1939 World's Fair and onward from ads in comic books (also see Tip Top)

	300	600	900	2010	3505	5000

NOTE: Li'l Abner reprinted from Tip Top.

COMICS READING LIBRARIES (See the Promotional Comics section)

COMICS REVUE
St. John Publ. Co. (United Features Synd.): June, 1947 - No. 5, Jan, 1948

1-Ella Cinders & Blackie	16	32	48	94	147	200
2,4: 2-Hap Hopper (7/47). 4-Ella Cinders (9/47)	10	20	30	58	79	100
3,5: 3-Iron Vic (8/47). 5-Gordo No. 1 (1/48)	10	20	30	56	76	95

COMIC STORY PAINT BOOK
Samuel Lowe Co.: 1943 (Large size, 68 pgs.)

1055-Captain Marvel & a Captain Marvel Jr. story to read & color; 3 panels in color per pg. (reprints)	93	186	279	591	1021	1450

COMING OF RAGE
Liquid Comics: 2015 - No. 5, 2016 ($3.99, limited series)

1-5-Wes Craven & Steve Niles-s/Francesco Biagini-a. 1-Afterword by Wes Craven						4.00

COMIX BOOK
Marvel Comics Group/Krupp Comics Works No. 4,5: 1974 - No. 5, 1976 ($1.00, B&W, magazine) (#1-3 newsstand; #4,5 were direct distribution only)

1-Underground comic artists; 2 pgs. Wolverton-a	3	6	9	15	22	28
2,3: 2-Wolverton-a (1 pg.)	3	6	9	14	19	24
4(2/76), 4(5/76), 5 (Low distribution)	3	6	9	16	23	30

NOTE: Print run No. 1-3: 200,000-250,000; No. 4&5: 10,000 each.

COMIX INTERNATIONAL
Warren Magazines: Jul, 1974 - No. 5, Spring, 1977 (Full color, stiff-c, mail only)

1-Low distribution; all Corben story remainders from Warren; Corben-c on all	9	18	27	62	126	190
2,4: 2-Two Dracula stories; Wood, Wrightson-r; Crandall-a; Maroto-a. 4-Printing w/ 3 Corben sty	6	12	18	37	66	95
3-5: 3-Dax story. 4-(printing without Corben story). 4-Crandall-a. 4,5-Vampirella stories. 5-Spirit story; Eisner-a	5	10	15	33	57	80

NOTE: No. 4 had two printings with extra Corben story in one. No. 3 may also have a variation. No. 3 has two Jeff Jones reprints from Vampirella.

COMMANDER BATTLE AND THE ATOMIC SUB
Amer. Comics Group (Titan Publ. Co.): Jul-Aug, 1954 - No. 7, Aug-Sep, 1955

1 (3-D effect)-Moldoff flying saucer-c	84	168	252	538	919	1300
2,4-7: 2-Moldoff-c. 4-(1-2/55)-Last pre-code; Landau-a. 5-3-D effect story (2 pgs.). 6,7-Landau-a. 7-Flying saucer-c	45	90	135	284	480	675
3-H-Bomb-c; Atomic Sub races atomic Spaceship	52	104	156	328	552	775

COMMANDERS IN CRISIS
Image Comics: Oct, 2020 - No. 12, Sept, 2021 ($3.99)

1-12-Steve Orlando-s/Davide Tinto-a						4.00

COMMANDO ADVENTURES
Atlas Comics (MMC): June, 1957 - No. 2, Aug, 1957

1-Severin-c	21	42	63	122	199	275
2-Severin-c; Reinman & Romita-a; Drucker-a?	15	30	45	84	127	170

COMMANDOS
DC Comics: Oct. 1942

1-Ashcan comic, not distributed to newsstands, only for in-house use. Cover art is Boy Commandos #1 with interior being a Boy Commandos story from an unidentified issue of Detective Comics (a VF copy sold for $2629 in 2018)						

COMMANDO YANK (See The Mighty Midget Comics & Wow Comics)

COMMON GROUNDS
Image Comics (Top Cow): Feb, 2004 - No. 6, July, 2004 ($2.99)

1-6: 1-Two covers; art by Jurgens and Oeming. 3-Bachalo, Jurgens-a. 4-Peréz-a						3.00
...: Baker's Dozen TPB (12/04, $14.99) r/#1-6; cover gallery; Holey Crullers pages						15.00

COMPASS
Image Comics: Jun, 2021 - No. 5, Oct, 2021 ($3.99)

1-5-MacKenzie & Walker-s/Greenwood-a						4.00

COMPLETE ALICE IN WONDERLAND (Adaptation of Carroll's original story)
Dynamite Entertainment: 2009 - No. 4 ($4.99, limited series)

1-4-Leah Moore & John Reppion-s/Erica Awano-a/John Cassaday-c						5.00

COMPLETE BOOK OF COMICS AND FUNNIES
William H. Wise & Co.: 1944 (25¢, one-shot, 196 pgs.)

1-Origin Brad Spencer, Wonderman; The Magnet, The Silver Knight by Kinstler; & Zudo the Jungle Boy app.	81	162	243	518	884	1250

COMPLETE BOOK OF TRUE CRIME COMICS
William H. Wise & Co.: No date (Mid 1940's) (25¢, 132 pgs.)

nn-Contains Crime Does Not Pay rebound (includes #22)	206	412	618	1318	2259	3200

COMPLETE COMICS (Formerly Amazing Comics No. 1)
Timely Comics (EPC): No. 2, Winter, 1944-45

2-The Destroyer, The Whizzer, The Young Allies & Sergeant Dix; Schomburg-c	206	412	618	1318	2259	3200

COMPLETE DRACULA (Adaptation of Stoker's original story)
Dynamite Entertainment: 2009 - No. 5, 2009 ($4.99, limited series)

1-5-Leah Moore & John Reppion-s/Colton Worley-a/John Cassaday-c						5.00

COMPLETE FRANK MILLER BATMAN, THE
Longmeadow Press: 1989 ($29.95, hardcover, silver gilded pages)

HC-Reprints Batman: Year One, Wanted: Santa Claus--Dead or Alive, and The Dark Knight

	GD	VG	FN	VF	VF/NM	NM-
	2.0	4.0	6.0	8.0	9.0	9.2

Returns ... 50.00

COMPLETE GUIDE TO THE DEADLY ARTS OF KUNG FU AND KARATE
Marvel Comics: 1974 (68 pgs., B&W magazine)

V1#1-Bruce Lee-c and 5 pg. story (scarce)	7	14	21	49	92	135

COMPLETE LOVE MAGAZINE (Formerly a pulp with same title)
Ace Periodicals (Periodical House): V26#2, May-June, 1951 - V32#4(#191), Sept, 1956

	GD	VG	FN	VF	VF/NM	NM-
V26#2-Painted-c (52 pgs.)	39	78	117	231	378	525
V26#3-6(2/52), V27#1(4/52)-6(1/53)	15	30	45	84	127	170
V28#1(3/53), V28#2(5/53), V29#3(7/53)-6(12/53)	14	28	42	78	112	145
V30#1(2/54), V30#1(#176, 4/54),2,4-6(#181, 1/55)	14	28	42	78	112	145
V30#3(#178)-Rock Hudson photo-c	14	28	42	82	121	160
V31#1(#182, 3/55)-Last precode	14	28	42	76	108	140
V31#2(5/55)-6(#187, 1/56)	13	26	39	74	105	135
V32#1(#188, 3/56)-4(#191, 9/56)	13	26	39	74	105	135

NOTE: (34 total issues). Photo-c V27#5-on. Painted-c V26#3.

COMPLETE MYSTERY (True Complete Mystery No. 5 on)
Marvel Comics: Aug, 1948 - No. 4, Feb, 1949 (Full length stories)

1-Seven Dead Men	71	142	213	454	777	1100
2-4: 2-Jigsaw of Doom!; Shores-a. 3-Fear in the Night; Burgos-c/a (28 pgs.).						
4-A Squealer Dies Fast	53	106	159	334	567	800

COMPLETE ROMANCE
Avon Periodicals: 1949

1-(Scarce)-Reprinted as Women to Love	71	142	213	454	777	1100

CONAN (See Chamber of Darkness #4, Giant-Size..., Handbook of..., King Conan, Marvel Graphic Novel #19, 28, Marvel Treasury Ed., Power Record Comics, Robert E. Howard's..., Savage Sword of Conan, and Savage Tales)

CONAN
Dark Horse Comics: Feb, 2004 - No. 50, May, 2008 ($2.99)

0-(11/03, 25¢-c) Busiek-s/Nord-a						3.00
1-($2.99) Linsner-c/Busiek-s/Nord-a	1	2	3	5	6	8
1-(2nd printing) J. Scott Campell-c						3.00
1-(3rd printing) Nord-c						3.00
2-49: 18-Severin & Timm-a. 22-Kaluta-a (6 pgs.) 24-Harris-c. 29-31-Mignola-a						3.00
24-Variant-c with nude woman (also see Conan and the Demons of Khitai #3 for ad)						175.00
50-($4.99) Harris-c; new story and reprint from Conan the Barbarian #30	1	2	3	5	6	8
... and the Daughters of Midora (10/04, $4.99) Texiera-a/c						5.00
...: Born on the Battlefield TPB (6/08, $17.95) r/#0,8,15,23,32,45,46; Ruth sketch pages						18.00
...: FCBD 2006 Special (5/06) Paul Lee-a; flip book with Star Wars FCBD 2006 Special						3.00
...: One For One (8/10, $1.00) r/#1 with red cover frame						3.00
...: The Blood-Stained Crown and Other Stories TPB (1/08, $14.95) r/#18,26-28,39						15.00
...: The Weight of the Crown (1/10, $3.50) Darick Robertson-a; 2 covers by Robertson						3.50
HC Vol. 1: The Frost Giant's Daughter and Other Stories (2005, $24.95) r/#1-6, partial #7; signed by Busiek; Nord sketch pages						25.00
Vol. 1: The Frost Giant's Daughter and Other Stories (2005, $15.95) r/#1-6, partial #7						16.00
Vol. 2: The God in the Bowl and Other Stories HC (2005, $24.95) r/#9-14						25.00
Vol. 2: The God in the Bowl and Other Stories SC (2006, $15.95) r/#9-14						16.00
Vol. 3: The Tower of the Elephant and Other Stories HC (5/06, $24.95) r/#0,16,17,19-22						25.00
Vol. 3: The Tower of the Elephant and Other Stories SC (6/06, $15.95) r/#0,16,17,19-22						16.00
Vol. 4: The Hall of the Dead and Other Stories HC (5/07, $24.95) r/#0,24,25,29-31,33,34						25.00
Vol. 4: The Hall of the Dead and Other Stories SC (6/07, $17.95) r/#0,24,25,29-31,33,34						18.00
Vol. 5: Rogues in the House and Other Stories SC (3/08, $17.95) r/#0,37,38,41-44						18.00
Vol. 6: The Hand of Nergal HC (10/08, $24.95) r/#0,47-50; sketch pages						25.00

CONAN AND THE DEMONS OF KHITAI
Dark Horse Comics: Oct, 2005 - No. 4, Jan, 2006 ($2.99, limited series)

1,2,4-Paul Lee-a/Akira Yoshida-s/Pat Lee-c						4.00
3-1st printing with red cover logo; letters page has image of Conan #24 nude variant-c						6.00
3-2nd printing with black cover logo; letters page has image of Conan #24 regular-c						3.00
TPB (7/06, $12.95) r/series						13.00

CONAN AND THE JEWELS OF GWAHLUR
Dark Horse Comics: Apr, 2005 - No. 3, June, 2005 ($2.99, limited series)

1-3-P. Craig Russell-a/c						3.00
HC (12/05, $13.95) r/series; P. Craig Russell interview and sketch pages						14.00

CONAN AND THE MIDNIGHT GOD
Dark Horse Comics: Dec, 2006 - No. 5, May, 2007 ($2.99, limited series)

1-5-Dysart-s/Conrad-a/Alexander-c						3.00
TPB (10/07, $14.95) r/#1-5 and Age of Conan: Hyborian Adventures one-shot						15.00

CONAN AND THE PEOPLE OF THE BLACK CIRCLE
Dark Horse Comics: Oct, 2013 - No. 4, Jan, 2014 ($3.50, limited series)

1-4-Van Lente-s/Olivetti-a/c						3.50

CONAN AND THE SONGS OF THE DEAD
Dark Horse Comics: July, 2006 - No. 5, Nov, 2006 ($2.99, limited series)

1-5-Timothy Truman-a/c; Joe Lansdale-s						3.00
TPB (4/07, $14.95) r/series; Truman sketch pages						15.00

CONAN: (Title Series): Marvel Comics

CONAN, 8/95 - No. 11, 6/96 ($2.95), 1-11: 4-Malibu Comic's Rune app.						5.00
...CLASSIC, 6/94 - No. 11, 4/95 ($1.50), 1-11: 1-r/Conan #1 by B. Smith, r/covers w/changes. 2-11-r/Conan #2-11 by Smith. 2-Bound w/cover to Conan The Adventurer #2 by mistake						5.00
...DEATH COVERED IN GOLD, 9/99 - No. 3, 11/99 ($2.99), 1-3-Roy Thomas-s/John Buscema-a						5.00
...FLAME AND THE FIEND, 8/00 - No. 3, 10/00 ($2.99), 1-3-Thomas-s						5.00
...RETURN OF STYRM, 9/98 - No. 3, 11/98 ($2.99), 1-3-Parente & Soresina-a; painted-c						5.00
...RIVER OF BLOOD, 6/98 - No. 3, 8/98 ($2.50), 1-3						5.00
...SCARLET SWORD, 12/98 - No. 3, 2/99 ($2.99), 1-3-Thomas-s/Raffaele-a						5.00

CONAN: BATTLE FOR THE SERPENT CROWN
Marvel Comics: Apr, 2020 - No. 5, Nov, 2020 ($3.99, limited series)

1-5-Saladin Ahmed-s/Luke Ross-a; set in the present; Black Cat & Mephisto app.						

	GD	VG	FN	VF	VF/NM	NM-
	2.0	4.0	6.0	8.0	9.0	9.2

3-Black Panther app. 4-Namor app.						4.00

CONAN: ISLAND OF NO RETURN
Dark Horse Comics: Jun, 2011 - No. 2, Jul, 2011 ($3.50, limited series)

1,2-Marz-s/Sears-a						4.00

CONAN RED SONJA
Dark Horse Comics: Jan, 2015 - No. 4, Apr, 2015 ($3.99, limited series)

1-4-Gail Simone & Jim Zub-s/Dan Panosian-a/c						6.00

CONAN: ROAD OF KINGS
Dark Horse Comics: Dec, 2010 - No. 12, Jan, 2012 ($3.50)

1-12: 1-Roy Thomas-s/Mike Hawthorne-a; covers by Wheatley & Keown						4.00

CONAN SAGA, THE
Marvel Comics: June, 1987 - No. 97, Apr, 1995 ($2.00/$2.25, B&W, magazine)

1-Barry Smith-r; new Smith-c	2	4	6	9	13	16
2-27: 2-9,11-new Barry Smith-c. 13,15-Boris-c. 17-Adams-r.18,25-Chaykin-r. 22-r/Giant-Size Conan 1,2						4.00
28-90: 28-Begin $2.25-c. 31-Red Sonja-r by N. Adams/SSOC #1; 1 pg. Jeff Jones-r. 32-Newspaper strip-r begin by Buscema. 33-Smith/Conrad-a. 39-r/Kull #1('71) by Andru & Wood. 44-Swipes-c/Savage Tales #1. 57-Brunner-r/SSOC #30. 66-r/Conan Annual #2 by Buscema. 79-r/Conan #43-45 w/Red Sonja. 85-Based on Conan #57-63						3.00
91-96						5.00
97-Last issue	1	2	3	5	6	8

NOTE: J. Buscema r-32-on; c-86. Chaykin r-34. Chiodo painted c-63, 65, 66, 82. G. Colan a-47p. Jusko painted c-64, 83. Kaluta c-84. Nino a-37. Ploog a-50. N. Redondo painted c-48, 50, 51, 53, 57, 62. Simonson r-50-54, 56. B. Smith r-51. Starlin c-34. Williamson r-50i.

CONAN: SERPENT WAR
Marvel Comics: Feb, 2020 - No. 4, Mar, 2020 ($4.99/$3.99, limited series)

1-($4.99) Jim Zub-s/Scot Eaton-a; Moon Knight, Solomon Kane and Dark Agnes app.; back-up Solomon Kane text serial						5.00
2-4-($3.99) Solomon Kane text serial in each. 2-Segovia-a. 3-Pizzari-a. 4-Guara-a						4.00

CONAN THE ADVENTURER
Marvel Comics: June, 1994 - No. 14, July, 1995 ($1.50)

1-($2.50)-Embossed foil-c; Kayaran-a						5.00
2-14						4.00
2-Contents are Conan Classics #2 by mistake						4.00

CONAN THE AVENGER
Dark Horse Comics: Apr, 2014 - No. 25, Apr, 2016 ($3.99/$3.50)

1-25: 1-Van Lente-s/Ching-a. 4-Staples-c. 13-15-Powell-a. 25-Bisley-c						4.00

CONAN THE BARBARIAN
Marvel Comics: Oct, 1970 - No. 275, Dec, 1993

1-Origin/1st app. Conan (in comics) by Barry Smith; 1st brief app. Kull; #1-9 are 15¢ issues	38	76	114	285	641	1000
2	10	20	30	69	147	225
3-(Low distribution in some areas)	13	26	39	89	195	300
4,5	8	16	24	52	99	145
6-9: 8-Hidden panel message, pg. 14. 9-Last 15¢-c	6	12	18	38	69	100
10,11 (25¢ 52 pg. giants): 10-Black Knight-r; Kull story by Severin	7	14	21	48	89	130
12,13: 12-Wrightson-c(i)	5	10	15	35	63	90
14,15-Elric app.	6	12	18	42	79	115
16,19,20: 16-Conan-r/Savage Tales #1	5	10	15	34	60	85
17,18-No Barry Smith-a	4	8	12	28	47	65
21,22: 22-Has reprint from #1	5	10	15	30	50	70
23-1st app. Red Sonja (2/73)	14	28	42	93	204	315
24-1st full Red Sonja story; last Smith-a	12	24	36	82	179	275
25-John Buscema-c/a begins	3	6	9	19	30	40
26-30: 28-Centerfold ad by Mark Jewelers	3	6	9	14	19	24
31-36,38-40	2	4	6	10	14	18
37-Neal Adams-c/a; last 20¢ issue; contains pull-out subscription form	3	6	9	21	33	45
41-43,46-50: 48-Origin retold	2	4	6	8	11	14
44,45-N. Adams-i(Crusty Bunkers). 45-Adams-c	2	4	6	9	13	16
51-57,59,60: 59-Origin Belit	1	3	4	6	8	10
58-2nd Belit app. (see Giant-Size Conan #1)	2	4	6	11	16	20
61-65-(Regular 25¢ editions)(4-8/76)	1	3	4	6	8	10
61-65-(30¢-c variants, limited distribution)	5	10	18	38	69	100
66-99: 68-Red Sonja story cont'd from Marvel Feature #7. 75-79-(Reg. 30¢-c). 84-Intro. Zula. 85-Origin Zula. 87-r/Savage Sword of Conan #3 in color	1	2	3	5	6	8
75-79-(35¢-c variants, limited distribution)	8	16	24	54	102	150
100-(52 pg. Giant)-Death of Belit	2	4	6	9	13	16
101-114						6.00
115-Double size	1	2	3	5	6	8
116-199,201-231,233-249: 116-r/Power Record Comic PR31. 244-Zula returns						6.00
200,232: 200-(52 pgs.). 232-Young Conan storyline begins; Conan is born						6.00
250-(60 pgs.)	1	2	3	5	6	8
251-270: 262-Adapted from R.E. Howard story						6.00
271-274	1	3	4	6	8	10
275-($2.50, 68 pgs.)-Final issue; painted-c (low print)	4	8	12	28	47	65
King Size 1(1973, 35¢)-Smith-r/#2,4; Smith-c	6	12	18	41	76	110
Annual 2(1976, 50¢)-New full length story	3	6	9	15	22	28
Annual 3,4: 3('78)-Chaykin/N. Adams-r/SSOC #2. 4('78)-New full length story	2	4	6	8	11	14
Annual 5,6: 5(1979)-New full length Buscema story & part-c, 6(1981)-Kane-c/a	2	4	6	8	10	12
Annual 7-12: 7('82)-Based on novel "Conan of the Isles" (new-a). 8(1984). 9(1984). 10(1986). 11(1986). 12(1987)						5.00
No. 1 Facsimile Edition (2/22, $3.99) Reprints #1 with original ads and Bullpen pages						4.00
Special Edition 1 (Red Nails)						5.00
The Chronicles of Conan Vol. 1: Tower of the Elephant and Other Stories (Dark Horse, 2003, $15.95) r/#1-8; afterword by Roy Thomas						16.00
The Chronicles of Conan Vol. 2: Rogues in the House and Other Stories (Dark Horse, 2003, $15.95) r/#9-13,16; afterword by Roy Thomas						16.00

Conan (2008 series) #47 © CPI

Conan the Barbarian #17 © CPI

Conan the Barbarian (2019 series) #17 © CPI

	GD 2.0	VG 4.0	FN 6.0	VF 8.0	VF/NM 9.0	NM- 9.2

The Chronicles of Conan Vol. 3: The Monster of the Monoliths and Other Stories (Dark Horse, 2003, $15.95) r/#14,15,17-21; afterword by Roy Thomas ... 16.00

The Chronicles of Conan Vol. 4: The Song of Red Sonja and Other Stories (Dark Horse, 2004, $15.95) r/#23-26 & "Red Nails" from Savage Tales; afterword by Roy Thomas ... 16.00

The Chronicles of Conan Vol. 5: The Shadow in the Tomb and Other Stories (Dark Horse, 2004, $15.95) r/#27-34; afterword by Roy Thomas ... 16.00

The Chronicles of Conan Vol. 6: The Curse of the Skull and Other Stories (Dark Horse, 2004, $15.95) r/#35-42; afterword by Roy Thomas ... 16.00

The Chronicles of Conan Vol. 7: The Dweller in the Pool and Other Stories (Dark Horse, 2005, $15.95) r/#43-51; afterword by Roy Thomas ... 16.00

The Chronicles of Conan Vol. 8: Brothers of the Blade and Other Stories (Dark Horse, 2005, $16.95) r/#52-59; afterword by Roy Thomas ... 17.00

The Chronicles of Conan Vol. 9: Riders of the River-Dragons and Other Stories (Dark Horse, 11/05, $16.95) r/#60-63,65,69-71; afterword by Roy Thomas ... 17.00

The Chronicles of Conan Vol. 10: When Giants Walk the Earth and Other Stories (Dark Horse, 3/06, $16.95) r/#72-77,79-82; afterword by Roy Thomas ... 17.00

The Chronicles of Conan Vol. 11: The Dance of the Skull and Other Stories (Dark Horse, 2/07, $16.95) r/#82-86,88-90; afterword by Roy Thomas ... 17.00

The Chronicles of Conan Vol. 12: The King Beast of Abombi and Other Stories (Dark Horse, 7/07, $16.95) r/#91,93-100; afterword by Roy Thomas ... 17.00

The Chronicles of Conan Vol. 13: Whispering Shadows and Other Stories (Dark Horse, 12/07, $16.95) r/#92,100-107; afterword by Roy Thomas ... 17.00

The Chronicles of Conan Vol. 14: Shadow of the Beast and Other Stories (Dark Horse, 3/08, $16.95) r/#92,108-115; afterword by Roy Thomas ... 17.00

The Chronicles of Conan Vol. 15: The Corridor of Mullah-Kajar and Other Stories (Dark Horse, 7/08, $16.95) r/#116-121 & Annual #2; afterword by Roy Thomas ... 17.00

NOTE: Arthur Adams c-248, 249. Neal Adams a-116(r); c-49i. Austin a-125, 126; c-125i, 126i. Brunner c-17i. c-40. Buscema a-25-36p, 38, 39, 41-56p, 58-62p, 65-67p, 68, 70-78p, 84-86p, 88-91p, 93-126p, 136p, 140, 141-144p, 146-158p, 159, 161, 162, 163p, 165-185p, 187-190p, Annual 2(3pgs.). 3-5p, 7p; c(p)-26, 36, 44, 46, 52, 56, 58, 59, 64, 65, 72, 78-80, 83, 91, 93-103, 105-126, 136-151, 155-159, 161, 162, 168, 169, 171, 172, 174, 175, 178-185, 188, 189, Annual 4, 5, 7. Chaykin a-79-83. Golden c-152. Kaluta c-167. Gil Kane a-12p, 17p, 18p, 127-130, 131-134p; c-12p, 17p, 18p, 23, 25, 27-32, 34, 35, 38, 39, 41-43, 45-51, 53-55, 57, 60-63, 65-71, 73p, 76p, 127-134. Jim Lee c-242. McFarlane c-241p. Ploog a-57. Russell a-21; c-251i. Simonson c-135. B. Smith a-1-11p, 12, 13-15p, 16, 19-21, 23, 24; c-1-11, 13-16, 19-24p. Starlin a-64. Wood a-47r. Issue Nos. 3-5, 7-9, 11, 16-18, 21, 23, 26, 27-30, 35, 37, 38, 42, 45, 52, 57, 58, 65, 69-71, 73, 79-83, 99, 100, 104, 114, Annual 2 have original Robert E. Howard stories adapted. Issues #32-34 adapted from Norvell Page's novel Flame Winds.

CONAN THE BARBARIAN (Volume 2)
Marvel Comics: July, 1997 - No. 3, Oct, 1997 ($2.50, limited series)
1-3-Castellini-a ... 5.00

CONAN THE BARBARIAN
Dark Horse Comics: Feb, 2012 - No. 25, Feb, 2014 ($3.50)
1-Brian Wood-s/Becky Cloonan-a; two covers by Carnevale & Cloonan

		1	2	3	5	6	8

2-25: 2,3-Brian Wood-s/Becky Cloonan-a ... 4.00
One for One: Conan the Barbarian #1 (1/14, $1.00) r/#1 ... 4.00

CONAN THE BARBARIAN
Marvel Comics: Mar, 2019 - No. 25, Nov, 2021 ($4.99/$3.99)
1-($4.99) Jason Aaron-s/Mahmud Asrar-a; part 1 of a bonus text novella ... 5.00
2-24-($3.99)-Bonus text novella continues: 2,3,5-7,9-12-Asrar-a. 4,8-Zaffino-a ... 4.00
25-($4.99) 300th legacy issue; Belit app.; stories by Zub, Hama, Slott, Owsley ... 5.00
...: Exodus 1 (10/19, $3.99) Esad Ribic-s/a; bonus thumbnails of layout sketches ... 4.00

CONAN: THE BARBARIAN
Titan Comics: Aug, 2023 - Present ($3.99)
1-8: 1-Jim Zub-s/Rob De La Torre-a ... 4.00

CONAN THE BARBARIAN MOVIE SPECIAL (Movie)
Marvel Comics Group: Oct, 1982 - No. 2, Nov, 1982
1,2-Movie adaptation; Buscema-a

		1	2	3	5	6	8

CONAN THE BARBARIAN: THE MASK OF ACHERON (Based on the 2011 movie)
Dark Horse Comics: Jul, 2011 ($6.99, one-shot)
1-Stuart Moore-s/Gabriel Guzman-a/c ... 7.00

CONAN THE BARBARIAN: THE USURPER
Marvel Comics: Dec, 1997 - No. 3, Feb, 1998 ($2.50, limited series)
1-3-Dixon-s ... 4.00

CONAN: THE BOOK OF THOTH
Dark Horse Comics: Mar, 2006 - No. 4, June, 2006 ($4.99, limited series)
1-4-Origin of Thoth-amon; Len Wein & Kurt Busiek-s/Kelley Jones-a/c ... 5.00
TPB (12/06, $17.95) r/#1-4 ... 18.00

CONAN THE CIMMERIAN
Dark Horse Comics: No. 0, Jun, 2008 - No. 25, Nov, 2010 (99¢/$2.99)
0-Follows Conan #50; Truman-s/Giorello-a/c ... 4.00
1-(7/08, $2.99) Two covers by Joe Kubert and Cho; Giorello & Corben-a ... 4.00

2-25: 2-7-Cho-c; Giorello & Corben-a. 8-18-Linsner-c. 14-Joe Kubert-a (7 pgs.) ... 4.00

CONAN THE DESTROYER (Movie)
Marvel Comics Group: Jan, 1985 - No. 2, Mar, 1985
1,2-r/Marvel Super Special ... 6.00

CONAN THE FRAZETTA COVER SERIES
Dark Horse Comics: Dec, 2007 - No. 8 ($3.50/$5.99/$6.99)
1-($3.50) Reprints from Dark Horse series with Frazetta covers

	2	4	6	9	12	15
2,3-($5.99)	1	3	4	6	8	10
4-8-($6.99)	2	4	6	10	12	

CONAN THE KING (Formerly King Conan)
Marvel Comics Group: No. 20, Jan, 1984 - No. 55, Nov, 1989

	2	4	6	9	12	15
20-49						5.00
50-54						6.00
55-Last issue	2	4	6	9	12	15

NOTE: Kaluta c-20-23, 24i, 26, 27, 30, 50, 52. Williamson a-37i; c-37i, 38i.

CONAN: THE LEGEND (See Conan 2004 series)

CONAN: THE LORD OF THE SPIDERS
Marvel Comics: Mar, 1998 - No. 3, May, 1998 ($2.50, limited series)
1-3-Roy Thomas-s/Raffaele-a ... 5.00

CONAN THE SAVAGE
Marvel Comics: Aug, 1995 - No. 10, May, 1996 ($2.95, B&W, Magazine)
1-10: 1-Bisley-c. 4-vs. Malibu Comics' Rune. 5,10-Brereton-c ... 5.00

CONAN THE SLAYER
Dark Horse Comics: Jul, 2016 - No. 12, Aug, 2017 ($3.99)
1-12: 1-Bunn-s/Dávila-a/Bermejo-c. 11-Verma-a ... 4.00

CONAN 2099
Marvel Comics: Jan, 2020 ($4.99, one-shot)
1-Duggan-s/Antonio-a; Morgan Le Fay app. ... 5.00

CONAN VS. RUNE (Also See Conan #4)
Marvel Comics: Nov, 1995 ($2.95, one-shot)
1-Barry Smith-c/a/scripts

	2	4	6	8	10	12

CONCRETE (Also see Dark Horse Presents & Within Our Reach)
Dark Horse Comics: March, 1987 - No. 10, Nov, 1988 ($1.50, B&W)
1-Paul Chadwick-c/a in all

	2	4	6	9	13	15

1-2nd print ... 4.00
2 ... 6.00
3-Origin ... 5.00
4-10 ... 4.00
A New Life 1 (1989, $2.95, B&W)-r/#3,4 plus new-a (11 pgs.) ... 4.00
Celebrates Earth Day 1990 ($3.50, 52 pgs.) ... 6.00
Color Special 1 (2/89, $2.95, 44 pgs.)-r/1st two Concrete apps. from Dark Horse Presents #1,2 plus new-a ... 6.00
Depths TPB (7/05, $12.95)-r/#1-5, stories from DHP #1,8,10,150; other short stories ... 13.00
Land And Sea 1 (2/89, $2.95, B&W)-r/#1,2 ... 6.00
Odd Jobs 1 (7/90, $3.50)-r/5,6 plus new-a ... 4.00
...Vol. 1: Depths ('05, $12.95, 9"x6") r/#1-5 & short stories ... 13.00
...Vol. 2: Heights ('05, $12.95, 9"x6") r/#6-10 & short stories ... 13.00
...Vol. 3: Fragile Creatures (3/06, $12.95, 9"x6") r/mini-series & short stories from DHP ... 13.00
...Vol. 4: Killer Smile (3/06, $12.95, 9"x6") r/mini-series & short stories from various ... 13.00
...Vol. 5: Think Like a Mountain (5/06, $12.95, 9"x6") r/mini-series & short stories ... 13.00
...Vol. 6: Strange Armor (7/06, $12.95, 9"x6") r/mini-series & short stories ... 13.00
...Vol. 7: The Human Dilemma (4/06, $12.95, 9"x6") r/mini-series ... 13.00

CONCRETE: (Title series), **Dark Horse Comics**
--ECLECTICA, 4/93 - No. 2, 5/93 ($2.95) 1,2 ... 4.00
--FRAGILE CREATURE, 6/91 - No. 4, 2/92 ($2.50) 1-4 ... 4.00
--KILLER SMILE, (Legend), 7/94 - No. 4, 10/94 ($2.95) 1-4 ... 4.00
--STRANGE ARMOR, 12/97 - No. 5, 5/98 ($2.95, color) 1-5-Chadwick-s/c/a; retells origin ... 4.00
--THE HUMAN DILEMMA, 12/04 - No. 6, 5/05 ($3.50)
1-6: Chadwick-a/c & scripts; Concrete has a child ... 3.50
--THINK LIKE A MOUNTAIN, (Legend), 3/96 - No. 6, 8/96 ($2.95)
1-6: Chadwick-a/scripts & Darrow-c in all ... 4.00

CONDORMAN (Walt Disney)
Whitman Publishing: Oct, 1981 - No. 3, Jan, 1982
1-3: 1,2-Movie adaptation; photo-c

	1	3	4	6	8	10

CONEHEADS

	GD 2.0	VG 4.0	FN 6.0	VF 8.0	VF/NM 9.0	NM- 9.2

Marvel Comics: June, 1994 - No. 4, 1994 ($1.75, limited series)

1	1	3	4	6	8	10
2-4						5.00

CONFESSIONS ILLUSTRATED (Magazine)
E. C. Comics: Jan-Feb, 1956 - No. 2, Spring, 1956

1-Craig, Kamen, Wood, Orlando-a	37	74	111	222	361	500
2-Craig, Crandall, Kamen, Orlando-a	28	56	84	165	270	375

CONFESSIONS OF LOVE
Artful Publ.: Apr, 1950 - No. 2, July, 1950 (25¢, 7-1/4x5-1/4", 132 pgs.)

1-Bakerish-a	97	194	291	621	1061	1500
2-Art & text; Bakerish-a	58	116	174	371	636	900

CONFESSIONS OF LOVE (Formerly Startling Terror Tales #10; becomes Confessions of Romance No. 7 on)
Star Publications: No. 11, 7/52 - No. 14, 1/53; No. 4, 3/53- No. 6, 8/53

11-13: 12,13-Disbrow-a	47	94	141	296	498	700
14,5,6	37	74	111	222	361	500
4-Disbrow-a	40	80	120	246	411	575

NOTE: All have **L. B. Cole** covers.

CONFESSIONS OF ROMANCE (Formerly Confessions of Love)
Star Publications: No. 7, Nov, 1953 - No. 11, Nov, 1954

7	34	68	102	199	325	450
8	23	46	69	138	227	315
9-Wood-a	30	60	90	177	289	400
10,11-Disbrow-a	22	44	66	132	216	300

NOTE: All have **L. B. Cole** covers.

CONFESSIONS OF THE LOVELORN (Formerly Lovelorn)
American Comics Group (Regis Publ./Best Synd. Features): No. 52, Aug, 1954 - No. 114, June-July, 1960

52 (3-D effect)	90	180	270	576	988	1400
53,55	30	60	90	177	289	400
54 (3-D effect)	47	94	141	296	498	700
56-Anti-communist propaganda story, 10 pgs; last pre-code (2/55)	24	48	72	142	234	325
57-90,100	14	28	42	82	121	160
91-Williamson-a	15	30	45	86	133	180
92-99,101-114	12	24	36	69	97	125

NOTE: **Whitney** a-most issues; c-52, 53. Painted c-106, 107.

CONFIDENTIAL DIARY (Formerly High School Confidential Diary; Three Nurses #18 on)
Charlton Comics: No. 12, May, 1962 - No. 17, Mar, 1963

12-17	3	6	9	17	26	35

CONGO BILL (See Action Comics & More Fun Comics #56)
National Periodical Publication: Aug-Sept, 1954 - No. 7, Aug-Sept, 1955

1	215	430	645	1700	--	--
2,7	131	262	393	1050	--	--
3-6: 4-Last pre-Code issue	106	212	318	850	--	--

NOTE: (Rarely found in fine to mint condition.) Nick Cardy c-1-7.

CONGO BILL
DC Comics (Vertigo): Oct, 1999 - No. 4, Jan, 2000 ($2.95, limited series)

1-4-Corben-c						4.00

CONGORILLA (Also see Action Comics #224)
DC Comics: Nov, 1992 - No. 4, Feb, 1993 ($1.75, limited series)

1-4: 1,2-Brian Bolland-c						4.00

CONJURORS
DC Comics: Apr, 1999 - No. 3, Jun, 1999 ($2.95, limited series)

1-3-Elseworlds; Phantom Stranger app.; Barreto-c/a						4.00

CONNECTICUT YANKEE, A (See Classic Classics)

CONNOR HAWKE: DRAGON'S BLOOD (Also see Green Arrow titles)
DC Comics: Jan, 2007 - No. 6, Jun, 2007 ($2.99, limited series)

1-6-Chuck Dixon-s/Derec Donovan-a/c						3.00
SC (2008, $19.99) r/#1-6						20.00

CONQUEROR, THE
Dell Publishing Co.: No., 690, Mar, 1956

Four Color 690-Movie, John Wayne photo-c	15	30	45	103	227	350

CONQUEROR COMICS
Albrecht Publishing Co.: Winter, 1945

nn	28	56	84	165	270	375

CONQUEROR OF THE BARREN EARTH (See The Warlord #63)
DC Comics: Feb, 1985 - No. 4, May, 1985 (Limited series)

1-4: Back-up series from Warlord						4.00

CONQUEST
Store Comics: 1953 (6¢)

1-Richard the Lion Hearted, Beowulf, Swamp Fox	14	28	42	82	121	160

CONQUEST
Famous Funnies: Spring, 1955

1-Crandall-a, 1 pg.; contains contents of 1953 ish.	18	36	54	105	165	225

CONSPIRACY
Marvel Comics: Feb, 1998 - No. 2, Mar, 1998 ($2.99, limited series)

1,2-Painted art by Korday/Abnett-s						4.00

CONSTANTINE (Also see Hellblazer)
DC Comics (Vertigo): 2005 (Based on the 2005 Keanu Reeves movie)

...: The Hellblazer Collection (2005, $14.95) Movie adaptation and r/#1, 27, 41; photo-c						15.00
...: The Official Movie Adaptation (2005, $6.95) Seagle-s/Randall-a/photo-c						7.00

CONSTANTINE (Also see Justice League Dark)
DC Comics: May, 2013 - No. 23, May, 2015 ($2.99)

1-Lemire & Fawkes-s/Guedes-a; two covers by Reis & Guedes						4.00
2-20: 2-The Spectre app. 5-Trinity War tie-in; Shazam app. 9-Forever Evil tie-in. 20-23-Constantine on Earth 2. 23-Darkseid app.						3.00
...: Futures End 1 (11/14, $2.99, regular-c) Five years later; Ferreyra-a/c						3.00
...: Futures End 1 (11/14, $3.99, 3-D cover)						4.00
.../Hellblazer Special Edition 1 (12/14, $1.00) Flipbook r/#1 and Hellblazer #1						3.00

CONSTANTINE: THE HELLBLAZER
DC Comics: Aug, 2015 - No. 13, Aug, 2016 ($2.99)

1-13: 1-Doyle & Tynion IV-s/Rossmo-a, covers by Rossmo & Doyle. 3,4-Doyle-a. 7-Swamp Thing app. 8-12-Neron app. 10,11-Foreman-a.						3.00

CONSUMED
Platinum Studios: July, 2007 - No. 4, Oct, 2007 ($2.99, limited series)

1-4-Linsner-c/Budd-a/Shumskas-Tait-a						3.00

CONTACT COMICS
Aviation Press: July, 1944 - No. 12, May, 1946

nn-Black Venus, Flamingo, Golden Eagle, Tommy Tomahawk begin	103	206	309	659	1130	1600
2-Classic sci-fi-c	103	206	309	659	1130	1600
3-5: 3-Last Flamingo. 3,4-Black Venus by L. B. Cole. 5-The Phantom Flyer app.	63	126	189	403	689	975
6,11-Kurtzman's Black Venus; 11-Last Golden Eagle, last Tommy Tomahawk; Feldstein-a	87	174	261	553	952	1350
7-10	55	110	165	352	601	850
12-Sky Rangers, Air Kids, Ace Diamond app.; L.B. Cole sci-fi cover	757	1514	2271	5526	9763	14,000

NOTE: **L. B. Cole** a-3, 9; c-1-12. **Giunta** a-3. **Hollingsworth** a-5, 7, 10. **Palais** a-11, 12.

CONTAGION
Marvel Comics: Dec, 2019 - No. 5, Dec, 2019 ($3.99, weekly limited series)

1-5-Brisson-s; Fantastic Four, Iron Fist, Luke Cage, Avengers app.						4.00

CONTEMPORARY MOTIVATORS
Pendelum Press: 1977 - 1978 ($1.45, 5-3/8x8", 31 pgs., B&W)

14-3002 The Caine Mutiny; 14-3010 Banner in the Sky; 14-3029 God Is My Co-Pilot; 14-3037 Guadalcanal Diary; 14-3045 Hiroshima; 14-3053 Hot Rod; 14-3061 Just Dial a Number; 14-3088 The Diary of Anne Frank; 14-3096 Lost Horizon	2	4	6	8	10	12

NOTE: Also see Pendelum Illustrated Classics. Above may have been distributed the same.

CONTEST OF CHAMPIONS (See Marvel Super-Hero...)

CONTEST OF CHAMPIONS
Marvel Comics: Dec, 2015 - No. 10, Sept, 2016 ($4.99/$3.99, limited series)

1-($4.99) The Collector, Venom, Mr. Fixit, Iron Man, Gamora & Maestro app.; Medina-a						5.00
2-9-($3.99) 2-Ares and Punisher 2099 app. 3-5-The Sentry app. 7,8-Ultimates app. 9-Revisits Civil War						4.00
10-($4.99) Finale; Ewing-s/Marcellius-a						5.00

CONTEST OF CHAMPIONS II
Marvel Comics: Sept, 1999 - No. 5, Nov, 1999 ($2.50, limited series)

1-5-Claremont-s/Jimenez-a						4.00

CONTRACT WITH GOD, A
Baronet Publishing Co./Kitchen Sink Press: 1978 ($4.95/$7.95, B&W, graphic novel)

nn-Will Eisner-s/a	3	6	9	17	26	35
Reprint (DC Comics, 2000, $12.95)						13.00

CONVERGENCE
DC Comics: No. 0, Jun, 2015 - No. 8, July, 2015 ($4.99/$3.99, weekly limited series)

0-Superman & multiple Brainiacs app.; intro Telos; Van Sciver-a/Jurgens & King-s						5.00
1-($4.99) Earth-2 heroes vs. Telos; Pagulayan-a; wraparound-c by Reis						5.00
2-7-($3.99) 2-Intro. Deimos; Pagulayan-a. 4,5-Warlord app. 5-Andy Kubert-a						4.00
8-($4.99) Conclusion; art by Segovia, Pagulayan, Pansica & Van Sciver						5.00

CONVERGENCE
DC Comics: June, 2015 - July, 2015 ($3.99, 2-part tie-in miniseries, each issue has a variant cover designed by Chip Kidd)

... Action Comics 1,2 - Pre-Crisis Earth Two Superman & Power Girl; Red Son Superman, Wonder Woman & Lex Luthor app.; Conner-c. 2-Bonus preview of Sinestro #12						4.00
... Adventures of Superman 1,2 - Pre-Crisis Earth One Superman & Supergirl app.; Wolfman-s. 2-Kamandi app.; bonus preview of Martian Manhunter #1						4.00
... Aquaman 1,2 - Harpoon-hand Aquaman & Deathblow app.; Cloonan-c; Richards-a. 2-Bonus preview of Doctor Fate #1						4.00
... Atom 1,2 - Pre-Flashpoint Ray Palmer & Deathstroke app.; Dillon-c/Yeowell-a. 2-Ryan Choi app.; bonus preview of Green Lantern #41						4.00
... Batgirl 1,2 - Stephanie Brown, Cassadra Cain, Tim Drake & Catman app; Leonardi-a. 2-Grodd app.; bonus preview of Prez #1						4.00
... Batman and Robin 1,2 - Pre-Flashpoint Batman, Damian & Red Hood app; Cowan & Janson-a. 2-Superman app.; bonus preview of Omega Men #1						4.00
... Batman and The Outsiders 1,2 - Pre-Crisis Outsiders and Omac app.; Andy Kubert-c. 2-Bonus preview of Batman Beyond #1						4.00
... Batman: Shadow of the Bat 1,2 - Pre-Zero Hour Batman & Azrael app. 1-Philip Tan-a/c. 2-Leonardi-a; bonus preview of Deathstroke #7						5.00
... Blue Beetle 1,2 - Charlton Blue Beetle, Captain Atom & The Question app.; Blevins-c. 2-Legion of Super-Heroes app.; bonus preview of Black Canary #1						4.00
... Booster Gold 1,2 - Rip Hunter & the Legion of Super-Heroes app.; Jurgens-c. 2-Blue Beetle app.; bonus preview of Earth-2: Society #1						4.00
... Catwoman 1,2 - Pre-Zero Hour purple suit Catwoman & Kingdom Come Batman app.; Ron Randall-a. 2-Bonus preview of Gotham By Midnight #6						4.00
... Crime Syndicate 1,2 - Earth-Three villains & 853rd Century JLA app.; Winslade-a. 2-Cyborg app.; bonus preview of Cyborg #1						4.00
... Detective Comics 1,2 - Earth-Two pre-Crisis Robin & Huntress vs. Red Son Superman; Cowan & Sienkiewicz-a. 2-Red Son Batman app.; bonus preview of Flash #41						4.00
... Flash 1,2 - Earth-One pre-Crisis Barry Allen vs. Tangent Superman; Abnett-s/Dallocchio-a. 2-Bonus preview of New Suicide Squad #9						4.00
... Green Arrow 1,2 - Pre-Zero Hour Oliver Queen & Connor Hawke app.; Black Canary & Dinah Lance; Morales-a. 2-Bonus preview of G.L.C. Lost Army #1						4.00
... Green Lantern Corps 1,2 - Earth-One pre-Crisis Guy Gardner, John Stewart & Hal Jordan;						

Constantine #19 © DC

Convergence Harley Quinn #1 © DC

Cosmic Ghost Rider #4 © MAR

	GD 2.0	VG 4.0	FN 6.0	VF 8.0	VF/NM 9.0	NM- 9.2

Hercules from Durvale app. 2-Bonus preview of Gotham Academy #7 ... 4.00

... Green Lantern/Parallax 1,2 - Pre-Zero Hour Hal Jordan & Kyle Rayner; Ron Wagner-a. Princess Fern of Electropolis app. 2-Bonus preview of Lobo #7 ... 4.00

... Harley Quinn 1,2 - Pre-Flashpoint Harley, Poison Ivy & Catwoman; Winslade-a. 2-Harley battles Captain Carrot. 2-Bonus preview of Section Eight #1 ... 4.00

... Hawkman 1,2 - Earth-One pre-Crisis Katar Hol & Shayera; Parker-s/Truman-a. 2-Bonus preview of Grayson #9 ... 4.00

... Infinity Inc. 1,2 - Earth-Two pre-Crisis Infinity Inc. vs. Future Jonah Hex & The Dogs of War; Ordway-s, 1-Ben Caldwell-a. 2-Bonus preview of Batgirl #41 ... 4.00

... Justice League 1,2 - Pre-Flashpoint female Justice League vs. Flashpoint Aquaman; Buckingham-c. 2-Bonus preview of Detective Comics #41 ... 4.00

... Justice League International 1,2 - Pre-Zero Hour JLI vs. Kingdom Come; Manley-a. 2-Bonus preview of Justice League #1 ... 4.00

... Justice League of America 1,2 - Earth-One pre-Crisis Detroit JLA vs. Tangent Secret Six; ChrisCross-a. 2-Bonus preview of Superman/Wonder Woman #18 ... 4.00

... Justice Society of America 1,2 - Earth-Two pre-Crisis JSA vs. Weaponers of Qward; Derenick-a. 2-Bonus preview of Superman/Wonder Woman #18 ... 4.00

... New Teen Titans 1,2 - Earth-One pre-Crisis Teen Titans vs. Tangent Doom Patrol; Nicola Scott-a. 2-Bonus preview of Robin: Son of Batman #1 ... 4.00

... Nightwing and Oracle 1,2 - Pre-Flashpoint version vs. Flashpoint Hawkman; Duursema-a/Thompson-c. 2-Bonus preview of Midnighter #1 ... 4.00

... Plastic Man and the Freedom Fighters 1,2 - Earth-X team vs. Futures End cyborgs; Silver Ghost app.; McCrea-a/Barta-c. 2-Bonus preview of Harley Quinn #17 ... 4.00

... The Question 1,2 - Pre-Flashpoint Question (Renee Montoya); Huntress, Batwoman & Two-Face app.; Rucka-s/Hamner-a. 2-Bonus preview of Starfire #1 ... 4.00

... Shazam! 1,2 - Earth-S Marvel Family vs. Gotham By Gaslight Batman; Shaner-a Sivana, Ibac, Mr. Atom app. 2-Bonus preview of Constantine The Hellblazer #1 ... 4.00

... Speed Force 1,2 - Pre-Flashpoint Flash (Wally West) vs. Flashpoint Wonder Woman Grummett-a; Fastback (Zoo Crew) app. 2-Bonus preview of Green Arrow #41 ... 4.00

... Suicide Squad 1,2 - Pre-Zero Hour vs. Kingdom Come Green Lantern Mandrake-a. 2-Bonus preview of Aquaman #41 ... 4.00

... Superboy 1,2 - Pre-Zero Hour Kon-El vs. Kingdom Come Superman, Flash & Red Robin; Moline-a/Tarr-c. 2-Bonus preview of Action Comics #41 ... 4.00

... Superboy and the Legion of Super-Heroes 1,2 - Pre-Crisis Legion vs. The Atomic Knights; Storms-a/Guerra-c. 2-Bonus preview of Teen Titans #9 ... 4.00

... Supergirl 1,2 - Matrix 1,2 - Pre-Zero Hour Supergirl vs. Lady Quark (Electropolis); Ambush Bug app.; Giffen-s/Green II-a/Porter-c. 2-Bonus preview of Bat-Mite #1 ... 4.00

... Superman 1 - Pre-Flashpoint Superman & Lois vs. Flashpoint heroes; Jurgens-s/Weeks-a ... 4.00

2-Birth of Jonathan Kent (Superman: Son of Kal-El); bonus preview of Doomed #1 (See Superman: Lois & Clark series) 3 6 9 21 33 45

... Superman: Man of Steel 1,2 - Pre-Zero Hour Steel vs. Gen-13; Parasite app.; Louise Simonson-s/June Brigman-a/Walt Simonson-c. 2-Bonus preview of Bizarro #1 ... 4.00

... Swamp Thing 1,2 - Earth-One pre-Crisis Swamp Thing vs. Red Rain vampire Batman; Len Wein-s/Kelley Jones-a. 2-Bonus preview of Catwoman #41 ... 4.00

... Titans 1,2 - Pre-Flashpoint Titans vs. The Extremists; Nicieza-s/Wagner-a; 2-Bonus preview of Red Hood & Arsenal #1 ... 4.00

... Wonder Woman 1,2 - Earth-One pre-Crisis Wonder Woman vs. Red Rain vampire Joker, Catwoman & Poison Ivy. 1-Middleton-a/c. 2-Lopresti-a; bonus preview of Secret Six ... 6.00

... World's Finest 1,2 - Earth-Two pre-Crisis Seven Soldiers of Victory vs. Weaponers of Qward; Scribbly Jibbet app.; Levitz-s. 2-Bonus preview of We Are Robin #1 ... 4.00

CONVOCATIONS: A MAGIC THE GATHERING GALLERY
Acclaim Comics (Armada): Jan, 1996 ($2.50, one-shot)

1-pin-ups by various artists including Kaluta, Vess, and Dringenberg ... 5.00

COO COO COMICS (...the Bird Brain No. 57 on)
Nedor Publ. Co./Standard (Animated Cartoons): Oct, 1942 - No. 62, Apr, 1952

1-Origin/1st app. Super Mouse & begin series (cloned from Superman); the first funny animal super hero series (see Looney Tunes #5 for this funny animal super hero)
68 136 204 435 743 1050

2 ... 25 50 75 150 245 340

3-10: 10-(3/44) ... 18 36 54 105 165 225

11-33: 33-1 pg. Ingels-a ... 13 30 45 84 127 170

34-40,43-46,48-50Text illos by Frazetta in all. 36-Super Mouse covers begin 18 36 54 107 169 230

41-Frazetta-a (6-pg. story & 3 text illos) 34 68 102 199 325 450

42,47-Frazetta-a & text illos. 23 46 69 136 223 310

51-62: 56-58,61-Super Mouse app. 14 28 42 80 115 150

"COOKIE" (Also see Topsy-Turvy)
Michel Publ./American Comics Group(Regis Publ.): Apr, 1946 - No. 55, Aug-Sept, 1955

1-Teen-age humor 37 74 111 222 361 500

2-1st app. Tee-Pee Tim who takes over Ha Ha Comics later 20 40 60 117 189 260

3-10: 8-Bing Crosby app. 15 30 45 88 137 185

11-20: 12-Hedy Lamarr app. 13-Jackie Robinson mentioned. 15-Gregory Peck cover app. 16-Ub Iwerks (a creator of Mickey Mouse) name used. 18-Jane Russell-type Jane Bustle. 19-Cookie takes a dog to see Lassie movie 14 28 42 81 118 155

21-23,26,28-30: 26-Milt Gross & Starlett O'Hara stories. 28,30-Starlett O'Hara stories 13 26 39 72 101 130

24,25,27-Starlett O'Hara stories 13 26 39 74 105 135

31-34,37-48,52-55 10 20 30 58 79 100

35,36-Starlett O'Hara stories 12 24 36 67 94 120

49-51: 49-(6-7/54)-3-D effect-c/s. 50-3-D effect. 51-(10-11/54) 8pg. TrueVision 3-D effect story 17 34 51 100 158 215

COOL CAT (What's Cookin' With...) (Formerly Black Magic)
Prize Publications: V8#6, Mar-Apr, 1962 - V9#2, July-Aug, 1962

V8#6, nn(V9#1, 5-6/62), V9#2 3 6 9 21 33 45

COOL WORLD (Movie by Ralph Bakshi)
DC Comics: Apr, 1992 - No. 4, Sept, 1992 ($1.75, limited series)

1-4: Prequel to animated/live action movie. 1-Bakshi-c. Bill Wray inks in all 1 3 4 6 8 10

Movie Adaptation nn ('92, $3.50, 68pg.)-Bakshi-c 2 4 6 9 12 15

COPPER CANYON (See Fawcett Movie Comics)

COPPERHEAD
Image Comics: Sept, 2014 - No. 19, Jun, 2018 ($3.50/$3.99)

1-19: 1-Faerber-s/Godlewski-a; multiple covers. 11-$3.99-c begins. 11-18-Moss-a ... 4.00

COPS (TV)
DC Comics: Aug, 1988 - No. 15, Aug, 1989 ($1.00)

1 ($1.50, 52 pgs.)-Based on Hasbro Toys ... 5.00

2-15: 14-Orlando-c(p) ... 4.00

COPS: THE JOB
Marvel Comics: June, 1992 - No. 4, Sept, 1992 ($1.25, limited series)

1-4: All have Jusko scripts & Golden-c ... 4.00

CORBEN SPECIAL, A
Pacific Comics: May, 1984 (one-shot)

1-Corben-c/a; E.A. Poe adaptation ... 6.00

CORE, THE
Image Comics: July, 2008 ($3.99)

Pilot Season - Hickman-s/Rocafort-a ... 4.00

CORKY & WHITE SHADOW (Disney, TV)
Dell Publishing Co.: No. 707, May, 1956 (Mickey Mouse Club)

Four Color 707-Photo-c 8 16 24 51 96 140

CORLISS ARCHER (See Meet Corliss Archer)

CORMAC MAC ART (Robert E. Howard's...)
Dark Horse Comics: 1990 - No. 4, 1990 ($1.95, B&W, mini-series)

1-4: All have Bolton painted-c; Howard adapts. ... 4.00

CORONAVIRUS BOOK (Cerebus in Hell)
Aardvark-Vanaheim: Dec, 2021 ($8.00, B&W)

1-Cerebus figures placed over original Gustave Doré artwork of Hell ... 8.00

CORPORAL RUSTY DUGAN (See Holyoke One-Shot #2)

CORPSES OF DR. SACOTTI, THE (See Ideal a Classical Comic)

CORSAIR, THE (See A-1 Comics No. 5, 7, 10 under Texas Slim)

CORUM: THE BULL AND THE SPEAR (See Chronicles Of Corum)
First Comics: Jan, 1989 - No. 4, July, 1989 ($1.95)

1-4: Adapts Michael Moorcock's novel ... 4.00

COSMIC BOOK, THE
Ace Comics: Dec, 1986 ($1.95)

1-(44pgs.)-Wood, Toth-a 1 3 4 6 8 10

COSMIC BOY (Also see The Legion of Super-Heroes)
DC Comics: Dec, 1986 - No. 4, Mar, 1987 (limited series)

1-4: Legends tie-ins all issues ... 4.00

COSMIC GHOST RIDER (See Thanos 2017 series #13 for debut)
Marvel Comics: Sept, 2018 - No. 5, Jan, 2019 ($3.99)

1-Cates-s/Burnett-a; Frank Castle as Ghost Rider; Odin and baby Thanos app. ... 4.00

2-5: 2,3-Galactus app. 5-Leads into Guardians of the Galaxy 2019 series ... 4.00

COSMIC GHOST RIDER
Marvel Comics: May, 2023 - No. 5, Sept, 2023 ($4.99/$3.99, limited series)

	GD 2.0	VG 4.0	FN 6.0	VF 8.0	VF/NM 9.0	NM- 9.2

1-($4.99) Stephanie Phillips-s/Juann Cabal-a ... 5.00
2-5-($3.99) Valkyrie app. ... 4.00

COSMIC GHOST RIDER DESTROYS MARVEL HISTORY
Marvel Comics: May, 2019 - No. 6, Oct, 2019 ($3.99, limited series)

1-6: 1-Scheer & Giovannetti-s/Sandoval-a: Uato the Watcher app. 2,4,6-Nauck-a ... 4.00

COSMIC GUARD
Devil's Due Publ.: Aug, 2004 - No. 6, Dec, 2005 ($2.99)

1-6-Jim Starlin-s/a ... 3.00

COSMIC HEROES
Eternity/Malibu Graphics: Oct, 1988 - No. 11, Dec, 1989 ($1.95, B&W)

1-11: Reprints 1934-1936's Buck Rogers newspaper strips #1-728 ... 4.00

COSMIC ODYSSEY
DC Comics: 1988 - No. 4, 1988 ($3.50, limited series, squarebound)

1-4: Reintro. New Gods into DC continuity; Superman, Batman, Green Lantern (John
Stewart) app; Starlin scripts, Mignola-c/a in all. 2-Darkseid merges Demon & Jason Blood
(separated in Demon limited series #4) ... 5.00
TPB (1992,2009, $19.99) r/#1-4; Robert Greenberger intro. ... 20.00

COSMIC POWERS
Marvel Comics: Mar, 1994 - No. 6, Aug, 1994 ($2.50, limited series)

1,2-Thanos app. 1-Ron Lim-c/a(p). 2-Terrax ... 5.00
3-6: 3-Ganymede & Jack of Hearts app. ... 4.00

COSMIC POWERS UNLIMITED
Marvel Comics: May, 1995 - No. 5, May, 1996 ($3.95, quarterly)

1-5 ... 4.00

COSMIC SLAM
Ultimate Sports Entertainment: 1999 ($3.95, one-shot)

1-McGwire, Sosa, Bagwell, Justice battle aliens; Sienkiewicz-c ... 4.00

COSMO (The Merry Martian)
Archie Comic Publications: Feb, 2018 - No. 5, Jul, 2018 ($2.99, limited series)

1-5-Cosmo, Astra, and Orbi app.; Ian Flynn-s/Tracy Yardley-a; multiple covers ... 3.00

COSMO CAT (Becomes Sunny #11 on; also see All Top & Wotalife Comics)
Fox Publications/Green Publ. Co./Norlen Mag.: July-Aug, 1946 - No. 10, Oct, 1947; 1957; 1959

1	37	74	111	218	354	490
2	17	34	51	100	158	215
3-Origin (11-12/46)	20	40	60	120	195	270
4-Robot-c	17	34	51	98	154	210
5-10	12	24	36	67	94	120
2-4(1957-Green Publ. Co.)	6	12	18	28	34	40
2-4(1959-Norlen Mag.)	5	10	15	24	30	35
I.W. Reprint #1	3	6	9	14	19	24

COSMO THE MERRY MARTIAN
Archie Publications (Radio Comics): Sept, 1958 - No. 6, Oct, 1959

1-Bob White-a in all	21	42	63	124	202	280
2-6	14	28	42	78	112	145

COSMO THE MIGHTY MARTIAN
Archie Comic Publications: Jan, 2020 - No. 5, Jun, 2020 ($3.99)

1-5-Ian Flynn-s/Tracy Yardley-a; multiple covers ... 4.00

COTTON WOODS (All-American athlete)
Dell Publishing Co.: No. 837, Sept, 1957

Four Color 837	5	10	15	33	57	80

COUGAR, THE (Cougar No. 2)
Seaboard Periodicals (Atlas): April, 1975 - No. 2, July, 1975

1,2: 1-Vampire; Adkins-a(p). 2-Cougar origin; werewolf-s; Buckler-c(p)					
	2	4	6	11	16	20

COUNT CROWLEY: AMATEUR MIDNIGHT MONSTER HUNTER
Dark Horse Comics: Mar, 2022 - No. 4, Nov, 2022 ($3.99, limited series)

1-4-David Dastmalchian-s/Lukas Ketner-a. 3-EC-style cover ... 4.00

COUNT CROWLEY: MEDIOCRE MIDNIGHT MONSTER HUNTER
Dark Horse Comics: Nov, 2023 - No. 4 ($4.99, limited series)

1,2-David Dastmalchian-s/Lukas Ketner-a ... 5.00

COUNT CROWLEY: RELUCTANT MIDNIGHT MONSTER HUNTER
Dark Horse Comics: Oct, 2019 - No. 4, Jan, 2020 ($3.99, limited series)

1-4-David Dastmalchian-s/Lukas Ketner-a ... 4.00

COUNTDOWN (See Movie Classics)

COUNTDOWN
DC Comics (WildStorm): June, 2000 - No. 8, Jan, 2001 ($2.95)

1-8-Mariotte-s/Lopresti-a ... 3.00

COUNTDOWN (Continued from 52 weekly series)
DC Comics: No. 51, July, 2007 - No. 1, June, 2008 ($2.99, weekly, limited series)
(issue #s go in reverse)

51-Gatefold wraparound-c by Andy Kubert; Duela Dent killed; the Monitors app. ... 3.00
50-1: 50-Joker-c. 48-Lightray dies. 47-Mary Marvel gains Black Adam's powers. 46-Intro.
Forerunner. 43-Funeral for Bart Allen. 39-Karate Kid-c ... 3.00
Countdown to Final Crisis Vol. 1 TPB (2008, $19.99) r/#51-39 ... 20.00
Countdown to Final Crisis Vol. 2 TPB (2008, $19.99) r/#38-26 ... 20.00
Countdown to Final Crisis Vol. 3 TPB (2008, $19.99) r/#25-13 ... 20.00
Countdown to Final Crisis Vol. 4 TPB (2008, $19.99) r/#12-1 ... 20.00

COUNTDOWN: ARENA (Takes place during Countdown #21-18)
DC Comics: Feb, 2008 - No. 4, Feb, 2008 ($3.99, weekly, limited series)

1-4-Battles between alternate Earth heroes; McDaniel-a; Andy Kubert variant-c on each ... 4.00
TPB (2008, $17.99) r/#1-4; variant covers ... 18.00

COUNTDOWN PRESENTS: LORD HAVOK & THE EXTREMISTS
DC Comics: Dec, 2007 - No. 8 ($2.99, limited series)

1-6: 1-Tieri-s/Sharp-a/c; Challengers From Beyond app. ... 3.00
TPB (2008, $17.99) r/#1-6 ... 18.00

COUNTDOWN PRESENTS THE SEARCH FOR RAY PALMER (Leads into Countdown #18)
DC Comics: Nov, 2007 - Feb, 2008 ($2.99, series of one-shots)

...: Wildstorm (11/07) Part 1; The Authority app.; Art Adams-c/Unzueta-a ... 3.00
...: Crime Society (12/07) Earth-3 Owlman & Jokester app.; Igle-a ... 3.00
...: Red Rain (1/08) Vampire Batman app.; Kelley Jones-c; Jones, Battle & Unzueta-a ... 3.00
...: Gotham By Gaslight (1/08) Victorian Batman app.; Tocchini-a/Nguyen-a ... 3.00
...: Red Son (2/08) Soviet Superman app.; Foreman-a ... 3.00
...: Superwoman/Batwoman (2/08) Conclusion; gender-reversed heroes; Sook-c ... 3.00
TPB (2008, $17.99) r/one-shots ... 18.00

COUNTDOWN SPECIAL
DC Comics: Dec, 2007 - Jun, 2008 ($4.99, collection of reprints related to Countdown)

...: Eclipso (5/08) r/Eclipso #10 & Spectre #17,18 (1994); Sook-c ... 5.00
...: Jimmy Olsen (1/08) r/Superman's Pal, Jimmy Olsen #136,147,148; Kirby-s/a; Sook-c ... 5.00
...: Kamandi (6/08) r/Kamandi: The Last Boy on Earth #1,10,29; Kirby-s/a; Sook-c ... 5.00
...: New Gods (3/08) r/Forever People #1, Mr. Miracle #1, New Gods #7; Kirby-s/a; Sook-c ... 5.00
...: Omac (4/08) r/Omac (1974) #1, Warlord #37-39, DC Comics Presents #61; Sook-c ... 5.00
...: The Atom 1,2 (2/08) r/stories from Super-Team Family #11-14; Sook-c on both ... 5.00
...: The Flash (12/07) r/Rogues Gallery in Flash (1st series) #106,113,155,174; Sook-c ... 5.00

COUNTDOWN TO ADVENTURE
DC Comics: Oct, 2007 - No. 8, May, 2008 ($3.99, limited series)

1-8: 1-Adam Strange, Animal Man and Starfire app.; origin of Forerunner ... 4.00
TPB (2008, $17.99) r/#1-8 ... 18.00

COUNTDOWN TO INFINITE CRISIS (See DC Countdown)

COUNTDOWN TO MYSTERY (See Eclipso: The Music of the Spheres TPB for reprint)
DC Comics: Nov, 2007 - No. 8, Jun, 2008 ($3.99, limited series)

1-8: 1-Doctor Fate, Eclipso, The Spectre and Plastic Man app. ... 4.00
TPB (2008, $17.99) r/#1-8 ... 18.00

COUNT DUCKULA (TV)
Marvel Comics: Nov, 1988 - No. 15, Jan, 1991 ($1.00)

1,8: 1-Dangermouse back-up. 8-Geraldo Rivera photo-c/& app.; Sienkiewicz-a(i)					
	1	3	4	6	8	10
2-7,9-15: Dangermouse back-ups in all					6.00

COUNT OF MONTE CRISTO, THE
Dell Publishing Co.: No. 794, May, 1957

Four Color 794-Movie, Buscema-a	8	16	24	51	96	140

COUP D'ETAT (Oneshots)
DC Comics (WildStorm): April, 2004 ($2.95, weekly limited series)

...: Sleeper 1 (part 1 of 4) Jim Lee-a; 2 covers by Lee and Bermejo ... 3.00
...: Stormwatch 1 (part 2 of 4) D'Anda-a; 2 covers by D'Anda and Bermejo ... 3.00
...: Wildcats Version 3.0 1 (part 3 of 4) Garza-a; 2 covers by Garza and Bermejo ... 3.00
...: The Authority 1 (part 4 of 4) Portacio-a; 2 covers by Portacio and Bermejo ... 3.00
...: Afterword 1 (5/04) Profile pages and prelude stories for Sleeper & Wetworks ... 3.00
TPB (2004, $12.95) r/series and profile pages from Afterword ... 13.00

COURAGE COMICS
J. Edward Slavin: No. 77, 1945 - No. 2, 1946

77-(1945), 2-(1946)	20	40	60	117	189	260

COURTNEY CRUMRIN
Oni Press: Apr, 2012 - No. 10, Feb, 2013 ($3.99)

1-10-Ted Naifeh-s/a ... 4.00
#1 (5/14, Free Comic Book Day giveaway) r/#1 ... 3.00

COURTNEY CRUMRIN...
Oni Press: July, 2005; July 2007; Dec, 2008 ($5.95, B&W, series of one-shots)

... And The Fire Thief's Tale (7/07) Naifeh-s/a ... 6.00
... And The Prince of Nowhere (12/08) Naifeh-s/a ... 6.00
... Tales (5/11) sequel to Tales Portrait of the Warlock...; Naifeh-s/a ... 6.00
... Tales Portrait of the Warlock as a Young Man (7/05) origin Uncle Aloysius; Naifeh-s/a ... 6.00

COURTNEY CRUMRIN & THE COVEN OF MYSTICS
Oni Press: Dec, 2002 - No. 4, March, 2003 ($2.95, B&W, limited series)

1-4-Ted Naifeh-s/a ... 3.00
TPB (9/03, $11.95, 8" x 5-1/2") r/#1-4 ... 12.00

COURTNEY CRUMRIN & THE NIGHT THINGS
Oni Press: Mar, 2002 - No. 4, June, 2002 ($2.95, B&W, limited series)

1-4-Ted Naifeh-s/a ... 3.00
Free Comic Book Day Edition (5/03) Naifeh-s/a ... 3.00
TPB (12/02, $11.95) r/#1-4 ... 12.00

COURTNEY CRUMRIN IN THE TWILIGHT KINGDOM
Oni Press: Dec, 2003 - No. 4, May, 2004 ($2.99, B&W, limited series)

1-4-Ted Naifeh-s/a ... 3.00
TPB (9/04, $11.95, digest-size) r/#1-4 ... 12.00

COURTSHIP OF EDDIE'S FATHER (TV)
Dell Publishing Co.: Jan, 1970 - No. 2, May, 1970

1-Bill Bixby photo-c on both	5	10	15	34	60	85
2	4	8	12	23	37	50

COVEN
Awesome Entertainment: Aug, 1997 - No. 5, Mar, 1998 ($2.50)

Preview	1	2	3	5	6	8
1-Loeb-s/Churchill-a; three covers by Churchill, Liefeld, Pollina					
	1	2	3	5	6	8
1-Fan Appreciation Ed.(3/98); new Churchill-c					3.00
1+ :Includes B&W art from Kaboom	1	3	4	6	8	10
2-Regular-c w/leaping Fantom						6.00
2-Variant-c w/circle of candles	1	2	3	5	6	8
3-6-Contains flip book preview of ReGex					3.00
3-White variant-c	1	2	3	4	5	7
3,4: 3-Halloween wraparound-c. 4-Purple variant-c					3.00

Cosmo #1 © ACP

Countdown #45 © DC

Cowboy Bebop #2 © Netflix

	GD 2.0	VG 4.0	FN 6.0	VF 8.0	VF/NM 9.0	NM- 9.2

...Black & White (9/98) Short stories — 3.00
...Fantom Special (2/98) w/sketch pages — 5.00

COVEN
Awesome Entertainment: Jan, 1999 - No. 3, June, 1999 ($2.50)

	GD 2.0	VG 4.0	FN 6.0	VF 8.0	VF/NM 9.0	NM- 9.2
1-3: 1-Loeb-s/Churchill-a; 6 covers by various. 2-Supreme-c/app. 3-Flip book w/Kaboom preview						3.00
... Dark Origins (7/99, 2.50) w/Lionheart gallery						3.00

COVENANT, THE
Image Comics (Top Cow): 2005 ($9.99, squarebound, one-shot)

nn-Tone Rodriguez-a/Aron Coleite-s						10.00

COVENANT, THE
Image Comics: Jun, 2015 - No. 5, Dec, 2015 ($3.99)

1-5-Rob Liefeld-s/c; Matt Horak-a; story of the Ark of the Covenant						4.00

COVER
DC Comics (Jinxworld): Nov, 2018 - No. 6, May, 2019 ($3.99)

1-6-Brian Michael Bendis-s/David Mack-a/c; comic creator as spy						4.00

COVERED WAGONS, HO (Disney, TV)
Dell Publishing Co.: No. 814, June, 1957 (Donald Duck)

	GD 2.0	VG 4.0	FN 6.0	VF 8.0	VF/NM 9.0	NM- 9.2
Four Color 814-Mickey Mouse app.	7	14	21	46	86	125

COWBOY ACTION (Formerly Western Thrillers No. 1-4; Becomes Quick-Trigger Western No. 12 on)
Atlas Comics (ACI): No. 5, March, 1955 - No. 11, March, 1956

	GD 2.0	VG 4.0	FN 6.0	VF 8.0	VF/NM 9.0	NM- 9.2
5	16	32	48	94	147	200
6-10: 6-8-Heath-a	13	26	39	72	101	130
11-Williamson-a (4 pgs.); Baker-a	14	28	42	80	115	150

NOTE: *Ayers* a-8. *Drucker* a-6. *Maneely* c/a-5, 6. *Severin* c-10. *Shores* a-7.

COWBOY BEBOP (Based on the Netflix adaptation of the animated series)
Titan Comics: Feb, 2022 - No. 4, Jul, 2022 ($3.99, limited series)

1-4-Dan Watters-s/Lamar Mathurin-a						4.00

COWBOY COMICS (Star Ranger #12, Stories #14)(Star Ranger Funnies #15)
Centaur Publishing Co.: No. 13, July, 1938 - No. 14, Aug, 1938

	GD 2.0	VG 4.0	FN 6.0	VF 8.0	VF/NM 9.0	NM- 9.2
13-(Rare)-Ace and Deuce, Lyin Lou, Air Patrol, Aces High, Lee Trent, Trouble Hunters begin	314	628	942	2198	3849	5500
14-(Rare)-Filchock-c	271	542	813	1734	2967	4200

NOTE: *Guardineer* a-13, 14. *Gustavson* a-13, 14.

COWBOY IN AFRICA (TV)
Gold Key: Mar, 1968

	GD 2.0	VG 4.0	FN 6.0	VF 8.0	VF/NM 9.0	NM- 9.2
1(10219-803)-Chuck Connors photo-c	4	8	12	27	44	60

COWBOY LOVE (Becomes Range Busters?)
Fawcett Publications/Charlton Comics No. 28 on: 7/49 - V2#10, 6/50; No. 11, 1951; No. 28, 2/55 - No. 31, 8/55

	GD 2.0	VG 4.0	FN 6.0	VF 8.0	VF/NM 9.0	NM- 9.2
V1#1-Rocky Lane photo back-c	21	42	63	122	199	275
2	10	20	30	56	76	95
V1#3,4,6 (12/49)	9	18	27	47	61	75
5-Bill Boyd photo back-c (11/49)	10	20	30	56	76	95
V2#7-Williamson/Evans-a	11	22	33	62	86	110
V2#8-11	8	16	24	42	54	65
V1#28 (Charlton)-Last precode (2/55) (Formerly Romantic Story?)						
	8	16	24	40	50	60
V1#29-31 (Charlton)-becomes Sweetheart Diary (#32 on)						
	7	14	21	37	46	55

NOTE: *Powell* a-10. *Marcus Swayze* a-2, 3. Photo c-11. No. 1-3, 5-7, 9, 10 are 52 pgs.

COWBOY ROMANCES (Young Men No. 4 on)
Marvel Comics (IPC): Oct, 1949 - No. 3, Mar, 1950 (All photo-c & 52 pgs.)

	GD 2.0	VG 4.0	FN 6.0	VF 8.0	VF/NM 9.0	NM- 9.2
1-Photo-c	32	64	96	188	307	425
2-William Holden, Mona Freeman "Streets of Laredo" photo-c						
	20	40	60	117	189	260
3-Photo-c	17	34	51	98	154	210

COWBOYS 'N' INJUNS (...and Indians No. 6 on)
Compix No. 1-5/Magazine Enterprises No. 6 on: 1946 - No. 5, 1947; No. 6, 1949 - No. 8, 1952

	GD 2.0	VG 4.0	FN 6.0	VF 8.0	VF/NM 9.0	NM- 9.2
1-Funny animal western	18	36	54	107	169	230
2-5-All funny animal western	11	22	33	62	86	110
6(A-1 23)-Half violent, half funny; Ayers-a	16	32	48	92	144	195
7(A-1 41, 1950), 8(A-1 48)-All funny	10	20	30	56	76	95
I.W. Reprint No. 1,7,10 (Reprinted in Canada by Superior, No. 7), 10('63)						
	3	6	9	15	22	28

COWBOY WESTERN COMICS (TV)(Formerly Jack In The Box; Becomes Space Western No. 40-45 & Wild Bill Hickok & Jingles No. 68 on; title: Cowboy Western Heroes No. 47 & 48; Cowboy Western No. 49 on)
Charlton (Capitol Stories): No. 17, 7/48 - No. 39, 8/52; No. 46, 10/53; No. 47, 12/53; No. 48, Spr, '54; No. 49, 5-6/54 - No. 67, 3/58 (nn 40-45)

	GD 2.0	VG 4.0	FN 6.0	VF 8.0	VF/NM 9.0	NM- 9.2
17-Jesse James, Annie Oakley, Wild Bill Hickok begin; Texas Rangers app.						
	20	40	60	120	195	270
18,19-Orlando-c/a. 18-Paul Bunyan begins. 19-Wyatt Earp story						
	11	22	33	62	86	110
20-25: 21-Buffalo Bill story. 22-Texas Rangers-c/story. 24-Joel McCrea photo-c & adaptation from movie "Three Faces West". 25-James Craig photo-c & adaptation from movie "Northwest Stampede"	10	20	30	54	72	90
26-George Montgomery photo-c and adaptation from movie "Indian Scout"; 1 pg. bio on Will Rogers	11	22	33	62	86	110
27-Sunset Carson photo-c & adapts movie "Sunset Carson Rides Again" plus 1 other Sunset Carson story	40	80	120	246	411	575
28-Sunset Carson line drawn-c; adapts movies "Battling Marshal" & "Fighting Mustangs" starring Sunset Carson	20	40	60	120	195	270
29-Sunset Carson line drawn-c; adapts movies "Rio Grande" with Sunset Carson & "Winchester '73" w/James Stewart plus 5 pg. life history of Sunset Carson featuring Tom Mix	20	40	60	120	195	270
30-Sunset Carson photo-c; adapts movie "Deadline" starring Sunset Carson plus 1 other Sunset Carson story	39	78	117	240	395	550
31-34,38,39,47-50 (no #40-45): 50-Golden Arrow, Rocky Lane & Blackjack (r?) stories						
	9	18	27	50	65	80
35,36-Sunset Carson-c/stories (2 in each). 35-Inside front-c photo of Sunset Carson plus photo on-c	20	40	60	120	195	270
37-Sunset Carson stories (2)	15	30	45	94	147	200
46-(Formerly Space Western)-Space western story	15	30	45	94	147	200
51-57,59-66: 51-Golden Arrow(r?) & Monte Hale-r renamed Rusty Hall. 53,54-Tom Mix-r. 55-Monte Hale story(r?). 66-Young Eagle story. 67-Wild Bill Hickok and Jingles-c/story						
	7	14	21	37	46	55
58-(1/56)-Wild Bill Hickok, Annie Oakley & Jesse James stories; Forgione-a						
	9	18	27	47	61	75
67-(15¢, 68 pgs.)-Williamson/Torres-a, 5 pgs.	9	18	27	52	69	85

NOTE: *Many issues trimmed 1" shorter. Maneely a-67(5). Inside front/back photo c-29.*

COWGIRL ROMANCES
Marvel Comics (CCC): No. 28, Jan, 1950 (52 pgs.)

	GD 2.0	VG 4.0	FN 6.0	VF 8.0	VF/NM 9.0	NM- 9.2
28(#1)-Photo-c	25	50	75	150	245	340

COWGIRL ROMANCES
Fiction House Magazines: 1950 - No. 12, Winter, 1952-53 (No. 1-3: 52 pgs.)

	GD 2.0	VG 4.0	FN 6.0	VF 8.0	VF/NM 9.0	NM- 9.2
1-Kamen-a	63	126	189	403	689	975
2	37	74	111	222	361	500
3-5: 5-12-Whitman-c (most)	30	60	90	177	289	400
6-9,11,12	30	54	84	165	270	375
10-Frazetta?/Williamson?-a; Kamen?/Baker?-a; r/Mitzi story from Movie Comics #4 w/all new dialogue	58	116	174	371	636	900

C.O.W.L.
Image Comics: May, 2014 - No. 11, Jul, 2015 ($3.50)

1-11: 1-Higgins & Siegel-s/Reis-a. 6-Origin of Grey Raven; Charretier-a						3.50

COW PUNCHER (...Comics)
Avon Periodicals: Jan, 1947; No. 2, Sept, 1947 - No. 7, 1949

	GD 2.0	VG 4.0	FN 6.0	VF 8.0	VF/NM 9.0	NM- 9.2
1-Clint Cortland, Texas Ranger, Kit West, Pioneer Queen begin; Kubert-a; Alabam stories begin	84	168	252	538	919	1300
2-Kubert, Kamen/Feldstein-a; bondage & torture cover by Kamen						
	161	322	483	1030	1765	2500
3-5,7: 3-Kiefer story	43	86	129	271	461	650
6-Opium drug mention story; bondage, headlight-c; Reinman-a						
	97	194	291	621	1061	1500

COWPUNCHER
Realistic Publications: 1953 (nn) (Reprints Avon's No. 2)

	GD 2.0	VG 4.0	FN 6.0	VF 8.0	VF/NM 9.0	NM- 9.2
nn-Kubert-a	19	38	57	111	176	240

COWSILLS, THE (See Harvey Pop Comics)

COW SPECIAL, THE
Image Comics (Top Cow): Spring-Summer 2000; 2001 ($2.95)

1-Previews upcoming Top Cow projects; Yancy Butler photo-c						3.00
Vol. 2 #1-Witchblade-c; previews and interviews						3.00

COYOTE
Marvel Comics (Epic Comics): June, 1983 - No. 16, Mar, 1986

1-10,15: 7-10-Ditko-a						4.00

	GD	VG	FN	VF	VF/NM	NM-
	2.0	4.0	6.0	8.0	9.0	9.2

	GD 2.0	VG 4.0	FN 6.0	VF 8.0	VF/NM 9.0	NM- 9.2
11-1st McFarlane-a.	5	10	15	33	57	80
12-14,16: 12-14-McFarlane-a. 14-Badger x-over.						
16-Reagan c/app.						6.00
Coyote Collection Vol. 1 (2005, $14.99) reprints from Coyote #1-7 & Scorpio Rose #1,2 plus Rogers layout pages for unpublished #3; Englehart intro.						15.00
Coyote Collection Vol. 2 (2005, $12.99) reprints from Coyote #1-4						15.00
Coyote Collection Vol. 3 (2006, $12.99) reprints from Coyote #5-8						13.00
Coyote Collection Vol. 4 (2007, $14.99) reprints from Coyote #9-12						15.00
Coyote Collection Vol. 5 (2007, $12.99) reprints from Coyote #13-16						13.00

COYOTES
Image Comics: Nov, 2017 - No. 8, Nov, 2018 ($3.99, limited series)

	GD	VG	FN	VF	VF/NM	NM-
1-8-Sean Lewis-s/Caitlin Yarsky-a						4.00

CRACKAJACK FUNNIES (Also see The Owl)
Dell Publishing Co.: June, 1938 - No. 43, Jan, 1942

	GD 2.0	VG 4.0	FN 6.0	VF 8.0	VF/NM 9.0	NM- 9.2
1-Dan Dunn, Freckles, Myra North, Wash Tubbs, Apple Mary, The Nebbs, Don Winslow, Tom Mix, Buck Jones, Major Hoople, Clyde Beatty, Boots begin	206	412	618	1318	2259	3200
2	84	168	252	538	919	1300
3	61	122	183	390	670	950
4	50	100	150	315	533	750
5-Nude woman on cover (10/38)	65	130	195	416	708	1000
6-8,10: 8-Speed Bolton begins (1st app.)	43	86	129	271	461	650
9-(3/39)-Red Ryder strip-r begin by Harman; 1st app. in comics & 1st cover app.	187	374	561	1197	2049	2900
11-14	37	74	111	222	361	500
15-Tarzan text feature begins by Burroughs (9/39); not in #26,35	40	80	120	246	411	575
16-24: 18-Stratosphere Jim begins (1st app., 12/39). 23-Ellery Queen begins plus-c (1st comic book app.)	33	66	99	194	317	440
25-The Owl begins (1st app., 7/40); in new costume #26 by Frank Thomas (also see Popular Comics #72)	103	206	309	659	1130	1600
26,27,29,30	53	106	159	334	567	800
28-Part Owl-c	68	136	204	435	743	1050
31-Owl covers begin, end #42	77	154	231	493	847	1200
32-Origin Owl Girl	84	168	252	538	919	1300
33-37: 36-Last Tarzan issue. 37-Cyclone & Midge begin (1st app.)	58	116	174	371	636	900
38-(scarce) Classic giant gorilla vs. Owl-c	100	200	300	635	1093	1550
39-Andy Panda begins (intro/1st app., 9/41)	90	180	270	576	988	1400
40-42: 42-Last Owl-c.	55	110	165	352	601	850
43-Terry & the Pirates-r	28	56	84	165	270	375

NOTE: *McWilliams a-1* at most issues.

CRACK COMICS (Crack Western No. 63 on)
Quality Comics Group: May, 1940 - No. 62, Sept, 1949

	GD 2.0	VG 4.0	FN 6.0	VF 8.0	VF/NM 9.0	NM- 9.2
1-Origin & 1st app. The Black Condor by Lou Fine, Madame Fatal, Red Torpedo, Rock Bradden & The Space Legion; The Clock, Alias the Spider (by Gustavson), Wizard Wells, & Ned Brant begin; Powell-a; Note: Madame Fatal is a man dressed as a woman	476	952	1428	3475	6138	8800
2	239	478	717	1530	2615	3700
3	181	362	543	1158	1979	2800
4	142	284	426	909	1555	2200
5-10: 5-Molly The Model begins. 10-Tor, the Magic Master begins	119	238	357	762	1306	1850
11-20: 13-1 pg. J. Cole-a. 15-1st app. Spitfire	100	200	300	635	1093	1550
21-24: 23-Pen Miller begins; continued from National Comics #22. 24-Last Fine Black Condor	77	154	231	493	847	1200
25	61	122	183	390	670	950
26-Flag-c	77	154	231	493	847	1200
27-(1/43)-Intro & origin Captain Triumph by Alfred Andriola (Kerry Drake artist) & begin series	123	246	369	787	1344	1900
28-30	47	94	141	296	498	700
31-39: 31-Last Black Condor	27	54	81	158	259	360
40-46	20	40	60	114	182	250
47-57,59,60-Capt. Triumph by Crandall	20	40	60	117	189	260
58,61,62-Last Captain Triumph	16	32	48	92	144	195

NOTE: *Black Condor by Fine: No. 1, 2, 5, 6, 8, 10-24; by Sultan: No. 3, 7; by Fugitani: No. 9. Cole a-34. Crandall a-61(unsigned); c-48, 49, 51-61. Guardineer a-17. Gustavson a-1, 2, 4, 7, 13, 17, 23. McWilliams a-15-27. Black Condor c-2, 4, 6, 8, 10, 12, 14, 16, 18, 20-26. Capt. Triumph c-27-62. The Clock c-1, 3, 5, 7, 9, 11, 13, 15, 17, 19.*

CRACK COMICS (Next Issue Project)
Image Comics: No. 63, Oct, 2011 ($4.99, one-shot)

	GD	VG	FN	VF	VF/NM	NM-
63-Mimics style & format of a 1949 issue; Weiss-c; s/a by various; Capt. Triumph app.						5.00

CRACK COMICS
Quality Comics: May 1940

1-Ashcan comic, not distributed to newsstands, only for in-house use. Cover art is the same as published version of Crack Comics #1 with exception of text panel on bottom left of cover. A CGC certified 4.0 copy sold for $1,495 in 2005.

CRACKDOWN (Based on the videogame)
Dynamite Entertainment: 2018 - No. 4, 2018 ($3.99)

	GD	VG	FN	VF	VF/NM	NM-
1-4-Jonathan Goff-s/Ricardo Jaime-a						4.00

CRACKED (Magazine) (Satire) (Also see The 3-D Zone #19)
Major Magazines(#1-212)/Globe Communications(#213-346/American Media #347 on):
Feb-Mar, 1958 - No. 365, Nov, 2004

	GD 2.0	VG 4.0	FN 6.0	VF 8.0	VF/NM 9.0	NM- 9.2
1-One pg. Williamson-a; Everett-c; Gunsmoke-s	44	88	132	326	738	1150
2-1st Shut-Ups & Bonus Cut-Outs; Superman parody-c by Severin (his 1st cover on the title) Frankenstein-s	20	40	60	138	307	475
3-5	14	28	42	96	211	325
6-10: 7-Reprints his 6 covers on-c. 8-Frankenstein-c. 10-Wolverton-a	10	20	30	68	144	220
11-12, 13(nn,3/60)	8	16	24	54	102	150
14-Kirby-a	9	18	27	59	117	175
15-17, 18(nn,2/61), 19,20	7	14	21	46	86	125
21-27(11/62), 27(No.28, 2/63; mis-#'d), 29(5/63)	6	12	18	37	66	95
30-40(11/64): 37-Beatles and Superman cameos	4	8	12	28	47	65
41-45,47-56,59,60: 47,49,52-Munsters. 51-Beatles inside-c. 59-Laurel and Hardy photos						

	GD 2.0	VG 4.0	FN 6.0	VF 8.0	VF/NM 9.0	NM- 9.2
46,57,58: 46,58-Man From U.N.C.L.E. 46-Beatles.	4	8	12	25	40	55
57-Rolling Stones	4	8	12	27	44	60
61-80: 62-Beatles cameo. 69-Batman, Superman app. 70-(8/68) Elvis cameo.						
71-Garrison's Gorillas; W.C. Fields photos	3	6	9	16	23	30
81-99: 99-Alfred E. Neuman on-c	3	6	9	14	20	25
100	3	6	9	17	26	35
101-119: 104-Godfather-c/s. 108-Archie Bunker-s. 112,119-Kung Fu (TV). 113-Tarzan-s. 115-MASH. 117-Cannon. 118-The Sting-c.	2	4	6	10	14	18
120(12/74) Six Million Dollar Man-c/s; Ward-a	2	4	6	13	18	22
121,122,124-126,128-133,136-140: 121-American Graffiti. 122-Korak-c/s. 124,131-Godfather-c/s. 128-Capone-c. 129,131-Jaws. 132-Baretta-c/s. 133-Space 1999. 136-Laverne and Shirley/Fonz-c. 137-Travolta/Kotter-c/s. 138-Travolta/Laverne and Shirley/Fonz-c. 139-Barney Miller-c. 140-King Kong-c/s; Fonz-s	2	4	6	10	14	18
123-Planet of the Apes-c/s; Six Million Dollar Man	3	6	9	15	22	28
127,134,135: 127-Star Trek-c/s; Ward-a. 134-Fonz-c/s. 135-Starsky and Hutch. 135-Bionic Woman-c/s; Ward-a	3	6	9	14	20	25
141,151-Charlie's Angels-c/s. 151-Frankenstein	3	6	9	14	20	25
142,143,150,152-155,157: 142-MASH-c/s. 143-Rocky-c/s; King Kong-s. 150-(5/78) Close Encounters-c/s. 152-Close Enc./Star Wars-c/s. 153-Close Enc./Fonz-c/s. 154-Jaws II-c/s. Star Wars-s. 155-Star Wars/Fonz-c	2	4	6	9	13	16
144,149,156,158-160: 144-Fonz/Happy Days-c. 149-Star Wars/Six Mil.$ Man-c/s. 156-Grease/Travolta-c. 158-Mork & Mindy. 159-Battlestar Galactica-c/s. MASH-s. 160-Superman-c/s	2	4	6	11	16	20
145,147-Both have insert postcards: 145-Fonz/Rocky/L&S-c/s. 147-Star Wars-c; Farrah photo page (missing postcards-1/2 price)						
146,148: 46-Star Wars-c/s with stickers insert (missing stickers-1/2 price). 148-Star Wars-c/s with inside-c color poster	3	6	9	18	28	38
161,170-Ward-a: 161-Mork & Mindy-c/s. 170-Dukes of Hazzard-c/s	2	4	6	8	11	14
162,165-168,171,172,175-178,180-Ward-a: 162-Sherlock Holmes-s. 165-Dracula-c/s. 167-Mork-c/s. 168,175-MASH-c/s. 168-Mork-s. 172-Dukes of Hazzard/CHiPs-c/s.	2	4	6	8	10	12
176-Barney Miller-c/s	2	4	6	8	11	14
163,179:163-Postcard insert; Mork & Mindy-c/s. 179-Insult cards insert; Popeye, Dukes of Hazzard-c/s	3	6	9	14	19	24
164,169: 164-Alien movie-c/s; Mork & Mindy-s. 169-Star Trek	3	6	9	13	19	24
173,174-Star Wars-Empire Strikes Back. 173-SW poster	3	6	9	20	25	
181,182,185-191,193,194,196-198-most Ward-a: 182-MASH-c/s. 185-Dukes of Hazzard-c/s; Jefferson-s. 187-Love Boat. 188-Fall Guy-s. 189-Fonz/Happy Days-c/s. 190,194-MASH-c/s. 191-Magnum P.I./Rocky-c; Magnum-s. 193-Knight Rider-s. 196-Dukes of Hazzard/Knight Rider-c/s. 198-Jaws III-c/s; Fall Guy-s	1	2	3	5	7	9
183,184,192,195,199,200-Ward-a in all: 183-Superman-c/s. 184-Star Trek-c/s. 192-E.T.-c/s. Rocky-s. 195-E.T.-c/s. 199-Jabba-c/s; Star Wars-s. 200-(12/83)				4	8	10
201,203,210-A-Team-c/s						6.00
202,204-206,211-224,226,227,230-233: 202-Knight Rider-s. 204-Magnum P.I. A-Team-s. 206-Michael Jackson/Mr. T-c/s. 212-Prince-c; Cosby-s. 213-Monsters issue-c/s. 215-Hulk Hogan/Mr. T-c/s. 216-Miami Vice-s; James Bond-s. 217-Rambo-s; Cosby-s; A-Team-s. 218-Rocky-s. 219-Arnold/Commando-c; Rocky-s; Godzilla. 220-Rocky-c/s. 221-Stephen King-app. 223-Miami Vice-s. 224-Cosby-s. 226-29th Anniv.; Tarzan-s; Aliens-s; Family Ties-s. 227-Cosby, Family Ties. 229-Monkees-c/s; Elvis on-c. 232-Alf, Cheers, StarTrek-s. 233-Superman/James Bond-c/s; Robocop, Predator-s						6.00
207-209,225,234: 207-Michael Jackson-c/s. 208-Indiana Jones-c/s. 209-MichaelJackson/Gremlins-c/s; Star Trek III-s. 225-Schwarzenegger/Stallone/G.I. Joe-c/s. 234-Don Martin-a begins; Batman/Robocop/Clint Eastwood-c/s						6.00
228,229: 228-Star Trek-c/s; Alf, Pee Wee Herman-s. 229-Monsters issue-c/s; centerfold with many superheroes						6.00
235,239,243,249: 235-1st Martin-c; Star Trek:TNG-s; Alf-s. 239-Beetlejuice-c/s; Mike Tyson-s. 243-X-Men and other heroes app. 249-Batman/Indiana Jones/Ghostbusters-c/s						6.00
236,244,245,248: 236-Madonna/Stallone-c/s; Twilight Zone-s. 244-Elvis-c/s; Martin-c. 245-Roger Rabbit-c/s. 248-Batman issue						6.00
237,238,240-242,246,247,250: 237-Robocop-s. 238-Rambo-c/s; Star Trek-s. 242-Dirty Harry-s. Ward-a. 246-Alf-s; Star Trek-s., Ward-a. 247-Star Trek-s. 250-Batman/Ghostbusters-s						4.00
251-253,255,256,259,261-265,275-278,281,284,286-297,299: 252-Star Trek-s. 253-Back to the future-c/s. 256-TMNT-c/s. Batman, Bart Simpson on-c. 259-Die Hard II, Robocop-s. 261-TMNT, Twin Peaks-s. 262-Rocky-c/s; Rocky Horror-s. 265-TMNT-s. 276-Aliens III, Batman-s. 277-Clinton-s. 284-Bart Simpson-c/s. 90210-s. 297-Van Damme-s/photo-c. 299-Dumb & Dumber-c/s						5.00
254,257,266,267,272,280,282,285,298,300: 254-Back to the Future, Punisher-s; Wolverton-a. Batman-s, Ward-a. 257-Batman, Simpsons-s; Spider-Man and other heroes app. 266-Terminator-c/s. 267-Toons-c/s. 272-Star Trek VI-s. 280-Swimsuit issue. 282-Cheers-c/s. 285-Jurassic Park-c/s. 298-Swimsuit issue; Martin-c. 300-(8/95) Brady Bunch-c/s						5.00
258,260,274,279,283: 258-Simpsons-c/s; Back to the Future-s. 260-Spider-Man-c/s; Simpsons-s. 274-Batman-c/s. 279-Madonna-c/s. 283-Jurassic Park-c/s; Wolverine app. inside back-c						5.00
301-305,307-365: 365-Freas-c						3.00
306-Toy Story-c/s						4.00
Biggest... (Winter, 1977)	2	4	6	13	18	22
Biggest, Greatest... nn('65)	5	10	15	30	50	70
Biggest, Greatest... 2('66/67) - #5('69/70)	3	6	9	19	30	40
Biggest, Greatest...6 ('70) - #12(Wint. '77)	3	6	9	14	19	24
Biggest, Greatest...13(Fall '78) - #21(Fall/Wint. '86)	2	4	6	8	11	14
...Blockbuster 1(Sum '87), 2('88), 3(Sum. '89)	1	3	4	6	8	10
...Blockbuster 4 - 6(Sum. '92)						6.00
...Collectors' Edition 4 ('73; formerly ...Special)	2	4	6	13	18	22
5-9,10(10/75)	2	4	6	11	15	18
11-19,20(11/17)	2	4	6	8	11	14
21,22,23(5/78): 23-Ward-a	2	4	6	8	11	14
(#24-62,64 not numbered)						
1978 (nn; July, Sept, Nov, Dec) (#24-27)	2	4	6	8	11	14
1979 (nn; May, July, Sept, Nov, Dec) (#28-33)	2	4	6	8	11	14
1980 (nn; Feb, May, July, Sept, Nov, Dec) (#34-39)1	3	4	6	8	10	
1981 (nn; Feb, May, July, Sept, Nov, Dec) (#40-45)1	3	4	6	8	10	
1982 (nn; Feb, May, July, Sept, Nov, Dec) (#46-51)1	3	4	6	8	10	

Crackdown #4 © Microsoft

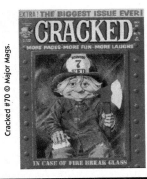

Cracked #70 © Major Mags.

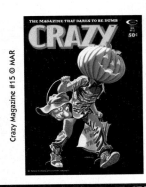

Crazy Magazine #15 © MAR

Grade columns: GD 2.0 · VG 4.0 · FN 6.0 · VF 8.0 · VF/NM 9.0 · NM- 9.2

(CRACKED, cont.)

1983 (nn; Feb, May, Sept, Nov, Dec) (#52-56) 1 3 4 6 8 10
1984 (nn; Feb, May, July, Nov) (#57-60) 1 2 3 4 5 7
1985 (nn; Feb) (#61) 1 2 3 4 5 7
62(9/85), nn(#63,11/85), 64(12/85), 65-69, 70(4/87) 1 2 3 4 5.00
71,72,73(100 pgs., 1/88), 74-79, 80(9/89) 5.00
81-96, 97(two diff. issues), 98-115: 83-Elvis, Batman parodies
116('98)-Last issue? 6.00
...Digest 1(Fall, '86, 148 pgs.), 2(1/87) 1 2 3 6 8 10
...Digest 3-5 1 2 3 4 5 7
...Party Pack 1,2('88) - 4('90) 4.00
...Shut-Ups 1(2/72) 3 6 9 17 26 35
...Shut-Ups (2/72) becomes Cracked Spec. #3 3 6 9 14 19 24
...Special 3('73; formerly Cracked Shut-Ups; ...Collectors' Edition#4 on) 2 4 6 13 18 22
... Summer Special 1(Sum. '91), 2(Sum. '92)-Don Martin-a 4.00
... Summer Special - 2(Sum. '93) - 8(Sum. '98) 3.00
... Super (Vol. 2, formerly Super Cracked) 5(Wint. '91/92) - 14(Wint.'97/98) 3.00
Extra Special... 1(Spr. '76) 2 4 6 11 16 20
Extra Special... 2(Spr./Sum. '77) 2 4 6 10 14 18
Extra Special... 2(Wint. '79) - 9(Wint. '86) 1 2 3 4 5 7
Giant... nn('65) 5 10 15 33 57 80
Giant... 2('66) - 5('69) 3 6 9 21 33 45
Giant...6('70) - 12('76) 3 6 9 16 24 32
Giant...nn(9/77, #13), nn(1/78, #14), nn(3/78, #15), nn(5/78, #16), nn(7/78, #17), nn(11/78, #18),
    nn(3/79, #19), nn(7/79, #20), nn(10/79, #21), nn(12/79, #22), nn(3/80, #23),
    nn(7/80, #24) 2 4 6 11 16 20
Giant...nn(10/80, #25), nn(12/80, #26), nn(3/81, #27), nn(7/81, #28), nn(10/81, #29),
    nn(12/81, #30), nn(7/82, #31), nn(10/82, #32), nn(12/82, #33), nn(7/83, #34),
    2 4 6 8 11 14
Giant...nn(10/83, #35), nn(12/83, #36), nn(3/84, #37), nn(7/84, #38), nn(10/84, #39),
    nn(3/85, #40), nn(7/85, #41), nn(10/85, #42) 1 2 3 5 7 9
Giant...43(3/86) - 46(1/87), 47(Wint. '88), 48(Wint. '89) 1 2 3 4 5 7
King Sized... 1('67) 4 8 12 25 40 55
King Sized... 2('68) - 5('71) 3 6 9 17 26 35
King Sized... 6('72) - 11('77) 3 6 9 14 20 26
King Sized... 12(Fall '78) - 17(Sum. '83) 2 4 6 8 11 14
King Sized... 18-20 (Sum'86) (#21,22 exist?) 1 3 4 6 8 10
Spaced Out... 1-4 ('93 - '94) 5.00
Super... 1('68) 4 8 12 25 40 55
Super... 2('69) 3 6 9 19 30 40
Super... 7('74), 8(Spr. '75) - 10(Spr. '77) 3 6 9 15 22 28
Super... 11(Sum. '78) - 16(Fall '81) 2 4 6 11 16 20
Super... 17(Spr. '82) - 22(Fall '83) 2 4 6 8 11 14
Super... 23(Sum. '84, mis-numbered as #24) 2 4 6 8 11 14
Super... 24(Fall '84, correctly numbered) 2 4 6 8 11 14
Super... 25(Wint. '85) - 32(Fall '86) 2 4 6 8 10 12
Super... (Vol. 2) 1('87, 100 pgs.)-Severin & Elder-a 1 3 4 6 8 10
Super... (Vol. 2) 2(Sum. '88), 3(Wint. '89), 4(exist?)(Becomes Cracked Super) 6.00
NOTE: *Burgos* a-1-10. *Colan* a-257. *Davis* a-5, 11-17, 24, 40, 80; c-12-14, 16. *Elder* a-5, 6, 10-13; c-10. *Everett* a-1-10, 23-25, 61; c-1. *Heath* a-1-3, 6, 13, 14, 17, 110; c-6. *Jaffee* a-5, 6. *Don Martin* a-235, 244, 247, 259, 261, 264. *Morrow* a-8-10. *Reinman* a-1-4. *Severin* c/a-in most all issues. *Shores* a-3-7. *Torres* a-7-10. *Ward* a-22-24, 27, 35, 40, 120-193, 195, 197-205, 242, 244, 246, 247, 250, 252-257. *Williamson* a-1 (1 pg.). *Wolverton* a-10 (2 pgs.). *Giant* nn('65). *Wood* a-27, 35, 40. Alfred E. Neuman a-177, 200, 202. Batman a-234, 248, 249, 256, 274. Captain America a-256. Christmas a-234, 243. Spider-Man a-260. Star Trek a-127, 169, 207, 228. Star Wars a-145, 146, 148, 149, 152, 155, 173, 174, 199. Superman a-183, 233. #144, 146 have free full-color pre-glued stickers. #145, 147, 155, 163 have free full-color postcards. #123, 137, 154, 157 have free iron-ons.

CRACKED MONSTER PARTY
Globe Communications: July, 1988 - No. 27, Wint. 1999/2000
1 3 6 9 14 20 25
2-4: 2-Wolfman, Frankenstein, Dracula, Nosferatu, The Mummy, Invisible Man & Mole Man-c. 2 4 6 10 14 18
    3-Darth Vader/Chewbacca-c. 4-Elvira vs. Nanny 2 4 6 8 10 12
5-10 1 2 3 4 5 7
11-26 1 2 3 4 5 7
27-Interview with a Vampire-c/s 2 4 6 8 10 12

CRACKED'S FOR MONSTERS ONLY
Major Magazines: Sept, 1969 - No. 9, Sept, 1969; June, 1972
1 5 10 15 33 57 80
2-9, nn(6/72) 4 8 12 23 37 50

CRACK WESTERN (Formerly Crack Comics; Jonesy No. 85 on)
Quality Comics Group: No. 63, Nov, 1949 - No. 84, May, 1953 (36 pgs., 63-68,74-on)
63(#1)-Ward-c; Two-Gun Lil (origin & 1st app.)(ends #84), Arizona Ames, his horse Thunder
    (with sidekick Spurs & his horse Calico), Frontier Marshal (ends #70), & Dead Canyon
    Days (ends #69) begin; Crandall-a 20 40 60 117 189 260
64,65: 64-Ward-c. Crandall-a in both. 15 30 45 85 130 175

66,68-Photo-c. 66-Arizona Ames becomes A. Raines (ends #84)
    14 28 42 76 108 140
67-Randolph Scott photo-c; Crandall-a 15 30 45 84 127 170
69(52pgs.)-Crandall-a 14 28 42 76 108 140
70(52pgs.)-The Whip (origin & 1st app.) & his horse Diablo begin (ends #84);
    Crandall-a 14 28 42 76 108 140
71(52pgs.)-Frontier Marshal becomes Bob Allen F. Marshal (ends #84);
    Crandall-c/a 14 28 42 82 121 160
72(52pgs.)-Tim Holt photo-c 13 26 39 72 101 130
73(52pgs.)-Photo-c 11 22 33 62 86 110
74-76,78,79,81,83-Crandall-c. 83-Crandall-a(p) 12 24 36 67 94 120
77,80,82 9 18 27 47 61 75
84-Crandall-c/a 13 26 39 72 101 130
NOTE: *Crandall* c-71p, 74-81, 83p(w/Cuidera-i).

CRASH COMICS (Cat-Man Comics No. 6 on)
Tem Publishing Co.: May, 1940 - No. 5, Nov, 1940
1-The Blue Streak, Strongman (origin), The Perfect Human, Shangra begin
    (1st app. of each); Kirby-a 394 788 1182 2758 4829 6900
2-Simon & Kirby-a 239 478 717 1530 2615 3700
3-Simon & Kirby-a 213 426 639 1363 2332 3300
4-Origin & 1st app. The Cat-Man; S&K-a 514 1028 1542 3750 6625 9500
5-1st Cat-Man c & 2nd app.; Simon & Kirby-a 300 600 900 1950 3375 4800
NOTE: Solar Legion by *Kirby* No. 1-5 (5 pgs. each). Strongman c-1-4. Catman c-5.

CRASH DIVE (See Cinema Comics Herald)
CRASH METRO AND THE STAR SQUAD
Oni Press: May, 1999 ($2.95, B&W, one-shot)
1-Allred-s/Ontiveros-a 4.00

CRASH RYAN (Also see Dark Horse Presents #44)
Marvel Comics (Epic): Oct, 1984 - No. 4, Jan, 1985 (Baxter paper, lim. series)
1-4 4.00

CRAVE
Image Comics: Nov, 2023 - No. 6 ($3.99, lim. series)
1-3-Maria Llovet-s/a 4.00

CRAZY (Also see This Magazine is Crazy)
Atlas Comics (CSI): Dec, 1953 - No. 7, July, 1954
1-Everett-c/a 90 180 270 576 988 1400
2 41 82 123 256 428 600
3-7: 4-I Love Lucy satire. 5-Satire on censorship 39 78 117 231 378 525
NOTE: *Ayers* a-5. *Berg* a-1, 2. *Burgos* a-6. *Drucker* a-6. *Everett* a-1-4. *Al Hartley* a-4. *Heath* a-3, 7; c-7. *Maneely* a-1-7, c-3, 4. *Post* a-3-6. Funny monster c-1-4.

CRAZY (Satire)
Marvel Comics Group: Feb, 1973 - No. 3, June, 1973
1-Not Brand Echh-r; Beatles cameo (r) 3 6 9 19 30 40
2,3-Not Brand Echh-r; Kirby-a 2 4 6 13 18 22

CRAZY MAGAZINE (Satire)
Marvel Comics: Oct, 1973 - No. 94, Apr, 1983 (40-90¢, B&W magazine) (#1, 44 pgs; #2-97,
    reg. issues, 52 pgs.; #92-95, 68 pgs)'
1-Wolverton(1 pg.), Bode-a; 3 pg. photo story of Neal Adams & Dick Giordano;
    Harlan Ellison story; TV Kung Fu sty. 12 18 32 57 80
2-"Live & Let Die"; 8pgs; Adams/Buscema-a; McCloud w5 pgs. Adams-a;
    Kurtzman's "Hey Look" 2 pg.-r 3 6 9 18 30 40
3-5: 3-"High Plains Drifter" w/Clint Eastwood c/s; Waltons app; Drucker, Reese-a. 4-Shaft-c/s;
    Ploog-a; Nixon 3 pg. app. Freas-a. 5-Michael Crichton's "Westworld" c/s; Nixon app.
    3 6 9 16 24 32
6,7,18: 6-Exorcist c/s; Nixon app. 7-TV's Kung Fu c/s; Nixon app.; Ploog & Freas-a.
    18-Six Million Dollar Man/Bionic Woman c/s; Welcome Back Kotter story 3 6 9 15 22 28
8-10: 8-Serpico c/s; Casper parody. 10-Playboy Bunny-c; Has 1st 4 covers on-c. 10-Playboy Bunny-c; M. Severin-a; Lee Marrs-a
    begins; "Deathwish" story 3 6 9 14 20 26
11-17,19: 11-Towering Inferno. 12-Rhoda. 13-"Tommy" the Who Rock Opera. 14-Mandingo.
    15-Jaws story. 16-Santa/Xmas-c; "Good Times" TV story; Jaws. 17-Bicentennial issue;
    Baretta; Woody Allen. 19-King Kong; Reagan, J. Carter, Howard the Duck cameos;
    "Laverne & Shirley" 2 4 6 11 16 20
20,24,27: 20-Bicentennial issue; Space 1999 sty; Superheroes song sheet, 4pgs. 24-Charlie's
    Angels. 27-Charlie's Angels/Travolta/Fonz-c; Bionic Woman sty 3 6 9 14 19 24
21-23,25,26,28-30: 21-Starsky & Hutch. 22-Mount Rushmore/J. Carter-c; TV's Barney Miller;
    Superheroes spoof. 23-Santa/Xmas-c; "Happy Days" sty; "Omen" sty. 25-J. Carter story;
    Grandenetti-a begins; TV's Alice; Logan's Run. 26-TV Stars-c; Mary Hartman, King Kong.
    28-Donny & Marie Osmond c/s; Marathon Man. 29-Travolta/Kotter-c; "One Day at a Time",
    3 6 9 14 19 24

	GD	VG	FN	VF	VF/NM	NM-		GD	VG	FN	VF	VF/NM	NM-
	2.0	4.0	6.0	8.0	9.0	9.2		2.0	4.0	6.0	8.0	9.0	9.2

Gong Show. 30-1977, 84 pgs. w/bonus: Jaws, Baretta, King Kong, Happy Days

31,33-35,38,40: 31-"Rocky"-c/s; TV game shows. 33-Peter Benchley's "Deep". 34-J. Carter-c; TV's "Fish". 35-Xmas-c with Fonz/Six Million Dollar Man/Wonder Woman/Darth Vader/Travolta, TV's "Mash" & "Family Matters". 38-Close Encounters of the Third Kind-c/s. 40-"Three's Company-c/s

| | 1 | 3 | 4 | 6 | 8 | 11 |

32-Star Wars/Darth Vader-c/s; "Black Sunday"

| | 3 | 6 | 9 | 15 | 22 | 28 |

36,42,47,49: 36-Farrah Fawcett/Six Million Dollar Man-c; TV's Nancy Drew & Hardy Boys; 1st app. Howard The Duck in Crazy, 2 pgs. 42-84 pgs. w/bonus; TV Hulk/Spider-Man-c; Mash, Gong Show, One Day at a Time, Disco, Alice. 47-Battlestar Galactica xmas-c; movie "Foul Play". 49-1979, 84 pgs. w/bonus; Mork & Mindy-c; Jaws, Saturday Night Fever, Three's Company

| | 2 | 4 | 6 | 9 | 12 | 15 |

37-1978, 84 pgs. w/bonus. Darth Vader-c; Barney Miller, Laverne & Shirley, Good Times, Rocky, Donny & Marie Osmond, Bionic Woman

| | 2 | 4 | 6 | 13 | 18 | 22 |

39,44: 39-Saturday Night Fever-c/s. 44-"Grease"-c w/Travolta/O. Newton-John

| | 2 | 4 | 6 | 11 | 16 | 20 |

41-Kiss-c & 1pg. photos; Disaster movies, TV's "Family", Annie Hall

| | 5 | 10 | 15 | 31 | 53 | 75 |

43,45,46,48,51: 43-Jaws-c; Saturday Night Fever. 43-E.C. swipe from Mad #131. 45-Travolta/O. Newton-John/J. Carter-c; Eight is Enough. 46-TV Hulk-c/s; Punk Rock. 48-"Wiz"-c, Battlestar Galactica-c. 51-Grease/Mork & Mindy/D&M Osmond-c, Mork & Mindy-sty. "Boys from Brazil"

| | 1 | 3 | 4 | 6 | 8 | 11 |

50,58: 50-Superman movie-c/sty, Playboy Mag., TV Hulk, Fonz; Howard the Duck, 1 pg. 58-1980, 84 pgs. w/32 pg. color comic bonus insert-Full reprint of Crazy Comic #1, Battlestar Galactica, Charlie's Angels, Starsky & Hutch

| | 2 | 4 | 6 | 11 | 16 | 20 |

52,59,60,64: 52-1979, 84 pgs. w/bonus. Marlon Brando-c; TV Hulk, Grease. Kiss, 1 pg. photos. 59-Santa Ptd-c by Larkin; "Alien", "Moonraker", Rocky-2, Howard the Duck, 1 pg. 60-Star Trek w/Muppets-c; Star Trek sty. 64-Star Wars. Severin-a. 64-84 pgs. w/bonus Monopoly game satire. "Empire Strikes Back", 8 pgs., One Day at a Time

| | 2 | 4 | 6 | 11 | 16 | 20 |

53,54,65,67-70: 53- "Animal House"-c/sty; TV's "Vegas", Howard the Duck, 1 pg. 54-Love at First Bite-c/sty, Fantasy Island sty, Howard the Duck 1 pg. 65-(Has #66 on-c, Aug/'80). "Black Hole" w/Janson-a; Kirby,Wood/Severin-a/r, 5 pgs. Howard the Duck, 3 pgs.; Broderick-a; Buck Rogers, Mr. Rogers. 67-84 pgs. w/bonus; TV's Kung Fu, Exorcist; Ploog-a(r). 68-American Gigolo, Dukes of Hazzard, Teen Hulk; Howard the Duck, 3 pgs. Broderick-a; Monster sty/5 pg. Ditko-a(r). 69-Obnoxio the Clown-c/sty; Stephen King's "Shining", Teen Hulk, Richie Rich, Howard the Duck, 3pgs; Broderick-a. 70-84 pgs. Towering Inferno, Daytime TV; Trina Robbins-a

| | 1 | 3 | 4 | 6 | 8 | 10 |

55-57,61,63: 55-84 pgs. w/bonus; Love Boat, Mork & Mindy, Fonz, TV Hulk. 56-Mork/Rocky/J. Carter-c; China Syndrome. 57-TV Hulk with Miss Piggy-c, Dracula, Taxi, Muppets. 61-1980, 84 pgs. Adams-a(r), McCloud, Pro wrestling, Casper, TV's Police Story. 63-Apocalypse Now-Coppola's cult movie; 3rd app. Teen Hulk, Howard the Duck, 3 pgs.

| | 2 | 4 | 6 | 8 | 11 | 14 |

62-Kiss-c & 2 pg. app; Quincy, 2nd app. Teen Hulk

| | 4 | 8 | 12 | 28 | 47 | 65 |

66-Sept/'80, Empire Strikes Back-c/sty; Teen Hulk by Severin, Howard the Duck, 3pgs. by Broderick

| | 3 | 6 | 9 | 14 | 20 | 25 |

71,72,75-77,79: 71-Blues Brothers parody, Teen Hulk, Superheroes parody, WKRP in Cincinnati, Howard the Duck, 3pgs. by Broderick. 72-Jackie Gleason/Smokey & the Bandit II-c/sty, Shogun, Teen Hulk. Howard the Duck 3pgs. by Broderick. 75-Flash Gordon movie c/sty; Teen Hulk, Cat in the Hat, Howard the Duck 3pgs. by Broderick. 76-84 pgs. w/bonus; Monster-sty w/ Crandall-a(r), Monster-stys(2) w/Kirby-a(r), 5pgs. ea; Mash, TV Hulk, Chinatown. 77-Popeye movie/R. Williams-c/sty; Teen Hulk, Love Boat, Howard the Duck 3 pgs. 79-84 pgs. w/bonus color stickers; has new material; "9 to 5" w/Dolly Parton, Teen Hulk, Magnum P.I., Monster-sty w/5pgs, Ditko-a(r), "Rat" w/Sutton-a(r), Everett-a, 4 pgs.(r)

| | 1 | 3 | 4 | 6 | 8 | 10 |

73,74,78,80: 73-84 pgs. w/bonus Hulk/Spiderman Finger Puppets-c & sty; "Live & Let Die, Jaws, Fantasy Island. 74-Dallas/"Who Shot J.R."-c/sty; Elephant Man, Howard the Duck 3pgs. by Broderick. 78-Clint Eastwood-c/sty; Teen Hulk, Superheroes parody, Lou Grant. 80-Star Wars, 2 pg. app; "Howling", TV's "Greatest American Hero"

| | 2 | 4 | 6 | 8 | 11 | 14 |

81,84,86,87,89: 81-.Superman Movie II-c/sty; Wolverine cameo, Mash, Teen Hulk. 84-American Werewolf in London, Johnny Carson app; Teen Hulk. 86-Time Bandits-c/sty; Private Benjamin. 87-Rubix Cube-c; Hill Street Blues, "Ragtime", Origin Obnoxio the Clown; Teen Hulk. 89-Burt Reynolds "Sharkey's Machine", Teen Hulk

| | 2 | 4 | 6 | 8 | 11 | 14 |

82-X-Men-c w/new Byrne-a, 84 pgs. w/new material; Fantasy Island, Teen Hulk, "For Your Eyes Only", Spiderman/Human Torch-r by Kirby/Ditko; Sutton-a(r); Rogers-a(r); Hunchback of Notre Dame, 5 pgs.

| | 3 | 6 | 9 | 14 | 19 | 24 |

83-Raiders of the Lost Ark-c/sty; Hart to Hart; Reese-a; Teen Hulk

| | 2 | 4 | 6 | 9 | 13 | 16 |

85,88: 85-84 pgs; Escape from New York, Teen Hulk; Kirby-a(r), 5 pgs, Poseidon Adventure, Flintstones, Sesame Street. 88-84 pgs. w/bonus Dr. Strange Game; some new material; Jeffersons, X-Men/Wolverine, 10 pgs.; Byrne-a; Apocalypse Now, Teen Hulk

| | 2 | 4 | 6 | 8 | 11 | 14 |

90-94: 90-Conan-c/sty; M. Severin-a; Teen Hulk. 91-84 pgs. some new material; Bladerunner-c/sty, "Deathwish-II, Teen Hulk, Black Knight, 10 pgs.-'50s-r w/Maneely-a. 92-Wrath of Khan Star Trek-c/sty; Joanie & Chachi, Teen Hulk. 93-"E.T."-c/sty, Teen Hulk, Archie Bunkers Place, Dr. Doom Game. 94-Poltergeist, Smurfs, Teen Hulk, Casper, Avengers parody-8pgs. Adams-a

| | 2 | 4 | 6 | 9 | 13 | 18 |

Crazy Summer Special #1 (Sum, '75, 100 pgs.)-Nixon, TV Kung Fu, Babe Ruth, Joe Namath, Waltons, McCloud, Chariots of the Gods

| | 3 | 6 | 9 | 14 | 20 | 26 |

NOTE: **N. Adams** a-2, 61r, 94p. **Austin** a-82i. **Buscema** a, 82. **Byrne** c-82p. **Nick Cardy** c-7, 8, 10, 12-16, Super Special 1. **Crandall** a-76r. **Ditko** a-68r, 79r, 82r. **Drucker** a-93. **Eisner** a-9-16. **Kelly Freas** c-1-6, 9, 11; a-7. **Kirby/Wood** a-66r. **Ploog** a-1, 4, 7, 67r, 73r. **Rogers** a-82. **Sparling** a-92. **Wood** a-65r. Howard the Duck in 36, 50, 51, 53, 54, 59, 63, 65, 68-78, 81, 84, 91, 72, 74, 75, 77, Teen Hulk in 46, c-42, 46, 57, 73. Star Wars in 32, 66r; c-37.

CRAZY (Homage to the humor magazine)
Marvel Comics: Dec, 2019 ($4.99, one-shot)

1-Short stories by various incl. Duggan, Macchio, Koblish, Simpson, Bill Morrison 5.00

CRAZYMAN
Continuity Comics: Apr, 1992 - No. 3, 1992 ($2.50, high quality paper)

1-($3.95, 52 pgs.)-Embossed-c; N. Adams part-i 5.00
2,3 ($2.50)- 2- N. Adams/Bolland-c 4.00

CRAZYMAN
Continuity Comics: V2#1, 5/93 - No. 4, 1/94 ($2.50, high quality paper)

V2#1-4: 1-Entire book is die-cut. 2-(12/93)-Adams-c(p) & part scripts. 3-(12/93).

4-Indicia says #3, Jan. 1993 | 4.00

CRAZY, MAN, CRAZY (Magazine) (Becomes This Magazine is...?) (Formerly From Here to Insanity)
Humor Magazines (Charlton): V2#1, Dec, 1955 - V2#2, June, 1956

V2#1,V2#2-Satire; Wolverton-a, 3 pgs. | 22 | 44 | 66 | 132 | 216 | 300

CREATOR-OWNED HEROES
Image Comics: Jun, 2012 - No. 8, Jan, 2013 ($3.99)

1-8-Anthology of short stories by various and creator interviews 4.00

CREATURE, THE (See Movie Classics)

CREATURE COMMANDOS (See Weird War Tales #93 for 1st app.)
DC Comics: May, 2000 - No. 8, Dec, 2000 ($2.50, limited series)

1-8: Truman-s/Eaton-a 3.00

CREATURES OF THE ID
Caliber Press: 1990 ($2.95, B&W)

1-Frank Einstein (Madman) app.; Allred-a | 10 | 20 | 30 | 64 | 132 | 200

CREATURES OF THE NIGHT
Dark Horse Books: Nov, 2004 ($12.95, hardcover graphic novel)

HC-Neil Gaiman-s/Michael Zulli-a/c 13.00

CREATURES ON THE LOOSE (Formerly Tower of Shadows No. 1-9)(See Kull)
Marvel Comics: No. 10, March, 1971 - No. 37, Sept, 1975 (New-a & reprints)

10-(15¢)-1st full app. King Kull; see Kull the Conqueror; Wrightson-a
| | 8 | 16 | 24 | 56 | 108 | 160
11-Classic story about an underground comic artist going to Hell
| | 4 | 8 | 12 | 27 | 44 | 60
12-15: 13-Last 15¢ issue | 4 | 8 | 12 | 23 | 37 | 50
16-Origin Warrior of Mars (begins, ends #21) | 3 | 6 | 9 | 15 | 22 | 28
17-20 | 2 | 4 | 6 | 9 | 13 | 16
21-Steranko-c | 3 | 6 | 9 | 17 | 26 | 35
22-Steranko-c; Thongor stories begin | 3 | 6 | 9 | 18 | 28 | 38
23-29-Thongor-c/stories | 1 | 3 | 4 | 6 | 8 | 10
30-Manwolf begins | 3 | 6 | 9 | 21 | 33 | 45
31-33 | 2 | 4 | 6 | 9 | 13 | 16
34-37 | 2 | 4 | 6 | 8 | 10 | 12

NOTE: **Crandall** a-13. **Ditko** r-15, 17, 18, 20, 22, 24, 27, 28. **Everett** a-16i(new). **Matt Fox** r-21i. **Howard** a-26i. **Gil Kane** a-16p, 17p, 19i; c-16, 17, 19, 20, 25, 29, 33p, 35p, 36p. **Kirby** a-10-15r, 16(2)r, 17r, 19r. **Morrow** a-20, 21. **Perez** a-33-37; c-34p. **Shores** a-11. **innott** r-21. **Sutton** c-10. **Tuska** a-30-32p.

CREECH, THE
Image Comics: Oct, 1997 - No. 3, Dec, 1997 ($1.95/$2.50, limited series)

1-3: 1-Capullo-s/c/a(p) 4.00
TPB (1999, $9.95) r/#1-3, McFarlane intro. 10.00
Out for Blood 1-3 (7/01 - No. 3, 11/01; $4.95) Capullo-s/c/a 5.00

CREED
Hall of Heroes Comics: Dec, 1994 - No. 2, Jan, 1995 ($2.50, B&W)

1-Trent Kaniuga-s/a | 4 | 8 | 12 | 23 | 37 | 50
2 | 2 | 4 | 6 | 11 | 16 | 20

CREED
Lightning Comics: June, 1995 - No. 3 ($2.75/$3.00, B&W/color)

1-($2.75) 4.00
1-($3.00, color) 5.00
1-($9.95)-Commemorative Edition 10.00
1-TwinVariant Edition (1250? print run) 10.00
1-Special Edition; polybagged w/certificate 4.00
1 Gold Collectors Edition; polybagged w/certificate 10.00
2,3-($3.00, color)-Butt Naked Edition & regular-c 3.00
3-($9.95)-Commemorative Edition; polybagged w/certificate & card 10.00

CREED: CRANIAL DISORDER
Lightning Comics: Oct, 1996 ($3.00, limited series)

1-3-Two covers 4.00
1-($5.95)-Platinum Edition 10.00
2,3-($9.95) Ltd. Edition 10.00

CREED/TEENAGE MUTANT NINJA TURTLES
Lightning Comics: May, 1996 ($3.00, one-shot)

1-Kaniuga-a(p)/scripts; Laird-c; variant-c exists 6.00
1-($9.95)-Platinum Edition 12.00
1-Special Edition; polybagged w/certificate 6.00

CREED: THE NEXT ROUND
BOOM! Studios: Jun, 2023 - No. 4, Sept, 2023 ($4.99, limited series)

1-4-Adonis Creed and his daughter Amara 5.00

CREEP, THE
Dark Horse Books: No. 0, Aug, 2012 - No. 4, Dec, 2012 ($2.99/$3.50)

0-Frank Miller-c; Arcudi-s/Case-a 4.00
1-4-($3.50): 1-Mignola-c. 2-Sook-c 4.00

CREEPER BY STEVE DITKO, THE
DC Comics: 2010 ($39.99, hardcover with dustjacket)

HC-Reprints Showcase #73, Beware the Creeper #1-6, First Issue Special #7 and apps. in World's Finest #249-255 and Cancelled Comic Cavalcade #2; intro. by Steve Niles 40.00

CREEPER, THE (See Beware... , Showcase #73 & 1st Issue Special #7)
DC Comics: Dec, 1997 - No. 11; #1,000,000 Nov, 1998 ($2.50)

1-11-Kaminski-s/Martinbrough-a(p). 7,8-Joker-c/app. 4.00
#1,000,000 (11/98) 853rd Century x-over 4.00

CREEPER, THE (See DCU Brave New World)
DC Comics: Oct, 2006 - No. 6, Mar, 2007 ($2.99, limited series)

1-6-Niles-s/Justiniano-a/c; Jack Ryder becomes the Creeper. 2-6-Batman app. 3.00
... - Welcome to Creepsville TPB ('07, $19.99) r/#1-6 & story from DCU Brave New World 20.00

CREEPS
Image Comics: Oct, 2001 - No. 4, May, 2002 ($2.95)

The Creeper by Steve Ditko HC © DC

Creepy (2013 series) #11 © New Comic Co.

Crime and Punishment #19 © LEV

	GD 2.0	VG 4.0	FN 6.0	VF 8.0	VF/NM 9.0	NM- 9.2

1-4-Mandrake-a/Mishkin-s   3.00

CREEPSHOW
Plume/New American Library Pub.: July, 1982 (softcover graphic novel)
1st edition-nn-(68 pgs.) Kamen-c/Wrightson-a; screenplay by Stephen King for
the George Romero movie   10   20   30   66   138   210
2nd-7th printings   3   6   9   17   26   35

CREEPSHOW
Image Comics (Skybound): Sept, 2022 - No. 5, Jan, 2023 ($3.99)
1-5-Horror anthology. 2-Lapham-s/a. 3-Francavilla-a   4.00

CREEPSHOW VOLUME 2
Image Comics (Skybound): Sept, 2023 - No. 5, Jan, 2023 ($3.99)
1-5-Horror anthology. 1-Ennis-s/Cloonan-a. Hester-s/a. 2-Walsh-s/a   4.00
...: Holiday Special 2023 1 (12/23, $3.99) Christmas-themed horror   4.00
....: Joe Hill & Jason Ciaramella-s/Walsh-a   5.00

CREEPY (See Warren Presents)
Warren Publishing Co./Harris Publ. #146: 1964 - No. 145, Feb, 1983; No. 146, 1985 (B&W, magazine)

1-Frazetta-a (his last story in comics?); Jack Davis-c; 1st Warren all comics magazine:
  1st app. Uncle Creepy   18   36   54   128   284   440
2-Frazetta-c & 1 pg. strip   15   30   45   100   220   340
3-8,11-13,15-17: 3-7,9-11,15-17-Frazetta-c. 7-Frazetta 1 pg. strip.
  15,16-Adams-a. 16-Jeff Jones-a   6   12   18   38   69   100
9-Creepy fan club sketch by Wrightson (1st published-a); has 1/2 pg. anti-smoking strip by
  Frazetta; Frazetta-c; 1st Wood and Ditko art on this title; Toth-a (low print)
    9   18   27   61   123   185
10-Brunner fan club sketch (1st published work)   8   16   24   52   99   145
14-Neal Adams 1st Warren work   8   16   24   54   102   150
18-28,30,31: 27-Frazetta-c   5   10   15   33   57   80
29,34: 29-Jones-a   5   10   15   33   57   80
32-(scarce) Frazetta-c; Harlan Ellison sty   9   18   27   63   129   195
33,35,37,39,40,42-47,49: 35-Hitler/Nazi-s. 39-1st Uncle Creepy solo-s; Cousin Eerie app.;
  early Brunner-a. 42-1st San Julian-a. 44-1st Ploog-a. 46-Corben-a
    4   8   12   27   44   60
36-(11/70)1st Corben art at Warren   5   10   15   33   57   75
38,41-(scarce): 38-1st Kelly-a. 41-Corben-a   5   10   15   35   63   90
48,55,65-(1972, 1973, 1974 Annuals) #55 & 65 contain an 8 pg. slick comic insert.
  48-(84 pgs.). 55-Color poster bonus (1/2 price if missing). 65-(100 pgs.)
  Summer Giant   5   10   15   31   53   75
50-Vampirella/Eerie/Creepy-c   6   12   18   42   79   115
51,54,56-61,64: All contain an 8 pg. slick comic insert in middle. 59-Xmas horror.
  54,64-Chaykin-a   4   8   12   28   47   65
52,53,66,71,72,75,76,78-80: 71-All Bermejo-a; Space & Time issue. 72-Gual-a. 78-Fantasy
  issue. 79,80-Monsters issue   3   6   9   21   33   45
62,63-1st & 2nd full Wrightson story art; Corben-a; 8 pg. color comic insert
    4   8   12   28   47   65
67,73   4   8   12   23   37   50
68-"Twas the Night Before Christmas"   5   10   15   31   53   75
69,70-Edgar Allan Poe issues; Corben-a   4   8   12   25   40   55
74,77: 74-All Crandell-a. 77-Xmas Horror issue; Corben-a,Wrightson-a
    5   10   15   25   40   55
81,84,85,88-90,92-94,96-99,102,104-112,114-118,120,122-130: 84,93-Sports issue.
  85,97,102-Monster issue. 89-All war issue; Nino-a. 94-Weird Children issue. 96,109-Aliens
  issue. 99-Disasters. 103-Corben-a. 104-Robots issue. 106-Sword & Sorcery.107-Sci-fi.
  116-End of Man. 125-Xmas Horror   2   4   6   11   16   20
82,100,101: 82-All Maroto issue. 100-(8/78) Anniversary. 101-Corben-a
    3   6   9   16   23   30
83,95-Wrightson-a. 83-Corben-a. 95-Gorilla/Apes.   3   6   9   14   20   25
86,87,91,103-Wrightson-a. 86-Xmas Horror   3   6   9   14   20   25
113-All Wrightson-r issue   3   6   9   19   30   40
119,121: 119-All Nino issue.121-All Severin-r issue   3   6   9   14   20   25
131,133-136,138,140: 135-Xmas issue   3   6   9   14   20   25
137,139: 132-Corben. 137-All Williamson-r issue. 139-All Toth-r issue
    3   6   9   16   23   30
141,143,144 (low dist.): 144-Giant, $2.25; Frazetta-c   3   6   9   18   28   38
142,145 (low dist.): 142-(10/82, 100 pgs.) All Torres issue. 145-(2/83) last Warren issue
    3   6   9   21   33   45
146 ($2.95)-1st from Harris; resurrection issue   7   14   21   48   89   130
Year Book '68-'70: '70-Neal Adams, Ditko-a(r)   5   10   15   34   60   85
Annual 1971,1972   5   10   15   33   57   70
1993 Fearbook ($3.95)-Harris Publ.; Brereton-c; Vampirella by Busiek-s/Art Adams-a;
  David-s; Paquette-a   35
....The Classic Years TPB (Harris/Dark Horse, '91, $12.95) Kaluta-r; art by Frazetta,Torres,

---

Crandall, Ditko, Morrow, Williamson, Wrightson   25.00
NOTE: *All issues contain many good artists works:* **Neal Adams, Brunner, Corben, Craig (Taycee), Crandall, Ditko, Evans, Frazetta, Heath, Jeff Jones, Krenkel, McWilliams, Morrow, Nino, Orlando, Ploog, Severin, Torres, Toth, Williamson, Wood, & Wrightson**; covers by **Crandall, Davis, Frazetta, Morrow, San Julian, Todd/Bode**; *Otto Binder's "Adam Link" stories in No. 2, 4, 6, 8, 9, 12, 13, 15 with Orlando art. Frazetta c-2-7, 9-11, 15-17, 27, 32, 83r, 89r, 91r.* **E.A. Poe** *adaptations in No. 69, 70.*

CREEPY (Mini-series)
Harris Comics/Dark Horse: 1992 - Book 4, 1992 (48 pgs, B&W, squarebound)
Book 1-4: Brereton painted-c on all. Stories and art by various incl. David (all), Busiek(2),
  Infantino(2), Guice(3), Colan(1)   2   4   6   8   10   12

CREEPY
Dark Horse Comics: July, 2009 - No. 24, Jun, 2016 ($4.99/$3.99, 48 pgs, B&W, quarterly)
1-13: 1-Powell-c; art by Wrightson, Toth, Alexander. 8,12-Corben-a   5.00
14-24-($3.99) 18-Nguyen-c. 20,23,24-Corben-a   4.00

CREEPY THINGS
Charlton Comics: July, 1975 - No. 6, June, 1976
1-Sutton-c/a   3   6   9   16   24   32
2-6: Ditko-a in 3,5. Sutton c-3,4. 6-Zeck-c   2   4   6   9   12   15
Modern Comics Reprint 2-6(1977)   5.00
NOTE: *Larson a-2,6. Sutton a-1,2,4,6. Zeck a-2.*

CREW, THE
Marvel Comics: July, 2003 - No. 7, Jan, 2004 ($2.50)
1-7-Priest-s/Bennett-a; James Rhodes (War Machine) app.   3.00

CRIME AND JUSTICE (Badge Of Justice #22 on; Rookie Cop No. 27 on)
Capitol Stories/Charlton Comics: March, 1951 - No. 21, Nov, 1954; No. 23, Mar, 1955 - No. 26, Sept, 1955 (No #22)
1   52   104   156   328   552   775
2   27   54   81   158   259   360
3-8,10-13: 6-Negligee panels   22   44   66   132   216   300
9-Classic story "Comics Vs. Crime"   41   82   123   256   428   600
14-Color illos in POP; story of murderer who beheads women
    36   72   108   211   343   475
15-17,19-21,23,24: 15-Negligee panels. 23-Rookie Cop (1st app.)
    30   60   90   86   133   180
18-Ditko-a   37   74   111   222   361   500
25,26: (scarce)   23   46   69   136   223   310
NOTE: *Alascia c-20. Ayers a-17. Shuster a-19-21; c-19. Bondage c-11, 12.*

CRIME AND PUNISHMENT (Title inspired by 1935 film)
Lev Gleason Publications: April, 1948 - No. 74, Aug, 1955
1-Mr. Crime app. on-c   52   104   156   328   552   775
2-Narrator, Officer Common Sense (a ghost) begins, ends #27? (see Crime Does
  Not Pay #41)   27   54   81   158   259   360
3-(6/48)-Used in SOTI, pg. 112; contains Biro & Gleason self
  censorship code of 12 listed restrictions   29   58   87   172   281   390
4,5   20   40   60   114   182   250
6-10   15   30   45   88   137   185
11-20   14   28   42   82   121   160
21-30   13   26   39   74   105   135
31-38,40-44,46: 46-One pg. Frazetta-a   12   24   36   67   94   120
39-Drug mention story "The Five Dopes"   20   40   60   117   189   260
45- "Hophead Killer" drug story   20   40   60   117   189   260
47-53,55,57,60-65,70-74:   11   22   33   62   86   110
54-Electric Chair-c   14   28   42   80   115   150
56-Classic dagger/torture-c   43   86   129   271   461   650
58-Used in POP, pg. 79   15   30   45   83   124   165
59-Used in SOTI, illo "What comic-book America stands for"
    42   84   126   265   445   625
66-Toth-c/a(4); 3-D effect issue (3/54); 1st "Deep Dimension" process
    47   94   141   296   498   700
67- "Monkey on His Back" heroin story; 3-D effect issue
    41   82   123   256   428   600
68-3-D effect issue; Toth-c (7/54)   39   78   117   231   378   525
69- "The Hot Rod Gang" dope crazy kids   19   38   57   111   176   240
NOTE: *Belfi a- 2, 3, 5. Biro c-most. Al Borth a-9, 35. Cooper a-9. Joe Certa a-8. Tony Diprata a-3, 5, 15, 34. Everett a-31. Bob Fujitani (Fuje) a-20, 26, 27. Joseph Gaguardi a-5, 18, 20. Fred Gardineer a-5, 12, 14, 15, 17, 18, 20, 26-28, 32, 34, 35, 38-44, 51, 54. Jack Keller a-18. Kinstler c-69. Martinott a-13. Al McWilliams a-36, 41, 48, 49. William Overgard a-36. Dick Rockwell a-35, 51. Robert Q. Sale a-43. George Tuska a-28, 30, 51, 64, 70. Painted c-31.*

CRIME AND PUNISHMENT: MARSHALL LAW TAKES MANHATTAN
Marvel Comics (Epic Comics): 1989 ($4.95, 52 pgs., direct sales only, mature)
nn-Graphic album featuring Marshall Law   5.00

CRIME BIBLE: THE FIVE LESSONS (Aftermath of DC's 52 series)

	GD	VG	FN	VF	VF/NM	NM-		GD	VG	FN	VF	VF/NM	NM-
	2.0	4.0	6.0	8.0	9.0	9.2		2.0	4.0	6.0	8.0	9.0	9.2

DC Comics: Dec, 2007 - No. 5, Apr, 2008 ($2.99, limited series)

	GD	VG	FN	VF	VF/NM	NM-
1-5-Rucka-s; The Question (Renee Montoya) app. 3-Batwoman app.						3.00
The Question: The Five Books of Blood HC (2008, $19.99) r/#1-5						20.00
The Question: The Five Books of Blood SC (2009, $14.99) r/#1-5						15.00

CRIME CAN'T WIN (Formerly Cindy Smith)
Marvel/Atlas Comics (TCI 41/CCC 42,43,4-12): No. 41, 9/50 - No. 43, 2/51; No. 4, 4/51 - No. 12, 9/53

	GD	VG	FN	VF	VF/NM	NM-
41(#1)-"The Girl Who Planned Her Own Murder"	39	78	117	231	378	525
42(#2)	23	46	69	136	223	310
43(#3)-Horror story	33	66	99	194	317	440
4(4/51),5-12: 10-Possible use in SOTI, pg. 161	19	38	57	112	179	240

NOTE: *Robinson* a-9-11. *Tuska* a-43.

CRIME CASES COMICS (Formerly Willie Comics)
Marvel/Atlas Comics(CnPC No.24-8/MJMC No.9-12): No. 24, 8/50 - No. 27, 3/51; No. 5, 5/51 - No. 12, 7/52

	GD	VG	FN	VF	VF/NM	NM-
24 (#1, 52 pgs.)-True police cases	30	60	90	177	289	400
25-27(#2)- 27-Maneely & Morisi-a	23	46	69	136	223	310
5-12: 11-Robinson-a. 12-Tuska-a	20	40	60	114	182	250

CRIME CLINIC
Ziff-Davis Publishing Co.: No. 10, July-Aug, 1951 - No. 5, Summer, 1952

	GD	VG	FN	VF	VF/NM	NM-
10(#1)-Painted-c; origin Dr. Tom Rogers	48	96	144	302	514	725
11(#2),4,5: 4,5-Painted-c	36	72	108	214	347	480
3-Used in SOTI, pg. 18	41	82	123	256	428	600

NOTE: All have painted covers by *Saunders. Starr* a-10.

CRIME CLINIC
Slave Labor Graphics: May, 1995 - No. 2, Oct, 1995 ($2.95, B&W, limited series)

	GD	VG	FN	VF	VF/NM	NM-
1,2						4.00

CRIME DETECTIVE COMICS
Hillman Periodicals: Mar-Apr, 1948 - V3#8, May-June, 1953

	GD	VG	FN	VF	VF/NM	NM-
V1#1-The Invisible 6, costumed villains app; Fuje-c/a, 15 pgs.						
	53	106	159	334	567	800
2,5: 5-Krigstein-a	26	52	78	154	252	350
3,4,6,7,10-12: 6-McWilliams-a	21	42	63	122	199	275
8-Kirbyish-a by McCann	21	42	63	122	199	275
9-Used in SOTI, pg. 16 & "Caricature of the author in a position comic book publishers wish he were in permanently" illo.	55	110	165	352	601	850
V2#1,4,7-Krigstein-a: 1-Tuska-a	18	36	54	107	169	230
2,3,5,6,8-12 (1-2/52)	17	34	51	98	154	210
V3#1-Drug use-c	18	36	54	105	165	225
2-8	15	30	45	85	130	175

NOTE: *Briefer* a-11, V3#1. *Kinstlerish*-a by McCann-V2#7, V3#2. *Powell* a-10, 11. *Starr* a-10.

CRIME DETECTOR
Timor Publications: Jan, 1954 - No. 5, Sept, 1954

	GD	VG	FN	VF	VF/NM	NM-
1	39	78	117	231	378	525
2-Headlights-c	58	116	174	371	636	900
3,4	18	36	54	105	165	225
5-Disbrow-a (classic)	34	68	102	199	325	450

CRIME DOES NOT PAY (Formerly Silver Streak Comics No. 1-21)
Comic House/Lev Gleason/Golfing: No. 22, June, 1942 - No. 147, July, 1955 (1st crime comic)(Title inspired by film)

	GD	VG	FN	VF	VF/NM	NM-
22 (23 on cover, 22 on indicia)-Origin The War Eagle & only app.; Chip Gardner begins; #22 was rebound in Complete Book of True Crime (Scarce)						
	838	1676	2514	6117	10,809	15,500
23-(9/42) (Scarce)	326	652	978	2282	3991	5700
24-(11/42) Intro. & 1st app. Mr. Crime; classic Biro-c showing woman's head on fire being pushed onto hot stovetop burner	2400	4800	7200	12,000	21,000	30,000
25-(1/43) 2nd app. Mr. Crime; classic '40s crime-c	161	322	483	1030	1765	2500
26-(3/43) 3rd app. Mr. Crime	135	270	405	864	1482	2100
27-Classic Biro-c pushing man into hot oven	161	322	483	1030	1765	2500
28-30: 30-Wood and Biro app.	93	186	279	591	1021	1450
31,32,34-40	53	106	159	334	567	800
33-(5/44) Classic Biro hanging & hatchet-c	486	972	1458	3550	6275	9000
41-(9/44) Origin 1st app. Officer Common Sense	50	100	150	315	533	750
42-(11/45) Classic electrocution-c	129	258	387	826	1413	2000
43-46,48-50: 44-50 are 68 pg. issues. 44-"Legs" Diamond story. 50-3/(47)-1st issue to advertise 5 million readers on front-c. 58-(12/47)-shows 6 million readers (these ads believed to have influenced the crime comic wave of 1948)						
	36	72	108	211	343	475
47-(9/46)-Electric chair-c	65	130	195	416	708	1000
51-70: 58(12/47)-Thomas Dun, killer of thousands (1565) story. 63,64-Possible use in SOTI, pg. 306. 63-Contains Biro & Gleason self censorship code of 12 listed restrictions (5/48)	27	54	81	158	259	360
71-99: 87-Chip Gardner begins, ends #100. 87-99-Painted-c						
	20	40	60	120	195	270
100-Painted-c	21	42	63	126	206	285
101-104,107-110: 101,102-Painted-c. 102-Chip Gardner app.						
	16	32	48	92	144	195
105-Used in POP, pg. 84	20	40	60	114	182	250
106,114-Frazetta-a, 1 pg.	17	34	51	100	158	215
111-Used in POP, pgs. 80 & 81; injury-to-eye sty illo	21	42	63	122	199	275
112,113,115-130	14	28	42	81	118	155
131-140	14	28	42	76	108	140
141,142-Last pre-code issue; Kubert-a	14	28	42	82	121	160
143-Kubert-a in one story	14	28	42	82	121	160
144-146	14	28	42	76	108	140
147-Last issue (scarce); Kubert-a	20	40	60	117	189	260
1-(Golfing-1945)	13	26	39	72	101	130
The Best of...(1944, 128 pgs.)-Series contains 4 rebound issues						
	148	296	444	947	1624	2300
...1945 issue	97	194	291	621	1061	1500
...1946-48 issues	71	142	213	454	777	1100
...1949-50 issues	57	114	171	362	619	875

...1951-53 issues (25¢)

	GD	VG	FN	VF	VF/NM	NM-
	53	106	159	334	567	800

NOTE: Many issues contain violent covers and stories. Who Dunit by *Guardineer*-39-42, 44-105, 108-110; Chip Gardner by *Bob Fujitani (Fuge)*-88-103. *Alderman* a-29, 41-44, 49. *Dan Barry* a-67, 75. *Charles Biro* c-1-76, 122, 142. *Dick Briefer* a-29(2), 30, 31, 33, 37, 39. *G. Colan* a-105. *Tony Dipreta* a-79, 90, 92. *Fuje* c-88, 89, 91-94, 96, 98, 99, 102, 103. *Fred Guardineer* a-51, 57, 58(2), 66-68, 71, 74, 79, 81, 90, 92. *Joe Kubert* c-143. *Landau* a-118. *Al Mandell* a-37. *Norman Maurer* a-29. *McWilliams* a-91, 93, 95, 100-103. *Rudy Palais* a-30, 33. *Bob Powell* a-146, 147. *George Tuska* a-48-50(2ea.), 51, 52 56, 57(2), 58, 60-64, 66-68, 71, 74, 81. *Painted c*-87-103. Bondage c-43, 62, 98.

CRIME EXPOSED
Marvel Comics (PPI)/Marvel Atlas Comics (PrPI): June, 1948; Dec, 1950 - No. 14, June, 1952

	GD	VG	FN	VF	VF/NM	NM-
1(6/48)	53	106	159	334	567	800
1(12/50)	37	74	111	222	361	500
2	21	42	63	122	199	275
3-9,11,14	18	36	54	105	165	225
10-Used in POP, pg. 81	21	42	63	124	202	280
12-Krigstein & Robinson-a	20	40	60	117	189	260
13-Used in POP, pg. 81; Krigstein-a	21	42	63	124	202	280

NOTE: *Keller* a-8, 10. *Maneely* c-8. *Robinson* a-11, 12. *Sale* a-4. *Tuska* a-3, 4.

CRIMEFIGHTERS
Marvel Comics (CmPS 1-3/CCC 4-10): Apr, 1948 - No. 10, Nov, 1949

	GD	VG	FN	VF	VF/NM	NM-
1-Some copies are undated & could be reprints	40	80	120	246	411	575
2,3: 3-Morphine addict story	21	42	63	126	206	285
4-10: 4-Early John Buscema-a. 6-Anti-Wertham editorial. 9,10-Photo-c						
	18	36	54	107	169	230

CRIME FIGHTERS (...Always Win)
Atlas Comics (CnPC): No. 11, Sept, 1954 - No. 13, Jan, 1955

	GD	VG	FN	VF	VF/NM	NM-
11-13: 11-Maneely-a,13-Pakula, Reinman, Severin-a						
	19	38	57	109	172	235

CRIME-FIGHTING DETECTIVE (Shock Detective Cases No. 20 on; formerly Criminals on the Run)
Star Publications: No. 11, Apr-May, 1950 - No. 19, June, 1952 (Based on true crime cases)

	GD	VG	FN	VF	VF/NM	NM-
11-L. B. Cole-c/a (2 pgs.); L. B. Cole-c on all	41	82	123	256	428	600
12,13,15-19: 17-Young King Cole & Dr. Doom app.	22	44	66	132	216	300
14-L. B. Cole-c/a, r/Law-Crime #2	26	52	78	154	252	350

CRIME FILES
Standard Comics: No. 5, Sept, 1952 - No. 6, Nov, 1952

	GD	VG	FN	VF	VF/NM	NM-
5-1pg. Alex Toth-a; used in SOTI, pg. 4 (text)	39	78	117	240	395	550
6-Sekowsky-a	20	40	60	114	182	250

CRIME ILLUSTRATED (Magazine)
E. C. Comics: Nov-Dec, 1955 - No. 2, Spring, 1956 (25¢, Adult Suspense Stories on-c)

	GD	VG	FN	VF	VF/NM	NM-
1-Ingels & Crandall-a	39	78	117	231	378	525
2-Ingels & Crandall-a	21	42	63	122	199	275

NOTE: *Craig* a-2. *Crandall* a-1, 2; c-2. *Evans* a-1. *Davis* a-1. *Ingels* a-1, 2. *Krigstein/Crandall* a-1. *Orlando* a-1, 2; c-1.

CRIME INCORPORATED (Formerly Crimes Incorporated)
Fox Feature Syndicate: No. 2, Aug, 1950 - No. 3, Aug, 1951

	GD	VG	FN	VF	VF/NM	NM-
2	37	74	111	222	361	500
3(1951)-Hollingsworth-a	24	48	72	142	234	325

CRIME MACHINE (Magazine reprints pre-code crime and gangster comics)
Skywald Publications: Feb, 1971 - No. 2, May, 1971 (B&W, 68 pgs., roundbound)

	GD	VG	FN	VF	VF/NM	NM-
1-Kubert-a(2)(r)(Avon); bikini girl in cake-c	6	12	18	42	79	115
2-Torres, Wildey-a; violent-c/a	4	8	12	28	47	65

CRIME MUST LOSE! (Formerly Sports Action?)
Sports Action (Atlas Comics): No. 4, Oct, 1950 - No. 12, April, 1952

	GD	VG	FN	VF	VF/NM	NM-
4-Ann Brewster-a in all; c-used in N.Y. Legis. Comm. documents						
	34	68	102	199	325	450
5-10,12: 9-Robinson-a	20	40	60	120	195	270
11-Used in POP, pg. 89	21	42	63	124	202	280

CRIME MUST PAY THE PENALTY (Formerly Four Favorites; Penalty #47, 48)
Ace Magazines (Current Books): No. 33, Feb, 1948; No. 2, Jun, 1948 - No. 48, Jan, 1956

	GD	VG	FN	VF	VF/NM	NM-
33(#1, 2/48)-Becomes Four Teeners #34?	65	130	195	416	708	1000
2(6/48)-Extreme violence; Palais-a	45	90	135	284	480	675
3,4,8: 3- "Frisco Mary" story used in Senate Investigation report, pg. 7. 4,8-Transvestism stories	26	52	78	154	252	350
5-7,9,10	20	40	60	115	185	255
11-19	19	38	57	109	172	235
20-Drug story "Dealers in White Death"	30	60	90	177	289	400
21-32,34-40,42-48: 44-Last pre-code	15	30	45	86	133	180
33(7/53)- "Dell Fabry-Junk King" drug story; mentioned in Love and Death						
	22	44	66	132	216	300
41-reprints "Dealers in White Death"	15	30	45	90	140	190

NOTE: *Cameron* a-29-31, 34, 35, 39-41. *Colan* a-20, 31. *Kremer* a-3, 37; *Larsen* a-32. *Palais* a-5?,37.

CRIME MUST STOP
Hillman Periodicals: October, 1952 (52 pgs.)

	GD	VG	FN	VF	VF/NM	NM-
V1#1(Scarce)-Similar to Monster Crime; Mort Lawrence, Krigstein-a						
	161	322	483	1030	1765	2500

CRIME MYSTERIES (Secret Mysteries #16 on; combined with Crime Smashers #7 on)
Ribage Publ. Corp. (Trojan Magazines): May, 1952 - No. 15, Sept, 1954

	GD	VG	FN	VF	VF/NM	NM-
1-Transvestite story; crime & terror stories begin	295	590	885	1888	3244	4600
2-Marijuana story (7/52)	226	452	678	1435	2468	3500
3-One pg. Frazetta-a	103	206	309	659	1130	1600
4-Cover shows girl in bondage having her blood drained; 1 pg. Frazetta-a						
	432	864	1296	3154	5577	8000
5-10	61	122	183	390	670	950
11,12,14	55	108	162	343	574	825
13-(5/54)-Angelo Torres 1st comic work (inks over Check's pencils); Check-a						
	161	322	483	1030	1765	2500
15-Acid in face-c	168	336	504	1075	1838	2600

NOTE: *Fass* a-13; c-4, 6, 10. *Hollingsworth* a-10-13, 15; c-2, 12, 13, 15. *Kiefer* a-4. *Woodbridge* a-13? Bondage-c-1, 8, 12.

CRIME ON THE RUN (See Approved Comics #8)

Crime Exposed #11 © MAR

Crime SuspenStories #26 © WMG

Crime Syndicate #6 © DC

	GD 2.0	VG 4.0	FN 6.0	VF 8.0	VF/NM 9.0	NM- 9.2

CRIME ON THE WATERFRONT (Formerly Famous Gangsters)
Realistic Publications: No. 4, May, 1952 (Painted cover)

4	41	82	123	256	428	600

CRIME PATROL (Formerly International #1-5; International Crime Patrol #6; becomes Crypt of Terror #17 on)
E. C. Comics: No. 7, Summer, 1948 - No. 16, Feb-Mar, 1950

7-Intro. Captain Crime	123	246	369	787	1344	1900
8-14: 12-Jewels-a	93	186	279	591	1021	1450
15-Intro. of Crypt Keeper (inspired by Witches Tales radio show) & Crypt of Terror (see Tales From the Crypt #33 for origin); used by N.Y. Legis. Comm.; last pg. Feldstein-a	331	662	993	2317	4059	5800
	811	1622	2433	5920	10,460	15,000
16-2nd Crypt Keeper app.; Roussos-a	331	662	993	2317	4059	5800

NOTE: *Craig c/a in most issues.* **Feldstein** *a-9-16.* **Kiefer** *a-8, 10, 11.* **Moldoff** *a-7.*

CRIME PATROL
Gemstone Publishing: Apr, 2000 - No. 10, Jan, 2001 ($2.50)

1-10: E.C. reprints						4.00

Volume 1,2 (2000, $13.50) 1-r/#1-5. 2-r/#6-10 ... 14.00

CRIME PHOTOGRAPHER (See Casey...)

CRIME REPORTER
St. John Publ. Co.: Aug, 1948 - No. 3, Dec, 1948 (Indicia shows Oct.)

1-Drug club story	116	232	348	742	1271	1800
2-Used in **SOTI**: illo- "Children told me what the man was going to do with the red-hot poker;" r/Dynamic #17 with editing; Baker-c; Tuska-a	314	628	942	2198	3849	5500
3-Baker-c; Tuska-a	129	258	387	826	1413	2000

CRIMES BY WOMEN
Fox Feature Syndicate: June, 1948 - No. 15, Aug, 1951; 1954 (True crime cases)

1-True story of Bonnie Parker	161	322	483	1030	1765	2500
2	103	206	309	659	1130	1600
3-Used in **SOTI**, pg. 234	161	322	483	1030	1765	2500
4,5,7-9,11-15: 8-Used in **POP**. 14-Bondage-c	97	194	291	621	1061	1500
6-Classic girl fight-c; acid-in-face panel	194	388	582	1242	2121	3000
10-Used in **SOTI**, pg. 72; girl fight-c	129	258	387	826	1413	2000
54(M.S. Publ.-'54)-Reprint; (formerly My Love Secret)	53	106	159	334	567	800

CRIMES INCORPORATED (Formerly My Past)
Fox Feature Syndicate: No. 12, June, 1950 (Crime Incorporated No. 2 on)

12	37	74	111	222	361	500

CRIMES INCORPORATED (See Fox Giants)

CRIME SMASHER (See Whiz #76)
Fawcett Publications: Summer, 1948 (one-shot)

1-Formerly Spy Smasher	50	100	150	315	533	750

CRIME SMASHERS (Becomes Secret Mysteries No. 16 on)
Ribage Publishing Corp.(Trojan Magazines): Oct, 1950 - No. 15, Mar, 1953

1-Used in **SOTI**, pg. 19,20, & illo "A girl raped and murdered;" Sally the Sleuth begins	116	232	348	742	1271	1800
2-Kubert-c	57	114	171	362	619	875
3,4	47	94	141	296	498	700
5-Wood-a	58	116	174	371	636	900
6,8-11: 8-Lingerie panel	39	78	117	231	378	525
7-Female heroin junkie story	65	130	195	416	708	1000
12-Injury to eye panel. 1 pg. Frazetta-a	53	106	159	334	567	800
13-Used in **POP**, pgs. 79,80; 1 pg. Frazetta-a	53	106	159	334	567	800
14,15	37	74	111	222	361	500

NOTE: **Hollingsworth** *a-14.* **Kiefer** *a-15. Bondage c-7, 9.*

CRIME SUSPENSTORIES (Formerly Vault of Horror No. 12-14)
E. C. Comics: No. 15, Oct-Nov, 1950 - No. 27, Feb-Mar, 1955

15-Identical to #1 in content: #1 printed on outside front cover. #15 (formerly "The Vault of Horror") printed and blackened out on inside front cover with Vol. 1, No. 1 printed over it. Evidently, several of No. 15 were printed before a decision was made not to drop the Vault of Horror and Haunt of Fear series. The print run was stopped on No. 15 and continued on No. 1. All of the No. 15 issues were changed as described above.

	234	468	702	1872	2986	4100
1	194	388	582	1552	2476	3400
2	97	194	291	776	1238	1700
3-5: 3-Poe adaptation. 3-Old Witch stories begin	69	138	207	552	876	1200
6-10: 9-Craig bio.	57	114	171	456	728	1000
11,12,14,15: 15-The Old Witch guest stars	46	92	138	368	584	800
13,16-Williamson-a	60	120	180	480	765	1050
17-Classic "bullet in the head" cover; Williamson/Frazetta-a (6 pgs.) Williamson bio.	171	342	513	1368	2184	3000
18,19: 19-Used in **SOTI**, pg. 235	50	100	150	400	638	875

20-Classic hanging cover used in SOTI, illo "Cover of a children's comic book"; issue was on display at the 1954 Senate hearing

	857	1714	2571	6856	10,928	15,000

21,24-26: 24- "Food For Thought" similar to "Cave In" in Amazing Detective Cases #13 (1952)

	37	74	111	296	473	650

22-Classic ax decapitation-c; likely the single most notorious cover of the pre-Code era; exhibited in the 1954 Senate Investigation on juvenile delinquency trial; decapitation story

	1700	3400	5100	13,600	21,800	30,000

NOTE: *Senator Kefauver questioning Bill Gaines: "Here is your May issue. This seems to be a man with a bloody ax holding a woman's head up which has been severed from her body. Do you think that's in good taste?" Gaines: "Yes I do - for the cover of a horror comic. A cover in bad taste, for example, might be defined as holding her head a little higher so that blood could be seen dripping from it and moving the body over a little further so that the neck of the body could be seen to be bloody." It was actually drawn this way first and Gaines had Craig change it to the published version.*

23-Used in Senate investigation on juvenile delinquency

	143	286	429	1144	1822	2500
27-Last issue (Low distribution)	71	142	213	568	909	1250

NOTE: *Craig a-1-21; c-1-18, 20-22. Crandall a-18-26. Davis a-4, 5, 7, 9-12, 20. Elder a-17,18. Evans a-15, 19, 21, 23, 25, 27; c-23, 24. Feldstein c-19. Ingels a-1-12, 14, 15, 27. Kamen a-2, a-18, 20-27; c-25-27. Krigstein a-22, 24, 25, 27. Kurtzman a-1, 3. Orlando a-16, 22, 24, 26. Wood a-1. Issues No. 1-3 were printed in Canada as "Weird Suspenstories." Issues No. 11-15 have E. C. "quickie" stories. No. 25 contains the famous "Are You a Red Dupe?" editorial. Ray Bradbury adaptations-15, 17.*

CRIME SUSPENSTORIES
Russ Cochran/Gemstone Publ.: Nov, 1992 - No. 27, May, 1999 ($1.50/$2.00/$2.50)

1-27: Reprints Crime SuspenStories series						4.00

CRIME SYNDICATE (Legion of Justice cover logo on #5)
DC Comics: May, 2021 - No. 6, Oct, 2021 ($3.99, limited series)

1-6-Earth-3 villains vs. Starro; Schmidt-s/McKeown-a; back-up origins; Hitch-a						4.00

CRIMINAL (Also see Criminal: The Sinners)
Marvel Comics (Icon): Oct, 2006 - No. 10, Oct, 2007 ($2.99)
Volume 2: Feb, 2008 - No. 7, Nov, 2008 ($3.50)

1-10-Ed Brubaker-s/Sean Phillips-a/c						3.00
Volume 2: 1-7-Brubaker-s/Phillips-a						3.50
...: Tenth Anniversary Special Edition (Image Comics, 4/16, $5.99) Brubaker-s/Phillips-a; 1970s Kung Fu magazine pastishe within story; intro. Fang the Kung Fu Werewolf						6.00
...: The Special Edition (Image Comics, 2/15, $4.99) Brubaker-s/Phillips-a; 1970s Conan B&W magazine pastishe within story						5.00
... Vol. 1: Coward TPB (2007, $14.99) r/#1-5; intro. by Tom Fontana						15.00
... Vol. 2: Lawless TPB (2007, $14.99) r/#6-10; intro. by Frank Miller						15.00
... Vol. 3: The Dead and the Dying TPB (2008, $11.99) r/V2#1-4; intro. by John Singleton						12.00

CRIMINAL
Image Comics: Jan, 2019 - No. 12, Jan, 2020 ($3.99)

1-12-Ed Brubaker-s/Sean Phillips-a/c						4.00

CRIMINAL MACABRE (limited series and one-shots)
Dark Horse Comics: ($2.99/$3.99)

...: Cellblock 666 (9/08 - No. 4, 5/09)(#25-28 in series) 1-4-Niles-s/Stakal-a/Bradstreet-c						3.00
.../ Count Crowley: From the Pit They Came (10/22, $3.99) Ketner-a						4.00
...: Die, Die, My Darling (4/12, $3.50) reprints serial from DHP #4-6; Staples-c						3.50
...: Feat of Clay (6/06, $2.99) Niles-s/Hotz-a/c						3.00
Free Comic Book Day: Criminal Macabre - Call Me Monster (5/11) flip book w/Baltimore						3.00
...: My Demon Baby (9/07 - No. 4, 4/08)(#21-24 in series) 1-4-Niles-s/Stakal-a						3.00
...: No Peace For Dead Men (9/11, $3.99) Niles-s/Mitten-a/Staples-c						4.00
...: The Big Bleed Out (12/19 - No. 4, 3/20 $3.99) 1-4-Niles-s/Mitten-a						4.00
...: The Eyes of Frankenstein (9/13 - No. 4, 12/13 $3.99) 1-4-Niles-s/Mitten-a						4.00
...: The Goon (7/11, $3.99) Niles-s/Mitten-a; covers by Powell & Staples						4.00
...: They Fight By Night (11/12, $3.99) reprints serial from DHP #10-13; Staples-c						4.00
...: Two Red Eyes (12/06 - No. 4, 3/07) 1-4-Niles-s/Hotz-a/Bradstreet-c						3.00

CRIMINAL MACABRE: A CAL MCDONALD MYSTERY (Also see Last Train to Deadsville)
Dark Horse Comics: May, 2003 - No. 5, Sept, 2003 ($2.99)

1-5-Niles-s/Templesmith-a						3.00

CRIMINAL MACABRE: FINAL NIGHT - THE 30 DAYS OF NIGHT CROSSOVER
Dark Horse Comics: Dec, 2012 - No. 4, Mar, 2013 ($3.99, limited series)

1-4-Niles-s/Mitten-a/Erickson-c						4.00

CRIMINAL MACABRE:THE THIRD CHILD
Dark Horse Comics: Sept, 2014 - No. 4, Dec, 2014 ($3.99, limited series)

1-4-Niles-s/Mitten-a/Erickson-c						4.00

CRIMINALS ON THE RUN (Formerly Young King Cole) (Crime Fighting Detective No. 11 on)
Premium Group (Novelty Press): V4#1, Aug-Sep, 1948-#10, Dec-Jan, 1949-50

V4#1-Young King Cole continues	47	94	141	296	498	700
2-6: 6-Dr. Doom app.	34	68	102	199	325	450
7-Classic "Fish in the Face" c by L. B. Cole	290	580	870	1856	3178	4500
V5#1,2 (#8,9),10: 9,10-L. B. Cole-c	28	56	84	168	274	380

	GD	VG	FN	VF	VF/NM	NM-
	2.0	4.0	6.0	8.0	9.0	9.2

NOTE: Most issues have **L. B. Cole** covers. **McWilliams** a-V4#6, 7, V5#2, 10; c-V4#5.

CRIMINAL: THE LAST OF THE INNOCENT
Marvel Comics (Icon): Jun, 2011 - No. 4, Sept, 2011 ($3.50)

1-4-Ed Brubaker-s/Sean Phillips-a/c						3.50

CRIMINAL: THE SINNERS
Marvel Comics (Icon): Sept, 2009 - No. 5, Mar, 2010 ($3.50)

1-5-Ed Brubaker-s/Sean Phillips-a/c						3.50

CRIMSON (Also see Cliffhanger #0)
Image Comics (Cliffhanger Productions): May, 1998 - No. 7, Dec, 1998;
DC Comics (Cliffhanger Prod.): No. 8, Mar, 1999 - No. 24, Apr, 2001 ($2.50)

1-Humberto Ramos-a/Augustyn-s						5.00
1-Variant-c by Warren						8.00
1-Chromium-c						15.00
2-Ramos-c with street crowd, 2-Variant-c by Art Adams						4.00
2-Dynamic Forces CrimsonChrome cover						15.00
3-7: 3-Ramos Moon background-c. 7-Three covers by Ramos, Madureira, & Campbell						3.50
8-23: 8-First DC issue						3.00
24-($3.50) Final issue; wraparound-c						4.00
DF Premiere Ed. 1998 ($6.95) covers by Ramos and Jae Lee						7.00
Crimson: Scarlet X Blood on the Moon (10/99, $3.95)						4.00
Crimson Sourcebook (11/99, $2.95) Pin-ups and info						3.00
Earth Angel TPB (2001, $14.95) r/#13-18						15.00
Heaven and Earth TPB (1/00, $14.95) r/#7-12						15.00
Loyalty and Loss TPB ('99, $12.95) r/#1-6						15.00
Redemption TPB ('01, $14.95) r/#19-24						15.00

CRIMSON AVENGER, THE (See Detective Comics #20 for 1st app.)(Also see Leading Comics #1 & World's Best/Finest Comics)
DC Comics: June, 1988 - No. 4, Sept, 1988 ($1.00, limited series)

1-4						4.00

CRIMSON CAGE, THE
Artists Writers & Artisans: Dec, 2021 - No. 5, Apr, 2022 ($3.99, limited series)

1-5-Horror tale told with professional wrestling; John Lees-s/Alex Cormack-a						4.00

CRIMSON DYNAMO
Marvel Comics (Epic): Oct, 2003 - No. 6, Apr, 2004 ($2.50/$2.99)

1-4,6: 1-John Jackson Miller-s/Steve Ellis-a/c						3.00
5-($2.99) Iron Man-c/app.						4.00

CRIMSON LOTUS
Dark Horse Comics: Nov, 2018 - No. 5, Mar, 2019 ($3.99, limited series)

1-5-John Arcudi-s/Mindy Lee-a/Tonci Zonjic-c						4.00

CRIMSON PLAGUE
Event Comics: June, 1997 ($2.95, unfinished mini-series)

1-George Perez-a						4.00

CRIMSON PLAGUE (George Pérez's...)
Image Comics (Gorilla): June, 2000 - No. 2, Aug, 2000 ($2.95, mini-series)

1-George Pérez-a; reprints 6/97 issue with 16 new pages						3.00
2-($2.50)						3.00

CRISIS AFTERMATH: THE BATTLE FOR BLUDHAVEN (Also see Infinite Crisis)
DC Comics: Jun, 2006 - No. 6, Sept, 2006 ($2.99, limited series)

1-Atomic Knights return; Teen Titans app.; Jurgens-a/Acuna-c						4.00
1-2nd printing with pencil cover						3.00
2-6: 2-Intro S.H.A.D.E. (new Freedom Fighters)						3.00
TPB (2007, $12.99) r/#1-6						13.00

CRISIS AFTERMATH: THE SPECTRE (Also see Infinite Crisis, Gotham Central and Tales of the Unexpected)
DC Comics: Jul, 2006 - No. 3, Sept, 2006 ($2.99, limited series)

1-3-Crispus Allen becomes the Spectre; Pfeifer-s/Chiang-a/c						3.00
TPB (12.99) r/#1-3 and Tales of the Unexpected #1-3						13.00

CRISIS IN INFINITE QUARANTINE (Cerebus in Hell)
Aardvark-Vanaheim: Aug, 2021 ($4.00, B&W)

1-Cerebus figures placed over original Gustave Doré artwork of Hell						4.00

CRISIS OF INFINITE CEREBI (Cerebus figures placed over original Gustave Doré artwork)
Aardvark-Vanaheim: Sept, 2018 ($4.00, B&W, one-shot)

1-Crisis on Infinite Earths #7-c swipe						4.00

CRISIS ON INFINITE EARTHS (Also see Official... Index and Legends of the DC Universe)
DC Comics: Apr, 1985 - No. 12, Mar, 1986 (maxi-series)

	GD	VG	FN	VF	VF/NM	NM-
1-1st DC app. Blue Beetle & Detective Karp from Charlton; Pérez-c on all	3	6	9	17	26	35
2	2	4	6	11	16	20
3-6: 6-Intro Charlton's Capt. Atom, Nightshade, Question, Judomaster, Peacemaker & Thunderbolt into DC Universe	2	4	6	9	13	16
7-Double size; death of Supergirl	3	6	9	19	30	40
8-Death of the Flash (Barry Allen)	3	6	9	18	28	38
8-Facsimile Edition (2019, $3.99) Reprints issue with original ads and letter column						4.00
9-11: 9-Intro. Charlton's Ghost into DC Universe. 10-Intro. Charlton's Banshee, Dr. Spectro, Image, Punch & Jewelee into DC Universe; Starman (Prince Gavyn) dies	2	4	6	8	10	12
12-(52 pgs.)-Deaths of Dove, Kole, Lori Lemaris, Sunburst, G.A. Robin & Huntress; Kid Flash becomes new Flash; 3rd & final DC app. of the 3 Lt. Marvels; Green Fury gets new look (becomes Green Flame in Infinity, Inc. #32)	2	4	6	9	13	16
Slipcased Hardcover (1998, $99.95) Wraparound dust-jacket cover pencilled by Pérez and painted by Alex Ross; sketch pages by Pérez; Wolfman intro.; afterword by Giordano						100.00
TPB (2000, $29.95) Wraparound-c by Pérez and Ross						30.00

NOTE: Crossover issues: All Star Squadron 50-56,60; Amethyst 13; Blue Devil 17,18; DC Comics Presents 78,86-88,95; Detective Comics 558; Fury of Firestorm 41,42; G.I. Combat 274; Green Lantern 194-196,198; Infinity, Inc. 18-25 & Annual 1, Justice League of America 244,245 & Annual 3; Legion of Super-Heroes 16,18; Losers Special 1; New Teen Titans 13,14; Omega Men 31,33; Superman 413-415; Swamp Thing 44,46; Wonder Woman 327-329.

CRISIS ON INFINITE EARTHS GIANT
DC Comics: 2019 - No. 2, 2020 ($4.99, 100 pgs., squarebound, Mass Market & Direct Market

editions exist for each issue, with different covers)

1,2: 1-Two new stories tied to TV event plus reprints #1,7. 2-Include reprints #8,11						5.00

CRISIS ON MULTIPLE EARTHS
DC Comics: 2002 - 2010 ($14.95, trade paperbacks)

TPB-(2003) Reprints 1st 4 Silver Age JLA/JSA crossovers from J.L.ofA. #21,22; 29,30; 37,38; 46,47; new painted-c by Alex Ross; intro. by Mark Waid						15.00
Volume 2 (2003, $14.95) r/J.L.ofA. #55,56; 64,65; 73,74; 82,83; new Ordway-c						15.00
Volume 3 (2004, $14.95) r/J.L.ofA. #91,92; 100-102; 107,108; 113; Wein intro., Ross-c						15.00
Volume 4 (2006, $14.99) r/J.L.ofA. #123-124 (Earth-Prime),135-137 (Fawcett's Shazam characters), 147-148 (Legion of Super-Heroes); Ross-c						15.00
Volume 5 (2010, $19.99) r/J.L.ofA. #159-160 (Jonah Hex, Enemy Ace), #171-172 (Murder of Mr. Terrific), 1#83-185 (New Gods & Darkseid); Pérez-c						20.00
... The Team-Ups Volume 1 (2005, $14.99) r/Flash #123,129,137,151; Showcase #55,56; Green Lantern #40, Brave and the Bold #61 and Spectre #7; new Ordway-c						15.00

CRITICAL MASS (See A Shadowline Saga: Critical Mass)

CRITICAL ROLE: THE TALES OF EXANDRIA: THE BRIGHT QUEEN (Based on characters from the D&D web series)
Dark Horse Comics: Oct, 2021 - No. 4, Mar, 2022 ($3.99, limited series)

1-4-Poelgeest-s/CoupleofKooks-a						4.00

CRITICAL ROLE: THE TALES OF EXANDRIA II: ARTAGAN
Dark Horse Comics: Jan, 2024 - Present ($3.99, limited series)

1,2-Sam Maggs-s/Aviv Or-a						4.00

CRITICAL ROLE VOX MACHINA ORIGINS (Based on characters from the D&D web series)
Dark Horse Comics: Jul, 2019 - No. 6, Apr, 2020 ($3.99, limited series)

1-6-Matthew Mercer & Jody Houser-s/Olivia Samson-a						4.00
(Series) III 1-6-(2/21 - No. 6, 5/22, $3.99) Mercer & Houser-s/Samson-a						4.00

CRITTER
Big Dog Press: Jul, 2011 - No. 4, 2011; Jun, 2012 - No. 20, Apr, 2014 ($3.50)

1-4-Multiple covers on all						3.50
Vol. 2 1-20-Multiple covers on all						3.50

CRITTER
Aspen MLT: Jul, 2015 - No. 4, Oct, 2015 ($3.99)

1-4-Reprints the 2011 series; multiple covers on all						4.00

CRITTERS (Also see Usagi Yojimbo Summer Special)
Fantagraphics Books: 1986 - No. 50, 1990 ($1.70/$2.00, B&W)

	GD	VG	FN	VF	VF/NM	NM-
1-Cutey Bunny, Usagi Yojimbo app.	4	8	12	23	37	50
2,4,5,8,9	1	2	3	5	6	8
3,6,7,10-Usagi Yojimbo app.	2	4	6	9	12	15
11,14-Usagi Yojimbo app. 11-Christmas Special (68 pgs.)						6.00
12,13,15-22,24-37,39,40: 22-Watchmen parody; two diff. covers exist						3.00
23-With Alan Moore Flexi-disc ($3.95)						5.00
38-($2.75-c) Usagi Yojimbo app.						5.00
41-49						4.00
50 ($4.95, 84 pgs.)-Neil the Horse, Capt. Jack, Sam & Max & Usagi Yojimbo app.; Quagmire, Shaw-a	2	4	6	8	10	12
Special 1 (1/88, $2.00)						4.00

CRONE
Dark Horse Comics: Nov, 2019 - No. 5, Mar, 2020 ($3.99, limited series)

1-5-Dennis Culver-s/Justin Greenwood-a						4.00

CROSS
Dark Horse Comics: No. 0, Oct, 1995 - No. 6, Apr, 1995 ($2.95, limited series, mature)

0-6: Darrow-c & Vachss scripts in all						4.00

CROSS AND THE SWITCHBLADE, THE
Spire Christian Comics (Fleming H. Revell Co.): 1972 (35-49¢)

	GD	VG	FN	VF	VF/NM	NM-
1-Some issues have nn	3	6	9	21	33	45

CROSS BRONX, THE
Image Comics: Sept, 2006 - No. 4, Dec, 2006 ($2.99, limited series)

1-4: 1-Oeming-a/c; Oeming & Brandon-s; Ribic var-c. 2-Johnson var-c. 4-Mack var-c						3.00

CROSSFIRE
Spire Christian Comics (Fleming H. Revell Co.): 1973 (39/49¢)

	GD	VG	FN	VF	VF/NM	NM-
nn	2	4	6	13	18	22

CROSSFIRE (Also see DNAgents)
Eclipse Comics: 5/84 - No. 17, 3/86; No. 18, 1/87 - No. 26, 2/88 ($1.50, Baxter paper) (#18-26 are B&W)

	GD	VG	FN	VF	VF/NM	NM-
1-11,14-26: 1-DNAgents x-over; Spiegle-c/a begins						4.00
12-Death of Marilyn Monroe; Dave Stevens-c	5	10	15	31	53	75
13-Death of Marilyn Monroe	1	3	4	6	8	10

CROSSFIRE AND RAINBOW (Also see DNAgents)
Eclipse Comics: June, 1986 - No. 4, Sept, 1986 ($1.25, deluxe format)

	GD	VG	FN	VF	VF/NM	NM-
1-3: Spiegle-a						4.00
4-Elvis cover by Dave Stevens	3	6	9	14	20	25

CROSSGEN...
CrossGeneration Comics

CrossGenesis (1/00) Previews CrossGen universe; cover gallery						3.00
...Primer (1/00) Wizard supplement; intro. to the CrossGen universe						3.00
...Sampler (2/00) Retailer preview book						3.00

CROSSGEN CHRONICLES
CrossGeneration Comics: June, 2000 - No. 8, Jul, 2002 ($3.95)

1-Intro. to CrossGen characters & company						4.00
1-(no cover price) same contents, customer preview						4.00
2-8: 2-(3/01) George Pérez-c/a. 3-5-Pérez-a/Waid-s. 6,8-Maroto-c/a. 7-Nebres-c/a						4.00

CROSSGEN TALES
Marvel Comics: Jan, 2023 ($8.99, squarebound, one-shot)

1-Reprints Ruse #1, Mystic #1, Sigil #1, Sojourn #1; intro. by Ron Marz						9.00

CROSSING MIDNIGHT

Crimson Lotus #1 © Mike Mignola

CrossGen Tales #1 © MAR

The Crow: Memento Mori #4 © James O'Barr

	GD 2.0	VG 4.0	FN 6.0	VF 8.0	VF/NM 9.0	NM- 9.2

DC Comics (Vertigo): Jan, 2007 - No. 19, Jul, 2008 ($2.99)

1-19: 1-Carey-s/Fern-a/Williams III-c. 10-12-Nguyen-a ... 3.00
...: Cut Here TPB (2007, $9.99) r/#1-5 ... 10.00
...: A Map of Midnight TPB (2008, $14.99) r/#6-12; afterword by Carey ... 15.00
...: The Sword in the Soul TPB (2008, $14.99) r/#13-19 ... 15.00

CROSSING THE ROCKIES (See Classics Illustrated Special Issue)

CROSSOVER
Image Comics: Nov, 2020 - Present ($3.99)

1-13: 1-Donny Cates-s/Geoff Shaw-a. 3-5-Madman app. 7-Zdarsky-s/Hester-a. 8-10-Walker & Pilgrim from Powers app. 10-13-Donny Cates app. 11-13-Negan app. ... 4.00
... #1 3-D Special (8/22, $8.99) Reprints #1 with 3-D effects; bagged with glasses ... 9.00

CROSSOVERS, THE
CrossGeneration Comics: Feb, 2003 - No. 9, Dec, 2003 ($2.95)

1-9-Robert Rodi-s. 1-6-Mauricet & Ernie Colon-a. 7-Staton-a begins ... 3.00
Vol. 1: Cross Currents (2003, $9.95) digest-sized reprints #1-6 ... 10.00

CROSS TO BEAR
AfterShock Comics: Oct, 2021 - No. 4 ($4.99, limited series)

1-3-Stojanovic-s/Banovic-a ... 5.00

CROSSWIND
Image Comics: Jun, 2017 - No. 6, Jan, 2018 ($3.99)

1-6-Gail Simone-s/Cat Staggs-a ... 4.00

CROW, THE (Also see Caliber Presents)
Caliber Press: Feb, 1989 - No. 4, 1989 ($1.95, B&W, limited series)

1-James O'Barr-c/a/scripts	40	80	120	296	673	1050
1-2nd printing	18	36	54	124	275	425
2	10	20	30	69	147	225
2,3-2nd printing	3	6	9	19	30	40
2-3rd printing	3	6	9	14	20	25
3,4	8	16	24	54	102	150

CROW, THE
Tundra Publishing, Ltd.: Jan, 1992 - No. 3, 1992 ($4.95, B&W, 68 pgs.)

1-r/#1,2 of Caliber series	3	6	9	21	33	45
2,3- 2-r/#3 of Caliber series w/new material. 3-All new material	3	6	9	14	20	25

CROW, THE
Kitchen Sink Press: Jan, 1996 - No. 3, Mar, 1996 ($2.95, B&W)

1-James O'Barr-c/scripts in all	2	4	6	8	11	14
2,3	1	2	3	5	6	8
#0-A Cycle of Shattered Lives (12/98, $3.50) new story by O'Barr						
	1	3	4	6	8	10

CROW, THE
Image Comics (Todd McFarlane Prod.): Feb, 1999 - No. 10, Nov, 1999 ($2.50)

1-Two covers by McFarlane and Kent Williams; Muth-s in all						
	1	3	4	6	8	10
2-10: 2-6,10-Paul Lee-a						4.00
Book 1 - Vengeance (2000, $10.95, TPB) r/#1-3,5,6						15.00
Book 2 - Evil Beyond Reach (2000, $10.95, TPB) r/#4,7-10						15.00
Todd McFarlane Presents The Crow Magazine 1 (3/00, $4.95)						
	1	2	3	5	6	8

CROW, THE: CITY OF ANGELS (Movie)
Kitchen Sink Press: July, 1996 - No. 3, Sept, 1996 ($2.95, limited series)

1-Adaptation of film; two-c (photo & illos.); Vincent Perez interview						
	1	3	4	6	8	10
2,3-Adaptation continues						5.00

CROW, THE: CURARE
IDW Publishing: Jun, 2013 - No. 3, Aug, 2013 ($3.99, limited series)

1-3-James O'Barr-s/Antoine Dodé-a; multiple covers on each ... 4.00

CROW, THE: DEATH AND REBIRTH
IDW Publishing: Jul, 2012 - No. 5, Nov, 2012 ($3.99, limited series)

1-5-Shirley-s/Colden-a; multiple covers on each ... 4.00

CROW, THE: FLESH AND BLOOD
Kitchen Sink Press: May, 1996 - No. 3, July, 1996 ($2.95, limited series)

1-James O'Barr-c on all	1	3	4	6	8	10
2,3						4.00

CROW: HACK / SLASH
IDW Publishing: Jun, 2019 - No. 4, Sept, 2019 ($3.99, limited series)

1-4-Tim Seeley-s/Jim Terry-a; multiple covers on each ... 4.00

CROW: HARK THE HERALD
IDW Publishing: Nov, 2019 ($4.99, one-shot)

1-Tim Seeley-s/Meredith Laxton-a; four covers ... 5.00

CROW: LETHE
IDW Publishing: Feb, 2020 - Present ($3.99, limited series)

1-Tim Seeley-s/Ilias Kyriazis-a; four covers ... 4.00

CROW, THE: MEMENTO MORI
IDW Publishing: Mar, 2018 - No. 4, Jun, 2018 ($3.99, limited series)

1-4-Recchioni-s/Dell'edera-a in all; back-up short stories in each by various ... 4.00

CROW, THE: PESTILENCE
IDW Publishing: Mar, 2014 - No. 4, Jun, 2014 ($3.99, limited series)

1-4-Frank Bill-s/Drew Moss-a; two covers ... 4.00

CROW, THE: RAZOR - KILL THE PAIN
London Night Studios: Apr, 1998 - No. 3, July, 1998 ($2.95, B&W, lim. series)

1-Hartsoe-s/O'Barr-painted-c	1	2	3	5	6	8
2,3-Hartsoe-s/O'Barr-painted-c						4.00
0(10/98) Dorien painted-c, Finale (2/99)						4.00
The Lost Chapter (2/99, $4.95), Tour Book-(12/97) pin-ups; 4 diff.-c						
	1	2	3	5	6	8

CROW, THE: SKINNING THE WOLVES
IDW Publishing: Dec, 2012 - No. 3, Feb, 2013 ($3.99, limited series)

1-3-James O'Barr-s/Jim Terry-s/a; multiple covers on each ... 4.00

CROW, THE: WAKING NIGHTMARES
Kitchen Sink Press: Jan, 1997 - No. 4, 1998 ($2.95, B&W, limited series)

1-Miran Kim-c on all	1	3	4	6	8	10
2-4						5.00

CROW, THE: WILD JUSTICE
Kitchen Sink Press: Oct, 1996 - No. 3, Dec, 1996 ($2.95, limited series)

1-Prosser-s/Adlard-a in all	1	3	4	6	8	10
2,3						5.00

CROWN COMICS (Also see Vooda)
Golfing/McCombs Publ.: Wint, 1944-45; No. 2, Sum, 1945 - No. 19, July, 1949

1- "The Oblong Box" E.A. Poe adaptation	68	136	204	435	743	1050
2-Baker-a	39	78	117	240	395	550
3-Baker-a; Voodah by Baker; racist-c	58	116	174	371	636	900
4-6-Baker-c/a; Voodah app. #4,5	48	96	144	302	514	725
7-Feldstein, Baker, Kamen-a; Baker-c	194	388	582	1242	2121	3000
8-Baker-a; Voodah app.	39	78	117	240	395	550
9-11,13-19: Voodah in #10-19. 13-New logo	24	48	72	142	234	325
12-Master Marvin by Feldstein, Starr-a; Voodah-c	32	64	96	188	307	425

NOTE: *Bolle* a-11, 13-16, 18, 19; c-11p, 15. *Powell* a-19. *Starr* a-11-13; c-11l.

CRUCIBLE
DC Comics (Impact): Feb, 1993 - No. 6, July, 1993 ($1.25, limited series)

1-6: 1-(99c)-Neon ink-c. 1,2-Quesada-c(p). 1-4-Quesada layouts ... 4.00

CRUDE
Image Comics (Skybound): Apr, 2018 - No. 6, Sept, 2018 ($3.99, limited series)

1-6-Steve Orlando-s/Garry Brown-a ... 4.00

CRUEL AND UNUSUAL
DC Comics (Vertigo): June, 1999 - No. 4, Sept, 1999 ($2.95, limited series)

1-4-Delano & Peyer-s/McCrea-c/a ... 4.00

CRUSADER FROM MARS (See Tops in Adventure)
Ziff-Davis Publ. Co.: Jan-Mar, 1952 - No. 2, Fall, 1952 (Painted-c)

1-Cover is dated Spring	97	194	291	621	1061	1500
2-Bondage-c	68	136	204	435	743	1050

CRUSADER RABBIT (TV)
Dell Publishing Co.: No. 735, Oct, 1956 - No. 805, May, 1957

Four Color 735 (#1)	23	46	69	161	356	550
Four Color 805	17	34	51	119	265	410

CRUSADERS, THE (Religious)
Chick Publications: 1974 - Vol. 17, 1988 (39/69c, 36 pgs.)

Vol.1-Operation Bucharest ('74). Vol.2-The Broken Cross ('74). Vol.3-Scarface ('74). Vol.4-Exorcists ('75). Vol.5-Chaos ('75)	3	6	9	16	23	30

Vol.6-Primal Man? ('76)-(Disputes evolution theory). Vol.7-The Ark-(claims proof of existence, destroyed by Bolsheviks). Vol.8-The Gift-(Life story of Christ). Vol.9-Angel of Light-(Story of

	GD 2.0	VG 4.0	FN 6.0	VF 8.0	VF/NM 9.0	NM- 9.2

the Devil). Vol.10-Spellbound?-(Tells how rock music is Satanic & produced by witches). 11-Sabotage?. 12-Alberto. 13-Double Cross. 14-The Godfathers. (No. 6-14 low in distribution; loaded with religious propaganda). 15-The Force. 16-The Four Horsemen

	3	6	9	16	23	30
Vol. 17-The Prophet (low print run)	3	6	9	17	26	35

CRUSADERS (Southern Knights No. 2 on)
Guild Publications: 1982 (B&W, magazine size)

1-1st app. Southern Knights	2	4	6	11	16	20

CRUSADERS, THE (Also see Black Hood, The Jaguar, The Comet, The Fly, Legend of the Shield, The Mighty… & The Web)
DC Comics (Impact): May, 1992 - No. 8, Dec, 1992 ($1.00/$1.25)

1-8-Contains 3 Impact trading cards						4.00

CRUSADES, THE
DC Comics (Vertigo): 2001 - No. 20, Dec, 2002 ($3.95/$2.50)

…: Urban Decree ('01, $3.95) Intro. the Knight; Seagle-s/Kelley Jones c/a		4.00
1-(5/01, $2.50) Sienkiewicz-c		3.00
2-20: 2-Moeller-c. 18-Begin $2.95-c		3.00

CRUSH
Dark Horse Comics: Oct, 2003 - No. 4, Jan, 2004 ($2.99, limited series)

1-4-Jason Hall-s/Sean Murphy-a		3.00

CRUSH, THE
Image Comics (Motown Machineworks): Jan, 1996 - No. 5, July, 1996 ($2.25, limited series)

1-5: Baron scripts		4.00

CRUSH & LOBO
DC Comics: Aug, 2021 - No. 8, Mar, 2022 ($3.99, limited series)

1-8-Lobo & his daughter from Teen Titans; Tamaki-s/Nahuelpan-a		4.00

CRUX
CrossGeneration Comics: May, 2001 - No. 33, Feb, 2004 ($2.95)

1-33: 1-Waid-s/ Epting & Magyar-a/c. 6-Pelletier-a. 13-Dixon-s begin. 25-Cover has fake creases and other aging		3.00
Atlantis Rising Vol. 1 TPB (2002, $15.95) r/#1-6		16.00
Test of Time Vol. 2 TPB (12/02, $15.95) r/#7-12		16.00
Vol. 3: Strangers in Atlantis (2003, $15.95) r/#13-18		16.00
Vol. 4: Chaos Reborn (2003, $15.95) r/#19-24		16.00

CRY FOR DAWN
Cry For Dawn Pub.: 1989 - No. 9 ($2.25, B&W, mature)

1	11	22	33	73	157	240
1-2nd printing	4	8	12	28	47	65
1-3rd printing	3	6	9	16	23	30
2	4	8	12	23	37	50
2-2nd printing	2	4	6	11	16	20
3	3	6	9	16	23	30
3a-HorrorCon Edition (1990, less than 400 printed, signed inside-c)						200.00
4-6	2	4	6	11	16	20
5-2nd printing	1	2	3	5	6	8
7-9	2	4	6	9	12	15
4-9-Signed & numbered editions	3	6	9	14	20	25
Angry Christ Comix HC (4/03, $29.99) reprints various stories; and 30 pgs. new material						30.00
…Calendar (1993)						35.00

CRY HAVOC
Image Comics: Jan, 2016 - No. 6, Jun, 2016 ($3.99)

1-6-Simon Spurrier-s/Ryan Kelly-a; 2 covers on each		4.00

CRYIN' LION COMICS
William H. Wise Co.: Fall, 1944 - No. 3, Spring, 1945

1-Funny animal	18	36	54	107	169	230
2-Hitler and Tojo app.	15	30	45	88	137	185
3	11	22	33	62	86	110

CRYPT
Image Comics (Extreme): Aug, 1995 - No. 2, Oct. 1995 ($2.50, limited series)

1,2-Prophet app.		4.00

CRYPTIC WRITINGS OF MEGADETH
Chaos! Comics: Sept, 1997 - No. 4, Jun, 1998 ($2.95, quarterly)

1-4-Stories based on song lyrics by Dave Mustaine		4.00

CRYPTOCRACY
Dark Horse Comics: Jun, 2016 - No. 6, Nov, 2016 ($3.99)

1-6: 1-Van Jensen-s/Pete Woods-a		4.00

CRYPT OF DAWN (see Dawn)
Sirius: 1996 ($2.95, B&W, limited series)

1-Linsner-c/s; anthology	1	3	4	6	8	10
2, 3 (2/98)						5.00
4,5: 4- (6/98), 5-(11/98)						4.00
Ltd. Edition						20.00

CRYPT OF SHADOWS
Marvel Comics Group: Jan, 1973 - No. 21, Nov, 1975 (#1-9 are 20¢)

1-Wolverton-r/Advs. Into Terror #7	6	12	18	37	66	95
2-10: 2-Starlin/Everett-c	3	6	9	18	27	36
11-21: 18,20-Kirby-a	3	6	9	16	23	30

NOTE: *Briefer a-2r. Ditko a-13r, 18-20r. Everett a-6, 14r; c-2i. Heath a-1r. Gil Kane c-1, 6. Mort Lawrence a-1r, 8r. Maneely a-2r. Moldoff a-8. Powell a-12r, 14r. Tuska a-2r.*

CRYPT OF SHADOWS (Marvel 80th Anniversary salute to horror comics)
Marvel Comics: Mar, 2019 ($3.99, one-shot)

1-Al Ewing-s; art by Garry Brown, Stephen Green, Djibril Morissett-Phan; Kyle Hotz-c		4.00

CRYPT OF SHADOWS
Marvel Comics: Dec, 2022; Dec, 2023 ($5.99/$4.99, one-shots)

1-($5.99) Short stories featuring Moon Knight, Man-Thing, Werewolf By Night & others		6.00
1-(12/23, $4.99) Short stories featuring Hulk, Scarlet Witch, Daredevil, Deadpool & others		5.00

CRYPT OF TERROR (Formerly Crime Patrol; Tales From the Crypt No. 20 on) (Also see EC Archives • Tales From the Crypt)
E. C. Comics: No. 17, Apr-May, 1950 - No. 19, Aug-Sept, 1950

17-1st New Trend to hit stands	486	972	1458	3888	6194	8500
18,19	229	458	687	1832	2916	4000

NOTE: *Craig c/a-17-19. Feldstein a-17-19. Ingels a-19. Kurtzman a-18. Wood a-18. Canadian reprints known; see Table of Contents.*

CRYPTOZOIC MAN (Comic Book Men)
Dynamite Entertainment: 2013 - No. 4, 2014 ($3.99, limited series)

1-Bryan Johnson-s/Walt Flanagan-a/c	2	4	6	11	16	20
2-4	2	4	6	8	10	12

CRYSIS (Based on the EA videogame)
IDW Publishing: Jun, 2011 - No. 6, Oct, 2011 ($3.99, limited series)

1-6: 1-Richard K. Moran-s/Peter Bergting-a; two covers		4.00

CSI: CRIME SCENE INVESTIGATION (Based on TV series)
IDW Publishing: Jan, 2003 - No. 5, May, 2003 ($3.99, limited series)

1-Two covers (photo & Ashley Wood); Max Allan Collins-s		4.00
2-5		4.00
Free Comic Book Day edition (7/04) Previews CSI: Bad Rap; The Shield: Spotlight; 24: One Shot; and 30 Days of Night		3.00
…: Case Files Vol. 1 TPB (8/06, $19.99) B&W rep/Serial TPB, CSI - Bad Rap and CSI - Demon House limited series		20.00
…: Serial TPB (2003, $19.99) r/#1-5; bonus short story by Collins/Wood		20.00
…: Thicker Than Blood (7/03, $6.99) Mariotte-s/Rodriguez-a		7.00

CSI: CRIME SCENE INVESTIGATION - BAD RAP
IDW Publishing: Aug, 2003 - No. 5, Dec, 2003 ($3.99, limited series)

1-5-Two photo covers; Max Allan Collins-s/Rodriguez-a		4.00
TPB (3/04, $19.99) r/#1-5		20.00

CSI: CRIME SCENE INVESTIGATION - DEMON HOUSE
IDW Publishing: Feb, 2004 - No. 5, Jun, 2004 ($3.99, limited series)

1-5-Photo covers on all; Max Allan Collins-s/Rodriguez-a		4.00
TPB (10/04, $19.99) r/#1-5		20.00

CSI: CRIME SCENE INVESTIGATION - DOMINOS
IDW Publishing: Aug, 2004 - No. 5, Dec, 2004 ($3.99, limited series)

1-5-Photo covers on all; Oprisko-s/Rodriguez-a		4.00

CSI: CRIME SCENE INVESTIGATION - DYING IN THE GUTTERS
IDW Publishing: Aug, 2006 - No. 5, Dec, 2006 ($3.99, limited series)

1-5-"Rich Johnston" murdered; comic creators (Quesada, Rucka, David, Brubaker, Silvestri and others) appear as suspects; Stephen Mooney-a; photo-c		4.00

CSI: CRIME SCENE INVESTIGATION - SECRET IDENTITY
IDW Publishing: Feb, 2005 - No. 5, Jun, 2005 ($3.99, limited series)

1-5-Photo covers on all; Steven Grant-s/Gabriel Rodriguez-a		4.00

CSI: MIAMI
IDW Publishing: Oct, 2003; Apr, 2004 ($6.99, one-shots)

… - Blood Money (9/04)-Oprisko-s/Guedes & Perkins-a		7.00
… - Smoking Gun (10/03)-Mariotte-s/Avilés & Wood-a		7.00
… - Thou Shalt Not… (4/04)-Oprisko-s/Guedes & Wood-a		7.00
TPB (2/05, $19.99) reprints one-shots		20.00

CSI: NY - BLOODY MURDER
IDW Publishing: July, 2005 - No. 5, Nov, 2005 ($3.99, limited series)

1-5-Photo covers on all; Collins-s/Woodward-a		4.00

C-23 (Jim Lee's…) (Based on Wizards of the Coast card game)
Image Comics: Apr, 1998 - No. 8, Nov, 1998 ($2.50)

1-8: 1,2-Choi & Mariotte-s/ Charest-c. 2-Variant-c by Jim Lee. 4-Ryan Benjamin-c. 5,8-Corben var.-c. 6-Flip book with Planetary preview; Corben-c		4.00

CUD
Fantagraphics Books: 8/92 - No. 8, 12/94 ($2.25-$2.75, B&W, mature)

1-8: Terry LaBan scripts & art in all. 6-1st Eno & Plum		4.00

CUD COMICS
Dark Horse Comics: Jan, 1995 - No. 8, Sept, 1997 ($2.95, B&W)

1-8: Terry LaBan-c/a/scripts. 5-Nudity; marijuana smoke		4.00
Eno and Plum TPB (1997, $12.95) r/#1-4, DHP #93-95		13.00

CULL, THE
Image Comics: Aug, 2023 - Present ($3.99)

1-5-Kelly Thompson-s/Mattia De Iulis-a		4.00

CULT OF CARNAGE: MISERY
Image Comics: Jul, 2023 - No. 5, Nov, 2023 ($4.99/$3.99)

1-($4.99) Liz Allan as a Carnage symbiote; Pirzada-s/Mortarino-a		5.00
2-5-($3.99)		4.00

CUPID
Marvel Comics (U.S.A.): Dec, 1949 - No. 2, Mar, 1950

1-Photo-c	30	60	90	177	289	400
2-Bettie Page ('50s pin-up queen) photo-c; Powell-a (see My Love #4)	87	174	261	553	952	1350

CURB STOMP
BOOM! Studios: Feb, 2015 - No. 4, May, 2015 ($3.99, limited series)

1-4-Ryan Ferrier-s/Devaki Neogi-a		4.00

CURIO
Harry 'A' Chesler: 1930's(?) (Tabloid size, 16-20 pgs.)

nn	23	52	78	154	252	350

CURLY KAYOE COMICS (Boxing)
United Features Syndicate/Dell Publ. Co.: 1946 - No. 8, 1950; Jan, 1958

1 (1946)-Strip-r (Fritzi Ritz); biography of Sam Leff, Kayoe's artist	28	56	84	168	274	380

Cult of Carnage: Misery #2 © MAR

Curse Words #2 © Silent E Prods

Cyber Force V4 #4 © TCOW

	GD 2.0	VG 4.0	FN 6.0	VF 8.0	VF/NM 9.0	NM- 9.2
2	19	38	57	111	176	240
3-8	15	30	45	84	127	170
United Presents…(Fall, 1948)	15	30	45	85	130	175
Four Color 871 (Dell, 1/58)	5	10	15	34	60	85

CURSED
Image Comics (Top Cow): Oct, 2003 - No. 4, Feb, 2004 ($2.99)
1-4-Avery & Blevins-s/Molenaar-a 3.00

CURSED COMICS CAVALCADE
DC Comics: Dec, 2018 ($9.99, square-bound one-shot)
1-Short stories of DC heroes facing ghosts and monsters by various; Mahnke-c 10.00

CURSE OF BRIMSTONE, THE
DC Comics: Jun, 2018 - No. 12, May, 2019 ($2.99)
1-12: 1-Philip Tan-a/Philip Tan-a. 6,11,12-Cowan-a. 9-Dr. Fate app. 3.00
Annual 1 (3/19, $4.99) Swamp Thing & Constantine app.; Perkins-a 5.00

CURSE OF DRACULA, THE
Dark Horse Comics: July, 1998 - No. 3, Sept, 1998 ($2.95, limited series)
1-3-Marv Wolfman-s/Gene Colan-a 4.00
TPB (2005, $9.95) r/series; intro. by Marv Wolfman 10.00

CURSE OF RUNE (Becomes Rune, 2nd Series)
Malibu Comics (Ultraverse): May, 1995 - No. 4, Aug, 1995 ($2.50, lim. series)
1-4: 1-Two covers form one image 4.00

CURSE OF THE SPAWN
Image Comics (Todd McFarlane Prod.): Sept, 1996 - No. 29, Mar, 1999 ($1.95)

1-Dwayne Turner-a(p)	2	4	6	10	14	18
1-B&W Edition	4	8	12	23	37	50
2-3	1	2	3	5	6	8

4-29: 12-Movie photo-c of Melinda Clarke (Priest) 4.00
Blood and Sutures ('99, $9.95, TPB) r/#5-8 .... 10.00
Lost Values ('00, $10.95, TPB) r/#12-14,22; Ashley Wood-c 11.00
Sacrifice of the Soul ('99, $9.95, TPB) r/#1-4 .... 10.00
Shades of Gray ('00, $9.95, TPB) r/#9-11,29 .... 10.00
The Best of the Curse of the Spawn (6/06, $16.99, TPB) B&W r/#1-8,12-16,20-29 .. 17.00

CURSE OF THE WEIRD
Marvel Comics: Dec, 1993 - No. 4, Mar, 1994 ($1.25, limited series)
(Pre-code horror-r)

1-4: 1,3,4-Wolverton-r(1-Eye of Doom; 3-Where Monsters Dwell; 4-The End of the World).						
2-Orlando-r. 4-Zombie-r by Everett; painted-c	1	2	3	5	6	8

NOTE: *Briefer* r-2. *Davis* a-4r. *Ditko* a-1r, 2r, 4r; c-1r. *Everett* r-1, 3, 4; c-4r. *Heath* r-1-3. *Kubert* r-3. *Wolverton* a-1r, 3r, 4r.

CURSE WORDS
Image Comics: Jan, 2017 - Present ($3.99)
1-25-Charles Soule-s/Ryan Browne-a 4.00
Holiday Special (12/17, $3.99) Mike Norton-a 4.00
... Spring Special (4/19, $3.99) Norton-a; takes place after #20; Ascender #1 preview . 4.00
... Summer Swimsuit Special (8/18, $3.99) Joe Quinones-a; takes place after #15 .. 4.00

CUSTER'S LAST FIGHT
Avon Periodicals: 1950

nn-Partial reprint of Cowpuncher #1	30	60	90	177	289	400

CUTEY BUNNY (See Army Surplus Komikz Featuring...)

CUTIE PIE
Junior Reader's Guild (Lev Gleason): May, 1955 - No. 3, Dec, 1955; No. 4, Feb, 1956; No. 5, Aug. 1956

1	12	24	36	69	97	125
2-5: 4-Misdated 2/55	8	16	24	42	54	65

CUTTING EDGE
Marvel Comics: Dec, 1995 ($2.95)
1-Hulk-c/story; Messner-Loebs scripts 4.00

CVO: COVERT VAMPIRIC OPERATIONS
IDW Publishing: June, 2003 ($5.99, one-shot)
1-Alex Garner-s/Mindy Lee-a(p) 6.00
... - Human Touch 1 (8/04, $3.99, one-shot) Hernandez & Garner-a 4.00
... - 100-Page Spectacular (4/11, $7.99) r/#1, African Blood #2 Rogue State #5 . 8.00
TPB (9/04, $19.99) r/#1 and ... - Artifact #1-3; intro. by Garner 20.00

CVO: COVERT VAMPIRIC OPERATIONS - AFRICAN BLOOD
IDW Publishing: Sept, 2006 - No. 4, May, 2007 ($3.99, limited series)
1-4-El Torres-s/Luis Czerniawski-a 4.00

CVO: COVERT VAMPIRIC OPERATIONS - ARTIFACT

IDW Publishing: Oct, 2003 - No. 3, Dec, 2003 ($3.99, limited series)
1-3-Jeff Mariotte-s/Gabriel Hernandez-a/Alex Garner-c 4.00

CVO: COVERT VAMPIRIC OPERATIONS - ROGUE STATE
IDW Publishing: Nov, 2004 - No. 5, Mar, 2005 ($3.99, limited series)
1-5-Jeff Mariotte-s/Vazquez-a 4.00
TPB (7/05, $19.99) r/#1-5; cover gallery 20.00

CYBERELLA
DC Comics (Helix): Sept, 1996 - No. 12, Aug, 1997 ($2.25/$2.50)(1st Helix series)
1-12: 1-5-Chaykin & Cameron-a. 1,2-Chaykin-c. 3-5-Cameron-c 4.00

CYBERFORCE
Image Comics (Top Cow Productions): Oct, 1992 - No. 4, 1993; No. 0, Sept, 1993 ($1.95, limited series)
1-Silvestri-c/a in all; coupon for Image Comics #0; 1st Top Cow Productions title .. 6.00
1-With coupon missing 2.00
2-4,0: 2-(3/93). 3-Pitt-c/story. 4-Codename: Stryke Force back-up (1st app.); foil-c. 0-(9/93)-Walt Simonson-c/a/scripts 4.00
...#1 30th Anniversary Edition (6/22, $4.99) R/#1 with creator interviews; cover gallery . 5.00

CYBERFORCE
Image Comics (Top Cow Productions)/Top Cow Comics No. 28 on:
V2#1, Nov, 1993 - No. 35, Sept. 1997 ($1.95)
V2#1-24: 1-7-Marc Silvestri/Keith Williams-c/a. 8-McFarlane-c/a. 10-Painted variant-c exists. 18-Variant-c exists. 23-Velocity-c. 4.00
1-3: 1-Gold Logo-c. 2-Silver embossed-c. 3-Gold embossed-c 10.00
1-(99¢, 3/96, 2nd printing) 3.00
25-($3.95)-Wraparound, foil-c 5.00
26-35: 28-(11/96)-1st Top Cow Comics iss. Quesada & Palmiotti's Gabriel app.
27-Quesada & Palmiotti's Ash app. 4.00
Annual 1,2 (3/95, 8/96, $2.50, $2.95) 5.00
NOTE: *Annuals read Volume One in the indica.*

CYBERFORCE (Volume 3)
Image Comics (Top Cow): Apr, 2006 - No. 6, Nov, 2006 ($2.99)
1-6: 1-Pat Lee-a/Ron Marz-s; three covers by Pat Lee, Marc Silvestri and Dave Finch . 3.00
#0-(6/06, $2.99) reprints origin story from Image Comics Hardcover Vol. 1 .. 3.00
.../X-Men 1 (1/07, $3.99) Pat Lee-a/Ron Marz-s; 2 covers by Lee and Silvestri . 4.00
Vol. 1 TPB (12/06, $14.99) r/#1-6, #0 & story from The Cow Quarterly; cover gallery . 15.00

CYBER FORCE (Volume 4)
Image Comics (Top Cow): Dec, 2012 - No. 11 (no cover price)
1-11: 1-Silvestri & Hawkins-s/Pham-a; multiple covers on each 3.00
...: Artifacts #0 (12/16, $3.99) Short stories by various; Khoi Pham-c 4.00

CYBER FORCE (Volume 5) (See Aphrodite IX and Ninth Generation)
Image Comics (Top Cow): Mar, 2018 - Present ($3.99)
1-11: 1-Matt Hawkins & Bryan Hill-s/Atilio Rojo-a; two covers; origin story . 4.00

CYBERFORCE/HUNTER-KILLER
Image Comics (Top Cow Productions): July, 2009 - No. 5, Mar, 2010 ($2.99)
1-5-Waid-s/Rocafort-a; multiple covers on each 3.00

CYBERFORCE ORIGINS
Image Comics (Top Cow Productions): Jan, 1995 - No. 3, Nov, 1995 ($2.50)
1-Cyblade (1/95) 5.00
1-Cyblade (3/96, 99¢, 2nd printing) 3.00
1A-Exclusive Ed.; Tucci-c 4.00
2,3: 2-Stryker (2/95)-1st Mike Turner-a. 3-Impact 3.00
(#4) Misery (12/95, $2.95) 3.00

CYBERFORCE/STRYKEFORCE: OPPOSING FORCES (See Codename: Stryke Force #15)
Image Comics (Top Cow Productions): Sept, 1995 - No. 2, Oct, 1995 ($2.50, limited series)
1,2: 2-Stryker disbands Strykeforce. 3.00

CYBERFORCE UNIVERSE SOURCEBOOK
Image Comics (Top Cow Productions): Aug, 1994/Feb, 1995 ($2.50)
1,2-Silvestri-c 3.00

CYBERFROG
Hall of Heroes: June, 1994 - No. 2, Dec, 1994 ($2.50, B&W, limited series)

1-Ethan Van Sciver-c/a/scripts	9	18	27	62	126	190
2	5	10	15	35	63	90

CYBERFROG
Harris Comics: Feb, 1996 - No. 3, Apr, 1996 ($2.95)

0-3: Van Sciver-c/a/scripts. 2-Variant-c exists	2	4	6	8	11	14

CYBERFROG: (Title series), **Harris Comics**

	GD 2.0	VG 4.0	FN 6.0	VF 8.0	VF/NM 9.0	NM- 9.2

--RESERVOIR FROG, 9/96 - No. 2, 10/96 ($2.95) 1,2: Van Sciver-c/a/scripts; wraparound-c

| | 2 | 4 | 6 | 9 | 12 | 15 |

--3RD ANNIVERSARY SPECIAL, 1/97 - #2, ($2.50, B&W) 1,2

| | 2 | 4 | 6 | 8 | 10 | 12 |

--VS. CREED, 7/97 ($2.95, B&W)1

| | 2 | 4 | 6 | 11 | 16 | 20 |

CYBERNARY (See Deathblow #1)
Image Comics (WildStorm Productions): Nov, 1995 - No.5, Mar, 1996 ($2.50)

| 1-5 | | | | | | 4.00 |

CYBERNARY 2.0
DC Comics (WildStorm): Sept, 2001 - No. 6, Apr, 2002 ($2.95, limited series)

| 1-6: Joe Harris-s/Eric Canete-a. 6-The Authority app. | | | | | | 3.00 |

CYBERPUNK
Innovation Publishing: Sept, 1989 - No. 2, Oct, 1989 ($1.95, 28 pgs.) Book 2, #1, May, 1990 - No. 2, 1990 ($2.25, 28 pgs.)

| 1-Ken Steacy painted-cover (Adults) | 2 | 4 | 6 | 9 | 12 | 15 |
| 2, Book 2 #1,2: 2-Ken Steacy painted-covers (Adults) | | | | | | 6.00 |

CYBERPUNK: THE SERAPHIM FILES
Innovation Publishing: Nov, 1990 - No. 2, Dec, 1990 ($2.50, 28 pgs., mature)

| 1,2: 1-Painted-c; story cont'd from Seraphim | | | | | | 5.00 |

CYBERPUNK 2077: BLACKOUT (Based on the video game Cyberpunk 2077)
Dark Horse Comics: Jun, 2022 - No. 4, Sept, 2022 ($3.99, limited series)

| 1-3-Bartosz Sytybor-s/Roberto Ricci-a | | | | | | 4.00 |

CYBERPUNK 2077: TRAUMA TEAM (Based on the video game Cyberpunk 2077)
Dark Horse Comics: Sept, 2020 - No. 4, Dec, 2020 ($3.99, limited series)

| 1-4-Cullen Bunn-s/Miguel Valderrama-a | | | | | | 4.00 |

CYBERPUNK 2077: XOXO (Based on the video game Cyberpunk 2077)
Dark Horse Comics: Oct, 2023 - No. 4, Jan, 2024 ($3.99, limited series)

| 1-4-Bartosz Sztybor-s/Jakub Rebelka-a | | | | | | 4.00 |

CYBERPUNK 2077: YOU HAVE MY WORD (Based on the video game Cyberpunk 2077)
Dark Horse Comics: Apr, 2021 - No. 4, Nov, 2022 ($3.99, limited series)

| 1-4-Bartosz Sztybor-s/Jesús Hervás-a | | | | | | 4.00 |

CYBERRAD
Continuity Comics: 1991 - No. 7, 1992 ($2.00)(Direct sale & newsstand-c variations)
V2#1, 1993 ($2.50)

1-7: 5-Glow-in-the-dark-c by N. Adams (direct sale only). 6-Contains a 4 pg. fold-out poster; N. Adams layouts						4.00
V2#1-($2.95, direct sale ed.)-Die-cut-c w/B&W hologram on-c; Neal Adams sketches						4.00
V2#1-($2.50, newsstand ed.)-Without sketches						4.00

CYBERRAD DEATHWATCH 2000 (Becomes CyberRad w/#2, 7/93)
Continuity Comics: Apr, 1993 - No. 2, 1993 ($2.50)

| 1,2: 1-Bagged w/2 cards; Adams-c & layouts & plots. 2-Bagged w/card; Adams scripts | | | | | | 4.00 |

CYBER 7
Eclipse Comics: Mar, 1989 - #7, Sept, 1989; V2#1, Oct, 1989 - #10, 1990 ($2.00, B&W)

| 1-7, Book 2 #1-10: Stories translated from Japanese | | | | | | 4.00 |

CYBLADE
Image Comics (Top Cow Productions): Oct, 2008 - No. 4, Mar, 2009 ($2.99)

1-4: 1,2-Mays-a/Fialkov-s. 1-Two covers. 3,4-Ferguson-a						3.00
.../ Ghost Rider 1 (Marvel/Top Cow, 1/97, $2.95) Devil's Reign pt. 2						4.00
...: Pilot Season 1 (9/07, $2.99) Rick Mays-a						3.00

CYBLADE/SHI (Also see Battle For The Independents & Shi/Cyblade: The Battle For The Independents)
Image Comics (Top Cow Productions): 1995 ($2.95, one-shot)

San Diego Preview	2	4	6	13	18	22
1-($2.95)-1st app. Witchblade	2	4	6	9	13	16
1-($2.95)-variant-c; Tucci-a						6.00

CYBORG (From Justice League)
DC Comics: Sept, 2015 - No. 12, Aug, 2016 ($2.99)

| 1-12: 1-Walker-s/Reis-a. 3-6-Metal Men app. 9,10-Shazam app. | | | | | | 3.00 |

CYBORG (DC Rebirth)
DC Comics: Nov, 2016 - No. 23, Aug, 2018 ($2.99/$3.99)

1-10: 1-Semper Jr.-s/Pelletier-a; Kilg%re app. 6-Intro. Variant						3.00
11-23: 11-Begin $3.99-c. 15-Metal Men app. 15-17-Beast Boy app.						4.00
...: Rebirth 1 (11/16, $2.99) Semper Jr.-s/Pelletier-a; origin retold						3.00

CYBORG (Dawn of DC)
DC Comics: Jul, 2023 - No. 6, Feb, 2024 ($3.99)

| 1-6: 1-Morgan Hampton-s/Tom Raney-a; Mammoth & Gizmo app. | | | | | | 4.00 |

CYBRID
Maximum Press: July, 1995 - No. 0, Jan, 1997 ($2.95/$3.50)

| 1-(7/95) | | | | | | 4.00 |
| 0-(1/97)-Liefeld-a/script; story cont'd in Avengelyne #4 | | | | | | 4.00 |

CYCLONE COMICS (Also see Whirlwind Comics)
Bilbara Publishing Co.: June, 1940 - No. 5, Nov, 1940

1-Origin Tornado Tom; Volton (the human generator), Tornado Tom, Kingdom of the Moon, Mister Q begin (1st app. of each)	110	220	330	704	1202	1700
2	81	162	243	518	884	1250
3-Classic-c (scarce)	155	310	465	992	1696	2400
4-(9/40)	84	168	252	538	919	1300
5-(Scarce)	116	232	348	742	1271	1800

Ashcan - (5/40) Not distributed to newsstands, for in house use. Cover produced on green stock paper. A CGC certified FN (6.0) copy sold for $2,000 in 2006.

CYCLOPS (X-Men)
Marvel Comics: Oct, 2001 - No. 4, Jan, 2002 ($2.50, limited series)

| 1-4-Texeira-c/a. 1,2-Black Tom and Juggernaut app. | | | | | | 4.00 |
| 1-(5/11, $2.99, one-shot) Haspiel-a; Batroc and the Circus of Crime app. | | | | | | 4.00 |

CYCLOPS (All-New X-Men)
Marvel Comics: Jul, 2014 - No. 12, Jun, 2015 ($3.99)

| 1-10: 1-Rucka-s/Dauterman-a; Corsair app. 6-12-Layman-s. 12-Black Vortex x-over | | | | | | 4.00 |

CYCLOPS: RETRIBUTION
Marvel Comics: 1994 ($5.95, trade paperback)

| nn-r/Marvel Comics Presents #17-24 | 2 | 4 | 6 | 8 | 11 | 14 |

CY-GOR (See Spawn #38 for 1st app.)
Image Comics (Todd McFarlane Prod.): July, 1999 - No. 6, Dec, 1999 ($2.50)

| 1-6-Veitch-s | | | | | | 4.00 |

CYNTHIA DOYLE, NURSE IN LOVE (Formerly Sweetheart Diary)
Charlton Publications: No. 66, Oct, 1962 - No. 74, Feb, 1964

| 66-74 | 4 | 8 | 12 | 23 | 37 | 50 |

DAFFODIL
Marvel Comics (Soleil): 2010 - No. 3, 2010 ($5.99, limited series)

| 1-3-English version of French comic; Brrémaud-s/Rigano-a | | | | | | 6.00 |

DAFFY (Daffy Duck No. 18 on)(See Looney Tunes)
Dell Publishing Co./Gold Key No. 31-127/Whitman No. 128 on: #457, 3/53 - #30, 7-9/62; #31, 10-12/62 - #145, 6/84 (No #132,133)

Four Color 457(#1)-Elmer Fudd x-overs begin	13	26	39	89	195	300
Four Color 536,615('55)	8	16	24	52	99	145
4(1-3/56)-11('57)	5	10	15	33	57	80
12-19(1958-59)	4	8	12	28	47	65
20-40(1960-64)	3	6	9	20	31	42
41-60(1964-68)	3	6	9	16	23	30
61-90(1969-74)-Road Runner in most. 76-82-"Daffy Duck and the Road Runner" on-c	2	4	6	11	16	20
90-Whitman variant	3	6	9	14	19	24
91-110	2	4	6	8	11	14
111-127	1	3	4	6	8	10
128,134-141: 139(2/82), 140(2-3/82), 141(4/82)	2	4	6	8	10	12
129(8/80),130,131 (pre-pack?) (scarce). 129-Sherlock Holmes parody-s	4	8	12	28	47	65
142-145(#90029 on-c; nd, nd code, pre-pack): 142(6/83), 143(8/83), 144(3/84), 145(6/84)	3	6	9	17	26	35
Mini-Comic 1 (1976: 3-1/4x6-1/2")	1	3	4	6	8	10

NOTE: Reprint issues-No.41-46, 48, 50, 53-55, 58, 59, 65, 67, 69, 73, 81, 96, 103-108; 136-142, 144, 145(1/3-2/3-r). (See March Comics for No. 277, 288, 303, 313, 334, 347, 357,375, 387, 397, 402, 413, 425, 437, 460).

DAFFY DUCK (Digest-size reprints from Looney Tunes)
DC Comics: 2005 ($6.99, digest)

| Vol. 1: You're Despicable! - Reprints from Looney Tunes #38,43,45,47,51,53,54,58,61,62,66,70 | | | | | | 7.00 |

DAFFY TUNES COMICS
Four-Star Publications: June, 1947; No. 12, Aug, 1947

| nn | 14 | 28 | 42 | 80 | 115 | 150 |
| 12-Al Fago-c/a; funny animal | 12 | 24 | 36 | 67 | 94 | 120 |

DAGAR, DESERT HAWK (Captain Kidd No. 24 on; formerly All Great)
Fox Feature Syndicate: No. 14, Feb, 1948 - No. 23, Apr, 1949 (No #17,18)

14-Tangi & Safari Cary begin; Good bondage-c/a	142	284	426	909	1555	2200
15,16-E. Good-a; 15-Headlight-c	74	148	222	470	810	1150
19,20,22: 19-Used in SOTI, pg. 180 (Tangi)	71	142	213	454	777	1100
21,23: 21-Bondage-c; "Bombs & Bums Away" panel in "Flood of Death" story used in SOTI. 23-Bondage-c	84	168	252	538	919	1300

NOTE: Tangi by Kamen-14-16, 19, 20; c-20, 21.

DAGAR THE INVINCIBLE (Tales of Sword & Sorcery…) (Also see Dan Curtis Giveaways & Gold Key Spotlight)
Gold Key: Oct, 1972 - No. 18, Dec, 1976; No. 19, Apr, 1982

1-Origin; intro. Villains Olstellon & Scor	4	8	12	23	37	50
2-5: 3-Intro. Graylin; Dagar's woman; Jarn x-over	3	6	9	14	19	24
6-1st Dark Gods story	2	4	6	9	13	16
7-10: 9-Intro. Torgus. 10-1st Three Witches story	2	4	6	9	13	16
11-18: 13-Durak & Torgus x-over; story continues in Dr. Spektor #15.						
14-Dagar's origin retold. 18-Origin retold	2	4	6	8	10	12
19(4/82)-Origin-r/#18						6.00

NOTE: Durak app. in 7, 12, 13. Tragg app. in 5, 11.

DAGWOOD (Chic Young's) (Also see Blondie Comics)
Harvey Publications: Sept, 1950 - No. 140, Nov, 1965

1	21	42	63	147	324	500
2	10	20	30	69	147	225
3-10	7	14	21	48	89	130
11-20	6	12	18	37	66	95
21-30	5	10	15	33	57	80
31-50: 33-Sci-Fi-c	4	8	12	28	47	65
51-70	3	6	9	21	33	45
71-100	3	6	9	17	26	35
101-121,123-128,130,135	3	6	9	16	23	30
122,129,131-134,136-140-All are 68-pg. issues	3	6	9	21	33	45

NOTE: Popeye and other one page strips appeared in early issues.

DAI KAMIKAZE!
Now Comics: June, 1987 - No. 12, Aug, 1988 ($1.75)

1-1st app. Speed Racer	2	4	6	8	10	12
1-Second printing						4.00
2-12						3.00

DAILY BUGLE (See Spider-Man)
Marvel Comics: Dec, 1996 - No. 3, Feb, 1997 ($2.50, B&W, limited series)

| 1-3-Paul Grist-s | | | | | | 4.00 |

DAISY
Dark Horse Comics: Dec, 2021 - No. 5, Apr, 2022 ($3.99)

| 1-5-Colin Lorimer-s/a | | | | | | 4.00 |

DAISY AND DONALD (See Walt Disney Showcase No. 8)

Cyborg (2023 series) #1 © DC

Dagwood #34 © HARV

Damage Control (2022 series) #4 © MAR

	GD	VG	FN	VF	VF/NM	NM-
	2.0	4.0	6.0	8.0	9.0	9.2

Gold Key/Whitman No. 42 on: May, 1973 - No. 59, July, 1984 (no No. 48)

	GD	VG	FN	VF	VF/NM	NM-
1-Barks-r/WDC&S #280,308	5	10	15	30	50	70
2-5: 4-Barks-r/WDC&S #224	2	4	6	11	16	20
6-10	2	4	6	9	12	15
11-20	1	3	4	6	8	10
21-41: 32-r/WDC&S #308	1	2	3	5	6	8
36,42-44 (Whitman)	2	4	6	8	11	14
45 (8/80),46-(pre-pack?)(scarce)	4	8	12	27	44	60
47-(12/80)-Only distr. in Whitman 3-pack (scarce)	5	10	15	35	63	90
48(3/81)-50(8/81): 50-r/#3	2	4	6	10	14	18
51-54: 51-Barks-r/4-Color 1150. 52-r/#2. 53(2/82), 54(4/82)						
	2	4	6	9	13	16
55-59-(all #90284 on-c, nd, nd code, pre-pack): 55(5/83), 56(7/83), 57(8/83),						
58(8/83), 59(7/84)	3	6	9	19	30	40

DAISY & HER PUPS (Dagwood & Blondie's Dogs)(Formerly Blondie Comics #20)
Harvey Publications: No. 21, 7/51 - No. 27, 7/52; No. 8, 9/52 - No. 18, 5/54

21 (#1)-Blondie's dog Daisy and her 5 pups led by Elmer begin. Rags Rabbit app.						
	6	12	18	38	69	100
22-27 (#2-7): 26 has No. 6 on cover but No. 26 on inside. 23,25-The Little King app.						
24-Bringing Up Father by McManus app. 25-27-Rags Rabbit app.						
	4	8	12	28	47	65
8-18: 8,9-Rags Rabbit app. 8,17-The Little King app. 11-The Flop Family Swan begins.						
22-Cookie app. 11-Felix The Cat app. by 17,18-Popeye app.						
	4	8	12	27	44	60

DAISY DUCK & UNCLE SCROOGE PICNIC TIME (See Dell Giant #33)
DAISY DUCK & UNCLE SCROOGE SHOW BOAT (See Dell Giant #55)
DAISY DUCK'S DIARY (See Dynabrite Comics, & Walt Disney's C&S #298)
Dell Publishing Co.: No. 600, Nov, 1954 - No. 1247, Dec-Feb, 1961-62 (Disney)

Four Color 600 (#1)	9	18	27	59	117	175
Four Color 659, 743 (11/56)	6	12	18	42	79	115
Four Color 858 (11/57), 948 (11/58), 1247 (12-2/61-62)						
	5	10	15	35	63	90
Four Color 1055 (11-1/59-60), 1150 (12-1/60-61)-By Carl Barks						
	9	18	27	59	117	175

DAISY HANDBOOK
Daisy Manufacturing Co.: 1946; No. 2, 1948 (10¢, pocket-size, 132 pgs.)

1-Buck Rogers, Red Ryder; Wolverton-a (2 pgs.)	28	56	84	168	274	380
2-Captain Marvel & Ibis the Invincible, Red Ryder, Boy Commandos & Robotman;						
Wolverton-a (2 pgs.); contains 8 pg. color catalog	28	56	84	168	274	380

DAISY MAE (See Oxydol-Drěft)
DAISY'S RED RYDER GUN BOOK
Daisy Manufacturing Co.: 1955 (25¢, pocket-size, 132 pgs.)

nn-Boy Commandos, Red Ryder; 1pg. Wolverton-a	18	36	54	105	165	225

DAKEN: DARK WOLVERINE
Marvel Comics: Nov, 2010 - No. 23, May, 2012 ($3.99/$2.99)

1-Camuncoli-a/c; Way & Liu-s; back-up history of the character						5.00
2-9, 9.1, 10-23-($2.99) 3,4-Fantastic Four app. 7-9-Crossover with X-23 #8,9; Gambit app.						
9.1-Avengers app. 13-16-Moon Knight app. 17-19-Runaways app.						3.00

DAKKON BLACKBLADE ON THE WORLD OF MAGIC: THE GATHERING
Acclaim Comics (Armada): June, 1996 ($5.95, one-shot)

1-Jerry Prosser scripts; Rags Morales-c/a.						6.00

DAKOTA LIL (See Fawcett Movie Comics)
DAKTARI (Ivan Tors) (TV)
Dell Publishing Co.: July, 1967 - No. 3, Oct, 1968; No. 4, Oct, 1969

1-Marshall Thompson photo-c on all	4	8	12	25	40	55
2-4	3	6	9	18	28	38

DALE EVANS COMICS (Also see Queen of the West...)(See Boy Commandos #32)
National Periodical Publications: Sept-Oct, 1948 - No. 24, Jul-Aug, 1952 (No. 1-19: 52 pgs.)

1-Dale Evans & her horse Buttermilk begin; Sierra Smith begins by Alex Toth						
	63	126	189	403	689	975
2-Alex Toth-a	31	62	93	186	303	420
3-11-Alex Toth-a	20	40	60	114	182	250
12-20: 12-Target-c	14	28	42	80	115	150
21-24	14	28	42	82	121	160

NOTE: Photo-c-1, 2, 4-14.

DALGODA
Fantagraphics Books: Aug, 1984 - No. 8, Feb, 1986 (High quality paper)

1,8: 1- Fujitake-c/a in all. 8-Alan Moore story						5.00

	GD	VG	FN	VF	VF/NM	NM-
	2.0	4.0	6.0	8.0	9.0	9.2

2-7: 2,3-Debut Grimwood's Daughter.						4.00

DALTON BOYS, THE
Avon Periodicals: 1951

1-(Number on spine)-Kinstler-c	28	56	84	165	270	375

DAMAGE
DC Comics: Apr, 1994 - No. 20, Jan, 1996 ($1.75/$1.95/$2.25)

1-20: 6-(9/94)-Zero Hour. 0-(10/94). 7-(11/94). 14-Ray app.						4.00

DAMAGE
DC Comics: Mar, 2018 - No. 16, Jun, 2019 ($2.99/$3.99)

1-12: 1-Venditti-s/Daniel-a; intro. Ethan Avery. 2-Suicide Squad app. 2,3-Wonder Woman app.						
4,5-Poison Ivy app. 4-Nord-a. 8,9-Unknown Soldier app. 10-12-Justice League app.						3.00
13-16-($3.99) 13-Batman app. 14-16-Congo Bill app.						4.00
Annual 1 (10/18, $4.99) Takes place between #8&9; Lopresti-a						5.00

DAMAGE CONTROL (See Marvel Comics Presents #19)
Marvel Comics: 5/89 - No. 4, 8/89; V2#1, 12/89 - No. 4, 2/90 ($1.00)
V3#1, 6/91 - No. 4, 9/91 ($1.25, all are limited series)

V1#1-4, V2#1-4,V3#1-4: V1#4-Wolverine app. V2#2,4-Punisher app. 1-Spider-Man app.						
2-New Warriors app. 3,4-Silver Surfer app. 4-Infinity Gauntlet parody						4.00

DAMAGE CONTROL
Marvel Comics: Oct, 2022 - No. 5, Feb, 2023 ($4.99/$3.99)

1-($4.99) Adam Goldberg & Hans Rodinoff-s/Will Robson-a						5.00
2-5-($3.99) 4-Wrecking Crew app. 5-Sentinels app.						4.00

DAMAGED
Radical Comics: Jul, 2011 - No. 6 ($3.99/$3.50, limited series)

1-($3.99) Lapham-s/Manco-a; covers by Maleev & Manco						4.00
2-4-($3.50) Maleev-c						3.50

DAMIAN: SON OF BATMAN
DC Comics: Dec, 2013 - No. 4, Mar, 2014 ($3.99, limited series)

1-4-Andy Kubert-s/c/a; near-future Damian; Ra's al Ghul & Talia app.						4.00
1-Variant-c by Tony Daniel						8.00

DAMNATION: JOHNNY BLAZE - GHOST RIDER
Marvel Comics: May, 2018 ($3.99, one-shot)

1-Part of x-over with Doctor Strange: Damnation; Sebela-s/Noto-a/Crain-c						4.00

DAMNED
Image Comics (Homage Comics): June, 1997 - No. 4, Sept, 1997 ($2.50, limited series)

1-4-Steven Grant-s/Mike Zeck-c/a in all						4.00

DAMN NATION
Dark Horse Comics: Feb, 2005 - No. 3, Apr, 2005 ($2.99, limited series)

1-3-J. Alexander-a/Andrew Cosby-s						3.00

DAMN THEM ALL
BOOM! Studios: Oct, 2022 - No. 12, Jan, 2024 ($3.99)

1-12-Spurrier-s/Adlard-a						4.00

DAMSELS
Dynamite Entertainment: 2012 - No. 13, 2014 ($3.99)

1-13: 1-Leah Moore & John Reppion-s/Aneke-a. 1-Campbell-c. 2-8-Linsner-c						4.00
... Giant Killer One Shot (2013, $4.99) Leah Moore & John Reppion-s/Dietrich Smith-a						5.00

DAMSELS IN EXCESS
Aspen MLT: Jul, 2014 - No. 5, May, 2015 ($3.99, limited series)

1-5-Vince Hernandez-s/Mirka Andolfo-a; multiple covers on each						4.00

DAMSELS: MERMAIDS
Dynamite Entertainment: No. 0, 2013 - No. 5, 2013 ($3.99)

0-Free Comic Book Day giveaway; Sturges-s/Deshong-a/Hans-c						3.00
1-5-($3.99) Sturges-s/Deshong-a. 1-Two covers by Anacleto & Renaud. 2-5-Renaud-c						4.00

DANCES WITH DEMONS (See Marvel Frontier Comics Unlimited)
Marvel Frontier Comics: Sept, 1993 - No. 4, Dec, 1993 ($1.95, limited series)

1-($2.95)-Foil embossed-c; Charlie Adlard & Rod Ramos-a						5.00
2-4						4.00

DAN DARE
Virgin Comics: Nov, 2007 - No. 7, July, 2008 ($2.99/$5.99)

1-6-Ennis-s/Erskine-a. 1-Two covers by Talbot and Horn. 2-6-Two covers on each						3.00
7-($5.99) Double sized finale with wraparound Erskine-c; Gibbons variant-c						6.00

DAN DARE
Titan Comics: Nov, 2017 - No. 4, Jan, 2018 ($3.99)

1-4-MIlligan-s/Foche-a; multiple covers on each						4.00

	GD 2.0	VG 4.0	FN 6.0	VF 8.0	VF/NM 9.0	NM- 9.2

DANDEE: Four Star Publications: 1947 (Advertised, not published)

DAN DUNN (See Crackajack Funnies, Detective Dan, Famous Feature Stories & Red Ryder)

DANDY COMICS (Also see Happy Jack Howard)
E. C. Comics: Spring, 1947 - No. 7, Spring, 1948

	GD 2.0	VG 4.0	FN 6.0	VF 8.0	VF/NM 9.0	NM- 9.2
1-Funny animal; Vince Fago-a in all; Dandy in all	58	116	174	371	636	900
2	39	78	117	231	378	525
3-7: 3-Intro Handy Andy who is c-feature #3 on	34	68	102	199	325	450

DANGER
Comic Media/Allen Hardy Assoc.: Jan, 1953 - No. 11, Aug, 1954

1-Heck-c/a	39	78	117	231	378	525
2,3,5,7,9-11:	21	42	63	122	199	275
4-Marijuana cover/story	24	48	72	142	234	325
6- "Narcotics" story; begin spy theme	22	44	66	130	213	295
8-Bondage/torture/headlights panels	34	68	102	199	325	450

NOTE: *Morisi* a-2, 5, 6(3), 10; c-2. Contains some reprints from Danger & Dynamite.

DANGER (Formerly Comic Media title)
Charlton Comics Group: No. 12, June, 1955 - No. 14, Oct, 1955

12(#1)	18	36	54	103	162	220
13,14: 14-r/#12	14	28	42	80	115	150

DANGER
Super Comics: 1964

Super Reprint #10-12 (Black Dwarf; #10-r/Great Comics #1 by Novack. #11-r/Johnny Danger #1. #12-r/Red Seal #14), #15-r/Spy Cases #26. #16-Unpublished Chesler material (Yankee Girl), #17-r/Scoop #8 (Capt. Courage & Enchanted Dagger), #18(nd)-r/Guns Against Gangsters #5 (Gun-Master, Annie Oakley, The Chameleon; L.B. Cole-r)

	3	6	9	14	20	25

DANGER AND ADVENTURE (Formerly This Magazine Is Haunted; Robin Hood and His Merry Men No. 28 on)
Charlton Comics: No. 22, Feb, 1955 - No. 27, Feb, 1956

22-Ibis the Invincible-c/story (last G.A. app.); Nyoka app.; last pre-code issue						
	15	30	45	83	124	165
23-Lance O'Casey-c/sty; Nyoka app.; Ditko-a thru #27						
	15	30	45	88	137	185
24-27: 24-Mike Danger & Johnny Adventure begin	12	24	36	67	94	120

DANGER GIRL (Also see Cliffhanger #0)
Image Comics (Cliffhanger Productions): Mar, 1998 - No. 4, Dec, 1998;
DC Comics (Cliffhanger Prod.): No. 5, July, 1999 - No. 7, Feb, 2001

Preview-Bagged in DV8 #14 Voyager Pack	2	4	6	11	16	20
Preview Gold Edition	4	8	12	22	35	50
1-($2.95) Hartnell & Campbell-s/Campbell/Garner-a	2	4	6	9	12	15
1-($4.95) Chromium cover	5	10	15	34	60	85
1-American Entertainment Ed.	1	3	4	6	8	10
1-American Entertainment Gold Ed., 1-Tourbook Ed.	2	4	6	11	16	20
1-"Danger-sized" ed.; over-sized format	3	6	9	16	24	32
2-($2.50)	1	2	3	5	6	8
2-Smoking Gun variant cover	7	14	21	48	89	130
2-Platinum ed.	11	22	33	73	157	240
2-Dynamic Forces Omnichrome variant-c	3	6	9	16	23	30
2-Gold foil cover	3	6	9	14	20	25
2-Ruby red foil cover	15	30	45	103	227	350
3,4: 3-c by Campbell, Charest and Adam Hughes. 4-Big knife variant-c						4.00
3,5: 3-Gold foil cover. 5-DF Bikini variant-c	1	3	4	6	8	10
4-6						4.00
7-($5.95) Wraparound gatefold-c; Last issue						6.00
...: Dangerous Visions 3-D (IDW, 2/19, $6.99) r/#1 & Preview; bagged with glasses						7.00
...: Danger-Sized Treasury Edition #1 (IDW, 1/12, $9.99, 13" x 8-1/2") r/#1,2 & Preview						10.00
...: Hawaiian Punch (5/03, $4.95) Campbell-a; Phil Noto-a						5.00
...: Odd Jobs TPB (2004, $14.95) r/one-shots Hawaiian Punch, Viva Las Danger & Special; Campbell-a						15.00
San Diego Preview (8/98, B&W) flip book w/Wildcats preview						5.00
Sketchbook (2001, $6.95) Campbell-a; sketches for comics, toys, games						7.00
...Special (2/00, $3.50) art by Campbell, Chiodo, and Art Adams						3.50
... 3-D #1 (4/03, $4.95, bagged with 3-D glasses) r/ Preview & #1 in 3-D						5.00
...: Viva Las Danger (1/04, $4.95) Noto-a/Campbell-c						5.00
...: The Dangerous Collection nn (8/98; r/#1)						6.00
...: The Dangerous Collection 2,3: 2-(11/98, $5.95) r/#2,3. 3-('99) r/#4,5						6.00
...: The Dangerous Collection nn, 2-($10.00) Gold foil logo						10.00
...: The Ultimate Collection HC ($29.95) r/#1-7; intro by Bruce Campbell						30.00
...: The Ultimate Collection SC ($19.95) r/#1-7; intro by Bruce Campbell						20.00

DANGER GIRL AND THE ARMY OF DARKNESS
Dynamite Entertainment/ IDW Publ.: 2011 - No. 6, 2012 ($3.99, limited series)

1-6-Hartnell-s/Bolson-a. 1,2 Covers by Campbell, Bradshaw & Renaud						4.00

DANGER GIRL: BACK IN BLACK
DC Comics (Cliffhanger): Jan, 2006 - No. 4, Apr, 2006 ($2.99, limited series)

1-Hartnell-s/Bradshaw-a; Campbell-c	1	3	4	6	8	10
2-4-Hartnell-s/Bradshaw-a						3.00
TPB (2007, $12.99) r/series & covers						13.00

DANGER GIRL: BODY SHOTS
DC Comics (WildStorm): Jun, 2007 - No. 4, Sept, 2007 ($2.99, limited series)

1-4-Hartnell-s/Bradshaw-a						5.00
TPB (2007, $12.99) r/series & covers						13.00

DANGER GIRL/ G.I. JOE
IDW Publishing: Jul, 2012 - No. 5, Nov, 2012 ($3.99, limited series)

1-Hartnell-s/Royle-a; 2 covers by Campbell on each	1	3	4	6	8	10
2-5-Hartnell-s/Royle-a						6.00

DANGER GIRL KAMIKAZE
DC Comics (Cliffhanger): Nov, 2001 - No. 2, Dec., 2001 ($2.95, lim. series)

1,2-Tommy Yune-s/a						3.00

DANGER GIRL: MAYDAY

IDW Publishing: Apr, 2014 - No. 4, Aug, 2014 ($3.99, limited series)

1-4-Hartnell-s/Royle-a; 2 covers by Royle on each						4.00

DANGER GIRL: RENEGADE
IDW Publishing: Sept, 2015 - No. 4, Jan, 2016 ($3.99, limited series)

1-4-Hartnell-s/Molnar-a/Campbell-c						4.00

DANGER GIRL: REVOLVER
IDW Publishing: Jan, 2012 - No. 4, Apr, 2012 ($3.99, limited series)

1-4-Hartnell-s/Madden-a; covers by Campbell & Madden						5.00

DANGER GIRL: THE CHASE
IDW Publishing: Sept, 2013 - No. 4, Dec, 2013 ($3.99, limited series)

1-4-Hartnell-s/Tolibao-a. 1-Three covers (Panosian, Wallace & photo)						5.00

DANGER GIRL: TRINITY
IDW Publishing: Apr, 2013 - No. 4, Jul, 2013 ($3.99, limited series)

1-Hartnell-s/Campbell-c; art by Royle, Tolibao, & Molnar; variant-c by Garner			2	4	6	10	14	18
2-4	1	3	4	6	8	10

DANGER IS OUR BUSINESS!
Toby Press: 1953(Dec.) - No. 10, June, 1955

1-Captain Comet by Williamson/Frazetta, 6 pgs. (science fiction)						
	74	148	222	470	810	1150
2	20	40	60	117	189	260
3-10	16	32	48	94	147	200
I.W. Reprint #9('64)-Williamson/Frazetta-r/#1; Kinstler-c						
	9	18	27	57	111	165

DANGER IS THEIR BUSINESS (Also see A-1 Comic)
Magazine Enterprises: No. 50, 1952

A-1 50-Powell-a	20	40	60	117	189	260

DANGER MAN (TV)
Dell Publishing Co.: No. 1231, Sept-Nov, 1961

Four Color 1231-Patrick McGoohan photo-c	11	22	33	77	166	255

DANGER STREET (Characters from 1st Issue Special series '74-'75)
DC Comics (Black Label): Feb, 2023 - No. 12, Feb, 2024 ($4.99, limited series)

1-12-King-s/Fornés-a; Lady Cop, Creeper, Starman, Warlord, Metamorpho, Atlas app.						5.00

DANGER TRAIL (Also see Showcase #50, 51)
National Periodical Publ.: July-Aug, 1950 - No. 5, Mar-Apr, 1951 (52 pgs.)

1-King Faraday begins, ends #4; Toth-a in all	161	322	483	1030	1765	2500
2	113	226	339	718	1234	1750
3-(Rare) one of the rarest early '50s DCs	174	348	522	1114	1907	2700
4,5: 5-Johnny Peril-c/story (moves to Sensation Comics #107); new logo (also see Comic Cavalcade #15-29)	81	162	243	518	884	1250

DANGER TRAIL
DC Comics: Apr, 1993 - No. 4, July, 1993 ($1.50, limited series)

1-4- Gulacy-c on all						4.00

DANGER UNLIMITED (See San Diego Comic Con Comics #2 & Torch of Liberty Special)
Dark Horse (Legend): Feb, 1994 - No. 4, May, 1994 ($2.00, limited series)

1-4: Byrne-c/a/scripts in all; origin stories of both original team (Doc Danger, Thermal, Miss Mirage, & Hunk) & future team (Thermal, Belebet, & Caucus). 1-Intro Torch of Liberty & Golgotha (cameo) in back-up story. 4-Hellboy & Torch of Liberty cameo in lead story						4.00
TPB (1995, $14.95)-r/#1-4; includes last pg. originally cut from #4						15.00

DAN HASTINGS (See Syndicate Features)

DANIEL BOONE (See The Exploits of..., Fighting... Frontier Scout...,The Legends of... & March of Comics No. 306)
Dell Publishing Co.: No. 1163, Mar-May, 1961

Four Color 1163-Marsh-a	5	10	15	35	63	90

DANIEL BOONE (TV) (See March of Comics No. 306)
Gold Key: Jan, 1965 - No. 15, Apr, 1969 (All have Fess Parker photo-c)

1-Back-c and last eight pages fold in half to form "Official Handbook Fess Parker as Daniel Boone Trail Blazers Club"	8	16	24	54	102	150
2-Back-c pin-up	5	10	15	30	50	70
3-5-Back-c pin-ups	4	8	12	25	40	55
6-15: 7,8-Back-c pin-up	3	6	9	19	30	40

DAN'L BOONE
Sussex Publ. Co.: Sept, 1955 - No. 8, Sept, 1957

1	15	30	45	86	133	180
2	10	20	30	54	72	90
3-8	8	16	24	40	50	60

DANNY BLAZE (...Firefighter) (Nature Boy No. 3 on)
Charlton Comics: Aug, 1955 - No. 2, Oct, 1955

1-Authentic stories of fire fighting	16	32	48	94	147	200
2	13	26	39	72	101	130

DANNY DINGLE (See Sparkler Comics)
United Features Syndicate: No. 17, 1940

Single Series 17	34	68	102	199	325	450

DANNY KETCH: GHOST RIDER
Marvel Comics: Jul, 2023 - No. 4, Oct, 2023 ($4.99/$3.99)

1-($4.99) Mackie-s/Picciotto-a; Johnny Blaze app.; intro The Broker						5.00
2-4-($3.99) 2-Blackout & The Scarecrow app.						4.00

DANNY THOMAS SHOW, THE (TV)
Dell Publishing Co.: No. 1180, Apr-June, 1961 - No. 1249, Dec-Feb, 1961-62

Four Color 1180-Toth-a, photo-c	16	32	48	111	246	380
Four Color 1249-Manning-a, photo-c	12	24	36	80	173	265

DANTE'S INFERNO (Based on the video game)
DC Comics (WildStorm): Feb, 2010 - No. 6, Jul, 2010 ($3.99, limited series)

Danger Girl: Renegade #3 © JS Campbell

Daredevil #41 © LEV

Daredevil #13 © MAR

	GD 2.0	VG 4.0	FN 6.0	VF 8.0	VF/NM 9.0	NM- 9.2

1-6-Christos Gage-s/Diego Latorre-a 4.00
TPB (2010, $19.99) r/#1-6 .... 20.00

DAOMU (Based on a novel series from China)
Image Comics: Feb, 2011 - No. 8, Dec, 2011 ($2.99)

1-8-Kennedy Xu-s/Ken Chou-a 3.00

DAPHNE BYRNE
DC Comics (Hill House Comics): Mar, 2020 - No. 6, Sept, 2020 ($3.99)

1-6-Laura Marks-s/Kelley Jones-a; back-up Sea Dogs serial 4.00

DARBY O'GILL & THE LITTLE PEOPLE (Movie)(See Movie Comics)
Dell Publishing Co.: 1959 (Disney)

Four Color 1024-Toth-a; photo-c. .... 9 ... 18 ... 27 ... 59 ... 117 ... 175

DAREDEVIL ("Daredevil Comics" on cover of #2) (See Silver Streak Comics)
Lev Gleason Publications (Funnies, Inc. No. 1): July, 1941 - No. 134, Sept, 1956
(52 pgs. #52-80; 64 pgs. #35-41)(Charles Biro stories)

1-No. 1 titled "Daredevil Battles Hitler," Classic battle issue as Daredevil teams up in each
strip - The Silver Streak, Lance Hale, Cloud Curtis, Dickey Dean & Pirate Prince to battle
Hitler; The Claw unites with Hitler and Japanese and battles Daredevil; Origin of Hitler
feature story "The Man of Hate." Classic Hitler photo app. on-c
1650 ... 3300 ... 4950 ... 12,300 ... 21,650 ... 31,000

2-London (by Jerry Robinson), Pat Patriot (by Reed Crandall), Nightro, Real American
No. 1 (by Briefer #2-11), Dash Dillon, Whirlwind begin; Dickie Dean, Pirate Prince
end; intro. & only app. Pioneer, Champion of America & Times Square. The Claw
continues #2-4 .... 415 ... 830 ... 1245 ... 2905 ... 5103 ... 7300

3-Intro./origin of 13. Newspaper editor has name "Roussos." Daredevil battles
the Claw ill. text story .... 284 ... 568 ... 852 ... 1818 ... 3109 ... 4400

4-The Claw captured and taken to New York Central Park Zoo. Whirlwind, the Blond Bomber
begins, ends #6 .... 245 ... 490 ... 735 ... 1568 ... 2684 ... 3800

5-Ghost vs. Claw begins by Bob Wood, ends #20; 13 & Jinx begin; origin 13 retold in text;
intro./origin Jinx, 13's sidekick; intro. Sniffer in Daredevil
232 ... 464 ... 696 ... 1485 ... 2543 ... 3600

6-(12/41)-Classic horror-c; Daredevil battles wolf with human brain; Dash Dillon ends
219 ... 438 ... 657 ... 1402 ... 2401 ... 3400

7,9: 7-(2/42), shows #6 on cover; delayed one month due to Pearl Harbor attack.
9-Daredevil on-c; Sniffer strip begins, ends #69
142 ... 284 ... 426 ... 909 ... 1555 ... 2200

8-Nazi WWII war-c. Nightro ends. Sniffer/Daredevil fight Nazi insurgents;
181 ... 362 ... 543 ... 1158 ... 1979 ... 2800

10-(5-42), "Remember Pearl Harbor" Japanese WWII-c; classic splash page w/American
flag. Daredevil joins Air Corps. to fight Japanese. Ghost Battles Claw & Japanese.
Last Whirlwind .... 314 ... 628 ... 942 ... 2198 ... 3849 ... 5500

11-Classic Quasimodo (hunchback of Notre Dame) on-c/story/torture-c/story. London,
Pat Patriot, Real America #1 end .... 1022 ... 2044 ... 3066 ... 6541 ... 10,271 ... 14,000

12-Origin of The Claw; Scoop Scuttle by Wolverton begins (2-4 pgs.), ends #22, not in #21.
Charles Biro biography. Dickey Dean, Pirate Prince return (both end #32)
161 ... 322 ... 483 ... 1030 ... 1765 ... 2500

13-Intro of Little Wise Guys (10/42)(also see Boy #4); Daredevil fights Nazi hooded
cult; Ghost battles the Claw, Hitler & Nazis in Britain; Bob Wood biography
119 ... 238 ... 357 ... 762 ... 1306 ... 1850

14-Classic Daredevil facial portrait-c; Hitler app.; "Slap the Jap" game included
110 ... 220 ... 330 ... 704 ... 1202 ... 1700

15-Death of Meatball .... 126 ... 252 ... 378 ... 806 ... 1378 ... 1950

16-WWII-c w/freighter hit by German torpedo. Meatball is buried & Curly joins
Little Wise Guys team .... 103 ... 206 ... 309 ... 659 ... 1130 ... 1600

17-Little Wise Guys hanging and beating Japanese soldiers on cover
258 ... 516 ... 774 ... 1651 ... 2826 ... 4000

18-New origin of Daredevil (not same as Silver Streak #6). Hitler, Mussolini Tojo and Mickey
Mouse app. on-c at carnival .... 168 ... 336 ... 504 ... 1075 ... 1838 ... 2600

19,20: Last Ghost vs. Claw .... 77 ... 154 ... 231 ... 493 ... 847 ... 1200

21-Reprints cover of Silver Streak #6 (on inside) plus intro. of The Claw from Silver Streak #1.
The Claw strip begins by Bob Q. Siege, ends #31 106 ... 212 ... 318 ... 673 ... 1162 ... 1650

22,23: 22-Daredevil trips the Tramp. 23-Dickie Dean by Bob Montana
52 ... 104 ... 156 ... 328 ... 552 ... 775

24-Bloody puppet show-c; classic Claw splash pg. .... 61 ... 122 ... 183 ... 390 ... 670 ... 950

25-1st Little Wise Guys-c without Daredevil .... 39 ... 78 ... 117 ... 240 ... 395 ... 550

26,28-30 .... 43 ... 86 ... 129 ... 271 ... 461 ... 650

27-Bondage/torture-c .... 155 ... 310 ... 465 ... 792 ... 1696 ... 2400

31-Death of The Claw .... 103 ... 206 ... 309 ... 659 ... 1130 ... 1600

32-34: 32,33-Egbert app. 33-Roger Wilco begins, ends #35
37 ... 74 ... 111 ... 222 ... 361 ... 500

35-37,39-41: 35-Two Daredevil stories begin, end #68; Chauncey app. 37-39-Go Along
Gallagher app. (#35-41 are 64 pgs.); 41-Dickie Dean begins
39 ... 78 ... 117 ... 231 ... 378 ... 525

38-Origin Daredevil retold from #18 .... 53 ... 106 ... 159 ... 334 ... 567 ... 800

42-Intro. Kilroy in Daredevil who unveils Daredevil's I.D.-c/sty
34 ... 68 ... 102 ... 199 ... 325 ... 450

43-45,47,48-All Daredevil-c. 43-Daredevil in costume on-c & 1 panel only inside;
44-DD back in costume; i.d. revealed on-c. .... 32 ... 64 ... 96 ... 188 ... 307 ... 425

46,50: DD not on-c .... 27 ... 54 ... 81 ... 158 ... 259 ... 360

49-Wise Guys fight secret hooded group c/sty. DD not on-c
32 ... 64 ... 96 ... 188 ... 307 ... 425

51,52,56-60,63-66,68,69-Last Daredevil & Sniffer (12/50). 56-Wise Guys start
their own circus. DD not on-c .... 21 ... 42 ... 63 ... 124 ... 202 ... 280

53-Daredevil/Wise Guys find lost palace of Zanzarah, an underground Egyptian tomb
w/mummy & treasure; classic c/story. DD-c .... 24 ... 48 ... 72 ... 142 ... 234 ... 325

54,55-Daredevil-c .... 22 ... 44 ... 66 ... 132 ... 216 ... 300

61-Daredevil & Wise Guys in haunted house classic c/story. Daredevil/Wise Guys
fly rocket into stratosphere. DD not on-c .... 24 ... 48 ... 72 ... 142 ... 234 ... 325

62-Wise Guys in medieval times, a dream by Peewee locked in a medieval museum;
classic c/story. DD not on-c .... 22 ... 44 ... 66 ... 132 ... 216 ... 300

67-Last Daredevil-c .... 23 ... 46 ... 69 ... 136 ... 223 ... 310

70-Little Wise Guys take over book without Daredevil. Daredevil removed from-c & logo;
Air Devils w/Hot Rock Flanagan begins, ends #80 15 ... 30 ... 45 ... 84 ... 127 ... 170

71-78,81: 81-Dilly Duncan begins, ends #134 .... 12 ... 24 ... 36 ... 69 ... 97 ... 125

79,80: 79-(10/51)-Daredevil returns; Wise Guys go to Africa. 80-Daredevil & Wise Guys blast
into space & land on Mars; last Daredevil app. in title
14 ... 28 ... 42 ... 78 ... 112 ... 145

82,90: One pg. Frazetta ad in both .... 12 ... 24 ... 36 ... 69 ... 97 ... 125

83-89,91-99,101-134 .... 11 ... 22 ... 33 ... 62 ... 86 ... 110

100-(7/53) .... 14 ... 28 ... 42 ... 78 ... 112 ... 145

NOTE: Biro a-1-22, 38; c-1-134; script-1-134. Dan Barry a(Daredevil) 40-48; Roy Belfi-a (Daredevil) 49-55. Bolle
a-125. Al Borth-a(Daredevil) #57-59. Briefer a-1-11 (Real American #1); Pirate Prince-#1, 2, 12-31. Tony Dipreta-
a(Daredevil) #108-110, 112-134. R.W. Hall a-22. Carl Hubbell a-9-21, 23-26, 27(Daredevil), 28-32. Al Mandel
a-13; Hy Mankin-a(Wise Guys)-#80, 81. Maurer-a(Daredevil)-23, 31, 37, 38, 41, 43-51, 53-67, 69; (Little Wise
Guys)-70-89. McWilliams a-70, 73-80. Bob Montana a-12, 23, 27, 28, 31-33. Wm. Overgard-a(Daredevil)-#67,
(Wise Guys)-74-79, 83-85, 87. Jerry Robinson a(London) #2-8. Roussos a(Nightro)-2-8. Bob Q. Siege-a(Claw)
27-31; (Daredevil)-#35. Wolverton a-12-22. Bob Wood-a(The Claw)-1-20; (The Ghost)-5-20. Dick Wood sty-2-10,
13-22, 27-32. Daredevil not on-c #46,49-52,56-66,68-134.

DAREDEVIL (...& the Black Widow #92-107 on-c only; see Giant-Size..., Marvel Advs., Marvel
Graphic Novel #24, Marvel Super Heroes, '66 & Spider-Man &...)
Marvel Comics Group: Apr, 1964 - No. 380, Oct, 1998

1-Origin/1st app. Daredevil; intro Foggy Nelson & Karen Page; death of Battling Murdock;
Bill Everett-c/a; reprinted in Marvel Super Heroes #1 (1966)
1600 ... 3200 ... 4800 ... 11,200 ... 20,600 ... 30,000

2-Fantastic Four cameo; 2nd app. Electro (Spidey villain); Thing guest star
118 ... 236 ... 354 ... 944 ... 2122 ... 3300

3-Origin & 1st app. The Owl (villain) .... 55 ... 110 ... 165 ... 440 ... 995 ... 1550

4-Origin & 1st app. The Purple Man .... 50 ... 100 ... 150 ... 400 ... 900 ... 1400

5-Minor costume change; Wally Wood-a begins .... 36 ... 72 ... 108 ... 266 ... 596 ... 925

6-Mr. Fear app. .... 38 ... 76 ... 114 ... 285 ... 641 ... 1000

7-Daredevil battles Sub-Mariner & dons red costume for 1st time (4/65); Marvel Masterwork
pin-up by Wood .... 52 ... 250 ... 375 ... 1000 ... 2250 ... 3500

8-10: 8-Origin/1st app. Stilt Man. 10-1st app. Cat Man, Bird Man, Ape Man & Frog Man
18 ... 36 ... 54 ... 124 ... 275 ... 425

11,13-15: 11-Last Wally Wood. 13-Facts about Ka-Zar's origin; vs. the Plunderer;
Kirby/Romita-a. 14-Romita-a begins; Ka-Zar & the Plunderer app. 15-1st app. the Ox
12 ... 24 ... 36 ... 83 ... 182 ... 280

12-1st app. Plunderer; Ka-Zar app. Kirby/Romita-a begins
18 ... 36 ... 54 ... 128 ... 284 ... 440

16-1st Romita-a on Spider-Man (5/66) .... 66 ... 132 ... 198 ... 528 ... 1189 ... 1850

17-Spider-Man x-over continues .... 23 ... 46 ... 69 ... 164 ... 362 ... 560

18-Origin 1st app. Gladiator .... 18 ... 36 ... 54 ... 124 ... 275 ... 425

19-DD vs. the Gladiator .... 10 ... 20 ... 30 ... 46 ... 86 ... 210

20-DD vs. the Owl; 1st Gene Colan-a .... 12 ... 24 ... 36 ... 84 ... 185 ... 285

21-DD vs. the Owl .... 9 ... 18 ... 27 ... 60 ... 120 ... 180

22-26,28-30: 22-DD vs. the Owl, Gladiator & and Masked Marauder; 1st app the Tri-Man.
23-Owl, Gladiator, Masked Marauder & Tri-Man app. 24-Ka-Zar app. 25-1st app. Leap-Frog;
1st app. 'Mike Murdock' Daredevil's fake twin brother. 26-Stilt-Man app. 30-Thor app. vs.
Cobra and Mr. Hyde .... 12 ... 24 ... 36 ... 56 ... 108 ... 160

27-Spider-Man x-over; Stilt-Man & the Masked Marauder app.
9 ... 18 ... 27 ... 62 ... 126 ... 190

31-36,39,40: 31,32-DD vs. Cobra & Mr. Hyde. 33,34-DD vs. the Beetle. 35-DD vs. the
Trapster. 36-DD vs. the Trapster; Dr. Doom cameo. 39-1st app. Exterminator (later
becomes Death-Stalker); Ape Man, Cat Man & Bird Man app. as the Unholy Three.
40-DD vs. the Unholy Three .... 7 ... 14 ... 21 ... 46 ... 86 ... 125

37,38: 37-Daredevil vs. Dr. Doom. 38-Dr. Doom app; Fantastic Four x-over; continued in
Fantastic Four #73 .... 12 ... 24 ... 36 ... 80 ... 173 ... 265

41,42,44-49: 41- 'Death' of Mike Murdock; Daredevil drops the fake twin persona; DD vs.
the Exterminator and the Unholy Three. 42-1st app. Jester. 44-46-DD vs. the Jester.

	GD 2.0	VG 4.0	FN 6.0	VF 8.0	VF/NM 9.0	NM- 9.2

48-DD vs. Stilt-Man. **49**-1st app. Star Saxon & the Plastoid
6 · 12 · 18 · 40 · 73 · 105

43-Daredevil vs. Captain America; origin partially retold; Kirby-c
12 · 24 · 36 · 79 · 170 · 260

50-51,53: 50-Barry Smith-a; last Stan Lee-s; vs. Star Saxon & the Plastoid. **51**-1st Roy Thomas-s; Barry Smith-a; vs. Star Saxon & the Plastoid. **53**-Gene Colan returns; origin retold
6 · 12 · 18 · 42 · 79 · 115

52-Barry Smith-a; Black Panther app.; learns Daredevil's secret identity
8 · 16 · 24 · 56 · 108 · 160

54-56,58-60: 54-Spider-Man cameo; vs. Mr. Fear. **55**-DD vs. Mr. Fear. **56**-1st app. Death's Head (Star Saxon) (9/69); story continued in #57. **58**-1st app. Stunt-Master.
59-1st app. Torpedo (dies this issue)
5 · 10 · 15 · 31 · 53 · 75

57-Reveals i.d. to Karen Page; Death's Head app.
6 · 12 · 18 · 48 · 89 · 130

61,63-68,70-72,74-76,78-80: 61-DD vs. the Jester, Cobra & Mr. Hyde. **63**-vs. Gladiator. **64**-Stunt-Master app. **67**-Stilt-Man app. **71**-Last Roy Thomas-s. **72**-1st app Tagak 'Lord of Leopards'; 1st Gerry Conway-s. **75**-1st app. El Condor. **76**-Death El Condor. **78**-1st app. Man-Bull. **79**-DD vs. Man-Bull. **80**-vs the Owl
6 · 12 · 18 · 28 · 47 · 65

62,69,73: 62-Origin of Nighthawk (Kyle Richmond). **69**-Black Panther app. **73**-Continued in Iron Man #35; Nick Fury app. vs. the Zodiac; concluded in Iron Man #36.
5 · 10 · 15 · 33 · 57 · 80

77-Spider-Man & Sub-Mariner app.; story continues in Sub-Mariner #40
6 · 12 · 18 · 41 · 76 · 110

81-(52 pgs.)-Black Widow becomes regular guest star (11/71); receives co-billing w/issue #92 through issue #107; vs. Mr. Kline and the Owl
8 · 16 · 24 · 56 · 108 · 160

82,84-87,89-98: 82-DD vs. Mr. Kline. **84**-Conclusion of the Mr. Kline story; see Iron Man #41-45 & Sub-Mariner #42. **85**-DD vs. Gladiator. **86**-Death of the Ox. **87**-Daredevil & the Black Widow relocate to San Francisco; Electro app. **89**-Purple Man & Electro app. **90**-Mr. Fear app. **91**-Death of Mr. Fear. **92**-Black Widow gets co-billing as of this issue. **93,94**-DD vs. the Indestructible Man. **95,96**-DD vs. the Man-Bull. **97-99**-DD vs. the Dark Messiah; Steve Gerber co-script; **98**-Last Conway-s
4 · 8 · 12 · 25 · 40 · 55

83,99: 83-Barry Smith layouts/Weiss-p. **99**-Hawkeye app; Steve Gerber-s begin; plot continues in Avengers #111
4 · 8 · 12 · 27 · 44 · 60

88-Purple Man app; early life of Black Widow revealed
5 · 10 · 15 · 33 · 57 · 80

100-1st app. Angar the Screamer; origin retold; Jann Wenner, editor of Rolling Stone app.
6 · 12 · 18 · 41 · 76 · 110

101,102,104,106,108-110: 101-vs Angar the Screamer. **102**-vs. Stilt-Man. **104**-Kraven the Hunter app. **106**-Moondragon app; vs. Terrex. **108**-Title returns to 'Daredevil'. Moondragon app.; 1st app. Black Spectre; Beetle app; Daredevil and Black Widow break-up.
109-Shanna the She-Devil app.; vs. Nekra & Black Spectre; story continues in Marvel Two-in-One #3. **110**-Continued from Marvel Two-in-One #3; vs. the Mandrill, Nekra & Black Spectre; brief Thing app.
3 · 6 · 9 · 21 · 33 · 45

103-1st app. & origin of Ramrod; Spider-Man app.
5 · 10 · 15 · 33 · 57 · 75

105-Origin of Moondragon by Starlin (12/73) Thanos cameo in flashback (early app.)
9 · 18 · 27 · 59 · 117 · 175

107-Starlin-c; Thanos cameo; Moondragon & Captain Marvel app; death of Terrex
4 · 8 · 12 · 27 · 44 · 60

111-1st app. Silver Samurai; Shanna the She-Devil, Mandrill, Nekra & Black Spectre app.
10 · 20 · 30 · 64 · 132 · 200

112,113,116-120: 112-Conclusion of the Black Spectre story; Mandrill & Nekra app. **113**-1st brief app. Death-Stalker; Gladiator app. **116,117**-DD vs. the Owl; **117**-Last Gerber-s. **118**-1st app. Blackwing; vs. the Circus of Crime. **119**-Tony Isabella-s begin. **120**-1st app. El Jaguar Agent of HYDRA
3 · 6 · 9 · 19 · 30 · 40

114-1st full Death-Stalker app; Man-Thing & Gladiator app.
4 · 8 · 12 · 27 · 44 · 60

115-Death-Stalker app.; advertisement for Wolverine in Incredible Hulk #181 (on pg. 19)
9 · 18 · 27 · 59 · 117 · 175

121-123,125-130,137: 121-vs. HYDRA; El Jaguar and the Dreadnaught; Nick Fury app. **122**-Return of Silvermane as the new Supreme HYDRA. **123**-Silvermane; El Jaguar, Dreadnaught, Mentallo & HYDRA app; Nick Fury and SHIELD app; last Isabella-s. **125**-Death of Copperhead; Wolfman-s begin. **126**-1st app. the second and third Torpedos; 1st app. Heather Glenn. **127**-vs. the third Torpedo (Brock Jones). **128**-Death-Stalker app. **129**-vs the Man-Bull
3 · 6 · 9 · 17 · 26 · 35

124-1st app. Copperhead; Black Widow leaves; Len Wein & Marv Wolfman co-plot
4 · 8 · 12 · 28 · 47 · 65

131-Origin/1st app. Bullseye (see Nick Fury #15)
20 · 40 · 60 · 138 · 307 · 475

132-2nd Bullseye app. new Bullseye (regular 25c edition)
6 · 12 · 18 · 41 · 76 · 110

132-(30¢-c variant, limited distribution)(4/76)
11 · 22 · 33 · 76 · 163 · 250

133-136: 133-Uri Geller & the Jester app. **134**-Torpedo app. vs. the Chameleon. **135,136**-vs. the Jester
3 · 6 · 9 · 16 · 23 · 30

133-136-(30¢-c variants, limited distribution)(5-8/76)
5 · 10 · 15 · 33 · 57 · 80

138-Ghost Rider-c/story; Death's Head is reincarnated; Byrne-a
3 · 6 · 9 · 21 · 33 · 45

139,140,142-145,147-154: 140-vs the Beetle & Gladiator. **142**-vs. Cobra & Hyde; Nova cameo. **143**-Cobra & Hyde app; last Wolfman-s. **144**-vs the Man-Bull & Owl. **145**-vs the Owl. **147**-Purple Man app. **148**-Death-Stalker app. **149**-1st app. the third Smasher. **150**-1st app. Paladin. **151**-Reveals i.d. to Heather Glenn. **152**-vs Death-Stalker; Roger McKenzie-s begin. **153**-vs Cobra & Hyde. **154**-vs Purple Man, Cobra & Hyde & Jester
3 · 6 · 9 · 15 · 22 · 28

141,146-Bullseye app.
4 · 8 · 12 · 28 · 47 · 65

146-(35¢-c variant, limited distribution)
12 · 24 · 36 · 83 · 182 · 280

147,148-(35¢-c variants, limited distribution)
9 · 18 · 27 · 59 · 117 · 175

155-157-DD vs. Death-Stalker; Black Widow, Hercules, Captain America & the Beast app.
3 · 6 · 9 · 16 · 24 · 32

158-Frank Miller-a begins (5/79) origin/death of Death-Stalker (see Captain America #235 & Spectacular Spider-Man #27)
9 · 18 · 27 · 59 · 117 · 175

159-Brief Bullseye app.
5 · 10 · 15 · 31 · 53 · 75

160,161-Bullseye and Black Widow app.
4 · 8 · 12 · 27 · 44 · 60

162-Ditko-a; no Miller-a; origin retold
3 · 6 · 9 · 15 · 22 · 28

163-Daredevil vs. the Hulk
6 · 12 · 18 · 41 · 76 · 110

164-Origin retold and expanded
4 · 8 · 12 · 23 · 37 · 50

165-167,170: 165-1st Miller co-plot w/McKenzie; Dr. Octopus app. **166**-vs. Gladiator. **167**-Last McKenzie co-plot; 1st app. Mauler. **170**-Kingpin app.
3 · 6 · 9 · 17 · 25 · 34

168-(1/81) Origin/1st app. Elektra; 1st Miller scripts
15 · 30 · 45 · 103 · 227 · 350

169-2nd Elektra app; Bullseye app.
5 · 10 · 15 · 30 · 50 · 70

171-173: 171,172-vs. the Kingpin
3 · 6 · 9 · 18 · 28 · 38

174-1st app. the Hand (Ninjas who trained Elektra)
4 · 8 · 12 · 25 · 40 · 55

175-Elektra & Daredevil vs. the Hand
3 · 6 · 9 · 20 · 31 · 42

176-1st app. Stick (Daredevil's mentor)
4 · 8 · 12 · 27 · 44 · 60

177-180-Elektra app: **177**-Kingpin & the Hand app. **178**-Kingpin & Power Man & Iron Fist app.
179-Anti-smoking issue mentioned in the Congressional Record
3 · 6 · 9 · 17 · 26 · 35

181-(4/82, 52-pgs)-Death of Elektra; Punisher cameo out of costume
4 · 8 · 12 · 28 · 47 · 65

182-184: 182-Bullseye app. **183,184** -'Angel Dust' drug story; Punisher app.
3 · 6 · 9 · 16 · 24 · 32

185-191: 186-Stilt-Man app. **187**-New Black Widow app.
189-Death of Stick; Black Widow app. **190**-Elektra returns, part origin; 2 pin-ups.
191-Classic 'Russian Roulette' story with Bullseye; last Miller Daredevil
2 · 4 · 6 · 8 · 11 · 14

192-195,198,199: 192-Alan Brennert story; Klaus Janson (p&i) begin. **193**-Larry Hama-s. **194**-Denny O'Neil-s begin. **198**-Bullseye receives Adamantium bones. **199**-Bullseye app; death of Dark Wind
1 · 2 · 3 · 5 · 6 · 8

196-Wolverine-c/app; 1st app. Dark Wind. Bullseye app.
3 · 6 · 9 · 17 · 26 · 35

197-Bullseye-c/app; 1st app, Yuriko Oyama (becomes Lady Deathstrike in Alpha Flight #33)
3 · 6 · 9 · 16 · 23 · 30

200-Bulleye vs. Daredevil; Byrne-c
2 · 4 · 6 · 8 · 11 · 14

201-207,209-218: 201-Black Widow solo story. **202**-1st app. Micah Synn. **203**-1st app. the Trump; Byrne-c. **204**-1st app. Crossbow (Green Arrow homage?) **205**-1st app. Gael (Irish Republican Army hitman). **206**-DD vs. Micah Synn; 1st Mazzucchelli-p on DD. Kingpin app. **207**-HYDRA & Black Widow app. **209**-Harlan Ellison plot. **210**-Crossbow & Kingpin app. **211,212**-DD & Kingpin team-up w/ Micah Synn. **215**-Two-Gun Kid flashback. **216**-Gael app. **217**-Gael app; 1st app. the Cossack; Barry-Windsor-Smith-c.
218-DD appears as the Jester
6.00

208,219: 208-Harlan Ellison and Arthur Byron Cover scripts borrowed from Avengers TV episode 'House that Jack Built'. **219**-Miller-c/script
7.00

220-226,234-237: 220-Death of Heather Glenn. **222**-Black Widow app. **223**-Secret Wars II crossover; Beyonder gives DD his sight back; DD rejects the gift. **225**-Vulture app. **226**-Gladiator app.; last Denny O'Neil-s. **234**-Madcap app. **235**-DD vs. Mr. Hyde. **237**-DD vs. Klaw; Black Widow app.
6.00

227-(2/86, 36 pgs.)-Miller scripts begin; classic 'Born Again' Pt.1 story begins; Kingpin learns DD's secret identity.
1 · 2 · 3 · 5 · 6 · 8

228-233: **'Born Again'; Kingpin ruins Matt Murdock's life. **232-1st app Nuke. **233**-Last Miller script; Captain America app.; death of Nuke
5.00

238-Mutant massacre; Sabretooth app; 1st Ann Nocenti-s
6.00

239,240,242-247: 239-1st app. Rotgut. **243**-1st app. Nameless One. **245**-Black Panther app. **246**-1st app. Chance. **247**-Black Widow app.
4.00

241-Todd McFarlane-a(p)
5.00

248-Wolverine cameo; 1st app. Bushwacker. **249**-DD vs. Wolverine; Bushwacker app.
6.00

250,251,253,258: 250-1st app. Bullet; Romita Jr-a begins. **251**-vs. Bullet. **253**-Kingpin app. **258**-1st app. Bengal
4.00

252-(52 pgs)-Fall of the Mutants tie-in; 1st app. Ammo. **260**-(52 pgs)-Bushwacker, Bullet, Ammo & Typhoid Mary vs. DD
5.00

254-Origin & 1st app. Typhoid Mary (5/88)
4 · 8 · 12 · 27 · 44 · 60

255,256: 2nd&3rd app. Typhoid Mary. **259**-Typhoid Mary app.
5.00

257-Punisher app. (x-over w/Punisher #10)
2 · 4 · 6 · 10 · 14 · 18

261-269,271-281: 261-Typhoid Mary & Human Torch app. **262**-Inferno tie-in. **263**-Inferno tie-in; 1st new look 'monstrous' Mephisto. **264**-vs the Hand. **265**-Inferno tie-in; Mephisto app. **266**-Mephisto app. **267**-Bullet app. **269**-Blob & Pyro (from Freedom Force) app. **272**-1st app. Shotgun; Inhumans app. **273**-DD vs. Shotgun; Inhumans app. **274**-Black Bolt & the Inhumans app. **275,276**-'Acts of Vengeance' x-over; Ultron app. **278**-Mephisto & Blackheart app. **279**-Mephisto app. **280**-DD in Hell; Mephisto app. **281**-Silver Surfer cameo; Mephisto & Blackheart app.
4.00

270-1st app. Blackheart (the son of Mephisto); Spider-Man app.
4 · 8 · 12 · 25 · 40 · 55

282-DD escapes Hell; Silver Surfer, Mephisto & Blackheart app.
5.00

283-287,289,291-299: 283-Captain America app. **284-287,289**-Bullseye impersonates DD; **284**-1st Lee Weeks-a. **291**-vs. Bullet; last Nocenti-s. **292,293**-Punisher app. **295**-Ghost Rider app. **297**-'Last Rights' Pt.1; Typhoid Mary app. **298**-Pt.2; Nick Fury & SHIELD app.
299-Pt. 3; Baron Strucker & Hydra vs. the Kingpin
4.00

288-Bullseye-c/s; Kingpin app; Elektra dream sequence
5.00

290-Bullseye vs. Daredevil
1 · 2 · 3 · 4 · 6 · 8

300-(52 pgs.)-'Last Rights' Pt.4; Kingpin loses criminal empire; last Weeks-a
5.00

301-318: 301-303-vs. the Owl. **305-306**-Spider-Man app. **307**-'Dead Man's Hand' Pt. 1; Nomad & Tombstone app.; continued in Nomad #4. **308**-'Dead Man's Hand' Pt. 5; continued from Punisher War Journal #45; Punisher app; continues in Punisher War Journal #46. **309**-'Dead Man's Hand' Pt. 7; continued from Nomad #5; continued in Punisher War Journal #47. **310**-Infinity War tie-in; Calypso vs. DD doppelganger. **311**-Calypso & Brother Voodoo app. **314,315**-Shock & Mr. Fear app. **317,318**-Taskmaster, Stilt-Man & Tatterdemalion app.
4.00

319-Prologue to Fall From Grace Pt. 1; Elektra returns; Silver Sable app.
6.00

319-2nd printing w/black-c
6.00

320-(9/93) Fall From Grace Pt. 1; Silver Sable app.
5.00

321-Fall From Grace regular ed; Pt. 2 new armored costume; Venom app.
4.00

321-($2.00)-Wraparound Glow-in-the-dark-c
5.00

322-325: 322-Fall From Grace Pt. 3; Eddie Brock app. **323,324:** Fall From Grace Pts. 4,5. **323**-vs. Venom-c/story. **324**-Morbius-c/story. **325**-($2.50, 52 pgs.) Fall From Grace ends; contains bound-in poster; Elektra app.
5.00

326-338: 326-New logo; Captain America app. **327**-Captain America-c/story. **328**-Captain America & Baron Strucker app. **329**-Iron Fist app. **330**-Gambit app. **331,332**-vs. Baron Strucker. **334-336**-Bushwacker app. **338**-Kingpin app.
4.00

339-343: 339-342-Kingpin app.
5.00

344-(9/95)-Title becomes part of the 'Marvel Edge' imprint; story continued from Double Edge: Alpha; Punisher & Nick Fury app.; continued in Ghost Rider #65
5.00

345-Original red costume returns; Marvel Overpower card insert
4.00

346-350: 348-1st app Cary Nord-a in DD (1/96) 'Dec' on-c. **350**-($2.95)-Double-Sized
4.00

350-($3.50)-Variant gold ink-c
5.00

351-353,355-360,362-364: 351-Last 'Marvel Edge' imprint issue. **353**-Karl Kessel scripts; Nord-c/a begins. **354**-Bullseye (illusion)-c. **355**-Pyro app. **357**-Enforcers app. **358**-Mysterio app. **360**-Absorbing Man app. **363**-Colan-c/a. **364**-Mr. Fear app.
4.00

Daredevil #102 © MAR

Daredevil V2 #5 © MAR

Daredevil (2011 series) #8 © MAR

	GD 2.0	VG 4.0	FN 6.0	VF 8.0	VF/NM 9.0	NM- 9.2

354-Spider-Man app.; $1.50-c begins — 1 3 4 6 8 10
361,365-367: 361-Black Widow & DD vs. Grey Gargoyle. 365-367: 365-Molten Man & Mr. Fear app. 366-Mr. Fear app.; Colan-c/a. 367-Colan-c/a; Mr. Fear & Gladiator app. — 5.00
368-Omega Red & Black Widow app. — 1 3 4 6 8 10
369-Black Widow app. — 6.00
370-374: 370-Darkstar, Vanguard & Ursa Major app; last Colan-a. 371-Black Widow app. 372-Ghost Rider (Daniel Ketch) app. 373,374-Mr. Fear app. — 5.00
375-($2.99)-Wraparound-c; Mr. Fear-c/app. — 5.00
376-379: "Flying Blind", DD goes undercover for SHIELD — 4.00
380-($2.99) Final issue; flashback story; Kingpin, Bullseye & Bushwacker app. — 2 4 8 11 16 20
#(-1) Flashback issue (7/97, $1.95); Gene Colan-a — 4.00
No. 181 Facsimile Edition (11/19, $4.99) r/#181 with original 1982 ads and letter column — 5.00
No. 183 Facsimile Edition (12/23, $3.99) r/#183 with original 1982 ads and letter column — 4.00
Special 1 (9/67, 25c, 68-pgs)-New art/story by Lee/Colan; DD vs. the 'Emissaries of Evil' (Electro, Leapfrog, Stilt-Man, Matador & Gladiator) — 11 22 33 76 163 250
Special 2,3: 2 (2/71, 25c, 52 pgs.) Reprints issues #10-11 by Wood. 3-(1/72, 25c, 52 pgs.) Reprints issues #16-17 — 5 10 15 30 50 70
Annual 4 (10/76, squarebound) Sub-Mariner & Black Panther app. — 4 8 12 27 44 60
Annual 4 (#5, 1989) Atlantis Attacks; continued from Spectacular Spider-Man Annual #9; Spider-Man app.; continued in Avengers Annual #18 — 6.00
Annual 6-9: 6-('90) Lifeform Pt. 2; continued from Punisher Annual #3; continues in Silver Surfer Annual #3. 7-('91) The Von Strucker Gambit Pt. 1; continued in Punisher Annual #4. Guice-a (7 pgs.). 8-('92) System Bites Pt. 2; Deathlok & Bushwacker app; continued in Wonder Man Annual #1. 9-('93) Polybagged w/card; 1st app. Devourer — 6.00
Annual 10-('94) Elektra, Nick Fury, Shang-Chi (Master of Kung-Fu) vs. Ghostmaker — 1 2 3 5 6 8
...: Born Again TPB ($17.95)-r/#227-233; Miller's/Mazzuchelli-a & new-c — 20.00
... By Frank Miller and Klaus Janson Omnibus HC (2007, $99.99, dustjacket) r/#158-161, 163-191 and What If...? #28; intros by Miller and Janson; interviews, bonus art — 100.00
... By Frank Miller and Klaus Janson Omnibus Companion HC (2007, $59.99, die-cut d.j.) r/#219,226-233, Daredevil: The Man Without Fear #1-5, Daredevil: Love and War, and Peter Parker, the Spect. Spider-Man #27-28; bonus materials — 60.00
...Deadpool Annual '97, $2.99)-Wraparound-c — 6.00
...: Fall From Grace TPB ($19.95)-r/#319-325 — 20.00
...: Gang War TPB ($15.95)-r/#169-172,180; Miller-a/p — 16.00
... Legends: (Vol. 4) Typhoid Mary TPB (2003, $19.95) r/#254-257,259-263 — 20.00
... :Love's Labors Lost TPB ($19.99)-r/#215-217,219-222,225,226; Mazzuchelli-c — 20.00
.../Punisher TPB (1988, $4.95)-r/D.D. #182-184 (all printings) — 6.00
...Visionaries: Frank Miller Vol. 1 TPB ($17.95)-r/#158-161,163-167 — 18.00
...Visionaries: Frank Miller Vol. 2 TPB ($24.95) r/#168-182; new Miller-c — 25.00
...Visionaries: Frank Miller Vol. 3 TPB ($24.95) r/#183-191, What If? #28,35 & Bizarre Adventures #28; Miller-c — 25.00
... Vs. Bullseye TPB Vol. 1 (2004, $15.99) r/#131-132,146,169,181,191 — 16.00
Wizard Ace Edition: Daredevil (Vol. 1) #1 (4/03, $13.99) Acetate Campbell-c — 14.00
NOTE: Art Adams-c238p, 239. Austin-a191; c-151i, 200i. John Buscema-a136, 137p, 234p, 235p; c-86p, 136i, 137p, 142, 219. Byrne-c200p, 201, 203, 223. Capullo-a286p. Colan-a(p)-20-49, 53-82; c(p)-20-42, 44-49, 53-60, 71, 92, 98, 138, 153, 154, 156, 157, 363, 366-370, Spec. 1r; c(p)-20-42, 44-49, 53-60, 71, 92, 98, 138, 153, 154, 156, 157, Annual 1. Craig-a50, 52i. Ditko-a-162, 234p, 235p, 264p; c-162. Everett-c130, 132i; inks-21, 83. Garney c/a-304. Gil Kane-a141p, 146-148p, 151p; c(p)-85, 90, 91, 93, 94, 115, 116, 119, 120, 125-128, 133, 139, 147, 152. Kirby-c2-4, 12p, 13p, 43. Layton-c202. Miller scripts-168-182, 183(part), 184-191, 219, 227-233; a-158-161p, 163-184p, 191p; c-158-161p, 163-184p, 185-189, 190p, 191. Orlando-a-2-4p. Powell-a9p, 11p, Special 1r, 2r. Simonson-c-199, 236p. B. Smith-a236p; c-51p, 52p, 217. Starlin-a155p, 169. Steranko-c145p, 146p. Tuska-a39i, 145p. Williamson-a(i)-237, 239, 240, 243, 248-257, 259-282, 283(part), 284, 285, 287, 288(part), 289(part), 293-300; c(i)-237, 243, 244, 248-257, 259-263, 265-278, 280-289, Annual 4. Wood-a-5-8, 9, 10, 11i, Spec. 2i; c-5-11, 164i.

DAREDEVIL (Volume 2)(Marvel Knights)(Becomes Black Panther: The Man Without Fear #513)
Marvel Comics: Nov, 1998 - No. 512, Feb, 2011 ($2.50/$2.99)

1-Kevin Smith-s/Quesada & Palmiotti-a — 2 4 6 11 16 20
1-($6.95) DF Edition w/Quesada & Palmiotti var-c — 3 6 9 14 19 24
1-($6.00) DF Sketch Ed. w/B&W-c — 15.00
2-Two covers by Campbell and Quesada/Palmiotti — 12.00
3-8: 4,5-Daredevil app. 5-Variant-c exists. 8-Spider-Man-c/app.; last Smith-s — 6.00
9-15: 9-11-David Mack-s; intro Echo. 12-Begin $2.99-c; Haynes-a. 13,14-Quesada-a. — 4.00
16-19-Direct editions; Bendis-s/Mack-c/painted-a — 4.00
18,19,21,22-Newsstand editions with variant cover logo "Marvel Unlimited Featuring..." — 5.00
20-($3.50) Gale-s/Winslade-a; back-up by Stan Lee/Colan-a; Mack-c — 5.00
21-40: 21-25-Gale-s. 26-38-Bendis-s/Maleev-a. 32-Daredevil's ID revealed. 35-Spider-Man-c/app. 38-Iron Fist & Luke Cage. 40-Dodson-a — 3.50
41-(25c-c) Begins "Lowlife" arc; Maleev-a; intro Milla Donovan — 3.00
41-(Newsstand edition with 2.99c-c) — 3.00
42-45-"Lowlife" arc; Maleev-a — 3.00
46-50-($2.99). 46-Typhoid Mary returns. 49-Bullseye app. 50-Art panels by various incl. Romita, Colan, Mack, Janson, Oeming, Quesada — 4.00
51-64,66-74,76-81: 54-55-Mack-s/a; Echo app. 54-Wolverine-c/app. 61-64-Black Widow app. 71-Decalogue begins. 76-81-The Murdock Papers. 81-Last Bendis-s/Maleev-a — 3.00

65-($3.99) 40th Anniversary issue; Land-c; art by Maleev, Horn, Bachalo and others — 4.00
75-($3.99) Decalogue ends; Jester app. — 4.00
82-99,101-119: 82-Brubaker-s/Lark-a begin; Foggy "killed". 84-86-Punisher app. 87-Other Daredevil ID revealed. 94-Romita-c. 111-Lady Bullseye debut — 3.00
82-Variant-c by McNiven — 4.00
100-($3.99) Three covers (Djurdjevic, Bermejo and Turner); art by Romita Sr., Colan, Lark, Sienkiewicz, Maleev, Bermejo & Djurdjevic; sketch art gallery; r/Daredevil #90 (1972) — 4.00
(After Vol. 2 #119, Aug, 2009, numbering reverts to original Vol. 1 with #500)
500-(10/09, $4.99) Kingpin, Lady Bullseye app.; back-up stories, pin-up & cover galleries; r/#191; five covers by Djurdjevic, Darrow, Dell'Otto, Ross and Zircher — 5.00
501-512: 501-Daredevil takes over The Hand; Diggle-s begins; Ribic-c. 508-Shadowland begins. 512-Black Panther app. — 3.00
Annual 1 (12/07, $3.99) Brubaker-s/Fernandez-a/Djurdjevic-a; Black Tarantula app. — 3.00
... & Captain America: Dead on Arrival (2008, $4.99) English version of Italian story — 5.00
... Black & White 1 (10/10, $3.99) B&W short stories by various; Aja-c — 4.00
... Blood of the Tarantula (6/08, $3.99) Parks & Brubaker-s/Samnee-a/Djurdjevic-c — 4.00
... By Brian Michael Bendis Omnibus Vol. 1 HC (2008, $99.99) oversized r/#16-19,26-50, and 56-80 — 100.00
... By Ed Brubaker Saga (2008, giveaway) synopsis of issues #82-110, preview of #111 — 3.00
... Cage Match 1 (7/10, $3.99) flashback early Luke Cage team-up; Chen-a — 3.00
... MGC #26 (8/10, $1.00) r/#26 with "Marvel's Greatest Comics" logo on cover — 3.00
...2099 #1 (11/04, $2.99) Kirkman-s/Moline-a — 10.00
TPB ($9.95) r/#1-3 — 10.00
...Vol. 1 HC (2001, $29.99, with dustjacket) r/#1-11,13-15 — 30.00
...Vol. 1 HC (2003, $29.99, with dustjacket) r/#1-11,13-15; larger page size — 30.00
...Vol. 2 HC (2002, $29.99, with dustjacket) r/#26-37; afterword by Bendis — 30.00
...Vol. 3 HC (2004, $29.99, with dustjacket) r/#38-50; Maleev sketch pages — 30.00
...Vol. 4 HC (2005, $29.99, with dustjacket) r/#56-65; Vol. 1 #81 (1971) Black Widow — 30.00
...Vol. 5 HC (2006, $29.99, with dustjacket) r/#66-75 — 30.00
...Vol. 6 HC (2006, $34.99, with dustjacket) r/#76-81 & What If Karen Page Had Lived? — 35.00
(Vol. 1) Visionaries TPB ($19.95) r/#1-8; Ben Affleck intro. — 20.00
(Vol. 2) Parts of a Hole TPB (1/02, $17.95) r/#9-15; David Mack intro. — 18.00
(Vol. 3) Wake Up TPB (2/02, $9.99) r/#16-19 — 10.00
...Vol. 4: Underboss TPB (8/02, $14.99) r/#26-31 — 15.00
...Vol. 5: Out TPB (2003, $19.99) r/#32-40 — 20.00
...Vol. 6: Lowlife TPB (2003, $13.99) r/#41-45 — 14.00
...Vol. 7: Hardcore TPB (2003, $13.99) r/#46-50 — 14.00
...Vol. 8: Echo - Vision Quest TPB (2004, $13.99) r/#51-55; David Mack-s/a — 14.00
...Vol. 9: King of Hell's Kitchen TPB (2004, $13.99) r/#56-60 — 14.00
...Vol. 10: The Widow TPB (2004, $16.99) r/#61-65 & Vol. 1 #81 — 17.00
...Vol. 11: Golden Age TPB (2005, $13.99) r/#66-70 — 14.00
...Vol. 12: Decalogue TPB (2005, $14.99) r/#71-75 — 15.00
...Vol. 13: The Murdock Papers TPB (2006, $14.99) r/#76-81 — 15.00
...: The Devil Inside and Out Vol. 1 (2006, $14.99) r/#82-87; Brubaker & Lark interview — 15.00
...: The Devil Inside and Out Vol. 2 (2007, $14.99) r/#88-93; Bermejo cover sketches — 15.00
... Hell To Pay TPB 1 (2007, $14.99) r/#94-99; Djurdjevic cover sketches — 15.00
... Hell To Pay TPB 2 (2008, $15.99) r/#100-105 — 16.00

DAREDEVIL (Volume 3)
Marvel Comics: Sept, 2011 - No. 36, Apr, 2014 ($3.99/$2.99)

1-($3.99) Mark Waid-s/Paolo Rivera-a; back-up tale with Marcos Martin-a — 4.00
1-Variant-c by Marcos Martin — 8.00
1-Variant-c by Neal Adams — 10.00
2-10,10.1,11-20,23,24,25,27-36-($2.99) 2-Capt. America app. 3-Klaw returns. 4-6-Marcos Martin-a. 8-X-over w/Amazing Spider-Man #677; Spider-Man and Black Cat app. 11-Spider-Man app. 17-Allred-a. 30-Silver Surfer app. 32,33-Satana & monsters app. — 3.00
21,22-1st app Superior Spider-Man (cameo). 22-Superior Spider-Man app. — 5.00
26-($3.99) Bullseye and Lady Bullseye app.; back-up "Fighting Cancer" story — 5.00
Annual 1 (10/12, $4.99) Alan Davis-s/a/c; Dr. Strange & ClanDestine app. — 5.00

DAREDEVIL (Volume 4)
Marvel Comics: May, 2014 - No. 18, Nov, 2015 ($3.99)

1-18-($3.99) Mark Waid-s/Chris Samnee-a; Murdock moves to San Francisco. 6,7-Original Sin tie-in. 8-10-Purple Man app. 14-Owl's daughter app. 15-18-Kingpin app. — 4.00
#0.1-(9/14, $4.99) Waid-s/Krause-a/Samnee-c — 4.00
#1.50-($4.99) 50th Anniversary issue; Murdock at 50; back-up Bendis-s/Maleev-a — 5.00
#15.1-(7/15, $4.99) Waid-s/Samnee-a; Guggenheim-s/Krause-a — 5.00

DAREDEVIL (Follows Secret Wars)
Marvel Comics: Feb, 2016 - No. 28, Dec, 2017; No. 595, Jan, 2018 - No. 612, Jan, 2019 ($3.99)

1-28: 1-Soule-s/Garney-a; Blindspot app. 2,3-The Hand app. 4-Steve Rogers app. 6,7-Elektra app.; Sienkiewicz-c. 9-Spider-Man app. 16-Spider-Man app. 18,19-Purple Man app. 23-She-Hulk app. 28-Kingpin becomes mayor of New York — 4.00
[Title switches to legacy numbering after #28 (12/17)]
595-599,601-611: 595-(1/18) Soule-s/Landini-a. 603,609-Elektra app. — 4.00

	GD 2.0	VG 4.0	FN 6.0	VF 8.0	VF/NM 9.0	NM- 9.2

600-(5/18, $5.99) Soule-s/Garney-a; Spider-Man and The Defenders app. — 6.00
612-($4.99) Soule-s/Noto-a; leads into Man Without Fear 2019 series — 5.00
Annual 1 (10/16, $4.99) Echo returns; Vanesa Del Ray-a — 5.00
Annual 1 (10/18, $4.99) Schultz-s/Takara-a; flashback to 1st meeting with Misty Knight — 5.00

DAREDEVIL (Follows Man Without Fear)
Marvel Comics: Apr, 2019 - No. 36, Jan, 2022 ($4.99/$3.99)
1-($4.99) Zdarsky-s/Checchetto-a; Kingpin app.; intro Det. Cole North — 5.00
2-24,26-35 ($3.99) 3,4-Punisher app. 10-16-Elektra app. 19,20-Bullseye, Crossbones, Rhino app. 20,22,24,26-Typhoid Mary app. 23-Spider-Man app. 26-King in Black tie-in — 4.00
25-Daredevil goes to jail; Elektra dons Daredevil costume — 5.00
36-(4.99) Murdock leaves jail; leads into Devil's Reign #1 — 5.00
Annual 1 (10/20, $4.99) Zdarsky-s/Garcia-a; spotlight on Mike Murdock; The Hood app. — 5.00

DAREDEVIL
Marvel Comics: Sept, 2022 - No. 14, Oct, 2023 ($4.99/$3.99)
1-($4.99) Zdarsky-s/Checchetto-a; Spider-Man app. — 5.00
2-($5.99) Legacy #650; back-up stories and bonus cover gallery — 6.00
3-10, 12,13-($3.99) 3-De Latorre-a; Luke Cage app. 6-Iron Man app. 7,8-Punisher app. — 4.00
11,14-($4.99) 11-Back-up story with Iron Fist — 5.00

DAREDEVIL
Marvel Comics: Nov, 2023 - Present ($6.99/$4.99)
1-($6.99) Ahmed-s/Kuder-a — 7.00
2-6-($4.99) 4-Bullseye app. 5-She-Hulk app. 5,6-Doctor Strange app. — 5.00

DAREDEVIL & ECHO (Also see Batman/Daredevil)
Marvel Comics: Jan, 2024 - No. 4, Oct, 2023 ($4.99/$3.99, limited series)
1-($4.99) Taboo & B. Earl-s/Phil Noto-a; Elektra app. — 5.00
2-4-($3.99) Ghost Rider app. — 4.00

DAREDEVIL/ BATMAN (Also see Batman/Daredevil)
Marvel Comics/ DC Comics: 1997 ($5.99, one-shot)
nn-McDaniel-c/a — 2 — 4 — 6 — 8 — 11 — 14

DAREDEVIL BATTLES HITLER (See Daredevil #1 [1941 series])

DAREDEVIL: BATTLIN' JACK MURDOCK
Marvel Comics: Aug, 2007 - No. 4, Nov, 2007 ($3.99, limited series)
1-4-Wells-s/DiGiandomenico-a; flashback to the fixed fight — 4.00
TPB (2007, $12.99) r/#1-4; page layouts and cover inks — 13.00

DAREDEVIL: BLACK ARMOR
Marvel Comics: Jan, 2024 - No. 4, Apr, 2024 ($4.99/$3.99, limited series)
1-($4.99) Story from the black armor era; Chichester-s/Diaz-a; Sabretooth app. — 5.00
2-4-($3.99) Hobgoblin and Baron Von Strucker app. — 4.00

DAREDEVIL COMICS (Golden Age title) (See Daredevil)

DAREDEVIL: DARK NIGHTS
Marvel Comics: Aug, 2013 - No. 8, Mar, 2014 ($3.99, limited series)
1-8: 1-3-Lee Weeks-s/a. 4,5-David Lapham-s/a; The Shocker app. 6-8-Conner-c — 4.00

DAREDEVIL/ ELEKTRA: LOVE AND WAR
Marvel Comics: 2003 ($29.99, hardcover with dust jacket)
HC-Larger-size reprints of Daredevil: Love and War (Marvel Graphic Novel #24) & Elektra: Assassin; Frank Miller-s; Bill Sienkiewicz-a — 30.00

DAREDEVIL: END OF DAYS
Marvel Comics: Dec, 2012 - No. 8, Aug, 2013 ($3.99, limited series)
1-8-Bendis-s/ Mack-s/Janson & Sienkiewicz-a; death of Daredevil in the future — 4.00

DAREDEVIL: FATHER
Marvel Comics: June, 2004 - No. 6, Feb, 2007 ($3.50/$2.99, limited series)
1-Quesada-s/a; Isanove-painted color — 3.50
1-Director's Cut ($2.99) cover and page development art; partial sketch-c — 3.00
2-6: 2-($2.99,10/05). 3-Santerians app. — 3.00
HC (2006, $24.99) r/series; Lindelof intro.; sketch pages, cover pencils and bonus art — 25.00

DAREDEVIL: GANG WAR (Tie-in to Spider-Man crossover event)
Marvel Comics: Feb, 2024 - No. 4, May, 2024 ($4.99/$3.99, limited series)
1-($4.99) Elektra as Daredevil; Spider-Man app.; Schultz-s/Davila-a — 5.00
2-4-($3.99) Madame Masque, Bellona, The Owl app. — 4.00

DAREDEVIL: NINJA
Marvel Comics: Dec, 2000 - No. 3, Feb, 2001 ($2.99, limited series)
1-3: Bendis-s/Haynes-a — 3.00
1-Dynamic Forces foil-c — 10.00
TPB (7/01, $12.99) r/#1-3 with cover and sketch gallery — 13.00

DAREDEVIL NOIR
Marvel Comics: June, 2009 - No. 4, Sept, 2009 ($3.99, limited series)
1-4-Irvine-s/Coker-a; covers by Coker and Calero — 4.00

DAREDEVIL / PUNISHER: SEVENTH CIRCLE
Marvel Comics: Jul, 2016 - No. 4, Oct, 2016 ($4.99, limited series)
1-4-Soule-s/Kudranski-a; Blindspot app. 3,4-Crimson Dynamo app. — 5.00

DAREDEVIL: REBORN (Follows Shadowland x-over)
Marvel Comics: Mar, 2011 - No. 4, Jul, 2011 ($3.99, limited series)
1-4-Diggle-s/Gianfelice-a — 4.00

DAREDEVIL: REDEMPTION
Marvel Comics: Apr, 2005 - No. 6, Aug, 2005 ($2.99, limited series)
1-6-Hine-s/Gaydos-a/Sienkiewicz-c — 3.00
TPB (2005, $14.99) r/#1-6 — 15.00

DAREDEVIL: SEASON ONE
Marvel Comics: 2012 ($24.99, hardcover graphic novel)
HC - Story of early career, yellow costume; Johnston-s/Alves-a/Tedesco painted-c — 25.00

DAREDEVIL/ SHI (See Shi / Daredevil)
Marvel Comics/ Crusade Comics: Feb,1997 ($2.95, one-shot)
1 — 4.00

DAREDEVIL/ SPIDER-MAN
Marvel Comics: Jan, 2001 - No. 4, Apr, 2001 ($2.99, limited series)
1-4-Jenkins-s/Winslade-a/Alex Ross-c; Stilt Man app. — 3.00
TPB (8/01, $12.95) r/#1-4; Ross-c — 13.00

DAREDEVIL THE MAN WITHOUT FEAR
Marvel Comics: Oct, 1993 - No. 5, Feb, 1994 ($2.95, limited series) (foil embossed covers)
1-Miller scripts; Romita, Jr./Williamson-c/a — 6.00
2-5 — 5.00
Hardcover — 100.00
Trade paperback — 20.00

DAREDEVIL: THE MOVIE (2003 movie adaptation)
Marvel Comics: March, 2003 ($3.50/$12.95, one-shot)
1-Photo-c of Ben Affleck; Bruce Jones-s/Manuel Garcia-a — 3.50
TPB ($12.95) r/movie adaptation; Daredevil #32; Ultimate Daredevil & Elektra #1 and Spider-Man's Tangled Web #4; photo-c of Ben Affleck — 13.00

DAREDEVIL: THE TARGET (Daredevil Bullseye on cover)
Marvel Comics: Jan, 2003 ($3.50, unfinished limited series)
1-Kevin Smith-s/Glenn Fabry-c/a — 3.50

DAREDEVIL VS. PUNISHER
Marvel Comics: Sept, 2005 - No. 6, Jan, 2006 ($2.99, limited series)
1-5-David Lapham-s/a — 3.00
TPB (2005, $15.99) r/#1-6 — 16.00

DAREDEVIL: WOMAN WITHOUT FEAR (Takes place during Devil's Reign series)
Marvel Comics: Mar, 2022 - No. 3, May, 2022 ($4.99/$3.99, limited series)
1-($4.99) Elektra continues as Daredevil; Zdarsky-s/De Latorre-a — 5.00
2,3-($3.99) Kraven app.; prelude to Punisher #1 — 4.00

DAREDEVIL: YELLOW
Marvel Comics: Aug, 2001 - No. 6, Jan, 2002 ($3.50, limited series)
1-6-Jeph Loeb-s/Tim Sale-a/c; origin & yellow costume days retold — 3.50
HC (5/02, $29.95) r/#1-6 with dustjacket; intro by Stan Lee; sketch pages — 30.00
Daredevil Legends Vol. 1: Daredevil Yellow (2002, $14.99, TPB) r/#1-6 — 15.00

DARING ADVENTURES (Also see Approved Comics)
St. John Publishing Co.: Nov, 1953 (25¢, 3-D, came w/glasses)
1 (3-D)-Reprints lead story from Son of Sinbad #1 by Kubert — 31 — 62 — 93 — 182 — 296 — 410

DARING ADVENTURES
I.W. Enterprises/Super Comics: 1963 - 1964
I.W. Reprint #8-r/Fight Comics #53; Matt Baker-a — 5 — 10 — 15 — 35 — 63 — 90
I.W. Reprint #9-r/Blue Bolt #115; Disbrow-a(3) — 6 — 12 — 18 — 37 — 66 — 95
Super Reprint #10,11('63)-r/Dynamic #24,16; 11-Marijuana story; Yankee Boy app.;
   Mac Raboy-a — 4 — 8 — 12 — 25 — 40 — 55
Super Reprint #12('64)-Phantom Lady from Fox (r/#14 only? w/splash pg. omitted);
   Matt Baker-a — 10 — 20 — 30 — 69 — 147 — 225
Super Reprint #15('64)-r/Hooded Menace #1 — 7 — 14 — 21 — 44 — 82 — 120
Super Reprint #16('64)-r/Dynamic #12 — 4 — 8 — 12 — 23 — 37 — 50
Super Reprint #17('64)-r/Green Lama #3 by Raboy — 4 — 8 — 12 — 28 — 47 — 65
Super Reprint #18-Origin Atlas from unpublished Atlas Comics #1 — 4 — 8 — 12 — 27 — 44 — 60

DARING COMICS (Formerly Daring Mystery) (Jeanie Comics No. 13 on)
Timely Comics (HPC): No. 9, Fall, 1944 - No. 12, Fall, 1945
9-Human Torch, Toro & Sub-Mariner app. — 400 — 800 — 1200 — 2800 — 4900 — 7000
10-12: 10-The Angel only app. 11,12-The Destroyer app. — 271 — 542 — 813 — 1734 — 2967 — 4200
NOTE: Schomburg c-9-11. Sekowsky c-12? Human Torch, Toro & Sub-Mariner c-9-12.

DARING CONFESSIONS (Formerly Youthful Hearts)
Youthful Magazines: No. 4, 11/52 - No. 7, 5/53; No. 8, 10/53
4-Doug Wildey-a; Tony Curtis story — 25 — 50 — 75 — 150 — 245 — 340
5-8: 5-Ray Anthony photo on-c. 6,8-Wildey-a — 19 — 38 — 57 — 109 — 172 — 235

DARING ESCAPES
Image Comics: Sept, 1998 - No. 4, Mar, 1999 ($2.95/$2.50, mini-series)
1-Houdini; following app. in Spawn #19,20 — 4.00
2-4-($2.50) — 4.00

DARING LOVE (Radiant Love No. 2 on)
Gilmor Magazines: Sept-Oct, 1953
1—Steve Ditko's 1st published work (1st drawn was Fantastic Fears #5)(Also see Black Magic #27)(scarce) — 454 — 908 — 1362 — 3314 — 5857 — 8400

DARING LOVE (Formerly Youthful Romances)
Ribage/Pix: No. 15, 12/52; No. 16, 2/53-c, 4/53-Indicia; No. 17-4/53-c & indicia
15 — 20 — 40 — 60 — 117 — 189 — 260
16,17: 17-Photo-c — 18 — 36 — 54 — 103 — 162 — 220
NOTE: Colletta a-15. Wildey a-17.

DARING LOVE STORIES (See Fox Giants)

DARING MYSTERY COMICS (Comedy Comics No. 9 on; title changed to Daring Comics with No. 9)
Timely Comics (TPI 1-6/TCI 7,8): 1/40 - No. 5, 6/40; No. 6, 9/40; No. 7, 4/41 - No. 8, 1/42
1-Origin The Fiery Mask (1st app.) by Joe Simon; Monako, Prince of Magic (1st app.), John Steele, Soldier of Fortune (1st app.), Doc Denton (1st app.) begin; Flash Foster & Barney Mullen, Sea Rover only app; bondage-c — 2750 — 5500 — 8250 — 21,300 — 43,150 — 65,000
2-(Rare)-Origin The Phantom Bullet (1st & only app.); The Laughing Mask & Mr. E only app.; Trojak the Tiger Man begins, ends #6; Zephyr Jones & K-4 & His Sky Devils app., also #4 — 1567 — 3134 — 4700 — 11,800 — 22,900 — 34,000
3-The Phantom Reporter, Dale of FBI, Captain Strong only app.; Breeze Barton, Marvex the Super-Robot, The Purple Mask begin — 865 — 1730 — 2595 — 6315 — 11,158 — 16,000
4,5: 4-Last Purple Mask; Whirlwind Carter begins; Dan Gorman, G-Man app. 5-The Falcon begins (1st app.); The Fiery Mask, Little Hercules app. by Sagendorf in the Segar style; bondage-c — 519 — 1038 — 1557 — 3789 — 6695 — 9600

Daredevil & Echo #1 © MAR

Dark Avengers #184 © MAR

Dark Crisis #1 © DC

DA

	GD 2.0	VG 4.0	FN 6.0	VF 8.0	VF/NM 9.0	NM- 9.2

6-Origin & only app. Marvel Boy by S&K; Flying Flame, Dynaman, & Stuporman only app.;
The Fiery Mask by S&K; S&K-c — 622 1244 1866 4541 8021 11,500

7-Origin and 1st app. The Blue Diamond, Captain Daring by S&K, The Fin by Everett,
The Challenger, The Silver Scorpion & The Thunderer by Burgos; Mr. Millions app — 459 918 1377 3350 5925 8500

8-Origin Citizen V; Last Fin, Silver Scorpion, Capt. Daring by Borth, Blue Diamond &
The Thunderer; Kirby & part solo Simon-c; Rudy the Robot only app.; Citizen V, Fin &
Silver Scorpion continue in Comedy #9 — 423 846 1269 3000 5250 7500

NOTE: *Schomburg c-1-4, 7. Simon a-2, 3, 5. Cover features: 1-Fiery Mask; 2-Phantom Bullet; 3-Purple Mask; 4-G-Man; 5-The Falcon; 6-Marvel Boy; 7, 8-Multiple characters.*

DARING MYSTERY COMICS 70th ANNIVERARY SPECIAL
Marvel Comics: Nov, 2009 ($3.99, one-shot)
1-New story of The Phantom Reporter; r/app. in Daring Mystery #3 (1940); 2 covers — 5.00

DARING NEW ADVENTURES OF SUPERGIRL, THE
DC Comics: Nov, 1982 - No. 13, Nov, 1983 (Supergirl No. 14 on)
1-Origin retold; Lois Lane back-ups in #2-12 — 3 6 9 16 23 30
2-13: 8,9-Doom Patrol app. 13-New costume; flag-c — 5.00
NOTE: *Buckler c-1p, 2p. Giffen c-3p, 4p. Gil Kane c-6,8, 9, 11-13.*

DARK, THE
Continuum Comics: Nov, 1990 - No. 4, Feb, 1993; V2#1, May, 1993 - V2#7, Apr?, 1994 ($1.95)
1-4: 1-Bright-p; Panosian, Hanna-i; Stroman-c. 2-(1/92)-Stroman-c/a(p).
4-Perez-c & part-i — 4.00
V2#1,V2#2-6: V2#1-Red foil Bart Sears-c. V2#1-Red non-foil variant-c. V2#1-2nd printing
w/blue foil Bart Sears-c. V2#2-Stroman/Bryant-a. 3-Perez-c(i). 3-6-Foil-c. 4-Perez-c & part-i;
bound-in trading cards. 5,6-(2,3/94)-Perez-c(i). 7-(B&W)-Perez-c(i) — 4.00
Convention Book 1 ,2(Fall/94, 10/94)-Perez-c — 4.00

DARK AGES
Dark Horse Comics: Aug, 2014 - No. 4, Nov, 2014 ($3.99, limited series)
1-4-Abnett-s/Culbard-a/c — 4.00

DARK AGES
Marvel Comics: Mar, 2022 - No. 6, May, 2022 ($4.99/$3.99, limited series)
1-($4.99) Taylor-s/Coello-a; Marvel heroes in a world without electricity — 5.00
2-6 ($3.99) Apocalypse & The Purple Man app. 4-Fin Fang Foom app. — 4.00

DARK AGNES (Robert E. Howard character)
Marvel Comics: Apr, 2020 - No. 5 ($3.99, limited series)
1,2-Becky Cloonan-s/Luca Pizzari-a; set in 1521 France — 4.00

DARK AND BLOODY, THE
DC Comics (Vertigo): Apr, 2016 - No. 6, Sept, 2016 ($3.99, limited series)
1-6-Aldridge-s/Godlewski-a — 4.00

DARK ANGEL (Formerly Hell's Angel)
Marvel Comics UK, Ltd.: No. 6, Dec, 1992 - No. 16, Dec, 1993 ($1.75)
6-8,13-16: 6-Excalibur-c/story. 8-Psylocke app. — 4.00
9-12-Wolverine/X-Men app. — 5.00

DARK ANGEL: PHOENIX RESURRECTION (Kia Asamiya's...)
Image Comics: May, 2000 - No. 4, Oct, 2001 ($2.95)
1-4-Kia Asamiya-s/a. 3-Van Fleet variant-c — 3.00

DARK ARK
AfterShock Comics: Sept, 2017 - No. 15, Mar, 2019 ($3.99)
1-15-Cullen Bunn-s/Juan Doe-a — 4.00

DARK ARK: AFTER THE FLOOD
AfterShock Comics: Oct, 2019 - No. 5, July, 2020 ($3.99, limited series)
1-5: 1-Cullen Bunn-s/Juan Doe-a. 3-5-Jesus Hervas-a — 4.00

DARK AVENGERS (See Secret Invasion and Dark Reign titles)
Marvel Comics: Mar, 2009 - No. 16, Jul, 2010 ($3.99)
1-Norman Osborn assembles his Avengers; Bendis-s/Deodato-a/c — 2 4 6 9 12 15
1-Variant Iron Patriot armor cover by Djurdjevic — 4 8 12 23 37 50
2-16: 2-6-Bendis-s/Deodato-a/c. 2-4 Dr. Doom app. 7,8-Utopia x-over; X-Men app.
9-Nick Fury app. 11,12-Deodato & Horn-a. 13-16-Siege. 13-Sentry origin — 4.00
Annual 1 (2/10, $4.99) Bendis-s/Bachalo-a; Marvel Boy new costume; Siege preview — 5.00
.../ Uncanny X-Men: Exodus (11/09, $3.99) Conclusion of x-over; Deodato & Dodson-a — 4.00
.../ Uncanny X-Men: Utopia (8/09, $3.99) Part 1 of x-over w/Uncanny X-Men #513,514 — 4.00

DARK AVENGERS (Title continues from Thunderbolts #174)
Marvel Comics: No. 175, Aug, 2012 - No. 190, Jul, 2013 ($2.99)
175-190: 175-New team assembles; Parker-s/Shalvey-a/Deodato-c — 3.00

DARK AVENGERS: ARES
Marvel Comics: Dec, 2009 - No. 3, Feb, 2010 ($3.99, limited series)

1-Garcia-a/Gillen-s/Nord-c — 1 3 4 6 8 10
2,3: 2-Tan-c. 3-McGuinness-c — 4.00

DARK BLOOD
BOOM! Studios: Jul, 2021 - No. 6, Jan, 2022 ($3.99, limited series)
1-6-Latoya Morgan-s. 1,2-Walt Barna-a. 3-6-Moisés Hidalgo-a — 4.00

DARKCHYLDE (Also see Dreams of the Darkchylde)
Maximum Press #1-3/ Image Comics #4 on: June, 1996 - No. 5, Sept, 1997 ($2.95/ $2.50)
1-Randy Queen-c/a/scripts; "Roses" cover — 1 3 4 6 8 10
1-American Entertainment Edition-wraparound-c — 1 3 4 6 8 10
1-"Fashion magazine-style" variant-c — 1 3 4 6 8 10
1-Special Comicon Edition (contents of #1) Winged devil variant-c — 2 4 6 9 12 15
1-($2.50)-Remastered Ed.-wraparound-c — 5.00
2(Reg-c),2-Spiderweb and Moon variant-c — 1 3 4 6 8 10
3(Reg-c),3-"Kalvin Clein" variant-c by Drew — 4.00
4,5(Reg-c), 4-Variant-c — 4.00
5-B&W Edition, 5-Dynamic Forces Gold Ed. — 8.00
0-(3/98, $2.50) — 6.00
0-Remastered (1/01, $2.95) includes Darkchylde: Redemption preview — 6.00
1/2-Wizard offer — 1 2 3 5 6 8
1/2 Variant-c — 1 3 4 6 8 10
... The Descent TPB ('98, $19.95) r/#1-5; bagged with Darkchylde The Legacy
Preview Special 1998; listed price is for TPB only — 20.00

DARKCHYLDE LAST ISSUE SPECIAL
Darkchylde Entertainment: June, 2002 ($3.95)
1-Wraparound-c; cover gallery — 5.00

DARKCHYLDE REDEMPTION
Darkchylde Entertainment: Feb, 2001 - No. 2, Dec, 2001 ($2.95)
1,2: 1-Wraparound-c — 3.00
1-Dynamic Forces alternate-c — 6.00
1-Dynamic Forces chrome-c — 16.00

DARKCHYLDE SKETCH BOOK
Image Comics (Dynamic Forces): 1998
1-Regular-c — 8.00
1-DarkChrome cover — 16.00

DARKCHYLDE SUMMER SWIMSUIT SPECTACULAR
DC Comics (WildStorm): Aug, 1999 ($3.95, one-shot)
1-Pin-up art by various — 5.00

DARKCHYLDE SWIMSUIT ILLUSTRATED
Image Comics: 1998 ($2.50, one-shot)
1-Pin-up art by various — 1 2 3 5 6 8
1-(6.95) Variant cover — 1 3 4 6 8 10
1-Chromium cover — 15.00

DARKCHYLDE THE DIARY
Image Comics: June, 1997 ($2.50, one-shot)
1-Queen-c/s/ art by various — 4.00
1-Variant-c — 5.00
1-Holochrome variant-c — 8.00

DARKCHYLDE THE LEGACY
Image Comics/DC (WildStorm) #3 on: Aug, 1998 - No. 3, June, 1999 ($2.50)
1-3: 1-Queen-c. 2-Two covers by Queen and Art Adams — 4.00

DARK CLAW ADVENTURES
DC Comics (Amalgam): June, 1997 ($1.95, one-shot)
1-Templeton-c/s/a & Burchett-a — 4.00

DARK CRISIS (Title changes to Dark Crisis on Infinite Earths for #4-7)(See Justice League #75 from 2022)
DC Comics: No. 0, Jun, 2022 - No. 7, Feb, 2023 ($5.99/$4.99)
0 FCBD Special Edition 2022 (6/22, giveaway) Cheung-a; preview of Dark Crisis #1 — 3.00
1-(8/22, $5.99) Williamson-s/Sampere-a; Jon Kent forms a new Justice League — 6.00
2-6 ($4.99) 2-Deathstroke vs. Nightwing. 4-Legion of Doom app. 6-Justice League returns — 5.00
7 ($5.99) Conclusion; s/a by various — 6.00
...: Big Bang 1 (2/23, $3.99) Waid-s/Jurgens-a; Flash vs. Anti-Monitor across Multiverse — 4.00
...: The Dark Army 1 (1/23, $5.99) Damian Wayne vs. The Darkness — 6.00
...: The Deadly Green 1 (12/22, $5.99) Jon Kent with Swamp Thing, Constantine, Raven — 6.00
...: War Zone 1 (2/23, $5.99) Short battle stories with Wally West, various Green Lanterns — 6.00
...: Worlds Without a Justice League - Batman 1 (1/23, $4.99) w/Zatanna — 5.00
...: Worlds Without a Justice League - Green Arrow 1 (12/22, $4.99) Black Canary app. — 5.00
...: Worlds Without a Justice League - Green Lantern 1 (10/22, $4.99) Back-up w/Hawkgirl — 5.00

	GD	VG	FN	VF	VF/NM	NM-
	2.0	4.0	6.0	8.0	9.0	9.2

...: Worlds Without a Justice League - Superman 1 (9/22, $4.99) Back-up with Aquaman 5.00

...: Worlds Without a Justice League - Wonder Woman 1 (11/22, $4.99) Martian Manhunter 5.00

DARK CRISIS: YOUNG JUSTICE
DC Comics: Aug, 2022 - No. 6, Jan, 2023 ($3.99, liimted series)

1-6-Fitzmartin-s/Braga-a. 4-6-Mickey Mxyzptlk app. 4.00

DARK CROSSINGS: DARK CLOUDS RISING
Image Comics (Top Cow): June, 2000; Oct, 2000 ($5.95, limited series)

1-Witchblade, Darkness, Tomb Raider crossover; Dwayne Turner-a 6.00
1-(Dark Clouds Overhead) 6.00

DARK CRYSTAL, THE (Movie)
Marvel Comics Group: April, 1983 - No. 2, May, 1983

| 1,2-Adaptation of film | 2 | 4 | 6 | 11 | 16 | 20 |

DARK DAYS (See 30 Days of Night)
IDW Publishing: June, 2003 - No. 6, Dec, 2003 ($3.99, limited series)

1-6-Sequel to 30 Days of Night; Niles-s/Templesmith-a 4.00
1-Retailer variant (Diamond/Alliance Fort Wayne 5/03 summit) 15.00
TPB (2004, $19.99) r/#1-6; cover gallery; intro. by Eric Red 20.00

DARK DAYS (Tie-ins to Dark Nights: Metal series)
DC Comics: Aug, 2017 - Sept, 2017 ($4.99, one-shots)

...: The Casting 1 (9/17, $4.99) Snyder & Tynion IV-s; Jim Lee, Andy Kubert & Romita Jr.-a; Joker, Green Lantern & Hawkman app. 5.00
...: The Forge (8/17, $4.99) Lee, Kubert & Romita Jr.-a; Mister Miracle, Mr. Terrific app. 5.00
...: The Forge/The Casting Director's Cut (1/18, $7.99) reprints 2 issues with B&W pencil-a; original script for The Forge 8.00

DARKDEVIL (See Spider-Girl)
Marvel Comics: Nov, 2000 - No. 3, Jan, 2001 ($2.99, limited series)

1-3: 1-Origin of Darkdevil; Kingpin-c/app. 3.00

DARK DOMINION
Defiant: Oct, 1993 - No. 10, July, 1994 ($2.50)

1-10-Len Wein scripts begin. 1-Intro Chasm. 4-Free extra 16 pgs. 7-9-J.G. Jones-c/a (his 1st pro work). 10-Pre-Schism issue; Shooter/Wein script; John Ridgway-a 4.00

DARKER IMAGE (Also see Deathblow, The Maxx, & Bloodwulf)
Image Comics: Mar, 1993 ($1.95, one-shot)

1-The Maxx by Sam Kieth begins; Bloodwulf by Rob Liefeld & Deathblow by Jim Lee begin (both 1st app.); polybagged w/1 of 3 cards by Kieth, Lee or Liefeld 4.00
1-B&W interior pgs. w/silver foil logo 6.00

DARK FANG
Image Comics: Nov, 2017 - No. 5, Mar, 2018 ($3.99)

1-5-Gunter-s/Shannon-a 4.00

DARK FANTASIES
Dark Fantasy: 1994 - No. 8, 1995 ($2.95)

1-Test print Run (3,000)-Linsner-c	1	2	3	5	6	8
1-Linsner-c						5.00
2-8: 2-4 (Deluxe), 2-4 (Regular), 5-8 (Deluxe) ($3.95)						4.00
5-8 (Regular; $3.50)						4.00

DARK GUARD
Marvel Comics UK: Oct, 1993 - No. 4, Jan, 1994 ($1.75)

1-($2.95)-Foil stamped-c 5.00
2-4 4.00

DARKHAWK (See Marvel Age #97 {Feb. 1991} for debut, and War of Kings)
Marvel Comics: Mar, 1991 - No. 50, Apr, 1995 ($1.00/1.25/1.50)

1-Origin of Darkhawk; Hobgoblin cameo	3	6	9	17	26	35
2,3,13,14: 2-Spider-Man & Hobgoblin app. 3-Spider-Man & Hobgoblin app. 13,14-Venom-c/story						5.00
4-12,15-24,26-49: 6-Capt. America & Daredevil x-over. 9-Punisher app. 11,12-Tombstone app. 19-Spider-Man & Brotherhood of Evil Mutants-c/story. 20-Spider-Man app. 22-Ghost Rider-c/story. 23-Origin begins, ends #25. 27-New Warriors-c/story. 35-Begin 3 part Venom story. 39-Bound-in trading card sheet						4.00
25,50: (52 pgs.)-Red holo-grafx foil-c w/double gatefold poster; origin of Darkhawk armor						5.00
Annual 1,2 ('92, '93, 68 pgs.): 1-Vs. Iron Man. 2-Polybagged w/card						5.00
Annual 3 ('94, 68 pgs.) Low print run	2	4	6	9	14	20

DARKHAWK (Marvel Legacy)
Marvel Comics: No. 51, Jan, 2018 ($3.99, one-shot)

51-Bowers & Sims-s/Kev Walker-a/Nakayama-c 6.00

DARKHAWK (Marvel)
Marvel Comics: Oct, 2021 - No. 5, Mar, 2022 ($4.99/$3.99, limited series)

1-($4.99) Higgins-s/Ramirez-a; intro. Connor Young as the new Darkhawk 5.00
2-5-($3.99) 3-5-Spider-Man (Miles) app. 4-Captain America app. 4.00
...: Heart of the Hawk (6/21, $4.99) Three short stories of the original Darkhawk 5.00

DARKHOLD, THE
Marvel Comics: Nov, 2021 - Mar, 2022 ($4.99/$3.99, series of one-shots)

... Alpha 1 (11/21, $4.99) 1st part; Orlando-s/Tormey-a; Scarlet Witch & Doom app. 5.00
... Black Bolt 1 (1/22, $3.99) Russell-s/Cutler-a; Maximus app. 4.00
... Blade 1 (12/21, $3.99) Kibblesmith-s/Sabbatini-a; vampire Amadeus Cho app. 4.00
... Iron Man 1 (12/21, $3.99) North-s/Sanna-a; alternate past with grey armor shown 4.00
... Omega 1 (3/22, $4.99) Conclusion; Orlando-s/Tormey-a; Chthon arrives 5.00
... Spider-Man 1 (2/22, $3.99) Paknadel-s/Neves-a; alternate past shown 4.00
... Wasp 1 (1/22, $3.99) Bellaire-s/Roe-a; alternate past with shown; Tigra app. 4.00

DARKHOLD: PAGES FROM THE BOOK OF SINS (See Midnight Sons Unlimited)
Marvel Comics (Midnight Sons imprint #15 on): Oct, 1992 - No. 16, Jan, 1994

1-($2.75, 52 pgs.)-Polybagged w/poster by Andy & Adam Kubert; part 4 of Rise of the Midnight Sons storyline	1	2	3	5	6	8
2-10,12-16: 3-Reintro Modred the Mystic (see Marvel Chillers #1). 4-Sabertooth-c/sty.						
5-Punisher & Ghost Rider app. 15-Spot varnish-c. 15,16-Siege of Darkness pt. 4&12						3.00
11-($2.25)-Outer-c is a Darkhold envelope made of black parchment w/gold ink						4.00

DARK HORSE BOOK OF... , THE
Dark Horse Comics: Aug, 2003 - Nov, 2006 ($14.95/$15.95, HC, 9 1/4" x 6 1/4")

... Hauntings (8/03, $14.95)-Short stories by various incl. Mignola (Hellboy), Thompson, Dorkin, Russell; Gianni-c 15.00
... Monsters (11/06, $15.95)-Short-s by Mignola, Thompson, Dorkin, Giffen, Busiek; Gianni-c 16.00
... The Dead (6/05, $14.95)-Short-s by Mignola, Thompson, Dorkin, Powell; Gianni-c 15.00
... Witchcraft (6/04, $14.95)-Short-s by Mignola, Thompson, Dorkin, Millionaire; Gianni-c 15.00

DARK HORSE CLASSICS (Title series), Dark Horse Comics

1992 $3.95, B&W, 52 pgs. nn's): The Last of the Mohicans. 20,000 Leagues Under the Sea 4.00

DARK HORSE CLASSICS
Dark Horse Comics: May, 1996 ($2.95, limited series)

| 1-Reprints Predator: Jungle Tales | 1 | 2 | 3 | 5 | 6 | 8 |

DARK HORSE CLASSICS: ALIENS VERSUS PREDATOR
Dark Horse Comics: Feb, 1997 - No. 6, Jul, 1997 ($2.95, limited series)

| 1-Reprints Aliens Versus Predator series | 1 | 3 | 4 | 6 | 8 | 10 |
| 2-6: R/Aliens Versus Predator | | | | | | 5.00 |

DARK HORSE CLASSICS: GODZILLA: KING OF THE MONSTERS
Dark Horse Comics: Apr, 1998 - No. 6, Sept, 1998 ($2.95, limited series)

| 1-Reprints Godzilla: Color Special; Art Adams-a | 2 | 4 | 6 | 11 | 16 | 20 |
| 2-6 | | | | | | 5.00 |

DARK HORSE CLASSICS: GODZILLA: TERROR OF GODZILLA
Dark Horse Comics: Aug, 1998 - No. 6, Jan, 1999 ($2.95, limited series)

| 1-Reprints manga Godzilla in color; Art Adams-c | 2 | 4 | 6 | 11 | 16 | 20 |
| 2-6 | 1 | 2 | 3 | 5 | 6 | 8 |

DARK HORSE CLASSICS – STAR WARS: DARK EMPIRE
Dark Horse Comics: Mar, 1997 - No. 6, Aug, 1997 ($2.95, limited series)

| 1,3-Reprints Star Wars: Dark Empire | 2 | 4 | 6 | 8 | 11 | 14 |
| 2,4-6: R/Star Wars: Dark Empire | | | | | | 5.00 |

DARK HORSE COMICS
Dark Horse Comics: Aug, 1992 - No. 25, Sept, 1994 ($2.50)

1-Dorman double gategold painted-c; Predator, Robocop, Timecop (3-part) & Renegade stories begin	1	2	3	5	6	8
2-6,11-25: 2-Mignola-c. 3-Begin 3-part Aliens story; Aliens-c. 4-Predator-c. 6-Begin 4 part Robocop story. 12-Begin 2-part Aliens & 3-part Predator stories. 13-Thing From Another World begins w/Nino-a(i). 15-Begin 2-part Aliens: Cargo story. 16-Begin 3-part Predator story. 17-Begin 3-part Star Wars: Droids story & 3-part Aliens: Alien story; Droids-c. 19-Begin 2-part X story						4.00
7-Begin Star Wars: Tales of the Jedi 3-part story	2	4	6	8	10	12
8-1st app. X and begins; begin 4-part James Bond	1	2	3	5	6	8
9,10: 9-Star Wars ends. 10-X ends; Begin 3-part Predator & Godzilla stories						5.00

NOTE: *Art Adams* c-11.

DARK HORSE DAY SAMPLER 2016
Dark Horse Comics: Jun, 2016 (no price, promotional one-shot)

nn-New Buffy the Vampire Slayer story; reprint stories of Sin City, AvP, Umbrella Academy 3.00

DARK HORSE DOWN UNDER
Dark Horse Comics: Jun, 1994 - No. 3, Oct, 1994 ($2.50, B&W, limited series)

1-3 4.00

DARK HORSE MAVERICK
Dark Horse Comics: July, 2000; July, 2001; Sept, 2002 (B&W, annual)

2000-($3.95) Short stories by Miller, Chadwick, Sakai, Pearson 4.00
2001-($4.99) Short stories by Sakai, Wagner and others; Miller-c 5.00
...: Happy Endings (9/02, $9.95) Short stories by Bendis, Oeming, Mahfood, Mignola, Miller, Kieth and others; Miller-c 10.00

DARK HORSE MONSTERS
Dark Horse Comics: Feb, 1997 ($2.95, one-shot)

1-Reprints 4.00

DARK HORSE PRESENTS
Dark Horse Comics: July, 1986 - No. 157, Sept, 2000 ($1.50-$2.95, B&W)

1-1st app. Concrete by Paul Chadwick	3	6	9	17	25	34
1-2nd printing (1988, $1.50)						4.00
1-Silver ink 3rd printing (1992, $2.25)-Says 2nd printing inside						4.00
2-9: 2-6,9-Concrete app.						6.00
10-1st app. The Mask; Concrete app.	4	8	12	25	40	55
11-19,21-23: 11-19,21-Mask stories. 12,14,16,18,22-Concrete app. 15(2/88).						
17-All Roachmill issue						6.00
20-(68 pgs.)-Concrete, Flaming Carrot, Mask	2	4	6	8	10	12
24-Origin Aliens-c/story (11/88); Mr. Monster app.	3	6	9	19	30	40
25-27,29-31,37-39,41,45,47-49: 38-Concrete. 44-Crash Ryan. 48,49-Contain 2 trading cards						3.00
28,33,40: 28-(52 pgs.)-Concrete app.; Mr. Monster story (homage to Graham Ingels). 33-(44 pgs.). 40-(52 pgs.)-1st Argosy story						4.00
32,34,35: 32-(68 pgs.)-Concrete, American. 34-Aliens-c/story. 35-Predator-c/app.						5.00
36-1st Aliens Vs. Predator story; painted-c	3	6	9	15	22	28
36-Variant line drawn-c	3	6	9	19	30	40
42,43,46: 42,43-Aliens-c/stories. 46-Prequel to new Predator II mini-series						3.00
50-S/F story by Perez; contains 2 trading cards						4.00
51-53-Sin City by Frank Miller, parts 2-4; 51,53-Miller-c (see D.H.P. Fifth Anniversary Special for pt. 1)	1	3	4	6	8	10
54-61: 54-(9/91) The Next Men begins (1st app.) by Byrne; Miller-a/Morrow-c. Homocide by Morrow (also in #55). 55-2nd app. The Next Men; parts 5 & 6 of Sin City by Miller; Miller-c. 56-(68 pg. annual)-part 7 of Sin City by Miller; part prologue to Aliens: Genocide; Next Men by Byrne. 57-(52 pgs.)-Part 8 of Sin City by Miller; Next Men by Byrne; Byrne & Miller-c; Alien Fire story; swipes cover to Daredevil #1. 58,59-Alien Fire stories. 58-61- Part 9-12 Sin City by Miller						5.00
62-Last Sin City (entire book by Miller)	2	4	6	9	13	16
63-66,68-79,81-84-($2.25): 64-Dr. Giggles begins (1st app.), ends #66; Boris the Bear story. 66-New Concrete-c/story by Chadwick. 71-Begin 3 part Dominque story by Jim Balent; Balent-c. 72-(3/93)-Begin 3-part Eudaemon (1st app.) story by Nelson						3.00
67-($3.95, 68 pgs.)-Begin 3-part prelude to Predator: Race War mini-series;						

Darkhawk (2021 series) #1 © MAR

Dark Horse Presents #13 © DH

Dark Knights of Steel #6 © DC

	GD 2.0	VG 4.0	FN 6.0	VF 8.0	VF/NM 9.0	NM- 9.2
Oscar Wilde adapt. by Russell						4.00
80-Art Adams-c/a (Monkeyman & O'Brien)						4.00
85-87,92-99: 85-Begin $2.50-c. 92, 93, 95-Too Much Coffee Man						3.00
88-Hellboy by Mignola.	2	4	6	9	13	16
89-91-Hellboy by Mignola.	1	2	3	5	6	8

NOTE: *There are 5 different Dark Horse Presents #100 issues*

	GD 2.0	VG 4.0	FN 6.0	VF 8.0	VF/NM 9.0	NM- 9.2
100-1-Intro Lance Blastoff by Miller; Milk & Cheese by Evan Dorkin						5.00
100-2-Hellboy-c by Wrightson; Hellboy story by Mignola; includes Roberta Gregory & Paul Pope stories	1	2	3	5	6	8
100-3-100-5: 100-3-Darrow-c, Concrete by Chadwick; Pekar story. 100-4-Gibbons-c: Miller story, Geary story/a. 100-5-Allred-c, Adams, Dorkin, Pope						3.00
101-125: 101-Aliens c/a by Wrightson, story by Pope. 103-Kirby gatefold-c. 106-Big Blown Baby by Bill Wray. 107-Mignola-c/a. 109-Begin $2.95-c; Paul Pope-c. 110-Ed Brubaker-a/s. 114-Flip books begin; Lance Blastoff by Miller; Star Slammers by Simonson. 115-Miller-c. 117-Aliens-c/app. 118-Evan Dorkin-c/a. 119-Monkeyman & O'Brien. 124-Predator. 125-Nocturnals						3.00
126-($3.95, 48 pgs.)-Flip book: Nocturnals, Starship Troopers						4.00
127-134,136-140: 127-Nocturnals. 129-The Hammer. 132-134-Warren-a						3.00
135-($3.50) The Mark						3.50
141-All Buffy the Vampire Slayer issue						4.00
142-149: 142-Mignola-a. 143-Tarzan. 146,147-Aliens vs. Predator. 148-Xena						3.00
150-($4.50) Buffy-c by Green; Buffy, Concrete, Fish Police app.						4.50
151-157: 151-Hellboy-c/app. 153-155-Angel flic-c. 156,157-Witch's Son						3.00
Annual 1997 ($4.95, 64 pgs.)-Flip book; Body Bags, Aliens. Pearson-c; stories by Allred & Stephens, Pope, Smith & Morrow	1	2	3	5		8
Annual 1998 ($4.95, 64 pgs.) 1st Buffy the Vampire Slayer comic app.; Hellboy story and cover by Mignola	4	8	12	25	40	55
Annual 1999 (7/99, $4.95) Stories of Xena, Hellboy, Ghost, Luke Skywalker, Groo, Concrete, the Mask and Usagi Yojimbo in their youth.	1	2	3	5		8
Annual 2000 ($4.95) Girl sidekicks; Chiodo-c and flip photo Buffy-c	1	3	4	6	8	10
...Aliens Platinum Edition (1992)-r/DHP #24,43,56 & Special	3	6	9	12	15	
...Fifth Anniversary Special nn (4/91, $9.95)-Part 1 of Sin City by Frank Miller (c/a); Aliens, Aliens vs. Predator, Concrete, Roachmill, Give Me Liberty & The American stories					40.00	
The One Trick Rip-off (1997, $12.95, TPB)-r/stories from #101-112						13.00

NOTE: *Geary a-59, 60. Miller a-Special, 51-53, 55-62; c-59-62, 100-1; c-51, 53, 55, 59-62, 100-1. Moebius a-63; c-63, 70. Vess a-78; c-75, 78.*

DARK HORSE PRESENTS
Dark Horse Comics: Apr, 2011 - No. 36, May, 2014 ($7.99, anthology)

	GD 2.0	VG 4.0	FN 6.0	VF 8.0	VF/NM 9.0	NM- 9.2
1-36: 1-Frank Miller-c & Xerxes preview; Neal Adams-s/a. 1-3-Concrete by Chadwick. 1-8-Chaykin-s/a. 2,3,9-Corben-a. 3-Steranko interview. 7-Hellboy app. 10-Milk & Cheese. 12-17-Aliens; Kieth-a. 14-Flipbook. 18-Capt. Midnight. 23-26,29-34-Nexus. 25,26-Buffy. 28,29-Neal Adams-s/a. 31,32-Hellboy; McMahon-a						8.00

DARK HORSE PRESENTS (Volume 3)
Dark Horse Comics: Aug, 2014 - No. 33, Apr, 2017 ($4.99, anthology)

	GD 2.0	VG 4.0	FN 6.0	VF 8.0	VF/NM 9.0	NM- 9.2
1-6: 1-Two covers. 1,2-Rusty & Big Guy by Darrow-s/a. 2-Aliens. 5-Alex Ross-c						5.00
7-(2/15) 200th Issue; Hellboy by Mignola & Bá, Groo, Mind Mgmt; Gibbons, Darrow-a						5.00
8-15,17-33: 8-10-Tarzan by Grell. 14,15-The Rook; Gulacy-a. 17,18-Levitz-s						5.00
16-($5.99) Flip book with Hellboy by Mignola; art by Calero, Ordway, McCarthy						6.00

DARK HORSE TWENTY YEARS
Dark Horse Comics: 2006 (25c, one-shot)

	GD 2.0	VG 4.0	FN 6.0	VF 8.0	VF/NM 9.0	NM- 9.2
nn-Pin-ups by Dark Horse artists of other artists' Dark Horse characters; Mignola-c						3.00

DARK IVORY
Image Comics: Mar, 2008 - No. 4, Jan, 2009 ($2.99, limited series)

	GD 2.0	VG 4.0	FN 6.0	VF 8.0	VF/NM 9.0	NM- 9.2
1-4-Eva Hopkins & Joseph Michael Linsner-s/Linsner-a/c						3.00

DARK KNIGHT (See Batman: The Dark Knight Returns & Legends of the...)

DARK KNIGHT RETURNS: THE GOLDEN CHILD
DC Comics (Black Label): Feb, 2020 ($5.99, squarebound, one-shot)

	GD 2.0	VG 4.0	FN 6.0	VF 8.0	VF/NM 9.0	NM- 9.2
1-Frank Miller-s/Rafael Grampá-a; Lara & Carrie from DK III vs. Joker & Darkseid						6.00
1-Retailer incentive-c by Miller (limited 1 for 100)						40.00

DARK KNIGHT RETURNS, THE: THE LAST CRUSADE
DC Comics: Aug, 2016 ($6.99, squarebound, one-shot)

	GD 2.0	VG 4.0	FN 6.0	VF 8.0	VF/NM 9.0	NM- 9.2
1-Miller & Azzarello-s/Romita Jr.-a; Jason Todd Robin vs. The Joker; Poison Ivy app.						7.00

DARK KNIGHTS OF STEEL
DC Comics: Jan, 2022 - No. 12, Oct, 2023 ($3.99, limited series)

	GD 2.0	VG 4.0	FN 6.0	VF 8.0	VF/NM 9.0	NM- 9.2
1-12: 1-The El family's rocket lands in Medieval times; Taylor-s/Putri-a. 4-Bengal-a						4.00
...: Tales From the Three Kingdoms 1 (11/22, $5.99) Short stories; origin of the Robins						6.00
...: The Gathering Storm 1 (2022, $6.99) Reprints #1-3						7.00
...: The Gathering Storm 1 (2/24, $5.99) Reprints #1-3						6.00

DARK KNIGHTS RISING: THE WILD HUNT (See Dark Nights: Metal series and other tie-ins)
DC Comics: Apr, 2018 ($4.99, one-shot)

	GD 2.0	VG 4.0	FN 6.0	VF 8.0	VF/NM 9.0	NM- 9.2
1-Snyder & Morrison-s/Porter & Mahnke-a; Detective Chimp app.; foil-c						5.00

DARK KNIGHT STRIKES AGAIN, THE (Also see Batman: The Dark Knight Returns)
DC Comics: 2001 - No. 3, 2002 ($7.95, prestige format, limited series)

	GD 2.0	VG 4.0	FN 6.0	VF 8.0	VF/NM 9.0	NM- 9.2
1-Frank Miller-s/a/c; sequel set 3 years after Dark Knight Returns; 2 covers						10.00
2,3						10.00
HC (2002, $29.95) intro. by Miller; sketch pages and exclusive artwork; cover has 3 1/4" tall partial dustjacket						30.00
SC (2002, $19.95) intro. by Miller; sketch pages						20.00

DARK KNIGHT III: THE MASTER RACE (Also see Batman: The Dark Knight Returns)
DC Comics: Jan, 2016 - No. 9, Jul, 2017 ($5.99, cardstock cover, limited series)

	GD 2.0	VG 4.0	FN 6.0	VF 8.0	VF/NM 9.0	NM- 9.2
1-9: 1-Miller & Azzarello-s/Andy Kubert-a; Dark Knight Universe Presents: The Atom mini-comic attached at centerfold, Miller-a. 2-Wonder Woman mini-comic. 3-Superman returns; Green Lantern mini-comic. 4-Batgirl mini-comic. 5-Lara mini-comic. 6-World's Finest mini-comic. 7-Strange Adventures mini-comic. 8-Detective mini. 9-Action mini						6.00
1-8-Deluxe Edition ($12.99, HC) reprints story plus mini-comic at full size; cover gallery						13.00
9-Deluxe Edition ($12.99, HC) Sold with slipcase fitting all 9 Deluxe Edition HCs						13.00
... Book One - Director's Cut (11/16, $7.99) r/ #1 in B&W art; script, variant cover gallery						8.00

DARKLING (See Mighty Crusaders #3)
Archie Comic Publications: Jan, 2024 ($3.99, one-shot)

	GD 2.0	VG 4.0	FN 6.0	VF 8.0	VF/NM 9.0	NM- 9.2
1-Sarah Kuhn-s/Carola Borelli-a; covers by Maria Sanapo and David Mack						4.00

DARKLON THE MYSTIC (Also see Eerie Magazine #79,80)
Pacific Comics: Oct, 1983 (one-shot)

	GD 2.0	VG 4.0	FN 6.0	VF 8.0	VF/NM 9.0	NM- 9.2
1-Starlin-c/a(r)						4.00

DARKMAN (Movie)
Marvel Comics: Sept, 1990; Oct, 1990 - No. 3, Dec, 1990 ($1.50)

	GD 2.0	VG 4.0	FN 6.0	VF 8.0	VF/NM 9.0	NM- 9.2
1 (9/90, $2.25, B&W mag., 68 pgs.)-Adaptation of film						5.00
1-3: Reprints B&W magazine						4.00

DARKMAN
Marvel Comics: V2#1, Apr, 1993 -No. 6, Sept, 1993 ($2.95, limited series)

	GD 2.0	VG 4.0	FN 6.0	VF 8.0	VF/NM 9.0	NM- 9.2
V2#1 ($3.95, 52 pgs.)						5.00
2-6						4.00

DARK MANSION OF FORBIDDEN LOVE, THE (Becomes Forbidden Tales of Dark Mansion No. 5 on)
National Periodical Publ.: Sept-Oct, 1971 - No. 4, Mar-Apr, 1972 (52 pgs.)

	GD 2.0	VG 4.0	FN 6.0	VF 8.0	VF/NM 9.0	NM- 9.2
1-Greytone-c on all	17	34	51	119	265	410
2-4: 2-Adams-c. 3-Jeff Jones-c	9	18	27	60	120	180

DARKMAN VS. THE ARMY OF DARKNESS (Movie crossover)
Dynamite Entertainment: 2006 - No. 4, 2007 ($3.50)

	GD 2.0	VG 4.0	FN 6.0	VF 8.0	VF/NM 9.0	NM- 9.2
1-4: 1-Busiek & Stern-s/Fry-a; photo-c and Perez and Bradshaw covers						3.50

DARK MATTER (Inspired 2015 TV series on SyFy channel)
Dark Horse Comics: Jan, 2012 - No. 4, Apr 2012 ($3.50, limited series)

	GD 2.0	VG 4.0	FN 6.0	VF 8.0	VF/NM 9.0	NM- 9.2
1-4-Joseph Mallozzi & Paul Mullie-s/Garry Brown-a						4.00

DARKMINDS
Image Comics (Dreamwave Prod.): July, 1998 - No. 8, Apr, 1999 ($2.50)

	GD 2.0	VG 4.0	FN 6.0	VF 8.0	VF/NM 9.0	NM- 9.2
1-Manga; Pat Lee-s/a; 2 covers	1	3	4	6	8	10
1-2nd printing						3.00
2, 0-(1/99, $5.00) Story and sketch pages						5.00
3-8, 1/2-(5/99, $2.50) Story and sketch pages						3.00
... Collected 1,2 (1/99,3/99, $7.95) r/#1-3. 2-r/#4-6						8.00
... Collected 3 (5/99, $5.95) r/#7,8						6.00

DARKMINDS (Volume 2)
Image Comics (Dreamwave Prod.): Feb, 2000 - No. 10, Apr, 2001 ($2.50)

	GD 2.0	VG 4.0	FN 6.0	VF 8.0	VF/NM 9.0	NM- 9.2
1-10-Pat Lee-c						3.00
0-(7/00) Origin of Mai Murasaki; sketchbook						3.00

DARKMINDS: MACROPOLIS
Image Comics (Dreamwave Prod.): Jan, 2002 - No. 4, Dec, 2002 ($2.95)

	GD 2.0	VG 4.0	FN 6.0	VF 8.0	VF/NM 9.0	NM- 9.2
Preview (8/01) Flip book w/Banished Knights preview						3.00
1-4-Jo Chen-a						3.00

DARKMINDS: MACROPOLIS (Volume 2)
Dreamwave Prod.: Sept, 2003 - No. 4, Jul, 2004 ($2.95)

	GD 2.0	VG 4.0	FN 6.0	VF 8.0	VF/NM 9.0	NM- 9.2
1-4-Chris Sarraceni-s/Kwang Mook Lim-a						3.00

DARKMINDS / WITCHBLADE (Also see Witchblade/Dark Minds)
Image Comics (Top Cow/Dreamwave Prod.): Aug, 2000 ($5.95, one-shot)

	GD	VG	FN	VF	VF/NM	NM-		GD	VG	FN	VF	VF/NM	NM-
	2.0	4.0	6.0	8.0	9.0	9.2		2.0	4.0	6.0	8.0	9.0	9.2

1-Wohl-s/Pat Lee-a; two covers by Silvestri and Lee ... 6.00

DARK MYSTERIES (Thrilling Tales of Horror & Suspense)
"Master" - "Merit" Publications: June-July, 1951 - No. 24, July, 1955

	GD	VG	FN	VF	VF/NM	NM-
1-Wood-c/a (8 pgs.)	174	348	522	1114	1907	2700
2-Classic skull-c; Wood/Harrison-c/a (8 pgs.)	290	580	870	1856	3178	4500
3-9: 7-Dismemberment, hypo blood drainage stys	87	174	261	552	951	1350
10-Cannibalism story; witch burning	514	1028	1542	3750	6625	9500
11-13,15-17: 11-Severed head panels. 13-Dismemberment-c/story. 17-The Old Gravedigger host	78	148	222	470	810	1150
14-Several E.C. Craig swipes	87	174	261	552	951	1350
18-Bondage, skeletons-c	129	258	387	826	1413	2000
19-Injury-to-eye panel; E.C. swipe; torture-c	459	918	1377	3350	5925	8500
20-Female bondage, blood drainage story	90	180	270	576	988	1400
21,22: 21-Devil-c. 22-Last pre-code issue, misdated 3/54 instead of 3/55	58	116	174	371	636	900
23,24	43	86	129	271	461	650

NOTE: *Cameron* a-1, 2. *Myron Fass* c/a-21. *Harrison* a-3, 7; c-3. *Hollingsworth* a-7-17, 20, 21, 23. *Wildey* a-5. *Woodish art by* *Fleishman*-9; c-10, 14-17. *Bondage* c-9, 10, 18, 19.

DARK NEMESIS (VILLAINS) (See Teen Titans)
DC Comics: Feb, 1998 ($1.95, one-shot)

1-Jurgens-s/Pearson-c ... 4.00

DARKNESS, THE (See Witchblade #10)
Image Comics (Top Cow Productions): Dec, 1996 - No. 40, Aug, 2001 ($2.50)

Special Preview Edition-(7/96, B&W)-Ennis script; Silvestri-a(p)	2	4	6	9	13	16
0	2	4	6	8	10	12
0-Gold Edition						16.00
1/2	1	3	4	6	8	10
1/2-Christmas-c	3	6	9	14	19	24
1/2-(3/01, $2.95) r/#1/2 w/new 6 pg. story & Silvestri-c						3.00
1-Ennis-s/Silvestri-a, 1-Black variant-c	2	4	6	9	12	15
1-Platinum variant-c						20.00
1-DF Green variant-c						12.00
1-25th Anniversary Commemorative Edition (11/20, $4.99) r/#1 with creator interviews						5.00
1,2: 1-Fan Club Ed.	1	3	4	6	8	10
3-5						6.00
6-10: 9,10-Witchblade "Family Ties" x-over pt. 2,3						4.00
7-Variant-c w/concubine	1	2	3	5	7	9
8-American Entertainment						6.00
8-10-American Entertainment Gold Ed.						7.00
11-Regular Ed.; Ennis-s/Silvestri & D-Tron-c						3.00
11-Nine (non-chromium) variant-c (Benitez, Cabrera, the Hildebrandts, Finch, Keown, Peterson, Portacio, Tan, Turner						4.50
11-Chromium-c by Silvestri & Batt						20.00
12-19: 13-Begin Benitez-a(p)						3.00
20-24,26-40: 34-Ripclaw app.						3.00
25-($3.99) Two covers (Benitez, Silvestri)						4.00
25-Chromium-c variant by Silvestri						8.00
.../ Batman (8/99, $5.95) Silvestri, Finch, Lansing-a(p)						6.00
...Collected Editions #1-4 ($4.95,TPB) 1- r/#1,2. 2- r/#3,4. 3- r/#5,6. 4- r/#7,8						6.00
...Collected Editions #5,6 ($5.95, TPB)5- r/#11,12. 6- r/#13,14						6.00
Deluxe Collected Editions #1 (12/98, $14.95, TPB) r/#1-6 & Preview						15.00
...: Heart of Darkness (2001, $14.95, TPB) r/ #7,8, 11-14						15.00
Holiday Pin-up-American Entertainment						5.00
Holiday Pin-up Gold Ed.-American Entertainment						7.00
Image Firsts: Darkness #1 (9/10, $1.00) r/#1 with "Image Firsts" logo on cover						3.00
Infinity #1 (8/99, $3.50) Lobdell-s						3.50
Prelude-American Entertainment						4.00
Prelude Gold Ed.-American Entertainment						9.00
Volume 1 Compendium (2006, $59.99) r/#1-40, V2 #1, Tales of the Darkness #1-4; #1/2, Darkness/Witchblade #1/2, Darkness: Wanted Dead; cover and sketch gallery						60.00
....: Wanted Dead 1 (8/03, $2.99) Texiera-a/Tieri-s						3.00
Wizard ACE Ed.- Reprints #1	2	4	6	8	10	12

DARKNESS (Volume 2)
Image Comics (Top Cow Productions): Dec, 2002 - No. 24, Oct, 2004 ($2.99)

1-24: 1-6-Jenkins-s/Keown-a. 17-20-Lapham-s. 23,24-Magdalena app.	3.00
... Black Sails (3/05, $2.99) Marz-s/Cha-a; Hunter-Killer app.	3.00
... and Tomb Raider (4/05, $2.99) r/Darkness Prelude & Tomb Raider/Darkness Special	3.00
...: Resurrection TPB (2/04, $16.99) r/#1-6 & Vol. 1 #40	17.00
.../ The Incredible Hulk (7/04, $2.99) Keown-a/Jenkins-s	3.00
.../ Vampirella (7/05, $2.99) Terry Moore-s; two covers by Basaldua and Moore	3.00
... Vol. 5 TPB (2006, $19.99) r/#7-16 & The Darkness: Wanted Dead #1; cover gallery	20.00
... vs. Mr Hyde Monster War 2005 (9/05, $2.99) x-over w/Witchblade, Tomb Raider and Magdalena; two covers	3.00
.../ Wolverine (2006, $2.99) Kirkham-a/Tieri-s	3.00

DARKNESS (Volume 3) (Numbering jumps from #10 to #75)
Image Comics (Top Cow Productions): Dec, 2007 - No. 116, Dec, 2013 ($2.99)

1-10: 1-Hester-s/Broussard-a. 1-Three covers. 7-9-Lucas-a. 8-Aphrodite IV app.	3.00
75 (2/09, $4.99) Four covers; Hester-s/art by various	5.00
76-99,101-113,115-($2.99) 76-99,101-Multiple covers on each	3.00
100 (2/12, $4.99) Four covers; Hester-s/art by various; cover gallery; series timeline	5.00
114-($4.99) The Age of Reason Part 1; Hine-s/Haun-a; bonus Darkness timeline	5.00
116-($3.99) The Age of Reason Part 3; Hine-s/Haun-a	4.00
... : Butcher (4/08, $3.99) Story of Butcher Joyce; Levin-s/Broussard-a/c	4.00
... : Close Your Eyes (6/14, $3.99) Story of Adelmo Estacado in 1912; Kot-s/Oleksicki-a/c	4.00
... : Confession (5/11) Free Comic Boy Day giveaway; Broussard & Molnar-a	3.00
... / Darkchylde: Kingdom Pain 1 (5/10, $4.99) Randy Queen-s/a	5.00
... First Look (11/07, 99c) Previews series; sketch pages	3.00
... : Hope (4/16, $3.99) Harmon-s/Dwyer-a/Linda Sejic-c	4.00
... : Lodbrok's Hand (12/08, $2.99) Hester-s/Oeming-a/c; variant-c by Carnevale	3.00
... : Shadows and Flame 1 (1/10, $2.99) Lucas-a/c	3.00
... : Vicious Traditions 1 (3/14, $3.99) Ales Kot-s/Dean Ormston-a/Dale Keown-c	4.00

DARKNESS: FOUR HORSEMEN
Image Comics (Top Cow): Aug, 2010 - No. 4, May, 2011 ($3.99, limited series)

1-4-Hine-s/Wamester-a ... 4.00

DARKNESS: LEVEL...
Image Comics (Top Cow): No. 0, Dec, 2006 - No. 5, Aug, 2007 ($2.99, limited series)

0-5: 0-Origin of The Darkness in WW1; Jenkins-s. 1-Jackie's origin retold; Sejic-a ... 3.00

DARKNESS/ PITT
Image Comics (Top Cow): Dec, 2006; Aug, 2009 - No. 3, Nov, 2009 ($2.99)

...: First Look (12/06) Jenkins script pages with Keown B&W and color art	3.00
1-3: 1-(8/09) Jenkins-s/Keown-a; covers by Keown and Sejic. 2,3-Two covers	3.00

DARKNESS/ SUPERMAN
Image Comics (Top Cow Productions): Jan, 2005 - No. 2, Feb, 2005 ($2.99, limited series)

1,2-Marz-s/Kirkham & Banning-a/Silvestri-c ... 3.00

DARKNESS VISIBLE
IDW Publishing: Feb, 2017 - No. 6, 2017 ($3.99)

1-6: 1-Mike Carey & Arvind David-s/Brendan Cahill-a. 3,6-Ramondelli-a ... 4.00

DARKNESS VS. EVA: DAUGHTER OF DRACULA
Dynamite Entertainment: 2008 - No. 4, 2008 ($3.50, limited series)

1-4-Leah Moore & John Reppion-s/Salazar-a; three covers on each ... 3.50

DARK NIGHT: A TRUE BATMAN STORY
DC Comics: 2016 ($22.99, HC Graphic Novel)

HC - Paul Dini-s/Eduardo Risso-a ... 23.00

DARK NIGHTS: DEATH METAL
DC Comics: Jul, 2020 - No. 7, Mar, 2021 ($4.99/$5.99, limited series)

1-6-Snyder-s/Capullo-a; sequel to Dark Nights: Metal; Batman Who Laughs app.						5.00
7-($5.99) Multiverse restored; leads into Future State titles	2	4	6	9	12	15
... - Guidebook 1 (10/20, $5.99) short s/a by various; Harley Quinn app.						6.00
... Infinite Hour Exxxtreme 1 (1/21, $5.99) Extremely violent stories hosted by Lobo						6.00
... Legends of the Dark Knights 1 (10/20, $5.99) Origin Robin King & other Batmen						6.00
... Multiverse's End 1 (1/21, $5.99) Capt. Carrot, Owlman. Pres. Superman & others						6.00
... Rise of the New God 1 (11/20, $5.99) Perpetua vs. The Batman Who Laughs						6.00
... Robin King 1 (11/20, $5.99) Robin King vs. the Robins; Rossmo & Sampere-a						6.00
... Speed Metal 1 (11/20, $5.99) Barrows-s; Wally West and other Flashes app.						6.00
... The Last 52: War of the Multiverses 1 (2/21, $8.99) Short stories by various						9.00
... The Last Stories of the DC Universe 1 (2/21, $8.99) Short stories by various						9.00
... The Multiverse That Laughs 1 (1/21, $5.99) Twisted humor short stories by various						6.00
... The Secret Origin 1 (2/21, $5.99) Origin/spotlight on Superboy-Prime						6.00
... Trinity Crisis 1 (11/20, $5.99) Snyder-s/Manapul-a; Batman, Superman, Wonder Woman						6.00

DARK NIGHTS: METAL (Also see Dark Days prelude one-shots)
DC Comics: Nov, 2017 - No. 6, May, 2018 ($4.99/$3.99)

1-($4.99) Snyder-s/Capullo-a; Justice League & Dream of the Endless app.; foil logo-c	1	3	4	6	8	10
1-Second printing; red title logo on cover						5.00
2-5-($3.99) 2-Barbatos app.						6.00
6-($4.99) Finale; leads into Justice League: No Justice series	1	2	3	5	6	8
Director's Cut 1 (2/18, $6.99) r/#1 pencil art; gallery of variant covers	1	3	4	6	8	10

DARK NIGHTS: THE BATMAN WHO LAUGHS (Dark Nights: Metal) (Also see Teen Titans #12 [11/17])
DC Comics: Jan, 2018 ($3.99, one-shot)

1-Tynion IV-s/Rossmo-a; Fabok foil-c; Bruce Wayne as Dark Multiverse Joker	3	6	9	14	20	25

DARK RED
AfterShock Comics: Mar, 2019 - No. 10, Jul, 2020 ($3.99)

1-10-Vampire Nazis in North Dakota; Tim Seeley-s/Corin Howell-a	4.00
1-Special Edition; r/#1 with bonus creator interviews and sketch art	4.00
...: Where Roads Lead 1 (1/22, $6.99, oversized 8-1/2" x 10-7/8") Seeley-s/Howell-a	7.00

DARK REIGN (Follows Secret Invasion crossover)
Marvel Comics: 2009 ($3.99/$4.99, one-shots)

...: Files 1 (2009, $4.99) profile pages of villains tied in to Dark Reign x-over	5.00
...: Made Men 1 (11/09, $3.99) short stories by various incl. Pham, Leon, Oliver	4.00
...: New Nation 1 (2/09, $3.99) previews of various series tied in to Dark Reign x-over	4.00
...: The Cabal 1 (6/09, $3.99) Cabal members stories by various incl. Granov, Acuña	4.00
...: The Goblin Legacy 1 (2009, $3.99) r/ASM #39,40; Osborn history; Mayhew-a	4.00

DARK REIGN: ELEKTRA
Marvel Comics: May, 2009 - No. 5, Oct, 2009 ($3.99, limited series)

1-5-Mann-s/Bermejo-c; Elektra after the Skrull replacement. 2,3-Bullseye app. ... 4.00

DARK REIGN: FANTASTIC FOUR
Marvel Comics: May, 2009 - No. 5, Sept, 2009 ($2.99, limited series)

1-5-Chen-a ... 3.00

DARK REIGN: HAWKEYE
Marvel Comics: June, 2009 - No. 5, Mar, 2010 ($3.99, limited series)

1-5-Bullseye on the Dark Avengers; Raney-a/Langley-c. 5-Guinaldo-a ... 4.00

DARK REIGN: LETHAL LEGION
Marvel Comics: Aug, 2009 - No. 3, Nov, 2009 ($3.99, limited series)

1-3-Santolouco-a/Edwards-c; Grim Reaper and Wonder Man app. ... 4.00

DARK REIGN: MR. NEGATIVE (Also see Amazing Spider-Man #546)
Marvel Comics: Aug, 2009 - No. 3, Oct, 2009 ($3.99, limited series)

1-3-Jae Lee-c/Gugliotta-a; Spider-Man app. ... 4.00

DARK REIGN: SINISTER SPIDER-MAN
Marvel Comics: Aug, 2009 - No. 4, Nov, 2009 ($3.99, limited series)

1-4-Bachalo-c/a; Venom/Scorpion as Dark Avenger Spider-Man ... 4.00

DARK REIGN: THE HOOD
Marvel Comics: Jul, 2009 - No. 5, Nov, 2009 ($3.99, limited series)

The Darkness #84 © TCOW

Dark Reign: The Cabal #1 © MAR

Dark Shadows (2011 series) #1 © Curtis

	GD 2.0	VG 4.0	FN 6.0	VF 8.0	VF/NM 9.0	NM- 9.2		GD 2.0	VG 4.0	FN 6.0	VF 8.0	VF/NM 9.0	NM- 9.2
1-5-Hotz-a/Djurdjevic-c						4.00							

DARK REIGN: THE LIST
Marvel Comics: 2009 - 2010 ($3.99, one-shots)

	GD 2.0	VG 4.0	FN 6.0	VF 8.0	VF/NM 9.0	NM- 9.2
... - Amazing Spider-Man (1/10, $3.99) Adam Kubert-c/a; back-up r/Pulse #5						4.00
... - Avengers (11/09, $3.99) Bendis-s/Djurdjevic-c/a; Ronin (Hawkeye) app.						4.00
... - Daredevil (11/09, $3.99) Diggle-s/Tan-c/a; Bullseye app.; leads into Daredevil #501						4.00
... - Hulk (12/09, $3.99) Pak-s/Oliver-a; Skaar app.; back-up r/Amaz. Spider-Man #14						4.00
... - Punisher (12/09, $3.99) Romita Jr.-a/c; Castle killed by Daken; preview of Franken-Castle in Punisher #11						6.00
... - Secret Warriors (12/09, $3.99) McGuinness-a/c; Nick Fury; back-up r/Steranko-a						4.00
... - Wolverine (12/09, $3.99) Ribic-a/c; Marvel Boy and Fantomex app.						4.00
... - X-Men (11/09, $3.99) Alan Davis-a/c; Namor app.; back-up r/Kieth-a						4.00

DARK REIGN: YOUNG AVENGERS
Marvel Comics: Jul, 2009 - No. 5, Dec, 2009 ($3.99, limited series)

	GD 2.0	VG 4.0	FN 6.0	VF 8.0	VF/NM 9.0	NM- 9.2
1-Brooks-a; Osborn's Young Avengers vs. original Young Avengers	2	4	6	9	12	15
2-5						4.00

DARK REIGN: ZODIAC
Marvel Comics: Aug, 2009 - No. 3, Nov, 2009 ($3.99, limited series)

	GD 2.0	VG 4.0	FN 6.0	VF 8.0	VF/NM 9.0	NM- 9.2
1-3-Casey-s/Fox-a. 1-Human Torch app.						4.00

DARK RIDE
Image Comics (Skybound): Oct, 2022 - Present ($3.99)

	GD 2.0	VG 4.0	FN 6.0	VF 8.0	VF/NM 9.0	NM- 9.2
1-10-Williamson-s/Bressan-a						4.00

DARK ROOM, THE
Image Comics: Jun, 2022 ($19.99, HC graphic novel)

	GD 2.0	VG 4.0	FN 6.0	VF 8.0	VF/NM 9.0	NM- 9.2
HC-Duggan-s/Buoncristiano-a						20.00

DARKSEID SPECIAL (Jack Kirby 100th Birthday tribute)
DC Comics: Oct, 2017 ($4.99, one-shot)

	GD 2.0	VG 4.0	FN 6.0	VF 8.0	VF/NM 9.0	NM- 9.2
1-Evanier/Kolins-a; Omac story with Levitz-s/Hester-a; r/Forever People #6 (4 pgs)						5.00

DARKSEID (VILLAINS) (See Jack Kirby's New Gods and New Gods)
DC Comics: Feb, 1998 ($1.95, one-shot)

	GD 2.0	VG 4.0	FN 6.0	VF 8.0	VF/NM 9.0	NM- 9.2
1-Byrne-s/Pearson-c						5.00

DARKSEID VS. GALACTUS: THE HUNGER
DC Comics: 1995 ($4.95, one-shot) (1st DC/Marvel x-over by John Byrne)

	GD 2.0	VG 4.0	FN 6.0	VF 8.0	VF/NM 9.0	NM- 9.2
nn-John Byrne-c/a/script	2	4	6	10	14	18

DARK SHADOWS
Steinway Comic Publ. (Ajax)(America's Best): Oct, 1957 - No. 3, May, 1958

	GD 2.0	VG 4.0	FN 6.0	VF 8.0	VF/NM 9.0	NM- 9.2
1	37	74	111	222	361	500
2,3	24	48	72	142	234	325

DARK SHADOWS (TV) (See Dan Curtis Giveaways)
Gold Key: Mar, 1969 - No. 35, Feb, 1976 (Photo-c: 1-7)

	GD 2.0	VG 4.0	FN 6.0	VF 8.0	VF/NM 9.0	NM- 9.2
1(30039-903)-With pull-out poster (25c)	25	50	75	175	388	600
1-With poster missing	7	14	21	48	89	130
2	8	16	24	54	102	150
3-With pull-out poster	9	18	27	62	126	190
3-With poster missing	5	10	15	35	63	90
4-7: 7-Last photo-c	6	12	18	38	69	100
8-10	5	10	15	30	50	70
11-20	4	8	12	27	44	60
21-35: 30-Last painted-c	4	8	12	23	37	50
Story Digest 1 (6/70, 148pp.)-Photo-c (low print)	7	14	21	46	86	125

DARK SHADOWS (TV) (See Nightmare on Elm Street)
Innovation Publishing: June, 1992 - No. 4, Spring, 1993 ($2.50, limited series, coated stock)

	GD 2.0	VG 4.0	FN 6.0	VF 8.0	VF/NM 9.0	NM- 9.2
1-Based on 1991 NBC TV mini-series; painted-c						5.00
2-4						4.00

DARK SHADOWS: BOOK TWO
Innovation Publishing: 1993 - No. 4, July, 1993 ($2.50, limited series)

	GD 2.0	VG 4.0	FN 6.0	VF 8.0	VF/NM 9.0	NM- 9.2
1-4-Painted-c. 4-Maggie Thompson scripts						4.00

DARK SHADOWS: BOOK THREE
Innovation Publishing: Nov, 1993 ($2.50)

	GD 2.0	VG 4.0	FN 6.0	VF 8.0	VF/NM 9.0	NM- 9.2
1-(Whole #9)						4.00

DARK SHADOWS/VAMPIRELLA
Dynamite Entertainment: 2012 - No. 5, 2012 ($3.99, limited series)

	GD 2.0	VG 4.0	FN 6.0	VF 8.0	VF/NM 9.0	NM- 9.2
1-5-Andreyko-s/Berkenkotter-a/Neves-c						5.00

DARK SHADOWS, VOLUME 1
Dynamite Entertainment: 2011 - No. 23, 2013 ($3.99)

	GD 2.0	VG 4.0	FN 6.0	VF 8.0	VF/NM 9.0	NM- 9.2
1-23-Set in 1971. 1-Aaron Campbell-a; covers by Campbell & Francavilla						4.00

DARK SHADOWS: YEAR ONE
Dynamite Entertainment: 2013 - No. 6, 2013 ($3.99, limited series)

	GD 2.0	VG 4.0	FN 6.0	VF 8.0	VF/NM 9.0	NM- 9.2
1-6-Origin of Barnabas Collins; Andreyko-s/Vilanova-a						4.00

DARK SOULS: LEGENDS OF THE FLAME (Based on the Bandai Namco video game)
Titan Comics: Sept, 2016 - No. 2, Nov, 2016 ($3.99, limited series)

	GD 2.0	VG 4.0	FN 6.0	VF 8.0	VF/NM 9.0	NM- 9.2
1,2-Short stories by various; multiple covers on each						4.00

DARK SOULS: THE AGE OF FIRE (Based on the Bandai Namco video game)
Titan Comics: May, 2018 - No. 4, Oct, 2018 ($3.99, limited series)

	GD 2.0	VG 4.0	FN 6.0	VF 8.0	VF/NM 9.0	NM- 9.2
1-4-O'Sullivan-s/Kokarev-a; multiple covers on each						4.00

DARK SOULS: THE BREATH OF ANDOLUS (Based on the Bandai Namco video game)
Titan Comics: May, 2016 - No. 4, Sept, 2016 ($3.99, limited series)

	GD 2.0	VG 4.0	FN 6.0	VF 8.0	VF/NM 9.0	NM- 9.2
1-4-George Mann-s/Alan Quah-a; multiple covers on each						4.00

DARK SOULS: THE WILLOW KING (Based on the Bandai Namco video game)
Titan Comics: Feb, 2024 - Present ($3.99, limited series)

	GD 2.0	VG 4.0	FN 6.0	VF 8.0	VF/NM 9.0	NM- 9.2
1-George Mann-s; multiple covers on each						4.00

DARK SOULS: WINTER'S SPITE (Based on the Bandai Namco video game)
Titan Comics: Dec, 2016 - No. 4, Apr, 2017 ($3.99, limited series)

	GD 2.0	VG 4.0	FN 6.0	VF 8.0	VF/NM 9.0	NM- 9.2
1-4-George Mann-s/Alan Quah-a; multiple covers on each						4.00

DARK SPACES: DUNGEON
IDW Publishing: Oct, 2023 - No. 5, Apr, 2024 ($4.99, limited series)

	GD 2.0	VG 4.0	FN 6.0	VF 8.0	VF/NM 9.0	NM- 9.2
1-5-Scott Snyder-s/Hayden Sherman-a						5.00

DARK SPACES: THE HOLLYWOOD SPECIAL
IDW Publishing: Aug, 2023 - No. 6, Feb, 2024 ($3.99, limited series)

	GD 2.0	VG 4.0	FN 6.0	VF 8.0	VF/NM 9.0	NM- 9.2
1-6-Jeremy Lambert-s/Claire Roe-a						4.00

DARK SPACES: WILDFIRE
IDW Publishing: Jul, 2022 - No. 5, Nov, 2022 ($3.99, limited series)

	GD 2.0	VG 4.0	FN 6.0	VF 8.0	VF/NM 9.0	NM- 9.2
1-5-Scott Snyder-s/Hayden Sherman-a						4.00

DARKSTAR AND THE WINTER GUARD
Marvel Comics: Aug, 2010 - No. 3, Oct, 2010 ($3.99, limited series)

	GD 2.0	VG 4.0	FN 6.0	VF 8.0	VF/NM 9.0	NM- 9.2
1-3-Gallaher-s/Ellis-a/Henry-c; back-up reprint from X-Men Unlimited #28						4.00

DARKSTARS, THE
DC Comics: Oct, 1992 - No. 38, Jan, 1996 ($1.75/$1.95)

	GD 2.0	VG 4.0	FN 6.0	VF 8.0	VF/NM 9.0	NM- 9.2
1-1st app. The Darkstars						5.00
2-24,25-38: 5-Hawkman & Hawkwoman app. 18-20-Flash app. 24-(9/94)-Zero Hour. 25-(11/94). 30-Green Lantern app. 31-...vs. Darkseid. 32-Green Lantern app.						4.00
#0-(10/94) Zero Hour issue released between #24 and #25						4.00

NOTE: *Travis Charest* a(p)-4-7; c(p)-2-5; c-6-11. **Stroman** a-1-3; c-1.

DARK TALES FROM THE VOKESVERSE
American Mythology: 2016 ($4.99, B&W)

	GD 2.0	VG 4.0	FN 6.0	VF 8.0	VF/NM 9.0	NM- 9.2
1-Short horror stories by Neil Vokes and various; 2 covers						5.00

DARK TOWER: THE BATTLE OF JERICHO HILL (Based on Stephen King's Dark Tower)
Marvel Comics: Feb, 2010 - No. 5, Jun, 2010 ($3.99, limited series)

	GD 2.0	VG 4.0	FN 6.0	VF 8.0	VF/NM 9.0	NM- 9.2
1-5-Peter David & Robin Furth-s/Jae Lee & Richard Isanove-a/c; variant-c for each						4.00

DARK TOWER: THE DRAWING OF THE THREE - BITTER MEDICINE (Stephen King)
Marvel Comics: Jun, 2016 - No. 5, Oct, 2016 ($3.99, limited series)

	GD 2.0	VG 4.0	FN 6.0	VF 8.0	VF/NM 9.0	NM- 9.2
1-5-Peter David & Robin Furth-s/Jonathan Marks-a/Nimit Malavia-c						4.00

DARK TOWER: THE DRAWING OF THE THREE - HOUSE OF CARDS (Stephen King)
Marvel Comics: May, 2015 - No. 5, Sept, 2015 ($3.99, limited series)

	GD 2.0	VG 4.0	FN 6.0	VF 8.0	VF/NM 9.0	NM- 9.2
1-5-Peter David & Robin Furth-s/Piotr Kowalski-a/J.T. Tedesco-c						4.00

DARK TOWER: THE DRAWING OF THE THREE - LADY OF SHADOWS (Stephen King)
Marvel Comics: Nov, 2015 - No. 5, Mar, 2016 ($3.99, limited series)

	GD 2.0	VG 4.0	FN 6.0	VF 8.0	VF/NM 9.0	NM- 9.2
1-5-Peter David & Robin Furth-s/Jonathan Marks-a/Nimit Malavia-c						4.00

DARK TOWER: THE DRAWING OF THE THREE - THE PRISONER (Stephen King)
Marvel Comics: Nov, 2014 - No. 5, Feb, 2015 ($3.99, limited series)

	GD 2.0	VG 4.0	FN 6.0	VF 8.0	VF/NM 9.0	NM- 9.2
1-5-Peter David & Robin Furth-s/Piotr Kowalski-a/J.T. Tedesco-c						4.00

DARK TOWER: THE DRAWING OF THE THREE - THE SAILOR (Stephen King)
Marvel Comics: Dec, 2016 - No. 5, Apr, 2016 ($3.99, limited series)

	GD 2.0	VG 4.0	FN 6.0	VF 8.0	VF/NM 9.0	NM- 9.2
1-5-Peter David & Robin Furth-s/Ramirez-a/Anacleto-c						4.00

DARK TOWER: THE FALL OF GILEAD (Based on Stephen King's Dark Tower)
Marvel Comics: July, 2009 - No. 6, Jan, 2010 ($3.99, limited series)

	GD 2.0	VG 4.0	FN 6.0	VF 8.0	VF/NM 9.0	NM- 9.2

1-6-Peter David & Robin Furth-s/Richard Isanove-a/Jae Lee-c; variant-c for each — 4.00
Dark Tower: Guide to Gilead (2009, $3.99) profile pages of people and places — 4.00

DARK TOWER: THE GUNSLINGER BORN (Based on Stephen King's Dark Tower series)
Marvel Comics: Apr, 2007 - No. 7, Oct, 2007 ($3.99)

1-Peter David & Robin Furth-s/Jae Lee & Richard Isanove-a; boyhood of Roland Deschain;
  afterword by Ralph Macchio; map of New Canaan — 6.00
1-Variant cover by Quesada — 10.00
1-Second printing with variant-c by Quesada — 5.00
1-Sketch cover variant by Jae Lee — 30.00
2-6-Jae Lee-c — 4.00
2-Second printing with variant-c by Immonen — 4.00
2-7-Variant covers. 2-Finch-c. 3-Yu-c. 4-McNiven-c. 5-Land-c. 6-Campbell. 7-Coipel — 6.00
2-7-B&W sketch-c by Jae Lee — 20.00
... MGC #1 (5/11, $1.00) r/#1 with "Marvel's Greatest Comics" logo on cover — 3.00
... Sketchbook (2006, no cover price) pencil art and designs by Lee; coloring process — 5.00
Dark Tower: Gunslinger's Guidebook (2007, $3.99) profile pages with Jae Lee-a — 4.00
HC (2007, $24.99) r/#1-7; variant covers and sketch pages; Macchio intro. — 25.00

DARK TOWER: THE GUNSLINGER - EVIL GROUND (Stephen King's Dark Tower)
Marvel Comics: Jun, 2013 - No. 2, Aug, 2013 ($3.99, limited series)

1,2-Robin Furth & Peter David-s/Richard Isanove-a/c — 4.00

DARK TOWER: THE GUNSLINGER - SHEEMIE'S TALE (Stephen King's Dark Tower)
Marvel Comics: Mar, 2013 - No. 2, Apr, 2013 ($3.99, limited series)

1,2-Robin Furth-s/Richard Isanove-a/c — 4.00

DARK TOWER: THE GUNSLINGER - SO FELL LORD PERTH (Stephen King's Dark Tower)
Marvel Comics: Sept, 2013 ($3.99, one-shot)

1-Robin Furth & Peter David-s/Richard Isanove-a/c — 4.00

DARK TOWER: THE GUNSLINGER - THE BATTLE OF TULL (Stephen King's Dark Tower)
Marvel Comics: Aug, 2011 - No. 5, Dec, 2011 ($3.99, limited series)

1-5-Peter David & Robin Furth-s/Michael Lark-a/c — 4.00

DARK TOWER: THE GUNSLINGER - THE JOURNEY BEGINS (Stephen King's Dark Tower)
Marvel Comics: Jul, 2010 - No. 5, Nov, 2010 ($3.99, limited series)

1-5-Peter David & Robin Furth-s/Sean Phillips-a/c — 4.00
1-Variant cover by Jae Lee — 5.00

DARK TOWER: THE GUNSLINGER - THE LITTLE SISTERS OF ELURIA (Stephen King)
Marvel Comics: Feb, 2011 - No. 5, Jun, 2011 ($3.99, limited series)

1-5: 1-Peter David & Robin Furth-s/Luke Ross-a/c — 4.00

DARK TOWER: THE GUNSLINGER - THE MAN IN BLACK (Stephen King)
Marvel Comics: Aug, 2012 - No. 5, Dec, 2012 ($3.99, limited series)

1-5-Peter David & Robin Furth-s/Maleev-a/c — 4.00

DARK TOWER: THE GUNSLINGER - THE WAY STATION (Stephen King)
Marvel Comics: Feb, 2012 - No. 5, Jun, 2012 ($3.99, limited series)

1-5-Peter David & Robin Furth-s/Laurence Campbell-a/c — 4.00

DARK TOWER: THE LONG ROAD HOME (Based on Stephen King's Dark Tower series)
Marvel Comics: May, 2008 - No. 5, Sept, 2008 ($3.99, limited series)

1-Peter David & Robin Furth-s/Jae Lee & Richard Isanove-a — 4.00
1-Variant cover by Deodato — 6.00
1-Sketch cover variant by Jae Lee — 30.00
2-5-Jae Lee-c — 4.00
2-5: 2-Variant-c by Quesada. 3-Djurdjevic var-c. 4-Garney var-c. 5-Bermejo var-c. — 6.00
2-5-B&W sketch-c by Jae Lee — 20.00
2-Second printing with variant-c by Lee — 4.00
Dark Tower: End-World Almanac (2008, $3.99) guide to locations and inhabitants — 4.00

DARK TOWER: THE SORCEROR (Based on Stephen King's Dark Tower)
Marvel Comics: June, 2009 ($3.99, one-shot)

1-Robin Furth-s/Richard Isanove-a/c; the story of Marten Broadcloak — 4.00

DARK TOWER: TREACHERY (Based on Stephen King's Dark Tower series)
Marvel Comics: Nov, 2008 - No. 6, Apr, 2009 ($3.99, limited series)

1-6-Peter David & Robin Furth-s/Jae Lee & Richard Isanove-a — 4.00
1-Variant cover by Dell'otto — 10.00

DARK WEB (Spider-Man x-over event)
Marvel Comics: Feb, 2023 - Apr, 2023 ($4.99)

1-(2/23) Zeb Wells-s/Adam Kubert-a; Ben Reilly, Madelyne Pryor & Venom app. — 5.00
...: Finale-(4/23) Wells-s/Adam Kubert-a; X-Men & Ms. Marvel app. — 5.00

DARK WEB: MS. MARVEL
Marvel Comics: Feb, 2023 - No. 2, Mar, 2023 ($3.99, limited series)

1,2-Pirzada-s/Mortarino-a. 2-Miles Morales app. — 4.00

DARK WEB: X-MEN
Marvel Comics: Feb, 2023 - No. 3, Mar, 2023 ($3.99, limited series)

1-3-Duggan-s. 1,2-Rod Reis-a. 2,3-Phil Noto-a — 4.00

DARKWING DUCK (TV cartoon) (Also see Cartoon Tales)
Disney Comics: Nov, 1991 - No. 4, Feb, 1992 ($1.50, limited series)

1-Adapts hour-long premiere TV episode	5	10	15	33	57	80
2-4: Adaptation continues	2	4	6	8	10	12

...Facsimile Edition, Issue 1 (Dynamite Ent., 2023, $3.99) Reprints #1 without original ads — 4.00

DARKWING DUCK (TV cartoon)
BOOM! Studios (KABOOM!): Jun, 2010 - No. 18, Nov, 2011 ($3.99)

1-Silvani-a; Launchpad McQuack app.; 3 covers	2	4	6	11	16	20
2	1	3	4	6	8	10

3-18-Multiple covers on all. 7-Batman #1 cover swipe. 8-Detective #31 cover swipe — 6.00

Annual 1 (3/11, $4.99) 3 covers; Quackerjack app.	3	6	9	16	23	30

... Free Comic Book Day Edition (5/11) Flip book with Chip 'N' Dale Rescue Rangers

	1	2	3	4	6	8

DARKWING DUCK (TV cartoon)
Dynamite Entertainment: 2023 - Present ($3.99)

1-10-Deibert-s/Lauro-a; multiple covers on each — 4.00

DARKWING DUCK: JUSTICE DUCKS
Dynamite Entertainment: 2024 - Present ($3.99)

1-Langridge-s/Lauro-a; multiple covers — 4.00

DARKWING DUCK: NEGADUCK
Dynamite Entertainment: 2023 - Present ($3.99)

1-4-Jeff Parker-a/Ciro Cangialosi-a; multiple covers on each — 4.00

DARK WOLVERINE (See Wolverine 2003 series)

DARK X-MEN (See Dark Avengers and the Dark Reign mini-series)
Marvel Comics: Jan, 2010 - No. 5, May, 2010 ($3.99, limited series)

1-5-Cornell-s/Kirk-a. 1-3-Bianchi-c. 1-Nate Grey returns — 4.00
...: The Confession (11/09, $3.99) Cansino-a; Paquette-a — 4.00

DARK X-MEN (Follows the 2023 Hellfire Gala)
Marvel Comics: Oct, 2023 - No. 5, Feb, 2024 ($4.99, limited series)

1-Steve Foxe-s/Jonas Scharf & Nelson Daniel-a — 5.00
2-5-($3.99) Ben Reilly app. — 4.00

DARK X-MEN: THE BEGINNING (See Dark Avengers and the Dark Reign mini-series)
Marvel Comics: Sept, 2009 - No. 3, Oct, 2009 ($3.99, limited series)

1-3: 1-Cornell-s/Kirk-a; Jae Lee-c on all. 2-Daken app. 3-Mystique app.; Jock-a — 4.00

DARLING LOVE
Close Up/Archie Publ. (A Darling Magazine): Oct-Nov, 1949 - No. 11, 1952 (no month)
(52 pgs.)(Most photo-c)

1-Photo-c	33	66	99	194	317	440
2-Photo-c	19	38	57	111	176	240
3-8,10,11: 3-6-photo-c	15	30	45	85	130	175
9-Krigstein-a	15	30	45	88	137	185

DARLING ROMANCE
Close Up (MLJ Publications): Sept-Oct, 1949 - No. 7, 1951 (All photo-c)

1-(52 pgs.)-Photo-c	39	78	117	231	378	525
2	18	36	54	107	169	230
3-7	15	30	45	90	140	190

DARQUE PASSAGES (See Master Darque)
Acclaim (Valiant): April, 1998 - No. 4, Mar, 1998 ($2.50)

1-4-Christina Z.-s/Manco-c/a — 4.00

DART (Also see Freak Force & Savage Dragon)
Image Comics (Highbrow Entertainment): Feb, 1996 - No. 3, May, 1996 ($2.50, lim. series)

1-3 — 4.00

DARTH MAUL (See Star Wars: Darth Maul)

DARTH VADER (Follows after the end of Star Wars Episode IV)
Marvel Comics: Apr, 2015 - No. 25, Dec, 2016 ($4.99/$3.99)

1-($4.99) Gillen-s/Larroca-a/Granov-c; intro. Wookiee bounty hunter Black Krrsantan; Jabba the Hut & Boba Fett app.	3	6	9	21	33	45
2	2	4	6	11	16	20
3-Intro. Doctor Aphra and Triple Zero	5	10	15	35	63	90
3-Second printing	4	8	12	28	47	65
4-12-($3.99) 6-Boba Fett app.	1	2	3	5	6	8
13-19,21-24: 13-15-Vader Down x-over pts. 2,4,6. 24-Flashbacks to Episode III						6.00
20-($4.99) The Emperor app.; back-up Triple-Zero & Beetee story w/Norton-a	1	3	4	6	8	10
25-($5.99) Gillen-s/Larroca-a; back-up story with Fiumara-c; bonus cover gallery						6.00
Annual 1 (2/16, $4.99) Gillen-s/Yu-a/c	1	2	3	5	6	8
...: Doctor Aphra No. 1 Halloween Comic Fest 2016 (12/16, giveaway) r/#3	1	3	4	6	8	10

DARTH VADER (Follows after the end of Star Wars Episode III)
Marvel Comics: Aug, 2017 - No. 25, Feb, 2019 ($4.99/$3.99)

1,2: 1-($4.99) Soule-s/Camuncoli-a/Cheung-c; back-up by Eliopoulos-s/a. 2-($3.99)	1	3	4	6	8	10
3-5,7-18,20-24-($3.99) Soule-s/Camuncoli-a. 5-Vader acquires the red light saber						5.00
6-1st app. Grand Inquisitor	3	6	9	19	30	40
19-1st app. Trilla Suduri (Second Sister)	2	4	6	9	12	15
25-($4.99) Camuncoli-a/c; recap of Vader's life	1	3	4	6	8	10
Annual 2 (9/18, $4.99) Wendig-s/Kirk-a/Deodato-c; Commander Krennic app.						5.00

DASTARDLY & MUTTLEY (See Fun-In No. 1-4, 6 and Kite Fun Book)
DC Comics: Nov, 2017 - No. 6, Apr, 2018 ($3.99, limited series)

1-6: 1-New origin for the pair; Ennis-s/Mauricet-a — 4.00

DATE WITH DANGER
Standard Comics: No. 5, Dec, 1952 - No. 6, Feb, 1953

5-Secret agent stories in both	77	154	231	493	847	1200
6-Atom bomb story	40	80	120	246	411	575

DATE WITH DEBBI (Also see Debbi's Dates)
National Periodical Publ.: Jan-Feb, 1969 - No. 17, Sept-Oct, 1971; No. 18, Oct-Nov, 1972

1-Teenage	10	20	30	68	144	220
2-5,17-(52 pgs) James Taylor sty.	5	10	15	31	53	75
6-12,18-Last issue	4	8	12	27	44	60
13-16-(68 pgs.) 14-1 pg. story on Jack Wild. 15-Marlo Thomas/"That Girl" story						
	5	10	15	30	50	70

DATE WITH JUDY, A (Radio/TV, and 1948 movie)
National Periodical Publications: Oct-Nov, 1947 - No. 79, Oct-Nov, 1960 (No. 1-25: 52 pgs.)

1-Teenage	58	116	174	371	636	900
2	22	44	66	132	216	300
3-10	17	34	51	98	154	210
11-20	14	28	42	82	121	160
21-40	14	28	42	78	112	145
41-45: 45-Last pre-code (2-3/55)	13	26	39	72	101	130
46-79: 79-Drucker-c/a	12	24	36	67	94	120

DATE WITH MILLIE, A (Life With Millie No. 8 on)(Teenage)
Atlas/Marvel Comics (MPC): Oct, 1956 - No. 7, Aug, 1957; Oct, 1959 - No. 7, Oct, 1960

Dark Web #1 © MAR

Darkwing Duck (2010 series) #8 © DIS

Dawn/Vampirella #3 © JML & DYN

	GD 2.0	VG 4.0	FN 6.0	VF 8.0	VF/NM 9.0	NM- 9.2
1(10/56)-(1st Series)-Dan DeCarlo-a in #1-7	155	310	465	992	1696	2400
2	55	110	165	352	601	850
3-7	34	68	102	204	332	460
1(10/59)-(2nd Series)	63	126	189	403	689	975
2-7	20	40	60	117	189	260

DATE WITH PATSY, A (Also see Patsy Walker)
Atlas Comics: Sept, 1957 (One-shot)

	GD 2.0	VG 4.0	FN 6.0	VF 8.0	VF/NM 9.0	NM- 9.2
1-Starring Patsy Walker	36	72	108	211	343	475

DAUGHTERS OF THE DRAGON (See Heroes For Hire)
Marvel Comics: 2005; Mar, 2006 - No. 6, Aug, 2006 ($2.99, limited series)

1-6-Palmiotti & Gray-s/Evans-a. 1-Rhino app. 5,6-Iron Fist app. 3.00
... Deadly Hands Special (2005, $3.99) reprints app. from Deadly Hands of Kung Fu #32,33 & Bizarre Adventures #25; Claremont-s/Rogers-a; new Rogers-c & interview 4.00
.... Deep Cuts MPGN (2018, $19.99, SC) printing of digital-first story; MacKay-s 20.00
...: Samurai Bullets TPB (2006, $15.99) r/#1-6 16.00

DAVID AND GOLIATH (Movie)
Dell Publishing Co.: No. 1205, July, 1961

	GD 2.0	VG 4.0	FN 6.0	VF 8.0	VF/NM 9.0	NM- 9.2
Four Color 1205-Photo-c	7	14	21	48	89	130

DAVID BORING (See Eightball)
Pantheon Books: 2000 ($24.95, hardcover w/dust jacket)
Hardcover - reprints David Boring stories from Eightball; Clowes-s/a 25.00

DAVID CASSIDY (TV)(See Partridge Family, Swing With Scooter #33 & Time For Love #30)
Charlton Comics: Feb, 1972 - No. 14, Sept, 1973

	GD 2.0	VG 4.0	FN 6.0	VF 8.0	VF/NM 9.0	NM- 9.2
1-Most have photo covers	7	14	21	48	89	130
2-5	4	8	12	27	44	60
6-14	4	8	12	23	37	50

DAVID LADD'S LIFE STORY (See Movie Classics)

DAVY CROCKETT (See Dell Giants, Fightin..., Frontier Fighters, It's Game Time, Power Record Comics, Western Tales & Wild Frontier)

DAVY CROCKETT (Frontier Fighter...)
Avon Periodicals: 1951

	GD 2.0	VG 4.0	FN 6.0	VF 8.0	VF/NM 9.0	NM- 9.2
nn-Tuska?, Reinman-a; Fawcette-c	28	56	84	165	270	375

DAVY CROCKETT (...King of the Wild Frontier No. 1,2)(TV)
Dell Publishing Co./Gold Key: 5/55 - No. 671, 12/55; No. 1, 12/63; No. 2, 11/69 (Walt Disney)

	GD 2.0	VG 4.0	FN 6.0	VF 8.0	VF/NM 9.0	NM- 9.2
Four Color 631(#1)-Fess Parker photo-c	16	32	48	108	239	370
Four Color 639-Photo-c	12	24	36	82	179	275
Four Color 664(#1)-Fess Parker photo-c	11	22	33	75	160	245
1(12/63-Gold Key)-Fess Parker photo-c; reprints	8	16	24	51	96	140
2(11/69)-Fess Parker photo-c; reprints	4	8	12	28	44	60

DAVY CROCKETT (...Frontier Fighter 1,2; Kid Montana #9 on)
Charlton Comics: Aug, 1955 - No. 8, Jan, 1957

	GD 2.0	VG 4.0	FN 6.0	VF 8.0	VF/NM 9.0	NM- 9.2
1	14	28	42	76	108	140
2	7	14	21	37	46	55
3-8	6	12	18	28	34	40

DAWN
Sirius Entertainment/Image Comics: June, 1995 - No. 6, 1996 ($2.95)

	GD 2.0	VG 4.0	FN 6.0	VF 8.0	VF/NM 9.0	NM- 9.2
1/2-w/certificate	1	2	3	5	6	8
1/2-Variant-c	2	4	6	10	14	18
1-Linsner-c/a	2	4	6	8	10	12
1-Black Light Edition	2	4	6	11	16	20
1-White Trash Edition	3	6	9	17	25	34
1-Look Sharp Edition	3	6	9	19	30	40
2-4: 1-Linsner-c/a						4.50
2-Variant-c, 3-Limited Edition	2	4	6	13	18	22
4-6-Vibrato-c						3.50
4, 5-Limited Edition	2	4	6	8	10	12
6-Limited Edition	2	4	6	8	10	12

...Convention Sketchbook (Image Comics, 2002, $2.95) pin-ups 6.00
...2003 Convention Sketchbook (Image Comics, 3/03, $2.95) pin-ups 4.00
...2004 Convention Sketchbook (Image Comics, 4/04, $2.95) pin-ups 4.00
...2005 Convention Sketchbook (Image Comics, 5/05, $2.95) pin-ups 4.00
Genesis Edition ('99, Wizard supplement) previews Return of the Goddess 4.00
Lucifer's Halo TPB (11/97, $19.95) r/Drama, Dawn #1-6 plus 12 pages of new artwork 20.00
... Not to Touch The Earth (9/10, $5.99) Linsner-s/c/a; pin-ups by various incl. Turner 6.00
...: Tenth Anniversary Special (9/99, $2.95) Interviews 3.00
The Portable Dawn ($9.95, 5"x4", 64 pgs.) Pocket-sized cover gallery 10.00
...: The Swordmaster's Daughter & Other Stories (2013, $3.99) Linsner-s/c/a 4.00

DAWN OF DC KNIGHT TERRORS FCBD SPECIAL EDITION 2023
DC Comics: Jul, 2023 (FCBD giveaway)(Continues in Knight Terrors: First Blood)
nn - Part 1 of Knight Terrors event; Williamson-s/Bachalo-a; checklist and cover previews 3.00

DAWN OF DC PRIMER SPECIAL EDITION 2023
DC Comics: Jul, 2023 (Promotional giveaway)
nn - Amanda Waller story; Williamson-s/Fernandez-a; bonus character profiles 3.00

DAWN OF THE DEAD (George A. Romaro's...)
IDW Publishing: Apr, 2004 - No. 3, Jun, 2004 ($3.99, limited series)

	GD 2.0	VG 4.0	FN 6.0	VF 8.0	VF/NM 9.0	NM- 9.2
1-3-Adaptation of the 2004 movie; Niles-s	2	4	6	8	10	12

TPB (9/04, $17.99) r/#1-3; intro. by George A. Romero 24.00

DAWN OF THE PLANET OF THE APES
BOOM! Studios: Nov, 2014 - No. 6, Apr, 2015 ($3.99, limited series)
1-6: 1-Takes place between the 2011 and 2014 movies; Moreci-s/McDaid-a 4.00

DAWN: THE RETURN OF THE GODDESS
Sirius Entertainment: Apr, 1999 - No. 4, July, 2000 ($2.95, limited series)
1-4-Linsner-s/a 4.00
TPB (4/02, $12.95) r/#1-4; intro. by Linsner 13.00

DAWN: THREE TIERS
Image Comics: Jun, 2003 - No. 6, Aug, 2005 ($2.95, limited series)
1-6-Linsner-s/a. 2-Preview of Vampire's Christmas 4.00

DAWN / VAMPIRELLA
Dynamite Entertainment: 2014 - No. 5, 2015 ($3.99, limited series)
1-5-Linsner-s/a/c. 3-Vampirella origin re-told 5.00

DAYDREAMERS (See Generation X)
Marvel Comics: Aug, 1997 - No. 3, Oct, 1997 ($2.50, limited series)
1-3-Franklin Richards, Howard the Duck, Man-Thing app. 4.00

DAY MEN
BOOM! Studios: Jul, 2013 - No. 8, Oct, 2015 ($3.99)
1-Stelfreeze-a/c; Gagnon & Nelson-s 5.00
2-8: 2-Covers by Stelfreeze & Pérez 4.00
...: Pen & Ink No. 1 (12/13, $9.99, 11"x17") Pen and ink art for #1&2 with commentary 10.00

DAY OF JUDGMENT
DC Comics: Nov, 1999 - No. 5, Nov, 1999 ($2.95/$2.50, limited series)
1-($2.95) Spectre possessed; Matt Smith-a 5.00
2-5: Parallax returns. 5-Hal Jordan becomes the Spectre 4.00
...Secret Files 1 (11/99, $4.95) Harris-c 5.00

DAY OF VENGEANCE (Prelude to Infinite Crisis)(Also see Birds of Prey #76 for 1st app. of Black Alice)
DC Comics: June, 2005 - No. 6, Nov, 2005 ($2.50, limited series)
1-6: 1-Jean Loring becomes Eclipso; Spectre, Ragman, Enchantress, Detective Chimp, Shazam app.; Justiniano-a. 2,3-Capt. Marvel app. 4-6-Black Alice app. 3.00
.... Infinite Crisis Special 1 (3/06, $4.99) Justiniano-a/Simonson-c 5.00
TPB (2005, $12.99) r/series & Action #826, Advs. of Superman #639, Superman #216 13.00

DAYS OF HATE
Image Comics: Jan, 2018 - No. 12, Jan, 2019 ($3.99)
1-12-Ales Kot-s/Danijel Zezelj-a 4.00

DAYS OF THE DEFENDERS (See Defenders, The)
Marvel Comics: Mar, 2001 ($3.50, one-shot)
1-Reprints early team-up of members, incl. Marvel Feature #1; Larsen-c 3.50

DAYS OF THE MOB (See In the Days of the Mob)

DAYTRIPPER
DC Comics (Vertigo): Feb, 2010 - No. 10, Nov, 2010 ($2.99, limited series)
1-10-Gabriel Bá & Fábio Moon-s/a 3.00
TPB (2010, $19.99) r/#1-10; sketch art pages 20.00

DAZEY'S DIARY
Dell Publishing Co.: June-Aug, 1962

	GD 2.0	VG 4.0	FN 6.0	VF 8.0	VF/NM 9.0	NM- 9.2
01-174-208: Bill Woggon-a	5	10	15	33	57	80

DAZZLER (Also see Marvel Graphic Novel & X-Men #130)
Marvel Comics Group: Mar, 1981 - No. 42, Mar, 1986

	GD 2.0	VG 4.0	FN 6.0	VF 8.0	VF/NM 9.0	NM- 9.2
1-X-Men app.; DeFalco-s/Romita Jr.-a	3	6	9	19	30	40

2-20,23,25,26,29-32,34-37,39-41: 2-X-Men app. 10,11-Galactus app. 23-Rogue/Mystique 1 pg. app. 26-Jusko-c. 40-Secret Wars II 5.00
21,22,24,27,28,38,42: 21-Double size; photo-c. 22 (12/82)-vs. Rogue Battle-c/sty. 24-Full app. Rogue w/Powerman (Iron Fist). 27-Rogue app. 28-Rogue app. Rogue; Mystique app. 38-Wolverine-c/app.; X-Men app. 42-Beast-c/app. 6.00

	GD	VG	FN	VF	VF/NM	NM-
	2.0	4.0	6.0	8.0	9.0	9.2

33-Michael Jackson "Thriller" swipe-c/sty 3 6 9 17 26 35
... No. 1 Facsimile Edition (4/19, $3.99) reprints #1 with original ads
        1 2 3 5 6 8
One-shot (7/10, $3.99) Andrasofszky-a/c; Arcade app. 6.00
...: X-Song 1 (8/18, $3.99) Visaggio-s/Braga-a
NOTE: No. 1 distributed only through comic shops. **Alcala** a-1i, 2i. **Chadwick** a-38-42p; c(p)-39, 41, 42. **Guice** a-38i, 42i; c-38, 40.

DC CHALLENGE (Most DC superheroes appear)
DC Comics: Nov. 1985 - No. 12, Oct. 1986 ($1.25/$2.00, maxi-series)

1-11: 1-Colan-a. 2,8-Batman-c/app. 4-Gil Kane-c/a 4.00
12-($2.00-c) Giant; low print 5.00
NOTE: Batman app. in 1-4, 6-12. Joker app. in 7. **Infantino** a-3. **Ordway** c-12. **Swan/Austin** c-10.

DC CLASSICS: THE BATMAN ADVENTURES
DC Comics: Aug. 2020 - No. 7, Feb. 2021 ($1.99)

1-7-Reprints The Batman Adventures series. 2-Catwoman app. 3-Joker app. 3.00

DC COMICS: BOMBSHELLS (Continues in Bombshells: United)
DC Comics: Oct. 2015 - No. 33, Oct. 2017 ($3.99, printings of digital-first stories)

1-Bennett-s/Sauvage-a/Lucia-a; set in 1940 WWII 2 4 6 8 10 12
2-13: 4-Harley Quinn-c/app. 1 2 3 5 6 8
14-Harley Quinn/Joker's Daughter-c 3 6 9 14 19 24
15-24: 15-18-Harley Quinn app. 5.00
25-($4.99) Suicide Squad app.; intro. Faora Hu-Ul; Aneke-a
        1 2 3 5 6 8
26-33: 27,32,33-Harley Quinn/Poison Ivy-c. 29-Superman app. 5.00
Annual 1 (10/16, $4.99) Bennett-s/Charretier-a; origin of vampire Batgirl 8.00

DC COMICS CLASSICS LIBRARY (Hardcover collections of classic DC stories)
DC Comics: 2009 - 2010 ($39.99, hardcover with dustjacket)

Batman: A Death in the Family ('09)- r/Batman #426-429, 440-442, New Titans #60,61 40.00
Batman Annuals ('09)- r/Batman Annual #1-3; afterword by Richard Bruning 40.00
Batman Annuals Volume 2 ('10)- r/Batman Annual #4-7; intro. by Michael Uslan 40.00
Flash of Two Worlds ('09)- r/Flash #123,129,137,151,170&173 team-ups with G.A. Flash 40.00
Justice League of America by George Pérez ('09) r/J.L.of A. #184-186, 192-194 40.00
Justice League of America by George Pérez Vol. 2 ('10) r/J.L.of A. #195-197,200 40.00
Legion of Super-Heroes: The Life and Death of Ferro Lad ('09) - r/Adventure Comics #346, 347,352-355,357; intro. by Paul Levitz; afterword by Jim Shooter 40.00
Roots of the Swamp Thing - r/House of Secrets #92 & Swamp Thing 1-13; Wein intro. 40.00
Superman: Kryptonite Nevermore ('09)- r/Superman #233-238,240-242; afterword by Denny O'Neil 40.00

DC COMICS ESSENTIALS
DC Comics: ($1.00, flipbooks with DC Graphic Novel catalog of recommended titles)

...: Action Comics #1 (2/14, $1.00) Reprints Action #1 (2011) with flipbook of DC GNs 3.00
...: Batman #1 (12/13, $1.00) Reprints Batman #1 (2011) with flipbook of DC GNs 3.00
...: Batman and Robin #1 (4/16, $1.00) Reprints Batman and Robin #1 (2011) with flipbook 3.00
...: Batman and Son Special Ed. ('14, $1.00) Reprints Batman #655 with flipbook 3.00
...: Batman: Death of the Family (6/16, $1.00) Reprints Batman #13 (2011) with flipbook 3.00
...: Batman: Hush Spec. Ed. ('14, $1.00) Reprints Batman #608 with flipbook of DC GNs 3.00
...: Batman: The Black Mirror Special Ed. ('14, $1.00) Reprints Detective #871 w/flipbook 3.00
...: Batman: The Dark Knight Returns #1 (5/16, $1.00) with flipbook 3.00
...: Batman: The Dark Knight Returns Special Ed. ('14, $1.00) Reprints #1 with flipbook 3.00
...: Batman: Year One ('14, $1.00) Reprints Batman #404 with flipbook of DC GNs 3.00
...: DC: The New Frontier #1 (3/16, $1.00) Reprints first issue with flipbook 3.00
...: Green Lantern #1 (1/14, $1.00) Reprints Green Lantern #1 (2011) with flipbook 3.00
...: JLA #1 (6/16, $1.00) Reprints JLA #1 with flipbook of DC GNs 3.00
...: Justice League #1 (1/14, $1.00) Reprints Justice League #1 (2011) with flipbook 3.00
...: Superman Unchained #1 (5/16, $1.00) Reprints Superman Unchained #1 with flipbook 3.00
...: Watchmen #1 (2/14, $1.00) Reprints Watchmen #1 (1986) with flipbook 3.00
...: Wonder Woman #1 (12/13, $1.00) Reprints Wonder Woman #1 (2011) with flipbook 3.00

DC COMICS MEGA SAMPLER
DC Comics: 2009; Jul. 2010 (6-1/4" x 9-1/2", FCBD giveaways)

1, 2010- Short stories of kid-friendly titles; Tiny Titans, Billy Batson, Super Friends app. 3.00

DC COMICS PRESENTS
DC Comics: July-Aug. 1978 - No. 97, Sept. 1986 (Superman team-ups in all)

1-4th Superman/Flash race 4 8 12 28 47 65
1-(Whitman variant) 5 10 15 35 63 90
2-Part 2 of Superman/Flash race 3 6 9 15 22 28
2-(Whitman variant) 4 8 12 19 28 35
3,4,9-12,14-16,19,21,22-(Whitman variants, low print run, none have issue # on cover) 3 6 9 14 20 25
3-10: 3-Adam Strange. 4-Metal Men. 5-Aquaman. 7-Red Tornado.
    8-Swamp Thing. 9-Wonder Woman. 10-Sgt. Rock 2 4 6 8 10 12
11-25,28-40: 12-Mister Miracle. 13-Legion of Super-Heroes. 19-Batgirl. 21-Elongated Man.
    23-Dr. Fate. 24-Deadman. 30-Black Canary. 31-Robin. 34-Marvel Family. 35-Man-Bat.
    36-Starman. 37-Hawkgirl. 38-The Flash 6.00
26-(10/80)-Green Lantern; intro Cyborg, Starfire, Raven (1st app. New Teen Titans in 16 pg.
    preview) Starlin-c/a; Sargon the Sorcerer back-up 11 22 33 76 163 250
27-1st app. Mongul 5 10 15 33 57 80
41-Superman/Joker-c/story; 1st app. New Wonder Woman in 16 pg. preview; Colan-a
    2 4 6 9 12 15
42-46,48,50,52-71,73-76,79-83: 42-Sandman. 43,80-Legion of Super-Heroes. 52-Doom Patrol;
    1st app. Ambush Bug. 58-Robin. 64-Kamandi. 82-Adam Strange. 83-Batman & Outsiders 4.00
47-(7/82) He-Man-c/s (1st app. in comics) 11 22 33 76 163 250
49-Black Adam & Captain Marvel app. 6 12 18 41 76 110
51-Preview insert (16 pgs.) of He-Man (2nd app.) 2 4 6 10 14 18
72,77,78,97: 72-Joker/Phantom Stranger-c/story. 77,78-Animal Man app. (77-c also).
    97-Phantom Zone 4.00
84-Challengers of the Unknown; Kirby-c/s. 6.00
85-Swamp Thing; Alan Moore scripts 6.00
86,88,96: 88-Crisis x-over. 88-Creeper 4.00
87-Origin/1st app. Superboy of Earth Prime 3 6 9 21 33 45
Annual 1(9/82)-G.A. Superman; 1st app. Alexander Luthor
    2 4 6 8 10 12
Annual 2,3: 2(7/83)-Intro/origin Superwoman. 3(9/84)-Shazam 4.00

Annual 4(10/85)-Superwoman 4.00
NOTE: **Adkins** a-25, 54; c-2. **Buckler** a-33, 34; c-30, 33, 34. **Giffen** a-39; c-59. **Gil Kane** a-28, 35, Annual 3; c-48p, 56, 58, 60, 62, 64, 68, Annual 2, 3. **Kirby** c/a-84. **Kubert** c/a-66. **Morrow** c/a-65. **Newton** c/a-54p. **Orlando** c-53i. **Perez** a-26p, 61p; c-38, 61, 94. **Starlin** a-26-29p, 36p, 37p; c-26-29, 36, 37, 93. **Toth** a-84. **Williamson** i-79, 85, 87.

DC COMICS PRESENTS: ...(Julie Schwartz tribute series of one-shots based on classic covers)
DC Comics: Sept. 2004 - Oct. 2004 ($2.50)

The Atom -(Based on cover of Atom #10) Gibbons-s/Oliffe-a; Waid-s/Jurgens-a; Bolland-c 3.00
Batman -(Batman #183) Johns-s/Infantino-a; Wein-s/Kuhn-a; Hughes-c 3.00
The Flash -(Flash #163) Loeb-s/McGuinness-a; O'Neil-s/Mahnke-a; Ross-c 3.00
Green Lantern -(Green Lantern #31) Azzarello-s/Breyfogle-a; Pasko-s/McDaniel-a; Bolland-c 3.00
Hawkman -(Hawkman #6) Bates-s/Byrne-a; Busiek-s/Simonson-a; Garcia-Lopez-c 3.00
Justice League of America -(J.L. of A. #53) Ellison & David-s/Giella/-a; Wolfman-s/Nguyen-a;
    Garcia-Lopez-c 3.00
Mystery in Space -(M.I.S. #82) Maggin-s/Williams-a; Morrison-s/Ordway-a; Ross-c 3.00
Superman -(Superman #264) Stan Lee-s/Cooke-a; Levitz-s/Giffen-a; Hughes-c 3.00

DC COMICS PRESENTS: ...
DC Comics: Dec. 2010 - Feb. 2016 ($7.99/$9.99, squarebound, one-shot reprints)

The Atom 1 (3/11) r/various DC Universe #28,29,40,41; Gil Kane-a 8.00
Batman 1 (12/10) r/Batman #582-585,600 8.00
Batman 2 (1/11) r/Batman #591-594 8.00
Batman 3 (2/11) r/Batman #595-598 8.00
Batman Adventures 1 (9/14) reprints; Burchett, Parobeck, Templeton, Timm-a 8.00
Batman: Arkham 1 (6/11) r/Batman Chronicles #6, Batman; Arkham Asylum - Tales of
    Madness #1, Batman Villains Secret Files #1 & Justice Leagues: J.L. of Arkham #1 8.00
Batman - Bad 1 (1/12) r/Batman: Legends of the D.K. #146-148 8.00
Batman Beyond 1 (2/11) r/Batman Beyond #13,14,21,22 8.00
Batman: Blaze of Glory 1 (2/12) r/Batman: Legends of the D.K. #197-199,212 8.00
Batman - Blink 1 (11/11) r/Batman: Legends of the D.K. #156-158 8.00
Batman/Catwoman 1 (12/10) r/Batman and Catwoman: Trail of the Gun 8.00
Batman - Conspiracy 1 (12/11) r/Batman: Legends of the D.K. #86-88; Detective #821 8.00
Batman - Dark Knight, Dark City 1 (7/11) r/Batman #452-454; Detective #633 8.00
Batman - Don't Blink 1 (1/12) r/Batman: Legends of the D.K. #164-167 8.00
Batman: Gotham Noir 1 (9/11) r/Batman: Gotham Noir #1 & Batman #604 8.00
Batman - Irresistible 1 (9/11) r/Batman: Legends of the D.K. #169-171; Hourman #22 8.00
Batman: The Demon Laughs 1 (12/11) r/Batman: Legends of the D.K. #142-145; Aparo-a 8.00
Batman: The Secret City 1 (2/12) r/Batman: Legends of the D.K. #180,181,190,191 8.00
Batman: Urban Legends 1 (2/12) r/Batman: Legends of the D.K. #168,177-179 8.00
Brightest Day 1 (2/11) r/Batman #205, Hawkman #27,34,36, Solo #8, DC Hol. '09 8.00
Brightest Day 2 (1/11) r/Firestorm #11-13 & Martian Manhunter #11,24 8.00
Brightest Day 3 (2/11) r/Legends of the DC Univ. #25-27 & Teen Titans #27,28 8.00
Captain Atom 1 (2/12) r/back-up stories from Action Comics #879-889 8.00
Catwoman - Guardian of Gotham 1 (12/11) r/Catwoman: Guardian of Gotham 1,2 8.00
Chase 1 (1/11) r/Chase #1,6-8 8.00
Darkseid War 1 (2/16, $7.99) r/New Gods 1,7, Mister Miracle #1 & Forever People #1 8.00
Demon Driven Out, The 1 (7/14, $9.99) r/The Demon: Driven Out #1-6 10.00
Elseworlds 80-Page Giant 1 (1/12) r/Elseworlds 80-Page Giant (pulled from distribution) 8.00
Flash 1 (7/11) r/Showcase #14 and Flash #125,130,139 8.00
Flash/Green Lantern: Faster Friends 1 (11/11) r/G.L./Flash: Faster Friends & Flash/G.L.: FF 8.00
Green Lantern 1 (12/10) r/Green Lantern #137-140 (2001) 8.00
Green Lantern - Fear Itself 1 (4/11) r/Green Lantern: Fear Itself GN 8.00
Green Lantern - Willworld 1 (7/11) r/Green Lantern: Willworld GN 8.00
Harley Quinn 1 (4/14) r/Batman: Harley Quinn #1, Joker's Asylum II: HQ #1 and others 8.00
Impulse 1 (8/11) r/Impulse #50-53 8.00
Jack Kirby Omnibus Sampler 1 (12/11) r/Kirby art stories from 1957,1958 8.00
JLA 1 (2/11) r/JLA #90-93 8.00
JLA - Age of Wonder 1 (12/11) r/JLA: Age of Wonder 8.00
JLA: Black Baptism 1 (8/11) r/JLA: Black Baptism #1-4 8.00
JLA Heaven's Ladder 1 (10/11) comic-sized reprint; and r/Green Lantern #1,000,000 8.00
Legion of Super-Heroes 1 (6/11) r/Legion of Super-Heroes #122,123 & Legionnaires 79,80 8.00
Legion of Super-Heroes 2 (2/12) r/Adv. #247 and recent Legion short stories 8.00
Lobo 1 (3/11) r/Lobo #63,64 & DC First: Superman/Lobo #1 8.00
Metal Men 1 (4/11) r/Doom Patrol ('09) #1-7 and Silver Age: The Brave and the Bold #1 8.00
Night Force 1 (4/11) r/Night Force #1-4; Gene Colan-a 8.00
Ninja Boy 1 (6/11) r/Ninja Boy #1-4 8.00
Robin War 100-Page Super Spectacular 1 (2/16) Ryan Sook-c 8.00
Shazam! 1,2 (9/11,10/11) 1-r/Power of Shazam #38-41. 2-r/ #42-46 8.00
Son of Superman 1 (7/11) r/Son of Superman 8.00
Superboy's Legion 1 (12/11) r/Superboy's Legion 1,2 (Elseworlds) 8.00
Superman 1 (12/10) r/Superman: The Man of Steel #121 & Superman #179,180,185 8.00
Superman 2 (1/11) r/Action #798, Superman: The Man of Steel #133, Superman #189 &
    Advs. of Superman #611 8.00
Superman 3 (2/11) r/Superman #177,178,181,182 8.00
Superman 4 (9/11) r/Action #768,771-773 8.00
Superman Adventures 1 (8/12) r/Superman Adventures #16,19,22,23 8.00
Superman/Doomsday 1 (5/11) r/Doomsday Annual #1 & Superman #175 8.00
Superman - Infestation 1 (8/11) r/Action #778, Advs. of Superman #591, Superman #169 and
    Superman: The Man of Steel #113 8.00
Superman: Lois and Clark 100-Page S.S. 1 (1/16) r/Superman: The Wedding Album 8.00
Superman - Secret Identity 1 (12/11) r/Superman: Secret Identity #1,2 8.00
Superman - Secret Identity 2 (1/12) r/Superman: Secret Identity #3,4 8.00
Superman - Sole Survivor 1 (3/11) r/Legends of the DC Universe #1-3,39 8.00
Superman - The Kents 1,2 (1/12, 2/12) 1-r/The Kents #1-4. 2-The Kents #5-8 8.00
Teen Titans 1 (11/11) r/Teen Titans Lost Annual #1 and Solo #7; Allred-a 8.00
Titans Hunt 100-Page Super Spectacular 1 (1/16) r/Teen Titans early apps.; Sook-a 8.00
The Life Story of the Flash 1 (1/12) r/The Life Story of the Flash GN 8.00
T.H.U.N.D.E.R. Agents 1 (2/11) r/T.H.U.N.D.E.R. Agents #1,2,7 (1966) 8.00
Wonder Woman 1 (4/11) r/Wonder Woman #139-142 (1998) 8.00
Wonder Woman Adventures 1 (9/12) r/Advs. in the DC Universe #1,3,11,19 8.00
Young Justice 1 (12/10) r/JLA World Without Grownups #1,2 8.00
Young Justice 2 (1/11) r/Y.J.: The Secret, Y.J. Secret Files #1, Y.J. In No Man's Land 8.00
Young Justice 3 (2/11) r/Young Justice #7 & YJ Secret Origins 80-Page Giant #1 8.00

DC COMICS - THE NEW 52 FCBD SPECIAL EDITION
DC Comics: Jun. 2012 (giveaway one-shot)

1-Origin of The Trinity of Sin (Pandora, The Question, Phantom Stranger); Justice League
    app.; Jim Lee, Reis, Ha, Rocafort-a; previews Earth 2, G.I. Combat, Ravagers 3.00

DC Comics: Bombshells #8 © DC

DCeased #4 © DC

DC: Mech #1 © DC

	GD	VG	FN	VF	VF/NM	NM-
	2.0	4.0	6.0	8.0	9.0	9.2

DC COMICS THE NEW 52 PRESENTS: ...
DC Comics: Mar, 2012 ($7.99, squarebound, one-shot reprints)
The Dark 1 (3/12) r/Animal Man #1, Swamp Thing #1, I, Vampire #1, and J.L. Dark #1 — 8.00

DC COUNTDOWN (To Infinite Crisis)
DC Comics: May, 2005 ($1.00, 80 pages, one-shot)
1-Death of Blue Beetle; prelude to OMAC Project, Day of Vengeance, Rann/Thanagar War
and Villains United mini-series; s/a by various; Jim Lee/Alex Ross-c — 4.00

DCEASED
DC Comics: Jul, 2019 - No. 6, Dec, 2019 ($3.99, limited series)
1-5-Zombie apocalypse in DC universe; Taylor-s/Hairsine-a. 1-Darkseid app. — 4.00
3,5-($4.99) 3-Variant digital Wonder Woman-c by Mattina. 5-Zombie Harley Quinn-c — 5.00
6-($4.99) Continues in DCeased: A Good Day to Die — 5.00
6-($5.99) Variant Darkseid-c by Mattina — 6.00
...: A Good Die to Die (11/19, $4.99) Taylor-s/Braga-a; Mr Miracle, Barda, Mr. Terrific app. — 5.00
...: Hope at World's End SC (2022, $17.99) Collects Chapters #1-15 of digital series — 18.00

DCEASED: DEAD PLANET
DC Comics: Sept, 2020 - No. 7, Mar, 2021 ($4.99/$3.99, limited series)
1-($4.99)-Zombie apocalypse; Damian Wayne, Jon Kent, Cassie Sandsmark app. — 5.00
2-6-($3.99) John Constantine, Swamp Thing, Zatanna app. — 4.00
7-($4.99)-Justice League vs. Amazo army; Constantine & Zatanna vs. Trigon — 5.00

DCEASED: UNKILLABLES
DC Comics: Apr, 2020 - No. 3, Jul, 2020 ($4.99, limited series)
1-3-Zombie apocalypse continues; Deathstroke with a team of villains; Red Hood app. — 5.00

DCEASED: WAR OF THE UNDEAD GODS
DC Comics: Oct, 2022 - No. 8, Jun, 2023 ($3.99/$4.99, limited series)
1-7: 1-Intro. Supergirl & Brainiac; Superman cured. 3-Lobo app. — 4.00
8-($4.99) Heroes vs. Erebos — 5.00

DC FESTIVAL OF HEROES: THE ASIAN SUPERHERO CELEBRATION
DC Comics: 2021 ($9.99, square-bound, one-shot)
1-Short stories of Asian characters incl. Batgirl, Katana, The Atom; intro Monkey Prince — 10.00

DC FIRST: ...(series of one-shots)
DC Comics: July, 2002 ($3.50)
Batgirl/Joker 1-Sienkiewicz & Terry Moore-a; Nowlan-c — 5.00
Green Lantern/Green Lantern 1-Alan Scott & Hal Jordan vs. Krona — 3.50
Flash/Superman 1-Superman races Jay Garrick; Abra Kadabra app. — 3.50
Superman/Lobo 1-Giffen-s; Nowlan-c — 3.50

DC GOES APE
DC Comics: 2008 ($19.99, trade paperback)
Vol. 1 - Reprints app. of Grodd, Beppo, Titano and other monkey tales; Art Adams-c — 20.00

DC GRAPHIC NOVEL (Also see DC Science Fiction...)
DC Comics: Nov, 1983 - No. 7, 1986 ($5.95, 68 pgs.)

		GD	VG	FN	VF	VF/NM	NM-
1-3,5,7: 1-Star Raiders; García-López-c/a; prequel to Atari Force #1. 2-Warlords; not from							
regular Warlord series. 3-The Medusa Chain; Ernie Colon story/a. 5-Me and Joe Priest;							
Chaykin-c. 7-Space Clusters; Nino-c/a			2	4	6	9	12	15
4-The Hunger Dogs by Kirby; Darkseid kills Himon from Mister Miracle & destroys New							
Genesis		5	10	15	33	57	80
6-Metalzoic; Sienkiewicz-c ($6.95)		2	4	6	9	12	15

DC HOLIDAY SPECIAL
DC Comics: Feb, 2010 ($5.99/$9.99, one-shots)
...'09 (2/10, $5.99) 1-Christmas short stories by various incl. Tucci, Chaykin; Nguyen-c — 6.00
...2017 (2/18, $9.99) 1-Story/art by various incl. Rucka, King, Francavilla; Andy Kubert-c — 10.00

DC HORROR PRESENTS: SGT. ROCK VS. THE ARMY OF THE DEAD
DC Comics: Nov, 2022 - No. 6, Apr, 2023 ($3.99, limited series)
1-6-Easy Company vs. zombies; Bruce Campbell-s/Eduardo Risso-a/Gary Frank-c — 4.00

DC HORROR PRESENTS: SOUL PLUMMER
DC Comics: Jan, 2022 - No. 6, May, 2022 ($3.99, limited series)
1-6: 1-Parks & Zebrowski-s/McCrea-a — 4.00

DC HORROR PRESENTS: THE CONJURING: THE LOVER
DC Comics: Aug, 2021 - No. 5, Dec, 2021 ($3.99, limited series)
1-5-Johnson-McGoldrick & Ogle-s/Garry Brown-a — 4.00

DC HOUSE OF HORROR
DC Comics: Dec, 2017 ($9.99, square-bound one-shot)
1-Horror short stories by various incl. Giffen, Porter, Baker, Raney, Chaykin, Kaluta-c — 10.00

DC INFINITE HALLOWEEN SPECIAL
DC Comics: Dec, 2007 ($5.99, one-shot)
1-Halloween short stories by various incl. Dini, Waid, Hairsine, Kelley Jones; Gene Ha-c — 6.00

DC LEAGUE OF SUPER-PETS FCBD SPECIAL EDITION 2022
DC Comics: Jun, 2022 (Free Comic Book Day giveaway, one-shot)
1-Characters from the 2022 movie; preview of the graphic novel; preview of Primer — 3.00

DC LOVE IS A BATTLEFIELD
DC Comics: Apr, 2021 ($9.99, squarebound, 80 pgs., one-shot)
1-Romance short stories by various; Harley Quinn, Poison Ivy, Batman, Catwoman app. — 10.00

DC/MARVEL: ALL ACCESS (Also see DC Versus Marvel & Marvel Versus DC)
DC Comics: 1996 - No. 4, 1997 ($2.95, limited series)
1-4: 1-Superman & Spider-Man app. 2-Robin & Jubilee app. 3-Dr. Strange & Batman-c/app.,
X-Men, JLA app. 4-X-Men vs. JLA-c/app. rebirth of Amalgam — 4.00

DC/MARVEL: CROSSOVER CLASSICS
DC Comics: 1998; 2003 ($14.95, TPB)
Vol. II-Reprints Batman/Punisher: Lake of Fire, Punisher/Batman: Deadly Knights,
Silver Surfer/Superman, Batman & Capt. America — 15.00
Vol. 4 (2003, $14.95) Reprints Green Lantern/Silver Surfer: Unholy Alliances, Darkseid/
Galactus: The Hunger, Batman & Spider-Man, and Superman/Fantastic Four — 15.00

DC: MECH
DC Comics: Sept, 2022 - No. 6, Feb, 2023 ($3.99, limited series)
1-6-Kenny Porter-s/Baldemar Rivas-a Justice League of giant robots vs. Darkseid — 4.00

DC NATION
DC Comics: Jul, 2018 (25¢, one-shot)
0-Short stories; Joker by King-s/Mann-a; Superman by Bendis-s/García-López-a; prelude to
Justice League: No Justice series; Jimenez-a — 3.00

DC NATION FCBD SUPER SAMPLER
DC Comics: (Giveaway)
.../ Superman Adventures Flip Book (6/12) stories from Superman Family Adventures,
Young Justice, Green Lantern: The Animated Series — 3.00
... (7/13) Stories from Beware the Batman and Teen Titans Go! — 3.00

DC NUCLEAR WINTER SPECIAL
DC Comics: Jan, 2019 ($9.99, square-bound, one-shot)
1-Wasteland short stories by various incl. Russell, Duce, Ordway, Hester; Paquette-c — 10.00

DC 100 PAGE SUPER SPECTACULAR
(Title is 100 Page... No. 14 on)(Square bound) (Reprints, 50¢)
National Periodical Publications: No. 4, Summer, 1971 - No. 13, 6/72; No. 14, 2/73 - No. 22, 11/73 (No #1-3)

	GD	VG	FN	VF	VF/NM	NM-
4-Weird Mystery Tales; Johnny Peril & Phantom Stranger; cover & splashes by Wrightson;						
origin Jungle Boy of Jupiter	28	56	84	202	451	700
5-Love Stories; Wood inks (7 pgs.)(scarcer)	55	110	165	440	995	1550
6- "World's Greatest Super-Heroes"; JLA, JSA, Spectre, Johnny Quick, Vigilante & Hawkman;						
contains unpublished Wildcat story; N. Adams wrap-around-c; r/JLA #21,22						
	18	38	57	133	297	460
6-Replica Edition (2004, $6.95) complete reprint w/wraparound-c						
	2	4	6	9	12	15
7-(Also listed as Superman #245) Air Wave, Kid Eternity, Hawkman-r; Atom-r/Atom #3						
	10	20	30	68	144	220
8-(Also listed as Batman #238) Batman, Legion, Aquaman-r; G.A. Atom, Sargon						
(r/Sensation #57), Plastic Man (r/Police #14) stories; Doom Patrol origin-r; Neal Adams						
wraparound-c	18	36	54	124	275	425
9-(Also listed as Our Army at War #242) Kubert-c 10		20	30	64	132	200
10-(Also listed as Adventure Comics #416) Golden Age-reprints; r/1st app. Black Canary						
from Flash #86; no Zatanna	11	22	33	75	160	245
11-(Also listed as Flash #214) origin Metal Men-r/Showcase #37; never before published						
G.A. Flash story.	9	18	27	58	114	170
12-(Also listed as Superboy #185) Legion-c/story; Teen Titans, Kid Eternity (r/Hit #46),						
Star Spangled Kid-r(S.S. #55)	8	16	24	56	108	160
13-(Also listed as Superman #252) Ray(r/Smash #17), Black Condor, (r/Crack #18),						
Hawkman(r/Flash #24); Starman-r/Adv. #67; Dr. Fate & Spectre-r/More Fun #57;						
Neal Adams-c	11	22	33	76	163	250
14-Batman-r/Detective #31,32,156; Atom-r/Showcase #34						
	8	16	24	54	102	150
15,16,18,19,21,22: 15-r/2nd app Newsboy Legion/Det. #64. 16-Sgt. Rock; r/Capt. Storm #1,						
1st Johnny Cloud/All-American Men of War #82. 18-Superman. 21-Superboy; r/Brave &						
the Bold #54. 22-r/All-Flash #13	9	18	27	58	114	170
17,20: 17-JSA-r/All Star #37 (10-11/47, 38 pgs.), Sandman-r/Adv. #65 (8/41), JLA #23 (11/63)						
& JLA #43 (3/66). 20-Batman-r/Det. #66,68, Spectre; origin Two-Face						
	6	12	18	41	76	110
... : Love Stories Replica Edition (2000, $6.95) reprints #5						7.00

NOTE: *Anderson* r-11, 14, 18i, 22. *B. Baily* r-18, 20. *Burnley* r-18, 20. *Crandall* r-14p, 20. *Drucker* r-4. *Grandenett*

	GD 2.0	VG 4.0	FN 6.0	VF 8.0	VF/NM 9.0	NM- 9.2

a-22(2)r. Heath a-22r. Infantino r-17, 20, 22. **G. Kane** r-18. Kirby r-15. Kubert r-6, 7, 16, 17; c-16, 19. **Manning** a-19r. **Meskin** r-4, 22. **Mooney** r-15, 21. **Toth** r-17, 20.

DC ONE MILLION (Also see crossover #1,000,000 issues and JLA One Million TPB)
DC Comics: Nov, 1998 - No. 4, Nov, 1998 ($2.95/$1.99, weekly lim. series)

1-($2.95) JLA travels to the 853rd century; Morrison-s					5.00
2-4-($1.99)					4.00
... Eighty-Page Giant (8/99, $4.95)					5.00
TPB ('99, $14.95) r/#1-4 and several x-over stories					15.00

DC POWER: A CELEBRATION
DC Comics: Mar, 2023 ($9.99, squarebound, one-shot)

1-Spotlight on DC's black heroes; short stories by various; Cyborg, John Stewart, Aqualad, Kid Flash, Batwing, Vixen, Amazing-Man and more app.; John Ridley intro.					10.00
... 2024 1(3/24, $9.99) Jo Mullein, Val-Zod, The Signal and more; Morgan Hampton intro.					10.00

DC PRIDE
DC Comics: Aug, 2021 ($9.99, squarebound, one-shot)

1-Spotlight on DC's LGBQT characters; short stories by various; Aqualad, Batwoman, Green Lantern Alan Scott, Renee Montoya, Midnighter & Apollo app.					10.00
... 2022 1-(8/22) Short stories by various incl. "Finding Batman" by Kevin Conroy-s					10.00
... 2023 1-(2023) Short stories by various incl. Morrison, Maines; bonus pin-ups					10.00
...: Through the Years 1 (8/23, $9.99) Reprints plus new Alan Scott story					10.00
...: Tim Drake Special 1 (8/22, $5.99) R/stories from Batman: Urban Legends #4-6 & 10					6.00

DC REBIRTH HOLIDAY SPECIAL
DC Comics: Feb, 2017 ($9.99, one-shot)

1-Short stories by various; framing pages of Harley Quinn by Dini-s/Charretier-a	2	4	6	8	11	14

DC RETROACTIVE (New stories done in old style plus reprint from decade)
DC Comics: Sept, 2011 - Oct, 2011 ($4.99, series of one-shots)

...: Batman - The '70s (9/11, $4.99) Len Wein-s/Tom Mandrake-a; r/Batman #307					5.00
...: Batman - The '80s (10/11, $4.99) Mike Barr-s/Jerry Bingham-a; The Reaper app.					5.00
...: Batman - The '90s (10/11, $4.99) Grant-s/Breyfogle-a; Scarface & Ventriloquist app.					5.00
...: Flash - The '70s (9/11, $4.99) Bates-s/Gallego-a; r/DC Comics Presents #2					5.00
...: Flash - The '80s (10/11, $4.99) Messner-Loebs-s/LaRocque-a; r/Flash v2 #18					5.00
...: Flash - The '90s (10/11, $4.99) Augustyn-s/Bowden-a; r/Flash v2 #142					5.00
...: Green Lantern - The '70s (9/11, $4.99) O'Neil-s/Grell-a; r/Green Lantern #76					5.00
...: Green Lantern - The '80s (10/11, $4.99) Wein-s/Staton-a; r/Green Lantern #172					5.00
...: Green Lantern - The '90s (10/11, $4.99) Marz-s/Banks-a; r/Green Lantern v3 #78					5.00
...: JLA - The '70s (9/11, $4.99) Bates-s; Adam Strange app.; r/J.L. of A. #123					5.00
...: JLA - The '80s (10/11, $4.99) Conway-s/Randall-a; Felix Faust app.; r/J.L.of A. #239					5.00
...: JLA - The '90s (10/11, $4.99) Giffen & DeMatteis-s/Maguire-a; r/J.L.A. #4					5.00
...: Superman - The '70s (9/11, $4.99) Pasko-s/Barreto-a; r/Action Comics #484					5.00
...: Superman - The '80s (10/11, $4.99) Wolfman-s/Cariello-a; r/Superman #352					5.00
...: Superman - The '90s (10/11, $4.99) L. Simonson-s/Bogdanove-a; Guardian app.					5.00
...: Wonder Woman - The '70s (9/11, $4.99) O'Neil-s/J. Bone-a; r/Wonder Woman #201					5.00
...: Wonder Woman - The '80s (10/11, $4.99) Thomas-s/Buckler-a; r/W.W. #288					5.00
...: Wonder Woman - The '90s (10/11, $4.99) Messner-Loebs-s/Moder-a; r/W.W. v2 #66					5.00

DC/RWBY (Based on the online series from Rooster Teeth)
DC Comics: Apr, 2023 - No. 7, Oct, 2023 ($3.99)

1-7: 1-Marguerite Bennett/Meghan Hetrick-a; Batman app.					4.00

DC'S BEACH BLANKET BAD GUYS SUMMER SPECIAL
DC Comics: Sept, 2018 ($9.99, 80 pgs, square-bound, one-shot)

1-Summer short stories by various; Conner-c; Joker, Mr. Freeze, Black Manta app.					10.00

DC SCIENCE FICTION GRAPHIC NOVEL
DC Comics: 1985 - No. 7, 1987 ($5.95)

SF1-SF7: SF1-Hell on Earth by Robert Bloch; Giffen-p. SF2-Nightwings by Robert Silverberg; G. Colan-p. SF3-Frost & Fire by Bradbury. SF4-Merchants of Venus. SF5-Demon With A Glass Hand by Ellison; M. Rogers-a. SF6-The Magic Goes Away by Niven. SF7-Sandkings by George R.R. Martin	2	4	6	8	11	14

DC'S CRIMES OF PASSION
DC Comics: Apr, 2020 ($9.99, 80 pgs, square-bound, one-shot)

1-Romance-themed short stories by various; Yasmine Putri-c					10.00

DC'S GHOULS JUST WANNA HAVE FUN
DC Comics: Dec, 2023 ($9.99, 80 pgs, square-bound, one-shot)

1-Halloween & horror-themed short stories by various					10.00

DC'S GRIFTER GOT RUN OVER BY A REINDEER
DC Comics: Jan, 2023 ($9.99, 80 pgs, square-bound, one-shot)

1-Winter & Christmas-themed short stories by various; D'Anda-c; Harley Quinn app.					10.00

DC'S HARLEY QUINN ROMANCES
DC Comics: Mar, 2023 ($9.99, square-bound, one-shot)

1-Romance-themed short stories by various; Amanda Conner-c					10.00

DC'S HOW TO LOSE A GUY GARDNER IN 10 DAYS
DC Comics: Mar, 2024 ($9.99, 80 pgs, square-bound, one-shot)

1-Romance-themed short stories by various; Plastic Man, Red Tornado app.; Conner-c					10.00

DC SILENT TALES
DC Comics: Jun, 2023 ($5.99, one-shot)

1-Gustavo Duarte-s/a; no dialogue stories; Harley Quinn, Cyborg, Lobo, Zatanna app.					6.00

DC SILVER AGE CLASSICS
DC Comics: 1992 ($1.00, all reprints)

...Action Comics #252-r/1st Supergirl. Adventure Comics #247-r/1st Legion of Super-Heroes. The Brave and the Bold #28-r/1st JLA. Detective Comics #225-r/1st Martian Manhunter. Detective Comics #327-r/1st new look Batman. Green Lantern #76-r/1st Green Lantern/ Green Arrow. House of Secrets #92-r/1st Swamp Thing. Showcase #4-r/1st S.A. Flash. Showcase #22-r/1st S.A. Green Lantern					4.00
...Sugar and Spike #99; includes 2 unpublished stories					5.00

DC'S LEGION OF BLOOM
DC Comics: May, 2023 ($9.99, square-bound, one-shot)

1-Plant-themed short stories by various; Swamp Thing, Floronic Man, Poison Ivy app.					10.00

DC SPECIAL (Also see Super DC Giant)
National Per. Publ.: 10-12/68 - No. 15, 11-12/71; No. 16, Spr/75 - No. 29, 8-9/77

	GD 2.0	VG 4.0	FN 6.0	VF 8.0	VF/NM 9.0	NM- 9.2
1-All Infantino issue; Flash, Batman, Adam Strange-r; begin 68 pg. issues, end #21	8	18	24	54	102	150
2-Teen humor; Binky, Buzzy, Harvey app.	9	18	27	62	126	190
3-All-Girl issue; unpubl. GA Wonder Woman story	9	18	27	60	120	180
4,11: 4-Horror (1st Abel, brief). 11-Monsters	5	10	15	35	63	90
5-10,12-15: 5-All Kubert issue; Viking Prince, Sgt. Rock-r. 6-Western. 7,9,13-Strangest Sports. 7-Viking Prince; Kubert-c/a (r/B&B almost entirely). 15-G.A. Plastic Man origin-r/ Police #1; origin Woozy by Cole; 14,15-(52 pgs.)	4	8	12	28	47	65
16-27: 16-Super Heroes Battle Super Gorillas. 17-Early S.A. Green Lantern-r. 22-Origin Robin Hood. 26-Enemy Ace. 27-Captain Comet story	3	6	9	16	23	30
28-Earth Shattering Disaster Stories; Legion of Super-Heroes story	3	6	9	17	25	34
29-New "The Untold Origin of the Justice Society"; Staton-a/Neal Adams-c; Hitler app. in story and on cover	5	10	15	34	60	85

NOTE: **N. Adams** c-3, 4, 6, 11, 29. **Grell** a-20; c-17, 20. **Heath** a-22r. **G. Kane** a-6p, 13r, 17r, 19-21r. **Kirby** a-4,11. **Kubert** a-6r, 12r, 22. **Meskin** a-10. **Moreira**-a-10. **Staton** a-29p. **Toth** a-13, 20r. #1-15: 25c; 16-27: 50c; 28, 29: 60c; #1-13, 16-21: 68 pgs; 14-15: 52 pgs; 25-27: oversized.

DC SPECIAL BLUE RIBBON DIGEST
DC Comics: Mar-Apr, 1980 - No. 24, Aug, 1982

	GD 2.0	VG 4.0	FN 6.0	VF 8.0	VF/NM 9.0	NM- 9.2
1,2,4: 1-Legion reprints. 2-Flash. 4-Green Lantern	3	6	9	13	16
3-Justice Society reprints; new Dr. Fate story	2	4	6	11	16	20
5-Secret Origins; new Zatara and Zatanna	2	4	6	11	16	20
6,8-10: 6-Ghosts. 8-Legion. 9-Secret Origins. 10-Warlord-"The Deimos Saga"-Grell-s/c/a	2	4	6	9	13	16
7-Sgt. Rock's Prize Battle Tales	3	6	9	14	19	24
11,16: 11-Justice League. 16-Green Lantern/Green Arrow-r; all Adams-a	2	4	6	9	13	16
12-Haunted Tank; reprints 1st app.	3	6	9	14	19	24
13-15,17-19: 13-Strange Sports Stories. 14-UFO Invaders; Adam Strange app. 15-Secret Origins of Super Villains; JLA app. 17-Ghosts. 18-Sgt. Rock; Kubert front & back-c. 19-new Perez-a	2	4	6	10	14	18
20-Dark Mansion of Forbidden Love (scarce)	5	10	15	30	50	70
21-Our Army at War	3	6	9	14	23	30
22-24: 22-Secret Origins. 23-Green Arrow; w/new 7 pg. story (Spiegle-a). 24-House of Mystery; new Kubert wraparound-c	3	6	9	14	19	24

NOTE: **N. Adams** a-16(6)r, 17r, 23r; c-16. **Aparo** a-6r, 24r; c-23. **Grell** a-8, 10; c-10. **Heath** a-14. **Infantino** a-15r. **Kaluta** a-17r. **Gil Kane** a-15r, 22r. **Kirby** a-5, 9r. **Kubert** a-3, 18, 21r; c-1, 7, 11, 14, 17, 18, 21, 24. **Morrow** a-24r. **Orlando** a-17r, 22r; c-1, 20. **Toth** a-21r, 24r. **Wood** a-3, 17r, 24r. **Wrightson** a-16r, 17r, 24r.

DC SPECIAL: CYBORG (From Teen Titans) (See Teen Titans 2003 series for TPB collection)
DC Comics: Jul, 2008 - No. 6, Dec, 2008 ($2.99, limited series)

1-6: 1-Sable-s/Lashley-a; origin re-told. 3-6-Magno-a					3.00

DC SPECIAL: RAVEN (From Teen Titans) (See Teen Titans 2003 series for TPB collection)
DC Comics: May, 2008 - No. 5, 2008 ($2.99, limited series)

1-5-Marv Wolfman-s/Damion Scott-a					3.00

DC SPECIAL SERIES
National Periodical Publications/DC Comics: 9/77 - No. 16, Fall, 1978; No. 17, 8/79 - No. 27, Fall, 1981 (No. 18, 19, 23, 24 - digest size, 100 pgs.; No. 25-27 - Treasury sized)

	GD 2.0	VG 4.0	FN 6.0	VF 8.0	VF/NM 9.0	NM- 9.2
1-"5-Star Super-Hero Spectacular 1977"; Batman, Atom, Flash, Green Lantern, Aquaman, in solo stories, Kobra app.; 1st app. Patty Spivot in Flash story; N. Adams-c	5	10	15	35	63	90
2(#1)-"The Original Swamp Thing Saga 1977"-r/Swamp Thing #1&2 by Wrightson; new Wrightson wraparound-c.	3	6	9	17	26	35
3,4,6-8: 3-Sgt Rock. 4-Unexpected. 6-Secret Society of Super Villains, Jones-a. 7-Ghosts Special. 8-Brave and Bold w/ new Batman, Deadman & Sgt Rock team-up	3	6	9	14	20	25
5-"Superman Spectacular 1977"-(84 pg, $1.00)-Superman vs. Brainiac & Lex Luthor, new 63 pg. story	3	6	9	17	26	35
9-Wonder Woman; Ditko-a (11 pgs.); Hitler-c	3	6	9	19	37	50
10-"Secret Origins of Superheroes Special 1978"-(52 pgs.)-Dr. Fate, Lightray & Black Canary on-c/new origin stories; Staton, Newton-a	3	6	9	14	20	25
11-"Flash Spectacular 1978"-(84 pgs.) Flash, Kid Flash, GA Flash & Johnny Quick vs. Grodd; Wood-i on Kid Flash chapter	2	4	6	13	18	22
12-"Secrets of Haunted House Special Spring 1978"	2	4	6	13	18	22
13-"Sgt. Rock Special Spring 1978", 50 pg new story	3	6	9	14	19	24
14,17,20-"Original Swamp Thing Saga", Wrightson-a: 14-Sum '78, r/#3,4. 17-Sum '79 r/#5-7. 20-Jan/Feb '80, r/#8-10	2	4	6	9	13	16
15-"Batman Spectacular Summer 1978", Ra's Al Ghul-app.; Golden-a; Rogers-a/front & back-c	4	8	12	27	44	60
16-"Jonah Hex Spectacular Fall 1978"; death of Jonah Hex, Heath-a; Bat Lash and Scalphunter stories	6	12	18	41	76	110
18,19-Digest size: 18-"Sgt. Rock's Prize Battle Tales Fall 1979". 19-"Secret Origins of Super-Heroes Fall 1979"; origins Wonder Woman (new-a),r/Robin, Batman-Superman team, Aquaman, Hawkman and others	2	4	6	10	14	18
21-"Super-Star Holiday Special Spring 1980", Frank Miller-a in "Batman--Wanted Dead or Alive" (1st Batman story); Jonah Hex, Sgt. Rock, Superboy & LSH and House of Mystery/ Witching Hour-c/stories	5	10	15	33	57	80
22-"G.I. Combat Sept. 1980", Kubert-c. Haunted Tank-s	3	6	9	14	19	24
23,24-Digest size: 23-World's Finest-r. 24-Flash	2	4	6	11	16	20
V5#25-($2.95)-"Superman II, the Adventure Continues Summer 1981"; photos from movie & photo-c (see All-New Coll. Ed. C-62 for first Superman movie)						
26-($2.50)-"Superman and His Incredible Fortress of Solitude Summer 1981"	3	6	9	17	26	35
27-($2.50)-"Batman vs. The Incredible Hulk Fall 1981"	9	18	27	59	117	175

NOTE: **Aparo** a-8. **Heath** a-12i, 16. **Infantino** a-23r. **Kubert** c-13, 19r. **Nasser/Netzer** a-1, 10i, 15. **Newton** a-10. **Nino** a-4, 7. **Starlin** c-12. **Staton** a-1. **Tuska** a-19r. #25 & 26. were advertised as All-New Collectors' Edition C-63, C-64. #63 was originally planned as All-New Collectors' Ed. C-30?; has C-630 & A.N.C.E. on cover.

DC SPECIAL: THE RETURN OF DONNA TROY
DC Comics: Aug, 2005 - No. 4, Late Oct, 2005 ($2.99, limited series)

1-4-Jimenez-s/Garcia-Lopez-a(p)/Pérez-i					3.00

DC Power: A Celebration #1 © DC

DC Special Series #9 © DC

DC Universe Presents #13 © DC

	GD	VG	FN	VF	VF/NM	NM-
	2.0	4.0	6.0	8.0	9.0	9.2

DC'S SAVED BY THE BELLE REVE
DC Comics: Oct, 2022 ($9.99, 80 pgs, square-bound, one-shot)
1-School-themed short stories by various; Juni Ba-c; Super Sons & Tiny Titans app. 10.00

DC'S TERROR THROUGH TIME
DC Comics: Dec, 2022 ($9.99, 80 pgs, square-bound, one-shot)
1-Tales of traumatizing time travel; short stories by various; John McCrea-c 10.00

DC'S 'TWAS THE 'MITE BEFORE CHRISTMAS
DC Comics: Feb, 2024 ($9.99, 80 pgs, square-bound, one-shot)
1-Short holiday stories by various; Damian meets Bat-Mite; Ben Caldwell-c 10.00

DC SUPERHERO GIRLS
DC Comics: May, 2016; May, 2017; May 2018 (All-ages FCBD giveaway)
1 FCBD 2017 Special Edition (5/17); teenage girl heroes; Fontana-s/Labat-a		3.00
1 FCBD 2018 Special Edition (5/18); Date With Disaster; Fontana-s/Labat-a		3.00
1 Special Edition (5/16); teenage girl heroes at Super Hero High; Fontana-s/Labat-a		3.00
... 2017 Halloween Comic Fest Special Edition (11/17); Labat & Garbowska-a		3.00
... Halloween Fest Special Edition (12/16); teenage girl heroes at Super Hero High		3.00

DC SUPERHERO GIRLS GIANT
DC Comics: 2019 - No. 2, 2020 ($4.99, 100 pgs., squarebound, Mass Market & Direct Market editions exist for each issue, with different covers)
1,2-Direct Market Edition - New stories and reprints from graphic novels 5.00

DC SUPER-STARS
National Periodical Publ./DC Comics: March, 1976 - No. 18, Winter, 1978 (No. 3-18: 52 pgs.)
	GD	VG	FN	VF	VF/NM	NM-
1-(68 pgs.)-Re-intro Teen Titans (predates T. T. #44 (11/76); tryout iss.) plus r/Teen Titans; W.W. as girl was original Wonder Girl	3	6	9	21	33	45
2-6,9,12,16: 2,4,6,8-Adam Strange; 2-(68 pgs.)-r/1st Adam Strange/Hawkman team-up from Mystery in Space #90 plus Atomic Knights origin-r. 3-Legion issue.						
4-r/Tales/Unexpected #45.	2	4	6	8	11	14
7-Aquaman spotlight; Aqualad, Aquagirl, Ocean Master & Black Manta app.; Aparo-c	3	6	9	21	33	45
8-r/1st Space Ranger from Showcase #15, Adam Strange-r/Mystery in Space #89 & Star Rovers-r/M.I.S. #80	2	4	6	9	13	16
10-Strange Sports Stories; Batman/Joker-c/story	3	6	9	15	22	28
11-Magic; Zatanna-c/reprint from Adv. #413-415 with Morrow-a; Morrow-c; Flash vs. Abra Kadabra (r/Flash #128)	12	24	36	79	170	260
13-Sergio Aragonés Special	3	6	9	15	22	28
14,15,18: 15-Sgt. Rock	2	4	6	9	13	16
17-Secret Origins of Super-Heroes (origin of The Huntress); origin Green Arrow by Grell; Legion app.; Earth 1I Batman & Catwoman marry (1st revealed; also see B&B #197 & Superman Family #211)	9	18	27	62	126	190
#17 (Facsimile Edition) (2020, $4.99) Reprints #17 with original ads						5.00

NOTE: **M. Anderson** r-2, 4, 6. **Aparo** c-7, 14, 18. **Austin** a-11. **Buckler** a-14p; c-10. **Grell** a-17. **G. Kane** a-1r, 10r. **Kubert** c-15. **Layton** c/a-16i, 17i. **Mooney** a-4r, 6r. **Morrow** c/a-11r. **Nasser** a-11. **Newton** c/a-16p. **Staton** a-17; c-17. No. 10, 12-18 contain all new material; the rest are reprints. #1 contains new and reprint material.

DC'S VERY MERRY MULTIVERSE
DC Comics: Feb, 2021 ($9.99, one-shot)
1-Short Holiday stories; Batman, Harley Quinn, Capt. Carrot, Lobo and others app. 10.00

DC'S YEAR OF THE VILLAIN SPECIAL
DC Comics: Jul, 2019 (25c, one-shot)
1-Short preludes; Legion of Doom, Leviathan, Batman Who Laughs app.; Capullo-c 3.00

DC: THE DOOMED AND THE DAMNED
DC Comics: Dec, 2020 ($9.99, one-shot)
1-Short horror stories; Batman, Madame Xanadu, Man-Bat, Etrigan, Green Lantern app. 10.00

DC: THE NEW FRONTIER (Also see Justice League: The New Frontier Special)
DC Comics: Mar, 2004 - No. 6, Nov, 2004 ($6.95, limited series)
1-6-DCU in the 1940s-60s; Darwyn Cooke-c/s/a in all. 1-Hal Jordan and The Losers app.
2-Origin Martian Manhunter; Barry Allen app. 3-Challengers of the Unknown 7.00
...Volume One (2004, $19.95, TPB) r/#1-3; cover gallery & intro. by Paul Levitz 20.00
...Volume Two (2005, $19.95, TPB) r/#4-6; cover gallery & afterword by Cooke 20.00

DC TOP COW CROSSOVERS
DC Comics/Top Cow Productions: 2007 ($14.99, TPB)
SC-r/The Darkness/Batman; JLA/Witchblade; The Darkness/Superman; JLA/Cyberforce 15.00

DC 2000
DC Comics: 2000 - No. 2, 2000 ($6.95, limited series)
1,2-JLA visit 1941 JSA; Semeiks-a 7.00

DCU BRAVE NEW WORLD (See Infinite Crisis and tie-ins)
DC Comics: Aug, 2006 ($1.00, 80 pgs., one-shot)
1-Previews 2006 series Martian Manhunter, OMAC, The Creeper, The All-New Atom, The

Trials of Shazam, and Uncle Sam and the Freedom Fighters; the Monitor app. 4.00

DCU (Halloween and Christmas one-shot anthologies)
DC Comics
... Halloween Special '09 (12/09, $5.99) Ha-c; art from Bagley, Tucci, K. Jones, Nguyen		6.00
... Halloween Special 2010 (12/10, $4.99) Ha-c; art from Tucci, Garbett; I....Vampire app.		5.00
... Holiday Special (2/09, $5.99) Christmas by various incl. Dini, Maguire, Reis; Quitely-c		6.00
... Holiday Special 2010 (2/11, $4.99) Jonah Hex, Spectre, Legion of S.H., Anthro app.		5.00
... Infinite Halloween Special (12/08, $5.99) Ralph & Sue Dibny app.; Gene Ha-c		6.00
... Infinite Holiday Special (2/07, $4.99) by various; Batwoman app.; Porter-c		5.00

DCU HEROES SECRET FILES
DC Comics: Feb, 1999 ($4.95, one-shot)
1-Origin-s and pin-ups; new Star Spangled Kid app. 5.00

DCU: LEGACIES
DC Comics: Jul, 2010 - No. 10, Apr, 2011 ($3.99, limited series)
1-10: 1,2-Andy Kubert-c; JSA app.; two covers on each. 3-JLA app.; Garcia-Lopez-a.
4-Sgt. Rock back-up; Joe Kubert-a. 5-Pérez-a. 8-Back-up Quitely-a. 4.00

DC UNIVERSE CHRISTMAS, A
DC Comics: 2000 ($19.95)
TPB-Reprints DC Christmas stories by various 20.00

DC UNIVERSE: DECISIONS
DC Comics: Early Nov, 2008 - No. 4, Late Dec, 2008 ($2.99, limited series)
1-4-Assassination plot in the Presidential election; Winick & Willingham-s/Porter-a 3.00

DC UNIVERSE HOLIDAY BASH
DC Comics: 1997- 1999 ($3.95)
I,II-(X-mas '96,'97) Christmas stories by various 5.00
III (1999, for Christmas '98, $4.95) 5.00

DC UNIVERSE ILLUSTRATED BY NEAL ADAMS (Also see Batman Illustrated by Neal Adams HC Vol. 1-3)
DC Comics: 2008 ($39.99, hardcover with dustjacket)
Vol. 1 - Reprints Adams' non-Batman/non-Green Lantern work from 1967-1972; incl. Teen Titans, DC war, Enemy Ace, Superman and PSAs; promo art; Levitz foreword 40.00

DC UNIVERSE: LAST WILL AND TESTAMENT
DC Comics: Oct, 2008 ($3.99, one-shot)
1-Geo-Force vs. Deathstroke; DC heroes prepare for Final Crisis; Brad Meltzer-s; Adam Kubert & Joe Kubert-a; two covers 4.00

DC UNIVERSE ONLINE LEGENDS (Based on the online game)
DC Comics: Early Apr, 2011 - Late May, 2012 ($2.99)
1-26: 1-Wolfman & Bedard-s/Porter-a; DC heroes & Luthor vs. Brainiac. 1-Wraparound-c 3.00

DC UNIVERSE: ORIGINS
DC Comics: 2009 ($14.99, TPB)
nn-Reprints 2-page origins of DC characters from back-ups in 52, Countdown and Justice League: Cry For Justice #1-3; s/a by various; Alex Ross-c 15.00

DC UNIVERSE PRESENTS (DC New 52)
DC Comics: Nov, 2011 - No. 19, Jun, 2013 ($2.99)
1-5-Deadman. 1-Deadman origin re-told; Jenkins-s/Chang-a/Sook-c		3.00
6-8-Challengers of the Unknown; DiDio-s/Ordway-a/Sook-c		3.00
9-19: 9-11-Savage; Chang-a. 12-Kid Flash. 13-16-Black Lightning & Blue Devil		3.00
#0 (11/12, $5.99) O.M.A.C., Mr. Terrific, Hawk & Dove, Blackhawks, Deadman origins		6.00

DC UNIVERSE: REBIRTH
DC Comics: Jul, 2016 ($2.99, one-shot)
1-($2.99) Wally West returns; Johns-s; art by Frank, Van Sciver, Reis & Jimenez; wraparound-c by Gary Frank		3.00
1-2nd printing ($5.99, squarebound) same wraparound-c by Gary Frank		6.00
1-3rd printing ($5.99, squarebound) variant Kid Flash cover by Gary Frank		6.00

DC UNIVERSE SPECIAL
DC Comics: July, 2008 - Aug, 2008 ($4.99, collection of reprints related to Final Crisis)
...: Justice League of America (7/08) r/J.L. of A. #111,166-168 & Detective #274; Sook-c		5.00
...: Reign in Hell (8/08) r/Blaze/Satanus War x-over; Sook-c		5.00
...: Superman (7/08) r/Mongul app. in Superman #32, Showcase '95 #7,8, Flash #102		5.00

DC UNIVERSE: THE STORIES OF ALAN MOORE (Also see Across the Universe:...)
DC Comics: 2006 ($19.99)
TPB-Reprints Batman: The Killing Joke, "Whatever Happened to the Man of Tomorrow", "For The Man Who Has Everything", and other classic Moore DC stories; Bolland-c 20.00

DC UNIVERSE: TRINITY
DC Comics: Aug, 1993 - No. 2, Sept, 1993 ($2.95, 52 pgs, limited series)

	GD	VG	FN	VF	VF/NM	NM-
	2.0	4.0	6.0	8.0	9.0	9.2

1,2-Foil-c; Green Lantern, Darkstars, Legion app. — 4.00

DC UNIVERSE VS. MASTERS OF THE UNIVERSE
DC Comics: Oct, 2013 - No. 6, May, 2014 ($2.99, limited series)
1-6: 1-3-Giffen-s/Soy-a/Benes-c; Constantine app. 4-6-Mhan-a — 3.00

DCU VILLAINS SECRET FILES
DC Comics: Apr, 1999 ($4.95, one-shot)
1-Origin-s and profile pages — 5.00

DC VERSUS MARVEL (See Marvel Versus DC) (Also see Amazon, Assassins, Bruce Wayne: Agent of S.H.I.E.L.D., Bullets & Bracelets, Doctor Strangefate, JLX, Legend of the Dark Claw, Magneto & The Magnetic Men, Speed Demon, Spider-Boy, Super Soldier, X-Patrol)
DC Comics: No. 1, 1996, No. 4, 1996 ($3.95, limited series)
1,4: 1-Marz script, Jurgens-a(p); 1st app. of Access. — 5.00
.../Marvel Versus DC ($12.95, trade paperback) r/1-4 — 13.00

DC VS. VAMPIRES
DC Comics: Dec, 2021 - No. 12, Feb, 2023 ($3.99, limited series)
1-12-Tynion IV & Rosenberg-s/Schmidt-a. 1-I, Vampire (Andrew Bennett) app. — 4.00
... Coffin Edition 1 (9/22, $5.99) Reprints #1-3; cover homage to Lost Boys movie poster — 6.00
... Crypt Edition 1 (9/22, $5.99) Reprints #4-6; cover homage to Breakfast Club poster — 6.00
... - Hunters 1 (7/22, $3.99) Damian in Gotham City; Googe-a — 4.00
... - Killers 1 (8/22, $3.99) Harley Quinn & Catwoman app.; Bowden-a — 4.00

DC VS. VAMPIRES: ALL-OUT WAR
DC Comics: Sept, 2022 - No. 6, Feb, 2023 ($3.99, B&W&red, limited series)
1-6-Rosenberg-s/Paknadel-a; John Constantine, Deathstroke, and Mary Marvel app. — 4.00

DC/WILDSTORM DREAMWAR
DC Comics: Jun, 2008 - No. 6, Nov, 2008 ($2.99, limited series)
1-6-Giffen-s; Silver Age JLA, Teen Titans, JSA, Legion app. on WildStorm Earth — 3.00
1-Variant-c of Superman & Midnighter by Garbett — 6.00
TPB (2009, $19.99) r/series — 20.00

DC: WORLD WAR III (See 52/WWIII)

D-DAY (Also see Special War Series)
Charlton Comics (no no. 3): Sum/63; No. 2, Fall/64; No. 4, 9/66; No. 5, 10/67; No. 6, 11/68

1,2: 1(1963)-Montes/Bache-a; 2(Fall '64)-Wood-a(4)	4	8	12	27	44	60
4-6('66-'68)-Montes/Bache-a #5	3	6	9	14	20	25

DEAD AIR
Slave Labor Graphics: July, 1989 ($5.95, graphic novel)

nn-Mike Allred's 1st published work	3	6	9	17	26	35

DEAD BODY ROAD: BAD BLOOD
Image Comics (Skybound): Jun, 2020 - No. 6, Dec, 2020 ($3.99)
1-6-Justin Jordan-s/Benjamin Tiesma-a/Matthew Scalera-c — 4.00

DEADBOX
Vault Comics: Sept, 2021 - Present ($3.99, limited series)
1-3-Russell-s/Tiesma-a — 4.00

DEAD BOY DETECTIVES
DC Comics (Vertigo): Feb, 2014 - No. 12, Feb, 2015 ($2.99, limited series)
1-12-Litt-s/Buckingham-a. 1-Covers by Buckingham & Chiang — 3.00

DEAD CORPSE
DC Comics (Helix): Sept, 1998 - No. 4, Dec, 1998 ($2.50, limited series)
1-4-Pugh-a/Hinz-s — 4.00

DEAD DAY
AfterShock Comics: May, 2020 - No. 5, Nov, 2020 ($3.99)
1-5-Ryan Parrott-s/Evgeniy Bornyakov-a — 4.00

DEAD DOG'S BITE
Dark Horse Comics: Mar, 2021 - No. 4, Jun, 2021 ($4.99, limited series)
1-4-Tyler Boss-s/a — 5.00

DEAD DROP
Valiant Entertainment: May, 2015 - No. 4, Aug, 2015 ($3.99, limited series)
1-4-Ales Kot-s/Adam Gorham-a; X-O Manowar app. 2-Archer app. — 4.00

DEAD END CRIME STORIES
Kirby Publishing Co.: April, 1949 (52 pgs.)

nn-(Scarce)-Powell, Roussos-a; painted-c	81	162	243	518	884	1250

DEAD ENDERS
DC Comics (Vertigo): Mar, 2000 - No. 16, June, 2001 ($2.50)
1-16-Brubaker-s/Pleece & Case-a — 3.00
Stealing the Sun (2000, $9.95, TPB) r/#1-4, Vertigo Winter's Edge #3 — 10.00

DEAD EYES (Copies recalled due to trademark dispute, cancelled after #2)(See Dead Rabbit)
Image Comics: Oct, 2019 ($3.99)
1-Duggan-s/McCrea-a — 6.00

DEAD-EYE WESTERN COMICS
Hillman Periodicals: Nov-Dec, 1948 - V3#1, Apr-May, 1953

V1#1-(52 pgs.)-Krigstein, Roussos-a	28	56	84	165	270	375
V1#2,3-(52 pgs.)	15	30	45	88	137	185
V1#4-12-(52 pgs.)	13	26	39	72	101	130
V2#1,2,5-8,10-12: 1-7-(52 pgs.)	9	18	27	52	69	85
3,4-Krigstein-a	10	20	30	56	76	95
9-One pg. Frazetta ad	9	18	27	52	69	85
V3#1	9	18	27	52	69	85

NOTE: *Briefer* a-V1#8. Kinstleresque stories by *McCann*-12, V2#1, 2, V3#1. *McWilliams* a-V1#5. *Ed Moore* a-V1#4.

DEADFACE: DOING THE ISLANDS WITH BACCHUS
Dark Horse Comics: July, 1991 - No. 3, Sept, 1991 ($2.95, B&W, lim. series)
1-3: By Eddie Campbell — 4.00

DEADFACE: EARTH, WATER, AIR, AND FIRE
Dark Horse Comics: July, 1992 - No. 4, Oct, 1992 ($2.50, B&W, limited series; British-r)
1-4: By Eddie Campbell — 4.00

DEAD HAND, THE
Image Comics: Apr, 2018 - No. 6, Sept, 2018 ($3.99)
1-6-Kyle Higgins-s/Stephen Mooney-a — 4.00

DEAD INSIDE
Dark Horse Comics: Dec, 2016 - No. 5, May, 2017 ($3.99)
1-5-Arcudi-s/Fejzula-a/Dave Johnson-c — 4.00

DEAD IN THE WEST
Dark Horse Comics: Oct, 1993 - No. 2, Mar, 1994 ($3.95, B&W, 52 pgs.)
1,2-Timothy Truman-c — 4.00

DEAD IRONS
Dynamite Entertainment: 2009 - No. 4, 2009 ($3.99)
1-4-Kuhoric-s/Alexander-a/Jae Lee-c — 4.00

DEAD KINGS
AfterShock Comics: Oct, 2018 - No. 5, May, 2019 ($3.99)
1-5-Steve Orlando-s/Matthew Dow Smith-a — 4.00

DEADLANDER (Becomes Dead Rider for #2)
Dark Horse Comics: Oct, 2007 - No. 4, ($2.99, limited series)
1-2-Kevin Ferrara-s/a — 3.00

DEADLANDS (Old West role playing game)
Image Comics: Jul, 2011; Aug, 2011; Jan, 2012 ($2.99, one-shots)
...: Black Water (1/12) Mariotte-s/Brook Turner-a — 3.00
...: Death Was Silent (8/11) Marz-s/Sears-a/c — 3.00
...: Massacre at Red Wing (7/11) Palmiotti & Gray-a/c — 3.00

DEADLIEST BOUQUET, THE
Image Comics: Aug, 2022 - No. 5, Dec, 2022 ($3.99)
1-5-Erica Schultz-s/Carola Borelli-a — 4.00

DEADLIEST HEROES OF KUNG FU (Magazine)
Marvel Comics Group: Summer, 1975 (B&W)(76 pgs.)

1-Bruce Lee vs. Carradine painted-c; TV Kung Fu, 4pgs. photos/article; Enter the Dragon, 24 pgs. photos/article w/ Bruce Lee; Bruce Lee photo pinup	6	12	18	38	69	100

DEADLINE
Marvel Comics: June, 2002 - No. 4, Sept, 2002 ($2.99, limited series)
1-4: 1-Intro. Kat Farrell; Bill Rosemann-s/Guy Davis-a; Horn painted-c — 3.00
TPB (2002, $9.99) r/#1-4 — 10.00

DEAD LUCKY, THE
Image Comics: Aug, 2022 - Present ($3.99)
1-11-Flores-s/Carlomagno-a — 4.00

DEADLY CLASS (Inspired the 2018 SYFY Channel TV show)
Image Comics: Jan, 2014 - No. 56, 2022 ($3.99)

1-Remender-s/Craig-a	2	4	6	11	16	20
2-6						6.00
7-56: 40-44-Bone Machine						4.00
.... Killer Set, FCBD Special (5/19, giveaway) New story by Remender-s/Craig-a						3.00

DEADLY DUO, THE
Image Comics (Highbrow Entertainment): Nov, 1994 - No. 3, Jan, 1995 ($2.50, lim. series)
1-3: 1-1st app. of Kill Cat — 4.00

DEADLY DUO, THE
Image Comics (Highbrow Entertainment): June, 1995 - No. 4, Oct, 1995 ($2.50, lim. series)
1-4: 1-Spawn app. 2-Savage Dragon app. 3-Gen 13 app. — 4.00

DEADLY FOES OF SPIDER-MAN (See Lethal Foes of...)
Marvel Comics: May, 1991 - No. 4, Aug, 1991 ($1.00, limited series)
1-4: 1-Punisher, Kingpin, Rhino app. — 4.00

DEADLY HANDS OF KUNG FU, THE (See Master of Kung Fu)
Marvel Comics Group: April, 1974 - No. 33, Feb, 1977 (75¢) (B&W, magazine)

1(V1#4 listed in error)-Origin Sons of the Tiger; Shang-Chi, Master of Kung Fu begins (ties w/Master of Kung Fu #17 as 3rd app. Shang-Chi); Bruce Lee painted-c by Neal Adams; 2pg. memorial photo pinup w/8 pgs. photos/articles; TV Kung Fu, 9 pgs. photos/articles; 15 pgs. Starlin-a	8	16	24	56	108	160
2-Adams painted-c; 1st time origin of Shang-Chi, 34 pgs. by Starlin. TV Kung Fu, 6 pgs. photos & article w/2 pg. pinup. Bruce Lee, 11 pgs. ph/a	6	12	18	37	66	95
3,4,7,10: 3-Adams painted-c; Gulacy-a. Enter the Dragon, photos/articles, 8 pgs. 4-TV Kung Fu painted-c by Neal Adams; TV Kung Fu 7 pg. article/art; Fu Manchu; Enter the Dragon, 10 pg. photos article w/Bruce Lee. 7-Bruce Lee painted-c & 9 pgs. photos/articles-Return of Dragon plus 1 pg. photo pinup. 10-(3/75)-Iron Fist painted-c & 34 pg. sty-Early app.	4	8	12	27	44	60
5,6: 5-1st app. Manchurian, 6 pgs. Gulacy-a. TV Kung Fu, 4 pg. article; reprints books w/Barry Smith-a. Capt. America-sty, 10 pgs. Kirby-a(r). 6-Bruce Lee photos/article, 6 pgs.; 5 pgs. early Perez-a	4	8	12	23	37	50
8,9,11: 9-Iron Fist, 2 pg. Preview pinup; Nebres-a. 11-Billy Jack painted-c by Adams; 17 pgs. photos/article	3	6	9	19	30	40
12,13: 12-James Bond painted-c by Adams; 14 pg. photos/article. 13-16 early Perez-a; Piers Anthony, 7 pgs.	3	6	9	17	26	35
14-Classic Bruce Lee painted-c by Adams. Lee pinup by Chaykin. Lee 16 pg. photos/article w/Bruce Lee. Green Hornet TV	9	18	27	58	114	170
15-Sum. '75 Giant Annual #1; 20pgs. Gulacy-a. Bruce Lee photo pinup & 3 pg. photos/article re book; Man-Thing app. Iron Fist-c/sty; Gulacy-a 18pgs.	4	8	12	23	37	50
16,18,20: 16-1st app. Corpse Rider, a Samurai w/Sanho Kim-a. 20-Chuck Norris painted-c & 16 pgs. interviews article/art w/Bruce Lee; Bruce Lee vs. C. Norris pinup by Ken Barr. Origin The White Tiger, Perez-a	4	8	12	23	37	50
17-Bruce Lee painted-c by Adams; interview w/R. Clouse, director Enter Dragon 7 pgs. w/B. Lee app. 1st Giffen-a (1pg. 11/75)	5	10	15	35	63	90
19-Iron Fist painted-c & series begins; 1st White Tiger	6	12	18	37	66	95

DC vs. Vampires #5 © DC

Dead Boy Detectives #9 © DC

Deadpool (1994 series) #3 © MAR

	GD	VG	FN	VF	VF/NM	NM-			GD	VG	FN	VF	VF/NM	NM-
	2.0	4.0	6.0	8.0	9.0	9.2			2.0	4.0	6.0	8.0	9.0	9.2

25 50 75 175 388 600
21-Bruce Lee 1pg. photos/article
3 6 9 19 30 40
22-1st brief app. Jack of Hearts. 1st Giffen sty-a (along w/Amazing Adv. #35, 3/76)
7 14 21 46 86 125
23-1st full app. Jack of Hearts
5 10 15 35 63 90
24-26,29: 24-Iron Fist-c & centerfold pinup. early Zeck-a; Shang Chi pinup; 6 pgs. Piers Anthony text sty w/Pérez/Austin-a; Jack of Hearts app. early Giffen-a. 25-1st app. Shimuru, "Samurai", 20 pgs. Mantlo-sty/Broderick-a; "Swordquest"-c & begins 17 pg. sty by Sanho Kim; 11 pg. photos/article; partly Bruce Lee. 26-Bruce Lee painted-c & pinup; 16 pgs. interviews w/Kwon & Clouse; talk about Bruce Lee re-filming of Lee legend. 29-Ironfist vs. Shang Chi battle-c/sty; Jack of Hearts app.
3 6 9 18 28 38
27
3 6 9 15 22 28
28-All Bruce Lee Special Issue; (1st time in comics). Bruce Lee painted-c by Ken Barr & pinup. 36 pgs. comics chronicling Bruce Lee's life; 15 pgs. B. Lee photos/article (Rare in high grade)
9 18 27 59 117 175
30-32: 30-Swordquest-c/sty & conclusion; Jack of Hearts app. 31-Jack of Hearts app; Staton-a. 32-1st Daughters of the Dragon-c/sty, 21 pgs. M. Rogers-a/Claremont-sty; Iron Fist pinup
5 10 15 33 57 80
33-Shang Chi-c/sty; Classic Daughters of the Dragon, 21 pgs. M. Rogers-a/Claremont-story with nudity; Bob Wall interview, photos/article, 14 pgs.
4 8 12 28 47 65
...Special Album Edition 1(Summer, '74)-Iron Fist-c/story (early app., 3rd?); 10 pgs. Adams-i; Shang Chi/Fu Manchu, 10 pgs.; Sons of Tiger, 11 pgs.; TV Kung Fu, 6 pgs. photos/article
5 10 15 33 57 80

NOTE: **Bruce Lee:** *1-7, 14, 15, 17, 25, 26, 28.* **Kung Fu (TV):** *1, 2, 4.* **Jack of Hearts:** *22, 23, 29-33.* **Shang Chi Master of Kung Fu:** *1-9, 11-18, 29, 31, 33.* **Sons of Tiger:** *1, 3, 4, 6-14, 16-19.* **Swordquest:** *25-27, 29-33.* **White Tiger:** *19-24, 26, 27, 29-33.* **N. Adams** *a-1i(part), 27i; c-1, 2-4, 11, 12, 14, 17.* **Giffen** *a-22p, 24p.* **G. Kane** *a-23p.* **Kirby** *a-5r.* **Nasser** *a-27p, 28.* **Perez** *a(p)-6-14, 16, 17, 19, 21.* **Rogers** *a-26, 32, 33.* **Starlin** *a-1, 2r, 15r.* **Staton** *a-28p, 31, 32.*

DEADLY HANDS OF KUNG FU
Marvel Comics: Jul, 2014 - No. 4, Oct, 2014 ($3.99, limited series)
1-4-Benson-s/Huat-a/Johnson-c. 2-4-Misty Knight & Colleen Wing app.   4.00

DEADLY HANDS OF KUNG FU: GANG WAR (Tie-in to Spider-Man crossover event)
Marvel Comics: Feb, 2024 - No. 3, Apr, 2024 ($4.99/$3.99, limited series)
1-($4.99) Greg Pak-s/Caio Majado-a; Spider-Man app.   5.00
2-4-($3.99) 3-Spider-Man & She-Hulk app.   4.00

DEADLY NEIGHBORHOOD SPIDER-MAN
Marvel Comics: Dec, 2022 - No. 5, Apr, 2023 ($4.99/$3.99, limited series)
1-($4.99) B. Earl & Taboo-s/Juan Ferreyra-a   5.00
2-5-($3.99)   4.00

DEAD MALL
Dark Horse Comics: Oct, 2022 - No. 4, Feb, 2023 ($3.99)
1-4-Adam Cesare-s/David Stoll-a   4.00

DEADMAN (See The Brave and the Bold & Phantom Stranger #39)
DC Comics: May, 1985 - No. 7, Nov, 1985 ($1.75, Baxter paper)
1-7: 1-Deadman-r by Infantino, N. Adams in all. 5-Batman-r/story-r/Strange Adventures. 7-Batman-r   6.00
... Book One TPB (2011, $19.99) r/apps. in Strange Adventures #205-213   20.00

DEADMAN
DC Comics: Mar, 1986 - No. 4, June, 1986 (75¢, limited series)
1-4: Lopez-c/a. 4-Byrne-c(p)   5.00

DEADMAN
DC Comics: Feb, 2002 - No. 9, Oct, 2002 ($2.50)
1-9: 1-4-Vance-s/Beroy-a. 3,4-Mignola-c. 5,6-Garcia-Lopez-a   4.00

DEADMAN
DC Comics (Vertigo): Oct, 2006 - No. 13, Oct, 2007 ($2.99)
1-13: 1-Bruce Jones-s/John Watkiss-a/c; intro Brandon Cayce   3.00
...: Deadman Walking TPB (2007, $9.99) r/#1-5   10.00

DEADMAN
DC Comics: Jan, 2018 - No. 6, Jun, 2018 ($3.99, limited series)
1-6-Neal Adams-s/a; Zatanna, The Spectre, Hook and Commissioner Gordon app.   4.00

DEADMAN: DARK MANSION OF FORBIDDEN LOVE
DC Comics: Dec, 2016 - No. 3, Apr, 2017 ($5.99, limited series, squarebound)
1-3-Sarah Vaughn-s/Lan Medina-a/Stephanie Hans-c   6.00

DEADMAN: DEAD AGAIN (Leads into 2002 series)
DC Comics: Oct, 2001 - No. 5, Oct, 2001 ($2.50, weekly limited series)
1-5: Deadman at the deaths of the Flash, Robin, Superman, Hal Jordan   3.00

DEADMAN: EXORCISM

DC Comics: 1992 - No. 2, 1992 ($4.95, limited series, 52 pgs.)
1,2: Kelley Jones-c/a in both   6.00

DEAD MAN LOGAN (Follows Old Man Logan series)
Marvel Comics: Jan, 2019 - No. 12, Dec, 2019 ($4.99/$3.99, limited series)
1-Ed Brisson-s/Mike Henderson-a; Mysterio, Miss Sinister & Hawkeye app.   5.00
2-10-($3.99) 2,3-Avengers app. 5-Mysterio app.   4.00
11,12: 11-1st Dani Cage. 12-Dani Cage becomes Thor   2 4 6 8 10 12

DEADMAN: LOVE AFTER DEATH
DC Comics: 1989 - No. 2, 1990 ($3.95, 52 pgs., limited series, mature)
Book One, Two: Kelley Jones-c/a in both. 1-Contains nudity   5.00

DEAD MAN'S RUN
Aspen MLT: No. 0, Dec, 2011 - No. 6, Jul, 2013 ($2.50/$3.50)
0-($2.50) Greg Pak-s/Tony Parker-a; 3 covers; bonus design sketch art   3.00
1-6: 1-(2/12, $3.50) Greg Pak-s/Tony Parker-a; 2 covers   3.50

DEAD OF NIGHT
Marvel Comics Group: Dec, 1973 - No. 11, Aug, 1975
1-Horror reprints   7 14 21 46 86 125
2-10: 10-Kirby-a. 6-Jack the Ripper-c/s   3 6 9 21 33 45
11-Intro Scarecrow; Kane/Wrightson-c   7 14 21 48 89 130
NOTE: **Ditko** *r-7, 10.* **Everett** *c-2.* **Sinnott** *r-1.*

DEAD OF NIGHT FEATURING DEVIL-SLAYER
Marvel Comics (MAX): Nov, 2008 - No. 4, Feb, 2009 ($3.99, limited series)
1-4-Keene-s/Samnee-a/Andrews-c   4.00

DEAD OF NIGHT FEATURING MAN-THING
Marvel Comics (MAX): Apr, 2008 - No. 4, July, 2008 ($3.99, limited series)
1-4: 1-Man-Thing origin re-told; Kano-a. 2-4-Jennifer Kale app.   4.00

DEAD OF NIGHT FEATURING WEREWOLF BY NIGHT
Marvel Comics (MAX): Mar, 2009 - No. 4, June, 2009 ($3.99, limited series)
1-4: 1-Werewolf By Night origin re-told; Swierczynski-s/Suayan-a   4.00

DEADPOOL (See New Mutants for 1st app.)
Marvel Comics: Aug, 1994 - No. 4, Nov, 1994 ($2.50, limited series)
1-Mark Waid's 1st Marvel work; Ian Churchill-c/a   3 6 9 15 23 30
2-4   1 3 4 6 8 10

DEADPOOL (... : Agent of Weapon X on cover #57-60) (title becomes Agent X)
Marvel Comics: Jan, 1997 - No. 69, Sept, 2002 ($2.95/$1.95/$1.99)
1-($2.95)-Wraparound-c; Kelly-s/McGuinness-a   6 12 18 38 69 100
2-Begin-$1.95-c.   2 4 6 10 14 18
3,5-10,12,13,15-22,24: 12-Variant-c. 22-Cable app.   6.00
4-Hulk-c/app.   3 6 9 16 24 32
11-($3.99)-Deadpool replaces Spider-Man from Amazing Spider-Man #47; Kraven, Gwen Stacy app.   3 6 9 21 33 45
14-1st Ajax; begin McDaniel-a   3 6 9 14 20 25
23,25-($2.99); 23-Dead Reckoning pt. 1; wraparound-c   1 2 3 4 5 7
26-40: 27-Wolverine-c/app. 37-Thor app.   5.00
41,43-49,51-53,56-60: 41-Begin $2.25-c. 44-Black Panther-c/app. 46-49-Chadwick-a. 51-Cover swipe of Detective #38. 57-60-BWS-c   4.00
42-G.I. Joe #21 cover swipe; silent issue   3 6 9 15 22 28
50-1st Kid Deadpool   3 6 9 14 20 25
54,55-Punisher-c/app. 54-Dillon-a. 55-Bradstreet-c   3 6 9 14 20 25
61-64,66-68: 61-64-Funeral For a Freak on cover. 66-69-Udon Studios-a. 67-Dazzler-c/app.   6 8 10
65-Girl in bunny suit-c; Udon Studios-a   4 8 12 28 47 65
69-Udon Studios-a   2 4 6 10 14 18
#(-1) Flashback (7/97) Lopresti-a; Wade Wilson's early days   2 4 6 13 18 22
.../Death '98 Annual ($2.99) Kelly-s   3 6 9 16 23 30
... Team-Up (12/98, $2.99) Widdle Wade-c/app.   2 4 6 10 14 18
Baby's First Deadpool Book (12/98, $2.99)   3 6 9 16 23 30
Encyclopædia Deadpoolica (12/98, $2.99) Synopses   3 6 9 15 22 28
.../GLI – Summer Fun Spectacular #1 (9/07, $3.99) short stories; Pelletier-c   6 8 10 12
... Classic Vol. 1 TPB (2008, $29.99) r/#1, New Mutants #98, Deadpool: The Circle Chase #1-4 and Deadpool (1994 series) #1-4   30.00
Mission Improbable TPB (9/98, $14.95) r/#1-5   20.00
Wizard #0 ('98, bagged with Wizard #87)   6.00

DEADPOOL
Marvel Comics: Nov, 2008 - No. 63, Dec, 2012 ($3.99/$2.99)

	GD	VG	FN	VF	VF/NM	NM-
	2.0	4.0	6.0	8.0	9.0	9.2

1-($3.99) Medina-a; Secret Invasion x-over; Crain-c

	3	6	9	16	24	32
1-Variant cover by Liefeld	4	8	12	27	44	60
2		1	3	4	6	8

3-10: 4-10-Pearson-a. 8,9-Thunderbolts x-over. 10-Dark Reign 6.00
11-24,26-33, 33.1, 34-44,46-49-($2.99): 11-20-Pearson-c. 16-18-X-Men app.
  19-21-Spider-Man & Hit-Monkey app. 26-Ghost Rider app. 27-29-Secret Avengers app.
  30,31-Curse of the Mutants. 37-39-Hulk app. 4.00
25-($3.99) 3-D cover, fake 3-D glasses on back-c; back-up story w/Bond-a 5.00

| 45-1st full app. of Evil Deadpool | 2 | 4 | 6 | 11 | 16 | 20 |

49.1, 51-63 ($2.99) 49-McCrea-a. 51-Garza-a. 61-Hit-Monkey app. 4.00
50-($3.99) Uncanny X-Force & Kingpin app.; Barberi-a

		1	2	3	5	6	8

900-(12/09, $4.99) Stories by various incl. Liefeld, Baker; wraparound-c by Johnson 6.00
1000-(10/10, $4.99) Stories by various; gallery of variant covers; Johnson-c 6.00
Annual 1 (7/11, $3.99) "Identity Wars" crossover; Spider-Man & Hulk app. 5.00
...& Cable #26 (4/11, $3.99) Swierczynski-s/Fernandez-a 4.00
...Family 1 (6/11, $3.99) short stories by various; Pearson-c 4.00
...'Games of Death 1 (5/09, $3.99) Benson-s/Crystal-a/Land-c 4.00
...MCG (7/10, $1.00) r/#1 with "Marvel's Greatest Comics" logo on cover 3.00

DEADPOOL
Marvel Comics: Jan, 2013 - No. 45, Jun, 2015 ($2.99)

1-Posehn & Duggan-s/Tony Moore-a/Darrow-c; Deadpool vs. Zombie ex-Presidents

		2	4	6	9	13	16
2-5							6.00

6-26: 7-Iron Man app.; spoof in 1980s style; Koblish-a/Maguire-a. 10-Spider-Man app.
  13-Spoof in 1970s style; Heroes For Hire app. 15-19-Wolverine & Capt. America app.
27-($9.99) Wedding of Deadpool & Shiklah; wraparound-c with 236 characters 15.00
28-33,35-44-($3.99): 30-32-Dazzler app. 36-39-AXIS tie-in. 40-Gracking issue 4.00
34-($4.99) Original Sin tie-in; flashback in 1990s style; Sabretooth & Alpha Flight app.

		1	2	3	5	6	8

45-($250 on cover, 5/15, $9.99) Death of Deadpool; back-up short stories by various 10.00
Annual 1 (1/14, $4.99) Madcap and Avengers app.; Acker & Blacker-s/Shaner-a 5.00
Annual 2 (7/14, $4.99) Spider-Man and The Chameleon app.; Camagni-a/Nakayama-a 5.00
Bi-Annual 1 (11/14, $4.99) Scheer & Giovannetti-s/Espin-a; Brute Force app. 5.00
...: The Gauntlet (3/14, giveaway) printing of Marvel digital comics content; Cho-c 3.00

DEADPOOL (Continues in Despicable Deadpool #287)
Marvel Comics: Jan, 2016 - No. 36, Nov, 2017 ($4.99/$3.99)

1-($4.99) Duggan-s/Hawthorne-a; Deadpool starts a Heroes For Hire

		1	2	3	5	6	8

2-6,8-12-($3.99) 3,4-Steve Rogers app. 6-Intro. Deadpool 2099; Koblish-a. 8-11-Sabretooth
  app. 12-Deadpool 2099 app. 4.00
7-($9.99) 25th Anniversary issue; back-up short stories about the Mercs For Money 10.00
13-($9.99) Crossover with Daredevil & Power Man and Iron Fist 10.00
14-20,22-24,26-29: 14-17-Civil War II tie-in. 14-Ulysses app. 15-Black Panther app. 4.00
21-($9.99) Duggan-s/Lolli-a; Shakespeare-style story by Doescher-s/Oliveira-a 10.00
25-($9.99) Duggan-s/Koblish-a; Deadpool 2099 story 6.00
30-($9.99) Duggan-s/Hawthorne-a; Deadpool in space; Agent Adsit & Rocket app. 10.00
31-36: 31-35-Secret Empire tie-in 4.00
#3.1-(2/16, $3.99) All-Spanish issue about the Mexican Deadpool Masacre; Koblish-a 4.00
Annual 1 (11/16, $4.99) Spoof of Spider-Man and His Amazing Friends cartoon; Koblish-a 5.00
...: Last Days of Magic 1 (7/16, $4.99) Koblish-a/Ramos-c; Doctor Strange app. 5.00
...: Masacre 1 (7/16, $3.99) Reprints #3.1 in English 4.00

DEADPOOL
Marvel Comics: Aug, 2018 - No. 15, Sept, 2019 ($4.99/$3.99)

1-($4.99) Skottie Young-s/Nic Klein-a; Scott Hepburn-a; Guardians of the Galaxy app. 5.00
2-14-($3.99) 2-Avengers and Champions app. 13,14-War of The Realms tie-in 4.00
15-($4.99) Mephisto app.; Young-s/Klein & Hepburn-a 5.00
Annual 1 (10/19, $4.99) "Acts of Evil" tie-in; Nightmare & Dr. Strange app. 5.00

DEADPOOL
Marvel Comics: Jan, 2020 - No. 10, Mar, 2021 ($4.99/$3.99)

1-($4.99) Kelly Thompson-s/Chris Bachalo-a; Elsa Bloodstone app. 5.00
2-10-($3.99) 2-4-Kraven The Hunter app. 2-Captain America app. 10-King in Black tie-in 4.00
...: Nerdy 30 #1 (5/21, $5.99) 30th Anniversary short stories by various 6.00
...: The End 1 (3/20, $4.99) Various "endings" to Deadpool; Kelly-s/Hawthorne-a 5.00

DEADPOOL
Marvel Comics: Jan, 2023 - No. 10, Oct, 2023 ($4.99/$3.99)

1-($4.99) Wong-s/Coccolo-a; Doctor Octopus & Carnage app. 5.00
2-10-($3.99) Lady Deathstrike app. 4.00
...: Seven Slaughters 1 (1/24, $9.99) Short stories by various incl. Liefeld, Land, Bunn 10.00

DEADPOOL & CABLE: SPLIT SECOND
Marvel Comics: Feb, 2016 - No. 3, Apr, 2016 ($3.99, limited series)

1-3-Nicieza-s/Reilly Brown-a 4.00

DEADPOOL & THE MERCS FOR MONEY
Marvel Comics: Apr, 2016 - No. 5, Aug, 2016 ($3.99)

1-5: 1-Bunn-s/Espin-a; bonus reprint of Spidey #1 4.00

DEADPOOL & THE MERCS FOR MONEY
Marvel Comics: Sept, 2016 - No. 10, Jun, 2017 ($3.99)

1-10: 1-Bunn-s/Coello-a; Negasonic Teenage Warhead app. 10-Dracula app. 4.00

DEADPOOL: ASSASSIN
Marvel Comics: Aug, 2018 - No. 6, Oct, 2018 ($3.99)

1-($4.99) Bunn-s/Bagley-a; Weasel app. 5.00
2-6-($3.99) 4.00

DEADPOOL: BACK IN BLACK (Deadpool with the Venom symbiote right before ASM #300)
Marvel Comics: Dec, 2016 - No. 5, Feb, 2017 ($3.99, limited series)

1-5: 2-Power Pack app. 5-Spider-Man in black costume app.; Eddie Brock app. 4.00

DEADPOOL: BAD BLOOD
Marvel Comics: 2017 ($24.99, HC, original graphic novel)

1-Rob Liefeld-s/a/c; Cable, Domino and X-Force app. 25.00

DEADPOOL: BAD BLOOD (Reprints original 2017 HC graphic novel)
Marvel Comics: Jun, 2022 - No. 4, Oct, 2022 ($3.99, limited series)

1-4-Rob Liefeld-s/a/c; Cable, Domino and X-Force app. 4.00

DEADPOOL: BADDER BLOOD
Marvel Comics: Aug, 2023 - No. 5, Dec, 2023 ($4.99, limited series)

1-5-Rob Liefeld-s/a/c; Cable and Wolverine app. 5.00

DEADPOOL: BLACK, WHITE & BLOOD
Marvel Comics: Oct, 2021 - No. 4, Jan, 2022 ($4.99, B&W&red anthology)

1-4: 1-Noto, Stokoe, Portacio-a. 3-Baruchel-s/Medina-a; Sakai-s/a. 4-Allred-s/a 5.00

DEADPOOL: DRACULA'S GAUNTLET (Printing of Marvel digital comic mini-series)
Marvel Comics: Sept, 2014 - No. 7, Oct, 2014 ($3.99, weekly limited series)

1-7-Duggan & Posehn-s; Deadpool meets Shiklah. 2,3,6-Blade app. 4-Frightful Four app. 4.00

DEADPOOL CORPS (Continues from Prelude to Deadpool Corps series)
Marvel Comics: Jun, 2010 - No. 12, May, 2011 ($3.99/$2.99)

1-($3.99) Liefeld-a/c; Gischler-s; 2 covers by Liefeld	1	2	3	5	6	8

2-12-($2.99) 2-5,7,9-Liefeld-a. 6-Mychaels-a 3.00
...: Rank and Foul 1 (5/10, $3.99) Handbook-style profile pages of allies and enemies 4.00

DEADPOOL KILLS DEADPOOL
Marvel Comics: Sept, 2013 - No. 4, Dec, 2013 ($2.99, limited series)

1-Bunn-s/Espin-a; Deadpool Corps app.	1	2	3	5	6	8
2-4						3.00

DEADPOOL KILLS THE MARVEL UNIVERSE
Marvel Comics: Oct, 2012 - No. 4, Oct, 2012 ($2.99, weekly limited series)

1-Bunn-s/Talajic-a/Andrews-c	3	6	9	19	30	40
2-4	2	4	6	8	10	12

DEADPOOL KILLS THE MARVEL UNIVERSE AGAIN
Marvel Comics: Sept, 2017 - No. 5, Nov, 2017 ($3.99, limited series)

1-5-Bunn-s/Talajic-a/Johnson-c. 3-Gwenpool app. 1,5-Red Skull app. 4.00

DEADPOOL KILLUSTRATED
Marvel Comics: Mar, 2013 - No. 4, Jun, 2013 ($2.99, limited series)

1-Bunn-s/Lolli-a/Del Mundo-c; stories/covers styled like Classics Illustrated

		1	2	3	5	6	8
2-4							4.00

DEADPOOL MAX
Marvel Comics (MAX): Dec, 2010 - No. 12, Nov, 2011 ($3.99)

1-12: 1-8,10-12-David Lapham-s/Kyle Baker-a/c. 6,7-Domino app. 9-Crystal-a 4.00
...X-Mas Special 1 (2/12, $4.99) Lapham-s; art by Lapham, Baker & Crystal; Baker-c 4.00

DEADPOOL MAX 2
Marvel Comics (MAX): Dec, 2011 - No. 6, May, 2012 ($3.99)

1-6: 1,2-David Lapham-s/Kyle Baker-a/c. 3-Crystal-a 4.00

DEADPOOL: MERC WITH A MOUTH
Marvel Comics: Sept, 2009 - No. 13, Sept, 2010 ($3.99/$2.99)

1-($3.99) Suydam-c/Dazo-a; Zombie-head Deadpool & Ka-Zar app.; r/Deadpool #4 ('97)	2	4	6	10	14	18

2-6,8-12-($2.99) Suydam-c on all. 8-Deadpool goes to Zombie dimension 4.00
7-($3.99) Covers by Suydam & Liefeld; art by Liefeld, Baker, Pastoras, Dazo;

1st app. Lady Deadpool	4	8	12	28	47	65
13-($3.99) Silence of the Lambs-c	2	4	6	11	16	20

DEADPOOL PULP
Marvel Comics: Nov, 2010 - No. 4, Feb, 2011 ($3.99, limited series)

1-4-Alternate Deadpool in 1955; Glass & Benson-s/Laurence Campbell-a/Jae Lee-c 4.00

DEADPOOL'S ART OF WAR
Marvel Comics: Dec, 2014 - No. 4, Mar, 2015 ($3.99, limited series)

1-4-David-s/Koblish-a; Loki and Thor app. 4.00

DEADPOOL'S SECRET SECRET WARS (Secret Wars tie-in)
Marvel Comics: Jul, 2015 - No. 4, Oct, 2015 ($4.99/$3.99, limited series)

1-($4.99) Deadpool inserts himself into the 1984 Secret Wars; Bunn-s/Harris-c 5.00
2-4-($3.99) Spider-Man, Avengers & X-Men app. 3-Black costume created 4.00
2-Gwenpool variant-c by Bachalo; 1st app. of Gwenpool 20.00

DEADPOOL: SUICIDE KINGS
Marvel Comics: Jun, 2009 - No. 5, Oct, 2009 ($3.99, limited series)

1-Barberi-a; Punisher, Daredevil, & Spider-Man app.	2	4	6		10	12
2-5						5.00

DEADPOOL TEAM-UP
Marvel Comics: No. 899, Jan, 2010 - No. 883, May, 2011 ($2.99, numbering runs in reverse)

899-883: 899-Hercules app.; Ramos-c. 897-Ghost Rider app. 894-Franken-Castle app.
  887-Thor app. 883-Galactus & Silver Surfer app. 3.00

DEADPOOL: THE CIRCLE CHASE (See New Mutants #98)
Marvel Comics: Aug, 1993 - No. 4, Nov, 1993 ($2.00, limited series)

1-($2.50)-Embossed-c	3	6	9	16	24	32
2-4	1	3	4	6	8	10

DEADPOOL: THE DUCK
Marvel Comics: Mar, 2017 - No. 5, May, 2017 ($3.99, limited series)

1-5-Deadpool & Howard the Duck merge; Rocket Raccoon app.; Camagni-a 4.00

DEADPOOL: TOO SOON
Marvel Comics: Dec, 2016 - No. 4, Mar, 2017 ($4.99, limited series)

1-4-Corin-s/Nauck-a; Squirrel Girl, Howard the Duck, Punisher, Forbush Man app. 5.00

DEADPOOL V GAMBIT
Marvel Comics: Aug, 2016 - No. 5, Nov, 2016 ($3.99, limited series)

1-5-Acker & Blacker-s/Beyruth-s. 1-Spider-Man & Daredevil app. 4.00

DEADPOOL VS. CARNAGE
Marvel Comics: Jun, 2014 - No. 4, Aug, 2014 ($3.99, limited series)

1-Bunn-s/Espin-a/Fabry-c	2	4	6	8	10	12

Deadpool (2016 series) #36 © MAR

Deadpool Max #2 © MAR

Dear Lonely Heart #2 © CM

	GD 2.0	VG 4.0	FN 6.0	VF 8.0	VF/NM 9.0	NM- 9.2
2-4						6.00

DEADPOOL VS. OLD MAN LOGAN
Marvel Comics: Dec, 2017 - No. 5, Apr, 2018 ($3.99, limited series)

	GD 2.0	VG 4.0	FN 6.0	VF 8.0	VF/NM 9.0	NM- 9.2
1-5-Declan Shalvey-s/Mike Henderson-a						4.00

DEADPOOL VS. THANOS
Marvel Comics: Nov, 2015 - No. 4, Dec, 2015 ($3.99, limited series)

1-4-Seeley-s/Bondoc-a; Death app. 2-Guardians of the Galaxy app.						4.00

DEADPOOL VS. THE PUNISHER
Marvel Comics: Jun, 2017 - No. 5, Aug, 2017 ($3.99, limited series)

1-5-Van Lente-s/Pere Pérez-a/Shalvey-c						4.00

DEADPOOL VS. X-FORCE
Marvel Comics: Sept, 2014 - No. 4, Nov, 2014 ($3.99, limited series)

1-4-Swierczynski-s/Larraz-a/Shane Davis-c						4.00

DEADPOOL: WADE WILSON'S WAR
Marvel Comics: Aug, 2010 - No. 4, Nov, 2010 ($3.99, limited series)

1-4-Swierczynski-s/Pearson-a/c; Bullseye, Domino & Silver Sable app.						4.00

DEAD RABBIT (Issues recalled due to trademark dispute, cancelled after #2)(See Dead Eyes)
Image Comics: Oct, 2018 - No. 2, Nov, 2018 ($3.99)

1-Duggan-s/McCrea-a						6.00
2-Bonus preview of Self/Made #1						4.00

DEAD RIDER (See Deadlander)

DEAD ROMANS
Image Comics (Shadowline): Mar, 2023 - No. 6, Aug, 2023 ($3.99, limited series)

1-6-Fred Kennedy-s/Nick Marinkovich-a						4.00

DEAD ROMEO
DC Comics: June, 2009 - No. 6, Nov, 2009 ($2.99, limited series)

1-6-Ryan Benjamin-a/Jesse Snider-s						3.00
TPB (2010, $19.99) r/#1-6; cover gallery						20.00

DEAD, SHE SAID
IDW Publishing: May, 2008 - No. 3, Sept, 2008 ($3.99, limited series)

1-3-Bernie Wrightson-a/Steve Niles-s						4.00

DEADSHOT (See Batman #59, Detective Comics #474, & Showcase '93 #8)
DC Comics: Nov, 1988 - No. 4, Feb, 1989 ($1.00, limited series)

1-Ostrander & Yale-s/Luke McDonnell-a	1	2	3	5	6	8
2-4						5.00

DEADSHOT
DC Comics: Feb, 2005 - No. 5, June 2005 ($2.95, limited series)

1-5-Zeck-c/Gage-s/Cummings-a. 3-Green Arrow app.						4.00

DEAD SPACE (Based on the Electronics Arts videogame)
Image Comics: Mar, 2008 - No. 6, Sept, 2008 ($2.99, limited series)

1-6-Templesmith-a/Johnston-s						3.00
... Extraction (9/09, $3.50) Templesmith-a/Johnston-s						3.50

DEAD VENGEANCE
Dark Horse Comics: Oct, 2015 - No. 4, Jan, 2016 ($3.99, limited series)

1-4-Bill Morrison-s. 1-Morrison-a. 2-4-Tone Rodriguez-a						4.00

DEAD WHO WALK, THE (See Strange Mysteries-Super Reprint #15,16 {1963-64})
Realistic Comics: 1952 (one-shot)

nn	168	336	504	1075	1838	2600

DEADWORLD (Also see The Realm)
Arrow Comics/Caliber Comics: Dec, 1986 - No. 26 ($1.50/$1.95/#15-28: $2.50, B&W)

1-4						4.00
5-26-Graphic cover version						4.00
5-26-Tame cover version						3.00
...Archives 1-3 (1992, $2.50)						3.00

DEAD X-MEN
Marvel Comics: Mar, 2024 - Present ($4.99/$3.99)

1-($4.99) Foxe-s/Scharf & Chang-a; Jubilee, Dazzler & Cannonball app.						5.00
2-($3.99)						4.00

DEAN KOONTZ'S FRANKENSTEIN: STORM SURGE
Dynamite Entertainment: 2015 - No. 6, 2016 ($3.99)

1-6-Chuck Dixon-s/Andres Ponce-a						4.00

DEAN MARTIN & JERRY LEWIS (See Adventures of...)

DEAR BEATRICE FAIRFAX

Best/Standard Comics (King Features): No. 5, Nov, 1950 - No. 9, Sept, 1951 (Vern Greene art)

	GD 2.0	VG 4.0	FN 6.0	VF 8.0	VF/NM 9.0	NM- 9.2
5-All have Schomburg air brush-c	22	44	66	132	216	300
6-9	15	30	45	90	140	190

DEAR HEART (Formerly Lonely Heart)
Ajax: No. 15, July, 1956 - No. 16, Sept, 1956

15,16	13	26	39	74	105	135

DEAR LONELY HEART (...Illustrated No. 1-6)
Artful Publications: Mar, 1951; No. 2, Oct, 1951 - No. 8, Oct, 1952

1	27	54	81	158	259	360
2	15	30	45	86	133	180
3-Matt Baker Jungle Girl story	34	68	102	204	332	460
4-8	14	28	42	81	118	155

DEAR LONELY HEARTS (Lonely Heart #9 on)
Harwell Publ./Mystery Publ. Co. (Comic Media): Aug, 1953 -No. 8, Oct, 1954

1	20	40	60	117	189	260
2-8	15	30	45	84	127	170

DEARLY BELOVED
Ziff-Davis Publishing Co.: Fall, 1952

1-Photo-c	24	48	72	142	234	325

DEAR NANCY PARKER
Gold Key: June, 1963 - No. 2, Sept, 1963

1-Painted-c on both	4	8	12	27	44	60
3	3	6	9	17	26	35

DEATH, THE ABSOLUTE... (From Neil Gaiman's Sandman titles)
DC Comics (Vertigo): 2009 ($99.99, oversized hardcover in slipcase)

nn-Reprints 1st app. in Sandman #8, Sandman #20, Death: The High Cost of Living #1-3, Death: the Time of Your Life #1-3, Death Talks About Life; short stories and pin-ups; merchandise pics; script and sketch art for Sandman #8; Gaiman afterword						100.00

DEATH: AT DEATH'S DOOR (See Sandman: The Season of Mists)
DC Comics (Vertigo): 2003 ($9.95, graphic novel one-shot, B&W, 7-1/2" x 5")

1-Jill Thompson-s/a/c; manga-style; Morpheus and the Endless app.						10.00

DEATHBED
DC Comics (Vertigo): Apr, 2018 - No. 6, Sept, 2018 ($3.99)

1-6-Joshua Williamson-s/Riley Rossmo-a						4.00

DEATH BE DAMNED
BOOM! Studios: Feb, 2017 - No. 4, May, 2017 ($3.99, limited series)

1-4-Ben Acker, Ben Blacker & Andrew Miller-s/Hannah Christenson-a						4.00

DEATHBLOW (Also see Batman/Deathblow and Darker Image)
Image Comics (WildStorm Productions): May (Apr. inside), 1993 - No. 29, Aug, 1996 ($1.75/$1.95/$2.50)

0-(8/96, $2.95, 32 pgs.)-r/Darker Image w/new story & art; Jim Lee & Trevor Scott-a; new Jim Lee-c						4.00
1-($2.50)-Red foil stamped logo on black varnish-c; Jim Lee-c/a; flip-book side has Cybernary -c/story (#2 also)						4.00
1-($1.95)-Newsstand version w/o foil-c & varnish						3.00
2-29: 2-(8/93)-Lee-a; with bound-in poster. 2-($1.75)-Newsstand version w/o poster. 4-Jim Lee-c/Tim Sale-a begin. 13-W/pinup poster by Tim Sale & Jim Lee. 16-($1.95 Newsstand & $2.50 Direct Market editions)-Wildstorm Rising Pt. 6. 17-Variant "Chicago Comicon" edition exists. 20,21-Gen 13 app. 23-Backlash-c/app. 24,25-Grifter-c/app; Gen 13 & Dane from Wetworks app. 28-Deathblow dies. 29-Memorial issue						3.00
5-Alternate Portacio-c (Forms larger picture when combined with alternate-c for Gen 13 #5, Kindred #3, Stormwatch #10, Team 7 #1, Union #0, Wetworks #2 & WildC.A.T.S #11)						6.00
...Sinners and Saints TPB ('99, $19.95) r/#1-12; Sale-c						20.00

DEATHBLOW (Volume 2)
DC Comics (WildStorm): Dec, 2006 - No. 9, Apr, 2008 ($2.99)

1-9: 1-Azzarello-s/D'Anda-a; two covers by D'Anda & Platt						3.00
...: And Then You Live! TPB (2008, $19.99) r/#1-9						20.00

DEATHBLOW BY BLOWS
DC Comics (WildStorm): Nov, 1999 - No. 3, Jan, 2000 ($2.95, limited series)

1-3-Alan Moore-s/Jim Baikie-a						4.00

DEATHBLOW/WOLVERINE
Image Comics (WildStorm Productions)/ Marvel Comics: Sept, 1996 - No. 2, Feb, 1997 ($2.50, limited series)

1,2: Wiesenfeld-s/Bennett-a						4.00

	GD	VG	FN	VF	VF/NM	NM-
	2.0	4.0	6.0	8.0	9.0	9.2

TPB (1997, $8.95) r/#1,2 .... 9.00

DEATH DEALER (Also see Frank Frazetta's...)
Verotik: July, 1995 - No. 4, July, 1997 ($5.95)

1-Frazetta-c; Bisley-a	3	6	9	16	23	30
1-2nd print, 2-4-($6.95)-Frazetta-c; embossed logo	1	2	3	4	5	7

DEATH-DEFYING 'DEVIL, THE (Also see Project Superpowers)
Dynamite Entertainment: 2008 - No. 4, 2009 ($3.50, limited series)

1-4-Casey & Ross-s/Salazar-a; multiple covers; the Dragon app. 3.50

DEATH-DEFYING 'DEVIL (Volume 2)
Dynamite Entertainment: 2019 - No. 5, 2020 ($3.99, limited series)

1-5-Gail Simone-s/Walter Giovani-a; multiple covers 4.00

DEATH-DEFYING DOCTOR MIRAGE, THE
Valiant Entertainment: Sept, 2014 - No. 5, Jan, 2015 ($3.99, limited series)

1-5-Van Meter-s/de la Torre-a. 1-3-Foreman-c. 4,5-Wada-c 4.00

DEATH-DEFYING DOCTOR MIRAGE, THE: SECOND LIVES
Valiant Entertainment: Dec, 2015 - No. 4, Mar, 2016 ($3.99, limited series)

1-4-Van Meter-s/de La Torre-a 4.00

DEATH HEAD
Dark Horse Comics: Jul, 2015 - No. 6, Feb, 2016 ($3.99, limited series)

1-6-Zach & Nick Keller-s/Joanna Estep-a 4.00

DEATH, JR.
Image Comics: Apr, 2005 - No. 3, Aug, 2005 ($4.99, squarebound, limited series)

1-3-Gary Whitta-s/Ted Naifeh-a	5.00
Vol. 1 TPB (2005, $14.99) r/series; concept and promotional art	15.00

DEATH, JR. (Volume 2)
Image Comics: Jul, 2006 - No. 3, May, 2007 ($4.99, squarebound, limited series)

1-3-Gary Whitta-s/Ted Naifeh-a. 1-Dan Brereton-c	5.00
... Halloween Special (10/06, 8-1/2"x 5-1/2", Halloween giveaway) Guy Davis-a	3.00
Vol. 2 TPB (2007, $14.99) r/series; Halloween story w/Guy Davis-a; promotional art	15.00

DEATHLOK (Also see Astonishing Tales #25)
Marvel Comics: July, 1990 - No. 4, Oct, 1990 ($3.95, 52 pgs.)

1-4: 1,2-Guice-a(p). 3,4-Denys Cowan-a, c-4 .... 5.00

DEATHLOK
Marvel Comics: July, 1991 - No. 34, Apr, 1994 ($1.75)

1-Silver ink cover; Denys Cowan-c/a(p) begins	1	3	4	6	8	10
2-18,20-24,26-34: 2-Forge (X-Men) app. 3-Vs. Dr. Doom. 5-X-Men & F.F. x-over.						
6,7-Punisher x-over. 9,10-Ghost Rider-c/story. 16-Infinity War x-over. 17-Jae Lee-c.						
22-Black Panther app. 27-Siege app.						4.00
19-($2.25)-Foil-c						5.00
25-($2.95, 52 pgs.)-Holo-grafx foil-c						5.00
Annual 1 (1992, $2.25, 68 pgs.)-Guice-p; Quesada-c(p)						5.00
Annual 2 (1993, $2.95, 68 pgs.)-Bagged w/card; intro Tracer						4.00

NOTE: *Denys Cowan a(p)-9-13, 15, Annual 1; c-9-12, 13p, 14. Guice/Cowan c-8.*

DEATHLOK
Marvel Comics: Sept, 1999 - No. 11, June, 2000 ($1.99)

1-11: 1-Casey-s/Manco-a. 2-Two covers. 4-Canete-a 4.00

DEATHLOK (...The Demolisher on cover)
Marvel Comics: Jan, 2010 - No. 7, Jul, 2010 ($3.99, limited series)

1-7-Huston-s/Medina-a/Peterson-c 4.00

DEATHLOK
Marvel Comics: Dec, 2014 - No. 10, Sept, 2015 ($3.99)

1-10: 1-Edmonson/Perkins-a; intro. Henry Hayes. 2-5,8-10-Domino app. 4.00

DEATHLOK SPECIAL
Marvel Comics: May, 1991 - No. 4, June, 1991 ($2.00, bi-weekly lim. series)

1-4: r/1-4(1990) w/new Guice-c #1,2; Cowan c-3,4	4.00
1-2nd printing w/white-c	4.00

DEATHMASK
Future Comics: Mar, 2003 - No. 3, June, 2003 ($2.99)

1-3-Giordano-a(p)/Michelinie & Layton-s 3.00

DEATHMATCH
BOOM! Studios: Dec, 2012 - No. 12, Nov, 2013 ($2.99)

1-($1.00) Jenkins-s/Magno-a; multiple covers	3.00
2-12 ($3.99) Multiple covers on each	4.00

DEATHMATE
Valiant (Prologue/Yellow/Blue)/Image Comics (Black/Red/Epilogue):
Sept, 1993 - Epilogue (#6), Feb, 1994 ($3.95/$4.95, limited series)

Preview-(Advance Comics ed., 7/93, 8 pgs.)	1	3	4	6	8	10
Preview-(Comic Defense System ed., 7/93, 8 pgs.)	1	3	4	6	8	10
Preview-(Previews orange ed., 8/93, 8 pgs.)	4	8	12	23	37	50
Preview-(Previews pink ed., 8/93, 8 pgs.)	2	4	6	10	14	18
Prologue (#1)–Silver foil; Jim Lee/Layton-c; B. Smith/Lee-a						4.00
Prologue–Special gold foil ed. of silver ed.	1	2	3	5	6	8
Black (#2)-(9/93, $4.95, 52 pgs.)-Silvestri/Jim Lee-c; pencils by Peterson/Silvestri/Capullo/						
Jim Lee/Portacio; 1st story app. Gen 13 telling their rebellion against the Troika						
(see WildC.A.T.S. Trilogy)	1	2	3	5	6	8
Black-Special gold foil edition	2	4	6	9	12	15
Yellow (#3)-(10/93, $4.95, 52 pgs.)-Yellow foil-c; Indicia says Prologue Sept 1993 by mistake;						
3rd app. Ninjak; Thibert-c(i)						5.00
Yellow-Special gold foil edition	1	2	3	5	6	8
Blue (#4)-(10/93, $4.95, 52 pgs.)-Thibert blue foil-c(i); Reese-a(i)						5.00
Blue-Special gold foil edition						6.00
Red (#5), Epilogue (#6)-(2/94, $2.95)-Silver foil Quesada/Silvestri-c; Silvestri-a(p)						4.00

DEATH METAL
Marvel Comics UK: Jan, 1994 - No. 4, Apr, 1994 ($1.95, limited series)

1-4: 1-Silver ink-c. Alpha Flight app. 4.00

DEATH METAL VS. GENETIX
Marvel Comics UK: Dec, 1993 - No. 2, Jan, 1994 (Limited series)

1-($2.95)-Polybagged w/2 trading cards	4.00
2-($2.50)-Polybagged w/2 trading cards	4.00

DEATH OF CAPTAIN MARVEL (See Marvel Graphic Novel #1)

DEATH OF DOCTOR STRANGE
Marvel Comics: Nov, 2021 - No. 5, Mar, 2022 ($4.99/$3.99, limited series)

1-($4.99) MacKay-s/Garbett-a; Strange murdered; replaced with temporal remnant	5.00
2-5-($3.99) 2-Clea & the Avengers app.; intro The Three Mothers	4.00
...: Avengers 1 (12/21, $4.99) Paknadel-s/Bodenheim-a	5.00
...: Blade 1 (2/22, $4.99) Lore-s/Burnett-a; Dracula app.	5.00
...: Bloodstone 1 (3/22, $4.99) Howard-s/Guara-a	5.00
...: Spider-Man 1 (1/22, $4.99) MacKay-s/Ferreira-a; Ben Reilly Spidey & Black Cat app.	5.00
...: White Fox 1 (1/22, $4.99) Alyssa Wong-s/Andie Tong & Luciano Vecchio-a	5.00
...: X-Men / Black Knight 1 (3/22, $4.99) Spurrier-s/Quinn-a; Rogue, Jean Grey, Synch app.	5.00

DEATH OF DRACULA
Marvel Comics: Aug, 2010 ($3.99, one shot)

1-Gischler-s/Camuncoli-a/c 4.00

DEATH OF HAWKMAN, THE
DC Comics: Dec, 2016 - No. 6, May, 2017 ($3.99, limited series)

1-6-Andreyko-s/Lopresti-a; Adam Strange app. 2-6-Despero app. 4.00

DEATH OF MR. MONSTER, THE (See Mr. Monster #8)

DEATH OF SUPERMAN (See Superman, 2nd Series)

DEATH OF SUPERMAN 30TH ANNIVERSARY SPECIAL, THE
DC Comics: Oct, 2022 ($10.99, square-bound, one-shot)

1-Four new stories by the creators of the original event; Doomsday app. 11.00

DEATH OF THE INHUMANS
Marvel Comics: Sept, 2018 - No. 5, Jan, 2019($4.99/$3.99, limited series)

1-($4.99) Cates-s/Olivetti-a; Vox app.	5.00
2-5-($3.99) Karnak app. 4-Beta Ray Bill app.	4.00

DEATH OF THE NEW GODS (Tie-in to the Countdown series)
DC Comics: Early Dec, 2007 - No. 8, Jun, 2008 ($3.50, limited series)

1-8-Jim Starlin-s/a/c. 1-Barda killed. 6-Orion dies. 7-Scott Free and Metron die	3.50
TPB (2009, $19.99) r/#1-8; Starlin intro.; cover gallery	20.00

DEATH OF THE VENOMVERSE (Also see Kid Venom: Origins #1)
Marvel Comics: Oct, 2023 - No. 5, Nov, 2023 ($3.99, limited series)

1-5-Bunn-s/Sandoval-a; Carnage vs. multiverse of Venoms. 2-5-Back-up with Kid Venom 5.00

DEATH OF WOLVERINE
Marvel Comics: Nov, 2014 - No. 4, Dec, 2014 ($4.99, limited series)

1-4-Soule-s/McNiven-a; multiple covers on each; bonus art & commentary in each	5.00
...: Deadpool & Captain America (12/14, $4.99) Duggan-s/Kolins-a	5.00
...: Life After Logan (1/15, $4.99) Short stories by various; Cyclops, Nightcrawler app.	5.00

DEATH OF WOLVERINE: THE LOGAN LEGACY (Continues in Wolverines #1)
Marvel Comics: Dec, 2014 - No. 7, Feb, 2015 ($3.99, bi-weekly limited series)

1-7: 1-Soule-s; X-23, Daken, Deathstrike, Mystique & Sabretooth app. 4.00

DEATH OF WOLVERINE: THE WEAPON X PROGRAM
Marvel Comics: Jan, 2015 - No. 5, Mar, 2015 ($3.99, bi-weekly limited series)

1-5-Soule-s. 1-3-Larroca-a. 3-Sabretooth app. 4.00

DEATH OF X (Leads into X-Men vs. Inhumans)
Marvel Comics: Oct, 2016 - No. 4, Jan, 2017 ($4.99/$3.99, limited series)

1-($4.99) Soule & Lemire-s; Kuder-a; X-Men, Inhumans & Hydra app.	5.00
2-4-($3.99) 2-Kuder-a. 3,4-Kuder & Garrón-a. 4-Death of Cyclops	4.00

DEATH ORB
Dark Horse Comics: Oct, 2018 - No. 5, Feb, 2019 ($3.99, limited series)

1-5-Ryan Ferrier-s/Alejandro Aragon-a 4.00

DEATH OR GLORY
Image Comics: May, 2018 - No. 11, Jul, 2020 ($4.99/$3.99)

1-Remender-s/Bengal-a; three covers by Bengal, Fegredo & Harren	5.00
2-11-($3.99) 2-Three covers. 3-11-Two covers	4.00

DEATH RACE 2020
Roger Corman's Cosmic Comics: Apr, 1995 - No. 8, Nov, 1995 ($2.50)

1-8: Sequel to the Movie 4.00

DEATH RATTLE (Formerly an Underground)
Kitchen Sink Press: Oct, 1985 - No. 18, 1988, 1994 ($1.95, Baxter paper, mature); V3#1, 11/95 - No. 5, 6/96 ($2.95, B&W)

V2#1-Corben-c	1	3	4	6	8	10
V2#2-7,9-18: 2-Unpubbed Spirit story by Eisner. 5-Robot Woman-r by Wolverton.						
6-B&W issues begin. 10-Savage World-r by by Williamson/Torres/Krenkel/Frazetta from						
Witzend #1. 16-Wolverton Spacehawk-r						5.00
8-(12/86)-1st app. Mark Schultz's Xenozoic Tales/Cadillacs & Dinosaurs						
	4	8	12	28	47	65
8-(1994)-r plus interview w/Mark Schultz						4.00
V3#1-5 ($2.95-c): 1-Mark Schultz-c						4.00

DEATH SENTENCE
Titan Comics: Nov, 2003 - No. 6, Apr, 2014 ($3.99)

1-6-Montynero-s/c; Dowling-a 4.00

DEATH SENTENCE LONDON
Titan Comics: Jun, 2015 - No. 6, Jan, 2016 ($3.99)

1-6-Montynero-s/c; Simmonds-a 4.00

DEATH'S HEAD (See Daredevil #56, Dragon's Claws #5 & Incomplete...)(See Amazing Fantasy (2004) for Death's Head 3.0)
Marvel Comics: Dec, 1988 - No. 10, Sept, 1989 ($1.75)

1-Dragon's Claws spin-off	4.00
2-Fantastic Four app.; Dragon's Claws x-over	4.00

Death Dealer #1 © Frazetta

Deathstroke (2016 series) #30 © DC

Death Vigil #1 © Stjepan Sejic

	GD	VG	FN	VF	VF/NM	NM-
	2.0	4.0	6.0	8.0	9.0	9.2

3-10: 8-Dr. Who app. 9-F. F. x-over; Simonson-c(p)   4.00

DEATH'S HEAD
Marvel Comics: Sept, 2019 - No. 4, Dec, 2019 ($3.99, limited series)
1-4-Tini Howard-s/Kei Zama-a; Wiccan, Hulkling & Hawkeye (Kate) app.   4.00

DEATH'S HEAD II (Also see Battletide)
Marvel Comics UK, Ltd.: Mar, 1992 - No. 4, June (May inside), 1992 ($1.75, color, lim. series)
1-4: 2-Fantastic Four app. 4-Punisher, Spider-Man, Daredevil, Dr. Strange, Capt. America
  & Wolverine in the year 2020   4.00
1,2-Silver ink 2nd printiings   4.00

DEATH'S HEAD II (Also see Battletide)
Marvel Comics UK, Ltd.: Dec, 1992 - No. 16, Mar, 1994 ($1.75/$1.95)
V2#1-13,15,16: 1-Gatefold-c. 1-4-X-men app. 15-Capt. America & Wolverine app.   4.00
V2# 14-($2.95)-Foil flip-c w/Death's Head II Gold #0   4.00
...Gold 1 (1/94, $3.95, 68 pgs.)-Gold foil-c   4.00

DEATH'S HEAD II & THE ORIGIN OF DIE CUT
Marvel Comics UK, Ltd.: Aug, 1993 - No. 2, Sept, 1993 (limited series)
1-($2.95)-Embossed-c   5.00
2 ($1.75)   4.00

DEATHSTROKE (DC New 52)
DC Comics: Nov, 2011 - No. 20, Jul, 2013 ($2.99)
1-Higgins-s/Bennett/Bisley-c   6.00
2-20: 4-Blackhawks app. 9-12-Liefeld-s/a/c; Lobo app.   3.00
#0 (11/12, $2.99) Origin story, Team 7 app.; Liefeld-s/a/c   3.00

DEATHSTROKE (DC New 52)
DC Comics: Dec, 2014 - No. 20, Sept, 2016 ($2.99)
1-20: 1-Tony Daniel-s/a; I Ching app. 3-6-Harley Quinn app. 7-10-Wonder Woman app.
11-13-Harley Quinn & Suicide Squad app.   3.00
Annual 1 (9/15, $4.99) Takes place between #8 & 9; Wonder Woman app.; Kirkham-a   5.00
Annual 1 (8/16, $4.99) Hester-s/Colak & Viacava-a   5.00

DEATHSTROKE (DC Rebirth)
DC Comics: Oct, 2016 - No. 50, Feb, 2020 ($2.99/$3.99)
1-19: 1-Priest-s/Pagulayan-a; Clock King app. 4,5-Batman & Robin (Damian) app.
8-Superman app. 11-The Creeper app.; Cowan & Sienkiewicz-a. 19-Lazarus Contract tie-in
  with Teen Titans and Titans   3.00
20-49-($3.99) The Defiance team forms; Terra app. 22-Dr. Light app. 32-35-Vs. Batman.
  37-40-Two-Face app. 42,43-Crossover with Teen Titans #28-30. 44-Funeral   4.00
50-($4.99) Pagulayan & Pasarin-a; Raven app.   5.00
Annual 1 (3/18, $4.99) Priest/Cowan & Sienkiewicz-a; Power Girl app.   5.00
... Rebirth 1 (10/16, $2.99) Priest-s/Pagulayan-a; Clock King app.   3.00
.../ Yogi Bear Special 1 (12/18, $4.99) Texeira-a; Kirkham-c; Secret Squirrel back-up   5.00

DEATHSTROKE INC.
DC Comics: Nov, 2021 - No. 15, Jan, 2023 ($3.99)
1-15: 1-Black Canary app.; Williamson-s/Porter-a. 10-Year One begins   4.00

DEATHSTROKE: THE TERMINATOR (Deathstroke: The Hunted #0-47; Deathstroke #48-60)
(Also see Marvel & DC Present, New Teen Titans #2, New Titans, Showcase '93 #7,9 & Tales of
the Teen Titans #42-44)
DC Comics: Aug, 1991 - No. 60, June, 1996 ($1.75-$2.25)

1-New Titans spin-off; Mike Zeck c-1-28	3	6	9	16	23	30
1-Gold ink 2nd printing ($1.75)	2	4	6	9	12	15
2						5.00

3-49,51-60: 6,8-Batman cameo. 7,9-Batman-c/story. 9-1st brief app. new Vigilante (female).
  10-1st full app. new Vigilante; Perez-i. 13-Vs. Justice League; Team Titans cameo on last pg.
  14-Total Chaos, part 1; story cont'd in New Titans #90. 15-1st app. Rose Wilson   4.00
50 ($3.50)   5.00
#0-(10/94) Zero Hour; begin Deathstroke, The Hunted; released between #40&41   4.00
Annual 1-4 ('92-'95, 68 pgs.): 1-Nightwing & Vigilante app. 2-Bloodlines
  Deathstorm; 1st app. Gunfire. 3-Elseworlds story. 4-Year One story   5.00
NOTE: *Golden* a-12. *Perez* a-11i. *Zeck* c-Annual 1, 2.

DEATH: THE HIGH COST OF LIVING (See Sandman #8) (Also see the Books of Magic
limited & ongoing series)
DC Comics (Vertigo): Mar, 1993 - No. 3, May, 1993 ($1.95, limited series)
1-Bachalo/Buckingham-a; Dave McKean-c; Neil Gaiman scripts in all

	1	2	3	5	6	8
1-Platinum edition	4	8	12	27	44	60

2   4.00
3-Pgs. 19 & 20 had wrong placement   4.00
3-Corrected version w/pgs. 19 & 20 facing each other   4.00
Death Talks About Life-giveaway about AIDS prevention   5.00
Hardcover (1994, $19.95)-r/#1-3 & Death Talks About Life; intro. by Tori Amos   20.00

Trade paperback (6/94, $12.95, Titan Books)-r/#1-3 & Death Talks About Life; prism-c   13.00

DEATH: THE TIME OF YOUR LIFE (See Sandman #8)
DC Comics (Vertigo): Apr, 1996 - No. 3, July, 1996 ($2.95, limited series)
1-3: Neil Gaiman story & Bachalo/Buckingham-a; Dave McKean-c. 2-(5/96)   4.00
Hardcover (1997, $19.95)-r/#1-3 w/3 new pages & gallery art by various   20.00
TPB (1997, $12.95)-r/#1-3 & Visions of Death gallery; Intro. by Claire Danes   13.00

DEATH 3
Marvel Comics UK: Sept, 1993 - No. 4, Dec, 1993 ($1.75, limited series)
1-($2.95)-Embossed-c   5.00
2-4   4.00

DEATH TO THE ARMY OF DARKNESS
Dynamite Entertainment: 2020 - No. 5, 2020 ($3.99, limited series)
1-5-Ryan Parrott-s/Jacob Edgar-a; intro. Lady Ash, dog Ash, skeleton Ash, mini Ash   4.00

DEATH VALLEY (Cowboys and Indians)
Comic Media: Oct, 1953 - No. 6, Aug, 1954

1-Billy the Kid; Morisi-a; Andru/Esposito-c/a	32	64	96	188	307	425
2-Don Heck-c	19	38	57	111	176	240
3-6,Morisi-a. 5-Discount-a	16	32	48	94	147	200

DEATH VALLEY (Becomes Frontier Scout, Daniel Boone No.10-13)
Charlton Comics: No. 7, 6/55 - No. 9, 10/55 (Cont'd from Comic Media series)

7-9-Wolverton-a (half pg.)	14	28	42	81	118	155

DEATH VIGIL
Image Comics (Top Cow): Jul, 2014 - No. 8, Sept, 2015 ($3.99)
1-8-Stjepan Sejic-s/a/c   4.00

DEATHWISH
DC Comics (Milestone Media): Dec, 1994 - No. 4, Mar, 1995 ($2.50, lim. series)
1-4   4.00

DEATH WRECK
Marvel Comics UK: Jan, 1994 - No. 4, Apr, 1994 ($1.95, limited series)
1-4: 1-Metallic ink logo; Death's Head II app.   4.00

DEBBIE DEAN, CAREER GIRL
Civil Service Publ.: April, 1945 - No. 2, July, 1945

1,2-Newspaper reprints by Bert Whitman	26	52	78	154	252	350

DEBBI'S DATES (Also see Date With Debbi)
National Periodical Publications: Apr-May, 1969 - No. 11, Dec-Jan, 1970-71

1	9	18	27	59	117	175
2,3,5,7-11: 2-Last 12¢ issue	5	10	15	30	50	70
4-Neal Adams text illo	5	10	15	33	57	80
6-Superman cameo	6	12	18	41	76	110

DECADE OF DARK HORSE, A
Dark Horse Comics: Jul, 1996 - No. 4, Oct, 1996 ($2.95, B&W/color, lim. series)
1-4: 1-Sin City-c/story by Miller; Grendel by Wagner; Predator. 2-Star Wars wraparound-c.
  3-Aliens-c/story; Nexus, Mask stories   6.00

DECAPITATOR (Randy Bowen's...)
Dark Horse Comics: Jun, 1998 - No. 4, ($2.95)
1-4-Bowen-s/art by various. 1-Mahnke-c. 3-Jones-c   4.00

DECEPTION, THE
Image Comics (Flypaper Press): 1999 - No. 3, 1999 ($2.95, B&W, mini-series)
1-3-Horley painted-c   4.00

DECIMATION: THE HOUSE OF M
Marvel Comics: Jan, 2006 ($3.99)
... - The Day After (one-shot) Claremont-s/Green-a   4.00

DECISION 2012 (Biographies of the main 2012 presidential candidates)
BOOM! Studios: Nov, 2011 ($3.99, series of one-shots)

...: Barack Obama 1 (11/11, $3.99) biography; Damian Couceiro-a; 2 covers	1	2	3	5	6	8
...: Michelle Bachman 1 (11/11) biography; Aaron McConnell-a; 2 covers						4.00
...: Ron Paul 1 (11/11) biography; Dean Kotz-a; 2 covers						4.00
...: Sarah Palin 1 (11/11) biography; Damian Couceiro-a; 2 covers						4.00

DECORUM
Image Comics: Mar, 2020 - No. 8, Nov, 2021 ($4.99/$3.99)
1,5,8-($4.99): 1-Hickman-s/Huddleston-a. 8-Squarebound w/wraparoiund-c   5.00
2-4,6,7-($3.99)   4.00

DEEP, THE (Movie)

	GD 2.0	VG 4.0	FN 6.0	VF 8.0	VF/NM 9.0	NM- 9.2

Marvel Comics Group: Nov, 1977 (Giant)

1-Infantino-c/a	2	4	6	8	11	14

DEEP BEYOND
Image Comics: Feb, 2021 - No. 12, Feb, 2022 ($3.99, limited series)

1-12-Andolfo & Goy-s/Broccardo-a ... 4.00

DEEP GRAVITY
Dark Horse Comics: Jul, 2014 - No. 4, Oct, 2014 ($3.99, limited series)

1-4-Hardman & Bechko-s/Baldó-a/Hardman-c ... 4.00

DEEP SLEEPER
Oni Press/Image Comics: Feb, 2004 - No. 4, Sept, 2004 ($3.50/$2.95, B&W, limited series)

1,2-(Oni Press, $3.50)-Hester-s/Huddleston-a ... 3.50
3,4-(Image Comics, $2.95) ... 3.00
... Omnibus (Image, 8/04, $5.95) r/#1,2 ... 6.00
... Vol. 1 TPB (2005, $12.95) r/#1-4; cover gallery ... 13.00

DEEP STATE
BOOM! Studios: Nov, 2014 - No. 8, Jul, 2015 ($3.99)

1-8-Justin Jordan-s/Ariela Kristantina-a ... 4.00

DEFCON 4
Image Comics (WildStorm Productions): Feb, 1996 - No. 4, Sept, 1996 ($2.50, lim. series)

1/2	1	2	3	5	7	9
1/2 Gold-(1000 printed)						14.00
1-Main Cover by Mat Broome & Edwin Rosell						4.00
1-Hordes of Cymulants variant-c by Michael Golden						5.00
1-Backs to the Wall variant-c by Humberto Ramos & Alex Garner						5.00
1-Defcon 4-Way variant-c by Jim Lee	1	2	3	4	5	7
2-4						4.00

DEFEND COMICS (The CBLDF Presents...)
Comic Book Legal Defense Fund: May, 2015 - Present (giveaway)

FCBD Edition - (5/15) Short stories incl. Kevin Keller, Beanworld; art by Liew, Parent ... 3.00
...: FCBD 2016 Edition - Short stories by various incl. James Kochalka; Craig Thompson-c ... 3.00
...: FCBD 2017 Edition - Short stories by various incl. Ryan North; Jeffrey Brown-c ... 3.00
...: FCBD 2018 Edition - Reading Without Walls ... 3.00
...: FCBD 2019 Edition - Short stories by various incl. Bill Griffith; Derek Charm-c ... 3.00

DEFENDERS, THE (TV)
Dell Publishing Co.: Sept-Nov, 1962 - No. 2, Feb-Apr, 1963

12-176-211(#1)	4	8	12	27	44	60
12-176-304(#2)	3	6	9	21	33	45

DEFENDERS, THE (Also see Giant-Size..., Marvel Feature, Marvel Treasury Edition, Secret Defenders & Sub-Mariner #34, 35; The New...#140-on)
Marvel Comics Group: Aug, 1972 - No. 152, Feb, 1986

1-Englehart-s/Sal Buscema-a begins; The Hulk, Doctor Strange, Sub-Mariner app.; last app. as Defenders in Marvel Feature #3; 1st Necrodamus; plot continued from Incredible Hulk #126; minor Omegatron app.

	17	34	51	117	259	400

2-Silver Surfer x-over; 1st Calizuma (a wizard in the service of the Nameless Ones)

	9	18	27	62	126	190

3,5: 3-Silver Surfer x-over; vs. The Nameless Ones; Barbara Norris app. from Incredible Hulk #126. 5-vs. The Omegatron (destroyed)

	5	10	15	34	60	85

4-Barbara Norris becomes the third incarnation of the Valkyrie (previously seen in Avengers #83 & Incredible Hulk #142); Enchantress, the Executioner & The Black Knight app. (turned to stone); Valkyrie joins the Defenders

	12	24	36	83	182	280

6,7: 6-Silver Surfer x-over. 7-Silver Surfer, Hawkeye app. vs. Red Ghost & Attuma

	4	8	12	23	37	50

8,9: 8-Silver Surfer & Hawkeye app. vs. Red Ghost & Attuma; 4-pg story begins "Avengers/Defenders War"; Dormammu & Loki team-up; story continues in Avengers #116. 9-Continued from Avengers #116; Iron Man vs. Hawkeye, Dr. Strange vs. Mantis; continued in Avengers #117.

	5	10	15	30	50	70

10-Hulk vs. Thor; continued in Avengers #118

	10	20	30	64	132	200

11-"Avengers/Defenders War" concludes; Silver Surfer, Black Knight & King Richard app.; last Englehart-s

	5	10	15	31	53	75

12-Last 20¢ issue; Wein-s begin; brief origin Valkyrie retold; vs. Xemnu the Titan; Defenders app. next in Giant-Size Defenders #1

	3	6	9	15	22	28

13,14: 13-Nighthawk app. vs. The Squadron Sinister (Hyperion, Dr. Spectrum & the Whizzer); 1st app. Nebulon the Celestial Man. 14-vs. The Squadron Sinister & Nebulon; Sub-Mariner leaves; Nighthawk joins

	3	6	9	17	26	35

15,16: 15-Magneto & Brotherhood of Evil Mutants app.; first Alpha the Ultimate Mutant; Professor X app. 16-Magneto & Brotherhood of Evil mutants turned into children; Defenders app. next in Giant-Size Defenders #2

	3	6	9	19	30	40

17-Power Man x-over (11/74); 1st app. of the Wrecking Crew (Thunderball, Bulldozer & Piledriver); Valkyrie leaves

	8	16	24	54	102	150

18-1st full app. of the Wrecking Crew

	7	14	21	46	86	125

19-20: 19-vs. the Wrecking Crew. 20-Continued from Marvel Two-in-one #7; Valkyrie returns (origin retold) 1st Gerber-s

	2	4	6	10	14	18

21-25: 21-1st Headmen (Chondu the Mystic, Dr. Arthur Nagan, Jerold Morgan); Valkyrie origin continued last issue; Hulk returns; story continued in Giant-Size Defenders #4. 22-25-vs. Sons of the Serpent. 23-Yellowjacket app. 24-25-Son of Satan, Daredevil, Yellowjacket & Power Man app.; story continues in Giant-Size Defenders #5; 25-1st app. "Elf with a gun"

	2	4	6	8	10	12

26-Continued from Giant-Size Defenders #5; Guardians of the Galaxy app. (pre-dates Marvel Presents #3); origin of Vance Astro; Killraven & Badoon x-over

	3	6	9	19	30	40

27-1st brief app. Starhawk (unnamed); Guardians of the Galaxy & Defenders vs. the Badoon

	3	6	9	12	27	40

28-1st full app. Starhawk; Guardians of the Galaxy & Badoon app.

	4	8	12	21	44	120

29-Starhawk joins the Guardians of the Galaxy; 1st app. Aleta (Starhawks wife); Guardians story continues in Marvel Presents #3

	2	4	6	9	30	40

30-Mantlo-s (fill-in issue)

	2	4	6	8	10	12

31-40: 31-Headman app. 32-Origin of Nighthawk; Headmen & Son of Satan app; 1st app. Ruby Thursday; 2nd app. "Elf with a gun". 33-Origin Nighthawk continued; return of Nebulon. 34-38-(Regular 25¢ editions). 34-vs. Nebulon. 35-1st new Red Guardian (Dr. Tania Belinsky); Headmen & Nebulon app. 36-Red Guardian & Plant Man app.

37-Power Man guest app.; vs. Plant Man, Eel & Porcupine; Nebulon app. 38-Power Man app.; vs. Eel & Porcupine; "Elf with a gun" app. 39-Power Man app. 40-1st new Valkyrie (gold) costume; "Elf with a gun" app.; story continued in Defenders Annual #1

	1	3	6	8		10

34-38-(30¢-c variants, limited distribution 4-8/76)

	5	10	15	30	50	70

41-46: 41-Last Gerber-s/Sal Buscema-a. 42,43-Egg Head, Rhino, Solarr & Cobalt Man app.; Giffen-a; 43-1st Red Rajah; Power Man app. 44-Power Man & Hellcat app. 45-Power Man & Hellcat app. 46-Dr. Strange & Red Guardian leave; "Elf with a gun" app.; vs. Scorpio

47-50-Moon Knight guest app. 47,48-Wonder Man app. 47-49-vs. Scorpio (Jacob Fury). 48-50-Death Scorpio; SHIELD app.

	1	2	3	5		8

48-52-(35¢-c variants, limited distribution)(6-10/77)

	8	16	24	57	96	140

51-60: 51,52-(Regular 30¢ editions). 51-Nighthawk vs. The Ringer. 52-Hulk vs. Sub-Mariner. 53-1st brief app. Lunatik (Lobo lookalike) created by Roger Slifer & Keith Giffen, six years before they create Lobo in Omega Men #3; 1st app. Sergie Krylov (The Presence). 54,55-vs. the Presence. 54-last Giffen-a. 55-Origin Red Guardian; Lunatik cameo. 56-Red Guardian leaves; Valkyrie vs. Lunatik. 57-Ms. Marvel (Carol Danvers) app. 58-60-Devil Slayer app.

	1	2	3	5		8

61-vs. Lunatik; Spider-Man app.

	1	2	3	5	6	8

62-"Defender for a day" issue; Jack of Hearts, Ms. Marvel (Carol Danvers) Hercules, Iron Man, White Tiger, Nova, Marvel Man (later Quasar), Son of Satan, Havok, Prowler, Paladin, Falcon, Torpedo, Black Goliath, Stingray, Polaris, Captain Ultra, Iron Fist, Captain Marvel (Mar-Vell), Tagak app. (all try to join Defenders)

	1	2	3	5		8

63-93,97-99: 63-Various villains form their own Defenders team. 64-Villains defeated; the various new Defenders leave. 66-68-Defenders in Asgard. 66-Hulk returns. 68-Hela app. 69-Omegatron app. 70-vs. Lunatik. 71-Origin Lunatik; Dr. Strange returns. 72,73-Lunatik app. 73-Foolkiller app. 74-Nighthawk resigns as leader; Foolkiller app. 75-vs. Foolkiller. 76-Wasp, Omega the Unknown & Ruby Thursday app. 77-Origin Omega the Unknown; Moondragon & Wasp app. 78-Original Defenders return (Hulk, Dr. Strange & Namor; continue thru #101); Wasp, Yellowjacket & Moondragon app. 79-Mandrill app. 81-Wasp & Yellowjacket app. 84-Atlantis vs. Wakanda; Namor vs. Black Panther. 85,86-Black Panther app. 87-Origin Hellcat retold. 90,91-vs. Mandrill; Daredevil app. 97,98-Devil Slayer & Man-Thing app. 98-Nighthawk leaves; Avengers app. 99-Mephisto app.

						5.00

94-1st Gargoyle (Isaac Christians)

	2	4	6	11	16	20

95,96: Ghost Rider app. 95-Dracula app.

						6.00

100-(52-pgs.)-Hellcat (Patsy Walker) revealed as Satan's daughter; Silver Surfer app.

	2	4	6	9	12	15

101-Silver Surfer app.

						6.00

102-111,115-119-124: 104-Beast joins. 105-Son of Satan joins; Mr. Fantastic app. 106-Captain America app.; death of Nighthawk. 107-Daredevil & Captain America app. 109-Spider-Man app.; Defenders app. next in Avengers Annual #11. 111-Overmind cameo. 120-122-Son of Satan-c/stories. 122-"Elf with a gun" returns; Silver Surfer & Iceman app. 123-"Elf with a Gun" app.; Moondragon cameo; 1st app. Cloud; Vision & Scarlet Witch app. 124-Origin of the "Elf with a gun"

						5.00

112-114-Overmind & Squadron Supreme app.

						5.00

125-(52 pgs)-Intro new Defenders (Angel, Beast, Iceman, Valkyrie, Gargoyle & Moondragon); Hulk, Dr. Strange, Namor & Silver Surfer app.; "Elf with a Gun" mystery resolved

						6.00

126-149,151: 126-130-Secret Empire story. 129-New Mutants cameo (3/84, early x-over). 134-1st full app. Manslaughter. 139-Odin app. 140-New Moondragon costume. 145-Johnny Blaze (Ghost Rider) app. 147-1st app. Interloper; Sgt. Fury app. 151-Manslaughter app.

						4.00

150-(52 pgs.)-Origin Cloud

						6.00

152-(52-pgs.)-Continued from Secret Wars II #7; Beyonder app.; vs. The Dragon of the Moon; leads into X-Factor #1

						6.00

Annual 1 (1976, 52 pgs.) Continued from Defenders #40; Power Man app.; vs. Nebulon, the Bozos and the Headmen

	3	6	9	22	35	45

...: Marvel Feature No. 1 Facsimile Edition (7/19, $4.99) r/Marvel Feature #1 w/orig. ads ... 5.00

NOTE: *Art Adams* c-142p. *Austin* a-53i; c-55i, 119i, 145i. *Frank Bolle* a-79, 10i, 11i. *Buckler* c(p)-34, 38, 76, 77, 79-86, 90, 91. *J. Buscema* c-66. *Giffen* a-42-49p, 50, 51-54p. *Golden* a-53p, 54p; c-94, 96. *Guice* c-129. *G. Kane* c(p)-13, 16, 18, 19, 21-26, 31-33, 35-37, 40, 41, 52, 55. *Kirby* c-42-45. *Mooney* a-3i, 31-34i, 62i, 63i, 85i. *Nasser* c-88p. *Perez* c(p)-51, 53, 54. *Rogers* c-89. *Starlin* c-91. *Tuska* a-57p. *Silver Surfer* in No. 2, 3, 5, 6, 8-11, 92, 98-101, 107, 112-115, 122-125.

DEFENDERS, THE (Volume 2) (Continues in The Order)
Marvel Comics: Mar, 2001 - No. 12, Feb, 2002 ($2.99/$2.25)

1-Busiek & Larsen-s/Larsen & Janson-a/c ... 3.00
2-11: 2-Two covers by Larsen & Art Adams; Valkyrie app. 4-Frenz-a ... 3.00
12-($3.50) 'Nuff Said issue; back-up-s Reis-a ... 4.00
...: From the Vault (9/11, $2.99) Previously unpublished story; Bagley-a ... 3.00

DEFENDERS, THE
Marvel Comics: Sept, 2005 - No. 5, Jan, 2006 ($2.99, limited series)

1-5-Giffen & DeMatteis-s/Maguire-a. 2-Dormammu app. ... 3.00
...: Indefensible HC (2006, $19.99, dust jacket) r/#1-5; Giffen & Maguire sketch page ... 20.00
...: Indefensible SC (2007, $13.99) r/#1-5; Giffen & Maguire sketch page ... 14.00

DEFENDERS, THE
Marvel Comics: Feb, 2012 - No. 12, Jan, 2013 ($3.99)

1-12: 1-Dr. Strange, Namor, Silver Surfer, Red She-Hulk, Iron Fist team; Dodson-a ... 4.00
...: Strange Heroes 1 (2/12, $4.99) Handbook-style profiles of team members and foes ... 5.00
...: The Coming of the Defenders 1 (2/12, $5.99) r/Marvel Feature #1-3; recolored-c of #1 ... 6.00
...: Tournament of Heroes 1 (3/12, $5.99) r/Defenders #62-65 (1978); recolored-c of #62 ... 6.00

DEFENDERS
Marvel Comics: Aug, 2017 - No. 10, Apr, 2018 ($4.99/$3.99)

1-($4.99) Luke Cage, Jessica Jones, Daredevil, Iron Fist team; Bendis-s/Marquez-a ... 5.00
2-10-($3.99) 3-Punisher app. 6-8-Deadpool app. ... 4.00

DEFENDERS
Marvel Comics: Oct, 2021 - No. 5, March, 2022 ($3.99)

1-5-Masked Raider, Dr. Strange, Silver Surfer, Harpy & Cloud team vs. Omnimax ... 4.00

DEFENDERS: BEYOND
Marvel Comics: Sept, 2022 - No. 5, Jan, 2023 ($3.99, limited series)

1-5-Loki, Blue Marvel, America Chavez, Tigra, Taaia team; Ewing-s/Rodriguez-a ... 4.00

DEFENDERS OF DYNATRON CITY
Marvel Comics: Feb, 1992 - No. 6, July, 1992 ($1.25, limited series)

1-6-Lucasarts characters. 2-Origin ... 4.00

Defenders (2017 series) #1 © MAR

Dejah of Mars #1 © ERB

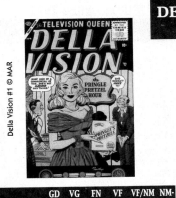

Della Vision #1 © MAR

	GD	VG	FN	VF	VF/NM	NM-		GD	VG	FN	VF	VF/NM	NM-
	2.0	4.0	6.0	8.0	9.0	9.2		2.0	4.0	6.0	8.0	9.0	9.2

DEFENDERS OF THE EARTH (TV)
Marvel Comics (Star Comics): Jan, 1987 - No. 4, July, 1987
  1-4: The Phantom, Mandrake The Magician, Flash Gordon begin. 3-Origin
    Phantom. 4-Origin Mandrake ... 4.00
DEFENDERS: THE BEST DEFENSE
Marvel Comics: Feb, 2019 ($4.99)
  1-Doctor Strange, Immortal Hulk, Silver Surfer, Namor app.; Ewing-s/Bennett-a ... 5.00
DEFEX
Devil's Due Publ.: Oct, 2004 - No. 6, Apr, 2005 ($2.95)
  1-6: 1-Wolfman-s/Caselli-a. 6-Pérez-c ... 3.00
DEFIANCE
Image Comics: Feb, 2002 - No. 8, Jun, 2003 ($2.95)
  Preview Edition (12/01) ... 3.00
  1-8-Barré-s/Kang & Suh-a ... 3.00
DEFINITIVE DIRECTORY OF THE DC UNIVERSE, THE (See Who's Who...)
DEJAH OF MARS (Warlord of Mars)
Dynamite Entertainment: 2014 - No. 4, 2014 ($3.99)
  1-4-Rahner-s/Morales-a; multiple covers on each ... 4.00
DEJAH THORIS (Warlord of Mars)
Dynamite Entertainment: 2016 - No. 6, 2016 ($3.99)
  1-6-Barbarie-s/Manna-a; multiple covers ... 4.00
DEJAH THORIS AND THE GREEN MEN OF MARS (Warlord of Mars)
Dynamite Entertainment: 2013 - No. 12, 2014 ($3.99)
  1-12: 1-8-Rahner-s/Antonio-a; multiple covers on each. 9-12-Morales-a ... 4.00
DEJAH THORIS AND THE WHITE APES OF MARS (Warlord of Mars)
Dynamite Entertainment: 2012 - No. 3, 2012 ($3.99)
  1-3-Rahner-s/Antonio-a; 2 covers by Peterson & Garza ... 4.00
DEJAH THORIS VERSUS JOHN CARTER
Dynamite Entertainment: 2021 - No. 6, 2021 ($3.99, limited series)
  1-6-Abnett-s/Miracolo-a; multple covers on each ... 4.00
DEJAH THORIS, VOLUME 2
Dynamite Entertainment: No. 0, 2018 - No. 10, 2018 ($3.99)
  0-(25¢-c) Amy Chu-s/Pasquale Qualano-a; multiple covers ... 3.00
  1-10-($3.99) Chu-s/Qualano-a; multiple covers ... 4.00
DEJAH THORIS, VOLUME 3 (Leads into Dejah Thoris Versus John Carter)
Dynamite Entertainment: 2019 - No. 12, 2021 ($3.99)
  1-12: 1-6-Dan Abnett-s/Vasco Georgiev-a; multiple covers on each. 7-10-Piriz-a ... 4.00
  ...: Fairy Tales 1 (2022, $4.99) Ron Marz-s/Andres Labrada-a; Snow White homage ... 5.00
  ...: Winter's End 1 (2021, $4.99) Short stories of Dejah Thoris and John Carter ... 5.00
DEJAH THORIS, VOLUME 4
Dynamite Entertainment: 2023 - No. 6, 2023 ($3.99)
  1-6-Chuck Brown-s/Emiliana Pinna-a; multiple covers ... 4.00
DELECTA OF THE PLANETS (See Don Fortune & Fawcett Miniatures)
DELETE
1First Comics: 2016 - No. 4, 2016 ($4.99, limited series)
  1-4-Palmiotti & Gray-s/Timms-a/Conner-c ... 5.00
DELICATE CREATURES
Image Comics (Top Cow): 2001 ($16.95, hardcover with dust jacket)
  nn-Fairy tale storybook; J. Michael Straczynski-s; Michael Zulli-a ... 17.00
DELINQUENTS
Valiant Entertainment: Aug, 2014 - No. 4, Nov, 2014 ($3.99, limited series)
  1-4-Quantum & Woody meet Archer & Armstrong; Asmus & Van Lente-s/Kano-a ... 4.00
DELIRIUM'S PARTY: A LITTLE ENDLESS STORYBOOK (Characters from The Sandman titles and The Little Endless Storybook)
DC Comics: 2011 ($14.99, hardcover, one-shot)
  HC-Jill Thompson-s/painted-a/c; Little Delirium throws a party; watercolor page process ... 15.00
DELLA VISION (...The Television Queen) (Patty Powers #4 on)
Atlas Comics: April, 1955 - No. 3, Aug, 1955

	GD	VG	FN	VF	VF/NM	NM-
1-Al Hartley-c	90	180	270	576	988	1400
2,3	48	96	144	302	514	725

DELLEC
Aspen MLT.: Aug, 2009 - No. 6, Oct, 2011 ($2.50)
  1-6-Gunnell-a/c ... 3.00

DELLEC VOLUME 2
Aspen MLT.: Sept, 2018 - No. 4, Jan, 2019 ($3.99)
  1-4-Frank Mastromauro & Vince Hernandez-s ... 4.00
  ... 2018 Primer 1 (9/18, 25¢) New short story and recap of Volume 1 ... 3.00
DELL GIANT COMICS
    Dell Publishing began to release square bound comics in 1949 with a 132-page issue called Christmas Parade #1. The covers were of a heavier stock to accommodate the increased number of pages. The books proved profitable at 25 cents, but the average number of pages was quickly reduced to 100. Ten years later they were converted to a numbering system similar to the Four Color Comics, for greater ease in distribution and the page counts cut back to mostly 84 pages. The label "Dell Giant" began to appear on the covers in 1954. Because of the size of the books and the heavier, less pliant cover stock, they are rarely found in high grade condition, and with the exception of a small quantity of copies released from Western Publishing's warehouse–are almost never found in near mint.

	GD 2.0	VG 4.0	FN 6.0	VF 8.0	VF/NM 9.0	NM- 9.2
Abraham Lincoln Life Story 1(3/58)	9	18	27	72	129	185
Bugs Bunny Christmas Funnies 1(11/50, 116pp)	23	46	69	184	322	460
...Christmas Funnies 2(11/51, 116pp)	13	26	39	104	180	225
...Christmas Funnies 3-5(11/52-11/54,)-Becomes Christmas Party #6						
	10	20	30	80	140	200
...Christmas Funnies 7-9(12/56-12/58)	9	18	27	72	124	175
...Christmas Party 6(11/55)-Formerly Bugs Bunny Christmas Funnies						
	9	18	27	72	124	175
...County Fair 1(9/57)	11	22	33	88	149	210
...Halloween Parade 1(10/53)-Trick 'N' Treat Halloween Fun #3 on	15	30	60	120	205	290
...Halloween Parade 2(10/54)-Trick 'N' Treat Halloween Fun #3 on						
	11	22	33	88	152	215
...Trick 'N' Treat Halloween Fun 3,4(10/55-10/56)-Formerly Halloween Parade #2						
	11	22	33	88	149	210
...Vacation Funnies 1(7/51, 112pp)	21	42	63	168	297	425
...Vacation Funnies 2('52)	14	28	42	112	191	270
...Vacation Funnies 3-5('53-'55)	10	20	30	80	138	195
...Vacation Funnies 6,7('56-'59)	9	18	27	72	124	175
...Vacation Funnies 8('58) 1st app. Beep Beep the Road Runner, Wile E. Coyote (1st meeting), Mathilda (Mrs. Beep Beep) and their 3 children who hatch from eggs; one month before Four Color #918	11	22	33	88	157	225
Cadet Gray of West Point 1(4/58)-Williamson-a, 10pgs.; Buscema-a; photo-c						
	8	16	24	64	107	150
Christmas In Disneyland 1(12/57)-Barks-a, 18 pgs.	25	50	75	200	350	500
Christmas Parade 1(11/49)(132 pgs.)(1st Dell Giant)-Donald Duck (25 pgs. by Barks, r-in G.K. Christmas Parade #5); Mickey Mouse & other film oriented stories; Cinderella (prior to movie), 7 Dwarfs, Bambi & Thumper, So Dear To My Heart, Flying Mouse, Dumbo, Cookieland & others	70	140	210	560	980	1400
Christmas Parade 2('50)-Donald Duck (132 pgs.) by Barks, r-in Gold Key's Christmas Parade #6). Mickey, Pluto, Chip & Dale, etc. Contents shift to a holiday expansion of W.D. C&S story	45	90	135	360	630	900
Christmas Parade 3-7('51-'55, #3-116pgs.; #4-7, 100 pgs.)						
	14	28	42	112	196	280
Christmas Parade 8(12/56)-Barks-a, 8 pgs.	23	46	69	184	317	450
Christmas Parade 9(12/58)-Barks-a, 20 pgs.	25	50	75	200	350	500
Christmas Treasury, A 1(11/54)	10	20	30	80	135	190
Davy Crockett, King Of The Wild Frontier 1(9/55)-Fess Parker photo-c; Marsh-a						
	19	38	57	152	269	385
Disneyland Birthday Party 1(10/58)-Barks-a, 16 pgs. r-by Gladstone						
	25	50	75	200	350	500
Donald and Mickey In Disneyland 1(5/58)	13	26	39	104	177	250
Donald Duck Beach Party 1(7/54)-Has an Uncle Scrooge story (not by Barks) that prefigures the later rivalry with Flintheart Glomgold and tells of Scrooge's wild rivalry with another millionaire	18	36	54	144	252	360
...Beach Party 2(1955)-Lady & Tramp	13	26	39	104	182	260
...Beach Party 3-5(1956-58)	11	22	33	88	152	215
...Beach Party 6(8/59, 84pp)-Stapled	8	16	24	64	115	165
Donald Duck Fun Book 1,2 (1953 & 10/54)-Games, puzzles, comics & cut-outs (very rare in unused condition)(most copies commonly have defaced interior pgs.)	63	126	189	504	877	1250
Donald Duck In Disneyland 1(9/55)-1st Disneyland Dell Giant						
	16	32	48	128	227	325
Golden West Rodeo Treasury 1(10/57)	10	20	30	80	135	190
Huey, Dewey and Louie Back to School 1(9/58)	9	18	27	72	126	180
Lady and The Tramp 1(6/55)	20	40	60	160	275	390
Life Stories of American Presidents 1(11/57)-Buscema-a						
	9	18	27	72	124	175
Lone Ranger Golden West 3(8/55)-Formerly Lone Ranger Western Treasury						
	18	36	54	144	255	365
Lone Ranger Movie Story nn(3/56)-Origin Lone Ranger in text; Clayton Moore photo-c						

	GD 2.0	VG 4.0	FN 6.0	VF 8.0	VF/NM 9.0	NM- 9.2

	GD 2.0	VG 4.0	FN 6.0	VF 8.0	VF/NM 9.0	NM- 9.2
	36	72	108	288	507	725

...Western Treasury 1(9/53)-Origin Lone Ranger, Silver, & Tonto; painted cover — 23 46 69 184 325 465

...Western Treasury 2(8/54)-Becomes Lone Ranger Golden West #3 — 18 36 54 144 255 365

Marge's Little Lulu & Alvin Story Telling Time 1(3/59)-r/#2,5,3,11,30,10,21,17,8, 14,16; Stanley-a — 14 28 42 112 196 280

...& Her Friends 4(3/56)-Tripp-a — 14 28 42 112 191 270

...& Her Special Friends 3(3/55)-Tripp-a — 16 32 48 128 219 310

...& Tubby At Summer Camp 5,2: 5(10/57)-Tripp-a. 2(10/58)-Tripp-a — 13 26 39 104 182 260

...& Tubby Halloween Fun 6,2: 6(10/57)-Tripp-a. 2(10/58)-Tripp-a — 14 28 42 112 191 270

...& Tubby In Alaska 1(7/59)-Tripp-a — 13 26 39 104 182 260

...On Vacation 1(7/54)-r/4C-110,14,4C-146,5,4C-97,4,4C-158,3,1;Stanley-a — 25 50 75 200 350 500

...& Tubby Annual 1(3/53)-r/4C-165,4C-74,4C-146,4C-97,4C-158, 4C-139, 4C-131; Stanley-a (1st Lulu Dell Giant) — 30 60 90 240 420 600

...& Tubby Annual 2('54)-r/4C-139,6,4C-115,4C-74,5,4C-97,3,4C-146,18; Stanley-a — 25 50 75 200 350 500

Marge's Tubby & His Clubhouse Pals 1(10/56)-1st app. Gran'pa Feeb;1st app. Janie; written by Stanley; Tripp-a — 15 30 45 120 210 300

Mickey Mouse Almanac 1(12/57)-Barks-a, 8pgs. — 27 54 81 216 378 540

...Birthday Party 1(9/53)-r/entire 48pgs. of Gottfredson's "Mickey Mouse in Love Trouble" from WDC&S 36-39. Quality equal to original. Also reprints one story each from Four Color 27, 79, & 181 plus 6 panels of highlights in the career of Mickey Mouse — 31 62 93 248 434 620

...Club Parade 1(12/55)-r/4-Color 16 with some death trap scenes redrawn by Paul Murry & recolored with night turned into day; quality less than original — 22 44 66 176 308 440

...In Fantasy Land 1(5/57) — 13 26 39 104 180 255

...In Frontier Land 1(5/56)-Mickey Mouse Club title — 13 26 39 104 180 255

...Summer Fun 1(8/58)-Mobile cut-outs on back-c; becomes Summer Fun with #2; Canadian version exists with 30¢-c price — 13 26 39 104 180 255

Moses & The Ten Commandments 1(8/57)-Not based on movie; Dell's adaptation; Sekowsky-a; variant version has "Gods of Egypt" comic back-c — 8 16 24 64 107 150

Nancy & Sluggo Travel Time 1(9/58) — 8 16 24 64 115 165

Peter Pan Treasure Chest 1(1/53, 212pp)-Disney; contains 54-page movie adaptation & other Peter Pan stories; plus Donald & Mickey stories w/P. Pan; a 32-page retelling of "D. Duck Finds Pirate Gold" with yellow beak, called "Capt. Hook & the Buried Treasure" — 145 290 435 1160 2030 2900

Picnic Party 6,7(7/55-6/56) (Formerly Vacation Parade)-Uncle Scrooge, Mickey & Donald — 12 24 36 96 166 235

Picnic Party 8(7/57)-Barks-a, 6pgs — 21 42 63 168 289 410

Pogo Parade 1(9/53)-Kelly-a(r-/Pogo from Animal Comics in this order: #11,13,21,14,27,16,23,9,18,15,17) — 25 50 75 200 350 500

Raggedy Ann & Andy 1(2/55) — 17 34 51 136 238 340

Santa Claus Funnies 1(11/52)-Dan Noonan -A Christmas Carol adaptation — 12 24 36 96 168 240

Silly Symphonies 1(9/52)-Redrawing of Gotfredson's Mickey Mouse strip of "The Brave Little Tailor;" 2 Good Housekeeping pages (from 1943); Lady and the Two Siamese Cats, three years before "Lady & the Tramp;" & Donald Duck's first app. in "The Wise Little Hen" & other stories based on 1930's Silly Symphony cartoons — 35 70 105 280 490 700

Silly Symphonies 2(9/53)-M. Mouse in "The Sorcerer's Apprentice", 2 Good Housekeeping pages (from 1944); The Pelican and the Snipe, Elmer Elephant, Peculiar Penguins, Little Hiawatha, & others — 24 48 72 192 339 485

Silly Symphonies 3(2/54)-r/Mickey & The Beanstalk (4-Color #157, 39pgs.), Little Minnehaha, Pablo, The Flying Gauchito, Pluto, & Bongo, & 2 Good Housekeeping pages (1944) — 20 40 60 160 275 390

Silly Symphonies 4(8/54)-r/Dumbo (4-Color 234), Morris The Midget Moose, The Country Cousin, Bongo, & Clara Cluck — 20 40 60 160 275 390

Silly Symphonies 5-8: 5(2/55)-r/Cinderella (4-Color 272), Bucky Bug, Pluto, Little Hiawatha, The 7 Dwarfs & Dumbo. 6(8/55)-r/Pinocchio (WDC&S 63), The 7 Dwarfs & Thumper (WDC&S 45), M. Mouse "Adventures With Robin Hood" (40 pgs.), Johnny Appleseed, Pluto & Peter Pan, & Bucky Bug; Cut-out on back-c. 7(2/57)-r/Reluctant Dragon, Ugly Duckling, M. Mouse & Peter Pan, Jiminy Cricket, Peter & The Wolf, Brer Rabbit, Bucky Bug; Cut-out on back-c. 8(2/58)-r/Thumper Meets The 7 Dwarfs (4-Color #19), Jiminy Cricket, Niok, Brer Rabbit; Cut-out on back-c — 16 32 48 128 224 320

Silly Symphonies 9(2/59)-r/Paul Bunyan, Humphrey Bear, Jiminy Cricket, The Social Lion, Goliath II; cut-out on back-c — 15 30 45 120 210 300

Sleeping Beauty 1(4/59) — 28 56 84 224 387 550

Summer Fun 2(8/59, 84pp, stapled binding)(Formerly Mickey Mouse...)-Barks-a(2), 24 pgs. — 25 50 75 200 350 500

Tarzan's Jungle Annual 1(8/52)-Lex Barker photo on-c of #1,2 — 16 32 48 128 227 325

...Annual 2(8/53) — 11 22 33 88 152 215

...Annual 3-7('54-9/58)(two No. 5s)-Manning-a-No. 3,5-7; Marsh-a in No. 1-7 plus painted-c 1-7 — 9 18 27 72 124 175

Tom and Jerry Back To School 1(9/56) 2 different back-c, variant has "Apple for the Teacher" cut-out — 12 24 36 96 168 240

...Picnic Time 1(7/58) — 10 20 30 80 135 190

...Summer Fun 1(7/54)-Droopy written by Barks — 15 30 45 120 205 290

...Summer Fun 2-4(7/55-7/57) — 8 16 24 64 107 150

...Toy Fair 1(9/58) — 9 18 27 72 126 180

...Winter Carnival 1(12/52)-Droopy written by Barks — 21 42 63 168 297 425

...Winter Carnival 2(12/53)-Droopy written by Barks — 16 32 48 128 224 320

...Winter Fun 3(12/54) — 8 16 24 64 115 165

...Winter Fun 4-7(12/55-11/58) — 7 14 21 56 101 145

Treasury of Dogs, A 1(10/56) — 8 16 24 64 107 150

Treasury of Horses, A (9/55) — 8 16 24 64 107 150

Uncle Scrooge Goes To Disneyland 1(8/57p)-Barks-a, 20 pgs. r-by Gladstone; 2 different back-c; variant shows 6 snapshots of Scrooge — 28 56 84 224 387 550

Vacation In Disneyland 1(8/58) — 11 22 33 88 157 225

Vacation Parade 1(7/50, 132pp)-Donald Duck & Mickey Mouse; Barks-a, 55 pgs. — 100 200 300 800 1400 2000

Vacation Parade 2(7/51,116pp) — 26 52 78 208 367 525

Vacation Parade 3-5(7/52-7/54)-Becomes Picnic Party No. 6 on. #4-Robin Hood Advs. — 14 28 42 112 194 275

Western Roundup 1(6/52)-Photo-c; Gene Autry, Roy Rogers, Johnny Mack Brown, Rex Allen, & Bill Elliott begin; photo back-c begin, end No. 14,16,18 — 25 50 75 200 350 500

Western Roundup 2(2/53)-Photo-c — 14 28 42 112 196 280

Western Roundup 3-5(7-9/53 - 1/54)-Photo-c — 11 22 33 88 157 225

Western Roundup 6-10(4-6/54 - 4-6/55)-Photo-c — 11 22 33 88 149 210

Western Roundup 11-17,25: 11-17-Photo-c; 11-13,16,17-Manning-a. 11-Flying A's Range Rider, Dale Evans begin — 9 18 27 72 129 185

Western Roundup 18-Toth-a; last photo-c; Gene Autry ends — 11 22 33 88 149 210

Western Roundup 19-24-Manning-a. 19-Buffalo Bill Jr. begins (7-9/57; early app.). 19,20,22-Toth-a. 21-Rex Allen, Johnny Mack Brown end. 22-Jace Pearson's Texas Rangers, Rin Tin Tin, Tales of Wells Fargo app., 4-6/58) & Wagon Train (2nd app.) begin — 9 18 27 72 129 185

Woody Woodpecker Back To School 1(10/52) — 10 20 30 80 140 200

...Back To School 2-4,6('53-10/57)-County Fair No. 5 — 8 16 24 64 112 160

...County Fair 5(9/56)-Formerly Back To School — 8 16 24 64 112 160

...County Fair 2(11/58) — 7 14 21 56 101 145

DELL GIANTS (Consecutive numbering)
Dell Publishing Co.: No. 21, Sept, 1959 - No. 55, Sept, 1961 (Most 84 pgs., 25¢)

21-(#1)-M.G.M.'s Tom & Jerry Picnic Time (84pp, stapled binding)-Painted-c — 11 22 33 88 157 225

22-Huey, Dewey & Louie Back to School (Disney; 10/59, 84pp, square binding begins) — 9 18 27 72 129 185

23-Marge's Little Lulu & Tubby Halloween Fun (10/59)-Tripp-a — 12 24 36 96 168 240

24-Woody Woodpecker's Family Fun (11/59)(Walter Lantz) — 8 16 24 64 112 160

25-Tarzan's Jungle World(11/59)-Marsh-a; painted-c — 11 22 33 88 152 215

26-Christmas Parade(Disney; 12/59)-Barks-a, 16pgs.; Barks draws himself on wanted poster on pg.13 — 21 42 63 168 289 410

27-Walt Disney's Man in Space (10/59) r-/4-Color 716,866, & 954 (100 pgs., 35¢)(TV) — 9 18 27 72 129 185

28-Bugs Bunny's Winter Fun (2/60) — 9 18 27 72 126 180

29-Marge's Little Lulu & Tubby in Hawaii (4/60)-Tripp-a — 12 24 36 96 166 235

30-Disneyland USA(Disney; 6/60) — 9 18 27 72 124 175

31-Huckleberry Hound Summer Fun (7/60)(TV)(HannaBarbera)-Yogi Bear & Pixie & Dixie app. — 12 24 36 96 173 250

32-Bugs Bunny Beach Party — 7 14 21 56 101 145

33-Daisy Duck & Uncle Scrooge Picnic Time (Disney; 9/60) — 9 18 27 72 124 175

34-Nancy & Sluggo Summer Camp (8/60) — 7 14 21 56 101 145

35-Huey, Dewey & Louie Back to School (Disney; 10/60)-1st app. Daisy Duck's Nieces, April, May & June — 12 24 36 96 163 230

36-Marge's Little Lulu & Witch Hazel Halloween Fun (10/60)-Tripp-a — 11 22 33 88 157 225

37-Tarzan, King of the Jungle (11/60)-Marsh-a; painted-c — 9 18 27 72 129 185

38-Uncle Donald & His Nephews Family Fun (Disney; 11/60)-Cover painting based on a pencil sketch by Barks — 12 24 36 96 166 235

39-Walt Disney's Merry Christmas (Disney; 12/60)-Cover painting based on a pencil sketch by Barks — 12 24 36 96 173 250

40-Woody Woodpecker Christmas Parade (12/60)(Walter Lantz) — 6 12 18 48 87 125

41-Yogi Bear's Winter Sports (12/60)(TV)(Hanna-Barbera)-Huckleberry Hound, Pixie & Dixie, Augie Doggie app. — 12 24 36 96 173 250

42-Marge's Little Lulu & Tubby in Australia (4/61) — 12 24 36 96 171 245

43-Mighty Mouse in Outer Space (5/61) — 20 40 60 160 275 390

44-Around the World with Huckleberry and His Friends (7/61)(TV)(Hanna-Barbera)-Yogi Bear, Pixie & Dixie, Quick Draw McGraw, Augie Doggie app.; 1st app. Yakky Doodle — 13 26 39 104 182 260

45-Nancy & Sluggo Summer Camp (8/61) — 7 14 21 56 96 135

46-Bugs Bunny Beach Party (8/61) — 7 14 21 56 96 135

47-Mickey & Donald in Vacationland (Disney; 8/61) — 8 16 24 64 115 165

48-The Flintstones (No. 1)(Bedrock Bedlam; 7/61)(TV)(Hanna-Barbera) 1st app. in comics — 35 70 105 280 490 700

49-Huey, Dewey & Louie Back to School (Disney; 9/61) — 9 18 27 72 124 175

50-Marge's Little Lulu & Witch Hazel Trick 'N' Treat (10/61) — 11 22 33 88 157 225

51-Tarzan, King of the Jungle by Jesse Marsh (11/61)-Painted-c — 8 16 24 64 110 155

52-Uncle Donald & His Nephews Dude Ranch (Disney; 11/61) — 8 16 24 64 115 165

53-Donald Duck Merry Christmas (Disney; 12/61) — 8 16 24 64 112 160

54-Woody Woodpecker's Christmas Party (12/61)-Issued after No. 55 — 7 14 21 56 98 140

55-Daisy Duck & Uncle Scrooge Showboat (Disney; 9/61) — 8 16 24 64 117 170

NOTE: All issues printed with & without an ad on back cover.

DELL JUNIOR TREASURY
Dell Publishing Co.: June, 1955 - No. 10, Oct, 1957 (15¢) (All painted-c)

1-Alice in Wonderland; r/4-Color #331 (52 pgs.) — 8 16 24 56 108 160

2-Aladdin & the Wonderful Lamp — 6 12 18 41 76 110

3-Gulliver's Travels (1/56) — 6 12 18 41 76 110

4-Adventures of Mr. Frog & Miss Mouse — 6 12 18 37 66 95

5-The Wizard of Oz (7/56) — 6 12 18 41 76 110

6-10: 6-Heidi (10/56). 7-Santa and the Angel. 8-Raggedy Ann and the Camel with the Wrinkled Knees. 9-Clementina the Flying Pig. 10-Adventures of Tom Sawyer — 6 12 18 37 66 95

DELTA 13

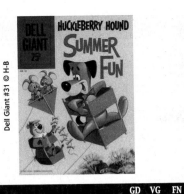

Dell Giant #31 © H-B

The Demon #15 © DC

Demon Wars: Scarlet Sin #1 © MAR

	GD	VG	FN	VF	VF/NM	NM-
	2.0	4.0	6.0	8.0	9.0	9.2

IDW Publishing: May, 2018 - No. 4, Aug, 2018 ($3.99, limited series)

1-4-Steve Niles-s/Nat Jones-a ... 4.00

DEMOLITION MAN
DC Comics: Nov, 1993 - No. 4, Feb, 1994 ($1.75, limited series)

1-4-Movie adaptation ... 4.00

DEMON, THE (See Detective Comics No. 482-485)
National Periodical Publications: Aug-Sept, 1972 - V3#16, Jan, 1974

1-Origin; Kirby-s/c/a in all; 1st Morgaine Le Fey	19	38	57	131	291	450
2-5	4	8	12	28	47	65
6-16: 7-1st app. Klarion the Witch Boy	3	6	9	21	33	45

DEMON, THE (1st limited series)(Also see Cosmic Odyssey #2)
DC Comics: Nov, 1986 - No. 4, Feb, 1987 (75¢, limited series)(#2 has #4 of 4 on-c)

1-4: Matt Wagner-a(p) & scripts in all. 4-Demon & Jason Blood become separate entities 4.00

DEMON, THE (2nd Series)
DC Comics: July, 1990 - No. 58, May, 1995 ($1.50/$1.75/$1.95)

1-Grant scripts begin, ends #39: 1-4-Painted-c ... 5.00
2-18,20,27-39,41,42: 3,8-Batman app. (cameo #4). 12-Bisley painted-c.
12-15,21-Lobo app. (1 pg. cameo #11). 23-Robin app. 29-Superman app.
31,33-39-Lobo app. ... 4.00
19-($2.50, 44 pgs.)-Lobo poster stapled inside ... 5.00
28,40: 28-Superman-c/story; begin $1.75-c. 40-Garth Ennis scripts begin ... 5.00

43-45-Hitman app.		1	2	3	5	7
46-48 Return of The Haunted Tank-c/s. 48-Begin $1.95-c.						5.00

49,51,55-58: 51-(9/94) Followed by Demon #0 issue ... 3.00
50 ($2.95, 52 pgs.) ... 4.00
52-54-Hitman-s ... 5.00
#0-(10/94) Zero Hour issue released between #51&52 ... 4.00
Annual 1 (1992, $3.00, 68 pgs.)-Eclipso-c/story ... 5.00

Annual 2 (1993, $3.50, 68 pgs.)-1st app. of Hitman	3	6	9	18	27	36

NOTE: *Alan Grant* scripts in #1-16, 20, 21, 23-25, 30-39, Annual 1. *Wagner* a/scripts-22.

DEMON DAYS (Reimagined Marvel characters set in Japanese folklore)
Marvel Comics: May, 2021 - May, 2022 ($4.99)

...: Blood Feud 1 (5/22) Part 4 of The Yashida Saga; Peach Momoko-s/a; Hulk app. ... 5.00
...: Cursed Web 1 (11/21) Part 2 of The Yashida Saga; Peach Momoko-s/a; Mystique app. ... 5.00
...: Mariko 1 (8/21) Part 1 of The Yashida Saga; Peach Momoko-s/a; Black Widow app. ... 5.00
...: Rising Storm 1 (2/22) Part 3 of The Yashida Saga; Momoko-s/a; Thor & Storm app. ... 5.00
...: X-Men 1 (5/22) Momoko-s/a; Psylocke & Venom app. ... 5.00
...: X-Men Creator Cut 1 (2/22, $5.99) Shows B&W inked story with character & sketch art ... 6.00

DEMON DREAMS
Pacific Comics: Feb, 1984 - No. 2, May, 1984

1,2-Mostly r-/Heavy Metal ... 4.00

DEMON: DRIVEN OUT
DC Comics: Nov, 2003 - No. 6, Apr, 2004 ($2.50, limited series)

1-6-Dysart-s/Mhan-a ... 3.00

DEMON, THE: HELL IS EARTH (Etrigan)
DC Comics: Jan, 2018 - No. 6, Jun, 2018 ($2.99, limited series)

1-6-Andrew Constant-s/Brad Walker-a; Xanadu app. ... 3.00

DEMON-HUNTER (See Marvel Spotlight #33)
Seaboard Periodicals (Atlas): Sept, 1975

1-Origin/1st app. Demon-Hunter; Buckler-c/a	3	6	9	16	23	30

DEMON KNIGHT: A GRIMJACK GRAPHIC NOVEL
First Publishing: 1990 ($8.95, 52 pgs.)

nn-Flint Henry-a ... 9.00

DEMON KNIGHTS (New DC 52) (Set in the Dark Ages)
DC Comics: Nov, 2011 - No. 23, Oct, 2013 ($2.99)

1-23: 1-Cornell-s/Neves-a/Daniel-c; Etrigan, Madame Xanadu & The Shining Knight app. ... 3.00
#0 (11/12, $2.99) Origin of Etrigan The Demon; Merlin app.; Cornell-s/Chang-a ... 3.00

DEMON WARS (Reimagined Marvel characters set in Japanese folklore)
Marvel Comics: Oct, 2022 - Jul, 2023 ($4.99)

...: Down in Flames 1 (4/23) Into the Spirit World pt. 3; Peach Momoko-s/a ... 5.00
...: Scarlet Sin 1 (7/23) Into the Spirit World pt. 4; Peach Momoko-s/a ... 5.00
...: Shield of Justice 1 (1/23) Into the Spirit World pt. 2; Peach Momoko-s/a ... 5.00
...: The Iron Samurai 1 (10/22) Into the Spirit World pt. 1; Peach Momoko-s/a ... 5.00

DENNIS THE MENACE (TV with 1959 issues) (Becomes ...Fun Fest Series;
See The Best of... & The Very Best of...)(...Fun Fest on-c only to #156-166)
Standard Comics/Pines No.15-31/Hallden (Fawcett) No.32 on: 8/53 - #14, 1/56; #15, 3/56 -
#31, 11/58; #32, 1/59 - #166, 11/79

	GD	VG	FN	VF	VF/NM	NM-
	2.0	4.0	6.0	8.0	9.0	9.2

1-1st app. Dennis, Mr. & Mrs. Wilson, Ruff & Dennis' mom & dad; Wiseman-a, written by Fred Toole-most issues	290	580	870	1856	3178	4500
2	81	162	243	518	884	1250
3-5	42	84	126	265	445	625
6-10: 8-Last pre-code issue	36	72	108	214	347	480
11-20	24	48	72	142	234	325
21,23-30	15	30	45	85	130	175
22-1st app. Margaret w/blonde hair	19	38	57	111	176	240
31-1st app. Joey	20	40	60	118	192	265
32-38,40(1/60): 37-A-Bomb blast panel	10	20	30	58	79	100
39-1st app. Gina (11/59)	14	28	42	76	108	140
41-60(7/62)	4	8	12	25	40	55
61-80(9/65),100(1/69)	3	6	9	16	23	30
81-99	2	4	6	11	16	20
101-117: 102-Last 12¢ issue	2	4	6	9	12	15
118(1/72)-131 (All 52 pages)	2	4	6	10	14	18
132(1/74)-142,144-160	1	2	3	5	7	9
143(3/76) Olympic-c/s; low print	2	4	6	11	16	20
161-166	1	3	4	6	8	10

NOTE: *Wiseman* c/a-1-46, 53, 68, 69.

DENNIS THE MENACE (Giants) (No. 1 titled Giant Vacation Special;
becomes Dennis the Menace Bonus Magazine No. 76 on)
(#1-8,18,23,25,30,38; 100 pgs.; rest to #41: 84 pgs.)(#42-75: 68 pgs.)
Standard/Pines/Hallden(Fawcett): Summer, 1955 - No. 75, Dec, 1969

nn-Giant Vacation Special(Summ/55-Standard)	21	42	63	122	199	275
nn-Christmas issue (Winter '55)	19	38	57	109	172	235
2-Giant Vacation Special (Summer '56-Pines)	15	30	45	86	133	180
3-Giant Christmas issue (Winter '56-Pines)	14	28	42	81	118	155
4-Giant Vacation Special (Summer '57-Pines)	14	28	42	78	112	145
5-Giant Christmas issue (Winter '57-Pines)	14	28	42	78	112	145
6-In Hawaii (Giant Vacation Special)(Summer '58-Pines)						
	13	26	39	74	105	135
6-In Hawaii (Summer '59-Hallden)-2nd printing; says 3rd large printing on-c						
6-In Hawaii (Summer '60)-3rd printing; says 4th large printing on-c						
6-In Hawaii (Summer '62)-4th printing; says 5th large printing on-c						
each....	9	18	27	50	65	80
6-Giant Christmas issue (Winter '58)	13	26	39	74	105	135
7-In Hollywood (Winter '59-Hallden)	5	10	15	33	57	80
7-In Hollywood (Summer '61)-2nd printing	3	6	9	21	33	45
8-In Mexico (Winter '60, 100 pgs.-Hallden/Fawcett)	5	10	15	33	57	80
8-In Mexico (Summer '62, 2nd printing)	3	6	9	21	33	45
9-Goes to Camp (Summer '61, 84 pgs.)-1st CCA approved issue						
	5	10	15	31	53	75
9-Goes to Camp (Summer '62)-2nd printing	3	6	9	21	33	45
10-12: 10-X-Mas issue (Winter '61), 11-Giant Christmas issue (Winter '62), 12-Triple Feature (Winter '62)						
13-17: 13-Best of Dennis the Menace (Spring '63)-Reprints, 14-And His Dog Ruff (Summer '63), 15-In Washington, D.C. (Summer '63), 16-Goes to Camp (Summer '63)-Reprints No. 9, 17-& His Pal Joey (Winter '63)	4	8	12	25	40	55
18-In Hawaii (Reprints No. 6)	3	6	9	21	33	45
19-Giant Christmas issue (Winter '63)	4	8	12	25	40	55
20-Spring Special (Spring '64)	4	8	12	25	40	55
21-40 (Summer '66): 30-r/#6. #35-Xmas spec.Wint.'65						
	3	6	9	19	30	40
41-60 (Fall '68)	3	6	9	15	22	28
61-75 (12/69): 68-Partial-r/#6	3	6	9	14	19	24

NOTE: *Wiseman* c/a-1-8, 12, 14, 15, 17, 20, 22, 27, 28, 31, 35, 36, 41, 49.

DENNIS THE MENACE
Marvel Comics Group: Nov, 1981 - No. 13, Nov, 1982

1-New-a	2	4	6	10	14	18
2-13: 2-New art. 3-Part-r. 4,5-r. 5-X-Mas-c & issue, 7-Spider Kid-c/sty						
	1	2	3	4	5	7

NOTE: *Hank Ketcham* c-most; a-3, 12. *Wiseman* a-4, 5.

DENNIS THE MENACE AND HIS DOG RUFF
Hallden/Fawcett: Summer, 1961

1-Wiseman-a	6	12	18	42	79	115

DENNIS THE MENACE AND HIS FRIENDS
Fawcett Publ.: 1969; No. 5, Jan, 1970 - No. 46, April, 1980 (All reprints)

Dennis the Menace & Joey No. 2 (7/69)	2	4	6	13	18	22
Dennis the Menace & Ruff No. 2 (9/69)	2	4	6	13	18	22
Dennis the Menace & Mr. Wilson No. 1 (10/69)	3	6	9	15	22	28
Dennis & Margaret No. 1 (Winter '69)	3	6	9	15	22	28
5-12: 5-Dennis the Menace & Margaret. 6-...& Joey. 7-...& Ruff. 8-...& Mr. Wilson						

	GD 2.0	VG 4.0	FN 6.0	VF 8.0	VF/NM 9.0	NM- 9.2

	GD 2.0	VG 4.0	FN 6.0	VF 8.0	VF/NM 9.0	NM- 9.2
13-21-(52 pg Giants): 13-(1/72). 21-(1/74)	2	4	6	8	11	14
22-37	2	4	6	10	14	18
38-46 (Digest size, 148 pgs., 4/78, 95¢)	1	3	4	6	8	10

NOTE: Titles rotate every four issues, beginning with No. 5. Joey issues: #2(7/69)6,10,14,18,22,26,30,34. Ruff issues: #2(9/69),7,11,15,19,23,27,31,35. Mr. Wilson issues: #1(10/69),8,12,16,20,24,28,32,36. Margaret issues: #1 (Wint./69),5,9,13,17,21,25,29,33,37.

DENNIS THE MENACE AND HIS PAL JOEY
Fawcett Publ.: Summer, 1961 (10¢) (See Dennis the Menace Giants No. 45)

1-Wiseman-c/a	6	12	18	42	79	115

DENNIS THE MENACE AND THE BIBLE KIDS
Word Books: 1977 (36 pgs.)

1-6: 1-Jesus. 2-Joseph. 3-David. 4-The Bible Girls. 5-Moses. 6-More About Jesus	2	4	6	10	14	18
7-9-Low print run: 7-The Lord's Prayer. 8-Stories Jesus told. 9-Paul, God's Traveller	3	6	9	20	31	42
10-Low print run; In the Beginning	5	10	15	34	60	85

NOTE: Ketcham c/a in all.

DENNIS THE MENACE BIG BONUS SERIES
Fawcett Publications: No. 10, Feb, 1980 - No. 11, Apr, 1980

10,11	1	2	3	5	6	8

DENNIS THE MENACE BONUS MAGAZINE (Formerly Dennis the Menace Giants Nos. 1-75)
(...Big Bonus Series on-c for #174-194)
Fawcett Publications: No. 76, 1/70 - No. 95, 7/71; No. 95, 7/71; No. 97, '71; No. 194, 10/79; (No. 76-124: 68 pgs.; No. 125-163: 52 pgs.; No. 164 on: 36 pgs.)

76-90(3/71)	2	4	6	10	14	18
91-95, 97-110(10/72): Two #95's with same date(7/71) A-Summer Games, and B-That's Our Boy. No #96	2	4	9	13	16	
111-124	2	4	6	8	10	12
125-163-(52 pgs.)	2	4	6	8	10	12
164-194: 166-Indicia printed backwards	1	2	3	4	5	7

DENNIS THE MENACE COMICS DIGEST
Marvel Comics Group: April, 1982 - No. 3, Aug, 1982 ($1.25, digest-size)

1-3-Reprints	1	3	4	6	8	10
1-Mistakenly printed with DC emblem on cover	2	4	6	10	12	15

NOTE: Ketcham c-all. Wiseman a-all. A few thousand #1's were published with a DC emblem on cover.

DENNIS THE MENACE FUN BOOK
Fawcett Publications/Standard Comics: 1960 (100 pgs.)

1-Part Wiseman-a	7	14	21	46	86	125

DENNIS THE MENACE FUN FEST SERIES (Formerly Dennis the Menace #166)
Hallden (Fawcett): No. 16, Jan, 1980 - No. 17, Mar, 1980 (40¢)

16,17-By Hank Ketcham	1	2	3	4	5	7

DENNIS THE MENACE POCKET FULL OF FUN!
Fawcett Publications (Hallden): Spring, 1969 - No. 50, March, 1980 (196 pgs.) (Digest size)

1-Reprints in all issues	5	10	15	34	60	85
2-10	4	8	12	23	37	50
11-20	3	6	9	15	22	28
21-28	2	4	6	11	16	20
29-50: 35,40,46-Sunday strip-r	1	4	6	8	11	14

NOTE: No. 1-28 are 196 pgs.; No. 29-36: 164 pgs.; No. 37: 148 pgs.; No. 38 on: 132 pgs. No. 8, 11, 15, 21, 25, 29 all contain strip reprints.

DENNIS THE MENACE TELEVISION SPECIAL
Fawcett Publ. (Hallden Div.): Summer, 1961 - No. 2, Spring, 1962 (Giant)

1	7	14	21	46	86	125
2	3	6	9	21	33	45

DENNIS THE MENACE TRIPLE FEATURE
Fawcett Publications: Winter, 1961 (Giant)

1-Wiseman-c/a	7	14	21	46	86	125

DEPT. H
Dark Horse Comics: Apr, 2016 - No. 24, Mar, 2018 ($3.99)

1-24-Matt Kindt-s/a. 1-Two covers						4.00

DEPARTMENT OF TRUTH
Image Comics: Sept, 2020 - Present ($3.99)

1-James Tynion IV-s/Martin Simmonds-a	3	6	9	14	20	25
2-4-Tynion IV-s/Simmonds-a	1	3	4	6	8	10
5-22: 6-Elsa Charretier-a						4.00

DEPUTY, THE (TV)
Dell Publishing Co.: No. 1077, Feb-Apr, 1960 - No. 1225, Oct-Dec, 1961 (all-Henry Fonda photo-c)

Four Color 1077 (#1)-Buscema-a	10	20	30	64	132	200
Four Color 1130 (9-11/60)-Buscema-a,1225	8	16	24	54	102	150

DEPUTY DAWG (TV) (Also see New Terrytoons)
Dell Publishing Co./Gold Key: Oct-Dec, 1961 - No. 1299, 1962; No. 1, Aug, 1965

Four Color 1238,1299	9	18	27	63	129	195
1(10164-508)(8/65)-Gold Key	9	18	27	63	129	195

DEPUTY DAWG PRESENTS DINKY DUCK AND HASHIMOTO-SAN (TV)
Gold Key: August, 1965

1(10159-508)	9	18	27	57	111	165

DESCENDENT, THE
AfterShock Comics: May, 2019 - No. 5, Sept, 2019 ($3.99)

1-5-Stephanie Phillips-s/Evgeniy Bornyakov-a						4.00

DESCENDER (Also see Ascender)
Image Comics: Mar, 2015 - No. 32, Jul, 2018 ($2.99/$3.99)

1-Lemire-s/Nguyen-a/c in all; bonus concept-a						5.00
1-Variant-c by Lemire						6.00
2-18-Lemire-s/Nguyen-a/c						3.00
19-32-($3.99)						4.00

	GD 2.0	VG 4.0	FN 6.0	VF 8.0	VF/NM 9.0	NM- 9.2
DESERT GOLD (See Zane Grey 4-Color 467)						
DESIGN FOR SURVIVAL (Gen. Thomas S. Power's...)						
American Security Council Press: 1968 (36 pgs. in color) (25¢)						
nn-Propaganda against the Threat of Communism-Aircraft cover; H-Bomb panel	3	6	9	20	31	42
Twin Circle Edition-Cover shows panels from inside	3	6	9	15	22	28

DESOLATION JONES
DC Comics (WildStorm): July, 2005 - No. 8, Feb, 2007 ($2.95/$2.99)

1-8: 1-6-Warren Ellis-s/J.H. Williams-a. 7,8-Zezelj-a						3.00

DESPERADO (Becomes Black Diamond Western No. 9 on)
Lev Gleason Publications: June, 1948 - No. 8, Feb, 1949 (All 52 pgs.)

1-Biro-c on all; contains inside photo-c of Charles Biro, Lev Gleason & Bob Wood	21	42	63	122	199	275
2	13	26	39	72	101	130
3-Story with over 20 killings	13	26	39	74	105	135
4-8	9	18	27	52	69	85

NOTE: Barry a-2. Fuje a-4, 8. Guardineer a-5-7. Kida a-3-7. Ed Moore a-4, 6.

DESPERADO PRIMER
Image Comics (Desperado): Apr, 2005 ($1.99, one-shot)

1-Previews of Roundeye, World Traveler, A Mirror To The Soul; Bolland-c						3.00

DESPERADOES
Image Comics (Homage): Sept, 1997 - No. 5, June, 1998 ($2.50/$2.95)

1-5-Mariotte-s/Cassaday-c/a. 1-5-(2.50-c). 2-5-(2.95)						4.00
...: A Moment's Sunlight TPB ('98, $16.95) r/#1-5						17.00
...: Epidemic! (11/99, $5.95) Mariotte-s						6.00

DESPERADOES: BANNERS OF GOLD
IDW Publishing: Dec, 2004 - No. 5, Apr, 2005 ($3.99, limited series)

1-5: Mariotte-s/Haun-a. 1-Cassaday-c						4.00

DESPERADOES: BUFFALO DREAMS
IDW Publishing: Jan, 2007 - No. 4, Apr, 2007 ($3.99, limited series)

1-4: Mariotte-s/Dose-a/c						4.00

DESPERADOES: QUIET OF THE GRAVE
DC Comics (Homage): Jul, 2001 - No. 5, Nov, 2001 ($2.95)

1-5-Jeff Mariotte-s/John Severin-c/a						3.00
TPB (2002, $14.95) r/#1-5; intro. by Brian Keene						15.00

DESPERATE TIMES (See Savage Dragon)
Image Comics: Jun, 1998 - No. 4, Dec, 1998; Nov, 2000 - No. 4, July, 2001 ($2.95, B&W)

1-Chris Eliopoulos-s/a in all	1	2	3	5	6	8
2-4						5.00
(Vol. 2) 1-4						3.00
(Vol. 3) 0-(1/04, $3.50) Pages read sideways						3.50
(Vol. 3) 1-Pages read sideways						3.00

DESPICABLE DEADPOOL (Marvel Legacy)
Marvel Comics: No. 287, Dec, 2017 - No. 300, Jul, 2018 ($3.99)

287-299: 287-Duggan-s/Koblish-a; Cable app. 293-Rogue app. 296-Capt. America app.						4.00
300-($5.99) Avengers and Champions app.						6.00

DESTINATION MOON (See Fawcett Movie Comics, Space Adventures #20, 23, & Strange Adventures #1)

DESTINY: A CHRONICLE OF DEATHS FORETOLD (See Sandman)
DC Comics (Vertigo): 1997 - No. 3, 1998 ($5.95, limited series)

1-3-Alisa Kwitney-s in all: 1-Kent Williams & Michael Zulli-a, Williams painted-c. 2-Williams & Scott Hampton-painted-c/a. 3-Williams & Guay-a						6.00
TPB (2000, $14.95) r/series	2	4	6	11	16	20

DESTROY!!
Eclipse Comics: 1986 ($4.95, B&W, magazine-size, one-shot)

1-Scott McCloud-s/a	4	8	12	23	37	50
3-D Special 1-r-/#1 ($2.50)	2	4	6	9	12	15

DESTROY ALL MONSTERS: A RECKLESS BOOK
Image Comics: Oct, 2021 ($24.99, HC graphic novel)

HC - Ed Brubaker-s/Sean Phillips-a; 3rd book in the Reckless series						25.00

DESTROYER
Marvel Comics: June, 2009 - No. 5, Oct, 2009 ($3.99, limited series)

1-5-Kirkman-s/Walker-a/Pearson-c						4.00

DESTROYER, THE
Marvel Comics (MAX): Nov, 1989 - No. 9, Jun, 1990 ($2.25, B&W, magazine, 52 pgs.)

1-Based on Remo Williams movie, paperbacks						6.00
2-9: 2-Williamson part inks. 4-Ditko-a						4.00

DESTROYER, THE
Marvel Comics: V2#1, March, 1991 ($1.95, 52 pgs.) V3#1, Dec, 1991 - No. 4, Mar, 1992 ($1.95, mini-series)

V2#1, V3#1-4: Based on Remo Williams paperbacks. V3#1-4-Simonson-c. 3-Morrow-a						4.00

DESTROYER, THE (Also see Solar, Man of the Atom)
Valiant: Apr, 1995 ($2.50/$2.95, color, one-shot)

0-($2.50-c) Indicia indicates #1						4.00
0-($2.95-c) Indicia indicates #1	2	4	6	9	12	15

DESTROYER (VICTOR LAVALLE'S...)
BOOM! Studios: May, 2017 - No. 6, Oct, 2017 ($3.99, limited series)

1-6-LaValle-s/Dietrich Smith-a; Frankenstein's monster app.						4.00

DESTROYER DUCK
Eclipse Comics: Feb, 1982 - No. 7, May, 1984 (#2-7: Baxter paper) ($1.50)

1-Origin Destroyer Duck; 1st app. Groo; Kirby-c/a(p)	6	12	18	38	69	100
2-5: 2-Starling back-up begins; Kirby-c/a(p) thru #5						6.00
6,7						5.00

NOTE: Neal Adams c-1i. Kirby c/a-1-5p. Miller c-7.

DESTRUCTOR, THE

Dept. H #7 © Matt Kindt

Desperado #4 © LEV

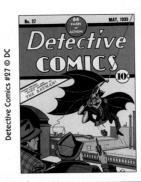

Detective Comics #97 © DC

	GD 2.0	VG 4.0	FN 6.0	VF 8.0	VF/NM 9.0	NM- 9.2

Atlas/Seaboard: February, 1975 - No. 4, Aug, 1975

	GD 2.0	VG 4.0	FN 6.0	VF 8.0	VF/NM 9.0	NM- 9.2
1-Origin/1st app.; Ditko/Wood-a; Wood-c(i)	3	6	9	16	23	30
2-4: 2-Ditko/Wood-a. 3,4-Ditko-a(p)	2	4	6	9	13	16

DETECTIVE COMICS (Also see other Batman titles)
National Periodical Publications/DC Comics: Mar, 1937 - No. 881, Oct, 2011

	GD 2.0	VG 4.0	FN 6.0	VF 8.0	VF/NM 9.0	NM- 9.2
1-(Scarce)-Slam Bradley & Spy by Siegel & Shuster, Speed Saunders by Stoner and Flessel, Cosmo, the Phantom of Disguise, Buck Marshall, Bruce Nelson begin; Chin Lung in 'Claws of the Red Dragon' serial begins; Vincent Sullivan-c	22,300	44,600	66,900	165,000	--	--
2 (Rare)-Creig Flessel-c begin; new logo	6770	13,540	20,310	44,000	--	--
3 (Rare)	4700	9400	14,100	36,000	--	--
4	3100	6200	9300	17,000	24,000	31,000
5-Larry Steele begins	2400	4800	7200	13,200	18,600	24,000
6,7,9,10	1800	3600	5400	9900	13,950	18,000
8-Mister Chang-c; classic-c	3000	6000	9000	16,500	23,250	30,000
11-14,17,19: 17-1st app. Fu Manchu in Detective	1600	3200	4800	8800	12,400	16,000
15,16-Have interior ad for Action Comics #1	1800	3600	5400	9900	13,950	18,000
18-Classic Fu Manchu-c; last Flessel-c	2500	5000	7500	13,700	19,350	25,000
20-The Crimson Avenger begins (1st app.)	1850	3700	5550	10,200	14,350	18,500
21,23-25	1300	2600	3900	7150	10,075	13,000
22-1st Crimson Avenger-c by Chambers (12/38)	1650	3300	4950	9100	12,800	16,500
26	1650	3300	4950	9100	12,800	16,500
27-The Bat-Man & Commissioner Gordon begin (1st app.), created by Bill Finger & Bob Kane (5/39); Batman-c (1st)(by Kane). Bat-Man's secret identity revealed as Bruce Wayne in six pg. story. Signed Rob't Kane (also see Det. Picture Stories #1 & Funny Pages V3#1)	327,200	654,400	981,600	2,182,000	3,491,000	4,800,000

27-Reprint, Oversize 13-1/2x10". WARNING: This comic is an exact duplicate reprint of the original except for its size. DC published it in 1974 with a second cover titling it as Famous First Edition. There have been many reported cases of the outer cover being removed and the interior sold as the original edition. The reprint with the new outer cover removed is practically worthless; see Famous First Edition for value.

	GD 2.0	VG 4.0	FN 6.0	VF 8.0	VF/NM 9.0	NM- 9.2
28-2nd app. The Batman (6 pg. story); non-Bat-Man-c; signed Rob't Kane	12,000	24,000	36,000	66,600	108,000	150,000
29-1st app. Doctor Death-c/story, Batman's 1st name villain. 1st 2 part story (10 pgs.) 2nd Batman-c	28,700	57,400	86,100	157,800	276,400	395,000
30-Dr. Death app. Story concludes from issue #29. Classic Batman splash panel by Kane.	3125	6250	9375	21,900	35,950	50,000
31-Classic Batman over castle cover; 1st app. The Monk & 1st Julie Madison (Bruce Wayne's 1st love interest); 1st Batplane (Bat-Gyro) and Batarang; 2nd 2-part Batman adventure. Gardner Fox takes over script from Bill Finger. 1st mention of locale (New York City) where Batman lives	48,800	97,600	146,400	273,000	399,000	525,000
32-Batman story concludes from issue #31. 1st app. Dala (Monk's assistant). Batman uses gun for 1st time to slay The Monk and Dala. This was the 1st time a costumed hero used a gun in comic books. 1st Batman head logo on cover	2170	4340	6510	14,900	26,450	38,000
33-Origin The Batman (2 pgs.)(1st told origin); Batman gun holster-c; Batman w/smoking gun panel at end of story. Batman story now 12 pgs. Classic Batman-c	18,125	36,250	54,375	113,300	201,650	290,000
34-2nd Crimson Avenger-c by Creig Flessel and last non Batman-c. Story from issue #32 x-over as Bruce Wayne sees Julie Madison off to America from Paris. Classic Batman splash panel used later in Batman #1 for origin story. Steve Malone begins	2240	4480	6720	16,100	27,050	38,000
35-Classic Batman hypodermic needle-c that reflects story in issue #34. Classic Batman with smoking .45 automatic splash panel. Batman-c	19,700	39,400	59,100	126,100	183,050	240,000
36-Batman-c that reflects adventure in issue #35. Origin/1st app. of Dr. Hugo Strange (1st major villain, 2/40). 1st finned-gloves worn by Batman	8950	17,900	26,850	64,900	97,450	130,000
37-Last solo Golden-Age Batman adventure in Detective Comics. Panel at end of story reflects adventure in Batman #1 that was originally planned for Detective #38. Cliff Crosby begins	5600	11,200	16,800	39,750	63,375	87,000
38-Origin/1st app. Robin the Boy Wonder (4/40); Batman and Robin-c begin; cover by Kane	17,000	34,000	51,000	119,000	174,500	230,000
39-Opium story; Clayface app. in 1 panel ad at the end of the Batman story	1500	3000	4500	11,400	20,700	30,000
40-Origin & 1st app. Clayface (Basil Karlo); 1st Joker cover app. (6/40); Joker story intended for this issue was used instead in Batman #1 instead; cover is similar to splash page in 2nd Joker story in Batman #1	4500	9000	13,500	30,000	52,500	75,000
41-Robin's 1st solo	541	1082	1623	3950	6975	10,000
42-44: 44-Crimson Avenger-new costume	423	846	1269	3088	5444	7800
45-1st Joker story in Det. (3rd book app. & 4th story app. over all, 11/40)	892	1784	2676	6512	11,506	16,500
46-50: 46-Death of Hugo Strange. 48-1st time car called Batmobile (2/41); Gotham City 1st mention in Detective (1st mentioned in Wow in #9); also see Batman #4). 49-Last Clayface	400	800	1200	2800	4900	7000

	GD 2.0	VG 4.0	FN 6.0	VF 8.0	VF/NM 9.0	NM- 9.2
51-53,55-57	309	618	927	2163	3782	5400
54-Cover mimics Detective #33 cover	354	708	1062	2478	4339	6200
58-1st Penguin app. (12/41); last Speed Saunders; Fred Ray-c	3000	6000	9000	22,500	33,750	45,000
59-Last Steve Malone; 2nd Penguin; Wing becomes Crimson Avenger's aide.	300	600	900	2070	3635	5200
60-Intro. Air Wave; Joker app. (2nd in Det.)	371	742	1113	2600	4550	6500
61,63: 63-Last Cliff Crosby; 1st app. Mr. Baffle	300	600	900	1920	3310	4700
62-Joker-c/story (2nd Joker-c, 4/42)	1500	3000	4500	11,400	20,700	30,000
64-Origin & 1st app. Boy Commandos by Simon & Kirby (7/42); Joker app.	541	1082	1623	3950	6975	10,000
65-1st Boy Commandos-c (S&K-a on Boy Commandos & Ray/Robinson-a on Batman & Robin on one-c); 4 artists on one-c	354	708	1062	2478	4339	6200
66-Origin & 1st app. Two-Face (originally named Harvey Kent)	3030	6060	9090	21,500	34,250	47,000
67-1st Penguin-c (9/42)	1250	2500	3750	9500	17,250	25,000
68-Two-Face-c/story; 1st Two-Face-c	919	1938	2757	6770	11,855	17,000
69-Classic Joker with 2 guns in his hands-c	3750	7500	11,250	26,600	42,300	58,000
70	331	662	993	2317	4059	5800
71-Classic Joker black background calendar-c	1675	3350	5025	11,150	19,825	28,500
72,74,75: 74-1st Tweedledum & Tweedledee plus-c; S&K-a	258	516	774	1651	2826	4000
73-Scarecrow-c/story (1st Scarecrow-c)	2230	4460	6690	14,900	26,450	38,000
76-Newsboy Legion & The Sandman x-over in Boy Commandos; S&K-a; Joker-c/story	486	972	1458	3550	6275	9000
77-79: All S&K-a	219	438	657	1402	2401	3400
80-Two-Face-c/story; S&K-a	300	600	900	2070	3635	5200
81,82,84,86-90: 81-1st Cavalier-c & app. 87-Penguin app. 89-Last Crimson Avenger; 2nd Cavalier-c & app.	177	354	531	1124	1937	2750
83-1st "skinny" Alfred (1/44)(see Batman #21; last S&K Boy Commandos (also #92,128); most issues #84-on signed S&K are not by them	206	412	618	1318	2259	3200
85-Joker-c/story; last Spy; Kirby/Klech Boy Commandos	470	940	1410	3431	6066	8700
91-Joker-c/story	366	732	1098	2562	4481	6400
92-98: 96-Alfred's last name 'Beagle' revealed, later changed to 'Pennyworth' in #214	142	284	426	909	1555	2200
99-Penguin-c/story	213	426	639	1363	2332	3300
100 (6/45)	177	354	531	1124	1937	2750
101-103,107,110-113,115-117,119	123	246	369	787	1344	1900
102-Joker-c/story	308	616	924	2156	3773	5400
108-1st Bat-signal-c (2/46)	470	940	1410	3431	6066	8700
109-Penguin app.	354	708	1062	2478	4339	6200
114,118-Joker-c/stories. 114-1st small logo (8/46)	331	662	993	2317	4059	5800
120-Penguin-c/story	245	490	735	1568	2684	3800
121,123,125,127,129,130	123	246	369	787	1344	1900
122-1st Catwoman-c (4/47)	1000	2000	3000	7600	13,800	20,000
124,128-Joker-c/stories	300	600	900	1920	3310	4700
126-Penguin-c	194	388	582	1242	2121	3000
131-134,136,139	116	232	348	742	1271	1800
135-Frankenstein-c/story	181	362	543	1158	1979	2800
137-Joker-c/story; last Air Wave	314	628	942	2198	3849	5500
138-Origin Robotman (see Star Spangled #7 for 1st app.); series ends #202	181	362	543	1158	1979	2800
140-The Riddler-c/story (1st app., 10/48)	3750	7500	11,250	25,000	42,500	60,000
141,143-148,150: 150-Last Boy Commandos	116	232	348	742	1271	1800
142-2nd Riddler-c/story	703	1406	2109	5132	9066	13,000
149-Joker-c/story	258	516	774	1651	2826	4000
151-Origin & 1st app. Pow Wow Smith, Indian lawman (9/49) & begins series	138	276	414	876	1513	2150
152,154,155,157-160: 152-Last Slam Bradley	116	232	348	742	1271	1800
153-1st app. Roy Raymond TV Detective (11/49); origin The Human Fly	135	270	405	864	1482	2100
156(2/50)-The new classic Batmobile	394	788	1182	2758	4829	6900
161-167,169,170,172-176: Last 52 pg. issue	116	232	348	742	1271	1800
168-Origin the Joker	4300	8600	12,900	26,900	42,450	58,000
171-Penguin-c	206	412	618	1318	2259	3200
177-179,181-186,188,189,191,192,194-199,201,202,204,206-210,212,214-216: 184-1st app. Fire Fly. 185-Secret of Batman's utility belt. 202-Last Robotman & Pow Wow Smith. 215-1st app. of Batmen of all Nations. 216-Last precode (2/55)	110	220	330	704	1202	1700
180,193-Joker-c/story	245	490	735	1568	2684	3800
187-Two-Face-c/story	371	742	1113	2600	4550	6500
190-Origin Batman retold	148	296	444	947	1628	2300
200(10/53), 205: 205-Origin Batcave	126	252	378	806	1378	1950

	GD 2.0	VG 4.0	FN 6.0	VF 8.0	VF/NM 9.0	NM- 9.2

203,211-Catwoman-c/stories — 168 336 504 1075 1838 2600
213-Origin & 1st app. Mirror Man — 155 310 465 992 1696 2400
217-224: 218-Batman Jr. & Robin Sr. app. — 93 186 279 591 1021 1450
225-(11/55)-1st app. Martian Manhunter (J'onn J'onzz); origin begins; also see Batman #78 — 1850 3700 5550 13,750 32,850 52,000
226-Origin Martian Manhunter cont'd (2nd app.) — 226 452 678 1446 2473 3500
227-229: Martian Manhunter stories in all — 103 206 309 659 1130 1600
230-1st app. Mad Hatter (imposter, not the one from Batman #49, this one's appearance inspired the 1966 TV version); brief recap origin of Martian Manhunter — 423 846 1269 3067 5384 7700
231-Brief origin recap Martian Manhunter — 81 162 243 518 884 1250
232,234,237,238,240 — 71 142 213 454 777 1100
233-Origin & 1st app. Batwoman (7/56) — 892 1784 2676 6512 11,506 16,500
235-Origin Batman & his costume; tells how Bruce Wayne's father (Thomas Wayne) wore Bat costume & fought crime (reprinted in Batman #255) — 135 270 405 864 1482 2100
236-1st S.A. issue; J'onn J'onzz talks to parents and Mars-1st since being stranded on Earth; 1st app. Bat-Tank? — 84 168 252 538 919 1300
239-Early DC grey tone-c — 110 220 330 704 1202 1700
241-Rainbow Batman cover and story — 181 362 543 1158 1979 2800
242-260: 246-Intro. Diane Meade, John Jones' girl. 249-Batwoman-c/app. 253-1st app. The Terrible Trio. 254-Bat-Hound-c/story. 257-Intro. & 1st app. Whirly Bats. 259-1st app. The Calendar Man — 55 110 165 352 601 850
261-264,266,268-271: 261-J. Jones tie-in to sci/fi movie "Incredible Shrinking Man"; 1st app. Dr. Double X. 262-Origin Jackal. 268,271-Manhunter origin recap — 43 86 129 271 461 650
265-Batman's origin retold with new facts — 63 126 189 403 689 975
267-Origin & 1st app. Bat-Mite (5/59) — 276 552 828 4753 3027 4300
272,274,275,277-280 — 37 74 111 222 361 500
273-J'onn J'onzz i.d. revealed for 1st time — 40 80 120 246 411 575
276-2nd app. Bat-Mite — 58 116 174 371 636 900
281-292, 294-297: 286,292-Batwoman-c/app. 287-Origin J'onn J'onzz retold. 289-Bat-Mite-c/story. 292-Last Roy Raymond. 297-Late 10c issue (11/61) — 30 60 90 177 289 400
293-(7/61)-Aquaman begins (pre #1); ends #300 — 37 74 111 218 354 490
298-(12/61)-1st modern Clayface (Matt Hagen) — 258 516 774 1651 2826 4000
299 — 30 60 90 177 289 400
300-(2/62)-1st Polka-Dot Man; Aquaman ends — 103 206 309 659 1130 1600
301-(3/62)-J'onn J'onzz returns to Mars (1st time since landed on Earth six years before) — 16 32 48 110 243 375
302-Batwoman-c/app. — 19 38 57 131 291 450
303-306,308-310,312-317,319-321,323,324,326,329,330: 321-2nd Terrible Trio. 326-Last J'onn J'onzz, story cont'd in House of Mystery #143; intro. Idol-Head of Diabolu — 11 22 33 76 163 250
307-Batwoman-c/app. — 13 26 39 86 188 290
311-1st app. Cat-Man; intro. Zook in John Jones — 30 60 90 216 483 750
318-Cat-Man-c/story (2nd app.); also 1st app. Batwoman as the Cat-Woman — 26 52 78 182 404 625
322,325: 322-Bat-Girl's 1st/only app. in Det. (6th in all); Batman cameo in J'onn J'onzz (only hero to app. in series). 325-Cat-Man-c/story (3rd app.); also 2nd app. Batwoman as the Cat-Woman — 15 30 45 100 220 340
327-(5/64)-Elongated Man begins, ends #383; 1st new look Batman with new costume; Infantino/Giella new look-a begins; Batman with gun — 19 38 57 131 291 450
328-Death of Alfred; Bob Kane biog, 2 pgs. — 15 30 45 100 220 340
331,333-340: 334-1st app. The Outsider — 9 18 27 63 129 195
332,341,345-Joker-c/stories — 13 26 39 86 188 290
342-358,360,361,366-368: 345-Intro Block Buster. 347-"What If" theme story (1/66). —
350-Elongated Man new costume. 355-Zatanna x-over in Elongated Man. 356-Alfred brought back in Batman, early SA app. — 9 18 27 61 123 185
359-Intro/origin (Barbara Gordon)-c/story (1/67); 1st Silver Age app. Killer Moth; classic Batgirl-c — 203 406 609 1675 3788 5900
359-Facsimile Edition (2020, $3.99) Reprints issue with original ads and letter column — 2 4 6 11 16 20
362,364-S.A. Riddler app. (early) — 10 20 30 66 138 210
363-2nd app. new Batgirl — 27 54 81 189 420 650
369(11/67)-N. Adams-a (Elongated Man); 3rd app. S.A. Catwoman (cameo; leads into Batman #197); 4th app. new Batgirl — 20 40 60 138 307 475
370-1st Neal Adams-a on Batman (cover only, 12/67) — 12 24 36 80 173 265
371-(1/68) 1st new Batmobile on TV show; classic Batgirl-c — 17 34 51 117 259 400
372,378,382,386,389,390: 375-New Batmobile-c — 8 16 24 51 96 140
377-S.A. Riddler-c/sty — 9 18 27 59 117 175
387-r/1st Batman story from #27 (30th anniversary, 5/69); Joker-c; last 12c issue — 12 24 36 79 170 260
388-Joker-c/story — 13 26 39 86 188 290
391-394,396,398,399,401,403,406,409: 392-1st app. Jason Bard. 401-2nd Batgirl/Robin team-up — 7 14 21 49 92 135
395-1st Neal Adams art on Detective — 21 42 63 147 324 500
397,402,404,407,408,410-Neal Adams-a. 402-Man-Bat-c/app. (2nd app.). — 12 24 36 80 173 265
404-Tribute to Enemy Ace —
400-(6/70)-Origin & 1st app. Man-Bat; 1st Batgirl/Robin team-up (cont'd in #401); Neal Adams-a — 42 84 126 311 706 1100
405-Debut League of Assassins — 31 62 93 223 499 775
411-(5/71) Intro. Talia, daughter of Ra's al Ghul (Ra's mentioned, but doesn't appear until Batman #232 (6/71); Bob Brown-a — 42 84 126 311 706 1100
412-413: 413-Last 15c issue — 7 14 21 49 92 135
414-424: All-25c, 52 pgs. 418-Creeper x-over. 424-Last Batgirl. — 16 24 51 96 140
425-436: 426,430,436-Elongated Man app. 428,434-Hawkman begins, ends #467 — 5 10 15 35 63 90
437-New Manhunter begins (10-11/73, 1st app.) by Simonson, ends #443 — 6 12 18 41 76 110
438-440,442-445 (All 100 Page Super Spectaculars): 438-Kubert Hawkman-r. 439-Origin Manhunter. 440-G.A. Manhunter(Adv. #79) by S&K, Hawkman, Dollman, Green Lantern; Toth-a. 442-G.A. Newsboy Legion, Black Canary, Elongated Man, Dr. Fate-r. 443-Origin The Creeper-r; death of Manhunter; G.A. Green Lantern, Spectre-r; Batman-r/Batman #18. — 8 16 24 54 110 165

444-G.A. Kid Eternity-r. 445-G.A. Dr. Midnite-r — 7 14 21 44 82 120
441-(6,7/74)(100 Page S.S.) 1st app. Lt. (Harvey) Bullock, first name not given, appears in only 3 panels; G.A. Plastic Man, Batman, Ibis-r — 8 16 24 51 96 140
446-456,458-460 — 3 6 9 19 30 40
457-Classic origin-c; origin retold & updated; 1st app. Leslie Thompkins — 11 22 33 73 157 240
461,462,464,465,470,480: 480-(44 pgs.). 470-Intro. Silver St. Cloud — 3 6 9 17 26 35
463-1st app. Black Spider — 5 10 15 33 57 80
466-468,471-473,478,479-Rogers-a in all: 466-1st app. Signalman since Batman #139. 470,471-1st modern app. Hugo Strange. 478-1st app. 3rd Clayface (Preston Payne). 479-(44 pgs.) — 4 8 12 27 44 60
469-Intro/origin Dr. Phosphorous; Simonson-a — 5 10 15 33 57 80
474-1st app. new Deadshot — 7 14 21 48 89 130
475-Joker-c/story; Rogers-a — 9 18 27 62 126 190
475-Facsimile Edition (2020, $3.99) Reprints issue with original ads and letter column — 2 4 6 8 10 12
476-Joker-c/story; Rogers-a — 6 12 18 42 79 115
477-Neal Adams-a(r); Rogers-a (3 pgs.) — 4 8 12 25 40 55
481-(Combined with Batman Family, 12-1/78-79, begin $1.00, 68 pg. issues, ends #495); 481-495-Batgirl, Robin solo stories — 4 8 12 25 40 55
482,483: 482-Starlin/Russell, Golden-a; The Demon begins (origin-r), ends #485 (by Ditko #483-485). 483-40th Anniversary issue; origin retold in brief; Newton Batman begins; Human Target with Chaykin-a; Batman Family pin-up on back-c — 3 6 9 16 23 30
484-495 (68 pgs.): 484-Origin Robin. 485-Death of Batwoman. 486-Killer Moth app. 487-The Odd Man by Ditko. 489-Robin/Batgirl team-up. 490-Black Lightning begins. 491-(#492 on inside). 493-Intro. The Swashbuckler — 3 6 9 14 19 24
496-499: 496-Clayface app. — 2 4 6 10 13 16
500-($1.50, 52 pgs.)-Batman/Deadman team-up with Infantino-a; new Hawkman story by Joe Kubert; incorrectly says 500th Anniv. of Det. — 5 10 15 38 28 38
501-503,505-522: 509-Catman-c. 510-Mad Hatter-c. 512-2nd app. new Dr. Death. 513-Two-Face app. 519-Last Batgirl. 521-Green Arrow series begins — 2 4 6 8 10 12
504-Joker-c/story — 3 6 9 14 19 24
523-1st Killer Croc (cameo); Solomon Grundy app. — 4 8 12 28 47 65
524-2nd app. Jason Todd (cameo)(3/83) — 4 8 12 28 47 65
525-3rd app. Jason Todd (See Batman #357) — 4 8 12 28 47 65
526-Batman's 500th app. in Detective Comics ($1.50, 68 pgs.); Death of Jason Todd's parents, Joker-c/story (1st); Bob Kane pin-up — 3 6 9 14 22 38
527-531,533,534,536-553,555-568,571,573: 538-Cat-Man-c/story cont'd from Batman #371. —
542-Jason Todd quits as Robin (becomes Robin again #547). 549,550-Alan Moore scripts (Green Arrow). 566-Batman villains profiled. 567-Harlan Ellison scripts — 1 3 4 6 8 10
532,569,570-Joker-c/stories — 3 6 9 16 23 30
535-Intro new Robin (Jason Todd)-1st appeared in Batman — 2 4 6 8 10 12
554-Intro new Black Canary (9/85) — 2 4 6 10 14 18
572-(3/87, $1.25, 60 pgs.)-50th Anniv. of Det. Comics — 2 4 6 10 14 18
574-Origin Batman & Jason Todd retold — 2 4 6 10 14 18
575-578: Year 2; McFarlane-c/a; The Reaper app. — 3 6 9 17 30 40
579-584,586-597,599,601-607,609,610: 579-New bat wing logo. 583-1st app. villains Scarface & Ventriloquist. 589,595-(52 pgs.)-Each contain free 16 pg. Batman stories. — 1 2 3 5 6 8
604-607-Mudpack storyline. 604,607-Contain Batman mini-posters. 610-Faked death of Penguin; artists names app. on tombstone on-c — 1 2 3 5 6 8
585-The Ratcatcher debut (4/88) — 1 2 3 6 8 10
598-($2.95, 84 pgs.)- "Blind Justice" storyline begins by Batman movie writer Sam Hamm, ends #600 — 2 4 6 11 15 18
600-(5/89, $2.95, 84 pgs)-50th Anniv. of Batman in Det.; 1 pg. Neal Adams pin-up, among other artists — 3 6 9 13 17 21
608-1st app. Anarky — 3 6 9 14 19 24
611-626,628-646,649-658: 612-1st new look Cat-Man; Catwoman app. 615-"The Penguin Affair" part 2 (See Batman #448,449). 617-Joker-c/story. 624-1st new Catwoman (w/death) & 1st new Batwoman. 626-Batman's 600th app. in Detective. 642-Return of Scarface, part 2. 644-Last $1.00-c. 644-646-The (2nd) Electrocutioner (Lester Buchinsky) app. 652,653-Huntress-c/story w/new costume plus Charest-c on both — 1 3 4 6 8
627-($2.95, 84 pgs.)-Batman's 601st app. in Det.; reprints 1st story/#27 plus 3 versions (2 new) of same story — 2 4 6 8 10 12
647-1st app. Stephanie Brown — 3 6 9 17 26 35
648-1st full app. Spoiler (Stephanie Brown) — 2 4 6 8 11 14
659-664: 659-Knightfall part 2; Kelley Jones-c. 660-Knightfall part 4; Bane-c by Sam Kieth. 661-Knightfall part 6; brief Joker & Riddler app. 662-Knightfall part 8; Riddler app.; Sam Kieth-c. 663-Knightfall part 10; Kelley Jones-c. 664-Knightfall part 12; Bane-c/story; Joker app.; continued in Showcase 93 #7 & 8; James-c — 1 2 3 4 6 8 10
665-675: 665,666-Knightfall parts 16 & 18; 666-Bane-c/story. 667-Knightquest: The Crusade & new Batman begins (1st app. in Batman #500). 669-Begin $1.50-c; Knightquest, cont'd in Robin #1. 671,673-Joker app. — 6.00
675-($2.95)-Collectors edition w/foil-c — 1 2 3 5 6
676-($2.50, 52 pgs.)-KnightsEnd pt. 2 — 1 2 3 5 6
677,678: 677-KnightsEnd pt. 9. 678-(9/94)-Zero Hour tie-in — 6.00
679-685: 679-(11/94) 682-Troika pt. 3 — 5.00
682-($2.50) Embossed-c Troika pt. 3 — 6.00
686-699,701-719: 686-Begin $1.95-c. 693,694-Poison Ivy-c/app. 695-Contagion pt. 2; Catwoman, Penguin app. 696-Contagion pt. 8. 698-Two-Face-c/app. 701-Legacy pt. 6; Batman vs. Bane-c/app. 702-Legacy Epilogue. 703-Final Night x-over. — 5.00
700-($4.95, Collectors Edition)-Legacy pt. 1; Ra's Al Ghul-c/app; Talia & Bane app; book displayed at shops in envelope — 1 3 4 6 8 11 14
700-($2.95, Regular Edition)-Different-c — 2 4 6 8 11 14
720-736,738,739: 720,721-Cataclysm pts. 5,14. 723-Green Arrow app. 730-740-No Man's Land stories. 735-1st app. Mercy Graves in regular DCU — 5.00
737-Harley Quinn-c/app. (1st app. in Detective); No Man's Land — 2 4 6 8 11 14
740-Joker, Bane-c/app.; Harley Quinn app.; No Man's Land — 4 9 14 23 30
741-($2.50) Endgame; Joker-c/app.; Harley Quinn app. — 2 4 6 8 11 14
741-($2.50) Endgame; Joker-c/app.; Harley Quinn app. — 1 3 4 6 8 10

Detective Comics #327 © DC

Detective Comics #831 © DC

Detective Comics #1062 © DC

	GD	VG	FN	VF	VF/NM	NM-
	2.0	4.0	6.0	8.0	9.0	9.2

742-749,751-765: 742-New look Batman begins; 1st app. Crispus Allen (who later becomes the Spectre). 751,752-Poison Ivy app. 756-Superman-c/app. 759-762-Catwoman back-up ... 4.00
750-($4.95, 64 pgs.) Ra's al Ghul-c 1 2 3 4 5 7
766-772: 766,767-Bruce Wayne: Murderer pt. 1,8. 769-772-Bruce Wayne: Fugitive pts. 4,8,12,16 ... 4.00
773,774,776-782,784-799: 773-Begin $2.75-c; Sienkiewicz-c. 777-784-Sale-c ... 4.00
784-786-Alan Scott app. 787-Mad Hatter app. 797-799-War Games ... 5.00
775-($3.50) Sienkiewicz-c ... 4.00
783-Nyssa 1 3 4 6 8 10
800-($3.50) Jock-c; aftermath of War Games; back-up by Lapham ... 5.00
801-830,832-836,838-849,851,852: 801-814-Lapham-s. 804-Mr. Freeze app. 809-War Crimes.
817-820: One Year Later 8-part x-over with Batman #651-654; Robinson-s/Bianchi-c.
819-Begin $2.99-c. 820-Dini-s/Williams III-a. 821-Harley Quinn app. 825-Dr. Phosphorus app.
827-Debut of new Scarface. 833,834-Zatanna & Joker app. 838,839-Resurrection of Ra's al Ghul x-over. 846-847-Batman R.I.P. x-over ... 4.00
817,818,838,839-2nd printings. 817-Combo-c of #817&#819 cover images. 818-Combo-c of #818 and Batman #653 cover images. 838-Andy Kubert variant-c. 839-Red bkgd-c ... 4.00
831,837-Harley Quinn app. 831-Dini-s 1 3 4 6 8 10
850-($3.50) Batman vs. Hush; Dini-s/Nguyen-a ... 6.00
853-Gaiman-s/Andy Kubert-a; continued from Batman #686; Kubert sketch pgs. ... 4.00
853-Variant-c with red background by Andy Kubert 3 6 9 14 20 25
854-872-($3.99) 854-Batwoman features begin; Rucka-a/J.H. Williams-a/c; The Question back-ups begin. 858-860-Batwoman origin. 871-1st Scott Snyder Batman-s ... 5.00
854,858,859,860-Variant-c: 854-JG Jones. 858-Hughes. 859-Jock. 860-Alex Ross ... 6.00
854-Special Edition (8/10, $1.00) reprints issue with "What's Next?" logo on cover ... 3.00
873-879-($2.99) 874,875,879-Francavilla-a ... 4.00
880-Joker-c/app.; Jock-c/a 10 20 30 64 132 200
881-(10/11) Last issue of first volume; Snyder-s/Jock & Francavilla-a 2 4 6 11 16 20
... 4.00
#0-(10/94) Zero Hour tie-in, released between #678 & #679 ... 4.00
#27-Facsimile Edition (2022, $6.99) Reprints entire issue with original ads ... 7.00
#38-Facsimile Edition (2020, $3.99) Reprints Robin's debut issue with original ads ... 7.00
#38-Facsimile Edition (2022, $6.99) Reprints Robin's debut issue with original ads ... 7.00
#58-Facsimile Edition (11/23, $6.99) Reprints Penguin's debut issue with original ads ... 5.00
#140-Facsimile Edition (12/23, $4.99) Reprints Riddler's debut issue with original ads ... 5.00
#411-Facsimile Edition (11/23, $6.99) Reprints Talia's debut issue with original ads ... 5.00
#1,000,000 (11/98) 853rd Century x-over
Annual 1 (1988, $1.50) 1 3 4 6 8 10
Annual 2-7.9 ('89-'94, '96, 68 pgs.)-4-Painted-c. 5-Joker-c/story (54 pgs.) continued in Robin Annual #1; Sam Kieth-c; Eclipso app. 6-Azrael as Batman in new costume; story ties the Twilight Man; Bloodlines storyline. 7-Elseworlds story. 9-Legends of the Dead Earth story
1 2 3 4 5 7
Annual 8 (1995, $3.95, 68 pgs.)-Year One story ... 5.00
Annual 10 (1997, $3.95)-Pulp Heroes story ... 5.00
Annual 11 (12/09, $4.99)-Azrael & The Question app.; continued from Batman Ann. #27 ... 5.00
Annual 12 (2/11, $4.99)-Nightrunner & The Question app.; continued in Batman Ann. #28 ... 5.00
NOTE: Neal Adams c-370, 372, 385, 389, 391, 392, 394-422, 439. Aparo a-437, 438, 444-446, 500, 625-632p. 638-643p; c-430, 437, 440-446, 448, 468-470, 480, 484(back), 492-502,508, 509, 515, 518-522, 641, 716, 719, 722, 724. Austin a-(i)450, 451, 463-468, 471-476; c(i)-474-476, 478. Baily a-443r. Buckler a-434, 446p; 479p; c(p)-467, 482, 505-507, 511, 513-516, 518. Burnley a(Batman)-65, 75, 78, 83, 100, 103, 125; c-62i, 63i, 64, 73i, 78, 83p, 96p, 103p, 105p, 106, 108, 121p, 123p, 125p. Chaykin a-441. Colan a(p)-510, 512, 517, 523, 528-538, 540-546, 555-567; c(p)-510, 512, 528, 530-535, 537, 538, 540, 541, 543-545, 556-558, 560-564. J. Craig a-488. Ditko a-443. Alan Grant scripts-584-597, 601-621, 641, 642, 483-485, 487. Golden a-482p; c-625, 626, 628-631, 633, 644-646. Alan Grant scripts-584-597, 601-621, 641, 642, 483-485, 487. Golden a-482p; c-625, 626, 628-631, 633, 644-646. Alan Grant scripts-584-597, 601-621, 641, 642. Infantino a-354, 442(2)r, 500, 572. Infantino/Anderson c-333, 337-340, 343, 344, 347, 351, 352, 359, 361-368, 371. Kelley Jones c-651, 657i, 658i, 659, 661, 663-675. Kaluta c-423, 426-428, 431, 434, 438, 446, 572. Bob Kane a-Most early issues #27 on, 297r, 356r, 438-440r, 442r, 443r. Kane/Robinson c-33. Gil Kane a(p)-368, 370-374, 384, 385, 388-407, 439. Kane/Anderson c-369. Sam Kieth c-654-656 (657, 658 w/Kelley Jones), 660, 662, Annual #5. Kubert a-438r, 439r, 500; c-348-350. McFarlane c/a(p)-576-578. Meskin a-420r. Mignola c-583. Moldoff c-233-354, 259, 266, 267, 275, 287, 289, 290, 297, 300. Moldoff/Giella a-328, 330, 332, 334, 336, 338, 340, 342, 344, 346, 348, 350, 352, 354, 356. Mooney a-444r. Moreira a-153-300, 419r, 444r, 445r. Nasser/Netzer a-654, 655, 657, 658. Newton a(p)-481, 483-499, 501-509, 511, 513-516, 518-520, 524, 526, 530; c-526p. Irv Novick c-375-377, 383. Robbins a-426p, 429p. Robinson a-part: 66, 68, 71-73; all: 74-76, 79, 80; c-62, 64, 66, 68-74, 79, 82, 86-88, 448, 471-479p, 481(?)-c-479, 472p, 473, 474-479p. Roussos Airwave-76-105(most); c(i)-71, 72, 74-76, 79, 107. Russell a-481i, 482i. Simon/Kirby a(Sandman)-76p, 79p, 82, 84, 85, 87, 89-93, 95-100, 102, 103i, 104i, 106, 108, 114, 117, 118, 122, 123, 469, 470, 500. Dick Sprang c-77, 82, 84, 85, 87, 89-93, 95-100, 102, 103i, 104i, 106, 108, 114, 117, 118, 122, 123, 128, 129, 131, 133, 135, 141, 148, 149, 168, 622-624. Starlin a-481p, 482p; c-503, 504, 567p. Starr a-444r. Toth a-442; r-414, 416, 418, 424, 440-441, 443, 444. Tuska a-486p, 490p. Matt Wagner c-647-649. Wrightson c-425.

DETECTIVE COMICS (DC New 52)(Numbering reverts to original series #934 after #52)
DC Comics: Nov, 2011 - No. 52, Jul, 2016 ($2.99/$3.99)

1-Joker app.; Tony Daniel-s/a/c 3 6 9 16 23 30
2-7: 2-Intro of the Dollmaker. 5-7-Penguin app. ... 5.00
8,10-14,16-18: 8-($3.99) Catwoman & Scarecrow app.; back-up Two-Face story begins ... 4.00
9-Night of the Owls ... 5.00
15-Die-cut Joker cover; Death of the Family tie-in ... 8.00
19-(6/13, $7.99) 900th issue of Detective; bonus back-up stories and pin-up art ... 8.00
20-24,26: 21-23-Man-Bat back-up story. 26-Man-Bat app. ... 4.00
23.1, 23.2, 23.3, 23.4 (11/13, $2.99, regular covers) 1 2 3 5 6 8

23.1 (11/13, $3.99, 3-D cover) "Poison Ivy #1" on cover; Fridolfs-s/Pina-a
2 4 6 9 12 15
23.2 (11/13, $3.99, 3-D cover) "Harley Quinn #1" on cover; Googe-a/Kindt-s; origin
2 4 6 13 18 22
23.3 (11/13, $3.99, 3-D cover) "Scarecrow #1" on cover; Kudranski-a ... 15.00
23.4 (11/13, $3.99, 3-D cover) "Man-Bat #1" on cover; Tieri-s/Eaton-a ... 15.00
25-($3.99) Zero Year focus on Lt. Gordon; Fabok-a/c; Man-Bat back-up ... 4.00
27-($7.99) Start of Gothtopia; short stories by Meltzer, Hitch, Neal Adams, Francavilla, Murphy ... 8.00
28-49,51,52: 28,29-Gothtopia. 30-34,37-40-Manupul-a. 37-40-Anarky app. 43,44-Joker's Daughter. 45,46-Justice League app. 47-"Robin War" tie-in ... 4.00
50-($4.99) Bonus pin-up swipes of classic Detective covers by various ... 5.00
#0 (11/12, $3.99) Flashback to training and return to Alfred ... 4.00
Annual 1 (10/12, $4.99) Black Mask app.; Daniel-s/c; Molenaar-a ... 5.00
Annual 2 (9/13, $4.99) The Wrath app.; Eaton-a/Clarke-c ... 5.00
Annual 3 (9/14, $4.99) March-c ... 5.00
...: Endgame 1 (5/15, $2.99) Tie-in to Endgame story in Batman #35-40; Anarky app. ... 3.00
...: Futures End 1 (11/14, $2.99, regular-c) Five years later; Riddler app. ... 3.00
...: Futures End 1 (11/14, $3.99, 3-D cover) ... 4.00

DETECTIVE COMICS (Numbering reverts to original V1 #934 after #52 from 2011-2016 series)
DC Comics: No. 934, Aug, 2016 - Present ($2.99/$3.99)

934-Tynion IV-s/Barrows-a; Batwoman, Spoiler, Red Robin, Clayface app.
1 2 3 5 6 8
935-949,951-974: 936-938-Alvaro Martinez-a. 937-Intro. Ulysses Armstrong. 940-Apparent death of Tim Drake. 941,942-Night of the Monster Men x-over. 944-Batwing returns. 948,949-Batwoman begins. 951-956-"League of Shadows". 958-961-Zatanna app.
965-Tim Drake vs. Mr. Oz. 965-967-Future Batman (Tim Drake) app. ... 3.00
950-($3.99) Prologue to "League of Shadows"; Takara-a; Shiva & Azrael app. ... 4.00
975-($3.99) Trial of Batwoman; Tynion IV-s/Martinez-a ... 4.00
976-987: 976-Batmen Eternal begins. 983-987-Black Lightning app. ... 3.00
988-999-($3.99) 989-993-Two-Face app. 994-999-Mahnke-a ... 4.00
1000-(5/19, $9.99) Short stories and pin-ups by various incl. Snyder/Capullo, Kevin Smith/ Jim Lee, Dini/Nguyen, Ellis/Cloonan, O'Neil/Epting, Priest/Adams, Bendis/Maleev; Johns/Kelley Jones, Tynion IV/Martinez-Bueno, Daniel/Joëlle Jones, Slam Bradley app.; intro. The Arkham Knight by Tomasi-s/Mahnke-a; 10 regular covers ... 15.00
1001-1023: 1001-1005-Arkham Knight app. 1004-Arkham Knight origin. 1006,1007-Spectre app.; Kyle Hotz-a 1008-Joker app. 1008-1016-Mr. Freeze app. 1009-1011-Deadshot app. 1013-Nora Fries revived. 1023-Joker War tie-in ... 4.00
1024-1026-Joker War tie-ins. 1026-Killer Croc app. 2 4 6 8 10 12
1027-(11/20, $9.99) Short stories by various incl. Bendis-s/Marquez-a, Fraction-s/Zdarsky-a, Rucka-s/Risso-a, King-s/Simonson-a, Snyder-s/Reis-a; Jurgens-s/a with 1930s Batman meets Kamandi (leads into Generations Shattered #1); bonus pin-ups; multiple covers 12.00
1028-1033: 1029-Debut The Mirror. 1131-1133-Hush app. ... 4.00
1034-1049, 1051-1075-($4.99): 1044-1046-"Fear State" tie-ins. 1047-1049-Reis-a ... 5.00
1050-($5.99)-Shadows of the Bat; Psycho Pirate app.; bonus preview of World's Finest #1 ... 6.00
1076-($5.99)-Alexander-a; The Question & Azrael app. ... 6.00
1077-1082-($4.99): 1077-1080-Alexander-a ... 5.00
Annual 1 (3/18, $4.99) Tynion IV-s/Barrows-a; Clayface origin re-told ... 5.00
Annual 2 (7/19, $4.99) Tomasi-s/Travis Moore-a; The Reaper app. ... 5.00
Annual 3 (Late March/20, $4.99) Spotlight on Alfred; back-up with Risso-a; Rude-c ... 6.00
2021 Annual 1 (1/22, $5.99) Prelude to Shadows of the Bat; Lapham-a ... 6.00
2022 Annual 1 (1/22, $5.99) Flashback to the Gathome Settlement in 1776; Mitten-a ... 6.00

DETECTIVE COMICS: BATMAN 80TH ANNIVERSARY GIANT
DC Comics: 2019 ($4.99, 100 pgs., squarebound, Walmart exclusive)

1-New story Venditti-s/Segovia-a; Two-Face app.; reprints 1st apps. of Batman, Robin, Batgirl, Leslie Thompkins, plus stories from Detective #500 and Batman Black and White #4
8 16 24 56 108 160

DETECTIVE DAN, SECRET OP. 48 (Also see Adventures of Detective Ace King and Bob Scully, The Two-Fisted Hick Detective)
Humor Publ. Co. (Norman Marsh): 1933 (10¢, 10x13", 36 pgs., B&W, one-shot) (3 color, cardboard-c)

nn-By Norman Marsh, 1st comic w/ original art; 1st newsstand-c; Dick Tracy look-alike; forerunner of Dan Dunn. (Title and Wu Fang character inspired Detective Comics #1 four years later.) (1st comic of a single theme) 2250 4500 6750 13,500 -- --

DETECTIVE EYE (See Keen Detective Funnies)
Centaur Publications: Nov, 1940 - No. 2, Dec, 1940

1-Air Man (see Keen Detective) & The Eye Sees begins; The Masked Marvel & Dean Denton app. 300 600 900 2070 3635 5200
2-Origin Don Rance and the Mysticape; Binder-a; Frank Thomas-c
258 516 774 1651 2826 4000

DETECTIVE PICTURE STORIES (Keen Detective Funnies No. 8 on?)
Comics Magazine Company: Dec, 1936 - No. 5, Apr, 1937

	GD 2.0	VG 4.0	FN 6.0	VF 8.0	VF/NM 9.0	NM- 9.2

1 (All issues are very scarce) — 730 / 1460 / 2190 / 4160 / 6830 / 9500
2-The Clock app. (1/37, early app.) — 370 / 740 / 1110 / 2100 / 3450 / 4800
3,4: 4-Eisner-a — 310 / 620 / 930 / 1770 / 2885 / 4000
5-The Clock-c/story (4/37); "The Case of the Missing Heir" 1st detective/adventure art by Bob Kane; Bruce Wayne prototype app. (story reprinted in Funny Pages V3 #1) — 525 / 1050 / 1575 / 3000 / 4900 / 6800

DETECTIVES, THE (TV)
Dell Publishing Co.: No. 1168, Mar-May, 1961 - No. 1240, Oct-Dec, 1961
Four Color 1168 (#1)-Robert Taylor photo-c — 10 / 20 / 30 / 66 / 138 / 210
Four Color 1219-Robert Taylor, Adam West photo-c — 10 / 20 / 30 / 66 / 138 / 210
Four Color 1240-Tufts-a; Robert Taylor photo-c; 2 different back-c — 8 / 16 / 24 / 51 / 96 / 140

DETECTIVES, INC. (See Eclipse Graphic Album Series)
Eclipse Comics: Apr, 1985 - No. 2, Apr, 1985 ($1.75, both w/April dates)
1,2: 2-Nudity — 4.00

DETECTIVES, INC.: A TERROR OF DYING DREAMS
Eclipse Comics: Jun, 1987 - No. 3, Dec, 1987 ($1.75, B&W& sepia)
1-3: Colan-a — 4.00
TPB ('99, $19.95) r/series — 20.00

DETENTION COMICS
DC Comics: Oct, 1996 ($3.50, 56 pgs., one-shot)
1-Robin story by Dennis O'Neil & Norm Breyfogle; Superboy story by Ron Marz & Ron Lim; Warrior story by Ruben Diaz & Joe Phillips; Phillips-c — 5.00

DETHKLOK (Based on the animated series Metalocalypse)
Dark Horse Comics: Oct, 2010 - No. 3, Feb, 2011 ($3.99, limited series)
1-3-Small & Schnepp-s; covers by Schnepp & Eric Powell — 4.00
...: Versus the Goon 1-(7/09, $3.50) Powell-s/a/c; Dethklok visits the Goon universe — 2 / 4 / 6 / 8 / 10 / 12
...: Versus the Goon 1-Variant cover by Jon Schnepp — 2 / 4 / 6 / 9 / 12 / 15
HC (7/11, $19.99) r/#1-3 & Dethklok: Versus the Goon — 20.00

DETONATOR (Mike Baron's...)
Image Comics: Nov, 2004 - No. 4 ($2.50/$2.95)
1-4-Mike Baron-s/Mel Rubi-a — 3.00

DEUS EX (Based on the Square Enix videogame)
DC Comics: Apr, 2011 - No. 6, Sept, 2011 ($2.99, limited series)
1-6-Robbie Morrison-s/Trevor Hairsine-a — 3.00

DEUS EX: CHILDREN'S CRUSADE (Based on the Square Enix videogame)
Titan Comics: Mar, 2016 - No. 5, Jul, 2016 ($3.99, limited series)
1-5-Alex Irvine-s/John Aggs-a; 3 covers on each — 4.00

DEVASTATOR
Image Comics/Halloween: 1998 - No. 3 ($2.95, B&W, limited series)
1,2-Hudnall-s/Horn-c/a — 4.00

DEVI (Shekhar Kapur's...)
Virgin Comics: July, 2006 - No. 20, Jun, 2008 ($2.99)
1-20: 1-Mukesh Singh-a/Siddharth Kotian-s. 2-Greg Horn-c — 3.00
.../Witchblade (4/08, $2.99) Singh-a/Land-c; continued from Witchblade/Devi — 3.00
... Vol. 1 TPB (5/07, $14.99) r/#1-5 and Story from Virgin Comics Preview #0 — 15.00
... Vol. 2 TPB (9/07, $14.99) r/#6-10; character and cover sketches — 15.00

DEVIL CHEF
Dark Horse Comics: July, 1994 ($2.50, B&W, one-shot)
nn — 4.00

DEVIL DINOSAUR
Marvel Comics Group: Apr, 1978 - No. 9, Dec, 1978
1-Kirby/Royer-a in all; all have Kirby-c — 5 / 10 / 15 / 30 / 50 / 70
2-9: 4-7-UFO/sci. fic. 8-Dinoriders-c/sty — 2 / 4 / 6 / 11 / 16 / 20
... By Jack Kirby Omnibus HC (2007, $29.99, dustjacket) r/#1-9; intro. by Brevoort — 70.00

DEVIL DINOSAUR SPRING FLING
Marvel Comics: June, 1997 ($2.99. one-shot)
1-(48 pgs.) Moon-Boy-c/app. — 4.00

DEVIL-DOG DUGAN (Tales of the Marines No. 4 on)
Atlas Comics (OPI): July, 1956 - No. 3, Nov, 1956
1-Severin-c — 28 / 56 / 84 / 168 / 274 / 380
2-Iron Mike McGraw x-over; Severin-c — 15 / 30 / 45 / 85 / 130 / 175
3 — 15 / 30 / 45 / 83 / 124 / 165

DEVIL DOGS
Street & Smith Publishers: 1942
1-Boy Rangers, U.S. Marines; WWII Japanese slaughter-c — 77 / 154 / 231 / 493 / 847 / 1200

DEVILERS
Dynamite Entertainment: 2014 - No. 7, 2015 ($2.99)
1-7-Fialkov-s/Triano-a/Jock-c — 3.00

DEVILINA (Magazine)
Atlas/Seaboard: Feb, 1975 - No. 2, May, 1975 (B&W)
1-Art by Reese, Marcos; "The Tempest" adapt. — 5 / 10 / 15 / 31 / 53 / 75
2 (Low printing) — 5 / 10 / 15 / 34 / 60 / 85

DEVIL KIDS STARRING HOT STUFF
Harvey Publications (Illustrated Humor): July, 1962 - No. 107, Oct, 1981 (Giant-Size #41-55)
1 (12¢ cover price #1-#41-9/69) — 33 / 66 / 99 / 238 / 532 / 825
2 — 10 / 20 / 30 / 69 / 147 / 225
3-10 (1/64) — 8 / 16 / 24 / 51 / 96 / 140
11-20 — 5 / 10 / 15 / 33 / 57 / 80
21-30 — 4 / 8 / 12 / 25 / 40 / 55
31-40: 40-(6/69) — 3 / 6 / 9 / 19 / 30 / 40
41-50: All 68 pg. Giants — 3 / 6 / 9 / 21 / 33 / 45
51-55: All 52 pg. Giants — 3 / 6 / 9 / 19 / 30 / 40
56-70 — 2 / 4 / 6 / 11 / 16 / 20
71-90 — 2 / 4 / 6 / 8 / 11 / 14
91-107 — 1 / 2 / 3 / 5 / 6 / 8

DEVIL'S DUE FREE COMIC BOOK DAY
Devil's Due Publ.: May, 2005 (Free Comic Book Day giveaway)
nn-Short stories of G.I. Joe, Defex and Darkstalkers; Darkstalkers flip cover — 3.00

DEVIL'S FOOTPRINTS, THE
Dark Horse Comics: March, 2003 - No. 4, June, 2003 ($2.99, limited series)
1-4-Paul Lee-c/a; Scott Allie-s — 3.00

DEVIL'S HIGHWAY
AWA Studios: Jul, 2020 - No. 5, Nov, 2020 ($3.99, limited series)
1-5-Benjamin Percy-s/Brent Schoonover-a — 4.00
Vol. 2 (5/22 - No. 5, 9/22) 1-5-Percy-s/Schoonover-a — 4.00

DEVIL'S REIGN
Marvel Comics: Feb, 2022 - No. 6, Jun, 2022 ($5.99/$4.99, limited series)
1-($5.99) Zdarsky-s/Checchetto-a; Wilson Fisk outlaws heroes in New York City — 6.00
2-5-($4.99) 2-Spider-Man vs. Taskmaster. 3-Superior Four app. — 5.00
6-($5.99) Daredevil vs. Kingpin; Avengers vs. The Purple Man — 6.00
...: Moon Knight 1 (5/22, $4.99) MacKay-s/Sabbatini-a — 5.00
...: Omega 1 (7/22, $4.99) Coda to the series; leads into Daredevil #1 (2022) — 5.00
...: Spider-Man 1 (4/22, $4.99) Ben Reilly Spidey; Anthony Piper-s/Zé Carlos-a — 5.00
...: Winter Soldier 1 (3/22, $4.99) Nico Leon-a; leads into Captain America #0 (2022) — 5.00
...: X-Men 1 (3/22, $4.99) Duggan-s/Noto-a; Emma Frost & Thunderbolts app. — 5.00

DEVIL'S REIGN: SUPERIOR FOUR
Marvel Comics: Mar, 2022 - No. 3, May, 2022 ($3.99, limited series)
1-3-Doc Ock w/multiverse Octaviuses as Wolverine, Hulk and Ghost Rider — 4.00

DEVIL'S REIGN: VILLAINS FOR HIRE
Marvel Comics: Mar, 2022 - No. 3, May, 2022 ($3.99, limited series)
1-3-New Thunderbolts team; U.S.Agent app.; Chapman-s/Garcia-a — 4.00

DEVIL'S REIGN: X-MEN
Marvel Comics: Mar, 2022 - No. 3, May, 2022 ($4.99/$3.99, limited series)
1-Duggan-s/Noto-a; Emma Frost & Thunderbolts app. — 5.00
2,3-($3.99) 2-Spider-Man app. 3-Union Jack app. — 4.00

DEVI / WITCHBLADE
Graphic India Pte, Ltd.: Jan, 2016 ($4.99, one-shot)
1-Ron Marz & Samit Basu-s/Eric & Rick Basuldua & Mukesh Singh-a; multiple covers — 5.00

DEVOLUTION
Dynamite Entertainment: 2016 - No. 5, 2016 ($3.99)
1-5-Remender-s/Wayshak/Jae Lee-c — 4.00

DEXTER (Character from the novels and Showtime series)
Marvel Comics: Sept, 2013 - No. 5, Jan, 2014 ($3.99, limited series)
1-Lindsay-s/Talajic/Mike Del Mundo-c in all — 3 / 6 / 9 / 14 / 12 / 25
2-5 — 6.00

DEXTER COMICS
Dearfield Publ.: Summer, 1948 - No. 5, July, 1949
1-Teen-age humor — 32 / 64 / 96 / 188 / 307 / 425
2-Junie Prom app. — 19 / 38 / 57 / 111 / 176 / 240
3-5 — 15 / 30 / 45 / 85 / 130 / 175

DEXTER DOWN UNDER (Character from the novels and Showtime series)
Marvel Comics: Apr, 2014 - No. 5, Aug, 2014 ($3.99, limited series)
1-5-Jeff Lindsay-s/Dalibor Talajic-a/Mike Del Mundo-c — 4.00

DEXTER'S LABORATORY (Cartoon Network)
DC Comics: Sept, 1999 - No. 34, Apr, 2003 ($1.99/$2.25)
1 — 3 / 6 / 9 / 15 / 22 / 28
2-10: 2-McCracken-s — 6.00
11-24, 26-34: 31-Begin $2.25-c. 32-34-Wray-c — 4.00
25-(50¢-c) Tartakovsky-s/a; Action Hank-c/app. — 4.00

DEXTER'S LABORATORY (Cartoon Network)
IDW Publishing: Apr, 2014 - No. 4, Jul, 2014 ($3.99)
1-4-Fridolfs-s/Jampole-a; three covers each — 4.00

DEXTER THE DEMON (Formerly Melvin The Monster)(See Cartoon Kids & Peter the Little Pest)
Atlas Comics (HPC): No. 7, Sept, 1957
7 — 15 / 30 / 45 / 85 / 130 / 175

DHAMPIRE: STILLBORN
DC Comics (Vertigo): 1996 ($5.95, one-shot, mature)
1-Nancy Collins script; Paul Lee-c/a — 6.00

DIABLO
DC Comics: Jan, 2012 - No. 5, Oct, 2012 ($2.99, limited series)
1-5-Aaron Williams-s/Joseph Lacroix-a/c — 3.00

DIABLO HOUSE
IDW Publishing: Jul, 2017 - No. 4, Dec, 2017 ($3.99)
1-4-Horror anthology; Ted Adams-s/Santipérez-a — 4.00

DIAL H (Dial H for HERO)(Also see Justice League #23.3)
DC Comics: Jul, 2012 - No. 15, Oct, 2013 ($2.99/$4.99)
1-14: 1-6-China Miéville-s/Mateus Santolouco-a/Brian Bolland-c. 1-Variant-c by Finch — 3.00
15-($4.99) Mieville-s/Ponticelli-a/Bolland-c — 5.00
#0 (11/12, $2.99) Origin of the dial; Miéville-s/Burchielli-a/Bolland-c — 3.00

DIAL H FOR HERO
DC Comics: May, 2019 - No. 12, Apr, 2020 ($3.99)
1-12: 1-Intro. Miguel Montez; Humphries-s/Quinones-a. 3-Robby Reed returns — 4.00

DIARY CONFESSIONS (Formerly Ideal Romance)
Stanmor/Key Publ.(Medal Comics): No. 9, May, 1955 - No. 14, Apr, 1955
9 — 15 / 30 / 45 / 90 / 140 / 190

Dethklok #2 © CN

Devil's Reign #1 © MAR

Dick Tracy #67 © UFS

	GD 2.0	VG 4.0	FN 6.0	VF 8.0	VF/NM 9.0	NM- 9.2
10-14	13	26	39	72	101	130

DIARY LOVES (Formerly Love Diary #1; G. I. Sweethearts #32 on)
Quality Comics Group: No. 2, Nov, 1949 - No. 31, April, 1953

	GD 2.0	VG 4.0	FN 6.0	VF 8.0	VF/NM 9.0	NM- 9.2
2-Ward-c/a, 9 pgs.	30	60	90	177	289	400
3 (1/50)-Photo-c begin, end #27?	15	30	45	88	137	185
4-Crandall-a	16	32	48	94	147	200
5-7,10	14	28	42	81	118	155
8,9-Ward-a 6,8 pgs. 8-Gustavson-a: Esther Williams photo-c	18	36	54	105	165	225
11,13,14,17-20	14	28	42	80	115	150
12,15,16-Ward-a 9,7,8 pgs.	17	34	51	98	154	210
21-Ward-a, 7 pgs.	15	30	45	90	140	190
22-31: 31-Whitney-a	14	28	42	78	112	145

NOTE: Photo c-3-10, 12-28.

DIARY OF HORROR
Avon Periodicals: December, 1952

	GD 2.0	VG 4.0	FN 6.0	VF 8.0	VF/NM 9.0	NM- 9.2
1-Hollingsworth-c/a; bondage-c	300	600	900	1950	3375	4800

DIARY SECRETS (Formerly Teen-Age Diary Secrets.)(See Giant Comics Ed.)
St. John Publishing Co.: No. 10, Feb, 1952 - No. 30, Sept, 1955

	GD 2.0	VG 4.0	FN 6.0	VF 8.0	VF/NM 9.0	NM- 9.2
10-Baker-c/a most issues	155	310	465	992	1696	2400
11-16,18,19: 12,13,15-Baker-c	103	206	309	659	1130	1600
17,20: Kubert-r/Hollywood Confessions #1. 17-r/Teen Age Romances #9	116	232	348	742	1271	1800
21-30: 22,27-Signed stories by Estrada. 28-Last precode (3/55)	77	154	231	493	847	1200
nn-(25¢ giant, nd (1950?)-Baker-c & rebound St. John comics	206	412	618	1318	2259	3200

DICK COLE (Sport Thrills No. 11 on)(See Blue Bolt & Four Most #1)
Curtis Publ./Star Publications: Dec-Jan, 1948-49 - No. 10, June-July, 1950

	GD 2.0	VG 4.0	FN 6.0	VF 8.0	VF/NM 9.0	NM- 9.2
1-Sgt. Spook; L. B. Cole-c; McWilliams-a; Curt Swan's 1st work	41	82	123	256	428	600
2,5	19	38	57	111	176	240
3,4,6-10: All-L.B. Cole-c. 10-Joe Louis story	25	50	75	150	245	340
Accepted Reprint #7(V1#6 on-c)(1950's)-Reprints #7; L.B. Cole-c	9	18	27	52	69	85
Accepted Reprint #9(nd)-(Reprints #9 & #8-c)	9	18	27	52	69	85

NOTE: L. B. Cole c-1, 3, 4, 6-10. Al McWilliams a-6. Dick Cole in 1-9. Baseball c-10. Basketball c-9. Football c-8.

DICKIE DARE
Eastern Color Printing Co.: 1941 - No. 4, 1942 (#3 on sale 6/15/42)

	GD 2.0	VG 4.0	FN 6.0	VF 8.0	VF/NM 9.0	NM- 9.2
1-Caniff-a, bondage-c by Everett	74	148	222	470	810	1150
2	34	68	102	199	325	450
3,4-Half Scorchy Smith by Noel Sickles who was very influential in Milton Caniff's development	36	72	108	211	343	475

DICK POWELL (Also see A-1 Comics)
Magazine Enterprises: No. 22, 1949 (one shot)

	GD 2.0	VG 4.0	FN 6.0	VF 8.0	VF/NM 9.0	NM- 9.2
A-1 22-Photo-c	24	48	72	142	234	325

DICK QUICK, ACE REPORTER (See Picture News #10)

DICKS
Caliber Comics: 1997 - No. 4, 1998 ($2.95, B&W)

	NM- 9.2
1-4-Ennis-s/McCrea-c/a; r/Fleetway	4.00
TPB ('98, $12.95) r/series	13.00

DICK'S ADVENTURES
Dell Publishing Co.: No. 245, Sept, 1949

	GD 2.0	VG 4.0	FN 6.0	VF 8.0	VF/NM 9.0	NM- 9.2
Four Color 245	6	12	18	41	76	110

DICK TRACY (See Famous Feature Stories, Harvey Comics Library, Limited Collectors' Ed., Mammoth Comics, Merry Christmas, The Original..., Popular Comics, Super Book No. 1, 7, 13, 25, Super Comics & Tastee-Freez)

DICK TRACY
David McKay Publications: May, 1937 - Jan, 1938

	GD 2.0	VG 4.0	FN 6.0	VF 8.0	VF/NM 9.0	NM- 9.2
Feature Books nn - 100 pgs., partially reprinted as 4-Color No. 1 (appeared before Large Feature Comics, 1st Dick Tracy comic book) (Very Rare-five known copies; two incomplete)	1850	3700	5550	13,900	25,450	37,000
Feature Books 4 - Reprints nn issue w/new-c	168	336	504	1075	1838	2600
Feature Books 6,9	110	220	330	704	1202	1700

DICK TRACY (...Monthly #1-24)
Dell Publishing Co.: 1939 - No. 24, Dec, 1949

	GD 2.0	VG 4.0	FN 6.0	VF 8.0	VF/NM 9.0	NM- 9.2
Large Feature Comic 1 (1939) -Dick Tracy Meets The Blank	258	516	774	1651	2826	4000
Large Feature Comic 4,8	129	258	387	826	1413	2000
Large Feature Comic 11,13,15	106	212	318	673	1162	1650
Four Color 1(1939)('35-r)	1160	2320	3480	8800	16,900	25,000
Four Color 6(1940)('37-r)-(Scarce)	290	580	870	1856	3178	4500
Four Color 8(1940)('38-'39-r)	161	322	483	1030	1765	2500
Large Feature Comic 3(1941, Series II)	116	232	348	742	1271	1800
Four Color 21('42)('38-r)	103	206	309	659	1130	1600
Four Color 34('44)('39-'40-r)	42	84	126	311	706	1100
Four Color 56('44)('40-r)	34	68	102	247	554	860
Four Color 96('46)('40-r)	23	46	69	161	356	550
Four Color 133('47)('40-'41-r)	18	36	54	124	275	425
Four Color 163('47)('41-r)	16	32	48	110	243	375
1(1/48)('34-r)	52	104	156	416	933	1450
2,3	24	48	72	168	377	585
4-10	19	38	57	133	297	460
11-18: 13-Bondage-c	14	28	42	97	214	330
19-1st app. Sparkle Plenty, B.O. Plenty & Gravel Gertie in a 3-pg. strip not by Gould	16	32	48	110	243	375
20-1st app. Sam Catchem; c/a not by Gould	13	26	39	91	201	310
21-24-Only 2 pg. Gould-a in each	13	26	39	89	195	300

NOTE: No. 19-24 have a 2 pg. biography of a famous villain illustrated by Gould: 19-Little Face; 20-Flattop; 21-Breathless Mahoney; 22-Measles; 23-Itchy; 24-The Brow.

DICK TRACY (Continued from Dell series)(...Comics Monthly #25-140)
Harvey Publications: No. 25, Mar, 1950 - No. 145, April, 1961

	GD 2.0	VG 4.0	FN 6.0	VF 8.0	VF/NM 9.0	NM- 9.2
25-Flat Top-c/story (also #26,27)	12	24	36	80	173	265
26-28,30: 28-Bondage-c. 28,29-The Brow-c/stories	9	18	27	61	123	185
29-1st app. Gravel Gertie in a Gould-r	10	20	30	69	147	225
31,32,34,35,37-40: 40-Intro/origin 2-way wrist radio (6/51)	8	16	24	52	99	145
33- "Measles the Teen-Age Dope Pusher"	10	20	30	64	132	200
36-1st app. B.O. Plenty in a Gould-r	9	18	27	61	123	185
41-50	7	14	21	46	86	125
51-56,58-80: 51-2pgs Powell-a	6	12	18	40	73	105
57-1st app. Sam Catchem in a Gould-r	7	14	21	46	86	125
81-99,101-140: 99-109-Painted-c	6	12	18	37	66	95
100, 141-145 (25¢)(titled "Dick Tracy")	6	12	18	40	73	105

NOTE: Powell a(1-2pgs.)-43, 44, 104, 108, 109, 145. No. 110-120, 141-145 are all reprints from earlier issues.

DICK TRACY ("Reuben Award" series)
Blackthorne Publishing: 12/84 - No. 24, 6/89 (1-12: $5.95; 13-24: $6.95, B&W, 76 pgs.)

	NM- 9.2
1-8-1st printings; hard-c ed. ($14.95)	20.00
1-3-2nd printings, 1986; hard-c ed.	20.00
1-12-1st & 2nd printings; squarebound. thick-c	12.00
13-24 ($6.95): 21,22-Regular-c & stapled	14.00

NOTE: Gould daily & Sunday strip-r in all. 1-12 r-12/31/45-4/5/49; 13-24 r-7/13/41-2/20/44.

DICK TRACY (Disney)
WD Publications: 1990 - No. 3, 1990 (color) (Book 3 adapts 1990 movie)

	NM- 9.2
Book One ($3.95, 52pgs.)-Kyle Baker-c/a	6.00
Book Two, Three ($5.95, 68pgs.)-Direct sale	6.00
Book Two, Three ($2.95, 68pgs.)-Newsstand	4.00

DICK TRACY ADVENTURES
Gladstone Publishing: May, 1991 ($4.95, 76 pgs.)

	NM- 9.2
1-Reprints strips 2/1/42-4/18/42	5.00

DICK TRACY: DEAD OR ALIVE
IDW Publishing: Sept, 2018 - No. 4, Dec, 2018 ($3.99, limited series)

	NM- 9.2
1-4-Lee & Michael Allred-s/Rich Tommaso-a	4.00

DICK TRACY, EXPLOITS OF
Rosdon Books, Inc.: 1946 ($1.00, hard-c strip reprints)

	GD 2.0	VG 4.0	FN 6.0	VF 8.0	VF/NM 9.0	NM- 9.2
1-Reprints the near complete case of "The Brow" from 6/12/44 to 9/24/44 (story starts a few weeks late)	26	52	78	154	252	350
with dust jacket...	40	80	120	246	411	575

DICK TRACY FOREVER
IDW Publishing: Apr, 2019 - No. 4, Jul, 2019 ($3.99, limited series)

	NM- 9.2
1-4-Michael A. Oeming-s/a. 1-Set in 1931. 2-Set in 1951. 3-Set in 2021. 4-Set in 2031	4.00

DICK TRACY MONTHLY/WEEKLY
Blackthorne Publishing: May, 1986 - No. 99, 1989 ($2.00, B&W)
(Becomes Weekly #26 on)

	GD 2.0	VG 4.0	FN 6.0	VF 8.0	VF/NM 9.0	NM- 9.2
1-60: Gould-r. 30,31-Mr. Crime app.						4.00
61-90						4.00
91-95						6.00
96-99-Low print	1	2	3	5	7	9

NOTE: #1-10 reprint strips 3/10/40-7/13/41; #10(pg.8)-51 reprint strips 4/6/49-12/31/55; #52-99 reprint strips 12/26/56-4/26/64.

	GD 2.0	VG 4.0	FN 6.0	VF 8.0	VF/NM 9.0	NM- 9.2

DICK TRACY SPECIAL
Blackthorne Publ.: Jan, 1988 - No. 3, Aug. (no month), 1989 ($2.95, B&W)
1-3: 1-Origin D. Tracy; 4/strips 10/12/31-3/30/32 — 4.00

DICK TRACY: THE EARLY YEARS
Blackthorne Publishing: Aug, 1987 - No. 4, Aug (no month) 1989 ($6.95, B&W, 76 pgs.)
1-3: 1-4-r/strips 10/12/31(1st daily)-8/31/32 & Sunday strips 6/12/32-8/28/32;
Big Boy apps. in #1-3 — 1 2 3 4 5 7
4 ($2.95, 52pgs.) — 4.00

DICK TRACY UNPRINTED STORIES
Blackthorne Publishing: Sept, 1987 - No. 4, June, 1988 ($2.95, B&W)
1-4: Reprints strips 1/1/56-12/25/56 — 4.00

DICK TURPIN (See Legend of Young...)

DIE (Singular of dice)
Image Comics: Dec, 2018 - No. 20, Sept, 2021 ($3.99)
1-20-Kieron Gillen-s/Stephanie Hans-a; Dungeons & Dragons-themed story — 4.00

DIE-CUT
Marvel Comics UK, Ltd: Nov, 1993 - No. 4, Feb, 1994 ($1.75, limited series)
1-4: 1-Die-cut-c; The Beast app. — 4.00

DIE-CUT VS. G-FORCE
Marvel Comics UK, Ltd: Nov, 1993 - No. 2, Dec, 1993 ($2.75, limited series)
1,2-($2.75)-Gold foil-c on both — 4.00

DIE!DIE!DIE!
Image Comics (Skybound): Jul, 2018 - Present ($3.99)
1-14: 1-Robert Kirkman-s/Chris Burnham-a. 14-Obama cover; Superman vs. Ali homage — 4.00

DIE HARD: YEAR ONE (Based on the John McClane character)
BOOM! Studios: Aug, 2009 - No. 8, Mar, 2010 ($3.99, limited series)
1-8-Chaykin-s; Officer McClane in 1976 NYC; multiple covers on each — 4.00

DIE KITTY DIE!
Chapterhouse Comics: Oct, 2016 - 2017 ($3.99/$4.99)
1,3,4-($3.99) Fernando Ruiz-s/Dan Parent-a; Harvey-style spoof — 5.00
2-($4.99) Bonus faux 1969 reprint; Li'l Satan app. — 6.00
... Christmas Special 1 (12/07, $4.99) Christmas stories — 1 2 3 5 6 8
... Summer Vacation 1 (7/17, $3.99) Parent, Ruiz & Lagace-a — 6.00

DIE KITTY DIE! HEAVEN & HELL
Chapterhouse Comics: No. 0, May, 2018 - No. 4, Jan, 2019 ($3.99/$4.99)
0-4-($3.99) Fernando Ruiz-s/Dan Parent-a — 4.00
...: 2018 Halloween Special (10/18, $3.99) Art by Parent, Lagace, Bone, Pepoy — 4.00

DIE KITTY DIE! HOLLYWOOD OR BUST
Chapterhouse Comics: Jul, 2017 - No. 4, Sept, 2017 ($3.99/$4.99)
1,2-($3.99) Fernando Ruiz/Dan Parent-a — 4.00
3,4-($4.99) — 5.00

DIE, MONSTER, DIE (See Movie Classics)

DIE!NAMITE
Dynamite Entertainment: 2020 - No. 5, 2021 ($3.99, limited series)
1-5-Vampirella, Red Sonja, Dejah Thoris, Peter Cannon Thunderbolt vs. zombies — 4.00
... Valentine's Special, Our Bloody Valentine (2021, $4.99) short stories by various — 5.00

DIE!NAMITE LIVES!
Dynamite Entertainment: 2021 - No. 5, 2021 ($3.99, limited series)
1-5-Ash (Evil Dead), Vampirella, Jennifer Blood, Project: Superpowers team vs. zombies — 4.00

DIE!NAMITE NEVER DIES!
Dynamite Entertainment: 2022 - No. 5, 2022 ($3.99, limited series)
1-5-Tarzan, Vampirella, Evil Sonja, Pantha team vs. zombie John Carter & Dejah Thoris — 4.00

DIESEL (TYSON HESSE'S...)
Boom Entertainment (BOOM! Box): Sept, 2015 - No. 4, Dec, 2015 ($3.99, limited series)
1-4-Tyson Hesse-s/a in all. 1-Three covers — 4.00

DIGIMON DIGITAL MONSTERS (TV)
Dark Horse Comics: May, 2000 - No. 12, Nov, 2000 ($2.95/$2.99)
1 — 3 6 9 14 19 24
2-12 — 4.00
Sealed 4-pack ($9.99) — 3 6 9 19 30 40

DIGITEK
Marvel UK, Ltd: Dec, 1992 - No. 4, Mar, 1993 ($1.95/$2.25, mini-series)
1-4: 3-Deathlock-c/story — 4.00

DILLY (Dilly Duncan from Daredevil Comics; see Boy Comics #57)
Lev Gleason Publications: May, 1953 - No. 3, Sept, 1953
1-Teenage; Biro-c — 13 26 39 74 105 135
2,3-Biro-c — 8 16 24 44 57 70

DILTON'S STRANGE SCIENCE (See Pep Comics #78)
Archie Comics: May, 1989 - No. 5, May, 1990 (75c/$1.00)
1-5 — 4.00

DIME COMICS
Newsbook Publ. Corp.: 1945; 1951
1-(32 pgs.) Silver Streak/Green Dragon-c/sty; Japanese WWII-c by L. B. Cole (Rare)
— 389 778 1167 2723 4762 6800
1(1951) — 27 54 81 158 259 360

DINGBATS (See 1st Issue Special)

DING DONG
Compix/Magazine Enterprises: Summer?, 1946 - No. 5, 1947 (52 pgs.)
1-Funny animal — 43 86 129 271 461 650
2 (9/46) — 21 42 63 122 199 275
3 (Wint '46-'47) - 5 — 17 34 51 98 154 210

DINKY DUCK (Paul Terry's...) (See Approved Comics, Blue Ribbon, Giant

---

Comics Edition #5A & New Terrytoons)
St. John Publishing Co./Pines No. 16 on: Nov, 1951 - No. 16, Sept, 1955; No. 16, Fall, 1956;
No. 17, May, 1957 - No. 19, Summer, 1958
1-Funny animal — 17 34 51 100 158 215
2 — 10 20 30 54 72 90
3-10 — 7 14 21 35 43 50
11-16(9/55) — 6 12 18 31 38 45
16 (Fall, '56) - 19 — 5 10 15 24 30 35

DINKY DUCK & HASHIMOTO-SAN (See Deputy Dawg Presents...)

DINO (TV)(The Flintstones)
Charlton Publications: Aug, 1973 - No. 20, Jan, 1977 (Hanna-Barbera)
1 — 4 8 12 23 37 50
2-10 — 2 4 6 10 14 18
11-20 — 2 4 6 8 10 12
Digest nn (w/Xerox Pub., 1974) (low print run) — 2 4 6 11 16 20

DINO ISLAND
Mirage Studios: Feb, 1994 - No. 2, Mar, 1994 ($2.75, limited series)
1,2-By Jim Lawson — 4.00

DINO RIDERS
Marvel Comics: Feb, 1989 - No. 3, 1989 ($1.00)
1-3: Based on toys — 4.00

DINOSAUR REX
Upshot Graphics (Fantagraphics): 1986 - No. 3, 1986 ($2.00, limited series)
1-3 — 4.00

DINOSAURS, A CELEBRATION
Marvel Comics (Epic): Oct, 1992 - No. 4, Oct, 1992 ($4.95, lim. series, 52 pgs.)
1-4: 2-Bolton painted-c — 5.00

DINOSAURS ATTACK! (Based on Topps trading card set)
IDW Publishing: Jul, 2013 - No. 5, Nov, 2013 ($3.99, limited series)
1-5: 1,2-Remastered version of 1991 graphic novel. 3-5-New continuation of story — 4.00

DINOSAURS ATTACK! THE GRAPHIC NOVEL
Eclipse Comics: 1991 ($3.95, coated stock, stiff-c)
Book One- Based on Topps trading cards — 5.00

DINOSAURS FOR HIRE
Malibu Comics: Feb, 1993 - No. 12, Feb, 1994 ($1.95/$2.50)
1-12: 1,10-Flip bk. 8-Bagged w/Skycap; Staton-c. 10-Flip book — 4.00

DINOSAURS GRAPHIC NOVEL (TV)
Disney Comics: 1992 - No. 2, 1993 ($2.95, 52 pgs.)
1,2-Staton-a; based on Dinosaurs TV show — 4.00

DINOSAURUS
Dell Publishing Co.: No. 1120, Aug, 1960
Four Color 1120-Movie, painted-c — 8 16 24 51 96 140

DIPPY DUCK
Atlas Comics (OPI): October, 1957
1-Maneely-a; code approved — 19 38 57 111 176 240

DIRECTORY TO A NONEXISTENT UNIVERSE
Eclipse Comics: Dec, 1987 ($2.00, B&W)
1 — 4.00

DIRK GENTLY'S HOLISTIC DETECTIVE AGENCY
IDW Publishing: May, 2015 - No. 5, Oct, 2015 ($3.99, limited series)
1-5: 1-Ryall-s/Kyriazis-a; multiple covers on each — 4.00
...: A Spoon Too Short 1-5 (2/16 - No. 5, 6/16, $3.99) A.E. David-s/Kyriazis-a — 4.00
...: The Salmon of Doubt 1-9 (10/16 - No. 9, 6/17, $3.99) A.E. David-s/Kyriazis-a — 4.00

DIRTY DOZEN (See Movie Classics)

DIRTY PAIR (Manga)
Eclipse Comics: Dec, 1988 - No. 4, Apr, 1989 ($2.00, B&W, limited series)
1-4: Japanese manga with original stories — 5.00
...: Start the Violence (Dark Horse, 9/99, $2.95) r/B&W stories in color from Dark
Horse Presents #132-134; covers by Warren & Pearson — 4.00

DIRTY PAIR: FATAL BUT NOT SERIOUS
Dark Horse Comics: July, 1995 - No. 5, Nov, 1995 ($2.95, limited series)
1-5 — 4.00

DIRTY PAIR: RUN FROM THE FUTURE (Manga)
Dark Horse Comics: Jan, 2000 - No. 4, Mar, 2000 ($2.95, limited series)
1-Warren-s/c/a — 3 6 9 19 30 40
1-Variant cover by Adam Hughes — 8 16 24 54 102 150
2-4-Warren-s/c/a — 1 3 4 6 8 10
2-4-Variant-c by Stelfreeze(2), Timm(3), Ramos(4) — 2 4 6 11 16 20

DIRTY PAIR: SIM HELL (Manga)
Dark Horse Comics: May, 1993 - No. 4, Aug, 1993 ($2.50, B&W, limited series)
1-4 — 4.00
...Remastered #1-4 (5/01 - 8/01) reprints in color, with pin-up gallery — 3.00

DIRTY PAIR II (Manga)
Eclipse Comics: June, 1989 - No. 5, Mar, 1990 ($2.00, B&W, limited series)
1-5: 3-Cover is misnumbered as #1 — 4.00

DIRTY PAIR III, THE (A Plague of Angels) (Manga)
Eclipse Comics: Aug, 1990 - No. 5, Aug, 1991 ($2.00/$2.25, B&W, lim. series)
1-5 — 4.00

DISASTER INC.
AfterShock Comics: Apr, 2020 - No. 5, Dec, 2020 ($4.99/$3.99)
1-($4.99)-Joe Harris-s/Sebastian Piriz-a — 5.00
2-5-($3.99) — 4.00

Die Hard: Year One #1 © 20Fox

Dinosaurs For Hire #2 © Tom Mason

Disney Comics and Stories #1 © DIS

	GD 2.0	VG 4.0	FN 6.0	VF 8.0	VF/NM 9.0	NM- 9.2

DISCIPLINE
Image Comics: Mar, 2016 - No. 6, Aug, 2016 ($2.99)

1-6-Peter Milligan-s/Leandro Fernández-a — 3.00

DISNEY AFTERNOON, THE (TV)
Marvel Comics: Nov, 1994 - No. 10?, Aug, 1995 ($1.50)

1-10: 3-w/bound-in Power Ranger Barcode Card — 6.00

DISNEY AFTERNOON GIANT
IDW Publishing: Oct, 2018 - No. 8, Dec, 2019 ($5.99)

1-8: 1-4-DuckTales and Chip 'n' Dale stories. 5-Darkwing Duck and Chip 'n' Dale — 6.00

DISNEY COMIC ALBUM
Disney Comics: 1990(no month, year) - No. 8, 1991 ($6.95/$7.95)

1,2 ($6.95): 1-Donald Duck and Gyro Gearloose by Barks(r). 2-Uncle Scrooge by Barks(r); Jr. Woodchucks app. — 9.00
3-8: 3-Donald Duck-r/F.C. 308 by Barks; begin $7.95-c. 4-Mickey Mouse Meets the Phantom Blot; r/M.M Club Parade (censored 1956 version of story). 5-Chip 'n' Dale Rescue Rangers; new-a. 6-Uncle Scrooge. 7-Donald Duck in Too Many Pets; Barks-r(4) including F.C. #29. 8-Super Goof; r/S.G. #1, D.D. #102 — 9.00

DISNEY COMIC HITS
Marvel Comics: Oct, 1995 - No. 16, Jan, 1997 ($1.50/$2.50)

1-16: 4-Toy Story. 6-Aladdin. 7-Pocahontas. 10-The Hunchback of Notre Dame (Same story in Disney's The Hunchback of Notre Dame). 13-Aladdin and the Forty Thieves — 4.00

DISNEY COMICS
Disney Comics: June, 1990

Boxed set of #1 issues includes Donald Duck Advs., Ducktales, Chip 'n Dale Rescue Rangers, Roger Rabbit, Mickey Mouse Advs. & Goofy Advs.; limited to 10,000 sets
2 — 4 — 6 — 11 — 16 — 20

DISNEY COMICS AND STORIES
IDW Publishing: Sept, 2018 - No. 13, May, 2020 ($5.99)

1-13-Reprints of Danish and Italian stories — 6.00

DISNEY GIANT HALLOWEEN HEX
IDW Publishing: Oct, 2016 ($6.99)

1-Halloween-themed reprints of U.S., Dutch and Italian stories; three covers — 7.00

DISNEY KINGDOMS: FIGMENT 2 (Sequel to Figment series)
Marvel Comics: Nov, 2015 - No. 5, Mar, 2016 ($3.99)

1-5: 1-Jim Zub-s/Ramon Bachs-a/J. T. Christopher-c — 4.00

DISNEY KINGDOMS: SEEKERS OF THE WEIRD
Marvel Comics: Mar, 2014 - No. 5, Jul, 2014 ($3.99)

1-5: 1-Seifert-s/Moline-a/Del Mundo-c. 3-Andrade-a — 4.00

DISNEYLAND BIRTHDAY PARTY (Also see Dell Giants)
Gladstone Publishing Co.: Aug, 1985 ($2.50)

1-Reprints Dell Giant with new-photo-c — 2 — 4 — 6 — 8 — 10 — 12
...Comics Digest #1-(Digest) — 2 — 4 — 6 — 8 — 11 — 14

DISNEYLAND MAGAZINE
Fawcett Publications: Feb. 15, 1972 - 1974 (10-1/4"x12-5/8", 20 pgs, weekly)

1-One or two page painted art features on Dumbo, Snow White, Lady & the Tramp, the Aristocats, Brer Rabbit, Peter Pan, Cinderella, Jungle Book, Alice & Pinocchio. Most standard characters app. — 3 — 6 — 9 — 17 — 25 — 34

DISNEYLAND, USA (See Dell Giant No. 30)

DISNEY MAGIC KINGDOM COMICS
IDW Publishing: May, 2016 - No. 2, Aug, 2016 ($6.99, squarebound, quarterly)

1,2-Reprints inspired by the theme parks; Barks-a — 7.00

DISNEY MOVIE BOOK
Walt Disney Productions (Gladstone): 1990 ($7.95, 8-1/2"x11", 52 pgs.) (w/pull-out poster)

1-Roger Rabbit in Tummy Trouble; from the cartoon film strips adapted to the comic format. Ron Dias-c — 2 — 4 — 6 — 8 — 10 — 12

DISNEY'S ACTION CLUB
Acclaim Books: 1997 - No. 4 ($4.50, digest size)

1-4: 1-Hercules. 4-Mighty Ducks — 4.50

DISNEY'S ALADDIN (Movie)
Marvel Comics: no date (Oct, 1994) - No. 11, 1995 ($1.50)

1 — 1 — 3 — 4 — 6 — 8 — 10
2-11 — 4.00

DISNEY'S BEAUTY AND THE BEAST (Movie)
Marvel Comics: Sept, 1994 - No. 13, 1995 ($1.50)

1-13 — 4.00

DISNEY'S BEAUTY AND THE BEAST HOLIDAY SPECIAL
Acclaim Books: 1997 ($4.50, digest size, one-shot)

1-Based on The Enchanted Christmas video — 6.00

DISNEY'S COLOSSAL COMICS COLLECTION
Disney Comics: 1991 - No. 10, 1993 ($1.95, digest-size, 96/132 pgs.)

1,4,6,9: 4;6,9-Darkwing Duck-r. 4-r/Darkwing Duck #1-4. 6-Goofy begins — 2 — 4 — 6 — 8 — 10
2,3,5,7,8,10: Ducktales, Talespin, Chip 'n Dale's Rescue Rangers. 8-Little Mermaid — 5.00

DISNEY'S COMICS IN 3-D
Disney Comics: 1992 ($2.95, w/glasses, polybagged)

1-Infinity-c; Barks, Rosa, Gottfredson-r — 5.00

DISNEY'S ENCHANTING STORIES
Acclaim Books: 1997 - No. 5 ($4.50, digest size)

1-5: 1-Hercules. 2-Pocahontas — 4.50

DISNEY'S HERO SQUAD
BOOM! Studios: Jan, 2010 - No. 8, Aug, 2010 ($2.99)

1-8: 1-3-Phantom Blot app. 1-Back-up reprint of Super Goof #1 — 3.00

DISNEY'S NEW ADVENTURES OF BEAUTY AND THE BEAST (Also see Beauty and the Beast & Disney's Beauty and the Beast)
Disney Comics: 1992 - No. 2, 1992 ($1.50, limited series)

1,2-New stories based on movie — 5.00

DISNEY'S POCAHONTAS (Movie)
Marvel Comics: 1995 ($4.95, one-shot)

1-Movie adaptation — 1 — 3 — 4 — 6 — 8 — 10

DISNEY'S TALESPIN LIMITED SERIES: "TAKE OFF" (TV) (See Talespin)
W. D. Publications (Disney Comics): Jan, 1991 - No. 4, Apr, 1991 ($1.50, lim. series, 52 pgs.)

1-4: Based on animated series; 4 part origin — 5.00

DISNEY'S TARZAN (Movie)
Dark Horse Comics: June, 1999 - No. 2, July, 1999 ($2.95, limited series)

1,2-Movie adaptation — 4.00

DISNEY'S THE LION KING (Movie)
Marvel Comics: July, 1994 - No. 2, July, 1994 ($1.50, limited series)

1,2: 2-part movie adaptation — 1 — 2 — 3 — 5 — 6 — 8
1-($2.50, 52 pgs.)-Complete story — 1 — 3 — 4 — 6 — 8 — 10

DISNEY'S THE LITTLE MERMAID (Movie)
Marvel Comics: Sept, 1994 - No. 12, 1995 ($1.50)

1 — 2 — 4 — 6 — 8 — 10 — 12
2-12 — 5.00

DISNEY'S THE LITTLE MERMAID LIMITED SERIES (Movie)
Disney Comics: Feb, 1992 - No. 4, May, 1992 ($1.50, limited series)

1-4: Peter David scripts; takes place before the movie — 1 — 2 — 3 — 5 — 6 — 8
Set of #1-4 in unopened 4-issue Collector's Pack — 65.00

DISNEY'S THE LITTLE MERMAID: UNDERWATER ENGAGEMENTS
Acclaim Books: 1997 ($4.50, digest size)

1-Flip book — 1 — 3 — 4 — 6 — 8 — 10

DISNEY'S THE HUNCHBACK OF NOTRE DAME (Movie)(See Disney's Comic Hits #10)
Marvel Comics: July, 1996 ($4.95, squarebound, one-shot)

1-Movie adaptation — 1 — 2 — 3 — 4 — 5 — 9
NOTE: A different edition of this series was sold at Wal-Mart stores with new covers depicting scenes from the 1989 feature film. Inside contents and price were identical.

DISNEY'S THE PRINCE AND THE PAUPER
W. D. Publications: no date ($5.95, 68 pgs., squarebound)

nn-Movie adaptation — 1 — 2 — 3 — 5 — 6 — 8

DISNEY'S THE THREE MUSKETEERS (Movie)
Marvel Comics: Jan, 1994 - No. 2, Feb, 1994 ($1.50, limited series)

1,2-Morrow-c; Spiegle-a; Movie adaptation — 4.00

DISNEY'S TOY STORY (Movie)
Marvel Comics: Dec, 1995 ($4.95, one-shot)

nn-Adaptation of film — 2 — 4 — 6 — 11 — 16 — 20

DISNEY TSUM TSUM KINGDOM ONE-SHOT (Based on the Japanese collectible stuffed toys)
IDW Publishing: Sept, 2018 ($7.99, squarebound, one-shot)

1-Short stories by various; Baldari-c — 8.00

	GD 2.0	VG 4.0	FN 6.0	VF 8.0	VF/NM 9.0	NM- 9.2

DISNEY VILLAINS: CRUELLA DE VIL (From 101 Dalmations movie)
Dynamite Entertainment: 2024 - Present ($3.99, limited series)

1-Sweeney Boo-s/Miriana Publia-a; multiple covers ... 4.00

DISNEY VILLAINS: HADES (From the Hercules movie)
Dynamite Entertainment: 2023 - No. 5, 2024 ($3.99, limited series)

1-5-Kalan-s/Ranaldi-a; multiple covers ... 4.00

DISNEY VILLAINS: MALEFICENT (From the Sleeping Beauty movie)
Dynamite Entertainment: 2023 - No. 5, 2023 ($3.99, limited series)

1-5-Soo Lee-s/a; multiple covers ... 4.00

DISNEY VILLAINS: SCAR (From The Lion King movie)
Dynamite Entertainment: 2023 - No. 4, 2023 ($3.99, limited series)

1-4-Chuck Brown-s/Trevor Fraley-a; multiple covers ... 4.00

DISSENSION: WAR ETERNAL
Aspen MLT: Jul, 2018 - No. 5, Jan, 2019 ($3.99)

1-5-Fielder-s/Gunderson-a; Aspen Mascots bonus back-up story in each ... 4.00

DISTANT SOIL, A (1st Series)
WaRP Graphics: Dec, 1983 - No. 9, Mar 1986 ($1.50, B&W)

1-Magazine size ... 6.00
2-9: 2-4 are magazine size ... 4.00
NOTE: Second printings exist of #1, 2, 3 & 6.

DISTANT SOIL, A
Donning (Star Blaze): Mar, 1989 ($12.95, trade paperback)

nn-new material ... 13.00

DISTANT SOIL, A (2nd Series)
Aria Press/Image Comics (Highbrow Entertainment) #15 on:
June, 1991 - No. 42, Oct, 2013 ($1.75/$2.50/$2.95/$3.50/$3.95, B&W)

1-27: 13-$2.95-c begins. 14-Sketchbook. 15-(8/96)-1st Image issue ... 4.00
29-33,35,37-($3.95) ... 4.00
34-($4.95, 64 pages) includes sketchbook pages ... 5.00
36,38-($4.50) 36-Back-up story by Darnall & Doran. 38-Includes sketch pages ... 4.50
39-42-($3.50) ... 3.50
The Aria ('01, $16.95,TPB) r/#26-31 ... 17.00
The Ascendant ('98, $18.95,TPB) r/#13-25 ... 19.00
The Gathering ('97, $18.95,TPB) r/#1-13; intro. Neil Gaiman ... 19.00
Vol. 4: Coda (2005, $17.99, TPB) r/#32-38 ... 18.00
NOTE: Four separate printings exist for #1 and are clearly marked. Second printings exist of #2-4 and are also clearly marked.

DISTANT SOIL, A: IMMIGRANT SONG
Donning (Star Blaze): Aug, 1987 ($6.95, trade paperback)

nn-new material ... 7.00

DISTRICT X (Also see X-Men titles) (Also see Mutopia X)
Marvel Comics: July, 2004 - No. 14, Aug, 2005 ($2.99)

1-14: 1-3-Bishop app.; Yardin-a/Hine-s ... 3.00
...Vol. 1: Mr. M (2005, $14.99) r/#1-6; sketch page by Yardin ... 15.00
...Vol. 2: Underground (2005, $19.99) r/#7-14; prologue from X-Men Unlimited #2 ... 20.00

DIVER DAN (TV)
Dell Publishing Co.: Feb-Apr, 1962 - No. 2, June-Aug, 1962

Four Color 1254(#1), 2 | 10 | 20 | 30 | 69 | 147 | 225

DIVERGENCE FCBD SPECIAL EDITION
DC Comics: Jun, 2015 (Free Comic Book Day giveaway)

1-Previews Batman #41, Superman #41, Justice League Darkseid War ... 6.00

DIVIDED STATES OF HYSTERIA
Image Comics: Jun, 2017 - No. 6, Nov, 2017 ($3.99)

1-6-Howard Chaykin-s/a ... 4.00

DIVINE RIGHT
Image Comics (WildStorm Prod.): Sept, 1997 - No. 12, Nov, 1999 ($2.50)

Preview ... 5.00
1,2: 1-Jim Lee-s/a(p)/c, 1-Variant-c by Charest ... 4.00
1-($3.50)-Voyager Pack w/Stormwatch preview ... 4.00
1-American Entertainment Ed. ... 6.00
2-Variant-c of Exotica & Blaze ... 5.00
3-Chromium-c by Jim Lee ... 5.00
3-12: 3-5-Fairchild & Lynch app. 4-American Entertainment Ed. 8-Two covers. 9-1st DC issue. 11,12-Divine Intervention pt. 1,4 ... 4.00
5-Pacific Comicon Ed. ... 6.00
6-Glow in the dark variant-c, European Tour Edition ... 20.00
...Book One TPB (2002, $17.95) r/#1-7 ... 18.00
...Book Two TPB (2002, $17.95) r/#8-12 & Divine Intervention Gen13, ...Wildcats ... 18.00
...Collected Edition #1-3 ($5.95, TPB) 1-r/#1,2. 2-r/#3,4. 3-r/#5,6 ... 6.00
Divine Intervention/Gen 13 (11/99, $2.50) Part 3; D'Anda-a ... 4.00
Divine Intervention/Wildcats (11/99, $2.50) Part 2; D'Anda-a ... 4.00

DIVINITY
Valiant Entertainment: Feb, 2015 - No. 4, May, 2015 ($3.99, limited series)

1-4-Kindt-s/Hairsine-a ... 4.00
#0 (8/17, $3.99) Kindt-s/Guedes-a; bonus preview of Eternity #1 ... 4.00

DIVINITY II
Valiant Entertainment: Apr, 2016 - No. 4, Jul, 2016 ($3.99, limited series)

1-4-Kindt-s/Hairsine-a; 4-Origin of Myshka ... 4.00

DIVINITY III: STALINVERSE
Valiant Entertainment: Dec, 2016 - No. 4, Mar, 2017 ($3.99, limited series)

1-4-Kindt-s/Hairsine-a ... 4.00
Divinity III: Aric, Son of the Revolution 1 (1/17, $3.99) Joe Harris-s/Cafu-a ... 4.00
Divinity III: Escape From Gulag 396 1 (3/17, $3.99) Eliot Rahal-s/Francis Portela-a ... 4.00
Divinity III: Komandar Bloodshot 1 (12/16, $3.99) Jeff Lemire-s/Clayton Crain-a ... 4.00
Divinity III: Shadowman and the Battle for New Stalingrad 1 (2/17, $3.99) Robert Gill-a ... 4.00

DIVISION 13 (See Comic's Greatest World)

Dark Horse Comics: Sept, 1994 - Jan, 1995 ($2.50, color)

1-4: Giffen story in all. 1-Art Adams-c ... 4.00

DIXIE DUGAN (See Big Shot, Columbia Comics & Feature Funnies)
McNaught Syndicate/Columbia/Publication Ent.: July, 1942 - No. 13, 1949
(Strip reprints in all)

1-Joe Palooka x-over by Ham Fisher	37	74	111	222	361	500
2	20	40	60	118	192	265
3(1943)	15	30	45	83	124	165
4,5(1945-46)-Bo strip-r	12	24	36	67	94	120
6-13(1/47-49): 6-Paperdoll cut-outs	10	20	30	58	79	100

DIXIE DUGAN
Prize Publications (Headline): V3#1, Nov, 1951 - V4#4, Feb, 1954

V3#1	14	28	42	78	112	145
2-4	8	16	24	44	57	70
V4#1-4(#5-8)	8	16	24	40	50	60

DIZZY DAMES
American Comics Group (B&M Distr. Co.): Sept-Oct, 1952 - No. 6, Jul-Aug, 1953

1-Whitney-c	97	194	291	621	1061	1500
2	53	106	159	334	567	800
3-6	32	64	96	188	307	425

DIZZY DON COMICS
F. E. Howard Publications/Dizzy Don Ent. Ltd (Canada): 1942 - No. 22, Oct, 1946; No. 3, Apr, 1947 - No. 4, Sept./Oct., 1947 (Most B&W)

1 (B&W)	61	122	183	390	670	950
2 (B&W)	39	78	117	240	395	550
4-21 (B&W)	34	68	102	199	325	450
22-Full color, 52 pgs.	37	74	111	222	361	500
3 (4/47), 4 (9-10/47)-Full color, 52 pgs.	37	74	111	222	361	500

DIZZY DUCK (Formerly Barnyard Comics)
Standard Comics: No. 32, Nov, 1950 - No. 39, Mar, 1952

32-Funny animal	14	28	42	76	108	140
33-39	8	16	24	44	57	70

DJANGO UNCHAINED (Adaptation of the 2012 movie)
DC Comics (Vertigo): Feb, 2013 - No. 7, Oct, 2013 ($3.99, limited series)

1-Adaptation of Quentin Tarantino's script; Guéra-a; Tarantino foreword; sketch pages	2	4	6	11	16	20
1-Variant-c by Jim Lee	5	10	15	33	57	80
2-Cowan-c; bonus concept art and cover sketch art	1	2	3	5	6	8
2-Variant-c by Mark Chiarello	3	6	9	17	26	35
3-7: 5-Quitely-c. 7-Alex Ross-c						5.00

DJANGO / ZORRO (Django from the 2012 Taratino movie)
Dynamite Entertainment: 2014 - No. 7, 2015 ($3.99/$5.99, limited series)

1-6-Tarantino & Matt Wagner-s/Esteve Polls-a; multiple covers on each ... 4.00
7-($5.99) Covers by Jae Lee & Francesco Francavilla ... 6.00

DMZ
DC Comics (Vertigo): Jan, 2006 - No. 72, Feb, 2012 ($2.99)

1-Brian Wood-s/Riccardo Burchielli-a ... 4.00
1-(2008, no cover price) Convention Exclusive promotional edition ... 3.00
2-49,51-72: 2-10-Brian Wood-s/Riccardo Burchielli-a. 11-Donaldson-a. 12-Wood-s/a ... 3.00
50-($3.99) Short stories by various incl. Risso, Moon, Gibbons, Bermejo, Jim Lee ... 4.00
... Blood in the Game (2009, $12.99) r/#29-34; intro. by Greg Palast ... 13.00
... Body of a Journalist TPB (2007, $12.99) r/#6-12; intro. by D. Randall Blythe ... 13.00
... Collective Punishment TPB (2011, $14.99) r/#55-59 ... 15.00
... Friendly Fire TPB (2008, $12.99) r/#18-22; intro. by Sgt. John G. Ford ... 13.00
... Hearts and Minds TPB (2010, $16.99) r/#42-49; intro. by Morgan Spurlock ... 17.00
... M.I.A. TPB (2011, $14.99) r/#50-54 ... 15.00
... On the Ground TPB (2006, $9.99) r/#1-5; intro. by Brian Azzarello ... 10.00
... Public Works TPB (2007, $12.99) r/#13-17; intro. by Cory Doctorow ... 13.00
... The Hidden War TPB (2008, $12.99) r/#23-28 ... 13.00
... War Powers TPB (2009, $14.99) r/#35-41 ... 15.00

DNAGENTS (The New DNAgents V2/1 on)(Also see Surge)
Eclipse Comics: March, 1983 - No. 24, July, 1985 ($1.50, Baxter paper)

1-Origin						5.00
2-23: 4-Amber app. 8-Infinity-c						4.00
24-Dave Stevens-c	6	12	18	38	69	100
... Industrial Strength Edition TPB (Image, 2008, $24.99) B&W r/#1-14; Evanier intro.						25.00

DOBERMAN (See Sgt. Bilko's Private...)

DOBERMAN
IDW Publishing (Darby Pop): Jul, 2014 - No. 5, Jan, 2015 ($3.99)

1-5-Marder, Rosell, & Lambert-s/McKinney-a ... 4.00

DOBIE GILLIS (See The Many Loves of...)

DOC FRANKENSTEIN
Burlyman Entertainment: Nov, 2004 - No. 6 ($3.50)

1-6-Wachowski brothers-s/Skroce-a ... 3.50

DOCK WALLOPER (Ed Burns' ...)
Virgin Comics: Nov, 2007 - No. 5, Jun, 2008 ($2.99)

1-5-Burns & Palmiotti-s/Siju Thomas-a; Prohibition time ... 3.00

DOC MACABRE
IDW Publishing: Dec, 2010 - No. 3, Feb, 2011 ($3.99)

1-3-Steve Niles-s/Bernie Wrightson-a/c ... 4.00

DOC SAMSON (Also see Incredible Hulk)
Marvel Comics: Jan, 1996 - No. 4, Apr, 1996 ($1.95, limited series)

1-4: 1-Hulk c/app. 2-She-Hulk-c/app. 3-Punisher-c/app. 4-Polaris-c/app. ... 4.00

DOC SAMSON (Incredible Hulk)
Marvel Comics: Mar, 2006 - No. 5, July, 2006 ($2.99, limited series)

1-5: 1-DiFilippo-s/Fiorentino-a. 3-Conner-c ... 3.00

Disney Villains: Hades #1 © DIS

DMZ #67 © Wood & Burchelli

The Five Nations of New York

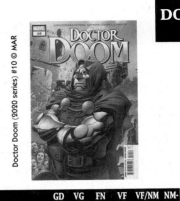
Doctor Doom (2020 series) #10 © MAR

	GD 2.0	VG 4.0	FN 6.0	VF 8.0	VF/NM 9.0	NM- 9.2

DOC SAVAGE
Gold Key: Nov, 1966

	GD 2.0	VG 4.0	FN 6.0	VF 8.0	VF/NM 9.0	NM- 9.2
1-Adaptation of the Thousand-Headed Man; James Bama c-r/1964 Doc Savage paperback	15	30	45	103	227	350

DOC SAVAGE (Also see Giant-Size...)
Marvel Comics Group: Oct, 1972 - No. 8, Jan, 1974

1	5	10	15	33	57	80
2,3-Steranko-c	4	8	12	23	37	50
4-8	2	4	6	10	14	18
...: The Man of Bronze TPB (DC Comics, 2010, $17.99) r/#1-8						18.00

NOTE: Gil Kane c-5, 6. Mooney a-1i. No. 1, 2 adapts pulp story "The Man of Bronze"; No. 3, 4 adapts "Death in Silver"; No. 5, 6 adapts "The Monsters"; No. 7, 8 adapts "The Brand of The Werewolf".

DOC SAVAGE (Magazine) (See Showcase Presents for reprint)
Marvel Comics Group: Aug, 1975 - No. 8, Spring, 1977 ($1.00, B&W)

1-Cover from movie poster; Ron Ely photo-c	3	6	9	21	33	45
2-5: 3-Buscema-a. 5-Adams-a(1 pg.), Rogers-a(1 pg)	2	4	6	9	13	16
6-8	2	4	6	10	14	18

DOC SAVAGE
DC Comics: Nov, 1987 - No. 4, Feb, 1988 ($1.75, limited series)

1-4: Dennis O'Neil-s/Adam & Andy Kubert-a/c in all						4.00
...: The Silver Pyramid TPB (2009, $19.99) r/#1-4						20.00

DOC SAVAGE
DC Comics: Nov, 1988 - No. 24, Oct, 1990 ($1.75/$2.00: #13-24)

1-16,19-24						4.00
17,18-Shadow x-over						5.00
Annual 1 (1989, $3.50, 68 pgs.)						5.00

DOC SAVAGE (First Wave)
DC Comics: Jun, 2010 - No. 18, Nov, 2011 ($3.99/$2.99)

1-9: 1-4-Malmont-s/Porter-a/J.G. Jones-c. Justice Inc. back-up; S. Hampton-a						4.00
1-6-Variant covers by Cassaday						5.00
10-17-($2.99) 10,16,17-Winslade-a						3.00

DOC SAVAGE
Dynamite Entertainment: 2013 - No. 8, 2014 ($3.99)

1-8: 1-Roberson-s/Evely-a; covers by Ross & Cassaday						4.00
Annual 2014 ($5.99) Denton-s/Castro-a						6.00
Special 2014: Woman of Bronze ($7.99, squarebound) Walker-s/Baal-a; Patricia Savage						8.00

DOC SAVAGE COMICS (Also see Shadow Comics)
Street & Smith Publ.: May, 1940 - No. 20, Oct, 1943 (1st app. in Doc Savage pulp, 3/33)

1-Doc Savage, Cap Fury, Danny Garrett, Mark Mallory, The Whisperer, Captain Death, Billy the Kid, Sheriff Pete & Treasure Island begin; Norgil, the Magician app.			730	1460	2190	5229	9365	13,500
2-Origin & 1st app. Ajax, the Sun Man; Danny Garrett, The Whisperer end; classic sci-fi cover	275	550	825	1746	3023	4300
3	187	374	561	1197	2049	2900
4-Treasure Island ends; Tuska-a	148	296	444	947	1624	2300
5-Origin & 1st app. Astron, the Crocodile Queen, not in #9 & 11; Norgi the Magician app.; classic-c	129	258	387	826	1413	2000
6-10: 6-Cap Fury ends; origin & only app. Red Falcon in Astron story. 8-Mark Mallory ends; Charlie McCarthy app. on-c plus true life story. 9-Supersnipe app. 10-Origin & only app. The Thunderbolt	81	162	243	518	884	1250
11,12	63	126	189	403	689	975
V2#1-6,8(#13-18,20): 15-Origin of Ajax the Sun Man; Jack Benny on-c; Hitler app. 16-The Pulp Hero, The Avenger app.; Fanny Brice story. 17-Sun Man ends; Nick Carter begins; Duffy's Tavern part photo-c & story. 18-Huckleberry Finn part-c/story. 19-Henny Youngman part photo-c & life story. 20-Only all funny-c w/Huckleberry Finn	60	120	180	381	653	925
V2#7-Classic Devil-c	74	148	222	470	810	1150

DOC SAVAGE: CURSE OF THE FIRE GOD
Dark Horse Comics: Sept, 1995 - No. 4, Dec, 1995 ($2.95, limited series)

1-4						4.00

DOC SAVAGE: THE MAN OF BRONZE
Skylark Pub: Mar, 1979, 68pgs. (B&W comic digest, 5-1/4x7-5/8")(low print)

15406-0: Whitman-a, 60 pgs., new comics	4	8	12	23	37	50

DOC SAVAGE: THE MAN OF BRONZE
Millennium Publications: 1991 - No. 4, 1991 ($2.50, limited series)

1-4: 1-Bronze logo						4.00
...: The Manual of Bronze 1 ($2.50, B&W, color, one-shot)-Unpublished proposed Doc Savage strip in color, B&W strip-r						4.00

DOC SAVAGE: THE MAN OF BRONZE, DOOM DYNASTY
Millennium Publ.: 1992 (Says 1991) - No. 2, 1992 ($2.50, limited series)

1,2						4.00

DOC SAVAGE: THE MAN OF BRONZE - REPEL
Innovation Publishing: 1992 ($2.50)

1-Dave Dorman painted-c						4.00

DOC SAVAGE: THE MAN OF BRONZE THE DEVIL'S THOUGHTS
Millennium Publ.: 1992 (Says 1991) - No. 3, 1992 ($2.50, limited series)

1-3						4.00

DOC SAVAGE: THE RING OF FIRE
Dynamite Entertainment: 2017 - No. 4, 2017 ($3.99, limited series)

1-4-Avallone-s/Acosta-a; multiple covers on each						4.00

DOC SAVAGE: THE SPIDER'S WEB
Dynamite Entertainment: 2015 - No. 5, 2016 ($3.99, limited series)

1-5-Roberson-s/Razek-a. 1-Multiple covers						4.00

DOC STEARN...MR. MONSTER (See Mr. Monster)

DR. ANTHONY KING, HOLLYWOOD LOVE DOCTOR
Minoan Publishing Corp./Harvey Publications No. 4: 1952(Jan) - No. 3, May, 1953; No. 4, May, 1954

1	24	48	72	142	234	325
2-4: 4-Powell-a	14	28	42	82	121	160

DR. ANTHONY'S LOVE CLINIC (See Mr. Anthony's...)

DOCTOR APHRA (Star Wars)(Title changes to Star Wars: Doctor Aphra with #7)
(See Darth Vader #3 for debut)
Marvel Comics: Feb, 2017 - No. 6, Jun, 2017 ($4.99/$3.99)

1-Gillen-s/Walker-a; back-up with Larroca-a; BT-1, Triple-Zero and Black Krrsantan app.	3	6	9	14	20	25
2-6-($3.99) Walker-a						4.00

DOCTOR APHRA (Star Wars)(2nd series)(Listed under Star Wars: Doctor Aphra)

DR. BOBBS
Dell Publishing Co.: No. 212, Jan, 1949

Four Color 212	7	14	21	49	92	135

DOCTOR DOOM
Marvel Comics: Dec, 2019 - No. 10, Feb, 2021 ($4.99/$3.99)

1-($4.99) Cantwell-s/Larroca-a; Kang the Conqueror app.						5.00
2-10-($3.99) Blue Marvel, Morgan Le Fay, Mephisto app.						4.00

DOCTOR DOOM AND THE MASTERS OF EVIL (All ages title)
Marvel Comics: Mar, 2009 - No. 4, Jun, 2009 ($2.99)

1-4: 1-Sinister Six app. 4-Magneto app.						3.00

DR. DOOM'S REVENGE
Marvel Comics: 1989 (Came w/computer game from Paragon Software)

V1#1-Spider-Man & Captain America fight Dr. Doom	4	8	12	28	47	65

DR. FATE (See 1st Issue Special, The Immortal..., Justice League, More Fun #55, & Showcase)

DOCTOR FATE
DC Comics: July, 1987 - No. 4, Oct, 1987 ($1.50, limited series, Baxter paper)

1-Giffen-c/a in all	1	3	4	6	8	10
2-4						6.00

DOCTOR FATE
DC Comics: Winter, 1988-'89 - No. 41, June, 1992 ($1.25/$1.50 #5 on)

1,15: 15-Justice League app.						5.00
2-14,16-41: 25-1st new Dr. Fate. 36-Original Dr. Fate returns						4.00
Annual 1(1989, $2.95, 68 pgs.)-Sutton-a						5.00

DOCTOR FATE
DC Comics: Oct, 2003 - No. 5, Feb, 2004 ($2.50, limited series)

1-5-Golden-s/Kramer-a						4.00

DOCTOR FATE
DC Comics: Aug, 2015 - No. 18, Jan, 2017 ($2.99)

1-18: 1-Levitz-s/Liew-a; Khalid Nassour chosen as new Doctor. 12-15-Kent Nelson app.						3.00

DR. FU MANCHU (See The Mask of...)
I.W. Enterprises: 1964

1-r/Avon's "Mask of Dr. Fu Manchu"; Wood-a	9	18	27	57	111	165

DR. GIGGLES (See Dark Horse Presents #64-66)
Dark Horse Comics: Oct, 1992 - No. 2, Oct, 1992 ($2.50, limited series)

	GD 2.0	VG 4.0	FN 6.0	VF 8.0	VF/NM 9.0	NM- 9.2

	GD 2.0	VG 4.0	FN 6.0	VF 8.0	VF/NM 9.0	NM- 9.2
1,2-Based on movie	1	3	4	6	8	10

DOCTOR GRAVES (Formerly The Many Ghosts of…)
Charlton Comics: No. 73, Sept, 1985 - No. 75, Jan, 1986

73-75-Low print run. 73,74-Ditko-a	2	4	6	8	10	12
… Magic Book nn (Charlton Press/Xerox Education, 1977, 68 pgs., digest) Ditko-c/a; Staton-a	4	8	12	23	37	50

DR. HORRIBLE (Based on Joss Whedon's internet feature)
Dark Horse Comics: Nov, 2009 ($3.50, one-shot)

1-Zack Whedon-s/Joëlle Jones-a; Captain Hammer pin-up by Gene Ha; 3 covers		3.50
… and other Horrible Stories TPB (9/10, $9.99) r/#1 and 3 stories from MySpace DHP		10.00
…: Best Friends Forever one-shot (11/18, $3.99) Whedon-s/Beroy & Soler-a/Fabio Moon-a		4.00

DR. JEKYLL AND MR. HYDE (See A Star Presentation & Supernatural Thrillers #4)

DR. KILDARE (TV)
Dell Publishing Co.: No. 1337, 4-6/62 - No. 9, 4-6/65 (All Richard Chamberlain photo-c)

Four Color 1337(#1, 1962)	10	20	30	64	132	200
2-9	6	12	18	41	76	110

DR. MASTERS (See The Adventures of Young…)

DOCTOR MID-NITE (Also see All-American #25)
DC Comics: 1999 - No. 3, 1999 ($5.95, square-bound, limited series)

1-3-Matt Wagner-s/John K. Snyder III-painted art		6.00
TPB (2000, $19.95) r/series		20.00

DOCTOR MIRAGE (Also see Death-Defying Doctor Mirage)
Valiant Entertainment: Aug, 2019 - No. 5, Dec, 2019 ($3.99, limited series)

1-5-Visaggio-s/Robles-a		4.00

DOCTOR OCTOPUS: NEGATIVE EXPOSURE
Marvel Comics: Dec, 2003 - No. 5, Apr, 2004 ($2.99, limited series)

1-5-Vaughan-s/Staz Johnson-a; Spider-Man app.		3.00
Spider-Man/Doctor Octopus: Negative Exposure TPB (2004, $13.99) r/series		14.00

DR. ROBOT SPECIAL
Dark Horse Comics: Apr, 2000 ($2.95, one-shot)

1-Bernie Mireault-s/a; some reprints from Madman Comics #12-15		3.00

DOCTOR SOLAR, MAN OF THE ATOM (See The Occult Files of Dr. Spektor #14 & Solar)
Gold Key/Whitman No. 28 on: 10/62 - No. 27, 4/69; No. 28, 4/81 - No. 31, 3/82 (1-27 have painted-c)

1-(#10000-210)-Origin/1st app. Dr. Solar (1st original Gold Key character)	68	136	204	544	1222	1900
2-Prof. Harbinger begins	15	30	45	100	220	340
3,4	9	18	27	59	117	175
5-Intro. Man of the Atom in costume	11	22	33	76	163	250
6-10	6	12	18	38	69	100
11-14,16-20	5	10	15	31	53	75
15-Origin retold	6	12	18	37	66	95
21-23: 23-Last 12¢ issue	4	8	12	28	47	65
24-27	4	8	12	25	40	55

		3	6	9	17	25	34
28-31: 29-Magnus Robot Fighter begins. 31-(3/82)The Sentinel app.						
Hardcover Vol. One (Dark Horse Books, 2004, $49.95) r/#1-7; creator bios						50.00
Hardcover Vol. Two (Dark Horse Books, 6/05, $49.95) r/#8-14; Jim Shooter foreword						50.00
Hardcover Vol. Three (Dark Horse Books, 9/05, $49.95) r/#15-22; Mike Baron foreword						50.00
Hardcover Vol. Four (Dark Horse Books, 11/07, $49.95) r/#23-31 and The Occult Files of Dr. Spektor #14; Batton Lash foreword						50.00

NOTE: *Frank Bolle* a-6-19, 29-31; c-29i, 30i. *Bob Fujitani* a-1-5. *Spiegle* a-29-31i. *Al McWilliams* a-20-23.

DOCTOR SOLAR, MAN OF THE ATOM
Valiant Comics: 1990 - No. 2, 1991 ($7.95, card stock-c, high quality, 96 pgs.)

1,2: Reprints Gold Key series	1	3	4	6	8	10

DOCTOR SOLAR, MAN OF THE ATOM
Dark Horse Comics: Jul, 2010 - No. 8, Sept, 2011 ($3.50)

1-(48 pgs.) Shooter-s/Calero-a; back-up reprint of origin/1st app. in D.S. #1 (1962)		4.00
2-8: 2-7-Roger Robinson-a		3.50
Free Comic Book Day Doctor Solar, Man of the Atom & Magnus, Robot Fighter (5/10, free) short story re-intros of Solar & Magnus; Shooter-s/Swanland-c; Calero & Reinhold-a		3.00

DOCTOR SPECTRUM (See Supreme Power)
Marvel Comics: Oct, 2004 - No. 6, Mar, 2005 ($2.99, limited series)

1-6-Origin; Sara Barnes-s/Travel Foreman-a		3.00
TPB (2005, $16.99) r/#1-6		17.00

DOCTOR SPEKTOR (See The Occult Files of…, & Spine-Tingling Tales)

DOCTOR SPEKTOR: MASTER OF THE OCCULT
Dynamite Entertainment: 2014 - No. 4, 2014 ($3.99)

1-4-Mark Waid-s; multiple covers on each		4.00

DOCTOR STAR AND THE KINGDOM OF LOST TOMORROW (Also see Black Hammer)
Dark Horse Comics: Mar, 2018 - No. 4, Jun, 2018 ($3.99, limited series)

1-4-Lemire-s/Fiumara-a		4.00

DOCTOR STRANGE (Formerly Strange Tales #1-168) (Also see The Defenders, Giant-Size…, Marvel Fanfare, Marvel Graphic Novel, Marvel Premiere, Marvel Treasury Edition, Strange & Strange Tales, 2nd Series)
Marvel Comics Group: No. 169, Jun, 1968 - No. 183, Nov, 1969

169(#1)-Origin retold; continued from Strange Tales #167; Roy Thomas-s/Dan Adkins-a; panel swipe/M.D. #1-c	50	100	150	400	900	1400
170-vs. Nightmare	10	20	30	69	147	225
171-176: 171-173-vs. Dormammu. 172-1st Colan-a. 174-1st Sons of Satannish						
	8	16	24	56	108	160
177-New masked costume	10	20	30	69	147	225
178-181: 178-Black Knight app.; continues in Avengers #61. 179-Spider-Man & Dr. Strange story from Amazing Spider-Man Annual #2. 180-Nightmare & Eternity app.; photo montage-c. 181-Brunner-c(part-i), last 12¢ issue	6	12	18	38	69	100
182-Juggernaut app.	8	16	24	54	102	150
183-Intro. The Undying Ones; cont'd in Sub-Mariner #22; concludes in Incredible Hulk #126;						

Dr. Strange returns in Marvel Feature #1 (second story)	8	16	24	54	102	150

DOCTOR STRANGE (2nd series)(Follows from Marvel Premiere #14)
Marvel Comics Group: Jun, 1974 - No. 81, Feb, 1987

1-Englehart-s/Brunner-c/a; 1st Silver Dagger	11	22	33	75	160	245
2-Silver Dagger app.; Defenders-c	6	12	18	41	76	110
3-5: 3-Mostly reprints; r-Strange Tales #126-127; 1 pg. original art. 4-5-Silver Dagger app.						
5-Last Brunner-a	3	6	9	19	30	40
6-10: 6-Dormammu app; Colan-a begins. 7-Dormammu app. 8-Dormammu app.; continued from Giant-Size Avengers #4. 9-Dormammu app. 10-Baron Mordo & Eternity app.						
	3	6	9	13	18	22
11,12,15-20: 13,15-17-(Regular 25¢ editions). 15,16-Strange vs. Satan. 17-1st Stygyro. 18-vs. Stygyro; last Englehart-s. 19-Wolfman-s begin; 1st Xander & the Creators. 20-vs. Xander and the Creators; slight x-over w/Annual #1	2	4	6	10	14	18
13-Nightmare app.; slight x-over with Tomb of Dracula #44						
	6	12	18	41	76	110
13,15-17-(30¢ variants, limited distribution)	5	10	15	33	57	80
14-(5/76) (Regular 25¢ edition) Dracula app.; story continues from Tomb of Dracula #44 and leads into Tomb of Dracula #45	2	4	6	11	16	20
14-(30¢-c variant, limited distribution)	6	12	18	37	66	95
21,22: 21-Reprints origin from Dr. Strange #169. 22-1st Apalla, Queen of the Sun	2	4	6	9	12	16
23-25,30,32-40: 23-25-(Regular 30¢ editions). 23-Starlin layouts; last Wolfman-s. 24-Starlin-s. 25-Starlin-c/s. 30-1st full app. Dweller in Darkness. 32-vs. Dweller in Darkness; 1st Dream Weaver. 33-Dweller in Darkness & Dream Weaver app. 34-vs. Cyrus Black & Nightmare. 35-Captain America & Iron Man app; Black Knight statue app. 36-Ningal app. (from Chamber of Chills #3). 37-Ningal, Dweller in Darkness & D'Spayre app. 38-Claremont-s begin. 40-Baron Mordo app.; continues in Man-Thing Vol. 2 #4						
		3	4	6	8	10
23-25-(35¢-c variants, limited distribution)(6,8,10/77)	9	18	27	58	114	170
26-29,31: 26-Starlin-a (p). Ancient One & In-Betweener app. 27-vs. Stygyro; Roger Stern-s begin; Ancient One & In-Betweener app. 28-vs. In-Betweener; Brunner-c/a. 29-vs. Deathstalker; Nighthawk app; Brunner-c/a. 31-Sub-Mariner app.						
		3	4	6	8	10
41-57,63-77,79-81: 41-Continued from Man-Thing Vol. 2 #4; Man-Thing & Baron Mordo app. 46-Miller-c/p. 48,49-Brother Voodoo app; 48-Marshall Rogers-p begin. 49-Baron Mordo app. 50-vs. Baron Mordo. 51-Dormammu app. 52-Nightmare. 53-Fantastic Four & Rama-Tut app.; takes place during FF #19. 55-D'Spayre app.; Golden-c. 56-Paul Smith-c; origin retold. 67-Hannibal King, Blade & Frank Drake app. 68,69-Black Knight app. 71-73-vs. Umar. 74-Secret Wars II x-over; Beyonder app. 75-Mignola-c; continued from FF #277; vs. Mephisto; last Stern-s. 79-1st Urthona. 80-1st Rintrah. 81-Last issue; Rintrah app; story continued in Strange Tales Vol. 2 #1						5.00
58-62: 58-Re-intro Hannibal King (cameo). 59-Hannibal King full app. 59-62-Dracula app. (Darkhold storyline). 61,62-Doctor Strange, Blade, Hannibal King & Frank Drake team-up to battle Dracula. 62-Death of Dracula & Lilith	1	2	3	5	6	8
78-New costume; Cloak (from Cloak & Dagger) app.	1	3	4	6	8	10
Annual 1 (1976, 52 pgs.)-New Russell-a (35 pgs.)	4	8	12	22	35	48
…: From the Marvel Vault (4/11, $2.99) Stern-s/Vokes-a						3.00
…/Silver Dagger Special Edition 1 (3/83, $2.50)-r/#1,2,4,5; Wrightson-c						5.00
… Vs. Dracula TPB (2006, $19.99) r/#14,58-62 and Tomb of Dracula #44						20.00
…What Is It That Disturbs You, Stephen? #1 (10/97, $5.99, 48 pgs.) Russell-a/Andreyko & Russell-s, retelling of Annual #1 story						6.00

NOTE: *Adkins* a-169, 170, 171i; c-169-171, 172i, 173. *Adams* a-4i. *Austin* a(i)-48-60, 66, 68, 70, 73; c(i)-48-53, 55, 58-60, 70. *Brunner* a-1-5p; c-1-6, 22, 28-30, 33. *Colan* a(p)-172-178, 180-183, 6-18, 36-45, 47; c(p)-172, 174-183, 11-21, 23, 27, 35, 36, 47. *Ditko* a-179r, 3r. *Everett* c-183. *Golden* a-46p, 55p; c-42-44, 46, 55p. *Kane* c(p)-8-10. *Miller* c-46p. *Nebres* a-20, 23, 24i, 26i, 32i; c-32i, 34. *Rogers* a-48-53p; c-47p-53p. *Russell* a-34i, 46i, Annual 1. *B. Smith* c-179. *Paul Smith* a-54p, 56p, 65, 66p, 68p, 69, 71-73; c-56, 65, 66, 68, 71. *Starlin* a-23p, 26; c-25, 26. *Sutton* a-27-29p, 31i, 33, 34p. Painted c-62, 63.

DOCTOR STRANGE (Volume 2)
Marvel Comics: Feb, 1999 - No. 4, May, 1999 ($2.99, limited series)

1-4: 1,2-Tony Harris-a/painted cover. 3,4-Chadwick-a		4.00

DOCTOR STRANGE (Follows Secret Wars event)
Marvel Comics: Dec, 2015 - No. 26, Dec, 2017; No. 381, Jan, 2018 - No. 390, Jul, 2018 ($4.99/$3.99)

1-($4.99) Aaron-s/Bachalo-a; back-up with Nowlan-a		5.00
2-5,7-19-($3.99) Aaron-s/Bachalo-a. 7-10-The Last Days of Magic		4.00
6-($4.99) The Last Days of Magic		5.00
20-($4.99) Doctor Strange in Weirdworld; art by Bachalo & Nowlan; last Aaron-s		5.00
21-24,26: 21-24-Empire tie-ins; Kingpin & Baron Mordo app.; Henrichon-a		4.00
25-($4.99) Barber-s/Nowlan-a/c		5.00
[Title switches to legacy numbering after #26 (12/17)]		
381-390: 381-385-Walta-a; Loki as Sorcerer Supreme. 383-385-The Sentry app. 386-Mephisto app.; Henrichon-a. 387-389-Damnation tie-ins. 390-Irving-a		4.00
#1.MU (4/17, $4.99) Monsters Unleashed tie-in; Chip Zdarsky/Julian Lopez-a		5.00
Annual 1 (11/16, $4.99) K. Immonen-s/Romero-a; Clea app.		5.00
…: Last Days of Magic 1 (6/16, $5.99) Story between #6 & 7; Doctor Voodoo & The Wu		6.00
…: Mystic Apprentice 1 (12/16, $3.99) New story w/Di Vito-a; r/Strange Tales #115, 110		5.00

DOCTOR STRANGE
Marvel Comics: Aug, 2018 - No. 20, Dec, 2019 ($3.99)

1-9,11-20: 1-Waid-s/Saiz-a; Strange goes to space. 2-Intro. Kanna. 3-Super-Skrull app. 11-17-Galactus app. 19-Strange's hands healed		4.00
10-($5.99) 400th issue; The Ancient One app.; bonus flashback with Nowlan-a		6.00
Annual 1 (12/19, $4.99) Scarlet Witch, Clea-man & Agatha Harkness app.		5.00
…: Nexus of Nightmares 1 (6/22, $3.99) Baron Mordo app.; Macchio-s/Moustafa-a		4.00
…: The Best Defense 1 (2/19, $4.99) Duggan-s/Smallwood-a; x-over with other Defenders		5.00
…: The End 1 (3/20, $4.99) Leah Williams-s/Filipe Andrade-a; Illyana Rasputin app.		5.00

DR. STRANGE (… Surgeon Supreme on cover)
Marvel Comics: Feb, 2020 - No. 6, Oct, 2020 ($3.99)

1-6: 1-Waid-s/Walker-a; The Wrecker app. 2-6-Dr. Druid app. 5,6-Madame Masque app.		4.00

DOCTOR STRANGE
Marvel Comics: May, 2023 - Present ($4.99/$3.99)

1-($4.99) Jed McKay-s/Pasqual Ferry-a; main cover by Alex Ross; Clea app.		5.00
2,4-12-($3.99) 4-Wong and Pandora Peters app. 6-Gedeon-a. 11,12-Beyruth-a		4.00

Doctor Mirage (2019 series) #4 © VAL

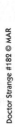

Doctor Strange #182 © MAR

Doctor Strange (2023 series) #1 © MAR

	GD 2.0	VG 4.0	FN 6.0	VF 8.0	VF/NM 9.0	NM- 9.2

3-($4.99) Dormammu app.; back-up story with Sister Grimm ... 5.00

DOCTOR STRANGE AND THE SORCERERS SUPREME (Prelude in Doctor Strange Annual #1)
Marvel Comics: Dec, 2016 - No. 12, Nov, 2017 ($3.99)
1-12: 1-9-Thompson-s/Rodriguez-a: The Ancient One, Wiccan & Merlin app. ... 5.00

DOCTOR STRANGE CLASSICS
Marvel Comics: Mar, 1984 - No. 4, June, 1984 ($1.50, Baxter paper)
1-4: Ditko-r; Byrne-c. 4-New Golden pin-up ... 5.00
NOTE: *Byrne c-1, 2-4.*

DOCTOR STRANGE: DAMNATION
Marvel Comics: Apr, 2018 - No. 4, Jun, 2018 ($3.99, limited series)
1-4-Spencer & Cates-s; Las Vegas is restored; Mephisto app. 1,2,4-Rod Reis-a ... 4.00

DOCTOR STRANGE: FALL SUNRISE
Marvel Comics: Jan, 2023 - No. 4, April 2023 ($4.99, limited series)
1-4-Tradd Moore-s/a ... 5.00

DOCTOR STRANGEFATE (See Marvel Versus DC #3 & DC Versus Marvel #4)
DC Comics (Amalgam): Apr, 1996 ($1.95)
1-Ron Marz script w/José Garcia-Lopez-(p) & Kevin Nowlan-(i). Access & Charles Xavier app. ... 6.00

DOCTOR STRANGE MASTER OF THE MYSTIC ARTS (See Fireside Book Series)

DOCTOR STRANGE/PUNISHER: MAGIC BULLETS
Marvel Comics: Feb, 2017 - No. 4, May, 2017 ($4.99, limited series)
1-4-Barber-s/Broccardo-a ... 5.00

DOCTOR STRANGE, SORCERER SUPREME
Marvel Comics (Midnight Sons imprint #60 on): Nov, 1988 - No. 90, June, 1996
($1.25/$1.50/$1.75/$1.95, direct sales only, Mando paper)
1-Continued from Strange Tales Vol. 2 #19; Fantastic Four, Avengers, Spider-Man, Silver Surfer, Hulk, Daredevil app. (cameos); Dormammu app.

	2	4	6	10	14	18

2-5,7-9: 2-Dormammu app. 3-New Defenders app. (Valkyrie, Andromeda, Interloper & Manslaughter.) 4-New Defenders becomes Dragoncircle; vs. Dragon of the Moon. 5-Roy & Dan Thomas-s & Guice-p begin; Rintrah app; vs. Baron Mordo. 7-Agamotto, Satannish, Mephisto app.; origin of Baron Mordo Pt. 2 (in back-up). 8-Mephisto vs. Satannish; origin of Baron Mordo Pt. 3 (in back-up). 9-History of Dr. Strange

	1	2	3	5	6	8

6-1st Mephista (daughter of Mephisto); Satannish & Mephisto app; Rintrah appears as Howard the Duck this issue; origin of Baron Mordo Pt. 1 (in back-up)

	3	6	9	15	22	28

10-45,48,49: 10-Re-intro Morbius w/new costume (11/89). 14-Origin Morbius. 15-Unauthorized Amy Grant photo-c. 16-vs. Baron Blood; Brother Voodoo app. also in back-up story (origin). 17-Morbius & Brother Voodoo app.; origin of Zombies in back-up. 19-Origin of the 1st Brother Voodoo back-up. 20-Dormammu app. 21-24: Dormammu & Baron Mordo app.; last Guice-a. 26-Werewolf by Night app. 28-Ghost Rider story continued from Ghost Rider #12; published at the same time as Dr. Strange/Ghost Rider special (4/91). 31-Infinity Gauntlet x-over; continued from Infinity Gauntlet #1; Silver Surfer app. 33-Thanos app. 34-36-Infinity Gauntlet x-overs. 34-Dr. Doom app. 35-Scarlet Witch & Thor app. 41-Wolverine app. 42-Infinity War x-overs. 42-Galactus app.; continued in Silver Surfer #67. 43-Continued from Infinity War #2; Galactus vs. Agamotto. 44-Galactus, Silver Surfer & Juggernaut app. 45-Galactus, Silver Surfer & Death app.

	1	2	3	5	6	8

46-1st app. Necromancer; Dr. Druid, Scarlet Witch & Agatha Harkness app.

	3	6	9	16	23	30

47-1st cover app. Necromancer

	3	6	9	14	20	25

50-($2.95, 52 pgs.)-Holo-grafx foil-c; Hulk, Ghost Rider & Silver Surfer app.; leads into new Secret Defenders series

	2	4	6	9	13	16

51-74: 52,53-Nightmare & Morbius app. 54-56: Infinity Crusade x-overs. 61-Siege of Darkness Pt. 15; new Dr. Strange begins (cameo, 1st app. 'Strange'; continued from Marvel Comics Presents #146; continued in Ghost Rider/Blaze Spirits of Vengeance #18. 62-Dr. Doom vs. Strange. 64,65-Sub-Mariner app. 65-Begin $1.95-c; bound-in card sheet. 66-Midnight Sons app.; continued in Dr. Strange Annual #4. 67-Clea returns; continued from Dr. Strange Annual #4. 69-Polaris & Forge app.; story takes place between X-Factor #105,106. 70,71-Hulk app. 72-Silver ink-c; Last Rites Pt. 1. 73-Last Rites Pt. 2.; Salom app.
74-Last Rites Pt. 3; Salom app. ... 6.00

75-($3.50) Foil-c; Last Rites Pt. 4; death of 'Strange'
| | 1 | 3 | 4 | 6 | 8 | 10 |
75-($2.50) Reg-c ... 5.00

76-89: 76-New look Dr. Strange. 80-Warren Ellis-s begin; another new look for Dr. Strange. 81-Begins "Over the Edge" branding. 82-Last Ellis-s. 84-DeMatteis-s begin; Baron Mordo app. 85-Baron Mordo revealed to have cancer. 86-Baron Mordo app. 87-'Death' of Baron Mordo ... 5.00

90-Last issue; Chthon app.

	2	4	6	11	16	20

Annual 1 (See Doctor Strange 2nd series)

Annual 2 ('92, $2.25, 68 pgs.) Return of the Defenders Pt. 4; continued from Silver Surfer Annual #5; Hulk, Sub-Mariner, Silver Surfer app.; vs. Wild One ... 6.00
Annual 3 ('93, $2.95, 68 pgs.) Polybagged w/card; 1st Kyllian ... 6.00
Annual 4 ('94, $2.95, 68 pgs.) Story occurs between Doctor Strange #66-67 ... 6.00
Ashcan (1995, 75¢) ... 4.00
.../Ghost Rider Special 1 (4/91, $1.50)-Same book as Doctor Strange, Sorcerer Supreme #28
| | 1 | 3 | 4 | 6 | 8 | 10 |
...Vs. Dracula 1 (3/94, $1.75, 52 pgs.)-r/Tomb of Dracula #44 & Dr. Strange #14
| | 1 | 3 | 4 | 6 | 8 | 10 |
NOTE: *Colan c/a-19. Golden c-28. Guice a-5-16, 18, 20-24; c-5-12, 20-24.*

DOCTOR STRANGE: THE OATH
Marvel Comics: Dec, 2006 - No. 5, Apr, 2007 ($2.99, limited series)
1-5-Vaughan-s/Martin-a; Night Nurse app. 1-Origin re-told ... 4.00
1-Halloween Comic Fest 2015 (12/15, giveaway) r/#1 with logo on cover ... 4.00
TPB (2007, $13.99) r/#1-5; sketch pages and promotional art ... 14.00

DR. TOM BRENT, YOUNG INTERN
Charlton Publications: Feb, 1963 - No. 5, Oct, 1963
| 1 | 3 | 6 | 9 | 21 | 33 | 45 |
| 2-5 | 3 | 6 | 9 | 14 | 21 | 26 |

DR. TOMORROW
Acclaim Comics (Valiant): Sept, 1997 - No. 12, Aug, 1998 ($2.50)
1-12: 1-Mignola-c ... 4.00

DOCTOR TOMORROW
Valiant Entertainment: Feb, 2020 - No. 5, Aug, 2020 ($3.99, limited series)
1-5-Arbona-s/Towe-a; intro. new Doctor Tomorrow ... 4.00

DR. VOLTZ (See Mighty Midget Comics)

DOCTOR VOODOO: AVENGER OF THE SUPERNATURAL
Marvel Comics: Dec, 2009 - No. 5, Apr, 2010 ($2.99, limited series)
1-5-Dr. Doom, Son of Satan & Ghost Rider app.; Palo-a ... 3.00
Doctor Voodoo: The Origin of Jericho Drumm (1/10, $4.99) r/Strange Tales #169,170 ... 5.00

DR. WEIRD
Big Bang Comics: Oct, 1994 - No. 2, May, 1995 ($2.95, B&W)
1,2: 1-Frank Brunner-a ... 4.00
... Special (2/94, $3.95, B&W, 68 pgs.) Origin-r by Starlin; Starlin-c ... 4.00

DOCTOR WHO (Also see Marvel Premiere #57-60)
Marvel Comics Group: Oct, 1984 - No. 23, Aug, 1986 ($1.50, direct sales, Baxter paper)
1-British-r
| | 2 | 4 | 6 | 10 | 14 | 18 |
2-15-British-r ... 5.00
16-23 ... 6.00
Graphic Novel Voyager (1985, $8.95) color reprints of B&W comic pages from Doctor Who Magazine #88-99; Colin Baker afterword ... 15.00

DOCTOR WHO (Based on the 2005 TV series with David Tennant)
IDW Publishing: Jan, 2008 - No. 6, Jun, 2008 ($3.99)
1-6: 1-Nick Roche-a/Gary Russell-s; two covers ... 4.00

DOCTOR WHO (Based on the 2005 TV series with David Tennant)
IDW Publishing: Jul, 2009 - No. 16, Oct, 2010 ($3.99)
1-16-Grist-c on all. 3-5,13-16-Art by Matt Smith (not the actor) ... 4.00
... Annual 2010 (7/10, $7.99) short stories by various; Yates-c; cameo by 11th Doctor ... 8.00
...: Autopia (6/09, $3.99) Ostrander-s; Yates-a/c; variant photo-c ... 4.00
...: Black Death White Life (9/09, $3.99) Mandrake-a; Guy Davis- c; variant photo-c ... 4.00
...: Cold-Blooded War (8/09, $3.99) Salmon-a/c; variant photo-c ... 4.00
...: Room With a Déjà View (6/09, $3.99) Eric J-a; Mandrake-c; variant photo-c ... 4.00
...: The Whispering Gallery (2/09, $3.99) Moore & Reppion-s; Templesmith-a/2 covers ... 4.00
...: Time Machination (5/09, $3.99) Paul Grist-a/c; variant photo-c ... 4.00

DOCTOR WHO (Based on the 2010 TV series with Matt Smith)
IDW Publishing: Jan, 2011 - No. 12, Apr, 2012 ($3.99)
1-16: 1-Edwards-a photo-c; Currie-a. 5-Buckingham-a. 12-Grist-a ... 4.00
Annual 2011 (8/11, $7.99) short stories by Fialkov, Shedd, Smith, McDaid and others ... 8.00
... Convention Special (7/11, no cover price, BBC America Shop Exclusive) The Doctor, Amy, and Rory at the San Diego Comic-Con; Matthew Dow Smith-s/Domingues-a ... 15.00
... 100 Page Spectacular 1 (7/12, $7.99) Short story reprints from various eras ... 8.00

DOCTOR WHO (Volume 3)(Based on the 2010 TV series with Matt Smith)
IDW Publishing: Sept, 2012 - No. 16, Dec, 2013 ($3.99)
1-16-Regular & photo-c on each: 1,2-Diggle-s/Buckingham-a. 3,4-Bond-a ... 4.00
...: 2016 Convention Exclusive (7/16, $10.00) Short stories of the various doctors ... 10.00
... Special 2012 (8/12, $7.99) Short stories by various incl. Wein, Diggle; Buckingham-c ... 8.00
... Special 2013 (12/13, $7.99) Cornell-s/Broxton-a; The Doctor visits the real world ... 8.00

	GD 2.0	VG 4.0	FN 6.0	VF 8.0	VF/NM 9.0	NM- 9.2

DOCTOR WHO (Based on the TV series with Jodie Whittaker)
Titan Comics: Dec, 2020 - No. 4, Mar, 2021 ($3.99)

1-4-The 13th and 10th Doctors team up; Rose app. 4.00

DOCTOR WHO: A FAIRYTALE LIFE (Based on the 2010 TV series with Matt Smith)
IDW Publishing: Apr, 2011 - No. 4, Jul, 2011 ($3.99, limited series)

1-4: 1-Sturges-s/Yeates-a; covers by Buckingham & Mebberson. 3-Shearer-a 4.00

DR. WHO & THE DALEKS (See Movie Classics)

DOCTOR WHO CLASSICS
IDW Publishing: Nov, 2005 - Oct, 2013 ($3.99)

1-10: Reprints from Doctor Who Weekly (1979); art by Gibbons, Neary and others 4.00
Series 2 (12/08 - No. 12, 11/09, $3.99) 1-12 .... 4.00
Series 3 (3/10 - No. 6, 8/10, $3.99) 1-6 .... 4.00
Series 4 (2/12 - No. 6, 7/12, $3.99) 1-6: Colin Baker era 4.00
Series 5 (3/13 - No. 5, 10/13 $3.99) 1-5: Sylvester McCoy era 4.00
...: The Seventh Doctor (2/11, $3.99) 1-5: 1-Furman-s/Ridgway-a; Sylvester McCoy-era 4.00

DOCTOR WHO: DOOM'S DAY
Titan Comics: Aug, 2023 - No. 2, Aug, 2023 ($3.99, limited series)

1,2-Houser-s/Ingranata-a; 12th Doctor, Missy and Doom app. 4.00

DOCTOR WHO: EMPIRE OF THE WOLF
Titan Comics: Dec, 2021 - No. 4, Mar, 2022 ($3.99, limited series)

1-4-Houser-s/Ingranata-a; 8th & 11th Doctors and Rose Tyler app. 4.00

DOCTOR WHO EVENT 2015: FOUR DOCTORS
Titan Comics: Sept, 2015 - No. 5, Oct, 2015 ($3.99, weekly limited series)

1-5-Paul Cornell-s/Neil Edwards-a; 10th, 11th, 12th and War Doctor app. 4.00

DOCTOR WHO EVENT 2016: SUPREMACY OF THE CYBERMEN
Titan Comics: Nov, 2016 - No. 5, Dec, 2016 ($3.99, limited series)

1-5-Mann & Scott-s; 9th, 10th, 11th, 12th Doctors app.; multiple covers on each 4.00

DOCTOR WHO FREE COMIC BOOK DAY
Titan Comics: Jun, 2015; Jun, 2016; Jun, 2017, 2019 (giveaways)

1-Short stories with the 10th, 11th & 12th Doctors; Paul Cornell interview 3.00
2016 - (6/16) Short stories with the 9th, 10th, 11th & 12th Doctors 3.00
2017 - (6/17) 12th Doctor and Bill; flashbacks with the 9th, 10th, 11th Doctors 3.00
2018 - (2018) 7th, 10th, 11th, 12th and 13th Doctors app.; photo-c 3.00
2019 - (2019) 13th Doctor and companions; Houser-s/Angiolini-c 3.00

DOCTOR WHO: GHOST STORIES (Sequel to the 2016 Christmas episode with The Ghost)
IDW Publishing: May, 2017 - No. 4, Aug, 2017 ($3.99, limited series)

1-4-George Mann-s; Grant and Lucy app.; multiple covers on each. 3-Calero-a 4.00

DOCTOR WHO: MISSY
Titan Comics: May, 2021 - No. 4, Aug, 2021 ($3.99, limited series)

1-4-Houser-s/Ingranata-a; Missy teams with the original Master 4.00

DOCTOR WHO: ORIGINS (Based on the Jo Martin version)
Titan Comics: Jul, 2022 - No. 4, Oct, 2022 ($3.99, limited series)

1-4-Houser-s/Ingranata-a; features the Fugitive Doctor; multiple covers 4.00

DOCTOR WHO: PRISONERS OF TIME
IDW Publishing: Feb, 2013 - No. 12, Nov, 2013 ($3.99, limited series)

1-50th Anniversary series with each issue spotlighting one Doctor; Francavilla-c 6.00
1-12-Photo covers 5.00
2-12: Francavilla-c on all. 5-12-Dave Sim variant-c. 8-Langridge-a 4.00

DOCTOR WHO: SPECIAL (Also see Doctor Who: The Lost Dimension)
IDW Publishing: Nov, 2017 - No. 2, Nov, 2017 ($4.99)

1,2-The Lost Dimension x-over parts 5 & 7; River Song and the 4th Doctor app. 5.00

DOCTOR WHO: THE EIGHTH DOCTOR (Based on the Paul McGann version)
Titan Comics: Nov, 2015 - No. 5, Apr, 2016 ($3.99, limited series)

1-5: 1-Intro. Josephine; Vieceli-a; multiple covers on each 4.00

DOCTOR WHO: THE ELEVENTH DOCTOR (Based on the Matt Smith version)
Titan Comics: Aug, 2014 - No. 15, Sept, 2015 ($3.99)

1-15: 1-Intro. Alice; Fraser-a; multiple covers on each 4.00

DOCTOR WHO: THE ELEVENTH DOCTOR YEAR TWO (Matt Smith version)
Titan Comics: Oct, 2015 - No. 15, Oct, 2016 ($3.99)

1-15: 1-War Doctor & Absolm Daak app.; multiple covers on each 4.00

DOCTOR WHO: THE ELEVENTH DOCTOR YEAR THREE (Matt Smith version)
Titan Comics: Feb, 2017 - No. 13, Feb, 2018 ($3.99)

1-13: 1-The Doctor and Alice; Rob Williams-s; multiple covers on each. 10-Lost Dimension x-over part 4 .... 4.00

DOCTOR WHO: THE FORGOTTEN (Based on the 2005 TV series with David Tennant)
IDW Publishing: Aug, 2008 - No. 6, Jan, 2009 ($3.99)

1-6: 1,2-Pia Guerra-a/Tony Lee-s; two covers 4.00

DOCTOR WHO: THE FOURTH DOCTOR (Based on the Tom Baker version)
Titan Comics: Apr, 2016 - No. 5, Oct, 2016 ($3.99)

1-5: Sarah Jane app.; Brian Williamson-a; multiple covers on each 4.00

DOCTOR WHO: THE LOST DIMENSION (Eight part x-over with 2017 Doctor Who titles)
Titan Comics: Sept, 2017 - Nov, 2017 ($3.99)

... Alpha (9/17, $3.99) Part one; multiple doctors and Capt. Jack app.; Stott-a 4.00
... Omega (11/17, $3.99) Concluding Part eight; multiple doctors and Jenny app. 4.00

DOCTOR WHO: THE NINTH DOCTOR (Based on the Christopher Eccleston version)
Titan Comics: Apr, 2015 - No. 5, Dec, 2015 ($3.99)

1-5: 1-Rose & Capt. Jack app.; Cavan Scott-s; multiple covers on each 4.00

DOCTOR WHO: THE NINTH DOCTOR ONGOING (Christopher Eccleston version)
Titan Comics: May, 2016 - No. 15, Sept, 2017 ($3.99)

1-15: 1-Rose & Capt. Jack app.; Cavan Scott-s; multiple covers on each 4.00
Doctor Who: The Ninth Special (Lost Dimension Part 2) (10/17, $3.99) Vastra app. 4.00

DOCTOR WHO: THE ROAD TO THE THIRTEEN DOCTOR

Titan Comics: Aug, 2018 - No. 3, Oct, 2018 ($3.99, limited series)

1-3: 1-The Tenth Doctor & companions; Peaty-s/Zanfardino-a. 2-Eleventh. 3-Twelfth 4.00

DOCTOR WHO: THE SEVENTH DOCTOR: OPERATION VOLCANO (Sylvester McCoy)
Titan Comics: Jul, 2018 - No. 3, Sept, 2018 ($5.99/$3.99)

1-($5.99) Ace & Gilmore app.; Andrew Cartmel-s/Christopher Jones-a 6.00
2,3-($3.99) 4.00

DOCTOR WHO: THE TENTH DOCTOR (Based on the David Tennant version)
Titan Comics: Aug, 2014 - No. 15, Sept, 2015 ($3.99)

1-15: 1-5-Casagrande-a; multiple covers on each. 1-Intro. Gabby. 6,7-Weeping Angels 4.00

DOCTOR WHO: THE TENTH DOCTOR YEAR TWO (David Tennant version)
Titan Comics: Oct, 2015 - No. 17, Jan, 2017 ($3.99)

1-17: 1-Abadzis-s/Carlini-a; multiple covers on each. 3-Captain Jack app. 4.00

DOCTOR WHO: THE TENTH DOCTOR YEAR THREE (David Tennant version)
Titan Comics: Feb, 2017 - No. 14, Mar, 2018 ($3.99)

1-14: 1-The Doctor & Gabby; Abadzis-s; multiple covers on each. 9-Lost Dimension x-over part 3 .... 4.00

DOCTOR WHO: THE THIRD DOCTOR (Based on the Jon Pertwee version)
Titan Comics: Oct, 2016 - No. 5, Mar, 2017 ($3.99)

1-5-Jo and The Brigadier app.; multiple covers on each 4.00

DOCTOR WHO: THE THIRTEENTH DOCTOR (Jodie Whittaker version)
Titan Comics: No. 0, Oct, 2018; No. 1, Dec, 2018 - No. 12, Oct, 2019 ($3.99)

0 - The Many Lives of Doctor Who ($7.99); short stories of each of the previous Doctors 8.00
1-12: 1-Houser-s/Stott-a; Ryan, Yasmin & Graham app. 4.00
... Holiday Special #1, (12/19, 1/20, $5.99) Houser-s/Ingranata-a 6.00
(Season 2) 2.1-2.4: 2.1-(2/20) Tenth Doctor & Martha app. 4.00

DOCTOR WHO: THE TWELFTH DOCTOR (Based on the Peter Capaldi version)
Titan Comics: Nov, 2014 - No. 15, Jan, 2016 ($3.99)

1-15: 1-The Doctor and Clara; Dave Taylor-a; multiple covers on each 4.00

DOCTOR WHO: THE TWELFTH DOCTOR YEAR TWO (Based on the Peter Capaldi version)
Titan Comics: Feb, 2016 - No. 15, Apr, 2017 ($3.99)

1-15: 1-The Doctor and Clara. 6-Intro. Hattie 4.00

DOCTOR WHO: THE TWELFTH DOCTOR YEAR THREE (The Peter Capaldi version)
Titan Comics: May, 2017 - No. 13, Apr, 2018 ($3.99)

1-13: 5-Bill Potts comic debut. 8-Lost Dimension x-over part 6; 9th & 10th Doctors app. 4.00

DOCTOR WHO: TIME LORD VICTORIOUS
Titan Comics: Oct, 2020 - No. 2, Nov, 2020 ($5.99, limited series)

1,2-The 10th Doctor and the Daleks app.; Jody Houser-s 6.00

DR. WONDER
Old Town Publishing: June, 1996 - No. 5 ($2.95, B&W)

1-5: 1-Intro & origin of Dr. Wonder; Dick Ayers-c/a; Irwin Hasen-a 4.00

DOCTOR ZERO
Marvel Comics (Epic Comics): Apr, 1988 - No. 8, Aug, 1989 ($1.25/$1.50)

1-8: 1-Sienkiewicz-c. 6,7-Spiegle-a 4.00
NOTE: *Sienkiewicz-3i, 4i; c-1.*

DO-DO (Funny Animal Circus Stories)
Nation-Wide Publishers: 1950 - No. 7, 1951 (5¢, 5x7-1/4" Miniature)

1 (52 pgs.)	22	44	66	132	216	300
2-7	12	24	36	69	97	125

DODO & THE FROG, THE (Formerly Funny Stuff; also see It's Game Time #2)
National Periodical Publications: No. 80, 9-10/54 - No. 88, 1-2/56; No. 89, 8-9/56; No. 90, 10-11/56; No. 91, 9/57; No. 92, 11/57 (See Comic Cavalcade and Captain Carrot)

80-1st app. Doodles Duck by Sheldon Mayer	20	40	60	114	182	250
81-91: Doodles Duck by Mayer in #81,83-90	11	22	33	62	86	110
92-(Scarce)-Doodles Duck by S. Mayer	18	36	54	105	165	225

DOG DAYS OF SUMMER
DC Comics: Jul, 2019 ($9.99, one-shot, squarebound)

1-Short stories by various; Krypto, Beast Boy, Batcow, Killer Croc, Animal Man app. 10.00

DOGFACE DOOLEY
Magazine Enterprises: 1951 - No. 5, 1953

1(A-1 40)	34	68	102	199	325	450
2(A-1 43), 3(A-1 49), 4(A-1 53)	21	42	63	126	206	285
5(A-1 64) Classic good girl-c	53	106	159	334	567	800
I.W. Reprint #1('64), Super Reprint #17	3	6	9	16	23	30

DOG MOON
DC Comics (Vertigo): 1996 ($6.95, one-shot)

1-Robert Hunter-scripts; Tim Truman-c/a 7.00

DOG OF FLANDERS, A
Dell Publishing Co.: No. 1088, Mar, 1960

Four Color 1088-Movie, photo-c	5	10	15	33	57	80

DOGPATCH (See Al Capp's... & Mammy Yokum)

DOGS OF WAR (Also see Warriors of Plasm #13)
Defiant: Apr, 1994 - No. 5, Aug, 1994 ($2.50)

1-5: 5-Schism x-over 4.00

DOGS-O-WAR
Crusade Comics: June, 1996 - No. 3, Jan, 1997 ($2.95, B&W, limited series)

1-3: 1,2-Photo-c 4.00

DOLLAR COMICS
DC Comics: 2019 - 2020 ($1.00, reprints with new house ads)

...: Amethyst 1 - ('20) Reprints Amethyst, Princess of Gemworld #1; Estrada & Colón-a 3.00
...: Batman 386 - ('20) Reprints intro/origin of Black Mask; Moench-s/Mandrake-a 3.00
...: Batman 428 - ('20) Reprints Death of Jason Todd; Starlin-s/Aparo/Mignola-a 3.00
...: Batman 497 - ('19) Reprints Bane breaking Batman's back; Moench-s/Aparo/Jones-a 3.00

Doctor Who (2020 series) #2 © BBC · **Doll Man #24 © QUA** · **Domino (2018 series) #6 © MAR**

	GD 2.0	VG 4.0	FN 6.0	VF 8.0	VF/NM 9.0	NM- 9.2

...: Batman 567 - ('20) Reprints 1st app. of Cassandra Cain Batgirl; Damion Scott-a 3.00
...: Batman 608 - ('19) Reprints 1st issue of Hush storyline; Loeb-s/Jim Lee-a 3.00
...: Batman 613 - ('19) Reprint from Hush storyline; Harley Quinn & Catwoman app. 3.00
...: Batman 663 - ('19) Reprints Joker storybook issue; Morrison-s/Van Fleet-a 3.00
...: Batman Adventures 12 - ('19) Reprints comic book debut of Harley Quinn; Batgirl app. 3.00
...: Batman/Huntress: Cry For Blood 1 ('20) The Question app.; Rucka-s/Burchett-a; The Question app. 3.00
...: Batman: Shadow of the Bat 1 - ('20) The Last Arkham; Grant-s/Breyfogle-a 3.00
...: Birds of Prey 1 - ('19) Reprints 1st 1999 Black Canary/Oracle issue; Dixon-s/Land-a 3.00
...: Blackest Night 1 - ('19) Reprints 1st issue of series; Johns-s/Reis-a 3.00
...: Catwoman 1 - ('20) Reprints 1st issue of 2002 series; Darwyn Cooke & Mike Allred-a 3.00
...: Crisis of Infinite Earths 1 - ('19) 1st issue of series; Wolfman-s/Pérez-a; Alex Ross-c 3.00
...: Detective Comics 554 - ('20) Reprints 1st new look Black Canary 3.00
...: Detective Comics 854 - (11/19) Early Batwoman spotlight; Williams III-a; photo-c 3.00
...: Flashpoint 1 - (1/20) Reprints 1st issue of series; Johns-s/Andy Kubert-a/c 3.00
...: Green Lantern 1 - ('20) Reprints 2011 New 52 issue 3.00
...: Green Lantern: Rebirth 1 - ('20) Reprints 2004 issue; Johns-s/Van Sciver-a 3.00
...: Harley Quinn 1 - ('19) Reprints 1st issue of 2013 series; Conner-a 3.00
...: Infinite Crisis 1 - ('19) Reprints 1st issue of series; Johns-s/Jimenez-a/Jim Lee-a 3.00
...: JLA 1 - ('20) Reprints 1996 issue; Morrison-s/Porter-a 3.00
...: JLA: Year One 1 - ('20) Reprints 1998 issue; Waid & Augustyn-s/Kitson-a 3.00
...: Justice League 1 - ('20) Reprints 1987 issue; Giffen & DeMatteis-s/Maguire-a 3.00
...: Justice League 1 - ('20) Reprints 2011 New 52 issue; Geoff Johns-s/Jim Lee-a 3.00
...: Justice League of America 1 - ('20) Reprints 2006 issue; Meltzer-s/Benes-a 3.00
...: Luthor 1 - ('19) Reprints Lex Luthor: Man of Steel #1; Azzarello-s/Bermejo-a/c 3.00
...: New Teen Titans 2 - ('20) Reprints debut of Deathstroke; Wolfman-s/Pérez-a 3.00
...: Robin 1 - ('20) Reprints 1991 issue; Tim Drake; Dixon-s/Lyle-a 3.00
...: Sandman 23 - ('20) Lucifer loses his wings and leaves Hell; Gaiman-s/Kelley Jones-a 3.00
...: Superman 75 - ('19) Reprints Death of Superman issue from 1993 3.00
...: Swamp Thing 1 - ('19) Reprints 1st issue of 1972 series; Wein-s/Wrightson-a 3.00
...: Swamp Thing 57 - ('20) Reprints #57 from '82 series; Adam Strange app.; Moore-s 3.00
...: Tales of the Teen Titans 44 - ('20) Conclusion of The Judas Contract; Pérez-a 3.00
...: The Brave and the Bold 197 - (3/20) Golden Age Batman and Catwoman team-up 3.00
...: The Flash 1 - ('20) Reprints 1987 issue with Wally West as the Flash; Guice-a 3.00
...: The Flash 164 - ('19) Reprints 2000 issue; Johns-s/Unzueta-a/Bolland-c 3.00
...: The Flash: Rebirth 1 - ('20) Reprints 2009 issue; Johns-s/Van Sciver-a 3.00
...: The Joker 1 - ('19) Reprints 1st issue of 1975 series; O'Neil-s/Novick-a 3.00
...: Watchmen 1 - ('19) Reprints 1st issue of series; Alan Moore-s/Dave Gibbons-a 3.00

DOLLFACE & HER GANG (Betty Betz'...)
Dell Publishing Co.: No. 309, Jan, 1951

	GD	VG	FN	VF	VF/NM	NM-
Four Color 309	9	18	27	59	117	175

DOLLHOUSE
Dark Horse Comics: Mar, 2011; Jul, 2011 - No. 5, Nov, 2011 ($3.50, limited series)
1-5-Richards-a; two covers on each 4.00
...: Epitaphs (3/11, $3.50) reprints story from DVD collection; covers by Noto & Morris 4.00

DOLLHOUSE FAMILY, THE
DC Comics (Hill House Comics): Jan, 2020 - No. 6, Jun, 2020 ($3.99)
1-6-Carey-s/Gross-a; back-up serial Sea Dogs in each 4.00

DOLLMAN (Movie)
Eternity Comics: Sept, 1991 - No. 4, Dec, 1991 ($2.50, limited series)
1-4: Adaptation of film 4.00

DOLL MAN QUARTERLY, THE (Doll Man #17 on; also see Feature Comics #27 & Freedom Fighters)
Quality Comics: Fall, 1941 - No. 7, Fall, '43; No. 8, Spr, '46 - No. 47, Oct, 1953

	GD	VG	FN	VF	VF/NM	NM-
1-Dollman (by Cassone), Justin Wright begin	349	698	1047	2443	4272	6100
2-The Dragon begins; Crandall-a(5)	158	316	474	1003	1727	2450
3,4	97	194	291	621	1061	1500
5-Crandall-a	97	194	291	621	1061	1500
6,7(1943)	55	110	165	352	601	850
8(1946)-1st app. Torchy by Bill Ward	194	388	582	1242	2121	3000
9(Summer 1946)	57	114	171	362	619	875
10-20	42	84	126	265	445	625
21-26,28-30: 28-Vs. The Flame	39	78	117	240	395	550
27-Sci-fi bondage-c	47	94	141	296	498	700
31-(12/50)-Intro Elmo, the wonder dog (Dollman's faithful dog)	50	100	150	315	533	750
32-35,38,40: 32-34-Jeb Rivers app. 34-Crandall-a(2)	40	80	120	246	411	575
36-Giant shark-c	48	96	144	302	514	725
37-Origin & 1st app. Dollgirl; Dollgirl bondage-c	110	220	330	704	1202	1700
39-"Narcotics...the Death Drug" c/story	60	120	180	381	653	925
41-47	34	68	102	199	325	450
Super Reprint #11('64, r/#20),15(r/#23),17(r/#28): 15,17-Torchy app.; Andru/Esposito-c	4	8	12	23	37	50

NOTE: Ward Torchy in 8, 9, 11, 12, 14-24, 27; by Fox-#26, 30, 35-47. Crandall a-2, 5, 10, 13 & Super #11, 17, 18. Crandall/Cuidera c40-42. Guardineer a-3. Bondage c-27, 37, 38, 39.

DOLLY
Ziff-Davis Publ. Co.: No. 10, July-Aug, 1951 (Funny animal)

	GD	VG	FN	VF	VF/NM	NM-
10-Painted-c	15	30	45	83	124	165

DOLLY DILL
Marvel Comics/Newsstand Publ.: 1945

	GD	VG	FN	VF	VF/NM	NM-
1	42	84	126	265	445	625

DOLLZ, THE
Image Comics: Apr, 2001 - No. 2, June, 2001 ($2.95)
1,2: 1-Four covers; Sniegoski & Green-s/Green-a 3.00

DOMINATION FACTOR
Marvel Comics: Nov, 1999 - 4.8, Feb, 2000 ($2.50, interconnected mini-series)
1.1, 2.3, 3.5, 4.7-Fantastic Four; Jurgens-s/a 4.00
1.2, 2.4, 3.6, 4.8-Avengers; Ordway-s/a 4.00

DOMINIC FORTUNE
Marvel Comics (MAX): Oct, 2009 - No. 4, Jan, 2010 ($3.99, limited series)
1-4-Howard Chaykin-s/a/c 4.00

DOMINION
Image Comics: Jan, 2003 - No. 2 ($2.95)
1,2-Keith Giffen-s/a 5.00

DOMINION (Manga)
Eclipse Comics: Dec, 1990 - No. 6., July, 1990 ($2.00, B&W, limited series)
1-6 4.00

DOMINION: CONFLICT 1 (Manga)
Dark Horse Comics: Mar, 1996 - No. 6, Aug, 1996 ($2.95, B&W, limited series)
1-6: Shirow-c/a/scripts 4.00

DOMINIQUE LAVEAU: VOODOO CHILD
DC Comics (Vertigo): May, 2012 - No. 7, Nov, 2012 ($2.99, limited series)
1-7-Selwyn Seyfu Hinds-s/Denys Cowan-a 3.00

DOMINO (See X-Force)
Marvel Comics: Jan, 1997 - No. 3, Mar, 1997 ($1.95, limited series)
1-3: 2-Deathstrike/app. 4.00

DOMINO (See X-Force)
Marvel Comics: Jun, 2003 - No. 4, Aug, 2003 ($2.50, limited series)
1-4-Stelfreeze-c/a; Pruett-s 3.00

DOMINO (X-Force)
Marvel Comics: Jun, 2018 - No. 10, Mar, 2019 ($3.99)
1-10-Simone-s/Baldeón-a. 4-6-Shang-Chi app. 8-Morbius app. 9,10-Longshot app. 4.00
Annual 1 (11/18, $4.99) Short flashback stories by various incl. Simone, Nicieza, Kirk 5.00

DOMINO CHANCE
Chance Enterprises: May-June, 1982 - No. 9, May, 1985 (B&W)
1-9: 7-1st app. Gizmo, 2 pgs. 8-1st full Gizmo story. 1-Reprint, May, 1985 4.00

DOMINO: HOTSHOTS (X-Force)
Marvel Comics: May, 2019 - No. 5, Sept, 2019 ($3.99, limited series)
1-5-Simone-s/Baldeón-a; Black Widow and Deadpool app. 4.00

DONALD AND MICKEY
IDW Publishing: Aug, 2017 - No. 4, May, 2018 ($5.99)
1-4-Reprints from European stories; 2 covers on each 6.00

DONALD AND MICKEY IN DISNEYLAND (See Dell Giants)

DONALD AND SCROOGE
Disney Comics: 1992 ($8.95, squarebound, 100 pgs.)

	GD	VG	FN	VF	VF/NM	NM-
nn-Don Rosa reprint special; r/U.S., D.D. Advs.	1	3	4	6	8	10

1-3 (1992, $1.50)-r/D.D. Advs. Donald Duck #1,22,24 & U.S. #261-263,269 3.00

DONALD AND THE WHEEL (Disney)
Dell Publishing Co.: No. 1190, Nov, 1961

	GD	VG	FN	VF	VF/NM	NM-
Four Color 1190-Movie, Barks-a	9	18	27	59	117	175

DONALD DUCK (See Adventures of Mickey Mouse, Cheerios, Donald & Mickey, Ducktales, Dynabrite Comics, Gladstone Comic Album, Mickey & Donald, Mickey Mouse Mag., Story Hour Series, Uncle Scrooge, Walt Disney's Comics & Stories, W. D.'s Donald Duck, Wheaties & Whitman Comic Books, Wise Little Hen, The)

DONALD DUCK
Whitman Publishing Co./Grosset & Dunlap/K.K.: 1935, 1936 (All pages on heavy linen-like

	GD 2.0	VG 4.0	FN 6.0	VF 8.0	VF/NM 9.0	NM- 9.2

finish cover stock in color;1st book ever devoted to Donald Duck; see Advs. of Mickey Mouse for 1st app.) (9-1/2x13")

Item	GD 2.0	VG 4.0	FN 6.0	VF 8.0	VF/NM 9.0	NM- 9.2
978(1935)-16 pgs.; Illustrated text story book	219	438	657	1402	2401	3400
nn(1936)-36 pgs.plus hard cover & dust jacket. Story completely rewritten with B&W illos added. Mickey appears and his nephews are named Morty & Monty						
Book only	213	426	639	1363	2332	3300
Dust jacket only...	40	80	120	246	411	575

DONALD DUCK (Walt Disney's) (10¢)
Whitman/K.K. Publications: 1938 (8-1/2x11-1/2", B&W, cardboard-c)
(Has D. Duck with bubble pipe on-c)

Item	GD 2.0	VG 4.0	FN 6.0	VF 8.0	VF/NM 9.0	NM- 9.2
nn-The first Donald Duck & Walt Disney comic book; 1936 & 1937 Sunday strip-r(in B&W); same format as the Feature Books; 1st strips with Huey, Dewey & Louie from 10/17/37; classic bubble pipe cover	514	1028	1542	3750	6625	9500

DONALD DUCK (Walt Disney's...#262 on; see 4-Color listings for titles & Four Color No. 1109 for origin story)
Dell Publ. Co./Gold Key #85-216/Whitman #217-245/Gladstone #246 on: 1940 - No. 84, Sept-Nov, 1962; No. 85, Dec, 1962 - No. 245, July, 1984; No. 246, Oct, 1986 - No. 279, May, 1990; No. 280, Sept, 1993 - No. 307, Mar,1998

Item	GD 2.0	VG 4.0	FN 6.0	VF 8.0	VF/NM 9.0	NM- 9.2
Four Color 4(1940)-Daily 1939 strip-r by Al Taliaferro	2700	5400	8100	20,250	37,125	54,000
Large Feature Comic 16(1/41)-1940 Sunday strips-r in B&W	1000	2000	3000	7600	13,800	20,000
Large Feature Comic 20('41)-Comic Paint Book, r-single panels from Large Feature #16 at top of each pg. to color; daily strip-r across bottom of each page. (Rare)	1250	2500	3750	9500	17,250	25,000
Four Color 9('42)- "Finds Pirate Gold"; 64 pgs. by Carl Barks & Jack Hannah (pgs. 1,2,5,12-40 are by Barks, his 1st Donald Duck comic book art work; © 8/17/42)	1250	2500	3150	8000	14,500	21,000
Four Color 29(9/43)- "Mummy's Ring" by Barks; reprinted in Uncle Scrooge & Donald Duck #1('65), W. D. Comics Digest #44('73) & Donald Duck Advs. #14	811	1622	2433	5920	10,460	15,000
Four Color 62(1/45)- "Frozen Gold"; 52 pgs. by Barks, reprinted in The Best of W.D. Comics & Donald Duck Advs. #4	241	482	723	1988	4494	7000
Four Color 108(1946)- "Terror of the River"; 52 pgs. by Carl Barks; reprinted in Gladstone Comic Album #2	107	214	321	856	1928	3000
Four Color 147(5/47)-in "Volcano Valley" by Barks	89	178	267	712	1606	2500
Four Color 159(8/47)-in "The Ghost of the Grotto"; 52 pgs. by Carl Barks; reprinted in Best of Uncle Scrooge & Donald Duck #1 ('66) & The Best of W.D. Comics & D.D. Advs. #9; two Barks stories	93	186	279	744	1672	2600
Four Color 178(12/47)-1st app. Uncle Scrooge by Carl Barks; reprinted in Gold Key Christmas Parade #3 & The Best of Walt Disney Comics	224	448	672	1848	4174	6500
Four Color 189(6/48)-by Carl Barks; reprinted in Best of Donald Duck & Uncle Scrooge #1('64) & D.D. Advs. #19	100	200	300	800	1800	2800
Four Color 199(10/48)-by Carl Barks; mentioned in Love and Death; r/in Gladstone Comic Album #5	96	192	288	768	1734	2700
Four Color 203(12/48)-by Barks; reprinted as Gold Key Christmas Parade #4	64	128	192	512	1156	1800
Four Color 223(4/49)-by Barks; reprinted as Best of Donald Duck #1 & Donald Duck Advs. #3	82	164	246	656	1478	2300
Four Color 238(8/49)-in "Voodoo Hoodoo" by Barks	61	122	183	488	1094	1700
Four Color 256(6/49)-by Barks; reprinted in Best of Donald Duck #1 & Uncle Scrooge #2('67), Gladstone Comic Album #16 & W.D. Comics Digest 44('73)	54	108	162	432	966	1500
Four Color 263(2/50)-Two Barks stories; r-in D.D. #278	50	100	150	400	900	1400
Four Color 275(5/50), 282(7/50), 291(9/50), 300(11/50)-All by Carl Barks; 275, 282 reprinted in W. D. Comics Digest #44('73). #275 r/in Gladstone Comic Album #10. #291 r/in D. Duck Advs. #16	48	96	144	374	862	1350
Four Color 308(1/51), 318(3/51)-by Barks; #318-reprinted in W.D. Comics Digest #34 & D.D. Advs. #2,19	46	92	138	359	805	1250
Four Color 328(5/51)-by Carl Barks	46	92	138	340	770	1200
Four Color 339(7-8/51), 379-2nd Uncle Scrooge-c; art not by Barks.	33	66	99	238	532	825
Four Color 356,394-Barks-c only	24	48	72	168	372	575
Four Color 367(1-2/52)-by Barks; reprinted as Gold Key Christmas Parade #2 & #8	38	76	114	285	641	1000
26(11-12/52)-In "Trick or Treat" (Barks-a, 36pgs.) 1st story r-in Walt Disney Digest #16 & Gladstone C.A. #23	42	84	126	311	706	1100
27-30-Barks-c only	13	26	39	91	201	310
31-44,47-50	7	14	21	46	86	125
45-Barks-a (6 pgs.)	13	26	39	89	195	300
46- "Secret of Hondorica" by Barks, 24 pgs.; reprinted in Donald Duck #98 & 154	17	34	51	119	265	410
51-Barks-a,1/2 pg.	7	14	21	46	86	125
52- "Lost Peg-Leg Mine" by Barks, 10 pgs.	14	28	42	96	211	325
53,55-59	6	12	18	38	69	100
54- "Forbidden Valley" by Barks, 26 pgs. (10¢ & 15¢ versions exist)	15	30	45	105	233	360
60- "Donald Duck & the Titanic Ants" by Barks, 20 pgs. plus 6 more pgs.	14	28	42	98	217	335
61-67,69,70	5	10	15	34	60	85
68-Barks-a, 5 pgs.	9	18	27	62	126	190
71-Barks-r, 1/2 pg.	5	10	15	34	60	85
72-78,80,82-97,99,100: 96-Donald Duck Album	5	10	15	33	57	80
79,81-Barks-a, 1pg.	5	10	15	34	60	85
98-Reprints #46 (Barks)	5	10	15	34	60	85
101,103-111,113-135: 120-Last 12¢ issue. 134-Barks-r/#52 & WDC&S 194.	4	8	12	22	35	48
135-Barks-r/WDC&S #98, 19 pgs.	4	8	12	23	37	50
102-Super Goof. 112-1st Moby Duck	4	8	12	23	37	50
136-153,155,156,158: 149-20¢-c begin	3	6	9	14	20	26
154-Barks-r(#46)	4	8	12	16	24	32
157,159,160,164: 157-Barks-r(#45); 25¢-c begin. 159-Reprints/WDC&S #192 (10 pgs.).						
160-Barks-r(#26). 164-Barks-r(#79).	3	6	9	14	20	26
161-163,165-173,175-187,189-191: 175-30¢-c begin. 187-Barks r/#68.	3	6	9	14	18	22
174,188: 174-r/4-Color #394.	3	6	9	14	19	24
175-177-Whitman variants	3	6	9	14	19	24
192-Barks-r(40 pgs.) from Donald Duck #60 & WDC&S #226,234 (52 pgs.)	3	6	9	15	22	28
193-200,202-207,209-211,213-216	2	4	6	9	13	16
201,208,212: 201-Barks-r/Christmas Parade #26, 16pgs. 208-Barks-r/#60 (6 pgs.). 212-Barks-r/WDC&S #130	3	6	9		13	16
217-219: 217 has 216 on-c. 219-Barks-r/#106,107, 10 pgs. ea.	2	4	6	10	14	18
220,225-228: 228-Barks-r/F.C. #275	2	4	6	10	14	18
221,223,224: Scarce; only sold in pre-packs. 221(8/80), 223(11/80), 224(12/80)	5	10	15	35	63	90
222-(9-10/80)-(Very low distribution)	17	34	51	119	265	410
229-240: 229-Barks-r/F.C. #282. 230-Barks-r/ #52 & WDC&S #194. 236(2/82), 237(2-3/82), 238(3/82), 239(4/82), 240(5/82).	3	6	9	13	18	22
241-245: 241(4/83), 242(5/83), 243(3/84), 244(4/84), 245(7/84)(low print)	3	6	9	14	19	24
246-(1st Gladstone issue)-Barks-r/FC #422	3	6	9	15	21	26
247-249,251: 248,249-Barks-r/DD #54 & 26. 251-Barks-r/1945 Firestone	2	4	6		13	16
250-($1.50, 68 pgs.)-Barks-r/4-Color #9	2	4	6		13	18
252-277,280: 254-Barks-r/FC #328. 256-Barks-r/FC #147. 257-($1.50, 52 pgs.)-Barks-r/Vacation Parade #1. 261-Barks-r/FC #300. 275-Kelly-r/FC #92. 280 (#1, 2nd Series)	1	2	3	5	6	8
278,279,286: 278,279 ($1.95, 68 pgs.): 278-Rosa-a; Barks-r/FC #263. 279-Rosa-c; Barks-r/MOC #4. 286-Rosa-a	1	2	3	5	7	9
281,282,284	1	2	3	5	6	7
283-Don Rosa-a, part-c & scripts	1	2	3		6	8
285,287-307						5.00
286 ($2.95, 68 pgs.)-Happy Birthday, Donald						6.00
Mini-Comic #1(1976)-(3-1/4x6-1/2"); r/D.D. #150	2	4	6	8	11	14

NOTE: Carl Barks wrote all issues he illustrated, but #117, 126, 138 contain his script only. Issues 4-Color #189, 199, 203, 223, 238, 256, 263, 275, 282, 308, 348, 356, 367, 394, 408, 422, 26-30, 35, 44, 46, 52, 55, 57, 60, 65, 70-73, 77-80, 83, 101, 103, 105, 106, 111, 126, 246r, 261r, 268r, 269r, 271r, 275r, 278r(F.C. 263) all have Barks covers. Barks r-263-267, 269-278-282, 284, 285. #96 titled "Comic Album", #99-"Christmas Album". New art issues (not reprints)-106-46, 148-63, 167, 169, 170, 172, 173, 175, 178, 179, 196, 209, 223, 225, 236. Taliaferro daily newspaper strips #258-260, 264, 284, 285; Sunday strips#247, 280-283.

DONALD DUCK (Numbering continues from Donald Duck and Friends #362)
BOOM! Studios (Kaboom!): No. 363, Feb, 2011 - No. 367, Jun, 2011 ($3.99)

Item	GD 2.0	VG 4.0	FN 6.0	VF 8.0	VF/NM 9.0	NM- 9.2
363-367: 363-Barks reprints incl. "Mystery of the Loch". 364-Rosa-c						4.00

DONALD DUCK
IDW Publishing: May, 2015 - No. 21, Jun, 2017 ($3.99)

Item	GD 2.0	VG 4.0	FN 6.0	VF 8.0	VF/NM 9.0	NM- 9.2
1-Legacy numbered #368; art by Scarpa and others; multiple covers						4.00
2-21-Reprints of Italian & Dutch stories; multiple covers on each. 8-Christmas issue						4.00
...'s Halloween Scream (10/15, Halloween giveaway) r/Donald Duck Advs. #7,8 (1990)						3.00

DONALD DUCK ADVENTURES (See Walt Disney's Donald Duck Adventures)
DONALD DUCK ALBUM (See Comic Album No. 1,3 & Dell Album)
Dell Publishing Co./Gold Key: 5-7/59 - F.C. No. 1239, 10-12/61; 1962; 8/63 - No. 2, Oct, 1963

Item	GD 2.0	VG 4.0	FN 6.0	VF 8.0	VF/NM 9.0	NM- 9.2
Four Color 995 (#1)	7	14	21	44	82	120
Four Color 1099,1140,1239-Barks-c	7	14	21	44	82	120
Four Color 1182, 01204-207 (1962-Dell)	5	10	15	34	60	85
1(8/63-Gold Key)-Barks-c	5	10	15	34	60	85
2(10/63)	4	8	12	28	47	65

DONALD DUCK AND FRIENDS (Numbering continues from Walt Disney's ...)
BOOM! Studios: No. 347, Oct, 2009 - No. 362, Jan, 2011 ($2.99)

Item	GD 2.0	VG 4.0	FN 6.0	VF 8.0	VF/NM 9.0	NM- 9.2
347-362: Two covers on most. Retitled "Donald Duck" with #363						3.00

DONALD DUCK AND THE BOYS (Also see Story Hour Series)
Whitman Publishing Co.: 1948 (5-1/4x5-1/2", 100pgs., hard-c; art & text)

Item	GD 2.0	VG 4.0	FN 6.0	VF 8.0	VF/NM 9.0	NM- 9.2
845-(49) new illos by Barks based on his Donald Duck 10-pager in WDC&S #74, Expanded text not written by Barks; covers not by Barks	50	100	150	350	600	850

(Prices vary widely on this book)

DONALD DUCK AND THE CHRISTMAS CAROL
Whitman Publishing Co.: 1960 (A Little Golden Book, 6-3/8"x7-5/8", 28 pgs.)

Item	GD 2.0	VG 4.0	FN 6.0	VF 8.0	VF/NM 9.0	NM- 9.2
nn-Story book pencilled by Carl Barks with the intended title "Uncle Scrooge's Christmas Carol." Finished art adapted by Norman McGary. (Rare)-Reprinted in Uncle Scrooge in Color.	20	40	60	100	185	270

DONALD DUCK BEACH PARTY (Also see Dell Giants)
Gold Key: Sept, 1965 (12¢)

Item	GD 2.0	VG 4.0	FN 6.0	VF 8.0	VF/NM 9.0	NM- 9.2
1(#10158-509)-Barks-r/WDC&S #45; painted-c	6	12	18	38	69	100

DONALD DUCK BOOK (See Story Hour Series)
DONALD DUCK COMICS DIGEST
Gladstone Publishing: Nov, 1986 - No. 5, July, 1987 ($1.25/$1.50, 96 pgs.)

Item	GD 2.0	VG 4.0	FN 6.0	VF 8.0	VF/NM 9.0	NM- 9.2
1,3: 1-Barks-c/a-r	1	3	4	6	8	10
2,4,5: 4.5-$1.50-c						6.00

DONALD DUCK FUN BOOK (See Dell Giants)
DONALD DUCK IN DISNEYLAND (See Dell Giants)
DONALD DUCK MARCH OF COMICS (See March of Comics #4,20,41,56,69,263)
DONALD DUCK MERRY CHRISTMAS (See Dell Giant No. 53)
DONALD DUCK PICNIC PARTY (See Picnic Party listed under Dell Giants)
DONALD DUCK TELLS ABOUT KITES (See Kite Fun Book)
DONALD DUCK, THIS IS YOUR LIFE (Disney, TV)
Dell Publishing Co.: No. 1109, Aug-Oct, 1960

Item	GD 2.0	VG 4.0	FN 6.0	VF 8.0	VF/NM 9.0	NM- 9.2
Four Color 1109-Gyro flashback to WDC&S #141; origin Donald Duck (1st told)	12	24	36	81	176	270

Donald Duck #35 © DIS

Don Winslow of the Navy #1 © FAW

Doom Patrol (2009 series) #1 © DC

	GD 2.0	VG 4.0	FN 6.0	VF 8.0	VF/NM 9.0	NM- 9.2

DONALD DUCK XMAS ALBUM (See regular Donald Duck No. 99)

DONALD IN MATHMAGIC LAND (Disney)
Dell Publishing Co.: No. 1051, Oct-Dec, 1959 - No. 1198, May-July, 1961

	GD	VG	FN	VF	VF/NM	NM-
Four Color 1051 (#1)-Movie	8	16	24	56	108	160
Four Color 1198-Reprint of above	6	12	18	37	66	95

DONALD QUEST (Donald Duck in parallel universe of Feudarnia)
IDW Publishing: Nov, 2016 - No. 5, Mar, 2017 ($3.99, limited series)

1-5-English version of Italian story; multiple covers on each. 1-Ambrosio-s/Freccero-a4.00

DONATELLO, TEENAGE MUTANT NINJA TURTLE
Mirage Studios: Aug, 1986 ($1.50, B&W, one-shot, 44 pgs.)

1	3	6	9	19	30	40

DONDI
Dell Publishing Co.: No. 1176, Mar-May, 1961 - No. 1276, Dec, 1961

Four Color 1176 (#1)-Movie; origin, photo-c	6	12	18	37	66	95
Four Color 1276	4	8	12	28	47	65

DON FORTUNE MAGAZINE
Don Fortune Publishing Co.: Aug, 1946 - No. 6, Feb, 1947

1-Delecta of the Planets by C.C. Beck in all	36	72	108	211	343	475
2	18	36	54	103	162	220
3-6: 3-Bondage-c	15	30	45	86	133	180

DONG XOAI, VIETNAM 1965
DC Comics: 2010 ($19.95, B&W graphic novel)

SC-Joe Kubert-s/a/c; includes report of actual events that inspired the story   20.00

DONKEY KONG (See Blip #1)

DONNA MATRIX
Reactor, Inc.: Aug, 1993 ($2.95, 52 pgs.)

1-Computer generated-c/a by Mike Saenz; 3-D effects   4.00

DON NEWCOMBE
Fawcett Publications: 1950 (Baseball)

nn-Photo-c	54	108	162	343	574	825

DON ROSA'S COMICS AND STORIES
Fantagraphics Books (CX Comics): 1983 ($2.95)

1,2: 1-(68 pgs.) Reprints Rosa's The Pertwillaby Papers episodes #128-133.						
2-(60 pgs.) Reprints episodes #134-138	2	4	6	11	16	20

DON SIMPSON'S BIZARRE HEROES (Also see Megaton Man)
Kitchen Sink Press/Fiasco Comics: May, 1990 - No. 17, Sept, 1996 ($2.50/$2.95, B&W)

1-(5/90, Kitchen Sink) Don Simpson-s/a	1	3	4	6	8	10
1-(5/94, Fiasco) Features Megaton Man	2	4	6	10	14	18
2-10: 9-Title changes to Bizarre Heroes	2	4	6	10	14	18
0,11-17: 0-(12/94) Begin $2.95-c; r/Bizarre Heroes #. 16-Indicia also reads Megaton Man vs. Forbidden Frankenstein #1. 17-(9/96)-Indicia also reads Megaton Man #0; intro Megaton Man and the Fiascoverse to new readers	1	2	3	5	6	8

DON'T GIVE UP THE SHIP
Dell Publishing Co.: No. 1049, Aug, 1959

Four Color 1049-Movie, Jerry Lewis photo-c	9	18	27	58	114	170

DON WINSLOW OF THE NAVY
Merwil Publishing Co.: Apr, 1937 - No. 2, May, 1937 (96 pgs.) (A pulp/comic book cross; stapled spine)

V1#1-Has 16 pgs. comics in color. Captain Colorful & Jupiter Jones by Sheldon Mayer; complete Don Winslow novel	705	1410	2114	5300	--	--
2-Sheldon Mayer-a	205	410	615	1550	--	--

DON WINSLOW OF THE NAVY (See Crackajack Funnies, Famous Feature Stories, Popular Comics & Super Book #5,6)
Dell Publishing Co.: No. 2, Nov, 1939 - No. 22, 1941

Four Color 2 (#1)-Rare	265	530	795	1694	2897	4100
Four Color 22	61	122	183	390	670	950

DON WINSLOW OF THE NAVY (See TV Teens; Movie, Radio, TV) (Fightin' Navy No. 74 on)
Fawcett Publications/Charlton No. 70 on: 2/43 - #64, 12/48; #65, 1/51 - #69, 9/51; #70, 3/55 - #73, 9/55

1-(68 pgs.)-Captain Marvel on cover	142	284	426	909	1555	2200
2	45	90	135	284	480	675
3	37	74	111	222	361	500
4-6: 6-Flag-c	30	60	90	177	289	400
7-10: 8-Last 68 pg. issue?	22	44	66	132	216	300
11-20	19	38	57	111	176	240

	GD	VG	FN	VF	VF/NM	NM-
21-40	16	32	48	94	147	200
41-43,45-64: 51,60-Singapore Sal (villain) app. 64-(12/48)	15	30	45	85	130	175
44-Classic spider-c	45	90	135	284	480	675
65(1/51)-Flying Saucer attack; photo-c	23	46	69	136	223	310
66 - 69(9/51): All photo-c. 66-sci-fi story	15	30	45	85	130	175
70(3/55)-73: 70-73 r-/#26,58 & 59	10	20	30	56	76	95

DOODLE JUMP (Based on the game app)
Dynamite Entertainment: 2014 - No. 6, 2015 ($3.99, limited series)

1-6-Steve Uy-a; multiple covers on each   4.00

DOOM
Marvel Comics: Oct, 2000 - No. 3, Dec, 2000 ($2.99, limited series)

1-3-Dr. Doom; Dixon-s/Manco-a   4.00

DOOMED (Also see Teen Titans #14 (2016))
DC Comics: Aug, 2015 - No. 6, Jan, 2016 ($2.99, limited series)

1-6: 1-Lobdell-s/Fernandez-a. 3-Alpha Centurion app. 4-6-Superman app.   3.00

DOOM FORCE SPECIAL
DC Comics: July, 1992 ($2.95, 68 pgs., one-shot, mature) (X-Force parody)

1-Morrison scripts; Simonson, Steacy, & others-a; Giffen/Mignola-c   4.00

DOOM PATROL, THE (Formerly My Greatest Adventure No. 1-85; see Brave and the Bold, DC Special Blue Ribbon Digest 19, Official... Index & Showcase No. 94-96)
National Periodical Publ.: No. 86, 3/64 - No. 121, 9-10/68; No. 122, 2/73 - No. 124, 6-7/73

86-1 pg. origin (#86-121 are 12¢ issues)	36	72	108	266	596	925
87-98: 88-Origin The Chief. 91-Intro. Mento	10	20	30	67	141	215
99-Intro. Beast Boy (later becomes the Changeling in New Teen Titans)	46	92	138	359	805	1250
100-Origin Beast Boy; Robot-Maniac series begins (12/65)	14	28	42	93	204	315
101-110: 102-Challengers of the Unknown app. 104-Wedding issue. 105-Robot-Maniac series ends. 106-Negative Man begins (origin)	7	14	21	46	86	125
111-120	6	12	18	37	66	95
121-Death of Doom Patrol; Orlando-c	14	28	42	96	211	325
122-124: All reprints	2	4	6	8	11	14
... No. 99 (Facsimile Edition) (1/24, $4.99) Reprints Beast Boy intro with original ads						5.00

DOOM PATROL
DC Comics (Vertigo imprint #64 on): Oct, 1987 - No, 87, Feb, 1995 (75¢-$1.95, new format)

1-Wraparound-c; Lightle-a	2	4	6	10	14	18
2-18: 3-1st app. Lodestone. 4-1st app. Karma. 8,15,16-Art Adams-c(i). 18-Invasion tie-in						4.00
19-(2/89)-Grant Morrison scripts begin, ends #63; 1st app Crazy Jane; $1.50-c & new format begins.	3	6	9	14	19	24
20-30: 29-Superman app. 30-Night Breed fold-out						6.00
31-34,37-41,45-49,51-56,58-60: 39-World Without End preview						4.00
35-1st brief app. of Flex Mentallo	2	4	6	11	16	20
36-1st full app. of Flex Mentallo	2	4	6	8	11	14
42-44-Origin of Flex Mentallo						4.00
50,57 ($2.50, 52 pgs.)						5.00
61-87: 61,70-Photo-c. 73-Death cameo (2 panels)						4.00
...And Suicide Squad 1 (3/88, $1.50, 52 pgs.)-Wraparound-c						5.00
Annual 1 (1988, $1.50, 52 pgs.)						5.00
Annual 2 (1994, $3.95, 68 pgs.)-Children's Crusade tie-in.						5.00
...: Crawling From the Wreckage TPB (2004, $19.95) r/#19-25; Morrison-s						20.00
...: Down Paradise Way TPB (2005, $19.99) r/#35-41; Morrison-s						20.00
...: Magic Bus TPB (2007, $19.99) r/#51-57; Morrison-s						20.00
...: Musclebound TPB (2006, $19.99) r/#42-50; Morrison-s; new Bolland-c						20.00
...: Planet Love TPB (2008, $19.99) r/#58-63 & Doom Force Special #1; Morrison-s						20.00
...: The Painting That Ate Paris TPB (2004, $19.95) r/#26-34; Morrison-s						20.00

NOTE: *Bisley* painted c-26-48, 55-58. *Bolland* c-64, 75. *Dringenberg* a-42(p). *Steacy* a-53.

DOOM PATROL
DC Comics: Dec, 2001 - No. 22, Sept, 2003 ($2.50)

1-Intro. new team with Robotman; Tan Eng Huat-c/a; John Arcudi-s						4.00
2-22: 4,5-Metamorpho & Elongated Man app. 13,14-Fisher-a. 20-Geary-a						3.00

DOOM PATROL (see JLA #94-99)
DC Comics: Aug, 2004 - No. 18, Jan, 2006 ($2.50)

1-18-John Byrne-s/a. 1-Green Lantern, Batman app.   3.00

DOOM PATROL
DC Comics: Oct, 2009 - No. 22, Jul, 2011 ($3.99/$2.99)

1-7: 1-Giffen-s/Clark-a; back-up Metal Men feature w/Maguire-a. 2-Two covers. 4-5-Blackest Night. 6-Negative Man origin re-told						4.00
8-22($2.99) 11,12-Ambush Bug app. 16-Giffen-a. 21-Robotman origin retold						3.00

	GD	VG	FN	VF	VF/NM	NM-
	2.0	4.0	6.0	8.0	9.0	9.2

...: Brotherhood TPB (2011, $17.99) r/#7-13 — 18.00
...: We Who Are About to Die TPB (2010, $14.99) r/#1-6; cover gallery; design art — 15.00

DOOM PATROL
DC Comics (Young Animal): Nov, 2016 - No. 12, Dec, 2018 ($3.99)
1-12: 1-Gerald Way-s/Nick Derington-a; main cover has peel-off gyro sticker. 8-Allred-a — 4.00
1-Director's Cut (5/17, $5.99) Pencil/ink art; original script with thumbnails — 6.00
.../ JLA Special 1 (4/18, $4.99) Part 5 of Milk Wars crossover; Eaglesham-a/Mann-a — 5.00

DOOM PATROL (See Tangent Comics/ Doom Patrol)

DOOM PATROL: WEIGHT OF THE WORLDS
DC Comics (Young Animal): Sept, 2019 - No. 7, Sept, 2020 ($3.99)
1-7: 1-Gerald Way-s/James Harvey-a. 3-Shaner-a. 5-Cloonan-a — 4.00

DOOMSDAY
DC Comics: 1995 ($3.95, one-shot)
1-Year One story by Jurgens, L. Simonson, Ordway, and Gil Kane; Superman app. — 5.00

DOOMSDAY CLOCK (See Watchmen)
DC Comics: Jan, 2018 - No. 12, Feb, 2020 ($4.99/$5.99, limited series)
1-Follows end of Watchmen; intro new Rorschach; Johns-s/Frank-a; 2 covers by Frank — 5.00
1-($5.99) Lenticular cover — 6.00
2-11: Two covers on each. 2-Comedian returns; Nathaniel Dusk makes DCU return as fictional 1940s - '50s film noir detective. 5-7-Joker app.; origin of Marionette — 5.00
12-($5.99) Superman vs. Dr. Manhattan; intro of the Metaverse — 6.00

DOOMSDAY + 1 (Also see Charlton Bullseye)
Charlton Comics: July, 1975 - No. 6, June, 1976; No. 7, June, 1978 - No. 12, May, 1979
1: #1-5 are 25¢ issues	4	8	12	25	40	55
2-6: 4-Intro Lor. 5-Ditko-a(1 pg.) 6-Begin 30¢-c	2	4	6	10	14	18
V3#7-12 (reprints #1-6)						6.00
5 (Modern Comics reprint, 1977)						6.00
NOTE: Byrne c/a-1-12; Painted covers-2-7.

DOOMSDAY.1
IDW Publishing: May, 2013 - No. 4, Aug, 2013 ($3.99)
1-4-John Byrne-s/a/c — 4.00

DOOMSDAY SQUAD, THE
Fantagraphics Books: Aug, 1986 - No. 7, 1987 ($2.00)
1,2,4-7: 2-New Byrne-a. 4-Neal Adams-c. 5-7-Gil Kane-c — 4.00
3-Usagi Yojimbo app. (1st in color); new Byrne-c — 6.00

DOOM'S IV
Image Comics (Extreme): July, 1994 - No.4, Oct, 1994 ($2.50, limited series)
1-4-Liefeld story — 4.00
1,2-Two alternate Liefeld-c each, 4 covers form 1 picture — 5.00

DOOM: THE EMPEROR RETURNS
Marvel Comics: Jan, 2002 - No. 3, Mar, 2002 ($2.50, limited series)
1-3-Dixon-s/Manco-a; Franklin Richards app. — 4.00

DOOM 2099 (See Marvel Comics Presents #118 & 2099: World of Tomorrow)
Marvel Comics: Jan, 1993 - No. 44, June, 1996 ($1.25/$1.50/$1.95)
1-Metallic foil stamped-c — 6.00
1-2nd printing — 4.00
2-24,26-44: 4-Ron Lim-c(p). 17-bound-in trading card sheet. 40-Namor & Doctor Strange app. 41-Daredevil app., Namor-c/app. 44-Intro The Emissary; story contin'd in 2099: World of Tomorrow — 4.00
18-Variant polybagged with Sega Sub-Terrania poster — 5.00
25 ($2.25, 52 pgs.) — 5.00
25 ($2.95, 52pgs.) Foil embossed cover — 6.00
29 ($3.50)-acetate-c. — 5.00
No. 1 (2/20, $4.99) Zdarsky-s/Castiello-a; tie-in to 2099 specials and ASM #33-36 (2020) — 5.00

DOOMWAR
Marvel Comics: Apr, 2010 - No. 6, Sept, 2010 ($3.99, limited series)
1-6-Doctor Doom invades Wakanda; Black Panther & X-Men app.; Romita Jr.-c/Eaton-a — 4.00

DOORWAY TO NIGHTMARE (See Cancelled Comic Cavalcade and Madame Xanadu)
DC Comics: Jan-Feb, 1978 - No. 5, Sept-Oct, 1978
| 1-Madame Xanadu in all | 6 | 12 | 18 | 38 | 69 | 100 |
| 2-5: 4-Craig-a | 2 | 4 | 6 | 10 | 14 | 18 |
NOTE: Kaluta covers on all. Merged into The Unexpected with No. 190.

DOPEY DUCK COMICS (Wacky Duck No. 3) (See Super Funnies)
Timely Comics (NPP): Fall, 1945 - No. 2, Apr, 1946
| 1-Casper Cat, Krazy Krow | 52 | 104 | 156 | 328 | 552 | 775 |
| 2-Casper Cat, Krazy Krow | 36 | 72 | 108 | 211 | 343 | 475 |

DORK
Slave Labor: June, 1993 - No. 11 ($2.50-$3.50, B&W, mature)
1-7,9-11: Evan Dorkin-c/a/scripts in all. 1(8/95),2(1/96)-(2nd printings). 1(3/97) (3rd printing). 1-Milk & Cheese app. 3-Eltingville Club starts. 6-Reprints 1st Eltingville Club app. from Instant Piano #1 — 4.00
8-($3.50) — 4.00
Who's Laughing Now? TPB (2001, $11.95) reprints most of #1-5 — 12.00
The Collected Dork, Vol. 2: Circling the Drain (6/03, $13.95) r/most of #7-10 & other-s — 14.00

DOROTHY & THE WIZARD IN OZ (Adaptation of the original 1908 L. Frank Baum book) (Also see Wonderful Wizard of Oz, Marvelous Land of Oz and Ozma of Oz)
Marvel Comics: Nov, 2011 - No. 8, Aug, 2012 ($3.99, limited series)
1-8-Eric Shanower-a/Skottie Young-a/c — 4.00

DOROTHY LAMOUR (Formerly Jungle Lil)(Stage, screen, radio)
Fox Feature Syndicate: No. 2, June, 1950 - No. 3, Aug, 1950
| 2-Wood-a(3), photo-c | 42 | 84 | 126 | 265 | 445 | 625 |
| 3-Wood-a(3), photo-c | 34 | 68 | 102 | 199 | 325 | 450 |

DOROTHY OF OZ PREQUEL
IDW Publishing: Mar, 2012 - No. 4, Aug, 2012 ($3.99, limited series)
1-4-Tipton-s/Shedd-a — 4.00

DOT DOTLAND (Formerly Little Dot Dotland)
Harvey Publications: No. 62, Sept, 1974 - No. 63, Nov, 1974
| 62,63 | 3 | 6 | 9 | 14 | 19 | 24 |

DOTTY (…& Her Boy Friends)(Formerly Four Teeners; Glamorous Romances No. 41 on)
Ace Magazines (A. A. Wyn): No. 35, June, 1948 - No. 40, May, 1949
| 35-Teen-age | 17 | 34 | 51 | 98 | 154 | 210 |
| 36-40: 37-Transvestism story | 12 | 24 | 36 | 69 | 97 | 125 |

DOTTY DRIPPLE (Horace & Dotty Dripple No. 25 on)
Magazine Ent.(Life's Romances)/Harvey No. 3 on: 1946 - No. 24, June, 1952 (Also see A-1 No. 1, 3-8, 10)
1 (nd) (10¢)	18	36	54	105	165	225
2	11	22	33	60	83	105
3-10: 3,4-Powell-a	7	14	21	37	46	55
11-24	6	12	18	31	38	45

DOTTY DRIPPLE AND TAFFY
Dell Publishing Co.: No. 646, Sept, 1955 - No. 903, May, 1958
| Four Color 646 (#1) | 6 | 12 | 18 | 37 | 66 | 95 |
| Four Color 691,718,746,801,903 | 4 | 8 | 12 | 28 | 47 | 65 |

DOUBLE ACTION COMICS
National Periodical Publications: No. 2, Jan, 1940 (68 pgs., B&W)
2-Contains original stories(?); pre-hero DC contents; same cover as Adventure No. 37. (seven known copies, four in high grade) (not an ashcan)
| | 4400 | 8800 | 13,200 | 28,600 | 35,200 | 44,000 |
NOTE: The cover to this book was probably reprinted from Adventure #37. #1 exists as an ash can copy with B&W cover; contains a coverless comic on inside with 1st & last page missing. There is proof of at least limited newsstand distribution. #2 cover proof only sold in 2005 for $4,000.

DOUBLE COMICS
Elliot Publications: 1940 - 1943 (132 pgs.)
1940 issues; Masked Marvel-c	343	686	1029	2400	4200	6000
1941 issues; Masked Marvel-c & the Mad Mong vs. the White Flash-c, Tornado Tim-c (attached), Nordac-c, & Green Light covers known	295	590	885	1888	4244	4600
1942 issues	295	590	885	1888	4244	4600
1943 issues	226	452	678	1446	2473	3500
NOTE: Double Comics consisted of an almost endless combination of pairs of remaindered, unsold issues of various comics representing most publishers and usually mixed publishers in the same book; e.g., a Captain America with a Silver Streak, or a Feature with a Detective, etc., could appear inside the same cover. The actual contents would have to determine its price. Prices listed are for average contents. Any containing rare origin or first issues are worth much more. Covers also vary in same year. Value would be approximately 50 percent of contents.

DOUBLE-CROSS (See The Crusaders)

DOUBLE-DARE ADVENTURES
Harvey Publications: Dec, 1966 - No. 2, Mar, 1967 (35¢/25¢, 68 pgs.)
| 1-Origin Bee-Man, Glowing Gladiator, & Magic-Master; Simon/Kirby-a | 6 | 12 | 18 | 40 | 73 | 105 |
| 2-Torres-a; r/Alarming Adv. #3('63) | 5 | 10 | 15 | 31 | 53 | 75 |
NOTE: Powell a-1. Simon/Sparling c-1, 2.

DOUBLE DRAGON
Marvel Comics: July, 1991 - No. 6, Dec, 1991 ($1.00, limited series)
1-6: Based on video game. 2-Art Adams-c — 4.00

DOUBLE EDGE
Marvel Comics: Alpha, 1995; Omega, 1995 ($4.95, limited series)
Alpha ($4.95)- Punisher story, Nick Fury app. — 5.00
Omega ($4.95)-Punisher, Daredevil, Ghost Rider app. Death of Nick Fury — 5.00

DOUBLE IMAGE
Image Comics: Feb, 2001 - No. 5, July, 2001 ($2.95)
1-5: 1-Flip covers of Codeflesh (Casey-s/Adlard-a) and The Bod (Young-s). 2-Two covers. 5-"Trust in Me" begins; Chaudhary-a — 3.00

DOUBLE LIFE OF PRIVATE STRONG, THE
Archie Publications/Radio Comics: June, 1959 - No. 2, Aug, 1959
| 1-Origin & re-intro The Shield; Simon & Kirby-c/a, their re-entry into the super-hero genre; intro./1st app. The Fly; 1st S.A. super-hero for Archie Publ. | 36 | 72 | 108 | 266 | 596 | 925 |
| 2-S&K-c/a; Tuska-a; The Fly app. (2nd or 3rd?) | 18 | 36 | 54 | 126 | 281 | 435 |

DOUBLE TROUBLE
St. John Publishing Co.: Nov, 1957 - No. 2, Jan-Feb, 1958
| 1,2: Tuffy & Snuffy by Frank Johnson; dubbed "World's Funniest Kids" | 10 | 20 | 30 | 54 | 72 | 90 |

DOUBLE TROUBLE WITH GOOBER
Dell Publishing Co.: No. 417, Aug, 1952 - No. 556, May, 1954
| Four Color 417 | 5 | 10 | 15 | 34 | 60 | 85 |
| Four Color 471,516,556 | 4 | 8 | 12 | 27 | 44 | 60 |

DOUBLE UP COMICS
Elliott Publications: 1941 (Pocket size, 192 pgs., 10¢)
| 1-Contains rebound copies of digest sized issues of Pocket Comics, Speed Comics, & Spitfire Comics; Japanese WWII-c | 331 | 662 | 993 | 2317 | 4059 | 5800 |

DOVER & CLOVER (See All Funny & More Fun Comics #93)

DOVER BOYS (See Adventures of the...)

DOVER THE BIRD
Famous Funnies Publishing Co.: Spring, 1955
| 1-Funny animal; code approved (10¢-c) | 13 | 26 | 39 | 72 | 101 | 130 |
| 1-Same cover; not code approved (6¢-c, 3 for 15¢) | 11 | 22 | 33 | 64 | 90 | 115 |

DOWN
Image Comics (Top Cow): Dec, 2005 - No. 4, Mar, 2006 ($2.99)
1-4-Warren Ellis-s. 1-Tony Harris-a/c. 2-4-Cully Hamner-a — 3.00
Down & Top Cow's Best of Warren Ellis TPB (6/06, $15.99) r/#1-4 & Tales of the Witchblade #3,4; Ellis-s; script for Down #1 with Harris sketch pages — 16.00

DOWN WITH CRIME
Fawcett Publications: Nov, 1952 - No. 7, Nov, 1953

Doomsday +1 #4 © CC

Dracula Lives! #8 © MAR

Draculina: Blood Simple #1 © DYN

	GD 2.0	VG 4.0	FN 6.0	VF 8.0	VF/NM 9.0	NM- 9.2

1 — 48 | 96 | 144 | 302 | 514 | 725
2,4,5: 2,4-Powell-a in each. 5-Bondage-c — 28 | 56 | 84 | 165 | 270 | 375
3-Used in **POP**, pg. 106; "H is for Heroin" drug story
  — 34 | 68 | 102 | 199 | 325 | 450
6,7: 6-Used in **POP**, pg. 80 — 28 | 56 | 84 | 165 | 270 | 375

DO YOU BELIEVE IN NIGHTMARES?
St. John Publishing Co.: Nov, 1957 - No. 2, Jan, 1958
1-Mostly Ditko-c/a — 81 | 162 | 243 | 518 | 884 | 1250
2-Ayers-a — 43 | 86 | 129 | 271 | 461 | 650

D.P. 7
Marvel Comics Group (New Universe): Nov, 1986 - No. 32, June, 1989
1-20, — 4.00
21-32-Low print — 5.00
Annual #1 (11/87)-Intro. The Witness — 5.00
... Classic Vol. 1 TPB (2007, $24.99) r/#1-9; Mark Gruenwald-s/Paul Ryan-a in all — 25.00
NOTE: *Williamson* a-9i, 11i; c-9i.

DRACULA (See Bram Stoker's Dracula, Giant-Size..., Little Dracula, Marvel Graphic Novel, Requiem for Dracula, Spider-Man Vs...., Stoker's..., Tomb of... & Wedding of...; also see Movie Classics under Universal Presents as well as Dracula)

DRACULA (See Movie Classics for #1)(Also see Frankenstein & Werewolf)
Dell Publ. Co.: No. 2, 11/66 - No. 4, 3/67; No. 6, 7/72 - No. 8, 7/73 (No #5)
2-Origin & 1st app. Dracula (11/66) (super hero) — 5 | 10 | 15 | 33 | 57 | 80
3,4: 4-Intro. Fleeta ('67) — 3 | 6 | 9 | 21 | 33 | 45
6-('72)-r/#2 w/origin — 3 | 6 | 9 | 15 | 22 | 28
7,8-r/#3, #4 — 2 | 4 | 6 | 13 | 18 | 22

DRACULA (Magazine)
Warren Publishing Co.: 1979 (120 pgs., full color)
Book 1-Maroto art; Spanish material translated into English (mail order only)
  — 6 | 12 | 18 | 37 | 66 | 95

DRACULA
Marvel Comics: Jul, 2010 - No. 4, Sept, 2010 ($3.99, limited series)
1-4-Colored reprint of Bram Stoker's Classic Dracula adapt. from Dracula Lives!, Legion of Monsters and Stoker's Dracula; Thomas-s/Giordano-a; J. Djurdjevic-c — 4.00

DRACULA CHRONICLES
Topps Comics: Apr, 1995 - No. 3, June, 1995 ($2.50, limited series)
1-3-Linsner-c — 4.00

DRACULA LIVES! (Magazine)(Also see Tomb of Dracula) (Reprinted in Stoker's Dracula)
Marvel Comics Group: 1973(no month) - No. 13, July, 1975 (75¢, B&W) (76 pgs.)
1-Boris painted-c — 8 | 16 | 24 | 56 | 108 | 160
2 (7/73)-1st time origin Dracula; Adams, Starlin-a — 5 | 10 | 15 | 34 | 60 | 85
3-1st app. Robert E. Howard's Soloman Kane; Adams-c/a
  — 5 | 10 | 15 | 31 | 53 | 75
4,5: 4-Ploog-a. 5(V2#1)-Bram Stoker's Classic Dracula adapt. begins
  — 4 | 8 | 12 | 23 | 37 | 50
6-9: 6-8-Bram Stoker adapt. 9-Bondage-c — 4 | 8 | 12 | 23 | 37 | 50
10 (1/75)-Lilith solo (1st?) — 4 | 8 | 12 | 27 | 44 | 60
11-13: 11-21 pg. Lilith solo sty. 12-31 pg. Dracula sty — 4 | 8 | 12 | 23 | 37 | 50
Annual 1(Summer, 1975, $1.25, 92 pgs.)-Morrow painted-c; 6 Dracula stys.
  25 pgs. Adams-a(r) — 4 | 8 | 12 | 25 | 40 | 55
NOTE: *N. Adams* a-2, 3i, 10i, Annual 1r(2, 3i). *Alcala* a-9. *Buscema* a-3p, 6p, Annual 1p. *Colan* a(p)-1, 2, 5, 6, 8. *Evans* a-7. *Gulacy* a-9. *Heath* a-1r, 13. *Pakula* a-6r. *Sutton* a-13. *Weiss* r-Annual 1p. 4 Dracula stories each in 1, 609; 3 Dracula stories each in 2, 4, 5,, 13.

DRACULA: LORD OF THE UNDEAD
Marvel Comics: Dec, 1998 - No. 3, Dec, 1998 ($2.99, limited series)
1-3-Olliffe & Palmer-a — 4.00

DRACULA: RETURN OF THE IMPALER
Slave Labor Graphics: July, 1993 - No. 4, Oct, 1994 ($2.95, limited series)
1-4 — 4.00

DRACULA'S REVENGE
IDW Publishing: Apr, 2004 - No. 3 ($3.99, limited series)
1,2-Forbeck-s/Kudranski-a — 4.00

DRACULA: THE COMPANY OF MONSTERS
BOOM! Studios: Aug, 2010 - No. 12, Jul, 2011 ($3.99)
1-12: 1-5-Busiek & Gregory-s/Godlewski-a. 1-Two covers by Brereton and Salas — 4.00

DRACULA VERSUS ZORRO
Topps Comics: Oct, 1993 - No. 2, Nov, 1993 ($2.95, limited series)
1,2: 1-Spot varnish & red foil-c. 2-Polybagged w/16 pg. Zorro #0 — 4.00

	GD 2.0	VG 4.0	FN 6.0	VF 8.0	VF/NM 9.0	NM- 9.2

DRACULA VERSUS ZORRO
Dark Horse Comics: Sept, 1998 - No. 2, Oct, 1998 ($2.95, limited series)
1,2 — 4.00

DRACULA: VLAD THE IMPALER (Also see Bram Stoker's Dracula)
Topps Comics: Feb, 1993 - No. 3, Apr, 1993 ($2.95, limited series)
1-3-Polybagged with 3 trading cards each; Maroto-c/a — 4.00

DRACULINA (From Vampirella)
Dynamite Entertainment: 2021 - No. 6, 2022 ($3.99, limited series)
1-6-Christopher Priest-s/Michael Sta. Maria-a; multiple covers on each — 4.00

DRACULINA: BLOOD SIMPLE
Dynamite Entertainment: 2023 - No. 6, 2023 ($3.99, limited series)
1-6-Christopher Priest-s/Michael Sta. Maria-a; multiple covers on each — 4.00

DRAFT, THE
Marvel Comics: 1988 ($3.50, one-shot, squarebound)
1-Sequel to "The Pitt" — 4.00

DRAFTED: ONE HUNDRED DAYS
Devil's Due Publishing: June, 2009 ($5.99, one-shot)
1-Barack Obama on a post-galactic-war Earth; Powers-s — 6.00

DRAG 'N' WHEELS (Formerly Top Eliminator)
Charlton Comics: No. 30, Sept, 1968 - No. 59, May, 1973
30 — 4 | 8 | 12 | 28 | 47 | 65
31-40-Scot Jackson begins — 3 | 6 | 9 | 18 | 28 | 38
41-50 — 3 | 6 | 9 | 16 | 24 | 32
51-59: Scot Jackson — 2 | 4 | 6 | 13 | 18 | 22
Modern Comics Reprint 58('78) — 5.00

DRAGON, THE (Also see The Savage Dragon)
Image Comics (Highbrow Ent.): Mar, 1996 - No. 5, July, 1996 (99¢, lim. series)
1-5: Reprints Savage Dragon limited series w/new story & art. 5-Youngblood app; includes 5 pg. Savage Dragon story from 1984 — 4.00

DRAGON AGE (Based on the EA videogame)
IDW Publishing (EA Comics): Mar, 2010 - No. 6, Nov, 2010 ($3.99)
1-6-Orson Scott Card & Aaron Johnston-s; Ramos-c — 4.00

DRAGON AGE: BLUE WRAITH (Based on the EA videogame)
Dark Horse Comics: Jan, 2020 - No. 3, Mar, 2020 ($3.99, limited series)
1-3-DeFilippis & Weir-s/Furukawa-a/Teng-c — 4.00

DRAGON AGE: DECEPTION (Based on the EA videogame)
Dark Horse Comics: Oct, 2018 - No. 3, Dec, 2018 ($3.99, limited series)
1-3-DeFilippis & Weir-s/Furukawa-a/Teng-c — 4.00

DRAGON AGE: DARK FORTRESS (Based on the EA videogame)
Dark Horse Comics: Mar, 2021 - No. 3, May, 2022 ($3.99, limited series)
1-3-DeFilippis & Weir-s/Furukawa-a/Teng-c — 4.00

DRAGON AGE: KNIGHT ERRANT (Based on the EA videogame)
Dark Horse Comics: May, 2017 - No. 5, Sept, 2017 ($3.99, limited series)
1-5-DeFilippis & Weir-s/Furukawa-a/Teng-c — 4.00

DRAGON AGE: MAGEKILLER (Based on the EA videogame)
Dark Horse Comics: Dec, 2015 - No. 5, Apr, 2016 ($3.99, limited series)
1-3-Rucka-s/Carnero/Teng-a — 4.00

DRAGON AGE: THE MISSING (Based on the EA videogame)
Dark Horse Comics: Jan, 2023 - No. 4, Apr, 2023 ($3.99, limited series)
1-4: 1-Mann-s/McKeown-a — 4.00

DRAGON AGE: THOSE WHO SPEAK (Based on the EA videogame)
Dark Horse Comics: Aug, 2012 - No. 3, Nov, 2012 ($3.50, limited series)
1-3-Gaider-s/Hardin-a/Palumbo-c — 3.50

DRAGON ARCHIVES, THE (Also see The Savage Dragon)
Image Comics: Jun, 1998 - No. 4, Jan, 1999 ($2.95, B&W)
1-4: Reprints early Savage Dragon app. — 4.00

DRAGON BALL
Viz Comics: Mar, 1998 - Part 6: #2, Feb, 2003($2.95, B&W, Manga reprints read right to left)
Part 1: 1-Akira Toriyama-s/a — 11 | 22 | 33 | 76 | 163 | 250
2 — 3 | 6 | 9 | 17 | 26 | 35
3-12 — 1 | 3 | 4 | 6 | 8 | 10
1-12 (2nd & 3rd printings) — 4.00
Part 2: 1-(4/99) — 2 | 4 | 6 | 11 | 16 | 20

	GD 2.0	VG 4.0	FN 6.0	VF 8.0	VF/NM 9.0	NM- 9.2

2-15: 15-($3.50-c) — 1, 2, 3, 5, 6, 8
Part 3: 1-14 — 5.00
Part 4: 1-10 — 5.00
Part 5: 1-7 — 5.00
Part 6: 1,2 — 5.00

DRAGON BALL Z
Viz Comics: Mar, 1998 - Part 5: #10, Oct, 2002 ($2.95, B&W, Manga reprints read right to left)
Part 1: 1-Akira Toriyama-s/a — 8, 16, 24, 51, 96, 140
2 — 3, 6, 9, 14, 19, 24
3-9 — 1, 3, 4, 6, 8, 10
1-9 (2nd & 3rd printings) — 4.00
Part 2: 1 — 2, 4, 6, 10, 14, 18
2-14 — 6.00
Part 3: 1-10 — 4.00
Part 4: 1-15 — 4.00
Part 5: 1-10 — 4.00

DRAGON, THE: BLOOD & GUTS (Also see The Savage Dragon)
Image Comics (Highbrow Entertainment): Mar, 1995 - No. 3, May, 1995 ($2.50, lim. series)
1-3: Jason Pearson-c/a/scripts — 4.00

DRAGON CHIANG
Eclipse Books: 1991 ($3.95, B&W, squarebound, 52 pgs.)
nn-Timothy Truman-c/a(p) — 4.00

DRAGONFLIGHT
Eclipse Books: Feb, 1991 - No. 3, 1991 ($4.95, 52 pgs.)
Book One - Three: Adapts 1968 novel — 5.00

DRAGONFLY (See Americomics #4)
Americomics: Sum, 1985 - No. 8, 1986 ($1.75/$1.95)
1 — 5.00
2-8 — 4.00

DRAGONFLY & DRAGONFLYMAN (See The Wrong Earth)
AHOY Comics: 2019 - No. 5, 2020 ($3.99, limited series)
1-5-Each hero versus Devil Man; Peyer-s/Krause-a — 4.00
1-Free Comic Book Day 2019 Edition; Russ Braun-a; back-up Captain Ginger story — 3.00

DRAGONFORCE
Aircel Publishing: 1988 - No. 13, 1989 ($2.00)
1-Dale Keown-c/a/scripts in #1-12 — 5.00
2-13: 13-No Keown-a — 4.00
...Chronicles Book 1-5 ($2.95, B&W, 60 pgs.): Dale Keown-r/Dragonring & Dragonforce — 5.00

DRAGONHEART (Movie)
Topps Comics: May, 1996 - No. 2, June, 1996 ($2.95/$4.95, limited series)
1-($2.95, 24 pgs.)-Adaptation of the film; Hildebrandt Bros-c; Lim-a. — 4.00
2-($4.95, 64 pgs.) — 5.00

DRAGONLANCE (Also see TSR Worlds)
DC Comics: Dec, 1988 - No. 34, Sept, 1991 ($1.25/$1.50, Mando paper)
1-Based on TSR game — 5.00
2-34: Based on TSR game. 30-32-Kaluta-c — 4.00

DRAGONLANCE: CHRONICLES
Devil's Due Publ.: Aug, 2005 - No. 8, Mar, 2006 ($2.95)
1-8-Dabb-s/Kurth-a — 3.00
...: Dragons of Autumn Twilight TPB (2006, $17.95) r/#1-8 — 18.00

DRAGONLANCE: CHRONICLES (Volume 2)
Devil's Due Publ.: July, 2006 - No. 4, Jan, 2007 ($4.95/$4.99, 48 pgs.)
1-4-Dragons of Winter Night; Dabb-s/Kurth-a — 5.00
...: Dragons of Winter Night TPB (3/07, $18.99) r/#1-4; cover gallery — 19.00

DRAGONLANCE: CHRONICLES (Volume 3)
Devil's Due Publ.: Mar, 2007 - No. 12, 2007 ($3.50)
1-11-Dragons of Spring Dawning; Dabb-s/Cope-a — 3.50

DRAGONLANCE: THE LEGEND OF HUMA
Devil's Due Publ.: Jan, 2004 - No. 6, Oct, 2005 ($2.95)
1-6-Mike Miller & Rael-a — 3.00

DRAGON LINES
Marvel Comics (Epic Comics/Heavy Hitters): May, 1993 - No. 4, Aug, 1993 ($1.95, lim. series)
1-($2.50)-Embossed-c; Ron Lim-c/a in all — 5.00
2-4 — 4.00

DRAGON LINES: WAY OF THE WARRIOR
Marvel Comics (Epic Comics/ Heavy Hitters): Nov, 1993 - No. 2, Jan, 1994 ($2.25, limited series)
1,2-Ron Lim-c/a(p) — 4.00

DRAGONQUEST
Silverwolf Comics: Dec, 1986 - No. 2, 1987 ($1.50, B&W, 28 pgs.)
1,2-Tim Vigil-c/a in all — 5.00

DRAGON'S CLAWS
Marvel UK, Ltd.: July, 1988 - No. 10, Apr, 1989 ($1.25/$1.50/$1.75, British)
1-10: 3-Death's Head 1 pg. strip on back-c (1st app.). 4-Silhouette of Death's Head on last pg. 5-1st full app. new Death's Head — 4.00

DRAGON'S LAIR: SINGE'S REVENGE (Based on the Don Bluth video game)
CrossGen Comics: Sept, 2003 - No. 3 ($2.95, limited series)
1-3-Mangels-s/Laguna-a — 3.00

DRAGONSLAYER (Movie)
Marvel Comics Group: October, 1981 - No. 2, Nov, 1981
1,2-Paramount Disney movie adaptation — 4.00

DRAGOON WELLS MASSACRE
Dell Publishing Co.: No. 815, June, 1957
Four Color 815-Movie, photo-c — 8, 16, 24, 51, 96, 140

DRAGSTRIP HOTRODDERS (World of Wheels No. 17 on)
Charlton Comics: Sum, 1963; No. 2, Jan, 1965 - No. 16, Aug, 1967
1 — 7, 14, 21, 49, 92, 135
2-5 — 4, 8, 12, 25, 40, 55
6-16 — 3, 6, 9, 21, 33, 45

DRAIN
Image Comics: Nov, 2006 - No. 6, Mar, 2008 ($2.99)
1-6: 1-Cebulski-s/Takeda-a; two covers by Takeda and Finch — 3.00
Vol. 1 TPB (2008, $16.99) r/#1-6; cover gallery and Takeda sketch art gallery — 17.00

DRAKUUN
Dark Horse Comics: Feb, 1997 - No. 25, Mar, 1999 ($2.95, B&W, manga)
1-25; 1-6- Johji Manabe-s/a in all. Rise of the Dragon Princess series. 7-12-Revenge of Gustav. 13-18-Shadow of the Warlock. 19-25-The Hidden War — 4.00

DRAMA
Sirius: June, 1994 ($2.95, mature)
1-1st full color Dawn app. in comics — 2, 4, 6, 9, 12, 15
1-Limited edition (1400 copies); signed & numbered; fingerprint authenticity — 3, 6, 9, 19, 30, 40
NOTE: Dawn's 1st full color app. was a pin-up in Amazing Heroes' Swimsuit Special #5.

DRAMA OF AMERICA, THE
Action Text: 1973 ($1.95, 224 pgs.)
1- "Students' Supplement to History" — 2, 4, 6, 8, 10, 12

DRAWING BLOOD
Kevin Eastman Studios: May, 2019 - No. 4, Aug, 2019 ($3.99, limited series)
1-4-Avallone-s/Bishop & Eastman-a — 4.00

DRAWING ON YOUR NIGHTMARES
Dark Horse Comics: Oct, 2003 ($2.99, one-shot)
1-Short stories; The Goon, Criminal Macabre, Tales of the Vampires; Templesmith-c — 3.00

DRAX (Guardians of the Galaxy)
Marvel Comics: Jan, 2016 - No. 11, Nov, 2016 ($3.99)
1-11-CM Punk & Cullen Bunn-s/Hepburn-a. 1-Guardians app. 4,5-Fin Fang Foom app. — 4.00

DRAX THE DESTROYER (Guardians of the Galaxy)
Marvel Comics: Nov, 2005 - No. 4, Feb, 2006 ($2.99, limited series)
1-4-Giffen-s/Breitweiser-a — 5.00
...: Earthfall TPB (2006, $10.99) r/#1-4; character design page — 11.00

DREAD GODS
IDW Publishing: Jul, 2017 - No. 4, Oct, 2018 ($3.99)
1-4-Marz-s/Raney-a — 4.00

DREADLANDS (Also see Epic)
Marvel Comics (Epic Comics): 1992 - No. 4, 1992 ($3.95, lim. series, 52 pgs.)
1-4: Stiff-c — 4.00

DREADSTAR (See Epic Illustrated #3 for 1st app. and Eclipse Graphic Album Series #5)
Marvel Comics (Epic Comics)/First Comics No. 27 on: Nov, 1982 - No. 64, Mar, 1991
1 — 2, 4, 6, 11, 16, 20
2-5,8-49 — 5.00
6,7,51-64: 6,7-1st app. Interstellar Toybox; 8pgs. ea.; Wrightson-a. 51-64-Lower print run — 5.00
50 — 6.00
Annual 1 (12/83) r/The Price (Eclipse Graphic Album Series #5) — 5.00

DREADSTAR
Malibu Comics (Bravura): Apr, 1994 - No. 6, Jan, 1995 ($2.50, limited series)
1-6-Peter David scripts; 1,2-Starlin-c — 4.00
NOTE: Issues 1-6 contain Bravura stamps.

DREADSTAR AND COMPANY
Marvel Comics (Epic Comics): July, 1985 - No. 6, Dec, 1985
1-6: 1,3,6-New Starlin-a; 2-New Wrightson-c; reprints of Dreadstar series — 4.00

DREAM BOOK OF LOVE (Also see A-1 Comics)
Magazine Enterprises: No. 106, June-July, 1954 - No. 123, Oct-Nov, 1954
A-1 106 (#1)-Powell, Bolle-a; Montgomery Clift, Donna Reed photo-c — 23, 46, 69, 136, 223, 310
A-1 114 (#2)-Guardineer, Bolle-a; Piper Laurie, Victor Mature photo-c — 17, 34, 51, 98, 154, 210
A-1 123 (#3)-Movie photo-c — 15, 30, 45, 90, 140, 190

DREAM BOOK OF ROMANCE (Also see A-1 Comics)
Magazine Enterprises: No. 92, 1954 - No. 124, Oct-Nov, 1954
A-1 92 (#5)-Guardineer-a; photo-c — 21, 42, 63, 122, 199, 275
A-1 101 (#6)(4-6/54)-Marlon Brando photo-c; Powell, Bolle, Guardineer-a — 39, 78, 117, 240, 395, 550
A-1 109,110,124: 109 (#7)(7-8/54)-Powell-a; movie photo-c. 110 (#8)(1/54)-Movie photo-c. 124 (#9)(10-11/54) — 15, 30, 45, 90, 140, 190

DREAMER, THE
Kitchen Sink Press: 1986 ($6.95, B&W, graphic novel)
nn-Will Eisner-s/a — 20.00
DC Comics Reprint ($7.95, 6/00) — 8.00

DREAMERY, THE
Eclipse Comics: Dec, 1986 - No. 14, Feb, 1989 ($2.00, B&W, Baxter paper)
1-14: 2-7-Alice In Wonderland adapt. — 4.00

DREAMING, THE (See Sandman, 2nd Series)
DC Comics (Vertigo): June, 1996 - No. 60, May, 2001 ($2.50)
1-McKean-c on all; LaBan scripts & Snejbjerg-a — 5.00
2-30,32-60: 2,3-LaBan scripts & Snejbjerg-a. 4-7-Hogan scripts; Parkhouse-a. 8-Zulli-a. 9-11-Talbot-s/Taylor-a(p). 41-Previews Sandman: The Dream Hunters. 50-Hempel, Fegredo, McManus, Totleben-a — 4.00
31-($3.95) Art by various — 5.00
...Beyond The Shores of Night TPB ('97, $19.95) r/#1-8 — 20.00
...Special (7/98, $5.95, one-shot) Trial of Cain — 6.00

Drawing Blood #2 © Eastman & Avallone

The Dreaming (2018 series) #8 © DC

Duck Avenger #5 © DIS

	GD 2.0	VG 4.0	FN 6.0	VF 8.0	VF/NM 9.0	NM- 9.2
...Through The Gates of Horn and Ivory TPB ('99, $19.95) r/#15-19,22-25						20.00
DREAMING, THE (The Sandman Universe)						
DC Comics (Vertigo): Nov, 2018 - No. 20, Jun, 2020 ($3.99)						
1-20: 1-Spurrier-s/Evely-a/Jae Lee-c; Lucien & Merv Pumpkinhead app. 7,8-Larson-a						4.00
DREAMING EAGLES						
AfterShock Comics: Dec, 2015 - No. 6, Jun, 2016 ($3.99)						
1-6-Ennis-s/Coleby-a; Tuskegee Airmen in WWII						4.00
DREAMING, THE: WAKING HOURS (The Sandman Universe)						
DC Comics (Vertigo): Oct, 2020 - No. 12, Sept, 2021 ($3.99)						
1-12: 1-G. Willow Wilson-s/Nick Robles-a; intro Ruin						4.00
DREAM OF LOVE						
I. W. Enterprises: 1958 (Reprints)						
1,2,8: 1-r/Dream Book of Love #1; Bob Powell-a. 2-r/Great Lover's Romances #10. 8-Great Lover's Romances #1; also contains 2 Jon Juan stories by Siegel & Schomburg; Kinstler-c.	3	6	9	19	30	40
9-Kinstler-c; 1pg. John Wayne interview & Frazetta illo from John Wayne Adv. Comics #2	3	6	9	19	30	40
DREAM POLICE						
Marvel Comics (Icon): Aug, 2005 ($3.99)						
1-Straczynski-s/Deodato-a/c						4.00
DREAM POLICE						
Image Comics (Joe's Comics): Apr, 2014 - No. 12, Sept, 2016 ($2.99)						
1-12-Straczynski-s/Kotian-a						3.00
DREAMS OF THE DARKCHYLDE						
Darkchylde Entertainment: Oct, 2000 - No. 6, Sept, 2001 ($2.95)						
1-6-Randy Queen-s in all. 1-Brandon Peterson-c/a						3.00
DREAM TEAM (See Battlezones: Dream Team 2)						
Malibu Comics (Ultraverse): July, 1995 ($4.95, one-shot)						
1-Pin-ups teaming up Marvel & Ultraverse characters by various artists including Allred, Romita, Darrow, Balent, Quesada & Palmiotti						5.00
DREAM THIEF						
Dark Horse Comics: May, 2013 - No. 5, Sept, 2013 ($3.99, limited series)						
1-5-Nitz-s/Smallwood-a. 1-Alex Ross-c. 2-Ryan Sook-c. 4-Dan Brereton-c						4.00
DREAM THIEF: ESCAPE						
Dark Horse Comics: Jun, 2014 - No. 4, Sept, 2014 ($3.99, limited series)						
1-4-Nitz-s/Smallwood-a. 1,2-Smallwood-a. 3,4-Galusha-a						4.00
DREAMWAVE PRODUCTIONS PREVIEW						
Dreamwave Productions: May, 2002 ($1.00, one-shot)						
nn-Previews Arkanium, Transformers: The War Within and other series						3.00
DRESDEN FILES (See Jim Butcher's...)						
DRIFTER						
Image Comics: Nov, 2014 - No. 19, Jun, 2017 ($3.50/$3.99)						
1-19-Ivan Brandon-s/Nic Klein-a; multiple covers on each. 15-Start $3.99-c						4.00
DRIFT FENCE (See Zane Grey 4-Color 270)						
DRIFT MARLO						
Dell Publishing Co.: May-July, 1962 - No. 2, Oct-Dec, 1962 (Painted-c)						
01-232-207 (#1)	5	10	15	34	60	85
2 (12-232-212)	4	8	12	27	44	60
DRISCOLL'S BOOK OF PIRATES						
David McKay Publ.: 1934 (B&W, hardcover with dust jacket; 124 pgs, 7x9")						
nn-"Pieces of Eight" strip by Montford Amory	27	54	81	158	259	360
DRIVER: CROSSING THE LINE (Based on the Ubisoft videogame)						
DC Comics: Oct, 2011 ($2.99, one-shot)						
1-David Lapham-s/Greg Scott-a/ Jock-c; bonus character design art						3.00
DROIDS (Based on Saturday morning cartoon) (Also see Dark Horse Comics)						
Marvel Comics (Star Comics): April, 1986 - No. 8, June, 1987						
1-R2D2 & C-3PO from Star Wars app. in all	3	6	9	19	30	40
2-8: 2,5,7,8-Williamson-a(i)	2	4	6	8	10	12
NOTE: *Romita a-3p. Sinnott a-3i.*						
DROOPY (see Tom & Jerry #60)						
DROOPY (Tex Avery's…)						
Dark Horse Comics: Oct, 1995 - No. 3, Dec, 1995 ($2.50, limited series)						
1-Characters created by Tex Avery; painted-c on all	1	3	4	6	8	10

	GD 2.0	VG 4.0	FN 6.0	VF 8.0	VF/NM 9.0	NM- 9.2
2						4.00
3-Headlights Christmas-c	1	3	4	6	8	10
DROPSIE AVENUE: THE NEIGHBORHOOD						
Kitchen Sink Press: June, 1995 ($15.95/$24.95, B&W)						
nn-Will Eisner (softcover)						18.00
nn-Will Eisner (hardcover)						30.00
DROWNED GIRL, THE						
DC Comics (Piranha Press): 1990 ($5.95, 52 pgs, mature)						
nn	1	2	3	5	6	8
DRUG WARS						
Pioneer Comics: 1989 ($1.95)						
1-Grell-c						4.00
DRUID						
Marvel Comics: May, 1995 - No. 4, Aug, 1995 ($2.50, limited series)						
1-4: Warren Ellis scripts.						4.00
DRUM BEAT						
Dell Publishing Co.: No. 610, Jan, 1955						
Four Color 610-Movie, Alan Ladd photo-c	8	16	24	55	105	155
DRUMS OF DOOM						
United Features Syndicate: 1937 (25¢)(Indian)(Text w/color illos.)						
nn-By Lt. F.A. Methot; Golden Thunder app.; Tip Top Comics ad in comic; nice-c	50	100	150	315	533	750
DRUNKEN FIST						
Jademan Comics: Aug, 1988 - No. 54, Jan, 1993 ($1.50/$1.95, 68 pgs.)						
1	1	2	3	5	6	8
2-50						4.00
51-54						4.00
DUCK ALBUM (See Donald Duck Album)						
Dell Publishing Co.: No. 353, Oct, 1951 - No. 840, Sept, 1957						
Four Color 353 (#1)-Barks-c; 1st Uncle Scrooge-c (also appears on back-c).	15	30	45	100	220	340
Four Color 450-Barks-c	10	20	30	69	147	225
Four Color 492,531,560,586,611,649,686,	7	14	21	46	86	125
Four Color 726,782,840	6	12	18	37	66	95
DUCK AVENGER						
IDW Publishing: No. 0, Aug, 2016; Oct, 2016 - No. 5, Jun, 2017 ($4.99/$5.99/$6.99)						
0-Reprints of Italian Donald Duck costumed super-hero stories						6.00
1-(10/16, $5.99) Three covers; Red Raider app.	2	4	6	8	10	12
2-($4.99) Three covers; Xadhoom app.						6.00
3-5: 3-($5.99). 4,5-($6.99)	1	2	3	5	6	8
DUCKMAN						
Dark Horse Comics: Sept, 1990 ($1.95, B&W, one-shot)						
1-Story & art by Everett Peck	6	12	18	37	66	95
DUCKMAN						
Topps Comics: Nov, 1994 - No. 5, May, 1995; No. 0, Feb, 1996 ($2.50)						
0 (2/96, $2.95, B&W)-r/Duckman #1 from Dark Horse Comics						5.00
1-5: 1- w/ coupon #A for Duckman trading card. 2-w/Duckman 1st season episode guide						5.00
DUCKMAN: THE MOB FROG SAGA						
Topps Comics: Nov, 1994 - No. 3, Feb, 1995 ($2.50, limited series)						
1-3: 1-w/coupon #B for Duckman trading card. S. Shaw!-c						5.00
DUCKTALES						
Gladstone Publ.: Oct, 1988 - No. 13, May, 1990 (1,2,9-11: $1.50; 3-8: 95¢)						
1-Barks-r	3	6	9	15	22	28
2-Barks-r	2	4	6	8	10	12
3-11: 2-7,9-11-Barks-r						5.00
12,13 ($1.95, 68 pgs)-Barks-r; 12-r/F.C. #495						6.00
Disney Presents Carl Barks' Greatest DuckTales Stories Vol. 1 (Gemstone Publ., 2006, $10.95) r/stories adapted for the animated TV series including "Back to the Klondike"						11.00
Disney Presents Carl Barks' Greatest DuckTales Stories Vol. 2 (Gemstone Publ., 2006, $10.95) r/stories adapted for the animated TV series; "Robot Robbers" app.						11.00
DUCKTALES (TV)						
Disney Comics: June, 1990 - No. 18, Nov, 1991 ($1.50)						
1-All new stories; Marv Wolfman-s	2	4	6	10	14	18
2-18						5.00
Disney's DuckTales by Marv Wolfman: Scrooge's Quest TPB (Gemstone, 9/07, $15.99) r/#1-7; intro. by Wolfman						16.00

	GD 2.0	VG 4.0	FN 6.0	VF 8.0	VF/NM 9.0	NM- 9.2

Disney's DuckTales: The Gold Odyssey TPB (Gemstone, 10/08, $15.99) 16.00
The Movie nn (1990, $7.95, 68 pgs.)-Graphic novel adapting animated movie 8.00

DUCKTALES (TV)
Boom Entertainment (KABOOM!): May, 2011 - No. 6, Nov, 2011 ($3.99)

1-Three covers; Spector-s/Massaroli-a	1	2	3	5	6	8

2-6: 2-4-Three covers on each; Spector-s/Massaroli-a. 5,6-Two covers; crossover with
  Darkwing Duck #17,18 .... 4.00

DUCKTALES (Based on the 2017 TV series)
IDW Publishing: No. 0, Jul, 2017 - No. 1, Sept, 2017 - No. 20, Apr, 2019 ($3.99)

0-20: 0,1-Caramagna-s; multiple covers 4.00

DUCKTALES: FAIRES AND SCARES
IDW Publishing: Dec, 2019 - No. 3, Feb, 2020 ($3.99, limited series)

1-3: 1,2-Behling-s. 3-Caramagna-s 4.00

DUCKTALES: SCIENCE AND SILENCE
IDW Publishing: Aug, 2019 - No. 3, Oct, 2019 ($3.99, limited series)

1-3-Behling-s 4.00

DUDLEY (Teen-age)
Feature/Prize Publications: Nov-Dec, 1949 - No. 3, Mar-Apr, 1950

1-By Boody Rogers	34	68	102	199	325	450
2,3	1	32	48	94	147	200

DUDLEY DO-RIGHT (TV)
Charlton Comics: Aug, 1970 - No. 7, Aug, 1971 (Jay Ward)

1	9	18	27	59	117	175
2-7	6	12	18	37	66	95

DUEL MASTERS (Based on a trading card game)
Dreamwave Productions: Nov, 2003 - No. 8, Sept, 2004 ($2.95)

1-8: 1-Bagged with card; Augustyn-s 3.00

DUKE (From G.I. Joe)
Image Comics (Skybound): Dec, 2023 - Present ($4.99/$3.99)

1-($4.99) Williamson-s/Reilly-a 5.00
2,3-($3.99) 3-Baroness app. 4.00

DUKE NUKEM: GLORIOUS BASTARD (Based on the video game)
IDW Publishing: Jul, 2011 - No. 4, Nov, 2011 ($3.99)

1-4: 1-Three covers; Waltz-s/Xermanico-a 4.00

DUKE OF THE K-9 PATROL
Gold Key: Apr, 1963

1 (10052-304)	4	8	12	25	40	55

DUMBO (Disney; see Movie Comics, & Walt Disney Showcase #12)
Dell Publishing Co.: No. 17, 1941 - No. 668, Jan, 1958

Four Color 17 (#1)-Mickey Mouse, Donald Duck, Pluto app.

	290	580	870	1856	3178	4500
Large Feature Comic 19 ('41)-Part-r 4-Color 17	300	600	900	2040	3570	5100
Four Color 234 ('49)	15	30	45	105	233	360

Four Color 668 (12/55)-1st of two printings. Dumbo on-c with starry sky. Same-c as #234

	11	22	33	73	157	240

Four Color 668 (1/58)-2nd printing. Same cover altered with Timothy Mouse added. Same
  contents

	8	16	24	51	96	140

DUMBO COMIC PAINT BOOK (See Dumbo, Large Feature Comic No. 19)

DUNC AND LOO (#1-3 titled "Around the Block with Dunc and Loo")
Dell Publishing Co.: Oct-Dec, 1961 - No. 8, Oct-Dec, 1963

1	5	10	15	35	63	90
2	4	8	12	27	44	60
3-8	3	6	9	21	33	45

NOTE: Written by *John Stanley*; *Bill Williams* art.

DUNE (Movie)
Marvel Comics: Apr, 1985 - No. 3, June, 1985

1-r/Marvel Super Special; movie adaptation	3	6	9	19	30	40
2,3-Adaptation continues	2	4	6	8	11	14

DUNE
BOOM! Studios: Jul, 2021 - Dec, 2021 ($7.99, series of one-shots)

...: A Whisper of Caladan Seas 1 (12/21) Herbert & Anderson-s/Rebelka-a 8.00
...: Blood of the Sardaukar 1 (7/21) Herbert & Anderson-s/Gorham-a 8.00

DUNE: HOUSE ATREIDES
BOOM! Studios: Oct, 2020 - No. 12, Dec, 2021 ($4.99)

1-12-Prequel to the original novel; Brian Herbert & Kevin J. Anderson-s/Dev Pramanik-a 5.00

DUNE: HOUSE HARKONNEN
BOOM! Studios: Jan, 2023 - No. 12, Jan, 2024 ($4.99)

1-12-Prequel to the novel; Brian Herbert & Kevin J. Anderson-s. 1-4-Michael Shelfer-a 5.00

DUNE: THE WATERS OF KANLY
BOOM! Studios: May, 2022 - No. 4, Aug, 2022 ($4.99)

1-4-Set during the events of the novel; Brian Herbert & Kevin J. Anderson-s/Mortarino-a 5.00

DUNGEONS & DRAGONS
IDW Publishing: No. 0, Aug, 2010 - No. 15, Jan, 2012 ($1.00/$3.99)

0-(8/10, $1.00) Five covers; previews D&D series and Dark Sun mini-series 3.00
1-15: 1-(11/10, $3.99) Di Vito-a/Rogers-s; two covers 4.00
Annual 2012: Eberron (3/12, $7.99) Crilley-s/Diaz & Rojo-a 8.00
Annual 2022 (8/22, $7.99) Zub-s/Mello & Clodfelter-a 8.00
... 100 Page Giant (9/19, $5.99) Reprints by various incl. Zub & Dunbar 6.00
... 100 Page Spectacular (1/12, $7.99) Reprints by various incl. Duursema & Morales 8.00
...: The Best of Minsc & Boo 1 (4/22, $5.99) Reprints highlighting the characters 6.00

DUNGEONS & DRAGONS: A DARKENED WISH
IDW Publishing: Feb, 2019 - No. 5, June, 2019 ($3.99, limited series)

1-5-B. Dave Walters-a/Tess Fowler-a; multiple covers on each 4.00

DUNGEONS & DRAGONS: AT THE SPINE OF THE WORLD
IDW Publishing: Oct, 2020 - No. 4, Jan, 2021 ($3.99, limited series)

1-4-Garcia & Mendez-s/Coccolo-a; multiple covers on each 4.00

DUNGEONS & DRAGONS: CUTTER
IDW Publishing: Apr, 2013 - No. 5, Sept, 2013 ($3.99, limited series)

1-5-R.A. & Geno Salvatore-s/Baldeon-a; 2 covers on each 4.00

DUNGEONS & DRAGONS: EVIL AT BALDUR'S GATE
IDW Publishing: Apr, 2018 - No. 5, Aug, 2018 ($3.99, limited series)

1-5: 1-Jim Zub-s/Dean Kotz-a 4.00

DUNGEONS & DRAGONS: FORGOTTEN REALMS
IDW Publishing: Apr, 2012 - No. 5, Sept, 2012 ($3.99, limited series)

1-5-Greenwood-s/Ferguson-a 4.00
... 100 Page Spectacular (4/12, $7.99) Reprints by various incl. Rags Morales 8.00

DUNGEONS & DRAGONS: FROST GIANT'S FURY
IDW Publishing: Dec, 2016 - No. 5, Apr, 2017 ($3.99, limited series)

1-5-Jim Zub-s/Netho Diaz-a 4.00

DUNGEONS & DRAGONS: FORTUNE FINDER
IDW Publishing: Nov, 2023 - No. 5, Mar, 2024 ($3.99, limited series)

1-5: 1-Jim Zub-s/Jose Jaro-a 4.00

DUNGEONS & DRAGONS: INFERNAL TIDES
IDW Publishing: Nov, 2019 - No. 5 ($3.99, limited series)

1,2-Jim Zub-s/Max Dunbar-a; multiple covers on each 4.00

DUNGEONS & DRAGONS: LEGENDS OF BALDUR'S GATE
IDW Publishing: Oct, 2014 - No. 5, Feb, 2016 ($3.99, limited series)

1-5-Jim Zub-s/Max Dunbar-a 4.00
... #1 Greatest Hits Collection (4/16, $1.00) reprints #1 .... 3.00

DUNGEONS & DRAGONS: MINDBREAKER
IDW Publishing: Oct, 2021 - No. 5, Feb, 2022 ($3.99, limited series)

1-5-Jim Zub-s/Eduardo Mello-a 4.00

DUNGEONS & DRAGONS: RAVENLOFT – ORPHAN OF AGONY ISLE
IDW Publishing: Jun, 2022 - No. 4, Sept, 2023 ($3.99, limited series)

1-4-Quinn-s/Underwood-a 5.00

DUNGEONS & DRAGONS: SATURDAY MORNING ADVENTURES
IDW Publishing: Mar, 2023 - No. 4, Jun, 2023 ($3.99, limited series)

1-4-Booher-s/Kambadais-a 5.00

DUNGEONS & DRAGONS: SATURDAY MORNING ADVENTURES II
IDW Publishing: Jan, 2024 - No. 4, Apr, 2024 ($3.99, limited series)

1-4-Booher-s/Kambadais-a 5.00

DUNGEONS & DRAGONS: SHADOWS OF THE VAMPIRE
IDW Publishing: Apr, 2016 - No. 5, Aug, 2016 ($4.99/$3.99, limited series)

1-($4.99) Jim Zub-s/Nelson Dániel-a; 4 covers 5.00
2-5-($3.99) Three covers on each 4.00

DUNGEONS & DRAGONS: THE LEGEND OF DRIZZT: NEVERWINTER TALES
IDW Publishing: Aug, 2011 - No. 5, Dec, 2011 ($3.99)

1-5-R.A. & Geno Salvatore-s/Agustin Padilla-a 4.00

DUO
DC Comics: Jul, 2022 - No. 6, Dec, 2022 ($3.99, limited series)

1-6-Greg Pak-s/Khoi Pham-a 4.00

DURANGO KID, THE (Also see Best of the West, Great Western & White Indian)
(Charles Starrett starred in Columbia's Durango Kid movies)
Magazine Enterprises: Oct-Nov, 1949 - No. 41, Oct-Nov, 1955 (All 36 pgs.)

1-Charles Starrett photo-c; Durango Kid & his horse Raider begin; Dan Brand & Tipi (origin) begin by Frazetta & continue through #16	74	148	222	470	810	1150
2-Starrett photo-c.	34	68	102	199	325	450
3-5-All have Starrett photo-c.	29	58	87	172	281	390
6-10: 7-Atomic weapon-c/story	16	32	48	94	147	200
11-16-Last Frazetta issue	14	28	42	80	115	150
17-Origin Durango Kid	16	32	48	94	147	200

18-30: 18-Fred Meagher-a on Dan Brand begins.19-Guardineer-c/a(3) begins,

end #41. 23-Intro. The Red Scorpion	10	20	30	54	72	90
31-Red Scorpion returns	9	18	27	52	69	85

32-41-Bolle/Frazetta*ish*-a (Dan Brand; true in later issues?)

	9	18	27	50	65	80

NOTE: #6, 8, 14, 15 contain *Frazetta* art not reprinted in White Indian. *Ayers* c-18. *Guardineer* a(3)-19-41; c-19-41. *Fred Meagher* a-18-29 at least.

DURANGO KID, THE
AC Comics: 1990 - #2, 1990 ($2.50,$2.75, half-color)

1,2: 1-Starrett photo front/back-c; Durango Kid-r; Starrett photo-c; White Indian-r
  by Frazetta; Guardineer-r (50th anniversary of films) 4.00

DUSTCOVERS: THE COLLECTED SANDMAN COVERS 1989-1997
DC Comics (Vertigo): 1997 ($39.95, Hardcover)

Reprints Dave McKean's Sandman covers with Gaiman text 40.00
Softcover (1998, $24.95) 25.00

DUSTY STAR
Image Comics (Desperado Studios): No. 0, Apr, 1997 - No. 1 ($2.95, B&W)

0,1-Pruett-s/Robinson-a 4.00

DUSTY STAR
Image Comics (Desperado Publishing): June, 2006 ($3.50)

1-Pruett-s/Robinson-s/a 3.50

DUTCH
Image Comics: No. 0, Nov, 2023 - Present ($3.99)

0,1: 0-Joe Casey-s/Nathan Fox. 1-Simon Gane-a 4.00

DV8 (See Gen 13)

DV8
Image Comics (WildStorm Productions): Aug, 1996 - No. 25, Dec, 1998;

Duck Tales (2017 series) #18 © DIS

Dynamic Comics #24 © CHES

Earth Prime: The Flash #5 © DC

	GD	VG	FN	VF	VF/NM	NM-
	2.0	4.0	6.0	8.0	9.0	9.2

DC Comics (WildStorm Prod.): No. 0, Apr, 1999 - No. 32, Nov, 1999 ($2.50)

1/2						6.00
1-Warren Ellis scripts & Humberto Ramos-c/a(p)						5.00
1-(7-variant covers, w/1 by Jim Lee) ...each						5.00
2-4: 3-No Ramos-a						4.00
5-32: 14-Regular-c, 14-Variant-c by Charest. 26-(5/99)-McGuinness-c						4.00
14-($3.50) Voyager Pack w/Danger Girl preview						5.00
0-(4/99, $2.95) Two covers (Rio and McGuinness)						4.00
Annual 1 (1/98, $2.95)						4.00
Annual 1999 ($3.50) Slipstream x-over with Gen13						4.00
Rave-(7/96, $1.75)-Ramos-c; pinups & interviews						4.00
...: Neighborhood Threat TPB (2002, $14.95) r/#1-6 & #1/2; Ellis intro.; Ramos-c						15.00

DV8: GODS AND MONSTERS
DC Comics (WildStorm): June, 2010 - No. 8, Jan, 2011 ($2.99, limited series)

1-8-Wood-s/Issacs-a						3.00
TPB (2011, $17.99) r/#1-8						18.00

DV8 VS. BLACK OPS
Image Comics (WildStorm): Oct, 1997 - No. 3, Dec, 1997 ($2.50, limited series)

1-3-Bury-s/Norton-a						4.00

DWIGHT D. EISENHOWER
Dell Publishing Co.: December, 1969

01-237-912 - Life story	5	10	15	35	63	90

DYING IS EASY
IDW Publishing: Dec, 2019 - No. 5, Apr, 2020 ($3.99)

1-5-Joe Hill-s/Martin Simmonds-a/c						4.00

DYNABRITE COMICS
Whitman Publishing Co.: 1978 - 1979 (69¢, 10x7-1/8", 48 pgs., cardboard-c)
(Blank inside covers)
11350 - Walt Disney's Mickey Mouse & the Beanstalk (4-C 157). 11350-1 - Mickey Mouse Album (4-C 1057, 1151,1246). 11351 - Mickey Mouse & His Sky Adventure (4-C 214, 343). 11354 - Goofy: A Gaggle of Giggles. 11354-1 - Super Goof Meets Super Thief. 11356 - (?). 11359 - Bugs Bunny-r. 11360 - Winnie the Pooh Fun and Fantasy (Disney-r).

each....		2	4	10	14	18

11352 - Donald Duck (4-C 408, Donald Duck 45,52)-Barks-a. 11352-1 - Donald Duck (4-C 318, 10 pg. Barks/ WDC&S 105,128)-Barks-a. 11353 - Daisy Duck's Diary (4-C 1055,1150) Barks-a. 11355 - Uncle Scrooge (Barks-a/U.S. 12,33). 11355-1 - Uncle Scrooge (Barks-a/U.S. 3,16) - Barks-c(r). 11357 - Star Trek (r/-Star Trek 33,41). 11358 - Star Trek (r/-Star Trek 34,36). 11361 - Gyro Gearloose and the Disney Ducks (r/4-C 1047,1184)-Barks-c(r)

each....		2	4	11	16	20

DYNAMIC ADVENTURES
I. W. Enterprises: No. 8, 1964 - No. 9, 1964

8-Kayo Kirby-r by Baker?/Fight Comics 53.	3	6	9	16	23	30
9-Reprints Avon's "Escape From Devil's Island"; Kinstler-c	3	6	9	17	26	35

DYNAMIC CLASSICS (See Cancelled Comic Cavalcade)
DC Comics: Sept-Oct, 1978 (44 pgs.)

1-Neal Adams Batman, Simonson Manhunter-r	2	4	6	9	12	15

DYNAMIC COMICS (No #4-7)(No #25-29)
Harry 'A' Chesler: Oct, 1941 - No. 3, Feb, 1942; No. 8, Mar, 1944 - No. 30, May, 1948

1-Origin Major Victory by Charles Sultan (reprinted in Major Victory #1), Dynamic Man & Hale the Magician; The Black Cobra only app.; Major Victory & Dynamic Man begin	300	600	900	1950	3375	4800
2-Origin Dynamic Boy & Lady Satan; intro. The Green Knight & sidekick Lance Cooper	194	388	582	1242	2121	3000
3-1st small logo, resumes with #10	155	310	465	992	1696	2400
8-Classic-c; Dan Hastings, The Echo, The Master Key, Yankee Boy begin; Yankee Doodle Jones app.; hypo story	1700	3400	5100	11,300	18,150	25,000
9-Mr. E begins; Mac Raboy-c	194	388	582	1242	2121	3000
10-Small logo begins	135	270	405	864	1482	2100
11-Classic-c	811	1622	2433	5920	10,460	15,000
12-16: 15-The Sky Chief app. 16-Marijuana story	103	206	309	659	1130	1600
17(1/46)-Illustrated in SOTI, "The children told me what the man going to do with the hot poker." saw Wertham this in Crime Reporter #2	103	206	309	659	1130	1600
18-Classic Airplanehead monster-c	300	600	900	1950	3375	4800
19-Classic puppeteer-c by Gattuso	103	206	309	659	1130	1600
20-Bare-breasted woman-c	187	374	561	1197	2049	2900
21-Dinosaur-c; new logo	77	154	231	493	847	1200
22,30	58	116	174	371	636	900
23,24-(68 pgs.): 23-Yankee Girl app.	55	110	165	352	601	850
I.W. Reprint #1,8('64): 1-r/#23. 8-Exist?	4	8	12	22	35	48

NOTE: Kinstler c-IW #1. Tuska art in many issues, #3, 9, 11, 12, 16, 19. Bondage c-16.

DYNAMITE (Becomes Johnny Dynamite No. 10 on)
Comic Media/Allen Hardy Publ.: May, 1953 - No. 9, Sept, 1954

1-Pete Morisi-a; Don Heck-c; r-as Danger #6	53	106	159	334	567	800
2	28	56	84	165	270	375
3-Marijuana story; Johnny Dynamite (1st app.) begins by Pete Morisi(c/a); Heck text-a; man shot in face at close range	36	72	108	211	343	475
4-Injury-to-eye, prostitution; Morisi-c/a	34	68	102	199	325	450
5-9-Morisi-c/a in all. 7-Prostitute story & reprints	26	52	78	154	252	350

DYNAMO (Also see Tales of Thunder & T.H.U.N.D.E.R. Agents)
Tower Comics: Aug, 1966 - No. 4, June, 1967 (25¢)

1-Crandall/Wood, Ditko/Wood-a; Weed series begins; NoMan & Lightning cameos; Wood-c/a	8	16	24	56	108	160
2-4: Wood-c/a in all	5	10	15	35	63	90

NOTE: Adkins/Wood a-2. Ditko a-4?. Tuska a-2, 3.

DYNAMO 5 (See Noble Causes: Extended Family #2 for debut of Captain Dynamo)
Image Comics: Jan, 2007 - No. 25, Oct, 2009 ($3.50/$2.99)

1-Intro. the offspring of Captain Dynamo; Faerber-s/Asrar-a						8.00
2						5.00
3-7,11-24: 5-Intro. Synergy. 13-Origin of Myriad. 21-Firebird app.						3.50
8-10-($2.99)						3.50
25-($4.99) Back-up short stories of team members						5.00
Annual #1 (4/08, $5.99) r/Captain Dynamo app. in Nobel Causes: Extended Family #2 and three new stories by Faerber & various; pin-up gallery						6.00
#0 (2/09, 99¢) short story leading into #20; text synopsis of story so far						3.00
...: Holiday Special 2010 (12/10, $3.99) Faerber-s/Takara-a						4.00
... Vol. 1: Post-Nuclear Family TPB (2007, $9.99) r/#1-7; Kirkman intro.						10.00
... Vol. 2: Moments of Truth TPB (2008, $14.99) r/#8-13						15.00

DYNAMO 5: SINS OF THE FATHER
Image Comics: Jun, 2010 - No. 5, Oct, 2010 ($3.99, limited series)

1-5-Faerber-s/Brilha-a. 2-4-Invincible app.						4.00

DYNAMO JOE (Also see First Adventures & Mars)
First/Comics: May, 1986 - No. 15, 1988 ($1.75)

1-15: 4-Cargonauts begin, Special 1(1/87)-Mostly-r/Mars						4.00

DYNOMUTT (TV)(See Scooby-Doo (3rd series))
Marvel Comics Group: Nov, 1977 - No. 6, Sept, 1978 (Hanna-Barbera)

1-The Blue Falcon, Scooby Doo app.	5	10	15	34	60	85
2-6-All newsstand only	3	6	9	17	26	35

EAGLE, THE (1st Series) (See Science Comics & Weird Comics #8)
Fox Feature Syndicate: July, 1941 - No. 4, Jan, 1942

1-The Eagle begins; Rex Dexter of Mars app. by Briefer; all issues feature German war covers	514	1028	1542	3750	6625	9500
2-The Spider Queen begins (origin)	275	550	825	1746	3023	4300
3,4: 3-Joe Spook begins (origin)	245	490	735	1568	2684	3800

EAGLE COMICS (2nd Series)
Rural Home Publ.: Feb-Mar, 1945 - No. 2, Apr-May, 1945

1-Aviation stories	155	310	465	992	1696	2400
2-Lucky Aces	103	206	309	659	1130	1600

NOTE: L. B. Cole c/a in each.

EARTH 4 (Also see Urth 4)
Continuity Comics: Dec, 1993 - No. 4, Jan, 1994 ($2.50)

1-4: 1-3 all listed as Dec, 1993 in indicia						4.00

EARTH 4 DEATHWATCH 2000
Continuity Comics: Apr, 1993 - No. 3, Aug, 1993 ($2.50)

1-3						4.00

EARTH MAN ON VENUS (An...) (Also see Strange Planets)
Avon Periodicals: 1951

nn-Wood-a (26 pgs.) / Fawcette	290	580	870	1856	3178	4500

EARTH-PRIME (Set in the continuity of the CW television shows)
DC Comics: Jun, 2022 - No. 6, Aug, 2022 ($5.99, limited series)

...: Batwoman 1 (6/22) Takes place during season 3; Clayton Henry-a						6.00
...: Superman & Lois 2 (6/22) Grummett-a						6.00
...: Legends of Tomorrow 3 (7/22) Pelletier-a; back-up story with Booster Gold						6.00
...: Stargirl 4 (7/22) Robinson & Sevenbergen-s/Ordway-a; The Needle app.						6.00
...: The Flash 5 (8/22) Spotlight on Impulse, XS and Kid Flash; LaFuente-a						6.00
...: Hero's Twilight 6 (8/22) Heroes vs. Magog; Robson-a; back-up with Cisco						6.00

EARTH 2
DC Comics: Jul, 2012 - No. 32, May, 2015 ($3.99/$2.99)

	GD	VG	FN	VF	VF/NM	NM-
	2.0	4.0	6.0	8.0	9.0	9.2

1-($3.99) James Robinson-s/Nicola Scott-a/Ivan Reis-c; ... 4.00
1-Variant-c by Hitch ... 6.00
2-15-($2.99) 2-New Flash. 3-New Green Lantern. 4-New Atom ... 3.00
15.1, 15.2 (11/13, $2.99, regular covers) ... 3.00
15.1 (11/13, $3.99, 3-D cover) "Desaad #1" on cover; Levitz-s/Cinar-a ... 5.00
15.2 (11/13, $3.99, 3-D cover) "Solomon Grundy #1" on cover; Kindt-s/Lopresti-a ... 5.00
16-24,26-30: 16-Superman returns. 17-Batman returns. 20-Jae Lee-a. 28-Lobo app. ... 3.00
25-($3.99) New Superman revealed ... 3.00
#0 (11/12, $2.99) Superman, Batman, Wonder Woman, Terry Sloan app.; Giorello-a ... 3.00
Annual 1 (7/13, $4.99) Robinson/Cafu-a; new Batman app. ... 3.00
Annual 2 (3/14, $4.99) Taylor-s/Rocha-a; origin of new Batman ... 5.00
...: Futures End 1 (11/14, $2.99, regular-c) Five years later; Barrows-a ... 3.00
...: Futures End 1 (11/14, $3.99, 3-D cover) ... 4.00

EARTH 2: SOCIETY
DC Comics: Aug, 2015 - No. 22, May, 2017 ($2.99)
1-22: 1-Johnny Sorrow app.; Dick Grayson as Batman. 4-Anarky app. 6-Intro. Hourman. 15-Tony Harris-a (8 pgs.) ... 3.00
Annual 1 (10/16, $4.99) Abnett/Redondo & Neves-a; The Ultra-Humanite app. ... 5.00

EARTH 2: WORLD'S END
DC Comics: Dec, 2014 - No. 26, Jun, 2015 ($2.99, weekly series)
1-25: 1-Prelude to Darkseid's first attack. 3,7,8,10-Constantine app. ... 3.00
26-($3.99) Andy Kubert-c; leads into Convergence #1 ... 4.00

EARTHWORM JIM (TV, cartoon)
Marvel Comics: Dec, 1995 - No. 3, Feb, 1996 ($2.25)

1-Based on video game and toys	5	10	15	33	57	80
2,3	2	4	6	9	12	15

EARTH X
Marvel Comics: No. 0, Mar, 1999 - No. 12, Apr, 2000 ($3.99/$2.99, lim. series)
nn- (Wizard supplement) Alex Ross sketchbook; painted-c ... 6.00
Sketchbook (2/99) New sketches and previews ... 6.00

0-(3/99)-Prelude; Leon-a(p)/Ross-c	1	2	3	4	5	7
1-(4/99)-Leon-a(p)/Ross-c	1	2	3	4	5	7

1-2nd printing ... 4.00
2-12 ... 4.00
#1/2 (Wizard) Nick Fury on cover; Reinhold-a ... 4.00
#X (6/00, $3.99) ... 4.00
... Trilogy Companion TPB (2008, $29.99) r/#1/2; artwork and content from the Earth X, Paradise X and Universe X series; gallery of variant covers and promotional art ... 30.00
HC (2005, $49.95) r/#0,1-12, #1/2, X; foreward by Joss Whedon; Ross sketch pages ... 50.00
TPB (12/00, $24.95) r/#0,1-12, X; foreward by Joss Whedon ... 25.00

EASTER BONNET SHOP (See March of Comics No. 29)

EASTER WITH MOTHER GOOSE
Dell Publishing Co.: No. 103, 1946 - No. 220, Mar, 1949

Four Color 103 (#1)-Walt Kelly-a	22	44	66	154	340	525
Four Color 140 ('47)-Kelly-a	16	32	48	107	236	365
Four Color 185 ('48), 220-Kelly-a	14	28	42	96	211	325

EAST MEETS WEST
Innovation Publishing: Apr, 1990 - No. 2, 1990 ($2.50, limited series, mature)
1,2: 1-Stevens part-i; Redondo-c(i). 2-Stevens-c(i); 1st app. Cheech & Chong in comics 4.00

EAST OF WEST
Image Comics: Mar, 2013 - Present ($3.50/$3.99)
1-Hickman-s/Dragotta-a ... 6.00
2-26-Hickman-s/Dragotta-a ... 3.50
27-44-($3.99) ... 4.00
45-($4.99) ... 5.00
... : The World (12/14, $3.99) Source book for characters, events, settings, timelines ... 4.00

EAT THE RICH
BOOM! Studios: Aug, 2021 - No. 5, Dec, 2021 ($3.99, limited series)
1-5-Sarah Gailey-s/Pius Bak-a ... 4.00

EC ARCHIVES
Gemstone Publishing/Dark Horse Books: 2006 - Present ($49.95/$49.99, hardcover with dustjacket)
Crime SuspenStories Vol. 1 - Recolored reprints of #1-6; foreward by Max Allan Collins 50.00
Frontline Combat Vol. 1 - Recolored reprints of #1-6; foreward by Henry G. Franke III 50.00
Haunt of Fear Vol. 1 - Recolored reprints of #15-17,4-6; foreward by Robert Englund 50.00
Haunt of Fear Vol. 2 - Recolored reprints of #7-12; foreward by Tim Sullivan 50.00
Panic Vol. 1 - Recolored reprints of #1-6; foreward by Bob Fingerman 50.00
Shock SuspenStories Vol. 1 - Recolored reprints of #1-6; foreward by Steven Spielberg 50.00
Shock SuspenStories Vol. 2 - Recolored reprints of #7-12; foreward by Dean Kamen 50.00
Shock SuspenStories Vol. 3 - Recolored reprints of #13-18; foreward by Brian Bendis 50.00
Tales From the Crypt Vol. 1 - Recolored reprints of Crypt of Terror #17-19 and Tales From the Crypt #20-22; foreward by John Carpenter; Al Feldstein behind-the-scenes info 100.00
Tales From the Crypt Vol. 2 - Recolored reprints of #23-28; foreward by Joe Dante 50.00
Tales From the Crypt Vol. 3 - Recolored reprints of #29-34; foreward by Bob Overstreet 50.00
Tales From the Crypt Vol. 4 - (DH) Recolored reprints of #35-40; foreward by Russ Cochran 50.00
Tales From the Crypt Vol. 5 - (DH) Recolored reprints of #41-46; foreward by Bruce Campbell 50.00
Two-Fisted Tales Vol. 1 - Recolored reprints of #18-23; foreward by Stephen Geppi 50.00
Two-Fisted Tales Vol. 2 - Recolored reprints of #24-29; foreward by Rocco Versaci, Ph.D. 50.00
Two-Fisted Tales Vol. 3 - (DH) Recolored reprints of #30-35; foreward by Joe Kubert 50.00
Vault of Horror Vol. 1 - Recolored reprints of #12-17; foreward by R.L. Stine 50.00
Vault of Horror Vol. 2 - Recolored reprints of #18-23; foreward by John Landis 80.00
Vault of Horror Vol. 3 - (DH) Recolored reprints of #24-29; foreward by Mike Richardson 50.00
Vault of Horror Vol. 4 - (DH) Recolored reprints of #30-35; foreward by Jonathan Maberry 50.00
Weird Fantasy Vol. 1 - (DH) Recolored reprints of #13-17; foreward by Walt Simonson 50.00
Weird Science Vol. 1 - Recolored reprints of #1-6; foreward by George Lucas 75.00
Weird Science Vol. 2 - Recolored reprints of #7-12; foreward by Paul Levitz 50.00
Weird Science Vol. 3 - Recolored reprints of #13-18; foreward by Jerry Weist 50.00

E. C. CLASSIC REPRINTS
East Coast Comix Co.: May, 1973 - No. 12, 1976 (E.C. Comics reprinted in color minus ads)

1-The Crypt of Terror #1 (Tales from the Crypt #46)	2	4	6	11	16	20

2-12: 2-Weird Science #15('52). 3-Shock SuspenStories #12. 4-Haunt of Fear #12. 5-Weird Fantasy #13('52). 6-Crime SuspenStories #25. 7-Vault of Horror #26. 8-Shock SuspenStories #6. 9-Two-Fisted Tales #34. 10-Haunt of Fear #23. 11-Weird Science 12(#1).

12-Shock SuspenStories #2	2	4	6	8	11	14

EC CLASSICS
Russ Cochran: Aug, 1985 - No. 12, 1986? (High quality paper; each-r 8 stories in color)
(#2-12 were resolicited in 1990)($34.95, 56 pgs., 8x11")
1-12: 1-Tales From the Crypt. 2-Weird Science. 3-Two-Fisted Tales (r/31); Frontline Combat (r/9). 4-Shock SuspenStories. 5-Weird Fantasy. 6-Vault of Horror. 7-Weird Science-Fantasy (r/23,24). 8-Crime SuspenStories (r/17,18). 9-Haunt of Fear (r/14,15). 10-Panic (r/1,2). 11-Tales From the Crypt (r/23,24). 12-Weird Science (r/20,22)

	1	2	3	4	5	7

ECHO
Abstract Studio: Mar, 2008 - No. 30, May, 2011 ($3.50)
1-Terry Moore-s/a/c ... 8.00
2-30 ... 3.50
Terry Moore's Echo: Moon Lake TPB (2008, $15.95) r/#1-5; Moore sketch pages ... 16.00

ECHOLANDS
Image Comics: Aug, 2021 - No. 6, Feb, 2022 ($4.99, printed sideways for landscape view)
1-6-JH Williams III & W. Haden Blackman-s/Williams III-a; two covers on each ... 5.00
...: Raw Cut Edition 1-6 (9/21 - No. 6, 2/22, $4.99) Reprints with B&W art; creator bonuses 5.00

ECHO OF FUTUREPAST
Pacific Comics/Continuity Com.: May, 1984 - No. 9, Jan, 1986 ($2.95, 52 pgs.)
1-9: Neal Adams-c/a in all? ... 6.00
NOTE: N. Adams a-1-6,7i,9i; c-1-3, 5p,7i,8,9i. Golden a-1-6 (Bucky O'Hare); c-6. Toth a-6,7.

ECLIPSE GRAPHIC ALBUM SERIES
Eclipse Comics: Oct, 1978 - 1989 (8-1/2x11") (B&W #1-5)
1-Sabre (10/78, B&W, 1st print.); Gulacy-a; 1st direct sale graphic novel ... 16.00
1-Sabre (2nd printing, 1/79) ... 8.00
1-Sabre (3rd printing, $5.95) ... 6.00
1-Sabre 30th Anniversary Edition (2008, $14.99, 9x6" HC) new McGregor & Gulacy intros. original script with sketch art ... 15.00
2,6,7: 2-Night Music (11/79, B&W)-Russell-a. 6-I Am Coyote (11/84, color)-Rogers-c/a. 7-The Rocketeer (9th print,$7.95). 7-The Rocketeer (3rd print, 1991, $8.95) ... 10.00
3,4: 3-Detectives, Inc. (5/80, B&W, $6.95)-Rogers-a. 4-Stewart The Rat (1980, B&W) -G. Colan-a ... 10.00
5-The Price (10/81, B&W)-Starlin-a ... 20.00
7-The Rocketeer (9/85, color)-Dave Stevens-a (r/chapters 1-5)(see Pacific Presents & Starslayer); has 7 pgs. new-a ... 25.00
7-The Rocketeer, signed & limited HC ... 90.00
7-The Rocketeer, hardcover (1986, $19.95) ... 40.00
7-The Rocketeer, unsigned HC (3rd, $32.95) ... 33.00
8-Zorro In Old California ('86, color) ... 14.00
8,12-Hardcover ... 18.00
9,10: 9-Sacred And The Profane ('86)-Steacy-a. 10-Somerset Holmes ('86, $15.95)-Adults, soft-c ... 16.00
9,10,12-Hardcover ($24.95). 12-signed & #'d ... 25.00
11-Floyd Farland, Citizen of the Future ('87, $2.95, B&W) Chris Ware-s/a ... 15.00
12,28,31,35: 12-Silverheels ('87, $7.95, color). 28-Miracleman Book I ($5.95). 31-Pigeons From Hell by R. E. Howard (11/88). 35-Rael: Into The Shadow of the Sun ('88, $7.95) 10.00
13-The Sisterhood of Steel ('87, $8.95, color) ... 10.00
14,16,18,20,23,24: 14-Samurai, Son of Death ('87, $4.95, B&W). 16,18,20,23-See Airfighters Classics #1-4. 24-Heartbreak ($4.95, B&W) ... 7.00
14 (2nd pr.),17,21: 14-Samurai, Son of Death ($3.95, 2nd printing). 17-Valkyrie, Prisoner of the Past SC ('88, $3.95, color). 21-XYR-Multiple ending comic ('88, $3.95, B&W) ... 6.00
15,22,27: 15-Twisted Tales (11/87, color)-Dave Stevens-c. 22-Alien Worlds #1 (5/88, $3.95, 52 pgs.)-Nudity. 27-Fast Fiction (She) ($5.95, B&W) ... 10.00
17-Valkyrie, Prisoner of the Past S&N Hardcover ('88, $19.95) ... 25.00
19-Scout: The Four Monsters ('88, $14.95, color)-r/Scout #1-7; soft-c ... 15.00
25,30,32-34: 25-Alex Toth's Zorro Vol. 1,2($10.95, B&W). 30-Brought To Light; Alan Moore scripts ('89). 32-Teenaged Dope Slaves and Reform School Girls. 33-Bogie.
34-Air Fighters Classics #5 ... 12.00
29-Real Love: Best of Simon & Kirby Romance Comics (10/88, $12.95) ... 15.00
30,31: Limited hardcover set ($29.95). 31-signed ... 30.00
36-Dr. Watchstop: Adventures in Time and Space ('89, $8.95) ... 10.00

ECLIPSE MAGAZINE (Becomes Eclipse Monthly)
Eclipse Publishing: May, 1981 - No. 8, Jan, 1983 ($2.95, B&W, magazine)
1-8: 1-1st app. Cap'n Quick and a Foozle by Rogers, Ms. Tree by Beatty, and Dope by Trina Robbins. 2-1st app. I Am Coyote by Rogers. 7-1st app. Masked Man by Boyer ... 4.00
NOTE: Colan a-3, 5, 8. Golden c/a-2. Gulacy a-6, c-1, 6. Kaluta c/a-5. Mayerik a-2, 3. Rogers a-1-8. Starlin a-1. Sutton a-6.

ECLIPSE MONTHLY
Eclipse Comics: Aug, 1983 - No. 10, Jul, 1984 (Baxter paper, $2.00/$1.50/$1.75)
1-10: ($2.00, 52 pgs.)-Cap'n Quick and a Foozle by Rogers, Static by Ditko, Dope by Trina Robbins, Rio by Wildey, The Masked Man by Boyer begin. 3-Ragamuffins begins ... 4.00
NOTE: Boyer c-6. Ditko a-1-3. Rogers a-1-4; c-2, 4, 7. Wildey a-1, 2, 5, 9, 10; c-5, 10.

ECLIPSO (See Brave and the Bold #64, House of Secrets #61 & Phantom Stranger, 1987)
DC Comics: Nov, 1992 - No. 18, Apr, 1994 ($1.25)
1-18: 1-Giffen plots/breakdowns begin. 10-Darkseid app. Creeper in #3-6,9,11-13. 18-Spectre-c/s ... 4.00
Annual 1 (1993, $2.50, 68 pgs.)-Intro Prism ... 5.00
...: The Music of the Spheres TPB (2009, $19.99) r/stories from Countdown to Mystery #1-8 20.00

ECLIPSO: THE DARKNESS WITHIN
DC Comics: July, 1992 - No. 2, Oct, 1992 ($2.50, 68 pgs.)
1,2: 1-With purple gem attached to-c, 1-Without gem; Superman, Creeper app., 2-Concludes Eclipso storyline from annuals ... 4.00

EC SAMPLER - FREE COMIC BOOK DAY
Gemstone Publishing: May, 2008
Reprinted stories with restored color from Weird Science #6, Two-Fisted Tales #22, Crypt of Terror #17, Shock Suspenstories #6 ... 3.00

Earth 2: Society #1 © DC

East of West #38 © Hickman & Dragotta

Echo #16 © Terry Moore

	GD	VG	FN	VF	VF/NM	NM-
	2.0	4.0	6.0	8.0	9.0	9.2

E. C. 3-D CLASSICS (See Three Dimensional...)

ECTOKID (See Razorline)
Marvel Comics: Sept, 1993 - No. 9, May, 1994 ($1.75/$1.95)

1-($2.50)-Foil embossed-c; created by C. Barker						5.00
2-9: 2-Origin. 5-Saint Sinner x-over						4.00
...: Unleashed! 1 (10/94, $2.95, 52 pgs.)						5.00

ED "BIG DADDY" ROTH'S RATFINK COMIX (Also see Ratfink)
World of Fandom/ Ed Roth: 1991 - No. 3, 1991 ($2.50)

1-3: Regular Ed., 1-Limited double cover	2	4	6	11	16	20

EDDIE CAMPBELL'S BACCHUS
Eddie Campbell Comics: May, 1995 - No. 60, May, 2001 ($2.95, B&W)

1-Cerebus app.	1	2	3	5	6	8
1-2nd printing (5/97)						3.00
2-10: 9-Alex Ross back-c						5.00
11-60						3.00
Doing The Islands With Bacchus ('97, $17.95)						18.00
Earth, Water, Air & Fire ('98, $9.95)						10.00
King Bacchus ('99, $12.95)						13.00
The Eyeball Kid ('98, $8.50)						8.50

EDDIE STANKY (Baseball Hero)
Fawcett Publications: 1951 (New York Giants)

nn-Photo-c	41	82	123	256	428	600

EDEN
AfterShock Comics: May, 2021 ($6.99, oversized 8-1/2" x 10-7/8", one shot)

1-Cullen Bunn-s/Dalibor Talajic-a						7.00

EDEN'S FALL (Characters from Postal, The Tithe, and Think Tank)
Image Comics (Top Cow): Jan, 2017 - No. 3 ($3.99)

1-3-Matt Hawkins & Bryan Hill-s/Atilio Rojo-a						4.00

EDEN'S TRAIL
Marvel Comics: Jan, 2003 - No. 5, May 2003 ($2.99, unfinished lim. series, printed sideways)

1-5-Chuck Austen-s/Steve Uy-a						3.00

EDENWOOD
Image Comics: Sept, 2023 - Present ($3.99)

1-4-Tony Daniel-s/a						4.00

EDGAR ALLAN POE'S MORELLA AND THE MURDERS IN THE RUE MORGUE
Dark Horse Comics: Jun, 2015 ($3.99, one-shot)

1-Adaptation of Poe's poems; story and art by Richard Corben						4.00

EDGAR ALLAN POE'S SNIFTER OF BLOOD
AHOY Comics: 2020 - No. 6, 2021 ($4.99)

1-6-Short stories; adaptations and paradies of Poe by various. 2-Monster Serials						5.00

EDGAR ALLAN POE'S SNIFTER OF DEATH
AHOY Comics: 2021 - No. 6, 2022 ($4.99)

1-6-Short stories; adaptations and paradies of Poe by various. 1-Monster Serials						5.00

EDGAR ALLAN POE'S SNIFTER OF TERROR
AHOY Comics: 2018 - 2020 ($3.99)

1-6-Short stories; adaptations and paradies of Poe by various						4.00
Season Two 1-6: 2-Action Comics #1 cover spoof; Russell-s. 3-Medley-s/a						4.00

EDGAR ALLAN POE'S THE CONQUEROR WORM
Dark Horse Comics: Nov, 2012 ($3.99, one-shot)

1-Adaptation of Poe's poem; story and art by Richard Corben; Corben sketch pages						4.00

EDGAR ALLAN POE'S THE FALL OF THE HOUSE OF USHER
Dark Horse Comics: May, 2013 - No. 2, Jun, 2013 ($3.99, limited series)

1,2-Adaptation of Poe's poem; story and art by Richard Corben; Corben sketch pages						4.00

EDGAR ALLAN POE'S - THE FALL OF THE HOUSE OF USHER AND OTHER TALES OF HORROR
Catlan Communications Pub.: Sept. 1985 (hardcover graphic novel)

nn-Reprints of Poe story issues from Warren comic mags; all Richard Corben-a; numbered edition of 350 signed by Corben; 60 pgs.						130.00
nn-Softcover edition						60.00

EDGAR ALLAN POE'S THE PREMATURE BURIAL
Dark Horse Comics: Apr, 2014 ($3.99, one-shot)

1-Adaptation of The Premature Burial and The Cask of Amontillado; Corben-s/a/c						4.00

EDGAR ALLAN POE'S THE RAVEN AND THE RED DEATH
Dark Horse Comics: Oct, 2013 ($3.99, one-shot)

	GD	VG	FN	VF	VF/NM	NM-
	2.0	4.0	6.0	8.0	9.0	9.2

1-Adaptation of The Raven and The Masque of the Red Death; Corben-s/a/c						4.00

EDGAR BERGEN PRESENTS CHARLIE McCARTHY
Whitman Publishing Co. (Charlie McCarthy Co.): No. 764, 1938 (36 pgs.; 15x10-1/2"; color)

764	90	180	270	576	988	1400

EDGAR RICE BURROUGHS' CARSON OF VENUS
American Mythology Prods.: 2018 - Present ($3.99)

...Fear on Four Worlds 1 - part 1 of crossover; Mills-s/Mesarcia-a						4.00
...: Pirates of Venus 1,2 - Reprints from Korak, Son of Tarzan #46-53; Wein-s/Kaluta-a						4.00
...: The Flames Beyond 1-3: 1-Kaluta-c/Carey/s/Mesarcia-a						4.00
.../ Warlord of Mars 1-Kaluta-c/Avallone-s/Mesarcia-a						4.00

EDGAR RICE BURROUGHS' PELLUCIDAR
American Mythology Prods.: 2018 - 2019 ($3.99)

1-At the Earth's Core; Wolfer-s/Rearte-a						4.00
1-Fear on Four Worlds; part 3 of crossover; Wolfer-s/Mesarcia-a						4.00
1-Wings of Death; Wolfer-s/Büll-a						4.00

EDGAR RICE BURROUGHS' TARZAN: A TALE OF MUGAMBI
Dark Horse Comics: 1995 ($2.95, one-shot)

1						4.00

EDGAR RICE BURROUGHS' TARZAN: IN THE LAND THAT TIME FORGOT AND THE POOL OF TIME
Dark Horse Comics: 1996 ($12.95, trade paperback)

nn-r/Russ Manning-a						13.00

EDGAR RICE BURROUGHS' TARZAN OF THE APES
Dark Horse Comics: May, 1999 ($12.95, trade paperback)

nn-reprints						13.00

EDGAR RICE BURROUGHS' TARZAN: THE LOST ADVENTURE
Dark Horse Comics: Jan, 1995 - No. 4, Apr, 1995 ($2.95, B&W, limited series)

1-4: ERB's last Tarzan story, adapted by Joe Lansdale						4.00
Hardcover (12/95, $19.95)						20.00
Limited Edition Hardcover ($99.95)-signed & numbered						100.00

EDGAR RICE BURROUGHS' TARZAN: THE RETURN OF TARZAN
Dark Horse Comics: May, 1997 - No. 3, July, 1997 ($2.95, limited series)

1-3						4.00

EDGAR RICE BURROUGHS' TARZAN: THE RIVERS OF BLOOD
Dark Horse Comics: Nov, 1999 - No. 4, Feb, 2000 ($2.95, limited series)

1-4-Kordey-c/a						4.00

EDGAR RICE BURROUGHS' THE LAND THAT TIME FORGOT
American Mythology Prods.: 2016 - No. 3, 2016 ($3.99, limited series)

1-3-Wolfer-s/Caracuzzo-a						4.00
1-Fear on Four Worlds; part 4 of crossover; Wolfer-s/Büll-a						4.00
.../ Pellucidar: Terror From the Earth's Core 1-3 ('17, $3.99) Wolfer-s/Magora & Cuesta-a						4.00
... See-Ta The Savage 1,2 (2017, $3.99) Wolfer-s/a						4.00

EDGAR RICE BURROUGHS' THE MOON MAID
American Mythology Prods.: 2018 - 2019 ($3.99)

1-3-Catacombs of the Moon						4.00
1-Fear on Four Worlds; part 2 of x-over; Mills-s/Rearte-a						4.00

EDGE
Malibu Comics (Bravura): July, 1994 - No. 3, Apr, 1995 ($2.50/$2.95, unfinished lim.series)

1-3-S. Grant-story & Gil Kane-c/a; w/Bravura stamp. 3-($2.95-c)						4.00

EDGE (Re-titled as Vector starting with #13)
CrossGeneration Comics: May, 2002 - No. 12, Apr, 2003 ($9.95/$11.95/$7.95, TPB)

1-3: Reprints from various CrossGen titles						10.00
4-8-($11.95)						12.00
9-12-($7.95, 8-1/4" x 5-1/2") digest-sized reprints						8.00

EDGE OF CHAOS
Pacific Comics: July, 1983 - No. 3, Jan, 1984 (Limited series)

1-3-Morrow c/a; all contain nudity						4.00

EDGE OF DOOM (Horror anthology)
IDW Publishing: Oct, 2010 - No. 5, Mar, 2011 ($3.99)

1-5-Steve Niles-s/Kelley Jones-a						4.00

EDGE OF SPIDER-GEDDON (Leads into Spider-Geddon #0)
Marvel Comics: Oct, 2018 - No. 4, Dec, 2018 ($3.99, limited series)

1-4: 1-Anarchic Spider-Man app.; Sandoval-a. 2- Peni Parker, SP//dr app. 4-Kuder-s/a						4.00

EDGE OF SPIDER-VERSE (See Amazing Spider-Man 2014 series #7-14)

	GD	VG	FN	VF	VF/NM	NM-
	2.0	4.0	6.0	8.0	9.0	9.2

Marvel Comics: Nov, 2014 - No. 5, Dec, 2014 ($3.99, limited series)

1-Spider-Man Noir; Isanove-a	2	4	6	9	13	16
2-Gwen Stacy Spider-Woman 1st app.; Robbi Rodriguez-a/c						
	18	36	54	122	271	420
2 Facsimile Edition (4/22, $3.99) r/#2 with original 2014 ads						5.00
3,4: 3-Weaver-s/a	1	3	4	6	8	10
5-1st app. Sp//dr & Peni Parker; Gerard Way-s	3	6	9	19	30	40

EDGE OF SPIDER-VERSE (2nd series)
Marvel Comics: Oct, 2022 - No. 5, Dec, 2022 ($4.99, limited series)

1-5: 1-Spider-Man Noir, Araña, Spider-Rex app. 2-Spider-Gwen, Spider-UK app.						
5-Intro Web-Weaver						5.00

EDGE OF SPIDER-VERSE (3rd series)
Marvel Comics: Jul, 2023 - No. 4, Sept, 2023 ($4.99, limited series)

1-4: 1-Spider-Rex & Spider-Killer app. 2-Spinstress & Sky-Spider app. 3-Spider-Boy; Ramos-a; Spider-Smasher app. 4-Dream-Spider, Headline & Araña app.						5.00

EDGE OF VENOMVERSE (Leads into Venomverse series)
Marvel Comics: Aug, 2017 - No. 5, Oct, 2017 ($3.99, limited series)

1-5: Venom merges with X-23; Boschi-a. 2-Gwenpool/Venom; Daredevil app. 3-Ghost Rider. 4-Old Man Logan. 5-Deadpool; Stokoe-a						4.00

EDWARD SCISSORHANDS (Based on the movie)
IDW Publishing: Oct, 2014 - No. 10, Jul, 2015 ($3.99)

1-Kate Leth-s/Drew Rausch-a; multiple covers	2	4	6	8	11	14
2-10-Multiple covers on each						4.00

ED WHEELAN'S JOKE BOOK STARRING FAT & SLAT (See Fat & Slat)

EERIE (Strange Worlds No. 18 on)
Avon Per.: No. 1, Jan, 1947; No. 1, May-June, 1951 - No. 17, Aug-Sept, 1954

1(1947)-1st supernatural comic; Kubert, Fugitani-a; bondage-c						
	1100	2200	3300	8360	15,180	22,000
1(1951)-Reprints story from 1947 #1	194	388	582	1242	2121	3000
2-Wood-c/a; bondage-c	194	388	582	1242	2121	3000
3-Wood-c; Kubert, Wood/Orlando-a	148	296	444	947	1624	2300
4,5-Wood-c	106	212	318	673	1162	1650
6,8,13,14: 8-Kinstler-a; bondage-c; Phantom Witch Doctor story						
	58	116	174	371	636	900
7-Wood/Orlando-c; Kubert-a	97	194	291	621	1061	1500
9-Kubert-a; Check-c	103	206	309	659	1130	1600
10,11: 10-Kinstler-a. 11-Kinstlerish by McCann	61	122	183	390	670	950
12-Dracula story from novel, 25 pgs.	90	180	270	576	988	1400
15-Reprints No. 1('51) minus-c(bondage)	53	106	159	334	567	800
16-Wood-a r/No. 3	71	110	165	352	601	850
17-Wood/Orlando & Kubert-a; reprints #3 minus inside & outside Wood-c						
	58	116	174	371	636	900

NOTE: *Hollingsworth a-9-11; c-10, 11.*

EERIE
I. W. Enterprises: 1964

I.W. Reprint #1('64)-Wood-c(r); r-story/Spook #1	5	10	15	31	53	75
I.W. Reprint #2,6,8: 8-Dr. Drew by Grandenetti from Ghost #9						
	4	8	12	28	47	65
I.W. Reprint #9-r/Tales of Terror #1(Toby); Wood-c	5	10	15	33	57	80

EERIE (Magazine)(See Warren Presents)
Warren Publ. Co.: No. 1, Sept, 1965; No. 2, Mar, 1966 - No. 139, Feb, 1983

1-24 pgs., black & white, small size (5-1/4x7-1/4"), cover from inside back cover of Creepy No. 2; stories reprinted from Creepy No. 7, 8. At least three different versions exist.
First Printing - B&W, 5-1/4" wide x 7-1/4" high, evenly trimmed. On page 18, panel 5, in the upper left-hand corner, the large rear view of a bald headed man blends into solid black and is unrecognizable. Overall printing quality is poor.

	64	128	192	512	1156	1800

Second Printing - B&W, 5-1/4x7-1/4", with uneven, untrimmed edges (if one of these were trimmed evenly, the size would be less than as indicated). The figure of the bald headed man on page 18, panel 5 is clear and discernible. The staples have a 1/4" blue stripe.

	17	34	51	117	259	400

Other unauthorized reproductions for comparison's sake would be practically worthless. One known version was probably shot off a first printing copy with some loss of detail; the finer lines tend to disappear in this version which can be determined by looking at the lower right-hand corner of page one, first story. The roof of the house is shaded with straight lines. These lines are sharp and distinct on the original, but broken on this version.

NOTE: **The Overstreet Comic Book Price Guide** recommends that, before buying a 1st issue, you consult an expert.

2-Frazetta-c; Toth-a; 1st app. host Cousin Eerie	13	26	39	86	188	290
3-Frazetta-c & half pg. ad (rerun in #4); Toth, Williamson, Ditko-a						
	10	20	30	68	144	220
4,6: 4-Frazetta-a (1/2 pg. ad)	7	14	21	48	89	130
5,7-Frazetta-a. Ditko-a in all	8	16	24	55	105	155
8-Frazetta-c; Ditko-a	9	18	27	59	117	175
9-11,25: 9,10-Neal Adams-a, Ditko-a. 11-Karloff Mummy adapt.-Wood-s/a. 25-Steranko-c						
	7	14	21	44	82	120
12-16,18-22,24,32-35,40,45: 12,13,20-Poe-s. 12-Bloch-s. 15,25-Jones-a. 13-Lovecraft-s. 14,16-Toth-a. 16,19,24-Stoker-s. 16,32,33,43-Corben-a. 34-Early Boris-a. 35-Early Brunner-a. 35,40-Early Ploog-a. 40-Frankenstein; Ploog-a (6/72, 6 months before Marvel's series)						
	5	10	15	30	50	70
17-(low distribution)	22	44	66	154	340	525
23-Classic Frazetta-c; Adams-a(reprint)	34	68	102	245	548	850
26-31,36-38,43,44	4	8	12	27	44	60
39,41: 39-1st Dax the Warrior; Maroto-a. 41-(low distribution)						
	5	10	15	34	60	85
42,51: 42-('73 Annual, 84 pgs.) Spooktacular; Williamson-a. 51-('74 Annual, 76 pgs.) Color poster insert; Toth-a						
	5	10	15	30	50	70
46,48: 46-Dracula story by Sutton begins; 2pgs. Vampirella. 48-Begin "Mummy Walks" and "Curse of the Werewolf" series (both continue in #49,50,52,53)						
	4	8	12	27	44	60
47,49,50,52,53: 47-Lilith. 49-Marvin the Dead Thing. 50-Satanna, Daughter of Satan. 52-Hunter by Neary begins. 53-Adams-a						
	4	8	12	25	40	55
54,55-Color insert Spirit story by Eisner, reprints sections 12/21/47 & 6/16/46 54-Dr. Archaeus series begins	3	6	9	17	33	45
56,57,59,63,69,77,78: All have 8 pg. slick color insert. 56,57,77-Corben-a. 59-(100 pgs.)						

		Summer Special, all Dax issue. 69-Summer Special, all Hunter issue, Neary-a.				
78-All Mummy issue	3	6	9	21	33	45
58,60,62,68,72,: 8 pg. slick color insert & Wrightson-a in all. 58,60,62-Corben-a. 60-Summer Giant (9/74, $1.25) 1st Exterminator One; Wood-a. 62-Mummies Walk. 68-Summer Special (84 pgs.)						
	4	8	12	23	37	50
61,64-67,71: 61-Mummies Walk-a, Wood-a. 64-Corben-a. 64,65,67-Toth-a. 65,66-El Cid. 67-Hunter II. 71-Goblin-c/1st app.						
	3	6	9	17	26	35
70,73-75	3	6	9	14	20	26
76-1st app. Darklon the Mystic by Starlin-s/a	3	6	9	20	31	42
79,80-Origin Darklon the Mystic by Starlin	3	6	9	17	26	35
81,86,97: 81-Frazetta-a. King Kong; Corben-a. 86-(92 pgs.) All Corben issue. 97-Time Travel/ Dinosaur issue; Corben,Adams-a						
	3	6	9	18	28	38
82-Origin/1st app	3	6	9	18	28	38
83,85,88,89,91-93,98,99: 98-Rook (31 pgs.). 99-1st Horizon Seekers						
	2	4	6	10	14	18
84,87,90,96,100: 84,100-Starlin-a. 87-Hunter 3; Nino-a. 87,90-Corben-a. 96-Summer Special (92 pgs.) 100-(92 pgs.) Anniverary issue; Rook (30 pgs.)						
	2	4	6	13	18	22
94,95-The Rook & Vampirella team-up. 95-Vampirella-c; 1st MacTavish						
	3	6	9	16	24	32
101,106,112,115,118,120,121,128: 101-Return of Hunter II, Starlin-a. 106-Hard John Nuclear Hit Parade Special, Corben-a. 112-All Maroto issue, Luana-s. 115-All José Ortiz issues. 118-1st Haggarth. 120-1st Zud Kamish. 121-Hunter/Darklon. 128-Starlin-a, Hsu-a						
	2	4	6	10	14	18
102-105,107-111,113,114,116,117,119,122-124,126,127,129: 103-105,109-111-Gulacy-a. 104-Beast World.						
	2	4	6	9	13	16
125-(10/81, 84 pgs.) all Neal Adams issue	2	4	6	9	14	19
130-(76 pgs.) Vampirella-c/sty (54 pgs.); Pantha, Van Helsing, Huntress, Dax, Schreck, Hunter, Exterminator One, Rook app.						
	3	6	9	16	23	30
131-(Lower distr.); all Wood issue	3	6	9	14	20	26
132-134,136: 132-Rook returns. 133-All Ramon Torrents-a issue. 134,136-Color comic insert						
	2	4	6	10	14	18
135-(Lower distr.) 10/82, 100 pgs.) All Ditko issue	3	6	9	14	20	26
137-139 (lower distr.):137-All Super-Hero issue. 138-Sherlock Holmes. 138,139-Color comic insert						
	2	4	6	13	18	22
Yearbook '70-Frazetta-c	5	10	15	35	63	90
Annual '71, '72-Reprints in both	4	8	12	25	40	55
... Archives - Volume One HC (Dark Horse, 3/09, $49.95; dustjacket) r/#1-5						50.00
... Archives - Volume Two HC (Dark Horse, 9/09, $49.95; dustjacket) r/#6-10; interview with Frank Frazetta from 1985						50.00

NOTE: *The above books contain by many good artists: N. Adams, Brunner, Corben, Craig (Taycee), Crandall, Ditko, Eisner, Evans, Jeff Jones, Krenkel, McWilliams, Morrow, Orlando, Ploog, Severin, Starlin, Torres, Toth, Williamson, Wood, and Wrightson; covers by Bode', Corben, Davis, Frazetta, Morrow, and Orlando. Frazetta c-2, 3, 7, 8, 23. Annuals from 1973-on are included in regular numbering. 1970-74 Annuals are complete reprints. Annuals from 1975-on are in the format of the regular issues.*

EERIE
Dark Horse Comics: Jul, 2012 - No. 8, Dec, 2015 ($2.99, B&W)

1-8-Sci-fi anthology by various. 2-Allred-a. 3-Wood-a(r). 4,6-Kelley Jones-a						3.00

EERIE ADVENTURES (Also see Weird Adventures)
Ziff-Davis Publ. Co.: Winter, 1951 (Painted-c)

1-Powell-a(2), McCann-a; used in **SOTI**; bondage-c; Krigstein back-c						
	155	310	465	992	1696	2400

NOTE: *Title dropped due to similarity to Avon's Eerie & legal action.*

EERIE TALES (Magazine)
Hastings Associates: 1959 (Black & White)

1-Williamson, Torres, Tuska-a, Powell(2), & Morrow(2)-a						
	27	54	81	158	259	360

EERIE TALES
Super Comics: 1963-1964

Super Reprint No. 10,11,12,18: 10('63)-r/Spook #27. Purple Claw in #11,12 ('63); #12-r/Avon's Eerie #1('51)-Kida-r						
	3	6	9	17	26	35
15-Wolverton-a, Spacehawk-r/Blue Bolt Weird Tales #113; Disbrow-a						
	5	10	15	31	53	75

EFFIGY
DC Comics (Vertigo): Mar, 2015 - No. 7, Sept, 2015 ($2.99/$3.99)

1-5: 1-Tim Seeley-s/Marley Zarcone-a						3.00
6,7-($3.99)						4.00

EGBERT
Arnold Publications/Quality Comics Group: Spring, 1946 - No. 20, Aug, 1950

1-Funny animal; intro Egbert & The Count	28	56	84	168	274	380
2	15	30	45	84	127	170
3-10	10	20	30	58	79	100
11-20	9	18	27	50	65	80

EGYPT
DC Comics (Vertigo): Aug, 1995 - No.7, Feb, 1996 ($2.50, lim. series, mature)

1-7: Milligan scripts in all.						4.00

EH! (...Dig This Crazy Comic) (From Here to Insanity No. 8 on)
Charlton Comics: Dec, 1953 - No. 7, Nov-Dec, 1954 (Satire)

1-Davis-ish-c/a by Ayers, Wood-ish-a by Giordano; Atomic Mouse app.						
	50	100	150	315	533	750
2-Ayers-c/a	30	60	90	177	289	400
3,5,7	28	56	84	165	270	375
4,6: Sexual innuendo-c. 6-Ayers-a	37	74	111	222	361	500

EI8HT
Dark Horse Comics: Feb, 2015 - No. 5, Jun, 2015 ($3.50)

1-5-Rafael Albuquerque-a/c; Mike Johnson-s						3.50

EIGHTBALL (Also see David Boring)
Fantagraphics Books: Oct, 1989 - Present ($2.75/$2.95/$3.95, semi-annually, mature)

1 (1st printing) Daniel Clowes-s/a in all	11	22	33	76	163	250
2,3	3	6	9	15	22	28
4-19: 17-(8/96)	2	4	6	8	11	14

Edge of Spider-Verse (2023 series) #2 © MAR

Eerie #47 © Warren

Eight Billion Genies #4 © Silent E Prods.

	GD 2.0	VG 4.0	FN 6.0	VF 8.0	VF/NM 9.0	NM- 9.2

	GD	VG	FN	VF	VF/NM	NM-
20,21: 21-($4.95) Concludes David Boring 3-parter	2	4	6	8	10	12
22-($5.95) 29 short stories	2	4	6	8	10	12
23-($7.00, 9" x 12") The Death Ray	2	4	6	9	12	15
Twentieth Century Eightball (2002, $19.00) r/Clowes strips						20.00

EIGHT BILLION GENIES
Image Comics: May, 2022 - No. 8, Apr, 2023 ($3.99, limited series)
1-8: Charles Soule-s/Ryan Browne-a — 4.00

EIGHTH WONDER, THE
Dark Horse Comics: Nov, 1997 ($2.95, one-shot)
nn-Reprints stories from Dark Horse Presents #85-87 — 4.00

EIGHT IS ENOUGH KITE FUN BOOK (See Kite Fun Book 1979 in the Promotional Comics section)

EIGHT LEGGED FREAKS
DC Comics (WildStorm): 2002 ($6.95, one-shot, squarebound)
nn-Adaptation of 2002 mutant spider movie; Joe Phillips-a; intro by Dean Devlin — 7.00

1872 (Secret Wars tie-in)
Marvel Comics: Sept, 2015 - No. 4, Dec, 2015 ($3.99, limited series)
1-4-Red Wolf in the western town of Timely in 1872. 4-Avengers of the West — 4.00

80 PAGE GIANT (...Magazine No. 2-15)
National Periodical Publications: 8/64 - No. 15, 10/65; No. 16, 11/65 - No. 89, 7/71 (25¢)
(All reprints) (#1-56: 84 pgs.; #57-89: 68 pgs.)

	GD	VG	FN	VF	VF/NM	NM-
1-Superman Annual; originally planned as Superman Annual #9 (8/64)	34	68	102	245	548	850
2-Jimmy Olsen	18	36	54	125	276	430
3,4: 3-Lois Lane. 4-Flash-G.A.-r; Infantino-a	15	30	45	103	227	350
5-Batman; has Sunday newspaper strip; Catwoman-r; Batman's Life Story-r (25th anniversary special)	15	30	45	103	227	350
6-Superman	13	26	39	91	201	310
7-Sgt. Rock's Prize Battle Tales; Kubert-c/a	26	52	78	182	404	625
8-More Secret Origins-origins of JLA, Aquaman, Robin, Atom, & Superman; Infantino-a	26	52	78	182	404	625
9-15: 9-Flash (r/Flash #106,117,123 & Showcase #14). 10-Superboy. 11-Superman; all Luthor issue. 12-Batman; has Sunday newspaper strip. 13-Jimmy Olsen. 14-Lois Lane. 15-Superman and Batman; Joker-c/story	12	24	36	82	179	275

Continued as part of regular series under each title in which that particular book came out, a Giant being published instead of the regular size. Issues No. 16 to 89 are listed here for your information. See individual titles for prices.
16-JLA #39 (11/65), 17-Batman #176, 18-Superman #183, 19-Our Army at War #164, 20-Action #334, 21-Flash #160, 22-Superboy #129, 23-Superman #187, 24-Batman #182, 25-Jimmy Olsen #95, 26-Lois Lane #68, 27-Batman #185, 28-World's Finest #161, 29-JLA #48, 30-Batman #187, 31-Superman #193, 32-Our Army at War #177, 33-Action #347, 34-Flash #169, 35-Superboy #138, 36-Superman #197, 37-Batman #193, 38-Jimmy Olsen #104, 39-Lois Lane #77, 40-World's Finest #170, 41-JLA #58, 42-Superman #202, 43-Batman #198, 44-Our Army at War #190, 45-Action #360, 46-Flash #178, 47-Superboy #147, 48-Superman #207, 49-Batman #203, 50-Jimmy Olsen #113, 51-Lois Lane #86, 52-World's Finest #179, 53-JLA #67, 54-Superman #212, 55-Batman #208, 56-Our Army at War #203, 57-Action #373, 58-Flash #187, 59-Superboy #156, 60-Superman #217, 61-Batman #213, 62-Jimmy Olsen #122, 63-Lois Lane #95, 64-World's Finest #188, 65-JLA #76, 66-Superman #222, 67-Batman #218, 68-Our Army at War #216, 69-Adventure #390, 70-Flash #196, 71-Superboy #165, 72-Superman #227, 73-Batman #223, 74-Jimmy Olsen #131, 75-Lois Lane #114, 76-World's Finest #197, 77-JLA #85, 78-Superman #232, 79-Batman #228, 80-Our Army at War #229, 81-Adventure #403, 82-Flash #205, 83-Superboy #174, 84-Superman #239, 85-Batman #233, 86-Jimmy Olsen #140, 87-Lois Lane #113, 88-World's Finest #206, 89-JLA #93.

87TH PRECINCT (TV) (Based on the Ed McBain novels)
Dell Publishing Co.: Apr-June, 1962 - No. 2, July-Sept, 1962

	GD	VG	FN	VF	VF/NM	NM-
Four Color 1309(#1)-Krigstein-a	9	18	27	60	120	180
2-Photo-c	7	14	21	43	89	130

E IS FOR EXTINCTION (Secret Wars tie-in)
Marvel Comics: Aug, 2015 - No. 4, Nov, 2015 ($4.99/$3.99, limited series)
1-($4.99) New X-Men in Mutopia; Burnham-s/Villalobos-a — 5.00
2-4-($3.99) Cassandra Nova returns — 4.00

EL BOMBO COMICS
Standard Comics/Frances M. McQueeny: 1946

	GD	VG	FN	VF	VF/NM	NM-
nn(1946), 1(no date)	22	44	66	132	216	300

EL CAZADOR
CrossGen Comics: Oct, 2003 - No. 6, Jun, 2004 ($2.95)
1-Dixon-s/Epting-a — 5.00
2-6: 5-Lady Death preview — 3.00
...: The Bloody Ballad of Blackjack Tom 1 (4/04, $2.95, one-shot) Cariello-a — 3.00

EL CID
Dell Publishing Co.: No. 1259, 1961

	GD	VG	FN	VF	VF/NM	NM-
Four Color 1259-Movie, photo-c	8	16	24	51	96	140

EL DIABLO (See All-Star Western #2 & Weird Western Tales #12)
DC Comics: Aug, 1989 - No. 16, Jan, 1991 ($1.50-$1.75, color)

	NM-
1 ($2.50, 52pgs.)-Masked hero	5.00
2-16	4.00

EL DIABLO
DC Comics (Vertigo): Mar, 2001 - No. 4, Jun, 2001 ($2.50, limited series)
1-4-Azzarello-s/Zezelj-a/Sale-c — 3.00
TPB (2008, $12.99) r/#1-4 — 13.00

EL DIABLO
DC Comics: Nov, 2008 - No. 6, Apr, 2009 ($2.99, limited series)
1-6-Nitz-s/Hester-a/c. 4,5-Freedom Fighters app. — 3.00

EL DORADO (See Movie Classics)

ELEANOR & THE EGRET
AfterShock Comics: Apr, 2017 - No. 5, Nov, 2017 ($3.99)
1-5-John Layman-s/Sam Kieth-a/c — 4.00

ELECTRIC ANT
Marvel Comics: Jun, 2010 - No. 5, Oct, 2010 ($3.99, Baxter paper)
1-5-Based on a Philip K. Dick story; David Mack-s/Pascal Alixe-a; Paul Pope-c — 4.00

ELECTRIC SUBLIME
IDW Publishing: Oct, 2016 - No. 4, Jan, 2017 ($3.99, limited series)
1-4-W. Maxwell Prince-s/Martin Morazzo-a; two covers on each — 4.00

ELECTRIC UNDERTOW (See Strikeforce Morituri: Electric Undertow)

ELECTRIC WARRIOR
DC Comics: May, 1986 - No. 18, Oct, 1987 ($1.50, Baxter paper)
1-18 — 4.00

ELECTRIC WARRIORS
DC Comics: Jan, 2019 - No. 6, Jun, 2019 ($3.99, limited series)
1-6-Steve Orlando-s/Travel Foreman-a — 4.00

ELECTROPOLIS
Image Comics: May, 2001 - No. 4, Jan, 2003 ($2.95/$5.95)
1-3-Dean Motter-s/a. 3-(12/01) — 3.00
4-(1/03, $5.95, 72 pages) The Infernal Machine pts. 4-6 — 6.00

ELEKTRA (Also see Daredevil #319-325)
Marvel Comics: Mar, 1995 - No. 4, June, 1995 ($2.95, limited series)
1-4-Embossed-c; Scott McDaniel-a — 5.00

ELEKTRA (Also see Daredevil)
Marvel Comics: Nov, 1996 - No. 19, Jun, 1998 ($1.95)
1-Peter Milligan scripts; Deodato-c/a — 5.00
1-Variant-c — 6.00
1-Dr. Strange-c/app. 10-Logan-c/app. — 4.00
#(-1) Flashback (7/97) Matt Murdock-c/app.; Deodato-c/a — 4.00
.../Cyblade (Image, 3/97,$2.95) Devil's Reign pt. 7 — 4.00

ELEKTRA (Vol. 2) (Marvel Knights)
Marvel Comics: Sept, 2001 - No. 35, Jun, 2004 ($3.50/$2.99)
1-Bendis-s/Austen-a/Horn-c — 4.00
2-6: 2-Two covers (Sienkiewicz and Horn) 3,4-Silver Samurai app. — 3.00
3-Initial printing with panel of nudity; most copies pulped

	GD	VG	FN	VF	VF/NM	NM-
	6	12	18	42	79	115

7-35: 7-Rucka-s begin. 9,10,17-Bennett-a. 19-Meglia-a. 23-25-Chen-a; Sienkiewicz-c — 3.00
...Vol. 1: Introspect TPB (2002, $16.99) r/#10-15; Marvel Knights: Double Shot #3 — 17.00
...Vol. 2: Everything Old is New Again TPB (2003, $16.99) r/#16-22 — 17.00
...Vol. 3: Relentless TPB (2004, $14.99) r/#23-28 — 15.00
...Vol. 4: Frenzy TPB (2004, $17.99) r/#29-35 — 18.00

ELEKTRA (All-New Marvel Now!)
Marvel Comics: Jun, 2014 - No. 11, May, 2015 ($3.99)
1-11: 1-Blackman-s/Del Mundo-a; multiple covers. 2,6,7-Lady Bullseye app. — 4.00

ELEKTRA
Marvel Comics: Apr, 2017 - No. 5, Aug, 2017 ($3.99, limited series)
1-5: Matt Owens-s/Juann Cabal-a; Arcade app. — 4.00

ELEKTRA
Marvel Comics: No. 100, Jun, 2022 ($4.99, one-shot)
100-Main story by Nocenti-s/Kotian-a; Typhoid Mary app.; bonus cover gallery — 5.00

ELEKTRA & WOLVERINE: THE REDEEMER
Marvel Comics: Jan, 2002 - No. 3, Mar, 2002 ($5.95, square-bound, lim. series)
1-3-Greg Rucka-s/Yoshitaka Amano-a/c — 6.00
HC (5/02, $29.95, with dustjacket) r/#1-3, interview with Greg Rucka — 30.00

	GD 2.0	VG 4.0	FN 6.0	VF 8.0	VF/NM 9.0	NM- 9.2

ELEKTRA: ASSASSIN (Also see Daredevil)
Marvel Comics (Epic Comics): Aug, 1986 - No. 8, June, 1987 (Limited series, mature)

1,8-Miller scripts in all; Sienkiewicz-c/a	1	3	4	6	8	10
2-7						5.00
Signed & numbered hardcover (Graphitti Designs, $39.95, 2000 print run)- reprints 1-8						60.00
TPB (2000, $24.95)						25.00

ELEKTRA: BLACK, WHITE & BLOOD
Marvel Comics: Mar, 2022 - No. 4, Jul, 2022 ($4.99, B&W with red, limited series)

1-4-Short story anthology by various. 1-Art by Bagley, Romero & D'Armini 5.00

ELEKTRA: GLIMPSE & ECHO
Marvel Comics: Sept, 2002 - No. 4, Dec, 2002 ($2.99, limited series)

1-4-Scott Morse-s/painted-a 3.00

ELEKTRA LIVES AGAIN (Also see Daredevil)
Marvel Comics (Epic Comics): 1990 ($24.95, oversize, hardcover, 76 pgs.)(Produced by Graphitti Designs)

nn-Frank Miller-a/scripts; Lynn Varley painted-a; Matt Murdock & Bullseye app. 40.00
2nd printing (9/02, $24.99) 25.00

ELEKTRA MEGAZINE
Marvel Comics: Nov, 1996 - No. 2, Dec, 1996 ($3.95, 96 pgs., reprints, limited series)

1,2: Reprints Frank Miller's Elektra stories in Daredevil 4.00

ELEKTRA SAGA, THE
Marvel Comics Group: Feb, 1984 - No. 4, June, 1984 ($2.00, limited series, Baxter paper)

1-4-r/Daredevil #168-190; Miller-c/a 5.00

ELEKTRA: THE HAND
Marvel Comics: Nov, 2004 - No. 5, Feb, 2005 ($2.99, limited series)

1-5-Gossett-a/Sienkiewicz-c/Yoshida-s; origin of the Hand in the 16th century 3.00

ELEKTRA: THE MOVIE
Marvel Comics: Feb, 2005 ($5.99)

1-Movie adaptation; McKeever-s/Perkins-a; photo-c 6.00
TPB (2005, $12.95) r/movie adaptation, Daredevil #168, 181 & Elektra #(-1) 13.00

ELEMENTALS, THE (See The Justice Machine, Morningstar Special, and Vortex)
Comico The Comic Co.: Jun, 1984 - No. 29, Sept, 1988; V2#1, Mar, 1989 - No. 26, Apr, 1993 ($1.50/$2.50, Baxter paper); V3#1, Dec, 1995 - No. 3 ($2.95)

1-Willingham-c/a, 1-8 ..... 5.00
2-29: 9-Bissette-a(p). 10-Photo-c. 18-Prelude to Avalon mini-series 4.00
V2#1-26: 16-1st app. Strikeforce America 4.00
V3#1-3: 1-Daniel-a(p), bagged w/gaming card 4.00
Lingerie (5/96, $2.95) 4.00
Special 1,2 (3/86, 1/89)-1-Willingham-a(p) 4.00

ELEMENTALS (Title series), **Comico**

--GHOST OF A CHANCE, 12/95 ($5.95)-graphic novel, nn-Ross-c. 6.00
--HOW THE WAR WAS WON, 6/96 - No. 2, 8/96 ($2.95) 1,2-Tony Daniel-a, &
  1-Variant-c; no logo 4.00
--SEX SPECIAL, 1991 - No. 4, Feb, 1993 ($2.95, color) 2 covers for each 4.00
--SEX SPECIAL, 5/97 - No. 2, 6/97 ($2.95, B&W) 1-Tony Daniel, Jeff Moy-a, 2-Robb
  Phipps, Adam McDaniel-a 4.00
--SWIMSUIT SPECTACULAR 1996, 6/96 ($2.95), 1-pin-ups, 1-Variant-c; no logo 4.00
--THE VAMPIRE'S REVENGE, 6/96 - No. 2 8/96 ($2.95) 1,2-Willingham-s,
  1-Variant-c; no logo 4.00

ELEPHANTMEN
Image Comics: July, 2006 - No. 80, Jan, 2018 ($2.99/$3.50/$3.99) (Flip covers on most)

1-16: 1-Starkings-s/Moritat-a/Ladronn-c. 6-Campbell flip-c. 15-Sale flip-c 4.00
17-30-($3.50) 25-Flip book preview of Marineman 4.00
31-49,51-80-($3.99) 32-Conan/Red Sonja homage. 42-44-Dave Sim-a (5 pgs.) 4.00
50-($5.99) Flip book with reprint of #1; cover gallery 6.00
...: Man and Elephantman 1 (3/11, $3.99) Three covers 4.00
... Shots (5/15, $5.99) Reprints short stories from anthologies; art by Sim, Sale, & others 6.00
...: The Pilot (5/07, $2.99) short stories and pin-ups by various incl. Sale, Jim Lee, Jae Lee 4.00
... War Toys (11/07 - No. 3, 4/08, $2.99) 1-3-Mappo war; Starkings-s/Moritat-a 4.00
... War Toys: Yvette (7/09, $3.50) Starkings-s/Moritat-a 4.00
Giant-Size Elephantman 1 (10/11, $5.99) r/#31,32 & Man and Elephantman; Campbell-c 6.00

1111 (ELEVEN ELEVEN)
Crusade Entertainment: Oct, 1996 ($2.95, B&W, one-shot)

1-Wrightson-c/a 4.00

ELEVEN OR ONE
Sirius: Apr, 1995 ($2.95)

1-Linsner-c/a	1	3	4	6	8	10
1-(6/96) 2nd printing						4.00

ELFLORD
Nightwind Productions: Jun, 1980 - Vol. 2 #1, 1982 (B&W, magazine-size)

1-1st Barry Blair-s/c/a in comics; B&W-c; limited print run for all	10	20	30	69	147	225
2-5-B&W-c	5	10	15	31	53	75
6-14: 9-14-Color-c	4	8	12	27	44	60
Vol. 2 #1 (1982)	4	8	12	23	37	50

ELFLORD
Aircel Publ.: 1986 - No. 6, Oct, 1989 ($1.70, B&W); V2#1- V2#31, 1995 ($2.00)

1 ..... 6.00
2-4,V2#1-20,22-30: 4-6: Last B&W. V2#1-Color-a begin. 22-New cast. 25-Begin B&W 4.00
1,2-2nd printings 4.00
21-Double size ($4.95) 5.00

ELFLORD
Warp Graphics: Jan, 1997-No.4, Apr, 1997 ($2.95, mini-series)

1-4 ..... 4.00

ELFLORD (CUTS LOOSE) (Vol. 2)

Warp Graphics: Sept, 1997 - No. 7, Apr, 1998 ($2.95, B&W, mini-series)

1-7 ..... 4.00

ELFLORD: DRAGON'S EYE
Night Wynd Enterprises: 1993 ($2.50, B&W)

1 ..... 4.00

ELFLORD: THE RETURN
Mad Monkey Press: 1996 ($6.95, magazine size)

1 ..... 7.00

ELFQUEST (Also see Fantasy Quarterly & Warp Graphics Annual)
Warp Graphics, Inc.: No. 2, Aug, 1978 - No. 21, Feb, 1985 (All magazine size)
No. 1, Apr, 1979
NOTE: Elfquest was originally published as one of the stories in Fantasy Quarterly #1. When the publisher went out of business, the creative team, Wendy and Richard Pini, formed WaRP Graphics and continued the series, beginning with Elfquest #2. Elfquest #1, which reprinted the story from Fantasy Quarterly, was published about the same time Elfquest #4 was released. Thereafter, most issues were reprinted as demand warranted, until Marvel announced it would reprint the entire series under its Epic imprint (Aug., 1985).

1(4/79)-Reprints Elfquest story from Fantasy Quarterly No. 1						
1st printing ($1.00-c)	9	18	27	57	111	165
2nd printing ($1.25-c)	2	4	6	10	14	18
3rd printings ($1.50-c)	1	2	3	5	6	8
4th printing; different-c ($1.50-c)						5.00
2(8/78) 1st printing ($1.00-c)	5	10	15	31	53	75
2nd printings ($1.25-c)						6.00
3rd & 4th printings ($1.50-c)(all 4th prints 1989)						5.00
3-5: 1st printings ($1.00-c)	3	6	9	17	26	35
6-9: 1st printings ($1.25-c)	3	6	9	15	22	28
2nd & 3rd printings ($1.50-c)						5.00
10-21: 1st printings ($1.50-c); 16-8pg. preview of A Distant Soil	2	4	6	11	16	20
10-14: 2nd printings ($1.50)						5.00

ELFQUEST
Marvel Comics (Epic Comics): Aug, 1985 - No. 32, Mar, 1988

1-Reprints in color the Elfquest epic by Warp Graphics	1	2	3	5	6	8
2-32						4.00

ELFQUEST
DC Comics: 2003 - 2005

Archives Vol. 1 (2003, $49.95, HC) r/#1-5 ..... 50.00
Archives Vol. 2 (2005, $49.95, HC) r/#6-10 & Epic Illustrated #1 ..... 50.00
25th Anniversary Special (2003, $2.95) r/Elfquest #1 (Apr, 1979); interview w/Pinis 4.00

ELFQUEST (Title series), Warp Graphics
'89 - No. 4, '89 ($1.50, B&W) 1-4: R-original Elfquest series 4.00

ELFQUEST (Volume 2),Warp Graphics: V2#1, 5/96 - No. 33, 2/99 ($4.95/$2.95, B&W)
V2#1-31: 1-3,5,8,10,12,13,18,21,23,25-Wendy Pini-c 6.00
32,33-($2.95-c) 6.00

--BLOOD OF TEN CHIEFS, 7/93 - No. 20, 9/95 ($2.00/$2.50)
1-20-By Richard & Wendy Pini 4.00
--HIDDEN YEARS, 5/92 - No. 29, 3/96 ($2.00/$2.25)1-9,9 1/2, 10-29 ..... 4.00
--JINK, 11/94 - No. 12, 2/6 ($2.25/$2.50) 1-12-W. Pini/John Byrne-back-c 4.00
--KAHVI, 10/95 - No. 6,3/96 ($2.25, B&W) 1-6 ..... 4.00
--KINGS CROSS, 11/97 - No. 2, 12/97 ($2.95, B&W) 1,2 ..... 4.00
--KINGS OF THE BROKEN WHEEL, 6/90 - No. 9, 2/92 ($2.00, B&W) (3rd Elfquest saga)
1-9-By R. & W. Pini; 1-Color insert 5.00
1-2nd printing 4.00
--METAMORPHOSIS, 4/96 ($2.95, B&W) 1 ..... 4.00
--NEW BLOOD (...Summer Special on-c #1 only), 8/92 - No. 35, 1/96 ($2.00-$2.50, color/
  B&W) 1-($3.95, 68 pgs.,....Summer Special on-c)-Byrne-a/scripts (16 pgs.) 5.00
2-35: Barry Blair-a in all 4.00
1993 Summer Special ($3.95) Byrne-a/scripts 4.00
--SHARDS, 8/94 - No. 16, 3/96 ($2.25/$2.50) 1-16 ..... 4.00
--SIEGE AT BLUE MOUNTAIN, WaRP Graphics/Apple: 3/87 - No. 8, 12/88 (1.75/ $1.95, B&W)

1-Staton-a(i) in all; 2nd Elfquest saga	1	2	3	5	6	8
1-3-2nd printing						4.00
2-8						5.00

--THE REBELS, 11/94 - No. 12, 3/96 ($2.25/$2.50, B&W/color) 1-12 ..... 4.00
--TWO-SPEAR, 10/95 - No. 5, 2/96 ($2.25, B&W) 1-5 ..... 4.00
--WAVE DANCERS, 12/93 - No. 6, 3/96, 1-6: 1-Foil-c & poster 4.00
Special 1 ($2.95) 4.00
--WORLDPOOL, 7/97 ($2.95, B&W) 1-Richard Pini-s/Barry Blair-a 4.00

ELFQUEST: STARGAZER'S HUNT
Dark Horse Comics: Nov, 2019 - No. 4, Oct, 2020 ($3.99)

1-4-Wendy & Richard Pini-s/Sonny Strait-a 4.00

ELFQUEST: THE DISCOVERY
DC Comics: Mar, 2006 - No. 4, Sept, 2006 ($3.99, limited series)

1-4-Wendy Pini-a/Wendy & Richard Pini-s 5.00
TPB (2006, $14.99) r/#1-4 ..... 15.00

ELFQUEST: THE FINAL QUEST
Dark Horse Comics: Oct, 2013; No. 1, Jan, 2014 - No. 24, Feb, 2018 ($3.50/$3.99)

1-14-Wendy Pini-a/Wendy & Richard Pini-s 3.50
15-24-($3.99) 4.00
... Special (10/13, $5.99) Wendy Pini-a/Wendy & Richard Pini-s; prologue to series 6.00

ELFQUEST: THE GRAND QUEST
DC Comics: 2004 - No. 14, 2006 ($9.95/$9.99, B&W, digest-size)

Vol. 1-6 ('04) 1-r/Elfquest #1-5; new W. Pini-c. 2-r/#5-8. 3-r/#8-11. 4-r/#11-15. 5-r/#15-18
  6-r/#18-20 ..... 10.00
Vol. 7-9 ('05) 1-r/Siege At Blue Mountain #1-3. 8-r/SABM #3-5. 9-r/SABM #6-8 ..... 10.00
Vol. 10-14 ('05) 10-r/Kings of the Broken Wheel #1-3. 11-KotBW #5-7 & Frazetta Fant. Ill.
  12-r/Kings of the Broken Wheel #8&9. 13-r/Elfquest V2 #4-18. 14-r/Hidden Years #4-9 1/2 ..... 10.00

Elektra: Black, White & Blood #1 © MAR

ElfQuest: The Final Quest #5 © Warp

Elsewhere #1 © Faerber & Kesgin

	GD	VG	FN	VF	VF/NM	NM-
	2.0	4.0	6.0	8.0	9.0	9.2

ELFQUEST: THE SEARCHER AND THE SWORD
DC Comics: 2004 ($24.95/$14.99, graphic novel)
HC (2004, $24.95, with dust jacket)-Wendy and Richard Pini-s/a/c ... 25.00
SC (2004, $14.99) ... 15.00

ELFQUEST: WOLFRIDER
DC Comics: 2003 - No. 2, 2003 ($9.95, digest-size)
Volume 1 ('03, $9.95, digest-size) r/Elfquest V2#19,21,23,25,27,29,31; Blood of Ten Chiefs #2;
Hidden Years #5; New Blood Special #1; New Blood 1993 Special #1; new W. Pini-c ... 10.00
Volume 2 ('03, $9.95, digest-size) r/Elfquest V2#33; Blood of Ten Chiefs #10,11,19; Warp
Graphics Annual #1 ... 10.00

ELIMINATOR (Also see The Solution #16 & The Night Man #16)
Malibu Comics (Ultraverse): Apr, 1995 - No. 3, Jul, 1995 ($2.95/$2.50, lim. series)
0-Mike Zeck-a in all ... 4.00
1-3-($2.50): 1-1st app. Siren ... 4.00
1-($3.95)-Black cover edition ... 5.00

ELIMINATOR FULL COLOR SPECIAL
Eternity Comics: Oct, 1991 ($2.95, one-shot)
1-Dave Dorman painted-c ... 4.00

ELLA CINDERS (See Comics On Parade, Comics Revue #1,4, Famous Comics Cartoon Book, Giant Comics
Editions, Sparkler Comics, Tip Top & Treasury of Comics)

ELLA CINDERS
United Features Syndicate: 1938 - 1940
Single Series 3(1938)	50	100	150	315	533	750
Single Series 21(#2 on-c, #21 on inside), 28('40)	41	82	123	256	428	600

ELLA CINDERS
United Features Syndicate: Mar, 1948 - No. 5, Mar, 1949
1-(#2 on cover)	19	38	57	111	176	240
2	14	28	42	76	108	140
3-5	10	20	30	54	72	90

ELLERY QUEEN
Superior Comics Ltd.: May, 1949 - No. 4, Nov, 1949
1-Kamen-c; L.B. Cole-a; r-in Haunted Thrills	68	136	204	435	743	1050
2-4: 3-Drug use stories(2)	47	94	141	296	498	700
NOTE: Iger shop art in all issues.

ELLERY QUEEN (TV)
Ziff-Davis Publishing Co.: 1-3/52 (Spring on-c) - No. 2, Summer/52 (Saunders painted-c)
1-Saunders-c	58	116	174	371	636	900
2-Saunders bondage, torture-c	43	86	129	271	461	650

ELLERY QUEEN (Also see Crackajack Funnies No. 23)
Dell Publishing Co.: No. 1165, Mar-May, 1961 - No.1289, Apr, 1962
Four Color 1165 (#1)	9	18	27	58	114	175
Four Color 1243 (11/61-1/62), 1289	7	14	21	48	89	130

ELMER FUDD (Also see Camp Comics, Daffy, Looney Tunes #1 & Super Book #10, 22)
Dell Publishing Co.: No. 470, May, 1953 - No. 1293, Mar-May, 1962
Four Color 470 (#1)	10	20	30	67	141	215
Four Color 558,628,689('56)	6	12	18	38	69	100
Four Color 725,783,841,888,938,977,1032,1081,1131,1171,1222,1293('62)	5	10	15	33	57	80

ELMO COMICS
St. John Publishing Co.: Jan, 1948 (Daily strip-r)
1-By Cecil Jensen	15	30	45	90	140	190

ELONGATED MAN (See Flash #112 & Justice League of America #105)
DC Comics: Jan, 1992 - No. 4, Apr, 1992 ($1.00, limited series)
1-4: 3-The Flash app. ... 4.00

ELRIC (Of Melnibone)(See First Comics Graphic Novel #6 & Marvel Graphic Novel #2)
Pacific Comics: Apr, 1983 - No. 6, Apr, 1984 ($1.50, Baxter paper)
1-6: Russell-c/a(i) in all ... 4.00

ELRIC
Topps Comics: 1996 ($2.95, one-shot)
0-One Life: Russell-c/a; adapts Neil Gaiman's short story "One Life--Furnished
in Early Moorock." ... 4.00

ELRIC, SAILOR ON THE SEAS OF FATE
First Comics: June, 1985 - No. 7, June, 1986 ($1.75, limited series)
1-7: Adapts Michael Moorcock's novel ... 4.00

ELRIC, STORMBRINGER

Dark Horse Comics/Topps Comics: 1997 - No. 7, 1997 ($2.95, limited series)
1-7: Russell-c/s/a; adapts Michael Moorcock's novel ... 4.00

ELRIC: THE BALANCE LOST
BOOM! Studios: Jul, 2011 - No. 12, Jun, 2012 ($3.99)
1-12: 1-Roberson-s/Biagini-a; four covers. 2-11-Three covers ... 4.00

ELRIC: THE BANE OF THE BLACK SWORD
First Comics: Aug, 1988 - No. 6, June, 1989 ($1.75/$1.95, limited series)
1-6: Adapts Michael Moorcock's novel ... 4.00

ELRIC: THE DREAMING CITY
Titan Comics: Sept, 2021 - No. 2, Oct, 2021 ($3.99, limited series)
1,2: Adapts Michael Moorcock's novel ... 4.00

ELRIC: THE VANISHING TOWER
First Comics: Aug, 1987 - No. 6, June, 1988 ($1.75, limited series)
1-6: Adapts Michael Moorcock's novel ... 4.00

ELRIC: WEIRD OF THE WHITE WOLF
First Comics: Oct, 1986 - No. 5, June, 1987 ($1.75, limited series)
1-5: Adapts Michael Moorcock's novel ... 4.00

EL SALVADOR - A HOUSE DIVIDED
Eclipse Comics: March, 1989 ($2.50, B&W, Baxter paper, stiff-c, 52 pgs.)
1-Gives history of El Salvador ... 4.00

ELSEWHERE
Image Comics: Aug, 2017 - No. 8, Jul, 2018 ($3.99)
1-8: 1-Jay Faerber-s/Sumeyye Kesgin-a; Amelia Earhart & DB Cooper app. ... 4.00

ELSEWHERE PRINCE, THE (Moebius' Airtight Garage)
Marvel Comics (Epic): May, 1990 - No. 6, Oct, 1990 ($1.95, limited series)
1-6: Moebius scripts & back-up-a in all ... 4.00

ELSEWORLDS 80-PAGE GIANT (See DC Comics Presents: ... for reprint)
DC Comics: Aug, 1999 ($5.95, one-shot)
1-Most copies destroyed by DC over content of the "Superman's Babysitter" story; some UK
shipments sold before recall ... 13 26 39 86 188 290

ELSEWORLD'S FINEST
DC Comics: 1997 - No. 2, 1997 ($4.95, limited series)
1,2: Elseworld's story-Superman & Batman in the 1920's ... 5.00

ELSEWORLD'S FINEST: SUPERGIRL & BATGIRL
DC Comics: 1998 ($5.95, one-shot)
1-Haley-a ... 1 3 4 6 8 10

ELSIE THE COW
D. S. Publishing Co.: Oct-Nov, 1949 - No. 3, July-Aug, 1950
1-(36 pgs.)	36	72	108	211	343	475
2,3	24	48	72	142	234	325

ELSON'S PRESENTS
DC Comics: 1981 (100 pgs., no cover price)
Series 1-6: Repackaged 1981 DC comics; 1-DC Comics Presents #29, Flash #303, Batman
#331. 2-Superman #335, Ghosts #96, Justice League of America #186. 3-New Teen Titans
#3, Secrets of Haunted House #32, Wonder Woman #275. 4-Secrets of the LSH #1,
Brave & the Bold #170, New Adv. of Superboy #13. 5-LSH #271, Green Lantern #136,
Super Friends #40. 6-Action #515, Mystery in Space #115, Detective #498
... 2 4 6 11 16 20

ELTINGVILLE CLUB, THE (Characters from Dork)
Dark Horse Comics: Apr, 2014 - No. 2, Aug, 2015 ($3.99, B&W, limited series)
1,2-Evan Dorkin-s/a ... 4.00
HC-(2/16, $19.99) Reprints #1,2 and stories from Dork, Instant Piano, DHP ... 20.00

ELVEN (Also see Prime)
Malibu Comics (Ultraverse): Oct, 1994 - No. 4, Feb, 1995 ($2.50, lim. series)
0 ($2.95)-Prime app. ... 4.00
1-4: 2,4-Prime app. 3-Primevil app. ... 4.00
1-Limited Foil Edition- no price on cover ... 5.00

ELVIRA IN HORRORLAND
Dynamite Entertainment: 2022 - No. 5, 2022 ($3.99, limited series)
1-5-Avallone-s/Califano-a; multiple covers. 1-Elvira in Bates Motel ... 4.00

ELVIRA IN MONSTERLAND
Dynamite Entertainment: 2023 - No. 5, 2023 ($3.99, limited series)
1-5-Avallone-s/Baal-a; multiple covers; multiverse of Draculas app. 4-Godzilla app. ... 4.00

	GD 2.0	VG 4.0	FN 6.0	VF 8.0	VF/NM 9.0	NM- 9.2

ELVIRA MEETS VINCENT PRICE
Dynamite Entertainment: 2021 - No. 5, 2022 ($3.99, limited series)

| 1-5-Avallone-s/Samu-a; multiple covers | | | | | | 4.00 |

ELVIRA MISTRESS OF THE DARK
Marvel Comics: Oct, 1988 ($2.00, B&W, magazine size)

| 1-Movie adaptation | 3 | 6 | 9 | 19 | 30 | 40 |

ELVIRA MISTRESS OF THE DARK
Claypool Comics (Eclipse): May, 1993 - No. 166, Feb, 2007 ($2.50, B&W)

1-Austin-a(i). Spiegle-a	2	4	6	9	12	15
2-6: Spiegle-a						5.00
7-99,101-166-Photo-c						4.00
100-(8/01) Kurt Busiek back-ups; art by DeCarlo and others						4.00
TPB ($12.95)						13.00

ELVIRA MISTRESS OF THE DARK
Dynamite Entertainment: 2018 - No. 12, 2020 ($3.99)

| 1-12: 1-Avallone-s/Acosta-a; multiple covers; Mary Wollstonecraft app. 2-E.A. Poe app. | | | | | | 4.00 |
| ... Spring Special One-Shot (2019, $4.99) Ruiz & Parent-s/a | | | | | | 5.00 |

ELVIRA'S HOUSE OF MYSTERY
DC Comics: Jan, 1986 - No. 11, Jan, 1987

| 1,11: 11-Dave Stevens-c | 3 | 6 | 9 | 19 | 30 | 40 |
| 2-10: 9-Photo-c, Special 1 (3/87, $1.25) | 1 | 2 | 3 | 5 | 6 | 8 |

ELVIRA THE SHAPE OF ELVIRA
Dynamite Entertainment: 2019 - No. 4, 2019 ($3.99, limited series)

| 1-4: 1-3-Avallone-s/Strukan-a; multiple covers. 4-Qualano-a | | | | | | 4.00 |

ELVIS MANDIBLE, THE
DC Comics (Piranha Press): 1990 ($3.50, 52 pgs., B&W, mature)

| nn | | | | | | 4.00 |

ELVIS PRESLEY (See Career Girl Romances #32, Go-Go, Howard Chaykin's American Flagg #10, Humbug #8, I Love You #60 & Young Lovers #18)

EL ZOMBO FANTASMA
Dark Horse Comics (Rocket Comics): Apr, 2004 - No. 3, June, 2004 ($2.99)

| 1-3-Wilkins-s&a/Munroe-s | | | | | | 3.00 |

E-MAN
Charlton Comics: Oct, 1973 - No. 10, Sept, 1975 (Painted-c No. 7-10)

1-Origin & 1st app. E-Man; Staton-c/a in all	6	9	17	25	34	
2-5: 2,4,5-Ditko-a. 3-Howard-a. 5-Miss Liberty Belle app. by Ditko		2	4	6	9	12	15
6-10: 6,7,9,10-Early Byrne-a (#6 is 1/75). 6-Disney parody. 8-Full-length story; Nova begins as E-Man's partner		2	4	6	11	16	20
1-4,9,10 (Modern Comics reprints, '77)						5.00

NOTE: Killjoy app.-No. 2, 4. Liberty Belle app.-No. 5. Rog 2000 app.-No. 6, 7, 9, 10. Travis app.-No. 3. Sutton a-1.

E-MAN
Comico: Sept, 1989 ($2.75, one-shot, no ads, high quality paper)

| 1-Staton-c/a; Michael Mauser story | | | | | | 4.00 |

E-MAN
Comico: V4#1, Jan, 1990 - No. 3, Mar, 1990 ($2.50, limited series)

| 1-3: Staton-c/a | | | | | | 4.00 |

E-MAN
Alpha Productions: Oct, 1993 ($2.75)

| V5#1-Staton-c/a; 20th anniversary issue | | | | | | 4.00 |

E-MAN COMICS (Also see Michael Mauser & The Original E-Man)
First Comics: Apr, 1983 - No. 25, Aug, 1985 ($1.00/$1.25, direct sales only)

| 1-25: 2-X-Men satire. 3-X-Men/Phoenix satire. 6-Origin retold. 8-Cutey Bunny app. 10-Origin Nova Kane. 24-Origin Michael Mauser | | | | | | 4.00 |

NOTE: Staton a-1-5, 6-25p; c-1-25.

E-MAN RETURNS
Alpha Productions: 1994 ($2.75, B&W)

| 1-Joe Staton-c/a(p) | | | | | | 4.00 |

EMERALD CITY OF OZ, THE (Dorothy Gale from Wonderful Wizard of Oz)
Marvel Comics: Sept, 2013 - No. 5, Feb, 2014 ($3.99, limited series)

| 1-5-Eric Shanower-s/Skottie Young-a/c | | | | | | 4.00 |

EMERALD DAWN
DC Comics: 1991 ($4.95, trade paperback)

| nn-Reprints Green Lantern: Emerald Dawn #1-6 | 1 | 2 | 3 | 5 | 6 | 8 |

EMERALD DAWN II (See Green Lantern...)

EMERGENCY (Magazine)
Charlton Comics: Jul, 1976 - No. 4, Jan, 1977 (B&W)

1-Neal Adams-c/a; Heath, Austin-a	4	8	12	28	47	65
2,3: 2-N. Adams-c. 3-N. Adams-a	3	6	9	19	30	40
4-Alcala-a	3	6	9	15	22	28

EMERGENCY (TV)
Charlton Comics: Jun, 1976 - No. 4, Dec, 1976

| 1-Staton-c; early Byrne-a (22 pages) | 4 | 8 | 12 | 27 | 44 | 60 |
| 2-4: 2-Staton-c. 2,3-Byrne text illos. | 3 | 6 | 9 | 15 | 22 | 28 |

EMERGENCY DOCTOR
Charlton Comics: Summer, 1963 (one-shot)

| 1 | 4 | 8 | 12 | 23 | 37 | 50 |

EMIL & THE DETECTIVES (See Movie Comics)

EMISSARY (Jim Valentino's...)
Image Comics (Shadowline): May, 2006 - No. 6 ($3.50)

| 1-6: 1-Rand-s/Ferreyra-a. 4-6-Long-s | | | | | | 3.50 |

EMMA (Adaptation of the Jane Austen novel)
Marvel Comics: May, 2011 - No. 5, Sept, 2011 ($3.99)

| 1-5-Nancy Butler-s/Janet K. Lee-a | | | | | | 4.00 |

EMMA FROST
Marvel Comics: Aug, 2003 - No. 18, Feb, 2005 ($2.50/$2.99)

1-7-Emma in high school; Bollers-s/Green-a/Horn-c						3.00
8-18-($2.99)						3.00
... Vol. 1: Higher Learning TPB (2004, $7.99, digest size) r/#1-6						8.00
... Vol. 2: Mind Games TPB (2005, $7.99, digest size) r/#7-12						8.00
... Vol. 3: Bloom TPB (2005, $7.99, digest size) r/#13-18						8.00

EMMA PEEL & JOHN STEED (See The Avengers)

EMPEROR'S NEW CLOTHES, THE
Dell Publishing Co.: 1950 (10¢, 68 pgs., 1/2 size, oblong)

| nn - (Surprise Books series) | 7 | 14 | 21 | 37 | 46 | 55 |

EMPIRE
Image Comics (Gorilla): May, 2000 - No. 2, Sept, 2000 ($2.50)
DC Comics: Aug, 2003; Sept, 2003 - No. 6, Feb, 2004 ($4.95/$2.50, limited series)

1,2: 1 (5/00)-Waid-s/Kitson-a; w/Crimson Plague prologue						3.00
0-(8/03) reprints #1,2						5.00
1-6: 1-(9/03) new Waid-s/Kitson-a/c						3.00
TPB (DC, 2004, $14.95) r/series; Kitson sketch pages; Waid intro.						15.00

EMPIRE OF THE DEAD: ACT ONE (George Romero's...)
Marvel Comics: Mar, 2014 - No. 5, Aug, 2014 ($3.99)

| 1-5-George Romero-s/Alex Maleev-a/c; zombies & vampires | | | | | | 4.00 |

EMPIRE OF THE DEAD: ACT TWO (George Romero's...)
Marvel Comics: Nov, 2014 - No. 5, Mar, 2015 ($3.99)

| 1-5-George Romero-s/Dalibor Talajic-a; zombies & vampires | | | | | | 4.00 |

EMPIRE OF THE DEAD: ACT THREE (George Romero's...)
Marvel Comics: Jun, 2015 - No. 5, Nov, 2015 ($3.99)

| 1-5-George Romero-s/Andrea Mutti-a; zombies & vampires | | | | | | 4.00 |

EMPIRE STRIKES BACK, THE (See Marvel Comics Super Special #16 & Marvel Special Edition)

EMPIRE: UPRISING
IDW Publishing: Apr, 2015 - No. 4, Jul, 2015 ($3.99)

| 1-4: Sequel to the 2003-2004 series; Waid-s/Kitson-a; two covers on each | | | | | | 4.00 |

EMPRESS
Marvel Comics (Icon): Jun, 2016 - No. 7, Jan, 2017 ($3.99/$5.99)

| 1-6-Millar-s/Immonen-a | | | | | | 4.00 |
| 7-($5.99) | | | | | | 6.00 |

EMPTY, THE
Image Comics: Feb, 2015 - No. 6, Sept, 2015 ($3.50/$3.99)

| 1-3-Jimmie Robinson-s/a | | | | | | 3.50 |
| 4-6-($3.99) | | | | | | 4.00 |

EMPTY LOVE STORIES
Slave Labor #1 & 2/Funny Valentine Press: Nov, 1994 - No. 2 ($2.95, B&W)

1,2: Steve Darnall scripts in all. 1-Alex Ross-c. 2-(8/96)-Mike Allred-c						5.00
1,2-2nd printing (Funny Valentine Press)						4.00
... 1999-Jeff Smith-c; Doran-a						4.00
..."Special" (2.95) Ty Templeton-c						4.00

EMPTY ZONE
Image Comics: Jun, 2015 - No. 10, Jul, 2016 ($3.50/$3.99)

| 1-8-Jason Shawn Alexander-s/a | | | | | | 3.50 |
| 9,10-($3.99) | | | | | | 4.00 |

EMPYRE (Also see Road to Empyre)
Marvel Comics: Sept, 2020 - No. 6 ($5.99/$4.99, weekly limited series)

1-($5.99) Ewing & Slott-s/Schiti-a; multiple covers; Fantastic Four & the Avengers app.						6.00
2-5-($4.99) 2-Carol Danvers gains the Accuser hammer. 3-Black Panther app.						5.00
6-($5.99) Ewing & Slott-s/Schiti-a; FF, Avengers, Spider-Man, Wolverine app.						6.00
...: Aftermath Avengers #1 (11/20, $4.99) Wedding of Hulkling and Wiccan						5.00
...: Fallout Fantastic Four #1 (11/20, $3.99) Slott-s/Izaakse-a; Uatu returns						5.00
...: Fantastic Four #0 (6/20, $4.99) Slott-s/Silva-a; leads into Empyre #1; The Profiteer app.						5.00
...: Handbook 1 (6/20, $4.99) Profile pages of participants, teams, alien races						5.00
...: Savage Avengers 1 (9/20, $4.99) Duggan-s/Smallwood-a; Conan & Venom app.						5.00

EMPYRE: AVENGERS
Marvel Comics: No. 0, Jul, 2020; Sept, 2020 - No. 3 Oct, 2020 ($4.99/$3.99 limited series)

| 0-($4.99) Ewing-s/Larraz-a | | | | | | 5.00 |
| 1-3-($3.99) Zub-s/Magno-a; Avengers & Ka-Zar app. | | | | | | 4.00 |

EMPYRE: CAPTAIN AMERICA
Marvel Comics: Sept, 2020 - No. 3, Oct, 2020 ($3.99 limited series)

| 1-3-P.K. Johnson-s/Olivetti-a | | | | | | 4.00 |

EMPYRE: X-MEN
Marvel Comics: Sept, 2020 - No. 4, Oct, 2020 ($4.99 limited series)

| 1-4: 1-Hickman & Howard-s/Buffagni-a. 2-Werneck-a; Hordeculture app. | | | | | | 5.00 |

ENCHANTED APPLES OF OZ, THE (See First Comics Graphic Novel #5)

ENCHANTED TIKI ROOM
Marvel Comics (Disney Kingdoms): Dec, 2016 - No. 5, Apr, 2017 ($3.99)

| 1-5-Jon Adams-s/Horacio Domingues-a | | | | | | 4.00 |

ENCHANTER
Eclipse Comics: Apr, 1987 - No. 3, Aug. 1987 ($2.00, B&W, limited series)

| 1-3 | | | | | | 4.00 |

ENCHANTING LOVE
Kirby Publishing Co.: Oct, 1949 - No. 6, July, 1950 (All 52 pgs.)

1-Photo-c	27	54	81	158	259	360
2-Photo-c; Powell-a	16	32	48	92	144	195
3,4,6: 3-Jimmy Stewart photo-c. 4-Photo-c	15	30	45	88	137	185
5-Ingels-a, 9 pgs.; photo-c	22	44	66	128	209	290

E-Man #8 © CC

Empyre #4 © MAR

Equilibrium #1 © Miramax

ER

	GD 2.0	VG 4.0	FN 6.0	VF 8.0	VF/NM 9.0	NM- 9.2

ENCHANTMENT VISUALETTES (Magazine) **World Editions:** Dec, 1949 - No. 5, Apr, 1950 (Painted c-1)

1-Contains two romance comic strips each	30	60	90	177	289	400
2	20	40	60	117	189	260
3-5	18	36	54	103	162	220

ENDER IN EXILE (Orson Scott Card's...)
Marvel Comics: Aug, 2010 - No. 5, Dec, 2010 ($3.99, limited series)
1-5-Sequel to Ender's Game; Johnston-s/Mhan-a/Fiumara-c 4.00

ENDER'S GAME: BATTLE SCHOOL
Marvel Comics: Dec, 2008 - No. 5, Jun, 2009 ($3.99, limited series)
1-5-Adaptation of Orson Scott Card novel Ender's Game; Yost-s/Ferry-a. 1-Two covers 4.00
Ender's Game: Mazer in Prison Special (4/10, $3.99) Johnston-s/Mhan-a 4.00
Ender's Game: Recruiting Valentine (8/09, $3.99) Timothy Green-a 4.00
Ender's Game: The League War (6/10, $3.99) Aaron Johnston-s/Timothy Green-a 4.00
Ender's Game: War of Gifts Special (2/10, $4.99) Timothy Green-a 5.00

ENDER'S GAME: COMMAND SCHOOL
Marvel Comics: Nov, 2009 - No. 5, Apr, 2010 ($3.99, limited series)
1-5-Adaptation of Orson Scott Card novel Ender's Game; Yost-s/Ferry-a 4.00

ENDER'S SHADOW: BATTLE SCHOOL
Marvel Comics: Feb, 2009 - No. 5, Jun, 2009 ($3.99, limited series)
1-5-Adaptation of O.S. Card novel Ender's Shadow; Carey-s/Fiumara-a. 1-Two covers 4.00

ENDER'S SHADOW: COMMAND SCHOOL
Marvel Comics: Nov, 2009 - No. 5, Apr, 2010 ($3.99, limited series)
1-5-Adaptation of O.S. Card novel Ender's Shadow; Carey-s/Fiumara-a 4.00

END LEAGUE, THE
Dark Horse Comics: Dec, 2007 - No. 9, Nov, 2009 ($2.99/$3.99)
1-8: 1-Broome-c/a; Remender-s. 5,6-Canete-a 3.00
9-($3.99) MacDonald-a/Canete-c 4.00

END OF NATIONS
DC Comics: Jan, 2012 - No. 4, Apr, 2012 ($2.99, limited series)
1-4-Based on the Trion Worlds videogame; Sanchez-s/Guichet-a/Sprouse-c 3.00

END TIMES OF BRAM AND BEN
Image Comics: Jan, 2013 - No. 4, Apr, 2013 ($2.99, limited series)
1-4: 1-Rapture parody; Asmus & Festante-s/Broo-a. 1-Mahfood-c 3.00

ENEMY ACE SPECIAL (Also see Our Army at War #151, Showcase #57, 58 & Star Spangled War Stories #138)
DC Comics: 1990 ($1.00, one-shot)
1-Kubert-r/Our Army #151,153; c-r/Showcase 57 .... 5.00

ENEMY ACE: WAR IDYLL
DC Comics: 1990 (Graphic novel)
Hardcover-George Pratt-s/painted-a/c 30.00
Softcover (1991, $14.95) 15.00

ENEMY ACE: WAR IN HEAVEN
DC Comics: 2001 - No. 2, 2001 ($5.95, squarebound, limited series)
1,2-Ennis-s; Von Hammer in WW2. 1-Weston & Alamy-a. 2-Heath-a 6.00
TPB (2003, $14.95) r/#1,2 & Star Spangled War Stories #139; Jim Dietz-painted-c 15.00

ENFIELD GANG MASSACRE, THE (That Texas Blood)
Image Comics: Aug, 2023 - No. 6, Jan, 2024 ($3.99, limited series)
1-6-Chris Condon-s/Jacob Phillips-a; six covers form one image 4.00

ENGINEHEAD
DC Comics: June, 2004 - No. 6, Nov, 2004 ($2.50, limited series)
1-6-Joe Kelly-s/Ted McKeever-a/c. 6-Metal Men app. 3.00

ENIAC
Bad Idea: Mar, 2021 - No. 4, Jun, 2021 ($3.99, limited series)

1-Kindt-s/Braithwaite-a; first printing with white logo	3	6	9	16	23	30
1-Not First Printing edition with dark title logo						4.00
2-4-Kindt-s/Braithwaite-a in all						4.00

ENIGMA
DC Comics (Vertigo): Mar, 1993 - No. 8, Oct, 1993 ($2.50, limited series)
1-8: Milligan scripts 4.00
Trade paperback ($19.95)-reprints 20.00

ENO AND PLUM (Also see Cud Comics)
Oni Press: Mar, 1998 ($2.95, B&W)
1-Terry LaBan-s/c/a 4.00

ENSIGN O'TOOLE (TV)
Dell Publishing Co.: Aug-Oct, 1963

1	4	8	12	23	37	50

ENSIGN PULVER (See Movie Classics)

ENTER: THE COMICS (Victorian Age content, see Victorian section for other Töpffer works)
University of Nebraska Press: 1965 (6-7/8 x 9-1/4", 120 pgs, hard-c)

nn - By Ellen Weisse	6	12	18	38	69	100

NOTE: Contains overview of Töpffer's life and career plus only published English translation of Töpffer's Monsieur Crepin (1837); appears to have been re-drawn by Weisse in the days before xerox machines.

ENTER THE HEROIC AGE
Marvel Comics: July, 2010 ($3.99, one-shot)
1-Short stories of Avengers Academy, Atlas, Black Widow, Thunderbolts; Hitch-c 4.00

ENTER THE HOUSE OF SLAUGHTER
BOOM! Studios: Aug, 2021 (Free Comic Book Day giveaway)
nn - Previews House of Slaughter series; Tynion IV & Brombal-s/Shehan-a 3.00

EPIC
Marvel Comics (Epic Comics): 1992 - Book 4, 1992 ($4.95, lim. series, 52 pgs.)
Book One-Four: 2-Dorman painted-c 5.00
NOTE: Alien Legion in #3. Cholly & Flytrap by Burden(scripts) & Suydam(art) in 3, 4. Dinosaurs in #4. Dreadlands in #1. Heliraiser in #1. Nightbreed in #2. Sleeze Brothers in #2. Stalkers in #1-4. Wild Cards in #1-4.

EPIC ANTHOLOGY
Marvel Comics (Epic Comics): Apr, 2004 ($5.99)
1-Short stories by various; debut 2nd Sleepwalker by Kirkman-s 6.00

EPIC ILLUSTRATED (Magazine)
Marvel Comics Group: Spring, 1980 - No. 34, Feb, 1986 ($2.00/$2.50, B&W/color, mature)

1-Frazetta-c; Silver Surfer/Galactus-sty; Wendy Pini-s/a; Suydam-s/a; Metamorphosis Odyssey begins (thru #9) Starlin-a	4	8	12	27	44	60
2,4-10: 2-Bissette/Veitch-a. 4-Ellison 15 pg. story w/Steacy-a; Hempel-s/a; Veitch-s/a. 5-Hildebrandts-c/interview; Jusko-a; Vess-s/a. 6-Ellison-s (26 pgs.) 7-Adams-s/a(16 pgs.). BWS interview. 8-Suydam-s/a. 9-Conrad-c. 10-Marada the She-Wolf-s/sty(21 pgs.) by Claremont/Bolton	2	4	6	8	11	14
3-1st app. Dreadstar (face apps. in 1 panel in #2)	5	10	15	33	57	80
11-20: 11-Wood-a; Jusko-a. 12-Wolverton Spacehawk-r edited & recolored w/article on him; Muth-a. 13-Blade Runner preview by Williamson. 14-Elric of Melnibone by Russell; Revenge of the Jedi preview. 15-Vallejo-c & interview; 1st Dreadstar solo story (cont'd in Dreadstar #1). 16-B. Smith-c/a(2); Sim-s/a. 17-Starslammers preview. 18-Go Nagai; Williams-a. 19-Jabberwocky w/Hampton-a; Cheech Wizard-s. 20-The Sacred & the Profane begins by Ken Steacy; Elric by Gould; Williams-a	1	3	4	6	8	10
21-30: 21-Vess-s/a. 22-Frankenstein w/Wrightson-a. 26-Galactus series begins (thru #34); Cerebus the Aardvark story by Dave Sim. 27-Groo. 28-Cerebus. 29-1st Sheeva. 30-Cerebus; History of Dreadstar, Starlin-s/a; Williams-a; Vess-a	2	4	6	8	10	12
	2	4	6	8	11	14
31-33: 31-Bolton-c/a. 32-Cerebus portfolio.	2	4	6	8	11	14
34-R.E.Howard tribute by Thomas-s/Plunkett-a; Moore-s/Veitch-a; Cerebus; Cholly & Flytrap w/Suydam-a; BWS-a	3	6	9	14	19	24
Sampler (early 1980 8 pg. preview giveaway) same cover as #1 with "Sampler" text						6.00

NOTE: N. Adams a-7; c-6. Austin a-15-20i. Bode a-19, 23, 27r. Bolton a-7, 10-12, 15, 18, 22-25; c-10, 18, 22, 23. Boris a-2-9, 13. Brunner c-12. Buscema a-1p, 9p, 11-13p. Byrne/Austin a-26-34. Chaykin a-2-5, 7-9, 25-34; c-17. Corben a-15; c-2. Frazetta c-1. Golden a-3r. Gulacy c/a-3. Jeff Jones c-25. Kaluta a-17r, 21, 24r, 26; c-4, 28. Nebres a-1. Reese a-12. Russell a-2-4, 9, 14, 33; c-14. Simonson a-17. B. Smith c/a-7, 16. Starlin a-1-9, 14, 15, 34. Steranko c-19. Williamson a-13, 27, 34. Wrightson a-13p, 22, 25, 27, 34; c-20.

EPIC LITE
Marvel Comics (Epic Comics): Sept, 1991 ($3.95, 52 pgs., one-shot)
1-Bob the Alien, Normalman by Valentino 4.00

EPICURUS THE SAGE
DC Comics (Piranha Press): Vol. 1, 1991 - Vol. 2, 1991 ($9.95, 8-1/8x10-7/8")

Volume 1,2-Sam Kieth-c/a; Messner-Loebs-s	2	4	6	11	16	20
TPB (2003, $19.95) r/ #1,2, Fast Forward Rising the Sun; new story						20.00

EPILOGUE
IDW Publishing: Sept, 2008 - No. 4, Dec, 2008 ($3.99)
1-4-Steve Niles-s/Kyle Hotz-a/c 4.00

EQUILIBRIUM (Based on the 2002 movie)
American Mythology Prods.: 2016 - No. 3, 2017 ($3.99)
1-3-Pat Shand-s/Jason Craig-a; multiple covers 4.00
...: Deconstruction 1 (2017, $3.99) Moroney-s/Dela Cuesta-a 4.00
...: Gunkata Casebook 1 (2018, $3.99) Mell-s/Hilinski-a 4.00

ERADICATOR
DC Comics: Aug, 1996 - No. 3, Oct, 1996 ($1.75, limited series)
1-3: Superman app. 4.00

	GD	VG	FN	VF	VF/NM	NM-
	2.0	4.0	6.0	8.0	9.0	9.2

E-RATIC
AWA Studios: Dec, 2020 - No. 5, Apr, 2021 ($3.99, limited series)
1-5-Kaare Andrews-s/a/c. 1-Variant-c by Mike Deodato ... 4.00

E-RATIC: RECHARGED
AWA Studios: Sept, 2022 - No. 4, Feb, 2023 ($3.99, limited series)
1-4-Kaare Andrews-s/a/c. 1-Variant-c by Mike Deodato ... 4.00

ERNIE COMICS (Formerly Andy Comics #21; All Love Romances #26 on)
Current Books/Ace Periodicals: No. 22, Sept, 1948 - No. 25, Mar, 1949

| nn (9/48,11/48; #22,23)-Teenage humor | 20 | 40 | 60 | 114 | 182 | 250 |
| 24,25 | 15 | 30 | 45 | 85 | 130 | 175 |

EROS / PSYCHE
Ablaze Publishing: 2021 - No. 5, 2021 ($3.99, limited series)
1-5-Maria Llovet-s/a; multiple covers on each ... 4.00

ERRAND BOYS
Image Comics: Oct, 2018 - No. 5, Feb, 2019 ($3.99, limited series)
1-5-Kirkbridge-s/Koutsis-a ... 4.00

ESCAPADE IN FLORENCE (See Movie Comics)

ESCAPE FROM DEVIL'S ISLAND
Avon Periodicals: 1952

| 1-Kinstler-c; r/as Dynamic Adventures #9 | 52 | 104 | 156 | 328 | 552 | 775 |

ESCAPE FROM NEW YORK (Based on the Kurt Russell movie)
BOOM! Studios: Dec, 2014 - No. 16, Apr, 2016 ($3.99)
1-16: 1-8-Christopher Sebela-s/Diego Barreto-a; multiple covers on each. 9-16-Simic-a ... 4.00

ESCAPE FROM THE PLANET OF THE APES (See Power Record Comics)

ESCAPE TO WITCH MOUNTAIN (See Walt Disney Showcase No. 29)

ESCAPISTS, THE (See Michael Chabon Presents The Amazing Adventures of the Escapist)
Dark Horse Comics: July, 2006 - No. 6, Dec, 2006 ($1.00/$2.99, limited series)
1-($1.00) Frank Miller-c; r/Vaughan story from Michael Chabon... #8 ... 3.00
2-6($2.99) Vaughan-s/Rolston & Alexander-a. 2-James Jean-c. 3-Cassaday-c ... 3.00

ESPERS (Also see Interface)
Eclipse Comics: July, 1986 - No. 5, Apr, 1987 ($1.25/$1.75, Mando paper)
1-5-James Hudnall story & David Lloyd-a. ... 4.00

ESPERS
Halloween Comics: V2#1, 1996 - No. 6, 1997 ($2.95, B&W) (1st Halloween Comics series)
V2#1-6: James D. Hudnall scripts ... 4.00
Undertow TPB ('98, $14.95) r/#1-6 ... 15.00

ESPERS
Image Comics: V3#1, 1997 - No. 7, 1998 ($2.95, B&W, limited series)
V3#1-7: James D. Hudnall scripts ... 4.00
Black Magic TPB ('98, $14.95) r/#1-4 ... 15.00

ESPIONAGE (TV)
Dell Publishing Co.: May-July, 1964

| 1 | | 3 | 6 | 9 | 21 | 33 | 45 |

ESSENTIAL (Title series), **Marvel Comics**
--**ANT-MAN**, '02 (B&W- r) V1-Reprints app. from Tales To Astonish #27, #35-69; Kirby-c ... 15.00
--**AVENGERS**, '98 (B&W-r) V1-R-Avengers #1-24; new Immonen-c ... 15.00
  V2(6/00)-Reprints Avengers #25-46, King-Size Special #1; Immonen-c ... 15.00
  V3(3/01)-Reprints Avengers #47-68, Annual #2; Immonen-c ... 15.00
  V4('04)-Reprints Avengers #69-97, Incredible Hulk #140; Neal Adams-c ... 15.00
  V5('06)-Reprints Avengers #98-119, Daredevil #99, Defenders #8-11 ... 17.00
  V6('08)-Reprints Avengers #120-140, Giant Size #4, Capt. Marvel #33 & FF #150 ... 17.00
--**CAPTAIN AMERICA**, '00 (B&W- r) V1-Reprints stories from Tales of Suspense
  #59-99, Captain America #100-102; new Romita & Milgrom-c ... 15.00
  V2(1/02)-Reprints #103-126; Steranko-c ... 15.00
  V3('06)-Reprints #127-153 ... 17.00
  V4('07)-Reprints #157-186 ... 17.00
--**CLASSIC X-MEN**, '06 (B&W- r) (See Essential Uncanny X-Men for V1)
  V2-($16.99) R-X-Men #25-53 & Avengers #53; Gil Kane-c ... 17.00
--**CONAN**, '00 (B&W- r) V1-R-Conan the Barbarian#1-25; new Buscema-c ... 15.00
--**DAREDEVIL**, '02 - V4 (B&W-r)
  V1-Reprints Daredevil #1-25 ... 15.00
  V2-($16.99) R-Daredevil #26-48, Special #1, Fantastic Four #73 ... 17.00
  V3-($16.99) R-Daredevil #49-74, Iron Man #35-38 ... 17.00
  V4-($16.99) R-Daredevil #75-101, Avengers #111 ... 17.00
--**DAZZLER**, '07 (B&W- r) V1-R/#1-21, X-Men #130-131, Amaz. Spider-Man #203 ... 17.00
--**DEFENDERS**, '05 (B&W-r) V1-Reprints Doctor Strange #183, Sub-Mariner #22,34,35,
  Incredible Hulk #126, Marvel Feature #1-3, Defenders #1-14, Avengers #115-118 ... 17.00
  V2-($16.99) R- Defenders #15-30, Giant-Size Defenders #1-4, Marvel Two-In-One #6,7,
  Marvel Team-Up #33-35 and Marvel Treasury Edition #12 ... 17.00
  V3-($16.99) R- Defenders #31-60 and Annual #1 ... 17.00
--**DOCTOR STRANGE**, '04 - V3 (B&W-r)
  V1-($15.95) Reprints Strange Tales #110,111,114-168 ... 17.00
  V1 (2nd printing)-(2006, $16.99) Reprints Strange Tales #110,111,114-168 ... 17.00
  V2-($16.99) R-Doctor Strange #169-178,180-183; Avengers #61, Sub-Mariner #22,
  Marvel Feature #1, Incredible Hulk #126 and Marvel Premiere #3-14 ... 17.00
  V3-($16.99) R-Doctor Strange #1-29 & Annual #1;Tomb of Dracula #44,45 ... 17.00
--**FANTASTIC FOUR**, '98 - V6 (B&W-r)
  V1-Reprints FF #1-20, Annual #1; new Alan Davis-c; multiple printings exist ... 17.00
  V2-Reprints FF #21-40, Annual #2; Davis and Farmer-c ... 15.00
  V3-Reprints FF #41-63, Annual #3,4; Davis-c ... 15.00
  V4-Reprints FF #64-83, Annual #5,6 ... 17.00
  V5-Reprints FF #84-110 ... 17.00
  V6-Reprints FF #111-137 ... 17.00
--**GHOST RIDER**, '05 (B&W-r) V1-Reprints Marvel Spotlight #5-12, Ghost Rider #1-20 and

Daredevil #138 ... 17.00
  V2-Reprints Ghost Rider #21-50 ... 17.00
--**GODZILLA**, '06 (B&W-r) V1-Godzilla #1-24 ... 20.00
--**HOWARD THE DUCK**, '02 (B&W- r) V1-Reprints #1-27, Annual #1; plus stories from Marvel
  Treasury Ed. #12, Man-Thing #1, Giant-Size Man-Thing #4,5, Fear #19; Bolland-c ... 15.00
--**HULK**, '99 (B&W-r) V1-R-Incred. Hulk #1-6, Tales To Astonish stories; new Timm-c ... 15.00
  V2-Reprints Tales To Astonish #102-117, Annual #1 ... 15.00
  V3-Reprints Incredible Hulk #118-142, Capt. Marvel #20&21, Avengers #88 ... 17.00
  V4-Reprints Incredible Hulk #143-170 ... 17.00
  V5-Reprints Incredible Hulk #171-200, Annual #5 ... 17.00
--**HUMAN TORCH**, '03 (B&W-r) V1-Strange Tales #101-134 & Ann. 2; Kirby-c ... 15.00
--**IRON MAN**, '00 - V3 (B&W-r)
  V1-Reprints Tales Of Suspense #39-72; new Timm-c and back-c ... 15.00
  V2-Reprints Tales Of Suspense #73-99, Tales To Astonish #82 & Iron Man #1-11 ... 17.00
  V3-Reprints Iron Man #12-38 & Daredevil #73 ... 17.00
--**KILLRAVEN**, '05 (B&W-r) V1-Reprints Amazing Adventures V2 #18-39, Marvel Team-Up #45,
  Marvel Graphic Novel #7, Killraven #1 (2001) ... 17.00
--**LUKE CAGE, POWER MAN**, '05 (B&W-r) V1-Hero for Hire #1-16 & Power Man #17-27 ... 17.00
  V2-Reprints Power Man #28-49 & Annual #1 ... 17.00
--**MAN-THING**, '06 (B&W-r) V1-Reprints Savage Tales #1, Astonishing Tales #12-13,
  Adventure Into Fear #10-19, Man-Thing #1-14, Giant-Size Man-Thing #1-2 & Monsters
  Unleashed #5,8,9 ... 17.00
  V2-R/Man-Things #15-22 & #1-11 ('79 series), Giant-Size Man-Thing #3-5, Rampaging
  Hulk #7, Marvel Team-Up #68, Marvel Two-In-One #43 & Doctor Strange #41 ... 17.00
--**MARVEL HORROR**, '06 (B&W-r) V1-R/#Ghost Rider #1-2, Marvel Spotlight #12-24, Son of
  Satan #1-8, Marvel Two-In-One #14, Marvel Team-Up #32,80,81, Vampire Tales #2-3,
  Haunt of Horror #2,4,5, Marvel Premiere #27, & Marvel Preview #7 ... 17.00
--**MARVEL SAGA**, '08 (B&W-r) V1 ... 17.00
--**MARVEL TEAM-UP**, '02 - V2 (B&W-r) V1('02, '06)-R/#1-24 ... 17.00
  V2-R/#25-51 and Marvel Two-In-One #17 ... 17.00
--**MARVEL TWO-IN-ONE**, '05 - V2 (B&W-r)
  V1-Reprints Marvel Feature #11&12, Marvel Two-In-One #1-20,22-25 & Annual #1,
  Marvel Team-Up #47 and Fantastic Four Ann. #11 ... 17.00
  V2-R/#26-52 & Annual #2,3 ... 17.00
--**MONSTER OF FRANKENSTEIN**, '04 (B&W-r) V1-Reprints Monster of Frankenstein #1-5,
  Frankenstein Monster #6-18, Giant-Size Werewolf #2, Monsters Unleashed #2,4-10 &
  Legion of Monsters #1 ... 17.00
--**MOON KNIGHT**, '06 (B&W-r) V1-Reprints Moon Knight #1-10 and early apps. ... 17.00
  V2-R/#1-30 ... 17.00
--**MS. MARVEL**, '07 (B&W-r) V1-Reprints Ms. Marvel #1-23, Marvel Super-Heroes
  Magazine #10,11, and Avengers Annual #10 ... 17.00
--**NOVA**, '06 (B&W-r) V1-Reprints Nova #1-25, AS-M #171, Marvel Two-In-One Ann. #3 ... 17.00
--**OFFICIAL HANDBOOK OF THE MARVEL UNIVERSE**, '06 (B&W-r) V1-Reprints #1-15
  profiling Abomination through Zzzax; dead and inactive characters; weapons & hardware;
  wraparound-c by Byrne ... 17.00
--**OFFICIAL HANDBOOK OF THE MARVEL UNIVERSE - DELUXE EDITION**, '06 (B&W-r)
  V1-Reprints #1-7 profiling Abomination through Magneto; wraparound-c by Byrne ... 17.00
  V2-Reprints #8-14 profiling Magus through Wolverine; wraparound-c by Byrne ... 17.00
  V3-Reprints #15-20 profiling Wonder Man through Zzzax & Book of the Dead ... 17.00
--**OFFICIAL HANDBOOK OF THE MARVEL UNIVERSE - MASTER EDITION**, '08 (B&W-r)
  V1-Reprints profiling Abomination through Gargoyle ... 17.00
  V2-Reprints profiles ... 17.00
--**OFFICIAL HANDBOOK OF THE MARVEL UNIVERSE - UPDATE '89**, '06 (B&W-r)
  V1-Reprints #1-8; wraparound-c by Frenz ... 17.00
--**PETER PARKER, THE SPECTACULAR SPIDER-MAN**, '05 (B&W-r) V1-Reprints #1-31 ... 17.00
  V2-Reprints #32-53 & Annual #1,2; Amazing Spider-Man Annual #13 ... 17.00
  V3-Reprints #54-74 & Annual #3; Frank Miller-c ... 17.00
--**POWER MAN AND IRON FIST**, '07 (B&W-r) V1-R/#50-72,74-75 ... 17.00
--**PUNISHER**, '04, '06 - '12 (B&W-r) V1-Reprints early app. in Amazing Spider-Man,
  Captain America, Daredevil, Marvel Preview and Punisher #1-5 (2 printings) ... 17.00
  V2-Punisher #1-20, Annual #1 and Daredevil #257 ... 17.00
  V3-Punisher #21-40, Annual #2,3 ... 17.00
  V4-Punisher #41-59 ... 17.00
--**RAMPAGING HULK**, '08 (B&W-r) V1-R/#1-9, The Hulk! #10-15 & Incredible Hulk #269 ... 17.00
--**SAVAGE SHE-HULK**, '06 (B&W-r) V1-R/#1-25 ... 17.00
--**SILVER SURFER**, '98 - Present (B&W-r)
  V1-R-material from SS#1-18 and Fantastic Four Ann. #5 ... 15.00
  V2-R-SS#1(1982), SS#1-18 & Ann#1(1987), Epic Illustrated #1, Marvel Fanfare #51 ... 17.00
--**SPIDER-MAN**, '96 - V8 (B&W-r)
  V1-R-AF #15, Amaz. S-M #1-20, Ann. #1 (2 printings) ... 15.00
  V2-R-Amaz. Spider-Man #21-43, Annual #2,3 ... 15.00
  V3-R-Amaz. Spider-Man #44-68 ... 15.00
  V4-R-Amaz. Spider-Man #69-89; Annual #4,5; new Timm-f&b-c ... 15.00
  V5-R-Amaz. Spider-Man #90-113; new Romita-c ... 15.00
  V6-R-Amaz. Spider-Man #114-137, Giant-Size Super-Heroes #1 G-S S-M #1,2 ... 17.00
  V7-R-Amaz. Spider-Man #138-160, Annual #10; Giant-Size Spider-Man #3-5 ... 17.00
  V8-R-Amaz. Spider-Man #161-185, Annual #11; G-S Spider-Man #6; Nova #12 ... 17.00
--**SPIDER-WOMAN**, '05 (B&W-r) V1-Reprints Marvel Spotlight #32, Marvel Two-In-One #29-33,
  Spider-Woman #1-25 ... 17.00
  V2-R-Spider-Woman #26-50, Marvel Team-Up #97 & Uncanny X-Men #148 ... 17.00
--**SUPER-VILLAIN TEAM-UP**, '04 (B&W-r) V1-r/S-V T-U #1-14 & 16-17, Giant-Size S-V T-U #1,2;
  Avengers #154-156; Champions #16, & Astonishing Tales #1-8 ... 17.00
--**TALES OF THE ZOMBIE**, '06 (B&W-r) V1-($16.99) r/#1-10 & Dracula Lives #1,2 ... 17.00
--**THOR**, '01 (B&W-r) V1-R-Journey Into Mystery #83-112 ... 15.00
  V2-($16.99) R-Thor #113-136 & Annual #1,2 ... 17.00
  V3-($16.99) R-Thor #137-166 ... 17.00

Eros/Psyche #4 © Maria Llovet

EROS/PSYCHE

Eternals (2021 series) #2 © MAR

ETERNALS

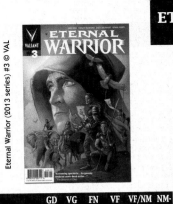

Eternal Warrior (2013 series) #3 © VAL

ETERNAL WARRIOR

	GD	VG	FN	VF	VF/NM	NM-
	2.0	4.0	6.0	8.0	9.0	9.2

--TOMB OF DRACULA, '03 - V4 (B&W-r) V1-R-Tomb of Dracula #1-25,
Werewolf By Night #15, Giant-Size Chillers #1 .... 15.00
   V2-($16.99) R-Tomb of Dracula #26-49, Giant-Size Dracula #2-5, Dr. Strange #14 ... 17.00
   V3-($16.99) R-Tomb of Dracula #50-70, Tomb of Dracula Magazine #1-4 ... 17.00
   V4-($16.99) R/Stories from Tomb of Dracula Magazine #2-6, Dracula Lives! #1-13, and
   Frankenstein Monster #7-9 .... 17.00
--UNCANNY X-MEN, '99 (B&W reprints) (See Essential Classic X-Men for V2)
   V1-Reprints X-Men (1st series) #1-24; Timm-c 15.00
ESSENTIAL VERTIGO: SWAMP THING
DC Comics: Nov, 1996 - No. 24, Oct, 1998 ($1.95/$2.25,B&W, reprints)
   1-11,13-24: 1-9-Reprints Alan Moore's Swamp Thing stories 4.00
   12-($3.50) r/Annual #2 .... 5.00
ESSENTIAL VERTIGO: THE SANDMAN
DC Comics (Vertigo): Aug, 1996 - No. 32, Mar, 1999 ($1.95/$2.25, reprints)
   1-13,15-31: Reprints Sandman, 2nd series 4.00
   14-($2.95) 4.00
   32-($4.50) Reprints Sandman Special #1 .... 4.50
ESSENTIAL WEREWOLF BY NIGHT
Marvel Comics: 2005 - V2 (B&W reprints)
   V1-($16.99) r/Marvel Spotlight #2-4, Werewolf By Night 1-23, Marvel Team-Up #12, Tomb of
   Dracula #18, Giant-Size Creatures #1 .... 17.00
   V2-R/#22-43, Giant-Size Werewolf #2-5 and Marvel Premiere #28 ... 17.00
ESSENTIAL WOLVERINE
Marvel Comics: 1999 - V4 (B&W reprints)
   V1-r/#1-23, V2-r/#24-47, V3-R/#48-69, V4-R/#70-90 .... 17.00
ESSENTIAL X-FACTOR
Marvel Comics: 2005 - V2 (B&W reprints)
   V1-($16.99) r/X-Factor #1-16 & Annual #1, Avengers #262, Fantastic Four #286,
   Thor #373&374 and Power Pack #27 .... 17.00
   V2-Reprints X-Factor #17-35 & Annual #2, Thor #378 .... 17.00
ESSENTIAL X-MEN
Marvel Comics: 1996 - V8 (B&W reprints)
   V1-V4: V1-R/Giant Size X-Men #1, X-Men #94-119. V2-R-X-Men #120-144. V3-R-Uncanny
   X-Men #145-161, Ann. #3-5. V4-Uncanny X-Men #162-179, Ann. #6 ... 15.00
   V5-($16.99) R/Uncanny X-Men #180-198, Ann. #7-8 .... 17.00
   V6-($16.99) R/Uncanny X-Men #199-213, Ann. #9, New Mutants Special Edition #1,
   X-Factor #9-11, New Mutants #46, Thor #373-374 and Power Pack #27 ... 17.00
   V7-($16.99) R/Uncanny X-Men #214-228, Ann. #10,11, and F.F. vs. The X-Men #1-4 ... 17.00
   V8-($16.99) R/Uncanny X-Men #229-243, Ann. #12 & X-Factor #36-39 ... 17.00
ESTABLISHMENT, THE (Also see The Authority and The Monarchy)
DC Comics (WildStorm): Nov, 2001 - No. 13, Nov, 2002 ($2.50)
   1-13-Edginton-s/Adlard-a 3.00
ET-ER (Extraterrestrial Emergency Room)
AWA Studios: Oct, 2021; Jun, 2022 ($3.99)
   1,2: 1-McComsey-s/Pulido-a; Panosian-c/Crystal-a. 2-Cho-c ... 4.00
ETERNAL
BOOM! Studios: Dec, 2014 - No. 4, Apr, 2015 ($3.99)
   1-4: 1-Harms-s/Valletta-a/Irving-c 4.00
ETERNAL, THE (MAX)
Marvel Comics (MAX): Aug, 2003 - No. 6, Jan, 2004 ($2.99, mature)
   1-6-Austen-s/Walker-a 3.00
ETERNAL BIBLE, THE
Authentic Publications: 1946 (Large size) (16 pgs. in color)

1		16	32	48	94	147	200

ETERNAL EMPIRE
Image Comics: May, 2017 - No. 10, Aug, 2018 ($3.99)
   1-9-Sarah Vaughn & Jonathan Luna-s/Luna-a/c 4.00
   10-($4.99) Conclusion 5.00
ETERNALS, THE
Marvel Comics Group: July, 1976 - No. 19, Jan, 1978

	GD	VG	FN	VF	VF/NM	NM-
1-(Regular 25¢ edition)-Origin & 1st app. Ikaris & The Eternals	6	12	18	41	76	110
1-(30¢-c variant, limited distribution)	15	30	45	103	227	350
2-Reg. 25¢ edition)-1st app. Ajak & The Celestials	4	8	12	28	47	65
2-(30¢-c variant, limited distribution)	10	20	30	69	147	225

   3-19: 3-1st app. Sersi. 5-1st app. Makarri, Domo, Zuras, & Thena. 11-1st app. Kingo.

	GD	VG	FN	VF	VF/NM	NM-
14,15-Cosmic powered Hulk-c/story	3	6	9	14	19	24
12-16-(35¢-c variants, limited distribution)	9	18	27	61	123	185
Annual 1(10/77)	3	6	9	14	20	25

   ... No. 1 Facsimile Edition (2/20, $3.99) Reprints #1 with original 1976 ads 4.00
   ...: Secrets From the Marvel Universe 1 (2/20, $4.99) Reprints from What If? #23-30 ... 5.00
   Eternals by Jack Kirby HC (2006, $75.00, dust jacket) r/#1-19 & Annual #1; intro by Royer;
   letter pages from #1,2,Annual #1; afterwords by Robert Greenberger ... 75.00
NOTE: *Kirby c/a(p) in all.*
ETERNALS, THE
Marvel Comics: Oct, 1985 - No. 12, Sept, 1986 (Maxi-series, mando paper)
   1,12 (52 pgs.): 12-Williamson-a(i) 5.00
   2-11 .... 4.00
ETERNALS
Marvel Comics: Aug, 2006 - No. 7, Mar, 2007 ($3.99, limited series)
   1-7-Neil Gaiman-s/John Romita Jr.-a/Rick Berry-c 4.00
   1-7-Variant covers by Romita Jr. 4.00
   1-Variant cover by Coipel 4.00
   ... Sketchbook (2006, $1.99, B&W) character sketches and sketch pages from #1 ... 4.00
   HC (2007, $29.99, dustjacket) r/#1-7; gallery of variant covers; sketches, Gaiman interview,
   Gaiman's original proposal; background essay on Kirby's Eternals ... 30.00
ETERNALS
Marvel Comics: Aug, 2008 - No. 9, May, 2009 ($2.99)
   1-9: 1-6-Acuña-a; Knauf-s. 7,8-Nguyen-a. 7,9-Iron Man app. ... 3.00
   Annual 1 (1/09, $3.99) Alixe-a/McGuinness-a; & reprint from Eternals #7 ('77) Kirby-s/a ... 4.00
ETERNALS
Marvel Comics: Mar, 2021 - No. 12, Jul, 2022 ($4.99/$3.99)
   1-($4.99) Kieron Gillen-s/Esad Ribic-a; Ikaris returns; Iron Man & Thanos app. ... 5.00
   2-12-($3.99) 2-Ikaris battles Thanos. 5-12-Thanos app. 11-Vilanova-a ... 4.00
   ...: Celestia 1 (12/21, $3.99) Gillen-s/Zama-a; history of the city ... 4.00
   ...: Forever 1 (12/21, $3.99) Macchio-s/Bachs-a/Nauck-c ... 4.00
   ...: Thanos Rises 1 (11/21, $3.99) Gillen-s/Weaver-a; parents of Thanos and his birth ... 4.00
   ...: The Heretic 1 (5/22, $3.99) Gillen-s/Bodenheim & Salazar-a; Uranos app. ... 4.00
ETERNAL SOULFIRE (Also see Soulfire)
Aspen MLT, Inc.: Jul, 2015 - No. 6, Feb, 2016 ($3.99, limited series)
   1-6-Multiple covers on each. 1-Krul-s/Konat-a. 3-Tovar & Konat-a ... 4.00
ETERNALS: THE HEROD FACTOR
Marvel Comics: Nov, 1991 ($2.50, 68 pgs.)
   1 .... 4.00
ETERNAL WARRIOR (See Solar #10 & 11)
Valiant/Acclaim Comics (Valiant): May, 1992 - No. 50, Mar, 1996 ($2.25/$2.50)

	GD	VG	FN	VF	VF/NM	NM-
1-Unity x-over; Miller-c; origin Eternal Warrior & Aram (Armstrong)	2	4	6	8	10	12
1-($2.25-c) Gold logo	3	6	9	15	22	28
1-Gold foil logo on embossed cover; no cover price	4	8	12	25	40	55

   2,3,5,8: 2-Unity x-over; Simonson-c. 3-Archer & Armstrong x-over. 5-2nd full app. Bloodshot
   (12/92; see Rai #0). 6,7: 6-2nd app. Master Darque. 8-Flip book w/Archer & Armstrong #8

	GD	VG	FN	VF	VF/NM	NM-
4-1st brief app. Bloodshot (last pg.); see Rai #0 for 1st full app.; Cowan-c	3	6	9	18	28	38

   9-25,27-34: 9-1st Book of Geomancer. 14-16-Bloodshot app. 18-Doctor Mirage cameo.
   19-Doctor Mirage app. 22-W/bound-in trading card. 25-Archer & Armstrong app.;
   cont'd from A&A #25 .... 3.00
   26-($2.75, 44 pgs.)-Flip book w/Archer & Armstrong 4.00
   35-50: 35-Double-c; $2.50-c begins. 50-Geomancer app. 3.00
   Special 1 (2/96, $2.50)-Wings of Justice; Art Holcomb script ... 3.00
   Yearbook 1 (1993, $3.95), 2(1994, $3.95) 3.95
ETERNAL WARRIOR (Also see Wrath of the Eternal Warrior)
Valiant Entertainment: Sept, 2013 - No. 8, Apr, 2014 ($3.99)
   1-8: 1-Pak-s/Hairsine-a; 2 covers. 2-Hairsine & Crain-a ... 4.00
   ...: Awakening 1 (5/17, $3.99) Venditti-s/Guedes-a 4.00
ETERNAL WARRIORS (Series of one-shots)
Acclaim Comics (Valiant Heroes)
   ... Archer & Armstrong 1 (12/97, $3.95) Teranishi-a 4.00
   ... Blackworks 1 (3/98, $3.95) Doug Wheatley-a 4.00
   ... Digital Alchemy Vol. 2 (9/97, $3.95, 64 pgs.) Holcomb-s/Eaglesham-a(p) ... 4.00
   ... Mog (8/98, $3.95, 64 pgs.) Holcomb-s/Morales-a(p) 4.00
   ... The Immortal Enemy (6/98, $3.95, 64 pgs.) Holcomb-s/Jimenez-a(p) ... 4.00
   ... Time and Treachery Vol. 1 (6/97, $3.95, 64 pgs.) Reintro Aram, Archer, Ivar the Timewalker,
   & Gilad the Warmaster; 1st app. Shalla Redburn; Holcomb script; 2 covers ...

	GD	VG	FN	VF	VF/NM	NM-
	2.0	4.0	6.0	8.0	9.0	9.2

ETERNAL WARRIOR: DAYS OF STEEL
Valiant Entertainment: Nov, 2014 - No. 3, Jan, 2015 ($3.99)

1-3-Milligan-s/Nord-a						4.00

ETERNAL WARRIORS: FIST AND STEEL
Acclaim Comics (Valiant): May, 1996 - No. 2, June, 1996 ($2.50, lim. series)

1,2: Geomancer app. in both. 1-Indicia reads "June." 2-Bo Hampton-a						4.00

ETERNITY (Also see Divinity)
Valiant Entertainment: Oct, 2017 - No. 4, Jan, 2018 ($3.99, limited series)

1-4: 1-Kindt-s/Hairsine-a; 5 covers						4.00

ETERNITY GIRL
DC Comics (Young Animal): May, 2018 - No. 6, Oct, 2018 ($3.99)

1-6-Visaggio-s/Liew-a. 1-Intro. Caroline Sharp						4.00

ETERNITY SMITH
Renegade Press: Sept, 1986 - No. 5, May, 1987 ($1.25/$1.50, 36 pgs.)

1-5: 1st app. Eternity Smith. 5-Death of Jasmine						4.00

ETERNITY SMITH
Hero Comics: Sept, 1987 - No. 9, 1988 ($1.95)

V2#1-9: 8-Indigo begins						4.00

ETHER
Dark Horse Comics: Nov, 2016 - No. 5, Mar, 2017 ($3.99)

1-5-Matt Kindt-s/David Rubin-a						4.00

ETHER ("The Copper Golems" on cover)
Dark Horse Comics: May, 2018 - No. 5, Sept, 2018 ($3.99)

1-5-Matt Kindt-s/David Rubin-a						4.00

ETHER: THE DISAPPEARANCE OF VIOLET BELL
Dark Horse Comics: Sept, 2019 - No. 5, Jan, 2020 ($3.99)

1-5-Matt Kindt-s/David Rubin-a						4.00

ETTA KETT
King Features Syndicate/Standard: No. 11, Dec, 1948 - No. 14, Sept, 1949

11-Teenage	18	36	54	105	165	225
12-14	14	28	42	80	115	150

EUTHANAUTS
IDW Publishing (Black Crown): Jul, 2018 - No. 5, Nov, 2018 ($3.99)

1-5-Tini Howard-s/Nick Robles-a						4.00

EVA: DAUGHTER OF THE DRAGON
Dynamite Entertainment: 2007 ($4.99, one-shot)

1-Two covers by Jo Chen and Edgar Salazar; Jerwa-s/Salazar-a						5.00

EVANESCENCE
Opus: Aug, 2022 - Present ($4.99, limited series)

1-3-Stories inspired by the band's music. 1-Kelly McKernan-s/a						5.00
...: My Heart is Broken 1 (2/23, $6.99) Maura McHugh-s/V.R. TenagaComics-a						7.00

EVANGELINE (Also see Primer)
Comico/First Comics V2#1 on/Lodestone Publ.: 1984 - #2, 6/84; V2#1, 5/87 - V2#12, Mar, 1989 (Baxter paper)

1,2, V2#1 (5/87) - 12, Special #1 (1986, $2.00)-Lodestone Publ.						4.00

EVA THE IMP
Red Top Comic/Decker: 1957 - No. 2, Nov, 1957

1,2	8	16	24	44	57	70

EVE
BOOM! Studios: May, 2021 - No. 5, Sept, 2021 ($3.99, limited series)

1-5-Victor LaValle-s/Jo Mi-Gyeong-a; multiple covers on each						4.00

EVE: CHILDREN OF THE MOON
BOOM! Studios: Oct, 2022 - No. 5, Feb, 2023 ($3.99, limited series)

1-5-Victor LaValle-s/Jo Mi-Gyeong-a; multiple covers on each						4.00

EVEN MORE FUND COMICS (Benefit book for the Comic Book Legal Defense Fund)
(Also see More Fund Comics)
Sky Dog Press: Sept, 2004 ($10.00, B&W, trade paperback)

nn-Anthology of short stories and pin-ups by various; Spider-Man-c by Cho						10.00

EVENT LEVIATHAN (See Action Comics #1007-1012 and Leviathan Dawn one-shot)
DC Comics: Aug, 2019 - No. 6, Jan, 2020 ($3.99, limited series)

1-6-Bendis-s/Maleev-a; Batman, Lois Lane, The Question, Green Arrow, Manhunter app.						4.00

E.V.E. PROTOMECHA
Image Comics (Top Cow): Mar, 2000 - No. 6, Sept, 2000 ($2.50)

Preview ($5.95) Flip book w/Soul Saga preview	2	4	6	8	10	12
1-6: 1-Covers by Finch, Madureira, Garza. 2-Turner var-c						3.00
1-Another Universe variant-c						5.00
TPB (5/01, $17.95) r/#1-6 plus cover galley and sketch pages						18.00

EVERAFTER (See Fables)
DC Comics (Vertigo): Nov, 2016 - No. 12, Oct, 2017 ($3.99)

1-12: 1-Justus & Sturges-s/Travis Moore-a; Snow & Bigby app. 7-Buckingham-a						4.00

EVERQUEST: ... (Based on online role-playing game)
DC Comics (WildStorm): 2002 ($5.95, one-shots)

The Ruins of Kunark - Jim Lee & Dan Norton-a; McQuaid & Lee-s; Lee-c						6.00
Transformations - Philip Tan-a; Devin Grayson-s; Portacio-c						6.00

EVER THE WAY OUT
Abstract Studio: 2020 ($17.99, B&W, graphic novel)

GN - Terry Moore-s/a; intro. Everly; Rachel & Lilith app.						18.00

EVERYBODY'S COMICS (See Fox Giants)

EVERYMAN, THE
Marvel Comics (Epic Comics): Nov, 1991 ($4.50, one-shot, 52 pgs.)

1-Mike Allred-a	1	2	3	4	5	7

EVERYTHING
Dark Horse Comics (Berger Books): Sept, 2019 - No. 5, Jan, 2020 ($3.99)

1-5-Christopher Cantwell-s/I.N.J. Culbard-a						4.00

EVERYTHING HAPPENS TO HARVEY
National Periodical Publications: Sept-Oct, 1953 - No. 7, Sept-Oct, 1954

1	47	94	141	296	498	700
2	24	48	72	142	234	325
3-7	20	40	60	117	189	260

EVERYTHING'S ARCHIE
Archie Publications: May, 1969 - No. 157, Sept, 1991 (Giant issues No. 1-20)

1-(68 pages)	9	18	27	59	117	175
2-(68 pages)	4	8	12	28	47	65
3-5-(68 pages)	4	8	12	25	40	55
6-13-(68 pages)	3	6	9	17	26	35
14-31-(52 pages)	2	4	6	13	18	22
32 (7/74)-50 (8/76)	2	4	6	8	10	12
51-80 (12/79),100 (4/82)	1	2	3	5	6	8
81-99						6.00
101-103,105,106,108-120						5.00
104,107-Cheryl Blossom app.	1	2	3	4	5	7
121-156: 142,148-Gene Colan-a						4.00
157-Last issue						5.00

EVERYTHING'S DUCKY (Movie)
Dell Publishing Co.: No. 1251, 1961

Four Color 1251-Mickey Rooney & Buddy Hackett photo-c	7	14	21	49	92	135

EVE STRANGER
IDW Publishing (Black Crown): Apr, 2019 - No. 5, Aug, 2019 ($3.99)

1-5-David Barnett-s/Philip Bond-a						4.00

EVE: VALKYRIE (Based on the video game)
Dark Horse Comics: Oct, 2015 - No. 4, Jan, 2016 ($3.99, limited series)

1-4-Brian Wood-s/Eduardo Francisco-a						4.00

EVIL DEAD, THE (Movie)
Dark Horse Comics: Jan, 2008 - No. 4, Apr, 2008 ($2.99, limited series)

1-4-Adaptation of the Sam Raimi/Bruce Campbell movie; Bolton painted-a/c						4.00

EVIL DEAD 2 (Movie)
Space Goat Productions: 2016 ($3.99, one-shots)

...: Revenge of Hitler 1 - Edginton-s/Watts-a						4.00
...: Revenge of Jack the Ripper 1 - Ball-s/Mauriz-a						4.00
...: Revenge of Krampus 1 - Edginton-s/Youkovich-a						4.00

EVIL DEAD 2: BEYOND DEAD BY DAWN (Movie)
Space Goat Productions: 2015 - No. 3, 2015 ($3.99, limited series)

1-3-Sequel to the Sam Raimi/Bruce Campbell movie; Hannah-s/Bagenda & Bazaldua-a						4.00

EVIL DEAD 2: CRADLE OF THE DAMNED (Movie)
Space Goat Productions: 2016 - No. 3, 2016 ($3.99, limited series)

1-3-Hannah-s/Bagenda & Bazaldua-a						4.00

EVIL DEAD 2: DARK ONES RISING (Movie)
Space Goat Productions: 2016 - No. 3, 2016 ($3.99, limited series)

1-3-Sequel to the Sam Raimi/Bruce Campbell movie; Hannah-s/Valdes-a						4.00

EVIL DEAD 2: REVENGE OF EVIL ED (Movie)
Space Goat Productions: 2017 - No. 2, 2017 ($3.99, limited series)

1,2-Edginton-s/Riccardi-a; Hitler, Rasputin, Bin Laden & Dracula app.						4.00

EVIL ERNIE
Eternity Comics: Dec, 1991 - No. 5, 1992 ($2.50, B&W, limited series)

1-1st app. Lady Death by Steven Hughes (12,000 print run); Lady Death app. in all issues	17	34	51	117	259	400
2-1st Lady Death-c (7,000 print run)	9	18	27	63	129	195
3-(7,000 print run)	5	10	15	33	57	80
4-(8,000 print run)	5	10	15	30	50	70
5	4	8	12	25	40	55
Special Edition 1	3	6	9	21	33	45
Youth Gone Wild! ($9.95, trade paperback)-r/#1-5	2	4	6	8	10	12
Youth Gone Wild! Director's Cut ($4.95)-Limited to 15,000, shows the making of the comic						6.00

EVIL ERNIE (Monthly series)
Chaos! Comics: July, 1998 - No. 10, Apr, 1999 ($2.95)

1-Pulido & Nutman-s/Brewer-a	1	3	4	6	8	10
1-($10.00) Premium Ed.	2	4	6	8	10	12
2-10-Pulido & Nutman-s/Brewer-a						4.00
... Baddest Battles (1/97, $1.50) Pin-ups; 2 covers						5.00
... Pieces of Me (11/00, $2.95, B&W) Flashback story; Pulido-s/Beck-a						4.00
... Relentless (5/02, $4.99, B&W) Pulido-s/Beck, Bonk, & Brewer-a						5.00
... Returns (10/01, $3.99, B&W) Pulido-s/Beck-a						4.00

EVIL ERNIE
Dynamite Entertainment: 2012 - No. 6, 2013 ($3.99)

1-6: 1-Origin re-told; Snider-s/Craig-a; covers by Brereton, Seeley, Syaf & Bradshaw						4.00

EVIL ERNIE (Volume 2)
Dynamite Entertainment: 2014 - No. 6, 2015 ($3.99)

1-6-Tim & Steve Seeley-s/Rafael Lanhellas-a; multiple covers						4.00

EVIL ERNIE (Volume 3)
Dynamite Entertainment: 2021 - No. 5, 2022 ($3.99, limited series)

1-5-Scott Lobdell-s/Ariel Medel-a; multiple covers; rebirth of Ernie						4.00

EVIL ERNIE: DEPRAVED
Chaos! Comics: Jul, 1999 - No. 3, Sept, 1999 ($2.95, limited series)

1-3-Pulido-s/Brewer-a						4.00

EVIL ERNIE: DESTROYER

Evangeline #1 © ECL

Evil Ernie #1 © Chaos!

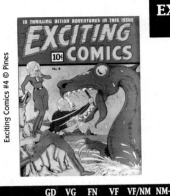

Exciting Comics #4 © Pines

	GD 2.0	VG 4.0	FN 6.0	VF 8.0	VF/NM 9.0	NM- 9.2

Chaos! Comics: Oct, 1997 - No. 9, Jun, 1998 ($2.95, limited series)
Preview ($2.50), 1-9-Flip cover — 4.00

EVIL ERNIE: GODEATER
Dynamite Entertainment: 2016 - No. 5, 2016 ($3.99)
1-5-Jordan-s/Worley-a; Davidsen-s/Razek-a; multiple covers — 4.00

EVIL ERNIE: IN SANTA FE
Devil's Due Publ.: Sept, 2005 - No. 4, Mar, 2006 ($2.95, limited series)
1-4-Alan Grant-s/Tommy Castillo-a/Alex Horley-c — 4.00

EVIL ERNIE: REVENGE
Chaos! Comics: Oct, 1994 - No. 4, Feb, 1995 ($2.95, limited series)

1-Glow-in-the-dark-c; Lady Death app. 1-3-flip book w. Kilzone Preview (series of 3)	2	4	6	8	10	12
1-Commemorative-(4000 print run)	2	4	6	9	13	16
2-4						4.00
Trade paperback (10/95, $12.95)						13.00

EVIL ERNIE: STRAIGHT TO HELL
Chaos! Comics: Oct, 1995 - No. 5, May, 1996 ($2.95, limited series)

1-Fold-out-c	2	4	6	8	10	12
1,3:1-($19.95) Chromium Ed. 3-Chastity Chase-c-(4000 printed)						20.00
2-5						4.00
Special Edition (10,000)						20.00

EVIL ERNIE: THE RESURRECTION
Chaos! Comics: 1993 - No. 4, 1994 (Limited series)

0						5.00
1	2	4	6	8	10	12
1A-Gold	3	6	9	16	23	30
2-4	1	2	3	5	6	8

EVIL ERNIE VS. THE MOVIE MONSTERS
Chaos! Comics: Mar, 1997 ($2.95, one-shot)

1						4.00
1-Variant-"Chaos-Scope•Terror Vision" card stock-c	1	3	4	6	8	10

EVIL ERNIE VS. THE SUPER HEROES
Chaos! Comics: Aug, 1995; Sept, 1998 ($2.95)

1-Lady Death poster						5.00
1-Foil-c variant (limited to 10,000)	2	4	6	11	16	20
1-Limited Edition (1000)	2	4	6	11	16	20
2-(9/98) Ernie vs. JLA and Marvel parodies						4.00

EVIL ERNIE: WAR OF THE DEAD
Chaos! Comics: Nov, 1999 - No. 3, Jan, 2000 ($2.95, limited series)
1-3-Pulido & Kaminski-s/Brewer-a. 3-End of Evil Ernie — 4.00

EVIL EYE
Fantagraphics Books: June, 1998 - No. 12, Jun, 2004 ($2.95/$3.50/$3.95, B&W)

1-7-Richard Sala-s/a						4.00
8-10-($3.50)						4.00
11,12-($3.95)						4.00

EVO (Crossover from Tomb Raider #25 & Witchblade #60)
Image Comics (Top Cow): Feb, 2003 ($2.99, one-shot)
1-Silvestri-c/a(p); Endgame x-over pt. 3; Sara Pezzini & Lara Croft app. — 3.00

EWOKS (Star Wars) (TV) (See Star Comics Magazine)
Marvel Comics (Star Comics): June, 1985 - No. 14, Jul, 1987 (75¢/$1.00)

1	4	8	12	25	40	55
2-9	2	4	6	9	12	15
10-Williamson-a (From Star Wars)	5	10	15	33	57	80
11-14: 14-($1.00-c)	2	4	6	11	16	20

EXCALIBUR (Also see Marvel Comics Presents #31)
Marvel Comics: Apr, 1988; Oct, 1988 - No. 125, Oct, 1998 ($1.50/$1.75/$1.99)

Special Edition nn (The Sword is Drawn)(4/88, $3.25)-1st Excalibur comic	1	2	3	5	6	8
Special Edition nn (4/88)-no price on-c	2	4	6	8	10	12
Special Edition nn (2nd & 3rd print, 10/88, 12/89)						5.00
...The Sword is Drawn (Apr, 1992, $4.50)						5.00
1($1.50, 10/88)-X-Men spin-off; Nightcrawler, Shadowcat (Kitty Pryde), Capt. Britain, Phoenix & Meggan begin						6.00
2-4						5.00
5-10						4.00

11-49,51-70,72-74,76: 10,11-Rogers/Austin-a. 21-Intro Crusader X. 22-Iron Man x-over.

24-John Byrne app. in story. 26-Ron Lim-c/a. 27-B. Smith-a(p). 37-Dr. Doom & Iron Man app. 41-X-Men (Wolverine) app.; Cable cameo. 49-Neal Adams c-swipe. 52,57-X-Men (Cyclops, Wolverine) app. 53-Spider-Man-c/story. 58-X-Men (Wolverine, Gambit, Cyclops, etc.)-c/story. 61-Phoenix returns. 68-Starjammers-c/story — 4.00

50-($2.75, 56 pgs.)-New logo						5.00
71-($3.95, 52 pgs.)-Hologram on-c; 30th anniversary						5.00
75-($3.50, 52 pgs.)-Holo-grafx foil-c						5.00
75-($2.25, 52 pgs.)-Regular edition						5.00

77-81,83-86: 77-Begin $1.95-c; bound-in trading card sheet. 83-86-Deluxe Editions and Standard Editions. 86-1st app. Pete Wisdom — 4.00

82-($2.50)-Newsstand edition						4.00
82-($3.50)-Enhanced edition						5.00

87-89,91-99,101-110: 87-Return from Age of Apocalypse. 92-Colossus-c/app. 94-Days of Future Tense 95-X-Man-c/app. 96-Sebastian Shaw & the Hellfire Club app. 99-Onslaught app. 101-Onslaught tie-in. 102-w/card insert. 103-Last Warren Ellis scripts; Belasco app. 104,105-Hitch & Neary-c/a. 109-Spiral-c/app. — 4.00

90,100-($2.95)-double-sized. 100-Onslaught tie-in; wraparound-c						5.00
111-124: 111-Begin $1.99-c, wraparound-c. 119-Calafiore-a						4.00
125-($2.99) Wedding of Capt. Britain and Meggan						5.00
Annual 1,2 ('93, '94, 68 pgs.)-1st app. Khaos. 2-X-Men & Psylocke app.						4.00
#(-1) Flashback (7/97)						6.00
...Air Apparent nn (12/91, $4.95)-Simonson-c						6.00
...Mojo Mayhem nn (12/89, $4.50)-Art Adams/Austin-c/a						6.00
...The Possession nn (7/91, $2.95, 52 pgs.)						5.00
...XX Crossing (7/92, 5/92-inside, $2.50)-vs. The X-Men						4.00
...Classic Vol. 1: The Sword is Drawn TPB (2005, $19.99) r/#1-5 & Special Edition nn (The Sword is Drawn)						20.00
...Classic Vol. 2: Two-Edged Sword TPB (2006, $24.99) r/#6-11						25.00
...Classic Vol. 3: Cross-Time Caper Book 1 TPB (2007, $24.99) r/#12-20						25.00
...Classic Vol. 4: Cross-Time Caper Book 2 TPB (2007, $24.99) r/#21-28						25.00
...Classic Vol. 5 TPB (2008, $24.99) r/#29-34 & Marvel GN Excalibur: Weird War III						25.00

EXCALIBUR
Marvel Comics: Feb, 2001 - No. 4, May, 2001 ($2.99)
1-4-Return of Captain Britain; Raimondi-a — 3.00

EXCALIBUR (X-Men Reloaded title) (Leads into House of M series, then New Excalibur)
Marvel Comics: July, 2004 - No. 14, July, 2005 ($2.99)

1-14: 1-Claremont-s/Lopresti-a/Park-c; Magneto returns. 6-11-Beast app. 13,14-Prelude to House of M; Dr. Strange app.						3.00
House of M Prelude: Excalibur TPB (2005, $11.99) r/#11-14						12.00
... Vol. 1: Forging the Sword (2004, $9.99) r/#1-4						10.00
... Vol. 2: Saturday Night Fever (2005, $14.99) r/#5-10						15.00

EXCALIBUR (Follows from House of X & Powers of X series)
Marvel Comics: Dec, 2019 - No. 26, Feb, 2022 ($4.99/$3.99)

1-($4.99) Tini Howard-s/Marcus To-a; Betsy Braddock, Rogue, Gambit, Jubilee app.						5.00
2-26-($3.99): 10,11-Kitty Pryde app. 12-15-"X of Swords" tie-ins. 21-Hellfire Gala						4.00

EXCELLENCE
Image Comics (Skybound): May, 2019 - Present ($3.99)
1-12-Brandon Thomas-s/Khary Randolph-a — 4.00

EXCITING COMICS
Nedor/Better Publications/Standard Comics: Apr, 1940 - No. 69, Sept, 1949

	GD 2.0	VG 4.0	FN 6.0	VF 8.0	VF/NM 9.0	NM- 9.2
1-Origin & 1st app. The Mask, Jim Hatfield, Sgt. Bill King, Dan Williams begin; early Robot-c (same as Smash #1)	524	1048	1572	3825	6763	9700
2-The Sphinx begins; The Masked Rider app.; Son of the Gods begins, ends #8	258	516	774	1651	2826	4000
3-Classic Science Fiction Robot-c	300	600	900	2010	3505	5000
4-6: All have Sci-Fi covers by Max Plaisted	219	438	657	1402	2401	3400
7,8-Schomburg jungle covers	174	348	522	1114	1907	2700
9-Origin/1st app. of The Black Terror & sidekick Tim, begin series (5/41) (Black Terror c-9-21,23-52,54,55)	1930	3860	5790	14,500	27,250	40,000
10-2nd app. Black Terror (6/41)	415	830	1245	2905	5103	7300
11-3rd app. Black Terror (7/41)	271	542	813	1734	2967	4200
12,13-Bondage covers	206	412	618	1318	2259	3200
14-Last Sphinx, Dan Williams	168	336	504	1075	1838	2600
15-The Liberator begins (origin); WWII-c	213	426	639	1363	2332	3300
16,19,20: 20-The Mask ends	142	284	426	909	1555	2200
17,18-WWII-c	168	336	504	1075	1838	2600
21,23,24	113	226	339	718	1234	1750
22-Origin The Eaglet; The American Eagle begins	161	322	483	1030	1765	2500
25-Robot-c	239	478	717	1530	2615	3700
26-Schomburg-c begin; Nazi WWII-c	245	490	735	1568	2684	3800
27,30-Japanese WWII-c	226	452	678	1446	2473	3500

28-(Scarce) Crime Crusader begins, ends #58; Nazi WWII-c

	GD	VG	FN	VF	VF/NM	NM-
	2.0	4.0	6.0	8.0	9.0	9.2

	1070	2140	3210	6400	10,700	15,000
29-Nazi WWII-c	258	516	774	1651	2826	4000

31,35,36-Japanese WWII-c. 35-Liberator ends, not in 31-33

	187	374	561	1197	2049	2900
32-34,37-Nazi WWII-c	187	374	561	1197	2049	2900
38 Gangster-c	135	270	405	864	1482	2100

39-WWII-c; Nazis giving poison candy to kids on cover; origin Kara, Jungle Princess

	1600	3200	4800	10,000	15,000	20,000

40,41-Last WWII covers in this title; Japanese WWII-c

	181	362	543	1158	1979	2800

42-50: 42-The Scarab begins. 45-Schomburg Robot-c. 49-Last Kara, Jungle Princess.

50-Last American Eagle	103	206	309	659	1130	1600
51-Miss Masque begins (1st app.)	142	284	426	909	1555	2200
52,54- 54-Miss Masque ends	93	186	279	591	1021	1450
53-Miss Masque-c	295	590	885	1888	3244	4600

55-58: 55-Judy of the Jungle begins (origin), ends #69; 1 pg. Ingels-a; Judy of the Jungle

c-56-66. 57,58-Airbrush-c	93	186	279	591	1021	1450

59-Frazetta art in Caniff style; signed Frank Frazeta (one!), 9 pgs.

	220	330	704	1202	1700	

60-66: 60-Rick Howard, the Mystery Rider begins. 66-Robinson/Meskin-a

	84	168	252	538	919	1300
67-69-All western covers	34	68	102	199	325	450

NOTE: Schomburg (Xela) c-26-68; airbrush c-57-66. Black Terror by R. Moreira-#65. Roussos a-62. Bondage-c 9, 12, 13, 20, 23, 25, 30, 59.

EXCITING ROMANCES
Fawcett Publications: 1949 (nd); No. 2, Spring, 1950 - No. 5, 10/50; No. 6 (1951, nd); No. 7, 9/51 -No. 12, 1/53 (Photo-c on #1-3)

1,3: 1(1949). 3-Wood-a	19	38	57	111	176	240
2,4,5-(1950)	13	26	39	72	101	130
6-12	10	20	30	56	76	95

NOTE: Powell a-8-10. Marcus Swayze a-5, 6, 9. Photo c-1-7, 10-12.

EXCITING ROMANCE STORIES (See Fox Giants)

EXCITING WAR (Korean War)
Standard Comics (Better Publ.): No. 5, Sept. 1952 - No. 8, May, 1953; No. 9, Nov. 1953

5	41	82	123	256	428	600
6-Flame thrower/burning body-c	97	194	291	621	1061	1500
7,9	26	52	78	154	252	350
8-Toth-a	41	82	123	256	428	600

EXCITING X-PATROL
Marvel Comics (Amalgam): June, 1997 ($1.95, one-shot)

1-Barbara Kesel-s/Bryan Hitch-a 4.00

EX-CON
Dynamite Entertainment: 2014 - No. 5, 2015 ($2.99, limited series)

1-5-Swierczynski-s/Burns-a/Bradstreet-c 3.00

EXECUTIONER, THE (Don Pendleton's...)
IDW Publishing: Apr, 2008 - No. 5, Aug, 2008 ($3.99)

1-5-Mack Boian origin re-told; Gallant-a/Wojtowicz-s 4.00

EXECUTIVE ASSISTANT: ASSASSINS
Aspen MLT: Jul, 2012 - No. 18, Feb, 2014 ($3.99)

1-18: 1-Five covers; Hernandez-s/Gunderson-a 4.00

EXECUTIVE ASSISTANT: IRIS (Also see All New Executive Assistant: Iris)
Aspen MLT: No. 0, Apr, 2009 - No. 6, Nov, 2010 ($2.50/$2.99)

0-($2.50) Wohl-s/Francisco-a; 3 covers 3.00
1-6-($2.99) Multiple covers on each 3.00
Annual 2015 (3/15, $5.99) Three stories by various; Benitez-c ... 6.00
... Sourcebook 1 (1/16, $4.99) Character profiles & storyline summaries ... 5.00

EXECUTIVE ASSISTANT: IRIS (Volume 2) (The Hit List Agenda x-over)
Aspen MLT: No. 0, Jul, 2011 - No. 5, Dec, 2011 ($2.99/$3.50)

0-($2.50) Wohl-s/Francisco-a; sketch page art; 3 covers 3.00
1-4-($2.99) Multiple covers on each. 1-Francisco-a. 2-4-Odagawa-a ... 3.00
5-($3.50) Odagawa-a 3.00

EXECUTIVE ASSISTANT: IRIS (Volume 3) (See All New Executive Assistant: Iris for Vol. 4)
Aspen MLT: Dec, 2012 - No. 5, Sept, 2013 ($3.99)

1-5-Multiple covers on each. 1-Wohl-s/Lei-a 4.00

EXECUTIVE ASSISTANT: IRIS (Volume 5)
Aspen MLT: May, 2018 - No. 5, Sept, 2018 ($3.99)

1-5-Multiple covers on each. 1-Northcott-s/Tran-a 4.00
... Primer 1 (5/18, 25¢) Origin re-told; recaps of previous volumes ... 3.00

EXECUTIVE ASSISTANT: LOTUS (The Hit List Agenda x-over)
Aspen MLT: Aug, 2011 - No. 3, Oct, 2011 ($2.99, limited series)

1-3-Multiple covers on each. Hernandez-s/Nome-a 3.00

EXECUTIVE ASSISTANT: ORCHID (The Hit List Agenda x-over)
Aspen MLT: Aug, 2011 - No. 3, Oct, 2011 ($2.99, limited series)

1-3: 1-Lobdell-s/Gunnell-a; multiple covers 3.00

EXECUTIVE ASSISTANT: VIOLET (The Hit List Agenda x-over)
Aspen MLT: Aug, 2011 - No. 3, Oct, 2011 ($2.99, limited series)

1-3: 1-Andreyko-s/Mhan-a; multiple covers 3.00

EXILED (Part 1 of x-over with Journey Into Mystery #637,638 & New Mutants #42,43)
Marvel Comics: July, 2012 ($2.99, one-shot)

1-Thor, Loki and New Mutants app.; DiGiandomenico-a 3.00

EXILED, THE
Whatnot Publishing: Feb, 2023 - Present ($3.99)

1-4-Story by Wesley Snipes, Adam Lawson & Keith Arem; Gabriel Santos-a ... 4.00

EXILE ON THE PLANET OF THE APES
BOOM! Studios: Mar, 2012 - No. 4 ($3.99, limited series)

1-3-Bechko & Hardman-s/Laming-a 4.00

EXILES (Also see Break-Thru)
Malibu Comics (Ultraverse): Aug, 1993 - No. 4, Nov, 1993 ($1.95)

1,2,4: 1,2-Bagged copies of each exist. 4-Team dies; story cont'd in Break-Thru #1 ... 4.00
3-($2.50, 40 pgs.)-Rune flip-c/story by B. Smith (3 pgs.) 5.00
1-Holographic-c edition 5.00

EXILES (All New, The) (2nd Series) (Also see Black September)
Malibu Comics (Ultraverse): Sept, 1995 - V2#11, Aug, 1996 ($1.50)

Infinity (9/95, $1.50)-Intro new team including Marvel's Juggernaut & Reaper ... 4.00

Infinity (2000 signed), V2#1 (2000 signed)	1	3	4	6	8	10

V2 #1-(10/95, 64 pgs.)-Reprint of Ultraforce V2#1 follows lead story ... 5.00
V2#2-4,6-11: 2-1st app. Hellblade. 8-Intro Maxis. 11-Vs. Maxis; Ripfire app.; cont'd in Ultraforce #12 ... 4.00
V2#5-($2.50) Juggernaut returns to the Marvel Universe. 4.00

EXILES (Also see X-Men titles) (Leads into New Exiles series)
Marvel Comics: Aug, 2001 - No. 100, Feb, 2008 ($2.99/$2.25)

1-($2.99) Blink and parallel world X-Men; Winick-s/McKone & McKenna-a						
	2	4	6	10	14	18

2-10-($2.25) 2-Two covers (McKone & JH Williams III). 5-Alpha Flight app. ... 4.00
11-24: 20-Blink leaves; Magik joins. 23,24-Walker-a; alternate Weapon-X app. ... 3.00
25-99: 25-Begin $2.99-c; Inhumans app.; Walker-a. 26-30-Austen-s. 33-Wolverine app. 35-37-Fantastic Four app. 37-Sunfire dies, Blink returns. 38-40-Hyperion app. 69-71-House of M. 77,78-Squadron Supreme app. 85,86-Multiple Wolverines. 90-Claremont-s begin; Psylocke app. 97-Shadowcat joins ... 3.00
100-($3.99) Last issue; Blink leaves; continues in Exiles (Days of Then and Now); r/#1 ... 4.00
Annual 1 (2/07, $3.99) Bedard-s/Raney-a/c 4.00
Exiles #1 (Days of Then and Now) (3/08, $3.99) short stories by various ... 4.00

EXILES
Marvel Comics: Jun, 2009 - No. 6, Nov, 2009 ($2.99/$3.99)

1,6-($3.99) Blink and parallel world Scarlet Witch, Beast and others; Bullock-c ... 4.00
2-5-($2.99) 3.00

EXILES
Marvel Comics: Jun, 2018 - No. 12, Mar, 2019 ($3.99)

1,4-12-Blink and parallel world Ms. Marvel, Iron Lad, Valkyrie & Wolvie; Nick Fury app. 4-The Thing & Falcon app. 8-Quinones-a ... 4.00

2-Intro Tessa Thompson	2	4	6	10	14	18
3-Intro Peggy Carter (Captain America)	4	8	12	23	37	50

EXILES VS. THE X-MEN (Titled All-New Exiles vs. X-Men on cover)
Malibu Comics (Ultraverse): Oct, 1995 (one-shot)

0-Limited Super Premium Edition; signed w/certificate; gold foil logo,						
0-Limited Premium Edition	1	3	4	6	8	10

EXIT STAGE LEFT: THE SNAGGLEPUSS CHRONICLES
DC Comics: Mar, 2018 - No. 6, Aug, 2018 ($3.99)

1-6-Russell-s/Feehan-a; Snagglepuss as a 1950s playwright; Huckleberry Hound app. ... 4.00

EX MACHINA
DC Comics: Aug, 2004 - No. 50, Sept, 2010 ($2.95/$2.99)

1-Intro. Mitchell Hundred; Vaughan-s/Harris-a/c 6.00
1-Special Edition (6/10, $1.00) Reprints #1 with "What's Next?" logo on cover ... 3.00
2-49: 12-Intro. Automaton. 33-Mitchell meets the Pope 3.00
50-($4.99) Wraparound-c 5.00
...: The Deluxe Edition Book One HC (2008, $29.99, dustjacket) r/#1-11; Vaughan's original proposal, Harris sketch pages; Brad Meltzer intro. ... 30.00
...: The Deluxe Edition Book Two HC (2009, $29.99, dustjacket) r/#12-20; Special #1,2; script and pencil art for #20; Wachowski Bros. intro. ... 30.00
...: The Deluxe Edition Book Three HC (2010, $29.99, dustjacket) r/#21-29; Special #3 and Ex Machina: Inside the Machine ... 30.00
...: The Deluxe Edition Book Four HC (2010, $29.99, dustjacket) r/#30-40 ... 30.00
...: The Deluxe Edition Book Five HC (2011, $29.99, dustjacket) r/#41-50; Special #4 ... 30.00
...: Inside the Machine (4/07, $2.99) script pages and Harris art and cover process ... 3.00
...: Masquerade Special (#3) (10/07, $3.50) John Paul Leon-a; Harris-c ... 3.50
... Special 1,2 (6/06 - No. 2, 8/06, $2.99) Sprouse-a; flashback to the Great Machine ... 3.00
... Special 4 (5/09, $3.99) Leon-a; Great Machine flashback; covers by Harris & Leon ... 4.50
... Dirty Tricks TPB (2009, $12.99) r/#35-39 and Masquerade Special #3 ... 13.00
... Ex Cathedra TPB (2008, $12.99) r/#30-34 .... 13.00
... March To War TPB (2006, $12.99) r/#17-20 and Special #1,2 ... 13.00
... Power Down TPB (2008, $12.99) r/#26-29 & ...: Inside the Machine ... 13.00
... Ring Out the Old TPB (2010, $14.99) r/#40-44 and Special #4 ... 15.00
... Smoke Smoke TPB (2007, $12.99) r/#21-25 .... 13.00
... The First Hundred Days TPB ('05, $9.95) r/#1-5; photo reference and sketch pages ... 10.00
... Tag TPB (2005, $12.99) r/#6-10; Harris sketch pages 13.00
... Term Limits TPB (2010, $14.99) r/#45-50 .... 15.00

EX-MUTANTS
Malibu Comics: Nov, 1992 - No. 18, Apr, 1994 ($1.95/$2.25/$2.50)

1-18: 1-Polybagged w/Skycap; prismatic cover 4.00

EXORCISTS (See The Crusaders)

EXORSISTERS
Image Comics: Oct, 2018 - Present ($3.99)

1-6-Ian Boothby-s/Gisele Lagacé-a. 1-Four covers. 2-6-Two covers ... 4.00

EXOSQUAD (TV)
Topps Comics: No. 0, Jan, 1994 ($1.00)

0-($1.00, 20 pgs.)-1st app.; Staton-a(p); wraparound-c 4.00

EXOTIC ROMANCES (Formerly True War Romances)
Quality Comics Group (Comic Magazines): No. 22, Oct, 1955 - No. 31, Nov, 1956

22	20	40	60	117	189	260
23-26,29	15	30	45	84	127	170
27,31-Baker-c/a	37	74	111	222	361	500
28,30-Baker-a	24	48	72	142	234	325

EXPANSE, THE (Based on the books of James S.A. Corey)
BOOM! Studios: Dec, 2020 - No. 4, Mar, 2021 ($3.99, limited series)

Ex Machina #24 © Vaughan & Harris

Extermination (2018 series) #3 © MAR

Extreme Venomverse #1 © MAR

	GD	VG	FN	VF	VF/NM	NM-
	2.0	4.0	6.0	8.0	9.0	9.2

1-4-Bechko-s/Aragon-a 4.00

EXPANSE, THE : DRAGON TOOTH (Based on the books of James S.A. Corey)
BOOM! Studios: Apr, 2023 - No. 12 ($4.99, limited series)
1-9-Diggle-s/Rubine-a 5.00

EXPENDABLES, THE (The Movie)
Dynamite Entertainment: 2010 - No. 4, 2010 ($3.99, limited series)
1-4-Chuck Dixon-s/Esteve Polls-a/Lucio Parrillo-c; prelude to the 2010 movie 4.00

EXPLOITS OF DANIEL BOONE
Quality Comics Group: Nov, 1955 - No. 6, Oct, 1956

1-All have Cuidera-c(i)	21	42	63	124	202	280
2 (1/56)	15	30	45	84	127	170
3-6	14	28	42	78	112	145

EXPLOITS OF DICK TRACY (See Dick Tracy)

EXPLORER JOE
Ziff-Davis Comic Group (Approved Comics): Win, 1951 - No. 2, Oct-Nov, 1952

1-Saunders painted cover	37	74	111	222	361	500
2-Krigstein-a; Saunders painted cover	19	38	57	111	176	240

EXPLORERS OF THE UNKNOWN (See Archie Giant Series #587, 599)
Archie Comics: June, 1990 - No. 6, Apr, 1991 ($1.00)
1-6: Featuring Archie and the gang 4.00

EXPOSED (...True Crime Cases; ...Cases in the Crusade Against Crime #5-9)
D. S. Publishing Co.: Mar-Apr, 1948 - No. 9, July-Aug, 1949

1	290	580	870	1856	3178	4500
2-Giggling killer story with excessive blood; two injury-to-eye panels; electrocution panel	54	108	162	343	574	825
3,8,9	24	48	72	142	234	325
4-Orlando-a	26	52	78	154	252	350
5-Breeze Lawson, Sky Sheriff by E. Good	26	52	78	154	252	350
6,7: 6-Ingels-a; used in **SOTI**, illo. "How to prepare an alibi" 7-Illo. in **SOTI**, "Diagram for housebreakers;" used by N.Y. Legis. Committee	160	159	334	567		800

EXTERMINATION
BOOM! Studios: Jun, 2012 - No. 8, Jan, 2013 ($1.00/$3.99)
1-($1.00) Nine covers; Spurrier-s/Jeffrey Edwards-a 4.00
2-8-($3.99) 4.00

EXTERMINATION
Marvel Comics: Oct, 2018 - No. 5, Feb, 2019 ($4.99, limited series)
1-($4.99)-Brisson-s/Larraz-a; the original five X-Men and Cable app.; Bloodstorm killed ... 5.00
2-4-($3.99) 4.00
5-($4.99) Brisson-s/Larraz-a; original X-Men return to their past 5.00

EXTERMINATORS, THE
DC Comics (Vertigo): Mar, 2006 - No. 30, Aug, 2008 ($2.99)
1-30: Simon Oliver-s/Tony Moore-a in most. 11,12-Hawthorne-a 3.00
...: Bug Brothers TPB (2006, $9.99) r/#1-5; intro. by screenwriter Josh Olson ... 10.00
...: Bug Brothers Forever TPB (2008, $14.99) r/#24-30; intro. by Simon Oliver ... 15.00
...: Crossfire and Collateral TPB (2008, $14.99) r/#17-23 .... 15.00
...: Insurgency TPB (2007, $12.99) r/#6-10 .... 13.00
...: Lies of Our Fathers TPB (2007, $14.99) r/#11-16 .... 15.00

EXTINCT!
New England Comics Press: Wint, 1991-92 - No. 2, Fall, 1992 ($3.50, B&W)
1,2-Reprints and background info of "perfectly awful" Golden Age stories ... 4.00

EXTINCTION EVENT
DC Comics (WildStorm): Sept, 2003 - No. 5, Jan, 2004 ($2.50, limited series)
1-5-Booth-a/Weinberg-s 3.00

EXTRA!
E. C. Comics: Mar-Apr, 1955 - No. 5, Nov-Dec, 1955

1-Not code approved	29	58	87	232	366	500
2-5: 3-1st EC Picto-Fiction story	17	34	51	136	218	300

NOTE: *Craig, Crandall, Severin* art in all.

EXTRA!
Gemstone Publishing: Jan, 2000 - No. 5, May, 2000 ($2.50)
1-5-Reprints E.C. series 4.00

EXTRA COMICS
Magazine Enterprises: 1948 (25¢, 3 comics in one)

1-Giant; consisting of rebound ME comics. Two versions known; (1)-Funnyman by Siegel & Shuster, Space Ace, Undercover Girl, Red Fox by L.B. Cole, Trail Colt & (2)-All Funnyman	90	180	270	576	988	1400

EXTRAORDINARY X-MEN
Marvel Comics: Jan, 2016 - No. 20, May, 2017 ($4.99/$3.99)
1-($4.99) Team of Old Man Logan, Storm, Jean Grey & others; Lemire-s/Ramos-a ... 5.00
2-7,9-20-($3.99) 2-Mister Sinister returns. 6,7,13-16-Ibanez-a. 9-12-Apocalypse Wars ... 4.00
8-($4.99) Apocalypse Wars x-over; Ramos-a; back-up story with Doctor Strange ... 5.00
Annual 1 (11/16, $4.99) Masters-s/Barberi-a; Montclare-s/Kämpe-a; Moon Girl app. ... 5.00

EXTREME
Image Comics (Extreme Studios): Aug, 1993 (Giveaway)
0 .... 4.00

EXTREME CARNAGE
Marvel Comics: Sept, 2021 - Nov, 2021 ($4.99/$3.99, 8-part series)
... Agony 1 (11/21, $3.99) Part 7; Wong-s/Galán-a 4.00
... Alpha 1 (9/21, $4.99) Part 1; P.K. Johnson-s/Garcia-a; Flash Thompson app. ... 5.00
... Lasher 1 (10/21, $3.99) Part 4; Chapman-s/Mooneyham-a 4.00
... Omega 1 (11/21, $4.99) Part 8; P.K. Johnson-s/Garcia-a 5.00
... Phage 1 (9/21, $3.99) Part 3; Orlando-s/Sandoval-a 4.00
... Riot 1 (10/21, $3.99) Part 5; Wong-s/Galán-a 4.00
... Scream 1 (9/21, $3.99) Part 2; Chapman-s/Mooneyham-a 4.00
... Toxin 1 (11/21, $3.99) Part 6; Orlando-s/Sandoval-a 4.00

EXTREME DESTROYER
Image Comics (Extreme Studios): Jan, 1996 ($2.50)
Prologue 1-Polybagged w/card; Liefeld-c, Epilogue 1-Liefeld-c 4.00

EXTREME JUSTICE
DC Comics: No. 0, Jan, 1995 - No. 18, July, 1996 ($1.50/$1.75)
0-18 .... 4.00

EXTREMELY YOUNGBLOOD
Image Comics (Extreme Studios): Sept, 1996 ($3.50, one-shot)
1 .... 4.00

EXTREME SACRIFICE
Image Comics (Extreme Studios): Jan, 1995 ($2.50, limited series)
Prelude (#1)-Liefeld wraparound-c; polybagged w/ trading card 4.00
Epilogue (#2)-Liefeld wraparound-c; polybagged w/trading card 4.00
Trade paperback (6/95, $16.95)-Platt-a 17.00

EXTREME SUPER CHRISTMAS SPECIAL
Image Comics (Extreme Studios): Dec, 1994 ($2.95, one-shot)
1 .... 4.00

EXTREME VENOMVERSE
Marvel Comics: Jul, 2023 - No. 5, Sept, 2023 ($4.99, limited series)
1-5: 1-Doc Ock app. 2-Black Cat app. 4-Momoko-s/a. 5-Jeff the Shark app. ... 5.00

EXTREMIST, THE
DC Comics (Vertigo): Sept, 1993 - No. 4, Dec, 1993 ($1.95, limited series)
1-4-Peter Milligan scripts; McKeever-c/a 4.00
1-Platinum Edition 5.00

EYE OF NEWT
Dark Horse Comics: Jun, 2014 - No. 4, Sept, 2014 ($3.99, limited series)
1-4-Michael Hague-s/a/c 4.00

EYE OF THE STORM
DC Comics (WildStorm): Sept, 2003 ($4.95)
Annual 1-Short stories by various incl. Portacio, Johns, Coker, Pearson, Arcudi ... 5.00

FABLES
DC Comics (Vertigo): July, 2002 - No. 149, Apr, 2015; No. 151, Jul, 2022 - No. 162, May, 2024 ($2.50/$2.75/$2.99/$3.99)

1-Willingham-s/Medina-a; two covers by Maleev & Jean		5	10	15	30	50	70
1: Special Edition (12/06, 25¢) r/#1 with preview of 1001 Nights of Snowfall							3.00
1: Special Edition (9/09, $1.00) r/#1 with preview of Peter & Max							3.00
1-Special Edition (8/10, $1.00) Reprints #1 with "What's Next?" logo on cover							3.00
1-Special Edition (3/16, $3.99) Reprints #1 with new cover by Dave McKean							3.00
2-Medina-a		2	4	6	9	12	15
3-5		1	3	4	6	8	10
6-37: 6-10-Buckingham-a. 11-Talbot-a. 18-Medley-a. 26-Preview of The Witching							5.00
6-RRP Edition wraparound variant-c; promotional giveaway for retailers (200 printed)		10	20	30	70	150	230
38-49,51-74,76-99,101-149: 38-Begin $2.75-c. 49-Begin $2.99-c. 57,58,76-Allred-a. 83-85-X-over with Jack of Fables & The Literals. 101-Shanower-a. 147-Terry Moore-a							
113-Back-up art by Russell, Cannon, Hughes. 147-Terry Moore-a (3 pgs.)							3.00
50-($3.99) Wedding of Snow White and Bigby Wolf; preview of Jack of Fables series							5.00

	GD 2.0	VG 4.0	FN 6.0	VF 8.0	VF/NM 9.0	NM- 9.2

75-($4.99) Geppetto surrenders; pin-up gallery by Powell, Nowlan, Cooke & others 5.00
100-(1/11, $9.99, squarebound) Buckingham-a; short stories art by Hughes & others 10.00
(#150) Fables: Farewell (2015, $17.99) Main story with Buckingham-a; numerous short stories with art by various incl. Neal Adams, Allred, Leialoha, Medina, Dodson 18.00
151-162: 151-(7/22, $3.99) Buckingham-a 4.00
Animal Farm (2003, $12.95, TPB) r/#6-10; sketch pages by Buckingham & Jean 13.00
... : Arabian Nights (And Days) (2006, $14.99, TPB) r/#42-47 15.00
... : Homelands (2005, $14.99, TPB) r/#34-41 15.00
Legends in Exile (2002, $9.95, TPB) r/#1-5; new short story Willingham-s/a 15.00
... : March of the Wooden Soldiers (2004, $17.95, TPB) r/#19-21 & ... : The Last Castle 15.00
... : 1001 Nights of Snowfall HC (2006, $19.99) short stories by Willingham with art by various incl. Bolton, Kaluta, Jean, McPherson, Thompson, Vess, Wheatley, Buckingham 20.00
... : 1001 Nights of Snowfall (2008, $14.99, TPB) short stories with art by various 15.00
... : Rose Red (2011, $17.99, TPB) r/#94-100; Buckingham design and sketch pages 18.00
... : Sons of Empire (2007, $17.99, TPB) r/#52-59 18.00
... : Storybook Love (2004, $14.95, TPB) r/#11-18 15.00
... : The Dark Ages (2009, $17.99, TPB) r/#76-82 18.00
... : The Deluxe Edition Book One HC (2009, $29.99, DJ) r/#1-10; character sketch-a 30.00
... : The Deluxe Edition Book Two HC (2010, $29.99, DJ) r/#11-18 & ... : The Last Castle 30.00
... : The Good Prince (2008, $17.99, TPB) r/#60-69 18.00
... : The Great Fables Crossover (2010, $17.99, TPB) r/#83-85, Jack of Fables #33-35 and The Literals #1-3; sneak preview of Peter & Max: A Fables Novel 18.00
... : The Last Castle (2003, $5.95) Hamilton-a/Willingham-s; prequel to title 6.00
... : The Mean Seasons (2005, $14.99, TPB) r/#22,28-33 15.00
... : War and Pieces (2008, $17.99, TPB) r/#70-75; sketch and pin-up pages 18.00
... : Witches (2010, $17.99, TPB) r/#86-93 18.00
... : Wolves (2006, $17.99, TPB) r/#48-51; script to #50 18.00

FABLES: THE WOLF AMONG US (Based on the Telltale Games video game)
DC Comics (Vertigo): Mar, 2015 - No. 16, Jun, 2016 ($3.99, printing of digital first stories)
1-16-Prequel to Fables; Sturges & Justus-s 4.00

FACE, THE (Tony Trent, the Face No. 3 on) (See Big Shot Comics)
Columbia Comics Group: 1941 - No. 2, 1943

1-The Face; Mart Bailey WWII-c	113	226	339	718	1234	1750
2-Bailey WWII-c	77	154	231	493	847	1200

FACES OF EVIL
DC Comics: Mar, 2009 ($2.99, series of one-shots)
... : Deathstroke 1 - Jeanty-a/Ladronn-c; Ravager app. 3.00
... : Kobra 1 - Jason Burr returns; Julian Lopez-a 3.00
... : Prometheus 1 - Gates-s/Dallacchio-a; origin re-told; Anima killed 3.00
... : Solomon Grundy 1 - Johns-s/Kolins-a; leads into Solomon Grundy mini-series 3.00

FACTOR X
Marvel Comics: Mar, 1995 - No. 4, July, 1995 ($1.95, limited series)
1-Age of Apocalypse 5.00
2-4 4.00

FACULTY FUNNIES
Archie Comics: June, 1989 - No. 5, May, 1990 (75¢/95¢ #2 on)
1-5: 1,2,4,5-The Awesome Foursome app. 4.00

FADE FROM GRACE
Beckett Comics: Aug, 2004 - No. 5, Mar, 2005 (99¢/$1.99)
1-(99¢) Jeff Amano-a/c; Gabriel Benson-s; origin of Fade 3.00
2-5-($1.99) 3.00
TPB (2005, $14.99) r/#1-5; cover gallery, afterword by David Mack 15.00

FADE OUT, THE
Image Comics: Aug, 2014 - No. 12, Jan, 2016 ($3.50/$3.99)
1-12-Ed Brubaker-s/Sean Phillips-a/c. 12-($3.99) 4.00

FAFHRD AND THE GREY MOUSER (Also see Sword of Sorcery & Wonder Woman #202)
Marvel Comics: Oct, 1990 - No. 4, 1991 ($4.50, 52 pgs., squarebound)
1-4: Mignola/Williamson-a; Chaykin scripts 5.00

FAGIN THE JEW
Doubleday: Oct, 2003 ($15.95, softcover graphic novel)
nn-Will Eisner-s/a; story of Fagin from Dickens' Oliver Twist 16.00

FAIREST (Characters from Fables)
DC Comics (Vertigo): May, 2012 - No. 33, Mar, 2015 ($2.99)
1-33: 1-6-Willingham-s/Jimenez-a. 1-Wraparound-c by Hughes & variant-c by Jimenez 3.00
... : In All The Land HC (2013, $24.99, dustjacket) New short stories by various; Hughes-c 25.00

FAIRLADY
Image Comics: Apr, 2019 - No. 5, Aug, 2019 ($3.99)
1-5-Brian Schirmer-s/Claudio Balboni-a 4.00

FAIRY QUEST: OUTCASTS
BOOM! Studios: Nov, 2014 - No. 2, Dec, 2014 ($3.99, limited series)
1,2-Jenkins-s/Ramos-a/c 4.00

FAIRY QUEST: OUTLAWS
BOOM! Studios: Feb, 2013 - No. 2, Mar, 2013 ($3.99, limited series)
1,2-Jenkins-s/Ramos-a/c 4.00

FAIRY TALE PARADE (See Famous Fairy Tales)
Dell Publishing Co.: June-July, 1942 - No. 121, Oct, 1946 (Most by Walt Kelly)

1-Kelly-a begins	86	172	258	688	1544	2400
2(8-9/42)	38	76	114	285	641	1000
3-5 (10-11/42 - 2-4/43)	29	58	87	196	441	685
6-9 (5-7/43 - 11.1/43-44)	22	44	66	154	340	525
Four Color 50('44), 69('45), 87('45)	21	42	63	147	324	500
Four Color 104('44)-Last Kelly issue	16	32	48	112	249	385
Four Color 121('46)-Not by Kelly	10	20	30	69	147	225

NOTE: #1-9, 4-Color 50, 69 have Kelly c/a; 4-Color #87, 104, 114-**Kelly** art only. #9 has a redrawn version of The Reluctant Dragon. This series contains all the classic fairy tales from Jack In The Beanstalk to Cinderella.

FAIRY TALES
Ziff-Davis Publ. Co. (Approved Comics): No. 10, Apr-May, 1951 - No. 11, June-July, 1951

	GD 2.0	VG 4.0	FN 6.0	VF 8.0	VF/NM 9.0	NM- 9.2
10,11-Painted-c	26	52	78	154	252	350

FAITH
DC Comics (Vertigo): Nov, 1999 - No. 5, Mar, 2000 ($2.50, limited series)
1-5-Ted McKeever-s/c/a 4.00

FAITH (Zephyr from Harbinger)
Valiant Entertainment: Jan, 2016 - No. 4, Apr, 2016 ($3.99, limited series)
1-4-Houser-s/Portela-a. 3,4-Torque app. 4.00

FAITH (Harbinger)
Valiant Entertainment: Jul, 2016 - No. 12, Jun, 2017 ($3.99)
1-12: 1-4-Houser-s/Pere Pérez-a. 5-Hillary Clinton app. 7-12-Eisma-a 4.00
Faith's Winter Wonderland Special 1 (12/17, $3.99) Sauvage-s/Portela & Kim-a 4.00

FAITH AND THE FUTURE FORCE (Harbinger)
Valiant Entertainment: Jul, 2017 - No. 4, Oct, 2017 ($3.99, limited series)
1-4-Houser-s. 1-Segovia & Kitson-a. 2-Kitson & Bernard-a. 3-Most Valiant heroes app. 4.00

FAITH DREAMSIDE (Harbinger)
Valiant Entertainment: Sept, 2018 - No. 4, Jan, 2019 ($3.99, limited series)
1-4-Houser-s/MJ Kim-a; Doctor Mirage app. 4.00

FAITHFUL
Marvel Comics/Lovers' Magazine: Nov, 1949 - No. 2, Feb, 1950 (52 pgs.)

1-Photo-c	34	68	102	199	325	450
2-Photo-c	19	38	57	111	176	240

FAITHLESS (Also see Heartbeat)
BOOM! Studios: Apr, 2019 - No. 6, Sept, 2019 ($3.99, limited series)
1-6-Brian Azzarello-s/Maria Llovet-a 4.00

FAITHLESS II
BOOM! Studios: Jun, 2020 - No. 6, Nov, 2020 ($3.99, limited series)
1-6-Brian Azzarello-s/Maria Llovet-a 4.00

FAITHLESS III
BOOM! Studios: Feb, 2022 - No. 6, Jul, 2022 ($3.99, limited series)
1-6-Brian Azzarello-s/Maria Llovet-a 4.00

FAKER
DC Comics (Vertigo): Sept, 2007 - No. 6, Feb, 2008 ($2.99, limited series)
1-6-Mike Carey-s/Jock-a/c 3.00
TPB (2008, $14.99) r/#1-6; Jock sketch pages 15.00

FALCON (See Marvel Premiere #49, Avengers #181 & Captain America #117 & 133)
Marvel Comics Group: Nov, 1983 - No. 4, Feb, 1984 (Mini-series)

1-Paul Smith-a(p)	2	4	6	9	13	16
2-4: 2-Paul Smith-c/Mark Bright-a. 3-Kupperberg-c						6.00

FALCON (Marvel Legacy)
Marvel Comics: Dec, 2017 - No. 8, Jul, 2018 ($3.99)
1-8: 1-Sam Wilson back as the Falcon after Secret Empire; Barnes-s/Cassara-a. 6-8-Misty Knight app. 7,8-Blade app. 4.00

FALCON & WINTER SOLDIER
Marvel Comics: Apr, 2020 - No. 5, Jan, 2021 ($3.99, limited series)
1-5-Derek Landy-s/Federico Vicentini-a; intro. The Natural 4.00

FALL AND RISE OF CAPTAIN ATOM, THE
DC Comics: Mar, 2017 - No. 6, Aug, 2017 ($2.99, limited series)
1-6-Bates-s/Conrad-a 3.00

FALLEN ANGEL
DC Comics: Sept, 2003 - No. 20, July, 2005 ($2.50/$2.95)
1-9-Peter David-s/David Lopez-a/Stelfreeze-c; intro. Lee 3.00
10-20: 10-Begin $2.95-c. 13,17-Kaluta-c. 20-Last issue; Pérez-c 3.00
TPB (2004, $12.95) r/#1-6; intro. by Harlan Ellison 13.00
Down to Earth TPB (2007, $14.99) r/#7-12 15.00

FALLEN ANGEL
IDW Publ.: Dec, 2005 - No. 33, Dec, 2008 ($3.99)
1-33: 1-14-Peter David-s/J.K Woodward-a. Retailer variant-c for each. 15-Donaldson-a. 17-Flip cover with Shi story; Tucci-a. 25-Wraparound-c; character gallery 4.00
... Reborn 1-4 (7/09 - No. 4, 10/09, $3.99) David-s/Woodward-a; Illyria (from Angel) app. 4.00
... Return of the Son 1-4 (1/11 - No. 4, 4/11, $3.99) David-s/Woodward-a; 4.00
... : To Serve in Heaven TPB (8/06, $19.99) r/#1-5; gallery of reg & variant covers 20.00

FALLEN ANGEL ON THE WORLD OF MAGIC: THE GATHERING
Acclaim (Armada): May, 1996 ($5.95, one-shot)
1-Nancy Collins story 6.00

FALLEN ANGELS
Marvel Comics Group: April, 1987 - No. 8, Nov, 1987 (Limited series)
1-8 4.00

FALLEN ANGELS (Follows from House of X & Powers of X series)
Marvel Comics: Jan, 2020 - No. 6, Mar, 2020 ($4.99/$3.99, limited series)
1-($4.99) Bryan Hill-s/Szymon Kudranski-a; Psylocke, Magneto, Cable, X-23 app. 5.00
2-6-($3.99) Havok-a. 5,6-Bling! and Husk app. 4.00

FALLEN FRIEND (The Death of Ms. Marvel) (See 2023's Amazing Spider-Man #26)
Marvel Comics: Sept, 2023 ($4.99, one-shot)
1-Wilson-s/Miyazawa-a; Waid-s/Ramos-a; Ahmed-s/Di Vito-a 5.00

FALLEN SON: THE DEATH OF CAPTAIN AMERICA
Marvel Comics: June, 2007 - No. 5, Aug, 2007 ($2.99, limited series)
1-5: Loeb-s in all. 1-Wolverine; Yu-a/c. 2-Avengers; McGuinness-a/c. 3-Captain America; Romita Jr.-a/c; Hawkeye app. 4-Spider-Man; Finch-c/a. 5-Cassaday-c/a 3.00
1-5-Variant covers by Turner 3.00
HC (2007, $19.99, dustjacket) r/#1-5 20.00
TPB (2007, $13.99) r/#1-5 14.00

FALLEN WORLD
Valiant Entertainment: May, 2019 - No. 5, Sept, 2019 ($3.99, limited series)

Fables #140 © Willingham & DC

Falcon (2017 series) #7 MAR

Famous Funnies #15 © EAS

	GD 2.0	VG 4.0	FN 6.0	VF 8.0	VF/NM 9.0	NM- 9.2
1-5-Abnett-s/Pollina-a; cyborg samurai Rai in New Japan in 4002 AD						4.00

FALLING IN LOVE
Arleigh Pub. Co./National Per. Pub.: Sept-Oct, 1955 - No. 143, Oct-Nov, 1973

	GD 2.0	VG 4.0	FN 6.0	VF 8.0	VF/NM 9.0	NM- 9.2
1	61	122	183	390	670	950
2	32	64	96	188	307	425
3-10	20	40	60	120	195	270
11-20	16	32	48	94	147	200
21-40	14	28	42	82	121	160
41-47: 47-Last 10¢ issue	14	28	42	78	112	145
48-70	6	12	18	38	69	100
71-99,108: 108-Wood-a (4 pgs., 7/69)	5	10	15	30	50	70
100 (7/68)	5	10	15	31	53	75
101-107,109-124	3	6	9	21	33	45
125-133: 52 pgs.	4	8	12	27	44	60
134-143	3	6	9	16	23	30

NOTE: *Colan* c/a-75, 81. 52 pgs.-#125-133.

FALLING MAN, THE
Image Comics: Feb, 1998 ($2.95)

1-McCorkindale-s/Hester-a						4.00

FALL OF THE HOUSE OF USHER, THE (See A Corben Special & Spirit section 8/22/48)

FALL OF THE HOUSE OF X (X-Men)
Marvel Comics: Mar, 2024 ($5.99/$4.99, limited series)

1-($5.99) Duggan-s/Werneck-a; the trial of Cyclops						6.00
2-($4.99) Polaris app.						5.00

FALL OF THE HULKS (Also see Hulk and Incredible Hulk)
Marvel Comics: Feb, 2010 - July, 2010 ($3.99, one-shots & limited series)

Alpha (2/10) Pelletier-a; The Leader, Dr. Doom, MODOK and The Thinker app.						4.00
Gamma (2/10) Romita Jr. -a; funeral for General Ross						4.00
Red Hulk (3/10 - No. 4, 6/10) 1-4: 1-A-Bomb app.						4.00
Savage She-Hulks (5/10 - No. 3, 7/10) 1-3: Cover tryptich by Campbell; Espin-a						4.00

FALL OF THE ROMAN EMPIRE (See Movie Comics)

FALL OUT TOY WORKS
Image Comics: Sept, 2009 - No. 5, Jun, 2010 ($3.99)

1-5-Co-created by Pete Wentz of the band Fall Out Boy; Basri-a. 5-Lau-c						4.00

FAMILY AFFAIR (TV)
Gold Key: Feb, 1970 - No. 4, Oct, 1970 (25¢)

	GD 2.0	VG 4.0	FN 6.0	VF 8.0	VF/NM 9.0	NM- 9.2
1-With pull-out poster; photo-c	6	12	18	37	66	95
1-With poster missing	3	6	9	17	26	35
2-4-Photo-c	3	6	9	21	33	45

FAMILY DYNAMIC, THE
DC Comics: Aug, 2008 - No. 3, Dec, 2008 ($2.25)

1-3-J. Torres-s/Tim Levins-a						3.00

FAMILY FUNNIES
Parents' Magazine Institute: No. 9, Aug-Sept, 1946

	GD 2.0	VG 4.0	FN 6.0	VF 8.0	VF/NM 9.0	NM- 9.2
9	8	16	24	42	54	65

FAMILY FUNNIES (Tiny Tot Funnies No. 9)
Harvey Publications: Sept, 1950 - No. 8, Apr, 1951

	GD 2.0	VG 4.0	FN 6.0	VF 8.0	VF/NM 9.0	NM- 9.2
1-Mandrake (has over 30 King Feature strips)	13	26	39	74	105	135
2-Flash Gordon, 1 pg.	8	16	24	44	57	70
3-8: 4,5,7-Flash Gordon, 1 pg.	7	14	21	37	46	55

FAMILY GUY (TV)
Devil's Due Publ.: 2006 ($6.95)

nn-101 Ways to Kill Lois; 2-Peter Griffin's Guide to Parenting; 3-Books Don't Taste Very Good						7.00
... A Big Book o' Crap TPB (10/06, $16.95) r/nn,2,3						17.00

FAMILY MATTER
Kitchen Sink Press: 1998 ($24.95/$15.95, graphic novel)

Hardcover ($24.95) Will Eisner-s/a						25.00
Softcover ($15.95)						16.00

FAMILY TREE
Image Comics: Nov, 2019 - No. 12, Jun, 2021 ($3.99)

1-12-Jeff Lemire-s/Phil Hester-a/c						4.00

FAMOUS AUTHORS ILLUSTRATED (See Stories by...)

FAMOUS CRIMES
Fox Feature Syndicate/M.S. Dist. No. 51,52: June, 1948 - No. 19, Sept, 1950; No. 20, Aug, 1951; No. 51, 52, 1953

	GD 2.0	VG 4.0	FN 6.0	VF 8.0	VF/NM 9.0	NM- 9.2
1-Blue Beetle app. & crime story-r/Phantom Lady #16	174	348	522	1114	1907	2700
2-Has woman dissolved in acid; lingerie-c/panels	181	362	543	1158	1979	2800
3-Injury-to-eye story used in SOTI, pg. 112; has two electrocution stories	90	180	270	576	988	1400
4-6	36	72	108	211	343	475
7- "Tarzan, the Wyoming Killer" (SOTI, pg. 44)	57	114	171	362	619	875
8-20: 17-Morisi-a. 20-Same cover as #15	28	56	84	165	270	375
51 (nd, 1953)	22	44	66	132	216	300
52 (Exist?)	24	48	72	142	234	325

FAMOUS FEATURE STORIES
Dell Publishing Co.: 1938 (7-1/2x11", 68 pgs.)

	GD 2.0	VG 4.0	FN 6.0	VF 8.0	VF/NM 9.0	NM- 9.2
1-Tarzan, Terry & the Pirates, King of the Royal Mtd., Buck Jones, Dick Tracy, Smilin' Jack, Dan Dunn, Don Winslow, G-Man, Tailspin Tommy, Mutt & Jeff, Little Orphan Annie reprints - all illustrated text	81	162	243	518	884	1250

FAMOUS FIRST EDITION (See Limited Collectors' Edition)
National Periodical Publications/DC Comics: ($1.00, 10x13-1/2", 72 pgs.) (No.6-8, 68 pgs.)
1974 - No. 8, Aug-Sept, 1975; C-61, 1979
(Hardbound editions with dust jackets are from Lyle Stuart, Inc.)

	GD 2.0	VG 4.0	FN 6.0	VF 8.0	VF/NM 9.0	NM- 9.2
C-26-Action Comics #1; gold ink outer-c	6	12	18	40	73	105
C-26-Hardbound edition w/dust jacket	15	30	45	105	233	360
C-28-Detective #27; silver ink outer-c	6	12	18	42	79	115
C-28-Hardbound edition w/dust jacket	15	30	45	105	233	360
C-30-Sensation #1(1974); bronze ink outer-c	5	10	15	33	57	80
C-30-Hardbound edition w/dust jacket	13	26	39	89	195	300
F-4-Whiz Comics #2(#1)(10-11/74)-Cover not identical to original (dropped "Gangway for Captain Marvel" from cover); gold ink on outer-c	5	10	15	30	50	70
F-4-Hardbound edition w/dust jacket	13	26	39	89	195	300
F-5-Batman #1(F-6 inside); silver ink on outer-c	5	10	15	34	60	85
F-5-Hardbound edition w/dust jacket (exist?)	13	26	39	89	195	300
V2#F-6-Wonder Woman #1	5	10	15	35	63	90
F-6-Wonder Woman #1 Hardbound w/dust jacket	13	26	39	89	195	300
F-7-All-Star Comics #3	5	10	15	31	53	75
F-8-Flash Comics #1(8-9/75)	5	10	15	31	53	75
V8#C-61-Superman #1(1979, $2.00)	4	8	12	28	47	65
V8#C-61 (Whitman variant)	5	10	15	30	50	70
V8#C-61 (Softcover in plain grey slipcase, edition of 250 copies) Each signed by Jerry Siegel and Joe Shuster at the bottom of the inside front cover						600.00

Warning: The above books are almost **exact** reprints of the originals that they represent except for the Giant-Size format. None of the originals are Giant-Size. The first five issues and C-61 were printed with two covers. Reprint information can be found on the outside cover, but not on the inside cover which was reprinted exactly like the original (inside and out).

FAMOUS FUNNIES
Eastern Color: 1934; July, 1934 - No. 218, July, 1955

A Carnival of Comics (See Promotional Comics section)

Series 1-(Very rare)(nd-early 1934)(68 pgs.) No publisher given (Eastern Color PrintingCo.); sold in chain stores for 10¢. 35,000 print run. Contains Sunday strip reprints of Mutt & Jeff, Reg'lar Fellers, Nipper, Hairbreadth Harry, Strange As It Seems, Joe Palooka, Dixie Dugan, The Nebbs, Keeping Up With the Jones, and others. Inside front and back covers and pages 1-16 of Famous Funnies Series 1, #s 49-64 reprinted from **Famous Funnies, A Carnival of Comics**, and most of pages 17-48 reprinted from **Funnies on Parade**.

	GD 2.0	VG 4.0	FN 6.0	VF 8.0	VF/NM 9.0	NM- 9.2
	7700	15,400	23,100	46,000	--	--
No. 1 (Rare)(7/34-on stands 5/34) - Eastern Color Printing Co. First monthly newsstand comic book. Contains Sunday strip reprints of Toonerville Folks, Mutt & Jeff, Hairbreadth Harry, S'Matter Pop, Nipper, Dixie Dugan, The Bungle Family, Connie, Ben Webster, Tailspin Tommy, The Nebbs, Joe Palooka, & others.	3530	7060	10,590	26,500	--	--
2 (Rare, 9/34)	840	1680	2520	6300	--	--
3-Buck Rogers Sunday strip-r by Rick Yager begins, ends #218; not in #191-208; 1st comic book app. of Buck Rogers; the number of the 1st strip reprinted is pg. 190, Series No. 1	1000	2000	3000	7500	--	--
4	360	720	1080	2700	--	--
5-1st Christmas-c on a newsstand comic	425	850	1275	3200	--	--
6-10	260	520	780	1950	--	--
11,12,18-Four pgs. of Buck Rogers in each issue, completes stories in Buck Rogers #1 which lacks these pages. 18-Two pgs. of Buck Rogers reprinted in Daisy Comics #1	129	258	387	826	1413	2000
13-17,19,20: 14-Has two Buck Rogers panels missing. 17-2nd Christmas-c on a newsstand comic (12/35)	97	194	291	621	1061	1500
21,23-30: 27-(10/36)-War on Crime begins (4 pgs.); 1st true crime in comics (reprints); other photo-c. 29-X-Mas-c (12/36)	74	148	222	470	810	1150
22-Four pgs. of Buck Rogers needed to complete stories in Buck Rogers #1	87	174	261	553	952	1350
31,33,34,36,37,39,40: 33-Careers of Baby Face Nelson & John Dillinger traced	52	104	156	328	552	775
32-(3/37) 1st app. the Phantom Magician (costume hero) in Advs. of Patsy						

	GD 2.0	VG 4.0	FN 6.0	VF 8.0	VF/NM 9.0	NM- 9.2
35-Two pgs. Buck Rogers omitted in Buck Rogers #2	57	114	171	362	619	875
38-Full color portrait of Buck Rogers	60	120	180	381	653	925
41-60: 41,53-X-Mas-c. 55-Last bottom panel, pg. 4 in Buck Rogers redrawn in Buck Rogers #3	39	78	117	240	395	550
61,63,64,66,67,69,70	28	56	84	165	270	375
62,65,68,73-78-Two pgs. Kirby-"Lightnin' & the Lone Rider". 65,77-X-Mas-c	30	60	90	177	289	400
71,79,80: 80-(3/41)-Buck Rogers story continues from Buck Rogers #5	25	50	75	150	245	340
72-Speed Spaulding begins by Marvin Bradley (artist), ends #88. This series was written by Edwin Balmer & Philip Wylie (later appeared as film & book "When Worlds Collide")	28	56	84	154	252	350
81-Origin & 1st app. Invisible Scarlet O'Neil (4/41); strip begins #82, ends #167; 1st non-funny-c (Scarlet O'Neil)	168	336	504	1075	1838	2600
82-Buck Rogers-c	41	82	123	256	428	600
83-87,90: 86-Connie vs. Monsters on the Moon-c (sci/fi). 87 has last Buck Rogers full page-r. 90-Bondage-c	24	44	66	128	209	290
88,89: 88-Buck Rogers in "Moon's End" by Calkins, 2 pgs.(not reprints). Beginning with #88, all Buck Rogers pgs. have been rearranged panels. 89-Origin & 1st app. Fearless Flint, the Flint Man	27	54	81	158	259	360
91-93,95,96,98-99,101,103-110: 98-Hitler, Tojo and Mussolini on inside back-c. 101-Christmas cover. 105-Series 2 begins (Strip Page #1)	18	36	54	105	165	225
94-Buck Rogers in "Solar Holocaust" by Calkins, 3 pgs.(not reprints)	20	40	60	117	189	260
97-War Bond promotion, Buck Rogers by Calkins, 2 pgs.(not reprints)	20	40	60	114	182	250
100-1st comic to reach #100; 100th Anniversary cover features 11 major Famous Funnies characters, including Buck Rogers	28	56	84	165	270	375
102-Chief Wahoo vs. Hitler,Tojo & Mussolini-c (1/43)	100	200	300	635	1093	1550
111-130 (5/45): 113-X-Mas-c	14	28	42	80	115	150
131-150 (1/47): 137-Strip page No. 110 omitted; Christmas-c. 144-(7/46) 12th Anniversary cover	13	26	39	74	105	135
151-162,164-168: 162-New Year's Eve-c	12	24	36	69	97	125
163-St. Valentine's Day-c (2/48)	14	28	42	81	118	155
169,170-Two text illos. by Al Williamson, his 1st comic book work	15	30	45	83	124	165
171-190: 171-Strip pgs. 227,229,230, Series 2 omitted. 172-Strip Pg. 232 omitted. 173-Christmas-c. 190-Buck Rogers ends with start of strip pg. 302, Series 2; Oaky Doaks-c/story	11	22	33	64	90	115
191-197,199,201,203,206-208: No Buck Rogers. 191-Barney Carr, Space detective begins, ends #192.	11	22	33	62	86	110
198,200,202,205-One pg. Frazetta ads; no B. Rogers	11	22	33	64	90	115
204-Used in POP, 7/8/99; war cover, pg #208	14	28	42	81	115	150
209-211,215,216: Frazetta-c. 209-Buck Rogers begins (12/53) with strip pg. 480, Series 2; 211-Buck Rogers ads by Anderson begins, ends #217. #215-Contains B. Rogers strip pg. 515-518, series 3 followed by pgs.179-181, Series 3	309	618	927	2163	3782	5400
212-214-Frazetta-c	514	1028	1542	3750	6625	9500
217-Buck Rogers-c	28	56	84	165	270	375
218-Buck Rogers ends with pg. 199, Series 3; Wee Three-c/story	12	24	36	69	97	125

NOTE: Rick Yager did the Buck Rogers Sunday strips reprinted in Famous Funnies. The Sundays were formerly done by Russ Keaton and Lt. Dick Calkins did the dailies, but would sometimes assist Yager on a panel or two from time to time. Strip No. 169 is Yager's first full Buck Rogers page. Yager did the strip until 1958 when Murphy Anderson took over. Tuska art from 4/26/59 - 1965. Virtually every panel was rewritten for Famous Funnies but not identical to the original Sunday page. The Buck Rogers reprints run continuously through Famous Funnies Issue No. 190 (Strip No. 302) with no break in story line. The story line has no continuity after No. 190. The Buck Rogers newspaper strips came out in four series: Series 1, 3/30/30 - 9/21/41 (No. 1 - 600); Series 2, 9/28/41 -10/21/51 (No. 1 -525)/Strip No. 110-1/2 (1/2 pg.) published in only a few newspapers); Series 3, 10/28/51 -2/9/58 (No. 100-428) (No No.1-99); Series 4, 2/16/58 - 6/13/65 (No numbers, dates only). Everett c-85, 86. Moulton a-100. Chief Wahoo c-93, 97, 102, 116, 130, 136, 139, 151. Dickie Dare c-83, 88. Fearless Flint c-89. Invisible Scarlet c-81, 87, 95, 121(part), 132. Scorchy Smith c-84, 90.

FAMOUS FUNNIES
Eastern Color: 1936

nn-2-color cvr/reprint of #10 w/issue #21(4/36) on inside. Blank back & interior cvrs. A CGC 5.5 copy sold in 2018 for $1920

FAMOUS FUNNIES
Super Comics: 1964

	GD 2.0	VG 4.0	FN 6.0	VF 8.0	VF/NM 9.0	NM- 9.2
Super Reprint Nos. 15-18:17-r/Double Trouble #1. 18-Space Comics #?	2	4	6	11	16	20

FAMOUS GANGSTERS (Crime on the Waterfront No. 4)
Avon Periodicals/Realistic No. 3: Apr, 1951 - No. 3, Feb, 1952

	GD 2.0	VG 4.0	FN 6.0	VF 8.0	VF/NM 9.0	NM- 9.2
1-3: 1-Capone, Dillinger; c/Avon paperback #329. 2-Dillinger Machine Gun Killer; Wood-c/a (1 pg.); r/Saint #7 & retitled "Mike Strong". 3-Lucky Luciano & Murder, Inc; c/Avon paperback #66	53	106	159	334	567	800

FAMOUS INDIAN TRIBES
Dell Publishing Co.: July-Sept, 1962; No. 2, July, 1972

	GD 2.0	VG 4.0	FN 6.0	VF 8.0	VF/NM 9.0	NM- 9.2
12-264-209(#1) (The Sioux)	3	6	9	16	23	30
2(7/72)-Reprints above	1	3	4	6	8	10

FAMOUS STARS
Ziff-Davis Publ. Co.: Nov-Dec, 1950 - No. 6, Spring, 1952 (All have photo-c)

	GD 2.0	VG 4.0	FN 6.0	VF 8.0	VF/NM 9.0	NM- 9.2
1-Shelley Winters, Susan Peters, Ava Gardner, Shirley Temple; Jimmy Stewart & Shelley Winters photo-c; Whitney-a	42	84	126	265	445	625
2-Betty Hutton, Bing Crosby, Colleen Townsend, Gloria Swanson; Betty Hutton photo-c; Everett-a(2)	37	74	111	188	307	425
3-Farley Granger, Judy Garland's ordeal (life story; she died 6/22/69 at the age of 47), Alan Ladd; Farley Granger photo-c; Whitney-a	47	74	111	222	361	500
4-Al Jolson, Bob Mitchum, Ella Raines, Richard Conte, Vic Damone; Jane Russell and Bob Mitchum photo-c; Crandall-a, 6pgs.	26	52	78	154	252	350
5-Liz Taylor, Betty Grable, Esther Williams, George Brent, Mario Lanza; Liz Taylor photo-c; Krigstein-a	60	120	180	381	653	925
6-Gene Kelly, Hedy Lamarr, June Allyson, William Boyd, Janet Leigh, Gary Cooper; Gene Kelly photo-c	26	52	78	154	252	350

FAMOUS STORIES (...Book No. 2)
Dell Publishing Co.: 1942 - No. 2, 1942

	GD 2.0	VG 4.0	FN 6.0	VF 8.0	VF/NM 9.0	NM- 9.2
1,2: 1-Treasure Island. 2-Tom Sawyer	34	68	102	199	325	450

FAMOUS TV FUNDAY FUNNIES
Harvey Publications: Sept, 1961 (25¢ Giant)

	GD 2.0	VG 4.0	FN 6.0	VF 8.0	VF/NM 9.0	NM- 9.2
1-Casper the Ghost, Baby Huey, Little Audrey	5	10	15	34	60	85

FAMOUS WESTERN BADMEN (Formerly Redskin)
Youthful Magazines: No. 13, Dec, 1952 - No. 15, Apr, 1953

	GD 2.0	VG 4.0	FN 6.0	VF 8.0	VF/NM 9.0	NM- 9.2
13-Redskin story	16	32	48	92	144	195
14,15: 15-The Dalton Boys story	12	24	36	69	97	125

FAN BOY
DC Comics: Mar, 1999 - No. 6, Aug, 1999 ($2.50, limited series)

1-6: 1-Art by Aragonés and various in all. 2-Green Lantern-c/a by Gil Kane. 3-JLA. 4-Sgt. Rock art by Heath, Marie Severin. 5-Batman art by Sprang, Adams, Miller, Timm. 6-Wonder Woman; art by Rude, Grell — 4.00

TPB (2001, $12.95) r/#1-6 — 13.00

FANBOYS VS. ZOMBIES
BOOM! Studios: Apr, 2012 - No. 20, Nov, 2013 ($1.00/$3.99)

1-($1.00) Eight covers; Humphries-s/Gaylord-a; zombies at San Diego Comic-Con — 3.00

2-20-($3.99) 2-12-Multiple covers on each. 17-Bryan Turner-a — 4.00

FANTASTIC (Formerly Captain Science; Beware No. 10 on)
Youthful Magazines: No. 8, Feb, 1952 - No. 9, Apr, 1952

	GD 2.0	VG 4.0	FN 6.0	VF 8.0	VF/NM 9.0	NM- 9.2
8-Capt. Science by Harrison	90	180	270	576	988	1400
9-Harrison-a; decapitation, shrunken head panels	61	122	183	390	670	950

FANTASTIC ADVENTURES
Super Comics: 1963 - 1964 (Reprints)

	GD 2.0	VG 4.0	FN 6.0	VF 8.0	VF/NM 9.0	NM- 9.2
9,10,12,15,16,18: 9-r/? 10-r/He-Man #2(Toby). 11-Disbrow-a. 12-Unpublished Chesler material? 15-r/Spook #23. 16-r/Dark Shadows #2(Steinway); Briefer-a.18-r/Superior Stories?	3	6	9	17	26	35
11-Wood-a; r/Blue Bolt #118	4	8	12	23	37	50
17-Baker-a(2) r/Seven Seas #6	4	8	12	23	37	50

FANTASTIC COMICS
Fox Feature Syndicate: Dec, 1939 - No. 23, Nov, 1941

	GD 2.0	VG 4.0	FN 6.0	VF 8.0	VF/NM 9.0	NM- 9.2
1-Intro/origin Samson; Stardust, The Super Wizard, Sub Saunders (by Kiefer), Space Smith, Capt. Kidd app	1000	2000	3000	7500	13,500	19,500
2-Powell text illos	411	822	1233	2877	5039	7200
3-Classic Lou Fine Robot-c; Powell text illos	15,000	30,000	45,000	82,500	101,250	120,000
4-Lou Fine-c	514	1028	1542	3750	6625	9500
5-Classic Lou Fine-c	383	766	1149	2681	4691	6700
6,7-Simon-c. 6-Bondage/torture-c	514	708	1062	2478	4339	6200
8-Bondage/torture-c	300	600	900	2070	3635	5200
9,10: 9-Bondage-c. 10-Intro/origin David, Samson's aide	206	412	618	1318	2259	3200
11-16,18-20: 11-Bondage/torture on a bed of nails-c. 16-Stardust ends	161	322	483	1030	1765	2500
17,23: 17-1st app. Black Fury & sidekick Chuck; ends #23. 23-Origin The Gladiator	194	388	582	1242	2121	3000
21-The Banshee begins(origin); ends #23; Hitler-c	458	972	1458	3550	6275	9000
22-WWII Holocaust bondage torture-c (likeness of Hitler as furnace on-c)	784	1568	2352	5723	10,112	14,500

NOTE: Lou Fine c-1-5. Tuska a-3-5, 8. Issue #11 has indicia in Mystery Men Comics #15. All issues feature Samson covers.

FANTASTIC COMICS (Imagining of a 1941 issue by modern creators in Golden Age style)
Image Comics: Jan, 2008 ($5.99, Golden Age sized, one-shot)

24-Samson, Yank Wilson, Stardust, Sub Saunders, Space Smith, Capt. Kidd app.; Larsen-c/a; art by Allred, Sienkiewicz, Yeates, Scioli, Hembeck, Ashley Wood & others — 6.00

FANTASTIC COMICS (Fantastic Fears #1-9; Becomes Samson #12)
Ajax/Farrell Publ.: No. 10, Nov-Dec, 1954 - No. 11, Jan-Feb, 1955

	GD 2.0	VG 4.0	FN 6.0	VF 8.0	VF/NM 9.0	NM- 9.2
10 (#1)	37	74	111	222	361	500
11-Robot-c	45	90	135	284	480	675

FANTASTIC FABLES
Silverwolf Comics: Feb, 1987 - No. 2, 1987 ($1.50, 28 pgs., B&W)

1,2: 1-Tim Vigil-a (6 pgs.). 2-Tim Vigil-a (7 pgs.) — 4.00

FANTASTIC FEARS (Formerly Captain Jet) (Fantastic Comics #10 on)
Ajax/Farrell Publ.: No. 7, May, 1953 - No. 9, Sept-Oct, 1954

	GD 2.0	VG 4.0	FN 6.0	VF 8.0	VF/NM 9.0	NM- 9.2
7(#1, 5/53)-Tales of Stalking Terror	110	220	330	704	1202	1700
8(#2, 7/53)	68	136	204	435	743	1050
3,4	58	116	174	371	636	900
5-(1-2/54)-Ditko story (1st drawn) is written by Bruce Hamilton; r-in Weird V2#8 but Daring Love #1 was published 1st; 1st pro work for Ditko	284	568	852	1818	3109	4400
6-Decapitation-girl's head w/paper cutter (classic)	174	348	522	1114	1907	2700
7(5-6/54), 9(9-10/54)	50	100	150	315	533	750
8(7-8/54)-Contains story intended for Jo-Jo; name changed to Kaza; decapitation story	54	108	162	343	574	825

FANTASTIC FIVE
Marvel Comics: Oct, 1999 - No. 5, Feb, 2000 ($1.99)

1-5: 1-M2 Universe; recaps origin; Ryan-a. 2-Two covers — 4.00

Spider-Girl Presents Fantastic Five: In Search of Doom (2006, $7.99, digest) r/#1-5 — 8.00

FANTASTIC FIVE
Marvel Comics: Sept, 2007 - No. 5, Nov, 2007 ($2.99, limited series)

1-5-DeFalco-s/Lim-a; Dr. Doom returns vs. the future Fantastic Five — 3.00

...: The Final Doom TPB (2007, $13.99) r/#1-5; cover sketches with inks — 14.00

FANTASTIC FORCE
Marvel Comics: Nov, 1994 - No. 18, Apr, 1996 ($1.75)

1-($2.50)-Foil wraparound-c; intro Fantastic Force w/Huntara, Devlor, Psi-Lord & Vibraxas — 5.00

2-18: 13-She-Hulk app. — 4.00

FANTASTIC FORCE (See Fantastic Four #558, Nu-World heroes from 500 years in the

Fanboys vs. Zombies #18 © BOOM!

Fantastic Comics #23 © FOX

Fantastic Four #115 © MAR

FA

	GD	VG	FN	VF	VF/NM	NM-
	2.0	4.0	6.0	8.0	9.0	9.2

future)
Marvel Comics: Jun, 2009 - No. 4, Sept, 2009 ($3.99/$2.99, limited series)
1-($3.99)-Ahearne-s/Kurth-a/Hitch-c; Fantastic Four app. 4.00
2-4-($2.99) 3,4-Ego the Living Planet app. 3.00

FANTASTIC FOUR (See America's Best TV…, Fireside Book Series, Giant-Size…, Giant Size Super-Stars, Marvel Age…, Marvel Collectors Item Classics, Marvel Knights 4, Marvel Milestone Edition, Marvel's Greatest, Marvel Treasury Edition, Marvel Triple Action, Official Marvel Index to…, Power Record Comics & Ultimate…)

FANTASTIC FOUR (See Volume Three for issues #500-611)
Marvel Comics Group: Nov, 1961 - No. 416, Sept, 1996 (Created by Stan Lee & Jack Kirby)
1-Origin & 1st app. The Fantastic Four (Reed Richards: Mr. Fantastic, Johnny Storm: The Human Torch, Sue Storm: The Invisible Girl, & Ben Grimm: The Thing–Marvel's 1st superhero group since the G.A.; 1st app. S.A. Human Torch); origin/1st app. The Mole Man.
7800 15,600 31,200 78,000 214,000 350,000
1-Golden Record Comic Set Reprint (1966)-cover not identical to original
46 92 138 340 770 1200
with Golden Record 59 118 177 472 1061 1650
2-Vs. The Skrulls (last 10¢ issue); (should have a pin-up of The Thing which many copies are missing) 630 1260 1890 5200 13,100 21,000
3-Fantastic Four don costumes & establish Headquarters; brief 1pg. origin; intro. The Fantasti-Car; Human Torch drawn w/two left hands on-c
660 1320 1980 5450 13,725 22,000
4-1st S. A. Sub-Mariner app. (5/62) 720 1440 2160 5950 14,975 24,000
5-Origin & 1st app. Doctor Doom 3280 6560 9840 26,200 54,100 82,000
6-Sub-Mariner, Dr. Doom team up; 1st Marvel villain team-up; (2nd S.A. Sub-Mariner app.
367 734 1100 3120 7060 11,000
7,9,10: 7-1st app. Kurrgo. 9-3rd Sub-Mariner app. 10-Stan Lee & Jack Kirby app. in story
169 338 507 1394 3147 4900
8-1st app. Puppet-Master & Alicia Masters 179 358 537 1477 3339 5200
11-Origin/1st app. The Impossible Man (2/63) 172 344 516 1419 3210 5000
12-Fantastic Four vs. The Hulk (1st meeting); 1st Hulk x-over & ties w/Amazing Spider-Man #1 as 1st Marvel x-over; (3/63) 415 830 1245 3700 9850 16,000
13-Intro. The Watcher; 1st app. The Red Ghost 317 634 951 2695 6098 9500
14,15,17,19: 14-Sub-Mariner x-over. 15-1st app. Mad Thinker. 19-Intro. Rama-Tut (Kang).
68 136 204 544 1222 1900
16-1st Ant-Man x-over (7/63); Wasp cameo 100 200 300 800 1900 2800
18-Origin/1st app. The Super Skrull 129 258 387 1032 2316 3600
20-Origin/1st app. The Molecule Man 89 178 267 712 1606 2500
21-Intro. The Hate Monger; 1st Sgt. Fury x-over (12/63)
50 100 150 400 900 1400
22-24: 22-Sue Storm gains more powers 40 80 120 296 673 1050
25-The Hulk vs. The Thing (their 1st battle); 3rd Avengers x-over (1st time w/Captain America)(cameo, 4/64); 2nd S.A. app. Cap (takes place between Avengers #4 & 5)
155 310 465 1279 2890 4500
26-The Hulk vs. The Thing (continued); 4th Avengers x-over
69 138 207 552 1251 1950
27-1st Doctor Strange x-over (6/64) 52 104 156 416 933 1450
28-Early X-Men x-over (7/64); same date as X-Men #6
61 122 183 488 1094 1700
29,30: 30-Intro. Diablo 36 72 108 266 596 925
31,32,34,35,37-40: 31-Early Avengers x-over (10/64). 35-Intro/1st app. Dragon Man. 39-Wood inks on Daredevil (early x-over) 26 52 78 182 404 625
33-1st app. Attuma; part photo-c 54 108 162 432 966 1500
36-Intro/1st app. Madam Medusa & the Frightful Four (Sandman, Wizard, Paste Pot Pete)
75 150 225 600 1350 2100
41-44: 41-43-Frightful Four app. 44-Intro. Gorgon 51 102 153 411 1246 380
45-Intro/1st app. The Inhumans (c/story, 12/65); also see Incredible Hulk Special #1 &
Thor #146, & 147 136 272 408 1088 2444 3800
46-1st Black Bolt-c (Kirby) & 1st full app. 71 142 213 568 1284 2000
47-3rd app. The Inhumans 23 46 69 151 356 500
48-Partial origin/1st app. The Silver Surfer & Galactus (3/66) by Lee & Kirby; Galactus brief app. in last panel; 1st of 3 part story 414 828 1242 3602 7800 12,000
49-2nd app./1st cover Silver Surfer & Galactus 241 482 723 1988 4494 7000
50-Silver Surfer battles Galactus; full S.S.-c 241 482 723 1988 4494 7000
51-Classic "This Man…This Monster" story 42 84 126 311 706 1100
52-1st app. The Black Panther (7/66) 367 734 1100 3100 7050 11,000
53-Origin & 2nd app. The Black Panther; origin/1st app. of Klaw
31 62 93 223 499 775
54-Inhumans cameo 16 32 48 110 243 375
55-Thing battles Silver Surfer; 4th app. Silver Surfer 46 92 138 359 805 1250
56-Silver Surfer cameo 17 34 51 117 259 400
57-Dr. Doom steals Silver Surfer's powers (also see Silver Surfer: Loftier Than Mortals); Dr. Doom & Silver Surfer-c 36 72 108 259 580 900
58-60: Dr. Doom with Silver Surfer's powers. 59,60-Inhumans cameo

	13	26	39	89	195	300

61-63,: 61-Silver Surfer cameo; Sandman app. (new costume). 62-1st Blastaar; Sandman app. 63-Sandman & Blastaar team-up 12 24 36 82 179 275
64-1st Kree Sentry #459 15 30 45 103 227 350
65-1st app. Ronan the Accuser; 1st Kree Supreme Intelligence
32 64 96 230 515 800
66-Begin 2 part origin of Him (Warlock); does not app. (9/67)
34 68 102 245 548 850
66,67-2nd printings (1994) 3 6 9 16 23 30
67-Origin/1st brief app. Him (Warlock); 1 page; see Thor #165,166 for 1st full app.; white cover scarcer in true high grade 64 128 192 512 1156 1800
68-71 9 18 27 63 129 195
72-Silver Surfer-c/story (pre-dates Silver Surfer #1) 38 76 114 285 641 1000
73-Spider-Man, D.D., Thor x-over; cont'd from Daredevil #38
30 45 100 220 340
74-Silver Surfer app. 19 38 57 131 291 450
75-Galactus and Silver Surfer app. 26 52 78 182 404 625
76,77: Silver Surfer app.(#77 is same date/S.S. #1) 10 20 30 70 150 230
78-80: 78-Wizard app. 80-1st Tomazooma, the Living Totem
9 18 27 57 111 165
81,84-88: 81-Crystal joins don costume; vs. the Wizard. 84-87-Dr. Doom app.
8 16 24 54 102 150
88-Mole Man app. 8 16 24 54 102 180
82,83-Black Bolt & the Inhumans app.; vs. Maximus 9 18 27 63 120 180
89-93,95-98,101: 89-Mole Man app. 91-Skrulls disguised as 1930s era gangsters; 1st app. Torgo. 92-The Thing app. as a space gladiator. 95-vs. Torgo. 95-1st app. the Monocle. 96-Mad-Thinker app. 98-Neil Armstrong Moon landing issue. 101-Last Kirby-a issue
7 14 21 49 92 135
94-(1/70) Intro Agatha Harkness; Frightful Four app. 21 42 63 147 324 500
99-Black Bolt & the Inhumans app. 8 16 24 54 102 150
100 (7/70) F.F. vs Thinker and Puppet-Master 10 20 30 70 150 230
102-104: 102-Romita Sr-a; 102-Sub-Mariner & Magneto app.
7 14 21 48 89 130
105,106,108,109,111: 108-Features Kirby & Buscema-a; Kirby material produced after issue #101, his last official issue before leaving Marvel. 109-Annihilus app. 111-Hulk cameo 6 12 18 41 76 110
107-Classic Thing transformation-c; 1st John Buscema-a on FF (2/71); 1st app. Janus
8 16 24 54 102 150
110-Initial version w/green Thing and blue faces and pink uniforms on-c
48 96 144 365 858 1350
110-Corrected-c w/accurately colored faces and uniforms and orange Thing
9 18 27 61 123 185
112-Hulk Vs. Thing (7/71) 71 142 213 568 1284 2000
113-115: 113-1st app. The Overmind; Watcher app. 114-vs the Overmind. 115-Origin of the Overmind; plot by Stan Lee, Archie Goodwin script; last 15¢ issue
5 10 15 33 63 90
116 (52 pgs.) FF and Dr. Doom vs. the Overmind; the Stranger app.; Goodwin story
8 16 24 57 106 140
117-119: 117,118-Diablo app; Goodwin's 119-Black Panther app. vs Klaw; 1st Roy Thomas FF story 5 10 15 34 60 85
120-1st app. Gabriel the Air-Walker (new herald of Galactus); Stan Lee story
14 28 42 96 211 325
121,123: 121-Silver Surfer vs. Gabriel; Galactus app. 123-Silver Surfer & Galactus app.
6 12 18 38 69 110
122-Silver Surfer & Galactus app; black cover, scarcer in higher grade
7 14 21 49 92 135
124,125,127,130,134-140: 125-Last Stan Lee-s. 127-Mole Man & Tyrannus app. 130-vs the new Frightful Four (Thundra, Sandman, Trapster and Wizard; Black Bolt & Inhumans app.). 134,135-Dragon Man app. 134-1st full Gerry Conway issue. 136-Shaper of Worlds app; Dragon Man cameo. 137-Shaper of Worlds app. 138-Return of the Miracle Man. 139-vs. Miracle Man. 140-Annihilus app. 5 10 15 30 50 70
126-Origin FF retold; cover swipe of FF #1; Roy Thomas scripts begin
5 10 15 35 63 90
128-Four page glossy insert of FF Friends & Foes; Mole Man app.
5 10 15 34 60 85
129-1st app. Thundra (super-strong Femizon) joins new Frightful Four
13 26 39 89 195 300
131-133: 131-Black Bolt, Medusa, Crystal, Quicksilver app; New Frightful Four app; Ross Andru-a; Steranko-c. 132-Black Bolt & Inhumans app; vs. Maximus; last Roy Thomas-s (returns in issue #158). 133-Thing vs Thundra battle issue; Ramona Fradon-a; Gerry Conway script 5 10 15 35 63 90
141-146,148-149: 141-Franklin Richards 'depowered;' Annihilus app.; FF break-up; last Buscema-a. 142-1st Darkoth the Demon; Dr. Doom app; Kirby/ish-a by Buckler begins. 143,144-vs. Dr. Doom. 145,146-vs. Ternak the Abominable Snowman. 148-vs. Wizard, Sandman, Trapster. 149-Sub-Mariner app. 4 8 12 27 44 60
147-Thing vs. Sub-Mariner-c/s 5 10 15 31 53 75

	GD	VG	FN	VF	VF/NM	NM-
	2.0	4.0	6.0	8.0	9.0	9.2

150-Crystal & Quicksilver's wedding; Avengers, Ultron-7 and Black Bolt & the Inhumans app; story continued from Avengers #127

5 10 15 33 57 80

151-154,158-160: 151-1st Mahkizmo the Nuclear Man; origin Thundra. 152,153-Thundra & Mahkizmo app. 154-Nick Fury app; part-r issue (Strange Tales #127). 158,159 vs. Xemu; Black Bolt & Inhumans app. 160-Arkon app.

3 6 9 17 26 35

155-157: Silver Surfer & Dr. Doom app.

4 8 12 28 47 65

161-163,168-171: 162,163-Arkon app. 168-Luke Cage, Power Man joins the FF (to replace the Thing). 169-Luke Cage app; 1st app. Thing exoskeleton. 170-Luke Cage leaves the FF; Puppet Master app. 171-1st Gorr the Golden Gorilla; Pérez-a

3 6 9 14 20 25

164-Re-intro Marvel Boy (as the Crusader); 1st George Pérez-a on FF

6 12 18 42 79 115

165-Origin of Marvel Boy & the Crusader; 1st app Frankie Ray. Pérez-a; death of the Crusader (a new Marvel Boy appears in Captain America #217)

3 6 9 21 33 45

166,167-vs the Hulk; Pérez-a. 167-The Thing loses his powers

4 8 12 25 40 55

169-173-(30¢-¢, limited distribution)(4-8/76)

6 12 18 40 73 105

172-175: 172-Galactus & High Evolutionary app. 175-Galactus vs. High Evolutionary; the Thing regains his powers

3 6 9 15 22 28

176-180: 176-Re-intro Impossible Man; Marvel artists app. 177-1st app. the Texas Twister & Captain Ultra; Impossible Man & Brute app. 178-179-Impossible Man, Tigra & Thundra app; Reed loses his stretching ability. 180-r/#101 by Kirby

3 6 9 14 19 24

181-199: 181-183-The Brute, Mad Thinker & Annihilus app; last Roy Thomas-s. 184-1st Eliminator; Len Wein-s begin. (co-plotter in #183-182) 185,186-New Salem Witches app.; part origin Agatha Harkness. 187,188-vs. Klaw & the Molecule Man. 189-G.A Human Torch app.; r-FF Annual #4. 190-1st Marv Wolfman FF. 191-FF break-up; Wolfman/Wein-s. 192-Last Pérez-a; Texas Twister app. 193,194-Diablo & Darkoth the Death Demon app. 195-Sub-Mariner app.; Wolfman begins as full plotter & scripter. 196-1st full app. of the clone of Dr. Doom. 197-vs. the Red Ghost; Reed regains his stretching ability. 198-vs Dr. Doom. 199-Origin & death of the clone of Doom; Dr. Doom app.

2 4 6 10 14 18

200-(11/78 52 pgs)-FF reunited vs Dr. Doom

4 8 12 27 44 60

201-203,219,222-231: 202-vs. Quasimodo. 219-Sub-Mariner app.; Moench & Sienkiewicz 1st FF work. 222-Agatha Harkness & Gabriel the Devil Hunter app. 224-Contains unused alternate-c for #3 and pin-ups. 225-Thor & Odin app. 226-1st Samurai Destroyer. 229-1st Ebon-Seeker. 230-vs. Ebon Seeker; Avengers app. 231-1st Stygorr of the Negative Zone

1 3 4 6 8 10

204-1st Nova Corps (cameo); 1st app. Queen Adora of Xandar; 1st app. of Xandar; FF vs. the Skrulls

3 6 9 19 30 40

205-1st full app. Nova Corps; Xandarian/Skrull war

3 6 9 17 26 35

206-208: 206-Nova app.; story continued from Nova #25; Sphinx & Skrulls app. 207-Spider-Man app. 208-Nova & the New Champions app. (Powerhouse, Diamondhead, the Comet & Crimebuster); Sphinx app.

2 4 6 9 12 15

209-210,213,214: 209-1st byrne-a on FF; 1st Herbie the Robot. 210-Galactus app. 213-Galactus vs. the Sphinx; Terrax app.

2 4 6 10 14 18

211-1st app. Terrax (new Herald of Galactus)

7 14 21 46 86 125

212-Byrne-a; Galactus vs. the High Evolutionary

3 6 9 17 26 35

215-218,220-221: Byrne-a in all. 215-Blastaar app; 1st app. the Futurist. 216-Blastaar & Futurist app; last Wolfman-s. 217-Early app. Dazzler (4/80); by Byrne; vs Herbie the Robot (destroyed). 218-Spider-Man app.; Frightful Four; continued from Spectacular Spider-Man #42. 220-1st byrne story on FF; origin retold; Avengers and Vindicator app.

1 2 3 5 6 8

232-Byrne story & art begins (7/81); vs. Diablo; brief Dr. Strange app; re-intro Frankie Raye

2 4 6 11 16 20

233-235,237-241,245-249,251,253-256: 233-Hammerhead app. 234,235-Ego the Living Planet. 238-Origin & 1st app. of Frankie Raye's flame powers, joins the FF. The Thing is 'devolved' into an 'uglier' version. 239-1st app. Aunt Petunia. 240-Black Bolt & the Inhumans app; Attilan (home of the Inhumans) relocated to the Moon. 241-Black Panther app. 245-Thing returns to his rocky-look. 246-Dr. Doom app. 247-Doom and FF team-up vs. Prince Zorba; Doom regains rule of Latveria; app. Kristoff. 248-Black Bolt & the Inhumans app. 249-vs Gladiator (of the Sh'iar). 251-FF explore the Negative Zone; Annihilus app. 254-1st Mantracora. 255-Brief Daredevil app; Annihilus app. 256-FF return from the Negative Zone; vs Annihilus; Avengers, Galactus and Nova (Frankie Raye) app.

1 2 3 5 6 8

236-20th Anniversary issue (11/81, 68 pgs, $1.00)-brief origin FF; Byrne-c(p)a; new Kirby-a; Marvel Super-Heroes & Stan Lee app.; cover Dr. Doom and Puppet Master app.; 1st 'Liddleville'

2 4 6 10 14 18

242-vs. Terrax; Thor, Iron Man & Daredevil cameos

2 4 6 8 10 12

243-Classic Galactus-c by Byrne; Thor, Captain America, Dr. Strange, Spider-Man & Daredevil app.

4 8 12 25 40 55

244-Frankie Raye becomes Nova – the new Herald of Galactus

3 6 9 28 47 65

250,257-260: 250-(52 pgs)-Spider-Man x-over; Byrne-a; Skrulls impersonate New X-Men; Gladiator app. 257-Galactus devours the Skrull homeworld; Sue announces pregnancy; Vision & Scarlet Witch cameo. 258-Dr. Doom team-up with Terrax; Kristoff app. 259-Dr. Doom & Terrax. vs FF; Silver Surfer cameo. 260-Terrax, Silver Surfer & Sub-Mariner app.; 'death' of Dr. Doom

1 2 3 5 6 8

252-Reads sideways; Annihilus app. Contains skin 'Tattooz' decals (no 'Tattooz' were included in Canadian editions, also in Amazing Spider-Man #238)

with Tattooz 1 3 4 6 8 10

without Tattooz 1 2 3 5 6 8

261-262: The Trial of Reed Richards. 261-Silver Surfer & the Watcher app. 262-Origin Galactus; John Byrne writes himself into story; the Watcher, Odin, Eternity app.

1 2 3 5 6 8

263-285: 263-Mole Man app. Vision cameo. 264-vs Mole Man; swipes-c of FF #1. 265-Secret Wars x-over; She-Hulk replaces the Thing; Vision & Scarlet Witch app. 267-Dr. Octopus, Michael Morbius, Donald Blake & Bruce Banner app; Sue loses her baby. 268-Origin She-Hulk retold; Hulk and Dr. Octopus app. 269-1st app. Terminus; re-intro Wyatt Wingfoot. 270-vs Terminus. 271-1st app Gormuu (flashback story pre-FF #1). 272-1st app. Nathaniel Richards the Warlord (Reed's father). 273-Nathaniel Richards app. 274-Spider-Man's alien costume app; (4th app. 1/85, 2 pgs.) the Thing app. on Battleworld. 275-She-Hulk solo story. 276-Mephisto & Dr. Strange app. 277-Split story format - the Thing returns to Earth and battles Dire Wraiths; FF battle Mephisto; Dr. Strange app. 278-Origin Dr. Doom retold; Kristoff becomes new Dr. Doom. 279-Baxter Building destroyed by Kristoff; new Hate Monger app. 280-New Hate Monger & Psycho Man app.;

1st app. Sue as Malice. 281-New Hate Monger, Malice & Psycho Man app. 282-Power Pack cameo; Secret Wars II x-over; Psycho Man app.; infinity cover. 283,284-vs. Psycho Man. 285-Secret Wars II x-over; Beyonder app.

6.00

286-2nd app. X-Factor

2 4 6 11 16 20

287-295: 287-Return of Dr. Doom. 288-Secret Wars II x-over; Dr. Doom vs. the Beyonder. 289-Blastaar app; Basilisk killed by Scourge; Nick Fury app; Annihilus returns. 290-Blastaar, Annihilus & Nick Fury app. 291-Action Comics #1 cover swipe; Nick Fury app. 292-Hitler-c; West Coast Avengers app; last Byrne-a. 294-Byrne plot only (last); Ordway-a; Roger Stern script. 295-Stern-s begin (over brief Byrne plot)

6.00

296-($1.50, 64-pgs)-Barry Smith-c/a (pgs 1-10); Shooter plot; Stan Lee script; Gammill, Frenz, Milgrom, John Buscema, Silvestri and Ordway-a; Sinnott & Colletta-inks; Mole Man app; returns to the FF

1 3 4 6 8 10

297-318,321-330: 297-Roger Stern-s begins; John Buscema-a returns. 299-Black costume Spider-Man app. 300-Wedding of Johnny Storm and 'Alicia'- see issue #358. 301-Wizard & Mad-Thinker app. 303-Thundra app. 304-Steve Englehart-s begins; the Thing becomes leader of the FF. 305-Quicksilver & Kristoff app ; Crystal rejoins FF; Dr. Doom app; leads into FF Annual #20. 306-v.s Diablo; Black Bolt & the Inhumans app; Captain America cameo; Ms. Marvel (Sharon Ventura) app. 307-Ms. Marvel joins the FF. vs. Diablo; Reed and Sue leave the FF. 308-1st Fasaud; last Buscema-a. 310-Keith Pollard-a begins; 1st mutated Thing; Ms. Marvel becomes 'She-Thing'. 311-Black Panther & Dr. Doom app. 312-Dr. Doom, Black Panther & X-Factor app. 313-Mole Man app. 314-Belasco & Master Pandemonium app. 315-Master Pandemonium & Comet Man app; Morbius the Living Vampire cameo. 316-Ka-Zar & Shanna the She-Devil app.; origin of the Savage Land. 317-Comet Man app. 318-Molecule Man & Dr. Doom app. 322-Ron Lim guest-a; She-Hulk vs. Ms. Marvel; Dragon Man app; Aron the Renegade Watcher app. 322-Inferno x-over; Graviton, Aron & Dragon Man app. 323-Inferno x-over; Mantis & Kang app. 324-Kang, Mantis & Necrodamus app; Silver Surfer cameo. 325-Mantis, Kang & Silver Surfer app. 326-vs new Frightful Four (Wizard, Hydroman, Klaw and Titania); Reed & Sue return; the Thing becomes human; Englehart-as 'John Harkness'. 327-vs Frightful Four; Aron the Renegade Watcher & Dragon Man app. 328-1st app. Aron's evil version of the FF; Frightful Four & Dragon Man app. 329-Evil FF vs. Mole Man; Aron app.

6.00

319,320: 319-(Double-size, 39 pgs); Secret Wars III; origin of the Beyonder; Dr. Doom, Molecule Man, Shaper of Worlds, Kubik app. 320-Grey Hulk vs. Thing; Dr. Doom; x-over w/Incredible Hulk #350

1 2 3 5 6 8

331-346, 351,352,354-357,359,360: 331-Ultron app. in dream sequence; Aron the Renegade Watcher app. 333-Avengers & Dr. Strange app. Evil FF vs real FF. 333-Aron the Renegade Watcher app. 334-Acts of Vengeance x-over; Simonson-s begins; Buckler-a; Thor & Captain America app. 335-Acts of Vengeance x-over; Apocalypse cameo. 336-Acts of Vengeance x-over. 337-Simonson art and begins; Thor & Iron Man join FF's mission. 338-Iron Man & Thor app. Death's Head app. Galactus cameo. 339-Thor vs. Gladiator; Galactus & the Black Celestial app. 340-Iron Man, Thor & Galactus app; death of the Black Celestial. 341-Thor, Iron Man & Galactus app. 342-Spider-Man cameo; no Simonson-a or art. 343-President Dan Quayle app. 346-T.V.A (Time Variance Authority) app. 351-Kubik & Kosmos app; Mark Bagley-a. 352-Reed vs Dr. Doom; Kristoff app; Justice Peace & the T.V.A app. 354-FF on trial by the T.V.A; Justice Peace and Mark Gruenwald (as Mr. Chairman) app. 354-Last Simonson issue. 355-vs. the Wrecker. 356-1st Tom Defalco-s & Paul Ryan-a (begin four-year run); Puppet Master & New Warriors app. 357-Alicia Masters revealed to be a Skrull (since issue #265); Puppet Master app.

6.00

347-Ghost Rider, Wolverine, Spider-Man, Hulk-c/stories thru #349; Arthur Adams-c/a(p) in each

2 4 6 8 10 12

347,348-Gold second printings

1 2 3 4 5 6

348-350: 348-349-Arthur Adams-c/a(p). 350-($1.50, 52 pgs)-The 'real' Dr. Doom returns; Kristoff app. Sharon Ventura becomes human again. Ben becomes the Thing again

1 2 3 5 6 8

353-FF on trial by the T.V.A.; Mr. Mobius app.

3 6 9 19 30 40

358-(11/91, $2.25, 88 pgs)-30th anniversary issue; gives history of the FF; die-cut-c; Art Adams back-up story-a; origin of Lyja the Skull as Alicia Masters; 1st app. Paibok the Power Skrull

2 4 6 9 12 15

361-368, 372-373: 361-Dr. Doom & the Yancy Street gang app. 362-Spider-Man app; 1st app. of the Innerverse. 363-1st app. Occulus. 364,365-vs. Occulus; 365-Sharon Ventura returns. 366-Infinity War x-over; Magus / Paibok & Devos team-up. 367-Infinity War x-over; Magus app. numerous super-heroes app. 368-Infinity War x-over; Human Torch vs. X-Men doppelgangers. 372-Spider-Man, Molecule Man, Puppet Master & Aron the Renegade Watcher app.; Silver Sable & the Wild Pack cameo; Devos, Paibok & Lyja app. 373-Human Torch vs. Silver Sable & the Wild Pack; Molecule Man vs. the Rogue Watcher; Dr. Doom app. (steals the power of Aron)

6.00

369,370-Infinity War x-over. 369-Thanos & Warlock and the Infinity Watch app; Aron the Renegade Watcher app.; the Magus gains the Infinity Gauntlet. 370-Warlock vs. the Magus for the Infinity Gauntlet; 1st app. Lyja the Lazer-first

1 2 3 5 6 8

371-All-white embossed-c ($2.00); 1st new (revealing) Invisible Woman costume; Paibok, Devos & Lyja vs. Human Torch; Aron the Renegade Watcher app; Ms. Marvel (Sharon Ventura) rejoins the FF

1 2 3 5 6 8

371-All-red 2nd printing ($2.00)

374,375: 374-vs Wolverine, Dr. Strange, Ghost Rider, the Hulk and Spider-Man (as the Secret Defenders); Thing's face injured by Wolverine; Dr. Doom app; Black Bolt & the Inhumans cameo; Uatu the Watcher app. 375-($2.95, 52-pgs)-Holo-Grafx foil-c; Secret Defenders app.; Black Bolt & the Inhumans app; cosmic powered Dr. Doom app. Uatu app.; re-intro Nathaniel Richards (from issue #273); Lyja changes allegiance to the FF

6.00

376-($2.95)-Variant polybagged w/Dirt Magazine #4 and music tape; harder to find in true NM- 9.2 due to being packaged with a tape cassette

1 2 3 5 6 8

376-380,382-386: 376-Nathaniel Richards and Dr. Doom app; Franklin becomes an adult (Psi-Lord). 377-1st app. Huntara; origin Devos; Paibok, Dr. Doom & Klaw app. 378-vs. Devos, Paibok & Huntara; Avengers, Spider-Man & Daredevil app. 379-Devos, Paibok, Huntara & Dr. Doom app. 380-Dr. Doom app. 382-Contains a coupon from Kaybee Toys for an exclusive Ghost Rider issue; also has 16-pg Midnight Sons 'Siege of Darkness' insert; Devos vs. the Skrull Empire. 383-Paibok vs. Devos. 384-Scott Lang app. as Ant-Man; Psi-Lord vs. Invisible Woman. 385-Starblast x-over; Ant-Man & Sub-Mariner app.; continues in Namor the Sub-Mariner #48. 386-Starblast x-over; Ant-Man & Sub-Mariner app.

5.00

381-'Death' of Reed Richards & Dr. Doom

1 2 3 5 6 8

387-Newsstand ed. ($1.25)

5.00

387-($2.95)-Collectors Ed. w/die-cut foil-c; Ant-Man app; Invisible Woman returns to her regular costume

1 2 3 5 6 8

388-393,396,397: 388-Bound in trading card sheet; Ant-Man, Sub-Mariner & Avengers app; 1st app. the Dark Raider. 389-Ant-Man, Sub-Mariner and the Collector app. 390- Ant-Man & Sub-Mariner app. Galactus & Silver Surfer app. in flashback to FF #48-50. 391-Ant-Man,

Fantastic Four #233 © MAR

Fantastic Four #395 © MAR

Fantastic Four V2 #12 © MAR

	GD	VG	FN	VF	VF/NM	NM-
	2.0	4.0	6.0	8.0	9.0	9.2

Sub-Mariner, Galactus & Silver Surfer app. 392-vs. the Dark Raider. 396-Power Rangers card insert. 397-Aron the Renegade Watcher & the Dark Raider app; return of Kristoff; Ant-Man app. 5.00

394-($2.95)-Collectors Edition-polybagged w/16-pg. Marvel; Action Hour book and acetate print; pink logo; Ant-Man, Wyatt Wingfoot & She-Hulk app.

	1	2	3		5	6	8

394-(Newsstand Edition-$1.50; white logo 5.00

395,398,399: 395-Wolverine-c/story; Ant-Man app. 398,399-($2.50)-Rainbow foil-c; Ant-Man, Uatu, Aron & the Dark Raider app. 6.00

400-($3.95, 64-pgs)-Rainbow foil-c; Stan Lee introduction; Celestials vs. the Watchers; Kristoff joins the FF. Ant-Man app.; Avengers & Spider-Man app. in back-up story; origin of the FF retold; Uatu vs. Aron (dies) 6.00

401-404,406-415: 401-Atlantis Rising x-over; Sub-Mariner & Thor app; Black Bolt cameo. 402-Atlantis Rising x-over; Sub-Mariner vs. Black Bolt; Thor vs. the FF. 404-1st brief app. Hyperstorm (arm only). 406-Return of Dr. Doom; Hyperstorm revealed, battles FF. 407-Return of Mr. Fantastic; x-over w/FF Unlimited #12; Hyperstorm app. 408-vs Hyperstorm; Dr. Doom app. 409-Dr. Doom & FF vs. Hyperstorm; Thing's facial injury cured (since #271). 410-Gorgon of the Inhumans app. 411-Black Bolt & the Inhumans app. 412-Mr. Fantastic vs. Sub-Mariner app. 413-Silver Surfer cameo; x-over w/Doom 2099 #42; Doom 2099 & Hyperstorm app; Franklin returns to being a child (Psi-Lord since #376). 414-Galactus vs. Hyperstorm; last Paul Ryan-a (since #356). 415-Onslaught tie-in; Pacheco-a; Professor X & Avengers app.; Apocalypse cameo; story continued in X-Men #55 ..... 5.00

405-Overpower card insert; scarcer in higher grades due to card indentation; new Ant-Man costume; Zarko the Tomorrow Man app; Conan cameo; 2nd app. Hyperstorm (cameo) 6.00

416-($2.50, 48 pgs)-Onslaught tie-in; Pacheco-a; Dr. Doom app; last issue; story continues in Onslaught Marvel Universe #1; Reed, Ben & Victor Von Doom app. in flashback in back-up story; Uatu the Watcher app. 6.00

#500-up (See Fantastic Four Vol. 3; series resumed original numbering after Vol. 3 #70)

Annual 1('63)-Origin of Sub-Mariner & 1st modern app of Atlantis & the Atlanteans incl. Lady Dorma; FF origin retold; Spider-Man app. in detailed retelling of his app. from Amazing Spider-Man #1

	172	344	516	1419	3210	5000

Annual 2('64)-Dr. Doom origin & c/story; FF #5-r in 2nd story; Pharaoh Rama-Tut app. in 3rd story

	111	222	333	888	1994	3100

Annual 3('65)-Reed & Sue wed; r/#6,11

	29	58	87	209	467	725

Special 4(11/66)-G.A. Torch x-over (1st S.A. app.) & origin retold; r/#25,26 (Hulk vs. Thing); Torch vs. Torch battle; Mad-Thinker app.; 1st app Quasimodo

	14	28	42	94	207	320

Special 5(11/67)-New art; Intro. Psycho-Man; early Black Panther, Inhumans & Silver Surfer (1st solo story); Black Bolt & the Inhumans app; Sue is revealed to be pregnant; Quasimodo app.

	26	52	78	182	404	625

Special 6(11/68)-Intro. Annihilus; birth of Franklin Richards; new 48 pg. movie length epic; last non-reprint annual

	100	200	300	800	1800	2800

Annual No. 6 Facsimile Edition (3/20, $4.99) Reprints Special #6 with original 1968 ads 10.00

Special 7(11/69)-all reprint issue; r/FF #1; r/origin of Dr. Doom from FF #5 & Dr. Doom story from FF Annual #2; Marvel staff photos seen in 'Because you Demanded It' featurette; new-c by Kirby

	7	14	21	46	86	125

Special 8-10: All reprints. 8(12/70)-F.F. vs. Sub-Mariner plus gallery of F.F. foes. Special 9(12/71)-r/FF #43, Strange Tales #131 & FF Annual #3. Special 10('73)-r/FF Annual #3,4; new-c by John Buscema

	4	8	12	27	44	60

Special 11-('76)-New story & art begins; alternate Earth versions of the Invaders app; story continues into Marvel Two-In-One Annual #1; Kirby-c

	3	6	9	11	16	20

Annual 12-14: Annual 12 ('78)-Black Bolt & the Inhumans app; vs. the Sphinx. Annual 13 ('78)-vs the Mole Man; Daredevil app. Annual 14 ('79)-Pérez-a; Avengers cameo; Sandman & Salem's Seven app.

	2	4	6	9	13	16

Annual 15-17: 15-('80, 68 pgs.); Perez-a; Captain Marvel & Dr. Doom app. Annual 16-('81)-Ditko-a/c; 1st Dragon lord. Annual 17-('83)-Byrne-c/a; Skrulls app.

	1	2	3	5	6	8

Annual 18-23: 18-('84)-Minor x-over w/X-Men #137; Wolverine cameo; wedding of Black Bolt & Medusa; the Watcher app. Annual 19-('85)-vs the Skrulls; Kang app; Byrne-a. Annual 20-('87)-Dr. Doom & Mephisto app; continued from FF #305. Annual 21-('88, 64 pgs.)-Square bound; Evolutionary War x-over; Black Bolt & the Inhumans app. Aron the Watcher app. (unnamed). Annual 22-('89, 64 pgs.)-Square bound; Atlantis Attacks x-over; Avengers & Dr. Strange app. Annual 23-('90, 64 pgs.)-Squarebound; 'Days of Future Present' Pt. 1; 1st Ahab; story continues in New Mutants Annual #6 (not X-Factor Annual #5 as noted); Dr. Doom app. in back-up feature; Byrne-c 6.00

Annual 24-27 (all square bound editions): Annual 24-('91, 64 pgs.)-Korvac Quest Pt.1; Guardians of the Galaxy app; story continues in Thor Annual #16; Molecule Man & Super-Skrull app. in back-up features. Annual 25-('92, 64 pgs.)-Citizen Kang Pt.3; continued from Thor Annual #17; Avengers app.; story continues in Avengers Annual #21; Moondragon vs. Mantis solo story & Kang retrospective. Annual 26-('93, 64 pgs.)-Bagged w/card featuring a new character 'Wildstreak'; vs. Dreadface; Hulk & Kosmos app. in solo story featuring the Celestials. Annual 27-('94, 64 pgs.)-Justice Peace & the T.V.A (Time Variance Authority) app.; featuring the chairman (Mark Gruenwald); Molecule Man vs.

	GD	VG	FN	VF	VF/NM	NM-
	2.0	4.0	6.0	8.0	9.0	9.2

Beyonder solo story 6.00

... #1 Facsimile Edition (10/18, $3.99) reprints #1 with original 1961 ads; bonus essays and gallery of FF #1 cover swipes and homages

	2	4	6	11	16	20

... #52 Facsimile Edition (1/23, $3.99) reprints #52 with original 1966 ads 6.00

Best of the Fantastic Four Vol. 1 HC (2005, $29.99) oversized reprints of classic stories from FF#1,39,40,51,100,116,176,236,267, Ann.2, V3#56,60 and more; Brevoort intro. 30.00

Maximum Fantastic Four HC (2005, $49.99, dust jacket) r/Fantastic Four #1 with super-sized art; historical background from Walter Mosley and Mark Evanier; dust jacket unfolds to a poster; giant FF#1 cover on one side, gallery of interior pages on other 50.00

...: Monsters Unleashed nn (1992, $5.95)-r/F.F. #347-349 w/new Arthur Adams-c

	2	4	6	10	14	18

...: Nobody Gets Out Alive (1994, $15.95) TPB r/ #387-392 ..... 16.00

... Omnibus Vol. 1 HC (2005, $99.99) r/#1-30 & Annual 1 plus letter pages; 3 intros. and a 1974 essay by Stan Lee; original plot synopsis for FF #1; essays and Kirby art 100.00

... Omnibus Vol. 2 HC (2007, $99.99) r/#31-60, Annual 2-4 and Not Brand Echh plus letter pages and essays by Stan Lee, Reginald Hudlin, Roy Thomas and others 100.00

Special Edition 1(5/84)-r/Annual #1; Byrne-c/a 5.00

...: The Lost Adventure (4/08, $4.99) Lee & Kirby story partially used in flashback in FF #108 completed with additional art by Frenz & Sinnott; plus reprint of FF #108 ..... 5.00

... Visionaries: George Pérez Vol. 1 (2005, $19.99) r/#164-167,170,176-178,184-186 ..... 20.00

... Visionaries: George Pérez Vol. 2 (2006, $19.99) r/#187-188,191-192, Annual #14-15, Marvel Two-In-One #60 and back-up story from Adventures of the Thing #3 ..... 20.00

... Visionaries (11/01, $19.95) r/#232-240 by John Byrne 25.00

... Visionaries John Byrne Vol. 1 (2004, $24.99) r/#241-250 by John Byrne 25.00

... Visionaries John Byrne Vol. 2 (2004, $24.99) r/#251-257; Annual #17; Avengers #233 and Thing #2 ..... 25.00

... Visionaries John Byrne Vol. 3 (2004, $24.99) r/#258-267; Alpha Flight #4 & Thing #10 ..... 25.00

... Visionaries John Byrne Vol. 4 (2005, $24.99) r/#268-275; Annual #18 & Thing #19 ..... 25.00

... Visionaries John Byrne Vol. 6 ('06, $24.99) r/#276-284; Secret Wars II #2 & Thing #23 ..... 25.00

... Visionaries John Byrne Vol. 5 (2005, $24.99) r/#285-286, Ann. #19, Avengers #263 & Ann. #14, and X-Factor #1 ..... 25.00

... Visionaries John Byrne Vol. 8 ('07, $24.99) r/#287-295 ..... 25.00

... Visionaries: Walter Simonson Vol. 1 (2007, $19.99) r/#334-341 ..... 20.00

NOTE: **Arthur Adams** c/a-347-349p. **Austin** c(i)-232-236, 238, 240-242, 250i, 286i. **Buckler** c-151, 168. **John Buscema** a(p)-107, 108(w/Kirby, Sinnott & Romita), 109-130, 132, 134-141, 160, 175-185. **Byrne** a-209-218p, 220p, 221p, 232-265, 266i, 11, 13; c(p)-107-122, 124-129, 133-139, 202, Annual 14p, Special 10. **Byrne** a-209-218p, 220p, 221p, 232-265, 266i, 267-273, 274-293p; Annual 17, 19; c-211-214p, 220p, 232-236p, 237, 238p, 239, 240-242p, 243-249, 250p, 251-267, Annual 17-19, Special 1-7, 9. **Marcos** a(i)-144i. **Mooney** a-118i, 152i. **Perez** a(p)-164-167, 170-172, 176-178, 184-188, 191p, 192p, Annual 14p, 15p; c(p)-183-188, 191, 192, 194-197. **Simonson** a-337-341, 343, 344p, 345p, 346, 350p, 352-354; c-212, 334-341, 342p, 343-346, 350, 353, 354. **Steranko** c-130-132p. **Williamson** c-357i.

FANTASTIC FOUR (Volume Two)

Marvel Comics: V2#1, Nov. 1996 - No. 13, Nov. 1997 ($2.95/$1.95/$1.99) (Produced by WildStorm Productions)

1-($2.95)-Reintro Fantastic Four; Jim Lee-c/a; Brandon Choi scripts; Mole Man app. 5.00

1-($2.95)-Variant-c

	1	2	3	4	5	7

2-9-($2.95)-2-Namor-c/app. 3-Avengers-c/app. 4-Two covers; Dr. Doom cameo 3.00

10,11,13: All $1.99-c. 13-"World War 3"-pt. 1, x-over w/Image 3.00

12-($2.99) "Heroes Reunited"-pt. 1 ..... 4.00

...: Heroes Reborn (7/00, $17.95, TPB) r/#1-6 ..... 18.00

Heroes Reborn: Fantastic Four (2006, $29.99, TPB) r/#1-12; Jim Lee intro.; pin-ups 30.00

FANTASTIC FOUR (Volume Three)

Marvel Comics: V3#1, Jan. 1998 - No. 588, Apr. 2011 ($2.99/$1.99/$2.25) No. 600, Jan. 2012 - No. 611, Dec. 2012 (Issues #589-599 do not exist, see FF series)

1-($2.99)-Heroes Return; Lobdell's/Davis & Farmer-a

	2	3	4	5	6	8

1-Alternate Heroes Return-c

	1	3	4	6	8	10

2-4,12: 2-Two covers. 4-Claremont-s/Larroca-a begin; Silver Surfer c/app. 5.00

12-($2.99) Wraparound-c by Larroca 4.00

5-10: 6-Heroes For Hire app. 9-Spider-Man c/app. 4.00

11-1st app. Ayesha 4.00

13-25: 13,14-Ronan-c/app. 25-($2.99) Dr. Doom returns 4.00

26-49: 27-Dr. Doom marries Sue. 30-Begin $2.25-c. 32,42-Namor-c/app. 35-Regular cover; Pacheco-s/a begins. 37-Super-Skrull-c/app. 38-New Baxter Building 3.00

35-($3.50) Variant foil enhanced-c; Pacheco-s/a begins 4.00

50-($3.99, 64 pgs.) BWS-c; Grummett, Pacheco, Rude, Udon-a 4.00

51-53,55-59: 51-53-Bagley-a(p)/Wieringo-c; Inhumans app. 55,56-Immonen-a 57-59-Warren-s/Grant-a 3.00

54-($3.50, 100 pgs.) Birth of Valeria; r/Annual #6 birth of Franklin 4.00

60-(9c-c) Waid-s/Wieringo-a begin 3.00

60-($2.25 newsstand edition)(also see Promotional Comics section) 3.00

61-70: 62-64-FF vs. Modulus. 65,66-Buckingham-a. 68-70-Dr. Doom app. 3.00

(After #70 [Aug, 2003] numbering reverted back to original Vol. 1 with #500, Sept, 2003)

500-($3.50) Regular edition; concludes Dr. Doom app.; Dr. Strange app.; Rivera painted-c 4.00

500-($4.99) Director's Cut Edition; chromium-c by Wieringo; sketch and script pages 8.00

	GD 2.0	VG 4.0	FN 6.0	VF 8.0	VF/NM 9.0	NM- 9.2

501-516: 501,502-Casey Jones-a. 503-508-Porter-a. 509-Wieringo-c/a resumes.
512,513-Spider-Man app. 514-516-Ha-c/Medina-a ... 3.00
517-537: 517-Begin $2.99-c. 519-523-Galactus app. 527-Straczynski-s begins. 537-Dr. Doom. ... 3.00
527-Variant Edition with different McKone-c ... 3.00
527-Wizard World Philadelphia Edition with B&W McKone sketch-c ... 3.00
536-Variant cover by Bryan Hitch ... 5.00
537-B&W variant cover ... 4.00
538-542-Civil War. 538-Don Blake reclaims Thor's hammer ... 4.00
543-45th Anniversary; Black Panther and Storm replace Reed and Sue; Granov-c ... 4.00
544-553: 544-546-Silver Surfer app.; Turner-c ... 3.00
554-568-Millar-s/Hitch-a/c. 558-561-Doctor Doom-c/app. 562-Funeral & proposal ... 3.00
554-Variant-c by Bianchi ... 6.00
554-Variant Skrull-c by Suydam ... 15.00
569-($3.99) Wraparound-c; Immonen-a; Dr. Doom app. ... 4.00
570-1st Council of Reeds ... 2 ... 4 ... 6 ... 11 ... 16 ... 20
571-586: 570,572,575-578-Eaglesham-a. 574-Spider-Man app. 584-586-Galactus app. ... 3.00
587-(3/11, $3.99) Death of Human Torch; Epting-a; issue is in black polybag; Davis-c ... 4.00
587-Variant-c by Cassaday ... 10.00
588-($3.99) Last issue; Dragotta-a; preview of FF #1; back-up w/Spider-Man; Davis-c ... 4.00
589-599-Do not exist; story continues in FF series
600-(1/12, $7.99) Avengers app.; Human Torch returns, back-up short stories; Dell'Otto-c ... 8.00
600-Variant-c by John Romita, Jr. ... 10.00
600-Variant-c by Art Adams ... 15.00
601-603,605,605.1, 606-611: 601-603-Johnny Storm & Avengers app. 602,603-Galactus app.
   605.1-Alternate origin; Choi-a. 607,608-Black Panther app. 611-Doctor Doom app. ... 3.00
604-($3.99) Future Franklin and Valeria app. ... 4.00
...'98 Annual ($3.50) Immonen-a ... 4.00
...'99 Annual ($3.50) Ladronn-a ... 4.00
...'00 Annual ($3.50) Larocca-a; Marvel Girl back-up story ... 4.00
...'01 Annual ($2.99) Maguire-a; Thing back-up w/Yu-a ... 4.00
... Annual 32 (8/10, $4.99) Hitch-a/c ... 5.00
... Annual 33 (9/12, $4.99) Alan Davis-s/a/c; Dr. Strange & Clan Destine app. ... 5.00
... : A Death in the Family (7/06, $3.99, one-shot) Weeks-a/c; and r/F.F. #245 ... 4.00
... By J. Michael Straczynski Vol. 1 (2005, $19.99, HC) r/#527-532 ... 20.00
Civil War: Fantastic Four TPB (2007, $17.99) r/#538-543; 45th Anniversary Toasts ... 18.00
... Cosmic-Size Special 1 (2/09, $4.99) Cary Bates-s/Bing Cansino-a; r/F.F. #237 ... 3.00
Fantastic 4th Voyage of Sinbad (9/01, $5.95) Claremont-s/Ferry-a ... 6.00
Flesh and Stone (8/01, $12.95, TPB) r/#35-39 ... 13.00
... Giant-Size Adventures 1 (8/09, $3.99) Cifuentes & Coover-a; Egghead app. ... 4.00
... In...Ataque del M.O.D.O.K.! (11/10, $3.99) English & Spanish editions; Beland-a/Doe-a ... 4.00
... /Inhumans TPB (2007, $19.99) r/#51-54 and Inhumans ('00) #1-4 ... 20.00
... Isla De La Muerte! (2008, $3.99) English & Spanish editions; Beland-s/Doe-a ... 4.00
... MGC #570 (7/11, $1.00) r/#570 with "Marvel's Greatest Comics" cover banner ... 3.00
... Presents: Franklin Richards 1 (11/05, $2.99) r/back-up stories from Power Pack #1-4 plus
   new 5 pg. story; Sumerak-s/Eliopoulos-a (Also see Franklin Richards) ... 3.00
...Special (2/06, $2.99) McDuffie-s/Casey Jones-a; dinner with Dr. Doom ... 3.00
...Tales Vol. 1 (2005, $7.99, digest) r/Marvel Age: FF Tales #1, Tales of the Thing #1-3, and
   Spider-Man Team-Up Special ... 8.00
... : The Last Stand (8/11, $4.99) #574, 587 & 588 (death of Johnny Storm) ... 5.00
...: The New Fantastic Four HC (2007, $19.99) r/#544-550; variant covers & sketch pgs. ... 20.00
...: The New Fantastic Four SC (2008, $15.99) r/#544-550; variant covers & sketch pgs. ... 16.00
... : The Wedding Special 1 (1/06, $5.00) 40th Anniversary new story w/FF Annual #3 ... 5.00
... Vol. 1 HC (2004, $29.99, dust jacket) oversized reprint /#60-70, 500-502; Mark Waid intro
   and series proposal; cover gallery ... 30.00
... Vol. 2 HC (2005, $29.99, d.j.) oversized r/#503-513; Waid intro.; deleted scenes ... 30.00
... Vol. 3 HC (2005, $29.99, d.j.) oversized r/#514-524; Waid commentaries; cover sketches ... 30.00
... Vol. 1: Imaginauts (2003, $17.99, TPB) r/#56,60-66; Mark Waid's series proposal ... 18.00
... Vol. 2: Unthinkable (2003, $17.99, TPB) r/#67-70,500-502; #500 Director's Cut extras ... 18.00
... Vol. 3: Authoritative Action (2004, $12.99, TPB) r/#503-508 ... 13.00
... Vol. 4: Hereafter (2004, $11.99, TPB) r/#509-513 ... 12.00
... Vol. 5: Disassembled (2004, $14.99, TPB) r/#514-519 ... 15.00
... Vol. 6: Rising Storm (2005, $13.99, TPB) r/#520-524 ... 14.00
...: The Beginning of the End TPB (2008, $14.99) r/#525,526,551-553 & Fantastic Four: Isla
   De La Muerte! one-shot ... 15.00
...: The Life Fantastic TPB (2006, $16.99) r/#533-535; The Wedding Special, Special (2/06)
   and A Death in the Family one-shots ... 17.00
Wizard #1/2 -Lim-a ... 10.00

FANTASTIC FOUR (Volume Four) (Marvel NOW!) (Also see FF)
Marvel Comics: Jan, 2013 - No. 16, Mar, 2014 ($2.99)

1-5-Fraction-s/Bagley-a/c ... 3.00
5AU-(5/13, $3.99) Age of Ultron tie-in; Fraction-s/Araújo-a/Bagley-c ... 4.00
6-15: 6-13-Blastaar app. 9,13-15-Dr. Doom app. 14,15-Ienco-a ... 3.00
16-($3.99) Fantastic Four vs. Doom, The Annihilation Conqueror; back-up w/Quinones-a ... 4.00

FANTASTIC FOUR (Volume Five) (All-New Marvel NOW!)
Marvel Comics: Apr, 2014 - No. 14, Feb, 2015; No. 642, Mar, 2015 - No. 645, Jun, 2015 ($3.99)

1-4-Robinson-s/Kirk-a. 3,4-Frightful Four app. ... 4.00
5-($4.99) Trial of the Fantastic Four; flashback-a by various incl. Starlin, Allred, Samnee ... 5.00
6-14: 6-8-Original Sin tie-in. 10,11-Scarlet Witch app. 11,12-Spider-Man app. ... 4.00
642-(3/15)-644: Heroes Reborn Avengers app. 643,644-Sleepwalker app. ... 4.00
645-($5.99) Psycho Man & the Frightful Four app.; Kirk-a; bonus back-up stories ... 6.00
Annual 1 (11/14, $4.99) Sue vs. Doctor Doom in Latveria; Grummett-a ... 5.00
100th Anniversary Special: Fantastic Four 1 (9/14, $3.99) Van Meter-s/Estep-a ... 4.00

FANTASTIC FOUR (Volume Six)
Marvel Comics: Oct, 2018 - No. 48, Dec, 2022 ($5.99/$3.99)

1-($5.99) Slott-s/Pichelli & Bianchi-a; Ben proposes to Alicia ... 6.00
2-4,6-11,13-20-($3.99) 4-Wrecking Crew app.; intro The Fantastix. 6-9-Doom vs. Galactus.
   10-War of The Realms tie-in; Moon Girl app. 13-Thing vs. Hulk. 15-Intro. Sky ... 4.00
5-($7.99) Wedding of Ben and Alicia; art by Kuder, Allred (origin re-telling) and Hughes ... 8.00
12-($4.99) Thing battles the Immortal Hulk; Izaakse-a; Future Foundation back-up ... 5.00
21-24,26-31,33,34: 21-23-Tie-in to Empyre event; Wolverine and Spider-Man app. 24-Iceman
   app. 28-Silver Surfer app. 29,30-King in Black tie-ins ... 4.00
25-($5.99) She-Hulk & Doctor Doom app.; back-up story with Uatu & Nick Fury ... 6.00
32-($4.99) The Bride of Doom part 1; Doctor Doom and Lyja app. ... 5.00
35-($9.99) 60th Anniversary celebration; Romita Jr.-a; Kang, Immortus, Rama-Tut app.;

	GD 2.0	VG 4.0	FN 6.0	VF 8.0	VF/NM 9.0	NM- 9.2

   back-up story retelling origin; Waid-s/Renaud-a ... 10.00
36-43,45-48: 38-She-Hulk app. 40-45-Reckoning War. 48 Judgment Day tie-in ... 4.00
...: Anniversary Tribute 1 (1/22, $6.99) Remakes 1961's FF #1 and FF Annual #3 with current
   artists each redrawing a page in their style; McNiven-c swipe of FF #1 ... 5.00
44-($4.99) Reckoning War; Silver Surfer & Doctor Doom app. ... 5.00
... 4 Yancy Street 1 (10/19, $4.99) Duggan-s; the Terrible Trio app. ... 5.00
... Grimm Noir 1 (4/20, $4.99) Duggan-s/Garney-a ... 5.00
... Marvels Snapshots 1 (5/20, $4.99) Dorkin & Dyer-s/Dewey-a ... 5.00
... Negative Zone 1 (1/20, $4.99) Carey-s/Caselli-a; Blastaar app. ... 5.00
... Road Trip 1 (2/21, $4.99) Cantwell-s/Andrade-a ... 5.00
... The Prodigal Sun 1 (9/19, $4.99) Davis-s/Manna-a; Ka-Zar app. ... 5.00
... Wedding Special 1 (2/19, $4.99) Simone-s/Braga-a; Slott-s/Buckingham-s/a; Hembeck-s/a ... 5.00

FANTASTIC FOUR (Volume Seven)
Marvel Comics: Jan, 2023 - Present ($4.99/$3.99)

1-($4.99) North-s/Coello-a; main cover by Alex Ross ... 5.00
2-6,8-17-($3.99) 13-Doctor Doom app. 17-Rama-Tut app. ... 4.00
7-($5.99) 700th Legacy issue; Doctor Doom & Aunt Petunia app. ... 6.00
Annual 1 (10/23, $4.99) Contest of Chaos Part 1; Ghost Rider app. ... 5.00

FANTASTIC FOUR AND POWER PACK
Marvel Comics: Sept, 2007 - No. 4, Dec, 2007 ($2.99, limited series)

1-4-Gurihiru-a/Van Lente-s; the Wizard app. ... 3.00
...: Favorite Son TPB (2008, $7.99, digest size) r/#1-4 ... 8.00

FANTASTIC FOUR: ANTITHESIS
Marvel Comics: Oct, 2020 - No. 4, Jan, 2021 ($4.99, limited series)

1-4-Neal Adams-a/Mark Waid-s; Silver Surfer & Galactus app. ... 5.00

FANTASTIC FOUR: ATLANTIS RISING
Marvel Comics: June, 1995 - No. 2, July, 1995 ($3.95, limited series)

1,2: Acetate-c ... 5.00
Collector's Preview (5/95, $2.25, 52 pgs.) ... 4.00

FANTASTIC FOUR: BIG TOWN
Marvel Comics: Jan, 2001 - No. 4, Apr, 2001 ($2.99, limited series)

1-4-"What If?" story; McKone-a/Englehart-s ... 3.00

FANTASTIC FOUR: FIREWORKS
Marvel Comics: Jan, 1999 - No. 3, Mar, 1999 ($2.99, limited series)

1-3-Remix; Jeff Johnson-a ... 4.00

FANTASTIC FOUR: FIRST FAMILY
Marvel Comics: May, 2006 - No. 6, Oct, 2006 ($2.99, limited series)

1-6-Casey-s/Weston-a; flashback to the days after the accident ... 3.00
TPB (2006, $15.99) r/#1-6 ... 16.00

FANTASTIC FOUR: FOES
Marvel Comics: Mar, 2005 - No. 6, Aug, 2005 ($2.99, limited series)

1-6-Kirkman-s/Rathburn-a. 1-Puppet Master app. 3-Super-Skrull app. 4-Mole Man app. ... 3.00
TPB (2005, $16.99) r/#1-6 ... 17.00

FANTASTIC FOUR: FULL CIRCLE
Abrams ComicArts (Marvel Comics): 2022 ($24.99, hardcover with dust jacket)

nn-Silver Age version of the team goes to the Negative Zone; Alex Ross-s/a ... 25.00
Previews Exclusive Slipcase Edition (2022, $40.00, limited to 3,000); bonus print ... 40.00

FANTASTIC FOUR: GRAND DESIGN
Marvel Comics: Dec, 2019 - No. 2, Jan, 2020 ($5.99, limited series)

1,2-History of the Fantastic Four retold; Tom Scioli-s/a/c; bonus background text info ... 6.00

FANTASTIC FOUR: HOUSE OF M (Reprinted in House of M: Fantastic Four/ Iron Man TPB)
Marvel Comics: Sept, 2005 - No. 3, Nov, 2005 ($2.99, limited series)

1-3: Fearsome Four, led by Doom; Scot Eaton-a ... 3.00

FANTASTIC FOUR INDEX (See Official...)

FANTASTIC FOUR/ IRON MAN: BIG IN JAPAN
Marvel Comics: Dec, 2005 - No. 4, Mar, 2006 ($3.50, limited series)

1-4-Seth Fisher-a/c; Zeb Wells-s; wraparound-c on each ... 3.50
TPB (2006, $12.99) r/#1-4 and Seth Fisher illustrated story from Spider-Man Unlimited #8 ... 13.00

FANTASTIC FOUR: LIFE STORY
Marvel Comics: Jul, 2021 - No. 6, Apr, 2022 ($4.99, limited series)

1-6-The 1961 Fantastic Four ages in real time; Russell-s/Izaakse-a. 2-The '70s; intro Doom
   and Namor. 4-The '90s; Silver Surfer app. 5-The '00s; Galactus arrives ... 5.00

FANTASTIC FOUR: 1 2 3 4
Marvel Comics: Oct, 2001 - No. 4, Jan, 2002 ($2.99, limited series)

1-4-Morrison-s/Jae Lee-a. 2-4-Namor-c/app. ... 3.00
TPB (2002, $9.99) r/#1-4 ... 10.00

FANTASTIC FOUR ROAST
Marvel Comics Group: May, 1982 (75¢, one-shot, direct sales)

1-Celebrates 20th anniversary of F.F.#1; X-Men, Ghost Rider & many others cameo; Golden,
   Miller, Buscema, Rogers, Byrne, Anderson art; Hembeck/Austin-c ... 5.00

FANTASTIC FOUR: THE END
Marvel Comics: Jan, 2007 - No. 6, May, 2007 ($2.99, limited series)

1-6-Alan Davis-s/a; last adventure of the future FF. 1-Dr. Doom-c/app. ... 3.00
Roughcut #1 ($3.99) B&W pencil art for full story and text script; B&W sketch cover ... 4.00
HC (2007, $19.99, dustjacket) r/#1-6 ... 20.00
SC (2008, $14.99) r/#1-6 ... 15.00

FANTASTIC FOUR: THE LEGEND
Marvel Comics: Oct, 1996 ($3.95, one-shot)

1-Tribute issue ... 4.00

FANTASTIC FOUR: THE MOVIE
Marvel Comics: Aug, 2005 ($4.99/$12.99, one-shot)

1-($4.99) Movie adaptation; Jurgens-a; behind the scenes feature; Doom origin; photo-c ... 5.00
TPB-($12.99) Movie adaptation, r/Fantastic Four #5 & 190, and FF Vol. 3 #60, photo-c ... 13.00

FANTASTIC FOUR: TRUE STORY

Fantastic Four (2013 series) #1 © MAR

Fantastic Four (2018 series) #35 © MAR

Far Sector #1 © DC

FA

	GD	VG	FN	VF	VF/NM	NM-
	2.0	4.0	6.0	8.0	9.0	9.2

Marvel Comics: Sept, 2008 - No. 4, Jan, 2009 ($2.99, limited series)

1-4-Cornell-s/Domingues-a/Henrichon-c — — — — — 3.00

FANTASTIC FOUR 2099
Marvel Comics: Jan, 1996 - No. 8, Aug, 1996 ($3.95/$1.95)

1-($3.95)-Chromium-c; X-Nation preview — — — — — 5.00
2-8: 4-Spider-Man 2099-c/app. 5-Doctor Strange app. 7-Thibert-c — — — — — 4.00
... No. 1 (1/20, $4.99) Karla Pacheco-s/Steven Cummings-a; H.E.R.B.I.E. app. — — — — — 5.00
NOTE: *Williamson* a-1i; c-1i.

FANTASTIC FOUR UNLIMITED
Marvel Comics: Mar, 1993 - No. 12, Dec, 1995 ($3.95, 68 pgs.)

1-12: 1-Black Panther app. 4-Thing vs. Hulk. 5-Vs. The Frightful Four. 6-Vs. Namor.
7, 9-12-Wraparound-c — — — — — 4.00

FANTASTIC FOUR UNPLUGGED
Marvel Comics: Sept, 1995 - No. 6, Aug 1996 (99¢, bi-monthly)

1-6 — — — — — 4.00

FANTASTIC FOUR - UNSTABLE MOLECULES
(Indicia for #1 reads STARTLING STORIES: ... ; #2 reads UNSTABLE MOLECULES)
Marvel Comics: Mar, 2003 - No. 4, June, 2003 ($2.99, limited series)

1-4-Guy Davis-c/a — — — — — 3.00
Fantastic Four Legends Vol. 1 TPB (2003, $13.99) r/#1-4, origin from FF #1 (1963) — — — — — 14.00
TPB (2005, $13.99) r/#1-4 — — — — — 14.00

FANTASTIC FOUR VS. X-MEN
Marvel Comics: Feb, 1987 - No. 4, June, 1987 (Limited series)

1-4: 4-Austin-a(i) — — — — — 5.00

FANTASTIC FOUR: WORLD'S GREATEST COMICS MAGAZINE
Marvel Comics: Feb, 2001 - No. 12 (Limited series)

1-12: Homage to Lee & Kirby era of F.F.; s/a by Larsen & various. 5-Hulk-c/app.
10-Thor app. — — — — — 3.00

FANTASTIC GIANTS (Formerly Konga #1-23)
Charlton Comics: V2#24, Sept, 1966 (25¢, 68 pgs.)

V2#24-Special Ditko issue; origin Konga & Gorgo reprinted plus two new Ditko stories
9   18   27   59   117   175

FANTASTIC TALES
I. W. Enterprises: 1958 (no date) (Reprint, one-shot)

1-Reprints Avon's "City of the Living Dead"   5   10   15   31   53   75

FANTASTIC VOYAGE (See Movie Comics)
Gold Key: Aug, 1969 - No. 2, Dec, 1969

1 (TV)   4   8   12   28   47   65
2-Cover has the text "Civilian Miniaturized Defense Force" in yellow bar at top;
back cover has painted art   3   6   9   19   30   40
2-Variant cover has text "In This Issue Sweepstakes..." along top; ad on back-c
4   8   12   23   37   50

FANTASTIC VOYAGES OF SINDBAD, THE
Gold Key: Oct, 1965 - No. 2, June, 1967

1-Painted-c on both   7   14   21   46   86   125
2   5   10   15   33   57   80

FANTASTIC WORLDS
Standard Comics: No. 5, Sept, 1952 - No. 7, Jan, 1953

5-Toth, Anderson-a   53   106   159   334   567   800
6-Toth-c/a   39   78   117   240   395   550
7   34   68   102   199   325   450

FANTASY ILLUSTRATED
New Media Publ.: Spring 1982 ($2.95, B&W magazine)

1-P. Craig Russell-c/a; art by Ditko, Sekowsky, Sutton; Englehart-s
1   3   4   6   8   10

FANTASY MASTERPIECES (Marvel Super Heroes No. 12 on)
Marvel Comics Group: Feb, 1966 - No. 11, Oct, 1967; V2#1, Dec, 1979 - No. 14, Jan, 1981

1-Photo of Stan Lee (12¢-c #1,2)   9   18   27   60   120   180
2-r/1st Fin Fang Foom from Strange Tales #89   6   12   18   38   69   100
3-8: 3-G.A. Capt. America-r begin, end #11; 1st 25¢ Giant; Colan-r. 3-6-Kirby-c(p).
4-Kirby-c(p)(i). 7-Begin G.A. Sub-Mariner, Torch-r/M. Mystery. 8-Torch battles the
Sub-Mariner-r/Marvel Mystery #9   6   12   18   37   66   95
9-Origin Human Torch-r/Marvel Comics #1   6   12   18   41   76   110
10,11: 10-r/origin & 1st app. All Winners Squad from All Winners #19. 11-r/origin of Toro
(H.T. #1) & Black Knight 1   5   10   15   34   60   85
V2#1(12/79, 75¢, 52 pgs.)-r/origin Silver Surfer from Silver Surfer #1 with editing plus

reprints cover; J. Buscema-a   2   4   6   9   12   15
2-14-Reprints Silver Surfer #2-14 w/covers   — — — — — 6.00
NOTE: *Buscema* c-V2#7-9(in part). *Ditko* r-1-3, 7, 9. *Everett* r-1,7-9. *Matt Fox* r-9i. *Kirby* r-1-11; c(p)-3, 4i, 5, 6.
Starlin r-8-13. Some direct sale V2#14's had a 50¢ cover price. #3-11 contain Capt. America-r/Capt. America #3-10.
#7-11 contain G.A.Human Torch & Sub-Mariner-r.

FANTASY QUARTERLY (Also see Elfquest)
Independent Publishers Syndicate: Spring, 1978 (B&W)

1-1st app. Elfquest; Dave Sim-a (6 pgs.)   14   28   42   93   204   315

FANTOMAN (Formerly Amazing Adventure Funnies)
Centaur Publications: No. 2, Aug, 1940 - No. 4, Dec, 1940

2-The Fantom of the Fair, The Arrow, Little Dynamite-r begin; origin The Ermine by Filchock;
Burgos, J. Cole, Ernst, Gustavson-a   194   388   582   1242   2121   3000
3,4: Gustavson-r. 4-Red Blaze story   155   310   465   992   1696   2400

FANTOMEX MAX
Marvel Comics: Dec, 2013 - No. 4, Mar, 2014 ($3.99)

1-4-Hope-s/Crystal-a/Francavilla-c   — — — — — 4.00

FAR CRY: RITE OF PASSAGE (Based on the Far Cry videogame series)
Dark Horse Comics: May, 2021 - No. 3, Aug, 2021 ($3.99, limited series)

1-3-Bryan Edward Hill-s/Geraldo Borges-a   — — — — — 4.00

FAREWELL MOONSHADOW (See Moonshadow)
DC Comics (Vertigo): Jan, 1997 ($7.95, one-shot)

nn-DeMatteis-s/Muth-c/a   — — — — — 8.00

FARGO KID (Formerly Justice Traps the Guilty)(See Feature Comics #47)
Prize Publications: V11#3(#1), June-July, 1958 - V11#5, Oct-Nov, 1958

V11#3(#1)-Origin Fargo Kid, Severin-c/a; Williamson-a(2); Heath-a
19   38   57   111   176   240
V11#4,5-Severin-c/a   13   26   39   74   105   135

FARMER'S DAUGHTER, THE
Stanhall Publ./Trojan Magazines: Feb-Mar, 1954 - No. 3, June-July, 1954; No. 4, Oct, 1954

1-Lingerie, nudity panel   226   452   678   1446   2473   3500
2-4(Stanhall)   142   284   426   909   1555   2200

FARMHAND
Image Comics: Jul, 2018 - Present ($3.99)

1-20-Rob Guillory-s/a   — — — — — 4.00

FARSCAPE (Based on TV series)
BOOM! Studios: Nov, 2008 - No. 4, Feb, 2009 ($3.99)

1-4-O'Bannon-s/Patterson-a; multiple covers   — — — — — 4.00

FARSCAPE (Based on TV series)
BOOM! Studios: Nov, 2009 - No. 24, Oct, 2011 ($3.99)

1-24-O'Bannon-s/Sliney-a; multiple covers   — — — — — 4.00
.... D'Argo's Lament 1-4 (4/09 - No. 4, 7/09, $3.99) Edwards-a; three covers on each   — — — — — 4.00
.... D'Argo's Quest 1-4 (12/09 - No. 4, 3/10, $3.99) Cleveland-a; three covers on each   — — — — — 4.00
.... D'Argo's Trial 1-4 (8/09 - No. 4, 11/09, $3.99) Cleveland-a; multiple covers on each   — — — — — 4.00
.... Gone and Back 1-4 (7/09 - No. 4, 10/09, $3.99) Patterson-a; multiple covers on each   — — — — — 4.00
.... Scorpius 0-7 (4/10 - No. 7, 2010, $3.99) 0-3-Ruiz-a; multiple-c. 4-7-Purcell-a   — — — — — 4.00
.... Strange Detractors 1-4 (3/09 - No. 4, 6/09, $3.99) Sliney-a; three covers on each   — — — — — 4.00

FARSCAPE: WAR TORN (Based on TV series)
DC Comics (WildStorm): Apr, 2002 - No. 2, May, 2002 ($4.95, limited series)

1,2-Teranishi/a/Wolfman-s; photo-c   — — — — — 5.00

FAR SECTOR
DC Comics (Young Animal): Jan, 2020 - No. 12, Aug, 2021 ($3.99)

1-12: 1-Intro Green Lantern Sojourner Mullein; N.K. Jemisin-s/Jamal Campbell-a   — — — — — 4.00

FASHION IN ACTION
Eclipse Comics: Aug, 1986 - Feb, 1987 (Baxter paper)

Summer Special 1, Winter Special 1, each Snyder III-c/a   — — — — — 4.00

FASTBALL EXPRESS (Major League Baseball)
Ultimate Sports Force: 2000 ($3.95, one-shot)

1-Polybagged with poster; Johnson, Maddux, Park, Nomo, Clemens app.   — — — — — 4.00

FASTER THAN LIGHT
Image Comics (Shadowline): Sept, 2015 - No. 10, Sept, 2016 ($2.99)

1-10-Brian Haberlin-s/a   — — — — — 3.00

FASTEST GUN ALIVE, THE (Movie)
Dell Publishing Co.: No. 741, Sept, 1956 (one-shot)

Four Color 741-Photo-c   7   14   21   44   82   120

FAST FICTION (...Action) (Stories by Famous Authors Illustrated #6 on)

	GD 2.0	VG 4.0	FN 6.0	VF 8.0	VF/NM 9.0	NM- 9.2

Seaboard Publ./Famous Authors Ill.: Oct, 1949 - No. 5, Mar, 1950 (All have Kiefer-c)(48 pgs.)

1-Scarlet Pimpernel; Jim Lavery-c/a	37	74	111	222	361	500
2-Captain Blood; H. C. Kiefer-c/a	27	54	81	158	259	360
3-She, by Rider Haggard; Vincent Napoli-a	36	72	108	211	343	475
4-(1/50, 52 pgs.)-The 39 Steps; Lavery-c/a	20	40	60	117	189	260
5-Beau Geste; Kiefer-c/a	20	40	60	117	189	260

NOTE: *Kiefer a-2, 5; c-2, 3,5. Lavery a-1, 4. Napoli a-3.*

FAST FORWARD
DC Comics (Piranha Press): 1992 - No. 3, 1993 ($4.95, 68 pgs.)

1-3: 1-Morrison scripts; McKean-c/a. 3-Sam Kieth-a						5.00

FAST WILLIE JACKSON
Fitzgerald Periodicals, Inc.: Oct, 1976 - No. 7, 1977

1	13	26	39	89	195	300
2-7	4	8	12	28	47	65

FAT ALBERT (...& the Cosby Kids) (TV)
Gold Key: Mar, 1974 - No. 29, Feb, 1979

1	9	18	27	59	117	175
2-10	3	6	9	16	24	32
11-29	2	4	6	11	16	20

FATALE (Also see Powers That Be #1 & Shadow State #1,2)
Broadway Comics: Jan, 1996 - No. 6, Aug, 1996 ($2.50)

1-6: J.G. Jones-c/a in all, Preview Edition 1 (11/95, B&W)						4.00

FATALE
Image Comics: Jan, 2012 - No. 24, Jul, 2014 ($3.50)

1-Brubaker-s/Phillips-a/c						5.00
1-Variant-c of Demon with machine gun						8.00
1-Second through Fifth printings						4.00
2-23-Brubaker-s/Phillips-a/c in all						3.50
24-($4.99) Story conclusion; bonus preview of The Fade Out series						5.00

FAT AND SLAT (Ed Wheelan) (Becomes Gunfighter No. 5 on)
E. C. Comics: Summer, 1947 - No. 4, Spring, 1948

1-Intro/origin Voltage, Man of Lightning; "Comics" McCormick, the World's No. 1 Comic Book Fan begins, ends #4	58	116	174	371	636	900
2-4: 4-Comics McCormick-c feature	39	78	117	231	378	525

FAT AND SLAT JOKE BOOK
All-American Comics (William H. Wise): Summer, 1944 (52 pgs., one-shot)

nn-by Ed Wheelan	39	78	117	231	378	525

FATE (See Hand of Fate & Thrill-O-Rama)

FATE
DC Comics: Oct, 1994 - No. 22, Sept, 1996 ($1.95/$2.25)

0,1-22: 8-Begin $2.25-c. 11-14-Alan Scott (Sentinel) app. 10,14-Zatanna app. 21-Phantom Stranger app. 22-Spectre app.						4.00

FATHER'S DAY
Dark Horse Comics: Oct, 2014 - No. 4, Jan, 2015 ($3.99, limited series)

1-4-Mike Richardson-s/Gabriel Guzmán-a						4.00

FATHOM
Comico: May, 1987 - No. 3, July, 1987 ($1.50, limited series)

1-3						4.00

FATHOM
Image Comics (Top Cow Prod.): Aug, 1998 - No. 14, May, 2002 ($2.50)

Preview						12.00
0-Wizard supplement						7.00
0-($6.95) DF Alternate						7.00
1/2 (Wizard) origin of Cannon; Turner-a						6.00
1/2 (3/03, 2.99) origin of Cannon						3.00
1-Turner-s/a; three covers; alternate story pages						6.00
1-Reprint Edition (8/21, $1.99) Bonus preview of Fathom: The Core #1						3.00
1-Wizard World Edition						9.00
2-14: 12-14-Witchblade app. 13,14-Tomb Raider app.						3.00
9-Green foil-c edition						15.00
9,12-Holofoil editions						18.00
12,13-DFE alternate-c						6.00
13,14-DFE Gold edition						8.00
14-DFE Blue						15.00
... Collected Edition 1 (3/99, $5.95) r/Preview & all three #1's						6.00
... Collected Edition 2-4 (3-12/99, $5.95) 2-r/#2,3. 3-r/#4,5. 4-r/#6,7						6.00
... Collected Edition 5 (4/00, $5.95) 5-r/#8,9						6.00
... Primer (6/11, $1.00) Comic style summary of Volume 1; text summaries of Vol. 2 & 3						3.00
... Swimsuit Special (5/99, $2.95) Pin-ups by various						3.00
... Swimsuit Special 2000 (12/00, $2.95) Pin-ups by various; Turner-c						3.00
Michael Turner's Fathom HC ('01, $39.95) r/#1-9, black-c w/silver foil						40.00
Michael Turner's Fathom SC ('01, $24.95) r/#1-9, new Turner-a						25.00
Michael Turner's Fathom The Definitive Edition ('08, $49.95) r/Preview, #0,1/2,1-14, Swimsuit Special 1999 & 2000; cover gallery; foreword by Geoff Johns						50.00

FATHOM (MICHAEL TURNER'S...) (Volume 2)
Aspen MLT, Inc.: No. 0, Apr, 2005 - No. 11, Dec, 2006 ($2.50/$2.99)

0-($2.50) Turnbull-a/Turner-c						3.00
1-11-($2.99) 1-Five covers. 2-Two covers. 4-Six covers						3.00
... Beginnings (2005, $1.99) Two covers; Turnbull-a						3.00
...: Killian's Vessel 1 (7/07, $2.99) 3 covers; Odagawa-a						3.00
... Prelude (6/05, $2.99) Seven covers; Garza-a						3.00

FATHOM (MICHAEL TURNER'S...) (Volume 3)
Aspen MLT, Inc.: No. 0, Jun, 2008 - No. 10, Feb, 2010 ($2.50/$2.99)

0-($2.50) Garza-a/c						3.00
1-10-($2.99) Garza-a; multiple covers on each						3.00

FATHOM (MICHAEL TURNER'S...) (Volume 4)

	GD 2.0	VG 4.0	FN 6.0	VF 8.0	VF/NM 9.0	NM- 9.2

Aspen MLT, Inc.: No. 0, Jun, 2011 - No. 9, May, 2013 ($2.50/$2.99/$3.50)

0-($2.50) Lobdell-s/Konat-a/c; interview with Lobdell; sketch art						3.00
1-3-($2.99) 1-Five covers						3.00
4-9-($3.50)						3.50

FATHOM (MICHAEL TURNER'S...) (Volume 5)
Aspen MLT, Inc.: Jul, 2013 - No. 8, Sept, 2014 ($1.00/$3.99)

1-($1.00) Wohl-s/Konat-a; multiple covers						3.00
2-8-($3.99) Multiple covers on all						4.00
Annual 1 (6/14, $5.99) Turner-c; short stories by Turner, Wohl/Calero, Ruffino & others						6.00

FATHOM (ALL NEW MICHAEL TURNER'S...) (Volume 6)
Aspen MLT: Feb, 2017 - No. 8, Sept, 2017 ($3.99)

1-8-Northcott-c/Renna-a; multiple covers						4.00

FATHOM (ALL NEW MICHAEL TURNER'S...) (Volume 7)
Aspen MLT: Jun, 2018 - No. 8, Apr, 2019 ($3.99)

1-8-Multiple covers on each; Ron Marz-s/Siya Oum-a						4.00
... Primer 1 (6/18, 25¢) Origin re-told; recaps of previous volumes						3.00

FATHOM (ALL NEW MICHAEL TURNER'S...) (Volume 8)
Aspen MLT: May, 2019 - No. 6, Oct, 2019 ($3.99)

1-6-Multiple covers on each; Hernandez-s/Campetella-a						4.00

FATHOM BLUE (MICHAEL TURNER'S...)
Aspen MLT, Inc.: Jun, 2015 - No. 6, Dec, 2015 ($3.99, limited series)

1-6-Hernandez-s/Avella-a; multiple covers on all						4.00

FATHOM: BLUE DESCENT (MICHAEL TURNER'S...)
Aspen MLT, Inc.: Jun, 2010 - No. 4, Feb, 2012 ($2.50/$2.99, limited series)

0-($2.50) Scott Clark-a; covers by Clark & Benitez						3.00
1-4-($2.99) Alex Sanchez-a. 1-Covers by Clark & Finch						3.00

FATHOM: CANNON HAWKE (MICHAEL TURNER'S...)
Aspen MLT, Inc.: Nov, 2005 - No. 5, Feb, 2006 ($2.99)

1-5-To-a/Turner-c						3.00
... Prelude (11/05, $2.50) Turner-c						3.00

FATHOM: DAWN OF WAR (MICHAEL TURNER'S...)
Aspen MLT, Inc.: Oct, 2004 - No. 3, Dec, 2004 ($2.99, limited series)

0-Caldwell-a						3.00
1-3-Caldwell-a						3.00
...: Cannon Hawke #0 ('04, $2.50) Turner-c						3.00
... The Complete Saga Vol. 1 (2005, $9.99) r/series with cover gallery						10.00

FATHOM: KIANI (MICHAEL TURNER'S...)
Aspen MLT, Inc.: No. 0, Feb, 2007 - No. 4, Dec, 2007 ($2.99, limited series)

0-4-Marcus To-a. 1-Six covers						3.00
Vol. 2 (4/12, $2.50) 0-Four covers						3.00
Vol. 2 (5/12 - No. 4, 11/12, $3.50) 1-4-Hernandez-s/Nome-a; multiple covers on each						3.50
Vol. 3 (3/14 - No. 4, 6/14, $3.99) 1-4-Hernandez-s/Cafaro-a; multiple covers on each						4.00
Vol. 4 (2/15 - No. 4, 5/15, $3.99) 1-4-Hernandez-s/Cafaro-a; multiple covers on each						4.00

FATHOM: KILLIAN'S TIDE
Image Comics (Top Cow Prod.): Apr, 2001 - No. 4, Nov, 2001 ($2.95)

1-4-Caldwell-a(p); two covers by Caldwell and Turner. 2-Flip-book preview of Universe						3.00
1-DFE Blue, 1-Holographic logo						12.00
4-Foil-c						12.00

FATHOM: THE CORE (Leads into Soulfire: The Core)
Aspen MLT, Inc.: Nov, 2021 - No. 2, Dec, 2021 ($3.99, limited series)

1,2-Hernandez-s/Konat-a; multiple covers						4.00

FATHOM: THE ELITE SAGA (MICHAEL TURNER'S...)
Aspen MLT, Inc.: Jun, 2013 - No. 5, Jul, 2013 ($3.99, weekly limited series)

1-5-Hernandez-s/Marion-a; multiple covers; leads into Fathom Volume 5						4.00

FATIMA...CHALLENGE TO THE WORLD (Also see Our Lady of Fatima)
Catechetical Guild: 1951, 36 pgs. (15¢)

nn (not same as 'Challenge to the World')	8	16	24	44	57	70

FATMAN, THE HUMAN FLYING SAUCER
Lightning Comics (Milson Publ. Co.): April, 1967 - No. 3, Aug-Sept, 1967 (68 pgs.) (Written by Otto Binder)

1-Origin/1st app. Fatman & Tinman by C.C. Beck; 1st app. Anti-Man; 2-pg. Fatman pin-up by Beck	7	14	21	49	92	135
2-C. C. Beck-a	5	10	15	33	57	80
3-(Scarce)-Beck-a	6	12	18	41	76	110

FAUNTLEROY COMICS (Super Duck Presents...)
Close-Up/Archie Publications: 1950: No. 2, 1951; No. 3, 1952

1-Super Duck-c/stories by Al Fagaly in all	13	26	39	74	105	135
2,3	8	16	24	42	54	65

FAUST
Northstar Publishing/Rebel Studios #7 on: 1989 - No 13, 1997 ($2.00/$2.25, B&W, mature themes)

1-Decapitation-c; Tim Vigil-c/a in all	3	6	9	21	33	45
1-2nd - 4th printings						4.00
2	2	4	6	8	11	14
2-2nd & 3rd printings, 3,5-2nd printing						4.00
3	2	4	6	8	10	12
4-10: 7-Begin Rebel Studios series						5.00
11-13-Scarce	2	4	6	8	11	14

FAWCETT MOTION PICTURE COMICS (See Motion Picture Comics)

FAWCETT MOVIE COMIC
Fawcett Publications: 1949 - No. 20, Dec, 1952 (All photo-c)

nn- "Dakota Lil"; George Montgomery & Rod Cameron (1949)	20	40	60	120	195	270
nn- "Copper Canyon"; Ray Milland & Hedy Lamarr (1950)	15	30	45	90	140	190

Fatale #1 © Broadway

Fathom V4 #1 © AspenMLT

Fear Itself #1 © MAR

	GD	VG	FN	VF	VF/NM	NM-
	2.0	4.0	6.0	8.0	9.0	9.2

	GD	VG	FN	VF	VF/NM	NM-
	2.0	4.0	6.0	8.0	9.0	9.2

nn- "Destination Moon" (1950) · 71 · 142 · 213 · 454 · 777 · 1100
nn- "Montana"; Errol Flynn & Alexis Smith (1950) · 15 · 30 · 45 · 90 · 140 · 190
nn- "Pioneer Marshal"; Monte Hale (1950) · 15 · 30 · 45 · 90 · 140 · 190
nn- "Powder River Rustlers"; Rocky Lane (1950) · 20 · 40 · 60 · 117 · 189 · 260
nn- "Singing Guns"; Vaughn Monroe, Ella Raines & Walter Brennan (1950) · 14 · 28 · 42 · 82 · 121 · 160
7- "Gunmen of Abilene"; Rocky Lane; Bob Powell-a (1950) · 17 · 34 · 51 · 98 · 154 · 210
8- "King of the Bullwhip"; Lash LaRue; Bob Powell-a (1950) · 21 · 42 · 63 · 126 · 206 · 285
9- "The Old Frontier"; Monte Hale; Bob Powell-a (mis-dated 2/50) 2/51; · 15 · 30 · 45 · 90 · 140 · 190
10- "The Missourians"; Monte Hale (4/51) · 15 · 30 · 45 · 90 · 140 · 190
11- "The Thundering Trail"; Lash LaRue (6/51) · 19 · 38 · 57 · 111 · 176 · 240
12- "Rustlers on Horseback"; Rocky Lane (8/51) · 15 · 30 · 45 · 90 · 140 · 190
13- "Warpath"; Edmond O'Brien & Forrest Tucker (10/51) · 14 · 28 · 42 · 80 · 115 · 150
14- "Last Outpost"; Ronald Reagan (12/51) · 33 · 66 · 99 · 194 · 317 · 440
15-(Scarce)- "The Man From Planet X"; Robert Clark; Schaffenberger-a (2/52) · 265 · 530 · 795 · 1694 · 2897 · 4100
16- "Ten Tall Men"; Burt Lancaster · 13 · 26 · 39 · 74 · 105 · 135
17- "Rose of Cimarron"; Jack Buetel & Mala Powers · 10 · 20 · 30 · 58 · 79 · 100
18- "The Brigand"; Anthony Dexter & Anthony Quinn; Schaffenberger-a · 10 · 20 · 30 · 58 · 79 · 100
19- "Carbine Williams"; James Stewart; Costanza-a; James Stewart photo-c · 11 · 22 · 33 · 62 · 86 · 110
20- "Ivanhoe"; Robert Taylor & Liz Taylor photo-c · 18 · 36 · 54 · 105 · 165 · 225

FAWCETT'S FUNNY ANIMALS (No. 1-26, 80-on titled "Funny Animals"; becomes Li'l Tomboy No. 92 on?)
Fawcett Publications/Charlton Comics No. 84 on: 12/42 - #79, 4/53; #80, 6/53 - #83, 12?/53; #84, 4/54 - #91, 2/56

1-Capt. Marvel on cover; intro. Hoppy The Captain Marvel Bunny, cloned from Capt. Marvel; Billy the Kid & Willie the Worm begin · 71 · 142 · 213 · 454 · 777 · 1100
2-Xmas-c · 39 · 78 · 117 · 231 · 378 · 525
3-5: 3(2/43)-Spirit of '43-c · 27 · 54 · 81 · 162 · 266 · 370
6,7,9,10 · 16 · 32 · 48 · 92 · 144 · 195
8-Flag-c · 17 · 34 · 51 · 98 · 154 · 210
11-20: 25-Xmas-c. 26-St. Valentine's Day-c · 13 · 26 · 39 · 74 · 105 · 135
21-40: 25-Xmas-c. 26-St. Valentine's Day-c · 10 · 20 · 30 · 56 · 76 · 95
41-86,90,91 · 9 · 18 · 27 · 50 · 65 · 80
87-89(10-54-2/55)-Merry Mailman ish (TV/Radio)-part photo-c · 10 · 20 · 30 · 56 · 76 · 95

NOTE: Marvel Bunny in all issues to at least No. 68 (not in 49-54).

FAZE ONE FAZERS
AC Comics: 1986 - No. 4, Sept, 1986 (Limited series)
1-4 · · · · · 4.00

F.B.I., THE
Dell Publishing Co.: Apr-June, 1965
1-Sinnott-a · · 5 · 10 · 15 · 34 · 60 · 85

F.B.I. STORY, THE (Movie)
Dell Publishing Co.: No. 1069, Jan-Mar, 1960
Four Color 1069-Toth-a; James Stewart photo-c · 9 · 18 · 27 · 61 · 123 · 185

FBP: FEDERAL BUREAU OF PHYSICS (Titled Collider for issue #1)
DC Comics (Vertigo): Sept, 2013 - No. 24, Nov, 2015 ($2.99/$3.99)
Collider #1- Simon Oliver-s/Robbi Rodriguez-a/Nathan Fox-c · · · · · 3.00
2-20: 2-(10/13) · · · · · 3.00
21-24-($3.99) · · · · · 4.00

FEAR (Adventure into…)
Marvel Comics Group: Nov, 1970 - No. 31, Dec, 1975
1-Fantasy & Sci-Fi-r in early issues; 68 pg. Giant size; Kirby-a(r) · 9 · 18 · 27 · 61 · 123 · 185
2-6: 2-4-(68 pgs.) 5,6-(52 pgs.) Kirby-a(r) · 5 · 10 · 15 · 30 · 50 · 70
7-9-Kirby-a(r) · 3 · 6 · 9 · 20 · 31 · 42
10-Man-Thing begins (10/72, 4th app.), ends #19; see Savage Tales #1 for 1st app.; 1st solo series; Chaykin/Morrow-c/a; · 12 · 24 · 36 · 80 · 173 · 265
11-Neal Adams-c · 13 · 26 · 39 · 89 · 195 · 300
12,13,14,16-18: 12-Starlin/Buckler-a. 17-Origin/1st app. Wundarr · 3 · 6 · 9 · 17 · 26 · 35
15-1st full-length Man-Thing story (8/73) · 3 · 6 · 9 · 21 · 33 · 45
19-Intro. Howard the Duck; Val Mayerik-a (12/73) · 16 · 32 · 48 · 110 · 243 · 375
20-Morbius, the Living Vampire begins, ends #31; has history recap of Morbius

with X-Men & Spider-Man · 10 · 20 · 30 · 64 · 132 · 200
21-23,25 · 3 · 6 · 9 · 16 · 24 · 32
24-Blade-c/sty · 10 · 20 · 30 · 68 · 144 · 220
26-31 · 3 · 6 · 9 · 14 · 19 · 24
NOTE: Bolle a-13i. Brunner c-15-17. Buckler a-11p, 12i. Chaykin a-10i. Colan a-23r. Craig a-10p. Ditko a-6-8r. Evans a-30. Everett a-9, 10i, 21r. Gulacy a-20p. Heath a-12r. Heck a-8r, 13r. Gil Kane a-21p; c(p)-20, 21, 23-28, 31. Kirby a-1-9r. Maneely a-24r. Mooney a-11i, 26r. Morrow a-11i. Paul Reinman a-14r. Robbins a(p)-25-27, 31. Russell a-23p, 24p. Severin c-8. Starlin c-12p.

FEAR AGENT
Image Comics (#1-11)/Dark Horse Comics.: Oct, 2005 - No. 32, Nov, 2011 ($2.99/$3.50)
1-11: 1-Remender-s/Moore-a. 5-Opeña begins. 11-Francavilla-a · 3.00
… The Last Goodbye 1-4 (Dark Horse, 6/07 - No. 4, 9/07) (#12-15) · 3.00
Tales of the Fear Agent: Twelve Steps in One (#16), 17-27 · 3.00
28-32-($3.50) Hawthorne & Moore-a/Moore-c · 3.50
… Vol 1.: Re-Ignition TPB (2006, $9.99) r/#1-4 · 10.00
… Vol 2.: My War TPB (Dark Horse Books, 2007, $14.95) r/#5-10; Opeña sketch pages · 15.00

FEARBOOK
Eclipse Comics: April, 1986 ($1.75, one-shot, mature)
1-Scholastic Mag-r; Bissette-a · 6.00

FEAR CASE
Dark Horse Comics: Feb, 2021 - No. 4, May, 2021 ($3.99)
1-4-Matt Kindt-s/Tyler Jenkins-a · 4.00

FEAR EFFECT (Based on the video game)
Image Comics (Top Cow): May, 2000; March, 2001 ($2.95)
Retro Helix 1 (3/01), Special 1 (5/00) · 3.00

FEAR IN THE NIGHT (See Complete Mystery No. 3)

FEAR ITSELF
Marvel Comics: Jun, 2011 - No. 7, Dec, 2011 ($3.99/$4.99, limited series)
1-6-Fraction-s/Immonen-a/McNiven-c. 3-Bucky apparently killed · 4.00
1-Blank cover · 4.00
7-($4.99) Thor perishes; previews of ...: The Fearless, Incredible Hulk #1, Defenders #1 · 5.00
7.1 Captain America (1/12, $3.99) Brubaker-s/Guice-a; Bucky's fate · 4.00
7.2 Thor (1/12, $3.99) Fraction-s/Adam Kubert-a/c; Thor's funeral; Tanarus returns · 4.00
7.3 Iron Man (1/12, $3.99) Fraction-s/Larroca-a/c; Odin app. · 4.00
...: Black Widow (8/11, $3.99) Peter Nguyen-a; Peregrine app. · 4.00
...: Book of the Skull (5/11, $3.99) prequel to series; WWII flashback, Red Skull app. · 4.00
...: Fellowship of Fear (10/11, $3.99) profiles of hammer-wielders and fear thrivers · 4.00
... FF (9/11, $3.99) Reed & Sue vs. Ben Grimm; Grummett-a/Dell'Otto-c · 3.00
...: Sin's Past (6/11, $4.99) r/Captain America #355-357; Sisters of Sin app. · 5.00
... Spotlight (6/11, $3.99) Interviews with Fraction and Immonen; feature articles · 4.00
...: The Monkey King (11/11, $2.99) Joshua Fialkov-s/Juan Doe-a · 3.00
...: The Worthy (9/11, $3.99) Origins of the hammer wielders; s/a by various · 4.00

FEAR ITSELF: DEADPOOL
Marvel Comics: Aug, 2011 - No. 3, Oct, 2011 ($2.99, limited series)
1-3-Hastings-s/Dazo-a · 3.00

FEAR ITSELF: FEARSOME FOUR
Marvel Comics: Aug, 2011 - No. 4, Nov, 2011 ($2.99, limited series)
1-4-Art by Bisley and others; Man-Thing, She-Hulk & Howard the Duck app. · 3.00

FEAR ITSELF: HULK VS. DRACULA
Marvel Comics: Nov, 2011 - No. 3, Dec, 2011 ($2.99, limited series)
1-3-Gischler-s/Stegman-a; Dell'Otto-c · 3.00

FEAR ITSELF: SPIDER-MAN
Marvel Comics: Jul, 2011 - No. 3, Sept, 2011 ($2.99, limited series)
1-3-Yost-s/McKone-a; Vermin app. · 3.00

FEAR ITSELF: THE DEEP
Marvel Comics: Aug, 2011 - No. 4, Nov, 2011 ($2.99, limited series)
1-4-Bunn-s/Garbett-a; Sub-Mariner vs. Attuma; Doctor Strange & Silver Surfer app. · 3.00

FEAR ITSELF: THE FEARLESS (Follows Fear Itself #7)
Marvel Comics: Dec, 2011 - No. 12, Jun, 2012 ($2.99, limited series)
1-12: 1-Fate of the Hammers; Bagley & Pelletier-a; Art Adams-c. 7-Wolverine app. · 3.00

FEAR ITSELF: THE HOME FRONT
Marvel Comics: Jun, 2011 - No. 7, Dec, 2011 ($3.99, limited series)
1-7-Short story anthology; Speedball w/Mayhew-a in all; Chaykin-a; Djurdjevic-c · 4.00

FEAR ITSELF: UNCANNY X-FORCE
Marvel Comics: Sept, 2011 - No. 3, Nov, 2011 ($2.99, limited series)
1-3-Bianchi-a/c · 3.00

	GD	VG	FN	VF	VF/NM	NM-
	2.0	4.0	6.0	8.0	9.0	9.2

FEAR ITSELF: WOLVERINE
Marvel Comics: Sept. 2011 - No. 3, Nov. 2011 ($2.99, limited series)
1-3-Boschi-a; Wolverine vs. S.T.R.I.K.E. 1-Acuña-c. 2,3-Molina-c ... 3.00

FEAR ITSELF: YOUTH IN REVOLT
Marvel Comics: Jul. 2011 - No. 6, Dec. 2011 ($2.99, limited series)
1-6-Firestar and The Initiative app.; McKeever-s/Norton-a ... 3.00

FEARLESS
Marvel Comics: Sept. 2019 - No. 4, Dec, 2019 ($4.99, limited series)
1-4 Stories of Captain Marvel, Storm, Invisible Woman and other female heroes ... 5.00

FEARLESS DAWN MEETS HELLBOY
Albatross Funnybooks: 2020 ($3.99, one-shot)
1-Mike Mignola & Steve Mannion-s/a ... 4.00

FEARLESS DEFENDERS (Marvel NOW!)
Marvel Comics: Apr, 2013 - No. 12, Feb, 2014 ($2.99/3.99)
1-4,5-7: 1-Valkyrie & Misty Knight team-up; Bunns-a/Sliney-a. 2-Dani Moonstar app. ... 3.00
4AU-(7/13, $3.99) Age of Ultron tie-in; Dr. Doom & Ares app. ... 4.00
8-12-($3.99) ... 4.00

FEARLESS FAGAN
Dell Publishing Co.: No. 441, Dec, 1952 (one-shot)
Four Color 441 ... 5 · 10 · 15 · 31 · 53 · 75

FEAR OF A RED PLANET
AfterShock Comics: Nov, 2022 - No. 5 ($4.99, limited series)
1-($4.99)-Mark Sable-s/Andrea Olimpieri-a ... 5.00
2-4-($3.99) ... 4.00

FEAR THE FUNHOUSE
Archie Comics Publications: Dec, 2022 ($3.99, one-shot)
1-Short horror stories with the Archie gang ... 4.00
...: Toybox of Terror 1 (12/23, $3.99) Covers by Caskey and Boo ... 4.00

FEATHERS
Archaia (BOOM! Studios): Jan, 2015 - No. 6, Jun, 2015 ($3.99, limited series)
1-6-Jorge Corona-s/a ... 4.00

FEATURE BOOK (Dell) (See Large Feature Comic)

FEATURE BOOKS (Newspaper-r, early issues)
David McKay Publications: May, 1937 - No. 57, 1948 (B&W)
(Full color, 68 pgs. begin #26 on)
Note: See individual alphabetical listings for prices

nn-Popeye & the Jeep (#1, 100 pgs.); reprinted as Feature Books #3(Very Rare; only 3 known copies, 1-VF, 2-in low grade)
nn-Dick Tracy (#1)-Reprinted as Feature Book #4 (100 pgs.) & in part as 4-Color #1 (Rare, less than 10 known copies)
NOTE: Above books were advertised together with different covers than Feature. Books #3 & 4.
1-King of the Royal Mtd. (#1)
2-Popeye (6/37) by Segar same as nn issue but a new cover added
3-Popeye (7/37) by Segar;
4-Dick Tracy (8/37)-Same as nn issue but a new cover added
5-Popeye (9/37) by Segar
6-Dick Tracy (10/37)
7-Little Orphan Annie (#1, 11/37) (Rare)-Reprints strips from 12/31/34 to 7/17/35
8-Secret Agent X-9 (12/37) -Not by Raymond
9-Dick Tracy (1/38)
10-Popeye (2/38)
11-Little Annie Rooney (#1, 3/38)
12-Blondie (#1) (4/38) (Rare)
13-Inspector Wade (5/38)
14-Popeye (6/38) by Segar
15-Barney Baxter (#1) (7/38)
16-Red Eagle (8/38)
17-Gangbusters (#1, 9/38) (1st app.)
18,19-Mandrake
20-Phantom (#1, 12/38)
21-Lone Ranger
22-Phantom
23-Mandrake
24-Lone Ranger (1941)
25-Flash Gordon (#1)-Reprints not by Raymond
26-Prince Valiant (1941)-Hal Foster-c/a; newspaper strips reprinted, pgs. 1-28,30-63; color & 68 pg. issues begin; Foster cover is only original comic book artwork by him
27-29,31,34-Blondie
30-Katzenjammer Kids (#1, 1942)
32,35,41,44-Katzenjammer Kids
33(nn)-Romance of Flying; World War II photos
36('43),38,40('44),42,43, 45,47-Blondie
37-Katzenjammer Kids; his photo & biog. of Harold H. Knerr (1883-1949) who took over strip from Rudolph Dirks in 1914
39-Phantom
46-Mandrake in the Fire World-(58 pgs.)
48-Maltese Falcon by Dashiell Hammett('46)
49,50-Perry Mason; based on Gardner novels
51,54-Rip Kirby; Raymond-c/s; origin-#51
52,55-Mandrake
53,56,57-Phantom
NOTE: All Feature Books through #25 are over-sized 8-1/2x11-3/8" comics with color covers and black and white interiors. The covers are rough, heavy stock. The page counts, including covers, are as follows: nn, #3, 4-100 pgs.; #1, 2-52 pgs.; #5-25 are all 76 pgs. #33 was found in bound set from publisher. Reprints from 1980s exist.

FEATURE COMICS (Formerly Feature Funnies)
Quality Comics Group: No. 21, June, 1939 - No. 144, May, 1950

21-The Clock, Jane Arden & Mickey Finn continue from Feature Funnies ... 84 · 168 · 252 · 538 · 919 · 1300
22-26: 23-Charlie Chan begins (8/39, 1st app.) ... 52 · 104 · 156 · 328 · 552 · 775
26-(nn, nd)-Cover in one color, (10¢, 36 pgs.; issue No. blanked out. Two variations exist, each contain half of the regular #26) ... 54 · 108 · 162 · 343 · 574 · 825
27-(12/39, Rare)-Origin/1st app. Doll Man by Eisner (scripts) & Lou Fine (art); Doll Man begins, ends #139 ... 838 · 1676 · 2514 · 6117 · 10,809 · 15,500
28-(1/40, Rare)-2nd app. Doll Man by Lou Fine ... 265 · 530 · 795 · 1694 · 2897 · 4100
29-Clock-c ... 135 · 270 · 405 · 864 · 1482 · 2100
30-1st Doll Man-c ... 232 · 464 · 696 · 1485 · 2543 · 3600
31-Last Clock & Charlie Chan issue (4/40); Charlie Chan moves to Big Shot #1 following month (5/40) ... 97 · 194 · 291 · 621 · 1061 · 1500
32,34,36: Dollman covers. 32-Rusty Ryan & Samar begin. 34-Captain Fortune app. ... 97 · 194 · 291 · 621 · 1061 · 1500
33,35,37- 37-Last Fine Doll Man ... 55 · 110 · 165 · 352 · 601 · 850

NOTE: A 15¢ Canadian version of Feature Comics #37, made in the US, exists.
38,40-Dollman covers. 38-Origin the Ace of Space. 40-Bruce Blackburn in costume ... 61 · 122 · 183 · 390 · 670 · 950
39,41: 39-Origin The Destroying Demon, ends #40; X-Mas-c. ... 42 · 84 · 126 · 265 · 445 · 625
42,46,48,50-Dollman covers. 42-USA, the Spirit of Old Glory begins. 46-Intro. Boyville Brigadiers in Rusty Ryan. 48-USA ends ... 47 · 94 · 141 · 296 · 498 · 700
43,45,47,49: 47-Fargo Kid begins ... 34 · 68 · 102 · 199 · 325 · 450
44-Doll Man by Crandall begins, ends #63; Crandall-a(2) ... 61 · 122 · 183 · 390 · 670 · 950
51,53,55,57,59: 57-Spider Widow begins ... 24 · 48 · 72 · 142 · 234 · 325
52,54,56,58,60-Dollman covers. 56-Marijuana story in Swing Sisson strip. 60-Raven begins, ends #71 ... 34 · 68 · 102 · 204 · 332 · 460
61,63,65,67 ... 21 · 42 · 63 · 122 · 199 · 275
62,64,66,68-Dollman covers. 68-(5/43) ... 31 · 62 · 93 · 182 · 296 · 410
69,71-Phantom Lady x-over in Spider Widow ... 24 · 48 · 72 · 142 · 234 · 325
70-Dollman-c; Phantom Lady x-over ... 34 · 68 · 102 · 204 · 332 · 460
72,74,77-80,100-Dollman covers. 72-Spider Widow ends ... 25 · 50 · 75 · 150 · 245 · 340
73,75,76 ... 19 · 38 · 57 · 111 · 176 · 240
81-99-All Dollman covers ... 20 · 40 · 60 · 120 · 195 · 270
101-144: 139-Last Doll Man & last Doll Man cover. 140-Intro. Stuntman Stetson (Stuntman Stetson c-140-144) ... 18 · 36 · 54 · 107 · 169 · 230
NOTE: Celardo a-37-43. Crandall a-44-60, 62, 63-on(most). Gustavson a-(Rusty Ryan)-32-134. Powell a-34, 64-73. The Clock c-25, 28, 29. Doll Man c-30, 32, 34, 36, 38, 40, 42, 44, 46, 48, 50, 52, 54, 56, 58, 60, 62, 64, 66, 68, 70, 72, 74, 77-139. Joe Palooka c-21, 24, 27.

FEATURE FILMS
National Periodical Publ.: Mar-Apr, 1950 - No. 4, Sept-Oct, 1950 (All photo-c)
1- "Captain China" with John Payne, Gail Russell, Lon Chaney & Edgar Bergen ... 65 · 130 · 195 · 416 · 708 · 1000
2- "Riding High" with Bing Crosby ... 69 · 138 · 207 · 435 · 735 · 1035
3- "The Eagle & the Hawk" with John Payne, Rhonda Fleming & D. O'Keefe ... 66 · 132 · 198 · 416 · 701 · 985
4- "Fancy Pants"; Bob Hope & Lucille Ball ... 72 · 144 · 216 · 454 · 770 · 1085

FEATURE FUNNIES (Feature Comics No. 21 on)(Earliest Quality Comics title)
Comic Favorites Inc./Quality Comics Group: Oct. 1937 - No. 20, May, 1939
1(V9#1-indicia)-Joe Palooka, Mickey Finn (1st app.), The Bungles, Jane Arden, Dixie Dugan (1st app.), Big Top, Ned Brant, Strange As It Seems, & Off the Record strip reprints begin ... 280 · 560 · 840 · 1540 · 2520 · 3500
2-The Hawk app. (11/37); Goldberg-c ... 135 · 270 · 405 · 864 · 1482 · 2100
3-Hawks of Seas begins by Eisner, ends #12; The Clock begins; Christmas-c ... 110 · 220 · 330 · 704 · 1202 · 1700
4,5 ... 77 · 154 · 231 · 493 · 847 · 1200
6-12: 11-Archie O'Toole by Bud Thomas begins, ends #22 ... 57 · 114 · 171 · 362 · 619 · 875
13-Espionage, Starring Black X begins by Eisner, ends #20 ... 63 · 126 · 189 · 403 · 689 · 975
14-20 ... 47 · 94 · 141 · 296 · 498 · 700
NOTE: Joe Palooka covers 1, 6, 9, 12, 15, 18.

FEATURE PRESENTATION, A (Feature Presentations Magazine #6)
(Formerly Women in Love) (Also see Startling Terror Tales #11)
Fox Feature Syndicate: No. 5, April, 1950
5(#1)-Black Tarantula (scarce) ... 81 · 162 · 243 · 518 · 884 · 1250

FEATURE PRESENTATIONS MAGAZINE (Formerly A Feature Presentation #5; becomes Feature Stories Magazine #3 on)
Fox Feature Syndicate: No. 6, July, 1950
6(#2)-Moby Dick; Wood-c ... 36 · 72 · 108 · 211 · 343 · 475

FEATURE STORIES MAGAZINE (Formerly Feature Presentations Mag. #6)
Fox Feature Syndicate: No. 3, Aug, 1950
3-Jungle Lil, Zegra stories; bondage-c ... 45 · 90 · 135 · 284 · 480 · 675

FEDERAL MEN COMICS
DC Comics: 1936
nn-Ashcan comic, not distributed to newsstands, only for in house use (no known sales)

FEDERAL MEN COMICS (See Adventure Comics #32, The Comics Magazine, New Adventure Comics, New Book of Comics, New Comics & Star Spangled Comics #91)
Gerard Publ. Co.: No. 2, 1945 (DC reprints from 1930's)
2-Siegel/Shuster-a; cover redrawn from Det. #9 ... 53 · 106 · 159 · 334 · 567 · 800

FELICIA HARDY: THE BLACK CAT
Marvel Comics: July, 1994 - No. 4, Oct, 1994 ($1.50, limited series)
1-Spider-Man app. ... 2 · 4 · 6 · 11 · 16 · 20
2-4: 4-Spider-Man app. ... 5.00

FELIX'S NEPHEWS INKY & DINKY
Harvey Publications: Sept, 1957 - No. 7, Oct, 1958
1-Cover shows Inky's left eye with 2 pupils ... 14 · 28 · 42 · 81 · 118 · 155
2-7 ... 8 · 16 · 24 · 44 · 57 · 70
NOTE: Messmer art in 1-6. Oriolo a-1-7.

FELIX THE CAT (See Cat Tales 3-D, The Funnies, March of Comics #24,36,51, New Funnies & Popular Comics)
Dell Publ. No. 1-19/Toby No. 20-61/Harvey No. 62-118/Dell No. 1-12:
1943 - No. 118, Nov, 1961; Sept-Nov, 1962 - No. 12, July, 1965
Four Color 15 ... 89 · 178 · 267 · 712 · 1606 · 2500
Four Color 46('44) ... 46 · 92 · 138 · 368 · 834 · 1300
Four Color 77('45) ... 40 · 80 · 120 · 296 · 673 · 1050
Four Color 119('46)-All new stories begin ... 36 · 72 · 108 · 259 · 580 · 900
Four Color 135('46) ... 23 · 46 · 69 · 156 · 348 · 540
Four Color 162(9/47) ... 18 · 36 · 54 · 124 · 275 · 425
1(2-3/48)(Dell) ... 31 · 62 · 93 · 223 · 499 · 775
2 ... 12 · 24 · 36 · 84 · 185 · 285
3-5 ... 10 · 20 · 30 · 65 · 135 · 205
6-19(2-3/51-Dell) ... 8 · 16 · 24 · 56 · 102 · 150
20-30,32,33,36,38-61(6/55)-All Messmer issues.(Toby): 28-(2/52)-Some copies have #29

Fearless Defenders #2 © MAR

Felix the Cat #108 © HARV

The Ferret #3 © MAL

	GD	VG	FN	VF	VF/NM	NM-
	2.0	4.0	6.0	8.0	9.0	9.2

	GD	VG	FN	VF	VF/NM	NM-
on cover, #28 on inside (Rare in high grade)	15	30	45	100	220	340
31,34,35-No Messmer; Messmer-c only 31,34	8	16	24	54	102	150
37-(100 pgs., 25 ¢, 1/15/53, X-Mas-c, Toby; daily & Sunday-r (rare)						
	36	72	108	266	596	925
62(8/55)-80,100 (Harvey)	4	8	12	28	47	65
81-99	4	8	12	25	40	55
101-118(11/61): 101-117-Reprints. 118-All new-a	3	6	9	17	26	35
12-269-211(#1, 9-11/62)(Dell)-No Messmer	4	8	12	28	47	65
2-12(7-9/65)(Dell, TV)-No Messmer	4	8	12	23	37	50
3-D Comic Book 1(1953-One Shot, 25¢)-w/glasses	39	78	117	231	378	525
Summer Annual nn ('53, 25¢, 100 pgs., Toby)-Daily & Sunday-r						
	50	100	150	315	533	750
Winter Annual 2 ('54, 25¢, 100 pgs., Toby)-Daily & Sunday-r						
	47	94	141	296	498	700

(Special note: Despite the covers on Toby 37 and the Summer Annual above proclaiming "all new stories," they were actually reformatted newspaper strips)

NOTE: Otto Messmer went to work for Universal Film as an animator in 1915 and then worked for the Pat Sullivan animation studio in 1916. He created a black cat in the cartoon short, Feline Follies in 1919 that became known as Felix in the early 1920s. The Felix Sunday strip began Aug. 14, 1923 and continued until Sept. 19, 1943 when Messmer took the character to Dell (Western Publishing) and began doing Felix comic books, first adapting strips to the comic format. The first all new Felix comic was Four Color #119 in 1946 (#4 in the Dell run). The daily Felix was begun on May 9, 1927 by another artist, but by the following year, Messmer did it too. King Features took the daily away from Messmer in 1954 and he began doing some of his most dynamic art for Toby Press. The daily Felix continued by Joe Oriolo who drew it until it was discontinued Jan. 9, 1967. Oriolo was Messmer's assistant for many years and inked some of Messmer's pencils through the Toby run, as well as doing some of the stories by himself. Though Messmer continued to work for Dell until the Toby run, his contribuitons were limited, and no all Messmer stories appeared after the Toby run until some early Toby reprints were published in the 1990s Harvey revival of the title. 4-Color Nos. 15, 46, 77 and the Toby Annuals are all daily or Sunday newspaper reprints from the 1930's-1940's drawn by Otto Messmer. #101-r/#64; 102-r/#65; 103-r/#67; 104-117-r/#68-81. Messmer in all Dell/Toby/Harvey issues except #31, 34, 35, 97, 98, 100, 118. Oriolo a-20, 31-on.

FELIX THE CAT (Also see The Nine Lives of…)
Harvey Comics/Gladstone: Sept, 1991 - No. 7, Jan, 1993 ($1.25/$1.50, bi-monthly)

1: 1950s-r/Toby stories by Messmer begins. 1-Inky and Dinky back-up story (produced by Gladstone)						6.00
2-7, Big Book, V2#1 (9/92, $1.95, 52 pgs.)						4.00

FELIX THE CAT AND FRIENDS
Felix Comics: 1992 - No. 5, 1993 ($1.95)

1-5: 1-Contains Felix trading cards						4.00

FELIX THE CAT & HIS FRIENDS (Pat Sullivan's…)
Toby Press: Dec, 1953 - No. 3, 1954 (Indicia title for #2&3 as listed)

	GD	VG	FN	VF	VF/NM	NM-
1 (Indicia title, "Felix and His Friends," #1 only)	34	68	102	204	332	460
2-3	21	42	63	124	202	280

FELIX THE CAT DIGEST MAGAZINE
Harvey Comics: July, 1992 ($1.75, digest-size, 98 pgs.)

1-Felix, Richie Rich stories						6.00

FELIX THE CAT KEEPS ON WALKIN'
Hamilton Comics: 1991 ($15.95, 8-1/2"x11", 132 pgs.)

nn-Reprints 15 Toby Press Felix the Cat and Felix and His Friends stories in new color						16.00

FELL
Image Comics: Sept, 2005 - No. 9, Jan, 2008 ($1.99)

1-9-Warren Ellis-s/Ben Templesmith-a						3.00
…, Vol. 1: Feral City TPB (2007, $14.99) r/#1-8						15.00

FELON
Image Comics (Minotaur Press): Nov, 2001 - No. 4, Apr, 2002 ($2.95, B&W)

1-4-Rucka-s/Clark-a/c						3.00

FEMALE FURIES (See New Gods titles)
DC Comics: Apr, 2019 - No. 6, Sept, 2019 ($3.99, limited series)

1-6-Origin of the Granny Goodness & the Furies; Castellucci-s/Melo-a. 4-Simonson-c						4.00

FEM FANTASTIQUE
AC Comics: Aug, 1988 ($1.95, B&W)

	GD	VG	FN	VF	VF/NM	NM-
V2#1-By Bill Black; Bettie Page pin-up	2	4	6	8	10	12

FEMFORCE (Also see Untold Origin of the Femforce)
Americomics: Apr, 1985 - No. 109 (1.75-/2.95, B&W #16-56)

	GD	VG	FN	VF	VF/NM	NM-
1-Black-a in most; Nightveil, Ms. Victory begin	2	4	6	9	13	16
2-10						4.00
11-43: 25-Origin/1st app. new Ms. Victory. 28-Colt leaves. 29,30-Camilla-r by Mayo from Jungle Comics. 36-(2.95, 52 pgs.)						4.00
44,64: 44-W/mini-comic, Catman & Kitten #0. 64-Re-intro Black Phantom						5.00
45-49,51-63,65-99: 51-Photo-c from movie. 57-Begin color issues. 95-Photo-c						3.00
50 ($2.95, 52 pgs.)-Contains flexi-disc; origin retold; most AC characters app.						4.00
100-($3.95)						5.00

	GD	VG	FN	VF	VF/NM	NM-
100-($6.90)-Polybagged	1	2	3	5	6	8
101-109-($4.95)						5.00
Special 1 (Fall, '84)(B&W, 52pgs.)-1st app. Ms. Victory, She-Cat, Blue Bulleteer, Rio Rita & Lady Luger						4.00
Bad Girl Backlash-(12/95, $5.00)						5.00
Frightbook 1 ('92, $2.95, B&W)-Halloween special, In the House of Horror 1 ('89, 2.50, B&W), Night of the Demon 1 ('90, 2.75, B&W), Out of the Asylum Special 1 ('87, B&W, $1.95), Pin-Up Portfolio						4.00
Pin-Up Portfolio (5 issues)						4.00

FEMFORCE UP CLOSE
AC Comics: Apr, 1992 - No. 11, 1995 ($2.75, quarterly)

1-11: 1-Stars Nightveil; inside f/c photo from Femforce movie. 2-Stars Stardust. 3-Stars Dragonfly. 4-Stars She-Cat						4.00

FENCE
BOOM! Studios (Boom! Box): Nov, 2017 - No. 12, Nov, 2018 ($3.99)

1-12-C.S. Pacat-s/Johanna the Mad-a						4.00

FENCE: REDEMPTION
BOOM! Studios (Boom! Box): Jun, 2023 - No. 4, Sept, 2023 ($4.99)

1-4-C.S. Pacat-s/Johanna the Mad-a						5.00

FERDINAND THE BULL (See Mickey Mouse Magazine V4#3)(Walt Disney's)
Dell Publishing Co.: 1938 (10¢, large size (9-1/2" x 10"), some color w/rest B&W)

	GD	VG	FN	VF	VF/NM	NM-
nn		24	48	72	142	234	325

FERRET
Malibu Comics: Sept, 1992; May, 1993 - No. 10, Feb, 1994 ($1.95)

1-(1992, one-shot)						4.00
1-10: 1-Die-cut-c. 2-4-Collector's Ed. w/poster. 5-Polybagged w/Skycap						4.00
2-4-($1.95)-Newsstand Edition w/different-c						4.00

FERRYMAN
DC Comics (WildStorm): Early Dec, 2008 - No. 5, Mar, 2009 ($3.50)

1-5-Andreyko-s/Wayshak-a						3.50

FEVER RIDGE: A TALE OF MACARTHUR'S JUNGLE WAR
IDW Publishing: Feb, 2013 - No. 4, Oct, 2013 ($3.99)

1-4-Heimos-s/Runge-a/DeStefano-l; 1940s War stories on New Guinea						4.00

FF (Fantastic Four after Human Torch's death)
Marvel Comics: May, 2011 - No. 23, Dec, 2012 ($3.99)

1-Hickman-s/Epting-a; Spider-Man joins						4.00
1-Blank variant cover						4.00
1-Variant-c by Daniel Acuña						8.00
1-Variant-c by Stan Goldberg						6.00
2-23-($2.99) 2-Dr. Doom joins. 4,5-Kitson-a. 5-7-Black Bolt returns. 10,11-Avengers app.						3.00
…: Fifty Fantastic Years 1 (11/11, $4.99) Handbook format profiles of heroes and foes						5.00

FF (Marvel NOW!)
Marvel Comics: Jan, 2013 - No. 16, Mar, 2014 ($2.99)

1-15: 1-Fraction-s/Allred-a; new team forms (Ant-Man, She-Hulk, Medusa, Ms. Thing) 6,9-Quinones-a. 8-Impossible Man app.						3.00
16-($3.99) Ant-Man vs. Doom; back-up w/Quinones-a; Uatu & Silver Surfer app.						4.00

F5
Image Comics/Dark Horse: Jan, 2000 - No. 4, Oct, 2000 ($2.50/$2.95)

Preview (1/00, $2.50) Character bios and b&w pages; Daniel-s/a						3.00
1-($2.95, 48 pages) Tony Daniel-s/a						4.00
1-($20.00) Variant bikini-c						20.00
2-4-($2.50)						3.00
F5 Origin (Dark Horse Comics, 11/01, 2.99) w/cover gallery & sketches						3.00

FIBBER McGEE & MOLLY (Radio)(Also see A-1 Comics)
Magazine Enterprises: No. 25, 1949 (one-shot)

	GD	VG	FN	VF	VF/NM	NM-
A-1 25	15	30	45	88	137	185

FICTION ILLUSTRATED
Byron Preiss Visual Publ./Pyramid: No. 1, Jan, 1975 - No. 4, Jan, 1977 ($1.00, #1,2 are digest size, 132 pgs.; #3,4 are graphic novels for mail order and specialty bookstores only)

	GD	VG	FN	VF	VF/NM	NM-
1,2: 1-Schlomo Raven; Sutton-a. 2-Starfawn; Stephen Fabian-a.	2	4	6	13	18	22
3-($1.00-c, 4 3/4 x 6 1/2" digest size) Chandler; new Steranko-a	3	6	9	14	20	26
3-($4.95-c, 8 1/2 x 11" graphic novel; low print) same contents and indicia, but "Chandler" is the cover feature title	5	10	15	31	53	75
4-($4.95-c, 8 1/2 x 11" graphic novel; low print) Son of Sherlock Holmes; Reese-a	4	8	12	27	44	60

	GD 2.0	VG 4.0	FN 6.0	VF 8.0	VF/NM 9.0	NM- 9.2

FICTION SQUAD
BOOM! Studios: Oct, 2014 - No. 6, Mar, 2015 ($3.99, limited series)

1-6-Jenkins-s/Bachs-a						4.00

FIELD, THE
Image Comics: Apr, 2014 - No. 4, Sept, 2014 ($3.50, limited series)

1-4-Brisson-s/Roy-a						3.50

FIERCE
Dark Horse Comics (Rocket Comics): July, 2004 - No. 4, Dec, 2004 ($2.99, limited series)

1-4-Jeremy Love-s/Robert Love-a						3.00

15-LOVE
Marvel Comics: Aug, 2011 - No. 3, Oct, 2011 ($4.99, limited series)

1-3-Tennis academy story; Andi Watson-s/Tommy Ohtsuka-a/c; Sho Murase-c						5.00

50 GIRLS 50
Image Comics: Jun, 2011 - No. 4, Sept, 2011 ($2.99, limited series)

1-4-Frank Cho-c; Cho & Murray-s/Medellin-a						3.00

52 (Leads into Countdown series)
DC Comics: Week One, July, 2006 - Week Fifty-Two, Jul, 2007 ($2.50, weekly series)

1-Chronicles the year after Infinite Crisis; Johns, Morrison, Rucka & Waid-s; JG Jones-c						4.00
2-10: 2-History of the DC Universe back-up thru #11. 6-1st app. The Great Ten.						
7-Intro. Kate Kane. 10-Supernova						3.00
11-Batwoman debut (single panel cameo in #9)						4.00
12-52: 12-Isis gains powers; back-up 2 pg. origins begin. 15-Booster Gold killed. 17-Lobo						
returns. 30-Batman-c/Robin & Nightwing app. 37-Booster Gold returns. 38-The Question						
dies. 42-Ralph Dibny dies. 44-Isis dies. 48-Renee becomes The Question. 50-World						
War III. 51-Mister Mind evolves. 52-The Multiverse is re-formed; wraparound-c						3.00
...: The Companion TPB (2007, $19.99) r/solo stories of series' prominent characters						20.00
...: Volume One TPB (2007, $19.99) r/#1-13; sample of page development; cover gallery						20.00
...: Volume Two TPB (2007, $19.99) r/#14-26; creator notes and sketches; cover gallery						20.00
...: Volume Three TPB (2007, $19.99) r/#27-39; notes and sketches; cover gallery						20.00
...: Volume Four TPB (2007, $19.99) r/#40-52; creator commentary; cover gallery						20.00

52 AFTERMATH: THE FOUR HORSEMEN (Takes place during 52 Week Fifty)
DC Comics: Oct, 2007 - No. 6, Mar, 2008 ($2.99, limited series)

1-6-Giffen-s/Olliffe-a; Superman, Batman & Wonder Woman app. 2-4,6-Van Sciver-c						3.00
TPB (2008, $19.99) r/#1-6						20.00

52/WWIII (Takes place during 52 Week Fifty)
DC Comics: Part One, Jun, 2007 - Part Four, Jun, 2007 ($2.50, 4 issues came out same day)

Part One - Part Four: Van Sciver-c/-a. 1-Black Adam. 3-Terra dies						3.00
DC: World War III TPB (2007, $17.99) r/Part One - Four and 52 Week 50						18.00

55 DAYS AT PEKING (See Movie Comics)

FIGHT AGAINST CRIME (Fight Against the Guilty #22, 23)
Story Comics: May, 1951 - No. 21, Sept, 1954

1-True crime stories #1-4	68	136	204	435	743	1050
2	40	80	120	246	411	575
3,5: 5-Frazetta-a, 1 pg.; content change to horror & suspense	40	80	120	244	402	560
4-Drug story "Hopped Up Killers"	50	100	150	315	533	750
6,7: 6-Used in **POP**, pgs. 83,84	155	310	465	992	1696	2400
8-Last crime format issue	40	80	120	246	411	575

NOTE: 2-21 contain violent, gruesome stories with blood, dismemberment, decapitation, E.C. style plot twists and several E.C. swipes. Bondage-c-4, 6, 18, 19.

9-11,13	90	180	270	576	988	1400
12-Morphine drug story "The Big Dope"	168	336	504	1075	1838	2600
14-Tothish art by Ross Andru; electrocution-c	135	270	405	864	1482	2100
15-B&W & color illos in **POP**	81	162	243	518	884	1250
16-E.C. story swipe/Haunt of Fear #19; Tothish-a by Ross Andru; bondage-c	110	220	330	704	1202	1700
17-Wildey E.C. story swipe/Shock SuspenStories #9; knife through neck-c (1/54)	116	232	348	742	1271	1800
18,19: 19-Bondage/torture-c	84	168	252	538	919	1300
20-Decapitation cover; contains hanging, ax murder, blood & violence	1900	3800	5700	14,450	26,225	38,000
21-E.C. swipe	97	194	291	621	1061	1500

NOTE: Cameron a-4, 5, 8. Hollingsworth a-3-7, 9, 10, 13. Wildey a-6, 15, 16.

FIGHT AGAINST THE GUILTY (Formerly Fight Against Crime)
Story Comics: No. 22, Dec, 1954 - No. 23, Mar, 1955

22-Toth styled art by Ross Andru; Ditko-a; E.C. story swipe; electrocution-c (Last pre-code)	60	120	180	381	653	925
23-Hollingsworth-a	37	74	111	222	361	500

FIGHT CLUB 2 (Sequel to the movie)(Also see Free Comic Book Day 2015)
Dark Horse Comics: May, 2015 - No. 10, Mar, 2016 ($3.99)

1-10-Chuck Palahniuk-s/Cameron Stewart-a						4.00

FIGHT CLUB 3 (Sequel to the movie)
Dark Horse Comics: Jan, 2019 - No. 12, Dec, 2019 ($3.99)

1-12-Chuck Palahniuk-s/Cameron Stewart-a/David Mack-c						4.00

FIGHT COMICS
Fiction House Magazines: Jan, 1940 - No. 83, 11/52; No. 84, Wint, 1952-53; No. 85, Spring, 1953; No. 86, Summer, 1954

1-Origin Spy Fighter, Starring Saber; Jack Dempsey life story; Shark Brodie & Chip Collins begin; Eisner-a	423	846	1269	3057	5379	7700
2-Joe Louis life story; Fine/Eisner-c	200	400	600	1280	2190	3100
3-Rip Regan, the Power Man begins (3/40); classic-c	239	478	717	1530	2615	3700
4,5: 4-Fine-c	155	310	465	992	1696	2400
6-10: 6,7-Powell-c	135	270	405	864	1482	2100
11-14: Rip Regan ends	129	258	387	826	1413	2000
15-1st app. Super American plus-c (10/41)	314	628	942	2198	3849	5500
16-Captain Fight begins (12/41); Spy Fighter ends	155	310	465	992	1696	2400
17,18: Super American ends	113	226	339	718	1234	1750
19-Japanese WWII-c; Captain Fight ends; Senorita Rio begins (6/42, origin & 1st app.);						

	GD 2.0	VG 4.0	FN 6.0	VF 8.0	VF/NM 9.0	NM- 9.2
Rip Carson, Chute Trooper begins	135	270	405	864	1482	2100
20-Classic female decapitation-c	161	322	483	1030	1765	2500
21-27,29,30: 21-24,26,27-Japanese WWII-c	106	212	318	673	1162	1650
28-Classic Japanese WWII torture-c	187	374	561	1197	2049	2900
31-Classic Japanese WWII decapitation-c	530	1060	1590	3869	6835	9800
32-Tiger Girl begins (6/44, 1st app.?); Nazi WWII-c	300	600	900	2010	3505	5000
33,35-39,41,42: 42-Last WWII-c (2/46)	90	180	270	576	988	1400
34-Classic Japanese WWII bondage-c	181	362	543	1158	1979	2800
40-Classic Nazi vulture bondage-c	187	374	561	1197	2049	2900
43,45-50: 48-Used in Love and Death by Legman. 49-Jungle-c begin, end #81	52	104	156	328	552	775
44-Classic bondage/torture-c; Capt. Fight returns	226	452	678	1446	2473	3500
51-Origin Tiger Girl; Patsy Pin-Up app.	45	90	135	284	480	675
52-60,62-64-Last Baker issue	32	64	96	188	307	425
61-Origin Tiger Girl retold	34	68	102	199	325	450
65-78: 78-Used in **POP**, pg. 99	27	54	81	162	266	370
79-The Space Rangers app.	32	64	96	188	307	425
80-85: 81-Last jungle-c. 82-85-War-c/stories	24	48	72	142	234	325
86-Two Tigerman stories by Evans-r/Rangers Comics #40,41; Moreira-r/Rangers Comics #45	27	54	81	158	259	360

NOTE: Bondage covers, Lingerie, headlights panels are common. Captain Fight by **Kamen**-51-66. Kayo Kirby by **Baker**-#43-64, 67(not by Baker). Senorita Rio by **Kamen**-#57-64; by **Grandenetti**-#65, 66. Tiger Girl by **Baker**-#36-60, 62-64; **Eisner**-c-1-3, 5, 10, 11. **Kamen** a-54?, 57? **Tuska**-a-1-5, 8, 10, 21, 29, 34. **Whitman**-c-73-84. **Zolnerwich**-c-16, 17, 22. Power Man-c-5, 6, 9. Super American-c-15-17. Tiger Girl-c-49-81.

FIGHT FOR LOVE
United Features Syndicate: 1952 (no month)

nn-Abbie & Slats newspaper-r	14	28	42	81	118	155

FIGHT FOR TOMORROW
DC Comics (Vertigo): Nov, 2002 - No. 6, Apr, 2003 ($2.50, limited series)

1-6-Denys Cowan-a/Brian Wood-s. 1-Jim Lee-c. 5-Jo Chen-c						3.00
TPB (2008, $14.99) r/#1-6						15.00

FIGHT GIRLS
AWA Studios: Jul, 2021 - No. 5, Nov, 2021 ($3.99, limited series)

1-5-Frank Cho-s/a/c						4.00

FIGHTING AIR FORCE (See United States Fighting Air Force)

FIGHTIN' AIR FORCE (Formerly Sherlock Holmes?; Never Again? War and Attack #54 on)
Charlton Comics: No. 3, Feb, 1956 - No. 53, Feb-Mar, 1966

V1#3	11	22	33	64	90	115
4-10	8	16	24	40	50	60
11(3/58, 68 pgs.)	9	18	27	52	69	85
12 (100 pgs.)-U.S. Nukes Russia	15	30	45	90	140	190
13-30: 13,24-Glanzman-a. 24-Glanzman-c. 27-Area 51, UFO story	3	6	9	21	33	45
31-53: 50-American Eagle begins	3	6	9	16	23	30

FIGHTING AMERICAN
Headline Publ./Prize (Crestwood): Apr-May, 1954 - No. 7, Apr-May, 1955

1-Origin & 1st app. Fighting American & Speedboy (Capt. America & Bucky clones); S&K-c/a(3); 1st super hero satire series	219	438	657	1402	2401	3400
2-S&K-a(3)	110	220	330	704	1202	1700
3-5: 3,4-S&K-a(3). 5-S&K-a(2); Kirby/?-a	97	194	291	621	1061	1500
6-Origin-r (4 pgs.) plus 2 pgs. by S&K	97	194	291	621	1061	1500
7-Kirby-a	81	162	243	518	884	1250

NOTE: **Simon** & Kirby covers on all. 6 is last pre-code issue.

FIGHTING AMERICAN
Harvey Publications: Oct, 1966 (25¢)

1-Origin Fighting American & Speedboy by S&K-r; S&K-c/a(3); 1 pg. Neal Adams ad	6	12	18	38	69	100

FIGHTING AMERICAN
DC Comics: Feb, 1994 - No. 6, 1994 ($1.50, limited series)

1-6						4.00

FIGHTING AMERICAN (Vol. 3)
Awesome Entertainment: Aug, 1997 - No. 2, Oct, 1997 ($2.50)

Preview-Agent America (pre-lawsuit)	1	2	3	5	6	7
1-Four covers by Liefeld, Churchill, Platt, McGuinness						4.00
1-Platinum Edition, 1-Gold foil Edition						10.00
1-Comic Cavalcade Edition, 2-American Ent. Spice Ed.						4.00
2-Platt-c, 2-Liefeld variant-c						4.00

FIGHTING AMERICAN
Titan Comics: Oct, 2017 - No. 4, Jan, 2018 ($3.99)

1-4-Rennie-s/Mighten-a; multiple covers; Fighting American & Speedboy trapped in 2017						4.00

FIGHTING AMERICAN: DOGS OF WAR
Awesome-Hyperwerks: Sept, 1998 - No. 3, May, 1999 ($2.50)

Limited Convention Special (7/98, B&W) Platt-a						4.00
1-3-Starlin-s/Platt-a/-c						4.00

FIGHTING AMERICAN: RULES OF THE GAME
Awesome Entertainment: Nov, 1997 - No. 3, Mar, 1998 ($2.50, lim. series)

1-3: 1-Loeb-s/McGuinness-a/c. 2-Flip book with Swat! preview						4.00
1-Liefeld SPICE variant-c, 1-Dynamic Forces Ed.; McGuinness-c						4.00
1-Liefeld Fighting American & cast variant-c						4.00

FIGHTING AMERICAN: THE TIES THAT BIND
Titan Comics: Apr, 2018 - No. 4, Jul, 2018 ($3.99, limited series)

1-4-Rennie-s/Andie Tong-a; multiple covers						4.00

FIGHTIN' ARMY (Formerly Soldier and Marine Comics) (See Captain Willy Schultz)
Charlton Comics: No. 16, 1/56 - No. 127, 12/76; No. 128, 9/77 - No. 172, 11/84

16	11	22	33	62	86	110
17-19,21-23,25-30	8	16	24	40	50	60
20-Ditko-a	10	20	30	51	72	90
24 (3/58, 68 pgs.)	9	18	27	52	69	85
31-45	3	6	9	18	28	38

52 #33 © DC

Fighting American #2 © S&K

Fightin' Navy #80 © CC

	GD 2.0	VG 4.0	FN 6.0	VF 8.0	VF/NM 9.0	NM- 9.2
46-50,52-60	3	6	9	16	23	30
51-Hitler-c	3	6	9	21	33	45
61-75	3	6	9	14	19	24
76-1st The Lonely War of Willy Schultz	3	6	9	17	26	35
77-80: 77-92-The Lonely War of Willy Schultz. 79-Devil Brigade	3	6	9	14	19	24
81-88,91,93-99: 82,83-Devil Brigade	2	4	6	10	14	18
89,90,92-Ditko-a	3	6	9	14	20	26
100	2	4	6	13	18	22
101-127	2	4	6	8	11	14
128-140	1	2	3	5	7	9
141-165	1	2	3	4	5	7
166-172-Low print run	1	2	3	5	6	8
108 (Modern Comics-1977)-Reprint						5.00

NOTE: *Aparo* c-154. *Glanzman* a-77-88. *Montes/Bache* a-48, 49, 51, 69, 75, 76, 170r.

FIGHTING CARAVANS (See Zane Grey 4-Color 632)

FIGHTING DANIEL BOONE
Avon Periodicals: 1953

	GD 2.0	VG 4.0	FN 6.0	VF 8.0	VF/NM 9.0	NM- 9.2
nn-Kinstler-c/a, 22 pgs.	22	44	66	128	209	290
I.W. Reprint #1-Reprints #1 above; Kinstler-c/a; Lawrence/Alascia-a	3	6	9	15	22	28

FIGHTING DAVY CROCKETT (Formerly Kit Carson)
Avon Periodicals: No. 9, Oct-Nov, 1955

	GD 2.0	VG 4.0	FN 6.0	VF 8.0	VF/NM 9.0	NM- 9.2
9-Kinstler-c	13	26	39	74	105	135

FIGHTIN' FIVE, THE (Formerly Space War) (Also See The Peacemaker)
Charlton Comics: July, 1964 - No. 41, Jan, 1967; No. 42, Oct, 1981 - No. 49, Dec, 1982

	GD 2.0	VG 4.0	FN 6.0	VF 8.0	VF/NM 9.0	NM- 9.2
V2#28-Origin/1st app. Fightin' Five; Montes/Bache-a	7	14	21	48	89	130
29-39-Montes/Bache-a in all	4	8	12	27	44	60
40-Peacemaker begins (1st app.)	93	186	279	744	1672	2600
41-Peacemaker (2nd app.); Montes/Bache-a	13	26	39	86	188	290
42-49: Reprints						6.00

FIGHTING FRONTS!
Harvey Publications: Aug, 1952 - No. 5, Jan, 1953

	GD 2.0	VG 4.0	FN 6.0	VF 8.0	VF/NM 9.0	NM- 9.2
1	15	30	45	86	133	180
2-Extreme violence; Nostrand/Powell-a	15	30	45	90	140	190
3-5: 3-Powell-a	9	18	27	50	65	80

FIGHTING INDIAN STORIES (See Midget Comics)

FIGHTING INDIANS OF THE WILD WEST!
Avon Periodicals: Mar, 1952 - No. 2, Nov, 1952

	GD 2.0	VG 4.0	FN 6.0	VF 8.0	VF/NM 9.0	NM- 9.2
1-Geronimo, Chief Crazy Horse, Chief Victorio, Black Hawk begin; Larsen-a; McCann-a(2)	25	50	75	150	245	340
2-Kinstler-c & inside-c only; Larsen, McCann-a	17	34	51	100	158	215
100 Pg. Annual (1952, 25c)-Contains three comics rebound; Geronimo, Chief Crazy Horse, Chief Victorio; Kinstler-c	47	94	141	296	498	700

FIGHTING LEATHERNECKS
Toby Press: Feb, 1952 - No. 6, Dec, 1952

	GD 2.0	VG 4.0	FN 6.0	VF 8.0	VF/NM 9.0	NM- 9.2
1- "Duke's Diary"; full pg. pin-ups by Sparling	24	48	72	142	234	325
2-5: 2- "Duke's Diary" full pg. pin-ups. 3-5- "Gil's Gals"; full pg. pin-ups	15	30	45	83	124	165
6-(Same as No. 3-5?)	14	28	42	80	115	150

FIGHTING MAN, THE (War)
Ajax/Farrell Publications(Excellent Publ.): May, 1952 - No. 8, July, 1953

	GD 2.0	VG 4.0	FN 6.0	VF 8.0	VF/NM 9.0	NM- 9.2
1	26	52	78	154	252	350
2	16	32	48	94	147	200
3-8	15	30	45	83	124	165
Annual 1 (1952, 25c, 100 pgs.)	65	130	195	416	708	1000

FIGHTIN' MARINES (Formerly The Texan; also see Approved Comics)
St. John(Approved Comics)/Charlton Comics No. 14 on:
No. 15, 8/51 - No. 12, 3/53; No. 14, 5/55 - No. 132, 11/76; No. 133, 10/77 - No. 176, 9/84 (No #13?) (Korean War #1-3)

	GD 2.0	VG 4.0	FN 6.0	VF 8.0	VF/NM 9.0	NM- 9.2
15(#1)-Matt Baker c/a "Leatherneck Jack"; slightly large size; Fightin' Texan No. 16 & 17?	71	142	213	454	777	1100
2-1st Canteen Kate by Baker; slightly large size; partial Baker-c	113	226	339	718	1234	1750
3-9,11-Canteen Kate by Baker; Baker c-#2,3,5-11; 4-Partial Baker-c	47	94	141	296	498	700
10-Matt Baker-c	50	100	150	315	533	750
12-No Baker-a; Last St. John issue?	16	32	48	94	147	200

14 (5/55; 1st Charlton issue; formerly?)-Canteen Kate by Baker; all stories reprinted from #2

	GD 2.0	VG 4.0	FN 6.0	VF 8.0	VF/NM 9.0	NM- 9.2
	28	56	84	165	270	375
15-Baker-c	22	44	66	132	216	300
16,18-20-Not Baker-c. 16-Grey-tone-c	10	20	30	54	72	90
17-Canteen Kate by Baker	22	44	66	132	216	300
21-24	8	16	24	48	57	70
25-(68 pgs.)(3/58)-Check-a	13	26	39	72	101	130
26-(100 pgs.)(8/58)-Check-a(5)	16	32	48	72	144	195
27-50	3	6	9	21	33	45
51-81: 78-Shotgun Harker & the Chicken series begin	3	6	9	16	23	30
82-85: 85-Last 12¢ issue	3	6	9	15	22	28
86-94: 94-Last 15¢ issue	2	4	6	11	16	20
95-100,122: 122-(1975) Pilot issue for "War" title (Fightin' Marines Presents War?)	2	4	6	10	14	18
101-121	2	4	6	8	11	14
123-140: 132 Hitler-c	2	4	6	8	10	12
141-170	1	2	3	5	6	8
171-176-Low print run	1	3	4	6	8	10
120(Modern Comics reprint, 1977)	1	2	3	5	6	8

NOTE: No. 14 & 16 (CC) reprint St. John issues; No. 16 reprints St. John insignia on cover. *Colan* a-3, 7. *Glanzman* c/a-92, 94. *Montes/Bache* a-48, 53, 55, 64, 65, 72-74, 77-83, 176r.

FIGHTING MARSHAL OF THE WILD WEST (See The Hawk)

FIGHTIN' NAVY (Formerly Don Winslow)
Charlton Comics: No. 74, 1/56 - No. 125, 4-5/66; No. 126, 8/83 - No. 133, 10/84

	GD 2.0	VG 4.0	FN 6.0	VF 8.0	VF/NM 9.0	NM- 9.2
74	5	10	15	35	63	90
75-81	4	8	12	25	40	55
82-Sam Glanzman-a (68 pg. Giant)	5	10	15	33	57	80
83-(100 pgs.)	7	14	21	44	82	120
84-99,101: 101-UFO-c/story	3	6	9	17	26	35
100	3	6	9	18	28	38
102-105,106-125('66)	3	6	9	14	21	26
126-133 (1984)-Low print run	1	2	3	5	6	8

NOTE: *Montes/Bache* a-109. *Glanzman* a-82, 92, 96, 98, 100, 131r.

FIGHTIN' PRINCE OF DONEGAL, THE (See Movie Comics)

FIGHTIN' TEXAN (Formerly The Texan & Fightin' Marines?)
St. John Publishing Co.: No. 16, Sept, 1952 - No. 17, Dec, 1952

	GD 2.0	VG 4.0	FN 6.0	VF 8.0	VF/NM 9.0	NM- 9.2
16,17: Tuska-a each. 17-Cameron-c/a	14	28	42	80	115	150

FIGHTING UNDERSEA COMMANDOS (See Undersea Fighting...)
Avon Periodicals: May, 1952 - No. 5, April, 1953 (U.S. Navy frogmen)

	GD 2.0	VG 4.0	FN 6.0	VF 8.0	VF/NM 9.0	NM- 9.2
1-Cover title is Undersea Fighting... #1 only	22	44	66	132	216	300
2	15	30	45	85	130	175
3-5: 1,3-Ravielli-a. 4-Kinstler-c	14	28	42	76	108	140

FIGHTING WAR STORIES
Men's Publications/Story Comics: Aug, 1952 - No. 5, 1953

	GD 2.0	VG 4.0	FN 6.0	VF 8.0	VF/NM 9.0	NM- 9.2
1	21	42	63	122	199	275
2-5	14	28	42	80	115	150

FIGHTING YANK (See America's Best Comics & Startling Comics)
Nedor/Better Publ./Standard: Sept, 1942 - No. 29, Aug, 1949

	GD 2.0	VG 4.0	FN 6.0	VF 8.0	VF/NM 9.0	NM- 9.2
1-The Fighting Yank begins; Mystico, the Wonder Man app; bondage-c	400	800	1200	2800	4900	7000
2	226	452	678	1446	2473	3500
3,4: Nazi WWII-c. 4-Schomburg-c begin	187	374	561	1197	2049	2900
5,8,9: 5-Nazi-c. 8,9-Japan War-c	194	388	582	1242	2121	3000
6-Classic Japanese WWII-c	377	754	1131	2639	4620	6600
7-Classic Hitler special bomb-c; Grim Reaper app.	389	778	1167	2723	4762	6800
10-Nazi bondage/torture/hypo-c	343	686	1029	2400	4200	6000
11,14,15: 11-The Oracle app. 15-Bondage/torture-c	106	212	318	682	1166	1650
12-Hirohito bondage Japanese WWII-c	219	438	657	1402	2401	3400
13-Last War-c (Japanese)	300	600	900	2010	3505	5000
16-20: 18-The American Eagle app.	84	168	252	538	919	1300
21-Kara, Jungle Princess app.; lingerie-c	248	490	735	1568	2684	3800
22-Schomburg Miss Masque dinosaur-c	126	252	378	806	1378	1950
23-Classic Schomburg hooded vigilante-c	541	1082	1623	3950	6975	10,000
24-Miss Masque app.	93	194	291	621	1061	1500
25-Robinson/Meskin-a; strangulation, lingerie panel; The Cavalier app.	93	186	279	591	1021	1450
26-29-All-Robinson/Meskin-a. 28-One pg. Williamson-a	65	130	195	416	708	1000

NOTE: *Schomburg* (Xela) c-4-29; airbrush-c 28, 29. Bondage c-1, 4, 8, 10, 11, 12, 15, 17.

FIGHTMAN
Marvel Comics: June, 1993 ($2.00, one-shot, 52 pgs.)

	GD	VG	FN	VF	VF/NM	NM-
	2.0	4.0	6.0	8.0	9.0	9.2

1 .... 4.00

FIGHT THE ENEMY
Tower Comics: Aug, 1966 - No. 3, Mar, 1967 (25¢, 68 pgs.)

1-Lucky 7 & Mike Manly begin	5	10	15	35	63	90
2-1st Boris Vallejo comic art; McWilliams-a	4	8	12	25	40	55
3-Wood-a (1/2 pg.); McWilliams, Bolle-a	4	8	12	25	40	55

FIGMENT (Disney Kingdoms) (See Disney Kingdoms: Figment 2 for sequel)
Marvel Comics: Aug, 2014 - No. 5, Dec, 2014 ($3.99, limited series)

1-5-Jim Zub-s/Filipe Andrade-a 4.00

FILM FUNNIES
Marvel Comics (CPC): Nov, 1949 - No. 2, Feb, 1950 (52 pgs.)

1-Krazy Krow, Wacky Duck	28	56	84	168	274	380
2-Wacky Duck	20	40	60	120	195	270

FILM STARS ROMANCES
Star Publications: Jan-Feb, 1950 - No. 3, May-June, 1950 (True life stories of movie stars)

1-Rudy Valentino & Gregory Peck stories; L. B. Cole-c; lingerie panels	63	126	189	403	689	975
2-Liz Taylor/Robert Taylor photo-c & true life story	71	142	213	454	777	1100
3-Douglas Fairbanks story; photo-c	34	68	102	204	332	460

FILTH, THE
DC Comics (Vertigo): Aug, 2002 - No. 13, Oct, 2003 ($2.95, limited series)

1-13-Morrison-s/Weston & Erskine-a 3.00
TPB (2004, $19.95) r/#1-13 .... 20.00

FINAL CRISIS
DC Comics: July, 2008 - No. 7, Mar, 2009 ($3.99, limited series)

1-Grant Morrison-s/J.G. Jones-a/c; Martian Manhunter killed; 2 covers .. 4.00
1-Director's Cut (10/08, $4.99) B&W printing of #1 with creator commentary .. 5.00
2-7: 2-Barry Allen-c/cameo; intro Big Science action; two covers. 6-Batman zapped .. 4.00
SC (2010, $19.99) r/#1-7, FC: Superman Beyond #1,2; Submit & FC Sketchbook .. 20.00
...: Rage of the Red Lanterns (12/08, $3.99) Atrocitus app.; intro. Blue Lantern; 3 covers .. 4.00
...: Requiem (9/08, $3.99) History, death and funeral of the Martian Manhunter; 2 covers .. 4.00
...: Resist (12/08, $3.99) Checkmate app.; Rucka & Trautman-s/Cliff Chiang-a .. 4.00
...: Secret Files (2/09, $3.99) origin of Libra; Wein-s/Shasteen-a; JG Jones sketch-a .. 4.00
...: Sketchbook (7/08, $2) Jones development sketches with Morrison commentary .. 3.00
...: Submit (12/08, $3.99) Black Lightning & Tattooed Man team up; Morrison-s; 2 covers .. 4.00

FINAL CRISIS: DANCE (Final Crisis Aftermath)
DC Comics: Jul, 2009 - No. 6, Dec, 2009 ($2.99, limited series)

1-6-Super Young Team; Joe Casey-s/Chriscross-a/Stanley Lau-c 3.00
TPB (2009, $17.99) r/#1-6 .... 18.00

FINAL CRISIS: ESCAPE (Final Crisis Aftermath)
DC Comics: Jul, 2009 - No. 6, Dec, 2009 ($2.99, limited series)

1-6-Nemesis & Cameron Chase app.; Ivan Brandon-s/Marco Rudy-a/Scott Hampton-c .. 3.00
TPB (2010, $17.99) r/#1-6 .... 18.00

FINAL CRISIS: INK (Final Crisis Aftermath)
DC Comics: Jul, 2009 - No. 6, Dec, 2009 ($2.99, limited series)

1-6-The Tattooed Man; Eric Wallace-s/Fabrizio Florentino-a/Brian Stelfreeze-c .. 3.00
TPB (2010, $17.99) r/#1-6 .... 18.00

FINAL CRISIS: LEGION OF THREE WORLDS
DC Comics: Oct, 2008 - No. 5, Sept, 2009 ($3.99, limited series)

1-Johns-s/Pérez-a; R.J. Brande killed; Time Trapper app.; two covers on each issue .. 5.00
2-5-Three Legions meet; two covers. 3-Bart Allen returns. 4-Superboy (Conner) returns .. 4.00
HC (2009, $19.99) r/#1-5; variant covers 20.00
SC (2010, $14.99) r/#1-5; variant covers 15.00

FINAL CRISIS: REVELATIONS
DC Comics: Oct, 2008 - No. 5, Feb, 2009 ($3.99, limited series)

1-5-Spectre and The Question; 2 covers on each. 1-Dr. Light killed; Rucka-s/Tan-a .. 4.00
HC (2009, $19.99, d.j.) r/#1-5; variant covers 20.00
SC (2009, $14.99) r/#1-5; variant covers 15.00

FINAL CRISIS: ROGUE'S REVENGE
DC Comics: Sept, 2008 - No. 3, Nov, 2008 ($3.99, limited series)

1-3-Johns-s/Kolins-a; Flash's Rogues, Zoom and Inertia app. 4.00
HC (2009, $19.99, d.j.) r/#1-3 & Flash #182,197; variant covers 20.00
SC (2009, $14.99) r/#1-3 & Flash #182,197; variant covers 15.00

FINAL CRISIS: RUN (Final Crisis Aftermath)
DC Comics: Jul, 2009 - No. 6, Dec, 2009 ($2.99, limited series)

1-6-The Human Flame on the run; Sturges-s/Williams-a/Kako-c 3.00
TPB (2010, $17.99) r/#1-6 .... 18.00

FINAL CRISIS: SUPERMAN BEYOND
DC Comics: Oct, 2008 - No. 2, Mar, 2009 ($4.50, limited series)

1,2-Morrison-s/Mahnke-a; parallel-Earth Supermen app.; 3-D pages and glasses .. 4.50

FINAL NIGHT, THE (See DC related titles and Parallax: Emerald Night)
DC Comics: Nov, 1996 - No. 4, Nov, 1996 ($1.95, weekly limited series)

1-4: Kesel-s/Immonen-a(p) in all. 4-Parallax's final acts 4.00
Preview 4.00
TPB-(1998, $12.95) r/#1-4, Parallax: Emerald Night #1, and preview .. 13.00

FINALS (See Vertigo Resurrected:... for collected reprint)
DC Comics (Vertigo): Sept, 1999 - No. 4, Dec, 1999 ($2.95, limited series)

1-4-Will Pfeifer-s/Jill Thompson-a 4.00

FINDING NEMO (Based on the Pixar movie)
BOOM! Studios: Jul, 2010 - No. 4, Oct, 2010 ($2.99, limited series)

1-4-Michael Raicht & Brian Smith-s/Jake Myler-a.1-Three covers 4.00

FINDING NEMO: REEF RESCUE (Based on the Pixar movie)
BOOM! Studios: May, 2009 - No. 4, Aug, 2009 ($2.99, limited series)

1-4-Marie Croall-s/Erica Leigh Currey-a; 2 covers 4.00

FIN FANG FOUR RETURN!

Marvel Comics: Jul, 2009 ($3.99, one-shot)

1-Fin Fang Foom, Googam, Elektro, Gorgilla and Doc Samson app. 5.00

FIRE
Caliber Press: 1993 - No. 2, 1993 ($2.95, B&W, limited series, 52 pgs.)

1,2-Brian Michael Bendis-s/a 4.00
TPB (1999, 2001, $9.95) Restored reprints of series 10.00

FIRE AND ICE
Dynamite Entertainment: 2023 - No. 2, 2023 ($3.99, limited series)

1,2-Willingham-s/Manco-a 4.00
... Teegra One-shot (2024, $5.99) Willingham-s/Di Caro-a/Panosian-c .. 6.00

FIRE AND ICE: WELCOME TO SMALLVILLE (See Power Girl Special #1)
DC Comics: Nov, 2023 - No. 6, Apr, 2024 ($3.99, limited series)

1-6-Starer-s/Bustos-a; Martha Kent and Ambush Bug app. 4-Lobo app. .. 4.00

FIREARM (Also see Codename: Firearm, Freex #15, Night Man #4 & Prime #10)
Malibu Comics (Ultraverse): Sept, 1993 - No. 18, Mar, 1995 ($1.95/$2.50)

0 ($14.95)-Came w/ video containing 1st half of story (comic contains 2nd half);
   1st app. Duet 15.00
1,3-6: 1-James Robinson scripts begin; Cully Hamner-a; Chaykin-c; 1st app. Alec Swan.
   3-Intro The Sportsmen; Chaykin-c. 4-Break-Thru x-over; Chaykin-c. 5-1st app. Ellen (Swan's
   girlfriend); 2 pg. origin of Prime. 6-Prime app. (story cont'd in Prime #10); Brereton-c .. 4.00
1-($2.50)-Newsstand edition polybagged w/card 5.00

1-Ultra Limited silver foil-c			1	2	3	5
2 ($2.50, 44 pgs.)-Hardcase app.;Chaykin-c; Rune flip-c/story by B. Smith (3 pgs.)						5

7-10,12-17: 12-The Rafferty Saga begins, ends #18; 1st app. Rafferty. 15-Night Man &
   Freex app. 17-Swan marries Ellen 4.00
11-($3.50, 68 pgs.)-Flip book w/Ultraverse Premiere #5 .... 4.00
18-Death of Rafferty; Chaykin-c 4.00
NOTE: *Brereton* c-6. *Chaykin* c-1-4, 14, 16, 18. *Hamner* a-1-4. *Herrera* a-12. *James Robinson* scripts-0-18.

FIRE BALL XL5 (See Steve Zodiac & The ...)

FIREBIRDS (See Noble Causes)
Image Comics: Nov, 2004 ($5.95)

1-Faerber-s/Ponce-a/c; intro. Firebird 6.00

FIREBRAND (Also see Showcase '96 #4)
DC Comics: Feb, 1996 - No. 9, Oct, 1996 ($1.75)

1-9: Brian Augustyn scripts; Velluto-c/a in all. 9-Daredevil #319-c/swipe .. 4.00

FIREBREATHER
Image Comics: Jan, 2003 - No. 4, Apr, 2003 ($2.95)

1-4-Hester-s/Kuhn-a 3.00
...: The Iron Saint (12/04, $6.95, squarebound) Hester-s/Kuhn-a 7.00
TPB (7/04, $13.95) r/#1-4; foreword by Brad Meltzer; gallery and sketch pages .. 14.00

FIREBREATHER
Image Comics: Jun, 2008 - No. 4, Feb, 2009 ($2.99)

1-4-Hester-s/Kuhn-a 3.00

FIREBREATHER (Vol.3): HOLMGANG
Image Comics: Nov, 2010 - No. 4, ($3.99, limited series)

1-4-Hester-s/Kuhn-a 4.00

FIREFLY (Based on the 2002 TV series)(Also see Serenity)
BOOM! Studios: Nov, 2018 - No. 36, Jan, 2022 ($3.99)

1-24,26-36: 1-Greg Pak-s/Dan McDaid-a. 20-24-Blue Sun Rising 4.00
25-($4.99) Pius Bak-a; time-jumps to after the movie 5.00
... Bad Company 1 (3/19, $7.99) Back story on Saffron; Gordon-s/Mortarino-a .. 8.00
... Blue Sun Rising 0 (9/20, $7.99) Leads into Firefly #21; Greg Pak-s/Dan McDaid-a .. 8.00
... Blue Sun Rising 1 (12/20, $7.99) Follows Firefly #24; Greg Pak-s/Dan McDaid-a .. 8.00
... Keep Flying 1 (11/22, $7.99) Jensen-s/Izzo-a 8.00
... River Run 1 (9/21, $7.99) River and Simon's escape from Osiris ... 8.00
... The Holiday Special 1 (12/21, $7.99) Christmas Carol homage by various; Inhyuk Lee-c .. 8.00
... The Outlaw Ma Reynolds 1 (1/20, $7.99) Takes place after #12; Paks-s/Gianfelice-a .. 8.00
... The Sting (11/19, $9.99) Saffron returns; Delilah S. Dawson-s; art by various .. 20.00
... 20th Anniversary Special 1 (8/22, $7.99) Two stories 8.00

FIREFLY: BRAND NEW 'VERSE (Based on the 2002 TV series)
BOOM! Studios: Mar, 2021 - No. 6, Aug, 2021 ($4.99)

1-6-Gordon-s/Mascolo-a; Zoë and a new crew 20 years after the events of Firefly .. 5.00

FIREFLY: THE FALL GUYS (Based on the 2002 TV series)
BOOM! Studios: Sept, 2023 - Present ($4.99)

1-5-Sam Humphries-s/Jordi Pérez-a 5.00

FIRE FROM HEAVEN
Image Comics (WildStorm Productions): Mar, 1996 ($2.50)

1,2-Moore-s 3.00

FIREHAIR COMICS (Formerly Pioneer West Romances #3-6; also see Rangers Comics)
Fiction House Magazines (Flying Stories): Winter/48-49; No. 2, Wint/49-50; No. 7, Spr/51 -
No. 11, Spr/52

1-Origin Firehair	55	110	165	352	601	850
2-Continues as Pioneer West Romances for #3-6	23	46	69	136	223	310
7-11	24	48	72	142	234	325
I.W. Reprint 8-(nd)-Kinstler-c; reprints Rangers #57; Dr. Drew story by Grandenetti	3	6	9	19	30	40

FIRE POWER
Image Comics: Aug, 2020 - No. 30, Feb, 2024 ($3.99)

1-11,13-24,26-29-Robert Kirkman-s/Chris Samnee-a 4.00
12,25-($4.99) 5.00
30-($5.99, squarebound) Series finale 7.00

FIRESIDE BOOK SERIES (Hard and soft cover editions)
Simon and Schuster: 1974 - 1980 (130-260 pgs.)

Amazing Spider-Man, The, 1979,	HC	7	14	21	48	89	130
130 pgs., $3.95, Bob Larkin-c	SC	5	10	15	33	57	80

Final Crisis #1 © DC

Firefly #29 © 20Fox

Firestar (2010 series) #1 © MAR

		GD 2.0	VG 4.0	FN 6.0	VF 8.0	VF/NM 9.0	NM- 9.2
America At War–The Best of DC War	HC	10	20	30	64	132	200
Comics, 1979, $6.95, 260 pgs, Kubert-c	SC	6	12	18	42	79	115
Best of Spidey Super Stories (Electric	HC	9	18	27	57	111	165
Company) 1978, $3.95,	SC	6	12	18	37	66	95
Bring On The Bad Guys (Origins of the	HC	7	14	21	46	86	125
Marvel Comics Villains) 1976, $6.95, 260 pgs.; Romita-c	SC	5	10	15	31	53	75
Captain America, Sentinel of Liberty,1979,	HC	7	14	21	48	89	130
130 pgs., $12.95, Cockrum-c	SC	5	10	15	33	57	80
Doctor Strange Master of the Mystic	HC	7	14	21	48	89	130
Arts, 1980, 130 pgs.	SC	5	10	15	33	57	80
Fantastic Four, The, 1979, 130 pgs.	HC	7	14	21	46	86	125
	SC	5	10	15	31	53	75
Heart Throbs–The Best of DC Romance	HC	13	26	39	86	188	290
Comics, 1979, 260 pgs., $6.95	SC	8	16	24	56	104	160
Incredible Hulk, The, 1978, 260 pgs.	HC	7	14	21	46	86	125
(8 1/4" x 11")	SC	5	10	15	31	53	75
Marvel's Greatest Superhero Battles,	HC	9	18	27	57	111	165
1978, 260 pgs., $6.95, Romita-c	SC	6	12	18	37	66	95
Mysteries in Space, 1980, $7.95,	HC	8	16	24	52	99	145
Anderson-c. r-DC sci/fi stories	SC	5	10	15	34	60	85
Origins of Marvel Comics, 1974, 260 pgs., $5.95. r-covers & origins of Fantastic	HC	7	14	21	49	92	135
Four, Hulk, Spider-Man, Thor, & Doctor Strange	SC	5	10	15	33	57	80
Silver Surfer, The, 1978, 130 pgs.,	HC	8	16	24	51	96	140
$4.95, Norem-c	SC	6	12	18	37	66	95
Son of Origins of Marvel Comics, 1975, 260 pgs., $6.95, Romita-c. Reprints							
covers & origins of X-Men, Iron Man,	HC	7	14	21	46	86	125
Avengers, Daredevil, Silver Surfer	SC	5	10	15	31	53	75
Superhero Women, The–Featuring the	HC	9	18	27	57	111	165
Fabulous Females of Marvel Comics, 1977, 260 pgs., $6.95, Romita-c	SC	6	12	18	37	66	95

Note: Prices listed are for all first printings. Later printings have lesser value.

FIRESTAR
Marvel Comics Group: Mar, 1986 - No. 4, June, 1986 (75¢)(From Spider-Man TV series)

	GD 2.0	VG 4.0	FN 6.0	VF 8.0	VF/NM 9.0	NM- 9.2
1,2: 1-X-Men & New Mutants app. 2-Wolverine-c (not really Wolverine?); Art Adams-a(p)						6.00
3,4: 3-Art Adams/Sienkiewicz-c. 4-B. Smith-c						4.00
X-Men: Firestar Digest (2006, $7.99, digest-size) r/#1-4; profile pages						8.00
1 (Jun, 2010, $3.99) Sean McKeever-s/Emma Rios-a						4.00

FIRESTONE (See Donald And Mickey Merry Christmas)

FIRESTORM (Also see The Fury of Firestorm, Cancelled Comic Cavalcade, DC Comics
Presents, Flash #289, & Justice League of America #179)
DC Comics: March, 1978 - No. 5, Oct-Nov, 1978

	GD	VG	FN	VF	VF/NM	NM-
1-Origin & 1st app.	6	12	18	28	69	100
2,4,5: 2-Origin Multiplex. 4-1st app. Hyena	2	4	6	11	16	20
3-Origin & 1st app. Killer Frost (Crystal Frost)	4	8	12	28	47	65
...: The Nuclear Man TPB (2011, $17.99) r/#1-5 and stories from Flash #289-293, plus story from Cancelled Comic Cavalcade (uncolored)						18.00

FIRESTORM
DC Comics: July, 2004 - No. 35, June, 2007 ($2.50/$2.99)

1-24: 1-Intro. Jason Rusch; Jolley-s/ChrisCross-a. 6-Identity Crisis tie-in. 7-Bloodhound x-over. 8-Killer Frost returns. 9-Ronnie Raymond returns. 17-Villains United tie-in. 21-Infinite Crisis. 24-One Year Later; Killer Frost app.						3.00
25-35: 25-Begin $2.99-c; Mr. Freeze app. 33-35-Mister Miracle & Orion app.						3.00
...: Reborn TPB (2007, $14.95) r/#23-27						15.00

FIRESTORM, THE NUCLEAR MAN (Formerly Fury of Firestorm)
DC Comics: No. 65, Nov, 1987 - No. 100, Aug, 1990

65-99: 66-1st app. Zuggernaut; Firestorm vs. Green Lantern. 67,68-Millennium tie-ins. 71-Death of Capt. X. 83-1st new look						4.00
100-($2.95, 68 pgs.)						5.00
Annual 5 (10/87)-1st app. new Firestorm						5.00

FIRST, THE
CrossGeneration Comics: Jan, 2001 - No. 37, Jan, 2004 ($2.95)

1-10: 1-Barbara Kesel-s/Bart Sears & Andy Smith-a						4.00
11-37						3.00
Preview (11/00, free) 8 pg. intro						3.00
Two Houses Divided Vol. 1 TPB (11/01, $19.95) r/#1-7; new Moeller-c						20.00

	GD 2.0	VG 4.0	FN 6.0	VF 8.0	VF/NM 9.0	NM- 9.2
Magnificent Tension Vol. 2 TPB (2002, $19.95) r/#8-13						20.00
Sinister Motives Vol. 3 TPB (2003, $15.95) r/#14-19						16.00
Vol. 4 Futile Endeavors (2003, $15.95) r/#20-25						16.00
Vol. 5 Liquid Alliances (2003, $15.95) r/#26-31						16.00
Vol. 6 Ragnarok (2004, $15.95) r/#32-37						16.00

FIRST AMERICANS, THE
Dell Publishing Co.: No. 843, Sept, 1957

Four Color 843-Marsh-a	9	18	27	57	111	165

FIRST BORN (See Witchblade and Darkness titles)
Image Comics (Top Cow): Aug, 2007 - No. 3 ($2.99, limited series)

... First Look (6/07, 99¢) Preview; The Darkness app.; Sejic-a; 2 covers (color & B&W)						3.00
1-3-($2.99) Two covers; Marz-s/Sejic-a. 3-Sara's baby is born						3.00
1-B&W variant Sejic cover						5.00
...: Aftermath (5/08, $3.99) short stories; Magdalena app.; two covers by Sook & Sejic						4.00

FIRST CHRISTMAS, THE (3-D)
Fiction House Magazines (Real Adv. Publ. Co.): 1953 (25¢, 8-1/4x10-1/4", oversize)(Came
w/glasses)

nn-(Scarce)-Kelly Freas painted-c; Biblical theme, birth of Christ; Nativity-c	39	78	117	240	395	550

FIRST COMICS GRAPHIC NOVEL
First Comics: Jan, 1984 - No. 21? (52 pgs./176 pgs., high quality paper)

1,2: 1-Beowulf ($5.95)(both printings). 2-Time Beavers						10.00
3($11.95, 100 pgs.)-American Flagg! Hard Times (2nd printing exists)						15.00
4-Nexus ($6.95)-r/B&W 1-3						15.00
5,7: 5-The Enchanted Apples of Oz ($7.95, 52 pgs.)-Intro by Harlan Ellison (1986). 7-The Secret Island Of Oz ($7.95)						10.00
6-Elric of Melnibone ($14.95, 176 pgs.)-Reprints with new color						18.00
8,10,14,18: Teenage Mutant Ninja Turtles Book I -IV ($9.95, 132 pgs.)-8-r/TMNT #1-3 in color w/12 pgs. new-a; origin. 10-r/TMNT #4-6 in color. 14-r/TMNT #7,8 in color plus new 12 pg. story. 18-r/TMNT #10,11 plus 3 pg. fold-out						20.00
9-Time 2: The Epiphany by Chaykin (11/86, $7.95, 52 pgs. - indicia says #8)						20.00
11-Sailor On The Sea of Fate ($14.95)						16.00
nn-Time 2: The Satisfaction of Black Mariah (9/87)						10.00
12-American Flagg! Southern Comfort (10/87, $11.95)						15.00
13,16,17,21: 13-The Ice King Of Oz. 16-The Forgotten Forest of Oz ($8.95). 17-Mazinger (68 pgs., $8.95). 21-Elric, The Weird of the White Wolf; r/#1-5						10.00
15,19: 15-Hex Breaker: Badger ($7.95). 19-The Original Nexus Graphic Novel ($7.95, 104 pgs.)-Reprints First Comics Graphic Novel #4						12.00
20-American Flagg! State of the Union ($11.95, 96 pgs.); r/A.F. #7-9						15.00

NOTE: Most or all issues have been reprinted.

1ST FOLIO (The Joe Kubert School Presents...)
Pacific Comics: Mar, 1984 ($1.50, one-shot)

1-Joe Kubert-c/a(2 pgs.); Adam & Andy Kubert-a						4.00

1ST ISSUE SPECIAL
National Periodical Publications: Apr, 1975 - No. 13, Apr, 1976 (Tryout series)

	GD	VG	FN	VF	VF/NM	NM-
1,6: 1-Intro. Atlas; Kirby-c/a/script. 6-Dingbats	3	6	9	18	27	36
2,12: 2-Green Team (see Cancelled Comic Cavalcade). 12-Origin/1st app. "Blue" Starman (2nd app. in Starman, 2nd Series #3); Kubert-c	2	4	6	8	11	14
3-Metamorpho by Ramona Fradon	2	4	6	11	16	20
4,10,11: 4-Lady Cop. 10-The Outsiders. 11-Code Name: Assassin; Grell-c	1	3	4	6	8	10
5-Manhunter; Kirby-c/a/script	3	6	9	18	27	36
7,9: 7-The Creeper by Ditko (c/a). 9-Dr. Fate; Kubert-c/Simonson-a.	2	4	6	11	16	20
8-Origin/1st app. The Warlord; Grell-c/a (11/75)	6	12	18	37	66	95
13-Return of the New Gods; Darkseid app.; 1st new costume Orion; predates New Gods #12 by more than a year	3	6	9	33	45	

FIRST KISS
Charlton Comics: Dec, 1957 - No. 40, Jan, 1965

V1#1	6	12	18	38	69	100
V1#2-10	4	8	12	23	37	50
11-40	3	6	9	16	23	30

FIRST LOVE ILLUSTRATED
Harvey Publications(Home Comics)(True Love): 2/49 - No. 9, 6/50; No. 10, 1/51 - No. 86,
3/58; No. 87, 9/58 - No. 88, 11/58; No. 89, 11/62, No. 90, 2/63

1-Powell-a(2)	25	50	75	150	245	340
2-Powell-a	15	30	45	83	124	165
3-"Was I Too Fat To Be Loved" story	17	34	51	98	154	210
4-10	11	22	33	62	86	110
11,12,14-30: 30-Lingerie panel	9	18	27	52	69	85

	GD 2.0	VG 4.0	FN 6.0	VF 8.0	VF/NM 9.0	NM- 9.2
13-"I Joined a Teen-age Sex Club" story	39	78	117	240	395	550
31-34,37,39-49: 49-Last pre-code (2/55)	9	18	27	47	61	75
35-Used in SOTI, illo "The title of this comic book is First Love"						
	25	50	75	150	245	340
36-Communism story, "Love Slaves"	15	30	45	85	130	175
38-Nostrand-a	10	20	30	56	76	95
50-66,71-90	8	16	24	42	54	65
67-70-Kirby-a	9	18	27	52	69	85

NOTE: *Disbrow* a-13. *Orlando* c-87. *Powell* a-1, 3-5, 7, 10, 11, 13-17, 19-24, 26-29, 33,35-41, 43, 45, 46, 50, 54, 55, 57, 58, 61-63, 65, 71-73, 76, 79r, 82, 84, 88.

FIRST MEN IN THE MOON (See Movie Comics)

FIRST ROMANCE MAGAZINE
Home Comics(Harvey Publ.)/True Love: 8/49 - #6, 6/50; #7, 6/51 - #50, 2/58; #51, 9/58 - #52, 11/58

1	20	40	60	120	195	270
2	12	24	36	67	94	120
3-5	10	20	30	54	72	90
6-10,28: 28-Nostrand-a(Powell swipe)	8	16	24	44	57	70
11-20	8	16	24	40	50	60
21-27,29-32: 32-Last pre-code issue (2/55)	7	14	21	37	46	55
33-40,44-52	7	14	21	35	43	50
41-43-Kirby-a	8	16	24	44	57	70

NOTE: *Powell* a-1-5, 8-10, 14, 18, 20-22, 24, 25, 28, 36, 46, 48, 51.

FIRST STRIKE (Hasbro heroes)
IDW Publishing: Aug, 2017 - No. 6, Oct, 2017 ($3.99, limited series)

1-6-Transformers, G.I. Joe, Rom, Micronauts and MASK app.; multiple covers on each						4.00

FIRST TRIP TO THE MOON (See Space Adventures No. 20)

FIRST WAVE (Based on Sci-Fi Channel TV series)
Andromeda Entertainment: Dec, 2000 - No. 4, Jun, 2001 ($2.99)

1-4-Kuhoric-a/Parsons-a/Busch-c						3.00

FIRST WAVE (Also see Batman/Doc Savage Special #1)
DC Comics: May, 2010 - No. 6, Nov, 2011 ($3.99, limited series)

1-6-Batman, Doc Savage and The Spirit app.; Azzarello-s/Morales-a/JG Jones-c						4.00
... Special 1 (6/11, $3.99) Winslade-a/Jones-c						4.00
HC (2011, $29.99, dustjacket) r/#1-6 & Batman/Doc Savage Special #1; sketch art						30.00

FIRST X-MEN
Marvel Comics: Oct, 2012 - No. 5, Mar, 2013 ($3.99, limited series)

1-5: 1-Neal Adams-c; Adams & Gage-s; Wolverine & Sabretooth 1st meet Xavier						4.00

FISHFLIES
Image Comics: Jul, 2023 - Present ($5.99)

1-4-Jeff Lemire-s/a						6.00

FISH POLICE (Inspector Gill of the...#2, 3)
Fishwrap Productions/Comico V2#5-17/Apple Comics #18 on:
Dec, 1985 - No. 11, Nov, 1987 ($1.50, B&W); V2#5, April, 1988 - V2#17, May, 1989 ($1.75, color) No. 18, Aug, 1989 - No. 26, Dec, 1990 ($2.25, B&W)

1-11, 1(5/86),2-2nd print, V2#5-17-(Color): V2#5-11. 12-17, new-a, 18-26 ($2.25-c, B&W)						4.00
18-Origin Inspector Gill						4.00
Special 1($2.50, 7/87, Comico)						5.00
Graphic Novel: Hairballs (1987, $9.95, TPB) r/#1-4 in color						10.00

FISH POLICE
Marvel Comics: V2#1, Oct, 1992 - No. 6, Mar, 1993 ($1.25)

V2#1-6: 1-Hairballs Saga begins; r/#1 (1985)						4.00

FISTFUL OF BLOOD
IDW Publishing: Oct, 2015 - No. 4, Jan, 2016 ($4.99, limited series)

1-4-Eastman-s/Bisley-a; remastering of series from Heavy Metal magazine						5.00

5 CENT COMICS (Also see Whiz Comics)
Fawcett Publ.: Feb, 1940 (5¢, reg. size, B&W)

nn - 1st app. Dan Dare. Ashcan comic, not distributed to newsstands, only for in-house use. A CGC certified 9.6 copy sold for $10,800 in 2003, and a CGC 9.4 sold for $11,500 in 2005.

5 RONIN (Marvel characters in Samurai setting)
Marvel Comics: May, 2011 - No. 5, May, 2011 ($2.99, weekly limited series)

1-Wolverine. 2-Hulk. 3-Punisher. 4-Psylocke; Mack-c. 5-Deadpool						5.00

5-STAR SUPER-HERO SPECTACULAR (See DC Special Series No. 1)

FIVE WEAPONS
Image Comics: Feb, 2013 - No. 10, Jul, 2014 ($3.50)

1-10-Jimmie Robinson-s/a/c						3.50

FIVE YEARS
Abstract Studio: 2019 - No. 10, 2020 ($3.99, B&W)

1-10-Terry Moore-s/a; characters from Strangers in Paradise, Rachel Rising, Echo app.						
7-David-c/app.						4.00

FIX, THE
Image Comics: Apr, 2016 - No. 12, Jun, 2018 ($3.99)

1-12-Nick Spencer-s/Steve Lieber-a						4.00

FLAILING AT LOVE
Aardvark-Vanaheim: Sept, 2022 ($4.00, B&W, one-shot)

1-Cerebus figures placed over original Gustave Doré artwork; Falling in Love #40 c-swipe						4.00

FLAME, THE (See Big 3 & Wonderworld Comics)
Fox Feature Syndicate: Sum, 1940 - No. 8, Jan, 1942 (#1,2: 68 pgs; #3-8: 44 pgs.)

1-Flame stories reprinted from Wonderworld #5-9; origin The Flame; Lou Fine-a (36 pgs.)						
	423	846	1269	3000	5250	7500
2-Fine-a(2); Wing Turner by Tuska; r/Wonderworld #3,10						
	219	438	657	1402	2401	3400
3-8: 3-Powell-a	148	296	444	947	1624	2300

FLAME, THE (Formerly Lone Eagle)
Ajax/Farrell Publications (Excellent Publ.): No. 5, Dec-Jan, 1954-55 - No. 3, April-May, 1955

	GD 2.0	VG 4.0	FN 6.0	VF 8.0	VF/NM 9.0	NM- 9.2
5(#1)-1st app. new Flame	77	154	231	493	847	1200
2,3	52	104	156	328	552	775

FLAMING CARROT COMICS (Also see Junior Carrot Patrol)
Killian Barracks Press: Summer-Fall, 1981 ($1.95, one shot) (Lg size, 8-1/2x11")

1-Bob Burden-c/a/scripts; serially #'ed to 6500	10	20	30	64	132	200

FLAMING CARROT COMICS (See Anything Goes, Cerebus, Teenage Mutant Ninja Turtles/Flaming Carrot Crossover & Visions)
Aardvark-Vanaheim/Renegade Press #6-17/Dark Horse #18-31:
May, 1984 - No. 5, Jan, 1985; No. 6, Mar, 1985 - No. 31, Oct, 1994 ($1.70/$2.00, B&W)

1-Bob Burden story/art	6	12	18	38	69	100
2	3	6	9	17	25	34
3	2	4	6	13	18	22
4-6	2	4	6	9	12	15
7-9	1	3	4	6	8	10
10-12						6.50
13-15						4.00
15-Variant without cover price						6.00
16-(6/87) 1st app. Mystery Men	3	6	9	19	30	40
17-23,25: 18-1st Dark Horse issue. 25-Contains trading cards; TMNT app.						4.00
24-(2.50, 52 pgs.)-10th anniversary issue						5.00
26,27-Teenage Mutant Ninja Turtles x-over. 26-Begin $2.25-c. 27-McFarlane-c						5.00
28-31: 29-Begin $2.50-c						4.00
Annual 1(1/97, $5.00)						5.00
... & Reid Fleming, World's Toughest Milkman (12/02, $3.99) listed as #32 in indicia						4.00
...:Fortune Favors the Bold (1998, $16.95, TPB) r/#19-24						17.00
...:Men of Mystery (7/97, $12.95, TPB) r/#1-3, + new material						13.00
...'s Greatest Hits (4/98, $17.95, TPB) r/#12-18, + new material						18.00
...:The Wild Shall Wild Remain (1997, $17.95, TPB) r/#4-11, + new s/a						18.00

FLAMING CARROT COMICS
Image Comics (Desperado): Dec, 2004 - 2006 ($2.95/$3.50, B&W)

1-3-Bob Burden story/art						6.00
4-($3.50-c)	1	2	3	4	5	7
... Special #1 (3/06, $3.50) All Photo comic						3.50
... Vol. 6 (2006, $14.99) r/1-4 & Special #1; intro. by Brian Bolland						15.00

FLAMING CEREBUS COMICS (Cerebus in Hell)
Aardvark-Vanaheim: Mar, 2021 ($4.00, B&W)

1-Cerebus figures placed over Gustave Doré artwork of Hell; Flaming Carrot #1-c swipe						4.00

FLAMING LOVE
Quality Comics Group (Comic Magazines): Dec, 1949 - No. 6, Oct, 1950 (Photo covers #2-6) (52 pgs.)

1-Ward-c/a (9 pgs.)	58	116	174	371	636	900
2	34	68	102	199	325	450
3-Ward-a (9 pgs.); Crandall-a	40	80	120	246	411	575
4-6: 4-Gustavson-a	26	52	78	154	252	350

FLAMING WESTERN ROMANCES (Formerly Target Western Romances)
Star Publications: No. 3, Mar-Apr, 1950

3-Robert Taylor, Arlene Dahl photo on-c with biographies inside; L. B. Cole-c						
	58	116	174	371	636	900

FLARE (Also see Champions for 1st app. & League of Champions)
Hero Comics/Hero Graphics Vol. 2 on: Nov, 1988 - No. 3, Jan, 1989 ($2.75, color, 52 pgs); V2#1, Nov, 1990 - No. 7, Nov, 1991 $2.95/$3.50, color, mature, 52 pgs.);V2#8, Oct, 1992 - No. 16, Feb, 1994 ($3.50/$3.95, B&W, 36 pgs.)

V1#1-3, V2#1-16: 5-Eternity Smith returns. 6-Intro The Tigress						4.00
Annual 1(1992, $4.50, B&W, 52 pgs.)-Champions-r						4.50

FLARE ADVENTURES
Hero Graphics: Feb, 1992 - No. 12, 1993? ($3.50/$3.95)

1 (90¢, color, 20 pgs.)						4.00
2-12-Flip book w/Champions Classics						4.00

FLASH, THE (See Adventure Comics, The Brave and the Bold, Crisis On Infinite Earths, DC Comics Presents, DC Special, DC Special Series, DC Super-Stars, The Greatest Flash Stories Ever Told, Green Lantern, Impulse, JLA, Justice League of America, Showcase, Speed Force, Super Team Family, Titans & World's Finest)

FLASH, THE (1st Series)(Formerly Flash Comics)(See Showcase #4,8,13,14)
National Periodical Publ./DC: No. 105, Feb-Mar, 1959 - No. 350, Oct, 1985

105-(2-3/59)-Origin Flash(retold), & Mirror Master (1st app.)						
	815	1630	2850	10,190	24,095	38,000
106-Origin Grodd & Pied Piper; Flash's 1st visit to Gorilla City; begin Grodd the Super Gorilla trilogy (Scarce)	400	800	1200	3400	7700	12,000
107-Grodd trilogy, part 2	145	290	435	1196	2698	4200
108-Grodd trilogy ends	125	250	375	1000	2250	3500
109-2nd app. Mirror Master	89	178	267	712	1606	2500
110-Intro/origin Kid Flash who later becomes Flash in Crisis On Infinite Earths #12; begin Kid Flash trilogy, ends #112 (also in #114,116,118); 1st app. & origin of The Weather Wizard	300	600	900	2495	5648	8800
111-2nd Kid Flash tryout; Cloud Creatures	93	186	279	744	1672	2600
112-Origin & 1st app. Elongated Man (4-5/60); also apps. in #115,119,130						
113-Origin & 1st app. Trickster	114	228	342	912	2056	3200
114-Captain Cold app. (see Showcase #8)	86	172	258	688	1544	2400
115,116,118,120: 119-Elongated Man marries Sue Dearborn. 120-Flash & Kid Flash team-up for 1st time	62	124	186	502	1126	1750
117-Origin & 1st app. Capt. Boomerang; 1st & only S.A. app. Winky Blinky & Noddy	46	92	138	359	805	1250
121,122: 122-Origin & 1st app. The Top	61	122	183	488	1094	1700
123-(9/61)-Re-intro. Golden Age Flash; origins of both Flashes; 1st mention of an Earth II where DC G.A. heroes live	34	68	102	245	548	850
124-Last 10¢ issue	333	666	1000	2831	6416	10,000
125-128,130: 127-Return of Grodd-c/story. 128-Origin & 1st app. Abra Kadabra. 130-(7/62)-1st Gauntlet of Super-Villains (Mirror Master, Capt. Cold, The Top, Capt. Boomerang & Trickster)	48	96	144	386	868	1350
129-2nd G.A. Flash x-over; J.S.A. cameo in flashback (1st S.A. app. G.A. Green Lantern, Hawkman, Atom, Black Canary & Dr. Mid-Nite. Wonder Woman (1st S.A. app.?) appears	27	54	81	194	435	675

Fishflies #1 © 171 Studios

The Flash #108 © DC

The Flash (2nd series) #92 © DC

	GD	VG	FN	VF	VF/NM	NM-
	2.0	4.0	6.0	8.0	9.0	9.2
	28	56	84	202	451	700
131-134,136,138: 131-Early Green Lantern x-over (9/62). 136-1st Dexter Miles	18	36	54	124	275	425.
135-1st app. of Kid Flash's yellow costume (3/63)	28	56	84	202	451	700
137-G.A. Flash x-over; J.S.A. cameo (1st S.A. app.)(1st real app. since 2-3/51); 1st S.A. app. Vandal Savage & Johnny Thunder; JSA team decides to re-form	42	84	126	311	706	1100
139-Origin & 1st app. Prof. Zoom	141	282	423	1142	2571	4000
140-Origin & 1st app. Heat Wave	24	48	72	168	372	575
141-146,148-150: 142-Trickster app.	13	26	39	87	191	295
147-2nd Prof. Zoom	22	44	66	154	340	525
151-Engagement of Barry Allen & Iris West; G.A. Flash vs. The Shade.	13	26	39	86	188	290
152-159: 159-Dr. Mid-Nite cameo	10	20	30	66	138	210
160-(80-Pg. Giant G-21); G.A. Flash & Johnny Quick-r	12	24	36	82	179	275
161-164,166,167: 167-New facts about Flash's origin	8	16	24	56	108	160
165-Barry Allen weds Iris West	9	18	27	58	114	170
168,170: 168-Green Lantern-c/app. 170-Dr. Mid-Nite, Dr. Fate, G.A. Flash x-over	8	16	24	56	108	160
169-(80-Pg. Giant G-34)-New facts about origin	9	18	27	57	111	165
171,172,174,176,177,179,180: 171-JLA, Green Lantern, Atom flashbacks. 174-Barry Allen reveals I.D. to wife. 179-(5/68)-Flash travels to Earth-Prime and meets DC editor Julie Schwartz; 1st unnamed app. Earth-Prime (See Justice League of America #123 for 1st named app. & 3rd app. overall)	7	14	21	48	89	130
173-G.A. Flash x-over	8	16	24	56	108	160
175-2nd Superman/Flash race (12/67) (See Superman #199 & World's Finest #198,199); JLA cameo; gold kryptonite used (on J'onn J'onzz impersonating Superman)	19	38	57	131	291	450
178-(80-Pg. Giant G-46)	9	18	27	57	111	165
181-186,188,189: 186-Re-intro Sargon. 189-Last 12c-c	5	10	15	34	60	85
187,196: (68-Pg. Giants G-58, G-70)	6	12	18	40	73	105
190,195,197-199: 198-Zatanna 1st solo story	4	8	12	27	44	60
200-(9/70)	5	10	15	35	60	90
201-204,206,207: 201-New G.A. Flash story. 206-Elongated Man begins 207-Last 15c issue	3	6	9	21	33	45
205-(68-Pg. Giant G-82)	5	10	18	41	76	110
208-213-(52 pg.): 211-G.A. Flash origin-r/#104; Roller Derby-c. 213-Reprints #137	3	6	12	25	40	55
214-DC 100 Page Super Spectacular DC-11; origin Metal Men-r/Showcase #37; never before published G.A. Flash story	9	18	27	58	114	170
215 (52 pgs.)-Flash-r/Showcase #4; G.A. Flash x-over, continued in #216	5	10	15	30	50	70
216,220: 220-1st app. Turtle since Showcase #4	3	6	9	17	26	35
217-219: Neal Adams-a all. 217-Green Lantern/Green Arrow series begins (9/72); 2nd G.L. & G.A. team-up series (see Green Lantern #76). 219-Last Green Arrow	5	10	15	34	60	85
221-224,227,228,230,231: 222-G. Lantern x-over. 228-(7-8/74)-Flash writer Cary Bates travels to Earth-One & meets Flash, Iris Allen & Trickster; 2nd unnamed app. Earth-Prime (See Justice League of America #123 for 1st named app. & 3rd app. overall)	3	6	9	14	19	24
225-Professor Zoom-c/app.	6	12	18	37	66	95
226-Neal Adams-c	3	6	9	17	26	35
229,232-(100 pg. issues)-G.A. Flash-r & new-a. 229-G.A. Flash & Rag Doll app. in new story	5	10	15	30	50	70
233-Professor Zoom-c/app.	3	6	9	21	33	45
234-236,238-250: 235-Green Lantern. 243-Death of The Top. 245-Origin The Floronic Man in Green Lantern back-up, ends #246. 246-Last Green Lantern. 247-Jay Garrick app. 250-Intro Golden Glider	2	4	6	10	14	18
237-Professor Zoom-c/app.	3	6	9	18	28	38
251-274: 256-Death of The Top retold. 265-267-(44 pgs.). 267-Origin of Flash's uniform. 270-Intro The Clown	2	4	6	10	14	18
268,273,274,278,283,286-(Whitman variants; low print run; no issue #s shown on covers)	2	4	6	8	11	14
275,276-Iris Allen dies	2	4	6	13	18	22
275,276-(Whitman variants; low print run; no issue #s shown on covers)	3	6	9	16	23	30
277-288,290: 286-Intro/origin Rainbow Raider	1	3	4	6	8	10
289-1st Pérez DC art (Firestorm); new Firestorm back-up series begins (9/80), ends #304	2	4	6	8	10	12
291-299,301-305: 291-1st app. Saber-Tooth (villain). 295-Gorilla Grodd-c/story. 298-Intro & origin new Shade. 301-Atomic bomb-c. 303-The Top returns. 304-Intro/origin Colonel Computron; 305-G.A. Flash x-over						6.00
300-(8/81, 52 pgs.)-25th Anniversary issue; Flash's origin and life story retold; wraparound-c						

	GD	VG	FN	VF	VF/NM	NM-
	2.0	4.0	6.0	8.0	9.0	9.2
by Infantino; no ads	1	3	4	6	8	10
306-313-Dr. Fate by Giffen. 309-Origin Flash retold						6.00
314-322,325-340: 318-322-Creeper back-ups. 319-Origin of Eradicator. 328-Iris West Allen's death retold. 329-JLA app. 340-Trial of the Flash begins						5.00
323,324-Two part Flash vs. Flash story. 323-Creeper back-up. 324-Death of Reverse Flash (Professor Zoom)	4	8	12	22	35	48
341-349: 344-Origin Kid Flash						6.00
350-Double size ($1.25) Final issue	1	2	3	5	6	8
Annual 1 (10-12/63, 80 pg. Giant)-Origin Elongated Man & Kid Flash-r; origin Grodd; G.A. Flash-r	35	70	105	252	564	875
Annual 1 Replica Edition (2001, $6.95)-Reprints the entire 1963 Annual						7.00
...Chronicles SC Vol. 1 (2009, $14.99)-r/Showcase #4,8,13,14 and Flash #105,106						15.00
...Chronicles SC Vol. 2 (2010, $14.99)-r/Flash #107-112						15.00
No. 105-(Facsimile Edition)(2020, $3.99) Reprints issue with original 1959 ads						4.00
No. 123-(Facsimile Edition)(2020, $3.99) Reprints issue with original 1961 ads & letters						5.00
No. 123-(Facsimile Edition)(12/22, $3.99) Reprints issue with original 1961 ads and letters						5.00
No. 123-(Facsimile Edition)(1/24, $3.99) Reprints issue with original 1961 ads and letters						4.00
The Flash Spectacular (See DC Special Series No. 11)						
The Flash vs. The Rogues TPB (2009, $14.99) r/1st app. of classic rogues in Showcase #8 and Flash #105,106,110,113,117,122,140,155; new Orbik-c						15.00
The Life Story of the Flash (1998, $12.95, Softcover) new Orbik-c						13.00
The Life Story of the Flash (1997, $19.95, Hardcover) "Iris Allen's" chronicle of Barry Allen's life; comic panels w/additional text; Waid & Augustyn-s/ Kane & Staton-a/Orbik painted-c						20.00

NOTE: **N. Adams** c-194, 195, 203, 204, 206-208, 211, 213, 215, 226p, 246. **M. Anderson** c-165, a(i)-195, 200-204, 206-208. **Austin** a-233i, 234i, 246i. **Buckler** a-271p; 272p; c(p)-247,292. 250, 252, 253p, 255, 256p, 258, 262, 265p, 267, 269-271. **Giffen** a-306-313p; c-310p, 315. **Giordano** a-226i. **Sid Greene** a-167-174i, 229i(r). **Grell** a-237p, 238p, 240-243p; c-236. **Heck** a-198p. **Infantino/Anderson** a-135. c-135, 170-174, 192, 200, 201, 328-333. **Infantino/Giella** c-105-112, 163, 164, 166-168. **G. Kane** a-195p; 197-199p, 229r, 232r; c-197-199, 312p. **Kubert** a-108p, 215i(r); c-189-191. **Lopez** c-272. **Meskin** a-229r; 232r. **Perez** a-289-293p; c-293. **Starlin** a-294-296p. **Staton** c-263p, 264p. Green Lantern x-over-131, 143, 168, 171, 191.

FLASH (2nd Series)(See Crisis on Infinite Earths #12 and All Flash #1)
DC Comics: June, 1987 - No. 230, Mar, 2006; No. 231, Oct, 2007 - No. 247, Feb, 2009

	GD	VG	FN	VF	VF/NM	NM-
	2.0	4.0	6.0	8.0	9.0	9.2
1-Guice-c/a begins; New Teen Titans app.	3	6	9	14	20	26
2-10: 3-Intro. Kilgore. 5-Intro. Speed McGee. 7-1st app. Blue Trinity. 8,9-Millennium tie-ins. 9-1st app. The Chunk						5.00
11-78,80: 12-Free extra 16 pg. Dr. Light story. 19-Free extra 14 pg. Flash story. 28-Capt. Cold app. 29-New Phantom Lady app. 40-Dr. Alchemy app. 50-($1.75, 52 pg.). 62-Flash: Year One begins, ends #65. 65-Last $1.00-c. 66-Aquaman app. 69,70-Green Lantern app. 70-Gorilla Grodd story, ends #73. 73-Re-intro Barry Allen & begin saga ("Barry Allen's" true ID revealed in #78). 76-Re-intro of Max Mercury (Quality Comics' Quicksilver), not in uniform until #77. 80-($1.25-c) Regular Edition						4.00
79,80 ($2.50): 79-(68 pg.) Barry Allen saga ends. 80-Foil-c						5.00
81-91,93-99,101: 81,82-Nightwing & Starfire app. 84-Razer app. 94-Zero Hour. 95-"Terminal Velocity" begins, ends #100. 96,98,99-Kobra app. 97-Origin Max Mercury; Chillblaine app.						4.00
92-1st Impulse	3	6	9	21	33	45
100 ($2.50)-Newstand edition; Kobra & JLA app.						4.00
100 ($3.50)-Foil-c edition; Kobra & JLA app.						5.00
102-131: 102-Mongul app.; begin-$1.75-c. 105-Mirror Master app. 107-Shazam app. 108-"Dead Heat" begins; 1st app. Savitar. 109-"Dead Heat" Pt. 2 (cont'd in Impulse #10). 110-"Dead Heat" Pt. 4 (cont'd in Impulse #11). 111-"Dead Heat" finale; Savitar disappears into the Speed Force; John Fox cameo (2nd app.). 112-"Race Against Time" begins, ends #118; re-intro John Fox. 113-Tornado Twins app. 119-Final Night x-over. 127-129-Rogue's Gallery & Neron. 128-Morrison & Millar-s begin						3.50
132-149: 135-GL & GA app. 138,140-Black Flash cameos. 141-1st full app. Black Flash. 142-Wally almost marries Linda; Waid-s return. 144-Cobalt Blue origin. 145-Chain Lightning begins. 147-Professor Zoom app. 149-Barry Allen app.						3.00
150-($2.95) Final showdown with Cobalt Blue						4.00
151-162: 151-Casey-s. 154-New Flash ID revealed. 159-Wally marries Linda. 162-Last Waid-s						3.00
163-169,171-187,189-196,201-206: 163-Begin $2.25-c. 164-186-Bolland-c. 183-1st app of 2nd Trickster (Axel Walker). 196-Winslade-a. 201-Dose-a begins. 205-Batman-c/app.						3.00
170-1st app. Dose-a						5.00
188-($2.95) Mirror Master, Weather Wizard, Trickster app.						4.00
197-Origin of Zoom (Hunter Zolomon) (6/03)	5	10	15	31	53	75
198,199-Zoom app.	1	3	4	6	8	10
200-($3.50) Flash vs. Zoom; Barry Allen & Hal Jordan app.; wraparound-c			3	5	6	8
207-230: 207-211-Turner-a/Porter-a. 209-JLA app. 210-Nightwing app. 212-Origin Mirror Master. 214-216-Identity Crisis x-over. 219-Wonder Woman app. 220-Rogue War. 224-Zoom & Prof. Zoom app. 225-Twins born; Barry Allen app.; last Johns-s						3.00
231-247: 231-(10/07) Waid-s/Acuña-a. 240-Grodd app.; "Dark Side Club"						3.00
#0-(10/94) Zero Hour issue released between #94 & 95						3.00
#1,000,000 (11/98) 853rd Century x-over						3.00
Annual 1-7,9: 2-('87-'94,'96, 98 pgs), 3-Gives history of G.A.,S.A., & Modern Age Flash in text.						

	GD	VG	FN	VF	VF/NM	NM-		GD	VG	FN	VF	VF/NM	NM-
	2.0	4.0	6.0	8.0	9.0	9.2		2.0	4.0	6.0	8.0	9.0	9.2

4-Armaggedon 2001. 5-Eclipso-c/story. 7-Elseworlds story. 9-Legends of the Dead Earth story; J.H. Williams-a(p); Mick Gray-a(i) **4.00**
Annual 8 (1995, $3.50)-Year One story **4.00**
Annual 10 (1997, $3.95)-Pulp Heroes stories **4.00**
Annual 11,12 ('98, '99)-11-Ghosts; Wrightson-c. 12-JLApe; Art Adams-c **4.00**
Annual 13 ('00, $3.50) Planet DC; Alcatena-c/a **4.00**
...: Blitz (2004, $19.95, TPB)-r/#192-200; Kolins-c **20.00**
...: Blood Will Run (2002, 2008; $17.95, TPB)-r/#170-176, Secret Files #3, Iron Heights **18.00**
...: Crossfire (2004, $17.95, TPB)-r/#183-191 & parts of Flash Secret Files #3 **18.00**
Dead Heat (2000, $14.95, TPB)-r/#108-111, Impulse #10,11 **15.00**
...80-Page Giant (8/98, $4.95) Flash family stories by Waid, Millar and others; Mhan-c **5.00**
...80-Page Giant 2 (4/99, $4.95) Stories of Flash family, future Kid Flash, original Teen Titans and XS **5.00**
...: Emergency Stop (2008, $12.99, TPB)-r/#130-135; Morrison & Millar-s **13.00**
...: Ignition (2005, $14.95, TPB)-r/#201-206 **15.00**
...: Iron Heights (2001, $5.95)-Van Sciver-c/a; 1st app. of the prison; intro. Girder, Murmur, Double Down and Blacksmith **6.00**
...: Mercury Falling (2009, $14.99, TPB)-r/Impulse #62-67 **15.00**
...: Our Worlds at War (10/01, $2.95)-Jae Lee-c; Black Racer app. **3.00**
...Plus 1 (1997, $2.95)-Nightwing-c/app. **4.00**
Race Against Time (2001, $14.95, TPB)-r/#112-118 **15.00**
...: Rogues (2003, $14.95, TPB)-r/#177-182 **15.00**
...: Rogue War (2006, $17.99, TPB)-r/#1/2,212,218,220-225; cover gallery **18.00**
...Secret Files 1 (11/97, $4.95) Origin-s & pin-ups **5.00**
...Secret Files 2 (11/99, $4.95) Origin of Replicant **5.00**
...Secret Files 3 (11/01, $4.95) Intro. Hunter Zolomon (who later becomes Zoom) **20.00**
Special 1 (1990, $2.95, 84 pgs.)-50th anniversary issue; Kubert-c; 1st Flash story by Mark Waid; 1st app. John Fox (27th Century Flash) **5.00**
Terminal Velocity (1996, $12.95, TPB)-r/#95-100. **13.00**
...: The Greatest Stories Ever Told (2007, $19.99, TPB) reprints; Ross-c/Waid intro. **20.00**
The Return of Barry Allen (1996, $12.95, TPB)-r/#74-79 **13.00**
The Secret of Barry Allen (2005, $19.99, TPB)-r/#207-211,213-217; Turner sketch page **20.00**
...: The Wild Ride HC (2008, $24.99, dustjacket)-r/#231-237 **25.00**
...: Time Flies (2002, $5.95)-Seth Fisher-c/a; Rozum-s **6.00**
TV Special 1 (1991, $3.95, 76 pgs.)-Photo-c plus behind the scenes photos of TV show; Saltares-a, Byrne scripts **5.00**
Wizard #1/2 (2005) prelude to Rogue Wars; Justiano-a **10.00**
...Wonderland TPB (2007, $12.99, TPB)-r/#164-169 **13.00**
NOTE: *Guice* a-1-9p, 11p, Annual 1p; c-1-9p, Annual 1p. *Perez* c-15-17, Annual 2i. *Charest* c/a-Annual 5p.

FLASH, THE (Brightest Day)(Leads into Flashpoint series)
DC Comics: Jun, 2010 - No. 12, Jul, 2011 ($3.99/$2.99)
1-($3.99) Barry Allen vs. the 25th Century Rogues; Johns-s/Manapul-a/c **4.00**
1-Variant-c by Tony Harris **10.00**
2-12-($2.99) Capt. Boomerang app. 8-Reverse Flash origin retold **3.00**
2-12-Variant covers. 2-Sook. 3-Horn. 4-Kolins. 5-Sook. 6-Garza. 7-Cooke **5.00**
...: Secret Files and Origins 1 (5/10, $3.99) Johns-s/Kolins-a; profiles of the Rogues **4.00**
...: The Dastardly Death of the Rogues HC (2011, $19.99, dj) r/#1-7 & Secret Files **20.00**

FLASH (New DC 52)
DC Comics: Nov, 2011 - No. 52, Jul, 2016 ($2.99/$3.99)

	GD		FN		VF/NM	NM-
1-Manapul & Buccellato-s; Manapul-a/c	2	4	6	8	10	12

1-Special Edition (12/14, $1.00) reprints #1 with Flash TV image above cover logo **3.00**
2-24: 6,7-Captain Cold app. 8,9,13-17-Grodd app. 17-24-Reverse Flash app. 18-Takara-a. 21-Kid Flash app. **3.00**
23.1, 23.2, 23.3 (11/13, $2.99, regular-c) **3.00**

23.1 (11/13, $3.99, 3-D cover) "Grodd #1" on cover; Batista-a/Manapul-c	1	3	4	6	8	10
23.2 (11/13, $3.99, 3-D cover) "Reverse Flash #1" on cover; origin; Hepburn-a/Manapul-c	1	3	4	6	8	10
23.3 (11/13, $3.99, 3-D cover) "The Rogues #1" on cover; Zircher-a/Manapul-c	1	3	4	6	8	10

25-($3.99) Zero Year; Sprouse & Manapul-a; first meeting of Barry and Iris **4.00**
26-39: 26-Googe-a. 27-Buccellato-s begin. 28-Deadman app. **3.00**
40-49,51,52: 40-($3.99) Professor Zoom cameo. 41-47-Prof. Zoom app. **4.00**
50-($4.99) The Rogues and The Riddler app.; back-up Kid Flash story **5.00**
#0 (11/12, $2.99) Barry's childhood and origin re-told; Manapul-a/c **3.00**
Annual #1 (10/12, $4.99) Continued from #12; origin of Glider; Kolins-a **5.00**
Annual #2 (9/13, $4.99) Green Lantern app.; Basri-a **5.00**
Annual #3 (6/14, $4.99) Intro. Wally West; Grodd app.; leads into Flash #31 **5.00**
Annual #4 (9/15, $4.99) Jensen-s/Dazo-a; background on Eobard Thawne; cont'd in #43 **5.00**
...: Futures End 1 (11/14, $2.99, reg.-c) Five years later; Wally West gains speed power **3.00**
...: Futures End 1 (11/14, $3.99, 3-D cover) **4.00**

FLASH, THE (DC Rebirth)(Reverts to legacy numbering with #750)
DC Comics: Aug, 2016 - No. 88, Early Apr, 2020; No. 750, Late Apr, 2020 - No. 800, Aug, 2023 ($2.99/$3.99)
1-20: 1-3-Williamson-s/Di Giandomenico-a. 3-Intro Godspeed. 8-Wally becomes the new Kid Flash in costume. 9-Flash of Two Worlds cover swipe; both Wallys app.
10-12-The Shade app. 14-17-Rogues Reloaded **3.00**
21,22-The Button x-over with Batman #21,22. 21-Flashpoint Thomas Wayne app.; Porter-a.
22-Reverse Flash app; Jay Garrick app.; leads into Doomsday Clock series **3.00**
23,24,26-49: 23-Reverse Flash & Hal Jordan app. 28-Intro. Negative Flash. 33-Dark Nights: Metal tie-in. 36-Preview of Damage #1. 39-44-Grodd app. 42-Panosian-a. 46-Zoom app.
47-49-Flash War; the Renegades app.; Porter-a **3.00**
25-($3.99) Reverse Flash origin re-told; art by Di Giandomenico, Sook & Googe **4.00**
50-74-($3.99) 50-Flash War comic.; Zoom app.; Impulse returns. 59-Intro. Fuerza.
64,65-X-over with Batman #64,65; Gotham Girl app. 70-74-Year One; origin re-told **4.00**
75-($4.99) Year of the Villain tie-in; Turtle app.; art by Porter, Duce & Kolins **5.00**
76-88: 76-83-Year of the Villain tie-in. 82-Acetate-c **4.00**
750-($7.99, 80 pages) The Flash Age pt. 1; short stories and pin-ups by various incl. Johns, Wolfman, & Manapul; Flash Forward epilogue; multiple covers **10.00**
751-774,776-799: 758-760-Tornado Twins app.; Jesse Quick & Max Mercury return.
759-762-Reverse Flash app. 763-766-Dr. Alchemy app. 768-Endless Winter pt. 2;
Black Adam app. 770-Jay Garrick & The Ray app. in WWII vs. Hitler. 771-Legion of Doom app.; Maguire-a. 772,773-Heat Wave app. 776-779-Dr. Fate & Justice League Dark app.
786-Dark Crisis tie-in. 790-796-One Minute War. 799-Granny Goodness app. **4.00**
760-($4.99) Wally West returns **5.00**

775-($4.99) Starbreaker and Eclipso return **5.00**
800-($4.99) "A Celebration of Wally West" s/a by various; prelude to Flash #1 (2023) **5.00**
Annual 1 (3/18, $4.99) Porter & Duce-a; leads into Flash War in Flash #47 **5.00**
Annual 2 (3/19, $4.99) Kolins-a; Godspeed & Impulse app. **5.00**
Annual 3 (3/23, $4.99) Segovia, Peterson & Pagulayan-a **6.00**
2021 Annual 1 (9/21, $5.99) Return to Sanctuary; Peterson & Pagulayan-a **6.00**
2022 Annual 1 (10/21, $5.99) Linda's romance novel **6.00**
...: One Minute War Special (3/23, $5.99) Tie-in with Flash #790-796 **6.00**
...: One Minute War: Start the Clock 1 (5/23, $5.99) Reprints Flash #790-792 **6.00**
...: Rebirth (8/16) Williamson-s/Di Giandomenico-a; Wally West & Batman app. **3.00**
...: Speed Buggy Special 1 (7/18, $4.99) Lobdell-s/Booth-a; Wally West & Savitar app. **5.00**

FLASH, THE (Dawn of DC)
DC Comics: Nov, 2023 - Present ($4.99/$3.99)
1-($4.99)-Spurrier-s/Deodato Jr.-a; Grodd app. **5.00**
2-6-($3.99) 2-Intro. The Stillness **4.00**

FLASH, THE (See Tangent Comics/ The Flash)

FLASH AND GREEN LANTERN: THE BRAVE AND THE BOLD
DC Comics: Oct, 1999 - No. 6, Mar, 2000 ($2.50, limited series)
1-6-Waid & Peyer-s/Kitson-a. 4-Green Arrow app.; Grindberg-a(p) **4.00**
TPB (2000, $12.95) r/#1-6 **13.00**

FLASH COMICS
DC Comics: Dec. 1939
1-Ashcan comic; not distributed to newsstands, only for in-house use. Cover art is Adventure Comics #41 and interior from All-American Comics #8. A CGC certified 9.6 sold for $11,500 in 2004. A CGC certified 9.4 sold for $6,572.50 in 2008. A CGC certified 9.6 sold for $8,513 in 2013. A CGC certified 9.4 sold for $20,315 in 2018.

FLASH COMICS (Whiz Comics No. 2 on)
Fawcett Publications: Jan, 1940 (12 pgs., B&W, regular size)
(Not distributed to newsstands; printed for in-house use)

NOTE: *Whiz Comics #2* was preceded by two books, *Flash Comics* and *Thrill Comics*, both dated Jan, 1940, (12 pgs, B&W, regular size). These two books are identical except for the title, and were both sent out to major distributors as ad copies to promote sales. It is believed that the complete 68 page issue of Fawcett's *Flash* and *Thrill Comics #1* was finished and ready for publication with the January date. Since DC Comics was also about to publish a book with the same date and title, Fawcett hurriedly printed up the black and white version of *Flash Comics* to secure copyright before DC. The inside covers are blank, with the covers and inside pages printed on a high quality uncoated paper stock. The eight page origin story of Captain Thunder is composed of pages 1-7 and 13 of the Captain Marvel story essentially as they appeared in the first issue of *Whiz Comics*. The balloon dialogue on page thirteen was relettered to tie the story into the end of page seven in *Flash* and *Thrill Comics* to produce a shorter version of the origin story for copyright purposes. Obviously, DC acquired the copyright and Fawcett dropped *Flash* as well as *Thrill* and came out with *Whiz Comics* a month later. Fawcett never used the cover to *Flash* and *Thrill #1*, designing a new cover for *Whiz Comics*. Fawcett also must have discovered that Captain Thunder had already been used by another publisher (Captain Terry Thunder by Fiction House). All references to Captain Thunder were relettered to Captain Marvel before appearing in *Whiz*.

1-(nn on-c, #1 on inside)-Origin & 1st app. Captain Thunder. Cover by C.C. Beck.
Eight copies of Flash and three copies of Thrill exist. All 3 copies of Thrill sold in 1986 for between $4,000-$10,000 each. A NM copy of Thrill sold in 1987 for $12,000. A VG copy of Thrill sold in 1987 for $9000 cash. A CGC certified 9.0 copy of the Flash Comics version sold for $10,117.50 in 2004. A CGC certified 9.4 copy of the Flash Comics version sold for $14,340 in 2008. A CGC certified 9.0 copy of the Thrill Comics version sold for $20,315 in 2008. A CGC certified 8.0 copy sold for $12,999 in 2012. A CGC certified 4.5 copy sold for $19,750 in 2017. A CGC certified 9.0 copy of Thrill Comics sold for $41,040 in 2017. A CGC certified 9.4 copy of Flash Comics sold for $85,000 in 2019.

FLASH COMICS (The Flash No. 105 on) (Also see All-Flash)
National Periodical Publ./All-American: Jan, 1940 - No. 104, Feb, 1949

	GD	VG	FN	VF	VF/NM	NM-
1-The Flash (origin/1st app.) by Harry Lampert, Hawkman (origin/1st app.) by Gardner Fox, The Whip, & Johnny Thunder (1st app.) by Stan Asch; Cliff Cornwall by Moldoff, Flash Picture Novelets (later Minute Movies w/#12) begin; Moldoff (Shelly) cover; 1st app. Shiera Sanders who later becomes Hawkgirl, #24; reprinted in Famous First Edition on sale 11/10/39); The Flash-c	28,600	57,200	85,800	208,800	304,400	400,000
1-Reprint, Oversize 13-1/2x10". **WARNING:** This comic is an exact reprint of the original except for its size. DC published it in 1974 with a second cover titling it as a Famous First Edition. There have been many reported cases of the outer cover being removed and the interior sold as the original edition. The reprint with the new outer cover removed is practically worthless. See Famous First Edition for value.						
2-Rod Rian begins, ends #11; Hawkman-c	1875	3750	5625	12,000	21,000	30,000
3-King Standish begins (1st app.), ends #41 (called The King #16-37,39-41); E.E. Hibbard-a begins on Flash	541	1082	1623	3950	6975	10,000
4-Moldoff (Shelly) Hawkman begins; The Whip-c	383	766	1149	2681	4691	6700
5-The King-c	300	600	900	2070	3635	5200
6-2nd Flash-c (alternates w/Hawkman #6 on)	919	1838	2757	6709	11,855	17,000
7-2nd Hawkman-c; 1st Moldoff Hawkman-c	730	1460	2190	5329	9415	13,500
8-New logo begins; classic Moldoff Flash-c	423	846	1269	3088	5444	7800
9,10: 9-Moldoff Hawkman-c. 10-Classic Moldoff Flash-c	423	846	1269	3000	5250	7500
11,13,15,20: 12-Les Watts begins; "Sparks" #16 on. 13-Has full page ad for All Star Comics #3. 17-Last Cliff Cornwall	271	342	813	1734	2967	4200
14-World War II cover	308	616	924	2156	3778	5400
21-Classic Hawkman-c	300	600	900	1920	3310	4700
22,23	245	490	735	1568	2684	3800
24-Shiera becomes Hawkgirl (12/41); see All-Star Comics #5 for 1st app.	300	600	900	1920	3310	4700
25-28,30: 28-Last Les Sparks.	161	322	483	1030	1765	2500
29-Ghost Patrol begins (origin/1st app.), ends #104	194	388	582	1242	2190	3000
31-Classic Hawkman dragon-c	206	412	618	1318	2259	3200
32,34,35,37-40:	161	322	483	1030	1765	2500
33-Classic Hawkman WWII-c; origin The Shade	314	628	942	2198	3849	5500
36-1st app. Rag Doll (see Flash #229)	181	362	543	1158	1979	2800
41-50	142	284	426	909	1555	2200
51-61: 52-1st computer in comics, c/s (4/44). 59-Last Minute Movies. 61-Last Moldoff Hawkman	113	226	339	718	1234	1750
62-Hawkman by Kubert begins	148	296	444	947	1624	2300
63-66,68-85: 66,68-Hop Harrigan app. 70-Mutt & Jeff app. 80-Atom begins, ends #104	148	296	444	947	1624	2300
67-Hawkman dinosaur-c; Hop Harrigan app.	103	206	309	659	1130	1600
86-Intro. The Black Canary in Johnny Thunder (8/47); see All-Star #38.	148	296	444	947	1624	2300

The Flash (2016 series) #73 © DC

Flash Comics #10 © DC

Flash Gordon (2014 series) #1 © KFS

	GD 2.0	VG 4.0	FN 6.0	VF 8.0	VF/NM 9.0	NM- 9.2
	4000	8000	12,000	24,000	32,000	40,000
87,88,90: 87-Intro. The Foil. 88-Origin Ghost.	155	310	465	992	1696	2400
89-Intro villain The Thorn. (scarce)	300	600	900	1920	3310	4700
91,93-99: 98-Atom & Hawkman don new costumes	161	322	483	1030	1765	2500
92-1st solo Black Canary plus-c; rare in Mint due to black ink smearing on white-c	1150	2300	3450	8700	15,850	23,000
100 (10/48),103(Scarce)-52 pgs. each	300	600	900	2010	3505	5000
101,102(Scarce)	314	628	942	2198	3849	5500
104-Origin the Flash retold (Scarce)	1000	2000	3000	7300	12,900	18,500

NOTE: *Irwin Hasen* a-Wheaties Giveaway. c-97, Wheaties Giveaway. *E.E. Hibbard* c-6, 12, 20, 24, 26, 28, 30, 44, 46, 48, 50, 62, 66, 68, 69, 72, 74, 76, 78, 80, 82. *Infantino* a-86p, 90, 93-95, 99-104; c-90, 92, 93, 97, 99, 101, 103. *Kinstler* c-87, 89(Hawkman)- c-87. *Chet Koziak* c-77, 79, 81. *Krigstein* a-94. *Kubert* a-62-76, 83, 85, 86, 88-104; c-63, 65, 67, 70, 71, 73, 75, 83, 85, 86, 88, 89, 91, 94, 96, 98, 100, 104. *Moldoff* a-3; c-3, 7-11, 13-17, plus odd #'s 19-61. *Martin Naydell* c-52, 54, 56, 58, 60, 64, 84.

FLASH DIGEST, THE (See DC Special Series #24)

FLASH FORCE 2000
DC Comics: 1984

	NM-
1-5	6.00

FLASH FORWARD (See Heroes in Crisis series)
DC Comics: Nov, 2019 - No. 6, Apr, 2020 ($3.99, limited series)

	NM-
1-6-Follows Wally West after Heroes in Crisis; Lobdell-s/Booth-a. 2-Jai & Iris app.	4.00

FLASH GIANT (Barry Allen)
DC Comics: 2019 - No. 7, 2019 ($4.99, 100 pgs., squarebound, Walmart exclusive)

	NM-
1-New story Simone-s/Henry-a; reprints from Flash #8 ('11), Adam Strange #1 ('04), and Shazam from Justice League #7 & 8('11)	8.00
2-7: 2-New story plus Flash, Adam Strange and Shazam reprints continue	5.00

FLASH GIANT
DC Comics: 2019 - No. 4, 2020 ($4.99, 100 pgs., squarebound, Mass Market & Direct Market editions exist for each issue, with different covers)

	NM-
1-4: 1-New stories vs. King Shark and Grodd; reprints. 3-The Atom app.	5.00

FLASH GORDON (See Defenders Of The Earth, Eat Right to Work..., Giant Comic Album, King Classics, King Classics, March of Comics #118, 133, 142, The Phantom #18, Street Comix & Wow Comics, 1st series)

FLASH GORDON
Dell Publishing Co.: No. 25, 1941; No. 10, 1943 - No. 512, Nov, 1953

	GD 2.0	VG 4.0	FN 6.0	VF 8.0	VF/NM 9.0	NM- 9.2
Feature Books 25 (#1)(1941)-r-not by Raymond	200	400	600	1280	2190	3100
Four Color 10(1942)-by Alex Raymond; reprints "The Ice Kingdom"	96	192	288	768	1734	2700
Four Color 84(1945)-by Alex Raymond; reprints "The Fiery Desert"	42	84	126	311	706	1100
Four Color 173	26	52	78	182	404	625
Four Color 190-Bondage-c; "The Adventures of the Flying Saucers"; 5th Flying Saucer story (6/48)- see The Spirit 9/28/47(1st), Shadow Comics V7#10 (2nd, 1/48), Captain Midnight #60 (3rd, 2/48) & Boy Commandos #26 (4th, 3-4/48)	31	62	93	223	499	775
Four Color 204,247	19	38	57	131	291	450
Four Color 424-Painted-c	13	26	39	89	195	300
2(5-7/53-Dell)-Painted-c; Evans-a?	10	20	30	69	147	225
Four Color 512-Painted-c	10	20	30	67	141	215

FLASH GORDON (See Tiny Tot Funnies)
Harvey Publications: Oct, 1950 - No. 4, April, 1951

	GD 2.0	VG 4.0	FN 6.0	VF 8.0	VF/NM 9.0	NM- 9.2
1-Alex Raymond-a; bondage-c; reprints strips from 7/14/40 to 12/8/40	60	120	180	381	653	925
2-Alex Raymond-a; r/strips 12/15/40-4/27/41	36	72	108	211	343	475
3,4-Alex Raymond-a; 3-bondage-c; r/strips 5/4/41-9/21/41. 4-r/strips 10/24/37-3/27/38	34	68	102	204	332	460
5-(Rare)-Small size-5-1/2x8-1/2"; B&W; 32 pgs.; Distributed to some mail subscribers only	103	206	309	659	1130	1600

(Also see All-New No. 15, Boy Explorers No. 2, and Stuntman No. 3)

FLASH GORDON
Gold Key: June, 1965

	GD 2.0	VG 4.0	FN 6.0	VF 8.0	VF/NM 9.0	NM- 9.2
1 (1947 reprint)-Painted-c	10	20	30	64	132	200

FLASH GORDON (Also see Comics Reading Libraries in the Promotional Comics section)
King #1-11/Charlton #12-18/Gold Key #19-23/Whitman #28 on:
9/66 - #11, 12/67; #12, 2/69 - #18, 1/70; #19, 9/78 - #37, 3/82 (Painted covers No. 19-30, 34)

	GD 2.0	VG 4.0	FN 6.0	VF 8.0	VF/NM 9.0	NM- 9.2
1-1st S.A. app Flash Gordon; Williamson c/a(s); E.C. swipe/Incredible S.F. #32; Mandrake story	14	28	42	84	117	150
1-Army giveaway(1968)("Complimentary" on cover)(Same as regular #1 minus Mandrake story & back-c)	5	10	15	30	50	70

2-8: 2-Bolle, Gil Kane-c; Mandrake story. 3-Williamson-a. 4-Secret Agent X-9 begins, Williamson-c/a(s). 5-Williamson-c/a(2). 6,8-Crandall-a. 7-Raboy-a (last in comics?).

	GD 2.0	VG 4.0	FN 6.0	VF 8.0	VF/NM 9.0	NM- 9.2
8-Secret Agent X-9-r	4	8	12	28	47	65
9-13: 9,10-Raymond-r. 10-Buckler's 1st pro work (11/67). 11-Crandall-a. 12-Crandall-c/a.	4	8	12	27	44	60
13-Jeff Jones-a (15 pgs.)	4	8	12	27	44	60
14,15: 15-Last 12¢ issue	3	6	9	19	30	40
16,17: 17-Brick Bradford story	3	6	9	16	24	32
18-Kaluta-a (3rd pro work?)(see Teen Confessions)	3	6	9	21	33	45
19(9/78, G.K.), 20-26	2	4	6	8	10	12
27-29,34,37: 34-37-Movie adaptation	2	4	6	8	11	14
30 (10/80)(scarce, from Whitman 3-pack only, 40¢-c)	4	8	12	27	44	60
30 (7/81; re-issue, 50c-c), 31-33-single issues	2	4	6	11	16	20
31-33 (Bagged 3-pack): Movie adaptation: Williamson-a.						60.00

NOTE: *Aparo* a-8. *Bolle* a-21, 22. *Boyette* a-14-18. *Briggs* c-10. *Buckler* a-10. *Crandall* c-6. *Estrada* a-3. *Gene Fawcette* a-29, 30, 34, 37. *McWilliams* a-31-33, 36.

FLASH GORDON
DC Comics: June, 1988 - No. 9, Holiday, 1988-'89 ($1.25, mini-series)

	NM-
1-9; 1,5-Painted-c	4.00

FLASH GORDON
Marvel Comics: June, 1995 - No. 2, July, 1995 ($2.95, limited series)

	NM-
1,2: Schultz scripts; Williamson-a	4.00

FLASH GORDON (The Mercy Wars)
Ardden Entertainment: Aug, 2008 - No. 6, Jul, 2009 ($3.99)

	NM-
1-6: 1-Deneen-s/Green-a; two covers	4.00
...: The Mercy Wars #0 (4/09, $2.99)	3.00

FLASH GORDON
Dynamite Entertainment: 2014 ($3.99)

	NM-
1-8: 1-Parker-s/Shaner-a; six covers. 2-8-Multiple covers on each	4.00
Annual 2014 ($7.99, squarebound) Short stories of the characters' pasts	8.00
Holiday Special 2014 ($5.99) Christmas-themed short stories by various	6.00

FLASH GORDON: INVASION OF THE RED SWORD
Ardden Entertainment: Jan, 2011 - No. 6, Nov, 2011 ($3.99)

	NM-
1-6-Deneen-s/Garcia-a. 1-Two covers	4.00

FLASH GORDON: KINGS CROSS
Dynamite Entertainment: 2016 - No. 5, 2017 ($3.99)

	NM-
1-5-Jeff Parker-s/Jesse Hamm-a; multiple covers on each; Mandrake & Phantom app.	4.00

FLASH GORDON THE MOVIE
Western Publishing Co.: 1980 (8-1/4 x 11", $1.95, 68 pgs.)

	GD 2.0	VG 4.0	FN 6.0	VF 8.0	VF/NM 9.0	NM- 9.2
11294-Williamson-c/a; adapts movie	2	4	6	11	16	20
13743-Hardback edition	3	6	9	16	23	30

FLASH GORDON: ZEITGEIST
Dynamite Entertainment: 2011 - No. 10, 2013 ($1.00/$3.99)

	NM-
1-($1.00) Flash, Dale and Zarkov head to Mongo; 4 covers by Ross, Renaud & others	4.00
2-10-($3.99) 2-8-Three covers. 9,10-Ross-c	4.00

FLASH/ GREEN LANTERN: FASTER FRIENDS (See Green Lantern/Flash...)
DC Comics: Oct, 1997 ($4.95, continuation of Green Lantern/Flash: Faster Friends #1)

	NM-
2-Waid/Augustyn-s	5.00

FLASHPOINT (Elseworlds Flash)
DC Comics: Dec, 1999 - No. 3, Feb, 2000 ($2.95, limited series)

	NM-
1-3-Paralyzed Barry Allen; Breyfogle-a/McGreal-s	4.00

FLASHPOINT (Leads into DC New 52 relaunches)
DC Comics: Jul, 2011 - No. 5, Late Oct, 2011 ($3.99, limited series)

	GD 2.0	VG 4.0	FN 6.0	VF 8.0	VF/NM 9.0	NM- 9.2
1-Johns-s/Andy Kubert-a; 2 covers on each	4	8	12	23	37	50
1 Special Edition (5/23, $3.99) Reprints #1 to promote The Flash movie						4.00
2-5-Johns-s/Andy Kubert-a. 2-4-Bonus design art. 5-New timeline	1	2	3	5	6	8
...: Abin Sur - The Green Lantern 1-3 (8/11 - No. 3, 10/11, $2.99) Massaferra-a/c						4.00
...: Batman Knight of Vengeance 1-3 (8/11 - No. 3, 10/11, $2.99) Risso-a/Johnson-c	1	3	4	6	8	10
...: Batman Knight of Vengeance 1 (6/22, $7.99) r/#1-3 & Flashpoint Beyond #0						8.00
...: Canterbury Cricket, The (8/11, $2.99, one-shot) Carlin-s/Morales-a						3.00
...: Citizen Cold 1-3 (8/11 - No. 3, 10/11, $2.99) Scott Kolins-s/a/c						3.00
...: Deadman and the Flying Grayson 1-3 (8/11 - No. 3, 10/11, $2.99) Chiang-c						3.00
...: Deathstroke & The Curse of the Ravager 1-3 (8/11 - No. 3, 10/11, $2.99) Bennett-a						3.00
...: Emperor Aquaman 1-3 (8/11 - No. 3, 10/11, $2.99) Bedard-s/Syaf-c						3.00
...: Frankenstein and the Creatures of the Unknown 1-3 (8/11 - No. 3, 10/11, $2.99)						3.00
...: Green Arrow Industries (8/11, $2.99, one-shot) Kalvachev-c						5.00
...: Grodd of War 1 (8/11, $2.99, one-shot) Manapul-c						5.00
...: Hal Jordan 1-3 (8/11 - No. 3, 10/11, $2.99) 1-Oliver-a. 2,3-Richards-a						3.00
...: Kid Flash Lost 1-3 (8/11 - No. 3, 10/11, $2.99) Gates-s/Manapul-c; Brainiac app.						3.00

	GD	VG	FN	VF	VF/NM	NM-
	2.0	4.0	6.0	8.0	9.0	9.2

...: Legion of Doom 1-3 (8/11 - No. 3, 10/11, $2.99) Glass-s/Sepulveda-c — 3.00
...: Lois Lane and the Resistance 1-3 (8/11 - No. 3, 10/11, $2.99) Abnett & Lanning-a — 3.00
...: Outsider, The 1-3 (8/11 - No. 3, 10/11, $2.99) Robinson/Nowlan-c — 3.00
...: Project Superman 1-3 (8/11 - No. 3, 10/11, $2.99) Gene Ha-c/a — 3.00
...: Reverse Flash (8/11, $2.99, one-shot) Kolins-s/Gomez-a

	1	3	4	6	8	10

...: Secret Seven 1-3 (8/11 - No. 3, 10/11, $2.99) Pérez-c on all. 1-Pérez-a. — 3.00
...: Wonder Woman and The Furies 1-3 (8/11 - No. 3, 10/11, $2.99) Aquaman app. — 4.00
...: World of Flashpoint 1-3 (8/11 - No. 3, 10/11, $2.99) Traci 13 app. — 3.00

FLASHPOINT BEYOND
DC Comics: No. 0, Jun, 2022 - No. 6, Dec, 2022 ($5.99/$4.99/$3.99, limited series)
0-($5.99) Johns-s-Risso-a; Thomas Wayne back in the Flashpoint Universe — 6.00
1-($4.99) Aquaman & Wonder Woman app.; Xermánico & Janin-a — 5.00
2-6-($3.99) 2,3-Subject 1 app. — 4.00

FLASH: REBIRTH
DC Comics: Jun, 2009 - No. 6, Apr, 2010 ($3.99/$2.99, limited series)
1-($3.99) Barry Allen's return; Johns-s/Van Sciver-a; Flash-c by Van Sciver

	1	2	3	5	6	8
1-Variant Barry Allen-c by Van Sciver	2	4	6	9	12	15

1-Second thru fourth printings — 4.00
1-Special Edition (8/10, $1.00) reprints #1 with "What's Next?" logo on cover — 3.00
2-6-($2.99) 3-Max Mercury returns — 3.00
2-6-Variant covers by Van Sciver — 3.00
HC (2010, $19.99, dustjacket) r/#1-6; Johns original proposal; sketch art; cover gallery — 20.00
SC (2011, $14.99) r/#1-6; Johns original proposal; sketch art; cover gallery — 15.00

FLASH: SEASON ZERO (Based on the 2014 TV series)
DC Comics: Dec, 2014 - No. 12, Nov, 2015 ($2.99, printings of digital-first stories)
1-12-Photo-c on #1-8. 1,4,6-9-Hester-a. 5-Felicity Smoak app. 7-9-Intro. Suicide Squad — 3.00

FLASH: THE FASTEST MAN ALIVE (3rd Series)(See Infinite Crisis)
DC Comics: Aug, 2006 - No. 13, Aug, 2007 ($2.99)
1-Bart Allen becomes the Flash; Lashley-a/Bilson & Demeo-s — 3.00
1-Variant-c by Joe and Andy Kubert — 5.00
2-12: 5-Cyborg app. 7-Inertia returns. 10-Zoom app. — 3.00
13-Bart Allen dies; 2 covers — 3.00
13-DC Nation Edition from the 2007 San Diego Comic-Con — 8.00
...: Full Throttle TPB (2007, $12.99) r/#7-13, All-Flash #1, DCU Infinite Holiday Spec. story — 13.00
...: Lightning in a Bottle TPB (2007, $12.99) r/#1-6 — 13.00

FLASH: THE FASTEST MAN ALIVE (Tie-in to the movie)
DC Comics: Nov, 2022 - No. 3, Jan, 2023 ($5.99, limited series)
1-3: 1-Batman & Girder app.; Barry gets the new costume. 2-Tarpit app.; Ferreyra-a — 6.00

FLAT-TOP
Mazie Comics/Harvey Publ.(Magazine Publ.) No. 4 on: 11/53 - No. 3, 5/54; No. 4, 3/55 - No. 7, 9/55

1-Teenage: Flat-Top, Mazie, Mortie & Stevie begin	15	30	45	84	127	170
2,3	9	18	27	52	69	85
4-7	8	16	24	42	54	65

FLAVOR
Image Comics: May, 2018 - No. 6, Oct, 2018 ($3.99)
1-6-Joseph Keatinge-s/Wook Jin Clark-a — 4.00

FLAWED
Image Comics: Sept, 2022 - No. 6, Apr, 2023 ($3.99)
1-6-Chuck Brown-s/Prenzy-a — 4.00

FLESH AND BONES
Upshot Graphics (Fantagraphics Books): June, 1986 - No. 4, Dec, 1986 (Limited series)
1-4: Alan Moore scripts (r) & Dalgoda by Fujitake — 4.00

FLESH CRAWLERS
Kitchen Sink Press: Aug, 1993 - No. 3, 1995 ($2.50, B&W, limited series, mature)
1-3 — 4.00

FLEX MENTALLO (Man of Muscle Mystery) (See Doom Patrol, 2nd Series)
DC Comics (Vertigo): Jun, 1996 - No. 4, Sept, 1996 ($2.50, lim. series, mature)
1-4: Grant Morrison scripts & Frank Quitely-c/a in all; banned from reprints due to Charles Atlas legal action

	2	4	6	9	13	16

FLINCH (Horror anthology)
DC Comics (Vertigo): Jun, 1999 - No. 16, Jan, 2001 ($2.50)
1-16: 1-Art by Jim Lee, Quitely, and Corben. 5-Sale-c. 11-Timm-a — 4.00

FLINTSTONE KIDS, THE (TV) (See Star Comics Digest)
Star Comics/Marvel Comics #5 on: Aug, 1987 - No. 11, Apr, 1989

	1	3	4	6	8	10
2-11						5.00

FLINTSTONES, THE (TV)(See Dell Giant #48 for No. 1)
Dell Publ. Co./Gold Key No. 7 (10/62) on: No. 2, Nov-Dec, 1961 - No. 60, Sept, 1970 (Hanna-Barbera)
2-2nd app. (TV show debuted on 9/30/60); 1st app. of Cave Kids; 15¢-c thru #5

	13	26	39	91	201	310
3-6(7-8/62): 3-Perry Gunnite begins. 6-1st 12¢-c	8	16	24	52	99	145
7 (10/62; 1st GK)	8	16	24	56	108	160
8-10	5	10	15	35	63	90
11-1st app. Pebbles (6/63)	9	18	27	62	126	190
12-15,17-20	4	8	12	28	47	65
16-1st app. Bamm-Bamm (1/64)	9	18	27	61	123	185
21-23,25-30,33: 26,27-2nd & 3rd app. The Grusomes. 30-1st app. Martian Mopheads (10/65).						
33-Meet Frankenstein & Dracula	4	8	12	27	44	60
24-1st app. The Grusomes	7	14	21	46	86	125
31,32,35-40: 31-Xmas-c. 36-Adaptation of "the Man Called Flintstone" movie. 39-Reprints						
34-1st app. The Great Gazoo	7	14	21	46	86	125
41-60: 46-Last 12¢ issue	3	6	9	20	31	42

At N. Y. World's Fair ('64)-J.W. Books (25¢)-1st printing; no date on-c (29¢ version exists,

---

2nd print?) Most H-B characters app.; including Yogi Bear, Top Cat, Snagglepuss and the Jetsons

	6	12	18	41	76	110

At N. Y. World's Fair (1965 on-c; re-issue; Warren Pub.)
NOTE: Warehouse find in 1984.

	3	6	9	14	20	25

Bigger & Boulder 1(#30013-211) (Gold Key Giant, 11/62, 25¢, 84 pgs.)

	8	16	24	56	108	160

Bigger & Boulder 2-(1966, 25¢)-Reprints B&B No. 1
...On the Rocks (9/61, $1.00, 6-1/4x9", cardboard-c, high quality paper,116 pgs.)

	4	8	12	25	40	55

B&W new material

	8	16	24	61	123	185

...With Pebbles & Bamm Bamm (100 pgs., G.K.)-30028-511 (paper-c, 25¢) (11/65)

	7	14	21	46	86	125

NOTE: (See Comic Album #16, Bamm-Bamm & Pebbles Flintstone, Dell Giant 48, Golden Comics Digest, March of Comics #229, 243, 271, 289, 299, 317, 327, 341, Pebbles Flintstone, Top Comics #2-4, and Whitman Comic Book.)

FLINTSTONES, THE (TV)(...& Pebbles)
Charlton Comics: Nov, 1970 - No. 50, Feb, 1977 (Hanna-Barbera)

1	7	14	21	44	82	120
2	4	8	12	27	44	60
3-7,9,10	3	6	9	19	30	40
8- "Flintstones Summer Vacation" (Summer, 1971, 52 pgs.)						
	5	10	15	31	53	75
11-20,36: 36-Mike Zeck illos (early work)	3	6	9	16	23	30
21-35,38-41,43-45	3	6	9	14	19	24
37-Byrne text illos (early work; see Nightmare #20)	3	6	9	16	23	30
42-Byrne-a (2 pgs.)	3	6	9	16	23	30
46-50	2	4	6	13	18	22
Digest nn (1972, B&W, 100 pgs.) (low print run)	3	6	9	19	30	40

(Also see Barney & Betty Rubble, Dino, The Great Gazoo, & Pebbles & Bamm-Bamm)

FLINTSTONES, THE (TV)(See Yogi Bear, 3rd series) (Newsstand sales only)
Marvel Comics Group: October, 1977 - No. 9, Feb, 1979 (Hanna-Barbera)

1-(30¢-c)	5	10	15	30	50	70
1-(35¢-c variant, limited distribution)	9	18	27	62	126	190
2,3,5,6: Yogi Bear app.	3	6	9	15	22	28
4-The Jetsons app.	3	6	9	16	24	32
7-9-Yogi Bear app.	3	6	9	19	30	40

FLINTSTONES, THE (TV)
Harvey Comics: Sept, 1992 - No. 13, Jun, 1994 ($1.25/$1.50) (Hanna-Barbera)

V2#1	1	3	4	6	8	10
V2#2-13						5.00
...Big Book 1,2 (11/92, 3/93; both $1.95, 52 pgs.)	2	4	6	11	16	20
...Giant Size 1-3 (10/92, 4/93, 11/93; $2.25, 68 pgs.)	1	3	4	6	8	10

FLINTSTONES, THE (TV)
Archie Publications: Sept, 1995 - No. 22, June, 1997 ($1.50)

1	1	3	4	6	8	10
2-22						4.00

FLINTSTONES, THE (TV)
DC Comics: Sept, 2016 - No. 12, Aug, 2017 ($3.99)
1-12: 1-6,8-12-Mark Russell-s/Steve Pugh-a; multiple covers. 2-Intro. Dino. 7-Leonardi-a; Great Gazoo app. 11-Jill Thompson-c. 11,12-Great Gazoo app. — 4.00

FLINTSTONES AND THE JETSONS, THE (TV)
DC Comics: Aug, 1997 - No. 21, May, 1999 ($1.75/$1.95/$1.99)

1	1	3	4	6	8	10
2-21: 19-Bizarro Elroy-c						4.00

FLINTSTONES CHRISTMAS PARTY, THE (See The Funtastic World of Hanna-Barbera No. 1)

FLIP
Harvey Publications: April, 1954 - No. 2, June, 1954 (Satire)

1-Nostrand-a	27	54	81	189	420	650
2-Nostrand & Powell-a	17	34	51	117	259	400

FLIPPER (TV)
Gold Key: Apr, 1966 - No. 3, Nov, 1967 (All have photo-c)

1	6	12	18	41	76	110
2,3	4	8	12	28	47	65

FLIPPITY & FLOP
National Per. Publ. (Signal Publ. Co.): 12-1/51-52 - No. 46, 8-10/59; No. 47, 9-11/60
1-Sam dog & his pets Flippity The Bird and Flop The Cat begin; Twiddle and Twaddle begin

	42	84	126	265	445	625
2	20	40	60	120	195	270
3-5	15	30	45	88	137	185
6-10	14	28	42	82	121	160
11-20: 20-Last precode (3/55)	12	24	36	69	97	125
21-47	10	20	30	58	79	100

FLOYD FARLAND (See Eclipse Graphic Album Series #11)

FLY, THE (Also see Adventures of..., Blue Ribbon Comics & Flyman)
Archie Enterprises, Inc.: May, 1983 - No. 9, Oct, 1984
1,2: 1-Mr. Justice app; origin Shield; Kirby-a; Steranko-c. 2-Ditko-c; Flygirl app. — 6.00
3-5: Ditko-a in all. 4,5-Ditko-c(p) — 5.00
6-9: Ditko-a in all. 6-8-Ditko-c(p) — 6.00
NOTE: Ayers c-9. Buckler a-1, 2. Kirby a-1. Nebres c-3, 4, 5i, 6, 7i. Steranko c-1, 2.

FLY, THE
Impact Comics (DC): Aug, 1991 - No. 17, Dec, 1992 ($1.00)
1 — 5.00
2-17: 4-Vs. The Black Hood. 9-Trading card inside — 4.00
Annual 1 ('92, $2.50, 68 pgs.)-Impact trading card — 5.00

FLYBOY (Flying Cadets)(Also see Approved Comics #5)
Ziff-Davis Publ. Co. (Approved): Spring, 1952 - No. 2, Oct-Nov, 1952

1-Saunders painted-c	26	52	78	154	252	350
2-(10-11/52) Saunders painted-c	17	34	51	100	158	215

FLYING ACES (Aviation stories)
Key Publications: July, 1955 - No. 5, Mar, 1956

Flash: Rebirth #5 © DC

Flintstones (2016 series) #3 © H-B

FOOM #22 © MAR

	GD 2.0	VG 4.0	FN 6.0	VF 8.0	VF/NM 9.0	NM- 9.2
1	14	28	42	78	112	145
2-5: 2-Trapani-a	9	18	27	47	61	75

FLYING A'S RANGE RIDER, THE (TV)(See Western Roundup under Dell Giants)
Dell Publishing Co.: #404, 6-7/52; #2, June-Aug, 1953 - #24, Aug, 1959 (All photo-c)

Four Color 404(#1)-Titled "The Range Rider"	10	20	30	68	144	220
2	6	12	18	38	69	100
3-10	5	10	15	34	60	85
11-16,18-24	5	10	15	30	50	70
17-Toth-a	5	10	15	34	60	85

FLYING CADET (WW II Plane Photos)
Flying Cadet Publ. Co.: Jan, 1943 - V2#8, Nov, 1944 (Half photos, half comics)

V1#1-Painted-c	22	44	66	132	216	300
2-Photo-c, P-47 Thunderbolt	14	28	42	76	108	140
3-9 (Two #6's, Sept. & Oct.): 4,5,6a,6b-Photo-c	13	26	39	72	101	130
V2#1-7 (1/44-9/44)(#10-16): 1,2,4,7-Photo-c	12	24	36	67	94	120
7 (#17 on cover)-Bare-breasted woman-c	55	110	165	352	601	850

FLYING COLORS 10th ANNIVERSARY SPECIAL
Flying Colors Comics: Fall 1998 ($2.95, one-shot)

1-Dan Brereton-c; pin-ups by Jim Lee and Jeff Johnson						4.00

FLYIN' JENNY
Pentagon Publ. Co./Leader Enterprises #2: 1946 - No. 2, 1947 (1945 strip-r)

nn-Marcus Swayze strip-r (entire insides)	28	56	84	168	274	380
2-Baker-c; Swayze strip reprints	65	130	195	416	708	1000

FLYING MODELS
H-K Publ. (Health-Knowledge Publs.): V61#3, May, 1954 (5¢, 16 pgs.)

V61#3 (Rare)	16	32	48	94	147	200

FLYING NUN (TV)
Dell Publishing Co.: Feb, 1968 - No. 4, Nov, 1968

1-Sally Field photo-c	9	18	27	58	114	170
2-4: 2-Sally Field photo-c	5	10	15	31	53	75

FLYING NURSES (See Sue & Sally Smith...)

FLYING SAUCERS (See The Spirit 9/28/47(1st app.), Shadow Comics V7#10 (2nd, 1/48), Captain Midnight #60 (3rd, 2/48), Boy Commandos #26 (4th, 3-4/48) & Flash Gordon Four Color 190 (5th, 6/48))

FLYING SAUCERS (See Out of This World Adventures #2)
Avon Periodicals/Realistic: 1950; 1952; 1953

1(1950)-Wood-a, 21 pgs.; Fawcette-c	145	290	435	921	1586	2250
nn(1952)-Cover altered plus 2 pgs. of Wood-a not in original						
	81	162	243	518	884	1250
nn(1953)-Reprints above (exist?)	74	148	222	470	810	1150

FLYING SAUCERS (Comics)
Dell Publishing Co.: April, 1967 - No. 4, Nov, 1967; No. 5, Oct, 1969

1-(12¢-c)	11	22	33	73	157	240
2-5: 5-Has same cover as #1, but with 15¢ price	5	10	15	31	53	75

FLY MAN (Formerly Adventures of The Fly; Mighty Comics #40 on)
Mighty Comics Group (Radio Comics) (Archie): No. 32, July, 1965 - No. 39, Sept, 1966 (Also see Mighty Crusaders)

32,33-Comet, Shield, Black Hood, The Fly & Flygirl x-over. 33-Re-intro wizard, Hangman (1st S.A. appearances)	6	12	18	37	66	95
34-39: 34-Shield begins. 35-Origin Black Hood. 36-Hangman x-over in Shield; re-intro. & origin of Web (1st S.A. app.). 37-Hangman, Wizard x-over in Flyman; last Shield issue. 38-Web story. 39-Steel Sterling (1st S.A. app.)	4	8	12	34	47	65

FLY, THE ; OUTBREAK (Sequel to the 1986 and 1989 movies)
IDW Publishing: Mar, 2015 - No. 5, Nov, 2015 ($3.99)

1-5-Martin Brundle's story continues; Brandon Seifert-s/Menton3-a; multiple covers						4.00

FOLKLORDS
BOOM! Studios: Nov, 2019 - No. 5 ($3.99, limited series)

1-5-Matt Kindt-s/Matt Smith-a						4.00

FOLLOW ME DOWN: A RECKLESS BOOK
Image Comics: Oct, 2022 ($24.99, HC graphic novel)

HC - Ed Brubaker-s/Sean Phillips-a; 5th book in the Reckless series						25.00

FOLLOW THE SUN (TV)
Dell Publishing Co.: May-July, 1962 - No. 2, Sept-Nov, 1962 (Photo-c)

01-280-207(No.1)	5	10	15	31	53	75
12-280-211(No.2)	4	8	12	28	47	65

FOODINI (TV)(The Great...; see Jingle Dingle & Pinhead &...)
Continental Publ. (Holyoke): March, 1950 - No. 4, Aug, 1950 (All have 52 pgs.)

	GD 2.0	VG 4.0	FN 6.0	VF 8.0	VF/NM 9.0	NM- 9.2
1-Based on TV puppet show (very early TV comic)	29	58	87	172	281	390
2-Jingle Dingle begins	16	32	48	94	147	200
3,4	14	28	42	80	115	150

FOOEY (Magazine) (Satire)
Scoff Publishing Co.: Feb, 1961 - No. 4, May, 1961

1	6	12	18	37	66	95
2-4	3	6	9	21	33	45

FOOFUR (TV)
Marvel Comics (Star Comics)/Marvel No. 5 on: Aug, 1987 - No. 6, Jun, 1988

1-6						5.00

FOOLKILLER (Also see The Amazing Spider-Man #225, The Defenders #73, Man-Thing #3 & Omega the Unknown #8)
Marvel Comics: Oct, 1990 - No. 10, Oct, 1991 ($1.75, limited series)

1-10: 1-Origin 3rd Foolkiller; Greg Salinger app; DeZuniga-a(i) in 1-4. 8-Spider-Man x-over						4.00

FOOLKILLER
Marvel Comics: Dec, 2007 - No. 5, Jul, 2008 ($3.99, limited series)

1-5-Hurwitz-s/Medina-a. 2-Origin						4.00

FOOLKILLER
Marvel Comics: Jan, 2017 - No. 5, May, 2017 ($3.99, limited series)

1-5-Max Bemis-s/Dalibor Talajic-a. 4-Deadpool app. 5-The Hood app.						4.00

FOOLKILLER: WHITE ANGELS
Marvel Comics: Sept, 2008 - No. 5, Jan, 2009 ($3.99, limited series)

1-5-Hurwitz-s/Azaceta-a						4.00

FOOM (Friends Of Ol' Marvel)
Marvel Comics: 1973 - No. 22, 1979 (Marvel fan magazine)

1	9	18	27	63	129	195
2-Hulk-c by Steranko; Wolverine prototype	21	42	63	147	324	500
3,4	6	12	18	38	69	100
5-Deathlok preview	6	12	18	42	79	115
6-9,11: 11-Kirby-a & interview	5	10	15	34	60	85
10-Article on new X-Men that came out before Giant-Size X-Men #1; new X-Men cover by Dave Cockrum	93	186	279	744	1672	2600
12-15: 11-Star-Lord preview. 12-Vision-c. 13-Daredevil-c. 14-Conan. 15-Howard the Duck; preview of Ms. Marvel & Capt. Britain	5	10	15	34	60	85
16-20: 16-Marvel bullpen. 17-Stan Lee issue. 19-Defenders	5	10	15	31	53	75
21-Star Wars	6	12	18	38	69	100
22-Spider-Man-c; low print run final issue	7	14	21	44	82	120

FOOTBALL THRILLS (See Tops In Adventure)
Ziff-Davis Publ. Co.: Fall-Winter, 1951-52 - No. 2, Fall, 1952 (Edited by "Red" Grange)

1-Powell a(2); Saunders painted-c; Red Grange, Jim Thorpe stories						
	37	74	111	222	361	500
2-Saunders painted-c	22	44	66	132	216	300

FOOT SOLDIERS, THE
Dark Horse Comics: Jan, 1996 - No. 4, Apr, 1996 ($2.95, limited series)

1-4: Krueger story & Avon Oeming-a. in all. 4-Alex Ross-c. 4-John K. Snyder, III-c						4.00

FOOT SOLDIERS, THE (Volume Two)
Image Comics: Sept, 1997 - No. 5, May, 1998 ($2.95, limited series)

1-5: 1-Yeowell-a. 2-McDaniel, Hester, Sienkiewicz, Giffen-a						4.00

FOR A NIGHT OF LOVE
Avon Periodicals: 1951

nn-Two stories adapted from the works of Emile Zola; Astarita, Ravielli-a; Kinstler-c						
	47	94	141	296	498	700

FORBIDDEN BRIDES OF THE FACELESS SLAVES IN THE SECRET HOUSE OF THE NIGHT OF DREAD DESIRE (Neil Gaiman's...)
Dark Horse Books: 2017 ($17.99, HC graphic novel)

HC-Neil Gaiman-s/Shane Oakley-a						18.00

FORBIDDEN KNOWLEDGE: ADVENTURE BEYOND THE DOORWAY TO SOULS WITH RADICAL DREAMER (Also see Radical Dreamer)
Mark's Giant Economy Size Comics: 1996 ($3.50, B&W, one-shot, 48 pgs.)

nn-Max Wrighter app.; Wheatley-c/a/script; painted infinity-c						4.00

FORBIDDEN LOVE
Quality Comics Group: Mar, 1950 - No. 4, Sept, 1950 (52 pgs.)

1-(Scarce)-Classic photo-c; Crandall-a	174	348	522	1114	1907	2700
2-(Scarce)-Classic photo-c	103	206	309	659	1130	1600
3-(Scarce)-Photo-c	90	180	270	576	988	1400

	GD	VG	FN	VF	VF/NM	NM-
	2.0	4.0	6.0	8.0	9.0	9.2

4-(Scarce)-Ward/Cuidera-a; photo-c 100 200 300 635 1093 1550

FORBIDDEN LOVE (See Dark Mansion of…)

FORBIDDEN PLANET
Innovation Publishing: May, 1992 - No. 4, 1992 ($2.50, limited series)
1-4: Adapts movie; painted-c 4.00

FORBIDDEN TALES OF DARK MANSION (Formerly Dark Mansion of Forbidden Love #1-4)
National Periodical Publ.: No. 5, May-June, 1972 - No. 15, Feb-Mar, 1974
5-(52 pgs.) 6 12 18 38 69 100
6-15: 13-Kane/Howard-a 3 6 9 17 26 35
NOTE: N. Adams c-9. Alcala a-9-11, 13. Chaykin a-7,15. Evans a-14. Heck a-5. Kaluta a-7i, 8-12; c-7, 8, 13. G. Kane a-13. Kirby a-6. Nino a-8, 12, 15. Redondo a-14.

FORBIDDEN WORLDS
American Comics Group: 7-8/51 - No. 34, 10-11/54; No. 35, 8/55 - No. 145, 8/67 (No. 1-5: 52 pgs.; No. 6-8: 44 pgs.)
1-Williamson/Frazetta-a (10 pgs.) 194 388 582 1242 2121 3000
2 81 162 243 518 884 1250
3-Williamson/Wood-a (7 pgs.); Frazetta (1 panel) 77 154 231 493 847 1200
4 53 106 159 334 567 800
5-Krenkel/Williamson-a (8 pgs.) 58 116 174 371 636 900
6-Harrison/Williamson (8 pgs.) 53 106 159 334 567 800
7,8,10: 7-1st monthly issue 39 78 117 231 378 525
9-A-Bomb explosion story 39 78 117 234 385 535
11-20 26 52 78 154 252 350
21-23,25-33 21 42 63 122 199 275
24-E.C. swipe by Landau 68 136 204 435 743 1050
34(10-11/54)(Scarce)(becomes Young Heroes #35 on)-Last pre-code issue; A-Bomb explosion story 28 56 84 165 270 375
35(8/55)-Scarce 24 48 72 142 234 325
36-62 14 28 42 82 121 160
63,69,76,78-Williamson-a in all; w/Krenkel #69 15 30 45 83 124 165
64,66-68,70-72,74,75,77,79-85,87-90 11 22 33 60 83 105
65- "There's a New Moon Tonight" listed in #114 as holding 1st record fan mail response 15 30 45 90 140 190
73-1st app. Herbie by Ogden Whitney 71 142 213 454 777 1100
86-Flying saucer-c by Schaffenberger 12 24 36 67 94 120
91-93,95-100 5 10 15 34 60 85
94-Herbie (2nd app.) 14 28 42 96 211 325
101-109,111-113,115,117-120 4 8 12 28 44 60
110,116-Herbie app. 116-Herbie goes to Hell; Elizabeth Taylor-c 8 16 24 56 108 160
114-1st Herbie-c; contains list of editor's top 20 ACG stories 12 24 36 82 179 275
121-123 3 6 9 21 33 45
124,127-130: 124-Magic Agent app. 4 8 12 23 37 50
125-Magic Agent app.; intro. & origin Magicman series, ends #141; Herbie app. 5 10 15 33 57 80
126-Herbie app. 4 8 12 28 47 65
131-139: 133-Origin/1st app. Dragonia in Magicman (1-2/66); returns in #138. 136-Nemesis x-over in Magicman 6 9 21 33 45
140-Mark Midnight app. by Ditko 4 8 12 23 37 50
141-145 3 6 9 19 30 40
NOTE: Buscema a-75, 79, 81, 82, 140r. Cameron a-5. Disbrow a-10. Ditko a-137p, 138, 140. Landau a-24, 27-29, 31-34, 48, 86r, 96, 143-45. Lazarus a-18, 23, 24, 57. Moldoff a-27, 31, 139r. Reinman a-93. Whitney a-70, 115, 116, 137; c-40, 46, 57, 60, 68, 70, 78, 79, 90, 93, 94, 100, 102, 103, 106-108, 114, 129.

FORCE, THE (See The Crusaders)

FORCE MAJEURE: PRAIRIE BAY (Also see Wild Stars)
Little Rocket Publications: May, 2002 ($2.95, B&W)
1-Tierney-s/Gil-c/a 3.00

FORCE OF BUDDHA'S PALM THE
Jademan Comics: Aug, 1988 - No. 55, Feb, 1993 ($1.50/$1.95, 68 pgs.)
1,55-Kung Fu stories in all 5.00
2-54 4.00

FORCE WORKS
Marvel Comics: July, 1994 - No. 22, Apr, 1996 ($1.50)
1-($3.95)-Fold-out pop-up-c; Iron Man, Wonder Man, Spider-Woman, U.S. Agent & Scarlet Witch (new costume) 5.00
2-11, 13-22: 5-Blue logo & pink logo versions. 9-Intro Dreamguard. 13-Avengers app. 4.00
5-Pink logo ($2.95)-polybagged w/ 16pg. Marvel Action Hour Preview & acetate print 5.00
12 ($2.50)-Flip book w/War Machine. 5.00

FORD ROTUNDA CHRISTMAS BOOK (See Christmas at the Rotunda)

FOREIGN INTRIGUES (Formerly Johnny Dynamite; becomes Battlefield Action #16 on)
Charlton Comics: No. 14, 1956 - No. 15, Aug, 1956
14,15-Johnny Dynamite continues 10 20 30 58 79 100

FOREMOST BOYS (See 4Most)

FOREVER DARLING (Movie)
Dell Publishing Co.: No. 681, Feb, 1956
Four Color 681-w/Lucille Ball & Desi Arnaz; photo-c 11 22 33 77 166 255

FOREVER EVIL (See Justice League #23 (2013))
DC Comics: Nov, 2013 - No. 7, Jul, 2014 ($3.99, limited series)
1-Earth Three Crime Syndicate takes over; Nightwing unmasked; Johns-s/Finch-a 4.00
1-Director's Cut 1 (12/13, $5.99) Pencil artwork with full script 6.00
2-6: 2-Luthor dons the green battlesuit. 4-Sinestro returns 4.00
7-($4.99) 5.00
… Aftermath: Batman vs. Bane 1 (6/14, $3.99) Tomasi-s/Eaton-a 4.00

FOREVER EVIL: A.R.G.U.S.
DC Comics: Dec, 2013 - No. 6, May, 2014 ($2.99, limited series)
1-6-Gates-s. Steve Trevor in search of missing heroes. 1,2-Deathstroke app. 3.00

FOREVER EVIL: ARKHAM WAR
DC Comics: Dec, 2013 - No. 6, May, 2014 ($2.99, limited series)

1-6-Tomasi-s/Eaton-a; Bane and the Arkham inmates. 4-6-The Talons app. 4.00

FOREVER EVIL: ROGUES REBELLION
DC Comics: Dec, 2013 - No. 6, May, 2014 ($2.99, limited series)
1-6-Buccellato-s/Hepburn/Shalvey-a. 2-Deathstorm & Power Ring app. 6-Grodd app. 3.00

FOREVER MAELSTROM
DC Comics: Jan, 2003 - No. 6, Jun, 2003 ($2.95, limited series)
1-6-Chaykin & Tischman-s/Lucas & Barreto-a 3.00

FOREVER PEOPLE, THE
National Periodical Publications: Feb-Mar, 1971 - No. 11, Oct-Nov, 1972 (Fourth World) (#1-3, 10-11 are 36 pgs.; #4-9 are 52 pgs.)
1-1st app. Forever People; Superman x-over; Kirby-c/a begins; 1st full app. Darkseid (3rd anywhere, 3 weeks before New Gods #1); Darkseid storyline begins, ends #8 (app. in 1-4,6,8; cameos in 5,11) 18 36 54 124 275 425
2-9: G.A. reprints thru #9. 9,10-Deadman app. 4 8 12 28 47 65
10,11 3 6 9 22 35 45
Jack Kirby's Forever People TPB (1999, $14.95, B&W&Grey) r/#1-11 plus bonus cover gallery 15.00
NOTE: Kirby c/a(p)-1-11; #4-9 contain Sandman reprints from Adventure #85, 84, 75, 80, 77, 74 in that order.

FOREVER PEOPLE
DC Comics: Feb, 1988 - No. 6, July, 1988 ($1.25, limited series)
1-6 4.00

FORGE
CrossGeneration Comics: Feb, 2002 - No. 13, May, 2003 ($9.95/$11.95/$7.95, TPB)
1-3: Reprints from various CrossGen titles 10.00
4-8-($11.95) 12.00
9-13-($7.95, 8-1/4" x 5-1/2") digest-sized reprints 8.00

FORGED, THE
Image Comics: Mar, 2023 - Present (oversized 10-7/8 x 8-1/2", $5.99/$6.99)
1-3-($5.99) Rucka-s/Trautmann-a 6.00
4-7-($6.99) 7.00

FOR GIRLS ONLY
Bernard Baily Enterprises: 11/53 - No. 2, 6/54 (100 pgs., digest size, 25¢)
1-25% comic book, 75% articles, illos, games 43 86 129 271 461 650
2-Eddie Fisher photo & story 37 74 111 222 361 500

FORGOTTEN FOREST OF OZ, THE (See First Comics Graphic Novel #16)

FORGOTTEN QUEEN, THE
Valiant Entertainment: Feb, 2019 - No. 4, May, 2019 ($3.99, limited series)
1-4-Tini Howard-s/Amilcar Pinna-a 4.00

FORGOTTEN REALMS (Also see Avatar & TSR Worlds)
DC Comics: Sept, 1989 - No. 25, Sept, 1991 ($1.50/$1.75)
1, Annual 1 (1990, $2.95, 68 pgs.) 5.00
2-25: Based on TSR role-playing game. 18-Avatar story 4.00

FORGOTTEN REALMS (Based on Wizards of the Coast game)
Devil's Due Publ.: June, 2005 - No. 3, Aug, 2005 ($4.95)
1-3-Salvatore-s/Seeley-a 5.00
…Exile (11/05 - No. 3, 1/06, $4.95) 1-3-Daab-s/Seeley-a. 1-Flip cover 5.00
…: Legacy (2/08 - No. 3, 6/08, $5.50) 1-3-Daab-s/Atkins-a 5.50
The Legend of Drizzt Book II: Exile (2006, $14.95, TPB) r/#1-3 15.00
…Sojourn (3/06 - No. 3, 6/06, $4.95) 1-3-Daab-s/Seeley-a 5.00
…: Streams of Silver (12/06 - No. 3, $5.50) 1-3-Daab-s/Semeiks-a 5.50
…The Crystal Shard (8/06 - No. 3, 12/06, $4.95) 1-3-Daab-s/Semeiks-a 5.00
…The Halfling's Gem (8/07 - No. 3, $5.50) 1-3-Daab-s/Seeley-a; two covers 5.50

FORLORN RIVER (See Zane Grey Four Color 395)

FOR LOVERS ONLY (Formerly Hollywood Romances)
Charlton Comics: No. 60, Aug, 1971 - No. 87, Nov, 1976
60 3 6 9 21 33 45
61-80,82-87: 67-Morisi-a 3 6 9 14 20 25
81-Psychedelic cover 3 6 9 17 26 35

FORMERLY KNOWN AS THE JUSTICE LEAGUE
DC Comics: Sept, 2003 - No. 6, Feb, 2004 ($2.50, limited series)
1-Giffen & DeMatteis-s/Maguire-a; Booster Gold, Blue Beetle, Captain Atom, Mary Marvel, Fire, and Elongated Man app. 4.00
2-6: 3,4-Roulette app. 6-JLA app. 3.00
TPB (2004, $12.95) r/#1-6 13.00

FORMIC WARS: BURNING EARTH
Marvel Comics: Apr, 2011 - No. 7, 2011 ($3.99, limited series)
1-7-Prequel to Orson Scott Card's novel Ender's Game. 1-Covers by Larroca & Hitch 4.00

FORMIC WARS: SILENT STRIKE (Follows Burning Earth limited series)
Marvel Comics: Feb, 2012 - No. 5, Jun, 2012 ($3.99, limited series)
1-5-Johnston-s/Caracuzzo-a/Camuncoli-c 4.00

FORTNITE X MARVEL: ZERO WAR (Polybagged with digital code)
Marvel Comics: Aug, 2022 - No. 5, Nov, 2022 ($5.99/$4.99, limited series)
1,5-($5.99) Spider-Man, Wolverine & Doctor Doom app.; Dávila-a 6.00
2-4-($4.99) 2,3-Avengers app. 5.00

FORT: PROPHET OF THE UNEXPLAINED
Dark Horse Comics: June, 2002 - No. 4, Sept, 2002 ($2.99, B&W, limited series)
1-4-Peter Lenkov-s/Frazer Irving-c/a 3.00
TPB (2003, $9.95) r/#1-4 10.00

FORTUNE AND GLORY
Oni Press: Dec, 1999 - No. 3, Apr, 2000 ($4.95, B&W, limited series)
1-3-Brian Michael Bendis in Hollywood 5.00
TPB ($14.95) 15.00

40 BIG PAGES OF MICKEY MOUSE
Whitman Publ. Co.: No. 945, Jan, 1936 (10-1/4x12-1/2", 44 pgs., cardboard-c)

Forever Evil #4 © DC

Forgotten Queen #1 © VAL

Four Color Comics #31 © DELL

	GD 2.0	VG 4.0	FN 6.0	VF 8.0	VF/NM 9.0	NM- 9.2

945-Reprints Mickey Mouse Magazine #1, but with a different cover; ads were eliminated and some illustrated stories had expanded text. The book is ¾" shorter than Mickey Mouse Mag. #1, but the reprints are same size (Rare)   200   400   600   1280   2190   3100

47 RONIN
Dark Horse Comics: Nov, 2012 - No. 5, Jul, 2013 ($3.99, limited series)
  1-5-Mike Richardson-s/Stan Sakai-a/c; 18th century samurai legend   4.00

FOR YOUR EYES ONLY (See James Bond...)

FOUNTAIN, THE (Companion graphic novel to the Darren Aronofsky film)
DC Comics (Vertigo): 2005 ($39.99, hardcover with dust jacket)
  1-Darren Aronofsky-s/Kent Williams-a   40.00

FOUR (Fantastic Four; See Marvel Knights 4 #28-30)

FOUR COLOR
Dell Publishing Co.: Sept?, 1939 - No. 1354, Apr-June, 1962
(Series I are all 68 pgs.)

NOTE: Four Color only appears on issues #19-25, 1-99,101. Dell Publishing Co. filed these as Series I, #1-25, and Series II, #1-1354. Issues beginning with #710? were printed with and without ads on back cover. Issues without ads are worth more.

SERIES I:
1(nn)-Dick Tracy   1160   2320   3480   8800   16,900   25,000
2(nn)-Don Winslow of the Navy (#1) (Rare) (11/39?)
    265   530   795   1694   2897   4100
3(nn)-Myra North (1/40)   135   270   405   864   1482   2100
4-Donald Duck by Al Taliaferro (1940)(Disney)(3/40?)
    2700   5400   8100   20,250   37,125   54,000
    (Prices vary widely on this book)
5-Smilin' Jack (#1) (5/40?)   103   206   309   659   1130   1600
6-Dick Tracy (Scarce)   290   580   870   1856   3178   4500
7-Gang Busters   77   154   231   493   847   1200
8-Dick Tracy   161   322   483   1030   1765   2500
9-Terry and the Pirates-r/Super #9-29   90   180   270   576   988   1400
10-Smilin' Jack   84   168   252   538   919   1300
11-Smitty (#1)   65   130   195   416   708   1000
12-Little Orphan Annie; reprints strips from 12/19/37 to 6/4/38
    90   180   270   576   988   1400
13-Walt Disney's Reluctant Dragon('41)-Contains 2 pgs. of photos from film; 2 pg. foreword to Fantasia by Leopold Stokowski; Donald Duck, Goofy, Baby Weems & Mickey Mouse (as the Sorcerer's Apprentice) app. (Disney)   239   478   717   1530   2615   3700
14-Moon Mullins (#1)   58   116   174   371   636   900
15-Tillie the Toiler (#1)   81   162   243   518   884   1250
16-Mickey Mouse (#1) (Disney) by Gottfredson   1550   3100   4650   20,150   --   --
17-Walt Disney's Dumbo, the Flying Elephant (#1)(1941)-Mickey Mouse, Donald Duck, & Pluto app. (Disney)   290   580   870   1856   3178   4500
18-Jiggs and Maggie (#1)(1936-38-r)   63   126   189   403   689   975
19-Barney Google and Snuffy Smith (#1)-(1st issue with Four Color on the cover)
    61   122   183   390   670   950
20-Tiny Tim   50   100   150   315   533   750
21-Dick Tracy   103   206   309   659   1130   1600
22-Don Winslow   61   122   183   390   670   950
23-Gang Busters   58   116   174   371   636   900
24-Captain Easy   65   130   195   416   708   1000
25-Popeye (1941)   123   246   369   787   1344   1900

SERIES II:
1-Little Joe (1942)   79   158   237   632   1416   2200
2-Harold Teen   38   76   114   285   641   1000
3-Alley Oop (#1)   57   114   171   456   1028   1600
4-Smilin' Jack   81   162   243   518   884   1250
5-Raggedy Ann and Andy (#1)   52   104   156   416   933   1450
6-Smitty   36   72   108   259   580   900
7-Smokey Stover (#1)   27   54   81   194   435   675
8-Tillie the Toiler   29   58   87   209   467   725
9-Donald Duck Finds Pirate Gold, by Carl Barks & Jack Hannah (Disney) (© 8/17/42)   1050   2100   3150   8000   14,500   21,000
10-Flash Gordon by Alex Raymond; reprinted from "The Ice Kingdom"
    96   192   288   768   1734   2700
11-Wash Tubbs   27   54   81   194   435   675
12-Walt Disney's Bambi (#1)   54   108   162   432   956   1500
13-Mr. District Attorney (#1)-See The Funnies #35 for 1st app.
    38   76   114   281   628   975
14-Smilin' Jack   35   70   105   252   564   875
15-Felix the Cat (#1)   89   178   267   712   1606   2500
16-Porky Pig (#1)(1942)- "Secret of the Haunted House"

| | 107 | 214 | 321 | 856 | 1928 | 3000 |

17-Popeye   54   108   162   432   966   1500
18-Little Orphan Annie's Junior Commandos; Flag-c; reprints strips from 6/14/42 to 11/21/42   71   142   213   454   777   1100
19-Walt Disney's Thumper Meets the Seven Dwarfs (Disney); reprinted in Silly Symphonies
    54   108   162   432   966   1500
20-Barney Baxter   29   58   87   209   467   725
21-Oswald the Rabbit (#1)(1943)   46   92   138   359   805   1250
22-Tillie the Toiler   20   40   60   138   307   475
23-Raggedy Ann and Andy   35   70   105   252   564   875
24-Gang Busters   34   68   102   245   548   850
25-Andy Panda (#1) (Walter Lantz)   46   92   138   340   770   1200
26-Popeye   54   108   162   432   966   1500
27-Walt Disney's Mickey Mouse and the Seven Colored Terror
    82   164   246   656   1478   2300
28-Wash Tubbs   19   38   57   131   291   450
29-Donald Duck and the Mummy's Ring, by Carl Barks (9/43)
    811   1622   2433   5920   10,460   15,000
30-Bambi's Children (1943)-Disney   44   88   132   326   738   1150
31-Moon Mullins   18   36   54   125   276   430
32-Smitty   18   36   54   128   284   440
33-Bugs Bunny "Public Nuisance #1"   136   272   408   1088   2444   3800
34-Dick Tracy   42   84   126   311   706   1100
35-Smokey Stover   17   34   51   119   265   410
36-Smilin' Jack   23   46   69   164   362   560
37-Bringing Up Father   21   42   63   147   324   500
38-Roy Rogers (#1, © 4/44)-1st western comic with photo-c (see Movie Comics #3)   155   310   465   1279   2890   4500
39-Oswald the Rabbit (1944)   29   58   87   209   467   725
40-Barney Google and Snuffy Smith   21   42   63   147   324   500
41-Mother Goose and Nursery Rhyme Comics (#1)-All by Walt Kelly
    27   54   81   189   420   650
42-Tiny Tim (1934-r)   19   38   57   133   294   460
43-Popeye (1938-'42-r)   30   60   90   216   483   750
44-Terry and the Pirates (1938-r)   32   64   96   230   515   800
45-Raggedy Ann   26   52   78   182   404   625
46-Felix the Cat and the Haunted Castle   46   92   138   368   834   1300
47-Gene Autry (copyright 6/16/44)   36   72   108   259   580   900
48-Porky Pig of the Mounties by Carl Barks (7/44)   107   214   321   856   1928   3000
49-Snow White and the Seven Dwarfs (Disney)   52   104   156   413   932   1450
50-Fairy Tale Parade-Walt Kelly art (1944)   21   42   63   147   324   500
51-Bugs Bunny Finds the Lost Treasure   41   82   123   303   689   1075
52-Little Orphan Annie; reprints strips from 6/18/38 to 11/19/38
    27   54   81   189   420   650
53-Wash Tubbs   15   30   45   103   227   350
54-Andy Panda   25   50   75   175   388   600
55-Tillie the Toiler   14   28   42   96   211   325
56-Dick Tracy   34   68   102   247   554   860
57-Gene Autry   30   60   90   216   483   750
58-Smilin' Jack   23   46   69   164   362   560
59-Mother Goose and Nursery Rhyme Comics-Kelly-c/a
    20   40   60   140   310   480
60-Tiny Folks Funnies   18   36   54   124   275   425
61-Santa Claus Funnies(11/44)-Kelly art   27   54   81   189   420   650
62-Donald Duck in Frozen Gold, by Carl Barks (1/45)
    241   482   723   1988   4494   7000
63-Roy Rogers; color photo-all 4 covers   40   80   120   296   673   1050
64-Smokey Stover   13   26   39   89   195   300
65-Smitty   15   30   45   100   220   340
66-Gene Autry   30   60   90   216   483   750
67-Oswald the Rabbit   16   32   48   112   249   385
68-Mother Goose and Nursery Rhyme Comics, by Walt Kelly
    20   40   60   140   310   480
69-Fairy Tale Parade, by Walt Kelly   21   42   63   147   324   500
70-Popeye and Wimpy   25   50   75   175   388   600
71-Walt Disney's Three Caballeros, by Walt Kelly (© 4/45)-(Disney)
    75   150   225   600   1350   2100
72-Raggedy Ann   21   42   63   147   324   500
73-The Gumps (#1)   14   28   42   96   211   325
74-Marge's Little Lulu (#1)   193   386   579   1592   3596   5600
75-Gene Autry and the Wildcat   23   46   69   164   362   560
76-Little Orphan Annie; reprints strips from 2/28/40 to 6/24/40
    20   40   60   144   317   490
77-Felix the Cat   40   80   120   296   673   1050
78-Porky Pig and the Bandit Twins   32   64   96   230   515   800

	GD 2.0	VG 4.0	FN 6.0	VF 8.0	VF/NM 9.0	NM- 9.2
79-Walt Disney's Mickey Mouse in The Riddle of the Red Hat by Carl Barks (8/45)	104	208	312	832	1866	2900
80-Smilin' Jack	14	28	42	93	204	315
81-Moon Mullins	12	24	36	81	176	270
82-Lone Ranger	40	80	120	296	673	1050
83-Gene Autry in Outlaw Trail	23	46	69	164	362	560
84-Flash Gordon by Alex Raymond-Reprints from "The Fiery Desert"	42	84	126	311	706	1100
85-Andy Panda and the Mad Dog Mystery	15	30	45	103	227	350
86-Roy Rogers; photo-c	29	58	87	209	467	725
87-Fairy Tale Parade by Walt Kelly; Dan Noonan-c	21	42	63	147	324	500
88-Bugs Bunny's Great Adventure (Sci/fi)	26	52	78	182	404	625
89-Tillie the Toiler	14	28	42	96	211	325
90-Christmas with Mother Goose by Walt Kelly (11/45)	16	32	48	111	246	380
91-Santa Claus Funnies by Walt Kelly (11/45)	18	36	54	128	284	440
92-Walt Disney's The Wonderful Adventures Of Pinocchio (1945); Donald Duck by Kelly, 16 pgs. (Disney)	54	108	162	432	966	1500
93-Gene Autry in The Bandit of Black Rock	19	38	57	133	297	460
94-Winnie Winkle (1945)	14	28	42	96	211	325
95-Roy Rogers Comics; photo-c	29	58	87	209	467	725
96-Dick Tracy	23	46	69	161	356	550
97-Marge's Little Lulu (1946)	71	142	213	568	1284	2000
98-Lone Ranger, The	28	56	84	202	451	700
99-Smitty	12	24	36	79	170	260
100-Gene Autry Comics; 1st Gene Autry photo-c	22	44	66	155	345	535
101-Terry and the Pirates	20	40	60	135	300	465

NOTE: No. 101 is last issue to carry "Four Color" logo on cover; all issues beginning with No. 100 are marked "…O.S." (One Shot) which can be found in the bottom left-hand panel on the first page; the numbers following "O. S." relate to the year/month issued.

	GD 2.0	VG 4.0	FN 6.0	VF 8.0	VF/NM 9.0	NM- 9.2
102-Oswald the Rabbit-Walt Kelly art, 1 pg.	15	30	45	100	220	340
103-Easter with Mother Goose by Walt Kelly	22	44	66	154	340	525
104-Fairy Tale Parade by Walt Kelly	16	32	48	112	249	385
105-Albert the Alligator and Pogo Possum (#1) by Kelly (4/46)	68	136	204	544	1222	1900
106-Tillie the Toiler (5/46)	10	20	30	70	150	230
107-Little Orphan Annie; reprints strips from 11/16/42 to 3/24/43	18	36	54	128	284	440
108-Donald Duck in The Terror of the River, by Carl Barks (Disney) (© 4/16/46)	107	214	321	856	1928	3000
109-Roy Rogers Comics; photo-c	22	44	66	154	340	525
110-Marge's Little Lulu	46	92	138	368	834	1300
111-Captain Easy	14	28	42	93	204	315
112-Porky Pig's Adventure in Gopher Gulch	18	36	54	128	284	440
113-Popeye; all new Popeye stories begin	15	30	45	105	233	360
114-Fairy Tale Parade by Walt Kelly	16	32	48	112	249	385
115-Marge's Little Lulu	44	88	132	326	738	1150
116-Mickey Mouse and the House of Many Mysteries (Disney)	27	54	81	194	435	675
117-Roy Rogers Comics; photo-c	17	34	51	119	265	410
118-Lone Ranger, The	28	56	84	202	451	700
119-Felix the Cat; all new Felix stories begin	36	72	108	259	580	900
120-Marge's Little Lulu	36	72	108	266	596	925
121-Fairy Tale Parade-(not Kelly)	10	20	30	69	147	225
122-Henry (#1) (10/46)	16	32	48	110	243	375
123-Bugs Bunny's Dangerous Venture	17	34	51	117	259	400
124-Roy Rogers Comics; photo-c	17	34	51	119	265	410
125-Lone Ranger, The	19	38	57	133	297	460
126-Christmas with Mother Goose (1946)	12	24	36	82	179	275
127-Popeye	15	30	45	105	233	360
128-Santa Claus Funnies- "Santa & the Angel" by Gollub; "A Mouse in the House" by Kelly	16	32	48	108	239	370
129-Walt Disney's Uncle Remus and His Tales of Brer Rabbit (#1) (1946)-Adapted from Disney movie "Song of the South"	36	72	108	259	580	900
130-Andy Panda (Walter Lantz)	10	20	30	70	150	230
131-Marge's Little Lulu	36	72	108	266	596	925
132-Tillie the Toiler (1947)	10	20	30	70	150	230
133-Dick Tracy	18	36	54	124	275	425
134-Tarzan and the Devil Ogre; Marsh-c/a	61	122	183	488	1094	1700
135-Felix the Cat	23	46	69	156	348	540
136-Lone Ranger, The	19	38	57	133	297	460
137-Roy Rogers Comics; photo-c	17	34	51	119	265	410
138-Smitty	10	20	30	67	141	215
139-Marge's Little Lulu (1947)	35	70	105	252	564	875
140-Easter with Mother Goose by Walt Kelly	16	32	48	107	236	365
141-Mickey Mouse and the Submarine Pirates (Disney)	26	52	78	182	404	625
142-Bugs Bunny and the Haunted Mountain	17	34	51	117	259	400
143-Oswald the Rabbit & the Prehistoric Egg	9	18	27	59	117	175
144-Roy Rogers Comics (1947)-Photo-c	17	34	51	119	265	410
145-Popeye	15	30	45	105	233	360
146-Marge's Little Lulu	35	70	105	252	564	875
147-Donald Duck in Volcano Valley, by Carl Barks (Disney) (5/47)	89	178	267	712	1606	2500
148-Albert the Alligator and Pogo Possum by Walt Kelly (5/47)	44	88	132	326	738	1150
149-Smilin' Jack	10	20	30	66	138	210
150-Tillie the Toiler (6/47)	10	20	30	66	138	210
151-Lone Ranger, The	12	24	36	112	249	385
152-Little Orphan Annie; reprints strips from 1/2/44 to 5/6/44	12	24	36	82	179	275
153-Roy Rogers Comics; photo-c	15	30	45	105	233	360
154-Walter Lantz Andy Panda	10	20	30	70	150	230
155-Henry (7/47)	10	20	30	70	150	230
156-Porky Pig and the Phantom	12	24	36	81	176	270
157-Mickey Mouse & the Beanstalk (Disney)	26	52	78	182	404	625

	GD 2.0	VG 4.0	FN 6.0	VF 8.0	VF/NM 9.0	NM- 9.2
158-Marge's Little Lulu	35	70	105	252	564	875
159-Donald Duck in the Ghost of the Grotto, by Carl Barks (Disney) (8/47)	93	186	279	744	1672	2600
160-Roy Rogers Comics; photo-c	15	30	45	105	233	360
161-Tarzan and the Fires Of Tohr; Marsh-c/a	48	96	144	374	862	1350
162-Felix the Cat (9/47)	18	36	54	124	275	425
163-Dick Tracy	16	32	48	110	243	375
164-Bugs Bunny Finds the Frozen Kingdom	17	34	51	117	259	400
165-Marge's Little Lulu	42	84	126	311	706	1100
166-Roy Rogers Comics (52 pgs.)-Photo-c	15	30	45	105	233	360
167-Lone Ranger, The	16	32	48	112	249	385
168-Popeye (10/47)	15	30	45	105	233	360
169-Woody Woodpecker (#1)- "Manhunter in the North"; drug use story	22	44	66	154	340	525
170-Mickey Mouse on Spook's Island (11/47)(Disney)-reprinted in Mickey Mouse #103	22	44	66	154	340	525
171-Charlie McCarthy (#1) and the Twenty Thieves	28	56	84	202	451	700
172-Christmas with Mother Goose by Walt Kelly (11/47)	12	24	36	82	179	275
173-Flash Gordon	26	52	78	182	404	625
174-Winnie Winkle	9	18	27	62	126	190
175-Santa Claus Funnies by Walt Kelly (1947)	16	32	48	108	239	370
176-Tillie the Toiler (12/47)	10	20	30	66	138	210
177-Roy Rogers Comics-(36 pgs.); Photo-c	15	30	45	100	220	340
178-Donald Duck "Christmas on Bear Mountain" by Carl Barks; 1st app. Uncle Scrooge (Disney)(12/47)	224	448	672	1848	4174	6500
179-Uncle Wiggily (#1)-Walt Kelly-c	17	34	51	114	252	390
180-Ozark Ike (#1)	13	26	39	89	195	300
181-Walt Disney's Mickey Mouse in Jungle Magic	22	44	66	154	340	525
182-Porky Pig in Never-Never Land (2/48)	12	24	36	81	176	270
183-Oswald the Rabbit (Lantz)	9	18	27	59	117	175
184-Tillie the Toiler	10	20	30	66	138	210
185-Easter with Mother Goose by Walt Kelly (1948)	14	28	42	96	211	325
186-Walt Disney's Bambi (4/48)-Reprinted as Movie Classic Bambi #3 (1956)	17	34	51	117	259	400
187-Bugs Bunny and the Dreadful Dragon	12	24	36	84	185	285
188-Woody Woodpecker (Lantz, 5/48)	13	26	39	86	188	290
189-Donald Duck in The Old Castle's Secret, by Carl Barks (Disney) (6/48)	100	200	300	800	1800	2800
190-Flash Gordon (6/48); bondage-c; "The Adventures of the Flying Saucers"; 5th Flying Saucer story- see The Spirit 9/28/47(1st), Shadow Comics V7#10 (2nd, 1/48),Captain Midnight #60 (3rd, 2/48) & Boy Commandos #26 (4th, 3-4/48)	31	62	93	223	499	775
191-Porky Pig to the Rescue	12	24	36	81	176	270
192-The Brownies (#1)-by Walt Kelly (7/48)	15	30	45	103	227	350
193-M.G.M. Presents Tom and Jerry (#1)(1948)	36	72	108	259	580	900
194-Mickey Mouse in The World Under the Sea (Disney)-Reprinted in Mickey Mouse #101	22	44	66	154	340	525
195-Tillie the Toiler	9	18	27	57	111	165
196-Charlie McCarthy in The Haunted Hide-Out; part photo-c	17	34	51	119	265	410
197-Spirit of the Border (#1) (Zane Grey) (1948)	13	26	39	91	201	310
198-Andy Panda	10	20	30	70	150	230
199-Donald Duck in Sheriff of Bullet Valley, by Carl Barks; Barks draws himself on wanted poster, last page; used in Love & Death (10/48)	96	192	288	768	1734	2700
200-Bugs Bunny, Super Sleuth	12	24	36	84	185	285
201-Christmas with Mother Goose by W. Kelly	10	20	30	66	138	210
202-Woody Woodpecker	9	18	27	62	126	190
203-Donald Duck in the Golden Christmas Tree, by Carl Barks (Disney) (12/48)	64	128	192	512	1156	1800
204-Flash Gordon (12/48)	19	38	57	131	291	450
205-Santa Claus Funnies by Walt Kelly	13	26	39	89	195	300
206-Little Orphan Annie; reprints strips from 11/10/40 to 1/11/41	8	16	24	52	99	145
207-King of the Royal Mounted (#1) (12/48)	18	36	54	100	220	340
208-Brer Rabbit Does It Again (Disney) (1/49)	14	28	42	96	211	325
209-Harold Teen	8	16	24	52	99	145
210-Tippie and Cap Stubbs	9	18	27	60	120	180
211-Little Beaver (#1)	12	24	36	79	170	260
212-Dr. Bobbs	7	14	21	49	92	135
213-Tillie the Toiler	9	18	27	57	111	165
214-Mickey Mouse and His Sky Adventure (2/49)(Disney)-Reprinted in Mickey Mouse #105	17	34	51	119	265	410
215-Sparkle Plenty (Dick Tracy-r by Gould)	12	24	36	82	179	275
216-Andy Panda and the Police Pup (Lantz)	8	16	24	55	105	155
217-Bugs Bunny in Court Jester	12	24	36	84	185	285
218-Three Little Pigs and the Wonderful Magic Lamp (Disney) (3/49)(#1)	13	26	39	89	195	300
219-Swee'pea	11	22	33	76	163	250
220-Easter with Mother Goose by Walt Kelly	14	28	42	96	211	325
221-Uncle Wiggily-Walt Kelly cover in part	10	20	30	68	144	220
222-West of the Pecos (Zane Grey)	9	18	27	57	111	165
223-Donald Duck "Lost in the Andes" by Carl Barks (Disney-4/49) (square egg story)	82	164	246	656	1478	2300
224-Little Iodine (#1), by Hatlo (4/49)	13	26	39	89	195	300
225-Oswald the Rabbit (Lantz)	7	14	21	46	86	125
226-Porky Pig and Spoofy, the Spook	9	18	27	62	129	195
227-Seven Dwarfs (Disney)	16	32	48	110	243	375
228-Mark of Zorro, The (#1) (1949)	32	64	96	230	515	800
229-Smokey Stover	7	14	21	46	86	125
230-Sunset Pass (Zane Grey)	9	18	27	57	111	165
231-Mickey Mouse and the Rajah's Treasure (Disney)	17	34	51	119	265	410
232-Woody Woodpecker (Lantz, 6/49)	23	46	69	161	356	550
233-Bugs Bunny, Sleepwalking Sleuth	12	24	36	84	185	285
234-Dumbo in Sky Voyage (Disney)	15	30	45	105	233	360

Four Color Comics #123 © WB

Four Color Comics #251 © KFS

Four Color Comics #332 © DELL

	GD 2.0	VG 4.0	FN 6.0	VF 8.0	VF/NM 9.0	NM- 9.2
235-Tiny Tim	8	16	24	52	99	145
236-Heritage of the Desert (Zane Grey) (1949)	9	18	27	57	111	165
237-Tillie the Toiler	9	18	27	57	111	165
238-Donald Duck in Voodoo Hoodoo, by Carl Barks (Disney) (8/49)	61	122	183	488	1094	1700
239-Adventure Bound (8/49)	6	12	18	41	76	110
240-Andy Panda (Lantz)	8	16	24	55	105	155
241-Porky Pig, Mighty Hunter	9	18	27	63	129	195
242-Tippie and Cap Stubbs	7	14	21	44	82	120
243-Thumper Follows His Nose (Disney)	15	30	45	105	233	360
244-The Brownies by Walt Kelly	11	22	33	73	157	240
245-Dick's Adventures (9/49)	6	12	18	41	76	110
246-Thunder Mountain (Zane Grey)	6	12	18	37	66	95
247-Flash Gordon	19	38	57	131	291	450
248-Mickey Mouse and the Black Sorcerer (Disney)	17	34	51	119	265	410
249-Woody Woodpecker in the "Globetrotter" (10/49)	9	18	27	62	126	190
250-Bugs Bunny in Diamond Daze; used in SOTI, pg. 309	16	32	48	110	243	375
251-Hubert at Camp Moonbeam	10	20	30	67	141	215
252-Pinocchio (Disney)-not by Kelly; origin	15	30	45	103	227	350
253-Christmas with Mother Goose by W. Kelly	10	20	30	66	138	210
254-Bugs Bunny Funnies by Walt Kelly; Pogo & Albert story by Kelly (11/49)	13	26	39	89	195	300
255-The Ranger (Zane Grey) (1949)	6	12	18	37	66	95
256-Donald Duck in "Luck of the North" by Carl Barks (Disney) (12/49)-Shows #257 on inside	54	108	162	432	966	1500
257-Little Iodine	9	18	27	58	114	170
258-Andy Panda and the Balloon Race (Lantz)	8	16	24	55	105	155
259-Santa and the Angel (Gollub art-condensed from #128) & Santa at the Zoo (12/49) -two books in one	9	18	27	62	126	190
260-Porky Pig, Hero of the Wild West (12/49)	9	18	27	63	129	195
261-Mickey Mouse and the Missing Key (Disney)	17	34	51	119	265	410
262-Raggedy Ann and Andy	9	18	27	57	111	165
263-Donald Duck in "Land of the Totem Poles" by Carl Barks (Disney) (2/50)-Has two Barks stories	50	100	150	400	900	1400
264-Woody Woodpecker in the Magic Lantern (Lantz)	9	18	27	62	126	190
265-King of the Royal Mounted (Zane Grey)	10	20	30	64	132	200
266-Bugs Bunny on the "Isle of Hercules" (2/50)-Reprinted in Best of Bugs Bunny #1	10	20	30	67	141	215
267-Little Beaver; Harmon-c/a	8	16	24	56	108	160
268-Mickey Mouse's Surprise Visitor (1950)(Disney)	17	34	51	117	259	400
269-Johnny Mack Brown (#1)-Photo-c	19	38	57	133	297	460
270-Drift Fence (Zane Grey) (3/50)	6	12	18	37	66	95
271-Porky Pig in Phantom of the Plains	9	18	27	63	129	195
272-Cinderella (Disney) (4/50)	15	30	45	105	233	360
273-Oswald the Rabbit (Lantz)	7	14	21	44	86	125
274-Bugs Bunny, Hare-brained Reporter	10	20	30	67	141	215
275-Donald Duck in "Ancient Persia" by Carl Barks (Disney) (5/50)	48	96	144	374	862	1350
276-Uncle Wiggily	7	14	21	49	92	135
277-Porky Pig in Desert Adventure (5/50)	9	18	27	63	129	195
278-(Wild) Bill Elliott Comics (#1)-Photo-c	15	30	45	100	220	340
279-Mickey Mouse and Pluto Battle the Giant Ants (Disney); reprinted in Mickey Mouse #102 & 245	13	26	39	89	195	300
280-Andy Panda in The Isle Of Mechanical Men (Lantz)	8	16	24	55	105	155
281-Bugs Bunny in The Great Circus Mystery	10	20	30	67	141	215
282-Donald Duck and the Pixilated Parrot by Carl Barks (Disney) (© 5/23/50)	48	96	144	374	862	1350
283-King of the Royal Mounted (7/50)	10	20	30	64	132	200
284-Porky Pig in The Kingdom of Nowhere	9	18	27	63	129	195
285-Bozo the Clown & His Minikin Circus (#1) (TV)	19	38	57	131	291	450
286-Mickey Mouse in The Uninvited Guest (Disney)	13	26	39	89	195	300
287-Gene Autry's Champion in The Ghost Of Black Mountain; photo-c	11	22	33	76	163	250
288-Woody Woodpecker in Klondike Gold (Lantz)	9	18	27	62	126	190
289-Bugs Bunny in "Indian Trouble"	10	20	30	67	141	215
290-The Chief (#1) (8/50)	9	18	27	60	120	180
291-Donald Duck in "The Magic Hourglass" by Carl Barks (Disney) (9/50)	48	96	144	374	862	1350
292-The Cisco Kid Comics (#1)	23	46	69	156	348	540
293-The Brownies-Kelly-c/a	11	22	33	73	157	240
294-Little Beaver	8	16	24	56	108	160
295-Porky Pig in President Porky (9/50)	9	18	27	63	129	195
296-Mickey Mouse in Private Eye for Hire (Disney)	13	26	39	89	195	300
297-Andy Panda in The Haunted Inn (Lantz, 10/50)	8	16	24	55	105	155
298-Bugs Bunny in Sheik for a Day	10	20	30	67	141	215
299-Buck Jones & the Iron Horse Trail (#1)	14	28	42	93	204	315
300-Donald Duck in "Big-Top Bedlam" by Carl Barks (Disney) (11/50)	48	96	144	374	862	1350
301-The Mysterious Rider (Zane Grey)	6	12	18	37	66	95
302-Santa Claus Funnies (11/50)	8	16	24	54	102	150
303-Porky Pig in The Land of the Monstrous Flies	8	16	24	54	102	150
304-Mickey Mouse in Tom-Tom Island (Disney) (12/50)	12	24	36	82	179	275
305-Woody Woodpecker (Lantz)	9	18	27	61	123	185
306-Raggedy Ann	7	14	21	48	86	125
307-Bugs Bunny in Lumber Jack Rabbit	9	18	27	59	117	175
308-Donald Duck in "Dangerous Disguise" by Carl Barks (Disney) (1/51)	46	92	138	359	805	1250
309-Betty Betz' Dollface and Her Gang (1951)	9	18	27	59	117	175
310-King of the Royal Mounted (1/51)	7	14	21	46	86	125
311-Porky Pig in Midget Horses of Hidden Valley	8	16	24	54	102	150
312-Tonto (#1)	11	22	33	75	160	245
313-Mickey Mouse in The Mystery of the Double-Cross Ranch (#1) (Disney) (2/51)	12	24	36	82	179	275

Note: Beginning with the above comic in 1951 Dell/Western began adding #1 in small print on the covers of several long running titles with the evident intention of switching these titles to their own monthly numbers, but when the conversions were made, there was no connection. It is thought that the post office may have stepped in and decreed the sequences should commence as though the first four colors printed had each begun with number one, or the first issues sold by subscription. Since the regular series' numbers don't correctly match to the numbers of earlier issues published, it's not known whether or not the numbering was in error.

	GD 2.0	VG 4.0	FN 6.0	VF 8.0	VF/NM 9.0	NM- 9.2
314-Ambush (Zane Grey)	6	12	18	37	66	95
315-Oswald the Rabbit (Lantz)	6	12	18	40	73	105
316-Rex Allen (#1)-Photo-c; Marsh-a	14	28	42	94	207	320
317-Bugs Bunny in Hair Today Gone Tomorrow (#1)	9	18	27	59	117	175
318-Donald Duck in "No Such Varmint" by Carl Barks (Disney) (#1)-Indicia shows #317 (Disney, © 1/23/51)	46	92	138	359	805	1250
319-Gene Autry's Champion; painted-c	6	12	18	41	76	110
320-Uncle Wiggily	7	14	21	49	92	135
321-Little Scouts (#1) (3/51)	7	14	21	48	89	130
322-Porky Pig in Roaring Rockets (#1 on-c)	8	16	24	54	102	150
323-Susie Q. Smith (#1) (3/51)	8	16	24	55	105	155
324-I Met a Handsome Cowboy (3/51)	8	16	24	56	108	160
325-Mickey Mouse in The Haunted Castle (#2) (Disney) (4/51)	12	24	36	82	179	275
326-Andy Panda (#1) (Lantz)	6	12	18	41	76	110
327-Bugs Bunny and the Rajah's Treasure (#2)	9	18	27	59	117	175
328-Donald Duck in Old California (#2) by Carl Barks-Peyote drug use issue (Disney) (5/51)	46	92	138	340	770	1200
329-Roy Roger's Trigger (#1)(5/51)-Painted-c	14	28	42	97	214	330
330-Porky Pig Meets the Bristled Bruiser (#2)	8	16	24	54	102	150
331-Alice in Wonderland (Disney) (1951)	19	38	57	131	291	450
332-Little Beaver	8	16	24	56	108	160
333-Wilderness Trek (Zane Grey) (5/51)	6	12	18	37	66	95
334-Mickey Mouse and Yukon Gold (Disney) (6/51)	12	24	36	82	179	275
335-Francis the Famous Talking Mule (#1, 6/51)-1st Dell non animated movie comic (all issues based on movie)	11	22	33	77	166	255
336-Woody Woodpecker (Lantz)	9	18	27	61	123	185
337-The Brownies-not by Walt Kelly	6	12	18	41	76	110
338-Bugs Bunny and the Rocking Horse Thieves	9	18	27	59	117	175
339-Donald Duck and the Magic Fountain-not by Barks (Disney) (7-8/51)	33	66	99	238	532	825
340-King of the Royal Mounted (7/51)	7	14	21	46	86	125
341-Unbirthday Party with Alice in Wonderland (Disney) (7/51)	19	38	57	131	291	450
342-Porky Pig the Lucky Peppermint Mine; r/in Porky Pig #3	6	12	18	54	102	115
343-Mickey Mouse in The Ruby Eye of Homar-Guy-Am (Disney)-Reprinted in Mickey Mouse #104	10	20	30	70	150	230
344-Sergeant Preston from Challenge of The Yukon (#1) (TV)	15	30	45	103	227	350
345-Andy Panda in Scotland Yard (8-10/51) (Lantz)	6	12	18	41	76	110
346-Hideout (Zane Grey)	6	12	18	37	66	95
347-Bugs Bunny the Frigid Hare (8-9/51)	9	18	27	59	117	175
348-Donald Duck "The Crocodile Collector"; Barks-c only (Disney) (9-10/51)	24	48	72	168	372	575
349-Uncle Wiggily	6	12	18	41	76	110

	GD 2.0	VG 4.0	FN 6.0	VF 8.0	VF/NM 9.0	NM- 9.2
350-Woody Woodpecker (Lantz)	9	18	27	61	123	185
351-Porky Pig & the Grand Canyon Giant (9-10/51)	6	12	18	54	102	115
352-Mickey Mouse in The Mystery of Painted Valley (Disney)	10	20	30	70	150	230
353-Duck Album (#1)-Barks-c (Disney)	15	30	45	100	220	340
354-Raggedy Ann & Andy	7	14	21	46	86	125
355-Bugs Bunny Hot-Rod Hare	9	18	27	59	117	175
356-Donald Duck in "Rags to Riches"; Barks-c only	24	48	72	168	372	575
357-Comeback (Zane Grey)	5	10	15	33	57	80
358-Andy Panda (Lantz) (11-1/52)	6	12	18	41	76	110
359-Frosty the Snowman (#1)	11	22	33	75	160	245
360-Porky Pig in Tree of Fortune (11-12/51)	6	12	18	54	102	115
361-Santa Claus Funnies	8	16	24	54	102	150
362-Mickey Mouse and the Smuggled Diamonds (Disney)	10	20	30	70	150	230
363-King of the Royal Mounted	6	12	18	40	73	105
364-Woody Woodpecker (Lantz)	6	12	18	37	66	95
365-The Brownies-not by Kelly	6	12	18	41	76	110
366-Bugs Bunny Uncle Buckskin Comes to Town (12-1/52)	9	18	27	59	117	175
367-Donald Duck in "A Christmas for Shacktown" by Carl Barks (Disney) (1-2/52)	38	76	114	285	641	1000
368-Bob Clampett's Beany and Cecil (#1)	26	52	78	182	404	625
369-The Lone Ranger's Famous Horse Hi-Yo Silver (#1); Silver's origin	11	22	33	72	154	235
370-Porky Pig in Trouble in the Big Trees	6	12	18	54	102	115
371-Mickey Mouse in The Inca Idol Case (1952) (Disney)	10	20	30	70	150	230
372-Riders of the Purple Sage (Zane Grey)	5	10	15	33	57	80
373-Sergeant Preston (TV)	9	18	27	61	123	185
374-Woody Woodpecker (Lantz)	6	12	18	37	66	95
375-John Carter of Mars (E. R. Burroughs)-Jesse Marsh-a; origin	37	74	111	274	612	950
376-Bugs Bunny, "The Magic Sneeze"	9	18	27	59	117	175
377-Susie Q. Smith	6	12	18	37	66	95
378-Tom Corbett, Space Cadet (#1) (TV)-McWilliams-a	20	40	60	140	315	490
379-Donald Duck in "Southern Hospitality"; 2nd Uncle Scrooge-c; not by Barks (Disney)	33	66	99	238	532	825
380-Raggedy Ann & Andy	7	14	21	46	86	125
381-Marge's Tubby (#1)	12	24	42	63	147	324
382-Snow White and the Seven Dwarfs (Disney)-origin; partial reprint of Four Color #49 (Movie)	13	26	39	86	188	290
383-Andy Panda (Lantz)	5	10	15	35	63	90
384-King of the Royal Mounted (3/52)(Zane Grey)	6	12	18	40	73	105
385-Porky Pig in The Isle of Missing Ships (3-4/52)	6	12	18	54	102	115
386-Uncle Scrooge (#1)-by Carl Barks (Disney) in "Only a Poor Old Man" (3/52)	195	390	585	1600	4200	6800
387-Mickey Mouse in High Tibet (Disney) (4-5/52)	10	20	30	70	150	230
388-Oswald the Rabbit (Lantz)	6	12	18	40	73	105
389-Andy Hardy Comics (#1)	8	16	24	54	102	150
390-Woody Woodpecker (Lantz)	6	12	18	37	66	95
391-Uncle Wiggily	6	12	18	41	76	110
392-Hi-Yo Silver	7	14	21	44	82	120
393-Bugs Bunny	9	18	27	59	117	175
394-Donald Duck in Malayalaya-Barks-c only (Disney)	24	48	72	168	372	575
395-Forlorn River(Zane Grey)-First Nevada (5/52)	5	10	15	33	57	80
396-Tales of the Texas Rangers(#1)(TV)-Photo-c	11	22	33	73	157	240
397-Sergeant Preston of the Yukon (TV) (5/52)	9	18	27	61	123	185
398-The Brownies-not by Kelly	6	12	18	41	76	110
399-Porky Pig in The Lost Gold Mine	6	12	18	54	102	115
400-Tom Corbett, Space Cadet (TV)-McWilliams-c/a	12	24	36	79	170	260
401-Mickey Mouse and Goofy's Mechanical Wizard (Disney) (6-7/52)	9	18	27	62	126	190
402-Mary Jane and Sniffles	10	20	30	69	147	225
403-Li'l Bad Wolf (Disney) (6/52)(#1)	10	20	30	66	138	210
404-The Range Rider (#1) (Flying A's...)(TV)-Photo-c	10	20	30	68	144	220
405-Woody Woodpecker (Lantz) (6-7/52)	6	12	18	37	66	95
406-Tweety and Sylvester (#1)	15	30	45	103	227	350
407-Bugs Bunny, Foreign-Legion Hare	8	16	24	54	102	150
408-Donald Duck and the Golden Helmet by Carl Barks (Disney) (7-8/52)	36	72	108	266	596	925
409-Andy Panda (7-9/52)	5	10	15	35	63	90
410-Porky Pig in The Water Wizard (7/52)	6	12	18	54	102	115
411-Mickey Mouse and the Old Sea Dog (Disney) (8-9/52)	9	18	27	62	126	190
412-Nevada (Zane Grey)	5	10	15	33	57	80
413-Robin Hood (Disney-Movie) (8/52)-Photo-c (1st Disney movie Four Color book)	10	20	30	60	132	200
414-Bob Clampett's Beany and Cecil (TV)	14	28	42	96	211	325
415-Rootie Kazootie (#1) (TV)	11	22	33	73	157	240
416-Woody Woodpecker (Lantz)	6	12	18	37	66	95
417-Double Trouble with Goober (#1) (8/52)	5	10	15	34	60	85
418-Rusty Riley, a Boy, a Horse, and a Dog (#1)-Frank Godwin-a (strip reprints) (8/52)	9	18	27	57	111	165
419-Sergeant Preston (TV)	9	18	27	61	123	185
420-Bugs Bunny in The Mysterious Buckaroo (8-9/52)	8	16	24	54	102	150
421-Tom Corbett, Space Cadet(TV)-McWilliams-a	12	24	36	79	170	260
422-Donald Duck and the Gilded Man, by Carl Barks (Disney) (9-10/52) (#423 on inside)	36	72	108	266	596	925
423-Rhubarb, Owner of the Brooklyn Ball Club (The Millionaire Cat) (#1)-Painted cover	8	16	24	52	99	145
424-Flash Gordon-Test Flight in Space (9/52)	13	26	39	89	195	300
425-Zorro, the Return of	13	26	39	86	188	290
426-Porky Pig in The Scalawag Leprechaun	6	12	18	54	102	115
427-Mickey Mouse and the Wonderful Whizzix (Disney) (10-11/52)-Reprinted						

	GD 2.0	VG 4.0	FN 6.0	VF 8.0	VF/NM 9.0	NM- 9.2
in Mickey Mouse #100	9	18	27	62	126	190
428-Uncle Wiggily	5	10	15	34	63	90
429-Pluto in "Why Dogs Leave Home" (Disney) (10/52)(#1)	12	24	36	83	182	280
430-Marge's Tubby, the Shadow of a Man-Eater	12	24	36	83	182	280
431-Woody Woodpecker (10/52) (Lantz)	6	12	18	37	66	95
432-Bugs Bunny and the Rabbit Olympics	8	16	24	54	102	150
433-Wildfire (Zane Grey) (11-1/52-53)	5	10	15	33	57	80
434-Rin Tin Tin "In Dark Danger" (#1) (TV) (11/52)-Photo-c	17	34	51	117	259	400
435-Frosty the Snowman (11/52)	7	14	21	48	89	130
436-The Brownies-not by Kelly (11/52)	6	12	18	37	66	95
437-John Carter of Mars (E.R. Burroughs)-Marsh-a	19	38	57	131	291	460
438-Annie Oakley (#1) (TV)	13	26	39	89	195	300
439-Little Hiawatha (Disney) (12/52)(#1)	9	18	27	58	114	170
440-Black Beauty (12/52)	6	12	18	35	69	100
441-Fearless Fagan	5	10	15	31	53	75
442-Peter Pan (Disney) (Movie)	12	24	36	83	182	280
443-Ben Bowie and His Mountain Men (#1)	9	18	27	63	129	195
444-Marge's Tubby	12	24	36	83	182	280
445-Charlie McCarthy	7	14	21	44	82	120
446-Captain Hook and Peter Pan (Disney)(Movie)(1/53)	10	20	30	69	147	225
447-Andy Hardy Comics	5	10	15	31	53	75
448-Bob Clampett's Beany and Cecil (TV)	14	28	42	96	211	325
449-Tappan's Burro (Zane Grey) (2-4/53)	5	10	15	33	57	80
450-Duck Album; Barks-c (Disney)	10	20	30	69	147	225
451-Rusty Riley-Frank Godwin-a (strip-r) (2/53)	5	10	15	35	63	90
452-Raggedy Ann & Andy (1953)	7	14	21	46	86	125
453-Susie Q. Smith (2/53)	6	12	18	37	66	95
454-Krazy Kat Comics; not by Herriman	6	12	18	42	79	115
455-Johnny Mack Brown Comics(3/53)-Photo-c	6	12	18	40	73	105
456-Uncle Scrooge Back to the Klondike (#2) by Barks (3/53) (Disney)	95	190	285	760	1955	3150
457-Daffy (#1)	13	26	39	89	195	300
458-Oswald the Rabbit (Lantz)	5	10	15	35	63	90
459-Rootie Kazootie (TV)	7	14	21	46	86	125
460-Buck Jones (4/53)	6	12	18	42	79	115
461-Marge's Tubby	11	22	33	76	163	250
462-Little Scouts	5	10	15	30	50	70
463-Petunia (4/53)	6	12	18	40	73	105
464-Bozo (4/53)	9	18	27	61	123	185
465-Francis the Famous Talking Mule	6	12	18	41	76	110
466-Rhubarb, the Millionaire Cat; painted-c	6	12	18	38	69	100
467-Desert Gold (Zane Grey) (5-7/53)	5	10	15	33	57	80
468-Goofy (#1) (Disney)	12	24	36	82	179	275
469-Beetle Bailey (#1) (5/53)	13	26	39	89	195	300
470-Elmer Fudd	10	20	30	67	141	215
471-Double Trouble with Goober	4	8	12	27	44	60
472-Wild Bill Elliott (6/53)-Photo-c	6	12	18	38	69	100
473-Li'l Bad Wolf (Disney) (6/53)(#2)	7	14	21	44	82	120
474-Mary Jane and Sniffles	8	16	24	55	105	155
475-M.G.M.'s The Two Mouseketeers (#1)	9	18	27	61	123	185
476-Rin Tin Tin (TV)-Photo-c	10	20	30	64	132	200
477-Bob Clampett's Beany and Cecil (TV)	14	28	42	96	211	325
478-Charlie McCarthy	7	14	21	44	82	120
479-Queen of the West Dale Evans (#1)-Photo-c	17	34	51	114	252	390
480-Andy Hardy Comics	5	10	15	31	53	75
481-Annie Oakley And Tagg (TV)	9	18	27	59	117	175
482-Brownies-not by Kelly	6	12	18	37	66	95
483-Little Beaver (7/53)	5	10	15	35	63	90
484-River Feud (Zane Grey) (8-10/53)	5	10	15	33	57	80
485-The Little People-Walt Scott (#1)	9	18	27	58	114	170
486-Rusty Riley-Frank Godwin strip-r	5	10	15	35	63	90
487-Mowgli, the Jungle Book (Rudyard Kipling's)	8	16	24	55	105	155
488-John Carter of Mars (Burroughs)-Marsh-a; painted-c	19	38	57	131	291	460
489-Tweety and Sylvester	9	18	27	61	123	185
490-Jungle Jim (#1)	10	20	30	64	132	200
491-Silvertip (#1) (Max Brand)-Kinstler-a (8/53)	9	18	27	59	117	175
492-Duck Album (Disney)	7	14	21	46	86	125
493-Johnny Mack Brown; photo-c	6	12	18	40	73	105
494-The Little King (#1)	10	20	30	64	132	200
495-Uncle Scrooge (#3) (Disney)-by Carl Barks (9/53)	60	120	180	480	1240	2000
496-The Green Hornet; painted-c	30	60	90	216	483	750
497-Zorro (Sword of...)-Kinstler-a	13	26	39	86	188	290
498-Bugs Bunny's Album (9/53)	6	12	18	41	76	110
499-M.G.M.'s Spike and Tyke (#1) (9/53)	9	18	27	58	114	170
500-Buck Jones	6	12	18	42	79	115
501-Francis the Famous Talking Mule	5	10	15	35	63	90
502-Rootie Kazootie (TV)	7	14	21	46	86	125
503-Uncle Wiggily (10/53)	5	10	15	34	63	90
504-Krazy Kat; not by Herriman	6	12	18	42	79	115
505-The Sword and the Rose (Disney) (10/53)(Movie)-Photo-c	9	18	27	61	123	185
506-The Little Scouts - Infinity cover	5	10	15	30	50	70
507-Oswald the Rabbit (Lantz)	5	10	15	35	63	90
508-Bozo (10/53)	9	18	27	61	123	185
509-Pluto (Disney) (10/53)	8	16	24	52	99	145
510-Son of Black Beauty	5	10	15	31	53	75
511-Outlaw Trail (Zane Grey)-Kinstler-a	5	10	15	35	63	90
512-Flash Gordon (9/53)	13	26	39	89	195	300
513-Ben Bowie and His Mountain Men	5	10	15	34	60	85
514-Frosty the Snowman (11/53)	7	14	21	48	89	130
515-Andy Hardy	5	10	15	31	53	75
516-Double Trouble With Goober	4	8	12	27	44	60

Four Color Comics #418 © DELL — RUSTY RILEY — A BOY, A HORSE, AND A DOG

Four Color Comics #535 © Desilu — I Love Lucy Comics — DELL

Four Color Comics #619 © DELL — Krazy Kat

Title	GD 2.0	VG 4.0	FN 6.0	VF 8.0	VF/NM 9.0	NM- 9.2
517-Chip 'N' Dale (#1) (Disney)	12	24	36	79	170	260
518-Rivets (11/53)	5	10	15	35	63	90
519-Steve Canyon (#1)-Not by Milton Caniff	9	18	27	59	117	175
520-Wild Bill Elliott-Photo-c	6	12	18	38	69	100
521-Beetle Bailey (12/53)	7	14	21	49	92	135
522-The Brownies	6	12	18	37	66	95
523-Rin Tin Tin (TV)-Photo-c (12/53)	10	20	30	64	132	200
524-Tweety and Sylvester	9	18	27	61	123	185
525-Santa Claus Funnies	8	16	24	54	102	150
526-Napoleon	7	14	21	46	86	125
527-Charlie McCarthy	7	14	21	44	82	120
528-Queen of the West Dale Evans; photo-c	9	18	27	62	126	190
529-Little Beaver	5	10	15	35	63	90
530-Bob Clampett's Beany and Cecil (TV) (1/54)	14	28	42	96	211	325
531-Duck Album (Disney)	7	14	21	46	86	125
532-The Rustlers (Zane Grey) (2-4/54)	5	10	15	33	57	80
533-Raggedy Ann and Andy	7	14	21	46	86	125
534-Western Marshal (Ernest Haycox's)-Kinstler-a	7	14	21	44	82	120
535-I Love Lucy (#1) (TV) (2/54)-Photo-c	48	96	144	374	862	1350
536-Daffy (3/54)	8	16	24	52	99	145
537-Stormy, the Thoroughbred… (Disney-Movie) on top 2/3 of each page; Pluto story on bottom 1/3 of each page (2/54)	6	12	18	42	79	115
538-The Mask of Zorro; Kinstler-a	13	26	39	86	188	290
539-Ben and Me (Disney) (3/54)	5	10	15	33	57	80
540-Knights of the Round Table (3/54) (Movie)-Photo-c	7	14	21	44	82	120
541-Johnny Mack Brown; photo-c	6	12	18	40	73	105
542-Super Circus Featuring Mary Hartline (TV) (3/54)	9	18	27	59	117	175
543-Uncle Wiggily (3/54)	5	10	15	34	63	90
544-Rob Roy (Disney-Movie)-Manning-a; photo-c	9	18	27	60	120	180
545-The Wonderful Adventures of Pinocchio-Partial reprint of Four Color #92 (Disney-Movie)	10	20	30	64	132	200
546-Buck Jones	6	12	18	42	79	115
547-Francis the Famous Talking Mule	5	10	15	35	63	90
548-Krazy Kat; not by Herriman (4/54)	5	10	15	31	53	75
549-Oswald the Rabbit (Lantz)	5	10	15	35	63	90
550-The Little Scouts	5	10	15	30	50	70
551-Bozo (4/54)	9	18	27	61	123	185
552-Beetle Bailey	7	14	21	49	92	135
553-Susie Q. Smith	6	12	18	37	66	95
554-Rusty Riley (Frank Godwin strip-r)	5	10	15	33	57	80
555-Range War (Zane Grey)	5	10	15	33	57	80
556-Double Trouble With Goober (5/54)	4	8	12	27	44	60
557-Ben Bowie and His Mountain Men	5	10	15	34	60	85
558-Elmer Fudd (5/54)	6	12	18	38	69	100
559-I Love Lucy (#2) (TV)-Photo-c	31	62	93	223	499	775
560-Duck Album (Disney) (5/54)	7	14	21	46	86	125
561-Mr. Magoo (5/54)	9	18	27	62	126	190
562-Goofy (Disney)(#2)	7	14	21	46	86	125
563-Rhubarb, the Millionaire Cat (6/54)	6	12	18	38	69	100
564-Li'l Bad Wolf (Disney)(#3)	7	14	21	44	82	120
565-Jungle Jim	5	10	15	35	63	90
566-Son of Black Beauty	5	10	15	31	53	75
567-Prince Valiant (#1)-By Bob Fuje (Movie)-Photo-c	11	22	33	73	157	240
568-Gypsy Colt (Movie) (6/54)	6	12	18	42	79	115
569-Priscilla's Pop	7	14	21	46	86	125
570-Bob Clampett's Beany and Cecil (TV)	14	28	42	96	211	325
571-Charlie McCarthy	7	14	21	44	82	120
572-Silvertip (Max Brand) (7/54); Kinstler-a	5	10	15	34	60	85
573-The Little People by Walt Scott	6	12	18	37	66	95
574-The Hand of Zorro; Kinstler-a	13	26	39	86	188	290
575-Annie Oakley and Tagg (TV)-Photo-c	9	18	27	59	117	175
576-Angel (#1) (8/54)	5	10	15	34	60	85
577-M.G.M.'s Spike and Tyke	6	12	18	41	76	110
578-Steve Canyon (8/54)	5	10	15	35	63	90
579-Francis the Famous Talking Mule	5	10	15	35	63	90
580-Six Gun Ranch (Luke Short-8/54)	6	12	18	37	66	95
581-Chip 'N' Dale (#2) (Disney)	6	12	18	42	79	115
582-Mowgli Jungle Book (Kipling) (8/54)	5	10	15	34	60	85
583-The Lost Wagon Train (Zane Grey)	5	10	15	33	57	80
584-Johnny Mack Brown-Photo-c	6	12	18	40	73	105
585-Bugs Bunny's Album	6	12	18	41	76	110
586-Duck Album (Disney)	7	14	21	46	86	125
587-The Little Scouts	5	10	15	30	50	70
588-King Richard and the Crusaders (Movie) (10/54) Matt Baker-a; photo-c	10	20	30	69	147	225
589-Buck Jones	6	12	18	42	79	115
590-Hansel and Gretel; partial photo-c	7	14	21	49	92	135
591-Western Marshal (Ernest Haycox's)-Kinstler-a	5	10	15	35	63	90
592-Super Circus (TV)	7	14	21	44	82	120
593-Oswald the Rabbit (Lantz)	5	10	15	35	63	90
594-Bozo (10/54)	9	18	27	61	123	185
595-Pluto (Disney)	7	14	21	46	86	125
596-Turok, Son of Stone (#1)	181	362	543	1158	1979	2800
597-The Little King	6	12	18	41	76	110
598-Captain Davy Jones	6	12	18	38	69	100
599-Ben Bowie and His Mountain Men	5	10	15	34	60	85
600-Daisy Duck's Diary (#1) (Disney) (11/54)	9	18	27	59	117	175
601-Frosty the Snowman	7	14	21	48	89	130
602-Mr. Magoo and Gerald McBoing-Boing	9	18	27	62	126	190
603-M.G.M.'s The Two Mouseketeers	7	14	21	44	82	120
604-Shadow on the Trail (Zane Grey)	5	10	15	33	57	80
605-The Brownies-not by Kelly (12/54)	6	12	18	37	66	95
606-Sir Lancelot (not TV)	7	14	21	46	86	125
607-Santa Claus Funnies	8	16	24	54	102	150
608-Silvertip- "Valley of Vanishing Men" (Max Brand)-Kinstler-a	5	10	15	34	60	85
609-The Littlest Outlaw (Disney-Movie) (1/55)-Photo-c	7	14	21	48	89	130
610-Drum Beat (Movie); Alan Ladd photo-c	8	16	24	55	105	155
611-Duck Album (Disney)	7	14	21	46	86	125
612-Little Beaver (1/55)	5	10	15	34	60	85
613-Western Marshal (Ernest Haycox's) (2/55)-Kinstler-a	5	10	15	35	63	90
614-20,000 Leagues Under the Sea (Disney) (Movie) (2/55)-Painted-c	10	20	30	69	147	225
615-Daffy	8	16	24	52	99	145
616-To the Last Man (Zane Grey)	5	10	15	33	57	80
617-The Quest of Zorro	13	26	39	86	188	290
618-Johnny Mack Brown; photo-c	6	12	18	40	73	105
619-Krazy Kat; not by Herriman	5	10	15	31	53	75
620-Mowgli Jungle Book (Kipling)	5	10	15	34	60	85
621-Francis the Famous Talking Mule (4/55)	5	10	15	33	57	800
622-Beetle Bailey	7	14	21	49	92	135
623-Oswald the Rabbit (Lantz)	5	10	15	33	57	80
624-Treasure Island(Disney-Movie)(4/55)-Photo-c	9	18	27	62	126	190
625-Beaver Valley (Disney-Movie)	6	12	18	37	66	95
626-Ben Bowie and His Mountain Men	5	10	15	34	60	85
627-Goofy (Disney) (5/55)	7	14	21	46	86	125
628-Elmer Fudd	6	12	18	38	69	100
629-Lady and the Tramp with Jock (Disney)	10	20	30	66	138	210
630-Priscilla's Pop	7	14	21	46	86	125
631-Davy Crockett, Indian Fighter (#1) (Disney) (5/55) (TV)-Fess Parker photo-c	16	32	48	108	239	370
632-Fighting Caravans (Zane Grey)	5	10	15	33	57	80
633-The Little People by Walt Scott (6/55)	6	12	18	37	66	95
634-Lady and the Tramp Album (Disney) (6/55)	8	16	24	52	99	145
635-Bob Clampett's Beany and Cecil (TV)	14	28	42	96	211	325
636-Chip 'N' Dale (Disney)	6	12	18	42	79	115
637-Silvertip (Max Brand)-Kinstler-a	5	10	15	34	60	85
638-M.G.M.'s Spike and Tyke (8/55)	6	12	18	41	76	110
639-Davy Crockett at the Alamo (Disney) (7/55) (TV)-Fess Parker photo-c	12	24	36	82	179	275
640-Western Marshal (Ernest Haycox's)-Kinstler-a	5	10	15	35	63	90
641-Steve Canyon (1955)-by Caniff	5	10	15	35	63	90
642-M.G.M.'s The Two Mouseketeers	7	14	21	44	82	120
643-Wild Bill Elliott; photo-c	5	10	15	34	60	85
644-Sir Walter Raleigh (5/55)-Based on movie "The Virgin Queen"; photo-c	6	12	18	42	79	115
645-Johnny Mack Brown; photo-c	6	12	18	40	73	105
646-Dotty Dripple and Taffy (#1)	6	12	18	37	66	95
647-Bugs Bunny's Album (9/55)	6	12	18	41	76	110
648-Jace Pearson of the Texas Rangers (TV)-Photo-c	6	12	18	40	73	105
649-Duck Album (Disney)	7	14	21	46	86	125
650-Prince Valiant; by Bob Fuje	8	16	24	55	105	155
651-King Colt (Luke Short) (9/55); Kinstler-a	6	12	18	37	66	95
652-Buck Jones	5	10	15	33	57	90

Title	GD 2.0	VG 4.0	FN 6.0	VF 8.0	VF/NM 9.0	NM- 9.2
653-Smokey the Bear (#1) (10/55)	10	20	30	67	141	215
654-Pluto (Disney)	7	14	21	46	86	125
655-Francis the Famous Talking Mule	5	10	15	33	57	80
656-Turok, Son of Stone (#2) (10/55)	42	84	126	311	706	1100
657-Ben Bowie and His Mountain Men	5	10	15	34	60	85
658-Goofy (Disney)	7	14	21	46	86	125
659-Daisy Duck's Diary (Disney)(#2)	6	12	18	42	79	115
660-Little Beaver	5	10	15	34	60	85
661-Frosty the Snowman	7	14	21	48	89	130
662-Zoo Parade (TV)-Marlin Perkins (11/55)	6	12	18	41	76	110
663-Winky Dink (TV)	10	20	30	64	132	200
664-Davy Crockett in the Great Keelboat Race (TV) (Disney) (11/55)-Fess Parker photo-c	11	22	33	75	160	245
665-The African Lion (Disney-Movie) (11/55)	5	10	15	35	63	90
666-Santa Claus Funnies	8	16	24	54	102	150
667-Silvertip and the Stolen Stallion (Max Brand) (12/55)-Kinstler-a	5	10	15	34	60	85
668-Dumbo (Disney) (12/55)-First of two printings. Dumbo on cover with starry sky. Reprints 4-Color #234?; same-c as #234	11	22	33	73	157	240
668-Dumbo (Disney) (1/58)-Second printing. Same cover altered, with Timothy Mouse added. Same contents as above	8	16	24	51	96	140
669-Robin Hood (Disney-Movie) (12/55)-Reprints #413 plus-c; photo-c	6	12	18	42	79	115
670-M.G.M's Mouse Musketeers (#1) (1/56)-Formerly the Two Mouseketeers	6	12	18	41	76	110
671-Davy Crockett and the River Pirates (TV) (Disney) (12/55)-Jesse Marsh-a; Fess Parker photo-c	11	22	33	75	160	245
672-Quentin Durward (1/56) (Movie)-Photo-c	6	12	18	42	79	115
673-Buffalo Bill, Jr. (#1) (TV)-James Arness photo-c	9	18	27	62	126	190
674-The Little Rascals (#1) (TV)	10	20	30	67	141	215
675-Steve Donovan, Western Marshal (#1) (TV)-Kinstler-a; photo-c	8	16	24	55	105	155
676-Will-Yum!	5	10	15	30	50	70
677-Little King	6	12	18	41	76	110
678-The Last Hunt (Movie)-Photo-c	6	12	18	42	79	115
679-Gunsmoke (#1) (TV)-Photo-c	21	42	63	147	324	500
680-Out Our Way with the Worry Wart (2/56)	5	10	15	35	63	90
681-Forever Darling (Movie) with Lucille Ball & Desi Arnaz (2/56)-; photo-c	11	22	33	77	166	255
682-The Sword & the Rose (Disney-Movie)-Reprint of #505; Renamed When Knighthood Was in Flower for the novel; photo-c	7	14	21	46	86	125
683-Hi and Lois (3/56)	6	12	18	42	79	115
684-Helen of Troy (Movie)-Buscema-a; photo-c	10	20	30	66	138	210
685-Johnny Mack Brown; photo-c	6	12	18	40	73	105
686-Duck Album (Disney)	7	14	21	46	86	125
687-The Indian Fighter (Movie)-Kirk Douglas photo-c	8	16	24	54	102	150
688-Alexander the Great (Movie) (5/56)-Buscema-a; photo-c	8	16	24	46	86	125
689-Elmer Fudd (3/56)	6	12	18	38	69	100
690-The Conqueror (Movie) - John Wayne photo-c	15	30	45	103	227	350
691-Dotty Dripple and Taffy	4	8	12	28	47	65
692-The Little People-Walt Scott	5	10	15	34	60	85
693-Song of the South (Disney) (1956)-Partial reprint of #129	11	22	33	76	163	250
694-Super Circus (TV)-Photo-c	7	14	21	44	82	120
695-Little Beaver	5	10	15	34	60	85
696-Krazy Kat; not by Herriman (4/56)	5	10	15	31	53	75
697-Oswald the Rabbit (Lantz)	5	10	15	33	57	80
698-Francis the Famous Talking Mule (4/56)	5	10	15	33	57	80
699-Prince Valiant-by Bob Fuje	8	16	24	55	105	155
700-Water Birds and the Olympic Elk (Disney-Movie) (4/56)	5	10	15	33	57	80
701-Jiminy Cricket (#1) (Disney) (5/56)	9	18	27	60	120	180
702-The Goofy Success Story (Disney)	7	14	21	46	86	125
703-Scamp (#1) (Disney)	11	22	33	73	157	240
704-Priscilla's Pop (5/56)	7	14	21	46	86	125
705-Brave Eagle (#1) (TV)-Photo-c	7	14	21	46	86	125
706-Bongo and Lumpjaw (Disney) (6/56)	6	12	18	41	76	110
707-Corky and White Shadow (Disney) (5/56)-Mickey Mouse Club (TV); photo-c	8	16	24	51	96	140
708-Smokey the Bear	6	12	18	40	73	105
709-The Searchers (Movie) - John Wayne photo-c	29	58	87	209	467	725
710-Francis the Famous Talking Mule	5	10	15	33	57	80
711-M.G.M's Mouse Musketeers	5	10	15	31	53	75
712-The Great Locomotive Chase (Disney-Movie) (9/56)-Photo-c	7	14	21	46	86	125
713-The Animal World (Movie) (8/56)	5	10	15	34	60	85
714-Spin and Marty (#1) (TV) (Disney)-Mickey Mouse Club (6/56); photo-c	12	24	36	79	170	260
715-Timmy (8/56)	6	12	18	41	76	110
716-Man in Space (Disney)(A science feature from Tomorrowland)	9	18	27	59	117	175
717-Moby Dick (Movie)-Gregory Peck photo-c	9	18	27	62	126	190
718-Dotty Dripple and Taffy	4	8	12	28	47	65
719-Prince Valiant; by Bob Fuje (8/56)	8	16	24	55	105	155
720-Gunsmoke (TV)-James Arness photo-c	10	20	30	66	138	210
721-Captain Kangaroo (TV)-Photo-c	13	26	39	91	201	310
722-Johnny Mack Brown-Photo-c	6	12	18	40	73	105
723-Santiago (Movie)-Kinstler-a (9/56); Alan Ladd photo-c	10	20	30	64	132	200
724-Bugs Bunny's Album	5	10	15	34	60	85
725-Elmer Fudd (5/56)	5	10	15	33	57	80
726-Duck Album (Disney) (9/56)	6	12	18	37	66	95
727-The Nature of Things (TV) (Disney)-Jesse Marsh-a	5	10	15	33	57	80
728-M.G.M's Mouse Musketeers	5	10	15	31	53	75
729-Bob Son of Battle (11/56)	5	10	15	30	50	70
730-Smokey Stover	5	10	15	35	63	90
731-Silvertip and The Fighting Four (Max Brand)-Kinstler-a	5	10	15	34	60	85
732-Zorro, the Challenge of (10/56)	13	26	39	86	188	290
733-Buck Jones	5	10	15	35	63	90
734-Cheyenne (#1) (TV) (10/56)-Clint Walker photo-c	13	26	39	89	195	300
735-Crusader Rabbit (#1) (TV)	23	46	69	161	356	550
736-Pluto (Disney)	7	14	21	46	86	125
737-Steve Canyon-Caniff-a	5	10	15	35	63	90
738-Westward Ho, the Wagons (Disney-Movie)-Fess Parker photo-c	8	16	24	54	102	150
739-Bounty Guns (Luke Short)-Drucker-a	5	10	15	30	50	70
740-Chilly Willy (#1) (Walter Lantz)	9	18	27	62	126	190
741-The Fastest Gun Alive (Movie)(9/56)-Photo-c	7	14	21	44	82	120
742-Buffalo Bill, Jr. (TV)-Photo-c	6	12	18	37	66	95
743-Daisy Duck's Diary (Disney) (11/56)	6	12	18	42	79	115
744-Little Beaver	5	10	15	34	60	85
745-Francis the Famous Talking Mule	5	10	15	33	57	80
746-Dotty Dripple and Taffy	4	8	12	28	47	65
747-Goofy (Disney)	7	14	21	46	86	125
748-Frosty the Snowman (11/56)	5	10	15	35	63	90
749-Secrets of Life (Disney-Movie)-Photo-c	5	10	15	31	53	75
750-The Great Cat Family (Disney-TV/Movie)-Pinocchio & Alice app.	6	12	18	42	79	115
751-Our Miss Brooks (TV)-Photo-c	9	18	27	59	117	175
752-Mandrake, the Magician	12	24	36	80	173	265
753-Walt Scott's Little People (11/56)	5	10	15	34	60	85
754-Smokey the Bear	5	10	15	40	73	105
755-The Littlest Snowman (12/56)	6	12	18	38	69	100
756-Santa Claus Funnies	8	16	24	54	102	150
757-The True Story of Jesse James (Movie)-Photo-c	9	18	27	58	114	170
758-Bear Country (Disney-Movie)	5	10	15	34	60	85
759-Circus Boy (TV)-The Monkees' Mickey Dolenz photo-c (12/56)	8	16	24	54	102	150
760-The Hardy Boys (#1) (TV) (Disney)-Mickey Mouse Club; photo-c	13	26	39	87	191	295
761-Howdy Doody (TV) (1/57)	9	18	27	61	123	185
762-The Sharkfighters (Movie) (1/57); Buscema-a; photo-c	9	18	27	62	126	190
763-Grandma Duck's Farm Friends (#1) (Disney)	8	16	24	51	96	140
764-M.G.M's Mouse Musketeers	5	10	15	31	53	75
765-Will-Yum!	5	10	15	30	50	70
766-Buffalo Bill, Jr. (TV)-Photo-c	6	12	18	37	66	95
767-Spin and Marty (TV) (Disney)-Mickey Mouse Club (2/57)	9	18	27	61	123	185
768-Steve Donovan, Western Marshal (TV)-Kinstler-a; photo-c	6	12	18	42	79	115
769-Gunsmoke (TV)-James Arness photo-c	10	20	30	66	138	210
770-Brave Eagle (TV)-Photo-c	5	10	15	33	57	80
771-Brand of Empire (Luke Short)(3/57)-Drucker-a	5	10	15	30	50	70
772-Cheyenne (TV)-Clint Walker photo-c	8	16	24	54	102	150
773-The Brave One (Movie)-Photo-c	5	10	15	35	63	90
774-Hi and Lois (3/56)	5	10	15	30	50	70
775-Sir Lancelot and Brian (TV)-Buscema-a; photo-c	9	18	27	59	117	175
776-Johnny Mack Brown; photo-c	6	12	18	40	73	105
777-Scamp (Disney) (3/57)	7	14	21	48	89	130
778-The Little Rascals (TV)	6	12	18	38	69	100
779-Lee Hunter, Indian Fighter (3/57)	6	12	18	40	73	105
780-Captain Kangaroo (TV)-Photo-c	12	24	36	79	170	260
781-Fury (#1) (TV) (3/57)-Photo-c	7	14	21	49	92	135
782-Duck Album (Disney)	6	12	18	37	66	95
783-Elmer Fudd	5	10	15	33	57	80
784-Around the World in 80 Days (Movie) (2/57)-Photo-c	7	14	21	46	86	125
785-Circus Boy (TV) (4/57)-The Monkees' Mickey Dolenz photo-c	10	20	30	64	132	200
786-Cinderella (Disney) (3/57)-Partial-r of #272	9	18	27	58	114	170
787-Little Hiawatha (Disney) (4/57)(#2)	6	12	18	41	76	110
788-Prince Valiant; by Bob Fuje	7	14	21	44	82	120
789-Silvertip-Valley Thieves (Max Brand) (4/57)-Kinstler-a	5	10	15	34	60	85
790-The Wings of Eagles (Movie) (John Wayne)-Toth-a; John Wayne photo-c; 10c & 15c eds exist	13	26	39	89	195	300
791-The 77th Bengal Lancers (TV)-Photo-c	7	14	21	44	82	120
792-Oswald the Rabbit (Lantz)	5	10	15	33	57	80
793-Morty Meekle	5	10	15	31	53	75
794-The Count of Monte Cristo (5/57) (Movie)-Buscema-a	8	16	24	51	96	140
795-Jiminy Cricket (Disney)(#2)	7	14	21	49	92	135
796-Ludwig Bemelman's Madeline and Genevieve	6	12	18	38	69	100
797-Gunsmoke (TV)-Photo-c	10	20	30	66	138	210
798-Buffalo Bill, Jr. (TV)-Photo-c	6	12	18	37	66	95
799-Priscilla's Pop	7	14	21	46	86	125
800-The Buccaneers (TV)-Photo-c	6	12	18	42	79	115
801-Dotty Dripple and Taffy	4	8	12	28	47	65
802-Goofy (Disney) (5/57)	7	14	21	46	86	125
803-Cheyenne (TV)-Clint Walker photo-c	8	16	24	54	102	150
804-Steve Canyon-Caniff-a (1957)	5	10	15	35	63	90
805-Crusader Rabbit (TV)	17	34	51	119	265	410
806-Scamp (Disney) (6/57)	7	14	21	48	89	130
807-Savage Range (Luke Short)-Drucker-a	5	10	15	30	50	70
808-Spin and Marty (TV) (Disney)-Mickey Mouse Club; photo-c	9	18	27	61	123	185
809-The Little People (Walt Scott)	5	10	15	34	60	85
810-Francis the Famous Talking Mule	5	10	15	31	53	75
811-Howdy Doody (TV) (7/57)	9	18	27	61	123	185

Four Color Comics #732 © DELL

Four Color Comics #823 © DELL

Four Color Comics #905 © DIS

	GD 2.0	VG 4.0	FN 6.0	VF 8.0	VF/NM 9.0	NM- 9.2
812-The Big Land (Movie); Alan Ladd photo-c	8	16	24	52	99	145
813-Circus Boy (TV)-The Monkees' Mickey Dolenz photo-c	10	20	30	64	132	200
814-Covered Wagons, Ho! (Disney)-Donald Duck (TV) (6/57); Mickey Mouse app.	7	14	21	46	86	125
815-Dragoon Wells Massacre (Movie)-photo-c	8	16	24	51	96	140
816-Brave Eagle (TV)-photo-c	5	10	15	33	57	80
817-Little Beaver	5	10	15	34	60	85
818-Smokey the Bear (6/57)	6	12	18	40	73	105
819-Mickey Mouse in Magicland (Disney) (7/57)	8	16	24	54	102	150
820-The Oklahoman (Movie)-Photo-c	9	18	27	60	120	180
821-Wringle Wrangle (Disney)-Based on movie "Westward Ho, the Wagons"; Marsh-a; Fess Parker photo-c	8	16	24	51	96	140
822-Paul Revere's Ride with Johnny Tremain (TV) (Disney)-Toth-a	9	18	27	57	111	165
823-Timmy	5	10	15	34	60	85
824-The Pride and the Passion (Movie) (8/57)-Frank Sinatra & Cary Grant photo-c	10	20	30	66	138	210
825-The Little Rascals (TV)	6	12	18	38	69	100
826-Spin and Marty and Annette (TV) (Disney)-Mickey Mouse Club; Annette Funicello photo-c	18	36	54	126	281	435
827-Silvertip Stover (8/57)	5	10	15	33	63	90
828-Buffalo Bill, Jr. (TV)-Photo-c	6	12	18	37	66	95
829-Tales of the Pony Express (TV) (8/57)-Painted-c	6	12	18	42	79	115
830-The Hardy Boys (Disney)-Mickey Mouse Club (8/57); photo-c	9	18	27	62	126	190
831-No Sleep 'Til Dawn (Movie)-Karl Malden photo-c	8	16	24	54	102	150
832-Lolly and Pepper (#1)	7	14	21	48	89	130
833-Scamp (Disney) (9/57)	7	14	21	48	89	130
834-Johnny Mack Brown; photo-c	6	12	18	40	73	105
835-Silvertip-The False Rider (Max Brand)	5	10	15	34	60	85
836-Man in Flight (Disney) (TV) (9/57)	7	14	21	48	89	130
837-Cotton Woods, (All-American Athlete...)	5	10	15	33	57	80
838-Bugs Bunny's Life Story Album (9/57)	5	10	15	34	60	85
839-The Vigilantes (Movie)	8	16	24	54	102	150
840-Duck Album (Disney) (9/57)	6	12	18	37	66	95
841-Elmer Fudd	5	10	15	33	57	80
842-The Nature of Things (Disney-Movie) ('57)-Jesse Marsh-a (TV series)	5	10	15	33	57	80
843-The First Americans (Disney) (TV)-Marsh-a	9	18	27	57	111	165
844-Gunsmoke (TV)-Photo-c	10	20	30	66	138	210
845-The Land Unknown (Movie)-Alex Toth-a	11	22	33	76	163	250
846-Gun Glory (Movie)-by Alex Toth; photo-c	8	16	24	51	96	140
847-Perri (squirrels) (Disney-Movie)-Two different covers published	6	12	18	42	79	115
848-Marauder's Moon (Luke Short)	5	10	15	30	50	70
849-Prince Valiant; by Bob Fuje	7	14	21	44	82	120
850-Buck Jones	5	10	15	35	63	90
851-The Story of Mankind (Movie) (1/58)-Hedy Lamarr & Vincent Price photo-c	8	16	24	54	102	150
852-Chilly Willy (2/58) (Lantz)	6	12	18	37	66	95
853-Pluto (Disney) (10/57)	7	14	21	46	86	125
854-The Hunchback of Notre Dame (Movie)-Photo-c	12	24	36	79	170	260
855-Broken Arrow (TV)-Photo-c	7	14	21	44	82	120
856-Buffalo Bill, Jr. (TV)-Photo-c	6	12	18	37	66	95
857-The Goofy Adventure Story (Disney) (11/57)	7	14	21	46	86	125
858-Daisy Duck's Diary (Disney) (11/57)	5	10	15	35	63	90
859-Topper and Neil (TV) (11/57)	8	16	24	51	96	140
860-Wyatt Earp (#1) (TV)-Manning-a; photo-c	11	22	33	76	163	250
861-Frosty the Snowman	5	10	15	35	63	90
862-The Truth About Mother Goose (Disney-Movie) (11/57)	8	16	24	51	96	140
863-Francis the Famous Talking Mule	5	10	15	31	53	75
864-The Littlest Snowman	6	12	18	38	69	100
865-Andy Burnett (TV) (Disney) (12/57)-Photo-c	9	18	27	57	111	165
866-Mars and Beyond (Disney-TV)(A science feature from Tomorrowland)	9	18	27	62	126	190
867-Santa Claus Funnies	8	16	24	54	102	150
868-The Little People (12/57)	5	10	15	34	60	85
869-Old Yeller (Disney-Movie)-Photo-c	6	12	18	42	73	115
870-Curly Kayoe (1/58)	5	10	15	34	60	85
871-Curly Kayoe	5	10	15	34	60	85
872-Captain Kangaroo (TV)-Photo-c	12	24	36	79	170	260
873-Grandma Duck's Farm Friends (Disney)	6	12	18	37	66	95
874-Old Ironsides (Disney-Movie with Johnny Tremain) (1/58)	8	16	24	51	96	140
875-Trumpets West (Luke Short) (2/58)	5	10	15	30	50	70
876-Tales of Wells Fargo (#1)(TV)(2/58)-Photo-c	9	18	27	62	126	190
877-Frontier Doctor with Rex Allen (TV)-Alex Toth-a; Rex Allen photo-c	9	18	27	61	123	185
878-Peanuts (#1)-Schulz-c only (2/58)	162	324	486	1337	3019	4700
879-Brave Eagle (TV) (2/58)-Photo-c	5	10	15	33	57	80
880-Steve Donovan, Western Marshal-Drucker-a (TV)-Photo-c	5	10	15	33	57	80
881-The Captain and the Kids (2/58)	5	10	15	30	50	70
882-Zorro (Disney)-1st Disney issue; by Alex Toth (TV) (2/58); photo-c	15	30	45	100	220	340
883-The Little Rascals (TV)	5	10	15	35	63	90
884-Hawkeye and the Last of the Mohicans (TV) (3/58); photo-c	7	14	21	44	82	120
885-Fury (TV) (3/58)-Photo-c	5	10	15	35	63	90
886-Bongo and Lumpjaw (Disney) (3/58)	5	10	15	31	53	75
887-The Hardy Boys (Disney) (TV)-Mickey Mouse Club (1/58)-Photo-c	9	18	27	62	126	190
888-Elmer Fudd (3/58)	5	10	15	33	57	80
889-Clint and Mac (Disney) (3/58)-Alex Toth-a; photo-c	10	20	30	67	141	215
890-Wyatt Earp (TV)-by Russ Manning; photo-c	8	16	24	56	108	160
891-Light in the Forest (Disney-Movie) (3/58)-Fess Parker photo-c	6	12	18	42	79	115
892-Maverick (TV) (4/58)-James Garner photo-c	21	42	63	147	324	500
893-Jim Bowie (TV)-Photo-c	7	14	21	44	82	120
894-Oswald the Rabbit (Lantz)	5	10	15	33	57	80
895-Wagon Train (#1) (TV) (3/58)-Photo-c	10	20	30	67	141	215
896-The Adventures of Tinker Bell (Disney)	14	28	42	96	211	325
897-Jiminy Cricket (Disney)	7	14	21	49	92	135
898-Silvertip (Max Brand)-Kinstler-a (5/58)	5	10	15	34	60	85
899-Goofy (Disney) (5/58)	5	10	15	35	63	90
900-Prince Valiant; by Bob Fuje	7	14	21	44	82	120
901-Little Hiawatha (Disney)	6	12	18	41	76	110
902-Will-Yum!	5	10	15	30	50	70
903-Dotty Dripple and Taffy	4	8	12	28	47	65
904-Lee Hunter, Indian Fighter	5	10	15	30	50	70
905-Annette (Disney) (TV) (5/58)-Mickey Mouse Club; Annette Funicello photo-c	24	48	72	168	372	575
906-Francis the Famous Talking Mule	5	10	15	31	53	75
907-Sugarfoot (#1) (TV)-Toth-a; photo-c	12	24	36	79	170	260
908-The Little People and the Giant-Walt Scott (5/58)	5	10	15	34	60	85
909-Smitty	4	8	12	27	44	60
910-The Vikings (Movie)-Buscema-a; Kirk Douglas photo-c	9	18	27	59	117	175
911-The Gray Ghost (TV)-Photo-c	8	16	24	55	105	155
912-Leave It to Beaver (#1) (TV)-Photo-c	17	34	51	117	259	400
913-The Left-Handed Gun (Movie) (7/58); Paul Newman photo-c	10	20	30	64	132	200
914-No Time for Sergeants (Movie)-Andy Griffith photo-c; Toth-a	10	20	30	66	138	210
915-Casey Jones (TV)-Alan Hale photo-c	6	12	18	40	73	105
916-Red Ryder Ranch Comics (7/58)	4	8	12	28	47	65
917-The Life of Riley (TV)-Photo-c	11	22	33	73	157	240
918-Beep Beep, the Roadrunner (#1) (7/58)-Published with two different back covers	15	30	45	103	227	350
919-Boots and Saddles (TV)-Photo-c	7	14	21	48	89	130
920-Zorro (Disney) (TV) (6/58)Toth-a; photo-c	10	20	30	69	147	225
921-Wyatt Earp (TV)-Manning-a; photo-c	8	16	24	56	108	160
922-Johnny Mack Brown by Russ Manning; photo-c	7	14	21	44	82	120
923-Timmy	5	10	15	34	60	85
924-Colt .45 (#1) (8/58)-W. Preston photo-c	10	20	30	64	132	200
925-Last of the Fast Guns (Movie) (8/58)-Photo-c	6	12	18	41	76	110
926-Peter Pan (Disney)-Reprint of #442	6	12	18	42	79	115
927-Top Gun (Luke Short) Buscema-a	5	10	15	30	50	70
928-Sea Hunt (#1) (9/58) (TV)-Lloyd Bridges photo-c	12	24	36	83	182	280
929-Brave Eagle (TV)-Photo-c	5	10	15	33	57	80
930-Maverick (TV) (7/58)-James Garner photo-c	11	22	33	73	157	240
931-Have Gun, Will Travel (#1) (TV)-Photo-c	15	30	45	103	227	350
932-Smokey the Bear (His Life Story)	6	12	18	40	73	105
933-Zorro (Disney, 9/58)-Alex Toth-a; photo-c	10	20	30	69	147	225
934-Restless Gun (#1) (TV)-Photo-c	10	20	30	64	132	200

	GD 2.0	VG 4.0	FN 6.0	VF 8.0	VF/NM 9.0	NM- 9.2
935-King of the Royal Mounted	5	10	15	31	53	75
936-The Little Rascals (TV)	5	10	15	35	63	90
937-Ruff and Reddy (#1) (9/58) (TV) (1st Hanna-Barbera comic book)	12	24	36	82	179	275
938-Elmer Fudd (9/58)	5	10	15	33	57	80
939-Steve Canyon - not by Caniff	5	10	15	35	63	90
940-Lolly and Pepper (10/58)	5	10	15	30	50	70
941-Pluto (Disney) (10/58)	5	10	15	35	63	90
942-Pony Express (Tales of the ...) (TV)	5	10	15	34	60	85
943-White Wilderness (Disney-Movie) (10/58)	6	12	18	37	66	95
944-The 7th Voyage of Sinbad (Movie) (9/58)-Buscema-a; photo-c	12	24	36	84	185	285
945-Maverick (TV)-James Garner/Jack Kelly photo-c	11	22	33	73	157	240
946-The Big Country (Movie)-Photo-c	6	12	18	42	79	115
947-Broken Arrow (TV) (11/58)	5	10	15	33	57	80
948-Daisy Duck's Diary (Disney) (11/58)	5	10	15	35	63	90
949-High Adventure(Lowell Thomas')(TV)-Photo-c	6	12	18	42	79	115
950-Frosty the Snowman	5	10	15	35	63	90
951-The Lennon Sisters Life Story (TV)-Toth-a, 32 pgs.; photo-c	11	22	33	76	163	250
952-Goofy (Disney) (11/58)	5	10	15	35	63	90
953-Francis the Famous Talking Mule	5	10	15	31	53	75
954-Man in Space-Satellites (TV)	8	16	24	51	96	140
955-Hi and Lois (11/58)	5	10	15	30	50	70
956-Ricky Nelson (#1) (TV)-Photo-c	17	34	51	119	265	410
957-Buffalo Bee (#1) (TV)	9	18	27	59	117	175
958-Santa Claus Funnies	7	14	21	44	82	120
959-Christmas Stories-(Walt Scott's Little People) (1951-56 strip reprints)	5	10	15	34	60	85
960-Zorro (Disney) (TV) (12/58)-Toth art; photo-c	10	20	30	69	147	225
961-Jace Pearson's Tales of the Texas Rangers (TV)-Spiegle-a; photo-c	5	10	15	34	60	85
962-Maverick (TV) (1/59)-James Garner/Jack Kelly photo-c	11	22	33	73	157	240
963-Johnny Mack Brown; photo-c	6	12	18	40	73	105
964-The Hardy Boys (TV) (Disney) (1/59)-Mickey Mouse Club; photo-c	9	18	27	62	126	190
965-Grandma Duck's Farm Friends (Disney)(1/59)	5	10	15	34	60	85
966-Tonka (starring Sal Mineo; Disney-Movie)-Photo-c	8	16	24	56	108	160
967-Chilly Willy (2/59) (Lantz)	6	12	18	37	66	95
968-Tales of Wells Fargo (TV)-Photo-c	8	16	24	54	102	150
969-Peanuts (2/59)	36	72	108	259	580	900
970-Lawman (#1) (TV)-Photo-c	12	24	36	79	170	260
971-Wagon Train (TV)-Photo-c	6	12	18	41	76	110
972-Tom Thumb (Movie)-George Pal (1/59)	8	16	24	56	105	160
973-Sleeping Beauty and the Prince(Disney)(5/59)	13	26	39	86	188	290
974-The Little Rascals (TV) (3/59)	5	10	15	35	63	90
975-Fury (TV)-Photo-c	5	10	15	35	63	90
976-Zorro (Disney) (TV)-Toth-a; photo-c	10	20	30	69	147	225
977-Elmer Fudd (3/59)	5	10	15	33	57	80
978-Lolly and Pepper	5	10	15	30	50	70
979-Oswald the Rabbit (Lantz)	5	10	15	33	57	80
980-Maverick (TV) (4-6/59)-James Garner/Jack Kelly photo-c	11	22	33	73	157	240
981-Ruff and Reddy (TV) (Hanna-Barbera)	8	16	24	52	99	145
982-The New Adventures of Tinker Bell (TV) (Disney)	10	20	30	70	150	230
983-Have Gun, Will Travel (TV) (4-6/59)-Photo-c	10	20	30	64	132	200
984-Sleeping Beauty's Fairy Godmothers (Disney)	10	20	30	69	147	225
985-Shaggy Dog (Disney-Movie)-Photo-all four covers; Annette on back-c(5/59)	9	18	27	57	111	165
986-Restless Gun (TV)-Photo-c	7	14	21	49	92	135
987-Goofy (Disney) (7/59)	5	10	15	35	63	90
988-Little Hiawatha (Disney)	6	12	18	41	76	110
989-Jiminy Cricket (Disney) (5-7/59)	7	14	21	49	92	135
990-Huckleberry Hound (#1)(TV)(Hanna-Barbera); 1st app. Huck, Yogi Bear, & Pixie & Dixie & Mr. Jinks	20	40	60	140	310	480
991-Francis the Famous Talking Mule	5	10	15	31	53	75
992-Sugarfoot (TV)-Toth-a; photo-c	10	20	30	66	138	210
993-Jim Bowie (TV)-Photo-c	5	10	15	35	63	90
994-Sea Hunt (TV)-Lloyd Bridges photo-c	9	18	27	59	117	175
995-Donald Duck Album (Disney) (5-7/59)(#1)	7	14	21	44	82	120
996-Nevada (Zane Grey)	5	10	15	33	57	80
997-Walt Disney Presents-Tales of Texas John Slaughter (#1) (TV) (Disney)-Photo-c; photo of W. Disney inside-c	8	16	24	51	96	140
998-Ricky Nelson (TV)-Photo-c	17	34	51	119	265	410
999-Leave It to Beaver (TV)-Photo-c	14	28	42	96	211	325
1000-The Gray Ghost (TV) (6-8/59)-Photo-c	8	16	24	55	105	155
1001-Lowell Thomas' High Adventure (TV) (8-10/59)-Photo-c	5	10	15	34	60	85
1002-Buffalo Bee (TV)	6	12	18	42	79	115
1003-Zorro (TV) (Disney)-Toth-a; photo-c	10	20	30	69	147	225
1004-Colt .45 (TV) (6-8/59)-Photo-c	8	16	24	51	96	140
1005-Maverick (TV)-James Garner/Jack Kelly photo-c	11	22	33	73	157	240
1006-Hercules (Movie)-Buscema-a; photo-c	11	22	33	73	157	240
1007-John Paul Jones (Movie)-Robert Stack photo-c	6	12	18	40	73	105
1008-Beep Beep, the Road Runner (7-9/59)	8	16	24	54	102	150
1009-The Rifleman (#1) (TV)-Photo-c	24	48	72	168	372	575
1010-Grandma Duck's Farm Friends (Disney)-by Carl Barks	11	22	33	73	157	240
1011-Buckskin (TV)	7	14	21	44	82	120
1012-Last Train from Gun Hill (Movie) (7/59)-Photo-c	8	16	24	56	108	160
1013-Bat Masterson (#1) (TV) (8/59)-Gene Barry photo-c	11	22	33	72	154	235
1014-The Lennon Sisters (TV)-Toth-a; photo-c	11	22	33	72	154	235
1015-Peanuts-Schulz-c	36	72	108	259	580	900
1016-Smokey the Bear Nature Stories	5	10	15	31	53	75
1017-Chilly Willy (Lantz)	6	12	18	37	66	95
1018-Rio Bravo (Movie)(6/59)-John Wayne; Toth-a; John Wayne, Dean Martin & Ricky Nelson photo-c	30	60	90	216	483	750
1019-Wagon Train (TV)-Photo-c	6	12	18	41	76	110
1020-Jungle Jim-McWilliams-a	5	10	15	33	57	80
1021-Jace Pearson's Tales of the Texas Rangers (TV)-Photo-c	5	10	15	34	60	85
1022-Timmy	5	10	15	34	60	85
1023-Tales of Wells Fargo (TV)-Photo-c	8	16	24	54	102	150
1024-Darby O'Gill and the Little People (Disney-Movie)-Toth-a; photo-c	9	18	27	59	117	175
1025-Vacation in Disneyland (8-10/59)-Carl Barks-a(24pgs.) (Disney)	15	30	45	103	227	350
1026-Spin and Marty (TV) (Disney) (9-11/59)-Mickey Mouse Club; photo-c	7	14	21	44	82	120
1027-The Texan (#1)(TV)-Photo-c	9	18	27	57	111	165
1028-Rawhide (#1) (9-11/59)-Clint Eastwood photo-c; Tufts-a	26	52	78	182	404	625
1029-Boots and Saddles (TV) (9/59)-Photo-c	5	10	15	34	60	85
1030-Spanky and Alfalfa, the Little Rascals (TV)	5	10	15	35	63	90
1031-Fury (TV)-Photo-c	5	10	15	35	63	90
1032-Elmer Fudd	5	10	15	33	57	80
1033-Steve Canyon-not by Caniff; photo-c	5	10	15	35	63	90
1034-Nancy and Sluggo Summer Camp (9-11/59)	5	10	15	30	50	70
1035-Lawman (TV)-Photo-c	8	16	24	55	105	155
1036-The Big Circus (Movie)	6	12	18	40	73	105
1037-Zorro (Disney) (TV)-Tufts-a; Annette Funicello photo-c	12	24	36	81	176	270
1038-Ruff and Reddy (TV)(Hanna-Barbera)(1959)	8	16	24	52	99	145
1039-Pluto (Disney) (11-1/60)	5	10	15	35	63	90
1040-Quick Draw McGraw (#1) (TV) (Hanna-Barbera) (12-2/60)	15	30	45	100	220	340
1041-Sea Hunt (TV) (10-12/59)-Toth-a; Lloyd Bridges photo-c	9	18	27	59	117	175
1042-The Three Chipmunks (Alvin, Simon & Theodore) (#1) (TV) (10-12/59)	12	24	36	79	170	260
1043-The Three Stooges (#1)-Photo-c	23	46	69	161	356	550
1044-Have Gun, Will Travel (TV)-Photo-c	10	20	30	64	132	200
1045-Restless Gun (TV)-Photo-c	7	14	21	49	92	135
1046-Beep Beep, the Road Runner (11-1/60)	8	16	24	54	102	150
1047-Gyro Gearloose (#1) (Disney)-All Barks-c/a	16	32	48	111	246	380
1048-The Horse Soldiers (Movie) (John Wayne)-Sekowsky-a; painted cover featuring John Wayne	12	24	36	80	173	265
1049-Don't Give Up the Ship (Movie) (8/59)-Jerry Lewis photo-c	9	18	27	58	114	170
1050-Huckleberry Hound (TV) (Hanna-Barbera) (10-12/59)	12	24	36	83	182	280
1051-Donald in Mathmagic Land (Disney-Movie)	8	16	24	56	108	160
1052-Ben-Hur (Movie) (11/59)-Manning-a	10	20	30	66	138	210
1053-Goofy (Disney) (11-1/60)	5	10	15	35	63	90
1054-Huckleberry Hound Winter Fun (TV) (Hanna-Barbera) (12/59)	12	24	36	83	182	280
1055-Daisy Duck's Diary (Disney)-by Carl Barks (11-1/60)	9	18	27	59	117	175
1056-Yellowstone Kelly (Movie)-Clint Walker photo-c	6	12	18	41	76	110
1057-Mickey Mouse Album (Disney)	7	14	21	46	86	125
1058-Colt .45 (TV)-Photo-c	8	16	24	51	96	140
1059-Sugarfoot (TV)-Photo-c	7	14	21	49	92	135
1060-Journey to the Center of the Earth (Movie)-Pat Boone & James Mason photo-c	13	26	39	89	195	300
1061-Buffalo Bee (TV)	6	12	18	42	79	115
1062-Christmas Stories (Walt Scott's Little People strip-r)	5	10	15	34	60	85
1063-Santa Claus Funnies	7	14	21	44	82	120
1064-Bugs Bunny's Merry Christmas (12/59)	5	10	15	34	60	85
1065-Frosty the Snowman	5	10	15	35	63	90
1066-77 Sunset Strip (#1) (TV)-Toth-a (1-3/60)-Efrem Zimbalist, Jr. & Edd "Kookie" Byrnes photo-c	9	18	27	63	129	195
1067-Yogi Bear (#1) (TV) (Hanna-Barbera)	14	28	42	96	211	325
1068-Francis the Famous Talking Mule	5	10	15	31	53	75
1069-The FBI Story (Movie)-Toth-a; James Stewart photo on-c	9	18	27	61	123	185
1070-Solomon and Sheba (Movie)-Sekowsky-a; photo-c	10	20	30	64	132	200
1071-The Real McCoys (#1) (TV) (1-3/60)-Toth-a; Walter Brennan photo-c	10	20	30	64	132	200
1072-Blythe (Marge's)	5	10	15	34	60	85
1073-Grandma Duck's Farm Friends-Barks-c/a (Disney)	11	22	33	73	157	240
1074-Chilly Willy (Lantz)	6	12	18	37	66	95
1075-Tales of Wells Fargo (TV)-Photo-c	8	16	24	54	102	150
1076-The Rebel (#1) (TV)-Sekowsky-a; photo-c	10	20	30	68	144	220
1077-The Deputy (#1) (TV)-Buscema-a; Henry Fonda photo-c	10	20	30	64	132	200
1078-The Three Stooges (2-4/60)-Photo-c	11	22	33	76	163	250
1079-The Little Rascals (TV) (Spanky & Alfalfa)	5	10	15	35	63	90
1080-Fury (TV) (2-4/60)-Photo-c	5	10	15	35	63	90
1081-Elmer Fudd	5	10	15	33	57	80
1082-Spin and Marty (Disney) (TV)-Photo-c	7	14	21	44	82	120
1083-Men into Space (TV)-Anderson-a; photo-c	6	12	18	41	76	110
1084-Speedy Gonzales	8	16	24	51	96	140
1085-The Time Machine (H.G. Wells) (Movie) (3/60)-Alex Toth-a; Rod Taylor photo-c	18	36	54	124	275	425
1086-Lolly and Pepper	5	10	15	30	50	70
1087-Peter Gunn (TV)-Photo-c	8	16	24	52	99	145

Four Color Comics #1015 © UFS

Four Color Comics #1087 © DELL

Four Color Comics #1187 © DELL

	GD 2.0	VG 4.0	FN 6.0	VF 8.0	VF/NM 9.0	NM- 9.2
1088-A Dog of Flanders (Movie)-Photo-c	5	10	15	33	57	80
1089-Restless Gun (TV)-Photo-c	7	14	21	49	92	135
1090-Francis the Famous Talking Mule	5	10	15	31	53	75
1091-Jacky's Diary (4-6/60)	5	10	15	34	60	85
1092-Toby Tyler (Disney-Movie)-Photo-c	6	12	18	41	76	110
1093-MacKenzie's Raiders (Movie/TV)-Richard Carlson photo-c from TV show	6	12	18	40	73	105
1094-Goofy (Disney)	5	10	15	35	63	90
1095-Gyro Gearloose (Disney)-All Barks-c/a	9	18	27	62	126	190
1096-The Texan (TV)-Rory Calhoun photo-c	7	14	21	46	86	125
1097-Rawhide (TV)-Manning-a; Clint Eastwood photo-c	13	26	39	91	201	310
1098-Sugarfoot (TV)-Photo-c	7	14	21	49	92	135
1099-Donald Duck Album (Disney) (5-7/60)-Barks-c	7	14	21	44	82	120
1100-Annette's Life Story (Disney-Movie) (5/60)-Annette Funicello photo-c	18	36	54	125	276	430
1101-Robert Louis Stevenson's Kidnapped (Disney-Movie) (5/60); photo-c	6	12	18	42	79	115
1102-Wanted: Dead or Alive (#1) (TV) (5-7/60); Steve McQueen photo-c	15	30	45	103	227	350
1103-Leave It to Beaver (TV)-Photo-c	14	28	42	96	211	325
1104-Yogi Bear Goes to College (TV) (Hanna-Barbera) (6-8/60)	9	18	27	59	117	175
1105-Gale Storm (Oh! Susanna) (TV)-Toth-a; photo-c	10	20	30	69	147	225
1106-77 Sunset Strip(TV)(6-8/60)-Toth-a; photo-c	7	14	21	49	92	135
1107-Buckskin (TV)-Photo-c	6	12	18	40	73	105
1108-The Troubleshooters (TV)-Keenan Wynn photo-c	6	12	18	42	79	115
1109-This Is Your Life, Donald Duck (Disney) (TV) (8-10/60)-Gyro flashback to WDC&S #141; origin Donald Duck (1st told)	12	24	36	81	176	270
1110-Bonanza (TV) (6-8/60)-Photo-c	32	64	96	230	515	800
1111-Shotgun Slade (TV)-Photo-c	6	12	18	40	73	105
1112-Pixie and Dixie and Mr. Jinks (#1) (TV) (Hanna-Barbera) (7-9/60)	8	16	24	54	102	150
1113-Tales of Wells Fargo (TV)-Photo-c	8	16	24	54	102	150
1114-Huckleberry Finn (Movie) (7/60)-Photo-c	6	12	18	42	79	115
1115-Ricky Nelson (TV)-Manning-a; photo-c	12	24	36	82	179	275
1116-Boots and Saddles (TV) (8/60)-Photo-c	5	10	15	34	60	85
1117-Boy and the Pirates (Movie)-Photo-c	6	12	18	37	66	95
1118-The Sword and the Dragon (Movie) (6/60)-Photo-c	9	18	27	57	111	165
1119-Smokey the Bear Nature Stories	5	10	15	31	53	75
1120-Dinosaurus (Movie)-Painted-c	8	16	24	51	96	140
1121-Hercules Unchained (Movie) (8/60)-Crandall/Evans-a	9	18	27	62	126	190
1122-Chilly Willy (Lantz)	6	12	18	37	66	95
1123-Tombstone Territory (TV)-Photo-c	7	14	21	49	92	135
1124-Whirlybirds (#1) (TV)-Photo-c	7	14	21	49	92	135
1125-Laramie (#1) (TV)-Photo-c; G. Kane/Heath-a	9	18	27	59	117	175
1126-Hotel Deparee - Sundance (TV) (8-10/60)-Earl Holliman photo-c	6	12	18	42	79	115
1127-The Three Stooges-Photo-c (8-10/60)	11	22	33	76	163	250
1128-Rocky and His Friends (TV) (Jay Ward) (8-10/60)	28	56	84	202	451	700
1129-Pollyanna (Disney-Movie)-Hayley Mills photo-c	8	16	24	52	99	145
1130-The Deputy (TV)-Buscema-a; Henry Fonda photo-c	8	16	24	54	102	150
1131-Elmer Fudd (9-11/60)	5	10	15	33	57	80
1132-Space Mouse (Lantz) (8-10/60)	6	12	18	37	66	95
1133-Fury (TV)-Photo-c	5	10	15	35	63	90
1134-Real McCoys (TV)-Toth-a; photo-c	10	20	30	64	132	200
1135-M.G.M.'s Mouse Musketeers (9-11/60)	4	8	12	28	47	65
1136-Jungle Cat (Disney-Movie)-Photo-c	6	12	18	40	73	105
1137-The Little Rascals (TV)	5	10	15	35	63	90
1138-The Rebel (TV)-Photo-c	8	16	24	55	105	155
1139-Spartacus (Movie) (11/60)-Buscema-a; Kirk Douglas photo-c	11	22	33	77	166	255
1140-Donald Duck Album (Disney)-Barks-c	7	14	21	44	82	120
1141-Huckleberry Hound for President (TV) (Hanna-Barbera) (10/60)	7	14	21	46	86	125
1142-Johnny Ringo (TV)-Photo-c	7	14	21	49	92	135
1143-Pluto (Disney) (11-1/60)	5	10	15	35	63	90
1144-The Story of Ruth (Movie)-Photo-c	9	18	27	57	111	165
1145-The Lost World (Movie)-Gil Kane-a; photo-c; 1 pg. Conan Doyle biography by Torres	9	18	27	61	123	185
1146-Restless Gun (TV)-Photo-c; Wildey-a	7	14	21	49	92	135
1147-Sugarfoot (TV)-Photo-c	7	14	21	49	92	135
1148-I Aim at the Stars-the Werner Von Braun Story (Movie) (11-1/61)-Photo-c	7	14	21	44	82	120
1149-Goofy (Disney) (11-1/61)	5	10	15	35	63	90
1150-Daisy Duck's Diary (Disney) (12-1/61) by Carl Barks	9	18	27	59	117	175
1151-Mickey Mouse Album (Disney) (11-1/61)	7	14	21	46	86	125
1152-Rocky and His Friends (TV) (Jay Ward) (12-2/61)	17	34	51	114	252	390
1153-Frosty the Snowman	5	10	15	35	63	90
1154-Santa Claus Funnies	7	14	21	44	82	120
1155-North to Alaska (Movie)-John Wayne photo-c	15	30	45	105	233	360
1156-Walt Disney Swiss Family Robinson (Movie) (12/60)-Photo-c	9	18	27	62	126	190
1157-Master of the World (Movie) (7/61)	8	16	24	55	105	155
1158-Three Worlds of Gulliver (2 issues exist with different covers) (Movie)-Photo-c	6	12	18	42	79	115
1159-77 Sunset Strip (TV)-Toth-a; photo-c	7	14	21	49	92	135
1160-Rawhide (TV)-Clint Eastwood photo-c	13	26	39	91	201	310
1161-Grandma Duck's Farm Friends (Disney) by Carl Barks	11	22	33	73	157	240
1162-Yogi Bear Joins the Marines (TV) (Hanna-Barbera) (5-7/61)	9	18	27	59	117	175
1163-Daniel Boone (3-5/61); Marsh-a	5	10	15	35	63	90
1164-Wanted: Dead or Alive (TV)-Steve McQueen photo-c	10	20	30	69	147	225
1165-Ellery Queen (#1) (3-5/61)	9	18	27	58	114	175
1166-Rocky and His Friends (TV) (Jay Ward)	17	34	51	114	252	390
1167-Tales of Wells Fargo (TV)-Photo-c	7	14	21	48	89	130
1168-The Detectives (TV)-Robert Taylor photo-c	10	20	30	66	138	210
1169-New Adventures of Sherlock Holmes	13	26	39	89	195	300
1170-The Three Stooges (3-5/61)-Photo-c	11	22	33	76	163	250
1171-Elmer Fudd	5	10	15	33	57	80
1172-Fury (TV)-Photo-c	5	10	15	35	63	90
1173-The Twilight Zone (#1) (TV) (5/61)-Crandall/Evans-c/a; Crandall tribute to Ingles	24	48	72	168	372	575
1174-The Little Rascals (TV)	5	10	15	33	57	80
1175-M.G.M.'s Mouse Musketeers (3-5/61)	4	8	12	28	47	65
1176-Dondi (Movie)-Origin; photo-c	6	12	18	37	66	95
1177-Chilly Willy (Lantz) (4-6/61)	6	12	18	37	66	95
1178-Ten Who Dared (Disney-Movie) (12/60)-Painted-c; cast member photo on back-c	7	14	21	46	86	125
1179-The Swamp Fox (TV) (Disney)-Leslie Nielsen photo-c	10	20	30	64	132	200
1180-The Danny Thomas Show (TV)-Toth-a; photo-c	16	32	48	111	246	380
1181-Texas John Slaughter (TV) (Walt Disney Presents...) (4-6/61)-Photo-c	6	12	18	42	79	115
1182-Donald Duck Album (Disney) (5-7/61)	5	10	15	34	60	90
1183-101 Dalmatians (Disney-Movie) (3/61)	12	24	36	79	170	260
1184-Gyro Gearloose; All Barks-c/a (Disney) (5-7/61) Two variations exist	9	18	27	62	126	190
1185-Sweetie Pie	5	10	15	38	69	100
1186-Yak Yak (#1) by Jack Davis (2 versions - one minus 3-pg. Davis-c/a)	8	16	24	56	108	160
1187-The Three Stooges (6-8/61)-Photo-c	11	22	33	76	163	250
1188-Atlantis, the Lost Continent (Movie) (5/61)-Photo-c	9	18	27	62	126	190
1189-Greyfriars Bobby (Disney-Movie) (11/61)-Photo-c (scarce)	6	12	18	41	76	110
1190-Donald and the Wheel (Disney) (11/61); Barks-c	9	18	27	59	117	175
1191-Leave It to Beaver (TV)-Photo-c	14	28	42	96	211	325
1192-Ricky Nelson (TV)-Manning-a; photo-c	12	24	36	82	179	275
1193-The Real McCoys (TV) (6-8/61)-Photo-c	7	14	21	48	89	130
1194-Pepe (Movie) (4/61)-Photo-c	5	10	15	33	57	80
1195-National Velvet (#1) (TV)-Photo-c	6	12	18	41	76	110
1196-Pixie and Dixie and Mr. Jinks (TV) (Hanna-Barbera) (7-9/61)	5	10	15	35	63	90
1197-The Aquanauts (TV) (5-7/61)-Photo-c	8	16	24	55	105	155
1198-Donald in Mathmagic Land (Disney-Movie)-Reprint of #1051	6	12	18	37	66	95
1199-The Absent-Minded Professor (Disney-Movie) (4/61)-Photo-c						

	GD 2.0	VG 4.0	FN 6.0	VF 8.0	VF/NM 9.0	NM- 9.2
	8	16	24	54	102	150
1199-Shaggy Dog & The Absent-Minded Professor (Disney-Movie) (8/67)-Photo-c						
1200-Hennessey (TV) (8-10/61)-Gil Kane-a; photo-c	8	16	24	54	102	150
	8	16	24	52	99	145
1201-Goofy (Disney) (8-10/61)	5	10	15	35	63	90
1202-Rawhide (TV)-Clint Eastwood photo-c	13	26	39	91	201	310
1203-Pinocchio (Disney) (3/62)	8	16	24	54	102	150
1204-Scamp (Disney)	4	8	12	27	44	60
1205-David and Goliath (Movie) (7/61)-Photo-c	7	14	21	48	89	130
1206-Lolly and Pepper (9-11/61)	5	10	15	30	50	70
1207-The Rebel (TV)-Sekowsky-a; photo-c	8	16	24	55	105	155
1208-Rocky and His Friends (Jay Ward) (TV)	17	34	51	114	252	390
1209-Sugarfoot (TV)-Photo-c (10-12/61)	7	14	21	49	92	135
1210-The Parent Trap (Disney-Movie) (8/61)-Hayley Mills photo-c						
	10	20	30	67	141	215
1211-77 Sunset Strip (TV)-Manning-a; photo-c	7	14	21	46	86	125
1212-Chilly Willy (Lantz) (7-9/61)	6	12	18	37	66	95
1213-Mysterious Island (Movie)-Photo-c	9	18	27	61	123	185
1214-Smokey the Bear	5	10	15	31	53	75
1215-Tales of Wells Fargo (TV) (10-12/61)	7	14	21	48	89	130
1216-Whirlybirds (TV)-Photo-c	7	14	21	46	86	125
1218-Fury (TV)-Photo-c	5	10	15	35	63	90
1219-The Detectives (TV)-Robert Taylor & Adam West photo-c						
	10	20	30	66	138	210
1220-Gunslinger (TV)-Photo-c	8	16	24	52	99	145
1221-Bonanza (TV) (9-11/61)-Photo-c	15	30	45	100	220	340
1222-Elmer Fudd (9-11/61)	5	10	15	33	57	80
1223-Laramie (TV)-Gil Kane-a; photo-c	6	12	18	37	66	95
1224-The Little Rascals (TV) (10-12/61)	5	10	15	33	57	80
1225-The Deputy (TV)-Henry Fonda photo-c	8	16	24	54	102	150
1226-Nikki, Wild Dog of the North (Disney-Movie) (9/61)-Photo-c						
	5	10	15	33	57	80
1227-Morgan the Pirate (Movie)-Photo-c	8	16	24	51	96	140
1229-Thief of Baghdad (Movie)-Crandall/Evans-a; photo-c						
	6	12	18	41	76	110
1230-Voyage to the Bottom of the Sea (#1) (Movie)-Photo insert on-c						
	12	24	36	83	182	280
1231-Danger Man (TV) (9-11/61)-Patrick McGoohan photo-c						
	11	22	33	77	166	255
1232-On the Double (Movie)	6	12	18	37	66	95
1233-Tammy Tell Me True (Movie) (1961)	8	16	24	56	108	160
1234-The Phantom Planet (Movie) (1961)	9	18	27	57	111	165
1235-Mister Magoo (#1) (12-2/62)	7	14	21	48	89	130
1235-Mister Magoo (3-5/65) 2nd printing; reprint of 12-2/62 issue						
	5	10	15	35	63	90
1236-King of Kings (Movie)-Photo-c	8	16	24	52	99	145
1237-The Untouchables (#1) (TV)-Not by Toth; photo-c						
	18	36	54	124	275	425
1238-Deputy Dawg (TV)	9	18	27	63	129	195
1239-Donald Duck Album (Disney) (10-12/61)-Barks-a						
	7	14	21	44	82	120
1240-The Detectives (TV)-Tufts-a; Robert Taylor photo-c						
	8	16	24	51	96	140
1241-Sweetie Pie	5	10	15	31	53	75
1242-King Leonardo and His Short Subjects (#1) (TV) (11-1/62)						
	10	20	30	67	141	215
1243-Ellery Queen	7	14	21	48	89	130
1244-Space Mouse (Lantz) (11-1/62)	6	12	18	37	66	95
1245-New Adventures of Sherlock Holmes	11	22	33	75	160	245
1246-Mickey Mouse Album (Disney)	7	14	21	46	86	125
1247-Daisy Duck's Diary (Disney) (12-2/62)	5	10	15	35	63	90
1248-Pluto (Disney)	5	10	15	35	63	90
1249-The Danny Thomas Show (TV)-Manning-a; photo-c						
	12	24	36	80	173	265
1250-The Four Horsemen of the Apocalypse (Movie)-Photo-c						
	9	18	27	59	117	175
1251-Everything's Ducky (Movie) (1961)	7	14	21	49	92	135
1252-The Andy Griffith Show (TV)-Photo-c; 1st show aired 10/3/60						
	42	84	126	311	706	1100
1253-Space Man (#1) (1-3/62)	9	18	27	62	126	190
1254- "Diver Dan" (#1) (TV) (2-4/62)-Photo-c	10	20	30	69	147	225
1255-The Wonders of Aladdin (Movie) (1961)	7	14	21	46	86	125
1256-Kona, Monarch of Monster Isle (#1) (2-4/62)-Glanzman-a						
	10	20	30	69	147	225
1257-Car 54, Where Are You? (#1) (TV) (3-5/62)-Photo-c						
	9	18	27	59	117	175
1258-The Frogmen (#1)-Evans-a	10	20	30	66	138	210
1259-El Cid (Movie) (1961)-Photo-c	8	16	24	51	96	140
1260-The Horsemasters (TV, Movie) (Disney) (12-2/62)-Annette Funicello photo-c						
	10	20	30	69	147	225
1261-Rawhide (TV)-Clint Eastwood photo-c	13	26	39	91	201	310
1262-The Rebel (TV)-Photo-c	8	16	24	55	105	155
1263-77 Sunset Strip (TV) (12-2/62)-Manning-a; photo-c						
	7	14	21	46	86	125
1264-Pixie and Dixie and Mr. Jinks (TV) (Hanna-Barbera)						
	5	10	15	35	63	90
1265-The Real McCoys (TV)-Photo-c	7	14	21	48	89	130
1266-M.G.M.'s Spike and Tyke (12-2/62)	5	10	15	30	50	70
1267-Gyro Gearloose; Barks-c/a, 4 pgs. (Disney) (12-2/62)						
	7	14	21	48	89	130
1268-Oswald the Rabbit (Lantz)	5	10	15	33	57	80
1269-Rawhide (TV)-Clint Eastwood photo-c	13	26	39	91	201	310
1270-Bullwinkle and Rocky (#1) (TV) (Jay Ward) (3-5/62)						
	16	32	48	112	249	385
1271-Yogi Bear Birthday Party (TV) (Hanna-Barbera) (11/61) (Given away for 1 box top from Kellogg's Corn Flakes)						
	6	12	18	40	73	105
1272-Frosty the Snowman	5	10	15	35	63	90
1273-Hans Brinker (Disney-Movie)-Photo-c (2/62)	6	12	18	37	66	95
1274-Santa Claus Funnies (12/61)	7	14	21	44	82	120
1275-Rocky and His Friends (Jay Ward)	17	34	51	114	252	390
1276-Dondi	4	8	12	28	47	65
1278-King Leonardo and His Short Subjects (TV)	10	20	30	67	141	215
1279-Grandma Duck's Farm Friends (Disney)	5	10	15	34	60	85
1280-Hennessey (TV)-Photo-c	6	12	18	42	79	115
1281-Chilly Willy (Lantz) (4-6/62)	6	12	18	37	66	95
1282-Babes in Toyland (Disney-Movie) (1/62); Annette Funicello photo-c						
	13	26	39	86	188	290
1283-Bonanza (TV) (2-4/62)-Photo-c	15	30	45	100	220	340
1284-Laramie (TV)-Heath-a; photo-c	6	12	18	37	66	95
1285-Leave It to Beaver (TV)-Photo-c	14	28	42	96	211	325
1286-The Untouchables (TV)-Photo-c	13	26	39	89	195	300
1287-Man from Wells Fargo (TV)-Photo-c	6	12	18	42	79	115
1288-Twilight Zone (TV) (4/62)-Crandall/Evans-c/a	12	24	36	83	182	280
1289-Ellery Queen	7	14	21	48	89	130
1290-M.G.M.'s Mouse Musketeers	4	8	12	28	47	65
1291-77 Sunset Strip (TV)-Manning-a; photo-c	7	14	21	46	86	125
1293-Elmer Fudd (3-5/62)	5	10	15	33	57	80
1294-Ripcord (TV)	7	14	21	46	86	125
1295-Mister Ed, the Talking Horse (#1) (TV) (3-5/62)-Photo-c						
	15	30	45	100	220	340
1296-Fury (TV) (3-5/62)-Photo-c	5	10	15	35	63	90
1297-Spanky, Alfalfa and the Little Rascals (TV)	5	10	15	33	57	80
1298-The Hathaways (TV)-Photo-c	6	12	18	37	66	95
1299-Deputy Dawg (TV)	9	18	27	63	129	195
1300-The Comancheros (Movie) (1961)-John Wayne						
	15	30	45	105	233	360
1301-Adventures in Paradise (TV) (2-4/62)	6	12	18	38	69	100
1302-Johnny Jason, Teen Reporter (2-4/62)	4	8	12	25	40	55
1303-Lad: A Dog (Movie)-Photo-c	5	10	15	33	57	80
1304-Nellie the Nurse (3-5/62)-Stanley-a	10	20	30	67	141	215
1305-Mister Magoo (3-5/62)	7	14	21	49	89	130
1306-Target: The Corruptors (#1) (TV) (3-5/62)-Photo-c						
	5	10	15	35	63	90
1307-Margie (TV) (3-5/62)	8	16	24	55	105	155
1308-Tales of the Wizard of Oz (TV) (3-5/62)	15	30	45	103	227	350
1309-87th Precinct (#1) (TV) (4-6/62)-Krigstein-a; photo-c						
	9	18	27	60	120	180
1310-Huck and Yogi Winter Sports (TV) (Hanna-Barbera) (3/62)						
	8	16	24	54	102	150
1311-Rocky and His Friends (TV) (Jay Ward)	17	34	51	114	252	390
1312-National Velvet (TV)-Photo-c	4	8	12	27	44	60
1313-Moon Pilot (Disney-Movie)-Photo-c	7	14	21	44	82	120
1328-The Underwater City (Movie) (1961)-Evans-a; photo-c						
	7	14	21	49	92	135
1329-See Gyro Gearloose #01329-207						
1330-Brain Boy (#1)-Gil Kane-a	10	20	30	69	147	225
1332-Bachelor Father (TV)	7	14	21	49	92	135
1333-Short Ribs (4-6/62)	6	12	18	42	79	115
1335-Aggie Mack (4-6/62)	6	12	18	37	66	95
1336-On Stage; not by Leonard Starr	5	10	15	34	60	85
1337-Dr. Kildare (#1) (TV) (4-6/62)-Photo-c	10	20	30	64	132	200
1341-The Andy Griffith Show (TV) (4-6/62)-Photo-c	36	72	108	266	596	925
1348-Yak Yak (#2)-Jack Davis-c/a	7	14	21	46	86	125
1349-Yogi Bear Visits the U.N. (TV) (Hanna-Barbera) (1/62)-Photo-c						
	8	16	24	54	102	150
1350-Comanche (Disney-Movie)(1962)-Reprints 4-Color #966 (title change from "Tonka" to "Comanche") (4-6/62)-Sal Mineo photo-c						
	6	12	18	38	69	100
1354-Calvin & the Colonel (#1) (TV) (4-6/62)	10	20	30	64	132	200

NOTE: Missing numbers probably do not exist.

4-D MONKEY, THE (Adventures of... #? on)
Leung's Publications: 1988 - No. 11, 1990 ($1.80/$2.00, 52 pgs.)

1-11: 1-Karate Pig, Ninja Flounder & 4-D Monkey (48 pgs., centerfold is a Christmas card).
2-4 (52 pgs.) 4.00

FOUR FAVORITES (Crime Must Pay the Penalty No. 33 on)
Ace Magazines: Sept, 1941 - No. 32, Dec, 1947

	GD 2.0	VG 4.0	FN 6.0	VF 8.0	VF/NM 9.0	NM- 9.2
1-Vulcan, Lash Lightning (formerly Flash Lightning in Sure-Fire), Magno the Magnetic Man & The Raven begin; flag/Hitler-c	331	662	993	2317	4059	5800
2-The Black Ace only app.; WWII flag-c	181	362	543	1158	1979	2800
3-Last Vulcan; V For Victory WWII-c	168	336	504	1075	1838	2600
4,5: 4-The Raven & Vulcan end; Unknown Soldier begins (see Our Flag), ends #28.						
5-Captain Courageous begins (5/42), ends #28 (moves over from Captain Courageous #6); not in #6. 5,6-Bondage/torture-c	181	362	543	1158	1979	2800
6-8: 6-The Flag app.; Mr. Risk begins (7/42)	148	296	444	947	1624	2300
9-Kurtzman-a (Lash Lightning); robot-c	168	336	504	1075	1838	2600
10-Classic Kurtzman-c/a (Magno & Davey)	371	742	1113	2600	4550	6500
11-Kurtzman-a; Hitler, Mussolini, Hirohito-c; L.B. Cole-a; Unknown Soldier by Kurtzman	377	754	1131	2639	4620	6600
12-L.B. Cole-a; Japanese WWII-c	174	348	522	1114	1907	2700
13-L.B. Cole-a (his first cover?); WWII-c	155	310	465	992	1696	2400
14,16-18,20: 18,20-Palais-c/a	84	168	252	538	919	1300
15-Japanese WWII-c	100	200	300	635	1093	1550
19-Nazi WWII bondage-c	161	322	483	1030	1765	2500
21-No Unknown Soldier; The Unknown app.	110	220	330	704	1202	1700
22-27: 22-Captain Courageous drops costume. 23-Unknown Soldier drops costume.						
25-29-Hap Hazard app. 26-Last Magno	61	122	183	390	670	950
28,29: Hap Hazard app. in all	43	86	129	271	461	650
30-32: 30-Funny-c begins (teen humor), end #32	23	46	69	136	223	310

NOTE: *Dave Berg* c-5. *Jim Mooney* a-6; c-1-3. *Palais* a-18-20; c-18-25.

FOUR HORSEMEN, THE (See The Crusaders)

FOUR HORSEMEN
DC Comics (Vertigo): Feb, 2000 - No. 4, May, 2000 ($2.50, limited series)

Four Color Comics #1258 © DELL

Four Favorites #12 © ACE

The Fox (2013 series) #1 © ACP

	GD 2.0	VG 4.0	FN 6.0	VF 8.0	VF/NM 9.0	NM- 9.2

1-4-Esad Ribic-c/a; Robert Rodi-s ... 3.00

FOUR HORSEMEN OF THE APOCALYPSE, THE (Movie)
Dell Publishing Co.: No. 1250, Jan-Mar, 1962 (one-shot)
Four Color 1250-Photo-c ... 9 18 27 59 117 175

4MOST (Foremost Boys No. 32-40; becomes Thrilling Crime Cases #41 on)
Novelty Publications/Star Publications No. 37-on:
Winter, 1941-42 - V8#(#36), 9-10/49; #37, 11-12/49 - #40, 4-5/50
V1#1-The Target by Sid Greene, The Cadet & Dick Cole begin with origins retold; produced by Funnies Inc.; quarterly issues begin, end V6#3; German WWII-c
... 219 438 657 1402 2401 3400
2-Last Target (Spr/42); WWII cover ... 77 154 231 847 1200
3-Dan'l Flannel begins; flag-c ... 53 106 159 334 567 800
4-1pg. Dr. Seuss (signed) (Aut/42); fish in the face-c ... 58 116 174 371 636 900
V2#1-3 ... 28 56 84 165 270 375
4-Hitler, Tojo & Mussolini app. as pumpkins on-c ... 77 154 231 493 847 1200
V3#1-4 ... 20 40 60 114 182 250
V4#1-4: 2-Walter Johnson-c ... 15 30 45 83 124 165
V5#1-4: 1-The Target & Targeteers app. ... 14 28 42 76 108 140
V6#1-4 ... 11 22 33 62 86 110
5-L.B. Cole-c ... 25 50 75 150 245 340
V7#1,3,5, V8#1, 37 ... 11 22 33 60 83 105
2,4,6-L.B. Cole-c. 6-Last Dick Cole ... 22 44 66 128 209 290
V8#2,3,5-L.B. Cole-c/a ... 25 50 75 150 245 340
4-L.B. Cole-a ... 16 32 48 92 144 195
38-40: 38-Johnny Weismuller (Tarzan) life story & Jim Braddock (boxer) life story.
38-40-L.B. Cole-c. 40-Last White Rider ... 17 34 51 98 154 210
Accepted Reprint 38-40 (nd): 40-r/Johnny Weismuller life story; all have L.B. Cole-c
... 10 20 30 56 76 95

411
Marvel Comics: June, 2003 - No. 2, Jul, 2003 ($3.50, limited series)
1,2-Tributes to peacemakers; s/a by various. 1-Millar, Quitely, Mack, Winslade & others-s/a.
2-Harris, Phillips, Manco, Bruce Jones. ... 3.50

FOUR POINTS, THE
Aspen MLT Inc.: Apr, 2015 - No. 5, Aug, 2015 ($3.99)
1-5-Lobdell-s/Gunderson-a; multiple covers ... 4.00

FOUR-STAR BATTLE TALES
National Periodical Publications: Feb-Mar, 1973 - No. 5, Nov-Dec, 1973
1-Reprints begin ... 3 6 9 16 24 32
2-5 ... 2 4 6 11 16 20
NOTE: Drucker r-1, 3-5. Heath r-2, 5; c-1. Krigstein r-5. Kubert r-4; c-2.

FOUR STAR SPECTACULAR
National Periodical Publications: Mar-Apr, 1976 - No. 6, Jan-Feb, 1977
1-Includes G.A. Flash story with new art ... 3 6 9 14 20 25
2-6: Reprints in all. 2-Infinity cover ... 2 4 6 8 11 14
NOTE: All contain DC Superhero reprints. #1 has 68 pgs.; #2-6, 52 pgs. #1, 4-Hawkman app.; #2-Kid Flash app.; #3-Green Lantern app; #2, 4, 5-Wonder Woman, Superboy app; #5-Green Arrow, Vigilante app; #6-Blackhawk G.A.-r.

FOUR TEENERS (Formerly Crime Must Pay The Penalty; Dotty No. 35 on)
A. A. Wyn: Jan-Feb, 1948 (52 pgs.)
34-Teen-age comic; Dotty app.; Curly & Jerry continue from Four Favorites
... 20 40 60 114 182 250

FOURTH MAN, THE
AWA Studios: Jan, 2022 - No. 4, Apr, 2022 ($3.99, limited series)
1-4-Jeff McComsly-s/Mike Deodato, Jr.-a ... 4.00

4001 A.D. (See Valiant 2016 FCBD edition for prelude)
Valiant Entertainment: May, 2016 - No. 4, Aug, 2016 ($3.99, limited series)
1-4-Matt Kindt-s/Clayton Crain-a. 1-David Mack-a (3 pages) ... 4.00
...: Bloodshot 1 (6/16, $3.99) Lemire-s/Braithwaite-a; Bloodshot reforms in 4001 A.D. ... 4.00
...: Shadowman 1 (7/16, $3.99) Houser & Roberts-s/Gill-a ... 4.00
...: War Mother 1 (8/16, $3.99) Van Lente-s/Giorello-a ... 4.00
...: X-O Manowar 1 (5/16, $3.99) Venditti-s/Henry-a; prelude to main series ... 4.00

FOURTH WORLD GALLERY (Jack Kirby's...)
DC Comics: 1996 (9/96) ($3.50, one-shot)
nn-Pin-ups of Jack Kirby's Fourth World characters (New Gods, Forever People & Mister Miracle) by John Byrne, Rick Burchett, Dan Jurgens, Walt Simonson & others ... 4.00

FOUR WOMEN
DC Comics (Homage): Dec, 2001 - No. 5, Apr, 2002 ($2.95, limited series)

1-5-Sam Kieth-s/a ... 3.00
TPB (2002, $17.95) r/series; foreward by Kieth ... 18.00

FOX, THE
Archie Comic Publications (Red Circle Comics): Dec, 2013 - No. 5, Apr, 2014 ($2.99)
1-5-Dean Haspiel-a/Haspiel and Mark Waid-s. 1-Three covers. 2-Two covers ... 3.00

FOX, THE
Archie Comic Publications (Dark Circle Comics): Jun, 2015 - No. 5, Oct, 2015 ($3.99)
1-5-Dean Haspiel-a/Haspiel and Mark Waid-s; multiple covers on each ... 4.00
...: Family Values 1 (7/22, $3.99. one-shot) Haspiel-s/a; reprint with Alex Toth-s/a ... 4.00

FOX AND THE CROW (Stanley & His Monster No. 109 on) (See Comic Cavalcade & Real Screen Comics)
National Periodical Publications: Dec-Jan, 1951-52 - No. 108, Feb-Mar, 1968
1 ... 135 270 387 826 1413 2100
2(Scarce) ... 58 116 174 371 636 900
3-5 ... 39 78 117 231 378 525
6-10 (6-7/53) ... 28 56 84 165 270 375
11-20 (10/54) ... 20 40 60 118 192 265
21-30: 22-Last precode issue (2/55) ... 15 30 45 85 130 175
31-40 ... 13 26 39 74 105 135
41-60 ... 6 12 18 38 69 100
61-80 ... 5 10 15 33 57 80
81-94: 94-(11/65)-The Brat Finks begin ... 8 8 12 27 44 60
95-Stanley & His Monster begins (origin & 1st app) ... 9 18 27 61 123 185
96-99,101-108 ... 3 6 9 21 33 45
100 (10-11/66) ... 4 8 12 23 37 50
NOTE: Many later covers by Mort Drucker.

FOX AND THE HOUND, THE (Disney)(Movie)
Whitman Publishing Co.: Aug, 1981 - No. 3, Oct, 1981
11292- Golden Press Graphic Novel ... 2 4 6 8 10 12
1-3-Based on animated movie ... 1 2 3 5 7 9

FOXFIRE (See The Phoenix Resurrection)
Malibu Comics (Ultraverse): Feb, 1996 - No. 4, May, 1996 ($1.50)
1-4: Sludge, Ultraforce app. 4-Punisher app. ... 4.00

FOX GIANTS (Also see Giant Comics Edition)
Fox Feature Syndicate: 1944 - 1950 (25¢, 132 - 196 pgs.)
Album of Crime nn(1949, 132p) ... 77 154 231 493 847 1200
Album of Love nn(1949, 132p) ... 84 168 252 538 919 1300
All Famous Crime nn(1949, 132p) ... 77 154 231 493 847 1200
All Good Comics 1(1944, 132p)(R.W. Voigt)-The Bouncer, Purple Tigress, Rick Evans, Puppeteer, Green Mask; Infinity-c ... 100 200 300 635 1093 1550
All Great nn(1944, 132p)-Capt. Jack Terry, Rick Evans, Jaguar Man ... 68 136 204 435 743 1050
All Great nn(Chicago Nite Life News)(1945, 132p)-Green Mask, Bouncer, Puppeteer, Rick Evans, Rocket Kelly ... 68 136 204 435 743 1050
All-Great Confession Magazine nn(1949, 132p) ... 81 162 243 518 884 1250
All-Great Confessions nn(1949, 132p) ... 81 162 243 518 884 1250
All Great Crime Stories nn(1949, 132p) ... 77 154 231 493 847 1200
All Great Jungle Adventures nn('49, 132p) ... 100 200 300 635 1093 1550
All Real Confession Magazine 3(1949, 132p) ... 81 162 243 518 884 1250
All Real Confession Magazine 4 (4/49, 132p) ... 81 162 243 518 884 1250
All Your Comics 1(1944, 132p)-The Puppeteer, Red Robbins, & Merciless the Sorcerer ... 65 130 195 416 708 1000
Almanac Of Crime nn(1948, 148p)-Phantom Lady ... 93 186 279 591 1021 1450
Almanac Of Crime 1(1950, 132p) ... 74 148 222 470 810 1150
Book Of Love nn(1950, 132p) ... 77 154 231 493 847 1200
Burning Romances 1(1949, 132p) ... 97 194 291 621 1061 1500
Crimes Incorporated nn(1950, 132p) ... 71 142 213 454 777 1100
Daring Love Stories nn(1950, 132p) ... 77 154 231 493 847 1250
Everybody's Comics 1(1944, 50¢, 196p)-The Green Mask, The Puppeteer, The Bouncer, Rocket Kelly, Rick Evans ... 77 154 231 493 847 1200
Everybody's Comics 1(1946, 196p)-Green Lama, The Puppeteer ... 65 130 195 416 708 1000
Everybody's Comics 1(1946, 196p)-Same as 1945 Ribtickler ... 52 104 156 328 552 775
Everybody's Comics 1(1947, 132p)-Jo-Jo, Purple Tigress, Cosmo Cat, Bronze Man ... 65 130 195 416 708 1000
Exciting Romance Stories nn(1949, 132p) ... 81 162 243 518 884 1250
Famous Love nn(1950, 132p)-Photo-c ... 77 154 231 493 847 1200
Intimate Confessions nn(1950, 132p) ... 77 154 231 493 847 1200
Journal Of Crime nn(1949, 132p) ... 77 154 231 493 847 1200
Love Problems nn(1949, 132p) ... 81 162 243 518 884 1250

	GD 2.0	VG 4.0	FN 6.0	VF 8.0	VF/NM 9.0	NM- 9.2
Love Thrills nn(1950, 132p)	77	154	231	493	847	1200
March of Crime nn('48, 132p)-Female w/rifle-c	81	162	243	518	884	1250
March of Crime nn('49, 132p)-Cop w/pistol-c	71	142	213	454	777	1100
March of Crime nn(1949, 132p)-Coffin & man w/machine-gun-c	71	142	213	454	777	1100
Revealing Love Stories nn(1950, 132p)	77	154	231	493	847	1200
Ribtickler nn(1945, 50¢, 196p)-Chicago Nite Life News; Marvel Mutt, Cosmo Cat, Flash Rabbit, The Nebbs app.	57	114	171	362	619	875
Romantic Thrills nn(1950, 132p)	77	154	231	493	847	1200
Secret Love Stories nn(1949, 132p)	81	162	243	518	884	1250
Strange Love nn(1950, 132p)-Photo-c	110	220	330	704	1202	1700
Sweetheart Scandals nn(1950, 132p)	77	154	231	493	847	1200
Teen-Age Love nn(1950, 132p)	77	154	231	493	847	1200
Throbbing Love nn(1950, 132p)-Photo-c; used in POP, pg. 107	103	206	309	659	1130	1600
Truth About Crime nn(1949, 132p)	77	154	231	493	847	1200
Variety Comics 1(1946, 132p)-Blue Beetle, Jungle Jo	74	148	222	470	810	1150
Variety Comics nn(1950, 132p)-Jungle Jo, My Secret Affair (w/Harrison/Wood-a), Crimes by Women & My Story	60	120	180	381	653	925
Western Roundup nn('50, 132p)-Hoot Gibson; Cody of the Pony Express app.	48	96	144	302	514	725

NOTE: Each of the above usually contain four remaindered Fox books minus covers. Since these missing covers often had the first page of the first story, most Giants therefore are incomplete. Approximate values are listed. Books with appearances of Phantom Lady, Rulah, Jo-Jo, etc. could bring more.

FOXHOLE (Becomes Never Again #8?)
Mainline/Charlton 5 on: 9-10/54 - No. 4, 3-4/55; No. 5, 7/55 - No. 7, 3/56

	GD 2.0	VG 4.0	FN 6.0	VF 8.0	VF/NM 9.0	NM- 9.2
1-Classic Kirby-c	206	412	618	1318	2259	3200
2-Kirby-c/a(2); Kirby scripts based on his war time experiences	53	106	159	334	567	800
3-5-Simon/Kirby-c only	39	78	117	231	378	525
6-Kirby-c/a(2)	45	90	135	284	480	675
7-Simon & Kirby-c	27	54	81	158	259	360
Super Reprints #10,15-17: 10-r/? 15,16-r/United States Marines #5,8. 17-r/Monty Hall #?	3	6	9	16	23	30
11,12,14-r/Foxhole #1,2,3; Kirby-c	3	6	9	21	33	45

NOTE: *Kirby* a(r)-Super #11, 12. *Powell* a(r)-Super #15, 16. Stories by actual veterans.

FOXY FAGAN COMICS (Funny Animal)
Dearfield Publishing Co.: Dec, 1946 - No. 7, Summer, 1948

	GD 2.0	VG 4.0	FN 6.0	VF 8.0	VF/NM 9.0	NM- 9.2
1-Foxy Fagan & Little Buck begin	17	34	51	98	154	210
2	10	20	30	54	72	90
3-7: 6-Rocket ship-c	9	18	27	50	65	80

FRACTION
DC Comics (Focus): June, 2004 - No. 6, Nov, 2004 ($2.50, limited series)
1-6-David Tischman-s/Timothy Green II-a — 3.00
SC (2011, $17.99) r/#1-6; cover gallery — 18.00

FRACTURED FAIRY TALES (TV)
Gold Key: Oct, 1962 (Jay Ward)

	GD 2.0	VG 4.0	FN 6.0	VF 8.0	VF/NM 9.0	NM- 9.2
1 (10022-210)-From Bullwinkle TV show	10	20	30	69	147	225

FRAGGLE ROCK (TV)
Marvel Comics (Star Comics)/Marvel V2 on: Apr, 1985 - No. 8, Sept, 1986; V2#1, Apr, 1988 - No. 5, Aug, 1988

	GD 2.0	VG 4.0	FN 6.0	VF 8.0	VF/NM 9.0	NM- 9.2
1 (75¢-c)	3	6	9	15	22	28
2-6 (75¢-c)	1	3	4	6	8	10
7,8	1	2	3	5	6	8
V2#1-5-($1.00): Reprints 1st series						4.00

FRAGGLE ROCK: JOURNEY TO THE EVERSPRING, (JIM HENSON'S...)
Archaia: Oct, 2014 - No. 4, Jan, 2015 ($3.99, limited series)
1-4-Kate Leth-s/Jake Myler-a. 1-Multiple covers — 5.00

FRANCIS, BROTHER OF THE UNIVERSE
Marvel Comics Group: 1980 (75¢, 52 pgs., one-shot)
1-John Buscema/Marie Severin-a; story of Francis Bernadone, celebrating his 800th birthday in 1982 — 6.00

FRANCIS THE FAMOUS TALKING MULE (All based on movie)
Dell Publishing Co.: No. 335 (#1), June, 1951 - No. 1090, March, 1960

	GD 2.0	VG 4.0	FN 6.0	VF 8.0	VF/NM 9.0	NM- 9.2
Four Color 335 (#1)	11	22	33	77	166	255
Four Color 465	6	12	18	41	76	110
Four Color 501,547,579	5	10	15	35	63	90
Four Color 621,655,698,710,745	5	10	15	33	57	80
Four Color 810,863,906,953,991,1068,1090	5	10	15	31	53	75

FRANK
Nemesis Comics (Harvey): Apr (Mar inside), 1994 - No. 4, 1994 ($1.75/$2.50, limited series)
1-4-($2.50, direct sale): 1-Foil-c Edition — 4.00
1-4-($1.75)-Newsstand Editions; Cowan-a in all — 4.00

FRANK
Fantagraphics Books: Sept, 1996 ($2.95, B&W)
1-Woodring-c/a/scripts — 4.00

FRANK BUCK (Formerly My True Love)
Fox Feature Syndicate: No. 70, May, 1950 - No. 3, Sept, 1950

	GD 2.0	VG 4.0	FN 6.0	VF 8.0	VF/NM 9.0	NM- 9.2
70-Wood a(p)(3 stories)-Photo-c	40	80	120	246	411	575
71-Wood-a (9 pgs.); photo/painted-c	22	44	66	128	209	290
3-Photo/painted-c	16	32	48	92	144	195

NOTE: Based on "Bring 'Em Back Alive" TV show.

FRANKEN-CASTLE (See The Punisher, 2009 series)

FRANKENSTEIN (See Dracula, Movie Classics & Werewolf)
Dell Publishing Co.: Aug-Oct, 1964; No. 2, Sept, 1966 - No. 4, Mar, 1967

	GD 2.0	VG 4.0	FN 6.0	VF 8.0	VF/NM 9.0	NM- 9.2
1(12-283-410)(1964)(2nd printing; see Movie Classics for 1st printing)	8	16	24	52	99	145
2-Intro. & origin super-hero character (9/66)	5	10	15	35	63	90
3,4	4	8	12	27	44	60

FRANKENSTEIN (The Monster of...; also see Monsters Unleashed #2, Power Record Comics, Psycho & Silver Surfer #7)
Marvel Comics Group: Jan, 1973 - No. 18, Sept, 1975

	GD 2.0	VG 4.0	FN 6.0	VF 8.0	VF/NM 9.0	NM- 9.2
1-Ploog-c/a begins, ends #6	11	22	33	73	157	240
2	5	10	15	35	63	90
3-5	4	8	12	23	37	50
6,7,10: 7-Dracula cameo	3	6	9	18	28	38
8,9-Dracula c/sty. 9-Death of Dracula	5	10	15	31	53	75
11-17	3	6	9	16	23	30
18-Wrightson-c(i)	3	6	9	17	26	35

NOTE: *Adkins* c-17i. *Buscema* a-7-10p. *Ditko* a-12r. *G. Kane* c-15p. *Orlando* a-8r. *Ploog* a-1-3, 4p, 5p, 6; c-1-6. *Wrightson* c-18i.

FRANKENSTEIN (Mary Wollstonecraft Shelley's...; A Marvel Illustrated Novel)
Marvel Pub.: 1983 ($8.95, B&W, 196 pgs., 8x11" TPB)

	GD 2.0	VG 4.0	FN 6.0	VF 8.0	VF/NM 9.0	NM- 9.2
nn-Wrightson-a; 4 pg. intro. by Stephen King	5	10	15	35	63	90
Limited HC Edition						175.00

FRANKENSTEIN, AGENT OF S.H.A.D.E. (New DC 52)
DC Comics: Nov, 2011 - No. 16, Mar, 2013 ($2.99)
1-16: 1-Lemire-s/Ponticelli-a/J.G. Jones-c; Ray Palmer & The Creature Commandos app. 5-Crossover with OMAC #5. 13-15-Rotworld — 3.00
#0 (11/12, $2.99) Kindt-s/Ponticelli-a; Frankenstein's origin — 3.00

FRANKENSTEIN ALIVE, ALIVE
IDW Publishing: May, 2012 - No. 4, Jan, 2018 ($3.99, B&W)
1-3-Niles-s/Wrightson-a; interview with creators; excerpt from M.W. Shelley writings — 4.00
4-($4.99) Art by Wrightson and Kelley Jones — 5.00
... Reanimated Edition (4/14, $5.99) r/#1,2; silver foil cover logo — 6.00
... Trio (1/18, $7.99) r/#1-3; silver foil cover logo — 8.00

FRANKENSTEIN COMICS (Also See Prize Comics)
Prize Publ. (Crestwood/Feature): Sum, 1945 - V5#5(#33), Oct-Nov, 1954

	GD 2.0	VG 4.0	FN 6.0	VF 8.0	VF/NM 9.0	NM- 9.2
1-Frankenstein begins by Dick Briefer (origin); Frank Sinatra parody	383	766	1149	2681	4691	6700
2	123	246	369	787	1344	1900
3-5	90	180	270	576	988	1400
6-10: 7-S&K a(r)/Headline Comics. 8(7-8/47)-Superman satire	81	162	243	518	884	1250
11-17(1-2/49)-11-Boris Karloff parody/c/story. 17-Last humor issue	61	122	183	390	670	950
18(3/52)-New origin, horror series begins	148	296	444	947	1624	2300
19,20(V3#4, 8-9/52)	110	220	330	704	1202	1700
21(V3#5), 22(V3#6), 23(V4#1) - #28(V4#6)	81	162	243	518	884	1250
29(V5#1) - #33(V5#5)	65	130	195	416	708	1000

NOTE: *Briefer* c/a-all. *Meskin* a-21, 29.

FRANKENSTEIN/DRACULA WAR, THE
Topps Comics: Feb, 1995 - No. 3, May, 1995 ($2.50, limited series)
1-3 — 4.00

FRANKENSTEIN, JR. (...& the Impossibles) (TV)
Gold Key: Jan, 1966 (Hanna-Barbera)

	GD 2.0	VG 4.0	FN 6.0	VF 8.0	VF/NM 9.0	NM- 9.2
1-Super hero (scarce)	12	24	36	83	182	280

FRANKENSTEIN MOBSTER
Image Comics: No. 0, Oct, 2003 - No. 7, Dec, 2004 ($2.95)
0-7: 0-Two covers by Wheatley and Hughes; Wheatley-s/a. 1-Variant-c by Wieringo — 3.00

FRANKENSTEIN: NEW WORLD (From Hellboy)
Dark Horse Comics: Aug, 2022 - No. 4, Dec, 2022 ($3.99, limited series)
1-4-Mignola, Golden & Sniegoski-s/Bergting-a — 4.00

FRANKENSTEIN: OR THE MODERN PROMETHEUS
Caliber Press: 1994 ($2.95, one-shot)
1 — 4.00

FRANKENSTEIN UNDERGROUND (From Hellboy)
Dark Horse Comics: Mar, 2015 - No. 5, Jul, 2015 ($3.50, limited series)
1-5-Mike Mignola-s/c; Ben Stenbeck-a — 3.50

FRANKENSTEIN UNDONE (From Hellboy)
Dark Horse Comics: Jan, 2020 - No. 2, Apr, 2020 ($3.99, limited series)
1,2-Mike Mignola & Scott Allie-s/Ben Stenbeck-a/c — 4.00

FRANK FRAZETTA FANTASY ILLUSTRATED (Magazine)
Quantum Cat Entertainment: Spring 1998 - No. 8 ($5.95, quarterly)

	GD 2.0	VG 4.0	FN 6.0	VF 8.0	VF/NM 9.0	NM- 9.2
1-Anthology; art by Corben, Horley, Jusko	1	2	3	4	6	8	10

1-Linsner variant-c — 15.00
2-Battle Chasers by Madureira; Harris-a — 8.00
2-Madureira Battle Chasers variant-c — 12.00
3-8-Frazetta-c — 6.00
3-Tony Daniel variant-c — 15.00
5,6-Portacio variant-c, 7,8-Alex Nino variant-c — 10.00
8-Alex Ross Chicago Comicon variant-c — 10.00

FRANK FRAZETTA'S DAWN ATTACK
Opus Comics: Nov, 2022 - Present ($4.99)
1-4: 1,2-Yapur & McDaid-a — 5.00

FRANK FRAZETTA'S DEATH DEALER
Image Comics: Mar, 2007 - No. 6, Jan, 2008 ($3.99)
1-6-Nat Jones; 3 covers (Frazetta, Jones, Jones sketch) — 4.00

FRANK FRAZETTA'S DEATH DEALER
Opus Comics: May, 2022 - No. 15, Sept, 2023 ($4.99)
1-15: 1-4-Iverson-s/Martino-a. 5-Gronbekk-s/Galindo-a — 5.00

FRANK FRAZETTA'S MOTHMAN
Opus Comics: May, 2023 - No. 3, Oct, 2023 ($4.99)
1-3: 1-Hedrick-s/Mutti & Guaragna-a — 5.00

Frankenstein Undone #1 © Mike Mignola

Frank Frazetta's Dawn Attack #1 © Frazetta

Frank Miller's Pandora #1 © FMP

	GD 2.0	VG 4.0	FN 6.0	VF 8.0	VF/NM 9.0	NM- 9.2

FRANK FRAZETTA'S TALES OF SCIENCE-FANTASY
Opus Comics: Apr, 2023 - Present ($4.99)

1,2: 1-Tipton-s/Ruiz-a						5.00

FRANK FRAZETTA'S...
Fantagraphics Books/Image Comics: one-shots

	1	3	4	6	8	
... Creatures 1 (Image Comics, 7/08, $3.99) Bergting-a; covers by Frazetta & Bergting	1	3	4	6	8	10
... Dark Kingdom 1-4 (Image, 4/08 - No. 4, 1/10, $3.99) Vigil-a; covers by Frazetta & Vigil	1	3	4	6	8	10
... Dracula Meets the Wolfman 1 (Image, 8/08, $3.99) Francavilla-a; 2 covers	1	3	4	6	8	10
... Moon Maid 1 (Image, 1/09, $3.99) Tim Vigil; covers by Frazetta & Vigil	1	3	4	6	8	10
... Neanderthal 1 (Image, 4/09, $3.99) Fotos & Vigil-a; covers by Frazetta & Fotos	1	3	4	6	8	10
... Sorcerer 1 (Image, 8/09, $3.99) Medors-a; covers by Frazetta & Medors	1	3	4	6	8	10
... Swamp Demon 1 (Image, 7/08, $3.99) Medors-a; covers by Frazetta & Medors	1	3	4	6	8	10
... Thun'da Tales 1 (Fantagraphics Books, 1987, $2.00) Frazetta-r	1	3	4	6	8	10
... Untamed Love 1 (Fantagraphics Books, 11/87, $2.00) r/1950's romance comics	1	3	4	6	8	10

FRANKIE COMICS (...& Lana No. 13-15) (Formerly Movie Tunes; becomes Frankie Fuddle No. 16 on)
Marvel Comics (MgPC): No. 4, Wint, 1946-47 - No. 15, June, 1949

	GD	VG	FN	VF	VF/NM	NM-
4-Mitzi, Margie, Daisy app.	32	64	96	188	307	425
5-9	20	40	60	118	192	265
10-15: 13-Anti-Wertham editorial	18	36	54	105	165	225

FRANKIE DOODLE (See Sparkler, both series)
United Features Syndicate: No. 7, 1939

	GD	VG	FN	VF	VF/NM	NM-
Single Series 7	39	78	117	240	395	550

FRANKIE FUDDLE (Formerly Frankie & Lana)
Marvel Comics: No. 16, Aug, 1949 - No. 17, Nov, 1949

	GD	VG	FN	VF	VF/NM	NM-
16,17	16	32	48	94	147	200

FRANKLIN RICHARDS (Fantastic Four)
Marvel Comics: April, 2006 - Jun, 2009 ($2.99/$3.99, one-shots)

...: A Fantastic Year 1 (2018, $7.99) reprints various one-shots; Eliopoulos-s/a						8.00
...: April Fools (6/09, $3.99) Eliopoulos-s/a						4.00
...: Collected Chaos (2008, $8.99, digest) reprints various one-shots						9.00
...: Fall Football Fiasco (1/08, $2.99) Eliopoulos-s/a						3.00
...: Happy Franksgiving (1/07, $2.99) Thanksgiving stories by Eliopoulos-a/Sumerak-s						3.00
...: It's Dark Reigning Cats & Dogs (4/09, $3.99) Eliopoulos-s/a						4.00
...: Lab Brat (2007, $7.99, digest) reprints one-shots and Masked Marvel back-ups						8.00
...: March Madness (5/07, $2.99) More science gone wrong by Eliopoulos-a/Sumerak-s						3.00
...: Monster Mash (11/07, $2.99) Science mishaps by Eliopoulos-a/Sumerak-s						3.00
...: Not-So-Secret Invasion (7/08, $2.99) Skrull cover; The Wizard app.						3.00
...: One Shot (4/06, $2.99) short stories by Eliopoulos-a/Sumerak-s						4.00
...: School's Out (4/09, $3.99) Eliopoulos-s/a; Katie Power app.						4.00
...: Sons of Geniuses (1/09, $3.99) parallel dimension alternate version hijinks						4.00
...: Spring Break (5/08, $2.99) short stories by Eliopoulos-a/Sumerak-s						3.00
...: Summer Smackdown (10/08, $2.99) short stories by Eliopoulos-a/Sumerak-s						3.00
...: Super Summer Spectacular (9/06, $2.99) short stories by Eliopoulos-a/Sumerak-s						3.00
...: World Be Warned (8/07, $2.99) short stories by Eliopoulos-a/Sumerak-s; Hulk app.						3.00

FRANK LUTHER'S SILLY PILLY COMICS (See Jingle Dingle...)
Children's Comics (Maltex Cereal): 1950 (10¢)

	GD	VG	FN	VF	VF/NM	NM-
1-Characters from radio, records, & TV	15	30	45	85	130	175

NOTE: Also printed as a promotional comic for Maltex cereal.

FRANK MERRIWELL AT YALE (Speed Demons No. 5 on?)
Charlton Comics: June, 1955 - No. 4, Jan, 1956 (also see Shadow Comics)

	GD	VG	FN	VF	VF/NM	NM-
1	9	18	27	52	69	85
2-4	7	14	21	35	43	50

FRANK MILLER'S PANDORA
Frank Miller Presents: 2022 - Present ($7.99/$3.99)

1-($7.99) Created by Frank Miller; Emma Kubert-a						8.00
2-6-($3.99)						4.00

FRANTIC (Magazine) (See Ratfink & Zany)
Pierce Publishing Co.: Oct, 1958 - V2#2, Apr, 1959 (Satire)

	GD	VG	FN	VF	VF/NM	NM-
V1#1	40	80	120	246	411	575

	GD	VG	FN	VF	VF/NM	NM-
2	15	30	45	90	140	190
V2#1,2: 1-Burgos-a; Severin-c/a; Powell-a?	13	26	39	72	101	130

FRAY (Also see Buffy the Vampire Slayer "season eight" #16-19)
Dark Horse Comics: June, 2001 - No. 8, July, 2003 ($2.99, limited series)

	GD	VG	FN	VF	VF/NM	NM-
1-Joss Whedon-s/Moline & Owens-a	1	2	3	5	6	8
1-DF Gold edition	2	4	6	9	12	15
2-8: 6-(3/02). 7-(4/03)						4.00
TPB (11/03, $19.95) r/#1-8; intros by Whedon & Loeb; Moline sketch pages						20.00

FREAK FORCE (Also see Savage Dragon)
Image Comics (Highbrow Ent.): Dec, 1993 - No. 18, July, 1995 ($1.95/$2.50)

1-18-Superpatriot & Mighty Man in all; Erik Larsen scripts in all. 4-Vanguard app. 8-Begin $2.50-c. 9-Cyberforce-c & app. 13-Variant-c						4.00

FREAK FORCE (Also see Savage Dragon)
Image Comics: Apr, 1997 - No. 3, July, 1997 ($2.95)

1-3-Larsen-s						4.00

FREAK OUT, USA (See On the Scene Presents...)

FREAK SHOW
Image Comics (Desperado): 2006 ($5.99, B&W, one-shot)

nn-Bruce Jones-s/Bernie Wrightson-c/a						6.00

FREAKS OF THE HEARTLAND
Dark Horse Comics: Jan, 2004 - No. 6, Nov, 2004 ($2.99)

1-6-Steve Niles-s/Greg Ruth-a						3.00

FRECKLES AND HIS FRIENDS (See Crackajack Funnies, Famous Comics Cartoon Book, Honeybee Birdwhistle... & Red Ryder)

FRECKLES AND HIS FRIENDS
Standard Comics/Argo: No. 5, 11/47 - No. 12, 8/49; 11/55 - No. 4, 6/56

	GD	VG	FN	VF	VF/NM	NM-
5-Reprints	20	40	60	114	182	250
6-12-Reprints. 7-9-Airbrush-c (by Schomburg?). 11-Lingerie panels	12	24	36	69	97	125

NOTE: Some copies of No. 8 & 9 contain a printing oddity. The negatives were elongated in the engraving process, probably to conform to page dimensions on the filler pages. Those pages only look normal when viewed at a 45 degree angle.

	GD	VG	FN	VF	VF/NM	NM-
1(Argo, '55)-Reprints (NEA Service)	8	16	24	40	50	60
2-4	5	10	15	22	26	30

FREDDY (Formerly My Little Margie's Boy Friends) (Also see Blue Bird)
Charlton Comics: V2#12, June, 1958 - No. 47, Feb, 1965

	GD	VG	FN	VF	VF/NM	NM-
V2#12-Teenage	5	10	15	33	57	80
13-15	3	6	9	18	28	38
16-47	3	6	9	14	19	24

FREDDY
Dell Publishing Co.: May-July, 1963 - No. 3, Oct-Dec, 1964

	GD	VG	FN	VF	VF/NM	NM-
1	3	6	9	21	33	45
2,3	3	6	9	16	23	30

FREDDY KRUEGER'S A NIGHTMARE ON ELM STREET
Marvel Comics: Oct, 1989 - No. 2, Dec, 1989 ($2.25, B&W, movie adaptation, magazine)

	GD	VG	FN	VF	VF/NM	NM-
1,2: Origin Freddy Krueger; Buckler/Alcala-a	3	6	9	21	33	45

FREDDY'S DEAD: THE FINAL NIGHTMARE
Innovation Publishing: Oct, 1991 - No. 3, Dec 1991 ($2.50, color mini-series, adapts movie)

	GD	VG	FN	VF	VF/NM	NM-
1-3: Dismukes (film poster artist) painted-c	2	4	6	9	12	15

FREDDY VS. JASON VS. ASH (Freddy Krueger, Friday the 13th, Army of Darkness)
DC Comics (WildStorm): Early Jan, 2008 - No. 6, May, 2008 ($2.99, limited series)

	GD	VG	FN	VF	VF/NM	NM-
1-Three covers by J. Scott Campbell; Kuhoric-s/Craig-a	3	6	9	17	26	35
1-Second printing with 3 covers combined sideways	1	3	4	6	8	10
2-6: 2-4-Eric Powell-c. 5,6-Richard Friend-c	1	3	4	6	8	10
2-4-Second printings with B&W covers						4.00
TPB (2008, $17.99) r/#1-6; creators' interviews	7	14	21	44	82	120

FREDDY VS. JASON VS. ASH: THE NIGHTMARE WARRIORS
DC Comics (WildStorm): Aug, 2009 - No. 6, Jan, 2010 ($3.99, limited series)

	GD	VG	FN	VF	VF/NM	NM-
1-Suydam-c; Katz & Kuhoric-s/Craig-a	1	3	4	6	8	10
2-6-Katz & Kuhoric-s/Craig-a						5.00
TPB (2010, $17.99) r/#1-6; cover gallery	5	10	15	33	57	80

FRED HEMBECK DESTROYS THE MARVEL UNIVERSE
Marvel Comics: July, 1989 ($1.50, one-shot)

1-Punisher app.; Staton-i (5 pgs.)						4.00

FRED HEMBECK SELLS THE MARVEL UNIVERSE

	GD 2.0	VG 4.0	FN 6.0	VF 8.0	VF/NM 9.0	NM- 9.2

Marvel Comics: Oct, 1990 ($1.25, one-shot)

1-Punisher, Wolverine parodies; Hembeck/Austin-c						4.00

FREE COMIC BOOK DAY
Various publishers

2013 (Avengers/Hulk)(Marvel, 5/13) Hulk and Avengers Assemble animated series						3.00
2014 (Guardians of the Galaxy)(Marvel, 5/14) r/#1; Thanos & Spider-Verse back-ups						3.00
2015 (Avengers)(Marvel, 6/15) All-New Avengers and Uncanny Humans						3.00
2015 (Dark Horse, 5/15) Previews Fight Club 2, The Goon, and The Strain						3.00
2015 (Secret Wars #1)(Marvel, 6/15) Prelude to Secret Wars series (#0 on cover); back-up with Avengers/Attack on Titan x-over; Alex Ross wraparound-c						3.00
2016 (Captain America #1)(Marvel, 5/16) Preview of Captain America: Steve Rogers #1 and Amazing Spider-Man "Dead No More" storyline						3.00
2016 (Civil War II #1)(Marvel, 5/16) Preview of Civil War II #1 and All-New All-Different Avengers #9; Nadia Pym (The Wasp) app.						3.00
2016 (Dark Horse, 5/16) Previews Serenity, Hellboy and Aliens: Defiance						3.00
2017 (Dark Horse, 5/17) Avatar (movie) w/Doug Wheatley-a; Briggs Land story - Wood-s/ Dell'Edera-a						3.00
2017 (All-New Guardians of the Galaxy)(Marvel, 7/17) 1-Duggan-s/Kuder-a; preview of Defenders #1; Bendis-s/Marquez-a						3.00
2017 (Secret Empire)(Marvel, 7/17) 1-Spencer-s/Sorrentino-a/Brooks-c; Steve Rogers vs. the Avengers; back-up prelude to Peter Parker: The Spectacular Spider-Man #1; Zdarsky-s/Siqueira-a; Vulture story						3.00
2018 (Amazing Spider-Man/Guardians of the Galaxy)(Marvel, 5/18) Ottley-s						3.00
2018 (Avengers/Captain America)(Marvel, 5/18) Aaron-s/Pichelli-a & Coates-s/Yu-a						3.00
2018 (Dark Horse, 5/18) Previews Overwatch and Black Hammer; Niemczyk-a						3.00
2019 (Dark Horse, 5/19) Previews Minecraft and Incredibles 2; Cassie Anderson-a						3.00
2019 (Dark Horse, 5/19) Stranger Things and Black Hammer; Chun Lo-c						3.00
2019 (Avengers/Savage Avengers)(Marvel, 7/19) Aaron-s/Caselli-a; McGuinness-a						3.00
2019 (Spider-Man/Venom)(Marvel, 7/19) Stegman-s; previews Absolute Carnage						3.00
2021 (Avengers/Hulk)(Marvel, 10/21) Ottley-c; previews Avengers #50 & Hulk #1 (2022)						3.00
2021 (AWA, 8/21) Previews The Resistance: Uprising, Moths, Not All Robots						3.00
2021 (Dark Horse, 8/21) Previews Critical Roll & The Witcher; Tyler Walpole-c						3.00
2021 (Spider-Man/Venom)(Marvel, 10/21) Gleason-c; also previews Daredevil						3.00
...: Dark Circle 1 (Archie Comic Pub., 6-7/15) Previews Black Hood, The Fox, The Shield						3.00
...: R.I.P.D. and The True Lives of the Fabulous Killjoys (Dark Horse, 5/13) Flipbook with Mass Effect						3.00

FREEDOM AGENT (Also see John Steele)
Gold Key: Apr, 1963 (12¢)

1 (10054-304)-Painted-c	4	8	12	28	47	65

FREEDOM FIGHTERS (See Justice League of America #107,108)
National Periodical Publ./DC Comics: Mar-Apr, 1976 - No. 15, July-Aug, 1978

1-Uncle Sam, The Ray, Black Condor, Doll Man, Human Bomb, & Phantom Lady begin (all former Quality characters)	4	8	12	23	37	50
2-9: 4,5-Wonder Woman x-over. 7-1st app. Crusaders?	2	4	6	9	12	15
10-15: 10-Origin Doll Man; Cat-Man-c/story (4th app; 1st revival since Detective #325). 11-Origin The Ray. 12-Origin Firebrand. 13-Origin Black Condor. 14-Batgirl & Batwoman app. 15-Batgirl & Batwoman app.; origin Phantom Lady	2	4	6	9	13	16

NOTE: *Buckler c-5-11p, 13p, 14p.*

FREEDOM FIGHTERS (Also see "Uncle Sam and the Freedom Fighters")
DC Comics: Nov, 2010 - No. 9, Jul, 2011 ($2.99)

1-9-Travis Moore-a. 1-6-Dave Johnson-c						3.00

FREEDOM FIGHTERS
DC Comics: Feb, 2019 - No. 12, Mar, 2020 ($3.99, limited series)

1-12: 1-Venditti-s/Barrows-a; intro. new Freedom Fighters on present day Earth-X						4.00

FREEDOM FORCE
Image Comics: Jan, 2005 - No. 6, June, 2005 ($2.95)

1-6-Eric Dieter-s/Tom Scioli-a						3.00

FREELANCERS
BOOM! Studios: Oct, 2012 - No. 6, Mar, 2013 ($1.00/$3.99)

1-($1.00) Brill-s/Covey-a; eight covers; back-up origin of Valerie & Cassie						3.00
2-6-($3.99) Multiple covers on each						4.00

FREEMIND
Future Comics: No. 0, Aug, 2002; Nov, 2002 - No. 7, June, 2003 ($3.50)

0-($2.25) Two covers by Giordano & Layton						3.00
1-7 ($3.50) 1-Two covers by Giordano & Layton; Giordano thru #3. 4,5-Leeke-a						3.50

FREEREALMS
DC Comics (WildStorm): Sept, 2009 - No. 12, Oct, 2010 ($3.99, limited series)

1-12-Based on the online game; Jon Buran-a						4.00
... Book One TPB (2010, $19.99) r/#1-6						20.00
... Book Two TPB (2010, $19.99) r/#7-12						20.00

FREEX
Malibu Comics (Ultraverse): July, 1993 - No. 18, Mar, 1995 ($1.95)

1-3,5-14,16-18: 1-Polybagged w/trading card. 2-Some were polybagged w/card. 6-Nightman-c/story. 7-2 pg. origin Hardcase by Zeck. 17-Rune app.						4.00
1-Holographic-c edition						8.00
1-Ultra 5,000 limited silver ink-c						5.00
4-($2.50, 48 pgs.)-Rune flip-c/story by B. Smith (3 pgs.); 3 pg. Night Man preview						4.00
15 ($3.50)-w/Ultraverse Premiere #9 flip book; Alec Swan & Rafferty app.						4.00
Giant Size 1 (7/94, $2.50)-Prime app.						4.00

NOTE: *Simonson c-1.*

FREEZE, THE
Image Comics: Dec, 2018 - No. 4, Mar, 2019 ($3.99)

1-4-Dan Wickline-s/Phillip Sevy-a						4.00

FRENEMY OF THE STATE
Oni Press: May, 2010 - No. 5, Dec, 2011 ($3.99)

1-5-Rashida Jones, Christina Weir & Nunzio DeFilippis-s						4.00

FRENZY (Magazine) (Satire)
Picture Magazine: Apr, 1958 - No. 7, Jun, 1959

1-Painted-c	18	36	54	105	165	225
2-7	9	18	27	52	69	85

FRESHMEN
Image Comics: Jul, 2005 - No. 6, Mar, 2006 ($2.99)

1-Sterbakov-s/Kirk-a; co-created by Seth Green; covers by Pérez, Migliari, Linsner						3.00
2-6-Migliari-c						3.00
... Yearbook (1/06, $2.99) profile pages of characters; art by various incl. Chaykin, Kirk						3.00
... Vol. 1 (3/06, TPB) r/#1-6 & Yearbook; cover gallery with concept art						17.00

FRESHMEN (Volume 2)
Image Comics: Nov, 2006 - No. 6, Aug, 2007 ($2.99)

1-6: 1-Sterbakov-s/Conrad-a; 4 covers						3.00
...: Summer Vacation Special (7/08, $4.99) Sterbakov-s; bonus pin-ups by various						5.00
... Vol. 2 Fundamentals of Fear (6/07, $16.99, TPB) r/#1-6; cover gallery, journals						17.00

FRIDAY FOSTER
Dell Publishing Co.: October, 1972

1-Black heroine; Jack Sparling-a	26	52	78	182	404	625

FRIDAY THE 13TH (Based on the horror movie franchise)
DC Comics (WildStorm): Feb, 2007 - No. 6, July, 2007 ($2.99, mature)

1-Gray & Palmiotti-s/Archer-a; cover by Sook	3	6	9	16	23	30
1-Variant-c by Bradstreet	4	8	12	23	37	50
2-6: Gray & Palmiotti-s/Archer-a/Sook-c						6.00
...: Abuser and The Abused (6/08, $3.50) Fialkov-s/Andy B.-a	2	4	6	11	16	20
...: Bad Land 1,2 (3/08 - No. 2, 4/08, $2.99) Marz-s/Huddleston-a/McKone-c	1	3	4	6	8	10
...: How I Spent My Summer Vacation 1,2 (11/07 - No. 2, 12/07, $2.99) Aaron-s/Archer-a	2	4	6	11	16	20
...: Pamela's Tale 1,2 (9/07 - No. 2, 10/07, $2.99) Andreyko-s/Moll-a/Nguyen-c	2	4	6	11	16	20

FRIENDLY GHOST, CASPER, THE (Becomes Casper... #254 on)
Harvey Publications: Aug, 1958 - No. 224, Oct, 1982; No. 225, Oct, 1986 - No. 253, June, 1990

1-Infinity-c	79	154	237	632	1416	2200
2	27	54	81	189	420	650
3-6: 6-X-Mas-c	12	24	36	80	173	265
7-10	9	18	27	62	126	190
11-20: 18-X-Mas-c	8	16	24	54	102	150
21-30	5	10	15	35	63	90
31-50	4	8	12	27	44	60
51-70,100: 54-X-Mas-c	3	6	9	19	30	40
71-99	3	6	9	16	23	30
101-131: 131-Last 12¢ issue	3	6	9	14	20	26
132-159	2	4	6	11	16	20
160-163: All 52 pg. Giants	3	6	9	14	20	26
164-199: 173,179,185-Cub Scout Specials	2	4	6	8	10	12
200	2	4	6	8	11	14
201-224	1	2	3	5	7	9
225-237: 230-X-mas-c. 232-Valentine's-c						5.00
238-253: 238-Begin $1.00-c. 238,244-Halloween-c. 243-Last new material						4.00

FRIENDLY NEIGHBORHOOD SPIDER-MAN
Marvel Comics: Dec, 2005 - No. 24, Nov, 2007 ($2.99)

1-Evolve or Die pt. 1; Peter David-s/Mike Wieringo-a; Morlun app.						4.00
1-Variant Wieringo-c with regular costume						5.00
2-4: 2-New Avengers app. 3-Spider-Man dies						3.00
2-4-var-c: 2-Bag-Head Fantastic Four costume. 3-Captain Universe. 4-Wrestler						5.00
5-10: 6-Red & gold costume. 8-10-Uncle Ben app.						3.00
11-23: 17-Black costume; Sandman app.						3.00
24-($3.99) "One More Day" part 2; Quesada-a; covers by Quesada & Djurdjevic						4.00
Annual 1 (7/07, $3.99) Origin of The Sandman; back-up w/Doran-a						4.00
... Vol. 1: Derailed (2006, $14.99) r/#5-10; Wieringo sketch pages						15.00
... Vol. 2: Mystery Date (2007, $13.99) r/#11-16						14.00

FRIENDLY NEIGHBORHOOD SPIDER-MAN
Marvel Comics: Mar, 2019 - No. 14, Feb, 2020 ($4.99/$3.99)

1-($4.99) Taylor-s/Cabal-a; Aunt May's diagnosis; Ferreira-a						5.00
2-14-($3.99) 2-Intro. The Rumor. 7-10-Lashley-a; Prowler app. 12,13-Fantastic Four app.						4.00

FRIEND OF THE DEVIL: A RECKLESS BOOK
Image Comics: Apr, 2021 ($24.99, HC graphic novel)

HC - Ed Brubaker-s/Sean Phillips-a; 2nd book in the Reckless series						25.00

FRIENDS OF MAXX (Also see Maxx)
Image Comics (I Before E): Apr, 1996 - No. 3, Mar, 1997 ($2.95)

1-3: Sam Kieth-c/a/scripts. 1-Featuring Dude Japan						4.00

FRIGHT
Atlas/Seaboard Periodicals: June, 1975 (Aug. on inside)

1-Origin/1st app. The Son of Dracula; Frank Thorne-c/a	3	6	9	19	30	40

FRIGHT NIGHT
Now Comics: Oct, 1988 - No. 22, 1990 ($1.75)

1-Adapts movie	2	4	6	9	12	15
2-22: 2-Movie adaptation cont. 8, 9-Evil Ed horror photo-c from movie						4.00

FRIGHT NIGHT
American Mythology Productions: 2021 - No. 4 ($3.99)

1-4-Based on the original novel; Kuhoric-s; art by Craig, Vokes, Geldhof & Webb						4.00

FRIGHT NIGHT II
Now Comics: 1989 ($3.95, 52 pgs.)

1-Adapts movie sequel						6.00

FRINGE (Based on the 2008 FOX television series)
DC Comics (WildStorm): Oct, 2008 - No. 6, Aug, 2009 ($2.99, limited series)

1-6-Anthology by various. 1-Mandrake & Coleby-a						4.00
TPB (2009, $19.99) r/#1-6; intro. by TV series co-creators Kurtzman & Orci						20.00

Freedom Fighters (2011 series) #9 © DC

Friendly Neighborhood Spider-Man #17 © MAR

Frogman Comics #8 © HILL

	GD	VG	FN	VF	VF/NM	NM-
	2.0	4.0	6.0	8.0	9.0	9.2

FRINGE: TALES FROM THE FRINGE (Based on the 2008 FOX television series)
DC Comics (WildStorm): Aug, 2010 - No. 6, Jan, 2011 ($3.99, limited series)

	GD	VG	FN	VF	VF/NM	NM-
1-6-Anthology by various; LaTorre-c. 1-Reg & photo-c						4.00

2-6-Variant covers from parallel world. 2-Death of Batman. 3-Superman/Dark Knight Returns.
  4-Crisis #7 Supergirl holding dead Superman. 5-Justice League #1 w/Jonah Hex.

	GD	VG	FN	VF	VF/NM	NM-
6-Red Lantern/Red Arrow #76						10.00
TPB (2011, $14.99) r/#1-6 with variant cover gallery and sketch art						15.00

FRISKY ANIMALS (Formerly Frisky Fables; Super Cat #56 on)
Star Publications: No. 44, Jan, 1951 - No. 55, Sept, 1953

	GD	VG	FN	VF	VF/NM	NM-
44-Super Cat; L.B. Cole	27	54	81	158	259	360
45-Classic L. B. Cole-c	39	78	117	231	378	525
46-51,53-55: Super Cat. 54-Super Cat-c begin	24	48	72	142	234	325
52-L. B. Cole-c/a, 3 1/2 pgs.; X-Mas-c	26	52	78	154	252	350

NOTE: All have **L. B. Cole-c.** No. 47-No Super Cat. Disbrow a-49, 52. Fago a-51.

FRISKY ANIMALS ON PARADE (Formerly Parade Comics; becomes Superspook)
Ajax-Farrell Publ. (Four Star Comic Corp.): Sept, 1957 - No. 3, Dec-Jan, 1957-1958

	GD	VG	FN	VF	VF/NM	NM-
1-L. B. Cole-c	21	42	63	124	202	280
2-No L. B. Cole-c	12	24	36	69	97	125
3-L. B. Cole-c	18	36	54	105	165	225

FRISKY FABLES (Frisky Animals No. 44 on)
Premium Group/Novelty Publ./Star Publ. V5#4 on: Spring, 1945 - No. 43, Oct, 1950

	GD	VG	FN	VF	VF/NM	NM-
V1#1-Funny animal; Al Fago-c/a #1-38	28	56	84	168	274	380
2,3(Fall & Winter, 1945)	16	32	48	94	147	200
V2#1(#4, 4/46) - 9,11,12(#15, 3/47): 4-Flag-c	14	28	42	76	108	140
10-Christmas-c. 12-Valentine's-c	14	28	42	78	112	145
V3#1(#16, 4/47) - 12(#27, 3/48): 4-Flag-c. 7,9-Infinity-c. 10-X-Mas-c. 12-Washington						
crossing the Delaware parody-c	12	24	36	69	97	125
V4#1(#28, 4/48) - 7(#34, 2-3/49)	11	22	33	62	86	110
V5#1(#35, 4-5/49) - 4(#38, 10-11/49)	10	20	30	58	79	100
39-43-L. B. Cole-c; 40-Xmas-c	24	48	72	142	234	325
Accepted Reprint No. 43 (nd); L.B. Cole-c; classic story "The Mad Artist"	12	24	36	67	94	120

FRITZI RITZ (See Comics On Parade, Single Series #5, 1(reprint), Tip Top & United Comics)

FRITZI RITZ (United Comics No. 8-26) (Also see Tip Topper for early Peanuts by Schulz)
United Features Synd./St. John No. 37-55/Dell No. 56 on:
1939; Fall, 1948; No. 3, 1949 - No. 7, 1949; No. 27, 3-4/53 - No. 36, 9-10/54; No. 37 - No. 55,
9-11/57; No. 56, 12-2/57-58 - No. 59, 9-11/58

	GD	VG	FN	VF	VF/NM	NM-
Single Series #5 (1939)	50	100	150	315	533	750
nn(1948)-Special Fall issue; by Ernie Bushmiller	30	60	90	177	289	400
3(#1)	24	48	72	142	234	325
4-7(1949): 6-Abbie & Slats app.	15	30	45	85	130	175
27(1953)-33,37-50,57-59-Early Peanuts (1-4 pgs.) by Schulz. 29-Five pg. Abbie & Slats; 1 pg.						
Mamie by Russell Patterson. 38(9/55)-41(4/56)-Low print run	22	44	66	128	209	290
34-36,51-56: 36-1 pg. Mamie by Patterson	13	26	39	74	105	135

NOTE: Abbie & Slats in #6,7, 27-31. Li'l Abner in #32-36.

FROGMAN COMICS
Hillman Periodicals: Jan-Feb, 1952 - No. 11, May, 1953

	GD	VG	FN	VF	VF/NM	NM-
1	22	44	66	132	216	300
2	14	28	42	78	112	145
3,4,6-11: 4-Meskin-a	12	24	36	67	94	120
5-Krigstein-a	13	26	39	74	105	135

FROGMEN, THE
Dell Publishing Co.: No. 1258, Feb-Apr, 1962 - No. 11, Nov-Jan, 1964-65 (Painted-c)

	GD	VG	FN	VF	VF/NM	NM-
Four Color 1258(#1)-Evans-a	10	20	30	66	138	210
2,3-Evans-a; part Frazetta inks in #2,3	5	10	15	34	60	85
4,6-11	4	8	12	25	40	55
5-Toth-a	4	8	12	28	47	65

FROM BEYOND THE UNKNOWN
National Periodical Publications: 10-11/69 - No. 25, 11-12/73

	GD	VG	FN	VF	VF/NM	NM-
1	6	12	18	38	69	100
2-6	4	8	12	23	37	50
7-11: (64 pgs.) 7-Intro Col. Glenn Merrit	4	8	12	25	40	55
12-17: (52 pgs.) 13-Wood-a(i)(r). 17-Pres. Nixon-c	3	6	9	19	30	40
18-25: Star Rovers-r begin #18,19. Space Museum in #23-25	3	6	9	15	22	28

NOTE: N. Adams c-3, 6, 8, 9. Anderson c-2, 4, 5, 10, 11i, 15-17, 22; reprints-3, 4, 6-8, 10, 11, 13-16, 24, 25. Infantino r-1-5, 7-19, 23-25; c-11p. Kaluta c-18, 19. Gil Kane a-9r. Kubert c-1, 7, 12-14. Toth a-2r. Wood a-13i. Photo c-22.

FROM BEYOND THE UNKNOWN GIANT

DC Comics: 2020 ($4.99, one-shot, 100 pgs., squarebound, Mass Market & Direct Market editions exist with different covers)

	GD	VG	FN	VF	VF/NM	NM-
1-New stories of Green Lantern, Kamandi & Legion of Super-Heroes and reprints						5.00

FROM DUSK TILL DAWN (Movie)
Big Entertainment: 1996 ($4.95, one-shot)

	GD	VG	FN	VF	VF/NM	NM-
nn-Adaptation of the film; Brereton-c	2	4	6	8	10	12
nn-($9.95)Deluxe Ed. w/ new material	2	4	6	11	16	20

FROM HELL
Mad Love/Tundra Publishing/Kitchen Sink: 1991 - No. 11, Sept, 1998 (B&W)

	GD	VG	FN	VF	VF/NM	NM-
1-Alan Moore and Eddie Campbell's Jack The Ripper story collected from the Taboo						
anthology series	3	6	9	16	23	30
1-(2nd printing (11/99)	2	4	6	8	10	12
1-(3rd printing)	1	2	3	4	5	7
2	1	3	4	6	8	10
2-(2nd printing)						6.00
2-(3rd printing)						4.00
3-1st Kitchen Sink Press issue	1	3	4	6	8	10
3-(2nd printing)						5.00
4-10: 10-(8/96)	1	2	3	5	6	8
11-Dance of the Gull Catchers (9/98, $4.95) Epilogue	2	4	6	10	14	18
Tundra Publishing reprintings 1-5 ('92)	1	2	3	4	5	7
HC						125.00
HC Ltd. Edition of 1,000 (signed and numbered)						230.00
TPB-1st printing (11/99)						60.00
TPB-2nd printing (3/00)						50.00
TPB-3rd printing (11/00)						40.00
TPB-4th printing (7/01) Regular and movie covers						35.00
TPB-5th printing - Regular and movie covers						35.00

FROM HERE TO INSANITY (Satire) (Formerly Eh! #1-7) (See Frantic & Frenzy)
Charlton Comics: No. 8, Feb, 1955 - V3#1, 1956

	GD	VG	FN	VF	VF/NM	NM-
8	32	64	96	188	307	425
9	28	56	84	165	270	375
10-Ditko-c/a (3 pgs.)	37	74	111	222	361	500
11-All Kirby except 4 pgs.	47	94	141	296	498	700
12-(Mag. size) Marilyn Monroe, Jackie Gleason-c; all Kirby except 4 pgs.	51	102	153	321	546	750
V3#1(1956)-Ward-c/a(2) (signed McCartney); 5 pgs. Wolverton-a; 3 pgs. Ditko-a; magazine						
format (cover says "Crazy, Man, Crazy" and becomes Crazy, Man, Crazy with V2#2)	84	168	252	538	919	1300

FROM THE PIT
Fantagor Press: 1994 ($4.95, one-shot, mature)

	GD	VG	FN	VF	VF/NM	NM-
1-R. Corben-a; HP Lovecraft back-up story	5	10	15	33	57	80

FROM THE WORLD OF MINOR THREATS: THE ALTERNATES
Dark Horse Comics: Sept, 2023 - No. 4, Dec, 2023 ($4.99, limited series)

	GD	VG	FN	VF	VF/NM	NM-
1-4-Oswalt, Blum & Seeley-s/Mitten & Fowler-a						5.00

FRONTIER DOCTOR (TV)
Dell Publishing Co.: No. 877, Feb, 1958 (one-shot)

	GD	VG	FN	VF	VF/NM	NM-
Four Color 877-Toth-a, Rex Allen photo-c	9	18	27	61	123	185

FRONTIER FIGHTERS
National Periodical Publications: Sept-Oct, 1955 - No. 8, Nov-Dec, 1956

	GD	VG	FN	VF	VF/NM	NM-
1-Davy Crockett, Buffalo Bill (by Kubert), Kit Carson begin (Scarce)	66	132	198	419	722	1025
2	43	86	129	271	461	650
3-8	40	80	120	244	402	560

NOTE: Buffalo Bill by Kubert in all.

FRONTIER ROMANCES
Avon Periodicals/I. W.: Nov-Dec, 1949 - No. 2, Feb-Mar, 1950 (Painted-c)

	GD	VG	FN	VF	VF/NM	NM-
1-Used in SOTI, pg. 180 (General reference) & illo. "Erotic spanking in a western						
comic book"	90	180	270	576	988	1400
2 (Scarce)-Woodish-a by Stallman	52	104	156	328	552	775
I.W. Reprint #1-Reprints Avon's #1	4	8	12	27	44	60
I.W. Reprint #9-Reprints ?	4	8	12	25	40	55

FRONTIER SCOUT: DAN'L BOONE (Formerly Death Valley; The Masked Raider No. 14 on)
Charlton Comics: No. 10, Jan, 1956 - No. 13, Aug, 1956; V2#14, Mar, 1965

	GD	VG	FN	VF	VF/NM	NM-
10	10	20	30	56	76	95
11-13(1956)	7	14	21	35	43	50
V2#14(3/65)	3	6	9	16	23	30

FRONTIERSMAN
Image Comics: Sept, 2021 - Present ($3.99)

	GD 2.0	VG 4.0	FN 6.0	VF 8.0	VF/NM 9.0	NM- 9.2

1-5-Kindlon-s/Ferrari-a; wraparound-c on each — 4.00
....-Lock-Up Special 1 (5/22, $5.99) Kindlon-s/Assirelli-a; wraparound-c — 6.00

FRONTIER TRAIL (The Rider No. 1-5)
Ajax/Farrell Publ.: No. 6, May, 1958

6		7	14	21	35	43	50

FRONTIER WESTERN
Atlas Comics (PrPI): Feb, 1956 - No. 10, Aug, 1957

	GD	VG	FN	VF	VF/NM	NM-
1-The Pecos Kid rides	28	56	84	165	270	375
2,3,6-Williamson-a, 4 pgs. each	18	36	54	105	165	225
4,7,9,10: 10-Check-a	14	28	42	78	112	145
5-Crandall, Baker, Davis-a; Williamson text illos	15	30	45	90	140	190
8-Crandall, Morrow, & Wildey-a	14	28	42	80	115	150

NOTE: *Baker* a-9. *Colan* a-2, 6. *Drucker* a-3, 4. *Heath* c-5. *Maneely* c/a-2, 7, 9. *Maurera* a-7. *Romita* a-7. *Severin* c-6, 8, 10. *Tuska* a-2. *Wildey* a-5, 8. *Ringo Kid* in No. 4.

FRONTLINE COMBAT
E. C. Comics: July-Aug, 1951 - No. 15, Jan, 1954

	GD	VG	FN	VF	VF/NM	NM-
1-Severin/Kurtzman-a	114	228	342	912	1456	2000
2	50	100	150	400	638	875
3	40	80	120	320	510	700
4-Used in SOTI, pg. 257; contains "Air Burst" by Kurtzman which is his personal all-time favorite story; "Light Brigade!" story based on Tennyson's "Charge of the Light Brigade"	43	86	129	344	547	750
5-John Severin and Bill Elder bios.	33	66	99	264	420	575
6-10: 6-Kurtzman bio. 9-Civil War issue	26	52	78	208	334	460
11-15	22	44	66	176	278	380

NOTE: *Davis* a-in all; c-11, 12. *Evans* a-10-15. *Heath* a-1. *Kubert* a-14. *Kurtzman* a-1-5; c-1-9. *Severin* a-5-7, 9, 13, 15. *Severin/Elder* a-2-11; c-10. *Toth* a-8, 12. *Wood* a-1-4, 6-10, 12-15; c-13-15. Special issues: No. 7 (Iwo Jima), No. 9 (Civil War), No. 12 (Air Force).
(Canadian reprints known; see Table of Contents.)

FRONTLINE COMBAT
Russ Cochran/Gemstone Publishing: Aug, 1995 - No. 14 ($2.00/$2.50)

1-14-E.C. reprints in all — 4.00

FRONT PAGE COMIC BOOK
Front Page Comics (Harvey): 1945

	GD	VG	FN	VF	VF/NM	NM-
1-Kubert-a; intro. & 1st app. Man in Black by Powell; Fuje-c	219	438	657	1402	2401	3400

FROST AND FIRE (See DC Science Fiction Graphic Novel)

FROSTBITE
DC Comics (Vertigo): Nov, 2016 - No. 6, Apr, 2017 ($3.99)

1-6-Joshua Williamson-s/Jason Shawn Alexander-a — 4.00

FROSTY THE SNOWMAN
Dell Publishing Co.: No. 359, Nov, 1951 - No. 1272, Dec-Feb?/1961-62

	GD	VG	FN	VF	VF/NM	NM-
Four Color 359 (#1)	11	22	33	75	160	245
Four Color 435,514,601,661	7	14	21	48	89	130
Four Color 748,861,950,1065,1153,1272	5	10	15	35	63	90

FROZEN (Disney movie)
Joe Books Ltd.: Jul, 2016 - No. 5 ($2.99)

1-5-Georgia Ball-s/Benedetta Barone-a — 4.00

FROZEN... (Disney movie)
Dark Horse Comics: 2018 - Present ($3.99, limited series)

....: Breaking Boundaries (8/18 - No. 3, 10/18) 1-3: 1-Caranagna & Nitz-s — 4.00
....: Reunion Road (3/19 - No. 3, 5/19) 1-3-Caranagna-s/Francisco-a — 4.00
....: The Hero Within (6/19 - No. 3, 9/19) 1-3-Caranagna-s — 4.00
....: True Treasure (11/19 - No. 3, 1/20) 1-3-Caranagna-s; leads up to Frozen 2 movie — 4.00

FRUITMAN SPECIAL (See Bunny #2 for 1st app.)
Harvey Publications: Dec, 1969 (68 pgs.)

	GD	VG	FN	VF	VF/NM	NM-
1-Funny super hero	4	8	12	27	44	60

F-TROOP (TV)
Dell Publishing Co.: Aug, 1966 - No. 7, Aug, 1967 (All have photo-c)

	GD	VG	FN	VF	VF/NM	NM-
1	13	26	39	91	201	310
2-7	5	10	15	34	60	85

FUGITIVES FROM JUSTICE (True Crime Stories)
St. John Publishing Co.: Feb, 1952 - No. 5, Oct, 1952

	GD	VG	FN	VF	VF/NM	NM-
1	36	72	108	211	343	475
2-Matt Baker-r/Northwest Mounties #2; Vic Flint strip reprints begin	32	64	96	188	307	425
3-Reprints panel from Authentic Police Cases that was used in SOTI with changes; Tuska-a	30	60	90	177	289	400
4	18	36	54	103	162	220
5-Last Vic Flint-r; bondage-c	22	44	66	132	216	300

FUGITOID
Mirage Studios: 1985 (B&W, magazine size, one-shot)

	GD	VG	FN	VF	VF/NM	NM-
1-Ties into Teenage Mutant Ninja Turtles #5	5	10	15	33	57	80

FU JITSU
AfterShock Comics: Sept, 2017 - No. 5, Feb, 2018 ($3.99)

1-5-Jai Nitz-s/Wesley St. Claire-a — 4.00

FULL OF FUN
Red Top (Decker Publ.)(Farrell)/I. W. Enterprises: Aug, 1957 - No. 2, Nov, 1957; 1964

	GD	VG	FN	VF	VF/NM	NM-
1(1957)-Funny animal; Dave Berg-a	10	20	30	54	72	90
2-Reprints Bingo, the Monkey Doodle Boy	6	12	18	28	34	40
8-I.W. Reprint('64)	2	4	6	11	16	20

FUN AT CHRISTMAS (See March of Comics No. 138)

FUN CLUB COMICS (See Interstate Theatres...)

FUN COMICS (Formerly Holiday Comics #1-8; Mighty Bear #13 on)
Star Publications: No. 9, Jan, 1953 - No. 12, Oct, 1953

	GD	VG	FN	VF	VF/NM	NM-
9-(25¢ Giant)-L. B. Cole X-mas-c; X-Mas issue	30	60	90	177	289	400

	GD	VG	FN	VF	VF/NM	NM-
10-12-L. B. Cole-c. 12-Mighty Bear-c/story	22	44	66	128	209	290

FUNDAY FUNNIES (See Famous TV..., and Harvey Hits No. 35,40)

FUN-IN (TV)(Hanna-Barbera)
Gold Key: Feb, 1970 - No. 10, Jan, 1972; No. 11, 4/74 - No. 15, 12/74

	GD	VG	FN	VF	VF/NM	NM-
1-Dastardly & Muttley in Their Flying Machines; Perils of Penelope Pitstop in #1-4; It's the Wolf in all	6	12	18	41	76	110
2-4,6-Cattanooga Cats in 2-4	3	6	9	21	33	45
5,7-Motormouse & Autocat, Dastardly & Muttley in both; It's the Wolf in #7	4	8	12	23	37	50
8,10-The Harlem Globetrotters, Dastardly & Muttley in #10	4	8	12	23	37	50
9-Where's Huddles?, Dastardly & Muttley, Motormouse & Autocat app.	4	8	12	23	37	50
11-Butch Cassidy	3	6	9	19	30	40
12-15: 12,15-Speed Buggy. 13-Hair Bear Bunch. 14-Inch High Private Eye	3	6	9	19	30	40

FUNKY PHANTOM, THE (TV)
Gold Key: Mar, 1972 - No. 13, Mar, 1975 (Hanna-Barbera)

	GD	VG	FN	VF	VF/NM	NM-
1	5	10	15	33	57	80
2-5	3	6	9	18	28	38
6-13	3	6	9	15	22	28

FUNLAND
Ziff-Davis (Approved Comics): No date (1940s) (25¢)

	GD	VG	FN	VF	VF/NM	NM-
nn-Contains games, puzzles, cut-outs, etc.	27	54	81	158	259	360

FUNLAND COMICS
Croyden Publishers: 1945

	GD	VG	FN	VF	VF/NM	NM-
1-Funny animal	22	44	66	128	209	290

FUNNIES, THE (New Funnies No. 65 on)
Dell Publishing Co.: Oct, 1936 - No. 64, May, 1942

	GD	VG	FN	VF	VF/NM	NM-
1-Tailspin Tommy, Mutt & Jeff, Alley Oop (1st app.), Capt. Easy (1st app.), Don Dixon begin	385	770	1155	2300	3950	5600
2 (11/36)-Scribbly by Mayer begins (see Popular Comics #6 for 1st app.)	172	344	516	1030	1765	2500
3	130	260	390	780	1340	1900
4,5: 4(1/37)-Christmas-c	100	200	300	600	1025	1450
6-10	80	160	240	460	742	1025
11-20: 16-Christmas-c	73	146	219	420	685	950
21-29: 25-Crime Busters by McWilliams(4pgs.)	58	116	174	334	542	750
30-John Carter of Mars (origin/1st app.) begins by Edgar Rice Burroughs; Jim Gary-a Warner Bros.' Bosko-c (4/39)	300	600	900	1980	3440	4900
31-34,36-44: 31,32-Gary-a. 33-John Coleman Burroughs art begins on John Carter. 34-Last funny-c. 40-John Carter of Mars-c	116	232	348	742	1271	1800
35-(9/39)-Mr. District Attorney begins; based on radio show; 1st cover app. John Carter of Mars	258	516	774	1651	2826	4000
45-Origin/1st app. Phantasmo, the Master of the World (Dell's 1st super-hero, 7/40) & his sidekick Whizzer McGee	142	284	426	909	1555	2200
46-50: 46-The Black Knight begins, ends #62	69	138	207	442	759	1075
51-56-Last ERB John Carter of Mars	55	110	165	352	601	850
57-Intro. & origin Captain Midnight (7/41)	377	754	1131	2639	4620	6600
58-60: 58-Captain Midnight-c begin, end #63	103	206	309	659	1130	1600
61-Andy Panda begins by Walter Lantz; WWII-c	155	310	465	992	1696	2400
62,63: 63-Last Captain Midnight-c; bondage-c	84	168	252	538	919	1300
64-Format change; Oswald the Rabbit, Felix the Cat, Li'l Eight Ball app.; origin & 1st app. Woody Woodpecker in Oswald; last Capt. Midnight; Oswald, Andy Panda, Li'l Eight Ball-c	300	600	900	1980	3440	4900

NOTE: *Mayer* c-26, 48. *McWilliams* art in many issues on "Rex King of the Deep". Alley Oop c-17, 20. Captain Midnight c-57(1/2), 58-63. John Carter c-35-37, 40. Phantasmo c-45-56, 57(1/2), 58-61(part). Rex King c-38, 39, 42. Tailspin Tommy c-41.

FUNNIES ANNUAL, THE
Avon Periodicals: 1959 ($1.00, approx. 7x10", B&W; tabloid-size)

	GD	VG	FN	VF	VF/NM	NM-
1-(Rare)-Features the best newspaper comic strips of the year: Archie, Snuffy Smith, Beetle Bailey, Henry, Blondie, Steve Canyon, Buz Sawyer, The Little King, Hi & Lois, Popeye, & others. Also has a chronological history of the comics from 2000 B.C. to 1959.	58	116	174	371	636	900

FUNNIES ON PARADE (See Promotional Comics section)

FUNNY ANIMALS (See Fawcett's Funny Animals)
Charlton Comics: Sept, 1984 - No. 2, Nov, 1984

1,2-Atomic Mouse-r; low print — 6.00

FUNNYBONE (... The Laugh-Book of Comical Comics)
La Salle Publishing Co.: 1944 (25¢, 132 pgs.)

	GD	VG	FN	VF	VF/NM	NM-
nn	40	80	120	246	411	575

FUNNY BOOK (...Magazine for Young Folks) (Hocus Pocus No. 9)
Parents' Magazine Press (Funny Book Publishing Corp.):
Dec, 1942 - No. 9, Aug-Sept, 1946 (Comics, stories, puzzles, games)

	GD	VG	FN	VF	VF/NM	NM-
1-Funny animal; Alice In Wonderland app.	20	40	60	118	192	265
2-Gulliver in Giant-Land	14	28	42	78	112	145
3-9: 4-Advs. of Robin Hood. 9-Hocus-Pocus strip	10	20	30	58	79	100

FUNNY COMICS
Modern Store Publ.: 1955 (7¢, 5x7", 36 pgs.)

	GD	VG	FN	VF	VF/NM	NM-
1-Funny animal	7	14	21	46	86	125

FUNNY COMIC TUNES (See Funny Tunes)

FUNNY FABLES
Decker Publications (Red Top Comics): Aug, 1957 - V2#2, Nov, 1957

	GD	VG	FN	VF	VF/NM	NM-
V1#1	8	16	24	44	57	70
V1#2,V2#1,2: V1#2 (11/57)-Reissue of V1#1	6	12	18	31	38	45

FUNNY FILMS (Features funny animal characters from films)
American Comics Group(Michel Publ./Titan Publ.): Sept-Oct, 1949 - No. 29, May-June, 1954 (No. 1-4: 52 pgs.)

Frozen #4 © DIS

Funny Folks #11 © DC

Funny Tunes #17 © MAR

	GD	VG	FN	VF	VF/NM	NM-
	2.0	4.0	6.0	8.0	9.0	9.2
1-Puss An' Boots, Blunderbunny begin	21	42	63	124	202	280
2	13	26	39	74	105	135
3-10: 3-X-Mas-c	9	18	27	50	65	80
11-20	7	14	21	35	43	50
21-29	6	12	18	28	34	40

FUNNY FOLKS
DC Comics: Feb, 1946

nn-Ashcan comic, not distributed to newsstands, only for in house use   (no known sales)

FUNNY FOLKS (Hollywood... on cover only No. 16-26; becomes Hollywood Funny Folks No. 27 on)
National Periodical Publ.: April-May, 1946 - No. 26, June-July, 1950.(52 pgs., #15 on)

1-Nutsy Squirrel begins (1st app.) by Rube Grossman; Grossman-a in most issues	50	100	150	315	533	750
2	26	52	78	154	252	350
3-5: 4-1st Nutsy Squirrel-c	16	32	48	94	147	200
6-10: 6,9-Nutsy Squirrel-c begin	13	26	39	72	101	130
11-26: 15-Begin 52 pg. issues (8-9/48)	10	20	30	58	79	100

NOTE: **Sheldon Mayer** a-in some issues. **Post** a-18. Christmas c-12.

FUNNY FROLICS
Timely/Marvel Comics (SPI): Summer, 1945 - No. 5, Dec, 1946

1-Sharpy Fox, Puffy Pig, Krazy Krow	37	74	111	222	361	500
2-(Fall 1945)	21	42	63	122	199	275
3,4: 3-(Spring 1946)	17	34	51	100	158	215
5-Kurtzman-a	18	36	54	107	169	230

FUNNY FUNNIES
Nedor Publishing Co.: April, 1943 (68 pgs.)

1-Funny animals; Peter Porker app.	28	56	84	168	274	380

FUNNYMAN (Also see Cisco Kid Comics & Extra Comics)
Magazine Enterprises: Dec, 1947; No. 1, Jan, 1948 - No. 6, Aug, 1948

nn(12/47)-Prepublication B&W undistributed copy by Siegel & Shuster-(5-3/4x8"), 16 pgs.; Sold at auction in 1997 for $575.00

1-Siegel & Shuster-a in all; Dick Ayers 1st pro work (as assistant) on 1st few issues	68	136	204	435	743	1050
2	37	74	111	222	361	500
3-6	33	66	99	194	317	440

FUNNY MOVIES (See 3-D Funny Movies)

FUNNY PAGES (Formerly The Comics Magazine)
Comics Magazine Co./Ultem Publ.(Chesler)/Centaur Publications:
No. 6, Nov, 1936 - No. 42, Oct, 1940

V1#6 (nn, nd)-The Clock begins (2 pgs., 1st app.), ends #11; The Clock is the 1st masked comic book hero	486	972	1458	3550	6275	9000
7-11: 11-(6/37)	206	412	618	1318	2259	3200
V2#1-V2#5: V2#1 (9/37)(V2#2 on-c; V2#1 in indicia) V2#2 (10/37)(V2#3 on-c; V2#2 in indicia.	174	348	522	1114	1907	2700
V2#3(11/37 - 5	194	388	582	1242	2121	3000
6(1st Centaur, 3/38)	161	322	483	1030	1765	2500
7-9						
10(Scarce, 9/38)-1st app. of The Arrow by Gustavson (Blue costume)	649	1298	1947	4738	8369	12,000
11,12	194	388	582	1242	2121	3000
V3#1-Bruce Wayne prototype in "Case of the Missing Heir," by Bob Kane, 3 months before app. Batman (See Det. Pic. Stories #5)	320	640	960	2240	3920	5600
2-6,8: 6,8-Last funny covers	194	388	582	1242	2121	3000
7-1st Arrow-c (9/39)	481	962	1443	3511	6206	8900
9-Tarpe Mills jungle-c	206	412	618	1318	2259	3200
10-2nd Arrow-c (Rare)	486	972	1458	3550	6275	9000
V4#1(1/40, Arrow-c)-(Rare)-The Owl & The Phantom Rider app.; origin Mantoka, Maker of Magic by Jack Cole. Mad Ming begins, ends #42; Tarpe Mills-a	486	972	1458	3550	6275	9000
35-Classic Arrow-c (Scarce)	514	1028	1542	3750	6625	9500
36-38-Mad Ming-c	300	600	900	1950	3375	4800
39-41-Arrow-c	337	674	1011	2359	4131	5900
42 (Scarce,10/40)-Arrow-c	423	846	1269	3088	5444	7800

NOTE: **Biro** c-V3#9. **Burgos** c-V3#10. **Jack Cole** a-V2#3, 7, 8, 10, 11. V4#1, 37; c-V3#2, 4. **Eisner** a-V1#7, 8?, 10. **Ken Ernst** a-V1#7, 8. **Everett** a-V2#11 (illos). **Filchock** c-V2#10, V3#6. **Gill Fox** a-V2#11. **Sid Greene** a-39. **Guardineer** a-V2#5, 7. **Gustavson** a-V2#5, V2#2 on-c. c-V3#2, 35, 39-42. **Bob Kane** a-V3#1. **McWilliams** a-V2#12, V3#1, 3-6. **Tarpe Mills** a-V3#8-10, V4#1; c-V3#9. **Ed Moore Jr.** a-V2#12. **Schwab** c-V3#1. **Bob Wood** a-V2#2, 3, 8. V3-c-V2#6. 7. Arrow c-V3#7, 10, V4#1, 35, 40-42.

FUNNY PICTURE STORIES (Comic Pages V3#4 on)
Comics Magazine Co./Centaur Publications: Nov, 1936 - V3#3, May, 1939

V1#1-The Clock begins (c-feature)(see Funny Pages for 1st app.)	649	1298	1947	4738	8369	12,000

	GD	VG	FN	VF	VF/NM	NM-
	2.0	4.0	6.0	8.0	9.0	9.2
2	271	542	813	1734	2967	4200
3-6(4/37): 4-Eisner-a	200	400	600	1280	2190	3100
7-(6/37) (Rare) Racial humor-c	423	846	1269	3088	5444	7800
V2#1 (9/37): V1#10 on-c; V2#1 in indicia)-Jack Strand begins	155	310	465	992	1696	2400
2 (10/37; V1#11 on-c; V2#2 in indicia	168	336	504	1075	1838	2600
3-5,7-11(11/38): 4-Christmas-c	142	284	426	909	1555	2200
6-(1st Centaur, 3/38)	161	322	483	1030	1765	2500
V3#1(1/39)-3	129	258	387	826	1413	2000

NOTE: **Biro** c-V2#1, 8, 9, 11. **Guardineer** a-V1#11; c-V2#6, V3#5. **Bob Wood** c/a-V1#11, V2#2; c-V2#3, 5.

FUNNY STUFF (Becomes The Dodo & the Frog No. 80)
All-American/National Periodical Publications No. 7 on: Summer, 1944 - No. 79, July-Aug, 1954 (#1-7 are quarterly)

1-The Three Mouseketeers (ends #28) & The "Terrific Whatzit" begin; Sheldon Mayer-a; Grossman-a in most issues	103	206	309	659	1130	1600
2-Sheldon Mayer-a	47	94	141	296	498	700
3-5: 3-Flash parody. 5-All Mayer-a/scripts issue	32	64	96	188	307	425
6-10 10-(6/46)	20	40	60	117	189	260
11-17,19	15	30	45	90	140	190
18-The Dodo & the Frog (2/47, 1st app?) begin?; X-Mas-c	28	56	84	165	270	375
19-1st Dodo & the Frog-c (3/47)	20	40	60	117	189	260
20-2nd Dodo & the Frog-c (4/47)	15	30	45	84	127	170
21,23-30: 24-Infinity-c. 30-Christmas-c	11	22	33	62	86	110
22-Superman cameo	40	80	120	246	411	575
31-79: 62-Bo Bunny app. by Mayer. 70-Bo Bunny series begins	10	20	30	56	76	95

NOTE: **Mayer** a-1-8, 55, ,57, 58, 61, 62, 64, 65, 68, 70, 72, 74-79; c-2, 5, 6, 8.

FUNNY STUFF STOCKING STUFFER
DC Comics: Mar, 1985 ($1.25, 52 pgs.)

1-Almost every DC funny animal featured						4.00

FUNNY 3-D
Harvey Publications: December, 1953 (25¢, came with 2 pair of glasses)

1-Shows cover in 3-D on inside	13	26	39	74	105	135

FUNNY TUNES (Animated Funny Comic Tunes No. 16-22; Funny Comic Tunes No. 23, on covers only; Oscar No. 24 on)
U.S.A. Comics Magazine Corp. (Timely): No. 16, Summer, 1944 - No. 23, Fall, 1946

16-Silly Seal, Ziggy Pig, Krazy Krow begin	30	60	90	177	289	400
17 (Fall/44)-Becomes Gay Comics #18 on?	23	46	69	138	227	315
18-22: 21-Super Rabbit app.	21	42	63	126	206	285
23-Kurtzman-a	22	44	66	132	216	300

FUNNY TUNES (Becomes Space Comics #4 on)
Avon Periodicals: July, 1953 - No. 3, Dec-Jan, 1953-54

1-Space Mouse, Peter Rabbit, Merry Mouse, Spotty the Pup, Cicero the Cat begin; all continue in Space Comics	15	30	45	88	137	185
2,3	10	20	30	54	72	90

FUNNY WORLD
Marbak Press: 1947 - No. 3, 1948

1-The Berrys, The Toodles & other strip-c begin	11	22	33	64	90	115
2,3	8	16	24	42	54	65

FUNTASTIC WORLD OF HANNA-BARBERA, THE (TV)
Marvel Comics Group: Dec, 1977 - No. 3, June, 1978 ($1.25, oversized)

1-3: 1-The Flintstones Christmas Party(12/77). 2-Yogi Bear's Easter Parade(3/78). 3-Laff-a-lympics(6/78)	4	8	12	25	40	55

FUN TIME
Ace Periodicals: Spring, 1953; No. 2, Sum, 1953; No. 3(nn), Fall, 1953; No. 4, Wint, 1953-54

1-(25¢, 100 pgs.)-Funny animal	26	52	78	154	252	350
2-4 (All 25¢, 100 pgs.)	19	38	57	111	176	240

FUN WITH LITTLE ARCHIE AND FRIENDS SPECIAL
Archie Comic Publications: Jun, 2022 ($3.99, one-shot)

1-Sabrina & Salem app.						4.00

FUN WITH SANTA CLAUS (See March of Comics No. 11, 108, 325)

FURTHER ADVENTURES OF CYCLOPS AND PHOENIX (Also see Adventures of Cyclops and Phoenix, Uncanny X-Men & X-Men)
Marvel Comics: June, 1996 - No. 4, Sept, 1996 ($1.95, limited series)

1-4: 1-Origin of Mr. Sinister; Milligan scripts; John Paul Leon-c/a(p). 2-4-Apocalypse app.						4.00
Trade Paperback (1997, $14.99) r/1-4						15.00

FURTHER ADVENTURES OF INDIANA JONES, THE (Movie) (Also see

	GD	VG	FN	VF	VF/NM	NM-
	2.0	4.0	6.0	8.0	9.0	9.2

Indiana Jones and the Last Crusade & Indiana Jones and the Temple of Doom)
Marvel Comics Group: Jan, 1983 - No. 34, Mar, 1986

1-Byrne/Austin-a; Austin-c	3	6	9	15	22	28
2-34: 2-Byrne/Austin-c/a						4.00

NOTE: *Austin* a-1i, 2i, 9i; c-1, 2i, 6i, 9i. *Byrne* a-1p, 2p; c-2p. *Chaykin* a-6p; c-6p, 8p-10p. *Ditko* a-21p, 25-28, 34. *Golden* c-24, 25. *Simonson* c-9. Painted c-14.

FURTHER ADVENTURES OF NICK WILSON, THE
Image Comics: Jan, 2018 - No. 5, May 2018 ($3.99)

1-5-Gorodetsky & Andreyko-s/Sadowski-a						4.00

FURTHER ADVENTURES OF NYOKA, THE JUNGLE GIRL, THE (See Nyoka)
AC Comics: 1988 - No. 5, 1989 ($1.95, color; $2.25/$2.50, B&W)

1-5 : 1,2-Bill Black-a plus reprints. 3-Photo-c. 5-(B&W)-Reprints plus movie photos						4.00

FURY (Straight Arrow's Horse...) (See A-1 No. 119)

FURY (TV) (See March Of Comics #200)
Dell Publishing Co./Gold Key: No. 781, Mar, 1957 - Nov, 1962 (All photo-c)

Four Color 781	7	14	21	49	92	135
Four Color 885,975,1031,1080,1133,1172,1218,1296	5	10	15	35	63	90
01292-208(#1-'62), 10020-211(11/62-G.K.)	5	10	15	33	57	80

FURY
Marvel Comics: May, 1994 ($2.95, one-shot)

1-Iron Man, Red Skull, FF, Hatemonger, Logan app.; origin Nick Fury						4.00

FURY (Volume 3)
Marvel Comics (MAX): Nov, 2001 - No. 6, Apr, 2002 ($2.99, mature content)

1-6-Ennis-s/Robertson-a						4.00

FURY
Marvel Comics: Jul, 2023 ($5.99, one-shot)

1-Stories in the present, the 1960s and World War II; art by Eaton, Reilly & Adam Kubert						6.00

FURY/ AGENT 13
Marvel Comics: June, 1998 - No. 2, July, 1998 ($2.99, limited series)

1,2-Nick Fury returns						4.00

FURY MAX (Nick Fury)("My War Gone By" on cover)
Marvel Comics (MAX): Jul, 2012 - No. 13, Aug, 2013 ($3.99, mature content)

1-13: 1-Ennis-s/Parlov-a/Johnson-c; Nick Fury in 1954 Indochina. 7-9-Frank Castle app.						4.00

FURY OF FIRESTORM, THE (Becomes Firestorm The Nuclear Man on cover with #50, in indicia with #65) (Also see Firestorm)
DC Comics: June, 1982 - No. 64, Oct, 1987 (75¢ on)

1-Intro The Black Bison; brief origin	3	6	9	18	28	38
2-6,8-22,25-40,43-64: 4-JLA x-over. 6-Masters of the Universe preview insert. 17-1st app. Firehawk. 21-Death of Killer Frost. 22-Origin. 27-Firestorm pin-up by Gil Kane. 34-1st app./origin Killer Frost II. 39-Weasel's ID revealed. 48-Intro. Moonbow. 53-Origin & 1st app. Silver Shade. 55,56-Legends x-over. 58-1st app./origin new Parasite						5.00
7-1st app. Plastique	2	4	6	9	12	15
23-(5/84) 1st app. Felicity Smoak (Byte)	3	6	9	15	22	28
24-(6/84)-1st app. Bug (origin); origin Byte; 1st app. Blue Devil in a prevue pull-out	3	6	9	16	23	30
41,42-Crisis x-over. 41-Harbinger, Psycho Pirate-c/app.						5.00
61-Test cover variant; Superman logo	4	8	12	27	44	60
Annual 1-4: 1(1983), 2(1984), 3(1985), 4(1986)						5.00

NOTE: *Colan* a-19p, Annual 4p. *Giffen* a-Annual 4p. *Gil Kane* c-30. *Nino* a-37. *Tuska* a-(p)-17, 18, 32, 45.

FURY OF FIRESTORM: THE NUCLEAR MEN (New DC 52)
DC Comics: Nov, 2011 - No. 20, Jul, 2013 ($2.99)

1-18: 1-Van Sciver & Simone-s/Cinar-a/Van Sciver-c. 7,8-Van Sciver-a. 9-JLI app.						3.00
19,20-Killer Frost app.						5.00
#0 (11/12, #2.99) Cinar-a/c						3.00

FURY OF SHIELD
Marvel Comics: Apr, 1995 - No. 4, July, 1995 ($2.50/$1.95, limited series)

1 ($2.50)-Foil-c						5.00
2-4: 4-Bagged w/ decoder						4.00

FURY: PEACEMAKER
Marvel Comics: Apr, 2006 - No. 6, Sept, 2006 ($3.50, limited series)

1-6-Flashback to WW2; Ennis-s/Robertson-a. 1-Deodato-c. 2-Texeira-c. 5-Dillon-c.						3.50
TPB (2006, $17.99) r/#1-6						18.00

FURY: S.H.I.E.L.D. 50TH ANNIVERSARY
Marvel Comics: Nov, 2015 ($3.99, one-shot)

1-Walker-s/Ferguson-a/Deodato-c; Nick Fury Jr. time travels to meet 1965 Nick Fury						4.00

FUSED
Image Comics: Mar, 2002 - No. 4, Jan, 2003 ($2.95)

1-4-Steve Niles-s. 1,2-Paul Lee-a. 3-Brad Rader-a. 4-Templesmith-a						3.00

FUSED
Dark Horse Comics: Dec, 2003 - No. 4, Mar, 2004 ($2.95)

1-4-Steve Niles/Josh Medors-a. 1-Powell-c						3.00

FUSION
Eclipse Comics: Jan, 1987 - No. 17, Oct, 1989 ($2.00, B&W, Baxter paper)

1-17: 11-The Weasel Patrol begins (1st app.?)						4.00

FUSION
Image Comics (Top Cow): May, 2009 - No. 3, Jul, 2009 ($2.99, limited series)

1-3-Avengers, Thunderbolts, Cyberforce and Hunter-Killer meet; Kirkham-a						3.00

FUTURAMA (TV)
Bongo Comics: 2000 - No. 81, 2016 ($2.50/$2.99/$3.99, bi-monthly)

1-Based on the FOX-TV animated series; Groening/Morrison-c						
	5	10	15	34	60	85
1-San Diego Comic-Con Premiere Edition	6	12	18	41	76	110
2-10: 8-CGC cover spoof; X-Men parody	2	4	6	8	10	12
11-30						6.00
31-81: 40,64-Santa app. 50-55-Poster included						4.00

Annual 1 (2018, $4.99) Wacky Races spoof; Pinocchio homage						5.00
Futurama Adventures TPB (2004, $14.95) r/#5-9						15.00
Futurama Conquers the Universe TPB (2007, $14.95) r/#10-13						15.00
Futurama-O-Rama TPB (2002, $12.95) r/#1-4; sketch pages of Fry's development						15.00
...: The Time Bender Trilogy TPB (2006, $14.95) r/#16-19; cover gallery						15.00

FUTURAMA/SIMPSONS INFINITELY SECRET CROSSOVER CRISIS (TV) (See Simpsons/Futurama Crossover Crisis II for sequel)
Bongo Comics: 2002 - No. 2, 2002 ($2.50, limited series)

1-Evil Brain Spawns put Futurama crew into the Simpsons' Springfield						
	3	6	9	16	23	30
2	2	4	6	8	10	12

FUTURE COMICS
David McKay Publications: June, 1940 - No. 4, Sept, 1940

1-(6/40, 64 pgs.)-Origin The Phantom (1st in comics) (4 pgs.); The Lone Ranger (8 pgs.) & Saturn Against the Earth (4 pgs.) begin						
	331	662	993	2317	4059	5800
2	168	336	504	1075	1838	2600
3,4	129	258	387	826	1413	2000

FUTURE COP L.A.P.D. (Electronic Arts video game) (Also see Promotional Comics section)
DC Comics (WildStorm): Jan, 1999 ($4.95, magazine sized)

1-Stories and art by various						5.00

FUTURE FIGHT FIRSTS (Also see Agents of Atlas 2019 series)
Marvel Comics: Dec, 2019 - Jan, 2020 ($4.99, limited series of one-shots)

...: Crescent and Io 1 (1/20) Origin stories; Alyssa Wong-s/Jon Lam-a						5.00
...: Luna Snow 1 (12/19) Origin story; Alyssa Wong-s/Gang Hyuk Lim-a						5.00
...: White Fox 1 (12/19) Origin story; Alyssa Wong-s/Kevin Libranda & Geoffo-a						5.00

FUTURE FOUNDATION (From Fantastic Four)
Marvel Comics: Oct, 2019 - No. 5, Feb, 2020 ($3.99, limited series)

1-5-Whitley-s; Alex & Julie Power, Dragon Man, Onome, Bentley-23 app. 1-3-Robson-a						4.00

FUTURE IMPERFECT (Secret Wars tie-in)
Marvel Comics: Aug, 2015 - No. 5, Nov, 2015 ($3.99, limited series)

1-5-Peter David-s/Greg Land-a; Maestro (Hulk) and The Thing (Thaddeus Ross) app.						4.00

FUTURE QUEST
DC Comics: Jul, 2016 - No. 12, Jul, 2017 ($3.99)

1-12: 1-Jonny Quest; Space Ghost, Birdman and Dr. Zin app.; Shaner & Rude-a. 8-Olivetti-a; The Impossibles app.						4.00

FUTURE QUEST PRESENTS
DC Comics: Oct, 2017 - No. 12, Sept, 2018 ($3.99)

1-4: 1-3-Space Ghost and the Herculoids; Parker-s/Olivetti-a/c. 4-Galaxy Trio; Randall-a						4.00
5-12: 5-7-Birdman; Hester-s/Rude-a; Mentok app. 8-Mightor. 9-11-Herculoids						4.00

FUTURE SHOCK
Image Comics: 2006 (Free Comic Book Day giveaway)

...: FCBD 2006 Edition; Spawn, Invincible, Savage Dragon & others short stories						3.00

FUTURE STATE: AQUAMAN
DC Comics: Mar, 2021 - No. 2, Apr, 2021 ($3.99, limited series)

1,2-Aquaman (Jackson Hyde) & Aquawoman (Andy Curry) app.; Thomas-s/Sampere-a						4.00

FUTURE STATE: BATMAN / SUPERMAN
DC Comics: Mar, 2021 - No. 2, Apr, 2021 ($3.99, limited series)

1,2-Batman & Superman vs. False Face Society in the near future; Yang-s/Oliver-a						4.00

FUTURE STATE: CATWOMAN
DC Comics: Mar, 2021 - No. 2, Apr, 2021 ($3.99, limited series)

1,2-Catwoman (Selina Kyle) in the near future; Talia app.; Ram V-s/Schmidt-a						4.00

FUTURE STATE: DARK DETECTIVE
DC Comics: Mar, 2021 - No. 4, Late Apr, 2021 ($5.99, limited series)

1-4-Bruce Wayne in the near future; Tamaki-s/Mora-a. 1,3-Back-up with Grifter and Huntress. 2,4-Back-up with Red Hood & Ravager. 4-White Rabbit app.						6.00

FUTURE STATE: GOTHAM
DC Comics: Jul, 2021 - No. 18, Dec, 2022 ($3.99, B&W)

1-18: 1-Red Hood featured; manga-style B&W art by Milogiannis; back-up (r) w/Otomo-s/a. 2-Back-up (r) w/Coipel-a. 3-5-Punchline app. 4-Harley Quinn-a. 8,9-Cizmesija-a						4.00

FUTURE STATE: GREEN LANTERN
DC Comics: Mar, 2021 - No. 2, Apr, 2021 ($5.99, limited series)

1,2-The Corps without rings. 1-Back-up with Jessica Cruz vs. Lyssa Drak; Guy Gardner. 2-Back-ups with Hal Jordan, Mogo, Keli Quintela, & Jo Mullein						6.00

FUTURE STATE: HARLEY QUINN
DC Comics: Mar, 2021 - No. 2, Apr, 2021 ($3.99, limited series)

1,2-Harley in the near future; Black Mask app.; Stephanie Phillips-s/Simone DiMeo-a						4.00

FUTURE STATE: IMMORTAL WONDER WOMAN
DC Comics: Mar, 2021 - No. 2, Apr, 2021 ($5.99, limited series)

1,2-Diana in the far future; Darkseid app.; Bartel-a; back-up with Nubia						6.00

FUTURE STATE: JUSTICE LEAGUE
DC Comics: Mar, 2021 - No. 2, Apr, 2021 ($5.99, limited series)

1,2-Superman (Jon Kent), Batman (Tim Fox), WW (Yara Flor), Aquawoman, G.L. (Jo Mullein), and Flash team; Hyperclan app.; back-up with J.L. Dark; Doctor Fate app.						6.00

FUTURE STATE: KARA ZOR-EL, SUPERWOMAN
DC Comics: Mar, 2021 - No. 2, Apr, 2021 ($3.99, limited series)

1,2-Kara on the Moon colony; intro. Lynari; Bennett-s/Sauvage-a						4.00

FUTURE STATE: LEGION OF SUPER-HEROES
DC Comics: Mar, 2021 - No. 2, Apr, 2021 ($3.99, limited series)

1,2-Bendis-s/Rossmo-a; Legion reunites in the farther future						4.00

FUTURE STATE: NIGHTWING
DC Comics: Mar, 2021 - No. 2, Apr, 2021 ($3.99, limited series)

1,2-Nightwing & Batman (Tim Fox) vs. Peacekeepers; Nicola Scott-a/Andrew Constant-s						4.00

Fury (2013 series) #12 © MAR

Future State: Dark Detective #2 © DC

Galactica 1980 #1 © Universal Studios

	GD	VG	FN	VF	VF/NM	NM-
	2.0	4.0	6.0	8.0	9.0	9.2

FUTURE STATE: ROBIN ETERNAL
DC Comics: Mar, 2021 - No. 2, Apr, 2021 ($3.99, limited series)
1,2-Tim Drake and Spoiler; Fitzmartin-s/Barrows-a — 4.00

FUTURE STATE: SHAZAM! (Continues in Future State: Black Adam)
DC Comics: Mar, 2021 - No. 2, Apr, 2021 ($3.99, limited series)
1,2-Vixen, Question, Miss Martian, Powerhouse, Creeper, Giganta app.; Pansica-a — 4.00

FUTURE STATE: SUICIDE SQUAD
DC Comics: Mar, 2021 - No. 2, Apr, 2021 ($5.99, limited series)
1,2-Team with Superman (Conner Kent), Batman (Talon), Martian Manhunter (Clayface), Aquaman (Fisherman), Flash (Bolt); back-up with Black Adam & Justice Legion-A — 6.00

FUTURE STATE: SUPERMAN: HOUSE OF EL
DC Comics: Apr, 2021 ($5.99, one-shot)
1-P.K. Johnson-s/Scott Godlewski-a; set in the far future with Kal-El's descendants — 6.00

FUTURE STATE: SUPERMAN OF METROPOLIS
DC Comics: Mar, 2021 - No. 2, Apr, 2021 ($5.99, limited series)
1,2-Jon Kent vs. Supergirl; Timms-a; back-ups with Mister Miracle and The Guardian — 6.00

FUTURE STATE: SUPERMAN VS. IMPERIOUS LEX
DC Comics: Mar, 2021 - No. 3, May, 2021 ($3.99, limited series)
1-Lexor joining the United Planets; Mark Russell-s/Steve Pugh-a — 4.00

FUTURE STATE: SUPERMAN / WONDER WOMAN
DC Comics: Mar, 2021 - No. 2, Apr, 2021 ($3.99, limited series)
1,2-Jon Kent & Yara Flor vs. Solaris; Watters-s/Del Duca-a — 4.00

FUTURE STATE: SUPERMAN: WORLDS OF WAR (Continues in Superman: House of El)
DC Comics: Mar, 2021 - No. 2, Apr, 2021 ($7.99, limited series)
1,2-Janin-a; back-ups with Mr. Miracle, Midnighter and Black Racer — 8.00

FUTURE STATE: SWAMP THING
DC Comics: Mar, 2021 - No. 2, Apr, 2021 ($3.99, limited series)
1,2-Ram V-s/Mike Perkins-a; Jason Woodrue & Obsidian app. — 4.00

FUTURE STATE: TEEN TITANS (Leads into Teen Titans Academy)
DC Comics: Mar, 2021 - No. 2, Apr, 2021 ($3.99, limited series)
1,2-Sheridan-s/Sandoval-a; Red X app.; Dick Grayson as Death-Wing — 4.00

FUTURE STATE: THE FLASH (Prelude to Future State: Teen Titans)
DC Comics: Mar, 2021 - No. 3, May, 2021 ($3.99, limited series)
1,2-Vietti-s. 1-Eaglesham-a; Flashes vs. Wally West as Famine. 2-Peterson-a — 4.00

FUTURE STATE: THE NEXT BATMAN
DC Comics: Mar, 2021 - No. 4, Apr, 2021 ($7.99, limited series)
1-4-Tim Fox as Batman; Ridley-s. 1-Derington-a. 1,3-Back-ups with Outsiders, Arkham Knights. 2,4-Back-ups with Batgirls & Gotham City Sirens — 8.00

FUTURE STATE: THE FLASH (Prelude to Future State: Teen Titans)
DC Comics: Mar, 2021 - No. 2, Apr, 2021 ($3.99, limited series)
1,2-Yara Flor from the Amazon Rainforest; Jöelle Jones-s/a — 4.00

FUTURE WORLD COMICS
George W. Dougherty: Summer, 1946 - No. 2, Fall, 1946

	GD	VG	FN	VF	VF/NM	NM-
1,2: H.C. Kiefer-c; preview of the World of Tomorrow	39	78	117	240	395	550

FUTURE WORLD COMIX (Warren Presents...)
Warren Publications: Sept, 1978 (B&W magazine, 84 pgs.)

1-Corben, Maroto, Morrow, Nino, Sutton-a; Todd-c/a; contains nudity panels	2	4	6	9	13	16

FUTURIANS, THE (See Marvel Graphic Novel #9)
Lodestone Publishing/Eternity Comics: Sept, 1985 - No. 3, 1985 ($1.50)
1-3: Indicia title "Dave Cockrum's..." — 4.00
Graphic Novel 1 ($9.95, Eternity)-r/#1-3, plus never published #4 issue — 10.00

FX
IDW Publishing: Mar, 2008 - No. 6, Aug, 2008 ($3.99)
1-6-John Byrne-a/c; Wayne Osborne-s — 4.00

G-8 (Listed at G-Eight)

GABBY (Formerly Ken Shannon) (Teen humor)
Quality Comics Group: No. 11, Jul, 1953; No. 2, Sep, 1953 - No. 9, Sep, 1954

	GD	VG	FN	VF	VF/NM	NM-
11(#1)(7/53)	14	28	42	82	121	160
2	10	20	30	54	72	90
3-9	9	18	27	50	65	80

GABBY GOB (See Harvey Hits No. 85, 90, 94, 97, 100, 103, 106, 109)

GABBY HAYES ADVENTURE COMICS
Toby Press: Dec, 1953

	GD	VG	FN	VF	VF/NM	NM-
1-Photo-c	18	36	54	103	162	220

GABBY HAYES WESTERN (Movie star)(See Monte Hale, Real Western Hero & Western Hero)
Fawcett Publications/Charlton Comics No. 51 on: Nov, 1948 - No. 50, Jan, 1953; No. 51, Dec, 1954 - No. 59, Jan, 1957

	GD	VG	FN	VF	VF/NM	NM-
1-Gabby & his horse Corker begin; photo front/back-c begin	42	84	126	265	445	625
2	21	42	63	124	202	280
3-5	15	30	45	88	137	185
6-10: 9-Young Falcon begins	14	28	42	78	112	145
11-20: 19-Last photo back-c	11	22	33	64	90	115
21-49: 20,22,24,26,28,29-(52 pgs.)	9	18	27	52	69	85
50-(1/53)-Last Fawcett issue; last photo-c?	10	20	30	58	79	100
51-(12/54)-1st Charlton issue; photo-c	11	22	33	60	83	105
52-59(1955-57): 53,55-Photo-c. 58-Swayze-a	8	16	24	42	54	65

GAGS
United Features Synd./Triangle Publ. No. 9 on: Jul, 1937 - V3#10, Oct, 1944 (13-3/4x10-3/4")

	GD	VG	FN	VF	VF/NM	NM-
1(7/37)-52 pgs.; 20 pgs. Grin & Bear It, Fellow Citizen	36	72	108	211	343	475
V1#9 (36 pgs.) (7/42)	14	28	42	80	115	150
V3#10	11	22	33	62	86	110

GALACTA: DAUGHTER OF GALACTUS
Marvel Comics: July, 2010 ($3.99, one-shot)
1-Adam Warren-s/Hector Sevilla-a; Warren & Sevilla-c : Wolverine and the FF app. — 4.00

GALACTICA 1980 (Based on the Battlestar Galactica TV series)
Dynamite Entertainment: 2009 - No. 4, 2009 ($3.50)
1-4-Guggenheim-s/Razek-a — 3.50

GALACTICA: THE NEW MILLENNIUM
Realm Press: Sept, 1999 ($2.99)
1-Stories by Shooter, Braden, Kuhoric — 4.00

GALACTIC GUARDIANS
Marvel Comics: July, 1994 - No. 4, Oct, 1994 ($1.50, limited series)
1-4 — 4.00

GALACTIC WARS COMIX (Warren Presents... on cover)
Warren Publications: Dec, 1978 (B&W magazine, 84 pgs.)

	GD	VG	FN	VF	VF/NM	NM-
nn-Wood, Williamson-r; Battlestar Galactica/Flash Gordon photo/text stories	2	4	6	9	13	16

GALACTUS THE DEVOURER
Marvel Comics: Sept, 1999 - No. 6, Mar, 2000 ($3.50/$2.50, limited series)

	GD	VG	FN	VF	VF/NM	NM-
1-($3.50) L. Simonson-s/Muth-a	2	4	6	8	10	12
2-5-($2.50) Buscema & Sienkiewicz-a						6.00
6-($3.50) Death of Galactus; Buscema & Sienkiewicz-a	1	2	3	5	6	8

GALAKTIKON
Albatross Funnybooks: 2017 - No. 6, 2018 ($3.99, limited series)
1-6-Brendon Small-s/Steve Mannion-a. 1-5-Eric Powell-c. 6-Mannion-c — 4.00

GALAXIA (Magazine)
Astral Publ.: 1981 ($2.50, B&W, 52 pgs.)

	GD	VG	FN	VF	VF/NM	NM-
1-Buckler/Giordano-c; Texeira/Guice-a; 1st app. Astron, Sojourner, Bloodwing, Warlords; Buckler-s/a	2	4	11	16	20	

GALAXY QUEST: GLOBAL WARNING! (Based on the 1999 movie)
IDW Publishing: Aug, 2008 - No. 5, Dec, 2008 ($3.99)
1-5-Lobdell-s/Kyriazis-a — 4.00

GALAXY QUEST: THE JOURNEY CONTINUES (Based on the 1999 movie)
IDW Publishing: Jan, 2015 - No. 4, Apr, 2015 ($3.99)
1-4-Erik Burnham-s/Nacho Arranz-a — 4.00

GALLANT MEN, THE (TV)
Gold Key: Oct, 1963 (Photo-c)

	GD	VG	FN	VF	VF/NM	NM-
1(1008-310)-Manning-a	3	6	9	21	33	45

GALLEGHER, BOY REPORTER (Disney, TV)
Gold Key: May, 1965

	GD	VG	FN	VF	VF/NM	NM-
1(10149-505)-Photo-c	3	6	9	17	26	35

GAMBIT (See X-Men #266 & X-Men Annual #14)
Marvel Comics: Dec, 1993 - No. 4, Mar, 1994 ($2.00, limited series)

	GD	VG	FN	VF	VF/NM	NM-
1-($2.50)-Lee Weeks-c/a in all; gold foil stamped-c	3	6	9	15	24	32

	GD 2.0	VG 4.0	FN 6.0	VF 8.0	VF/NM 9.0	NM- 9.2
1 (Gold)		8	16	24	51	96	140
2-4							6.00

GAMBIT
Marvel Comics: Sept, 1997 - No. 4, Dec, 1997 ($2.50, limited series)

1-4-Janson-a/Mackie & Kavanagh-s	1	2	3	5	6	8

GAMBIT
Marvel Comics: Feb, 1999 - No. 25, Feb, 2001 ($2.99/$1.99)

1-($2.99) Five covers; Nicieza-a/Skroce-a	1	2	3	5	6	8
2-11,13-16-($1.99) 2-Two covers (Skroce & Adam Kubert)						3.00
12-($2.99)						4.00
17-24: 17-Begin $2.25-c. 21-Mystique-c/app.						3.00
25-($2.99) Leads into "Gambit & Bishop"						4.00
...1999 Annual ($3.50) Nicieza-s/McDaniel-a						4.00
...2000 Annual ($3.50) Nicieza-s/Derenick & Smith-a						4.00

GAMBIT
Marvel Comics: Nov, 2004 - No. 12, Aug, 2005 ($2.99)

1-12: 1-Jeanty-a/Land-a/Layman-s. 5-Wolverine-c/app. 9-Brother Voodoo-c/app.						3.00
... and the Champions: From the Marvel Vault 1 (10/11, $2.99) George Tuska's last art						3.00
...: Hath No Fury TPB (2005, $14.99) r/#7-12						15.00
...: House of Cards TPB (2005, $14.99) r/#1-6; Land cover sketches; unused covers						15.00

GAMBIT
Marvel Comics: Oct, 2012 - No. 17, Nov, 2013 ($2.99)

1-17: 1-Asmus-s/Mann-a; covers by Mann & Bachalo. 6,7-Pete Wisdom app.						3.00

GAMBIT
Marvel Comics: Jul, 2022 - No. 5, Jan, 2023 ($3.99)

1-5-Claremont-s/Kotian-a; untold story from era with de-aged amnesiac Storm						4.00

GAMBIT & BISHOP (... : Sons of the Atom on cover)
Marvel Comics: Feb, 2001 - No. 6, May, 2001 ($2.25, bi-weekly limited series)

Alpha (2/01) Prelude to series; Nord-a						3.00
1-6-Jeanty-a/Williams-c						3.00
Genesis (3/01, $3.50) reprints their first apps. and first meeting						4.00

GAMBIT AND THE X-TERNALS
Marvel Comics: Mar, 1995 - No. 4, July, 1995 ($1.95, limited series)

1-4-Age of Apocalypse						4.00

GAME BOY (Super Mario covers on all)
Valiant: 1990 - No. 4, 1990 ($1.95, coated-c)

1		4	8	12	28	47	65
2		3	6	9	24	33	45
3,4-Layton-a. 4-Morrow-a		3	6	9	14	20	25

GAMEKEEPER (Guy Ritchie's...)
Virgin Comics: Mar, 2007 - No. 5, Sept, 2007; Mar, 2008 - No. 5, Jul, 2008 ($2.99)

1-5-Andy Diggle-s/Mukesh Singh-a; 2 covers on each						3.00
1-Extended Edition (6/07, $2.99) r/#1 with script excerpt and sketch art						3.00
Series 2 (3/08 - No. 5, 7/08) 1-5-Parker-s/Randle-a						3.00
Vol. 1 TPB (10/07, $14.99) r/#1-5; script and sketch pages; Guy Ritchie intro.						15.00

GAME OF THRONES, A (George R.R. Martin's...) (Based on A Song of Ice and Fire)
Dynamite Entertainment: 2011 - No. 24, 2014 ($3.99)

1-Covers by Alex Ross and Mike Miller		3	6	9	17	26	35
2-24: 2-Covers by Alex Ross and Mike Miller							6.00

GAMERA
Dark Horse Comics: Aug, 1996 - No. 4, Nov, 1996 ($2.95, limited series)

1-4						4.00

GAMMA FLIGHT (From Immortal Hulk)
Marvel Comics: Aug, 2021 - No. 5, Dec, 2021 ($3.99, limited series)

1-5-Ewing & Frasier-s/Medina-a; Puck, Titania, Absorbing Man & Doc Sasquatch team						4.00

GAMMARAUDERS
DC Comics: Jan, 1989 - No. 10, Dec, 1989 ($1.25/$1.50/$2.00)

1-10-Based on TSR game						4.00

GAMORA (Guardians of the Galaxy)
Marvel Comics: Feb, 2017 - No. 5, Jul, 2017 ($3.99, limited series)

1-5-Perlman-s/Checchetto-a. 1,5-Thanos & Nebula app.						4.00

GAMORRA SWIMSUIT SPECIAL
Image Comics (WildStorm Productions): June, 1996 ($2.50, one-shot)

1-Campbell wraparound-c; pinups						4.00

GANDY GOOSE (Movies/TV)(See All Surprise, Giant Comics Edition #5A &10, Paul Terry's Comics & Terry-Toons)
St. John Publ. Co./Pines No. 5,6: Mar, 1953 - No. 5, Nov, 1953; No. 5, Fall, 1956 - No. 6, Sum/58

1-All St. John issues are pre-code	15	30	45	86	133	180
2	9	18	27	52	69	85
3-5(1953)(St. John)	8	16	24	40	50	60
5,6(1956-58)(Pines)-CBS Television Presents...	6	12	18	28	34	40

GANG BUSTERS (See Popular Comics #38)
David McKay/Dell Publishing Co.: 1938 - 1943

Feature Books 17(McKay)('38)-1st app.	100	200	300	635	1093	1550
Large Feature Comic 10('39)-(Scarce)	97	194	291	621	1061	1500
Large Feature Comic 17('41)	63	126	189	403	689	975
Four Color 7(1940)	77	154	231	493	847	1200
Four Color 23('42)	58	116	174	371	636	900
Four Color 24('43)	34	68	102	245	548	850

GANG BUSTERS (Radio/TV)(Gangbusters #14 on)
National Periodical Publ.: Dec-Jan, 1947-48 - No. 67, Dec-Jan, 1958-59 (No. 1-23: 52 pgs.)

1	103	206	309	659	1130	1600
2	41	82	123	256	428	600
3-5	28	56	84	165	270	375

6-10: 9-Dan Barry-a. 9,10-Photo-c	21	42	63	122	199	275
11-13-Photo-c	17	34	51	100	158	215
14,17-Frazetta-a, 8 pgs. each. 14-Photo-c	37	74	111	222	361	500
15,16,18-20,26: 26-Kirby-a	15	30	45	85	130	175
21-25,27-30	14	28	42	76	108	140
31-44: 44-Last Pre-code (2-3/55)	12	24	36	67	94	120
45-67	10	20	30	54	72	90

NOTE: Barry a-6, 8, 10. Drucker a-51. Moreira a-48, 50, 59. Roussos a-8.

GANGLAND
DC Comics (Vertigo): Jun, 1998 - No. 4, Sept, 1998 ($2.95, limited series)

1-4: Crime anthology by various. 2-Corben-a						4.00
TPB-(2000, $12.95) r/#1-4; Bradstreet-c						13.00

GANGSTERS AND GUN MOLLS
Avon Per./Realistic Comics: Sept, 1951 - No. 4, June, 1952 (Painted c-1-3)

1-Wood-a, 1 pg; c-/Avon paperback #292	90	180	270	576	988	1400
2-Check-a, 8 pgs.; Kamen-a; Bonnie Parker story	77	154	231	493	847	1200
3-Marijuana mentioned; used in POP, pg. 84,85	60	120	180	381	653	925
4-Syd Shores-c	58	116	174	371	636	900

GANGSTERS CAN'T WIN
D. S. Publishing Co.: Feb-Mar, 1948 - No. 9, June-July, 1949 (All 52 pgs?)

1-True crime stories	53	106	159	334	567	800
2-Skull-c	331	662	993	2317	4059	5800
3,5,6	27	54	81	158	259	360
4-Acid in face story	36	72	108	211	343	475
7-9	21	42	63	124	202	280

NOTE: Ingles a-5, 6. McWilliams a-5, 7, 8. Reinman c-6.

GANG WORLD
Standard Comics: No. 5, Nov, 1952 - No. 6, Jan, 1953

5-Bondage-c	28	56	84	168	274	380
6	20	40	60	120	195	270

GARBAGE PAIL KIDS COMIC BOOK (Based on the trading cards)
IDW Publishing: Dec, 2014 - Feb, 2015 ($3.99, series of one-shots)

... Love Stinks (2/15) short stories by various incl. Haspiel, Wheeler, Bagge; 3 covers						
		1	2	3	4	6	8	10
... Puke-tacular (12/14) short stories by various incl. Bagge, Wray, Barta; 3 covers						
		2	4	6	9	12	15

GARBAGE PAIL KIDS: ORIGINS (Based on the trading cards)
Dynamite Entertainment: 2022 - No. 3, 2022 ($3.99)

1-3-Zapata-a. 1-Origin of Adam Bomb						4.00

GARBAGE PAIL KIDS: TRASHIN' THROUGH TIME (Based on the trading cards)
Dynamite Entertainment: 2023 - No. 3, 2024 ($4.99, bagged with trading card)

1-3-Zapata						4.00

GARFIELD (Newspaper/cartoon cat)(Also see Grumpy Cat)
Boom Entertainment (KaBOOM!): May, 2012 - No. 36, Apr, 2015 ($3.99)

1-24-Evanier-s. 1-Two covers by Barker. 8-Christmas-c. 13,20-Pet Force app.						4.00
1-4-First Appearance Variants by Jim Davis. 1-Garfield. 2-Odie. 3-Jon. 4-Nermal						10.00
25-($4.99) Covers by George Pérez and Barker; bonus pin-ups						5.00
26-36: 30-EC-style horror cover. 33-36-His 9 Lives						4.00
... 2016 Summer Special 1 (7/16, $7.99) Evanier & Nickel-s; Batman spoof						
			1	2	3	5	6	8
... 2018 Vacation Times Blues 1 (5/18, $7.99) Evanier & Nickel-s; Hirsch-a						
			1	2	3	5	6	8
... Cheesy Holiday Special 1 (12/15, $4.99) Christmas stories; Evanier & Nickel-s						5.00
...: Pet Force Special 1 (8/13, $4.99) Cover swipe of Amazing Spider-Man #50						5.00
...: Pet Force 2014 Special (4/14, $4.99) The Pet Force multiverse; bonus sketch art						5.00
... TV or Not TV? 1 (10/18, $7.99) Halloween stories; Evanier & Nickel-s; Hirsch-a						8.00

GARFIELD: HOMECOMING (Newspaper/cartoon cat)
Boom Entertainment (KaBOOM!): Jun, 2018 - No. 4, Sept, 2018 ($3.99, limited series)

1-4-Scott Nickel-s. 1-Talmadge & Alfaro-a. 2-Paroline, Lamb & Alfaro-a						4.00

GARGOYLE (See The Defenders #94)
Marvel Comics Group: June, 1985 - No. 4, Sept, 1985 (75¢, limited series)

1-Wrightson-a; character from Defenders						5.00
2-4						4.00

GARGOYLES (TV cartoon)
Marvel Comics: Feb, 1995 - No. 11, Dec, 1995 ($2.50)

1-11: Based on animated series						4.00
... Facsimile Edition Issue #1 (Dynamite Ent., 2023, $3.99) r/#1; preview of 2022 series						5.00

GARGOYLES (TV cartoon)
Dynamite Entertainment: 2022 - Present ($3.99)

1-11-Greg Weisman-s/George Kambadais-a						4.00
... Halloween Special 1 (2023, $4.99) Weisman-s/Bonesso-a						5.00

GARGOYLES: DARK AGES (TV cartoon)
Dynamite Entertainment: 2023 - Present ($3.99)

1-5-Greg Weisman-s/Drew Moss-a						4.00

GARRISON
DC Comics (WildStorm): Jun, 2010 - No. 6, Nov, 2010 ($2.99)

1-6-Mariotte-s/Francavilla-a/c						3.00

GARRISON'S GORILLAS (TV)
Dell Publishing Co.: Jan, 1968 - No. 4, Oct, 1968; No. 5, Oct, 1969 (Photo-c)

1		4	8	12	28	47	65
2-5: 5-Reprints #1		3	6	9	19	30	40

GARY GIANNI'S THE MONSTERMEN
Dark Horse Comics: Aug, 1999 ($2.95, one-shot)

1-Gianni-s/c/a; back-up Hellboy story by Mignola						4.00

GASM (Sci-Fi, Horror, Fantasy comics magazine)(Mature content)
Stories, Layouts & Press, Inc.: Nov, 1977 - nn (No. 5), Jun, 1978 (B&W/color)

Gambit (2013 series) #17 © MAR(VEL)

Gears of War #9 © Epic Comics

Geiger #6 © Johns & Frank

	GD 2.0	VG 4.0	FN 6.0	VF 8.0	VF/NM 9.0	NM- 9.2
1-Mark Wheatley-s/a; Gene Day-s/a; Workman-a	3	6	9	16	23	30
2 (12/77) Wheatley-a; Winnick-s/a; Workman-a	2	4	6	11	16	20
nn(#3, 2/78) Day-s/a; Wheatley-a; Workman-a	2	4	6	10	14	18
nn(#4, 4/78) Day-s/a; Wheatley-a; Corben-a	3	6	9	14	20	26
nn(#5, 6/78) Hempel-s/a; Howarth-a; Corben-a	3	6	9	16	23	30

GASOLINA
Image Comics (Skybound): Sept, 2017 - No. 18, May, 2019 ($3.99)

1-18-Sean Mackiewicz-s/Niko Walter-a						4.00

GASOLINE ALLEY (Top Love Stories No. 3 on?)
Star Publications: Sept-Oct, 1950 - No. 2, Dec, 1950 (Newspaper-r)

1-Contains 1 pg. intro. history of the strip (The Life of Skeezix); reprints 15 scenes of highlights from 1921-1935, plus an adventure from 1935 and 1936 strips; a 2-pg. filler is included on the life of the creator Frank King, with photo of the cartoonist.	26	52	78	154	252	350
2-(1936-37 reprints)-L. B. Cole-c	30	60	90	177	289	400

(See Super Book No. 21)

GASP!
American Comics Group: Mar, 1967 - No. 4, Aug, 1967 (12¢)

1	6	12	18	37	66	95
2-4	4	8	12	23	37	50

GATECRASHER
Black Bull Entertainment: Mar, 2000 - No. 4, Jun, 2000 ($2.50, limited series)

1,2-Waid-s/Conner & Palmiotti-c/a; 1,2-variant-c by J.G. Jones						3.00
3,4: 3-Jusko var-c. 4-Linsner-c						3.00
... Ring of Fire TPB (11/00, $12.95) r/#1-4; Hughes-a; Ennis intro.						13.00

GATECRASHER (Regular series)
Black Bull Entertainment: Aug, 2000 - No. 6, Jan, 2001 ($2.50, limited series)

1-6-Waid-s/Conner & Palmiotti-c/a; 1-3-Variant-c by Fabry. 4-Hildebrandts variant-c. 5-Art Adams var-c. 6-Texeira var-c						3.00

GAY COMICS (Honeymoon No. 41)
Timely Comics/USA Comic Mag. Co. No. 18-24: Mar, 1944 (no month); No. 18, Fall, 1944 - No. 40, Oct, 1949

1-Wolverton's Powerhouse Pepper; Tessie the Typist begins; 1st app. Willie (one shot)	123	246	369	787	1344	1900
18-(Formerly Funny Tunes #17?)-Wolverton-a	77	154	231	493	847	1200
19-29: Wolverton-a in all. 21,24-6 pg., 7 pg. Powerhouse Pepper; additional 2 pg. story in 24.)						
23-7 pg Wolverton story & 2 two pg stories (total of 11pgs.)	57	114	171	362	619	875
24,29-Kurtzman-a (24-"Hey Look"(2))	57	114	171	362	619	875
30,33,36,37-Kurtzman's "Hey Look"	32	64	96	188	307	425
31-Kurtzman's "Hey Look" (1), Giggles 'N' Grins (1-1/2)	34	68	102	199	325	450
32,35,38-40: 35-Nellie The Nurse begins?	28	56	84	168	274	380
34-Three Kurtzman's "Hey Look"	34	68	102	199	325	450

GAY COMICS (Also see Smile, Tickle, & Whee Comics)
Modern Store Publ.: 1955 (7¢, 5x7-1/4, 52 pgs.)

1	8	16	24	51	96	140

GAY PURR-EE (See Movie Comics)

GCPD: THE BLUE WALL (Gotham City Police Deptartment)
DC Comics: Dec, 2022 - No. 6, May, 2023 ($3.99, limited series)

1-6-John Ridley-s/Stefano Raffaele-a; intro. Officer Samantha Park						4.00

GEARS OF WAR (Based on the video game)
DC Comics (WildStorm): Dec, 2008 - No. 24, Aug, 2012 ($3.99/$2.99)

1-15: 1-Liam Sharp/Joshua Ortega-a. 1-Two covers						4.00
16-24-($2.99) 16-Traviss-s/Gopez-a. 18-20-Mhan-a. 19-24-Prelude to Gears of War 3						3.00
... Reader (4/09, $3.99) r/#1 & 2 in flipbook						4.00
... Sourcebook (8/09, $3.99) character pin-ups by various; Platt-c						4.00
Book One HC (2009, $19.99, dustjacket) r/#1-6 & Sourcebook						20.00
Book One SC (2010, $14.99) r/#1-6 & Sourcebook						15.00
Book Two HC (2011, $24.99, dustjacket) r/#7-13						25.00

GEARS OF WAR: HIVEBUSTERS (Based on the video game)
IDW Publishing: Mar, 2019 - No. 4, Jun, 2019 ($3.99)

1-4-Kurtis Wiebe-s. 1,2-Alan Quah-a. 3-Quah & Coccolo-a. 4-Padilla & Wagner Reis-a						4.00
Gears Pop One-Shot (7/19, $4.99) Art in the style of Funko Pop figures						5.00

GEARS OF WAR: THE RISE OF RAAM (Based on the video game)
IDW Publishing: Jan, 2018 - No. 4, Apr, 2018 ($3.99)

1-4-Kurtis Wiebe-s/Max Dunbar-a						4.00

GEAR STATION, THE
Image Comics: Mar, 2000 - No. 5, Nov, 2000 ($2.50)

	GD 2.0	VG 4.0	FN 6.0	VF 8.0	VF/NM 9.0	NM- 9.2
1-Four covers by Ross, Turner, Pat Lee, Fraga						3.00
1-($6.95) DF Cover						7.00
2-5: 2-Two covers by Fraga and Art Adams						3.00

GEEK, THE (See Brother Power... & Vertigo Visions)

GEEKSVILLE (Also see 3 Geeks, The)
3 Finger Prints/ Image: Aug, 1999 - No. 6, March, 2001 ($2.75/$2.95, B&W)

1,2,4-6-The 3 Geeks by Koslowski; Innocent Bystander by Sassaman						6.00
3-Includes "Babes & Blades" mini-comic	1	2	3	5	6	8
0-(3/00) First Image issue						3.00
(Vol. 2) 1-4-($2.95) 3-Mini-comic insert by the Geeks. 4-Steve Borock app.						3.00

GEIGER
Image Comics (Mad Ghost): Apr, 2021 - Present ($3.99)

1-5-Geoff Johns-s/Gary Frank-a						4.00
6-($4.99) Junkyard Joe app.						5.00
... 80-Page Giant 1 (2/22, $7.99) Stories of the Las Vegas casinos; s-a by various incl. Johns, Frank, Hitch, Kelley Jones, Pelletier, Prado; preview of Junkyard Joe #1						8.00

GEIGER: GROUND ZERO
Image Comics (Ghost Machine): Nov, 2023 - No. 2, Dec, 2023 ($3.99)

1,2-Geoff Johns-s/Gary Frank-a; leads into Ghost Machine #1						4.00

G-8 AND HIS BATTLE ACES (Based on pulps)
Gold Key: Oct, 1966

1 (10184-610)-Painted-c	4	8	12	28	47	65

G-8 AND HIS BATTLE ACES
Blazing Comics: 1991 ($1.50, one-shot)

1-Glanzman-a; Truman-a						4.00

NOTE: Flip book format with "The Spider's Web" #1 on other side w/Glanzman-a, Truman-c.

GEM COMICS
Spotlight Publishers: Apr, 1945 (52 pgs)

1-Little Mohee, Steve Strong app.; Jungle bondage-c	90	180	270	576	988	1400

GEMINI BLOOD
DC Comics (Helix): Sept, 1996 - No. 9, May, 1997 ($2.25, limited series)

1-9: 5-Simonson-c						4.00

GEN ACTIVE
DC Comics (WildStorm): May, 2000 - No. 6, Aug, 2001 ($3.95)

1-6: 1-Covers by Campbell and Madureira; Gen 13 & DV8 app. 5-Mahfood-a; Quitely and Stelfreeze-a. 6-Portacio-a-c						4.00

GENE AUTRY (See March of Comics No. 25, 28, 39, 54, 78, 90, 104, 120, 135, 150 in the Promotional Comics section & Western Roundup under Dell Giants)

GENE AUTRY COMICS (Movie, Radio star; singing cowboy)
Fawcett Publications: Jan, 1942 (On sale 12/17/41) - No. 10, 1943 (68 pgs.)
(Dell takes over with No. 11)

1 (Scarce)-Gene Autry & his horse Champion begin; photo back-c	354	708	1062	2478	4339	6200
2-(1942)	90	180	270	576	988	1400
3-5: 3-(11/1/42)	50	100	150	315	533	750
6-10	41	82	123	256	428	600

GENE AUTRY COMICS (...& Champion No. 102 on)
Dell Publishing Co.: No. 11, 1943 - No. 121, Jan-Mar, 1959 (TV - later issues)

11 (1943, 60 pgs.)-Continuation of Fawcett series; photo back-c; first Dell issue	33	66	99	238	532	825
12 (2/44, 60 pgs.)	29	58	87	209	467	725
Four Color 47 (1944, 60 pgs.)	36	72	108	259	580	900
Four Color 57 (11/44), 66 ('45)(52 pgs. each)	30	60	90	216	483	750
Four Color 75, 83 ('45, 36 pgs. each)	23	46	69	164	362	560
Four Color 93 ('45, 36 pgs.)	19	38	57	133	297	460
Four Color 100 ('46, 36 pgs.) First Gene Autry photo-c	22	44	66	155	345	535
1 (5-6/46, 52 pgs.)	34	68	102	245	548	850
2 (7-8/46)-Photo-c begin, end #111	15	30	45	100	220	340
3-5: 4-Intro Flapjack Hobbs	11	22	33	76	163	250
6-10	10	20	30	64	132	200
11-20: 20-Panhandle Pete begins	9	18	27	60	120	180
21-29 (36 pgs.)	8	16	24	52	99	145
30-40 (52 pgs.)	7	14	21	44	82	120
41-56 (52 pgs.)	6	12	18	38	69	100
57-66 (36 pgs.): 58-X-mas-c	5	10	15	34	60	85
67-80 (52 pgs.): 70-X-mas-c	5	10	15	34	60	85

	GD 2.0	VG 4.0	FN 6.0	VF 8.0	VF/NM 9.0	NM- 9.2

81-90 (52 pgs.): 82-X-mas-c. 87-Blank inside-c — 5 · 10 · 15 · 31 · 53 · 75
91-99 (36 pgs. Nos. 91-on). 94-X-mas-c — 4 · 8 · 12 · 28 · 47 · 65
100 — 5 · 10 · 15 · 30 · 50 · 70
101-111-Last Gene Autry photo-c — 4 · 8 · 12 · 27 · 44 · 60
112-121-All Champion painted-c, most by Savitt — 4 · 8 · 12 · 25 · 40 · 55
NOTE: Photo back covers 4-18, 20-45, 48-65. **Manning** a-118. **Jesse Marsh** art: 4-Color No. 66, 75, 93, 100, No. 1-25, 27-37, 39, 40.

GENE AUTRY'S CHAMPION (TV)
Dell Publ. Co.: No. 287, 8/50; No. 319, 2/51; No. 3, 8-10/51 - No. 19, 8-10/55
Four Color 287(#1)('50, 52 pgs.)-Photo-c — 11 · 22 · 33 · 76 · 163 · 250
Four Color 319(#2, '51), 3: 2-Painted-c begin, most by Sam Savitt — 6 · 12 · 18 · 41 · 76 · 110
4-19: 19-Last painted-c — 4 · 8 · 12 · 28 · 47 · 65

GENE COLAN TRIBUTE BOOK (Produced for The Hero Initiative)
Marvel Comics: 2008 ($9.99, one-shot)
1-Spotlighted stories from Tales of Suspense #89,90, Doctor Strange #174 and others — 12.00

GENE DOGS
Marvel Comics UK: Oct, 1993 - No. 4, Jan, 1994 ($1.75, limited series)
1-($2.75)-Polybagged w/4 trading cards — 5.00
2-4: 2-Vs. Genetix — 4.00

GENE POOL
IDW Publishing: Oct, 2003 ($6.99, squarebound)
nn-Wein & Wolfman-s/Cummings-a — 7.00

GENERAL DOUGLAS MACARTHUR
Fox Feature Syndicate: 1951
nn-True life story — 21 · 42 · 63 · 122 · 199 · 275

GENERATION HEX
DC Comics (Amalgam): June, 1997 ($1.95, one-shot)
1-Milligan-s/ Pollina & Morales-a — 4.00

GENERATION HOPE (See X-Men titles and Cable)
Marvel Comics: Jan, 2011 - No. 17, May, 2012 ($3.99/$2.99)
1-($3.99).Gillen-s/Espin-a; Coipel-c; back-up bio of Hope Summers — 4.00
1-Variant-c by Greg Land — 8.00
2-17-($2.99) 5,9-McKelvie-a. 10,11-Seeley-a. 11-X-Men: Schism tie-in — 3.00

GENERATION M (Follows House of M x-over)
Marvel Comics: Jan, 2006 - No. 5, May, 2006 ($2.99, limited series)
1-5-Jenkins-s/Bachs-a. 1-Chamber app. 2-Jubilee app. 3-Blob-c. 4-Angel-c — 3.00
Decimation: Generation M TPB (2006, $13.99) r/#1-5 — 14.00

GENERATION NEXT
Marvel Comics: Mar, 1995 - No. 4, June, 1995 ($1.95, limited series)
1-4-Age of Apocalypse; Scott Lobdell scripts & Chris Bachalo-c/a — 4.00

GENERATIONS: (Team-ups of legacy characters after Secret Empire)
Marvel Comics: Oct, 2017 (2017, $4.99, series of one-shots)
... Banner Hulk & The Totally Awesome Hulk 1 (10/17) Pak-s/Buffagni-a — 5.00
... Captain Marvel & Captain Mar-Vell 1 (11/17) Stohl-s/Schoonover-a; Annihilus app. — 5.00
... Hawkeye & Hawkeye 1 (10/17) Thompson-s/Raffaele-a; Swordsman app. — 5.00
... Iron Man & Ironheart 1 (11/17) Bendis-s; future Tony Stark as Sorceror Supreme app. — 5.00
... Miles Morales Spider-Man & Peter Parker Spider-Man 1 (11/17) Bendis-s — 5.00
... Ms. Marvel & Ms. Marvel 1 (11/17) Kamala meets younger Carol; Nightscream app. — 5.00
... Phoenix & Jean Grey 1 (11/17) Bunn-s/Silva-a; Galactus app. — 5.00
... Sam Wilson Captain America & Steve Rogers Captain America 1 (11/17) Spencer-s — 5.00
... The Unworthy Thor & The Mighty Thor 1 (10/17) Aaron-s/Asrar-a; Apocalypse app. — 5.00
... Wolverine & All-New Wolverine 1 (10/17) Taylor-s/Rosanas-a; Sabretooth app. — 5.00

GENERATIONS... (Follows events in Dark Nights: Death Metal)
DC Comics: Mar, 2021 - Apr, 2021 ($9.99, limited series)
... Forged 1 (4/21, 9.99) Conclusion vs. Dominus; Jor-El, O.M.A.C. app.; art by various — 10.00
... Shattered 1 (3/21, $9.99) Kamandi teams with Booster Gold, 1939 Batman, Steel, Sinestro, Starfire, Silver Age Superboy and Dr. Light; intro Dominus; art by various — 10.00

GENERATION X (See Gen ∕ Generation X)
Marvel Comics: Oct, 1994 - No. 75, Oct, 2001 ($1.50/$1.95/$1.99/$2.25)
Collectors Preview ($1.75, "Ashcan" Edition — 4.00
-1(7/97) Flashback story — 4.00
1/2 (San Diego giveaway) — 2 · 4 · 6 · 8 · 10 · 12
1-($3.95)-Wraparound chromium-c; Scott Lobdell scripts & Chris Bachalo-a begins — 1 · 3 · 4 · 6 · 8 · 10
2-($1.95)-Deluxe edition, Bachalo-a — 5.00
3,4-($1.95)-Deluxe Edition; Bachalo-a — 5.00
2-10: 2-4-Standard Edition. 5-Returns from "Age of Apocalypse", begin $1.95-c. 6-Bachalo-a(p) ends, returns #7. 7-Roger Cruz-a(p). 10-Omega Red-c/app. — 4.00
11-24, 26-28: 13,14-Bishop-app. 17-Stan Lee app. (Stan Lee scripts own dialogue); Bachalo/Buckingham-a. 17-Onslaught update. 18-Toad cameo. 20-Franklin Richards app; Howard the Duck cameo. 21-Howard the Duck app. 22-Nightmare app. — 4.00
25-($2.99)-Wraparound-c. Black Tom, Howard the Duck app. — 5.00
29-37: 29-Begin $1.99-c, "Operation Zero Tolerance". 33-Hama-s — 4.00
38-49: 38-Dodson-a begins. 40-Penance ID revealed. 49-Maggott app. — 4.00
50,57-($2.99): 50-Crossover w/X-Man #50 — 5.00
51-56, 58-62: 59-Avengers & Spider-Man app. — 3.00
63-74: 63-Ellis-s begin. 64-Begin $2.25-c. 69-71-Art Adams-c — 3.00
75-($2.99) Final issue; Chamber joins the X-Men; Lim-a — 4.00
'95 Special-($3.95) — 5.00
'96 Special-($2.95)-Wraparound-c; Jeff Johnson-c/a — 5.00
'97 Special-($2.99)-Wraparound-c; — 5.00
'98 Annual-($3.50)-vs. Dracula — 5.00
'99 Annual-($3.50)-Monet leaves — 4.00
75¢ Ashcan Edition — 3.00
...Holiday Special 1 (2/99, $3.50) Pollina-a — 4.00
...Underground Special 1 (5/98, $2.50, B&W) Mahfood-a — 4.00

GENERATION X
Marvel Comics: Jul, 2017 - No. 9, Jan, 2018; No. 85, Feb, 2018 - No. 87, Apr, 2018 ($3.99)

1-9: 1-Strain-s/Pinna-a — 4.00
[Title switches to legacy numbering after #9 (1/18)]
85-87: 85-(2/18) Monet app.; Dodson-a — 4.00

GENERATION X/ GEN ∕ (Also see Gen ∕ Generation X)
Marvel Comics: 1997 ($3.99, one-shot)
1-Robinson-s/Larroca-a(p) — 4.00

GENERATION ZERO (see Harbinger Wars)
Valiant Entertainment: Aug, 2016 - No. 9, Apr, 2017 ($3.99)
1-9: 1-Van Lente-s/Portela-a; multiple covers. 3-Archie-style art by Derek Charm — 4.00

GENERIC COMIC, THE
Marvel Comics Group: Apr, 1984 (one-shot)
1 — 4.00

GENE RODDENBERRY'S LOST UNIVERSE
Tekno Comix: Apr, 1995 - No. 7, Oct, 1995 ($1.95)
1-7: 1-3-w/ bound-in game piece & trading card. 4-w/bound-in trading card — 4.0

GENE RODDENBERRY'S XANDER IN LOST UNIVERSE
Tekno Comix: No. 0, Nov, 1995; No. 1, Dec, 1995 - No. 8, July, 1996 ($2.25)
0,1-8: 1-5-Jae Lee-c. 4-Polybagged. 8-Pt. 5 of The Big Bang x-over — 4.00

GENESIS (See DC related titles)
DC Comics: Oct, 1997 - No. 4, Oct, 1997 ($1.95, weekly limited series)
1-4: Byrne-s/Wagner-a(p) in all. — 4.00

GENESIS: THE #1 COLLECTION (WildStorm Archives)
WildStorm Productions: 1998 ($9.99, TPB, B&W)
nn-Reprints #1 issues of WildStorm titles and pin-ups — 10.00

GENETIX
Marvel Comics UK: Oct, 1993 - No. 6, Mar, 1994 ($1.75, limited series)
1-($2.75)-Polybagged w/4 cards; Dark Guard app. — 5.00
2-6: 2-Intro Tektos. 4-Vs. Gene Dogs — 4.00

GENEXT (Next generation of X-Men)
Marvel Comics: July, 2008 - No. 5, Nov, 2008 ($3.99, limited series)
1-5: 1-Claremont-s/Scherberger-a; character profile pages — 4.00

GENEXT: UNITED
Marvel Comics: July, 2009 - No. 5, Dec, 2009 ($3.99, limited series)
1-5: 1-Claremont-s/Meyers-a; Beast app. — 4.00

GENIS-VELL: CAPTAIN MARVEL
Marvel Comics: Sept, 2022 - No. 5, Jan, 2023 ($4.99/$3.99)
1-($4.99) Peter David-s/Juanan Ramirez-a; Genis-Vell & Rick Jones return — 5.00
2-5-($3.99) 2-Death app. 3-5-Shatterax app. — 4.00

GENIS-VELL: MARVEL TALES
Marvel Comics: Jan, 2022 ($7.99, one-shot)
1-Reprints Captain Marvel #0-3 (2000); Rick Jones with Captain Marvel (Genis-Vell) — 8.00

GENIUS
Image Comics (Top Cow): Aug, 2014 - No. 5, Aug, 2014 ($3.99, limited series)
1-5-Bernardin & Freeman-s/Afua Richardson-a — 4.00

GEN:LOCK (Based on the animated series) (Printings of stories that first appeared online)
(Issues #6 & #7 were solicited but not printed)
DC Comics (Rooster Teeth Productions): Jan, 2020 - No. 5, May, 2020 ($3.99)
1-5: 1,2,5-Kelly & Lanzing-s/Barberi-a. 3,4-Prasetya-a — 4.00

GEN 12 (Also see Gen 13 and Team 7)
Image Comics (WildStorm Productions): Feb, 1998 - No. 5, June, 1998 ($2.50, lim. series)
1-5: 1-Team 7 & Gen 13 app.; wraparound-c — 4.00

GEN 13 (Also see Wild C.A.T.S. #1 & Deathmate Black #2)
Image Comics (WildStorm Productions): Feb, 1994 - No. 5, July 1994 ($1.95, limited series)
0 (8/95, $2.50)-Ch. 1 w/Jim Lee-p; Ch. 4 w/Charest-p — 4.00
1/2 — 1 · 2 · 3 · 4 · 5 · 7
1-($2.50)-Created by Jim Lee — 1 · 3 · 4 · 6 · 8 · 10
1-2nd printing — 3.00
1-"3-D" Edition (9/97, $4.95)-w/glasses — 5.00
2-($2.50) — 1 · 2 · 3 · 4 · 5 · 7
3-Pitt-c & story — 4.00
4-Pitt-c & story; wraparound-c — 4.00
5 — 4.00
5-Alternate Portacio-c; see Deathblow #5 — 6.00
...Collected Edition ('94, $12.95)-r/#1-5 — 13.00
...Rave ($1.50, 3/95)-wraparound-c — 4.00
...: Who They Are And How They Came To Be... (2006, $14.99) r/#1-5; sketch gallery — 15.00
NOTE: Issues 1-4 contain coupons redeemable for the ashcan edition of Gen 13 #0. Price listed is for a complete book.

GEN 13
Image Comics (WildStorm Productions): Mar, 1995 - No. 36, Dec, 1998; **DC Comics (WildStorm):** Mar, 1999 - No. 77, Jul, 2002 ($2.95/$2.50)
1-A (Charge)-Campbell/Garner-c — 2 · 4 · 6 · 8 · 10 · 12
1-B (Thumbs Up)-Campbell/Garner-c — 1 · 3 · 4 · 6 · 8 · 10
1-C-1-F,1-I-1-M: 1-C (Lil' GEN 13)-Art Adams-c. 1-D (Barbari-GEN)-Simon Bisley-c. 1-E (Your Friendly Neighborhood Grunge)-Cleary-c. 1-F (GEN 13 Goes Madison Ave.)-Golden-c. 1-I (That's the way we became GEN 13)-Campbell/Gibson-c. 1-J (All Dolled Up)-Campbell/McWeeney-c. 1-K (Verti-GEN)-Dunn-c. 1-L (Picto-Fiction). 1-M (Do it Yourself Cover) — 1 · 2 · 3 · 4 · 5 · 7
1-G (Lin-GEN-re)-Michael Lopez-c — 3 · 6 · 9 · 18 · 28 · 38
1-H (GEN-et Jackson)-Jason Pearson-c — 4 · 8 · 12 · 23 · 37 · 50
1-Chromium-c by Campbell — 4 · 8 · 12 · 27 · 44 · 60
1-Chromium-c by Jim Lee — 5 · 10 · 15 · 33 · 57 · 80
1-"3-D" Edition (2/98, $4.95)-w/glasses — 5.00
2 ($1.95, Newsstand)-WildStorm Rising Pt. 4; bound-in card — 4.00
2-12: 2-($2.50, Direct Market)-WildStorm Rising Pt. 4, bound-in card. 6,7-Jim Lee-c/a(p). 9-Ramos-a. 10,11-Fire From Heaven Pt. 3. & Pt.9 — 4.00

Generation Hope #1 © MAR

Gen13 #1 © DC

Georgie Comics #25 © MAR

	GD	VG	FN	VF	VF/NM	NM-			GD	VG	FN	VF	VF/NM	NM-
	2.0	4.0	6.0	8.0	9.0	9.2			2.0	4.0	6.0	8.0	9.0	9.2

11-($4.95)-Special European Tour Edition; chromium-c		3	6	9	14	20	25	and Campbell/McWeeney						4.00
13A,13B,13C-($1.30, 13 pgs.): 13A-Archie & Friends app. 13B-Bone-c/app.;								1-($4.95) 3-D Edition w/glasses; Campbell-c						5.00
Teenage Mutant Ninja Turtles, Madman, Spawn & Jim Lee app.						5.00		**GEN 13 INTERACTIVE**							
14-24- 20-Last Campbell-a						4.00		Image Comics (WildStorm): Oct, 1997 - No. 3, Dec, 1997 ($2.50, lim. series)						
25-($3.50)-Two covers by Campbell and Charest						4.00		1-3-Internet voting used to determine storyline						4.00
25-($3.50)-Voyager Pack w/Danger Girl preview						5.00		... Plus! (7/98, $11.95) r/series & 3-D Special (in 2-D)						12.00
25-Foil-c						10.00		**GEN 13: MAGICAL DRAMA QUEEN ROXY**							
26-32,34: 26-Arcudi-s/Frank-a begins. 34-Back-up story by Art Adams						3.00		Image Comics (WildStorm): Oct, 1998 - No. 3, Dec, 1998 ($3.50, lim. series)						
33-Flip book w/Planetary preview						4.00		1-3-Adam Warren-s/c/a; manga style, 2-Variant-c by Hiroyuki Utatane						4.00
35-49: 36,38,40-Two covers. 37-First DC issue. 41-Last Frank-a						3.00		1-($6.95) Dynamic Forces Ed. w/Variant Warren-c						7.00
50-($3.95) Two covers by Lee and Benes; art by various						3.00		**GEN 13/MONKEYMAN & O'BRIEN**							
51-76: 51-Moy-a; Fairchild loses her powers. 60-Warren-s/a. 66-Art by various								Image Comics (WildStorm): Jun, 1998 - No. 2, July, 1998 ($2.50, lim. series)						
incl. Campbell (3 pgs.). 70,75,76-Mays-a. 76-Original team dies						3.00		1,2-Art Adams-s/a(p); 1-Two covers						4.00
77-($3.50) Mays, Andrews, Warren-a						4.00		1-($4.95) Chromium-c						5.00
Annual 1 (1997, $2.95) Ellis-s/ Dillon-c/a.						5.00		1-($6.95) Dynamic Forces Ed.						7.00
Annual 1999 ($3.50, DC) Slipstream x-over w/ DV8						5.00		**GEN 13: ORDINARY HEROES**							
Annual 2000 ($3.50) Devil's Night x-over w/WildStorm titles; Bermejo-c						4.00		Image Comics (WildStorm Publications): Feb, 1996 - No. 2, July, 1996 ($2.50, lim. series)						
...: A Christmas Caper (1/00, $5.95, one-shot) McWeeney-s/a						6.00		1,2-Adam Hughes-c/a/scripts						4.00
... Archives (4/98, $12.99) B&W reprints of mini-series, #0,1/2,1-13ABC; includes								TPB (2004, $14.95) r/series, Gen13 Bootleg #1&2 and Wildstorm Thunderbook; new						
cover gallery and sourcebook						13.00		Hughes-c and art pages						15.00
...: Carny Folk (2/00, $3.50) Collect back-up stories						3.50		**GENTLE BEN** (TV)							
... European Vacation TPB ($6.95) r/#6,7						7.00		Dell Publishing Co.: Feb, 1968 - No. 5, Oct, 1969 (All photo-c)						
.../ Fantastic Four (2001, $5.95) Maguire-s/c/a(p)						6.00		1		4	8	12	25	40	55
... Going West (5/99, $2.50, one-shot) Pruett-s						3.00		2-5: 5-Reprints #1		3	6	9	16	23	30
...: Grunge Saves the World (5/99, $5.95, one-shot) Altieri-c/a						6.00		**GEOMANCER** (Also see Eternal Warrior: Fist & Steel)							
... I Love New York TPB ($9.95) r/part #25, 26-29; Frank-c						10.00		Valiant: Nov, 1994 - No. 8, June, 1995 ($3.75/$2.25)						
... London, New York, Hell TPB ($6.95) r/Annual #1 & Bootleg Ann. #1						7.00		1 ($3.75)-Chromium wraparound-c; Eternal Warrior app.						5.00
... Lost in Paradise TPB ($6.95) r/#3-5						7.00		2-8						4.00
.../ Maxx (12/95, $3.50, one-shot) Messner-Loebs-s, 1st Coker-c/a.						4.00		**GEORGE OF THE JUNGLE** (TV)(See America's Best TV Comics)							
... Meanwhile (2003, $17.95) r/#43,44,66-70; all Warren-s; art by various						18.00		Gold Key: Feb, 1969 - No. 2, Oct, 1969 (Jay Ward)						
... Medicine Song (2001, $5.95) Brent Anderson-c/a(p)/Raab-s						6.00		1		9	18	27	59	117	175
... Science Friction (2001, $5.95) Haley & Lopresti-a						6.00		2		6	12	18	37	66	95
... Starting Over TPB ($14.95) r/#1-7						15.00		**GEORGE PAL'S PUPPETOONS** (Funny animal puppets)							
... Superhuman Like You TPB ($12.95) r/#60-65; Warren-c						13.00		Fawcett Publications: Dec, 1945 - No. 18, Dec, 1947; No. 19, 1950						
... #13 A,B&C Collected Edition ($6.95, TPB) r/#13A,B&C						7.00		1-Captain Marvel-c		52	104	156	328	552	775
...: 3-D Special (1997, $4.95, one-shot) Art Adams-s/a(p)						5.00		2		28	56	84	165	270	375
...: The Unreal World (7/96, $2.95, one-shot) Humberto Ramos-c/a						3.00		3-10		18	36	54	103	162	220
... We'll Take Manhattan TPB ($14.95) r/#45-50; new Benes-c						15.00		11-19		15	30	45	83	124	165
...: Wired (4/99, $2.50, one-shot) Richard Bennett-c/a						3.00		**GEORGE PEREZ'S SIRENS**							
...: Yearbook 1997 (6/97, $2.50) College-themed stories and pin-ups by various						3.00		BOOM! Studios: Sept, 2014 - No. 6, Dec, 2016 ($3.99, limited series)						
...: 'Zine (12/96, $1.95, B&W, digest size) Campbell/Garner-c						3.00		1-6-George Pérez-s/a; multiple covers						4.00
Variant Collection-Four editions (all 13 variants w/Chromium variant-limited, signed)						100.00		**GEORGE R.R. MARTIN'S A CLASH OF KINGS** (Based on A Song of Ice and Fire, Book 2)							
GEN 13								Dynamite Entertainment: 2017 - No. 16, 2019; 2020 - No. 16 ($3.99)						
DC Comics (WildStorm): No. 0, Sept, 2002 - No. 16, Feb, 2004 ($2.95)								1-16: 1-Landry Q. Walker-s/Mel Rubi-a; multiple covers						4.00
0-(13-c) Intro. new team; includes previews of 21 Down & The Resistance						3.00		Volume 2 (2020 - No. 16) 1-16-Landry Q.Walker-s/Mel Rubi-a						4.00
1-Claremont-s/Garza-c/a; Fairchild app.						3.00		**GEORGIE COMICS** (...& Judy Comics #20-35? see All Teen & Teen Comics)							
2-16: 8-First 13-Bachs-a. 16-Original team returns						3.00		Timely Comics/GPI No. 1-34: Spr, 1945 - No. 39, Oct, 1952 (#1-3 are quarterly)						
...: September Song TPB (2003, $19.95) r/#0-6; Garza sketch pages						20.00		1-Dave Berg-a		60	120	180	381	653	925
GEN 13 (Volume 4)								2		36	72	108	214	347	480
DC Comics (WildStorm): Dec, 2006 - No. 39, Feb, 2011 ($2.99)								3-5,7,8(11/46)		28	56	84	165	270	375
1-39: 1-Simone-s/Caldwell-a; re-intro the original team; Caldwell-a. 8-The Authority app.						3.00		6-Georgie visits Timely Comics		34	68	102	204	332	460
1-Variant-c by J. Scott Campbell						5.00		9,10-Kurtzman's "Hey Look" (1 & ?); Millie the Model & Margie app.						
...: Armageddon (1/08, $2.99) Gage-s/Meyers-a; future Gen13 app.						3.00				32	64	96	188	307	425
...: Best of a Bad Lot TPB (2007, $14.99) r/#1-6						15.00		11,12: 11-Margie, Millie app.		23	46	69	136	223	310
...: 15 Minutes TPB (2008, $14.99) r/#14-20						15.00		13-Kurtzman's "Hey Look", 3 pgs.		24	48	72	142	234	325
...: Road Trip TPB (2008, $14.99) r/#7-13						15.00		14-Wolverton-a(1 pg.); Kurtzman's "Hey Look"		25	50	75	150	245	340
...: World's End TPB (2009, $17.99) r/#21-26						18.00		15,16,18-20		21	42	63	122	199	275
GEN 13 BOOTLEG								17,29-Kurtzman's "Hey Look", 1 pg.		22	44	66	132	216	300
Image Comics (WildStorm): Nov, 1996 - No. 20, Jul, 1998 ($2.50)								21-24,27,28,30-39: 21-Anti-Wertham editorial. 33-38-Hy Rosen-c						
1-Alan Davis-a; alternate costumes-c						4.00				21	42	63	122	199	275
1-Team falling variant-c						5.00		25-Painted-c by classic pin-up artist Peter Driben		126	252	378	806	1378	1950
2-7: 2-Alan Davis-a. 5,6-Terry Moore-s. 7-Robinson/s/Scott Hampton-a						4.00		26-Logo design swipe from Archie Comics		42	84	126	265	445	625
8-10-Adam Warren-a						4.00		**GERALD McBOING-BOING AND THE NEARSIGHTED MR. MAGOO** (TV)							
11-20: 11,12-Lopresti-a & Simonson-s. 13-Wieringo-s/a. 14-Mariotte-s/Phillips-a.								(Mr. Magoo No. 6 on)						
15,16-Strnad-s/Shaw-a. 18-Altieri-s/a(p)/c, 18-Variant-c by Bruce Timm						4.00		Dell Publishing Co.: Aug-Oct, 1952 - No. 5, Aug-Oct, 1953						
... Grunge: The Movie (12/97, $4.95) r/#8-10, Warren-c						5.00		1		11	22	33	73	157	240
...Vol. 1 TPB (10/98, $11.95) r/#1-4						12.00		2-5		8	16	24	54	102	150
GEN 13/ GENERATION X (Also see Generation X / Gen 13)															
Image Comics (WildStorm Publications): July, 1997 ($2.95, one-shot)															
1-Choi-s/ Art Adams-p/Garner-i. Variant covers by Adams/Garner															

	GD 2.0	VG 4.0	FN 6.0	VF 8.0	VF/NM 9.0	NM- 9.2

GERONIMO (See Fighting Indians of the Wild West!)
Avon Periodicals: 1950 - No. 4, Feb, 1952

1-Indian Fighter; Maneely-a; Texas Rangers-r/Cowpuncher #1; Fawcette-c

	28	56	84	168	274	380

2-On the Warpath; Kit West app.; Kinstler-c/a

| | 18 | 36 | 54 | 107 | 169 | 230 |

3-And His Apache Murderers; Kinstler-c/a(2); Kit West-r/Cowpuncher #6

| | 18 | 36 | 54 | 107 | 169 | 230 |

4-Savage Raids of; Kinstler-c & inside front-c; Kinstlerish-a by McCann(3)

| | 18 | 36 | 54 | 103 | 162 | 220 |

GERONIMO JONES
Charlton Comics: Sept, 1971 - No. 9, Jan, 1973

| 1 | 3 | 6 | 9 | 15 | 22 | 28 |
| 2-9 | 2 | 4 | 6 | 8 | 10 | 12 |

Modern Comics Reprint #7('78)   5.00

GETALONG GANG, THE (TV)
Marvel Comics (Star Comics): May, 1985 - No. 6, Mar, 1986

1-6: Saturday morning TV stars   5.00

GET JIRO!
DC Comics (Vertigo): 2012 ($24.99, hardcover graphic novel with dust jacket)

HC - Anthony Bourdain & Joel Rose-s/Langdon Foss-a   25.00
SC - (2013, $14.99) Anthony Bourdain & Joel Rose-s/Langdon Foss-a   15.00

GET JIRO: BLOOD AND SUSHI
DC Comics (Vertigo): 2015 ($22.99, hardcover graphic novel with dust jacket)

HC - Prequel to Get Jiro!; Anthony Bourdain & Joel Rose-s/Alé Garza-a/Dave Johnson-c   23.00

GET LOST
Mikeross Publications/New Comics: Feb-Mar, 1954 - No. 3, June-July, 1954 (Satire)

1-Andru/Esposito-a in all?

| | 50 | 100 | 150 | 315 | 533 | 750 |

2-Andru/Esposito-c; has 4 pg. E.C. parody featuring "The Sewer Keeper"

| | 33 | 66 | 99 | 194 | 317 | 440 |

3-John Wayne 'Hondo' parody

| | 27 | 54 | 81 | 162 | 266 | 370 |

1,2 (10,12/87-New Comics)-B&W r-original   5.00

GET SMART (TV)
Dell Publ. Co.: June, 1966 - No. 8, Sept, 1967 (All have Don Adams photo-c)

1	11	22	33	76	163	250
2,3-Ditko-a	6	12	18	40	73	105
4-8: 8-Reprints #1 (cover and insides)	5	10	15	33	57	80

GHOST (...Comics #9)
Fiction House Magazines: 1951(Winter) - No. 11, Summer, 1954

1-Most covers by Whitman

| | 314 | 628 | 942 | 2198 | 3849 | 5500 |

2-Ghost Gallery & Werewolf Hunter stories; classic-c

| | 290 | 580 | 870 | 1856 | 3178 | 4500 |

3-9: 3,6,7,9-Bondage-a. 9-Abel, Discount-a

| | 206 | 412 | 618 | 1344 | 2259 | 3200 |

10,11-Dr. Drew by Grandenetti in each, reprinted from Rangers; 11-Evans-r/ Rangers #39; Grandenetti-r/Rangers #49

| | 168 | 336 | 504 | 1075 | 1838 | 2600 |

GHOST (See Comic's Greatest World)
Dark Horse Comics: Apr, 1995 - No. 36, Apr, 1998 ($2.50/$2.95)

1-Adam Hughes-a

| | 1 | 3 | 4 | 6 | 8 | 10 |

2,3-Hughes-a   5.00
4-24: 4-Barb Wire app. 5,6-Hughes-c. 12-Ghost/Hellboy preview. 15,21-X app. 18,19-Barb Wire app.   4.00
25-($3.50)-48 pgs. special   5.00
26-36: 26-Begin $2.95-c. 29-Flip book w/Timecop. 33-36-Jade Cathedral; Harris painted-c 4.00

Special 1 (7/94, $3.95, 48 pgs.)

| | 1 | 2 | 3 | 4 | 5 | 7 |

Special 2 (6/98, $3.95) Barb Wire app.   5.00
Special 3 (see Ghost Volume 2)
... Black October (1/99, $14.95, trade paperback)-r/#6-9,26,27   15.00
... Nocturnes (1996, $9.95, trade paperback)-r/#1-3 & 5   10.00
... Omnibus Vol. 1 (10/08, $24.95, 9x6")-r/#1-12; Special 1 and Decade of Dark Horse #2 25.00
... Stories (1995, $9.95, trade paperback)-r/Early Ghost app.   10.00

GHOST (Volume 2)
Dark Horse Comics: Sept, 1998 - No. 22, Aug, 2000 ($2.95)

1-22: 1-4-Ryan Benjamin-c/Zanier-a   4.00
Handbook (8/99, $2.95) guide to issues and characters   4.00
Special 3 (12/98, $3.95)   5.00

GHOST (3rd series)
Dark Horse Comics: No. 0, Sept, 2012 - No. 4, Mar, 2013 ($2.99)

0-4-DeConnick-s/Noto-a. 0-Frison-c. 1,2-Covers by Noto & Alex Ross   3.00

GHOST (4th series)
Dark Horse Comics: Dec, 2013 - No. 12, Feb, 2015 ($2.99)

1-12: 1,2-DeConnick & Sebela/Sook-a/Dodson-c. 3,4-Borges-a   3.00

GHOST AND THE SHADOW
Dark Horse Comics: Dec, 1995 ($2.95, one-shot)

1-Moench scripts   6.00

GHOST/BATGIRL
Dark Horse Comics: Aug, 2000 - No. 4, Dec, 2000 ($2.95, limited series)

1-4-Cassandra Cain Batgirl; Oracle & Bruce Wayne app.; Benjamin-c/a   4.00

GHOST/HELLBOY
Dark Horse Comics: May, 1996 - No. 2, June, 1996 ($2.50, limited series)

1,2: Mike Mignola-c/scripts & breakdowns; Scott Benefiel finished-a   5.00

GHOST BREAKERS (Also see Racket Squad in Action, Red Dragon & (CC) Sherlock Holmes Comics)
Street & Smith Publications: Sept, 1948 - No. 2, Dec, 1948 (52 pgs.)

1-Powell-c/a(3); Dr. Neff (magician) app.

| | 55 | 110 | 165 | 352 | 601 | 850 |

2-Powell-c/a(2); Maneely-a

| | 42 | 84 | 126 | 265 | 445 | 625 |

GHOSTBUSTERS (TV) (Also, see Real...and Slimer)
First Comics: Feb, 1987 - No. 6, Aug, 1987 ($1.25)

1-6: Based on new animated TV series   5.00

GHOSTBUSTERS
IDW Publishing: Sept, 2011 - No. 16, Dec, 2012 ($3.99)

1-16-Burnham-s/Schoening-a; multiple covers   4.00
...: 100-Page Spooktacular (10/12, $7.99) reprints of IDW stories   10.00

GHOSTBUSTERS
IDW Publishing: (one-shots)

Annual 2017 (1/17, $7.99) Burnham-s/Schoening-a and short stories by various   8.00
Annual 2018 (2/18, $7.99) Burnham-s/Schoening-a; Ghostbusters: Crossing Over prelude 8.00
Answer the Call Ghostbusters 35th Anniversary One-Shot (4/19, $3.99) Female team   4.00
...: Con-Volution (6/10, $3.99) Josh Howard-a   4.00
...: Deviations (3/16, $4.99) What If.. Ghostbusters never crossed the streams   5.00
... Funko Universe One Shot (5/17, $4.99) Story with Funko Pop-styled characters   4.00
... Halloween Comicfest 2017 (10/17, giveaway) Burnham-s/Schoening-a   3.00
...: Tainted Love (2/10, $3.99) Salgood Sam-a   4.00
... 35th Anniversary: Extreme: One Shot (4/20, $3.99) Comic team   4.00
... 35th Anniversary: Ghostbusters: One Shot (4/20, $3.99) Movie team; Schoening-a   4.00
... 35th Anniversary: Tthe Real Ghostbusters: One Shot (4/20, $3.99) Cartoon team   4.00
... 20/20 (1/19, $4.99) Set 20 years in the future; Sanctum of Slime team app.   5.00
...: What in Samhain Just Happened? (10/10, $3.99) Peter David-s/Dan Schoening-a   4.00

GHOSTBUSTERS
IDW Publishing: Feb, 2013 - No. 20, Sept, 2014 ($3.99)

1-20-Janine & the female Ghostbuster crew; Burnham-s/Schoening-a; multiple covers   4.00
Annual 2015 (11/15, $7.99) Burnham-s/Schoening-a and bonus 1-pagers by various   8.00

GHOSTBUSTERS: ANSWER THE CALL
IDW Publishing: Oct, 2017 - No. 5, Feb, 2018 ($3.99)

1-5-Female crew; Thompson-s/Howell-a   4.00

GHOSTBUSTERS: CROSSING OVER
IDW Publishing: Mar, 2018 - No. 8, Oct, 2018 ($3.99)

1-8-Meeting of movie, cartoon, comic Ghostbusters teams; Burnham-s/Schoening-a   4.00

GHOSTBUSTERS: DISPLACED AGGRESSION
IDW Publishing: Sept, 2009 - No. 4, Dec, 2009 ($3.99)

1-Lobdell-s/Kyriazis-a

| | 1 | 3 | 4 | 6 | 8 | 10 |

2,3   4.00
Hundred Penny Press: Ghostbusters: Displaced Aggression (3/11, $1.00) r/#1   5.00

GHOSTBUSTERS: GET REAL
IDW Publishing: Jun, 2015 - No. 4, Sept, 2015 ($3.99)

1-4-Burnham-s/Schoening-a; multiple-c; Real Ghostbusters meet comic Ghostbusters   4.00

GHOSTBUSTERS: INFESTATION (Zombie x-over with Star Trek, G.I. Joe & Transformers)
IDW Publishing: Mar, 2011 - No. 2, Mar, 2011 ($3.99, limited series)

1,2-Kyle Hotz-a; covers by Hotz and Snyder III

| | 1 | 2 | 3 | 5 | 6 | 8 |

GHOSTBUSTERS: INTERNATIONAL
IDW Publishing: Jun, 2016 - No. 11, Nov, 2016 ($3.99)

1-11-Burnham-s/Schoening-a; 2 covers on each   4.00

GHOSTBUSTERS: LEGION (Movie)
88 MPH Studios: Feb, 2004 - No. 4, May, 2004 ($2.95/$3.50)

1-Steve Kurth-a/Andrew Dabb-s

| | 1 | 3 | 4 | 6 | 8 | 10 |

1-3 ($3.50) Brereton variant-c

| | 2 | 4 | 6 | 11 | 16 | 20 |

2-4   5.00

GHOSTBUSTERS 101
IDW Publishing: Mar, 2017 - No. 6, Aug, 2017 ($3.99, limited series)

1-6-Burnham-s/Schoening-a; multiple covers on each; original and female teams meet   4.00

GHOSTBUSTERS: THE OTHER SIDE
IDW Publishing: Oct, 2008 - No. 4, Jan, 2009 ($3.99)

1-Champagne-s/Nguyen-a

| | 1 | 3 | 4 | 6 | 8 | 10 |

2-4   4.00

GHOSTBUSTERS II
Now Comics: Oct, 1989 - No. 3, Dec, 1989 ($1.95, mini-series)

1-3: Movie Adaptation

| | 2 | 4 | 6 | 9 | 12 | 15 |

GHOSTBUSTERS: YEAR ONE
IDW Publishing: Jan, 2020 - No. 4, ($3.99, limited series)

1,2-Burnham-s/Schoening-a; multiple-c; first year after the events of the first movie   4.00

GHOST CASTLE (See Tales of...)

GHOSTED
Image Comics (Skybound): Jul, 2013 - No. 20, May, 2015 ($2.99)

1-20: 1-Williamson-s/Sudzuka-a/Phillips-c. 6-10-Gianfelice-a. 16-Ryp-a   3.00

GHOSTED IN L.A.
BOOM! Studios (BOOM! Box): Jul, 2019 - No. 12, Aug, 2020 ($3.99)

1-12-Sina Grace-s/Siobhan Keenan-a. 10-Grace-a   4.00

GHOST IN THE SHELL (Manga)
Dark Horse: Mar, 1995 - No. 8, Oct, 1995 ($3.95, B&W/color, lim. series)

1	6	12	18	38	69	100
2	3	6	9	19	30	40
3	3	6	9	16	23	30
4-8	2	4	6	8	11	14

GHOST IN THE SHELL 2: MAN-MACHINE INTERFACE (Manga)
Dark Horse Comics: Jan, 2003 - No. 11, Dec, 2003 ($3.50, color/B&W, lim. series)

1-Masamune Shirow-a in all

| | 2 | 4 | 6 | 8 | 10 | 12 |

2-11: 5-B&W   5.00

GHOST IN YOU, THE: A RECKLESS BOOK
Image Comics: Apr, 2022 ($24.99, HC graphic novel)

HC - Ed Brubaker-s/Sean Phillips-a; 4th book in the Reckless series   25.00

GHOSTLORE
BOOM! Studios: May, 2023 - Present ($4.99)

Ghostbusters: Crossing Over #4 © Columbia

Ghostly Tales #70 © CC

Ghost Rider #11 © MAR

	GD 2.0	VG 4.0	FN 6.0	VF 8.0	VF/NM 9.0	NM- 9.2

1-8-Cullen Bunn-s/Leomacs-a ... 5.00

GHOSTLY HAUNTS (Formerly Ghost Manor)
Charlton Comics: #20, 9/71 - #53, 12/76; #54, 9/77 - #55, 10/77; #56, 1/78 - #58, 4/78

	GD	VG	FN	VF	VF/NM	NM-
20	4	8	12	18	37	50
21	3	6	9	14	19	24
22-25,27,31-34,36-Ditko-c/a. 27-Dr. Graves x-over. 32-New logo. 33-Back to old logo	3	6	9	16	23	30
26,29,30,35-Ditko-c	2	4	6	13	18	22
28,37-40-Ditko-a. 39-Origin & 1st app. Destiny Fox	2	4	6	11	16	20
41,42- Ditko-c/a; Ditko-a. 42-Newton-c/a	2	4	6	13	18	22
43-46,48,50,52-Ditko-a	2	4	6	10	14	18
47,54,56-Ditko-c/a. 56-Ditko-a(r).	3	6	9	14	19	24
49,51,53,55,57	2	4	6	8	10	12
58 (4/78) Last issue	3	6	9	14	19	24

40,41(Modern Comics-r, 1977, 1978) ... 6.00

NOTE: Ditko a-22-25, 27, 28, 31-34, 36-41, 43-48, 50, 52, 54, 56r; c-22-27, 29, 30, 33-36, 47, 54, 56. Glanzman a-20. Howard a-27, 30, 35, 40-43, 48, 54, 57. Kim a-38, 41, 57. Larson a-48, 50. Newton c/a-42. Staton a-32, 35; c-28, 46. Sutton c-33, 37, 39, 41.

GHOSTLY TALES (Formerly Blue Beetle No. 50-54)
Charlton Comics: No. 55, 4-5/66 - No. 124, 12/76; No. 125, 9/77 - No. 169, 10/84

	GD	VG	FN	VF	VF/NM	NM-
55-Intro. & origin Dr. Graves; Ditko-a	9	18	27	63	129	195
56-58,60,61,70,71,72,75-Ditko-a. 70-Dr. Graves ends. 75-Last 12¢ issue	5	10	15	31	53	75
59,62-66,68	4	8	12	23	37	50
67,69,73-Ditko-c/a	5	10	15	34	60	85
74,91,98,119,123,124,127-130: 127,130-Sutton-a	2	4	6	13	18	22
76,79-82,85-Ditko-a	3	6	9	16	24	32
77,78,83,84,86-90,92-95,97,99-Ditko-a	4	8	12	23	37	50
96-Ditko-a	3	6	9	16	24	32
100-Ditko-c; Sutton-a	3	6	9	17	26	35
101,103-105-Ditko-a	3	6	9	14	19	24
102,109-Ditko-a	3	6	9	16	23	30
110,113-Sutton-c; Ditko-a	3	6	9	14	19	24
106-Ditko & Sutton-a; Sutton-c	3	6	9	14	19	24
107-Ditko, Wood, Sutton-a	3	6	9	14	20	26
108,116,117,126-Ditko-a	3	6	9	14	19	24
111,118,120-122,125-Ditko-a	3	6	9	16	23	30
112,114,115: 112,114-Ditko, Sutton-a. 114-Newton-a. 115-Newton, Ditko-a.	3	6	9	14	19	24
131-134,151,157,163-Ditko-c/a	2	4	6	13	18	22
135,142,145-150,153,154,156,158-160	1	2	3	5	7	9
136-141,143,144,152,155-Ditko-a	2	4	6	8	10	12
161,162,164-168-Lower print run. 162-Nudity panel	2	4	6	9	12	15
169 (10/84) Last issue; lower print run.	2	4	6	11	16	20

NOTE: Aparo a-65, 66, 68, 72, 137, 141r, 142r; c-71, 72, 74-76, 81, 146r, 149. Ditko a-55-58, 60, 61, 67, 69-73, 75-90, 92-97, 99-118, 120-122, 125, 131-133, 147, 148, 151, 157-160, 163; c-67, 69, 73, 77, 78, 83, 84, 86-90, 92-97, 99, 102, 109, 111, 120-122, 125, 131-133, 147, 148, 151, 157-160, 163. Glanzman a-57. Howard a-95, 98, 99, 108, 117, 129. Kim c-98, 107, 120, 121, 161. Larson a-117, 119, 136, 159; c-136. Morisi a-83, 84, 86. Newton a-114; c-115(painted). Palais a-61. Staton a-161; c-117. Sutton c-106, 107, 111-114, 127, 130, 162; c-100, 106, 110, 113(painted). Wood a-107.

GHOSTLY WEIRD STORIES (Formerly Blue Bolt Weird)
Star Publications: No. 120, Sept. 1953 - No. 124, Sept. 1954

	GD	VG	FN	VF	VF/NM	NM-
120-Jo-Jo-r	194	388	582	1242	2121	3000
121,123,124: 121-Jo-Jo-r. 123-Jo-Jo; Disbrow-a(2). 124-Torpedo Man	168	336	504	1075	1838	2600
122-The Mask-r/Capt. Flight #5; Rulah-r; has 1pg. story 'Death and the Devil Pills' from Western Outlaws #17	343	686	1029	2400	4200	6000

NOTE: Disbrow a-120-124. L. B. Cole covers all issues (#122 is a sci-fi cover).

GHOST MACHINE
Image Comics (Ghost Machine): Jan, 2024 ($4.99, one-shot)

1-Geiger,Redcoat and Rook app.; Johns-s; art by Frank and Hitch ... 5.00

GHOST MANOR (Ghostly Haunts No. 20 on)
Charlton Comics: July, 1968 - No. 19, July, 1971

	GD	VG	FN	VF	VF/NM	NM-
1	9	18	27	60	120	180
2-7: 7-Last 12¢ issue	4	8	12	28	47	65
8-12,17: 17-Morisi-a	3	6	9	19	30	40
13,14,16-Ditko-a	3	6	9	22	35	48
15,18,19-Ditko-c/a	4	8	12	28	47	65

GHOST MANOR (2nd Series)
Charlton Comics: Oct, 1971-No. 32, Dec, 1976; No. 33, Sept, 1977-No. 77, 11/84

	GD	VG	FN	VF	VF/NM	NM-
1	6	12	18	38	69	100
2,3,5-7,9-Ditko-c	3	6	9	17	26	35
4,10-Ditko-c/a	3	6	9	21	33	45

	GD	VG	FN	VF	VF/NM	NM-
8-Wood, Ditko-a; Sutton-c	3	6	9	19	30	40
11,14-Ditko-c/a	3	6	9	16	24	32
12,17,27,30	2	4	6	9	13	16
13,15,16,23-26,29: 13-Ditko-a. 15,16-Ditko-c. 23-Sutton-a. 24-26,29-Ditko-a.	2	4	6	13	18	22
26-Early Zeck-a; Boyette-c	2	4	6	9	13	16
18-(3/74) Newton 1st pro art; Ditko-a; Sutton-c	3	6	9	15	22	28
19-21: 19-Newton, Sutton-a; nudity panels. 20-Ditko-a. 21-E-Man, Blue Beetle, Capt. Atom cameos; Ditko-a.	2	4	6	13	18	22
22-Newton-c/a; Ditko-a	3	6	9	14	19	24
25,28,31,37,38-Ditko-c/a: 28-Nudity panels	3	6	9	14	19	24
32-36,39,41,45,48-50,53: 34-Black Cat by Kim	2	4	6	8	10	12
40-Ditko-a; torture & drug use	2	4	6	13	18	22
42,43,46,47,51,52,60,62,69-Ditko-a	2	4	6	11	16	20
44,54,71-Ditko-a	2	4	6	8	11	14
55,56,58,59,61,63,65-68,70	1	2	3	5	7	9
57-Wood, Ditko, Howard-a	2	4	6	9	12	15
64-Ditko & Newton-a	2	4	6	8	11	14
71-76 (low print)	2	3	4	6	8	10
77-(11/84) Last issue Aparo-r/Space Adventures V3#60 (Paul Mann)	3	6	9	13	16	

19 (Modern Comics reprint, 1977) ... 6.00

NOTE: Ditko a-4, 8, 10, 11(2), 13, 14, 18, 20-22, 24-26, 28, 29, 31, 37r, 38r, 40r, 42-44r, 46r, 47, 51r, 52r, 54r, 57, 60, 62(4), 64r, 69, 71; c-2-7, 9-11, 14-16, 28, 31, 37, 38, 42, 43, 46, 47, 51, 52, 60, 62, 64. Howard a-4, 8, 12, 17, 19-21, 31, 41, 45, 57. Newton a-18-20, 22, 64; c-22. Staton a-13, 38, 44, 45. Sutton a-19, 23, 25, 45; c-8, 18.

GHOST RACERS (Secret Wars Battleworld tie-in)
Marvel Comics: Aug, 2015 - No. 4, Nov, 2015 ($3.99, limited series)

1-4-Johnny Blaze, Danny Ketch, Robbie Reyes, Carter Slade app.; Francavilla-c ... 4.00

GHOST RIDER (See A-1 Comics, Best of the West, Black Phantom, Bobby Benson, Great Western, Red Mask & Tim Holt)
Magazine Enterprises: 1950 - No. 14, 1954

NOTE: The character was inspired by Vaughn Monroe's "Ghost Riders in the Sky", and Disney's movie "The Headless Horseman."

	GD	VG	FN	VF	VF/NM	NM-
1(A-1 #27)-Origin Ghost Rider	168	336	504	1075	1838	2600
2-5: 2(A-1 #29), 3(A-1 #31), 4(A-1 #34), 5(A-1 #37)-All Frazetta only	126	252	378	806	1378	1950
6,7: 6(A-1 #44)-Loco weed story, 7(A-1 #51)	58	116	174	371	636	900
8,9: 8(A-1 #57)-Drug use story, 9(A-1 #69)	43	86	129	271	461	650
10(A-1 #71)-Vs. Frankenstein	53	106	159	334	567	800
11-14: 11(A-1 #75), 12(A-1 #80)-Bondage-c; one-eyed Devil-c. 13(A-1 #84). 14(A-1 #112)	39	78	117	240	395	550

NOTE: Dick Ayers art in all; c-1, 6-14.

GHOST RIDER, THE (See Night Rider & Western Gunfighters)
Marvel Comics Group: Feb, 1967 - No. 7, Nov, 1967 (Western hero)(12¢)

	GD	VG	FN	VF	VF/NM	NM-
1-Origin & 1st app. Ghost Rider; Kid Colt-reprints begin	46	92	138	340	770	1200
2	9	18	27	59	117	175
3-7: 6-Last Kid Colt-r; All Ayers-c/a(p)	8	16	24	55	105	155

GHOST RIDER (See The Champions, Marvel Spotlight #5, Marvel Team-Up #15, 58, Marvel Treasury Edition #18, Marvel Two-In-One #8, The Original Ghost Rider & The Original Ghost Rider Rides Again)
Marvel Comics Group: Sept, 1973 - No. 81, June, 1983 (Super-hero)

	GD	VG	FN	VF	VF/NM	NM-
1-Johnny Blaze, the Ghost Rider begins; brief app. Daimon Hellstrom (Son of Satan)	55	110	165	441	996	1550
2-1st full app. Daimon Hellstrom; gives glimpse of costume (1 panel); story continues in Marvel Spotlight #12	14	28	42	97	214	330
3-5: 3-Ghost Rider gains power to make cycle of fire; Son of Satan app.	7	14	21	44	82	120
6-9	4	8	12	28	47	65
10-Hulk on cover; reprints origin/1st app. from Marvel Spotlight #5; Ploog-a	6	12	18	37	66	95
11-16: 11-Hulk app.	3	6	9	16	23	30
17,19-(Reg. 25¢ editions)(4,8/76)	3	6	9	16	23	30
17,19-(30¢-c variants, limited distribution	6	12	18	42	79	115
18-(Reg. 25¢ edition)(6/76)-Spider-Man-c & app.	3	6	9	17	26	35
18-(30¢-c variant, limited distribution)	6	12	18	42	79	115
20-Daredevil x-over; ties into D.D. #138; Byrne-a	3	6	9	19	30	40
21-30: 22-1st app. Enforcer. 29,30-Vs. Dr. Strange	2	4	6	10	14	18
24-26-(35¢-c variants, limited distribution)	6	12	18	42	79	115
31-34,36-49: 40-Nuclear explosion-c	2	4	6	8	10	12
35-Death Race classic; Starlin-c/a/sty	3	6	9	15	22	28
50-Double size	3	6	9	14	20	25
51-76: 55-Werewolf by Night app. 68-Origin retold	1	2	3	5	6	8
77-80: 77-Origin retold. 80-Brief origin recap	1	3	4	6	8	10

	GD 2.0	VG 4.0	FN 6.0	VF 8.0	VF/NM 9.0	NM- 9.2

81-Death of Ghost Rider (Demon leaves Blaze)   4   8   12   23   37   50
... Team Up TPB (2007, $15.99) r/#27, 50, Marvel Team-Up #91, Marvel Two-In-One #80,
    Avengers #214 and Marvel Premiere #28; Night Rider app.: cover gallery   16.00
NOTE: *Anderson* c-64p. *Infantino* a(p)-43, 44, 51. *G. Kane* a-21p; c(p)-1, 2, 4, 5, 8, 9, 11-13, 19, 20, 24, 25. *Kirby*
c-21-23. *Mooney* a-2-9p, 30i. *Nebres* c-26i. *Newton* a-3i. *Perez* c-26p. *Shores* a-2i. *J. Sparling* a-62p, 64p, 65p.
Starlin a(p)-35. *Sutton* a-1p, 44i, 64i, 65i, 66, 67i. *Tuska* a-13p, 14p, 16p.

GHOST RIDER (Volume 2) (Also see Doctor Strange/Ghost Rider Special,
Marvel Comics Presents & Midnight Sons Unlimited)
Marvel Comics (Midnight Sons imprint #44 on): V2#1, May, 1990 - No. 93, Feb, 1998
($1.50/$1.75/$1.95)

1-($1.95, 52 pgs.)-Origin/1st app. new Ghost Rider; Kingpin app.   4   8   12   27   44   60
1-2nd printing (not gold)   5.00
2-5: 3-Kingpin app. 5-Punisher app.; Jim Lee-c   6.00
5-Gold background 2nd printing   4.00
6-14,16-24,29,30,32-39: 6-Punisher app. 6,17-Spider-Man/Hobgoblin-c/story. 9-X-Factor app.
    10-Reintro Johnny Blaze on the last pg. 11-Stroman-c/a(p). 12,13-Dr. Strange x-over cont'd
    in D.S. #28. 13-Painted-c. 14-Johnny Blaze vs. Ghost Rider; origin recap 1st Ghost Rider
    (Blaze). 18-Painted-c by Nelson. 29-Wolverine-c/story. 32-Dr. Strange x-over; Johnny Blaze
    app. 34-Williamson-a(i). 36-Daredevil app. 37-Archangel app.   4.00
15-Glow in the dark-c   1   3   4   6   8   10
25-27: 25-($2.75)-Double-size; contains pop-up scene insert. 26,27-X-Men x-over;
    Lee/Williams-c on both   5.00
28,31-($2.50, 52 pgs.)-Polybagged w/poster; part 1 & part 6 of Rise of the Midnight Sons
    storyline (see Ghost Rider/Blaze #1)   5.00
40-Outer-c is Darkhold envelope made of black parchment w/gold ink; Midnight Massacre;
    Demogoblin app.   6.00
41-48: 41-Lilith & Centurious app.; begin $1.75-c. 41-43-Neon ink-c. 43-Has free extra 16 pg.
    insert on Siege of Darkness. 44,45-Siege of Darkness parts 2 & 10. 44-Spot varnish-c.
    46-Intro new Ghost Rider. 48-Spider-Man app.   4.00
49,51-60,62-74: 49-Begin $1.95-c; bound-in trading card sheet; Hulk app. 55-Werewolf by
    Night app. 65-Punisher app. 67,68-Gambit app. 68-Wolverine app. 73,74-Blaze, Vengeance
    app.   4.00
50,61: 50-($2.50, 52 pgs.)-Regular edition   5.00
50-($2.95, 52 pgs.)-Collectors Ed. die cut foil-c   5.00
75-89: 76-Vs. Vengeance. 77,78-Dr. Strange-app. 78-New costume   4.00
90-92   6.00
93-($3.95)-Last issue; Saltares & Texeira-a   5   10   15   30   50   70
(#94, see Ghost Rider Finale for unpublished story)
#(-1) Flashback (7/97) Saltares-a   4.00
Annual 1,2 ('93, '94, $2.95, 68 pgs.)   4.00
...And Cable 1 (9/92, $3.95, stiff-c, 68 pgs.)-Reprints Marvel Comics Presents #90-98
    w/new Kieth-c   4.00
...:Crossroads (11/95, $3.95) Die cut cover; Nord-a   5.00
... Cycle of Vengeance 1 (3/12, $5.99) r/Marvel Spotlight #5, Ghost Rider (1990) #1 and
    Ghost Rider (2006) #1; Leinil Yu-c   6.00
... Finale (2007, $3.99) r/#93 and the story meant for the unpublished #94; Saltares-a   4.00
Highway to Hell (2001, $3.50) Reprints origin from Marvel Spotlight #5   3.50
...: Resurrected TPB (2001, $12.95) r/#1-7   13.00
NOTE: *Andy & Joe Kubert* c/a-28-31. *Quesada* c-21. *Williamson* a(i)-33-35; c-33i.

GHOST RIDER (Volume 3)
Marvel Comics: Aug, 2001 - No. 6, Jan, 2002 ($2.99, limited series)

1-6-Grayson-s/Kaniuga-a/c   3.00
...: The Hammer Lane TPB (6/02, $15.95) r/#1-6   16.00

GHOST RIDER
Marvel Comics: Nov, 2005 - No. 6, Apr, 2006 ($2.99, limited series)

1-6-Garth Ennis-s/Clayton Crain-a/c. 1-Origin retold   3.00
1 (Director's Cut) (2005, $3.99) r/#1 with Ennis pitch and script and Crain art process   4.00
...: Road to Damnation HC (2006, $19.99, dust jacket) r/#1-6; variant covers & concept-a   20.00
...: Road to Damnation SC (2007, $14.99) r/#1-6; variant covers & concept-a   15.00

GHOST RIDER
Marvel Comics: Sept, 2006 - No. 35, Jul, 2009 ($2.99)

1-11: 1-Daniel Way-s/Saltares & Texeira-a. 2-4-Dr. Strange app. 6,7-Corben-a   3.00
12-27,29-35: 12,13-World War Hulk; Saltares-a/Dell'Otto-c. 23-Danny Ketch returns   3.00
28-($3.99) Silvestri-c/Huat-a; back-up history of Danny Ketch   4.00
Annual 1 (1/08, $3.99) Ben Oliver-a/c/Stuart Moore-s   4.00
Annual 2 (10/08, $3.99) Spurrier-s/Robinson-a; r/Ghost Rider #35 (1979)   4.00
... Vol. 1: Vicious Cycle TPB (2007, $13.99) r/#1-5   14.00
... Vol. 2: The Life and Death of Johnny Blaze TPB (2007, $13.99) r/#6-11   14.00
... Vol. 3: Apocalypse Soon TPB (2008, $10.99) r/#12,13 & Annual #1   11.00
... Vol. 4: Revelations TPB (2008, $14.99) r/#14-19   15.00

GHOST RIDER
Marvel Comics: No. 0.1, Aug, 2011 - No. 9, May 2012 ($2.99/$3.99)

0.1-($2.99) Johnny Blaze gets rid of the Spirit of Vengeance; Matthew Clark-a   3.00
1-($3.99) Adam Kubert-c; Fear Itself tie-in; new female Ghost Rider; Mephisto app.   4.00
2-9: 2-4-($2.99) Fear Itself tie-in. 5-Garbett-a. 7,8-Hawkeye app.   3.00

GHOST RIDER (Robbie Reyes) (Also see All-New Ghost Rider)
Marvel Comics: Jan, 2017 - No. 5, May 2017 ($3.99)

1-5-Felipe Smith-s; Hulk (Amadeus Cho) and X-23 app. 1-Intro. Pyston Nitro. 3-5-Silk app.   4.00

GHOST RIDER (Danny Ketch)
Marvel Comics: Dec, 2019 - No. 7, Sept, 2020 ($4.99/$3.99)

1-($4.99) Brisson-s/Kuder-a; Johnny Blaze, Lilith & Mephisto app.   5.00
2-7-($3.99) 2-Johnny becomes the Rider. 5-7-Wolverine app. 6,7-Dr. Strange app.   4.00
...: Danny Ketch - Marvel Tales 1 (1/23, $7.99) Reprints Ghost Rider (1990) #1-3   8.00
...: Return of Vengeance 1 (2/21, $4.99) Howard Mackie-s/Javier Saltares-a   5.00

GHOST RIDER (Johnny Blaze)
Marvel Comics: Apr, 2022 - No. 21, Feb, 2024 ($5.99/$3.99)

1-($5.99) Benjamin Percy-s/Cory Smith-a; Johnny Blaze returns   6.00
2-13,15-19-($3.99) 5,6,17-Wolverine app.   4.00
14,20,21-($4.99) 14-Bonus back-up story with Taegukgi from Tiger Division   5.00
Annual 1 (12/23, $4.99) The Hood and Elsa Bloodstone app.; Percy-s/Danny Kim-a   5.00
...: Vengeance Forever (10/22, $4.99) Percy-s/Ryp-a; stories of previous Ghost Riders   5.00

.../Wolverine: Weapons of Vengeance Alpha (10/23, $4.99) Percy-s/Shaw-a   5.00
.../Wolverine: Weapons of Vengeance Omega (11/23, $4.99) Percy-s/Shaw-a   5.00

GHOST RIDER/BALLISTIC
Marvel Comics: Feb, 1997 ($2.95, one-shot)

1-Devil's Reign pt. 3   1   2   3   5   6   8

GHOST RIDER/BLAZE: SPIRITS OF VENGEANCE (Also see Blaze)
Marvel Comics (Midnight Sons imprint #17 on): Aug, 1992 - No. 23, June, 1994 ($1.75)

1-($2.75, 52 pgs.)-Polybagged w/poster; part 2 of Rise of the Midnight Sons
    storyline; Adam Kubert-a begins   1   2   3   5   6   8
2-11,14-21: 4-Art Adams & Joe Kubert-p. 5,6-Spirits of Venom parts 2 & 4 cont'd from Web
    of Spider-Man #95,96 w/Demogoblin. 14-17-Neon ink-c. 15-Intro Blaze's new costume &
    power. 17,18-Siege of Darkness parts 8 & 13. 17-Spot varnish-c   4.00
12-($2.95)-Glow-in-the-dark-c   6.00
13-($2.25)-Outer-c is Darkhold envelope made of black parchment w/gold ink; Midnight
    Massacre x-over   6.00
22,23: 22-Begin $1.95-c; bound-in trading card sheet   4.00
NOTE: *Adam & Joe Kubert* c-7, 8. *Adam Kubert/Steacy* c-6. *J. Kubert* a-13p(6 pgs.).

GHOST RIDER/CAPTAIN AMERICA: FEAR
Marvel Comics: Oct, 1992 ($5.95, 52 pgs.)

nn-Wraparound gatefold-c; Williamson inks   1   3   4   6   8   10

GHOST RIDER: DANNY KETCH
Marvel Comics: Dec, 2008 - No. 5, Apr, 2009 ($3.99, limited series)

1-5-Saltares-a   4.00

GHOST RIDER: HEAVEN'S ON FIRE
Marvel Comics: Oct, 2009 - No. 6, Mar, 2010 ($3.99, limited series)

1-6: 1-Jae Lee-c/Boschi-a/Aaron-s; Hellstorm app.; r/pages from Ghost Rider #1 ('73)   4.00

GHOST RIDER: TRAIL OF TEARS
Marvel Comics: Apr, 2007 - No. 6, Sept, 2007 ($2.99, limited series)

1-6-Garth Ennis-s/Clayton Crain-a/c; Civil War era tale   3.00
HC (2007, $19.99) r/series   20.00
SC (2008, $14.99) r/series   15.00

GHOST RIDER 2099
Marvel Comics: May, 1994 - No. 25, May, 1996 ($1.50/$1.95)

1 ($2.25)-Collector's Edition w/prismatic foil-c   2   4   6   9   12   15
1 ($1.50)-Regular Edition; bound-in trading card sheet   4.00
2-24: 7-Spider-Man 2099 app.   4.00
2-(Variant); polybagged with Sega Sub-Terrania poster)   5.00
25 ($2.95)   4.00
No. 1 (2/20, $4.99) Brisson-s/Couceiro-a; tie-in with 2099 one-shots   5.00

GHOST RIDER, WOLVERINE, PUNISHER: THE DARK DESIGN
Marvel Comics: Dec, 1994 ($5.95, one-shot)

nn-Gatefold-c   6.00

GHOST RIDER; WOLVERINE; PUNISHER: HEARTS OF DARKNESS
Marvel Comics: Dec, 1991 ($4.95, one-shot, 52 pgs.)

1-Double gatefold-c; John Romita, Jr.-c/a(p)   1   3   4   6   8   10

GHOSTS (See The World Around Us #24)

GHOSTS (Ghost No. 1)
National Periodical Publications/DC Comics: Sept-Oct, 1971 - No. 112, May, 1982 (No. 1-5:
52 pgs.)

	GD 2.0	VG 4.0	FN 6.0	VF 8.0	VF/NM 9.0	NM- 9.2
1-Aparo-a	13	26	39	89	195	300
2-Wood-a(i)	7	14	21	44	82	120
3-5-(52 pgs.)	6	12	18	38	69	100
6-10	4	8	12	27	44	60
11-20	3	6	9	14	20	25
21-39	2	4	6	9	13	16
40-(68 pgs.)	3	6	9	16	23	30
41-60	2	4	6	8	10	12
61-96	1	2	3	5	6	8

97-99-The Spectre vs. Dr. 13 by Aparo. 97,98-Spectre-c by Aparo.

	2	4	6	10	14	18
100-Infinity-c	2	4	6	8	10	12
101-112	1	2	3	5	6	8

NOTE: *B. Baily* a-77. *Buckler* c-99, 100. *J. Craig* a-108. *Ditko* a-77, 111. *Giffen* a-104p, 106p, 111p. *Glanzman*
a-2. *Golden* a-88. *Infantino* a-8. *Kaluta* c-7, 93, 101. *Kubert* a-8; c-89, 105-108, 111. *Mayer* a-111. *McWilliams*
a-99. *Win Mortimer* a-89, 91, 94. *Nasser/Netzer* a-97. *Newton* a-92p, 94p. *Nino* a-35, 37, 57. *Orlando* a-74i;
c-80. *Redondo* a-9, 13, 45. *Sparling* a(p)-90, 93, 94. *Spiegle* a-103, 105. *Tuska* a-2i. Dr. 13, the Ghostbreaker
back-ups in 95-99, 101.

GHOSTS
DC Comics (Vertigo): Dec, 2012 ($7.99, one-shot)

1-Short stories by various incl. Johns, Lemire, Pope, Lapham; Joe Kubert's last work   8.00

GHOSTS GIANT
DC Comics: 2019 ($4.99, 100-page, squarebound)

1-Short stories; new Spectre, Constantine and Gentleman Ghost plus reprints   8.00

GHOST-SPIDER (Also see Spider-Gwen)
Marvel Comics: Oct, 2019 - No. 10, Oct, 2020 ($3.99)

1-10: 1-McGuire-s/Miyazawa-a; Gwen goes to college on Earth-616; Jackal app.   4.00
Annual 1 (11/19, $4.99) Vita Ayala-a/Pere Pérez-a; Arcade app.   5.00

GHOSTS SPECIAL (See DC Special Series No. 7)

GHOST STATION ZERO (See Codename: Baboushka)
Image Comics: Aug, 2017 - No. 4, Nov, 2017 ($3.99)

1-4-Johnston-s/Chankhamma-a   4.00

GHOST STORIES (See Amazing Ghost Stories)

GHOST STORIES
Dell Publ. Co.: Sept-Nov, 1962; No. 2, Apr-June, 1963 - No. 37, Oct, 1973

	GD 2.0	VG 4.0	FN 6.0	VF 8.0	VF/NM 9.0	NM- 9.2
12-295-211(#1)-Written by John Stanley	8	16	24	54	102	150
2	5	10	15	30	50	70

3-10: Two No. 6's exist with different c/a(12-295-406 & 12-295-503)

Ghost Rider (2008 series) #29 © MAR

Ghosts Giant #1 © DC

Giant Days #50 © John Allison

	GD 2.0	VG 4.0	FN 6.0	VF 8.0	VF/NM 9.0	NM- 9.2
#12-295-503 is actually #9 with indicia to #6	3	6	9	21	33	45
11-21: 21-Last 12¢ issue	3	6	9	17	26	35
22-37	3	6	9	14	20	25

NOTE: #21-34, 36, 37 all reprint earlier issues.

GHOST WHISPERER (Based on the CBS television series)
IDW Publishing: Mar, 2008 - No. 5, July, 2008 ($3.99)

1-5: 1-Two covers by Casagrande & Ho; Casagrande-a	5.00

GHOST WHISPERER: THE MUSE
IDW Publishing: Dec, 2008 - No. 4, Mar, 2009 ($3.99)

1-4-Two covers (photo & art) for each; Barbara Kesel-s/ Adriano Loyola-a	5.00

GHOUL, THE
IDW Publishing: Nov, 2009 - No. 3, Mar, 2010 ($3.99, limited series)

1-3-Niles-s/Wrightson-a	4.00

GHOUL TALES (Magazine)
Stanley Publications: Nov, 1970 - No. 5, July, 1971 (52 pgs.) (B&W)

1-Aragon pre-code reprints; Mr. Mystery as host; bondage-c	9	18	27	58	114	170
2,3: 2-(1/71)Reprint/Climax #1. 3-(3/71)	5	10	15	31	53	75
4-(5/71) Reprints story "The Way to a Man's Heart" used in **SOTI**	5	10	15	35	63	90
5-ACG reprints	4	8	12	27	44	60

NOTE: No. 1-4 contain pre-code Aragon reprints.

GIANT BOY BOOK OF COMICS (Also see Boy Comics)
Newsbook Publications (Gleason): 1945 (240 pgs., hard-c)

1-Crimebuster & Young Robin Hood; Biro-c	142	284	426	909	1555	2200

GIANT COMIC ALBUM
King Features Syndicate: 1972 (59¢, 11x14", 52 pgs., B&W, cardboard-c)

Newspaper reprints: Barney Google, Little Iodine, Katzenjammer Kids, Henry, Beetle Bailey,

Blondie, & Snuffy Smith each...	3	6	9	19	30	40
Flash Gordon ('68-69 Dan Barry)	4	8	12	25	40	55
Mandrake the Magician ('59 Falk), Popeye	4	8	12	23	37	50

GIANT COMICS
Charlton Comics: Summer, 1957 - No. 3, Winter, 1957 (25¢, 96 pgs., not rebound material)

1-Atomic Mouse, Lil Genius, Lil Tomboy app.	34	68	102	199	325	450
2-(Fall '57) Romance	39	78	117	231	378	525
3-Christmas Book; Atomic Mouse, Atomic Rabbit, Li'l Genius, Li'l Tomboy & Atom the Cat stories	24	48	72	142	234	325

GIANT COMICS (See Wham-O Giant Comics)

GIANT COMICS EDITION (See Terry-Toons) (Also see Fox Giants)
St. John Publishing Co.: 1947 - No. 17, 1950 (25¢, 100-164 pgs.)

1-Mighty Mouse	71	142	213	454	777	1100
2-Abbie & Slats	41	82	123	256	428	600
3-Terry-Toons Album; 100 pgs.	54	108	162	343	574	825
4-Crime comics; contains Red Seal No. 16, used & illo. in SOTI	97	194	291	621	1061	1500
5-Police Case Book (4/49, 132 pgs.)-Contents varies; contains remaindered St. John books - some volumes contain 5 copies rather than 4, with 160 pages; Matt Baker-c	90	180	270	576	988	1400
5A-Terry-Toons Album (132 pgs.)-Mighty Mouse, Heckle & Jeckle, Gandy Goose & Dinky stories	47	94	141	296	498	700
6-Western Picture Stories; Baker-c/a(3); Tuska-a; The Sky Chief, Blue Monk, Ventrilo app., 132 pgs.	90	180	270	576	988	1400
7-Contains a teen-age romance plus 3 Mopsy comics	103	206	309	659	1130	1600
8-The Adventures of Mighty Mouse (10/49)	47	94	141	296	498	700
9-Romance and Confession Stories; Kubert-a(4); Baker-a; photo-c (132 pgs.)	206	412	618	1318	2259	3200
10-Terry-Toons Album (132 pgs.)-Mighty Mouse, Heckle & Jeckle, Gandy Goose stories	47	94	141	296	498	700
11-Western Picture Stories-Baker-c/a(4); The Sky Chief, Desperado, & Blue Monk app.; another version with Son of Sinbad by Kubert (132 pgs.)	90	180	270	576	988	1400
12-Diary Secrets; Baker prostitute-c; 4 St. John romance comics; Baker-a	2080	4160	6240	12,500	18,750	25,000
13-Romances; Baker, Kubert-a	232	464	696	1485	2543	3600
14-Mighty Mouse Album (132 pgs.)	48	96	144	302	514	725
15-Romances (4 love comics)-Baker-c	300	600	900	1950	3375	4800
16-Little Audrey; Abbott & Costello, Casper	68	136	204	435	743	1050
17-(nn)-Mighty Mouse Album (nn, no date, but did follow No. 16); 100 pgs. on cover but has 148 pgs.	50	100	150	315	533	750

NOTE: The above books contain remaindered comics and contents could vary with each issue. No. 11, 12 have part photo magazine insides.

GIANT COMICS EDITIONS
United Features Syndicate: 1940's (132 pgs.)

1-Abbie & Slats, Abbott & Costello, Jim Hardy, Ella Cinders, Iron Vic, Gordo, & Bill Bumlin	58	116	174	371	636	900
2-Jim Hardy, Ella Cinders, Elmo & Gordo	41	82	123	250	418	585

NOTE: Above books contain rebound copies; contents can vary.

GIANT DAYS
BOOM! Studios (BOOM! Box): Mar, 2015 - No. 54, Sept, 2019 ($3.99)

1-24,26-49,51-54: 1-6-John Allison-s/Lissa Treiman a/c. 7-Max Sarin-a begins. 38-Madrigal-a. Allison-a. 54-Esther & Daisy's graduations	4.00
25,50-($4.99) 25-Christmas story	5.00
...: As Time Goes By 1 (10/19, $7.99) Final issue; takes place a year after #54	8.00
... 2016 Holiday Special #1 (10/16, $7.99) Treiman-a/c; back-up w/Caanan Grall-a	8.00
... 2017 Holiday Special #1 (10/16, $7.99) St-Onge-a/c	8.00
...: Where Women Glow and Men Plunder 1 (12/18, $7.99) Ed visits Australia; Allison-a	8.00

GIANT GRAB BAG OF COMICS (See Archie All-Star Specials under Archie Comics)

GIANTKILLER
DC Comics: Aug, 1999 - No. 6, Jan, 2000 ($2.50, limited series)

1-6-Story and painted art by Dan Brereton	4.00
...A to Z: A Field Guide to Big Monsters (8/99)	4.00
...Vol. 1 TPB (Image Comics, 2006, $14.99) r/#1-6 & A-Z; gallery of concept art	15.00

GIANTKILLERS
IDW Publishing: No. 0, Nov, 2017 ($3.99)

0-Bart Sears-s/a; Ron Marz-s/Tom Raney-a	4.00
... One-Shot (3/19, $7.99) Sears-s; art by Leonardi/Pennington & Hetrick	8.00

GIANT-MAN (Tie-in to War of the Realms event)
Marvel Comics: Jul, 2019 - No. 3, Aug, 2019 ($3.99, limited series)

1-3-Williams-s/Castiello-a; Ant-Man, Giant-Man, Goliath & Atlas app. 3-Moonstone app.	4.00

GIANT ROBOT HELLBOY
Dark Horse Comics: Oct, 2023 - No. 3 ($3.99, limited series)

1-3-Mignola-s/Fegredo-a; Hellboy linked to a Pacific Rim giant robot	4.00

GIANTS (See Thrilling True Story of the Baseball...)

GIANTS
Dark Horse Comics: Dec, 2017 - No. 5, Apr, 2018 ($3.99)

1-5-Carlos & Miguel Valderrama-s/a	4.00

GIANT-SIZE ATOM
DC Comics: May, 2011 ($4.99, one-shot)

1-Gary Frank-c; Hawkman app.; Lemire-s/Asrar-a	5.00

GIANT-SIZE...
Marvel Comics Group: May, 1974 - Dec, 1975 (35/50¢, 52/68 pgs.)
(Some titles quarterly) (Scarce in strict NM or better due to defective cutting, gluing and binding; warping, splitting and off-center pages are common)

Avengers 1(8/74)-New-a plus G.A.H. Torch-r; 1st modern app. The Whizzer; 1st modern app. Miss America; 2nd app. Invaders; Kang, Rama-Tut, Mantis app.	8	16	24	54	102	150
Avengers 2(11/74)-Death of the Swordsman; origin of Rama-Tut	6	12	18	38	69	100
Avengers 3,5: 3(2/75).5(12/75)-Reprints Avengers Special #1	5	10	15	30	50	70
Avengers 4 (6/75)-Vision marries Scarlet Witch.	5	10	16	34	56	108	160
Captain America 1(12/75)-r/stories T.O.S. 59-63 by Kirby (#63 reprints origin)	5	10	15	31	53	75
Captain Marvel 1(12/75)-r/Capt. Marvel #17, 20, 21 by Gil Kane (p)	5	10	15	30	50	70
Chillers 1(6/74, 52 pgs)-Curse of Dracula; origin/1st app. Lilith, Dracula's daughter; Heath-r, Colan-c/a(p); becomes Giant-Size Dracula #2 on	13	26	39	89	195	300
Chillers 1(2/75, 50¢, 68 pgs.)-Alcala-a	5	10	15	35	63	90
Chillers 2(5/75)-All-r; Everett-r from Advs. into Weird Worlds	3	6	9	20	31	42
Chillers 3(8/75)-Wrightson-c(new)/a(r); Colan, Kirby, Smith-r	4	8	12	25	40	55
Conan 1(9/74)-B. Smith-r/#3; start adaptation of Howard's "Hour of the Dragon" (ends #4); 1st app. Belit (one-panel cameo with blonde hair); new-a begins	5	10	15	33	57	80
Conan 2(12/74)-B. Smith-r/#5; Sutton-a(i)(#1 also); Buscema-c	3	6	9	19	30	40
Conan 3-5: 3(4/75)-B. Smith-r/#6; Sutton-a(i). 4(6/75)-B. Smith-r/#7.						

	GD 2.0	VG 4.0	FN 6.0	VF 8.0	VF/NM 9.0	NM- 9.2

5(1975)-B. Smith-r/#14,15; Kirby-c — 3 · 6 · 9 · 16 · 24 · 32

Creatures 1(5/74, 52 pgs.)-Werewolf app; 1st app. Tigra (formerly Cat); Crandall-r; becomes Giant-Size Werewolf w/#2 — 12 · 24 · 36 · 82 · 179 · 275

Daredevil 1(1975)-Reprints Daredevil Annual #1 — 6 · 12 · 18 · 37 · 66 · 95

Defenders 1(7/74, 68-pgs.)-Dr. Strange, Hulk, Namor & Valkyrie app.; continued from Defenders #12; mostly reprint stories, with a few pages of new material by Jim Starlin; Hulk-r from Incredible Hulk #3; Sub-Mariner-r from Sub-Mariner (Golden Age) #41; Dr. Strange-r from Strange Tales #145; Silver Surfer-r from Fantastic Four Annual #5 — 14 · 28 · 42 · 84 · 86 · 125

Defenders 2(10/74, 68-pgs.)-New G. Kane-c/a/p; Son of Satan app. vs. Asmodeus; Sub-Mariner-r from Young Men #25; Black Knight-r from Black Knight #4 (1955); Dr. Strange-r from Strange Tales #119 — 4 · 8 · 12 · 27 · 44 · 60

Defenders 3(1/75, 68-pgs.)-1st app. Korvac; Grandmaster vs. The Prime Mover; Daredevil app.; G.A. Sub-Mariner-r from Sub-Mariner #38; Dr. Strange-r from Strange Tales #120 — 19 · 38 · 57 · 131 · 291 · 450

Defenders No. 3 Facsimile Edition (2/20, $4.99) Reprints issue with original ads — 3 · 4 · 6 · 8 · 10

Defenders 4(4/75, 68-pgs.)-Continued from Defenders #21; Yellowjacket & Wasp app.; vs. Egghead, Squadron Sinister (Hyperion, Dr. Spectrum and the Whizzer); Sub-Mariner-r from Human Torch Comics #4 (technically 3rd issue); Dr. Strange-r from Strange Tales #121 — 4 · 8 · 12 · 23 · 37 · 50

Defenders 5(7/75, 68-pgs.)-Continued from Defenders #25; Guardians of the Galaxy app.; (3rd app) continued from Marvel Two-in-One #5; story continued in Defenders #26; Nighthawk-r from Daredevil #62 — 4 · 8 · 12 · 23 · 37 · 50

Doc Savage 1(1975, 68 pgs.)-r/#1,2; Mooney-r — 3 · 6 · 9 · 21 · 42

Doctor Strange 1(11/75)-Reprints stories from Strange Tales #164-168; Lawrence, Tuska-r — 5 · 10 · 15 · 35 · 63 · 90

Dracula 2(9/74, 50¢)-Formerly Giant-Size Chillers — 4 · 8 · 12 · 25 · 40 · 55

Dracula 3(12/74)-Fox-r/Uncanny Tales #6 — 3 · 6 · 9 · 20 · 31 · 42

Dracula 4(3/75)-Ditko-r(2) — 3 · 6 · 9 · 20 · 31 · 42

Dracula 5(6/75)-1st Byrne art at Marvel — 5 · 10 · 15 · 33 · 57 · 80

Fantastic Four 2,3: 2(8/74)-Formerly Giant-Size Super-Stars; Ditko-r. 2-Buscema-a. 3(11/74)-Buckler-a — 4 · 8 · 12 · 27 · 44 · 60

Fantastic Four 4(2/75)-1st Madrox; Buscema-a — 25 · 50 · 75 · 175 · 388 · 600

Fantastic Four 5,6: 5(5/75)-All-r; Kirby, G. Kane-r. 6(10/75)-All-r; Kirby-r — 5 · 10 · 15 · 23 · 37 · 50

Hulk 1(1975) r/Hulk Special #1 — 5 · 10 · 15 · 31 · 53 · 75

Invaders 1(6/75, 50¢, 68 pgs.)-Origin; G.A. Sub-Mariner/Sub-Mariner #1; intro Master Man — 6 · 12 · 18 · 41 · 76 · 110

Iron Man 1(1975)-Ditko reprint — 5 · 10 · 15 · 35 · 63 · 90

Kid Colt 1-3: 1(1/75). 2(4/75). 3(7/75)-new Ayers-a — 7 · 14 · 21 · 48 · 89 · 130

Man-Thing 1(8/74)-New Ploog-c/a (25 pgs.); Ditko-r/Amazing Adv. #11; Kirby-r/ Strange Tales Ann. #2 & T.O.S. #15; (#1-5 all have new Man-Thing stories, pre-hero-r & are 68 pgs.) — 6 · 12 · 18 · 38 · 69 · 100

Man-Thing 2,3: 2(11/74)-Buscema-c/a(p); Kirby, Powell-r. 3(2/75)-Alcala-a; Ditko, Kirby, Sutton-r; Gil Kane-c — 3 · 6 · 9 · 21 · 33 · 45

Man-Thing 4,5: 4(5/75)-Howard the Duck by Brunner-c/a; Ditko-r. 5(8/75)-Howard the Duck by Brunner (p); Dracula cameo in Howard the Duck; Buscema-a(p); Sutton-a(i); G. Kane-c — 5 · 10 · 15 · 30 · 50 · 70

Marvel Triple Action 1,2: 1(5/75). 2(7/75) — 3 · 6 · 9 · 19 · 30 · 40

Master of Kung Fu 1(9/74)-Russell-a; Yellow Claw-r in #1-4; Gulacy-a in #1,2 — 5 · 10 · 15 · 33 · 57 · 80

Master of Kung Fu 2-4: 2-(12/74)-r/Yellow Claw-r. 3(3/75)-Gulacy-a; Kirby-a. 4(6/75)-Kirby-a — 4 · 8 · 12 · 23 · 37 · 50

Power Man 1(1975) — 4 · 8 · 12 · 28 · 47 · 65

Spider-Man 1(7/74)-Spider-Man /Human Torch-r by Kirby/Ditko; Byrne-r plus new-a (Dracula/story) — 9 · 18 · 27 · 59 · 117 · 175

Spider-Man 2,3: 2(10/74)-Shang-Chi/app. 3(1/75)-Doc Savage/app.; Daredevil/ Spider-Man-r w/Ditko-a — 5 · 10 · 15 · 30 · 50 · 70

Spider-Man 4(4/75)-3rd Punisher app.; Byrne, Ditko-r — 12 · 24 · 36 · 79 · 170 · 260

Spider-Man 5,6: 5(7/75)-Man-Thing/Lizard-c. 6(9/75) — 4 · 8 · 12 · 27 · 44 · 60

Super-Heroes Featuring Spider-Man 1(6/74, 35¢, 52 pgs.)-Spider-Man vs. Man-Wolf; Morbius, the Living Vampire app.; Ditko-r; G. Kane-c; Spidey villains app. — 8 · 16 · 24 · 56 · 108 · 160

Super-Stars 1(5/74, 35¢, 52 pgs.)-Fantastic Four; Thing vs. Hulk; Kirbyish-c/a by Buckler/Sinnott; F.F. villains profiled; becomes Giant-Size Fantastic Four 2 on — 6 · 12 · 18 · 41 · 76 · 110

Super-Stars No. 1 Facsimile Edition (2/24, $6.99) — 7.00

Super-Villain Team-Up 1(3/75, 68 pgs.)-Craig-r(i) (Also see Fantastic Four #6 for 1st super-villain team-up) — 5 · 10 · 15 · 30 · 50 · 70

Super-Villain Team-Up 2(6/75, 68 pgs.)-Dr. Doom, Sub-Mariner app.; Spider-Man-r from Amazing Spider-Man #8 by Ditko; Sekowsky(a)-p — 3 · 6 · 9 · 21 · 33 · 45

Thor 1(7/75) — 5 · 10 · 15 · 34 · 60 · 85

Werewolf 2(10/74, 68 pgs.)-Formerly Giant-Size Creatures; Ditko-r; Frankenstein app. — 4 · 8 · 12 · 27 · 44 · 60

Werewolf 3,5: 3(1/75, 68 pgs.). 5(7/75, 68 pgs.) — 3 · 6 · 9 · 19 · 30 · 40

Werewolf 4(4/75, 68 pgs.)-Morbius the Living Vampire app. — 4 · 8 · 12 · 27 · 44 · 60

X-Men 1(Summer, 1975, 50¢, 68 pgs.)-1st app. new X-Men; intro. Nightcrawler, Storm, Colossus & Thunderbird; 2nd full app. Wolverine after Incredible Hulk #181 — 600 · 1100 · 1800 · 3000 · 4500 · 6000

X-Men No. 1 Facsimile Edition (9/19, $4.99) Reprints issue with original ads — 10.00

X-Men No. 1 Facsimile Edition (10/23, $7.99) Reprints issue with original ads — 8.00

X-Men 2 (11/75)-N. Adams-r (51 pgs) — 10 · 20 · 30 · 66 · 138 · 210

Giant Size Marvel TPB (2005, $24.99) reprints stories from Giant-Size Avengers #1, G-S Fantastic Four #4, G-S Defenders #4, G-S Super-Heroes #1, G-S Invaders #1, G-S X-Men #1 and Giant-Size Creatures #1 — 25.00

GIANT-SIZE...
Marvel Comics: 2005 - Present ($4.99/$3.99)

Amazing Spider-Man: Chameleon Conspiracy 1 (8/21, $5.99) Follows ASM #69 (2021) — 6.00

Amazing Spider-Man: King's Ransom 1 (5/21, $5.99) Follows ASM #66 (2021) — 6.00

Astonishing X-Men 1 (7/08) Concludes story from Astonishing X-Men #24; Whedon-s/ Cassaday-a/wraparound-c; Spider-Man, FF, Dr. Strange app.; variant cover gallery — 5.00

Astonishing X-Men 1 (4/08, $4.99) Variant B&W cover — 5.00

Avengers 1 (2/08, $4.99) new short stories and r/Avengers #58, 201; Hitch-c — 5.00

Avengers/Invaders 1 ('08, $3.99) r/Avengers #71; Invaders #10, Ann. 1 & G-S #2 — 4.00

Black Cat: Infinity Score 1 (1/22, $4.99) Follows Black Cat V2 #10 (2021) — 5.00

Fantastic Four 1 (4/24, $6.99) Niceza-s/Creees Lee-a, reprint from Fantastic Four #33 — 7.00

Gwen Stacy 1 (10/22, $9.99) r/Gwen Stacy #1,2 and unpublished stories meant for #3-5 — 10.00

Hulk 1 (8/06, $4.99)-2 new stories; Planet Hulk (David-s/Santacruz-a) & Hulk vs. The Champions (Pak-s/Lopresti-a; r/Incredible Hulk: The End) — 5.00

Incredible Hulk 1 (7/08, $3.99)-1 new story; r/Incredible Hulk Annual #7; Frank-c — 5.00

Invaders 2 ('05, $4.99)-new Thomas-s/Weeks-a; r/Invaders #1&2 & All-Winners #1&2 — 5.00

Marvel Adventures The Avengers (9/07, $3.99) Agents of Atlas and Kang app.; Kirk-a: reprint of 1st Namora app. from Marvel Mystery Comics #82; reprint from Venus #1 — 4.00

Spider-Man (7/14, $4.99) origin retold, other short stories; Scherberger-a — 5.00

Spider-Man (3/24, $6.99) Miles Morales fights Venom; Hitch-c — 7.00

Spider-Woman (4/05, $4.99)-new story; r/Marvel Spotlight #32 & S-W #1,37,38 — 5.00

Wolverine (12/06, $4.99)-new Lapham-s/Aja-a; r/X-Men #6,7 — 5.00

X-Men 3 ('05, $4.99)-new Whedon-s/N. Adams-a; r/team-ups; Cockrum & Cassaday-c — 5.00

X-Men: Fantomex 1 (10/20, $4.99) Hickman-s/Rod Reis-a; history revealed — 5.00

X-Men: Jean Grey and Emma Frost 1 (4/20, $4.99) Hickman-s/Dauterman-a — 5.00

X-Men: Magneto 1 (4/20, $4.99) Hickman-s/Ramón Pérez-a; Namor app. — 5.00

X-Men: Nightcrawler 1 (5/20, $4.99) Hickman-s/Alan Davis-a; Magik & Lockheed app. — 5.00

X-Men: Storm 1 (3/20, $4.99) Hickman-s/Dauterman-a; Cypher & Fantomex app. — 5.00

X-Men: Thunderbird 1 (6/22, $4.99) John Proudstar returns in current time; new look — 5.00

X-Men: Tribute to Wein & Cockrum 1 (11/20, $5.99) Wein's original script re-drawn by modern artists (1 page each); bonus profiles of Wein, Cockrum & Claremont; Granov-c — 6.00

X-Statix 1 (9/19, $4.99) Milligan-s/Allred-a; intro new team members — 5.00

GIANT-SIZE JINGLES (Cerebus figures placed over original Gustave Doré artwork)
Aardvark-Vanaheim: 2019 ($4.00, B&W)

1-"Three Giant-Size Firsts worth noting" according to the cover; G:S X-Men #1-c swipe — 4.00

GIANT-SIZE LITTLE MARVEL: AVX (Secret Wars tie-in)
Marvel Comics: Aug, 2015 - No. 4, Nov, 2015 ($3.99, limited series)

1-4-Skottie Young-s/a; all ages kid-version Avengers vs. X-Men spoof. 4-GOTG app. — 4.00

GIANT-SIZE PUBLIC DEFENDERS (Cerebus)
Aardvark-Vanaheim: 2022 ($8.00, B&W)

1-Giant-Size Defenders #1-c swipe — 8.00

GIANT SPECTACULAR COMICS (See Archie All-Star Special under Archie Comics)

GIANT SUMMER FUN BOOK (See Terry-Toons...)

G. I. COMBAT
Quality Comics Group: Oct, 1952 - No. 43, Dec, 1956

	GD 2.0	VG 4.0	FN 6.0	VF 8.0	VF/NM 9.0	NM- 9.2
1-Crandall-c; Cuidera a-1-43i	290	580	870	1856	3178	4500
2	58	116	174	371	636	900
3-5,10-Crandall-c/a	53	106	159	334	567	800
6-Crandall-a	48	96	144	302	514	725
7-9	45	90	135	284	480	675
11-20	36	72	108	214	347	480
21-31,33,35-43: 41-1st S.A. issue	34	68	102	204	332	460
32-Nuclear attack-c/story "Atomic Rocket Assault"	50	100	150	315	533	750
34-Crandall-a	39	78	117	231	378	525

G. I. COMBAT (See DC Special Series #22)
National Periodical Publ./DC Comics: No. 44, Jan, 1957 - No. 288, Mar, 1987

	GD 2.0	VG 4.0	FN 6.0	VF 8.0	VF/NM 9.0	NM- 9.2
44-Grey tone-c	106	212	318	848	1899	2950
45	46	92	138	359	805	1250
46-50	38	76	114	281	628	975
51-Grey tone-c	44	88	132	326	738	1150
52-54,59,60	32	64	96	230	515	800
55-Minor Sgt. Rock prototype by Finger	36	72	108	266	596	925
56-Sgt. Rock prototype by Kanigher/Kubert	52	104	156	416	933	1450
57,58-Pre-Sgt. Rock Easy Co. stories	38	76	114	281	628	975
61-65,70-73	24	48	72	168	372	575
66-Pre-Sgt. Rock Easy Co. story	36	72	108	266	596	925
67-1st Tank Killer	46	92	138	359	805	1250
68-(1/59) "The Rock". Sgt. Rock prototype. Part of lead-up trio to 1st definitive Sgt. Rock. Character named Jimmy referred to as "The Rock" appears as a sergeant in the story and as a private in the story. In reprint (Our Army at War #242) DC edits Jimmy's name out; also see Our Army at War #81-84	169	338	507	1394	3147	4900
69-Grey tone-c	44	88	132	326	738	1150
74-American flag-c	31	62	93	223	499	775
75-80: 75-Grey tone-c begin, end #109	28	76	114	281	628	975
81,82,84-86-Grey tone-c	35	70	105	252	564	875
83-1st Big Al, Little Al & Charlie Cigar; grey tone-c	46	92	138	359	805	1250
87-(4-5/61) 1st Haunted Tank; series begins; classic Heath washtone-c	200	400	600	1650	3725	5800
88-(6-7/61) 2nd Haunted Tank	57	114	171	456	1028	1600
89,90: 90-Last 10¢ issue	34	68	102	245	548	850
91-(12/61-1/62)1st Haunted Tank-c; Grey tone-c	79	158	237	632	1416	2200
92-95,99-Grey tone-c. 94-Panel inspired a famous Roy Lichtenstein painting	29	58	87	209	467	725
96-98-Grey tone-c	24	44	66	154	340	525
100,108: 100-(6-7/63) Grey tone-c. 108-1st Sgt. Rock x-over	24	48	72	168	372	575
101-103,105-107-Grey tone-c	18	36	51	121	268	415
104,109-Grey tone-c	22	44	66	154	340	525
110-112,115-118,120	13	26	39	91	201	310
113-Grey tone-c	18	36	54	128	284	440
114-Origin Haunted Tank	38	76	114	285	641	1000
119-Grey tone-c	16	32	48	112	249	385
121-136: 121-1st app. Sgt. Rock's father. 125-Sgt. Rock app. 136-Last 12¢ issue	9	18	27	60	120	180
137,139,140	6	12	18	41	76	110
138-Intro. The Losers (Capt. Storm, Gunner/Sarge, Johnny Cloud) in Haunted Tank (10-11/69)	14	28	42	93	204	310
141-143	4	8	12	28	47	65
144-148 (68 pgs.)	5	10	15	33	57	80
149,151-154 (52 pgs.): 151-Capt. Storm story. 151,153-Medal of Honor series by Maurer	4	8	12	28	47	65

Giant-Size Daredevil #1 © MAR

G.I. Combat #91 © DC

G.I. Joe V2 #12 © Hasbro

	GD 2.0	VG 4.0	FN 6.0	VF 8.0	VF/NM 9.0	NM- 9.2
150- (52 pgs.) Ice Cream Soldier story (tells how he got his name); Death of Haunted Tank-c/s	5	10	15	33	57	80
155-167,169,170	3	6	9	15	22	28
168-Neal Adams-c	4	8	12	25	40	55
171-194,196-199	3	6	9	14	19	24
195-(10/76) Haunted Tank meets War That Time Forgot; Dinosaur-c/s; Kubert-a	3	6	9	16	24	32
200-(3/77) Haunted Tank-c/s; Sgt. Rock and the Losers app.; Kubert-c	3	6	9	17	25	34
201,202 ($1.00 size) Neal Adams-c	3	6	9	17	25	34
203-210 ($1.00 size)	3	6	9	15	22	28
211-230 ($1.00 size)	3	6	9	14	19	24
231-259 ($1.00 size).232-Origin Kana the Ninja. 244-Death of Slim Stryker. 246-(76 pgs., $1.50)-30th Anniversary issue. 257-Intro. Stuart's Raiders Mercenaries.	2	4	6	10	14	18
260-281: 260-Begin $1.25, 52 pg. issues, end #281. 264-Intro Sgt. Bullet; origin Kana. 269-Intro. The Bravos of Vietnam. 274-Cameo of Monitor from Crisis on Infinite Earths	2	4	6	8	11	14
282-288 (75¢): 282-New advs. begin	1	3	4	6	8	10

NOTE: **N. Adams** c-168, 201, 202. **Check** a-168, 173. **Drucker** a-48, 61, 63, 66, 71, 72, 76, 134, 140, 141, 144, 147, 148, 153. **Evans** a-135, 138, 158, 164, 168, 201, 202, 204, 205, 215, 256. **Giffen** a-267. **Glanzman** a-most issues. **Kubert/Heath** a-most issues; **Kubert** covers most issues. **Morrow** a-159-161(2 pgs.). **Redondo** a-189, 240i, 243i. **Sekowsky** a-162a. **Severin** a-147, 152, 154. **Simonson** a-169. **Thorne** a-152, 156. **Wildey** a-153. Johnny Cloud app.-112, 115, 120. Mlle. Marie app.-123, 132, 200. Sgt. Rock app.-111-113, 115, 120, 125, 141, 146, 147, 149, 200. USS Stevens by **Glanzman**-145, 150-153, 157. **Grandenetti** c-44-48.

G. I. COMBAT
DC Comics: Nov, 2010 ($3.99, one-shot)

1-Haunted Tank and General J.E.B. Stuart app.; Sturges-s/Winslade-a/Darrow-c	4.00

G. I. COMBAT
DC Comics: Jul, 2012 - No. 7, Feb, 2013 ($3.99)

1-7: 1-War That Time Forgot; Olivetti-a; Unknown Soldier; Panosian-a; two covers	4.00
#0 (11/12, $3.99) Unknown Soldiers through history; War That Time Forgot; Olivetti-a	4.00

GIDEON FALLS
Image Comics: Mar, 2018 - No. 27, Dec, 2020 ($3.99)

1-26-Lemire-s/Sorrentino-a	4.00
#1 Director's Cut (9/18, $4.99) r/#1 in B&W with original script	5.00
27-($7.99, 80 pgs.) Last issue; Lemire-s/Sorrentino-a	8.00

GIDGET (TV)
Dell Publishing Co.: Apr, 1966 - No. 2, Dec, 1966

	GD 2.0	VG 4.0	FN 6.0	VF 8.0	VF/NM 9.0	NM- 9.2
1-Sally Field photo-c	9	18	27	62	126	190
2	7	14	21	49	92	135

GIFT COMICS
Fawcett Publications: 1942 - No. 4, 1949 (50¢/25¢, 324 pgs./152 pgs.)

	GD 2.0	VG 4.0	FN 6.0	VF 8.0	VF/NM 9.0	NM- 9.2
1-Captain Marvel, Bulletman, Golden Arrow, Ibis the Invincible, Mr. Scarlet, & Spy Smasher begin; not rebound, remaindered comics, printed at same time as originals; 50¢-c & 324 pgs. begin, and #3.	343	686	1029	2400	4200	6000
2-Commando Yank, Phantom Eagle, others app.	226	452	678	1446	2473	3500
3 (50¢, 324 pgs.)	168	336	504	1075	1838	2600
4-(25¢, 152 pgs.)-The Marvel Family, Captain Marvel, etc.; each issue can vary in contents	110	220	330	794	1202	1700

GIFTS FROM SANTA (See March of Comics No. 137)

GIFTS OF THE NIGHT
DC Comics (Vertigo): Feb, 1999 - No. 4, May, 1999 ($2.95, limited series)

1-4-Bolton-c/a; Chadwick-s	4.00

GIGANTIC
Dark Horse Comics: Nov, 2008 - No. 5, Jan, 2010 ($3.50, limited series)

1-5-Remender-s/Nguyen-a; Earth as a reality show	3.50

GIGGLE COMICS (Spencer Spook No. 100) (Also see Ha Ha Comics)
Creston No.1-63/American Comics Group No. 64 on; Oct, 1943 - No. 99, Jan-Feb, 1955

	GD 2.0	VG 4.0	FN 6.0	VF 8.0	VF/NM 9.0	NM- 9.2
1-Funny animal	53	106	159	334	567	800
2	27	54	81	158	259	360
3-5: Ken Hultgren-a begins?	19	38	57	111	176	240
6-9: 9-1st Superkatt (6/44)	15	30	45	88	137	185
10-Superkatt shoots Japanese plane and fights Nazi robot	18	36	54	105	165	225
11-20	14	28	42	81	118	155
21-40: 22-Spencer Spook 2nd app. 32-Patriotic-c. 37-X-Mas-c. 39-St. Valentine's	14	28	42	76	108	140
41-54,56-59,62-99: Spencer Spook app. in many. 44-Mussel-Man app. (Superman parody). 45-Witch Hazel 1st app. 46-Bob Hope & Bing Crosby app. 49,69-X-Mas-c.	11	22	33	62	86	110
55,60,61-Milt Gross-a. 61-X-Mas-c	14	28	42	78	112	145

G-I IN BATTLE (G-I No. 1 only)
Ajax-Farrell Publ./Four Star: Aug, 1952 - No. 9, July, 1953; Mar, 1957 - No. 6, May, 1958

	GD 2.0	VG 4.0	FN 6.0	VF 8.0	VF/NM 9.0	NM- 9.2
1	39	78	117	240	395	550
2	32	64	96	188	307	425
3-9	15	30	45	88	137	185
Annual 1(1952, 25¢, 100 pgs.)	43	86	129	271	461	650
1(1957-Ajax)	12	24	36	67	94	120
2-6	8	16	24	40	50	60

G. I. JANE
Stanhall/Merit No. 11: May, 1953 - No. 11, Mar, 1955 (Misdated 3/54)

	GD 2.0	VG 4.0	FN 6.0	VF 8.0	VF/NM 9.0	NM- 9.2
1-PX Pete begins; Bill Williams-c/a	58	116	174	371	636	900
2-7(5/54)	41	82	123	256	428	600
8-10(12/54, Stanhall)	32	64	96	188	307	425
11 (3/55, Merit)	32	64	96	188	307	425

G. I. COMBAT (Also see Advs. of..., Showcase #53, 54 & The Yardbirds)
Ziff-Davis Publ. Co. (Korean War): No. 10, Feb/Mar, 1951; No. 11, Apr/May, 1951 - No. 51, Jun, 1957 (52 pgs.: #10-14, V2 #6-17?)

	GD 2.0	VG 4.0	FN 6.0	VF 8.0	VF/NM 9.0	NM- 9.2
10(#1)-Saunders painted-c begin	34	68	102	199	325	450
11-14(#2-5, 10/51): 11-New logo. 12-New logo	20	40	60	114	182	250
V2#6(12/51)-17-(11/52; Last 52 pgs.?)	15	30	45	90	140	190
18-(25¢, 100 pg. Giant, 12-1/52-53)	39	78	117	231	378	525
19-30: 20-22,24,28-31-The Yardbirds app.	14	28	42	82	121	160
31-47,49-51	14	28	42	78	112	145
48-Atom bomb story	14	28	42	80	115	150

NOTE: **Powell** a-V2#7, 8, 11. **Norman Saunders** painted c-10-14, V2#6-14, 26, 30, 31, 35, 38, 39. **Tuska** a-7. Bondage c-29, 35, 38.

G. I. JOE (America's Movable Fighting Man)
Custom Comics: 1967 (5-1/8x8-3/8", 36 pgs.)

	GD 2.0	VG 4.0	FN 6.0	VF 8.0	VF/NM 9.0	NM- 9.2
nn-Schaffenberger-a; based on Hasbro toy	5	10	15	34	60	85

G. I. JOE
Dark Horse Comics: Dec, 1995 - No. 4, Apr, 1996 ($1.95, limited series)

1-4: Mike W. Barr scripts. 1-Three Frank Miller covers with title logos in red, white and blue. 2-Breyfogle-c. 3-Simonson-a	5.00

G. I. JOE
Dark Horse Comics: V2#1, June, 1996 - V2#4, Sept, 1996 ($2.50)

V2#1-4: Mike W. Barr scripts. 4-Painted-c	5.00

G. I. JOE
Image Comics/Devil's Due Publishing: 2001 - No. 43, May, 2005 ($2.95)

	GD 2.0	VG 4.0	FN 6.0	VF 8.0	VF/NM 9.0	NM- 9.2
1-Campbell-c; back-c painted by Beck; Blaylock-s	2	4	6	8	10	12

1-2nd printing with front & back covers switched	6.00
2,3	5.00
4-($3.50)	5.00
5-20,22-41: 6-SuperPatriot preview. 18-Brereton-a. 31-33-Wraith back-up; Caldwell-a	3.00
21-Silent issue; Zeck-a; two covers by Campbell and Zeck	4.00
42,43-($4.50)-Dawn of the Red Shadows; leads into G.I. Joe Vol. 2	4.50
...: Cobra Reborn (1/04, $4.95) Bradstreet/Jenkins-s	5.00
...: G. I. Joe Reborn (2/04, $4.95) Bradstreet-c/Bennett & Saltares-a	5.00
...: Malfunction (2003, $15.95) r/#11-15	16.00
...: M. I. A. (2002, $4.95) r/#1&2; Beck back-c from #1 on cover	5.00
...: Players & Pawns (11/04, $12.95) r/#28-33; cover gallery	13.00
...: Reborn (2004, $9.95) r/Cobra Reborn & G.I. Joe Reborn	13.00
...: Reckonings (2002, $12.95) r/#6-9; Zeck-c	15.00
...: Reinstated (2002, $14.95) r/#1-4	13.00
...: The Return of Serpentor (2002, $12.95) r/#16,22-25; cover gallery	13.00
...Vol. 8: The Rise of the Red Shadows (1/06, $14.95) r/#42,43 & prologue pgs. from #37-41	15.00

G. I. JOE (Volume 2) (Also see Snake Eyes: Declassified)
Devil's Due Publishing: No. 0, June, 2005 - No. 36, June, 2008 (25¢/$2.95/$3.50/$4.50)

0-(25¢-c) Casey-s/Caselli-a	3.00
1-4,7-19: (2.95): 1-Four covers; Casey-s/Caselli-a. 4-R. Black-c	3.00
5,6-($4.50) 6-Wraparound-c	4.50
20-29,31-35-($3.50) 25-Wraparound-c World War III part 1	3.50
30,36-($5.50) 30-Double-sized World War III part 6. 36-Double-sized WW III part 12	5.50
...America's Elite Vol. 1: The Newest War TPB ('06, $14.95) r/#0-5; cover gallery	15.00
...America's Elite Vol. 2: The Ties That Bind TPB (8/06, $15.95) r/#6-12; cover gallery	16.00
...America's Elite Vol. 3: In Sheep's Clothing TPB (2007, $18.99) r/#13-18; cover gallery	19.00
...America's Elite Vol. 4: Truth and Consequences TPB (9/07, $18.99) r/#19-24; covers	19.00
... Data Desk Handbook (10/05, $2.95) character profile pages	3.00
... Data Desk Handbook A-M (10/07, $5.50) character profile pages	5.50

Grade scale (both columns): **GD 2.0 · VG 4.0 · FN 6.0 · VF 8.0 · VF/NM 9.0 · NM- 9.2**

... Data Desk Handbook N-Z (11/07, $3.50) character profile pages — 3.50
...: Scarlett: Declassified (7/06, $4.95) Scarlett's childhood and training; Noto-c/a — 5.00
... Special Missions (2/06, $4.95) short stories and profile pages by various — 5.00
... Special Missions Antarctica (12/06, $4.95) short stories and profile pages by various — 5.00
... Special Missions Brazil (4/07, $5.50) short stories and profile pages by various — 5.00
... Special Missions: The Enemy (9/07, $5.50) two stories and profile pages by various — 5.50
... Special Missions Tokyo (9/06, $4.95) short stories and profile pages by various — 5.00
...: The Hunt For Cobra Commander (5/06, 25¢) short story and character profiles — 3.00

G.I. JOE
IDW Publishing: No. 0, Oct, 2008; No. 1, Jan, 2009 - No. 27, Feb, 2011 ($1.00/$3.99)

0-($1.00) Short stories by Dixon & Hama; creator interviews and character sketches — 3.00
1-27-($3.99) 1-Dixon-s/Atkins-a; covers by Johnson, Atkins and Dell'Otto — 4.00
...: Cobra Commander Tribute - 100-Page Spectacular 1 (4/11, $7.99) reprints — 8.00
...: Special - Helix (8/09, $3.99) Reed-s/Suitor-a — 4.00

G.I. JOE, VOLUME 2 (Prelude in G.I. Joe: Cobra Civil War #0) (Season 2 in indicia)
IDW Publishing: May, 2011 - No. 21, Jan, 2013 ($3.99)

1-21: 1-Dixon-s/Saltares-a; three covers by Howard. 9-Cobra Command Part 1 — 4.00

G.I. JOE VOLUME 3
IDW Publishing: Feb, 2013 - No. 15, Apr, 2014 ($3.99)

1-15-Van Lente-s/Kurth-a in most; multiple covers. 6-Igle-a. 12-15-Allor-s — 4.00

G.I. JOE VOLUME 4
IDW Publishing: Sept, 2014 - No. 8, Apr, 2015 ($3.99)

1-4-The Fall of G.I. Joe; Karen Traviss-s/Steve Kurth-a; multiple covers — 4.00

G.I. JOE (Follows the Revolution x-over)
IDW Publishing: Jan, 2017 - No. 9, Oct, 2017 ($3.99)

1-9: 1-4-Reconstruction; Dreadnoks app.; Milonogiannis-a; multiple covers — 4.00
... First Strike 1 (9/17, $3.99) Tie-in to First Strike x-over series; Kyriazis-a; 3 covers — 4.00
...: Revolution 1 (10/16, $3.99) Tie-in to Revolution x-over; Sitterson-s/Milonogiannis-a — 4.00

G.I. JOE
IDW Publishing: Sept, 2019 - No. 5 ($3.99)

1-5: 1-Intro. Tiger; Allor-s/Evenhuis-a; multiple covers. 4-Walter-a — 4.00
...: Castle Fall (11/20, $7.99) Allor-s/Evenhuis-a — 8.00

G.I. JOE AND THE TRANSFORMERS
Marvel Comics Group: Jan, 1987 - No. 4, Apr, 1987 (Limited series)

	GD	VG	FN	VF	VF/NM	NM-
1	3	6	9	14	19	24
2-4	1	2	3	5	6	8

G.I. JOE, A REAL AMERICAN HERO (...Starring Snake-Eyes on-c #135 on)
Marvel Comics Group: June, 1982 - No. 155, Dec, 1994

	GD	VG	FN	VF	VF/NM	NM-
1-Printed on Baxter paper; based on Hasbro toy	10	20	30	69	147	225
2-Printed on regular paper; 1st app. Kwinn	6	12	18	38	69	100
3-10: 6-1st app. Oktober Guard	3	6	9	16	23	30
11-20: 11-Intro Airborne. 13-1st Destro (cameo). 14-1st full app. Destro. 15-1st app. Major Blood. 16-1st app. Cover Girl and Trip-Wire	2	4	6	13	18	22
21-1st app. Storm Shadow; silent issue	9	18	27	63	129	195
22-1st app. Duke and Roadblock	4	8	12	27	44	60
23,24,28-30,60-Todd McFarlane-a	4	8	12	27	40	55
25-1st full app. Zartan, 1st app of Cutter, Deep Six, Mutt and Junkyard, and The Dreadnoks	4	8	12	27	40	55
26,27-Origin Snake-Eyes parts 1 & 2	3	6	9	17	25	34
31-50: 31-1st Spirit Iron-Knife. 32-1st Blowtorch, Lady J, Recondo, Ripcord. 33-New headquarters. 40-1st app. of Shipwreck, Barbecue. 48-1st app. Sgt. Slaughter. 49-1st app. of Lift-Ticket, Slipstream, Leatherneck, Serpentor	1	2	3	5	6	8
51-59,61-90						6.00
91,92,94-99: 94-96-Snake Eyes Trilogy	1	2	3	5	6	9
93-Snake-Eyes' face first revealed	3	6	9	15	22	28
100,135-138: 135-138-($1.75)-Bagged w/trading card. 138-Transformers app.	2	4	6	10	14	18
101-122,124-133: 101-New Oktober Guard app. 110-1st Garney-a. 117- Debut G.I. Joe Ninja Force	2	4	6	8	10	12
123,134: 123-Cobra Commander. 134-Snake-Eyes	3	6	9	14	20	25
139-142-New Transformers app.	3	6	9	14	20	25
143,145-149: 145-Intro. G.I. Joe Star Brigade	2	4	6	10	14	18
144-Origin Snake-Eyes	3	6	9	14	20	26
150-Low print thru #155	3	6	9	21	33	45
151-154: 152-30th Anniversary (of doll) issue, original G.I. Joe General Joseph Colton app. (also app. in #151)	3	6	9	19	30	40
155-Last issue	9	18	27	62	126	190
All 2nd printings						4.00
Special #1 (2/95, $1.50) r/#60 w/McFarlane-a. Cover swipe from Spider-Man #1	10	20	30	69	147	225
Special Treasury Edition (1982)-r/#1	4	8	12	23	37	50

Volume 1 TPB (4/02, $24.95) r/#1-10; new cover by Michael Golden — 35.00
Volume 2 TPB (6/02, $24.95) r/#11-20; new cover by J. Scott Campbell — 35.00
Volume 3 TPB (2002, $24.99) r/#21-30; new cover by J. Scott Campbell — 35.00
Volume 4 TPB (2002, $25.99) r/#31-40; new cover by J. Scott Campbell — 35.00
Volume 5 TPB (2002, $24.99) r/#42-50; new cover by J. Scott Campbell — 35.00
Yearbook 1-4: (3/85-3/88)-r/#1; Golden-c/back-c. 2-Golden-c/a. 3-Zeck-c; silent story — 4.00
Yearbook #1 Reprint (1/21, $3.99) Reprints #1 with new cover by Netho Diaz — 4.00
Yearbook #2 Reprint (6/21, $5.99) Reprints #2 by Hama-s/Golden-a — 6.00
Yearbook #3 Reprint (9/21, $5.99) Reprints #3 silent story by Hama-s/Wagner-a — 6.00
Yearbook #4 Reprint (12/21, $5.99) Reprints #4 by Hama-s/Trimpe-a — 6.00
NOTE: *Garney* a(p)-110. *Golden* c-23, 29, 34, 36. *Heath* a-24. *Rogers* a(p)-75, 77-82, 84, 86; c-77.

G.I. JOE, A REAL AMERICAN HERO
IDW Publishing: No. 156, Jul, 2010 - No. 300, Nov, 2022 ($3.99)

156-199-Continuation of story from Marvel series #155 (1994); Hama-s — 4.00
200-(3/14, $5.99) Multiple covers; bonus interview with artist SL Gallant — 6.00
201-249,251-254,256-299: 201-214-Hama-s/Gallant-a. 213-Death of Snake Eyes. 216-218-Villanelli-a. 219-225-Cobra World Order — 4.00
250-($4.99) Hama-s/Diaz-a; Dawn of the Arashikage conclusion — 5.00
255-($4.99) Hama-s/Tolibao-a; IDW's 100th issue; Snake Eyes origin — 5.00
300-($6.99) Hama-s/Gallant-a; wraparound main-c — 7.00

Annual 2012 (2/12, $7.99) Hama-s; Frenz, Wagner & Trimpe-a — 8.00
... #1 Anniversary Edition (3/18, $3.99) r/#1(1982); silver foil cover logo — 4.00
...: Cobraaaa! (3/22, $7.99) Reprints of Cobra's most notorious stories; Daniel Maine-c — 8.00
... Cobra World Order Prelude (10/15, $3.99) Starts seven-part bi-weekly event — 4.00
... 40th Anniversary Special 1 (4/22, $7.99) Pages of #21 redrawn by current artists, plus reprint of original 1984 story; bonus sketch pages — 8.00
Hundred Penny Press: G.I. Joe: Real American Hero #1 (3/11, $1.00) r/#1 (1982) — 3.00
... Yearbook 2019 (1/19, $4.99) Dawn Moreno, new Snake Eyes app.; Hama-s — 5.00
... Yo, Joe! (2/22, $7.99) Reprints of greatest adventures; Daniel Maine-c — 8.00

G.I. JOE, A REAL AMERICAN HERO
Image Comics (Skybound): No. 301, Nov, 2023 - Present ($3.99)

301-304-Hama-s/Monneyham-a — 4.00
... #1 Larry Hama Cut (11/23, $3.99) Reprints 1982's #1 issue with Hama's unaltered script — 4.00

G.I. JOE, A REAL AMERICAN HERO – SATURDAY MORNING ADVENTURES
IDW Publishing: Feb, 2022 - No. 4, Jun, 2022 ($3.99, limited series)

1-4-Art style of the cartoon; Burnham-s/Schoening-a — 4.00

G.I. JOE, A REAL AMERICAN HERO: SILENT OPTION
IDW Publishing: Sept, 2018 - No. 4, Dec, 2018 ($4.99, limited series)

1-4-Hama-s/Diaz-a; spotlight on Snake Eyes (Dawn Moreno); Agent Helix back-up story — 5.00

G.I. JOE, A REAL AMERICAN HERO VS. THE SIX MILLION DOLLAR MAN
IDW Publishing: Feb, 2018 - No. 4, May, 2018 ($3.99, limited series)

1-4-Ferrier-s/Gallant-a; 5 covers — 4.00

G.I. JOE: BATTLE FILES
Image Comics: 2002 - No. 3, 2002 ($5.95)

1-3-Profile pages of characters and history; Beck-a — 6.00

G.I. JOE: COBRA (#5-on is continuation of G.I. Joe: Cobra II #4, not G.I. Joe: Cobra #4)
IDW Publishing: Mar, 2009 - No. 13, Feb, 2011 ($3.99)

1-4,5-13: 1-4-Gage & Costa-s/Fuso-a/covers by Chaykin & Fuso. 5-8-Carrera-a — 4.00
Hundred Penny Press: G.I. Joe: Cobra #1 (4/11, $1.00) r/#1 with Chaykin-c — 3.00
... Special (9/09, $3.99) Costa-s/Fuso-a — 4.00
... Special 2 - Chameleon (9/10, $3.99) Costa-s/Fuso-a — 4.00
... II (1/10 - No. 4, 4/10, $3.99) 1-4-Gage & Costa-s/Fuso-a/covers by Chaykin & Fuso — 4.00

G.I. JOE: COBRA CIVIL WAR
IDW Publishing: No. 0, Apr, 2011 ($3.99)

0-Prelude to G.I. Joe, Cobra & Snake Eyes Civil War series; four covers — 4.00
0-Muzzle Flash Edition (6/11, price not shown) r/#0 in B&W and partial color — 4.00

G.I. JOE: COBRA VOLUME 2 (Prelude in G.I. Joe: Cobra Civil War #0)
IDW Publishing: May, 2011 - No. 9, Jan, 2012 ($3.99)(Re-named Cobra with #10)

1-9: Multiple covers on all. 1-4-Costa/Fuso-a — 4.00

G.I. JOE COMICS MAGAZINE
Marvel Comics Group: Dec, 1986 - No. 13, 1988 ($1.50, digest-size)

	GD	VG	FN	VF	VF/NM	NM-
1-G.I. Joe reprints	3	6	9	14	20	25
2-13: G.I. Joe-r	1	3	4	6	8	10

G.I. JOE DECLASSIFIED
Devil's Due Publishing: June, 2006 - No. 3, 2006 ($4.95, bi-monthly)

1-3-New "early" adventures of the team; Hama-s; Quinn & DeLandro-a; var-c for each — 5.00
TPB (1/07, $18.99) r/#1-3; cover gallery — 19.00

G.I. JOE: DEVIATIONS
IDW Publishing: Mar, 2016 ($4.99, one-shot)

1-Paul Allor-s/Corey Lewis-a; What If Cobra defeated G.I. Joe and ruled the world — 5.00

G.I. JOE: DREADNOKS: DECLASSIFIED
Devil's Due Publishing: Nov, 2006 - No. 3, Mar, 2007 ($4.95/$4.99/$5.50, bi-monthly)

1,2-Secret history of the team; Blaylock-s; var-c for each — 5.00
3-($5.50) — 5.50

G.I. JOE EUROPEAN MISSIONS (Action Force in indicia) (Series reprints Action Force)
Marvel Comics Ltd. (British): Jun, 1988 - No. 15, Dec, 1989 ($1.50/$1.75)

	GD	VG	FN	VF	VF/NM	NM-
1,3-Snake Eyes & Storm Shadow-c/s	2	4	6	8	10	12
2,4-15						6.00

G.I. JOE: FRONT LINE
Image Comics: 2002 - No. 18, Dec, 2003 ($2.95)

1-18: 1-Jurgens-a/Hama-s. 1-Two covers by Dorman & Sharpe. 7,8-Harris-c — 3.00
...Vol. 1 - The Mission That Never Was TPB (2003, $14.95) r/ #1-4; script pages — 15.00
...Vol. 2 - Icebound TPB (3/04, $12.95) r/ #5-8 — 13.00
...Vol. 3 - History Repeating TPB (4/04, $9.95) r/#11-14 — 10.00
...Vol. 4 - One-Shots TPB (5/04, $15.95) r/#9,10,15-18 — 16.00

G.I. JOE: FUTURE NOIR SPECIAL
IDW Publishing: Nov, 2010 - No. 2, Dec, 2010 ($3.99, limited series, greytone art)

1,2-Schmidt-s/Bevilacqua-a — 4.00

G.I. JOE: HEARTS & MINDS
IDW Publishing: May, 2010 - No. 5, Sept, 2010 ($3.99)

1-5: Short origin stories; Brooks-s; Chaykin & Fuso-a — 4.00

G.I. JOE: INFESTATION (Zombie x-over with Star Trek, Ghostbusters & Transformers)
IDW Publishing: Mar, 2011 - No. 2, Mar, 2011 ($3.99, limited series)

1,2-Timpano-a; covers by Timpano and Snyder III — 4.00

G.I. JOE: MASTER & APPRENTICE
Image Comics: May, 2004 - No. 4, Aug, 2004 ($2.95)

1-4-Caselli-a/Jerwa-a — 3.00

G.I. JOE: MASTER & APPRENTICE 2
Image Comics: Feb, 2005 - No. 4, May, 2005, $2.95, limited series)

1-4: Stevens & Vedder-a/Jerwa-a — 3.00

G.I. JOE MOVIE PREQUEL...
IDW Publishing: Mar, 2009 - No. 4, June, 2009 ($3.99, limited series)

1-4-Two covers on each: 1-Duke. 2-Destro. 3-The Baroness. 4-SnakeEyes — 4.00

G.I. Joe, A Real American Hero #22 © Hasbro

G.I. Joe: Cobra V2 #6 © Hasbro

The Gimmick #3 © Starer & Gogou

	GD 2.0	VG 4.0	FN 6.0	VF 8.0	VF/NM 9.0	NM- 9.2

G.I. JOE: OPERATION HISS
IDW Publishing: Feb, 2010 - No. 5, Jun, 2010 ($3.99, limited series)
1-5: 1-4-Reed-s/Padilla-a; covers by Corroney & Padilla. 5-Guglotta-a — 4.00

G. I. JOE ORDER OF BATTLE, THE
Marvel Comics Group: Dec, 1986 - No. 4, Mar, 1987 (limited series)
1-4 — 6.00

G.I. JOE: ORIGINS
IDW Publishing: Feb, 2009 - No. 23, Jan, 2011 ($3.99)
1-23: 1-Origin of Snake Eyes; Hama-s. 12-Templesmith-a. 19-Benitez-a — 4.00

G.I. JOE: RELOADED
Image Comics: Mar, 2004 -No. 14, Apr, 2005 ($2.95)
1-14: 1-3-Granov-c/Ney Rieber-s. 5,6-Rieber-s/Saltares-a. 8-Origin of the Baroness — 4.00
Vol. 1 In the Name of Patriotism (11/04, $12.95) r/#1-6; cover gallery — 13.00

G.I. JOE: RISE OF COBRA MOVIE ADAPTATION
IDW Publishing: July, 2009 - No. 4, July, 2009 ($3.99, weekly limited series)
1-4-Tipton-s/Maloney-a; two covers — 4.00

G.I. JOE: SIERRA MUERTE
IDW Publishing: Feb, 2019 - No. 3, Apr, 2019 ($4.99, limited series)
1-3-Michel Fiffe-s/a — 5.00

G.I. JOE SIGMA 6 (Based on the cartoon TV series)
Devil's Due Publishing: Dec, 2005 - No. 6, May, 2006 ($2.95, limited series)
1-6-Andrew Daab-s — 3.00
TPB Vol. 1 (10/06, $10.95, 8-1/4" x 5-3/4") r/#1-6; cover gallery — 11.00

G.I. JOE: SNAKE EYES
IDW Publishing: Oct, 2009 - No. 4, Jan, 2010 ($3.99, limited series)
1-4-Ray Park & Kevin VanHook-s/Lee Ferguson-a; two covers — 4.00

G.I. JOE: SNAKE EYES, AGENT OF COBRA
IDW Publishing: Jan, 2015 - No. 5, May, 2015 ($3.99, limited series)
1-5-Costa-s/Villanelli-a — 4.00

G.I. JOE: SNAKE EYES, VOLUME 2 (Continues as Snake Eyes #8)
IDW Publishing: May, 2011 - No. 7, Nov, 2011 ($3.99)
1-7-Dixon-s/Atkins & Padilla-a; two covers — 4.00

G. I. JOE SPECIAL MISSIONS (Indicia title: Special Missions)
Marvel Comics Group: Oct, 1986 - No. 28, Dec, 1989 ($1.00)

1	1	3	4	6	8	10
2-20						5.00
21-28						6.00

G.I. JOE: SPECIAL MISSIONS
IDW Publishing: Mar, 2013 - No. 14, Apr, 2014($3.99)
1-14: 1-4-Dixon-s/Gulacy-a; covers by Chen and Gulacy. 5-7-Rosado-a. 10-13-Gulacy-a — 4.00

G. I. JOE: THE COBRA FILES
IDW Publishing: Apr, 2013 - No. 9, Dec, 2013 ($3.99)
1-9: 1-Costa-s/Fuso-a; multiple covers. 5,6-Dell'edera-a — 4.00

G.I. JOE 2 MOVIE PREQUEL...
IDW Publishing: Feb, 2012 - No. 4, Apr, 2012 ($3.99, limited series)
1-4-Barber-s/Navarro & Rojo-a — 4.00

G.I. JOE VS. THE TRANSFORMERS
Image Comics: Jun, 2003 - No. 6, Nov, 2003 ($2.95, limited series)
1-Blaylock-s/Mike Miller-a; three covers by Miller, Campbell & Andrews — 4.00
1-2nd printing; black cover with logo; back-c by Campbell — 3.00
2-6: 2-Two covers by Miller & Brooks — 3.00
TPB (3/04, $15.95) r/series; sketch pages — 16.00

G.I. JOE VS. THE TRANSFORMERS (Volume 2)
Devil's Due Publ.: Sept, 2004 - No. 4, Dec, 2004 ($4.95/$2.95, limited series)
1-($4.95) Three covers; Jolley-s/Su & Seeley-a — 5.00
2-4-($2.95) Two covers by Su & Pollina — 3.00
Vol. 2 TPB (4/05, $14.95) r/series; interview with creators; sketch pages and covers — 15.00

G.I. JOE VS. THE TRANSFORMERS (Volume 3) THE ART OF WAR
Devil's Due Publ.: Mar, 2006 - No. 5, July, 2006 ($2.95, limited series)
1-5: 1-Three covers; Seeley-s/Ng-a — 3.00
TPB (8/06, $14.95) r/series; cover gallery — 15.00

G.I. JOE VS. THE TRANSFORMERS (Volume 4) BLACK HORIZON
Devil's Due Publ.: Jan, 2007 - No. 2, Feb, 2007 ($5.50, limited series)

	GD 2.0	VG 4.0	FN 6.0	VF 8.0	VF/NM 9.0	NM- 9.2

1,2: 1-Three covers; Seeley-s/Wildman-a. 2-Two covers — 5.50

G. I. JUNIORS (See Harvey Hits No. 86,91,95,98,101,104,107,110,112,114,116,118,120,122)

GILES SEASON 11 (From Buffy the Vampire Slayer)
Dark Horse Comics: Feb, 2018 - No. 4, May, 2018 ($3.99, limited series)
1-4-Whedon & Alexander-s/Jon Lam-a — 5.00

GILGAMESH II
DC Comics: 1989 - No. 4, 1989 ($3.95, limited series, prestige format, mature)
1-4: Starlin-c/a/scripts — 5.00

GIL THORP
Dell Publishing Co.: May-July, 1963

1-Caniff-ish art		4	8	12	23	37	50

GIMMICK, THE
AHOY Comics: 2023 - No. 6, 2023 ($3.99)
1-6-Joanne Starer-s/Elena Gogou-a — 4.00

GINGER
Archie Publications: 1951 - No. 10, Summer, 1954

1-Teenage humor; headlights-c	252	504	756	1613	2757	3900
2-(1952)	40	80	120	246	411	575
3-6: 6-(Sum/53)	23	46	69	136	223	310
7-10-Katy Keene app.	41	82	123	256	428	600

GINGER FOX (Also see The World of Ginger Fox)
Comico: Sept, 1988 - No. 4, Dec, 1988 ($1.75, limited series)
1-4: Part photo-c on all — 4.00

GIRL
DC Comics (Vertigo Verite): Jul, 1996 - No. 3, 1996 ($2.50, lim. series, mature)
1-3: Peter Milligan scripts; Fegredo-c/a — 4.00

GIRL COMICS (Becomes Girl Confessions No. 13 on)
Marvel/Atlas Comics(CnPC): Oct, 1949 - No. 12, Jan, 1952 (#1-4: 52 pgs.)

1-Photo-c	39	78	117	240	395	550
2-Kubert-a; photo-c	21	42	63	122	199	275
3-Everett-a; Liz Taylor photo-c	43	86	129	271	461	650
4-11: 4-Photo-c. 10-12-Sol Brodsky-c	18	36	54	103	162	220
12-Krigstein-a; Al Hartley-c	18	36	54	107	169	230

GIRL COMICS
Marvel Comics: May, 2010 - No. 3, Sept, 2010 ($4.99, limited series)
1-3-Anthology of short stories by women creators. 1-Conner-c. 2-Thompson-c. 3-Chen-c — 5.00

GIRL CONFESSIONS (Formerly Girl Comics)
Atlas Comics (CnPC/ZPC): No. 13, Mar, 1952 - No. 35, Aug, 1954

13-Everett-a	21	42	63	124	202	280
14,15,19,20	17	34	51	98	154	210
16-18-Everett-a	19	38	57	111	178	240
21-35: Robinson-a	15	30	45	85	130	175

GIRL CRAZY
Dark Horse Comics: May, 1996 - No. 3, July, 1996 ($2.95, B&W, limited series)
1-3: Gilbert Hernandez-a/scripts — 4.00

GIRL FROM U.N.C.L.E., THE (TV) (Also see The Man From...)
Gold Key: Jan, 1967 - No. 5, Oct, 1967

1-McWilliams-a; Stephanie Powers photo front/back-c & pin-ups (no ads, 12c)	7	14	21	46	86	125
2-5-Leonard Swift-Courier No. 5. 4-Back-c pin-up	5	10	15	33	57	80

GIRL IN THE BAY, THE
Dark Horse Comics (Berger Books): Feb, 2019 - No. 4, May, 2019 ($3.99)
1-4-J.M. DeMatteis-s/Corin Howell-a — 4.00

GIRLS
Image Comics: May, 2005 - No. 24, Apr, 2007 ($2.95/$2.99)
1-Luna Brothers-s/a/c — 4.00
2-24 — 3.00
Image Firsts: Girls #1 (4/10, $1.00) r/#1 with "Image Firsts" cover logo — 3.00
...Vol. 1: Conception TPB (2005, $14.99) r/#1-6 — 15.00
...Vol. 2: Emergence TPB (2006, $14.99) r/#7-12 — 15.00
...Vol. 3: Survival TPB (2006, $14.99) r/#13-18 — 15.00
...Vol. 4: Extinction TPB (2007, $14.99) r/#19-24 — 15.00

GIRLS' FUN & FASHION MAGAZINE (Formerly Polly Pigtails)
Parents' Magazine Institute: V5#44, Jan, 1950 - V5#48, Sept., 1950

V5#44	9	18	27	52	69	85

	GD 2.0	VG 4.0	FN 6.0	VF 8.0	VF/NM 9.0	NM- 9.2

45-48   8   16   24   42   54   65

GIRLS IN LOVE
Fawcett Publications: May, 1950 - No. 2, July, 1950

	GD 2.0	VG 4.0	FN 6.0	VF 8.0	VF/NM 9.0	NM- 9.2
1-Photo-c	15	30	45	90	140	190
2-Photo-c	13	26	39	72	101	130

GIRLS IN LOVE
Quality Comics Group: No. 46, Sept, 1955 - No. 57, Dec, 1956

46	15	30	45	88	137	185
47-53,55,56	14	28	42	75	108	140
54- 'Commie' story	15	30	45	84	127	170
57-Matt Baker-c/a	21	42	63	126	206	285

GIRLS IN WHITE (See Harvey Comics Hits No. 58)

GIRLS' LIFE (Patsy Walker's Own Magazine For Girls!)
Atlas Comics (BFP): Jan, 1954 - No. 6, Nov, 1954

1	26	52	78	154	252	350
2-Al Hartley-c	16	32	48	92	144	195
3-6	15	30	45	86	133	180

GIRLS' LOVE STORIES
National Comics (Signal Publ. No. 9-65/Arleigh No. 83-117): Aug-Sept, 1949 - No. 180, Nov-Dec, 1971 (No. 1-13: 52 pgs.)

1-Toth, Kinstler-a, 8 pgs. each; photo-c	97	194	291	621	1061	1500
2-Kinstler-a?	43	86	129	271	461	650
3-10: 1-9-Photo-c	28	56	84	168	274	380
11-20	22	44	66	128	209	290
21-33: 21-Kinstler-a. 33-Last pre-code (1-2/55)	15	30	45	90	140	190
34-50	13	26	39	72	101	130
51-70	11	22	33	62	86	110
71-99: 83-Last 10¢ issue	5	10	15	34	60	85
100	5	10	15	35	63	90
101-146: 113-117-April O'Day app.	4	8	12	23	37	50
147-151- "Confessions" serial. 150-Wood-a	4	8	12	25	40	55
152-160,171-179	3	6	9	18	28	38
161-170 (52 pgs.)	4	8	12	25	40	55
180 Last issue	4	8	12	23	37	50

Ashcan (8-9/49) not distributed to newsstands   (a FN/VF copy sold for $836.50 in 2012)

GIRLS OF DIMENSION 13, THE
AfterShock Comics: Apr, 2021 - No. 5, Aug, 2021 ($4.99/$3.99, limited series)

1-($4.99) Graham Nolan-s/Bret Blevins-a						5.00
2-5-($3.99)						4.00

GIRLS' ROMANCES
National Periodical Publ.(Signal Publ. No. 7-79/Arleigh No. 84): Feb-Mar, 1950 - No. 160, Oct, 1971 (No. 1-11: 52 pgs.)

1-Photo-c	81	162	243	518	884	1250
2-Photo-c; Toth-a	40	80	120	244	402	560
3-10: 3-6-Photo-c	27	54	81	162	266	370
11,12,14-20	20	40	60	115	185	255
13-Toth-c	21	42	63	124	202	280
21-31: 31-Last pre-code (2-3/55)	15	30	45	86	133	180
32-50	7	14	21	49	92	135
51-99: 78-Panel inspired a famous Roy Lichtenstein painting. 80-Last 10¢ issue	5	10	15	35	63	90
100	6	12	18	37	66	95
101-108,110-120: 105-Panel inspired a famous Roy Lichtenstein painting	4	8	12	25	40	55
109-Beatles-c/story	20	40	60	138	307	475
121-133,135-140	4	8	12	23	37	50
134-Neal Adams-c (splash pg. is same as-c)	6	12	18	43	79	115
141-158	3	6	9	19	30	40
159,160-52 pgs.	5	10	15	31	53	75

GIRL WHO KICKED THE HORNETS NEST, THE
DC Comics (Vertigo): 2015 ($29.99, HC graphic novel, dustjacket)

HC-Adaptation of the novel; Mina-s/Mutti-a & Fuso-a/Bermejo-c						30.00

GIRL WHO WOULD BE DEATH, THE
DC Comics (Vertigo): Dec, 1998 - No. 4, March, 1999 ($2.50, lim. series)

1-4-Kiernan-s/Ormston-a						4.00

GIRL WITH THE DRAGON TATTOO, THE
DC Comics (Vertigo): Book One, 2012; Book Two, 2013 ($19.99, HC graphic novels)

Book One HC-First part of the adaptation of the novel; Mina-s/Manco-a/Bermejo-c						20.00
Book Two HC-Second part of the adaptation; Mina-s/Manco-a/Bermejo-c						20.00

G. I. SWEETHEARTS (Formerly Diary Loves; Girls In Love #46 on)
Quality Comics Group: No. 32, June, 1953 - No. 45, May, 1955

32	16	32	48	94	147	200
33-45: 44-Last pre-code (3/55)	13	26	39	74	105	135

G.I. TALES (Formerly Sgt. Barney Barker No. 1-3)
Atlas Comics (MCI): No. 4, Feb, 1957 - No. 6, July, 1957

4-Severin-a(4)	16	32	48	94	147	200
5	14	28	42	78	112	145
6-Orlando, Powell, & Woodbridge-a	14	28	42	80	115	150

GIVE ME LIBERTY (Also see Dark Horse Presents Fifth Anniversary Special, Dark Horse Presents #100-4, Happy Birthday Martha Washington, Martha Washington Goes to War, Martha Washington Stranded In Space & San Diego Comicon Comics #2)
Dark Horse Comics: June, 1990 - No. 4, 1991 ($4.95, limited series, 52 pgs.)

1-4: 1st app. Martha Washington; Frank Miller scripts, Dave Gibbons-c/a in all						6.00

G. I. WAR BRIDES
Superior Publishers Ltd.: Apr, 1954 - No. 8, June, 1955

1	21	42	63	124	202	280
2	15	30	45	83	124	165
3-8: 4-Kamenesque-a; lingerie panels	14	28	42	81	118	155

G. I. WAR TALES
National Periodical Publications: Mar-Apr, 1973 - No. 4, Oct-Nov, 1973

1-Reprints in all; dinosaur-c/s	4	8	12	28	47	65
2-N. Adams-a(r)	3	6	9	16	23	30
3,4: 4-Krigstein-a(r)	3	6	9	15	22	28

NOTE: *Drucker* a-3r, 4r. *Heath* a-4r. *Kubert* a-2, 3; c-4r.

GIZMO
Mirage Studios: 1986 - No. 6, July, 1987 ($1.50, B&W)

1-6						4.00

G.L.A. (Great Lakes Avengers)(Also see GLX-Mas Special)
Marvel Comics: June, 2005 - No. 4, Sept, 2005 ($2.99, limited series)

1-4-Slott-s/Pelletier-a						3.00
...: Misassembled TPB (2005, $14.99) r/#1-4, West Coast Avengers #46 (1st app.) and Marvel Super-Heroes #8 (1st app. Squirrel Girl; Ditko-a)						15.00

GLADSTONE COMIC ALBUM
Gladstone: 1987 - No. 28, 1990 ($5.95/$9.95, 8-1/2x11")(All Mickey albums are by Gottfredson)

1-25: 1-Uncle Scrooge; Barks-r; Beck-c. 2-Donald Duck; r/F.C. #108 by Barks. 3-Mickey Mouse-r by Gottfredson. 4-Uncle Scrooge; r/F.C. #456 by Barks w/unedited story. 5-Donald Duck Advs.; r/F.C. #199. 6-Uncle Scrooge-r by Barks. 7-Donald Duck-r by Barks. 8-Mickey Mouse-r. 9-Bambi; r/F.C. #186? 10-Donald Duck Advs.; r/F.C. #275. 11-Uncle Scrooge; r/U.S. #4. 12-Donald And Daisy; r/F.C. #1055, WDC&S. 13-Donald Duck Advs.; r/F.C. #408. 14-Uncle Scrooge; Barks-r/U.S #21. 15-Donald And Gladstone; Barks-r. 16-Donald Duck Advs.; r/F.C. #238. 17-Mickey Mouse strip-r (The World of Tomorrow, The Pirate Ghost Ship). 18-Donald Duck and the Junior Woodchucks; Barks-r. 19-Uncle Scrooge; r/U.S. #12. 20-Rosa-c. 21-F.C. #386; Barks-c/a-r. 21-Donald Duck Family; Barks-r/D.D. #26 w/unedited story. 23-Donald Duck; Barks-r/D.D. #26 w/unedited story. 24-Uncle Scrooge; Barks-r; Rosa-c. 25-D. Duck; Barks-c/a-r/F.C. #367						

    1   3   4   6   8   10

26-28: All have $9.95-c. 26-Mickey & Donald; Gottfredson-c/a(r). 27-Donald Duck; r/WDC&S by Barks. Barks painted-c. 28-Uncle Scrooge & Donald Duck; Rosa-c/a (4 stories)	1	3	4	6	8	10

Special 1-7: 1 ('89-'90, $9.95/13.95)-1-Donald Duck Finds Pirate Gold; r/F.C. #9. 2 ('89, $8.95)-Uncle Scrooge and Donald Duck; r/Uncle Scrooge #5; Rosa-c. 3 ('89, $8.95)-Mickey Mouse strip-r. 4 ('89, $11.95)-Uncle Scrooge; Rosa-c/a-r/Son of the Sun from U.S. #219 plus Barks-r/U.S. 5 ('90, $11.95)-Donald Duck Advs.; Barks-r/U.S. #282 & 422 plus Barks painted-c. 6 ('90, $12.95)-Uncle Scrooge; Barks-c/a-r/Uncle Scrooge. 7 ('90, $13.95)-Mickey Mouse; Gottfredson strip-r	2	4	6	9	11	14

GLADSTONE COMIC ALBUM (2nd Series)(Also see The Original Dick Tracy)
Gladstone Publishing: 1990 ($5.95, 8-1/2 x 11," stiff-c, 52 pgs.)

1,2-The Original Dick Tracy. 2-Origin of the 2-way wrist radio						6.00
3-D Tracy Meets the Mole-r by Gould ($6.95).	1	2	3	5	6	8

GLAMOROUS ROMANCES (Formerly Dotty)
Ace Magazines (A. A. Wyn): No. 41, July, 1949 - No. 90, Oct, 1956 (Photo-c 68-90)

41-Dotty app.	21	42	63	124	202	280
42-72,74-80: 44-Begin 52 pg. issues. 45,50-61-Painted-c. 80-Last pre-code (2/55)	15	30	45	85	130	175
73-L.B. Cole-r/All Love #27	15	30	45	86	133	180
81-90	14	28	42	78	112	145

GLAMOURPUSS
Aardvark-Vanaheim Inc.: Apr, 2008 - No. 26, Jul, 2012 ($3.00, B&W)

1-26: 1-Two covers: Dave Sim-s/a/c. 9,10-Gene Colan-c. 11-Heath-c. 19-Allred-c						3.00
1-Comics Industry Preview Edition (Diamond Dateline supplement)						4.00

GLOBAL FREQUENCY
DC Comics (WildStorm): Dec, 2002 - No. 12, Aug, 2004 ($2.95, limited series)

1-12-Warren Ellis-s. 1-Leach-a. 2-Fabry-a. 3-Dillon-a. 5-Muth-a. 7-Bisley-a. 12-Ha-a						3.00
1-RRP Edition variant-c; promotional giveaway for retailers (200 printed)						4.00
...: Detonation Radio TPB (2005, $14.95) r/#7-12						15.00
...: Planet Ablaze TPB (2003, $14.95) r/#1-6						15.00

GLORY
Image Comics (Extreme Studios)/Maximum Press: Mar, 1995 - No. 22, Apr, 1997 ($2.50)

0-Deodato-c/a. 1-(3/95)-Deodato-a						4.00
1A-Variant-c						5.00
2-11,13-22: 4-Variant-c by Quesada & Palmiotti. 5-Bagged w/Youngblood gaming card. 7,8-Deodato-c/a(p). 8-Babewatch x-over. 9-Cruz-c; Extreme Destroyer Pt. 5; polybagged w/card. 10-Angela/app. 11-Deodato-c.						4.00
12-($3.50)-Photo-c						5.00
...& Friends Christmas Special (12/95, $2.50) Deodato-c						4.00
...& Friends Lingerie Special (9/95, $2.95) Pin-ups w/photos; photo-c; variant-c exists						4.00
.../Angela: Angels in Hell (4/96, $2.50) Flip book w/Darkchylde #1						4.00
.../Avengelyne (10/95, $3.95) 1-Chromium-c, 1-Regular-c.						5.00
Trade Paperback (1995, $9.95)-r/#1-4						10.00

GLORY (Continues numbering from the 1995-1997 series)
Image Comics: Feb, 2012 - No. 34, Apr, 2013 ($2.99/$3.99)

23-28-Joe Keatinge-s/Ross Campbell-a. 23-Supreme app.						3.00
29-34-($3.99)						4.00

GLORY
Awesome Comics: Mar, 1999 ($2.50)

0-Liefeld-c; story and sketch pages						4.00

GLORY (ALAN MOORE'S...)
Avatar Press: Dec, 2001 - No. 2 ($3.50)

Preview-(9/01, $1.99) B&W pages and cover art; Alan Moore-s						3.00
0-Four regular covers						3.50
1,2: 1-Alan Moore-s/Mychaels & Gebbie-a; nine covers by various. 2-Five covers						3.50

GLORY & FRIENDS BIKINI FEST
Image Comics (Extreme): Sept, 1995 - No. 2, Oct, 1995 ($2.50, limited series)

1,2: 1-Photo-c; centerfold photo; pin-ups						4.00

GLORY/CELESTINE: DARK ANGEL
Image Comics/Maximum Press (Extreme Studios): Sept, 1996 - No. 3, Nov, 1996 ($2.50)

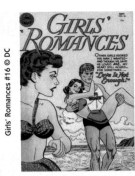

Girls' Romances #16 © DC

Glory #7 © Rob Liefeld

Godland #28 © Casey & Scioli

	GD 2.0	VG 4.0	FN 6.0	VF 8.0	VF/NM 9.0	NM- 9.2		GD 2.0	VG 4.0	FN 6.0	VF 8.0	VF/NM 9.0	NM- 9.2

1-3 ... 4.00

GLOW (Gorgeous Ladies of Wrestling)(Based on the Netflix series)
IDW Publishing: Mar, 2019 - No. 4, Jun, 2019 ($3.99, limited series)
1-4-Tini Howard-s/Hannah Templer-a; multiple covers on each ... 4.00
...: Summer Special (7/19, $3.99) Devin Grayson-s/Lisa Sterle-a ... 4.00

GLOW VS THE BABYFACE (Gorgeous Ladies of Wrestling)(Based on the Netflix series)
IDW Publishing: Nov, 2019 - No. 4, Feb, 2020 ($3.99, limited series)
1-4-Garcia & Mendez-s/Templer-a; multiple covers on each ... 4.00

GLX-MAS SPECIAL (Great Lakes Avengers)
Marvel Comics: Feb, 2006 ($3.99, one-shot)
1-Christmas themed stories by various incl. Haley, Templeton, Grist, Wieringo ... 4.00

G-MAN: CAPE CRISIS
Image Comics: Aug, 2009 - No. 5, Jan, 2010 ($2.99, limited series)
1-5-Chris Giarrusso-s/a; back-up short strips by various ... 3.00

GNOME MOBILE, THE (See Movie Comics)

G'NORT SWIMSUIT EDITION
DC Comics: Oct, 2023 ($5.99, one-shot)
1-Beach-themed short stories by various and a gallery of recent swimsuit variant covers 6.00

GOBBLEDYGOOK
Mirage Studios: 1984 - No. 2, 1984 (B&W)(1st Mirage comics, published at same time)
1-(24 pgs.)-(distribution of approx. 50) Teenage Mutant Ninja Turtles app. on full page back-
   ad; Teenage Mutant Ninja Turtles do not appear inside. 1st app of Fugitoid
   1200 2400 3600 10,200 23,100 36,000
2-(24 pgs.)-Teenage Mutant Ninja Turtles on full page back-c ad
   400 800 1200 3400 7700 12,000
NOTE: Counterfeit copies exist. Originals feature both black & white covers and interiors. Signed and numbered copies do not exist.

GOBBLEDYGOOK
Mirage Studios: Dec, 1986 ($3.50, B&W, one-shot, 100 pgs.)
1-New 8 pg. TMNT story plus a Donatello/Michaelangelo 7 pg. story & a Gizmo story;
   Corben-i(r)/TMNT #7 ... 5 10 15 34 60 85

GOBLIN, THE
Warren Publishing Co.: June, 1982 - No. 3, Dec, 1982 ($2.25, B&W magazine with 8 pg. color
insert comic in all)
1-The Gremlin app. Philo Photon & the Troll Patrol, Micro-Buccaneers & Wizard Wormglow
   begin & app. in all. Tin Man app. Golden-a(p). Nebres-c/a in all
   3 6 9 14 19 24
2,3: 2-1st Hobgoblin. 3-Tin Man app. ... 2 4 6 10 14 18
NOTE: Bermejo a-1-3. Elias a-1-3. Laxamana a-1-3. Nino a-3.

GO-BOTS (Based on the Hasbro toys)
IDW Publishing: Nov, 2018 - No. 5, Mar, 2019 ($3.99, limited series)
1-5-Tom Scioli-s/a/c ... 3.00

GOD COMPLEX
Image Comics: Dec, 2009 - No. 7, Jun, 2010 ($2.99)
1-7-Oeming & Berman-s/Broglia-a/Oeming-c ... 3.00

GOD COMPLEX: DOGMA
Image Comics (Top Cow): Oct, 2017 - No. 6, Jun, 2018 ($3.99)
1-6-Jenkins-s/Prasetya-a ... 4.00

GOD COUNTRY
Image Comics: Jan, 2017 - No. 6, Jun, 2017 ($3.99, limited series)
1-Donny Cates-s/Geoff Shaw-a ... 4 8 12 23 37 50
2-6 ... 1 2 3 5 6 8

GODDAMNED, THE
Image Comics: Nov, 2015 - No. 5, Nov, 2016 ($3.99)
1-5-Jason Aaron-s/r.m. Guéra-a; story of Cain and Noah ... 4.00

GODDAMNED, THE: THE VIRGIN BRIDES
Image Comics: Jul, 2020 - No. 5, May, 2021 ($3.99)
1-5-Jason Aaron-s/r.m. Guéra-a ... 4.00

GODDESS
DC Comics (Vertigo): Jun, 1995 - No. 8, Jan, 1996 ($2.95, limited series)
1-Garth Ennis scripts; Phil Winslade-c/a in all ... 5.00
2-8 ... 4.00

GODDESS MODE
DC Comics (Vertigo): Feb, 2019 - No. 6, Jul, 2019 ($3.99)
1-6-Zoë Quinn-s/Robbi Rodriguez-a ... 4.00

GODFATHERS, THE (See The Crusaders)

GOD HATES ASTRONAUTS
Image Comics: Sept, 2014 - No. 10, Jul, 2015 ($3.50)
1-10-Ryan Browne-s/a. 1-Covers by Browne & Darrow ... 3.50

GOD IS
Spire Christian Comics (Fleming H. Revell Co.): 1973, 1975 (35-49¢)
nn-(1973) By Al Hartley ... 3 6 9 14 19 24
nn-(1975) ... 2 4 6 10 14 18

GOD IS DEAD
Avatar Press: Aug, 2013 - No. 48, Feb, 2016 ($3.99)
1-24,26-46: 1-5-Hickman & Costa-s/Amorim-a ... 4.00
25,48-($5.99) 25-Costa-s/DiPascale, Nobile & Urdinola-a. 48-Last issue; cover gallery 6.00
...Book of Acts Alpha (7/14, $5.99) Short stories by Alan Moore and others ... 6.00
...Book of Acts Omega (7/14, $5.99) Short stories by various ... 6.00

GODKILLERS
AfterShock Comics: Feb, 2020 - No. 5, Aug, 2020 ($3.99, limited series)
1-5-Mark Sable-s/Maan House-a ... 4.00

GODLAND
Image Comics: July, 2005 - Finale, Dec, 2013 ($2.99)
1-35-Joe Casey-s; Kirby-esque art by Tom Scioli. 13-Var-c by Giffen & Larsen.
   33-"Dogland" on cover ... 3.00
16-(60¢-c) Re-cap/origin issue ... 3.00
36-($3.99) ... 4.00
... Finale (12/13, $6.99) Final issue ... 7.00
Image Firsts: Godland #1 (9/10, $1.00) r/#1 with "Image Firsts" cover logo ... 3.00
...: Celestial Edition One HC (2007, $34.99) r/#1-12 and story from Image Holiday Special;
   intro. by Grant Morrison; cover gallery, developmental art and original story pitches 35.00

GOD OF TREMORS
AfterShock Comics: Aug, 2021 ($6.99, over-sized 8-1/2" x 10-7/8", one-shot)
1-Peter Milligan-s/Piotr Kowalski-a ... 7.00

GOD OF WAR (Based on the Sony videogame)
DC Comics (WildStorm): May, 2010 - No. 6, Mar, 2011 ($3.99/$2.99, limited series)
1-6-Wolfman-s/Sorrentino-a/Park-c. 6-($2.99) ... 4.00

GOD OF WAR (Based on the Sony videogame)
Dark Horse Comics: Nov, 2018 - No. 4, Feb, 2019 ($3.99, limited series)
1-4-Chris Roberson-s/Tony Parker-a/E.M. Gist-c ... 4.00

GOD OF WAR: FALLEN GOD (Based on the Sony videogame)
Dark Horse Comics: Mar, 2021 - No. 4, Jun, 2021 ($3.99, limited series)
1-4-Chris Roberson-s/Tony Parker-a/Dave Rapoza-c ... 4.00

G.O.D.S.
Marvel Comics: Dec, 2023 - Present ($9.99/$4.99)
1-($9.99) Hickman-s/Schiti-a; intro Wyn and Aiko; Doctor Strange app. ... 10.00
2-5-($4.99) ... 5.00

GOD SAVE THE QUEEN
DC Comics (Vertigo): 2007 ($19.99, hardcover with dustjacket, graphic novel)
HC-Mike Carey-s/John Bolton-painted art ... 20.00
SC-(2008, $12.99) Different painted-c by Bolton ... 13.00

GOD'S COUNTRY (Also see Marvel Comics Presents)
Marvel Comics: 1994 ($6.95)
nn-P. Craig Russell-a; Colossus story; r/Marvel Comics Presents #10-17 ... 7.00

GOD'S HEROES IN AMERICA
Catechetical Guild Educational Society: 1956 (nn) (25¢/35¢, 68 pgs.)
307 ... 3 6 9 19 30 40

GOD'S SMUGGLER (Religious)
Spire Christian Comics/Fleming H. Revell Co.: 1972 (35¢/39¢/40¢)
1-Three variations exist ... 3 6 9 14 19 24

GODWHEEL
Malibu Comics (Ultraverse): No. 0, Jan, 1995 - No. 3, Feb, 1995 ($2.50, limited series)
0-3: 0-Flip-c. 1-1st app. Primevil; Thor cameo (1 panel). 3-Pérez-a in Ch. 3, Thor app. 4.00

GODZILLA (Movie)
Marvel Comics: August, 1977 - No. 24, July, 1979 (Based on movie series)
1-(Regular 30¢ edition)-Moench-s/Trimpe-a/Mooney-i ... 6 12 18 41 76 110
1-(35¢-c variant, limited distribution) ... 28 56 84 202 451 700

	GD	VG	FN	VF	VF/NM	NM-
	2.0	4.0	6.0	8.0	9.0	9.2

	GD	VG	FN	VF	VF/NM	NM-
2-(Regular 30¢ edition)-Tuska-i.	3	6	9	19	30	40
2,3-(35¢-c variant, limited distribution)	12	24	36	82	179	275
3-(30¢-c) Champions app.(w/o Ghost Rider)	3	6	9	17	26	35
4:10: 4,5-Sutton-a	3	6	9	14	19	24
11-23: 14-Shield app. 20-F.F. app. 21,22-Devil Dinosaur app.						
	2	4	6	9	13	16
24-Last issue	3	6	9	17	26	35

GODZILLA (Movie)
Dark Horse Comics: May, 1988 - No. 6, 1988 ($1.95, B&W, limited series) (Based on movie series)

	GD	VG	FN	VF	VF/NM	NM-
1	3	6	9	14	19	24
2-6	1	3	4	6	8	10
...Collection (1990, $10.95)-r/1-6 with new-c						16.00
...Color Special 1 (Sum, 1992, $3.50, color, 44 pgs.)-Arthur Adams wraparound-c/a & part scripts	2	4	6	8	10	12
...King Of The Monsters Special (8/87, $1.50)-Origin; Bissette-c/a						
	2	4	6	11	16	20
...Vs. Barkley nn (12/93, $2.95, color)-Dorman painted-c	3	6	9	17	26	35

GODZILLA (King of the Monsters) (Movie)
Dark Horse Comics: May, 1995 - No. 16, Sept, 1996 ($2.50) (Based on movies)

	GD	VG	FN	VF	VF/NM	NM-
0,1: 0-r/Dark Horse Comics #10,11. 1-Kevin Maguire scripts						
	2	4	6	9	12	15
2-16: 2,3-Maguire scripts. 3-8-Art Adams-c						5.00
...Vs. Hero Zero ($2.50)						5.00

GODZILLA
IDW Publishing: May, 2012 - Present ($3.99/$7.99)

	GD	VG	FN	VF	VF/NM	NM-
1-13: 1-5,7,8,10-Swierczynski/Gane-a; multiple covers on each. 6-Wachter-a						4.00
... Best of Gigan (12/23, $7.99) Reprints of 4 recent stories						8.00
... Best of Godzilla (6/22, $6.99) Reprints of 4 recent stories						7.00
... Best of King Ghidorah (3/23, $6.99) Reprints of 4 recent stories						7.00
... Best of MechaGodzilla (9/23, $6.99) Reprints of 4 recent stories						7.00
... Best of Mothra (10/22, $6.99) Reprints of 4 recent stories						7.00
... Rivals: Biollante vs. Destoroyah (5/23, $7.99) Bunn/Wachter-a						8.00
... Rivals: Mothra vs. M.O.G.U.E.R.A. (2/24, $7.99) Parker-s/Chan-a						8.00
... Rivals: Mothra vs. Titanosaurus (3/23, $7.99) Delliquanti/Feriowind-a						8.00
... Rivals: vs. Battra (8/22, $7.99) Rosie Knight/Oliver Ono-a; Mothra app.						8.00
... Rivals: vs. Gigan (11/22, $7.99) Davidsen-s/SidVenBlu-a						8.00
... Rivals: vs. Hedorah (6/21, $7.99) Battle in New York City in 1971; E.J. Su-a						8.00
... Rivals: vs. King Ghidorah (3/22, $7.99) Kidnapped to Mars; Adam Gorham-a						8.00
... Rivals: vs. MechaGodzilla (11/23, $7.99) Martinez-s/Huset & Sanchez-a						8.00
... Rivals: vs. Mothra (9/21, $7.99) Battle in Japan in 1984; Gallant-a						8.00
... Rivals: vs. SpaceGodzilla (8/23, $7.99) Matt Frank-s/a						8.00
... The IDW Era (5/14, $3.99) Plot synopses of mini-series and cover galleries						4.00
... Valentine's Day Special (2/24, $4.99) Zoe Tunnell-s/Sebastian Piriz-a						5.00

GODZILLA: CATACLYSM
IDW Publishing: Aug, 2014 - No. 5, Dec, 2014 ($3.99, limited series)

	GD	VG	FN	VF	VF/NM	NM-
1-5-Bunn/Wachter-a; multiple covers on each						4.00

GODZILLA: GANGSTERS AND GOLIATHS
IDW Publishing: Jun, 2011 - No. 5, Oct, 2011 ($3.99, limited series)

	GD	VG	FN	VF	VF/NM	NM-
1-5-Layman-s/Ponticelli-a; Mothra app. 1-Darrow-c						4.00

GODZILLA: HERE THERE BE DRAGONS
IDW Publishing: Jun, 2023 - No. 5, Nov, 2023 ($3.99, limited series)

	GD	VG	FN	VF	VF/NM	NM-
1-5-Tieri-s/Miranda-a; discovery of Monster Island in 1357, and later pirate visits						4.00

GODZILLA IN HELL
IDW Publishing: Jul, 2015 - No. 5, Nov, 2015 ($3.99, limited series)

	GD	VG	FN	VF	VF/NM	NM-
1-5: Two covers on each. 1-Stokoe-s/a. 5-Wachter-s/a						4.00

GODZILLA: KINGDOM OF MONSTERS
IDW Publishing: Mar, 2011 - No. 12, Feb, 2012 ($3.99)

	GD	VG	FN	VF	VF/NM	NM-
1-12: 1-Hester-a; covers by Ross & Powell. 2,3-Covers by Hester & Powell						4.00
...: 100 Cover Charity Spectacular (8/11, $7.99) Variant covers for Japan Disaster Relief						8.00

GODZILLA LEGENDS (Spotlight on other monsters)
IDW Publishing: Nov, 2011 - No. 5, Mar, 2012 ($3.99)

	GD	VG	FN	VF	VF/NM	NM-
1-5-Art Adams-c. 1-Anguirus. 2-Rodan. 3-Titanosaurus. 4-Hedorah. 5-Kumonga						4.00

GODZILLA: MONSTERS AND PROTECTORS
IDW Publishing: Apr, 2021 - No. 5, Aug, 2021 ($4.99/$3.99, limited series)

	GD	VG	FN	VF	VF/NM	NM-
1-($4.99) Burnham-s/Schoening-a						5.00
2-5-($3.99) 2,5-Mothra app. 3,5-Biollante app.						4.00
...— Summer Smash One Shot (7/23, $6.99) Burnham-s/Schoening-a						7.00

GODZILLA: MONSTERS AND PROTECTORS ALL HAIL THE KING
IDW Publishing: Oct, 2022 - No. 5, Feb, 2023 ($3.99, limited series)

	GD	VG	FN	VF	VF/NM	NM-
1-5-Burnham/Schoening-a						4.00

GODZILLA: OBLIVION
IDW Publishing: Mar, 2016 - No. 5, Jul, 2016 ($3.99, limited series)

	GD	VG	FN	VF	VF/NM	NM-
1-5-Fialkov-s/Churilla-a; Mechagodzilla & Ghidorah app.						4.00

GODZILLA: RAGE ACROSS TIME
IDW Publishing: Aug, 2016 - No. 5, Nov, 2016 ($3.99, limited series)

	GD	VG	FN	VF	VF/NM	NM-
1-5-Story & art by various						4.00

GODZILLA: RULERS OF EARTH
IDW Publishing: Jun, 2013 - No. 25, Jun, 2015 ($3.99)

	GD	VG	FN	VF	VF/NM	NM-
1-24: 1-8-Chris Mowry-s/Matt Frank-a						4.00
25-($7.99) Mowry-s/Frank & Zornow-a						8.00

GODZILLA: THE HALF-CENTURY WAR
IDW Publishing: Aug, 2012 - No. 5, Feb, 2013 ($3.99, limited series)

	GD	VG	FN	VF	VF/NM	NM-
1-5-James Stokoe-s/a						4.00

GODZILLA VS. THE MIGHTY MORPHIN POWER RANGERS
BOOM! Studios / IDW Publishing: Mar, 2022 - No. 5, Sept, 2022 ($3.99, limited series)

	GD	VG	FN	VF	VF/NM	NM-
1-5-Cullen Bunn-s/Freddie Williams III-a						4.00

GODZILLA: WAR FOR HUMANITY
IDW Publishing: Aug, 2023 - No. 5, May, 2024 ($4.99, limited series)

	GD	VG	FN	VF	VF/NM	NM-
1-5-Andrew MacLean-s/Jake Smith-a						5.00

GOG (VILLAINS) (See Kingdom Come)
DC Comics: Feb, 1998 ($1.95, one-shot)

	GD	VG	FN	VF	VF/NM	NM-
1-Waid-s/Ordway-a(p)/Pearson-c						4.00

GO GIRL!
Image Comics: Aug, 2000 - No. 5 ($3.50, B&W, quarterly)

	GD	VG	FN	VF	VF/NM	NM-
1-5-Trina Robbins-s/Anne Timmons-a; pin-up gallery						3.50

GO-GO
Charlton Comics: June, 1966 - No. 9, Oct, 1967

	GD	VG	FN	VF	VF/NM	NM-
1-Miss Bikini Luv begins; Rolling Stones, Beatles, Elvis, Sonny & Cher, Bob Dylan, Sinatra, parody; Herman's Hermits pin-ups; D'Agostino-c/a in #1-8						
	9	18	27	61	123	185
2-Ringo Starr, David McCallum & Beatles photos on cover; Beatles story and photos; Blooperman & parody of JLA heroes	9	18	27	57	111	165
3,4: 3-Blooperman, ends #6; 1 pg. Batman & Robin satire; full pg. photo pin-ups Lovin' Spoonful & The Byrds	5	10	15	33	57	80
5,7,9: 5 (2/67)-Super Hero & TV satire by Jim Aparo & Grass Green begins. 6-8-Aparo-a. 7-Photo of Brian Wilson of Beach Boys on-c & Beach Boys photo inside f/b-c. 9-Aparo-c/a						
	5	10	15	33	57	80
6-Parody of JLA & DC heroes vs. Marvel heroes; Aparo-a; Elvis parody; Petula Clark photo-c; first signed work by Jim Aparo	5	10	15	35	63	90
8-Monkees photo on-c & photo inside f/b-c	6	12	18	38	69	100

GO-GO AND ANIMAL (See Tippy's Friends...)

GOING STEADY (Formerly Teen-Age Temptations)
St. John Publ. Co.: No. 10, Dec, 1954 - No. 13, June, 1955; No. 14, Oct, 1955

	GD	VG	FN	VF	VF/NM	NM-
10(1954)-Matt Baker-c/a	232	464	696	1485	2543	3600
11(2/55, last precode), 12(4/55)-Baker-c	103	206	309	659	1130	1600
13(6/55)-Baker-c/a	155	310	465	992	1696	2400
14(10/55)-Matt Baker-c/a, 25 pgs.	161	322	483	1030	1765	2500

GOING STEADY (Formerly Personal Love)
Prize Publications/Headline: V3#3, Feb, 1960 - V3#6, Aug, 1960; V4#1, Sept-Oct, 1960

	GD	VG	FN	VF	VF/NM	NM-
V3#3-6, V4#1	8	16	24	52	99	145

GOING STEADY WITH BETTY (Becomes Betty & Her Steady No. 2)
Avon Periodicals: Nov-Dec, 1949 (Teen-age)

	GD	VG	FN	VF	VF/NM	NM-
1-Partial photo-c	50	100	150	315	533	750

GOLDEN AGE, THE (TPB also reprinted in 2005 as JSA: The Golden Age)
DC Comics (Elseworlds): 1993 - No. 4, 1994 ($4.95, limited series)

	GD	VG	FN	VF	VF/NM	NM-
1-4: James Robinson scripts; Paul Smith-c/a; gold foil embossed-c						6.00
Trade Paperback (1995, $19.95) intro by Howard Chaykin						20.00

GOLDEN AGE SECRET FILES
DC Comics: Feb, 2001 ($4.95, one-shot)

	GD	VG	FN	VF	VF/NM	NM-
1-Origins and profiles of JSA members and other G.A. heroes; Lark-c						5.00

GOLDEN ARROW (See Fawcett Miniatures, Mighty Midget & Whiz Comics)

GOLDEN ARROW (...Western No. 6)
Fawcett Publications: Spring,.1942 - No. 6, Spring, 1947 (68 pgs.)

	GD	VG	FN	VF	VF/NM	NM-
1-Golden Arrow begins	53	106	159	334	567	800
2-(1943)	28	56	84	168	274	380
3-5: 3-(Win/45-46). 4-(Spr/46). 5-(Fall/46)	18	36	54	103	162	220
6-Krigstein-a	18	36	54	105	165	225

Ashcan (1942) not distributed to newsstands, only for in house use. A CGC certified 9.0 sold for $3,734.38 in 2008.

GOLDEN COMICS DIGEST
Gold Key: May, 1969 - No. 48, Jan, 1976
NOTE: Whitman editions exist of many titles and are generally valued the same.

	GD	VG	FN	VF	VF/NM	NM-
1-Tom & Jerry, Woody Woodpecker, Bugs Bunny	5	10	15	33	57	80
2-Hanna-Barbera TV Fun Favorites; Space Ghost, Flintstones, Atom Ant, Jetsons, Yogi Bear, Banana Splits, others app.	6	12	18	41	76	110
3-Tom & Jerry, Woody Woodpecker	3	6	9	16	24	32
4-Tarzan; Manning & Marsh-a	4	8	12	28	47	65
5,8-Tom & Jerry, W. Woodpecker, Bugs Bunny	3	6	9	16	23	30
6-Bugs Bunny	3	6	9	16	23	30
7-Hanna-Barbera TV Fun Favorites	5	10	15	33	57	80
9-Tarzan	4	8	12	28	47	65
10,12-17: 10-Bugs Bunny. 12-Tom & Jerry, Bugs Bunny, W. Woodpecker Journey to the Sun. 13-Tom & Jerry. 14-Bugs Bunny Fun Packed Funnies. 15-Tom & Jerry, Woody Woodpecker, Bugs Bunny. 16-Woody Woodpecker Cartoon Special. 17-Bugs Bunny						
	3	6	9	16	23	30
11-Hanna-Barbera TV Fun Favorites	5	10	15	34	60	85
18-Tom & Jerry; Barney Bear-r by Barks	3	6	9	16	24	32
19-Little Lulu	4	8	12	25	40	55
20-22: 20-Woody Woodpecker Falltime Funtime. 21-Bugs Bunny Showtime. 22-Tom & Jerry Winter Wingding	3	6	9	16	23	30
23-Little Lulu & Tubby Fun Fling	4	8	12	25	40	55
24-26,28: 24-Woody Woodpecker Fun Festival. 25-Tom & Jerry. 26-Bugs Bunny Halloween Hulla-Boo-Loo; Dr. Spektor article, also #25. 28-Tom & Jerry						
	3	6	9	14	20	26
27-Little Lulu & Tubby in Hawaii	4	8	12	24	38	52
29-Little Lulu & Tubby	4	8	12	24	38	52
30-Bugs Bunny Vacation Funnies	3	6	9	14	20	26
31-Turok, Son of Stone; r/4-Color #596,656; c-r/#9	4	8	12	27	44	60
32-Woody Woodpecker Summer Fun	3	6	9	14	20	26
33,36: 33-Little Lulu & Tubby Halloween Fun; Dr. Spektor app. 36-Little Lulu & Her Friends						
	4	8	12	24	38	52
34,35,37-39: 34-Bugs Bunny Winter Funnies. 35-Tom & Jerry Snowtime Funtime. 37-Woody Woodpecker County Fair. 39-Bugs Bunny Summer Fun						
	3	6	9	14	20	26

Godzilla: Oblivion #1 © Toho

Gold Goblin #5 © MAR

Gomer Pyle #2 © Ashland

	GD	VG	FN	VF	VF/NM	NM-
	2.0	4.0	6.0	8.0	9.0	9.2

38-The Pink Panther

| | 3 | 6 | 9 | 16 | 24 | 32 |

40,43: 40-Little Lulu & Tubby Trick or Treat; all by Stanley. 43-Little Lulu in Paris

| | 4 | 8 | 12 | 24 | 38 | 52 |

41,42,44,47: 41-Tom & Jerry Winter Carnival. 42-Bugs Bunny. 44-Woody Woodpecker Family
Fun Festival. 47-Bugs Bunny

| | 3 | 6 | 9 | 14 | 20 | 25 |

45-The Pink Panther

| | 3 | 6 | 9 | 16 | 24 | 32 |

46-Little Lulu & Tubby

| | 4 | 8 | 12 | 21 | 33 | 45 |

48-The Lone Ranger

| | 3 | 6 | 9 | 17 | 26 | 35 |

NOTE: #1-30, 164 pgs.; #31 on, 132 pgs..

GOLDEN LAD
Spark/Fact & Fiction Publ.: July, 1945 - No. 5, June, 1946 (#4, 5: 52 pgs.)

1-Origin & 1st app. Golden Lad & Swift Arrow; Sandusky and the Senator begins

| | 74 | 148 | 222 | 470 | 810 | 1150 |

2-Mort Meskin-c/a

| | 34 | 68 | 102 | 204 | 332 | 460 |

3,4-Mort Meskin-c/a

| | 32 | 64 | 96 | 188 | 307 | 425 |

5-Origin & 1st app. Golden Girl; Shaman & Flame app.

| | 43 | 86 | 129 | 271 | 461 | 650 |

NOTE: All have **Robinson**, and **Roussos** art plus **Meskin** covers and art.

GOLDEN LEGACY
Fitzgerald Publishing Co.: 1966 - 1972 (Black History) (25¢)

1-12,14-16: 1-Toussaint L'Ouverture (1966), 2-Harriet Tubman (1967), 3-Crispus Attucks &
the Minutemen (1967), 4-Benjamin Banneker (1968), 5-Matthew Henson (1969),
6-Alexander Dumas & Family (1969), 7-Frederick Douglass, Part 1 (1969), 8-Frederick
Douglass, Part 2 (1970), 9-Robert Smalls (1970), 10-J. Cinque & the Amistad Mutiny
(1970), 11-Men in Action: White, Marshall J. Wilkins (1970), 12-Black Cowboys (1972),
14-The Life of Alexander Pushkin (1971), 15-Ancient African Kingdoms (1972),
16-Black Inventors (1972)   each....

| | 4 | 8 | 12 | 23 | 37 | 50 |

13-The Life of Martin Luther King, Jr. (1972)

| | 5 | 10 | 15 | 30 | 50 | 70 |

1-10,12,13,15,16(1976)-Reprints

| | 2 | 4 | 6 | 9 | 12 | 15 |

GOLDEN LOVE STORIES (Formerly Golden West Love)
Kirby Publishing Co.: No. 4, April, 1950

4-Powell-a; Glenn Ford/Janet Leigh photo-c

| | 20 | 40 | 60 | 120 | 195 | 270 |

GOLDEN PICTURE CLASSIC, A
Western Printing Co. (Simon & Shuster): 1956-1957 (Text stories w/illustrations in color; 100 pgs. each)

CL-401: Treasure Island

| | 11 | 22 | 33 | 64 | 90 | 115 |

CL-402,403: 402: Tom Sawyer. 403: Black Beauty

| | 10 | 20 | 30 | 54 | 72 | 90 |

CL-404, 405: CL-404: Little Women. CL-405: Heidi

| | 10 | 20 | 30 | 54 | 72 | 90 |

CL-406: Ben Hur

| | 8 | 16 | 24 | 44 | 57 | 70 |

CL-407: Around the World in 80 Days

| | 8 | 16 | 24 | 44 | 57 | 70 |

CL-408: Sherlock Holmes

| | 9 | 18 | 27 | 50 | 65 | 80 |

CL-409: The Three Musketeers

| | 8 | 16 | 24 | 44 | 57 | 70 |

CL-410: The Merry Advs. of Robin Hood

| | 8 | 16 | 24 | 44 | 57 | 70 |

CL-411,412: 411: Hans Brinker. 412: The Count of Monte Cristo

| | 9 | 18 | 27 | 50 | 65 | 80 |

(Both soft & hardcover editions are valued the same)

NOTE: Recent research has uncovered new information. Apparently #1-6 were issued in 1956 and #7-12 in 1957. But they can be found in the following series listings: CL-1 to CL-12 (softbound); CL-401 to CL-412 (also softbound); CL-101 to CL-112 (hardbound); plus two new series discoveries: A Golden Reading Adventure, publ. by Golden Press; edited down to 60 pages and reduced in size to 6x9"; only #s discovered so far are #381 (CL-4), #382 (CL-6) & #387 (CL-3). They have no reorder list and some have covers different from GPC. There have also been found British hardbound editions of GPC with dust jackets. Copies of all five listed series vary from scarce to very rare. Some editions of some series have not yet been found at all.

GOLDEN PICTURE STORY BOOK
Racine Press (Western): Dec, 1961 (50¢, Treasury size, 52 pgs.) (All are scarce)

ST-1-Huckleberry Hound (TV); Hokey Wolf, Pixie & Dixie, Quick Draw McGraw,
Snooper and Blabber, Augie Doggie app.

| | 15 | 30 | 45 | 103 | 227 | 350 |

ST-2-Yogi Bear (TV); Snagglepuss, Yakky Doodle, Quick Draw McGraw,
Snooper and Blabber, Augie Doggie app.

| | 15 | 30 | 45 | 103 | 227 | 350 |

ST-3-Babes in Toyland (Walt Disney's...)-Annette Funicello photo-c

| | 19 | 38 | 57 | 131 | 291 | 450 |

ST-4-(...of Disney Ducks)-Walt Disney's Wonderful World of Ducks (Donald Duck, Uncle
Scrooge, Donald's Nephews, Grandma Duck, Ludwig Von Drake, & Gyro Gearloose
stories)

| | 19 | 38 | 57 | 131 | 291 | 450 |

GOLDEN RECORD COMIC (See Amazing Spider-Man #1, Avengers #4, Fantastic Four #1, Journey Into Mystery #83) (Also see Superman Record Comic and Batman Record Comic in the Promotional section)

GOLDEN STORY BOOKS
Western Printing Co. (Simon & Shuster): 1949-1950 (Heavy covers, digest size, 128 pgs.)
(Illustrated text in color)

7-Walt Disney's Mystery in Disneyville, a book-length adventure starring Donald and Nephews,
Mickey and Nephews, and with Minnie, Daisy and Goofy. Art by Dick Moores and Manuel
Gonzales (scarce)

| | 31 | 93 | 182 | 296 | 410 |

10-Bugs Bunny's Treasure Hunt, a book-length adventure starring Bugs & Porky Pig, with

---

Petunia Pig & Nephew, Cicero. Art by Tom McKimson (scarce)

| | 21 | 42 | 63 | 122 | 199 | 275 |

11,12 ('50): 11-M-G-M's Tom & Jerry. 12-Walt Disney's "So Dear My Heart"

| | 20 | 40 | 60 | 114 | 182 | 250 |

GOLDEN WEST LOVE (Golden Love Stories No. 4)
Kirby Publishing Co.: Sept-Oct, 1949 - No. 3, Feb, 1950 (All 52 pgs.)

1-Powell-a in all; Roussos-a; painted-c

| | 30 | 60 | 90 | 177 | 289 | 400 |

2,3: Photo-c

| | 19 | 38 | 57 | 111 | 176 | 240 |

GOLDEN WEST RODEO TREASURY (See Dell Giants)

GOLDFISH (See A.K.A. Goldfish)

GOLD GOBLIN (Spider-Man)
Marvel Comics: Jan, 2023 - Present ($3.99)

1-4-Cantwell-s/Medina-a; Norman Osborn as a hero

| | | | | | 4.00 |

GOLDIE VANCE
Boom Entertainment (BOOM! Box): Apr, 2016 - No. 12, May, 2017 ($3.99)

1-12: 1-8-Hope Larson-s/Brittney Williams-a. 1-Five covers. 2-4-Two covers. 9-12-Hayes-a

| | | | | | 4.00 |

GOLDILOCKS (See March of Comics No. 1)

GOLD KEY: ALLIANCE
Dynamite Entertainment: 2016 - No. 5, 2016 ($3.99, limited series)

1-5: 1-Team up of Magnus, Turok, Solar & Samson; Hester-s/Peeples-a

| | | | | | 4.00 |

GOLD KEY CHAMPION
Gold Key: Mar, 1978 - No. 2, May, 1978 (50¢, 52 pgs.)

1-Space Family Robinson; half-r

| | 2 | 4 | 6 | 9 | 13 | 16 |

2-Mighty Samson; half-r

| | 1 | 3 | 4 | 6 | 8 | 10 |

GOLD KEY SPOTLIGHT
Gold Key: May, 1976 - No. 11, Feb, 1978

1-Tom, Dick & Harriet

| | | | | 8 | 11 | 14 |

2-11: 2-Wacky Advs. of Cracky. 3-Wacky Witch. 4-Tom, Dick & Harriet. 5-Wacky Advs. of
Cracky. 6-Dagar the Invincible; Santos-a; origin Demonomicon. 7-Wacky Witch & Greta
Ghost. 8-The Occult Files of Dr. Spektor, Simbar, Lu-sai; Santos-a. 9-Tragg.
10-O. G. Whiz. 11-Tom, Dick & Harriet

| | 2 | 4 | 6 | 8 | 10 | 12 |

GOLD MEDAL COMICS
Cambridge House: 1945 (25¢, one-shot, 132 pgs.)

nn-Captain Truth by Fujitani as well as Stallman and Howie Post, Crime Detector, The Witch
of Salem, Luckyman, others app.

| | 43 | 86 | 129 | 271 | 461 | 650 |

GOLEM WALKS AMONG US!, THE
Dark Horse Comics: Aug, 2021 - No. 2, Sept, 2021 ($3.99, limited series)

1,2-Mignola & Golden-s/Bergting-a; set in 1938 Italy

| | | | | | 4.00 |

GOMER PYLE (TV)
Gold Key: July, 1966 - No. 3, Oct, 1967

1-Photo front/back-c

| | 10 | 20 | 30 | 67 | 141 | 215 |

2,3-Photo-c

| | 6 | 12 | 18 | 37 | 66 | 95 |

GON
DC Comics (Paradox Press): July, 1996 - No. 4, Oct, 1996; No. 5, 1997 ($5.95, B&W, digest-size, limited series)

1-5: Misadventures of baby dinosaur; 1-Gon. 2-Gon Again. 3-Gon: Here Today,
Gone Tomorrow. 4-Gon: Going, Going...Gon. 5-Gon Swimmin'. Tanaka-c/a/scripts in all

| | 1 | 3 | 4 | 6 | 8 | 10 |

GON COLOR SPECTACULAR
DC Comics (Paradox Press): 1998 ($5.95, square-bound)

nn-Tanaka-c/a/scripts

| | 2 | 4 | 6 | 10 | 14 | 18 |

GONE
DSTLRY: Oct, 2023 - Present ($8.99, oversized 10-7/8 x 8-1/2")

1,2-Jock-s/a

| | | | | | 9.00 |

GONERS
Image Comics: Oct, 2014 - No. 6, Mar, 2015 ($2.99)

1-6-Semahn-s/Corona-a

| | | | | | 3.00 |

GON ON SAFARI
DC Comics (Paradox Press): 2000 ($7.95, B&W, digest-size)

nn-Tanaka-c/a/scripts

| | 1 | 3 | 4 | 6 | 8 | 10 |

GON UNDERGROUND
DC Comics (Paradox Press): 1999 ($7.95, B&W, digest-size)

nn-Tanaka-c/a/scripts

| | 1 | 3 | 4 | 6 | 8 | 10 |

GON WILD

	GD 2.0	VG 4.0	FN 6.0	VF 8.0	VF/NM 9.0	NM- 9.2

DC Comics (Paradox Press): 1997 ($9.95, B&W, digest-size)

nn-Tanaka-c/a/scripts in all. (Rep. Gon #3,4)	2	4	6	9	12	15

GOOD ASIAN, THE
Image Comics: May, 2021 - No. 10, Apr, 2022 ($3.99)

1-10-Pornsak Pichetshote-s/Alexandre Tefenkgi-a; Chinese-Americans in 1936 San Fran.						4.00

GOODBYE, MR. CHIPS (See Movie Comics)

GOOD GIRL ART QUARTERLY
AC Comics: Summer, 1990 - No. 15, Spring, 1994; No. 19, 2001 (B&W/color, 52 pgs.)

1-($3.50)-All have one new story (often FémForce) & rest reprints by Baker, Ward & other "good girl" artists	2	4	6	11	16	20
2-($3.95), 19-(2001) FX Convention Exclusive						8.00
3-15-($3.50)						8.00

GOOD GIRL COMICS (Formerly Good Girl Art Quarterly)
AC Comics: No. 16, Summer, 1994 - No. 18, 1995 (B&W)

16-18						6.00

GOOD GUYS, THE
Defiant: Nov, 1993 - No. 9, July, 1994 ($2.50/$3.25/$3.50)

1-($3.50, 52 pgs.)-Glory x-over from Plasm						5.00
2,3,5-9: 3-Chasm app. 9-Pre-Schism issue						4.00
4-($3.25, 52 pgs.) Nudge sends Chasm to Plasm						5.00

GOOD, THE BAD AND THE UGLY, THE (Also see Man With No Name)
Dynamite Entertainment: 2009 - No. 8 ($3.50)

1-8: 1-Character from the 1966 Clint Eastwood movie; Dixon-s/Polls-a; three covers						3.50

GOOD TRIUMPHS OVER EVIL! (Also see Narrative Illustration)
M.C. Gaines: 1943 (12 pgs., 7-1/4"x10", B&W) (not a comic book) (Rare)

nn-A pamphlet, sequel to Narrative Illustration	174	348	522	1114	1907	2700

NOTE: **Print, A Quarterly Journal of the Graphic Arts** Vol. 3 No. 3 (64 pg. square bound) features 1st printing of Good Triumphs Over Evil! A VG copy sold for $350 in 2005.

GOOFY (Disney)(See Dynabrite Comics, Mickey Mouse Magazine V4#7, Walt Disney Showcase #35 & Wheaties)
Dell Publishing Co.: No. 468, May, 1953 - Sept-Nov, 1962

Four Color 468 (#1)	12	24	36	82	179	275
Four Color 562,627,658,702,747,802,857	7	14	21	46	86	125
Four Color 899,952,987,1053,1094,1149,1201	5	10	15	35	63	90
12-308-211(Dell, 9-11/62)	5	10	15	31	53	75

GOOFY ADVENTURES
Disney Comics: June, 1990 - No. 17, 1991 ($1.50)

1-17: Most new stories. 2-Joshua Quagmire-a w/free poster. 7-WDC&S-r plus new-a. 9-Gottfredson-r. 14-Super Goof story. 15-All Super Goof issue. 17-Gene Colan-a(p)						4.00

GOOFY ADVENTURE STORY (See Goofy No. 857)

GOOFY COMICS (Companion to Happy Comics)(Not Disney)
Nedor Publ. Co. No. 1-14/Standard No. 14-48: June, 1943 - No. 48, 1953 (Animated Cartoons)

1-Funny animal; Oriolo-c	43	86	129	271	461	650
2	22	44	66	132	216	300
3-10	17	34	51	98	154	210
11-19	14	28	42	81	118	155
20-35-Frazetta text illos in all	15	30	45	84	127	170
36-48	12	24	36	69	97	125

GOOFY SUCCESS STORY (See Goofy No. 702)

GOON, THE
Avatar Press: Mar, 1999 - No. 3, July, 1999 ($3.00, B&W)

1-Eric Powell-s/a	20	40	60	138	307	475
2	5	10	15	34	60	85
3	6	12	18	37	66	95
...: Rough Stuff (Albatross, 1/03, $15.95) r/Avatar Press series #1-3						20.00
...: Rough Stuff (Dark Horse, 2/04, $12.95) r/Avatar Press series #1-3 newly colored						15.00

GOON, THE (2nd series)
Albatross Exploding Funny Books: Oct, 2002 - No. 4, Feb, 2003 ($2.95)

1-Eric Powell-s/a	5	10	15	35	63	90
2-4	3	6	9	14	20	25
...Color Special 1 (8/02)	3	6	9	17	25	34
...: Nothin' But Misery Vol. 1 (Dark Horse, 7/03, $15.95, TPB) - Reprints The Goon #1-4 (Albatross series), Color Special, and story from DHP #157						18.00

GOON, THE (3rd series) (Also see Dethklok Versus the Goon)
Dark Horse Comics: June, 2003 - No. 44, Nov, 2013 ($2.99/$3.50)

1-Eric Powell-s/a in all	4	8	12	23	37	50
2-4	2	4	6	8	10	12
5-31: 7-Hellboy-c/app; framing seq. by Mignola 14-Two covers						4.00
32-($3.99, 3/09) Tenth Anniversary issue; with sketch pages and pin-ups						5.00
33-44-($3.50) 33-Silent issue. 35-Dorkin-s. 39-Gimmick issue. 41-43-Buckingham-a.						
44-Spanish issue						3.50
...: 25¢ Edition (9/05, 25¢)						3.00
...: Chinatown and the Mystery of Mr. Wicker HC (11/07, $19.95) original GN; Powell-s/a						20.00
...: Fancy Pants Edition HC (10/05, $24.95, dust jacket) r/#1,2 of 2nd series & #1,3,5,9 of 3rd series; Powell intro.; sketch pages and cover gallery						25.00
...: Heaps of Ruination (5/05, $12.95, TPB) r/#5-8; intro. by Frank Darabont						13.00
...: My Murderous Childhood (And Other Grievous Yarns) (5/04, $13.95, TPB) r/#1-4 and short story from Drawing on Your Nightmares one-shot; intro. by Frank Cho						14.00
...: One For One (8/10, $1.00) r/#1 with red cover frame						3.00
...: One For The Road (6/14, $3.50) Jack Davis-c; EC horror hosts app.						3.50
...: Theater Bizarre (10/15, $3.99) Prelude to The Lords of Misery; Zombo app.						4.00
...: Virtue and the Grim Consequences Thereof (2/06, $16.95) r/#9-13						17.00
...: Wicked Inclinations (12/06, $14.95) r/#14-18; intro. by Mike Allred						15.00

GOON, THE (4th series)
Albatross Funnybooks: 2019 - Present ($3.99)

1-14: 1-4,13,14-Eric Powell-s/a. 5-8-Powell & Sniegoski-s/Parson-a. 9-12-Langridge/Norton-a 4.00						

GOON NOIR, THE (Dwight T. Albatross's...)
Dark Horse Comics: Sept, 2006 - No. 3, Jan, 2007 ($2.99, B&W, limited series)

1-3-Anthology 1-Oswalt-s/Ploog-a; Sniegoski-s/Powell-a; Morrison-s/a; Niles-s/Sook-a						4.00

GOON: OCCASION OF REVENGE, THE
Dark Horse Comics: Jul, 2014 - No. 4, Dec, 2014 ($3.50, limited series)

1-4-Powell-s/a. 3-Origin of Kid Gargantuan						3.50

GOON: ONCE UPON A HARD TIME, THE
Dark Horse Comics: Feb, 2015 - No. 4, Oct, 2015 ($3.50, limited series)

1-4-Powell-s/a						3.50

GOOSE (Humor magazine)
Cousins Publ. (Fawcett): Sept, 1976 - No. 3, 1976 (75¢, 52 pgs., B&W)

1-Nudity in all	3	6	9	18	28	38
2,3: 2-(10/76) Fonz-c/s; Lone Ranger story. 3-Wonder Woman, King Kong, Six Million Dollar Man stories	3	6	9	14	20	26

GOOSEBUMPS: DOWNLOAD AND DIE!
IDW Publishing: Feb, 2018 - No. 3, Apr, 2018 ($3.99, limited series)

1-3-Jen Vaughn-s/Michelle Wong-a						4.00

GOOSEBUMPS: HORRORS OF THE WITCH HOUSE
IDW Publishing: Mar, 2019 - No. 3, May, 2019 ($3.99, limited series)

1-3-Denton J. Tipton & Matthew Dow Smith-s/Chris Fenoglio-a						4.00

GOOSEBUMPS: MONSTERS AT MIDNIGHT
IDW Publishing: Oct, 2017 - No. 3, Dec, 2017 ($3.99, limited series)

1-3-Lambert-s/Fenoglio-a						4.00

GOOSEBUMPS: SECRETS OF THE SWAMP
IDW Publishing: Sept, 2020 - No. 5, Jan, 2021 ($3.99, limited series)

1-5-Nijkamp-s/Montanez-a						4.00

GORDO (See Comics Revue No. 5 & Giant Comics Edition)

GORGO (Based on M.G.M. movie) (See Return of...)
Charlton Comics: May, 1961 - No. 23, Sept, 1965

1-Ditko-a, 22 pgs.	33	66	99	238	532	825
2,3-Ditko-c/a	15	30	45	105	233	360
4-Ditko-c	10	20	30	70	150	230
5-11,13-16: 11,13-16-Ditko-a. 11-Ditko-c	9	18	27	59	117	175
12,17-23: 12-Reptisaurus x-over. 17-23-Montes/Bache-a. 20-Giordano-c	6	12	18	38	69	100
Gorgo's Revenge('62)-Becomes Return of...	8	16	24	51	96	140

GORILLA MAN (From Agents of Atlas)
Marvel Comics: Sept, 2010 - No. 3, Nov, 2010 ($3.99, limited series)

1-3-Parker-s/Caracuzzo-a. 1-Johnson-c. 3-Dell'Otto-c						4.00

GOSPEL BLIMP, THE
Spire Christian Comics (Fleming H. Revell Co.): 1974, 1975 (35¢/39¢, 36 pgs.)

nn-(1974)	3	6	9	14	19	24
nn-(1975)	2	4	6	9	13	16

GOTHAM ACADEMY
DC Comics: Dec, 2014 - No. 18, Jul, 2016 ($2.99)

1-18: 1-Cloonan & Fletcher-s/Kerschl-a. 4-6-Killer Croc. 6,7-Damian Wayne app.						3.00
Annual 1 (10/16, $4.99) Art by Archer, Wildgoose, Dialynas, Msassyk; Blight app.						5.00
...: Endgame 1 (5/15, $2.99) Tie-in to Joker story in Batman titles						3.00
...: Maps of Mystery 1 (7/23, $5.99) Maps Mizoguchi teams with Batman; Kerschl-s/a						6.00

GOTHAM ACADEMY: SECOND SEMESTER
DC Comics: Nov, 2016 - No. 12, Oct, 2017 ($2.99)

1-12: 1-3-Cloonan, Fletcher & Kerschl-s/Archer-a. 4-Jon Lam-a. 11-Damian app.						3.00

GOTHAM BY GASLIGHT (A Tale of the Batman)(See Batman: Master of...)
DC Comics: 1989 ($3.95, one-shot, squarebound, 52 pgs.)

nn-Mignola/Russell-a; intro by Robert Bloch	2	4	6	11	16	20

GOTHAM BY MIDNIGHT
DC Comics: Jan, 2015 - No. 12, Feb, 2016 ($2.99)

1-12: 1-5-Fawkes-s/Templesmith-a/c. 4,5,7-11-The Spectre app. 6-12-Ferreyra-a						3.00
Annual 1 (9/15, $4.99) Fawkes/Duce-a; The Gentleman Ghost origin						5.00

GOTHAM CENTRAL
DC Comics: Early Feb, 2003 - No. 40, Apr, 2006 ($2.50)

1-40-Stories of Gotham City Police. 1-Brubaker & Rucka-s/Lark-c/a. 10-Two-Face app. 13,15-Joker-c. 18-Huntress app. 27-Catwoman-c. 32-Poison Ivy app. 34-Teen Titans-c/app. 38-Crispus Allen killed (becomes The Spectre in Infinite Crisis #5)						3.00
... Special Edition 1 (11/14, $1.00) r/#1 with Gotham TV show banner on cover						3.00
... Book One: In the Line of Duty HC (2008, $29.99, dustjacket) r/#1-10; sketch pages						30.00
... Book One: In the Line of Duty SC (2008, $19.99) r/#1-10; sketch pages						20.00
... Book Two: Jokers and Madmen HC (2009, $29.99, dustjacket) r/#11-22						30.00
... Book Two: Jokers and Madmen SC (2011, $19.99) r/#11-22						20.00
... Book Three: On the Freak Beat HC (2010, $29.99, dustjacket) r/#23-31						30.00
... Book Four: Corrigan HC (2011, $29.99, dustjacket) r/#32-40						30.00
... Dead Robin (2007, $17.99, TPB) r/#33-40; cover gallery						18.00
...: Half a Life (2005, $14.99, TPB) r/#6-10, Batman Chronicles #16 and Detective #747						15.00
...: In The Line of Duty (2004, $9.95, TPB) r/#1-5, cover gallery & sketch pages						10.00
...: The Quick and the Dead TPB (2006, $14.99) r/#23-25,28-31						15.00
...: Unresolved Targets (2006, $14.99, TPB) r/#12-15,19-22, cover gallery						15.00

GOTHAM CITY GARAGE
DC Comics: Dec, 2017 - No. 12, May, 2018 ($2.99, printings of stories that first appeared online)

1-12: 1-Female heroes as a biker gang; Kelly & Lanzing-s/Ching-a/Albuquerque-c						3.00

GOTHAM CITY MONSTERS
DC Comics: Nov, 2019 - No. 6, Apr, 2020 ($3.99, limited series)

1-6-Orlando-s/Nahuelpan-a; Frankenstein, Killer Croc, Orca app. 3-6-Batwoman app.						4.00

GOTHAM CITY SIRENS (Batman: Reborn)
DC Comics: Aug, 2009 - No. 26, Oct, 2011 ($2.99)

The Goon #26 © Eric Powell

Gotham Academy #11 © DC

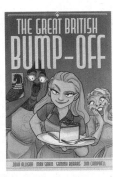

The Great British Bump-Off #4 © John Allison

	GD 2.0	VG 4.0	FN 6.0	VF 8.0	VF/NM 9.0	NM- 9.2
1-Catwoman, Harley Quinn and Poison Ivy; Dini-s/March-a/c	5	10	15	31	53	75
1-Variant-c by JG Jones	12	24	36	79	170	260
2-4	2	4	6	11	16	20
5-Full Harley Quinn cover	3	6	9	15	22	28
6-10	2	4	6	8	10	12
11-19	1	3	4	6	8	10
20,23-Joker, Harley Quinn cover	2	4	6	10	14	18
21-Full Harley Quinn cover	2	4	6	10	14	18
22,24-26						5.00
...: Song of the Sirens HC (2010, $19.99, dustjacket) r/#8-13 & Catwoman #83						20.00
...: Union HC (2010, $19.99, dustjacket) r/#1-7						20.00
...: Union SC (2011, $17.99) r/#1-7						18.00

GOTHAM CITY VILLAINS ANNIVERSARY GIANT
DC Comics: Jan, 2022 ($9.99, 100 pgs., squarebound, one-shot)

1-Short stories by various incl. Penguin/Catwoman by Danny DeVito-s/Mora-a; Bermejo-c	10.00

GOTHAM CITY: YEAR ONE
DC Comics: Dec, 2022 - No. 6, May, 2023 ($4.99, limited series)

1-6-Bruce Wayne's grandparents set in 1961; Slam Bradley app.; King-s/Hester-a	5.00

GOTHAM GAZETTE (Battle For The Cowl crossover in Batman titles)
DC Comics: May, 2009; Jul, 2009 ($2.99, one-shots)

1-Short stories of Gotham without Batman; Nguyen, March, ChrisCross & others-a	3.00
...: Batman Alive? (7/09) Vicki Vale app.; Nguyen, March, ChrisCross & others-a	3.00

GOTHAM GIRLS
DC Comics: Oct, 2002 - No. 5, Feb, 2003 ($2.25, limited series)

	GD	VG	FN	VF	VF/NM	NM-
1-Catwoman, Batgirl, Poison Ivy, Harley Quinn from animated series; Catwoman-c	3	6	9	15	22	28
2,4,5: 2-Poison Ivy-c. 4-Montoya-c. 5-Batgirl-c	2	4	6	10	14	18
3-Harley Quinn-c	4	8	12	27	44	60

GOTHAM NIGHTS (See Batman: Gotham Nights II)
DC Comics: Mar, 1992 - No. 4, June, 1992 ($1.25, limited series)

1-4: Featuring Batman	4.00

GOTHAM UNDERGROUND
DC Comics: Dec, 2007 - No. 9, Aug, 2008 ($2.99, limited series)

1-9-Nine covers interlock for single image; Tieri-s/Calafiore-a/c. 7,8-Vigilante app.	4.00
Batman: Gotham Underground TPB (2008, $19.99) r/#1-9; interlocked image cover	20.00

GOTHIC ROMANCES (Also see My Secrets)
Atlas/Seaboard Publ.: Dec, 1974 (75¢, B&W, magazine, 76 pgs.)

	GD	VG	FN	VF	VF/NM	NM-
1-Text w/ illos by N. Adams, Chaykin, Heath (2 pgs. ea.); painted cover from Ravenwood Gothic paperback "The Conservatory"(scarce)	36	72	108	259	580	900

GOTHIC TALES OF LOVE (Magazine)
Marvel Comics: Apr, 1975 - No. 3, 1975 (B&W, 76 pgs.)

1-3-Painted-c/a (scarce)	33	66	99	238	532	825

GOVERNOR & J. J., THE (TV)
Gold Key: Feb, 1970 - No. 3, Aug, 1970 (Photo-c)

1	4	8	12	25	40	55
2,3	3	6	9	18	28	38

GRACKLE, THE
Acclaim Comics: Jan, 1997 - No. 4, Apr, 1997 ($2.95, B&W)

1-4: Mike Baron scripts & Paul Gulacy-c/a. 1-4-Doublecross	4.00

GRAFIK MUSIK
Caliber Press: Nov, 1990 - No. 4, Aug, 1991 ($3.50/$2.50)

	GD	VG	FN	VF	VF/NM	NM-
1-($3.50, 48 pgs., color) Mike Allred-c/a/scripts-1st app. in color of Frank Einstein (Madman)	3	6	9	18	27	36
2-($2.50, 24 pgs., color)	3	6	9	14	20	25
3,4-($2.50, 24 pgs., B&W)	2	4	6	11	16	20

GRANDMA DUCK'S FARM FRIENDS(See Walt Disney's C&S 293 & Wheaties)
Dell Publishing Co.: No. 763, Jan, 1957 - No. 1279, Feb, 1962 (Disney)

Four Color 763 (#1)	8	16	24	51	96	140
Four Color 873	6	12	18	37	66	95
Four Color 965,1279	5	10	15	34	60	85
Four Color 1010,1073,1161-Barks-a; 1073,1161-Barks-c/a	11	22	33	73	157	240

GRAND PASSION
Dynamite Entertainment: 2016 - No. 5, 2017 ($3.99, limited series)

1-5-James Robinson-s/Tom Feister-a/John Cassaday-c	4.00

GRAND PRIX (Formerly Hot Rod Racers)
Charlton Comics: No. 16, Sept, 1967 - No. 31, May, 1970

	GD	VG	FN	VF	VF/NM	NM-
16-Features Rick Roberts	4	8	12	23	37	50
17-20	3	6	9	17	26	35
21-31	3	6	9	16	23	30

GRAPHIC FANTASY
Image Comics: Feb, 2021 - No. 2, Feb, 2021 ($9.99/$5.99, B&W)

1-Reprint of 1982 fanzine with the 1st app. of Savage Dragon by Erik Larsen	10.00
2-($5.99) Reprint of 1982 fanzine with the 2nd app. of Savage Dragon	6.00

GRAPHIQUE MUSIQUE
Slave Labor Graphics: Dec, 1989 - No. 3, May, 1990 ($2.95, 52 pgs.)

	GD	VG	FN	VF	VF/NM	NM-
1-Mike Allred-c/a/scripts	4	8	12	23	37	50
2,3	3	6	9	19	30	45

GRASS KINGS
BOOM! Studios: Mar, 2017 - No. 15, May, 2018 ($3.99)

1-14-Matt Kindt-s/Tyler Jenkins-a	4.00
15-($4.99) Last issue; Kindt-s/Jenkins-a	5.00

GRAVESLINGER
Image Comics (Shadowline): Oct, 2007 - No. 4, Mar, 2008 ($3.50, limited series)

1-4-Denton & Mariotte-s/Cboins-a	3.50

GRAVE TALES
Hamilton Comics: Oct, 1991 - No. 3, Feb, 1992 ($3.95, B&W, mag., 52 pgs.)

	GD	VG	FN	VF	VF/NM	NM-
1-Staton-c/a	2	3	4	6	8	10
2,3: 2-Staton-a; Morrow-c	1	2	3	5	6	8

GRAVEYARD SHIFT
Image Comics: Dec, 2014 - No. 4, Apr, 2015 ($3.50)

1-4: 1-Jay Faerber-s/Fran Bueno-a; wraparound-c	3.50

GRAVITY (Also see Beyond! limited series)
Marvel Comics: Aug, 2005 - No. 5, Dec, 2005 ($2.99, limited series)

1-5: 1-Intro. Gravity; McKeever-s/Norton-a. 2-Rhino-c/app. 5-Spider-Man app.	3.00
...: Big-City Super Hero (2005, $7.99, digest) r/#1-5	8.00

GRAY AREA, THE
Image Comics: Jun, 2004 - No. 3, Oct, 2004 ($5.95/$3.95, limited series)

1,3-($5.95) Romita, Jr.-a/Brunswick-s; sketch pages and script pages. 3-Pin-up pages	6.00
2-($3.95)	4.00
...Vol. 1: All Of This Can Be Yours (2005, $14.95) r/series & sketch,script & pin-up pages	15.00

GRAY GHOST, THE
Dell Publishing Co.: No. 911, July, 1958; No. 1000, June-Aug, 1959

	GD	VG	FN	VF	VF/NM	NM-
Four Color 911 (#1), 1000-Photo-c each	8	16	24	55	105	155

GRAYSON (See Forever Evil) (Leads into Nightwing: Rebirth)
DC Comics: Sept, 2014 - No. 20, Jul, 2016 ($2.99/$3.99)

1-8-Dick Grayson as secret agent; Seeley & King-s/Janin-a. 1,2,6,7-Midnighter app.	3.00
9-20-($3.99): 10-Lex Luthor app. 12-Return to Gotham; Batgirl, Red Robin.	4.00
15-"Robin War" tie-in	5.00
Annual 1 (2/15, $4.99) Mooney-a	5.00
Annual 2 (11/15, $4.99) Superman and Blockbuster app.; Alvaro Martinez-a	5.00
Annual 3 (8/16, $4.99) Harley Quinn, Constantine, Azrael, Simon Baz app.	5.00
...: Futures End 1 (11/14, $2.99, regular-c) Five years later; Mooney-a	3.00
...: Futures End 1 (11/14, $3.99, 3-D cover)	4.00

GREAT ACTION COMICS
I. W. Enterprises: 1958 (Reprints with new covers)

	GD	VG	FN	VF	VF/NM	NM-
1-Captain Truth reprinted from Gold Medal #1	3	6	9	17	25	34
8,9-Reprints Phantom Lady #15 & 23	8	16	24	56	108	160

GREAT AMERICAN COMICS PRESENTS - THE SECRET VOICE
Peter George 4-Star Publ./American Features Syndicate: 1945 (10¢)

1-Anti-Nazi; "What Really Happened to Hitler"	87	174	261	553	952	1350

GREAT AMERICAN WESTERN, THE
AC Comics: 1987 - No. 4, 1990? ($1.75/$2.95/$3.50, B&W with some color)

1-4: 1-Western-r plus Bill Black-a. 2-Tribute to ME comics; Durango Kid photo-c 3-Tribute to Tom Mix plus Roy Rogers, Durango Kid; Billy the Kid-r by Severin; photo-c. 4- ($3.50, 52 pgs., 16 pgs. color)-Tribute to Lash LaRue; photo-c & interior photos; Fawcett-r	4.00
...Presents 1 (1991, $5.00) New Sunset Carson; film history	5.00

GREAT BRITISH BUMP-OFF, THE
Dark Horse Comics: Apr, 2023 - No. 4, Jul, 2023 ($3.99, limited series)

1-4-John Allison-s/Max Sarin-a	4.00

	GD	VG	FN	VF	VF/NM	NM-
	2.0	4.0	6.0	8.0	9.0	9.2

GREAT CAT FAMILY, THE (Disney-TV/Movie)
Dell Publishing Co.: No. 750, Nov, 1956 (one-shot)

Four Color 750-Pinocchio & Alice app.	6	12	18	42	79	115

GREAT COMICS
Great Comics Publications: Nov, 1941 - No. 3, Jan, 1942

1-Origin/1st app. The Great Zarro; Madame Strange & Guy Gorham, Wizard of Science & The Great Zarro begin	161	322	483	1030	1765	2500
2-Buck Johnson, Jungle Explorer app.; X-Mas-c	87	174	261	553	952	1350
3-Futuro Takes Hitler to Hell-c/s; "The Lost City" movie story (starring William Boyd); continues in Choice Comics #3 (scarce)	3000	6000	9000	15,000	22,500	30,000

GREAT COMICS
Novack Publishing Co./Jubilee Comics/Knockout/Barrel O' Fun: 1945

1-(Four publ. variations: Barrel O-Fun, Jubilee, Knockout & Novack)-The Defenders, Capt. Power app.; L.B. Cole-c	74	148	222	470	810	1150
1-(Jubilee)-Same cover; Boogey Man, Satanas, & The Sorcerer & His Apprentice	39	78	117	240	395	550
1-(Barrel O' Fun)-L. B. Cole-c; Barrel O' Fun overprinted in indicia; Li'l Cactus, Cuckoo Sheriff (humorous)	34	68	102	199	325	450

GREAT DOGPATCH MYSTERY (See Mammy Yokum & the...)

GREATEST ADVENTURE, THE (Edgar Rice Burroughs characters)
Dynamite Entertainment: 2017 - No. 9, 2018 ($3.99)

1-9: 1-Tarzan & Jane, Korak, Jason Gridley, John Carter & Dejah Thoris app.; Razek-a						4.00

GREATEST AMERICAN HERO (Based on the 1981-1986 TV series)
Catastrophic Comics: Dec, 2008 - No. 3, May, 2009 ($3.50/$3.95)

1-3-Origin re-told; William Katt and others-a. 3-Obama-c/app.						4.00

GREATEST BATMAN STORIES EVER TOLD, THE
DC Comics

Hardcover ($24.95)		50.00
Softcover ($15.95) "Greatest DC Stories Vol. 2" on spine		20.00
Vol. 2 softcover (1992, $16.95) "Greatest DC Stories Vol. 7" on spine		20.00

GREATEST FLASH STORIES EVER TOLD, THE
DC Comics: 1991

nn-Hardcover ($29.95); Infantino-c		45.00
nn-Softcover ($14.95)		20.00

GREATEST GOLDEN AGE STORIES EVER TOLD, THE
DC Comics: 1990 ($24.95, hardcover)

nn-Ordway-c		60.00

GREATEST HITS
DC Comics (Vertigo): Dec, 2008 - No. 6, Apr, 2009 ($2.99, limited series)

1-6-Intro. The Mates superhero team in 1967 England; Tischman-s/Fabry-a/c		3.00

GREATEST JOKER STORIES EVER TOLD, THE (See Batman)
DC Comics: 1983

Hardcover ($19.95)-Kyle Baker painted-c		50.00
Softcover ($14.95)		20.00
Stacked Deck...Expanded Edition (1992, $29.95)-Longmeadow Press Publ.		35.00

GREATEST 1950s STORIES EVER TOLD, THE
DC Comics: 1990

Hardcover ($24.95)-Kubert-c		55.00
Softcover ($14.95) "Greatest DC Stories Vol. 5" on spine		22.00

GREATEST TEAM-UP STORIES EVER TOLD, THE
DC Comics: 1989

Hardcover ($24.95)-DeVries and Infantino painted-c		55.00
Softcover ($14.95) "Greatest DC Stories Vol. 4" on spine; Adams-c		22.00

GREATEST SUPERMAN STORIES EVER TOLD, THE
DC Comics: 1987

Hardcover ($24.95)		50.00
Softcover ($15.95)		22.00

GREAT EXPLOITS
Decker Publ./Red Top: Oct, 1957

1-Krigstein-a(2) (re-issue on cover); reprints Daring Advs. #6 by Approved Comics	9	18	27	52	69	85

GREAT FOODINI, THE (See Foodini)

GREAT GAZOO, THE (The Flintstones)(TV)
Charlton Comics: Aug, 1973 - No. 20, Jan, 1977 (Hanna-Barbera)

1	5	10	15	31	53	75
2-10	3	6	9	17	26	35
11-20	2	4	6	11	16	20

GREAT GRAPE APE, THE (TV)(See TV Stars #1)
Charlton Comics: Sept, 1976 - No. 2, Nov, 1976 (Hanna-Barbera)

1	5	10	15	33	57	80
2	3	6	9	14	20	25

GREAT GRIMMAX, THE
Defiant: Aug, 1994 (8 pgs.)

0-Hero Illustrated giveaway, Polgardy/Shooter story, J.G. Jones-c, Cockrum-a		4.00

GREAT LAKES AVENGERS (Also see G.L.A.)
Marvel Comics: Dec, 2016 - No. 7, Jun, 2017 ($3.99)

1-7: 1-Team reunites; Squirrel Girl cameo; Gorman-s/Robson-a. 7-Deadpool app.		4.00

GREAT LOCOMOTIVE CHASE, THE (Disney)
Dell Publishing Co.: No. 712, Sept, 1956 (one-shot)

Four Color 712-Movie, photo-c	7	14	21	46	86	125

GREAT LOVER ROMANCES (Young Lover Romances #4,5)
Toby Press: 3/51; #2, 1951 (nd); #3, 1952 (nd); #6, Oct?, 1952 - No. 22, May, 1955 (Photo-c #1-5, 10 ,13, 15, 17) (no #4, 5)

1-Jon Juan story-r/Jon Juan #1 by Schomburg; Dr. Anthony King app.	30	60	90	177	289	400
2-Jon Juan, Dr. Anthony King app.	18	36	54	103	162	220
3,7,9-14,16-22: 10-Rita Hayworth photo-c. 17-Rita Hayworth & Aldo Ray photo-c	14	28	42	81	118	155
6-Kurtzman-a (10/52)	16	32	48	92	144	195
8-Five pgs. of "Pin-Up Pete" by Sparling	15	30	45	88	137	185
15-Liz Taylor photo-c (scarce)	58	116	174	371	636	900

GREAT RACE, THE (See Movie Classics)

GREAT SCOTT SHOE STORE (See Bulls-Eye)

GREAT SOCIETY COMIC BOOK, THE (Political parody)
Pocket Books Inc./Parallax Pub.: 1966 ($1.00, 36 pgs., 7"x10", one-shot)

nn-Super-LBJ-c/story; 60s politicians app. as super-heroes; Tallarico-a	3	6	9	18	28	38

GREAT TEN, THE (Characters from Final Crisis)
DC Comics: Jan, 2010 - No. 9, Sept, 2010 ($2.99, limited series)

1-9-Super team of China; Bedard-s/McDaniel-a/Stanley Lau-c		3.00

GREAT WEST (Magazine)
M. F. Enterprises: 1969 (B&W, 52 pgs.)

V1#1	2	4	6	10	14	18

GREAT WESTERN
Magazine Enterprises: No. 8, Jan-Mar, 1954 - No. 11, Oct-Dec, 1954

8(A-1 93)-Trail Colt by Guardineer; Powell Red Hawk-r/Straight Arrow begins, ends #11; Durango Kid story	18	36	54	109	172	235
9(A-1 105), 11(A-1 127)-Ghost Rider, Durango Kid app. in each. 9-Red Mask-c, but no app.	15	30	45	85	130	175
10(A-1 113)-The Calico Kid by Guardineer-r/Tim Holt #8; Straight Arrow, Durango Kid app.	12	24	36	69	97	125
I.W. Reprint #1,2 9: 1,2-r/Straight Arrow #36,42. 9-r/Straight Arrow #?	3	6	9	15	22	28
I.W. Reprint #8-Origin Ghost Rider(r/Tim Holt #11); Tim Holt app.; Bolle-a	3	6	9	16	24	32

NOTE: *Guardineer c-8. Powell a(r)-8-11 (from Straight Arrow).*

GREEK STREET
DC Comics (Vertigo): Sept, 2009 - No. 16, Dec, 2010 ($1.00/$2.99)

1-16: 1-($1.00) Milligan-s/Gianfelice-a. 2: Begin $2.99-c		3.00
...: Blood Called For Blood SC (2010, $9.99) r/#1-5; Mike Carey intro.; sketch art		10.00
...: Cassandra Complex SC (2010, $14.99) r/#6-11		15.00

GREEN ARROW (See Action #440, Adventure, Brave & the Bold, DC Super Stars #17, Detective #521, Flash #217, Green Lantern #76, Justice League of America #4, Leading Comics, More Fun #73 (1st app.), Showcase '95 #9 & World's Finest Comics)

GREEN ARROW
DC Comics: May, 1983 - No. 4, Aug, 1983 (limited series)

1-Origin; Speedy cameo; Mike W. Barr scripts, Trevor Von Eeden-c/a.	3	6	9	17	26	35
2-4	1	3	4	6	8	10

GREEN ARROW
DC Comics: Feb, 1988 - No. 137, Oct, 1998 ($1.00-$2.50) (Painted-c #1-3)

1-Mike Grell scripts begin, ends #80	2	4	6	9	12	15
2-49,51-74,76-86: 27,28-Warlord app. 35-38-Co-stars Black Canary; Bill Wray-i. 40-Grell-a. 47-Begin $1.50-c. 63-No longer has mature readers on-c. 63-66-Shado app. 81-Aparo-a begins, ends #100; Nuklon app. 82-Intro & death of Rival. 83-Huntress-c/story. 84, 85-Deathstroke app. 86-Catwoman-c/story w/Jim Balent layouts						4.00
50,75-($2.50, 52 pgs.): Anniversary issues. 75-Arsenal (Roy Harper) & Shado app.						5.00
87-96: 87-$1.95-c begins. 88-Guy Gardner, Martian Manhunter, & Wonder Woman-c/app.; Flash-c. 89-Anarky app. 90-(9/94)-Zero Hour tie-in. 91-(11/94). 93-1st app. Camerouge. 95-Hal Jordan app. 96-Intro new Force of July; Hal Jordan (Parallax) app; Oliver Queen learns that Connor Hawke is his son						3.00
97-99,102-109: 97-Begin $2.25-c; no Aparo-a. 98-99-Arsenal app. 102,103-Underworld Unleashed x-over. 104-GL (Kyle Rayner)-c/app. 105-Robin-c/app. 107-109-Thorn app. 109-Lois Lane cameo; Weeks-c.						3.00
100-($3.95)-Foil-c; Superman app.	1	3	4	6	8	10
101-Death of Oliver Queen; Superman app.	3	6	9	11	16	23
110,111-124: 110,111-GL x-over. 110-Intro Hatchet. 114-Final Night. 115-117-Black Canary & Oracle app.						3.00
125-($3.50, 48 pgs.)-GL x-over cont. in GL #92						4.00
126-136: 126-Begin $2.50-c. 130-GL & Flash x-over. 132,133-JLA app. 134,135-Brotherhood of the Fist pts. 1,5. 136-Hal Jordan app.						3.00
137-Last issue; Superman app.; last panel cameo of Oliver Queen						4.00
#0 (10/94) Zero Hour; 1st app. Connor Hawke; Aparo-a(p); released between #90 & #91						4.00
#1,000,000 (11/98) 853rd Century x-over						
Annual 1-6 ('88-'94, 68 pgs.)-1-No Grell scripts. 2-No Grell scripts; recaps origin Green Arrow, Speedy, Black Canary & others. 3-Bill Wray-a. 4-50th anniversary issue. 5-Batman, Eclipso app. 6-Bloodlines; Hook app.						5.00
Annual 7-('95, $3.95)-Year One story						5.00

NOTE: *Aparo a-0, 81-85, 86 (partial),87p, 88p, 91-95, 96i, 98-100p, 109p; c-81,98-100p. Austin c-96i. Balent layouts-86. Burchett c-91-95. Campanella a-100-108i, 110-113i; c-99i, 101-108i,110-113i. Denys Cowan a-39p, 41-43p, 47p, 48p, 60p; c-41-43, Damaggio a(p)-97p, 100-108p, 110-112p; c-97-99p, 101-108p, 110-113p. Mike Grell c-1-4, 10p, 19, 30, 40, 44, 45, 47-80, Annual 4, 5. Nasser/Netzer a-89, 96. Sienkiewicz a-109i. Springer a-67, 68. Weeks c-109.*

GREEN ARROW
DC Comics: Apr, 2001 - No. 75, Aug, 2007 ($2.50/$2.99)

1-Oliver Queen returns; Kevin Smith-s/Hester/Wagner-painted-c	2	4	6	10	14	18
1-2nd-4th printings						3.00
2-Batman cameo	1	2	3	4	5	7
2-2nd printing						3.00
3-5: 4-JLA app.						5.00
6-15: 7-Barry Allen & Hal Jordan app. 9,10-Stanley & his Monster app. 10-Oliver regains his soul. 12-Hawkman-c/app.						4.00
16-25: 16-Brad Meltzer-s begin; The Shade app. 18-Solomon Grundy-c/app. 19-JLA app.						

Great Gazoo #12 © H-B

Green Arrow (2001 series) #46 © DC

Green Hornet #2 © Greenway

	GD	VG	FN	VF	VF/NM	NM-		GD	VG	FN	VF	VF/NM	NM-
	2.0	4.0	6.0	8.0	9.0	9.2		2.0	4.0	6.0	8.0	9.0	9.2

22-Beatty-s; Count Vertigo app. 23-25-Green Lantern app.; Raab-s/Adlard-a	3.00
26-49: 26-Winick-s begin. 35-37-Riddler app. 43-Mia learns she's HIV+. 45-Mia becomes	
the new Speedy. 46-Teen Titans app. 49-The Outsiders app.	3.00
50-($3.50) Green Arrow's team and the Outsiders vs. The Riddler and Drakon	4.00
51-59: 51-Anarky app. 52-Zatanna-c/app. 55-59-Dr. Light app.	3.00
60-74: 60-One Year Later starts. 62-Begin $2.99-c; Deathstroke app. 69-Batman app.	3.00
75-($3.50) Ollie proposes to Dinah (see Black Canary mini-series); JLA app.	4.00
... By Jack Kirby (2001, $5.95) Collects Green Arrow stories by Kirby from the 1950s;	
introduction by Evanier	6.00
...: City Walls SC (2005, $17.95) r/#32, 34-39	18.00
...: Crawling Through the Wreckage SC (2007, $12.99) r/#60-65	13.00
...: Heading Into the Light SC (2006, $12.99) r/#52,54-59	13.00
...: Moving Targets SC (2006, $17.99) r/#40-50	18.00
...: Quiver HC (2002, $24.95) r/#1-10; Smith intro.	25.00
...: Quiver SC (2003, $17.95) r/#1-10; Smith intro.	18.00
...: Road to Jericho SC (2007, $17.99) r/#66-75	18.00
...Secret Files & Origins 1-(1/02, $4.95) Origin stories and profiles; Wagner-c	5.00
...: Sounds of Violence HC (2003, $19.95) r/#11-15; Hester intro. & sketch pages	20.00
...: Sounds of Violence SC (2003, $12.95) r/#11-15; Hester intro. & sketch pages	13.00
...: Straight Shooter SC (2004, $12.95) r/#26-31	13.00
...: The Archer's Quest HC (2003, $19.95) r/#16-21; pitch, script and sketch pages	20.00
...: The Archer's Quest SC (2004, $14.95) r/#16-21; pitch, script and sketch pages	15.00

GREEN ARROW (Brightest Day)
DC Comics: Aug, 2010 - No. 15, Oct, 2011 ($3.99/$2.99)

1-Oliver Queen in the Star City forest; Green Lantern app.; Neves-a/Cascioli-c	5.00
1-Variant-c by Van Sciver	8.00
2-15-($2.99) 2-Green Lantern app. 7-Mayhew-a. 8-11-The Demon app. 12-Swamp Thing	3.00
...: Into the Woods HC (2011, $22.99) r/#1-7; variant cover gallery	23.00

GREEN ARROW (DC New 52)
DC Comics: Nov, 2011 - No. 52, Jul, 2016 ($2.99)

1-Krul-s/Jurgens & Pérez-a/Wilkins-c	1	3	4	6	8	10

2-24: 4,5-Giffen-s. 13,14-Hawkman app. 17-24-Lemire-s/Sorrentino-a/c. 22-Count Vertigo	
app. 23,24-Richard Dragon app.	3.00
23.1 (11/13, $2.99, regular cover) "Count Vertigo #1" on cover; Sorrentino-a/c	3.00
23.1 (11/13, $3.99, 3-D cover) "Count Vertigo #1" on cover; Sorrentino-a/c	5.00
25-($3.99) Zero Year tie-in; Batman app.; back-up with Cowan-a	4.00
26-49: 26-31-Outsiders War; Lemire-s/Sorrentino-a/c. 35-40-Hitch'-a; Felicity Smoak app.	3.00
50-($4.99) Kudranski-a; Deathstroke app.	5.00
51,52-Deathstroke app.	3.00
#0 (11/12) Origin story re-told; Nocenti-s/Williams II-a	3.00
Annual 1 (11/15, $4.99) Percy-s/Kudranski-a/Edwards-c	5.00
...: Futures End 1 (11/14, $2.99, regular-c) Five years later; Lemire-s/Sorrentino-a	3.00
...: Futures End 1 (11/14, $3.99, 3-D cover)	4.00

GREEN ARROW (DC Rebirth)
DC Comics: Aug, 2016 - No. 50, May, 2019 ($2.99/$3.99)

1-24: 1,2-Percy-s/Schmidt-a; Black Canary & Shado app. 3-5-Ferreyra-a. 14-Malcolm Merlyn	
returns. 21-24-Cheshire app.	3.00
25-($3.99) Schmidt-a; Kate Spencer app.; Moira Queen returns	4.00
26-33: 26,27-Flash app. 27-Wonder Woman app. 28-Superman app. 29-Batman app.	
30,31-Green Lantern app. 32-Dark Nights: Metal tie-in	3.00
34-49-($3.99) 41,42-The Parasite app. 45-Roy Harper's funeral	4.00
50-($4.99) Nowlan-c	
Annual 1 (1/18, $4.99) Count Vertigo app.; Percy-s/Carlini-a	5.00
Annual 2 (7/18, $4.99) Justice League: No Justice tie-in; Carnero-a	5.00
...: Rebirth 1 (8/16, $2.99) Percy-a/Schmidt-a; Black Canary app.	3.00

GREEN ARROW (Dawn of DC)(Continues from Dark Crisis on Infinite Earths #6)
DC Comics: Jun, 2023 - Present ($3.99)

1-9: 9-Williamson-s/Izaakse-a; Roy Harper & Connor Hawke app. 2,3-Peacemaker app.	4.00

GREEN ARROW/BLACK CANARY (Titled Green Arrow for #30-32)
DC Comics: Dec, 2007 - No. 32, Jun, 2010 ($3.50/$2.99)

1-($3.50) Connor Hawke & Black Canary; follows Wedding Special; Winick-s/Chang-a	6.00
2-21-($2.99) 3-Two covers; Connor shot. 5-Dinah & Ollie's real wedding	3.00
22-30-($3.99) Back-up stories begin. 28-Origin of Cupid. 30-Blackest Night	4.00
30-Variant cover by Mike Grell	8.00
31-32-($2.99) Rise and Fall; Dallocchio-a	3.00
...: A League of Their Own TPB (2009, $17.99) r/#11-14 & G.A. Secret Files & Origins	18.00
...: Big Game TPB (2010, $19.99) r/#21-26	20.00
...: Enemies List TPB (2009, $17.99) r/#15-20	18.00
...: Family Business TPB (2009, $17.99) r/#5-10	18.00
...: Five Stages TPB (2010, $17.99) r/#27-30	18.00
...: Road To The Altar TPB (2008, $17.99) r/proposal pages from Green Arrow #75, Birds of	
Prey #109, Black Canary #1-4 and Black Canary Wedding Planner #1	18.00

...: The Wedding Album HC (2008, $19.99, dustjacket) r/#1-5 & Wedding Special #1	20.00
...: The Wedding Album SC (2009, $17.99) r/#1-5 & Wedding Special #1	18.00
... Wedding Special 1 (11/07, $3.99) Winick-s/Conner-a/c; Dinah & Ollie's "wedding"	10.00
... Wedding Special 1 (11/07, $3.99) 2nd printing with Ryan Sook variant-c	4.00

GREEN ARROW 80TH ANNIVERSARY 100-PAGE SUPER SPECTACULAR
DC Comics: Aug, 2021 ($9.99, squarebound, one-shot)

1-Short stories & pin-ups by various; Denny O'Neil tribute; multiple covers	10.00

GREEN ARROW: THE LONG BOW HUNTERS
DC Comics: Aug, 1987 - No. 3, Oct, 1987 ($2.95, limited series, mature)

1-Grell-c/a in all	2	4	6	8	10	12
1,2-2nd printings						4.00
2,3						6.00
Trade paperback (1989, $12.95)-r/#1-3						15.00

GREEN ARROW: THE WONDER YEAR
DC Comics: Feb, 1993 - No. 4, May, 1993 ($1.75, limited series)

1-4: Mike Grell-a(p)/scripts & Gray Morrow-a(i)	4.00

GREEN ARROW: YEAR ONE
DC Comics: Early Sept, 2007 - No. 6, Late Nov, 2007 ($2.99, bi-weekly limited series)

1-6-Origin re-told; Diggle-s/Jock-a	3.00
1-Special Edition (12/14, $1.00) Reprints #1; Arrow TV show banner atop cover	3.00
HC (2008, $24.99) r/#1-6; intro. by Brian K. Vaughan; script and sketch pages	25.00
SC (2009, $14.99) r/#1-6; intro. by Brian K. Vaughan; script and sketch pages	15.00

GREEN BERET, THE (See Tales of...)

GREEN DANTE / GREEN VIRGIL
Aardvark-Vanaheim: Apr, 2020 ($4.00, B&W)

1-Cerebus figures with original Gustave Doré artwork; Green Lantern #76-c swipe	4.00

GREEN GIANT COMICS (Also see Colossus Comics)
Pelican Publ. (Funnies, Inc.): 1940 (No price on cover; distributed in New York City only)

1-Dr. Nerod, Green Giant, Black Arrow, Mundoo & Master Mystic app.; origin Colossus (Rare)						
	1720	3440	5160	12,500	24,750	37,000

NOTE: The idea for this book came from George Kapitan. Printed by Moreau Publ. of Orange, N.J. as an experiment to see if they could profitably use the idle time of their 40-page Hoe color press. The experiment failed due to the difficulty of obtaining good quality color registration and Mr. Moreau believes the book never reached the stands. The book has no price or date which lends credence to this. Contains five pages reprinted from Motion Picture Funnies Weekly.

GREEN GOBLIN
Marvel Comics: Oct, 1995 - No. 13, Oct, 1996 ($2.95/$1.95)

1-($2.95)-Scott McDaniel-c/a begins, ends #7; foil-c	5.00
2-13: 2-Begin $1.95-c. 4-Hobgoblin-c/app.; Thing app. 6-Daredevil-c/app. 8-Robertson-a;	
McDaniel-c. 12,13-Onslaught x-over. 13-Green Goblin quits; Spider-Man app.	4.00

GREENHAVEN
Aircel Publishing: 1988 - No. 3, 1988 ($2.00, limited series, 28 pgs.)

1-3	4.00

GREEN HORNET, THE (TV)
Dell Publishing Co./Gold Key: Sept, 1953; Feb, 1967 - No. 3, Aug, 1967

	GD	VG	FN	VF	VF/NM	NM-
Four Color 496-Painted-c.	30	60	90	216	483	750
1-Bruce Lee photo-c and back-c pin-up	27	54	81	189	420	650
2,3-Bruce Lee photo-c	14	28	42	96	211	325

GREEN HORNET, THE (Also see Kato of the... & Tales of the...)
Now Comics: Nov, 1989 - No. 14, Feb, 1991 ($1.75)
V2#1, Sept. 1991 - V2#40, Jan, 1995 ($1.95)

1 ($2.95, double-size)-Steranko painted-c; G.A. Green Hornet	6.00
1,2: 1-2nd printing ('90, $2.95)-New Butler-c	4.00
3-14: 5-Death of original ('30s) Green Hornet. 6-Dave Dorman painted-c. 11-Snyder-c	4.00
V2#1-11,13-21,24-26,28-30,32-37: 1-Butler painted-c. 9-Mayerik-c	4.00
12-($2.50)-Color Green Hornet button polybagged inside	5.00
22,23-($2.95)-Bagged w/color hologravure card	
27-($2.95)-Newsstand ed. polybagged w/multi-dimensional card (1993 Anniversary Special	
on cover), 27-($2.95)-Direct Sale ed. polybagged w/multi-dimensional card;	
cover variations	4.00
31,38: 31-($2.50)-Polybagged w/trading card	4.00
39,40-Low print run	6.00
1-($2.50) Polybagged w/button (same as #12)	5.00
2,3-($1.95)-Same as #13 & 14	4.00
Annual 1 (12/92, $2.50), Annual 1994 (10/94, $2.95)	5.00

GREEN HORNET (Becomes Green Hornet: Legacy with #34)
Dynamite Entertainment: 2010 - No. 33, 2013 ($3.99)

1-Kevin Smith-s/Jonathan Lau-a; multiple covers by Alex Ross, Cassaday, Campbell and	

	GD	VG	FN	VF	VF/NM	NM-
	2.0	4.0	6.0	8.0	9.0	9.2

Segovia 4.00
2-33-Multiple covers by Ross and others on each. 11-Hester-s begins 4.00
Annual 1 (2010, $5.99) Hester-s/Netzer & Rafael-a 6.00
Annual 2 (2012, $4.99) Hester-c/Rahner-s/Cliquet-a; back-up r/G.H. Comics #1 (1940) 5.00
... FCBD Edition; 5 previews of various new Green Hornet series; Cassaday-c 3.00

GREEN HORNET
Dynamite Entertainment: 2013 - No. 13, 2014 ($3.99)
1-13: 1-Set in 1941; Mark Waid-s/Daniel Indro-a; 2 covers by Alex Ross & Paolo Rivera 4.00
... One Night in Bangkok (2023, $4.99) Denton-s/Morales-a 5.00

GREEN HORNET: AFTERMATH
Dynamite Entertainment: 2011 - No. 4, 2011 $1.99/$3.99, limited series)
1-Nitz-s/Raynor-a; Green Hornet & Kato after the 2011 movie 3.00
2-4-($3.99) 4.00

GREEN HORNET: BLOOD TIES
Dynamite Entertainment: 2010 - No. 4, 2011 ($3.99)
1-4-Ande Parks-s/Johnny Desjardins-a; original Green Hornet & Kato 4.00

GREEN HORNET COMICS (...Racket Buster #44) (Radio, movies)
Helnit Publ. Co.(Holyoke) No. 1-6/Family Comics(Harvey) No. 7-on:
Dec, 1940 - No. 47, Sept, 1949 (See All New #13,14)(Early issues: 68 pgs.)

	GD	VG	FN	VF	VF/NM	NM-
1-1st app. Green Hornet & Kato; text origin of Green Hornet on inside front-c; intro the Black Beauty (Green Hornet's car); painted-c	990	1980	2970	7200	13,850	20,500
2-(3/41) Early issues based on radio adventures	290	580	870	1856	3178	4500
3	187	374	561	1197	2049	2900
4-6: 6-(8/41)	168	336	504	1075	1838	2600
7 (6/42)-1st app. of the Green Hornet villain The Murdering Clown; origin The Zebra & begins; Robin Hood, Spirit of '76, Blonde Bomber & Mighty Midgets begin; new logo	206	412	618	1318	2259	3200
8-Classic horror bondage killer dwarf-c	258	516	774	1651	2826	4000
9-Kirby-c	194	388	582	1242	2121	3000
10-(12/42) Hornet vs. The Murdering Clown-c/sty	148	296	444	947	1624	2300
11-Mr. Q app.	135	270	405	864	1482	2100
12-1st WWII cover for this title; Mr. Q app.	135	270	405	864	1482	2100
13-1st Nazi-c; shows Hitler poster on-c	300	600	900	1920	3310	4700
14-Bondage-c; Mr. Q app.	116	232	348	742	1271	1800
15-Nazi WWII-c	155	310	465	992	1696	2400
16-Nazi WWII prisoner of war cable car cover	155	310	465	992	1696	2400
17-Nazi WWII-c	142	284	426	909	1555	2200
18,19-Japanese WWII-c	142	284	426	909	1555	2200
20-Classic Japanese WWII-c	161	322	483	1030	1765	2500
21-23-Japanese WWII-c	110	220	330	704	1202	1700
24-Classic Japanese poison rockets Sci-Fi-c	161	322	483	1030	1765	2500
25,27,28,30	55	110	165	352	601	850
26-(9/45) Japanese WWII-c	65	130	195	416	708	1000
29-Jerry Robinson skull-c	61	122	183	390	670	950
31-The Man in Black Called Fate begins (11-12/45, early page.)	58	116	174	371	636	900
32-36	39	78	117	231	378	525
37,38: Shock Gibson app. by Powell. 37-S&K Kid Adonis reprinted from Stuntman #3.						
38-Kid Adonis app.	39	78	117	231	378	525
39-Stuntman story by S&K	43	86	129	271	461	650
40-47: 42-47-Kerry Drake in all. 45-Boy Explorers on-c only. 46- "Case of the Marijuana Racket" cover/story; Kerry Drake app.	31	62	93	182	296	410

NOTE: *Fuje* a-23, 24, 26. *Henkle* c-7-9. *Kubert* a-29, 30. *Powell* a-7-10, 12, 14, 16-21, 30, 31(2), 32(3), 33, 34(3), 35, 36, 37(2), 38. *Robinson* a-27. *Schomburg* c-17-20. *Kirbyish* c-7, 15. Bondage c-8, 11, 14, 18, 26, 36.

GREEN HORNET: DARK TOMORROW
Now Comics: June, 1993 - No. 3, Aug, 1993 ($2.50, limited series)
1-3: Future Green Hornet 4.00

GREEN HORNET: GOLDEN AGE RE-MASTERED
Dynamite Entertainment: 2010 - No. 8, 2011 ($3.99)
1-8-Re-colored reprints of 1940's Green Hornet Comics; new Rubenstein-c 4.00

GREEN HORNET: LEGACY (Numbering continues from Green Hornet 2010-2013 series)
Dynamite Entertainment: No. 34, 2013 - No. 42, 2013 ($3.99)
34-42: 34-Jai Nitz-s/Jethro Morales-a 4.00

GREEN HORNET: PARALLEL LIVES
Dynamite Entertainment: 2010 - No. 5, 2010 ($3.99, limited series)
1-5-Jai Nitz-s/Nigel Raynor-a; semi-prequel to the 2011 movie; Kato's origin 4.00

GREEN HORNET: REIGN OF THE DEMON
Dynamite Entertainment: 2016 - No. 4, 2017 ($3.99, limited series)
1-4-David Liss-s/Kewber Baal-a 4.00

GREEN HORNET '66 MEETS THE SPIRIT: VOLUME 1
Dynamite Entertainment: 2017 - No. 5, 2017 ($3.99, limited series)
1-5-Fred VanLente-s/Bob Q-a; The Octopus app. 4.00

GREEN HORNET: SOLITARY SENTINEL, THE
Now Comics: Dec, 1992 - No. 3, 1993 ($2.50, limited series)
1-3 4.00

GREEN HORNET STRIKES!
Dynamite Entertainment: 2010 - No. 10, 2012 ($3.99)
1-10: 1-Matthews-s/Padilla-a/Cassaday-c; future Green Hornet 4.00

GREEN HORNET, VOLUME 2
Dynamite Entertainment: 2018 - No. 5, 2018 ($3.99)
1-5-Amy Chu-s/German Erramouspe-a; new female Green Hornet 4.00

GREEN HORNET, VOLUME 3
Dynamite Entertainment: 2020 - No. 5, 2020 ($3.99, B&W & green tint)
1-5-Lobdell/Marques & Bona-a; regular Green Hornet & Kato 4.00

GREEN HORNET: YEAR ONE
Dynamite Entertainment: 2010 - No. 12, 2011 ($3.99, limited series)
1-12-Matt Wagner-s/Aaron Campbell-a; 1940's Green Hornet & Kato. 1-5-Cassaday-c 4.00

...: Special 1 (2013, $4.99) Crosby-s/Menna-a/Chen-c 5.00

GREEN JET COMICS, THE (See Comic Books, Series 1 in the Promotional Comics section)

GREEN LAMA (Also see Comic Books, Series 1, Daring Adventures #17 & Prize Comics #7)
Spark Publications/Prize No. 7 on: Dec, 1944 - No. 8, Mar, 1946

	GD	VG	FN	VF	VF/NM	NM-
1-Intro. Lt. Hercules & The Boy Champions; Mac Raboy-c/a #1-8						
	148	296	444	947	1624	2300
2-Lt. Hercules borrows the Human Torch's powers for one panel						
	93	186	279	591	1021	1450
3-5,8: 4-Dick Tracy take-off in Lt. Hercules story by H. L. Gold (science fiction writer); Japanese WWII-c; Emperor Hirohito app.; Hitler story; Lt. Hercules story; Little Orphan Annie, Smilin' Jack & Snuffy Smith take-off (5/45)						
	60	120	180	381	653	925
6-Classic Raboy swastika-c	116	232	348	742	1271	1800
7-Christmas-c; Raboy craft tint-c/a (note: a small quantity of NM copies surfaced)						
	36	72	108	211	343	475
... Archives Featuring the Art of Mac Raboy Vol. 1 HC (Dark Horse Books, 4/08, $49.95)						
r/#1-4 including back-up features; foreword by Chuck Rozanski						50.00
... Archives Featuring the Art of Mac Raboy Vol. 2 HC (Dark Horse Books, 1/09, $49.95)						
r/#5-8; foreword by Chuck Rozanski						50.00

NOTE: *Robinson* a-3-5, 8. *Roussos* a-8. Formerly a pulp hero who began in 1940.

GREEN LANTERN (1st Series) (See All-American, All Flash Quarterly, All Star Comics, The Big All-American & Comic Cavalcade)
National Periodical Publications/All-American: Fall, 1941 - No. 38, May-June, 1949 (#1-18 are quarterly)

	GD	VG	FN	VF	VF/NM	NM-
1-Origin retold; classic Purcell-c	3675	7350	11,025	29,400	53,700	98,000
2-1st book-length story	757	1514	2271	5526	9763	14,000
3-Classic German war-c by Mart Nodell	811	1622	2433	5920	10,460	15,000
4-Green Lantern & Doiby Dickles join the Army	415	830	1245	2905	5103	7300
5-WWII-c	365	730	1095	2555	4478	6400
6,8: 8-Hop Harrigan begins; classic-c	300	600	900	2010	3505	5000
7-Classic robot-c	320	640	960	2240	3920	5600
9-School for Vandals-s	258	516	774	1651	2826	4000
10-Origin/1st app. Vandal Savage	343	686	1029	2400	4200	6000
11,13-15	200	400	600	1280	2190	3100
12-Origin/1st app. Gambler	213	426	639	1363	2332	3300
16-Classic jungle-c (scarce in high grade)	206	412	618	1318	2259	3200
17,19,20	155	310	465	992	1696	2400
18-Christmas-c	200	400	600	1280	2190	3100
21-26	148	296	444	947	1624	2300
27-Origin/1st app. Sky Pirate	187	374	561	1197	2049	2900
28-1st Sportsmaster (Crusher Crock)	168	336	504	1075	1838	2600
29-All Harlequin issue; classic Harlequin-c	271	542	813	1734	2967	4200
30-Origin/1st app. Streak the Wonder Dog by Toth (2-3/48) (Rare)						
	514	1028	1542	3750	6625	9500
31-Harlequin-c/app.	194	388	582	1242	2121	3000
32-35: 35-Kubert-c. 35-38-New logo	135	270	405	864	1482	2100
36-38: 37-Sargon the Sorcerer app.	168	336	504	1075	1838	2600

NOTE: *Book-length stories #2-7. Mayer/Moldoff c-9. Mayer/Purcell c-8. Purcell c-1. Mart Nodell c-2, 3, 7. Paul Reinman c-11, 12, 15-22. Toth a-28, 30, 31, 34-38; c-28, 30, 34p, 36-38p. Cover to #8 says Fall while the indicia says Summer issue. Cover to the Streak the Wonder Dog c-30 by Robinson (Adventures), 34, 36, 38.*

GREEN LANTERN (See Action Comics Weekly, Adventure Comics, Brave & the Bold, Day of Judgment, DC Special, DC Special Comics, Flash, Guy Gardner, Guy Gardner Reborn, JLA, JSA, Justice League of America, Parallax: Emerald Night, Showcase, Showcase '93 #12 & Tales of The...Corps)

GREEN LANTERN (2nd Series) (Green Lantern Corps #206 on) (See Showcase #22-24)
National Periodical Publ./DC Comics: Jul/Aug. 1960 - No. 89, Apr/May 1972;
No. 90, Aug/Sept. 1976 - No. 205, Oct. 1986

	GD	VG	FN	VF	VF/NM	NM-
1-(7-8/60)-Origin retold; Gil Kane-c/a continues; 1st app. Guardians of the Universe						
	500	1000	1500	4650	12,075	19,500
2-1st Pieface	104	208	312	632	1866	2900
3-Contains readers poll	61	122	183	488	1094	1700
4,5: 5-Origin/1st app. Hector Hammond	46	92	138	368	834	1300
6-Intro Tomar-Re the alien G.L.	46	92	138	340	770	1200
7-Origin/1st app. Sinestro (7-8/61)	139	278	417	1112	2506	3900
8-1st 5700 A.D. story; grey tone-c	46	92	138	359	805	1250
9-1st Sinestro-c; 1st Jordan Brothers; last 10¢-c	57	114	171	456	1028	1600
10	40	80	120	296	673	1050
11,12	24	48	72	168	372	575
13-Flash x-over	38	76	114	285	641	1000
14,15,17-20: 14-Origin/1st app. Sonar. 20-Flash app.	19	38	57	131	291	450
16-Origin & 1st app. (Silver Age) Star Sapphire	54	108	162	432	966	1500
21,22,25-28,30: 21-Origin & 1st app. Dr. Polaris	14	28	42	96	211	325
23-1st Tattooed Man	16	32	48	110	243	375
24-Origin & 1st app. Shark	28	56	84	202	451	700
29-JLA cameo; 1st Blackhand	21	42	63	147	324	500
31-39: 37-1st app. Evil Star (villain)	11	22	33	76	163	250
40-Origin of Infinite Earths (10/65); 2nd solo G.A. Green Lantern in Silver Age (see Showcase #55); origin The Guardians; Doiby Dickles app.	48	96	138	368	834	1300
41-44,46-50: 50-Zatanna x-over. 43-Flash x-over	10	20	30	64	132	200
45-2nd S.A. app. G.A. Green Lantern in title (6/66)	14	28	42	94	207	320
51,53-58	8	16	24	54	102	150
52-G.A. Green Lantern x-over; Sinestro app.	11	22	33	76	163	250
59-1st app. Guy Gardner (3/68)	46	92	138	368	834	1300
60,62-69: 69-Wood inks; last 12¢ issue	6	12	18	41	76	110
61-G.A. Green Lantern x-over	8	16	24	52	99	145
70-75	5	10	15	33	63	90
76-(4/70)-Begin Green Lantern/Green Arrow series (by Neal Adams #76-89) ends #122 (see Flash #217 for 2nd series)	96	192	288	768	1734	2700
77-Neal Adams-c/a	12	24	36	82	179	275
78-80-Neal Adams-c/a	10	20	30	67	141	215
81-84: 82-Wrightson-i(1 pg.). 83-G.L. reveals i.d. to Carol Ferris. 84-N. Adams/Wrightson-a (22 pgs.); last 15¢-c; partial photo-c	9	18	27	59	117	175
85,86-(52 pgs.) Classic anti-drug covers/stories; Speedy as a heroin junkie						
86-G.A. Green Lantern-r; Toth-a	11	22	33	76	163	250
87-(52 pgs.) 1st app. John Stewart (12-1/71-72) (becomes 3rd Green Lantern in #182);						

Green Hornet (2010 series) #1 © GH Inc.

Green Lantern #17 © DC

Green Lantern (2nd series) #59 © DC

	GD	VG	FN	VF	VF/NM	NM-
	2.0	4.0	6.0	8.0	9.0	9.2

	GD	VG	FN	VF	VF/NM	NM-
	2.0	4.0	6.0	8.0	9.0	9.2

2nd app. Guy Gardner (cameo) — 38 76 114 285 641 1000

88-(2-3/72, 52 pgs.)-Unpubbed G.A. Green Lantern story; Green Lantern-r/Showcase #23. N. Adams-c/a (1 pg.) — 9 18 27 59 117 175

89-(4-5/72, 52 pgs.)-G.A. Green Lantern-r; Green Lantern & Green Arrow move to Flash #217 (2nd team-up series) — 8 16 24 56 108 160

90 (8-9/76)-Begin 3rd Green Lantern/Green Arrow team-up series; Mike Grell-c/a begins, ends #111 — 3 6 9 19 30 40

91-99 — 2 4 6 10 16 20

100-(1/78, Giant)-1st app. Air Wave II — 3 6 9 21 33 45

101-107,111,113-115,117-119: 107-1st Tales of the G.L. Corps story

108-110-(44 pgs)-G.A. Green Lantern back-ups in each. 111-Origin retold; G.A. Green Lantern app. — 2 4 6 10 14 18

112-G.A. Green Lantern origin retold — 3 6 9 16 23 30

116-1st app. Guy Gardner as a G.L. (5/79) — 4 8 12 28 47 65

116-Whitman variant; issue # on cover — 5 10 15 33 57 80

117-119,121-(Whitman variants; low print run; none have issue # on cover) — 2 4 6 10 14 18

120,121,123-140,142-150: 123-Last Green Lantern/Green Arrow team-up. 130-132-Tales of the G.L. Corps. 132-Adam Strange series begins, ends147. 136,137-1st app. Citadel; Space Ranger app. 142,143-Omega Men app.;Perez-c. 144-Omega Men cameo. 148-Tales of the G.L. Corps begins, ends #173. 150-Anniversary issue, 52 pgs.; no G.L. Corps — 1 2 3 5 7 9

122-2nd app. Guy Gardner as Green Lantern; Flash & Hawkman brief app. — 3 6 9 15 22 28

141-1st app. Omega Men (6/81) — 2 4 6 12 27 44

151-180,183,184,186,187: 159-Origin Evil Star. 160,161-Omega Men app. 172-Gibbons-c/a begins. 175-No issue number shown on cover — 6.00

181,182,185,188,191: 181-Hal Jordan resigns as G.L. 182-John Stewart becomes new G.L.; origin recap of Hal Jordan as G.L. 185-Origin (new G.L.). 188-I.D. revealed; 1st app; Moore/Gibbons art. 191-Re-intro Star Sapphire (cameo) — 1 2 3 5 8

189,190,193,196-199,202-205: 194,198-Crisis x-over. 199-Hal Jordan returns as a member of G.L. Corps (3 G.L.s now). — 5.00

192-Re-intro & origin of Star Sapphire (1st full app.) — 2 4 6 9 13 16

194-Hal Jordan/Guy Gardner battle; Guardians choose Guy Gardner to become new Green Lantern — 1 2 3 5 6 8

195-Guy Gardner becomes Green Lantern; Crisis on Infinite Earths x-over — 2 4 6 10 13 18

200-Double-size — 1 2 3 5 6 8

201-Green Lantern Corps begins (is cover title, says premiere issue); intro. Kilowog — 3 6 9 20 31 42

Annual 1 (Listed as Tales Of The Green Lantern Corps Annual 1)

Annual 2,3 (See Green Lantern Corps Annual #2,3)

... No. 1 (Facsimile Edition)(2020, $3.99) r/#1 with original 1960 ads and letter column — 4.00

... No. 85 (Facsimile Edition)(2019, $3.99) r/#85 with original ads and letter column — 4.00

... No. 87 (Facsimile Edition)(4/24, $4.99) r/#87 with original ads and letter column — 5.00

Special 1 (1988), 2 (1989)-(Both $1.50, 52 pgs.)

... Chronicles TPB (2009, $14.99) r/Showcase #22-24 & Green Lantern #1-3 — 15.00

... Chronicles Vol. 2 TPB (2009, $14.99) r/Green Lantern #4-9 — 15.00

... Chronicles Vol. 3 TPB (2010, $14.99) r/Green Lantern #10-14 and Flash #131 — 15.00

NOTE: N. Adams a-76, 77-87p, 89; c-63, 76-89. M. Anderson a-137i. Austin a-93i, 94i, 171i. Chaykin c-119. Greene a-39-49i, 58-63i; c-54-58i. Grell a-90-100, 106, 108-111; c-90-106, 108-112. Heck a-120-122p. Infantino a-137p, 145-147p, 151, 152p. Gil Kane a-149p, 50-57, 58-61p, 68-75p, 85p(r), 87p(r), 88p(r), 156, 177, 184p; c-1-52, 54-61p, 67-75, 123, 154, 156, 165-171, 177, 184. Newton a-148p, 149p, 181. Perez c-132p, 141-144. Sekowsky a-65p, 170p. Simonson c-200. Sparling a-63p. Starlin c-129, 133. Staton a-117p, 123-127p, 128, 129-131p, 132-139, 140p, 141-146, 147p, 148-150, 151-155p; c-107p, 117p, 135(i), 136p, 145p, 146, 147, 148-152p, 155p. Toth a-86r, 171p. Tuska a-166-168p, 170p.

GREEN LANTERN (3rd Series)

DC Comics: June, 1990 - No. 181, Nov, 2004 ($1.00/$1.25/$1.50/$1.75/$1.95/$1.99/$2.25)

| | | | 1 | 3 | 4 | 6 | 8 | 10 |

1-Hal Jordan, John Stewart & Guy Gardner return; Batman & JLA app. — 1 3 4 6 8 10

2-18,20-26: 9-12-Guy Gardner solo story. 13-(52 pgs.). 18-Guy Gardner solo story.

25-($1.75, 52 pgs.)-Hal Jordan/Guy Gardner battle — 5.00

19-($1.75, 52 pgs.)-50th anniversary issue; Mart Nodell (original G.A. artist) part-p on G.A. Green Lantern; G. Kane-c — 6.00

27-45,47: 30,31-Gorilla Grodd-c/story(see Flash #69). 38,39-Adam Strange-c/story.

28-Deathstroke-c/s. 47-Green Arrow x-over — 4.00

46,48,49,50: 46-Superman app. cont'd in Superman #82. 48-Emerald Twilight part 1.

50-($2.95)-Glow-in-the-dark-c — 6.00

51-62: 51-1st app. New Green Lantern (Kyle Rayner) with new costume. 53-Superman-c/story.

55-(9/94)-Zero Hour; leads into issue #0. 56-(11/94) — 4.00

63,64-Kyle Rayner vs. Hal Jordan. — 4.00

65-80,82-92: 63-Begin $1.75-c. 65-New Titans app. 66,67-Flash app. 71-Batman & Robin app. 72-Shazam!-c/app. 73-Wonder Woman-c/app. 76,77-Green Arrow x-over. 80-Final Night. 87-JLA x-over. 91-Genesis x-over. 92-Green Arrow x-over — 4.00

81-(Regular Ed.)-Memorial for Hal Jordan (Parallax); most DC heroes app. — 5.00

81-($3.95, Deluxe Edition)-Embossed prism-c — 6.00

93-99: 93-Begin $1.95-c; Deadman app. 94-Superboy app. 95-Starlin-a(p). 98,99-Legion of Super-Heroes-c/app. — 4.00

100-($2.95) Two covers (Jordan & Rayner); vs. Sinestro — 6.00

101-106: 101-106-Hal Jordan-c/app. 103-JLA-c/app. 104-Green Arrow app. — 4.00

105,106-Parallax app.

107-126: 107-Jade becomes a Green Lantern. 119-Hal Jordan/Spectre app. 125-JLA app. — 3.00

127-149: 127-Begin $2.25-c. 129-Winick-s begin. 134-136-JLA/c/app. 143-Joker: Last Laugh; Lee-c. 145-Kyle becomes The Ion. 149-Superman-c/app. — 3.00

150-($3.50) Jim Lee-c; Kyle becomes Green Lantern again; new costume — 4.00

151-181: 151-155-Jim Lee-c. 154-Terry attacked. 155-Spectre-c/app. 162-164-Crossover with Green Arrow #23-25. 165-Raab-s begin. 169-Kilowog returns — 3.00

#0 (10/94) Zero Hour; published between #55 & #56 — 3.00

#1,000,000 (11/98) 853rd Century x-over; Hitch & Neary-a/c — 3.00

Annual 1-3: ('92-'94, 68 pgs.)-1-Eclipso app. 2 -Intro Nightblade. 3-Elseworlds story — 5.00

Annual 4 (1995, $3.50)-Year One story — 5.00

Annual 5,7,8 ('96, '98, '99, $2.95): 5-Legends of the Dead Earth. 7-Ghosts; Wrightson-c. 8-JLApe; Art Adams-c — 5.00

Annual 6 (1997, $3.95)-Pulp Heroes story — 5.00

Annual 9 (2000, $3.50) Planet DC — 4.00

...80 Page Giant (12/98, $4.95) Stories by various — 5.00

...80 Page Giant 2 (6/99, $4.95) Team-up — 5.00

...80 Page Giant 3 (8/00, $5.95) Darkseid vs. the GL Corps — 6.00

...: 1001 Emerald Nights (2001, $6.95) Elseworlds; Guay-a/c; LaBan-s — 7.00

...-3-D #1 (12/98, $3.95) Jeanty-a — 4.00

...: A New Dawn TPB (1998, $9.95) r/#50-55 — 10.00

...: Baptism of Fire TPB (1999, $12.95)-r/#59,66,67,70-75 — 13.00

...: Brother's Keeper (2003, $12.95) r/#151-155; Green Lantern Secret Files #3 — 13.00

...: Emerald Allies TPB (2000, $14.95)-r/GL/GA team-ups — 15.00

...: Emerald Knights TPB (1998, $12.95)-r/Hal Jordan's return — 13.00

...: Emerald Twilight nn (1994, $5.95)-r/#48 — 6.00

...: Emerald Twilight/New Dawn TPB (2003, $19.95)-r/#48-55 — 20.00

...: Ganthet's Tale nn (1992, $5.95, 68 pgs.)-Silver foil logo; Niven scripts; Byrne-c/a — 13.00

.../Green Arrow Vol. 1 (2004, $12.95) -r/GL #76-82; intro. by O'Neil

.../Green Arrow Vol. 2 (2004, $12.95) -r/GL #83-87,89 & Flash #217-219, 226; cover gallery with 1983-84 GL/GA covers #1-7; intro. by Giordano — 13.00

.../Green Arrow Collection, Vol. 2-r/GL #84-87,89 & Flash #217-219 & GL/GA #5-7 by O'Neil/Adams/Wrightson — 13.00

...: New Journey, Old Path TPB (2001, $12.95)-r/#129-136 — 13.00

...: Our Worlds at War (2001, $2.95) Jae Lee-c; prelude to x-over — 3.00

...: Passing the Torch (2004, $12.95, TPB) r/#156,158-161 & GL Secret Files #2 — 13.00

...Plus 1 (12/1996, $2.95)-The Ray & Polaris-c/app. — 4.00

...: Secret Files 1-3 (7/98-7/02, $4.95)-1-Origin stories & profiles. 2-Grell-c — 5.00

.../Superman: Legend of the Green Flame (2000, $5.95) 1988 unpub. Neil Gaiman story of Hal Jordan with art by various; Frank Miller-c — 6.00

...: The Power of Ion (2003, $14.95, TPB) r/#142-150 — 15.00

...: The Road Back nn (1992, $8.95)-r/1-8 w/covers — 9.00

...: Traitor TPB (2001, $12.95) r/Legends of the DCU #20,21,28,29,37,38 — 13.00

...: Willworld (2001, $24.95, HC) Seth Fisher-a/J.M. DeMatteis-s; Hal Jordan — 25.00

...: Willworld (2003, $17.95, SC) Seth Fisher-a/J.M. DeMatteis-s; Hal Jordan — 18.00

NOTE: Staton a(p)-9-12; c-9-12.

GREEN LANTERN (See Tangent Comics/ Green Lantern)

GREEN LANTERN (4th Series) (Follows Hal Jordan's return in Green Lantern: Rebirth)

DC Comics: July, 2005 - No. 67, Aug, 2011 ($3.50/$2.99)

1-($3.50) Two covers by Pacheco and Ross; Johns/Van Sciver and Pacheco-a — 5.00

2-20-($2.99) 2-4-Manhunters app. 6-Bianchi-a. 7,8-Green Arrow app. 8-Bianchi-c. 9-Batman app.; two covers by Bianchi and Van Sciver. 10,11-Reis-a. 17-19-Star Sapphire returns. 18-Acuna-a; Sinestro Corps back-ups begin — 3.00

8-Variant-c by Neal Adams — 8.00

21-Sinestro Corps War pt. 2 — 5.00

21-2nd printing with variant green hued background-c — 3.00

22-24: 22-Sinestro Corps War pt. 4; green hued-c. 23-Part 6. 24-Part 8 — 4.00

22,23-2nd printings. 22-Yellow hued-c. 23-B&W Hal Jordan with colored rings — 3.00

25-($4.99) Sinestro Corps War conclusion; Ivan Reis-c — 6.00

25-($4.99) Variant cover by Gary Frank; Sinestro Corps War conclusion — 8.00

26-28,30-43: 26-Alpha Lanterns. 30-35-Childhood & origin re-told; Sinestro app. 41-Origin Larfleeze. 43-Prologue to Blackest Night, origin of Black Hand; Mahnke-a — 3.00

29-Childhood & origin re-told — 5.00

29-Special Edition (6/10, $1.00) reprints #29 with "What's Next?" logo on cover — 3.00

29-Special Edition (San Diego Comic-Con giveaway) reprints #29 with new Van Sciver cover and Geoff Johns intro on inside front cover — 3.00

39-43-Variant covers: 39,40-Migliari. 41-42-Barrows — 12.00

44-49,51,52-Blackest Night. 44-Flash app. 46-Sinestro vs. Mongul. 47-Black Lantern Abin Sur.

	GD 2.0	VG 4.0	FN 6.0	VF 8.0	VF/NM 9.0	NM- 9.2

49-Art by Benes & Ordway; Atom and Mera app. 51-Nekron app. — 3.00
44-49,51-Variant covers: 44-Tan. 45-Manapul. 46. Andy Kubert. 47-Benes. 48-Morales.
49-Migliari. 51-Horn. 52-Shane Davis — 8.00
50-($3.99)-Black Lantern Spectre & Parallax app.; Mahnke-a/c — 4.00
50-Variant-c by Jim Lee — 12.00
53-67: 53-62-Brightest Day. 54,55-Lobo app. 58-60-Flash app. 60-Krona returns.
64-67-War of the Green Lanterns x-over. 67-Sinestro becomes a Green Lantern — 3.00
FCBD 2011 Green Lantern Flashpoint Special Edition (6/11, giveaway) r/#30 and previews
Flashpoint x-over; Andy Kubert-a — 3.00
...: Larfleeze Christmas Special 1 (2/11, $3.99) Johns-s/Booth-a/Ha-c — 4.00
.../Plastic Man: Weapons of Mass Deception (2/11, $4.99) Brent Anderson-a — 5.00
...Secret Files and Origins 2005 (6/05, $4.99) Johns-s/Cooke & Van Sciver-a; profiles with
art by various incl. Chaykin, Gibbons, Gleason, Igle; Pacheco-c — 5.00
.../Sinestro Corps: Secret Files 1 (2/08, $4.99) Profiles of Green Lanterns and Corps info — 5.00
...: Agent Orange HC (2009, $19.99) r/#38-42 & Blackest Night #0; sketch art — 20.00
...: Agent Orange SC (2010, $14.99) r/#38-42 & Blackest Night #0; sketch art — 15.00
Blackest Night: Green Lantern HC (2010, $24.99) r/#43-52; variant covers; sketch art — 25.00
Blackest Night: Green Lantern SC (2011, $19.99) r/#43-52; variant covers; sketch art — 20.00
...: Brightest Day HC (2011, $22.99) r/#53-62; variant cover gallery — 23.00
...: In Brightest Day SC (2008, $19.99) r/stories selected by Geoff Johns w/commentary — 20.00
...: No Fear HC (2006, $24.99) r/#1-6 & Secret Files and Origins — 25.00
...: No Fear SC (2008, $12.99) r/#1-6 & Secret Files and Origins — 13.00
...: Rage of the Red Lanterns HC (2009, $24.99) r/#26-28,36-38 & Final Crisis: Rage... — 25.00
...: Rage of the Red Lanterns SC (2010, $14.99) r/#26-28,36-38 & Final Crisis: Rage... — 15.00
...: Revenge of the Green Lanterns HC (2006, $19.99) r/#7-13; variant cover gallery — 20.00
...: Revenge of the Green Lanterns SC (2008, $12.99) r/#7-13; variant cover gallery — 13.00
...: Secret Origin HC (2008, $19.99) r/#29-35 — 20.00
...: Secret Origin (New Edition) HC (2010, $19.99) r/#29-35; intro. by Ryan Reynolds — 20.00
...: Secret Origin SC (2008, $14.99) r/#29-35 — 15.00
...: Secret Origin (New Edition) SC (2011, $14.99) r/#29-35; intro. by Ryan Reynolds;
photo-c of Reynolds from movie; movie preview photo gallery — 15.00
... Super Spectacular (1/12, $7.99, magazine-size) r/Blackest Night #0,1, Green Lantern #76
from 1970 and Brave and the Bold #30 from 2009 — 8.00
...: Tales of the Sinestro Corps HC (2008, $29.99, d.j.) r/back-up stories from #18-20,
Tales of the Sinestro Corps series, Green Lantern: Sinestro Corps Special and
Sinestro Corps: Secret Files — 30.00
...: Tales of the Sinestro Corps SC (2009, $14.99) same contents as HC — 15.00
...: The Sinestro Corps War Vol. 1 HC (2008, $24.99, d.j.) r/#21-23, Green Lantern Corps
#14-15 and Green Lantern: Sinestro Corps Special — 25.00
...: The Sinestro Corps War 1 SC (2009, $14.99) same contents as HC — 15.00
...: The Sinestro Corps War Vol. 2 HC (2008, $24.99, d.j.) r/#24,25, Green Lantern Corps
#16-19; interview with the creators and sketch art — 25.00
... - Wanted: Hal Jordan HC (2007, $19.99) r/#14-20 with Sinestro Corps back-ups — 20.00
... - Wanted: Hal Jordan SC (2008, $14.99) r/#14-20 without Sinestro Corps back-ups — 15.00

GREEN LANTERN (DC New 52)
DC Comics: Nov, 2011 - No. 52, Jul, 2016 ($2.99/$3.99)

1-19: 1-Sinestro as Green Lantern; Johns-s/Mahnke-a/Reis-c (1st & 2nd print). 6-Choi-a.
9-Origin of the Indigo tribe. 14-Justice League app. 17-19-Wrath of the First Lantern — 3.00
1-9-Variant-c. 1-Capullo. 2-Finch. 3-Van Sciver. 4-Manapul. 5-Choi. 6-Reis. 8-Keown — 4.00
8-Combo pack ($3.99) polybagged with digital code — 4.00
20-($7.99, squarebound) Conclusion of "Wrath of the First Lantern"; last Johns-s — 8.00
21-23: 21-Venditti-s/Tan-a begin — 3.00
23.1, 23.2, 23.3, 23.4 (11/13, $2.99, regular covers) — 3.00
23.1 (11/13, $3.99, 3-D cover) "Relic #1" on cover; origin of Relic; Morales-a — 6.00
23.2 (11/13, $3.99, 3-D cover) "Mongul #1" on cover; origin; Starlin-s/Porter-a — 5.00
23.3 (11/13, $3.99, 3-D cover) "Black Hand #1" on cover; Soule-s/Ponticelli-a — 5.00
23.4 (11/13, $3.99, 3-D cover) "Sinestro #1" on cover; origin; Kindt-s/Eaglesham-a — 5.00
24-27,29-34: 24-Lights Out pt. 1; Relic app.; Central Battery destroyed — 3.00
28-Flip-book with Red Lanterns #28; Red Lantern Supergirl app. — 3.00
35-40: 35-37-Godhead x-over; New Gods, Orion & Metron app. 36,37-Black Hand app. — 3.00
41-49,51,52-($3.99) 42,43,45,46-Black Hand app. 43-Relic returns. 47-Parallax app. — 4.00
50-($4.99) Parallax app. — 5.00
#0 (11/12, $2.99) Simon Baz becomes a Green Lantern; Mahnke-a — 3.00
Annual 1 (10/12, $4.99) 1st print w/black-c; Rise of the Third Army prologue — 5.00
Annual 2 (12/13, $4.99) Lights Out pt. 5; Sean Chen-a — 5.00
Annual 3 (2/15, $4.99) Godhead conclusion; Van Sciver-c — 5.00
Annual 4 (11/15, $4.99) Venditti-s/Alixe-a — 5.00
...: Futures End 1 (11/14, $2.99, regular-c) Five years later; Relic app. — 3.00
...: Futures End 1 (11/14, $3.99, 3-D cover) — 4.00
.../New Gods: Godhead 1 (12/14, $4.99) Part 1 to Godhead x-over; Highfather app. — 5.00

GREEN LANTERN, THE
DC Comics: Jan, 2019 - No. 12, Dec, 2019 ($4.99/$3.99)

1-($4.99) Grant Morrison-s/Liam Sharp-a — 5.00
2-11-($3.99) 2-Evil Star app. 5,6-Adam Strange app. 8-Green Arrow app. — 4.00
12-($4.99) Leads into Green Lantern: Blackstars #1 — 5.00
Annual 1 (9/19, $4.99) Air Wave app.; Morrison-s/Camuncoli-a — 5.00

GREEN LANTERN
DC Comics: Jun, 2021 - No. 12, Jun, 2022 ($4.99)

1-12: 1-Teen Lantern & John Stewart featured; Thorne-s/Soy-a. 3-7-Raney-i; Jo Mullein app.
8-ChrisCross-a. 12-John Stewart becomes the Emerald Knight — 5.00
2021 Annual 1 (11/21, $5.99) Sinestro Corps app.; Cady-s/Basri & Derenick-a — 6.00

GREEN LANTERN (Dawn of DC)(Hal Jordan back on Earth)
DC Comics: Jul, 2023 - Present ($4.99)

1-9: 1-Jeremy Adams-s/Xermanico-a; back-up story with John Stewart — 5.00

GREEN LANTERN ANNUAL NO. 1, 1963
DC Comics: 1998 ($4.95, one-shot)

1-Reprints Golden Age & Silver Age stories in 1963-style 80 pg. Giant format;
new Gil Kane sketch art — 5.00

GREEN LANTERN: BLACKSTARS
DC Comics: Jan, 2020 - No. 3, Mar, 2020 ($3.99, limited series)

1-3-Morrison-s/Xermanico-a; Mongul app. — 4.00

GREEN LANTERN: BRIGHTEST DAY; BLACKEST NIGHT
DC Comics: 2002 ($5.95, squarebound, one-shot)

nn-Alan Scott vs. Solomon Grundy in 1944; Snyder III-c/a; Seagle-s

	1		2	3	5	6	8

GREEN LANTERN: CIRCLE OF FIRE
DC Comics: Early Oct, 2000 - No. 2, Late Oct, 2000 (limited series)

1-($4.95) Intro. other Green Lanterns — 5.00
2-($3.75) — 4.00
Green Lantern (x-overs)- .../Adam Strange; .../Atom; .../Firestorm; ... /Green Lantern,
Winick-s; .../Power Girl (all $2.50-c) — 3.00
TPB (2002, $17.95) r/#1,2 & x-overs — 18.00

GREEN LANTERN CORPS, THE (Formerly Green Lantern; see Tales of...)
DC Comics: No. 206, Nov, 1986 - No. 224, May, 1988

206-223: 212-Millennium tie-ins — 4.00
224-Double-size last issue — 5.00
...Corps Annual 2,3- (12/86,8/87) 1-Formerly Tales of ... Annual #1; Alan Moore scripts.
3-Indicia says Green Lantern Annual #3; Moore scripts; Byrne-a — 5.00
NOTE: *Austin* a-Annual 3i. *Gil Kane* a-223, 224p; c-223, 224, Annual 2. *Russell* a-223, 217p, 217p, 221p, 222p, Annual 3; c-207-213p, 217p, 221p, 222p. *Willingham* a-213p, 219p, 220p, 218p, 219p, Annual 2, 3p; c-218p, 219p.

GREEN LANTERN CORPS
DC Comics: Aug, 2006 - No. 63, Oct, 2011 ($2.99)

1,14-19: 1-Gibbons-s. 14-19-Sinestro Corps War pts. 3,5,7,9,10, Epilogue — 4.00
2-13: 2-6,10,11-Gibbons-s. 9-Darkseid app. — 3.00
20-38: 20-Mongul app. — 3.00
20-Second printing with sketch-c — 3.00
34-38: 34-37-Variant covers by Migliari. 38-Fabry var-c — 10.00
39-45-Blackest Night. 43-45-Red Lantern Guy Gardner — 3.00
39-45-Variant covers: 39-Jusko. 40-Tucci. 41,42,44-Horn. 43-Ladronn. 45 Bolland — 8.00
46,47-($3.99) 46-Blackest Night. 47-Brightest Day — 4.00
48-61-($2.99) 48-Migliari-c; Ganthet joins the Corps. 49-52-Cyborg Superman app.
58-60-War of the Green Lanterns x-over. 60-Mogo destroyed — 3.00
Blackest Night: Green Lantern Corps HC (2010, $24.99, d.j.) r/#39-47, cover gallery — 25.00
Blackest Night: Green Lantern Corps SC (2010, $19.99) r/#39-47, cover gallery — 20.00
...: Emerald Eclipse HC (2009, $24.99) r/#33-39; gallery of variant covers — 25.00
...: Emerald Eclipse SC (2010, $14.99) r/#33-39; gallery of variant covers — 15.00
...: Revolt of the Alpha-Lanterns HC (2011, $22.99) r/#21,22,48-52 — 23.00
...: Ring Quest TPB (2008, $14.99) r/#19,20,23-26 — 15.00
...: The Dark Side of Green TPB (2007, $12.99) r/#7-13 — 13.00
...: To Be a Lantern TPB (2007, $12.99) r/#1-6 — 13.00

GREEN LANTERN CORPS (DC New 52)
DC Comics: Nov, 2011 - No. 40, May, 2015 ($2.99)

1-23: 1-Tomasi-s/Pasarin-a/Mahnke-c; John Stewart & Guy Gardner-c — 3.00
24-39: 24-Lights Out pt. 2; Oa destroyed. 35-37-Godhead x-over — 3.00
40-($3.99) Chang-a — 4.00
#0 (11/12, $2.99) Origin of Guy Gardner; Tomasi-s/Pasarin-a — 3.00
Annual 1 (3/13, $4.99) Rise of the Third Army conclusion; Mogo returns — 5.00
Annual 2 (3/14, $4.99) Villains United; Evil Star, Bolphunga, Kanjar Ro app. — 5.00
...: Futures End 1 (11/14, $2.99, regular-c) Five years later; Indigo Tribe app. — 3.00
...: Futures End 1 (11/14, $3.99, 3-D cover) — 4.00

GREEN LANTERN CORPS: EDGE OF OBLIVION
DC Comics: Mar, 2016 - No. 6, Aug, 2016 ($2.99, limited series)

1-6: 1-3-Taylor-s/Van Sciver-a. 4,5-Syaf-a — 3.00

GREEN LANTERN CORPS QUARTERLY
DC Comics: Summer, 1992 - No. 8, Spring, 1994 ($2.50/$2.95, 68 pgs.)

1-G.A. Green Lantern story; Staton-a(p) — 4.00
2-8: 2-G.A. G.L.-c/story; Austin-c(i); Gulacy-a(p). 3-G.A. G.L. story. 4-Austin-i. 7-Painted-c;
Tim Vigil-a. 8-Lobo-c/s — 4.00

GREEN LANTERN CORPS: RECHARGE
DC Comics: Nov, 2005 - No. 5, Mar, 2006 ($3.50/$2.99, limited series)

1-($3.50) Kyle Rayner, Guy Gardner & Kilowog app.; Gleason-a — 4.00
2-5-($2.99) — 3.00
TPB (2006, $12.99) r/series — 13.00

GREEN LANTERN: DRAGON LORD
DC Comics: 2001 - No. 3, 2001 ($4.95, squarebound, limited series)

1-3: A G.L. in ancient China; Moench-s/Gulacy-c/a — 5.00

GREEN LANTERN: EARTH ONE
DC Comics: Mar, 2018 (Graphic novel)

Volume One HC ($24.95) Hardman & Bechko-s/Hardman-a; re-imagined origin — 25.00

GREEN LANTERN 80TH ANNIVERSARY 100-PAGE SUPER SPECTACULAR
DC Comics: Aug, 2020 ($9.99, squarebound, one-shot)

1-Short stories and pin-ups by various incl. Johns, O'Neil, Grell, Reis; multiple covers — 10.00

GREEN LANTERN: EMERALD DAWN (Also see Emerald Dawn)
DC Comics: Dec, 1989 - No. 6, May, 1990 ($1.00, limited series)

1-Origin retold; Giffen plots in all — 6.00
2-6: 4-Re-intro. Tomar-Re — 4.00

GREEN LANTERN: EMERALD DAWN II (Emerald Dawn II #1 & 2)
DC Comics: Apr, 1991 - No. 6, Sept, 1991 ($1.00, limited series)

1-6 — 4.00
TPB (2003, $12.95) r/#1-6; Alan Davis-c — 13.00

GREEN LANTERN: EMERALD WARRIORS
DC Comics: Oct, 2010 - No. 13, Oct, 2011 ($3.99/$2.99)

1-5-($3.99) Guy Gardner's exploits; Migliari-c. 1-Bermejo variant-c. 2-5-Massaferra var-c — 4.00
6-13-($2.99) 6,7-Covers by Migliari & Massaferra. 8-10-War of the Green Lanterns x-over — 3.00

GREEN LANTERN: EVIL'S MIGHT (Elseworlds)
DC Comics: 2002 - No. 3 ($5.95, squarebound, limited series)

1-3-Kyle Rayner in 19th century NYC; Rogers-a; Chaykin & Tischman-s — 6.00

GREEN LANTERN: FEAR ITSELF
DC Comics: 1999 (Graphic novel)

Green Lantern (2021 series) #12 © DC

Green Lantern: Emerald Warriors #11 © DC

Green Mask #11 © FOX

	GD	VG	FN	VF	VF/NM	NM-
	2.0	4.0	6.0	8.0	9.0	9.2

Hardcover ($24.95) Ron Marz-s/Brad Parker painted-a — 25.00
Softcover ($14.95) — 15.00

GREEN LANTERN/FLASH: FASTER FRIENDS (See Flash/Green Lantern...)
DC Comics: 1997 ($4.95, limited series)

1-Marz-s — 5.00

GREEN LANTERN GALLERY
DC Comics: Dec, 1996 ($3.50, one-shot)

1-Wraparound-c; pin-ups by various — 4.00

GREEN LANTERN/GREEN ARROW (Also see The Flash #217)
DC Comics: Oct, 1983 - No. 7, April, 1984 (52-60 pgs.)

1- Reprints Green Lantern #76, 77 — 2 — 4 — 6 — 8 — 10 — 12
2-7-Reprints from Green Lantern #78-89 — 5.00
NOTE: *Neal Adams* r-1-7; c-1-4. *Wrightson* r-4, 5.

GREEN LANTERN/HUCKLEBERRY HOUND SPECIAL
DC Comics: Dec, 2018 ($4.99, one-shot)

1-John Stewart and Huckleberry Hound meet in 1972; Russell-s/Leonardi-a — 5.00

GREEN LANTERN · LEGACY: THE LAST WILL & TESTAMENT OF HAL JORDAN
DC Comics: 2002 ($24.95, hardcover graphic novel)

Hardcover-Anderson & Sienkiewicz-a/c; Kelly-s; Return of Oa — 25.00
Softcover (2004, $17.95) — 18.00

GREEN LANTERN: LOST ARMY
DC Comics: Aug, 2015 - No. 6, Jan, 2016 ($2.99)

1-6: 1-Bunn-s/Saiz-a; featuring John Stewart, Guy Gardner, Kilowog, Arisia, Krona — 3.00

GREEN LANTERN: MOSAIC (Also see Cosmic Odyssey #2)
DC Comics: June, 1992 - No. 18, Nov, 1993 ($1.25)

1-18: Featuring John Stewart. 1-Painted-c by Cully Hamner — 4.00

GREEN LANTERN MOVIE PREQUEL (2011 movie)
DC Comics: July, 2011; April, 2011 ($2.99, one-shots)

...: Abin Sur 1 - Green-s/Gleason-a; movie photo-c — 3.00
...: Hal Jordan 1 - Johns & Berlanti-s/Ordway-a; movie photo-c; Sinestro & Tomar-Re app. — 3.00
...: Kilowog 1 - Tomasi-s/Ferreira-a; movie photo-c — 3.00
...: Sinestro 1 (10/11) - Johns-s/Tolibao, Richards & Ordway-a; movie photo-c — 3.00
...: Tomar-Re 1 - Guggenheim-s/Richards-a; movie photo-c — 3.00

GREEN LANTERN: NEW GUARDIANS (DC New 52)
DC Comics: Nov, 2011 - No. 40, May, 2015 ($2.99)

1-Bedard-s/Kirkham-a/c; Kyle origin flashback; Fatality app. — 6.00
2-23: 13-16-Third Army. 21-Relic freed. 22,23-Kyle vs. Relic. 23-Blue Lanterns destroyed — 3.00
24-34: 24-Lights Out pt. 3. — 3.00
35-39: 35-37-Godhead x-over; Highfather app. 38,39-Oblivion returns — 3.00
40-($3.99) Oblivion app.; the start of the White Lantern Corps — 4.00
#0 (11/12, $2.99) Bedard-s/Kuder-a; Zamarons app. — 3.00
Annual 1 (3/13, $4.99) Giffen-s/Kolins-a/c — 5.00
Annual 2 (6/14, $4.99) Segovia-a; takes place between #30 & #31 — 5.00
...: Futures End 1 (11/14, $2.99, regular-c) Five years later; intro. Saysoran — 3.00
...: Futures End 1 (11/14, $3.99, 3-D cover) — 4.00

GREEN LANTERN: REBIRTH
DC Comics: Dec, 2004 - No. 6, May, 2005 ($2.95, limited series)

1-Johns/Van Sciver-a; Hal Jordan as The Spectre on-c — 8.00
1-2nd printing; Hal Jordan as Green Lantern on-c — 4.00
1-3rd printing; B&W-c version of 1st printing — 3.00
1 Special Edition (9/09, $1.00) r/#1 with "After Watchmen" cover frame — 3.00
2-Guy Gardner becomes a Green Lantern again; JLA app. — 5.00
2-2nd & 3rd printings — 3.00
3-6: 3-Sinestro returns. 4-6-JLA & JSA app. — 3.00
HC (2005, $24.99, dust jacket) r/series & Wizard preview; intro. by Brad Meltzer — 25.00
SC (2007, 2010, $14.99) r/series & Wizard preview; intro. by Brad Meltzer — 15.00

GREEN LANTERNS (DC Rebirth) (Also see Hal Jordan and the Green Lantern Corps)
DC Comics: Aug, 2016 - No. 57, Dec, 2018 ($2.99/$3.99)

1-24: 1-Simon Baz and Jessica Cruz team up; Humphries-s/Rocha-a. 6-1st app. the Phantom Ring. 8-Dominators app.; Benes-a. 9-14-Phantom Lantern. 16,17-Batman app. — 3.00
25-($3.99) Lanterns vs. Volthoom; Rocha-a — 4.00
26-49: 28-31-The Ancient Lanterns app. 35-Intro. Singularity Jain. 35,36-Bolphunga app. — 3.00
50-57-($3.99) 50,51,55-57-Perkins-a. 53-57-Cyborg Superman app. — 4.00
Annual 1 (7/18, $4.99) Diggle-s/Perkins-a — 5.00
...: Rebirth 1 (8/16, $2.99) Van Sciver & Benes-a; Hal Jordan & Atrocitus app. — 3.00

GREEN LANTERN SEASON TWO, THE (Follows Green Lantern: Blackstars series)
DC Comics: Apr, 2020 - No. 12, May, 2021 ($4.99/$3.99)

1-($4.99) Grant Morrison-s/Liam Sharp-a; intro Young Guardians; Hal returns to Earth — 5.00
2-11-($3.99) 4-The Flash app. 11-Hector Hammond app. — 4.00
12-($4.99) Hector Hammond app. — 5.00

GREEN LANTERN/SENTINEL: HEART OF DARKNESS
DC Comics: Mar, 1998 - No. 3, May, 1998 ($1.95, limited series)

1-3-Marz-s/Pelletier-a — 4.00

GREEN LANTERN/SILVER SURFER: UNHOLY ALLIANCES
DC Comics: 1995 ($4.95, one-shot)(Prelude to DC Versus Marvel)

nn-Hal Jordan app. — 2 — 4 — 6 — 8 — 11 — 14

GREEN LANTERN SINESTRO CORPS SPECIAL (Continues in Green Lantern #21)
DC Comics: Aug, 2007 ($4.99, one-shot)

1-Kyle Rayner becomes Parallax; Cyborg Superman & Earth-Prime Superboy app.; Johns-s; Van Sciver-a/c; back-up story origin of Sinestro; Gibbons-a; Sinestro on cover — 2 — 4 — 6 — 8 — 10 — 12
1-(2nd printing) Kyle Rayner as Parallax on cover — 6.00
1-(3rd printing) Sinestro cover with muted colors — 5.00

GREEN LANTERN/ SPACE GHOST SPECIAL
DC Comics: May, 2017 ($4.99, one-shot)

1-Tynion IV-s/Olivetti-a/c; back-up Ruff 'n' Ready retro-intro. by Chaykin-s/a — 5.00

GREEN LANTERN: THE ANIMATED SERIES (Based on the Cartoon Network series)
DC Comics: No. 0, Jan, 2012 - No. 14, Sept, 2013 ($2.99)

0,1: 0-Baltazar & Franco-s/Brizuela-a; Kilowog and Red Lanterns app. — 5.00
2-14: 13-Lobo app. — 4.00

GREEN LANTERN: THE GREATEST STORIES EVER TOLD
DC Comics: 2006 ($19.99, TPB)

SC-Reprints Showcase #22; G.L. #1,31,74,87,172; ('90 series) #3, and others; Ross-c — 20.00

GREEN LANTERN: THE NEW CORPS
DC Comics: 1999 - No. 2, 1999 ($4.95, limited series)

1,2-Kyle recruits new GLs; Eaton-a — 5.00

GREEN LANTERN VS. ALIENS
Dark Horse Comics: Sept, 2000 - No. 4, Dec, 2000 ($2.95, limited series)

1-4: 1-Hal Jordan and GL Corps vs. Aliens; Leonardi-p. 2-4-Kyle Rayner — 3.00

GREEN LANTERN: WAR JOURNAL (John Stewart)
DC Comics: Nov, 2023 - Present ($3.99)

1-6-P.K. Johnson-s/Montos-a — 4.00

GREEN MASK, THE (See Mystery Men)
Summer, 1940 - No. 9, 2/42; No. 10, 8/44 - No. 11, 11/44;
Fox Feature Syndicate: V2#1, Spring, 1945 - No. 6, 10-11/46

V1#1-Origin The Green Mask & Domino; reprints/Mystery Men #1-3,5-7; Lou Fine-c	300	600	900	2010	3505	5000
2-Zanzibar The Magician by Tuska	148	296	444	947	1624	2300
3-Powell-a; Marijuana story	110	220	330	704	1202	1700
4-Navy Jones begins, ends #6	84	168	252	538	919	1300
5	65	130	195	416	708	1000
6-The Nightbird begins, ends #9; Good Girl bondage/torture-c	271	542	813	1734	2967	4200
7,9: 9(2/42)-Becomes The Bouncer #10(nn) on? & Green Mask #10 on	58	116	174	371	636	900
8-Classic Good Girl torture/bondage-c	300	600	900	2010	3505	5000
10,11: 10-Origin One Round Hogan & Rocket Kelly	41	82	123	256	428	600
V2#1	34	68	102	204	332	460
2-6	27	54	81	158	259	360

GREEN PLANET, THE
Charlton Comics: 1962 (one-shot) (12¢)

| nn-Giordano-c; sci-fi | 11 | 22 | 33 | 72 | 154 | 235 |

GREEN TEAM (See Cancelled Comic Cavalcade & 1st Issue Special)

GREEN TEAM: TEEN TRILLIONAIRES
DC Comics: Jul, 2013 - No. 8, Mar, 2014 ($2.99)

1-8-Baltazar & Franco-s/Guara-a. 1-3-Conner-c. 3-Deathstroke app. 8-Teen Titans app. — 3.00
1-Variant-c by Chiang — 3.00

GREEN VALLEY
Image Comics (Skybound): Oct, 2016 - No. 9, Jun, 2017 ($2.99/$3.99)

1-8-Max Landis-s/Giuseppe Camuncoli-a — 3.00
9-($3.99) — 4.00

GREEN WOMAN, THE

	GD 2.0	VG 4.0	FN 6.0	VF 8.0	VF/NM 9.0	NM- 9.2

DC Comics (Vertigo): 2010 ($24.99, HC graphic novel)
HC-John Bolton-a/Peter Straub & Michael Easton-s ... 25.00

GREETINGS FROM SANTA (See March of Comics No. 48)

GRENDEL (Also see Primer #2, Mage and Comico Collection)
Comico: Mar, 1983 - No. 3, Feb, 1984 ($1.50, B&W)(#1 has indicia to Skrog #1)

	GD	VG	FN	VF	VF/NM	NM-
1-Origin Hunter Rose	12	24	36	80	173	265
2,3: 2-Origin Argent	8	16	24	56	108	160

GRENDEL
Comico: Oct, 1986 - No. 40, Feb, 1990 ($1.50/$1.95/$2.50, mature)

	GD	VG	FN	VF	VF/NM	NM-
1	2	4	6	10	14	18
1,2: 2nd printings						3.00
2,3,5-13: 13-15-Ken Steacy-c						4.00
4,16: 4-Dave Stevens-c(i). 16-Re-intro Mage (series begins, ends #19)						6.00
17-40: 24-25,27-28,30-31-Snyder-c/a						3.00
Devil by the Deed (Graphic Novel, 8/86, $5.95, 52 pgs.)-r/Grendel back-ups/ Mage 6-14; Alan Moore intro.	1	3	4	6	8	10
Devil's Legacy ($14.95, 1988, Graphic Novel)	2	4	6	9	12	15
Devil's Vagary (10/87, B&W & red)-No price; included in Comico Collection	2	4	6	10		12

GRENDEL (Title series): **Dark Horse Comics**
--ARCHIVES, 5/07 ($14.95, HC) r/1st apps. in Primer #2 and Grendel #1-3; Wagner intro. 15.00
--BEHOLD THE DEVIL, No. 0, 7/07 - No. 8, 6/08 ($3.50/50¢, B&W&Red)
  0-(50¢-c) Prelude to series; Matt Wagner-s/a; interview with Wagner ... 3.00
  1-8-Matt Wagner-s/a/c in all ... 3.50
--BLACK, WHITE, AND RED, 11/98 - No. 4, 2/99 ($3.95, anthology)
  1-Wagner-s in all. Art by Sale, Leon and others ... 5.00
  2-4: 2-Mack, Chadwick-a. 3-Allred, Kristensen-a. 4-Pearson, Sprouse-a ... 4.00
--CLASSICS, 11/95 ($3.95, mature) 1,2-reprints; new Wagner-c ... 4.00
--CYCLE, 10/95 ($5.95) 1-nn-history of Grendel by M. Wagner & others ... 6.00
--DEVIL BY THE DEED, 7/93 ($3.95, varnish-c) 1-nn-M. Wagner-c/a/scripts;
  r/Grendel back-ups from Mage #6-14 ... 6.00
  Reprint (12/97, $3.95) w/pin-ups by various ... 4.00
  Hardcover (2007, $12.95) reprint recolored to B&W&red; includes covers and intros from
    previously reprinted editions ... 13.00
--DEVIL CHILD, 6/99 - No. 2, 7/99 ($2.95, mature) 1,2-Sale & Kristiansen-a/Schutz-s ... 4.00
--DEVIL QUEST, 11/95 ($2.95, mature) 1-nn-Prequel to Batman/Grendel II; M. Wagner
  story & art; r/back-up story from Grendel Tales series. ... 5.00
--DEVILS AND DEATHS, 10/94 - 11/94 ($2.95, mature) 1,2 ... 4.00
: DEVIL'S LEGACY, 3/00 - No. 12, 2/01 ($2.95, reprints 1986 series, recolored)
  1-12-Wagner-s/c; Pander Bros.-a ... 3.00
: DEVIL'S ODYSSEY, 10/19 - No. 8, 7/21 ($3.99) 1-8-Wagner-s/a; Grendel Prime returns ... 4.00
: DEVIL'S REIGN, 5/04 - No. 7, 12/04 ($3.50, repr. 1989 series #34-40, recolored)
  1-7-Sale-c/a. ... 3.50
: GOD AND THE DEVIL, No. 0, 1/03 - No. 10, 12/03 ($3.50/$4.99, repr. 1986 series, recolored)
  0-9: 0-Sale-c/a; r/#23. 1-9-Snyder-c ... 3.50
  10-($4.99) Double-sized; Snyder-c ... 5.00
--RED, WHITE & BLACK, 9/02 - No. 4, 12/02 ($4.99, anthology)
  1-4-Wagner-s in all. 1-Art by Thompson, Sakai, Mahfood and others. 2-Kelley Jones, Watson,
    Brereton, Hester & Parks-a. 3-Oeming, Noto, Cannon, Ashley Wood, Huddleston-a.
    4-Chiang, Dalrymple, Robertson, Snyder III and Zulli-a ... 5.00
  TPB (2005, $19.95) r/#1-4; cover gallery, artist bios ... 20.00
--TALES: DEVIL'S CHOICES, 3/95 - 6/95 ($2.95, mature) 1-4 ... 4.00
--TALES: FOUR DEVILS, ONE HELL, 8/93 - 1/94 ($2.95, mature)
  1-6-Wagner painted-c ... 4.00
  TPB (12/94, $17.95) r/#1-6 ... 18.00
--TALES: HOMECOMING, 12/94 - 2/95 ($2.95, mature) 1-3 ... 4.00
--TALES: THE DEVIL IN OUR MIDST, 5/94 - 9/95 ($2.95, mature) 1-5-Wagner painted-c ... 4.00
--TALES: THE DEVIL MAY CARE, 12/95 - No. 6, 5/96 ($2.95, mature)
  1-6-Terry LaBan scripts. 5-Batman/Grendel II preview ... 4.00
--TALES: THE DEVIL'S APPRENTICE, 9/97 - No. 3, 11/97 ($2.95, mature)
  1-3 ... 4.00
--TALES: THE DEVIL'S HAMMER, 2/94 - No. 3, 4/94 ($2.95, mature)
  1-3-Rob Walton-s/a; back-up stories by Wagner ... 4.00
: THE DEVIL INSIDE, 9/01 - No. 3, 11/01 ($2.99)
  1-3-r/#13-15 with new Wagner-c ... 4.00
VS. THE SHADOW, 9/14 - No. 3, 11/14 ($5.99, squarebound)
  Matt Wagner-s/a/c; Grendel time-travels to The Shadow's era ... 6.00
: WAR CHILD, 8/92 - No. 10, 6/93 ($2.50, lim. series, mature)
  1-9: 1-4-Bisley painted-c; Wagner-i & scripts in all ... 4.00
  10-($3.50, 52 pgs.) Wagner-a ... 5.00
  Limited Edition Hardcover ($99.95) ... 100.00

GRENDEL, KENTUCKY
AWA Studios: Sept, 2020 - No. 4, Dec, 2020 ($3.99, limited series)
1-4-Jeff McComsey-s/Tommy Lee Edwards-a ... 4.00

GREYFRIARS BOBBY (Disney)(Movie)
Dell Publishing Co.: No. 1189, Nov, 1961 (one-shot)

	GD	VG	FN	VF	VF/NM	NM-
Four Color 1189-Photo-c	6	12	18	41	76	110

GREYLORE
Sirius: 12/85 - No. 5, Sept, 1986 ($1.50/$1.75, high quality paper)
1-5: Bo Hampton-a in all ... 4.00

GREYSHIRT: INDIGO SUNSET (Also see Tomorrow Stories)
America's Best Comics: Dec, 2001 - No. 6, Aug, 2002 ($3.50, limited series)
1-6-Veitch-s/a. 4-Back-up w/John Severin-a. 6-Cho-a ... 3.50
TPB (2002, $19.95) r/#1-6; preface by Alan Moore ... 20.00

GRIDIRON GIANTS
Ultimate Sports Ent.: 2000 - No. 2 ($3.95, cardstock covers)
1,2-NFL players Sanders, Marino, Plummer, T. Davis battle evil ... 4.00

GRIFFIN, THE
DC Comics: 1991 - No. 6, 1991 ($4.95, limited series, 52 pgs.)
Book 1-6: Matt Wagner painted-c ... 5.00

GRIFTER (Also see Team 7 & WildC.A.T.S)
Image Comics (WildStorm Prod.): May, 1995 - No. 10, Mar, 1996 ($1.95)
1 ($1.95, Newsstand)-WildStorm Rising Pt. 5 ... 4.00
1-10:1 ($2.50, Direct)-WildStorm Rising Pt. 5, bound-in trading card ... 4.00
...: One Shot (1/95, $4.95) Flip-c ... 4.00

GRIFTER
Image Comics (WildStorm Prod.): V2#1, July, 1996 - No. 14, Aug, 1997 ($2.50)
V2#1-14: Steven Grant scripts ... 4.00

GRIFTER (DC New 52)
DC Comics: Nov, 2011 - No. 16, Mar, 2013 ($2.99)
1-16: 1-Grifter in the new DC universe; Edmondson/Cafu-a/c. 4-Green Arrow app. ... 3.00
#0 (11/12, $2.99) Liefeld-s/c; Clark-a ... 3.00

GRIFTER & MIDNIGHTER
DC Comics (WildStorm Prod.): May, 2007 - No. 6, Oct, 2007 ($2.99, limited series)
1-6-Dixon-s/Benjamin-a/c. 1,3-The Authority app. ... 3.00
TPB (2008, $17.99) r/#1-6 ... 18.00

GRIFTER AND THE MASK
Dark Horse Comics: Sept, 1996 - No. 2, Oct, 1996 ($2.50, limited series)
(1st Dark Horse Comics/Image x-over)
1,2: Steve Seagle scripts ... 4.00

GRIFTER/BADROCK (Also see WildC.A.T.S & Youngblood)
Image Comics (Extreme Studios): Oct, 1995 - No.2, Nov, 1995 ($2.50, unfinished lim. series)
1,2: 2-Flip book w/Badrock #2 ... 4.00

GRIFTER/SHI
Image Comics (WildStorm Productions): Apr, 1996 - No. 2, May, 1996 ($2.95, limited series)
1,2: 1-Jim Lee-c/a(p); Travis Charest-a(p). 2-Billy Tucci-c/a(p); Travis Charest-a(p) ... 4.00

GRIM
BOOM! Studios: May, 2022 - Present ($3.99)
1-15-Stephanie Phillips-s/Flaviano-a ... 4.00
...: Pen & Ink No. 1 (2/24, $6.99) Reprints #1 in B&W with artist commentary ... 7.00

GRIM GHOST, THE
Atlas/Seaboard Publ.: Jan, 1975 - No. 3, July, 1975

	GD	VG	FN	VF	VF/NM	NM-
1-3: Fleisher-s in all. 1-Origin. 2-Son of Satan; Colan-a. 3-Heath-c	2	4	6	13	18	22

GRIM GHOST
Ardden Entertainment (Atlas Comics): Mar, 2011 - No. 6, Nov, 2011 ($2.99)
1-6-Isabella & Susco-s/Kelley Jones-a. 1-Re-intro. Matthew Dunsinane ... 3.00
... Issue Zero - NY Comicon Edition (10/10, $2.99) Qing Ping Mui-a; prequel to #1 ... 3.00

GRIMJACK (Also see Demon Knight & Starslayer)
First Comics: Aug, 1984 - No. 81, Apr, 1991 ($1.00/$1.95/$2.25)

	GD	VG	FN	VF	VF/NM	NM-
1-John Ostrander scripts & Tim Truman-c/a begins	1	2	3	5	6	8
2-25: 20-Sutton-c/a begins. 22-Bolland-a						3.00
26-2nd color Teenage Mutant Ninja Turtles	2	4	6	10		12
27-74,76-81 (Later issues $1.95, $2.25): 30-Dynamo Joe x-over; 31-Mandrake-c/a begins. 73,74-Kelley Jones-a						3.00
75-($5.95, 52 pgs.)-Fold-out map; coated stock						6.00

The Legend of Grimjack Vol. 1 (IDW Publishing, 2004, $19.99) r/Starslayer #10-18;
  8 new pages & art ... 20.00
The Legend of Grimjack Vol. 2 (IDW, 2005, $19.99) r/#1-7; unpublished art ... 20.00
The Legend of Grimjack Vol. 3 (IDW, 2005, $19.99) r/#8-14; cover gallery ... 20.00
The Legend of Grimjack Vol. 4 (IDW, 2005, $24.99) r/#15-21; cover gallery ... 25.00
The Legend of Grimjack Vol. 5 (IDW, 5/06, $24.99) r/#22-30; cover gallery ... 25.00
The Legend of Grimjack Vol. 6 (IDW, 1/07, $24.99) r/#31-37; cover gallery ... 25.00
The Legend of Grimjack Vol. 7 (IDW, 4/07, $24.99) r/#38-46; covers; "Rough Trade" ... 25.00
NOTE: *Truman* c/a-1-17.

GRIMJACK CASEFILES
First Comics: Nov, 1990 - No. 5, Mar, 1991 ($1.95, limited series)
1-5 Reprints 1st stories from Starslayer #10 on ... 4.00

GRIMJACK: KILLER INSTINCT
IDW Publ.: Jan, 2005 - No. 6, June, 2005 ($3.99, limited series)
1-6-Ostrander-s/Truman-a ... 4.00

GRIMJACK: THE MANX CAT
IDW Publ.: Aug, 2009 - No. 6, Jan, 2010 ($3.99, limited series)
1-6-Ostrander-s/Truman-a ... 4.00

GRIMM (Based on the NBC TV series)
Dynamite Entertainment.: 2013 - No. 12, 2014 ($3.99)
1-11: 1-Two covers (Alex Ross & photo). 2-11-Pararillo & photo-c on each ... 4.00
12-($4.99) Gaffen & McVey-s/Rodolfo-a; Paririllo & photo-c ... 5.00
#0 (2013, Free Comic Book Day giveaway) Prequel to issue #1; Portacio-a ... 3.00
... Portland, WU (2014, $7.99) Gaffen & McVey-s/Govar-a ... 8.00
...: The Warlock 1-4 (2013 - No. 4, 2014, $3.99) Nitz-s/Malaga-a ... 4.00

GRIMM VOLUME 2 (Based on the NBC TV series)
Dynamite Entertainment.: 2016 - No. 5, 2017 ($3.99)
1-5-Kittredge-s/Sanapo-a; two covers ... 4.00

GRIMM FAIRY TALES
Zenescope Entertainment: Jun, 2005 - No. 125, Aug, 2016 ($2.99/$3.99)

	GD	VG	FN	VF	VF/NM	NM-
1-Al Rio-c; Little Red Riding Hood app.; multiple variant covers	6	12	18	38	69	100
2-Multiple variant covers	3	6	9	19	30	40

Grendel vs. The Shadow #1 © Conde Nast

Grifter (2011 series) #10 © DC

Grimm Fairy Tales #113 © ZEN

GR

	GD 2.0	VG 4.0	FN 6.0	VF 8.0	VF/NM 9.0	NM- 9.2
3-6-Multiple variant covers	2	4	6	10	14	18
7-12: Multiple covers on each						6.00
13-74,76-84,86-99,101,102: Multiple covers on each						3.00
75-(7/12, $5.99) Covers by Campbell, Sejic, Michaels and others						6.00
85-(5/13, $5.99) Unleashed part 2						6.00
100-(7/14, $5.99) Age of Darkness; covers by Neal Adams and others						6.00
103-124-($3.99)						4.00
125-(8/16, $9.99) Five covers						10.00
#0 Free Comic Book Day Special Edition (4/14, giveaway) Age of Darkness tie-in						3.00
2016 Annual (10/16, $5.99) Spotlight on Skylar; art by various; 4 covers						6.00
... Animated One Shot (10/12, $3.99) Schnepp-c; bonus design art						4.00
Grimm Tales of Terror 2016 Holiday Special (11/16, $5.99) 4 covers						6.00
Grimm Tales of Terror 2019 Halloween Special (10/19, $5.99) 5 covers						6.00
Grimm Universe Presents Fall 2019 (8/19, $7.99) 5 covers						8.00
... Halloween Special 1,2, 2013, 2014, 2015, 2016 (10/09, 10/10, 10/13, 10/14, 9/15, 10/16, $5.99) Multiple covers on each						6.00
... Holiday Edition (11/14, $5.99) The story of Krampus; multiple covers						6.00
... Presents Wounded Warriors (7/13, $6.99) Multiple military-themes covers						7.00
... The Dark Queen One Shot (1/14, $5.99) Sharma-a; 4 covers						6.00

GRIMM FAIRY TALES (Volume 2)
Zenescope Entertainment: Dec, 2016 - Present ($3.99)

1-Brusha-s/Silva-a; multiple covers	1	2	3			8
2-24,26-49,51-74,76-81: 2,3-Brusha-s/Silva-a. 37-Leads into 2020 Annual						4.00
25-($5.99) The War of the Grail; continues in Annual 2019; Goetten-a						6.00
50-($5.99) A Dark Conclusion; gatefold wraparound-c						6.00
75-($6.99) Rise of Cthulhu; gatefold wraparound-c						7.00
... 2017 Halloween Special (10/17, $5.99) Short stories by various; 4 covers						6.00
...: 2019 Annual (1/19, $5.99) Casallos-a; 4 covers						6.00
...: 2019 Giant-Size (2/19, $5.99) Casallos-a; 5 covers; continues in #26						6.00
...: 2019 Holiday Special (11/19, $5.99) Short stories by various; 5 covers						6.00
...: 2020 Annual (6/20, $5.99) Abrera-a; 4 covers; Skye vs. Merlin; follows #37						6.00
...: 2020 Holiday Special (12/20, $5.99) Short stories by various; 5 covers						6.00
...: 2022 Annual (8/22, $7.99) Abrera-a; 4 covers; follows #62						8.00
... Universus One-Shot (3/20, $4.99) Franchini-s/Garcia-a; two covers; includes cards						5.00
... Volume 2 Annual: The Last Dream (1/24, $7.99) Takes place before #79						8.00

GRIMM FAIRY TALES PRESENTS ALICE IN WONDERLAND
Zenescope Entertainment: Jan, 2012 - No. 6, May, 2012 ($2.99)

1-Multiple variant covers	3	6	9	15	22	28
2-6: Multiple covers on each	1	2	3	5	6	8

GRIMM FAIRY TALES MYTHS & LEGENDS
Zenescope Entertainment: Jan, 2011 - No. 25, Feb, 2013 ($2.99)

1-Campbell-c; multiple variant covers	2	4	6	9	12	15
2-5						6.00
6-24						3.00
25-(2/13, $5.99) Multiple variant covers						6.00

GRIMM FAIRY TALES PRESENTS WONDERLAND (Title changes to Wonderland with #43)
Zenescope Entertainment: Jul, 2012 - Finale, Sept, 2016 ($2.99)

1-Campbell-c; multiple variant covers	2	4	6	9	12	15
2,3						6.00
4-18						3.00
19-24,26-49-($3.99)						4.00
25-(7/14, $5.99) Multiple variant covers						6.00
50-(8/16, $5.99) Multiple variant covers						6.00
... Finale (9/16, $5.99) Last issue; 4 covers; Shand-s/Follini-a						6.00
Free Comic Book Day 2015 Special Edition (5/15, giveaway) Brescini-a						3.00

GRIMMISS ISLAND (Issue #1 titled Itty Bitty Comics #5: Grimmiss Island)
Dark Horse Comics: Mar, 2015 - No. 4, Jun, 2015 ($2.99, limited series)

1-4-All-ages humor story by Art Baltazar & Franco						3.00

GRIMM'S GHOST STORIES (See Dan Curtis)
Gold Key/Whitman No. 55 on: Jan, 1972 - No. 60, June, 1982 (Painted-c #1-42,44,46-56)

1	5	10	15	33	57	80
2-5,8: 5,8-Williamson-a	3	6	9	14	20	25
6,7,9,10	2	4	6	11	16	20
11-20	2	4	6	8	11	14
21-42,45-54: 32,34-Reprints. 45-Photo-c	1	3	4	6	8	10
43,44,55-60: 43,44-(52 pgs.). 43-Photo-c. 58(2/82). 59(4/82)-Williamson-a(r/#8). 60(6/82)						
Mini-Comic No. 1 (3-1/4x6-1/2", 1976)	1	3	4	6	8	10

NOTE: *Reprints-#32?, 34?, 39, 43, 44, 47?, 53; 56-60(1/3). Bolle a-8, 17, 22-25, 27, 29(2), 33, 35, 41, 45(2), 48(2), 50, 52, 57. Celardo a-17, 26, 28p, 30, 31, 43(2), 45. Lopez a-24, 25. McWilliams a-33, 44, 48, 54(2), 57, 58. Win Mortimer a-31, 33, 49, 51, 55, 56, 58(2), 59, 60. Roussos a-25, 30. Sparling a-23, 24, 28, 30, 31, 33, 43r, 44, 45, 51(2), 52, 56-58, 59(2), 60. Spiegle a-44.*

GRIN (The American Funny Book) (Satire)
APAG House Pubs: Nov, 1972 - No. 3, April, 1973 (Magazine, 52 pgs.)

1-Parodies-Godfather, All in the Family	3	6	9	17	26	35
2,3	2	4	6	13	18	22

GRIN & BEAR IT (See Gags)
Dell Publishing Co.: No. 28, 1941

Large Feature Comic 28	23	46	69	136	223	310

GRINDHOUSE: DOORS OPEN AT MIDNIGHT
Dark Horse Comics: Oct, 2013 - No. 8, May, 2014 ($3.99)

1-8: 1-Francavilla-c/DeCampi-s. 1,2-Bee Vixens From Mars. 3,4-Prison Ship Antares						4.00

GRINDHOUSE: DRIVE IN, BLEED OUT
Dark Horse Comics: Nov, 2014 - No. 8, Aug, 2015 ($3.99)

1-8: 1,2-Slay Ride; DeCampi-s/Guéra-a. 7,8-Nebulina. 8-Manara-c						4.00

GRIPS (Extreme violence)
Silverwolf Comics: Sept, 1986 - No. 4, Dec, 1986 ($1.50, B&W, mature)

1-Tim Vigil-c/a in all						6.00
2-4						4.00

GRIP: THE STRANGE WORLD OF MEN
DC Comics (Vertigo): Jan, 2002 - No. 5, May, 2002 ($2.50, limited series)

1-4-Gilbert Hernandez-s/a						3.00

GRIT GRADY (See Holyoke One-Shot No. 1)

GROO (Also see Sergio Aragonés' Groo...)

GROO (Sergio Aragonés'...)
Image Comics: Dec, 1994 - No. 12, Dec, 1995 ($1.95)

1-12: 2-Indicia reads #1, Jan, 1995; Aragonés-c/a in all						4.00

GROO (Sergio Aragonés'...)
Dark Horse Comics: Jan, 1998 - No. 4, Apr, 1998 ($2.95)

1-4-Aragonés-c/a in all						4.00
...: One For One (9/10, $1.00) reprints #1 with red cover frame						3.00

GROO CHRONICLES, THE (Sergio Aragonés)
Marvel Comics (Epic Comics): June, 1989 - No. 6, Feb, 1990 ($3.50)

Book 1-6: Reprints early Pacific issues						5.00

GROO: FRAY OF THE GODS (Sergio Aragonés'...)
Dark Horse Comics: Jul, 2016 - No. 4, Jan, 2017 ($3.99, limited series)

1-4-Aragonés-c/a; Evanier-s						4.00

GROO: FRIENDS AND FOES (Sergio Aragonés'...)
Dark Horse Comics: Jan, 2015 - No. 12, Jan, 2016 ($3.99)

1-12-Aragonés-c/a in all; spotlights on various characters. 1-Spotlight on Captain Ahax						4.00

GROO: GODS AGAINST GROO (Sergio Aragonés'...)
Dark Horse Comics: Dec, 2022 - No. 4, Mar, 2023 ($3.99, limited series)

1-4-Aragonés-c/a; Evanier-s						4.00

GROO: IN THE WILD (Sergio Aragonés'...)
Dark Horse Comics: Jul, 2023 - No. 4, Nov, 2023 ($4.99, limited series)

1-4-Aragonés-c/a; Evanier-s						5.00

GROO MEETS TARZAN (Sergio Aragonés'...)
Dark Horse Comics: Jul, 2021 - No. 4, Nov, 2021 ($3.99, limited series)

1-4-Aragonés & Evanier-s/Aragonés-a(Groo) & Thomas Yeates (Tarzan)						4.00

GROO: PLAY OF THE GODS (Sergio Aragonés'...)
Dark Horse Comics: Jul, 2017 - No. 4, Oct, 2017 ($3.99, limited series)

1-4-Aragonés-c/a; Evanier-s						4.00

GROO SPECIAL
Eclipse Comics: Oct, 1984 ($2.00, 52 pgs., Baxter paper)

1-Aragonés-c/a	3	6	9	16	23	30

GROOT (Guardians of the Galaxy)
Marvel Comics: Aug, 2015 - No. 6, Jan, 2016 ($3.99)

1-4,6: 1-Loveness/Kesinger-a; Rocket Raccoon app. 2-Flashback to Groot meeting Rocket. 3-Silver Surfer app.						4.00
5-Baby Groot app.	2	4	6	9	12	15

GROOT (Guardians of the Galaxy)
Marvel Comics: Jul, 2023 - No. 4, Oct, 2023 ($4.99/$3.99)

1-($4.99) Abnett-s/Couceiro-a; young Groot before joining the Guardians; Mar-Vell app.						5.00
2-4-($3.99)						4.00

	GD	VG	FN	VF	VF/NM	NM-
	2.0	4.0	6.0	8.0	9.0	9.2

GROO THE WANDERER (See Destroyer Duck #1 & Starslayer #5)
Pacific Comics: Dec, 1982 - No. 8, Apr, 1984

1-Aragonés-c/a(p)/Evanier-s in all; Aragonés bio.	3	6	9	21	33	45
2-5: 5-Deluxe paper (1.00-c)	2	4	6	9	13	16
6-8	2	4	6	10	14	18

GROO THE WANDERER (Sergio Aragonés'...) (See Marvel Graphic Novel #32)
Marvel Comics (Epic Comics): March, 1985 - No. 120, Jan, 1995

1-Aragonés-c/a in all	3	6	9	17	26	35
2-10	1	2	3	5	6	8
11-20,50-($1.50, double size)						5.00
21-49,51-99: 87-direct sale only, high quality paper						4.00
100-($2.95, 52 pgs.)						5.00
101-120						4.00
Groo Carnival, The (12/91, $8.95)-r/#9-12						11.00
Groo Garden, The (4/94, $10.95)-r/#25-28						11.00

GROO VS. CONAN (Sergio Aragonés'...)
Dark Horse Comics: Jul, 2014 - No. 4, Oct, 2014 ($3.50, limited series)

1-4: Aragonés & Evanier-s/Aragonés-c/a in all; Thomas Yeates on Conan art						3.50

GROOVY (Cartoon Comics - not CCA approved)
Marvel Comics Group: March, 1968 - No. 3, July, 1968

1-Monkees, Ringo Starr, Sonny & Cher, Mamas & Papas photos	9	18	27	59	117	175
2,3	6	12	18	37	66	95

GROSS POINT
DC Comics: Aug, 1997 - No. 14, Aug, 1998 ($2.50)

1-14: 1-Waid/Augustyn-s						4.00

GROUNDED
Image Comics: July, 2005 - No. 6, May, 2006 ($2.95/$2.99, limited series)

1-6-Mark Sable-s/Paul Azaceta-a. 1-Mike Oeming-c						3.00
Vol. 1: Powerless TPB (2006, $14.99) r/#1-6; sketch pages and creator bios						15.00

GRRL SCOUTS (Jim Mahfood-s)... (Also see 40 oz. Collected)
Oni Press: Mar,1999 - No. 4, Dec, 1999 ($2.95, B&W, limited series)

1-4-Mahfood-s/c/a						4.00
TPB (2003, $12.95) r/#1-4; pin-ups by Warren, Winick, Allred, Fegredo and others						13.00

GRRL SCOUTS: MAGIC SOCKS
Image Comics: May, 2017 - No. 6, Oct, 2017 ($3.99, limited series)

1-6-Mahfood-s/c/a						4.00

GRRL SCOUTS: STONE GHOST
Image Comics: Nov, 2021 - No. 6, Apr, 2022 ($3.99, limited series)

1-6-Mahfood-s/c/a						4.00

GRRL SCOUTS: WORK SUCKS
Image Comics: Feb, 2003 - No. 4, May, 2003 ($2.95, B&W, limited series)

1-4-Mahfood-s/c/a						3.00
TPB (2004, $12.95) r/#1-4; pin-ups by Oeming, Dwyer, Tennapel and others						13.00

GRUMBLE
Albatross Funnybooks: 2018 - Present ($3.99)

1-10-Rafer Roberts-s/Mike Norton-a						4.00
...: Memphis & Beyond the Infinite 1-5 (2020 - No 5, 2020, $3.99) Roberts-s/Norton-a						4.00
... vs. The Goon (2019, Free Comic Book Day giveaway) Mike Norton & Eric Powell-a						4.00

GRUMPY CAT
Dynamite Entertainment: 2015 - No. 3, 2015 ($3.99, limited series)

1-3-Short stories; Ben McCool & Ben Fisher-s/Steve Uy & Michelle Nguyen-a						4.00
..., Free Comic Book Day 2016 (giveaway) Short stories by various						3.00

GRUMPY CAT AND POKEY
Dynamite Entertainment: 2016 - No. 6, 2016 ($3.99, limited series)

1-6-Short stories. 1-McCool & Fisher-s/Uy, Haeser & Garbowska-a; multiple covers						4.00

GRUMPY CAT / GARFIELD
Dynamite Entertainment: 2017 - No. 3, 2017 ($3.99, limited series)

1-3-Mark Evanier-s/Steve Uy-a; multiple covers						4.00

GUADALCANAL DIARY (See American Library)

GUARDIAN ANGEL
Image Comics: May, 2002 - No. 2, July, 2002 ($2.95)

1,2-Peterson-s/Wiesenfeld-a						3.00

GUARDIANS
Marvel Comics: Sept, 2004 - No. 5, Dec, 2004 ($2.99, limited series)

1-5-Sumerak-s/Casey Jones-a						3.00

GUARDIANS OF INFINITY
Marvel Comics: Feb, 2016 - No. 8, Sept, 2016 ($4.99)

1-8-Guardians of the Galaxy & 31st century Guardians. 1-Back-up story with The Thing						5.00

GUARDIANS OF KNOWHERE (Secret Wars tie-in)
Marvel Comics: Sept, 2015 - No. 4, Nov, 2015 ($3.99, limited series)

1-4-Bendis-s/Deodato-a; Guardians of the Galaxy, Angela & Mantis app.						4.00
1-Variant Gwenom (Gwen/Venom) cover by Guillory						8.00

GUARDIANS OF METROPOLIS
DC Comics: Nov, 1995 - Feb, 1995 ($1.50, limited series)

1-4: 1-Superman & Granny Goodness app.						4.00

GUARDIANS OF THE GALAXY (Also see The Defenders #26, Marvel Presents #3, Marvel Super-Heroes #18, Marvel Two-In-One #5)
Marvel Comics: June, 1990 - No. 62, July, 1995 ($1.00/$1.25)

1-Valentino-c/a(p); Taserface	3	6	9	21	33	45
2-5: 2-Zeck-c(i). 5-McFarlane-c(i)	1	3	4	6	8	10
6-15: 7-Intro Malevolence (Mephisto's daughter); Perez-c(i). 8-Intro Rancor (descendant of Wolverine) in cameo. 9-1st full app. Rancor; Rob Liefeld-c(i). 10-Jim Lee-c(i).						

	GD	VG	FN	VF	VF/NM	NM-
	2.0	4.0	6.0	8.0	9.0	9.2

13,14-1st app. Spirit of Vengeance (futuristic Ghost Rider). 14-Spirit of Vengeance vs. The Guardians. 15-Starlin-c(i)						4.00
16-($1.50, 52 pgs.)-Starlin-c(i)						5.00
17-24,26-38,40-47: 17-20-31st century Punishers storyline. 20-Last $1.00-c. 21-Rancor app. 22-Reintro Starhawk. 24-Silver Surfer-c/story; Ron Lim-c. 26-Origin retold. 27-28-Infinity War x-over; 27-Inhumans app. 43-Intro Wooden (son of Thor)						4.00
25-($2.50)-Prism foil-c; Silver Surfer/Galactus-c/s						5.00
25-($2.50)-Without foil-c; newsstand edition						4.00
39-($2.95, 52 pgs.)-Embossed & holo-grafx foil-c; Dr. Doom vs. Rancor						5.00
48,49,51-56: 48-bound-in trading card sheet						4.00
50-($2.00, 52 pgs.)-Newsstand edition						5.00
50-($2.95, 52 pgs.)-Collectors ed. w/foil embossed-c						6.00
57-61	1	2	3	5	6	8
62	2	4	6	10	14	18
Annual 1-4: ('91-'94, 68 pgs.)-1-Origin. 2-Spirit of Vengeance-c/story. 3,4-Bagged w/card						5.00

GUARDIANS OF THE GALAXY (See Annihilation series)
Marvel Comics: July, 2008 - No. 25, Jun, 2010 ($2.99)

1-Continued from Annihilation Conquest #6; origin of the new Guardians: Star-Lord, Drax, Warlock, Rocket Raccoon, Quasar (female version: Phyla-Vell) and Gamora; Mantis and Groot are not official members; Cosmo the talking dog and Nova (Richard Rider) app.; Abnett & Lanning-s/Pelletier-a	6	12	18	38	69	100
1-Second printing; variant-c				14	20	25
2,3: 2-Vance Astro (Major Victory) app.; full-size Groot on the cover but still growing (potted plant-size) in story. 3-Starhawk app.; Guardians vs. the Universal Church of Truth	2	4	6	10	14	18
3-Variant cover	2	4	6	11	16	20
4,5-Secret Invasion x-overs; Skrulls app.	1	3	4	6	8	10
5-Monkey variant-c by Nic Klein	2	4	6	9	12	15
6-Secret Invasion x-over; Warlock, Gamora, Quasar and Star-Lord leave the team	1	3	4	6		10
7-Original Guardians app: Vance Astro, Charlie-27, Martinex & Yondu app; Groot, Mantis and Bug (from the Micronauts) join Rocket Raccoon, Vance Astro (Major Victory) and a re-grown Groot as the Guardians; Blastaar app.	2	4	6	8	10	12
7-Variant-c by Jim Valentino	2	4	6	11	16	20
8-War of Kings x-over; Blastaar & Ronan the Accuser app.	1	3	4	6		10
8-Variant-c; Thanos with the Infinity Gauntlet by Brandon Peterson	3	6	9	19	30	40
9-12: 9-War of Kings x-over; Star-Lord and Jack Flagg vs. Blastaar at the super-villain prison in the Negative Zone. 10-War of Kings x-over; Blastaar & Reed Richards app. Star-Lord reunited with the Guardians. 11-Drax and Quasar (Phyla-Vell) story; Maelstrom & Dragon of the Moon app. 12-Moondragon returns; Quasar (Wendell Vaughn) regains the Quantum-bands becomes Protector of the Universe; Maelstrom & Oblivion app; Phyla-Vell becomes new Avatar of Death	2	4	6	8		10
13-War of Kings x-over; Phyla-Vell changes name to 'Martyr'; Moondragon & Jack Flagg join the Guardians; Warlock, Drax & Gamora return to Guardians; Black Bolt & the Inhumans, Vulcan, ruler of the Shi'ar Empire and the Starjammers app.; story continues on War of Kings #3	2	4	6	8	10	12
14-20: 14-War of Kings x-over; Warlock vs. Vulcan; Guardians vs. the Inhumans. 15-War of Kings x-over; Guardians vs. the Sh'iar; Black Bolt & the Inhumans app. 16-War of Kings x-over; Star-Lord, Bug, Jack Flagg, Mantis & Cosmo vs. the Badoon; original Guardians: Martinex, Youndu, Charlie-27, Starhawk and Major Victory app. 17-War of Kings x-over; 'death' of Warlock & Martyr; return of the Magus. 18-Star-Lord, Mantis, Cosmo, Bug & Jack Flagg in alternate future 3000AD; Killraven & Hollywood (Wonder Man) app.; vs. the Martians; original Guardians app.; Starhawk, Charlie-27 & Nikki. 19-Kang app.; 'death' of Martyr & Warlock again; 'death' of Major Victory, Gamora, Cosmo & Mantis. 20-Realm of Kings x-over; Star-Lord, Groot, Rocket Raccoon, Bug, Jack Flagg, Drax & Moondragon appear as the Guardians	1	3	4	6	8	10
17-Variant 70th Anniversary Frame-c by Perkins	2	4	6	11	16	20
21-Realm of Kings x-over; brief appearance of the Cancerverse	2	4	6	8	10	12
22,23: 23-Realm of Kings x-over; the Magus returns. 23-Martyr, Gamora, Cosmo, Mantis & Major Victory return to life; Magus app.	2	4	6	9	12	15
23-Deadpool Variant-c by Alex Garner	3	6	9	17	26	35
24-Realm of Kings x-over; Thanos returns, kills Martyr; Maelstrom app.	2	4	6	9	12	15
	3	6	9	14	20	25
25-Last issue; Guardians vs. Thanos; leads into Thanos Imperative #1	3	6	9	16	23	30
25-Variant-c by Skottie Young	2	4	6	11	16	20

GUARDIANS OF THE GALAXY (Marvel NOW!) (Also see the 2013 Nova series)
(See Incredible Hulk #271, Iron Man #55, Marvel Preview #4,7, Strange Tales #180 and Tales to Astonish #13 for 1st app. of 2014 movie characters)
Marvel Comics: No. 0.1, Apr, 2013; No. 1, May, 2013 - No. 27, Jul, 2015 ($3.99)

0.1-(4/13) Origin of Star-Lord; Bendis-s/McNiven-a						5.00
1-Bendis-s/McNiven-a; Iron Man app.; at least 15 variant covers exist	2	4	6	8	10	12
2-4: Iron Man app.	1	2	3	5	6	8
5-Angela & Thanos app.						5.00
6-13: 8,9-Infinity tie-in; Francavilla-a/c. 10-Maguire-a. 11-13-Trial of Jean Grey						4.00
14-($4.99) Venom and Captain Marvel app.; Bradshaw-a; Guardians of 3014 app.						5.00
15-24,26,27: 16,17-Angela app. 18-20-Original Sin tie-in; Thanos app. 23-Origin of the Symbiotes. 24-Black Vortex crossover						4.00
25-($4.99)-Black Vortex crossover; Kree homeworld destroyed						5.00
Annual 1 (2/15, $4.99) Bendis-s/Cho-a; Nick Fury, Dum Dum, Skrulls app.						5.00
...: Best Story Ever 1 (6/15, $3.99) Tim Seeley-s; Nebula & Thanos app.						4.00
...: Galaxy's Most Wanted 1 (9/14, $3.99) Rocket & Groot; DiVito-a; r/Thor #314 Drax app.						4.00
100th Anniversary Special: Guardians of the Galaxy (9/14, $3.99) Future Guardians						4.00
...: Tomorrow's Avengers 1 (9/13, $4.99) Short stories; art by various						5.00
Marvel's Guardians of the Galaxy Prelude 1,2 (6/14 - No. 2, 7/14, $2.99) 1-Gamora & Nebula app. 2-Rocket & Groot						3.00

GUARDIANS OF THE GALAXY
Marvel Comics: Dec, 2015 - No. 19, Jun, 2017 ($3.99)

1-18: 1-Rocket, Groot, Drax, Venom, The Thing and Kitty Pryde team; Bendis-s. 12,13-Civil War II tie-ins. 12-Avengers app. 14-Spider-Man app.; Maguire-a						4.00
19-($4.99) Thanos and Anriihilus app.; Schiti, Noto, Pichelli, Bagley & others-a						5.00

Grrl Scouts: Magic Socks #3 © Jim Mahfood

Guardians of the Galaxy (2014 series) #17 © MAR

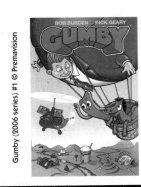

Gumby (2006 series) #1 © Premavision

	GD	VG	FN	VF	VF/NM	NM-
	2.0	4.0	6.0	8.0	9.0	9.2

1.MU (Monsters Unleashed) (5/17, $4.99) Baldeón-a/Walsh-c — 5.00
... Dream On 1 (6/17, $3.99) Death's Head app.; r/1st Taserface from GOTG #1 (1990) — 4.00
... Mission Breakout 1 (7/17, $4.99) Hastings-s/Salazar-a; The Collector app. — 5.00

GUARDIANS OF THE GALAXY (Marvel Legacy)
Marvel Comics: No. 146, Jan, 2018 - No. 150, Mar, 2018 ($3.99)
146-149: 146-Ant-Man joins; Nova Corps app.- Duggan-s/To-a — 4.00
150-($4.99) Lenticular-c by Ross; Adam Warlock returns — 5.00

GUARDIANS OF THE GALAXY
Marvel Comics: Mar, 2019 - No. 12, Feb, 2020 ($4.99/$3.99)
1-($4.99) Cates-s/Shaw-a; Cosmic Ghost Rider, Silver Surfer, Beta Ray Bill & others join — 5.00
2-11-($3.99) 2-Hela & The Collector app. — 4.00
12-($4.99) Donny Cates-s/Cory Smith-a — 5.00
Annual 1 (8/19, $4.99) Takes place before issue #7; Cosmo, Quasar, Adam Warlock app. — 5.00
...: Marvel Presents No. 3 Facsimile Ed. (3/19, $3.99) r/Marvel Presents #3 w/original ads — 4.00
...: The Prodigal Sun 1 (11/19, $4.99) Peter David-s/Francesco Manna-a — 5.00

GUARDIANS OF THE GALAXY
Marvel Comics: Mar, 2020 - No. 18, Nov, 2021 ($4.99/$3.99)
1-($4.99) Al Ewing-s/Juann Cabal-a; Nova (Richard Rider) and Marvel Boy app. — 5.00
2-12,14-18-($3.99) 3-5-Blackjack O'Hare app. 10-King in Black tie-in — 4.00
13-($4.99) Legacy issue #175; Doctor Doom cameo — 5.00
...: Bane of Blastaar 1 (6/23, $3.99) Macchio-s/Tinto-a — 4.00
...: Cosmic Rewind 1 (1/23, $3.99) Kevin Shinick-s/Gerardo Sandoval-a — 4.00

GUARDIANS OF THE GALAXY
Marvel Comics: Jun, 2023 - Present ($4.99/$3.99)
1-($4.99) Kelly & Lanzing-s/Kev Walker-a — 5.00
2-10-($3.99) — 4.00
Annual 1 (4/24, $4.99) Kelly & Lanzing-s/Kev Walker-a — 5.00

GUARDIANS OF THE GALAXY ADAPTATION ("... Vol. 2 Prelude" on cover)
Marvel Comics: Mar, 2017 - No. 2, Apr, 2017 ($3.99, limited series)
1,2-Adaptation of the 2014 movie; Corona Pilgrim-s/Chris Allen-a — 4.00

GUARDIANS OF THE GALAXY & X-MEN: THE BLACK VORTEX
Marvel Comics: Alpha, Apr, 2015 - Omega, Jun, 2015 ($4.99, bookends for crossover)
... Alpha (4/15) Part 1 of crossover; McGuinness-a — 5.00
... Omega (6/15) Part 13 of crossover; Ronan app.; McGuinness-a — 5.00

GUARDIANS OF THE GALAXY: MOTHER ENTROPY
Marvel Comics: Jul, 2017 - No. 5, Jul, 2017 (weekly limited series)
1-5-Starlin-s/Alan Davis-a; Pip the Troll app. 4-Gladiator app. — 4.00

GUARDIANS OF THE GALAXY: TELLTALE GAMES (Based on the videogame)
Marvel Comics: Sept, 2017 - No. 5, Jan, 2018 ($3.99, limited series)
1-5: 1-Van Lente/Espin-a. 2-5-Cosmo app. 5-Thanos app. — 4.00

GUARDIANS TEAM-UP
Marvel Comics: May, 2015 - No. 10, Oct, 2015 ($3.99)
1-10: 1-Bendis-s/Adams-a. 1,2-The Avengers app. 3-Black Vortex crossover. 4-Gamora & She-Hulk. 7-Drax & Ant-Man. 9-Spider-Man & Star-Lord; Pulido-s/a. 10-Deadpool & Rocket — 4.00

GUARDIANS 3000
Marvel Comics: Dec, 2014 - No. 8, Jul, 2015 ($3.99)
1-8: 1-Abnett-s/Sandoval-a; Alex Ross-c; Guardians vs. Badoon in 3014 A.D. 1-6-Ross-c. 6-Guardians meet the 2015 Guardians — 4.00

GUARDING THE GLOBE (See Invincible)
Image Comics: Aug, 2010 - No. 6, Oct, 2011 ($3.50)
1-6-Kirkman & Cereno-s/Getty-a. 1-Back-c swipe of Avengers #4 w/Obama — 3.50

GUARDING THE GLOBE (2nd series) (See Invincible Universe)
Image Comics: Sept, 2012 - No. 6, Feb, 2013 ($2.99)
1-6: 1-Wraparound-c; Hester-s/Nauck-a — 3.00

GUERRILLA WAR (Formerly Jungle War Stories)
Dell Publishing Co.: No. 12, July-Sept, 1965 - No. 14, Mar, 1966
12-14 — 3 — 6 — 9 — 16 — 23 — 30

GUIDEBOOK TO THE MARVEL CINEMATIC UNIVERSE
Marvel Comics: Dec, 2015 - Feb, 2017 ($3.99)
... - Marvel's Agents of S.H.I.E.L.D. Season One (8/16, $3.99) Profile pages — 4.00
... - Marvel's Agents of S.H.I.E.L.D. Season Two/Marvel's Agent Carter Season One (12/16, $3.99) Flipbook with character profile pages; both covers by Marcos Martin — 4.00
... - Marvel's Agents of S.H.I.E.L.D. Season Three/Marvel's Agent Carter Season Two (2/17, $3.99) Flipbook with character profile pages; covers by Del Mundo & Johnson — 4.00
... - Marvel's Avengers: Age of Ultron (11/16, $3.99) Profile pages of characters — 4.00

... - Marvel's Captain America: Civil War (3/17, $3.99) Profile pages — 4.00
... - Marvel's Captain America: The First Avenger (3/16, $3.99) Profile pages — 4.00
... - Marvel's Captain America: The Winter Soldier/Marvel's Ant-Man (7/16, $3.99) Flipbook — 4.00
... - Marvel's Doctor Strange (5/17, $3.99) Profile pages of characters, weapons, locations — 4.00
... - Marvel's Guardians of the Galaxy (9/16, $3.99) Profile pages of characters, locations — 4.00
... - Marvel's Incredible Hulk/Marvel's Iron Man 2 (1/16, $3.99) Flipbook; profile pages — 4.00
... - Marvel's Iron Man (12/15, $3.99) Profile pages of characters, weapons, locations — 4.00
... - Marvel's Iron Man 3/Marvel's Thor: The Dark World (6/16, $3.99) Flipbook profiles — 4.00
... - Marvel's The Avengers (4/16, $3.99) Profile pages of characters, weapons — 4.00
... - Marvel's Thor (2/16, $3.99) Profile pages of characters, weapons, locations — 4.00

GUILD, THE (Based on the web-series)
Dark Horse Comics: Mar, 2010 - No. 3, May, 2010 ($3.50, limited series)
1-3-Felicia Day-s/Jim Rugg-a; two covers on each — 3.50
... Bladezz 1 (6/11, $3.50) Currie-a/Kerschl-c; variant-c by Dalrymple — 3.50
... Clara 1 (9/11, $3.50) Chan-a/Chaykin-c; variant-c by Aronowitz — 3.50
... Fawkes 1 (5/12, $3.50) Day & Wheaton-s/McKelvie-a; variant-c by Rios — 3.50
... Tink 1 (3/11, $3.50) art by Donaldson, Warren, Seeley & others; variant-c by Bagge — 3.50
... Vork 1 (12/10, $3.50) Robertson-a/c; variant-c by Hernandez — 3.50
... Zaboo 1 (12/11, $3.50) Cloonan-a/Dorkin-c; variant-c by Jeanty — 3.50

GUILTY (See Justice Traps the Guilty)

GULLIVER'S TRAVELS (See Dell Jr. Treasury No. 3)
Dell Publishing Co.: Sept-Nov, 1965
1 — 5 — 10 — 15 — 33 — 57 — 80

GUMBY
Wildcard Ink: July, 2006 - No. 3 ($3.99)
1-3-Bob Burden & Rick Geary-s&a — 4.00

GUMBY'S SUMMER FUN SPECIAL
Comico: July, 1987 ($2.50)
1-Art Adams-c/a; B. Burden scripts — 6.00

GUMBY'S WINTER FUN SPECIAL
Comico: Dec, 1988 ($2.50, 44 pgs.)
1-Art Adams-c/a — 6.00

GUMPS, THE (See Merry Christmas..., Popular & Super Comics)
Dell Publ. Co./Bridgeport Herald Corp.: No. 73, 1945; Mar-Apr, 1947 - No. 5, Nov-Dec, 1947
Four Color 73 (Dell)(1945) — 14 — 28 — 42 — 96 — 211 — 325
1 (3-4/47) — 20 — 40 — 60 — 117 — 189 — 260
2-5 — 12 — 24 — 36 — 67 — 94 — 120

GUN CANDY (Also see The Ride)
Image Comics: July, 2005 - No. 2 ($5.99)
1,2-Stelfreeze-c/a; flip book with The Ride (1-Pearson-c. 2-Noto-c) — 6.00

GUNFIGHTER (Fat & Slat #1-4) (Becomes Haunt of Fear #15 on)
E. C. Comics (Fables Publ. Co.): No. 5, Sum, 1948 - No. 14, Mar-Apr, 1950
5,6-Moon Girl in each — 110 — 220 — 330 — 704 — 1202 — 1700
7-14: 13,14-Bondage-c — 54 — 108 — 162 — 343 — 574 — 825
NOTE: Craig & H. C. Kiefer art in most issues. Craig c-5, 6, 13, 14. Feldstein/Craig a-10. Feldstein a-7-11. Harrison/Wood a-13, 14. Ingels a-5-14; c-7-12.

GUNFIGHTERS, THE
Super Comics (Reprints): 1963 - 1964
10-12,15,16,18: 10,11-r/Billy the Kid #s? 12-r/The Rider #5(Swift Arrow). 15-r/Straight Arrow #42; Powell-r. 16-r/Billy the Kid #?(Toby). 18-r/The Rider #3; Severin-c — 2 — 4 — 6 — 10 — 14 — 18

GUNFIGHTERS, THE (Formerly Kid Montana)
Charlton Comics: No. 51, 10/66 - No. 52, 10/67; No. 53, 6/79 - No. 85, 7/84
51,52 — 2 — 4 — 6 — 11 — 16 — 20
53,54,56:53,54-Williamson/Torres-r/Six Gun Heroes #47,49. 56-Williamson/Severin-c; Severin-r/Sheriff of Tombstone 1 — 1 — 3 — 4 — 6 — 8 — 10
55,57-80 — — — — — — 6.00
81-84-Lower print run — 1 — 2 — 3 — 5 — 6 — 8
85-S&K-r/1955 Bullseye — 1 — 3 — 4 — 6 — 8 — 10

GUNFIRE (See Deathstroke Annual #2 & Showcase 94 #1,2)
DC Comics: May, 1994 - No. 13, June, 1995 ($1.75/$2.25)
1-13: 2-Ricochet-c/story. 5-(9/94). 6-(11/94) — 4.00
#0-(10/94) Zero Hour tie-in, released between #5 & #6 — 4.00

GUN GLORY (Movie)
Dell Publishing Co.: No. 846, Oct, 1957 (one-shot)
Four Color 846-Toth-a, photo-c. — 8 — 16 — 24 — 51 — 96 — 140

	GD	VG	FN	VF	VF/NM	NM-
	2.0	4.0	6.0	8.0	9.0	9.2

GUNHAND, THE
American Mythology Productions: 2024 - Present ($4.99)

1-Marty Grosser-s/Matthew Plog-a; the Frankenstein monster's story continues; 4 covers						5.00

GUNHAWK, THE (Formerly Whip Wilson)(See Wild Western and Two-Gun Western #5)
Marvel Comics/Atlas (MCI): No. 12, Nov, 1950 - No. 18, Dec, 1951

	GD	VG	FN	VF	VF/NM	NM-
12	24	48	72	144	237	330
13-18: 13-Tuska-a. 16-Colan-a. 18-Maneely-c	18	36	54	103	162	220

GUNHAWKS (Gunhawk No. 7)
Marvel Comics Group: Oct, 1972 - No. 7, October, 1973

1,6: 1-Reno Jones, Kid Cassidy; Shores-c/a(p). 6-Kid Cassidy dies	4	8	12	23	37	50
2-5,7: 7-Reno Jones solo	2	4	6	13	18	22

GUNHAWKS, THE (Marvel 80th Anniversary salute to western comics)
Marvel Comics: Apr, 2019 ($3.99, one shot)

1-David & Maria Lapham-s/Luca Pizzari-a						4.00

GUN HONEY
Titan Comics: Oct, 2021 - No. 4, Jan, 2022 ($3.99, limited series)

1-4-Charles Ardai-s/Ang Hor Kheng-a; multiple covers on each						4.00

GUN HONEY: BLOOD FOR BLOOD
Titan Comics: Sept, 2022 - No. 4, Jan, 2023 ($3.99, limited series)

1-4-Charles Ardai-s/Ang Hor Kheng-a; multiple covers on each						4.00

GUNMASTER (Becomes Judo Master #89 on)
Charlton Comics: 9/64 - No. 4, 1965; No. 84, 7/65 - No. 88, 3-4/66; No. 89, 10/67

V1#1	5	10	15	33	57	80
2-4, V5#84-86: 84-Formerly Six-Gun Heroes	3	6	9	15	22	28
V5#87-89	2	4	6	11	16	20

NOTE: Vol. 5 was originally cancelled with #88 (3-4/66). #89 on, became Judo Master, then later in 1967, Charlton issued #89 as Gunmaster one-shot.

GUNNING FOR HITS
Image Comics: Jan, 2019 - No. 6, Jun, 2019 ($3.99)

1-6-Jeff Rougvie-s/Moritat-a						4.00

GUN RUNNER
Marvel Comics UK: Oct, 1993 - No. 6, Mar, 1994 ($1.75, limited series)

1-($2.75)-Polybagged w/4 trading cards; Spirits of Vengeance app.						5.00
2-6: 2-Ghost Rider & Blaze app.						4.00

GUNS AGAINST GANGSTERS (True-To-Life Romances #8 on)
Curtis Publications/Novelty Press: Sept-Oct, 1948 - No. 6, July-Aug, 1949; V2#1, Sept-Oct, 1949

1-Toni & Greg Gayle begins by Schomburg; L.B. Cole-c	65	130	195	416	708	1000
2-L.B. Cole-c	42	84	126	265	445	625
3-5	37	74	111	222	361	500
6-Giant shark and Toni Gayle-c by Cole	194	388	582	1242	2121	3000
V2#1	36	72	108	211	343	475

NOTE: L. B. Cole c-1-6, V2#1, 2; a-1, 3(2), 4-6.

GUNSLINGER
Dell Publishing Co.: No. 1220, Oct-Dec, 1961 (one-shot)

Four Color 1220-Photo-c	8	16	24	52	99	145

GUNSLINGER (Formerly Tex Dawson...)
Marvel Comics Group: No. 2, Apr, 1973 - No. 3, June, 1973

2,3	2	4	6	13	18	22

GUNSLINGERS
Marvel Comics: Feb, 2000 ($2.99)

1-Reprints stories of Two-Gun Kid, Rawhide Kid and Caleb Hammer						3.00

GUNSLINGER SPAWN (Title changes to Gunslinger)
Image Comics (Todd McFarlane Prods.): Oct, 2021 - Present ($5.99/$2.99)

1-($5.99) Todd McFarlane-s/Brett Booth-a; back-up by Ales Kot-s/Philip Tan-a						6.00
2-28-($2.99) McFarlane-s/Booth-a. 3-6-Clown returns						3.00

GUNSMITH CATS: (Title series), Dark Horse Comics

--BAD TRIP (Manga), 6/98 - No. 6, 11/98 ($2.95, B&W) 1-6						4.00
--BEAN BANDIT (Manga), 1/99 - No. 9 ($2.95, B&W, limited series) 1-9						4.00
--GOLDIE VS. MISTY (Manga), 11/97 - No. 7, 5/98 ($2.95, B&W) 1-7						4.00
--KIDNAPPED (Manga), 11/99 - No. 10, 8/00 ($2.95, B&W) 1-10						4.00
--MISTER V (Manga), 10/00 - No. 11, 8/01 ($3.50/$2.99), B&W) 1-11						3.50
--THE RETURN OF GRAY (Manga), 8/96 - No. 7, 2/97 ($2.95, B&W) 1-7						4.00
--SHADES OF GRAY (Manga), 5/97 - No. 5, 9/97 ($2.95, B&W) 1-5						4.00
--SPECIAL (Manga) Nov, 2001 ($2.99, B&W, one-shot)						3.00

GUNSMOKE (Blazing Stories of the West)
Western Comics (Youthful Magazines): Apr-May, 1949 - No. 16, Jan, 1952

1-Gunsmoke & Masked Marvel begin by Ingels; Ingels bondage-c	60	120	180	381	653	925
2-Ingels-c/a(2)	39	78	117	231	378	525
3-Ingels bondage-c/a	34	68	102	204	332	460
4-6: Ingels-c	26	52	78	154	252	350
7-10	16	32	48	98	154	210
11-16: 15,16-Western/horror stories	15	30	45	94	147	200

NOTE: Stallman a-11, 14. Wildey a-15, 16.

GUNSMOKE (TV)
Dell Publishing Co./Gold Key (All have James Arness photo-c): No. 679, Feb, 1956 - No. 27, Feb, 1969 - No. 6, Feb, 1970

Four Color 679(#1)	21	42	63	147	324	500
Four Color 720,769,797,844 (#2-5),6(11-1/57-58)	10	20	30	66	138	210
7,8,9,11,12-Williamson-a in all, 4 pgs. each	8	16	24	54	102	150
10-Williamson/Crandall-a, 4 pgs.	8	16	24	54	102	150

13-27	7	14	21	44	82	120
1 (Gold Key)	7	14	21	44	82	120
2-6('69-70)	4	8	12	23	37	50

GUNSMOKE TRAIL
Ajax-Farrell Publ./Four Star Comic Corp.: June, 1957 - No. 4, Dec, 1957

1	11	22	33	64	90	115
2-4	7	14	21	35	43	50

GUNSMOKE WESTERN (Formerly Western Tales of Black Rider)
Atlas Comics No. 32-35(CPS/NPI); Marvel No. 36 on: No. 32, Dec, 1955 - No. 77, July, 1963

32-Baker & Drucker-a	28	56	84	165	270	375
33,35,36-Williamson-a in each; 5,6 & 4 pgs. plus Drucker-a #33. 33-Kinstler-a?	19	38	57	111	176	240
34-Baker-a, 4 pgs.; Severin-c	20	40	60	117	189	260
37-Davis-a(2); Williamson text illo	15	30	45	90	140	190
38,39: 39-Williamson text illo (unsigned)	14	28	42	82	121	160
40-Williamson/Mayo-a (4 pgs.)	15	30	45	84	127	170
41,42,45,46,48,49,50,52-54,57,58,60: 49,52-Kid from Texas story. 57-1st Two Gun Kid by Severin. 60-Sam Hawk app. in Kid Colt	13	26	39	74	105	135
43,44-Torres-a	13	26	39	74	105	135
47,51,59,61: 47,51,59-Kirby-a. 61-Crandall-a	14	28	42	80	115	150
50-Kirby, Crandall-a	15	30	45	84	127	170
55,56-Matt Baker-a	15	30	45	90	140	190
62-67,69,71-73,77-Kirby-a. 72-Origin Kid Colt	8	16	24	51	96	140
68,70,74-76: 68-(10¢-c)	7	14	21	46	86	125
68-(10¢ cover price blacked out, 12¢ printed on)	14	28	42	96	211	325

NOTE: Colan a-35-37, 39, 72, 76. Davis a-37, 52, 54, 55; c-50, 54. Ditko a-66; c-56p. Drucker a-32-34. Heath c-33. Jack Keller a-34, 35, 40, 51, 53, 55, 56, 60, 61, 65, 68, 69, 71, 72, 74, 75, 77; c-72. Kirby a-47, 50, 51, 59, 62(3), 63-67, 69, 71, 73, 77, c-56(w/Ditko), 60, 65, 66, 68, 69, 71-77. Ayers), 62, 63, 65, 66, 68, 69, 71-77. Maneely a-53; c-45. Robinson a-35. Severin a-35, 59-61; c-34, 35, 39, 42, 43. Tuska a-34. Wildey a-10, 37, 42, 56, 57. Kid Colt in all. Two-Gun Kid in No.57, 59, 60-63. Wyatt Earp in No.45, 48, 49, 51-56, 58.

GUNS OF FACT & FICTION (Also see A-1 Comics)
Magazine Enterprises: No. 13, 1948 (one-shot)

A-1 13-Used in SOTI, pg. 19; Ingels & J. Craig-a	37	74	111	222	361	500

GUNS OF THE DRAGON
DC Comics: Oct, 1998 - No. 4, Jan, 1999 ($2.50, limited series)

1-4-DCU in the 1920's; Enemy Ace & Bat Lash app.						4.00

GUNWITCH, THE : OUTSKIRTS OF DOOM (See The Nocturnals)
Oni Press: June, 2001 - No. 3, Oct, 2001 ($2.95, B&W, limited series)

1-3-Brereton-s/painted-c/Naifeh-s						3.00

GUY GARDNER (Guy Gardner: Warrior #17 on)(Also see Green Lantern #59)
DC Comics: Oct, 1992 - No. 44, July, 1996 ($1.25/$1.50/$1.75)

1-Staton-c/a(p) begins						5.00
2-24,26-30: 6-Guy vs. Hal Jordan. 8-Vs. Lobo-c/story. 15-JLA x-over, begin 1.50-c. 18-Begin 4-part Emerald Fallout story; splash page x-over GL #50. 18-21-Vs. Hal Jordan.						
24 (9/94)-Zero Hour						4.00
25 (11/94, $2.50, 52 pgs.)						5.00
29 ($2.95)-Gatefold-c						5.00
29-Variant-c (Edward Hopper's Nighthawks)						4.00
31-44: 31-$1.75-c begins. 40-Gorilla Grodd-c/app. 44-Parallax-app. (1 pg.)						4.00
#0-(10/94) Zero Hour tie-in; released between #24 & #25						4.00
Annual 1 (1995, $3.50)-Year One story						5.00
Annual 2 (1996, $2.95)-Legends of the Dead Earth story						5.00

GUY GARDNER: COLLATERAL DAMAGE
DC Comics: 2006 - No. 2 ($5.99, square-bound, limited series)

1,2-Howard Chaykin-s/a						6.00

GUY GARDNER REBORN
DC Comics: 1992 - Book 3, 1992 ($4.95, limited series)

1-3: Staton-c/a(p). 1-Lobo-c/cameo. 2,3-Lobo-c/s						6.00

GWAR: ORGASMAGEDDON (Based on the band GWAR)
Dynamite Entertainment: 2017 - No. 4, 2017 ($3.99, limited series)

1-4-Matt Maguire & Matt Miner-s/Sawyer & Maguire-a; multiple covers						4.00

GWENPOOL (Also see Unbelievable Gwenpool)
Marvel Comics: Feb, 2016; Feb, 2017 ($5.99, one-shots)

... Holiday Special: Merry Mix-Up (2/17, $5.99) 1-Deadpool, Squirrel Girl, Punisher app.						6.00
... Special (2/16, $5.99) 1-Christmas-themed short stories; She-Hulk, Deadpool app.						6.00

GWENPOOL STRIKES BACK
Marvel Comics: Oct, 2019 - No. 5, Feb, 2020 ($3.99)

1-5-Leah Williams-s/David Baldeón-a. 1-Spider-Man app. 3-5-Ms. Marvel app. 5-Photo-c						4.00

GWEN STACY (See Giant-Size Gwen Stacy for all 5 chapters)
Marvel Comics: Apr, 2020 - No. 2, May, 2020 ($4.99/$3.99, unfinished 5-issue series)

1-($4.99) Gage-s/Nauck-a; main cover by Adam Hughes; Gwen in high school						5.00
2-($3.99) Norman Osborn app.						4.00

GYPSY COLT
Dell Publishing Co.: No. 568, June, 1954 (one-shot)

Four Color 568-Movie	6	12	18	42	79	115

GYRO GEARLOOSE (See Dynabrite Comics, Walt Disney's C&S #140 & Walt Disney Showcase #18)
Dell Publishing Co.: No. 1047, Nov-Jan/1959-60 - May-July, 1962 (Disney)

Four Color 1047 (No. 1)-All Barks-c/a	16	32	48	111	246	380
Four Color 1095,1184-All by Carl Barks	9	18	27	62	126	190
Four Color 1267-Barks c/a, 4 pgs.	7	14	21	48	89	130
01329-207 (#1, 5-7/62)-Barks-c only (indexed as 4-Color 1329?)						
	5	10	15	35	63	90

HACKER FILES, THE
DC Comics: Aug, 1992 - No. 12, July, 1993 ($1.95)

1-12: 1-Sutton-a(p) begins; computer generated-c						4.00

HACK/SLASH

The Gunhand #1 © Martin Grosser

Gyro Gearloose #1 © DIS

Hack/Slash vs. Chaos #1 © DYN

	GD	VG	FN	VF	VF/NM	NM-
	2.0	4.0	6.0	8.0	9.0	9.2

Devil's Due Publishing: Apr. 2004 - No. 32, Mar, 2010 ($3.25/$4.95)

1-Seeley-s/Caselli-a/c		5	10	15	31	53	75
...: (The Series) 1-5,7-24,26,27,29-32 (5/07-No. 32, 3/10, $3.50) Flashack to Cassie's childhood and origin. 12-Milk & Cheese cameo. 15-Re-Animator app.						5.00
6,28-Archie parodies	2	4	6	11	16	20
25-($5.50) Double sized issue; Baugh-a; two covers						5.50
...: Comic Book Carnage (3/05) Manfredi-a/Seeley-s; Robert Kirkman & Steve Niles app.						
	1	3	4	6	8	10
...: First Cut TPB (10/05, $14.95) r/one-shots with sketch pages, designs, interviews						15.00
...: Girls Gone Dead (10/04, $4.95) Manfredi-a	1	3	4	6	8	10
...: Land of Lost Toys 1-3 (11/05 - No. 3, 1/06, $3.25) Crossland-a/Seeley-s						5.00
...: New Reader Halloween Treat #1 (10/08, $3.50) origin retold; Cassie's diary pages						5.00
...: The Final Revenge of Evil Ernie (6/05, $4.95) Salman-a; two covers						
	1	3	2	5	6	8
...: Trailers (2/05, $3.25) short stories by Seeley; art by various; three covers						6.00
...: Slice Hard (12/05, $4.95) Seeley-s						5.00
...: Slice Hard Pre-Sliced 25¢ Special (2/06, 25¢) origin story by Seeley; sketch pages						3.00
...: Vs Chucky (3/07, $5.50) Seeley-s/Merhoff-a; 3 covers						
	1	3	4	6	8	10
...: Vol. 2 Death By Sequel TPB (1/07, $18.99) r/Land of Lost Toys #1-3, Trailers, Slice Hard						19.00
...: Vol. 3 Friday the 31st TPB (10/07, $18.99) r/The Series #1-4 & ... Vs Chucky						19.00

HACK/SLASH
Image Comics: Feb, 2011 - No. 25, Mar, 2013 ($3.50)

1-Seeley-s/Leister-a		2	4	6	8	10	12
2-25: 5-Esquejo-c. 9-11-Bomb Queen app.						5.00
... Annual 2010: Murder Messiah (10/10, $5.99) Seeley-s/Morales-a						
	1	3	4	6	8	10
... Annual 2011: Hatchet/Slash (11/11, $5.99)						6.00
.../ Eva: Monster's Ball 1-4 (Dynamite Ent., 2011 - No. 4, 2011, $3.99) Jerwa-s/Razek-a						5.00
... 15th Anniversary Celebration (9/19, $5.99) Cassie appears in the real world; pin-ups						6.00
... Hot Shorts 1 (10/22, $3.99) Seeley-s; art by Seeley, Terry & Leister						5.00
... Me Without You (1/11, $3.50) Leister-a/Seeley-s; 2 covers						
	1	3	4	6	8	10
.../ Nailbiter 1 (3/15, $4.99) Flip book with Nailbiter / Hack/Slash 1						5.00
...: Trailers #2 (11/10, $6.99) short stories; story & art by various; Seeley-c						7.00
Image Firsts: Hack/Slash #1 (10/10, $1.00) r/#1 (2004) with "Image Firsts" cover frame						4.00

HACK SLASH: BACK TO SCHOOL
Image Comics: Oct, 2023 - No. 4, Apr, 2024 ($3.99)

1-4-Zoe Thorogood-s/a						4.00

HACK SLASH: MY FIRST MANIAC
Image Comics: Jun, 2010 - No. 4, Sept, 2010 ($3.99)

1-Leister-a/Seeley-s	2	4	6	8	10	12
2-4						5.00

HACK SLASH: RESURRECTION
Image Comics: Oct, 2017 - No. 12, Oct, 2018 ($3.99)

1-12-Tini Howard-s/Celor-a. 3-Vlad returns. 8-11-Vampirella app.						4.00

HACK/SLASH: SON OF SAMHAIN
Image Comics: Jul, 2014 - No. 5, Nov, 2014 ($3.99)

1-Laiso-a/Moreci & Seeley-s	2	4	6	8	10	12
2-5						5.00

HACK/SLASH VS. CHAOS
Dynamite Entertainment: 2018 - No. 5, 2019 ($3.99)

1-5-Seeley-s; multiple covers; Evil Ernie, Chastity, Purgatori app. 1-Lobosco-a						4.00

HACK/SLASH VS. VAMPIRELLA
Dynamite Entertainment: 2017 - No. 5, 2018 ($3.99)

1-5-Aldridge-s/Lobosco-a; multiple covers						4.00

HACKTIVIST
Archaia Black Label: Jan, 2014 - No. 4, Apr, 2014 ($3.99)

1-4-Kelly & Lanzing-s/To-a; created by Alyssa Milano						4.00
... Volume 2 (BOOM! Ent.; 7/15 - No. 6, 12/15, $3.99) 1-6-Kelly & Lanzing-s/To-a						4.00

HAGAR THE HORRIBLE (See Comics Reading Libraries in the Promotional Comics section)

HA HA COMICS (Teepee Tim No. 100 on; also see Giggle Comics)
Scope Mag.(Creston Publ.) No. 1-80/American Comics Group: Oct, 1943 - No. 99, Jan, 1955

1-Funny animal	47	94	141	296	498	700
2	25	50	75	150	245	340
3-5: Ken Hultgren-a begins?	20	40	60	114	182	250
6-10	15	30	45	88	137	185

11-20: 14-Infinity-c	14	28	42	80	115	150
21-40	13	26	39	72	101	130
41-43,45-94,97-99: 49,61-X-Mas-c	11	22	33	62	86	110
44-1st Tee-Pee Tim app.; begin series; Little Black Sambo app.						
	13	26	39	74	105	135
95,96-3-D effect-c/story	20	40	60	120	195	270

HAIL HYDRA (Secret Wars tie-in)
Marvel Comics: Sept, 2015 - No. 4, Jan, 2016 ($3.99, limited series)

1-4-Nomad (Ian Rogers) vs. Hydra; Remender-s/Boschi-a; Venom app.						4.00

HAIRBALL
Dark Horse Comics: Apr, 2023 - No. 4, Jul, 2023 ($5.99, limited series)

1-4-Cat horror; Matt Kindt-s/Tyler Jenkins-a						6.00

HAIR BEAR BUNCH, THE (TV) (See Fun-In No. 13)
Gold Key: Feb, 1972 - No. 9, Feb, 1974 (Hanna-Barbera)

1	4	8	12	23	37	50
2-9	3	6	9	16	24	32

HALCYON
Image Comics: Nov, 2010 - No. 5, May, 2011 ($2.99)

1-5-Guggenheim & Butters-s/Bodenheim-a						3.00

HALF PAST DANGER
IDW Publishing: May, 2013 - No. 6, Oct, 2013 ($3.99, limited series)

1-6: Dinosaurs and Nazis in 1943; Stephen Mooney-s/a/c						4.00

HALF PAST DANGER 2
IDW Publishing: Sept, 2017 - No. 5, Jan, 2018 ($3.99, limited series)

1-5-Nazis in 1948; Stephen Mooney-s/a/c						4.00

HAL JORDAN AND THE GREEN LANTERN CORPS (DC Rebirth) (Also see Green Lanterns)
DC Comics: Sept, 2016 - No. 50, Early Oct, 2018 ($2.99)

1-24: 1-Venditti-s/Sandoval-a; Sinestro app.; GL Corps returns. 4,5,17,22-24-Van Sciver-a. 10-12-Larfleeze app. Kyle becomes a Green Lantern again						3.00
						4.00
25-($3.99) Van Sciver-a						
26-49: 26,27-Orion of the New Gods app. 30,31-Superman app. 32-Dark Nights: Metal. 37-41-Zod app. 42-Darkstars return. 42,45-Van Sciver-a						3.00
50-($3.99) Sandoval-a; Zod app.						
...: Rebirth 1 (9/16, $2.99) Venditti/Van Sciver-a; Sinestro & Lyssa app.						3.00

HALLELUJAH TRAIL, THE (See Movie Classics)

HALL OF FAME FEATURING THE T.H.U.N.D.E.R. AGENTS
JC Productions(Archie Comics Group): May, 1983 - No. 3, Dec, 1983

1-3: Thunder Agents-r(Crandall, Kane, Tuska, Wood-a). 2-New Ditko-c						4.00

HALLOWEEN (Movie)
Chaos! Comics: Nov, 2000; Apr, 2001 ($2.95/$2.99, one-shots)

1-Brewer-a; Michael Myers childhood at the Sanitarium						4.00
...II: The Blackest Eyes (4/01, $2.99) Beck-a						4.00
...III: The Devil's Eyes (11/01, $2.99) Justiniano-a						4.00

HALLOWEEN (Halloween Nightdance on cover)(Movie)
Devils Due Publishing: Mar, 2008 - No. 4, May, 2008 ($3.50, limited series)

1-4-Seeley-a/Hutchinson-s; multiple covers on each						3.50
...: 30 Years of Terror (8/08, $5.50) short stories by various incl. Seeley						5.50

HALLOWEEN EVE
Image Comics: Oct, 2012 ($3.99, one-shot)

One-Shot - Brandon Montclare-s/Amy Reeder-a; two covers by Reeder						4.00

HALLOWEEN HORROR
Eclipse Comics: Oct, 1987 (Seduction of the Innocent #7)($1.75)

1-Pre-code horror-r						5.00

HALLOWEEN MEGAZINE
Marvel Comics: Dec, 1996 ($3.95, one-shot, 96 pgs.)

1-Reprints Tomb of Dracula						4.00

HALLOWEEN PARTY
Image Comics: Oct, 2022 ($4.99, one-shot)

1-Scotch McTiernan returns; Duggan & Posehn-s/Koblish-a						5.00

HALLOWS' EVE
Marvel Comics: May, 2023 - No. 5, Sept, 2023 ($3.99, limited series)

1-5-Janine Godbe from Amazing Spider-Man; Schultz-s/Dowling-a. 3-Spider-Man app.						4.00
...: The Big Night 1 (12/23, $4.99) Schultz-s/Dowling-a						5.00

HALO GRAPHIC NOVEL (Based on video game)

	GD	VG	FN	VF	VF/NM	NM-
	2.0	4.0	6.0	8.0	9.0	9.2

Marvel Publishing Inc.: 2006 ($24.99, hardcover with dust jacket)

HC-Anthology set in the Halo universe; art by Bisley, Moebius and others; pin-up gallery by various incl. Darrow, Pratt, Williams and Van Fleet; Phil Hale painted-c ... 25.00

HALO: BLOOD LINE (Based on video game)
Marvel Comics: Feb, 2010 - No. 5, Jul, 2010 ($3.99, limited series)

1-5-Van Lente-s/Portela-a ... 4.00

HALO: COLLATERAL DAMAGE (Based on video game)
Dark Horse Comics: Jun, 2018 - No. 3, Aug, 2018 ($3.99)

1-3-Alex Irvine-s/Dave Crossland-a ... 4.00

HALO: ESCALATION (Based on video game)
Dark Horse Comics: Dec, 2013 - No. 24, Nov, 2015 ($3.99)

1-24: 1-4-Chris Schlerf-s/Sergio Ariño-a ... 4.00

HALO: FALL OF REACH - BOOT CAMP (Based on video game)
Marvel Comics: Nov, 2010 - No. 4, Apr, 2011 ($3.99, limited series)

1-4-Reed-s/Ruiz-a ... 4.00

HALO: FALL OF REACH - COVENANT (Based on video game)
Marvel Comics: Jun, 2011 - No. 4, Dec, 2011 ($3.99, limited series)

1-4-Reed-s/Ruiz-a ... 4.00

HALO: FALL OF REACH - INVASION (Based on video game)
Marvel Comics: Mar, 2012 - No. 4, Aug, 2012 ($3.99, limited series)

1-4-Reed-s/Ruiz-a ... 4.00

HALO: HELLJUMPER (Based on video game)
Marvel Comics: Sept, 2009 - No. 5, Jan, 2010 ($3.99, limited series)

1-5-Peter David-s/Eric Nguyen-a ... 4.00

HALO: INITIATION (Based on video game)
Dark Horse Comics: Aug, 2013 - No. 3, Oct, 2013 ($3.99, limited series)

1-3-Brian Reed-s/Marco Castiello-a ... 4.00

HALO: LONE WOLF (Based on video game)
Dark Horse Comics: Jan, 2019 - No. 4, Apr, 2019 ($3.99, limited series)

1-4-Toole-s/McKeown-a; spotlight on Linda-058 ... 4.00

HALO: RISE OF ATRIOX (Based on video game)
Marvel Comics: Aug, 2017 - No. 5, Jan, 2018 ($3.99, limited series)

1-5: 1-Cullen Bunn-s/Eric Nguyen-a. 2-Houser-s/Gonzalez-a. 3-John Jackson Miller-s ... 4.00

HALO: UPRISING (Based on video game) (Also see Marvel Spotlight: Halo)
Marvel Comics: Oct, 2007 - No. 4, Jun, 2009 ($3.99, limited series)

1-4-Bendis-s/Maleev-a; takes place between the *Halo 2* and *Halo 3* video games ... 4.00

HALO JONES (See The Ballad of...)

HAMMER, THE
Dark Horse Comics: Oct, 1997 - No. 4, Jan, 1998 ($2.95, limited series)

1-4-Kelley Jones-s/c/a, ...: Uncle Alex (8/98, $2.95) ... 4.00

HAMMER, THE: THE OUTSIDER
Dark Horse Comics: Feb, 1999 - No. 3, Apr, 1999 ($2.95, limited series)

1-3-Kelley Jones-s/c/a ... 4.00

HAMMERLOCKE
DC Comics: Sept, 1992 - No. 9, May, 1993 ($1.75, limited series)

1-($2.50, 52 pgs.)-Chris Sprouse-c/a in all ... 5.00
2-9 ... 4.00

HAMMER OF GOD (Also see Nexus)
First Comics: Feb, 1990 - No. 4, May, 1990 ($1.95, limited series)

1-4 ... 4.00

HAMMER OF GOD: BUTCH
Dark Horse Comics: May, 1994 - No. 4, Aug, 1994 ($2.50, limited series)

1-3 ... 4.00

HAMMER OF GOD: PENTATHLON
Dark Horse Comics: Jan, 1994 ($2.50, one shot)

1-Character from Nexus ... 4.00

HAMMER OF GOD: SWORD OF JUSTICE
First Comics: Feb 1991 - Mar 1991 ($4.95, lim. series, squarebound, 52 pgs.)

V2#1,2 ... 5.00

HAMMER OF THE GODS
Insight Studio Groups: 2001 - No. 5, 2001 ($2.95, limited series)

1-Michael Oeming & Mark Wheatley-s/a; Frank Cho-c ... 6.00
1-(IDW, 7/11, $1.00) reprints #1 with "Hundred Penny Press" logo on Oeming cover ... 3.00
2-5: 3-Hughes-c. 5-Dave Johnson-c ... 3.00
The Color Saga (2002, $4.95) r/"Enemy of the Gods" internet strip ... 5.00
Mortal Enemy TPB (2002, $18.95) r/#1-5; intro. by Peter David; afterword by Raven ... 19.00

HAMMER OF THE GODS: HAMMER HITS CHINA
Image Comics: Feb, 2003 - No. 3, Sept, 2003 ($2.95, limited series)

1-3-Oeming & Wheatley-s/a; Oeming-c. 2-Frankenstein Mobster by Wheatley ... 3.00

HANDBOOK OF THE CONAN UNIVERSE, THE (Reprinted in The Official... Anniversary Ed.)
Marvel Comics: June, 1985; Jan, 1986 ($1.25, one-shot)

1-(6/85) Kaluta-c (2 printings) ... 6.00
1-(1/86) Kaluta-c ... 6.00

	1	2	3	5	6	8
nn-(no date, circa '87-88, B&W, 36 pgs.) reprints '86 with changes; new painted cover	1	2	3	5	6	8

HAND OF FATE (Formerly Men Against Crime)
Ace Magazines: No. 8, Dec, 1951 - No. 25, Dec, 1954 (Weird/horror stories) (Two #25's)

	2.0	4.0	6.0	8.0	9.0	9.2
8-Surrealistic text story	63	126	189	403	689	975
9,10,21-Necronomicon sty; drug belladonna used	42	84	126	265	445	625
11-18,20,22,23	37	74	111	222	361	500
19-Bondage, hypo needle scenes	48	96	144	302	514	725
24-Electric chair-c	54	108	162	343	574	825

	2.0	4.0	6.0	8.0	9.0	9.2
25a(11/54), 25b(12/54)-Both have Cameron-a	39	78	117	231	378	525

NOTE: *Cameron a-9, 10, 19-25a, 25b; c-13. Sekowsky a-8, 9, 13, 14.*

HAND OF FATE
Eclipse Comics: Feb, 1988 - No. 3, Apr, 1988 ($1.75/$2.00, Baxter paper)

1-3; 3-B&W ... 4.00

HANDS OF THE DRAGON
Seaboard Periodicals (Atlas): June, 1975

	2.0	4.0	6.0	8.0	9.0	9.2
1-Origin/1st app.; Craig-a(p)/Mooney inks	3	6	9	15	22	28

HANGMAN, THE
Archie Comic Publications: Dec, 2015 - No. 4, Dec, 2016 ($3.99)

1-4-Tieri-s/Ruiz-a; new Hangman recruited; multiple covers ... 4.00

HANGMAN COMICS (Special Comics No. 1; Black Hood No. 9 on)
(Also see Flyman, Mighty Comics, Mighty Crusaders & Pep Comics)
MLJ Magazines: No. 2, Spring, 1942 - No. 8, Fall, 1943

	2.0	4.0	6.0	8.0	9.0	9.2
2-The Hangman, Boy Buddies begin	428	856	1284	3124	5512	7900
3-Beheading splash pg.; Nazi war-c; classic-c	757	1514	2271	5526	9763	14,000
4-Classic Nazi WWII hunchback torture-c	514	1028	1542	3750	6625	9500
5-1st Japan war-c; bondage/torture-c	300	600	900	2070	3635	5200
6-Horror-c	300	600	900	1950	3375	4800
7,8: 8-2nd app. Super Duck (ties w/Jolly Jingles #11)	284	568	852	1818	3109	4400

NOTE: *Fuje a-7(3), 8(3); c-3. Reinman c/a-3. Sahle c-6.*

HANK
Pentagon Publishing Co.: 1946

	2.0	4.0	6.0	8.0	9.0	9.2
nn-Coulton Waugh's newspaper reprint	14	28	42	76	108	140

HANK HOWARD, PIZZA DETECTIVE IN CALIGULA'S SAFE
Bad Idea: May, 2021 ($1.00, one-shot)

1-Venditti-s/Lapham-a ... 5.00

HANK JOHNSON, AGENT OF HYDRA (Secret Wars tie-in)
Marvel Comics: Oct, 2015 ($3.99, one-shot)

1-Mandel-s/Walsh-a; Steranko cover swipe by Conner ... 4.00

HANNA-BARBERA (See Golden Comics Digest No. 2, 7, 11)

HANNA-BARBERA ALL-STARS
Archie Publications: Oct, 1995 - No. 4, Apr, 1996 ($1.50, bi-monthly)

1-4 ... 4.00

HANNA-BARBERA BANDWAGON (TV)
Gold Key: Oct, 1962 - No. 3, Apr, 1963

	2.0	4.0	6.0	8.0	9.0	9.2
1-Giant, 84 pgs. 1-Augie Doggie app.; 1st app. Lippy the Lion, Touché Turtle & Dum Dum, Wally Gator, Loopy de Loop,	11	22	33	73	157	240
2-Giant, 84 pgs. J. Mr. & Mrs. J. Evil Scientist (1st app.) in Snagglepuss story; Yakky Doodle, Ruff and Reddy and others app.	8	16	24	51	96	140
3-Regular size; Mr. & Mrs. J. Evil Scientist app. (pre-#1), Snagglepuss, Wally Gator and others app.	6	12	18	40	73	105

HANNA-BARBERA GIANT SIZE
Harvey Comics: Oct, 1992 - No. 3 ($2.25, 68 pgs.)

	2.0	4.0	6.0	8.0	9.0	9.2
V2#1-3:Flintstones, Yogi Bear, Magilla Gorilla, Huckleberry Hound, Quick Draw McGraw, Yakky Doodle & Chopper, Jetsons & others	1	2	3	5	6	8

HANNA-BARBERA HI-ADVENTURE HEROES (See Hi-Adventure...)

HANNA-BARBERA PARADE (TV)
Charlton Comics: Sept, 1971 - No. 10, Dec, 1972

	2.0	4.0	6.0	8.0	9.0	9.2
1	6	12	18	41	76	110
2,4-10	4	8	12	25	40	55
3-(52 pgs.)- "Summer Picnic"	5	10	15	33	57	80

NOTE: *No. 4 (1/72) went on sale late in 1972 with the January 1973 issues.*

HANNA-BARBERA PRESENTS
Archie Publications: Nov, 1995 - No. 8 ($1.50, bi-monthly)

1-8: 1-Atom Ant & Secret Squirrel. 2-Wacky Races. 3-Yogi Bear. 4-Quick Draw McGraw & Magilla Gorilla. 5-A Pup Named Scooby-Doo. 6-Superstar Olympics. 7-Wacky Races. 8-Frankenstein Jr. & the Impossibles ... 4.00

HANNA-BARBERA SPOTLIGHT (See Spotlight)

HANNA-BARBERA SUPER TV HEROES (TV)
Gold Key: Apr, 1968 - No. 7, Oct, 1969 (Hanna-Barbera)

	2.0	4.0	6.0	8.0	9.0	9.2
1-The Birdman, The Herculoids (ends #6; not in #3), Moby Dick, Young Samson & Goliath (ends #2,4), and The Mighty Mightor begin; Spiegle-a in all	14	28	42	96	211	325
2-The Galaxy Trio app.; Shazzan begins; 12¢ and 15¢ versions exist	9	18	27	61	123	185
3,6,7-The Space Ghost app.	8	16	24	55	105	155
4,5	7	14	21	48	89	130

NOTE: *Birdman in #1,2,4,5. Herculoids in #2,4-7. Mighty Mightor in #1,2,4-7. Moby Dick in all. Shazzan in #2-5. Young Samson & Goliath in #1,3.*

HANNA-BARBERA TV FUN FAVORITES (See Golden Comics Digest #2,7,11)

HANNA-BARBERA (TV STARS) (See TV Stars)

HANS BRINKER (Disney)
Dell Publishing Co.: No. 1273, Feb, 1962 (one-shot)

	2.0	4.0	6.0	8.0	9.0	9.2
Four Color 1273-Movie, photo-c	6	12	18	37	66	95

HANS CHRISTIAN ANDERSEN
Ziff-Davis Publ. Co.: 1953 (100 pgs., Special Issue)

	2.0	4.0	6.0	8.0	9.0	9.2
nn-Danny Kaye (movie)-Photo-c; fairy tales	20	40	60	114	182	250

HANSEL & GRETEL
Dell Publishing Co.: No. 590, Oct, 1954 (one-shot)

	2.0	4.0	6.0	8.0	9.0	9.2
Four Color 590-Partial photo-c	7	14	21	49	92	135

HANSI, THE GIRL WHO LOVED THE SWASTIKA
Spire Christian Comics (Fleming H. Revell Co.): 1973, 1976 (39¢/49¢)

	2.0	4.0	6.0	8.0	9.0	9.2
1973 edition with 39¢-c	12	24	36	81	176	270

Halo: Escalation #7 © Microsoft

Han Solo #4 © Lucasfilm

Harbinger (2012 series) #1 © VAL

	GD	VG	FN	VF	VF/NM	NM-
	2.0	4.0	6.0	8.0	9.0	9.2
1976 edition with 39¢-c	10	20	30	67	141	215
1976 edition with 49¢-c	15	30	45	100	220	340

HAN SOLO (Star Wars)
Marvel Comics: Aug, 2016 - No. 5, Jan, 2017 ($3.99, limited series)

1-5-Marjorie Liu-s/Mark Brooks-a/Lee Bermejo-c; takes place between Episodes 4 & 5						4.00

HAP HAZARD COMICS (Real Love No. 25 on)
Ace Magazines (Readers' Research): Summer, 1944 - No. 24, Feb, 1949
(#1-6 are quarterly issues)

	GD	VG	FN	VF	VF/NM	NM-
1	21	42	63	124	202	280
2	13	26	39	74	105	135
3-10	10	20	30	58	79	100
11,12,15,16,20-24	10	20	30	54	72	90
13,17-19-Good Girl covers	40	80	120	246	411	575
14-(4/47) Feldstein-c; Cary Grant, Frank Sinatra, Van Johnson, Guy Madison, Alan Ladd and Robert Taylor app.	47	94	141	296	498	700

HAP HOPPER (See Comics Revue No. 2)

HAPPIEST MILLIONAIRE, THE (See Movie Comics)

HAPPI TIM (See March of Comics No. 182)

HAPPY
Image Comics: Sept, 2012 - No. 4, Feb, 2013 ($2.99, limited series)

1-4-Grant Morrison-s/Darick Robertson-a. 1-Covers by Robertson & Allred						5.00

HAPPY BIRTHDAY MARTHA WASHINGTON (Also see Give Me Liberty, Martha Washington Goes To War, & Martha Washington Stranded In Space)
Dark Horse Comics: Mar, 1995 ($2.95, one-shot)

1-Miller script; Gibbons-c/a						4.00

HAPPY COMICS (Happy Rabbit No. 41 on)
Nedor Publ./Standard Comics (Animated Cartoons): Aug, 1943 - No. 40, Dec, 1950
(Companion to Goofy Comics)

	GD	VG	FN	VF	VF/NM	NM-
1-Funny animal	40	80	120	246	411	575
2	21	42	63	124	202	280
3-10	15	30	45	88	137	185
11-19	14	28	42	81	118	155
20-31,34-37-Frazetta text illos in all (2 in #34&35, 3 in #27,28,30). 27-Al Fago-a	15	30	45	85	130	175
32-Frazetta-a, 7 pgs. plus 2 text illos; Roussos-a	28	56	84	168	274	380
33-Frazetta-a(2), 6 pgs. each (Scarce)	37	74	111	222	361	500
38-40	13	26	39	74	105	135

HAPPYDALE: DEVILS IN THE DESERT
DC Comics (Vertigo): 1999 - No. 2, 1999 ($6.95, limited series)

1,2-Andrew Dabb-s/Seth Fisher-a						7.00

HAPPY DAYS (TV)(See Kite Fun Book)
Gold Key: Mar, 1979 - No. 6, Feb, 1980

	GD	VG	FN	VF	VF/NM	NM-
1-Photo-c of TV cast; 35¢-c	5	10	15	33	57	80
2-6-(40¢-c)	2	4	6	10	14	18

HAPPY HOLIDAY (See March of Comics No. 181)

HAPPY HORROR DAYS
Archie Comic Publications: Feb, 2023 ($3.99, one-shot)

1-Short Christmas-themed horror stories; Krampus app.						4.00

HAPPY HOULIHANS (Saddle Justice No. 3 on; see Blackstone, The Magician Detective)
E. C. Comics: Fall, 1947 - No. 2, Winter, 1947-48

	GD	VG	FN	VF	VF/NM	NM-
1-Origin Moon Girl (same date as Moon Girl #1)	113	226	339	718	1234	1750
2	40	80	120	246	411	575

HAPPY HOUR
AHOY Comics: 2020 - No. 6, 2021 ($3.99, limited series)

1-6-Peter Milligan-s/Michael Montenat-a						4.00

HAPPY JACK
Red Top (Decker): Aug, 1957 - No. 2, Nov, 1957

	GD	VG	FN	VF	VF/NM	NM-
V1#1,2	7	14	21	37	46	55

HAPPY JACK HOWARD
Red Top (Farrelly)/Decker: 1957

	GD	VG	FN	VF	VF/NM	NM-
nn-Reprints Handy Andy story from E. C. Dandy Comics #5, renamed "Happy Jack"	7	14	21	35	43	50

HAPPY RABBIT (Formerly Happy Comics)
Standard Comics (Animated Cartoons): No. 41, Feb, 1951 - No. 48, Apr, 1952

	GD	VG	FN	VF	VF/NM	NM-
41-Funny animal	13	26	39	72	101	130

	GD	VG	FN	VF	VF/NM	NM-
	2.0	4.0	6.0	8.0	9.0	9.2
42-48	9	18	27	52	69	85

HARBINGER (Also see Unity)
Valiant: Jan, 1992 - No. 41, June, 1995 ($1.95/$2.50)

	GD	VG	FN	VF	VF/NM	NM-
0-Prequel to the series; available by redeeming coupons in #1-6; cover image has pink sky; title logo is blue	5	10	15	31	53	75
0-(2nd printing) cover has blue sky & red logo	1	3	4	6	8	10
1-1st app. (with coupon)	6	12	18	38	69	100
1-Low print run	3	6	9	14	19	24
5,6-Solar app. 6-Torque dies	2	4	6	9	12	15
7-10: 8,9-Unity x-overs. 8-Miller-c. 9-Simonson-c. 10-1st app. H.A.R.D Corps (10/92)	1	2	3	5	6	8
11-24,26-41: 14-1st app. Stronghold. 18-Intro Screen. 19-1st app. Stunner. 22-Archer & Armstrong app. 24-Cover similar to #1. 26-Intro New Harbingers. 29-Bound-in trading card. 30-H.A.R.D. Corps app. 32-Eternal Warrior app. 33-Dr. Eclipse app.						4.00
25-($3.50, 52 pgs.)-Harada vs. Sting						5.00
...: Acts of God 1 (1/98, $3.95) Paco Diaz-a						4.00
...: Files 1,2 (8/94,2/95 $2.50)						4.00
...: The Beginning HC (2007, $24.95) recolored reprints #0-7 and Story of Harada from coupons from #1-6; new "Origin of Harada" story by Shooter and Bob Hall						30.00
Trade paperback nn (11/92, $9.95)-Reprints #1-4 & comes polybagged with a copy of Harbinger #0 w/new-c. Price for TPB only						15.00

NOTE: *Issues 1-6 have coupons with origin of Harada and are redeemable for Harbinger #0.*

HARBINGER
Valiant Entertainment: Jun, 2012 - No. 25, Jul, 2014 ($3.99)(#0 released between #8 & #9)

1-Dysart-s/Khari Evans-a; covers by Lozzi and Suayan (Pullbox variant)						4.00
1-Variant cover by Braithwaite						10.00
1-QR voice variant cover by Jelena Djurdjevic						45.00
2-24-Two covers on each (standard & pullbox). 2-Origin continues. 11-14-Harbinger Wars tie-in. 23-Flamingo dies						4.00
25-($4.99) Back-up story by Tiwary & Larosa; bonus features and cover gallery						5.00
#0 (2/13, $3.99) Origin of Harada; Suayan & Pere Pérez-a; covers by Crain & Suayan						4.00
#0-Variant gatefold-c by Lewis Larosa						15.00
... Bleeding Monk #0 (3/14, $3.99) Dysart-s; art by Evans, Suayan, Segovia & LaRosa						4.00
... Faith #0 (12/14, $3.99) Dysart-s; Robert Gill-a						4.00

HARBINGER, THE
Valiant Entertainment: Oct, 2021 - No. 8, May, 2022 ($3.99)

1-8-Kelly & Lansing-s/Rodriguez-a; Pete Stanchek returns. 4-Faith cameo						4.00

HARBINGER: OMEGAS
Valiant Entertainment: Jul, 2014 - No. 3, Oct, 2014 ($3.99, limited series)

1-3-Dysart-s/Sandoval-a						4.00

HARBINGER RENEGADE
Valiant Entertainment: Nov, 2016 - No. 8, Oct, 2017; No. 0 Nov, 2017 ($3.99, limited series)

1-8: 1-Rafer Roberts-s/Darick Robertson-a; intro Alexander Solomon. 6-Ryp-a						4.00
#0-(11/17) Follows #8; Ryp-a; H.A.R.D. Corps app.						4.00

HARBINGER WARS
Valiant Entertainment: Apr, 2013 - No. 4, Jul, 2013 ($3.99, limited series)

1-4: 1-Dysart-s/Henry, Crain & Suayan-a; covers by Larosa & Henry (Pullbox)						4.00
1-Variant cover by Crain						10.00
1-Variant cover by Zircher						50.00

HARBINGER WARS 2
Valiant Entertainment: May, 2018 - No. 4, Aug, 2018 ($3.99, limited series)

1-4-Kindt-s/Giorello-a; Bloodshot, Ninjak, X-O Manowar, Live Wire app.						4.00
...: Aftermath 1 (9/18, $3.99) Kindt-s/Pollina-a; X-O Manowar & Live Wire app.						4.00
...: Prelude (5/18, $3.99) Heisserer-s/Allén-a						4.00

HARD BOILED
Dark Horse Comics: Sept, 1990 - No. 3, Mar, 1992 ($4.95/$5.95, 8 1/2x11", lim. series)

	GD	VG	FN	VF	VF/NM	NM-
1-Frank Miller-s/Darrow-c/a in all; sexually explicit & violent	3	6	9	14	19	24
2,3	2	4	6	8	10	12
TPB (5/93, $15.95)						20.00
Big Damn Hard Boiled (12/97, $29.95, B&W) r/#1-3	5	10	15	33	57	80

HARDCASE (See Break Thru, Flood Relief & Ultraforce, 1st Series)
Malibu Comics (Ultraverse): June, 1993 - No. 26, Aug, 1995 ($1.95/$2.50)

1-Intro Hardcase; Dave Gibbons-c; has coupon for Ultraverse Premiere #0; Jim Callahan-a(p) begin, ends #3						5.00
1-With coupon missing						3.00
1-Platinum Edition						6.00
1-Holographic Cover Edition; 1st full-c holograph tied w/Prime 1 & Strangers 1						

	GD	VG	FN	VF	VF/NM	NM-
	2.0	4.0	6.0	8.0	9.0	9.2

1-Ultra Limited silver foil-c 6.00
2,3-Callahan-a, 2-($2.50)-Newsstand edition bagged w/trading card 5.00
4,6-15, 17-19: 4-Strangers app. 7-Break-Thru x-over. 8-Solution app. 9-Vs. Turf.
12-Silver foil logo, wraparound-c. 17-Prime app. 4.00
5-($2.50, 48 pgs.)-Rune flip-c/story by B. Smith (3 pgs.) 5.00
16 ($3.50, 68 pgs.)-Rune pin-up 5.00
20-26: 23-Loki app. 4.00
NOTE: *Perez a-8(2); c-20i.*

HARDCORE
Image Comics: May, 2012 ($2.99)

1-Kirkman-s/Stelfreeze-a/Silvestri-c	2	4	6	8	10	12

HARDCORE
Image Comics (Skybound): Dec, 2018 - No. 5, Apr, 2019 ($3.99)

1-5-Diggle-s/Vitti-a/Panosian-c 4.00

HARDCORE: RELOADED
Image Comics (Skybound): Dec, 2019 - No. 5, Jun, 2020 ($3.99)

1-5-Brandon Thomas-s/Francis Portela-a/Nic Klein-c 4.00

HARDCORE STATION
DC Comics: July, 1998 - No. 6, Dec, 1998 ($2.50, limited series)

1-6-Starlin-s/a(p). 3-Green Lantern-c/app. 5,6-JLA-c/app. 4.00

H.A.R.D. CORPS, THE (See Harbinger #10)
Valiant: Dec, 1992 - No. 30, Feb, 1995 ($2.25) (Harbinger spin-off)

1-($2.50)-Gatefold-c by Jim Lee & Bob Layton 5.00
1-Gold variant 15.00
2-30: 5-Bloodshot-c/story cont'd from Bloodshot #3. 5-Variant edition; came w/Comic Defense
System. 10-Turok app. 17-vs. Armorines. 18-Bound-in trading card. 20-Harbinger app. 4.00

HARD TIME
DC Comics (Focus): Apr, 2004 - No. 12, Mar, 2005 ($2.50)

1-12-Gerber-s/Hurtt-a; 1-Includes previews of other DC Focus series 3.00
... 50 to Life (2004, $9.95, TPB) r/#1-6; cover gallery with sketches 10.00

HARD TIME: SEASON TWO
DC Comics: Feb, 2006 - No. 7, Aug, 2006 ($2.50/$2.99)

1-5-Gerber-s/Hurtt-a 3.00
6,7-($2.99) 7-Ethan paroled in 2053 .... 3.00

HARDWARE
DC Comics (Milestone): Apr, 1993 - No. 50, Apr, 1997 ($1.50/$1.75/$2.50)

1-($2.95)-Collector's Edition polybagged w/poster & trading card (direct sale only)

1-Platinum Edition	5	10	15	33	57	80
1-Regular edition	1	3	4	6	8	10

2-15,17-19: 11-Shadow War x-over. 11,14-Simonson-c. 12-Buckler(a(p). 17-Worlds Collide
Pt. 2. 18-Simonson-c; Worlds Collide Pt. 9. 15-1st Humberto Ramos DC work 4.00
16,25: 16-($2.50, 52 pgs.)-Newsstand Ed. 25-($2.95, 52 pgs.) 5.00
16,50-($3.95, 52 pgs.)-16-Collector's Edition w/gatefold 2nd cover by Byrne; new armor;
Icon app. 6.00
20-24,26-48 .... 4.00

49-Moebius-c	5	10	15	35	63	90

...: The Man in the Machine TPB (2010, $19.99) r/#1-8 .... 20.00

HARDWARE: SEASON ONE (Milestone Returns)
DC Comics: Oct, 2021 - No. 6, Jul, 2022 ($3.99, lmited series)

1-6-Brandon Thomas-s/Denys Cowan-a 4.00

HARDY BOYS, THE (Disney)
Dell Publ. Co.: No. 760, Dec, 1956 - No. 964, Jan, 1959 (Mickey Mouse Club)

Four Color 760 (#1)-Photo-c	11	22	33	76	163	250
Four Color 830(8/57), 887(1/58), 964-Photo-c	9	18	27	62	126	190

HARDY BOYS, THE (TV)
Gold Key: Apr, 1970 - No. 4, Jan, 1971

1	4	8	12	27	44	60
2-4	3	6	9	17	26	35

HARLAN ELLISON'S DREAM CORRIDOR
Dark Horse Comics: Mar, 1995 - No. 5, July, 1995 ($2.95, anthology)

1-5: Adaptation of Ellison stories. 1-4-Byrne-a. 4.00
Special (1/95, $4.95) 6.00
Trade paperback (1996, $18.95, 192 pgs)-r/#1-5 & Special #1 .... 19.00

HARLAN ELLISON'S DREAM CORRIDOR QUARTERLY
Dark Horse Comics: V2#1, Aug, 1996 ($5.95, anthology, squarebound)

V2#1-Adaptations of Ellison's stories w/new material; Neal Adams-a 6.00
Volume 2 TPB (3/07, $19.95) r/V2#1 and unpublished material incl. last Swan-a 20.00

HARLEEN
DC Comics (Black Label): Nov, 2019 - No. 3, Feb, 2020 ($7.99, 10-3/4" x 8-1/2", lim. series)

1-3-Retelling of Harley Quinn's origin with Joker; Stjepan Sejic-s/a 8.00

HARLEM GLOBETROTTERS (TV) (See Fun-In No. 8, 10)
Gold Key: Apr, 1972 - No. 12, Jan, 1975 (Hanna-Barbera)

1	5	10	15	33	57	80
2-5	3	6	9	15	22	28
6-12	2	4	6	13	18	22

NOTE: *#4, 8, and 12 contain 16 extra pages of advertising.*

HARLEQUIN VALENTINE
Dark Horse Comics: Nov, 2001 ($10.95, hardcover, one-shot)

nn-Neil Gaiman-s; painted-a/c by John Bolton 11.00

HARLEY & IVY MEET BETTY & VERONICA (Archie Comics)
DC Comics: Dec, 2017 - No. 6, May, 2018 ($3.99, limited series)

1-6: 1-Harvey & Ivy go to Riverdale; Dini & Andreyko-s/Braga-a. 1-Conner-c. 2-Zatanna app.
3,4-The Joker app. 4.00
1-Variant-c by Adam Hughes 5.00

HARLEY QUINN (See Batman Adventures #12 for 1st app.)(Also see Gotham City Sirens,

Old Lady Harley, and Suicide Squad)
DC Comics: Dec, 2000 - No. 38, Jan, 2004 ($2.95/$2.25/$2.50)

1-Joker and Poison Ivy app.; Terry & Rachel Dodson/a/c

	5	10	15	33	57	80
2,3-($2.25): 2-Two-Face-c/app. 3-Slumber party	2	4	6	11	16	20
4-9,11-($2.25). 6,7-Riddler app.	1	3	4	6	8	10
10-Batgirl-c/s	2	4	6	10	14	18
12-($2.95) Batman app.	2	4	6	10	14	18

13,17-19: 13-Joker: Last Laugh. 17,18-Bizarro-c/app. 19-Superman-c

	2	4	6	11	16	20

14-16,20-24,26-31,33-37: 23-Begin $2.50-c. 23,24-Martian Manhunter app.

	1	2	3	5	6	8
25-Classic Joker-c/s	3	6	9	16	23	30
32-Joker-c/app.	2	4	6	11	16	20
38-Last issue; Adlard-a/Morse-c	3	6	9	14	20	25

Harley & Ivy: Love on the Lam (2001, $5.95) Winick-s/Chiodo-c/a

	3	6	9	14	20	26

...: Our Worlds at War (10/01, $2.95) Jae Lee-c; art by various

	2	4	6	10	14	18

HARLEY QUINN (DC New 52)
DC Comics: No. 0, Jan, 2014 - No. 30, Sept, 2016 ($2.99/3.99)

0-Conner & Palmiotti-s; art by Conner & various; Conner-c

	2	4	6	10	14	18
0-Variant-c by Stephane Roux	3	6	9	13	19	25
1-(2/14) Chad Hardin-a; Conner-c	3	6	9	17	25	34
1-Variant-c by Adam Hughes	13	26	39	89	195	300

1-Halloween Fest Special Edition (12/15, free) r/#1 with "Halloween ComicFest" logo 5.00

2-Poison Ivy app.	2	4	6	9	12	15
3-5: 4-Roux-a	1	2	3	5	6	8

6-16: 6,7-Poison Ivy app. 11-13-Power Girl app. 16-Intro. of The Gang of Harleys
17-30-($3.99) 17-19-Capt Strong app. 20,21-Deadshot app. 25-Joker app. 4.00
26-28-Red Tool app. 30-Charretier-a; Poison Ivy app. 4.00
Annual 1 (12/14, $5.99) Polybagged with "Rub 'N Smell" pages 6.00
... & The Suicide Squad April Fools' Special 1 (6/16, $4.99) Rob Williams-s/Jim Lee-a 5.00
...Director's Cut #0 (8/14, $4.99) With commentary by Conner & Palmiotti; cover gallery 5.00
...: Futures End 1 (11/14, $2.99, regular-c) Five years later; Joker app. 5.00
...: Futures End 1 (11/14, $3.99, 3-D cover) 8.00
... Holiday Special (2/15, $4.99) Christmas-themed stories; back-up Darwyn Cooke-a

	1	2	3	5	6	8

... Invades Comic-Con International: San Diego 1 (9/14, $4.99) Wraparound-c

	2	4	6	8	10	10

... Road Trip Special (11/15, $5.99) Harley, Catwoman & Poison Ivy road trip; Conner-c

	1	2	3	5	6	8

... Valentine's Day Special (4/15, $4.99) Bruce Wayne and Poison Ivy app.

	1	2	3	5	6	8

HARLEY QUINN (DC Rebirth)
DC Comics: Oct, 2016 - No. 75, Oct, 2020 ($2.99/$3.99)

1-Conner & Palmiotti-s/Hardin-a; Poison Ivy & Red Tool app.

	1	2	3	5	6	8

2-6: 4-Linsner-a. 6-Joker flashback w/Jill Thompson-a (4 pgs.) 4.00
7-24: 9-Kaluta-a (4 pgs.). 10-Linsner & Morital-a. 15,16-Power Girl & Atlee app.
17-Back-up stories by Dini & Palmiotti-s/Blevins-a begin, thru #25; Joker app. 3.00
25-($3.99) Back-up story w/Joker continues in Harley Loves Joker #1 .... 4.00
26-46: 27-Tieri-s/Carlini-a/Thompson-c. 29-Kaluta-a (5 pgs.) 34-Last Palmiotti & Conner-s.
35-39-Tieri-s. 36,37-Penguin app. 42-Old Lady Harley. 45,46-Granny Goodness & Female
Furies app. 3.00
47-49,51-74 ($3.99) 47-Harley on Apokolips. 48,49-Lord Death Man app. 51,52-Capt. Triumph
app. 57,58-Batman app. 71-74-Booster Gold app. 4.00
50-($4.99) Jonni DC app.; art by various; Conner infinity-c; Captain Triumph returns 5.00
63-($4.99) Variant Year of the Villain painted-c by Frank Cho 5.00
75-($5.99) Roast of Harley Quinn; back up story tie-in to Joker War; Punchline app. 5.00
... Batman Day Special Edition (10/17, giveaway) r/#7; Joker app. 5.00
...: Be Careful What You Wish For Special Edition 1 (3/18, $4.99) Reprints story from
Loot Crate edition plus 18 new pages; art by Conner, Hardin, Schmidt & Caldwell 5.00
.../Gossamer 1 (10/18, $4.99) Looney Tunes monster. 71-74-Booster Gold app. 5.00
... 25th Anniversary Special 1 (11/17, $4.99) Short stories by various incl. Dini, Conner,
Palmiotti, Zdarsky, Quinones, Hardin; 2 covers by Conner & Dodson 5.00
Harley Quinn's Greatest Hits TPB (2016, $9.99) r/Batman Advs. #12 & other stories 10.00
Harley Quinn's Villain of the Year (2019, $4.99) Russell-s/Norton-a/Conner-c 5.00

HARLEY QUINN (Infinite Frontier)
DC Comics: May, 2021 - Present ($3.99)

1-24: 1-Phillips-s/Rossmo-a. 7-9-"Fear State" tie-ins. 10-Braga-a. 23-Robin (Damian) app. 4.00
25-($4.99) Old Lady Harley and a multiverse of Harleys app. 5.00
26,27-($3.99) Batwoman app. 4.00
28-37-($3.99) 29-Zatanna app.; back-up Adam Warren-s/a. 30,31-Capt. Carrot app. 5.00
... 30th Anniversary Special 1 (11/22, $9.99) Short stories by various; multiple covers 10.00
... Uncovered 1 (11/22, $5.99) Gallery of recent variant covers by Chew, Hughes, others 6.00
2021 Annual 1 (11/21, $5.99) Phillips-s/Lafuente & Sommariva-a; Joker app. 6.00
2022 Annual 1 (10/22, $5.99) Phillips-s/Buonfantino & Duarte-a; Task Force XX app. 6.00

HARLEY QUINN AND HER GANG OF HARLEYS
DC Comics: Jun, 2016 - No. 6, Nov, 2016 ($3.99, limited series)

1-6-Palmiotti & Tieri-s/Mauricet-a/Conner-c; intro. Harley Sinn. 5-Origin of Harley Sinn 4.00

HARLEY QUINN & POISON IVY
DC Comics: Nov, 2019 - No. 6, Apr, 2020 ($3.99, limited series)

1-6-Houser-s/Melo-a. 1,2-Floronic Man app. 2,3-Mad Hatter app. 5-Batwoman app. 4.00

HARLEY QUINN AND POWER GIRL
DC Comics: Aug, 2015 - No. 6, Feb, 2016 ($3.99, limited series)

1-6-Takes place during Harley Quinn #11-13; Vartox app.; Roux-a 4.00

HARLEY QUINN & THE BIRDS OF PREY
DC Comics (Black Label): Apr, 2020 - No. 4, Mar, 2021 ($5.99, 8-1/2" x 10-3/4", lim. series)

1-4-Conner & Palmiotti-s/Conner-a; Power Girl, Huntress & Cassandra Cain app. 6.00

Hardware: Season One #3 © DC

Harley Quinn (2016 series) #17 © DC

Harvey Hits #37 © HARV

	GD	VG	FN	VF	VF/NM	NM-
	2.0	4.0	6.0	8.0	9.0	9.2

HARLEY QUINN: BLACK + WHITE + REDDER
DC Comics: Sept, 2023 - No. 6, Feb, 2024 ($4.99, limited series anthology in B&W&Red)

1-6: 1-Zdarsky-s/Maguire-a. 2-Zatanna app. 3-Simone-s — 5.00

HARLEY QUINN: HARLEY LOVES JOKER
DC Comics: Early Jul, 2018 - No. 2, Jul, 2018 ($3.99, limited series)

1,2-Dini-s/Blevins-a; covers by Conner & Cho; original costume Harley; intro The Grison — 4.00

HARLEY QUINN: THE ANIMATED SERIES
DC Comics: Oct, 2022 (Series of one-shots)

... The Real Sidekicks of New Gotham Special 1 (10/22, $9.99)-Short stories; Sarin-c — 10.00

HARLEY QUINN: THE ANIMATED SERIES: LEGION OF BATS! (Follows Season 3)
DC Comics: Dec, 2022 - No. 6, May, 2023 ($3.99, limited series)

1-6: 1-Tee Franklin-s/Shae Beagle-a; Harley joins the Bat-family — 4.00

HARLEY QUINN: THE ANIMATED SERIES: THE EAT. BANG! KILL. TOUR (Follows Season 2)
DC Comics: Nov, 2021 - No. 6, Apr, 2022 ($3.99)

1-6-Tee Franklin-s/Max Sarin-a; Poison Ivy, Catwoman & Vixen app. — 4.00

HARLEY'S LITTLE BLACK BOOK (Harley Quinn team-up book)
DC Comics: Feb, 2016 - No. 6, May, 2017 ($4.99, bi-monthly)

1-4,6: 1-Palmiotti & Conner-s; Wonder Woman app.; Conner-c. 2-Green Lantern app. 3-Zatanna app.; Linsner-a. 4-DC Bombshells app.; Tucci-a. 6-Lobo app.; Bisley-a — 5.00

	1	2	3	5	6	8
1-Polybagged variant-c by Campbell (3 versions: sketch, B&W, and color)						5.00

5-Neal Adams-a; homage to "Superman vs. Muhammad Ali" — 5.00

HAROLD TEEN (See Popular Comics, & Super Comics)
Dell Publishing Co.: No. 2, 1942 - No. 209, Jan, 1949

	GD	VG	FN	VF	VF/NM	NM-
Four Color 2	38	76	114	285	641	1000
Four Color 209	8	16	24	52	99	145

HARRIET TUBMAN: DEMON SLAYER
Massive Publishing: Sept, 2023 - No. 6, Feb, 2024 ($4.99)

1-6-David Crownson-s/Courtland Ellis-a — 5.00

HARROW COUNTY (Also see Tales From Harrow County)
Dark Horse Comics: May, 2015 - No. 32, Jun, 2018 ($3.99)

1-31: 1-8-Cullen Bunn-s/Tyler Crook-a. 9,17-Carla Speed McNeil-a — 4.00
1-Halloween ComicFest Edition (10/16, no price) r/#1 — 3.00
32-($4.99) Last issue; Bunn-s/Crook-a — 5.00

HARROWERS, THE (See Clive Barker's...)

HARSH REALM (Inspired 1999 TV series)
Harris Comics: 1993- No. 6, 1994 ($2.95, limited series)

1-6: Painted-c. Hudnall-s/Paquette & Ridgway-a — 4.00
TPB (2000, $14.95) r/series — 15.00

HARVESTER, THE
Legendary Comics: Feb, 2015 - No. 6, Jul, 2015 ($3.99)

1-6-Brandon Seifert-s/Eric Battle-a/c — 4.00

HARVEY
Marvel Comics: Oct, 1970; No. 2, 12/70; No. 3, 6/72 - No. 6, 12/72

	10	20	30	66	138	210
1-Teenage	10	20	30	66	138	210
2-6	7	14	21	46	86	125

HARVEY COLLECTORS COMICS (Titled Richie Rich Collectors Comics on cover of #6-on)
Harvey Publ.: Sept, 1975 - No. 15, Jan, 1978; No. 16, Oct, 1979 (52 pgs.)

	2	4	6	13	18	22
1-Reprints Richie Rich #1,2	2	4	6	13	18	22
2-10: 7-Splash pg. shows cover to Friendly Ghost Casper #1	2	4	6	8	11	14
11-16: 16-Sad Sack-r	1	2	3	5	7	9

NOTE: All reprints: Casper-#2, 7, Richie Rich-#1, 3, 5, 6, 8-15, Sad Sack-#16. Wendy-#4.

HARVEY COMICS HITS (Formerly Joe Palooka #50)
Harvey Publications: No. 51, Oct, 1951 - No. 62, Apr, 1953

51-The Phantom	43	86	129	271	461	650
52-Steve Canyon's Air Power(Air Force sponsored)	14	28	42	76	108	140
53-Mandrake the Magician	21	42	63	122	199	275
54-Tim Tyler's Tales of Jungle Terror	14	28	42	80	115	150
55-Love Stories of Mary Worth	13	26	39	74	105	135
56-The Phantom; bondage-c	37	74	111	222	361	500
57-Rip Kirby Exposes the Kidnap Racket; entire book by Alex Raymond	18	36	54	105	165	225
58-Girls in White (nurses stories)	15	30	45	85	130	175
59-Tales of the Invisible featuring Scarlet O'Neil	19	38	57	111	176	240

60-Paramount Animated Comics #1 (9/52) (3rd app. Baby Huey); 2nd Harvey app. Baby Huey

& Casper the Friendly Ghost (1st in Little Audrey #25 (8/52)); 1st app. Herman & Catnip (c/story) & Buzzy the Crow

	77	154	231	493	847	1200
61-Casper the Friendly Ghost #6 (3rd Harvey Casper, 10/52)-Casper-c	63	126	189	403	689	975
62-Paramount Animated Comics #2; Herman & Catnip, Baby Huey & Buzzy the Crow	21	42	63	122	199	275

HARVEY COMICS LIBRARY
Harvey Publications: Apr, 1952 - No. 2, 1952

1-Teen-Age Dope Slaves as exposed by Rex Morgan, M.D.; drug propaganda story; used in SOTI, pg. 27	486	972	1458	3550	6275	9000
2-Dick Tracy Presents Sparkle Plenty in "Blackmail Terror"	28	56	84	165	270	375

HARVEY COMICS SPOTLIGHT
Harvey Comics: Sept, 1987 - No. 4, Mar, 1988 (75¢/$1.00)

1-New material; begin 75¢-c, ends #3; Sad Sack — 5.00
2-4: 2,4-All new material. 2-Baby Huey. 3-Little Dot; contains reprints w/5 pg. new story. — 5.00
4-$1.00-c; Little Audrey — 4.00
NOTE: No. 5 was advertised but not published.

HARVEY HITS (Also see Tastee-Freez Comics in the Promotional Comics section)
Harvey Publications: Sept, 1957 - No. 122, Nov, 1967

1-The Phantom	36	72	108	266	596	925
2-Rags Rabbit (10/57)	7	14	21	48	89	130
3-Richie Rich (11/57)-r/Little Dot; 1st book devoted to Richie Rich; see Little Dot for 1st app.	155	310	465	1279	2890	4500
4-Little Dot's Uncles (12/57)	17	34	51	117	259	400
5-Stevie Mazie's Boy Friend (1/58)	5	10	15	35	63	90
6-The Phantom (2/58); 2pg. Powell-a	20	40	60	140	310	480
7-Wendy the Good Little Witch (3/58, pre-dates Wendy #1; 1st book devoted to Wendy)	61	122	183	488	1094	1700
8-Sad Sack's Army Life; George Baker-c	9	18	27	61	123	185
9-Richie Rich's Golden Deeds; (2nd book devoted to Richie Rich) reprints Richie Rich story from Tastee-Freez #1	86	172	258	688	1544	2400
10-Little Lotta's Lunch Box	13	26	39	89	195	300
11-Little Audrey Summer Fun (7/58)	9	18	27	61	123	185
12-The Phantom; 2pg. Powell-a (8/58)	17	34	51	114	252	390
13-Little Dot's Uncles (9/58); Richie Rich 1pg.	11	22	33	77	166	255
14-Herman & Katnip (10/58, TV/movies)	5	10	15	33	57	80
15-The Phantom (12/58)-1 pg. origin	17	34	51	119	265	410
16-Wendy the Good Little Witch (1/59); Casper app.	14	28	42	96	211	325
17-Sad Sack's Army Life (2/59)	5	10	15	34	66	85
18-Buzzy & the Crow	4	8	12	25	40	55
19-Little Audrey (4/59)	5	10	15	35	63	90
20-Casper & Spooky	7	14	21	48	89	130
21-Wendy the Witch	7	14	21	44	82	120
22-Sad Sack's Army Life	4	8	12	28	47	65
23-Wendy the Witch (8/59)	7	14	21	44	82	120
24-Little Dot's Uncles (9/59); Richie Rich 1pg.	8	16	24	54	102	150
25-Herman & Katnip (10/59)	3	6	9	21	33	45
26-The Phantom (11/59)	12	24	36	83	182	280
27-Wendy the Good Little Witch (12/59)	6	12	18	42	79	115
28-Sad Sack's Army Life (1/60)	4	8	12	25	40	55
29-Harvey-Toon (No.1)('60); Casper, Buzzy	5	10	15	31	53	75
30-Wendy the Witch (3/60)	7	14	21	44	82	120
31-Herman & Katnip (4/60)	3	6	9	19	30	45
32-Sad Sack's Army Life (5/60)	3	6	9	21	33	45
33-Wendy the Witch (6/60)	6	12	18	40	73	105
34-Harvey-Toon (7/60)	4	8	12	23	37	50
35-Funday Funnies (8/60)	3	6	9	19	30	40
36-The Phantom (1960)	12	24	36	81	176	270
37-Casper & Nightmare	6	12	18	38	69	100
38-Harvey-Toon	4	8	12	23	37	50
39-Sad Sack's Army Life (12/60)	3	6	9	20	31	42
40-Funday Funnies (1/61)	3	6	9	16	24	32
41-Herman & Katnip	3	6	9	16	24	32
42-Harvey-Toon (3/61)	3	6	9	18	28	38
43-Sad Sack's Army Life (4/61)	3	6	9	18	28	38
44-The Phantom (5/61)	11	22	33	76	163	250
45-Casper & Nightmare	5	10	15	30	50	70
46-Harvey-Toon (7/61)	3	6	9	16	24	32
47-Sad Sack's Army Life (8/61)	3	6	9	16	24	32
48-The Phantom (9/61)	11	22	33	76	163	250
49-Stumbo the Giant (1st app. in Hot Stuff)	9	18	27	58	114	170
50-Harvey-Toon (11/61)	3	6	9	16	23	30

	GD 2.0	VG 4.0	FN 6.0	VF 8.0	VF/NM 9.0	NM- 9.2
51-Sad Sack's Army Life (12/61)	3	6	9	16	23	30
52-Casper & Nightmare	4	8	12	28	47	65
53-Harvey-Toons (2/62)	3	6	9	16	23	30
54-Stumbo the Giant	5	10	15	33	57	80
55-Sad Sack's Army Life (4/62)	3	6	9	16	23	30
56-Casper & Nightmare	4	8	12	25	40	55
57-Stumbo the Giant	5	10	15	33	57	80
58-Sad Sack's Army Life	3	6	9	16	23	30
59-Casper & Nightmare (7/62)	4	8	12	25	40	55
60-Stumbo the Giant (9/62)	5	10	15	31	53	75
61-Casper & Nightmare	3	6	9	15	22	28
62-Casper & Nightmare	4	8	12	22	35	48
63-Stumbo the Giant	4	8	12	27	44	60
64-Sad Sack's Army Life (1/63)	3	6	9	15	22	28
65-Casper & Nightmare	4	8	12	22	35	48
66-Stumbo The Giant (3/63)	4	8	12	22	35	48
67-Sad Sack's Army Life (4/63)	3	6	9	15	22	28
68-Casper & Nightmare	4	8	12	22	35	48
69-Stumbo the Giant (6/63)	4	8	12	27	44	60
70-Sad Sack's Army Life (7/63)	3	6	9	15	22	28
71-Casper & Nightmare (8/63)	3	6	9	20	31	42
72-Stumbo the Giant	4	8	12	27	44	60
73-Little Sad Sack (10/63)	3	6	9	15	22	28
74-Sad Sack's Muttsy… (11/63)	3	6	9	15	22	28
75-Casper & Nightmare	4	8	12	18	28	38
76-Little Sad Sack	3	6	9	15	22	28
77-Sad Sack's Muttsy…	3	6	9	15	22	28
78-Stumbo the Giant (3/64); JFK caricature	4	8	12	28	44	60

79-87: 79-Little Sad Sack (4/64). 80-Sad Sack's Muttsy… (5/64). 81-Little Sad Sack. 82-Sad Sack's Muttsy… 83-Little Sad Sack(8/64). 84-Sad Sack's Muttsy… 85-Gabby Gob (#1) (10/64). 86-G. I. Juniors (#1)(11/64). 87-Sad Sack's Muttsy… (12/64)

	GD 2.0	VG 4.0	FN 6.0	VF 8.0	VF/NM 9.0	NM- 9.2
	3	6	9	15	22	28
88-Stumbo the Giant (1/65)	4	8	12	27	44	60

89-122: 89-Sad Sack's Muttsy… 90-Gabby Gob. 91-G. I. Juniors. 92-Sad Sack's Muttsy… (5/65). 93-Sadie Sack (6/65). 94-Gabby Gob. 95-G. I. Juniors (8/65). 96-Sad Sack's Muttsy… (9/65). 97-Gabby Gob (10/65). 98-G. I. Juniors (11/65). 99-Sad Sack's Muttsy… (12/65). 100-Gabby Gob(1/66). 101-G. I. Juniors (2/66). 102-Sad Sack's Muttsy… (3/66). 103-Gabby Gob. 104- G. I. Juniors. 105-Sad Sack's Muttsy… 106-Gabby Gob (7/66). 107-G. I. Juniors (8/66). 108-Sad Sack's Muttsy…109-Gabby Gob. 110-G. I. Juniors (11/66). 111-Sad Sack's Muttsy… (12/66). 112-G. I. Juniors. 113-Sad Sack's Muttsy… 114-G. I. Juniors. 115-Gabby Gob. 116-G. I. Juniors (5/67). 117-Sad Sack's Muttsy… 118-G. I. Juniors. 119-Sad Sack's Muttsy… (8/67). 120-G. I. Juniors (9/67). 121-Sad Sack's Muttsy… (10/67). 122-G. I. Juniors (11/67)

	GD 2.0	VG 4.0	FN 6.0	VF 8.0	VF/NM 9.0	NM- 9.2
	2	4	6	10	14	18

HARVEY HITS COMICS
Harvey Publications: Nov, 1986 - No. 6, Oct, 1987

	GD 2.0	VG 4.0	FN 6.0	VF 8.0	VF/NM 9.0	NM- 9.2
1-Little Lotta, Little Dot, Wendy & Baby Huey	1	2	3	4	5	7
2-6: 3-Xmas-c						4.50

HARVEY POP COMICS (Rock Happening) (Teen Humor)
Harvey Publications: Oct, 1968 - No. 2, Nov, 1969 (Both are 68 pg. Giants)

	GD 2.0	VG 4.0	FN 6.0	VF 8.0	VF/NM 9.0	NM- 9.2
1-The Cowsills	5	10	15	34	60	85
2-Bunny	5	10	15	31	53	75

HARVEY 3-D HITS (See Sad Sack)

HARVEY-TOON (…S) (See Harvey Hits No. 29, 34, 38, 42, 46, 50, 53)

HARVEY WISEGUYS (…Digest #? on)
Harvey Comics: Nov, 1987; #2, Nov, 1988; #3, Apr, 1989 - No. 4, Nov, 1989 (98 pgs., digest-size, $1.25/$1.75)

	GD 2.0	VG 4.0	FN 6.0	VF 8.0	VF/NM 9.0	NM- 9.2
1-Hot Stuff, Spooky, etc.	2	3	4	6	8	10
2-4: 2 (68 pgs.)	1	2	3	4	5	7

HASBRO HEROES SOURCEBOOK 2017
IDW Publishing: May, 2017 - No. 3, Jul, 2017 ($4.99, limited series)
1-3-Profile pages of characters from Transformers, G.I. Joe, Micronauts, Rom, M.A.S.K. ... 5.00

HASBRO TOYBOX QUARTERLY
IDW Publishing: Dec, 2017 ($5.99, one-shot)
1-Short stories of My Little Pony, Equestria Girls and Hanazuki by various; pin-ups ... 6.00

HASHTAG: DANGER (Also see back-ups in High Heaven and Captain Ginger)
IDW Publishing: 2019 - No. 5, 2019 ($3.99, limited series)
1-5-Peyer-s/Giarrusso-a; Snelson back-ups by Constant-s/Harper-a ... 4.00

HATARI (See Movie Classics)

HATCHET (Based on the 2007 movie)(Also see Victor Crowley's…)
American Mythology Productions: No. 0, 2017 - No. 3, 2018 ($3.99)
0-3-Kuhoric-s/Mangum-a; Victor Crowley app. ... 4.00

HATCHET: VENGEANCE (Based on the 2007 movie)
American Mythology Productions: 2018 - No. 3, 2021 ($3.99)
1-3-Kuhoric-s/Calzada-a; prelude to the first movie ... 4.00

HATE
Fantagraphics Books: Spr, 1990 - No. 30, 1998 ($2.50/$2.95, B&W/color)

	GD 2.0	VG 4.0	FN 6.0	VF 8.0	VF/NM 9.0	NM- 9.2
1	2	4	6	8	10	12
2-3						6.00
4-10						5.00
11-20: 16- color begins						5.00
21-29						5.00
30-($3.95) Last issue						4.00
Annual 1 (2/01, $3.95) Peter Bagge-s/a						5.00
Annual 2-9 (12/01 - No. 9, Spr, 2011; $4.95) Peter Bagge-s/a						5.00
Buddy Bites the Bullet! (2001, $16.95) r/Buddy stories in color						17.00
Buddy Go Home! (1997, $16.95) r/Buddy stories in color						17.00
Hate-Ball Special Edition ($3.95, giveaway)-reprints						4.00
Hate Jamboree (10/98, $4.50) old & new cartoons						4.50

HATHAWAYS, THE (TV)
Dell Publishing Co.: No. 1298, Feb-Apr, 1962 (one-shot)

	GD 2.0	VG 4.0	FN 6.0	VF 8.0	VF/NM 9.0	NM- 9.2
Four Color 1298-Photo-c	6	12	18	37	66	95

HAUNT
Image Comics: Oct, 2009 - No. 28, Dec, 2012 ($2.99)
1-McFarlane & Kirkman-s/Capullo & Ottley-a/McFarlane-a(i)/c; two variant-c ... 6.00
2-28: 2-Two covers. 13-($1.99). 19-Casey-s/Fox-a begins ... 3.00
Image Firsts: Haunt #1 (10/10, $1.00) r/#1 with "Image First" cover logo ... 3.00

HAUNTED (See This Magazine Is Haunted)

HAUNTED (Baron Weirwulf's Haunted Library on-c #21 on)
Charlton Comics: 9/71 - No. 30, 11/76; No. 31, 9/77 - No. 75, 9/84

	GD 2.0	VG 4.0	FN 6.0	VF 8.0	VF/NM 9.0	NM- 9.2
1-All Ditko issue	7	14	21	49	92	135
2-7-Ditko-c/a	4	8	12	23	37	50
8,12,28-Ditko-a	2	4	6	13	18	22
9,19	2	4	6	8	11	14
10,20,15,18: 10,20-Sutton-a. 15-Sutton-c	2	4	6	8	11	14
11,13,14,16-Ditko-c/a	3	6	9	16	23	30
17-Sutton-c/a; Newton-a	2	4	6	9	12	15
21-Newton-c/a; Sutton-a; 1st Baron Weirwulf	3	6	9	16	24	32
22-Newton-c/a; Sutton-a	2	4	6	9	13	16
23,24-Sutton-c; Ditko-a	2	4	6	9	13	16
25-27,29,32,33	2	4	6	8		10
30,41,47,49-52,60,74-Ditko-c/a: 51-Reprints #1	2	4	6	8		10
31,35,37,38-Sutton-a	1	3	4	6	11	20
34,36,39,40,42,57-Ditko-a	2	4	6	8	10	12
43-46,48,53-56,58,59,61-73: 59-Newton-a. 64-Sutton-c. 71-73-Low print	1	2	3	5	6	8
75 (9/84) Last issue; low print	1	3	6	9	13	16

NOTE: **Aparo** c-45. **Ditko** a-1-8, 11-16, 18, 23, 24, 28, 30, 34r, 36r, 39-42r, 47r, 49-52r, 57, 60, 74. c-1-7, 11, 13, 14, 16, 30, 41, 47, 49-52, 74. **Howard** a-6, 9, 18, 22, 25, 32. **Kim** a-9, 19. **Morisi** a-13. **Newton** a-17, 21, 59r; c-21, 22(painted). **Staton** a-11, 12, 18, 21, 22, 30, 33, 35, 38; c-18, 33, 38. **Sutton** a-10, 17, 20-22, 31, 35, 37, 38; c-15, 17, 18, 23(painted), 24(painted), 27, 64r. #49 reprints Tales of the Mysterious Traveler #4.

HAUNTED, THE
Chaos! Comics: Jan, 2002 - No. 4, Apr, 2002 ($2.99, limited series)
1-4-Peter David-s/Nat Jones-a ... 3.00
…: Gray Matters (7/02, $2.99) David-s/Jones-a ... 3.00

HAUNTED CITY
Aspen MLT: No. 0, Aug, 2011 - No. 2 ($2.50/$3.50)
0-($2.50)-Taylor & Johnson-s/Michael Ryan-a; four covers ... 3.00
1,2-($3.50) -Taylor & Johnson-s/Michael Ryan-a; four covers ... 3.50

HAUNTED LOVE
Charlton Comics: Apr, 1973 - No. 11, Sept, 1975

	GD 2.0	VG 4.0	FN 6.0	VF 8.0	VF/NM 9.0	NM- 9.2
1-Tom Sutton (16 pgs.)	8	16	24	52	99	145
2,3,6,7,10,11	3	6	9	21	33	45
4,5-Ditko-a	4	8	12	25	40	55
8,9-Newton-a	3	6	9	21	33	45
Modern Comics #1(1978)	2	4	6	8	10	12

NOTE: **Howard** a-8i. **Kim** a-7-9. **Newton** c-8, 9. **Staton** a-1-6. **Sutton** a-1, 3-5, 10, 11.

HAUNTED MANSION, THE (Disney Kingdoms)
Marvel Comics: May, 2016 - No. 5, Sept, 2016 ($3.99, limited series)
1-5-Joshua Williamson-s/Jorge Coelho-a/E.M. Gist-c ... 4.00
… No. 1 Halloween Comic Fest 2016 (giveaway, 12/16) r/#1 ... 3.00

HAUNTED TANK, THE
DC Comics (Vertigo): Feb, 2009 - No. 5, June, 2009 ($2.99, limited series)
1-5-Marraffino/Flint-a. 1-Two covers by Flint and Joe Kubert ... 3.00
TPB (2010, $14.99) r/#1-5 ... 15.00

HAUNTED THRILLS (Tales of Horror and Terror)
Ajax/Farrell Publications: June, 1952 - No. 18, Nov-Dec, 1954

	GD 2.0	VG 4.0	FN 6.0	VF 8.0	VF/NM 9.0	NM- 9.2
1-r/Ellery Queen #1	123	246	369	787	1344	1900
2-L. B. Cole-a r/Ellery Queen #1	81	162	243	518	884	1250
3,4: 3-Drug use story	61	122	183	390	670	950
5-Classic skull-c	459	918	1377	3350	5925	8500
6-Classic top hatted skull throwing dice-c	486	972	1458	3550	6275	9000
7,8,10,12: 7-Hitler story.	65	130	195	416	708	1000
9-Classic decapitated heads-c	206	412	618	1318	2259	3200
11-Nazi death camp story	187	374	561	1197	2049	2900
13-18: 14-Jesus Christ apps. in story by Webb. 15-Jo-Jo-r. 18-Lingerie panels; skull-c	57	114	171	362	619	875

NOTE: **Kamenish** art in most issues. **Webb** a-12.

HAUNT OF FEAR (Formerly Gunfighter)
E. C. Comics: No. 15, May-June, 1950 - No. 28, Nov-Dec, 1954

	GD 2.0	VG 4.0	FN 6.0	VF 8.0	VF/NM 9.0	NM- 9.2
15(#1, 1950)(Scarce)	457	914	1371	3656	5828	8000
16-1st app. "The Witches Cauldron" & the Old Witch (by Kamen); begin series as hostess of Haunt of Fear (also see Yellowjacket #7-10)	194	388	582	1552	2476	3400
17-Origin of Crypt of Terror, Vault of Horror, & Haunt of Fear; used in SOTI, pg. 43; last pg. Ingels-a used by N.Y. Legis. Comm.; story "Monster Maker" based on Frankenstein. Old Witch by Feldstein	194	388	582	1552	2476	3400
4-Ingels becomes regular artist for Old Witch. 1st Vault Keeper & Crypt Keeper app. in HOF; begin series	120	240	360	960	1530	2100
5-Injury-to-eye panel, pg. 4 of Wood story	103	206	309	824	1312	1800
6,7,9,10: 6-Crypt Keeper by Feldstein begins. 9-Crypt Keeper by Davis begins. 10-Ingels biog.	80	160	240	640	1020	1400
8-Classic Feldstein Shrunken Head-c	114	228	342	912	1460	2000
11,12: Classic Ingels-c; 11-Kamen biog. 12-Feldstein biog.; "Poetic Justice" story adapted for the 1972 Tales From the Crypt film	80	160	240	640	1020	1400
13,15,16,20: 16-Ray Bradbury adaptation. 20-Feldstein-r/Vault of Horror #12	69	138	207	552	876	1200
14-Origin Old Witch by Ingels; classic-Ingels-c	103	206	309	824	1312	1800
17-Classic Ingels-c and "Horror We? How's Bayou?" story, considered ECs best horror story	143	286	429	1144	1822	2500
18-Old Witch-c; Ray Bradbury adaptation & biography	94	188	282	752	1201	1650
19-Used in SOTI, ill. "A comic book baseball game" & Senate investigation on juvenile delinq. bondage/decapitation-c	91	182	273	728	1164	1600

Haunted Tank (2009 series) #1 © DC

Hawk & Dove (2011 series) #1 © DC

Hawkeye (2012 series) #1 © MAR

	GD	VG	FN	VF	VF/NM	NM-			GD	VG	FN	VF	VF/NM	NM-
	2.0	4.0	6.0	8.0	9.0	9.2			2.0	4.0	6.0	8.0	9.0	9.2

21-27: 22-"Wish You Were Here" story inspired by "The Monkey's Paw" by W.W. Jacobs, which is referenced in story; adapted for the 1972 Tales From the Crypt film; Snow White satire. 23-EC version of the Hansel and Gretel story; **SOTI**, pg. 241 discusses the original Grimm tale in relation to comics. 24-Used in Senate Investigative Report, pg.8. 26-Contains anti-censorship editorial, 'Are you a Red Dupe?' 27-Cannibalism story; Vault Keeper shown reading **SOTI**; brief text reference to unpublished 4th EC horror title The Crypt of Terror

		46	92	138	368	584	800

28-Low distribution

		77	154	231	616	983	1350

NOTE: (Canadian reprints known; see Table of Contents). **Craig** a-15-17, 5, 7, 10, 12, 13; c-15-17, 5-7. **Crandall** a-20, 21, 26, 27. **Davis** a-4-26, 28. **Evans** a-15-19, 22-25, 27. **Feldstein** a-15-17, 20; c-4, 8-10. **Ingels** a-16, 17, 4-28; c-11-28. **Kamen** a-16, 4, 6, 7, 9-11, 13-19, 21-28. **Krigstein** a-28. **Kurtzman** a-15(#1), 17(#3). **Orlando** a-9, 12. **Wood** a-15, 16, 4-6.

HAUNT OF FEAR, THE
Gladstone Publishing: May, 1991 - No. 2, July, 1991 ($2.00, 68 pgs.)

1,2: 1-Ghastly Ingels-c(r); 2-Craig-c(r)						4.00

HAUNT OF FEAR
Russ Cochran/Gemstone Publ.: Sept, 1991 - No. 5, 1992 ($2.00, 68 pgs.); Nov, 1992 - No. 28, Aug, 1998 ($1.50/$2.00/$2.50)

1-28: 1-Ingels-c(r). 1-3-r/HOF #15-17 with original-c. 4,5-r/HOF #4,5 with original-c						4.00
Annual 1-5: 1- r/#1-5. 2- r/#6-10. 3- r/#11-15. 4- r/#16-20. 5- r/#21-25						14.00
Annual 6-r/#26-28						9.00

HAUNT OF HORROR, THE (Digest)
Marvel Comics: Jun, 1973 - No. 2, Aug, 1973 (164 pgs.); text and art

1-Morrow painted skull-c; stories by Ellison, Howard, and Leiber; Brunner-a

	5	10	15	31	53	75

2-Kelly Freas painted bondage-c; stories by McCaffrey, Goulart, Leiber, Ellison; art by Simonson, Brunner, and Buscema

	3	6	9	19	30	40

HAUNT OF HORROR, THE (Magazine)
Cadence Comics Publ. (Marvel): May, 1974 - No. 5, Jan, 1975 (75¢) (B&W)

1,2: 2-Origin & 1st app. Gabriel the Devil Hunter; Satana begins

	4	8	12	25	40	55

3-5: 4-Neal Adams-a. 5-Evans-a(2)

	4	8	12	27	44	60

NOTE: **Alcala** a-2. **Colan** a-2p. **Heath** r-1. **Krigstein** r-3. **Reese** a-1. **Simonson** a-1.

HAUNT OF HORROR: EDGAR ALLAN POE
Marvel Comics (MAX): July, 2006 - No. 3, Sept, 2006 ($3.99, B&W, limited series)

1-3- Poe-inspired/adapted stories with Richard Corben-a						4.00
HC (2006, $19.99) r/series; cover sketches						20.00

HAUNT OF HORROR: LOVECRAFT
Marvel Comics (MAX): Aug, 2008 - No. 3, Oct, 2008 ($3.99, B&W, limited series)

1-3-Lovecraft-inspired/adapted stories with Richard Corben-a						4.00

HAUNT YOU TO THE END
Image Comics (Top Cow): Jun, 2023 - No. 5, Oct, 2023 ($3.99)

1-5-Ryan Cady-s/Andrea Mutti-a						4.00

HAVE GUN, WILL TRAVEL (TV)
Dell Publishing Co.: No. 931, 8/58 - No. 14, 7-9/62 (All Richard Boone photo-c)

Four Color 931 (#1)	15	30	45	103	227	350
Four Color 983,1044 (#2,3)	10	20	30	64	132	200
4 (1-3/60) - 10	7	14	21	46	86	125
11-14	7	14	21	44	82	120

HAVEN: THE BROKEN CITY (See JLA/Haven: Arrival and JLA/Haven: Anathema)
DC Comics: Feb, 2002 - No. 9, Oct, 2002 ($2.50, limited series)

1-9-Olivetti-c/a: 1- JLA app. Series concludes in JLA/Haven: Anathema						3.00

HAVOK & WOLVERINE - MELTDOWN (See Marvel Comics Presents #24)
Marvel Comics (Epic Comics): Mar, 1989 - No. 4, Oct, 1989 ($3.50, mini-series, squarebound, mature)

1-4- Art by Kent Williams & Jon J. Muth; story by Walt & Louise Simonson						6.00

HAWAIIAN DICK (Also see Aloha, Hawaiian Dick)
Image Comics: Dec, 2002 - No. 3, Feb, 2003 ($2.95, limited series)

1-3-B. Clay Moore-s/Steven Griffin-a						3.00
...: Byrd of Paradise TPB (8/03, $14.95) r/#1-3, script & sketch pages						15.00

HAWAIIAN DICK: SCREAMING BLACK THUNDER
Image Comics: Nov, 2007 - No. 5, Oct, 2008 ($2.99, limited series)

1-5-B. Clay Moore-s/Scott Chantler-a						3.00

HAWAIIAN DICK: THE LAST RESORT
Image Comics: Aug, 2004 - No. 4, June, 2006 ($2.95/$2.99, limited series)

1-4-B. Clay Moore-s/Steven Griffin-a						3.00
Vol. 2 TPB (10/06, $14.99) r/#1-4 & the original series pitch						15.00

HAWAIIAN EYE (TV)
Gold Key: July, 1963 (Troy Donahue, Connie Stevens photo-c)

1 (10073-307)	6	12	18	37	66	95

HAWAIIAN ILLUSTRATED LEGENDS SERIES
Hogarth Press: 1975 (B&W)(Cover printed w/blue, yellow, and green)

1-Kalelealuaka, the Mysterious Warrior						5.00

HAWK, THE (Also see Approved Comics #1, 7 & Tops In Adventure)
Ziff-Davis/St. John Publ. Co. No. 4 on: Wint/51 - No. 3, 11-12/52; No. 4, 1-2/53; No. 8, 9/54 - No. 12, 5/55 (Painted c-1-4)(#5-7 don't exist)

1-Anderson-a	34	68	102	204	332	460
2 (Sum, '52)-Kubert, Infantino-a	20	40	60	117	189	260
3-4	15	30	45	84	127	170
8-12: 8(9/54)-Reprints #3 w/different-c by Baker. 9-Baker-c/a; Kubert-a(r)/#2. 10-Baker-c/a; r/one story from #2. 11-Baker-c; Buckskin Belle & The Texan app. 12-Baker-c/a:						
Buckskin Belle app.	45	90	135	284	480	675
3-D (11/53, 25¢)-Came w/glasses; Baker-c	40	80	120	246	411	575

NOTE: **Baker** c-8-12. **Larsen** a-10. **Tuska** a-1, 9, 12. Painted c-1, 4, 7.

HAWK AND THE DOVE, THE (See Showcase #75 & Teen Titans) (1st series)
National Periodical Publications: Aug-Sept, 1968 - No. 6, June-July, 1969

1-Ditko-c/a	8	16	24	56	108	160
2-6: 5-Teen Titans cameo	5	10	15	31	53	75

NOTE: **Ditko** c/a-1, 2. **Gil Kane** a-3p, 4p, 5, 6p; c-3-6.

HAWK AND DOVE (2nd Series)
DC Comics: Oct, 1988 - No. 5, Feb, 1989 ($1.00, limited series)

1-Rob Liefeld-c/a(p) in all; 1st app. Dawn Granger as Dove	1	2	3	5	6	8
2-5						4.00
Trade paperback ('93, $9.95)-Reprints #1-5						12.00

HAWK AND DOVE
DC Comics: June, 1989 - No. 28, Oct, 1991 ($1.00)

1-28						4.00
Annual 1,2 ('90, '91; $2.00) 1-Liefeld pin-up. 2-Armageddon 2001 x-over						5.00

HAWK AND DOVE
DC Comics: Nov, 1997 - No. 5, Mar, 1998 ($2.50, limited series)

1-5-Baron-s/Zachary & Giordano-a						4.00

HAWK AND DOVE (DC New 52)
DC Comics: Nov, 2011 - No. 8, Jun, 2012 ($2.99)

1-8: 1-Gates-s/Liefeld-a/c; Deadman app. 6-Batman & Robin app.; Liefeld-s/a/c						3.00

HAWK AND WINDBLADE (See Elflord)
Warp Graphics: Aug, 1997 - No.2, Sept, 1997 ($2.95, limited series)

1,2-Blair-s/Chan-c/a						4.00

HAWKEN: MELEE (Based on the computer game Hawken)
Archaia Black Label: Dec, 2013 - No. 5 ($3.99, limited series)

1,2: 1-Abnett-s/Dallocchio-a. 2-Jim Mahfood-s/a						4.00

HAWKEYE (See The Avengers #16 & Tales Of Suspense #57)
Marvel Comics Group: Sept, 1983 - No. 4, Dec, 1983 (limited series)

1-Mark Gruenwald-a/scripts in all; origin Hawkeye	3	6	9	19	30	40
2-4: 3-Origin Mockingbird. 4-Hawkeye & Mockingbird elope	2	4	6	9	12	15

HAWKEYE
Marvel Comics: Jan, 1994 - No. 4, Apr, 1994 ($1.75, limited series)

1	1	3	4	6	8	10
2-4						5.00

HAWKEYE (Volume 2)
Marvel Comics: Dec, 2003 - No. 8, Aug, 2004 ($2.99)

1-8: 1-6-Nicieza-s/Raffaele-a. 7,8-Bennett-a; Black Widow app.						4.00

HAWKEYE (Also see All-New Hawkeye)
Marvel Comics: Oct, 2012 - No. 22, Sept, 2015 ($2.99)

1-Fraction-s/Aja-a; Kate Bishop app.	3	6	9	17	25	34
2,3	1	3	4	6	8	10
4-8: 7-Lieber & Hamm-a						6.00
9-21: 10,12-Francavilla-a. 11-Dog issue. 16-Released before #15						4.00
22-($4.99) Aja-a						5.00
Annual 1 (9/13, $4.99) Pulido-a; Kate Bishop in L.A.; Madame Mask app.						5.00

HAWKEYE (Kate Bishop as Hawkeye)
Marvel Comics: Feb, 2017 - No. 16, May, 2018 ($3.99)

	GD	VG	FN	VF	VF/NM	NM-
	2.0	4.0	6.0	8.0	9.0	9.2

1-16: 1-5,7-11-Thompson-s/Romero-a. 5,6-Jessica Jones app. ... 4.00

HAWKEYE AND MOCKINGBIRD (Avengers) (Leads into Widowmaker mini-series)
Marvel Comics: Aug, 2010 - No. 6, Jan, 2011 ($3.99/$2.99)

1-($3.99) Heroic Age; Jim McCann-s/David Lopez-a; history of the characters ... 4.00
2-6-($2.99) Phantom Rider, Dominic Fortune & Crossfire app. ... 3.00

HAWKEYE & THE LAST OF THE MOHICANS (TV)
Dell Publishing Co.: No. 884, Mar, 1958 (one-shot)

Four Color 884-Lon Chaney Jr. photo-c ... 7 ... 14 ... 21 ... 44 ... 82 ... 120

HAWKEYE: BLINDSPOT (Avengers)
Marvel Comics: Apr, 2011 - No. 4, Jul, 2011 (limited series)

1-4: 1-McCann-s/Diaz-a; Zemo app. 2-Diaz & Dragotta-a ... 3.00

HAWKEYE: EARTH'S MIGHTIEST MARKSMAN
Marvel Comics: Oct, 1998 ($2.99, one-shot)

1-Justice and Firestar app.; DeFalco-s ... 5.00

HAWKEYE: FREEFALL
Marvel Comics: Mar, 2020 - No. 6, Nov, 2020 ($3.99, limited series)

1-6-Rosenberg-s/Schmidt-a; The Hood app. 4-Daredevil app. ... 4.00

HAWKEYE: KATE BISHOP
Marvel Comics: Jan, 2022 - No. 5, May, 2022 ($3.99)

1-5-Marieke Nijkamp-s/Enid Balám-a ... 4.00

HAWKEYE VS. DEADPOOL
Marvel Comics: No. 0, Nov, 2014 - No. 4, Mar, 2015 ($4.99/$3.99, limited series)

0-($4.99) Duggan-s/Lolli-a; Black Cat app. ... 6 ... 9 ... 14 ... 19 ... 24
1-($3.99) Covers by Harren & Pearson; Kate Bishop & Typhoid Mary app. ... 1 ... 3 ... 4 ... 6 ... 8 ... 10
2-4 ... 4.00

HAWKGIRL (Title continued from Hawkman #49, Apr, 2006)
DC Comics: No. 50, May, 2006 - No. 66, Sept, 2007 ($2.50/$2.99)

50-66: 50-Chaykin-a/Simonson-s begin; One Year Later. 52-Begin $2.99-c. 57,58-Bennett-a. 59-Blackfire app. 63-Batman app. 64-Superman app. ... 3.00
...: Hath-Set TPB (2008, $17.99) r/#61-66 ... 18.00
...: Hawkman Returns TPB (2007, $17.99) r/#57-60 & JSA Classified #21,22 ... 18.00
...: The Maw TPB (2007, $17.99) r/#50-56 ... 18.00

HAWKGIRL (Dawn of DC)
DC Comics: Sept, 2023 - No. 6, Feb, 2024 ($3.99, limited series)

1-6: 1-Intro. Galaxy. 3-Batman app. ... 4.00

HAWKMAN (See Atom & Hawkman, The Brave & the Bold, DC Comics Presents, Detective Comics, Flash Comics, Hawkworld, JSA, Justice League of America #31, Legend of the Hawkman, Mystery in Space, Savage Hawkman, Shadow War Of…, Showcase, & World's Finest #256)

HAWKMAN (1st Series) (Also see The Atom #7 & Brave & the Bold #34-36, 42-44, 51)
National Periodical Publications: Apr-May, 1964 - No. 27, Aug-Sept, 1968

1-(4-5/64)-Anderson-c/a begins, ends #21 ... 66 ... 132 ... 198 ... 528 ... 1189 ... 1850
2 ... 20 ... 40 ... 60 ... 141 ... 313 ... 485
3,5: 5-2nd app. Shadow Thief ... 13 ... 26 ... 39 ... 89 ... 195 ... 300
4-Origin & 1st app. Zatanna (10-11/64) ... 190 ... 380 ... 570 ... 1500 ... 2900 ... 4300
6 ... 10 ... 20 ... 30 ... 66 ... 138 ... 210
7 ... 9 ... 18 ... 27 ... 62 ... 126 ... 190
8-10: 9-Atom cameo; Hawkman & Atom learn each other's I.D.; 3rd app. Shadow Thief ... 8 ... 16 ... 24 ... 54 ... 102 ... 150
11-15 ... 6 ... 12 ... 18 ... 40 ... 73 ... 105
16-27: 18-Adam Strange x-over (cameo #19). 25-G.A. Hawkman-r by Moldoff. 26-Kirby-a(r). 27-Kubert-c ... 5 ... 10 ... 15 ... 34 ... 60 ... 85

HAWKMAN (2nd Series)
DC Comics: Aug, 1986 - No. 17, Dec, 1987

1-Shadow-Thief app. ... 1 ... 2 ... 3 ... 5 ... 6 ... 8
2-17: 10-Byrne-c, Special #1 (1986, $1.25) ... 4.00
Trade paperback (1989, $19.95)-r/Brave and the Bold #34-36,42-44 by Kubert; Kubert-c ... 20.00

HAWKMAN (4th Series) (See both Hawkworld limited & ongoing series)
DC Comics: Sept, 1993 - No. 33, July, 1996 ($1.75/$1.95/$2.25)

1-($2.50)-Gold foil embossed-c; storyline cont'd from Hawkworld ongoing series; new costume & powers. ... 2 ... 3 ... 5 ... 6 ... 8
2-33: 2-Green Lantern x-over. 3-Airstryke app. 4,6-Wonder Woman app. 13-(9/94)-Zero Hour. 15-Aquaman-c app. 23-Wonder Woman app. 25-Kent Williams-c. 29,30-Chaykin-a. 32-Breyfogle-c ... 4.00
#0-(10/94) Zero Hour tie-in; released between #13 & #14 ... 4.00
Annual 1 (1993, $2.50, 68 pgs.)-Bloodlines Earthplague ... 5.00
Annual 2 (1995, $3.95)-Year One story ... 5.00

HAWKMAN (Title continues as Hawkgirl #50-on) (See JSA #23 for return)
DC Comics: May, 2002 - No. 49, Apr, 2006 ($2.50)

1-Johns & Robinson-s/Morales-a ... 5.00
1-2nd printing ... 3.00
2-40: 2-4-Shadow Thief app. 5,6-Green Arrow-c/app. 8-Atom-c/app. 13-Van Sciver-a. 14-Gentleman Ghost app. 15-Hawkwoman app. 16-Byth returns. 23-25-Black Reign x-over with JSA #56-58. 26-Byrne-c/a. 29,30-Land-c. 37-Golden Eagle returns ... 3.00
41-49: 41-Hawkman killed. 43-Golden Eagle origin. 46-49-Adam Kubert-c ... 3.00
...: Allies & Enemies TPB (2004, $14.95) r/#7-14 & pages from Secret Files and Origins ... 15.00
...: Endless Flight TPB (2003, $12.95) r/#1-6 & Secret Files and Origins ... 13.00
...: Rise of the Golden Eagle TPB (2006, $17.99) r/#37-45 ... 18.00
...: Secret Files and Origins (10/02, $4.95) profiles and pin-ups by various ... 5.00
...: Special 1 (10/08, $3.50) Tie-in to Rann-Thanagar Holy War series; Starlin-s/a(p) ... 3.50
...: Wings of Fury TPB (2005, $17.99) r/#15-22 ... 18.00

HAWKMAN
DC Comics: Aug, 2018 - No. 29, Jan, 2021 ($3.99)

1-29: 1-12-Venditti-s/Hitch-a. 1-2-Madame Xanadu app. 4-6-The Atom app. 13-Conrad-a 14-18-Year of the Villain tie-in. 14-17-Shadow Thief app. 18-22-The Infected. 27-Justice Society app. ... 4.00

HAWKMAN: FOUND (See Dark Nights: Metal series and other tie-ins)

DC Comics: Feb, 2018 ($3.99, one-shot)

1-Lemire-s/Hitch-a; foil-c ... 4.00

HAWKMOON: THE JEWEL IN THE SKULL
First Comics: May, 1986 - No. 4, Nov, 1986 ($1.75, limited series, Baxter paper)

1-4: Adapts novel by Michael Moorcock ... 4.00

HAWKMOON: THE MAD GOD'S AMULET
First Comics: Jan, 1987 - No. 4, July, 1987 ($1.75, limited series, Baxter paper)

1-4: Adapts novel by Michael Moorcock ... 4.00

HAWKMOON: THE RUNESTAFF
First Comics: Jun, 1988 - No. 4, Dec, 1988 ($1.75-$1.95, lim. series, Baxter paper)

1-4: ($1.75) Adapts novel by Michael Moorcock. 3,4 ($1.95) ... 4.00

HAWKMOON: THE SWORD OF DAWN
First Comics: Sept, 1987 - No. 4, Mar, 1988 ($1.75, lim. series, Baxter paper)

1-4: Dorman painted-c; adapts Moorcock novel ... 4.00

HAWKS OF THE SEAS (WILL EISNER'S…)
Dark Horse Comics: July, 2003 ($19.95, B&W, hardcover)

nn-Reprints 1937-1939 weekly Pirate serial by Will Eisner; Williamson intro. ... 20.00

HAWKWORLD
DC Comics: 1989 - No. 3, 1989 ($3.95, prestige format, limited series)

Book 1-3: 1-Tim Truman story & art in all; Hawkman dons new costume; reintro Byth ... 5.00
TPB (1991, $16.95) r/#1-3 ... 17.00

HAWKWORLD (3rd Series)
DC Comics: June, 1990 - No. 32, Mar, 1993 ($1.50/$1.75)

1-Hawkman spin-off; story cont'd from Hawkworld ... 5.00
2-32: 15,16-War of the Gods x-over. 22-J'onn J'onzz app. ... 4.00
Annual 1-3 ('90-'92, $2.95, 68 pgs.), 2-2nd printing with silver ink-c ... 5.00
NOTE: Truman a-30-32; c-27-32, Annual 1.

HAYWIRE
DC Comics: Oct, 1988 - No. 13, Sept, 1989 ($1.25, mature)

1-13 ... 4.00

HAZARD
Image Comics (WildStorm Prod.)**:** June, 1996 - No. 7, Nov, 1996 ($1.75)

1-7: 1-Intro Hazard; Jeff Mariotte scripts begin; Jim Lee-c(p) ... 4.00

HAZEL & CHA CHA SAVE CHRISTMAS: TALES FROM THE UMBRELLA ACADEMY
Dark Horse Comics: Nov, 2019 ($3.99, one-shot)

1-Gerald Way & Scott Allie-s/Tommy Lee Edwards-a; covers by Edwards & Mahfood ... 2 ... 4 ... 6 ... 8 ... 10 ... 12

HEADLESS HORSEMAN HALLOWEEN ANNUAL
Dark Horse Comics: Oct, 2023 ($7.99, one-shot)

1-Short stories by various incl. Dastmalchian, Crook & Sevy; covers by Ketner & Mignola 8.00

HEADLINE COMICS
DC Comics: Jan. 1942

nn - Ashcan comic, not distributed to newsstands, only for in-house use. Cover art is More Fun Comics #73, interior being Star Spangled Comics #1 (a FN copy sold for $2270.50 in 2012)

HEADLINE COMICS (…For the American Boy) (…Crime No. 32-39)
Prize Publ./American Boys' Comics: Feb, 1943 - No. 22, Nov-Dec, 1946; No. 23, 1947 - No. 77, Oct, 1956

1-WWII-c/sty.; Junior Rangers-c/stories begin; Yank & Doodle x-over in Junior Rangers (Junior Rangers are Uncle Sam's nephews) ... 116 ... 232 ... 348 ... 742 ... 1271 ... 1800
2-Japanese WWII-c; Junior Rangers "Nip the Nippons!"-c ... 77 ... 154 ... 231 ... 493 ... 847 ... 1200
3-Junior Rangers vs. Hitler sty.; 1st app. Invisible Boy; German WWII-c; used in POP, pg. 84 (scarce) ... 74 ... 148 ... 222 ... 470 ... 810 ... 1150
4-Junior Rangers vs. Hitler, Mussolini, Hirohito & Dr. Schmutz (1st app.); German WWII-c; (scarce) ... 81 ... 162 ... 243 ... 518 ... 884 ... 1250
5-7,9: 5-Junior Rangers invade Italy; WWII-c/sty. 6,7-Nazi WWII-c/sty. 7-1st app. Kinker Kinkaid (ends #12). 9-WWII Halloween-c/sty ... 65 ... 130 ... 195 ... 416 ... 708 ... 1000
8-Classic Hitler-c ... 3180 ... 6360 ... 9540 ... 19,100 ... 27,050 ... 35,000
10-Hitler story ... 71 ... 142 ... 213 ... 454 ... 777 ... 1100
11-Classic Mad Japanese scientist WWII-c ... 595 ... 1190 ... 1785 ... 4350 ... 7675 ... 11,000
12,13,15: 13,15-Blue Streak app. ... 33 ... 66 ... 99 ... 194 ... 317 ... 440
14-Japanese WWII-c ... 48 ... 96 ... 144 ... 302 ... 514 ... 725
16-Origin & 1st app. Atomic Man (11-12/45) ... 40 ... 80 ... 120 ... 246 ... 411 ... 575
17,18-Atomic Man-c/sty. ... 34 ... 68 ... 102 ... 199 ... 325 ... 450
19-Atomic Man-c/sty.; S&K-a ... 58 ... 116 ... 174 ... 371 ... 636 ... 900
20,21: 21-Atomic Man ends (9-10/46) ... 25 ... 50 ... 75 ... 150 ... 245 ... 340
22-Last Junior Rangers; Kiefer-c ... 21 ... 42 ... 63 ... 122 ... 199 ... 275
23,24: (All S&K-a). 23-Valentine's Day Massacre story; content changes to true crime.
24-Dope-crazy killer story ... 39 ... 78 ... 117 ... 240 ... 395 ... 550
25-35-S&K-c/a. 25-Powell-a ... 35 ... 70 ... 105 ... 208 ... 339 ... 470
36-S&K-a begin ... 31 ... 62 ... 93 ... 182 ... 296 ... 410
37-1 pg. S&K, Severin-a; rare Kirby photo-c app. ... 54 ... 108 ... 162 ... 343 ... 574 ... 825
38,40-Meskin-a ... 18 ... 36 ... 54 ... 103 ... 162 ... 220
39,41-43,46-56: 41-J. Edgar Hoover 26th Anniversary issue with photo on-c ...
43,49-Meskin-a. 48-Meskin ... 15 ... 30 ... 45 ... 90 ... 140 ... 190
44,45-S&K-c; Severin/Elder, Meskin-a ... 22 ... 44 ... 66 ... 132 ... 216 ... 300
57-77: 70-Roller Derby-c. 72-Meskin-c/a(i) ... 15 ... 30 ... 45 ... 84 ... 127 ... 170
NOTE: Hollingsworth a-30. Photo c-36-43. H. C. Kiefer c-12-16, 22. Atomic Man c-17-19.

HEAP, THE
Skywald Publications: Sept, 1971 (52 pgs.)

1-Kinstler-r/Strange Worlds #8; new-s w/Sutton-a ... 5 ... 10 ... 15 ... 34 ... 60 ... 85

HEART AND SOUL
Mikeross Publications: April-May, 1954 - No. 2, June-July, 1954

1,2 ... 15 ... 30 ... 45 ... 83 ... 124 ... 165

HEART ATTACK
Image Comics (Skybound)**:** Nov, 2019 - No. 6, Jun, 2020 ($3.99)

Hawkgirl (2023 series) #1 © DC

Headline Comics #27 © Prize

Heavy Vinyl #4 © Scheme Machine

	GD 2.0	VG 4.0	FN 6.0	VF 8.0	VF/NM 9.0	NM- 9.2
						4.00

1-6-Shawn Kittelsen-s/Eric Zawadzki-a 4.00

HEARTBEAT (Also see Faithless)
BOOM! Studios: Nov, 2019 - No 5, Mar, 2020 ($3.99, limited series)
1-5-Maria Llovet-s/a 4.00

HEARTBREAKERS (Also see Dark Horse Presents)
Dark Horse Comics: Apr, 1996 - No. 4, July, 1996 ($2.95, limited series)
1-4: 1-With paper doll & pin-up. 2-Alex Ross pin-up. 3-Evan Dorkin pin-ups. 4-Brereton-c;
Matt Wagner pin-up 4.00
...Superdigest (7/98, $9.95, digest-size) new stories 10.00

HEARTLAND (See Hellblazer)
DC Comics (Vertigo): Mar, 1997 ($4.95, one-shot, mature)
1-Garth Ennis-s/Steve Dillon-c/a 5.00

HEART OF EMPIRE
Dark Horse Comics: Apr, 1999 - No. 9, Dec, 1999 ($2.95, limited series)
1-9-Bryan Talbot-s/a 4.00

HEART OF THE BEAST, THE
DC Comics (Vertigo): 1994 ($19.95, hardcover, mature)
1-Dean Motter scripts 20.00

HEARTS OF DARKNESS (See Ghost Rider; Wolverine; Punisher: Hearts of...)

HEART THROBS (Love Stories No. 147 on)
Quality Comics/National Periodical #47(4-5/57) on (Arleigh #48-101): 8/49 - No. 8, 10/50;
No. 9, 3/52 - No. 146, Oct, 1972

	GD 2.0	VG 4.0	FN 6.0	VF 8.0	VF/NM 9.0	NM- 9.2
1-Classic Ward-c, Gustavson-a. 9 pgs.	58	116	174	371	636	900
2-Ward-c/a (9 pgs); Gustavson-a	37	74	111	222	361	500
3-Gustavson-a	21	42	63	122	199	275
4,6,8-Ward-a, 8-9 pgs.	24	48	72	142	234	325
5,7	17	34	51	100	158	215
9-Robert Mitchum, Jane Russell photo-c	20	40	60	117	189	260
10,15-Ward-a	20	40	60	117	189	260
11-14,16-20: 12 (7/52)	14	28	42	82	121	160
21-Ward-c	20	40	60	114	182	250
22,23-Ward-a(p)	15	30	45	86	133	180
24-33: 33-Last pre-code (3/55)	14	28	42	81	118	155
34-39,41-44,46 (12/56; last Quality issue)	14	28	42	78	112	145
40-Ward-a; r-7 pgs.#21	15	30	45	83	124	165
45-Baker-a	9	18	27	61	123	185
47-(4-5/57; 1st DC issue)	27	54	81	194	435	675
48-60, 100	10	20	30	67	141	215
61-70	8	16	24	52	99	145
71-99: 74-Last 10 cent issue	7	14	21	48	89	130
101-The Beatles app. on-c	20	40	60	138	307	475
102-119: 102-123-(Serial)-Three Girls, Their Lives, Their Loves						
	5	10	15	34	60	85
120-(6-7/69) Neal Adams-c	7	14	21	49	92	135
121-132,143-146	4	8	12	28	47	65
133-142-(52 pgs.)	5	10	15	33	57	80

NOTE: **Gustavson** a-8. **Tuska** a-128. Photo c-4, 5, 8-10, 15, 17.

HEART THROBS - THE BEST OF DC ROMANCE COMICS (See Fireside Book Series)

HEART THROBS
DC Comics (Vertigo): Jan, 1999 - No. 4, Apr, 1999 ($2.95, lim. series)
1-4-Romance anthology. 1-Timm-c. 3-Corben-a 4.00

HEATHCLIFF (See Star Comics Magazine)
Marvel Comics (Star Comics)/Marvel Comics No. 23 on: Apr, 1985 - No. 56, Feb, 1991
(#16-on, $1.00)

	GD 2.0	VG 4.0	FN 6.0	VF 8.0	VF/NM 9.0	NM- 9.2
1-Post-a most issues	2	4	6	9	12	15
2-10,47: 47-Batman parody (Catman vs. the Soaker)						5.00
11-46,48-56: 43-X-Mas issue						4.00
Annual 1 ('87)						5.00

HEATHCLIFF'S FUNHOUSE
Marvel Comics (Star Comics)/Marvel No. 6 on: May, 1987 - No. 10, 1988
1 .... 5.00
2-10 .... 4.00

HEATHENS, THE
AfterShock Comics: Nov, 2021 - No. 5, Mar, 2022 ($4.99/$3.99, limited series)
1-($4.99) Cullen Bunn & Heath Amodio-s/Sami Kivelä-a 5.00
2-5-($3.99) 4.00

HEAT SEEKER: A GUN HONEY SERIES
Titan Comics: Jul, 2023 - No. 4, Dec, 2023 ($3.99, limited series)

	GD 2.0	VG 4.0	FN 6.0	VF 8.0	VF/NM 9.0	NM- 9.2
						4.00

1-4-Charles Ardai-s/Ace Continuado-a 4.00

HEAVY HITTERS
Marvel Comics (Epic Comics): 1993 ($3.75, 68 pgs.)
1-Bound w/trading card; Lawdog, Feud, Alien Legion, Trouble With Girls, & Spyke 4.00

HEAVY LIQUID
DC Comics (Vertigo): Oct, 1999 - No. 5, Feb, 2000 ($5.95, limited series)
1-5-Paul Pope-s/a; flip covers 6.00
TPB (2001, $29.95) r/#1-5 .... 30.00
TPB (2009, $24.95) r/#1-5; development sketches and cover gallery; new cover 25.00
HC (2008, $39.99, dustjacket) r/#1-5; development sketches and cover gallery 40.00

HEAVY VINYL (Title changed from Hi-Fi Fight Club after #3)
Boom Entertainment (BOOM! Box): No. 4, Nov, 2017 ($3.99)
4-Carly Usdin-s/Nina Vakueva-a 4.00

HECKLE AND JECKLE (Paul Terry's...)(See Blue Ribbon, Giant Comics Edition #5A & 10,
Paul Terry's, Terry-Toons Comics)
St. John Publ. Co. No. 1-24/Pines No. 25 on: No. 3, 2/52 - No. 24, 10/55; No. 25, Fall/56 - No.
34, 6/59

	GD 2.0	VG 4.0	FN 6.0	VF 8.0	VF/NM 9.0	NM- 9.2
3(#1)-Funny animal	29	58	87	172	281	390
4(6/52), 5	15	30	45	84	127	170
6-10(4/53)	10	20	30	54	72	90
11-20	8	16	24	40	50	60
21-34: 25-Begin CBS Television Presents on-c	7	14	21	35	42	50

HECKLE AND JECKLE (TV) (See New Terrytoons)
Gold Key/Dell Publ. Co.: 11/62 - No. 4, 8/63; 5/66; No. 2, 10/66; No. 3, 8/67

	GD 2.0	VG 4.0	FN 6.0	VF 8.0	VF/NM 9.0	NM- 9.2
1 (11/62; Gold Key)	6	12	18	41	76	110
2-4	3	6	9	21	33	45
1 (5/66; Dell)	4	8	12	27	44	60
2,3	3	6	9	18	28	38

(See March of Comics 379, 472, 484)

HECKLE AND JECKLE 3-D
Spotlight Comics: 1987 - No. 2?, 1987 ($2.50)
1,2 .... 5.00

HECKLER, THE
DC Comics: Sept, 1992 - No. 6, Feb, 1993 ($1.25)
1-6-T&M Bierbaum-s/Keith Giffen-c/a 4.00

HECTIC PLANET
Slave Labor Graphics 1998 ($12.95/$14.95)
Book 1,2-r-Dorkin-s/a from Pirate Corp$ Vol. 1 & 2 .... 15.00

HECTOR COMICS (The Keenest Teen in Town)
Key Publications: Nov, 1953 - No. 3, 1954

	GD 2.0	VG 4.0	FN 6.0	VF 8.0	VF/NM 9.0	NM- 9.2
1-Teen humor	14	28	42	76	108	140
2,3	8	16	24	44	57	70

HECTOR HEATHCOTE (TV)
Gold Key: Mar, 1964

	GD 2.0	VG 4.0	FN 6.0	VF 8.0	VF/NM 9.0	NM- 9.2
1 (10111-403)	6	12	18	41	76	110

HECTOR THE INSPECTOR (See Top Flight Comics)

HEDGE KNIGHT, THE
Image Comics: Aug, 2003 - No. 6, Apr, 2004 ($2.95, limited series)
1-6-George R.R. Martin-s/Mike S. Miller-a. 1-Two covers by Kaluta and Miller 3.00
George R.R. Martin's The Hedge Knight HC (Marvel, 2006, $19.99) r/series; 2 covers 20.00
George R.R. Martin's The Hedge Knight SC (Marvel, 2007, $14.99) r/series 15.00
TPB (2004, $14.95) r/series plus new short story 15.00

HEDGE KNIGHT II: SWORN SWORD
Marvel Comics (Dabel Brothers): Jun, 2007 - No. 6, Jun, 2008 ($2.99, limited series)
1-6-George R.R. Martin-s/Mike Miller-a. 1-Two covers by Yu & Miller, plus Miller B&W-c 3.00
... HC (2008, $19.99) r/series; 2 covers 20.00

HEDY DE VINE COMICS (Formerly All Winners #21? or Teen #22?(6/47);
Hedy of Hollywood #36 on; also see Annie Oakley & Venus)
Marvel Comics (RCM): No. 22, Aug, 1947 - No. 35, Oct, 1949

	GD 2.0	VG 4.0	FN 6.0	VF 8.0	VF/NM 9.0	NM- 9.2
22-1st app. Hedy De Vine (also see Joker #32)	110	220	330	704	1202	1700
23,24,27-30: 23-Wolverton-a, 1 pg; Kurtzman's "Hey Look", 2 pgs. 24,27-30- "Hey Look" by Kurtzman, 1-3 pgs.	57	114	171	362	619	875
25-Classic "Hey Look" by Kurtzman, "Optical Illusion"	71	142	213	454	777	1100
26- "Giggles 'n' Grins" by Kurtzman	53	106	159	334	567	800
31-34: 32-Anti-Wertham editorial	39	78	117	231	378	525

	GD 2.0	VG 4.0	FN 6.0	VF 8.0	VF/NM 9.0	NM- 9.2
35-Four pgs. "Rusty" by Kurtzman	40	80	120	246	411	575

HEDY-MILLIE-TESSIE COMEDY (See Comedy Comics)

HEDY OF HOLLYWOOD (Formerly Hedy Devine Comics)
Marvel Comics (RCM)/Atlas #50: No. 36, Feb, 1950 - No. 50, Sept, 1952

	GD 2.0	VG 4.0	FN 6.0	VF 8.0	VF/NM 9.0	NM- 9.2
36(#1)	54	108	162	343	574	825
37-50	39	78	117	240	395	550

HEDY WOLFE (Also see Patsy & Hedy & Miss America Magazine V1#2)
Atlas Publishing Co. (Emgee): Aug, 1957

1-Patsy Walker's rival; Al Hartley-c	37	74	111	222	361	500

HEE HAW (TV)
Charlton Press: July, 1970 - No. 7, Aug, 1971

1	5	10	15	30	50	70
2-7	3	6	9	21	33	45

HEIDI (See Dell Jr. Treasury No. 6)

HEIDI SAHA (AN ILLUSTRATED HISTORY OF...)
Warren Publishing: 1973 (500 printed)
nn-Photo-c; an early Vampirella model for Warren (a FN/VF copy sold in 2011 for $776.75)

HELEN OF TROY (Movie)
Dell Publishing Co.: No. 684, Mar, 1956 (one-shot)

Four Color 684-Buscema-a, photo-c	10	20	30	66	138	210

HELL
Dark Horse Comics: July, 2003 - No. 4, Mar, 2004 ($2.99, limited series)
1-4-Augustyn-s/Demong-a/Meglia-c ... 3.00

HELLBLAZER (John Constantine) (See Saga of Swamp Thing #37 & 2013 Constantine title)
(Also see Books of Magic limited series and Sandman Universe Presents)
DC Comics (Vertigo #63 on): Jan, 1988 - No. 300, Apr, 2013 ($1.25-$2.99)

1-(44 pgs.)-John Constantine; McKean-c thru #21; 1st app. Papa Midnite	5	10	15	34	60	85
1-Special Edition (7/10, $1.00) r/#1 with "What's Next?" cover logo						5.00
2-5	1	2	3	5	7	9
6-8,10: 10-Swamp Thing cameo						6.00
9,19: 9-X-over w/Swamp Thing #76. 19-Sandman app.	1	2	3	6		8
11-18,20						6.00

21-26,28-30: 22-Williams-c. 24-Contains bound-in Shocker movie poster.
25,26-Grant Morrison scripts.
27-Neil Gaiman scripts; Dave McKean-a; low print run ... 5.00

31-39: 36-Preview of World Without End.	3	6	9	21	33	45

40-($2.25, 52 pgs.)-Dave McKean-a & colors; preview of Kid Eternity ... 5.00
41-Ennis scripts begin; ends #83 ... 5.00
42-49,51-74,76-99,101-119: 44,45-Sutton-a(i). 52-Glenn Fabry painted-c begin. 62-Special Death insert by McKean. 63-Silver metallic ink on-c. 77-Totleben-c. 84-Sean Phillips-c/a begins; Delano story. 85-88-Eddie Campbell story. 89-Paul Jenkins scripts begin. ... 4.00
50,75,100,120: 50-($3.00, 52 pgs.). 75-($2.95, 52 pgs.). 100,120 ($3.50,48 pgs.) ... 5.00
121-199, 201-249, 251-274,276-299: 129-Ennis-s. 141-Bradstreet-a. 146-150-Corben-a. 151-Azzarello-s begin. 175-Carey-s begin. 176-Begin a. 182,183-Bermejo-a. 216-Mina-s begins. 220-Begin $2.99-c. 229-Carey-s/Leon-a. 234-Initial printing (white title logo) has missing text; corrected printing has lt. blue title logo. 265,266,271-274-Bisley-a. 268-271-Shade the Changing Man app. ... 4.00
200-($4.50) Carey-s/Dillon, Frusin, Manco-a ... 4.00
250-($4.99) Short stories by various; art by Lloyd, Phillips, Milligan; Bermejo-c ... 5.00
275-($4.99) Constantine's wedding; Bisley-c ... 5.00
300-($4.99) Last issue; Bisley-c ... 5.00
Annual 1 (1989, $2.95, 68 pgs.)-Bryan Talbot's 1st work in American comics ... 6.00
Annual 1 (Annual 2011 on cover, 2/12, $4.99)-Milligan-s/Bisley-a/c ... 5.00
Special 1 (1993, $3.95, 68 pgs.)-Ennis story; w/pin-ups. ... 5.00
...Black Flowers (2005, $14.99, TPB) r/#181-186 ... 15.00
...Bloodlines (2007, $19.99, TPB) r/#47-50,52-55,59-61 ... 20.00
...Damnation's Flame (1999, $16.95, TPB) r/#72-77 ... 17.00
...Dangerous Habits (1997, $14.95, TPB) r/#41-46 ... 15.00
...Fear and Loathing (1997, $14.95, TPB) r/#62-67 ... 18.00
...Fear and Loathing (2nd printing, $17.95) ... 18.00
...Freezes Over (2003, $14.95, TPB) r/#157-163 ... 15.00
...Good Intentions (2002, $12.95, TPB) r/#151-156 ... 13.00
...Haunting (2003, $12.95, TPB) r/#134-139 ... 10.00
...Hard Time (2001, $9.95, TPB) r/#146-150 ... 13.00
...Highwater (2004, $19.95, TPB) r/#164-174 ... 20.00
John Constantine Hellblazer: All His Engines HC (2005, $24.95, with dustjacket) new graphic novel; Mike Carey-s/Leonardo Manco-a ... 25.00
John Constantine Hellblazer: All His Engines SC (2006, $14.99) new graphic novel ... 15.00
John Constantine Hellblazer: Bloody Carnations SC (2011, $19.99) r/#267-275 ... 20.00
John Constantine Hellblazer: Empathy is the Enemy SC (2006, $14.99) r/#216-222 ... 15.00
John Constantine Hellblazer: Hooked SC (2010, $14.99) r/#256-260 ... 15.00
John Constantine Hellblazer: India SC (2010, $14.99) r/#261-266 ... 15.00
John Constantine Hellblazer: Joyride SC (2008, $14.99) r/#230-237 ... 15.00
John Constantine Hellblazer: Pandemonium HC (2010, $24.99, with dustjacket) new graphic novel; Jamie Delano-s/Jock-a ... 25.00
John Constantine Hellblazer: Pandemonium SC (2011, $17.99) new graphic novel ... 18.00
John Constantine Hellblazer: Scab SC (2009, $14.99) r/#250-255 ... 15.00
John Constantine Hellblazer: The Devil You Know SC (2007, $19.99) r/#10-13, Annual #1 and The Horrorist miniseries #1,2 ... 20.00
John Constantine Hellblazer: The Family Plot SC (2008, $19.99, TPB) r/#23,24,28-33 ... 20.00
John Constantine Hellblazer: The Fear Machine SC (2008, $19.99, TPB) r/#14-22 ... 20.00
John Constantine Hellblazer: The Red Right Hand SC (2007, $14.99) r/#223-228 ... 15.00
John Const. Hellblazer: The Roots of Coincidence ('09, $14.99) r/#243,244,247-249 ... 15.00
Original Sins (1993, $19.95, TPB) r/#1-9 ... 20.00
Original Sins (2011, $19.95, TPB) r/#1-9 ... 20.00
Rake at the Gates of Hell (2003, $19.95, TPB) r/#78-83; Heartland #1 ... 20.00
: Rare Cuts (2014, $14.95, TPB) r/#11,25,26,35,56,84 & Vertigo Secret Files: Hellblazer ... 15.00
: Reasons To Be Cheerful (2007, $14.99, TPB) r/#201-206 ... 15.00
: Red Sepulchre (2005, $12.99, TPB) r/#175-180 ... 13.00

	GD 2.0	VG 4.0	FN 6.0	VF 8.0	VF/NM 9.0	NM- 9.2
...: Setting Sun (2004, $12.95, TPB) r/#140-143						13.00
...: Son of Man (2004, $12.95, TPB) r/#129-133						13.00
...: Stations of the Cross (2006, $14.99, TPB) r/#194-200						15.00
...: Staring At The Wall (2005, $14.99, TPB) r/#187-193						15.00
...: Tainted Love (1998, $16.95, TPB) r/#68-71, Vertigo Jam #1 and Hellblazer Special #1						17.00

NOTE: *Alcala* a-8i, 9i, 18-22i. *Gaiman* scripts-27. *McKean* a-27,40; c-1-21. *Sutton* a-44i, 45i. *Talbot* a-Annual 1.

HELLBLAZER (DC Rebirth)
DC Comics: Oct, 2016 - No. 24, Sept, 2018 ($2.99/$3.99)
1-8: 1-4-Simon Oliver-s/Moritat-a; Swamp Thing app. 5-7-Cassaday-c ... 3.00
9-24-($3.99): 9-12-Fabbri-a. 11,12-Lotay-c. 15-Justice League app. 20-24-Huntress app. ... 4.00
...: Rebirth 1 (9/16, $2.99) Oliver-s/Moritat-a; Swamp Thing, Wonder Woman app. ... 3.00

HELLBLAZER: CITY OF DEMONS
DC Comics (Vertigo): Early Dec, 2010 - No. 5, Feb, 2011 ($2.99, limited series)
1-5-Si Spencer-s/Sean Murphy-a/c ... 3.00
TPB (2011, $14.99) r/#1-5 & story from Vertigo Winter's Edge #3 ... 15.00

HELLBLAZER: RISE AND FALL
DC Comics (Black Label): Nov, 2020 - No. 2, Jan, 2021 ($6.99, limited series, over-sized 10-7/8" x 8-1/2")
1,2-Tom Taylor-s/Darick Robertson-a; 2 covers on each ... 7.00

HELLBLAZER SPECIAL: BAD BLOOD
DC Comics (Vertigo): Sept, 2000 - No. 4, Dec, 2000 ($2.95, limited series)
1-4-Delano-s/Bond-a; Constantine in 2025 London ... 3.00

HELLBLAZER SPECIAL: CHAS
DC Comics (Vertigo): Sept, 2008 - No. 5, Jan, 2009 ($2.99, limited series)
1-5-Story of Constantine's cab driver; Oliver-s/Sudzuka-a/Fabry-c ... 3.00
... - The Knowledge TPB (2009, $14.99) r/#1-5 ... 15.00

HELLBLAZER SPECIAL: LADY CONSTANTINE
DC Comics (Vertigo): Feb, 2003 - No. 4, May, 2003 ($2.95, limited series)
1-4-Story of Johanna Constantine in 1785; Diggle-s/Sudzuka-a/Noto-c ... 3.00

HELLBLAZER/THE BOOKS OF MAGIC
DC Comics (Vertigo): Dec, 1997 - No. 2, Jan, 1998 ($2.50, limited series)
1,2-John Constantine and Tim Hunter ... 4.00

HELLBOY (Also see Batman/Hellboy/Starman, Danger Unlimited #4, Dark Horse Presents, Gen¹³ #13B, Ghost/Hellboy, John Byrne's Next Men, San Diego Comic Con #2, Savage Dragon, & Young Hellboy)

HELLBOY
Dark Horse Comics: Apr, 2008
... - Free Comic Book Day; Three short stories; Mignola-c; art by Fegredo, Davis, Azaceta ... 4.00

HELLBOY: ALMOST COLOSSUS
Dark Horse Comics (Legend): Jun, 1997 - No. 2, Jul, 1997 ($2.95, lim. series)

1,2-Mignola-s/a	1	3	4	6	8	10

HELLBOY AND THE B.P.R.D.
Dark Horse Comics: Dec, 2014 - No. 5, Apr, 2015 ($3.50, limited series)
1-5-Mignola & Arcudi-s/Maleev-a/c; Hellboy's first mission; set in 1952 ... 3.50
...: Her Fatal Hour and The Sending (12/20, $3.99) Mignola-s/Trevallion-a ... 4.00
...: Long Night at Goloski Station (10/19, $3.99) Mignola-s/Matt Smith-a/Mignola-c ... 4.00
...: Night of the Cyclops (5/22, $3.99) Mignola-s/Vatine-a/c ... 4.00
...: 1953 - Beyond the Fences 1-3 (2/16 - No. 3, 4/16, $3.50) Paolo Rivera-a/c ... 3.50
...: 1953 - The Phantom Hand & The Kelpie (10/15, $3.50) Mignola-s/Stenbeck-a ... 3.50
...: 1953 - The Witch Tree & Rawhead and Bloody Bones (11/15, $3.50) Mignola-s/c; Stenbeck-a ... 3.50
...: 1953 - The Witch Tree & Rawhead and Bloody Bones, Halloween Comics Fest (10/17, giveaway) Mignola-s/c; Stenbeck-a ... 3.00
...: 1954 - Black Sun 1,2 (9/16 - No. 2, 10/16, $3.99) Stephen Green-a/c ... 4.00
...: 1954 - Ghost Moon 1,2 (3/17 - No. 2, 4/17, $3.99) Mignola & Roberson-s/Churilla-a ... 4.00
...: 1954 - The Unreasoning Beast (11/16, $3.99) Mignola & Roberson-s/Reynolds-a ... 4.00
...: 1955 - Burning Season (2/18, $3.99) Mignola & Roberson-s/Rivera-a ... 4.00
...: 1955 - Occult Intelligence 1-3 (9/17 - No. 3, 11/17, $3.99) Churilla-a ... 4.00
...: 1955 - Secret Nature (8/16, $3.99) Mignola & Roberson-s/Martinbrough-a ... 4.00
...: 1956 1-5 (1/19 - No. 5, 3/19, $3.99) Mignola & Roberson-s/Norton, Li & Oeming-a ... 4.00
...: 1957 - Falling Sky (8/22, $3.99) Mignola & Roberson-s/Martinbrough-a ... 4.00
...: 1957 - Family Ties (9/21, $3.99) Mignola & Roberson-s/Campbell-a ... 4.00
...: 1957 - Fearful Symmetry (6/23, $3.99) Mignola & Roberson-s/Sampson-a ... 4.00
...: 1957 - Forgotten Lives (2/22, $3.99) Mignola & Roberson-s/Green-a ... 4.00
...: 1957 - From Below (8/23, $3.99) Mignola & Roberson-s/Norton-a ... 4.00
...: Old Man Whittier (12/22, $3.99) Mignola-s/Walta-a/c ... 4.00
...: Saturn Returns 1-3 (8/19 - No. 3, 10/19, $3.99) Mignola & Allie-s/Mitten-a ... 4.00
...: The Beast of Vargu (6/19, $3.99) Mignola-s/Fegredo-a/c ... 4.00
...: The Return of Effie Kolb 1,2 (2/20 - No. 2, 10/20, $3.99) Mignola-s/Zach Howard-a ... 4.00
...: The Secret of Chesbro House 1,2 (7/21 - No. 2, 8/21, $3.99) McManus-a ... 4.00
...: The Seven Wives Club (11/20, $4.99) Mignola-s/Hughes-a; covers by Mignola & Hughes ... 4.00
...: Time is a River (7/22, $3.99) Mignola-s/László-a ... 4.00

HELLBOY/BEASTS OF BURDEN
Dark Horse Comics: Oct, 2010 ($3.50, one-shot)

... Sacrifice - Dorkin & Mignola-s/Jill Thompson-a	1	3	4	6	8	10

HELLBOY: BEING HUMAN
Dark Horse Comics: May, 2011 ($3.50, one-shot)

nn-Mignola-s; Richard Corben-a/c; Roger app.	2	4	6	8	10	12

HELLBOY: BOX FULL OF EVIL
Dark Horse Comics: Aug, 1999 - No. 2, Sept, 1999 ($2.95, lim. series)

1,2-Mignola-s/a; back-up story w/ Matt Smith-a	2	4	6	8	10	12

HELLBOY: BUSTER OAKLEY GETS HIS WISH
Dark Horse Comics: Apr, 2011 ($3.50, one-shot)

nn-Mignola-s; Kevin Nowlan-a; two covers by Mignola & Nowlan	1	3	4	6	8	10

HELLBOY CHRISTMAS SPECIAL
Dark Horse Comics: Dec, 1997 ($3.95, one-shot)

nn-Christmas stories by Mignola, Gianni, Darrow	3	6	9	14	19	24

Hellblazer (2016 series) #13 © DC

Hellboy in Hell #6 © Mike Mignola

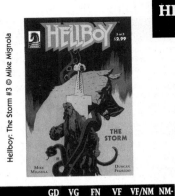

Hellboy: The Storm #3 © Mike Mignola

	GD 2.0	VG 4.0	FN 6.0	VF 8.0	VF/NM 9.0	NM- 9.2

HELLBOY: CONQUEROR WORM
Dark Horse Comics: May, 2001 - No. 4, Aug, 2001 ($2.99, limited series)
1-4-Mignola-s/a/c · 2 · 4 · 6 · 8 · 10 · 12

HELLBOY: DARKNESS CALLS
Dark Horse Comics: Apr, 2007 - No. 6, Nov, 2007 ($2.99, limited series)
1-6-Mignola-s/Fegredo-a · 1 · 2 · 3 · 5 · 6 · 8

HELLBOY: DOUBLE FEATURE OF EVIL
Dark Horse Comics: Nov, 2010 ($3.50, one-shot)
1-Mignola-s; Corben-a/c · 1 · 2 · 3 · 5 · 6 · 8

HELLBOY: HOUSE OF THE LIVING DEAD
Dark Horse Comics: Nov, 2011 ($14.99, hardcover graphic novel)
1-Mignola-a/c; Hellboy and Lucha Libre · 15.00

HELLBOY IN HELL (Follows Hellboy's death in Hellboy: The Fury)
Dark Horse Comics: Dec, 2012 - No. 10, Jun, 2016 ($2.99)
1-Mignola-s/a/c · 1 · 3 · 4 · 6 · 8 · 10
1-Variant "Year in Monsters" cover · 16.00
2-6 · 1 · 2 · 3 · 5 · 6 · 8
7-10 · 4.00

HELLBOY IN LOVE
Dark Horse Comics: Oct, 2022 - No. 5 ($3.99, limited series)
1-4-Christopher Golden-s/Matt Smith-a; set in 1979 · 4.00

HELLBOY IN MEXICO
Dark Horse Comics: May, 2010 ($3.50, one-shot)
1-Mignola-s; Corben-a/c; Mexican wrestlers vs. monsters · 2 · 4 · 6 · 8 · 10 · 12

HELLBOY: IN THE CHAPEL OF MOLOCH
Dark Horse Comics: Oct, 2008 ($2.99, one-shot)
nn-Mignola-s/a/c · 1 · 3 · 4 · 6 · 8 · 10

HELLBOY: INTO THE SILENT SEA
Dark Horse Comics: Apr, 2017 ($14.99, HC graphic novel)
nn-Mignola-s/c; Gianni-a · 15.00

HELLBOY, JR.
Dark Horse Comics: Oct, 1999 - No. 2, Nov, 1999 ($2.95, limited series)
1,2-Stories and art by various · 6.00
TPB (1/04, $14.95) r/#1&2, Halloween; sketch pages; intro. by Steve Niles; Bill Wray-c · 15.00

HELLBOY, JR., HALLOWEEN SPECIAL
Dark Horse Comics: Oct, 1997 ($3.95, one-shot)
nn-"Harvey" style renditions of Hellboy characters; Bill Wray, Mike Mignola & various-s/a; wraparound-c by Wray · 1 · 3 · 4 · 6 · 8 · 10

HELLBOY: KRAMPUSNACHT
Dark Horse Comics: Dec, 2017 ($3.99, one-shot)
nn-Krampus app.; Mike Mignola-s/Adam Hughes-a; covers by Mignola & Hughes · 2 · 4 · 6 · 8 · 10 · 12

HELLBOY: MAKOMA, OR A TALE TOLD...
Dark Horse Comics: Feb, 2006 - No. 2, Mar, 2006 ($2.99, lim. series)
1,2-Mignola-s/c; Mignola & Corben-a · 1 · 3 · 4 · 6 · 8 · 10

HELLBOY PREMIERE EDITION
Dark Horse Comics (Wizard): 2004 (no price, one-shot)
nn- Two covers by Mignola & Davis; Mignola-s/a; BPRD story w/Arcudi-s/Davis-a · 2 · 4 · 6 · 9 · 12 · 15
Wizard World Los Angeles-Movie photo-c; Mignola-s/a; BPRD story w/Arcudi-s/Davis-a · 2 · 4 · 6 · 9 · 13 · 16

HELLBOY: SEED OF DESTRUCTION (First Hellboy series)
Dark Horse Comics (Legend): Mar, 1994 - No. 4, Jun, 1994 ($2.50, lim. series)
1-Mignola-c/a w/Byrne scripts; Monkeyman & O'Brien back-up story
(origin) by Art Adams · 5 · 10 · 15 · 31 · 53 · 75
2-1st app. Abe Sapien & Liz Sherman · 3 · 6 · 9 · 21 · 33 · 45
3,4 · 2 · 4 · 6 · 10 · 14 · 18
Hellboy: One for One (8/10, $1.00) r/#1 Hellboy story with red cover frame · 6.00
Trade paperback (1994, $17.95)-collects all four issues plus r/Hellboy's 1st app. in San Diego Comic Con #2 & pin-ups · 20.00
Limited edition hardcover (1995, $99.95)-includes everything in trade paperback plus additional material. · 150.00

HELLBOY STRANGE PLACES
Dark Horse Books: Apr, 2006 ($17.95, TPB)

SC - Reprints Hellboy: The Third Wish #1,2 and Hellboy: The Island #1,2; sketch pages · 24.00

HELLBOY: THE BONES OF GIANTS
Dark Horse Comics: Nov, 2021 - No. 4, Feb, 2022 ($3.99, lim. series)
1-4-Mignola & Golden-s/Matt Smith-a · 4.00

HELLBOY: THE BRIDE OF HELL
Dark Horse Comics: Dec, 2009 ($3.50, one-shot)
1-Mignola-s/c; Corben-a; preview of The Marquis: Inferno · 1 · 2 · 3 · 5 · 6 · 8

HELLBOY: THE CHAINED COFFIN AND OTHERS
Dark Horse Comics (Legend): Aug, 1998 ($17.95, TPB)
nn-Mignola-c/a; reprints out-of-print one shots; pin-up gallery · 18.00

HELLBOY: THE COMPANION
Dark Horse Books: May, 2008 ($14.95, 9"x6", TPB)
nn-Overview of Hellboy history, characters, stories, mythology; text with Mignola panels · 15.00

HELLBOY: THE CORPSE
Dark Horse Comics: Mar, 2004 (25¢, one-shot)
nn-Mignola-c/a/scripts; reprints "The Corpse" serial from Capitol City's Advance Comics catalog; development sketches and photos of the Corpse from the Hellboy movie · 2 · 4 · 6 · 8 · 10 · 12

HELLBOY: THE CORPSE AND THE IRON SHOES
Dark Horse Comics (Legend): Jan, 1996 ($2.95, one-shot)
nn-Mignola-c/a/scripts; reprints "The Corpse" serial w/new story · 2 · 4 · 6 · 8 · 10 · 12

HELLBOY: THE CROOKED MAN
Dark Horse Comics: Jul, 2008 - No. 3, Sept, 2008 ($2.99, lim. series)
1-3-Mignola-s/Corben-a/c · 1 · 2 · 3 · 5 · 6 · 8

HELLBOY: THE FURY
Dark Horse Comics: Jun, 2011 - No. 3, Aug, 2011 ($2.99, lim. series)
1-3-Mignola-s/c; Fegredo-a. 1-Variant-c by Fegredo. 3-Hellboy dies · 1 · 2 · 3 · 5 · 6 · 8
3-Retailer Incentive Variant · 16 · 32 · 48 · 110 · 243 · 375

HELLBOY: THE GOLDEN ARMY
Dark Horse Comics: Jan, 2008 (no cover price)
nn-Prelude to the 2008 movie; Del Toro & Mignola-s/Velasco-a; 3 photo covers · 1 · 3 · 4 · 6 · 8 · 10

HELLBOY: THE ISLAND
Dark Horse Comics: June, 2005 - No. 2, July, 2005 ($2.99, lim. series)
1,2: Mignola-c/a & scripts · 1 · 2 · 3 · 5 · 6 · 8

HELLBOY: THE MIDNIGHT CIRCUS
Dark Horse Books: Oct, 2013 ($14.99, hardcover graphic novel)
nn-Mignola-s/c; Fegredo-a; young Hellboy runs away from BPRD in 1948 · 25.00

HELLBOY: THE RIGHT HAND OF DOOM
Dark Horse Comics (Legend): Apr, 2000 ($17.95, TPB)
nn-Mignola-c/a/s; reprints · 18.00

HELLBOY: THE SILVER LANTERN CLUB
Dark Horse Comics: Oct, 2021 - No. 5, Mar, 2022 ($3.99, limited series)
1-5-Mignola & Roberson-s/Mitten & Stenbeck-a · 4.00

HELLBOY: THE SLEEPING AND THE DEAD
Dark Horse Comics: Dec, 2010 - No. 2, Feb, 2011 ($3.50, lim. series)
1,2-Mignola-s/Scott Hampton-a · 1 · 2 · 3 · 5 · 6 · 8

HELLBOY: THE STORM
Dark Horse Comics: Jul, 2010 - No. 3, Sept, 2010 ($2.99, lim. series)
1-3-Mignola-s/Fegredo-a · 1 · 2 · 3 · 5 · 6 · 8

HELLBOY: THE THIRD WISH
Dark Horse Comics (Maverick): July, 2002 - No. 2, Aug, 2002 ($2.99, lim. series)
1,2-Mignola-c/a/s · 1 · 3 · 4 · 6 · 8 · 10

HELLBOY THE TROLL WITCH AND OTHERS
Dark Horse Books: Nov, 2007 ($17.95, TPB)
SC - Reprints Hellboy: Makoma, Hellboy Premiere Edition and stories from Dark Horse Book of Hauntings, DHB of Witchcraft, DHB of the Dead, DHB of Monsters · 18.00

HELLBOY: THE WILD HUNT
Dark Horse Comics: Dec, 2008 - No. 8, Nov, 2009 ($2.99, lim. series)
1-8: Mignola-c/s; Fegredo-a · 1 · 2 · 3 · 5 · 6 · 8

	GD	VG	FN	VF	VF/NM	NM-
	2.0	4.0	6.0	8.0	9.0	9.2

HELLBOY: THE WOLVES OF ST. AUGUST
Dark Horse Comics (Legend): 1995 ($4.95, squarebound, one-shot)
nn-Mignola--c/a/scripts; r/Dark Horse Presents #88-91 with additional story

	2	4	6	8	10	12

HELLBOY VS. LOBSTER JOHNSON: THE RING OF DEATH
Dark Horse Comics: May, 2019 ($3.99, one-shot)
1-Mignola & Roberson-s; art by Norton & Grist; Paolo Rivera-c

	2	4	6	8	10	12

HELLBOY: WAKE THE DEVIL (Sequel to Seed of Destruction)
Dark Horse Comics (Legend): Jun, 1996 - No. 5, Oct, 1996 ($2.95, lim. series)
1-5: Mignola-c/a & scripts; The Monstermen back-up story by Gary Gianni

	2	4	6	8	10	12
TPB (1997, $17.95) r/#1-5						18.00

HELLBOY: WEIRD TALES
Dark Horse Comics: Feb, 2003 - No. 8, Apr, 2004 ($2.99, limited series, anthology)
1-8-Hellboy stories from other creators. 1-Cassaday-c/s/a; Watson-s/a. 6-Cho-c

	1	2	3	5	6	8
... Vol. 1 (2004, 17.95) r/#1-4						18.00
... Vol. 2 (2004, 17.95) r/#5-8 and Lobster Johnson serial from #1-8						18.00

HELLBOY WINTER SPECIAL
Dark Horse Comics: Jan, 2016; Jan, 2017; Dec, 2018; Jan, 2020 ($3.99, one-shots)

1-Short stories by Mignola, Sale, Oeming, Allie, Roberson and others; Sale-c						4.00
nn (1/17)-Short stories; Mignola & Roberson-s, Mitten, Grist & Fiumara-a; Fiumara-c						4.00
... 2018 (12/18) Short stories; Mignola-s/Stenbeck-a; Bá & Moon-s/a; Zonjic-a						4.00
... 2019 (1/20) Short stories; Mignola-s/László-a; Roberson-s/Del Duca-a; Mutti-a						4.00
... The Yule Cat (12/23) Matt Smith-s/a						4.00

HELLCAT
Marvel Comics: Sept, 2000 - No. 3, Nov, 2000 ($2.99)

1-3-Englehart-s/Breyfogle-a; Hedy Wolfe app.						3.00

HELLCAT (Patsy Walker)
Marvel Comics: May, 2023 - No. 5, Sept, 2023 ($4.99/$3.99)

1-($4.99) Christopher Cantwell-s/Alex Lins-a						5.00
2-5-($3.99) Sleepwalker and Hellstrom app.						4.00

HELLCOP
Image Comics (Avalon Studios): Aug, 1998 - No. 4, Mar, 1999 ($2.50)

1-4: 1-(Oct. on-c) Casey-s						4.00

HELLCOP
Image Comics (Shadowline): Oct, 2021 - No. 10, Aug, 2022 ($3.99)

1-10-Brian Haberlin-s/a						4.00
...: Halloween Special 1 (10/21, $7.99, bagged with 3-D glasses) r/#1 with 3-D effects						8.00

HELL ETERNAL
DC Comics (Vertigo Verité): 1998 ($6.95, squarebound, one-shot)

1-Delano/-s/Phillips-a						7.00

HELLGATE: LONDON (Based on the video game)
Dark Horse Comics: No. 0, May 2006 - No. 3, Mar, 2007 ($2.99)

0-3-Edginton-s/Pugh-a/Briclot-c						3.00

HELLHOUNDS (...: Panzer Cops #3-6)
Dark Horse Comics: 1994 - No. 6, July, 1994 ($2.50, B&W, limited series)

1-6: 1-Hamner-c. 3-(4/94)						4.00

HELLHOUND, THE REDEMPTION QUEST
Marvel Comics (Epic Comics): Dec, 1993 - No. 4, Mar, 1994 ($2.25, lim. series, coated stock)

1-4						4.00

HELLIONS (See 2020 X-Men titles)
Marvel Comics: May, 2020 - No. 18, Feb, 2022 ($4.99/$3.99)

1-($4.99) Havok, Mr. Sinister, Psylocke, Scalphunter app.; Wells-s/Segovia-a						5.00
2-17-($3.99) 2-Scalphunter renamed Greycrow. 5,6-"X of Swords" tie-in. 12-Hellfire Gala						4.00
18-($4.99) Last issue; Wells-s/Carlos & Segovia-a						5.00

HELL IS A SQUARED CIRCLE
AfterShock Comics: Sept, 2022 ($7.99, oversized 8-1/2" x 10-7/8", one shot)

1-Chris Condon-s/Francesco Biagini-a						8.00

HELLMOUTH (Crossover with Buffy the Vampire Slayer and Angel)
BOOM! Studios: Oct, 2019 - No. 5, Feb, 2020 ($3.99, limited series)

1-5-Bellaire & Lambert-s/Carlini-a						4.00

HELLO BUDDIES
Harvey Publications: 1953 (25¢, small size)

1		5	10	15	35	63	90

HELLO BUDDY (see also HALT FRIENDS in the Platinum Era section)
???: 1944, 1945 (4-1/4 x 5-1/4", 32 pgs, color-c, B&W, 15¢)
nn - Military oriented jokes & cartoons. 1945-Christmas-c with soldiers

		3	6	9	16	23	30

NOTE: Says on front cover: "Comics of War Facts of Service Sold on its merits by Unemployed or Disabled Ex-Service Men." These are very common; contents vary widely.

HELL 'O DALI (Cerebus)
Aardvark-Vanaheim: Oct, 2022 ($4.00, B&W)

1-X-Men #42-c swipe						4.00

HELLO, I'M JOHNNY CASH
Spire Christian Comics (Fleming H. Revell Co.): 1976 (39¢/49¢)

nn-(39¢-c)		3	6	9	19	30	40
nn-(49¢-c)		3	6	9	16	23	30

HELL ON EARTH (See DC Science Fiction Graphic Novel)

HELLO PAL COMICS (Short Story Comics)
Harvey Publications: Jan, 1943 - No. 3, May, 1943 (Photo-c)
1-Rocketman & Rocketgirl begin; Yankee Doodle Jones app.; Mickey Rooney photo-c

	71	142	213	454	777	1100
2-Charlie McCarthy photo-c (scarce)	56	112	168	349	595	840
3-Bob Hope photo-c (scarce)	60	120	180	384	660	935

HELLRAISER (See Clive Barker's...)

HELLRAISER/NIGHTBREED – JIHAD (Also see Clive Barker's...)
Epic Comics (Marvel Comics): 1991 - Book 2, 1991 ($4.50, 52 pgs.)

Book 1,2		1	3	4	6	8	10

HELL-RIDER (Motorcycle themed magazine)
Skywald Publications: Aug, 1971 - No. 2, Oct, 1971 (B&W, 68 pgs.)

1-Origin & 1st app.; Butterfly & the Wild Bunch begin; 1st Hell-Rider by Andru, Esposito and Friedrich	9	18	27	59	117	175
2-Andru, Ayers, Buckler, Shores-a	5	10	15	35	63	90

NOTE: #3 advertised in Psycho #5 but did not come out. Buckler a-1, 2. Rosenbaum c-1,2.

HELL'S ANGEL (Becomes Dark Angel #6 on)
Marvel Comics UK: July, 1992 - No. 5, Nov, 1993 ($1.75)

1-5: X-Men (Wolverine, Cyclops)-c/stories. 1-Origin. 3-Jim Lee cover swipe						4.00

HELLSHOCK
Image Comics: July, 1994 - No. 4, Nov, 1994 ($1.95, limited series)

1-4-Jae Lee-c/a & scripts. 4-Variant-c.						4.00

HELLSHOCK
Image Comics: Jan, 1997 - No. 3, Jan, 1998 ($2.95/$2.50, limited series)

1-($2.95)-Jae Lee-c/s/a, Villarrubia-painted-a						5.00
2-($2.50)						4.00
Book 3: The Science of Faith (1/98, $2.50) Jae Lee-c/s/a, Villarrubia-painted-a						4.00
Vol. 1 HC (2006, $49.99) r/#1-3 re-colored, with unpublished 22 pg. conclusion; cover gallery and sketches; alternate opening art; intro. by Jim Lee						50.00

HELL SONJA
Dynamite Entertainment: 2021 - No. 5, 2022 ($3.99, limited series)

1-5: 1-4-Hastings-s/Qualano-a; multiple covers on each; the alternate Sonjas app.						4.00

HELLSPAWN
Image Comics: Aug, 2000 - No. 16, Apr, 2003 ($2.50)

1-Bendis-s/Ashley Wood-c/a; Spawn & Clown app.	1	2	3	5	6	8
2-9: 6-Last Bendis-s; Mike Moran (Miracleman app.). 7-Niles-s						4.00
10-15-Templesmith-a						4.00
16-Final issue; Templesmith-a	1	3	4	6	8	10
...: The Ashley Wood Collection Vol. 1 (4/06, $24.95, TPB) r/#1-10; sketch & cover gallery						25.00

HELLSTORM: PRINCE OF LIES (See Ghost Rider #1 & Marvel Spotlight #12)
Marvel Comics: Apr, 1993 - No. 21, Dec, 1994 ($2.00)

1-($2.95)-Parchment-c w/red thermographic ink						5.00
2-21: 14-Bound-in trading card sheet. 18-P. Craig Russell-c						4.00

HELLSTORM: SON OF SATAN
Marvel Comics (MAX): Dec, 2006 - No. 5, Apr, 2007 ($3.99, limited series)

1-5-Suydam-c/Irvine-s/Braun & Janson-a						4.00
... - Equinox TPB (2007, $17.99) r/#1-5; interviews with the creators						18.00

HELLSTROM: MARVEL TALES
Marvel Comics: Jan, 2021 ($7.99, one-shot)

1-Reprints notable apps. in Ghost Rider #1, Son of Satan #1, Marvel Fanfare #59 and Hellstrom, Prince of Lies #1; Ralph Macchio intro.						8.00

HELL TO PAY
Image Comics: Nov, 2022 - No. 6, Jun, 2023 ($3.99)

1-6-Soule-s/Sliney-a						4.00

HELMET OF FATE, THE (Series of one-shots following Doctor Fate's helmet)
DC Comics: Mar, 2007 - May 2007 ($2.99, one-shots)

...: Black Alice (5/07) Simone-s/Rouleau-a						3.00
...: Detective Chimp (3/07) Willingham-s/McManus-a/Bolland-c						3.00
...: Ibis the Invincible (3/07) Williams-s/Winslade-a; the Ibistick returns						3.00
...: Sargon the Sorcerer (4/07) Niles-s/Scott Hampton-s; debut new Sargon						3.00
...: Zauriel (4/07) Gerber-s/Snejbjerg-a/Kaluta-c; leads into new Doctor Fate series						3.00
TPB (2007, $14.99) r/one-shots						15.00

HELM GREYCASTLE
Image Comics (Top Cow): Apr, 2021 - No. 4, Sept, 2021 ($3.99, limited series)

1-4-Barajas-s/Handoko-a; bonus Role Playing Game pages in each						4.00

HELP US! GREAT WARRIOR
BOOM! Studios (BOOM! Box): Feb, 2015 - No. 6, Jul, 2015 ($3.99)

1-6-Madeleine Flores-s/a						4.00

HE-MAN (See Masters Of The Universe)

HE-MAN (Also see Tops In Adventure)
Ziff-Davis Publ. Co. (Approved Comics): Fall, 1952

1-Kinstler painted-c; Powell-a	21	42	63	124	202	280

HE-MAN
Toby Press: May, 1954 - No. 2, July, 1954 (Painted-c by B. Safran)

1-Gorilla-c	20	40	60	114	182	250
2-Shark-c	18	36	54	105	165	225

HE-MAN AND THE MASTERS OF THE UNIVERSE
DC Comics: Sept, 2012 - No. 6, Mar, 2013 ($2.99)

1-James Robinson-s/Philip Tan-a/c; Skeletor app.	2	4	6	8	10	12
2-6: 5-Adam gets the sword						5.00

HE-MAN AND THE MASTERS OF THE UNIVERSE
DC Comics: Jun, 2013 - No. 19, Jan, 2015 ($2.99)

1-Giffen-s/Mhan-a/Benes-c	1	3	4	6	8	10
2-12,15-17: 7,8-Abnett-s/Kayanan-a						5.00
13,14-Origin of She-Ra begins	3	6	9	14	20	25
18-Full app. of She-Ra	4	8	12	27	44	60
19-Origin of Skeletor	3	6	9	16	23	30

Hellions #15 © MAR

Hellstrom: Marvel Tales #1 © MAR

Heralds #4 © MAR

	GD 2.0	VG 4.0	FN 6.0	VF 8.0	VF/NM 9.0	NM- 9.2		GD 2.0	VG 4.0	FN 6.0	VF 8.0	VF/NM 9.0	NM- 9.2

HE-MAN AND THE MASTERS OF THE MULTIVERSE
DC Comics: Jan, 2020 - No. 6, Jul, 2020 ($3.99, limited series)
1-6: 1-3-Seeley-s/Fraga-a; He-Man of Hellskull app. 4-6-Derenick-a   4.00

HE-MAN: THE ETERNITY WAR
DC Comics: Feb, 2015 - No. 15, Apr, 2016 ($2.99)

1-Abnett-s/Mhan-a; Hordak invades; origin of Grayskull	1	3	4	6	8	10
2-15						3.00

HE-MAN / THUNDERCATS
DC Comics: Dec, 2016 - No. 6, May, 2017 ($3.99, limited series)

1-Freddie Williams II-a; Mumm-Ra & Skeletor app.	3	6	9	16	23	30
2-6						5.00

HENNESSEY (TV)
Dell Publishing Co.: No. 1200, Aug-Oct, 1961 - No. 1280, Mar-May, 1962

Four Color 1200-Gil Kane-a, photo-c	8	16	24	52	99	145
Four Color 1280-Photo-c	6	12	18	42	79	115

HENRY (Also see Little Annie Rooney)
David McKay Publications: 1935 (52 pgs.) (Daily B&W strip reprints)(10"x10" cardboard-c)

1-By Carl Anderson	45	90	135	284	480	675

HENRY (See King Comics & Magic Comics)
Dell Publishing Co.: No. 122, Oct, 1946 - No. 65, Apr-June, 1961

Four Color 122-All new stories begin	16	32	48	110	243	375
Four Color 155 (7/47), 1 (1-3/48)-All new stories	10	20	30	70	150	230
2	6	12	18	40	73	105
3-10	5	10	15	34	60	85
11-20: 20-Infinity-c	5	10	15	30	50	70
21-30	4	8	12	25	40	55
31-40	3	6	9	21	33	45
41-65	3	6	9	17	26	35

HENRY (See Giant Comic Album and March of Comics No. 43, 58, 84, 101, 112, 129, 147, 162, 178, 189)

HENRY ALDRICH COMICS (TV)
Dell Publishing Co.: Aug-Sept, 1950 - No. 22, Sept-Nov, 1954

1-Part series written by John Stanley; Bill Williams-a	9	18	27	62	126	190
2	5	10	15	35	63	90
3-5	5	10	15	31	53	75
6-10	4	8	12	27	44	60
11-22	4	8	12	23	37	50

HENRY BREWSTER
Country Wide (M.F. Ent.): Feb, 1966 - V2#7, Sept, 1967 (All 25¢ Giants)

1	3	6	9	19	30	40
2-6(12/66), V2#7-Powell-a in most	3	6	9	14	20	25

HEPCATS
Antarctic Press: Nov, 1996 - No. 12 ($2.95, B&W)
0-12-Martin Wagner-c/s-a; 0-color   4.00
0-($9.95) CD Edition   10.00

HERALDS
Marvel Comics: Aug, 2010 - No. 5, Aug, 2010 ($2.99, weekly limited series)
1-5-Kathryn Immonen-s/Zonjic & Harren-a; She-Hulk, Hellcat, Emma Frost, Photon app.   3.00

HERBIE (See Forbidden Worlds #73,94,110,114,116 & Unknown Worlds #20)
American Comics Group: April-May, 1964 - No. 23, Feb, 1967 (All 12¢)

1-Whitney-c/a in most issues	19	38	57	131	291	450
2-4	8	16	24	56	108	160
5-Beatles parody (10 pgs.), Dean Martin, Frank Sinatra app. (10-11/64)						
	9	18	27	61	123	185
6,7,9,10	7	14	21	48	89	130
8-Origin & 1st app. The Fat Fury	9	18	27	58	114	170
11-23: 14-Nemesis & Magicman app. 17-r/2nd Herbie from Forbidden Worlds #94. 21-r/1st Herbie from F.W. #73	6	12	18	37	66	95
... Archives Volume One HC (Dark Horse, 8/08, $49.95, dust jacket) r/earliest apps. in Forbidden Worlds, Unknown Worlds, and Herbie #1-5; Scott Shaw intro.						50.00

HERBIE
Dark Horse Comics: Oct, 1992 - No. 12, 1993 ($2.50, limited series)
1-Whitney-r plus new-c/a in all; Byrne-c/a & scripts   5.00
2-6: 3-Bob Burden-c/a. 4-Art Adams-c/a   4.00

HERBIE GOES TO MONTE CARLO, HERBIE RIDES AGAIN (See Walt Disney Showcase No. 24, 41)

HERC (Hercules from the Avengers)
Marvel Comics: Jun, 2011 - No. 10, Jan, 2012 ($2.99)
1-6, (6.1), 7-10: 1-Pak & Van Lente-s; Hobgoblin app. 3-6-Fear Itself tie-in. 6.1-Grell-a 7,8-Spider-Island tie-in; Herc gets Spider-powers. 10-Elektra app.   3.00

HERCULES (See Hit Comics #1-21, Journey Into Mystery Annual, Marvel Graphic Novel #37, Marvel Premiere #26 & The Mighty...)

HERCULES (See Charlton Classics)
Charlton Comics: Oct, 1967 - No. 13, Sept, 1969; Dec, 1968

1-Thane of Bagarth begins; Glanzman-a in all	5	10	15	31	53	75
2-13: 1-5,7-10-Aparo-a. 8-(12¢-c)	4	8	12	23	37	50
4-Magazine format (low distribution)	8	16	24	54	102	150
8-Magazine format (low distribution)(12/68, 35¢, B&W); new Hercules story plus-r story/#1; Thane-r/#1-3	5	10	15	33	57	80
Modern Comics reprint 10('77), 11('78)						6.00

HERCULES (Prince of Power) (Also see The Champions)
Marvel Comics Group: V1#1, Sept, 1982 - V1#4, Dec, 1982; V2#1, Mar, 1984 - V2#4, Jun, 1984 (color, both limited series)
1-4, V2#1-4: Layton-c/a. 4-Death of Zeus.   4.00
NOTE: *Layton a-1, 2, 3p, 4p, V2#1-4; c-1-4, V2#1-4.*

HERCULES
Marvel Comics: Jun, 2005 - No. 5, Sept, 2005 ($2.99, limited series)
1-5-Texeira-a/c; Tieri-s. 4-Capt. America, Wolverine and New Avengers app.   3.00
...: New Labors of Hercules TPB (2005, $13.99) r/#1-5   14.00

HERCULES
Marvel Comics: Jan, 2016 - No. 6, Jun, 2016 ($3.99)
1-6: 1-Dan Abnett-s/Luke Ross-a; Gilgamesh app.   4.00

HERCULES: FALL OF AN AVENGER (Continues in Heroic Age: Prince of Power)
Marvel Comics: May, 2010 - No. 2, June, 2010 ($3.99, limited series)
1,2-Follows Hercules' demise in Incredible Hercules #141; Olivetti-c/a   4.00

HERCULES: HEART OF CHAOS
Marvel Comics: Aug, 1997 - No. 3, Oct, 1997 ($2.50, limited series)
1-3-DeFalco-s, Frenz-a   4.00

HERCULES: OFFICIAL COMICS MOVIE ADAPTION
Acclaim Books: 1997 ($4.50, digest size)
nn-Adaptation of the Disney animated movie   4.50

HERCULES: THE LEGENDARY JOURNEYS (TV)
Topps Comics: June, 1996 - No. 5, Oct, 1996 ($2.95)

1-2: 1-Golden-c						4.00
3-Xena-c/app.	2	4	6	8	10	12
3-Variant-c	2	4	6	11	16	20
4,5: Xena-c/app.						5.00

HERCULES: TWILIGHT OF A GOD
Marvel Comics: Aug, 2010 - No. 4, Nov, 2010 ($3.99, limited series)
1-4-Layton-s/a(i); Lim-a; Galactus app.   4.00

HERCULES UNBOUND
National Periodical Publications: Oct-Nov, 1975 - No. 12, Aug-Sept, 1977

1-García-López-a/Wood-i begins	2	4	6	12	16	20
2-12: 2-6-García-López-a. 7-Adams ad. 10-Atomic Knights x-over	1	3	4	6	8	10

NOTE: *Buckler c-7p. Layton inks-9, 10. Simonson a-7-10p, 11, 12; c-8p, 9-12. Wood a-1-8i; c-7i, 8i.*

HERCULES (...Unchained #1121)
Dell Publishing Co.: No. 1006, June-Aug, 1959 - No.1121, Aug, 1960

Four Color 1006-Buscema-a, photo-c	11	22	33	73	157	240
Four Color 1121-Crandall/Evans-a	9	18	27	62	126	190

HERCULIAN
Image Comics: Mar, 2011 ($4.99, oversized, one-shot)
1-Golden Age style superhero stories and humor pages; Erik Larsen-s/a/c   5.00

HERE COMES SANTA (See March of Comics No. 30, 213, 340)

HERE'S HOWIE COMICS
National Periodical Publications: Jan-Feb, 1952 - No. 18, Nov-Dec, 1954

1	58	116	174	371	636	900
2	24	48	72	142	234	325
3-5: 5-Howie in the Army issues begin (9-10/52)	18	36	54	105	165	190
6-10	15	30	45	99	140	190
11-18	15	30	45	86	133	180
Ashcan (1,2/51) not distributed to newsstands			(a FN copy sold for $836.50 in 2012)			

	GD 2.0	VG 4.0	FN 6.0	VF 8.0	VF/NM 9.0	NM- 9.2

HERETIC, THE
Dark Horse (Blanc Noir): Nov, 1996 - No. 4, Mar, 1997 ($2.95, lim. series)

1-4:-w/back-up story 4.00

HERITAGE OF THE DESERT (See Zane Grey, 4-Color 236)

HERMAN & KATNIP (see Harvey Comics Hits #60 & 62, Harvey Hits #14,25,31,41 & Paramount Animated Comics #1)

HERMANN
Aardvark-Vanaheim: Dec, 2020 ($4.00, B&W)

1-Cerebus figures with original Gustave Doré artwork; homage to Watchmen's Rorschach 4.00

HERMES VS. THE EYEBALL KID
Dark Horse Comics: Nov, 1994 - No. 3, Feb, 1995 ($2.95, B&W, limited series)

1-3: Eddie Campbell-c/a/scripts 4.00

H-E-R-O (Dial H For HERO)
DC Comics: Apr, 2003 - No. 22, Jan, 2005 ($2.50)

1-Will Pfeiffer-s/Kano-a/Van Fleet-c 3.50
2-22: 2-6-Kano-a. 7,8-Gleason-a. 12-14-Kirk-a. 15-22-Robby Reed app. 3.00
...: Double Feature (6/03, $4.95) r/#1&2 .... 5.00
...: Powers and Abilities (2003, $9.95) r/#1-6; intro. by Geoff Johns 10.00

HERO (Warrior of the Mystic Realms)
Marvel Comics: May, 1990 - No. 6, Oct, 1990 ($1.50, limited series)

1-6: 1-Portacio-i 4.00

HERO ALLIANCE, THE
Sirius Comics: Dec, 1985 - No. 2, Sept, 1986 (B&W)

1,2: 2-($1.50), Special Edition 1 (7/86, color) 4.00

HERO ALLIANCE
Wonder Color Comics: May, 1987 ($1.95)

1-Ron Lim-a 4.00

HERO ALLIANCE
Innovation Publishing: V2#1, Sept, 1989 - V2#17, Nov, 1991 ($1.95, 28 pgs.)

V2#1-17: 1,2-Ron Lim-a 4.00
Annual 1 (1990, $2.75, 36 pgs.)-Paul Smith-c/a 4.00
Special 1 (1992, $2.50, 32 pgs.)-Stuart Immonen-a (10 pgs.) 4.00

HERO ALLIANCE: END OF THE GOLDEN AGE
Innovation Publ.: July, 1989 - No. 3, Aug, 1989 ($1.75, bi-weekly lim. series)

1-3: Bart Sears & Ron Lim-c/a; reprints & new-a 4.00

HEROBEAR AND THE KID
Boom Entertainment (KaBOOM!)

... 2013 Annual 1 (10/13, $3.99) Halloween-themed story 4.00
... 2016 Fall Special 1 (10/16, $5.99) Saving Time: Part Two 6.00
... Special (6/13, $3.99) Mike Kunkel-s/a/c 4.00
...: The Inheritance (8/13 - No. 5, 12/13, $3.99) 1-5-Mike Kunkel-s/a/c; origin re-told 4.00

HERO COMICS (Hero Initiative benefit book)
IDW Publishing: 2009 - Present ($3.99)

1-Short story anthology by various incl. Colan, Chaykin; covers by Wagner & Campbell 4.00
2011-Covers by Campbell & Hughes; Gaiman-s/Kieth-a; Chew & Elephantmen app. 4.00
2012-Cover by Campbell; TMNT by Eastman; art by Heath, Sim, Kupperberg, & others 4.00
2014-Covers by Campbell & Kieth; Sable by Grell; art by Kieth, Goldberg & others 4.00
...: A Hero Initiative Benefit Book SC (5/16, $19.99) reprints from previous editions 20.00

HEROES
Marvel Comics: Dec, 2001 ($3.50, magazine-size, one-shot)

1-Pin-up tributes to the rescue workers of the Sept. 11 tragedy; art and text by various; cover by Alex Ross 6.00
1-2nd and 3rd printings 4.00

HEROES (Also see Shadow Cabinet & Static)
DC Comics (Milestone): May, 1996 - No. 6, Nov, 1996 ($2.50, limited series)

1-Intro Heroes (Iota, Donner, Blitzen, Starlight, Payback & Static) 6.00
2-6 .... 4.00

HEROES (Based on the NBC TV series)
DC Comics (WildStorm): 2007; 2009 ($29.99, hardcover with dustjacket)

Vol. 1 - Collects 34 installments of the online graphic novel; art by various; two covers by Jim Lee and Alex Ross; intro. by Masi Oka; Jeph Loeb interview 30.00
Vol. 2 - (2009) Collects 46 installments of the online graphic novel; art by various incl. Gaydos, Grummett, Gunnell, Odagawa; two covers by Tim Sale and Gene Ha 30.00

HER-OES
Marvel Comics: Jun, 2010 - No. 4, Sept, 2010 ($2.99, limited series)

1-4-Randolph/Rousseau-a; Wasp, She-Hulk, Namora as teenagers 3.00

HEROES AGAINST HUNGER
DC Comics: 1986 ($1.50; one-shot for famine relief)

1-Superman, Batman app.; Neal Adams-c(p); includes many artists work; Jeff Jones assist (2 pg.) on B. Smith-a; Kirby-a 6.00

HEROES ALL CATHOLIC ACTION ILLUSTRATED
Heroes All Co.: 1943 - V6#5, Mar 10, 1948 (paper covers)

	GD 2.0	VG 4.0	FN 6.0	VF 8.0	VF/NM 9.0	NM- 9.2
V1#1-(16 pgs., 8x11")	24	48	72	142	234	325
V1#2-(16 pgs., 8x11")	19	38	57	111	176	240
V2#1(1/44)-3(3/44)-(16 pgs., 8x11")	15	30	45	94	147	200
V3#1(1/45)-10(12/45)-(16 pgs., 8x11")	15	30	45	85	130	175
V4#1-35 (12/20/46)-(16 pgs.)	14	28	42	80	115	150
V5#1(1/10/47)-8(2/28/47)-(16 pgs.), V5#9(3/7/47)-20(11/25/47)-(32 pgs.),						
V6#1(1/10/48)-5(3/10/48)-(32 pgs.)	.12	24	36	69	97	125

HEROES ANONYMOUS
Bongo Comics: 2003 - No. 6, 2004 ($2.99, limited series)

1-6-($2.99)-Bill Morrison-c. 2-Guerra-a. 3-Pepoy-a 3.00

HEROES AT HOME
Marvel Comics: 2020 ($9.99, 5" x 5", one-shot)

1-Zeb Wells-s/Gurihiru-a; humor strips of Marvel heroes quarantined at home 10.00

HEROES FOR HIRE
Marvel Comics: July, 1997 - No. 19, Jan, 1999 ($2.99/$1.99)

1-($2.99)-Wraparound cover 6.00
2-19: 2-Variant cover. 9-Thunderbolts app. 9-Punisher-c/app. 10,11-Deadpool-c/app. 18,19-Wolverine-c/app. 4.00
.../Quicksilver '98 Annual ($2.99) Siege of Wundagore pt.5 .... 5.00

HEROES FOR HIRE
Marvel Comics: Oct, 2006 - No. 15, Dec, 2007 ($2.99)

1-5-Tucci-a/c; Black Cat, Shang-Chi, Tarantula, Humbug & Daughters of the Dragon app. 3.00
6-15: 6-8-Sparacio-c. 9,10-Golden-c. 11-13-World War Hulk x-over. 13-Takeda-c 3.00
... Vol. 1: Civil War (2007, $13.99) r/#1-5 .... 14.00
... Vol. 2: Ahead of the Curve (2007, $13.99) r/#6-10 .... 14.00
... Vol. 3: World War Hulk (2008, $13.99) r/#11-15 .... 14.00

HEROES FOR HIRE
Marvel Comics: Feb, 2011 - No. 12, Nov, 2011 ($3.99/$2.99)

1-($3.99) Abnett & Lanning/Walker-a; back-up history of the various teams 4.00
2-12-($2.99) 2-Silver Sable & Ghost Rider app. 5-Punisher app. 9-11-Fear Itself tie-in 3.00

HEROES FOR HOPE STARRING THE X-MEN
Marvel Comics Group: Dec, 1985 ($1.50, one-shot, 52 pgs., proceeds donated to famine relief)

	GD 2.0	VG 4.0	FN 6.0	VF 8.0	VF/NM 9.0	NM- 9.2
1-Stephen King scripts; Byrne, Miller, Corben-a; Wrightson/J. Jones-a (3 pgs.); Art Adams-c; Starlin back-c	1	3	4	6	8	10

HEROES: GODSEND (Based on the NBC TV series)(Prelude to the 2015 revival)
Titan Comics: Apr, 2016 - No. 5, Aug, 2016 ($3.99, limited series)

1-5: 1-Origin of Farah Nazan; Roy Allan Martinez-a; multiple covers on each 4.00

HEROES, INC. PRESENTS CANNON
Wally Wood/CPL/Gang Publ.: 1969 - No. 2, 1976 (Sold at Army PXs)

	GD 2.0	VG 4.0	FN 6.0	VF 8.0	VF/NM 9.0	NM- 9.2
nn-Ditko, Wood-a; Wood-c; Reese-a(p)	3	6	9	14	20	25
2-Wood-c; Ditko, Byrne, Wood-a; 8-1/2x10-1/2"; B&W; $2.00	3	6	9	19	30	40

NOTE: *First issue not distributed by publisher; 1,800 copies were stored and 900 copies were stolen from warehouse. Many copies have surfaced in recent years.*

HEROES IN CRISIS
DC Comics: Nov, 2018 - No. 9, Jul, 2019 ($3.99, limited series)

1-9: 1-Tom King-s/Clay Mann-a; murder of Wally West, Arsenal and others 4.00

HEROES OF THE WILD FRONTIER (Formerly Baffling Mysteries)
Ace Periodicals: No. 27, Jan, 1956 - No. 2, Apr, 1956

	GD 2.0	VG 4.0	FN 6.0	VF 8.0	VF/NM 9.0	NM- 9.2
27(#1),2-Davy Crockett, Daniel Boone, Buffalo Bill	7	14	21	35	43	50

HEROES REBORN (one-shots)
Marvel Comics: Jan, 2000 ($1.99)

...: Ashema; ...: Doom; ...: Doomsday; ...: Masters of Evil; ...: Rebel; ...: Remnants; ...: Young Allies 3.00

HEROES REBORN
Marvel Comics: Jul, 2021 - No. 7, Aug, 2021 ($5.99/$4.99, weekly limited series)

1-($5.99) Squadron Supreme replaces the Avengers; Blade app.; Aaron-s/McGuinness-a 6.00
2-7-($4.99) 2-Captain America returns. 4-Stokoe-a. 7-Leads into Heroes Return #1 .... 5.00
...: American Knights 1 (8/21, $4.99) Spotlight on Luke Cage & Nighthawk; Grist-s/Allen-a 5.00
...: Hyperion & The Imperial Guard 1 (7/21, $4.99) Gady-s/Bandini-a 5.00
...: Magneto & The Mutant Force 1 (7/21, $4.99) Orlando-s/Chang-a 5.00
...: Marvel Double Action 1 (8/21, $4.99) Nighthawk & Falcon in '70s style team-up; Jurgens-a 5.00
...: Night-Gwen 1 (8/21, $4.99) Ayala-s/Karami-a; Misty Knight app. 5.00
...: Peter Parker, The Amazing Shutterbug 1 (7/21, $4.99) Lim & De Latorre-a 5.00
...: Siege Society 1 (7/21, $4.99) Ziglar-s/Medina-a; Hawkeye, Black Widow & others 5.00
...: Weapon X & Final Flight 1 (8/21, $4.99) Wolverine & Sasquatch app.; Boschi-a 5.00
...: Young Squadron 1 (7/21, $4.99) Kid Spectrum, Girl Power, Falcon & Deadpool app. 5.00

HEROES REBORN: THE RETURN (Also see Avengers, Fantastic Four, Iron Man & Captain America titles for issues and TPBs)
Marvel Comics: Dec, 1997 - No. 4, Dec, 1997 ($2.50, weekly mini-series)

1-4-Avengers, Fantastic Four, Iron Man & Captain America rejoin regular Marvel Universe; Peter David-s/Larocca-c/a 4.00
1-4-Variant-c for each 6.00

	GD 2.0	VG 4.0	FN 6.0	VF 8.0	VF/NM 9.0	NM- 9.2
Wizard 1/2	1	2	3	5	7	9

Return of the Heroes TPB ('98, $14.95) r/#1-4 .... 15.00

HEROES RETURN
Marvel Comics: Aug, 2021 ($5.99, conclusion to Heroes Reborn)

1-($5.99) Squadron Supreme vs. the Avengers & Blade; Aaron-s/McGuinness-a 6.00

HEROES: VENGEANCE (Based on the NBC TV series)(Prelude to the 2015 revival)
Titan Comics: Nov, 2015 - No. 5, Mar, 2016 ($3.99, limited series)

1-5: 1-Origin of El Vengador; Rubine-a; multiple covers on each 4.00

HERO FOR HIRE (Power Man No. 17 on; also see Cage)
Marvel Comics Group: June, 1972 - No. 16, Dec, 1973

	GD 2.0	VG 4.0	FN 6.0	VF 8.0	VF/NM 9.0	NM- 9.2
1-Origin & 1st app. Luke Cage; Tuska-a(p)	71	142	213	588	1284	2000
2-Tuska-a(p); 1st app. Claire Temple	7	14	21	48	89	130
3,4: 3-1st app. Mace. 4-1st app. Phil Fox of the Bugle	5	10	15	33	57	80
5-1st app. Black Mariah	5	10	15	35	63	90
6-10: 8,9-Dr. Doom app. 9-F.F. app. 10-1st app. Mr. Death	4	8	12	25	40	55
11-16: 14-Origin retold. 15-Everett Sub-Mariner-r('53). 16-Origin Stiletto; death of Rackham	3	6	9	20	31	42

HERO HOTLINE (1st app. in Action Comics Weekly #637)
DC Comics: April, 1989 - No. 6, Sept, 1989 ($1.75, limited series)

1-6: Super-hero humor; Schaffenberger-i 4.00

HEROIC ADVENTURES (See Adventures)

HEROIC AGE
Marvel Comics: Nov, 2010 ($3.99, limited series)

Her-oes #4 © MAR

Heroes For Hire (2007 series) #8 © MAR

Hex Wives #6 © Ben Blacker

	GD	VG	FN	VF	VF/NM	NM-
	2.0	4.0	6.0	8.0	9.0	9.2

... Heroes 1 (11/10, $3.99) profile of heroes, bios, pros, cons, "power grid"; Raney-c — 4.00
... Villains 1 (1/11, $3.99) profile of villains, bios, pros, cons, "power grid"; Jae Lee-c — 4.00
... X-Men 1 (2/11, $3.99) profile of members in Steve Rogers journal entries.; Jae Lee-c — 4.00

HEROIC AGE: PRINCE OF POWER (Continued from Hercules: Fall of an Avenger)
Marvel Comics: Jul, 2010 - No. 4, Oct, 2010 ($3.99, limited series)
1-4-Van Lente & Pak-s; Thor app.; leads into Chaos War #1 — 4.00

HEROIC COMICS (Reg'lar Fellers...#1-15; New Heroic #41 on)
Eastern Color Printing Co./Famous Funnies (Funnies, Inc. No. 1):
Aug, 1940 - No. 97, June, 1955

1-Hydroman (origin) by Bill Everett, The Purple Zombie (origin) & Mann of India by Tarpe Mills begins (all 1st apps.)	245	490	735	1568	2684	3800
2	103	206	309	659	1130	1600
3,4	57	114	171	362	619	875
5,6	50	100	150	315	533	750
7-Origin & 1st app. Man O'Metal (1 pg.)	52	104	156	328	552	775
8-10: 10-Lingerie panels	39	78	117	234	385	535
11,13	37	74	111	222	361	500
12-Music Master (origin/1st app.) begins by Everett, ends No. 31; last Purple Zombie & Mann of India	42	84	126	265	445	625
14,15-Hydroman x-over in Rainbow Boy. 14-Origin & 1st app. Rainbow Boy (super hero). 15-1st app. Downbeat	39	78	117	231	378	525
16-20: 16-New logo. 17-Rainbow Boy x-over in Hydroman. 19-Rainbow Boy x-over in Hydroman & vice versa	26	52	78	154	252	350
21-30:25-Rainbow Boy x-over in Hydroman. 28-Last Man O'Metal. 29-Last Hydroman	20	40	60	114	182	250
31,34,38	9	18	27	50	65	80
32,36,37-Toth-a (3-4 pgs. each)	10	20	30	58	76	95
33,35-Toth-a (8 & 9 pgs.)	10	20	30	58	79	100
39-42-Toth, Ingels-a	10	20	30	58	79	100
43,46,47,49-Toth-a (2-4 pgs.). 47-Ingels-a	10	20	30	54	72	90
44,45,50-Toth-a (6-9 pgs.)	10	20	30	56	76	95
48,53,54	9	18	27	47	61	75
51-Williamson-a	10	20	30	58	79	100
52-Williamson-a (3 pg. story)	9	18	27	50	65	80
55-Toth-a	10	20	30	54	72	90
56-60: 60-Everett-a	9	18	27	50	65	80
61-Everett-a	9	18	27	47	61	75
62,64-Everett-c/a	10	20	30	54	72	90
63-Everett-c	9	18	27	52	69	85
65-Williamson/Frazetta-a; Evans-a (2 pgs.)	13	26	39	72	101	130
66,75,94-Frazetta-a (2 pgs. each)	9	18	27	52	69	85
67,73-Frazetta-a (4 pgs. each)	11	22	33	62	86	110
68,74,76-80,84,85,88-93,95-97: 95-Last pre-code	9	18	27	47	61	75
69,72-Frazetta-a (6 & 8 pgs. each); 1st (?) app. Frazetta Red Cross ad	14	28	42	76	108	140
70,71,86,87-Frazetta, 3-4 pgs. each; 1 pg. ad by Frazetta in #70	11	22	33	60	83	105
81,82-Frazetta art (1 pg. each): 81-1st (?) app. Frazetta Boy Scout ad (tied w/ Buster Crabbe #9	9	18	27	52	69	85
83-Frazetta-a (1/2 pg.)	9	18	27	52	69	85

NOTE: **Evans** a-64, 65. **Everett** a-(Hydroman-c/a-No. 1-9), 44, 60-64; c-1-9, 62-64. **Harvey Fuller** c-28-35. **Sid Greene** a-38-43, 46. **Guardineer** a-42(3), 43, 44, 45(2), 49(3), 50, 60, 61(2), 65, 67(2) 70-72. **Ingels** c-41. **Kiefer** a-46, 48; c-19-22, 24, 44, 46, 48, 51-53, 65, 67-69, 71-74, 76, 77, 79, 80, 82, 85, 86, 88, 89, 94, 95. **Mort Lawrence** a-45. **Tarpe Mills** a-2(2), 3(2), 10. **Ed Moore** a-49, 52-54, 56-63, 65-69, 72-74, 76, 77. **H.G. Peter** a-58-74, 76, 77, 87. **Paul Reinman** a-49. **Rico** a-31. *Captain Tootsie* by **Beck**-31, 32. Painted-c #16 on. *Hydroman* c-1-11. *Music Master* c-12, 13, 15. *Rainbow Boy* c-14.

HERO INITIATIVE: MIKE WIERINGO BOOK (Also see Hero Comics)
Marvel Comics: Aug, 2008 ($4.99)
1-The "What If" Fantastic Four story with Wieringo-a (7 pgs.) finished by other artists after his passing; art by Davis, Immonen, Ramos, Kitson and others; written tributes — 5.00

HERO TRADE, THE (1st Bad Idea title)
Bad Idea: Sept, 2020 ($3.00, B&W, one-shot)

1-Matt Kindt-s/David Lapham-a	10	20	30	64	132	200

HERO TRADE: A BRIEF CASE (Bonus mailed with only 50 orders of Hero Trade)
Bad Idea: Feb, 2021 (limited edition of 50, B&W, one-shot)

1-Kindt-s/Lapham-a; r/story pages from Eniac #1	38	76	114	285	641	1000

HERO TRADE: PASSIVE / AGGRESSIVE
Bad Idea: Aug, 2021 ($5.99, same cover with 2 different lead stories)
Aggressive version-(noted on inside front cover) Kindt-s/Lapham-a; distributed to Eastern U.S.

	1	3	4	6	8	10

Passive version-(noted on inside front cover) Kindt-s/Lapham-a; distributed to Western U.S. (more rare than the Aggressive version)

	2	4	6	9	12	15

HERO WORSHIP
Avatar Press: Jun, 2012 - No. 6, Nov, 2012 ($3.99)
1-6: 1-Zak Penn & Scott Murphy-s/Michael DiPascale-a; 2 covers — 4.00

HERO ZERO (Also see Comics' Greatest World & Godzilla Versus Hero Zero)
Dark Horse Comics: Sept, 1994 ($2.50)
0 — 4.00

HE WHO FIGHTS WITH MONSTERS
Ablaze Publishing: 2021 - No. 5, 2022 ($3.99, limited series)
1-5-Francesco Artibani-s/Werther Dell'Edra-a; multiple covers on each — 4.00

HEX (Replaces Jonah Hex)
DC Comics: Sept, 1985 - No. 18, Feb, 1987 (Story cont'd from Jonah Hex # 92)
1-Hex in post-atomic war world — 6.00
2-10,14-18: 6-Origin Stiletta — 4.00
11-13: All contain future Batman storyline. 13-Intro The Dogs of War (origin #15) — 6.00
NOTE: **Giffen** a(p)-15-18; c(p)-15,17,18. **Texeira** a-1, 2p, 3p, 5-7p, 9p, 11-14p; c(p)-1, 2, 4-7, 12.

HEXBREAKER (See First Comics Graphic Novel #15)

HEXED
BOOM! Studios: Aug, 2014 - No. 12, Aug, 2015 ($3.99)
1-12: 1-Michael Alan Nelson-s/Dan Mora-a; 3 covers — 4.00

HEXWARE
Image Comics: Dec, 2022 - No. 6, May, 2023 ($3.99)
1-6-Tim Seeley-s/Zulema Scotto Lavina-a — 4.00

HEX WIVES
DC Comics (Vertigo): Dec, 2018 - No. 6, May, 2019 ($3.99)
1-6: 1-Ben Blacker-s/Mirka Andolfo/Joëlle Jones-a. 5-Lotay-c — 4.00

HEY KIDS! COMICS!
Image Comics: Aug, 2018 - No. 5, Dec, 2018 ($3.99, limited series)
1-5-Howard Chaykin-s/a — 4.00

HEY KIDS! COMICS! VOL. 2, PROPHETS & LOSS
Image Comics: May, 2021 - No. 6, Oct, 2021 ($3.99, limited series)
1-6-Howard Chaykin-s/a — 4.00

HEY KIDS! COMICS! VOL. 3
Image Comics: Apr, 2023 - No. 6, Sept, 2023 ($3.99, limited series)
1-6-Howard Chaykin-s/a — 4.00

HEY THERE, IT'S YOGI BEAR (See Movie Comics)

HI-ADVENTURE HEROES (TV)
Gold Key: May, 1969 - No. 2, Aug, 1969 (Hanna-Barbera)

1-Three Musketeers, Gulliver, Arabian Knights	5	10	15	30	50	70
2-Three Musketeers, Micro-Venture, Arabian Knights	4	8	12	27	44	60

HI AND LOIS
Dell Publishing Co.: No. 683, Mar, 1956 - No. 955, Nov, 1958

Four Color 683 (#1)	6	12	18	42	79	115
Four Color 774(3/57),955	5	10	15	30	50	70

HI AND LOIS
Charlton Comics: Nov, 1969 - No. 11, July, 1971

1	3	6	9	14	20	25
2-11	2	4	6	9	12	15

HICKORY (See All Humor Comics)
Quality Comics Group: Oct, 1949 - No. 6, Aug, 1950

1-Sahl-c/a in all; Feldstein?-a	34	68	102	204	332	460
2	22	44	66	128	209	290
3-6-Good Girl covers	58	116	174	371	636	900

HIDDEN CREW, THE (See The United States Air Force Presents:...)

HIDDEN SOCIETY
Dark Horse Comics: Feb, 2020 - No. 4, Oct, 2020 ($3.99, limited series)
1-4-Rafael Scavone-s/Rafael Albuquerque-a; two covers — 4.00

HIDE-OUT (See Zane Grey, Four Color No. 346)

HIDING PLACE, THE
Spire Christian Comics (Fleming H. Revell Co.): 1973 (39¢/49¢)

nn	3	6	9	17	26	35

HI-FI FIGHT CLUB (Title changes to Heavy Vinyl for #4)
Boom Entertainment (BOOM! Box): Aug, 2017 - No. 3, Oct, 2017 ($3.99)

	GD 2.0	VG 4.0	FN 6.0	VF 8.0	VF/NM 9.0	NM- 9.2

1-3-Carly Usdin-s/Nina Vakueva-a ... 4.00

HIGH ADVENTURE
Red Top(Decker) Comics (Farrell): Oct, 1957

	GD	VG	FN	VF	VF/NM	NM-
1-Krigstein-r from Explorer Joe (re-issue on-c)	6	12	18	31	38	45

HIGH ADVENTURE (TV)
Dell Publishing Co.: No. 949, Nov, 1958 - No. 1001, Aug-Oct, 1959 (Lowell Thomas)

	GD	VG	FN	VF	VF/NM	NM-
Four Color 949 (#1)-Photo-c	6	12	18	42	79	115
Four Color 1001-Lowell Thomas'...(#2)	5	10	15	34	60	85

HIGH CHAPARRAL (TV)
Gold Key: Aug, 1968 (Photo-c)

	GD	VG	FN	VF	VF/NM	NM-
1 (10226-808)-Tufts-a	6	12	18	38	69	100

HIGH HEAVEN
Ahoy Comics: 2018 - No. 5, 2019 ($3.99)

1-5-Tom Peyer-s/Greg Scott-a; back-up w/Giarusso-a ... 4.00

HIGHLANDER
Dynamite Entertainment: No. 0, 2006 - No. 12, 2007 (25¢/$2.99)

0-(25¢-c) Takes place after the first movie; photo-c and Dell'Otto painted-c ... 3.00
1-12: 1-($2.99) Three covers; Moder-a/Jerwa & Oeming-s. 2-Three covers ... 3.00
... Origins: The Kurgan 1,2 (2009 - No. 2, 2009, $4.99) Three covers; Rafael-a ... 5.00
...: Way of the Sword (2007 - No. 4, 2008, $3.50) Two interlocking covers for each ... 3.50

HIGHLANDER: THE AMERICAN DREAM
IDW Publishing: Feb, 2017 - No. 5, Jun, 2017 ($3.99)

1-5-Brian Ruckley-s/Andrea Mutti-a; multiple covers; MacLeod in 1985 New York ... 4.00

HIGH LEVEL
DC Comics (Vertigo): Apr, 2019 - No. 6, Nov, 2019 ($3.99)

1-6-Sheridan-s/Bagenda-a ... 4.00

HIGH ROADS
DC Comics (Cliffhanger): June, 2002 - No. 6, Nov, 2002 ($2.95, limited series)

1-6-Leinil Yu-c/a; Lobdell-s ... 3.00
TPB (2003, $14.95) r/#1-6; sketch pages ... 15.00

HIGH SCHOOL CONFIDENTIAL DIARY (Confidential Diary #12 on)
Charlton Comics: June, 1960 - No. 11, Mar, 1962

	GD	VG	FN	VF	VF/NM	NM-
1	5	10	15	34	60	85
2-11	3	6	9	19	30	40

HIGHWAYMEN
DC Comics (WildStorm): Aug, 2007 - No. 5, Dec, 2007 ($2.99)

1-5-Bernardin & Freeman-s/Garbett-a ... 3.00
TPB (2008, $17.99) r/#1-5 ... 18.00

HIGH WAYS, THE
IDW Publishing: Dec, 2012 - No. 4, Apr, 2013 ($3.99, limited series)

1-4-John Byrne-s/a/c ... 4.00

HI HI PUFFY AMIYUMI (Based on Cartoon Network animated series)
DC Comics: Apr, 2006 - No. 3, June, 2006 ($2.25, limited series)

1-3-Phil Moy-a ... 3.00

HI-HO COMICS
Four Star Publications: nd (2/46?) - No. 3, 1946

	GD	VG	FN	VF	VF/NM	NM-
1-Funny Animal; L.B. Cole-c	45	90	135	284	480	675
2-3: 2-L. B. Cole-c	33	66	99	194	317	440

HI-JINX (Teen-age Animal Funnies)
La Salle Publ. Co./B&I Publ. Co. (American Comics Group)/Creston: 1945; July-Aug, 1947 - No. 7, July-Aug, 1948

	GD	VG	FN	VF	VF/NM	NM-
nn-(© 1945, 25 cents, 132 Pgs.)(La Salle)	37	74	111	222	361	500
1-Teen-age, funny animal	25	50	75	150	245	340
2,3	15	30	45	90	140	190
4-7-Milt Gross. 4-X-Mas-c	23	46	69	136	223	310

HI-LITE COMICS
E. R. Ross Publishing Co.: Fall, 1945

	GD	VG	FN	VF	VF/NM	NM-
1-Miss Shady	28	56	84	165	270	375

HILLBILLY
Albatross Funnybooks: 2016 - No. 12, 2018 ($3.99)

1-12-Eric Powell-s/c; Powell-a in #1-7. 2-The Buzzard app. 5-Back-up with Mannion-a. 8-Di Meo-a ... 4.00

HILLBILLY (Red Eyed Witchery From Beyond on cover)
Albatross Funnybooks: 2019 - No. 4, 2019 ($3.99)

1-4-Eric Powell-s/c; Simone Di Meo-a ... 4.00

HILLBILLY COMICS
Charlton Comics: Aug, 1955 - No. 4, July, 1956 (Satire)

	GD	VG	FN	VF	VF/NM	NM-
1-By Art Gates	17	34	51	98	154	210
2-4	13	26	39	74	105	135

HILL HOUSE COMICS 2019 SAMPLER
DC Comics (Hill House Comics): Oct, 2019 (no price, promotional giveaway)

nn-Previews Basketful of Heads, The Dollhouse Family, and The Low, Low Woods ... 3.00

HILLY ROSE'S SPACE ADVENTURES
Astro Comics: May, 1995 - No. 9 ($2.95, B&W)

	GD	VG	FN	VF	VF/NM	NM-
1	1	2	3	5	7	9
2-9						5.00
Trade Paperback (1996, $12.95)-r/#1-5						13.00

HINTERKIND
DC Comics (Vertigo): Dec, 2013 - No. 18, Jul, 2015 ($2.99)

1-18: 1-Ian Edginton-s/Francesco Trifogli-a/Greg Tocchini-a ... 3.00

HIP FLASK (Also see Elephantmen)
Active Images/Image Comics

...: Ouroborous (12/12, $4.99) Starkings-s/Ladronn-a ... 5.00
... Unnatural Selection (9/02, $2.99) Casey & Starkings-s/Ladronn-a; var.-c by Madureira, Campbell, Churchill ... 3.00

HIP-IT-TY HOP (See March of Comics No. 15)

HIRE, THE (BMWfilms.com's...)
Dark Horse Comics: July, 2004 - No. 6 ($2.99)

1-4: 1-Matt Wagner-s/Wagner & Velasco-a. 2-Bruce Campbell-s/Plunkett-a. 3-Waid-s ... 3.00
TPB (4/06, $17.95) r/#1-4 ... 18.00

HI-SCHOOL ROMANCE (...Romances No. 41 on)
Harvey Publ./True Love(Home Comics): Oct, 1949 - No. 5, June, 1950; No. 6, Dec, 1950 - No. 73, Mar, 1958; No. 74, Sept, 1958 - No. 75, Nov, 1958

	GD	VG	FN	VF	VF/NM	NM-
1-Photo-c	20	40	60	117	189	260
2-Photo-c	13	26	39	74	105	135
3-9: 3-5-Photo-c	10	20	30	58	79	100
10-Rape story	18	36	54	107	169	230
11-20	9	18	27	50	65	80
21-31	8	16	24	42	54	65
32- "Unholy passion" story	12	24	36	69	97	125
33-36: 36-Last pre-code (2/55)	8	16	24	40	50	60
37-53,59-72,74,75	7	14	21	35	43	50
54-58,73-Kirby-a	8	16	24	42	54	65

HI-SCHOOL ROMANCE DATE BOOK
Harvey Publications: Nov, 1962 - No. 3, Mar, 1963 (25¢ Giants)

	GD	VG	FN	VF	VF/NM	NM-
1-Powell, Baker-a	7	14	21	44	82	120
2,3	4	8	12	23	37	50

HIS NAME IS SAVAGE (Magazine format)
Adventure House Press: June, 1968 (35¢, 52 pgs.)

	GD	VG	FN	VF	VF/NM	NM-
1-Gil Kane-a	5	10	15	34	60	85

HI-SPOT COMICS (Red Ryder No. 1 & No. 3 on)
Hawley Publications: No. 2, Nov, 1940

	GD	VG	FN	VF	VF/NM	NM-
2-David Innes of Pellucidar; art by J. C. Burroughs; written by Edgar Rice Burroughs	300	600	900	2070	3635	5200

HISTORY OF THE DC UNIVERSE (Also see Crisis on Infinite Earths)
DC Comics: Sept, 1986 - No. 2, Nov, 1986 ($2.95, limited series)

	GD	VG	FN	VF	VF/NM	NM-
1,2: 1-Perez-c/a						5.00
Limited Edition hardcover	4	8	12	26	41	55
Softcover (2002, $9.95) new Alex Ross wraparound-c						13.00
Softcover (12.99) Alex Ross wraparound-c						13.00

HISTORY OF THE MARVEL UNIVERSE
Marvel Comics: Sept, 2019 - No. 6, Feb, 2020 ($4.99, limited series)

1-6-Mark Waid-s/Javier Rodriguez-a chronological Marvel history & bonus annotations ... 5.00

HISTORY OF VIOLENCE, A (Inspired the 2005 movie)
DC Comics (Paradox Press) 1997 ($9.95, B&W graphic novel)

	GD	VG	FN	VF	VF/NM	NM-
nn-Paperback ($9.95) John Wagner-s/Vince Locke-a	3	6	9	14	20	25

HIT
BOOM! Studios: Sept, 2013 - No. 4, Dec, 2013 ($3.99, limited series)

1-4-Bryce Carlson-s/Vanesa R. Del Ray-a/Ryan Sook-c ... 4.00
...: 1957 (3/15 - No. 4, 7/15, $3.99) 1-4-Bryce Carlson-s/Vanesa R. Del Ray-a/c ... 4.00

HITCHHIKERS GUIDE TO THE GALAXY (See Life, the Universe and Everything & Restaurant at the End of the Universe)
DC Comics: 1993 - No. 3, 1993 ($4.95, limited series)

1-3: Adaptation of Douglas Adams book ... 5.00
TPB (1997, $14.95) r/#1-3 ... 15.00

HIT COMICS
Quality Comics Group: July, 1940 - No. 65, July, 1950

	GD	VG	FN	VF	VF/NM	NM-
1-Origin/1st app. Neon, the Unknown & Hercules; intro. The Red Bee; Bob & Swab, Blaze Barton, the Strange Twins, X-5 Super Agent, Casey Jones & Jack & Jill (ends #7) begin	1000	2000	3000	7600	13,800	20,000
2-The Old Witch begins, ends #14 (scarce)	389	778	1167	2723	4762	6800
3-Casey Jones ends; transvestism story "Jack & Jill"	365	730	1095	2555	4478	6400
4-Super Agent (ends #17); Betty Bates (ends #65) begin; X-5 ends	320	640	960	2240	3920	5600
5-Classic Lou Fine cover	1250	2500	3750	9500	17,250	25,000
6,8-10: 10-Old Witch by Crandall (4 pgs.); 1st work in comics (4/41)	295	590	885	1888	3244	4600
7-Skull bondage-c	486	972	1458	3550	6275	9000
11-Classic cover	383	766	1149	2681	4691	6700
12-16: 13-Blaze Barton ends	388	582	1242	2121	3000	
17-Last Neon; Crandall Hercules in all; last Lou Fine-c; skeleton-c	300	600	900	2010	3505	5000
18-Origin & 1st app. Stormy Foster, the Great Defender begins; Crandall-a	245	490	735	1568	2684	3800
19,20	155	310	465	992	1696	2400
21-24: 21-Last Hercules. 24-Last Red Bee & Strange Twins	142	284	426	909	1555	2200
25-Origin & 1st app. Kid Eternity and begins by Moldoff (12/42); 1st app. The Keeper (Kid Eternity's aide)	276	552	828	1753	3027	4300
26-Blackhawk x-over in Kid Eternity	123	246	369	787	1344	1900
27-29	57	114	171	362	619	875
30,31- "Bill the Magnificent" by Kurtzman, 11 pgs. in each	52	104	156	328	552	775
32-40: 32-Plastic Man x-over. 34-Last Stormy Foster	36	72	108	211	343	475
41-50	26	52	78	154	252	350
51-60-Last Kid Eternity	24	48	72	142	234	325
61-63-Crandall-c/a; 61-Jeb Rivers begins	25	50	75	150	245	340
64,65-Crandall-a	24	48	72	142	234	325

NOTE: *Crandall* a-11-17(Hercules), 23, 24(Stormy Foster); c-18-20, 23, 24. *Fine* c-1-14, 16,

High Heaven #1 © AHOY and Mary Siau

Hillbilly #3 © Eric Powell

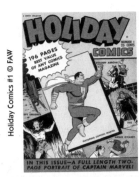
Holiday Comics #1 © FAW

	GD	VG	FN	VF	VF/NM	NM-
	2.0	4.0	6.0	8.0	9.0	9.2

17(most). **Ward** c-33. Bondage c-7, 64. Hercules c-3, 10-17. Jeb Rivers c-61-65. Kid Eternity c-25-60 (w/ Keeper-28-34, 36, 39-43, 45-55). Neon the Unknown c-2, 4, 8, 9. Red Bee c-1, 5-7. Stormy Foster c-18-24.

HIT-GIRL (Also see Kick-Ass)
Marvel Comics (Icon): Aug, 2012 - No. 5, Apr, 2013 ($2.99, limited series)

1-Takes place between Kick-Ass & Kick Ass 2 series; Millar-s/Romita Jr.-a/c
| | 1 | 2 | 3 | 5 | 6 | 8 |
2-5 .... 3.00

HIT-GIRL (Also see Kick-Ass)
Image Comics: Feb, 2018 - No. 12, Jan, 2019 ($3.99)

1-12: 1-4-Millar-s/Ortiz-a. 5-8-In Canada; Lemire-s/Risso-a. 9-12-Albuquerque-s/a ... 4.00

HIT-GIRL SEASON TWO (Also see Kick-Ass)
Image Comics: Feb, 2019 - No. 12, Jan, 2020 ($3.99)

1-12: 1-4-Kevin Smith-s/Pernille Orum-a. 5-8-Hong Kong; Parlov-a. 9-12-India ... 4.00

HITLER'S ASTROLOGER (See Marvel Graphic Novel #35)

HITMAN (Also see Bloodbath #2, Batman Chronicles #4, Demon #43-45 & Demon Annual #2)
DC Comics: May, 1996 - No. 60, Apr, 2001 ($2.25/$2.50)

1-Garth Ennis-s & John McCrea-c/a begin; Batman app.
| | | 2 | 4 | 6 | 10 | 14 | 18 |
2-Joker-c;Two Face, Mad Hatter, Batman app. | 1 | 2 | 3 | 5 | 6 | 8 |
3-5: 3-Batman-c/app.; Joker app. 4-1st app. Nightfist ... 5.00
6-20: 8-Final Night x-over. 10-GL cameo. 11-20: 11,12-GL-c/app. 15-20-"Ace of Killers". 16-18-Catwoman app. 17-19-Demon-app. ... 4.00
21-59: 34-Superman-c/app. ... 4.00
60-($3.95) Final issue; includes pin-ups by various ... 4.00
#1,000,000 (11/98) Hitman goes to the 853rd Century ... 5.00
Annual 1 (1997, $3.95) Pulp Heroes ... 4.00
.../Lobo: That Stupid Bastich (7/00, $3.95) Ennis-s/Mahnke-a ... 4.00
TPB-(1997, $9.95) r/#1-3, Demon Ann. #2, Batman Chronicles #4 ... 10.00
Ace of Killers TPB ('00/'11, $17.95/$17.99) r/#15-22 ... 18.00
Local Heroes TPB ('99, $17.95) r/#9-14 & Annual #1 ... 10.00
10,000 Bullets TPB ('98, $9.95) r/#4-8 ... 18.00
Ten Thousand Bullets TPB ('10, $17.99) r/#4-8 & Annual #1; intro. by Kevin Smith ... 18.00
Who Dares Wins TPB ('01, $12.95) r/#23-28 ... 13.00

HIT-MONKEY (See Deadpool)
Marvel Comics: Apr, 2010; Sept, 2010 - No. 3, Nov, 2010 ($3.99/$2.99)

1-(4/10, $3.99) Printing of story from Marvel Digital Comics; Frank Cho-c; origin revealed ... 4.00
1-3-Daniel Way-s/Talajic-a/Johnson-c; Bullseye app. ... 3.00

HI-YO SILVER (See Lone Ranger's Famous Horse... and The Lone Ranger; and March of Comics No. 215 in the Promotional Comics section)

HOBBIT, THE
Eclipse Comics: 1989 - No. 3, 1990 ($4.95, squarebound, 52 pgs.)

Book 1-Adapts novel; Wenzel-a | | 3 | 6 | 9 | 17 | 26 | 35 |
Book 1-Second printing ... 5.00
Book 2,3-Adaptation continues | | 2 | 4 | 6 | 8 | 11 | 14 |
Graphic Novel (1990, Ballantine)-r/#1-3 ... 25.00

HOCUS POCUS (See Funny Book #9)

HOGAN'S HEROES (TV) (Also see Wild!)
Dell Publishing Co.: June, 1966 - No. 8, Sept, 1967; No. 9, Oct, 1969

1: Photo-c on #1-7 | 9 | 18 | 27 | 61 | 123 | 185 |
2,3-Ditko-a(p) | 6 | 12 | 18 | 42 | 79 | 115 |
4-9: 9-Reprints #1 | 5 | 10 | 15 | 33 | 57 | 80 |

HOKUM & HEX (See Razorline)
Marvel Comics (Razorline): Sept, 1993 - No. 9, May, 1994 ($1.75/$1.95)

1-($2.50)-Foil embossed-c; by Clive Barker ... 5.00
2-9: 5-Hyperkind x-over ... 4.00

HOLIDAY COMICS
Fawcett Publications: 1942 (25¢, 196 pgs.)

1-Contains three Fawcett comics plus two page portrait of Captain Marvel; Capt. Marvel, Jungle Girl #1, & Whiz. Not rebound, remaindered comics; printed at the same time as originals (scarce in high grade) | 325 | 650 | 975 | 2300 | 4550 | 6800 |

HOLIDAY COMICS (Becomes Fun Comics #9-12)
Star Publications: Jan, 1951 - No. 8, Oct, 1952

1-Funny animal contents (Frisky Fables) in all; L. B. Cole X-Mas-c
| | 47 | 94 | 141 | 296 | 498 | 700 |
2-Classic L. B. Cole-c | 40 | 80 | 120 | 246 | 411 | 575 |
3-8: 5,8-X-Mas-c; all L.B.Cole-c | 24 | 48 | 72 | 142 | 242 | 325 |
Accepted Reprint 4 (nd)-L.B.Cole-c | 13 | 26 | 39 | 72 | 101 | 130 |

HOLIDAY DIGEST

Harvey Comics: 1988 ($1.25, digest-size)
1 | | 1 | 2 | 3 | 5 | 7 | 9 |

HOLIDAY PARADE (Walt Disney's...)
W. D. Publications (Disney): Winter, 1990-91(no year given) - No. 2, Winter, 1990-91 ($2.95, 68 pgs.)

1-Reprints 1947 Firestone by Barks plus new-a ... 5.00
2-Barks-r plus other stories ... 4.00

HOLIDAY PARTY (Scotch McTiernan's)
Image Comics: Jan, 2023 ($3.99, one-shot)

1-Duggan & Posehn-s/Koblish-a ... 4.00

HOLI-DAY SURPRISE (Formerly Summer Fun)
Charlton Comics: V2#55, Mar, 1967 (25¢ Giant)

V2#55 | 4 | 8 | 12 | 27 | 44 | 60 |

HOLLYWOOD COMICS
New Age Publishers: Winter, 1944 (52 pgs.)

1-Funny animal | 25 | 50 | 75 | 150 | 245 | 340 |

HOLLYWOOD CONFESSIONS
St. John Publishing Co.: Oct, 1949 - No. 2, Dec, 1949

1-Kubert-c/a (entire book) | 52 | 104 | 156 | 328 | 552 | 775 |
2-Kubert-c/a (entire book) (Scarce) | 55 | 110 | 165 | 352 | 601 | 850 |

HOLLYWOOD DIARY
Quality Comics Group: Dec, 1949 - No. 5, July-Aug, 1950

1-No photo-c | 36 | 72 | 108 | 214 | 347 | 480 |
2-Photo-c | 22 | 44 | 66 | 128 | 209 | 290 |
3-5-Photo-c. 3-Betty Carlin photo-c. 5-June Allyson/Peter Lawford photo-c | 20 | 40 | 60 | 114 | 182 | 250 |

HOLLYWOOD FILM STORIES
Feature Publications/Prize: April, 1950 - No. 4, Oct, 1950 (All photo-c; "Fumetti" type movie comic)

1-June Allyson photo-c | 28 | 56 | 84 | 168 | 274 | 380 |
2-4: 2-Lizabeth Scott photo-c. 3-Barbara Stanwick photo-c. 4-Betty Hutton photo-c | 20 | 40 | 60 | 117 | 189 | 260 |

HOLLYWOOD FUNNY FOLKS (Formerly Funny Folks; becomes Nutsy Squirrel #61 on)
National Periodical Publ.: No. 27, Aug-Sep, 1950 - No. 60, July-Aug, 1954

27-Nutsy Squirrel continues | 15 | 30 | 45 | 84 | 127 | 170 |
28-40 | 11 | 22 | 33 | 64 | 90 | 115 |
41-60 | 10 | 20 | 30 | 54 | 72 | 90 |
NOTE: **Rube Grossman** a-most issues. **Sheldon Mayer** a-27-35, 37-40, 43-46, 48-51, 53, 56, 57, 60.

HOLLYWOOD LOVE DOCTOR (See Doctor Anthony King...)

HOLLYWOOD PICTORIAL (...Romances on cover)
St. John Publishing Co.: No. 3, Jan, 1950

3-Matt Baker-a; photo-c | 47 | 94 | 141 | 296 | 498 | 700 |
(Becomes a movie magazine - Hollywood Pictorial Western with No. 4.)

HOLLYWOOD ROMANCES (Formerly Brides In Love; becomes For Lovers Only #60 on)
Charlton Comics: V2#46, 11/66; #47, 10/67; #48, 11/68;V3#49,11/69-V3#59, 6/71

V2#46-Rolling Stones-c/story | 10 | 20 | 30 | 68 | 144 | 220 |
V2#47-V3#59: 56- "Born to Heart Break" begins | 3 | 6 | 9 | 19 | 30 | 40 |

HOLLYWOOD SECRETS
Quality Comics Group: Nov, 1949 - No. 6, Sept, 1950

1-Ward-c/a (9 pgs.) | 54 | 108 | 162 | 343 | 574 | 825 |
2-Crandall, Ward-c/a (9 pgs.) | 43 | 86 | 129 | 271 | 461 | 650 |
3-6: All photo-c. 5-Lex Barker (Tarzan)-c | 21 | 42 | 63 | 122 | 199 | 275 |
...of Romance, I.W. Reprint #9; r/#2 above w/Kinstler-c | 3 | 6 | 9 | 15 | 22 | 28 |

HOLLYWOOD SUPERSTARS
Marvel Comics (Epic Comics): Nov, 1990 - No. 5, Apr, 1991 ($2.25)

1-($2.95, 52 pgs.)-Spiegle-c/a in all; Aragonés-a, inside front-c plus 2-4 pgs. ... 5.00
2-5 ($2.25) ... 4.00

HOLO-MAN (See Power Record Comics)

HOLYOKE ONE-SHOT
Holyoke Publishing Co. (Tem Publ.): 1944 - No. 10, 1945 (All reprints)

1,2: 1-Grit Grady (on cover only), Miss Victory, Alias X (origin)-All reprints from Captain Fearless. 2-Rusty Dugan (Corporal); Capt. Fearless (origin), Mr. Miracle (origin) app. | 39 | 78 | 117 | 231 | 378 | 525 |
3-Miss Victory; r/Crash #4; Cat Man (origin), Solar Legion by Kirby app.; Miss Victory on cover only (1945) | 58 | 116 | 174 | 371 | 636 | 900 |

	GD	VG	FN	VF	VF/NM	NM-
	2.0	4.0	6.0	8.0	9.0	9.2

4,6,8: 4-Mr. Miracle; The Blue Streak app.; reprints early Cat-Man story. 6-Capt. Fearless, Alias X, Capt. Stone (splash used as-c to #10); Diamond Jim & Rusty Dugan (splash from cover of #2). 8-Blue Streak, Strong Man (story matches cover to #7)-Crash reprints

	32	64	96	188	307	425

5,7: 5-U.S. Border Patrol Comics (Sgt. Dick Carter of the...), Miss Victory (story matches cover to #3), Citizen Smith, & Mr. Miracle app. 7-Secret Agent Z-2, Strong Man, Blue Streak (story matches cover to #8); Reprints from Crash #2

	33	66	99	194	317	440

9-Citizen Smith, The Blue Streak, Solar Legion by Kirby & Strongman, the Perfect Human app.; reprints from Crash #4 & 5; Citizen Smith on cover only-from story in #5 (1944-before #3)

	37	74	111	222	361	500
10-Captain Stone; r/Crash; Solar Legion by S&K	37	74	111	222	361	500

HOLY ROLLER, THE
Image Comics: Nov. 2023 - Present ($3.99)

1-4-Remender, Samburg & Trohman-s/Boschi-a						4.00

HOLY TERROR
Legendary Comics: Sept, 2011 ($29.95, HC graphic novel, 12-1/4" wide x 9-1/4" tall)

HC-Frank Miller-s/a/c; B&W art with spot color; The Fixer vs. Al-Qaeda in Empire City						30.00

HOME (Based on the DreamWorks movie)
Titan Comics: Aug, 2015 - No. 4, Nov, 2015 ($3.99)

1-4: 1-Davison-s/Hebb-a						4.00

HOMECOMING
Aspen MLT: Aug, 2012 - No. 4, Sept, 2013 ($3.99)

1-4: 1-Wohl-s/Laiso-a; covers by Michael Turner and Mike DeBalfo						4.00

HOMER COBB (See Adventures of...)

HOMER HOOPER
Atlas Comics: July, 1953 - No. 4, Dec, 1953

1-Teenage humor	19	38	57	111	176	240
2-4	14	28	42	80	115	150

HOMER, THE HAPPY GHOST (See Adventures of...)
Atlas(ACI/PPI/WPI)/Marvel: 3/55 - No. 22, 11/58; V2#1, 11/69 - V2#4, 5/70

V1#1-Dan DeCarlo-c/a begins, ends #22	40	80	120	246	411	575
2-1st code approved issue	23	46	69	136	223	310
3-10	21	42	63	124	202	280
11-20,22	20	40	60	117	189	260
21-Sci-fi cover	39	78	117	231	378	525
V2#1 (11/69)	13	26	39	91	201	310
2-4	8	16	24	56	108	160

HOME RUN (Also see A-1 Comics)
Magazine Enterprises: No. 89, 1953 (one-shot)

A-1 89 (#3)-Powell-a; Stan Musial photo-c	21	42	63	124	202	280

HOMICIDE (Also see Dark Horse Presents)
Dark Horse Comics: Apr, 1990 ($1.95, B&W, one-shot)

1-Detective story						4.00

HOMIES
Dynamite Entertainment: 2016 - No. 4, 2017 ($3.99)

1-4-Gonzales & Serrano-s/Huerta-a						4.00

HONEYMOON (Formerly Gay Comics)
A Lover's Magazine(USA) (Marvel): No. 41, Jan, 1950

41-Photo-c; article by Betty Grable	20	40	60	117	189	260

HONEYMOONERS, THE (TV)
Lodestone: Oct, 1986 ($1.50)

1-Photo-c						6.00

HONEYMOONERS, THE (TV)
Triad Publications: Sept, 1987 - No. 13? ($2.00)

1-13						5.00

HONEYMOON ROMANCE
Artful Publications (Canadian): Apr, 1950 - No. 2, July, 1950 (25¢, digest size)

1,2-(Rare)	380	760	1140	1900	2850	3800

HONEY WEST (TV)
Gold Key: Sept, 1966 (Photo-c)

1 (10186-609)	9	18	27	62	126	190

HONEY WEST (TV)
Moonstone: 2010 - No. 4 ($5.99/$3.99)

1-($5.99) Trina Robbins-s/Cynthia Martin-a; two art covers & two photo covers						6.00
2-4-($3.99)						4.00

HONG KONG PHOOEY (TV)
Charlton Comics: June, 1975 - No. 9, Nov, 1976 (Hanna-Barbera)

1	8	16	24	51	96	140
2	3	6	9	21	33	45
3-9	3	6	9	16	23	30

HONG ON THE RANGE
Image/Flypaper Press: Dec, 1997 - No. 3, Feb, 1998 ($2.50, lim. series)

1-3: Wu-s/Lafferty-a						4.00

HOOD, THE
Marvel Comics (MAX): Jul, 2002 - No. 6, Dec, 2002 ($2.99, limited series)

1-6-Vaughan-s/Hotz-c/a						3.00
Vol. 1 Blood From Stones HC (2007, $19.99, dustjacket) r/#1-6; production sketch art						20.00
Vol. 1 Blood From Stones TPB (2003, $14.99) r/#1-6						15.00

HOODED HORSEMAN, THE (Formerly Blazing West)
American Comics Group (Michel Publ.): No. 21, 1-2/52 - No. 27, 1-2/54; No. 18, 12-1/54-55 - No. 22, 8-9/55

21(1-2/52)-Hooded Horseman, Injun Jones cont.	19	38	57	111	176	240
22	20	40	60	117	189	260
23,24,27(1-2/54)	11	22	33	62	86	110
25 (9-10/53)-Cowboy Sahib on cover only; Hooded Horseman i.d. revealed	12	24	36	67	94	120
26-Origin/1st app. Cowboy Sahib by L. Starr	14	28	42	80	115	150
18(12-1/54-55)-Photo-c	12	24	36	67	94	120
19,21,22: 19-Last precode (1-2/55)	9	18	27	52	69	85
20-Origin Johnny Injun	10	20	30	56	76	95

NOTE: *Whitney* c/a-21('52), 20-22.

HOODED MENACE, THE (Also see Daring Adventures)
Realistic/Avon Periodicals: 1951 (one-shot)

nn-Based on a band of hooded outlaws in the Pacific Northwest, 1900-1906; reprinted in Daring Advs. #15	239	478	717	1530	2615	3700

HOODS UP (See the Promotional Comics section)

HOOK (Movie)
Marvel Comics: Early Feb, 1992 - No. 4, Late Mar, 1992 ($1.00, limited series)

1-4: Adapts movie; Vess-c; 1-Morrow-a(p)						4.00
nn (1991, $5.95, 84 pgs.)-Contains #1-4; Vess-c						6.00
1 (1991, $2.95, magazine, 84 pgs.)-Contains #1-4; Vess-c (same cover as nn issue)						4.00

HOOK JAW
Titan Comics: Jan, 2017 - No. 5, May, 2017 ($3.99)

1-5-Inspired by a 1976 British comic strip; Si Spurrier-s/Conor Boyle-a; multiple covers						4.00

HOOT GIBSON'S WESTERN ROUNDUP (See Western Roundup under Fox Giants)

HOOT GIBSON WESTERN (Formerly My Love Story)
Fox Feature Syndicate: No. 5, May, 1950 - No. 3, Sept, 1950

5,6(#1,2): 5-Photo-c. 6-Photo/painted-c	21	42	63	123	197	270
3-Wood-a; painted-c	22	44	66	131	211	290

HOPALONG CASSIDY (Also see Bill Boyd Western, Master Comics, Real Western Hero, Six Gun Heroes & Western Hero; Bill Boyd starred as Hopalong Cassidy in movies, radio & TV)
Fawcett Publications: Feb, 1943; No. 2, Summer, 1946 - No. 85, Nov, 1953

1 (1943, 68 pgs.)-H. Cassidy & his horse Topper begin (on sale 1/8/43)-Captain Marvel app. on-c	200	400	600	1280	2190	3100
2-(Sum, '46)	43	86	129	271	461	650
3,4: 3-(Fall, '46, 52 pgs. begin)	20	40	60	120	195	270
5- "Mad Barber" story mentioned in SOTI, pgs. 308,309; photo-c	22	44	66	128	209	290
6-10: 8-Photo-c	16	32	48	94	147	200
11-19: 11,13-19-Photo-c	14	28	42	80	115	150
20-29 (52 pgs.)-Painted-c	12	24	36	69	97	125
30,31,33,34,37-39,41 (52 pgs.)-Photo-c	11	22	33	60	83	105
32,40 (36pgs.)-Painted-c	10	20	30	54	72	90
35,42,43,45-47,49-51,53,54,56 (52 pgs.)-Photo-c	10	20	30	56	76	95
36,44,48 (36 pgs.)-Photo-c	9	18	27	52	69	85
52,55,57-70 (36 pgs.)-Photo-c	9	18	27	47	61	75
71-84-Photo-c	8	16	24	42	54	65
85-Last Fawcett issue; photo-c	9	18	27	52	69	85

NOTE: Line-drawn c-1-4, 6, 7, 9, 10, 12.

... & The 5 Men of Evil (AC Comics, 1991, $12.95) r/newspaper strips and Fawcett story "Signature of Death"						13.00

HOPALONG CASSIDY
National Periodical Publications: No. 86, Feb, 1954 - No. 135, May-June, 1959 (All-36 pgs.)

86-Gene Colan-a begins, ends #117; photo covers continue	36	72	108	216	351	485
87	20	40	60	118	189	260
88-91: 91-1 pg. Superboy-sty (7/54)	15	30	45	83	124	165
92-99 (98 has #93 on-c; last precode issue, 2/55). 95-Reversed photo-c to #52. 98-Reversed photo-c to #61. 99-Reversed photo-c to #60	14	28	42	76	108	140
100-Same cover as #50	15	30	45	83	124	165
101-108: 105-Same photo-c as #54. 107-Same photo-c as #51. 108-Last photo-c	6	12	18	38	69	100
109-130: 118-Gil Kane-a begins. 123-Kubert-a (2 pgs.). 124-Grey tone-c	5	10	15	35	63	90
131-135	6	12	18	37	66	95

HOPELESS SAVAGES (Also see Too Much Hopeless Savages)
Oni Press: Aug, 2001 - No. 4, Nov, 2001 ($2.95, B&W, limited series)

1-4-Van Meter-s/Norrie-a/Clugston-Major-a/Watson-c						3.00
Free Comic Book Day giveaway (5/02) #/1 with "Free Comic Book Day" banner on-c						3.00
TPB (2002, $13.95, 8" x 5.75") r/#1-4; plus color stories; Watson-c						14.00

HOPELESS SAVAGES: GROUND ZERO
Oni Press: June, 2002 - No. 4, Oct, 2002 ($2.95, B&W, limited series)

1-4-Van Meter-s/O'Malley-a/Dodson-a. 1-Watson-a						3.00
TPB (2003, $11.95, 8" x 5.75") r/#1-4; Dodson-c						12.00

HOPE SHIP
Dell Publishing Co.: June-Aug, 1963

1	3	6	9	16	24	32

HOPPY THE MARVEL BUNNY (See Fawcett's Funny Animals)
Fawcett Publications: Dec, 1945 - No. 15, Sept, 1947

1	36	72	108	211	343	475
2	16	32	48	94	147	200
3-15: 7-Xmas-c	14	28	42	80	115	150

HORACE & DOTTY DRIPPLE (Dotty Dripple No. 1-24)
Harvey Publications: No. 25, Aug, 1952 - No. 43, Oct, 1955

25-43	6	12	18	28	34	40

HORIZONTAL LIEUTENANT, THE (See Movie Classics)

HORIZON ZERO DAWN (Based on the Guerrilla Games videogame)
Titan Comics: Sept, 2020 - No. 4, Nov, 2020; Aug, 2021 - No. 2.4, Feb, 2022 ($3.99)

1-4-Anne Toole-s/Ann Maulina-a; multiple covers						4.00
(Volume 2, 8/21 - 2/22) 2.1-2.4: 2.1-2.3-Elmer Damaso-a. 2.4-Maulina-a						4.00

HOROBI

Hopalong Cassidy #1 © FAW

Horrific #12 © CM

Hotell #2 © AWA

	GD	VG	FN	VF	VF/NM	NM-
	2.0	4.0	6.0	8.0	9.0	9.2

Viz Premiere Comics: 1990 - No. 8, 1990 ($3.75, B&W, mature readers, 84 pgs.) V2#1, 1990 - No. 7, 1991 ($4.25, B&W, 68 pgs.)

1-8: Japanese manga, Part Two, #1-7						5.00

HORRIFIC (Terrific No. 14 on)
Artful/Comic Media/Harwell/Mystery: Sept, 1952 - No. 13, Sept, 1954

	GD	VG	FN	VF	VF/NM	NM-
1	300	600	900	1950	3375	4800
2	168	336	504	1075	1838	2600
3-Bullet in head-c	371	742	1113	2600	4550	6500
4,5,7,9,10: 4-Shrunken head-c. 7-Guillotine-c	116	232	348	742	1271	1800
6-Jack The Ripper story	135	270	405	864	1482	2100
8-Origin & 1st app. The Teller (E.C. parody)	219	438	657	1402	2401	3400
11-13: 11-Swipe/Witches Tales #6,27; Devil-c	71	142	213	454	777	1100

NOTE: *Don Heck a-8; c-3-13. Hollingsworth a-4. Morisi a-8. Palais a-5, 7-12.*

HORRORCIDE
IDW Publishing: Sept, 2004 ($6.99)

1-Steve Niles short stories; art by Templesmith, Medors and Chee						7.00

HORROR FROM THE TOMB (Mysterious Stories No. 2 on)
Premier Magazine Co.: Sept, 1954

	GD	VG	FN	VF	VF/NM	NM-
1-Woodbridge/Torres, Check-a; The Keeper of the Graveyard is host	300	600	900	2010	3505	5000

HORRORIST, THE (Also see Hellblazer)
DC Comics (Vertigo): Dec, 1995 - No. 2, Jan, 1996 ($5.95, lim. series, mature)

1,2: Jamie Delano scripts, David Lloyd-c/a; John Constantine (Hellblazer) app.						6.00

HORROR OF COLLIER COUNTY
Dark Horse Comics: Oct, 1999 - No. 5, Feb, 2000 ($2.95, B&W, limited series)

1-5-Rich Tommaso-s/a						4.00

HORRORS, THE (Formerly Startling Terror Tales #10)
Star Publications: No. 11, Jan, 1953 - No. 15, Apr, 1954

	GD	VG	FN	VF	VF/NM	NM-
11-Horrors of War; Disbrow-a(2)	116	232	348	742	1271	1800
12-Horrors of War; color illo in POP	77	154	231	493	847	1200
13-Horrors of Mystery; crime stories	232	464	696	1485	2543	3600
14,15-Horrors of the Underworld; crime stories	71	142	213	454	777	1100

NOTE: *All have L. B. Cole covers; a-12. Hollingsworth a-13. Palais a-13r.*

HORROR TALES (Magazine)
Eerie Publications: V1#7, 6/69 - V6#6, 12/74; V7#1, 2/75; V7#2, 5/76 - V8#5, 1977; V9#1-3, 8/78; V10#1(2/79) (V1-V6: 52 pgs.); V7, V8#2: 112 pgs.; V8#4 on: 68 pgs.) (No V5#3, V8#1,3)

	GD	VG	FN	VF	VF/NM	NM-
V1#7	10	20	30	64	132	200
V1#8,9	8	16	24	51	96	140
V2#1-6('70), V3#1-6('71), V4#1-3,5-7('72)	6	12	18	42	79	115
V4#4-LSD story reprint/Weird V3#5	8	16	24	51	96	140
V5#1,2,4,5(6/73),5(10/73),6(12/73),V6#1-6('74),V7#1,2,4('76),V7#3('76)-Giant issue,						
V8#2,4,5('77)	6	12	18	40	72	105
V9#1-3(11/78, $1.50), V10#1(2/79)	6	12	18	41	76	110

NOTE: *Bondage-c-V6#1, 3, V7#2.*

HORSE FEATHERS COMICS
Lev Gleason Publ.: Nov, 1945 - No. 4, July(Summer on-c), 1948 (52 pgs.) (#2,3 are oversized)

	GD	VG	FN	VF	VF/NM	NM-
1-Wolverton's Scoop Scuttle, 2 pgs.	24	48	72	142	234	325
2	14	28	42	82	121	160
3,4: 3-(5/48)	10	20	30	58	79	100

HORSEMAN
Crusade Comics/Kevlar Studios: Mar, 1996 - No. 3, Nov, 1997 ($2.95)

0-1st Kevlar Studios issue, 1-(3/96)-Crusade issue; Shi-c/app., 1-(11/96)-3-(11/97)-Kevlar Studios						4.00

HORSEMASTERS, THE (Disney)(TV, Movie)
Dell Publishing Co.: No. 1260, Dec-Feb, 1961/62

	GD	VG	FN	VF	VF/NM	NM-
Four Color 1260-Annette Funicello photo-c	10	20	30	69	147	225

HORSE SOLDIERS, THE
Dell Publishing Co.: No. 1048, Nov-Jan, 1959/60 (John Wayne movie)

	GD	VG	FN	VF	VF/NM	NM-
Four Color 1048-Painted-c, Sekowsky-a	12	24	36	80	173	265

HORSE WITHOUT A HEAD, THE (See Movie Comics)

HOT DOG
Magazine Enterprises: June-July, 1954 - No. 4, Dec-Jan, 1954-55

	GD	VG	FN	VF	VF/NM	NM-
1(A-1 #107)	14	28	42	80	115	150
2,3(A-1 #115),4(A-1 #136)	9	18	27	50	65	80

HOT DOG (See Jughead's Pal, Hotdog)

HOTEL DEPAREE - SUNDANCE (TV)

Dell Publishing Co.: No. 1126, Aug-Oct, 1960 (one-shot)

	GD	VG	FN	VF	VF/NM	NM-
Four Color 1126-Earl Holliman photo-c	6	12	18	42	79	115

HOTELL
AWA Studios: Mar, 2020 - No. 4, Aug, 2020 ($3.99, limited series)

1-4-John Lees-s/Dalibor Talajic-a						4.00

HOTELL VOL. 2
AWA Studios: Dec, 2021 - No. 5, Apr, 2022 ($3.99, limited series)

1-5-John Lees-s/Dalibor Talajic-a						4.00

HOT ROD AND SPEEDWAY COMICS
Hillman Periodicals: Feb-Mar, 1952 - No. 5, Apr-May, 1953

	GD	VG	FN	VF	VF/NM	NM-
1	34	68	102	199	325	450
2-Krigstein-a	21	42	63	126	206	285
3-5	14	28	42	78	112	145

HOT ROD COMICS (...Featuring Clint Curtis) (See XMas Comics)
Fawcett Publications: Nov, 1951 (no month given) - V2#7, Feb, 1953

	GD	VG	FN	VF	VF/NM	NM-
nn (V1#1)-Powell-c/a in all	37	74	111	222	361	500
2 (4/52)	20	40	60	120	195	270
3-6, V2#7	15	30	45	86	133	180

HOT ROD KING (Also see Speed Smith the Hot Rod King)
Ziff-Davis Publ. Co.: Fall, 1952

	GD	VG	FN	VF	VF/NM	NM-
1-Giacoia-a; Saunders painted-c	39	78	117	231	378	525

HOT ROD RACERS (Grand Prix No. 16 on)
Charlton Comics: Dec, 1964 - No. 15, July, 1967

	GD	VG	FN	VF	VF/NM	NM-
1	8	16	24	55	105	155
2-5	5	10	15	30	50	70
6-15	4	8	12	23	37	50

HOT RODS AND RACING CARS (Motor Mag. No. 1): Nov, 1951 - No. 120, June, 1973
Charlton Comics

	GD	VG	FN	VF	VF/NM	NM-
1-Speed Davis begins; Indianapolis 500 story	37	74	111	222	361	500
2	20	40	60	117	189	260
3-10	13	26	39	74	105	135
11-20	10	20	30	56	76	95
21-33,36-40	9	18	27	47	61	75
34, 35 (? & 6/58, 68 pgs.)	11	22	33	60	83	105
41-60	7	14	21	37	46	55
61-80	6	9	9	19	30	40
81-100	3	6	9	16	23	30
101-120	3	6	9	14	19	24

HOT SHOT CHARLIE
Hillman Periodicals: 1947 (Lee Elias)

	GD	VG	FN	VF	VF/NM	NM-
1	19	38	57	109	172	235

HOT SHOTS: AVENGERS
Marvel Comics: Oct, 1995 ($2.95, one-shot)

nn-pin-ups						4.00

HOTSPUR
Eclipse Comics: Jun, 1987 - No. 3, Sep, 1987 ($1.75, lim. series, Baxter paper)

1-3						4.00

HOT STUFF (See Stumbo Tinytown)
Harvey Comics: V2#1, Sept, 1991 - No. 12, June, 1994 ($1.00)

V2#1-Stumbo back-up story						5.00
2-12 ($1.50)						4.00
...Big Book 1 (11/92), 2 (6/93) (Both $1.95, 52 pgs.)						5.00

HOT STUFF CREEPY CAVES
Harvey Publications: Nov, 1974 - No. 7, Nov, 1975

	GD	VG	FN	VF	VF/NM	NM-
1	4	8	12	23	37	50
2-7	3	6	9	15	21	26

HOT STUFF DIGEST
Harvey Comics: July, 1992 - No. 5, Nov, 1993 ($1.75, digest-size)

V2#1-Hot Stuff, Stumbo, Richie Rich stories						6.00
2-5						4.00

HOT STUFF GIANT SIZE
Harvey Comics: Oct, 1992 - No. 3, Oct, 1993 ($2.25, 68 pgs.)

V2#1-Hot Stuff & Stumbo stories						5.00
2,3						4.00

HOT STUFF SIZZLERS

	GD	VG	FN	VF	VF/NM	NM-
	2.0	4.0	6.0	8.0	9.0	9.2

Harvey Publications: July, 1960 - No. 59, Mar, 1974; V2#1, Aug, 1992

1- 84 pgs. begin, ends #5; Hot Stuff, Stumbo begin	16	32	48	107	236	365
2-5	8	16	24	52	99	145
6-10- 6-68 pgs. begin, ends #45	5	10	15	35	63	90
11-20	4	8	12	27	44	60
21-45	3	6	9	19	30	40
46-52: 52 pgs. begin	3	6	9	16	23	30
53-59	2	4	6	10	14	18
V2#1-(8/92, $1.25)-Stumbo back-up						5.00

HOT STUFF, THE LITTLE DEVIL (Also see Devil Kids & Harvey Hits)
Harvey Publications (Illustrated Humor): 10/57 - No. 141, 7/77; No. 142, 2/78 - No. 164, 8/82; No. 165, 10/86 - No. 171, 11/87; No. 172, 11/88; No. 173, Sept, 1990 - No. 177, 1/91

1-1st app. Hot Stuff; UFO story	179	358	537	1477	3339	5200
2-Stumbo-like giant 1st app. (12/57)	40	80	120	296	673	1050
3-Stumbo the Giant debut (2/58)	20	40	60	138	307	475
4,5	17	34	51	117	259	400
6-10	10	20	30	66	138	210
11-20	8	16	24	51	96	140
21-40	5	10	15	34	60	85
41-60	4	8	12	25	40	55
61-80	3	6	9	19	30	40
81-105	3	6	9	15	22	28
106-112: All 52 pg. Giants	3	6	9	17	26	35
113-125	2	4	6	9	12	15
126-141	1	2	3	5	7	9
142-177: 172-177-($1.00)						6.00

Harvey Comics Classics Vol. 3 TPB (Dark Horse Books, 3/08, $19.95) Reprints Hot Stuff's earliest appearances in this title and Devil Kids, mostly B&W with some color stories; history, early concept drawings; foreword by Mark Arnold 20.00

HOT WHEELS (TV)
National Periodical Publications: Mar-Apr, 1970 - No. 6, Jan-Feb, 1971

1	12	24	36	79	170	260
2,4,5	6	12	18	38	69	100
3-Neal Adams-c	8	16	24	52	99	145
6-Neal Adams-c/a	9	18	27	59	117	175

NOTE: *Toth* a-1p, 2-5; c-1p, 5.

HOURMAN (Justice Society member, see Adventure Comics #48)

HOURMAN (See JLA and DC One Million)
DC Comics: Apr, 1999 - No. 25, Apr, 2001 ($2.50)

1-25: 1-JLA app.; McDaniel-c. 2-Tomorrow Woman-c/app. 6,7-Amazo app. 11-13-Justice Legion A app. 16-Silver Age flashback. 18,19-JSA-c/app. 22-Harris-c/a. 24-Hourman Vs. Rex Tyler						4.00

HOUSE OF CEREBUS
Aardvark-Vanaheim: Jan, 2020 ($4.00, B&W)

1-Swamp Thing parady; Dave Sim-s/a; House of Secrets #92-c swipe						4.00

HOUSE OF FUN
Dark Horse Comics: Dec, 2012 ($3.50)

0-Reprints Evan Dorkin humor strips from Dark Horse Presents #10-12						3.50

HOUSE OF GOLD AND BONES
Dark Horse Comics: Apr, 2013 - No. 4, Jul, 2013 ($3.99, limited series)

1-4-Corey Taylor-s/Richard Clark-a; 2 covers on each						4.00

HOUSE OF HEM
Marvel Comics: 2015 ($7.99, one-shot)

1-Reprints Fred Hembeck's Marvel highlights incl. Fantastic Four Roast; wraparound-c						8.00

HOUSE OF LOST HORIZONS, THE (A Sarah Jewell Mystery)
Dark Horse Comics: May, 2021 - No. 5, Sept, 2021 ($3.99, limited series)

1-5-Chris Roberson-s/Leila Del Duca-a						4.00

HOUSE OF M (Also see miniseries with Fantastic Four, Iron Man and Spider-Man)
Marvel Comics: Aug, 2005 - No. 8, Dec, 2005 ($2.99, limited series)

1-Bendis-s/Coipel-a/Ribic-c; Scarlet Witch changes reality; Quesada variant-c						5.00
2-8-Variant covers for each						3.00
... MGC #1 (6/11, $1.00) r/#1 with "Marvel's Greatest Comics" logo on cover						3.00
Secrets Of The House Of M (2005, $3.99, one-shot) profile pages and background info						4.00
... Sketchbook (6/05) B&W preview sketches by Coipel, Davis, Hairsine, Quesada						3.00
TPB (2006, $24.99) r/#1-8 and The Pulse: House of M Special Edition newspaper						25.00
...: Fantastic Four/ Iron Man TPB (2006, $13.99) r/ both House of M mini-series						14.00
....: World of M Featuring Wolverine TPB (2006, $13.99) r/2005 x-over issues Wolverine #33-35, Black Panther #7, Captain America #10 and The Pulse #10						14.00
HC (2008, $29.99, oversized with d.j.) r/#1-8, The Pulse: House of M Special Edition newspaper and Secrets Of The House Of M one-shot; script pages; cover gallery						30.00

HOUSE OF M (Secret Wars tie-in)
Marvel Comics: Oct, 2015 - No. 4, Dec, 2015 ($3.99, limited series)

1-4: 1,2-Hopeless & Bunn-s/Failla-a; Magneto & the House of Magnus. 3,4-Anindito-a						4.00

HOUSE OF M: AVENGERS
Marvel Comics: Jan, 2008 - No. 5, Apr, 2008 ($2.99, limited series)

1-5-Gage-s/Perkins-a; Luke Cage, Iron Fist, Hawkeye, Tigra, Misty Knight, Shang-Chi						3.00

HOUSE OF M: MASTERS OF EVIL
Marvel Comics: Oct, 2009 - No. 4, Jan, 2010 ($3.99, limited series)

1-4-Gage-s/Garcia-a/Perkins-c; The Hood app.						4.00

HOUSE OF MYSTERY
DC Comics: Dec/Jan. 1951

nn - Ashcan comic; not distributed to newsstands, only for in-house use. Cover art is Danger Trail #3 with interior being Star Spangled Comics #109. A VG+ copy sold for $2,357.50 in 2002.

HOUSE OF MYSTERY (See Brave and the Bold #93, Elvira's House of Mystery, Limited Collectors' Edition & Super DC Giant)

HOUSE OF MYSTERY, THE
National Periodical Publications/DC Comics: Dec-Jan, 1951-52 - No. 321, Oct, 1983 (No. 194-203: 52 pgs.)

1-DC's first horror comic	300	600	900	2010	3505	5000
2	135	270	405	864	1482	2100
3	77	154	231	493	847	1200
4,5	68	136	204	435	743	1050
6-10	60	120	180	381	653	925
11-15	52	104	156	328	552	775
16(7/53)-25	40	80	120	246	411	575
26-35(2/55)-Last pre-code issue; 30-Woodish-a	34	68	102	204	332	460
36-50: 50-Text story of Orson Welles' War of the Worlds broadcast	18	36	54	122	271	420
51-60: 55-1st S.A. issue	15	30	45	105	233	360
61,63,65,66,69,70,72,76,79,85-Kirby-a	17	34	51	117	259	400
62,64,67,68,71,73-75,77,78,80-83,86-99: 92-Grey tone-c	15	30	45	100	220	340
84-Prototype of Negative Man (Doom Patrol)	29	58	87	209	467	725
100 (7/60)	16	32	48	110	243	375
101-116: 109-Toth, Kubert-a. 116-Last 10¢ issue	11	22	33	77	166	255
117-130: 117-Swipes-c to HOS #20. 120-Toth-a	10	20	30	67	141	215
131-142	9	18	27	60	120	180
143-J'onn J'onzz, Manhunter begins (6/64), ends #173; story continues from Detective #326; intro. Idol-Head of Diabolu	20	40	60	135	300	465
144	9	18	27	57	111	165
145-155,157-159: 149-Toth-a. 155-The Human Hurricane app. (12/65), Red Tornado prototype. 158-Origin Diabolu Idol-Head	6	12	18	37	66	95
156-Robby Reed begins (origin/1st app.), ends #173	14	28	42	96	211	325
160-(7/66)-Robby Reed becomes Plastic Man in this issue only; 1st S.A. app. Plastic Man; intro Marco Xavier (Martian Manhunter) & Vulture Crime Organization; ends #173						
	19	38	57	131	291	450
161-173: 169-Origin/1st app. Gem Girl	5	10	15	31	53	75
174-Mystery format begins.	26	52	78	182	404	625
175-1st app. Cain (House of Mystery host); Adams-c	17	34	51	117	259	400
176,177-Neal Adams-c	10	20	30	67	141	215
178-Neal Adams-c (2/69)	11	22	33	76	163	250
179-Neal Adams/Orlando, Wrightson-a (1st pro work, 3 pgs.); Adams-c						
	22	44	66	154	340	525
180,181,183: Wrightson-a (3,10, & 3 pgs.); Adams-c. 180-Last 12¢ issue; Kane/Wood-a(2). 183-Wood-a	6	12	18	40	73	105
182,184-Adams-c. 182-Toth-a. 184-Kane/Wood, Toth-a						
	7	14	21	48	89	130
185-Williamson/Kaluta-a; Howard-a (3 pgs.); Adams-c	8	16	24	51	96	140
186-N. Adams-c/a; Wrightson-a (10 pgs.)	8	16	27	59	117	175
187,190: Adams-c. 187-Toth-a. 190-Toth-a(r)	6	12	18	42	79	115
188-Wrightson-a (8 & 3pgs.); Adams-c	8	16	24	55	105	155
189,192,197: Adams-c on all. 189-Wood-a(i). 192-Last 15¢-c						
	6	12	18	40	73	105
191-Wrightson-a (8 & 3pgs.); Adams-c	7	14	21	49	92	135
193-Wrightson-c	6	12	18	40	73	105
194-Wrightson-c; 52 pgs begin, end #203; Toth,Kirby-a						
	8	16	24	55	105	155
195-Wrightson-c. Swamp creature story by Wrightson similar to Swamp Thing (10 pgs.)(10/71)	11	22	33	73	157	240
196,198	5	10	15	35	63	90
199-Adams-c; Wood-a(8pgs.); Kirby-a	6	12	18	42	79	115
200-(25¢, 52 pgs.)-One third-r (3/72)	6	12	18	41	76	110
201-203-(25¢, 52 pgs.)-One third-r	5	10	15	33	57	80
204-Wrightson-c/a, 9 pgs.	6	12	18	38	69	100
205,206,208,210,212,215,216,218	4	8	12	23	37	50
207-Wrightson-c/a (8 pgs.); Starlin, Redondo-a	6	12	18	38	69	100
209,211,213,214,217,219-Wrightson-c	5	10	15	31	53	75
220,222,223	3	6	9	15	22	28
221-Wrightson/Kaluta-a(8 pgs.); Wrightson-c	6	12	18	37	66	95
224-Wrightson-r from Spectre #9; Dillin/Adams-r from House of Secrets #82; begin 100 pg. classics; Phantom Stranger-r. 225,227-(100 pgs.): 225-Spectre app. 226-Wrightson/Redondo-a Phantom Stranger-r. 228-N. Adams inks; Wrightson-r. 229-Wrightson-a(r); Toth-r; last 100 pg. issue	5	10	15	35	63	90
230,232-235,237-250: 230-UFO-c	3	6	9	16	23	30
231-Classic Wrightson-c	6	12	18	41	76	110
236-Wrightson-c; Ditko-a(p); N. Adams-i	5	10	15	35	63	90
251-254-(84 pgs.)-Adams-c. 251-Wood-a	4	8	12	27	44	60
255,256-(84 pgs.)-Wrightson-c	4	8	12	24	40	55
257-259-(84 pgs.)	3	6	9	18	28	38
260-289: 282-(68 pgs.)-Has extra story "The Computers That Saved Metropolis" Radio Shack giveaway by Jim Starlin	2	4	6	8	10	12
290-1st "I, Vampire"	6	12	18	36	68	100
291-299: 291,293,295-299-"I, Vampire"	3	6	9	11	16	20
300,319-"I, Vampire". 319-Death of Andrew Bennett	3	6	9	14	19	24
301-318,320: 301-318-"I, Vampire"	2	4	6	9	12	15
321-Final issue; Joe Orlando & Karen Berger app.	3	6	9	17	25	34
Welcome to the House of Mystery (7/98, $5.95) reprints stories with new framing story by Gaiman and Aragonés						6.00

NOTE: *Neal Adams* a-236i; c-175-192, 197, 199, 251-254. *Alcala* a-209, 217, 219, 224, 227. *M. Anderson* a-212; c/a-37. *Aparo* a-209. *Aragones* a-185, 186, 194, 196, 200, 202, 229, 251. *Baily* a-279p. *Cameron* a-76, 79. *Colan* a-202r. *Craig* a-263, 275, 295, 300. *Dillin/Adams*-r-224. *Ditko* a-236p, 247, 254, 258, 276; c-277. *Drucker* a-37. *Evans* c-218. *Fradon* a-251. *Giffen* a-284. *Giunta* a-199, 227r. *Golden* a-257, 259. *Heath* a-194r; c-203. *Howard* a-182, 185, 187, 196, 229r, 247r, 254, 279r. *Kaluta* a-195, 200, 250r; c-200-202, 210, 212, 233, 260, 261, 263, 265, 267, 268, 273, 276, 284, 293-295, 300, 302, 304, 305, 309-319, 321. *Bob Kane* a-84. *Gil Kane* a-196p, 253p, 300p. *Kirby* a-194r; 199r; c-65, 76, 78, 79, 85. *Kubert* c-282, 283, 285, 286, 289-292, 297-299, 301, 303, 306-308. *Maneely* a-60. *Mayer* a-317p. *Meskin* a-52-144 (most), 195r, 224r, 229r; c-63, 66, 124, 127. *Mooney* a-24, 159, 160. *Moreira* a-3, 4, 19-50, 52, 58, 59, 62, 68, 77, 79, 90, 108, 113, 123, 201r, 228; c-4-28, 44, 47, 50, 54, 59, 62, 64, 68, 70, 73. *Morrow* a-192, 196, 253, 260. *Mortimer* a-204(3 pgs.). *Nasser* a-276. *Newton* a-259. *Nino* a-204, 213, 220, 224, 225, 245, 246, 252-256, 283. *Orlando* a-175(2 pgs.), 178, 240i; c-240, 258p, 262, 264p, 270p, 271, 272, 274, 275, 278, 296. *Redondo* a-194, 195, 197, 202, 203, 207, 211, 214, 217, 219, 226, 227, 229, 236, 251-287(layout), 303r, 308; c-229. *Reese* a-195, 200, 205r. *Rogers* a-254, 274, 277. *Roussos* a-65, 84, 224i. *Sekowsky* a-282p. *Sparling* a-203. *Starlin* a-207(2 pgs.), 282p; c-281. *Leonard Starr* a-3. *Staton* a-300p. *Sutton* a-189, 271, 290, 291, 293, 295, 297-299, 302, 303, 306-309, 310-313i, 314. *Tuska* a-293p, 294p, 316p. *Wrightson* c-193-195, 204, 207, 209, 211, 213, 214, 217, 219, 221, 231, 236, 255, 256r; c-204.

HOUSE OF MYSTERY
DC Comics (Vertigo): Jul, 2008 - No. 42, Dec, 2011 ($2.99)

House of M: Avengers #4 © MAR

House of Slaughter #16 © Tynion IV & Dell'edera

House of Whispers #1 © DC

	GD 2.0	VG 4.0	FN 6.0	VF 8.0	VF/NM 9.0	NM- 9.2

1-Cain & Abel app.; Rossi-a/Weber-c ... 2 4 6 9 12 15
1-Variant-c by Bernie Wrightson ... 3 6 9 17 26 35
2-12,14-42: 9-Wrightson-a (6 pgs.). 16-Corben-a ... 3.00
13-Art by Neal Adams, Ralph Reese, Eric Powell, Sergio Aragonés ... 3.00
13-Variant-c by Neal Adams ... 5.00
... Halloween Annual #1 (12/09, $4.99) 1st app. I, Zombie in 7 pg. preview; short stories by
   various incl. Nowlan, Wagner, Willingham ... 3 6 9 14 20 25
... Halloween Annual #2 (12/10, $4.99) short stories by various incl. Carey, Allred, Gross ... 6.00
...: Love Stories for Dead People TPB (2009, $14.99) r/#6-10 ... 15.00
...: Room and Boredom TPB (2008, $9.99) r/#1-5 ... 10.00
...: Safe as Houses TPB (2011, $14.99) r/#26-30 ... 15.00
...: The Beauty of Decay TPB (2010, $17.99) r/#16-20 & Halloween Annual #1 ... 18.00
...: The Space Between TPB (2010, $14.99) r/#11-15; sketch pages ... 15.00
...: Under New Management TPB (2011, $14.99) r/#20-25 ... 15.00

HOUSE OF NIGHT (Based on the series of novels by P.C. Cast and Kristin Cast)
Dark Horse Comics: Nov, 2011 - No. 5, Mar, 2012 ($1.00/$2.99, limited series)
1-($1.00) Cast, Cast & Dalian-s/Joëlle Jones & Kerschl-a; Frison-c ... 3.00
1-($1.00) Variant-c by Steve Morris ... 4.00
2-5-($2.99) Jones-a; two covers by Jones & Ryan Hill on each ... 3.00

HOUSE OF PENANCE
Dark Horse Comics: Apr, 2016 - No. 5, Aug, 2016 ($3.99)
1-5: 1-Peter J. Tomasi-s/Ian Bertram-a ... 4.00

HOUSE OF SECRETS (Combined with The Unexpected after #154)
National Periodical Publications/DC Comics: 11-12/56 - No. 80, 9-10/66; No. 81, 8-9/69 - No. 140, 2-3/76; No. 141, 8-9/76 - No. 154, 10-11/78

	GD 2.0	VG 4.0	FN 6.0	VF 8.0	VF/NM 9.0	NM- 9.2
1-Drucker-a; Moreira-c	152	304	456	1254	2827	4400
2-Moreira-a	50	100	150	400	900	1400
3-Kirby-c/a	48	96	144	374	862	1350
4-Kirby-a	36	72	108	259	580	900
5-7	26	52	78	182	404	625
8-Kirby-a	27	54	81	194	435	675
9-11: 11-Lou Cameron-a (unsigned); Kirby-a	25	50	75	175	388	600
12-Kirby-c/a; Lou Cameron-a	26	52	78	182	404	625
13-15: 14-Flying saucer-c	18	36	54	124	275	425
16-20	17	34	51	114	252	390
21,22,24-30	15	30	45	100	220	340
23-1st app. Mark Merlin & begin series (8/59)	21	42	63	147	324	500
31-50: 40-Toth-a. 50-Last 10¢ issue	13	26	39	86	188	290
51-60: 58-Origin Mark Merlin	10	20	30	67	141	215
61-First Eclipso (7-8/63) and begin series	68	136	204	544	1222	1900
62	9	18	27	62	126	190
63-65-Toth-a on Eclipso (see Brave and the Bold #64)						
	8	16	24	51	96	140
66-1st Eclipso-c (also #67,70,78,79); Toth-a	10	20	30	67	147	225
67,73: 67-Toth-a on Eclipso. 73-Mark Merlin becomes Prince Ra-Man (1st app.)						
	7	14	21	48	89	130
68-72,74-80: 76-Prince Ra-Man vs. Eclipso. 80-Eclipso, Prince Ra-Man end						
	6	12	18	38	69	100
81-Mystery format begins; 1st app. Abel (House Of Secrets host);						
(cameo in DC Special #4)	25	50	75	175	388	600
82-84: 82-Neal Adams-c(i)	8	16	24	54	102	150
85,90: 85-N. Adams-a(i). 90-Buckler (early work)/N. Adams-a(i)						
	8	16	24	55	105	155
86,88,89,91	7	14	21	48	89	130
87-Wrightson & Kaluta-a	8	18	27	57	111	165
92-1st app. Swamp Thing-c/story (8 pgs.).(6-7/71) by Berni Wrightson(p) with ink assists by						
Jeff Jones, Kaluta & Weiss; classic-c	425	850	1700	3400	5100	6800
92 (Facsimile Edition)(2019, $3.99) r/#92 w/original ads and letter column			6	9	12	15
93,94,96-(52 pgs.)-Wrightson-c. 94-Wrightson-a(i); 96-Wood-a						
	9	18	27	57	111	165
95,97,98-(52 pgs.)	6	12	18	37	66	95
99-Wrightson splash pg.	6	12	18	37	66	95
100-Classic Wrightson-c	8	16	24	55	105	155
101,102,104,105,108-111,113-120	3	6	9	19	30	40
103,106,107-Wrightson-a	5	10	15	34	60	85
112-Grey tone-c	4	8	12	28	47	65
121-133	2	4	6	11	16	20
134-Wrightson-a	3	6	9	17	26	35
135,136,139-Wrightson-a/c	3	6	9	20	31	42
137,138,141-153	2	4	6	10	14	18
140-1st solo origin of the Patchworkman (see Swamp Thing #3)						
	3	6	9	16	23	30

	GD 2.0	VG 4.0	FN 6.0	VF 8.0	VF/NM 9.0	NM- 9.2
154 (10-11/78, 44 pgs.) Last issue	3	6	9	13		16

NOTE: *Neal Adams* c-81, 82, 84-88, 90, 91. *Alcala* a-104-107. *Anderson* a-91. *Aparo* a-93, 97, 105. *B. Bailey* a-107. *Cameron* a-13, 15. *Colan* a-63. *Ditko* a-139p, 148. *Elias* a-58. *Evans* a-118. *Finlay* a-7r(Real Fact?). *Glanzman* a-91. *Golden* a-151. *Heath* a-31. *Heck* a-85. *Kaluta* a-87, 98, 99; c-98, 99, 101, 102, 105, 149, 151, 154. *Bob Kane* a-18, 21. *G. Kane* a-85p. *Kirby* c-3, 11, 12. *Kubert* a-39. *Meskin* a-2-68 (most), 94r; c-55-60. *Moreira* a-7, 8, 51, 54, 102-104, 106, 108, 113, 116, 118, 121, 123, 127; c-1, 2, 4-10, 13-20. *Morrow* a-86, 89, 90; c-89, 146-148. *Nino* a-101, 103, 106, 144. *Orlando* a-73, 128, 131, 147, 153. *Redondo* a-95, 99, 102, 104p, 113, 116, 134, 136, 139, 140. *Reese* a-85. *Severin* a-91. *Starlin* c-150. *Sutton* a-154. *Toth* a-63-67, 83, 93r, 94r; 96r-98r, 123. *Tuska* a-90, 104. *Wrightson* a-134; c-92-94, 96, 100, 103, 106, 107, 135, 136, 139.

HOUSE OF SECRETS
DC Comics (Vertigo): Oct, 1996 - No. 25, Dec, 1998 ($2.50) (Creator-owned series)
1-Steven Seagle-s/Kristiansen-c/a. ... 5.00
2-25: 5,7-Kristiansen-c/a. 6-Fegrado-a ... 4.00
TPB-(1997, $19.95) ... 15.00

HOUSE OF SECRETS: FACADE
DC Comics (Vertigo): 2001 - No. 2, 2001 ($5.95, limited series)
1,2-Steven Seagle-s/Teddy Kristiansen-c/a. ... 6.00

HOUSE OF SLAUGHTER (See Something is Killing the Children & Enter the House of Slaughter)
BOOM! Studios: Oct, 2021 - Present ($3.99)
1-20: 1-4-Tynion IV & Brombal-s/Shehan-a. 6-10-Cadonici-a ... 4.00
...: Pen & Ink 1 (1/24, $6.99) Reprints #1 in B&W with Shehan commentary on each page ... 7.00

HOUSE OF TERROR (3-D)
St. John Publishing Co.: Oct, 1953 (25¢, came w/glasses)
1-Kubert, Baker-a ... 32 64 96 188 307 425

HOUSE OF WHISPERS (The Sandman Universe)(Issues #21 & #22 were only released digitally)
DC Comics (Vertigo): Nov, 2018 - No. 20, Jun, 2020 ($3.99)
1-20: 1-Hopkinson-s/Stanton-a; Abel & Goldie app. ... 4.00

HOUSE OF X (Weekly series alternating with Powers of X #1-6)
Marvel Comics: Sept, 2019 - No. 6, Dec, 2019 ($5.99/$4.99)
1-($5.99) Hickman-s/Larraz-a; Fantastic Four app. ... 6.00
2-6-($4.99) 2-Moira MacTaggart new origin. 3-Bonus Krakoan alphabet translation guide ... 5.00

HOUSE OF YANG, THE (See Yang)
Charlton Comics: July, 1975 - No. 6, June, 1976; 1978
1-Sanho Kim-a in all ... 2 4 6 13 18 22
2-6 ... 2 4 6 8 10 12
Modern Comics #1,2(1978) ... 6.00

HOUSE ON THE BORDERLAND
DC Comics (Vertigo): 2000 ($29.95, hardcover, one-shot)
HC-Adaptation of William Hope Hodgson book; Corben-a ... 30.00
SC (2003, $19.95) ... 20.00

HOUSE II: THE SECOND STORY
Marvel Comics: Oct, 1987 (One-shot)
1-Adapts movie ... 4.00

HOWARD CHAYKIN'S AMERICAN FLAGG (See American Flagg!)
First Comics: V2#1, May, 1988 - V2#12, Apr, 1989 ($1.75/$1.95, Baxter paper)
V2#1-9,11,12-Chaykin-c(p) in all ... 4.00
10-Elvis Presley photo-c ... 5.00

HOWARD THE DUCK (See Bizarre Adventures #34, Crazy Magazine, Fear, Man-Thing, Marvel Treasury Edition & Sensational She-Hulk #14-17)
Marvel Comics Group: Jan, 1976 - No. 31, May, 1979; No. 32, Jan, 1986; No. 33, Sept, 1986

	GD 2.0	VG 4.0	FN 6.0	VF 8.0	VF/NM 9.0	NM- 9.2
1-Brunner-a/c; Spider-Man x-over (low distr.)	8	16	24	55	105	155
2-Brunner-c/a	3	6	9	16	24	32
3,4-(Regular 25¢ edition). 3-Buscema-a(p). (7/76)	3	6	9	14	20	26
3,4-(30¢-c, limited distribution)	6	12	18	37	60	95
5	2	4	6	10	14	18
6-11: 8-Howard The Duck for president. 9-1st Sgt. Preston Dudley of RCMP.						
10-Spider-Man-c/sty	1	3	4	6	8	10
12-1st brief app. Kiss (3/77)	4	8	12	27	44	60
13-(30¢-c) 1st full app. Kiss (6/77); Daimon Hellstrom app. plus cameo of						
Howard as Son of Satan	4	8	12	28	47	65
13-(35¢-c, limited distribution)	10	20	30	67	141	215
14-32: 14-17-(Regular 30¢-c). 14-Howard as Son of Satan-c/story; Son of Satan app.						
16-Album issue; 3 pgs. comics. 22,23-Man-Thing-c/stories; Star Wars parody.						
30,32-P. Smith-a	1	2	3	5	6	8
14-17-(35¢-c, limited distribution)	7	14	21	46	86	125
33-Last issue; low print run	2	4	6	9	12	15
Annual 1 (1977, 52 pgs.)-Mayerik-a	2	4	6	10	14	18
... No. 1 Facsimile Ed. (8/19, $3.99) r/#1 w/original ads						4.00

... Omnibus HC (2008, $99.99, dustjacket) r/#1-33 & Annual #1, Adventure Into Fear #19,

	GD	VG	FN	VF	VF/NM	NM-		GD	VG	FN	VF	VF/NM	NM-
	2.0	4.0	6.0	8.0	9.0	9.2		2.0	4.0	6.0	8.0	9.0	9.2

Man-Thing #1, Giant-Size Man-Thing #4&5, Marvel Treasury Ed. #12, Marvel Team-Up #96 and FOOM #15; Gerber foreword; creator interviews; bonus art; 2 covers 100.00
NOTE: *Austin* c-29i. *Bolland* c-33. *Brunner* a-1p, 2p; c-1, 2. *Buckler* c-3p. *Buscema* a-3p. *Colan* (a)p-4-15, 17-20, 24-27, 30, 31; c(p)-4-31, Annual 1p. *Leialoha* a-1-13i; c(i)-3-5, 8-11. *Mayerik* a-22, 23, 33. *Paul Smith* a-30p, 32. Man-Thing app. in #22, 23.

HOWARD THE DUCK (Magazine)
Marvel Comics Group: Oct, 1979 - No. 9, Mar, 1981 (B&W, 68 pgs.)

1-Art by Colan, Janson, Golden. Kidney Lady app.	3	6	9	16	24	32
2,3,6-9 (nudity in most): 2-Mayerik-c. 3-Xmas issue; Jack Davis-c; Duck World flashback.						
6-1st Street People back-up story. 7-Has pin-up by Byrne; Man-Thing-c/s (46 pgs.)						
8-Batman parody w/Marshall Rogers-a; Dave Sim-a (1 pg.). 9-Marie Severin-a; John Pound painted-c	2	4	6	8	10	12
4,5- 4-Beatles, John Lennon, Elvis, Kiss & Devo cameos; Hitler app. 5-Undead Duck, Dracula app.	2	4	6	10	14	18
NOTE: *Buscema* a-4p. *Colan* a-1-5p, 7-9p. *Jack Davis* c-3. *Golden* a(p)-1, 5, 6(51pgs.) a-8. *Rogers* a-7, 8. *Simonson* a-7.

HOWARD THE DUCK (Volume 2)
Marvel Comics: Mar, 2002 - No. 6, Aug, 2002 ($2.99)

1-Gerber-s/Winslade-a/Fabry-c						6.00
2-6: 2,4,6-Gerber-s/Winslade-a/Fabry-c. 3-Fabry-a/c						4.00
TPB (9/02, $14.99) r/#1-6						15.00

HOWARD THE DUCK (Volume 3)
Marvel Comics: Dec, 2007 - No. 4, Feb, 2008 ($2.99, limited series)

1-4-Templeton-a/Bobillo-a/c. She-Hulk app.						4.00
....: Media Duckling TPB ($11.99) r/#1-4; Howard the Duck #1 (1/76) and pages from Civil War: Choosing Sides						12.00

HOWARD THE DUCK (Volume 4)
Marvel Comics: May 2015 - No. 5, Oct, 2015 ($3.99)

1-5-Zdarsky-s/Quinones-a. 1-Spider-Man app. 2-Guardians of the Galaxy app.						4.00

HOWARD THE DUCK (Volume 5)
Marvel Comics: Jan, 2016 - No. 11, Dec, 2016 ($4.99/$3.99)

1-($4.99) Zdarsky-s/Quinones-a; back-up with Gwenpool in #1-3	3	6	9	14	19	24
2-3-($4.99): 2-Fish-a						6.00
4-11-($3.99) 4,5-Silver Surfer, Galactus & the Guardians of the Galaxy app. 6-Squirrel Girl x-over. 7-Maguire-a. 8-Beverly app. 9-Lea Thompson app. 9-11-Mojo app.						4.00

HOWARD THE DUCK
Marvel Comics: Jan, 2024 ($5.99, one-shot)

1-($4.99) 50th anniversary celebration of short stories by various incl. Zdarsky, Quinones						6.00

HOWARD THE DUCK HOLIDAY SPECIAL
Marvel Comics: Feb, 1997 ($2.50, one-shot)

1-Wraparound-c; Hama-s	1	3	4	6	8	10

HOWARD THE DUCK: THE MOVIE
Marvel Comics Group: Dec, 1986 - No. 3, Feb, 1987 (Limited series)

1-3: Movie adaptation; r/Marvel Super Special						5.00

HOWARD THE HUMAN (Secret Wars tie-in)
Marvel Comics: Oct, 2015 ($3.99, one-shot)

1-Howard the Duck as human in all-animal world; Skottie Young-s/Jim Mahfood-a						4.00

HOW BOYS AND GIRLS CAN HELP WIN THE WAR
The Parents' Magazine Institute: 1942 (10¢, one-shot)

1-All proceeds used to buy war bonds	43	86	129	271	461	650

HOWDY DOODY (TV)(See Jackpot of Fun-- & Poll Parrot)(Some have stories by John Stanley)
Dell Publishing Co.: 1/50 - No. 38, 7-9/56; No. 761, 1/57; No. 811, 7/57

1-(Scarce)-Photo-c; 1st TV comic	79	158	237	632	1416	2200
2-Photo-c	34	68	102	241	541	840
3-5-All photo-c	19	38	57	133	297	460
6-Used in SOTI, pg. 309; classic; painted covers begin	26	52	78	182	404	625
7-10	12	24	36	84	185	285
11-20: 13-X-mas-c	10	20	30	70	150	230
21-38, Four Color 761,811	9	18	27	61	123	185

HOW IT BEGAN
United Features Syndicate: No. 15, 1939 (one-shot)

Single Series 15	40	80	120	246	411	575

HOWLING COMMANDOS OF S.H.I.E.L.D.
Marvel Comics: Dec, 2015 - No. 6, May, 2016 ($3.99)

1-6: 1-Barbiere-s/Schoonover-a; Dum Dum Dugan, Orrgo, Man-Thing, Hit-Monkey app.						4.00

HOW SANTA GOT HIS RED SUIT (See March of Comics No. 2)

HOW THE WEST WAS WON (See Movie Comics)

HOW TO DRAW FOR THE COMICS
Street and Smith: No date (1942?) (10¢, 64 pgs., B&W & color, no ads)

nn-Art by Robert Winsor McCay (recreating his father's art), George Marcoux (Supersnipe artist), Vernon Greene (The Shadow artist), Jack Binder (with biog.), Thorton Fisher, Jon Small, & Jack Farr; has biographies of each artist	43	86	129	271	461	650

H. P. LOVECRAFT'S CTHULHU
Millennium Publications: Dec, 1991 - No. 3, May, 1992 ($2.50, limited series)

1-3: 1-Contains trading cards on thin stock						4.00

H. R. PUFNSTUF (TV) (See March of Comics #360)
Gold Key: Oct, 1970 - No. 8, July, 1972

1-Photo-c	10	20	30	64	132	200
2-8-Photo-c on all. 6-8-Both Gold Key and Whitman editions exist	7	14	21	46	86	125

HUBERT AT CAMP MOONBEAM
Dell Publishing Co.: No. 251, Oct, 1949 (one shot)

Four Color 251	10	20	30	70	141	215

HUCK
Image Comics: Nov, 2015 - No. 6, Apr, 2016 ($3.50/$3.99)

1-5-Millar-s/Albuquerque-a; 2 covers on each						3.50
6-($3.99)						4.00

HUCK & YOGI JAMBOREE (TV)
Dell Publishing Co.: Mar, 1961 ($1.00, 6-1/4x9", 116 pgs., cardboard-c, high quality paper) (B&W original material)

nn (scarce)	9	18	27	62	126	190

HUCK & YOGI WINTER SPORTS (TV)
Dell Publishing Co.: No. 1310, Mar, 1962 (Hanna-Barbera) (one-shot)

Four Color 1310	8	16	24	54	102	150

HUCK FINN (See The New Adventures of... & Power Record Comics)

HUCKLEBERRY FINN (Movie)
Dell Publishing Co.: No. 1114, July, 1960

Four Color 1114-Photo-c	6	12	18	42	79	115

HUCKLEBERRY HOUND (See Dell Giant #31,44, Golden Picture Story Book, Kite Fun Book, March of Comics #199, 214, 235, Spotlight #1 & Whitman Comic Books)

HUCKLEBERRY HOUND (TV)
Dell/Gold Key No. 18 (10/62) on: No. 990, 5-7/59 - No. 43, 10/70 (Hanna-Barbera)

Four Color 990(#1)-1st app. Huckleberry Hound, Yogi Bear, & Pixie & Mr. Jinks	20	40	60	140	310	480
Four Color 1050,1054 (12/59)	12	24	36	83	182	280
3(1-2/60) - 7 (9-10/60), Four Color 1141 (10/60)	7	14	21	46	86	125
8-10	6	12	18	37	66	95
11,13-17 (6-8/62)	5	10	15	30	50	70
12-1st Hokey Wolf & Ding-a-Ling	5	10	15	33	57	80
18,19 (84pgs.): 18-20 titled ...Chuckleberry Tales	7	14	21	44	82	120
20-Titled Chuckleberry Tales	4	8	12	28	47	65
21-30: 28-30-Reprints	4	8	12	23	37	50
31-43: 31,32,35,37-43-Reprints	3	6	9	19	30	40

HUCKLEBERRY HOUND (TV)
Charlton Comics: Nov, 1970 - No. 8, Jan, 1972 (Hanna-Barbera)

1	5	10	15	34	60	85
2-8	3	6	9	17	26	35

HUEY, DEWEY, & LOUIE (See Donald Duck, 1938 for 1st app. Also see Mickey Mouse Magazine V4#2, V5#7 & Walt Disney's Junior Woodchucks Limited Series)

HUEY, DEWEY, & LOUIE BACK TO SCHOOL (See Dell Giant #22, 35, 49 & Dell Giants)

HUEY, DEWEY, AND LOUIE JUNIOR WOODCHUCKS (Disney)
Gold Key No. 1-61/Whitman No. 62 on: Aug, 1966 - No. 81, July, 1984
(See Walt Disney's Comics & Stories #125)

1	8	16	24	54	102	150
2,3(12/68)	4	8	12	23	37	50
4,5(4/70)-r/two WDC&S D.Duck stories by Barks	3	6	9	19	30	40
6-17	3	6	9	17	26	35
18,27-30	3	6	9	15	21	26
19-23,25-New storyboarded scripts by Barks, 13-25 pgs. per issue						
24,26: 26-r/Barks Donald Duck WDC&S stories	3	6	9	18	28	38
31-57,60,61: 35,41-r/Barks J.W. scripts	2	4	6	13	23	30
58,59: 58-r/Barks Donald Duck WDC&S stories	2	4	6	9	13	16
62-64 (Whitman)	2	4	6	9	13	16
65-(9/80), 66 (Pre-pack? scarce)	4	8	12	25	40	55
67 (1/81),68	2	4	6	9	13	16
67-60¢ cover variant	4	8	12	17	21	24
69-74: 72(2/82), 73(2-3/82), 74(3/82)	2	4	6	8	11	14
75-81 (all #90183; pre-pack; nd, nd code; scarce): 75(4/83), 76(5/83), 77(7/83), 78(8/83), 79(4/84), 80(5/84), 81(7/84)	3	6	9	16	23	30

HUGGA BUNCH (TV)
Marvel Comics (Star Comics): Oct, 1986 - No. 6, Aug, 1987

1-6						6.00

HULK (Magazine)(Formerly The Rampaging Hulk)(Also see The Incredible Hulk)
Marvel Comics: No. 10, Aug., 1978 - No. 27, June, 1981 ($1.50)

10-16,18: 10-Bill Bixby interview. 11-Moon Knight begins. 12-15,18-Moon Knight stories. 12-Lou Ferrigno interview.	3	6	9	14	20	25
17-Moon Knight story with 1st Randall Spector	3	6	9	21	46	86	125
19-27: 20-Moon Knight story. 23-Last full color issue; Banner is attacked. 24-Part color, Lou Ferrigno interview. 25-Part color. 26,27-are B&W	2	4	6	11	16	20
NOTE: #10-20 have fragile spines which split easily. *Alcala* a(i)-15, 17-20, 22, 24-27. *Buscema* a-23; c-26. *Chaykin* a-21-25. *Colan* a(p)-11, 19, 24-27. *Jusko* painted c-12. *Nebres* a-16. *Severin* a-19i. Moon Knight by *Sienkiewicz* in 13-15, 17, 18, 20. *Simonson* a-27; c-23. Dominic Fortune appears in #21-24.

HULK (Becomes Incredible Hulk Vol. 2 with issue #12)
Marvel Comics: Apr, 1999 - No. 11, Feb, 2000 ($2.99/$1.99)

1-($2.99) Byrne-s/Garney-a	1	2	3	5	6	8
1-Variant-c	2	4	6	8	10	12
1-DFE Remarked-c						50.00
1-Gold foil variant						10.00
2-7-($1.99): 2-Two covers. 5-Art by Jurgens, Buscema & Texeira. 7-Avengers app.						4.00
8-Hulk battles Wolverine	2	4	6	9	13	16
9-11: 11-She-Hulk app.						3.00
1999 Annual ($3.50) Chapter One story; Byrne-s/Weeks-a						4.00
Hulk Vs. The Thing (12/99, $3.99, TPB) reprints their notable battles						4.00

HULK (Also see Fall of the Hulks and King-Size Hulk) (Becomes Red She-Hulk with #58)
Marvel Comics: Mar, 2008 - No. 57, Oct, 2012 ($2.99)

1-Red Hulk app.; Abomination killed; Loeb-s/McGuinness-a/c	5	10	15	30	50	70
1-Variant-c by Acuña	5	10	15	31	53	75
1-Variant-c with Incredible Hulk #1 cover swipe by McGuinness	5	10	15	31	53	75

Howard the Duck (2016 series) #1 © MAR

Huckleberry Hound #32 © H-B

Hulk (2022 series) #1 © MAR

	GD	VG	FN	VF	VF/NM	NM-
	2.0	4.0	6.0	8.0	9.0	9.2

1,2-2nd printings with wraparound McGuinness variant-c 3.00

2-22: 2-Iron Man app.; Rick Jones becomes the new Abomination. 4,6-Red Hulk vs. green Hulk; two covers (each Hulk); Thor app. 7-9-Art Adams & Cho-a (2 covers) 10-Defenders re-form. 14,15-X-Force, Elektra & Deadpool app. 15-Red She-Hulk app.
19-21-Fall of the Hulks x-over. 19-FF app. 22-World War Hulks 4.00

2-9: 2-Variant-c by Djurdjevic. 3-Var-c by Finch. 5-Var-c by Coipel. 6,7-Var-c by Turner 8-Var-c by Sal Buscema. 9-Two covers w/Hulks as Santa 6.00

23-($4.99): Origin of the Red Hulk; art by Sale, Romita, Deodato, Trimpe, Yu, others 5.00

24-31-($3.99): 24-World war Hulks. 25,26-Iron Man app. 26-Thor app. 4.00

30.1, 32-49 ($2.99): 34-Planet Red Hulk begins. 37-38-Fear Itself tie-in 3.00

50-($3.99) Haunted Hulk; Dr. Strange app.; back-up w/Brereton-a; Pagulayan-a 4.00

50-Variant covers by Art Adams, Humberto Ramos & Walt Simonson 15.00

51-57: 53-57-Eaglesham-a; Alpha Flight app. 3.00

... Family: Green Genes 1 (2/09, $4.99) new She-Hulk, Scorpion, Skaar & Mr. Fixit stories 8

... Let the Battle Begin 1 (5/10, $3.99) Snider-s/Kurth-a; Del Mundo-c; McGuinness-a 4.00

... MGC #1 (6/10, $1.00) r/#1 with "Marvel's Greatest Comics" logo on cover

... Monster-Size Special (12/08, $3.99) monster-themed stories by Niles, David & others 4.00

...: Raging Thunder 1 (8/08, $3.99) Hulk vs. Thundra; Breitweiser-a; r/FF #133; Land-c

Hulk-Sized Mini-Hulks ('11, $2.99) Red, Green & Blue Hulks all-ages humor; Giarrusso-a

... Vs. Fin Fang Foom (2/08, $3.99) new re-telling of first meeting; r/Strange Tales #89

... Vs. Hercules (6/08, $3.99) Djurdjevic-c; new story w/art by various; r/Tales To Ast. #79

...: Winter Guard (2/10, $3.99) Darkstar, Crimson Dynamo app. Steve Ellis-a/c

Hulk 100 Project (2008, $10.00, SC, charity book for the HERO Initiative) collection of 100 variant covers by Adams, Romita Sr. & Jr., Cho, McGuinness and more 10.00

HULK (Follows Indestructible Hulk series)
Marvel Comics: Jun, 2014 - No. 16, Jul, 2015 ($3.99)

1-15: 1-4-Waid-s/Bagley-a; 3,4-Avengers app. 5-Alex Ross-c. 6-15-Duggan-s.
13,14-Deadpool app. 14-15-Hulk vs. Red Hulk 4.00

16-($4.99) Avengers app.; Duggan-s/Bagley-a; leads into Secret Wars 5.00

Annual 1 (11/14, $4.99) Monty Nero-s; art by Luke Ross, Goddard & Laming 5.00

HULK (Jennifer Walters as Hulk; follows events of Civil War II)(Continues as She-Hulk #159)
Marvel Comics: Feb, 2017 - No. 11, Dec, 2017 ($3.99)

1-11: 1-6-Mariko Tamaki-s/Nico Leon-a. 3,11-Hellcat app. 4.00

HULK (Follows Immortal Hulk series)
Marvel Comics: Jan, 2022 - No. 14, Jun, 2023 ($4.99/$3.99)

1-($4.99) Donny Cates-s/Ryan Ottley-a 5.00

2-14-($3.99) 2-Alternate dimension Wolverine app. 7,8-Iron Man & Thor app. 4.00

Annual 1 (7/23, $4.99) Pepose-s/Majado-a; bonus prelude to Incredible Hulk #1 (2023) 5.00

HULK AND POWER PACK (All ages series)
Marvel Comics: May, 2007 - No. 4, Aug, 2007 ($2.99, limited series)

1-4-Sumerak-s. 1,2,4-Williams-a. 1-Absorbing Man app. 3-Kuhn-a; Abomination app. 3.00

...: Pack Smash! (2007, $6.99, digest) r/#1-4 7.00

HULK & THING: HARD KNOCKS
Marvel Comics: Nov, 2004 - No. 4, Feb, 2005 ($3.50, limited series)

1-4-Bruce Jones-s/Jae Lee-a/c 3.50

TPB (2005, $13.99) r/#1-4 and Giant-Size Super-Stars #1 14.00

HULK: BROKEN WORLDS
Marvel Comics: May, 2009 -No. 2, July, 2009 ($3.99, limited series)

1,2-Short stories of alternate world Hulks by various, incl. Trimpe, David, Warren 4.00

HULK CHRONICLES: WWH
Marvel Comics: Oct, 2008 - No. 6, Mar, 2009 ($4.99, limited series)

1-6-Reprints stories from World War Hulk x-over. 1-R/Inc. Hulk #106 & WWH Prologue 5.00

HULK: DESTRUCTION
Marvel Comics: Sept, 2005 - No. 4, Dec, 2005 ($2.99, limited series)

1-4-Origin of the Abomination; Peter David-s/Jim Muniz-a 3.00

HULKED-OUT HEROES
Marvel Comics: Jun, 2010 - No. 2, Jun, 2010 ($3.99, limited series)

1,2-World War Hulks tie-in; Deadpool app.; Ramos-a 4.00

HULK: FUTURE IMPERFECT
Marvel Comics: Jan, 1993 - No. 2, Dec, 1992 (In error) ($5.95, 52 pgs., squarebound, limited series)

1,2: Embossed-c; Peter David story & George Perez-c/a. 1-1st app. Maestro. | 3 | 6 | 9 | 14 | 20 | 25

HULK: GRAND DESIGN
Marvel Comics: May, 2022 - Jun, 2022 ($5.99, limited series)

... - Madness 1 (6/22, $5.99) Jim Rugg-s/a; revisits events from Inc. Hulk #301-474 6.00

... - Monster 1 (5/22, $5.99) Jim Rugg-s/a; revisits highlights from Inc. Hulk #1-300 6.00

HULK: GRAY
Marvel Comics: Dec, 2003 - No. 6, Apr, 2004 ($3.50, limited series)

1-6-Hulk's origin & early days; Loeb-s/Sale-a/c 4.00

HC (2004, $21.99, with dust jacket) oversized r/#1-6 22.00

SC (2005, $19.99) r/#1-6 20.00

HULKLING & WICCAN
Marvel Comics: Aug, 2022 ($5.99, one-shot)

1-Trujillo-s/Nishijima-a 6.00

HULK: NIGHTMERICA
Marvel Comics: Aug, 2003 - No. 6, May, 2004 ($2.99, limited series)

1-6-Brian Ashmore painted-a/c 4.00

HULK/ PITT
Marvel Comics: 1997 ($5.99, one-shot)

1-David-s/Keown-c/a | 1 | 3 | 4 | 6 | 8 | 10

HULK: SEASON ONE
Marvel Comics: 2012 ($24.99, hardcover graphic novel)

HC - Origin and early days; Van Lente-s/Fowler-a/Tedesco painted-c 25.00

HULK SMASH
Marvel Comics: Mar, 2001 - No. 2, Apr, 2001 ($2.99, limited series)

1,2-Ennis-s/McCrea & Janson-a/Nowlan painted-c 3.00

HULK SMASH AVENGERS
Marvel Comics: Jul, 2012 - No. 5, July, 2012 ($2.99, weekly limited series)

1-5-Hulk vs. Avengers from various points in Marvel History. 1-Frenz-a. 5-Oeming-a 3.00

HULK: THE MOVIE
Marvel Comics

...Adaptation (8/03, $3.50) Bruce Jones-s/Bagley-a/Keown-c 4.00

TPB (2003, $12.99) r/Adaptation, Ultimates #5, Inc. Hulk #34, Ult. Marvel Team-Up #2&3 13.00

HULK 2099
Marvel Comics: Dec, 1994 - No. 10, Sept, 1995 ($1.50/$1.95)

1-($2.50)-Green foil-c | 1 | 2 | 3 | 5 | 6 | 8

2-10: 2-A. Kubert-a. 4.00

HULKVERINES
Marvel Comics: Apr, 2019 - No. 3, Jun, 2019 ($4.99)

1-3-Hulk, Weapon H, Wolverine and The Leader app.; Pak-s/Anindito-a 4.00

HULK VS. THOR: BANNER OF WAR ALPHA (Tie-in to Hulk #7,8, Thor #25,26 x-over)
Marvel Comics: Apr, 2022 ($5.99, one-shot)

1-Part 1 of x-over; Cates-s/Coccolo-a; The Watcher app.; continues in Thor #25 5.00

HULK/WOLVERINE: 6 HOURS
Marvel Comics: Mar, 2003 - No. 4, May, 2003 ($2.99, limited series)

1-4-Bruce Jones-s/Scott Kolins-a; Bisley-c 3.00

Hulk Legends Vol. 1: Hulk/Wolverine: 6 Hours (2003, $13.99, TPB) r/#1-4 & 1st Wolverine app. from Incredible Hulk #181 14.00

HUMAN BOMB
DC Comics: Feb, 2013 - No. 4, May, 2013 ($2.99, limited series)

1-4: 1-Re-intro/origin; Gray & Palmiotti-s/Ordway-a/c 3.00

HUMAN DEFENSE CORPS
DC Comics: Jul, 2003 - No. 6, Dec, 2003 ($2.50, limited series)

1-6-Ty Templeton-s/Sauve, Jr. & Vlasco-a. 1-Lois Lane app. 3.00

HUMAN FLY
I.W. Enterprises/Super: 1963 - 1964 (Reprints)

I.W. Reprint #1-Reprints Blue Beetle #44('46) | 3 | 6 | 9 | 15 | 22 | 28

Super Reprint #10-R/Blue Beetle #46('47) | 3 | 6 | 9 | 15 | 22 | 28

HUMAN FLY, THE
Marvel Comics Group: Sept, 1977 - No. 19, Mar, 1979

1-(Regular 30¢-c) Origin; Spider-Man x-over | 3 | 6 | 9 | 21 | 33 | 45

1-(35¢-c, limited distribution) | 10 | 20 | 30 | 64 | 132 | 200

2-(Regular 30¢-c)-Ghost Rider app. | 2 | 4 | 6 | 11 | 16 | 20

2-(35¢-c, limited distribution) | 6 | 12 | 18 | 41 | 76 | 110

HU

	GD	VG	FN	VF	VF/NM	NM-		GD	VG	FN	VF	VF/NM	NM-
	2.0	4.0	6.0	8.0	9.0	9.2		2.0	4.0	6.0	8.0	9.0	9.2

3-8,10-18 ... 5.00
9,19: 9-Daredevil x-over; Byrne-c(p). 19-Last issue 2 4 6 8 10 12
NOTE: *Austin* c-4i, 9i. *Elias* a-1, 3p, 4p, 7p, 10-12p, 15p, 18p, 19p. *Layton* c-19.

HUMANKIND
Image Comics (Top Cow): Sept, 2004 - No. 5, Mar, 2005 ($2.99, limited series)
1-5-Tony Daniel-a. 1-Three covers by Daniel, Silvestri, and Land 3.00

HUMAN RACE, THE
DC Comics: May, 2005 - No. 7, Nov, 2005 ($2.99, limited series)
1-7-Raab-s/Justiniano-a/c 3.00

HUMAN TARGET
DC Comics (Vertigo): Apr, 1999 - No. 4, July, 1999 ($2.95, limited series)
1-4-Milligan-s/Bradstreet-c/Biukovic-a 4.00
1-Special Edition (6/10, $1.00) r/#1 with "What's Next?" logo on cover 4.00
TPB (2000, $12.95) new Bradstreet-c 13.00
...: Chance Meetings TPB (2010, $14.99) r/#1-4 and Human Target: Final Cut GN 15.00

HUMAN TARGET
DC Comics (Vertigo): Oct, 2003 - No. 21, June, 2005 ($2.95)
1-21: 1-5-Milligan-s/Pulido-a/c. 6-Chiang-a 3.00
...: Living in Amerika TPB (2004, $14.95) r/#6-10; Chiang sketch pages 15.00
...: Second Chances TPB (2011, $19.99) r/#1-10; Chiang sketch pages 20.00
...: Strike Zones TPB (2004, $9.95) r/#1-5 10.00

HUMAN TARGET (Based on the Fox TV series)
DC Comics: Apr, 2010 - No. 6, Sept, 2010 ($2.99, limited series)
1-6-Wein-s/Redondo-a; back-up stories by various. 1-Bermejo-c. 5-Sook-c 3.00
TPB (2010, $17.99) r/#1-6 18.00

HUMAN TARGET, THE (Also see Tales of the Human Target)
DC Comics (Black Label): Jan, 2022 - No. 12, Apr, 2023 ($4.99, limited series)
1-12-Tom King-s/Greg Smallwood-a; Ice app. 3,6-Guy Gardner app. 8-Rocket Red app. 5.00

HUMAN TARGET: FINAL CUT
DC Comics (Vertigo): 2002 ($29.95/$19.95, graphic novel)
Hardcover (2002, $29.95) Milligan-s/Pulido-a/c 30.00
Softcover (2003, $19.95) 20.00

HUMAN TARGET SPECIAL (TV)
DC Comics: Nov, 1991 (52 pgs., one-shot)
1 4.00

HUMAN TORCH, THE (Red Raven #1)(See All-Select, All Winners, Marvel Mystery, Men's Adventures, Mystic Comics (2nd series), Sub-Mariner, USA & Young Men)
Timely/Marvel Comics (TP 2,3/TCI 4-9/SePI 10/SnPC 11-25/CnPC 26-35/Atlas Comics (CPC 36-38)): No. 2, Fall, 1940 - No. 15, Spring, 1944; No. 16, Fall, 1944 - No. 35, Mar, 1949 (Becomes Love Tales #36 on); No. 36, April, 1954 - No. 38, Aug, 1954

2(#1)-Intro & Origin Toro; The Falcon, The Fiery Mask, Mantor the Magician, & Microman only app.; Human Torch by Burgos, Sub-Mariner by Everett begin (origin of each in text); WWII-c 3075 6150 9225 21,500 50,700 82,000
3(#2)-40 pg. H.T. story; H.T. & S.M. battle over who is best artist in text-Everett or Burgos 838 1676 2514 6117 10,809 15,500
4(#3)-Origin The Patriot in text; last Everett Sub-Mariner; Sid Greene-a 649 1298 1947 4738 8369 12,000
5(#4)-The Patriot app; Angel x-over in Sub-Mariner (Summer, 1941); 1st Nazi war-c this title; back-c ad for Young Allies #1 with diff. cover-a 514 1028 1542 3750 6625 9500
5-Human Torch battles Sub-Mariner (Fall, '41); 60 pg. story 757 1514 2271 5526 9763 14,000
6-Schomburg hooded villain bondage-c 423 846 1269 3088 5444 7800
7-1st Japanese war-c 459 918 1377 3350 5925 8500
8-Human Torch battles Sub-Mariner; 52 pg. story; Wolverton-a, 1 pg.; Nazi WWII-c 757 1514 2271 5526 9763 14,000
9-Classic Human Torch vs. Gen. Rommel, "The Desert Rat"; Nazi WWII-c 514 1028 1542 3750 6625 9500
10-Human Torch battles Sub-Mariner, 45 pg. story; Wolverton-a, 1 pg.; Nazi WWII-c 508 1016 1524 3708 6554 9400
11,14,15: 11-Nazi WWII-c. 14-Nazi WWII-c; 1st Atlas Globe logo (Winter, 1943-44; see All Winners #11 also) 371 742 1113 2600 4550 6500
12-Classic Japanese WWII-c, Torch melts Japanese soldier's arm 1600 3200 4800 12,000 22,000 32,000
13-Classic Schomburg Japanese WWII bondage-c 420 840 1260 2940 5170 7400
16-20: 16-18,20-Japanese WWII-c. 19-Bondage-c. 20-Last War issue 300 600 900 1920 3310 4700
21,22,24-30: 27-2nd app. (1st-c) Asbestos Lady (see Capt. America Comics #63 for 1st app.) 232 464 696 1485 2543 3600
23 (Sum/46)-Becomes Junior Miss 24? Classic Schomburg Robot-c 389 778 1167 2723 4762 6800
31,32: 31-Namora x-over in Sub-Mariner (also #30); last Toro. 32-Sungirl, Namora app.; Sungirl-c 206 412 618 1318 2259 3200
33-Capt. America x-over 258 516 774 1651 2826 4000
34-Sungirl solo 206 412 618 1318 2259 3200
35-Captain America & Sungirl app. (1949) 206 412 618 1318 2259 3200
36-38(1954)-Sub-Mariner in all 174 348 522 1114 1907 2700
NOTE: *Ayers* Human Torch in 36(3). *Brodsky* c-25, 31-33?, 37, 38. *Burgos* c-36. *Everett* a-1-3, 27, 28, 30, 37, 38. *Powell* a-36(Sub-Mariner). *Schomburg* c-1-3, 5-8, 10-23. *Sekowsky* c-28, 34?, 35? *Shores* c-24, 26, 27, 29, 30. *Mickey Spillane* a-2, 12, 19.

HUMAN TORCH, THE (Also see Avengers West Coast, Fantastic Four, The Invaders, Saga of the Original... & Strange Tales #101)
Marvel Comics Group: Sept, 1974 - No. 8, Nov, 1975
1: 1-8-r/stories from Strange Tales #101-108 6 12 18 37 66 95
2-8: 1st H.T. title since G.A. 7-vs. Sub-Mariner 3 6 9 16 23 30
NOTE: *Golden Age & Silver Age Human Torch-r #1-8. Ayers r-6, 7. Kirby/Ayers r-1-5, 8.*

HUMAN TORCH (From the Fantastic Four)
Marvel Comics: June, 2003 - No. 12, Jun, 2004 ($2.50/$2.99)
1-7-Skottie Young-c/a; Karl Kesel-s 3.00
8-12 ($2.99) 8,10-Dodd-a. 9-Young-a. 11-Porter-a. 12-Medina-a 3.00
...: Vol. 1: Burn TPB (2005, $7.99, digest size) r/#1-6 8.00

HUMAN TORCH COMICS 70TH ANNIVERSARY SPECIAL
Marvel Comics: July, 2009 ($3.99, one-shot)
1-Covers by Granov and Martin; new story and r/1st app Toro from Human Torch #2 5.00

HUMBUG (Satire by Harvey Kurtzman)
Humbug Publications: Aug, 1957 - No. 9, May, 1958; No. 10, June, 1958; No. 11, Oct, 1958
1-Wood-a (intro pgs. only) 28 56 84 165 270 375
2 15 30 45 85 130 175
3-9: 8-Elvis in Jailbreak Rock 14 28 42 76 108 140
10,11-Magazine format. 10-Photo-c 15 30 45 90 140 190
Bound Volume(#1-9)(extremely rare) 65 130 195 416 708 1000
NOTE: *Davis* a-1-11. *Elder* a-2-4, 6-9, 11. *Heath* a-2, 4-8, 10. *Jaffee* a-2, 4-9. *Kurtzman* a-11.

HUMDINGER (Becomes White Rider and Super Horse #3 on?)
Novelty Press/Premium Group: May-June, 1946 - V2#2, July-Aug, 1947
1-Jerkwater Line, Mickey Starlight by Don Rico, Dink begin 39 78 117 240 395 550
2 18 36 54 105 165 225
3-6, V2#1,2 14 28 42 78 112 145

HUMONGOUS MAN
Alternative Press (Ikon Press): Sept, 1997 -No. 3 ($2.25, B&W)
1-3-Stepp & Harrison-c/s/a. 4.00

HUMOR (See All Humor Comics)

HUMPHREY COMICS (Joe Palooka Presents...; also see Joe Palooka)
Harvey Publications: Oct, 1948 - No. 22, Apr, 1952
1-Joe Palooka's pal (r); (52 pgs.)-Powell-a 17 34 51 100 158 215
2,3: Powell-a 10 20 30 54 72 90
4-Boy Heroes app.; Powell-a 11 22 33 62 86 110
5-8,10: 5,6-Powell-a. 7-Little Dot app. 8 16 24 42 54 65
9-Origin Humphrey 9 18 27 50 65 80
11-22 8 16 24 40 50 60

HUNCHBACK OF NOTRE DAME, THE
Dell Publishing Co.: No. 854, Oct, 1957 (one shot)
Four Color 854-Movie, photo-c 12 24 36 79 170 260

HUNGER (See Age of Ultron and Cataclysm titles)
Marvel Comics: Sept, 2013 - No. 4, Dec, 2013 ($3.99, limited series)
1-4-Fialkov-s/Kirk-a/Granov-c; Galactus in the Ultimate Universe. 2-4-Silver Surfer app. 4.00
1-Variant-c by Neal Adams 18.00

HUNGER, THE
Speakeasy Comics: May, 2005 ($2.99)
1-Andy Bradshaw-s/a; Eric Powell-c 3.00

HUNGER DOGS, THE (See DC Graphic Novel #4)

HUNGRY GHOSTS
Dark Horse Comics (Berger Books): Jan, 2018 - No. 4, Apr, 2018 ($3.99, limited series)
1-4-Anthony Bourdain & Joel Rose-s/Paul Pope-c. 1-Ponticella & Del Rey-a. 2-Manco & Santolouco-a. 3-Cabrol & Paul Pope-a. 4-Francavilla & Koh-a 4.00

HUNK
Charlton Comics: Aug, 1961 - No. 11, 1963
1 4 8 12 23 37 50
2-11 3 6 9 14 20 25

HUNT, THE
Image Comics (Shadowline): Jul, 2016 - No. 5, Dec, 2016 ($3.99)
1-5-Colin Lorimer-s/a 4.00

HUNTED (Formerly My Love Memoirs)
Fox Feature Syndicate: No. 13, Jul, 1950; No. 2, Sept, 1950
13(#1)-Used in SOTI, pg. 42 & illo. "Treating police contemptuously" (lower left); Hollingsworth bondage-c 77 154 231 493 847 1200
2 27 54 81 158 259 360

HUNTER-KILLER
Image Comics (Top Cow): Nov, 2004 - No. 12, Mar, 2007 ($2.99)
0-(11/04, 25c) Prelude with Silvestri sketch page and Waid afterword 3.00
1-12: 1-(3/05, $2.99) Waid-s/Silvestri-a; four covers. 2-Linsner variant-c 3.00
...: Collected Edition Vol. 1 (9/05, $4.99) r/#0-3 5.00
...Dossier 1 (9/05, $2.99) character profiles with art by various; Migliari-c 3.00
...: Volume 1 TPB (1/08, $24.99) r/#0-12; Dossier and Script Book; variant covers 25.00

HUNTER: THE AGE OF MAGIC (See Books of Magic)
DC Comics (Vertigo): Sept, 2001 - No. 25, Sept, 2003 ($2.50/$2.75)
1-25: Horrocks-s/Case-a. 1-8-Bolton-c. 14-Begin $2.75-c. 19-Bachalo-c 3.00

HUNT FOR THE SKINWALKER
BOOM! Studios: Sept, 2023 - No. 4, Dec, 2023 ($4.99, limited series)
1-4-Zac Thompson-s/Valeria Burzo-a 5.00

HUNT FOR WOLVERINE (Leads into Return of Wolverine series)
Marvel Comics: Jun, 2018 ($5.99)
1-Soule-s; Logan's removal from the statue; X-Men, Tony Stark, Daredevil app. 6.00
...: Dead Ends 1 (10/18, $4.99) Soule-s/Rosanas-a; conclusion to story 5.00

HUNT FOR WOLVERINE: ADAMANTIUM AGENGA
Marvel Comics: Jul, 2018 - No. 4, Oct, 2018 ($3.99, limited series)
1-4-Iron Man, Spider-Man, Jessica Jones & Luke Cage app.; Taylor-s/Silva-a 4.00

HUNT FOR WOLVERINE: CLAWS OF A KILLER
Marvel Comics: Jul, 2018 - No. 4, Oct, 2018 ($3.99, limited series)
1-4-Sabretooth, Daken & Lady Deathstrike app.; Tamaki-s/Guice-a 4.00

HUNT FOR WOLVERINE: MYSTERY IN MADRIPOOR
Marvel Comics: Jul, 2018 - No. 4, Oct, 2018 ($3.99, limited series)
1-4-Psylocke, Storm, Rogue, Jubilee, Kitty Pryde & Domino app.; Zub-s/Silas-a 4.00

HUNT FOR WOLVERINE: WEAPON LOST
Marvel Comics: Jul, 2018 - No. 4, Oct, 2018 ($3.99, limited series)

Human Target (2021 series) #7 © DC

Hungry Ghosts #4 © Bourdain & Rose

Ice Cream Man #17 © Prince & Morazzo

IC

	GD	VG	FN	VF	VF/NM	NM-
	2.0	4.0	6.0	8.0	9.0	9.2

1-4-Daredevil, Misty Knight & Cypher app.; Soule-s/Buffagni-a 4.00

HUNTRESS, THE (See All-Star Comics #69, Batman Family, DC Super Stars #17, Detective #652, Infinity, Inc. #1 & Wonder Woman #271)
DC Comics: Apr, 1989 - No. 19, Oct, 1990 ($1.00, mature)

1-Staton-c/a(p) in all	2	4	6	9	12	15

2-19: 17-19-Batman-c/stories 4.00
..: Darknight Daughter TPB (2006, $19.99) r/origin & early apps. in DC Super Stars #17,
Batman Family #18-20 & Wonder Woman #271-287,289,290,294,295; Bolland-c 20.00

HUNTRESS, THE
DC Comics: June, 1994 - No. 4, Sept, 1994 ($1.50, limited series)

1-4-Netzer-c/a: 2-Batman app. 4.00

HUNTRESS (Leads into 2012 World's Finest series)
DC Comics: Dec, 2011 - No. 6, May, 2012 ($2.99, limited series)

1-6-Levitz-s/To-a/March-c 3.00

HUNTRESS: YEAR ONE
DC Comics: Early July, 2008 - No. 6, Late Sept, 2008 ($2.99, limited series)

1-6-Origin re-told; Cliff Richards-a/Ivory Madison-s 3.00
TPB (2009, $17.99) r/#1-6; intro. by Paul Levitz 18.00

HURRICANE COMICS
Cambridge House: 1945 (52 pgs.)

1-(Humor, funny animal)	36	72	108	211	343	475

HYBRIDS
Continuity Comics: Jan, 1994 ($2.50, one-shot)

1-Neal Adams-c(p) & part-a(i); embossed-c 4.00

HYBRIDS DEATHWATCH 2000
Continuity Comics: Apr, 1993 - No. 3, Aug, 1993 ($2.50)

0-(Giveaway)-Foil-c; Neal Adams-c(i) & plots (also #1,2) 4.00
1-3: 1-Polybagged w/card; die-cut-c. 2-Thermal-c. 3-Polybagged w/card;
indestructible-c; Adams plot 4.00

HYBRIDS ORIGIN
Continuity Comics: 1993 - No. 5, Jan, 1994 ($2.50)

1-5: 2,3-Neal Adams-c. 4,5-Valeria the She-Bat app. Adams-c(i) 4.00

HYDE
IDW Publ.: Oct, 2004 ($7.49, one-shot)

1-Steve Niles-s/Nick Stakal 7.50

HYDE-25
Harris Publications: Apr, 1995 ($2.95, one-shot)

0-Coupon for poster; r/Vampirella's 1st app. 4.00

HYDROMAN (See Heroic Comics)

HYPERION (Squadron Supreme)
Marvel Comics: May, 2016 - No. 6, Oct, 2016 ($3.99)

1-6: 1-4,6-Wendig-s/Virella-a. 5-Anindito-a. 5,6-Iron Man & Thundra app. 4.00

HYPERKIND (See Razorline)
Marvel Comics: Sept, 1993 - No. 9, May, 1994 ($1.75/$1.95)

1-($2.50)-Foil embossed-c; by Clive Barker 5.00
2-9 .... 4.00
...Unleashed 1 (8/94, $2.95, 52 pgs., one-shot) 5.00

HYPER MYSTERY COMICS
Hyper Publications: May, 1940 - No. 2, June, 1940 (68 pgs.)

1-Hyper, the Phenomenal begins; Calkins-a	300	600	900	2010	3505	5000
2-H.G. Peter-a	187	374	561	1197	2049	2900

HYPERNATURALS
BOOM! Studios: Jul, 2012 - No. 12, Jun, 2013 ($3.99)

1-12: 1-Abnett & Lanning-s/Walker & Guinaldo-a; at least eight covers. 2-Two printings 4.00
... Free Comic Book Day Edition (5/12) Prelude to issue #1 .... 3.00

HYPERSONIC
Dark Horse Comics: Nov, 1997 - No. 4, Feb, 1998 ($2.95, limited series)

1-4: Abnett & White-s/Erskine-a 4.00

I AIM AT THE STARS (Movie)
Dell Publishing Co.: No. 1148, Nov-Jan/1960-61 (one-shot)

Four Color 1148-The Werner Von Braun Sty-photo-c	7	14	21	44	82	120

I AM AN AVENGER (See Avengers, Young Avengers and Pet Avengers)
Marvel Comics: Nov, 2010 - No. 5, Mar, 2011 ($3.99, limited series)

1-5-Short stories by various. 1-Yu-c. 2-Land-c. 2-4-Mayhew-a. 3-Noto-c. 4-Acuña-c 4.00

I AM BATMAN (Jace Fox from Future State)(Story continued from The Next Batman; Second Son)
DC Comics: No. 0, Oct, 2021 - No. 18, Apr, 2023 ($4.99/$3.99)

0-($4.99) John Ridley-s/Travel Foreman-a 5.00
1-18-($3.99) Ridley-s. 1-4-Segovia-a. 13,14-The Question app. 15-Sinestro app. 4.00

I AM CAPTAIN AMERICA
Marvel Comics: Jan, 2012 ($3.99, one-shot)

1-Collection of Captain America-themed 70th Anniversary covers with artist profiles 4.00

I AM COYOTE (See Eclipse Graphic Album Series & Eclipse Magazine #2)

I AM GROOT (Guardians of the Galaxy)
Marvel Comics: Jul, 2017 - No. 5, Nov, 2017 ($3.99, limited series)

1-Hastings-s/Flaviano-a; Guardians of the Galaxy app.	1	3	4	6	8	10

2-5: 5-Guardians of the Galaxy app. 4.00

I AM IRON MAN
Marvel Comics: May, 2023 - No. 5, Sept, 2023 ($3.99, limited series)

1-5-Murewa Ayodele-s/Dotun Akande-a. 4-Dr. Strange app. 4.00

I AM LEGEND
Eclipse Books: 1991 - No. 4, 1991 ($5.95, B&W, squarebound, 68 pgs.)

1-4: Based on 1954 novel by Richard Matheson	1	2	3	5	6	8

I AM LEGION (English version of French graphic novel Je Suis Légion)
Devils Due Publishing: Jan, 2009 - No. 6, July, 2009 ($3.50)

1-6-John Cassaday-a/Fabien Nury-s; two covers 3.50

IBIS, THE INVINCIBLE (See Fawcett Miniatures, Mighty Midget & Whiz)
Fawcett Publications: 1942 (Fall?); #2, Mar.,1943; #3, Wint, 1945 - #5, Fall, 1946; #6, Spring, 1948

1-Origin Ibis; Raboy-c; on sale 1/2/43	271	542	813	1734	2967	4200
2-Bondage-c (on sale 2/5/43)	116	232	348	742	1271	1800
3-Wolverton-a #3-6 (4 pgs. each)	77	154	231	493	847	1200
4-6: 5-Bondage-c	53	106	159	334	567	800

NOTE: *Mac Raboy c(p)-3-5. Schaffenberger c-6.*

I-BOTS (See Isaac Asimov's I-BOTS)

I CAN SELL YOU A BODY
IDW Publ.: Dec, 2019 - No. 4, Mar, 2020 ($3.99)

1-4-Ryan Ferrier-s/George Kambadais-a 4.00

ICE AGE ON THE WORLD OF MAGIC: THE GATHERING (See Magic The Gathering)

ICE CREAM MAN (Horror anthology)
Image Comics: Jan, 2018 - Present ($3.99)

1-Prince-s/Morazzo-a; 1st app. of the Ice Cream Man	9	18	27	59	117	175
1-2nd printing	5	10	15	33	57	80
2	4	8	12	23	37	50
3-15	2	4	6	10	14	18

16-24,26-38: 17-Action Comics #1 cover swipe. 20-Dr. Seuss homage (10 pgs.) 4.00
25-($4.99) Bonus back-up story 5.00

... Presents Quarantine Comix Special 1 (9/20, $5.99) Printing of online mini-comics	2	4	6	10	14	18

ICE KING OF OZ, THE (See First Comics Graphic Novel #13)

ICEMAN (Also see The Champions & X-Men #94)
Marvel Comics Group: Dec, 1984 - No. 4, June, 1985 (Limited series)

1,2,4: Zeck covers on all 4.00
3-The Defenders, Champions (Ghost Rider) & the original X-Men x-over 5.00

ICEMAN (X-Men)
Marvel Comics: Dec, 2001 - No. 4, Mar, 2002 ($2.50, limited series)

1-4-Abnett & Lanning-s/Kerschl-a 3.00

ICEMAN (X-Men)
Marvel Comics: Aug, 2017 - No. 11, May, 2018 ($3.99)

1-11: 1-Grace-s/Vitti-a. 2-Kitty Pryde app. 5-Juggernaut app. 4.00

ICEMAN (X-Men)
Marvel Comics: Nov, 2018 - No. 5, Mar, 2019 ($3.99, limited series)

1-5: 1-Grace-s/Stockman-a. 2-White Queen app. 4,5-Mr. Sinister app. 4.00

ICEMAN AND ANGEL (X-Men)
Marvel Comics: May, 2011 ($2.99, one-shot)

1-Brian Clevinger-s/Juan Doe-a; Goom & Googam app. 3.00

	GD	VG	FN	VF	VF/NM	NM-
	2.0	4.0	6.0	8.0	9.0	9.2

ICON
DC Comics (Milestone): May, 1993 - No. 42, Feb, 1997 ($1.50/$1.75/$2.50)

	GD	VG	FN	VF	VF/NM	NM-
1-($2.95)-Collector's Edition polybagged w/poster & trading card (direct sale only)						
	2	4	6	11	16	20
1-Regular edition	2	4	6	9	12	15
2-24,30-42: 9-Simonson-c. 15,16-Worlds Collide Pt. 4 & 11. 15-Superboy app.						
16-Superman-c/story. 40-Vs. Blood Syndicate						4.00
25-($2.95, 52 pgs.)						6.00
... A Hero's Welcome SC (2009, $19.99) r/#1-8; intro. by Reginald Hudlin						
	3	6	9	21	33	45
...: Mothership Connection SC (2010, $24.99) r/#13,19-22,24-27,30						25.00

ICON & ROCKET: SEASON ONE
DC Comics: Sept, 2021 - No. 6, May, 2022 ($3.99)

1-6-Hudlin-s/Braithwaite-a. 5,6-Static app.						4.00

ICON VS. HARDWARE
DC Comics: Apr, 2023 - Present ($4.99)

1-5-Hudlin & Chills-s/Cowan & Montanez-a. 4-Brainiac app.						5.00

IDAHO
Dell Publishing Co.: June-Aug, 1963 - No. 8, July-Sept, 1965

	GD	VG	FN	VF	VF/NM	NM-
1	3	6	9	18	27	36
2-8: 5-7-Painted-c	2	4	6	9	13	16

IDEAL (... a Classical Comic) (2nd Series) (Love Romances No. 6 on)
Timely Comics: July, 1948 - No. 5, March, 1949 (Feature length stories)

	GD	VG	FN	VF	VF/NM	NM-
1-Antony & Cleopatra	42	84	126	265	445	625
2-The Corpses of Dr. Sacotti	37	74	111	222	361	500
3-Joan of Arc; used in SOTI, pg. 310 'Boer War'	34	68	102	204	332	460
4-Richard the Lion-hearted; titled "...the World's Greatest Comics":						
The Witness story	47	94	141	296	498	700
5-Ideal Love & Romance; change to love; photo-c	24	48	72	142	234	325

IDEAL COMICS (1st Series) (Willie Comics No. 5 on)
Timely Comics (MgPC): Fall, 1944 - No. 4, Spring, 1946

	GD	VG	FN	VF	VF/NM	NM-
1-Funny animal; Super Rabbit in all	50	100	150	315	533	750
2	25	50	75	150	245	340
3,4	22	44	66	132	216	300

IDEAL LOVE & ROMANCE (See Ideal, A Classical Comic)

IDEAL ROMANCE (Formerly Tender Romance)
Key Publ.: No. 3, April, 1954 - No. 8, Feb, 1955 (Diary Confessions No. 9 on)

	GD	VG	FN	VF	VF/NM	NM-
3-Bernard Baily-c	15	30	45	85	130	175
4-8: 4-6-B. Baily-c	11	22	33	62	86	110

IDEALS (Secret Stories)
Ideals Publ., USA: 1981 (68 pgs, graphic novels, 7x10", stiff-c)

	GD	VG	FN	VF	VF/NM	NM-
Captain America - Star Spangled Super Hero	3	6	9	19	30	40
Fantastic Four - Cosmic Quartet	3	6	9	19	30	40
Incredible Hulk - Gamma Powered Goliath	3	6	9	19	30	40
Spider-Man - World Famous Wall Crawler	4	8	12	23	37	50

IDENTITY CRISIS
DC Comics: Aug, 2004 - No. 7, Feb, 2005 ($3.95, limited series)

1-Meltzer-s/Morales-a/Turner-c in all; Sue Dibny murdered						5.00
1-(Second printing) black-c with white sketch lines						5.00
1-(3rd & 4th) 3rd-Bloody broken photo glass image-c by Morales. 4th-Turner red-c						4.00
1-Diamond Retailer Summit Edition with sketch-c						30.00
1-Special Edition (6/09, $1.00) r/#1 with "After Watchmen" cover frame						3.00
2-7: 2-4-Deathstroke app. 5-Firestorm, Jack Drake, Capt. Boomerang killed						4.00
2-(Second printing) new Morales sketch-c						4.00
Final printings for all issues with red background variant covers						
HC (2005, $24.99, dust jacket) r/series; Director's Cut extras; cover gallery; Whedon intro.;						
2 covers: Direct Market-c by Turner, Bookstore-c with Morales-a						25.00
SC (2006, $14.99) r/series; Director's Cut extras; cover gallery; Whedon intro						15.00

IDENTITY DISC
Marvel Comics: Aug, 2004 - No. 5, Dec, 2004 ($2.99, limited series)

1-5-Sabretooth, Bullseye, Sandman, Vulture, Deadpool app.; Higgins-a						4.00
TPB (2004, $13.99) r/#1-5						14.00

IDES OF BLOOD
DC Comics (WildStorm): Oct, 2010 - No. 6, Mar, 2011 ($3.99/$2.99, limited series)

1-6-Stuart Paul-s/Christian Duce-a/Michael Geiger-c; Roman Empire vampires						4.00

I DIE AT MIDNIGHT (Vertigo V2K)
DC Comics (Vertigo): 2000 ($6.95, prestige format, one-shot)

1-Kyle Baker-s/a						7.00

IDOL
Marvel Comics (Epic Comics): 1992 - No. 3, 1992 ($2.95, mini-series, 52 pgs.)

Book 1-3						4.00

IDOLIZED
Aspen MLT: No. 0, Jun, 2012 - No. 5, Apr, 2013 ($2.50/$3.99)

0-($2.50) Schwartz-s/Gunnell-a; regular & photo covers; Superhero Idol background						3.00
1-5-($3.99) 1-Art Adams & photo covers; origin of Joule						4.00

I DREAM OF JEANNIE (TV)
Dell Publishing Co.: Apr, 1966 - No. 2, Dec, 1966 (Photo-c)

	GD	VG	FN	VF	VF/NM	NM-
1-Barbara Eden photo-c, each	23	46	69	161	356	550
2	10	20	30	68	144	220

IDW ENDLESS SUMMER
IDW Publishing: Aug, 2023 ($4.99, series of one-shots)

... – Dungeons & Dragons Saturdday Morning Adventures 1-Booher-s/Lawrence-a						5.00
... – My Little Pony 1-Williams-s/Haines-a; spotlight on Sunny						5.00
... – Sonic the Hedgehog 1-Galligan-s/Yardley & Rothlisberger-a						5.00
... – Teenage Mutant Ninja Turtles 1-Dave Baker-s/Tango-a; Krang app.						5.00

I FEEL SICK

Slave Labor Graphics: Aug, 1999 - No. 2, May, 2000 ($3.95, limited series)

1,2-Jhonen Vasquez-s/a						4.00

IGNITED
Humanoids, Inc.: 2019 - Present ($3.99)

1-8: 1-Waid & Osajvefo-s/Briones-a						4.00

I HATE FAIRYLAND (Also see I Hate Image, FCBD Special)
Image Comics: Oct, 2015 - No. 20, Jul, 2018 ($3.50/$3.99)

1-10-Skottie Young-s/a/c; each has variant cover with "F*** Fairyland" title						3.50
11-20-($3.99) 12-Lone Wolf & Cub homage-c. 13-Rankine-a. 20-Finale						4.00
...: I Hate Image Special Edition (10/17, $5.99) r/I Hate Image FCBD Special with 4 new pages; bonus script and sketch art; 2 covers						6.00

I HATE FAIRYLAND (Volume 2)
Image Comics: Nov, 2022 - Present ($3.99)

1-11-Skottie Young-s/Brett Bean-a; Gert as a young adult						4.00

I HATE GALLANT GIRL
Image Comics (Shadowline): Nov, 2008 - No. 3, Jan, 2009 ($3.50, limited series)

1-3-Kat Cahill-s/Seth Damoose-a						3.50

I HATE IMAGE, FCBD SPECIAL
Image Comics: May, 2017 (free giveaway)

1-Gert from I Hate Fairyland vs. Image characters from Walking Dead, Bitch Planet, Saga, Paper Girls, Chew, Spawn and others; Skottie Young-s/a/c						3.00

I (heart) MARVEL
Marvel Comics: Apr, 2006; May, 2006 ($2.99, one-shots)

...: Marvel AI 1 (4/06) Cebulski-s; manga art by various; Vision, Daredevil, Elektra app.						3.00
...: Masked Intentions 1 (5/06) Squirrel Girl, Speedball, Firestar, Justice app.; Nicieza-s						4.00
...: My Mutant Heart 1 (4/06) Wolverine, Cannonball, Doop app.						3.00
...: Outlaw Love 1 (4/06) Bullseye, The Answer, Ruby Thursday app.; Nicieza-s						3.00
...: Web of Romance 1 (4/06) Spider-Man, Mary Jane, The Avengers app.						3.00

ILLEGITIMATES, THE
IDW Publishing: Dec, 2013 - No. 6, May, 2014 ($3.99)

1-6: 1-Taran Killam & Marc Andreyko-a/Kevin Sharpe-a; covers by Ordway & Willington						4.00

ILLUMINATI
Marvel Comics: Jan, 2016 - No. 7, Jul, 2016 ($3.99)

1-7: 1-Williamson-s/Crystal-a; The Hood, Titania and others team. 4-Thor app.						4.00

ILLUMINATOR
Marvel Comics/Nelson Publ.: 1993 - No. 4, 1993 ($4.99/$2.95, 52 pgs.)

1,2-($4.99) Religious themed						5.00
3,4						4.00

ILLUSTRATED GAGS
United Features Syndicate: No. 16, 1940

	GD	VG	FN	VF	VF/NM	NM-
Single Series 16	28	56	84	165	270	375

ILLUSTRATED LIBRARY OF..., AN (See Classics Illustrated Giants)

ILLUSTRATED STORIES OF THE OPERAS
Baily (Bernard) Publ. Co.: 1943 (16 pgs., B&W) (25 cents) (covers are black & red ink on white or yellow paper, with scarcer editions having B&W with red)

	GD	VG	FN	VF	VF/NM	NM-
nn-(Rare)(4 diff. issues)-Faust (part-r in Cisco Kid #1, 2 cover versions: 25¢ & no price)						
nn-Aida, nn-Carmen, Baily-a, nn-Rigoletto	93	186	279	591	1021	1450

ILLUSTRATED STORY OF ROBIN HOOD & HIS MERRY MEN, THE (See Classics Giveaways, 12/44)

ILLUSTRATED TARZAN BOOK, THE (See Tarzan Book)

I LOVED (Formerly Rulah; Colossal Features Magazine No. 33 on)
Fox Feature Syndicate: No. 28, July, 1949 - No. 32, Mar, 1950

	GD	VG	FN	VF	VF/NM	NM-
28	27	54	81	158	259	360
29-32	20	40	60	117	189	260

I LOVE LUCY
Eternity Comics: 6/90 - No. 6, 1990;V2#1, 11/90 - No. 6, 1991 ($2.95, B&W, mini-series)

1-6: Reprints 1950s comic strip; photo-c						4.00
Book II #1-6: Reprints comic strip; photo-c						4.00
...In Full Color 1 (1991, $5.95, 52 pgs.)-Reprints I Love Lucy Comics #4,5,8,16; photo-c with embossed logo (2 versions exist, one with pgs. 18 & 19 reversed, the other corrected)						

	GD	VG	FN	VF	VF/NM	NM-
	1	2	3	4	5	6
...In 3-D 1 (1991, $3.95, w/glasses)-Reprints I Love Lucy Comics; photo-c; bagged						6.00

I LOVE LUCY COMICS (TV) (Also see The Lucy Show)
Dell Publishing Co.: No. 535, Feb, 1954 - No. 35, Apr-June, 1962 (Lucille Ball photo-c on all)

	GD	VG	FN	VF	VF/NM	NM-
Four Color 535(#1)	48	96	144	374	862	1350
Four Color 559(#2, 5/54)	31	62	93	223	499	775
3 (8-10/54) - 5	17	34	51	119	265	410
6-10	13	26	39	87	191	295
11-20	10	20	30	68	144	220
21-35	9	18	27	59	117	175

I LOVE NEW YORK
Linsner.com: 2002 ($2.95, B&W, one-shot)

1-Linsner-s/a; benefit book for the Sept. 11 charities						3.00

I LOVE YOU
Fawcett Publications: June, 1950 (one-shot)

	GD	VG	FN	VF	VF/NM	NM-
1-Photo-c	20	40	60	117	189	260

I LOVE YOU (Formerly In Love)
Charlton Comics: No. 7, 9/55 - No. 121, 12/76; No. 122, 3/79 - No. 130, 5/80

	GD	VG	FN	VF	VF/NM	NM-
7-Kirby-c; Powell-a	10	20	30	66	138	210
8-10	5	10	15	35	63	90
11-16,18-20	5	10	15	33	57	80
17-(68 pg. Giant)	8	16	24	52	99	145
21-50: 26-No Torres-a	4	8	12	27	44	60
51-59	4	8	12	23	37	50
60-(1/66)-Elvis Presley line drawn c/story	17	34	51	119	265	410

I Hate Fairyland #4 © Skottie Young

Imaginary Fiends #1 © Seeley & Molnar

Immortal Hulk #35 © MAR

	GD 2.0	VG 4.0	FN 6.0	VF 8.0	VF/NM 9.0	NM- 9.2
61-85	3	6	9	16	23	30
86-90,92-98,100-110	2	4	6	8	11	14
91-(5/71) Ditko-a (5 pgs.)	3	6	9	14	19	24
99-David Cassidy pin-up	2	4	6	11	16	20
111-113,115-130	2	4	6	8	10	12
114-Psychedelic cover	3	6	9	18	28	38

I, LUSIPHUR (Becomes Poison Elves, 1st series #8 on)
Mulehide Graphics: 1991 - No. 7, 1992 (B&W, magazine size)

	GD 2.0	VG 4.0	FN 6.0	VF 8.0	VF/NM 9.0	NM- 9.2
1-Drew Hayes-c/a/scripts	7	14	21	49	92	135
2,4,5	3	6	9	14	20	25
3-Low print run	4	8	12	27	44	60
6,7	2	4	6	8	11	14

Poison Elves: Requiem For An Elf (Sirius Ent., 6/96, $14.95, trade paperback)
-Reprints I, Lusiphur #1,2 as text, and 3-6 .... 15.00

I'M A COP
Magazine Enterprises: 1954 - No. 3, 1954

	GD 2.0	VG 4.0	FN 6.0	VF 8.0	VF/NM 9.0	NM- 9.2
1(A-1 #111)-Powell-c/a in all	20	40	60	117	189	260
2(A-1 #126), 3(A-1 #128)	14	28	42	78	112	145

IMAGE COMICS HARDCOVER
Image Comics: 2005 ($24.99, hardcover with dust jacket)
Vol. 1-New Spawn by McFarlane-s/a; Savage Dragon origin by Larsen; CyberForce by Silvestri; ShadowHawk by Valentino; intro by Marder; Image timeline 25.00

IMAGE COMICS SUMMER SPECIAL
Image Comics: July, 2004 (Free Comic Book Day giveaway)
1-New short stories of Spawn, Invincible, Savage Dragon and Witchblade 3.00

IMAGE FIRST
Image Comics: 2005 ($6.99, TPB)
Vol. 1 (2005) r/Strange Girl #1, Sea of Red #1, The Walking Dead #1 and Girls #1 .... 3 6 9 14 20 25

IMAGE FIRSTS (Reprints of first issues)
Image Comics: Feb, 2021 ($1.00, series of one-shots)
...: Ascender #1 - Lemire-s/Nguyen-a 3.00
...: Bitter Root #1 - Walker & Brown/Greene-a 3.00
...: Die #1 - Gillen-s/Hans-a 3.00
...: Killadelphia #1 - Barnes-s/Alexander-a 3.00
...: Mercy #1 - Mirka Andolfo-a 3.00
...: The Old Guard #1 - Rucka-s/Fernández-a 3.00
...: Undiscovered Country #1 - Snyder & Soule-s/Camuncoli-a 3.00

IMAGE GRAPHIC NOVEL
Image Int.: 1984 ($6.95)(Advertised as Pacific Comics Graphic Novel #1)
1-The Seven Samuroid; Brunner-c/a 12.00

IMAGE HOLIDAY SPECIAL 2005
Image Comics: 2005 ($9.99, TPB)
nn-Holiday-themed short stories by various incl. Walking Dead by Kirkman; Larsen, Kurtz, Valentino; Frank Cho-c 3 6 9 14 20 25

IMAGE INTRODUCES...
Image Comics: Oct, 2001 - June, 2002 ($2.95, anthology)
Believer #1-Schamberger-s/Thurman & Molder-a; Legend of Isis preview 3.00
Cryptopia #1-Raab-s/Quinn-a 3.00
Dog Soldiers #1-Hunter-s/Pachoumis-a 3.00
Legend of Isis #1-Valdez-a 3.00
Primate #1-Two covers; Beau Smith & Bernhardt-s/Byrd-a 3.00

IMAGES OF A DISTANT SOIL
Image Comics: Feb, 1997 ($2.95. B&W, one-shot)
1-Sketches by various 4.00

IMAGES OF SHADOWHAWK (Also see Shadowhawk)
Image Comics: Sept, 1993 - No. 3, 1994 ($1.95, limited series)
1-3: Keith Giffen-c/a; Trencher app. 4.00

IMAGE! 30TH ANNIVERSARY ANTHOLOGY
Image Comics: Apr, 2022 - No. 12, Apr, 2023 ($5.99, squarebound)
1-12: Short story anthology featuring Image characters; some serialized stories 6.00

IMAGE 20 (FREE COMIC BOOK DAY 2012....)
Image Comics: May, 2012 (giveaway)
nn-Previews of Revival, Guarding the Globe, It-Girl and the Atomics, Near Death 3.00

IMAGE TWO-IN-ONE
Image Comics: Mar, 2001 ($2.95, 48 pgs., B&W, one-shot)
1-Two stories; 24 pages produced in 24 hrs. by Larsen and Eliopoulos 4.00

IMAGE UNITED
Image Comics: No. 0, Mar, 2010; Nov, 2009 - No. 6 ($3.99, limited series)
0-(3/10, $2.99) Fortress and Savage Dragon app. 3.00
1-3-($3.99) Image character crossover; Kirkman-s; art by Larsen, Liefeld, McFarlane, Portacio, Silvestri and Valentino; Spawn, Witchblade, Savage Dragon, Youngblood, Cyberforce and Shadowhawk app. Multiple covers on each 4.00
1-Jim Lee variant-c 8.00

IMAGE ZERO
Image Comics: 1993 (Received through mail w/coupons from Image books)
0-Savage Dragon, StormWatch, Shadowhawk, Strykeforce; 1st app. Troll; 1st app. McFarlane's Freak, Blotch, Sweat and Budd 5.00

IMAGINARIES, THE
Image Comics: Mar, 2005 - No. 4, June, 2005 ($2.95, limited series)
1-4-Mike S. Miller & Ben Avery-s; Miller & Titus-a 3.00

IMAGINARY FIENDS
DC Comics (Vertigo): Jan, 2018 - No. 6, Jun, 2016 ($3.99, limited series)
1-6-Tim Seeley-s/Stephen Molnar-a/Richard Pace-c 4.00

IMAGINE AGENTS
BOOM! Studios: Oct, 2013 - No. 4, Jan, 2014 ($3.99, limited series)
1-4-Brian Joines-s/Bachan-a 4.00

I'M DICKENS - HE'S FENSTER (TV)
Dell Publishing Co.: May-July, 1963 - No. 2, Aug-Oct, 1963 (Photo-c)

	GD 2.0	VG 4.0	FN 6.0	VF 8.0	VF/NM 9.0	NM- 9.2
1	5	10	15	33	57	80
2	5	10	15	30	50	70

I MET A HANDSOME COWBOY
Dell Publishing Co.: No. 324, Mar, 1951

	GD 2.0	VG 4.0	FN 6.0	VF 8.0	VF/NM 9.0	NM- 9.2
Four Color 324	8	16	24	56	108	160

IMMORAL X-MEN
Marvel Comics: Apr 2023 - No. 3, Jun, 2023 ($4.99)
1-3: 1-Sins of Sinister part 4; Gillen-s/Medina-a. 2-Part 6; Di Vito-a. 3-Part 8; Vitti-a 5.00

IMMORTAL BROTHERS: THE TALE OF THE GREEN KNIGHT
Valiant Entertainment: Apr, 2017 ($4.99, one-shot)
1-Van Lente-s/Nord & Henry-a; Archer & Faith app.; bonus preview of Rapture 5.00

IMMORTAL DOCTOR FATE, THE
DC Comics: Jan, 1985 - No. 3, Mar, 1985 ($1.25, limited series)
1-3: 1-Reprints; Simonson-c/a. 2-R/back-ups from Flash #306-313; Giffen-c/a(p) 6.00

IMMORTAL HULK
Marvel Comics: Aug, 2018 - No. 50, Dec, 2021 ($4.99/$3.99)

	GD 2.0	VG 4.0	FN 6.0	VF 8.0	VF/NM 9.0	NM- 9.2
1-($4.99) Bruce Banner returns; intro Jackie McGee; Ewing-s/Bennett-a	3	6	9	17	26	35
2-($3.99) Intro Dr. Frye	3	6	9	21	33	45
3-15: 4,5-Sasquatch app. 6,7-Avengers app. 9-13-Absorbing Man app. 13,14-Betty app.	2	4	6	11	16	20
14-Kyle Hotz-a	1	3	4	6	8	10

16-Joe Fixit returns
17-24-($3.99) 4.00
25-($5.99) Hulk as the Breaker of Worlds; Germán Garcia-a 6.00
26-32,34-49: 26-Amadeus Cho app. 30-32-Xemnu app. 34-The Leader's origin retold. 46,47-Avengers app. 4.00
33-($5.99) 750th Legacy issue; Xemnu app.; art by Bennett & Pitarra 6.00
50-($9.99, squarebound) Fantastic Four app. 10.00
#0-(11/20, $4.99) Reprints Incredible Hulk #312 & #(-1) with new framing story; De Iulis-a 5.00
...: Flatline 1 (4/21, $4.99) Declan Shalvey-s/a 5.00
...: Great Power 1 (4/20, $4.99) Spider-Man gets Hulk powers; Fantastic Four app. 5.00
...: The Best Defense 1 (2/19, $4.99) Ewing-s/Di Meo-a; see Defenders: The Best Defense 5.00
...: The Threshing Place 1 (11/19, $4.99) Lemire-s/Del Mundo-a/c 5.00
...: Time of Monsters 1 (7/21, $4.99) Ewing & Paknadel-s/Ferreyra-a/c; back-up w/Nowlan-a 5.00

IMMORTAL HULK DIRECTOR'S CUT
Marvel Comics: Oct, 2019 - No. 6, Dec, 2019 ($5.99/$4.99)
1-($5.99) Reprints #1 with bonus pencil art, variant cover gallery; creator interviews 6.00
2-6-($4.99) Reprints with bonus pencil art or scripts and interviews 5.00

IMMORTAL IRON FIST, THE (Also see Iron Fist)
Marvel Comics: Jan, 2007 - No. 27, Aug, 2009 ($2.99/$3.99)

	GD 2.0	VG 4.0	FN 6.0	VF 8.0	VF/NM 9.0	NM- 9.2
1-Brubaker & Fraction-s/Aja-c/a; origin retold; intro. Orson Randall	1 2	3	4	6	8	10
1-Variant-c by Dell'Otto	3	6	9	17	26	35

	GD 2.0	VG 4.0	FN 6.0	VF 8.0	VF/NM 9.0	NM- 9.2

1-Director's Cut ($3.99) r/#1 and 8-page story from Civil War: Choosing Sides; script excerpt; character designs; sketch and inks art; cover variant and concepts — 4.00

2,3	1	2	3	5	6	8
4-7,9-13,15-26: 6,17-20-Flashback-by Heath. 21-Green-a						3.00
8-1st Immortal weapons & Fat Cobra	2	4	6	9	12	15

14,27: 14-($3.99) Heroes For Hire app. 27-Last issue; 2 covers; Foreman & Lapham-a — 4.00
Annual 1 (11/07, $3.99) Brubaker & Fraction-s/Chaykin, Brereton & J. Djurdjevic-a — 4.00
... Orson Randall and the Death Queen of California (11/08, $3.99) art by Camuncoli — 4.00
... Orson Randall and the Green Mist of Death (4/08, $3.99) art by Heath and various — 4.00
...: The Origin of Danny Rand (2008, $3.99) r/Marvel Premiere #15-16 recolored — 4.00
... Vol. 1: The Last Iron Fist Story HC (2007, $19.99, dustjacket) r/#1-6, story from Civil War: Choosing Sides; sketch pages — 20.00
... Vol. 1: The Last Iron Fist Story SC (2007, $14.99) same content as HC — 15.00
... Vol. 2: The Seven Capital Cities HC (2008, $24.99, dustjacket) r/#8-14 & Annual #1 — 25.00

IMMORTALIS (See Mortigan Goth: Immortalis)

IMMORTAL MEN, THE (Follows events of Dark Nights: Metal)
DC Comics: Jun, 2018 - No. 6, Nov, 2018 ($2.99)

1-6: 1-Jim Lee & Ryan Benjamin-a/Tynion IV-s; Batman Who Laughs cameo — 4.00

IMMORTAL RED SONJA
Dynamite Entertainment: 2022 - No. 10, 2022 ($3.99)

1-10: 1-Abnett-s/Miracolo-a. 2,3-Pinna-a — 4.00

IMMORTAL SHE-HULK
Marvel Comics: Nov, 2020 ($4.99, one-shot)

1-Ewing-s/Davis-Hunt-a; origin re-told, Wolverine, Thor, The Leader app. — 5.00

IMMORTAL THOR
Marvel Comics: Oct, 2023 - Present ($6.99/$4.99)

1-($6.99) Ewing-s/Cóccolo-a; Toranos, the Utgard Thor app. — 7.00
2-7-($4.99) 3-Loki app. 4-Storm app. 6,7-Loki app. — 5.00

IMMORTAL WEAPONS (Also see Immortal Iron Fist)
Marvel Comics: Sept, 2009 - No. 5, Jan, 2010 ($3.99, limited series)

1-5: Back-up Iron Fist stories in all. 1-Origin of Fat Cobra. 2-Brereton-a — 4.00

IMMORTAL X-MEN
Marvel Comics: May 2022 - No. 18, Feb, 2024 ($5.99/$3.99)

1-Gillen-s/Werneck-a; wraparound-c — 6.00
2-18-($3.99) — 4.00

IMOGEN OF THE WYRDING WAY (Tales From the Outerverse)
Dark Horse Comics: Jun, 2021 ($3.99, one-shot)

1-Mignola & Golden-s/Bergting-a — 4.00

IMPACT
E. C. Comics: Mar-Apr, 1955 - No. 5, Nov-Dec, 1955

1-Not code approved; classic Holocaust story	44	88	132	352	564	775

1-Variant printed by Charlton. Title logo is white instead of yellow and print quality is inferior. Distributed to newsstands before being destroyed & reprinted (scarce)

	46	92	138	368	584	800
2	21	42	63	168	264	360
3-5: 4-Crandall-a	17	34	51	136	213	290

NOTE: Crandall a-1-4. Davis a-2-4; c-1-5. Evans a-1, 4, 5. Ingels a-in all. Kamen a-3. Krigstein a-1, 5. Orlando a-2, 5.

IMPACT
Gemstone Publishing: Apr, 1999 - No. 5, Aug, 1999 ($2.50)

1-5-Reprints E.C. series — 4.00

IMPACT CHRISTMAS SPECIAL (!mpact W!nter Special on cover)
DC Comics (Impact Comics): 1991 ($2.50, 68 pgs.)

1-Gift of the Magi by Infantino/Rogers; The Black Hood, The Fly, The Jaguar, & The Shield stories — 4.00

IMPACT WINTER: ROOK (Based on the audible original series)
Image Comics (Skybound): Jul, 2023 ($4.99)

1-Beacham-s/Milana-a — 5.00

IMPACT WINTER SPECIAL (See Impact Christmas Special, the title used in the indicia)

IMPERIAL GUARD
Marvel Comics: Jan, 1997 - No. 3, Mar, 1997 ($1.95, limited series)

1-3: Augustyn-s in all; 1-Wraparound-c — 4.00

IMPERIUM
Valiant Entertainment: Mar, 2015 - No. 16, May, 2016 ($3.99)

1-16: 1-4-Dysart-s/Braithwaite-a. 5-8-Eaton-a. 9-12-The Vine Imperative; Cafu-a — 4.00

IMPOSSIBLE MAN SUMMER VACATION SPECTACULAR, THE
Marvel Comics: Aug, 1990; No. 2, Sept, 1991 ($2.00, 68 pgs.) (See Fantastic Four#11)

1-Spider Man, Quasar, Dr. Strange, She-Hulk, Punisher & Dr. Doom stories; Barry Crain, Guice-a; Art Adams-c(i) — 4.00
2-Ka Zar & Thor app.; Cable Wolverine-c app. — 4.00

IMPULSE (See Flash #92, 2nd Series for 1st app.) (Also see Young Justice)
DC Comics: Apr, 1995 - No. 89, Oct, 2002 ($1.50/$1.75/$1.95/$2.25/$2.50)

1-Mark Waid scripts & Humberto Ramos-c/a(p) begin; brief retelling of origin — 6.00
2-12: 9-XS from Legion (Impulse's cousin) comes to the 20th Century, returns to the 30th Century in #12. 10-Dead Heat Pt. 3 (cont'd in Flash #110). 11-Dead Heat Pt. 4 (cont'd in Flash #111); Johnny Quick dies. — 4.00
13-25: 14-Trickster app. 17-Zatanna-c/app. 21-Legion-c/app. 22-Jesse Quick-c/app. 24-Origin; Flash app. 25-Last Ramos-a. — 4.00
26-55: 26-Rousseau-a begins. 28-1st new Arrowette (see World's Finest #113). 30-Genesis x-over. 47-Superman-c/app. 50-Batman & Joker-c/app. Van Sciver-a begins. — 3.00
56-62: 56-Young Justice app. — 3.00
63-89: 63-Begin $2.50-c. 66-JLA,JSA-c/app. 68,69-Adam Strange, GL app. 77-Our Worlds at War x-over; Young Justice-c/app. 85-World Without Young Justice x-over pt. 2. — 3.00
#1,000,000 (11/98) John Fox app. — 3.00
Annual 1 (1996, $2.95)-Legends of the Dead Earth; Parobeck-a — 4.00
Annual 2 (1997, $3.95)-Pulp Heroes stories; Orbik painted-c — 4.00
.../Atom Double-Shot 1(2/98, $1.95) Jurgens-s/Mhan-a — 3.00

...: Bart Saves the Universe (4/99, $5.95) JSA app. — 6.00
...Plus (9/97, $2.95) w/Gross Out (Scare Tactics)-c/app. — 4.00
...Reckless Youth (1997, $14.95, TPB) r/Flash #92-94, Impulse #1-6 — 15.00

INCAL, THE
Marvel Comics (Epic): Nov, 1988 - No. 3, Jan, 1989 ($10.95/$12.95, mature)

1-Moebius-c/a in all; sexual content	4	8	12	27	44	60
2,3	2	4	6	11	16	20

INCOGNEGRO
DC Comics (Vertigo): 2008 ($19.99, B&W, hardcover graphic novel with dustjacket)

HC-Mat Johnson-s/Warren Pleece-a — 20.00

INCOGNEGRO: RENAISSANCE
Dark Horse Comics (Berger Books): Feb, 2018 - No. 5, Jun, 2018 ($3.99, B&W, lim. series)

1-5-Mat Johnson-s/Warren Pleece-a — 5.00

INCOGNITO
Marvel Comics (Icon): Dec, 2008 - No. 6, Aug, 2009 ($3.50/$3.99, limited series)

1-5-Brubaker-s/Phillips-a/c; pulp noir-style — 3.50
6-($3.99) Bonus history of the Zeppelin pulps — 4.00
...: Bad Influences (10/10 - No. 5, 4/11, $3.50) 1-5 Brubaker-s/Phillips-a/c — 3.50

INCOMING
Marvel Comics: Feb, 2020 ($9.99, one-shot)

1-Leads into the Empyre event; Masked Raider app.; connecting short stories by various — 10.00

INCOMPLETE DEATH'S HEAD (Also see Death's Head)
Marvel Comics UK: Jan, 1993 - No. 12, Dec, 1993 ($1.75, limited series)

1-($2.95, 56 pgs.)-Die-cut cover — 5.00
2-11: 2-Re-intro original Death's Head. 3-Original Death's Head vs. Dragon's Claws — 4.00
12-($2.50, 52 pgs.)-She Hulk app. — 5.00

INCORRUPTIBLE (Also see Irredeemable)
BOOM! Studios: Dec, 2000 - No. 30, May, 2012 ($3.99)

1-30: 1-Waid-s/Diaz-a; 3 covers — 4.00
1-Artist Edition (12/11, $3.99) r/#1 in B&W with bonus sketch and design art — 4.00

INCREDIBLE HERCULES (Continued from Incredible Hulk #112, Jan, 2008)
Marvel Comics: No. 113, Feb, 2008 - No. 141, Apr, 2010 ($2.99/$3.99)

113-125: 113-Ares and Wonder Man app.; Art Adams-c. 116-Romita Jr-c; Eternals app. — 3.00
113-Variant-c by Pham — 5.00
126-($3.99) Hercules origin retold; back-up story w/Miyazawa-a — 4.00
127-137: 128-Dark Avengers app. 132-Replacement Thor. 136-Thor app. — 3.00
138-141-($3.99) Assault on New Olympus; Avengers app. — 4.00

INCREDIBLE HULK, THE (See Aurora, The Avengers #1, The Defenders #1, Giant-Size..., Hulk, Marvel Collectors Item Classics, Marvel Comics Presents #26, Marvel Fanfare, Marvel Treasury Edition, Power Record Comics, Rampaging Hulk, She-Hulk, 2099 Unlimited & World War Hulk)

INCREDIBLE HULK, THE
Marvel Comics: May, 1962 - No. 6, Mar, 1963 (Hulk stories continue in Tales to Astonish #59)

1-Origin & 1st app. (skin is grey colored); Kirby pencils begin, end #5						
	7600	15,200	26,600	81,100	255,550	430,000
2-1st green skinned Hulk; Kirby/Ditko-a	800	1600	2400	6800	15,400	24,000
3-Origin retold; 1st app. Ringmaster (9/62)	286	572	858	2402	5451	8500
4-Brief origin retold	234	468	702	1931	4366	6800
5-1st app of Tyrannus	269	538	807	2219	5010	7800
6-(3/63) Intro. Teen Brigade; all Ditko-a	241	482	723	1988	4494	7000

INCREDIBLE HULK, THE
Marvel Comics: No. 102, Apr, 1968 - No. 474, Mar, 1999 (Numbering continued from Tales to Astonish #101)

102-(4/68) -Origin retold; Hulk in Asgard; Enchantress & Executioner app; Gary Friedrich-s begin; Marie Severin-c/a	38	76	114	285	641	1000
103-1st Space Parasite	12	24	36	83	182	280
104-Hulk vs. the Rhino	14	28	42	96	211	325
105-1st Missing Link	14	28	42	96	211	325
106-110: 106-vs. Missing Link; Nick Fury & SHIELD app; Trimpe pencils begin (continues through issue #193). 107,108-vs. the Mandarin. 108-Nick Fury & SHIELD app.; Stan Lee-s (continues through issue #120). 109,110-Ka-Zar app.						
	9	18	27	58	114	170
111-117: 111-Ka-Zar app.; 1st Galaxy Master. 112-Origin of the Galaxy Master. 113-vs. Sandman. 114-Sandman & Mandarin vs. the Hulk. 115-117-vs. the Leader						
	7	14	21	44	82	120
118-Hulk vs. Sub-Mariner	10	20	30	67	141	215
119,120,123-125: 119-Maximus (of the Inhumans) app. 120-Last Stan Lee plot, Roy Thomas script; Maximus app. 123,124-vs. The Leader. 124-1st Sal Buscema-p (as a fill-in).						
125-vs. the Absorbing Man	5	10	15	35	63	90
121-Roy Thomas-s begin; 1st app. and origin of the Glob						
	8	16	24	51	96	140
122-Hulk battles Thing (12/69); Fantastic Four app.	12	24	36	79	170	260
126-1st Barbara Norriss (becomes Valkyrie in Defenders #4); story continued from Sub-Mariner #22 (see Dr. Strange #183 for pt.1); Dr. Strange gives up being Sorcerer Supreme						
	9	18	27	48	89	130
127,129,130,132-139: 127-Tryannus & the Mole Man app; 1st app. Mogol. 129-Leader revives the Glob. 130-(story continues from Captain Marvel #21); 132-HYDRA app. 134-1st Golem. 135-Kang & Phantom Eagle app. 136-1st Xeron the Starslayer; Abomination cameo. 137-Xeron app. Hulk vs. Abomination. 138-Sandman app. 139-Leader app; Hulk story continues in Avengers #88						
	5	10	15	30	50	70
128-Avengers app.	6	12	18	38	69	100
131-1st Jim Wilson; Iron Man app.	6	12	18	40	73	105
140-Written by Harlan Ellison; 1st Jarella (Hulk's love); story continues from Avengers #88; battles Psyklop						
	7	14	21	46	86	125
140-2nd printing	2	4	6	8	11	14
141-1st app. Doc Samson (7/71)	23	46	69	156	348	540
142-Our Valkyrie app. (Samantha Parrington) (see Avengers #82 for 1st Marvel Valkyrie); Enchantress app.	7	14	21	46	86	125
143,144-Doctor Doom app.	6	12	18	38	69	100
145-(52-pgs)-Origin retold	6	12	18	41	76	110
146-151: 146,147-Richard Nixon & The Leader app. 148-Jarella app. 149-1st app.						

Immortal Thor #1 © MAR

Impulse #46 © DC

Incredible Hulk #325 © MAR

	GD	VG	FN	VF	VF/NM	NM-
	2.0	4.0	6.0	8.0	9.0	9.2

The Inheritor. 150-Havok app. 151-Has minor Ant-Man app.
| | 4 | 8 | 12 | 25 | 40 | 55 |

152,153: Hulk on trial; Daredevil, Fantastic Four, Avengers app.
| | 4 | 8 | 12 | 28 | 47 | 65 |

154-Ant-Man app; story coincides with Ant-Man's re-intro in Marvel Feature #4; Hydra & the Chameleon app.
| | 4 | 8 | 12 | 27 | 44 | 60 |

155-160: 155-1st Shaper of Worlds. 156-Jarella app. 157,158-the Leader & Rhino app.

158-Counter-Earth & the High Evolutionary app. 159-Steve Englehart-s begin; Hulk vs. Abomination. 160-vs. Tiger Shark
| | 4 | 8 | 12 | 22 | 35 | 48 |

161-The Mimic dies; Beast app.
| | 6 | 12 | 18 | 37 | 66 | 95 |

162-1st app. The Wendigo (4/73) Beast app.
| | 17 | 34 | 51 | 117 | 259 | 400 |

163-165,170,173,174,179: 163-1st app. The Gremlin. 164-1st Capt. Omen & Colonel John D. Armbuster. 165-Capt. Omen app; 1st Aquon. 173,174-vs. the Cobalt Man. 179-Return of the Missing Link; 1st Len Wein-s
| | 3 | 6 | 9 | 17 | 25 | 34 |

166-169,171: 166-1st Zzzax; Hawkeye app.; story continues into Defenders #7. 167-Hulk vs. MODOK. 168-1st Harpy (transformed Betty Ross; also seen briefly in nudity panels) 169-1st Bi-Beast; MODOK and A.I.M. app.; Harpy transformed back into Betty.
| | 3 | 6 | 9 | 18 | 27 | 36 |

171-vs. Abomination; last Englehart-s
| | 3 | 6 | 9 | 18 | 27 | 36 |

172-X-Men cameo; origin Juggernaut retold
| | 6 | 12 | 18 | 41 | 76 | 110 |

175-Black Bolt/Inhumans c/story
| | 4 | 8 | 12 | 23 | 37 | 50 |

176-Hulk on Counter-Earth; Man-Beast app; Warlock cameo (2 panels only)
| | 4 | 8 | 12 | 25 | 40 | 55 |

177-1st actual death of Warlock (last panel only); Man-Beast app.
| | 6 | 12 | 18 | 41 | 76 | 110 |

178-Rebirth of Warlock (story continues in Strange Tales #178)
| | 7 | 14 | 21 | 46 | 86 | 125 |

180-(10/74)-1st brief app. Wolverine (last pg.)
| | 89 | 178 | 367 | 712 | 1606 | 2500 |

181-(11/74)-1st full Wolverine story; Trimpe-a
| | 1200 | 2400 | 3600 | 6000 | 9000 | 12,000 |

182-Wolverine cameo; see Giant-Size X-Men #1 for next app.; 1st Crackajack Jackson
| | 19 | 38 | 57 | 131 | 291 | 450 |

183-Zzzax app.
| | 4 | 8 | 12 | 23 | 37 | 50 |

184-vs. Warlord Kraa
| | 3 | 6 | 9 | 18 | 27 | 36 |

185-192,194-196,199: 185-Death of Col. Armbuster. 186-1st Devastator. 187-188-vs. the Gremlin, Nick Fury app. 189-Mole Man app. 190-1st Glorian; Shaper of Worlds app. 191-vs. the Toad Men; Glorian & Shaper of Worlds app. 194-vs. the Locust; 1st Sal Buscema-p (through #309). 195-Abomination & Hulk team-up. 196-vs. Abomination. 199-Hulk vs. SHIELD & Doc Samson; Nick Fury app.
| | 3 | 6 | 9 | 15 | 22 | 28 |

193-vs. Doc Samson c/story; last regular Trimpe-a
| | 4 | 8 | 12 | 23 | 37 | 50 |

197-Collector, Man-Thing & Glob app; Wrightson-c
| | 7 | 14 | 21 | 44 | 82 | 120 |

198-Collector, Man-Thing & Glob app.
| | 3 | 6 | 9 | 19 | 30 | 40 |

198,199, 201,202-(30¢-c variants, lim. distribution)
| | 8 | 16 | 24 | 56 | 108 | 160 |

200-(25¢-c) Silver Surfer app. (illusion only); anniversary issue
| | 4 | 8 | 12 | 27 | 44 | 60 |

200-(30¢-c variant, limited distribution)(6/76)
| | 8 | 16 | 24 | 51 | 96 | 140 |

201-(30¢-c)-Conan swipe-c/sty (vs. Bronak the Barbarian)
| | 3 | 6 | 9 | 16 | 23 | 30 |

202-205,208-211,213,215-220: 202-Jarella cameo. 203-Jarella app.; death of Psyklop. 204-Trimpe-p; alternate Hulk origin. 205-Death of Jarella; vs. the Crypto Man. 208-Absorbing Man app. 209-Hulk vs. Absorbing Man. 210,211-Hulk team-up with Dr. Druid vs. the Maha Yogi. 213-1st Quintronic Man. 215,216-vs. the second Bi-Beast. 218-Doc Samson vs. the Rhino (no Hulk in story). 219-220-vs. Captain Barracuda
| | 2 | 4 | 6 | 10 | 14 | 18 |

206,207-Defenders app.
| | 3 | 6 | 9 | 14 | 19 | 24 |

212,214: 212-1st app. The Constrictor. 214-Hulk vs. Jack of Hearts (1st app. outside of B&W magazines)
| | 3 | 6 | 9 | 14 | 19 | 24 |

212-216-(35¢-c variant, limited distribution)
| | 7 | 14 | 24 | 36 | 82 | 179 | 275 |

221-227,230-231: 221-Stingray app. 222-Last Wein-s; Jim Starlin co-plot and (p). 223-The Leader returns; Roger Stern-s begin. 224-225-vs. The Leader. 227-Original Avengers app. (in dream sequence)
| | 2 | 4 | 6 | 8 | 10 | 12 |

228-1st female Moonstone (Karla Sofen) (10/78)
| | 5 | 10 | 15 | 31 | 53 | 75 |

229-2nd app. new Moonstone
| | 2 | 4 | 6 | 10 | 14 | 18 |

232,233: 232-Captain America x-over from Captain America #230; vs. Moonstone, Vamp and 'the Corporation'; Marvel Man (Quasar) app. 233-Marvel Man app. (Quasar)
| | 2 | 4 | 6 | 8 | 11 | 14 |

234-(4/79)-Marvel Man formally changes his name to Quasar
| | 5 | 10 | 15 | 34 | 60 | 85 |

235-249: 235-237-Machine Man app. 238-President Jimmy Carter app. 241-243-vs. Tyrannus. 243-Last Stern-s. 244-vs. the Living Colossus. 245-1st Mantlo-s (through #313); 1st app. The Super-Mandroid (Col. Talbot); Captain Mar-Vell cameo. 246-Captain Mar-Vell app.; Hulk vs. Super-Mandroid. 247-Minor Captain Mar-Vell app. 248-vs. the Gardener. 249-Steve Ditko-c
| | 2 | 4 | 6 | 8 | 10 | 12 |

250-Giant-Size (square-bound, 48-pgs)-Silver Surfer app.
| | 5 | 10 | 15 | 31 | 53 | 75 |

251-253,256-270: 251-3-D Man app. 252,253-Woodgod app. 256-1st Sabra (Israeli super-hero).

257-1st Arabian Knight. 258,259-Soviet Super-Soldiers, Red Guardian & the Presence app. 260-Death of Col. Talbot. 261-Absorbing Man app. 263-Landslide & Avalanche app. 264-Death of the Night Flyer; Corruptor app. 265-1st app. The Rangers (Firebird, Shooting Star, Night Rider, Red Wolf & Lobo, Texas Tornado); Corruptor app. 266-High Evolutionary app. 267-Glorian and the Shaper of Worlds app. 268-Pariah-c/s; origin of Rick Jones retold. 269-1st Marvel Universe app. of Bereet; 1st Hulk-Hunters (Amphibion, Torgo, Dark Crawler). 270-Hulk Hunters, Bereet & Galaxy Master app.
| | 1 | 3 | 4 | 6 | 8 | 10 |

254-1st app. the U-Foes (evil versions of the Fantastic Four)
| | 3 | 6 | 9 | 16 | 23 | 30 |

255-Hulk vs. Thor
| | 3 | 6 | 9 | 15 | 22 | 28 |

271-(5/82)-2nd app. & 1st full app. Rocket Raccoon (see Marvel Preview #7 for debut)
| | 12 | 24 | 36 | 79 | 170 | 260 |

272-3rd app Rocket Raccoon; Sasquatch & Wendigo app; Wolverine & Alpha Flight cameo in flashback; Bruce Banner's mind takes control of the Hulk
| | 4 | 8 | 12 | 27 | 44 | 60 |

273-277,280-299: 273-Sasquatch app. 275-vs. Megalith; U-Foes app. 276,277-U-foes app. 280,281-The Leader returns. 282-She-Hulk app. 283,284-Avengers app; vs. the Leader. 285-Zzzax app. 287-290-MODOK & Abomination app. 292-Circus of Crime & Dragon Man app. 293-Fantastic Four app. (in a dream). 294,295-Boomerang app. 296-Rom app.
| | 1 | 3 | 4 | 6 | 8 | 10 |

278,279-Most Marvel characters app. (Wolverine in both). 279-X-Men & Alpha Flight cameos
| | 1 | 3 | 4 | 6 | 8 | 10 |

297-299-Dr. Strange & Nightmare app.

300-(11/84, 52 pgs)-Spider-Man app. in new black costume on-c & 2 pg. cameo; Hulk reverts to savagery; Thor, Daredevil, Power Man & Iron Fist, Human Torch app; Dr. Strange banishes the Hulk from Earth
| | 3 | 6 | 9 | 19 | 30 | 40 |

301-313: 301-Hulk banished to the 'Crossroads' (through #313); Dr. Strange app. 302-Mignola-c. 304-U-Foes cameo; Mignola-c (through issue #309). 305-vs the U-Foes. 306-Return of Xeron the Starslayer. 307-Death of Xeron. 308-vs N'Garia demons. 309-Last Sal Buscema-a. 310-Blevins-a. 311-Mignola-a. 312-Secret Wars II x-over; Mignola-c/a; origin retold w/further detail regarding physical abuse at the hands of his father.
| | 2 | 3 | 5 | 6 | 7 | 8 |

313-Crossover w/Alpha Flight #29; Mignola-c/a
| | 1 | 3 | 4 | 6 | 8 | 10 |

314-Byrne-c/a begins; ends #319; Hulk returns to Earth; vs. Doc Samson
| | 1 | 3 | 4 | 6 | 8 | 10 |

315-319: 315-Hulk & Banner separated. 316-vs Hercules, Sub-Mariner, Wonder Man & Iron Man of the Avengers. 317-1st app. the new Hulkbusters; Hulk vs. Doc Samson. 318-Doc Samson vs. Hulkbusters. 319-Banner and Betty Ross wed
| | 1 | 2 | 3 | 5 | 6 | 8 |

320,325,327-329: 320-Al Milgrom story & art begin. 325-vs. Zzzax. 327-Zzzax app. 328-1st Peter David-s. 329-1st app. The Outcasts
| | | | | | | 6.00 |

321-323: 321-Avengers vs. Hulk. 322-Avengers & West Coast Avengers app. 323-East & West Coast Avengers app.
| | 1 | 2 | 3 | 5 | 6 | 8 |

324-Return of the Grey Hulk (Banner & Hulk rejoined) first since #1 (c-swipe of #1)
| | 3 | 6 | 9 | 19 | 30 | 40 |

326-Grey vs. Green (Rick Jones) Hulk
| | 2 | 4 | 6 | 8 | 11 | 14 |

330-1st McFarlane-c/p; last Milgrom-s; Thunderbolt Ross 'dies'
| | 3 | 6 | 9 | 20 | 31 | 42 |

331-Peter David begins as regular plotter; McFarlane-p
| | 6 | 9 | 17 | 25 | 34 |

332-Grey Hulk & Leader vs. Green Hulk (Rick Jones) 2 | 4 | 6 | 8 | 11 | 14 |

333-334,338-339: 338-1st app. Mercy. 339-The Leader app.
| | 1 | 2 | 3 | 4 | 8 | 10 |

335-No McFarlane-a
| | 1 | 3 | 5 | 6 | 8 |

336,337-X-Factor app.
| | 1 | 3 | 4 | 6 | 8 | 10 |

340-Classic Hulk vs. Wolverine-c by McFarlane
| | 10 | 20 | 30 | 69 | 147 | 225 |

341-344,346: 341-The Man-Bull; McFarlane begins pencils and inks. 342-The Leader app. 343-1st app. Rock & Redeemer. 344-McFarlane (p) only; vs. The Leader, Rock & Redeemer; Betty revealed to be pregnant. 346-The Leader app. Last McFarlane-p
| | 1 | 2 | 3 | 4 | 8 | 12 |

345-($1.50, 52 pgs) vs. The Leader; Gamma-Bomb explosion; World thinks the Hulk is dead; McFarlane (p) only
| | 3 | 6 | 9 | 21 | 33 | 45 |

347-349,351-366: 347-1st app. The Hulk as 'Mr. Fixit'; relocated to Las Vegas; 1st app. Marlo; Absorbing Man app. 348-vs. Absorbing Man. 349-Spider-Man app.; Dr. Doom cameo. 351-How the Hulk survived the Gamma-Bomb is revealed. 356-Glorian app. 356-Glorian & Shaper of Worlds app. 359-Wolverine-c (illusion) by John Byrne. 360-Nightmare & D'spayre app; Betty loses her baby. 361-Iron Man app. 362-Werewolf by Night app. 363-Acts of Vengeance tie-in; Dr. Strange & Grey Gargoyle app. 364-vs Abomination; 1st app. Madman. 365-Fantastic Four app. 366-Leader & Madman app.
| | | | | | | 6.00 |

350-Hulk/Thing battle
| | 3 | 6 | 9 | 11 | 14 |

367-1st Dale Keown on Hulk (3/90) Leader & Madman app.
| | 1 | 2 | 3 | 6 | 8 |

368-371,373-375: 368-Sam Kieth-c/a; 1st app. Pantheon. 369-Keown-a (becomes regular artist through #398). vs. the Freedom Force. 370,371-Dr. Strange & Namor app. (Defenders reunion). 374,375-vs. the Super-Skrull.
| | | | | | | 6.00 |

372-Green Hulk returns
| | 1 | 2 | 3 | 6 | 8 |

376-Green vs. Grey Hulk; 1st app. Agamemnon of the Pantheon

	GD 2.0	VG 4.0	FN 6.0	VF 8.0	VF/NM 9.0	NM- 9.2		GD 2.0	VG 4.0	FN 6.0	VF 8.0	VF/NM 9.0	NM- 9.2

	2	4	6	10	14	18

377-(1/91, $1.00) 1st all new Hulk; fluorescent green background-c

	3	9	19	30	40

377-($1.00) 2nd printing; black background-c

	3	7	9	14	20	25

377-($1.75) 3rd printing from 1994; low print run; muted green background-c

	15	30	45	103	227	350

378-392,394-399: 378,380,389-No Keown-a. 379-Contined from issue #377; new direction for the Hulk; 1st app. of Delphi, Ajax, Achilles, Paris & Hector of the Pantheon. 380-Doc Samson app. 381,382-Pantheon app. 383-Infinity Gauntlet x-over; Abomination app. 384-Infinity Gauntlet tie-in; Abomination. 385-Infinity Gauntlet tie-in. 386,387-Sabra app. 388-1st app. Speedfreak. 390-X-Factor cameo. 391,392-X-Factor app.394-1st app. Trauma; no Keown-a. 395,396-Punisher app. 397-399; Leader & U-Foes app. 398-Last Keown-a. — 5.00
393 ($2.50, 72 pgs) — 6.00
393-2nd print; silver-ink background — 5.00
400-($2.50, 68-pgs)-Holo-grafx foil-c & r/TTA #63 — 6.00
400-2nd print; yellow logo — 5.00
401-403,405-416: 401-U-Foes app. 402-Return of Doc Samson; Juggernaut & Red Skull app. 403-Gary Frank-a begins; Juggernaut & Red Skull app. 405-1st app. Piecemeal. 406-Captain America app. 407-vs. Piecemeal & Madman. 408-vs. Piecemeal & Madman; Motormouth & Killpower (Marvel UK characters) app. 409-vs. Madman; Motormouth & Killpower app. 410-Nick Fury & SHIELD app. 411-Pantheon vs. SHIELD; Nick Fury app. 412-Hulk & She-Hulk vs. Bi-Beast. 413-Trauma app; Pt. 1 (of 4) of the Troyjan War. 414-vs. Trauma; Silver Surfer app. 415-Silver Surfer & Starjammers app. 416-Final of the Troyjan War; death of Trauma. — 5.00
404-Avengers vs. Juggernaut & Red Skull app. — 6.00
417,419-424: 417-Begins $1.50-c; Rick Jones Bachelor party; many heroes from Avengers & Fantastic Four app; Hulk returns from "Future Imperfect". 419-No Frank-a. 420-Special AIDS awareness issue; death of Jim Wilson. 421-Hulk & the Pantheon in Asgard. 423-Hela app. — 4.00
418-($2.50)-Collectors Edition w/Gatefold die-cut-c; the wedding of Rick Jones & Marlo; includes cameo apps. of various Marvel characters as well as DC's Death & Peter David — 5.00
418-($1.50, Regular Edition) — 4.00
425-($2.25, 52 pgs); Last Frank-a; Liam Sharp-a begins; death of Achilles — 5.00

425-($3.50, 52 pgs)-Holographic-c

	1	2	3	5	6	8

426-433,442: 426-Nick Fury app. 427,428-Man-Thing app. 430-Speedfreak app. 431,432-Abomination app. 432-Last Sharp-a. 433-Punisher app; title becomes part of the 'Marvel Edge' titles (through #439). 442-She-Hulk & Doc Samson team-up; no Hulk app. — 4.00
434-Funeral for Nick Fury; Wolverine, Dr. Strange, Avengers app; Marvel Overpower card insert (harder to find above 9.2 due to card indentations) — 5.00
435-($2.50)-Rhino app; excerpt from "What Savage Beast" — 5.00
436-439: 436-"Ghosts of the Future" Pt.1 (of 5); Leader app. 439-Maestro app. — 5.00
440-"Ghosts of the Future" Pt. 5; Hulk vs. Thor — 6.00

441-She-Hulk-c/s; "Pulp Fiction" parody-c

	3	6	9	21	33	45

443,446-448: 443-Begin $1.50-c; re-app. of Hulk. 446-w/card insert. 447-Begin Deodato-c/a — 4.00
444,445: 444-Cable-c/app; Onslaught x-over. 445-Onslaught x-over; Avengers app. — 5.00
447-Variant-c — 5.00

449-1st app. Thunderbolts (1/97); Citizen V, Songbird, Mach-1, Techno, Atlas & Meteorite

	7	14	21	46	86	125

450-($2.95)-Thunderbolts app. 2 stories; Heroes Reborn versions of Hulk, Dr. Strange, Mr. Fantastic & Iron Man app. — 6.00
451-453, 458-470: 452-Heroes Reborn Hulk app. 453-Hulk vs. Heroes Reborn Hulk. 458-Mr. Hyde app. 459-Abomination app. 461-Maestro app. 463-Silver Surfer cameo. 464-Silver Surfer app. 465-Mr. Fantastic & Tony Stark app. 466-'Death' of Betty Banner. 467-Last Peter David issue. 468-Casey-s/Puilido-a begin. 469-Super-Adaptoid & Ringmaster app. 470-Ringmaster & the Circus of Crime app. — 4.00
454-Wolverine & Ka-Zar app.; Adam Kubert-a — 6.00
455-Wolverine, Storm, Cannonball & Cyclops of the X-Men app.; Adam Kubert-a — 6.00
456-Apocalypse enlists the Hulk as 'War'; Apocalypse app. — 6.00

457-Hulk (as Horseman of the Apocalypse 'War' vs. Juggernaut. Apocalypse app.

	1	3	4	6	8	10

471-473: 471-Circus of Crime app. 473-Watcher app; Abomination revealed as Betty's killer. — 5.00

474-($2.99) Last issue; Abomination app; c-homage to issue #1

	2	4	6	8	10	12

#(-1) Flashback (7/97) Kubert-a — 5.00

Special 1 (10/68, 25¢, 68 pg.)-New 51 pg. story; Hulk battles the Inhumans (early app)

	5	10	20	439	805	1250

Special 2 (10/69, 25¢, 68 pg.)-Origin retold (from issue #3) r-TTA #62-66

	7	14	21	48	89	130

Special 3,4: 3-(1/71, 25¢, 68 pg.)-r/TTA #70-74. 4-(1/72, 52 pg.)-r/TTA 75-77 & Not Brand Echh #5

	4	8	12	28	47	65

Annual 5 (1976) 2nd app. Groot

	8	16	24	56	108	160

Annual 6 (1977)-1st app. Paragon (later becomes Her, then later Ayesha); Dr. Strange app.

	5	10	15	31	53	75

Annual 7 ('78)-Byrne/Layton-c/a; Iceman & Angel app; vs. the Mastermold

	3	6	9	19	30	40

Annual 8 ('79)-Byrne/Stern-s; Hulk vs. Sasquatch

	2	4	6	8	11	14

Annual 9,10: 9-('80)-Ditko-a. 10-('81)-Captain Universe app.

	1	2	3	5	6	8

Annual 11 ('82)-Doc Samson back-up by Miller-(p)(5pg); Spider-Man & Avengers app.

		3	4	6	8	10

Annual 12-14: 12-('83)-Trimpe-a. 13-('84)-Story takes place at the 'Crossroads' (after Hulk was banished from Earth); takes place between pages of Incredible Hulk #301-302. 14-Byrne's; takes place between pages of Incredible Hulk #314 — 6.00
Annual 15-('86)-Zeck-c; Abomination & Tryannus app. — 6.00
Annual 16-20: 16-('90, $2.00, 68 pgs. "Lifeform" Pt. 3; continued from Daredevil Annual #6, continued in Silver Surfer Annual #3; Hulk app. in back-up story. 17-('91, $2.00)- "Subterranean Wars" Pt. 2; continued from Avengers Annual #20; continued in Namor the Sub-Mariner Annual #1. 18-('92)-"Return of the Defenders" Pt.1; continued in Namor the Sub-Mariner Annual #2. 19-('93)-Bagged w/card; 1st app. Lazarus — 6.00

...'97 ($2.99) Pollina-c

	1	2	3	5	6	8

...And Wolverine 1 (10/86, $2.50)-r/1st app. (#180-181)

		3	9	17	26	35

...: Beauty and the Behemoth ('98, $19.95, TPB) r/Bruce & Betty stories — 20.00

...Ground Zero ('95, $12.95) r/#340-346 — 15.00
...Hercules Unleashed (10/96, $2.50) David-s/Deodato-c/a — 4.00
... No. 1 Facsimile Edition (12/19, 12/23, $3.99) r/#1 with original 1962 ads — 4.00

... No. 180 Facsimile Edition (3/20, $3.99) r/#180 with original ads and letter column

	1	3	4	6	8	10

... No. 180 Facsimile Edition (9/23, $3.99) r/#180 with original ads and letter column — 4.00

... No. 180 Facsimile Edition (5/19, $3.99) r/#181 with original ads and letter column

	2	4	6	9	12	15

... No. 181 Facsimile Edition (9/23, $3.99) r/#181 with original ads and letter column — 4.00

... No. 181 Facsimile Edition (5/19, $3.99) r/#182 with original ads and letter column

	1	2	3	5	6	8

... No. 182 Facsimile Edition (9/23, $3.99) r/#182 with original ads and letter column — 4.00
... No. 347 Facsimile Edition (3/23, $3.99) r/#1 with original 1988 ads — 4.00
... Omnibus Vol. 1 HC (2008, $99.99, dustjacket) r/#1-6 & 102, Tales To Astonish #59-101 bonus art, cover reprints; afterword by Peter David; Kirby cover from #1 — 180.00
... Omnibus Vol. 1 HC (2008, $99.99, dustjacket) Variant-c swipe of #1 by Alex Ross — 140.00
.../Sub-Mariner '98 Annual ($2.99) — 6.00

...Versus Quasimodo 1 (3/83, one-shot)-Based on Saturday morning cartoon

	2	4	6	9	12	15

...Vs. Superman 1 (7/99, $5.95, one-shot)-painted-c by Rude

	3	6	9	14	19	24

...Versus Venom 1 (4/94, $2.50, one-shot)-Embossed-c; red foil logo — 40.00
... Visionaries: Peter David Vol. 1 (2005, $19.99) r/#331-339 written by Peter David — 25.00
... Visionaries: Peter David Vol. 2 (2005, $19.99) r/#340-348 — 20.00
... Visionaries: Peter David Vol. 3 (2006, $19.99) r/#349-354, Web of Spider-Man #44, and Fantastic Four #320 — 20.00
... Visionaries: Peter David Vol. 4 (2007, $19.99) r/#355-363 and Marvel Comics Presents #26,45 — 40.00
... Visionaries: Peter David Vol. 5 (2008, $19.99) r/#364-372 and Annual #16 — 40.00
Wizard #1 Ace Edition - Reprints #1 with new Adam Kubert-c — 14.00
Wizard #181 Ace Edition - Reprints #181 with new Chen-c — 25.00

(Also see titles listed under Hulk)

NOTE: Adkins a-111-116i. Austin a(i)-350, 351, 353, 354; c-302i, 350i. Ayers a-3-5i. Buckler a-Annual 5; c-252. John Buscema c-202p. Byrne a-314-319p; c-314-316, 318, 319, 359, Annual 14i. Colan c-363. Ditko a-2i, 6, 249, Annual 2r(5), 3r, 9p; c-2i, 6, 235, 249. Everett c-133i. Golden c-248, 251. Kane c(p)-193, 194, 196, 198. Dale Keown a(i)-367, 369-377, 379, 381-388, 390-393, 395-398; c-369-377p, 381, 382p, 384, 385, 386, 387p, 388, 390p, 391-393, 395p, 396, 397p, 398. Kirby a-1-5p, Special 2, 3r, Annual 5i; c-1-5. Annual 5i. McFarlane a-330-334p, 336-339p, 340-343, 344-346p; c-330p, 340p, 341-343, 344p, 345, 346p. Mignola c-302, 305, 313. Miller c-258p, 261, 264, 268. Mooney a-322p, 287i, 288i. Powell a-Special 3r(2). Romita a-Annual 17p. Severin a(i)-108-110, 131-133, 141-151, 153-155; c(i)-109, 110, 132, 142, 144-155. Simonson c-283, 364-367. Starlin a-222p; c-217. Staton a(i)-187-189, 191-209. Tuska a-102i, 105i, 106i, 218p. Williamson a-310i; c-310i, 311i. Wrightson c-197.

INCREDIBLE HULK (Vol. 2) (Formerly Hulk #1-11; becomes Incredible Hercules with #113) (Re-titled Incredible Hulks #612-on)(Also see World War Hulk)
Marvel Comics: No. 12, Mar, 2000 - No. 112, Jan, 2008 ($1.99-$3.50)
No. 600, Sept. 2009 - No. 611, Oct. 2010 ($3.99/$4.99)

12-Jenkins-s/Garney & McKone-a — 6.00

13,14-($1.99) Garney & Buscema-a

	1	2	3	5	6	8

15-24,26-32: 15-Begin $2.25-c. 21-Maximum Security x-over. 24-($1.99-c) — 3.00
25-($2.99) Hulk vs. The Abomination; Romita Jr.-a — 4.00
33-($3.50, 100 pgs.) new Bogdanove-a/Priest-s; reprints — 4.00
34-Bruce Jones-s begin; Romita Jr.-a — 4.00
35-49,51-54: 35-39-Jones-s/Romita Jr.-a. 40-43-Weeks-a. 44-49-Immonen-a. — 3.00
50-($3.50) Deodato-s begins; Abomination app. thru #54 — 4.00
55-74,77-91: 55(25¢-c) Abomination Returns; Fernandez-a. 60-65,70-72-Deodato-a. 66-69-Braithwaite-a. 71-74-Iron Man app. 77-($2.99) Peter David-s begin/Weeks-a. 80-Wolverine-c. 82-Jae Lee-c/a. 83-86-House of M x-over. 87-Scorpion app. — 3.00
75,76-($3.50) The Leader app. 75-Robertson-a/Frank-c. 76-Braithwaite-a — 4.00
92-Planet Hulk begins; Ladronn-c — 5.00
92-2nd printing with variant-c by Bryan Hitch — 4.00
93-99,101-105 Planet Hulk; Ladronn-c — 3.00
100-($3.99) Planet Hulk continues; back-up w/Frank-a; r/#152,153; Ladronn-c — 4.00
100-($3.99) Green Hulk variant-c by Michael Turner — 10.00
100-($3.99) Hulk variant-c by Michael Turner — 30.00
106-World War Hulk begins; Gary Frank-a/c — 6.00
106-2nd printing with new cover of Hercules and Angel — 3.00
107-112: 107-Hercules vs. Hulk. 108-Rick Jones app. 112-Art Adams-c. — 3.00
600-(9/09, $4.99) Covers by Ross, Sale and wraparound-c by McGuinness; back-up with Stan Lee-s; r/Hulk: Gray #1; cover gallery — 5.00
601-611-($3.99): 601-605-Olivetti-a. 603-Wolverine app. 606-608-Fall of the Hulks — 4.00
(Title becomes Incredible Hulks with #612, Nov, 2010)
Annual 2000 ($3.50) Texeira-a/Jenkins-s; Avengers app. — 4.00
Annual 2001 ($2.99) Thor-c/app.; Larsen-s/Williams III-c — 4.00
Annual 4 (8/11, $3.99) Identity Wars; Spider-Man and Deadpool app.; Barrionuevo-a — 4.00
... & The Human Torch: From the Marvel Vault 1 (8/11, $2.99) unpublished story w/Ditko-a — 4.00
...: Boiling Point (Volume 2, 2002, $8.99, TPB) r/#40-43; Andrews-c — 9.00
Dogs of War (6/01, $19.95, TPB) r/#12-20 — 20.00
House of M (2006, $13.99) r/House of M tie-in issues Incredible Hulk #83-87 — 14.00
Hulk: Planet Hulk HC (2007, $39.99, dustjacket) oversized r/#92-105, Planet Hulk: Gladiator Guidebook, stories from Amazing Fantasy (2004) #15 and Giant-Size Hulk #1 — 40.00
Hulk: Planet Hulk SC (2008, $34.99) same content as HC — 35.00
Planet Hulk: Gladiator Guidebook (2006, $3.99) bios of combatants and planet history
...: Prelude to Planet Hulk (2006, $13.99, TPB) r/#88-91 & Official Handbook: Hulk 2004 — 14.00
...: Return of the Monster (2002, $12.99, TPB) r/#34-39 — 13.00
...: The End (8/02, $5.95) David-s/Keown-a; Hulk in the far future — 6.00
...: The End HC (2008, $19.99, dustjacket) r/The End & Future Imperfect #1-2 — 20.00
...Volume 1 HC (2002, $29.99, oversized) r/#34-43 & Startling Stories: Banner #1-4 — 30.00
...Volume 2 HC (2003, $29.99, oversized) r/#44-54; sketch pages and cover gallery — 30.00
Volume 3: Transfer of Power (2003, $12.99, TPB) r/#44-49 — 13.00
Volume 4: Abominable (2003, $11.99, TPB) r/#50-54; Abomination app.; Deodato-a — 12.00
Volume 5: Hulk in Plain Sight (2003, $11.99, TPB) r/#55-59; Fernandez-a — 12.00
Volume 6: Split Decisions (2004, $12.99, TPB) r/#60-65; Deodato-a — 12.00
Volume 7: Dead Like Me (2004, $12.99, TPB) r/#66-69 & Hulk Smash #1&2 — 13.00
Volume 8: Big Things (2004, $17.99, TPB) r/#70-76; Iron Man app. — 18.00
Volume 9: Tempest Fugit (2005, $14.99, TPB) r/#77-82 — 15.00

INCREDIBLE HULK (Also see Indestructible Hulk)
Marvel Comics: Dec, 2011 - No. 15, Dec, 2012 ($3.99)
1-Aaron-s/Silvestri-a; bonus interview with Aaron; cover by Silvestri — 4.00

Incredible Hulk (2nd series) #106 © MAR

Incredible Hulks #612 © MAR

Indian Chief #23 © DELL

	GD	VG	FN	VF	VF/NM	NM-
	2.0	4.0	6.0	8.0	9.0	9.2

1-Variant covers by Neal Adams, Whilce Portacio & Ladronn | | | | | | 8.00
2-7: 2-Silvestri, Portacio & Tan-a. 7-Hulk & Banner merge; Portacio-a | | | | | | 4.00
7.1-(7/12, $2.99) Palo-a/Komarck-c; Red She-Hulk app. | | | | | | 3.00
8-15: 8-Punisher app.; Dillon-a. 12-Wolverine & The Thing app. | | | | | | 4.00

INCREDIBLE HULK (Marvel Legacy)(Continued from Totally Awesome Hulk #23)
Marvel Comics: No. 709, Dec, 2017 - No. 717, Jul, 2018 ($3.99)

709-717: 709-713-"Return to Planet Hulk"; Hulk goes to Sakaar; Pak-s/Land-a. 717-Cho-c | | | | | | 4.00
...: Last Call 1 (8/19, $4.99) Peter David-s/Dale Keown-a; Mister Hyde app. | | | | | | 5.00

INCREDIBLE HULK (See story prelude in Hulk Annual #1 (2023))
Marvel Comics: Aug, 2023 - Present ($4.99/$3.99)

1,5-($4.99) 1-P.K. Johnson-s/Nick Klein-a; Age of Monsters. 5-Bonus Power Man story | | | | | | 5.00
2-4,6-9-($3.99) 4-Man-Thing app. | | | | | | 4.00

INCREDIBLE HULKS (Continues from Incredible Hulk #611)
Marvel Comics: No. 612, Nov, 2010 - No. 635, Oct, 2011 ($2.99/$3.99)

612-615,617-621: 618-620-Chaos War. 621-Hercules app. | | | | | | 4.00
616-($4.99) Bonus She-Hulk story; Rio-a | | | | | | 5.00
622-634-($2.99) 623-625-Ka-Zar app.; Eaglesham-a. 626-629-Grummett-a | | | | | | 3.00
635-($3.99) Fin Fang Foom & Dr. Strange app.; Greg Pak interview | | | | | | 4.00
...: Chaos War (2011, $19.99, TPB) r/#618-622 | | | | | | 20.00
...: Dark Son (2011, $24.99, HC) r/#612-617 | | | | | | 25.00
...: Dark Son (2011, $19.99, TPB) r/#612-617 | | | | | | 20.00
...: Heart of the Monster (2011, $16.99, TPB) r/#630-635 | | | | | | 17.00
...: Planet Savage (2011, $15.99, TPB) r/#623-629 | | | | | | 16.00

INCREDIBLE HULKS: ENIGMA FORCE
Marvel Comics: Nov, 2010 - No. 3, Jan, 2011 ($3.99, limited series)

1-3-Reed-s/Munera-a/Pagulayan-c; Bug app. | | | | | | 4.00

INCREDIBLE MR. LIMPET, THE (See Movie Classics)

INCREDIBLES, THE
Image Comics: Nov, 2004 - No. 4, Feb, 2005 ($2.99, limited series)

1-4-Adaptation of 2004 Pixar movie; Ricardo Curtis-a | | | | | | 3.00
TPB (2005, $12.95) r/#1-4; cover gallery | | | | | | 13.00

INCREDIBLES, THE (Pixar characters)
BOOM! Studios: No. 0, Jul, 2009 - No. 15, Oct, 2010 ($2.99)

0-15: 0-3-City of Incredibles; Waid & Walker-s. 0,1-Wagner-c. 8-15-Walker-s | | | | | | 3.00
...: Family Matters 1-4 (3/09 - No. 4, 6/09) Waid-s/Takara-a. 1-Five covers | | | | | | 3.00

INCREDIBLES 2: CRISIS IN MID-LIFE! & OTHER STORIES (Pixar characters)
Dark Horse Comics: Jul, 2018 - No. 3, Sept, 2018 ($3.99, limited series)

1-3-Short stories by Gage, Gurihiru, Bone, Walker and Greppi | | | | | | 4.00

INCREDIBLES 2: SECRET IDENTITIES (Pixar characters)
Dark Horse Comics: Apr, 2019 - No. 3, Jun, 2019 ($3.99, limited series)

1-3-Christos Gage-s/Jean-Claudio Vinci-a | | | | | | 4.00

INCREDIBLES 2: SLOW BURN (Pixar characters)
Dark Horse Comics: Feb, 2020 - No. 3 ($3.99, limited series)

1-3-Christos Gage-s/Jean-Claudio Vinci-a; Jack loses his speed powers | | | | | | 4.00

INCREDIBLE SCIENCE FICTION (Formerly Weird Science-Fantasy)
E. C. Comics: No. 30, July-Aug, 1955 - No. 33, Jan-Feb, 1956

		GD	VG	FN	VF	VF/NM	NM-
30-Davis-c begin, end #32		69	138	207	552	876	1200
31-Williamson/Krenkel-a, Wood-a(2)		53	106	159	424	675	925
32-"Food For Thought" by Williamson/Krenkel		54	108	162	432	691	950
33-Classic Wood-c; "Judgment Day" story-r/Weird Fantasy #18; final issue & last E.C. comic book		74	148	222	592	946	1300

NOTE: **Davis** a-30, 32, 33; c-30-32. **Krigstein** a-in all. **Orlando** a-30, 32, 33. **Wood** a-30, 31, 33; c-33.

INCREDIBLE SCIENCE FICTION (Formerly Weird Science-Fantasy)
Russ Cochran/Gemstone Publ.: No. 8, Aug, 1994 - No. 11, May, 1995 ($2.00)

8-11: Reprints #30-33 of E.C. series | | | | | | 4.00

INCURSION
Valiant Entertainment: Feb, 2019 - No. 4, May, 2019 ($3.99, limited series)

1-4: 1-Diggle & Paknadel-s/Braithwaite-a; Geomancer app.; Punk Mambo preview | | | | | | 4.00

INDEPENDENCE DAY (Movie)
Marvel Comics: No. 0, June, 1996 - No. 2, Aug, 1996 ($1.95, limited series)

0-Special Edition; photo-c | | | | | | 5.00
0-2 | | | | | | 4.00

INDEPENDENCE DAY (Movie)
Titan Comics: Mar, 2016 - No. 5, Jul, 2016 ($3.99, limited series)

1-5: 1-Victor Gischler-s/Steve Scott-a; four covers. 2-5-Two covers | | | | | | 4.00

INDESTRUCTIBLE
IDW (Darby Pop): Dec, 2013 - No. 10, Dec, 2014 ($3.99)

1-10: 1-Kline-s/Garron & Garcia-a | | | | | | 4.00
...: Stingray One Shot (5/15, $3.99) Marsick-s/Reguzzoni-a | | | | | | 4.00

INDESTRUCTIBLE HULK (Marvel NOW!)(Follows Incredible Hulk 2011-2012 series)
Marvel Comics: Jan, 2013 - No. 20, May, 2014 ($3.99)

1-Waid-s/Yu-a; Banner hired by SHIELD; Maria Hill app. | | | | | | 4.00
2-20: 2-Iron Man app. 4,5-Attuma app. 6-8-Thor app.; Simonson-a/c. 9,10-Daredevil app.
12-Two-Gun Kid, Kid Colt, and Rawhide Kid app. 17,18-Iron Man app. | | | | | | 4.00
Annual 1 (2/14, $4.99) Parker-s/Asrar-a; Iron Man app. | | | | | | 5.00
...: Special 1 (12/13, $4.99) Original X-Men and Superior Spider-Man app. | | | | | | 5.00

INDIANA JONES (Title series), **Dark Horse Comics**

--ADVENTURES, 6/08 ($6.95, digest-sized) Vol. 1 - new all-ages adventures; Beavers-a | | | | | | 7.00
--AND THE ARMS OF GOLD, 2/94 - 5/94 ($2.50) 1-4 | | | | | | 4.00
--AND THE FATE OF ATLANTIS, 3/91 - 9/91 ($2.50) 1-4-Dorman painted-c on
all; contain trading cards (#1 has a 2nd printing, 10/91) | | | | | | 4.00
--AND THE GOLDEN FLEECE, 6/94 - 7/94 ($2.50) 1,2 | | | | | | 4.00
--AND THE IRON PHOENIX, 12/94 - 3/95 ($2.50) 1-4 | | | | | | 4.00

INDIANA JONES AND THE KINGDOM OF THE CRYSTAL SKULL
Dark Horse Comics: May, 2008 - No. 2, May, 2008 ($5.99, limited series, movie adaptation)

1,2-Luke Ross-a/John Jackson Miller-adapted-s; two covers by Struzan & Fleming | | | | | | 6.00
TPB (5/08, $12.95) r/#1,2; Struzan-c | | | | | | 13.00

INDIANA JONES AND THE LAST CRUSADE
Marvel Comics: 1989 - No. 4, 1989 ($1.00, limited series, movie adaptation)

1-4: Williamson-i assist | | | | | | 4.00
1-(1989, $2.95, B&W mag., 80 pgs.) | | | | | | 5.00
--AND THE SHRINE OF THE SEA DEVIL: Dark Horse, 9/94 ($2.50, one shot)
1-Gary Gianni-a | | | | | | 4.00
--AND THE SARGASSO PIRATES: Dark Horse, 12/95 - 3/96 ($2.50) 1-4: 1,2-Ross-c | | | | | | 4.00
--AND THE SPEAR OF DESTINY: Dark Horse, 4/95 - 8/95 ($2.50) 1-4 | | | | | | 4.00
--AND THE TOMB OF THE GODS, 6/08 - No. 4, 3/09 ($2.99) 1-4: 1-Tony Harris-c | | | | | | 3.00
--THUNDER IN THE ORIENT: Dark Horse, 9/93 - '94 ($2.50)
1-6: Dan Barry story & art in all; 1-Dorman painted-c | | | | | | 4.00

INDIANA JONES AND THE TEMPLE OF DOOM
Marvel Comics Group: Sept, 1984 - No. 3, Nov, 1984 (Movie adaptation)

1-3-r/Marvel Super Special; Guice-a | | | | | | 5.00

INDIANA JONES OMNIBUS
Dark Horse Books: Feb, 2008; June 2008; Feb, 2009 ($24.95, digest-size)

Volume One - Reprints Indiana Jones and the Fate of Atlantis, Indiana Jones: Thunder in the
Orient; and Indiana Jones and the Arms of Gold mini-series | | | | | | 25.00
Volume Two - Reprints I.J. and the Golden Fleece, I.J. and the Shrine of the Sea Devil, I.J. and
the Iron Phoenix, I.J. and the Spear of Destiny, I.J. and the Sargasso Pirates | | | | | | 25.00
The Further Adventures Volume One - r (2/09) r/Raiders of the Lost Ark #1-3 & The Further
Adventures of Indiana Jones #1-12 | | | | | | 25.00

INDIAN BRAVES (Baffling Mysteries No. 5 on)
Ace Magazines: March, 1951 - No. 4, Sept, 1951

		GD	VG	FN	VF	VF/NM	NM-
1-Green Arrowhole begins, apps. in all		30	60	90	177	289	400
2		14	28	42	76	108	140
3,4		9	18	27	50	65	80
I.W. Reprint #1 (nd)-r/Indian Braves #4		2	4	6	11	16	20

INDIAN CHIEF (White Eagle...) (Formerly The Chief, Four Color 290)
Dell Publ. Co.: No. 3, July-Sept, 1951 - No. 33, Jan-Mar, 1959 (All painted-c)

		GD	VG	FN	VF	VF/NM	NM-
3		5	10	15	35	63	90
4-11: 6-White Eagle app.		5	10	15	30	50	70
12-1st White Eagle (10-12/53)-Not same as earlier character							
		5	10	15	34	60	85
13-29		4	8	12	23	37	50
30-33-Buscema-a		4	8	12	25	40	55

INDIAN CHIEF (See March of Comics No. 94, 110, 127, 140, 159, 170, 187)

INDIAN FIGHTER, THE (Movie)
Dell Publishing Co.: No. 687, May, 1956 (one-shot)

		GD	VG	FN	VF	VF/NM	NM-
Four Color 687-Kirk Douglas photo-c		8	16	24	54	102	150

INDIAN FIGHTER
Youthful Magazines: May, 1950 - No. 11, Jan, 1952

		GD	VG	FN	VF	VF/NM	NM-
1		26	52	78	154	252	350

	GD 2.0	VG 4.0	FN 6.0	VF 8.0	VF/NM 9.0	NM- 9.2

2-Wildey-a/c(bondage) — 15 30 45 85 130 175
3-11: 3,4-Wildey-a. 6-Davy Crockett story — 12 24 36 67 94 120
NOTE: *Hollingsworth a-5. Walter Johnson c-1, 3, 4, 6. Palais a-10. Staliman a-5-8. Wildey a-2-4; c-2, 5.*

INDIAN LEGENDS OF THE NIAGARA (See American Graphics)

INDIANS
Fiction House Magazines (Wings Publ. Co.): Spring, 1950 - No. 17, Spr, 1953 (1-8: 52 pgs.)
1-Manzar The White Indian, Long Bow & Orphan of the Storm begin

		37	74	111	222	361	500
2-Starlight begins	19	38	57	109	172	235
3-5: 5-17-Most-c by Whitman	15	30	45	88	137	185
6-10	14	28	42	82	121	160
11-17	14	28	42	78	112	145

INDIANS OF THE WILD WEST
I. W. Enterprises: Circa 1958? (no date) (Reprints)
9-Kinstler-c; Whitman-a; r/Indians #? — 3 6 9 15 22 28

INDIANS ON THE WARPATH
St. John Publishing Co.: 1950 (no month) (132 pgs.)
nn-Matt Baker-c; contains St. John comics rebound. Many combinations possible
— 55 110 165 352 601 850

INDIAN TRIBES (See Famous Indian Tribes)

INDIAN WARRIORS (Formerly White Rider and Super Horse; becomes Western Crime Cases #9)
Star Publications: No. 7, June, 1951 - No. 8, Sept, 1951
7-White Rider & Superhorse continue; "Last of the Mohicans" serial begins;

L.B. Cole-c	25	50	75	150	245	340
8-L.B. Cole-c	22	44	66	132	216	300
3-D 1(12/53, 25¢)-Came w/glasses; L.B. Cole-c	37	74	111	222	361	500
Accepted Reprint(nn)(inside cover shows White Rider & Superhorse #11)-r/cover to #7; origin White Rider &...; L.B. Cole-c	8	16	24	44	57	70
Accepted Reprint #8 (nd); L.B. Cole-c (r-cover to #8)	8	16	24	44	57	70

INDOORS-OUTDOORS (See Wisco)

INDUSTRIAL GOTHIC
DC Comics (Vertigo): Dec, 1995 - No. 5, Apr, 1996 ($2.50, limited series)
1-5: Ted McKeever-c/a/scripts — 4.00

INFAMOUS (Based on the Sony videogame)
DC Comics: Early May, 2011 - No. 6, Late July, 2011 ($2.99, limited series)
1-6: 1-William Harms/s/Eric Nguyen-a/Doug Mahnke-c. 3-6-Benes-c — 3.00

INFAMOUS IRON MAN (Doctor Doom as Iron Man)
Marvel Comics: Dec, 2016 - No. 12, Nov, 2017 ($3.99)
1-12: 1-Bendis-s/Maleev-a; Diablo app. 1-9-The Thing app. 5-Doom's mother returns — 4.00

INFECTED, THE (Year of the Villain tie-ins)
DC Comics: Feb, 2020 ($3.99, series of one-shots)
...: Deathbringer (2/20) Donna Troy corrupted by The Batman That Laughs; Teen Titans app. 4.00
...: King Shazam (1/20) Billy Batson corrupted; Marvel Family app.; Bennett-a 4.00
...: Scarab (2019) Jaime Reyes Blue Beetle corrupted; Williams II-a 4.00
...: The Commissioner (2/20) Jim Gordon corrupted; Batgirl app; Herbert-a 4.00

INFERIOR FIVE, THE (Inferior 5 #11, 12) (See Showcase #62, 63, 65)
National Periodical Publications (#1-10: 12¢): 3-4/67 - No. 10, 9-10/68; No. 11, 8-9/72 - No. 12, 10-11/72

1-(3-4/67)-Sekowsky-a(p); 4th app.	6	12	18	37	66	95
2-5: 2-Plastic Man, F.F. app. 4-Thor app.	3	6	9	21	33	45
6-9: 6-Stars DC staff	3	6	9	16	23	30
10-Superman x-over; F.F., Spider-Man & Sub-Mariner app.						
		4	8	12	25	40	55
11,12: Orlando-c/a; both r/Showcase #62,63	2	4	6	11	16	20

INFERIOR FIVE
DC Comics: Nov, 2019 - No. 4, Feb, 2020 ($3.99, limited series originally planned for 12 issues)
1-4-Giffen & Lemire-s&a; back-up with Peacemaker — 4.00

INFERNAL MAN-THING (Sequel to story in Man-Thing #12 [1974])
Marvel Comics: Sept, 2012 - No. 3, Oct, 2012 ($3.99, limited series)
1-3-Gerber-s; painted-a by Nowlan; Art Adams-c. 1,2-Bonus reprint of Man-Thing #12 — 4.00

INFERNO (See Legion of Super-Heroes)

INFERNO
DC Comics: Oct, 1997 - No. 4, Feb, 1998 ($2.50, limited series)
1-Immonen-s/c/a in all — 5.00
2-4 — 4.00

INFERNO (Secret Wars tie-in)
Marvel Comics: Jul, 2015 - No. 5, Nov, 2015 ($3.99, limited series)
1-5-Hopeless-s/Garrón-a; Magik, Colossus, Nightcrawler, Madelyne Pryor app. — 4.00

INFERNO (X-Men on Krakoa)
Marvel Comics: Nov, 2021 - No. 4, Mar, 2022 ($5.99, limited series)
1-4-Hickman-s/Schiti & Caselli-a; Moira MacTaggert's role in building Krakoa — 6.00

INFERNO GIRL RED (See Radiant Black)
Image Comics: Jan, 2023 - No. 3, Mar, 2023 ($5.99, limited series)
1-3-D'Urso-a/Groom-a — 6.00

INFERNO: HELLBOUND
Image Comics (Top Cow): Jan, 2002 - No. 3 ($2.50/$2.99)
1,2: 1-Seven covers; Silvestri-a/Silvestri and Wohl-s — 3.00
3-($2.99) Tan-a — 3.00
#0 (7/02, $3.00) Tan-a — 3.00
Wizard #0- Previews series; bagged with Wizard Top Cow Special mag — 3.00

INFESTATION (Zombie crossover with G.I. Joe, Star Trek, Transformers and Ghostbusters)
IDW Publishing: Jan, 2011 - No. 2, Apr, 2011 ($3.99, limited series)
1,2-Abnett & Lanning-s/Messina-a; two covers by Messina & Snyder III — 4.00
...: Outbreak 1-4 (6/11 - No. 4, 9/11, $3.99) Messina-a; Covert Vampiric Operations app. — 4.00

INFESTATION 2 (IDW characters vs. H.P. Lovecraft's Elder Gods)

IDW Publishing: Jan, 2012 - No. 2, Apr, 2012 ($3.99, limited series)
1,2-Swierczynski-s/Messina-a; three covers by Garner, Ramondelli & Messina — 4.00
...: Dungeons & Dragons 1,2 (2/12 - No. 2, 2/12, $3.99) 3 covers — 4.00
...: G.I. Joe 1,2 (3/12 - No. 2, 3/12, $3.99) Raicht-s/De Landro-a; 3 covers — 4.00
...: Team-Up 1 (2/12, $3.99) Ryall-s/Robinson-a; covers by Powell & Morrison — 4.00
...: Teenage Mutant Ninja Turtles 1,2 (3/12 - No. 2, 3/12, $3.99) Mark Torres-a; 3 covers — 4.00
...: 30 Days of Night 1 (4/12, $3.99) Swierczynski-s/Sayger-a; 3 covers — 4.00
...: Transformers 1,2 (2/12 - No. 2, 2/12, $3.99) Dixon-s/Guidi-a; 3 covers — 4.00

INFIDEL
Image Comics: Mar, 2018 - No. 5, Jul, 2018 ($3.99, limited series)
1-5-Pornsak Pichetshote-s/Aaron Campbell-a — 4.00

INFINITE, THE
Image Comics (SkyBound): Aug, 2011 - No. 4, Nov, 2011 ($2.99)
1-4: 1-Robert Kirkman-s/Rob Liefeld-a; at least 11 covers. 2-Six covers — 3.00

INFINITE CRISIS
DC Comics: Dec, 2005 - No. 7, Jun, 2006 ($3.99, limited series)

1-Johns-s/Jimenez-a; two covers by Jim Lee and George Pérez		1	3	4	6	8	10
1-RRP Edition with Jim Lee sketch-c						100.00

2,4,6,7: 4-New Spectre; Earth-2 returns. 6-Superboy killed, new Earth formed.
7-Earth-2 Superman dies — 5.00

3-1st app. Jaime Reyes		1	3	4	6	8	10
5-1st Jaime Reyes as new Blue Beetle; Earth-2 Lois Lane dies						
		3	6	9	21	33	45

HC (2006, $24.99, dustjacket) r/#1-7; DiDio intro.; sketch cover gallery; interview/commentary with Johns, Jimenez and editors; sketch art — 25.00
... Companion TPB (2006, $14.99) r/Day of Vengeance: Infinite Crisis Special #1, Rann-Thanagar War: ICS #1, The Omac Project: ICS #1, Villains United: ICS #1 — 15.00
... Secret Files 2006 (4/06, $5.99) tie-in story with Earth-2 Lois and Superman, Earth-Prime Superboy and Alexander Luthor; art by various; profile pages — 6.00

INFINITE CRISIS AFTERMATH (See Crisis Aftermath:...)

INFINITE CRISIS: FIGHT FOR THE MULTIVERSE (Based on the video game)
DC Comics: Sept, 2014 - No. 12, Aug, 2015 ($3.99, limited series)
1-12: 1-Abnett-s; art by various. 2-6-Polybagged — 4.00

INFINITE DARK
Image Comics: Oct, 2018 - No. 8, Jul, 2019 ($3.99)
1-8-Ryan Cady-s/Andrea Mutti-a — 4.00

INFINITE FRONTIER
DC Comics: No. 0, May, 2021 - No. 6 ($5.99/$4.99)
0-($5.99) Short stories previewing the new DC Multiverse; Wonder Woman returns — 6.00
1-6-($4.99) Justice Incarnate app. (Calvin Ellis Superman, Flashpoint Batman, Mary Marvel, Captain Carrot, Aquawoman, Machinehead) — 5.00
...: Secret Files 1 (8/21, $9.99) Short stories featuring Director Bones, Calvin Ellis, Roy Harper, Jade, Psycho Pirate — 10.00

INFINITE LOOP
IDW Publishing: Apr, 2015 - No. 6, Sept, 2015 ($3.99)
1-6-Pierrick Colinet-s/Elsa Charretier-a — 4.00

INFINITE LOOP, VOLUME 2
IDW Publishing: Sept, 2017 - No. 4, Dec, 2017 ($3.99)
1-4-Colinet & Charretier-s/Di Nicuolo-a — 4.00

INFINITE VACATION
Image Comics (Shadowline): Jan, 2011 - No. 5, Jan, 2013 ($3.50/$5.99)
1-4-Nick Spencer-s/Christian Ward-a/c — 3.50
5-($5.99) Conclusion; gatefold centerfold — 6.00

INFINITY (Crossover with the Avengers titles)
Marvel Comics: Oct, 2013 - No. 6, Jan, 2014 ($4.99/$3.99/$5.99, limited series)
1-($4.99) Avengers, Inhumans and Thanos app.; Hickman-s/Cheung-a/Adam Kubert-c — 5.00
2-5-($3.99) Opeña-a. 3-Terragen bomb triggered — 4.00
6-($5.99) Cheung-a — 6.00
Free Comic Book Day 2013 (Infinity) 1 (5/13, giveaway) Previews series; Cheung-a — 3.00

INFINITY ABYSS (Also see Marvel Universe: The End)
Marvel Comics: Aug, 2002 - No. 6, Oct, 2002 ($2.99, limited series)
1-5-Starlin-s/a; Thanos, Captain Marvel, Spider-Man, Dr. Strange app. — 4.00
6-($3.50) — 4.00
Thanos Vol. 2: Infinity Abyss TPB (2003, $17.99) r/ #1-6 — 25.00

INFINITY COUNTDOWN
Marvel Comics: May, 2018 - No. 5, Sept, 2018 ($4.99, limited series with one-shots)
1-5-Duggan-s/Kuder-a; Guardians of the Galaxy app.; Groot restored — 5.00
... Adam Warlock 1 (4/18, $4.99) Prelude to series; Duggan-s/Allred-a — 5.00
... Black Widow 1 (8/18, $4.99) Duggan-s/Virella-a; Jamie Braddock app. — 5.00
... Captain Marvel 1 (7/18, $4.99) McCann-s/Olortegui-a; alternate Capt. Marvels app. — 5.00
... Champions 1,2 (8/18, 9/18, $4.99) 1-Zub-s/Laiso-a; Warbringer & Thanos app. — 5.00
... Daredevil 1 (7/18, $4.99) Duggan-s/Sprouse, Noto & Ferguson-a — 5.00
... Darkhawk 1-4 (7/18 - No. 4, 9/18, $4.99) Bowers & Sims-s/Gang Lim-a — 5.00
... Prime 1 (4/18, $4.99) Prelude; Duggan-s/Deodato-a; Wolverine, Magus, Ultron app. — 5.00

INFINITY CRUSADE
Marvel Comics: June, 1993 - No. 6, Nov, 1993 ($3.50/$2.50, limited series, 52 pgs.)
1-6: By Jim Starlin & Ron Lim. 1-($3.50). 2-6-($2.99) — 6.00

INFINITY ENTITY, THE (Concludes in Thanos: The Infinity Entity GN)
Marvel Comics: May, 2016 - No. 4, Jun, 2016 ($3.99, limited series)
1-4: Jim Starlin-s/Alan Davis-a. 1-Rebirth of Adam Warlock. 4-Mephisto app. — 4.00

INFINITY GAUNTLET (The... #2 on; see Infinity Crusade, The Infinity War & Warlock & the Infinity Watch)
Marvel Comics: July, 1991 - No. 6, Dec, 1991 ($2.50, limited series)

1-Thanos-c/stories in all; Starlin scripts in all	4	8	12	27	44	60
2-6: 5,6-Ron Lim-c/a	2	4	6	11	16	20

Infected: King Shazam #1 © DC

Infinity Entity #2 © MAR

Inhumanity #1 © MAR

	GD 2.0	VG 4.0	FN 6.0	VF 8.0	VF/NM 9.0	NM- 9.2

TPB (4/99, $24.95) r/#1-6 .... 30.00
NOTE: *Lim* a-3p(part), 5p, 6p; c-5i, 6i. *Perez* a-1-3p, 4p(part); c-1(painted), 2-4, 5i, 6i.

INFINITY GAUNTLET (Secret Wars tie-in)
Marvel Comics: Jul, 2015 - No. 5, Jan, 2016 ($3.99, limited series)
1-5-Duggan & Weaver-s/Weaver-a; Thanos & The Guardians of the Galaxy app. 4.00

INFINITY: HEIST (Tie-in to the Infinity crossover)
Marvel Comics: Nov, 2013 - No. 4, Feb, 2014 ($3.99, limited series)
1-4-Tieri-s/Barrionuevo-a; Spymaster, Titanium Man, Whirlwind app. 4.00

INFINITY, INC. (See All-Star Squadron #25)
DC Comics: Mar, 1984 - No. 53, Aug, 1988 ($1.25, Baxter paper, 36 pgs.)
1-Brainwave, Jr., Fury, The Huntress, Jade, Northwind, Nuklon, Obsidian, Power Girl, Silver Scarab & Star Spangled Kid begin 5.00
2-13,38-49,51-53: 2-Dr. Midnite, G.A. Flash, W. Woman, Dr. Fate, Hourman, Green Lantern, Wildcat app. 5-Nudity panels. 13-Re-intro Rose and Thorn. 46,47-Millennium tie-ins. 49-Hector Hall becomes The Sandman (1970s Kirby) 4.00
14-Todd McFarlane-a (5/85, 2nd full story) 3 6 9 19 30 40
15,17-37-McFarlane-a (20,23,24: 5 pgs. only; 33: 2 pgs.); 18-24-Crisis x-over. 21-Intro new Hourman & Dr. Midnight. 26-New Wildcat app. 31-Star Spangled Kid becomes Skyman. 32-Green Fury becomes Green Flame. 33-Origin Obsidian. 35-1st modern app. G.A. Fury 5.00
16-Mr. Bones debut 2 4 6 8 10 12
50 ($2.50, 52 pgs.) 5.00
Annual 1,2: 1(12/85)-Crisis x-over. 2('88, $2.00), Special 1 ('87, $1.50) 5.00
...: The Generations Saga Volume One HC (2011, $39.99) r/#1-4, All-Star Squadron #25,26 & All-Star Squadron Annual #2 .... 40.00
NOTE: *Kubert* r-4. *McFarlane* a-14-37p, Annual 1p; c(p)-14-19, 22, 25, 26, 31-33, 37, Annual 1. *Newton* a-12p, 13p(last work 4/85). *Tuska* a-11p. JSA app. 3-10.

INFINITY, INC. (See 52)
DC Comics: Nov, 2007 - No. 12, Oct, 2008 ($2.99)
1-12: 1-Milligan-s; Steel app. 3.00
...: Luthor's Monsters TPB (2008, $14.99) r/#1-5 .... 15.00
...: The Bogeyman TPB (2008, $14.99) r/#6-10 .... 15.00

INFINITY MAN AND THE FOREVER PEOPLE
DC Comics: Aug, 2014 - No. 9, May, 2015 ($2.99)
1-9: 1-DiDio-s/Giffen-a. 2,5,6-Grummett-a. 3-Starlin-a. 4-6-Guy Gardner app. 9-Giffen-a 3.00
...: Futures End 1 (11/14, $2.99, regular-c) Five years later; Philip Tan-a 3.00
...: Futures End 1 (11/14, $3.99, 3-D cover) 4.00

INFINITY: THE HUNT (Tie-in to the Infinity crossover)
Marvel Comics: Nov, 2013 - No. 4, Jan, 2014 ($3.99, limited series)
1-4-Kindt-s/Sanders-a; Avengers Academy, Wolverine & She-Hulk app. 4.00

INFINITY WAR, THE (Also see Infinity Gauntlet & Warlock and the Infinity...)
Marvel Comics: June, 1992 - No. 6, Nov, 1992 ($2.50, mini-series)
1-Starlin scripts, Lim-c/a(p), Thanos app. in all 1 3 4 6 8 10
2-6: All have wraparound gatefold covers 6.00
TPB (2006, $29.99) r/#1-6, Marvel Comics Presents #108-111, Warlock and the Infinity Watch #7-10; cover gallery and synopses of Infinity War crossovers 30.00

INFINITY WARS (Also see Infinity Countdown)
Marvel Comics: Oct, 2018 - No. 6 ($5.99/$4.99, limited series)
1-($5.99) Duggan-s/Deodato-a; Guardians of the Galaxy, Dr. Strange, Loki app. 6.00
2-5-($4.99) 3-Infinity Warps created; Deodato-a 5.00
6-($5.99) Duggan-s/Deodato-a; Adam Warlock app. 6.00
...: Fallen Guardian 1 (2/19, $4.99) MacDonald-a; takes place after #6 .... 5.00
... Infinity 1 (3/19, $3.99) Duggan-s/Bagley-a; The fate of the Time Stone; Loki app. 4.00
... Prime 1 (9/18, $4.99) Duggan-s/Deodato-a; prelude to series; Thanos killed 5.00

INFINITY WARS: ARACHKNIGHT
Marvel Comics: Dec, 2018 - No. 2, Jan, 2019 ($3.99, limited series)
1,2-Origin of Spider-Man/Moon Knight combo; Hopeless-s/Garza-a 4.00

INFINITY WARS: GHOST PANTHER
Marvel Comics: Jan, 2019 - No. 2, Feb, 2019 ($3.99, limited series)
1,2-Origin of Ghost Rider/Black Panther combo; MacKay-s/Palo-a; Killraven app. 4.00

INFINITY WARS: INFINITY WARPS
Marvel Comics: Jan, 2019 - No. 2, Feb, 2019 ($3.99, limited series)
1,2-Short stories of Observer-X, Moon Squirrel and Tippysaur, Green Widow and others 4.00

INFINITY WARS: IRON HAMMER
Marvel Comics: Nov, 2018 - No. 2, Dec, 2018 ($3.99, limited series)
1,2-Origin of Iron Man/Thor combo; Ewing-s/Rosanas-a 4.00

INFINITY WARS: SLEEPWALKER

Marvel Comics: Dec, 2018 - No. 4, Feb, 2019 ($3.99, limited series)
1-4-Bowers & Sims-s/Nauck-a 4.00

INFINITY WARS: SOLDIER SUPREME
Marvel Comics: Nov, 2018 - No. 2, Dec, 2018 ($3.99, limited series)
1,2: 1-Origin of Captain America/Doctor Strange combo; Duggan-s/Adam Kubert-a 4.00

INFINITY WARS: WEAPON HEX
Marvel Comics: Nov, 2018 - No. 2, Jan, 2019 ($3.99, limited series)
1,2-Origin of X-23/Scarlet Witch combo; Acker & Blacker-s/Sandoval-a 4.00

INFORMER, THE
Feature Television Productions: April, 1954 - No. 5, Dec, 1954

	GD 2.0	VG 4.0	FN 6.0	VF 8.0	VF/NM 9.0	NM- 9.2
1-Sekowsky-a begins	21	42	63	122	199	275
2	11	22	33	64	90	115
3-5	9	18	27	52	69	85

IN HIS STEPS
Spire Christian Comics (Fleming H. Revell Co.): 1973, 1977 (39/49¢)

	GD 2.0	VG 4.0	FN 6.0	VF 8.0	VF/NM 9.0	NM- 9.2
nn	2	4	6	11	16	20

INHUMAN (Also see Uncanny Inhumans)
Marvel Comics: Jun, 2014 - No. 14, Jun, 2015 ($3.99)
1-14: 1-3-Soule-s/Madureira-a; Medusa app. 4-7,9-11-Stegman-a. 10-Spider-Man app. 4.00
Annual 1 (7/15, $4.99) Soule-s/Stegman-a; continues from #14; Ms. Marvel app. 5.00
...: Special 1 (6/15, $4.99) Crossover with Amaz. Spider-Man & All-New Capt. America 5.00

INHUMANITY
Marvel Comics: Feb, 2014 - No. 2, Mar, 2014 ($3.99)
1,2: 1-After the fall of Attilan, origin of the Inhumans retold; Fraction/Coipel-a 4.00
...: Superior Spider-Man 1 (3/14, $3.99) Gage-s/Hans-a/c 4.00
...: The Awakening 1,2 (2/14 - No. 2, 3/14, $3.99) Kindt-s/Davidson-a 4.00

INHUMANOIDS, THE (TV)
Marvel Comics (Star Comics): Jan, 1987 - No. 4, July 1987
1-4: Based on Hasbro toys 4.00

INHUMANS, THE (See Amazing Adventures, Fantastic Four #54 & Special #5, Incredible Hulk Special #1, Marvel Graphic Novel & Thor #146)
Marvel Comics: Oct, 1975 - No. 12, Aug, 1977

	GD 2.0	VG 4.0	FN 6.0	VF 8.0	VF/NM 9.0	NM- 9.2
1: #1-4,6 are 25¢ issues	6	12	18	41	76	110
2-4-Peréz-a	3	6	9	14	20	25
5-12: 9-Reprints Amazing Adventures #1,2('70). 12-Hulk app.	2	4	6	10	14	18
4-(30¢-c variant, limited distribution)(4/76) Pérez-a	4	8	12	27	44	60
6-(30¢-c variant, limited distribution)(8/76)	4	8	12	27	44	60
11,12-(35¢-c variants, limited distribution)	6	12	18	41	76	110

Special 1(4/90, $1.50, 52 pgs.)-F.F. cameo 5.00
...: The Great Refuge (5/95, $2.95) 5.00
NOTE: *Buckler* c-2-4p, 5. *Gil Kane* a-5-7p; c-1p, 7p, 8p. *Kirby* a-9r. *Mooney* a-11i. *Perez* a-1-4p, 8p.

INHUMANS (Marvel Knights)
Marvel Comics: Nov, 1998 - No. 12, Oct, 1999 ($2.99, limited series)

	GD 2.0	VG 4.0	FN 6.0	VF 8.0	VF/NM 9.0	NM- 9.2
1-Jae Lee-c/a; Paul Jenkins-s	3	6	9	15	22	28
1-($6.95) DF Edition; Jae Lee variant-c	3	6	9	17	26	35

2-Two covers by Lee and Darrow 6.00
3,4,6-12 .... 4.00

	GD 2.0	VG 4.0	FN 6.0	VF 8.0	VF/NM 9.0	NM- 9.2
5-1st app. Yelena Belova (Black Widow)	5	10	15	31	53	75

TPB (10/00, $24.95) r/#1-12 .... 25.00

INHUMANS (Volume 3)
Marvel Comics: Jun, 2000 - No. 4, Oct, 2000 ($2.99, limited series)
1-4-Ladronn-c/Pacheco & Marin-s. 1-3-Ladronn-a. 4-Lucas-a 3.00

INHUMANS (Volume 6)
Marvel Comics: Jun, 2003 - No. 12, Jun, 2004 ($2.50/$2.99)
1-12: 1-6-McKeever-s/Clark-a/JH Williams III-c. 7-Begin $2.99-c. 7,8-Teranishi-a 3.00
Vol. 1: Culture Shock (2005, $7.99, digest) r/#1-6; story pitch and sketch pages 8.00

INHUMANS: ATTILAN RISING (Secret Wars tie-in)
Marvel Comics: Jul, 2015 - No. 5, Nov, 2015 ($3.99, limited series)
1-5-Soule-s/Timms-a/Johnson-a 4.00

INHUMANS: JUDGMENT DAY
Marvel Comics: Mar, 2018 ($4.99, one-shot)
1-Follows from Royals #12; Al Ewing-s/Del Mundo & Libranda-a; Acuna-c 5.00

INHUMANS: ONCE AND FUTURE KINGS
Marvel Comics: Oct, 2017 - No. 5, Feb, 2018 ($3.99, limited series)
1-5: 1-Priest-s/Noto-a; young Black Bolt, Maximus & Medusa. 4-Spider-Man app. 4.00

	GD 2.0	VG 4.0	FN 6.0	VF 8.0	VF/NM 9.0	NM- 9.2

INHUMANS PRIME
Marvel Comics: May, 2017 ($4.99, one-shot)

1-Follows IVX series; leads into Royals #1; Al Ewing-s/Ryan Sook & Chris Allen-a						5.00

INHUMANS 2099
Marvel Comics: Nov, 2004 ($2.99, one-shot)

1-Kirkman-s/Rathburn-a/Pat Lee-c						3.00

INHUMANS VS. X-MEN (See IVX)

INJECTION
Image Comics: May, 2015 - No. 15, Nov, 2017 ($2.99/$3.99)

1-10-Warren Ellis-s/Declan Shalvey-a						3.00
11-15-($3.99)						4.00

INJUSTICE: GODS AMONG US (Based on the video game)
DC Comics: Mar, 2013 - No. 12, Feb, 2014 ($3.99)

1-Lois Lane dies; Joker app.	3	6	9	19	30	40
1-Variant-c	4	8	12	23	37	50
1-Second printing						6.00
2-Joker killed						10.00
3-12: 6-Nightwing dies						4.00
Annual 1 (1/14, $4.99) Harley Quinn & Lobo app.; Ryp-c						5.00

INJUSTICE (Gods Among Us:) **YEAR TWO** (Based on the video game)
DC Comics: Mar, 2014 - No. 12, Late Nov, 2014 ($2.99)

1-Sinestro app.	1	2	3	5	6	8
2-12: 2-6,9-12-Sinestro app. 7-11-Harley Quinn app.						4.00
Annual 1 (12/14, $4.99) Stories of Oracle, Green Lantern & Sinestro; Raapack-c						5.00

INJUSTICE: GODS AMONG US: YEAR THREE (Based on the video game)
DC Comics: Early Dec, 2014 - No. 12, Late May, 2015 ($2.99, printings of digital-first stories)

1-12: 1-Constantine joins the fight. 5-New Deadman app.						3.00
Annual 1 (6/15, $4.99) Prequel to Year Three; Constantine app.; Titans vs. Superman						5.00

INJUSTICE: GODS AMONG US: YEAR FOUR (Based on the video game)
DC Comics: Early Jul, 2015 - No. 12, Late Dec, 2015 ($2.99, printings of digital-first stories)

1-12: 1-The Olympus Gods join the fight. 10-Harley Quinn cover						3.00

INJUSTICE: GODS AMONG US: YEAR FIVE (Based on the video game)
DC Comics: Early Mar, 2016 - No. 20, Late Dec, 2016 ($2.99, printings of digital-first stories)

1-20: 1-Doomsday & Bane app. 6-Solomon Grundy app. 7-Damian becomes Nightwing. 12-Alfred killed by Zsasz. 18-Deathstroke app.						3.00
Annual 1 (1/17, $4.99) Harley Quinn app.; leads into Injustice: Ground Zero						5.00

INJUSTICE: GROUND ZERO (Follows Year Five)
DC Comics: Early Feb, 2016 - No. 12, Jul, 2017 ($2.99, printings of digital-first stories)

1-12: 1-Mhan & Derenick-a; Harley & Joker app. 12-Superman vs. Superman						3.00

INJUSTICE 2 (Follows Ground Zero)(Prequel to the Injustice 2 video game)
DC Comics: Early Jul, 2017 - No. 36, Dec, 2018 ($2.99, printings of digital-first stories)

1-36: 1-Taylor-s/Redondo-a; Harley joins the Suicide Squad. 3-Intro. Athanasia. 6-Intro/origin Supergirl						3.00
Annual 1 (1/18, $4.99) Origin of Wonder Woman; back-up with Harley Quinn; Mhan-a						5.00
Annual 2 (1/19, $4.99) Follows #36; Ma & Pa Kent app.; Redondo-a						5.00

INJUSTICE VS. MASTERS OF THE UNIVERSE (Injustice: Gods Among Us)
DC Comics: Sept, 2018 - No. 6, Mar, 2019 ($3.99, limited series)

	1	2	3	5	6	8
1-Seeley-s/Williams II-a; Justice Leaguers & He-Man vs. Darkseid & Skeletor						
1-Variant-c by Tim Seeley	2	4	6	8	10	12
2-6						4.00

INKBLOT
Image Comics: Sept, 2020 - Present ($3.99)

1-15-Emma Kubert & Rusty Gladd-s/a						4.00

INKY & DINKY (See Felix's Nephews…)

IN LOVE (…Magazine on-c; I Love You No. 7 on)
Mainline/Charlton No. 5 (5/55)-on: Aug-Sept, 1954 - No. 6, July, 1955 ('Adult Reading' on-c)

1-Simon & Kirby-a; book-length novel in all issues	77	154	231	493	847	1200
2,3-S&K-a. 3-Last pre-code (12-1/54-55)	40	80	120	246	411	575
4-S&K-a.(Rare)	43	86	129	271	461	650
5-S&K-c only	24	48	72	142	234	325
6-No S&K-a	15	30	45	90	140	190

IN SEARCH OF THE CASTAWAYS (See Movie Comics)

INSEXTS
AfterShock Comics: Dec, 2015 - No. 13, Sept, 2017 ($3.99, mature)

1-13-Marguerite Bennett-s/Ariela Kristantina-a						4.00

INSIDE CRIME (Formerly My Intimate Affair)
Fox Feature Syndicate (Hero Books): No. 3, July, 1950 - No. 2, Sept, 1950

3-Wood-a (10 pgs.); L. B. Cole-c	41	82	123	256	428	600
2-Used in **SOTI**, pg. 182,183; r/Spook #24	31	62	93	182	296	410
nn (nd, M.S. Dist. Pub.) Wally Wood-c	14	28	42	82	121	160

INSPECTOR, THE (TV) (Also see The Pink Panther)
Gold Key: July, 1974 - No. 19, Feb, 1978

1	3	6	9	21	33	45
2-5	2	4	6	13	18	22
6-9	2	4	6	10	14	18
10-19: 11-Reprints	2	4	6	8	10	12

INSPECTOR, THE Volume 2 (The Pink Panther)
American Mythology: 2016 ($3.99, one-shot)

1-The Pink Files; new stories by Fridolfs & Gallagher; reprints						4.00

INSPECTOR GILL OF THE FISH POLICE (See Fish Police)

INSPECTOR WADE
David McKay Publications: No. 13, May, 1938

Feature Books 13	41	82	123	256	428	600

INSTANT PIANO
Dark Horse Comics: Aug, 1994 - No. 4, Feb, 1995 ($3.95, B&W, bimonthly, mature)

1-4						4.00

INSUFFERABLE
IDW Publishing: May, 2015 - No. 8, Dec, 2015 ($3.99)

1-8-Waid-s/Krause-a						4.00

INSUFFERABLE: HOME FIELD ADVANTAGE
IDW Publishing: Oct, 2016 - No. 4, Jan, 2017 ($3.99)

1-4-Waid-s/Krause-a						4.00

INSUFFERABLE: ON THE ROAD
IDW Publishing: Feb, 2016 - No. 6, Jul, 2016 ($3.99)

1-6-Waid-s/Krause-a						4.00

INSURGENT
DC Comics: Mar, 2013 - No. 3, May, 2013 ($2.99, limited series)

1-3-DeSanto & Farmer-s/Dallocchio-a						3.00

INTERFACE
Marvel Comics (Epic Comics): Dec, 1989 - No. 8, Dec, 1990 ($1.95, mature, coated paper)

1-8: Cont. from 1st ESPers series; painted-c/a						3.00
Espers: Interface TPB ('98, $16.95) r/#1-6						17.00

INTERNATIONAL COMICS (…Crime Patrol No. 6)
E. C. Comics: Spring, 1947 - No. 5, Nov-Dec, 1947

1-Schaffenberger-a begins, ends #4	161	322	483	1030	1765	2500
2	71	142	213	454	777	1100
3-5	58	116	174	371	636	900

INTERNATIONAL CRIME PATROL (Formerly International Comics #1-5; becomes Crime Patrol No. 7 on)
E. C. Comics: No. 6, Spring, 1948

6-Moon Girl app.	284	568	852	1818	3109	4400

INTERNATIONAL IRON MAN
Marvel Comics: May, 2016 - No. 7, Dec, 2016 ($3.99)

1-7-Bendis-s/Maleev-a. 1-4-Flashback to college years in London. 5-Intro. Amanda Armstrong. 6,7-Flashback to Stark's real parents meeting						4.00

INTERSECT
Image Comics: Nov, 2014 - No. 6, Apr, 2015 ($3.50)

1-6-Ray Fawkes-s/a. 1-Lemire-c. 2-Kindt-c						3.50

IN THE DAYS OF THE MOB (Magazine)
Hampshire Dist. Ltd. (National): Fall, 1971 (B&W)

1-Kirby-a; John Dillinger wanted poster inside (1/2 value if poster is missing)	7	14	21	48	89	130

IN THE PRESENCE OF MINE ENEMIES
Spire Christian Comics/Fleming H. Revell Co.: 1973 (35/49¢)

nn	3	6	9	15	22	28

IN THE SHADOW OF EDGAR ALLAN POE
DC Comics (Vertigo): 2002 (Graphic novel)

Hardcover (2002, $24.95) Fuqua-s/Phillips and Parke photo-a						25.00
Softcover (2003, $17.95)						18.00

INTIMATE
Charlton Comics: Dec, 1957 - No. 3, May, 1958

1	40	80	120	246	411	575
2,3	15	30	45	83	124	165

INTIMATE CONFESSIONS (See Fox Giants)

INTIMATE CONFESSIONS
Country Press Inc.: 1942

nn-Ashcan comic, not distributed to newsstands, only for in house use. A VF copy sold for $1,000 in 2007, and a VF+ copy sold for $1,525 in 2007.

INTIMATE CONFESSIONS
Realistic Comics: July-Aug, 1951 - No. 7, Aug, 1952; No. 8, Mar, 1953 (All painted-c)

1-Kinstler-a; c/Avon paperback #222	239	478	717	1530	2615	3700
2	58	116	174	371	636	900
3-c/Avon paperback #250; Kinstler-c/a	61	122	183	390	670	950
4-8: 4-c/Avon paperback #304; Kinstler-c. 6-c/Avon paperback #120.						
8-c/Avon paperback #375; Kinstler-a	52	104	156	328	552	775

INTIMATE CONFESSIONS
I. W. Enterprises/Super Comics: 1964

I.W. Reprint #9,10, Super Reprint #10,12,18	3	6	9	16	24	32

INTIMATE LOVE
Standard Comics: No. 5, 1950 - No. 28, Aug, 1954

5-8: 6-8-Severin/Elder-a	15	30	45	90	140	190
9	14	28	42	76	108	140
10-Jane Russell, Robert Mitchum photo-c	19	38	57	111	176	240
11-18,20,23,25,27,28	13	26	39	72	101	130
19,21,22,24,26-Toth-a	14	28	42	78	112	145

NOTE: *Celardo* a-8, 10. **Colletta** a-23. *Moreira* a-13(2). Photo-c-6, 7, 10, 12, 14, 15, 18-20, 24, 26, 27.

INTIMATES, THE
DC Comics (WildStorm): Jan, 2005 - No. 12, Dec, 2005 ($2.95/$2.99)

1-12: 1-Joe Casey-s/Jim Lee-c/Lee and Giuseppe Camuncoli-a						3.00

INTIMATE SECRETS OF ROMANCE
Star Publications: Sept, 1953 - No. 2, Apr, 1954

1,2-L. B. Cole-c	34	68	102	199	325	450

INTRIGUE
Quality Comics Group: Jan, 1955

1-Horror; Jack Cole reprint/Web of Evil	48	96	114	302	514	725

INTRIGUE

Injustice Year Two #1 © DC

Invaders #27 © MAR

Invincible #72 © Kirkman & Walker

	GD 2.0	VG 4.0	FN 6.0	VF 8.0	VF/NM 9.0	NM- 9.2

Image Comics: Aug, 1999 - No. 3, Feb, 2000 ($2.50/$2.95)
1,2: 1-Two covers (Andrews, Wieringo); Shum-s/Andrews-a — 4.00
3-($2.95) — 4.00

INTRUDER
TSR, Inc.: 1990 - No. 10, 1991 ($2.95, 44 pgs.)
1-10 — 5.00

INVADERS, THE (TV)(Aliens From a Dying Planet)
Gold Key: Oct, 1967 - No. 4, Oct, 1968 (All have photo-c)
1-Spiegle-a in all — 9 18 27 60 120 180
2-4: 2-Pin-up on back-c. 3-Has variant 15¢-c with photo back-c — 6 12 18 37 66 95

INVADERS, THE (Also see The Avengers #71, Giant-Size Invaders, and All-New Invaders)
Marvel Comics Group: August, 1975 - No. 40, May, 1979; No. 41, Sept, 1979
1-Captain America & Bucky, Human Torch & Toro, & Sub-Mariner begin; cont'd. from Giant
Size Invaders #1; #1-7 are 25¢ issues — 7 14 21 44 82 120
2-5: 2-1st app. Brain-Drain. 3-Battle issue; Cap vs. Namor vs. Torch; intro U-Man — 3 6 9 19 30 40
6,9,10: 6-(Regular 25¢ edition). 6-(7/76) Liberty Legion app. 9-Origin Baron Blood.
10-G.A. Capt. America-r/C.A #22 — 4 6 11 16 20
6-(30¢-c variant, limited distribution) — 6 12 18 38 69 100
7-(Reg. 25¢ edition) Intro Baron Blood & intro/1st app. Union Jack; Human Torch origin retold — 6 12 18 41 76 110
7-(30¢-c variant, limited distribution) — 11 22 33 73 157 240
8-Union Jack-c/story — 4 8 12 27 44 60
11,13-16,19: 11-Origin Spitfire. 14-1st app. The Crusaders. 16-Re-intro
The Destroyer. 19-Hitler-c/story — 2 4 6 9 13 16
12-1st Jacqueline as Spitfire — 5 10 15 31 53 75
17,18-(Regular 30¢-c): 17-Intro Warrior Woman. 18-Re-intro The Destroyer w/new origin — 3 6 9 21 33 45
17-19,21-(35¢-c variants, limited distribution) — 11 22 33 75 160 245
20-(Regular 30¢-c) Reprints origin/1st app. Sub-Mariner from Motion Picture Funnies Weekly
with color added & brief write-up about MPFW; 1st app. new Union Jack II — 5 10 15 31 53 75
20-(35¢-c variant, limited distribution) — 12 24 36 80 173 265
21-(Regular 30¢ edition)-r/Marvel Mystery #10 (battle issue) — 2 4 6 9 13 16
22-30,34-40: 22-New origin Toro. 24-r/Marvel Mystery #17 (team-up issue; all-r). 25-All new-a
begins. 28-Intro new Human Top & Golden Girl. 29-Intro Teutonic Knight. 34-Mighty
Destroyer joins. 35-The Whizzer app. — 1 3 4 6 8 10
31-33: 31-Frankenstein-c/sty. 32,33-Thor app. — 2 4 6 8 11 14
41-Double size last issue — 3 6 9 16 23 30
Annual 1 (9/77)-Schomburg, Rico stories (new); Schomburg-c/a (1st for Marvel in 30 years);
Avengers app.; re-intro The Shark & The Hyena — 5 10 15 33 57 80
... Classic Vol. 1 TPB (2007, $24.99) r/#1-9, Giant-Size Invaders #1 and Marvel
Premiere #29,30; cover pencils and cover inks — 25.00
NOTE: *Buckler* a-5. *Everett* r-20(`39), 21(1940), 24, Annual 1. *Gil Kane* c(p)-13, 17, 18, 20-27. *Kirby* c(p)-3-12, 14-16, 32, 33. *Mooney* a-5i, 16, 22. *Robbins* a-1-4, 6-9, 10(3 pg.), 11-15, 17-21, 23, 25-28; c-28.

INVADERS (See Namor, the Sub-Mariner #12)
Marvel Comics Group: May, 1993 - No. 4, Aug, 1993 ($1.75, limited series)
1-4 — 4.00

INVADERS (2004 title - see New Invaders)

INVADERS
Marvel Comics: Mar, 2019 - No. 12, Feb, 2020 ($4.99/$3.99)
1-($4.99) Zdarsky-s/Magno & Guice-a; Captain America, Namor & Winter Soldier — 5.00
2-12-($3.99) 2-Hydro-Man app. 5-7-Avengers app. — 4.00

INVADERS FROM HOME
DC Comics (Piranha Press): 1990 - No. 6, 1990 ($2.50, mature)
1-6 — 4.00

INVADERS NOW! (See Avengers/Invaders and The Torch series)
Marvel Comics: Nov, 2010 - No. 5, Mar, 2011 ($3.99, limited series)
1-5-Alex Ross-c; Steve Rogers, Bucky, Human Torch & Toro, Sub-Mariner app. — 4.00

INVADER ZIM
Oni Press: Jul, 2015 - Present ($3.99)
1-Jhonen Vasquez-s/Aaron Alexovich-a; multiple covers — 4.00
2-49: 40-Multiverse Zims; short stories by various — 4.00
50-($6.99) Vasquez & Trueheart-s/Wucinich-a — 7.00
... #1 Square One Edition (2/17, $1.00) r/#1 — 3.00
...: Free Comic Book Day Edition (5/18, giveaway) r/#20; Floopsy & Shmoopsy app. — 3.00
...: Oni 25th Anniversary Edition (11/22, $9.99) r/#1; silver foil cover enhancements — 10.00

INVADER ZIM QUARTERLY
Oni Press: Jun, 2020 - Sept, 2020 ($5.99)
...Dib's Dilemma 1 (9/20, $5.99) Logan-s/Wucinich-a; multiple covers — 6.00
...Gir's Big Day 1 (6/20, $5.99) Eric Trueheart-s/Aaron Alexovich-a; multiple covers — 6.00

INVASION
DC Comics: Holiday, 1988-'89 - No. 3, Jan, 1989 ($2.95, lim. series, 84 pgs.)
1-3: 1-McFarlane/Russell-a. 2-McFarlane/Russell & Giffen/Gordon-a — 5.00
Invasion! TPB (2008, $24.99) r/#1-3 — 25.00

INVINCIBLE (Also see The Pact #4)
Image Comics: Jan, 2003 - No. 144, Feb, 2018 ($2.95/$2.99)
1-Kirkman-s/Walker-a — 38 76 114 285 641 1000
2-Kirkman-s/Walker-a — 10 20 30 64 132 200
3-Kirkman-s/Walker-a — 4 8 12 25 40 55
4-8: 4-Preview of The Moth — 2 4 6 11 16 20
9,12-14: 14-Cho-c — 2 4 6 8 10 12
10 — 3 6 9 21 33 45
11-Origin of Omni-Man — 8 16 24 51 96 140
15-24,26-41,43-49: 33-Tie-in w/Marvel Team-Up #14 — 6.00
25-($4.95) Science Dog app.; back-up stories w/origins of Science Dog and teammates — 6.00
42-($1.99) Includes re-cap of the entire series — 5.00
50-(6/08, $4.99) Two covers; back-up origin of Cecil Stedman; Science Dog app. — 1 3 4 6 8 10
51-59,61-74: 51-Jim Lee-c; new costumes. 57-Continues in Astounding Wolf-Man #11. 71-74-Viltrumite War — 4.00
71-74-Viltrumite War — 3.00
76-99,101-109,111-117: 89-Intro. Zandale. 97-Origin of Bulletproof. 112-Baby born — 3.00
60-($3.99) Invincible War; Witchblade, Savage Dragon, Spawn, Youngblood app. — 1 3 5 6 8
75-($5.99) Viltrumite War; Science Dog back-up; 2 covers — 1 3 4 6 8 10
100-(1/13, $3.99) "The Death of Everyone" conclusion; multiple covers — 5.00
110-Rape issue — 6.00
118-141: 118-(25¢-c). 124-126-Reboot. 132-Oliver dies. 133-(25¢-c) Mark & Eve wedding — 3.00
142-143-($3.99) — 4.00
144-($5.99) Last issue; art by Ottley & Walker — 6.00
#0-(4/05, 50¢) Origin of Invincible; Ottley-a — 3.00
#1 Facsimile Edition-(1/23, $3.99) Reprints #1 — 4.00
Image Firsts: Invincible #1 (4/10, $1.00) r/#1 with "Image Firsts" cover logo — 3.00
Official Handbook of the Invincible Universe 1,2 (11/06, 1/07, $4.99) profile pages — 5.00
Official Handbook of the Invincible Universe Vol. 1 (2007, $14.99) r/#1-2; sketch pages — 13.00
... Presents Atom Eve 1,2 (12/07, 3/08, $2.99) origin of Atom Eve; Bellegarde-a — 3.00
... Presents Atom Eve & Rex Splode 1-3 (10/09 - 2/10, $2.99) origin of Rex — 3.00
... Returns (4/10, $3.99) Leads into Viltrumite War in #71; 4 covers — 4.00
... Undeluxe #1-(1/23, $3.99) Reprints #1 in B&W with bonus sketch art — 4.00
... Universe Primer 1 (5/08, $5.99) r/Invincible #1, Brit #1, Astounding Wolf-Man #1 — 6.00
The Complete Invincible Library Vol. 1 Slipcase HC (2006, $125.00) oversized r/#1-24, #0 and
story from Image Comics Summer Special (FCBD 2004); sketch pages; script for #1 — 125.00
..., Ultimate Collection Vol. 1 HC (2005, $34.95) oversized r/#1-13; sketch pages — 35.00
..., Ultimate Collection Vol. 2 HC (2006, $34.99) oversized r/#14-24, #0 and story from Image
Comics Summer Special (FCBD 2004); sketch pages and script for #23; intro by
Damon Lindelof; afterword by Robert Kirkman — 35.00
..., Ultimate Collection Vol. 3 HC (2007, $34.95) oversized r/#25-35 & The Pact #4; sketch
pages and script for #28; afterword by Robert Kirkman — 35.00
..., Ultimate Collection Vol. 4 HC (2008, $34.99) oversized r/#36-47; sketch & script pgs. — 35.00
Vol. 1: Family Matters TPB (8/03, $12.95) r/#1-4; intro. by Busiek; sketch pages — 13.00
Vol. 2: Eight in Enough TPB (3/04, $12.95) r/#5-8; intro. by Larsen; sketch pages — 13.00
Vol. 3: Perfect Strangers TPB (2004, $12.95) r/#9-12; intro. by Brevoort; sketch pages — 13.00
Vol. 4: Head of the Class TPB (1/05, $14.95) r/#14-19; intro. by Waid; sketch pages — 15.00
Vol. 5: The Facts of Life TPB (2005, $14.99) r/#20-24; intro. by Wieringo; sketch pages — 15.00
Vol. 6: A Different World TPB (2006, $14.99) r/#25-30; intro. by Brubaker; sketch pages — 15.00
Vol. 7: Three's Company TPB (2006, $14.99) r/#31-35 & The Pact #4; sketch pages — 15.00
Vol. 8: My Favorite Martian TPB (2007, $14.99) r/#36-41; sketch pages — 15.00
Vol. 9: Out of This World TPB (2008, $14.99) r/#42-47; sketch pages — 15.00

INVINCIBLE FOUR OF KUNG FU & NINJA
Leung Publications: April, 1988 - No. 6, 1989 ($2.00)
1-($2.75) — 5.00
2-6: 2-Begin $2.00-c — 4.00

INVINCIBLE IRON MAN
Marvel Comics: July, 2008 - No. 33, Feb, 2011;
No. 500, Mar, 2011 - No. 527, Dec, 2012 ($2.99/$3.99)
1-Fraction-s/Larroca-a; covers by Larroca & Quesada — 5.00
1-Downey movie photo wraparound — 6.00
1-Secret Movie Variant white-c with movie cast — 30.00

	GD	VG	FN	VF	VF/NM	NM-
	2.0	4.0	6.0	8.0	9.0	9.2

2-18: 2-War Machine and Thor app. 7-Spider-Man app. 8-10-Dark Reign. 11-War Machine
app.; Pepper gets her armor suit. 12-Namor app. — 3.00
19,20-($3.99) 20-Stark Disassembled starts; back-up synopsis of recent storylines — 4.00
21-24-Covers by Larocca and Zircher. 21-Thor & Capt. America app. 22-Dr. Strange app. — 3.00
25-($3.99) Fraction-s/Larroca-a; new armor — 4.00
26-31-($2.99) 29-New Rescue armor — 3.00
32,33-($3.99)-War Machine app.; back-up w/McKelvie-a — 4.00
(After #33, numbering reverts to original Vol. 1 as #500)
500-(3/11, $4.99) Two covers by Larroca; Mandarin & Spider-Man app.; cover gallery — 5.00
500-Variant-c by Romita Jr. — 10.00
500.1 (4/11, $2.99) History re-told; Fraction-s/Larroca-a/c — 3.00
501-527-($3.99) 501-503-Doctor Octopus app. 503-Back-up w/Chaykin-a. 504-509-Fear Itself
tie-in; Grey Gargoyle app. 517-New War Machine armor — 4.00
Annual 1 (8/10, $4.99) Larroca-c; history of the Mandarin; Di Giandomenico-a — 5.00
...MGC #1 (4/10, free) r/#1 with "Marvel's Greatest Comics" cover logo — 3.00

INVINCIBLE IRON MAN
Marvel Comics: Dec, 2015 - No. 14, Dec, 2016 ($3.99)

1-6,8,10-14: 1-Bendis-s/Marquez-a; Doctor Doom & Madame Masque app. 6-14-Deodato-a.						
8-Spider-Man app. 11-14-Civil War II tie-in						4.00
7-1st app. Riri Williams (cameo); Spider-Man app.	6	12	18	41	76	110
9-1st full app. of Riri Williams	6	12	18	41	76	110

INVINCIBLE IRON MAN (Riri Williams as Ironheart)
Marvel Comics: Jan, 2017 - No. 11, Nov, 2017 ($3.99)
1-11: 1-Bendis-s/Caselli-a; Riri Williams childhood origin; Animax app. — 4.00

INVINCIBLE IRON MAN (Marvel Legacy)(Also continued from Infamous Iron Man)
Marvel Comics: No. 593, Dec, 2017 - No. 600, Jul, 2018 ($3.99)
593-599-Bendis-s/Caselli & Maleev-a; Ironheart & Doctor Doom app. — 4.00
600-($5.99) James Rhodes returns; leads into Tony Stark: Iron Man series — 6.00

INVINCIBLE IRON MAN (Indicia lists title as Iron Man for #1-5)
Marvel Comics: Feb, 2023 - Present $4.99/$3.99)
1-($4.99) Duggan-s/Frigeri-a — 5.00
2-9-($3.99) 2-Ironheart app. 3-War Machine app. — 4.00
10-($4.99) Duggan-s/Frigeri-a; Emma Frost app. — 5.00
11-15-($3.99) 12-14-Ironheart app. — 4.00
Annual 1 (10/23, $4.99) Contest of Chaos tie-in with other Annuals; Storm app. — 5.00

INVINCIBLE RED SONJA, THE
Dynamite Entertainment: 2021 - No. 10, 2022 ($3.99)
1-10-Palmiotti & Conner-s/Moritat-a — 4.00

INVINCIBLE UNIVERSE (Characters from Invincible)
Image Comics: Apr, 2013 - No. 12, Apr, 2014 ($2.99)
1-12-Hester-s/Nauck-a. 1-Wraparound-c — 3.00

INVISIBLE BOY (See Approved Comics)

INVISIBLE KINGDOM
Dark Horse Comics (Berger Books): Mar, 2019 - Present ($3.99)
1-10-G. Willow Wilson-s/Christian Ward-a — 4.00

INVISIBLE MAN, THE (See Superior Stories #1 & Supernatural Thrillers #2)

INVISIBLE PEOPLE
Kitchen Sink Press: 1992 (B&W, lim. series)
Book One: Sanctum; Book Two: "The Power": Will Eisner-s/a in all — 4.00
Book Three: "Mortal Combat" — 4.00
Hardcover ($34.95) — 35.00
TPB (DC Comics, 9/00, $12.95) reprints series — 13.00

INVISIBLE REPUBLIC
Image Comics: Feb, 2015 - No. 15, Mar, 2017 ($2.99/$3.99)
1-10-Hardman & Bechko-s/Hardman-a — 3.00
11-15-($3.99) — 4.00

INVISIBLES, THE (1st Series)
DC Comics (Vertigo): Sept, 1994 - No. 25, Oct, 1996 ($1.95/$2.50; mature)

1-($2.95, 52 pgs.)-Intro King Mob, Ragged Robin, Boy, Lord Fanny & Dane (Jack Frost);						
Grant Morrison scripts in all	2	4	6	9	12	15
2-8: 4-Includes bound-in trading cards. 5-1st app. Orlando; brown paper-c						4.00
9-25: 10-Intro Jim Crow. 13-15-Origin Lord Fanny. 19-Origin King Mob; polybagged.						
20-Origin Boy. 21-Mister Six revealed. 25-Intro Division X						3.00

Apocalipstick (2001, $19.95, TPB)-r/#9-16; Bolland-a — 20.00
Entropy in the U.K. (2001, $19.95, TPB)-r/#17-25; Bolland-c — 20.00
Say You Want A Revolution (1996, $17.50, TPB)-r/#1-8 — 18.00
NOTE: *Buckingham* a-25p. *Rian Hughes* c-1, 5. *Phil Jimenez* a-17p-19p. *Paul Johnson* a-16, 21. *Sean Phillips*
c-2-4, 6-25. *Weston* a-10p. *Yeowell* a-1p-4p, 22p-24p.

INVISIBLES, THE (2nd Series)
DC Comics (Vertigo): V2#1, Feb, 1997 - No. 22, Feb, 1999 ($2.50; mature)
1-Intro Jolly Roger; Grant Morrison scripts, Phil Jimenez-a, & Brian Bolland-c begins — 6.00
2-22: 9,14-Weston-a — 4.00
Bloody Hell in America TPB ('98, $12.95) r/#1-4 — 13.00
Counting to None TPB ('99, $19.95) r/#5-13 — 20.00
Kissing Mr. Quimper TPB ('00, $19.95) r/#14-22 — 20.00

INVISIBLES, THE (3rd Series) (Issue #'s go in reverse from #12 to #1)
DC Comics (Vertigo): V3#12, Apr, 1999 - No. 1, June, 2000 ($2.95, mature)
1-12-Bolland-c; Morrison-s on all. 1-Quitely-a. 2-4-Art by various. 5-8-Phillips-a.
9-12-Phillip Bond-a — 4.00
The Invisible Kingdom TPB ('02, $19.95) r/#12-1; new Bolland-c — 20.00

INVISIBLE SCARLET O'NEIL (Also see Famous Funnies #81 & Harvey Comics Hits #59)
Famous Funnies (Harvey): Dec, 1950 - No. 3, Apr, 1951 (2-3 pgs. of Powell-a in each issue.)

1		28	56	84	168	274	380
2,3		20	40	60	120	195	270

INVISIBLE WOMAN (Fantastic Four)
Marvel Comics: Sept, 2019 - No. 5, Jan, 2020 ($3.99, limited series)
1-5-Mark Waid-s/Mattia De Iulis-a; main cover by Adam Hughes; Black Widow app. — 4.00

ION (Green Lantern Kyle Rayner) (See Countdown)
DC Comics: Jun, 2006 - No. 12, May, 2007 ($2.99)
1-12: 1-Marz-s/Tocchini-a. 3-Mogo app. 9,10-Tangent Green Lantern app. 12-Monitor app. — 3.00
...: The Torchbearer TPB (2007, $14.99) r/#1-6 — 15.00

I, PAPARAZZI
DC Comics (Vertigo): 2001 ($29.95, HC, digitally manipulated photographic art)
nn-Pat McGreal-s/Steven Parke-digital-a/Stephen John Phillips-photos — 30.00

IRON AGE
Marvel Comics: Aug, 2011 - No. 3, Oct, 2011 ($4.99, limited series)
1-3-Iron Man time travels. 1-Avengers. 2-Fantastic Four. 3-Dazzler & X-Men — 5.00
...: Alpha (8/11, $2.99) First part of the series; Dark Phoenix app.; Issacs-a — 3.00
...: Omega (10/11, $2.99) Conclusion of the series; Olivetti-a/Issacs-a — 3.00

IRON AND THE MAIDEN
Aspen MLT: Sept, 2007 - No. 4, Dec, 2007 ($3.99)
1-4: 1-Two covers by Manapul and Madureira/Matsuda; Jason Rubin-s — 4.00
...: Brutes, Bims and the City (2/08, $3.99) character backgrounds/development art — 3.00

IRON CAT
Marvel Comics: Aug, 2022 - No. 5, Dec, 2022 ($4.99/$3.99, limited series)
1-($4.99)-Jed MacKay-s Pere Pérez-a; Black Cat app. — 5.00
2-5-($3.99) Madame Menace app. — 4.00

IRON CORPORAL, THE (See Army War Heroes #22)
Charlton Comics: No. 23, Oct. 1985 - No. 25, Feb, 1986
23-25: Glanzman-a(r); low print — 6.00

IRON FIST (See Immortal Iron Fist, Deadly Hands of Kung Fu, Marvel Premiere & Power Man)
Marvel Comics: Nov, 1975 - No. 15, Sept, 1977

	GD	VG	FN	VF	VF/NM	NM-
1-Iron Fist battles Iron Man (#1-6: 25¢)	10	20	30	64	132	200
2	4	8	12	28	47	65
3-10: 4-6-(Regular 25¢ edition)(4-6/76). 8-Origin retold						
	3	6	9	19	30	40
4-6-(30¢-c variant, limited distribution)	6	12	18	41	76	110
11,13: 13-(30¢-c)	3	6	9	16	24	32
12-Capt. America app.	6	12	18	38	69	100
13-(35¢-c variant, limited distribution)	17	34	51	117	259	400
14-1st app. Sabretooth (8/77)(see Power Man)	28	56	84	202	451	700
14-(35¢-c variant, limited distribution)	172	344	516	1419	3210	5000
15-(Regular 30¢ ed.) X-Men app., Byrne-a	8	16	24	54	102	150
15-(35¢-c variant, limited distribution)	66	132	198	528	1189	1850

NOTE: *Adkins* a-8p, 10i, 13i; c-8i. *Byrne* a-1-15p; c-8p, 15p. *G. Kane* c-4-6p. *McWilliams* a-1i.

IRON FIST
Marvel Comics: Sept, 1996 - No. 2, Oct, 1996 ($1.50, limited series)
1,2 — 5.00

IRON FIST
Marvel Comics: Jul, 1998 - No. 3, Sept, 1998 ($2.50, limited series)
1-3: Jurgens-s/Guice-a — 4.00

IRON FIST (Also see Immortal Iron Fist)
Marvel Comics: May, 2004 - No. 6, Oct, 2004 ($2.99)
1-6: 1-4,6-Kevin Lau-c/a. 5-Mays-c/a — 4.00

IRON FIST
Marvel Comics: May, 2017 - No. 7, Nov, 2017; No. 73, Dec, 2017 - No. 80, Jun, 2018 ($3.99)
1-7: 1-Brisson-s/Perkins-a. — 4.00
[Title switches to legacy numbering after #7 (11/17)]
73-80: 73-77-Sabretooth app. 78-80-Damnation x-over; Orson Randall app. — 4.00

IRON FIST
Marvel Comics: Apr, 2022 - No. 5, Oct, 2022 ($3.99)
1-5: 1-Intro. Lin Lie, the new Iron Fist; Danny Rand app. 5-Loki app. — 4.00

IRON FIST: HEART OF THE DRAGON
Marvel Comics: Mar, 2021 - No. 6, Aug, 2021 ($3.99)
1-6-Hama-s/Wachter-a; Luke Cage, Taskmaster, and Lady Bullseye app. — 4.00

IRON FIST: PHANTOM LIMB (Printing of digital-first story)
Marvel Comics: 2018 ($19.99, square-bound TPB)
nn-Chapman-s/Sanna-a; Luke Cage app. — 20.00

IRON FIST: THE LIVING WEAPON
Marvel Comics: Jun, 2014 - No. 12, Jul, 2015 ($3.99)
1-12-Kaare Andrews-s/a/c; origin re-told in flashbacks — 4.00

IRON FIST: WOLVERINE
Marvel Comics: Nov, 2000 - No. 4, Feb, 2001 ($2.99, limited series)
1-4-Igle-c/a; Kingpin app. 2-Iron Man app. 3,4-Capt. America app. — 4.00

IRON GHOST
Image Comics: Apr, 2005 - No. 6, Mar, 2006 ($2.95/$2.99, limited series)
1-6-Chuck Dixon-s/Sergio Cariello-a; flip cover on each — 3.00

IRONHAND OF ALMURIC (Robert E. Howard's...)
Dark Horse Comics: Aug, 1991 - No. 4, 1991 ($2.00, B&W, mini-series)
1-4: 1-Conrad painted-c — 4.00

IRONHEART (Riri Williams) (See Invincible Iron Man #7)
Marvel Comics: Jan, 2019 - No. 12, Jan, 2020 ($4.99/$3.99)
1-($4.99) Eve L. Ewing-s/Libranda & Vecchio-a; Clash app. — 5.00
2-12-($3.99) 6-Miles (Spider-Man) app. 7,8-Nadia (Wasp) app. 8-Dr. Strange app. — 4.00

IRON HORSE (TV)
Dell Publishing Co.: March, 1967 - No. 2, June, 1967

	GD	VG	FN	VF	VF/NM	NM-
1-Dale Robertson photo covers on both	3	6	9	19	30	40
2	3	6	9	15	21	26

IRONJAW (Also see The Barbarians)
Atlas/Seaboard Publ.: Jan, 1975 - No. 4, July, 1975

Invisible Kingdom #1 © Wilson & Ward

Iron Fist (2017 series) #4 © MAR

Iron Man #74 © MAR

	GD 2.0	VG 4.0	FN 6.0	VF 8.0	VF/NM 9.0	NM- 9.2

1,2-Neal Adams-c. 1-1st app. Iron Jaw; Sekowsky-a(p); Fleisher-s
3 6 9 16 24 32
3,4-Marcos. 4-Origin
2 4 6 9 13 16

IRON LANTERN
Marvel Comics (Amalgam): June, 1997 ($1.95, one-shot)
1-Kurt Busiek-s/Paul Smith & Al Williamson-a ... 4.00

IRON MAIDEN LEGACY OF THE BEAST
Heavy Metal Inc.: Oct, 2017 - No. 5 ($3.99, limited series)
1-Llexi Leon & Edginton-s/West-a/Casas-c; Eddie app. ... 4.00

IRON MAN (Also see The Avengers #1, Giant-Size…, Marvel Collectors Item Classics, Marvel Double Feature, Marvel Fanfare, Tales of Suspense #39 & Uncanny Tales #52)
Marvel Comics: May, 1968 - No. 332, Sept, 1996

1-Origin; Colan-c/a(p); story continued from Iron Man & Sub-Mariner #1
250 500 750 1500 2300 3100
2
16 32 48 107 236 365
3-Iron Man vs. The Freak
12 24 36 82 179 275
4,5- 4-Unicorn app.
10 20 30 67 141 215
6-10: 7,8-Gladiator app. 9-Iron Man battles green Hulk-like android. 9,10-The Mandarin app.
8 16 24 55 105 155
11-15: 10,11-Mandarin app. 12-1st app. Controller. 15-Last 12c issue; vs Unicorn and the Red Ghost
7 14 21 44 82 120
16,18-20: 16-Vs. Unicorn and the Red Ghost. 18-Avengers app.
5 10 15 34 60 85
19-Captain America app.
17-1st Madame Masque & Midas (Mordecai Midas) 10 20 30 68 144 220
21-24,26-30: 21-Crimson Dynamo app. 22-Death of Janice Cord; Crimson Dynamo app.
27-Intro Firebrand. 28-Controller app.
4 8 12 28 47 65
25-Iron Man battles Sub-Mariner
7 14 21 44 82 120
31-42: 33-1st app. Spymaster. 35-Daredevil & Nick Fury vs Zodiak; x-over w/Daredevil #73.
36-Daredevil & Nick Fury vs Zodiak. 39-Avengers app. 42-Last 15c issue
4 8 12 25 40 55
43-Intro the Guardsman (25¢ Giant, 52 pgs); Giant-Man back-up (r) from TTA #52
7 14 21 48 89 130
44-46,48-53: 44-Capt. America app; back-up Ant-Man w/Andru-a. 46-The Guardsman dies.
48-Firebrand app. 49-Super-Adaptoid app. 50-Princess Python app. 53-1st Black Lama;
Starlin part pencils
4 8 12 37 50
47-Origin retold; Barry Smith-a(p)
12 24 36 79 170 260
54-Iron Man battles Sub-Mariner; 1st app. Moondragon (1/73) as Madame MacEvil;
Everett part-c
15 30 45 103 227 350
55-1st app. Thanos, Drax the Destroyer, Mentor, Starfox & Kronos (2/73); Starlin-c/a
160 320 480 960 1480 2000
56-Starlin-a
5 10 15 35 63 90
57-63: 57,58-Mandarin and Unicorn app. 59-Firebrand app. 60,61-Vs. the Masked Marauder.
62-Whiplash app. 63-Vs. Dr. Spectrum
3 6 9 17 26 35
64,65,67-70: 64,65-Dr. Spectrum app; origin is #65; Thor brief app. 67-Last 20c issue.
68-Sunfire, Mandarin and Unicorn app. 69,70-Mandarin, Yellow Claw & Ultimo app.
3 6 9 15 22 28
66-Iron Man vs. Thor
5 10 15 35 63 90
71-84: 71-Yellow Claw & Black Lama app. 72-Black Lama app; Iron Man at the San Diego
Comic Con. 73-Vs. Crimson Dynamo & Radioactive Man; Stark Industries renamed Stark
International. 74-Modok vs. Mad-Thinker; Black Lama app in "War of the Super-Villains".
75-Black Lama & Yellow Claw app. 76-r/#9. 77-Conclusion of the War of the
Super-Villains"; Black Lama app. 80-Origin of Black Lama. 81-Black Lama & Firebrand
app. 82,83-Red Ghost app.
2 4 6 11 16 20
85-89 (Regular 25c editions): 86-1st app. Blizzard. 87-Origin Blizzard. 88-Brief Thanos
cameo. 89-Daredevil app; last 25c-c
2 4 6 11 16 20
85-89-(30¢-c variants, limited dist.)(4-8/76)
6 12 18 40 73 105
90-99: 90,91-Blood Brothers & Controller app. 92-Vs. Melter. 95-Ultimo app. 96-1st new
Guardsman (Michael O' Brien). 98,99-Mandarin & Sunfire app.
2 4 6 10 14 18
99,101-103-(35c-c variants, limited dist.)
12 24 36 86 188 290
100-(7/77)-Starlin-c; Iron Man vs. The Mandarin
5 10 15 33 57 80
100-(35¢-c variant, limited dist.)
27 54 81 194 435 675
101-Intro DreadKnight; Frankenstein app.
3 6 9 16 23 30
102-2nd DreadKnight
2 4 6 11 16 20
103-117: 103-Jack of Hearts app; guest stars through issue #113. 104-107-Vs. Midas.
109-1st app. New Crimson Dynamo; 1st app. Vanguard. 110-Origin Jack of Hearts retold;
death of Count Nefaria. 113,114-Unicorn and Titanium Man app. 114,115-Avengers app;
1st John Romita Jr. pencils on Iron Man (10/78). 116-1st David Michelinie & Bob Layton
issue
2 4 6 12 15
118-Byrne(a(p); 1st app. Jim Rhodes
6 12 18 41 76 110
119,122-124,127: 122-Origin. 123-128-Tony treated for alcohol problem. 123,124-Vs. Blizzard,
Melter & Whiplash; Justin Hammer app. 127-Vs. Justin Hammer's "Super-Villain army"
3 6 9 14 19 24

120,121,126: 120,121-Sub-Mariner app. 126-Classic Tony becoming Iron Man-c
3 6 9 15 22 28
125-Avengers & Ant-Man (Scott Lang) app.
3 6 9 17 25 34
128-(11/79) Classic Tony Stark alcoholism cover
10 20 30 67 141 215
129,130,134-149: 134,135-Titanium Man app. 137-139-Spymaster app. 142-Intro. Space
Armor. 143-1st app. Sunturion. 146 Backlash app. (formally Whiplash). 148-Captain
America app. 149-Dr. Doom app.
2 4 6 8 10 12
131-133: 131,132-Hulk x-over. 133-Hulk/Ant Man-c
2 4 6 10 14 18
150-Double size; Dr. Doom; Merlin & Camelot
6 12 18 37 66 95
151-168: 151-Ant-Man (Scott Lang) app. 152-1st app stealth armor. 153-Living Laser app;
last Layton co-plot (returns in #215). 154-Unicorn app. 156-Intro the Mauler; last Michelinie
plot (returns in issue #215); last Romita Jr. art (p). 159-Paul Smith-a(p); Fantastic Four app.
160-Serpent Squad app. 161-Moon Knight app. 163-Intro. Obadiah Stane (hand only).
166-1st full app. Obadiah Stane. 167-Tony Stark alcohol problem resurfaces.
168-Machine Man app.
1 3 4 6 8 10
169-New Iron Man (Jim Rhodes replaces Tony Stark) 2 4 6 10 14 18
170-199: 172-Captain America x-over. 180-181-Vs. Mandarin. 191-198-Tony Stark returns as
original Iron Man. 197-Secret Wars II x-over; Byrne-c 1 2 3 5 6 8
200-($1.25, 52 pgs.)-Tony Stark returns as new Iron Man (red & white armor)
thru #230
3 6 9 16 23 30
201-213,215-224: 206-Hawkeye & Mockingbird app. 219-Intro. The Ghost. 220-Spymaster &
Ghost app. 224-Vs. Beetle, Backlash, Blizzard & Justin Hammer. 5.00
214-Spider-Woman (Julia Carpenter) app. in new black costume (1/87) 6.00
225-(12/87, $1.25, 40 pgs)- Armor Wars begins; Ant-Man app.
2 4 6 8 10 12
226-227,229-230: Armor Wars in all. 226-West Coast Avengers app. 227-Beetle app.;
Iron Man vs SHIELD Mandroids. 229-Vs. Crimson Dynamo & Titanium Man. 230-Armor
Wars conclusion; app. to Firepower 5.00
228-Armor Wars; Iron Man vs. Captain America (as the Captain) 6.00
231,234,247: 231-Intro. new Iron Man armor. 234-Spider-Man x-over. 247-Hulk x-over 5.00
232,233,235-243,245,246,248,249: 232-Barry Windsor Smith co-plot and (p). 233-Ant-Man app.
235,236-Vs. Grey Gargoyle. 238-Rhino & Capt. America app. 239,240-Vs. Justin Hammer.
241,242-Mandarin app. 243-Tony Stark loses use of legs. 249-Dr. Doom app. 4.00
244-($1.50, 52 pgs.)-New Armor makes him walk 5.00
250-($1.50, 52 pgs.)-Dr. Doom app.; Acts of Vengeance x-over; last Michelinie/Layton issue 5.00
251-274,276-281,283,285-287,289,292-299: 255-Intro new Crimson Dynamo (Valenyine
Shatalov). 258-Byrne script & Romita Jr.-a(p) begins. 261-264-Mandarin & Fin Fang
Foom app. 290-James Rhodes retains the War Machine armor. 292-Capt. America app.
295-Infinity Crusade x-over. 296,297-Omega Red app. 298,299-Return of Ultimo 4.00
275-($1.50, 52 pgs.) Mandarin & Fin Fang Foom app. 5.00
282-1st full app. War Machine (7/92) 6 12 18 41 76 110
284-Death of Iron Man (Tony Stark); James Rhodes becomes War Machine
1 2 3 5 6 8
288-($2.50, 52pg.)-Silver foil stamped-c; Iron Man's 350th app. in comics 5.00
290-($2.95, 52pg.)-Gold foil stamped-c; 30th ann. 5.00
291-Iron Man & War Machine team-up 5.00
300-($3.95, 68 pg.)-Collector's Edition w/embossed foil-c; anniversary issue;
War Machine-c/story 5.00
300-($2.50, 68 pgs.)-Newsstand Edition 5.00
301,303: 301-Venom cameo. 303-Captain America app. 2 4 6 8 10 12
302-Venom-c/story; Captain America app.
304-Thunderstrike app.; begin $1.50-c; bound-in-trading card sheet
3 6 9 17 26 35
305-Hulk-c/story
3 6 9 16 23 30
306-309-Mandarin app. 309-War Machine app. 4.00
310-($1.50) Polybagged w/16 pg Marvel Action Hour preview & acetate print 6.00
310-($1.50) Regular edition; white logo; "Hands of the Mandarin" x-over w/Force Works and
War Machine 5.00
311,312- "Hands of the Mandarin" x-over w/Force Works and War Machine. 312-w/bound-in
Power Ranger card 4.00
313,315,316,318: 315-316-Black Widow app. 316-Crimson Dynamo & Titanium Man app. 5.00
314-Crossover w/Captain America; Henry Pym app. 6.00
317-($2.95)-Flip book; Black Widow app; death of Titanium Man; Hawkeye, War Machine &
USAgent app. 6.00
319-Intro. new Iron Man armor; Force Works app; prologue to "The Crossing" story 6.00
320-325: 321-w/Overpower card insert. 322-324-Avengers app; x-over w/Avengers and
Force Works. 325-($2.95)-Wraparound-c; Tony Stark Iron Man vs "Teen" Tony Iron Man;
Avengers & Force Works x-over; continued in Avengers #395 5.00
326- "Teen" Tony app. as Iron Man thru #332; Avengers, Thor & Cap America x-over 6.00
327-330: 330-War Machine & Stockpile app; return of Morgan Stark 4.00
331-War Machine app; leads into the "Onslaught" x-over 5.00
332-(9/96) Onslaught x-over; last issue 6.00
Special 1 (8/70)-Sub-Mariner x-over; Everett-c 8 16 24 51 96 140
Special 2 (11/71, 52 pgs.)-r/TOS #81,82,91 (all-r) 4 8 12 23 37 50

	GD 2.0	VG 4.0	FN 6.0	VF 8.0	VF/NM 9.0	NM- 9.2

Annual 3 (1976)-Man-Thing app. — 3 6 9 16 23 30

King Size 4 (8/77)-The Champions (w/Ghost Rider) app.; Newton-a(i) — 3 6 9 14 20 26

Annual 5 ('82) Black Panther & Mandarin app. — 2 4 6 10 14 18

Annual 6-9: ('83-'86) 6-New Iron Man (J. Rhodes) app. 8-X-Factor app. — 6.00

Annual 10 ('89) Atlantis Attacks x-over; P. Smith-a; Layton/Guice-a; Sub-Mariner app. — 6.00

Annual 11-15 ('90-'94): 11-Terminus Factor pt. 2; origin of Mrs. Arbogast by Ditko (p&i).
12-1 pg. origin recap; Ant-Man back-up in: Subterranean Wars Pt. 4. 13-Darkhawk &
Avengers West Coast app.; Colan/Williamson-a. 14-Bagged w/card; 1st app. Face Thief
15- Iron Man vs. the Controller — 6.00

...: Armor Wars TPB (2007, $24.99) r/#225-232; Micheline intro. — 25.00

Manual 1 (1993, $1.75)-Operations handbook — 5.00

Graphic Novel: Crash (1988, $12.95, Adults, 72 pgs.)-Computer generated art & color;
violence & nudity — 13.00

...Collector's Preview (11/94, $1.95)-wraparound-c; text & illos-no comics — 4.00

...: Demon in a Bottle HC (2008, $24.99) r/#120-128; two covers — 25.00

...: Demon in a Bottle TPB (2006, $24.99) r/#120-128 — 25.00

...: Many Armors of Iron Man (2008, $24.99) r/#47, 142-144, 152-153, 200, 218 — 25.00

... No. 1 Facsimile Edition (7/23, $3.99) r/#1 with original 1968 ads — 4.00

...Vs. Dr. Doom (12/94, $12.95)-r/#149-150, 249,250. Julie Bell-c — 13.00

...Vs. Dr. Doom: Doomquest HC (2008, $19.99, dustjacket)-r/#149-150, 249,250;
new Micheline intro.; bonus art — 20.00

...: War Machine TPB (2008, $29.99) r/#280-291 — 30.00

The Invincible Iron Man Omnibus Vol. 1 HC (2008, $99.99, dustjacket) r/Iron Man stories from
Tales of Suspense #39-83 & Tales To Astonish #82; 1992 intro. by Stan Lee; 1975 essay
by Lee; 2008 essay by Layton; gallery of original art and covers; creator bios — 100.00

NOTE: Austin c-105i, 109-111i, 151i. Byrne a-118p; c-109p, 197, 253. Colan a-1p, 253, Special 1p(3); c-1p. Craig a-1i, 2-4, 5-13i, 14, 15-19i, 24p, 25p, 26i; c-2-4. Ditko a-160p. Everett c-29. Guice a-233-241p. G. Kane c(p)-52-54, 63, 67, 72-75, 77-79, 88, 98. Kirby a-Special 1p; 80p, 90, 92-95. Mooney a-40i, 43i, 47i. Perez c-103p. Simonson c-Annual 8. B. Smith a-232p, 243i; c-232. P. Smith a-159p, 245p, Annual 10p; c-159. Starlin a-53p(part), 55p, 56p; c-55p, 160, 163. Tuska a-5-13p, 15-23p, 24i, 32p, 38-46p, 48-54p, 57-61p, 63-69p, 70-72p, 78p, 86-92p, 95-106p, Annual 4p. Wood a-Special 1i.

IRON MAN (The Invincible...) (Volume Two)
Marvel Comics: Nov, 1996 - No. 13, Nov, 1997 ($2.95/$1.95/$1.99)
(Produced by WildStorm Productions)

V2#1-3-Heroes Reborn begins; Scott Lobdell scripts & Whilce Portacio-c/a begin;
new original Iron Man & Hulk. 2-Hulk app. 3-Fantastic Four app. — 5.00

1-Variant-c — 6.00

4-11: 4-Two covers. 6-Fantastic Four app.; Industrial Revolution; Hulk app. 7-Return of Rebel.
11-($1.99) Dr. Doom-c/app. — 4.00

12-($2.99) "Heroes Reunited"-pt. 3; Hulk-c/app. — 5.00

13-($1.99) "World War 3"-pt. 3, x-over w/Image — 4.00

Heroes Reborn: Iron Man (2006, $29.99, TPB) r/#1-12; Heroes Reborn #1/2; pin-ups — 30.00

IRON MAN (The Invincible...) (Volume Three)
Marvel Comics: Feb, 1998 - No. 89, Dec, 2004 ($2.99/$1.99/$2.25)

V3#1-($2.99)-Follows Heroes Return; Busiek scripts & Chen-c/a begin; Deathsquad app. — 6.00

1-Alternate Ed. — 1 2 3 5 7 9

2-12: 2-Two covers. 6-Black Widow-c/app. 7-Warbird-c/app. 8-Black Widow app. 9-Mandarin
returns — 4.00

13-($2.99) battles the Controller — 5.00

14-24: 14-Fantastic Four-c/app. — 3.00

25-($2.99) Iron Man and Warbird battle Ultimo; Avengers app. — 4.00

26-30-Quesada-a. 28-Whiplash killed. 29-Begin $2.25-c. — 3.00

31-45,47-49,51-54: 35-Maximum Security x-over; FF-c/app. 41-Grant-a begins.
44-New armor debut. 48-Ultron-c/app. — 3.00

46-($3.50, 100 pgs.) Sentient armor returns; r/V1#78,140,141 — 4.00

50-($3.50) Grell-s begin; Black Widow app. — 4.00

55-($3.50) 400th issue; Asamiya-c; back-up story Stark reveals ID; Grell-a — 4.00

56-66: 56-Reis-a. 57,58-Ryan-a. 59-61-Grell-c/a. 62,63-Ryan-a. 64-Davis-a; Thor-c/app. — 3.00

67-89: 67-Begin $2.99-c; Gene Ha-c. 75-83-Granov-c. 84-Avengers Disassembled prologue
85-89-Avengers Disassembled. 85-88-Harris-a. 86-89-Pat Lee-c. 87-Rumiko killed — 4.00

.../Captain America '98 Annual ($3.50) vs. Modok — 4.00

1999, 2000 Annual ($3.50) — 4.00

2001 Annual ($2.99) Claremont-s/Ryan-a — 4.00

Avengers Disassembled: Iron Man TPB (2004, $14.99) r/#84-89 — 15.00

Mask in the Iron Man (5/01, $14.95, TPB) r/#26-30, #1/2 — 15.00

IRON MAN (The Invincible...)
Marvel Comics: Jan, 2005 - No. 35, Jan, 2009 ($3.50/$2.99)

1-($3.50-c) Warren Ellis-s/Adi Granov-a; start of Extremis storyline — 5.00

2-6-($2.99): 5-Flashback to origin; Stark gets new abilities — 4.00

7-14: 7-Knauf-s/Zircher-a. 13,14-Civil War — 3.00

15-24,26,27,29-35: 15-Stark becomes Director of S.H.I.E.L.D. 19,20-World War Hulk.
33-Secret Invasion; War Machine app. 34,35-War Machine title logo — 3.00

25,28-($3.99)-Includes movie preview & armor showcase. 28-Red & white armor — 4.00

All-New Iron Manual (2/08, $4.99) Handbook-style guide to characters & armor suits — 5.00

... By Design 1 (11/10, $3.99) Gallery of 2010 variant covers with artist commentary — 4.00

.../Captain America: Casualties of War (2/07, $3.99) two covers; flashbacks — 4.00

...: Director of S.H.I.E.L.D. Annual 1 (1/08, $3.99) Madame Hydra app.; Cheung-a — 4.00

Free Comic Book Day 2010 (Iron Man: Supernova) #1 (5/10, 9-1/2" x 6-1/4") Nova app. — 4.00

Free Comic Book Day 2010 (Iron Man/Thor) #1 (5/10, 9-1/2" x 6-1/4") Romita Jr.-a/c — 3.00

...Golden Avenger 1 (11/08, $3.99) Santacruz-a; movie photo-c — 4.00

.../Hulk/Fury 1 (2/09, $3.99) crossover of movie-version characters — 4.00

Indomitable Iron Man (4/10, $3.99) B&W stories; Chaykin-s/a; Rosado-a; Parrillo-c — 4.00

Iron Manual Mark 3 (6/10, $3.99) Handbook-format profiles of characters — 4.00

...: Iron Protocols (12/09, $3.99) Olivetti-c/Nelson-a — 4.00

...: Kiss and Kill (8/10, $3.99) Black Widow and Wolverine app. — 4.00

Marvel Halloween Ashcan 2007 (8-1/2" x 5-3/8") updated design; Michael Golden-c — 3.00

...: Requiem (2009, $4.99) r/TOS #39, Iron Man #144 (1981); armor profiles — 5.00

...: The End (1/09, $4.99) future Tony Stark retires; Micheline-s/Chang & Layton-a — 5.00

...: Titanium! 1 (12/10, $4.99) short stories by various; Yardin-a — 5.00

Civil War: Iron Man TPB (2007, $11.99) r/#13,14, .../Captain America: Casualties of War,
and Civil War: The Confession — 12.00

HC (2006, $19.99, dust jacket) r/#1-6 and Granov covers from Iron Man V3 #75-83 — 20.00

...: Director of S.H.I.E.L.D. TPB (2007, $14.99) r/#15-18; Strange Tales #135 (1965) and Iron
Man #129; profile pages for Iron Man and S.H.I.E.L.D.; creator interviews — 15.00

...: Extremis SC (2007, $14.99) r/#1-6 and Granov covers from Iron Man V3 #75-83 — 15.00

...: Execute Program SC (2007, $14.99) r/#7-12; cover layouts and sketches — 15.00

IRON MAN (Marvel Now!)(Leads into Superior Iron Man)
Marvel Comics: Jan, 2013 - No. 28, Aug, 2014 ($3.99)

1-28: 1-8-Gillen-s/Land-c/a. 5-Stark heads out to space. 9-17-Secret Origin of Tony Stark.
9-12-Eaglesham-a. 17-Arno Stark revealed. 23-26-Malekith app. — 4.00

20.INH (3/12, $3.99) Inhumanity tie-in; origin The Exile; Padilla-a — 4.00

Annual 1 (4/14, $4.99) Gillen-s/Martinez, Padilla & Marz-a — 5.00

... Special 1 (9/14, $4.99) Cont'd from Uncanny X-Men Special #1; Ryan-s/Handoko-a — 5.00

IRON MAN (The Armor Wars)
Marvel Comics: No. 258.1, Jul, 2013 - No. 258.4, Jul, 2013 ($3.99, weekly limited series)

258.1-258.4 - Set after Iron Man #258 (1990); Micheline-s/Dave Ross & Bob Layton-a — 4.00

IRON MAN (Follows the Iron Man 2020 series)(Continues in Invincible Iron Man #1)
Marvel Comics: Nov, 2020 - No. 25, Jan, 2023 ($4.99/$3.99)

1-($4.99) Cantwell-s/Cafu-a; main wraparound cover by Alex Ross; Patsy Walker app. — 5.00

2-24-($3.99) Hellcat app. 2-Crusher Creel app. 8-Moondragon app. 16-Doctor Doom app. — 4.00

25-($5.99) Legacy issue #650; back-up with Thor app. & faux reprint in early '70s style — 6.00

Annual 1 (4/14, $4.99) MacKay-s/Roberson-a; Miles Morales app. — 5.00

.../Hellcat Annual 1 (8/22, $4.99) Chris Cantwell-s/Ruairi Coleman-a; Hedy Wolfe app. — 5.00

IRON MAN AND POWER PACK
Marvel Comics: Jan, 2008 - No. 4, Apr, 2008 ($2.99, limited series)

1-4-Gurihiru-a/Sumerak-s; Puppet Master app.; Mini Marvels back-ups in each — 3.00

...: Armored and Dangerous TPB (2008, $7.99, digest size) r/series — 8.00

IRON MAN & SUB-MARINER
Marvel Comics Group: Apr, 1968 (12¢, one-shot) (Pre-dates Iron Man #1 & Sub-Mariner #1)

1-Iron Man story by Colan/Craig continued from Tales of Suspense #99 & continued in
Iron Man #1; Sub-Mariner story by Colan continued from Tales to Astonish #101 &
continued in Sub-Mariner #1; Colan/Everett-c — 38 76 114 285 641 1000

IRON MAN AND THE ARMOR WARS
Marvel Comics: Oct, 2009 - No. 4, Jan, 2010 ($2.99, limited series)

1-4-Rousseau-a; Crimson Dynamo & Omega Red app. — 3.00

IRON MAN: ARMORED ADVENTURES
Marvel Comics: Sept, 2009 ($3.99, one-shot)

1-Based on the 2009 cartoon; Brizuela-a; Nick Fury & Living Laser app. — 4.00

IRON MAN: BAD BLOOD
Marvel Comics: Sept, 2000 - No. 4, Dec, 2000 ($2.99, limited series)

1-4-Micheline-s/Layton-a — 3.00

IRON MAN: ENTER THE MANDARIN
Marvel Comics: Nov, 2007 - No. 6, Apr, 2008 ($2.99, limited series)

1-6-Casey-s/Canete-a; retells first meeting — 3.00

TPB (2008, $14.99) r/#1-6 — 15.00

IRON MAN: EXTREMIS DIRECTOR'S CUT
Marvel Comics: Jun, 2010 - No. 6, Sept, 2010 ($3.99, limited series)

1-6-Reprints Iron Man #1-6 (2005 series) with script pages and design art — 4.00

IRON MAN: FATAL FRONTIER
Marvel Comics: 2014 ($34.99, hardcover)

HC - Printing of digital comic #1-13 and r/Iron Man Annual #1 (4/14) — 35.00

IRON MAN: HONG KONG HEROES
Marvel Comics: May, 2018 ($3.99, one-shot)

1-Howard Wong-s/Justice Wong-a; Hulk & Black Panther app.; intro Arwyn Wong — 4.00

IRON MAN: HOUSE OF M (Also see House of M and related x-overs)
(Reprinted in House of M: Fantastic Four/ Iron Man TPB)
Marvel Comics: Sept, 2005 - No. 3, Nov, 2005 ($2.99, limited series)

1-3-Pat Lee-a/c; Greg Pak-s — 3.00

IRON MAN: HYPERVELOCITY
Marvel Comics: Mar, 2007 - No. 6, Aug, 2007 ($2.99, limited series)

1-6-Adam Warren-s/Brian Denham-a/c — 3.00

TPB (2007, $14.99) r/#1-6; layout pages and armor design sketches — 15.00

IRON MAN: I AM IRON MAN
Marvel Comics: Mar, 2010 - No. 2, Apr, 2010 ($3.99, limited series)

1,2-Adaptation of the first movie; Peter David-s/Sean Chen-a/Adi Granov-c — 4.00

IRON MAN: INEVITABLE
Marvel Comics: Feb, 2006 - No. 6, July, 2006 ($2.99, limited series)

1-6-Joe Casey-s/Frazer Irving; Spymaster and the Living Laser app. — 3.00

TPB (2006, $14.99) r/#1-6; cover sketches — 15.00

IRON MAN: LEGACY
Marvel Comics: Jun, 2010 - No. 11, Apr, 2011 ($3.99/$2.99)

1-Van Lente-s/Kurth-a; Dr. Doom app.; back-up r/debut in Tales of Suspense #39 — 4.00

2-11-($2.99) 4-Titanium Man & Crimson Dynamo app. 6-The Pride app. — 3.00

IRON MAN: LEGACY OF DOOM
Marvel Comics: Jun, 2008 - No. 4, Sept, 2008 ($2.99, limited series)

1-4-Micheline-s/Lim & Layton-a; Dr. Doom app. — 3.00

IRON MAN NOIR
Marvel Comics: Jun, 2010 - No. 4, Sept, 2010 ($3.99, limited series)

1-4-Pulp-style set in 1939; Snyder-s/Garcia-a — 4.00

IRON MAN: RAPTURE
Marvel Comics: Jan, 2011 - No. 4, Feb, 2011 ($3.99, limited series)

1-4-Irvine-s/Medina-a/Bradstreet-c. 3,4-War Machine app. — 4.00

IRON MAN: SEASON ONE
Marvel Comics: 2013 ($24.99, hardcover graphic novel)

HC - Origin story and early days; Chaykin-s/Parel-a/Tedesco painted-c — 25.00

IRON MAN: THE COMING OF THE MELTER
Marvel Comics: Jul, 2013 ($3.99, one-shot)

Iron Man (2013 series) #1 © MAR

Iron Man: Legacy of Doom #1 © MAR

It Girl and The Atomics #1 © Mike Allred

	GD	VG	FN	VF	VF/NM	NM-
	2.0	4.0	6.0	8.0	9.0	9.2

1-Movie version; Ron Lim-a; back-up reprint of Iron Man #72 (1/75); 3 covers — 4.00

IRON MAN: THE IRON AGE
Marvel Comics: Aug, 1998 - No. 2, Sept, 1998 ($5.99, limited series)
1,2-Busiek-s; flashback story from gold armor days — 6.00

IRON MAN: THE LEGEND
Marvel Comics: Sept, 1996 ($3.95, one-shot)
1-Tribute issue — 5.00

IRON MAN/ THOR
Marvel Comics: Jan, 2011 - No. 4, Apr, 2011 ($3.99, limited series)
1-4-Eaton-a; Crimson Dynamo & Diablo app. — 4.00

IRON MANTICORE (Reprints from Cerebus in Hell)
Aardvark-Vanaheim: Sept, 2019 ($4.00, B&W)
1-Cerebus figures placed over original Doré artwork of Hell; Iron Man #128-c swipe — 4.00

IRON MAN 2: ... (Follows the first movie)
Marvel Comics: Jun, 2010 - Nov, 2010 ($3.99, limited series)
Agents of S.H.I.E.L.D. 1 (11/10, $3.99) Nick Fury, Agent Coulson & Black Widow app. — 4.00
Public Identity (6/10 - No. 3, 7/10, $3.99) 1-3-Kitson & Lim-a/Granov-c — 4.00
Spotlight (4/10, $3.99) Interviews with Granov, Guggenheim, Fraction, Ellis, Michelinie — 4.00

IRON MAN 2 ADAPTATION, (MARVEL'S...)
Marvel Comics: Jan, 2013 - No. 2, Feb, 2013 ($2.99, limited series)
1,2-Photo-c; Rosanas-a — 3.00

IRON MAN 2.0
Marvel Comics: Apr, 2011 - No. 12, Feb, 2012 ($3.99/$2.99)
1-($3.99) Spencer-s/Kitson-c; back-up history of War Machine — 4.00
1-Variant-c by Djurdjevic — 6.00
2-7,(7.1),8-12-($2.99) 2,3-Kitson, Kano & Di Giandomenico-a. 5-7-Fear Itself tie-in — 3.00
...: Modern Warfare 1 (10/11, $4.99) r/#1-3 with variant covers — 5.00

IRON MAN 3 PRELUDE, (MARVEL'S...)
Marvel Comics: Mar, 2013 - No. 2, Apr, 2013 ($2.99, limited series)
1,2-Photo-c; Gage-s/Kurth-a; War Machine app. — 3.00

IRON MAN 2020 (Also see Machine Man limited series)
Marvel Comics: June, 1994 ($5.95, one-shot)
nn — 6.00

IRON MAN 2020
Marvel Comics: Mar, 2020 - No. 6, Oct, 2020 ($4.99, limited series)
1-6-Slott & Gage-s/Woods-a; Arno Stark as Iron Man; Machine Man app. — 5.00

IRON MAN: VIVA LAS VEGAS
Marvel Comics: Jul, 2008 - No. 2 ($3.99, unfinished limited series)
1,2-Jon Favreau-s/Adi Granov-a/c — 4.00

IRON MAN VS WHIPLASH
Marvel Comics: Jan, 2010 - No. 4, Apr, 2010 ($3.99, limited series)
1-4-Briones-a/Peterson-c; origin of new Whiplash — 4.00

IRON MAN/X-O MANOWAR: HEAVY METAL (See X-O Manowar/Iron Man: In Heavy Metal)
Marvel Comics: Sept, 1996 ($2.50, one-shot) (1st Marvel/Valiant x-over)
1-Pt. II of Iron Man/X-O Manowar x-over; Fabian Nicieza scripts; 1st app. Rand Banion — 4.00

IRON MARSHALL
Jademan Comics: July, 1990 - No. 32, Feb, 1993 ($1.75, plastic coated-c)
1,32: Kung Fu stories. 1-Poster centerfold — 5.00
2-31-Kung Fu stories in all — 4.00

IRON PATRIOT (Marvel Now!)
Marvel Comics: May, 2014 - No. 5, Sept, 2014 ($3.99)
1-5-James Rhodes in the armor; Ales Kot-s/Garry Brown-a/c — 4.00

IRON VIC (See Comics Revue No. 3 & Giant Comics Editions)
United Features Syndicate/St. John Publ. Co.: 1940

	GD	VG	FN	VF	VF/NM	NM-
Single Series 22	41	82	123	256	428	600

IRONWOLF
DC Comics: 1986 ($2.00, one shot)
1-r/Weird Worlds #8-10; Chaykin story & art — 4.00

IRONWOLF: FIRES OF THE REVOLUTION (See Weird Worlds #8-10)
DC Comics: 1992 ($29.95, hardcover)
nn-Chaykin/Moore story, Mignola-a w/Russell inks. — 30.00

IRREDEEMABLE (Also see Incorruptible)

BOOM! Studios: Apr, 2009 - No. 37, May, 2012 ($3.99)
1-37: 1-Waid-s/Krause-a; 3 covers; Grant Morrison afterword. 2-32-Three covers — 4.00
1-Artist Edition (12/11, $3.99) r/#1 in B&W with bonus sketch and design art — 4.00
... Special 1 (4/10, $3.99) Art by Azaceta, Rios & Chaykin; three covers — 4.00

IRREDEEMABLE ANT-MAN, THE
Marvel Comics: Dec, 2006 - No. 12, Nov, 2007 ($2.99)
1-12-Kirkman-s/Hester-a/c; intro. Eric O'Grady as the new Ant-Man. 7-Ms. Marvel app. 10-World War Hulk x-over — 3.00
... Vol. 1: Lowlife (2007, $9.99, digest) r/#1-6 — 10.00
... Vol. 2: Small-Minded (2007, $9.99, digest) r/#7-12 — 10.00

ISAAC ASIMOV'S I-BOTS
Tekno Comix: Dec, 1995 - No. 7, May, 1996 ($1.95)
1-7: 1-6-Perez-c/a. 2-Chaykin variant-c exists. 3-Polybagged. 7-Lady Justice-c/app. — 4.00

ISAAC ASIMOV'S I-BOTS
BIG Entertainment: V2#1, June, 1996 - No. 9, Feb, 1997 ($2.25)
V2#1-9: 1-Lady Justice-c/app. 6-Gil Kane-c — 4.00

ISIS (TV) (Also see Shazam)

National Per.I Publ./DC Comics: Oct-Nov, 1976 - No. 8, Dec-Jan, 1977-78	GD	VG	FN	VF	VF/NM	NM-
1-Wood inks	5	10	15	31	53	75
2-8: 5-Isis new look. 7-Origin	2	4	6	9	13	16

ISLAND AT THE TOP OF THE WORLD (See Walt Disney Showcase #27)

ISLAND OF DR. MOREAU, THE (Movie)

Marvel Comics Group: Oct, 1977 (52 pgs.)	GD	VG	FN	VF	VF/NM	NM-
1-Gil Kane-c/a	1	3	4	6	8	10

ISLAND OF DR. MOREAU, THE (Adaptation of the novel)
IDW Publishing: Jul, 2019 - No. 2, Aug, 2019 ($4.99, limited series)
1,2-Ted Adams & Gabriel Rodríguez-s/Rodríguez-a — 5.00

ISOLA
Image Comics: Apr, 2018 - Present ($3.99)
1-10-Brenden Fletcher & Karl Kerschl & Msassyk-a — 4.00
... Prologue (1/19, no cover price) reprints pages from Motor Crush #1-5 — 3.00

I SPY (TV)

Gold Key: Aug, 1966 - No. 6, Sept, 1968 (All have photo-c)	GD	VG	FN	VF	VF/NM	NM-
1-Bill Cosby, Robert Culp photo covers	12	24	36	82	179	275
2-6: 3,4-McWilliams-a. 5-Last 12¢-c	6	12	18	38	69	100

IT! (See Astonishing Tales 21-24 & Supernatural Thrillers No. 1)

ITCHY & SCRATCHY COMICS (The Simpsons TV show)

Bongo Comics: 1993 - No. 3, 1993 ($1.95)	GD	VG	FN	VF	VF/NM	NM-
1-3: 1-Bound-in jumbo poster. 3-w/decoder screen trading card	2	4	6	9	13	16
Holiday Special ('94, $1.95)	2	4	6	8	10	14

IT GIRL (Also see Atomics, and Madman Comics)
Oni Press: May, 2002 ($2.95, one-shot)
1-Allred-s/Clugston-Major-c/a; Atomics and Madman app. — 3.00

IT GIRL! AND THE ATOMICS (Also see Atomics, and Madman Comics)
Image Comics: Aug, 2012 - No. 12, Jul, 2013 ($2.99)
1-12: 1-Rich-s/Norton-a/Allred-c. 2-Two covers (Allred & Cooke). 6-Clugston Flores-a — 3.00

IT REALLY HAPPENED

William H. Wise No. 1,2/Standard (Visual Editions): 1944 - No. 11, Oct, 1947	GD	VG	FN	VF	VF/NM	NM-
1-Kit Carson & Ben Franklin stories	36	72	108	214	347	480
2,3-Nazi WWII-c	19	38	57	111	176	240
4,6,9,11: 4-D-Day story. 6-Ernie Pyle WWII-c; Joan of Arc story. 9-Captain Kidd & Frank Buck stories	15	30	45	84	127	170
5-Lou Gehrig & Lewis Carroll stories	21	42	63	124	202	280
7-Teddy Roosevelt story	16	32	48	92	144	195
8-Story of Roy Rogers	20	40	60	115	185	255
10-Honus Wagner & Mark Twain stories	19	38	57	109	172	235

NOTE: Guardineer a-7(2), 8(2), 10, 11. Schomburg c-1-7, 9-11.

IT RHYMES WITH LUST (Also see Bold Stories & Candid Tales)

St. John Publishing Co.: 1950 (Digest size, 128 pgs., 25¢)	GD	VG	FN	VF	VF/NM	NM-
nn (Rare)-Matt Baker & Ray Osrin-a	400	800	1200	2800	4900	7000

IT'S A BIRD...
DC Comics: 2004 ($24.95, hardcover with dust jacket)
HC-Semi-autobiographical story of Steven Seagle writing Superman; Kristiansen-a — 25.00
SC-($17.95) — 18.00

	GD 2.0	VG 4.0	FN 6.0	VF 8.0	VF/NM 9.0	NM- 9.2

IT'S ABOUT TIME (TV)
Gold Key: Jan, 1967

1 (10195-701)-Photo-c	4	8	12	28	47	65

IT'S A DUCK'S LIFE
Marvel Comics/Atlas(MMC): Feb, 1950 - No. 11, Feb, 1952

1-Buck Duck, Super Rabbit begin	23	46	69	136	223	310
2	14	28	42	82	121	160
3-11	14	28	42	76	108	140

IT'S GAMETIME
National Periodical Publications: Sept-Oct, 1955 - No. 4, Mar-Apr, 1956

1-(Scarce)-Infinity-c; Davy Crockett app. in puzzle	126	252	378	806	1378	1950
2,3 (Scarce): 2-Dodo & The Frog	84	168	252	538	919	1300
4 (Rare)	93	186	279	591	1021	1450

IT'S JEFF
Marvel Comics: May, 2023 ($5.99, one-shot)

1-Short shark stories by Kelly Thompson & Gurihiru; Avengers app.						6.00
...: The Jeff-verse 1 (1/24, $5.99) More short shark stories; Gwenpool app.						6.00

IT'S LOVE, LOVE, LOVE
St. John Publishing Co.: Nov, 1957 - No. 2, Jan, 1958 (10c)

1,2	16	32	48	94	147	200

IT! THE TERROR FROM BEYOND SPACE
IDW Publishing: Jul, 2010 - No. 3, Sept, 2010 ($3.99, limited series)

1-3-Naraghi-s/Dos Santos-a/Mannion-c						4.00

ITTY BITTY COMICS (Issue #5, see Grimmiss Island; title changes to Grimmiss Island)
Dark Horse Comics: Nov, 2014 - No. 4, Feb, 2015 ($2.99, limited series)

1-4-All-ages humor stories of kid-version Mask by Art Baltazar & Franco						3.00

ITTY BITTY COMICS: THE MASK
Dark Horse Comics: Nov, 2014 - No. 4, Feb, 2015 ($2.99, limited series)

1-4-All-ages humor stories of kid-version Mask by Art Baltazar & Franco						3.00

ITTY BITTY HELLBOY
Dark Horse Comics: Aug, 2013 - No. 5, Dec, 2013 ($2.99, limited series)

1-5-All-ages humor stories of kid-version Hellboy characters by Art Baltazar & Franco						3.00

ITTY BITTY HELLBOY: THE SEARCH FOR THE WERE-JAGUAR
Dark Horse Comics: Nov, 2015 - No. 4, Feb, 2016 ($2.99, limited series)

1-4-All-ages humor stories of kid-version Hellboy characters by Art Baltazar & Franco						3.00

I, VAMPIRE (DC New 52)
DC Comics: Nov, 2011 - No. 19, Jun, 2013 ($2.99)

1-Fialkov-s/Sorrentino-a/Frison-c						6.00
2-19: 4-Constantine app. 5-7-Batman app. 7,8-Crossover with Justice League Dark #7,8. 12-Stormwatch app. 16-19-Constantine app.						4.00
#0-(11/12, $2.99) Origin of Andrew Bennett; Fialkov-s/Sorrentino-a/Crain-c						3.00

IVANHOE (See Fawcett Movie Comics No. 20)

IVANHOE
Dell Publishing Co.: July-Sept, 1963

1 (12-372-309)	3	6	9	20	31	42

IVAR, TIMEWALKER
Valiant Entertainment: Jan, 2015 - No. 12, Dec, 2015 ($3.99)

1-12: 1-4-Fred Van Lente-s/Clayton Henry-a. 5-8-Portela-a. 9-Pere Perez-a						4.00

IVX (Inhumans vs X-Men) (Also see Death of X)
Marvel Comics: No. 0, Jan, 2017 - No. 6, May, 2017 ($3.99/$4.99/$5.99)

0-($4.99) Soule-s/Rocafort-a: Beast, Medusa, Emma Frost, Magneto app.						5.00
1-($5.99) Soule & Lemire-s/Yu-a; multiple covers						6.00
2-5-($3.99) 2-Yu-a. 3-5-Garrón-a						5.00
6-($4.99) Yu-a; leads into Inhumans Prime #1, X-Men Prime #1 & Unc. Inhumans #20						5.00

IWO JIMA (See Spectacular Features Magazine)

IXTH GENERATION (See Ninth Generation)

I, ZOMBIE (Inspired the 2015 TV show)(See House of Mystery Halloween Annual #1 for 1st app.)
DC Comics (Vertigo): July, 2010 - No. 28, Oct, 2012 ($1.00/$2.99)

1-($1.00) Allred-a/Roberson-s; 2 covers by Allred & Cooke	3	6	9	16	23	30
2-28-($2.99) Allred-c/a in most. 12-Gilbert Hernandez-a. 18-Jay Stephens-a. 25-Rugg-a						4.00
... Special Edition 1 (1/15, $1.00) r/#1; new inteview with Allred						4.00
...: Dead to the World TPB (2011, $14.99) r/#1-5 & House of Mystery Hall. Ann. #1						15.00

JACE PEARSON OF THE TEXAS RANGERS (Radio/TV)(4-Color #396 is titled Tales of the Texas Rangers; ...'s Tales of ... #11-on)(See Western Roundup under Dell Giants)
Dell Publishing Co.: No. 396, 5/52 - No. 1021, 8-10/59 (No #10) (All-Photo-c)

Four Color 396 (#1)	11	22	33	73	157	240
2(5-7/53) - 9(2-4/55)	6	12	18	40	73	105
Four Color 648(#10, 9/55)	6	12	18	40	73	105
11(11-2/55-56) - 14,17-20(6-8/58)	5	10	15	33	57	80
15,16-Toth-a	5	10	15	34	60	85
Four Color 961,1021: 961-Spiegle-a	5	10	15	34	60	85

NOTE: Joel McCrea photo c-1-9, F.C. 648 (starred on radio show only); Willard Parker photo c-11-on (starred on TV series).

JACK ARMSTRONG (Radio)(See True Comics)
Parents' Institute: Nov, 1947 - No. 9, Sept, 1948; No. 10, Mar, 1949 - No. 13, Sept, 1949

nn (6/47) Ashcan edition; full color slick cover			(a FN/VF sold for $485 in 2011)			
1-(Scarce) (odd size) Cast intro. inside front-c; Vic Hardy's Crime Lab begins	50	100	150	315	533	750
2	21	42	63	126	206	285
3-5	15	30	45	90	140	190
6-13	14	28	42	81	118	155

JACK CROSS
DC Comics: Oct, 2005 - No. 4, Jan, 2006 ($2.50)

1-4-Warren Ellis-s/Gary Erskine-a						3.00

DC Comics Presents: Jack Cross #1 (12/10, $7.99, squarebound) r/#1-4

						8.00

JACKED
DC Comics (Vertigo): Jan, 2016 - No. 6, Jun, 2016 ($3.99)

1-6-Eric Kripke-s/John Higgins-a/Glenn Fabry-c						4.00

JACKIE CHAN'S SPARTAN X
Topps Comics: May, 1997 - No. 3 ($2.95, limited series)

1-3-Michael Golden-s/a; variant photo-c						3.00

JACKIE CHAN'S SPARTAN X: HELL BENT HERO FOR HIRE
Image Comics (Little Eva Ink): Mar, 1998 - No. 3 ($2.95, B&W)

1-3-Michael Golden-s/a: 1-variant photo-c						3.00

JACKIE GLEASON (TV) (Also see The Honeymooners)
St. John Publishing Co.: Sept, 1955 - No. 4, Dec, 1955?

1(1955)(TV)-Photo-c	93	186	279	591	1021	1450
2-4	55	110	165	352	601	850

JACKIE GLEASON AND THE HONEYMOONERS (TV)
National Periodical Publications: June-July, 1956 - No. 12, Apr-May, 1958

1-1st app. Ralph Kramden	168	336	504	1075	1838	2600
2	87	174	261	553	952	1350
3-11-Statue of Liberty-c	58	116	174	271	636	900
12 (Scarce)	84	168	252	538	919	1300

JACKIE JOKERS (Became Richie Rich &…)
Harvey Publications: March, 1973 - No. 4, Sept, 1973 (#5 was advertised, but not published)

1-1st app.	3	6	9	16	23	30
2-4: 2-President Nixon app.	2	4	6	8	11	14

JACKIE ROBINSON (Famous Plays of…) (Also see Negro Heroes #2 & Picture News #4)
Fawcett Publications: May, 1950 - No. 6, 1952 (Baseball hero) (All photo-c)

nn	116	232	348	742	1271	1800
2	58	116	174	371	636	900
3-6	50	100	150	315	533	750

JACK IN THE BOX (Formerly Yellowjacket Comics #1-10; becomes Cowboy Western Comics #17 on)
Frank Comunale/Charlton Comics No. 11 on: Feb, 1946; No. 11, Oct, 1946 - No. 16, Nov-Dec, 1947

1-Stitches, Marty Mouse & Nutsy McKrow	28	56	84	168	274	380
11-Yellowjacket (early Charlton comic)	31	62	93	182	296	410
12,14,15	19	38	57	111	176	240
13-Wolverton-a	40	80	120	246	411	575
16-12 pg. adapt. of Silas Marner; Kiefer-a	20	40	60	117	189	260

JACK KIRBY OMNIBUS, THE
DC Comics: 2011; 2013 ($49.99, hardcover with dustjacket)

Vol. 1 ('11) Recolored reprints of Kirby's DC work from 1946, 1957-1959; Evanier intro.						50.00
Vol. 2 ('13) Recolored reprints of Kirby's DC work from 1973-1987; Morrow intro.						50.00

JACK KIRBY'S FOURTH WORLD (See Mister Miracle & New Gods, 3rd Series)
DC Comics: Mar, 1997 - No. 20, Oct, 1998 ($1.95/$2.25)

1-20: 1-Byrne-a/scripts & Simonson-c begin; story cont'd from New Gods, 3rd Series #15; retells "The Pact" (New Gods, 1st Series #7); 1st brief DC app. Thor. 2-Thor vs. Big Barda; "Apokolips Then" back-up begins; Kirby-c/swipe (Thor #126) 8-Genesis x-over. 10-Simonson-a/s 13-Simonson back-up story. 20-Superman-c/app.						4.00

JACK KIRBY'S FOURTH WORLD OMNIBUS
DC Comics: 2007 - Vol. 4, 2008 ($49.99, hardcovers with dustjackets)

Vol. 1 ('07) Recolored reprints in chronological order of Superman's Pal, Jimmy Olsen #133-139, Forever People #1-3, New Gods #1-3, and Mister Miracle #1-3; Morrison intro, bonus art						80.00
Vol. 2 ('07) r/Jimmy Olsen #141-145, F.P. #4-6, N.G. #4-6 & M.M. #4-6; bonus art						50.00
Vol. 3 ('07) r/Jimmy Olsen #146-148, F.P. #7-10, N.G. #7-10 & M.M. #7-9; bonus art						50.00
Vol. 4 ('08) r/F.P. #11, M.M. #10-18, N.G. #11 & reprint series #6, & DC Graphic Novel #6 (The Hunger Dogs); Levitz intro.; Evanier afterword; character profile pages						50.00

JACK KIRBY'S GALACTIC BOUNTY HUNTERS
Marvel Comics (Icon): July, 2006 - No. 6, Nov, 2007 ($3.99)

1-6-Based on a Kirby concept; Mike Thibodeaux-a; Lisa Kirby, Thibodeaux and others-s						4.00
HC (2007, $24.99) r/series; pin-ups and supplemental art and interviews						25.00

JACK KIRBY'S SECRET CITY SAGA
Topps Comics (Kirbyverse): No. 0, Apr, 1993; No. 1, May, 1993 - No. 4, Aug, 1993 ($2.95, limited series)

0-(No cover price, 20 pgs.)-Simonson-c/a						4.00
0-Red embossed-c (limited ed.)						5.00
0-Gold foil-c (limited ed.)	1	3	4	6	8	10
1-4-Bagged w/3 trading cards; Ditko-c/a. 1-Ditko/Art Adams-c. 2-Ditko/Byrne-c; has coupon for Pres. Clinton.holo-foil trading card. 3-Dorman poster; has coupon for Gore holo-foil trading card. 4-Ditko/Perez-c						4.00

NOTE: Issues #1-4 contain coupons redeemable for Kirbychrome version of #1

JACK KIRBY'S SILVER STAR (Also see Silver Star)
Topps Comics (Kirbyverse): Oct, 1993 ($2.95)(Intended as a 4-issue limited series)

1-Silver ink-c; Austin-c/a(i); polybagged w/3 cards						4.00

JACK KIRBY'S STARR WARRIORS STARRING ADAM STARR AND THE SOLAR LEGION
Image Comics: Sept, 2023 ($9.99, one-shot)

1-Adaptation of early Kirby work in Crash Comics #1-3 by Tom Scioli						10.00

JACK KIRBY'S TEENAGENTS (See Satan's Six)
Topps Comics (Kirbyverse): Aug, 1993 - No. 4, Nov, 1993 ($2.95, limited series)

1-4: Bagged with/3 trading cards; Busiek/Austin-c(i); 3-Liberty Project app.						4.00

JACK KRAKEN
Dark Horse Comics: May, 2014 ($3.99, one-shot)

1-Tim Seeley; art by Ross Campbell & Jim Terry						4.00

JACK OF FABLES (See Fables)
DC Comics (Vertigo): Sept, 2006 - No. 50, Apr, 2011 ($2.99)

1-49: 1-Willingham & Sturges-s/Akins-a. 33-35-Crossover with Fables and The Literals						3.00

Itty Bitty Hellboy #1 © Mike Mignola

iZombie #14 © Monkey Brain & Allred

Jack Staff #15 © Paul Grist

	GD 2.0	VG 4.0	FN 6.0	VF 8.0	VF/NM 9.0	NM- 9.2
50-($4.99) Akins & Braun-a; Bolland-c						5.00
1-Special Edition (8/10, $1.00) r/#1 with "What's Next?" logo on cover						3.00
...: Americana TPB (2008, $14.99) r/#17-21						15.00
...: Jack of Hearts TPB (2007, $14.99) r/#6-11						15.00
...: The Bad Prince TPB (2008, $14.99) r/#12-16						15.00
...: The Big Book of War TPB (2009, $14.99) r/#28-32						15.00
...: The End TPB (2011, $17.99) r/#46-50						18.00
...: The Fulminate Blade TPB (2011, $14.99) r/#41-45						15.00
...: The (Nearly) Great Escape TPB (2007, $14.99) r/#1-5; Akins sketch pages						15.00
...: The New Adventures of Jack and Jack TPB (2010, $14.99) r/#36-40						15.00
...: Turning Pages TPB (2009, $14.99) r/#22-27						15.00

JACK OF HEARTS (Also see The Deadly Hands of Kung Fu #22 & Marvel Premiere #44)
Marvel Comics Group: Jan, 1984 - No. 4, Apr, 1984 (60¢, limited series)

	GD	VG	FN	VF	VF/NM	NM-
1-4						4.00

JACKPOT!
AfterShock Comics: Apr, 2016 - No. 6, Jun, 2017 ($3.99)

1-6-Ray Fawkes-s/Brian Stelfreeze-a. 1-4-Marco Failla-a. 5,6-Georges Duarte-a						4.00

JACKPOT (Mary Jane Watson)
Marvel Comics: Mar, 2024 ($4.99, one-shot)

1-Tie-in to the Amazing Spider-Man Gang War event; Bronfman-s/Vasquez-a						5.00

JACKPOT COMICS (Jolly Jingles #10 on)
MLJ Magazines: Spring, 1941 - No. 9, Spring, 1943

	GD	VG	FN	VF	VF/NM	NM-
1-The Black Hood, Mr. Justice, Steel Sterling & Sgt. Boyle begin; WWII sunburst-c by Biro	423	846	1269	3000	5250	7500
2-S. Cooper-c	187	374	561	1197	2049	2900
3-Hubbell-c; bondage -c	194	388	582	1242	2121	3000
4-Archie begins; (his face appears on cover in small circle) (Win/41; on sale 12/41)-(also see Pep Comics #22); 1st app. Mrs. Grundy, the principal; Novick-c	3900	7800	11,700	22,200	30,100	38,000
5-Hitler, Tojo, Mussolini-c by Montana; 1st definitive Mr. Weatherbee; 1st brief app. Reggie in 1 panel	919	1838	2757	6700	11,855	17,000
6,7-Bondage-c by Novick	320	640	960	2240	3920	5600
8,9-Sahle-c. 8-WWII-c. 9-WWII bondage-c	295	590	885	1888	3244	4600

JACK Q FROST (See Unearthly Spectaculars)

JACK STAFF (Vol. 2; previously published in Britain)
Image Comics: Feb, 2003 - No. 20, May, 2009 ($2.95/$3.50)

1-5-Paul Grist-s/a						3.50
6-20-($3.50) 6-Flashback to the WW2 Freedom Fighters						3.50
... Special 1 (1/08, $3.50) Molachi the Immortal app.						3.50
The Weird World of Jack Staff King Size Special 1 (7/07, $5.99, B&W) r/story serialized in Comics International magazine; afterword by Grist						6.00
Vol. 1: Everything Used to Be Black and White TPB (12/03, $19.95) r/British issues						20.00
Vol. 2: Soldiers TPB (2005, $15.95) r/#1-5; cover gallery						16.00
Vol. 3: Echoes of Tomorrow TPB (2006, $16.99) r/#6-12; cover gallery						17.00

JACK THE GIANT KILLER (See Movie Classics)

JACK THE GIANT KILLER (New Adventures of...)
Bimfort & Co.: Aug-Sept, 1953

	GD	VG	FN	VF	VF/NM	NM-
V1#1-H. C. Kiefer-c/a	36	72	108	211	343	475

JACKY'S DIARY
Dell Publishing Co.: No. 1091, Apr-June, 1960 (one-shot)

	GD	VG	FN	VF	VF/NM	NM-
Four Color 1091	5	10	15	34	60	85

JADEMAN COLLECTION
Jademan Comics: Dec, 1989 - No. 3, 1990 ($2.50, plastic coated-c, 68 pgs.)

1-3: 1-Wraparound-c w/fold-out poster						4.00

JADEMAN KUNG FU SPECIAL
Jademan Comics: 1988 ($1.50, 64 pgs.)

1						4.00

JADE WARRIORS (Mike Deodato's...)
Image Comics (Glass House Graphics): Nov, 1999 - No. 3, 2000 ($2.50)

1-3-Deodato-a						4.00
1-Variant-c						4.00

JAGUAR, THE (Also see The Adventures of...)
Impact Comics (DC): Aug, 1991 - No. 14, Oct, 1992 ($1.00)

1-14: 4-The Black Hood x-over. 7-Sienkiewicz-c. 9-Contains Crusaders trading card						4.00
Annual 1 (1992, $2.50, 68 pgs.)-With trading card						5.00

JAGUAR, THE (Mighty Crusaders)

Archie Comic Publications: Apr, 2024 ($3.99, one-shot)

	GD	VG	FN	VF	VF/NM	NM-
1-Keryl Brown Ahmed-s/Tango-a; two covers						4.00

JAGUAR GOD
Verotik: Mar, 1995 - No. 7, June, 1997 ($2.95, mature)

0 (2/96, $3.50)-Embossed Frazetta-c; Bisley-a; w/pin-ups.						5.00
1-Frazetta-c.						5.00
2-7: 2-Frazetta-c. 3-Bisley-c. 4-Emond-c. 7-($2.95)-Frazetta-c						4.00

JAKE THRASH
Aircel Publishing: 1988 - No. 3, 1988 ($2.00)

1-3						4.00

JAM, THE (...Urban Adventure)
Slave Labor Nos. 1-5/Dark Horse Comics Nos. 6-8/Caliber Comics No. 9 on:
Nov, 1989 - No. 14, 1997 ($1.95/$2.50/$2.95, B&W)

1-14: Bernie Mireault-c/a/scripts. 6-1st Dark Horse issue. 9-1st Caliber issue						4.00

JAMBOREE COMICS
Round Publishing Co.: Feb, 1946(no month given) - No. 3, Apr, 1946

	GD	VG	FN	VF	VF/NM	NM-
1-Funny animal	21	42	63	122	199	275
2,3	15	30	45	85	130	175

JAMES BOND
Dynamite Entertainment: 2015 - No. 12, 2016 ($3.99)

1-12-Warren Ellis-s/Jason Masters-a; multiple covers on each. 1-6-Vargr. 7-12-Eidolon						4.00
...: M (2018, $4.99) Shalvey-s/c; Holden-a						5.00
...: Moneypenny (2016, $4.99) Houser-s/Edgar-a/Lotay-c						5.00
...: Service (2017, $7.99) Kieron Gillen/Antonio Fuso-a/Jamie McKelvie-c						8.00
...: Solstice (2017, $4.99) Ibrahim Moustafa-s/a						5.00

JAMES BOND (Volume 2)
Dynamite Entertainment: 2017 - No. 6, 2017 ($3.99)

1-6-Black Box; Percy-s/Lobosco-a. 1-Five covers. 2-6-Multiple covers on each						4.00

JAMES BOND (Volume 3)
Dynamite Entertainment: 2019 - No. 6, 2020 ($3.99)

1-6: 1-Ayala & Lore-s/Gapstur-a						4.00

JAMES BOND (Volume 4)
Dynamite Entertainment: 2023 - Present ($4.99)

1,2-Ennis-s/Lobosco-a/Dave Johnson-c						5.00

JAMES BOND: AGENT OF SPECTRE
Dynamite Entertainment: 2021 - No. 5, 2021 ($3.99, limited series)

1-5-Gage-s/Casalanguida-a; Blofeld app.; multiple covers on each						4.00

JAMES BOND 007
Dynamite Entertainment: 2018 - No. 12, 2019 ($3.99, limited series)

1-12: 1-3-Greg Pak-s/Marc Laming-a; Oddjob app. 4-6-Stephen Mooney-a; Goldfinger app.						4.00

JAMES BOND: 007
Dynamite Entertainment: 2022 - No. 6, 2023 ($3.99)

1-6-Philip Kennedy Johnson-s/Marco Finnegan-a						4.00

JAMES BOND 007: A SILENT ARMAGEDDON
Dark Horse Comics/Acme Press: Mar, 1993 - Apr 1993 (limited series)

1,2						5.00

JAMES BOND: 007, FOR KING AND COUNTRY
Dynamite Entertainment: 2023 - No. 6, 2023 ($3.99, limited series)

1-6-Philip Kennedy Johnson-s/Giorgio Spalletta-a						4.00

JAMES BOND 007: GOLDENEYE (Movie)
Topps Comics: Jan, 1996 ($2.95, unfinished limited series of 3)

	GD	VG	FN	VF	VF/NM	NM-
1-Movie adaptation; Stelfreeze-c	1	3	4	6	8	10

JAMES BOND 007: SERPENT'S TOOTH
Dark Horse Comics/Acme Press: July 1992 - Aug 1992 ($4.95, limited series)

1-3-Paul Gulacy-c/a						5.00

JAMES BOND 007: SHATTERED HELIX
Dark Horse Comics: Jun 1994 - July 1994 ($2.50, limited series)

1,2						5.00

JAMES BOND 007: THE QUASIMODO GAMBIT
Dark Horse Comics: Jan 1995 - May 1995 ($3.95, limited series)

1-3						4.50

JAMES BOND: FELIX LEITER
Dynamite Entertainment: 2017 - No. 6, 2017 ($3.99)

	GD	VG	FN	VF	VF/NM	NM-
	2.0	4.0	6.0	8.0	9.0	9.2

1-6-James Robinson-s/Aaron Campbell-a ... 4.00

JAMES BOND FOR YOUR EYES ONLY
Marvel Comics Group: Oct, 1981 - No. 2, Nov, 1981

1,2-Movie adapt.; r/Marvel Super Special #19 ... 6.00

JAMES BOND: HAMMERHEAD
Dynamite Entertainment: 2016 - No. 6, 2016 ($3.99)

1-6-Diggle-s/Casalanguida-a. 1-Three covers ... 4.00

JAMES BOND: HIMEROS
Dynamite Entertainment: 2021 - No. 5, 2022 $3.99, limited series)

1-5: 1-Barnes-s/Fuso-a; covers by Francavilla & Guice. 3-Minotti-a ... 4.00

JAMES BOND JR. (TV)
Marvel Comics: Jan, 1992 - No. 12, Dec, 1992 (#1: $1.00, #2-on: $1.25)

1-12: Based on animated TV show ... 4.00

JAMES BOND: KILL CHAIN
Dynamite Entertainment: 2017 - No. 6, 2017 ($3.99)

1-6-Diggle-s/Casalanguida-a. 1-Three covers. 2-Felix Leiter app. ... 4.00

JAMES BOND: LICENCE TO KILL (See Licence To Kill)

JAMES BOND: ORIGIN
Dynamite Entertainment: 2018 - No. 12, 2019 ($3.99)

1-12: 1-Parker-s/Bob Q-a; multiple covers; young James Bond in 1941 WWII England ... 4.00

JAMES BOND: PERMISSION TO DIE
Eclipse Comics/ACME Press: 1989 - No. 3, 1991 ($3.95, lim. series, squarebound, 52 pgs.)

1-3: Mike Grell-c/a/scripts in all. 3-($4.95) ... 5.00

JAMES BOND: THE BODY
Dynamite Entertainment: 2018 - No. 6, 2018 ($3.99)

1-6: 1-Kot-s/Casalanguida-a. 2-Fuso-a ... 4.00

JAM, THE: SUPER COOL COLOR INJECTED TURBO ADVENTURE #1 FROM HELL!
Comico: May, 1988 ($2.50, 44 pgs., one-shot)

1 ... 4.00

JANE ARDEN (See Feature Funnies & Pageant of Comics)
St. John (United Features Syndicate): Mar, 1948 - No. 2, June, 1948

	GD	VG	FN	VF	VF/NM	NM-
1-Newspaper reprints	20	40	60	114	182	250
2	15	30	45	85	130	175

JANE FOSTER & THE MIGHTY THOR
Marvel Comics: Aug, 2022 - No. 5, Dec, 2022 ($3.99, limited series)

1-5-Gronbekk-s/Dowling-a; Sif & The Enchantress app. ... 4.00

JANE WIEDLIN'S LADY ROBOTIKA
Image Comics: Jul, 2010 - No. 2, Aug, 2010 ($3.50, unfinished limited series)

1,2-Wiedlin & Bill Morrison-s. 1-Morrison & Rodriguez-a. 2-Moy-a ... 3.50

JANN OF THE JUNGLE (Jungle Tales No. 1-7)
Atlas Comics (CSI): No. 8, Nov, 1955 - No. 17, June, 1957

	GD	VG	FN	VF	VF/NM	NM-
8(#1)	50	100	150	315	533	750
9,11-15	31	62	93	182	296	410
10-Williamson/Colletta-c	36	72	108	211	343	475
16,17-Williamson/Mayo-a(3), 5 pgs. each	33	66	99	194	317	440

NOTE: *Everett* c-15-17. **Heck** a-8, 15, 17. *Maneely* c-11. *Shores* a-8.

JASON & THE ARGOBOTS
Oni Press: Aug, 2002 - No. 4, Dec, 2002 ($2.95, B&W, limited series)

1-4-Torres-s/Norton-c/a ... 3.00
Vol. 1 Birthquake TPB (6/03, $11.95, digest size) r/#1-4, Sunday comic strips ... 12.00
Vol. 2 Machina Ex Deus TPB (9/03, $11.95, digest size) new story ... 12.00

JASON & THE ARGONAUTS (See Movie Classics)

JASON GOES TO HELL: THE FINAL FRIDAY (Movie)
Topps Comics: July, 1993 - No. 3, Sept, 1993 ($2.95, limited series)

	GD	VG	FN	VF	VF/NM	NM-
1-Adaptation of film. 1-Glow-in-the-dark-c	3	6	9	18	27	36
2,3-Adaptation continues	2	4	6	9	12	15

JASON'S QUEST (See Showcase #88-90)

JASON VS. LEATHERFACE
Topps Comics: Oct, 1995 - No. 3, Jan, 1996 ($2.95, limited series)

	GD	VG	FN	VF	VF/NM	NM-
1-Collins scripts; Bisley-c on all	3	6	9	17	26	35
2,3	2	4	6	11	16	20

JAWS 2 (See Marvel Comics Super Special, A)

JAY & SILENT BOB (See Clerks, Oni Double Feature, and Tales From the Clerks)
Oni Press: July, 1998 - No. 4, Oct, 1999 ($2.95, B&W, limited series)

1-Kevin Smith-s/Fegredo-a; photo-c & Quesada/Palmiotti-c

	GD	VG	FN	VF	VF/NM	NM-
	2	4	6	9	12	15

1-San Diego Comic Con variant covers (2 different covers, came packaged with action figures) ... 10.00
1-2nd & 3rd printings, 2-4: 2-Allred-a. 3-Flip-c by Jaime Hernandez ... 5.00
Chasing Dogma TPB (1999, $11.95) r/#1-4; Alanis Morissette intro. ... 13.00
Chasing Dogma TPB (2001, $12.95) r/#1-4 in color; Morissette intro. ... 13.00
Chasing Dogma HC (1999, $69.95, S&N) r/#1-4 in color; Morissette intro. ... 70.00

JAY GARRICK: THE FLASH (Justice Society)(See Stargirl: The Lost Children)
DC Comics: Dec, 2023 - No. 6, Jun, 2024 ($3.99)

1-6: 1-Jeremy Adams-s/Diego Olortegui-a; Judy Garrick (The Boom) app. 4-Origin ... 4.00

JCP FEATURES
J.C. Productions (Archie): Feb, 1982-c; Dec, 1981-indicia ($2.00, one-shot, B&W magazine)

1-T.H.U.N.D.E.R. Agents; Black Hood by Morrow & Neal Adams; Texeira-a; 2 pgs. S&K-a from Fly #1

	GD	VG	FN	VF	VF/NM	NM-
	2	4	6	10	14	18

JEAN GREY (X-Men) (Also see Phoenix Resurrection: The Return of Jean Grey)
Marvel Comics: Jul, 2017 - No. 11, Mar, 2018 ($3.99)

1-10: 1-Hopeless-s/Ibáñez-a. 4-Thor app. 6-Dr. Strange app. 7-Scarlet Witch app. ... 4.00

11-($4.99) Follows Phoenix Resurrection #5; leads into X-Men: Red #1 ... 5.00

JEAN GREY (Fall of X)
Marvel Comics: Oct, 2023 - Present ($4.99)

1-($4.99) Louise Simonson-s/Bernard Chang-a ... 5.00
2-4-($3.99) ... 4.00

JEANIE COMICS (Formerly All Surprise; Cowgirl Romances #28)
Marvel Comics/Atlas(CPC): No. 13, April, 1947 - No. 27, Oct, 1949

	GD	VG	FN	VF	VF/NM	NM-
13-Mitzi, Willie begin	43	86	129	271	461	650
14,15	30	60	90	177	289	400
16-Used in Love and Death by Legman; Kurtzman's "Hey Look"	37	74	111	222	361	500
17-19,21,22-Kurtzman's "Hey Look" (1-3 pgs. each)	24	48	72	144	237	330
20,23-27	22	44	66	130	213	295

JEEP COMICS (Also see G.I. Comics and Overseas Comics)
R. B. Leffingwell & Co.: Winter, 1944, No. 2, Spring, 1945 - No. 3, Mar-Apr, 1948

	GD	VG	FN	VF	VF/NM	NM-
1-Capt. Power, Criss Cross & Jeep & Peep (costumed) begin	103	206	309	659	1130	1600
2- Jeep & Peep-c	54	108	162	343	574	825
3-L. B. Cole dinosaur-c	74	148	222	470	810	1150

JEEPERS CREEPERS (Based on the 2001 horror movie)
Dynamite Entertainment: 2018 - No. 5, 2018 ($3.99, limited series)

1-5-Marc Andreyko-s/Kewber Baal-a; multiple covers on each ... 4.00

JEFF JORDAN, U.S. AGENT
D. S. Publishing Co.: Dec, 1947 - Jan, 1948

	GD	VG	FN	VF	VF/NM	NM-
1	22	44	66	132	216	300

JEFF STEINBERG: CHAMPION OF EARTH
Oni Press: Aug, 2016 - No. 6, Mar, 2017 ($4.99)

1-6: 1-Fialkov-s/Fleecs-a; covers by Fleecs & Burnham ... 5.00

JEM & THE HOLOGRAMS
IDW Publishing: Mar, 2015 - No. 26, Apr, 2017 ($3.99)

1-25: 1-Origin re-told; multiple covers ... 4.00
26-($4.99) Thompson-s/Lagace-a; previews Infinite x-over series; cover gallery ... 5.00
Annual 2017 (1/17, $7.99) Thompson-s; art by Lagace and others; 2 covers ... 8.00
... Holiday Special (12/15, $3.99) Mebberson-a ... 4.00
IDW Greatest Hits: Jem and the Holograms #1 (7/16, $1.00) r/#1 ... 4.00
... 20/20 #1 (1/19, $4.99) Set 20 years in the future; Sina Grace-s/Siobhan Keenan-a ... 5.00
... Valentine Special (2/16, $3.99) Thompson-s/Bartel-a ... 4.00

JEM AND THE HOLOGRAMS: DIMENSIONS
IDW Publishing: Nov, 2017 - No. 4, Feb, 2018 ($3.99, limited series)

1-4-Anthology by various; multiple covers on each. 1-Leth-s/Ford-a ... 4.00

JEM AND THE HOLOGRAMS: INFINITE
IDW Publishing: Jun, 2017 - No. 3, Aug, 2017 ($3.99, limited series)

1-3-Part 1,3,5 of the x-over series with Jem and the Holograms: The Misfits: Infinite ... 4.00

JEM AND THE HOLOGRAMS: THE MISFITS: INFINITE
IDW Publishing: Jun, 2017 - No. 3, Aug, 2017 ($3.99, limited series)

1-3-Part 2,4,6 of the x-over with Jem and the Holograms: Infinite ... 4.00

JEMM, SON OF SATURN
DC Comics: Sept, 1984 - No. 12, Aug, 1985 (Maxi-series, mando paper)

1-12: 3-Origin. 4-Superman app. ... 4.00
NOTE: *Colan* a-1-12p; c-1-5, 7-12p.

JEM: THE MISFITS (From Jem and the Holograms)
IDW Publishing: Dec, 2016 - No. 5, Apr, 2017 ($3.99)

1-5-Kelly Thompson-s/Jenn St-Onge-a ... 4.00

JENNIFER BLOOD
Dynamite Entertainment: 2011 - No. 36, 2014 ($3.99)

1-36: 1-3-Garth Ennis-s/Adriano Batista-a; four covers on each. 4-The Ninjettes app. ... 4.00
Annual 1 (2012, $4.99) Al Ewing-s/Igor Vitorino-a/Sean Chen-c; origin ... 5.00
... Presents Giulietta Romeo: Hitwoman 1 (2022, $4.99) Van Lente-s/Carey-a ... 5.00

JENNIFER BLOOD: BATTLE DIARY
Dynamite Entertainment: 2023 - Present ($4.99)

1-3-Fred Van Lente-s/Robert Carey-a ... 5.00

JENNIFER BLOOD: BORN AGAIN
Dynamite Entertainment: 2014 - No. 5, 2014 ($3.99)

1-5-Steven Grant-s/Kewber Baal-a/Stephen Segovia-c ... 4.00

JENNIFER BLOOD: FIRST BLOOD
Dynamite Entertainment: 2011 - No. 6, 2013 ($3.99)

1-6-Mike Carroll-s/Igor Vitorino-a/Mike Mayhew-c; origin & training ... 4.00

JENNIFER BLOOD, VOLUME 2
Dynamite Entertainment: 2021 - No. 10, 2022 ($3.99)

1-10: 1-Fred Van Lente-s/Vincenzo Federici-a; multiple covers on each ... 4.00

JENNIFER'S BODY (Based on the 2009 movie)
BOOM! Studios: Aug, 2009 ($24.99, hardcover graphic novel)

HC-Short stories of Jennifer and her victims; Spears-s/art by various; pin-up art ... 25.00

JENNY FINN
Oni Press: June, 1999 - No. 2, Sept, 1999 ($2.95, B&W, unfinished lim. series)

1,2-Mignola & Nixey-s/Nixey-a/Mignola-c ... 4.00
...: Doom (Atomeka, 2005, $6.99, TPB) r/#1 & 2 with new supplemental material ... 7.00

JENNY SPARKS: THE SECRET HISTORY OF THE AUTHORITY
DC Comics (WildStorm): Aug, 2000 - No. 5, Mar, 2001 (limited series)

1-Millar-s/McCrea & Hodgkins-a/Hitch & Neary-c ... 4.00

	GD	VG	FN	VF	VF/NM	NM-
1-Variant-c by McCrea	1	3	4	6	8	10

2-5: 2-Apollo & Midnighter. 3-Jack Hawksmoor. 4-Shen. 5-Engineer ... 3.00
TPB (2001, $14.95) r/#1-5; Ellis intro. ... 15.00

James Bond: Himeros #1 © Ian Fleming

Jay Garrick: The Flash #1 © DC

Jessica Jones #1 © MAR

	GD 2.0	VG 4.0	FN 6.0	VF 8.0	VF/NM 9.0	NM- 9.2

JERICHO (Based on the TV series)
Devil's Due Publishing/IDW Publishing: Oct, 2009 - Jan, 2014 ($3.99)

... Redux (IDW, 2/11, $7.99) r/Season 3: Civil War #1-3						8.00
... Season 3: Civil War 1-4: 1-Story by the show's writing staff						4.00
... Season 4: 1-5: 1-(7/12) Photo-c & Bradstreet-c						4.00

JERRY DRUMMER (Boy Heroes of the Revolutionary War) (Formerly Soldier & Marine V2#9)
Charlton Comics: V3#10, Apr, 1957 - V3#12, Oct, 1957

V3#10-12: 11-Whitman-c/a	7	14	21	37	46	55

JERRY IGER'S... (All titles, Blackthorne/First)(Value: cover or less)

JERRY LEWIS (See The Adventures of...)

JERSEY GODS
Image Comics: Feb, 2009 - No. 12, May, 2010 ($3.50)

1-11: 1-Brunswick-s/McDaid-a; two covers by McDaid and Allred						3.50
12-($4.99) Wraparound cover swipe of Superman #252 by Allred						5.00

JESSE JAMES (The True Story Of..., also seeThe Legend of...)
Dell Publishing Co.: No. 757, Dec, 1956 (one shot)

Four Color 757-Movie, photo-c	9	18	27	58	114	170

JESSE JAMES (See Badmen of the West & Blazing Sixguns)
Avon Periodicals: 8/50 - No. 9, 11/52; No. 15, 10/53 - No. 29, 8-9/56

1-Kubert Alabam-r/Cowpuncher #1	27	54	81	158	259	360
2-Kubert-a(3)	20	40	60	117	189	260
3-Kubert Alabam-r/Cowpuncher #2	18	36	54	105	165	225
4,9-No Kubert	14	28	42	80	115	150
5,6-Kubert Jesse James-a(3); 5-Wood-a(1pg.)	19	38	57	109	172	235
7-Kubert Jesse James-a(2)	16	32	48	94	147	200
8-Kinstler-a(3)	14	28	42	82	121	160
15-Kinstler-r/#3	13	26	39	74	105	135
16-Kinstler-r/#3 & story-r/Butch Cassidy #1	14	28	42	76	108	140
17-19,21: 17-Jesse James-r/#4; Kinstler-c idea from Kubert splash in #6. 18-Kubert Jesse James-r/#5. 19-Kubert Jesse James-r/#6. 21-Two Jesse James-r/#4, Kinstler-r/#4	12	24	36	69	97	125
20-Williamson/Frazetta-a; r/Chief Vic. Apache Massacre; Kubert Jesse James-r/#6; Kit West story by Larsen	19	38	57	111	176	240
22-29: 22,23-No Kubert. 24-New McCarty strip by Kinstler; Kinstler-r. 25-New McCarty Jesse James strip by Kinstler; Jesse James-r/#7,9. 26,27-New McCarty Jesse James strip plus a Kinstler/McCann Jesse James-r. 28-Reprints most of Red Mountain, Featuring Quantrells Raiders	12	24	36	69	97	125
Annual nn (1952; 25¢; 100 pgs.)- "...Brings Six-Gun Justice to the West"- 3 earlier issues rebound; Kubert, Kinstler-a(3)	40	80	120	246	411	575

NOTE: Mostly reprints #10 on. Fawcette c-1, Kida a-5. Kinstler a-3, 4, 7-9, 15r, 16r(2), 21-27; c-3, 4, 9, 17-27. Painted c-5-8. 22 has 2 stories r/Sheriff Bob Dixon's Chuck Wagon #1 with name changed to Sheriff Bob Trent.

JESSE JAMES
Realistic Publications: July, 1953

nn-Reprints Avon's #1; same-c, colors different	14	28	42	81	118	155

JESSICA JONES (Also see Alias)
Marvel Comics: Dec, 2016 - No. 18, May, 2018 ($3.99)

1-18-Bendis-s/Gaydos-a; Luke Cage app. 1-Misty Knight app. 13-17-Purple Man app.						4.00
...: Purple Daughter (2019, $19.99, square-bound) Printing of digital-first story; De Julis-a						20.00

JESSICA JONES: BLIND SPOT
Marvel Comics: Mar, 2020 - No. 6, May, 2020 ($3.99, printing of digital-first story)

1-6-Kelly Thompson-s/Mattia De Iulis-a. 2,3-Elsa Bloodstone app. 4-Spider-Man app.						4.00

JEST (Formerly Snap; becomes Kayo #12)
Harry 'A' Chesler: No. 10, 1944 - No. 11, 1944

10-Johnny Rebel & Yankee Boy app. in text	30	60	90	177	289	400
11-Little Nemo in Adventure Land	27	54	81	158	259	360

JESTER
Harry 'A' Chesler: No. 10, 1945

10	26	52	78	154	252	350

JESUS
Spire Christian Comics (Fleming H. Revell Co.): 1979 (49¢)

nn	2	4	6	11	16	20

JET (See Jet Powers)

JET (Crimson from Wildcore & Backlash)
DC Comics (WildStorm): Nov, 2000 - No. 4, Feb, 2001 ($2.50, limited series)

1-4-Nguyen-a/Abnett & Lanning-s						3.00

JET ACES

Fiction House Magazines: 1952 - No. 4, 1953

1- Sky Advs. of American War Aces (on sale 6/20/52)	26	52	78	154	252	350
2-4	15	30	45	90	140	190

JETCAT CLUBHOUSE (Also see Land of Nod, The)
Oni Press: Apr, 2001 - No. 3, Aug, 2001 ($3.25)

1-3-Jay Stephens-s/a. 1-Wraparound-c						3.25
TPB (8/02, $10.95, 8 3/4" x 5 3/4") r/#1-3 & stories from Nickelodeon mag. & other						11.00

JET DREAM (...and Her Stunt-Girl Counterspies)(See The Man from Uncle #7)
Gold Key: June, 1968 (12¢)

1-Painted-c	4	8	12	27	44	60

JET FIGHTERS (Korean War)
Standard Magazines: No. 5, Nov, 1952 - No. 7, Mar, 1953

5,7-Toth-a. 5-Toth-c	19	38	57	111	176	240
6-Celardo-a	15	30	45	84	127	170

JET POWER
I.W. Enterprises: 1963

I.W. Reprint 1,2-r/Jet Powers #1,2	3	6	9	19	30	40

JET POWERS (American Air Forces No. 5 on)
Magazine Enterprises: 1950 - No. 4, 1951

1(A-1 #30)-Powell-c/a begins	47	94	141	296	498	700
2(A-1 #32) Classic Powell dinosaur-c/a	47	94	141	296	498	700
3(A-1 #35)-Williamson/Evans-a	48	96	144	302	514	725
4(A-1 #38)-Williamson/Wood-a; "The Rain of Sleep" drug story	50	100	150	315	533	750

JET PUP (See 3-D Features)

JETSONS (See March of Comics #276, 330, 348 & Spotlight #3)
Gold Key: Jan, 1963 - No. 36, Oct, 1970 (Hanna-Barbera)

1-1st comic book app.	54	108	162	432	966	1500
2	12	24	36	79	170	260
3-10: 9-Flintstones x-over	9	18	27	58	114	170
11-22	7	14	21	48	89	130
23-36-Reprints: 23-(7/67)	5	10	15	31	53	75

JETSONS, THE (TV) (Also see Golden Comics Digest)
Charlton Comics: Nov, 1970 - No. 20, Dec, 1973 (Hanna-Barbera)

1	9	18	27	63	129	195
2	5	10	15	30	50	70
3-10: Flintstones x-over	3	6	9	20	31	42
11-20	3	6	9	16	24	32
nn (1973, digest, 60¢, 100 pgs.) B&W one page gags	4	8	12	23	37	50

JETSONS, THE (TV)
Harvey Comics: V2#1, Sept, 1992 - No. 5, Nov, 1993 ($1.25/$1.50) (Hanna-Barbera)

V2#1-5						5.00
...Big Book V2#1,2,3 ($1.95, 52 pgs.): 1-(11/92). 2-(4/93). 3-(7/93)						5.00
...Giant Size 1,2,3 ($2.25, 68 pgs): 1-(10/92). 2-(4/93). 3-(10/93)						5.00

JETSONS, THE (TV)
Archie Comics: Sept, 1995 - No. 8, Apr, 1996 ($1.50)

1-8						4.00

JETSONS, THE (TV)
DC Comics: Jan, 2018 - No. 6, Mar, 2018 ($3.99, limited series)

1-6: covers by Conner & Dave Johnson						4.00

JETTA OF THE 21ST CENTURY
Standard Comics: No. 5, Dec, 1952 - No. 7, Apr, 1953 (Teen-age Archie type)

5-Dan DeCarlo-a	110	220	330	704	1202	1700
6-Robot-c	87	174	261	553	952	1350
7	65	130	195	416	708	1000
TPB (Airwave Publ., 2006, $9.99) B&W reprint of series; Bill Morrison intro./back-c						10.00

JEW GANGSTER
DC Comics: 2005 ($14.99, SC graphic novel)

SC-Joe Kubert-s/a						15.00

JEZEBEL JADE (Hanna-Barbera)
Comico: Oct, 1988 - No. 3, Dec, 1988 ($2.00, mini-series)

1-3: Johnny Quest spin-off; early Adam Kubert-a						4.00

JEZEBELLE (See Wildstorm 2000 Annuals)
DC Comics (WildStorm): Mar, 2001 - No. 6, Aug, 2001 ($2.50, limited series)

	GD	VG	FN	VF	VF/NM	NM-
	2.0	4.0	6.0	8.0	9.0	9.2

1-6-Ben Raab-s/Steve Ellis-a   3.00

JIGGS & MAGGIE
Dell Publishing Co.: No. 18, 1941 (one shot)

Four Color 18 (#1)-(1936-38-r)	63	126	189	403	689	975

JIGGS & MAGGIE
Standard Comics/Harvey Publications No. 22 on: No. 11, 1949 (June) - No. 21, 2/53; No. 22, 4/53 - No. 27, 2-3/54

11	20	40	60	114	182	250
12-15,17-21	14	28	42	76	108	140
16-Wood text illos.	14	28	42	78	112	145
22-24-Little Dot app.	12	24	36	69	97	125
25,27	11	22	33	60	83	105
26-Four pgs. partially in 3-D	15	30	45	83	124	165

NOTE: *Sunday page reprints by McManus loosely blended into story continuity. Based on Bringing Up Father strip. Advertised on covers as "All New."*

JIGSAW (Big Hero Adventures)
Harvey Publ. (Funday Funnies): Sept, 1966 - No. 2, Dec, 1966 (36 pgs.)

1-Origin & 1st app.; Crandall-a (5 pgs.)	4	8	12	25	40	55
2-Man From S.R.A.M.	3	6	9	16	23	30

JIGSAW OF DOOM (See Complete Mystery No. 2)

JIM BOWIE (Formerly Danger?; Black Jack No. 20 on)
Charlton Comics: No. 16, Mar, 1956 - No. 19, Apr, 1957

16	8	16	24	44	57	70
17-19: 18-Giordano-c	6	12	18	29	36	42

JIM BOWIE (TV, see Western Tales)
Dell Publishing Co.: No. 893, Mar, 1958 - No. 993, May-July, 1959

Four Color 893 (#1)	7	14	21	44	82	120
Four Color 993-Photo-c	5	10	15	35	63	90

JIM BUTCHER'S THE DRESDEN FILES: DOG MEN (Based on the Dresden Files novels)
Dynamite Entertainment: 2017 - No. 6, 2017 ($3.99, limited series)

1-6: 1-Jim Butcher & Mark Powers-s/Diego Galindo-a/c   4.00

JIM BUTCHER'S THE DRESDEN FILES: DOWN TOWN (Based on the Dresden Files novels)
Dynamite Entertainment: 2015 - No. 6, 2015 ($3.99, limited series)

1-6: 1-Jim Butcher & Mark Powers-s/Carlos Gomez-a/Stjepan Sejic-c   4.00

JIM BUTCHER'S THE DRESDEN FILES: FOOL MOON
Dynamite Entertainment: 2011 - No. 8, 2012 ($3.99, limited series)

1-8: 1-Jim Butcher & Mark Powers-s/Chase Conley-a/Brett Booth-c   4.00

JIM BUTCHER'S THE DRESDEN FILES: GHOUL GOBLIN
Dynamite Entertainment: 2012 - No. 6, 2013 ($3.99, limited series)

1-6: 1-Jim Butcher & Mark Powers-s/Joseph Cooper-a; Syaf-c   4.00

JIM BUTCHER'S THE DRESDEN FILES: STORM FRONT (Based on the Dresden Files novels)
Dabel Bros. Productions: Oct, 2008 (Nov.-on-c) - No. 4, Apr, 2009 ($3.99, limited series)

1-4-Jim Butcher & Mark Powers-s/Ardian Syaf-a; covers by Syaf & Tsai   4.00
Vol. 2: 1,2 (7/09 - No. 4)   4.00

JIM BUTCHER'S THE DRESDEN FILES: WAR CRY
Dynamite Entertainment: 2014 - No. 5, 2014 ($3.99/$4.99, limited series)

1-4: 1-Jim Butcher & Mark Powers-s/Carlos Gomez-a; Sejic-c   4.00
5-($4.99) Wraparound-c by Sejic   5.00

JIM BUTCHER'S THE DRESDEN FILES: WELCOME TO THE JUNGLE
Dabel Bros. Productions: Mar, 2008 (Apr. on-c) - No. 4, Jul, 2008 ($3.99, limited series)

1-Jim Butcher-s/Ardian Syaf-a; Ardian Syaf-c   5.00
1-Variant-c by Chris McGrath   8.00
1-New York Comic-Con 2008 variant-c   15.00
1-Second printing   4.00
2-4-Two covers on each   4.00
HC (2008, $19.95, dustjacket) r/#1-4; Butcher intro.; concept art pages   20.00

JIM BUTCHER'S THE DRESDEN FILES: WILD CARD
Dynamite Entertainment: 2016 - No. 6, 2016 ($3.99, limited series)

1-6-Jim Butcher & Mark Powers-s/Carlos Gomez-a/c   4.00

JIM DANDY
Dandy Magazine (Lev Gleason): May, 1956 - No. 3, Sept, 1956 (Charles Biro)

1-Jim Dandy adventures w/Cup, an alien & his flying saucer (both invisible) from the planet Zikalug begins; ends #3. Biro-c. 1,2-Bammy Boozle app.

	15	30	45	90	140	190
2,3: 2-Two pg. actual flying saucer reports	11	22	33	64	90	115

JIM HARDY (See Giant Comics Eds., Sparkler & Treasury of Comics #2 & 5)
United Features Syndicate/Spotlight Publ.: 1939; 1942; 1947 - No. 2, 1947

Single Series 6 ('39)	53	106	159	334	567	800
Single Series 27('42)	40	80	120	246	411	575
1('47)-Spotlight Publ.	19	38	57	111	176	240
2	13	26	39	72	101	130

JIM HARDY
Spotlight/United Features Synd.: 1944 (25¢, 132 pgs.) (Tip Top, Sparkler-r)

nn-Origin Mirror Man; Triple Terror app.	47	94	141	296	498	700

JIM HENSON'S BENEATH THE DARK CRYSTAL
BOOM! Studios (Archaia): Jul, 2018 - No. 12, Aug, 2019 ($3.99, limited series)

1-12-Adam Smith-s/Alexandria Huntington-a   4.00

JIM HENSON'S LABYRINTH: CORONATION
BOOM! Studios (Archaia): Feb, 2018 - No. 12, Mar, 2019 ($3.99, limited series)

1-12: 1-Spurrier-s/Bayliss-a/Staples-c; Jareth before becoming the Goblin King   4.00

JIM HENSON'S LABYRINTH: UNDER THE SPELL
BOOM! Studios (Archaia): Nov, 2018 ($7.99, one-shot)

1-Short stories; Vidaurri-a/Webb-a; Grace-a/Sun-a; Dialynas-s/a; Issacs-c   8.00

JIM HENSON'S THE DARK CRYSTAL: AGE OF RESISTANCE

BOOM! Studios (Archaia): Sept, 2019 - No. 12, Oct, 2020 ($3.99, limited series)

1-12: 1-6,8-Addis & Matthews-s/Andelfinger-a. 7-Carlomagno-a. 9-12-Migyeong-a   4.00

JIM HENSON'S THE STORYTELLER: DRAGONS (Also see The Storyteller)
BOOM! Studios (Archaia): Dec, 2015 - No. 4, Mar, 2016 ($3.99, limited series)

1-4: 2-Pride-s/a   4.00

JIM HENSON'S THE STORYTELLER: GHOSTS
BOOM! Studios (Archaia): Mar, 2019 - No. 4, Aug, 2020 ($3.99, limited series)

1-4: 1-Márk László-s/a. 2-Jennifer Rostowsky-s/a. 3-Michael Walsh-s/a 4-VER-s/a   4.00

JIM HENSON'S THE STORYTELLER: SHAPESHIFTERS
BOOM! Studios (Archaia): Mar, 2022 - No. 4, Jun, 2022 ($3.99, limited series)

1-4   4.00

JIM HENSON'S THE STORYTELLER: TRICKSTERS
BOOM! Studios (Archaia): Mar, 2021 - No. 4, Jun, 2021 ($3.99, limited series)

1-4-Momoko main-c on all. 1-Rivera-s/Zhang-a. 2-Ifueko-s/Kubo-a   4.00

JIM HENSON'S THE STORYTELLER: WITCHES
BOOM! Studios (Archaia): Sept, 2014 - No. 4, Dec, 2014 ($3.99, limited series)

1-4: 1-Vidaurri-s/a. 2-Vanderklugt-s/a. 3-Matthew Dow Smith-s/a. 4-Stokely-s/a   4.00

JIMINY CRICKET (Disney., see Mickey Mouse Mag. V5#3 & Walt Disney Showcase #37)
Dell Publishing Co.: No. 701, May, 1956 - No. 989, May-July, 1959

Four Color 701	9	18	27	60	120	180
Four Color 795, 897, 989	7	14	21	49	92	135

JIM LEE SKETCHBOOK
DC Comics (WildStorm): 2002 (no price, 16 pgs.)

nn-Various DC and WildStorm character sketches by Lee	3	6	9	16	23	30

JIMMY CORRIGAN (See Acme Novelty Library)

JIMMY DURANTE (Also see A-1 Comics)
Magazine Enterprises: No. 18, Oct, 1949 - No. 20, Winter 1949-50

A-1 18,20-Photo-c (scarce)	52	104	156	328	552	775

JIMMY OLSEN (See Superman's Pal...)

JIMMY OLSEN
DC Comics: May, 2011 ($5.99, one-shot)

1-Reprints back-up feature from Action Comics #893-896 plus new material; Conner-c   6.00

JIMMY OLSEN: ADVENTURES BY JACK KIRBY
DC Comics: 2003, 2004 ($19.95, TPB)

nn-(2003) Reprints Jack Kirby's early issues of Superman's Pal Jimmy Olsen #133-139,141; Mark Evanier intro.; cover by Kirby and Steve Rude   20.00
Vol. 2 (2004) Reprints #142-148; Evanier intro.; cover gallery and sketch pages   20.00

JIMMY'S BASTARDS
AfterShock Comics: Jun, 2017 - No. 9, Jul, 2018 ($3.99)

1-9: 1-Garth Ennis/Russ Braun-a/Dave Johnson-c; intro. Secret Agent Jimmy Regent   4.00

JIMMY WAKELY (Cowboy movie star)
National Per. Publ.: Sept-Oct, 1949 - No. 18, July-Aug, 1952 (1-13: 52pgs.)

1-Photo-c, 52 pgs. begin; Alex Toth-a; Kit Colby Girl Sheriff begins	47	94	141	296	498	700
2-Toth-a	18	36	54	107	169	230
3,4,6,7-Frazetta-a in all, 3 pgs. each; Toth-a in all. 4-Last photo-c. 4-Kurtzman "Pot-Shot Pete", 1 pg; Toth-a	21	42	63	122	199	275
5,8-15-Toth-a; 12,14-Kubert-a (3 & 2 pgs.)	16	32	48	94	147	200
16-18	15	30	45	83	124	165

NOTE: *Gil Kane c-10-18p.*

JIM RAY'S AVIATION SKETCH BOOK
Vital Publishers: Mar-Apr, 1946 - No. 2, May-June, 1946 (15¢)

1-Picture stories of planes and pilots; atomic explosion panel	40	80	120	246	411	575
2-Story of General "Nap" Arnold	27	54	81	160	263	365

JIM SOLAR (See Wisco/Klarer in the Promotional Comics section)

JINGLE BELLE (Paul Dini's...)
Oni Press/Top Cow: Nov, 1999 - No. 2, Dec, 1999 ($2.95, B&W, limited series)

1,2-Paul Dini-s. 2-Alex Ross flip-c   4.00
Jingle Belle: Dash Away All (12/03, $11.95, digest-size) Dini-s/Garibaldi-a   12.00
Jingle Belle: Gift-Wrapped (Top Cow, 12/11, $3.99) Dini-s/Gladden-a   4.00
Jingle Belle: Santa Claus vs. Frankenstein (Top Cow, 12/08, $2.99) Dini-s/Gladden-a   3.00
Jingle Belle's Cool Yule (11/02, $13.95,TPB) r/All-Star Holiday Hullaballo, The Mighty Elves, and Jubilee; internet strips and a color section w/DeStefano-a   14.00
Jingle Belle: The Homemade's Tale (IDW, 11/18, $4.99) Dini-s/Baldari-a/Buscema-c   5.00
Paul Dini's Jingle Belle Jubilee (11/01, $2.95) Dini-s; art by Rolston, DeCarlo, Morrison and Bone; pin-ups by Thompson and Aragonés   3.00
Paul Dini's Jingle Belle's All-Star Holiday Hullaballoo (11/00, $4.95) stories by various including Dini, Aragonés, Jeff Smith, Bill Morrison; Frank Cho-c   5.00
Paul Dini's Jingle Belle: The Fight Before Christmas (12/05, $2.99) Dini-s/Bone & others-a   3.00
Paul Dini's Jingle Belle: The Mighty Elves (7/01, $2.95) Dini-s/Bone-a   3.00
Paul Dini's Jingle Belle Winter Wingding (11/02, $2.95) Dini-s/Clugston-Major-c   3.00
The Bakers Meet Jingle Belle (12/06, $2.99) Dini-s/Kyle Baker-a   3.00
TPB (10/00, $8.95) r/#1&2, and app. from Oni Double Feature #13   9.00

JINGLE BELLE (Paul Dini's...)
Dark Horse Comics: Nov, 2004 - No. 4, Apr, 2005 ($2.99, limited series)

1-4-Paul Dini-s/Jose Garibaldi-a   3.00
TPB (9/05, $12.95) r/#1-4   13.00

JINGLE BELLS (See March of Comics No. 65)

JINGLE DINGLE CHRISTMAS STOCKING COMICS (See Foodini #2)
Stanhall Publications: V2#1, 1951 (no date listed) (25¢, 100 pgs., giant-size) (Publ. annually)

V2#1-Foodini & Pinhead, Silly Pilly plus games & puzzles	30	60	90	177	289	400

Jimmy Wakely #7 © DC

Jirni V3 #1 © AspenMLT

JLA #24 © DC

	GD 2.0	VG 4.0	FN 6.0	VF 8.0	VF/NM 9.0	NM- 9.2

	GD 2.0	VG 4.0	FN 6.0	VF 8.0	VF/NM 9.0	NM- 9.2

JINGLE JANGLE COMICS (Also see Puzzle Fun Comics)
Eastern Color Printing Co.: Feb, 1942 - No. 42, Dec, 1949

1-Pie-Face Prince of Old Pretzleburg, Jingle Jangle Tales by George Carlson, Hortense, & Benny Bear begin	58	116	174	371	636	900
2-4: 2,3-No Pie-Face Prince. 4-Pie-Face Prince-c	27	54	81	158	259	360
5 (10/42)	22	44	66	132	216	300
6-10: 8-No Pie-Face Prince	18	36	54	103	162	220
11-15	14	28	42	82	121	160
16-30: 17,18-No Pie-Face Prince. 24,30-XMas-c	12	24	36	67	94	120
31-42: 36,42-Xmas-c	10	20	30	58	79	100

NOTE: *George Carlson* a-(2) in all except No. 2, 3, 8; c-1-6. *Carlson* 1 pg. puzzles in 9, 10, 12-15, 18, 20. *Carlson* illustrated a series of Uncle Wiggily books in 1930's.

JING PALS
Victory Publishing Corp.: Feb, 1946 - No. 4, Aug?, 1946 (Funny animal)

1-Wishing Willie, Puggy Panda & Johnny Rabbit begin	21	42	63	124	202	280
2-4	14	28	42	80	115	150

JINKS, PIXIE, AND DIXIE (See Kite Fun Book & Whitman Comic Books)

JINNY HEX SPECIAL (From Young Justice 2019 series)
DC Comics: Feb, 2021 ($4.99, one-shot)

1-Visaggio-s/Melnikov-a/Derington-c; Jonah Hex and Superman cameos		5.00

JINX
Caliber Press: 1996 - No. 7, 1996 ($2.95, B&W, 32 pgs.)

1-7: Brian Michael Bendis-c/a/scripts. 2-Photo-c		4.00

JINX (Volume 2)
Image Comics: 1997 - No. 5, 1998 ($2.95, B&W, bi-monthly)

1-4: Brian Michael Bendis-c/a/scripts.		4.00
5-($3.95) Brereton-c		5.00
...Buried Treasures ('98, $3.95) short stories, ...Confessions ('98, $3.95) short stories, ...Pop Culture Hoo-Hah ('98, $3.95) humor shorts		5.00
TPB (1997, $10.95) r/Vol 1,2		11.00
...: The Definitive Collection ('01, $24.95) remastered #1-5, sketch pages, art gallery, script excerpts, Mack intro.		25.00

JINX: TORSO
Image Comics: 1998 - No. 6, 1999 ($3.95/$4.95, B&W)

1-6-Based on Eliot Ness' pursuit of America's first serial killer; Brian Michael Bendis & Marc Andreyko-a/Bendis-s. 3-6-($4.95)		5.00
Softcover (2000, $24.95) r/#1-6; intro. by Greg Rucka; photo essay of the actual murders and police documents		25.00
Hardcover (2000, $49.95) signed & numbered		50.00

JINXWORLD SAMPLER
DC Comics: 2018 ($1.00)

nn-Reprints Scarlet #1, United States of Murder, Inc. #1 & Powers #1; Bendis-s		3.00

JIRNI
Aspen MLT: Apr, 2013 - No. 5, Oct, 2013 ($1.00/$3.99)

1-($1.00) J.T. Krul-s/Paolo Pantalena-a; multiple covers		3.00
2-5-($3.99) Multiple covers on each		4.00
Vol. 2 #1 (6/14, $3.99) Krul-s/Pantalena-a		4.00
Vol. 2 #1-5 (8/15 - No. 5, 12/15, $3.99) Krul-s/Marion-a; multiple covers on each		4.00
Vol. 3 #1-5 (3/18 - No. 5, 7/18, $3.99) Krul-s/Maria-a; multiple covers on each		4.00
... Primer (3/18, 25¢) Origin re-told with re-cap of Vol. 1 & 2; sketch art		4.00

JLA (See Justice League of America and Justice Leagues)
DC Comics: Jan, 1997 - No. 125, Apr, 2006 ($1.95/$1.99/$2.25/$2.50)

1-Morrison-s/Porter & Dell-a. The Hyperclan app.	2	4	6	9	12	15
2	1	3	4	6	8	10
3,4	1	2	3	5	7	9
5-Membership drive; Tomorrow Woman app.						6.00
6-9: 6-1st app. Zauriel. 8-Green Arrow joins.						6.00
10-21: 10-Rock of Ages begins. 11-Joker and Luthor-c/app. 12-Intro. Hourman from the 853rd century. 14-Darkseid app. 15-($2.95) Rock of Ages concludes; intro. Superman One Million. 16-New members join; Prometheus app. 17,20-Jorgensen-a. 18-21-Waid-s. 20,21-Adam Strange c/app.						5.00
22-40: 22-Begin $1.99-c; Sandman (Daniel) app. 23-1st app. Justice Legion A. 27-Amazo app. 28-31-JSA app. 35-Hal Jordan/Spectre app. 36-40-World War 3						4.00
41-($2.99) Conclusion of World War 3; last Morrison-s						5.00
42-49,51-74: 43-Waid-s; Ra's al Ghul app. 44-Begin $2.25-c. 46-Batman leaves. 47-Hitch & Neary-a begins; JLA battles Queen of Fables. 52-55-Hitch-a. 59-Joker: Last Laugh. 61-68-Kelly-s/Mahnke-a. 69-73-Hunt for Aquaman; bi-monthly with alternating art by Mahnke and Guichet						4.00

50-($3.75) JLA vs. Dr. Destiny; art by Hitch & various		5.00
75-(1/03, $3.95) leads into Aquaman (4th series) #1		5.00
76-99: 76-Firestorm app. 77-Banks-a. 79-Kanjar Ro app. 91-93-O'Neil-s/Huat-a. 94-99-Byrne & Ordway-a/Claremont-s; Doom Patrol app.		4.00
100-(1997, $3.50) Intro. Vera Black; leads into Justice League Elite #1		5.00
101-125: 101-106-Austen-s/Garney-a/c. 107-114-Crime Syndicate app.; Busiek-s. 115-Begin $2.50-c; Johns & Heinberg-s; Secret Society of Super-Villains app.		4.00
#1,000,000 (11/98) 853rd Century x-over		4.00
Annual 1 (1997, $3.95) Pulp Heroes; Augustyn-s/Olivetti & Ha-a		5.00
Annual 2 (1998, $2.95) Ghosts; Wrightson-c		5.00
Annual 3 (1999, $2.95) JLApe; Art Adams-c		5.00
Annual 4 (2000, $3.50) Planet DC x-over; Steve Scott-c/a		5.00
... American Dreams (1998, $7.95, TPB) r/#5-9		8.00
...: Crisis of Conscience TPB (2006, $12.99) r/#115-119		13.00
.../ Cyberforce (DC/Top Cow, 2005, $5.99) Kelly-s/Mahnke-a/Silvestri-c		6.00
Divided We Fall (2001, $17.95, TPB) r/#47-54		18.00
...80-Page Giant 1 (7/98, $4.95) stories & art by various		6.00
...80-Page Giant 2 (11/99, $4.95) Green Arrow & Hawkman app. Hitch-c		6.00
...80-Page Giant 3 (10/00, $5.95) Pariah & Harbinger; intro. Moon Maiden		6.00
...Foreign Bodies (1999, $5.95, one-shot) Kobra app.; Semeiks-a		6.00
...Gallery (1997, $2.95) pin-ups by various; Quitely-c		4.00
...God & Monsters (2001, $6.95, one-shot) Benefiel-a/c		7.00
Golden Perfect (2003, $12.95, TPB) r/#61-65		13.00
.../ Haven: Anathema (2002, $6.95) Concludes the Haven: The Broken City series		7.00
.../ Haven: Arrival (2001, $6.95) Leads into the Haven: The Broken City series		7.00
...In Crisis Secret Files 1 (11/98, $4.95) recap of JLA in DC x-overs		5.00
...: Island of Dr. Moreau, The (2002, $6.95, one-shot) Elseworlds; Pugh-c/a; Thomas-s		7.00
.../ JSA Secret Files & Origins (1/03, $4.95) prelude to JLA/JSA: Virtue & Vice; short stories and pin-ups by various; Pacheco-c		5.00
.../ JSA: Virtue and Vice HC (2002, $24.95) Teams battle Despero & Johnny Sorrow; Goyer & Johns-s/Pacheco-a/c		25.00
.../ JSA: Virtue and Vice SC (2003, $17.95)		18.00
Justice For All (1999, $14.95, TPB) r/#24-33		15.00
New World Order (1997, $5.95, TPB) r/#1-4		6.00
...: Obsidian Age Book One, The (2003, $12.95) r/#66-71		13.00
...: Obsidian Age Book Two, The (2003, $12.95) r/#72-76		13.00
One Million (2004, $19.95, TPB) r/#DC One Million #1-4 and other #1,000,000 x-overs		20.00
...: Our Worlds at War (9/01, $2.95) Jae Lee-c; Aquaman presumed dead		4.00
...: Pain of the Gods (2005, $12.99) r/#101-106		13.00
...Primeval (1999, $5.95, one-shot) Abnett & Lanning-s/Olivetti-a		6.00
...: Riddle of the Beast HC (2001, $24.95) Grant-s/painted-a by various; Sweet-c		25.00
...: Riddle of the Beast SC (2003, $14.95) Grant-s/painted-a by various; Kaluta-c		15.00
Rock of Ages (1998, $9.95, TPB) r/#10-15		10.00
Rules of Engagement (2004, $12.95, TPB) r/#77-82		13.00
...: Seven Caskets (2004, $5.95, one-shot) Brereton-s/painted-c/a		6.00
...: Shogun of Steel (2002, $6.95, one-shot) Elseworlds; Justiniano-c/a		7.00
...Showcase 80-Page Giant (2/00, $4.95) Hitch-c		5.00
Strength in Numbers (1998, $12.95, TPB) r/#16-23, Secret Files #2 and Prometheus #1		13.00
...Superpower (1999, $5.95, one-shot) Arcudi-s/Eaton-a; Mark Antaeus joins		6.00
Syndicate Rules (2005, $17.99, TPB) r/#107-114, Secret Files #4		18.00
Terror Incognita (2002, $12.95, TPB) r/#55-60		13.00
...: The Deluxe Edition Vol. 1 HC (2008, $29.99, dustjacket) oversized r/#1-9 and JLA Secret Files #1		30.00
...: The Deluxe Edition Vol. 2 HC (2009, $29.99, dustjacket) oversized r/#10-17, JLA/Wildcats, and Prometheus #1		30.00
...: The Deluxe Edition Vol. 3 HC (2010, $29.99, dustjacket) oversized r/#22-26, 28-31 & #1,000,000		30.00
...: The Deluxe Edition Vol. 4 HC (2010, $34.99, dustjacket) oversized r/#34, 36-41, JLA Classified #1-3 and JLA: Earth 2 GN		35.00
The Tenth Circle (2004, $12.95, TPB) r/#94-99		13.00
...: The Greatest Stories Ever Told TPB (2006, $19.99) r/Justice League of America #19,71, 122,166-168,200, Justice League #1, JLA Secret Files #3, 80-Page Giant #1		20.00
Tower of Babel (2001, $12.95, TPB) r/#42-46, Secret Files #3, 80-Page Giant #1		15.00
Trial By Fire (2004, $12.95, TPB) r/#84-89		13.00
...Vs. Predator (DC/Dark Horse, 2000, $5.95, one-shot) Nolan-c/a		10.00
...: Welcome to the Working Week (2003, $6.95, one-shot) Patton Oswalt-s		7.00
...: World War III (2000, $12.95, TPB) r/#34-41		13.00
...: World Without a Justice League (2006, $12.99, TPB) r/#120-125		13.00
...Zatanna's Search (2003, $12.95, TPB) rep. Zatanna's early app. & origin; Bolland-c		50.00

JLA: ACT OF GOD
DC Comics: 2000 - No. 3, 2001 ($4.95, limited series)

1-3-Elseworlds; metahumans lose their powers; Moench-s/Dave Ross-a		5.00

JLA: AGE OF WONDER
DC Comics: 2003 - No. 2, 2003 ($5.95, limited series)

	GD 2.0	VG 4.0	FN 6.0	VF 8.0	VF/NM 9.0	NM- 9.2

1,2-Elseworlds; Superman and the League of Science during the Industrial Revolution   6.00

JLA: A LEAGUE OF ONE
DC Comics: 2000 (Graphic novel)
Hardcover ($24.95) Christopher Moeller-s/painted-a   25.00
Softcover (2002, $14.95)   15.00

JLA/AVENGERS (See Avengers/JLA for #2 & #4)
Marvel Comics: Sept, 2003; No. 3, Dec, 2003 ($5.95, limited series)

	GD	VG	FN	VF	VF/NM	NM-
1-Busiek-s/Pérez-a; wraparound-c; Krona, Starro, Grandmaster, Terminus app.	3	6	9	14	20	25
3-Busiek-s/Pérez-a; wraparound-c; Phantom Stranger app.	3	6	9	16	23	30
SC (2008, $19.99) r/4-issue series; cover gallery; intros by Stan Lee & Julius Schwartz	9	16	24	54	102	150

JLA: BLACK BAPTISM
DC Comics: May, 2001 - No. 4, Aug, 2001 ($2.50, limited series)
1-4-Saiz-a(p)/Bradstreet-c; Zatanna app.   4.00

JLA: CLASSIFIED
DC Comics: Jan, 2005 - No. 54, May, 2008 ($2.95/$2.99)
1-3-Morrison-s/McGuinness-a/c; Ultramarines app.   3.00
4-9-"I Can't Believe It's Not The Justice League," Giffen & DeMatteis-s/Maguire-a   3.00
10-31,33-54: 10-15-New Maps of Hell; Ellis-s/Guice-a. 16-21-Garcia-Lopez-a. 22-25-Detroit League & Royal Flush Gang app.; Englehart-s. 26-28-Chaykin-a. 37-41-Kid Amazo. 50-54-Byrne-a/Middleston-c   3.00
32-($3.99) Dr. Destiny app.; Jurgens-a   4.00
I Can't Believe It's Not The Justice League TPB (2005, $12.99) r/#4-9   13.00
.... Kid Amazo TPB (2007, $12.99) r/#37-41   13.00
.... New Maps of Hell TPB (2006, $12.99) r/#10-15   13.00
.... That Was Now, This Is Then TPB (2008, $14.99) r/#50-54   15.00
.... The Hypothetical Woman TPB (2008, $12.99) r/#16-21   13.00
.... Ultramarine Corps TPB (2007, $14.99) r/#1-3, JLA/WildC.A.T.s #1 and JLA Secret Files 2004 #1   15.00

JLA CLASSIFIED: COLD STEEL
DC Comics: 2005 - No. 2, 2006 ($5.99, limited series, prestige format)
1,2-Chris Moeller-s/a; giant robot Justice League   6.00

JLA: CREATED EQUAL
DC Comics: 2000 - No. 2, 2000 ($5.95, limited series, prestige format)
1,2-Nicieza-s/Maguire-a; Elseworlds-Superman as the last man on Earth   6.00

JLA: DESTINY
DC Comics: 2002 - No. 4, 2002 ($5.95, prestige format, limited series)
1-4-Elseworlds; Arcudi-s/Mandrake-a   6.00

JLA / DOOM PATROL SPECIAL (Milk Wars DC/Young Animal crossover)
DC Comics: Mar, 2018 ($4.99, one-shot)
1-Part 1 of crossover; Orlando & Way-s/Aco-a/Quitely-c; Lord Manga Khan app.   5.00

JLA: EARTH 2
DC Comics: 2000 (Graphic novel)
Hardcover ($24.95) Morrison-s/Quitely-a; Crime Syndicate app.   25.00
Softcover ($14.95)   15.00

JLA: GATEKEEPER
DC Comics: 2001 - No. 3, 2001 ($4.95, prestige format, limited series)
1-3-Truman-s/a   5.00

JLA: HEAVEN'S LADDER
DC Comics: 2000 ($9.95, Treasury-size one-shot)
nn-Bryan Hitch & Paul Neary-c/a; Mark Waid-s   10.00

JLA/HITMAN (Justice League/Hitman in indicia)
DC Comics: Nov, 2007 - No. 2, Dec, 2007 ($3.99, limited series)
1,2-Ennis-s/McCrea-a; Bloodlines creatures return   4.00

JLA: INCARNATIONS
DC Comics: Jul, 2001 - No. 7, Feb, 2002 ($3.50, limited series)
1-7-Ostrander-s/Semeiks-a; different eras of the Justice League   4.00

JLA: LIBERTY AND JUSTICE
DC Comics: Nov, 2003 ($9.95, Treasury-size one-shot)
nn-Alex Ross-c/a; Paul Dini-s; story of the classic Justice League   10.00

JLA PARADISE LOST
DC Comics: Jan, 1998 - No. 3, Mar, 1998 ($1.95, limited series)
1-3-Millar-s/Olivetti-a   4.00

JLA: SCARY MONSTERS
DC Comics: May, 2003 - No. 6, Oct, 2003 ($2.50, limited series)
1-6-Claremont-s/Art Adams-c   4.00

JLA SECRET FILES
DC Comics: Sept, 1997 - 2004 ($4.95)
1-Standard Ed. w/origin-s & pin-ups   5.00
1-Collector's Ed. w/origin-s & pin-ups; cardstock-c   6.00
2,3: 2-(8/98) origin-s of JLA #16's newer members. 3-(12/00)   5.00
... 2004 (11/04) Justice League Elite app.; Mahnke & Byrne-a; Crime Syndicate app.   5.00

JLA: SECRET ORIGINS
DC Comics: Nov, 2002 ($7.95, Treasury-size one-shot)
nn-Alex Ross 2-page origins of Justice League members; text by Paul Dini   8.00

JLA: SECRET SOCIETY OF SUPER-HEROES
DC Comics: 2000 - No. 2, 2000 ($5.95, limited series, prestige format)
1,2-Elseworlds JLA; Chaykin and Tischman-s/McKone-a   6.00

JLA /SPECTRE: SOUL WAR
DC Comics: 2003 - No. 2, 2003 ($5.95, prestige format, limited series)
1,2-DeMatteis-s/Banks & Neary-a   6.00

JLA: THE NAIL (Elseworlds) (Also see Justice League of America: Another Nail)
DC Comics: Aug, 1998 - No. 3, Oct, 1998 ($4.95, prestige format)
1-3-JLA in a world without Superman; Alan Davis-s/a(p)   5.00
TPB ('98, $12.95) r/series w/new Davis-c   13.00

JLA / TITANS
DC Comics: Dec, 1998 - No. 3, Feb, 1999 ($2.95, limited series)
1-3-Grayson-s; P. Jimenez-c/a   4.00
....:The Technis Imperative ('99, $12.95, TPB) r/#1-3; Titans Secret Files   13.00

JLA: TOMORROW WOMAN (Girlfrenzy)
DC Comics: June, 1998 ($1.95, one-shot)
1-Peyer-s; story takes place during JLA #5   4.00

JLA / WILDC.A.T.S
DC Comics: 1997 ($5.95, one-shot, prestige format)
1-Morrison-s/Semeiks & Conrad-a   6.00

JLA /WITCHBLADE
DC Comics/Top Cow: 2000 ($5.95, prestige format, one-shot)
1-Pararillo-c/a   6.00

JLA / WORLD WITHOUT GROWN-UPS (See Young Justice)
DC Comics: Aug, 1998 - No. 2, Sept, 1998 ($4.95, prestige format)
1,2-JLA, Robin, Impulse & Superboy app.; Ramos & McKone-a   6.00
TPB ('98, $9.95) r/series & Young Justice: The Secret #1   10.00

JLA: YEAR ONE
DC Comics: Jan, 1998 - No. 12, Dec, 1998 ($2.95/$1.95, limited series)
1-($2.95)-Waid & Augustyn-s/Kitson-a   5.00
1-Platinum Edition   12.00
2-12-($1.95): 5-Doom Patrol-c/app. 7-Superman app.   4.00
TPB ('99,'09, $19.95/$19.99) r/#1-12; Busiek intro.   20.00

JLA-Z
DC Comics: Nov, 2003 - No. 3, Jan, 2004 ($2.50, limited series)
1-3-Pin-ups and info on current and former JLA members and villains; art by various   4.00

JLX
DC Comics (Amalgam): Apr, 1996 ($1.95, one-shot)
1-Mark Waid scripts   5.00

JLX UNLEASHED
DC Comics (Amalgam): June, 1997 ($1.95, one-shot)
1-Priest-s/Oscar Jimenez & Rodriguez-a   4.00

JOAN OF ARC (Also see A-1 Comics, Classics Illustrated #78, and Ideal a Classical Comic)
Magazine Enterprises: No. 21, 1949 (one shot)

	GD	VG	FN	VF	VF/NM	NM-
A-1 21-Movie adaptation; Ingrid Bergman photo-covers & interior photos; Whitney-a	32	64	96	188	307	425

JOE COLLEGE
Hillman Periodicals: Fall, 1949 - No. 2, Wint, 1950 (Teen-age humor, 52 pgs.)

	GD	VG	FN	VF	VF/NM	NM-
1-Powell-a; Briefer-a	18	36	54	105	165	225
2-Powell-a	13	26	39	72	101	130

JOE FIXIT (See Incredible Hulk #347)
Marvel Comics: Mar, 2023 - No. 5, Jul, 2023 ($3.99)
1-5-Set during Banner's Vegas era; Peter David-s/Yildiray Cinar-a. 2-5-Spider-Man app.   4.00

JOE FRANKENSTEIN
IDW Publishing: Feb, 2015 - No. 4, May, 2015 ($3.99)
1-4-Chuck Dixon & Graham Nolan-s/Graham Nolan-a   4.00

JOE GOLEM
Dark Horse Comics: Nov, 2015 - No. 5, Mar, 2016 ($3.50)
1-5-Mignola & Golden-s/Reynolds-a   4.00

JOE GOLEM: THE CONJURORS
Dark Horse Comics: May, 2019 - No. 5, Oct, 2019 ($3.99)
1-5-Mignola & Golden-s/Bergting-a   4.00

JOE GOLEM: THE DROWNING CITY
Dark Horse Comics: Sept, 2018 - No. 5, Jan, 2019 ($3.99)
1-5-Mignola & Golden-s/Bergting-a   4.00

JOE GOLEM: THE OUTER DARK
Dark Horse Comics: May, 2017 - No. 5, Jan, 2018 ($3.99)
1-5-Mignola & Golden-s/Reynolds-a. 4,5-Titled Joe Golem: Flesh and Blood #1,2   4.00

JOE JINKS
United Features Syndicate: No. 12, 1939

	GD	VG	FN	VF	VF/NM	NM-
Single Series 12	37	74	111	222	361	500

JOE KUBERT PRESENTS
DC Comics: Dec, 2012 - No. 6, May, 2013 ($4.99, limited series)
1-6: Anthology of short stories by Kubert, Buniak & Glanzman. 1-Hawkman app.   5.00

JOE LOUIS (See Fight Comics #2, Picture News #6 & True Comics #5)
Fawcett Publications: Sept, 1950 - No. 2, Nov, 1950 (Photo-c) (Boxing champ) (See Dick Cole #10)

	GD	VG	FN	VF	VF/NM	NM-
1-Photo-c; life story	66	132	198	419	722	1025
2-Photo-c	47	94	141	296	498	700

JOE PALOOKA (1st Series)(Also see Big Shot Comics, Columbia Comics & Feature Funnies)
Columbia Comic Corp. (Publication Enterprises): 1942 - No. 4, 1944

	GD	VG	FN	VF	VF/NM	NM-
1-1st to portray American president; gov't permission required	142	284	426	909	1555	2200
2 (1943)-Hitler-c	135	270	405	864	1482	2100
3-Nazi Sub-c	57	114	171	362	619	875
4	45	90	135	284	480	675

JOE PALOOKA (2nd Series) (Battle Adv. #68-74; ...Advs. #75, 77-81, 83-85, 87; Champ of the Comics #76, 82, 86, 89-93) (See All-New)

JLA: Classified #4 © DC

Joe Golem #1 © Mignola & Golden

John Carter of Mars #1 © DYN

	GD	VG	FN	VF	VF/NM	NM-
	2.0	4.0	6.0	8.0	9.0	9.2

Harvey Publications: Nov, 1945 - No. 118, Mar, 1961

1-By Ham Fisher	68	136	204	435	743	1050
2	34	68	102	204	332	460
3,4,6,7-1st Flyin' Fool, ends #25	20	40	60	117	189	260
5-Boy Explorers by S&K (7-8/46)	23	46	69	136	223	310
8-10	15	30	45	84	127	170

11-14,16,18-20: 14-Black Cat text-s(2). 18-Powell-a. 19-Freedom Train-c

	13	26	39	74	105	135
15-Origin & 1st app. Humphrey (12/47); Super-heroine Atoma app. by Powell	16	32	48	94	147	200
17-Humphrey vs. Palooka-c/s; 1st app. Little Max	15	30	45	90	140	190
21-26,29,30: 22-Powell-a. 30-Nude female painting	10	20	30	58	79	100
27-Little Max app.; Howie Morenz-s	10	20	30	56	76	95
28-Babe Ruth 4 pg. sty.	10	20	30	58	79	100

31,39,51: 31-Dizzy Dean 4 pg. sty. 39-(12/49) Humphrey & Little Max begin; Sonny Baugh football-s; Sherlock Max-s. 51-Babe Ruth 2 pg. sty; Jake Lamotta 1/2 pg. sty.

	9	18	27	50	65	80

32-38,40-50,52-61: 35-Little Max-c/story(4 pgs.); Joe Louis 1 pg. sty. 36-Humphrey story.

41-Bing Crosby photo on-c. 44-Palooka marries Ann Howe. 50-(11/51)-Becomes Harvey Comics Hits #51

	8	16	24	44	57	70
62-S&K Boy Explorers-r	9	18	27	50	65	80
63-65,73-80,100: 79-Story of 1st meeting with Ann	8	16	24	40	50	60
66,67-'Commie' torture story "Drug-Diet Horror"	14	28	42	81	118	155
68,70-72: 68,70-Joe vs. "Gooks". 71-Bloody bayonets-c. 72-Tank-c	14	28	42	78	112	145
69-1st "Battle Adventures" issue; torture & bondage	15	30	45	84	127	170
81-99,101-115: 104,107-Humphrey & Little Max-s	7	14	21	37	46	55
116-S&K Boy Explorers-r (Giant, '60)	9	18	27	47	61	75
117-(84 pg. Giant) r/Commie issues #66,67; Powell-a	9	18	27	52	69	85
118-(84 pg. Giant) Jack Dempsey 2 pg. sty. Powell-a	9	18	27	47	61	75

...Visits the Lost City nn (1945)(One Shot)(50¢)-164 page continuous story strip reprint.
Has biography & photo of Ham Fisher; possibly the single longest comic book story published in that era (159 pgs.?) (scarce)

	242	484	726	1537	2644	3750

NOTE: *Nostrand/Powell* a-73. *Powell* a-7, 8, 10, 12, 14, 17, 19, 26-45, 47-53, 70, 73 at least. Black Cat text stories #8, 12, 13, 19.

JOE PALOOKA
IDW Publishing: Dec, 2012 - No. 6, May, 2013 ($3.99, limited series)

1-6: 1-Bullock-s/Peniche-a; Joe Palooka updated as a MMA fighter						4.00

JOE PSYCHO & MOO FROG
Goblin Studios: 1996 - No. 5, 1997 ($2.50, B&W)

1-5: 4-Two covers						4.00
...Full Color Extravagarbonzo ($2.95, color)						4.00

JOE THE BARBARIAN
DC Comics (Vertigo): Mar, 2010 - No. 8, May, 2011 ($1.00/$2.99/$3.99)

1-($1.00) Grant Morrison-s/Sean Murphy-a						3.00
2-7-($2.99)						3.00
8-($3.99)						4.00

JOE YANK (Korean War)
Standard Comics (Visual Editions): No. 5, Mar, 1952 - No. 16, 1954

5-Toth, Celardo, Tuska-a	15	30	45	88	137	185
6-Toth, Severin/Elder-a	14	28	42	81	118	155
7-Pinhead Perkins by Dan DeCarlo (in all?)	12	24	36	67	94	120
8-Toth-c	14	28	42	76	108	140
9-16: 9-Andru-c. 12-Andru-a	12	24	36	67	94	120

JOHN BOLTON'S HALLS OF HORROR
Eclipse Comics: June, 1985 - No. 2, June, 1985 ($1.75, limited series)

1,2-British-r; Bolton-c/a						5.00

JOHN BOLTON'S STRANGE WINK
Dark Horse Comics: Mar, 1998 - No. 3, May, 1998 ($2.95, B&W, limited series)

1-3-Anthology; Bolton-s/c/a						5.00

JOHN BYRNE'S NEXT MEN (See Dark Horse Presents #54)
Dark Horse Comics (Legend imprint #19 on): Jan, 1992 - No. 30, Dec, 1994 ($2.50, mature)

1-Silver foil embossed-c; Byrne-c/a/scripts in all	1	3	4	6	8	10
1-4: 1st print with gold ink logo						3.00
0-(2/92)-r/chapters 1-4 from DHP w/new Byrne-c						4.00
5-20,22-30: 7-10-MA #1-4 mini-series on flip side. 16-Origin of Mark IV. 17-Miller-c. 19-22-Faith storyline. 23-26-Power storyline. 27-30-Lies storyline Pt. 1-4						4.00
21-(12/93) 2nd Hellboy; cover and Hellboy pages by Mike Mignola; Byrne other pages (see San Diego Comic Con Comics #2 for 1st app.)	8	16	24	54	102	150
...Parallel, Book 2 ($16.95)-TPB; r/#7-12						17.00

...Fame, Book 3($16.95)-TPB r/#13-18 17.00
...Faith, Book 4($14.95)-TPB r/#19-22 15.00
NOTE: Issues 1 through 6 contain certificates redeemable for an exclusive Next Men trading card set by Byrne. Prices are for complete books. *Cody* painted c-23-26. *Mignola* a-21(part); c-21.

JOHN BYRNE'S NEXT MEN (Continues in Next Men: Aftermath #40)
IDW Publishing: Dec, 2010 - No. 9, Aug, 2011 ($3.99)

1-9-John Byrne-s/a/c in all. 1-Origin retold. 6,7-Abraham Lincoln app.						4.00

JOHN BYRNE'S 2112
Dark Horse Comics (Legend): Oct, 1991 ($9.95, TPB)

1-Byrne-c/a/s						10.00

JOHN CARTER OF MARS (See The Funnies & Tarzan #207)
Dell Publishing Co.: No. 375, Mar-May, 1952 - No. 488, Aug-Oct, 1953
(Edgar Rice Burroughs)

Four Color 375 (#1)-Origin; Jesse Marsh-a	37	74	111	274	612	950
Four Color 437, 488-Painted-c	19	38	57	131	291	460

JOHN CARTER OF MARS
Gold Key: Apr, 1964 - No. 3, Oct, 1964

1(10104-404)-r/4-Color #375; Jesse Marsh-a	9	18	27	59	117	175
2(407), 3(410)-r/4-Color #437 & 488; Marsh-a	6	12	18	37	66	95

JOHN CARTER OF MARS
House of Greystroke: 1970 (10-1/2x16-1/2", 72 pgs., B&W, paper-c)

1941-42 Sunday strip-r; John Coleman Burroughs-a	4	8	12	23	37	50

JOHN CARTER OF MARS
Dynamite Entertainment: 2022 - No. 5, 2022 ($3.99)

1-5-Chuck Brown-s/George Kambadais-a; multiple covers						4.00

JOHN CARTER OF MARS: A PRINCESS OF MARS
Marvel Comics: Nov, 2011 - No. 3, Mar, 2012 ($2.99, limited series)

1-5: 1-Langridge-s/Andrade-a; covers by Young and Andrade. 2-4-Young-c						3.00

JOHN CARTER: THE END
Dynamite Entertainment: 2017 - No. 5, 2017 ($3.99)

1-5-Brian Wood-s/Alex Cox-a; multiple covers						4.00

JOHN CARTER: THE GODS OF MARS
Marvel Comics: May, 2012 - No. 5, Sept, 2012 ($3.99, limited series)

1-5-Sam Humphries-s/Ramón Pérez-a; Carter's 2nd trip to Mars						4.00

JOHN CARTER: THE WORLD OF MARS
Marvel Comics: Dec, 2011 - No. 4, Mar, 2012 ($3.99, limited series)

1-4-Movie prequel; Peter David-s/Luke Ross-a. 1-Ribic-c. 4-Olivetti-c						4.00

JOHN CARTER, WARLORD OF MARS (Also see Tarzan #207-209 and Weird Worlds)
Marvel Comics: June, 1977 - No. 28, Oct, 1979

1,18: 1-Origin. 18-Frank Miller-a(p)(1st publ. Marvel work)	4	8	12	23	37	50
1-(35¢-c variant, limited dist.)	11	22	33	76	163	250
2-5-(35¢-c variants, limited dist.)	7	14	21	48	89	130
2-17,19-28: 11-Origin Dejah Thoris	2	4	6	9	12	15
Annuals 1-3: 1(1977). 2(1978). 3(1979)-All 52 pgs. with new book-length stories	1	3	4	6	8	10

Edgar Rice Burroughs' John Carter of Mars: Weird Worlds TPB (Dark Horse Books, Jan. 2011, ($14.99) r/stories from Tarzan #207-209 and Weird Worlds #1-7; Marv Wolfman intro. 15.00
NOTE: *Austin* c-24i. *Gil Kane* a-1-10p; c-1p, 2p, 3, 4-9p, 10, 15p, Annual 1p. *Layton* a-17i. *Miller* c-25, 26p. *Nebres* a-24-i, 8-16i; c(i)-6-9, 11-22, Annual 1. *Perez* c-24p. *Simonson* a-15p. *Sutton* a-7i.

JOHN CARTER, WARLORD OF MARS
Dynamite Entertainment: 2014 - No. 14, 2015 ($3.99)

1-14: 1-5-Marz-s/Malsuni-s; multiple covers in all						4.00
... 2015 Special ($4.99) Napton-s/Rodolfo-a/Parillo-c						5.00

JOHN CONSTANTINE: HELLBLAZER
DC Comics (Black Label): Jan, 2020 - No. 12, Jan, 2021 ($3.99)

1-12: Simon Spurrier-s. 1-3,6-8-Aaron Campbell-a. 4,5,9-Matias Bergara-a						4.00

JOHN CONSTANTINE, HELLBLAZER: DEAD IN AMERICA
DC Comics (Black Label): Mar, 2024 - Present ($4.99)

1-3: Simon Spurrier-s/Aaron Campbell-a						5.00

JOHN CONSTANTINE - HELLBLAZER SPECIAL: PAPA MIDNITE
DC Comics (Vertigo): April, 2005 - No. 5, Aug, 2005 ($2.95/$2.99, limited series)

1-5-Origin of Papa Midnite; Akins-a/Johnson-s						5.00

JOHN F. KENNEDY, CHAMPION OF FREEDOM
Worden & Childs: 1964 (no month) (25¢)

	GD	VG	FN	VF	VF/NM	NM-
	2.0	4.0	6.0	8.0	9.0	9.2

	GD 2.0	VG 4.0	FN 6.0	VF 8.0	VF/NM 9.0	NM- 9.2
nn-Photo-c	9	18	27	61	123	185

JOHN F. KENNEDY LIFE STORY
Dell Publishing Co.: Aug-Oct, 1964; Nov, 1965; June, 1966 (12¢)

	GD 2.0	VG 4.0	FN 6.0	VF 8.0	VF/NM 9.0	NM- 9.2
12-378-410-Photo-c	9	18	27	61	123	185
12-378-511 (reprint, 11/65)	4	8	12	23	37	50
12-378-606 (reprint, 6/66)	3	6	9	20	31	42

JOHN FORCE (See Magic Agent)

JOHN HIX SCRAP BOOK, THE
Eastern Color Printing Co. (McNaught Synd.): Late 1930's (no date) (10¢, 68 pgs., regular size)

	GD 2.0	VG 4.0	FN 6.0	VF 8.0	VF/NM 9.0	NM- 9.2
1-Strange As It Seems (resembles Single Series books)	50	100	150	315	533	750
2-Strange As It Seems	36	72	108	211	343	475

JOHN JAKES' MULLKON EMPIRE
Tekno Comix: Sept, 1995 - No. 6, 1996 ($1.95)

	GD 2.0	VG 4.0	FN 6.0	VF 8.0	VF/NM 9.0	NM- 9.2
1-6						4.00

JOHN LAW DETECTIVE (See Smash Comics #3)
Eclipse Comics: April, 1983 ($1.50, Baxter paper)

	GD 2.0	VG 4.0	FN 6.0	VF 8.0	VF/NM 9.0	NM- 9.2
1-Three Eisner stories originally drawn in 1948 for the never published John Law #1; original cover pencilled in 1948 & inked in 1982 by Eisner						4.00

JOHN McCAIN (See Presidential Material: John McCain)

JOHNNY APPLESEED (See Story Hour Series)

JOHNNY CASH (See Hello, I'm...)

JOHNNY DANGER (See Movie Comics, 1946)
Toby Press: 1950 (Based on movie serial)

	GD 2.0	VG 4.0	FN 6.0	VF 8.0	VF/NM 9.0	NM- 9.2
1-Photo-c; Sparling-a	28	56	84	165	270	375

JOHNNY DANGER PRIVATE DETECTIVE
Toby Press: Aug, 1954 (Reprinted in Danger #11 by Super)

	GD 2.0	VG 4.0	FN 6.0	VF 8.0	VF/NM 9.0	NM- 9.2
1-Photo-c; Opium den story	24	48	72	142	234	325

JOHNNY DYNAMITE (Formerly Dynamite #1-9; Foreign Intrigues #14 on)
Charlton Comics: No. 10, June, 1955 - No. 12, Oct, 1955

	GD 2.0	VG 4.0	FN 6.0	VF 8.0	VF/NM 9.0	NM- 9.2
10-12	16	32	48	92	144	195

JOHNNY DYNAMITE
Dark Horse Comics: Sept, 1994 - Dec, 1994 ($2.95, B&W & red, limited series)

	GD 2.0	VG 4.0	FN 6.0	VF 8.0	VF/NM 9.0	NM- 9.2
1-4: Max Allan Collins scripts in all; Terry Beatty-a						4.00
...: Underworld GN (AiT/Planet Lar, 3/03, $12.95, B&W) r/#1-4 in B&W without red						13.00

JOHNNY HAZARD
Best Books (Standard Comics) (King Features): No. 5, Aug, 1948 - No. 8, May, 1949; No. 35, date?

	GD 2.0	VG 4.0	FN 6.0	VF 8.0	VF/NM 9.0	NM- 9.2
5-Strip reprints by Frank Robbins (c/a)	20	40	60	118	192	265
6,8-Strip reprints by Frank Robbins	17	34	51	103	162	220
7,35: 7-New art, not Robbins	14	28	42	78	112	145

JOHNNY JASON (...Teen Reporter)
Dell Publishing Co.: Feb-Apr, 1962 - No. 2, June-Aug, 1962

	GD 2.0	VG 4.0	FN 6.0	VF 8.0	VF/NM 9.0	NM- 9.2
Four Color 1302, 2(01380-208)	4	8	12	25	40	55

JOHNNY LAW, SKY RANGER
Good Comics (Lev Gleason): Apr, 1955 - No. 3, Aug, 1955; No. 4, Nov, 1955

	GD 2.0	VG 4.0	FN 6.0	VF 8.0	VF/NM 9.0	NM- 9.2
1-Edmond Good-c/a	14	28	42	81	118	155
2-4	10	20	30	56	76	95

JOHNNY MACK BROWN (Western star; see Western Roundup under Dell Giants)
Dell Publishing Co.: No. 269, Mar, 1950 - No. 963, Feb, 1959 (All Photo-c)

	GD 2.0	VG 4.0	FN 6.0	VF 8.0	VF/NM 9.0	NM- 9.2
Four Color 269(#1)(3/50, 52pgs.)-Johnny Mack Brown & his horse Rebel begin; photo front/back-c begin; Marsh-a in #1-9	19	38	57	133	297	460
2(10-12/50, 52pgs.)	10	20	30	66	138	210
3(1-3/51, 52pgs.)	8	16	24	54	102	150
4-10 (9-11/52)(36pgs.), Four Color 455,493,541,584,618,645,685,722,776,834,963	6	12	18	40	73	105
Four Color 922-Manning-a	7	14	21	44	82	120

JOHNNY PERIL (See Comic Cavalcade #15, Danger Trail #5, Sensation Comics #107 & Sensation Mystery)

JOHNNY RINGO (TV)
Dell Publishing Co.: No. 1142, Nov-Jan, 1960/61 (one shot)

	GD 2.0	VG 4.0	FN 6.0	VF 8.0	VF/NM 9.0	NM- 9.2
Four Color 1142-Photo-c	7	14	21	49	92	135

JOHNNY STARBOARD (See Wisco)

JOHNNY THE HOMICIDAL MANIAC (Also see Squee)
Slave Labor Graphics: Aug, 1995 - No. 7, Jan, 1997 ($2.95, B&W, lim. series)

	GD 2.0	VG 4.0	FN 6.0	VF 8.0	VF/NM 9.0	NM- 9.2
1-Jhonen Vasquez-c/s/a (1995)	10	20	30	64	132	200
1-Special Signed & numbered edition of 2,000 (1996)	5	10	15	35	63	90
2,3: 2-(11/95). 3-(2/96)	1	3	4	6	8	10
4-7: 4-(5-96). 5-(8/96)						5.00
Hardcover-($29.95) r/#1-7						35.00
TPB-($19.95)						25.00

JOHNNY THUNDER
National Periodical Publications: Feb-Mar, 1973 - No. 3, July-Aug, 1973

	GD 2.0	VG 4.0	FN 6.0	VF 8.0	VF/NM 9.0	NM- 9.2
1-Johnny Thunder & Nighthawk-r in all	3	6	9	17	26	35
2,3: 2-Trigger Twins app.	2	4	6	8	11	14

NOTE: All contain 1950s DC reprints from All-American Western. Drucker r-2, 3. G. Kane r-2, 3. Moreira r-1, 3; c-1r, 3r. Also see All-American, All-Star Western, Flash Comics, Western Comics, World's Best & World's Finest.

JOHN PAUL JONES
Dell Publishing Co.: No. 1007, July-Sept, 1959 (one-shot)

	GD 2.0	VG 4.0	FN 6.0	VF 8.0	VF/NM 9.0	NM- 9.2
Four Color 1007-Movie, Robert Stack photo-c	6	12	18	40	73	105

JOHN ROMITA JR. 30TH ANNIVERSARY SPECIAL
Marvel Comics: 2006 ($3.99, one-shot)

	GD 2.0	VG 4.0	FN 6.0	VF 8.0	VF/NM 9.0	NM- 9.2
nn-r/1st story in Amazing Spider-Man Annual #11; timeline, sketch pages, interviews						4.00

JOHN STEED & EMMA PEEL (See The Avengers, Gold Key series)

JOHN STEELE SECRET AGENT (Also see Freedom Agent)
Gold Key: Dec, 1964

	GD 2.0	VG 4.0	FN 6.0	VF 8.0	VF/NM 9.0	NM- 9.2
1-Freedom Agent	6	12	18	41	76	110

JOHN STEWART: THE EMERALD KNIGHT (Green Lantern)
DC Comics: Feb, 2023 ($5.99, one-shot)

	GD 2.0	VG 4.0	FN 6.0	VF 8.0	VF/NM 9.0	NM- 9.2
1-Geoffrey Thorne-s/Marco Santucci-a						6.00

JOHN WAYNE ADVENTURE COMICS (Movie star; See Big Tex, Oxydol-Dreft, Tim McCoy, & With The Marines...#1)
Toby Press: Winter, 1949-50 - No. 31, May, 1955 (Photo-c: 1-12,17,25-on)

	GD 2.0	VG 4.0	FN 6.0	VF 8.0	VF/NM 9.0	NM- 9.2
1 (36pgs.)-Photo-c begin (1st time in comics on-c)	265	530	795	1694	2597	4100
2-4: 2-(4/50, 36pgs.)-Williamson/Frazetta-a(2) 6 & 2 pgs. (one story-r/Billy the Kid #1); photo back-c. 3-(36pgs.)-Williamson/Frazetta-a(2), 16 pgs. total; photo back-c. 4-(52pgs.)-Williamson/Frazetta-a(2), 16 pgs. total	84	168	252	538	919	1300
5 (52pgs.)-Kurtzman-a-(Alfred "L" Newman in Potshot Pete)	71	142	213	454	777	1100
6 (52pgs.)-Williamson/Frazetta (10 pgs.); Kurtzman-a "Pot-Shot Pete", (5 pgs.); & "Genius Jones", (1 pg.)	81	162	243	518	884	1250
7 (52pgs.)-Williamson/Frazetta-a (10 pgs.)	66	132	198	419	722	1025
8 (36pgs.)-Williamson/Frazetta-a(2) (12 & 9 pgs.)	77	154	231	493	847	1200
9-11: Photo western-c	43	86	129	268	454	640
12,14-Photo war-c. 12-Kurtzman-a(2 pg.) "Genius"	43	86	129	271	461	650
13,15: 13,15-Line-drawn-c begin, end #24	39	78	117	236	388	540
16-Williamson/Frazetta-r/Billy the Kid #1	40	80	120	248	414	580
17-Photo-c	40	80	120	248	414	580
18-Williamson/Frazetta-a (r/#4 & 8, 19 pgs.)	43	86	129	268	454	640
19-24: 23-Evans-a?	36	72	108	214	347	480
25-Photo-c resume; end #31; Williamson/Frazetta-r/Billy the Kid #3	45	90	135	284	480	675
26-28,30-Photo-c	39	78	117	236	388	540
29,31-Williamson/Frazetta-a in each (r/#4, 2)	42	84	126	265	445	620

NOTE: Williamsonish art in later issues by Gerald McCann.

JOHN WICK (Based on the Keanu Reeves movies)
Dynamite Entertainment: 2018 - No. 5, 2019 ($3.99)

	GD 2.0	VG 4.0	FN 6.0	VF 8.0	VF/NM 9.0	NM- 9.2
1-Pak-s/Valletta-a; four covers	3	6	9	21	33	45
2-Three covers	2	4	6	9	12	15
3-5-Gaudio-a; three covers	1	2	3	5	6	8

JOIN THE FUTURE
AfterShock Comics: Mar, 2020 - No. 5, Sept, 2020 ($4.99/$3.99)

	GD 2.0	VG 4.0	FN 6.0	VF 8.0	VF/NM 9.0	NM- 9.2
1-($4.99) Zack Kaplan-s/Piotr Kowalski-a						5.00
2-5-($3.99)						4.00

JO-JO COMICS (...Congo King #7-29; My Desire #30 on)(Also see Fantastic Fears and Jungle Jo)
Fox Feature Syndicate: 1945 - No. 29, July, 1949 (Two No.7's; no #13)

	GD 2.0	VG 4.0	FN 6.0	VF 8.0	VF/NM 9.0	NM- 9.2
nn(1945)-Funny animal, humor	34	68	102	199	325	450
2(Sum, '46)-6(4-5/47): Funny animal. 2-Ten pg. Electro story (Fall/46)	20	40	60	117	189	260
7(7/47)-Jo-Jo, Congo King begins (1st app.); Bronze Man & Purple Tigress app.	116	232	348	742	1271	1800
7(#8) (9/47)	87	174	261	553	952	1350
8(#9) (9/47) Classic Kamen mountain of skulls-c; Tanee begin	135	270	405	864	1482	2100
9,10(#10,11)	77	154	231	493	847	1200
11,12(#12,13),14,16: 11,16-Kamen bondage-c	68	136	204	435	713	1050
15-Cited by Dr. Wertham in 5/47 Saturday Review of Literature	65	130	195	416	708	1000
17-Kamen bondage-c	129	258	387	826	1413	2000
18-20	60	120	180	381	653	925
21-24,26-29: 21-Hollingsworth-a (4 pgs.); 23-1 pg.	52	104	156	328	552	775
25-Classic bondage-c by Matt Baker	676	1352	2028	4935	8718	12,500

NOTE: Many bondage-c/a by Baker/Kamen/Feldstein/Good. No. 7's have Princesses Gwenna, Geesa, Yolda, & Safra before settling down on Tanee.

JOKEBOOK COMICS DIGEST ANNUAL (...Magazine No. 5 on)
Archie Publications: Oct, 1977 - No. 13, Oct, 1983 (Digest Size)

	GD 2.0	VG 4.0	FN 6.0	VF 8.0	VF/NM 9.0	NM- 9.2
1(10/77)-Reprints; Neal Adams-a	2	4	6	13	18	22
2(4/78)-5	2	4	6	9	12	15
6-13	1	3	4	6	8	10

JOKER
DC Comics: 2008 ($19.99, hardcover graphic novel with dustjacket)

	GD 2.0	VG 4.0	FN 6.0	VF 8.0	VF/NM 9.0	NM- 9.2
HC-Joker is released from Arkham; Azzarello-s/Bermejo-a						20.00

JOKER, THE (See Batman #1, Batman: The Killing Joke, Brave & the Bold, Detective, Greatest Joker Stories & Justice League Annual #2)
National Periodical Publications: May, 1975 - No. 9, Sept-Oct, 1976

	GD 2.0	VG 4.0	FN 6.0	VF 8.0	VF/NM 9.0	NM- 9.2
1-Two-Face app.	11	22	33	76	163	250
2-Willie the Weeper app.	6	12	18	41	76	110
3,4: 3-The Creeper app. 4-Green Arrow-c/sty	5	10	15	33	57	80
5-9: 6-Sherlock Holmes-c/sty. 7-Lex Luthor-c/story. 8-Scarecrow-c/story. 9-Catwoman-c/story	4	8	12	26	44	60
...: The Greatest Stories Ever Told TPB (2008, $19.99) r/Batman #1 and other apps.						20.00

JOKER, THE (See Tangent Comics/ The Joker)

JOKER, THE
DC Comics: May, 2021 - No. 15, Sept, 2022 ($4.99/$5.99)

	GD 2.0	VG 4.0	FN 6.0	VF 8.0	VF/NM 9.0	NM- 9.2
1-($4.99) Tynion IV-s/March-a; back-up Punchline story in all issues						5.00
2-14-($5.99) 2-Intro Vengeance (daughter of Bane), 5,10-Francavilla-a						6.00
15-($6.99) Bane and Vengeance app.						7.00
2021 Annual 1-(1/22, $5.99) Tynion IV & Rosenberg-s/Francavilla-a; Catman app.						6.00
.../ Harley Quinn: Uncovered 1-(2/24, $5.99) Gallery of recent variant covers						6.00
...: Uncovered 1-(8/23, $5.99) Gallery of variant covers from this title and from Joker: The Man Who Stopped Laughing; commentary pages w/Jorge Corona; Bermejo-c						6.00

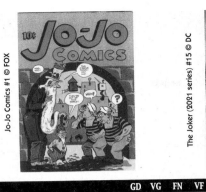
Jo-Jo Comics #1 © FOX

The Joker (2021 series) #15 © DC

Jonah Hex (2006 series) #6 © DC

	GD 2.0	VG 4.0	FN 6.0	VF 8.0	VF/NM 9.0	NM- 9.2

JOKER COMICS (Adventures Into Terror No. 43 on)
Timely/Marvel Comics No. 36 on (TCI/CDS): Apr, 1942 - No. 42, Aug, 1950

1-(Rare)-Powerhouse Pepper (1st app.) begins by Wolverton; Stuporman app. from Daring Comics	354	708	1062	2478	4339	6200
2-Wolverton-a; 1st app. Tessie the Typist & begin series	168	336	504	1075	1838	2600
3-5-Wolverton-a	110	220	330	704	1202	1700
6-10-Wolverton-a. 6-Tessie-c begin	61	122	183	390	670	950
11-20-Wolverton-a	57	114	171	362	619	875
21,22,24-27,29,30-Wolverton cont'd & Kurtzman's "Hey Look" in #23-27	50	100	150	315	533	750
23-1st "Hey Look" by Kurtzman; Wolverton-a	53	106	159	334	567	800
28,32,34,37-41: 28-Millie the Model begins. 32-Hedy begins. 41-Nellie the Nurse app.	28	56	84	168	274	380
31-Last Powerhouse Pepper; not in #28	43	86	129	271	461	650
33,35,36-Kurtzman's "Hey Look"	30	60	90	177	289	400
42-Only app. 'Patty Pinup,' clone of Millie the Model	34	68	102	199	325	450

JOKER / DAFFY DUCK
DC Comics: 2018 ($4.99, one-shot)

1-Lobdell-s/Booth-a/c; Daffy Duck as a Joker henchman; Batman app.						6.00
1-Variant-c by Sanford Greene	2	4	6	8	10	12

JOKER: DEVIL'S ADVOCATE
DC Comics: 1996 ($24.95/$12.95, one-shot)

nn-(Hardcover)-Dixon scripts/Nolan & Hanna-a	35.00
nn-(Softcover)	20.00

JOKER 80TH ANNIVERSARY 100-PAGE SUPER SPECTACULAR
DC Comics: Jun, 2020 ($9.99, squarebound, one-shot)

1-Short stories and pin-ups by various; origin Punchline; multiple covers	10.00

JOKER / HARLEY: CRIMINAL SANITY
DC Comics (Black Label): Dec, 2019 - No. 9 ($5.99, 10-3/4" x 8-1/2", lim. series)

1-7: 1,2-Kami Garcia-s/Mico Suayan & Mike Mayhew-a. 1-Three covers. 2-7-Two covers	6.00
... Secret Files 1 (9/20, $5.99) Covers by Mack & Sienkiewicz; art by Mack and others	6.00

JOKER: KILLER SMILE (See Batman: The Smile Killer one-shot for epilogue)
DC Comics (Black Label): Dec, 2019 - No. 3, Mar, 2020 ($5.99, 10-3/4" x 8-1/2", lim. series)

1-3-Jeff Lemire-s/Andrea Sorrentino-a; two covers by Sorrentino & Kaare Andrews	6.00

JOKER: LAST LAUGH (See Batman: The Joker's Last Laugh for TPB)
DC Comics: Dec, 2001 - No. 6, Jan, 2002 ($2.95, weekly limited series)

1-6: 1,6-Bolland-c						4.00
...Secret Files (12/01, $5.95) Short stories by various; Simonson-c	1	3	4	6	8	10

JOKER / MASK
Dark Horse Comics: May, 2000 - No. 4, Aug, 2000 ($2.95, limited series)

1-Batman, Harley Quinn, Poison Ivy app.	3	6	9	14	20	25
2-4	2	4	6	9	12	15

JOKER PRESENTS: A PUZZLEBOX, THE
DC Comics: Oct, 2021 - No. 7, Apr, 2022 ($4.99, printing of digital-first series)

1-7: 1-Rosenberg-s/Merino-a; main-c by Zdarsky; Riddler murdered	5.00

JOKER'S ASYLUM
DC Comics: Sept, 2008 ($2.99, weekly limited series of one-shots)

...: Joker - Andy Kubert-a, Sanchez-a; ...: Poison Ivy - Guillem March-a; ...: Scarecrow - Juan Doe-c/a; ...: Two-Face - Andy Clarke-c/a	5.00
Batman: The Joker's Asylum TPB (2008, $14.99) r/one-shots	15.00

JOKER'S ASYLUM II
DC Comics: Aug, 2010 ($2.99, weekly limited series of one-shots)

...: Clayface - Kelley Jones-c/a; ; ...: Killer Croc - Mattina-c; Mad Hatter - Giffen & Sienkiewicz-a, Sienkiewicz-c; ...: Riddler - Van Sciver-c	1	2	3	5	6	8
...: Harley Quinn - Quinones-a	3	6	9	15	22	28
Batman: The Joker's Asylum Volume 2 TPB (2011, $14.99) r/one-shots						15.00

JOKER, THE: THE MAN WHO STOPPED LAUGHING
DC Comics: Dec, 2022 - No. 12, Jan, 2024 ($5.99, limited series)

1-12-Rosenberg-s/DiGiandomenico & Francavilla-a. 4-Joker pregnancy story	6.00

JOKER, THE: YEAR OF THE VILLAIN
DC Comics: 2019 ($4.99, one-shot)

1-John Carpenter & Anthony Burch-s/Philip Tan-a; Enchantress app.	5.00

JOLLY CHRISTMAS, A (See March of Comics No. 269)

JOLLY COMICS: Four Star Publishing Co.: 1947 (Advertised, not published)

JOLLY COMICS
No publisher: No date (1930s-40s)(10¢, cover is black/red ink on yellow paper, blank inside-c)

nn-Snuffy Smith & Katzenjamer Kids on-c only. Buck Rogers, Dickey Dare, Napoleon & others app. Reprints Ace Comics #8-c. A GD copy sold in 2014 for $358.50	252	504	756	1613	2757	3900

JOLLY JINGLES (Formerly Jackpot Comics)
MLJ Magazines: No. 10, Sum, 1943 - No. 16, Wint, 1944/45

10-Super Duck begins (origin & 1st app.); Woody The Woodpecker begins (not same as Lantz character)	81	162	243	518	884	1250
11 (Fall, '43)-2nd Super Duck (see Hangman #8)	39	78	117	231	378	525
12-Hitler-c	194	388	582	1242	2121	3000
13-16: 13-Sahle-c. 15,16-Vigoda-c	28	56	84	165	270	375

JONAH HEX (See All-Star Western, Hex and Weird Western Tales)
National Periodical Pub./DC Comics: Mar-Apr, 1977 - No. 92, Aug, 1985

1-Garcia-Lopez-c/a	9	18	27	59	117	175
2-1st app. El Papagayo	5	10	15	33	57	80
3,4,9: 9-Wrightson-c	5	10	15	30	50	70
5,6,10: 5-Rep 1st app. from All-Star Western #10	4	8	12	28	47	65
7,8-Explains Hex's face disfigurement (origin)	5	10	15	33	57	80
11-20: 12-Starlin-a	3	6	9	17	26	35
21-32: 23-Intro. Mei Ling. 31,32-Origin retold	2	4	6	13	18	22
33-50	2	4	6	8	11	14
51-80	1	2	3	5	7	9
81-91: 89-Mark Texeira-a. 91-Cover swipe from Superman #243 (hugging a mystery woman)	2	4	6	8	10	12
92-Story cont'd in Hex #1	3	6	9	19	30	40

NOTE: Ayers a(p)-35-37, 40, 41, 44-53, 56, 58-82. Buckler a-11; c-11, 13-16. Kubert c-43-46. Morrow a-90-92; c-10. Spiegle(Tothish) a-34, 38, 40, 49, 52. Texeira a-89p. Batlash back-ups in 49, 52. El Diablo back-ups in 48, 56-60, 73-75. Scalphunter back-ups in 40, 41, 45-47.

JONAH HEX (Also see All Star Western [2011 DC New 52 title])
DC Comics: Jan, 2006 - No. 70, Oct, 2011 ($2.99)

1-Justin Gray & Jimmy Palmiotti-s/Luke Ross-a/Quitely-c	5.00
1-Special Edition (7/10, $1.00) r/#1 with "What's Next?" logo on cover	3.00
2-49,51-70: 3-Bat Lash app. 10,16,17,19,20,22-Noto-a. 11-El Diablo app.; Beck-a. 13-15-Origin retold. 21,23,27,30,32,37,38,42,52,54,57,59,61,63,67-Bernet-a.	3.00
33-Darwyn Cooke-a/c. 34-Sparacio-a. 51-Giordano-a. 53-Tucci-c/a. 62-Risso-a	3.00
50-($3.99) Darwyn Cooke-a/c	4.00
...: Bullets Don't Lie TPB (2009, $14.99) r/#31-36	15.00
...: Counting Corpses TPB (2011, $14.99) r/#43,50-54	15.00
...: Face Full of Violence TPB (2006, $12.99) r/#1-6	13.00
...: Guns of Vengeance TPB (2007, $12.99) r/#7-12	13.00
...: Lead Poisoning TPB (2009, $14.99) r/#37-42	15.00
...: Luck Runs Out TPB (2008, $12.99) r/#25-30	13.00
...: No Way Back HC (2010, $19.99) new GN; Gray & Palmiotti-s/DeZuniga-a	20.00
...: No Way Back SC (2011, $14.99) new GN; Gray & Palmiotti-s/DeZuniga-a	15.00
...: Only the Good Die Young TPB (2008, $12.99) r/#19-24	13.00
...: Origins TPB (2007, $12.99) r/#13-18	13.00
...: Tall Tales TPB (2011, $14.99) r/#55-60	15.00
...: The Six Gun War TPB (2010, $14.99) r/#44-49	15.00
...: Welcome to Paradise TPB (2010, $17.99) r/debut in All-Star Western #10 plus early apps. in Weird Western Tales and Jonah Hex #2,4 (1977 series)	18.00

JONAH HEX AND OTHER WESTERN TALES (Blue Ribbon Digest)
DC Comics: Sept-Oct, 1979 - No. 3, Jan-Feb, 1980 (100 pgs.)

1-3: 1-Origin Scalphunter-r, Ayers/Evans, Neal Adams-c; painted-c. 2-Weird Western Tales-r; Neal Adams, Toth, Aragonés-a. 3-Outlaw-r, Scalphunter-r; Gil Kane, Wildey-a	2	4	6	11	16	20

JONAH HEX: RIDERS OF THE WORM AND SUCH
DC Comics (Vertigo): Mar, 1995 - No. 5, July, 1995 ($2.95, limited series)

1-5-Lansdale story, Truman-a	4.00

JONAH HEX: SHADOWS WEST
DC Comics (Vertigo): Feb, 1999 - No. 3, Apr, 1999 ($2.95, limited series)

1-3-Lansdale-s/Truman-a	4.00

JONAH HEX SPECTACULAR (See DC Special Series No. 16)

JONAH HEX: TWO-GUN MOJO
DC Comics (Vertigo): Aug, 1993 - No. 5, Dec, 1993 ($2.95, limited series)

1-Lansdale scripts in all; Truman/Glanzman-a in all w/Truman-c	6.00
1-Platinum edition with no price on cover	20.00
2-5	4.00
TPB-(1994, $12.95) r/#1-5	13.00

JONAH HEX / YOSEMITE SAM

	GD 2.0	VG 4.0	FN 6.0	VF 8.0	VF/NM 9.0	NM- 9.2

DC Comics: Aug, 2017 ($4.99, one-shot)
1-Palmiotti-s/Teixeira-a; Foghorn Leghorn app. ... 5.00

JONESES, THE
AWA Studios: Apr, 2022 - No. 5, Sept, 2022 ($3.99, limited series)
1-5-Moreci-s/Vitti-a ... 4.00

JONESY (Formerly Crack Western)
Comic Favorite/Quality Comics Group: No. 85, Aug, 1953; No. 2, Oct, 1953 - No. 8, Oct, 1954

	GD 2.0	VG 4.0	FN 6.0	VF 8.0	VF/NM 9.0	NM- 9.2
85(#1)-Teen-age humor	14	28	42	78	112	145
2	9	18	27	47	61	75
3-8	8	16	24	40	50	60

JONESY
BOOM! Studios (BOOM! Box): Feb, 2016 - No. 12, Apr, 2017 ($3.99, originally a 4-part series)
1-12-Sam Humphries-s/Caitlin Rose Boyle-a. 1-Multiple covers ... 4.00

JON JUAN (Also see Great Lover Romances)
Toby Press: Spring, 1950

	GD 2.0	VG 4.0	FN 6.0	VF 8.0	VF/NM 9.0	NM- 9.2
1-All Schomburg-a (signed Al Reid on-c); written by Siegel; used in SOTI, pg. 38 (Scarce)	97	194	291	621	1061	1500

JONNI THUNDER (...A.K.A. Thunderbolt)
DC Comics: Feb, 1985 - No. 4, Aug, 1985 (75¢, limited series)
1-4: 1-Origin & 1st app. ... 4.00

JONNY DOUBLE
DC Comics (Vertigo): Sept, 1998 - No. 4, Dec, 1998 ($2.95, limited series)
1-4-Azzarello-s ... 4.00
TPB (2002, $12.95) r/#1-4; Chiarello-c ... 13.00

JONNY QUEST (TV)
Gold Key: Dec, 1964 (Hanna-Barbera)

	GD 2.0	VG 4.0	FN 6.0	VF 8.0	VF/NM 9.0	NM- 9.2
1 (10139-412)	40	80	120	296	673	1050

JONNY QUEST (TV)
Comico: June 1986 - No. 31, Dec, 1988 ($1.50/$1.75)(Hanna-Barbera)
1,3,5: 3,5-Dave Stevens-c ... 6.00
2,4,6-31: 30-Adapts TV episode ... 4.00
Special 1(9/88, $1.75), 2(10/88, $1.75) ... 4.00
NOTE: *M. Anderson a-9. Mooney a-Special 1. Pini a-2. Quagmire a-31p. Rude a-1; c-2i. Sienkiewicz c-11. Spiegle a-7, 12, 21; c-21 Staton a-2i, 11p. Steacy c-8. Stevens a-4i; c-3,5. Wildey a-1, c-1, 7, 12. Williamson a-4i; c-4i.*

JONNY QUEST CLASSICS (TV)
Comico: May, 1987 - No. 3, July, 1987 ($2.00) (Hanna-Barbera)
1-3: Wildey-c/a; 3-Based on TV episode ... 4.00

JON SABLE, FREELANCE (Also see Mike Grell's Sable & Sable)
First Comics: 6/83 - No. 56, 2/88 (#1-17, $1; #18-33, $1.25, #34-on, $1.75)
1-Mike Grell-c/a/scripts ... 5.00
2-56: 3-5-Origin, parts 1-3. 6-Origin, part 4. 11-1st app. of Maggie the Cat. 14-Mando paper begins. 16-Maggie the Cat. app. 25-30-Shatter app. 34-Deluxe format begins ($1.75) ... 4.00
The Complete Jon Sable, Freelance: Vol. 1 (IDW, 2005, $19.99) r/#1-6 ... 20.00
The Complete Jon Sable, Freelance: Vol. 2 (IDW, 2005, $19.99) r/#7-11 ... 20.00
The Complete Jon Sable, Freelance: Vol. 3 (IDW, 2005, $19.99) r/#12-16 ... 20.00
The Complete Jon Sable, Freelance: Vol. 4 (IDW, 2005, $19.99) r/#17-21 ... 20.00
NOTE: *Aragones a-33; c-33(part). Grell a-1-43;c-1-52, 53p, 54-56.*

JON SABLE, FREELANCE
IDW Publ.: (Limited series)
...: Ashes of Eden 1-5 (2009 - No. 5, 2/10, $3.99) Mike Grell-c/a/scripts ... 4.00
...: Bloodtrail 1-6 (4/05 - No. 6, 11/05, $3.99) Mike Grell-c/a/scripts ... 4.00
...: Bloodtrail TPB (4/06, $19.99) r/#1-6; cover gallery ... 20.00

JOOK JOINT
Image Comics: Oct, 2018 - No. 5 (2019, $3.99, limited series)
1,2-Tee Franklin-s/Alitha Martinez-a ... 4.00

JOSEPH & HIS BRETHREN (See The Living Bible)

JOSIE (She's... #1-16) (...& the Pussycats on) (See Archie's Pals 'n' Gals #23 for 1st app.) (Also see Archie Giant Series Magazine #528, 540, 551, 562, 571, 584, 597, 610, 622)
Archie Publ./Radio Comics: Feb, 1963; No. 2, Aug, 1963 - No. 106, Oct, 1982

	GD 2.0	VG 4.0	FN 6.0	VF 8.0	VF/NM 9.0	NM- 9.2
1	86	172	258	688	1544	2400
2	19	38	57	133	297	460
3-5	11	22	33	73	157	240
6-10: 6-(5/64) Book length Haunted Mansion-c/s. 7-(8/64) 1st app. Alexandra Cabot?	8	16	24	54	102	150
11-20	5	10	15	35	63	90
21, 23-30	5	10	15	31	53	75
22 (9/66)-Mighty Man & Mighty (Josie Girl) app.	5	10	15	34	60	85
31-44	4	8	12	27	44	60
45 (12/69)-Josie and the Pussycats begins (Hanna Barbera TV cartoon); 1st app. of the Pussycats	44	88	132	326	738	1150
46-2nd app./1st cover Pussycats	14	28	42	96	211	325
47-3rd app. of the Pussycats	8	16	24	56	108	160
48,49-Pussycats band-c/s	9	18	27	58	114	170
50-J&P-c; go to Hollywood, meet Hanna & Barbera	9	18	27	59	117	175
51-54	4	8	12	25	40	55
55-74 (2/74)(52 pg. issues). 73-Pussycats band-c	4	8	12	23	37	50
75-90(8/76)	3	6	9	14	20	26
91-99	2	4	6	11	16	20
100 (10/79)	3	6	9	14	19	24
101-106: 103-Pussycats band-c	2	4	6	13	18	22

JOSIE & THE PUSSYCATS (TV)
Archie Comics: 1993 - No. 2, 1994 ($2.00, 2 pgs.)(Published annually)

	GD 2.0	VG 4.0	FN 6.0	VF 8.0	VF/NM 9.0	NM- 9.2
1,2-Bound-in pull-out poster in each. 2-(Spr/94)	1	2	3		6	8

JOSIE AND THE PUSSYCATS
Archie Comic Publications: Nov, 2016 - No. 9, Oct, 2017 ($3.99)
1-9: 1-Bennett & Deordio-s/Audrey Mok-a; multiple covers; back-up classic reprints.
5,6-Riverdale TV previews. 9-Shannon-a ... 4.00

JOSIE ANNIVERSARY SPECTACULAR
Archie Comic Publications: Jan, 2024 ($3.99)
1- New story by Holly G! and reprints ... 4.00

JOURNAL OF CRIME (See Fox Giants)

JOURNEY
Aardvark-Vanaheim #1-14/Fantagraphics Books #15-on: 1983 - No. 14, Sept, 1984; No. 15, Apr, 1985 - No. 27, July, 1986 (B&W)

	GD 2.0	VG 4.0	FN 6.0	VF 8.0	VF/NM 9.0	NM- 9.2
1	1	3	4	6	8	10
2-27: 20-Sam Kieth-a						4.00

JOURNEY INTO FEAR
Superior-Dynamic Publications: May, 1951 - No. 21, Sept, 1954

	GD 2.0	VG 4.0	FN 6.0	VF 8.0	VF/NM 9.0	NM- 9.2
1-Baker-r(2)	168	336	504	1075	1838	2600
2	77	154	231	493	847	1200
3,4	58	116	174	371	636	900
5-10,15: 15-Used in SOTI, pg. 389	50	100	150	315	533	750
11-14,16-21	47	94	141	296	498	700

NOTE: *Kamenish 'headlight'-a most issues. Robinson a-10.*

JOURNEY INTO MYSTERY (1st Series) (Thor Nos. 126-502)
Atlas(CPS No. 1-48/AMI No. 49-68/Marvel No. 69 (6/61) on): 6/52 - No. 48, 8/57; No. 49, 11/58 - No. 125, 2/66; 503, 11/96 - No. 521, June, 1998

	GD 2.0	VG 4.0	FN 6.0	VF 8.0	VF/NM 9.0	NM- 9.2
1-Weird/horror stories begin	1850	3700	5550	13,000	19,500	26,000
2	271	542	813	1734	2967	4200
3,4	213	426	639	1363	2332	3300
5,7-11	194	388	582	1242	2121	3000
6-Classic Everett-c	300	600	900	2010	3505	5000
12-20,22: 15-Atomic explosion panel. 22-Davisesque-a; last pre-code issue (2/55)	123	246	369	787	1344	1900
21-Kubert-a; Tothish by Andru	129	258	387	826	1413	2000
23-32,35-38,40: 24-Torres?-a. 38-Ditko-a	93	183	279	591	1021	1450
33-Williamson-a; Ditko-a (his 1st for Atlas?)	123	246	369	787	1344	1900
34,39: 34-Krigstein-a. 39-1st S.A. issue; Wood-a	100	200	300	635	1093	1550
41-Crandall-a; Frazettaesque-a by Morrow	87	174	261	553	952	1350
42,46,48: 42,48-Torres-a. 46-Torres & Krigstein-a	46	92	138	340	770	1200
43,44-Williamson/Mayo-a in both. 43-Invisible Woman prototype	52	104	156	406	928	1450
45,47	44	88	132	326	738	1150
49-Matt Fox, Check-a	54	108	162	432	966	1500
50,52-54: 50-Davis-a. 54-Williamson-a	54	108	162	432	966	1500
51-Kirby/Wood-a	66	132	198	528	1189	1850
55-61,63-65,67-69,71,72,74,75: 74-Contents change to Fantasy. 75-Last 10¢ issue	44	88	132	326	738	1150
62-Prototype ish. (The Hulk); 1st app. Xemnu (Titan) called "The Hulk"	107	214	321	856	1928	3000
66-Prototype ish. (The Hulk)-Return of Xemnu "The Hulk"	82	164	246	656	1478	2300
70-Prototype ish. (The Sandman)(7/61); similar to Spidey villain	59	118	177	472	1061	1650
73-Story titled "The Spider" where a spider is exposed to radiation & gets powers of a human and shoots webbing; a reverse prototype of Spider-Man's origin	79	158	237	632	1416	2200
76,77,80,81: 80-Anti-communist propaganda story	37	74	111	274	612	950
76-(10¢ cover price blacked out, 12¢ printed on)	64	128	192	512	1156	1800
78-The Sorceror (Dr. Strange prototype) app. (3/62)	68	136	204	544	1222	1900
79-Prototype issue. (Mr. Hyde)	50	100	150	400	900	1400
82-Prototype ish. (Scorpion)	46	92	138	340	770	1200
83-Origin & 1st app. The Mighty Thor by Kirby (8/62) and begin series; Thor-c also begin	2660	5320	9310	26,600	75,800	125,000
83-Reprint from the Golden Record Comic Set	27	54	81	194	435	675
With the record (1966)	42	84	126	311	706	1100
84-2nd app. Thor	467	934	1400	3970	8985	14,000
85-1st app. Loki & Heimdall; 1st brief app. Odin (1 panel); 1st app. Asgard	2000	4000	6000	12,000	19,000	26,000
86-1st full app. Odin	114	228	342	912	2056	3200
87-Prisoner of the Reds	104	208	312	832	1866	2900
88-2nd Loki-c	114	228	342	912	2056	3200
89-Origin Thor retold; classic Thor-c	159	318	477	1312	2956	4600
90-No Kirby-a	71	142	213	568	1284	2000
91,92,94,96-Sinnott-a	54	108	162	432	966	1500
93,97-Kirby-a; Tales of Asgard series begins #97 (origin which concludes in #99); origin & 1st app. Lava Man. 97-1st app. Surtur (1 panel)	57	114	171	456	1028	1600
95-Sinnott-a; Thor vs. Thor	64	128	192	512	1156	1800
98,99-Kirby/Heck-a. 98-Origin/1st app. The Human Cobra. 99-1st app. Mr. Hyde; Surtur app.	42	84	126	311	706	1100
100-Kirby/Heck-a; Thor battles Mr. Hyde	40	80	120	296	673	1050
101,108: 101-(2/64)-2nd Avengers x-over (w/o Capt. America); see Tales Of Suspense #49 for 1st x-over. 108-(9/64)-Early Dr. Strange & Avengers x-over; ten extra pgs. Kirby-a	28	56	84	202	451	700
102-(3/64) 1st app. Sif, Balder and Hela	64	128	192	512	1156	1800
103-1st app. Enchantress	129	258	387	1032	2316	3600
104-107,110: 105-109-Ten extra pgs. Kirby-a in each. 107-1st app. Grey Gargoyle. 110,111-Two part battle vs. The Human Cobra & Mr. Hyde	27	54	81	194	435	675
109-Magneto-c & app. (1st x-over, 10/64)	50	100	150	400	900	1400
111,113: 113-Origin Loki	20	40	60	138	307	475
112-Thor Vs. Hulk (1/65); Origin Loki	75	150	225	600	1350	2100
114-Origin/1st app. Absorbing Man	46	92	138	340	770	1200
115-Detailed origin of Loki	26	52	78	182	404	625
116,117,120-123,125	16	32	48	110	243	375
118-1st app. Destroyer	33	66	99	238	532	825
119-Intro Hogun, Fandral, Volstagg; 2nd Destroyer	25	50	75	175	388	600
124-Hercules-c/story	17	34	51	114	250	390

503-521: 503-(11/96, $1.50)-The Lost Gods begin; Tom DeFalco scripts & Deodato

Josie and the Pussycats (2016 series) #2 © ACP

Journey into mystery #84 © MAR

JSA #46 © DC

	GD	VG	FN	VF	VF/NM	NM-
	2.0	4.0	6.0	8.0	9.0	9.2

Studios-c/a. 505-Spider-Man-c/app. 509-Loki-c/app. 514-516-Shang-Chi 4.00
#(-1) Flashback (7/97) Tales of Asgard Donald Blake app. 6.00
Annual 1(1965, 25¢, 72 pgs.)-New Thor vs. Hercules(1st app.)-c/story (see Incredible Hulk #3);
Kirby-c/a; r/#85,93,95,97 141 282 423 1142 2571 4000
NOTE: *Ayers* a-14, 39, 64i, 71i, 74i, 80i. *Bailey* a-43. *Briefer* a-5, 12. *Cameron* a-35. *Check* a-17. *Colan* a-23, 81; c-14. *Ditko* a-33, 38, 50-96; c-58, 67, 71, 88i. *Kirby/Ditko* a-50-83. *Everett* a-20, 48; c-4-7, 9, 36, 37, 39-42, 44, 45, 47. *Forte* a-19, 35, 40, 53. *Heath* a-4-6, 11, 14; c-1, 8, 11, 15, 51. *Heck* a-53, 58, 73. *Kirby* a(p)-51, 52, 56, 57-60, 62-64, 66, 67, 69-89, 93, 97, 98, 100(w/Heck), 101-125; c-50-57, 59-66, 68-70, 72-82, 88(w/Ditko), 83 & 84 (w/Sinnott), 85-96(w/Ayers), 97-125p. *Leiber/Fox* a-93, 98-102. *Maneely* c-20-22. *Morisi* a-42. *Morrow* a-41, 42. *Orlando* a-30, 45, 57. *Mac Pakula* (Tothish) a-9, 35, 41. *Powell* a-20, 27, 34. *Reinman* a-39, 70, 87, 92, 96i. *Robinson* a-9. *Roussos* a-39. *Robert Sale* a-14. *Severin* a-27; c-30. *Sinnott* a-41; c-50. *Tuska* a-9. *Wildey* a-16.

JOURNEY INTO MYSTERY (Series and numbering continue from Thor #621)
Marvel Comics: No. 622, Jun, 2011 - No. 655, Oct, 2013 ($3.99/$2.99)

622-Reincarnated young Loki; Thor app.; Braithwaite-s; Hans-c 4.00
622-Variant covers by Art Adams and Lee Weeks 6.00
623-626, 626.1, 627-630-($2.99) Fear Itself tie-in. 628,629-Portacio-a 3.00
631-655: 631-Portacio-a; Aftermath. 632-Hellstrom app. 637,638-Exiled x-over with New
    Mutants #41-43. 642-644-Crossover with Mighty Thor #19-21. 646-Features Sif 3.00

JOURNEY INTO MYSTERY (2nd Series)
Marvel Comics: Oct, 1972 - No. 19, Oct, 1975

1-Robert Howard adaptation; Starlin/Ploog-a 6 12 18 37 66 95
2-5: 2,3,5-Bloch adapt. 4-H. P. Lovecraft adapt. 3 6 9 18 28 38
6-19: Reprints 3 6 9 15 25 34
NOTE: *N. Adams* a-2i. *Ditko* r-7, 10, 12, 14, 15, 19; c-10. *Everett* r-9, 14. *G. Kane* r-9, 2p; c-1-3p. *Kirby* r-7, 13, 15, 18, 19; c-7. *Mort Lawrence* r-2. *Maneely* r-3. *Orlando* r-16. *Reese* a-1, 2i. *Starlin* a-1, 3p. *Torres* r-16. *Wildey* r-9, 14.

JOURNEY INTO MYSTERY: THE BIRTH OF KRAKOA
Marvel Comics: Nov, 2018 ($4.99, one-shot)

1-Nick Fury and the Howling Commandos app.; Hopeless-s/Morissette-Phan-a 5.00

JOURNEY INTO UNKNOWN WORLDS (Formerly Teen)
Atlas Comics (WFP): No. 36, Sept, 1950 - No. 38, Feb, 1951;
No. 4, Apr, 1951 - No. 59, Aug, 1957

36(#1)-Science fiction/weird; "End Of The Earth" c/story
    275 550 825 1750 3275 4800
37(#2)-Science fiction; "When Worlds Collide" c/story; Everett-c/a; Hitler story
    142 284 426 909 1555 2200
38(#3)-Science fiction 123 246 369 787 1344 1900
4-6,8,10-Science fiction/weird 77 154 231 493 847 1200
7-Wolverton-a "Planet of Terror", 6 pgs; electric chair c-inset/story
    113 226 339 718 1234 1750
9-Giant eyeball story 100 200 300 635 1093 1550
11,12-Krigstein-a 55 110 165 352 601 850
13,16,17,20 48 96 114 302 514 725
14-Wolverton-a "One of Our Graveyards Is Missing", 4 pgs; Tuska-a
    90 180 270 576 988 1400
15-Wolverton-a "They Crawl by Night", 5 pgs.; 2 pg. Maneely s/f story
    93 186 279 591 1021 1450
18,19-Matt Fox-a 55 110 165 352 601 850
21-33: 21-Decapitation-c. 24-Sci/fic story. 26-Atom bomb panel. 27-Sid Check-a.
    33-Last pre-code (2/55) 41 82 123 256 428 600
34-Kubert, Torres-a 37 74 111 222 361 500
35-Torres-a 36 72 108 211 343 475
36-45,48,50,53,55,59: 43-Krigstein-a. 44-Davis-a. 45,55,59-Williamson-a in all; with Mayo
    #55,59. 55-Crandall-a. 48,53-Crandall-a (4 pgs. #48). 48-Check-a. 50-Davis, Crandall-a
    33 66 99 194 317 440
46,47,49,52,54,56-58: 54-Torres-a 31 62 93 182 296 410
51-Ditko, Wood-a 36 72 108 214 347 480
NOTE: *Ayers* a-43. *Berg* a-38(#3), 43. *Lou Cameron* a-33. *Colan* a-37(#2), 6, 17, 19, 20, 23, 39. *Ditko* a-45, 51. *Drucker* a-35, 58. *Everett* a-37(#2), 11, 14, 41, 55, 56; c-37(#2), 11, 13, 14, 17, 22, 47, 48, 50, 53-55, 59. *Forte* a-49. *Fox* a-21, 49. *Heath* a-4(#1), 4, 6-8, 17, 20, 22, 36i; c-18. *Keller* a-15. *Mort Lawrence* a-38; c-38. *Maneely* a-7, 8, 15, 16, 22, 49, 58; c-8, 19, 25, 52. *Morrow* a-48. *Orlando* a-44, 57. *Pakula* a-36. *Powell* a-42, 53, 54. *Reinman* a-8i. *Rico* a-21. *Robert Sale* a-14, 49. *Sekowsky* a-4, 5, 9. *Severin* a-38, 51; c-38, 48i, 56i. *Sinnott* a-9, 21, 24. *Tuska* a-38(#3), 14. *Wildey* a-25, 43, 44.

JOURNEY INTO UNKNOWN WORLDS (Marvel 80th Anniversary salute to science fiction)
Marvel Comics: Mar, 2019 ($3.99, one-shot)

1-Bunn-s/Sanna-a; Chapman-s/Manna-a; McKone-c 4.00

JOURNEY TO STAR WARS: THE FORCE AWAKENS - SHATTERED EMPIRE
Marvel Comics: Nov, 2015 - No. 4, Dec, 2015 ($3.99, weekly limited series)

1-4-Rucka-s; takes place just after Episode 6 Battle of Endor; multiple covers on each 4.00

JOURNEY TO STAR WARS: THE LAST JEDI - CAPTAIN PHASMA
Marvel Comics: Sept, 2017 - No. 4, Dec, 2017 ($3.99, weekly limited series)

1-4-Checchetto-a/Renaud-c; takes place at the end of Episode 7 and just after 4.00

JOURNEY TO STAR WARS: THE RISE OF SKYWALKER - ALLEGIANCE
Marvel Comics: Dec, 2019 - No. 4, Dec, 2020 ($4.99/$3.99, weekly limited series)

1-($4.99) Ethan Sacks-s/Luke Ross-a; follows events after Episode 8 5.00
2-4-($3.99) Sacks-s/Ross-a; interlocking covers with #1 4.00

JOURNEY TO THE CENTER OF THE EARTH (Movie)
Dell Publishing Co.: No. 1060, Nov-Jan, 1959/60 (one-shot)

Four Color 1060-Pat Boone & James Mason photo-c 13 26 39 89 195 300

JOY OPERATIONS
Dark Horse Comics: Nov, 2021 - No. 5, Mar, 2022 ($3.99)

1-5-Bendis-s/Stephen Byrne-a/c. 1-Variant-c by Mack. 2-Variant-c by Oeming 4.00

JOYRIDE
BOOM! Studios: Apr, 2016 - No. 12, Apr, 2017 ($3.99, originally planned as a 4-part series)

1-12-Jackson Lanzing & Collin Kelly-s/Marcus To-a. 1-Multiple covers 4.00

JSA (Justice Society of America) (Also see All Star Comics)
DC Comics: Aug, 1999 - No. 87, Sept, 2006 ($2.50/$2.99)

1-Robinson and Goyer-s; funeral of Wesley Dodds 2 4 6 8 10 12
2-5: 4-Return of Dr. Fate 6.00
6-24: 6-Black Adam-c/app. 11,12-Kobra. 16-20-JSA vs. Johnny Sorrow. 19,20-Spectre app.
    4.00
25-($3.75) Hawkman rejoins the JSA 1 2 3 5 7 9
26-36, 38-49: 27-Capt. Marvel app. 29-Joker: Last Laugh. 31,32-Snejbjerg-a.
    33-Ultra-Humanite. 34-Intro. new Crimson Avenger and Hourman. 42-G.A. Mr. Terrific and
    the Freedom Fighters app. 46-Eclipso returns 3.00
37-($3.50) Johnny Thunder merges with the Thunderbolt; origin new Crimson Avenger 4.00
50-($3.95) Wraparound-c by Pacheco; Sentinel becomes Green Lantern again 4.00
51-74,76-82: 51-Kobra killed. 54-JLA app. 55-Ma Hunkle (Red Tornado) app. 56-58-Black
    Reign x-over with Hawkman #23-25. 64-Sand returns. 67-Identity Crisis tie-in; Gibbons-a.
    68,69,72-81-Ross-c. 73,74-Day of Vengeance tie-in. 76-OMAC tie-in. 82-Infinite Crisis
    x-over; Levitz-s/Pérez-a 3.00
75-($2.99) Day of Vengeance tie-in; Alex Ross Spectre-c 4.00
83-87: One Year Later; Pérez-c. 83-85,87-Morales-a; Gentleman Ghost app. 85-Begin $2.99-c;
    Earth-2 Batman, Atom, Sandman, Mr. Terrific app. 86,87-Ordway-a. 3.00
Annual 1 (10/00, $3.50) Planet DC; intro. Nemesis 4.00
... Black Reign TPB (2005, $12.99) r/#56-58, Hawkman #23-25; Watson cover gallery 13.00
... Black Vengeance TPB (2006, $19.99) r/#66-75 20.00
... Darkness Falls TPB (2002, $19.95) r/#6-15 20.00
... Fair Play TPB (2003, $14.95) r/#26-31 & Secret Files #2 15.00
... Ghost Stories TPB (2006, $14.99) r/#82-87 15.00
... Justice Be Done TPB (2000, $14.95) r/Secret Files & #1-5 20.00
... Lost TPB (2005, $19.99) r/#59-67 15.00
... Mixed Signals TPB (2006, $14.99) r/#76-81 3.00
... Our Worlds at War 1 (9/01, $2.95) Jae Lee-c; Saltares-a 4.00
... Presents Green Lantern TPB (2008, $14.99) r/JSA Classified #25,32,33 and Green Lantern:
    Brightest Day, Blackest Night 15.00
... Princes of Darkness TPB (2005, $19.95) r/#46-55 20.00
... Savage Times TPB (2004, $14.95) r/#39-45 15.00
... Secret Files 1 (8/99, $4.95) Origin stories and pin-ups; death of Wesley Dodds
    (G.A. Sandman); intro new Hawkgirl 2 4 6 11 16 20
... Secret Files 2 (9/01, $4.95) Short stories and profile pages
    1 2 3 5 6 8
... Stealing Thunder TPB (2003, $14.95) r/#32-38; JSA vs. The Ultra-Humanite 15.00
...: The Golden Age TPB (2005, $19.99) r/"The Golden Age" Elseworlds mini-series 20.00
...: The Return of Hawkman TPB (2002, $19.95) r/#16-26 & Secret Files #1 20.00

JSA: ALL STARS
DC Comics: July, 2003 - No. 8, Feb, 2004 ($2.50/$3.50, limited series, back-up stories in
Golden Age style)

1-3,5,6,8-Goyer & Johns-s/Cassaday-c. 1-Velluto-a; intro. Legacy. 2-Hawkman by Loeb/Sale
3-Dr. Fate by Cooke. 5-Hourman by Chaykin. 6-Dr. Mid-nite by Azzarello/Risso 3.00
4-Starman by Robinson/Harris; 1st app. Courtney Whitmore as Stargirl 4.00
7-($3.50) Mr. Terrific back-up story by Chabon; Lark-a 15.00
TPB (2004, $14.95) r/#1-8 3.00

JSA: ALL STARS
DC Comics: Feb, 2010 - No. 18, Jul, 2011 ($3.99/$2.99)

1-13-Younger JSA members form team. 1-Covers by Williams and Sook 4.00
14-18-($2.99) 3.00
... Constellations TPB (2010, $14.99) r/#1-6 and sketch art 15.00
...: Glory Days TPB (2011, $17.99) r/#7-13 18.00

JSA: CLASSIFIED (Issues #1-4 reprinted in Power Girl TPB)
DC Comics: Sept, 2005 - No. 39, Aug, 2008 ($2.50/$2.99)

1-(1st printing) Conner-c/a; origin of Power Girl 1 3 4 6 8 10

	GD	VG	FN	VF	VF/NM	NM-		GD	VG	FN	VF	VF/NM	NM-
	2.0	4.0	6.0	8.0	9.0	9.2		2.0	4.0	6.0	8.0	9.0	9.2

1-(1st printing) Adam Hughes variant-c 3 6 16 23 30
1-(2nd & 3rd printings) 2nd-Hughes B&W sketch-c. 3rd-Close-up of Conner-c 6.00
2-11: 2-JSA app. 4-Leads into Infinite Crisis #2. 5-7-Injustice Society app. 10-13-Vandal Savage origin retold; Gulacy-a/c 3.00
12-39: 12-Begin 99-c. 17,18-Bane app. 19,20-Morales-a. 21,22-Simonson-s/a 3.00
...: Honor Among Thieves TPB (2007, $14.99) r/#5-9 15.00

JSA LIBERTY FILES: THE WHISTLING SKULL
DC Comics: Feb, 2013 - No. 6, Jul, 2013 ($2.99, limited series)
1-6-Dr. Mid-Nite and Hourman in 1940; B. Clay Moore-s/Tony Harris-c/a 3.00

JSA STRANGE ADVENTURES
DC Comics: Oct, 2004 - No. 6, Mar, 2005 ($3.50, limited series)
1-6-Johnny Thunder as pulp writer; Kitson-a/Watson-c/ Kevin Anderson-s 3.50
TPB (2010, $14.99) r/#1-6 15.00

JSA: THE LIBERTY FILE (Elseworlds)
DC Comics: Feb, 2000 - No. 2, Mar, 2000 ($6.95, limited series)
1,2-Batman, Dr. Mid-Nite and Hourman vs. WW2 Joker; Tony Harris-c/a 7.00
JSA: The Liberty Files TPB (2004, $19.95) r/The Liberty File and The Unholy Three series 20.00

JSA: THE UNHOLY THREE (Elseworlds)(Sequel to JSA: The Liberty File)
DC Comics: 2003 - No. 2, 2003 ($6.95, limited series)
1,2-Batman, Superman and Hourman; Tony Harris-c/a 7.00

JSA VS. KOBRA
DC Comics: Aug, 2009 - No. 6, Jan, 2010 ($2.99, limited series)
1-6-Kramer-a/Ha-c; Jason Burr app. 3.00
TPB (2010, $14.99) r/#1-6; cover gallery 15.00

J2 (Also see A-Next and Juggernaut)
Marvel Comics: Oct, 1998 - No. 12, Sept, 1999 ($1.99)
1-12:1-Juggernaut's son; Lim-a. 2-Two covers; X-People app. 3-J2 battles the Hulk 4.00
Spider-Girl Presents Juggernaut Jr. Vol.1: Secrets & Lies (2006, $7.99, digest) r/#1-6 8.00

JUBILEE (X-Men)
Marvel Comics: Nov, 2004 - No. 6, Apr, 2005 ($2.99)
1-6: 1-Jubilee in a Los Angeles high school; Kirkman-s; Casey Jones-c 3.00

JUDAS
BOOM! Studios: Dec, 2017 - No. 4, Mar, 2018 ($3.99, limited series)
1-4-Judas' time with Jesus and in the Afterlife; Lucifer app.; Loveness-s/Rebelka-a 4.00

JUDAS COIN, THE
DC Comics: 2012 $22.99, hardcover graphic novel with dust jacket)
HC-Walt Simonson-s/a/c; Batman, Two-Face, Golden Gladiator, Viking Prince, Captain Fear, Bat Lash, Manhunter 2070 app.; bonus sketch gallery 23.00

JUDENHASS
Aardvark-Vanaheim Press: 2008 ($4.00, B&W, squarebound)
nn-Dave Sim-writer/artist; The Shoah and Jewish persecution through history 4.00

JUDE, THE FORGOTTEN SAINT
Catechetical Guild Education Soc.: 1954 (16 pgs., 8x11"; full color; paper-c)
nn 6 12 18 28 34 40

JUDGE COLT
Gold Key: Oct, 1969 - No. 4, Sept, 1970 (Painted cover)
1 3 6 9 16 23 30
2-4 2 4 6 9 13 16

JUDGE DREDD (...Classics #62 on; also see Batman - Judge Dredd, The Law of Dredd & 2000 A.D. Monthly)
Eagle Comics/IPC Magazines Ltd./Quality Comics #34-35, V2#1-37/ Fleetway #38 on: Nov, 1983 - No. 35, 1986; V2#1, 1986 - No. 77, 1993
1-Bolland-a 6 12 18 37 66 95
2-5 2 4 6 9 12 15
6-35 6.00
V2#1-('86)-New look begins 6.00
2-10 5.00
11-77: 20-Begin $1.50-c. 21/22, 23/24-Two issue numbers in one. 28-1st app. Megaman (super-hero). 39-Begin $1.75-c. 51-Begin $1.95-c. 53-Bolland-a. 57-Reprints 1st published Judge Dredd story 4.00
Special 1 5.00
NOTE: **Bolland** a-1-6, 8, 10; c-1-10, 15. **Guice** c-V2#23/24, 26, 27.

JUDGE DREDD (3rd Series)
DC Comics: Aug, 1994 - No. 18, Jan, 1996 ($1.95)
1-18: 12-Begin $2.25-c 4.00
nn ($5.95)-Movie adaptation, Sienkiewicz-c 6.00

JUDGE DREDD
IDW Publishing: Nov, 2012 - No. 30, May, 2015 ($3.99)
1-30: 1-Swierczynski-s; six covers 4.00

JUDGE DREDD
IDW Publishing: Dec, 2015 - No. 12, Nov, 2016 ($3.99)
1-12: 1-Farinas & Freitas-s/McDaid-a; multiple covers 4.00
Annual 1 (2/17, $7.99) Farinas & Freitas-s/McDaid-a; two covers 8.00
...: Cry of the Werewolf (3/17, $5.99) Reprint from 2000 AD; Steve Dillon-a/c; new pin-ups 6.00
...: Deviations (3/17, $4.99) McCrea-s/a; What If Dredd stayed a werewolf; bonus pin-ups 5.00
... Funko Universe (4/17, $4.99) Short stories w/characters styled like Pop! Vinyl figures 5.00
...: Mega-City Zero 1 (5/18, $1.00) reprints #1 3.00
...: 100-Page Giant (2/20, $5.99) Reprints stories from recent mini-series 6.00

JUDGE DREDD: ANDERSON, PSI-DIVISION
IDW Publishing: Aug, 2014 - No. 4, Dec, 2014 ($3.99)
1-4-Matt Smith-s/Carl Critchlow-a; three covers on each 4.00

JUDGE DREDD CLASSICS (Reprints)
IDW Publishing: Jul, 2013 - No. 6 ($3.99)
1-6-Wagner & Grant-s 4.00
Free Comic Book Day 2013 (5/13, free) Judge Death app.; Walter the Wobot back-ups 3.00

...: The Dark Judges 1-5 (1/15 - No. 5, 5/15, $3.99) Wagner & Grant-s/Bolland-a 4.00

JUDGE DREDD: LEGENDS OF THE LAW
DC Comics: Dec, 1994 - No. 13, Dec, 1995 ($1.95)
1-13: 1-5-Dorman-c 4.00

JUDGE DREDD: MEGA-CITY TWO
IDW Publishing: Jan, 2014 - No. 5, May, 2014 ($3.99)
1-5-Wolk-s/Farinas-a 4.00

JUDGE DREDD'S CRIME FILE
Eagle Comics: Aug, 1985 - No. 6, Feb, 1986 ($1.25, limited series)
1-6: 1-Byrne-a 5.00

JUDGE DREDD: THE BLESSED EARTH
IDW Publishing: Apr, 2017 - No. 8, Nov, 2017 ($3.99)
1-8-Farinas & Freitas-a; multiple covers on each 4.00

JUDGE DREDD: THE EARLY CASES
Eagle Comics: Feb, 1986 - No. 6, Jul, 1986 ($1.25, Mega-series, Mando paper)
1-6: 2000 A.D.-r 5.00

JUDGE DREDD: THE JUDGE CHILD QUEST (Judge Child in indicia)
Eagle Comics: Aug, 1984 - No. 5, Oct, 1984 ($1.25, Lim. series, Baxter paper)
1-5: 2000A.D.-r; Bolland-c/a 6.00

JUDGE DREDD: THE MEGAZINE
Fleetway/Quality: 1991 - No. 3 ($4.95, stiff-c, squarebound, 52 pgs.)
1-3 5.00

JUDGE DREDD: TOXIC
IDW Publishing: Oct, 2018 - No. 4, Jan, 2019 ($3.99)
1-4-Paul Jenkins-s/Marco Castiello-a 4.00

JUDGE DREDD: UNDER SIEGE
IDW Publishing: May, 2018 - No. 4, Aug, 2018 ($3.99)
1-4-Mark Russell-s/Max Dunbar-a 4.00

JUDGE DREDD VS. ALIENS: INCUBUS
Dark Horse Comics: March, 2003 - No. 4, June, 2003 ($2.99, limited series)
1-4-Flint-a/Wagner & Diggle-s 3.00

JUDGE DREDD: YEAR ONE
IDW Publishing: Mar, 2013 - No. 4, Jul, 2013 ($3.99)
1-4-Matt Smith-s/Simon Coleby-a 4.00

JUDGE PARKER
Argo: Feb, 1956 - No. 2, 1956
1-Newspaper strip reprints 9 18 27 47 61 75
2 6 12 18 31 38 45

JUDGMENT DAY
Awesome Entertainment: June, 1997 - No. 3, Oct, 1997 ($2.50, limited series)
1-3: 1 Alpha-Moore-s/Liefeld-c/a(p) flashback art by various in all. 2 Omega. 3 Final Judgment. All have a variant cover by Dave Gibbons 4.00
...Aftermath-($3.50) Moore-s/Kane-a; Youngblood, Glory, New Men, Maximage, Allies and Spacehunter short stories. Also has a variant cover by Dave Gibbons 4.00
TPB (Checker Books, 2003, $16.95) r/series 17.00

JUDO JOE
Jay-Jay Corp.: Aug, 1953 - No. 3, Dec, 1953 (Judo lessons in each issue)
1-Drug ring story 19 38 57 111 176 240
2,3-Hypo needle story 13 26 39 72 101 130

JUDOMASTER (Gun Master #84-89) (Also see Crisis on Infinite Earths, Sarge Steel #6, Special War Series, & Thunderbolt)
Charlton Comics: No. 89, May-June, 1966 - No. 98, Dec, 1967 (Two No. 89's)
89-3rd app. Judomaster 5 10 15 30 50 70
90-Origin of Thunderbolt 4 8 12 27 44 60
91-Sarge Steel begins 4 8 12 22 35 48
92-98: 93-Intro. Tiger 3 6 9 21 33 45
93,94,96,98-(Modern Comics reprint, 1977) 1 2 3 5 6 8
NOTE: **Morisi** Thunderbolt #90. #91 has 1 pg. biography on writer/artist Frank McLaughlin.

JUDY CANOVA (Formerly My Experience) (Stage, screen, radio)
Fox Feature Syndicate: No. 23, May, 1950 - No. 3, Sept, 1950
23(#1)-Wood-c,a(p)? 32 64 96 188 307 425
24-Wood-a(p) 30 60 90 177 289 400
3-Wood-c; Wood/Orlando-a 34 68 102 199 325 450

JUDY GARLAND (See Famous Stars)

JUDY JOINS THE WAVES
Toby Press: 1951 (For U.S. Navy)
nn 12 24 36 67 94 120

JUGGERNAUT (See X-Men)
Marvel Comics: Apr, 1997, Nov, 1999 ($2.99, one-shots)
1-(4/97) Kelly-s/ Rouleau-a 4.00
1-(11/99) Casey-s; Eighth Day x-over; Thor, Iron Man, Spidey app. 4.00

JUGGERNAUT (X-Men)
Marvel Comics: Nov, 2020 - Present ($3.99)
1-5-Nicieza-s/Garney-a. 2-Hulk app. 4,5-Arnim Zola app. 4.00

JUGHEAD (Formerly Archie's Pal...)
Archie Publications: No. 126, Nov, 1965 - No. 352, June, 1987
126-130: 129-LBJ on cover 3 6 9 18 28 38
131,133,135-160(9/68) 3 6 9 16 23 30
132,134: 132-Shield-c; The Fly & Black Hood app.; Shield cameo.
134-Shield-c 5 10 15 30 50 70
161-180 2 4 6 13 19 24
181-199 2 4 6 9 13 16
200(1/72) 2 4 6 11 16 20

Judge Dredd (2013 series) #16 © Rebellion

Judomaster #92 © CC

Jughead (2015 series) #11 © ACP

	GD 2.0	VG 4.0	FN 6.0	VF 8.0	VF/NM 9.0	NM- 9.2
201-240(5/75)	2	4	6	8	10	12
241-270(11/77)	1	2	3	5	7	9
271-299	1	2	3	4	5	7
300(5/80)-Anniversary issue; infinity-c	1	2	3	5	6	8
301-320(1/82)						5.00
321-324,326-352						4.00
325-(10/82) Cheryl Blossom app. (not on cover); same month as intro. (cover & story)						
in Archie's Girls, Betty & Veronica #320; Jason Blossom app.; DeCarlo-a	10	20	30	67	149	215

JUGHEAD (2nd Series)(Becomes Archie's Pal Jughead Comics #46 on)
Archie Enterprises: Aug, 1987 - No. 45, May, 1993 (.75/$1.00/$1.25)

1	1	2	3	4	5	7
2-10						4.00
11-45: 4-X-Mas issue. 17-Colan-c/a						3.00

JUGHEAD (Volume 3)
Archie Comic Publications: Nov, 2015 - No. 16, Aug, 2017 ($3.99)
1-16-Multiple covers and classic back-up reprints. 1-6-Chip Zdarsky-s/Erica Henderson-a. 5,6-Jughead as Captain Hero. 7-13-Derek Charm-a. 9-13-Ryan North-s; Sabrina app. 4.00

JUGHEAD AND ARCHIE DOUBLE DIGEST (Becomes Jughead & Archie Comics Digest)
Archie Comic Publ. Inc: Jun, 2014 - No. 27, Oct, 2017 ($3.99-$6.99, digest-size)
1-3: 1-Reprints; That Wilkin Boy app. 4.00
4,7-9,11-14,16,19,26-($4.99) 5.00
5,10,15,21,23,25-($6.99, 320 pgs.) Titled Jughead & Archie Jumbo Comics Digest 7.00
6,17,18,20,22,24,27-($5.99, 192 pgs.) Titled Jughead & Archie Comics Annual.
24-Winter Annual 6.00

JUGHEAD & FRIENDS DIGEST MAGAZINE
Archie Publ.: Jun, 2005 - No. 38, Aug, 2010 ($2.39/$2.49/$2.69, digest-size)
1-38: 1-That Wilkin Boy app. 3.00

JUGHEAD AS CAPTAIN HERO (See Archie as Pureheart the Powerful, Archie Giant Series Magazine #142 & Life With Archie)
Archie Publications: Oct, 1966 - No. 7, Nov, 1967

1-Super hero parody	9	18	27	57	111	165
2	5	10	15	34	60	85
3-7	4	8	12	28	47	65

JUGHEAD COMICS. NIGHT AT GEPPI'S ENTERTAINMENT MUSEUM
Archie Comic Publ. Inc: 2008
Free Comic Book Day giveaway - New story; Archie gang visits GEM; Steve Geppi app. 3.00

JUGHEAD JONES COMICS DIGEST, THE (...Magazine No. 10-64; Jughead Jones Digest Magazine #65)
Archie Publ.: June, 1977 - No. 100, May, 1996 ($1.35/$1.50/$1.75, digest-size, 128 pgs.)

1-Neal Adams-a; Capt. Hero-r	4	8	12	25	40	55
2(9/77)-Neal Adams-a	3	6	9	16	23	30
3-6,8-10	2	4	6	11	16	20
7-Origin Jaguar-r; N. Adams-a.	2	4	6	13	18	22
11-20: 13-r/1957 Jughead's Folly	2	4	6	8	10	12
21-50	1	2	3	4	5	7
51-70						5.00
71-100						3.00

JUGHEAD'S BABY TALES
Archie Comics: Spring, 1994 - No. 2, Wint. 1994 ($2.00, 52 pgs.)
1,2: 1-Bound-in pull-out poster 4.00

JUGHEAD'S DINER
Archie Comics: Apr, 1990 - No. 7, Apr, 1991 ($1.00)
1 5.00
2-7 4.00

JUGHEAD'S DOUBLE DIGEST (...Magazine #5)
Archie Comics: Oct, 1989 - No. 200, Apr, 2014 ($2.25 - $3.99/$5.99)

1		2	4	6	8	10	12
2-10: 2,5-Capt. Hero stories		1	2	3	5	6	8
11-25							5.00

26-195: 58-Begin $2.99-c. 66-Begin $3.19-c. 91-Begin $3.59-c. 138-Reprints entire Jughead #1 (1949). 139-142-"New Look" Jughead; Staton-a. 148-Begin $3.99-c 4.00
196-200-($5.99) Titled "Jughead's Double Double Digest" 6.00
Archie New Look Series Book 2, Jughead "The Matchmakers" TPB (2009, $10.95) r/new look series in #139-142; new cover by Staton & Milgrom 11.00

JUGHEAD'S EAT-OUT COMIC BOOK MAGAZINE (See Archie Giant Series Magazine No. 170)

JUGHEAD'S FANTASY

Archie Publications: Aug, 1960 - No. 3, Dec, 1960

	GD 2.0	VG 4.0	FN 6.0	VF 8.0	VF/NM 9.0	NM- 9.2
1	27	54	81	189	420	650
2	15	30	45	100	220	340
3	12	24	36	79	170	260

JUGHEAD'S FOLLY
Archie Publications (Close-Up): 1957 (36 pgs.)(one-shot)
1-Jughead a la Elvis (Rare) (1st reference to Elvis in comics?) 90 180 270 576 988 1400

JUGHEAD'S JOKES
Archie Publications: Aug, 1967 - No. 78, Sept, 1982
(No. 1-8, 38 on: reg. size; No. 9-23: 68 pgs.; No. 24-37: 52 pgs.)

1	8	16	24	54	102	150
2	5	10	15	30	50	70
3-8	3	6	9	17	26	35
9,10 (68 pgs.)	3	6	9	19	30	40
11-23(4/71) (68 pgs.)	3	6	9	16	23	30
24-37(1/74) (52 pgs.)	2	4	6	11	16	20
38-50(9/76)	1	3	4	6	8	10
51-78						6.00

JUGHEAD'S PAL HOT DOG (See Laugh #14 for 1st app.)
Archie Comics: Jan, 1990 - No. 5, Oct, 1990 ($1.00)
1 5.00
2-5 4.00

JUGHEAD'S SOUL FOOD
Spire Christian Comics (Fleming H. Revell Co.): 1979 (49¢/59¢)
nn-Low print run 3 6 9 15 22 28

JUGHEAD'S TIME POLICE
Archie Comics: July, 1990 - No. 6, May, 1991 ($1.00, bi-monthly)
1 5.00
2-6: Colan-a-3-6p; c-3-6 4.00

JUGHEAD: TIME POLICE
Archie Comic Publications: Aug, 2019 - No. 5, Dec, 2019 ($3.99, limited series)
1-5-Sina Grace-s/Derek Charm-a; multiple covers on each; January McAndrews app. 4.00

JUGHEAD: THE HUNGER (Continues in Jughead The Hunger vs Vampironica)
Archie Comic Publications: Dec, 2017 - No. 13, May, 2019 ($3.99)
1-13-Tieri-s; Jughead as a werewolf. 1-8-Pat & Tim Kennedy-a; 2-13-Eisma-a (partial) 4.00
Jughead The Hunger, One-Shot (5/17, $4.99) Tieri-s/Walsh-a; prelude to issue #1 5.00

JUGHEAD: THE HUNGER VS VAMPIRONICA
Archie Comic Publications: Jun, 2019 - No. 5, Dec, 2019 ($3.99, limited series)
1-5-Tieri-s/Pat & Tim Kennedy-a; Eisma-a (partial); multiple covers. 3-5 Sabrina app. 4.00

JUGHEAD WITH ARCHIE DIGEST (...Plus Betty & Veronica & Reggie Too No. 1,2; ...Magazine #33-?, 101-on; ...Comics Digest Mag.)
Archie Pub.: Mar, 1974 - No. 200, May, 2005 ($1.00-$2.39)

1		5	10	15	34	60	85
2		4	8	12	23	37	50
3-10		3	6	9	17	26	35
11-13,15-17,19,20: Capt. Hero-r in #14-16; Capt. Pureheart #17,19		2	4	6	10	14	18
14,18,21,22-Pureheart the Powerful in #18,21,22		2	4	6	11	16	20
23-30: 29-The Shield-r. 30-The Fly-r		1	3	4	6	8	10
31-50,100		1	2	3	5	6	8
51-99		1	2	3	4	5	7
101-121							4.00
122-200: 156-Begin $2.19-c. 180-Begin $2.39-c							3.00

JUICE SQUEEZERS
Dark Horse Comics: Jan, 2014 - No. 4, Apr, 2014 ($3.99, limited series)
1-4-David Lapham-s/a/c 4.00

JUKE BOX COMICS
Famous Funnies: Mar, 1948 - No. 6, Jan, 1949

1-Toth-c/a; Hollingsworth-a	43	86	129	271	461	650
2-Transvestism story	28	56	84	168	274	380
3-6: 3-Peggy Lee story. 4-Jimmy Durante line drawn-c. 6-Features Desi Arnaz plus Arnaz line drawn-c	21	42	63	122	199	275

JULES VERNE'S LIGHTHOUSE
Image Comics: Apr, 2021 - No. 5, Sept, 2021 ($4.99/$3.99, limited series)
1-($4.99) David Hine & Brian Haberlin-s/Haberlin-a 5.00

	GD	VG	FN	VF	VF/NM	NM-
	2.0	4.0	6.0	8.0	9.0	9.2

2-5-($3.99)   4.00

JUMBO COMICS (Created by S.M. Iger)
Fiction House Magazines (Real Adv. Publ. Co.): Sept, 1938 - No. 167, Mar, 1953 (No. 1-3: 68 pgs., No. 4-8: 52 pgs.)(No. 1-8 oversized-10-1/2x14-1/2"; black & white)

1-(Rare)-Sheena Queen of the Jungle(1st app.) by Meskin, Hawks of the Seas (The Hawk #10 on; see Feature Funnies #3) by Eisner, The Hunchback by Dick Briefer (ends #8), Wilton of the West (ends #24), Inspector Dayton (ends #67) & ZX-5 (ends #140) begin; 1st comic art by Jack Kirby (Count of Monte Cristo & Wilton of the West); Mickey Mouse appears (1 panel) with brief biography of Walt Disney; 1st Sheena by Peter Pupp by Bob Kane.
Note: Sheena was created by Iger for publication in England as a newspaper strip. The early issues of Jumbo contain Sheena strip-r; multiple panel-c 1,2,7

     4475   8950   13,425   35,800   --   --
2-(Rare)-Origin Sheena. Diary of Dr. Hayward by Fine plus 2 other stories; contains strip from Universal Film featuring Edgar Bergen & Charlie McCarthy plus-c (preview of film)   1550   3100   4650   12,400   --   --
3-Last Kirby issue   1075   2150   3225   8600   --   --
4-(Scarce)-Origin The Hawk by Eisner; Wilton of the West by Fine (ends #14)(1st comic work); Count of Monte Cristo by Fine (ends #15); The Diary of Dr. Hayward by Fine (cont'd #8,9)   1000   2000   3000   8000   --   --
5-Christmas-c   925   1850   2775   7400   --   --
6-8-Last B&W iss. #8 was a 1939 N.Y. World's Fair Special Edition; Frank Buck's Jungleland story   813   1626   2439   6500   --   --
9-Stuart Taylor begins by Fine (ends #140); Fine-c; 1st color issue (8-9/39)-1st Sheena (jungle) cover; 8-1/4x10-1/4" (oversized in width only)   1225   2450   3675   9800   --   --
10-Regular size 68 pg. issues begin; Sheena dons new costume w/origin costume; Stuart Taylor sci/fi-c; classic Lou Fine-c   595   1190   1784   4350   7675   11,000
11-13: 12-The Hawk-c by Eisner. 13-Eisner-c   271   542   813   1734   2967   4200
14-Intro. Lightning (super-hero) on only   271   542   813   1734   2967   4200
15-1st Lightning story and begins, ends #41   181   362   543   1158   1979   2800
16-Lightning-c   206   412   618   1318   2259   3200
17,18,20: 17-Lightning part-c   155   310   465   992   1696   2400
19-Classic Sheena Giant Ape-c by Powell   194   388   582   1242   2121   3000
21-30: 22-1st Tom, Dick & Harry; origin The Hawk retold. 25-Midnight the Black Stallion begins, ends #65   110   220   330   704   1202   1700
31-(9/41)-1st app. Mars God of War in Stuart Taylor story (see Planet Comics #15.) (scarce)   377   754   1131   2639   4620   6600
32-40: 35-Shows V2#11 (correct number does not appear)   90   180   270   576   988   1400
41-50: 42-Ghost Gallery begins, ends #167   55   110   165   352   601   850
51-60: 52-Last Tom, Dick & Harry   45   90   135   284   480   675
61-70: 68-Sky Girl begins, ends #130; not in #79   39   78   117   240   395   550
71-93,95-99: 89-ZX5 becomes a private eye.   34   68   102   199   325   450
94-Used in Love and Death by Legman   37   74   111   222   361   500
100   34   68   102   204   332   460
101-121   28   56   84   168   274   380
121-140,150-158: 155-Used in POP, pg. 98   25   50   75   150   245   340
141-149-Two Sheena stories. 141-Long Bow, Indian Boy begins, ends #160   26   52   78   154   252   350
159-163: Space Scouts serial in all. 160-Last jungle-c (6/52). 161-Ghost Gallery covers begin, end #167. 163-Suicide Smith app.   32   64   96   188   307   425
164-The Star Pirate begins of #165   63   126   189   403   689   975
165-167: 165,167-Space Rangers app.   54   108   162   343   574   825
NOTE: Bondage covers, negligee panels, torture, etc. are common in this series. Hawks of the Seas, Inspector Dayton, regular in action, Sports Shorts, & Uncle Otto by Eisner, #1-7. Hawk by Eisner-#10-13. Eisner-c 8, 12-14. Top. Patsy pin-ups in 92-97, 99-101. Sheena by Meskin-#1, 4; by Powell-#2, 3, 5-28; Powell C-14-16, 17, 19. Powell/Eisner c-15. Sky Girl by Matt Baker-#68, 80-130. ZX-5 & Ghost Gallery by Kamen-#90-130. Bailey a-3-8. Briefer a-1-8, 10. Fine a-14; c-9-11. Kamen a-101, 105, 123, 132; c-105, 121-145. Bob Kane a-1-8. Whitman a-146-167(most). Jungle c-9, 13,15, 17 on.

JUMPER: JUMPSCARS
Oni Press: Jan, 2008 ($14.95, graphic novel)
SC-Prelude to 2008 movie Jumper; Brian Hurtt-a/c   15.00

JUNGLE ACTION
Atlas Comics (IPC): Oct, 1954 - No. 6, Aug, 1955
1-Leopard Girl begins by Al Hartley (#1,3); Jungle Boy by Forte; Maneely-a in all   60   120   180   381   653   925
2-(3-D effect cover)   50   100   150   315   533   750
3-6: 3-Last precode (2/55)   36   72   108   214   347   480
NOTE: Maneely c-1, 2, 5, 6. Romita a-3, 6. Shores a-3, 6; c-3, 4?.

JUNGLE ACTION (…& Black Panther #18-21?)
Marvel Comics Group: Oct, 1972 - No. 24, Nov, 1976
1-Lorna, Jann-r (All reprints in 1-4)   5   10   15   33   57   80
2-4   3   6   9   17   25   34
5-Black Panther begins (r/Avengers #62)   24   48   72   144   235   325
6-New solo Black Panther stories begin; 1st app. Erik Killmonger   30   60   90   216   483   750
7,9,10: 9-Contains pull-out centerfold ad by Mark Jewelers   5   10   15   33   57   80
8-Origin Black Panther   5   10   15   41   46   125
11-18,23,24: 18-1st app. Madame Slay (Erik Killmonger's girlfriend). 23-r/Daredevil #69.
24-1st Wind Eagle; story cont'd in Marvel Premiere #51-#53   3   6   9   17   26   35
19,20-Black Panther vs. the Klan (cont'd in #21,22)   5   10   15   35   63   90
21(Regular 25¢ edition)(5/76) The Klan app.   10   20   30   64   132   200
21-(30¢-c variant, limited distribution   15   30   45   100   220   340
22-(Regular 25¢ edition)(7/76)   5   10   15   33   57   80
22-(30¢-c variant, limited distribution   10   20   30   69   147   225
NOTE: Buckler a-6-9p, 22; c-8p, 12p. Buscema a-5p; c-22. Byrne c-23. Gil Kane a-8p; c-2, 4, 10p, 11p, 13-17, 19, 24. Maneely r-1. Russell a-13i. Starlin c-3p.

JUNGLE ADVENTURES
Super Comics: 1963 - 1964 (Reprints)
10,12,15,17,18: 10-r/Terrors of the Jungle #4 & #10(Rulah). 12-r/Zoot #14(Rulah).15-r/Kaanga from Jungle #152 & Tiger Girl. 17-All Jo-Jo. 18-Reprints/White Princess of the Jungle #1; no Kinstler-a; origin of both White Princess & Cap'n Courage   3   6   9   19   30   40

JUNGLE ADVENTURES
Skywald Comics: Mar, 1971 - No. 3, June, 1971 (25¢, 52 pgs.) (Pre-code reprints & new-s)
1-Zangar origin; reprints of Jo-Jo, Blue Gorilla(origin)/White Princess #3, Kinstler-r/White Princess #2   3   6   9   19   30   40
2,3: 2-Zangar, Sheena-r/Sheena #17 & Jumbo #162, Jo-Jo, origin Slave Girl-r. 3-Zangar, Jo-Jo, White Princess, Rulah-r   3   6   9   15   22   28

JUNGLE BOOK (See King Louie and Mowgli, Movie Comics, Mowgli…, Walt Disney Showcase #45 & Walt Disney's The Jungle Book)

JUNGLE CAT (Disney)
Dell Publishing Co.: No. 1136, Sept-Nov, 1960 (one shot)
Four Color 1136-Movie, photo-c   6   12   18   40   73   105

JUNGLE COMICS
Fiction House Magazines: 1/40 - No. 157, 3/53; No. 158, Spr, 1953 - No. 163, Summer, 1954
1-Origin The White Panther, Kaanga, Lord of the Jungle, Tabu, Wizard of the Jungle; Wambi, the Jungle Boy, Camilla & Capt. Terry Thunder begin (1st app.). Lou Fine-c   703   1406   2109   5132   9066   13,000
2-Fantomah, Mystery Woman of the Jungle begins #51; The Red Panther begins, ends #26   258   516   774   1651   2826   4000
3,4   181   362   543   1158   1974   2800
5-Classic Eisner-c   245   490   735   1568   2684   3800
6-10: 7,8-Powell-c   110   220   330   704   1202   1700
11-Classic dinosaur-c   314   628   942   2198   3849   5500
12-20: 13-Tuska-c   81   162   243   518   884   1250
21-30: 25-Shows V2#1 (correct number does not appear). #27-New origin Fantomah, Daughter of the Pharoahs; Camilla dons new costume   63   126   189   403   689   975
31-40   48   96   144   302   514   725
41,43-50   43   86   129   271   461   650
42-Kaanga by Crandall, 12 pgs.   59   78   117   341   636   900

51-60   39   78   117   341   636   900
61-70: 67-Cover swipes Crandall splash pg. in #42   34   68   102   204   332   460
71-80: 79-New origin Tabu   30   60   90   177   289   400
81-97,99   28   56   94   168   274   380
98-Used in SOTI, pg. 185 & illo "In ordinary comic books, there are pictures within pictures for children who know how to look"; used by N.Y. Legis. Comm.   45   90   135   284   480   675
100   34   68   102   199   325   450
101-110: 104-In Camilla story, villain is Dr. Wertham   27   54   81   162   266   370
111-120: 118-Clyde Beatty app.   26   52   78   154   252   350
121-130   24   48   72   142   234   325
131-163: 135-Desert Panther begins in Terry Thunder (origin), not in #137; ends (dies) #138.
139-Last 52 pg. issue. 141-Last Tabu. 143,145-used in POP, pg. 99. 151-Last Camilla & Terry Thunder. 152-Tiger Girl begins. 158-Last Wambi; Sheena app.   22   44   66   132   216   300
I.W. Reprint #1,9: 1-r/? 9-r/#151   5   10   15   22   35   45
NOTE: Bondage covers, negligee panels, torture, etc. are common in this series. Camilla by Fran Hopper-#70-92; by Baker-#69, 100-113, 115, 116; by Lubbers-#97-99 by Tuska-#63, 65. Kaanga by John Celardo-#80-113; by Larsen-#71, 75-79; by Moreira-#58, 60, 61, 63-70, 72-74; by Tuska-#37, 62; by Whitman-#114-163. Tabu by Larsen-#59-75, 82-92; by Whitman-#93-113. Terry Thunder by Hopper-#71, 72; by Celardo-#78, 79; by Lubbers-#80-85. Tiger Girl by Baker-#49-130; #152, 155-157, 159. Wambi by Baker-#62-67, 74. Astarita c-45, 46. Celardo a-78; c-88-113. Crandall c-67 from splash pg. Eisner c-2, 5, 6. Fine c-1. Larsen a-65, 66, 71, 72, 74, 75, 79, 83, 84, 87-90. Moreira c-43, 44. Morisi a-51. Powell c-7, 8. Sultan c-3, 4. Tuska c-13. Whitman c-132-163(most). Zoinerovich c-11, 12, 18-41.

JUNGLE COMICS
Blackthorne Publishing: May, 1988 - No. 4 ($2.00, B&W/color)
1-Dave Stevens-c; B. Jones scripts in all   3   6   9   21   33   45
2-4: 2-B&W-a begins   6.00

JUNGLE GIRL (See Lorna, the…)

JUNGLE GIRL (Nyoka, Jungle Girl No. 2 on)
Fawcett Publications: Fall, 1942 (one-shot)(No month listed)
1-Bondage-c; photo of Kay Aldridge who played Nyoka in movie serial app. on-c. Adaptation of the classic Republic movie serial Perils of Nyoka. 1st comic to devote entire contents to a movie serial adaptation   155   310   465   992   1696   2400

JUNGLE GIRL
Dynamite Entertainment: No. 0, 2007 - 2009 (25¢/$2.99/$3.50)
.0-(25¢-c) Eight page preview; preview of Superpowers w/Alex Ross-a   3.00
1-5-Frank Cho-plot/cover; Batista-a/variant-c   3.00
… Season 2 ($3.50) 1-5-Two covers by Cho & Batista   3.50
… Season 3 ($3.99) 1-4-Cho-c/Jadson-a/Murray-s   4.00

JUNGLE JIM (Also see Ace Comics)
Standard Comics (Best Books): No. 11, Jan, 1949 - No. 20, Apr, 1951
11   15   30   45   90   140   190
12-20   11   22   33   62   86   110

JUNGLE JIM
Dell Publishing Co.: No. 490, 8/53 - No. 1020, 8-10/59 (Painted-c)
Four Color 490(#1)   10   20   30   64   132   200
Four Color 565(#2, 6/54)   5   10   15   35   63   90
3(10-12/54)-5   4   8   12   27   44   60
6-19(1-3/59)   4   8   12   25   40   55
Four Color 1020(#20)   5   10   15   33   57   80

JUNGLE JIM
King Features Syndicate: No. 5, Dec, 1967
5-Reprints Dell #5; Wood-c   2   4   6   10   14   18

JUNGLE JIM (Continued from Dell series)
Charlton Comics: No. 22, Feb, 1969 - No. 28, Feb, 1970 (#21 was an overseas edition only)
22-Dan Flagg begins; Ditko/Wood-a   9   18   27   11   33   45
23-26: 23-Last Dan Flagg; Howard-c. 24-Jungle People begin   3   6   9   15   21   26
27,28: 27-Ditko/Howard-a. 28-Ditko-a   3   6   9   16   24   32
NOTE: Ditko cover of #22 reprints story panels.

JUNGLE JO

Jungle Girl #1 © Jungle Girl LLC

Junkyard Joe #6 © Johns & Frank

Jurassic League #1 © DC

	GD 2.0	VG 4.0	FN 6.0	VF 8.0	VF/NM 9.0	NM- 9.2

Fox Feature Syndicate (Hero Books): Mar, 1950 - No. 3, Sept, 1950

nn-Jo-Jo blanked out in titles of interior stories, leaving Congo King; came out after Jo-Jo #29

(intended as Jo-Jo #30?) — 74 148 222 470 810 1150

1-Tangi begins; part Wood-a — 81 162 243 518 884 1250

2,3 — 54 108 162 343 574 825

JUNGLE LIL (Dorothy Lamour #2 on; also see Feature Stories Magazine)

Fox Feature Syndicate (Hero Books): April, 1950

1 — 68 136 204 435 743 1050

JUNGLE TALES (Jann of the Jungle No. 8 on)

Atlas Comics (CSI): Sept, 1954 - No. 7, Sept, 1955

1-Jann of the Jungle — 57 114 171 362 619 875

2-7: 3-Last precode (1/55) — 39 78 117 231 378 525

NOTE: *Heath* c-5. *Heck* a-6, 7. *Maneely* a-2; c-1, 3. *Shores* a-5-7; c-4, 6. *Tuska* a-2.

JUNGLE TALES OF TARZAN

Charlton Comics: Dec, 1964 - No. 4, July, 1965

1 — 6 12 18 37 66 95

2-4 — 4 8 12 25 40 55

NOTE: *Giordano* c-3p. *Glanzman* a-1-3. *Montes/Bache* a-4.

JUNGLE TERROR (See Harvey Comics Hits No. 54)

JUNGLE THRILLS (Formerly Sports Thrills; Terrors of the Jungle #17 on)

Star Publications: No. 16, Feb, 1952; Dec, 1953; No. 7, 1954

16-Phantom Lady & Rulah story-reprint/All Top No. 15; used in POP, pg. 98,99;
L. B. Cole-c — 77 154 231 493 847 1200

3-D 1(12/53, 25¢)-Came w/glasses; Jungle Lil & Jungle Jo appear; L. B. Cole-c — 54 108 162 343 574 825

7-Titled 'Picture Scope Jungle Adventures,' (1954, 36 pgs, 15¢)-3-D effect c/stories; story &
coloring book; Disbrow-a/script; L.B. Cole-c — 58 116 174 371 636 900

JUNGLE TWINS, THE (Tono & Kono)

Gold Key/Whitman No. 18: Apr, 1972 - No. 17, Nov, 1975; No. 18, May, 1982

1-All painted covers — 3 6 9 16 23 30

2-5 — 2 4 6 9 12 15

6-18: 18(Whitman, 5/82)-Reprints — 1 3 4 6 8 10

NOTE: UFO c/story No. 13. Painted-c No. 1-17. *Spiegle* c-18.

JUNGLE WAR STORIES (Guerrilla War No. 12 on)

Dell Publishing Co.: July-Sept, 1962 - No. 11, Apr-June, 1965 (Painted-c)

01-384-209 (#1) — 5 10 15 30 50 70

2-11 — 3 6 9 17 25 34

JUNIE PROM (Also see Dexter Comics)

Dearfield Publishing Co.: Winter, 1947-48 - No. 7, Aug, 1949

1-Teen-age — 45 90 135 284 480 675

2 — 32 64 96 188 307 425

3-7 — 25 50 75 150 245 340

JUNIOR

Fantagraphics Books: June, 2000 - No. 5, Jan, 2001 ($2.95, B&W)

1-5-Peter Bagge-s/a — 3.00

JUNIOR CARROT PATROL (Jr. Carrot Patrol #2)

Dark Horse Comics: May, 1989; No. 2, Nov, 1990 ($2.00, B&W)

1,2-Flaming Carrot spin-off. 1-Bob Burden-c(i) — 4.00

JUNIOR COMICS (Formerly Li'l Pan; becomes Western Outlaws with #17)

Fox Feature Syndicate: No. 9, Sept, 1947 - No. 16, July, 1948

9-Feldstein-c/a — 226 452 678 1446 2473 3500

10-16: 10-12,14-16-Feldstein-c/a; headlights-c — 206 412 618 1318 2259 3200

JUNIOR FUNNIES (Formerly Tiny Tot Funnies No. 9)

Harvey Publ. (King Features Synd.): No. 10, Aug, 1951 - No. 13, Feb, 1952

10-Partial reprints in all; Blondie, Dagwood, Daisy, Henry, Popeye, Felix,
Katzenjammer Kids — 8 16 24 42 54 65

11-13 — 7 14 21 37 46 55

JUNIOR HOPP COMICS

Stanmor Publ.: Feb, 1952 - No. 3, July, 1952

1-Teenage humor — 26 52 78 154 252 350

2,3: 3-Dave Berg-a — 17 34 51 98 154 210

JUNIOR MEDICS OF AMERICA, THE

E. R. Squire & Sons: No. 1359, 1957 (15¢)

1359 — 7 14 21 35 43 50

JUNIOR MISS

Timely/Marvel (CnPC): Wint, 1944; No. 24, Apr, 1947 - No. 39, Aug, 1950

1-Frank Sinatra & June Allyson life story — 53 106 159 234 567 800

24-Formerly The Human Torch #23? — 27 54 81 158 259 360

25-38: 29,31,32,34-Cindy-c/stories (others?) — 19 38 57 111 176 240

39-Kurtzman-a — 20 40 60 117 189 260

NOTE: Painted-c 35-37. 35, 37-all romance. 36, 38-mostly teen humor. *Louise Alston* c-36.

JUNIOR PARTNERS (Formerly Oral Roberts' True Stories)

Oral Roberts Evangelistic Assn.: No. 120, Aug, 1959 - V3#12, Dec, 1961

120(#1) — 4 8 12 25 40 55

2(9/59) — 3 6 9 17 26 35

3-12(7/60) — 2 4 6 13 18 22

V2#1(8/60)-5(12/60) — 2 4 6 9 13 16

V3#1(1/61)-12 — 2 4 6 8 10 12

JUNIOR TREASURY (See Dell Junior...)

JUNIOR WOODCHUCKS GUIDE (Walt Disney's...)

Danbury Press: 1973 (8-3/4"x5-3/4", 214 pgs., hardcover)

nn-Illustrated text based on the long-standing J.W. Guide used by Donald Duck's nephews
Huey, Dewey & Louie by Carl Barks. The guidebook was a popular plot device to enable
the nephews to solve problems facing their uncle or Scrooge McDuck (scarce) — 7 14 21 46 86 125

JUNIOR WOODCHUCKS LIMITED SERIES (Walt Disney's...)

W. D. Publications (Disney): July, 1991 - No. 4, Oct, 1991 ($1.50, limited series; new &
reprint-a)

1-The Beagle Boys app.; Barks-r — 1 3 4 6 8 10

2-4 — 4.00

JUNIOR WOODCHUCKS (See Huey, Dewey & Louie...)

JUNK RABBIT

Image Comics (Shadowline): Apr, 2023 - No. 5, Aug, 2023 ($3.99)

1-5-Jimmie Robinson-s/a — 4.00

JUNKYARD JOE

Image Comics (Mad Ghost): Oct, 2022 - Present ($4.99/$3.99)

1-Junkyard Joe in 1972 Vietnam War; Geoff Johns-s/Gary Frank-a; multiple covers — 5.00

2-5-Jumps to modern times; focus on Muddy Davis — 4.00

6-($4.99) — 5.00

JUPITER'S CIRCLE (Prequel to Jupiter's Legacy)

Image Comics: Apr, 2015 - No. 6, Sept, 2015 ($3.50/$3.99)

1-6-Mark Millar-s/Frank Quitely-a/c. 1-Three covers. 1-3,5-Torres-a. 4,5-Gianfelice-a — 4.00

Volume 2 (11/15 - No. 6, 5/16) 1-6-Covers by Quitely & Sienkiewicz. 1,2,6-Torres-a.

3-5-Spouse-a — 4.00

JUPITER'S LEGACY

Image Comics: Apr, 2013 - No. 5, Jan, 2015 ($2.99/$4.99)

1-4-Mark Millar-s/Frank Quitely-a/c — 3.00

1-Variant-c by Hitch — 4.00

5-($4.99) Covers by Hitch and Fegredo; bonus pin-ups and cosplay photos — 5.00

1-Studio Edition (12/13, $4.99) Quitely's B&W art and Millar's script; design art — 5.00

JUPITER'S LEGACY REQUIEM

Image Comics: Jun, 2021 - No. 6, Dec, 2021 ($5.99/$3.99)

1,6-($5.99)-Mark Millar-s. 1-Edwards-a. 6-Matt Smith-a — 6.00

2-5-($3.99) 2-4-Edwards-a. 5-Matt Smith-a — 4.00

JUPITER'S LEGACY 2

Image Comics: Jan, 2016 - No. 5, Jul, 2017 ($3.99)

1-5-Mark Millar-s/Frank Quitely-a/c — 4.00

JURASSIC LEAGUE

DC Comics: Jul, 2022 - No. 6 ($3.99, limited series)

1-5-Gedeon & Johnson-s/Gedeon-a; Justice League as dinosaurs in prehistoric era — 4.00

JURASSIC PARK

Topps Comics: June, 1993 - No. 4, Aug, 1993; No. 5, Oct, 1994 - No. 10, Feb, 1995

1-($2.50)-Newsstand Edition; Kane/Perez-a in all; 1-4: movie adaptation — 2 4 6 11 16 20

1-($2.95)-Collector's Ed.; polybagged w/3 cards — 3 6 9 14 20 25

1-Amberchrome Edition w/no price or ads — 8 16 24 56 108 160

2-4-($2.50)-Newsstand Edition — 5.00

2,3-($2.95)-Collector's Ed.; polybagged w/3 cards — 1 3 4 6 8 10

4-10: 4-($2.95)-Collector's Ed.; polybagged w/1 of 4 different action hologram trading card;
Gil Kane/Pérez-a. 5-becomes Advs. of .... — 5.00

Annual 1 ($3.95, 5/95) — 1 3 4 6 8 10

Trade paperback (1993, $9.95)-r/#1-4; bagged w/#0 — 3 6 9 14 20 25

JURASSIC PARK

	GD 2.0	VG 4.0	FN 6.0	VF 8.0	VF/NM 9.0	NM- 9.2

IDW Publishing: Jun, 2010 - No. 5, Oct, 2010 ($3.99, limited series)
1-5: Takes place 13 years after the first movie; Schreck-s. 1-Covers by Yeates & Miller ... 5.00

JURASSIC PARK: DANGEROUS GAMES
IDW Publishing: Sept, 2011 - No. 5, Jan, 2012 ($3.99, limited series)
1-5-Erik Bears/Jorge Jimenez-a, 1-Covers by Darrow & Zornow ... 4.00

JURASSIC PARK: RAPTOR
Topps Comics: Nov, 1993 - No. 2, Dec, 1993 ($2.95, limited series)
1,2: 1-Bagged w/3 trading cards & Zorro #0; Golden c-1,2 ... 6.00

JURASSIC PARK: RAPTORS ATTACK
Topps Comics: Mar, 1994 - No. 4, June, 1994 ($2.50, limited series)
1-4-Michael Golden-c/frontispiece ... 6.00

JURASSIC PARK: RAPTORS HIJACK
Topps Comics: July, 1994 - No. 4, Oct, 1994 ($2.50, limited series)
1-4: Michael Golden-c/frontispiece ... 5.00

JURASSIC PARK: THE DEVILS IN THE DESERT
IDW Publishing: Jan, 2011 - No. 4, Apr, 2011 ($3.99, limited series)
1-4-John Byrne-s/a/c ... 4.00

JUST A PILGRIM
Black Bull Entertainment: May, 2001 - No. 5, Sept, 2001 ($2.99)
Limited Preview Edition (12/00, $7.00) Ennis & Ezquerra interviews ... 7.00
1-Ennis-s/Ezquerra-a; two covers by Texeira & JG Jones ... 3.00
2-5: 2-Fabry-c. 3-Nowlan-c. 4-Sienkiewicz-c ... 3.00
TPB (11/01, $12.99) r/#1-5; Waid intro. ... 13.00

JUST A PILGRIM: GARDEN OF EDEN
Black Bull Entertainment: May, 2002 - No. 4, Aug, 2002 ($2.99, limited series)
Limited Preview Ed. (1/02, $7.00) Ennis & Ezquerra interviews; Jones-c ... 7.00
1-4-Ennis-s/Ezquerra-a ... 3.00
TPB (11/02, $12.99) r/#1-4; Gareb Shamus intro. ... 13.00

JUSTICE
Marvel Comics Group (New Universe): Nov, 1986 - No. 32, June, 1989
1-32: 26-32-$1.50-c (low print run) ... 4.00

JUSTICE
DC Comics: Oct, 2005 - No. 12, Aug, 2007 ($2.99/$3.50/$3.99, bi-monthly maxi-series)
1-Classic Justice League vs. The Legion of Doom; Alex Ross & Doug Braithwaite; Jim Krueger-s; two covers by Ross; Ross sketch pages ... 5.00
1-2nd & 3rd printings ... 4.00
2-($3.50) ... 4.00
2 (2nd printing), 3-11-($3.50) ... 3.50
12-($3.99) Two covers (Heroes & Villains) ... 4.00
Absolute Justice HC (2009, $99.99, slipcased book with dustjacket) oversized r/#1-12; afterwords by creators; Ross sketch and design art; photo gallery of action figures ... 100.00
HC (2011, $39.99, dustjacket) r/#1-12 ... 40.00
... Volume One HC (2006, $19.99, dustjacket) r/#1-4; Krueger intro.; sketch pages ... 20.00
... Volume One SC (2008, $14.99) r/#1-4; Krueger intro.; sketch pages ... 15.00
... Volume Two HC (2007, $19.99, dustjacket) r/#5-8; Krueger intro.; sketch pages ... 20.00
... Volume Two SC (2008, $14.99) r/#5-8; Krueger intro.; sketch pages ... 15.00
... Volume Three HC (2007, $19.99, dustjacket) r/#9-12; Ross intro.; sketch pages ... 20.00
... Volume Three SC (2007, $14.99) r/#9-12; Ross intro.; sketch pages ... 15.00

JUSTICE COMICS (Formerly Wacky Duck; Tales of Justice #53 on)
Marvel/Atlas Comics (NPP 7-9,4-19/CnPC 20-23/MjMC 24-38/Male 39-52):
No. 7, Fall/47 - No. 9, 6/48; No. 8, 4/48 - No. 52, 5/55

	GD 2.0	VG 4.0	FN 6.0	VF 8.0	VF/NM 9.0	NM- 9.2
7(#1, 1947)	47	94	141	296	498	700
8(#2)-Kurtzman-a "Giggles 'n' Grins" (3)	31	62	93	182	296	410
9(#3, 6/48)	25	50	75	150	245	340
4	22	44	66	128	209	290
5(9/48)-9: 8-Anti-Wertham editorial	20	40	60	117	189	260
10-15-Photo-c	17	34	51	98	154	210
16-30	15	30	45	90	140	190
31-40,42-52: 35-Gene Colan-a. 48-Last precode; Pakula & Tuska-a. 50-Sayers-a	15	30	45	86	133	180
41-Electrocution-c	30	60	90	177	289	400

NOTE: *Hartley* a-48. *Heath* a-24. *Maneely* c-44, 52. *Pakula* a-43, 45, 47, 48. *Louis Ravielli* a-39, 47. *Robinson* a-22, 25, 28, 41. *Sale* c-45. *Shores* c-7(#1), 8(#2)? *Tuska* a-41, 48. *Wildey* a-52.

JUSTICE: FOUR BALANCE
Marvel Comics: Sept, 1994 - No. 4, Dec, 1994 ($1.75, limited series)
1-4: 1-Thing & Firestar app. ... 4.00

JUSTICE, INC. (The Avenger) (Pulp)
National Periodical Publications: May-June, 1975 - No. 4, Nov-Dec, 1975

	GD 2.0	VG 4.0	FN 6.0	VF 8.0	VF/NM 9.0	NM- 9.2
1-McWilliams-a. Kubert-c; origin	2	4	6	11	16	20
2-4: 2-4-Kirby-a(p), c,2,3p. 4-Kubert-c	2	4	6	11	16	20

NOTE: *Adapted from Kenneth Robeson novel, creator of Doc Savage.*

JUSTICE, INC. (Pulp)
DC Comics: 1989 - No. 2, 1989 ($3.95, 52 pgs., squarebound, mature)
1,2: Re-intro The Avenger; Andrew Helfer scripts & Kyle Baker-c/a ... 5.00

JUSTICE, INC. (Pulp)
Dynamite Entertainment: 2014 - No. 6, 2015 ($3.99/$5.99)
1-5-The Shadow, Doc Savage and The Avenger app; Uslan-s/Timpano-a; multiple covers ... 4.00
6-($5.99) Covers by Ross, Francavilla, Hardman and Syaf ... 6.00

JUSTICE, INC.: THE AVENGER (Pulp)
Dynamite Entertainment: 2015 - No. 6, 2015 ($3.99)
1-6: 1-Waid-s/Freire-a; multiple covers incl. 1975 series #1 cover swipe by Ross ... 4.00

JUSTICE, INC.: THE AVENGER VOLUME 1 (Pulp)
Dynamite Entertainment: 2017 - No. 4, 2017 ($3.99)
1-4-Higgins & Gentile-s/Shibao-a. 1-Covers by Mandrake & Shibao ... 4.00

JUSTICE LEAGUE (...International #7-25; ...America #26 on)
DC Comics: May, 1987 - No. 113, Aug, 1996 (Also see Legends #6)

1-Batman, Green Lantern (Guy Gardner), Blue Beetle, Mr. Miracle, Capt. Marvel & Martian Manhunter begin; 1st app. Maxwell Lord

	GD 2.0	VG 4.0	FN 6.0	VF 8.0	VF/NM 9.0	NM- 9.2
	3	6	9	16	23	30

2,3: 3-Regular-c (white background) ... 6.00

3-Limited-c (yellow background, Superman logo)

	GD 2.0	VG 4.0	FN 6.0	VF 8.0	VF/NM 9.0	NM- 9.2
	5	10	15	30	50	70

4-6,8-10: 4-Booster Gold joins. 5-Origin Gray Man; Batman vs. Guy Gardner; Creeper app. 9,10-Millennium x-over ... 5.00
7-($1.25, 52 pgs.)-Capt. Marvel & Dr. Fate resign; Capt. Atom & Rocket Red join ... 5.00
11-17,22,23,25-49,51-68,71-82: 16-Bruce Wayne-c/story. 31,32-J. L. Europe x-over. 58-Lobo app. 61-New team begins; swipes-c to J.L. of A. #1('60). 70-Newsstand version w/o outer-c. 71-Direct sales version w/black outer-c. 71-Newsstand version w/o outer-c. 80-Intro new Booster Gold. 82,83-Guy Gardner-c ... 4.00
18-21,24,50: 18-21-Lobo app. 24-($1.50)-1st app. Justice League Europe. 50-($1.75, 52 pgs.) ... 5.00

69-Doomsday tie-in; takes place between Superman: The Man of Steel #18 & Superman #74

	GD 2.0	VG 4.0	FN 6.0	VF 8.0	VF/NM 9.0	NM- 9.2
	2	4	6	11	16	20

69,70-2nd printings ... 3.00
70-Funeral for a Friend part 1; red 3/4 outer-c ... 5.00
83-99,101-113: 92-(9/94)-Zero Hour x-over; Triumph app. 113-Green Lantern, Flash & Hawkman app. ... 4.00
100 ($3.95)-Foil-c; 52 pgs. ... 4.00
100 ($2.95)-Newsstand ... 4.00
#0-(10/94) Zero Hour (published between #92 & #93); new team begins (Hawkman, Flash, Wonder Woman, Metamorpho, Nuklon, Crimson Fox, Obsidian & Fire) ... 4.00
Annual 1-8,10 ('87-'94, '96, 68 pgs.): 2-Joker-c/story; Batman cameo. 5-Armageddon 2001 x-over; Silver ink 2nd print. 7-Bloodlines x-over. 8-Elseworlds story. 10-Legends of the Dead Earth ... 5.00
Annual 9 (1995, $3.50)-Year One story ... 5.00
Special 1,2 ('90,'91, 52 pgs.): 1-Giffen plots. 2-Staton-a(p) ... 5.00
Spectacular 1 (1992, $1.50, 52 pgs.)-Intro new JLI & JLE teams; ties into JLI #61 & JLE #37; two interlocking covers by Jurgens ... 5.00
A New Beginning Trade Paperback (1989, $12.95)-r/#1-7 ... 13.00
... International Vol. 1 HC (2008, $24.99) r/#1-7; new intro. by Giffen ... 25.00
... International Vol. 1 SC (2009, $17.99) r/#1-7; new intro. by Giffen ... 18.00
... International Vol. 2 HC (2009, $24.99) r/#8-13, Annual #1 and Suicide Squad #13 ... 25.00
... International Vol. 2 SC (2009, $17.99) r/#8-13, Annual #1 and Suicide Squad #13 ... 18.00
... International Vol. 3 SC (2009, $19.99) r/#14-22 ... 20.00
... International Vol. 4 SC (2010, $17.99) r/#23-30 ... 18.00
... International Vol. 5 SC (2011, $19.99) r/#Annual #2,3 & Justice League Europe #1-6 ... 20.00
... International Vol. 6 SC (2011, $24.99) r/#31-35 & Justice League Europe #7-11 ... 25.00
NOTE: *Anderson* c-61i. *Austin* a-19, 60i; c-1i. *Giffen* a-13; c-21p. *Guice* a-62i. *Maguire* a-1-12, 16-19, 22, 23. *Russell* a-Annual 1i; c-54i. *Willingham* a-30p, Annual 2.

JUSTICE LEAGUE (DC New 52)
DC Comics: Oct, 2011 - No. 52, Aug, 2016 ($3.99)

1-Johns-s/Jim Lee-a/c; Batman, Green Lantern & Superman app.; orange background-c

	GD 2.0	VG 4.0	FN 6.0	VF 8.0	VF/NM 9.0	NM- 9.2
	2	4	6	13	18	22

1-Combo-Pack edition ($4.99) polybagged with digital download code; blue background-c

	GD 2.0	VG 4.0	FN 6.0	VF 8.0	VF/NM 9.0	NM- 9.2
	1	3	4	6	8	10

1-Variant-c by Finch ... 25.00
1-Second printing ... 25.00
2-11,13-23: 3-Wonder Woman & Aquaman arrive. 4-Darkseid arrives. 6-Pandora back-up. 7-Gene Ha-a; back-up Shazam origin begins; Frank-a. 8-D'Anda-a. 13,14-Cheetah app. 15-17-Throne of Atlantis. 22,23-Trinity War. 23-Crime Syndicate arrives ... 4.00
12-Superman/Wonder Woman kiss-c ... 4.00
23.1, 23.2, 23.3, 23.4 (11/13), regular-c ... 3.00
23.1 (11/13, $3.99, 3-D cover) "Darkseid #1" on cover; origin; Kaiyo app.; Reis-c ... 5.00
23.2 (11/13, $3.99, 3-D cover) "Lobo #1" on cover; Bennett-s/Oliver-a/Kuder-c ... 5.00
23.3 (11/13, $3.99, 3-D cover) "Dial E #1" on cover; Miéville-s; art by various ... 5.00
23.4 (11/13, $3.99, 3-D cover) "Secret Society #1" on cover; Owlman app.; Kudranski-a ... 5.00
24-29-Forever Evil. 24-Origin of Ultraman. 25-Origin of Owlman. 27-Cyborg upgraded. 28,29-Metal Men return ... 4.00
30-39: 30-Lex Luthor app.; intro Jessica Cruz. 31-33-Doom Patrol app. 33-Luthor joins. 35-Amazo virus unleashed; intro Lena Luthor ... 4.00
40-Darkseid War prologue, continues in DC's 2015 FCBD edition; intro. Grail (cameo) ... 4.00
41-($4.99) Darkseid War pt 1; Mister Miracle & the Anti-Monitor app.; intro Myrina Black ... 5.00
42-49-Darkseid War. 45,46-Manapul-a ... 4.00
48-Coloring Book variant-c by Kolins ... 4.00
50-($5.99) Conclusion to Darkseid War; Jessica Cruz becomes a Green Lantern; first mention of the "3 Jokers"

	GD 2.0	VG 4.0	FN 6.0	VF 8.0	VF/NM 9.0	NM- 9.2
	3	6	9	14	20	25

51,52: 51-Flashback with Robin; Pelletier-a. Lex Luthor as Superman; Grummett-a ... 4.00
#0-(11/12, $3.99) Origin of Shazam; back-up with Pandora ... 4.00
...: Darkseid War: Batman (12/15, $3.99) Pasarin-a; Batman on Mobius chair; Joe Chill app. ... 4.00
...: Darkseid War: Flash (1/16, $3.99) Merino-a; Flash vs. the Black Racer ... 4.00
...: Darkseid War: Green Lantern (1/16, $3.99) Shaner-a; Hal Jordan becomes God of Light ... 4.00
...: Darkseid War: Lex Luthor (2/16, $3.99) Dazo-a; The God of Apocalypse ... 4.00
...: Darkseid War: Shazam (1/16, $3.99) Kolins-a ... 4.00
...: Darkseid War: Superman (6/16, $3.99) Reis, Jimenez & Pelletier-a; Grail's origin ... 4.00
...: Darkseid War: Superman (3/16, $3.99) Dazo-a; The God of Steel ... 4.00
...: Futures End 1 (11/14, $2.99, regular-c) Cont'd from Justice League United: FE #1 ... 3.00
...: Futures End 1 (11/14, $3.99, 3-D cover) ... 4.00
...: Trinity War Director's Cut 1 (10/13, $5.99) r/#22 pencil art and script ... 6.00

JUSTICE LEAGUE (DC Rebirth)
DC Comics: Sept, 2016 - No. 43, Jun, 2018 ($2.99)
1-11-Hitch-s/Daniel-a. 4-Merino-a. 6-Clark & Derenick-a. 11-Amazo app. ... 3.00
1 Director's Cut (12/16, $7.99) r/#1 with B&W art; original script; variant cover gallery ... 5.00
12-24,26-43: 12,13: Justice League vs. Suicide Squad tie-ins. 12-Max Lord returns. 20,21-Hitch-a. 24-Mera app. 26-Intro. Justice League's children. 32,33-Dark Nights: Metal 41-43-Deathstroke app. ... 3.00
25-($3.99) Hltch-a/Derenick-a. Mera app. ... 4.00
... Day Special Edition 1 (1/18, giveaway) r/Justice League #1 (2011) new Reis-c ... 3.00
...: Rebirth 1 (9/16, $2.99) Hitch-s/a; pre-New 52 Superman joins ... 4.00

JUSTICE LEAGUE (Follows Justice League: No Justice series)
DC Comics: Early Aug, 2018 - No. 75, Jun, 2022 ($3.99/$4.99)
1-24: 1-Snyder-s/Cheung-a; Legion of Doom app. 2-4-Jimenez-a. 5-Tynion IV-s/Mahnke-a. 7,8-Batman Who Laughs and Starman (Will Payton) app. 10,11-Manapul-a. 11,12-Drowned Earth x-over with Aquaman. 19-24-Mr. Mxyzptlk app. ... 4.00

Justice #4 © DC

Justice League (2018 series) #32 © DC

Justice League of America #4 © DC

	GD	VG	FN	VF	VF/NM	NM-
	2.0	4.0	6.0	8.0	9.0	9.2

25-($4.99) Year of the Villain prelude ... 5.00
26-49,51-58: 27-Amazo app. 30-37-Kamandi and the JSA app. 40-42-Madame Xanadu app.
45-The Spectre app. 48,49-Spurrier-s. 53-57-Death Metal tie-ins. 58-Endless Winter ... 4.00
50-($5.99) Conclusion of "The Rule of War"; Lopresti-a ... 6.00
59-74-($4.99): 59-Bendis-s/Marquez-a begins; Naomi app.; back-up JL Dark in all ... 5.00
75-($6.99) Death of the Justice League; acetate outer cover; prelude to Dark Crisis #1 ... 7.00
Annual 1 (3/19, $4.99) New Gods & Green Lantern Corps app.; Sampere-a/Paquette-a ... 5.00
Annual 2 (11/20, $4.99) JLA vs. The Hall of Justice; Venditti-s/Lopresti-a ... 5.00
2022 Annual 1 (4/22, $5.99) Bendis-s/Sanford Greene-a; OMAC app. ... 6.00
... /Aquaman: Drowned Earth 1 (12/18, $4.99) Porter-a; continues in Justice League #11 ... 6.00
...: Road to Dark Crisis 1 (7/22, $5.99) Follows events of Justice League #75 ... 6.00

JUSTICE LEAGUE ADVENTURES (Based on Cartoon Network series)
DC Comics: Jan, 2002 - No. 34, Oct, 2004 ($1.99/$2.25)

1-Timm & Ross-c ... 4.00
2-32: 3-Nicieza-s. 5-Starro app. 10-Begin $2.25-c. 14-Includes 16 pg. insert for VERB
with Haberlin CG-art. 15,29-Amancio-a. 16-McCloud-s. 20-Psycho Pirate app.
25,26-Adam Strange-c/app. 28-Legion of Super-Heroes app. 30-Kamandi app. ... 3.00
Free Comic Book Day giveaway - (5/02) r/#1 with "Free Comic Book Day" banner on-c ... 3.00
TPB (2003, $9.95) r/#1,3,6,10-13; Timm/Ross-c from #1 ... 10.00
...Vol. 1: The Magnificent Seven (2004, $6.95) digest-size reprints #3,6,10-12 ... 7.00
...Vol. 2: Friends and Foes (2004, $6.95) digest-size reprints #13,14,16,19,20 ... 7.00

JUSTICE LEAGUE: A MIDSUMMER'S NIGHTMARE
DC Comics: Sept, 1996 - No. 3, Nov, 1996 ($2.95, limited series, 38 pgs.)

1-3: Re-establishes Superman, Batman, Green Lantern, The Martian Manhunter, Flash,
Aquaman & Wonder Woman as the Justice League; Mark Waid & Fabian Nicieza
co-scripts; Jeff Johnson & Darick Robertson-a(p); Kevin Maguire-c ... 5.00
TPB-(1997, $8.95) r/1-3 ... 9.00

JUSTICE LEAGUE: CRY FOR JUSTICE
DC Comics: Sept, 2009 - No. 7, July, 2010 ($3.99, limited series)

1-7-James Robinson-s/Mauro Cascioli-a/c. 2-Two covers; Congorilla origin ... 4.00
HC (2010, $24.99, d.j.) r/#1-7, Face of Evil: Prometheus ... 25.00
SC (2011, $19.99) r/#1-7, Face of Evil: Prometheus ... 20.00

JUSTICE LEAGUE DARK (DC New 52)
DC Comics: Nov, 2011 - No. 40, May, 2015 ($2.99/$3.99)

1-23: 1-Milligan-s; Deadman, Madame Xanadu, Zatanna, Shade, John Constantine app.
7,8-Crossover with I,Vampire #6,7. 7-Batgirl app. 9-Black Orchid joins. 11,12-Tim Hunter
app. 13-Leads into J.L. Dark Annual #1. 19-21-Flash app. 22,23-Trinity War ... 3.00
23.1, 23.2 (11/13, $2.99, regular-c) ... 3.00
23.1 (11/13, $3.99, 3-D cover) "The Creeper #1" on cover; origin; Nocenti-s/Janin-c ... 5.00
23.2 (11/13, $3.99, 3-D cover) "Eclipso #1" on cover; origin; Tan-a/Janin-c ... 5.00
24-40: 24-29-Forever Evil tie-ins. 40-Constantine returns ... 4.00
#0-(11/12, $2.99) Constantine and Zatanna's 1st meeting; Garbett-a/Sook-c ... 3.00
Annual #1 (2/12, $4.99) Continued from #13; Frankenstein & Amethyst app. ... 5.00
Annual #2 (2/14, $4.99) Janson-a/March-c; House of Wonders app. ... 5.00
...: Futures End 1 (11/14, $2.99, regular-c) Five years later; Etrigan app. ... 3.00
...: Futures End 1 (11/14, $3.99, 3-D cover) ... 5.00

JUSTICE LEAGUE DARK (See back-up stories in Justice League #59-70)
DC Comics: Sept, 2018 - No. 29, Feb, 2021 ($3.99)

1-12: 1-Tynion IV-s; Wonder Woman, Zatanna, Swamp Thing, Detective Chimp app. ... 4.00
13-29: 13-18-Year of the Villain tie-ins. 13-Buckingham-a; origin Dr. Fate. 20-23-Animal Man
app. 20,23-Hotz-a. 29-Endless Winter part 7 ... 4.00
Annual 1 (9/19, $4.99) Jason Woodrue and Circe app. ... 5.00
2021 Annual 1 (1/22, $5.99) Ram V & Watters-s/Kingsland-a; Yuga Khan & Merlin app. ... 6.00
... and Wonder Woman: The Witching Hour 1 (12/18, $4.99) Black Orchid app.; Merino-a ... 5.00

JUSTICE LEAGUE ELITE (See JLA #100 and JLA Secret Files 2004)
DC Comics: Sept, 2004 - No. 12, Aug, 2005 ($2.50)

1-12-Flash, Green Arrow, Vera Black and others; Kelly-s/Mahnke-a. 5,6-JSA app. ... 3.00
JL Elite TPB (2005, $19.99) r/#1-4, Action #775, JLA #100, JLA Secret Files 2004 ... 20.00
...Vol. 2 TPB (2007, $19.99) r/#5-12 ... 20.00

JUSTICE LEAGUE EUROPE (Justice League International #51 on)
DC Comics: Apr, 1989 - No. 68, Sept., 1994 (75¢/$1.00/$1.25/$1.50)

1-Giffen plots in all, breakdowns in #1-8,13-30; Justice League #1-c/swipe ... 5.00
2-10: 7-9-Batman app. 7,8-JLA x-over. 8,9-Superman app. ... 4.00
11-49: 12-Metal Men app. 20-22-Rogers-c/a(p). 33,34-Lobo vs. Despero. 37-New team
begins; swipes-c to JLA #9; see JLA Spectacular ... 4.00
50-($2.50, 68 pgs.)-Battles Sonar ... 4.00
51-68: 68-Zero Hour x-over; Triumph joins Justice League Task Force (See JLTF #17) ... 4.00
Annual 1-5 ('90-'94, 68 pgs.)-1-Return of the Global Guardians; Giffen plots/breakdowns.
2-Armageddon 2001; Giffen-a(p); Rogers-a(p); Golden-a(i). 5-Elseworlds story ... 5.00
NOTE: *Phil Jimenez* a-68p. *Rogers* c/a-20-22. *Sears* a-1-12, 14-19, 23-29; c-1-10, 12, 14-19, 23-29.

JUSTICE LEAGUE: GENERATION LOST (Brightest Day)
DC Comics: Early July, 2010 - No. 24, Early Jun, 2011 ($2.99, bi-weekly limited series)

1-23: 1-Maxwell Lord's return; Winick & Giffen-s. 1-5,7-Harris-c. 13-Magog killed ... 3.00
24-($4.99) Wonder Woman vs. Omac Prime; Lopresti-a/Nguyen-c ... 5.00
... Volume One HC (2010, $39.99, dustjacket) r/#1-12; cover gallery ... 40.00

JUSTICE LEAGUE GIANT (See Wonder Woman Giant #1 for continued JL & Aquaman)
(See reprint of new stories in Wonder Woman: Come Back to Me)
DC Comics: 2018 - No. 7, 2019 ($4.99, 100 pgs., squarebound, Walmart exclusive)

1-New Wonder Woman story Seeley-s/Leonardi-a; reprints Justice League ('11),
The Flash ('11), and Aquaman ('11) in all ... 8.00
2-7: 2-New WW by Seeley-s/Watanabe-a. 3-New WW by Palmiotti & Conner-s/Hardin-a
begins. 4-7-Jonah Hex app. in new WW story ... 5.00

JUSTICE LEAGUE: GODS & MONSTERS (Tie-in to 2015 animated film)
DC Comics: Oct, 2015 - No. 3, Oct, 2015 ($3.99, weekly limited series)

1-3-DeMatteis & Timm-s/Silas-a; alternate Superman, Batman & Wonder Woman ... 4.00
... - Batman 1 (9/15, $3.99) origin of the Kirk Langstrom Batman; Matthew Dow Smith-a ... 4.00
... - Superman 1 (9/15, $3.99) origin of the Hernan Guerra Superman; Morital-a ... 4.00
... - Wonder Woman 1 (9/15, $3.99) origin of Bekka of New Genesis; Leonardi-a ... 4.00

JUSTICE LEAGUE INCARNATE (Story continues in 2022's Justice League #75)
DC Comics: Jan, 2022 - No. 5, May, 2022 ($4.99, limited series)

1-5-Earth-23 Superman, Flashpoint Batman, Capt. Carrot, Doctor Multiverse app. ... 5.00

JUSTICE LEAGUE INFINITY (Style of the Justice League 2001 animated series)
DC Comics: Jul, 2021 - No. 7, Mar, 2022 ($3.99, limited series)

1-7: 1-Amazo returns. 2-Overman app. 3,4-Darkseid app. 5-7 Justice Alliance app. ... 4.00

JUSTICE LEAGUE INTERNATIONAL (See Justice League Europe)

JUSTICE LEAGUE INTERNATIONAL (DC New 52)
DC Comics: Nov, 2011 - No. 12, Oct, 2012 ($2.99)

1-12: 1-Jurgens-s/Lopresti-a/c; Batman, Booster Gold, Guy Gardner, Vixen, Fire, Ice.
8-Batwing joins; OMAC app. ... 3.00
Annual 1 (10/12, $4.99) Fabok-a/c; JLI vs. OMAC; Blue Beetle joins ... 5.00

JUSTICE LEAGUE: LAST RIDE
DC Comics: Jul, 2021 - No. 7, Jan, 2022 ($3.99, limited series)

1-7-Zdarsky-s/Mendonca-a; set in the future; Darkseid, Brainiac, Cyborg Superman app. ... 4.00

JUSTICE LEAGUE: NO JUSTICE
DC Comics: Jul, 2018 - No. 4, Jul, 2018 ($3.99, weekly limited series)

1-4: 1-Brainiac app.; Justice League, Teen Titans, Titans, Suicide Squad team ups.
1,2,4-Manapul-a. 2-Vril Dox app. 3-Rossmo-a ... 4.00

JUSTICE LEAGUE ODYSSEY
DC Comics: Nov, 2018 - No. 25, Dec, 2020 ($3.99)

1-10: 1-Williamson-s/Sejic-a; Cyborg, Starfire, Jessica Cruz and Azrael vs. Darkseid ... 4.00
11-25: 11-15-Year of The Villain tie-ins. 16-Intro Gamma Knife ... 4.00

JUSTICE LEAGUE OF AMERICA (See Brave & the Bold #28-30, Mystery In Space #75 &
Official... Index) (See Crisis on Multiple Earths TPBs for reprints of JLA/JSA crossovers)
National Periodical Publ./DC Comics: Oct-Nov, 1960 - No. 261, Apr, 1987 (r/#1-99,139-157: 52 pgs.)

	GD	VG	FN	VF	VF/NM	NM-
	2.0	4.0	6.0	8.0	9.0	9.2

1-(10-11/60)-Origin & 1st app. Despero; Aquaman, Batman, Flash, Green Lantern, J'onn
J'onzz, Superman & Wonder Woman continue from Brave and the Bold

	GD	VG	FN	VF	VF/NM	NM-	
	650	1300	2600	8450	20,475	32,500	
2	125	250	375	1000	2250	3500	

3-Origin/1st app. Kanjar Ro (see Mystery in Space #75)(scarce in high grade due to black-c)
| | 121 | 242 | 363 | 968 | 2184 | 3450 |

4-Green Arrow joins JLA
| | 82 | 164 | 246 | 656 | 1478 | 2300 |

5-Origin of J.L. app. Dr. Destiny
| | 66 | 132 | 198 | 528 | 1189 | 1850 |

6-8,10: 6-Origin & 1st app. Prof. Amos Fortune. 7-(10-11/61)-Last 10¢ issue. 10-(3/62)-Origin
& 1st app. Felix Faust; 1st app. Lord of Time
| | 46 | 92 | 138 | 359 | 805 | 1250 |

9-(2/62)-Origin JLA (1st origin)
| | 53 | 106 | 159 | 424 | 950 | 1475 |

11-15: 12-(6/62)-Origin & 1st app. Dr. Light. 13-(8/62)-Speedy app.
| | 29 | 58 | 87 | 209 | 467 | 725 |

14-(9/62)-Atom joins JLA
| | 24 | 48 | 72 | 168 | 372 | 575 |

16-20: 17-Adam Strange flashback

21-(8/63)-"Crisis on Earth-One"; re-intro. of JSA in this title (see Flash #129)
(1st S.A. app. Hourman & Dr. Fate)
| | 55 | 110 | 165 | 440 | 995 | 1550 |

22- "Crisis on Earth-Two"; JSA x-over (story continued from #21)
| | 40 | 80 | 120 | 296 | 673 | 1050 |

23-28: 24-Adam Strange app. 27-Robin app.
| | 17 | 34 | 51 | 117 | 259 | 400 |

29-"Crisis on Earth-Three"; JSA x-over; 1st app. Crime Syndicate of America (Ultraman,
Owlman, Superwoman, Power Ring, Johnny Quick); 1st S.A. app. Starman
| | 36 | 72 | 108 | 266 | 596 | 925 |

30-JSA x-over; Crime Syndicate app.
| | 20 | 40 | 60 | 138 | 307 | 475 |

31-Hawkman joins JLA, Hawkgirl cameo (11/64)
| | 15 | 30 | 45 | 105 | 233 | 360 |

	GD 2.0	VG 4.0	FN 6.0	VF 8.0	VF/NM 9.0	NM- 9.2
32,34: 32-Intro & Origin Brain Storm. 34-Joker-c/sty	11	22	33	72	154	235
33,35,36,40,41: 40-3rd S.A. Penguin app. 41-Intro & origin The Key	10	20	30	66	138	210
37-39: 37,38-JSA x-over. 37-1st S.A. app. Mr. Terrific; Batman cameo. 38-"Crisis on Earth-A".						
39-Giant G-16; r/B&B #28,30 & JLA #5	12	24	36	83	182	280
42-45: 42-Metamorpho app. 43-Intro. Royal Flush Gang	8	16	24	56	108	160
46-JSA x-over; 1st S.A. app. Sandman; 3rd S.A. app. of G.A. Spectre (8/66)	14	28	42	96	211	325
47-JSA x-over; 4th S.A. app. of G.A. Spectre.	10	20	30	66	138	210
48-Giant G-29; r/JLA #2,3 & B&B #29	9	18	27	59	117	175
49,50,52-54,57,59,60	7	14	21	46	86	125
51-Zatanna app.	10	20	30	66	147	225
55-Intro. Earth 2 Robin (1st G.A. Robin in S.A.)	10	20	30	66	138	210
56-JLA vs. JSA (1st G.A. Wonder Woman in S.A.)	9	18	27	63	129	195
58-Giant G-41; r/JLA #6,8,1	9	18	27	57	111	165
61-63,66,68-72: 69-Wonder Woman quits. 71-Manhunter leaves. 72-Last 12¢ issue	5	10	15	35	63	90
64-(8/68)-JSA story; origin/1st app. S.A. Red Tornado	10	20	30	70	150	230
65-JSA story continues	6	12	18	38	69	100
67-Giant G-53; r/JLA #4,14,31	8	16	24	52	99	145
73-1st S.A. app. of G.A. Superman	8	16	24	51	96	140
74-Black Canary joins; Larry Lance dies; 1st meeting of G.A. & S.A. Superman; Neal Adams-c	10	20	30	70	150	230
75-2nd app. Green Arrow in new costume (see Brave & the Bold #85)	36	72	108	259	580	900
76-Giant G-65	6	12	18	42	79	115
77-80: 78-Re-intro Vigilante (1st S.A. app?)	4	8	12	28	47	65
81-90: 82-1st S.A. app. of G.A. Batman (cameo). 83-Apparent death of The Spectre. 87-Zatanna app. 90-Last 15¢ issue	4	8	12	27	44	60
91,92: 91-1st meeting of the G.A. & S.A. Robin; begin 25¢, 52 pg. issues, ends #99. 92-S.A. Robin costume on issue that is similar to that of G.A. Robin in All Star Comics #58	4	8	12	28	47	65
93-(Giant G-77,G-89; 68 pgs.)	6	12	18	41	76	110
94-1st app. Merlyn (Green Arrow villain); reprints first Sandman story (Adv. #40) & origin/1st app. Starman (Adv. #61); Deadman x-over; N. Adams-a (4 pgs.)		12	24	54	102	150
95,96: 95-Origin Dr. Fate & Dr. Midnight-r/ More Fun #67, All-American #25). 96-Origin Hourman (Adv. #48); Wildcat-r	5	10	15	30	50	70
97-99: 97-Origin JLA retold; Sargon, Starman-r. 98-S.A. Sargon, Starman-r. 99-S.A. Sandman, Atom-r; last 52 pg. issue	4	8	12	27	44	60
100-(8/72)-1st meeting of G.A. & S.A. W. Woman	7	14	21	44	82	120
101,102: JSA x-over. 102-Red Tornado destroyed	4	8	12	28	47	65
103-106,109: 103-Rutland Vermont Halloween x-over; Phantom Stranger joins. 105-Elongated Man joins. 106-New Red Tornado joins. 109-Hawkman resigns	3	6	9	19	26	32
107,108,116: 1st revival app. of G.A. Uncle Sam, Black Condor, The Ray, Dollman, Phantom Lady & The Human Bomb	4	8	12	28	47	65
110,112-116: All 100 pgs. 112-Amazo app.; Crimson Avenger, Vigilante-r; origin Starman-r/ Adv. #81. 115-Martian Manhunter app.	5	10	15	33	57	80
111-JLA vs. Injustice Gang; intro. Libra (re-appears in 2008's Final Crisis); Shining Knight, Green Arrow-r	5	10	15	33	60	85
117-122,125-134: 117-Hawkman rejoins. 120,121-Adam Strange app. 125,126-Two-Face-app. 128-Wonder Woman rejoins	3	6	9	16	23	30
123-(10/75),124: JLA/JSA x-over. DC editor Julie Schwartz & JLA writers Cary Bates & Elliot S! Maggin appear in story as themselves. 1st named app. Earth-Prime (3rd app. after Flash; 1st Series #179 & 228)	3	6	9	21	33	45
135-136: 135-137-G.A. Bulletman, Bulletgirl, Spy Smasher, Mr. Scarlet, Pinky & Ibis x-over, 1st appearances since #7	4	8	12	26	43	60
137-(12/76) Superman battles G.A. Captain Marvel	5	10	15	33	57	80
138-Adam Strange app. w/c by Neal Adams; 1st app. Green Lantern of the 73rd Century	4	8	12	28	40	55
139-157: 139-157-(52 pgs.): 139-Adam Strange app. 144-Origin retold; origin J'onn J'onzz. 145-Red Tornado resurrected. 147,148-Legion of Super-Heroes x-over	2	4	6	10	14	18
158-160-(44 pgs.)	2	4	6	8	11	14
158,160-162,169,171,172,173,176,179,181-(Whitman variants; low print run, none show issue # on cover)	2	4	6	10	14	18
161-165,169-182: 161-Zatanna joins & new costume. 171,172-JSA x-over. 171-Mr. Terrific murdered. 178-Cover similar to #1; J'onn J'onzz app. 179-Firestorm joins. 181-Green Arrow leaves JLA	1	2	3	5	6	8
166-168- "Identity Crisis (2004)" precursor; JSA app. vs. Secret Society of Super-Villains	3	6	9	16	23	30
166-168-Whitman variants (no issue # on covers)	4	8	12	23	37	50
183-185-JSA/New Gods/Darkseid/Mr. Miracle x-over	2	4	6	10	14	18
186-194,198,199: 192,193-Real origin Red Tornado. 193-1st app. All-Star Squadron as free 16 pg. insert	1	2	3	4	6	8
195-197-JSA app. vs. Secret Society of Super-Villains	1	2	3	4	6	8
200-($1.50, Anniversary issue, 76 pgs.)-JLA origin retold; Green Arrow rejoins; Bolland, Aparo, Giordano, Gil Kane, Infantino, Kubert-a; Pérez-c/a	2	4	6	10	14	18
201-206,209-243,246-259: 203-Intro/origin new Royal Flush Gang. 219,220-True origin Black Canary. 228-Re-intro Martian Manhunter. 228-230-War of the Worlds storyline; JLA Satellite destroyed by Martians. 233-Story cont'd from Annual #2. 243-Aquaman leaves. 250-Batman rejoins. 253-Origin Despero. 258-Death of Vibe. 258-261-Legends x-over						6.00
207,208-JSA, JLA, & All-Star Squadron team-up						8
244,245-Crisis x-over						6.00
260-Death of Steel	1	2	3	5	6	8
261-Last issue	1	3	4	6	8	10
Annual 1-3 ('83-'85), 2-Intro new J.L.A. (Aquaman, Martian Manhunter, Steel, Gypsy, Vixen, Vibe, Elongated Man & Zatanna). 3-Crisis x-over	1	2	3	5	6	8
... Hereby Elects (2006, $14.99, TPB) reprints issues where new members joined; JLofA #4,75,105,106,146,161,173 & 174; roster of various incarnations; Ordway-c						15.00

NOTE: *Neal Adams* c-63, 66, 67, 70, 74, 79, 81, 82, 86-89, 91, 138; reprints in annuals c-1-4, 6, 7, 10, 12-14. *Aparo* a-200. *Austin* a-200i. *Baily* a-96r. *Bolland* a-200. *Buckler* c-158, 163, 164. *Burnley* r-94, 98. *Greene* a-46-61i, 64-73i, 110i(r). *Grell* c-117, 122. *Kaluta* c-154p. *Gil Kane* a-200. *Krigstein* a-96i(r/Sensation #84). *Kubert* a-200; c-72, 73. *Nino* a-228i, 230i. *Orlando* c-151i. *Perez* a-184-186p, 192-197p, 200p; c-184p, 186, 192-195, 196p, 197p, 199, 200, 201p, 202, 203-205p, 207-209, 212-215, 217, 219, 220. *Reinman* c-97. *Roussos* a-62i. *Sekowsky* a-37, 38, 44-63p, 110-112p(r); c-46-48p, 51p. *Sekowsky/Anderson* c-5, 8, 9, 11, 15. *B. Smith* c-185i. *Starlin* c-178-180, 183, 185p. *Staton* a-244p; c-157p, 244p. *Toth* r-110. *Tuska* a-153, 228p, 241-243p. JSA x-overs-21, 22, 29, 30, 37, 38, 46, 47, 55, 56, 64, 65, 73, 74, 82, 83, 91, 92, 100, 101, 102, 107, 108, 110, 113, 115, 123, 124, 135-137, 147, 148, 159, 160, 171, 172, 183-185, 195-197, 207-209, 219, 220, 231, 232, 244.

JUSTICE LEAGUE OF AMERICA
DC Comics: No. 0, Sept, 2006 - No. 60, Oct, 2011 ($2.99/$3.99)

	NM- 9.2
0-Meltzer-s; history of the JLA; art by various incl. Lee, Giordano, Benes; Turner-c	5.00
0-Variant-c by Campbell	15.00
1-($3.99) Two interlocking covers by Benes; Benes-a	5.00
1-Variant-c by Turner	8.00
1-RRP Edition; sideways composite of both Benes covers	50.00
1-Second printing; Benes cover image between black bars	4.00
2-5-($2.99) Turner-c	4.00
2-5: Variant-c: 2-Jimenez. 3-Sprouse. 4-JG Jones. 5-Art Adams	5.00
6,7-($3.50) 6-JLA vs. Amazo; covers by Turner and Hughes. 7-Roster picked, new HQs; two Benes covers and Turner cover.	4.00
8-11,13-24,26-38-($2.99) 8-11-JLA/JSA team-up; covers by Turner & Jimenez. 10-Wally West returns. 13-Two covers. 14-15-Injustice Gang. 16-Tangent Flash. 20-Queen Bee app. 21-Libra app.; leads into Final Crisis #1. 35,36-Royal Flush Gang app. 38-Bagley-a begins	3.00
12-($3.50) Two Ross covers; origin retold with Wight-a; Benes-a	4.00
25-($3.99) McDuffie-s/art by various; Benes-c	4.00
39-49,51,52-($3.99) 39,40-Blackest Night. 41-New team; 2 covers. 44-48-Justice Society app. 44-Jade returns.	4.00
50-($4.99) Crime Syndicate app.; Bagley-a; wraparound-c by Van Sciver	5.00
50-Variant-c by Bagley, swipe of Quitely's JLA: Earth 2 cover	5.00
50-Variant-c by Jim Lee; swipe of Brave and the Bold #28 Starro cover	120.00
53-60-($2.99) 54-Booth-a; Eclipso returns. 55-Doomsday app.	3.00
... 80 Page Giant (11/09, $5.99) Anacleto-c; short stories by various; Ra's al Ghul app.	6.00
... 80 Page Giant 2011 (6/11, $5.99) Lau-c; chapters by various; JLA goes to Hell	6.00
Free Comic Book Day giveaway - (2007) r/#0 with "Free Comic Book Day" banner on-c	3.00
Justice League Wedding Special 1 (11/07, $3.99) McKone-a; Injustice League forms	4.00
...: Dark Things HC (2011, $24.99, dustjacket) r/#44-48 & J.S.A. #41,42	25.00
...: The Injustice Gang HC (2008, $19.99, dustjacket) r/#13-16; Wedding Special	20.00
...: The Lightning Saga HC (2008, $24.99, dustjacket) r/#0,8-12 & Justice Society of America #5,6; intro. by Patton Oswalt	25.00
...: The Lightning Saga SC (2008, $17.99) r/#0,8-12 & J.S.A. #5,6; intro. by Oswalt	18.00
...: Sanctuary SC (2009, $14.99) r/#17-21	15.00
...: Second Coming HC (2009, $19.99, dustjacket) r/#22-26	20.00
...: Second Coming SC (2010, $17.99) r/#22-26	18.00
...: Team History HC (2010, $19.99, dustjacket) r/#38-43	20.00
...: The Tornado's Path HC (2007, $24.99, dustjacket) r/#1-7; variant cover gallery; Lindelof intro.; commentary by Meltzer & Benes	25.00
...: The Tornado's Path SC (2008, $17.99) r/#1-7; variant cover gallery; Lindelof intro.; commentary by Meltzer & Benes	18.00
...: When Worlds Collide HC (2009, $24.99, dustjacket) r/#27,28,30-34	25.00
...: When Worlds Collide SC (2010, $14.99) r/#27,28,30-34	15.00

JUSTICE LEAGUE OF AMERICA (DC New 52) (Leads into Justice League United)
DC Comics: Apr, 2013 - No. 14, Jul, 2014 ($3.99)

	NM- 9.2
1-14: Hitch-s/Finch-a/c; Green Arrow, Catwoman, Martian Manhunter, Katana & others team; variant covers with U.S. flag and each of the 50 state flags plus DC and Puerto Rico. 2-Covers by Finch and Ryp. 3-7: 3-5-Martian Manhunter back-up. 4,5-Shaggy Man app. 6,7-Trinity War. 8-14-Forever Evil. 10-Stargirl origin. 11,12-Despero app.	4.00
7.1, 7.2, 7.3, 7.4 (11/13, $2.99, regular-c)	3.00
7.1 (11/13, $3.99, 3-D cover) "Deadshot #1" on cover; origin; Kindt-s/Daniel-c	5.00
7.2 (11/13, $3.99, 3-D cover) "Killer Frost #1" on cover; origin; Gates-s/Santacruz-a	5.00
7.3 (11/13, $3.99, 3-D cover) "Shadow Thief #1" on cover; origin; Hardin-s/Daniel-c	5.00
7.4 (11/13, $3.99, 3-D cover) "Black Adam #1" on cover; Black Adam returns	5.00

JUSTICE LEAGUE OF AMERICA
DC Comics: Aug, 2015 - No. 10, Jan, 2017 ($5.99/$3.99)

	NM- 9.2
1-($5.99) Bryan Hitch-s/a; the Parasite app.	6.00
2-10-($3.99) 2-4-Hitch-s/a. 5-Martian Manhunter spotlight; Kindt & Williams-s/Tan-a	4.00

JUSTICE LEAGUE OF AMERICA (DC Rebirth)
DC Comics: Apr, 2017 - No. 29, Jun, 2018 ($2.99)

	NM- 9.2
1-24,26-29: 1-Orlando-s/Reis-a; team of Batman, Black Canary, Lobo, Vixen, Killer Frost, The Atom & The Ray; Lord Havok app. 14-17-Ray Palmer app. 18-20-Prometheus app. 21-Intro new Aztek. 22-24-Queen of Fables app. 23,24-Prometheus app.	3.00
25-($3.99) Lord Havok app.	4.00
Annual 1 (1/18, $4.99) Lobo & Black Canary team-up; Kelley Jones-a	5.00
...: Killer Frost - Rebirth 1 (3/17, $2.99) Orlando-s/Andolfo-a; Amanda Waller app.	3.00
...: Rebirth 1 (4/17, $2.99) Orlando-s/Reis-a; team assembles	3.00
...: The Atom - Rebirth 1 (3/17, $2.99) Orlando-s; Ryan Choi as the new Atom	3.00
...: The Ray - Rebirth 1 (3/17, $2.99) Orlando-s; Stephen Byrne-a	3.00
...: Vixen - Rebirth 1 (3/17, $2.99) Orlando & Houser-s; Jamal Campbell-a; origin retold	3.00

JUSTICE LEAGUE OF AMERICA : ANOTHER NAIL (Elseworlds) (Also see JLA: The Nail)
DC Comics: 2004 - No. 3, 2004 ($5.95, prestige format)

	NM- 9.2
1-3-Sequel to JLA: The Nail; Alan Davis-s/a(p)	6.00
TPB (2004, $12.95) r/series	13.00

JUSTICE LEAGUE OF AMERICA SUPER SPECTACULAR
DC Comics: 1999 ($5.95, mimics format of DC 100 Page Super Spectaculars)

	NM- 9.2
1-Reprints Silver Age JLA and Golden Age JSA	6.00

JUSTICE LEAGUE OF AMERICA'S VIBE (DC New 52)
DC Comics: Apr, 2013 - No. 10, Feb, 2014 ($2.99)

	NM- 9.2
1-10: 1,2-Johns & Kreisberg-s/Woods-a/Finch-c; origin. 5-Suicide Squad app.	3.00

JUSTICE LEAGUE OF AMERICA/ THE 99
DC Comics: Dec, 2010 - No. 6, May, 2011 ($3.99/$2.99, limited series)

	NM- 9.2
1-3-($3.99) Derenick-a/Massaferra-a; JLA meets Teshkeel Comics characters	4.00
4-6-($2.99) Starro app.	3.00

JUSTICE LEAGUE OF AMERICA/ POWER RANGERS
DC Comics: Mar, 2017 - No. 6, Nov, 2017 ($3.99, limited series)

	NM- 9.2
1-6-Tom Taylor-s/Stephen Byrne-a; Lord Zedd app.; Power Rangers in JLA dimension	4.00

Justice League of America (2007 series) #8 © DC

Justice League United #14 © DC

Justice Society of America #54 © DC

	GD	VG	FN	VF	VF/NM	NM-		GD	VG	FN	VF	VF/NM	NM-
	2.0	4.0	6.0	8.0	9.0	9.2		2.0	4.0	6.0	8.0	9.0	9.2

JUSTICE LEAGUE QUARTERLY (...International Quarterly #6 on)
DC Comics: Winter, 1990-91 - No. 17, Winter, 1994 ($2.95/$3.50, 84 pgs.)

1-12,14-17: 1-Intro The Conglomerate (Booster Gold, Praxis, Gypsy, Vapor, Echo, Maxi-Man,
& Reverb); Justice League #1-c/swipe. 1,2-Giffen plots/breakdowns. 3-Giffen plot; 72 pgs.
4-Rogers/Russell-a in back-up. 5,6-Mark Waid scripts. 8,17-Global Guardians app.   4.00
13-Linsner-a   6.00
NOTE: Phil Jimenez a-17p. Sprouse a-1p.

JUSTICE LEAGUE: RISE AND FALL
DC Comics: 2010, 2011

Justice League of America: Rise and Fall Special #1 (5/10, $3.99) Hunt for Green Arrow   4.00
HC-(2011, $24.99) Reprints Justice League of America #43, Justice League: The Rise and Fall
Special #1, Green Arrow #31,32 and Justice League: The Rise of Arsenal #1-4   25.00

JUSTICE LEAGUES...
DC Comics: Mar, 2001 ($2.50, limited series)

JL?, Justice League of Amazons, Justice League of Atlantis, Justice League of Arkham,
Justice League of Aliens, JLA: JLA split by the Advance Man; Perez-c in all;
s&a by various   3.00

JUSTICE LEAGUE TASK FORCE
DC Comics: June, 1993 - No. 37, Aug, 1996 ($1.25/$1.50/$1.75)

1-37: Aquaman, Nightwing, Flash, J'onn J'onzz, & Gypsy form team. 5,6-Knight-quest
tie-ins (new Batman cameo #5, 1 pg.). 15-Triumph cameo. 16-(9/94)-Zero Hour x-over;
Triumph app.; leads into issue #0. 17-(11/94)-Triumph becomes part of Justice League Task
Force (See JLE #68). 26-Impulse app. 35-Warlord app. 37-Triumph quits team   4.00
#0 (10/94) Zero Hour; released between #16 & #17   4.00

JUSTICE LEAGUE: THE NEW FRONTIER SPECIAL (Also see DC: The New Frontier)
DC Comics: May, 2006 ($4.99, one-shot)

1-Short stories by Darwyn Cooke, J. Bone and Dave Bullock; bonus movie storyboards   5.00

JUSTICE LEAGUE: THE RISE OF ARSENAL (Follows Justice League: Cry For Justice)
DC Comics: May, 2010 - No. 4, Aug, 2010 ($3.99, limited series)

1-4-Horn-a/Borges-a/Krul-s. 2,3-Cheshire app.   4.00

JUSTICE LEAGUE 3000
DC Comics: Feb, 2014 - No. 15, May, 2015 ($2.99)

1-15-Justice League of the 31st century. 1-Giffen & DeMatteis-s/Porter-a/c. 10-Etrigan app.
11-Blue Beetle and Booster Gold cameo. 12-14-Blue Beetle and Booster Gold app.
14-Kamandi app.; Kuhn-a 14,15-Etrigan app. 15-Fire returns   3.00

JUSTICE LEAGUE 3001
DC Comics: Aug, 2015 - No. 12, Jul, 2016 ($2.99)

1-12: 1-Giffen & DeMatteis-s/Porter-a/c; Supergirl app. 4-Kolins-a. 5,6-Harley Quinn app. 3.00

JUSTICE LEAGUE UNITED (DC New 52)
DC Comics: No. 0, Jun, 2014 - No. 16, Feb, 2016 ($3.99)

0-16: 0-Lemire-s/McKone-a; Adam Strange, Lobo & Byth app. 3-Hawkman killed.
6-10-Legion of Super-Heroes app. 11-13,15-Harris-c. 13-15-Sgt Rock app.   4.00
Annual #1 (12/14, $4.99) Legion of Super-Heroes app.; continued in #6   5.00
...: Futures End (11/14, $2.99, reg-c) 5 years later; 2-parter with Justice League: FE #1   3.00
...: Futures End 1 (11/14, $3.99, 3-D cover)   4.00

JUSTICE LEAGUE UNLIMITED (Based on Cartoon Network animated series)
DC Comics: Nov, 2004 - No. 46, Aug, 2008 ($2.25)

1-46: 1-2,23,42-Royal Flush Gang app. 4-Adam Strange app.
10-Creeper app. 17-Freedom Fighters app. 18-Space Cabby app. 27-Black Lightning app.
34-Zod app. 41-Harley Quinn-c/app.   3.00
Free Comic Book Day giveaway (5/06) r/#1 with "Free Comic Book Day" banner on-c   3.00
Jam Packed Action (2005, $7.99, digest) adaptations of two TV episodes   8.00
... Vol. 1: United They Stand (2005, $6.99, digest) r/#1-5   7.00
... Vol. 2: World's Greatest Heroes (2006, $6.99, digest) r/#6-10   7.00
... Vol. 3: Champions of Justice (2006, $6.99, digest) r/#11-15   7.00
...: Heroes (2009, $12.99, full-size) r/#23-29   13.00
... The Ties That Bind (2008, $12.99, full-size) r/#16-22   13.00

JUSTICE LEAGUE VS. GODZILLA VS. KONG
DC Comics: Dec, 2023 - No. 7 ($4.99, limited series)

1-5-Buccellato-s/Duce-a; 1-Legion of Doom app.   5.00
...: Monster-Sized Edition 1 (3/24, $6.99) Reprints #1 & 2   7.00

JUSTICE LEAGUE VS. SUICIDE SQUAD (Leads into Justice League of America '17 series)
DC Comics: Feb, 2017 - No. 6, Mar, 2017 ($2.99, weekly limited series)

1-6: 1-Max Lord & Lobo app.; Fabok-a. 2-Daniel-a. 4-6-Eclipso app. 6-Porter-a   4.00

JUSTICE LEAGUE VS. THE LEGION OF SUPER-HEROES
DC Comics: Mar, 2022 - No. 6, Nov, 2022 ($3.99, limited series)

1-6-Bendis-s/Godlewski-a; teams face The Great Darkness   4.00

JUSTICE MACHINE, THE
Noble Comics: June, 1981 - No. 5, Nov, 1983 ($2.00, nos. 1-3 are mag. size)

1-Byrne-c(p)		3	6	9	15	21	26
2-Austin-c(i)		2	4	6	9	12	15
3		1	3	4	6	8	10
4,5							6.00

Annual 1 (1/84, 68 pgs.)(published by Texas Comics); 1st app. The Elementals; Golden-c(p);
new Thunder Agents story (43 pgs.)   2 4 6 8 10 12

JUSTICE MACHINE (Also see The New Justice Machine)
Comico/Innovation Publishing: Jan, 1987 - No. 29, May 1989 ($1.50/$1.75)

1-29   4.00
Annual 1(6/89, $2.50, 36 pgs.)-Last Comico ish.   4.00
Summer Spectacular 1 ('89, $2.75)-Innovation Publ.; Byrne/Gustovich-c   4.00

JUSTICE MACHINE, THE
Innovation Publishing: 1990 - No. 4, 1990 ($1.95/$2.25, deluxe format, mature)

1-4: Gustovich-c/a in all   4.00

JUSTICE MACHINE FEATURING THE ELEMENTALS
Comico: May, 1986 - No. 4, Aug, 1986 ($1.50, limited series)

1-4   4.00

JUSTICE RIDERS
DC Comics: 1997 ($5.95, one-shot, prestige format)

1-Elseworlds; Dixon-s/Williams & Gray-a   6.00

JUSTICE SOCIETY
DC Comics: 2006; 2007 ($14.99, TPB)

Vol. 1 - Rep. from 1976 revival in All Star Comics #58-67 & DC Special #29; Bolland-c   15.00
Vol. 2 - R/All Star Comics #68-74 & Adventure Comics #461-466; new Bolland-c   15.00

JUSTICE SOCIETY OF AMERICA (See Adventure #461 & All-Star #3)
DC Comics: April, 1991 - No. 8, Nov, 1991 ($1.00, limited series)

1-8: 1-Flash. 2-Black Canary. 3-Green Lantern. 4-Hawkman. 5-Flash/Hawkman.
6-Green Lantern/Black Canary. 7-JSA   4.00

JUSTICE SOCIETY OF AMERICA (Also see Last Days of the... Special)
DC Comics: Aug, 1992 - No. 10, May, 1993 ($1.25)

1-10: 1-1st app. Jesse Quick   4.00

JUSTICE SOCIETY OF AMERICA (Follows JSA series)
DC Comics: Feb, 2007 - No. 54, Oct, 2011 ($3.99/$2.99)

1-($3.99) New team selected; intro. Maxine Hunkle; Alex Ross-c
		2	4	6	9	12	15
		2	4	6	10	14	18

1-Variant-c by Eaglesham
2-22,24-49,51-54: 1-Covers by Ross & Eaglesham. 3,4-Vandal Savage app. 5,6-JLA/JSA
team-up. 9-22-Kingdom Come Superman app.18-Magog app. 22-Superman returns to
Kingdom Come Earth; Ross partial art. 23-25-Ordway-a. 26-Triptych cover by Ross.
33-Team splits. 34,35-Mordru app. 41,42-Justice League x-over. 52-54-Challengers of the
Unknown app. 54-Darwyn Cooke-c   3.00
23-Black Adam-c/app.   6.00
50-($4.99) Degaton app.; art by Derenick, Chaykin, Williams II, and Pérez; Massafera-c   5.00
JSA Annual 1 (9/08, $3.99) Power Girl on Earth-2; Ross-c/Ordway-a   5.00
JSA Annual 2 (4/10, $4.99) All Star team app.; Magog quits; Williams-a   5.00
... 80 Page Giant (1/10, $5.99) short stories by various incl. Ordway, S. Hampton   6.00
... 80 Page Giant 2010 (12/10, $5.99) short stories by various   6.00
... 80 Page Giant 2011 (8/11, $5.99) short stories by various incl. Chaykin, Hampton   6.00
...: Special (11/10, $4.99) Scott Kolins-s/a; spotlight on Magog   6.00
...: Axis of Evil SC (2010, $14.99) r/#34-40   15.00
...: Black Adam and Isis HC (2009, $19.99, d.j.) r/#23-28   20.00
...: Black Adam and Isis SC (2010, $14.99) r/#23-28   15.00
...: Kingdom Come Special: Magog (1/09, $3.99) Pasarin-a; origin re-told; 2 covers   4.00
...: Kingdom Come Special: Superman (1/09, $3.99) Lois' death re-told; Alex Ross-s/a/c;
thumbnails, photo references, sketch art   4.00
...: Kingdom Come Special: Superman (1/09, $3.99) Eaglesham variant cover   8.00
...: Kingdom Come Special: The Kingdom (1/09, $3.99) Pasarin-a; 2 covers   4.00
...: The Bad Seed SC (2010, $14.99) r/#29-33   15.00
...: The Next Age SC (2008, $14.99) r/#1-4; Ross and Eaglesham sketch pages   15.00
...: Thy Kingdom Come Part One HC (2008, $19.99, d.j.) r/#7-12; Ross sketch pages   20.00
...: Thy Kingdom Come Part One SC (2009, $14.99) r/#7-12; Ross sketch pages   15.00
...: Thy Kingdom Come Part Two HC (2008, $24.99, d.j.) r/#13-18 & Annual #1; Ross sketch
pages   25.00
...: Thy Kingdom Come Part Two SC (2009, $19.99) r/#13-18 & Ann. #1; Ross sketch-a   20.00
...: Thy Kingdom Come Part Three HC (2009, $24.99, d.j.) r/#19-22 & K.C. Specials -
Superman, Magog and The Kingdom; Ross sketch pages   25.00
...: Thy Kingdom Come Part Three SC (2010, $19.99) same contents as HC   20.00

	GD	VG	FN	VF	VF/NM	NM-
	2.0	4.0	6.0	8.0	9.0	9.2

JUSTICE SOCIETY OF AMERICA (Follows The New Golden Age one-shot)
DC Comics: Jan, 2023 - Present ($3.99)

	GD	VG	FN	VF	VF/NM	NM-
1-9: 1-Johns-s/Janin-a. 2-Huntress meets the 1940 JSA. 6,7-Young Justice Society app.						4.00
... Gold Edition 1 (12/23, $4.99) Reprints #1-3						5.00

JUSTICE SOCIETY OF AMERICA 100-PAGE SUPER SPECTACULAR
DC Comics: 2000 ($6.95, mimics format of DC 100 Page Super Spectaculars)

1-"1975 Issue" reprints Flash team-up and Golden Age JSA						7.00

JUSTICE SOCIETY RETURNS, THE (See All Star Comics (1999) for related titles)
DC Comics: 2003 ($19.95, TPB)

TPB-Reprints 1999 JSA x-over from All-Star Comics #1,2 and related one-shots						20.00

JUSTICE TRAPS THE GUILTY (Fargo Kid V11#3 on)
Prize/Headline Publications: Oct-Nov, 1947 - V11#(#92), Apr-May, 1958 (True FBI Cases)

	GD	VG	FN	VF	VF/NM	NM-
V2#1-S&K-c/a; electrocution-c	110	220	330	704	1202	1700
2-S&K-c/a	47	94	141	296	498	700
3-5-S&K-c/a	39	78	117	240	395	550
6-S&K-c/a; Feldstein-a	47	94	141	296	498	700
7,9-S&K-c/a. 7-9-V2#1-3 in indicia; #7-9 on-c	36	72	108	214	347	480
8-Krigstein-a; S&K-c; lie detector machine-a	34	68	102	199	325	450
10-Krigstein-a; S&K-c/a	36	72	108	214	347	480
11,18,19-S&K-c	21	42	63	124	202	280
12,14-17,20-No S&K. 14-Severin/Elder-a (8pg.)	15	30	45	83	124	165
13-Used in SOTI, pg. 110-111	18	36	54	103	162	220
21,30-S&K-c/a	22	44	66	132	216	300
22,23-S&K-c	17	34	51	98	154	210
24-26,27,29,31-50: 32-Meskin story	14	28	42	80	115	150
28-Kirby-c	17	34	51	98	154	210
51-55,57,59-70	13	26	39	72	101	130
56-Ben Oda, Joe Simon, Joe Genola, Mort Meskin & Jack Kirby app. in police line-up on classic-c	26	52	78	154	252	350
58-Illo. in SOTI, "Treating police contemptuously" (top left); text on heroin	37	74	111	222	361	500
71-92: 76-Orlando-a	10	20	30	56	76	95

NOTE: *Bailey* a-12, 13. *Elder* a-8. *Kirby* a-19p. *Meskin* a-22, 27, 63, 64; c-45, 46. *Robinson/Meskin* a-5, 19. *Severin* a-8, 11p. Photo c-12, 15-17.

JUST IMAGINE STAN LEE WITH... (Stan Lee re-invents DC icons)
DC Comics: 2001 - 2002 ($5.95, prestige format, one-shots)
(Adam Hughes back-c on all)(Michael Uslan back-up stories in all, diff. artists)

	GD	VG	FN	VF	VF/NM	NM-
Scott McDaniel Creating **Aquaman**- Back-up w/Ramona Fradon-a						6.00
Joe Kubert Creating **Batman**- Back-up w/Michael Kaluta-a						6.00
Chris Bachalo Creating **Catwoman**- Back-up w/Darwyn Cooke & Mike Allred-a	2	4	6	8	10	12
John Cassaday Creating **Crisis**- no back-up story						6.00
Kevin Maguire Creating **The Flash**- Back-up w/Sergio Aragonés-a						6.00
Dave Gibbons Creating **Green Lantern**- Back-up w/Dick Giordano-a						6.00
Jerry Ordway Creating **JLA**						6.00
John Byrne Creating **Robin**- Back-up w/John Severin-a						6.00
Walter Simonson Creating **Sandman**- Back-up w/Richard Corben-a						6.00
Gary Frank Creating **Shazam!**- Back-up w/Kano-a	1	2	3	5	6	8
John Buscema Creating **Superman**- Back-up w/Kyle Baker-a	2	4	6	8	10	12
Jim Lee Creating **Wonder Woman**- Back-up w/Gene Colan-a	2	4	6	8	11	14
Secret Files and Origins #1 (3/02, $4.95) Crisis prologue; Jurgens-a						5.00
TPB -Just Imagine Stan Lee Creating the DC Universe: Book One (2002, $19.95) r/Batman, Wonder Woman, Superman, Green Lantern						20.00
TPB -Just Imagine Stan Lee Creating the DC Universe: Book Two (2003, $19.95) r/Flash, JLA, Secret Files and Origins, Robin, Shazam; sketch pages						20.00
TPB -Just Imagine Stan Lee Creating the DC Universe: Book Three (2004, $19.95) r/Aquaman, Catwoman, Sandman, Crisis; profile pages						20.00

JUST MARRIED
Charlton Comics: January, 1958 - No. 114, Dec, 1976

	GD	VG	FN	VF	VF/NM	NM-
1	10	20	30	66	138	210
2	5	10	15	31	53	75
3-10	4	8	12	25	40	55
11-30	3	6	9	17	26	35
31-50	2	4	6	11	16	20
51-70	2	4	6	9	13	16
71-78,80-89	2	4	6	8	11	14
79-Ditko-a (7 pages)	2	4	6	10	14	18
90-Susan Dey and David Cassidy full page poster	2	4	6	11	16	20
91-114	2	4	6	8	10	12

KA'A'NGA COMICS (...Jungle King)(See Jungle Comics)
Fiction House Magazines (Glen-Kel Publ. Co.): Spring, 1949 - No. 20, Summer, 1954

	GD	VG	FN	VF	VF/NM	NM-
1-Ka'a'nga, Lord of the Jungle begins	71	142	213	454	777	1100
2 (Winter, '49-'50)	37	74	111	222	361	500
3,4	29	58	87	172	281	390
5-Camilla app.	31	62	93	182	295	410
6-10: 7-Tuska-a. 9-Tabu, Wizard of the Jungle app. 10-Used in POP, pg. 99	20	40	60	117	189	260
11-15: 15-Camilla-r by Baker/Jungle #106	15	30	45	90	140	190
16-Sheena app.	17	34	51	98	154	170
17-20	15	30	45	84	127	170
I.W. Reprint #1,8: 1-r/#18. Kinstler-c. 8-r/#10	3	6	9	16	23	30

NOTE: *Celardo* c-1. *Whitman* c-8-20(most).

KABOOM
Awesome Entertainment: Sept, 1997 - No. 3, Nov, 1997 ($2.50)

1-3: 1-Matsuda-a/Loeb-s; 4 covers exist (Matsuda, Sale, Pollina and McGuinness), 1-Dynamic Forces Edition, 2-Regular, 2-Alicia Watcher variant-c, 2-Gold logo variant-c, 3-Two covers by Liefeld & Matsuda, 3-Dynamic Forces Ed., Prelude Ed.						4.00
Prelude Gold Edition						5.00

KABOOM (2nd series)
Awesome Entertainment: July, 1999 - No. 3, Dec, 1999 ($2.50)

1-3: 1-Grant-a(p); at least 4 variant covers						4.00

KABOOM! SUMMER BLAST FREE COMIC BOOK DAY EDITION
Boom Entertainment (KaBOOM!): May 2013; May 2014 (free giveaways)

nn-(5/13) Short stories of Adventure Time, Regular Show, Herobear, Garfield, Peanuts						3.00
nn-(5/14) Adventure Time, Regular Show, Steven Universe, Uncle Grandpa and others						3.00

KABUKI
Caliber: Nov, 1994 ($3.50, B&W, one-shot)

	GD	VG	FN	VF	VF/NM	NM-
nn-(Fear The Reaper) 1st app.; David Mack-c/a/s	1	2	3	5	6	8
Color Special (1/96, $2.95)-Mack-c/a/scripts; pin-ups by Tucci, Harris & Quesada						4.00
Gallery (8/95, $2.95)- pinups from Mack, Bradstreet, Paul Pope & others						5.00

KABUKI
Image Comics: Oct, 1997 - No. 9, Mar, 2000 ($2.95, color)

	GD	VG	FN	VF	VF/NM	NM-
1-David Mack-c/s/a						5.00
1-($10.00)-Dynamic Forces Edition	1	3	4	6	8	10
2-5						4.00
6-9						4.00
#1/2 (9/01, $2.95) r/Wizard 1/2; Eclipse Mag. article; bio						3.00
...Classics (2/99, $3.95) Reprints Fear the Reaper						4.00
...Classics 2 (3/99, $3.95) Reprints Dance of Dance						3.00
...Classics 3-5 (3-6/99, $4.95) Reprints Circle of Blood-Acts 1-3						5.00
...Classics 6-12 (7/99-3/00, $3.25) Various reprints						3.25
...Images (6/98, $4.95) r/#1 with new pin-ups						5.00
...Images 2 (1/99, $4.95) r/#1 with new pin-ups						5.00
...Metamorphosis TPB (10/00, $24.95) r/#1-9; Sienkiewicz intro.; 2nd printing exists						25.00
...Reflections 1-4 (7/98-5/02, $4.95) new story plus art techniques						5.00
... The Ghost Play (11/02, $2.95) new story plus interview						3.00

KABUKI
Marvel Comics (Icon): July, 2004 - No. 9, Sept, 2007 ($2.99, color)

	GD	VG	FN	VF	VF/NM	NM-
1-9: 1-David Mack-c/s/a in all; variant-c by Alex Maleev. 4-Variant-c by Adam Hughes. 6-Variant-c by Mignola. 8-Variant-c by Kent Williams. 9-Allred var-c						3.00
...: The Alchemy HC (2008, $29.99, dust jacket) oversized r/#1-9; bonus art & content						30.00
... Reflections 5-15 (7/05-10/09, $5.99) paintings & sketches of recent work; photos						6.00

KABUKI AGENTS (SCARAB)
Image Comics: Aug, 1999 - No. 8, Aug, 2001 ($2.95, B&W)

1-8-David Mack-s/Rick Mays-a						4.00

KABUKI: CIRCLE OF BLOOD
Caliber Press: Jan, 1995 - No. 6, Nov, 1995 ($2.95, B&W)

1-David Mack story/a in all						5.00
2-6: 3-#1 on inside indicia.						4.00
6-Variant-c						4.00
TPB ($16.95) r/#1-6, intro. by Steranko						17.00
TPB (1997, $17.95) Image Edition-r/#1-6, intro. by Steranko						18.00
TPB ($24.95) Deluxe Edition						25.00

KABUKI: DANCE OF DEATH
London Night Studios: Jan, 1995 ($3.00, B&W, one-shot)

	GD	VG	FN	VF	VF/NM	NM-
1-David Mack-c/a/scripts	1	2	3	5	6	8

KABUKI: DREAMS
Image Comics: Jan, 1998 ($4.95, TPB)

nn-Reprints Color Special & Dreams of the Dead						5.00

KABUKI: DREAMS OF THE DEAD
Caliber: July, 1996 ($2.95, one-shot)

nn-David Mack-c/a/scripts						4.00

KABUKI FAN EDITION
Gemstone Publ./Caliber: Feb, 1997 (mail-in offer, one-shot)

nn-David Mack-c/a/scripts						4.00

KABUKI: MASKS OF THE NOH
Caliber: May, 1996 - No. 4, Feb, 1997 ($2.95, limited series)

1-4: 1-Three-c (1A-Quesada, 1B-Buzz, &1C-Mack). 3-Terry Moore pin-up						4.00
TPB (4/98, $10.95) r/#1-4; intro by Terry Moore						11.00

KABUKI: SKIN DEEP
Caliber Comics: Oct, 1996 - No. 3, May, 1997 ($2.95)

1-3:David Mack-c/a/scripts. 2-Two-c (1-Mack, 1-Ross)						4.00
TPB (5/98, $9.95) r/#1-3; intro by Alex Ross						10.00

KAMANDI: AT EARTH'S END
DC Comics: June, 1993 - No. 6, Nov, 1993 ($1.75, limited series)

1-6: Elseworlds storyline						4.00

KAMANDI CHALLENGE, THE (Commemoration for Jack Kirby's 100th birthday)
DC Comics: Mar, 2017 - No. 12, Feb, 2018 ($4.99/$3.99, limited series)

1-($4.99) DiDio-s/Giffen-a; Janson-a/Timm-c						5.00
2-11-($3.99) 2-Neal Adams-a; Tomasi-s; covers by Adams & Rocafort. 3-Palmiotti-s/Conner-a. 8-Giffen-s/Rude-a; Jim Lee-c. 10-Shane Davis-a. 11-Simonson-a						4.00
12-($4.99) Gail Simone-s; art by Jill Thompson and Ryan Sook; afterword by Paul Levitz						4.00
... Special 1 (3/17, $7.99) r/#1,32 and unpubl'd #60,61 from Cancelled Comic Cavalcade						8.00

KAMANDI, THE LAST BOY ON EARTH (Also see Alarming Tales #1, Brave and the Bold #120 & 157, Cancelled Comic Cavalcade & Wednesday Comics)
National Periodical Publ./DC Comics: Oct-Nov, 1972 - No. 59, Sept-Oct, 1978

	GD	VG	FN	VF	VF/NM	NM-
1-Origin & 1st app. Kamandi; intro Ben Boxer	7	14	21	46	86	125
2,3	4	8	12	28	47	65
4,5: 4-Intro. Prince Tuftan of the Tigers. 5-Intro. Flower	4	8	12	25	40	55
6-10	3	6	9	18	28	38
11-20	3	6	9	15	22	28
21-28,30,31,33-40: 24-Last 20¢ issue. 31-Intro Pyra.	2	4	6	11	16	22
29,32: 29-Superman x-over. 32-(68 pgs.)-r/origin from #1 plus one new story; 4 pg. biog. of Jack Kirby with B&W photos	3	6	9	20	30	40
41-57: 50 Kamandi becomes an OMAC	2	4	6	10	14	18
58-Karate Kid x-over from LSH (see Karate Kid #15)	3	6	9	14	19	24

Just Married #37 © CC

Kaptara #1 © Zdarsco & McLeod

Katy Keene #7 © ACP

	GD	VG	FN	VF	VF/NM	NM-
	2.0	4.0	6.0	8.0	9.0	9.2

59-(44 pgs.)-Story cont'd in Brave and the Bold #157; The Return of Omac back-up
by Starlin-c/a(p) cont'd in Warlord #37 ... 3 ... 6 ... 9 ... 16 ... 23 ... 30
NOTE: *Ayers* a(p)-48-59 (most). *Giffen* a-44p, 45p. *Kirby* a-1-40p; c-1-33. *Kubert* c-34-41. *Nasser* a-45p, 46p. *Starlin* a-59p; c-57, 59p.

KAMEN RIDER ZERO ONE
Titan Comics: Dec, 2022 - No. 4, May ($3.99)
1-4-Easton-s/Prasetya-a ... 4.00

KAMUI (Legend Of...#2 on)
Eclipse Comics/Viz Comics: May 12, 1987 - No. 37, Nov. 15, 1988 ($1.50, B&W, bi-weekly)
1-37: 1-3 have 2nd printings ... 4.00

KANAN - THE LAST PADAWAN (Star Wars)
Marvel Comics: Jun, 2015 - No. 12, May 2016 ($3.99)
1-12: 1-Weisman-s/Larraz-a; takes place after Episode 3; flashbacks to the Clone Wars.
9-11-General Grievous app. ... 4.00

KANE & LYNCH (Based on the video games)
DC Comics (WildStorm): Oct, 2010 - No. 6, Apr, 2011 ($3.99/$2.99, limited series)
1-4-($3.99) Templesmith-c/Edginton-s/Mitten-a ... 4.00
5,6-($2.99) ... 3.00
TPB (2011, $17.99) r/#1-6; cover gallery ... 18.00

KANG THE CONQUEROR (Leads into Timeless #1)
Marvel Comics: Oct, 2021 - No. 5, Feb, 2022 ($4.99/$3.99)
1-($4.99) Lanzing & Kelly-s/Magno-a; origin of young Kang (Nathaniel Richards) ... 5.00
2-5-($3.99) 2-Rama-Tut app. 3-Doctor Doom & the Avengers app. ... 4.00

KAOS MOON (Also see Negative Burn #34)
Caliber Comics: 1996 - No. 4, 1997 ($2.95, B&W)
1-4-David Boller-s/a ... 4.00
3,4-Limited Alternate-c ... 5.00
3,4-Gold Alternate-c, Full Circle TPB ($5.95) r/#1,2 ... 6.00

KAPTARA
Image Comics: Apr, 2015 - No. 5, Nov, 2015 ($3.50)
1-5-Chip Zdarsky-s/Kagan McLeod-a ... 3.50

KAPTARA: UNIVERSAL TRUTHS
Image Comics: Aug, 2023 - No. 6, JAn, 2024 ($3.99)
1-6-Chip Zdarsky-s/Kagan McLeod-a ... 4.00

KARATE KID (See Action, Adventure, Legion of Super-Heroes, & Superboy)
National Periodical Publications/DC Comics: Mar-Apr, 1976 - No. 15, July-Aug, 1978 (Legion of Super-Heroes spin-off)
1-Meets Iris Jacobs; Estrada/Staton-a ... 4 ... 8 ... 12 ... 23 ... 37 ... 50
2-14: 2-Major Disaster app. 14-Robin x-over ... 2 ... 3 ... 4 ... 6 ... 8 ... 10
15-Continued into Kamandi #58 ... 2 ... 4 ... 6 ... 11 ... 16 ... 20
NOTE: *Grell* c-1-4, 7, 8, 5p, 6p. *Staton* a-1-9i. Legion x-over-No. 1, 2, 4, 6, 10, 12, 13. *Princess Projectra* x-over-7, 9.

KARMEN
Image Comics: Mar, 2021 - No. 5, Jul, 2021 ($3.99, lim. series, English version of French comic)
1-5-Guillem March-s/a/c. 1-Variant-c by Manara ... 4.00

KARNAK (Inhumans)
Marvel Comics: Dec, 2015 - No. 6, Apr, 2017 ($3.99)
1-6: 1,2-Warren Ellis-s/Gerardo Zaffino-a. 3-6-Roland Boschi-a ... 4.00

KATANA (DC New 52) (From Justice League Of America 2013 series)
DC Comics: Apr, 2013 - No. 10, Feb, 2014 ($2.99)
1-10: 1,2-Nocenti-s/Sanchez-a/Finch-c; origin. 2-Steve Trevor app. 3-6-Creeper app. ... 3.00

KATHY
Standard Comics: Sept, 1949 - No. 17, Sept, 1955
1-Teen-age ... 47 ... 94 ... 141 ... 296 ... 498 ... 700
2-Schomburg-c ... 21 ... 42 ... 63 ... 124 ... 202 ... 280
3-5 ... 15 ... 30 ... 45 ... 88 ... 137 ... 185
6-17: 17-Code approved ... 15 ... 30 ... 45 ... 85 ... 130 ... 175

KATHY (The Teenage Tornado)
Atlas Comics/Marvel (ZPC): Oct, 1959 - No. 27, Feb, 1964 (most issues contain paper dolls and pin-up pages)
1-The Teen-age Tornado; Goldberg-c/a in all ... 39 ... 78 ... 117 ... 231 ... 378 ... 525
2 ... 21 ... 42 ... 63 ... 124 ... 202 ... 280
3-15 ... 19 ... 38 ... 57 ... 111 ... 176 ... 240
16-23,25,27: 22-(4/63) Elvis Presley & Ricky Nelson app. in story "A Song in Her Heart"
... 15 ... 30 ... 45 ... 90 ... 140 ... 190
24-(8/63) Frank Sinatra, Cary Grant, Ed Sullivan & Liz Taylor-c

	22	44	66	128	209	290
26-(12/63) Kathy becomes a model; Millie app. ... 17 ... 34 ... 51 ... 98 ... 154 ... 210

KAT KARSON
I. W. Enterprises: No date (Reprint)
1-Funny animals ... 2 ... 4 ... 6 ... 11 ... 16 ... 20

KATO (Also see The Green Hornet)
Dynamite Entertainment: 2010 - No. 14, 2011 ($3.99)
1-14: 1-Kato and daughter origin; Garza-a/Parks-s. 2-10 Bernard-a ... 4.00
Annual 1 (2011, $4.99) Parks-s/Salazar-a ... 5.00

KATO OF THE GREEN HORNET (Also see The Green Hornet)
Now Comics: Nov, 1991 - No. 4, Feb, 1992 ($2.50, mini-series)
1-4: Brent Anderson-c/a ... 5.00

KATO OF THE GREEN HORNET II (Also see The Green Hornet)
Now Comics: Nov, 1992 - No. 2, Dec, 1993 ($2.50, mini-series)
1,2-Baron-s/Mayerik & Sherman-a ... 5.00

KATO ORIGINS (See The Green Hornet: Year One)
Dynamite Entertainment: 2010 - No. 11, 2011 ($3.99)
1-11-Kato in 1942; Jai Nitz-s/Colton Worley-a; covers by Worley & Francavilla ... 4.00

KATY KEENE (Also see Kasco Komics, Laugh, Pep, Suzie, & Wilbur)
Archie Publ./Close-Up/Radio Comics: 1949 - No. 4, 1951; No. 5, 3/52 - No. 62, Oct, 1961 (50-53-Adventures of...on-c) (Cut and missing pages are common)
1-Bill Woggon-c/a begins; swipes-c to Mopsy #1 ... 271 ... 542 ... 813 ... 1734 ... 2967 ... 4200
2-(1950) ... 93 ... 186 ... 279 ... 591 ... 1021 ... 1450
3-5: 3-(1951). 5-(3/52) ... 65 ... 130 ... 195 ... 416 ... 708 ... 1000
6-10 ... 47 ... 94 ... 141 ... 296 ... 498 ... 700
11,13-21: 21-Last pre-code issue (3/55) ... 39 ... 78 ... 117 ... 240 ... 395 ... 550
12-(Scarce) ... 47 ... 94 ... 141 ... 296 ... 498 ... 700
22-40 ... 29 ... 58 ... 87 ... 172 ... 281 ... 390
41-60: 54-Wedding Album plus wedding pin-up ... 23 ... 46 ... 69 ... 136 ... 223 ... 310
61-Sci-fi-c ... 31 ... 62 ... 93 ... 182 ... 296 ... 410
62-Classic Robot-c ... 61 ... 122 ... 183 ... 390 ... 670 ... 950
Annual 1('54, 25¢)-All new stories; last pre-code ... 68 ... 136 ... 204 ... 435 ... 743 ... 1050
Annual 2-6('55-59, 25¢)-All new stories ... 39 ... 78 ... 117 ... 231 ... 378 ... 525
3-D (1953, 25¢, large size)-Came w/glasses ... 47 ... 94 ... 141 ... 296 ... 498 ... 700
Charm 1(9/58)-Woggon-c/a; new stories, and cut-outs
... 39 ... 78 ... 117 ... 240 ... 395 ... 550
Glamour 1(1957)-Puzzles, games, cut-outs ... 39 ... 78 ... 117 ... 231 ... 378 ... 525
Spectacular 1('56) ... 40 ... 80 ... 120 ... 246 ... 411 ... 575
NOTE: *Debby's Diary* in-No. 47-49, 52, 57.

KATY KEENE COMICS DIGEST MAGAZINE
Close-Up, Inc. (Archie Ent.): 1987 - No. 10, July, 1990 ($1.25/$1.35/$1.50, digest size)
1 ... 3 ... 6 ... 9 ... 14 ... 19 ... 24
2-10 ... 1 ... 3 ... 4 ... 6 ... 8 ... 10
NOTE: *Many used copies are cut-up inside.*

KATY KEENE FASHION BOOK MAGAZINE
Radio Comics/Archie Publications: 1955 - No. 13, Sum, '56 - N. 23, Wint, '58-59 (nn 3-10) (no #11,12)
1-Bill Woggon-c/a ... 69 ... 138 ... 207 ... 442 ... 759 ... 1075
2 ... 39 ... 78 ... 117 ... 231 ... 378 ... 525
13-18: 18-Photo Bill Woggon ... 30 ... 60 ... 90 ... 177 ... 289 ... 400
19-23 ... 25 ... 40 ... 75 ... 150 ... 245 ... 340

KATY KEENE HOLIDAY FUN (See Archie Giant Series Magazine No. 7, 12)

KATY KEENE MODEL BEHAVIOR
Archie Comic Publications: 2008 ($10.95, TPB)
Vol. 1 - New story and reprinted apps./pin-ups from Archie & Friends #101-112 ... 11.00

KATY KEENE PINUP PARADE
Radio Comics/Archie Publications: 1955 - No. 15, Summer, 1961 (25¢) (Cut-out & missing pages are common)
1-Cut-outs in all?; last pre-code issue ... 65 ... 130 ... 195 ... 416 ... 708 ... 1000
2-(1956) ... 35 ... 70 ... 105 ... 208 ... 339 ... 470
3-5: 3-(1957). 5-(1959) ... 30 ... 60 ... 90 ... 177 ... 289 ... 400
6-10,12-14: 8-Mad parody. 10-Bill Woggon photo ... 25 ... 50 ... 75 ... 150 ... 245 ... 340
11-Story of how comics get CCA approved, narrated by Katy
... 32 ... 64 ... 96 ... 188 ... 307 ... 425
15(Rare)-Photo artist & family ... 47 ... 94 ... 141 ... 296 ... 498 ... 700

KATY KEENE SPECIAL (Katy Keene #7; see Laugh Comics Digest)
Archie Ent.: Sept, 1983 - No. 33, 1990 (Later issues published quarterly)
1-10: 1-Woggon-r; new Woggon-c. 3-Woggon-r ... 1 ... 3 ... 4 ... 6 ... 8 ... 10

	GD 2.0	VG 4.0	FN 6.0	VF 8.0	VF/NM 9.0	NM- 9.2
11-25: 12-Spider-Man parody	1	2	3	5	6	8
26-32-(Low print run)	2	4	6	8	10	12
33	2	4	6	8	11	14

KATZENJAMMER KIDS, THE (See Captain & the Kids & Giant Comic Album)
David McKay Publ./Standard No. 12-21(Spring/'50 - 53)/Harvey No. 22, 4/53 on: 1945-1946; Summer, 1947 - No. 27, Feb-Mar, 1954

	GD 2.0	VG 4.0	FN 6.0	VF 8.0	VF/NM 9.0	NM- 9.2
Feature Books 30	21	42	63	126	206	285
Feature Books 32,35('45),41,44('46)	19	38	57	112	179	245
Feature Book 37-Has photos & biography of Harold Knerr	20	40	60	115	190	260
1(1947)-All new stories begin	20	40	60	115	190	260
2-5	12	24	36	69	97	125
6-11	10	20	30	56	76	95
12-14(Standard)	9	18	27	47	61	75
15-21(Standard)	8	16	24	44	57	70
22-25,27(Harvey): 22-24-Henry app.	7	14	21	35	43	50
26-Half in 3-D	16	32	48	98	154	210

KAYO (Formerly Bullseye & Jest; becomes Carnival Comics)
Harry 'A' Chesler: No. 12, Mar, 1945

	GD 2.0	VG 4.0	FN 6.0	VF 8.0	VF/NM 9.0	NM- 9.2
12-Green Knight, Capt. Glory, Little Nemo (not by McCay)	39	78	117	231	378	525

KA-ZAR (Also see Marvel Comics #1, Savage Tales #6 & X-Men #10)
Marvel Comics Group: Aug, 1970 - No. 3, Mar, 1971 (Giant-Size, 68 pgs.)

	GD 2.0	VG 4.0	FN 6.0	VF 8.0	VF/NM 9.0	NM- 9.2
1-Reprints earlier Ka-Zar stories; Avengers x-over in Hercules; Daredevil, X-Men app.; hidden profanity-c	5	10	15	34	60	85
2,3-Daredevil. 2-r/Daredevil #13 w/Kirby layouts; Ka-Zar origin, Angel-r from X-Men by Tuska. 3-Romita & Heck-a (no Kirby)	3	6	9	21	33	45

NOTE: *Buscema* r-2. *Colan* a-1p(r). *Kirby* c/a-1, 2. #1-Reprints X-Men #10 & Daredevil #24.

KA-ZAR
Marvel Comics Group: Jan, 1974 - No. 20, Feb, 1977 (Regular Size)

	GD 2.0	VG 4.0	FN 6.0	VF 8.0	VF/NM 9.0	NM- 9.2
1	4	8	12	25	40	55
2-10	2	4	6	8	11	14
11-14,16,18-20: 16-Only a 30 ¢ edition exists	1	2	3	5	6	8
15,17-(Regular 25¢ edition)(8/76)	1	2	3	5	6	8
15,17-(30¢-c variants, limited distribution)	4	8	12	23	37	50

NOTE: *Alcala* a-15p, 16i. *Brunner* a-6-10p; c-1, 5, 7. *Heath* a-12. *G. Kane* c(p)-3, 5, 8-11, 15, 20. *Kirby* c-12p. *Reinman* a-1p.

KA-ZAR (Volume 2)
Marvel Comics: May, 1997 - No. 20, Dec, 1998 ($1.95/$1.99)
1-Waid-s/Andy Kubert-c/a. thru #4 — 5.00
1-2nd printing; new cover — 4.00
2,4: 2-Two-c — 4.00
3-Alpha Flight #1 preview — 5.00
5-13,15-20: 8-Includes Spider-Man Cybercomic CD-ROM. 9-11-Thanos app. 15-Priest-s/Martinez & Rodriguez-a; Punisher app. — 4.00
14-($2.99) Last Waid/Kubert issue; flip book with 2nd story previewing new creative team of Priest-s/Martinez & Rodriguez-a — 5.00
'97 Annual ($2.99)-Wraparound-c — 5.00

KA-ZAR
Marvel Comics: Aug, 2011 - No. 5, Dec, 2011 ($2.99, limited series)
1-5-Jenkins-s/Alixe-a/c — 3.00

KA-ZAR LORD OF THE SAVAGE LAND (Follows Empyre: Avengers #1-3)
Marvel Comics: Nov, 2021 - Present ($3.99)
1-4: 1-Zac Thompson-s/Germán Garcia-a — 4.00

KA-ZAR: MARVEL TALES
Marvel Comics: Nov, 2021 ($7.99, one-shot)
1-Reprints Marvel Tales (1982) #1-4; X-Men app.; intro. by Ralph Macchio — 8.00

KA-ZAR OF THE SAVAGE LAND
Marvel Comics: Feb, 1997 ($2.50, one-shot)
1-Wraparound-c — 4.00

KA-ZAR: SIBLING RIVALRY
Marvel Comics: July, 1997 ($1.95, one-shot)
(# -1) Flashback story w/Alpha Flight #1 preview — 4.00

KA-ZAR THE SAVAGE (See Marvel Fanfare)
Marvel Comics Group: Apr, 1981 - No. 34, Oct, 1984 (Regular size)(Mando paper #10 on)

	GD 2.0	VG 4.0	FN 6.0	VF 8.0	VF/NM 9.0	NM- 9.2
1-Bruce Jones-s begin	1	3	4	6	8	10

2-20,24,27,28,30-34: 11-Origin Zabu. 12-One of two versions with panel missing on pg. 10. 20-Kraven the Hunter-c/story (also apps. in #21) — 4.00

	GD 2.0	VG 4.0	FN 6.0	VF 8.0	VF/NM 9.0	NM- 9.2
12-Version with panel on pg. 10 (1600 printed)	1	3	4	6	8	10

21-23, 25,26-Spider-Man app. 26-Photo-c. — 4.00
29-Double size; Ka-Zar & Shanna wed — 5.00

NOTE: *B. Anderson* a-1-15p, 18, 19; c-1-17, 18p, 20(back). *G. Kane* a(back-up)-11, 12, 14.

KEEN DETECTIVE FUNNIES (Formerly Detective Picture Stories?)
Centaur Publications: No. 8, July, 1938 - No. 24, Sept, 1940

	GD 2.0	VG 4.0	FN 6.0	VF 8.0	VF/NM 9.0	NM- 9.2
V1#8-The Clock continues-r/Funny Picture Stories #1; Roy Crane-a (1st?)	411	822	1233	2877	5039	7200
9-Tex Martin by Eisner; The Gang Buster app.	308	616	924	2156	3778	5400
10,11: 11-Dean Denton story (begins?)	300	600	900	1920	3310	4700
V2#1,2-The Eye Sees by Frank Thomas begins; ends #23(Not in V2#3&5). 2-Jack Cole-a	219	438	657	1402	2401	3400
3-6: 3-TNT Todd begins. 4-Gabby Flynn begins. 5,6-Dean Denton story	181	362	543	1158	1979	2800
7-The Masked Marvel by Ben Thompson begins (7/39, 1st app.)(scarce)	354	708	1062	2478	4339	6200
8-Nudist ranch panel w/four girls	258	516	774	1651	2826	4000
9-11	161	322	483	1030	1765	2500
12(12/39)-Origin The Eye Sees by Frank Thomas; death of Masked Marvel's sidekick ZL	219	438	657	1402	2401	3400
V3#1	161	322	483	1030	1765	2500
18-Bondage/torture-c	232	464	696	1485	2543	3600

	GD 2.0	VG 4.0	FN 6.0	VF 8.0	VF/NM 9.0	NM- 9.2
19,21,22	155	310	465	992	1696	2400
20-Classic Eye Sees-c by Thomas	331	662	993	2317	4059	5800
23-Air Man begins (intro); Air Man-c	226	452	678	1446	2473	3500
24-(scarce) Air Man-c	245	490	735	1568	2684	3800

NOTE: *Burgos* a-V2#2. *Jack Cole* a-V2#2. *Eisner* a-10, V2#6r. *Ken Ernst* a-V2#4-7; 9, 10, 19, 21; c-V2#4. *Everett* a-V2#2, 9, 11, 12, 20. *Guardineer* a-V2#5, 66. *Gustavson* a-V2#4-6. *Simon* c-V3#1. *Thompson* c-V2#7, 9, 10, 22.

KEEN KOMICS
Centaur Publications: V2#1, May, 1939 - V2#3, Nov, 1939

	GD 2.0	VG 4.0	FN 6.0	VF 8.0	VF/NM 9.0	NM- 9.2
V2#1(Large size)-Dan Hastings (s/f), The Big Top, Bob Phantom the Magician, The Mad Goddess app.	411	822	1233	2877	5039	7200
V2#2(Reg. size)-The Forbidden Idol of Machu Picchu; Cut Carson by Burgos begins	181	362	543	1158	1979	2800
V2#3-Saddle Sniffl by Jack Cole, Circus Pays, Kings Revenge app.	148	296	444	947	1624	2300

NOTE: *Binder* a-V2#2. *Burgos* a-V2#2, 3. *Ken Ernst* a-V2#2. *Gustavson* a-V2#2. *Jack Cole* a-V2#3.

KEEN TEENS (Girls magazine)
Life's Romances Publ./Leader/Magazine Ent.: 1945; nn, 1946; No. 3, Feb-Mar, 1947 - No. 6, Aug-Sept, 1947

	GD 2.0	VG 4.0	FN 6.0	VF 8.0	VF/NM 9.0	NM- 9.2
nn (#1, 1945)-Claire Voyant (cont'd. in other nn issue) movie photos, Dotty Dripple, Gertie O'Grady & Sissy; Van Johnson, Sinatra photo-c	63	130	195	416	708	1000
nn (#2, 1946)-16 pgs. Claire Voyant & 16 pgs. movie photos	41	82	123	256	428	600
3-6: 4-Glenn Ford photo-c. 5-Perry Como-c	22	44	66	132	216	300

KELLYS, THE (Formerly Rusty Comics; Spy Cases No. 26 on)
Marvel Comics (HPC): No. 23, Jan, 1950 - No. 25, June, 1950 (52 pgs.)

	GD 2.0	VG 4.0	FN 6.0	VF 8.0	VF/NM 9.0	NM- 9.2
23-Teenage	23	46	69	136	223	310
24,25: 24-Margie app.	15	30	45	90	140	190

KEN MAYNARD WESTERN (Movie star)(See Wow Comics, 1936)
Fawcett Publ.: Sept, 1950 - No. 8, Feb, 1952 (All 36 pgs.; photo front/back-c)

	GD 2.0	VG 4.0	FN 6.0	VF 8.0	VF/NM 9.0	NM- 9.2
1-Ken Maynard & his horse Tarzan begin	31	62	93	182	296	410
2	18	36	54	105	165	225
3-8: 6-Atomic bomb explosion panel	14	28	42	80	115	150

KENNEL BLOCK BLUES
BOOM! Studios: Feb, 2016 - No. 4, May, 2016 ($3.99, limited series)
1-4-Ryan Ferrier-s/Daniel Bayliss-a — 4.00

KEN SHANNON (Becomes Gabby #11 on) (Also see Police Comics #103)
Quality Comics Group: Oct, 1951 - No. 10, Apr, 1953 (A private eye)

	GD 2.0	VG 4.0	FN 6.0	VF 8.0	VF/NM 9.0	NM- 9.2
1-Crandall-a	57	114	171	362	619	875
2-Crandall c/a(2)	42	84	126	265	445	625
3-Horror-c; Crandall-a	52	104	156	328	552	775
4,5-Crandall-a	33	66	99	194	317	440
6-Crandall-c/a; "The Weird Vampire Mob"-c/s	61	122	183	390	670	950
7-"The Ugliest Man Alive"-c; Crandall-a	52	104	156	328	552	775
8,9: 8-Opium den drug use story	28	56	84	168	274	380
10-Crandall-a	30	60	90	177	289	400

NOTE: *Crandall/Cuidera* c-1-10. *Jack Cole* a-1-9. #1-15 published after title change to Gabby.

KEN STUART
Publication Enterprises: Jan, 1949 (Sea Adventures)

	GD 2.0	VG 4.0	FN 6.0	VF 8.0	VF/NM 9.0	NM- 9.2
1-Frank Borth-c/a	16	32	48	94	147	200

KENT BLAKE OF THE SECRET SERVICE (Spy)
Marvel/Atlas Comics (20CC): May, 1951 - No. 14, July, 1953

	GD 2.0	VG 4.0	FN 6.0	VF 8.0	VF/NM 9.0	NM- 9.2
1-Injury to eye, bondage, torture; Brodsky-c	41	82	123	256	428	600
2-Drug use w/hypo scenes; Brodsky-c	23	46	69	136	223	310
3-14: 8-R.Q. Sale-a (2 pgs.)	16	32	48	94	147	200

NOTE: *Heath* c-5, 7, 8. *Infantino* c-12. *Maneely* c-3. *Sinnott* a-2(3). *Tuska* a-8(3pg.).

KENT MENACE
Brilliant Entertainment/American Mythology Prods.: Autumn 2020; May, 2021 ($5.00/$3.99)
#0 ($5.00) Intro. story with Braden-s/Malbrough-a; bonus pin-ups — 5.00
#0: The Director's Cut (AMP, 5/21, $3.99) r/#0 with new story with Braden-s/Malbrough-a; 2 new text stories by Meggan Groves Robinson & Marty Grosser — 4.00
Gods and Monsters Promotional Edition (11/22, $3.99) Short stories and text stories — 4.00
...Vs Technofreak (Spring 2024, $6.99) Scott Braden & John Charles-s — 7.00

KENT MENACE QUARTERLY
Brilliant Enterprise, LLC: Summer 2023 - Present ($9.99)
1-Short stories, text tales and bonus pin-ups by various; Plog-c — 10.00

KENTS, THE
DC Comics: Aug, 1997 - No. 12, July, 1998 ($2.50, limited series)
1-12-Ostrander-s by Truman and Bair (#1-8), Mandrake (#9-12) — 4.00
TPB ($19.95) r/#1-12 — 20.00

KERRY DRAKE (Also see A-1 Comics)
Argo: Jan, 1956 - No. 2, March, 1956

	GD 2.0	VG 4.0	FN 6.0	VF 8.0	VF/NM 9.0	NM- 9.2
1,2-Newspaper-r	10	20	30	54	72	90

KERRY DRAKE DETECTIVE CASES (...Racket Buster No. 32,33)
(Also see Chamber of Clues & Green Hornet Comics #42-47)
Life's Romances/Compix/Magazine Ent. No.1-5/Harvey No.6 on: 1944 - No. 5, 1944; No. 6, Jan, 1948 - No. 33, Aug, 1952

	GD 2.0	VG 4.0	FN 6.0	VF 8.0	VF/NM 9.0	NM- 9.2
nn(1944) (A-1 Comics)(slightly over-size)	39	78	117	240	395	550
2	24	48	72	142	234	325
3,4(1944)	20	40	60	117	189	260
5(1944)-Bondage headlight-c	71	142	213	454	777	1100
6,8(1948): Lady Crime by Powell. 8-Bondage-c	15	30	45	86	133	180
7-Kubert-a; biog of Andriola (artist)	15	30	45	90	140	190
9,10-Two-part marijuana story; Kerry smokes marijuana in #10	20	40	60	117	189	260
11-15	14	28	42	78	112	145
16-33	10	20	30	58	79	100

NOTE: *Andiola* c-6-9. *Berg* a-5. *Powell* a-10-23, 28, 29.

KEVIN KELLER (Also see Veronica #202 for 1st app. & #207-210 for first mini-series)

Ka-Zar (2011 series) #1 © MAR

Kent Menace Quarterly #1 © Braden & Malbrough

Kick-Ass (2018 series) #15 © D&E & JRJr

	GD	VG	FN	VF	VF/NM	NM-
	2.0	4.0	6.0	8.0	9.0	9.2

Archie Comics Publications: Apr, 2012 - No. 15, Nov, 2014 ($2.99)
1-14-Two covers on each. 5-Action #1 swipe-c. 6-George Takei app. ... 3.00
15-($3.99) The Equalizer app.; 3 covers incl. Sensation #1 and X-Men #141 swipes ... 4.00

KEWPIES
Will Eisner Publications: Spring, 1949
1-Feiffer-a; Kewpie Doll ad on back cover; used in **SOTI**, pg. 35
  81 162 243 518 884 1250

KEY COMICS
Consolidated Magazines: Jan, 1944 - No. 5, Aug, 1946
1-The Key, Will-O-The-Wisp begin 65 130 195 416 708 1000
2 (3/44) 36 72 108 214 347 480
3,4: 3 (Winter 45/46). 4-(5/46)-Origin John Quincy The Atom (begins); Walter Johnson c-3-5
  32 64 96 188 307 425
5-4pg. Faust Opera adaptation; Kiefer;-a; back-c advertises "Masterpieces Illustrated" by Lloyd Jacquet after he left Classic Comics (no copies of Masterpieces Illustrated known)
  39 78 117 240 395 550

KEY OF Z
BOOM! Studios: Oct, 2011 - No. 4, Jan, 2012 ($3.99, limited series)
1-4: 1-Claudio Sanchez & Chondra Echert-s/Aaron Kuder-a; covers by Fox & Moore ... 4.00

KEY RING COMICS
Dell Publishing Co.: 1941 (16 pgs.; two colors) (sold 5 for 10¢)
1-Sky Hawk, 1-Features Sleepy Samson, 1-Origin Greg Gilday; r/War Comics #2
  20 40 60 117 189 260
1-Radior (Super hero) 22 44 66 128 209 290
1-Viking Carter (WWII Nazi-c) 21 42 63 124 202 280
NOTE: Each book has two holes in spine to put in binder.

KICK-ASS
Marvel Comics (Icon): April, 2008 - No. 8, Mar, 2010 ($2.99)
1-Mark Millar-s/John Romita Jr.-a/c ... 24.00
1-Red variant cover by McNiven ... 25.00
1-2nd printing ... 4.00
1-Director's Cut (8/08, $3.99) r/#1 with script and sketch pages; Millar afterword ... 5.00
2 ... 8.00
3-8: 3-1st app. Hit-Girl. 5-Intro. Red Mist ... 4.00
NOTE: Multiple printings exist for most issues.

KICK-ASS
Image Comics: Feb, 2018 - No. 18, Oct, 2019 ($3.99)
1-18: 1-Mark Millar-s/John Romita Jr.-a/c. 1-Intro. Patience Lee. 7-18-Niles-s/Frusin-a ... 4.00

KICK-ASS 2
Marvel Comics (Icon): Dec, 2010 - No. 7, May, 2012 ($2.99/$4.99)
1-6-Mark Millar-s/John Romita Jr.-a/c ... 3.00
1-6-Variant covers. 1-Edwards. 2-Yu. 5-Photo & Hitch. 6-Photo-c ... 5.00
7-($4.99) Extra-sized finale; bonus preview of Secret Service #1 ... 5.00
7-($4.99) Variant photo-c ... 7.00

KICK-ASS 3
Marvel Comics (Icon): Jul, 2013 - No. 8, Oct, 2014 ($2.99/$3.99/$4.99/$5.99)
1-5-($2.99) Mark Millar-s/John Romita Jr.-a/c ... 3.00
1-5-Variant covers. 1-Hughes. 2-Fegredo. 3-Mack. 5-Bond ... 5.00
6-($4.99) Secret origin of Hit-Girl ... 4.00
7-($3.99) ... 5.00
8-($5.99) ... 6.00

KICK-ASS VS. HIT-GIRL
Image Comics: Nov, 2020 - No. 5, Mar, 2021 ($3.99)
1-5-Patience Lee vs. Mindy McCready; Niles-s/Frusin-a ... 4.00

KID CARROTS
St. John Publishing Co.: September, 1953
1-Funny animal 14 28 42 78 112 145

KID COLT ONE-SHOT
Marvel Comics: Sept, 2009 ($3.99)
1-DeFalco-s/Burchett-a/Luke Ross-c ... 4.00

KID COLT OUTLAW (Kid Colt #1-4; ...Outlaw #5-on)(Also see All Western Winners, Best Western, Black Rider, Giant-Size..., Two-Gun Kid, Two-Gun Western, Western Winners, Wild Western, Wisco)
Marvel Comics(LCC) 1-16; Atlas(LMC) 17-102; Marvel 103-on: 8/48 - No. 139, 3/68; No. 140, 11/69 - No. 229, 4/79
1-Kid Colt & his horse Steel begin 284 568 852 1818 3109 4400
2 113 226 339 718 1234 1750

3-5: 4-Anti-Wertham editorial; Tex Taylor app. 5-Blaze Carson app.
  71 142 213 454 777 1100
6-8: 6-Tex Taylor app; 7-Nimo the Lion begins, ends #10
  43 86 129 271 461 650
9,10 (52 pgs.) 48 96 144 302 514 725
11-Origin (10/50) 48 96 144 302 514 725
12-20 30 60 90 177 289 400
21-32 25 50 75 150 245 340
33-45: Black Rider in all 22 44 66 128 209 290
46,47,49,50 20 40 60 117 189 260
48-Kubert-a 20 40 60 120 195 270
51-53,55,56 19 38 57 111 176 240
54-Williamson/Maneely-c 20 40 60 117 189 260
57-60,66: 4-pg. Williamson-a in all 11 22 33 76 163 240
61-63,67-78,80-86: 69,73-Maneely-c. 70-Severin-c. 86-Kirby-a(r).
  11 22 33 73 157 240
64,65-Crandall-a 12 24 36 81 176 270
79,87: 79-Origin retold. 87-Davis-a(r) 11 22 33 76 163 250
88,89-Williamson-a in both (4 pgs). 89-Redrawn Matt Slade #2
  11 22 33 76 163 250
90-99,101-106,108,109: 91-Kirby/Ayers-c. 95-Kirby/Ayers-c/story. 102-Last 10¢ issue
  13 26 39 89 195 300
100 19 38 57 131 291 450
107-Only Kirby sci-fi cover of title 46 92 138 368 834 1300
110-(5/63)-1st app. Iron Mask (Iron Man type villain) 18 36 54 124 275 425
111-113,115-120 10 20 30 64 132 200
114-(1/64)-2nd app. Iron Mask 13 26 39 89 195 300
121-129,133-139: 121-Rawhide Kid x-over. 125-Two-Gun Kid x-over. 139-Last 12¢ issue
  7 14 21 49 86 125
130-132 (68 pgs.)-one new story each. 130-Origin 8 16 24 54 102 150
140-155: Reprints begin (later issues mostly-r). 155-Last 15¢ issue
156-Giant; reprints (52 pgs.) 3 6 9 16 24 32
157-180,200: 170-Origin retold. 4 8 12 22 35 48
181-199 3 6 9 15 22 28
201-229: 201-New material w/Rawhide Kid app; Kane-c. 229-Rawhide Kid-r
  3 6 9 14 19 24
  2 4 6 11 16 20
205-209-(30¢-c variants, limited dist.) 13 26 39 86 188 290
218-220-(35¢-c variants, limited dist.) 13 26 39 89 195 300
...Album (no date; 1950's; Atlas Comics)-132 pgs.; cardboard cover, B&W stories: (Rare)
  181 362 543 1158 1979 2800
NOTE: Ayers a-many. Colan a-52, 53, 84, 112, 114; c(p)-223, 228, 229. Crandall a-140r, 167r. Everett a-90, 137i, 225i(r). Heath a-8(2); c-34, 35, 39, 44, 46, 48, 49, 50, 52, 64. Heck a-135, 139. Jack Keller a-25(2), 26-68(3-4), 73, 78, 82, 84, 85, 88, 92, 94p, 98, 99, 101, 102, 106-130, 132, 140-150r. Kirby a-86r, 93, 96, 119, 176(part); c-87, 92-95, 97, 99-112, 114-117, 121-123, 197r; w/Ditko c-89. Maneely a-12, 68, 81; c-9, 17, 19, 40-43, 47, 52, 69-78, 80-86, 89. Morrow a-173r, 216r. Rico a-13, 18. Severin c-55, 58, 59, 84, 143, 148, 149i. Shores 68, 73, 78, 81, 142r, 150r. Sutton a-136, 137p, 225p(r). Wildey a-47, 54, 82, 144r. Williamson r-147, 170, 172, 216. Woodbridge a-64, 81. Black Rider in #33-45, 74, 86. Iron Mask in #110, 114, 121, 127. Sam Hawk in #80, 84, 101, 111, 121, 146, 174, 181, 188.

KID COWBOY (Also see Approved Comics #4 & Boy Cowboy)
Ziff-Davis Publ./St. John (Approved Comics) #11,14: 1950 - No. 11, Wint, '52-'53; No. 13, April 1953; No. 14, June, 1954 (No #12) (Painted covers #1-10,13,14)
1-Lucy Belle & Red Feather begin 26 52 78 154 252 350
2-Maneely-a 15 30 45 86 166 180
3-11,13,14: (#3, spr. '51). 5-Berg-a. 14-Code approved
  14 28 42 82 121 145

KID DEATH & FLUFFY HALLOWEEN SPECIAL
Event Comics: Oct, 1997 ($2.95, B&W, one-shot)
1-Variant-c by Cebollero & Quesada/Palmiotti ... 4.00

KID DEATH & FLUFFY SPRING BREAK SPECIAL
Event Comics: July, 1996 ($2.50, B&W, one-shot)
1-Quesada & Palmiotti-c/scripts ... 4.00

KIDDIE KAPERS
Kiddie Kapers Co., 1945/Decker Publ. (Red Top-Farrell): 1945?(nd); Oct, 1957; 1963 - 1964
1(nd, 1945-46?, 36 pgs.)-Infinity-c; funny animal 13 26 39 72 101 130
1(10/57)(Decker)-Little Bit-r from Kiddie Karnival 5 10 15 24 30 35
Super Reprint #7, 10('63), 12, 14('63), 15,17('64), 18('64): 10, 14-r/Animal Adventures #1.
15-Animal Advs. #? 17-Cowboys 'N' Injuns #? 2 4 6 9 13 16

KIDDIE KARNIVAL
Ziff-Davis Publ. Co. (Approved Comics): 1952 (25¢, 100 pgs.) (One Shot)
nn-Rebound Little Bit #1,2; painted-c 39 78 117 240 395 550

KID ETERNITY (Becomes Buccaneers) (See Hit Comics)
Quality Comics Group: Spring, 1946 - No. 18, Nov, 1949

	GD 2.0	VG 4.0	FN 6.0	VF 8.0	VF/NM 9.0	NM- 9.2
1	90	180	270	576	988	1400
2	40	80	120	246	411	575
3-Mac Raboy-a	41	82	123	256	428	600
4-10	26	52	78	154	252	350
11-18	20	40	60	115	185	255

KID ETERNITY
DC Comics: 1991 - No. 3, Nov, 1991 ($4.95, limited series)

1-3: Grant Morrison scripts/Duncan Fegredo-a/c						6.00
TPB (2006, $14.99) r/#1-3						15.00

KID ETERNITY
DC Comics (Vertigo): May, 1993 - No. 16, Sept, 1994 ($1.95, mature)

1-16: 1-Gold ink-c. 6-Photo-c. All Sean Phillips-c/i except #15 (Phillips-c/i only)						4.00

KID FROM DODGE CITY, THE
Atlas Comics (MMC): July, 1957 - No. 2, Sept, 1957

1-Don Heck-a	20	40	60	114	182	250
2-Everett-c	14	28	42	81	118	155

KID FROM TEXAS, THE (A Texas Ranger)
Atlas Comics (CSI): June, 1957 - No. 2, Aug, 1957

1-Powell-a; Severin-c	18	36	54	105	165	225
2	13	26	39	74	105	135

KID KOKO
I. W. Enterprises: 1958

Reprint #1,2-(r/M.E.'s Koko & Kola #4, 1947)	4	7	10	14	17	20

KID KOMICS (Kid Movie Komics No. 11)
Timely Comics (USA 1,2/FCI 3-10): Feb, 1943 - No. 10, Spring, 1946

1-Origin Captain Wonder & sidekick Tim Mullrooney, & Subbie; intro the Sea-Going Lad, Pinto Pete, & Trixie Trouble; Knuckles & Whitewash Jones (from Young Allies) app.; Wolverton-a (7 pgs.)	775	1550	2325	5650	10,325	15,000
2-The Young Allies, Red Hawk, & Tommy Tyme begin; last Captain Wonder & Subbie; Schomburg Japanese WWII bondage-c	314	628	942	2198	3849	5500
3-The Vision, Daredevils & Red Hawk app.	245	490	735	1568	2684	3800
4-The Destroyer begins; Sub-Mariner app.; Red Hawk & Tommy Tyme end; classic Schomburg WWII human meat grinder-c	300	600	900	1950	3375	4800
5,6: 5-Tommy Tyme begins, ends #10	161	322	483	1030	1765	2500
7-10: 7,10-The Whizzer app. Destroyer not in #7,8. Young Allies & Whizzer	129	258	387	826	1413	2000

NOTE: **Brodsky** c-5. **Schomburg** c-2-4, 6-10. **Shores** c-1. Captain Wonder c-1, 2. The Young Allies c-3-10.

KID LOBOTOMY
IDW Publishing (Black Crown): Oct, 2017 - No. 6, Mar, 2018 ($3.99)

1-6: 1-Milligan-s/Fowler-a; covers by Fowler & Quitely						4.00

KID MONTANA (Formerly Davy Crockett Frontier Fighter; The Gunfighters No. 51 on)
Charlton Comics: V2#9, Nov, 1957 - No. 50, Mar, 1965

V2#9 (#1)	5	10	15	30	50	70
10	3	6	9	21	33	45
11,12,14-20	3	6	9	15	22	28
13-Williamson-a	3	6	9	21	33	45
21-35: 25,31-Giordano-c. 32-Origin Kid Montana. 34-Geronimo-c/s. 35-Snow Monster-c/s	2	4	6	11	16	20
36-50: 36-Dinosaur-c/s. 37,48-Giordano-c	2	4	6	9	12	15

NOTE: Title change to Montana Kid on cover only #44 & 45; remained Kid Montana on inside. **Chasal** a-29,30. **Giordano** c-25,31,37,48. **Giordano/Alascia** c-12. **Mastroserio** a-9,11,13,14,22; c-11,14. **Masulli/Mastroserio** c-13. **Montes/Bache** a-42. **Morisi** c-16,32-34,36,37,40,41,44,46; a-13,15,16,31-50. **Nicholas/Alascia** a-44,48.

KID MOVIE KOMICS (Formerly Kid Komics; Rusty Comics #12 on)
Timely Comics: No. 11, Summer, 1946

11-Silly Seal & Ziggy Pig; 2 pgs. Kurtzman "Hey Look" plus 6 pg. "Pigtales" story	39	78	117	231	378	525

KIDNAPPED (See Marvel Illustrated: Kidnapped)

KIDNAPPED (Robert Louis Stevenson's...also see Movie Comics)(Disney)
Dell Publishing Co.: No. 1101, May, 1960

Four Color 1101-Movie, photo-c	6	12	18	42	79	115

KIDNAP RACKET (See Harvey Comics Hits No. 57)

KID SLADE, GUNFIGHTER (Formerly Matt Slade...)
Atlas Comics (SPI): No. 5, Jan, 1957 - No. 8, July, 1957

5-Maneely, Roth, Severin-a in all; Maneely-c	16	32	48	94	147	200
6,8-Severin-c	13	26	39	74	105	135
7-Williamson/Mayo-a, 4 pgs.; Maneely-c	14	28	42	82	121	160

KID SUPREME (See Supreme)
Image Comics (Extreme Studios): Mar, 1996 - No. 3, July, 1996 ($2.50)

1-3: Fraga-a/scripts. 3-Glory-c/app.						4.00

KID VENOM: ORIGINS
Marvel Comics: Mar, 2024 ($4.99, one-shot)

1-Collects the short stories from Death of the Venomverse #2-5; Taigami-s/a						5.00

KID ZOO COMICS
Street & Smith Publications: July, 1948 (52 pgs.)

1-Funny Animal	36	72	108	211	343	475

KILLADELPHIA
Image Comics: Nov, 2019 - Present ($3.99)

1-33-Philadelphia vampires; Rodney Barnes-s/Jason Shawn Alexander-a/c. 30-Spawn app.						4.00

KILL ALL PARENTS
Image Comics: June, 2008 ($3.99, one-shot)

1-Marcelo Di Chiara-a/Mark Andrew Smith-s						4.00

KILLAPALOOZA
DC Comics (WildStorm): July, 2009 - No. 6, Dec, 2009 ($2.99, limited series)

1-6: 1-Beechen-s/Hairsine-a/c						3.00
TPB (2010, $19.99) r/#1-6						20.00

KILLER (...Tales By Timothy Truman)
Eclipse Comics: March, 1985 ($1.75, one-shot, Baxter paper)

1-Timothy Truman-c/a						4.00

KILLER INSTINCT (Video game)
Acclaim Comics: June, 1996 - No. 6 ($2.50, limited series)

1-6: 1-Bart Sears-a(p). 4-Special #1. 5-Special #2. 6-Special #3						4.00

KILLER INSTINCT (Video game)
Dynamite Entertainment: 2017 - No. 6, 2018 ($3.99, limited series)

1-6: 1,2-Ian Edginton-s/Cam Adams-a; multiple covers. 3-6-Ediano Silva-a						4.00

KILLER QUEENS
Dark Horse Comics: Aug, 2021 - No. 4, Nov, 2021 ($3.99, limited series)

1-4-David M. Booher-s/Claudia Balboni-a; 3 covers on each						4.00

KILLER QUEENS (Second series)
Dark Horse Comics: Aug, 2023 - No. 4, Jan, 2024 ($3.99, limited series)

1-David M. Booher-s/Bradley Clayton-a						4.00

KILLERS
Valiant Entertainment: Jul, 2019 - No. 5, Nov, 2019 ($3.99, limited series)

1-5-B. Clay Moore-s/Fernando Dagnino-a; origin of KI-6						4.00

KILLERS, THE
Magazine Enterprises: 1947 - No. 2, 1948 (No month)

1-Mr. Zin, the Hatchet Killer; mentioned in **SOTI**, pgs. 179,180; used by N.Y. Legis. Comm.; L. B. Cole-c	226	452	678	1446	2473	3500
2-(Scarce)-Hashish smoking story; "Dying, Dying, Dead" drug story; Whitney, Ingels-a; Whitney hanging-c	181	362	543	1158	1979	2800

KILLING GIRL
Image Comics: Aug, 2007 - No. 5, Dec, 2007 ($2.99, limited series)

1-5: 1-Frank Espinosa-a/Glen Brunswick-s; covers by Espinosa and Frank Cho						3.00

KILLING JOKE, THE (See Batman: The Killing Joke under Batman one-shots)

KILLING RED SONJA, VOLUME 1 (Follows Red Sonja Volume 5 #12)
Dynamite Entertainment: 2020 - No. 5, 2020 ($3.99)

1-5-Russell & Ingman-s/Rousseau-a. 4-Sorcerors of Wigur-Nomadene app.						4.00

KILL LOCK, THE
IDW Publishing: Dec, 2019 - No. 6, May, 2020 ($3.99)

1-3-Livio Ramondelli-s/a						4.00

KILL LOCK, THE: THE ARTISAN WRAITH
IDW Publishing: Mar, 2022 - No. 6, Aug, 2022 ($3.99/$7.99)

1-5-Livio Ramondelli-s/a						4.00
6-($7.99) Double size finale						8.00

KILLMONGER (From Black Panther)
Marvel Comics: Feb, 2019 - No. 5, May, 2019 ($4.99/$3.99, limited series)

1-($4.99) Bryan Hill-s/Juan Ferreyra-a; N'Jadaka's rise to Killmonger; Kingpin app.						5.00
2-5-($3.99) 2,3-Bullseye app. 3-5-Black Widow app.						4.00

KILL OR BE KILLED
Image Comics: Aug, 2016 - No. 20, Jun, 2018 ($3.99)

1-20-Ed Brubaker-s/Sean Phillips-a						4.00

KILLPOWER: THE EARLY YEARS
Marvel Comics UK: Sept, 1993 - No. 4, Dec, 1993 ($1.75, mini-series)

1-($2.95)-Foil embossed-c						5.00
2-4: 2-Genetix app. 3-Punisher app.						4.00

KILLRAVEN (See Amazing Adventures #18 (5/73))
Marvel Comics: Feb, 2001 ($2.99, one-shot)

1-Linsner-s/a/c						3.00

KILLRAVEN
Marvel Comics: Dec, 2002 - No. 6, May, 2003 ($2.99, limited series)

1-6-Alan Davis-s/a(p)/Mark Farmer-i						3.00
HC (2007, $19.99) r/#1-6; cover gallery, pencil art; foreward by Alan Davis						20.00

KILLRAZOR
Image Comics (Top Cow Productions): Aug, 1995 ($2.50, one-shot)

1						4.00

KILL WHITEY DONOVAN
Dark Horse Comics: Dec, 2019 - No. 5, Apr, 2020 ($3.99, limited series)

1-5-Sydney Duncan-s/Natalie Barahona-a; 2 covers by Pearson and Barahona						4.00

KILL YOUR BOYFRIEND
DC Comics (Vertigo): June, 1995 ($4.95, one-shot)

1-Grant Morrison story						6.00
1 ($5.95, 1998) 2nd printing						6.00

KILL YOUR DARLINGS
Image Comics: Sept, 2023 - Present ($3.99)

1-6-Parker & Sheridan-s/Quinn-a						4.00

KILROY (Volume 2)
Caliber Press: 1998 ($2.95, B&W)

1-Pruett-s						4.00

KILROY IS HERE
Caliber Press: 1995 ($2.95, B&W)

1-10						4.00

KILROYS, THE
B&I Publ. Co. No. 1-19/American Comics Group: June-July, 1947 - No. 54, June-July, 1955

1	30	60	90	177	289	400
2	15	30	45	92	144	195
3-5: 5-Gross-a	15	30	45	83	124	165
6-10: 8-Milt Gross's Moronica (1st app.)	12	24	36	69	97	125
11-20: 14-Gross-a	10	20	30	56	76	95

Kid Komics #1 © MAR

Kill or Be Killed #1 © Basement Gang

King Conan (2021 series) #1 © CPI

	GD 2.0	VG 4.0	FN 6.0	VF 8.0	VF/NM 9.0	NM- 9.2
21-30	9	18	27	52	69	85
31-47,50-54	9	18	27	47	61	75
48,49-(3-D effect-c/stories)	19	38	57	112	179	245

KILROY: THE SHORT STORIES
Caliber Press: 1995 ($2.95, B&W)

1						4.00

KIM REAPER
Oni Press: Apr, 2017 - No. 4, Jul, 2017 ($3.99, limited series)

1-4-Sarah Graley-s/a/c						4.00

KIM REAPER: VAMPIRE ISLAND
Oni Press: Sept, 2018 - No. 4, Nov, 2018 ($3.99, limited series)

1-4-Sarah Graley-s/a/c						4.00

KIN
Image Comics (Top Cow): Mar, 2000 - No. 6, Sept, 2000 ($2.95)

1-5-Gary Frank-s/c/a						3.00
1-($6.95) DF Alternate footprint cover						7.00
6-($3.95)						4.00
... Descent of Man TPB (2002, $19.95) r/ #1-6						20.00

KINDRED, THE
Image Comics (WildStorm Productions): Mar, 1994 - No. 4, July, 1995 ($1.95, lim. series)

1-($2.50)-Grifter & Backlash app. in all; bound-in trading card						5.00
2-4						4.00
2,3: 2-Variant-c. 3-Alternate-c by Portacio, see Deathblow #5						10.00
Trade paperback (2/95, $9.95)						

NOTE: **Booth** c/a-1-4. The first four issues contain coupons redeemable for a Jim Lee Grifter/Backlash print.

KINDRED II, THE
DC Comics (WildStorm): Mar, 2002 - No. 4, June, 2002 ($2.50, limited series)

1-4-Booth-s/Booth & Regla-a						3.00

KINETIC
DC Comics (Focus): May, 2004 - No. 8, Dec, 2004 ($2.50)

1-8-Puckett-s/Pleece-a/c						3.00
TPB (2005, $9.99) r/#1-8; cover gallery and sketch pages						10.00

KING (Magazine)
Skywald Publ.: Mar, 1971 - No. 2, July, 1971

1-Violence; semi-nudity; Boris Vallejo-a (2 pgs.)	5	10	15	33	57	80
2-Photo-c	3	6	9	21	33	45

KING ARTHUR AND THE KNIGHTS OF JUSTICE
Marvel Comics UK: Dec, 1993 - No. 3, Feb, 1994 ($1.25, limited series)

1-3: TV adaptation						4.00

KING CLASSICS
King Features: 1977 (36 pgs., cardboard-c) (Printed in Spain for U.S. distr.)

1-Connecticut Yankee, 2-Last of the Mohicans, 3-Moby Dick, 4-Robin Hood, 5-Swiss Family Robinson, 6-Robinson Crusoe, 7-Treasure Island, 8-20,000 Leagues, 9-Christmas Carol, 10-Huck Finn, 11-Around the World in 80 Days, 12-Davy Crockett, 13-Don Quixote, 14-Gold Bug, 15-Ivanhoe, 16-Three Musketeers, 17-Baron Munchausen, 18-Alice in Wonderland, 19-Black Arrow, 20-Five Weeks in a Balloon, 21-Great Expectations, 22-Gulliver's Travels, 23-Prince & Pauper, 24-Lawrence of Arabia (Originals, 1977-78)

each....		2	4	6	10	14	18
Reprints (1979; HRN-24)		2	4	6	8	10	12

NOTE: The first eight issues were not numbered. Issues No. 25-32 were advertised but not published. The 1977 originals have HRN 32a; the 1978 originals have HRN 32b.

KING COLT (See Luke Short's Western Stories)

KING COMICS (Strip reprints)
David McKay Publications/Standard #156-on: 4/36 - No. 155, 11-12/49; No. 156, Spr/50 - No. 159, 2/52 (Winter on-c)

1-1st app. Flash Gordon by Alex Raymond; Brick Bradford (1st app.), Popeye, Henry (1st app.) & Mandrake the Magician (1st app.) begin; Popeye-c begin	1750	3500	5250	14,000	--	--
2	390	780	1170	2150	3325	4500
3	267	534	800	1600	2400	3200
4	205	410	615	1130	1765	2400
5	155	310	465	850	1325	1800
6-10: 9-X-Mas-c	107	214	321	590	920	1250
11-20	80	160	240	440	683	925
21-30: 21-X-Mas-c	60	120	180	330	515	700
31-40-33-Last Segar Popeye	50	100	150	275	420	625
41-50: 46-Text illos by Marge Buell contain characters similar to Lulu, Alvin & Tubby.						
50-The Lone Ranger begins	39	78	117	231	378	525
51-60: 52-Barney Baxter begins?	36	72	108	211	343	475
61-The Phantom begins	37	74	111	222	361	500
62-80: 76-Flag-c. 79-Blondie begins	20	40	60	118	192	265
81-99	15	30	45	88	137	185
100	20	40	60	114	182	250
101-114: 114-Last Raymond issue (1 pg.); Flash Gordon by Austin Briggs begins, ends #155	14	28	42	81	118	155
115-145: 117-Phantom origin retold	10	20	30	58	79	100
146,147-Prince Valiant in both	9	18	27	52	69	85
148-155: 155-Flash Gordon ends (11-12/49)	9	18	27	52	69	85
156-159: 156-New logo begins (Standard)	9	18	27	50	65	80

NOTE: Marge Buell text illos in No. 24-46 at least.

KING CONAN (Conan The King No. 20 on)
Marvel Comics Group: Mar, 1980 - No. 19, Nov, 1983 (52 pgs.)

1	3	6	9	14	19	24
2-19: 4-Death of Thoth Amon. 7-1st Paul Smith-a, 1 pg. pin-up (9/81)						5.00

NOTE: **J. Buscema** c-1-9p, 17p; c(p)-1-5, 7-9, 14, 17. **Kaluta** c-19. **Nebres** a-17i, 18, 19i. **Severin** c-18. **Simonson** c-6.

KING CONAN
Marvel Comics: Feb, 2022 - No. 6, Sept, 2022 ($4.99/$3.99)

1-($4.99) Jason Aaron-s/Mahmud Asrar-a; Thoth-Amon app.						5.00
2-6-($3.99) 5-Thoth-Amon origin re-told						4.00

KING CONAN: THE CONQUEROR
Dark Horse Comics: Feb, 2014 - No. 6, Jul, 2014 ($3.50, limited series)

1-6-Truman-s/Giorello-a/c						3.50

KING CONAN: THE HOUR OF THE DRAGON
Dark Horse Comics: May, 2013 - No. 6, Oct, 2013 ($3.50, limited series)

1-6-Truman-s/Giorello-a/Parel-c						3.50

KING CONAN: THE PHOENIX ON THE SWORD
Dark Horse Comics: Jan, 2012 - No. 4, Apr, 2012 ($3.50, limited series)

1-4-Truman-s/Giorello-a/Robinson-c. 1-Variant-c by Parel						3.50

KING CONAN: THE SCARLET CITADEL
Dark Horse Comics: Feb, 2011 - No. 4, May, 2011 ($3.50, limited series)

1-4-Truman-s/Giorello-a/Robertson-c. 1-Variant-c by Parel						3.50

KING CONAN: WOLVES BEYOND THE BORDER
Dark Horse Comics: Dec, 2015 - No. 4, Mar, 2016 ($3.99, limited series)

1-4-Truman-s/Giorello-a/c. 1-Kull app. 4-Bran Mak Morn app.						4.00

KING DAVID
DC Comics (Vertigo): 2002 ($19.95, 8 1/2" x 11")

nn-Story of King David; Kyle Baker-s/a						20.00

KINGDOM, THE
DC Comics: Feb, 1999 - No. 2, Feb, 1999 ($2.95/$1.99, limited series)

1,2-Waid-s; sequel to Kingdom Come; introduces Hypertime	1	3	4	6	8	10
...: Kid Flash 1 (2/99, $1.99) Waid-s/Pararillo-a, ...: Nightstar 1 (2/99, $1.99) Waid-s/Haley-a, ...: Offspring 1 (2/99, $1.99) Waid-s/Quitely-a, ...: Planet Krypton 1 (2/99, $1.99) Waid-s/Kitson-a, ...: Son of the Bat 1 (2/99, $1.99) Waid-s/Apthorp-a						4.00

KINGDOM COME (Also see Justice Society of America #9-22)
DC Comics: 1996 - No. 4, 1996 ($4.95, painted limited series)

1-Mark Waid scripts & Alex Ross-painted c/a in all; tells the last days of the DC Universe; 1st app. Magog	3	6	9	14	19	24
2-Superman forms new Justice League	3	6	9	14	19	24
3-Return of Captain Marvel	2	4	6	8	10	12
4-Final battle of Superman and Captain Marvel	2	4	6	8	11	14
Deluxe Slipcase Edition-($89.95) w/Revelations companion book, 12 new story pages, foil stamped covers, signed and numbered						120.00
Hardcover Edition-($29.95)-Includes 12 new story pages and artwork from Revelations, new cover artwork with gold foil inlay						40.00
Hardcover 2nd printing						30.00
Softcover Ed.-($14.95)-Includes 12 new story pgs. & artwork from Revelations, new c-artwork						20.00
Softcover Ed.-(2008, $17.99)-New wraparound gatefold cover by Ross						18.00

KING: FLASH GORDON
Dynamite Entertainment: 2015 - No. 4, 2015 ($3.99)

1-4: 1-Acker & Blacker-s/Ferguson-c/Cooke-c; variant-c by Liefeld. 2-Zdarsky-c						4.00

KING IN BLACK (See Venom and Knull: Marvel Tales)
Marvel Comics: Feb, 2021 - No. 5, Jun, 2021 ($5.99/$4.99)

1-($5.99) Cates-s/Stegman-a; Knull arrives on Earth; Venom & the Avengers app.						6.00
2-4-($4.99) 2-Namor & Spider-Man app. 3-Thor returns. 4-Enigma Force app.						5.00
5-($5.99) Cates-s/Stegman-a; Silver Surfer, Venom & the Avengers app.						6.00

	GD 2.0	VG 4.0	FN 6.0	VF 8.0	VF/NM 9.0	NM- 9.2

...: Black Knight 1 (4/21, $4.99) Spurrier-s/Saiz-a — 5.00
...: Black Panther 1 (4/21, $4.99) Thorne-s/Peralta-a; Shuri & Storm app. — 5.00
...: Captain America 1 (5/21, $4.99) Lore-s/Colak & Leon-a; Falcon & Winter Soldier app. — 5.00
...: Ghost Rider 1 (5/21, $4.99) Brisson-s/Frigeri-a; Mephisto app. — 5.00
... Handbook 1 (5/21, $4.99) Profiles for the symbiotes and major characters — 5.00
...: Immortal Hulk 1 (2/21, $4.99) Ewing-s/Kuder-a; Savage Hulk vs. symbiotes — 5.00
...: Iron Man/Doom 1 (2/21, $3.99) Cantwell-s/Larroca-a; battle a symbiote Santa Claus — 4.00
...: Marauders 1 (4/21, $4.99) Gerry Duggan-s/Luke Ross-a — 5.00
...: Scream 1 (5/21, $4.99) Clay Chapman-s/Garry Brown-a — 5.00
...: Spider-Man 1 (5/21, $4.99) MacKay-s/Bandini-a; Reptil app. — 5.00
...: Wiccan and Hulkling 1 (5/21, $4.99) Tini Howard-s/Luciano Vecchio-a — 5.00

KING IN BLACK: GWENOM VS. CARNAGE
Marvel Comics: Mar, 2021 - No. 3, May, 2021 ($3.99, limited series)
1-3-McGuire-s/Flaviano-a; Ghost-Spider & Mary Jane Watson app. — 4.00

KING IN BLACK: NAMOR
Marvel Studios: Feb, 2021 - No. 5, Jun, 2021 ($3.99, limited series)
1-5-Busiek-s/Dewey-a; flashback to Namor's youth — 4.00

KING IN BLACK: PLANET OF THE SYMBIOTES
Marvel Comics: Mar, 2021 - No. 3, May, 2021 ($3.99, limited series)
1-3-Scream app.; Knull attacks Ravencroft; Misty Knight & John Jameson app. — 4.00

KING IN BLACK: RETURN OF THE VALKYRIES
Marvel Comics: Feb, 2021 - No. 4, May, 2021 ($3.99, limited series)
1-4-Aaron & Gronbekk-s/Vakueva-a; Jane Foster, The Sentry & Dani Moonstar app. — 4.00

KING IN BLACK: THUNDERBOLTS
Marvel Comics: Mar, 2021 - No. 3, May, 2021 ($3.99, limited series)
1-3-Rosenberg-s/Ferreyra-a; Star, Rhino, Batroc, Taskmaster app. — 4.00

KING: JUNGLE JIM
Dynamite Entertainment: 2015 - No. 4, 2015 ($3.99)
1-4: 1-Tobin-s/Jarrell-a/Cooke-c; variant-c by Liefeld. 2-Zdarsky-c — 4.00

KING KONG (See Movie Comics)

KING KONG: THE 8TH WONDER OF THE WORLD (Adaptation of 2005 movie)
Dark Horse Comics: Dec, 2005 ($3.99, planned limited series completed in TPB)

	GD 2.0	VG 4.0	FN 6.0	VF 8.0	VF/NM 9.0	NM- 9.2
1-Photo-c; Dustin Weaver-a/Christian Gossett-s	1	3		4	6	8	10

TPB (11/06, $12.95) r/#1 and unpublished parts 2&3; photo-c; Dorman paintings — 13.00

KING LEONARDO & HIS SHORT SUBJECTS (TV)
Dell Publishing Co./Gold Key: Nov-Jan, 1961-62 - No. 4, Sept, 1963

	GD 2.0	VG 4.0	FN 6.0	VF 8.0	VF/NM 9.0	NM- 9.2
Four Color 1242,1278	10	20	30	67	141	215
01390-207(5-7/62)(Dell)	8	16	24	52	99	145
1 (10/62)	9	18	27	60	120	180
2-4	7	14	21	48	89	130

KING LOUIE & MOWGLI (See Jungle Book under Movie Comics)
Gold Key: May, 1968 (Disney)

	GD 2.0	VG 4.0	FN 6.0	VF 8.0	VF/NM 9.0	NM- 9.2
1 (#10223-805)-Characters from Jungle Book	4	8	12	23	37	50

KING: MANDRAKE THE MAGICIAN
Dynamite Entertainment: 2015 - No. 4, 2015 ($3.99)
1-4: 1-Langridge-s/Treece-a/Cooke-c; variant-c by Liefeld. 2-Zdarsky-c — 4.00

KING OF DIAMONDS (TV)
Dell Publishing Co.: July-Sept, 1962

	GD 2.0	VG 4.0	FN 6.0	VF 8.0	VF/NM 9.0	NM- 9.2
01-391-209-Photo-c	5	10	15	30	50	70

KING OF KINGS (Movie)
Dell Publishing Co.: No. 1236, Oct-Nov, 1961

	GD 2.0	VG 4.0	FN 6.0	VF 8.0	VF/NM 9.0	NM- 9.2
Four Color 1236-Photo-c	8	16	24	52	99	145

KING OF NOWHERE
BOOM! Studios: Mar, 2020 - No. 5, Sept, 2020 ($3.99, limited series)
1-5-W. Maxwell Prince-s/Tyler Jenkins-a — 4.00

KING OF SPIES
Image Comics: Dec, 2021 - No. 4, Mar, 2022 ($4.99/$3.99, limited series)
1-($4.99) Mark Millar-s/Matteo Scalera-a; intro. Roland King — 5.00
2,3-($3.99) — 4.00
4-($5.99) — 6.00

KING OF THE BAD MEN OF DEADWOOD
Avon Periodicals: 1950 (See Wild Bill Hickok #16)

	GD 2.0	VG 4.0	FN 6.0	VF 8.0	VF/NM 9.0	NM- 9.2
nn-Kinstler-c; Kamen/Feldstein-a/Cowpuncher #2	24	48	72	142	234	325

KING OF THE ROYAL MOUNTED (See Famous Feature Stories, King Comics, Red Ryder #3 & Super Book #2, 6)

KING OF THE ROYAL MOUNTED (Zane Grey's...)
David McKay/Dell Publishing Co.: No. 1, May, 1937; No. 9, 1940; No. 207, Dec, 1948 - No. 935, Sept-Nov, 1958

	GD 2.0	VG 4.0	FN 6.0	VF 8.0	VF/NM 9.0	NM- 9.2
Feature Books 1 (5/37)(McKay)	110	220	330	704	1202	1700
Large Feature Comic 9 (1940)	55	110	165	352	601	850
Four Color 207(#1, 12/48)	18	36	54	100	220	340
Four Color 265,283	10	20	30	64	132	200
Four Color 310,340	7	14	21	46	86	125
Four Color 363,384, 8(6-8/52)-10	6	12	18	40	73	105
11-20	5	10	15	31	53	75
21-28(3-5/58)	4	8	12	27	44	60
Four Color 935(9-11/58)	5	10	15	31	53	75

NOTE: 4-Color Nos. 207, 265, 283, 310, 340, 363, 384 are all newspaper reprints with Jim Gary art. No. 8 on are all Dell originals. Painted c-No. 9-on.

KINGPIN
Marvel Comics: Nov, 1997 ($5.99, squarebound, one-shot)
nn-Spider-Man & Daredevil vs. Kingpin; Stan Lee-s/ John Romita Sr.-a — 6.00

KINGPIN
Marvel Comics: Aug, 2003 - No. 7, Jan, 2004 ($2.50/$2.99, limited series)
1-6-Bruce Jones-s/Sean Phillips & Klaus Janson-a — 3.00

7-($2.99) — 3.00

KINGPIN
Marvel Comics: Apr, 2017 - No. 5, Aug, 2017 ($3.99, limited series)
1-Wilson Fisk goes legit; Matthew Rosenberg-s/Ben Torres-a. 2-5-Tombstone app. — 4.00

KING: PRINCE VALIANT
Dynamite Entertainment: 2015 - No. 4, 2015 ($3.99)
1-4: 1-Cosby-s/Salasi-a/Cooke-c; variant-c by Liefeld. 2-Zdarsky-c — 4.00

KING RICHARD & THE CRUSADERS
Dell Publishing Co.: No. 588, Oct, 1954

	GD 2.0	VG 4.0	FN 6.0	VF 8.0	VF/NM 9.0	NM- 9.2
Four Color 588-Movie, Matt Baker-a, photo-c	10	20	30	69	147	225

KING-SIZE CABLE SPECTACULAR (Takes place between Cable (2008 series) #6 & #7)
Marvel Comics: Nov, 2008 ($4.99, one-shot)
1-Lashley-a; Deadpool #1 preview; cover gallery of variants from 2008 series — 5.00

KING-SIZE CONAN
Marvel Comics: Feb, 2021 ($6.99, one-shot)
1-Short stories by various incl. Roy Thomas, Eastman, Busiek, McNiven, Woods — 7.00

KING-SIZE HULK (Takes place between Hulk (2008 series) #3 & #4)
Marvel Comics: July, 2008 ($4.99, one-shot)

	GD 2.0	VG 4.0	FN 6.0	VF 8.0	VF/NM 9.0	NM- 9.2
1-Art Adams, Frank Cho, & Herb Trimpe-a; double-c by Cho & Adams; Red Hulk, She-Hulk & Wendigo app.; origin Abomination; r/Incr. Hulk #180,181 & Avengers #83	2	4	6	9	12	15

KING-SIZE SPIDER-MAN SUMMER SPECIAL
Marvel Comics: Oct, 2008 ($4.99, one-shot)
1-Short stories by various; Falcon app.; Burchett, Giarrusso & Coover-a — 5.00

KINGSMEN: THE RED DIAMOND (Sequel to Secret Service)(Inspired Kingsmen movies)
Image Comics: Sept, 2017 - No. 6, Feb, 2018 ($3.99, limited series)
1-6-Rob Williams-s/Simon Fraser-a. 1-Multiple covers — 4.00

KINGS OF THE NIGHT
Dark Horse Comics: 1990 - No. 2, 1990 ($2.25, limited series)
1,2-Robert E. Howard adaptation; Bolton-c — 4.00

KING SOLOMON'S MINES (Movie)
Avon Periodicals: 1951

	GD 2.0	VG 4.0	FN 6.0	VF 8.0	VF/NM 9.0	NM- 9.2
nn (#1 on 1st page)	55	110	165	352	601	850

KING SPAWN
Image Comics: Aug, 2021 - Present ($5.99/$2.99)
1-($5.99) Sean Lewis-s/Javi Fernandez-a; back-ups with Haunt, Nightmare, Gunslinger Spawn; stories by McFarlane; art by various; multiple covers — 6.00
2-30-($2.99) 4-She-Spawn app. 9,13-15-Nachlik-a. 18-Mack-c — 3.00

KINGS QUEST
Dynamite Entertainment: 2016 - No. 5, 2016 ($3.99, limited series)
1-5-Flash Gordon, Mandrake, Prince Valiant, The Phantom team; multiple-c on each — 4.00

KING'S ROAD
Dark Horse Comics: Feb, 2016 - No. 3, Apr, 2016 ($3.99, limited series)
1-3-Peter Hogan-s/Phil Winslade & Staz Johnson-a; Johnson-c — 4.00

KINGS WATCH
Dynamite Entertainment: 2013 - No. 5, 2014 ($3.99)
1-5-Flash Gordon, Mandrake and The Phantom team up; Parker-s/Laming-a — 4.00

KINGSWAY WEST
Dark Horse Comics: Aug, 2016 - No. 4, Feb, 2017 ($3.99)
1-4-Greg Pak-s/Mirko Colak-a/c — 4.00

KING TANK GIRL
Albatross Funnybooks: 2020 - No. 5, 2021 ($3.99, limited series)
1-5-Alan Martin-s/Brett Parson-a; Tank Girl and crew go to England — 4.00

KING: THE PHANTOM
Dynamite Entertainment: 2015 - No. 4, 2015 ($3.99)
1-4: 1-Clevinger-s/Schoonover-a/Cooke-c; var-c by Liefeld; Mandrake app. 2-Zdarsky-c — 4.00

KING THOR
Marvel Comics: Nov, 2019 - No. 4, Feb, 2020 ($3.99/$5.99)
1-3-($3.99) Jason Aaron-s/Esad Ribic-a; set in the far future; Frigg, Ellisiv & Atli app. — 4.00
4-($5.99) Leads into 2020 Thor series; art by Ribic, Del Mundo, Coipel & others — 6.00

KING TIGER
Dark Horse Comics: Aug, 2015 - No. 4, Nov, 2015 ($3.99, limited series)
1-4-Randy Stradley-s/Doug Wheatley-a/c — 4.00

KIPLING, RUDYARD (See Mowgli, The Jungle Book)

KIRBY: GENESIS
Dynamite Entertainment: No. 0, 2011 - No. 8, 2012 ($1.00/$3.99)
0-($1.00) Busiek-s; art by Alex Ross & Jack Herbert; series preview, sketch-a — 3.00
1-8-($3.99) Ross & Herbert-a. 1-Seven covers. 2-8-Covers by Ross & Sook — 4.00

KIRBY: GENESIS - CAPTAIN VICTORY
Dynamite Entertainment: 2011 - No. 6, 2012 ($3.99)
1-6: 1-Origin retold; four covers; Sterling Gates-s/Wagner Reis-a — 4.00

KIRBY: GENESIS - DRAGONSBANE
Dynamite Entertainment: 2012 - No. 4, 2013 ($3.99, unfinished limited series)
1-4-Rodi & Ross-s/Casas-a; covers by Ross and Herbert — 4.00

KIRBY: GENESIS - SILVER STAR
Dynamite Entertainment: 2011 - No. 6, 2012 ($3.99)
1-6-Jai Nitz-s/Johnny Desjardins-a. 1-Four covers. 2-6-Three covers — 4.00

KISS (See Crazy Magazine, Howard the Duck #12, 13, Marvel Comics Super Special #1, 5, Rock Fantasy Comics #10 & Rock N' Roll Comics #9)

KISS
Dark Horse Comics: June, 2002 - No. 13, Sept, 2003 ($2.99, limited series)

King of Spies #5 © Netflix

King Spawn #16 © TMP

KISS (2019 series) #4 © KISS Nation

	GD 2.0	VG 4.0	FN 6.0	VF 8.0	VF/NM 9.0	NM- 9.2
1-Photo-c and J. Scott Campbell-c; Casey-s						6.00
2-13: 2-Photo-c and J. Scott Campbell-c. 3-Photo-c and Leinil Yu-c						4.00
...: Men and Monsters TPB (9/03, $12.95) r/#7-10						13.00
...: Rediscovery TPB (2003, $9.95) r/#1-3						10.00
...: Return of the Phantom TPB (2003, $9.95) r/#4-6						10.00
...: Unholy War TPB (2004, $9.95) r/#11-13						10.00
KISS						
IDW Publishing: June, 2012 - No. 8, Jan, 2013 ($3.99)						
1-8-Multiple covers on each. 1,2-Ryall-s/Igle-a						4.00
KISS (Volume 1)						
Dynamite Entertainment: 2016 - No. 10, 2017 ($3.99)						
1-10-Amy Chu-s/Kewber Baal-a; multiple covers						4.00
...: Blood and Stardust 1-5 (2018 - No. 5, 2019, $3.99) Bryan Hill-s/Rodney Buscemi-a						4.00
...: Forever (2017, $7.99, squarebound) Burnham-s/Daniel HDR-a/Cinar-c						8.00
...: The Demon 1-4 (2017, $3.99) prequel to 2016 series; Chu & Burnham/Casallos-a						4.00
KISS 4K						
Platinum Studios Comics: May, 2007 - No. 6, Apr, 2008 ($3.99/$2.99)						
1-Sprague-s/Crossley & Campos-a/Migliari-c						4.00
1-B&W sketch-c						6.00
1-Destroyer Edition ($50.00, 30"x18", edition of 5000)						50.00
2-6-($2.99)						3.00
KISSMAS (12/07, $4.99) Christmas-themed issue; re-cap of issues #1-4						5.00
KISSING CHAOS						
Oni Press: Sept, 2001 - No. 8, Mar, 2002 ($2.25, B&W, 6" x 9", limited series)						
1-8-Arthur Dela Cruz-s/a						3.00
...: Nine Lives (12/03, $2.99, regular comic-sized)						3.00
...: 1000 Words (7/03, $2.99, regular comic-sized)						3.00
TPB (9/02, $17.95) r/#1-8						18.00
KISSING CHAOS: NONSTOP BEAUTY						
Oni Press: Oct, 2002 - No. 4, March, 2003 ($2.95, B&W, 6" x 9", limited series)						
1-4-Arthur Dela Cruz-s/a						3.00
TPB (9/03, $11.95) r/#1-4						12.00
KISS KIDS						
IDW Publishing: Aug, 2013 - No. 4, Nov, 2013 ($3.99, limited series)						
1-4-Short stories of KISS members as grade-school kids; Ryall & Waltz-s						4.00
KISS KISS BANG BANG						
CrossGen Comics: Feb, 2004 - No. 5, Jun, 2004 ($2.95)						
1-5-Bedard-s/Perkins-a						3.00
KISS ME, SATAN						
Dark Horse Comics: Sept, 2013 - No. 5, Jan, 2014 ($3.99, limited series)						
1-5-Gischler-s/Ferreyra-a; Dave Johnson-c						4.00
KISS: PHANTOM OBSESSION						
Dynamite Entertainment: 2021 - No. 5, 2021 ($3.99)						
1-5-Edginton-s/Celor-a; multiple covers						4.00
KISS SOLO						
IDW Publishing: Mar, 2013 - No. 4, Jun, 2013 ($3.99, limited series)						
1-4-Multiple covers on each. 1-Ryall-s/Medina-a. 2-Waltz-s/Rodriguez-a						4.00
KISS THE ARMY OF DARKNESS						
Dynamite Entertainment: 2018 ($3.99, one-shot)						
1-Bowers & Sims-s/Coleman-a; multiple covers; KISS meets Ash						4.00
KISS: THE END						
Dynamite Entertainment: 2019 - No. 5, 2019 ($3.99, limited series)						
1-5-Amy Chu-s/Edu Menna-a; multiple covers. 2-Flashback to 1973						4.00
KISS: THE PSYCHO CIRCUS						
Image Comics: Aug, 1997 - No. 31, June, 2000 ($1.95/$2.25/$2.50)						
1-Holguin-s/Medina-a(p)	2	4	6	8	10	12
1-2nd & 3rd printings						3.00
2						6.00
3,4: 4-Photo-c						5.00
5-8: 5-Begin $2.25-c						4.00
9-29						4.00
30,31: 30-Begin $2.50-c						4.00
Book 1 TPB ('98, $12.95) r/#1-6						13.00
Book 2 Destroyer TPB (8/99, $9.95) r/#10-13						10.00
Book 3 Whispered Scream TPB ('00, $9.95) r/#7-9,18						10.00
...Magazine 1 ($6.95) r/#1-3 plus interviews						7.00
...Magazine 2-5 ($4.95) 2-r/#4,5 plus interviews. 3-r/#6,7. 4-r/#8,9						5.00
Wizard Edition ('98, supplement) Bios, tour preview and interviews						3.00
KISS / VAMPIRELLA						
Dynamite Entertainment: 2017 - No. 5, 2017 ($3.99)						
1-5-Sebela-s/Martello-a; multiple covers; Vampirella meets KISS in 1974						4.00
KISSYFUR (TV)						
DC Comics: 1989 (Sept.) ($2.00, 52 pgs., one-shot)						
1-Based on Saturday morning cartoon						4.00
KISS: ZOMBIES						
Dynamite Entertainment: 2019 - No. 5, 2020 ($3.99, limited series)						
1-5-Ethan Sacks-s/Rodney Buchemi-a; multiple covers; KISS in the zombie future						4.00
KIT CARSON (Formerly All True Detective Cases No. 4; Fighting Davy Crockett No. 9; see Blazing Sixguns & Frontier Fighters)						
Avon Periodicals: 1950; No. 2, 8/51 - No. 3, 12/51; No. 5, 11-12/54 - No. 8, 9/55 (No #4)						
nn(#1) (1950)- "...Indian Scout" ; r-Cowboys 'N' Injuns #?	16	32	48	96	151	205
2(8/51)	14	28	42	78	112	145
3(12/51)- "...Fights the Comanche Raiders"	12	24	36	69	97	125
5-6,8(11-12/54-9/55): 5-Formerly All True Detective Cases (last pre-code);						
titled "...and the Trail of Doom"	11	22	33	60	83	105
7-McCann-a?	11	22	33	60	83	105
I.W. Reprint #10('63)-r/Kit Carson #1; Severin-c	2	4	6	11	16	20
NOTE: **Kinstler** c-1-3, 5-8.						
KIT CARSON & THE BLACKFEET WARRIORS						
Realistic: 1953						
nn-Reprint; Kinstler-c	14	28	42	78	112	145
KITCHEN, THE						
DC Comics (Vertigo): Jan, 2015 - No. 8, Aug, 2015 ($2.99, limited series)						
1-8-Masters-s/Doyle-a/Cloonan-c						3.00
KIT KARTER						
Dell Publishing Co.: May-July, 1962						
1	3	6	9	19	30	40
KITTY						
St. John Publishing Co.: Oct, 1948						
1-Teenage; Lily Renee-c/a	28	56	84	165	270	375
KITTY PRYDE, AGENT OF S.H.I.E.L.D. (Also see Excalibur and Mekanix)						
Marvel Comics: Dec, 1997 - No. 3, Feb, 1998 ($2.50, limited series)						
1-3-Hama-s						4.00
KITTY PRYDE AND WOLVERINE (Also see Uncanny X-Men & X-Men)						
Marvel Comics Group: Nov, 1984 - No. 6, Apr, 1985 (Limited series)						
1-Characters from X-Men	3	6	9	14	19	24
2-6						5.00
X-Men: Kitty Pryde and Wolverine HC (2008, $19.99) r/series						20.00
KLARER GIVEAWAYS (See Wisco in the Promotional Comics section)						
KLARION (The Witchboy)						
DC Comics: Dec, 2014 - No. 6, May, 2015 ($2.99)						
1-6: 1-3-Nocenti-s/McCarthy-a. 4-Fiorentino-a						3.00
KLAUS						
BOOM! Studios: Nov, 2015 - No. 7, Aug, 2016 ($3.99)						
1-7: 1-Origin of Santa Claus; Grant Morrison-s/Dan Mora-a; multiple covers						4.00
... and the Crisis in Xmasville 1 (12/17, $7.99) Morrison-s/Mora-a; Snowmaiden app.						8.00
... and the Crying Snowman 1 (12/18, $7.99) Morrison-s/Mora-a;						8.00
... and the Life & Times of Joe Christmas 1 (12/19, $7.99) Morrison-s/Mora-a; calendar printed sideways showing Joe Christmas from 1930-2001						8.00
... and the Witch of Winter 1 (12/16, $7.99) Morrison-s/Mora-a; Geppetto app.						8.00
KLAWS OF THE PANTHER (Also see Black Panther)						
Marvel Comics: Dec, 2010 - No. 4, Feb, 2011 ($3.99, limited series)						
1-Maberry-s/Gugliotta-a/Del Mundo-c; Ka-Zar & Shanna app.	3	6	9	14	20	25
2-4: 3-Spider-Man app.	1	2	3	5	6	8
KNEEL BEFORE ZOD						
DC Comics: Mar, 2024 - Present ($4.99/$3.99, limited series)						
1-($4.99) Casey-s/McDaid-a; Ursa and Lor-Zod app.						5.00
2,3-($3.99) 3-Ursa killed						4.00
KNIGHT AND SQUIRE (Also see Batman #667-669)						

	GD	VG	FN	VF	VF/NM	NM-
	2.0	4.0	6.0	8.0	9.0	9.2

DC Comics: Dec, 2010 - No. 6, May, 2011 ($2.99, limited series)

1-6-Cornell-s/Broxton-a. 1-Two covers by Paquette & Tucci. 5,6-Joker app.						4.00
TPB (2011, $14.99) r/#1-6; sketch and design art						15.00

KNIGHT AND THE LADY OF PLAY, THE
Image Comics: Nov, 2022 ($3.99, one-shot)

1-Jonathan Luna-s/a						4.00

KNIGHTED
AWA Studios: Nov, 2021 - No. 5, Apr, 2022 ($3.99, limited series)

1-5-Gregg Hurwitz-s/Mark Texeira-a						4.00

KNIGHTHAWK
Acclaim Comics (Windjammer): Sept, 1995 - No. 6, Nov, 1995 ($2.50, lim. series)

1-6: 6-origin						4.00

KNIGHTMARE
Image Comics (Extreme Studios): Feb, 1995 - No. 5, June, 1995 ($2.50)

0 ($3.50)						5.00
1-5: 4-Quesada & Palmiotti variant-c, 5-Flip book w/Warcry						4.00

KNIGHTS 4 (See Marvel Knights 4)

KNIGHTS OF PENDRAGON, THE (Also see Pendragon)
Marvel Comics Ltd.: July, 1990 - No. 18, Dec, 1991 ($1.95)

1-18: 1-Capt. Britain app. 2,8-Free poster inside. 9,10-Bolton-c. 11,18-Iron Man app.						4.00

KNIGHTS OF THE ROUND TABLE
Dell Publishing Co.: No. 540, Mar, 1954

	GD	VG	FN	VF	VF/NM	NM-
Four Color 540-Movie, photo-c	7	14	21	44	82	120

KNIGHTS OF THE ROUND TABLE
Pines Comics: No. 10, April, 1957

	GD	VG	FN	VF	VF/NM	NM-
10-Features Sir Lancelot	6	12	18	31	38	45

KNIGHTS OF THE ROUND TABLE
Dell Publishing Co.: Nov-Jan, 1963-64

	GD	VG	FN	VF	VF/NM	NM-
1 (12-397-401)-Painted-c	3	6	9	20	31	42

KNIGHTS OF X (X-Men)
Marvel Comics: Jun, 2022 - No. 5, Oct, 2022 ($4.99/$3.99)

1-($4.99) Tini Howard-s/Bob Quinn-a; Captain Britain, Gambit, King Arthur app.						5.00
2-5-($3.99)						4.00

KNIGHTS TEMPORAL
AfterShock Comics: Jul, 2019 - No. 5, Jan, 2020 ($3.99, limited series)

1-5-Cullen Bunn-s/Fran Galán-a						4.00

KNIGHTSTRIKE (Also see Operation: Knightstrike)
Image Comics (Extreme Studios): Jan, 1996 ($2.50)

1-Rob Liefeld & Eric Stephenson story; Extreme Destroyer Part 6						4.00

KNIGHT TERRORS (See Dawn of DC Knight Terrors FCBD Special Edition 2023 for Part 1)
DC Comics: Sept, 2023 - No. 4, Oct, 2023 ($3.99, limited series)

...: First Blood (9/23, $5.99) **Part 2 of event**; Williamson-s/Porter-a; Dr. Destiny app.						6.00
1-4-Williamson-s/Camuncoli-a; Deadman, Wesley Dodds vs. God of Nightmares						4.00
...: Night's End (10/23, $5.99) **Conclusion of event**; Deadman vs. Insomnia						6.00
..... Action Comics 1,2 (9/23, 10/23, $4.99) Features Power Girl and Cyborg Superman						5.00
...: Angel Breaker 1,2 (9/23, 10/23, $4.99) Seeley-s/Bright-a						5.00
...: Batman 1,2 (9/23, 10/23, $4.99) Williamson-s/March-a; back-up Damian story						5.00
...: Black Adam 1,2 (9/23, 10/23, $4.99) Jeremy Haun-a						5.00
...: Catwoman 1,2 (9/23, 10/23, $4.99) Tini Howard-s/Leila Leiz-a						5.00
...: Detective Comics 1,2 (9/23, 10/23, $4.99) Watters-s/Federici-a; Jim Gordon's nightmare						5.00
...: Green Lantern 1,2 (9/23, 10/23, $4.99) Parallax and Sinestro app.						5.00
...: Harley Quinn 1,2 (9/23, 10/23, $4.99) Tini Howard-s/Hayden Sherman-a						5.00
...: Nightwing 1,2 (9/23, 10/23, $4.99) Cloonan & Conrad-s/Di Nicuolo-a						5.00
...: Poison Ivy 1,2 (9/23, 10/23, $4.99) Harley Quinn app.						5.00
...: Punchline 1,2 (9/23, 10/23, $3.99) Danny Lore-s/Lucas Meyer-a						4.00
...: Ravager 1,2 (9/23, 10/23, $3.99) Ed Brisson-s/Dexter Soy-a						4.00
...: Robin 1,2 (9/23, 10/23, $4.99) Tim Drake and Jason Todd						5.00
...: Shazam! 1,2 (9/23, 10/23, $4.99) Mary Marvel's nightmare; Mark Waid-s/Roger Cruz-a						5.00
...: Superman 1,2 (9/23, 10/23, $4.99) Williamson-s/Reilly-a; Aquaman app.						5.00
...: The Flash 1,2 (9/23, 10/23, $4.99) Paknadel-s/Bayliss-a						5.00
...: The Joker 1,2 (9/23, 10/23, $4.99) Rosenberg-s/Raffaele-a						5.00
...: Titans 1,2 (9/23, 10/23, $4.99) Constant-s/Godlewski-a; focus on Donna Troy						5.00
...: Wonder Woman 1,2 (9/23, 10/23, $4.99) Detective Chimp & Constantine app.						5.00
...: Zatanna 1,2 (9/23, 10/23, $3.99) Robotman (Doom Patrol) app.						5.00

KNIGHT WATCHMAN (See Big Bang Comics & Dr. Weird)
Image Comics: June, 1998 - No. 4, Oct, 1998 ($2.95/$3.50, B&W, lim. series)

1-4-Ben Torres-c/a in all. 4-($3.50)						4.00

KNIGHT WATCHMAN: GRAVEYARD SHIFT
Caliber Press: 1994 ($2.95, B&W)

1,2-Ben Torres-a						4.00

KNOCK EM DEAD
AfterShock Comics: Dec, 2020 - No. 5, Apr, 2021 ($4.99/$3.99)

1-($4.99) Eliot Rahal-s/Mattia Monaco-a						5.00
2-5-($3.99)						4.00

KNOCK KNOCK (...Who's There?)
Dell Publ./Gerona Publications: No. 801, 1936 (52 pgs.) (8x9", B&W)

	GD	VG	FN	VF	VF/NM	NM-
801-Joke book; Bob Dunn-a	16	32	48	94	147	200

KNOCKOUT ADVENTURES
Fiction House Magazines: Winter, 1953-54

	GD	VG	FN	VF	VF/NM	NM-
1-Reprints Fight Comics #53 w/Rip Carson-c/s	18	36	54	107	169	230

KNUCKLES (Spin-off of Sonic the Hedgehog)
Archie Publications: Apr, 1997 - No. 32, Feb, 2000 ($1.50/$1.75/$1.79)

	GD	VG	FN	VF	VF/NM	NM-
1	2	4	6	8	11	14
2-32						4.00

KNUCKLES' CHAOTIX
Archie Publications: Jan, 1996 ($2.00, annual)

	GD	VG	FN	VF	VF/NM	NM-
1	2	4	6	8	10	12

KNULL
Marvel Comics: Feb, 2021 ($7.99, one-host)

1-Reprints Venom (2018) #3,4,25 & Web of Venom: Carnage Born #1						8.00

KOBALT
DC Comics (Milestone): June, 1994 - No. 16, Sept, 1995 ($1.75/$2.50)

	GD	VG	FN	VF	VF/NM	NM-
1-15: 1-Byrne-c. 4-Intro Page						4.00
16-Kent Williams-c	2	4	6	9	12	15

KOBRA (Unpublished #8 appears in DC Special Series No. 1)
National Periodical Publications: Feb-Mar, 1976 - No. 7, Mar-Apr, 1977

	GD	VG	FN	VF	VF/NM	NM-
1-1st app.; Kirby-a redrawn by Marcos; only 25¢-c	3	6	9	19	30	40
2-7: (All 30¢ issues) 3-Giffen-a	1	3	4	6	8	10
...: Resurrection TPB (2010, $19.99) r/#1, DC Special Series No. 1 and later apps. in Checkmate #23-25, Faces of Evil: Kobra #1 and various Who's Who issues						20.00

NOTE: *Austin* a-3i. *Buckler* a-5p; c-5p. *Kubert* c-4. *Nasser* a-6p, 7; c-7.

KOKEY KOALA (...and the Magic Button)
Toby Press: May, 1952

	GD	VG	FN	VF	VF/NM	NM-
1-Funny animal	18	36	54	107	169	230

KOKO AND KOLA (Also see A-1 Comics #16 & Tick Tock Tales)
Com/Magazine Enterprises: Fall, 1946 - No. 5, May, 1947; No. 6, 1950

	GD	VG	FN	VF	VF/NM	NM-
1-Funny animal	20	40	60	117	189	260
2-X-mas-c	14	28	42	80	115	150
3-6: 6(A-1 28)	12	24	36	67	94	120

KO KOMICS
Gerona Publications: Oct, 1945 (scarce)

	GD	VG	FN	VF	VF/NM	NM-
1-The Duke of Darkness & The Menace (hero); Kirby-c	113	226	339	718	1234	1750

KOLCHAK: THE NIGHT STALKER (TV)
Moonstone: 2002 - 2007 ($6.50/$6.95)

1-($6.50) Jeff Rice-s/Gordon Purcell-a						6.50
... Black & White & Read All Over (2005, $4.95) short stories by various; 2 covers						5.00
... Devil in the Details (2003, $6.95) Trevor Von Eeden-a						7.00
... Eve of Terror (2005, $5.95) Gentile-s/Figueroa-a/Beck-c						6.00
... Fever Pitch (2002, $6.95) Christopher Jones-a						7.00
... Get of Belial (2002, $6.95) Art Nichols-a						7.00
... Lambs to the Slaughter (2003, $6.95) Trevor Von Eeden-a						7.00
... Pain Most Human (2004, $6.95) Greg Scott-a						7.00
... Tales: The Frankenstein Agenda 1 (2007 - No. 3, $3.50) Michelinie-s						3.50
... Tales of the Night Stalker 1-7 (2003 - No. 7, $3.50) two covers by Moore & Ulanski						3.50
TPB (2004, $17.95) r/#1, Get of Belial & Fever Pitch						18.00
Vol. 2: Terror Within TPB (2006, $16.95) r/Pain Most Human, Pain Without Tears & Devil in the Details						17.00

KOMIC KARTOONS
Timely Comics (EPC): Fall, 1945 - No. 2, Winter, 1945

	GD	VG	FN	VF	VF/NM	NM-
1,2-Andy Wolf, Bertie Mouse	39	78	117	231	378	525

KOMIK PAGES (Formerly Snap; becomes Bullseye #11)
Harry 'A' Chesler, Jr. (Our Army, Inc.): Apr, 1945 (All reprints)

	GD	VG	FN	VF	VF/NM	NM-
10(#1 on inside)-Land O' Nod by Rick Yager (2 pgs.), Animal Crackers, Foxy GrandPa, Tom, Dick & Mary, Cheerio Minstrels, Red Starr plus other 1-2 pg. strips; Cole-a	32	64	96	188	307	425

KONA (...Monarch of Monster Isle)
Dell Publishing Co.: Feb-Apr, 1962 - No. 21, Jan-Mar, 1967 (Painted-c)

	GD	VG	FN	VF	VF/NM	NM-
Four Color 1256 (#1)	10	20	30	69	147	225
2-10: 4-Anak begins. 6-Gil Kane-c	5	10	15	34	60	85
11-21	4	8	12	28	47	65

NOTE: *Glanzman* a-all issues.

KONGA (Fantastic Giants No. 24) (See Return of...)
Charlton Comics: June, 1960 - No. 2, Aug, 1961 - No. 23, Nov, 1965

	GD	VG	FN	VF	VF/NM	NM-
1(1960)-Based on movie; Giordano-c	28	56	84	202	451	700
2-5: 2-Giordano-c; no Ditko-a	12	24	36	79	170	260
6-9-Ditko-c/a	9	18	27	60	120	180
10-15	8	16	24	56	108	160
16-23	6	12	18	37	66	95

NOTE: *Ditko* a-1, 3-15; c-4, 6-9, 11. *Glanzman* a-12. *Montes* & *Bache* a-16-23.

KONGA'S REVENGE (Formerly Return of...)
Charlton Comics: No. 2, Summer, 1963 - No. 3, Fall, 1964; Dec, 1968

	GD	VG	FN	VF	VF/NM	NM-
2,3: 2-Ditko-c/a	7	14	21	49	92	135
1(12/68)-Reprints Konga's Revenge #3	3	6	9	16	24	32

KONG: GODS OF SKULL ISLAND
BOOM! Studios: Oct, 2017 ($7.99, one-shot)

1-Phillip Kennedy Johnson-s/Chad Lewis-a						8.00

KONG OF SKULL ISLAND
BOOM! Studios: Jul, 2016 - No. 12, Jun, 2017 ($3.99, limited series)

1-12-James Asmus-s/Carlos Magno-a; multiple covers on each						4.00
... 2018 Special 1 (5/18, $7.99) Paul Allor-s/Carlos Magno-a						8.00

KONG ON THE PLANET OF THE APES
BOOM! Studios: Nov, 2017 - No. 6, Apr, 2018 ($3.99, limited series)

1-6-Ryan Ferrier-s/Carlos Magno-a; multiple covers on each						4.00

KONG: THE GREAT WAR
Dynamite Entertainment: 2023 - Present ($3.99, limited series)

1-4-Alex Cox-s/Tommaso Bianchi-a						4.00

KONG THE UNTAMED
National Periodical Publications: June-July, 1975 - V2#5, Feb-Mar, 1976

Knight Terrors: Shazam! #2 © DC

Kong: The Great War #1 © DeVito Artworks

Krazy Komics #23 © MAR

	GD 2.0	VG 4.0	FN 6.0	VF 8.0	VF/NM 9.0	NM- 9.2
1-1st app. Kong; Wrightson-c; Alcala-a	3	6	9	16	23	30
2-Wrightson-c; Alcala-a	2	4	6	11	16	20
3-5: 3-Alcala-a	1	3	4	6	8	10

KOOKABURRA K
Marvel Comics (Soleil): 2009 - No. 3, 2010 ($5.99, limited series)

1-3-Humberto Ramos-a/c						6.00

KOOKIE
Dell Publishing Co.: Feb-Apr, 1962 - No. 2, May-July, 1962 (15 cents)

	GD 2.0	VG 4.0	FN 6.0	VF 8.0	VF/NM 9.0	NM- 9.2
1-Written by John Stanley; Bill Williams-a	7	14	21	49	92	135
2	6	12	18	41	76	110

KOOSH KINS
Archie Comics: Oct, 1991 - No. 3, Feb, 1992 ($1.00, bi-monthly, limited series)

1-3						4.00

NOTE: No. 4 was planned, but cancelled.

KORAK, SON OF TARZAN (Edgar Rice Burroughs)(See Tarzan #139)
Gold Key: Jan, 1964 - No. 45, Jan, 1972 (Painted-c No. 1-?)

	GD 2.0	VG 4.0	FN 6.0	VF 8.0	VF/NM 9.0	NM- 9.2
1-Russ Manning-a	9	18	27	60	120	180
2-5-Russ Manning-a	5	10	15	33	57	80
6-11-Russ Manning-a	5	10	15	30	50	70
12-23: 12,13-Warren Tufts-a. 14-Jon of the Kalahari ends. 15-Mabu, Jungle Boy begins. 21-Manning-a. 23-Last 12¢ issue	4	8	12	27	44	60
24-30	3	6	9	21	33	45
31-45	3	6	9	17	26	35

KORAK, SON OF TARZAN (Tarzan Family #60 on; see Tarzan #230)
National Periodical Publications: V9#46, May-June, 1974 - V12#56, Feb-Mar, 1974; No. 57, May-June, 1975 - No. 59, Sept-Oct, 1975 (Edgar Rice Burroughs)

	GD 2.0	VG 4.0	FN 6.0	VF 8.0	VF/NM 9.0	NM- 9.2
46-(52 pgs.)-Carson of Venus begins (origin), ends #56; Pellucidar feature; Weiss-a	3	6	9	15	22	28
47-59: 49-Origin Korak retold	2	4	6	8	11	14

NOTE: All have covers by Joe Kubert. Manning strip reprints-No. 57-59. Murphy Anderson a-52,56. Michael Kaluta a-46-56. Frank Thorne a-46-51.

KORE
Image Comics: Apr, 2003 - No. 5, Sept, 2003 ($2.95)

1-5: 1-Two covers by Capullo and Seeley; Seeley-a (p)						3.00

KORG: 70,000 B.C. (TV)
Charlton Publications: May, 1975 - No. 9, Nov, 1976 (Hanna-Barbera)

	GD 2.0	VG 4.0	FN 6.0	VF 8.0	VF/NM 9.0	NM- 9.2
1,2: 1-Boyette-c/a. 2-Painted-c; Byrne text illos	2	4	6	13	18	22
3-9	2	4	6	8	11	14

KORNER KID COMICS: Four Star Publications: 1947 (Advertised, not pub.)

KORVAC SAGA (Secret Wars tie-in)
Marvel Comics: Aug, 2015 - No. 4, Nov, 2015 ($3.99, limited series)

1-4-Guardians 3000, Avengers and Wonder Man app.; Abnett-s/Schmidt-a						4.00

KOSHCHEI IN HELL
Dark Horse Comics: Nov, 2022 - No. 4, Apr, 2023 ($3.99, limited series)

1-4-Mignola-s/c; Stenbeck-a						4.00

KOSHCHEI THE DEATHLESS
Dark Horse Comics: Dec, 2017 - No. 6, Jun, 2018 ($3.99, limited series)

1-6-Mignola-s/c; Stenbeck-a; Hellboy app.						4.00

KRAMPUS
Image Comics: Dec, 2013 - No. 5, May, 2014 ($2.99)

1-5-Sinterklaas' assistant; Joines-s/Kotz-a						3.00

KRAZY KAT
Holt: 1946 (Hardcover)

	GD 2.0	VG 4.0	FN 6.0	VF 8.0	VF/NM 9.0	NM- 9.2
Reprints daily & Sunday strips by Herriman	57	114	171	362	619	875
dust jacket only	42	84	126	265	450	635

KRAZY KAT (See Ace Comics & March of Comics No. 72, 87)

KRAZY KAT COMICS (...& Ignatz the Mouse early issues)
Dell Publ. Co./Gold Key: May-June, 1951 - F.C. #696, Apr, 1956; Jan, 1964 (None by Herriman)

	GD 2.0	VG 4.0	FN 6.0	VF 8.0	VF/NM 9.0	NM- 9.2
1(1951)	10	20	30	70	150	230
2-5 (#5, 8-10/52)	5	10	15	35	63	90
Four Color 454,504	6	12	18	42	79	115
Four Color 548,619,696 (4/56)	5	10	15	31	53	75
1(10098-401)(1/64-Gold Key)(TV)	4	8	12	25	40	55

KRAZY KOMICS (1st Series) (Cindy Comics No. 27 on) (Also see Ziggy Pig)
Timely Comics (USA No. 1-21/JPC No. 22-26): July, 1942 - No. 26, Spr, 1947

	GD 2.0	VG 4.0	FN 6.0	VF 8.0	VF/NM 9.0	NM- 9.2
1-Toughy Tomcat, Ziggy Pig (by Jaffee) & Silly Seal begin	161	322	483	1030	1765	2500
2	57	114	171	362	619	875
3-8,10	40	80	120	246	411	575
9-Hitler parody-c	155	310	465	992	1696	2400
11,13,14	30	60	90	177	289	400
12-Timely's entire art staff drew themselves in a Creeper story	43	86	129	271	461	650
15-(8-9/44)-Has "Super Soldier" by Pfc. Stan Lee	32	64	96	186	307	425
16-24,26: 16-(10-11/44). 26-Super Rabbit-c/story	24	48	72	144	237	330
25-Wacky Duck-c/story & begin; Kurtzman-a (6pgs.)	32	64	96	188	307	425

KRAZY KOMICS (2nd Series)
Timely/Marvel Comics: Aug, 1948 - No. 2, Nov, 1948

	GD 2.0	VG 4.0	FN 6.0	VF 8.0	VF/NM 9.0	NM- 9.2
1-Wolverton (10 pgs.) & Kurtzman (8 pgs.)-a; Eustice Hayseed begins (Li'l Abner swipe)	71	142	213	454	777	1100
2-Wolverton-a (10 pgs.); Powerhouse Pepper cameo	48	96	144	302	514	725

KRAZY KROW (Also see Dopey Duck, Film Funnies, Funny Frolics & Movie Tunes)
Marvel Comics (ZPC): Summer, 1945 - No. 3, Wint, 1945/46

	GD 2.0	VG 4.0	FN 6.0	VF 8.0	VF/NM 9.0	NM- 9.2
1	39	78	117	231	378	525
2,3	24	48	72	142	234	325
I.W. Reprint #1('57), 2('58), 7	3	6	9	16	23	30

KRAZYLIFE (Becomes Nutty Life #2)
Fox Feature Syndicate: 1945 (no month)

	GD 2.0	VG 4.0	FN 6.0	VF 8.0	VF/NM 9.0	NM- 9.2
1-Funny animal	34	68	102	199	325	450

KREE/SKRULL WAR STARRING THE AVENGERS, THE
Marvel Comics: Sept, 1983 - No. 2, Oct, 1983 ($2.50, 68 pgs., Baxter paper)

1,2						6.00

NOTE: Neal Adams p-1r, 2. Buscema a-1r, 2r. Simonson a-1p; c-1p.

KROFFT SUPERSHOW (TV)
Gold Key: Apr, 1978 - No. 6, Jan, 1979

	GD 2.0	VG 4.0	FN 6.0	VF 8.0	VF/NM 9.0	NM- 9.2
1-Photo-c	3	6	9	17	26	35
2-6: 6-Photo-c	3	6	9	14	19	24

KRRSANTAN: STAR WARS TALES
Marvel Comics: Jul, 2022 ($7.99, squarebound, one-shot)

	GD 2.0	VG 4.0	FN 6.0	VF 8.0	VF/NM 9.0	NM- 9.2
1-Reprints early apps. in Star Wars (2015) #14,15,20 and Star Wars: Doctor Aphra Annual #1	1	2	3	5	6	8

KRULL
Marvel Comics Group: Nov, 1983 - No. 2, Dec, 1983

1,2-Adaptation of movie; r/Marvel Super Special. 1-Photo-c from movie						5.00

KRUSTY COMICS (TV)(See Simpsons Comics)
Bongo Comics: 1995 - No. 3, 1995 ($2.25, limited series)

1-3						5.00

KRYPTON CHRONICLES
DC Comics: Sept, 1981 - No. 3, Nov, 1981

1-3: 1-Buckler-c(p)						4.00

KRYPTO THE SUPERDOG (TV)
DC Comics: Nov, 2006 - No. 6, Apr, 2007 ($2.25)

1-6-Based on Cartoon Network series. 1-Origin retold						3.00

KULL
Dark Horse Comics: Nov, 2008 - No. 6, May, 2009 ($2.99)

1-6: 1-Nelson-s/Conrad-a; two covers by Andy Brase and Joe Kubert						3.00

KULL AND THE BARBARIANS
Marvel Comics: May, 1975 - No. 3, Sept, 1975 ($1.00, B&W, magazine)

	GD 2.0	VG 4.0	FN 6.0	VF 8.0	VF/NM 9.0	NM- 9.2
1-(84 pgs.) Andru/Wood-r/Kull #1; 2 pgs. Neal Adams; Gil Kane(r), Marie & John Severin-a(r); Krenkel text illo.	4	8	12	22	35	48
2,3: 2-(84 pgs.) Red Sonja by Chaykin begins; Solomon Kane begins; Gil Kane-a; Solomon Kane pin-up by Wrightson. 3-(76 pgs.) Origin Red Sonja by Chaykin; Adams-a; Solomon Kane app.	3	6	9	17	26	35

KULL: ETERNAL
IDW Publishing: Jun, 2017 - No. 3, Apr, 2018 ($3.99, limited series)

1-3-Waltz-s/Pizzari-a; multiple covers on each; Kull travels through history						4.00

KULL: THE CAT AND THE SKULL
Dark Horse Comics: Oct, 2011 - No. 4, Jan, 2012 ($3.50, limited series)

1-4-Lapham-s/Guzman-a/Chen-c. 1-Variant-c by Hans						3.50

KULL THE CONQUEROR (...the Destroyer #11 on; see Conan #1, Creatures on the Loose

	GD 2.0	VG 4.0	FN 6.0	VF 8.0	VF/NM 9.0	NM- 9.2

#10, Marvel Preview, Monsters on the Prowl)
Marvel Comics Group: June, 1971 - No. 2, Sept, 1971; No. 3, July, 1972 - No. 15, Aug, 1974;
No. 16, Aug, 1976 - No. 29, Oct, 1978

1-Andru/Wood-a; 2nd app. & origin Kull; 15¢ issue	6	12	18	42	79	115
2-5: 2-3rd Kull app. Last 15¢ iss. 3-13: 20¢ issues. 3-Thulsa Doom-c/app.						
	3	6	9	19	30	40
6-10: 7-Thulsa Doom-c/app	2	4	6	10	14	18
11-15: 11-15-Ploog-a. 14,15: 25¢ issues	2	4	6	8	11	14
16-(Regular 25¢ edition)(8/76)	2	3	4	6	8	10
16-(30¢-c variant, limited distribution)	3	6	9	19	30	40
17-29: 21-23-(Reg. 30¢ editions)	2	3	4	6	8	10
21-23-(35¢-c variants, limited distribution)	10	20	30	70	150	230

NOTE: No. 1, 2, 7-9, 11 are based on Robert E. Howard stories. *Alcala* a-17p, 18-20i; c-24. *Ditko* a-12r, 15r. *Gil Kane* c-15p, 21. *Nebres* a-22i-27i; c-25i, 27i. *Ploog* c-11i, 12p, 13. *Severin* a-2-9i; c-2-10i, 19. *Starlin* 21.

KULL THE CONQUEROR
Marvel Comics Group: Dec, 1982 - No. 2, Mar, 1983 (52 pgs., Baxter paper)

1,2: 1-Buscema-a(p)						4.00

KULL THE CONQUEROR (No. 9,10 titled "Kull")
Marvel Comics Group: 5/83 - No. 10, 6/85 (52 pgs., Baxter paper)

V3#1-10: Buscema-a in #1-3,5-10						4.00

NOTE: *Bolton* a-4. *Golden* painted c-3-8. *Guice* a-4p. *Sienkiewicz* a-4; c-2.

KULL: THE HATE WITCH
Dark Horse Comics: Nov, 2010 - No. 4, Feb, 2011 ($3.50)

1-4-Lapham/s/Guzman/Fleming-a						3.50

KUNG FU (See Deadly Hands of…, & Master of…)

KUNG FU FIGHTER (See Richard Dragon…)

KUNG FU PANDA
Titan Comics: Nov, 2015 -No. 4, Jan, 2016 ($3.99, limited series)

1-4-Simon Furman-s. 1,2-Lee Robinson-a						4.00

KUNG FU PANDA 2
Ape Entertainment: 2011 - No. 6, 2012 ($3.95/$3.99, limited series)

1-6-Short stories by various						4.00

KURT BUSIEK'S ASTRO CITY (Limited series) (Also see Astro City: Local Heroes)
Image Comics (Juke Box Productions): Aug, 1995 - No. 6, Jan, 1996 ($2.25)

1-Kurt Busiek scripts, Brent Anderson-a & Alex Ross front & back-c begins; 1st app. Samaritan & Honor Guard (Cleopatra, MHP, Beautie, The Black Rapier, Quarrel & N-Forcer)	3	6	9	14	19	24
2-6: 2-1st app. The Silver Agent, The Old Soldier, & the "original" Honor Guard (Max O'Millions, Starwoman, the "original" Cleopatra, the "original" N-Forcer, the Bouncing Beatnik, Leopardman & Kitkat). 3-1st app. Jack-in-the-Box & The Deacon. 4-1st app. Winged Victory (cameo), The Hanged Man & The First Family. 5-1st app. Crackerjack, The Astro City Irregulars, Nightingale & Sunbird. 6-Origin Samaritan; 1st full app. Winged Victory	1	3	4	6		8
Life In The Big City-(8/96, $19.95, trade paperback)-r/Image Comics limited series w/sketchbook & cover gallery; Ross-/a						20.00
Life In The Big City-(8/96, $49.95, hardcover, 1000 print run)-r/Image Comics limited series w/sketchbook & cover gallery; Ross-/a						50.00

KURT BUSIEK'S ASTRO CITY (1st Homage Comics series)
Image Comics (Homage Comics): V2#1, Sept, 1996 - No. 15, Dec, 1998;
DC Comics (Homage Comics): No. 16, Mar, 1999 - No. 22, Aug, 2000 ($2.50)

1/2-(10/96)-The Hanged Man story; 1st app. The All-American & Slugger, The Lamplighter, Time-Keeper & Eterneon	1	3	4	6		8
1/2-(1/98) 2nd printing w/new cover						3.00
1- Kurt Busiek scripts, Alex Ross-c, Brent Anderson-a & Will Blyberg-i begin; intro The Gentleman, Thunderhead & Helia.	1	2	3	5	6	8
1-(12/97, $4.95) "3-D Edition" w/glasses						5.00
2-Origin The First Family; Astra story	1	2	3	4	5	7
3-5: 4-1st app. The Crossbreed, Ironhorse, Glue Gun & The Confessor (cameo)						6.00
6-10						5.00
11-22: 14-20-Steeljack story arc. 16-(3/99) First DC issue						3.00
TPB-($19.95) Ross-c, r/#4-9, #1/2 w/sketchbook						20.00
Family Album TPB ($19.95) r/#1-3,10-13						20.00
The Tarnished Angel HC ($29.95) r/#14-20; new Ross dust jacket; sketch pages by Anderson & Ross; cover gallery with reference photos						30.00
The Tarnished Angel SC ($19.95) r/#14-20; new Ross-c						20.00

KURTZ VS. KURTZ (Cerebus)
Aardvark-Vanaheim: Aug, 2022 ($4.00, B&W)

1-Two-Fisted Tales #18-c swipe						4.00

LABMAN
Image Comics: Nov, 1996 ($3.50, one-shot)

1-Allred-c						4.00

LAB RATS
DC Comics: June, 2002 - No. 8, Jan, 2003 ($2.50)

1-8-John Byrne-s/a. 5,6-Superman app.						3.00

LABYRINTH
Marvel Comics Group: Nov, 1986 - No. 3, Jan, 1987 (Limited series)

1-3: David Bowie movie adaptation; r/Marvel Super Special #40	3	6	9	17	23	35

LABYRINTH (Jim Henson's…)
Boom Entertainment (Archaia): (one-shots)

… Masquerade 1 (12/21, $7.99)-Donnelly-s/Bak, Dodge, & Carlomagno-a						
	2	4	6	9	12	15
… 30th Anniversary Special 1 (8/16, $9.99)-Short stories by various; multiple covers						
	3	6	9	14	20	25
… 2017 Special 1 (11/17, $7.99) Short stories by various incl. Katie Cook & Landridge						
	2	4	6	8	10	12

LA COSA NOSTROID (See Scud: The Disposible Assassin)
Fireman Press: Mar, 1996 - No. 9, 1998 ($2.95, B&W)

1-9-Dan Harmon-s/Rob Schrab-c/a						4.00

LAD: A DOG (Movie)
Dell Publishing Co.: 1961 - No. 2, July-Sept, 1962

Four Color 1303	5	10	15	33	57	80
2	4	8	12	23	37	50

LA DIABLA (Prelude to The Lords of Misery)
Albatross Funnybooks: 2020 ($3.99, one-shot)

1-Eric Powell-s/a; various origins of La Diabla						4.00

LADY AND THE TRAMP (Disney, See Dell Giants & Movie Comics)
Dell Publishing Co.: No. 629, May, 1955 - No. 634, June, 1955

Four Color 629 (#1)-…with Jock	10	20	30	66	138	210
Four Color 634-…Album	8	16	24	52	99	145

LADY BALTIMORE
Dark Horse Comics: Mar, 2021 - No. 5, Oct, 2021 ($3.99, limited series)

1-5-Mike Mignola & Christopher Golden-s/Bridgit Connell-a						4.00
…: The Dream of Ikelos 1 (3/23, $3.99) Mignola & Golden-s/Connell-a						4.00

LADY CASTLE
BOOM! Studios: Jan, 2017 - No. 4, May, 2017 ($3.99, limited series)

1-4: Delilah Dawson-s/Ashley Woods-a. 2-4-Farrow-a						4.00

LADY COP (See 1st Issue Special)

LADY DEADPOOL
Marvel Comics: Sept, 2010 ($3.99, one-shot)

1-Land-c/Lashley-a	2	4	6	11	16	20

LADY DEATH (See Evil Ernie)
Chaos! Comics: Jan, 1994 - No. 3, Mar, 1994 ($2.75, limited series)

1/2-Steven Hughes-c/a in all	1	3	6	6	8	10
1/2 Gold	1	3	4	6	8	10
1/2 Signed Limited Edition	2	4	6	8	10	12
1/2 Velvet	3	6	9	14	19	24
1-($3.50)-Chromium-c	2	4	6	11	16	20
1-Commemorative	2	4	6	10	14	18
1-(9/96, $2.95) "Encore Presentation"; r/#1						5.00
2	1	3	4	6		8
3						5.00
…And Jade (4/02, $2.99) Augustyn-s/Reis-a						3.00
…And The Women of Chaos! Gallery #1 (11/96, $2.25) pin-ups by various						3.00
…/Bad Kitty (9/01, $2.99) Mota-c/a						3.00
…/Bedlam (6/02, $2.99) Augustyn-s/Reis-c						3.00
…By Steven Hughes (6/00, $2.95) Tribute issue to Steven Hughes						3.00
…By Steven Hughes Deluxe Edition(6/00, $15.95)						16.00
…/Chastity (1/02, $2.99) Mota-c/a; Augustyn-s						3.00
…Death Becomes Her #0 (11/97, $2.95) Hughes-c/a						3.00
…FAN Edition: All Hallow's Eve #1 (1/97, mail-in)						5.00
…In Lingerie #1 (8/95, $2.95) pin-ups, wraparound-c						3.00
…In Lingerie #1-Leather Edition (10,000)						12.00
…In Lingerie #1-Micro Premium Edition; Lady Demon-c (2,000)						35.00
…: Love Bites (3/01, $2.99) Kaminski-s/Luke Ross-a						3.00
…/Medieval Witchblade (8/01, $3.50) covers by Molenaar and Silvestri						3.50
…/Medieval Witchblade Preview Ed. (8/01, $1.99) Molenaar-c						3.00
…: Mischief Night (11/01, $2.99) Ostrander-s/Reis-a						3.00
…: Re-Imagined (7/02, $2.99) Gossett-c						3.00
…: River of Fear (4/01, $2.99) Bennett-a(p)/Cleavenger-c						3.00
…: Swimsuit Special #1-($2.50)-Wraparound-c						3.00
…: Swimsuit Special #1-Red velvet-c						14.00
…: Swimsuit 2001 #1-(2/01, $2.99)-Reis-c; art by various						3.00
…: The Reckoning (7/94, $6.95)-r/#1-3						7.00
…: The Reckoning (8/95, $12.95)- new printing including Lady Death 1/2 & Swimsuit Special #1						13.00
…/Vampirella (3/99, $3.50) Hughes-c/a						3.50
…/Vampirella 2 (3/00, $3.50) Deodato-c/a						3.50
…Vs. Purgatori (3/99, $3.50) Deodato-a						3.50
…Vs. Vampirella Preview (2/00, $1.00) Deodato-a/c						3.00

LADY DEATH (Ongoing series)
Chaos! Comics: Feb, 1998 - No. 16, May, 1999 ($2.95)

1-Pulido-s/Steven Hughes-c/a	2	4	6	9	12	15
2-16: 2-4: Pulido-s/Hughes-c/a. 5-8,13-16-Deodato-a. 9-11-Hughes-a						4.00
…Retribution (8/98, $2.95) Jadsen-a						4.00
…Retribution Premium Ed.						6.00

LADY DEATH
Boundless Comics: No. 0, Nov, 2010 - No. 26 ($3.99)

0-26-Pulido & Wolfer-s/Mueller-a on most; multiple covers on all. 25-Borstel-a						4.00
… Free Comic Book Day 2012 (5/12, free) "The Beginning" on cover; Mueller-a						3.00
… Origins Annual 1 (8/11, $4.99) Martin-a/Pulido-s						5.00
… Premiere (7/10, free) previews series; five covers						3.00

LADY DEATH…
Coffin Comics (One-shots)

… #1 - 25th Anniversary Edition (2/19, $4.99) remastered reprint of Lady Death #1 ('94)						5.00
… Chaos Rules 1 (5/16, $7.99) Pulido & Augustyn-s/Verma-a						8.00
… Hellraiders 1 (1/19, $4.99) Pulido & Maclean-s/Verma-a; multiple covers						5.00
… Merciless Onslaught 1 (8/17, $7.99) Pulido & Maclean-s/Verma-a; multiple covers						8.00
… Oblivion Kiss 1 (4/17, $7.99) Pulido & Maclean-s/Verma-a; multiple covers						8.00
… Revelations 1 (2/17, $3.99) Pin-up gallery of covers						4.00
… Zodiac 1 (12/16, $3.99) 12 pin-up images of the 12 zodiac signs by Nei Ruffino						4.00

LADY DEATH: ALIVE
Chaos! Comics: May, 2001 - No. 4, Aug, 2001 ($2.99, limited series)

1-4-Ivan Reis-a; Lady Death becomes mortal						3.00

LADY DEATH: A MEDIEVAL TALE (Brian Pulido's…)
CG Entertainment: Mar, 2003 - No. 12, Apr, 2004 ($2.95)

Kung Fu Panda 2 #1 © DW

Lady Baltimore #1 © Mignola & Golden

Lady Death: Chaos Rules #1 © LD LLC

	GD	VG	FN	VF	VF/NM	NM-			GD	VG	FN	VF	VF/NM	NM-
	2.0	4.0	6.0	8.0	9.0	9.2			2.0	4.0	6.0	8.0	9.0	9.2

1-12: 1-Brian Pulido-s/Ivan Reis-a; Lady Death in the CrossGen Universe   3.00
Vol.1 TPB (2003, $9.95) digest-sized reprint of #1-6   10.00

LADY DEATH: APOCALYPSE
Boundless Comics: Jan, 2015 - No. 6, Jun, 2015 ($4.99)

1-6: 1-4-Wolfer-s/Borstel-a; multiple covers. 5,6-Wickline-s/Mueller-a   5.00
#0 (8/15, $6.99) Pulido-s/Valenzuela-a; bonus art gallery   7.00

LADY DEATH: APOCALYPTIC ABYSS
Coffin Comics: Feb, 2019 - No. 2, Apr, 2019 ($4.99, limited series)

1,2-Pulido & Maclean-s/Verma-a   5.00

LADY DEATH: BLASPHEMY ANTHEM
Coffin Comics: 2020 - No. 2, Feb, 2021 ($4.99, limited series)

1,2-Pulido & Maclean-s/Bernard-a; The Trinity app.   5.00

LADY DEATH: CATACLYSMIC MAJESTY
Coffin Comics: Feb, 2022 - No. 2, Apr, 2022 ($4.99, limited series)

1,2-Pulido & Maclean-s/Bernard-a   5.00

LADY DEATH: CYBERNETIC DESECRATION
Coffin Comics: Nov, 2023 - No. 2, Jan, 2024 ($5.99, limited series)

1,2-Pulido & Maclean-s/Bernard-a; Cyber-Lady Death vs. Empress Death   6.00

LADY DEATH: DARK ALLIANCE
Chaos! Comics: July, 2002 - No. 5, ($2.99, limited series)

1-3-Reis-a/Ostrander-s   3.00

LADY DEATH: DARK MILLENNIUM
Chaos! Comics: Feb, 2000 - No. 3, Apr, 2000 ($2.95, limited series)

Preview (6/00, $5.00)   5.00
1-3-Ivan Reis-a   3.00

LADY DEATH: DIABOLICAL HARVEST
Coffin Comics: May, 2023 - No. 2, Mar, 2023 ($5.99, limited series)

1,2-Pulido & Maclean-s/Bernard-a   6.00

LADY DEATH: GODDESS RETURNS
Chaos! Comics: Jun, 2002 - No. 2, Aug, 2002 ($2.99, limited series)

1,2-Mota-a/Ostrander-s   3.00

LADY DEATH: HEARTBREAKER
Chaos! Comics: Mar, 2002 - No. 4, ($2.99, limited series)

1-Molenaar-a/Ostrander-s   3.00

LADY DEATH: JUDGEMENT WAR
Chaos! Comics: Nov, 1999 - No. 3, Jan, 2000 ($2.95, limited series)

Prelude (10/99) two covers   4.00
1-3-Ivan Reis-a   4.00

LADY DEATH: LAST RITES
Chaos! Comics: Oct, 2001 - No. 4, Feb, 2001 ($2.99, limited series)

1-4-Ivan Reis-a/Ostrander-s   3.00

LADY DEATH: MALEVOLENT DECIMATION
Coffin Comics: Apr, 2021 - No. 2, May, 2021 ($4.99, limited series)

1,2-Pulido & Maclean-s/Bernard-a   5.00

LADY DEATH: NECROTIC GENESIS
Coffin Comics: Jan, 2023 - No. 2, Mar, 2023 ($5.99, limited series)

1,2-Pulido & Maclean-s/Bernard-a   6.00

LADY DEATH: NIGHTMARE SYMPHONY
Coffin Comics: Nov, 2018 - No. 2, Dec, 2019 ($4.99, limited series)

1,2-Pulido & Maclean-s/Spay-a   5.00

LADY DEATH ORIGINS: CURSED
Boundless Comics: Mar, 2012 - No. 3, May, 2012 ($4.99/$3.99, limited series)

1-($4.99)-Pulido-s/Guzman; multiple covers   5.00
2,3-($3.99)   4.00

LADY DEATH: SACRIFICIAL ANNIHILATION
Coffin Comics: Jun, 2022 - No. 2, Aug, 2022 ($5.99, limited series)

1,2-Pulido & Maclean-s/Bernard-a   6.00

LADY DEATH: SCORCHED EARTH
Coffin Comics: Feb, 2020 - No. 2, Nov, 2020 ($4.99, limited series)

1,2-Pulido & Maclean-s/Bernard-a   5.00

LADY DEATH: THE CRUCIBLE
Chaos! Comics: Nov, 1996 - No. 6, Oct, 1997 ($3.50/$2.95, limited series)

1/2   4.00
1/2 Cloth Edition   8.00
1-Wraparound silver foil embossed-c   5.00
2-6-($2.95)   4.00

LADY DEATH: THE GAUNTLET
Chaos! Comics: Apr, 2002 - No. 2, May, 2002 ($2.99, limited series)

1,2: 1-J. Scott Campbell-c/redesign of Lady Death's outfit; Mota-a   4.00

LADY DEATH: THE ODYSSEY
Chaos! Comics: Apr, 1996 - No. 4, Aug, 1996 ($3.50/$2.95)

1-($1.50)-Sneak Peek Preview   4.00

1-($1.50)-Sneak Peek Preview Micro Premium Edition (2500 print run)		2	4	6	9	12	15
1-($3.50)-Embossed, wraparound goil foil-c							5.00
1-Black Onyx Edition (200 print run)		5	10	15	33	57	80
1-($19.95)-Premium Edition (10,000 print run)							20.00
2-4-($2.95)							3.00

LADY DEATH: THE RAPTURE
Chaos! Comics: Jun, 1999 - No. 4, Sept, 1999 ($2.95, limited series)

1-4-Ivan Reis-c/a; Pulido-s   4.00

LADY DEATH: THE WILD HUNT (Brian Pulido's...)
CG Entertainment: Apr, 2004 - No. 2, May, 2005 ($2.95)

1-2: 1-Brian Pulido-s/Jim Cheung-a   3.00

LADY DEATH: TREACHEROUS INFAMY
Coffin Comics: Jul, 2021 - No. 2, Sept, 2021 ($4.99, limited series)

1,2-Pulido & Maclean-s/Bernard-a   5.00

LADY DEATH: TRIBULATION
Chaos! Comics: Dec, 2000 - No. 4, Mar, 2001 ($2.95, limited series)

1-4-Ivan Reis-a; Kaminski-s   3.00

LADY DEATH II: BETWEEN HEAVEN & HELL
Chaos! Comics: Mar, 1995 - No. 4, July, 1995 ($3.50, limited series)

1-Chromium wraparound-c; Evil Ernie cameo	1	2	3	5	6	8
1-Commemorative (4,000), 1-Black Velvet-c	2	4	6	10	14	18
1-Gold	1	3	4	6	8	10
1-"Refractor" edition (5,000)	2	4	6	11	16	20
2-4						4.00
4-Lady Demon variant-c	1	2	3	5	7	9
Trade paperback-($12.95)-r/#1-4						13.00

LADY DEATH: UNHOLY RUIN
Coffin Comics: Apr, 2018 - No. 2, Jun, 2018 ($4.99, limited series)

1,2-Pulido & Maclean-s/Verma-a   5.00

LADY DEMON
Chaos! Comics: Mar, 2000 - No. 3, May, 2000 ($2.95, limited series)

1-3-Kaminski-s/Brewer-a   3.00

LADY DEMON
Dynamite Entertainment: 2014 - No. 4, 2015 ($3.99)

1-4: 1-3-Gillespie-s/Andolfo-a; multiple covers. 1-Origin retold. 4-Ramirez-a   4.00

LADY FOR A NIGHT (See Cinema Comics Herald)

LADY HEL
Dynamite Entertainment: 2022 - No. 4, 2022 ($3.99)

1-4-Burnham-s/Tasbolatov-a; multiple covers; Purgatori app.   4.00

LADY JUSTICE (See Neil Gaiman's...)

LADY KILLER
Dark Horse Comics: Jan, 2015 - No. 5, May, 2015 ($3.50)

1-5-Joëlle Jones-a/Jones and Jamie Rich-s   3.50

LADY KILLER 2
Dark Horse Comics: Aug, 2016 - No. 5, Sept, 2017 ($3.99)

1-5-Joëlle Jones-s/a   4.00

LADY LUCK (Formerly Smash #1-85) (Also see Spirit Sections #1)
Quality Comics Group: No. 86, Dec, 1949 - No. 90, Aug, 1950

86(#1)	161	322	483	1030	1765	2500
87-90	100	200	300	635	1093	1550

LADY MECHANIKA
Aspen MLT: No. 0, Oct, 2010 - No. 5, Mar, 2015 ($2.50/$2.99)

0-Joe Benitez-s/a; two covers; Benitez interview and sketch pages   3.00

	GD 2.0	VG 4.0	FN 6.0	VF 8.0	VF/NM 9.0	NM- 9.2

0-(Benitez Productions, 8/15, $1.00) — 3.00
1-(1/11, $2.99) Multiple covers — 10.00
2-5-Multiple covers on each. 5-($4.99) — 5.00
... FCBD Vol. 1 Issue 1 (5/16, giveaway) r/#0; excerpt from mini-series — 3.00
... FCBD 2019 Vol. 1 Issue 1 (5/19, giveaway) r/#0; excerpts from mini-series — 3.00

LADY MECHANIKA: LA BELLE DAME SANS MERCI
Benitez Productions: Jul, 2018 - No. 3, Oct, 2018 ($3.99, limited series)
1-3-Joe Benitez-a/s; M.M. Chen-s; multiple covers on each — 4.00

LADY MECHANIKA: LA DAMA DE LA MUERTE
Benitez Productions: Sept, 2016 - No. 3, Dec, 2016 ($3.99, limited series)
1-3-Joe Benitez-a/s; M.M. Chen-s; multiple covers on each — 4.00

LADY MECHANIKA: SANGRE
Benitez Productions: Jun, 2019 - No. 5, Jan, 2020 ($3.99, limited series)
1-5-Joe Benitez-a/s; M.M. Chen-s; Brian Ching-a; multiple covers on each — 4.00

LADY MECHANIKA: THE CLOCKWORK ASSASSIN
Benitez Productions: Jul, 2017 - No. 3, Oct, 2017 ($3.99, limited series)
1-3-Joe Benitez-a/M.M. Chen-s; multiple covers on each — 4.00

LADY MECHANIKA: THE LOST BOYS OF WEST ABBEY
Benitez Productions: May, 2016 - No. 2, Jun, 2016 ($3.99)
1,2-Joe Benitez-a/M.M. Chen-s; multiple covers on each — 4.00

LADY MECHANIKA: THE MONSTER OF THE MINISTRY OF HELL
Benitez Productions: Dec, 2021 - No. 4, May, 2022 ($3.99, limited series)
1-4-Joe Benitez-s/a; multiple covers on each — 4.00

LADY MECHANIKA: THE TABLET OF DESTINIES
Benitez Productions: Apr, 2015 - No. 6, Oct 2015 ($3.99, limited series)
1-6-Joe Benitez-s/a; multiple covers on each — 4.00

LADY PENDRAGON
Maximum Press: Mar, 1996 ($2.50)
1-Matt Hawkins script — 4.00

LADY PENDRAGON
Image Comics: Nov, 1998 - No. 3, Jan, 1999 ($2.50, mini-series)
Preview (6/98) Flip book w/ Deity preview — 4.00
1-3: 1-Matt Hawkins/Stinsman-a — 4.00
1-($6.95) DF Ed. with variant-c by Jusko — 7.00
2-($4.95) Variant edition — 5.00
0-(3/99) Origin; flip book — 4.00

LADY PENDRAGON (Volume 3)
Image Comics: Apr, 1999 - No. 9, Mar, 2000 ($2.50, mini-series)
1,2,4-6,8-10: 1-Matt Hawkins-s/Stinsman-a. 2-Peterson-c — 4.00
3-Flip book w/Alley Cat preview (1st app.) — 5.00
7-($3.95) Flip book; Stinsman-a/Cleavenger painted-a — 5.00
Gallery Edition (10/99, $2.95) pin-ups — 4.00
...Merlin (1/00, $2.95) Stinsman-a — 3.00
.../ More Than Mortal (5/99, $2.50) Scott-s/Norton-a; 2 covers by Norton & Finch — 4.00
.../ More Than Mortal Preview (5/99) Diamond Dateline supplement — 4.00
Pilot Season: Lady Pendragon (5/08, $3.99) Hawkins-s/Eru-a; wraparound-c by Struzan — 4.00

LADY RAWHIDE
Topps Comics: July, 1995 - No. 5, Mar, 1996 ($2.95, bi-monthly, limited series)
1-5: Don McGregor scripts & Mayhew-a. in all. 2-Stelfreeze-c. 3-Hughes-c. 4-Golden-c. 5-Julie Bell-c. — 4.00
It Can't Happen Here TPB (8/99, $16.95) r/#1-5 — 17.00
Mini Comic 1 (7/95) Maroto-a; Zorro app. — 4.00
Special Edition 1 (6/95, $3.95)-Reprints — 4.00

LADY RAWHIDE (Volume 2)
Topps Comics: Oct, 1996 - No. 5, June, 1997 ($2.95, limited series)
1-5: 1-Julie Bell-c. — 4.00

LADY RAWHIDE (Volume 1)
Dynamite Entertainment: 2013 - No. 5, 2014 ($3.99)
1-5-Trautmann-s/Estevam-a/Linsner-c — 4.00

LADY RAWHIDE / LADY ZORRO
Dynamite Entertainment: 2015 - No. 4, 2015 ($3.99, limited series)
1-4-Denton-s/Villegas-a. 1-Mayhew-c. 2-4-Chin-c — 4.00

LADY RAWHIDE OTHER PEOPLE'S BLOOD (ZORRO'S ...)
Image Comics: Mar, 1999 - No. 5, July, 1999 ($2.95, B&W)
1-5-Reprints Lady Rawhide series in B&W — 4.00

LADY SUPREME (See Asylum)(Also see Supreme & Kid Supreme)
Image Comics (Extreme): May, 1996 - No. 2, June, 1996 ($2.50, limited series)
1,2-Terry Moore -s; 1-Terry Moore-c. 2-Flip book w/Newmen preview — 4.00

LADY ZORRO
Dynamite Entertainment: 2014 - No. 4, 2014 ($3.99, limited series)
1-4-de Campi-s/Villegas-a/Linsner-c — 4.00

LADY ZORRO (Also see Zorro: Galleon of the Dead)
American Mythology Prods.: 2020 ($3.99, one-shot)
1-Pat Shand-s/Vincenzo Carratu-a; origin of Muat — 4.00
... Final Fight 1 (2023, $3.99) Shand-s/Gambone-a — 4.00

LAFF-A-LYMPICS (TV)(See The Funtastic World of Hanna-Barbera)
Marvel Comics: Mar, 1978 - No. 13, Mar, 1979 (Newsstand sales only)

	GD 2.0	VG 4.0	FN 6.0	VF 8.0	VF/NM 9.0	NM- 9.2
1-Yogi Bear, Scooby Doo, Pixie & Dixie, etc.	4	8	12	23	37	50
2-8	3	6	9	14	19	24
9-13: 11-Jetsons x-over; 1 pg. illustrated bio of Mighty Mightor, Herculoids, Shazzan, Galaxy Trio & Space Ghost	3	6	9	16	23	30

LAFFY-DAFFY COMICS
Rural Home Publ. Co.: Feb, 1945 - No. 2, Mar, 1945

	GD 2.0	VG 4.0	FN 6.0	VF 8.0	VF/NM 9.0	NM- 9.2
1-Funny animal	15	30	45	86	133	180

	GD 2.0	VG 4.0	FN 6.0	VF 8.0	VF/NM 9.0	NM- 9.2
2-Funny animal	13	26	39	74	105	135

LAGUARDIA
Dark Horse Comics (Berger Books): Dec, 2018 - No. 4, Mar, 2019 ($4.99, limited series)
1-4-Nnedi Okorafor-s/Tana Ford-a — 5.00

LAKE OF FIRE
Image Comics: Aug, 2016 - No. 5, Dec, 2016 ($3.99)
1-5-Nathan Fairbairn-s/Matt Smith-a — 4.00

LAMENTATION
Oni Press: May, 2023 - Present ($6.99)
1,2-Cullen Bunn-s/Arjuna Susini-a — 7.00

LA MUERTA...
Coffin Comics (One-shots)
...: Ascension 1 (1019 $7.99) Maclean-s/Gomez-a — 8.00
...: Descent 1 (7/16, $7.99) Maclean-s/Gomez-a; origin — 8.00
...: Last Rites 1 (9/16, $7.99) Maclean-s/Gomez-a — 8.00
...: Onslaught 1 (5/22, $7.99) Maclean-s/Gomez-a — 8.00
...: Vengeance 1 (9/17, $7.99) Maclean-s/Gomez-a — 8.00

LA MUERTA: RETRIBUTION
Coffin Comics: Sept, 2018 - No. 2, Sept, 2018 ($4.99, limited series)
1,2-Mike Maclean-s/Joel Gomez-a — 5.00

LANA (Little Lana No. 8 on)
Marvel Comics (MjMC): Aug, 1948 - No. 7, Aug, 1949 (Also see Annie Oakley)

	GD 2.0	VG 4.0	FN 6.0	VF 8.0	VF/NM 9.0	NM- 9.2
1-Rusty, Millie begin	74	148	222	470	810	1150
2-Kurtzman's "Hey Look" (1); last Rusty	36	72	108	214	347	480
3-7: 3-Nellie begins	27	54	81	158	259	360

LANCELOT & GUINEVERE (See Movie Classics)

LANCELOT LINK, SECRET CHIMP (TV)
Gold Key: Apr, 1971 - No. 8, Feb, 1973 (All photo-c)

	GD 2.0	VG 4.0	FN 6.0	VF 8.0	VF/NM 9.0	NM- 9.2
1	5	10	15	35	63	90
2-8	4	8	12	23	37	50

LANCELOT STRONG (See The Shield)

LANCE O'CASEY (See Mighty Midget & Whiz Comics)
Fawcett Publications: Spring, 1946 - No. 3, Fall, 1946; No. 4, Summer, 1948

	GD 2.0	VG 4.0	FN 6.0	VF 8.0	VF/NM 9.0	NM- 9.2
1-Captain Marvel app. on-c	36	72	108	211	343	475
2	20	40	60	117	189	260
3,4	15	30	45	88	137	185

NOTE: The cover for the 1st issue was done in 1942 but was not published until 1946. The cover shows 68 pages but actually has only 36 pages.

LANCER (TV)(Western)
Gold Key: Feb, 1969 - No. 3, Sept, 1969 (All photo-c)

	GD 2.0	VG 4.0	FN 6.0	VF 8.0	VF/NM 9.0	NM- 9.2
1	4	8	12	25	40	55
2,3	3	6	9	17	26	35

LANDO (Star Wars)
Marvel Comics: Sept, 2015 - No. 5, Dec, 2015 ($3.99, limited series)
1-5-Soule-s/Maleev-a; Lobot & Emperor Palpatine app. — 4.00

LAND OF NOD, THE
Dark Horse Comics: July, 1997 - No. 3, Feb, 1998 ($2.95, B&W)
1-3-Jetcat; Jay Stephens-s/a — 4.00

LAND OF OZ
Arrow Comics: 1998 - No. 9 ($2.95, B&W)
1-9-Bishop-s/Bryan-s/a — 4.00

LAND OF THE DEAD (George A. Romaro's...)
IDW Publishing: Aug, 2005 - No. 5 ($3.99, limited series)
1-4-Adaptation of 2005 movie; Ryall-s/Rodriguez-a — 4.00
TPB (3/06, $19.99) r/#1-5; cover gallery — 20.00

LAND OF THE GIANTS (TV)
Gold Key: Nov, 1968 - No. 5, Sept, 1969 (All have photo-c)

	GD 2.0	VG 4.0	FN 6.0	VF 8.0	VF/NM 9.0	NM- 9.2
1	6	12	18	42	79	115
2-5	4	8	12	28	47	65

LAND OF THE LOST COMICS (Radio)
E. C. Comics: July-Aug, 1946 - No. 9, Spring, 1948

	GD 2.0	VG 4.0	FN 6.0	VF 8.0	VF/NM 9.0	NM- 9.2
1	50	100	150	315	533	750
2	32	64	96	190	310	430
3-9	26	52	78	154	252	350

LAND THAT TIME FORGOT, THE (Movie)
Amercan Mythology Productions: 2019 - No. 2, 2019 ($3.99, B&W)
1,2-Reprints movie adaptation from Marvel Movie Premiere #1; Wolfman-s/Cardy-c —

LAND THAT TIME FORGOT, THE : FEARLESS
Amercan Mythology Productions: 2020 - No. 3, 2021 ($3.99)
1-3-Wolfer-s/Casas-a — 4.00

LAND UNKNOWN, THE (Movie)
Dell Publishing Co.: No. 845, Sept, 1957

	GD 2.0	VG 4.0	FN 6.0	VF 8.0	VF/NM 9.0	NM- 9.2
Four Color 845-Alex Toth-a	11	22	33	76	163	250

LANTERN CITY (TV)
BOOM! Studios (Archaia): May, 2015 - No. 12, Apr, 2016 ($3.99)
1-12: 1-Jenkins & Daley-s/Magno-a. 3-Daley & Scott-s — 4.00

LA PACIFICA
DC Comics (Paradox Press): 1994/1995 ($4.95, B&W, limited series, digest size, mature)
1-3 — 5.00

LARA CROFT AND THE FROZEN OMEN (Also see Tomb Raider titles)
Dark Horse Comics: Oct, 2015 - No. 5, Feb, 2016 ($3.99)
1-5: 1-Corinna Bechko-s/Randy Green-a — 4.00

Lady Mechanika #5 © Joe Benitez

Lance O'Casey #1 © FAW

Larfleeze #1 © DC

	GD	VG	FN	VF	VF/NM	NM-		GD	VG	FN	VF	VF/NM	NM-
	2.0	4.0	6.0	8.0	9.0	9.2		2.0	4.0	6.0	8.0	9.0	9.2

LARAMIE (TV)
Dell Publishing Co.: Aug, 1960 - July, 1962 (All photo-c)

Four Color 1125-Gil Kane/Heath-a	9	18	27	59	117	175
Four Color 1223,1284, 01-418-207 (7/62)	6	12	18	37	66	95

LAREDO (TV)
Gold Key: June, 1966

1 (10179-606)-Photo-c	3	6	9	21	33	45

LARFLEEZE (Orange Lantern) (Story continued from back-ups in Threshold #1-5)
DC Comics: Aug, 2013 - No. 12, Aug, 2014 ($2.99)

1-12: 1-Giffen & DeMatteis-s/Kolins-a/Porter-c; origin told	3.00

LARGE FEATURE COMIC (Formerly called Black & White in previous guides)
Dell Publishing Co.: 1939 - No. 13, 1943

Note: See individual alphabetical listings for prices

1 (Series I)-Dick Tracy Meets the Blank
3-Heigh-Yo Silver! The Lone Ranger (text & ill.)(76 pgs.); also exists as a Whitman #710; based on radio
6-Terry & the Pirates & The Dragon Lady; reprints dailies from 1936
8-Dick Tracy the Racket Buster
9-King of the Royal Mounted (Zane Grey's...)
10-(Scarce) Gang Busters (No. appears on inside front cover); first slick cover (based on radio program)
13-Dick Tracy and Scottie of Scotland Yard
15-Dick Tracy and the Kidnapped Princes
17-Gang Busters (1941)
18-Phantasmo (see The Funnies #45)
20-Donald Duck Comic Paint Book (rarer than #16) (Disney)
21,22: 21-Private Buck. 22-Nuts & Jolts
24-Popeye in "Thimble Theatre" by Segar
26-Smitty
28-Grin and Bear It
30-Tillie the Toiler
2-Winnie Winkle (#1)
3-Dick Tracy
4-Tiny Tim (#1)
6-Terry and the Pirates; Caniff-a
8-Bugs Bunny (#1)('42)
9-Bringing Up Father
10-Popeye (Thimble Theatre)
11-Barney Google and Snuffy Smith
13-(nn)-1001 Hours Of Fun; puzzles & games; by A. W. Nugent. This book was bound as #13 with Large Feature Comic in publisher's files

2-Terry and the Pirates (#1)
4-Dick Tracy Gets His Man
5-Tarzan of the Apes (#1) by Harold Foster (origin); reprints 1st Tarzan dailies from 1929
7-(Scarce, 52 pgs.)-Hi-Yo Silver the Lone Ranger to the Rescue; also exists as a Whitman #715; based on radio program
11-Dick Tracy Foils the Mad Doc Hump
12-Smilin' Jack; no number on-c
14-Smilin' Jack Helps G-Men Solve a Case!
16-Donald Duck; 1st app. Daisy Duck on back cover (6/41-Disney)
19-Dumbo Comic Paint Book (Disney); partial-r from 4-Color #17
23-The Nebbs
25-Smilin' Jack-1st issue to show title on-c
27-Terry and the Pirates; Caniff-c/a
29-Moon Mullins
1 (Series II)-Peter Rabbit by Harrison Cady; arrival date-3/27/42
5-Toots and Casper
7-Pluto Saves the Ship (#1) (Disney)-Written by Carl Barks, Jack Hannah, & Nick George (Barks' 1st comic book work)
12-Private Buck

NOTE: The Black & White Feature Books are oversized 8-1/2x11-3/8" comics with color covers and black and white interiors. The first nine issues all have rough, heavy stock covers, and, except for #7, all have 76 pages, including covers. #7 and #10-on all have 52 pages. Beginning with #10 the covers are slick and thin and, because of their size, are difficult to handle without damaging. For this reason, they are seldom found in fine to mint condition. The paper stock, unlike Wow #1 and Capt. Marvel #1, is itself not unstable ...just thin. Many issues were reprinted in the early 1980s, identical except for the copyright notice on the first page.

LARRY DOBY, BASEBALL HERO
Fawcett Publications: 1950 (Cleveland Indians)

nn-Bill Ward-a; photo-c	90	180	270	576	988	1400

LARRY HARMON'S LAUREL AND HARDY (...Comics)
National Periodical Publ.: July-Aug, 1972 (Digest advertised, not published)

1-Low print run	9	18	27	59	117	175

LARS OF MARS
Ziff-Davis Publishing Co.: No. 10, Apr-May, 1951 - No. 11, July-Aug, 1951 (Painted-c) (Created by Jerry Siegel, editor)

10-Origin; Anderson-a(3) in each; classic robot-c	129	258	387	826	1413	2000
11-Gene Colan-a; classic-c	97	194	291	621	1061	1500

LARS OF MARS 3-D
Eclipse Comics: Apr, 1987 ($2.50)

1-r/Lars of Mars #10,11 in 3-D plus new story	5.00
2-D limited edition (B&W, 100 copies)	20.00

LASER ERASER & PRESSBUTTON (See Axel Pressbutton & Miracle Man 9)
Eclipse Comics: Nov, 1985 - No. 6, 1987 (95¢/$2.50, limited series)

1-6: 5,6-(95¢)	4.00
...In 3-D 1 (8/86, $2.50)	5.00
2-D 1 (B&W, limited to 100 copies signed & numbered)	20.00

LASH LARUE WESTERN (Movie star; King of the bullwhip)(See Fawcett Movie Comic, Motion Picture Comics & Six-Gun Heroes)
Fawcett Publications: Sum, 1949 - No. 46, Jan, 1954 (36 pgs., 1-6,9,13,16-on)

1-Lash & his horse Black Diamond begin; photo front/back-c begin	58	116	174	371	636	900
2(11/49)	29	58	87	172	281	390
3-5	22	44	66	130	213	295
6,9: 6-Last photo back-c; intro. Frontier Phantom (Lash's twin brother)	19	38	57	109	172	235
7,8,10 (52pgs.)	20	40	60	114	182	250
11,12,14,15 (52pgs.)	15	30	45	84	127	170
13,16-20 (36pgs.)	14	28	42	80	115	150
21-30: 21-The Frontier Phantom app.	12	24	36	69	97	125
31-45	11	22	33	60	83	105
46-Last Fawcett issue & photo-c	11	22	33	64	90	115

LASH LARUE WESTERN (Continues from Fawcett series)
Charlton Comics: No. 47, Mar-Apr, 1954 - No. 84, June, 1961

47-Photo-c	14	28	42	80	115	150
48	11	22	33	60	83	105
49-60, 67,68-(68 pgs.). 68-Check-a	9	18	27	52	69	85
61-66,69,70: 52-r/#8; 53-r/#22	9	18	27	47	61	75
71-83	8	16	24	40	50	60
84-Last issue	9	18	27	47	61	75

LASH LARUE WESTERN
AC Comics: 1990 ($3.50, 44 pgs) (24 pgs. of color, 16 pgs. of B&W)

1-Photo covers; r/Lash #6; r/old movie posters	4.00
Annual 1 (1990, $2.95, B&W, 44 pgs.)-Photo covers	4.00

LASSIE (TV)(M-G-M's... #1-36; see Kite Fun Book)
Dell Publ. Co./Gold Key No. 59 (10/62) on: June, 1950 - No. 70, July, 1969

1 (52 pgs.)-Photo-c; inside lists One Shot #282 in error	27	54	81	189	420	650
2-Painted-c begin	8	16	24	56	108	160
3-10	6	12	18	37	66	95
11-19: 12-Rocky Langford (Lassie's master) marries Gerry Lawrence. 15-1st app. Timbu	5	10	15	30	50	70
20-22-Matt Baker-a	5	10	15	33	57	80
23-38: 33-Robinson-a.	4	8	12	28	47	65
39-1st app. Timmy as Lassie picks up her TV family; photo-c	5	10	15	35	63	90
40-50-Photo-c on all	4	8	12	28	47	65
51-58-Photo-c on all	4	8	12	27	44	60
59 (10/62)-1st Gold Key	4	8	12	28	47	65
60-70: 63-Last (10/63). 64-r/#19. 65-Forest Ranger Corey Stuart begins, ends #69. 70-Forest Rangers Bob Ericson & Scott Turner app. (Lassie's new masters)	4	8	12	25	40	55
11193(1978, $1.95, 224 pgs., Golden Press)-Baker-r (92 pgs.)	4	8	12	25	40	55

NOTE: Also see March of Comics #210, 217, 230, 254, 266, 278, 296, 308, 324,334, 346, 358, 370, 381, 394, 411, 432.

LAST AMERICAN, THE
Marvel Comics (Epic): Dec, 1990 - No. 4, March, 1991 ($2.25, mini-series)

1-4: Alan Grant scripts	4.00

LAST ANNIHILATION, THE
Marvel Comics: Nov, 2021 ($4.99, series of one-shots)

...: Wakanda & Vibranium & Vibraxas app.	5.00
...: Wiccan & Hulkling 1 (11/21) Bazaldua-a; Dormammu app.	5.00

LAST AVENGERS STORY, THE (Last Avengers #1)
Marvel Comics: Nov, 1995 - No. 2, Dec, 1995 ($5.95, painted, limited series) (Alterniverse)

1,2: Peter David story; acetate-c in all. 1-New team (Hank Pym, Human Torch, Cannonball, She-Hulk, Hotshot, Bombshell, Tommy Maximoff, Hawkeye & Mockingbird) forms to battle Ultron 59, Kang the Conqueror, The Grim Reaper & Oddball	6.00
...: Marvel Tales 1 (2/22, $7.99) Reprints 1,2; intro. by Ralph Macchio	8.00

LAST BARBARIANS, THE
Image Comics: Feb, 2023 - No. 5, Jun, 2023 ($3.99)

1-5-Brian Haberlin-s/a	4.00

	GD 2.0	VG 4.0	FN 6.0	VF 8.0	VF/NM 9.0	NM- 9.2

LAST BATTLE, THE
Image Comics: Dec, 2011 ($7.99, square-bound, one-shot)
1-Facari-s/Brereton-painted art/c; Roman gladiator story; bonus Brereton sketch pages — 8.00

LAST CHRISTMAS, THE
Image Comics: May, 2006 - No. 5, Oct, 2006 ($2.99, limited series)
1-5-Gerry Duggan & Brian Posehn-s/Rick Remender & Hilary Barta-a — 3.00
TPB (2006, $14.99) r/#1-5; Patton Oswalt intro.; sketch pages and art — 15.00

LAST CONTRACT, THE
BOOM! Studios: Jan, 2016 - No. 4, Apr, 2016 ($3.99, limited series)
1-4-Brisson-s/Estherren-a/c — 4.00

LAST DAY IN VIETNAM
Dark Horse Books: July, 2000 ($10.95, graphic novel)
nn-Will Eisner-s/a/c — 11.00

LAST DAYS OF ANIMAL MAN, THE
DC Comics: July, 2009 - No. 6, Dec, 2009 ($2.99, limited series)
1-6: 1-Conway-s/Batista-a/Bolland-c. 3,4-Starfire app. 5,6-Future Justice League app. — 3.00
TPB (2010, $17.99) r/#1-6 — 18.00

LAST DAYS OF THE JUSTICE SOCIETY SPECIAL
DC Comics: 1986 ($2.50, one-shot, 68 pgs.)
1-62 pg. JSA story plus unpubbed G.A. pg. — 2 — 4 — 6 — 8 — 10 — 12

LAST DEFENDERS, THE
Marvel Comics: May, 2008 - No. 6, Oct, 2008 ($2.99, limited series)
1-6-Nighthawk, She-Hulk, Colossus, and Blazing Skull; Muniz-a. 2-Deodato-c — 3.00

LAST FANTASTIC FOUR STORY, THE
Marvel Comics: Oct, 2007 ($4.99, one-shot)
1-Stan Lee-s/John Romita, Jr.-a/c; Galactus app. — 5.00

LAST GANG IN TOWN
DC Comics (Vertigo): Feb, 2016 - No. 6, Aug, 2016 ($3.99, limited series)
1-6: 1-Simon Oliver-s/Rufus Dayglo-a/Rob Davis-c — 4.00

LAST GENERATION, THE
Black Tie Studios: 1986 - No. 5, 1989 ($1.95, B&W, high quality paper)
1-5 — 4.00
Book 1 (1989, $6.95)-By Caliber Press — 7.00

LAST GOD, THE
DC Comics (Black Label): Dec, 2019 - No. 12, Mar, 2021 ($4.99)
1-12-Phillip Kennedy Johnson-s/Riccardo Federici-a — 5.00
...: Songs of Lost Children 1 (12/20, $4.99) Dan Watters-s/Steve Beach-a — 5.00
...: Tales From the Book of Ages 1 (8/20, $4.99) Roleplaying sourcebook — 5.00

LAST HERO STANDING (Characters from Spider-Girl's M2 universe)
Marvel Comics: Aug, 2005 - No. 5, Aug, 2005 ($2.99, weekly limited series)
1-5: 1-DeFalco-s/Olliffe-a. 4-Thor app. 5-Capt. America dies — 3.00
TPB (2005, $13.99) r/#1-5 — 14.00

LAST HUNT, THE
Dell Publishing Co.: No. 678, Feb, 1956
Four Color 678-Movie, photo-c — 6 — 12 — 18 — 42 — 79 — 115

LAST KISS
ACME Press (Eclipse): 1988 ($3.95, B&W, squarebound, 52 pgs.)
1-One story adapts E.A. Poe's The Black Cat — 5.00

LAST OF THE COMANCHES (Movie) (See Wild Bill Hickok #28)
Avon Periodicals: 1953
nn-Kinstler-c/a, 21pgs.; Ravielli-a — 22 — 44 — 66 — 132 — 216 — 300

LAST OF THE ERIES, THE (See American Graphics)

LAST OF THE FAST GUNS, THE
Dell Publishing Co.: No. 925, Aug, 1958
Four Color 925-Movie, photo-c — 6 — 12 — 18 — 41 — 76 — 110

LAST OF THE MOHICANS (See King Classics & White Rider and...)

LAST OF THE VIKING HEROES, THE (Also see Silver Star #1)
Genesis West Comics: Mar, 1987 - No. 12 ($1.50/$1.95)
1-4,5A,5B,6-12: 4-Intro The Phantom Force, 1-Signed edition ($1.50) 5A-Kirby/Stevens-c.
   5B,6 ($1.95). 7-Art Adams-c. 8-Kirby back-c. — 4.00
Summer Special 1-3: 1-(1988)-Frazetta-c & illos. 2 (1990, $2.50)-A TMNT app.
   3 (1991, $2.50)-Teenage Mutant Ninja Turtles — 4.00
Summer Special 1-Signed edition (sold for $1.95) — 4.00
NOTE: Art Adams c-7. Byrne c-3. Kirby c-1p, 5p. Perez c-2i. Stevens c-5Ai.

LAST ONE, THE
DC Comics (Vertigo): July, 1993 - No. 6, Dec, 1993 ($2.50, lim. series, mature)
1-6 — 4.00

LAST PHANTOM, THE (Lee Falk's Phantom)
Dynamite Entertainment: 2010 - No. 12, 2012 ($3.99)
1-12-Beatty-s/Ferigato-a; 1-Two covers by Alex Ross; Neves & Prado var. covers — 4.00
Annual 1 (2011, $4.99) Beatty-s/Desjardins-a; two covers by Desjardins & Ross — 5.00

LAST PLANET STANDING
Marvel Comics: July, 2006 - No. 5, Sept, 2006 ($2.99, limited series)
1-5-Galactus threatens Spider-Girl & Fantastic Five's M2 Earth; Avengers app.; Olliffe-a — 3.00
TPB (2006, $13.99) r/series — 14.00

LAST RONIN, THE (See TMNT: The Last Ronin)

LAST SHADOWHAWK, THE
Image Comics: Aug, 2022 ($3.99)
1-Philip Tan-s/a — 4.00
... 3D #1 (9/22, $7.99)-Printed with 3D effects; bagged with 3D glasses — 8.00

LAST SHOT
Image Comics: Aug, 2001 - No. 4, Mar, 2002 ($2.95, limited series)

1-4: 1-Wraparound-c; by Studio XD — 3.00
...: First Draw (5/01, $2.95) Introductory one-shot — 3.00

LAST SIEGE, THE
Image Comics: May, 2018 - No. 8, Jan, 2019 ($3.99)
1-8-Landry Q. Walker-s/Justin Greenwood-a — 4.00

LAST SONS OF AMERICA
BOOM! Studios: Nov, 2015 - No. 4, Apr, 2016 ($3.99, limited series)
1-4-Phillip Johnson-s/Matthew Dow Smith-a — 4.00

LAST SPACE RACE, THE
AfterShock Comics: Oct, 2018 - No. 5, Jul, 2019 ($3.99, limited series)
1-5-Peter Calloway-s/Alex Shibao-a — 4.00

LAST STARFIGHTER, THE
Marvel Comics Group: Oct, 1984 - No. 3, Dec, 1984 (75¢, movie adaptation)
1-3: r/Marvel Super Special; Guice-c — 4.00

LAST STOP ON THE RED LINE
Dark Horse Comics: May, 2019 - No. 4, Oct, 2019 ($3.99, limited series)
1-4-Paul Maybury-s/Sam Lotfi-a — 4.00

LAST TEMPTATION, THE
Marvel Comics: 1994 - No. 3, 1994 ($4.95, limited series)
1-3-Alice Cooper story; Neil Gaiman scripts; McKean-c; Zulli-a: 1-Two covers — 5.00
HC (Dark Horse Comics, 2005, $14.95) r/#1-3; Gaiman intro. — 15.00

LAST TRAIN FROM GUN HILL
Dell Publishing Co.: No. 1012, July, 1959
Four Color 1012-Movie, photo-c — 8 — 16 — 24 — 56 — 108 — 160

LAST TRAIN TO DEADSVILLE: A CAL McDONALD MYSTERY (See Criminal Macabre)
Dark Horse Comics: May, 2004 - No. 4, Sept, 2004 ($2.99, limited series)
1-4-Steve Niles-s/Kelley Jones-a/c — 3.00
TPB (2005, $14.95) r/series — 15.00

LATEST ADVENTURES OF FOXY GRANDPA (See Foxy Grandpa)

LATEST COMICS (Super Duper No. 3?)
Spotlight Publ./Palace Promotions (Jubilee): Mar, 1945 - No. 2, 1945?
1-Super Duper — 24 — 48 — 72 — 142 — 234 — 325
2-Bee-29 (nd); Jubilee in indicia blacked out — 16 — 32 — 48 — 94 — 147 — 200

LAUGH
Archie Enterprises: June, 1987 - No. 29, Aug, 1991 (75¢/$1.00)
V2#1 — 5.00
2-10,14,24: 5-X-Mas issue. 14-1st app. Hot Dog. 24-Re-intro Super Duck — 4.00
11-13,15-23,25-29: 19-X-Mas issue — 4.00

LAUGH COMICS (Teenage) (Formerly Black Hood #9-19) (Laugh #226 on)
Archie Publications (Close-Up): No. 20, Fall, 1946 - No. 400, Apr, 2005
20-Archie begins; Katy Keene & Taffy begin by Woggon; Suzie & Wilbur also begin;
   Archie covers begin — 187 — 374 — 561 — 1197 — 2049 — 2900
21-23,25 — 74 — 148 — 222 — 470 — 810 — 1150
24- "Pipsy" by Kirby (6 pgs.) — 84 — 168 — 252 — 538 — 919 — 1300
26-30 — 48 — 96 — 144 — 302 — 514 — 725
31-40 — 39 — 78 — 117 — 240 — 395 — 550
41-60: 41,54-Debbi by Woggon — 28 — 56 — 84 — 168 — 274 — 385
61-80: 67-Debbi by Woggon — 20 — 40 — 60 — 114 — 182 — 250
81-99 — 10 — 20 — 30 — 64 — 132 — 200
100 — 10 — 20 — 30 — 69 — 147 — 225
101-105,110,112,114-126: 125-Debbi app. — 8 — 16 — 24 — 52 — 99 — 145
106-109,111,113-Neal Adams-a (1 pg.) in each — 8 — 16 — 24 — 54 — 102 — 150
127-144: Super-hero app. in all (see note) — 9 — 18 — 27 — 58 — 114 — 170
145-(4/63) Josie by DeCarlo begins — 9 — 18 — 27 — 61 — 123 — 185
146-149-early Josie app. by DeCarlo — 6 — 12 — 18 — 41 — 76 — 110
150,162,163,165,167,169,170-No Josie — 5 — 10 — 15 — 30 — 50 — 70
151-161,164,168-Josie app. by DeCarlo — 5 — 10 — 15 — 34 — 60 — 85
166-Beatles-c (1/65) — 10 — 20 — 30 — 64 — 132 — 200
171-180, 200 (11/67) — 4 — 8 — 12 — 25 — 40 — 55
181-199 — 3 — 6 — 9 — 16 — 24 — 32
201-240(3/74) — 3 — 6 — 9 — 14 — 19 — 24
241-280(7/74) — 2 — 4 — 6 — 8 — 10 — 12
281-299 — 2 — 4 — 6 — 8 — 11 — 14
300(3/76) — 2 — 4 — 6 — 8 — 11 — 14
301-340 (7/79) — 1 — 2 — 3 — 5 — 7 — 9
341-370 (1/82) — 1 — 2 — 3 — 4 — 5 — 7
371-379,385-399 — — — — — — 5.00
380-Cheryl Blossom app. — 2 — 4 — 6 — 11 — 16 — 20
381-384,400: 381-384-Katy Keene app.; by Woggon-381,382 — — — — — — 6.00
NOTE: The Fly app. in 128, 129, 132, 134, 138, 139. Flygirl app. in 136, 137, 143. Flyman app. in 137. The Jaguar app. in 127, 130, 131, 133, 135, 140-142, 144. Josie app. in 145-149, 151-161, 164, 168. Katy Keene app. in 20-125, 129, 130, 133. Horror/Sci-Fi covers on 128-135, 137, 139. Many issues contain paper dolls. Al Fagaly c-20-29. Montana c-33, 36, 37, 42. Bill Vigoda c-30, 50.

LAUGH COMICS DIGEST (...Magazine #23-89; Laugh Digest Mag. #90 on)
Archie Publ. (Close-Up No. 1, 3 on): 8/74; No. 2, 9/75; No. 3, 3/76 - No. 200, Apr, 2005
(Digest-size) (Josie and Sabrina app. in most issues)
1-Neal Adams-a — 5 — 10 — 15 — 31 — 53 — 75
2,7,8,19-Neal Adams-a — 3 — 6 — 9 — 19 — 30 — 40
3-6,9,10 — 3 — 6 — 9 — 15 — 22 — 28
11-18,20 — 2 — 4 — 6 — 11 — 16 — 20
21-40 — 1 — 3 — 4 — 6 — 9 — 13
41-60 — 1 — 3 — 4 — 6 — 8 — 10
61-80 — 1 — 2 — 3 — 5 — 6 — 8
81-99 — — — — — — 5.00
100 — — — — — — 6.00
101-138 — — — — — — 4.00
139-200: 139-Begin $1.95-c. 148-Begin $1.99-c. 156-Begin $2.19-c. 180-Begin $2.39-c. — — — — — — 3.00
NOTE: Katy Keene in 23, 25, 27, 32-38, 40, 45-48, 50. The Fly-r in 19, 20. The Jaguar-r 25, 27. Mr. Justice-r in 21. The Web-r in 23.

Last Defenders #3 © MAR

Lawbreakers #8 © CC

Lazarus Planet: Omega #1 © DC

	GD	VG	FN	VF	VF/NM	NM-		GD	VG	FN	VF	VF/NM	NM-
	2.0	4.0	6.0	8.0	9.0	9.2		2.0	4.0	6.0	8.0	9.0	9.2

LAUGH COMIX (Laugh Comics inside)(Formerly Top Notch Laugh; Suzie Comics No. 49 on)

							161	322	483	1030	1765	2500

MLJ Magazines: No. 46, Summer, 1944 - No. 48, Winter, 1944-45

46-Wilbur & Suzie in all; Harry Sahle-c	43	86	129	271	461	650
47,48: 47-Sahle-c. 48-Bill Vigoda-c	31	62	93	182	296	410

LAUGH-IN MAGAZINE (TV)(Magazine)
Laufer Publ. Co.: Oct, 1968 - No. 12, Oct, 1969 (50¢) (Satire)

V1#1	5	10	15	30	50	70
2-12	3	6	9	21	33	45

LAUREL & HARDY (See Larry Harmon's... & March of Comics No. 302, 314)

LAUREL AND HARDY (...Comics)
St. John Publ. Co.: 3/49 - No. 3, 9/49; No. 26, 11/55 - No. 28, 3/56 (No #4-25)

1	116	232	346	742	1271	1800
2	48	96	144	302	514	725
3	40	80	120	246	411	575
26-28 (Reprints)	20	40	60	117	189	260

LAUREL AND HARDY (TV)
Dell Publishing Co.: Oct, 1962 - No. 4, Sept-Nov, 1963

12-423-210 (8-10/62)	6	12	18	42	79	115
2-4 (Dell)	4	8	12	28	47	65

LAUREL AND HARDY (Larry Harmon's...)
Gold Key: Jan, 1967 - No. 2, Oct, 1967

1-Photo back-c	5	10	15	30	50	70
2	4	8	12	21	33	45

LAUREL AND HARDY
American Mythology Productions: 2019 - No. 2, 2019 ($3.99)

1,2-New stories and reprints						4.00
... Christmas Follies 1 (2020, $3.99) New stories; Check-s/Tapié-a; Pacheco-s/a						4.00
... Gold Key Edition #1 (2019, $3.99) Reprints #1 from Jan, 1967						4.00
.../ The Three Stooges 1 (2020, $3.99) New story; Check & Kuhoric-s/Tapié-a						4.00

L.A.W., THE (LIVING ASSAULT WEAPONS)
DC Comics: Sept, 1999 - No. 6, Feb, 2000 ($2.50, limited series)

1-6-Blue Beetle, Question, Judomaster, Capt. Atom app.; Giordano-a. 5-JLA app.						4.00

LAW AGAINST CRIME (Law-Crime on cover)
Essenkay Publishing Co.: April, 1948 - No. 3, Aug, 1948 (Real Stories from Police Files)

1-(#1-3 are half funny animal, half crime stories)-L. B. Cole-c/a in all; electrocution-c						
	314	628	942	2198	3849	5500
2-L. B. Cole-c/a	142	284	426	909	1555	2200
3-Used in **SOTI**, pg. 180,181 & illo "The wish to hurt or kill couples in lovers' lanes"; reprinted in All-Famous Crime #9	181	362	543	1158	1979	2800

LAW AND ORDER
Maximum Press: Sept, 1995 - No. 2, 1995 ($2.50, unfinished limited series)

1,2						4.00

LAWBREAKERS (...Suspense Stories No. 10 on)
Law and Order Magazines (Charlton): Mar, 1951 - No. 9, Oct-Nov, 1952

1	53	106	159	334	567	800
2	32	64	96	190	310	430
3,5,6,8,9: 6-Anti-Wertham editorial	27	54	81	158	259	360
4- "White Death" junkie story	39	78	117	231	378	525
7- "The Deadly Dopesters" drug story	42	84	126	265	445	625

LAWBREAKERS ALWAYS LOSE!
Marvel Comics (CBS): Spring, 1948 - No. 10, Oct, 1949

1-2pg. Kurtzman-a, "Giggles 'n' Grins"	50	100	150	315	533	750
2	28	56	84	168	274	380
3-5: 4-Vampire story	21	42	63	124	202	280
6(2/49)-Has editorial defense against charges of Dr. Wertham	23	46	69	136	223	310
7-Used in **SOTI**, illo "Comic-book philosophy"	52	104	156	328	552	775
8-10: 9,10-Photo-c	20	40	60	117	189	260

NOTE: **Brodsky** c-4, 5. **Shores** c-1-3, 6-8.

LAWBREAKERS SUSPENSE STORIES (Formerly Lawbreakers; Strange Suspense Stories No. 16 on)
Capitol Stories/Charlton Comics: No. 10, Jan, 1953 - No. 15, Nov, 1953

10	97	194	291	621	1061	1500
11 (3/53)-Severed tongues-c/story & woman negligee scene						
	514	1028	1542	3750	6625	9500
12-14: 13-Giordano-c begin, end #15	50	100	150	315	533	750
15-Acid-in-face-c/story; hands dissolved in acid story						

LAW-CRIME (See Law Against Crime)

LAWDOG
Marvel Comics (Epic Comics): May, 1993 - No. 10, Feb, 1993

1-10						4.00

LAWDOG/GRIMROD: TERROR AT THE CROSSROADS
Marvel Comics (Epic Comics): Sept, 1993 ($3.50)

1						4.00

LAWMAN (TV)
Dell Publishing Co.: No. 970, Feb, 1959 - No. 11, Apr-June, 1962 (All photo-c)

Four Color 970(#1) John Russell, Peter Brown photo-c	12	24	36	79	170	260
Four Color 1035('60), 3(2-4/60)-Toth-a	8	16	24	55	105	155
4-11	6	12	18	38	69	100

LAW OF DREDD, THE (Also see Judge Dredd)
Quality Comics/Fleetway#8 on: 1989 - No. 33, 1992 ($1.50/$1.75)

1-33: Bolland a-1-6,8,10-12,14(2 pg),15,19						4.00

LAWRENCE (See Movie Classics)

LAZARUS (Also see Lazarus: X +66)
Image Comics: Jun, 2013 - Present ($2.99/$3.50/$3.99)

1-9-Rucka-s/Lark-a/c						3.50
10-21-($3.50) 19-Bonus preview of Black Magic #1						3.50
22-28-($3.99)						4.00
Image Firsts Lazarus #1 (11/15, $1.00) reprints #1; afterword by Rucka; Lark sketch art						3.00
... Sourcebook, Volume 1: Carlyle (4/16, $3.99) Dossier of politics, locations, weapons						4.00
... Sourcebook, Volume 2: Hock (5/17, $3.99) Dossier of politics, locations, weapons						4.00
... Sourcebook, Volume 3: Vassalovka (2/18, $3.99) Dossier of politics, locations						4.00

LAZARUS CHURCHYARD
Tundra Publishing: June, 1992 - No. 3, 1992 ($3.95/$4.50, 44 pgs., coated stock)

1-3						5.00
The Final Cut (Image, 1/01, $14.95, TPB) Reprints Ellis/D'Israeli strips						15.00

LAZARUS FIVE
DC Comics: July, 2000 - No. 5, Nov, 2000 ($2.50, limited series)

1-5-Harris-c/Abell-a(p)						3.00

LAZARUS PLANET
DC Comics: Mar, 2023 - Apr, 2023 ($4.99/$5.99, series of one-shots)

...: Alpha (3/23, $5.99) Heroes vs. King Fire Bull; Waid-s/Federici-a						6.00
...: Assault on Krypton (3/23, $4.99) Dreamer, Power Girl, Mercy Graves app.						5.00
...: Dark Fate (4/23, $4.99) Dreamer, Power Girl app.						5.00
...: Legends Reborn (3/23, $4.99) Titans, Firestorm, City Boy & The Question app.						5.00
...: Next Evolution (4/23, $4.99) The Vigil, Flatline, Deadeye, Red Canary, Sideways app.						5.00
...: Omega (4/23, $5.99) Black Alice, Monkey Prince, Zatanna app.; back-up w/Darkseid						6.00
...: We Once Were Gods (3/23, $4.99) Aquaman, Wonder Woman, Shazam family app.						5.00

LAZARUS PLANET: REVENGE OF THE GODS (Leads into 2023's Shazam! #1)
DC Comics: May, 2023 - No. 4, Jun, 2023 ($4.99, limited series)

1-4-Wonder Woman, Shazam family app.						5.00

LAZARUS: RISEN (Characters from Lazarus)
Image Comics: Mar, 2019 - Present ($7.99, squarebound, limited series)

1-7-Rucka-s/Lark-a; takes place in the year X +68						8.00

LAZARUS: X +66 (Characters from Lazarus)
Image Comics: Jul, 2017 - No. 6, Feb, 2018 ($3.99, limited series)

1-6: 1-Lieber-a. 2-Chater-a. 5-Evely-a						4.00

LCSD 2021 FRIDAY (Local Comic Shop Day edition)
Image Comics: Nov, 2021 ($3.99, one-shot)

1-Ed Brubaker-s/Marcos Martin-a						4.00

LEADING COMICS
DC Comics: Jan, 1942

nn - Ashcan comic, not distributed to newsstands, only for in-house use. Cover art is Detective Comics #57, interior is Star Spangled Comics #2 (a FN+ copy sold for $1015.75 in 2012)						

LEADING COMICS (...Screen Comics No. 42 on)
National Periodical Publications: Winter, 1941-42 - No. 41, Feb-Mar, 1950

1-Origin The Seven Soldiers of Victory; Green Arrow & Speedy, Crimson Avenger, Shining Knight, The Vigilante, Star Spangled Kid & Stripesy begin; The Dummy (Vigilante villain)						
1st app.; 1st Green Arrow-c	470	940	1410	3431	6066	8700
2-Meskin-a; Fred Ray-c	155	310	465	992	1696	2400

	GD 2.0	VG 4.0	FN 6.0	VF 8.0	VF/NM 9.0	NM- 9.2
3	116	232	348	742	1271	1800
4,5	77	154	231	493	847	1200
6-10	55	110	165	352	601	850
11,12,14(Spring, 1945)	47	94	141	296	498	700
13-Classic robot-c	129	258	387	826	1413	2000
15-(Sum, '45)-Contents change to funny animal	31	62	93	182	296	410
16-22,24-30: 16-Nero Fox-c begin, end #22	15	30	45	86	133	180
23-1st app. Peter Porkchops by Otto Feuer & begins	31	62	93	182	296	410
31,32,34-41: 34-41-Leading Screen… on-c only	14	28	42	80	115	150
33-(Scarce)	22	44	66	128	209	290

NOTE: *Otto Feuer*-a most #15-on; *Rube Grossman*-a most (#15-on)c-15-41. *Post* a-23-37, 39, 41.

LEADING MAN
Image Comics: June, 2006 - No. 5, Feb, 2007 ($3.50, limited series)

1-5-B. Clay Moore-s/Jeremy Haun-a						3.50
TPB (2/07, $14.95) r/#1-5; sketch gallery						15.00

LEADING SCREEN COMICS (Formerly Leading Comics)
National Periodical Publ.: No. 42, Apr-May, 1950 - No. 77, Aug-Sept, 1955

42-Peter Porkchops-c/stories continue	14	28	42	81	118	155
43-77	13	26	39	74	105	135

NOTE: *Grossman* a-most. *Mayer* a-45-48, 50, 54-57, 60, 62-74, 75(3), 76, 77.

LEAGUE OF CHAMPIONS, THE (Also see The Champions)
Hero Graphics: Dec, 1990 - No. 12, 1992 ($2.95, 52 pgs.)

1-12: 1-Flare app. 2-Origin Malice						5.00

LEAGUE OF EXTRAORDINARY CEREBI, THE (Cerebus in Hell)
Aardvark-Vanaheim: Oct, 2018 ($4.00, B&W)

1-Cerebus figures placed over original Gustave Doré artwork of Hell						4.00

LEAGUE OF EXTRAORDINARY CORONA, THE (Cerebus in Hell)
Aardvark-Vanaheim: Nov, 2021 ($4.00, B&W)

1-Cerebus figures placed over original Gustave Doré artwork of Hell						4.00

LEAGUE OF EXTRAORDINARY GENTLEMEN, THE
America's Best Comics: Mar, 1999 - No. 6, Sept, 2000 ($2.95, limited series)

1-Alan Moore-s/Kevin O'Neill-a	3	6	9	14	20	26
1-DF Edition ($10.00) O'Neill-c	3	6	9	16	24	32
2,3						6.00
4-6: 5-Revised printing with "Amaze 'Whirling Spray' Syringe" parody ad						4.00
5-Initial printing recalled because of "Marvel Co. Syringe" parody ad						
	14	28	42	93	204	315
… Compendium 1,2: 1-r/#1,2. 2-r/#3,4						6.00
Hardcover (2000, $24.95) r/#1-6 plus cover gallery						25.00

LEAGUE OF EXTRAORDINARY GENTLEMEN, THE (Volume 2)
America's Best Comics: Sept, 2002 - No. 6, Nov, 2003 ($3.50, limited series)

1-6-Alan Moore-s/Kevin O'Neill-a						5.00
… Bumper Compendium 1,2: 1-r/#1,2. 2-r/#3,4						6.00
… Black Dossier (HC, 2007, $29.99) new graphic novel; 3-D section with glasses; extras						30.00

LEAGUE OF EXTRAORDINARY GENTLEMEN
Top Shelf Productions/Knockabout Comics: 2009; 2011; 2012 ($7.95/$9.95, squarebound)

… Century: 1910 (2009, $7.95) Alan Moore-s/Kevin O'Neill-a						8.00
… Century #2 "1969" (2011, $9.95) Alan Moore-s/Kevin O'Neill-a						10.00
… Century #3 "2009" (2012, $9.95) Alan Moore-s/Kevin O'Neill-a						10.00

LEAGUE OF EXTRAORDINARY GENTLEMEN VOLUME 4: THE TEMPEST
Top Shelf Productions: Jun, 2018 - No. 6, Jun, 2019 ($4.99, limited series)

1-6-Alan Moore-s/Kevin O'Neill-a. 3-Includes 3-D pages and glasses						5.00

LEAGUE OF JUSTICE
DC Comics (Elseworlds): 1996 - No. 2, 1996 ($5.95, 48 pgs., squarebound)

1,2: Magic-based alternate DC Universe story; Giordano-i						6.00

LEATHERFACE
Arpad Publishing: May (April on-c), 1991 - No. 4, May, 1992 ($2.75, painted-c)

1-Based on Texas Chainsaw movie; Dorman-c	3	6	9	17	26	35
2-4-Dorman-c on all	2	4	6	8	10	12

LEATHERNECK THE MARINE (See Mighty Midget Comics)

LEAVE IT TO BEAVER (TV)
Dell Publishing Co.: No. 912, June, 1958; May-July, 1962 (All photo-c)

Four Color 912	17	34	51	117	259	400
Four Color 999,1103,1191,1285, 01-428-207	14	28	42	96	211	325

LEAVE IT TO BINKY (Binky No. 72 on) (Super DC Giant) (No. 1-22: 52 pgs.)
National Periodical Publs.: 1-2/3/48 - #60, 10/58; #61, 6-7/68 - #71, 2-3/70 (Teen-age humor)

1-Lucy wears Superman costume	57	114	171	362	619	875
2	28	56	84	168	274	380
3,4	20	40	60	117	189	260
5-Superman cameo	24	48	72	142	234	325
6-10	15	30	45	86	133	180
11-14,16-22: Last 52 pg. issue	14	28	42	76	108	140
15-Scribbly story by Mayer	14	28	42	82	121	160
23-28,30-45: 45-Last pre-code (2/55)	11	22	33	62	86	110
29-Used in **POP**, pg. 78	12	24	36	67	94	120
46-60: 60-(10/58)	6	12	18	38	69	100
61 (6-7/68) 1950's reprints with art changes	6	12	18	37	66	95
62-69: 67-Last 12c issue	5	10	15	30	50	70
70-7pg. app. Bus Driver who looks like Ralph from Honeymooners						
	5	10	15	33	57	80
71-Last issue	5	10	15	31	53	75

NOTE: *Aragones* a-61, 62, 67. *Drucker* a-28. *Mayer* a-1, 2, 15. Created by *Mayer*.

LEAVE IT TO CHANCE
Image Comics (Homage Comics): Sept, 1996 - No. 11, Sept, 1998; No. 13, July, 2002
DC Comics (Homage Comics): No. 12, Jun, 1999 ($2.50/$2.95/$4.95)

1-3: 1-Intro Chance Falconer & St. George; James Robinson scripts & Paul Smith-c/a						5.00
4-12: 12-(6/99)						4.00
13-(7/02, $4.95) includes sketch pages and pin-ups						5.00

Free Comic Book Day Edition (2003) - James Robinson-s/Paul Smith-a						3.00
Shaman's Rain TPB (1997, $9.95) r/#1-4						10.00
Shaman's Rain HC (2002, $14.95. over-sized 8 1/4" x 12") r/#1-4						15.00
Trick or Threat TPB (1997, $12.95) r/#5-8						13.00
Trick or Threat HC (2002, $14.95. over-sized 8 1/4" x 12") r/#5-8						15.00
Vol. 3: Monster Madness and Other Stories HC (2003, $14.95, 8 1/4" x 12") r/#9-11						15.00

LEAVING MEGALOPOLIS: SURVIVING MEGALOPOLIS
Dark Horse Comics: Jan, 2016 - No. 6, Sept, 2016 ($3.99)

1-6-Gail Simone-s/Jim Calafiore-a						4.00

LEE HUNTER, INDIAN FIGHTER
Dell Publishing Co.: No. 779, Mar, 1957; No. 904, May, 1958

Four Color 779 (#1)	6	12	18	40	73	105
Four Color 904	5	10	15	30	50	70

LEFT-HANDED GUN, THE (Movie)
Dell Publishing Co.: No. 913, July, 1958

Four Color 913-Paul Newman photo-c	10	20	30	64	132	200

LEGACY
Majestic Entertainment: Oct, 1993 - No. 2, Nov, 1993; No. 0, 1994 ($2.25)

1-2,0: 1-Glow-in-the-dark-c. 0-Platinum						

LEGACY
Image Comics: May, 2003 - No. 4, Feb, 2004 ($2.95)

1-4: 1-Francisco-a/Treffiletti-s						3.00

LEGACY OF KAIN (Based on the Eidos video game)
Top Cow Productions: Oct, 1999; Jan, 2004 ($2.99)

…Defiance 1 (1/04, $2.99) Cha-c; Kirkham-a	2	4	6	9	12	15
…Soul Reaver 1 (10/99, Diamond Dateline supplement) Benitez-c						
	2	4	6	9	12	15

LEGACY OF LUTHER STRODE, THE (Also see Legend of Luther Strode)
Image Comics: Apr, 2015 - No. 6, May, 2016 ($3.99/$3.50)

1-($3.99) Justin Jordan-s/Tradd Moore-a						4.00
2-6-($3.50)						3.50

LEGEND
DC Comics (WildStorm): Apr, 2005 - No. 4, July, 2005 ($5.95/$5.99, limited series)

1-4-Howard Chaykin-s/Russ Heath-a; inspired by Philip Wylie's novel "Gladiator"						6.00

LEGENDARY STAR-LORD (Guardians of the Galaxy)
Marvel Comics: Sept, 2014 - No. 12, Jul, 2015 ($3.99)

1-12: 1-Humphries-s/Medina-a. 4-Thanos app. 9-11-Black Vortex x-over						4.00

LEGENDARY TALESPINNERS
Dynamite Entertainment: 2010 - No. 3, 2010 ($3.99)

1-3-Kuhoric-s/Bond-a; two covers						4.00

LEGENDERRY: A STEAMPUNK ADVENTURE
Dynamite Entertainment: 2014 - No. 7, 2014 ($3.99)

1-7-Willingham-s/Davila-a/Benitez-c.						4.00

LEGENDERRY: GREEN HORNET
Dynamite Entertainment: 2015 - No. 5, 2015 ($3.99)

1-5-Gregory-s/Peeples-a; multiple covers						4.00

LEGENDERRY: RED SONJA
Dynamite Entertainment: 2015 - No. 5, 2015 ($3.99)

1-5: 1-Andreyko-s/Aneke-a; multiple covers; Steampunk Sonja; Bride of Frankenstein app.						4.00

LEGENDERRY: RED SONJA (Volume 2)
Dynamite Entertainment: 2018 - No. 5, 2018 ($3.99)

1-5-Andreyko-s/Lima-a; multiple covers; Kulan Gath app.						4.00
nn-(12/23, $5.99) Collins-s/Baal-a; Dorian Gray app.						6.00

LEGENDERRY: VAMPIRELLA
Dynamite Entertainment: 2015 - No. 5, 2015 ($3.99)

1-5-Avallone-s/Cabrera-a; Steampunk Vampirella						4.00

LEGEND OF CUSTER, THE (TV)
Dell Publishing Co.: Jan, 1968

1-Wayne Maunder photo-c	3	6	9	17	26	35

LEGEND OF ISIS
Alias Entertainment: May, 2005 - No. 5 ($2.99)

1-5: 1-Three covers; Ottney-s/Fontana-a						3.00
…: Beginnings TPB (5/05, $9.99) Ottney-s						10.00

LEGEND OF JESSE JAMES, THE (TV)
Gold Key: Feb, 1966

10172-602-Photo-c	3	6	9	19	30	40

LEGEND OF KAMUI, THE (See Kamui)

LEGEND OF LOBO, THE (See Movie Comics)

LEGEND OF LUTHER STRODE, THE (Sequel to Strange Talent of Luther Strode)
Image Comics: Dec, 2012 - No. 6, Aug, 2013 ($3.50, limited series)

1-5: Justin Jordan-s/Tradd Moore-a						3.50

LEGEND OF OZ: TIK-TOK AND THE KALIDAH
Aspen MLT: Apr, 2016 - No. 3, Jul, 2016 ($3.99)

1-3-Rob Anderson-s/Renato Rei-a. 1-Three covers. 2,3-Two covers						4.00

LEGEND OF OZ: THE WICKED WEST
Big Dog Press: Oct, 2011 - No. 6, Aug, 2012; Oct, 2012 - No. 18, May 2014 ($3.50)

1-6-Multiple covers on all						3.50
Vol. 2 1-18-Multiple covers on all						3.50

LEGEND OF OZ: THE WICKED WEST
Aspen MLT: Oct, 2015 - No. 6, Mar, 2016 ($3.99)

1-6-Reprints 2011 series						4.00

League of Extraordinary Gentlemen V2 #1 © Moore & O'Neill

Legenderry Red Sonja V2 #2 © DYN

Legends of the Dark Knight #1 © DC

	GD 2.0	VG 4.0	FN 6.0	VF 8.0	VF/NM 9.0	NM- 9.2

LEGEND OF SHANG-CHI, THE
Marvel Comics: Apr, 2021 ($3.99, one-shot)

	GD 2.0	VG 4.0	FN 6.0	VF 8.0	VF/NM 9.0	NM- 9.2
1-Alyssa Wong-s/Andie Tong-a; Lady Deathstrike app.						4.00

LEGEND OF SUPREME
Image Comics (Extreme): Dec, 1994 - No. 3, Feb, 1995 ($2.50, limited series)

1-3						4.00

LEGEND OF THE ELFLORD
DavDez Arts: July, 1998 - No. 2, Sept, 1998 ($2.95)

1,2-Barry Blair & Colin Chin-s/a						4.00

LEGEND OF THE HAWKMAN
DC Comics: 2000 - No. 3, 2000 ($4.95, limited series)

1-3-Raab-s/Lark-c/a						5.00

LEGEND OF THE SHADOW CLAN
Aspen MLT: Feb, 2013 - No. 5, Jul, 2013 ($1.00/$3.99)

1-($1.00) David Wohl-s/Cory Smith-a; mutiple covers						3.00
2-5-($3.99)						4.00

LEGEND OF THE SHIELD, THE
DC Comics (Impact Comics): July, 1991 - No. 16, Oct, 1992 ($1.00)

1-16; 6,7-The Fly x-over. 12-Contains trading card						4.00
Annual 1 (1992, $2.50, 68 pgs.)-Snyder-a; w/trading card						4.00

LEGEND OF THE SWAMP THING HALLOWEEN SPECTACULAR
DC Comics: Dec, 2020 ($5.99, one-shot)

1-Six short stories by various; art by Perkins, Timms, Stanton, Ward, Rios; Perkins-c						6.00

LEGEND OF WONDER WOMAN, THE
DC Comics: May, 1986 - No. 4, Aug, 1986 (75¢, limited series)

1		2	4	6	8	10	12
2-4		1	3	4	6	8	10

LEGEND OF WONDER WOMAN, THE (Printing of digital-first stories)
DC Comics: Mar, 2016 - No. 9, Oct, 2016 ($3.99)

1-9; Childhood/origin flashbacks of Diana; Renae de Liz-s/a. 2-Steve Trevor app.						4.00

LEGEND OF YOUNG DICK TURPIN, THE (Disney)(TV)
Gold Key: May, 1966

1 (10176-605)-Photo/painted-c		3	6	9	19	30	40

LEGEND OF ZELDA, THE (Link: The Legend... in indicia)
Valiant Comics: 1990 - No. 4, 1990 ($1.95, coated stiff-c) V2#1, 1990 - No. 5, 1990 ($1.50)

1		10	20	30	69	147	225
2-4; 4-Layton-c(i)		3	6	9	17	25	34
V2#1-5		2	4	6	8	10	12

LEGENDS
DC Comics: Nov, 1986 - No. 6, Apr, 1987 (75¢, limited series)

1-Byrne-c/a(p) in all; 1st app. Amanda Waller and the new Captain Marvel		3	6	9	14	20	25
2,4,5							6.00
3-1st app. new Suicide Squad; death of Blockbuster	3	6	9	17	26	35
6-1st app. new Justice League	2	4	6	9	13	16

LEGENDS OF DANIEL BOONE, THE (...Frontier Scout)
National Periodical Publications: Oct-Nov, 1955 - No. 8, Dec-Jan, 1956-57

1 (Scarce)-Nick Cardy c-1-8	63	126	189	403	689	975
2 (Scarce)	50	100	150	315	533	750
3-8 (Scarce)	39	78	117	231	378	525

LEGENDS OF NASCAR, THE
Vortex Comics: Nov, 1990 - No. 14, 1992? (#1 3rd printing (1/91) says 2nd printing inside)

1-Bill Elliott biog.; Trimpe-a ($1.50)						5.00
1-2nd printing (11/90, $2.00)						4.00
1-3rd print; contains Maxx racecards ($3.00)						4.00
2-14: 2-Richard Petty. 3-Ken Schrader (7/91). 4-Bobby Allison; Spiegle-a(p); Adkins part-i. 5-Sterling Marlin. 6-Bill Elliott. 7-Junior Johnson; Spiegle-c/a. 8-Benny Parsons; Heck-a						4.00
1-13-Hologram cover versions. 2-Hologram shows Bill Elliott's car by mistake (all are numbered & limited)						5.00
2-Hologram corrected version						5.00
Christmas Special ($5.95)						6.00

LEGENDS OF RED SONJA
Dynamite Entertainment: 2013 - No. 5, 2014 ($3.99)

1-5-Short stories by various incl. Simone, Grayson; covers by Anacleto & Thorne						4.00

LEGENDS OF THE DARK CLAW

DC Comics (Amalgam): Apr, 1996 ($1.95)

1-Jim Balent-c/a	1	3	4	6	8	10

LEGENDS OF THE DARK KNIGHT (See Batman: ...)

LEGENDS OF THE DARK KNIGHT
DC Comics: Dec, 2012 - No. 13, Dec, 2013 ($3.99, printings of digital first stories)

1-13: 1-Lindelof-s. 2-4-Joker app. 5-Hester-a						4.00
... 100 Page Super Spectacular 1-5 (2/14 - No. 5, 3/15, quarterly, $9.99) 1-(2/14)						10.00

LEGENDS OF THE DARK KNIGHT
DC Comics: Jul, 2021 - No. 8, Feb, 2022 ($3.99, printings of digital first stories)

1-8: 1-3-Darick Robertson-s/a. 1,2-Joker app. 7-Azrael app.						4.00

LEGENDS OF THE DC UNIVERSE
DC Comics: Feb, 1998 - No. 41, June, 2001 ($1.95/$1.99/$2.50)

1-13,15-21: 1-3-Superman; Robinson-s/Semeiks-a/Orbik-painted-c. 4,5-Wonder Woman; Deodato-a/Rude painted-c. 8-GL/GA, O'Neil-s. 10,11-Batgirl; Dodson-a. 12,13-Justice League. 15-17-Flash. 18-Kid Flash; Guice-a. 19-Impulse; prelude to JLApe Annuals. 20,21-Abin Sur						4.00
14-($3.95) Jimmy Olsen; Kirby-esque-c by Rude						5.00
22-27,30: 22,23-Superman; Rude-c/Ladronn-a. 26,27-Aquaman/Joker						3.00
28,29: Green Lantern & the Atom; Gil Kane-a; covers by Kane and Ross						3.00
31,32: 32-Begin $2.50-c; Wonder Woman; Texeira-a						3.00
33-36-Hal Jordan as The Spectre; DeMatteis-s/Zulli-a; Hale painted-c						3.00
37-41: 37,38-Kyle Rayner. 39-Superman. 40,41-Atom; Harris-c						3.00
... Crisis on Infinite Earths 1 (2/99, $4.95) Untold story during and after Crisis on Infinite Earths #4; Wolfman-s/Ryan-a/Orbik-c						5.00
... 80 Page Giant 1 (9/98, $4.95) Stories and art by various incl. Ditko, Perez, Gibbons, Mumy; Joe Kubert-c						5.00
... 80 Page Giant 2 (1/00, $4.95) Stories and art by various incl. Challengers by Art Adams; Sean Phillips-c						5.00
... 3-D Gallery (12/98, $2.95) Pin-ups w/glasses						4.00

LEGENDS OF THE LEGION (See Legion of Super-Heroes)
DC Comics: Feb, 1998 - No. 4, May, 1998 ($2.25, limited series)

1-4:1-Origin-s of Ultra Boy. 2-Spark. 3-Umbra. 4-Star Boy						4.00

LEGENDS OF THE STARGRAZERS (See Vanguard Illustrated #2)
Innovation Publishing: Aug, 1989 - No. 6, 1990 ($1.95, limited series, mature)

1-6: 1-Redondo part inks						4.00

LEGENDS OF THE WORLD'S FINEST (See World's Finest)
DC Comics: 1994 - No. 3, 1994 ($4.95, squarebound, limited series)

1-3: Simonson scripts; Brereton-c/a; embossed foil logos						6.00
TPB-(1995, $14.95) r/#1-3						15.00

LEGENDS OF TOMORROW
DC Comics: May, 2016 - No. 6, Oct, 2016 ($7.99, squarebound)

1-6: Short stories of Firestorm, Metal Men, Metamorpho and Sugar & Spike. 6-Legion of Super-Heroes app.						8.00

LEGION (David Haller from X-Men)
Marvel Comics: Mar, 2018 - No. 5, Jul, 2018 ($3.99)

1-5: 1-3-MIlligan-s/Torres-a. 4-Ferguson-a						4.00

L.E.G.I.O.N. (The # to right of title represents year of print)(Also see Lobo & R.E.B.E.L.S.)
DC Comics: Feb, 1989 - No. 70, Sept, 1994 ($1.50/$1.75)

1-Giffen plots/breakdowns in #1-12,28						6.00
2-22,24-47: 3-Lobo app. #3 on. 4-1st Lobo-c this title. 5-Lobo joins L.E.G.I.O.N. 13-Lar Gand app. 16-Lar Gand joins L.E.G.I.O.N., leaves #19. 31-Capt. Marvel app. 35-L.E.G.I.O.N. '92 begins						4.00
23,70-($2.50, 52 pgs.)-L.E.G.I.O.N. '91 begins. 70-Zero Hour						5.00
48,49,51-69: 48-Begin $1.75-c. 63-L.E.G.I.O.N. '94 begins; Superman x-over						4.00
50-($3.50, 68 pgs.)						5.00
Annual 1-5 ('90-94, 68 pgs.): 1-Lobo, Superman app. 2-Alan Grant scripts. 5-Elseworlds story; Lobo app.						5.00
NOTE: *Alan Grant* scripts in #1-39, 51, Annual 1, 2.						

LEGION, THE (Continued from Legion Lost & Legion Worlds)
DC Comics: Dec, 2001 - No. 38, Oct, 2004 ($2.50)

1-Abnett & Lanning-s; Coipel & Lanning-c/a						4.00
2-24: 3-8-Ra's al Ghul app. 5-Snejbjerg-a. 9-DeStefano-a. 12-Legion vs. JLA. 16-Fatal Five app.; Walker-a 17,18-Ra's al Ghul app. 20-23-Universo app.						3.00
25-($3.95) Art by Harris, Cockrum, Rivoche; teenage Clark Kent app.; Harris-c						4.00
26-38-Superboy in classic costume. 26-30-Darkseid app. 31-Giffen-a. 35-38-Jurgens-a.						3.00
...Secret Files 3003 (1/04, $4.95) Kirk-a, Harris-a; Superboy app.						5.00
...Foundations TPB (2004, $19.95) r/#25-30 & Secret Files 3003; Harris-c						20.00

LEGION LOST (Continued from Legion of Super-Heroes [4th series] #125)

	GD	VG	FN	VF	VF/NM	NM-
	2.0	4.0	6.0	8.0	9.0	9.2

DC Comics: May, 2000 - No. 12, Apr, 2001 ($2.50, limited series)

1-Abnett & Lanning-s. Coipel & Lanning-c/a	1	2	3		5	7
2-12-Abnett & Lanning-s. Coipel & Lanning-c/a in most. 4,9-Alixe-a						3.00
HC (2011, $39.99, dustjacket) r/#1-12						40.00

LEGION LOST (DC New 52)
DC Comics: Nov, 2011 - No. 16, Mar, 2013 ($2.99)

1-16: 1-Nicieza-s/Woods-a/c; Legionnaires trapped in the 21st century. 7,8-DeFalco-s. 8-Prelude to The Culling; Ravagers app. 9-The Culling x-over with Teen Titans. 14-16-Superboy & the Ravagers app.						3.00
#0 (11/12, $2.99) Origin of Timber Wolf; DeFalco-s/Woods-a						3.00

LEGIONNAIRES (See Legion of Super-Heroes #40, 41 & Showcase 95 #6)
DC Comics: Apr, 1992 - No. 81, Mar, 2000 ($1.25/$1.50/$2.25)

1-49,51-77: 1-(4/92)-Chris Sprouse-c/a; polybagged w/SkyBox trading card. 11-Kid Quantum joins. 18-(9/94)-Zero Hour; leads into #0. 19-(11/94). 37-Valor (Lar Gand) becomes M'onel. 43-Legion tryouts; reintro Princess Projectra, Shadow Lass & others. 47-Some one cover image with LSH #91. 60-Karate Kid & Kid Quantum join. 61-Silver Age & 70's Legion app. 76-Return of Wildfire. 79,80-Coipel-c/a; Legion vs. the Blight						4.00
50-($3.95) Pullout poster by Davis/Farmer						5.00
#0-(10/94)-Zero Hour restart of Legion; released between #18 & #19						4.00
#1,000,000 (11/98) Sean Phillips-a						4.00
Annual 1,3 ('94,'96 $2.95)-1-Elseworlds-s. 3-Legends of the Dead Earth-s						5.00
Annual 2 (1995, $3.95)-Year One-s						5.00

LEGIONNAIRES THREE
DC Comics: Jan, 1986 - No. 4, May, 1986 (75¢, limited series)

1-4						4.00

LEGION OF MONSTERS (Also see Marvel Premiere #28 & Marvel Preview #8)
Marvel Comics Group: Sept, 1975 ($1.00, B&W, magazine, 76 pgs.)

1-Origin & 1st app. Legion of Monsters; Neal Adams-c; Morrow-a; origin & only app. The Manphibian; Frankenstein by Mayerik; Bram Stoker's Dracula adaptation; Reese-a; painted-c (#2 was advertised with Morbius & Satana, but was never published)	12	24	36	80	173	265

LEGION OF MONSTERS (One-shots)
Marvel Comics: Apr, 2007 - Sept, 2007 ($2.99)

... Man-Thing (5/07) Huston-s/Janson-a/Land-c; Simon Garth: Zombie by Ted McKeever	2	4	6	9	12	15
... Morbius (9/07) Cahill-s/Gaydos-a/Land-c; Dracula w/Finch-a/Cebulski-s	2	4	6	9	12	15
... Satana (8/07) Furth-s/Andrasofszky-a/Land-c; Living Mummy by Hickman	2	4	6	9	12	15
... Werewolf By Night (4/07) Carey-s/Land-a/c; Monster of Frankenstein by Skottie Young	2	4	6	9	12	15
HC (2007, $24.99, dustjacket) oversized r/series and classic stories; sketch pages						35.00

LEGION OF MONSTERS
Marvel Comics: Dec, 2011 - No. 4, Mar, 2012 ($3.99, limited series)

1-Hopeless-s/Doe-a/c; Morbius, Manphibian, Elsa Bloodstone app.	2	4	6	11	16	20
2-4						4.00

LEGION OF NIGHT, THE
Marvel Comics: Oct, 1991 - No. 2, Oct, 1991 ($4.95, 52 pgs.)

1,2-Whilce Portacio-c/a(p)						5.00

LEGION OF SUBSTITUTE HEROES SPECIAL (See Adventure Comics #306)
DC Comics: July, 1985 ($1.25, one-shot, 52 pgs.)

1-Giffen-c/a						4.00

LEGION OF SUPER-HEROES (See Action Comics, Adventure, All New Collectors Edition, Legionnaires, Legends of the Legion, Limited Collectors Edition, Secrets of the..., Superboy & Superman)
National Periodical Publications: Feb, 1973 - No. 4, July-Aug, 1973

1-Legion & Tommy Tomorrow reprints begin	3	6	9	21	33	45
2-4: 2-Forte-r. 3-r/Adv. #340. Action #240. 4-r/Adv. #341, Action #233; Mooney-r	2	4	6	13	18	22

LEGION OF SUPER-HEROES, THE (Formerly Superboy and...; Tales of The Legion #314 on)
DC Comics: No. 259, Jan, 1980 - No. 313, July, 1984

259(#1)-Superboy leaves Legion	2	4	6	8	11	14
260-270: 265-Contains 28 pg. insert "Superman & the TRS-80 computer"; origin Tyroc; Tyroc leaves Legion						6.00
261,263,264,266-(Whitman variants; low print run; no cover #'s)						
	2	4	6	8	11	14
271-289: 272-Blok joins; origin; 20 pg. insert-Dial 'H' For Hero. 277-Intro. Reflecto. 280-Superboy re-joins Legion. 282-Origin Reflecto. 283-Origin Wildfire						6.00
290-294-Great Darkness saga. 294-Double size (52 pgs.)						
	1	2	3	5	7	9
295-299,301-313: 297-Origin retold. 298-Free 16 pg. Amethyst preview. 306-Brief origin Star Boy (Swan art). 311-Colan-a						4.00
Annual 1-3(82-84, 52 pgs.)-1-Giffen-c/a; 1st app./origin new Invisible Kid who joins Legion. 2-Karate Kid & Princess Projectra wed & resign						5.00
...The Great Darkness Saga (1989, $17.95, 196 pgs.)-r/LSH #287,290-294 & Annual #3; Giffen-c/a	4	8	12	23	37	50
...The Great Darkness Saga The Deluxe Edition HC (2010, $39.99, dj)-r/LSH #284-296 & Annual #1; new intro. by Levitz, script for #290, Giffen design sketches						
	5	10	15	30	50	70

NOTE: **Aparo** c-282, 283, 300(part). **Austin** c-268i. **Buckler** c-273p, 274p, 276p. **Colan** a-311p. **Ditko** a(p)-267, 268, 272, 274, 276, 281. **Giffen** a-285-313p, Annual 1p; c-287p, 288p, 289, 290p, 291p, 292, 293, 294-299p, 300, 301-313p, Annual 1p, 2p. **Perez** c-268p, 277-280, 281p. **Staton** a-259p, 260p, 280. **Tuska** a-308p.

LEGION OF SUPER-HEROES (3rd Series) (Reprinted in Tales of the Legion)
DC Comics: Aug, 1984 - No. 63, Aug, 1989 ($1.25/$1.75, deluxe format)

1-Silver ink logo	1	3	4	6	8	10
2-36,39-44,46-49,51-62: 4-Death of Karate Kid. 5-Death of Nemesis Kid. 12-Cosmic Boy, Lightning Lad, & Saturn Girl resign. 14-Intro new members: Tellus, Sensor Girl, Quislet. 15-17-Crisis tie-ins. 18-Crisis x-over. 25-Sensor Girl i.d. revealed as Princess Projectra.						

35-Saturn Girl rejoins. 42,43-Millennium tie-ins. 44-Origin Quislet						3.00
37,38-Death of Superboy			8	9	13	16
45,50: 45 ($2.95, 68 pgs.)-Anniversary ish. 50-Double size ($2.50-c)						4.00
63-Final issue						4.00
Annual 1-4 (10/85-'88, 52 pgs.)-1-Crisis tie-in						4.00
...: An Eye For An Eye TPB (2007, $17.99)-r/#1-6; intro by Paul Levitz; cover gallery						18.00
...: The More Things Change TPB (2008, $17.99)-r/#7-13; cover gallery						18.00

NOTE: **Byrne** c-36p. **Giffen** a(p)-1, 2, 50-55, 57-63, Annual 1p, 2; c-1-5p, 54p, Annual 1. **Orlando** a-6p. **Steacy** c-45-50, Annual 3.

LEGION OF SUPER-HEROES (4th Series)
DC Comics: Nov, 1989 - No. 125, Mar, 2000 ($1.75/$1.95/$2.25)

1-Giffen-c/a(p)/scripts begin (4 pg.-a only #18)						6.00
2-20,26-49,51-53,55-58: 4-Mon-El (Lar Gand) destroys Time Trapper, changes reality. 5-Alt. reality story where Mordru rules all; Ferro Lad app. 6-1st app. of Laurel Gand (Lar Gand's cousin). 8-Origin. 13-Free poster by Giffen showing new costumes. 15-(2/91)-1st reference of Lar Gand as Valor. 17-Tornado Twins app. 26-New map of headquarters. 34-Six pg. preview of Timber Wolf mini-series. 40-Minor Legionnaires app. 41-(3/93)-SW6 Legion renamed Legionnaires w/new costumes and some new code-names						3.00
21-25: 21-24-Lobo & Darkseid storyline. 24-Cameo SW6 younger Legion duplicates. 25-SW6 Legion full intro.						5.00
50-($3.50, 68 pgs.)						5.00
54-($2.95)-Die-cut & foil stamped-c						5.00
59-99: 61-(9/94)-Zero Hour. 62-(11/94). 75-XS travels back to the 20th Century (cont'd in Impulse #9). 77-Origin of Braniac 5. 81-Reintro Sun Boy. 85-Half of the Legion sent to the 20th century, Superman-c/app. 86-Final Night. 87-Deadman-c/app. 88-Impulse-c/app. Adventure Comics #247 cover swipe. 91-Forms one cover image with Legionnaires #47. 96-Wedding of Ultra Boy and Apparition. 99-Robin, Impulse, Superboy app.						3.00
100-($5.95, 96 pgs.)-Legionnaires return to the 30th Century; gatefold-c; 5 stories-art by Simonson, Davis and others	1	2	3	4	5	7
101-121: 101-Armstrong-a(p) begins. 105-Legion past & present vs. Time Trapper. 109-Mordru-a. 110-Thunder joins. 114,115-Bizarro Legion. 120,121-Fatal Five.						3.00
122-124: 122,123-Coipel-c/a. 124-Coipel-c						4.00
125-Leads into "Legion Lost" maxi-series; Coipel-c						5.00
#0-(10/94)-Zero Hour restart of Legion; released between #61 & #62						3.00
#1,000,000 (11/98) Giffen-a						3.00
Annual 1-5 (1990-1994, $3.50, 68 pgs.): 4-Bloodlines. 5-Elseworlds story						4.00
Annual 6 (1995,$3.95)-Year One story						4.00
Annual 7 (1996, $3.50, 48 pgs.)-Legends of the Dead Earth story; intro 75th Century Legion of Super-Heroes; Wildfire app.						4.00
Legion: Secret Files 1 (1/98, $4.95) Retold origin & pin-ups						5.00
Legion: Secret Files 2 (6/99, $4.95) Story and profile pages						5.00
The Beginning of Tomorrow TPB ('99, $17.95) r/post-Zero Hour reboot						18.00

NOTE: **Giffen** a-1-24; breakdowns-26-32, 34-36; c-1-7, 8(part), 9-24. **Brandon Peterson** a(p)-15(1st for DC), 16, 18, Annual 2(54 pgs.). **Swan/Anderson** c-8(part).

LEGION OF SUPER-HEROES (5th Series) (Title becomes Supergirl and the Legion of Super-Heroes #16-36) (Intro. in Teen Titans/Legion Special)
DC Comics: Feb, 2005 - No. 15, Apr, 2006; No. 37, Feb, 2008 - No. 50, Mar, 2009 ($2.95/$2.99)

1-15: 1-Waid-s/Kitson-a/c. 4-Kirk & Gibbons-a. 9-Jeanty-a. 15-Dawnstar, Tyroc, Blok-c						3.00
37-50: 37-Shooter-s/Manapul-a begin; two interlocking covers. 50-Wraparound cover						3.00
44-Variant-c by Neal Adams						5.00
... Death of a Dream TPB ('06, $14.99) r/#7-13						15.00
... Enemy Manifest HC ('09, $24.99, dustjacket) r/#45-50						25.00
... Enemy Manifest SC ('10, $14.99) r/#45-50						15.00
... Enemy Rising HC ('08, $19.99, dustjacket) r/#37-44						20.00
... Enemy Rising SC ('09, $14.99) r/#37-44						15.00
...: 1050 Years of the Future TPB ('08, $19.99) r/greatest tales of their 50 year history						20.00
... Teenage Revolution TPB ('05, $14.99) r/#1-6 & Teen Titans/Legion Spec.; sketch pages						15.00

LEGION OF SUPER-HEROES (6th Series)
DC Comics: Jul, 2010 - No. 16, Oct, 2011 ($3.99/$2.99)

1-9: 1-Earth-Man app. Titan destroyed; Levitz-s/Cinar-a/c. 6-Jimenez back-up-a						4.00
1-6-Variant covers by Jim Lee						8.00
10-16-($2.99) 12-16-Legion of Super-Villains app.						3.00
Annual 1 (2/11, $4.99) New Emerald Empress; Levitz-s/Giffen-a						5.00
...: The Choice HC (2011, $24.99, dustjacket) r/#1-6; variant-c gallery and Cinar art						25.00

LEGION OF SUPER-HEROES (DC New 52)(Also see Legion Lost)
DC Comics: Nov, 2011 - No. 23, Oct, 2013 ($2.99)

1-23: 1-4-Levitz-s/Portela-a. 5-Simonson-c/a. 8-Lightle-a. 17-Giffen-a. 23-Maguire-a						3.00
#0 (11/12, $2.99) Story of Brainiac 5 joining the Legion; Levitz-s/Kolins-a						3.00

LEGION OF SUPER-HEROES (See Superman (2018 series) #14,15)
DC Comics: Jan, 2020 - Present ($3.99)

1-12: 1-Bendis-s/Sook-a; Superboy (Jon Kent) joins the Legion; Mordru app. 3-Robin app. 4,5-Origin retold. 4-Sook & Janin-a. 5-Sook & Godlewski-a. 6-Intro Gold Lantern & Dr. Fate. 8,9-Different artist each page; 8-Mack, Allred, Maleev. 9-Grell, Nowlan, Romita, Jr.						4.00
... Millennium 1,2 ($4.99, 11/19 - No. 2, 12/19) Bendis-s; Rose & Thorn, Kamandi app.						5.00

LEGION OF SUPER-HEROES/BUGS BUNNY SPECIAL
DC Comics: Aug, 2017 ($4.99, one-shot)

1-Humphries-s/Grummett-a/c; Bugs Bunny in the 31st century; Supergirl & Validus app.						5.00

LEGION OF SUPER-HEROES IN THE 31ST CENTURY (Based on the animated series)
DC Comics: June, 2007 - No. 20, Jan, 2009 ($2.25)

1-20: 1-Chynna Clugston-a; Fatal Five app. 6-Green Lantern Corps app. 15-Impulse app.						3.00
1-(6/07) Free Comic Book Day giveaway						
...: Tomorrow's Heroes (2008, $14.99) r/#1-7; cover gallery						15.00

LEGION OF SUPER-VILLAINS
DC Comics: May, 2011 ($4.99, one-shot)

1-Levitz-s/Portela-a; Saturn Queen, Lightning Lord, Sun-Killer, Micro Lad app.						5.00

LEGION OF X (Legion and the X-Men)
Marvel Comics: Jun, 2022 - No. 10, Apr, 2023 ($4.99/$3.99)

1-($4.99) Spurrier-s/Bazaldua-a						5.00
2-10-($3.99) 2-Banshee app. 6-Judgment Day tie-in						4.00

LEGION: PROPHETS (Prelude to 2010 movie)

Legion of Super-Heroes (1989 series) #13 © DC

Legion of X #1 © MAR

Lenore V2 #11 © Roman Dirge

	GD	VG	FN	VF	VF/NM	NM-
	2.0	4.0	6.0	8.0	9.0	9.2

IDW Publishing: Nov, 2009 - No. 4, Dec, 2009 ($3.99, limited series)
1-4: Stewart & Waltz-s. 1-Muriel-a. 2-Holder-a. 3-Paronzini-a. 4-Gaydos-a 4.00

LEGION: SCIENCE POLICE (See Legion of Super-Heroes)
DC Comics: Aug, 1998 - No. 4, Nov, 1998 ($2.25, limited series)
1-4-Ryan-a 4.00

LEGION: SECRET ORIGIN (Legion of Super-Heroes)
DC Comics: Dec, 2011 - No. 6, May, 2012 ($2.99, limited series)
1-6-Levitz-s/Batista-a; formation of the Legion retold 3.00

LEGION WORLDS (Follows Legion Lost series)
DC Comics: Jun, 2001 - No. 6, Nov, 2001 ($3.95, limited series)
1-6-Abnett & Lanning-s; art by various. 5-Dillon-a. 6-Timber Wolf app. 4.00

LEGO NINJAGO: GARMADON
Image Comics: Apr, 2022 - No. 5, Oct, 2022 ($3.99, limited series)
1-5-Lego-style story; Tri Vuong-s/a 4.00

LEMONADE KID, THE (See Bobby Benson's B-Bar-B Riders)
AC Comics: 1990 ($2.50, 28 pgs.)
1-Powell-c(r); Red Hawk-r by Powell; Lemonade Kid-r/Bobby Benson by Powell (2 stories) 4.00

LENNON SISTERS LIFE STORY, THE
Dell Publishing Co.: No. 951, Nov, 1958 - No. 1014, Aug, 1959
| Four Color 951 (#1)-Toth-a, 32pgs, photo-c | 11 | 22 | 33 | 76 | 163 | 250 |
| Four Color 1014-Toth-a, photo-c | 11 | 22 | 33 | 72 | 154 | 235 |

LENORE
Slave Labor Graphics/Titan Comics: Feb, 1998 - Present ($2.95/$3.95, B&W, color #13-on)
1-12: 1-Roman Dirge-s/a, 1,2-2nd printing 4.00
13-($3.95, color) 4.00
Vol. 2 (8/09 - No. 11) 1-11: 1st and 2nd printings; Lenore's origin 4.00
Vol. 3 (9/19, $3.99)-Two covers 4.00
...: Cooties TPB (3/06, $13.95) r/#9-12; pin-ups by various 14.00
...: Noogies TPB ($11.95) r/#1-4 .... 12.00
...: Pink Bellies HC (Titan, 3/15, $17.99) Vol. 2 #8-11 .... 18.00
...: Purple Nurples HC (8/13, $17.95) Vol. 2 #4-7 .... 18.00
...: Swirlies HC (8/12, $17.95) r/#13 & Vol. 2 #1-3 .... 18.00
...: Wedgies TPB (2000, $13.95) r/#5-8 .... 14.00

LEONARD NIMOY'S PRIMORTALS
Tekno Comix: Mar, 1995 - No. 15, May, 1996 ($1.95)
1-15: Concept by Leonard Nimoy & Isaac Asimov 1-3-w/bound-in game piece & trading card. 4-w/Teknophage Steel Edition coupon. 13,14-Art Adams-c. 15-Simonson-c 4.00

LEONARD NIMOY'S PRIMORTALS
BIG Entertainment: V2#0; June, 1996 - No. 8, Feb, 1997 ($2.25)
V2#0-8: 0-Includes Pt. 9 of "The Big Bang" x-over. 0,1-Simonson-c. 3-Kelley Jones-c 4.00

LEONARD NIMOY'S PRIMORTALS ORIGINS
Tekno Comix: Nov, 1995 - No. 2, Dec, 1995 ($2.95, limited series)
1,2: Nimoy scripts; Art Adams-c; polybagged 4.00

LEONARDO (Also see Teenage Mutant Ninja Turtles)
Mirage Studios: Dec, 1986 ($1.50, B&W, one-shot)
| 1 | | 4 | 8 | 12 | 28 | 47 | 65 |

LEONIDE THE VAMPYR
Dark Horse Comics: Oct, 2022; Dec, 2022 ($3.99, one-shots)
...: A Christmas For Crows (12/22); Mike Mignola-s/Rachele Aragno-a 4.00
...: Miracle at the Crows Head (10/22); Mike Mignola-s/Rachele Aragno-a 4.00

LEO THE LION
I. W. Enterprises: No date (1960s) (10¢)
| 1-Reprint | 2 | 4 | 6 | 9 | 13 | 16 |

LEROY (Teen-age)
Standard Comics: Nov, 1949 - No. 6, Nov, 1950
1	24	48	72	144	237	330
2-Frazetta text illo.	18	36	54	103	162	220
3-6: 3-Lubbers-a	14	28	42	81	118	155

LESTER OF THE LESSER GODS
Albatross Funnybooks: 2021 ($3.99, one-shot)
1-Eric Powell, Lucky Yates & Mac Cushing/Gideon Kendall-a 4.00

LETHAL (Also see Brigade)
Image Comics (Extreme Studios): Feb, 1996 ($2.50, unfinished limited series)

1-Marat Mychaels-c/a. 4.00

LETHAL FOES OF SPIDER-MAN (Sequel to Deadly Foes of Spider-Man)
Marvel Comics: Sept, 1993 - No. 4, Dec, 1993 ($1.75, limited series)
1-4 .... 4.00

LETHARGIC LAD
Crusade Ent.: June, 1996 - No. 3, Sept, 1996 ($2.95, B&W, limited series)
1,2 .... 4.00
3-Alex Ross-c/swipe (Kingdom Come) 5.00
...Jumbo Sized Annual #1 (Summer 2002, $3.99) prints comic stories from internet 4.00

LETHARGIC LAD ADVENTURES
Crusade Ent./Destination Ent.#3 on: Oct, 1997 - No. 12, Sept./Oct. 1999 ($2.95, B&W)
1-12-Hyland-s/a. 9-Alex Ross sketch page & back-c 4.00

LET ME IN: CROSSROADS (Based on the 2010 movie Let Me In)
Dark Horse Comics: Dec, 2010 - No. 4, Mar, 2011 ($3.99, limited series)
1-4-Prelude to the film; Andreyko-s/Reynolds-a/Phillips-c 4.00
1-4 Variant photo-c 8.00

LET'S PRETEND (CBS radio)
D. S. Publishing Co.: May-June, 1950 - No. 3, Sept-Oct, 1950
| 1 | 23 | 46 | 69 | 136 | 223 | 310 |
| 2,3 | 18 | 36 | 54 | 103 | 162 | 220 |

LET'S READ THE NEWSPAPER
Charlton Press: 1974
| nn-Features Quincy by Ted Shearos | 1 | 3 | 4 | 6 | 8 | 10 |

LET'S TAKE A TRIP (TV) (CBS Television Presents)
Pines Comics: Spring, 1958
| 1-Marv Levy-c/a | 6 | 12 | 18 | 27 | 33 | 38 |

LETTER 44
Oni Press: Oct, 2013 - No. 35, Aug, 2017 ($1.00/$3.99)
1-($1.00)-Soule-a/Alberto Alburquerque-a 5.00
2-35-($3.99) 7-Joëlle Jones-a. 14-Drew Moss-a. 28-Gluskova-a 4.00
... #1 Square One Edition (2/17, $1.00) r/#1 .... 3.00

LETTERS TO SANTA (See March of Comics No. 228)

LEV GLEASON PRESENTS
Comic House: Apr, 2021 - Present ($9.99)
1,2: 1-New stories of Silver Streak, Captain Canuck. 2-Golden Age Daredevil 10.00

LEVIATHAN DAWN (Also see Event Leviathan)
DC Comics: 2020 ($4.99, one-shot)
1-Follows Event Leviathan series; Bendis-s/Maleev-a 5.00

LEX LUTHOR: MAN OF STEEL
DC Comics: May, 2005 - No. 5, Sept, 2005 ($2.99, limited series)
1-5: 1-Azzarello-s/Bermejo-a/c in all. 3-Batman-c/app. 3.00
TPB (2005, $12.99) r/series 13.00
Luthor HC (2010, $19.99, d.j.) r/#1-5 with 10 new story pages; cover gallery & sketch-a 20.00

LEX LUTHOR/PORKY PIG
DC Comics: Oct, 2018 ($4.99, one-shot)
1-Mark Russell-s/Brad Walker-a/Ben Oliver-c; back-up story in classic cartoon style 5.00

LEX LUTHOR: THE UNAUTHORIZED BIOGRAPHY
DC Comics: 1989 ($3.95, 52 pgs., one-shot, squarebound)
1-Painted-c; Clark Kent app. 6.00

LEX LUTHOR: YEAR OF THE VILLAIN
DC Comics: 2019 ($4.99, one-shot)
1-Latour-s/Hitch-a; multiverse of Luthors app. 5.00

LGBTQ ETC PEOPLE (Reprints from Cerebus in Hell)
Aardvark-Vanaheim: Jun, 2019 ($4.00, B&W)
1-Cerebus figures placed over original Gustave Doré artwork of Hell; X-Men #1-c swipe 4.00

LIBERTY COMICS (Miss Liberty No. 1)
Green Publishing Co.: No. 5, May, 1945 - No. 15, July, 1946 (MLJ & other-r)
5 (5/45)-The Prankster app; Starr-a	37	74	111	222	361	500
10-Hangman & Boy Buddies app.; reprints 3 Hangman stories, incl. Hangman #8	43	86	129	271	461	650
11 (V2#2, 1/46)-Wilbur in women's clothes	19	38	57	111	176	240
12 (V2#4)-Black Hood & Suzie app.; classic Skull-c	290	580	870	1856	3178	4500
14,15-Patty of Airliner; Starr-a in both	32	64	96	188	307	425

LIBERTY COMICS (The CBLDF Presents...)

	GD 2.0	VG 4.0	FN 6.0	VF 8.0	VF/NM 9.0	NM- 9.2

Image Comics: July, 2008; Oct, 2009 ($3.99/$4.99, Comic Book Legal Defense Fund benefit)
- 1-Two covers by Campbell & Mignola; art by Cooke, Aragones, A. Adams & others — 4.00
- 1-(12/08) Second printing with Thor-c by Simonson — 4.00
- 2-(10/09, $4.99) two covers by Romita Jr. & Sale; art by Allred, Templesmith, Jim Lee — 5.00
- Liberty Annual 2010 (10/10, $4.99) Covers by Gibbons & Robertson — 5.00
- Liberty Annual 2011 (10/11, $4.99) Covers by Wagner & Cassaday — 5.00
- Liberty Annual 2012 (10/12, $4.99) Covers by Dodson & Bá; Walking Dead story — 5.00
- Liberty Annual 2013 (10/13, $4.99) Covers by Corben & Marquez — 5.00
- Liberty Annual 2014 (10/14, $4.99) Covers by Allred, Simonson, & Charm — 5.00
- Liberty Annual 2015 (10/15, $4.99) Covers by Fegredo, Fowler & Del Rey — 5.00
- Liberty Annual 2016 (11/16, $4.99) Stories by Guinan, Pope, Wimberly, Schkade & others — 5.00

LIBERTY COMICS
Heroic Publishing: Sept, 2007 ($4.50)
- 1-Mark Sparacio-c — 4.50

LIBERTY GIRL
Heroic Publishing: Aug, 2006 - No. 3, May, 2007 ($3.25/$2.99)
- 1-3-Mark Sparacio-c/a — 3.25

LIBERTY GUARDS
Chicago Mail Order: 1942 (Centaur Publ.)
- nn-Reprints Man of War #1 with cover of Liberty Scouts #1; Nazi subs pulling into the harbor in front of the Capitol building & Washington Monument cover by Gustavson — 226 | 452 | 678 | 1446 | 2473 | 3500

LIBERTY MEADOWS
Insight Studios Group/Image Comics #27 on: 1999 - No. 37 ($2.95, B&W)
- 1-Frank Cho-s/a; reprints newspaper strips — 3 | 6 | 9 | 17 | 26 | 35
- 1-2nd & 3rd printings — 1 | 2 | 3 | 4 | 5 | 7
- 2,3 — 2 | 4 | 6 | 8 | 11 | 14
- 4-10 — 1 | 2 | 3 | 4 | 5 | 7
- 11-25,27-37: 20-Adam Hughes-c. 22-Evil Brandy vs. Brandy. 27-1st Image issue, printed sideways — 3.00
- ..., Cover Girl HC (Image, 2006, $24.99, with dustjacket) r/color covers of #1-19,21-37 along with B&W inked versions, sketches and pin-up art — 25.00
- ...: Eden Book 1 SC (Image, 2002, $14.95) r/#1-9; sketch gallery — 15.00
- ...: Eden Book 1 SC 2nd printing (Image, 2004, $19.95) r/#1-9; sketch gallery — 20.00
- ...: Eden Book 1 HC (Image, 2003, $24.95, with dustjacket) r/#1-9; sketch gallery — 25.00
- ...: Creature Comforts Book HC (Image, 2004, $24.95, with d.j.) r/#10-18; sketch gallery — 25.00
- ...: Creature Comforts Book 2 SC (Image, 12/04, $14.95) r/#10-18; sketch gallery — 15.00
- ...Book 3: Summer of Love HC (Image, 12/04, $24.95) r/#19-27; sketch gallery — 25.00
- ...Book 3: Summer of Love SC (Image, 7/05, $14.95) r/#19-27; sketch gallery — 15.00
- ...Book 4: Cold, Cold Heart HC (Image, 9/05, $24.95) r/#28-36; sketch gallery — 25.00
- ...Book 4: Cold, Cold Heart SC (Image, 2006, $14.99) r/#28-36; sketch gallery — 15.00
- Image Firsts: Liberty Meadows #1 (9/10, $1.00) r/#1 — 3.00
- ... Sourcebook (5/04, $4.95) character info and unpublished strips — 5.00
- ... Wedding Album (#26) (2002, $2.95) — 3.00

LIBERTY PROJECT, THE
Eclipse Comics: June, 1987 - No. 8, May, 1988 ($1.75, color, Baxter paper)
- 1-8: 6-Valkyrie app. — 4.00

LIBERTY SCOUTS (See Liberty Guards & Man of War)
Centaur Publications: No. 2, June, 1941 - No. 3, Aug, 1941
- 2(#1)-Origin The Fire-Man, Man of War; Vapo-Man & Liberty Scouts begin; intro Liberty Scouts; Gustavson-c/a in both — 206 | 412 | 618 | 1318 | 2259 | 3200
- 3(#2)-Origin & 1st app. The Sentinel — 206 | 412 | 618 | 1318 | 2259 | 3200

LIBRARIANS, THE (Based on the TV series)
Dynamite Entertainment: 2017 - No. 4, 2018 ($3.99)
- 1-4-Pfeiffer-s/Buchemi-a; multiple covers — 4.00

LICENCE TO KILL (James Bond 007) (Movie)
Eclipse Comics: 1989 ($7.95, slick paper, 52 pgs.)
- nn-Movie adaptation; Timothy Dalton photo-c — 1 | 3 | 4 | 6 | 8 | 10
- Limited Hardcover ($24.95) — 25.00

LIDSVILLE (TV)
Gold Key: Oct, 1972 - No. 5, Oct, 1973
- 1-Photo-c on all — 5 | 10 | 15 | 31 | 53 | 75
- 2-5 — 3 | 6 | 9 | 21 | 33 | 45

LIEUTENANT, THE (TV)
Dell Publishing Co.: April-June, 1964
- 1-Photo-c — 3 | 6 | 9 | 17 | 26 | 35

LIEUTENANT BLUEBERRY (Also see Blueberry)
Marvel Comics (Epic Comics): 1991 - No. 3, 1991 (Graphic novel)
- 1-($8.95)-Moebius-a in all — 4 | 8 | 12 | 28 | 47 | 65
- 2-($8.95) — 3 | 6 | 9 | 21 | 33 | 45
- 3-($14.95) — 4 | 8 | 12 | 27 | 44 | 60

LT. ROBIN CRUSOE, U.S.N. (See Movie Comics & Walt Disney Showcase #26)

LIFE AND DEATH OF TOYO HARADA, THE
Valiant Entertainment: Mar, 2019 - No. 6, Jul, 2019 ($3.99, limited series)
- 1-6-Dysart-s/Cafu-a. 2-Flashback-a by Guice. 3-Albert Einstein app. — 4.00

LIFE EATERS, THE
DC Comics (WildStorm): 2003 ($29.95, hardcover with dust jacket)
- HC-David Brin-s; Scott Hampton-painted-a/c; Norse Gods team with the Nazis — 30.00
- SC-(2004, $19.95) — 20.00

LIFE IS STRANGE (Based on the Square Enix video game)
Titan Comics: Dec, 2018 - No. 12, Feb, 2020 ($3.99)
- 1-12-Emma Vieceli-s/Claudia Leonardi-a — 4.00

LIFE IS STRANGE (Based on the Square Enix video game)
Titan Comics: Nov, 2020 - No. 2.4 ($3.99)
- 2.1-2.4-Emma Vieceli-s/Claudia Leonardi-a — 4.00

LIFE IS STRANGE: COMING HOME (Based on the Square Enix video game)

Titan Comics: Aug, 2021 - No. 2, Sept, 2021 ($5.99, limited series)
- 1,2-Emma Vieceli-s/Claudia Leonardi-a — 6.00

LIFE IS STRANGE: FORGET-ME-NOT (Based on the Square Enix video game)
Titan Comics: Jan, 2024 - No. 2, Mar, 2024 ($3.99, limited series)
- 1,2-Zoe Thorogood-s/Claudia Leonardi-a — 4.00

LIFE IS STRANGE: SETTLING DUST (Based on the Square Enix video game)
Titan Comics: Oct, 2021 - No. 4, Apr, 2022 ($3.99, limited series)
- 1-4-Emma Vieceli-s/Claudia Leonardi-a — 4.00

LIFE OF CAPTAIN MARVEL, THE
Marvel Comics Group: Aug, 1985 - No. 5, Dec, 1985 ($2.00, Baxter paper)
- 1-5-All reprint Starlin issues of Iron Man #55, Capt. Marvel #25-34 plus Marvel Feature #12 (all with Thanos). 4-New Thanos back-c by Starlin — 6.00

LIFE OF CAPTAIN MARVEL, THE (Carol Danvers)
Marvel Comics: Sept, 2018 - No. 5, Feb, 2019 ($4.99/$3.99, limited series)
- 1-($4.99) Childhood flashbacks; Stohl-s/Pacheco & Sauvage-a — 5.00
- 2-5-($3.99) 4-Origin of Carol's mother — 4.00

LIFE OF CHRIST, THE
Catechetical Guild Educational Society: No. 301, 1949 (35¢, 100 pgs.)
- 301-Reprints from Topix(1949)-V5#11,12 — 10 | 20 | 30 | 58 | 79 | 100

LIFE OF CHRIST: THE CHRISTMAS STORY, THE
Marvel Comics/Nelson: Feb, 1993 ($2.99, slick stock)
- nn — 5.00

LIFE OF CHRIST: THE EASTER STORY, THE
Marvel Comics/Nelson: 1993 ($2.99, slick stock)
- nn — 5.00

LIFE OF CHRIST VISUALIZED
Standard Publishers: 1942 - No. 3, 1943
- 1-3: All came in cardboard case, each... — 9 | 18 | 27 | 50 | 65 | 80
- Case only..... — 10 | 20 | 30 | 54 | 72 | 90

LIFE OF CHRIST VISUALIZED
The Standard Publ. Co.: 1946? (48 pgs. in color)
- nn — 7 | 14 | 21 | 37 | 46 | 55

LIFE OF ESTHER VISUALIZED
The Standard Publ. Co.: No. 2062, 1947 (48 pgs. in color)
- 2062 — 7 | 14 | 21 | 37 | 46 | 55

LIFE OF JOSEPH VISUALIZED
The Standard Publ. Co.: No. 1054, 1946 (48 pgs. in color)
- 1054 — 7 | 14 | 21 | 37 | 46 | 55

LIFE OF PAUL (See The Living Bible)

LIFE OF POPE JOHN PAUL II, THE
Marvel Comics Group: Jan, 1983 ($1.50/$1.75)
- 1 — 3 | 6 | 9 | 14 | 19 | 24

LIFE OF RILEY, THE (TV)
Dell Publishing Co.: No. 917, July, 1958
- Four Color 917-William Bendix photo-c — 11 | 22 | 33 | 73 | 157 | 240

LIFE ON ANOTHER PLANET
Kitchen Sink Press: 1978 (B&W, graphic novel, magazine size)
- nn-Will Eisner-s/a — 20.00
- Reprint (DC Comics, 5/00, $12.95) — 13.00

LIFE'S LIKE THAT
Croyden Publ. Co.: 1945 (25¢, B&W, 68 pgs.)
- nn-Newspaper Sunday strip-r by Neher — 8 | 16 | 24 | 44 | 57 | 70

LIFE STORIES OF AMERICAN PRESIDENTS (See Dell Giants)

LIFE STORY
Fawcett Publications: Apr, 1949 - V8#46, Jan, 1953; V8#47, Apr, 1953 (All have photo-c?)
- V1#1 — 20 | 40 | 60 | 120 | 195 | 270
- 2 — 12 | 24 | 36 | 67 | 94 | 120
- 3-6, V2#7-12 (3/50) — 10 | 20 | 30 | 54 | 72 | 90
- V3#13-Wood-a (4/50) — 15 | 30 | 45 | 94 | 147 | 200
- V3#14-18, V4#19-24, V6#25-30, V6#31-35 — 9 | 18 | 27 | 50 | 65 | 80
- V6#36- "I sold drugs" on-c — 15 | 30 | 45 | 85 | 130 | 175
- V7#37,40-42, V8#44,45 — 9 | 18 | 27 | 47 | 61 | 75
- V7#38, V8#43-Evans-a — 9 | 18 | 27 | 50 | 65 | 80
- V7#39-Drug Smuggling & Junkie story — 14 | 28 | 42 | 76 | 108 | 140
- V8#46,47 (Scarce) — 11 | 22 | 33 | 62 | 86 | 110
- NOTE: Powell a-13, 23, 24, 26, 28, 30, 32, 39. Marcus Swayze a-1-3, 10-12, 15, 16, 20, 21, 23-25, 31, 35, 37, 40, 44, 46.

LIFE, THE UNIVERSE AND EVERYTHING (See Hitchhikers Guide to the Galaxy & Restaurant at the End of the Universe)
DC Comics: 1996 - No. 3, 1996 ($6.95, squarebound, limited series)
- 1-3: Adaptation of novel by Douglas Adams. — 1 | 2 | 3 | 4 | 5 | 7

LIFE WITH ARCHIE
Archie Publications: Sept, 1958 - No. 286, Sept, 1991
- 1 — 82 | 164 | 246 | 656 | 1478 | 2300
- 2-(9/59) — 36 | 72 | 108 | 206 | 596 | 925
- 3-5: 3-(7/60) — 19 | 38 | 57 | 133 | 297 | 460
- 6-8,10 — 13 | 26 | 39 | 91 | 201 | 310
- 9,11-Horror/SciFi-c — 19 | 38 | 57 | 131 | 291 | 450
- 12-20 — 9 | 18 | 27 | 60 | 120 | 180
- 21(7/63)-30 — 8 | 16 | 24 | 56 | 108 | 160
- 31-34,36-38,40,41 — 7 | 14 | 21 | 49 | 92 | 135
- 35,39-Horror/Sci-Fi-c — 10 | 20 | 30 | 69 | 147 | 225
- 42-Pureheart begins (1st app.-c/s, 10/65) — 15 | 30 | 45 | 100 | 220 | 340
- 43,44 — 8 | 16 | 24 | 54 | 102 | 150

Life of Captain Marvel (2018 series) #5 © MAR

Life With Archie #162 © ACP

Limited Collectors' Edition C-41 © DC

	GD	VG	FN	VF	VF/NM	NM-
	2.0	4.0	6.0	8.0	9.0	9.2

	GD	VG	FN	VF	VF/NM	NM-
	2.0	4.0	6.0	8.0	9.0	9.2

45(1/66) 1st Man From R.I.V.E.R.D.A.L.E. 9 18 27 59 117 175
46-Origin Pureheart 9 18 27 57 111 165
47-49 7 14 21 44 82 120
50-United Three begin: Pureheart (Archie), Superteen (Betty), Captain Hero (Jughead)
 10 20 30 64 132 200
51-59: 59-Pureheart ends 6 12 18 37 66 95
60-Archie band begins, ends #66 7 14 21 46 86 125
61-66: 61-Man From R.I.V.E.R.D.A.L.E.-c/s 5 10 15 33 57 80
67-80 4 8 12 27 44 60
81-99 4 8 12 23 37 50
100 (8/70), 113-Sabrina & Salem app. 4 8 12 28 47 65
101-112, 114-130(2/73), 139(11/73)-Archie Band c/s 3 6 9 16 23 30
131,134-138,140-146,148-161,164-170(6/76) 3 6 9 14 19 24
132,133,147,163-all horror-c/s 3 6 9 18 28 38
162-UFO c/s 3 6 9 17 25 34
171,173-175,177-184,186,189,191-194,196 2 4 6 8 11 14
172,185,197 : 172-(9/77)-Bi-Cent. spec. ish, 185-2nd 24th cent.-c/s, 197-Time machine/
 SF-c/s 2 4 6 10 14 18
176(12/76)-1st app. Capt. Archie of Starship Rivda, in 24th century c/s; 1st app.
 Stella the Robot 3 6 9 17 25 34
187,188,195,198,199-all horror-c/s 3 6 9 14 19 24
190-1st Dr. Doom-c/s 3 6 9 15 22 28
200 (12/78) Maltese Pigeon-s 2 4 6 11 16 20
201-203,205-237,239,240(1/84): 208-Reintro Veronica 1 3 4 6 8 10
204-Flying saucer-c/s 2 4 6 8 11 14
238-(9/83)-25th anniversary issue; Ol' Betsy (jalopy) replaced
 2 4 6 8 10 12
241-278,280-285: 250-Comic book convention-s 5.00
279,286: 279-Intro Mustang Sally ($1.00, 7/90) 6.00
NOTE: *Gene Colan* a-272-279, 285, 286. Horror/Sci-Fi-c 9, 11, 35, 39, 162.

LIFE WITH ARCHIE (The Married Life) (Magazine)
Archie Publications: Sept, 2010 - No. 37, Sept, 2014 ($3.99, magazine-size)
1-Continuation of Married Life stories from Archie #600-605; articles/interviews
 1 3 4 6 8 10
2-10 5.00
11-15,17-34 4.00
16-Kevin Keller gay wedding 10.00
36-($4.99, comic-size) Death of Archie; 5 covers by Allred, Francavilla, Hughes,
 Ramon Perez & Staples 3 5 6 8
37-($4.99, comic-size) One Year Later aftermath; 5 covers by Chiang, Edwards, Alex Ross,
 Simonson & Thompson 5.00
...: The Death of Archie: A Life Celebrated Commemorative Issue (2014, $9.99) reprints #36
 & #37 in magazine size; afterword by Jon Goldwater; cover gallery w/artist quotes 10.00

LIFE WITH MILLIE (Formerly A Date With Millie) (Modeling With Millie #21 on)
Atlas/Marvel Comics Group: No. 8, Dec, 1960 - No. 20, Dec, 1962
8-Teenage 13 26 39 104 201 310
9-11 10 20 30 88 144 220
12-20 9 18 27 52 126 190

LIFE WITH SNARKY PARKER (TV)
Fox Feature Syndicate: Aug, 1950
1-Early TV comic; photo-c from TV puppet show 36 72 108 211 343 475

LIFE ZERO
Ablaze Publishing: 2022 - No. 6, 2022 ($3.99)
1-5-Stefano Vietti-s/Marco Checchetto-a 4.00

LIGHT AND DARKNESS WAR, THE
Marvel Comics (Epic Comics): Oct, 1988 - No. 6, Dec, 1989 ($1.95, lim. series)
1-6 4.00

LIGHT BRIGADE, THE
DC Comics: 2004 - No. 4, 2004 ($5.95, limited series)
1-4-Archangels in World War II; Tomasi-s/Snejbjerg-a 6.00
TPB (2005, 2009, $19.99) r/series; cover galery 20.00

LIGHT FANTASTIC, THE (Terry Pratchett's)
Innovation Publishing: June, 1992 - No. 4, Sept, 1992 ($2.50, mini-series)
1-4: Adapts 2nd novel in Discworld series 4.00

LIGHTHOUSE (see Jules Verne's Lighthouse)

LIGHT IN THE FOREST (Disney)
Dell Publishing Co.: No. 891, Mar, 1958
Four Color 891-Movie, Fess Parker photo-c 6 12 18 42 79 115

LIGHTNING COMICS (Formerly Sure-Fire No. 1-3)

Ace Magazines: No. 4, Dec, 1940 - No. 13(V3#1), June, 1942
4-Characters continue from Sure-Fire 271 542 813 1734 2967 4200
5,6: 6-Dr. Nemesis begins 194 388 582 1242 2121 3000
V2#1-6: 2- "Flash Lightning" becomes "Lash..." 148 296 444 947 1624 2300
V3#1-Intro. Lightning Girl & The Sword 161 322 483 1030 1765 2500
NOTE: *Anderson* a-V2#6. *Mooney* c-V1#5, 6, V2#1-6, V3#1. Bondage c-V2#6. Lightning-c on all.

LIGHTNING COMICS PRESENTS
Lightning Comics: May, 1994 ($3.50)
1-Red foil-c distr. by Diamond Distr., 1-Black/yellow/blue-c distrib. by Capital Distr.,
 1-Red/yellow-c distributed by H. World, 1-Platinum 4.00

LIGHTSTEP
Dark Horse Comics (Eipix Comics): Nov, 2018 - No. 5, Apr, 2019 ($3.99, limited series)
1-5-Milos Slavkovic-s/a; Mirko Topalski-s 4.00

LI'L (These titles are listed under Little ...)

LILI
Image Comics: No. 0, 1999 ($4.95, B&W)
0-Bendis & Yanover-s 5.00

LILLITH (See Warrior Nun...)
Antarctic Press: Sept, 1996 - No. 3, Feb, 1997 ($2.95, limited series)
1-3: 1-Variant-c 5.00

LILO & STITCH (Disney)
Dynamite Entertainment: 2024 - Present ($3.99)
1-Greg Pak-s/Giulia Giacomino-a; multiple covers 4.00

LIMITED COLLECTORS' EDITION (See Famous First Edition, Marvel Treasury #28, Rudolph
The Red-Nosed Reindeer, & Superman Vs. The Amazing Spider-Man; becomes All-New
Collectors' Edition)
National Periodical Publications/DC Comics:
(#21-34,51-59: 84 pgs.; #35-41: 68 pgs.; #42-50: 60 pgs.)
C-21, Summer, 1973 - No. C-59, 1978 ($1.00) (10x13-1/2")
(Rudolph...C-20 (implied), 12/72)-See Rudolph The Red-Nosed Reindeer
C-21: Shazam (TV); r/Captain Marvel Jr. #11 by Raboy; C.C. Beck-c, biog. & photo
 3 6 9 21 33 45
C-22: Tarzan; complete origin reprinted from #207-210; all Kubert-c/a; Joe Kubert biography &
 photo inside 3 6 9 17 26 35
C-23: House of Mystery; Wrightson, N. Adams/Orlando. G. Kane/Wood, Toth, Aragones,
 Sparling reprints 4 8 12 28 47 65
C-24: Rudolph The Red-Nosed Reindeer 6 12 18 42 79 115
C-25: Batman; Neal Adams-c/a(r); G.A. Joker-r; Batman/Enemy Ace-r; Novick-a(r); has
 photos from TV show 4 8 12 28 47 65
C-26: See Famous First Edition C-26 (same contents)
C-27,C-29,C-31: C-27: Shazam (TV); G.A. Capt. Marvel & Mary Marvel-r; Beck-r.
 C-29: Tarzan; reprints "Return of Tarzan" from #219-223 by Kubert; Kubert-c.
 C-31: Superman; origin-r; Giordano-a; photos of George Reeves from 1950s TV show on
 inside b/c; Burnley, Boring-r 3 6 9 16 23 30
C-32: Ghosts (new-a) 4 8 12 23 37 50
C-33: Rudolph The Red-Nosed Reindeer(new-a) 6 12 18 37 66 95
C-34: Christmas with the Super-Heroes; unpublished Angel & Ape story by Oksner & Wood;
 Batman & Teen Titans-r 4 8 12 26 47 65
C-35: Shazam (TV); photo cover features TV's Captain Marvel, Jackson Bostwick; Beck-r;
 TV photos inside b/c 3 6 9 15 22 28
C-36: The Bible; all new adaptation beginning with Genesis by Kubert, Redondo & Mayer;
 Kubert-c 3 6 9 15 22 28
C-37: Batman; r-1946 Sundays; inside b/c photos of Batman TV show villains (all villain issue);
 r/G.A. Joker, Catwoman, Penguin, Two-Face, & Scarecrow stories plus 1946 Sundays-r)
 3 6 9 20 31 42
C-38: Superman; 1 pg. N. Adams; part photo-c; photos from TV show on inside back-c
 3 6 9 16 26 35
C-39: Secret Origins of Super-Villains; N. Adams-i(r); collection reprints 1950's Joker origin,
 Luthor origin from Adv. Comics #271, Captain Cold origin from Showcase #8 among others;
 G.A. Batman-r; Beck-r 3 6 9 17 26 35
C-40: Dick Tracy by Gould featuring Flattop; newspaper-r from 12/21/43 - 5/17/44;
 biog. of Chester Gould 6 12 18 36 63 90
C-41: Super Friends (TV); JLA-r(1965); Toth-c/a 3 6 9 16 24 32
C-42: Rudolph 3 6 9 18 28 38
C-43-C-47: C-43: Christmas with the Super-Heroes; Wrightson, S&K, Neal Adams-a.
 C-44: Batman; N. Adams-p(r) & G.A.-r; painted-c. C-45: More Secret Origins of
 Super-Villains; Flash-r/#105; G.A. Wonder Woman & Batman/Catwoman-r. C-46: Justice
 League of America(1963-r); 3 pgs. Toth-a. C-47: Superman Salutes the Bicentennial
 (Tomahawk interior); 2 pgs. new-a 3 6 9 14 20 26
C-48,C-49: C-48: Superman Vs. The Flash (Superman/Flash race); swipes-c to Superman
 #199; r/Superman #199 & Flash #175; 6 pgs. Neal Adams-a. C-49: Superboy & the Legion

	GD 2.0	VG 4.0	FN 6.0	VF 8.0	VF/NM 9.0	NM- 9.2
of Super-Heroes	3	6	9	16	23	30
C-50: Rudolph The Red-Nosed Reindeer; contains poster attached at the centerfold with a cardstock flap (1/2 price if poster is missing)	4	8	12	28	47	65
C-51: Batman; Neal Adams-c/a	3	6	9	24	33	45
C-52,C-57: C-52: The Best of DC; Neal Adams-c/a; Toth, Kubert-a. C-57: Welcome Back, Kotter-r(TV)(5/78) includes unpublished #11	3	6	9	16	23	30
C-53 thru C-56, C-58, C-60 thru C-62 (See All-New Collectors' Edition)						
C-59: Batman's Strangest Cases; N. Adams-r; Wrightson-r/Swamp Thing #7; N. Adams/Wrightson-c	3	6	9	17	26	35

NOTE: *All-r with exception of some special features and covers. Aparo a-52r; c-37. Grell c-49. Infantino a-25, 39, 44, 45, 52. Bob Kane r-25. Robinson r-25, 44. Sprang r-44. Issues #21-31, 35-39, 45, 48 have back cover cut-outs.*

LINDA (Everybody Loves…) (Phantom Lady No. 5 on)
Ajax-Farrell Publ. Co.: Apr-May, 1954 - No. 4, Oct-Nov, 1954

	GD 2.0	VG 4.0	FN 6.0	VF 8.0	VF/NM 9.0	NM- 9.2
1-Kamenish-a	26	52	78	154	252	350
2-Lingerie panel	16	32	48	94	147	200
3,4	14	28	42	82	121	160

LINDA CARTER, STUDENT NURSE (Also see Night Nurse)
Atlas Comics (AMI): Sept, 1961 - No. 9, Jan, 1963

	GD 2.0	VG 4.0	FN 6.0	VF 8.0	VF/NM 9.0	NM- 9.2
1-Al Hartley-c; 1st app. character who becomes Night Nurse in Daredevil V2 #58 (2004)	194	388	582	1242	2121	3000
2-9	32	64	96	188	307	425

LINDA LARK
Dell Publishing Co.: Oct-Dec, 1961 - No. 8, Aug-Oct, 1963

	GD 2.0	VG 4.0	FN 6.0	VF 8.0	VF/NM 9.0	NM- 9.2
1	4	8	12	23	37	50
2-8	3	6	9	15	22	28

LINE OF DEFENSE 3000AD (Based on the video game)
DC Comics: No. 0, 2012 (no price)

0-Brian Ching-a						3.00

LINUS, THE LIONHEARTED (TV)
Gold Key: Sept, 1965

	GD 2.0	VG 4.0	FN 6.0	VF 8.0	VF/NM 9.0	NM- 9.2
1 (10155-509)	6	12	18	38	69	100

LION, THE (See Movie Comics)

LION & THE EAGLE, THE
AfterShock Comics: Feb, 2022 - No. 4, Jun, 2022 ($7.99, 8-1/2" x 10-7/8", limited series)

1-4-Garth Ennis-s/PJ Holden-a						8.00

LIONHEART
Awesome Comics: Sept, 1999 - No. 2, Dec, 1999 ($2.99/$2.50)

1-Ian Churchill-story/a, Jeph Loeb-s; Coven app.						5.00
2-Flip book w/Coven #4						4.00

LION OF SPARTA (See Movie Classics)

LIPPY THE LION AND HARDY HAR HAR (TV)
Gold Key: Mar, 1963 (12¢) (See Hanna-Barbera Band Wagon #1)

	GD 2.0	VG 4.0	FN 6.0	VF 8.0	VF/NM 9.0	NM- 9.2
1 (10049-303)	7	14	21	49	92	135

LISA COMICS (TV)(See Simpsons Comics)
Bongo Comics: 1995 ($2.25)

	GD 2.0	VG 4.0	FN 6.0	VF 8.0	VF/NM 9.0	NM- 9.2
1-Lisa in Wonderland	2	4	6	9	12	15

LITERALS, THE (See Fables and Jack of Fables)
DC Comics (Vertigo): June, 2009 - No. 3, Aug, 2009 ($2.99)

1-3-Crossover with Fables #83-85 and Jack of Fables #33-35; Buckingham-c/a						3.00

LI'L ABNER (See Comics on Parade, Sparkle, Sparkler Comics, Tip Top Comics & Tip Topper)
United Features Syndicate: 1939 - 1940

	GD 2.0	VG 4.0	FN 6.0	VF 8.0	VF/NM 9.0	NM- 9.2
Single Series 4 ('39)	90	180	270	576	988	1400
Single Series 18 ('40) (#18 on inside, #2 on-c)	68	136	204	435	743	1050

LI'L ABNER (Al Capp's; continued from Comics on Parade #58)
Harvey Publ. No. 61-69 (2/49)/Toby Press No. 70 on: No. 61, Dec, 1947 - No. 97, Jan, 1955 (See Oxydol-Dreft in Promotional Comics section)

	GD 2.0	VG 4.0	FN 6.0	VF 8.0	VF/NM 9.0	NM- 9.2
61(#1)-Wolverton & Powell-a	30	60	90	177	289	400
62-65: 63-The Wolf Girl app. 65-Powell-a	16	32	48	92	144	195
66,67,69,70	15	30	45	86	133	180
68-Full length Fearless Fosdick-c/story	17	34	51	98	154	210
71-74,76,80	13	26	39	74	105	135
75,77-79,86,91-All with Kurtzman art; 86-Sadie Hawkins Day. 91-r/#77	15	30	45	83	124	165
81-85,87-90,92-94,96,97: 83-Evil-Eye Fleegle & Double Whammy app. 88-Cousin Weakeyes goes hunting. 94-Six lessons from Adam Lazonga. 96-Football issue	12	24	36	69	97	125
95-Full length Fearless Fosdick story	14	28	42	76	108	140

LI'L ABNER
Toby Press: 1951

	GD 2.0	VG 4.0	FN 6.0	VF 8.0	VF/NM 9.0	NM- 9.2
1	20	40	60	117	189	260

LI'L ABNER'S DOGPATCH (See Al Capp's...)

LITTLE AL OF THE F.B.I.
Ziff-Davis Publications: No. 10, 1950 (no month) - No. 11, Apr-May, 1951 (Saunders painted-c)

	GD 2.0	VG 4.0	FN 6.0	VF 8.0	VF/NM 9.0	NM- 9.2
10(1950)	24	48	72	142	234	325
11(1951)	18	36	54	105	165	225

LITTLE AL OF THE SECRET SERVICE
Ziff-Davis Publications: No. 10, 7-8/51; No, 2, 9-10/51; No. 3, Winter, 1951 (Saunders painted-c)

	GD 2.0	VG 4.0	FN 6.0	VF 8.0	VF/NM 9.0	NM- 9.2
10(#1)	21	42	63	124	202	280
2,3	16	32	48	92	144	195

LITTLE AMBROSE
Archie Publications: September, 1958

	GD 2.0	VG 4.0	FN 6.0	VF 8.0	VF/NM 9.0	NM- 9.2
1-Bob Bolling-c	20	40	60	120	195	270

LITTLE ANGEL
Standard (Visual Editions)/Pines: No. 5, Sept, 1954; No. 6, Sept, 1955 - No. 16, Sept, 1959

	GD 2.0	VG 4.0	FN 6.0	VF 8.0	VF/NM 9.0	NM- 9.2
5-Last pre-code issue	9	18	27	52	69	85
6-16	7	14	21	37	46	55

LITTLE ANNIE ROONEY (Also see Henry)
David McKay Publ.: 1935 (25¢, B&W dailies, 48 pgs.)(10"x10", cardboard-c)

	GD 2.0	VG 4.0	FN 6.0	VF 8.0	VF/NM 9.0	NM- 9.2
Book 1-Daily strip-r by Darrell McClure	39	78	117	231	378	525

LITTLE ANNIE ROONEY (See King Comics & Treasury of Comics)
David McKay/St. John/Standard: 1938; Aug, 1948 - No. 3, Oct, 1948

	GD 2.0	VG 4.0	FN 6.0	VF 8.0	VF/NM 9.0	NM- 9.2
Feature Books 11 (McKay, 1938)	40	80	120	244	402	560
1 (St. John)	17	34	51	98	154	210
2,3	10	20	30	56	76	95

LITTLE ARCHIE (The Adventures of... #13-on) (See Archie Giant Series Mag. #527, 534, 538, 545, 549, 556, 560, 566, 570, 583, 594, 596, 607, 609, 619)
Archie Publications: 1956 - No. 180, Feb, 1983 (Giants No. 3-84)

	GD 2.0	VG 4.0	FN 6.0	VF 8.0	VF/NM 9.0	NM- 9.2
1-(Scarce)	145	290	435	1196	2698	4200
2 (1957)	50	100	150	400	900	1400
3-5: 3-(1958)-Bob Bolling-c & giant issues begin	27	54	81	189	420	650
6-10	18	36	54	128	284	440
11-17,19,21 (84 pgs.)	13	26	39	91	201	310
18,20,22 (84 pgs.)-Horror/Sci-Fi-c	19	38	57	133	297	460
23-39 (68 pgs.)	9	18	27	58	114	170
40 (Fall/66)-Intro. Little Pureheart-c/s (68 pgs.)	8	16	24	62	126	190
41,44-Little Pureheart (68 pgs.)	7	14	21	48	89	130
42-Intro The Little Archies Band, ends #66 (68 pgs.)	8	16	24	52	99	145
43-1st Boy From R.I.V.E.R.D.A.L.E. (68 pgs.)	7	14	21	49	92	135
45-58 (68 pgs.)	6	12	18	37	66	95
59 (68 pgs.)-Little Sabrina begins	8	18	27	59	117	175
60-66 (68 pgs.)	6	12	18	37	66	75
67(9/71)-84: 84-Last 52pg. Giant-Size (2/74)	3	6	9	21	33	45
85-99	3	6	9	14	20	26
100	3	6	9	16	23	30
101-112,114-116,118-129	2	4	6	9	13	16
113,117,130: 113-Halloween Special issue(12/76). 117-Donny Osmond-c cameo 130-UFO cover (5/78)	2	4	6	11	16	20
131-150(1/80), 180(Last issue, 2/83)	2	4	6	8	10	12
151-179	1	3	4	6	8	10
…In Animal Land 1 (1957)	33	66	99	238	532	825
…In Animal Land 17 (Winter, 1957-58)-19 (Summer,1958)-Formerly Li'l Jinx	13	26	39	91	201	310
Archie Classics-The Adventures of Little Archie Vol. 1 TPB (2004, $10.95) reprints						11.00
Vol. 2 TPB (2008, $9.95) reprints plus new 22 pg. story with Bolling-a						10.00

NOTE: *Little Archie Band app. 42-66. Little Sabrina in 59-78,80-180*

LITTLE ARCHIE CHRISTMAS SPECIAL (See Archie Giant Series #581)

LITTLE ARCHIE COMICS DIGEST ANNUAL (…Magazine #5 on)
Archie Publications: 10/77 - No. 48, 5/91 (Digest-size, 128 pgs., later issues $1.35-$1.50)

	GD 2.0	VG 4.0	FN 6.0	VF 8.0	VF/NM 9.0	NM- 9.2
1(10/77)-Reprints	3	6	9	19	30	40
2(4/78,3(11/78)-Neal Adams-a. 3-The Fly-r by S&K	3	6	9	14	20	26
4(4/79) - 10	2	4	6	10	14	18
11-20	2	4	6	8	10	12
21-30: 28-Christmas-c	1	2	3	5	6	8
31-48: 40,46-Christmas-c						5.00

NOTE: *Little Jinx, Little Jughead & Little Sabrina in most issues.*

LITTLE ARCHIE DIGEST MAGAZINE
Archie Comics: July, 1991 - No. 21, Mar, 1998 ($1.50/$1.79/$1.89, digest size, bi-annual)

V2#1						6.00
2-10						4.00
11-21						4.00

LITTLE ARCHIE MYSTERY
Archie Publications: Aug, 1963 - No. 2, Oct, 1963 (12¢ issues)

	GD 2.0	VG 4.0	FN 6.0	VF 8.0	VF/NM 9.0	NM- 9.2
1	19	38	57	131	291	450
2	10	20	30	64	132	200

LITTLE ARCHIE, ONE SHOT
Archie Comic Publications: May, 2017 ($4.99, one-shot)

nn-Art Baltazar & Franco-s/a; 3 covers; Sabrina app.						5.00

LITTLE ASPIRIN (See Little Lenny & Wisco)
Marvel Comics (CnPC): July, 1949 - No. 3, Dec, 1949 (52 pgs.)

	GD 2.0	VG 4.0	FN 6.0	VF 8.0	VF/NM 9.0	NM- 9.2
1-Oscar app.; Kurtzman-a (4 pgs.)	26	52	78	154	252	350
2-Kurtzman-a (4 pgs.)	15	30	45	84	127	170
3-No Kurtzman-a	11	22	33	62	86	110

LITTLE AUDREY (Also see Playful…)
St. John Publ.: Apr, 1948 - No. 24, May, 1952

	GD 2.0	VG 4.0	FN 6.0	VF 8.0	VF/NM 9.0	NM- 9.2
1-1st app. Little Audrey	168	336	504	1075	1838	2600
2	50	100	150	315	533	750
3-5	28	56	84	165	270	375
6-10	20	40	60	115	190	260
11-20: 16-X-Mas-c	15	30	45	85	130	175
21-24	14	28	42	80	115	150

LITTLE AUDREY (See Harvey Hits #11, 19)
Harvey Publications: No. 25, Aug, 1952 - No. 53, April, 1957

	GD 2.0	VG 4.0	FN 6.0	VF 8.0	VF/NM 9.0	NM- 9.2
25-(Paramount Pictures Famous Star- on-c); 1st Harvey Casper and Baby Huey (1 month earlier than Harvey Comic Hits #60(9/52))	29	58	87	209	467	725
26-30: 26-28-Casper app.	9	18	27	60	120	180
31-40: 32-35-Casper app.	7	14	21	44	82	120
41-53	5	10	15	33	57	80
…Clubhouse 1 (9/61, 68 pg. Giant)-New stories & reprints	9	18	27	57	111	165

LITTLE AUDREY
Harvey Comics: Aug, 1992 - No. 8, July, 1994 ($1.25/$1.50)

V2#1						5.00
2-8						4.00

LITTLE AUDREY (...Yearbook)

Little Audrey #34 © HARV

Li'l Depressed Boy #4 © S. Struble

Little Eva #14 © STJ

	GD	VG	FN	VF	VF/NM	NM-
	2.0	4.0	6.0	8.0	9.0	9.2

St. John Publishing Co.: 1950 (50¢, 260 pgs.)

Contains 8 complete 1949 comics rebound; Casper, Alice in Wonderland, Little Audrey, Abbott & Costello, Pinocchio, Moon Mullins, Three Stooges (from Jubilee), Little Annie Rooney app. (Rare)

	206	412	618	1318	2259	3200

(Also see All Good & Treasury of Comics)

NOTE: *This book contains remaindered St. John comics; many variations possible.*

LITTLE AUDREY & MELVIN (Audrey & Melvin No. 62)
Harvey Publications: May, 1962 - No. 61, Dec, 1973

	GD	VG	FN	VF	VF/NM	NM-
1	9	18	27	63	129	195
2-5	4	8	12	25	40	55
6-10	3	6	9	21	33	45
11-20	3	6	9	16	23	30
21-40: 22-Richie Rich app.	2	4	6	13	18	22
41-50,55-61	2	4	6	9	13	16
51-54: All 52 pg. Giants	2	4	6	13	18	22

LITTLE AUDREY TV FUNTIME
Harvey Publ.: Sept, 1962 - No. 33, Oct, 1971 (#1-31: 68 pgs.; #32,33: 52 pgs.)

	GD	VG	FN	VF	VF/NM	NM-
1-Richie Rich app.	9	18	27	63	129	195
2,3: Richie Rich app.	4	8	12	27	44	60
4,5: 5-25¢ & 35¢ issues exist	4	8	12	23	37	50
6-10	3	6	9	17	26	35
11-20	3	6	9	14	19	24
21-33	2	4	6	11	16	20

LITTLE BAD WOLF (Disney; see Walt Disney's C&S #52, Walt Disney Showcase #21 & Wheaties)
Dell Publishing Co.: No. 403, June, 1952 - No. 564, June, 1954

	GD	VG	FN	VF	VF/NM	NM-
Four Color 403 (#1)	10	20	30	66	138	210
Four Color 473 (6/53), 564	7	14	21	44	82	120

LI'L BATTLESTAR GALACTICA (Classic 1978 TV series)
Dynamite Entertainment: 2014 ($3.99, one-shot)

1-Kid version spoof by Franco & Art Baltazar; covers by Baltazar & Garbowska						4.00

LITTLE BEAVER
Dell Publishing Co.: No. 211, Jan, 1949 - No. 870, Jan, 1958 (All painted-c)

	GD	VG	FN	VF	VF/NM	NM-
Four Color 211('49)-All Harman-a	12	24	36	79	170	260
Four Color 267,294,332(5/51)	8	16	24	56	108	160
3(10-12/51)-8(1-3/53)	5	10	15	31	53	75
Four Color 483(8-10/53),529	5	10	15	35	63	90
Four Color 612,660,695,744,817,870	5	10	15	34	60	85

LI'L BIONIC KIDS (Six Million Dollar Man and Bionic Woman)
Dynamite Entertainment: 2014 ($3.99, one-shot)

1-Kid version spoof; Bigfoot app.; Jerwa-s/McGinty-a; covers by Baltazar & Garbowska						4.00

LITTLE BIT
Jubilee/St. John Publishing Co.: Mar, 1949 - No. 2, June, 1949

	GD	VG	FN	VF	VF/NM	NM-
1-Kid humor	15	30	45	86	133	180
2	11	22	33	62	86	110

LI'L DEPRESSED BOY
Image Comics: Feb, 2011 - No. 16, Apr, 2013 ($2.99/$3.99)

1-12-S. Steven Struble-s/Sina Grace-a. 5-Guillory-c. 6-Adlard-c. 10-Childish Gambino app.						3.00
13-16-($3.99)						4.00
Vol. 0 (12/11, $9.99) reprints earlier stories from webcomics & anthologies; various-a						10.00

LI'L DEPRESSED BOY: SUPPOSED TO BE THERE TOO
Image Comics: Oct, 2014 - No. 5, Jun, 2015 ($3.99)

1-5-S. Steven Struble-s/Sina Grace-a						4.00

LITTLE DOT (See Humphrey, Li'l Max, Sad Sack, and Tastee-Freez Comics)
Harvey Publications: Sept, 1953 - No. 164, Apr, 1976

	GD	VG	FN	VF	VF/NM	NM-
1-Intro/1st app. Richie Rich & Little Lotta	1000	2000	3000	7500	13,500	19,500
2-1st app. Freckles & Pee Wee (Little Dot's poor friends)	187	374	561	1197	2049	2900
3	106	212	318	678	1164	1650
4	94	188	282	597	1025	1450
5-Origin dots on Little Dot's dress	106	212	318	678	1164	1650
6-Richie Rich, Little Lotta, & Little Dot all on cover; 1st Richie Rich cover featured	258	516	774	1651	2826	4000
7-10: 9-Last pre-code issue (1/55)	71	142	213	454	777	1100
11-20	39	78	117	231	378	525
21-30	18	36	54	107	169	230
31-40	14	28	42	80	115	150
41-50	11	22	33	62	86	110

	GD	VG	FN	VF	VF/NM	NM-
	2.0	4.0	6.0	8.0	9.0	9.2
51-60	9	18	27	52	69	85
61-80	4	8	12	27	44	60
81-100	3	6	9	19	30	40
101-141: 122-Richie Rich, Little Lotta, & Little Dot birthday-c. 134-Richie Rich, Little Lotta, Little Audrey & Little Dot lemonade-c	3	6	9	16	23	30
142-145: All 52 pg. Giants	3	6	9	17	26	35
146-164	2	4	6	11	16	20

NOTE: *Richie Rich & Little Lotta in all.*

LITTLE DOT
Harvey Comics: Sept, 1992 - No. 7, June, 1994 ($1.25/$1.50)

V2#1-Little Dot, Little Lotta, Richie Rich in all						5.00
2-7 ($1.50)						4.00

LITTLE DOT DOTLAND (Dot Dotland No. 62, 63)
Harvey Publications: July, 1962 - No. 61, Dec, 1973

	GD	VG	FN	VF	VF/NM	NM-
1-Richie Rich begins	12	24	36	83	182	280
2,3	7	14	21	44	82	120
4,5	5	10	15	35	63	90
6-10	4	8	12	23	37	50
11-20	3	6	9	17	26	35
21-30	3	6	9	16	23	30
31-50	3	6	9	17	26	35
51-54: All 52 pg. Giants	3	6	9	16	23	30
55-61	2	4	6	11	16	20

LITTLE DOT'S UNCLES & AUNTS (See Harvey Hits No. 4, 13, 24)
Harvey Enterprises: Oct, 1961; No. 2, Aug, 1962 - No. 52, Apr, 1974

	GD	VG	FN	VF	VF/NM	NM-
1-Richie Rich begins; 68 pgs. begin	15	30	45	103	227	350
2,3	8	16	24	51	96	140
4,5	5	10	15	35	63	90
6-10	5	10	15	31	53	75
11-20	4	8	12	23	37	50
21-37: Last 68 pg. issue	3	6	9	18	28	38
38-52: All 52 pg. Giants	3	6	9	16	23	30

LITTLE DRACULA
Harvey Comics: Jan, 1992 - No. 3, May, 1992 ($1.25, quarterly, mini-series)

1-3						4.00

LITTLE ENDLESS STORYBOOK, THE (See The Sandman titles and Delirium's Party)
DC Comics: 2001 ($5.95, Prestige format, one-shot)

nn-Jill Thompson-s/painted-a/c; puppy Barnabas searches for Delirium						10.00
HC (2011, $14.99) r/story plus original character sketches and merchandise design						15.00

LI'L ERNIE (Evil Ernie)
Dynamite Entertainment: 2014 ($3.99, one-shot)

1-Kid version spoof; Roger Langridge-s/a; covers by Baltazar & Garbowska						4.00

LITTLE EVA
St. John Publishing Co.: May, 1952 - No. 31, Nov, 1956

	GD	VG	FN	VF	VF/NM	NM-
1	23	46	69	136	223	310
2	14	28	42	81	118	155
3-5	10	20	30	58	79	100
6-10	9	18	27	50	65	80
11-31	8	16	24	44	57	70
3-D 1,2(10/53, 11/53, 25¢)-Both came w/glasses. 1-Infinity-c	19	38	57	112	179	245
I.W. Reprint #1-3,6-8: 1-r/Little Eva #28. 2-r/Little Eva #29. 3-r/Little Eva #24	2	4	6	10	14	18
Super Reprint #10,12('63),14,16,18('64): 18-r/Little Eva #25.	2	4	6	10	14	18

LI'L GENIUS (Formerly Super Brat; Summer Fun No. 54) (See Blue Bird & Giant Comics #3)
Charlton Comics: No. 6, 1954 - No. 52, 1/65; No. 53, 10/65; No. 54, 10/85 - No. 55, 1/86

	GD	VG	FN	VF	VF/NM	NM-
6 (#1)	11	22	33	62	86	110
7-10	7	14	21	37	46	55
11-1st app. Li'l Tomboy (10/56); same month as 1st issue of Li'l Tomboy (V14#92)	8	16	24	40	50	60
12-15,19,20	6	12	18	29	36	42
16,17-(68 pgs.)	6	12	18	40	50	60
18-(100 pgs., 10/58)	11	22	33	60	83	105
21-35: 34-Atomic bomb explosion	3	6	9	15	22	28
36-53	2	4	6	10	14	18
54,55 (Low print)						6.00

LI'L GHOST
St. John Publ. Co./Fago No. 1 on: 2/58; No. 2,1/59 - No. 3, Mar, 1959

	GD 2.0	VG 4.0	FN 6.0	VF 8.0	VF/NM 9.0	NM- 9.2

1(St. John) — 14, 28, 42, 76, 108, 140
2,3 — 9, 18, 27, 47, 61, 75

LITTLE GIANT COMICS
Centaur Publications: 7/38 - No. 3, 10/38; No. 4, 2/39 (132 pgs.) (6-3/4x4-1/2")

	GD 2.0	VG 4.0	FN 6.0	VF 8.0	VF/NM 9.0	NM- 9.2
1-B&W with color-c; stories, puzzles, magic	300	600	900	2010	3505	5000
2,3-B&W with color-c	258	516	774	1651	2826	4000
4 (6-5/8x9-3/8")(68 pgs., B&W inside)	271	542	813	1734	2967	4200

NOTE: Filchock c-2, 4. Gustavson a-1. Pinajian a-4. Bob Wood a-1.

LITTLE GIANT DETECTIVE FUNNIES
Centaur Publ.: Oct. 1938; No. 4, Jan, 1939 (6-3/4x4-1/2", 132 pgs., B&W)

	GD 2.0	VG 4.0	FN 6.0	VF 8.0	VF/NM 9.0	NM- 9.2
1-B&W with color-c	300	600	900	2010	3505	5000
4(1/39, B&W; color-c; 68 pgs., 6-1/2x9-1/2")-Eisner-r	258	516	774	1651	2826	4000

LITTLE GIANT MOVIE FUNNIES
Centaur Publ.: Aug, 1938 - No. 2, Oct, 1938 (6-3/4x4-1/2", 132 pgs., B&W)

	GD 2.0	VG 4.0	FN 6.0	VF 8.0	VF/NM 9.0	NM- 9.2
1-Ed Wheelan's "Minute Movies" reprints	271	542	813	1734	2967	4200
2-Ed Wheelan's "Minute Movies" reprints	206	412	618	1318	2259	3200

LITTLE GROUCHO (...the Red-Headed Tornado; ...Grouchy No. 2)
Reston Publ. Co.: No. 16; Feb-Mar, 1955 - No. 2, June-July, 1955 (See Tippy Terry)

	GD 2.0	VG 4.0	FN 6.0	VF 8.0	VF/NM 9.0	NM- 9.2
16, 1 (2-3/55)	12	24	36	67	94	120
2(6-7/55)	8	16	24	47	61	75

LITTLE HIAWATHA (Disney; see Walt Disney's C&S #143)
Dell Publishing Co.: No. 439, Dec, 1952 - No. 988, May-July, 1959

	GD 2.0	VG 4.0	FN 6.0	VF 8.0	VF/NM 9.0	NM- 9.2
Four Color 439 (#1)	9	18	27	58	114	170
Four Color 787 (4/57), 901 (5/58), 988	6	12	18	41	76	110

LITTLE IKE
St. John Publishing Co.: April, 1953 - No. 4, Oct, 1953

	GD 2.0	VG 4.0	FN 6.0	VF 8.0	VF/NM 9.0	NM- 9.2
1-Kid humor	15	30	45	84	127	170
2	9	18	27	47	61	75
3,4	8	16	24	40	50	60

LITTLE IODINE (See Giant Comic Album)
Dell Publ. Co.: No. 224, 4/49 - No. 257, 1949: 3-5/50 - No. 56, 4-6/62 (1-4-52pgs.)

	GD 2.0	VG 4.0	FN 6.0	VF 8.0	VF/NM 9.0	NM- 9.2
Four Color 224-By Jimmy Hatlo	13	26	39	89	195	300
Four Color 257	9	18	27	58	114	170
1(3-5/50)	10	20	30	66	138	210
2-5	5	10	15	35	63	90
6-10	5	10	15	30	50	70
11-20	4	8	12	27	44	60
21-30: 27-Xmas-c	4	8	12	23	37	50
31-40	3	6	9	21	33	45
41-56	3	6	9	19	30	40

LITTLE JACK FROST
Avon Periodicals: 1951

	GD 2.0	VG 4.0	FN 6.0	VF 8.0	VF/NM 9.0	NM- 9.2
1	18	36	54	103	162	220

LI'L JINX (Little Archie in Animal Land #17) (Also see Pep Comics #62)
Archie Publications: No. 1(#11), Nov, 1956 - No. 16, Sept, 1957

	GD 2.0	VG 4.0	FN 6.0	VF 8.0	VF/NM 9.0	NM- 9.2
1(#11)-By Joe Edwards; "First Issue" on cover	22	44	66	132	216	300
12(1/57)-16	14	28	42	82	121	160

LI'L JINX (See Archie Giant Series Magazine No. 223)

LI'L JINX CHRISTMAS BAG (See Archie Giant Series Mag. No. 195, 206, 219)

LI'L JINX GIANT LAUGH-OUT (See Archie Giant Series Mag. No. 176, 185)
Archie Publications: No. 33, Sept, 1971 - No. 43, Nov, 1973 (52 pgs.)

	GD 2.0	VG 4.0	FN 6.0	VF 8.0	VF/NM 9.0	NM- 9.2
33-43 (52 pgs.)	2	4	6	13	18	22

LITTLE JOE (See Popular Comics & Super Comics)
Dell Publishing Co.: No. 1, 1942

	GD 2.0	VG 4.0	FN 6.0	VF 8.0	VF/NM 9.0	NM- 9.2
Four Color 1	79	158	237	632	1416	2200

LITTLE JOE
St. John Publishing Co.: Apr, 1953

	GD 2.0	VG 4.0	FN 6.0	VF 8.0	VF/NM 9.0	NM- 9.2
1	11	22	33	62	86	110

LI'L KIDS (Also see Li'l Pals)
Marvel Comics Group: 8/70 - No. 2, 10/70; No. 3, 11/71 - No. 12, 6/73

	GD 2.0	VG 4.0	FN 6.0	VF 8.0	VF/NM 9.0	NM- 9.2
1	8	16	24	55	105	155
2-9	4	8	12	28	47	65
10-12-Calvin app.	5	10	15	30	50	70

LITTLE KING
Dell Publishing Co.: No. 494, Aug, 1953 - No. 677, Feb, 1956

	GD 2.0	VG 4.0	FN 6.0	VF 8.0	VF/NM 9.0	NM- 9.2
Four Color 494 (#1)	10	20	30	64	132	200
Four Color 597, 677	6	12	18	41	76	110

LITTLE LANA (Formerly Lana)
Marvel Comics (MjMC): No. 8, Nov, 1949; No. 9, Mar, 1950

	GD 2.0	VG 4.0	FN 6.0	VF 8.0	VF/NM 9.0	NM- 9.2
8,9	22	44	66	132	216	300

LITTLE LENNY
Marvel Comics (CDS): June, 1949 - No. 3, Nov, 1949

	GD 2.0	VG 4.0	FN 6.0	VF 8.0	VF/NM 9.0	NM- 9.2
1-Little Aspirin app.	19	38	57	111	176	240
2,3	13	26	39	74	105	135

LITTLE LIZZIE
Marvel Comics (PrPl)/Atlas (OMC): 6/49 - No. 5, 4/50; 9/53 - No. 3, Jan, 1954

	GD 2.0	VG 4.0	FN 6.0	VF 8.0	VF/NM 9.0	NM- 9.2
1-Kid humor	21	42	63	124	202	280
2-5	12	24	36	67	94	120
1 (9/53, 2nd series by Atlas)-Howie Post-c	14	28	42	78	112	145
2,3	10	20	30	54	72	90

LITTLE LOTTA (See Harvey Hits No. 10)
Harvey Publications: 11/55 - No. 110, 11/73; No. 111, 9/74 - No. 120, 5/76
V2#1, Oct, 1992 - No. 4, July, 1993 ($1.25)

1-Richie Rich (r) & Little Dot begin — 69, 138, 207, 552, 1251, 1950

	GD 2.0	VG 4.0	FN 6.0	VF 8.0	VF/NM 9.0	NM- 9.2
2,3	19	38	57	133	297	460
4,5	11	22	33	73	157	240
6-10	7	14	21	46	86	125
11-20	5	10	15	35	63	90
21-40	4	8	12	23	37	50
41-60	3	6	9	18	28	38
61-80: 62-1st app. Nurse Jenny	3	6	9	15	22	28
81-99	2	4	6	11	16	20
100-103: All 52 pg. Giants	3	6	9	14	19	24
104-120	2	4	6	8	10	12
V2#1-4 (1992-93)						4.00

NOTE: No. 121 was advertised, but never released.

LITTLE LOTTA FOODLAND
Harvey Publications: 9/63 - No. 14, 10/67; No. 15, 10/68 - No. 29, Oct, 1972

	GD 2.0	VG 4.0	FN 6.0	VF 8.0	VF/NM 9.0	NM- 9.2
1-Little Lotta, Little Dot, Richie Rich, 68 pgs. begin	11	22	33	73	157	240
2,3	6	12	18	38	69	100
4,5	5	10	15	30	50	70
6-10	4	8	12	23	37	50
11-20	3	6	9	16	23	30
21-26: 26-Last 68 pg. issue	3	6	9	14	20	25
27,28: Both 52 pgs.	2	4	6	11	16	20
29-(36 pgs.)	2	4	6	8	11	14

LITTLE LULU (Formerly Marge's Little Lulu)
Gold Key 207-257/Whitman 258 on: No. 207, Sept, 1972 - No. 268, Mar, 1984

	GD 2.0	VG 4.0	FN 6.0	VF 8.0	VF/NM 9.0	NM- 9.2
207,209,220-Stanley-r. 207-1st app. Henrietta	2	4	6	13	18	22
208,210-219: 208-1st app. Snobbily, Wilbur's butler	2	4	6	9	13	16
221-240,242-249, 250(r/#166), 251-254(r/#206)	2	4	6	8	10	12
241,263-Stanley-r	2	4	6	8	11	14
255-257(Gold Key): 256-r/#212	1	3	4	6	8	10
258,259,262(50¢-c),264(2/82),265(3/82) (Whitman)	2	4	6	11	16	20
260-(9/80)(Whitman pre-pack only - low distribution)	15	30	45	103	227	350
261-(11/80)(Whitman pre-pack only)	7	14	21	44	82	120
262-(1/81) Variant 40¢-c price error (reg. ed. 50¢-c)	5	9	14	15	22	28
266-268 (All #90028 on-c; no date, no date code; 3-pack): 266(7/83). 267(8/83).						
268(3/84)-Stanley-r	3	6	9	17	26	35

LITTLE MARY MIXUP (See Comics On Parade)
United Features Syndicate: No. 10, 1939 - No. 26, 1940

	GD 2.0	VG 4.0	FN 6.0	VF 8.0	VF/NM 9.0	NM- 9.2
Single Series 10, 26	39	78	117	231	378	525

LITTLE MAX COMICS (Joe Palooka's Pal; see Joe Palooka)
Harvey Publications: Oct, 1949 - No. 73, Nov, 1961

	GD 2.0	VG 4.0	FN 6.0	VF 8.0	VF/NM 9.0	NM- 9.2
1-Infinity-c; Little Dot begins; Joe Palooka on-c	32	64	96	190	310	430
2-Little Dot app.; Joe Palooka on-c	15	30	45	86	133	180
3-Little Dot app.; Joe Palooka on-c	10	20	30	58	79	100
4-10: 5-Little Dot app., 1pg.	9	18	27	47	61	75
11-20	8	16	24	40	50	60
21-40: 23-Little Dot app. 38-r/#20	6	12	18	31	38	45
41-62,66	3	6	9	17	26	35
63-65,67-73-Include new five pg. Richie Rich stories. 70-73-Little Lotta app.	3	6	9	18	28	38

LI'L MENACE
Fago Magazine Co.: Dec, 1958 - No. 3, May, 1959

	GD 2.0	VG 4.0	FN 6.0	VF 8.0	VF/NM 9.0	NM- 9.2
1-Peter Rabbit app.	12	24	36	69	97	125
2-Peter Rabbit (Vincent Fago's)	8	16	24	42	54	65
3	7	14	21	35	43	50

LITTLE MERMAID, THE (Walt Disney's...; also see Disney's...)
W. D. Publications (Disney): 1990 (no date given)($5.95, no ads, 52 pgs.)

	GD 2.0	VG 4.0	FN 6.0	VF 8.0	VF/NM 9.0	NM- 9.2
nn-Adapts animated movie	3	4	6	8	10	
nn-Comic version ($2.50)	1	2	3	5	6	8

LITTLE MERMAID, THE (Also see Disney's The Little Mermaid Limited Series)
Disney Comics: 1992 - No. 4, 1992 ($1.50, mini-series)

1-Based on movie						6.00
2-4						4.00
1-4: 2nd printings sold at Wal-Mart w/different-c						4.00
Set of #1-4 in unopened 4-issue Collector's Pack						60.00

LITTLE MERMAID, THE
Disney Comics: Oct, 2019 - No. 3, Feb, 2020 ($3.99, limited series)

1-3-Adapts the movie; Castellucci-s/Lavina-a/c						4.00

LITTLE MISS MUFFET
Best Books (Standard Comics)/King Features Synd.: No. 11, Dec, 1948 - No. 13, March, 1949

	GD 2.0	VG 4.0	FN 6.0	VF 8.0	VF/NM 9.0	NM- 9.2
11-Strip reprints; Fanny Cory-c/a	15	30	45	83	124	165
12,13-Strip reprints; Fanny Cory-a	10	20	30	54	72	90

LITTLE MISS SUNBEAM COMICS
Magazine Enterprises/Quality Bakers of America: June-July, 1950 - No. 4, Dec-Jan, 1950-51

	GD 2.0	VG 4.0	FN 6.0	VF 8.0	VF/NM 9.0	NM- 9.2
1	21	42	63	124	202	280
2-4	14	28	42	78	112	145
...Advs. In Space ('55)	8	16	24	44	57	70

LITTLE MONSTERS, THE (See March of Comics #423, Three Stooges #17)
Gold Key: Nov, 1964 - No. 44, Feb, 1978

	GD 2.0	VG 4.0	FN 6.0	VF 8.0	VF/NM 9.0	NM- 9.2
1	6	12	18	38	69	100
2	3	6	9	20	31	42
3-10	3	6	9	16	24	32
11-20	3	6	9	15	21	26
21-30: 19-21-Reprints	2	4	6	11	16	20
31-44: 34-39,43-Reprints	2	4	6	8	11	14

LITTLE MONSTERS (Movie)
Now Comics: 1989 - No. 6, June, 1990 ($1.75)

1-6: Photo-c from movie						5.00

Little Lotta #27 © HARV

The Little Monsters #1 © GK

Livewire #6 © VAL

	GD	VG	FN	VF	VF/NM	NM-
	2.0	4.0	6.0	8.0	9.0	9.2

LITTLE MONSTERS
Image Comics: Mar, 2022 - No. 13, May, 2023 ($3.99)

	GD	VG	FN	VF	VF/NM	NM-
1-13-Jeff Lemire-s/Dustin Nguyen-a/c						4.00

LITTLE NEMO (See Cocomalt, Future Comics, Help, Jest, Kayo, Punch, Red Seal, & Superworld; most by Winsor McCay Jr., son of famous artist) (Other McCay books: see Little Sammy Sneeze & Dreams of the Rarebit Fiend)

LITTLE NEMO (…in Slumberland)
McCay Features/Nostalgia Press('69): 1945 (11x7-1/4", 28 pgs., B&W)

	GD	VG	FN	VF	VF/NM	NM-
1905 & 1911 reprints by Winsor McCay	14	28	42	76	108	140
1969-70 (Exact reprint)	2	4	6	9	12	15

LITTLE NEMO: RETURN TO SLUMBERLAND
IDW Publishing: Aug, 2014 - No. 4, Feb, 2015 ($3.99)

	GD	VG	FN	VF	VF/NM	NM-
1-4-New stories in McCay style; Shanower-s/Rodriguez-a in all. 1-Multiple covers						4.00

LITTLE ORPHAN ANNIE (See Annie, Famous Feature Stories, Marvel Super Special, Merry Christmas…, Popular Comics, Super Book #7, 11, 23 & Super Comics)

LITTLE ORPHAN ANNIE
David McKay Publ./Dell Publishing Co.: No. 7, 1937 - No. 3, Sept-Nov, 1948; No. 206, Dec, 1948

	GD	VG	FN	VF	VF/NM	NM-
Feature Books(McKay) 7-(1937) (Rare)	142	284	426	909	1555	2200
Four Color 12(1941)	90	180	270	576	988	1400
Four Color 18(1943)-Flag-c	71	142	213	454	777	1100
Four Color 52(1944)	27	54	81	189	420	650
Four Color 76(1945)	20	40	60	144	317	490
Four Color 107(1946)	18	36	54	128	284	440
Four Color 152(1947)	12	24	36	82	179	275
1(3-5/48)-r/strips from 5/7/44 to 7/30/44	12	24	36	81	176	270
2-r/strips from 7/21/40 to 9/9/40	9	18	27	57	111	165
3-r/strips from 9/10/40 to 11/9/40	8	16	24	55	105	155
Four Color 206(12/48)	8	16	24	52	99	145

LI'L PALS (Also see Li'l Kids)
Marvel Comics Group: Sept, 1972 - No. 5, May, 1973

	GD	VG	FN	VF	VF/NM	NM-
1	8	16	24	54	102	150
2-5: 5-Super Rabbit story	5	10	15	30	50	70

LI'L PAN (Formerly Rocket Kelly; becomes Junior Comics with #9)(Also see Wotalife Comics)
Fox Feature Syndicate: No. 6, Dec-Jan, 1946-47 - No. 8, Apr-May, 1947

	GD	VG	FN	VF	VF/NM	NM-
6	16	32	48	92	144	195
7,8: 7-Atomic bomb story; robot-c	14	28	42	81	118	155

LITTLE PEOPLE (Also see Darby O'Gill & the…)
Dell Publishing Co.: No. 485, Aug-Oct, 1953 - No. 1062, Dec, 1959 (Walt Scott's)

	GD	VG	FN	VF	VF/NM	NM-
Four Color 485 (#1)	9	18	27	58	114	170
Four Color 573(7/54), 633(6/55)	6	12	18	37	66	95
Four Color 692(3/56),753(11/56),809(7/57),868(12/57),908(5/58),959(12/58),1062						
	5	10	15	34	60	85

LITTLE RASCALS
Dell Publishing Co.: No. 674, Jan, 1956 - No. 1297, Mar-May, 1962

	GD	VG	FN	VF	VF/NM	NM-
Four Color 674 (#1)	10	20	30	67	141	215
Four Color 778(3/57),825(8/57)	6	12	18	34	69	100
Four Color 883(3/58),936(9/58),974(3/59),1030(9/59),1079(2-4/60),1137(9-11/60)						
	5	10	15	35	63	90
Four Color 1174(3-5/61),1224(10-12/61),1297	5	10	15	33	57	80

LI'L RASCAL TWINS (Formerly Nature Boy)
Charlton Comics: No. 6, 1957 - No. 18, Jan, 1960

	GD	VG	FN	VF	VF/NM	NM-
6-Li'l Genius & Tomboy in all	7	14	21	37	46	55
7-18: 7-Timmy the Timid Ghost app.	4	8	12	18	22	25

LITTLE RED HOT (CHANE OF FOOLS)
Image Comics: Feb, 1999 - No. 3, Apr, 1999 ($2.95/$3.50, B&W, limited series)

	GD	VG	FN	VF	VF/NM	NM-
1-3-Dawn Brown-s/a. 2,3-($3.50-c)						4.00
The Foolish Collection TPB ($12.95) r/#1-3						13.00

LITTLE RED HOT: BOUND
Image Comics: July, 2001 - No. 3, Nov, 2001 ($2.95, color, limited series)

	GD	VG	FN	VF	VF/NM	NM-
1-3-Dawn Brown-s/a.						4.00

LITTLE ROQUEFORT COMICS (See Paul Terry's Comics #105)
St. John Publishing Co.(all pre-code)/Pines No. 10: June, 1952 - No. 9, Oct, 1953; No. 10, Summer, 1958

	GD	VG	FN	VF	VF/NM	NM-
1-By Paul Terry; Funny Animal	15	30	45	90	140	190
2	9	18	27	50	65	80
3-10: 10-CBS Television Presents on-c	7	14	21	37	46	55

LITTLE SAD SACK (See Harvey Hits No. 73, 76, 79, 81, 83)

Harvey Publications: Oct, 1964 - No. 19, Nov, 1967

	GD	VG	FN	VF	VF/NM	NM-
1-Richie Rich app. on cover only	5	10	15	34	60	85
2-10	3	6	9	17	26	35
11-19	3	6	9	15	22	28

LITTLE SCOUTS
Dell Publishing Co.: No. 321, Mar, 1951 - No. 587, Oct, 1954

	GD	VG	FN	VF	VF/NM	NM-
Four Color 321 (#1, 3/51)	7	14	21	48	89	130
2(10-12/51) - 6(10-12/52)	4	8	12	25	40	55
Four Color 462,506,550,587: 506-Infinity cover	5	10	15	30	50	70

LITTLE SHOP OF HORRORS SPECIAL (Movie)
DC Comics: Feb, 1987 ($2.00, 68 pgs.)

	GD	VG	FN	VF	VF/NM	NM-
1-Colan-c/a	2	4	6	11	16	20

LI'L SONJA (Red Sonja)
Dynamite Entertainment: 2014 ($3.99, one-shot)

	GD	VG	FN	VF	VF/NM	NM-
1-Kid version spoof; Jim Zub-s/Joel Carroll-a; covers by Baltazar & Garbowska						4.00

LITTLE SPUNKY
I. W. Enterprises: No date (1958) (10¢)

	GD	VG	FN	VF	VF/NM	NM-
1-r/Frisky Fables #1	3	6	9	14	19	24

LITTLE STAR
Oni Press: Feb, 2005 - No. 6, Dec, 2005 ($2.99, B&W, limited series)

	GD	VG	FN	VF	VF/NM	NM-
1-6-Andi Watson-s/a						3.00
TPB (4/06, $19.95) r/#1-6						20.00

LITTLE STOOGES, THE (The Three Stooges' Sons)
Gold Key: Sept, 1972 - No. 7, Mar, 1974

	GD	VG	FN	VF	VF/NM	NM-
1-Norman Maurer cover/stories in all	3	6	9	18	28	38
2-7	2	4	6	13	18	22

LITTLEST OUTLAW (Disney)
Dell Publishing Co.: No. 609, Jan, 1955

	GD	VG	FN	VF	VF/NM	NM-
Four Color 609-Movie, photo-c	7	14	21	48	89	130

LITTLEST PET SHOP (Based on the Hasbro toys)
IDW Publishing: May, 2014 - No. 5, Sept, 2014 ($3.99)

	GD	VG	FN	VF	VF/NM	NM-
1-5: 1-Ball-s/Peña-a; multiple covers. 2-5-Two covers on each						4.00
… Spring Cleaning (4/15, $7.99) Four short stories; Ball-s; art by various						8.00

LITTLEST SNOWMAN, THE
Dell Publishing Co.: No. 755, 12/56; No. 864, 12/57; 12-2/1963-64

	GD	VG	FN	VF	VF/NM	NM-
Four Color 755,864, 1(1964)	6	12	18	38	69	100

LI'L TOMBOY (Formerly Fawcett's Funny Animals; see Giant Comics #3)
Charlton Comics: V14#92, Oct, 1956; No. 93, Mar, 1957 - No. 107, Feb, 1960

	GD	VG	FN	VF	VF/NM	NM-
V14#92-Ties as 1st app. with Li'l Genius #11	7	14	21	37	46	55
93-107: 97-Atomic Bunny app.	5	10	15	24	29	34

LI'L VAMPI (Vampirella)
Dynamite Entertainment: 2014 ($3.99, one-shot)

	GD	VG	FN	VF	VF/NM	NM-
1-Kid version spoof; Trautmann-s/Garbowska-a; covers by Baltazar & Garbowska						4.00

LI'L WILLIE COMICS (Formerly & becomes Willie Comics #22 on)
Marvel Comics: No. 20, July, 1949 - No. 21, Sept, 1949

	GD	VG	FN	VF	VF/NM	NM-
20,21: 20-Little Aspirin app.	19	38	57	111	176	240

LITTLE WOMEN (See Power Record Comics)

LIVE IT UP
Spire Christian Comics (Fleming H. Revell Co.): 1973, 1974,1976 (39-49 cents)

	GD	VG	FN	VF	VF/NM	NM-
nn-1973 Edition	2	4	6	13	18	22
nn-1974,1976 Editions	2	4	6	8	11	14

LIVEWIRE
Valiant Entertainment: Dec, 2018 - No. 12, Nov, 2019 ($3.99)

	GD	VG	FN	VF	VF/NM	NM-
1-12: 1-Vita Ayala-s/Raúl Allén-a. 5-8-Kano-a. 9-12-Tana Ford-a						4.00

LIVEWIRES
Marvel Comics: Apr, 2005 - No. 6, Sept, 2005 ($2.99, limited series)

	GD	VG	FN	VF	VF/NM	NM-
1-6-Adam Warren-s/c; Rick Mays-a						3.00
…: Clockwork Thugs, Yo (2005, $7.99, digest) r/#1-6						8.00

LIVING BIBLE, THE
Living Bible Corp.: Fall, 1945 - No. 3, Spring, 1946

	GD	VG	FN	VF	VF/NM	NM-
1-The Life of Paul; all have L. B. Cole-c	53	106	159	334	567	800
2-Joseph & His Brethren; Jonah & the Whale	37	74	111	222	361	500
3-Chaplains At War (classic-c)	55	110	165	352	601	850

	GD 2.0	VG 4.0	FN 6.0	VF 8.0	VF/NM 9.0	NM- 9.2			GD 2.0	VG 4.0	FN 6.0	VF 8.0	VF/NM 9.0	NM- 9.2

LIVING WITH THE DEAD
Dark Horse Comics: Oct, 2007 - No. 3, Nov, 2007 ($2.99, limited series)
1-3-Zombies; Mike Richardson-s/Ben Stenbeck-a/Richard Corben-c ... 3.00

LOADED BIBLE
Image Comics: Apr, 2006; May, 2007; Feb, 2008 ($4.99)
...: Jesus vs. Vampires (4/06) Tim Seeley-s/Nate Bellegarde-a ... 5.00
...2: Blood of Christ (5/07) Seeley/Mike Norton-a. ...3: Communion (2/08) 5.00

LOADED BIBLE: BLOOD OF MY BLOOD
Image Comics: Mar, 2022 - No. 6, Jul, 2022 ($3.99, limited series)
1-6-Tim Seeley & Steve Orlando-s/Giuseppe Cafaro-a ... 4.00

LOBO
Dell Publishing Co.: Dec, 1965; No. 2, Oct, 1966
1-1st black character to have his own title ... 52 104 156 446 933 1450
2 ... 25 50 75 175 388 600

LOBO (Also see Action #650, Adventures of Superman, Demon (2nd series), Justice League, L.E.G.I.O.N., Mister Miracle, Omega Men #3 & Superman #41)
DC Comics: Nov, 1990 - No. 4, Feb, 1991 ($1.50, color, limited series)
1-(99c)-Giffen plots/Breakdowns in all ... 2 4 6 11 16 20
1-2nd printing ... 4.00
2-4: 2-Legion '89 spin-off. 1-4 have Bisley painted covers & art ... 6.00
... Blazing Chain of Love 1 (9/92, $1.50)-Denys Cowan-c/a; Alan Grant scripts, ...Convention Special 1 (1993, $1.75), ...: Portrait of a Victim 1 (1993, $1.75) ... 4.00
... Paramilitary Christmas Special 1 (1991, $2.39, 52 pgs.) Bisley-c/a ... 5.00
...: Portrait of a Bastich TPB (2008, $19.99) r/#1-4 & Lobo's Back 1-4 ... 20.00

LOBO (Also see Showcase '95 #9)
DC Comics: Dec, 1993 - No. 64, Jul, 1999 ($1.75/$1.95/$2.25/$2.50, mature)
1 ($2.95)-Foil enhanced-c; Alan Grant scripts begin ... 1 3 4 6 8 10
2-64: 2-7-Alan Grant scripts. 50-Lobo vs. the DCU. 58-Giffen-a ... 4.00
#0-(10/94)-Origin retold; published between #9 & #10 ... 4.00
#1,000,000 (11/98) 853rd Century x-over ... 4.00
Annual 1 (1993, $3.50, 68 pgs.)-Bloodlines x-over ... 5.00
Annual 2 (1994, $3.50)-21 artists (20 listed on-c); Alan Grant script; Elseworlds story ... 5.00
Annual 3 (1995, $3.95)-Year One story ... 5.00
.../Authority: Holiday Hell TPB (2006, $17.99) r/Lobo Paramilitary Christmas Special; Authority/Lobo: Jingle Hell and Spring Break Massacre; WildStorm Winter Special ... 18.00
...Big Babe Spring Break Special (Spr., '95, $1.95)-Balent-a ... 6.00
...Bounty Hunting for Fun and Profit ('95)-Bisley-c ... 6.00
... Chained (5/97, $2.50)-Alan Grant story ... 5.00
.../Deadman: The Brave And The Bald (2/95, $3.50) ... 5.00
.../Demon: Helloween (12/96, $2.25)-Giarrano-a ... 4.00
...Fragtastic Voyage 1 ('97, $5.95)-Mejia painted-c/a 1 3 4 6 8 10
...Gallery (9/95, $3.50)-pin-ups. ... 1 3 4 6 8 10
...In the Chair 1 (8/94, $1.95, 36 pgs.), ...I Quit-(12/95, $2.25) ... 4.00
.../Judge Dredd ('95, $4.95). ... 5.00
...Lobocop 1 (2/94, $1.95)-Alan Grant scripts; painted-c ... 4.00

LOBO (Younger version from New 52 Justice League #23.2)
DC Comics: Dec, 2014 - No. 13, Feb, 2016 ($2.99)
1-Bunn-s/Brown-a ... 6.00
2-13: 2-5-Bunn-s/Brown-a. 4-Superman app. 10,11-Sinestro app. 13-Hal Jordan app. ... 4.00
Annual 1 (9/15, $4.99) Bunn-s/Rocha-a; the Sinestro Corps app.; leads into Lobo #10 ... 5.00

LOBO: (Title Series), DC Comics
--A CONTRACT ON GAWD, 4/94 - 7/94 (mature) 1-4: Alan Grant scripts. 3-Groo cameo ... 4.00
--DEATH AND TAXES, 10/96 - No. 4, 1/97, 1-4-Giffen/Grant scripts ... 4.00
--GOES TO HOLLYWOOD, 8/96 ($2.25), 1-Grant scripts ... 6.00
--HIGHWAY TO HELL, 1/10 - No. 2, 2/10 ($6.99), 1,2-Scott Ian-s/Sam Kieth-a/c ... 7.00
TPB (2010, $19.99) r/#1,2; intro. by Scott Ian; Kieth B&W art pages ... 20.00
--INFANTICIDE, 10/92 - 1/93 ($1.50, mature), 1-4-Giffen-c/a; Grant scripts ... 4.00
--/ MASK, 2/97 - No. 2, 3/97 ($5.95), 1,2 ... 1 3 4 6 8 10
--/ ROAD RUNNER, 8/17 ($4.99), 1-Bill Morrison-s/Kelley Jones-a/c; Wile E. Coyote app.
 ... 1 3 4 6 8 10
--'S BACK, 5/92 - No. 4, 11/92 ($1.50, mature), 1-4: 1-Has 3 outer covers. Bisley painted-c 1,2. 4-Sam Kieth-c; all have Giffen plots/breakdown & Grant scripts ... 4.00
Trade paperback (1993, $9.95)-r/1-4 ... 10.00
--THE DUCK, 6/97 ($1.95), 1-A. Grant-s/V. Semeiks & R. Kryssing-a
 ... 1 3 4 6 8 10
--UNAMERICAN GLADIATORS, 6/93 - No. 4, 9/93 ($1.75, mature), 1-4-Mignola-c; Grant/Wagner scripts
 ... 4.00
--UNBOUND, 8/03 - No. 6, 5/04 ($2.95), 1-6-Giffen/Horley-c/a. 4-6-Ambush Bug app. ... 4.00

LOBSTER JOHNSON (One-shots) (See B.P.R.D. and Hellboy titles)
Dark Horse Comics
...: A Chain Forged in Life (7/15, $3.50) Mignola & Arcudi-s; Nixey & Nowlan-a ... 4.00
...: Caput Mortuum (9/12, $3.50) Mignola & Arcudi-s; Zonjic-c/a ... 4.00
...: Garden of Bones (1/17, $3.99) Mignola & Arcudi-s; Stephen Green-a/Zonjic-c ... 4.00
...: Mangekyo (8/17, $3.99) Mignola & Arcudi-s; Stenbeck-a/Zonjic-c ... 4.00
...: Satan Smells a Rat (5/13, $3.50) Mignola & Arcudi-s; Nowlan-c/a ... 4.00
...: The Forgotten Man (4/16, $3.50) Mignola & Arcudi-s; Snejbjerg-a/Zonjic-c ... 4.00
...: The Glass Mantis (12/15, $3.50) Mignola & Arcudi-s; Fejzula-a/Zonjic-c ... 4.00

LOBSTER JOHNSON: A SCENT OF LOTUS (See B.P.R.D. and Hellboy titles)
Dark Horse Comics: Jul, 2013 - No. 2, Aug, 2013 ($3.50, limited series)
1,2-Mignola & Arcudi-s; Fiumara-a/Zonjic-c ... 4.00

LOBSTER JOHNSON: GET THE LOBSTER
Dark Horse Comics: Feb, 2014 - No. 5, Aug, 2014 ($3.99, limited series)
1-5-Mignola & Arcudi-s; Zonjic-a/c ... 4.00

LOBSTER JOHNSON: METAL MONSTERS OF MIDTOWN
Dark Horse Comics: May, 2016 - No. 3, Jul, 2016 ($3.50/$3.99, limited series)
1-3-Mignola & Arcudi-s; Zonjic-a/c. 1-$3.50. 2,3-$3.99 ... 4.00

LOBSTER JOHNSON: THE BURNING HAND
Dark Horse Comics: Jan, 2012 - No. 5, May, 2012 ($3.50, limited series)
1-5-Mignola & Arcudi-s; Zonjic-a. 1-Two covers by Dave Johnson & Mignola ... 4.00

LOBSTER JOHNSON: THE IRON PROMETHEUS
Dark Horse Comics: Sept, 2007 - No. 5, Jan, 2008 ($2.99, limited series)
1-Mignola-s/c; Armstrong-a ... 1 3 4 6 8 10
2-5-Mignola-s/c; Armstrong-a ... 5.00

LOBSTER JOHNSON: THE PIRATE'S GHOST
Dark Horse Comics: Mar, 2017 - No. 3, May, 2017 ($3.99, limited series)
1-3-Mignola & Arcudi-s; Zonjic-a/c ... 4.00

LOCAL MAN
Image Comics: Feb, 2023 - Present ($3.99)
1-9-Seeley-s/Fleecs-a; flip-cover and story on all ... 4.00
...: Gold (8/23, $4.99) Gold foil cover homage to Deathmate series ... 5.00

LOCKE & KEY
IDW Publ.: Feb, 2008 - No. 6, July, 2008 ($3.99, limited series)
1-Joe Hill-s/Gabriel Rodriguez-a ... 4 8 12 23 37 50
1-Second printing ... 1 2 3 5 6 8
2 ... 1 3 4 6 8 10
3-6 ... 1 2 3 5 6 8
...: 15th Anniversary - Only Bad Edition #1 (7/23, $7.99) r/#1; bonus art, cover gallery
 ... 1 2 3 5 6 8
...: Free Comic Book Day Edition (5/11) r/story from Crown of Shadows ... 4.00
...: Grindhouse (8/12, $3.99) EC-style; Hill-s/Rodriguez-a; bonus Guide to the Keyhouse
 ... 2 4 6 11 16 20
...: Guide to the Known Keys (1/12, $3.99) Key to the Moon; bonus Guide to the Keys
 ... 2 4 6 9 12 15
...: Welcome to Lovecraft Legacy Edition #1 (8/10, $1.00) r/#1; synopsis of later issues 4.00
...: Welcome to Lovecraft Special Edition #1 SC (9/09, $5.99) Hill-s/Rodriguez-a; script; back-up story with final art from Seth Fisher 1 3 4 6 8 10

LOCKE & KEY: ALPHA
IDW Publ.: Aug, 2013 - No. 2, Oct, 2013 ($7.99, limited series)
1,2-Series conclusion; Joe Hill-s/Gabriel Rodriguez-a ... 8.00

LOCKE & KEY: CLOCKWORKS
IDW Publ.: Jun, 2011 - No. 6, Apr, 2012 ($3.99, limited series)
1-6: 1-Hill-s/Rodriguez-a; set in 1776 ... 4.00

LOCKE & KEY: CROWN OF SHADOWS
IDW Publ.: Nov, 2009 - No. 6, Apr, 2010 ($3.99, limited series)
1-6-Joe Hill-s/Gabriel Rodriguez-a ... 6.00

LOCKE & KEY: DOG DAYS
IDW Publ.: Oct, 2019 ($4.99, one-shot)
nn - Joe Hill-s/Gabriel Rodriguez-a; bonus preview of Dying is Easy #1 ... 5.00

LOCKE & KEY: HEAD GAMES
IDW Publ.: Jan, 2009 - No. 6, Jun, 2009 ($3.99, limited series)
1-6-Joe Hill-s/Gabriel Rodriguez-a. 3-EC style-c ... 6.00

LOCKE & KEY: ...IN PALE BATTALIONS GO...
IDW Publ.: Aug, 2020 - No. 3, Oct, 2020 ($3.99, limited series)
1-3-Joe Hill-s/Gabriel Rodriguez-a ... 4.00

LOCKE & KEY: KEYS TO THE KINGDOM
IDW Publ.: Sept, 2010 - No. 6, Mar, 2011 ($3.99, limited series)
1-6-Joe Hill-s/Gabriel Rodriguez-a ... 4.00

LOCKE & KEY: OMEGA
IDW Publ.: Nov, 2012 - No. 5, May, 2013 ($3.99, limited series)
1-5-Next to Final series; Joe Hill-s/Gabriel Rodriguez-a ... 4.00

LOCKE & KEY: SMALL WORLD
IDW Publ.: Dec, 2016 ($4.99, one-shot)
1-Set in early 1900s; Joe Hill-s/Gabriel Rodriguez-a; multiple covers ... 5.00

LOCKE & KEY / THE SANDMAN UNIVERSE
IDW Publ.: No. 0, Oct, 2020 - Nov, 2021 ($3.99/$6.99)
0-"Open the Moon" by Joe Hill-s/Gabriel Rodriguez-a; r/Sandman #1 ... 4.00
...: Hell & Gone 1 (IDW, 4/21, $6.99) Hill-s/Rodriguez-a; the imprisoned Dream app. ... 7.00
...: Hell & Gone 2 (DC, 11/21, $6.99) Hill-s/Rodriguez-a ... 7.00

LOCKJAW (From the Inhumans)
Marvel Comics: Apr, 2018 - No. 4, Jul, 2018 ($3.99, limited series)
1-4-Kibblesmith-s/Villa-a; D-Man app. 1,2-Ka-Zar app. 3-Spider-Ham app. ... 4.00

LOCKJAW AND THE PET AVENGERS (Also see Tails of the Pet Avengers)
Marvel Comics: July, 2009 - No. 4, Oct, 2009 ($2.99, limited series)
1-4-Lockheed, Frog Thor, Zabu, Lockjaw and Redwing team up; 2 covers on each ... 3.00

LOCKJAW AND THE PET AVENGERS UNLEASHED
Marvel Comics: May, 2010 - No. 4, Aug, 2010 ($2.99, limited series)
1-4-Eliopoulos-s/Guara-a; 2 covers on each ... 3.00

LOCO (Magazine) (Satire)
Satire Publications: Aug, 1958 - V1#3, Jan, 1959
V1#1-Chic Stone-a ... 9 18 27 50 65 80
V1#2,3-Severin-a, 2 pgs. Davis; 3-Heath-a ... 7 14 21 37 46 55

LODGER
IDW Publishing (Black Crown): Oct, 2018 - No. 5, Feb, 2019 ($3.99, B&W)
1-5-Davis & Maria Lapham-s/David Lapham-a. 1-Covers by Lapham & Sienkiewicz ... 4.00

LOGAN (Wolverine)
Marvel Comics: May, 2008 - No. 3, Jul, 2008 ($3.99, limited series)
1-3-Vaughan-s/Risso-a/c; regular & B&W editions for each ... 4.00

LOGAN: PATH OF THE WARLORD
Marvel Comics: Feb, 1996 ($5.95, one-shot)

Local Man #4 © Seeley & Fleecs

Logan #2 © MAR

Loki (2023 series) #1 © MAR

	GD 2.0	VG 4.0	FN 6.0	VF 8.0	VF/NM 9.0	NM- 9.2
1-John Paul Leon-a	1	2	3	5	6	8

LOGAN: SHADOW SOCIETY
Marvel Comics: 1996 ($5.95, one-shot)

1						6.00

LOGAN'S RUN
Marvel Comics Group: Jan, 1977 - No. 7, July, 1977

	GD 2.0	VG 4.0	FN 6.0	VF 8.0	VF/NM 9.0	NM- 9.2
1: 1-5-Based on novel & movie	3	6	9	14	20	26
2-5,7: 6,7-New stories adapted from novel	2	4	6	8	10	12
6-1st Thanos solo story (back-up) by Zeck (6/77)(See Iron Man #55 for debut)	4	8	12	28	47	65
6-(35c-c variant, limited distribution)	14	28	42	96	211	325
7-(35c-c variant, limited distribution)	10	20	30	69	147	225

NOTE: *Austin* a-6i. *Gulacy* c-6. *Kane* c-7p. *Perez* a-1-5p; c-1-5p. *Sutton* a-6p, 7p.

LOIS & CLARK, THE NEW ADVENTURES OF SUPERMAN
DC Comics: 1994 ($9.95, one-shot)

	GD 2.0	VG 4.0	FN 6.0	VF 8.0	VF/NM 9.0	NM- 9.2
1-r/Man of Steel #2, Superman Ann. 1, Superman #9 & 11, Action #600 & 655, Adventures of Superman #445, 462 & 466	1	3	4	6	8	10

LOIS LANE (Also see Daring New Adventures of Supergirl, Showcase #9,10 & Superman's Girlfriend...)
DC Comics: Aug, 1986 - No. 2, Sept, 1986 ($1.50, 52 pgs.)

1,2-Morrow-c/a in each						4.00

LOIS LANE
DC Comics: Sept, 2019 - No. 12, Sept, 2020 ($3.99)

1-12: 1-Rucka-s/Perkins-a; The Question (Renee) app. 3-The Question (Charlie) app. 6-Event Leviathan tie-in						4.00

LOKI (Thor)(Also see Vote Loki)
Marvel Comics: Sept, 2004 - No. 4, Nov, 2004 ($3.50)

	GD 2.0	VG 4.0	FN 6.0	VF 8.0	VF/NM 9.0	NM- 9.2
1-Rodi-s/Ribic-a/c in all	2	4	6	8	10	12
2-4						4.00
HC (2005, $17.99, with dustjacket) oversized r/#1-4; original proposal and sketch pages						18.00
SC (2007, $12.99) r/#1-4; original proposal and sketch pages						13.00

LOKI (Thor)
Marvel Comics: Dec, 2010 - No. 4, May, 2011 ($3.99, limited series)

1-4-Aguirre-Sacasa-s/Fiumara-a. 2-Balder dies						4.00

LOKI (Thor)
Marvel Comics: Sept, 2019 - No. 5, Jan, 2020 ($3.99, limited series)

1-5: 1-4-Kibblesmith-s/Bazaldua-a. 2,4-Tony Stark app. 5-Wolverine app.						4.00

LOKI (Thor)
Marvel Comics: Aug, 2023 - No. 4, Nov, 2023 ($4.99/$3.99, limited series)

1-($4.99) Watters-s/Peralta-a; Thor app.						5.00
2-4-($3.99) 3-Wiccan & Hulkling app. 4-Bullseye app.						4.00

LOKI: AGENT OF ASGARD (Thor)
Marvel Comics: Apr, 2014 - No. 17, Oct, 2015 ($2.99/$3.99)

1-5: 1-Ewing-s/Garbett-a/Frison-c; Avengers app.						3.00
6-17-($3.99) 6-9-Axis tie-ins. 6,7-Doctor Doom app. 14-17-Secret Wars tie-ins						4.00

LOKI: RAGNAROK AND ROLL (not the character from Thor)
BOOM! Studios: Feb, 2014 - No. 4, Jun, 2014 ($3.99, limited series)

1,2-Esquivel-s/Gaylord-a/Ziritt-c						4.00

LOLA XOXO
Aspen MLT: Apr, 2014 - No. 6, Mar, 2015 ($3.99)

1-6-Siya Oum-s/a; multiple covers						4.00
The Art of Lolo XOXO 1 (9/16, $5.99) Siya Oum sketch pages and cover gallery						6.00

LOLA XOXO VOLUME 2
Aspen MLT: Jul, 2017 - No. 6, Jan, 2018 ($3.99)

1-6-Siya Oum-s/a; multiple covers						4.00

LOLA XOXO VOLUME 3
Aspen MLT: Jul, 2019 - No. 6, Aug, 2020 ($3.99)

1-6-Siya Oum-s/a; multiple covers						4.00

LOLA XOXO: WASTELAND MADAM
Aspen MLT: Apr, 2015 - No. 4, Feb, 2016 ($3.99)

1-4-Vince Hernandez-s/Siya Oum-a; multiple covers						4.00

LOLLIPOP KIDS, THE
AfterShock Comics: Oct, 2018 - No. 5, Apr, 2019 ($3.99)

1-5-Adam Glass-s/Diego Yapur-a/Robert Hack-c						4.00

LOLLY AND PEPPER
Dell Publishing Co.: No. 832, Sept, 1957 - July, 1962

	GD 2.0	VG 4.0	FN 6.0	VF 8.0	VF/NM 9.0	NM- 9.2
Four Color 832(#1)	7	14	21	48	89	130
Four Color 940,978,1086,1206	5	10	15	30	50	70
01-459-207 (7/62)	3	6	9	18	28	38

LOMAX (See Police Action)

LONE
Dark Horse Comics: Sept, 2003 - No. 6, Mar, 2004 ($2.99)

1-6-Stuart Moore-s/Jerome Opeña-a/Templesmith-c						3.00

LONE EAGLE (The Flame No. 5 on)
Ajax/Farrell Publications: Apr-May, 1954 - No. 4, Oct-Nov, 1954

	GD 2.0	VG 4.0	FN 6.0	VF 8.0	VF/NM 9.0	NM- 9.2
1	16	32	48	94	147	200
2-4: 3-Bondage-c	10	20	30	58	79	100

LONE GUNMEN, THE (From the X-Files)
Dark Horse Comics: June, 2001 ($2.99, one-shot)

1-Paul Lee-a; photo-c						3.00

LONELY HEART (Formerly Dear Lonely Hearts; Dear Heart #15 on)
Ajax/Farrell Publ. (Excellent Publ.): No. 9, Mar, 1955 - No. 14, Feb, 1956

	GD 2.0	VG 4.0	FN 6.0	VF 8.0	VF/NM 9.0	NM- 9.2
9-Kamen-*esque*-a; (Last precode)	18	36	54	105	165	225
10-14	14	28	42	78	112	145

LONELY RECEIVER
AfterShock Comics: Sept, 2020 - No. 5, Jan, 2021 ($4.99/$3.99)

1-($4.99) Zac Thompson-s/Jen Hickman-a/c						5.00
2-5-($3.99)						4.00

LONE RANGER, THE (See Ace Comics, Aurora, Dell Giants, Future Comics, Golden Comics Digest #48, King Comics, Magic Comics & March of Comics #165, 174, 193, 208, 225, 238, 310, 322, 338, 350)

LONE RANGER, THE
Dell Publishing Co.: No. 3, 1939 - No. 167, Feb, 1947

	GD 2.0	VG 4.0	FN 6.0	VF 8.0	VF/NM 9.0	NM- 9.2
Large Feature Comic 3(1939)-Heigh-Yo Silver; text with illus. by Robert Weisman; also exists as a Whitman #710 (scarce)	284	568	852	1818	3109	4400
Large Feature Comic 7(1939)-Illustr. by Henry Vallely; Hi-Yo Silver the Lone Ranger to the Rescue; also exists as Whitman #715 (scarce)	265	530	795	1694	2897	4100
Feature Book 21(1940), 24(1941)	106	212	318	673	1162	1650
Four Color 82(1945)	40	80	120	296	673	1050
Four Color 98(1945),118(1946)	28	56	84	202	451	700
Four Color 125(1946),136(1947)	19	38	57	133	297	460
Four Color 151,167(1947)	16	32	48	112	249	385

LONE RANGER, THE (Movie, radio & TV; Clayton Moore starred as Lone Ranger in the movies; No. 1-37: strip reprints)(See Dell Giants)
Dell Publishing Co.: Jan-Feb, 1948 - No. 145, May-July, 1962

	GD 2.0	VG 4.0	FN 6.0	VF 8.0	VF/NM 9.0	NM- 9.2
1 (36 pgs.)-The Lone Ranger, his horse Silver, companion Tonto & his horse Scout begin	71	142	213	568	1284	2000
2 (52 pgs. begin, end #41)	27	54	81	194	435	675
3-5	22	44	66	154	340	525
6,7,9,10	16	32	48	112	249	385
8-Origin retold; Indian back-c begin, end #35	19	38	57	131	291	450
11-20: 11- "Young Hawk" Indian boy serial begins, ends #145	12	24	36	80	173	265
21,22,24-31: 51-Reprint. 31-1st Mask logo	10	20	30	64	132	200
23-Origin retold	12	24	36	80	173	265
32-37: 32-Painted-c begin. 36-Animal photo back-c begin, end #49. 37-Last newspaper-r issue; new outfit; red shirt becomes blue; most known copies show the blue shirt on-c and inside	9	18	27	58	114	170
37-Variant issue; Long Ranger wears a red shirt on-c and inside. A few copies of the red shirt outfit were printed before catching the mistake and changing the color to blue (rare)	16	32	48	110	243	375
38-41 (All 52 pgs.) 38-Paul S. Newman-s (wrote most of the stories #38-on)	8	16	24	54	102	150
42-50 (36 pgs.)	7	14	21	46	86	125
51-74 (52 pgs.): 56-One pg. origin story of Lone Ranger & Tonto. 71-Blank inside-c	6	12	18	42	79	115
75,77-99: 79-X-mas-c	6	12	18	40	73	105
76-Classic flag-c	7	14	21	44	82	120
100	7	14	21	46	86	125
101-111: Last painted-c	6	12	18	37	66	95
112-Clayton Moore photo-c begin, end #145	15	30	45	103	227	350
113-117: 117-10¢ &15¢-c exist	9	18	27	60	120	180
118-Origin Lone Ranger, Tonto, & Silver retold; Dan Reid origin; Special Silver anniversary issue	19	38	57	131	291	450
119-140: 139-Fran Striker-s	8	16	24	56	108	160

	GD 2.0	VG 4.0	FN 6.0	VF 8.0	VF/NM 9.0	NM- 9.2

141-145 | 9 | 18 | 27 | 58 | 114 | 170

NOTE: *Hank Hartman* painted c(signed)-65, 66, 70, 75, 82; unsigned-64?, 67-69?, 71, 72, 73?, 74?, 76-78, 80, 81, 83-91, 92?, 93-111. *Ernest Nordli* painted c(signed)-42, 50, 52, 53, 56, 59, 60; unsigned-39-41, 44-49, 51, 54, 55, 57, 58, 61-63?

LONE RANGER, THE
Gold Key (Reprints in #13-20): 9/64 - No. 16, 12/69; No. 17, 11/72; No. 18, 9/74 - No. 28, 3/77

1-Retells origin	7	14	21	46	86	125
2	3	6	9	21	33	45
3-10: Small Bear-r in #6-12. 10-Last 12¢ issue	3	6	9	19	30	40
11-17	3	6	9	15	22	28
18-28	2	4	6	11	16	20
Golden West 1(30029-610, 10/66)-Giant; r/most Golden West #3 including Clayton Moore photo front/back-c	6	12	18	40	73	105

LONE RANGER
Dynamite Entertainment: 2006 - No. 25, 2011 ($2.99/$3.50/$3.99)

1-Retells origin; Carriello-a/Matthews-s; badge cover by Cassaday						4.00
1-Variant mask cover by Cassaday						5.00
1-Baltimore Comic-Con 2006 variant cover with masked face and horse silhouette						12.00
1-Directors' Cut ($4.99) r/#1 with comments at page bottoms, script and sketches						5.00
2-23: 2-Origin continues; Tonto app.						3.50
24-($3.99)						4.00
25-($4.99) Carriello-a						5.00
... and Tonto 1-4 (200-2010, $4.99) Cassaday-c						5.00
... Volume 1: Now and Forever TPB (2007, $19.99) r/#1-6; sketch pages						20.00

LONE RANGER: VOLUME 1
Dynamite Entertainment: 2018 - No. 5, 2019 ($3.99, limited series)

1-5-Mark Russell-s/Bob Q-a. 1-Cover by Cassaday, Allred & Francavilla						4.00

LONE RANGER, THE (Volume 2)
Dynamite Entertainment: 2012 - No. 25, 2014 ($3.99)

1-25: 1-Parks-s/Polls-a; two covers by Ross & Francavilla. 2-21-Francavilla-c						4.00
Annual 2013 ($4.99) Denton-s/Triano-a/Worley-c						5.00

LONE RANGER AND TONTO, THE
Topps Comics: Aug, 1994 - No. 4, Nov, 1994 ($2.50, limited series)

1-4: 3-Origin of Lone Ranger; Tonto leaves; Lansdale story, Truman-c/a in all.						4.00
1-4: Silver logo. 1-Signed by Lansdale and Truman						6.00
Trade paperback (1/95, $9.95)						10.00

LONE RANGER AND ZORRO: THE DEATH OF ZORRO, THE
Dynamite Entertainment: 2011 - No. 5, 2011 ($3.99, limited series)

1-5: 1-Four covers by Alex Ross and others; Parks-s/Polls-a						4.00

LONE RANGER GREEN HORNET
Dynamite Entertainment: 2016 - No. 5, 2016 ($3.99, limited series)

1-5-Uslan-s/Timpano-a. 3-Jesse Owens as the new Lone Ranger						4.00

LONE RANGER'S COMPANION TONTO, THE (TV)
Dell Publishing Co.: No. 312, June, 1951 - No. 33, Nov-Jan/58-59 (All painted-c)

Four Color 312(#1, 1/51)	11	22	33	75	160	245
2(8-10/51),3: #2 titled "Tonto"	6	12	18	42	79	115
4-10	5	10	15	35	63	90
11-20	5	10	15	31	53	75
21-33	4	8	12	28	47	65

NOTE: *Ernest Nordli* painted c(signed)-2, 7; unsigned-3-6, 8-11, 12?, 13, 14, 18?, 22-24? See Aurora Comic Booklets.

LONE RANGER'S FAMOUS HORSE HI-YO SILVER, THE (TV)
Dell Publishing Co.: No. 369, Jan, 1952 - No. 36, Oct-Dec, 1960 (All painted-c, most by Sam Savitt) (Lone Ranger appears in most issues)

Four Color 369(#1)-Silver's origin as told by The Lone Ranger	11	22	33	72	154	235
Four Color 392(#2, 4/52)	7	14	21	44	82	120
3(7-9/52)-10(4-6/52)	5	10	15	31	53	75
11-36	4	8	12	27	44	60

LONE RANGER, THE : SNAKE OF IRON
Dynamite Entertainment: 2012 - No. 4, 2013 ($3.99, limited series)

1-4: 1-Dixon-s/Polls-a/Calero-a						4.00

LONE RANGER, THE : VINDICATED
Dynamite Entertainment: 2014 - No. 4, 2015 ($3.99, limited series)

1-4-Justin Gray-s/Rey Villegas-a. 1-Cassaday-c. 2-4-Laming-c						4.00

LONE RIDER (Also see The Rider)
Superior Comics(Farrell Publ.): Apr, 1951 - No. 26, Jul, 1955 (#3-on: 36 pgs.)

1 (52 pgs.)-The Lone Rider & his horse Lightnin' begin; Kamen-*ish*-a begins	39	78	117	231	378	525
2 (52 pgs.)-The Golden Arrow begins (origin)	20	40	60	117	189	260
3-6: 6-Last Golden Arrow	19	38	57	109	172	235
7-Golden Arrow becomes Swift Arrow; origin of his shield	20	40	60	114	182	250
8-Origin Swift Arrow	18	36	54	107	169	230
9,10	12	24	36	69	97	125
11-14	10	20	30	54	72	90
15-Golden Arrow origin-r from #2, changing name to Swift Arrow	12	24	36	67	94	120
16-20,22-26: 23-Apache Kid app.	9	18	27	50	65	80
21-3-D effect-c	18	36	54	105	165	225

LONERS, THE
Marvel Comics: June, 2007 - No. 6, Jan, 2008 ($2.99, limited series)

1-6-Cebulski-s/Moline-a/Pearson-c; Lightspeed, Spider-Woman, Ricochet app.						3.00
...: The Secret Lives of Super Heroes TPB (2008, $14.99) r/#1-6; sketch pages						15.00

LONE WOLF AND CUB
First Comics: May, 1987 - No. 45, Apr, 1991 ($1.95-$3.25, B&W, deluxe size)

1-Frank Miller-c & intro.; reprints manga series by Koike & Kojima	3	6	9	14	19	24

1-2nd print, 3rd print, 2-2nd print						4.00
2-12: 6-72 pgs. origin issue	1	3	4	6	8	10
13-38,40: 40-Ploog-c						6.00
39-($5.95, 120 pgs.)-Ploog-c	1	2	3	5	6	8
41-44: 41-($3.95, 84 pgs.)-Ploog-c. 42-Ploog-c						6.00
45-Last issue; low print	3	6	9	16	23	30
Deluxe Edition ($19.95, B&W)						20.00

NOTE: *Sienkiewicz* c-13-24. *Matt Wagner* c-25-30.

LONE WOLF AND CUB (Trade paperbacks)
Dark Horse Comics: Aug, 2000 - No. 28 ($9.95, B&W, 4" x 6", approx. 300 pgs.)

1-Collects First Comics reprint series; Frank Miller-c						18.00
1-(2nd printing)						12.00
1-(3rd-5th printings)						10.00
2,3-(1st printings)						12.00
2,3-(2nd printings)						10.00
4-28						10.00

LONE WOLF 2100 (Also see Reveal)
Dark Horse Comics: May, 2002 - No. 11, Dec, 2003 ($2.99, color)

1-New homage to Lone Wolf and Cub; Kennedy-s/Velasco-a						4.00
2-11						3.00
...: The Red File (1/03, $2.99) character and story background files						3.00
... Vol. 1 - Shadows on Saplings TPB (2003, $12.95, 6" x 9") r/#1-4						13.00
... Vol. 2 - The Language of Chaos TPB (2003, $12.95, 6" x 9") r/#5-8, Dirty Tricks short story from Reveal						13.00

LONE WOLF 2100: CHASE THE SETTING SUN
Dark Horse Comics: Jan, 2016 - No. 4, Apr, 2016 ($3.99, color)

1-4-Heisserer-s/Sepulveda-a						4.00

LONG BOW (...Indian Boy)(See Indians & Jumbo Comics #141)
Fiction House Mag. (Real Adventures Publ.): 1951 - No. 8, Fall, 1952; No. 9, Spring, 1953

1-Most covers by Maurice Whitman	22	44	66	132	216	300
2	12	24	36	69	97	125
3-9	10	20	30	58	79	100

LONG HOT SUMMER, THE
DC Comics (Milestone): Jul, 1995 - No. 3, Sept, 1995 ($2.95/$2.50, lim. series)

1-3: 1-($2.95-c). 2,3-($2.50-c)	1	3	4	6	8	10

LONG JOHN SILVER & THE PIRATES (Formerly Terry & the Pirates)
Charlton Comics: No. 30, Aug, 1956 - No. 32, March, 1957 (TV)

30-32: Whitman-c	14	28	42	76	108	140

LONGSHOT (Also see X-Men, 2nd Series #10)
Marvel Comics: Sept, 1985 - No. 6, Feb, 1986 (60¢, limited series)

1-Art Adams/Whilce Portacio-c/a in all	4	8	12	27	44	60
2-5: 4-Spider-Man app.	3	6	9	11	16	20
6-Double size	3	6	9	14	20	26
Trade Paperback (1989, $16.95)-r/#1-6						17.00

LONGSHOT
Marvel Comics: Feb, 1998 ($3.99, one-shot)

1-DeMatteis-s/Zulli-a						4.00

LONGSHOT SAVES THE MARVEL UNIVERSE
Marvel Comics: Jan, 2014 - No. 4, Feb, 2014 ($2.99, limited series)

1-4-Hastings-s/Camagni-a/Nakayama-a. 3,4-Superior Spider-Man app.						3.00

LOOKING GLASS WARS: HATTER M
Image Comics (Desperado): Dec, 2005 - No. 4, Nov, 2006 ($3.99)

1-4-Templesmith-a/c						4.00

LOONEY TUNES (2nd Series) (TV)
Gold Key/Whitman: April, 1975 - No. 47, June, 1984

1-Reprints	3	6	9	21	33	45
2-10: 2,4-reprints	2	4	6	13	18	22
11-20: 16-reprints	2	4	6	9	12	15
21-30	2	4	6	8	8	10
31,32,36-42(2/82)	1	2	3	5	6	8
33-(8/80)-35 (Whitman pre-pack only; scarce)	3	6	9	21	33	45
43(4/82),44(6/83) (low distribution)	2	4	6	9	13	16
45-47 (All #90296 on-c; nd, nd code, pre-pack)	5(8/83)	46(3/84)	47(6/84)			
	3	6	9	14	20	26

LOONEY TUNES (3rd Series) (TV)
DC Comics: Apr, 1994 - Present ($1.50/$1.75/$1.95/$1.99/$2.25/$2.50/$2.99)

1-10,120: 1-Marvin Martian-c/sty; Bugs Bunny, Roadrunner, Daffy begin. 120-($2.95-C)						5.00
11-119,121-187: 23-34-($1.75-c). 35-43-($1.95-c). 44-Begin $1.99-c. 93-Begin $2.25-c. 100-Art by various incl. Kyle Baker, Marie Severin, Darwyn Cooke, Jill Thompson						4.00
188-277: 188-Begin $2.99-c; Scooby-Doo spoof. 193-Christmas-c. 237-Duck Dodgers						4.00
...Back In Action Movie Adaptation (12/03, $3.95) photo-c						4.00

LOONEY TUNES AND MERRIE MELODIES COMICS ("Looney Tunes" #166(8/55) on) (Also see Porky's Duck Hunt)
Dell Publishing Co.: 1941 - No. 246, July-Sept, 1962

1-Porky Pig, Bugs Bunny, Daffy Duck, Elmer Fudd, Mary Jane & Sniffles, Pat Patsy and Pete begin (1st comic book app. of each). Bugs Bunny story by Win Smith (early Mickey Mouse artist)	1390	2780	4170	10,600	22,300	34,000
2 (11/41)	200	400	600	1650	3725	5800
3-Kandi the Cave Kid begins by Walt Kelly; also in #4-6,8,11,15	139	278	417	1112	2506	3900
4-Kelly-a	129	258	387	1032	2316	3600
5-Bugs Bunny The Super-Duper Rabbit story (1st funny animal super hero, 3/42; also see Coo Coo); Kelly-a	100	200	300	800	1800	2800
6,8: 8-Kelly-a	79	158	237	632	1416	2200
7,9,10: 9-Painted-c. 10-Flag-c	54	108	162	432	966	1500
11,15-Kelly-a; 15-Christmas-c	54	108	162	432	966	1500
12-14,16-19	40	80	120	296	673	1050
20-25: Pat, Patsy & Pete by Walt Kelly in all. 20-War Bonds-c						

Lone Ranger (2006 series) #14 © Classic Media

Looney Tunes #219 © WB

Lords of the Jungle #1 © DYN

	GD 2.0	VG 4.0	FN 6.0	VF 8.0	VF/NM 9.0	NM- 9.2
	34	68	102	245	548	850
26-30	24	48	72	168	372	575
31-40: 33-War Bonds-c. 39-Christmas-c	19	38	57	133	297	460
41-50: 45-War Bonds-c	15	30	45	100	220	340
51-60: 51-Christmas-c	12	24	36	81	176	270
61-80	9	18	27	58	114	170
81-99: 87,99-Christmas-c	7	14	21	49	92	135
100-New Year's-c	8	16	24	55	105	155
101-120	9	18	27	60	120	180
121-150: 124-New Year's-c. 133-Tattoo-c	5	10	15	35	63	90
151-200: 159-Christmas-c	5	10	15	33	57	80
201-240	5	10	15	31	53	75
241-246	5	10	15	33	57	80

LOONY SPORTS (Magazine)
3-Strikes Publishing Co.: Spring, 1975 (68 pgs.)

1-Sports satire	2	4	6	8	11	14

LOOSE CANNON (Also see Action Comics Annual #5 & Showcase '94 #5)
DC Comics: June, 1995 - No. 4, Sept, 1995 ($1.75, limited series)

1-4: Adam Pollina-a. 1-Superman app. 4.00

LOOY DOT DOPE
United Features Syndicate: No. 13, 1939

Single Series 13	37	74	111	218	354	490

LORD JIM (See Movie Comics)

LORD OF THE JUNGLE
Dynamite Entertainment: 2012 - No. 15, 2013 ($1.00/$3.99)

1-($1.00) Retelling of Tarzan's origin; Nelson-s/Castro-a; four covers 3.00
2-15-($3.99) 2-6-Three covers. 7-13-Two covers 4.00
Annual 1 (2012, $4.99) Rahner-a/Davila-a/Parrillo-c 5.00

LORD OF THE JUNGLE VOLUME 3
Dynamite Entertainment: 2022 - No. 6, 2023 ($3.99)

1-6-Dan Jurgens-s/Benito Gallego-a; retelling of Tarzan's origin 4.00

LORD PUMPKIN
Malibu Comics (Ultraverse): Oct, 1994 ($2.50, one-shot)

0-Two covers 4.00

LORD PUMPKIN/NECROMANTRA
Malibu Comics (Ultraverse): Apr, 1995 - No. 4, July, 1995 ($2.95, limited series, flip book)

1-4 .... 4.00

LORDS OF AVALON: KNIGHT OF DARKNESS
Marvel Comics: Jan, 2008 - No. 6, July, 2009 ($3.99, limited series)

1-6-($3.99)-Kenyon & Furth-s; Ohtsuka-a/c 4.00

LORDS OF AVALON: SWORD OF DARKNESS
Marvel Comics: Apr, 2008 - No. 6, Sept, 2008 ($3.99/$2.99, limited series)

1-($3.99)-Adaptation of Sherrilyn Kenyon's Arthurian fantasy; Ohtsuka-a/c 4.00
2-6-($2.99) 3.00
HC (2008, $19.99) r/#1-6; two covers 20.00

LORDS OF EMPYRE (Tie-in to Empyre series)
Marvel Comics: Sept, 2020 - Oct, 2020 ($4.99, series of one-shots)

...: Celestial Messiah 1 (10/20) Paknadel-s/Lins-a; leads into Empyre #3 .... 5.00
...: Emperor Hulkling 1 (9/20) Zdarsky & Oliveira-s/Garcia-a; prelude to events of Empyre 5.00
...: Swordsman 1 (10/20) Paknadel-s/Nachlik-a 5.00

LORDS OF MARS
Dynamite Entertainment: 2013 - No. 6, 2014 ($3.99, limited series)

1-6-Tarzan and Jane meet John Carter on Mars; Nelson-s/Castro-a; multiple covers 4.00

LORDS OF THE JUNGLE
Dynamite Entertainment: 2016 - No. 6, 2016 ($3.99, limited series)

1-6-Tarzan and Sheena app.; Bechko-s/Castro-a; covers by Castro & Massafera 4.00

LORNA, RELIC WRANGLER
Image Comics: Mar, 2011 ($3.99, one-shot)

1-Micah Harris-s; J. Bone-c 4.00

LORNA THE JUNGLE GIRL (...Jungle Queen #1-5)
Atlas Comics (NPI 1/OMC 2-11/NPI 12-26): July, 1953 - No. 26, Aug, 1957

1-Origin & 1st app.	68	136	204	435	743	1050
2-Intro. & 1st app. Greg Knight	36	72	108	211	343	475
3-5	32	64	96	188	307	425
6-11: 11-Last pre-code (1/55)	28	56	84	165	270	375

	GD 2.0	VG 4.0	FN 6.0	VF 8.0	VF/NM 9.0	NM- 9.2
12-17,19-26: 14-Colletta & Maneely-c	25	50	75	150	245	340
18-Williamson/Colletta-c	26	52	78	154	252	350

NOTE: *Brodsky* c-1-3, 5, 9. *Everett* c-21, 23-26. *Heath* c-6, 7. *Maneely* c-12, 15. *Romita* a-18, 20, 22, 24, 26. *Shores* a-14-16, 18, 24, 26; c-11, 13, 16. *Tuska* a-6.

LOSERS (Inspired the 2010 movie)
DC Comics (Vertigo): Aug, 2003 - No. 32, Mar, 2006 ($2.95/$2.99)

1-Andy Diggle-s/Jock-a	2	4	6	8	10	12
1-Special Edition (6/10, $1.00) r/#1 with "What's Next?" logo on cover						
	1	2	3	5	6	8

2-32: 15-Bagged with Sky Captain CD. 20-Oliver-a. 27-Wilson-a 3.00
...: Ante Up TPB (2004, $9.95) r/#1-6 .... 10.00
...: Book Two TPB (2010, $24.99) r/#13-32; Ian Rankin intro.; preliminary art pages 25.00
...: Close Quarters TPB (2005, $14.99) r/#20-25 .... 15.00
...: Double Down TPB (2004, $12.95) r/#7-12 .... 13.00
...: Endgame TPB (2006, $14.99) r/#26-32 .... 15.00
...: Trifecta TPB (2005, $14.99) r/#13-19 .... 15.00
...: Volumes One and Two TPB (2010, $19.99) r/#1-12; new intro. by Diggle 20.00

LOSERS SPECIAL (See Our Fighting Forces #123)(Also see G.I. Combat & Our Fighting Forces)
DC Comics: Sept, 1985 1.25, one-shot)

1-Capt. Storm, Gunner & Sarge; Crisis on Infinite Earths x-over						
	1	3	4	6	8	10

LOST, THE
Chaos! Comics: Dec, 1997 - No. 3 ($2.95, B&W, unfinished limited series)

1-3-Andreyko-script: 1-Russell back-c 4.00

LOST BOYS, THE (Sequel to the 1987 vampire movie)
DC Comics (Vertigo): Dec, 2016 - No. 6, May, 2017 ($3.99)

1-6-Tim Seeley-s/Scott Godlewski-a/Tony Harris-c; Frog Bros. app. 4.00

LOST BOYS: REIGN OF FROGS (Based on the 1987 vampire movie)
DC Comics (WildStorm): Jul, 2008 - No. 4, Oct, 2008 ($3.50, limited series)

1-4-Rodionoff-s/Gomez-a; Edgar Frog app. 3.50
TPB (2009, $12.99) r/#1-4 .... 13.00

LOST CITY EXPLORERS
AfterShock Comics: Jun, 2018 - No. 5, Oct, 2018 ($3.99, limited series)

1-5-Zack Kaplan-s/Alvaro Sarrasece-a 4.00

LOST CONTINENT
Eclipse Int'l: Sept, 1990 - No. 6, 1991 ($3.50, B&W, squarebound, 60 pgs.)

1-6: Japanese story translated to English 5.00

LOST IN SPACE (Movie)
Dark Horse Comics: Apr, 1998 - No. 3, July, 1998 ($2.95, limited series)

1-3-Continuation of 1998 movie; Erskine-c 4.00

LOST IN SPACE (TV)(Also see Space Family Robinson)
Innovation Publishing: Aug, 1991 - No. 12, Jan, 1993 ($2.50, limited series)

1-Bill Mumy (Will Robinson) script	1	2	3	5	6	8
1,2-Special Ed.: r/#1,2 plus new art & new-c						3.00
2-12: 9-Perez-c; Mumy script						3.00
Annual 1 (1991, $2.95, 52 pgs.) Good Girl bondage-c	3	6	9	14	19	24
Annual 2 (1992, $2.95, 52 pgs.)						4.00
...: Project Robinson (11/93, $2.50) 1st & only part of intended series						3.00

LOST IN SPACE: COUNTDOWN TO DANGER (Based on the 2018 Netflix series)
Legendary Comics: Oct, 2018 ($17.95, hardcover, one-shot)

HC-Short stories occuring before and during events of the series; Zid-a 18.00

LOST IN SPACE: THE LOST ADVENTURES (IRWIN ALLEN'S...) (TV)
American Gothic Press: Mar, 2016 - No. 6, Nov, 2016 ($3.99, limited series)

1-6-Adaptation of unused scripts. 1-3-The Curious Galactics. 4-6-Malice in Wonderland 6.00

LOST IN SPACE: VOYAGE TO THE BOTTOM OF THE SOUL
Innovation Publishing: No. 13, Aug, 1993 - No. 18, 1994 ($2.50, limited series)

13(V1#1, $2.95)-Embossed silver logo edition; Bill Mumy scripts begin; painted-c						
	2	4	6	8	9	10
13(V1#1, $4.95)-Embossed gold logo edition bagged w/poster						
	4	8	12	18	24	30
14-18: Painted-c	2	4	6	11	16	20
	1	2	3	5	6	8

NOTE: Originally intended to be a 12 issue limited series.

LOST PLANET
Eclipse Comics: 5/87 - No. 5, 2/88; No. 6, 3/89 (Mini-series, Baxter paper)

1-6-Bo Hampton-c/a in all 4.00

LOST SOLDIERS

	GD 2.0	VG 4.0	FN 6.0	VF 8.0	VF/NM 9.0	NM- 9.2

Image Comics: Jul, 2020 - No. 5, Dec, 2020 ($3.99, limited series)

| 1-5-Alex Kot-s/Luca Casalanguida-a | | | | | | 4.00 |

LOST WAGON TRAIN, THE (See Zane Grey Four Color 583)

LOST WORLD, THE
Dell Publishing Co.: No. 1145, Nov-Jan, 1960-61

| Four Color 1145-Movie, Gil Kane-a, photo-c; 1pg. Conan Doyle biography by Torres | | | | | | |
| | 9 | 18 | 27 | 61 | 123 | 185 |

LOST WORLD, THE (See Jurassic Park)
Topps Comics: May, 1997 - No. 4, Aug, 1997 ($2.95, limited series)

| 1-Movie adaptation | 3 | 6 | 9 | 14 | 20 | 25 |
| 2-4-Movie adaptation continues | 1 | 3 | 4 | 6 | 8 | 10 |

LOST WORLDS (Weird Tales of the Past and Future)
Standard Comics: No. 5, Oct, 1952 - No. 6, Dec, 1952

| 5- "Alice in Terrorland" by Alex Toth; J. Katz-a | 77 | 154 | 231 | 493 | 847 | 1200 |
| 6-Toth-a | 47 | 94 | 141 | 296 | 498 | 700 |

LOT, THE
Bad Idea: Jul, 2021 - No. 4, Oct, 2021 ($5.99, limited series)

| 1-4-Lead story with Marguerite Bennett-s/Renato Guedes-a; back-ups by various | | | | | | 6.00 |

LOTS 'O' FUN COMICS
Robert Allen Co.: 1940s? (5¢, heavy stock, blue covers)

nn-Contents can vary; Felix, Planet Comics known; contents would determine value. Similar to Up-To-Date Comics. Remainders - re-packaged.

LOT 13
DC Comics: Dec, 2012 - No. 5, Apr, 2013 ($2.99, limited series)

| 1-5-Niles-s/Fabry-a/c | | | | | | 3.00 |

LOU GEHRIG (See The Pride of the Yankees)

LOVE ADVENTURES (Actual Confessions #13)
Marvel (IPS)/Atlas Comics (MPI): Oct, 1949; No. 2, Jan, 1950; No. 3, Feb, 1951 - No. 12, Aug, 1952

1-Photo-c	34	68	102	199	325	450
2-Powell-a; Tyrone Power, Gene Tierney photo-c	26	52	78	154	252	350
3-8,10-12: 8-Robinson-a	18	36	54	103	162	220
9-Everett-a	18	36	54	107	169	230

LOVE AND AARDVARKS (Reprints from Cerebus in Hell)
Aardvark-Vanaheim: Apr, 2018 ($4.00, B&W)

| 1-Cerebus figures placed over original Doré artwork; Love and Rockets #1 cover swipe | | | | | | 4.00 |

LOVE AND MARRIAGE
Superior Comics Ltd. (Canada): Mar, 1952 - No. 16, Sept, 1954

1	27	54	81	158	259	360
2	15	30	45	86	133	180
3-10	15	30	45	83	124	165
11-16	14	28	42	76	108	140
I.W. Reprint #1,2,8,11,14: 8-r/Love and Marriage #3. 11-r/Love and Marriage #11						
	3	6	9	15	22	28
Super Reprint #10('63),15,17('64):15-Love and Marriage #?						
	3	6	9	15	22	28

NOTE: *All issues have Kamenish art.*

LOVE AND ROCKETS
Fantagraphics Books: 1981 - No. 50, May, 1996 ($2.95/$2.50/$4.95, B&W, mature)

1-B&W-c (1981, $1.00; publ. by Hernandez Bros.)(800 printed)						
	13	26	39	91	201	310
1 (Fall '82; Fantagraphics, color-c)	9	18	27	63	129	195
1-2nd & 3rd printing, 2-11,29-31: 2nd printings	2	4	6	9	12	15
2	3	6	9	21	39	45
3-10	2	4	6	8	10	12
11-49: 30 ($2.95, 52 pgs.)						5.00
50-($4.95)						6.00

LOVE AND ROCKETS (Volume 2)
Fantagraphics Books: Spring, 2001 - No. 20, Summer, 2007 ($3.95-$7.99, B&W, mature)

1-Gilbert, Jaime and Mario Hernandez-s/a	1	3	4	6	8	10
2-9						5.00
10-($5.95)						6.00
11-19-($4.50)						4.50
20-($7.99)						8.00
...: Stories • Free Comic Book Day 2016 Edition (giveaway)						3.00

LOVE AND ROMANCE
Charlton Comics: Sept, 1971 - No. 24, Sept, 1975

1	3	6	9	21	33	45
2-5,7-10	2	4	6	10	14	18
6-David Cassidy pin-up; grey-tone cover	3	6	9	14	19	24
11,13-24	2	4	6	8	10	12
12-Susan Dey poster	2	4	6	10	14	18

LOVE AT FIRST SIGHT
Ace Magazines (RAR Publ. Co./Periodical House): Oct, 1949 - No. 43, Nov, 1956 (Photo-c: 18-42)

1-Painted-c	41	82	123	256	428	600
2-Painted-c	21	42	63	122	199	275
3-10: 4,7-Painted-c	18	36	54	103	162	220
11-20	15	30	45	88	137	185
21-33: 33-Last pre-code	15	30	45	85	130	175
34-43	14	28	42	81	118	155

LOVE BUG, THE (See Movie Comics)

LOVEBUNNY AND MR. HELL
Devil's Due Publ./Image Comics: 2002 - 2004 ($2.95, B&W, one-shots)

1-Tim Seeley-s						6.00
...: A Day in the Lovelife (Image, 2003) Blaylock-a						3.00
...: Savage Love (Image, 2003) Seeley-s/a; Savage Dragon app.; Seeley & Larsen-c						3.00

| TPB (4/04, $9.95, digest-sized) reprints | | | | | | 10.00 |

LOVE CLASSICS
A Lover's Magazine/Marvel: Nov, 1949 - No. 2, Feb, 1950 (Photo-c, 52 pgs.)

| 1,2: 2-Virginia Mayo photo-c; 30 pg. story "I Turned Into a Small-Town Flirt" | | | | | | |
| | 37 | 74 | 111 | 222 | 361 | 500 |

LOVE CONFESSIONS
Quality Comics: Oct, 1949 - No. 54, Dec, 1956 (Photo-c: 3,4,6,7,9,11-18,21,24,25)

1-Ward-c/a, 9 pgs; Gustavson-a	53	106	159	334	567	800
2-Gustavson-a; Ward-c	27	54	81	158	259	360
3	20	40	60	117	189	260
4-Crandall-a	20	40	60	120	195	270
5-Ward-a, 7 pgs.	22	44	66	128	209	290
6,7,9,11-13,15,16,18: 7-Van Johnson photo-c. 8-Robert Mitchum & Jane Russell photo-c						
	16	32	48	92	144	195
8,10-Ward-a (2 stories in #10)	22	44	66	132	216	300
14,17,19,22-Ward-a; 17-Faith Domerque photo-c	20	40	60	120	195	270
20-Ward-a(2)	21	42	63	124	202	280
21,23-28,30-38,40-42: Last precode, 4/55	15	30	45	85	130	175
29-Ward-a	19	38	57	111	176	240
39,53-Matt Baker-a	18	36	54	103	162	220
43,44,46,47,50,52-54: 47-Ward-c?	15	30	45	83	124	165
45,48-Ward-a	18	36	54	105	165	225
49-Baker-c/a	28	56	84	165	270	375

LOVECRAFT
DC Comics: 2003 (graphic novel)

| Hardcover ($24.95) Rodionoff & Giffen-s/Breccia-a; intro. by John Carpenter | | | | | 25.00 | |
| Softcover ($17.95) | | | | | 18.00 | |

LOVE DIARY
Our Publishing Co./Toytown/Patches: July, 1949 - No. 48, Oct, 1955 (Photo-c: 1-30) (52 pgs. #1-11?)

1-Krigstein-a	39	78	117	240	395	550
2,3-Krigstein & Mort Leav-a in each	22	44	66	132	216	300
4-8	19	38	57	111	176	240
9,10-Everett-a	20	40	60	117	189	260
11-15,17-20	18	36	54	103	162	220
16- Mort Leav-a, 3 pg. Baker-sty. Leav-a	19	38	57	111	176	240
21-30,32-48: 45-Leav-a. 47-Last precode(12/54)	16	32	48	94	147	200
31-John Buscema headlights-c	28	56	84	165	270	375

LOVE DIARY (Diary Loves #2 on; title change due to previously published title)
Quality Comics Group: Sept, 1949

| 1-Ward-c/a, 9 pgs. | 55 | 110 | 165 | 352 | 601 | 850 |

LOVE DIARY
Charlton Comics: July, 1958 - No. 102, Dec, 1976

1	15	30	45	85	130	175
2	9	18	27	52	69	85
3-5,7-10	8	16	24	42	54	65
6-Torres-a	8	16	24	44	57	70
11-20	4	8	12	25	40	55
21-40	3	6	9	17	26	35
41-60	3	6	9	14	20	26
61-78,80,100-102	2	4	6	11	16	20
79-David Cassidy pin-up	3	6	9	15	22	28
81,83,84,86-99	2	4	6	8	11	14
82,85: 82-Partridge Family poster. 85-Danny poster	3	6	9	14	19	24

LOVE DOCTOR (See Dr. Anthony King...)

LOVE DRAMAS (True Secrets No. 3 on?)
Marvel Comics (IPS): Oct, 1949 - No. 2, Jan, 1950

| 1-Jack Kamen-a; photo-c | 34 | 68 | 102 | 199 | 325 | 450 |
| 2-Photo-c | 21 | 42 | 63 | 122 | 199 | 275 |

LOVE EVERLASTING
Image Comics: Aug, 2022 - Present ($3.99)

| 1-12-Romance stories; Tom King-s/Elsa Charretier-a | | | | | | 4.00 |

LOVE EXPERIENCES (Challenge of the Unknown No. 6)
Ace Periodicals (A.A. Wyn/Periodical House): Oct, 1949 - No. 5, June, 1950; No. 6, Apr, 1951 - No. 38, June, 1956

1-Painted-c	39	78	117	231	378	525
2	20	40	60	117	189	260
3-5: 5-Painted-c	17	34	51	98	154	210
6-10	15	30	45	90	140	190
11-30: 30-Last pre-code (2/55)	15	30	45	85	130	175
31-38: 38-Indicia date-6/56; c-date-8/56	14	28	42	82	121	160

NOTE: *Anne Brewster a-15. Photo c-4, 15-35, 38.*

LOVE FIGHTS
Oni Press: June, 2003 - No. 12, Aug, 2004 ($2.99, B&W)

| 1-12-Andi Watson-s/a | | | | | | 3.00 |
| Vol. 1 TPB (4/04, $14.95, digest-size) r/#1-6 | | | | | | 15.00 |

LOVE IS LOVE
IDW Publishing/DC Comics: 2016 ($9.99, TPB)

| SC-Anthology to benefit the survivors of the Orlando Pulse shooting; Charretier-c | | | | | | |
| | 3 | 6 | 9 | 14 | 19 | 24 |

LOVE JOURNAL
Our Publishing Co.: No. 10, Oct, 1951 - No. 25, July, 1954

10-Woman on-c "Branded"	161	322	483	1030	1765	2500
11-15,17-25: 19-Mort Leav-a	37	74	111	222	361	500
16-Buscema headlight-c	47	94	141	296	498	700

LOVELAND
Mutual Mag./Eye Publ. (Marvel): Nov, 1949 - No. 2, Feb, 1950 (52 pgs.)

| 1,2-Photo-c | 23 | 46 | 69 | 136 | 223 | 310 |

Love Confessions #25 © QUA

Love Romances (2019 series) #1 © MAR

Lovers #61 © MAR

	GD 2.0	VG 4.0	FN 6.0	VF 8.0	VF/NM 9.0	NM- 9.2

LOVELESS
DC Comics: Dec, 2005 - No. 24, Jun, 2008 ($2.99)

1-24: 1-Azzarello-s/Frusin-a. 6-8,15,22,23,24-Zezelj-a. 11,12,16-21-Dell'Edera-a						3.00
...: A Kin of Homecoming TPB (2006, $9.99) r/#1-5						10.00
...: Blackwater Falls TPB (2008, $19.99) r/#13-24						20.00
...: Thicker Than Blackwater TPB (2007, $14.99) r/#6-12						15.00

LOVE LESSONS
Harvey Comics/Key Publ. No. 5: Oct, 1949 - No. 5, June, 1950

	GD	VG	FN	VF	VF/NM	NM-
1-Metallic silver-c printed over the cancelled covers of Love Letters #1; indicia title is "Love Letters"	22	44	66	132	216	300
1-Non-metallic version	20	40	60	114	182	250
2-Powell-a; photo-c	14	28	42	76	108	140
3-5: 3,4-Photo-c	10	20	30	58	79	100

LOVE LETTERS (10/49, Harvey; advertised but never published; covers were printed before cancellation and were used as the cover to Love Lessons #1)

LOVE LETTERS (Love Secrets No. 32 on)
Quality Comics: 11/49 - #6, 9/50; #7, 3/51 - #31, 6/53; #32, 2/54 - #51, 12/56

	GD	VG	FN	VF	VF/NM	NM-
1-Ward-c, Gustavson-a	39	78	117	240	395	550
2-Ward-c, Gustavson-a	31	62	93	182	296	410
3-Gustavson-a	21	42	63	122	199	275
4-Ward-a, 9 pgs.; photo-c	26	52	78	154	252	350
5-8,10	15	30	45	90	140	190
9-One pg. Ward "Be Popular with the Opposite Sex"; Robert Mitchum photo-c	17	34	51	98	154	210
11-Ward-r/Broadway Romances #2 & retitled	17	34	51	98	154	210
12-15,18-20	15	30	45	85	130	175
16,17-Ward-a; 16-Anthony Quinn photo-c. 17-Jane Russell photo-c	21	42	63	124	202	280
21-29	15	30	45	84	127	170
30,31(6/53)-Ward-a	15	30	45	90	140	190
32(2/54)-39: 37-Ward-a. 38-Crandall-a. 39-Last precode (4/55)	14	28	42	81	118	155
40-48	14	28	42	78	112	145
49-51: 49,50-Baker-a. 51-Baker-c	20	40	60	117	189	260

NOTE: Photo-c on most 3-28.

LOVE LIFE
P. L. Publishing Co.: Nov, 1951

	GD	VG	FN	VF	VF/NM	NM-
1	18	36	54	105	165	225

LOVELORN (Confessions of the Lovelorn #52 on)
American Comics Group (Michel Publ./Regis Publ.): Aug-Sept, 1949 - No. 51, July, 1954 (No. 1-26: 52 pgs.)

	GD	VG	FN	VF	VF/NM	NM-
1	28	56	84	168	274	380
2	18	36	54	103	162	220
3-10	15	30	45	84	127	170
11-20,22-48: 18-Drucker-a(2 pgs.). 46-Lazarus-a	14	28	42	81	118	155
21-Prostitution story	19	38	57	111	176	240
49-51-Has 3-D effect-c/stories	24	48	72	142	234	325

LOVE MEMORIES
Fawcett Publications: 1949 (no month) - No. 4, July, 1950 (All photo-c)

	GD	VG	FN	VF	VF/NM	NM-
1	22	44	66	128	209	290
2-4: 2-(Win/49-50)	14	28	42	80	115	150

LOVE ME TENDERLOIN: A CAL McDONALD MYSTERY
Dark Horse Comics: Jan, 2004 ($2.99, one-shot)

1-Niles-s/Templesmith-a/c						3.00

LOVE MYSTERY
Fawcett Publications: June, 1950 - No. 3, Oct, 1950 (All photo-c)

	GD	VG	FN	VF	VF/NM	NM-
1-George Evans-a	29	58	87	172	281	390
2,3-Evans-a. 3-Powell-a	20	40	60	115	185	255

LOVE PROBLEMS (See Fox Giants)

LOVE PROBLEMS AND ADVICE ILLUSTRATED (see True Love...)

LOVE ROMANCES (Formerly Ideal #5)
Timely/Marvel/Atlas(TCI No. 7-71/Male No. 72-106): No. 6, May, 1949 - No. 106, July, 1963

	GD	VG	FN	VF	VF/NM	NM-
6-Photo-c	34	68	102	204	332	460
7-Photo-c; Kamen-a	20	40	60	117	189	260
8-Kubert-a; photo-c	20	40	60	117	189	260
9-20: 9-12-Photo-c	18	36	54	103	162	220
21,24-Krigstein-a	19	38	57	111	176	240
22,23,25-35,37,39,40	17	34	51	98	154	210
36,38-Krigstein-a	18	36	54	103	162	220
41-44,46,47: Last precode (2/55)	16	32	48	94	147	200
45,57-Matt Baker-a	22	44	66	128	209	290
48,50-52,54-56,58-74	9	18	27	60	120	180
49,53-Toth-a, 6 & ? pgs.	9	18	27	62	126	190
75,77,82-Matt Baker-a	13	26	39	86	188	290
76,78-81,86,88-90,92-95: 80-Heath-a. 95-Last 10¢-c?	10	20	30	70	150	230
83,84,87,91,106-Kirby-c. 83-Severin-a	13	26	39	91	201	310
85,96,99-105-Kirby-c/a	16	32	48	108	239	370
97-10¢ cover price blacked out, 12¢ printed on cover; Kirby-c/a	24	54	81	189	420	650
98-Kirby-c/a	17	34	51	117	259	400

NOTE: Anne Brewster a-67, 72. Colletta a-37, 40, 42, 44, 46, 67(2); c-42, 44, 46, 49, 54, 80. Everett c-70. Hartley c-20, 21, 30, 31. Heath a-87. Kirby c-80, 85, 88. Robinson a-29.

LOVE ROMANCES (Marvel 80th Anniversary salute to romance comics)
Marvel Comics: Apr, 2019 ($3.99, one-shot)

1-Short stories by various incl. Simone, Antonio, Hopeless, Martello, Jon Adams						4.00

LOVERS (Formerly Blonde Phantom)
Marvel Comics No. 23,24/Atlas No. 25 on (ANC): No. 23, May, 1949 - No. 86, Aug?, 1957

	GD	VG	FN	VF	VF/NM	NM-
23-Photo-c begin, end #29	34	68	102	199	325	450
24-Toth-ish plus Robinson-a	20	40	60	114	182	250
25,30-Kubert-a; 7, 10 pgs.	20	40	60	117	189	260
26-29,31-36,39,40: 35-Maneely-c	17	34	51	98	154	210
37,38-Krigstein-a	18	36	54	107	169	230
41-Everett-a(2)	18	36	54	107	169	230
42,44-65: 65-Last pre-code (1/55)	15	30	45	85	130	175
43-Frazetta 1 pg. ad	15	30	45	86	133	180
66,68-80,82-86	15	30	45	84	127	170
67-Toth-a	15	30	45	86	133	180
81-Baker-a	16	32	48	94	147	200

NOTE: Anne Brewster a-86. Colletta a-54, 59, 62, 64, 65, 69, 85; c-61, 64, 65, 75. Hartley c-37, 53, 54. Heath a-61. Maneely a-57. Powell a-27, 30. Robinson a-42, 54, 56.

LOVERS' LANE
Lev Gleason Publications: Oct, 1949 - No. 41, June, 1954 (No. 1-18: 52 pgs.)

	GD	VG	FN	VF	VF/NM	NM-
1-Biro-c	26	52	78	154	252	350
2-Biro-c	15	30	45	90	140	190
3-20: 3,4-Painted-c. 20-Frazetta 1 pg. ad	14	28	42	81	118	155
21-38,40,41	13	26	39	74	105	135
39-Story narrated by Frank Sinatra	15	30	45	88	137	185

NOTE: Briefer a-6, 13, 21. Esposito a-5. Fuje a-4, 16; c-many. Guardineer a-1, 3. Kinstler c-41. Sparling a-3. Tuska a-6. Fantastic c-3-18. Photo c-19-22, 26-28.

LOVE SCANDALS
Quality Comics: Feb, 1950 - No. 5, Oct, 1950 (Photo-c #2-5) (All 52 pgs.)

	GD	VG	FN	VF	VF/NM	NM-
1-Ward-c/a, 9 pgs.	40	80	120	246	411	575
2,3: 2-Gustavson-a	20	40	60	117	189	260
4-Ward-a, 18 pgs; Gil Fox-a	31	62	93	182	296	410
5-C. Cuidera-a; tomboy story "I Hated Being a Woman"	25	50	75	150	245	340

LOVE SECRETS
Marvel Comics(IPC): Oct, 1949 - No. 2, Jan, 1950 (52 pgs., photo-c)

	GD	VG	FN	VF	VF/NM	NM-
1	27	54	81	158	259	360
2	19	38	57	111	176	240

LOVE SECRETS (Formerly Love Letters #31)
Quality Comics Group: No. 32, Aug, 1953 - No. 56, Dec, 1956

	GD	VG	FN	VF	VF/NM	NM-
32	24	48	72	142	234	325
33,35-39	15	30	45	85	130	175
34-Ward-a	19	38	57	111	176	240
40-Matt Baker-c	21	42	63	124	200	280
41-43: 43-Last precode (3/55)	15	30	45	85	130	175
44,47-50,53,54	14	28	42	82	121	160
45-Ward-a	16	32	48	92	144	195
46-Ward-a; Baker-a	18	36	54	107	169	230
51,52-Ward(r). 52-r/Love Confessions #17	15	30	45	85	130	175
55-Baker-a	18	36	54	103	165	225
56-Baker-c	21	42	63	124	202	280

LOVE STORIES (See Top Love Stories)

LOVE STORIES (Formerly Heart Throbs)
National Periodical Publ.: No. 147, Nov, 1972 - No. 152, Oct-Nov, 1973

	GD	VG	FN	VF	VF/NM	NM-
147-152	3	6	9	17	26	35

LOVE STORIES OF MARY WORTH (See Harvey Comics Hits #55 & Mary Worth)
Harvey Publications: Sept, 1949 - No. 5, May, 1950

	GD 2.0	VG 4.0	FN 6.0	VF 8.0	VF/NM 9.0	NM- 9.2
1-1940's newspaper reprints-#1-4	13	26	39	74	105	135
2-5: 3-Kamen/Baker-a?	9	18	27	52	69	85

LOVE TALES (Formerly The Human Torch #35)
Marvel/Atlas Comics (ZPC No. 36-50/MMC No. 67-75): No. 36, 5/49 - No. 58, 8/52; No. 59, date? - No. 75, Sept, 1957

	GD 2.0	VG 4.0	FN 6.0	VF 8.0	VF/NM 9.0	NM- 9.2
36-Photo-c	34	68	102	199	325	450
37	18	36	54	107	169	230
38-44,46-50: 39-41-Photo-c. 48-Maneely-c	16	32	48	94	147	200
45,51,52,69: 45-Powell-a. 51,69-Everett-a. 52-Krigstein-a	17	34	51	98	154	210
53-60: 60-Last pre-code (2/55)	15	30	45	86	133	180
61-68,70-75: 75-Brewster, Cameron, Colletta-a	15	30	45	84	127	170

LOVE THRILLS (See Fox Giants)

LOVE TRAILS (Western romance)
A Lover's Magazine (CDS)(Marvel): Dec, 1949 - No. 2, Mar, 1950 (52 pgs.)

	GD 2.0	VG 4.0	FN 6.0	VF 8.0	VF/NM 9.0	NM- 9.2
1,2: 1-Photo-c	23	46	69	136	223	310

LOW
Image Comics: Aug, 2014 - No. 26, Feb, 2021 ($3.99/$3.50)

	NM- 9.2
1,11-26-($3.99) Remender-s/Tocchini-a	4.00
2-10-($3.50) Remender-s/Tocchini-a	3.50

LOWELL THOMAS' HIGH ADVENTURE (See High Adventure)

LOWLIFES
IDW Publishing: Jun, 2018 - No. 4, Sept, 2018 ($3.99, limited series)

	NM- 9.2
1-3-Buccellato-s/Sentenac-a	4.00

LOW, LOW WOODS, THE
DC Comics (Hill House Comics): Feb, 2020 - No. 6, Aug, 2020 ($3.99)

	NM- 9.2
1-6-Carmen Machado-s/Dani-a	4.00

LT. (See Lieutenant)

LUCAS STAND
BOOM! Studios: Jun, 2016 - No. 6, Nov, 2016 ($3.99, limited series)

	NM- 9.2
1-6-Kurt Sutter & Caitlin Kittredge-s/Jesús Hervás-a. 1-Multiple covers	4.00

LUCAS STAND: INNER DEMONS
BOOM! Studios: Feb, 2018 - No. 4, May, 2018 ($3.99, limited series)

	NM- 9.2
1-4-Kurt Sutter & Caitlin Kittredge-s/Jesús Hervás-a	4.00

LUCIFER (See The Sandman #4)
DC Comics (Vertigo): Jun, 2000 - No. 75, Aug, 2006 ($2.50/$2.75)

	GD 2.0	VG 4.0	FN 6.0	VF 8.0	VF/NM 9.0	NM- 9.2
1-Carey-s/Weston-a/Fegredo-c	4	8	12	28	47	65
2,3-Carey-s/Weston-a/Fegredo-c	1	3	4	6	8	10
4-10: 4-Pleece-a. 5-Gross-a						3.00
11-49,51-73: 16-Moeller-c begin. 25,26-Death app. 45-Naifeh-a. 53-Kaluta-c begin.						
62-Doran-a. 63-Begin $2.75-c						3.00
50-($3.50) P. Craig Russell-a; Mazikeen app.						4.00
74-($2.99) Kaluta-c						3.00
75-($3.99) Last issue; Lucifer's origins retold; Morpheus app.; Gross-a/Moeller-a						4.00
Preview-16 pg. flip book w/Swamp Thing Preview						3.00
Vertigo Essentials: Lucifer #1 Special Edition (3/16, $1.00) Flipbook with GN promos						3.00
...: A Dalliance With the Damned TPB ('02, $14.95) r/#14-20						15.00
...: Children and Monsters TPB ('01, $17.95) r/#5-13						18.00
...: Crux TPB (2006, $14.99) r/#55-61						15.00
...: Devil in the Gateway TPB ('01, $14.95) r/#1-4 & Sandman Presents:...#1-3						15.00
...: Evensong TPB (2007, $14.99) r/#70-75 & Lucifer: Nirvana one-shot						15.00
...: Exodus TPB (2005, $14.95) r/#42-44,46-49						15.00
...: Inferno TPB (2003, $14.95) r/#29-35						15.00
...: Mansions of the Silence TPB (2004, $14.95) r/#36-41						15.00
...: Morningstar TPB (2006, $14.99) r/#62-69						15.00
...: Nirvana (2002, $5.95) Carey-s/Muth-painted-c/a; Daniel app.						6.00
...: The Divine Comedy TPB (2003, $17.95) r/#21-28						18.00
...: The Wolf Beneath the Tree TPB (2005, $14.99) r/#45,50-54						15.00

LUCIFER (See The Sandman #4)
DC Comics (Vertigo): Feb, 2016 - No. 19, Aug, 2017 ($3.99)

	NM- 9.2
1-19: 1-Holly Black-s/Lee Garbett-a/Dave Johnson-c. 6-Stephanie Hans-a	4.00

LUCIFER (The Sandman Universe)
DC Comics (Vertigo): Dec, 2018 - No. 18, May, 2020 ($3.99)

	NM- 9.2
1-18: 1-Dan Watters-s/Max & Sebastian Fiumara-a/Jock-c. 9-Kelley Jones-a	4.00

LUCIFER'S HAMMER (Larry Niven & Jerry Pournelle's…)
Innovation Publishing: Nov, 1993 - No. 6, 1994 ($2.50, painted, limited series)

	NM- 9.2
1-6: Adaptation of novel, painted-c & art	4.00

LUCKY COMICS
Consolidated Magazines: Jan, 1944; No. 2, Sum, 1945 - No. 5, Sum, 1946

	GD 2.0	VG 4.0	FN 6.0	VF 8.0	VF/NM 9.0	NM- 9.2
1-Lucky Starr & Bobbie begin	54	108	162	343	574	825
2-4	32	64	96	188	307	425
5-Devil-c by Walter Johnson	97	194	291	621	1061	1500

LUCKY DEVIL
Dark Horse Comics: Aug, 2021 - No. 4, Nov, 2021 ($3.99)

	NM- 9.2
1-4-Cullen Bunn-s/Fran Galán-a	4.00

LUCKY DUCK
Standard Comics (Literary Ent.): No. 5, Jan, 1953 - No. 8, Sept, 1953

	GD 2.0	VG 4.0	FN 6.0	VF 8.0	VF/NM 9.0	NM- 9.2
5-Funny animal; Irving Spector-a	15	30	45	86	133	180
6-Irving Spector-a	13	26	39	74	105	135

NOTE: Harvey Kurtzman tried to hire Spector for Mad #1.

LUCKY "7" COMICS
Howard Publishers Ltd.: 1944 (No date listed)

	GD 2.0	VG 4.0	FN 6.0	VF 8.0	VF/NM 9.0	NM- 9.2
1-Pioneer, Sir Gallagher, Dick Royce, Congo Raider, Punch Powers; bondage-c	71	142	213	454	777	1100

LUCKY STAR (Western)
Nation Wide Publ. Co.: 1950 - No. 7, 1951; No. 8, 1953 - No. 14, 1955 (5x7-1/4"; full color, 5¢)

	GD 2.0	VG 4.0	FN 6.0	VF 8.0	VF/NM 9.0	NM- 9.2
nn (#1)-(5¢, 52 pgs.)-Davis-a	22	44	66	128	209	290
2,3-(5¢, 52 pgs.)-Davis-a	14	28	42	82	121	160
4-7-(5¢, 52 pgs.)-Davis-a	14	28	42	80	115	150
Given away with Lucky Star Western Wear by the Juvenile Mfg. Co. (SanTone)	7	14	21	37	46	55

LUCY CLAIRE: REDEMPTION
Image Comics: Dec, 2019 - Present ($3.99)

	NM- 9.2
1-4-John Upchurch-s/a	4.00

LUCY SHOW, THE (TV) (Also see I Love Lucy)
Gold Key: June, 1963 - No. 5, June, 1964 (Photo-c: 1,2)

	GD 2.0	VG 4.0	FN 6.0	VF 8.0	VF/NM 9.0	NM- 9.2
1	12	24	36	81	176	270
2	6	12	18	41	76	110
3-5: Photo back c-1,2,4,5	6	12	18	37	66	95

LUCY, THE REAL GONE GAL (Meet Miss Pepper #5 on)
St. John Publishing Co.: June, 1953 - No. 4, Dec, 1953

	GD 2.0	VG 4.0	FN 6.0	VF 8.0	VF/NM 9.0	NM- 9.2
1-Negligee panels	43	86	129	271	461	650
2	23	46	69	136	223	310
3,4: 3-Drucker-a	22	44	66	128	209	290

LUDOCRATS, THE
Image Comics: Apr, 2020 - Present ($3.99)

	NM- 9.2
1-5-Kieron Gillen & Jim Rossignol-s/Jeff Stokely-a	4.00

LUDWIG BEMELMAN'S MADELEINE & GENEVIEVE
Dell Publishing Co.: No. 796, May, 1957

	GD 2.0	VG 4.0	FN 6.0	VF 8.0	VF/NM 9.0	NM- 9.2
Four Color 796	6	12	18	38	69	100

LUDWIG VON DRAKE (TV)(Disney)(See Walt Disney's C&S #256)
Dell Publishing Co.: Nov-Dec, 1961 - No. 4, June-Aug, 1962

	GD 2.0	VG 4.0	FN 6.0	VF 8.0	VF/NM 9.0	NM- 9.2
1	6	12	18	38	69	100
2-4	5	10	15	30	50	70

LUFTWAFFE: 1946 (Volume 1)
Antarctic Press: July, 1996 - No. 4, Jan, 1997 ($2.95, B&W, limited series)

	NM- 9.2
1-4-Ben Dunn & Ted Nomura-s/a, ...Special Ed.	4.00

LUFTWAFFE: 1946 (Volume 2)
Antarctic Press: Mar, 1997 - No. 18 ($2.95/$2.99, B&W, limited series)

	NM- 9.2
1-18: 8-Reviews Tigers of Terra series	4.00
Annual 1 (4/98, $2.95)-Reprints early Nomura pages	5.00
...Color Special (4/98)	4.00
...Technical Manual 1,2 (2/98, 4/99)	4.00

LUGER
Eclipse Comics: Oct, 1986 - No. 3, Feb, 1987 ($1.75, miniseries, Baxter paper)

	NM- 9.2
1-3: Bruce Jones scripts; Yeates-c/a	4.00

LUKE CAGE (Also see Cage & Hero for Hire)
Marvel Comics: Jul, 2017 - No. 5, Nov, 2017; No. 166, Dec, 2017 - No. 170, Apr, 2018 ($3.99)

	NM- 9.2
1-5-Walker-s/Blake-a; Cloak and Dagger app.	4.00
[Title switches to legacy numbering after #5 (11/17)]	
166-170: 166-Sanna-a; The Ringmaster app.; bonus origin re-cap w/Bagley-a	4.00

LUKE CAGE: GANG WAR (Tie-in to Gang War in Amazing Spider-Man)
Marvel Comics: Jan, 2024 - No. 4, Apr, 2024 ($4.99/$3.99, limited series)

	NM- 9.2
1-($4.99) Rodney Barnes-s/Ramón F. Bachs-a; Cloak and Dagger app.	5.00
2-4-($3.99) Jessica Jones and Danny Rand app.	4.00

LUKE CAGE NOIR
Marvel Comics: Oct, 2009 - No. 4, Jan, 2010 ($3.99, limited series)

	NM- 9.2
1-4-Glass & Benson-a/Martinbrough-a; covers by Bradstreet and Calero	4.00

LUKE SHORT'S WESTERN STORIES
Dell Publishing Co.: No. 580, Aug, 1954 - No. 927, Aug, 1958

	GD 2.0	VG 4.0	FN 6.0	VF 8.0	VF/NM 9.0	NM- 9.2
Four Color 580(8/54), 651(9/55)-Kinstler-a	6	12	18	37	66	95
Four Color 739,771,807,848,875,927	5	10	15	30	50	70

LUMBERJANES
BOOM! Box: Apr, 2014 - Present ($3.99/$6.99)

	NM- 9.2
1-Noelle Stevenson & Grace Ellis-s/Brooke Allen-a; multiple covers	10.00
2	6.00
3-24,26-49,51-72	4.00
25-($4.99) Two covers by Allen & Wiedle; preview of Lumberjanes/Gotham Academy	5.00
50-($4.99) Four covers by Leyh and Fish	5.00
73-75-($6.99)	7.00
...: A Midsummer Night's Scheme 1 (8/18, $7.99) Andelfinger-s/Gonzalez-a	8.00
...: Beyond Bay Leaf (10/15, $4.99) Faith Erin Hicks-s/Rosemary Valero-O'Connell-a	5.00
...: End of Summer (12/20, $6.99) Watters & Leyh-s/Bosy & Bryant-a	7.00
...: Faire and Square 2017 Special 1 (6/17, $7.99) Black-s/Julia-a; 3 covers	8.00
...: Making the Ghost of It 2016 Special 1 (9/16, $7.99) Wang-s/Norrie-a; Ganucheau-a	8.00
...: Somewhere That's Green 1 (5/19, $7.99) McGuire-s/Bosy-a	8.00
...: The Shape of Friendship GN (11/19, $14.99, SC) Lilah Sturges-s/Polterink-a	15.00
...: The Shape of Friendship Free Comic Book Day Special 2019 (5/19, giveaway)	3.00

LUMBERJANES / GOTHAM ACADEMY
BOOM! Box: Jun, 2016 - No. 6, Nov, 2016 ($3.99)

	NM- 9.2
1-6: 1-Chynna Clugston Flores-s/Rosemary Valero-O'Connell-a; multiple covers	4.00

LUNA
BOOM! Studios: Feb, 2021 - No. 5, Jun, 2021 ($3.99, limited series)

	NM- 9.2
1-5-Maria Llovet-s/a	4.00

LUNA MOON-HUNTER
WaterWalker Studios: Jul, 2012 - No. 2, Aug, 2012 ($5.95, limited series)

	NM- 9.2
1,2-Rob Hughes-s/Jeff Slemons-a. 1-Posada-c. 2-Buzz-c	6.00
SC-($24.95, 180 pgs.) Painted-c by Buzz & Parrillo; art by Slemons, Buzz & LaRocque	25.00
HC-($49.95, limited edition of 1000) Signed by Hughes & Slemons; 2 bonus articles	50.00

LUNATIC FRINGE, THE
Innovation Publishing: July, 1989 - No. 2, 1989 ($1.75, deluxe format)

Lucifer (2018 series) #6 © DC

Lumberjanes #33 © BOOM!

Mad #2 © WMG

	GD	VG	FN	VF	VF/NM	NM-
	2.0	4.0	6.0	8.0	9.0	9.2

1,2 — 4.00

LUNATICKLE (Magazine) (Satire)
Whitstone Publ.: Feb, 1956 - No. 2, Apr, 1956

| 1,2-Kubert-a (scarce) | 10 | 20 | 30 | 56 | 76 | 95 |

LUNATIK
Marvel Comics: Dec, 1995 - No. 3, Feb, 1996 ($1.95, limited series)

1-3 — 4.00

LURKERS, THE
IDW Publ.: Oct, 2004 - No. 4, Jan, 2005 ($3.99)

1-4-Niles-s/Casanova-a — 4.00

LUST FOR LIFE
Slave Labor Graphics: Feb, 1997 - No. 4, Jan, 1998 ($2.95, B&W)

1-4: 1-Jeff Levin-s/a — 4.00

LUTHOR (See Lex Luthor: Man of Steel)

LYCANTHROPE LEO
Viz Communications: 1994 - No. 7($2.95, B&W, limited series, 44 pgs.)

1-7 — 5.00

LYNCH (See Gen ¹³)
Image Comics (WildStorm Productions): May, 1997 ($2.50, one-shot)

1-Helmut-c/app. — 4.00

LYNCH MOB
Chaos! Comics: June, 1994 - No. 4, Sept, 1994 ($2.50, limited series)

1-4 — 5.00
| 1-Special edition full foil-c | 1 | 2 | 3 | 5 | 6 | 8 |

LYNDON B. JOHNSON
Dell Publishing Co.: Mar, 1965

| 12-445-503-Photo-c | 4 | 8 | 12 | 23 | 37 | 50 |

M
Eclipse Books: 1990 - No. 4, 1991 ($4.95, painted, 52 pgs.)

1-Adapts movie; contains flexi-disc ($5.95) — 6.00
2-4 — 5.00

MACE GRIFFIN BOUNTY HUNTER (Based on video game)
Image Comics (Top Cow): May, 2003 ($2.99, one-shot)

1-Nocon-a — 3.00

MACGYVER: FUGITIVE GAUNTLET (Based on TV series)
Image Comics: Oct, 2012 - No. 5, Feb, 2013 ($3.50, limited series)

1-5-Lee Zlotoff & Tony Lee-s/Will Sliney-a — 3.50

MACHETE (Based on the Robert Rodriguez movie)
IDW Publishing: No. 0, Sept, 2010 ($3.99)

0-Origin story; Rodriguez & Kaufman-s/Sayger-a; 3 covers — 4.00

MACHINE, THE
Dark Horse Comics: Nov, 1994 - No. 4, Feb, 1995 ($2.50, limited series)

1-4 — 4.00

MACHINE GUN WIZARDS (See Tommy Gun Wizards)

MACHINE MAN (Also see 2001, A Space Odyssey)
Marvel Comics Group: Apr, 1978 - No. 9, Dec, 1978; No. 10, Aug, 1979 - No. 19, Feb, 1981

1-Jack Kirby-c/a/scripts begin; end #9	3	6	9	21	33	46
2-9-Kirby-c/a/s. 9-(12/78)	2	4	6	9	12	15
10-17: 10-(8/79) Marv Wolfman scripts & Ditko-a begins						
	1	3	4	6	8	10
18-Wendigo, Alpha Flight-ties into X-Men #140	3	6	9	17	26	35
19-Intro/1st app. Jack O'Lantern (Macendale), later becomes 2nd Hobgoblin						
	5	10	15	30	50	70

NOTE: Austin c-7i, 19i. Buckler c-17p, 18p. Byrne c-14p. Ditko a-10-19; c-10-13, 14i, 15, 16. Kirby a-1-9p; c-1-5, 7-9p. Layton c-7i. Miller c-19p. Simonson c-6.

MACHINE MAN (Also see X-51)
Marvel Comics Group: Oct, 1984 - No. 4, Jan, 1985 (limited series)

1-4-Barry Smith-c/a(i) & colors in all; Jocasta app. 1-3-Trimpe-a(p). 2-1st app. Arno Stark (Iron Man 2020) — 5.00
TPB (1988, $6.95) r/ #1-4; Barry Smith-c — 10.00
.../Bastion '98 Annual ($2.99) wraparound-c — 4.00

MACHINE MAN 2020 (Also see 2020 Machine Man)
Marvel Comics: Aug, 1994 - No. 2, Sept, 1994 ($2.00, 52 pgs., limited series)

1,2: Reprints Machine Man limited series; Barry Windsor-Smith-c/i(r) — 5.00

MACHINE TEEN
Marvel Comics: July, 2005 - No. 5, Nov, 2005 ($2.99, limited series)

1-5-Sumerak-s/Hawthorne-a. 1-James Jean-c — 3.00
...: History (2005, $7.99, digest) r/#1-5 — 8.00

MACK BOLAN: THE EXECUTIONER (Don Pendleton's...)
Innovation Publishing: July, 1993 ($2.50)

1-3-($2.50) — 4.00
1-($3.95)-Indestructible Cover Edition — 5.00
1-($2.95)-Collector's Gold Edition; foil stamped — 4.00
1-($3.50)-Double Cover Edition; red foil outer-c — 5.00

MACKENZIE'S RAIDERS (Movie, TV)
Dell Publishing Co.: Apr-June, 1960

| Four Color 1093-Richard Carlson photo-c from TV show | | | | | | |
| | 6 | 12 | 18 | 40 | 73 | 105 |

MACROSS (Becomes Robotech: The Macross Saga #2 on)
Comico: Dec, 1984 ($1.50)(Low print run)

| 1-Early manga app. | 6 | 12 | 18 | 38 | 69 | 100 |

MACROSS II
Viz Select Comics: 1992 - No. 10, 1993 ($2.75, B&W, limited series)

1-10: Based on video series — 4.00

MAD (Tales Calculated to Drive You...)
E. C. Comics (Educational Comics): Oct-Nov, 1952 - No. 550, Apr, 2018
(No. 24-on are magazine format) (Kurtzman editor No. 1-28, Feldstein No. 29 - No. ?)

1-Wood, Davis, Elder start as regulars	543	1086	1629	4344	6922	9500
2-Dick Tracy cameo	240	360	960	1530	2100
3,4: 3-Stan Lee mentioned. 4-Reefer mention story "Flob Was a Slob" by Davis; Superman parody	97	194	291	776	1238	1700
5-W.M. Gaines biog.	189	378	567	1512	2406	3300
6-11: 6-Popeye cameo. 7,8- "Hey Look" reprints by Kurtzman. 11-Wolverton-a; Davis story was-r/Crime SuspenStories #12 w/new Kurtzman dialogue						
	66	132	198	528	839	1150
12-15: 12-Archie parody. 15,18-Pot Shot Pete-r by Kurtzman						
	51	102	153	408	654	900
16-23(5/55): 18-Alice in Wonderland by Jack Davis. 21-1st app. Alfred E. Neuman on-c in fake ad. 22-All by Elder plus photo-montages by Kurtzman. 23-Special cancel announcement						
	41	82	123	328	527	725
24(7/55)-1st magazine issue (25¢); Kurtzman logo & border on-c; 1st "What? Me Worry?" on-c; 2nd printing exists	94	188	282	752	1201	1650
25-Jaffee starts as regular writer	44	88	132	352	564	775
26,27: 27-Jaffee starts as story artist; new logo	39	78	117	312	499	685
28-Last issue edited by Kurtzman; (three cover variations exist with different wording on contents banner on lower right of cover; value of each the same)						
	39	78	117	240	395	550
29-Kamen-a; Don Martin starts as regular; Feldstein editing begins						
	36	72	108	216	351	485
30-1st A. E. Neuman cover by Mingo; last Elder-a; Bob Clarke starts as regular; Disneyland & Elvis Presley spoof	57	114	171	362	619	875
31-Freas starts as regular; last Davis-a until #99	34	68	102	204	332	460
32,33: 32-Orlando, Drucker, Woodbridge start as regulars; Wood back-a. 33-Orlando back-c						
	27	54	81	162	266	370
34-Berg starts as regular	22	44	66	132	216	300
35-Mingo wraparound-c; Crandall-a	22	44	66	132	216	300
36-40 (7/58): 39-Beall-c	18	36	54	105	165	225
41-50: 42-Danny Kaye-s. 44-Xmas-c. 47-49-Sid Caesar-s. 48-Uncle Sam-c. 50 (10/59)-Peter Gunn-s	15	30	45	90	140	190
51-59: 52-Xmas-c; 77 Sunset Strip. 53-Rifleman-s. 54-Jaffee-a begins. 55-Sid Caesar-s. 59-Strips of Superman, Flash Gordon, Donald Duck & others. 58-Halloween/Headless Horseman-c	14	28	42	80	115	150
60 (1/61)-JFK/Nixon flip-c; 1st Spy vs. Spy by Prohias, who starts as regular						
	15	30	45	94	147	200
61-70: 64-Rickard starts as regular. 65-JFK-s. 66-JFK-c. 68-Xmas-c by Martin. 70-Route 66-s	6	12	18	41	76	110
71-75,77-80 (7/63): 72-10th Anniv. special; 1/3 pg. strips of Superman, Tarzan & others. 73-Bonanza-s. 74-Dr. Kildare-s	6	12	18	38	69	100
76-Aragonés starts as regular	6	12	18	38	69	100
81-85: 81-Superman strip. 82-Castro-c. 85-Lincoln-c	8	12	28	47	65
86-1st Fold-in; commonly creased back covers makes these and later issues scarcer in NM						
	5	10	15	35	63	90
87,88	5	10	15	31	53	75
89,90: 89-One strip by Walt Kelly; Frankenstein-c. Fugitive-s. 90-Ringo back-c by Frazetta; Beatles app.	5	10	15	34	60	85

	GD 2.0	VG 4.0	FN 6.0	VF 8.0	VF/NM 9.0	NM- 9.2			GD 2.0	VG 4.0	FN 6.0	VF 8.0	VF/NM 9.0	NM- 9.2

91,94,96,100: 94-King Kong-c. 96-Man From U.N.C.L.E. 100-(1/66)-Anniversary issue

| | 4 | 8 | 12 | 28 | 47 | 65 |

92,93,95,97-99: 99-Davis-a resumes

| | 4 | 8 | 12 | 27 | 44 | 60 |

101,104,106,108,114,115,119,121: 101-Infinity-c; Voyage to the Bottom of the Sea-s. 104-Lost in Space-s. 106-Tarzan Bat-c by Frazetta; 2-pg. Batman by Aragonés. 108-Hogan's Heroes by Davis. 114-Rat Patrol-s. 115-Star Trek. 119-Invaders (TV). 121-Beatles-c; Ringo pin-up; flip-c of Silk-Teen; Flying Nun-s

| | 4 | 8 | 12 | 20 | 31 | 42 |

102,103,107,109-113,116-118,120(7/68): 118-Beatles cameo

| | 3 | 6 | 9 | 18 | 28 | 38 |

105-Batman-c/s, TV show parody (9/66)

| | 6 | 12 | 18 | 37 | 66 | 95 |

122,124,126,128,129,131-134,136,137,139,140: 122-Ronald Reagan photo inside; Drucker & Mingo-a. 126-Family Affair-s. 128-Last Orlando. 131-Reagan photo back-c. 132-Xmas-c. 133-John Wayne/True Grit. 136-Room 222

| | 3 | 6 | 9 | 15 | 22 | 30 |

123-Four different covers

| | 3 | 6 | 9 | 18 | 24 | 30 |

125,127,130,135,138: 125-2001 Space Odyssey; Hitler back-c. 127-Mod Squad-c/s. 130-Land of the Giants-s; Torres begins as reg. 135-Easy Rider-c by Davis. 138-Snoopy-c; MASH-s

| | 3 | 6 | 9 | 16 | 24 | 32 |

141-149,151-156,158-165,167-170: 141-Hawaii Five-0. 147-All in the Family-s. 153-Dirty Harry-s. 155-Godfather-c/s. 156-Columbo-s. 159-Clockwork Orange-s. 161-Tarzan-s. 164-Kung Fu (TV)-s. 165-James Bond-s; Dean Martin-c. 169-Drucker-c; McCloud-s. 170-Exorcist-s

| | 3 | 6 | 9 | 14 | 19 | 24 |

150-(4/72) Partridge Family-s

| | 3 | 6 | 9 | 16 | 23 | 30 |

157-(3/73) Planet of the Apes-c/s

| | 3 | 6 | 9 | 16 | 23 | 30 |

166-(4/74) Classic finger-c

| | 3 | 6 | 9 | 21 | 33 | 45 |

171-185,187,189-192,194,195,198,199: 172-Six Million Dollar Man-s; Hitler back-c. 178-Godfather II-c/s. 180-Jaws-c/s (1/76). 182-Bob Jones starts as regular. 185-Starsky & Hutch-s. 187-Fonz/Happy Days-c/s; Harry North starts as regular. 189-Travolta/Kotter-c/s. 190-John Wayne-s. 192-King Kong-c/s. 194-Rocky-c/s. Laverne & Shirley-s. 199-James Bond-s

| | 2 | 4 | 6 | 10 | 14 | 18 |

186,188,197,200: 186-Star Trek-c. 188-Six Million Dollar Man/ Bionic Woman. 197-Spock-c; Star Wars-s. 200-Close Encounters

| | 3 | 6 | 9 | 14 | 20 | 25 |

193,196: 193-Farrah/Charlie's Angels. 196-Star Wars-c/s

| | 3 | 6 | 9 | 16 | 23 | 30 |

201,203,205,220: 201-Sat. Night Fever-c/s. 203-Star Wars. 205-Travolta/Grease. 220-Yoda-c, Empire Strikes Back-s

| | 2 | 4 | 6 | 9 | 13 | 16 |

202,204,206,207,209,211-219,221-227,229,230: 204-Hulk TV show. 206-Tarzan. 208-Superman movie. 209-Mork & Mindy. 212-Spider-Man-s; Alien (movie)-s. 213-James Bond, Dracula, Rocky II-s Star Trek. 219-Martin-c. 223-Dallas-c/s. 225-Popeye. 226-Superman II. 229-James Bond. 230-Star Wars

| | 2 | 4 | 6 | 8 | | 10 |

208,228: 208-Superman movie-c/s; Battlestar Galactica-s. 228-Raiders of the Lost Ark-s

| | 2 | 4 | 6 | 10 | 14 | 18 |

210-Lord of the Rings

| | 2 | 4 | 6 | 10 | 14 | 18 |

231-235,237-241,243-249,251-260: 233-Pac-Man-c. 234-MASH-c/s. 235-Flip-c with Rocky III & Conan; Boris-a. 239-Mickey Mouse-c. 241-Knight Rider-s. 243-Superman III. 245- Last Rickard-a. 247-Seven Dwarfs-c. 253-Supergirl movie-c/s; Prince/Purple Rain-s. 254-Rock stars-s. 255-Reagan-c; Cosby-s. 256-Last issue edited by Feldstein; Dynasty, Bev. Hills Cop. 259-Rambo. 260-Back to the Future-c/s; Honeymooners-s

| | | 1 | 2 | 3 | 5 | 8 |

236,242,250: 236-E.T.-c/s;Star Trek II-s. 242-Star Wars/A-Team-s. 250-Temple of Doom/ Tarzan-s

| | | 1 | 2 | 3 | 5 | 8 |

261-267,269-276,278-288,290-297: 261-Miami Vice. 262-Rocky IV-c/s, Leave It To Beaver-s. 263-Young Sherlock Holmes-s. 264-Hulk Hogan-c; Rambo-s. 267-Top Gun. 271-Star Trek IV-c/s. 272-ALF-c; Get Smart-s. 273-Pee Wee Herman-c/s. 274-Last Marvin-s. 281-California Raisins-c. 282-Star Trek:TNG-s; ALF-s. 283-Rambo III-c/s. 284-Roger Rabbit-c/s. 285-Hulk Hogan-c. 287-3 pgs. Eisner-a. 291-TMNT-c. 292-Indiana Jones-s. 292-Super Mario Bros.-c; Married with Children-s. 295-Back to the Future II.

| | | 1 | 2 | 3 | 4 | 5 |

297-Mike Tyson-c

| | | 1 | 2 | 3 | 4 | 5 | 7 |

268,277,289,298-300: 268-Aliens-c/s. 277-Michael Jackson-c/s; Robocop-c. 289-Batman movie parody. 298-Gremlins II-c/s; Robocop II. Batman-s. 299-Simpsons-c/story; Total Recall-s. 300(1/91) Casablanca-s, Dick Tracy-s, Wizard of Oz-s, Gone With The Wind-s

| | | 1 | 2 | 3 | 5 | 8 |

300-303 (1/91-6/91)-Special Hussein Asylum Editions; only distributed to the troops in the Middle East (see Mad Super Spec.)

| | 3 | 6 | 9 | 19 | 30 | 40 |

301-310,312,313,315-320,322,324,326-334,337-349: 303-Home Alone-c/s. 305-Simpsons-s. 306-TMNT II movie. 308-Terminator II. 315-Tribute to William Gaines. 316-Photo-c. 319-Dracula-c/s. 320-Disney's Aladdin-s. 322-Batman Animated Series. 327-Seinfeld-s; X-Men-s. 331-Flintstones-c/s. 332-O.J. Simpson-s; Simpsons app. in Lion King. 334-Frankenstein-c/s. 338-Judge Dredd-c for Frazetta. 341-Pocahontas-s. 345-Beatles app. (1 pg.) 347-Broken Arrow & Mission Impossible

| | | | | | | 5.00 |

311,314,321,323,325,335,336,350,354,358: 311-Addams Family-c/story, Home Improvement-s. 314-Batman Returns-c/story. 321-Star Trek DS9-c/s. 323-Jurassic Park-c/s. 325,336-Beavis & Butthead-c/s. 335-X-Files-s; Pulp Fiction-s; Interview with the Vampire-s. 336-Lois & Clark-s. 350-Polybagged w/CD Rom. 354-Star Wars; Beavis & Butthead-s. 358-X-Files 1/5

| | | | | | | 5.00 |

351-353,355-357,359-500

| | | | | | | 5.00 |

501-550-($5.99)

| | | | | | | 6.00 |

Mad About Super Heroes (2002, $9.95) n/super hero app.; Alex Ross-c

| | | | | | | 10.00 |

NOTE: **Aragonés** a-210, 293. **Beall** c-39. **Davis** c-2, 27, 135, 139, 178, 213, 219, 246, 260, 296, 308. **Drucker** a-35-62; c-122, 169, 176, 225, 234, 266, 274, 280, 285, 297, 299, 303, 314, 315, 321. **Elder** c-5, 259, 261, 268. **Elder/Kurtzman** a-37-42. **Freas** c-40-59, 62-67, 69-70, 73-74. **Heath** a-14, 27. **Jaffee** c-199, 217, 224, 259. **Kamen** a-29. **Krigstein** a-12, 17, 24, 26. **Kurtzman** c-1, 3, 4, 6-10, 13, 16, 18. **Martin** a-29-62; c-68, 165, 229. **Mingo** c-30-37, 61, 71, 75-80, 82-114, 117-124, 126, 129, 131, 133, 134, 136, 140, 150-162, 164, 166-168, 171, 172, 174, 177, 179, 181, 183, 185, 198, 206, 209, 211, 214, 218, 221, 222, 300. **John Severin** a-1-6, 9, 10. **Wolverton** c-11; a-11, 17, 29, 31, 36, 40, 82, 137. **Wood** a-1-23, 23-62; c-56, 28, 29. **Woodbridge** a-35-62. Issues 1-23 are 36 pgs.; 24-28 are 58 pgs.; 29 on are 52 pgs.

MAD (See Mad Follies, ...Special, More Trash from..., and The Worst from...)

MAD ABOUT MILLIE (Also see Millie the Model)
Marvel Comics Group: April, 1969 - No. 16, Nov, 1970

1-Giant issue	12	24	36	81	176	270
2,3 (Giants)	8	16	24	51	96	140
4-10	6	12	18	37	66	95
11-16: 16-r	5	10	15	35	63	90
Annual 1(11/71, 52 pgs.)	7	14	21	44	82	120

MADAME FRANKENSTEIN
Image Comics: May, 2014 - No. 7, Nov, 2014 ($2.99, B&W, limited series)

| 1-7-Jamie Rich-s/Megan Levens-a/Joëlle Jones-c. 1-Variant-c by Mittens | | | | | | 3.00 |

MADAME MIRAGE
Image Comics (Top Cow): June, 2007 - No. 6, May, 2008 ($2.99)

1-6: 1-Paul Dini-s/Kenneth Rocafort-a; two covers by Horn and Rocafort						3.00
... First Look (5/07, 99¢) preview of series; Dini interview; cover gallery						3.00
Volume 1 TPB (7/08, $14.99) r/#1-6; cover gallery; cover and design sketches						15.00

MADAME XANADU
DC Comics: July, 1981 ($1.00, no ads, 36 pgs.)

| 1-Marshall Rogers-a (25 pgs.); Kaluta-c/a (2pgs.); pin-up | | | | | | |
| | 2 | 4 | 6 | 10 | 14 | 18 |

MADAME XANADU (Also see Doorway to Nightmare)
DC Comics (Vertigo): Aug, 2008 - No. 29, Jan, 2011 ($2.99)

1-Matt Wagner-s/Amy Reeder Hadley-a/c; Phantom Stranger app.						4.00
1,2-Variant covers. 1-Wagner. 2-Kaluta						5.00
2-29: 2-10-Amy Reeder Hadley-a/c; Phantom Stranger app. 6-Death (from The Sandman) app.; covers by Hadley & Quitely. 9-Zatara app. 10-Jim Corrigan becomes The Spectre. 11-15-Kaluta-a. 14,15-Sandman (Wesley Dodds) app. 16-18-Hadley-a; Det. Jones app. 3.00						
...: Broken House of Cards TPB (2011, $17.99) r/#16-23 and story from House of Mystery Halloween Annual #1						18.00
...: Disenchanted TPB (2009, $12.99) r/#1-10; James Robinson intro.; Hadley sketch-a						13.00
...: Exodus TPB (2010, $12.99) r/#11-15; Chris Roberson intro.						13.00
...: Extra-Sensory TPB (2011, $17.99) r/#24-29						18.00

MADAM SATAN (From Chilling Adventures of Sabrina)
Archie Comics: Dec, 2020 ($3.99, one-shot)

| 1-Eliot Rahal-s/Julius Ohta-a; Madam Satan before becoming Greendale High principal | | | | | | 4.00 |
| ... Hell on Earth 1 (10/23, $3.99) Rahal-s/Federici-a; Jinx app. | | | | | | 4.00 |

MADBALLS
Star Comics/Marvel Comics #9 on: Sept, 1986 - No. 3, Nov, 1986; No. 4, June, 1987 - No. 10, June, 1988

| 1-10: Based on toys. 9-Post-a | | | | | | 5.00 |

MADBALLS VS. GARBAGE PAIL KIDS
Dynamite Entertainment: 2022 - No. 4, 2022 ($3.99, limited series)

| 1-4-Sholly Fisch-s/Jason Crosby-a | | | | | | 4.00 |

MADBALLS VS. GARBAGE PAIL KIDS: TIME AGAIN, SLIME AGAIN
Dynamite Entertainment: 2023 - No. 4, 2023 ($3.99, limited series)

| 1-4-Sholly Fisch-s/Jason Crosby-a | | | | | | 4.00 |

MAD DISCO
E.C. Comics: 1980 (one-shot, 36 pgs.)

| 1-Includes 30 minute flexi-disc of Mad disco music | 3 | 6 | 9 | 14 | 19 | 24 |

MAD-DOG
Marvel Comics: May, 1993 - No. 6, Oct, 1993 ($1.25)

| 1-6-Flip book w/2nd story "created" by Bob Newhart's character from his TV show "Bob" set at a comic book company; actual s/a-Ty Templeton | | | | | | 4.00 |

MAD DOGS
Eclipse Comics: Feb, 1992 - No. 3, July, 1992 ($2.50, B&W, limited series)

| 1-3 | | | | | | 4.00 |

MAD 84 (Mad Extra)
E.C. Comics: 1984 (84 pgs.)

| 1 | | 1 | 3 | 4 | 6 | 8 | 10 |

MADE IN KOREA
Image Comics: May, 2021 - No. 6, Dec, 2021 ($3.99, limited series)

| 1-6-Jeremy Holt-s/George Schall-a | | | | | | 4.00 |

MAD FOLLIES (Special)
E. C. Comics: 1963 - No. 7, 1969

nn(1963)-Paperback book covers	23	46	69	161	356	550
2(1964)-Calendar	16	32	48	111	246	380
3(1965)-Mischief Stickers	11	22	33	76	163	250
4(1966)-Mobile; Frazetta-r/back-c Mad #90	9	18	27	57	111	165
5,6: 5(1967)-Stencils. 6(1968)-Mischief Stickers	7	14	21	44	82	120
7(1969)-Nasty Cards	7	14	21	44	82	120

(If bonus is missing, issue is half price)
NOTE: **Clarke** c-4. **Frazetta** r-4, 6 (1 pg. ea.). **Mingo** c-1-3. **Orlando** a-5.

MAD HATTER, THE (Costumed Hero)
O. W. Comics Corp.: Jan-Feb, 1946 - No. 2, Sept-Oct, 1946

| 1-Freddy the Firefly begins; Giunta-c/a | 84 | 168 | 252 | 538 | 919 | 1300 |
| 2-Has ad for E.C.'s Animal Fables #1 | 50 | 100 | 150 | 315 | 533 | 750 |

MADHOUSE
Ajax/Farrell Publ. (Excellent Publ./4-Star): 3-4/54 - No. 4, 9-10/54; 6/57 - No. 4, Dec?, 1957

1(1954)	43	86	129	271	461	650
2,3	25	50	75	150	245	340
4-Surrealistic-c	34	68	102	204	332	460
1(1957, 2nd series)	20	40	60	117	189	260
2-4 (#4 exist?)	14	28	42	80	115	150

MAD HOUSE (Formerly Madhouse Glads; ...Comics #104? on)
Red Circle Productions/Archie Publications: No. 95, 9/74 - No. 97, 1/75; No. 98, 8/75 - No. 130, 10/82

95,96-Horror stories through #97; Morrow-c	3	6	9	15	22	28
97-Intro. Henry Hobson; Morrow-a/c, Thorne-a	2	4	6	10	16	20
98,99,101-120-Satire/humor stories. 110-Sabrina app.,1pg.						
	2	4	6	8	10	12
100	2	4	6	8	11	14
121-129	2	4	6	8	11	14
130	2	4	6	8	11	14
Annual 8(1970-71)-Formerly Madhouse Ma-ad Annual; Sabrina app. (6 pgs.)						
	4	8	12	28	47	65
Annual 9-12(1974-75): 11-Wood-a(r)	4	8	12	28	47	65
...Comics Digest (′75-76) r/1st & 2nd Sabrina app.	2	4	6	11	16	20
2-8(8/82)(...Mag. #5 on)-Sabrina in many	2	4	6	9	13	16

Madam Satan #1 © ACP

Madman Atomic Comics #2 © Allred

Maestros #1 © Steve Skroce

	GD	VG	FN	VF	VF/NM	NM-
	2.0	4.0	6.0	8.0	9.0	9.2

NOTE: **B. Jones** a-96. **McWilliams** a-97. **Wildey** a-95, 96. See Archie Comics Digest #1, 13.

MADHOUSE GLADS (Formerly ...Ma-ad; Madhouse #95 on)
Archie Publ.: No. 73, May, 1970 - No. 94, Aug, 1974 (No. 78-92: 52 pgs.)

73-77,93,94: 74-1 pg. Sabrina	2	4	6	9	13	16
78-92 (52 pgs.)	2	4	6	11	16	20

MADHOUSE MA-AD (...Jokes #67-70; ...Freak-Out #71-74)
(Formerly Archie's Madhouse) (Becomes Madhouse Glads #73 on)
Archie Publications: No. 67, April, 1969 - No. 72, Jan, 1970

67-71: 70-1 pg. Sabrina	3	6	9	16	23	30
72-6 pgs. Sabrina	4	8	12	28	47	65
...Annual 7(1969-70)-Formerly Archie's Madhouse Annual; becomes Madhouse Annual; 6 pgs. Sabrina	5	10	15	30	50	70

MADMAN (See Creatures of the Id #1)
Tundra Publishing: Mar, 1992 - No. 3, 1992 ($3.95, duotone, high quality, lim. series, 52 pgs.)

1-Mike Allred-c/a in all	2	4	6	9	13	16
1-2nd printing						5.00
2,3						6.00

MADMAN ADVENTURES
Tundra Publishing: 1992 - No. 3, 1993 ($2.95, limited series)

1-Mike Allred-c/a in all	1	3	4	6	8	10
2,3						5.00
TPB (Oni Press, 2002, $14.95) r/#1-3 & first app. of Frank Einstein from Creatures of the Id in color; gallery pages						15.00

MADMAN ATOMIC COMICS (Also see The Atomics)
Image Comics: Apr, 2007 - No. 17, Sept, 2009 ($2.99/$3.50)

1-12-Mike Allred-s/c/a. 1-Origin re-told; pin-ups by Rivoche and Powell. 3-Sale back-c.		3.50
13-17-($3.50) Wraparound-c. 14-Back-up w/Darwyn Cooke-a		3.50
All-New Giant-Size Super Ginchy Special (4/11, $5.99) Allred-s/a; back-ups/pin-ups		6.00
Madman In Your Face 3D Special (11/14, $9.99) Classic stories converted to 3D plus a new short story by Mike Allred and pin-ups by various; glasses included		10.00
... Vol. 1 (2008, $19.99) r/#1-7; bonus art; Jamie Rich intro.		20.00

MADMAN COMICS (Also see The Atomics)
Dark Horse Comics (Legend No. 2 on): Apr, 1994 - No. 20, Dec, 2000 ($2.95/$2.99)

1-Allred-c/a; F. Miller back-c.	1	3	4	6	8	10
2-3: 3-Alex Toth back-c.						5.00
4-11: 4-Dave Stevens back-c. 6,7-Miller/Darrow's Big Guy app. 6-Bruce Timm back-c. 7-Darrow back-c. 8-Origin?; Bagge back-c. 10-Allred/Ross-c; Ross back-c.						4.00
11-Frazetta back-c						4.00
12-16: 12-(4/99)						
17-20: 17-The G-Men From Hell #1 on cover; Brereton back-c. 18-(#2). 19,20-($2.99-c).						3.50
20-Clowes back-c						
... Boogaloo TPB (6/99, $8.95) r/Nexus Meets Madman & Madman: The Jam						9.00
... Gargantua! (2007, $125.00, HC with dustjacket) r/Madman#1-3, Madman Adventures #1-3, Madman Comics #1-20 and Madman King-Size Super Groovy Special; pin-ups						125.00
Image Firsts: Madman #1 (10/10, $1.00) r/#1						3.00
Ltd. Ed. Slipcover (1997, $99.95, signed and numbered) w/Vol.1 & Vol. 2.						100.00
Vol.1- reprints #1-5; Vol. 2- reprints #6-10						
The Complete Madman Comics: Vol. 2 (11/96, $17.95, TPB) r/#6-10 plus new material						18.00
Madman King-Size Super Groovy Special (Oni Press, 7/03, $6.95) new short stories by Allred, Derington, Krall and Weissman						7.00
Madman Picture Exhibition No. 1-4 (4-7/02, $3.95) pin-ups by various						4.00
Madman Picture Exhibition Limited Edition (10/02, $29.95) Hardcover collects MPE #1-4						30.00
... Volume 2 SC (2007, $17.99) r/#1-11; Erik Larsen intro.						18.00
... Volume 3 SC (2007, $17.99) r/#12-20 and story from King-Size Groovy; Allred intro.						18.00
Yearbook '95 (1996, $17.95, TPB)-r/#1-5, intro by Teller						18.00

MADMAN / THE JAM
Dark Horse Comics: Jul, 1998 - No. 2, Aug, 1998 ($2.95, mini-series)

1,2-Allred & Mireault-s/a		4.00

MAD MAX: FURY ROAD (Based on the 2015 movie)
DC Comics (Vertigo): Jul, 2015 - Oct, 2015 ($4.99, series of one-shots)

... :Furiosa (8/15, $4.99) Origin of Furiosa; Tristan Jones-a; Edwards-c		5.00
...: Max 1,2 (9/15, 10/15, $4.99) Recap of Max's history & prelude to movie		5.00
...: Nux & Immortan Joe (7/15, $4.99) Origins of Nux & Immortan Joe; Edwards-c		5.00

MAD MONSTER PARTY (See Movie Classics)

MADNESS, THE
Artists, Writers & Artisans, Inc.: Aug, 2023 - No. 6, Jan, 2024 ($3.99)

1-Straczynski-s/-Aco-a		4.00

MADNESS IN MURDERWORLD
Marvel Comics: 1989 (Came with computer game from Paragon Software)

V1#1-Starring The X-Men	3	6	9	16	23	30

MADRAVEN HALLOWEEN SPECIAL
Hamilton Comics: Oct, 1995 ($2.95, one-shot)

nn-Morrow-a		4.00

MADROX (from X-Factor)
Marvel Comics (Marvel Knights): Nov, 2004 - No. 5, Mar, 2005 ($2.99)

1-5-Peter David-s/Pablo Raimondi-a; Strong Guy app.		3.00
...: Multiple Choice TPB (2005, $13.99) r/#1-5		14.00
X-Factor: Madrox - Multiple Choice HC (2008, $19.99) r/#1-5		20.00

MAD SPECIAL (...Super Special)
E. C. Publications, Inc.: Fall, 1970 - No. 141, Nov, 1999 (84 - 116 pgs.)
(If bonus is missing, issue is one half price)

Fall 1970(#1)-Bonus-Voodoo Doll; contains 17 pgs. new material	10	20	30	68	138	210
Spring 1971(#2)-Wall Nuts; 17 pgs. new material	5	10	15	34	60	85
3-Protest Stickers	5	10	15	33	57	80
4-8: 4-Mini Posters. 5-Mad Flag. 6-Mad Mischief Stickers. 7-Presidential candidate posters, Wild Shocking Message posters. 8-TV Guise	5	10	15	30	50	70
9(1972)-Contains Nostalgic Mad #1 (28 pgs.)	4	8	12	27	44	60
10-13: 10-Nonsense Stickers (Don Martin). 13-Sickie Stickers; 3 pgs. Wolverton-r/Mad #137. 11-Contains 33-1/3 RPM record. 12-Contains Nostalgic Mad #2 (36 pgs.); Davis, Wolverton-a	3	6	9	19	30	40
14,16-21,24: 4-Vital Message posters & Art Depreciation paintings. 16-Mad-hesive Stickers. 17-Don Martin posters. 20-Martin Stickers. 18-Contains Nostalgic Mad #4 (36 pgs.). 21,24-Contains Nostalgic Mad #5 (28 pgs.) & #6 (28 pgs.)	3	6	9	16	23	30
15-Contains Nostalgic Mad #3 (28 pgs.)	3	6	9	16	24	32
22,23,25,27-29,30: 22-Diplomas. 23-Martin Stickers. 25-Martin Shock-Sticks. 28-Contains Nostalgic Mad #7 (36 pgs.). 29-Mad Collectable-Connectables Posters. 30-The Movies	2	4	6	9	13	16
26-Has 33-1/3 RPM record	2	4	6	13	18	22
31,33-35,37-50	2	4	6	8	11	14
32-Contains Nostalgic Mad #8. 36-Has 96 pgs. of comic book & comic strip spoofs: titles "The Comics" on-c	2	4	6	9	13	16
51-70	1	3	4	6	8	10
71-88,90-100: 71-Batman parodies-r by Wood, Drucker. 72-Wolverton-c-from 1st panel in Mad #11; Wolverton-s/ r/new dialogue. 83-All Star Trek spoof issue	1	3	5	6	8	
76-(Fall, 1991)-Special Hussein Asylum Edition; distributed only to the troops in the Middle East (see Mad #300-303)	2	4	6	13	18	22
89-($3.95)-Polybagged w/1st of 3 Spy vs. Spy hologram trading cards (direct sale only issue) (other cards came w/card set)	2	4	6	8	10	
101-141: 117-Sci-fi parodies-r.	1	3	4	6	8	10

NOTE: #28-30 have no number on cover. **Freas** c-76. **Mingo** c-9, 11, 15, 19, 23.

MAE
Dark Horse Comics/Lion Forge #7-on: May, 2016 - Present ($3.99)

1-Gene Ha-s/a/c; intro. by Bill Willingham; bonus pin-ups by Graham & Conner		5.00
2-9: 2-5-Ha-s/a/c. 3-Pin-up by Katie Cook. 6-Ha-s/Ganucheau-a. 8-Waid-s. 9-Kremer-s		4.00

MAESTRO
Marvel Comics: Oct, 2020 - No. 5, Feb, 2021 ($4.99/$3.99)

1-($4.99)-Origin of future Hulk; Peter David-s/Germán Peralta; M.O.D.O.K. app.	1	2	3	5	6	8
2-5-($3.99) Hercules app.						4.00

MAESTRO: FUTURE IMPERFECT – MARVEL TALES
Marvel Comics: Oct, 2020 ($7.99, one-shot)

1-Reprints intro. of Maestro in Hulk: Future Imperfect #1,2; Peter David-s/George Pérez-a		8.00

MAESTROS
Image Comics: Oct, 2017 - No. 7, Aug, 2018 ($3.99)

1-7-Steve Skroce-s/a		4.00

MAESTRO: WAR AND PAX (Follows Maestro series)
Marvel Comics: Mar, 2021 - No. 5, Jul, 2021 ($4.99/$3.99)

1-($4.99)-Future Hulk; Peter David-s/Javier Pina; Machine Man app.		5.00
2-5-($3.99) Doctor Doom app.		4.00

MAESTRO: WORLD WAR M (Follows Maestro: War and Pax series)
Marvel Comics: Apr, 2022 - No. 5, Sept, 2022 ($4.99/$3.99)

1-($4.99)-Future Hulk; Peter David-s/German Peralta-a; The Abomination app.		5.00
2-5-($3.99) Sub-Mariner app. 3,4-Giganto returns. 5-Cabrol-a		4.00

MAGDALENA, THE (See The Darkness #15-18)
Image Comics (Top Cow): Apr, 2000 - No. 3, Jan, 2001 ($2.50)

	GD 2.0	VG 4.0	FN 6.0	VF 8.0	VF/NM 9.0	NM- 9.2

Preview Special ('00, $4.95) Flip book w/Blood Legacy preview ... 5.00
1-Benitez-c/a; variant covers by Silvestri & Turner ... 3.00
2,3: 2-Two covers ... 3.00
.../Angelus #1/2 (11/01, $2.95) Benitez-c/Ching-a ... 3.00
...Blood Divine (2002, $9.95) r/#1-3 & #1/2; cover gallery ... 10.00
.../Vampirella (7/03, $2.99) Wohl-s/Benitez-a; two covers ... 3.00

MAGDALENA, THE (Volume 2)
Image Comics (Top Cow): Aug, 2003 - No. 4, Dec, 2003 ($2.99)
Preview (6/03) B&W preview; Wizard World East logo on cover ... 3.00
1-4-Holguin-s/Basaldua-a ... 3.00
1-Variant-c by Jim Silke benefitting ACTOR charity ... 3.00
TPB Volume 1 (12/06, $19.99) r/both series, Darkness #15-18 & Magdalena/Angelus ... 20.00
.../Daredevil (5/08, $3.99) Phil Hester-s; Hester & Sejic-c ... 4.00
.../Vampirella (12/04, $2.99) Kirkman-s/Manapul-a; two covers by Manapul and Bachalo ... 3.00
... Vs. Dracula Monster War 2005 (6/05, $2.99) four covers; Joyce Chin-a ... 3.00

MAGDALENA, THE (Volume 3)
Image Comics (Top Cow): Apr, 2010 - No. 12, May, 2012 ($3.99)
1-12: 1-Marz-s/Blake-a/Sook-c. 7,8-Keu Cha-a ... 4.00
... Seventh Sacrament 1 (12/14, $3.99) Tini Howard-s/Aileen Oracion-a ... 4.00

MAGDALENA (Volume 4)
Image Comics (Top Cow): Mar, 2017 - No. 4, Jun, 2017 ($3.99, limited series)
1-4-Howard & Cady-s/DiBari-a ... 4.00

MAGE (The Hero Discovered...; also see Grendel #16)
Comico: Feb, 1984 (no month) - No. 15, Dec, 1986 ($1.50, Mando paper)

	GD 2.0	VG 4.0	FN 6.0	VF 8.0	VF/NM 9.0	NM- 9.2
1-Comico's 1st color comic	3	6	9	16	23	30
2-5: 3-Intro Edsel						6.00
6-Grendel begins (1st in color)	3	6	9	17	26	35
7-1st new Grendel story	2	4	6	8	10	12
8-14: 13-Grendel dies. 14-Grendel story ends						6.00
15-($2.95) Double size w/pullout poster	1	2	3	5	6	8

Image Firsts: Mage - The Hero Discovered #1 (10/10, $1.00) r/#1 w/"Image Firsts" logo ... 3.00
TPB Volume 1-4 (Image, $5.95) 1- r/#1,2. 2- r/#3,4. 3- r/#5,6. 4- r/#7,8 ... 7.00
TPB Volume 5-7 (Image, $6.95) 5- r/#9,10. 6- r/#11,12. 7- r/#13,14 ... 7.00
TPB Volume 8 (Image, 9/99, $7.50) r/#15 ... 7.50
..., Vol. 1 TPB (Image, 2004, $29.99) r/#1-15; cover gallery, promo artwork, bonus art ... 30.00

MAGE (The Hero Defined) (Volume 2)
Image Comics: July, 1997 - No. 15, Oct, 1999 ($2.50)
0-(7/97, $5.00) American Ent. Ed. ... 5.00
1-14: Matt Wagner-c/s/a in all. 13-Three covers ... 4.00
1-"3-D Edition" (2/98, $4.95) w/glasses ... 5.00
15-($5.95) Acetate cover ... 6.00
Volume 1,2 TPB ('98,'99, $9.95) 1- r/#1-4. 2-r/#5-8 ... 10.00
Volume 3 TPB ('00, $12.95) r/#9-12 ... 13.00
Volume 4 TPB ('01, $14.95) r/#13-15 ... 15.00
Hardcover Vol. 2 (2005, $49.95) r/#1-15; cover gallery, character design & sketch pages ... 50.00

MAGE, BOOK THREE: THE HERO DENIED
Image Comics: No. 0 July, 2017 - No. 15, Feb, 2019 ($1.99/$3.99)
0-(7/17, $1.99) Return of Kevin Matchstick ... 3.00
1-14-Matt Wagner-c/s/a ... 4.00
15-($7.99) Finale of the trilogy ... 8.00

MAGE KNIGHT: STOLEN DESTINY (Based on the fantasy game Mage Knight)
Idea + Design Works: Oct, 2002 - No. 5, Feb, 2003 ($3.50, limited series)
1-5: 1-J. Scott Campbell-c; Cabrera-a/Dezago-s, 2-Dave Johnson-c ... 3.50

MAGGIE AND HOPEY COLOR SPECIAL (See Love and Rockets)
Fantagraphics Books: May, 1997 ($3.50, one-shot)
1 ... 4.00

MAGGIE THE CAT (Also see Jon Sable, Freelance #11 & Shaman's Tears #12)
Image Comics (Creative Fire Studio): Jan, 1996 - No. 2, Feb, 1996 ($2.50, unfinished limited series)
1,2: Mike Grell-c/a/scripts ... 4.00

MAGIC (Magic the Gathering)
BOOM! Studios: Apr, 2021 - No. 25, Apr, 2023 ($4.99)
1-25: 1-MacKay-s/Guara-a ... 5.00
...: Ajani Goldmane 1 (8/22, $8.99) McGuire-s/Olivetti-c ... 9.00
...: Master of Metal 1 (11/21, $8.99) Scott-s/Carlomagno & Coelho-a ... 9.00
...: Nahiri the Lithomancer 1 (11/22, $8.99) McGuire-s/Lobo-a ... 9.00
...: Planeswalkers: Noble 1 (6/23, $7.99) Caballero & Locatelli-a ... 8.00
...: Planeswalkers: Notorious 1 (8/23, $7.99) Short stories by various; 3 covers ... 8.00

MAGICA DE SPELL GIANT HALLOWEEN HEX (Also see Walt Disney Showcase #30)
IDW Publishing: No. 2, Sept, 2018 ($5.99, numbering continues from Disney Giant Halloween Hex)
2-Reprints from Italian & Danish editions; art by Cavazzano & Alfonso ... 6.00

MAGIC AGENT (See Forbidden Worlds & Unknown Worlds)
American Comics Group: Jan-Feb, 1962 - No. 3, May-June, 1962

	GD 2.0	VG 4.0	FN 6.0	VF 8.0	VF/NM 9.0	NM- 9.2
1-Origin & 1st app. John Force	5	10	15	30	50	70
2,3	3	6	9	21	33	45

MAGIC COMICS
David McKay Publications: Aug, 1939 - No. 123, Nov-Dec, 1949

	GD 2.0	VG 4.0	FN 6.0	VF 8.0	VF/NM 9.0	NM- 9.2
1-Mandrake the Magician, Henry, Popeye, Blondie, Barney Baxter, Secret Agent X-9 (not by Raymond), Bunky by Billy DeBeck & Thornton Burgess text stories illustrated by Harrison Cady begin; Henry covers begin	380	760	1140	2240	3870	5500
2	145	290	435	856	1478	2100
3	103	206	309	608	1054	1500
4	80	160	240	470	810	1150
5	65	130	195	384	667	950
6-11: 8-11-Mandrake/Henry funny covers	53	106	159	315	545	775
12-16,18,20: 12-20,22-24-Serious Mandrake mystery covers	75	150	225	440	770	1100
17-The Lone Ranger begins (scarce)	100	200	300	590	1020	1450

	GD 2.0	VG 4.0	FN 6.0	VF 8.0	VF/NM 9.0	NM- 9.2
19-Classic robot-c (scarce)	186	372	558	1100	1900	2700
21-Mandrake/Henry funny cover	40	80	120	246	411	575
22-24	52	104	156	328	552	775
25-1st Blondie-c	42	84	126	265	445	625
26-30: 26-Dagwood-c begin	30	60	90	177	289	400
31-40: 36-Flag-c	21	42	63	122	199	275
41-50	16	32	48	94	147	200
51-60	14	28	42	80	115	150
61-70	12	24	36	67	94	120
71-99, 107,108-Flash Gordon app; not by Raymond	10	20	30	54	72	90
100	11	22	33	60	83	105
101-106,109-123: 123-Last Dagwood-c	9	18	27	50	65	80

MAGIC FLUTE, THE (See Night Music #9-11)

MAGICIAN: APPRENTICE
Dabel Brothers/Marvel Comics (Dabel Brothers) #3 on: Mar, 2007 - No. 12, Dec, 2007 ($2.95/$2.99)
1-12-Adaptation of the Raymond E. Feist Riftwar Saga series ... 3.00
1,2-($5.95) 1-Wraparound variant-c by Maitz. 2-Wraparound variant-c by Booth ... 6.00
Collected Edition (10/06, $3.99) r/#182 ... 4.00
Vol. 1 HC (2007, $19.99, dustjacket) r/#1-6; foreword by Feist ... 20.00
Vol. 1 SC (2007, $15.99) r/#1-6; foreword by Feist ... 16.00
Vol. 2 HC (2008, $19.99, dustjacket) r/#7-12 ... 20.00

MAGICIANS, THE (Based on the series of novels by Lev Grossman)
Archaia: Nov, 2019 - No. 5, Mar, 2020 ($3.99, limited series)
1-5-Lilah Sturges-s/Pius Bak-a ... 4.00

MAGIC ORDER, THE
Image Comics: Jun, 2018 - No. 6, Feb, 2019 ($3.99, limited series)
1-6-Mark Millar-s/Olivier Coipel-a/c ... 4.00

MAGIC ORDER 2, THE
Image Comics: Oct, 2021 - No. 6, Mar, 2022 ($3.99/$4.99, limited series)
1-5-Mark Millar-s/Stuart Immonen-a/c ... 4.00
6-($4.99) ... 5.00

MAGIC ORDER 3, THE
Image Comics: Jul, 2022 - No. 6, Dec, 2022 ($3.99/$4.99)
1-5-Mark Millar-s/Gigi Cavenago-a/c ... 4.00
6-($4.99) ... 5.00

MAGIC ORDER 4, THE
Image Comics: Jan, 2023 - No. 6, Aug, 2023 ($4.99/$3.99, limited series)
1-($4.99)-Mark Millar-s/Dike Ruan-a/c ... 5.00
2-6-($3.99) ... 4.00

MAGIC PICKLE
Oni Press: Sept, 2001 - No. 4, Dec, 2001 ($2.95, limited series)
1-4-Scott Morse-s/a; Mahfood-a (2 pgs.) ... 3.00

MAGIC SWORD, THE (See Movie Classics)

MAGIC THE GATHERING (Title Series), **Acclaim Comics (Armada)**

	GD 2.0	VG 4.0	FN 6.0	VF 8.0	VF/NM 9.0	NM- 9.2
...ANTIQUITIES WAR, 11/95 - 2/96 ($2.50), 1-4-Paul Smith-a(p)						4.00
...ARABIAN NIGHTS, 12/95 - 1/96 ($2.50), 1,2	1	3	4	6	8	10
...COLLECTION, '95 ($4.95), 1,2-polybagged						5.00
...CONVOCATIONS, '95 ($2.50), 1-nn-pin-ups						4.00
...ELDER DRAGONS, '95 ($2.50)-Doug Wheatley-a	1	3	4	6	8	10
...FALLEN ANGEL, '95 ($5.95), nn	1	2	3	5	6	8
...FALLEN EMPIRES ,9/95 - 10/95 ($2.75), 1,2						4.00
...Collection ($4.95)-polybagged	1	3	4	6	8	10
...HOMELANDS, '95 ($5.95), nn-polybagged w/card; Hildebrandts-c	1	3	4	6	8	10
... ICE AGE (On The World of...) ,7/95 -11/95 ($2.50), 1-4: 1,2-bound-in Magic Card. 3,4-bound-in insert						5.00
...LEGEND OF JEDIT OJANEN, '96 ($2.50), 1,2						5.00
...NIGHTMARE, '95 ($2.50, one shot), 1						5.00
...THE SHADOW MAGE, 7/95 - 10/95 ($2.50), 1-4-bagged w/Magic The Gathering card	3	6	9	14	20	25
...Collection 1,2 (1995, $4.95)-Trade paperback; polybagged	1	3	4	6	8	10
...SHANDALAR, '96 ($2.50), 1,2	1	3	4	6	8	10
...WAYFARER ,11/95 - 2/96 ($2.50), 1-5						5.00

MAGIC: THE GATHERING
IDW Publishing: Dec, 2011 - No. 4, Mar, 2012 ($3.99, limited series)
1-4-Forbeck-s/Cóccolo-a ... 4.00

MAGIC: THE GATHERING: CHANDRA
IDW Publishing: Nov, 2018 - No. 4, Feb, 2019 ($3.99, limited series)
1-4-Ayala-s/Tolibao-a ... 4.00

MAGIC: THE GATHERING: GERRARD'S QUEST
Dark Horse Comics: Mar, 1998 - No. 4, June, 1998 ($2.95, limited series)
1-4: Grell-s/Mhan-a ... 5.00

MAGIC: THE GATHERING - PATH OF VENGEANCE
IDW Publishing: Oct, 2012 - No. 4, Feb, 2013 ($4.99, limited series, bagged with card)
1-4-Forbeck-s/Cóccolo-a ... 5.00

MAGIC: THE GATHERING - THEROS
IDW Publishing: Oct, 2013 - No. 5 ($4.99, limited series, bagged with card)
1-5-Ciaramella-s/Cóccolo-a ... 5.00

MAGIC: THE GATHERING - THE SPELL THIEF
IDW Publishing: May, 2012 - No. 4, Aug, 2012 ($4.99, limited series, bagged with card)

Mage, Book 3: The Hero Denied #15 © Matt Wagner

Magneto (2014 series) #1 © MAR

Magnificent Ms. Marvel #3 © MAR

	GD 2.0	VG 4.0	FN 6.0	VF 8.0	VF/NM 9.0	NM- 9.2

1-4-Forbeck-s/Cóccolo-a 5.00

MAGIC: THE HIDDEN PLANESWALKER (Magic the Gathering)
BOOM! Studios: Apr, 2022 - No. 4, Jul, 2022 ($4.99)
1-4-Mairghread Scott-s/Fabiana Mascolo-a 5.00

MAGIK (Illyana and Storm Limited Series)
Marvel Comics Group: Dec, 1983 - No. 4, Mar, 1984 (60¢, limited series)
1-4: 1-Characters from X-Men; Inferno begins; X-Men cameo (Buscema pencils in #1,2; c-1p. 2-4: 2-Nightcrawler app. & X-Men cameo 5.00

MAGIK (See Black Sun mini-series)
Marvel Comics: Dec, 2000 - No. 4, Mar, 2001 ($2.99, limited series)
1-4-Liam Sharp-a/Abnett & Lanning-s; Nightcrawler app. 3.00

MAGILLA GORILLA (TV) (See Kite Fun Book)
Gold Key: May, 1964 - No. 10, Dec, 1968 (Hanna-Barbera)

	GD	VG	FN	VF	VF/NM	NM-
1-1st comic app.	11	22	33	73	157	240
2-4: 3-Vs. Yogi Bear for President. 4-1st Punkin Puss & Mushmouse, Ricochet Rabbit & Droop-a-Long	5	10	15	35	63	90
5-10: 10-Reprints	5	10	15	30	50	70

MAGILLA GORILLA (TV)(See Spotlight #4)
Charlton Comics: Nov, 1970 - No. 5, July, 1971 (Hanna-Barbera)

	GD	VG	FN	VF	VF/NM	NM-
1	7	14	21	48	89	130
2-5	3	6	9	21	33	45

MAGNETIC MEN FEATURING MAGNETO
Marvel Comics (Amalgam): June, 1997 ($1.95, one-shot)
1-Tom Peyer-s/Barry Kitson & Dan Panosian-a 5.00

MAGNETO (See X-Men #1)
Marvel Comics: nd (Sept, 1993) (Giveaway) (one-shot)
0-Embossed foil-c by Sienkiewicz; r/Classic X-Men #19 & 12 by Bolton 5.00

MAGNETO
Marvel Comics: Nov, 1996 - No. 4, Feb, 1997 ($1.95, limited series)
1-4: Peter Milligan scripts & Kelley Jones-a(p) 4.00

MAGNETO
Marvel Comics: Mar, 2011 ($2.99, one-shot)
1-Howard Chaykin-s/a; Roger Cruz-c 3.00

MAGNETO
Marvel Comics: May, 2014 - No. 21, Oct, 2015 ($3.99)
1-21: 1-Bunn-s/Walta-a/Rivera-c. 9-12-AXIS tie-ins. 18-21-Secret Wars tie-ins 4.00

MAGNETO
Marvel Comics: Oct, 2023 - No. 4, Jan, 2024 ($4.99/$3.99)
1-($4.99) DeMatteis-s/Nauck-a; New Mutants app. 5.00
2-4-($3.99) 4.00

MAGNETO AND THE MAGNETIC MEN
Marvel Comics (Amalgam): Apr, 1996 ($1.95, one-shot)
1-Jeff Matsuda-a(p) 4.00

MAGNETO ASCENDANT
Marvel Comics: May, 1999 ($3.99, squarebound one-shot)
1-Reprints early Magneto appearances 4.00

MAGNETO: DARK SEDUCTION
Marvel Comics: Jun, 2000 - No. 4, Sept, 2000 ($2.99, limited series)
1-4: Nicieza-s/Cruz-a. 3,4-Avengers-c/app. 3.00

MAGNETO: NOT A HERO (X-Men Regenesis)
Marvel Comics: Jan, 2012 - No. 4, Apr, 2012 ($2.99, limited series)
1-4-Skottie Young-s/Clay Mann-a; Joseph returns 3.00

MAGNETO REX
Marvel Comics: Apr, 1999 - No. 3, July, 1999 ($2.50, limited series)
1-3-Rogue, Quicksilver app.; Peterson-a(p) 4.00

MAGNIFICENT MS. MARVEL
Marvel Comics: May, 2019 - Present ($3.99)
1-17: 1-Saladin Ahmed-s/Minkyu Jung-a. 5-New costume. 10-Intro. Stormranger 13-Intro. Amulet. 17-Dum Dum Dugan app. 4.00
18-($4.99) 75th issue of Ms. Marvel; battles Stormranger 5.00
Annual 1 (9/19, $4.99) Visaggio-s/Lam-a; The Super-Skrull app. 5.00

MAGNUS (Robot Fighter)(Volume 1)
Dynamite Entertainment: 2017 - No. 5, 2017 ($3.99)

1-5-Higgins-s/Fornés-a. 1,2-Turok back-up. 3-5-Doctor Spektor back-up 4.00

MAGNUS, ROBOT FIGHTER (...4000 A.D.)(See Doctor Solar)
Gold Key: Feb, 1963 - No. 46, Jan, 1977 (All painted covers except #5,30,31)

	GD	VG	FN	VF	VF/NM	NM-
1-Origin & 1st app. Magnus; Aliens (1st app.) series begins	89	178	267	712	1606	2500
2,3	15	30	45	103	227	350
4-10: 10-Simonson fan club illo (5/65, 1st-a?)	8	16	24	55	105	155
11-20	5	10	15	34	60	85
21,24-28: 28-Aliens ends	4	8	12	27	44	60
22,23: 22-Origin-r/#1; last 12¢ issue	4	8	12	28	47	65
29-46-Mostly reprints	3	6	9	15	22	28

...: One For One (Dark Horse Comics, 9/10, $1.00) r/#1 .... 3.00
Russ Manning's Magnus Robot Fighter - Vol. 1 HC (Dark Horse, 2004, $49.95) r/#1-7 .... 100.00
Russ Manning's Magnus Robot Fighter - Vol. 2 HC (DH, 6/05, $49.95) r/#8-14; forward by Steve Rude 50.00
Russ Manning's Magnus Robot Fighter - Vol. 3 HC (Dark Horse, 10/06, $49.95) r/#15-21 60.00
NOTE: *Manning* a-1-22, 28-43(r). *Spiegle* a-23, 44r.

MAGNUS ROBOT FIGHTER (Also see Vintage Magnus)
Valiant/Acclaim Comics: May, 1991 - No. 64, Feb, 1996 ($1.75/$1.95/$2.25/$2.50)

	GD	VG	FN	VF	VF/NM	NM-
1-Nichols/Layton-c/a; 1-8 have trading cards	3	6	9	14	19	24
2-4,6,8: 4-Rai cameo. 6-1st Solar x-over.	1	3	4	6	8	10
5-Origin & 1st full app. Rai (10/91); #5-8 are in flip book format and back-c & half of book are Rai #1-4 mini-series	3	6	9	16	23	30
7-Magnus vs. Rai-c/story; 1st X-O Armor	2	4	6	11	16	20
0-Origin issue; Layton-a; ordered through mail w/coupons from 1st 8 issues plus 50¢; B. Smith trading card						40
0-Sold thru comic shops without trading card	3	6	9	14	19	24
9-11						6.00
12-(3.25, 44 pgs.)-Turok-c/story (1st app. in Valiant universe, 5/92); has 8 pg. Magnus story insert	3	6	9	17	26	35
13-24,26-48: 14-1st app. Isak. 15,16-Unity x-overs. 15-Miller-c. 16-Birth of Magnus. 21-New direction & new logo.24-Story cont'd in Rai & the Future Force #9. 33-Timewalker app. 36-Bound-in trading cards. 37-Rai, Starwatchers & Psi-Lords cont. 44-Bound-in sneak peek card						4.00
21-Gold ink variant	2	4	6	11	16	20
25-($2.95)-Embossed silver foil-c; new costume						5.00
49-63						4.00
64-($2.50): 64-Magnus dies?	2	4	6	11	16	20

...Invasion (1994, $9.95)-r/Rai #1-4 & Magnus #5-8 16.00
Magnus Steel Nation (1994, $9.95) r/#1-4 16.00
Yearbook (1994, $3.95, 52 pgs.) 4.00
NOTE: *Ditko/Reese* a-18. *Layton* a(i)-5; c-6-9i, 25; back(i)-5-8. *Reese* a(i)-22, 25, 28; c(i)-22, 24, 28. *Simonson* c-16. Prices for issues 1-8 are for trading cards and coupons intact.

MAGNUS ROBOT FIGHTER
Acclaim Comics (Valiant Heroes): V2#1, May, 1997 - No. 18, Jun, 1998 ($2.50)
1-18: 1-Reintro Magnus; Donavon Wylie (X-O Manowar) cameo; Tom Peyer scripts & Mike McKone-c/a begin; painted variant-c exists 4.00

MAGNUS ROBOT FIGHTER
Dark Horse Comics: Aug, 2010 - No. 4, May, 2011 ($3.50)
1-4: 1-Shooter-s/Reinhold-a; covers by Swanland & Reinhold; back-up r/#1 (1963) 3.50

MAGNUS ROBOT FIGHTER
Dynamite Entertainment: 2014 - No. 12, 2015 ($3.99)
1-12: 1-8-Fred Van Lente-s/Cory Smith-a; multiple covers on each 4.00
#0 (2014, $3.99) Takes place between #2 & #3; Roberto Castro-a 4.00

MAGNUS ROBOT FIGHTER/NEXUS
Valiant/Dark Horse Comics: Dec, 1993 - No. 2, Apr, 1994 ($2.95, lim. series)
1,2: Steve Rude painted-c & pencils in all 4.00

MAGOG (See Justice Society of America 2007 series)(Continues in Justice Society Special #1)
DC Comics: Nov, 2009 - No.12, Ot. 2010 ($2.99)
1-12: 1-Giffen-s/Porter-a/Fabry-c; variant-c by Porter. 7-Zatanna app. 3.00
...: Lethal Force TPB (2010, $14.99) r/#1-5 15.00

MAID OF THE MIST (See American Graphics)

MAI, THE PSYCHIC GIRL
Eclipse Comics: May, 1987 - No. 28, July, 1989 ($1.50, B&W, bi-weekly, 44pgs.)
1-28, 1,2-2nd print 4.00

MAJESTIC (Mr. Majestic from WildCATS)
DC Comics: Oct, 2004 - No. 4, Jan, 2005 ($2.95, limited series)
1-4-Kerschl-a/Abnett & Lanning-s. 1-Superman app.; Superman #1 cover swipe 3.00
...: Strange New Visitor TPB (2005, $14.99) r/#1-4 & Action #811, Advs. of Superman #624

	GD	VG	FN	VF	VF/NM	NM-
	2.0	4.0	6.0	8.0	9.0	9.2

& Superman #201   15.00

MAJESTIC (Mr. Majestic from WildCATS)
DC Comics (WildStorm): Mar, 2005 - No. 17, July, 2006 ($2.95/$2.99)
1-17: 1-Googe-a/Abnett & Lanning-s; Superman app. 9-Jeanty-a; Zealot app.   3.00
....: Meanwhile, Back on Earth... TPB (2006, $14.99) r/#8-12   15.00
....: The Final Cut TPB (2007, $14.99) r/#13-17 & story fro WildStorm Winter Special 15.00
....: While You Were Out TPB (2006, $12.99) r/#1-7   13.00

MAJOR BUMMER
DC Comics: Aug, 1997 - No. 15, Oct, 1998 ($2.50)
1-15: 1-Origin and 1st app. Major Bummer   4.00

MAJOR HOOPLE COMICS (See Crackajack Funnies)
Nedor Publications: nd (Jan, 1943)
1-Mary Worth, Phantom Soldier app. by Moldoff   41   82   123   256   428   600

MAJOR VICTORY COMICS (Also see Dynamic Comics)
H. Clay Glover/Service Publ./Harry 'A' Chesler: 1944 - No. 3, Summer, 1945
1-Origin Major Victory (patriotic hero) by C. Sultan (reprint from Dynamic #1);
  1st app. Spider Woman; Nazi WWII-c   168   336   504 1075 1838 2600
2-Dynamic Boy app.; WWII-c   90   180   270   576   988 1400
3-Rocket Boy app.; WWII-c   81   162   243   518   884 1250

MAJOR X
Marvel Comics: Jun, 2019 - No. 6, Aug, 2019 ($4.99/$3.99)
1-($4.99) Rob Liefeld-s/a; Cable, Domino, Deadpool, Wolverine app.   5.00
2-6-($3.99) 2,4,5-Liefeld-s/Peeples-a. 3-Portacio-a. 6-Rob Liefeld-s/a   4.00
No. 0 (10/19, $4.99) r/Wolverine #154,155 with new framing pages; Liefeld-s/a 5.00

MALIBU ASCHAN: RAFFERTY (See Firearm #12)
Malibu Comics (Ultraverse): Nov, 1994 (99¢, B&W w/color-c; one-shot)
1-Previews "The Rafferty Saga" storyline in Firearm; Chaykin-c   4.00

MALTESE FALCON
David McKay Publications: No. 48, 1946
Feature Books 48-by Dashiell Hammett   103   206   309   659 1130 1600

MALU IN THE LAND OF ADVENTURE
I. W. Enterprises: 1964 (See White Princess of Jungle #2)
1-r/Avon's Slave Girl Comics #1; Severin-c   5   10   15   31   53   75

MAMMOTH COMICS
Whitman Publishing Co.(K. K. Publ.): 1938 (84 pgs.) (B&W, 8-1/2x11-1/2")
1-Alley Oop, Terry & the Pirates, Dick Tracy, Little Orphan Annie, Wash Tubbs, Moon Mullins,
  Smilin' Jack, Tailspin Tommy, Don Winslow, Dan Dunn, Smokey Stover & other reprints
  (scarce)   271   542   813 1734 2967 4200

MAN AGAINST TIME
Image Comics (Motown Machineworks): May, 1996 - No. 4, Aug, 1996 ($2.25, lim. series)
1-4: 1-Simonson-c. 2,3-Leon-a. 4-Barreto & Leon-c   4.00

MAN AMONG YE, A
Image Comics (Top Cow): Jun, 2020 - No. 8, Feb, 2022 ($3.99)
1-8-Stephanie Phillips-s/Craig Cermak-a; Caribbean pirates in 1720   4.00

MAN AND SUPERMAN 100-PAGE SUPER SPECTACULAR
DC Comics: Apr, 2019 ($9.99, squarebound, one-shot)
1-Wolfman-s/Castellini-a; Clark Kent's first days in Metropolis re-told   10.00

MAN-BAT (See Batman Family, Brave & the Bold, & Detective #400)
National Periodical Publ./DC Comics: Dec-Jan, 1975-76 - No. 2, Feb-Mar, 1976; Dec, 1984
1-Ditko-a(p); Aparo-c; Batman app.; 1st app. She-Bat?; 1st app. Baron Tyme
                                            3   6   9   21   33   45
2-Aparo-c   2   4   6   10   14   18
1 (12/84)-N. Adams-r(3)/Det.(Vs. Batman on-c)   1   2   3   5   6   8

MAN-BAT
DC Comics: Feb, 1996 - No. 3, Apr, 1996 ($2.25, limited series)
1-3: Dixon scripts in all. 2-Killer Croc-c/app.   4.00

MAN-BAT
DC Comics: Jun, 2006 - No. 5, Oct, 2006 ($2.99, limited series)
1-5: Bruce Jones-s/Mike Huddleston-a/c. 1-Hush app.   3.00

MAN-BAT
DC Comics: Apr, 2021 - No. 5, Aug, 2021 ($3.99, limited series)
1-5: 1-Dave Wielgosz-s/Sumit Kumar-a; covers by Hotz & Nowlan. 1-3-Task Force X 4.00

MAN CALLED A-X, THE
Malibu Comics (Bravura): Nov, 1994 - No. 4, Jun, 1995 ($2.95, limited series)
0-4: Marv Wolfman scripts & Shawn McManus-c/a. 0-(2/95). 1-"1A" on cover   4.00

MAN CALLED A-X, THE
DC Comics: Oct, 1997 - No. 8, May, 1998 ($2.50)
1-8: Marv Wolfman scripts & Shawn McManus-c/a.   4.00

MAN CALLED KEV, A (See The Authority)
DC Comics (WildStorm): Sept, 2006 - No. 5, Feb, 2007 ($2.99, limited series)
1-5-Ennis-s/Ezquerra-a/Fabry-c   3.00
TPB (2007, $14.99) r/#1-5; cover gallery   15.00

MAN COMICS
Marvel/Atlas Comics (NPI): Dec, 1949 - No. 28, Sept, 1953 (#1-6: 52 pgs.)
1-Tuska-a   43   86   129   271   461   650
2-Tuska-a   23   46   69   136   223   310
3-6   19   38   57   111   176   240
7,8   18   36   54   103   162   220
9-13,15: 9-Format changes to war   18   36   54   103   162   220
14-Henkel (3 pgs.); Pakula-a   20   40   60   114   182   250
16-21,23-28: 28-Crime issue (Bob Brant)   17   34   51   98   154   210
22-Krigstein-a, 5 pgs.   20   40   60   117   189   260
NOTE: **Berg** a-14, 15, 19. **Colan** a-9, 13, 21, 23. **Everett** a-8, 22; c-22, 25. **Heath** a-11, 13, 16, 17, 21. **Henkel** a-7.
Kubertish a-by **Bob Brown**-a. **Maneely** a-5, 11-13; c-5, 10, 11, 16. **Reinman** a-11. **Robinson** a-7, 10, 14. **Robert**

Sale a-9, 11. **Sinnott** a-22, 23. **Tuska** a-14, 23.

MANDRAKE THE MAGICIAN (See Defenders Of The Earth, 123, 46, 52, 55, Giant Comic Album,
King Comics, Magic Comics, The Phantom #21, Tiny Tot Funnies & Wow Comics, '36)

MANDRAKE THE MAGICIAN (See Harvey Comics Hits #53)
David McKay Publ./Dell/King Comics (All 12¢): 1938 - 1948; Sept, 1966 - No. 10, Nov, 1967
Feature Books 18,19,23 (1938)   129   258   387   826 1413 2000
Feature Books 46   77   154   231   493   847 1200
Feature Books 52,55   58   116   174   371   636   900
Four Color 752 (11/56)   12   24   36   80   173   265
1-Begin S.O.S. Phantom, ends #3   8   16   24   56   108   160
2-7,9- 4-Girl Phantom app. 5-Flying Saucer-c/story. 5,6-Brick Bradford app. 7-Origin Lothar.
  9-Brick Bradford app.   4   8   12   25   40   55
8-Jeff Jones (4 pgs.)   4   8   12   27   44   60
10-Rip Kirby app.; Raymond-a (14 pgs.)   5   10   15   30   50   70

MANDRAKE THE MAGICIAN
Marvel Comics: Apr, 1995 - No. 2, May, 1995 ($2.95, unfinished limited series)
1,2: Mike Barr scripts   4.00

MAN-EATERS
Image Comics: Sept, 2018 - No. 12, May, 2019 ($3.99)
1-12-Chelsea Cain-s/Kate Niemczyk-a   4.00
....: Tomorrow Belongs to You! (3/20, $4.99)   5.00

MAN-EATERS: THE CURSED
Image Comics: Jul, 2021 - No. 5, Nov, 2021 ($3.99)
1-5-Chelsea Cain-s/Kate Niemczyk & Lia Miternique-a   4.00

MAN-EATING COW (See Tick #7,8)
New England Comics: July, 1992 - No. 10, 1994? ($2.75, B&W, limited series)
1-10   4.00
Man-Eating Cow Bonanza (6/96, $4.95, 128 pgs.)-r/#1-4.   5.00

MAN FROM ATLANTIS (TV)
Marvel Comics: Feb, 1978 - No. 7, Aug, 1978
1-(84 pgs.)-Sutton-a(p), Buscema-c; origin & cast photos
                                            3   6   9   15   22   28
2-7   6.00

MAN FROM PLANET X, THE
Planet X Productions: 1987 (no price; probably unlicensed)
1-Reprints Fawcett Movie Comic   4.00

MAN FROM U.N.C.L.E., THE (TV) (Also see The Girl From Uncle)
Gold Key: Feb, 1965 - No. 22, Apr, 1969 (All photo-c)
1   15   30   45   100   20   340
2-Photo back c-2-8   7   14   21   44   82   120
3-10: 7-Jet Dream begins (1st app., also see Jet Dream) (all new stories)
                                            5   10   15   33   50   80
11-22: 19-Last 12¢ issue. 21,22-Reprint #10 & 7   5   10   15   30   50   70

MAN FROM U.N.C.L.E., THE (TV)
Entertainment Publishing: 1987 - No. 11 ($1.50/$1.75, B&W)
1-7 ($1.50), 8-11 ($1.75)   4.00

MAN FROM WELLS FARGO (TV)
Dell Publishing Co.: No. 1287, Feb-Apr, 1962 - May-July, 1962 (Photo-c)
Four Color 1287, #01-495-207   6   12   18   42   79   115

MANGA DARKCHYLDE (Also see Darkchylde titles)
Dark Horse Comics: Feb, 2005 - No. 5 ($2.99, limited series)
1,2-Randy Queen-s/a; manga-style pre-teen Ariel Chylde   3.00

MANGA SHI (See Tomoe)
Crusade Entertainment: Aug, 1996 ($2.95)
1-Printed back to front (manga-style)   4.00

MANGA SHI 2000
Crusade Entertainment: Feb, 1997 - No. 3, June, 1997 ($2.95, mini-series)
1-3: Two covers   4.00

MANHATTAN PROJECTS, THE
Image Comics: Mar, 2012 - No. 25, Nov, 2014 ($3.50)
1-Hickman-s/Pitarra-a; intro. Robert and Joseph Oppenheimer   15.00
2   10.00
3   6.00
4-6   4.00
7-25: 10,15,19-Browne-a.   4.00

MANHATTAN PROJECTS, THE : THE SUN BEYOND THE STARS
Image Comics: Mar, 2015 - No. 4, Feb, 2016 ($3.50)
1-4-Hickman-s/Pitarra-a   3.50

MANHUNT! (Becomes Red Fox #15 on)
Magazine Enterprises: 10/47 - No. 11, 8/48; No. 12 (no date); No. 13,14, 1953
1-Red Fox by L. B. Cole, Undercover Girl by Whitney, Space Ace begin (1st app.);
  negligee panels   181   362   543 1158 1979 2800
2-Electrocution-c   295   590   885 1888 3244 4600
3-5   74   148   222   470   810 1150
6-Bondage, torture-c   284   568   852 1818 3109 4400
7-10: 7-Space Ace ends. 8-Trail Colt begins (intro/1st app., 5/48) by Guardineer; Trail Colt-c.
  10-G. Ingels-a   55   110   165   352   601   850
11(8/48)-Frazetta-a, 7 pgs.; The Duke, Scotland Yard begin
                                      77   154   231   493   847 1200
12 (no indicia, no date) Same content as Trail Colt nn (A-1 #24); 7 pg. Frazetta which were
  reprinted in Manhunt! No. 11; Undercover Girl app.; The Red Fox by L.B. Cole; Whitney-c/a;
  published in Canada   514 1028 1542 3750 6625 9500
13(A-1 #63)-Frazetta, r-/Trail Colt #1, 7 pgs.   63   126   189   403   689   975
14(A-1 #77)-Bondage/hypo-c; last L. B. Cole Red Fox; Ingels-a
                                     314   628   942 2198 3849 5500
NOTE: **Guardineer** a-1-5; c-8. **Paul Parker** c-9, 11. **Whitney** a-2-14; c-1-6, 10, 12. **Red Fox** by L. B. **Cole** c-1-14.

716

A Man Called Kev #1 © WSP

Manhunter Special #1 © DC

Manifest Destiny #29 © Skybound

	GD	VG	FN	VF	VF/NM	NM-
	2.0	4.0	6.0	8.0	9.0	9.2

#15 was advertised but came out as Red Fox #15.

MANHUNTER (See Adventure #58, 73, Brave & the Bold, Detective Comics, 1st Issue Special, House of Mystery #143 and Justice League of America)
DC Comics: 1984 ($2.50, 76 pgs; high quality paper)

1-Simonson-c/a(r)/Detective; Batman app. 5.00

MANHUNTER
DC Comics: July, 1988 - No. 24, Apr, 1990 ($1.00)

1-24: 8,9-Flash app. 9-Invasion. 17-Batman-c/sty 4.00

MANHUNTER
DC Comics: No. 0, Nov, 1994 - No. 12, Nov, 1995 ($1.95/$2.25)

0-12 . . . . 4.00

MANHUNTER (Also see Batman: Streets of Gotham)
DC Comics: Oct, 2004 - No. 38, Mar, 2009 ($2.50/$2.99)

1-21: 1-Intro. Kate Spencer; Saiz-a/Jae Lee-c/Andreyko-s. 2,3 Shadow Thief app.
  13,14-Omac x-over. 20-One Year Later 3.00
22-30: 22-Begin $2.99-c. 23-Sandra Knight app. 27-Chaykin-c. 28-Batman app. 3.00
31-38: 31-(8/08) Gaydos-a. 33,34-Suicide Squad app. . . . 3.00
... Forgotten (2009, $17.99) r/#31-38 . . . . 18.00
... Origins (2007, $17.99) r/#15-23 . . . . 18.00
... Street Justice (2005, $12.99) r/#1-5; Andreyko intro. . . 13.00
... Trial By Fire (2007, $17.99) r/#6-14 . . . . 18.00
...: Unleashed (2008, $17.99) r/#24-30 . . . . 18.00

MANHUNTER: ...
DC Comics: 1979, 1999

The Complete Saga TPB (1979) Reprints stories from Detective Comics #437-443 by
  Goodwin and Simonson 40.00
The Special Edition TPB (1999, $9.95) r/stories from Detective Comics #437-443 12.00

MANHUNTER SPECIAL (Jack Kirby 100th Birthday tribute)
DC Comics: Oct, 2017 ($4.99, one-shot)

1-Paul Kirk Manhunter & Sandman and Sandy app.; Giffen-s/Buckingham-a; Demon back-up
  w/Rude-a; bonus Kirby reprint from Tales of the Unexpected #13; Bruce Timm-c 5.00

MANIAC OF NEW YORK
AfterShock Comics: Feb, 2021 - No. 5, Jun, 2021 ($4.99/$3.99)

1-($4.99) Elliott Kalan-s/Andrea Mutti-a 5.00
2-5-($3.99) 4.00

MANIAC OF NEW YORK: VOLUME 2 (The Bronx is Burning)
AfterShock Comics: Dec, 2021 - No. 4, Mar, 2022 ($4.99)

1-4-Elliott Kalan-s/Andrea Mutti-a 5.00

MANIAC OF NEW YORK: VOLUME 3 (Don't Call It a Comeback)
AfterShock Comics: Jan, 2023 - Present ($4.99)

1,2-Elliott Kalan-s/Andrea Mutti-a 5.00

MANIFEST DESTINY
Image Comics (Skybound): Nov, 2013 - No. 48, Dec, 2022 ($2.99/$3.99)

1-Lewis & Clark in 1804 American Frontier encountering zombies & other creatures;						
Chris Dingess-s/Matthew Roberts-a	3	6	9	16	24	32
2	1	3	4	6	8	10

3-30: 25-Back-up Sacagawea story 3.00
31-48-($3.99) 4.00

MANIFEST ETERNITY
DC Comics: Aug, 2006 - No. 6, Jan, 2007 ($2.99)

1-6-Lobdell-s/Nguyen-a/c 3.00

MAN IN BLACK (See Thrill-O-Rama) (Also see All New Comics, Front Page, Green Hornet #31, Strange Story and Tally-Ho Comics)
Harvey Publications: Sept, 1957 - No. 4, Mar, 1958

1-Bob Powell-c/a	22	44	66	128	209	290
2-4: Powell-c/a	15	30	45	90	140	190

MAN IN BLACK
Lorne-Harvey Publications (Recollections): 1990 - No. 2, July, 1991 (B&W)

1,2 . . . . 4.00

MAN IN FLIGHT (Disney, TV)
Dell Publishing Co.: No. 836, Sept, 1957

Four Color 836	7	14	21	48	89	130

MAN IN SPACE (Disney, TV, see Dell Giant #27)
Dell Publishing Co.: No. 716, Aug, 1956 - No. 954, Nov, 1958

Four Color 716-A science feat. from Tomorrowland	9	18	27	59	117	175

	GD	VG	FN	VF	VF/NM	NM-
	2.0	4.0	6.0	8.0	9.0	9.2

Four Color 954-Satellites	8	16	24	51	96	140

MANKIND (WWF Wrestling)
Chaos Comics: Sept, 1999 ($2.95, one-shot)

1-Regular and photo-c 5.00
1-Premium Edition ($10.00) Dwayne Turner & Danny Miki-c 10.00

MANN AND SUPERMAN
DC Comics: 2000 ($5.95, prestige format, one-shot)

nn-Michael T. Gilbert-s/a 6.00

MANN'S WORLD
AWA Studios: Jan, 2021 - No. 4, Apr, 2021 ($3.99, limited series)

1-4-Victor Gischler-s/Niko Walter-a 4.00

MAN OF STEEL, THE (Also see Superman: The Man of Steel)
DC Comics: 1986 (June release) - No. 6, 1986 (75¢, limited series)

1-6: Silver only; Byrne-c/a/scripts in all; origin, 1-Alternate-c for newsstand sales,1-Distr. to						
toy stores by So Much Fun, 2-6: 2-Intro. Lois Lane, Jimmy Olsen. 3-Intro/origin Magpie;						
Batman-c/story. 4-Intro. new Lex Luthor	1	2	3	5	6	8
1-6-Silver Editions (1993, $1.95)-r/1-6						3.00
...The Complete Saga nn (SC)-Contains #1-6, given away in contest; limited edition						
	4	8	12	28	47	65

NOTE: *Issues 1-6 were released between Action #583 (9/86) & Action #584 (1/87) plus Superman #423 (9/86) & Advs. of Superman #424 (1/87).*

MAN OF STEEL, THE (Also see Action Comics #1000)(Leads into Superman #1)
DC Comics: Jul, 2018 - No. 6, Sept, 2018 ($3.99, weekly limited series)

1-6-Bendis-s; Rogol Zaar app.; interlocking covers by Reis. 1-Reis-a; intro. Melody Moore.
  2-Shaner & Rude-a. 3-Sook-a. 4-Maguire-a. 5-Hughes-a. 6-Fabok-a . 4.00

MAN OF THE ATOM (See Solar, Man of the Atom Vol. 2)

MAN OF WAR (See Liberty Guards & Liberty Scouts)
Centaur Publications: Nov, 1941 - No. 2, Jan, 1942

1-The Fire-Man, Man of War, The Sentinel, Liberty Guards, & Vapo-Man begin;						
Gustavson-c/a; Flag-c	239	478	717	1530	2615	3700
2-Intro The Ferret; Gustavson-c/a	187	374	561	1197	2049	2900

MAN OF WAR
Eclipse Comics: Aug, 1987 - No. 3, Feb, 1988 ($1.75, Baxter paper)

1-3: Bruce Jones scripts 4.00

MAN OF WAR (See The Protectors)
Malibu Comics: 1993 - No. 8, Feb, 1994 ($1.95/$2.50/$2.25)

1-5 ($1.95)-Newsstand Editions w/different-c 4.00
1-8: 1-5-Collector's Edi. w/poster. 6-8 ($2.25): 6-Polybagged w/Skycap. 8-Vs. Rocket
  Rangers 5.00

MAN O' MARS
Fiction House Magazines: 1953; 1964

1-Space Rangers; Whitman-c	181	362	543	1158	1979	2800
I.W. Reprint #1-r/Man O'Mars #1 & Star Pirate; Murphy Anderson-a						
	9	18	27	58	114	170

MANOR BLACK
Dark Horse Comics: Jul, 2019 - No. 4, Oct, 2019 ($3.99, limited series)

1-4-Cullen Bunn & Brian Hurtt-s/Tyler Crook-a 4.00

MANOR BLACK: FIRE IN THE BLOOD
Dark Horse Comics: Feb, 2022 - No. 4, Jul, 2022 ($3.99, limited series)

1-4-Cullen Bunn & Brian Hurtt-s/Brian Hurtt-a 4.00

MANTECH ROBOT WARRIORS
Archie Enterprises, Inc.: Sept, 1984 - No. 4, Apr, 1985 (75¢)

1-4: Ayers-c/a(p). 1-Buckler-c(i) 4.00

MAN-THING (See Fear, Giant-Size..., Marvel Comics Presents, Marvel Fanfare, Monsters Unleashed, Power Record Comics & Savage Tales)
Marvel Comics Group: Jan, 1974 - No. 22, Oct, 1975; V2#1, Nov, 1979 - V2#11, July, 1981

1-Howard the Duck (2nd app.) cont'd/Fear #19	14	28	42	94	207	320
2	4	8	12	25	40	55
3-1st app. original Foolkiller	3	6	9	17	26	35
4-Origin Foolkiller; last app. 1st Foolkiller	3	6	9	16	24	32
5-11-Ploog-a. 11-Foolkiller cameo (flashback)	3	6	9	16	23	30
12-22: 19-1st app. Scavenger. 20-Spidey cameo. 21-Origin Scavenger, Man-Thing.						
22-Howard the Duck cameo	2	4	6	10	14	18
V2#1(1979)	2	4	6	13	18	22
						6.00
V2#2-11: 4-Dr. Strange-c/app. 11-Mayerik-a						

NOTE: *Alcala a-14. Brunner c-1. J. Buscema a-12p, 13p, 16p. Gil Kane c-4p, 10p, 12-20p, 21. Mooney a-17, 18, 19p, 20-22, V2#1-3p. Ploog Man-Thing-5p, 6p, 7, 8, 9-11p; c-5, 6, 8, 9, 11. Sutton a-13i. No. 19 says #10 in*

	GD 2.0	VG 4.0	FN 6.0	VF 8.0	VF/NM 9.0	NM- 9.2

indicia.

MAN-THING (Volume Three, continues in Strange Tales #1 (9/98))
Marvel Comics: Dec, 1997 - No. 8, July, 1998 ($2.99)
1-8-DeMatteis-s/Sharp-a. 2-Two covers. 6-Howard the Duck-c/app. — 5.00

MAN-THING (Prequel to 2005 movie)
Marvel Comics: Sept, 2004 - No. 3, Nov, 2004 ($2.99, limited series)
1-3-Hans Rodionoff-s/Kyle Hotz-a — 3.00
...: Whatever Knows Fear... (2005, $12.99, TPB) r/#1-3, Savage Tales #1, Adv. Into Fear #16 — 13.00

MAN-THING
Marvel Comics: May, 2017 - No. 5, Aug, 2017 ($3.99, limited series)
1-5-R.L. Stein-s/German Peralta-a; back-up horror short stories; Stein-s. 1-Origin re-told — 4.00

MANTLE
Image Comics: May, 2015 - No. 5, Sept, 2015 ($3.99)
1-5-Brisson-s/Level-a — 4.00

MANTRA
Malibu Comics (Ultraverse): July, 1993 - No. 24, Aug, 1995 ($1.95/$2.50)

	GD 2.0	VG 4.0	FN 6.0	VF 8.0	VF/NM 9.0	NM- 9.2
1-Polybagged w/trading card & coupon						5.00
1-Newsstand edition w/o trading card or coupon						4.00
1-Full cover holographic edition	2	4	6	8	11	14
1-Ultra-limited silver foil-c	1	3	4	6	8	10

2,3,5-9,11-24: 2-($2.50-Newsstand edition bagged w/card. 3-Intro Warstrike & Kismet.
6-Break-Thru x-over. 7-Prime app.; origin Prototype by Jurgens/Austin (2 pgs.)
11-New costume. 17-Intro NecroMantra & Pinnacle; prelude to Godwheel — 4.00
4-($2.50, 48 pgs.)-Rune flip-c/story by B. Smith (3 pgs.) — 5.00
10-($3.50, 68 pgs.)-Flip-c w/Ultraverse Premiere #2 — 5.00
Giant Size 1 (7/94, $2.50, 44 pgs.) — 5.00
...Spear of Destiny 1,2 (4/95, $2.50, 36pgs.) — 4.00

MANTRA (2nd Series) (Also See Black September)
Malibu Comics (Ultraverse): Infinity, Sept, 1995 - No. 7, Apr, 1996 ($1.50)
Infinity (9/95, $1.50)-Black September x-over, Intro new Mantra — 4.00
1-7: 1-(10/95). 5-Return of Eden (original Mantra). 6,7-Rush app. — 4.00

MAN WHO F#%ED UP TIME, THE
AfterShock Comics: Feb, 2020 - No. 5, Aug, 2020 ($3.99)
1-5-John Layman-s/Karl Mostert-a — 4.00

MAN WITH NO NAME, THE (Based on the Clint Eastwood gunslinger character)
Dynamite Entertainment: 2008 - No. 11, 2009 ($3.50)
1-11: 1-Gage-s/Dias-a/Isanove-c. 7-Bernard-a — 3.50

MAN WITHOUT FEAR (Follows Daredevil #612)
Marvel Comics: Feb, 2019 - No. 5, Mar, 2019 ($3.99, weekly limited series)
1-5-Jed McKay-s/Kyle Hotz-a. 1,5-Beyruth-a. 3-Defenders app. 4-Kingpin app. — 4.00

MAN WITH THE SCREAMING BRAIN (Based on screenplay by Bruce Campbell & David Goodman)
Dark Horse Comics: Apr, 2005 - No. 4, July, 2005 ($2.99, limited series)
1-4-Campbell-Goodman-s; Remender-a/c. 1-Variant-c by Noto. 3-Powell var-c.
4-Mignola var-c. — 3.00
TPB (11/05, $13.95) r/#1-4; David Goodman intro.; cover gallery — 14.00

MAN WITH THE X-RAY EYES, THE (See X... under Movie Comics)

MANY DEATHS OF LAILA STARR, THE
BOOM! Studios: Apr, 2021 - No. 5, Sept, 2021 ($3.99, limited series)
1-5-Ram V-s/Filipe Andrade-a — 4.00

MANY GHOSTS OF DR. GRAVES, THE (Doctor Graves #73 on)
Charlton Comics: 5/67 - No. 60, 12/76; No. 61, 9/77 - No. 62, 10/77; No. 63, 2/78 - No. 65, 4/78; No. 66, 6/81 - No. 72, 5/82

	GD 2.0	VG 4.0	FN 6.0	VF 8.0	VF/NM 9.0	NM- 9.2
1-Ditko-a; Palais-c; early issues 12¢-c	9	18	27	61	123	185
2-6,8,10	3	6	9	21	33	45
7,9-Ditko-a	4	8	12	25	40	55
11-13,16-18-Ditko-c/a	3	6	9	20	31	42
14,19,23,25	2	4	6	11	16	20
15,20,21-Ditko-a	3	6	9	15	22	28
22,24,26,27,29-35,38,40-Ditko-c/a	3	6	9	16	23	30
28-Ditko-c	2	4	6	9	15	22
36,46,56,57,59,61,66,67,69,71	2	4	6	8	11	14
37,41,43,51,60-Ditko-a	2	4	6	9	13	16
39,58-Ditko-c. 39-Sutton-a. 58-Ditko-a	2	4	6	9	13	16
42,44,53-Sutton-c; Ditko-a. 42-Sutton-a	2	4	6	9	13	16
45-(5/74) 2nd Newton comic work (8 pgs.); new logo; Sutton-c	2	4	6	11	16	20
47-Newton, Sutton, Ditko-a	2	4	6	10	14	18
48-Ditko, Sutton-a	2	4	6	9	13	16
49-Newton-c/a; Sutton-a.	2	4	6	9	13	16
50-Sutton-a	2	4	6	8	10	12
52-Newton-c; Ditko-a	2	4	6	9	13	16
54-Early Byrne-c; Ditko-a	2	4	6	10	14	18
55-Ditko-c; Sutton-a	2	4	6	9	13	16
62-65,68-Ditko-c/a. 65-Ditko-a	2	4	6	11	16	20
70,72-Ditko-a	2	4	6	9	13	16
Modern Comics Reprint 12,25 (1978)						6.00

NOTE: Aparo a-4, 5, 7, 8, 66r, 69r; c-8, 14, 19, 66r, 67r. Byrne c-54. Ditko a-1, 7, 9, 11-13, 15-18, 20-22, 24, 26, 27, 29, 30-35, 37, 38, 40-44, 47, 48, 50r, 60-65r, 70, 72; c-11-13, 16-18, 22, 24, 26-35, 38, 40, 55, 58, 62-65. Howard a-38, 39, 45i, 65; c-48. Kim a-36, 46, 52. Larson a-68. Morisi a-13, 14, 23, 26. Newton a-45, 47p, 49p; c-49, 52. Staton a-36, 37, 41, 43. Sutton a-39, 42, 47-50, 55, 65; c-42, 44, 45; painted c-53. Zeck a-56, 59.

MANY LOVES OF DOBIE GILLIS (TV)
National Periodical Publications: May-June, 1960 - No. 26, Oct, 1964

	GD 2.0	VG 4.0	FN 6.0	VF 8.0	VF/NM 9.0	NM- 9.2
1-Most covers by Bob Oksner	30	60	90	216	483	750
2-5	16	32	48	110	243	375
6-10: 10-Last 10¢-c	11	22	33	75	160	245
11-26: 20-Drucker-a. 24-(3-4/64). 25-(9/64)	10	20	30	65	135	205

MANY WORLDS OF TESLA STRONG, THE (Also see Tom Strong)

America's Best Comics: July, 2003 ($5.95, one-shot)
1-Two covers by Timm & Art Adams; art by various incl. Campbell, Cho, Noto, Hughes — 6.00

MARA
Image Comics: Dec, 2012 - No. 6, Oct, 2013 ($2.99)
1-6-Brian Wood-s/Ming Doyle-a — 3.00

MARAUDERS
Marvel Comics: Dec, 2019 - No. 27, Mar, 2022 ($4.99/$3.99)
1-($4.99) Duggan-s/Lolli-a; Kitty Pryde, Storm, Iceman, Emma Frost, Pyro app. — 5.00
2-12-($3.99) 2-Kate becomes the Red Queen. 3-Shinobi Shaw returns — 4.00
13-($4.99) "X of Swords" tie-in; Black Panther and Shuri app. — 5.00
14-20,22-26: 14,15- "X of Swords" tie-ins — 4.00
21-($4.99) Hellfire Gala; bonus reprint of Classic X-Men #7 — 4.00
27-($4.99) Duggan-s/Lolli & Noto-a — 5.00
Annual 1-(3/22, $4.99) Orlando-s/Creees Lee-a; Daken app. — 5.00

MARAUDERS
Marvel Comics: Jun, 2022 - No. 12, May, 2023 ($4.99/$3.99)
1-($4.99) Orlando-s/Carlini-a; Kate Pryde, Bishop, Psylocke, Daken, Aurora app. — 5.00
2-12-($3.99) 6-Judgment Day tie-in — 4.00

MARAUDER'S MOON (See Luke Short, Four Color #848)

MARCH OF COMICS (See Promotional Comics section)

MARCH OF CRIME (Formerly My Love Affair #1-6) (See Fox Giants)
Fox Feature Synd.: No. 7, July, 1950 - No. 2, Sept, 1950; No. 3, Sept, 1951

	GD 2.0	VG 4.0	FN 6.0	VF 8.0	VF/NM 9.0	NM- 9.2
7(#1)(7/50)-True crime stories; Wood-a	53	106	159	334	567	800
2(9/50)-Wood-a (exceptional)	53	106	159	334	567	800
3(9/51)	29	58	87	172	281	390

MARCO POLO (Also see Classic Comics #27)
Charlton Comics Group: 1962 (Movie classic)

	GD 2.0	VG 4.0	FN 6.0	VF 8.0	VF/NM 9.0	NM- 9.2
nn (Scarce)-Glanzman-c/a (25 pgs.)	12	24	36	82	179	275

MARC SILVESTRI SKETCHBOOK
Image Comics (Top Cow): Jan, 2004 ($2.99, one-shot)
1-Character sketches, concept artwork, storyboards of Witchblade, Darkness & others — 5.00

MARC SPECTOR: MOON KNIGHT (Also see Moon Knight)
Marvel Comics: June, 1989 - No. 60, Mar, 1994 ($1.50/$1.75, direct sales)

	GD 2.0	VG 4.0	FN 6.0	VF 8.0	VF/NM 9.0	NM- 9.2
1	3	6	9	16	23	30
2,3,5-10: 8,9-Punisher app.	1	3	4	6	8	10
4-Intro new Midnight	2	4	6	11	16	20

11-24,26-34,37-49,51-54: 15-Silver Sable app. 19-21-Spider-Man & Punisher app.
32,33-Hobgoblin II (Macendale) & Spider-Man (in black costume) app. 35-38-Punisher story.
42-44-Infinity War x-over. 46-Demogoblin app. 51,53-Gambit app. — 6.00
25,50: 25-(52 pgs.)-Ghost Rider app. 50-(56 pgs.)-Special die-cut-c

	GD 2.0	VG 4.0	FN 6.0	VF 8.0	VF/NM 9.0	NM- 9.2
35-Randall Spector app. (1st app. in Hulk magazine #17); Punisher app.	2	4	6	10	14	18
36-Shadow Knight app.; Punisher app.	3	6	9	14	20	25
55-New look; Platt-c/a	6	12	18	37	66	95
56-Platt-c/a	3	6	9	19	30	40
57-Spider-Man-c/app.; Platt-c/a	6	12	18	38	69	100
58,59-Platt-c	2	4	6	11	16	20
60-Platt-c/a; Moon Knight dies	2	4	6	11	16	22
...: Divided We Fall (4.95, 52 pgs.)	2	4	6	11	16	20
Special 1 (1992, $2.50)	1	2	3	6	9	12

NOTE: Cowan c(p) 20-23. Guice c-20. Heath c/a-4. Platt-a 55-57,60; c-55-60.

MARGARET O'BRIEN (See The Adventures of...)

MARGE'S LITTLE LULU (Continues as Little Lulu from #207 on)
Dell Publishing Co./Gold Key #165-206: No. 74, 6/45 - No. 164, 7-9/62; No. 165, 10/62 - No. 206, 8/72
Marjorie Henderson Buell, born in Philadelphia, Pa., in 1904, created Little Lulu, a cartoon character that appeared weekly in the Saturday Evening Post from Feb. 23, 1935 through Dec. 30, 1944. She was not responsible for any of the comic books. **John Stanley** did pencils only on all Little Lulu comics through at least #135 (1959). He did pencils and inks on Four Color #74 & 97. **Irving Tripp** began inking stories from #1 on, and remained the comic's illustrator throughout its entire run. Stanley did storyboards (layouts), pencils, and scripts in all cases and inking only on covers. His word balloons were written in cursive. Tripp and occasionally other artists at Western Publ. in Poughkeepsie, N.Y. blew up the pencilled pages, inked the blowups, and lettered them. **Arnold Drake** did storyboards, pencils and scripts starting with #197 (1970) on, amidst reprinted issues. Buell sold her rights exclusively to Western Publ. in Dec., 1971. The earlier issues had to be approved by Buell prior to publication.

	GD 2.0	VG 4.0	FN 6.0	VF 8.0	VF/NM 9.0	NM- 9.2
Four Color 74('45)-Intro Lulu, Tubby & Alvin	193	386	579	1592	3596	5600
Four Color 97(2/46)	71	142	213	568	1284	2000

(Above two books are all John Stanley - cover, pencils, and inks.)

	GD 2.0	VG 4.0	FN 6.0	VF 8.0	VF/NM 9.0	NM- 9.2
Four Color 110('46)-1st Alvin Story Telling Time; 1st app. Willy; variant cover exists	46	92	138	368	834	1300
Four Color 115-1st app. Boys' Clubhouse	44	88	132	326	738	1150
Four Color 120, 131: 120-1st app. Eddie	36	72	108	266	596	925
Four Color 139('47),146,158	35	70	105	252	564	875
Four Color 165 (10/47)-Smokes doll hair & has wild hallucinations. 1st Tubby detective story	42	84	126	311	706	1100
1(1-2/48)-Lulu's Diary feature begins	79	158	237	632	1416	2200
2-1st app. Gloria; 1st app. Miss Feeny	31	62	93	223	499	775
3-5	27	54	81	194	435	675
6-10: 7-1st app. Annie; Xmas-c	21	42	63	150	330	510
11-20: 18-X-Mas-c. 19-1st app. Wilbur. 20-1st app. Mr. McNabbem	17	34	51	114	252	390
21-30: 26-r/F.C. 110. 30-Xmas-c	15	30	45	100	220	340
31-38,40: 35-1st Mumday story	12	24	36	81	176	270
39-Intro. Witch Hazel in "That Awful Witch Hazel"	13	26	39	86	188	290
41-60: 42-Xmas-c. 45-2nd Witch Hazel app. 49-Gives Stanley & others credit	10	20	30	69	147	225
61-80: 63-1st app. Chubby (Tubby's cousin). 68-1st app. Prof. Cleff. 78-Xmas-c. 80-Intro. Little Itch (2/55)	9	18	27	57	111	165
81-99: 90-Xmas-c	7	14	21	46	86	125
100	7	14	21	49	92	135
101-130: 123-1st app. Fifi	6	12	18	37	66	95
131-164: 135-Last Stanley-p	5	10	15	33	57	80

Mara #1 © Brian Wood

Marineman #4 © Ian Churchill

Marmaduke Mouse #47 © QUA

	GD 2.0	VG 4.0	FN 6.0	VF 8.0	VF/NM 9.0	NM- 9.2
165-Giant; ...in Paris ('62)	9	18	27	61	123	185
166-Giant; ...Christmas Diary (1962 - '63)	9	18	27	61	123	185
167-169	4	8	12	28	47	65
170,172,175,176,178-196,198-200-Stanley-r. 182-1st app. Little Scarecrow Boy						
	3	6	9	17	26	35
171,173,174,177,197	3	6	9	16	23	30
201,203,206-Last issue to carry Marge's name	3	6	9	14	20	26
202,204,205-Stanley-r	3	6	9	16	23	30
...Summer Camp 1(8/67-G.K.-Giant) '57-58-r	5	10	15	35	63	90
...Trick 'N' Treat (12¢)(12/62-Gold Key)	6	12	18	40	73	105
Marge's Lulu and Tubby in Japan (15¢)(5-7/62) 01476-207						
	8	16	24	51	96	140

NOTE: See Dell Giant Comics #23, 29, 36, 42, 50, & Dell Giants for annuals. All Giants not by Stanley from L.L. on Vacation (7/54) on. Irving Tripp a-#1-on. Christmas c-7, 18, 30, 42, 78, 90, 126, 146, 250. Summer Camp issues #173, 177, 181, 189, 197, 201, 206.

MARGE'S LITTLE LULU (See Golden Comics Digest #19, 23, 27, 29, 33, 36, 40, 43, 46, & March of Comics #251, 267, 275, 293, 307, 323, 335, 349, 355, 369, 385, 406, 417, 427, 439, 456, 468, 475, 488)

MARGE'S TUBBY (Little Lulu)(See Dell Giants)
Dell Publishing Co./Gold Key: No. 381, Aug, 1952 - No. 49, Dec-Feb, 1961-62

Four Color 381(#1)-Stanley script; Irving Tripp-a	21	42	63	147	324	500
Four Color 430,444-Stanley-a	12	24	36	83	182	280
Four Color 461 (4/53)-1st Tubby & Men From Mars story; Stanley-a						
	11	22	33	76	163	250
5 (7-9/53)-Stanley-a	8	16	24	56	108	160
6-10	7	14	21	48	89	130
11-20	5	10	15	35	63	90
21-30	5	10	15	30	50	70
31-49	4	8	12	27	44	60
...& the Little Men From Mars No. 30020-410(10/64-G.K.)-25¢, 68 pgs.						
	7	14	21	44	82	120

NOTE: John Stanley did all storyboards & scripts through at least #35 (1959). Lloyd White did all art except F.C. 381, 430, 444, 461 & #5.

MARGIE (See My Little...)

MARGIE (TV)
Dell Publ. Co.: No. 1307, Mar-May, 1962 - No. 2, July-Sept, 1962 (Photo-c)

Four Color 1307(#1)	8	16	24	55	105	155
2	5	10	15	31	53	75

MARGIE COMICS (Formerly Comedy Comics; Reno Browne #50 on)
(Also see Cindy & Teen Comics)
Marvel Comics (ACI): No. 35, Winter, 1946-47 - No. 49, Dec, 1949

35	40	80	120	246	411	575
36-38,42,45,47-49	21	42	63	124	202	280
39,41,43(2),44,46-Kurtzman's "Hey Look"	22	44	66	132	216	300
40-Three "Hey Looks", three "Giggles 'n' Grins" by Kurtzman						
	24	48	72	142	234	325

MARINEMAN (Ian Churchill's...)
Image Comics: Dec, 2010 - No. 6, Jun, 2011 ($3.99/$4.99)

1-5-Ian Churchill-s/a/c						4.00
6-($4.99) Origin revealed						5.00

MARINES (See Tell It to the...)

MARINES ATTACK
Charlton Comics: Aug, 1964 - No. 9, Feb-Mar, 1966

1-Glanzman-a begins	4	8	12	28	47	65
2-9: 8-1st Vietnam war-c/story	3	6	9	18	28	38

MARINES AT WAR (Formerly Tales of the Marines #4)
Atlas Comics (OPI): No. 5, Apr, 1957 - No. 7, Aug, 1957

5-7	18	36	54	107	169	230

NOTE: Colan a-5. Drucker a-5. Everett a-5. Maneely a-5. Orlando a-7. Severin c-5.

MARINES IN ACTION
Atlas News Co.: June, 1955 - No. 14, Sept, 1957

1-Rock Murdock, Boot Camp Brady begin	27	54	81	158	259	360
2-14	18	36	54	105	165	225

NOTE: Berg a-2, 8, 9, 11, 14. Heath c-2, 9. Maneely c-1, 3. Severin a-4; c-7-11, 14.

MARINES IN BATTLE
Atlas Comics (ACI 1-12/WPI No. 13-25): Aug, 1954 - No. 25, Sept, 1958

1-Heath-c; Iron Mike McGraw by Heath; history of U.S. Marine Corps. begins						
	47	94	141	296	498	700
2-Heath-c	24	48	72	142	234	325
3-6,8-10: 4-Last precode (2/55); Romita-a	18	36	54	107	169	230
7-Kubert/Moskowitz-a (6 pgs.)	19	38	57	111	176	240

	GD 2.0	VG 4.0	FN 6.0	VF 8.0	VF/NM 9.0	NM- 9.2
11-16,18-21,24	17	34	51	98	154	210
17-Williamson-a (3 pgs.)	20	40	60	114	182	250
22,25-Torres-a	17	34	51	98	154	210
23-Crandall-a; Mark Murdock app.	18	36	54	105	165	225

NOTE: Berg a-22. G. Colan a-22, 23. Drucker a-6. Everett a-4, 15; c-21. Heath c-1, 2, 4. Maneely c-23, 24. Orlando a-14. Pakula a-6, 23. Powell a-14. Severin a-22; c-12. Sinnott a-23. Tuska a-15.

MARINE WAR HEROES (Charlton Premiere #19 on)
Charlton Comics: Jan, 1964 - No. 18, Mar, 1967

1-Montes/Bache-c/a	5	10	15	31	53	75
2-16,18: 11-Vietnam sty w/VC tunnels & moles.14,18-Montes/Bache-a						
	3	6	9	17	25	34
17-Tojo's plan to bomb Pearl Harbor & 1st Atomic bomb blast on Japan						
	5	10	15	34	60	85

MARJORIE FINNEGAN, TEMPORAL CRIMINAL
Artists, Writers & Artisans: May, 2021 - No. 8, Dec, 2021 ($3.99, limited series)

1-8-Garth Ennis-s/Goran Sudzuka-a/Andy Clarke-c						4.00

MARK, THE (Also see Mayhem)
Dark Horse Comics: Dec, 1993 - No. 4, Mar, 1994 ($2.50, limited series)

1-4						4.00

MARKED, THE
Image Comics (Shadowline): Oct, 2019 - No. 10, Dec, 2020 ($3.99, limited series)

1-10: 1-Hine & Haberlin-s/Haberlin-a						4.00
...: Halloween Special 1 (10/22, $5.99) Hine & Haberlin-s/Haberlin-a						6.00

MARK HAZZARD: MERC
Marvel Comics Group: Nov, 1986 - No. 12, Oct, 1987 (75¢)

1-Morrow-a	2	4	6	8	10	12
2-12: Morrow-a						4.00
Annual 1 (11/87, $1.25)						5.00

MARK OF CHARON (See Negation)
CG Entertainment: Apr, 2003 - No. 5, Aug, 2003 ($2.95, limited series)

1-5-Bedard-s/Bennett-a						3.00

MARK OF ZORRO (See Zorro, Four Color #228)

MARK OF ZORRO, THE
American Mythology Prods.: 2019 ($3.99, one-shot)

1-Reprints Four Color #228 (5/49); Bill Ely-a						4.00

MARK 1 COMICS (Also see Shaloman)
Mark 1 Comics: Apr, 1988 - No. 3, Mar, 1989 ($1.50)

1-3: Early Shaloman app. 2-Origin						4.00

MARKSMAN, THE (Also see Champions)
Hero Comics: Jan, 1988 - No. 5, 1988 ($1.95)

1-5: 1-Rose begins. 1-3-Origin The Marksman						4.00
Annual 1 ('88, $2.75, 52 pgs.)-Champions app.						5.00

MARK TRAIL
Standard Magazines (Hall Syndicate)/Fawcett Publ. No. 5: Oct, 1955; No. 5, Summer, 1959

1(1955)-Sunday strip-r	9	18	27	50	65	80
5(1959) By Ed Dodd	6	12	18	28	34	40
...Adventure Book of Nature 1 (Summer, 1958, 25¢, Pines)-100 pg. Giant; Special Camp Issue; contains 78 Sunday strip-r by Ed Dodd						
	10	20	30	54	72	90

MARMADUKE MONK
I. W. Enterprises/Super Comics: No date; 1963 (10¢)

I.W. Reprint 1 (nd)	2	4	6	8	11	14
Super Reprint 14 (1963)-r/Monkeyshines Comics #?	2	4	6	8	10	12

MARMADUKE MOUSE
Quality Comics Group (Arnold Publ.): Spring, 1946 - No. 65, Dec, 1956 (Early issues: 52 pgs.)

1-Funny animal	23	46	69	136	223	310
2	14	28	42	82	121	160
3-10	11	22	33	62	86	110
11-30	9	18	27	47	61	75
31-65: Later issues are 36 pgs.	8	16	24	40	50	60
Super Reprint #14(1963)	2	4	6	11	16	20

MARQUIS, THE
Oni Press

...: A Sin of One ($2.99, 5/03) Guy Davis-s/a; Michael Gaydos-c						3.00
...: Intermezzo TPB ($11.95, 12/03) r/A Sin of One and Hell's Courtesan #1,2						12.00

MARQUIS, THE: DANSE MACABRE
Oni Press: May, 2000 - No. 5, Feb, 2001 ($2.95, B&W, limited series)

	GD 2.0	VG 4.0	FN 6.0	VF 8.0	VF/NM 9.0	NM- 9.2

1-5-Guy Davis-s/a. 1-Wagner-c. 2-Mignola-c. 3-Vess-c. 5-K. Jones-c — 3.00
TPB (8/2001, $18.95) r/1-5 & Les Preludes; Seagle intro. — 19.00

MARQUIS, THE: DEVIL'S REIGN: HELL'S COURTESAN
Oni Press: Feb, 2002 - No. 2, Apr, 2002 ($2.95, B&W, limited series)
1,2-Guy Davis-s/a — 3.00

MARRIAGE OF HERCULES AND XENA, THE
Topps Comics: July, 1998 ($2.95, one-shot)
1-Photo-c; Lopresti-a; Alex Ross pin-up, 1-Alex Ross painted-c — 4.00
1-Gold foil logo-c — 5.00

MARRIED ... WITH CHILDREN (TV)(Based on Fox TV show)
Now Comics: June, 1990 - No. 7, Feb, 1991(12/90 inside) ($1.75)
V2#1, Sept, 1991 - No. 7, Apr, 1992 ($1.95)

1	2	4	6	9	13	16
2-7: 2-Photo-c, 1,2-2nd printing, V2#2-7: 1,4,6-Photo-c						5.00
V2#1	1	3	4	6	8	10
...Buck's Tale (6/94, $1.95)	1	2	3	5	6	8
...1994 Annual nn (2/94, $2.50, 52 pgs.)-Flip book format						5.00
Special 1 (7/92, $1.95)-Kelly Bundy photo-c/poster	1	3	4	6	8	10

MARRIED ... WITH CHILDREN: KELLY BUNDY
Now Comics: Aug, 1992 - No. 3, Oct, 1992 ($1.95, limited series)
1-3: Kelly Bundy photo-c & poster in each — 6.00

MARRIED ... WITH CHILDREN: QUANTUM QUARTET
Now Comics: Oct, 1993 - No. 4, 1994, ($1.95, limited series)
1-4: Fantastic Four parody — 6.00

MARRIED ... WITH CHILDREN: 2099
Now Comics: June, 1993 - No. 3, Aug, 1993 ($1.95, limited series)

1,2	1	3	4	6	8	10
3-Star Wars parody	2	4	6	11	16	20

MARS
First Comics: Jan, 1984 - No. 12, Jan, 1985 ($1.00, Mando paper)
1-12: Marc Hempel & Mark Wheatley story & art. 2-The Black Flame begins.
10-Dynamo Joe begins — 4.00
TPB (IDW Publ., 8/05, $39.99) r/#1-12, creator commentary; bonus art; new Hempel-c — 40.00

MARS & BEYOND (Disney, TV)
Dell Publishing Co.: No. 866, Dec, 1957

Four Color 866-A Science feat. from Tomorrowland	9	18	27	62	126	190

MARS ATTACKS
Topps Comics: May, 1994 - No. 5, Sept, 1994 ($2.95, limited series)

1-5-Giffen story; flip books	2	4	6	8	10	12
Gold Edition (5/94)	3	6	9	16	23	30
Special Edition (5/94)	2	4	6	9	12	15
Trade paperback (12/94, $12.95)-r/limited series plus new 8 pg. story						15.00

MARS ATTACKS
Topps Comics: V2#1, 8/95 - V2#3, 10/95; V2#4, 1/96 - No. 7, 5/96($2.95, bi-monthly #6 on)
V2#1-7: 1-Counterstrike storyline begins. 4-(1/96). 5-(1/96). 5,7-Brereton-c.
6-(3/96)-Simonson-c. 7-Story leads into Baseball Special #1 — 5.00
Baseball Special 1 (6/96, $2.95)-Bisley-c. — 5.00

MARS ATTACKS
IDW Publishing: Jun, 2012 - No. 10, May, 2013 ($3.99, issues #6-10 polybagged with card)
1-10: 1-Layman-s/McCrea-a; 58 covers including all 54 cards from 1962 set — 4.00
... #1 IDW's Greatest Hits Edition (3/16, $1.00) reprints #1 — 3.00
... Art Gallery (9/14, $3.99) Trading card style art by various — 4.00
...: Classics Obliterated (6/13, $7.99) Spoofs of Moby Dick, Jekyll & Hyde, Robinson Crusoe — 8.00
... KISS (1/13, $3.99) Ryall-s/Robinson-a; 2 variant-c with Judge Dredd & Star Slammers — 4.00
... Popeye (1/13, $3.99) Beatty-a; 2 variant-c with Miss Fury & Opus — 4.00
... The Holidays (10/12, $7.99) short stories for Halloween-Christmas; 5 covers — 8.00
... The Real Ghostbusters (1/13, $3.99) Holder-a; 2 variant-c with Chew & Madman — 4.00
... : The Transformers (1/13, $3.99) 2 variant-c with Spike & Strangers in Paradise — 4.00
... Zombie vs. Robots (1/13, $3.99) Ryall-s; 2 variant-c with Rog-2000 & Cerebus — 4.00

MARS ATTACKS
Dynamite Entertainment: 2018 - No. 5, 2019 ($3.99, limited series)
1-5-Kyle Starks-s/Chris Schweizer-a; multiple covers on each — 4.00

MARS ATTACKS FIRST BORN
IDW Publishing: May, 2014 - No. 4, Aug, 2014 ($3.99, limited series)
1-4-Chris Ryall-s/Sam Kieth-a; multiple covers on each — 4.00

MARS ATTACKS HIGH SCHOOL
Topps Comics: May, 1997 - No. 2, Sept, 1997 ($2.95, B&W, limited series)
1,2-Stelfreeze-c — 4.00

MARS ATTACKS JUDGE DREDD
IDW Publishing: Sept, 2013 - No. 4, Dec, 2013 ($3.99, limited series)
1-4-Al Ewing-s/John McCrea-a/Greg Staples-c — 4.00

MARS ATTACKS IMAGE
Topps Comics: Dec, 1996 - No. 4, Mar, 1997 ($2.50, limited series)
1-4-Giffen-s/Smith & Sienkiewicz-a — 4.00

MARS ATTACKS: OCCUPATION
IDW Publishing: Mar, 2016 - No. 5, Jul, 2016 ($3.99, limited series)
1-5-John Layman-s/Andy Kuhn-a; multiple covers — 4.00

MARS ATTACKS / RED SONJA
Dynamite Entertainment: 2020 - No. 5, 2020 ($3.99, limited series)
1-5-John Layman-s/Fran Strukan-a; multiple covers. 3-Intro. Green Sonja — 4.00

MARS ATTACKS THE SAVAGE DRAGON
Topps Comics: Dec, 1996 - No. 4, Mar, 1997 ($2.95, limited series)
1-4: 1-w/bound-in card — 4.00

MARSHAL BLUEBERRY (See Blueberry)

Marvel Comics (Epic Comics): 1991 ($14.95, graphic novel)

1-Moebius-a	4	8	12	25	40	55

MARSHAL LAW (Also see Crime And Punishment: Marshall Law...)
Marvel Comics (Epic Comics): Oct, 1987 - No. 6, May, 1989 ($1.95, mature)
1-6 — 4.00

M.A.R.S. PATROL TOTAL WAR (Formerly Total War #1,2)
Gold Key: No. 3, Sept, 1966 - No. 10, Aug, 1969 (All-Painted-c except #7)

3-Wood-a; aliens invade USA	6	12	18	42	79	115
4-10	4	8	12	23	37	50
Wally Wood's M.A.R.S. Patrol Total War TPB (Dark Horse, 9/04, $12.95) r/#3 & Total War #1&2; foreward by Batton Lash; afterword by Dan Adkins						13.00

MARTHA WASHINGTON (Also see Dark Horse Presents Fifth Anniversary Special, Dark Horse Presents #100-4, Give Me Liberty, Happy Birthday Martha Washington & San Diego Comicon Comics #2)

MARTHA WASHINGTON... (one-shots)
Dark Horse Comics (Legend): ($2.95/$3.50, one-shots)
... Dies (7/07, $3.50) Miller-s/Gibbons-a; r/Miller's original outline for Give Me Liberty — 4.00
... Stranded in Space (11/95, $2.95) Miller-s/Gibbons-a; Big Guy app. — 5.00

MARTHA WASHINGTON GOES TO WAR
Dark Horse Comics (Legend): May, 1994 - No. 5, Sep, 1994 ($2.95, lim. series)
1-5-Miller scripts; Gibbons-c/a — 5.00
TPB ($17.95) r/#1-5 — 18.00

MARTHA WASHINGTON SAVES THE WORLD
Dark Horse Comics: Dec, 1997 - No. 3, Feb, 1998 ($2.95/$3.95, lim. series)
1,2-Miller scripts; Gibbons-c/a in all — 5.00
3-($3.95) — 5.00

MARTHA WAYNE (See The Story of...)

MARTIAN MANHUNTER (See Detective Comics & Showcase '95 #9)
DC Comics: May, 1988 - No. 4, Aug,. 1988 ($1.25, limited series)
1-4: 1,4-Batman app. 2-Batman cameo — 4.00
Special 1-(1996, $3.50) — 5.00

MARTIAN MANHUNTER (See JLA)
DC Comics: No. 0, Oct, 1998 - No. 36, Nov, 2001 ($1.99)
0-(10/98) Origin retold; Ostrander-s/Mandrake-c/a — 4.00
1-36: 1-(12/98). 6-9-JLA app. 18,19-JSA app. 24-Mahnke-a — 4.00
#1,000,000 (11/98) 853rd Century x-over — 4.00
Annual 1,2 (1998,1999; $2.95) 1-Ghosts; Wrightson-c. 2-JLApe — 5.00

MARTIAN MANHUNTER (See DCU Brave New World)
DC Comics: Oct, 2006 - No. 8, May, 2007 ($2.99, limited series)
1-8-Lieberman-s/Barrionuevo-a/c — 3.00
...: The Others Among Us TPB (2007, $19.99) r/#1-8 & story from DCU Brave New World 20.00

MARTIAN MANHUNTER
DC Comics: Aug, 2015 - No. 12, Jul, 2016 ($2.99)
1-12: 1-Rob Williams-s/Eddy Barrows-a. 1-3-JLA app. 10-Origin — 3.00

MARTIAN MANHUNTER
DC Comics: Feb, 2019 - No. 12, Apr, 2020 ($3.99)
1-12: 1-Orlando-s/Rossmo-a; Earth detective and flashbacks to Mars. 3-Origin retold — 4.00

MARTIAN MANHUNTER: AMERICAN SECRETS
DC Comics: 1992 - Book Three, 1992 ($4.95, limited series, prestige format)
1-3: Barreto-a — 5.00

MARTIAN MANHUNTER/ MARVIN THE MARTIAN SPECIAL
DC Comics: 2017 ($4.99, one-shot)
1-Orlando & Barbiere-s/Lopresti-a; covers by Lopresti & DeStefano — 5.00

MARTIN KANE (William Gargan as... Private Eye)(Stage/Screen/Radio/TV)
Fox Feature Syndicate (Hero Books): No. 4, June, 1950 - No. 2, Aug, 1950 (Formerly My Secret Affair)

4(#1)-True crime stories; Wood-c/a(2); used in SOTI, pg. 160; photo back-c		43	86	129	271	461	650
2-Wood/Orlando story, 5 pgs; Wood-a(2)	33	66	99	194	317	440

MARTIN LUTHER KING AND THE MONTGOMERY STORY (See Promotional Comics section)

MARTIN MYSTERY
Dark Horse (Bonelli Comics): Mar, 1999 - No. 6, Aug, 1999 ($4.95, B&W, digest size)
1-6-Reprints Italian series in English; Gibbons-c on #1-3 — 5.00

MARTY MOUSE
I. W. Enterprises: No date (1958?) (10¢)

1-Reprint	3	6	9	16	23	30

MARVEL
Marvel Comics: May, 2020 - No. 6, May, 2021 ($4.99)
1-6-Short story anthology; Alex Ross-s/a. 1-Busiek-s/Rude-a. 2-Powell-s/a; Brereton-s/a. 3-Weiss-s/a. 4-Acuña-s/a; Barta-s/a, Dr. Droom app. 5-Hughes-a/s — 5.00

MARVEL ACTION: AVENGERS (All ages)(Title changed from Avengers after #5)
IDW Publishing: No. 6, May, 2019 - No. 9, Sept, 2019 ($3.99)
6-9-Iron Man, Captain America, Thor, Hawkeye, Black Widow, Black Panther & Hulk app. 4.00

MARVEL ACTION: CAPTAIN MARVEL (All ages)
IDW Publishing: 2019 - No. 3, Oct, 2019 ($3.99)
1-3-Spider-Woman app.; Sam Maggs-s/Sweeney Boo-a — 4.00

MARVEL ACTION: CAPTAIN MARVEL (2nd series)(All ages)
IDW Publishing: Jan, 2021 - No. 5, May, 2021 ($3.99)
1-5: 1,2-Ghost-Spider app.; Sam Maggs-s — 4.00

MARVEL ACTION: CHILLERS (All ages)
IDW Publishing: Oct, 2020 - No. 4, Dec, 2020 ($3.99)
1-4-Iron Man, Ironheart & Dr. Strange app. 2-Elsa Bloodstone app. 3-Venom app. — 4.00

MARVEL ACTION CLASSICS (All ages)

Mars Attacks Judge Dredd #2 © Topps & Rebellion

Marvel Action: Origins #1 © MAR

Marvel Age #63 © MAR

MA

	GD	VG	FN	VF	VF/NM	NM-
	2.0	4.0	6.0	8.0	9.0	9.2

IDW Publishing: May, 2019 - Present ($4.99)

... Ant-Man 1 (11/19, $4.99) Ant-Man reprints; Van Lente-s/Lolli-a; Clayton Henry-c						5.00
... Avengers Featuring Doctor Strange 1 (1/20, $4.99) Reprints; Spider-Man app.						5.00
... Hulk 1 (7/19, $4.99) Reprints; Doctor Strange, Iron Man and Spider-Man app.						5.00
... Spider-Man 1 (5/19, $4.99) Reprints; Doctor Strange and Thor app.						5.00
... Spider-Man Two-In-One 2-4 (12/19 - No. 4, 10/21, $4.99) Reprints						5.00

MARVEL ACTION HOUR FEATURING IRON MAN (TV cartoon)
Marvel Comics: Nov, 1994 - No. 8, June, 1995 ($1.50/$2.95)

1-8: Based on cartoon series						4.00
1 ($2.95)-Polybagged w/16 pg Marvel Action Hour Preview & acetate print						5.00

MARVEL ACTION HOUR FEATURING THE FANTASTIC FOUR (TV cartoon)
Marvel Comics: Nov, 1994 - No. 8, June, 1995 ($1.50/$2.95)

1-8: Based on cartoon series						4.00
1-($2.95)-Polybagged w/ 16 pg Marvel Action Hour Preview & acetate print						5.00

MARVEL ACTION: ORIGINS (All ages stories)
IDW Publishing (Marvel): Dec, 2020 - No. 4, Oct, 2021 ($3.99)

1-Origins of Spider-Man & Thanos. 2-Captain Marvel. 3-Incredible Hulk & Venom. 4-Miles Morales Spider-Man						4.00

MARVEL ACTION: SPIDER-MAN (All ages stories)
IDW Publishing (Marvel): Nov, 2018 - No. 12, Nov, 2019 ($3.99)

1-12: 1-3-Dawson-s/Ossio-a; teen-age Peter Parker, Miles and Spider-Gwen app.						4.00
Volume 2 (1/20 - No. 3, 7/20) 1-3-Teen-age Peter Parker, Miles and Spider-Gwen app.						4.00
Volume 3 (3/21 - No. 5, 8/21) 1-5-Teen-age Peter Parker. 1,2-Scorpion app.						4.00

MARVEL ACTION UNIVERSE (TV cartoon)
Marvel Comics: Jan, 1989 ($1.00, one-shot)

1-r/Spider-Man And His Amazing Friends						4.00

MARVEL ADVENTURES
Marvel Comics: Apr, 1997 - No. 18, Sept, 1998 ($1.50)

1-18-"Animated style": 1,4,7-Hulk-c/app. 2,11-Spider-Man. 3,8,15-X-Men. 5-Spider-Man & X-Men. 6-Spider-Man & Human Torch. 9,12-Fantastic Four. 10,16-Silver Surfer. 13-Spider-Man & Silver Surfer. 14-Hulk & Dr. Strange. 18-Capt. America						4.00

MARVEL ADVENTURES...
Marvel Comics: 2007, 2008 (Free Comic Book Day giveaways)

... Free Comic Book Day 2007 (6/07) 1-Iron Man, Hulk and Franklin Richards app.						3.00
... Free Comic Book Day 2008 - Iron Man, Hulk, Ant-Man and Spider-Man app.						3.00

MARVEL ADVENTURES FANTASTIC FOUR (All ages title)
Marvel Comics: No. 0, July, 2005 - No. 48, July, 2009 ($1.99/$2.50/$2.99)

0-($1.99) Movie version characters; Doc. Doom app.; Eaton-a						3.00
1-10-($2.50) 1-Skrulls app. 7-Namor app.						3.00
11-48-($2.99) 12,42-Dr. Doom app. 24-Namor app. 26,28-Silver Surfer app.						3.00
... Vol. 1: Family of Heroes (2005, $6.99, digest) r/#1-4						7.00
... Vol. 2: Fantastic Voyages (2006, $6.99, digest) r/#5-8						7.00
... Vol. 3: World's Greatest (2006, $6.99, digest) r/#9-12						7.00
... Vol. 4: Cosmic Threats (2006, $6.99, digest) r/#13-16						7.00
... Vol. 5: All 4 One, 4 For All (2007, $6.99, digest) r/#17-20						7.00
... Vol. 6: Monsters & Mysteries (2007, $6.99, digest) r/#21-24						7.00
... Vol. 7: The Silver Surfer (2007, $6.99, digest) r/#25-28						7.00
... Vol. 8: Monsters, Moles, Cowboys & Coupons (2008, $7.99, digest) r/#29-32						8.00

MARVEL ADVENTURES FLIP MAGAZINE (All ages title)
Marvel Comics: Aug, 2005 - No. 26, Sept, 2007 ($3.99/$4.99)

1-11: 1-10-Rep. Marvel Advs. Fantastic Four and Marvel Advs. Spider-Man in flip format						4.00
12-14-($4.99) Reprints Marvel Advs. Spider-Man & X-Men/Power Pack in flip format						5.00
15-26-Rep. Marvel Advs. Fantastic Four and Marvel Advs. Spider-Man in flip format						5.00

MARVEL ADVENTURES HULK (All ages title)
Marvel Comics: Sept, 2007 - No. 16, Dec, 2008 ($2.99)

1-16: 1-New version of Hulk's origin; Pagulayan-c. 2-Jamie Madrox app. 13-Mummies						3.00
... Vol. 1: Misunderstood Monster (2007, $6.99, digest) r/#1-4						7.00

MARVEL ADVENTURES IRON MAN (All ages title)
Marvel Comics: July, 2007 - No. 13, Jul, 2008 ($2.99)

1-13: 1-4-Michael Golden-c. 1-New version of Iron Man's origin. 2-Intro. the Mandarin						3.00
... Vol. 1: Heart of Steel (2007, $6.99, digest) r/#1-4						7.00
... Vol. 2: Iron Armory (2008, $7.99, digest) r/#5-8						8.00

MARVEL ADVENTURES SPIDER-MAN (All ages title)
Marvel Comics: May, 2005 - No. 61, May, 2010 ($2.50/$2.99)

1-13-Lee & Ditko stories retold with new art. 13-Conner-c						3.00
14-48: 14-Begin $2.99-c. 14-16-Conner-c. 22,23-Black costume. 35-Venom app.						3.00
50-($3.99) Sinister Six app.; back-up w/Sonny Liew-a						4.00

51-61: 53-Emma Frost becomes a regular; intro. Chat; Skottie Young-c begin						3.00
... Vol. 1 HC (2006, $19.99, with dustjacket) r/#1-8; plot for #7; sketch pages from #6,8						20.00
... Vol. 1: The Sinister Six (2005, $6.99, digest) r/#1-4						7.00
... Vol. 2: Power Struggle (2005, $6.99, digest) r/#5-8						7.00
... Vol. 3: Doom With a View (2006, $6.99, digest) r/#9-12						7.00
... Vol. 4: Concrete Jungle (2006, $6.99, digest) r/#13-16						7.00
... Vol. 5: Monsters on the Prowl (2007, $6.99, digest) r/#17-20						7.00
... Vol. 6: The Black Costume (2007, $6.99, digest) r/#21-24						7.00
... Vol. 7: Secret Identity (2007, $6.99, digest) r/#25-28						7.00
... Vol. 8: Forces of Nature (2008, $7.99, digest) r/#29-32						8.00
... Vol. 9: Fiercest Foes (2008, $7.99, digest) r/#33-36						8.00

MARVEL ADVENTURES SPIDER-MAN (All ages title)
Marvel Comics: June, 2010 - No. 24, May, 2012 ($3.99/$2.99)

1-($3.99) Tobin-s; Franklin Richards back-up						4.00
2-23-($2.99): 3,7-Wolverine app. 3,4-Bullseye app. 6-Doctor Octopus app.						3.00

MARVEL ADVENTURES STARRING DAREDEVIL (...Adventure #3 on)
Marvel Comics Group: Dec, 1975 - No. 6, Oct, 1976

	GD	VG	FN	VF	VF/NM	NM-
1	3	6	9	16	23	30
2-6-r/Daredevil #22-27 by Colan. 3-5-(25¢-c)	1	3	4	6	8	10
3-5-(30¢-c variants, limited distribution) (4,6,8/76)	6	12	18	42	79	115

MARVEL ADVENTURES SUPER HEROES (All ages title)
Marvel Comics: Sept, 2008 - No. 21, May, 2010 ($2.99)

1-21: 1-4: Spider-Man, Hulk and Iron Man team-ups. 1-Hercules app. 5-Dr. Strange app. 6-Ant-Man origin re-told. 7-Thor. 8,12-Capt. America. 17-Avengers begin						3.00

MARVEL ADVENTURES SUPER HEROES (All ages title)
Marvel Comics: June, 2010 - No. 24, May, 2012 ($3.99/$2.99)

1-($3.99) Iron Man and Avengers vs. Magneto						4.00
2-24-($2.99) 4-Deadpool app. 5-Rhino app. 11,12,22-Hulk app. 13,14,19-Thor						3.00

MARVEL ADVENTURES THE AVENGERS (All ages title)
Marvel Comics: July, 2006 - No. 39, Oct, 2009 ($2.99)

1-39-Spider-Man, Wolverine, Hulk, Iron Man, Capt. America, Storm, Giant-Girl app.						3.00
... Vol. 1: Heroes Assembled (2006, $6.99, digest) r/#1-4						7.00
... Vol. 2: Mischief (2007, $6.99, digest) r/#5-8						7.00
... Vol. 3: Bizarre Adventures (2007, $6.99, digest) r/#9-12						7.00
... Vol. 4: The Dream Team (2007, $6.99, digest) r/#13-15 & Giant-Size #1						7.00
... Vol. 5: Some Assembling Required (2008, $7.99, digest) r/#16-19						8.00

MARVEL ADVENTURES TWO-IN-ONE
Marvel Comics: Oct, 2007 - No. 18 ($4.99, bi-weekly)

1-18: 1-9-Reprints Marvel Adventures Spider-Man and Fantastic Four stories. 10-Hulk						5.00

MARVEL AGE (The Official Marvel News Magazine)
(A low priced news Magazine in comic format to promote coming issues)
Marvel Publications: Apr, 1983 - No. 140, Sept, 1994

	GD	VG	FN	VF	VF/NM	NM-
1-Saga of Crystar-c/s	2	4	6	8	11	14
2-5,9,11,14,15						5.00
6-Beta Ray Bill preview (9/83)	3	6	9	14	20	25
7-Spider-Ham preview	1	3	4	6	8	10
8-Stan Lee/Jim Shooter-c/interviews	2	4	6	8	11	14
10-Star Wars-c, preview Spider-Man vs. Hobgoblin	2	4	6	8	10	12
12-(3/84) 2 pg. preview/1st app. of Spider-Man in Alien Venom black costume, 2 months before Amazing Spider-Man #252	5	10	15	34	60	85
13,16: 16-New Mutants-c/s						6.00
17-Transformers preview (8/84)	2	4	6	9	13	16
18-24,26-28,30,32-37,39,40						4.00
25(4/85)-Rocket Raccoon-c/preview art one month before Rocket Raccoon #1						6.00
29-Longshot preview (8/85)	2	4	6	9	12	15
31-Thundercats preview (10/85)	2	4	6	11	16	20
38-He-Man & Masters of the Universe-c/preview	2	4	6	8	12	15
41(8/86)-Classic Stan Lee-c/sty	4	8	12	28	47	65
42-66: 53-Girls of Marvel swimsuits-c						4.00
67-Jim Lee-c, Wolverine/punisher/Sub-Mariner-c/s						6.00
68-86,88,89: 76-She-Hulk swimsuit-c by John Byrne						5.00
87-Danny Ketch as Ghost Rider	2	4	6	11	16	20
90(7/90)-Spider-Man-c by Todd McFarlane; Jim Lee Interview	3	6	9	16	23	30
91-Thanos and Silver Surfer-c	2	4	6	8	11	14
92-94,96,98,101-103,105-137,139						4.00
95-Captain America 50th Anniversary-c/issue						6.00
97(2/91)-Darkhawk-c/preview; Infinity Gauntlet	4	8	12	25	40	55
99(4/91)-Black Panther Returns-c	2	4	6	9	12	15
100-Sleepwalker	1	3	4	6	8	10

	GD 2.0	VG 4.0	FN 6.0	VF 8.0	VF/NM 9.0	NM- 9.2
104-Wolverine-c by Jim Lee; Psylocke cameo	3	6	9	19	30	40
138(7/94)-Deadpool, Cable-c	2	4	6	11	16	20
140-Last issue	1	3	4	6	8	10
Annual 1(9/85)	2	4	6	8	10	12
Annual 2, 3(9/87)						5.00
Annual 4(6/88)-1st app. Damage Control	2	4	6	8	11	14
No. 1000 (10/23, $9.99) Short stories by various incl. Allred, McNiven, Sauvage, Waid						10.00

MARVEL AGE FANTASTIC FOUR (All ages title)
Marvel Comics: Jun, 2004 - No. 12, Mar, 2005 ($2.25)

1-12-Lee & Kirby stories retold with new art by various. 11-Impossible Man app.						3.00
...Tales (4/05, $2.25) retells first meeting with the Black Panther; O'Hare & Lim-a						3.00
Vol. 1: All For One TPB (2004, $5.99, digest size) r/#1-4						6.00
Vol. 2: Doom TPB (2004, $5.99, digest size) r/#5-8						6.00
Vol. 3: The Return of Doctor Doom TPB (2005, $5.99, digest size) r/#9-12						6.00

MARVEL AGE HULK (All ages title)
Marvel Comics: Nov, 2004 - No. 4, Feb, 2005 ($1.75)

1-3-Lee & Kirby stories retold with new art by various						3.00
Vol. 1: Incredible TPB (2005, $5.99, digest) r/#1-4						6.00
Vol. 2: Defenders (2008, $7.99, digest) r/#5-8						8.00

MARVEL AGE SPIDER-MAN (All ages title)
Marvel Comics: May, 2004 - No. 20, Mar, 2005 ($2.25)

1-20-Lee & Ditko stories retold with new art. 4-Doctor Doom app. 5-Lizard app.						3.00
1-(Free Comic Book Day giveaway, 8/04) Spider-Man vs. The Vulture; Brooks-a						3.00
Vol. 1 TPB (2004, $5.99, digest) 1-r/#1-4						6.00
Vol. 2: Everyday Hero TPB (2004, $5.99, digest) r/#5-8						6.00
Vol. 3: Swingtime TPB (2004, $5.99, digest) r/#9-12						6.00
Spidey Strikes Back TPB (2005, 5.99, digest) r/#17-20						6.00

MARVEL AGE SPIDER-MAN TEAM-UP (Marvel Adventures on cover)
Marvel Comics: June, 2005 (Free Comic Book Day giveaway)

1-Spider-Man meets the Fantastic Four						3.00

MARVEL AGE SPIDER-MAN TEAM-UP (All ages Spider-Man team-ups) (Also see Free Comic Book Day edition in the Promotional Comics section)
Marvel Comics: Jan, 2005 - No. 5, Apr, 2005 ($1.75)

1-5-Stories retold with new art by various. 1-Fantastic Four app. 3-Kitty Pryde app.						3.00
... Vol. 1: A Little Help From My Friends (2005, $7.99, digest) r/#1-5						8.00

MARVEL AND DC PRESENT FEATURING THE UNCANNY X-MEN AND THE NEW TEEN TITANS
Marvel Comics/DC Comics: 1982 ($2.00, 68 pgs., one-shot, Baxter paper)

1-3rd app. Deathstroke the Terminator; Darkseid app.; Simonson/Austin-a	3	6	9	21	33	45

MARVEL APES
Marvel Comics: Nov, 2008 - No. 4, Dec, 2008 ($3.99, limited series)

1-4: 1-Kesel-s/Bachs-a; back-up history story with Peyer-s/Kitson-a; two covers						4.00
1-($10.00) Hero limited edition with Daredevil gorilla cover by Mike Wieringo						10.00
#0-(2008, $3.99) r/Amazing Spider-Man #110,111; gallery of Marvel Apes variant covers						4.00
...: Amazing Spider-Monkey Special 1 (6/09, $3.99) Sandman and the Apevengers app.						4.00
...: Grunt Line 1 (7/09, $3.99) Kesel-s; Charles Darwin app.						4.00
...: Speedball Special 1 (5/09, $3.99) Bachs & Hardin-a						4.00

MARVEL ASSISTANT-SIZED SPECTACULAR
Marvel Comics: Jun, 2009 - No. 2, Jun, 2009 ($3.99, limited series)

1,2-Short stories by various incl. Isanove, Giarrusso, Nauck, Wyatt Cenak, Warren						4.00

MARVEL ATLAS (Styled after the Official Marvel Handbooks)
Marvel Comics: 2007 - No. 2, 2008 ($3.99, limited series)

1,2-Profiles and maps of countries in the Marvel Universe						4.00

MARVEL BOY (Astonishing #3 on; see Marvel Super Action #4)
Marvel Comics (MPC): Dec, 1950 - No. 2, Feb, 1951

1-Origin Marvel Boy by Russ Heath	226	452	678	1446	2473	3500
2-Everett-a; Washington D.C. under attack	181	362	543	1158	1979	2800

MARVEL BOY (Marvel Knights)
Marvel Comics: Aug, 2000 - No. 6, Mar, 2001 ($2.99, limited series)

1-Intro. Marvel Boy; Morrison-s/J.G. Jones-c/a						4.00
1-DF Variant-c						5.00
2-6						3.00
TPB (6/01, $15.95)						16.00

MARVEL BOY: THE URANIAN (Agents of Atlas)
Marvel Comics: Mar, 2010 - No. 3, May, 2010 ($3.99, limited series)

1-3-Origin re-told; back-up reprints from 1950s; Heath & Everett-a						4.00

MARVEL CHILLERS (Also see Giant-Size Chillers)
Marvel Comics Group: Oct, 1975 - No. 7, Oct, 1976 (All 25¢ issues)

1-Intro. Modred the Mystic, ends #2; Kane-c(p)	8	16	24	52	99	145
2-2nd Modred	4	8	9	17	26	35
3-Tigra, the Were-Woman begins (origin), ends #7 (see Giant-Size Creatures #1); Chaykin/Wrightson-c	6	12	18	41	76	110
4,5,7: 4-Kraven app. 5,6-Red Wolf app. 7-Kirby-c; Tuska-a	2	4	6	11	16	20
4-6-(30¢-c variants, limited distribution)(4-8/76)	5	10	15	34	60	85
6-Byrne-a(p); Buckler-c(p)	3	6	9	14	20	26

NOTE: *Bolle* a-1. *Buckler* c-2. *Kirby* c-7.

MARVEL CLASSICS COMICS SERIES FEATURING...
(Also see Pendulum Illustrated Classics)
Marvel Comics Group: 1976 - No. 36, Dec, 1978 (52 pgs., no ads)

1-Dr. Jekyll and Mr. Hyde	2	4	6	13	18	22
2-10,18: 28-1st Golden-c/a; Pit and the Pendulum	2	4	6	8	11	14
11-27,29-36	1	3	4	6	8	10

NOTE: *Adkins* c-1i, 4i, 12i. *Alcala* a-34i; c-34. *Bolle* a-35. *Buscema* c-17p, 19p, 26p. *Golden* c/a-28. *Gil Kane* c-16p, 21p, 22p, 24p, 32p. *Nebres* a-5; c-24i. *Nino* a-2, 8. *No. 1-12 were reprinted from Pendulum Illustrated Classics.*

MARVEL COLLECTIBLE CLASSICS: AVENGERS

	GD 2.0	VG 4.0	FN 6.0	VF 8.0	VF/NM 9.0	NM- 9.2
Marvel Comics: 1998 ($10.00, reprints with chromium wraparound-c)						
1-Reprints Avengers Vol.3, #1; Perez-c	3	6	9	16	24	32

MARVEL COLLECTIBLE CLASSICS: SPIDER-MAN
Marvel Comics: 1998 ($10.00, reprints with chromium wraparound-c)

1-Reprints Amazing Spider-Man #300; McFarlane-c	72	144	216	360	505	650
2-Reprints Spider-Man #1; McFarlane-c	29	58	87	145	203	260

MARVEL COLLECTIBLE CLASSICS: X-MEN
Marvel Comics: 1998 ($10.00, reprints with chromium wraparound-c)

1-Reprints (Uncanny) X-Men #1 & 2; Adam Kubert-c 3	6	9	21	33	45	
2-6: 2-Reprints Uncanny X-Men #141 & 142; Byrne-c. 3-Reprints (Uncanny) X-Men #137; Larroca-c. 4-Reprints X-Men #25; Andy Kubert-c. 5-Reprints Giant Size X-Men #1; Gary Frank-c. 6-Reprints X-Men V2#1; Ramos-c	3	6	9	16	24	32

MARVEL COLLECTOR'S EDITION
Marvel Comics: 1992 (Ordered thru mail with Charleston Chew candy wrapper)

1-Flip-book cover: Spider-Man, Silver Surfer, Wolverine (by Sam Kieth), & Ghost Rider stories; Wolverine back-c by Kieth	2	4	8	10	12	

MARVEL COLLECTORS' ITEM CLASSICS (Marvel's Greatest #23 on)
Marvel Comics Group(ATF): Feb, 1965 - No. 22, Aug, 1969 (25¢, 68 pgs.)

1-Fantastic Four, Spider-Man, Thor, Hulk, Iron Man-r begin	15	30	45	100	220	340
2 (4/66)	7	14	21	46	86	125
3,4	5	10	15	37	66	95
5-10	5	10	15	34	60	85
11-22: 22-r/The Man in the Ant Hill/TTA #27	5	10	15	30	50	70

NOTE: *All reprints; Ditko, Kirby art in all.*

MARVEL COMICS (Marvel Mystery Comics #2 on)
Timely Comics (Funnies, Inc.): Oct, Nov, 1939

NOTE: The first issue was originally dated October 1939. Most copies have a black circle stamped over the date (on cover and inside) with "November" printed over it. However, some copies do not have the November overprint and could have a higher value. Most No. 1's have printing defects, i.e., tilted pages which caused trimming into the panels usually on right side and bottom. Covers exist with and without gloss finish.

1-Origin Sub-Mariner by Bill Everett(1st newsstand app.); 1st 8 pgs. were produced for Motion Picture Funnies Weekly #1 which was probably not distributed outside of advance copies; intro Human Torch by Carl Burgos, Kazar the Great (1st Tarzan clone), & Jungle Terror(only app.); intro. The Angel by Gustavson, The Masked Raider & his horse Lightning (ends #12); cover by sci/fi pulp illustrator Frank R. Paul						
	79,300	158,600	237,900	475,800	749,400	1,400,000

MARVEL COMICS
Marvel Comics: 1990 ($17.95, hardcover)

1-Reprint of entire Marvel Comics #1	2	4	6	10	14	18

MARVEL COMICS
Marvel Comics

... No. 1 Halloween Comic Fest 2014 (giveaway) Re-colored reprint of Human Torch and Sub-Mariner stories from Marvel Comics #1; cover swipe by Jelena Djurdjevic						3.00
... 70th Anniversary Special (10/09, $4.99) Re-colored reprint of entire Marvel Comics #1; cover swipe by Jelena Djurdjevic						6.00

MARVEL COMICS
Marvel Comics: No. 1000, Oct, 2019 - No. 1001, Dec, 2019 ($9.99/$4.99)

1000-($9.99, square-bound) Single page stories tied in to each year of Marvel from 1939-2020; intro. The Eternity Mask; s/a by various; main cover by Alex Ross						10.00
1001-($4.99) Single page stories; s/a by various						5.00

MARVEL COMICS DIGEST (All-ages Marvel reprint stories printed by Archie Comics)
Archie Comics Publications: Jul, 2017 - No. 8, Oct, 2018 ($6.99, digest-size)

1-8: 1-Spider-Man reprints. 2,6-Avengers. 3-Thor. 4-X-Men. 5-Avengers/Black Panther. 7-Avengers/Ant-Man. 8-Spider-Man & Venom						7.00

MARVEL COMICS PRESENTS
Marvel Comics (Midnight Sons imprint #143 on): Early Sept, 1988 - No. 175, Feb, 1995 ($1.25/$1.50/$1.75, bi-weekly)

1-Wolverine by Buscema in #1-10	3	6	9	16	23	30
2-5	1	3	4	6	8	10
6-10: 6-Sub-Mariner app. 10-Colossus begins						5.00
11-18,20-47,51-71: 17-Cyclops begins. 24-Havok begins. 25-Origin/1st app. Nth Man. 26-Hulk begins by Rogers. 29-Quasar app. 31-Excalibur begins by Austin (i). 32-McFarlane-a(p). 33-Capt. America; Jim Lee-a. 37-Devil-Slayer app. 38-Wolverine begins by Buscema; Hulk app. 39-Spider-Man app. 46-Liefeld Wolverine-c. 51-53-Wolverine by Rob Liefeld. 54-61-Wolverine/Hulk story: 54-Werewolf by Night begins; The Shroud by Ditko. 58-Iron Man by Ditko. 59-Punisher. 62-Deathlok & Wolverine stories 63-Wolverine. 64-71-Wolverine/Ghost Rider 8-part story. 70-Liefeld Ghost Rider/Wolverine-c						4.00
19-1st app. Damage Control	2	4	6	8	10	12
48-50-Wolverine & Spider-Man team-up by Erik Larsen-c/a. 48-Wasp app. 49,50-Savage Dragon prototype app.? by Larsen. 50-Silver Surfer. 50-53-Comet Man; Mumy scripts						6.00
72-Begin 13-part Weapon-X story (Wolverine origin) by B. Windsor-Smith (prologue)	3	6	9	17	25	34
73-Weapon-X part 1; Black Knight, Sub-Mariner	2	4	6	8	11	14
74-84: 74-Weapon-X part 2; Black Knight, Sub-Mariner. 76-Death's Head story. 77-Mr. Fantastic story. 78-Iron Man by Steacy. 80,81-Capt. America by Ditko/Austin. 81-Daredevil by Rogers/Williamson. 82-Power Man. 83-Human Torch by Ditko(a&scripts); $1.00-c direct, $1.25 newsstand. 84-Last Weapon-X (24 pg. conclusion)						4.00
85-Begin 8-part Wolverine story by Sam Kieth (c/a); 1st Kieth-a on Wolverine; begin 8-part Beast story by Jae Lee(p) with Liefeld part pencils #85,86; 1st Jae Lee-a (assisted w/Liefeld, 1991)						5.00
86-90: 86-89-Wolverine, Beast stories continue. 90-Begin 8-part Ghost Rider & Cable story, ends #97; begin flip book format w/two-c						4.00
91-111: 93-Begin 6-part Wolverine story app #98. 98-Begin 2-part Ghost Rider story. 99-Spider-Man story. 100-Full-length Ghost Rider/Wolverine story by Sam Kieth w/Tim Vigil assists; anniversary issue, non flip-book. 101-Begin 6-part Ghost Rider/Dr. Strange story & begin 8-part Wolverine/Nightcrawler story by Colan/Williamson; Punisher story. 107-Begin 6-part Ghost Rider/Werewolf by Night story. 109-Begin 8 part Wolverine/Typhoid Mary story. 111-Iron Fist. 113-Begin 6-part Giant-Man & begin 6-part Ghost Rider/Iron Fist						

Marvel Chillers #5 © MAR

Marvel Divas #1 © MAR

The Marvel Family #13 © FAW

	GD	VG	FN	VF	VF/NM	NM-		GD	VG	FN	VF	VF/NM	NM-
	2.0	4.0	6.0	8.0	9.0	9.2		2.0	4.0	6.0	8.0	9.0	9.2

stories. 117-Preview of Ravage 2099 (1st app.); begin 6 part Wolverine/Venom story w/Kieth-a. 118-Preview of Doom 2099 (1st app.). 119-Begin Ghost Rider/Cloak & Dagger by Colan. 120,136,138-Spider-Man. 123-Begin 8-part Ghost Rider/Typhoid Mary story; begin 4-part She Hulk story; begin 8-part Wolverine/Lynx story. 125-Begin 6-part Iron Fist story. 130-Begin 6-part Ghost Rider/ Cage story. 136-Daredevil. 137-Begin 6-part Wolverine story & 6-part Ghost Rider story. 147-Begin 2-part Vengeance-c/story w/new Ghost Rider. 149-Vengeance-c/story w/new Ghost Rider. 150-Silver ink-c; begin 2-part Bloody Mary story w/Typhoid Mary,Wolverine, Daredevil, new Ghost Rider; intro Steel Raven. 152-Begin 4-part Wolverine, 4-part War Machine, 4-part Vengeance, 3-part Moon Knight stories; same date as War Machine #1. 143-146: Siege of Darkness parts 3,6,11,14; all have spot-varnished-c. 143-Ghost Rider/Scarlet Witch; intro new Werewolf. 144-Begin 2-part Morbius story. 145-Begin 2-part Nightstalkers story. 153-155-Bound-in Spider-Man trading card sheet. 172-Flip-book; intro new Lunatik, Giffen-c/a. 173-Flip-book; Lunatik story; Fabry-c/Giffen-a. 174-Lunatik story, Giffen-a ... 4.00

175-Flip-book with New Genix-c; Lunatik story, Giffen-a

	2	4	6	10	14	18
...Colossus: God's Country (1994, $6.95) r/#10-17	1	2	3	4	5	7

...: Wolverine Vol. 1 TPB (2005, $12.99) r/Wolverine stories from #1-10 ... 13.00
...: Wolverine Vol. 2 TPB (2006, $12.99) r/from #39-50 and Marvel Age Annual #4 ... 13.00
...: Wolverine Vol. 3 TPB (2006, $12.99) r/#51-61 ... 13.00
...: Wolverine Vol. 4 TPB (2006, $12.99) r/from #62-71 ... 13.00
NOTE: Austin a-31-37i; c(i)-48, 50, 99, 122. Buscema a-1-10, 38-47; c-6. Byrne a-79; c-71. Colan a(p)-36, 37. Colan/Williamson a-101-108. Ditko a-7p, 10, 56p, 58, 80, 81, 83. Guice a-62. Sam Kieth a-85-92, 117-122; c-85-98, 99p, 100, 108, 117, 118, 120-122; back c-109-113, 117. Jae Lee c-129(back). Liefeld a-51, 52, 53p(2), 85p; c-46, 70. McFarlane c-32. Mooney a-73. Rogers a-26, 38, 46i, 81p. Russell a-10-14,16,17i; c-4,19, 30,31i. Saltares a-8p(early), 38-45p. Simonson c-1. B. Smith a-72-84; c-72-84. P. Smith a-34. Sparling a-33. Starlin a-89i. Staton a-74. Steacy a-78. Sutton a-101-105. Williamson c-62i. Two Gun Kid by Gil Kane in #116, 122.

MARVEL COMICS PRESENTS
Marvel Comics: Nov, 2007 - No. 12, Oct, 2008 ($3.99)

1-12-Short stories by various. 1-Wraparound-c by Campbell ... 4.00

MARVEL COMICS PRESENTS
Marvel Comics: Mar, 2019 - No. 9, Nov, 2019 ($4.99)

1-9: 1-Wolverine serialized story begins; Namor & Capt. America stories. 2-Gorilla Man app. 3-Crusher Hogan app. 4-Moon Knight. 5-Venom app. 6-Intro. Wolverine's daughter Jonah 8-White Fox ... 5.00

MARVEL COMICS SUPER SPECIAL, A (Marvel Super Special #5 on)
Marvel Comics: Sept, 1977 - No. 41(?), Nov, 1986 (nn 7) ($1.50, magazine)

1-Kiss, 40 pgs. comics plus photos & features; John Buscema-a(p); also see Howard the Duck #12; ink contains real KISS blood; Dr. Doom, Spider-Man, Avengers, Fantastic Four, Mephisto app.

	20	40	60	138	307	475
2-Conan (1978)	3	6	9	21	33	45

3-Close Encounters of the Third Kind (1978); Simonson-a

	3	6	9	16	24	32

4-The Beatles Story (1978)-Perez/Janson-a; has photos & articles

	7	14	21	49	92	135
5-Kiss (1978)-Includes poster	26	39	89	195	300	
6-Jaws II (1978)	5	10	15	33	57	80

7-Sgt. Pepper; Beatles movie adaptation; withdrawn from U.S. distribution (French ed. exists) 8-Battlestar Galactica; tabloid size ($1.50) 1978; adapts TV show

	3	6	9	16	23	30
8-Modern-r of tabloid size	2	4	6	11	16	20

8-Battlestar Galactica; publ. in regular magazine format; low distribution ($1.50, 8-1/2x11")

	3	6	9	16	24	32
9-Conan	3	6	9	16	24	32
10-Star-Lord (1st color story)	5	10	15	30	50	70

11-13-Weirdworld begins #11; 25 copy special press run of each with gold seal and signed by artists (Proof quality), Spring-June, 1979

	18	27	57	111	165	

11-14: 11-13-Weirdworld (regular issues): 11-Fold-out centerfold. 14-Miller-c(p); adapts movie "Meteor."

	2	4	6	8	11	14

15-Star Trek with photos & pin-ups ($1.50-c)

	3	6	9	15	22	28

15-With $2.00 price; the price was changed at tail end of a 200,000 press run

	3	6	9	16	24	32
16-Empire Strikes Back adaptation; Williamson-a	10	20	30	64	132	200
17-Xanadu (movie adaptation)	5	10	15	24	30	35
18-Raiders of the Lost Ark (movie adaptation)	6	12	18	31	38	45

19,20 (Movie adaptations): 19-For Your Eyes Only (James Bond). 20-Dragonslayer

	3	6	9	12	16	20

21,23,25,26,28-30 (Movie adaptations): 21-Conan. 23-Annie. 25-Rock and Rule-w/photos; artwork is from movie. 26-Octopussy (James Bond). 28-Krull; photo-c. 29-Tarzan of the Apes (Greystoke movie). 30-Indiana Jones and the Temple of Doom

	2	4	6	8	10	12
22-Blade Runner; Williamson-a/Steranko-c	7	14	21	44	82	120
24-The Dark Crystal	3	6	9	14	19	24
27-Return of the Jedi	6	12	18	41	76	110

31-39,41: 31-The Last Star Fighter. 32-The Muppets Take Manhattan. 33-Buckaroo Banzai. 34-Sheena. 35-Conan The Destroyer. 36-Dune. 37-2010. 38-Red Sonja. 39-Santa Claus:The Movie. 41-Howard The Duck

	2	4	6	8	10	12
40-Labyrinth	5	10	15	34	60	85

NOTE: J. Buscema a-1, 2, 9, 11-13, 18p, 21, 35, 40; c-11(part), 12. Chaykin a-3, 19p; c-18, 19. Colan a(p)-6, 10, 14. Morrow a-34; c-1i, 34. Nebres a-11. Spiegle a-29. Stevens a-27. Williamson a-27. #22-28 contain photos from movies.

MARVEL COMICS: 2001
Marvel Comics: 2001 (no cover price, one-shot)

1-Previews new titles for Fall 2001; Wolverine-c ... 3.00

MARVEL DABEL BROTHERS SAMPLER
Marvel Comics: Dec, 2006 (no cover price, one-shot)

1-Profiles and sample pages of Anita Blake, Magician: Apprentice, Red Prophet, Ptolus ... 3.00

MARVEL DIVAS
Marvel Comics: Sept, 2009 - No. 4, Dec, 2009 ($3.99, limited series)

1-4-Black Cat, Firestar, Hellcat and Photon app. 1-Campbell-c ... 4.00

MARVEL DOUBLE FEATURE
Marvel Comics Group: Dec, 1973 - No. 21, Mar, 1977

1-Capt. America, Iron Man-r/T.O.S. begin	5	10	15	33	57	80
2-10: 3-Last 20¢ issue	2	4	6	10	14	18

11-17,20,21:17-Story-r/Iron Man & Sub-Mariner #1; last 25¢ issue

	3	4	6	8	10	12
15-17-(30¢-c variants, limited distribution)(4,6,8/76)	5	10	15	30	50	70
18,19-Colan/Craig-r from Iron Man #1 in both	2	4	6	8	11	14

NOTE: Colan r-1-19p. Craig r-17-19i. G. Kane r-15p; c-15p. Kirby r-1-16p, 20, 21; c-17-20.

MARVEL DOUBLE SHOT
Marvel Comics: Jan, 2003 - No. 4, April, 2003 ($2.99, limited series)

1-4: 1-Hulk by Haynes; Thor w/Asamiya-a; Jusko-c. 2-Dr. Doom by Rivera; Simpsons-style Avengers by Bill Morrison ... 3.00

MARVEL FAMILY (Also see Captain Marvel Adventures No. 18)
Fawcett Publications: Dec, 1945 - No. 89, Jan, 1954

1-Origin Captain Marvel, Captain Marvel Jr., Mary Marvel, & Uncle Marvel retold; origin/1st app. Black Adam

	2580	5160	7740	17,200	28,600	40,000
2-The 3 Lt. Marvels & Uncle Marvel app.	87	174	261	533	952	1350
3	60	120	180	381	653	925
4,5	53	106	159	334	567	800

6-10: 6-Classic portrait-c with Uncle Marvel. 7-Shazam app.

	41	82	123	256	428	600
11-20	34	68	102	204	332	460
21-30	31	62	93	182	296	410
31-40	27	54	81	158	259	360
41-46,48-50	25	50	75	150	245	340
47-Flying Saucer-c/story (5/50)	36	72	108	211	343	475
51-76	24	48	72	140	230	320
77-Communist Threat-c	53	106	159	334	567	800
78,81-Used in POP, pg. 92,93.	27	54	81	162	266	370
79,80,82-88: 79-Horror satire-c	26	52	78	154	252	350

89-Last issue; last Fawcett Captain Marvel app. (low distribution)

	52	104	156	328	552	775

MARVEL FAMILY
DC Comics: Oct, 2022 ($3.99, one-shot)

1-Reprint of the full 1945 issue with original ads; r/origin & 1st app. Black Adam ... 6.00

MARVEL FANFARE (1st Series)
Marvel Comics Group: Mar, 1982 - No. 60, Jan, 1992 ($1.25/$2.25, slick paper, direct sales)

1-Spider-Man/Angel team-up; 1st Paul Smith-a (1st full story; see King Conan #7); Daredevil app. complete missing the centerfold)

	2	4	6	11	16	20
2-Spider-Man, Ka-Zar, The Angel. F.F. origin retold	2	4	6	8	10	12
3,4-X-Men & Ka-Zar. 4-Deathlok, Spidey app.	1	3	4	6	8	10

5-14: 5-Dr. Strange, Capt. America. 6-Spider-Man, Scarlet Witch. 7-Incredible Hulk; D.D. back-up(also 15). 8-Dr. Strange; Wolf Boy begins. 9-Man-Thing. 10-13-Black Widow. 14-The Vision ... 6.00
15,24,33: 15-The Thing by Barry Smith, c/a. 24-Weirdworld; Wolverine back-up. 33-X-Men, Wolverine app.

	1	2	3	5	6	8

16-23,25-32,34,44-46,50: 16,17-Skywolf. 16-Sub-Mariner back-up. 17-Hulk back-up. 18-Capt. America by Miller. 19-Cloak and Dagger. 20-Thing/Dr. Strange. 21-Thing/Dr. Strange /Hulk. 22,23-Iron Man vs. Dr. Octopus. 25,26-Weirdworld. 27-Daredevil/Spider-Man. 28-Alpha Flight. 29-Hulk. 30-Moon Knight. 31,32-Captain America. 34-37-Warriors Three. 38-Moon Knight/Dazzler. 39-Moon Knight/Hawkeye.

	GD	VG	FN	VF	VF/NM	NM-		GD	VG	FN	VF	VF/NM	NM-
	2.0	4.0	6.0	8.0	9.0	9.2		2.0	4.0	6.0	8.0	9.0	9.2

40-Angel/Rogue & Storm. 41-Dr. Strange. 42-Spider-Man. 43-Sub-Mariner/Human Torch.
44-Iron Man vs. Dr. Doom by Ken Steacy. 46-Fantastic Four. 47-Hulk. 48-She-Hulk/Vision.
49-Dr. Strange/Nick Fury. 50-X-Factor ... 5.00
45-All pin-up issue by Steacy, Art Adams & others   2 4 6 8 10 12
51-($2.95, 52 pgs.)-Silver Surfer; Fantastic Four & Capt. Marvel app.; 51,52-Colan/Williamson back-up (Dr. Strange) ... 6.00
52,53,56-60: 52,53-Black Knight; 53-Iron Man back up. 56-59-Shanna the She-Devil.
58-Vision & Scarlet Witch back-up. 60-Black Panther/Rogue/Daredevil stories ... 4.00
54,55-Wolverine back-ups. 54-Black Knight. 55-Power Pack ... 5.00
... No. 10 Facsimile Edition (12/20, $3.99) Reprints #10 with original ads ... 4.00
... Vol. 1 TPB (2008, $24.99) r/#1-7 ... 25.00
NOTE: **Art Adams** c-13. **Austin** a-1i, 4i, 33i, 38i; c-6i, 33i. **Buscema** a-51p. **Byrne** a-1p, 29, 48; c-29. **Chiodo** painted c-56-59. **Colan** a-51p. **Cowan/Simonson** c-60. **Golden** a-1, 2, 4p, 47; c-1, 2, 47. **Infantino** c/a)p-8. **Gil Kane** a-8-11p. **Miller** a-18; c-1(Back-c), 18. **Perez** a-10, 11p, 12, 13p; c-10-13p. **Rogers** a-5p; c-5p. **Russell** a-5i, 6i, 8-11i, 43i; c-5i, 6. **Paul Smith** a-1p, 4p, 32, 60; c-4p. **Staton** c/a-50(p). **Williamson** a-30i, 51i.

MARVEL FANFARE (2nd Series)
Marvel Comics: Sept, 1996 - No. 6, Feb, 1997 (99¢)
1-6: 1-Capt. America & The Falcon-c/story; Deathlok app. 2-Wolverine & Hulk-c/app.
3-Ghost Rider & Spider-Man-c/app. 5-Longshot-c/app. 6-Sabretooth, Power Man, & Iron Fist-c/app ... 4.00

MARVEL FEATURE (See Marvel Two-In-One)
Marvel Comics: Dec, 1971 - No. 12, Nov, 1973 (1,2: 25¢, 52 pg. giants) (#1-3: quarterly)
1-Origin/1st app. The Defenders (Sub-Mariner, Hulk & Dr. Strange); see Sub-Mariner #34,35 for prequel; Dr. Strange solo story (predates Dr. Strange #1) plus 1950s Sub-Mariner-r; Neal Adams-c   36 72 108 259 580 900
2-2nd app. Defenders; 1950s Sub-Mariner-r. Rutland, Vermont Halloween x-over   10 20 30 64 132 200
3-Defenders ends   6 12 18 40 73 105
4-Re-intro Antman (1st app. since 1960s), begin series; brief origin; Spider-Man app.   8 16 24 54 102 150
5-7,9,10: 6-Wasp app. & begins team-ups. 9-Iron Man app. 10-Last Antman   4 8 12 23 37 50
8-Origin Antman & Wasp-r/TTA #44; Kirby-a   4 8 12 27 44 60
11-Thing vs. Hulk; 1st Thing solo book (9/73); origin Fantastic Four retold   8 16 24 56 108 160
12-Thing/Iron Man; early Thanos app.; occurs after Capt. Marvel #33; Starlin-a(p)   5 10 15 35 63 90
NOTE: **Bolle** a-9i. **Everett** a-1i, 3i. **Hartley** r-10. **Kane** c-3p, 7p. **Russell** a-7-10p. **Starlin** a-8, 11, 12; c-8.

MARVEL FEATURE (Also see Red Sonja)
Marvel Comics: Nov, 1975 - No. 7, Nov, 1976 (Story cont'd in Conan #68)
1-Red Sonja begins (pre-dates Red Sonja #1); adapts Howard short story; Adams-r/Savage Sword of Conan #1   5 10 15 30 50 70
2   3 6 9 14 20 25
3-6: Thorne-c/a in #2-7. 4,5-(Regular 25¢ edition)(5,7/76)   2 4 6 8 10 12
4,5-(30¢-c variants, limited distribution)   6 12 18 37 66 95
7-Red Sonja battles Conan   4 8 12 23 37 50

MARVEL FRONTIER COMICS UNLIMITED
Marvel Frontier Comics: Jan, 1994 ($2.95, 68 pgs.)
1-Dances with Demons, Immortalis, Children of the Voyager, Evil Eye, The Fallen stories 5.00

MARVEL FUMETTI BOOK
Marvel Comics Group: Apr, 1984 ($1.00, one-shot)
1-All photos; Stan Lee photo-c; Art Adams touch-ups ... 5.00

MARVEL FUN & GAMES
Marvel Comics Group: 1979/80 (color comic for kids)
1,11: 1-Games, puzzles, etc. 11-X-Men-c   2 4 6 8 10 12
2-10,12,13: (beware marked pages)   1 2 3 4 5 7

MARVEL GIRL
Marvel Comics: Apr, 2011 ($2.99, one-shot)
1-Early X-Men days of Jean Grey; Fialkov-s/Plati-a/Cruz-c ... 3.00

MARVEL GRAPHIC NOVEL
Marvel Comics Group (Epic Comics): 1982 - No. 38, 1990? ($5.95/$6.95)
1-Death of Captain Marvel (2nd Marvel graphic novel); Capt. Marvel battles Thanos by Jim Starlin (c/a/scripts)   7 14 21 44 82 120
1 (2nd & 3rd printings)   2 4 6 13 18 22
2-Elric: The Dreaming City   3 6 9 15 22 28
3-Dreadstar; Starlin-c/a, 52 pgs.   3 6 9 14 20 25
4-Origin/1st app. The New Mutants (1982)   9 18 27 59 117 175
4,5-2nd printings   2 4 6 11 16 20
5-X-Men; book-length story (1982)   5 10 15 33 57 80
6-15,20,25,30,31: 6-The Star Slammers. 7-Killraven. 8-Super Boxers; Byrne scripts. 9-The Futurians. 10-Heartburst. 11-Void Indigo. 12-Dazzler. 13-Starstruck. 14-The Swords Of The Swashbucklers. 15-The Raven Banner (a Tale of Asgard). 20-Greenberg the Vampire. 25-Alien Legion. 30-A Sailor's Story. 31-Wolfpack   2 4 6 8 11 14
16,17,21,29: 16-The Aladdin Effect (Storm, Tigra, Wasp, She-Hulk). 17-Revenge Of The Living Monolith (Spider-Man, Avengers, FF app.). 21-Marada the She-Wolf. 29-The Big Chance (Thing vs. Hulk)   2 4 6 10 14 18
18-She Hulk   4 8 12 27 44 60
19,26-28: 19-Witch Queen of Acheron (Conan). 26-Dracula. 27-Avengers (Emperor Doom). 28-Conan the Reaver   2 4 6 11 16 20
22-Amaz. Spider-Man in Hooky by Wrightson   3 6 9 17 26 35
23,24: 23-Dr. Strange. 24-Love and War (Daredevil); Miller scripts   3 6 9 14 19 24
32-Death of Groo   3 6 9 14 19 24
32-2nd printing ($5.95)   2 4 6 8 10 12
33,34,36,37: 33-Thor. 34-Predator & Prey (Cloak & Dagger). 36-Willow (movie adapt.). 37-Hercules   2 4 6 8 11 14
35-Hitler's Astrologer (The Shadow, $12.95, HC)   2 4 6 11 16 20
35-Soft-c reprint (1990, $10.95)   2 4 6 9 12 15
38-Silver Surfer (Judgement Day)($14.95, HC)   2 4 6 13 18 24
38-Soft-c reprint (1990, $10.95)   2 4 6 9 12 15

nn-Abslom Daak: Dalek Killer (1990, $8.95) Dr. Who   2 4 6 9 12 15
nn-Arena by Bruce Jones (1989, $5.95) Dinosaurs   2 4 6 8 10 12
nn- A-Team Storybook Comics Illustrated (1983) r/ A-Team mini-series #1-3   2 4 6 8 10 12
nn-Ax (1988, $5.95) Ernie Colan-s/a   2 4 6 8 10 12
nn-Black Widow Coldest War (4/90, $9.95)   2 4 6 9 12 15
nn-Chronicles of Genghis Grimtoad (1990, $8.95)-Alan Grant-s   2 4 6 8 10 12
nn-Conan the Barbarian in the Horn of Azoth (1990, $8.95)   2 4 6 8 10 12
nn-Conan of Isles ($8.95)   2 4 6 8 11 16
nn-Conan Ravagers of Time (1992, $9.95) Kull & Red Sonja app.   2 4 6 8 11 16
nn-Conan -The Skull of Set   2 4 6 8 11 16
nn-Doctor Strange and Doctor Doom Triumph and Torment (1989, $17.95, HC)   3 6 9 17 26 35
nn-Dreamwalker (1989, $6.95)-Morrow-a   2 4 6 8 10 12
nn-Excalibur Weird War III (1990, $9.95)   2 4 6 8 10 12
nn-G.I. Joe - The Trojan Gambit (1983, 68 pgs.)   2 4 6 10 14 18
nn-Harvey Kurtzman Strange Adventures (Epic, $19.95, HC) Aragonés, Crumb   3 6 9 16 23 30
nn-Hearts and Minds (1990, $6.95) Heath-a   2 4 6 8 10 12
nn-Inhumans (1988, $7.95)-Williamson-i   3 6 9 14 20 25
nn-Jhereg (Epic, 1990, $8.95)   2 4 6 8 10 12
nn-Kazar-Guns of the Savage Land (7/90, $8.95)   2 4 6 8 10 12
nn-Kull-The Vale of Shadow ('89, $6.95)   2 4 6 8 10 12
nn-Last of the Dragons (1988, $6.95) Austin-a(i)   2 4 6 8 10 12
nn-Nightraven: House of Cards (1991, $14.95)   2 4 6 10 14 18
nn-Nightraven: The Collected Stories (1990, $9.95) Bolton-r/British Hulk mag.; David Lloyd-c/a   2 4 6 8 10 12
nn-Original Adventures of Cholly and Flytrap (Epic, 1991, $9.95) Suydam-s/c/a   2 4 6 10 14 18
nn-Rick Mason Agent (1989, $9.95)   2 4 6 8 10 12
nn-Roger Rabbit In The Resurrection Of Doom (1989, $8.95)   4 8 12 23 37 50
nn-A Sailor's Story Book II: Winds, Dreams and Dragons ('86, $6.95, softcover) Glansman-s/c/a   2 4 6 8 10 12
nn-Squadron Supreme: Death of a Universe (1989, $9.95) Gruenwald-s; Ryan & Williamson-a   3 6 9 14 20 25
nn-Who Framed Roger Rabbit (1989, $6.95)   2 4 6 9 12 15
NOTE: **Aragones** c-27, 32. **Buscema** a-38. **Byrne** c/a-18. **Heath** a-35i. **Kaluta** a-13, 35p; c-13. **Miller** a-24p. **Simonson** a-1. **Starlin** c/a-1,3. **Williamson** a-1. **Wrightson** c-29i.

MARVEL HEARTBREAKERS
Marvel Comics: Apr, 2010 ($3.99, one-shot)
1-Romance short stories; Spider-Man, MJ & Gwen app.; Casagrande-a; Beast app. ... 4.00

MARVEL - HEROES & LEGENDS
Marvel Comics: Oct, 1996; 1997 ($2.95)
nn-Wraparound-c, ...1997 ($2.99) -Original Avengers story ... 6.00

MARVEL HEROES FLIP MAGAZINE
Marvel Comics: Aug, 2005 - No. 26, Sept, 2007 ($3.99/$4.99)
1-11-Reprints New Avengers and Captain America (2005 series) in flip format thru #13 ... 4.00
12-26: 14-19-Reprints New Avengers and Young Avengers in flip format. 20-Ghost Rider 5.00

MARVEL HOLIDAY SPECIAL
Marvel Comics: No. 1, 1991 - 2011
1-($2.25, 84 pgs.) X-Men, Fantastic Four, Punisher, Thor, Capt. America, Ghost Rider, Capt. Ultra, Spidey stories; Art Adams-c/a   1 3 4 6 8 10
nn (1992, 1/93 on-c)-Wolverine, Thanos (by Starlin/Lim/Austin) ... 4.00
nn (1993, 1/94 on-c)-Spider-Man vs. Mephisto; Nick Fury by Chaykin; Hulk app. ... 4.00
nn (1994)-Capt. America, X-Men, Silver Surfer ... 4.00
... 1996-Spider-Man by Waid & Olliffe; X-Men, Silver Surfer ... 4.00
... 2004-Spider-Man by DeFalco & Miyazawa; X-Men, Fantastic Four ... 4.00
... 2004 TPB ($15.99) r/M.H.S. 2004 & past Christmas-themed stories ... 16.00
1 (1/06, $3.99) new Christmas-themed stories by various; Immonen-c ... 4.00
... 2006 (2/07, $3.99) Fin Fang Foom, Hydra, AIM app.; gallery of past covers; Irving-c ... 4.00
... 2007 (2/08, $3.99) Spider-Man & Wolverine stories; Hembeck-a ... 4.00
... 2011 (2/12, $3.99) Seeley-c; Spider-Man, Wolverine, Nick Fury, The Thing app. ... 4.00
Marvel Holiday (2006, $7.99, digest) reprints from M.H.S. 2004, 2006 & TPB ... 8.00
Marvel Holiday Spectacular Magazine (2009, $9.99, magazine) reprints from M.H.S. '93, '94, & Amazing Spider-Man #166; and new material w/Doe, Semeiks & Nauck-a ... 10.00
NOTE: **Art Adams** a-'92. **Golden** a-'93. **Kaluta** c-'93. **Perez** c-'94.

MARVEL ILLUSTRATED...
Marvel Comics: 2007 ($2.99)
...Jungle Book - reprints from Marvel Fanfare #8-11; Gil Kane-s/a(p); P. Craig Russell-i ... 3.00

MARVEL ILLUSTRATED: KIDNAPPED (Title changes to Kidnapped with #5)
Marvel Comics: Jan, 2009 - No. 5, May, 2009 ($3.99, limited series)
1-5-Adaptation of the Stevenson novel; Roy Thomas-s/Mario Gully-a/Parel-c ... 4.00

MARVEL ILLUSTRATED: LAST OF THE MOHICANS
Marvel Comics: July, 2007 - No. 6, Dec, 2007 ($2.99, limited series)
1-6-Adaptation of the Cooper novel; Roy Thomas-s/Steve Kurth-a. 1-Jo Chen-c ... 3.00
HC (2008, $19.99) r/#1-6 ... 20.00

MARVEL ILLUSTRATED: MOBY DICK
Marvel Comics: Apr, 2008 - No. 6, Sept, 2008 ($2.99, limited series)
1-6-Adaptation of the Melville novel; Roy Thomas-s/Alixe-a/Watson-c ... 3.00

MARVEL ILLUSTRATED: PICTURE OF DORIAN GRAY
Marvel Comics: Jan, 2008 - No. 6, July, 2008 ($2.99, limited series)
1-6-Adaptation of the Wilde novel; Roy Thomas-s/Fiumara-a. 1-Parel-c ... 3.00

MARVEL ILLUSTRATED: SWIMSUIT ISSUE (Also see Marvel Swimsuit Special)
Marvel Comics: 1991 ($3.95, magazine, 52 pgs.)
V1#1-Parody of Sports Illustrated swimsuit issue; Mary Jane Parker centerfold pin-up by Jusko; 2nd print exists   3 6 9 14 20 25

Marvel Graphic Novel #18 © MAR

Marvel Illustrated: The Iliad #1 © MAR

Marvel Knights 20th #3 © MAR

	GD	VG	FN	VF	VF/NM	NM-		GD	VG	FN	VF	VF/NM	NM-
	2.0	4.0	6.0	8.0	9.0	9.2		2.0	4.0	6.0	8.0	9.0	9.2

MARVEL ILLUSTRATED: THE ILIAD
Marvel Comics: Feb, 2008 - No. 8, Sept, 2008 ($2.99, limited series)

1-8-Adaptation of Homer's Epic Poem; Roy Thomas-s/Sepulveda-a/Rivera-c   3.00

MARVEL ILLUSTRATED: THE MAN IN THE IRON MASK
Marvel Comics: Sept, 2007 - No. 6, Feb, 2008 ($2.99, limited series)

1-6-Adaptation of the Dumas novel; Roy Thomas-s/Hugo Petrus-a. 1-Djurdjevic-c   3.00
HC (2008, $19.99) r/#1-6   20.00

MARVEL ILLUSTRATED: THE ODYSSEY (Title changes to The Odyssey with #7)
Marvel Comics: Nov, 2008 - No. 8, June, 2009 ($3.99, limited series)

1-8-Adaptation of Homer's Epic Poem; Roy Thomas-s/Greg Tocchini-a/c   4.00

MARVEL ILLUSTRATED: THE THREE MUSKETEERS
Marvel Comics: Aug, 2008 - No. 6, Jan, 2009 ($3.99, limited series)

1-6-Adaptation of the Dumas novel; Roy Thomas-s/Hugo Petrus-a/Parel-c   4.00

MARVEL ILLUSTRATED: TREASURE ISLAND
Marvel Comics: Aug, 2007 - No. 6, Jan, 2008 ($2.99, limited series)

1-6-Adaptation of the Stevenson novel; Roy Thomas-s/Mario Gully-a/Greg Hildebrandt-c   3.00
HC (2008, $19.99) r/#1-6   20.00

MARVEL KNIGHTS (See Black Panther, Daredevil, Inhumans, & Punisher)
Marvel Comics: 1998 (Previews for upcoming series)

Sketchbook-Wizard suppl.; Quesada & Palmiotti-c   4.00
Tourbook-($2.99) Interviews and art previews   4.00

MARVEL KNIGHTS
Marvel Comics: July, 2000 - No. 15, Sept, 2001 ($2.99)

1-Daredevil, Punisher, Black Widow, Shang-Chi, Dagger app.   4.00
2-15-Two covers by Barreto & Quesada   3.00
.../Marvel Boy Genesis Edition (6/00) Sketchbook preview   3.00
...: Millennial Visions (2/02, $3.99) Pin-ups by various; Harris-c   4.00

MARVEL KNIGHTS (Volume 2)
Marvel Comics: May, 2002 - No. 6, Oct, 2002 ($2.99)

1-6-Daredevil, Punisher, Black Widow app.; Ponticelli-a   3.00

MARVEL KNIGHTS: DOUBLE SHOT
Marvel Comics: June, 2002 - No. 4, Sept, 2002 ($2.99, limited series)

1-4: 1-Punisher by Ennis & Quesada; Daredevil by Haynes; Fabry-c   3.00

MARVEL KNIGHTS 4 (Fantastic Four) (Issues #1&2 are titled **Knights 4**) (#28-30 titled **Four**)
Marvel Comics: Apr, 2004 - No. 30, July, 2006 ($2.99)

1-30: 1-7-McNiven-c/a; Aguirre-Sacasa-a. 8,9-Namor app. 13-Cho-c. 14-Land-c.   3.00
    21-Flashback meeting with Black Panther. 30-Namor app.   17.00
...Vol. 1: The Wolf at the Door (2004, $16.99, TPB) r/#1-7   14.00
...Vol. 2: The Stuff of Nightmares (2005, $13.99, TPB) r/#8-12   15.00
...Vol. 3: Divine Time (2005, $14.99, TPB) r/#13-18   15.00
...Vol. 4: Impossible Things Happen Every Day (2006, $14.99, TPB) r/#19-24   15.00
Fantastic Four: The Resurrection of Nicholas Scratch TPB (2006, $14.99) r/#25-30   15.00

MARVEL KNIGHTS: HULK
Marvel Comics: Feb, 2014 - No. 4, May, 2104 ($3.99, limited series)

1-4-Keatinge-s/Kowalski-a; Banner in Paris   4.00

MARVEL KNIGHTS MAGAZINE
Marvel Comics: May, 2001 - No. 6, Oct, 2001 ($3.99, magazine size)

1-6-Reprints of recent Daredevil, Punisher, Black Widow, Inhumans   4.00

MARVEL KNIGHTS SPIDER-MAN (Title continues in Sensational Spider-Man #23)
Marvel Comics: Jun, 2004 - No. 22, Mar, 2006 ($2.99)

1-Wraparound-c by Dodson; Millar-s/Dodson-a; Green Goblin app.   4.00
2-12: 2-Avengers app. 2,3-Vulture & Electro app. 5,8-Cho-c/a. 6-8-Venom app.   3.00
13-18-Reginald Hudlin-s/Billy Tan-a. 13,14,18-New Avengers app. 15-Punisher app.   3.00
19-22-The Other x-over pts. 2,5,8,11; Pat Lee-a   3.00
19-22-var-c: 19-Black costume. 20-Scarlet Spider. 21-Spider-Armor. 22-Peter Parker   5.00
... Vol. 1 HC (2005, $29.99, over-sized with d.j.) r/#1-12; Stan Lee intro.; Dodson & Cho
    sketch pages   30.00
... Vol. 1: Down Among the Dead Men (2004, $9.99, TPB) r/#1-4   10.00
... Vol. 2: Venomous (2005, $9.99, TPB) r/#5-8   10.00
... Vol. 3: The Last Stand (2005, $9.99, TPB) r/#9-12   10.00
... Vol. 4: Wild Blue Yonder (2005, $14.99, TPB) r/#13-18   15.00

MARVEL KNIGHTS: SPIDER-MAN
Marvel Comics: Dec, 2013 - No. 5, Apr, 2014 ($3.99, limited series)

1-5-Matt Kindt-s/Marco Rudy-a; Arcade app.   4.00

MARVEL KNIGHTS 20TH
Marvel Comics: Jan, 2019 - No. 6, Mar, 2019 ($4.99/$3.99, bi-weekly limited series)

1,6-($4.99) Cates-s/Foreman-a; Daredevil, Frank Castle, Kingpin & Doctor Doom app.   5.00
2-5-($3.99) 2-Henrichon-a. 3-Couceiro-a. 4,5-Black Panther app.   4.00

MARVEL KNIGHTS 2099
Marvel Comics: 2005 ($13.99, TPB)

nn-Reprints one shots: Daredevil 2099, Punisher 2099, Black Panther 2099, Inhumans 2099
    and Mutant 2099; Pat Lee-c   14.00

MARVEL KNIGHTS: X-MEN
Marvel Comics: Jan, 2014 - No. 5, May, 2014 ($3.99, limited series)

1-4-Brahm Revel-s/Cris Peter-a; Sabretooth app.   4.00

MARVEL LEGACY
Marvel Comics: Nov, 2017 ($5.99, one-shot)

1-Leads into Marvel's Legacy title re-boot following Secret Empire; Aaron-s/Ribic &
    McNiven main art, plus art by various; wraparound gatefold front-c by Quesada   6.00

MARVEL LEGACY: ...
Marvel Comics: 2006, 2007 ($4.99, one-shots)

... The 1960s Handbook - Profiles of 1960s iconic and minor characters; info thru 1969   5.00
... The 1970s Handbook - Profiles of 1970s iconic and minor characters; info thru 1979   5.00
... The 1980s Handbook - Profiles of 1980s iconic and minor characters; info thru 1989   5.00
... The 1990s Handbook - Profiles of 1990s iconic and minor characters; Lim-c   5.00
...: The 1960s-1990s Handbook TPB (2007, $19.99) r/one-shots   20.00

MARVELMAN CLASSIC
Marvel Comics: 2010 ($34.99, B&W)

HC-(2010, $34.99) Reprints of 1950s British Marvelman stories; character history   35.00
... Primer (8/10, $3.99) Character history; Mick Anglo interview; Quesada-c   4.00

MARVELMAN FAMILY'S FINEST
Marvel Comics: 2010 - No. 6, Jan, 2011 ($3.99, B&W, limited series)

1-6-Reprints of 1950s Marvelman, Young Marvelman and Marvelman Family stories   4.00

MARVEL MANGAVERSE:... (one-shots)
Marvel Comics: March, 2002 ($2.25, manga-inspired one-shots)

Avengers Assemble! - Udon Studio-s/a   3.00
Eternity Twilight ($3.50) - Ben Dunn-s/a/wrap-around-c   4.00
Fantastic Four - Adam Warren-s/Keron Grant-a   3.00
Ghost Riders - Chuck Austen-s/a   3.00
Punisher - Peter David-s/Lea Hernandez-a   3.00

Spider-Man - Kaare Andrews-s/a	2	4	6	11	16	20

X-Men - C.B. Cebulski-s/Jeff Matsuda-a   3.00

MARVEL MANGAVERSE (Manga series)
Marvel Comics: June, 2002 - No. 6, Nov., 2002 ($2.25)

1-6: 1-Ben Dunn-a; intro. manga Captain Marvel   3.00
Vol. 1 TPB (2002, $24.95) r/one-shots   25.00
Vol. 2 TPB (2002, $12.99) r/#1-6   13.00
Vol. 3: Spider-Man-Legend of the Spider-Clan (2003, $11.99, TPB) r/series   12.00

MARVEL MASTERPIECES COLLECTION, THE
Marvel Comics: May, 1993 - No. 4, Aug, 1993 ($2.95, coated paper, lim. series)

1-4-Reprints Marvel Masterpieces trading cards w/ new Jusko paintings in each;
    Jusko painted-c/a   4.00

MARVEL MASTERPIECES 2 COLLECTION, THE
Marvel Comics: July, 1994 - No. 3, Sept, 1994 ($2.95, limited series)

1-3: 1-Kaluta-c; r/trading cards; new Steranko centerfold   4.00

MARVEL MEOW
Marvel Comics: Mar, 2024 ($5.99, one-shot)

1-Nao Fujii-s/a; short cat-centric humor stories with cats and the Marvel heroes & villains   6.00

MARVEL MILESTONE EDITION
Marvel Comics: 1991 - 1999 ($2.95, coated stock)(r/originals with original ads w/silver ink-c)

...: Amazing Fantasy #15 (3/92); ....:Hulk #181 (8/99, $2.99)						
	3	6	9	18	28	38

...: Amazing Spider-Man #1 (1/93), ...: Amazing Spider-Man #1 (1/93) variation- no price on-c,
    ...: Amazing Spider-Man #3 (3/95, $2.95), ...: Amazing Spider-Man #129 (11/92),
    ...: Avengers #1 (9/93), ...:Avengers #4 (3/95, $2.95), ...: Captain America #1 (3/95, $3.95),
    ...: Fantastic Four #1 (11/91), ...: Fantastic Four #5 (11/92), ...: Giant Size X-Men #1
    (1991, $3.95, 68 pgs.), ...: Incredible Hulk #1 (3/92, says 3/91 by error), ...: Iron Man #55
    (11/92), ...: Strange Tales-r/Dr. Strange stories from #110, 111, 114, & 115; ...: Tales of

Suspense #39 (3/93), ...: X-Men #1-Reprints X-Men #1 (1991)						
	2	4	6	8	11	14

...: Amazing Spider-Man #149 (11/94, $2.95), ...: Avengers #16 (10/93), ...: X-Men #9 (10/93),						
...:X-Men #28 (11/94, $2.95)	1	2	3	5	6	8
...: Iron Fist #14 (11/92)	2	4	6	8	10	12

MA

	GD	VG	FN	VF	VF/NM	NM-
	2.0	4.0	6.0	8.0	9.0	9.2

MARVEL MILESTONES
Marvel Comics: 2005 - 2006 ($3.99, coated stock)(r/originals w/silver ink-c)

...: Beast & Kitty Pryde-r/from Amazing Adventures #11 & Uncanny X-Men #153						5.00
...: Black Panther, Storm & Ka-Zar-r/from Black Panther #26, Marvel Team-Up #100 and Marvel Mystery Comics #2						5.00
...: Blade, Man-Thing & Satana-r/from Tomb of Dracula #10, Adv. Into Fear #16 and Vampire Tales #2						5.00
...: Captain Britain, Psylocke & Sub-Mariner-r/from Spect. Spidey #114, Uncanny X-Men #213 and Human Torch #2						5.00
...: Doom, Sub-Mariner & Red Skull -r/from FF Ann. #2, Sub-Mariner Comics #1, Captain America Comics #1						5.00
...: Dragon Lord, Speedball and The Man in the Sky -r/from Marvel Spotlight #5, Speedball #1 and Amazing Adult Fantasy #14; Ditko-a on all						5.00
...: Dr. Strange, Silver Surfer, Sub-Mariner, & Hulk -r/from Marvel Premiere #3, FF Ann. #5, Marvel Comics #1, Incredible Hulk #3						5.00

| ...: Ghost Rider, Black Widow & Iceman -r/from Marvel Spotlight #5, Daredevil #81, X-Men #47 | 1 | 3 | 4 | 6 | 8 | 10 |

...: Iron Man, Ant-Man & Captain America -r/from TOS #39,40, TTA #27, Capt. America #1	1	2	3	5	6	8

...: Legion of Monsters, Spider-Man and Brother Voodoo -r/from Marvel Premiere #28 & others						5.00
...: Millie the Model & Patsy Walker-r/from Millie the Model #100, Defenders #65						5.00
...: Onslaught -r/Onslaught: Marvel; wraparound-c						5.00
...: Rawhide Kid & Two-Gun Kid-r/Two-Gun Kid #60 and Rawhide Kid #17						5.00
...: Special: Bloodstone, X-51 & Captain Marvel II ($4.99) -r/from Marvel Presents #1, Machine Man #1, Amazing Spider-Man Ann. #19, and Bloodstone #1						6.00
...: Star Brand & Quasar -r/from Star Brand #1 & Quasar #1						5.00
...: Ultimate Spider-Man, Ult. X-Men, Microman & Mantor -r/from Ultimate Spider-Man #1/2, Ultimate X-Men #1/2 and Human Torch #2						5.00
...: Venom & Hercules -r/Marvel S-H Secret Wars #8, Journey Into Mystery Ann. #1	2	4	6	11	16	20
...: Wolverine, X-Men & Tuk: Caveboy -r/from Marvel Comics Presents #1, Uncanny X-Men #201, Capt. America Comics #1,2						5.00
...: (Jim Lee and Chris Claremont): X-Men and the Starjammers Pt. 1 -r/Unc. X-Men #275						5.00
...: X-Men and the Starjammers Pt. 2 -r/Unc. X-Men #276,277						5.00

MARVEL MINI-BOOKS (See Promotional Comics section)

MARVEL MONSTERS:... (one-shots)
Marvel Comics: Dec, 2005; Oct, 2019 ($3.99/$4.99)

...Devil Dinosaur 1 - Hulk app.; Eric Powell-c/a; Sniegoski-s; r/Journey Into Mystery #62						5.00
...Fin Fang Four 1 - FF app.; Powell-c; Langridge-s/Gray-a; r/Strange Tales #89						5.00
...From the Files of Ulysses Bloodstone 1 - Guide to classic Marvel monsters; Powell-c						5.00
...Monsters on the Prowl 1 - Niles-s/Fegredo-a/Powell-c; Thing, Hulk, Giant-Man & Beast app.						5.00
...Where Monsters Dwell 1 - Giffen-s/a; David-s/Pander-a; Parker-s/Braun-s; Powell-c						5.00
HC (2006, $20.99, dust jacket) r/one-shots						21.00
... No. 1 (10/19, $4.99) Bunn-s/Hepburn-a; monster pin-ups & profiles by various						5.00

MARVEL MOVIE PREMIERE (Magazine)
Marvel Comics Group: Sept, 1975 (B&W, one-shot)

1-Burroughs' "The Land That Time Forgot" adapt.	3	6	9	15	22	28

MARVEL MOVIE SHOWCASE FEATURING STAR WARS
Marvel Comics Group: Nov, 1982 - No. 2, Dec, 1982 ($1.25, 68 pgs.)

1-Star Wars movie adaptation; reprints Star Wars #1-3 by Chaykin; reprints-c to Star Wars #1	6	12	18	41	76	110
2-Reprints Star Wars #4-6; Stevens-r	8	12	25	40	55	

MARVEL MOVIE SPOTLIGHT FEATURING RAIDERS OF THE LOST ARK
Marvel Comics: Nov, 1982 ($1.25, 68 pgs.)

1-Edited-r/Raiders of the Lost Ark #1-3; Buscema-c/a(p); movie adapt.						6.00

MARVEL MUST HAVES (Reprints of recent sold-out issues)
Marvel Comics: Dec, 2001 - 2005 ($2.99/$3.99/$4.99)

1,2,4-6: 1-r/Wolverine: Origin #1, Startling Stories: Banner #1, Tangled Web #4 and Cable #97. 2-Amazing Spider-Man #36 and others. 4-Truth #1, Capt. America V4 #1, and The Ultimates #1. 5-r/Ultimate War #1, Ult. X-Men #26, Ult Spider-Man #33.						
6-Ult. Spider-Man #33-36						4.00
3-r/Call of Duty: The Brotherhood #1 & Daredevil #32,33						3.00
Amazing Spider-Man #30-32; Incredible Hulk #34-36; The Ultimates #1-3; Ultimate Spider-Man #1-3; Ultimate X-Men #1-3; (New) X-Men #114-116 each...						4.00
NYX #1-3	3	6	9	21	33	45
NYX #4-5 with sketch & cover gallery; Ultimates 2 #1-3 each...	2	4	6	10	14	18
Spider-Man and the Black Cat #1-3; preview of #4						5.00

MARVEL MYSTERY COMICS (Formerly Marvel Comics) (Becomes Marvel Tales No. 93 on)
Timely /Marvel Comics (TP #2-17/TCI #18-54/MCI #55-92): No. 2, Dec, 1939 - No. 92, June, 1949 (Some material from #8-10 reprinted in 2004's Marvel 65th Anniversary Special #1)

2-(Rare)-American Ace begins, ends #3; Human Torch (blue costume) by Burgos, Sub-Mariner by Everett continue; 2 pg. origin recap of Human Torch; Angel-c	4540	9080	13,620	34,400	76,000	118,000
3-New logo from Marvel pulp begins; 1st app. of television in comics? in Human Torch story (1/40); Angel-c	3370	6740	10,110	25,300	50,150	75,000
4-Intro. Electro, the Marvel of the Age (ends #19), The Ferret, Mystery Detective (ends #9); 1st Sub-Mariner-c by Schomburg; 2nd German swastika on-c of a comic (2/40); one month after Top-Notch Comics #2	4050	8100	12,150	30,400	60,200	90,000
5 Classic Schomburg Torch-c, his 1st ever (Scarce)	4250	8500	12,750	31,450	65,700	100,000
6-Angel-c; Gustavson Angel story	1500	3000	4500	11,400	20,700	30,000
7-Sub-Mariner attacks N.Y. city & Torch joins police force setting up battle in #8-10. Classic Schomburg Torch-c, his 2nd ever	1600	3200	4800	12,200	22,100	32,000
8-1st Human Torch & Sub-Mariner battle(6/40)	1780	3560	5340	13,300	28,650	44,000
9-(Scarce)-Human Torch & Sub-Mariner battle (cover/story); classic-c by Schomburg	5700	11,400	17,100	42,200	83,600	125,000
10-Human Torch & Sub-Mariner battle, conclusion, 1 pg.; Terry Vance, the Schoolboy Sleuth begins, ends #57	1550	3100	4645	11,550	24,775	38,000
11-Schomburg Torch-c, his 3rd ever	649	1298	1947	1738	8369	12,000
12-Classic Angel-c by Kirby	622	1244	1866	4541	8021	11,500
13-Intro. of The Vision by S&K (11/40); Sub-Mariner dons new costume, ends #15;						

Schomburg's 4th Human Torch-c	1200	2400	3600	9100	16,550	24,000
14-16: 14-Shows-c to Human Torch #1 on-c (12/40). 15-S&K Vision, Gustavson Angel story	486	972	1458	3550	6275	9000
17-Human Torch/Sub-Mariner team-up by Burgos/Everett; Human Torch pin-up on back-c; shows-c to Human Torch #2 on-c	568	1136	1744	4146	7323	10,500
18-1st app. villain "The Cat's Paw"	465	930	1395	3395	5998	8600
19,20: 19-Origin Toro in text; shows-c to Sub-Mariner #1 on-c. 20-Origin The Angel in text	443	886	1329	3234	5717	8200
21-The Patriot begins, (intro. in Human Torch #4 (#3)); not in #46-48; Sub-Mariner pin-up on back-c; Gustavson Angel story (7/41)	486	972	1458	3550	6275	9000
22-25: 23-Last Gustavson Angel; origin The Vision in text. 24-Injury-to-eye story	432	864	1296	3154	5577	8000
26-29: 27-Ka-Zar ends; last S&K Vision who battles Satan. 28-Jimmy Jupiter in the Land of Nowhere begins, ends #48; Sub-Mariner vs. The Flying Dutchman	429	858	1287	3132	5516	7900
30-"Remember Pearl Harbor" Japanese war-c	584	1168	1752	4263	7532	10,800
31,32-"Remember Pearl Harbor" Japanese war-c. 31-Sub-Mariner by Everett ends, resumes #84. 32-1st app. The Boobes	429	858	1287	3132	5516	7900
33,35,36,38,39: 36-Nazi invasion of NYC cover. 39-WWII Nazi-c	423	846	1269	3046	5323	7600
34-Everett, Burgos, Martin Goodman, Funnies, Inc. office appear in story & battles Hitler; last Burgos Human Torch	443	886	1329	3234	5717	8200
37-Classic Hitler-c	541	1082	1623	3950	6975	10,000
40-Classic Zeppelin-c	1900	3800	5700	14,400	26,200	38,000
41-Hirohito & Tojo-c	486	972	1458	3550	6275	9000
42,43,47	415	830	1245	2905	5103	7300
44-Classic Super Plane-c	2500	5000	7500	19,000	34,500	50,000
45-Red Skull, Nazi hooded Vigilante war-c	703	1406	2109	5132	9066	13,000
46-Classic Hitler-c	2600	5200	7800	19,800	35,900	52,000
48-Last Vision; flag-c	454	908	1362	3314	5857	8400
49-Origin Miss America	454	908	1362	3314	5857	8400
50-Mary becomes Miss Patriot (origin)	432	864	1296	3154	5577	8000
51-60: 54-Bondage-c	331	662	993	2317	4059	5800
61,62,64-Last German war-c	300	600	900	2070	3635	5200
63-Classic Hitler-c; The Villainess Cat-Woman only app.	622	1244	1866	4541	8021	11,500
65,66-Last Japanese War-c	300	600	900	2070	3635	5200
67-78: 74-Last Patriot. 75-Young Allies begin. 76-Ten Chapter Miss America serial begins, ends #85	200	400	600	1280	2190	3100
79-New cover format; Super Villains begin on cover; last Angel	219	438	657	1402	2401	3400
80-1st app. Capt. America in Marvel Comics	258	516	774	1651	2826	4000
81-Captain America app.	219	438	657	1402	2401	3400
82-Origin & 1st app. Namora (5/47); 1st Sub-Mariner/Namora team-up; Captain America app.	514	1028	1542	3750	6625	9500
83,85: 83-Last Young Allies. 85-Last Miss America; Blonde Phantom app.	200	400	600	1280	2190	3100
84-Blonde Phantom begins (on-c of #84,88,89); Sub-Mariner by Everett begins; Captain America app.; Everett-c	271	542	813	1734	2967	4200
86-Blonde Phantom i.d. revealed; Captain America app.; last Bucky app.	213	426	639	1363	2332	3300
87-1st Capt. America/Golden Girl team-up; last Toro app. (8/48)	213	426	639	1363	2332	3300
88-Golden Girl, Namora, & Sun Girl (1st in Marvel Comics) x-over; Captain America, Blonde Phantom app.	290	580	870	1856	3178	4500
89-1st Human Torch/Sun Girl team-up; 1st Captain America solo; Blonde Phantom app.	213	426	639	1363	2332	3300
90,91: 90-Blonde Phantom un-masked; Captain America app. 91-Capt. America app.; Blonde Phantom & Sub-Mariner end; early Venus app. (4/49) (scarce)	258	516	774	1651	2826	4000
92-Feature story on the birth of the Human Torch and the death of Professor Horton (his creator); last Sub-Mariner in Marvel Comics; Captain America app. (scarce)	438	876	1314	3197	5649	8100
132 Pg. issue, B&W, 25¢ (1943-44)-printed in N. Y.; square binding, blank inside covers); has Marvel No. 33-c in color; contains Capt. America #18 & Marvel Mystery Comics #33; same contents as Captain America Annual	8400	16,800	25,200	52,000	—	—
132 Pg. issue (with variant contents), B&W, 25¢ (1942-'43)- square binding, blank inside covers; has same Marvel No. 33-c in color but contains Capt. America #22 & Marvel Mystery Comics #41 instead	8400	16,800	25,200	52,000	—	—

NOTE: *Brodsky* c-49, 72, 86, 88-92. *Crandall* a-26i. *Everett* c-9, 87, 84. *Gabrielle* c-30-32. *Schomburg* c-3-11, 13-29, 33-36, 39-48, 50-59, 63-69, 74, 76, 132 pg. issue. *Shores* c-37, 38, 75p, 77, 78p, 79p, 80, 81p, 82-84, 85p, 87p. *Sekowsky* c-73. Bondage covers-3, 4, 7, 12, 28, 29, 49, 50, 52, 56, 57, 58, 59, 65. Angel c-2, 3, 8, 12. Remember Pearl Harbor issues-#30-32.

MARVEL MYSTERY COMICS
Marvel Comics: Dec, 1999 ($3.95, reprints)

1-Reprints original 1940s stories; Schomburg-c from #74						5.00

MARVEL MYSTERY COMICS 70th ANNIVERARY SPECIAL
Marvel Comics: Jul, 2009 ($3.99, one-shot)

1-Rivera-c; new Sub-Mariner/Human Torch team-up set in 1941; reps. from #4 & 5						5.00

MARVEL MYSTERY HANDBOOK: 70th ANNIVERARY SPECIAL
Marvel Comics: 2009 ($4.99, one-shot)

1-Official Handbook-style profile pages of characters from Marvel's first year						5.00

MARVEL NEMESIS: THE IMPERFECTS (EA Games characters)
Marvel Comics: July, 2005 - No. 6, Dec, 2005 ($2.99, limited series)

1-6-Jae Lee-c/Greg Pak-s/Renato Arlem-a; Spider-Man, Thing, Wolverine, Elektra app						3.00
Digest (2005, $7.99) r/#1-6						8.00

MARVEL 1985
Marvel Comics: July, 2008 - No. 6, Dec, 2008 ($3.99, limited series)

1-6: 1-Marvel villains come to the real world; Millar-s/Edwards-a; three covers						4.00
HC (2009, $24.99) r/#1-6; intro. by Lindelof; Edwards production art						25.00

MARVEL NO-PRIZE BOOK, THE (The Official… on-c)
Marvel Comics Group: Jan, 1983 (one-shot, direct sales only)

1-Stan Lee as Doctor Doom cover by Golden; Kirby-a	2	4	6	10	14	18

Marvel Mystery Comics #3 © MAR

Marvel Now! Point One #1 © MAR

Marvel Premiere #13 © MAR

	GD	VG	FN	VF	VF/NM	NM-
	2.0	4.0	6.0	8.0	9.0	9.2

MARVEL NOW! POINT ONE
Marvel Comics: Dec, 2012 ($5.99, one-shot)

1-Short story lead-ins to new Marvel Now! series; Nick Fury, Nova, Star-Lord, Ant-Man & others app.; s/a by various; Granov-c and baby variant-c by Skottie Young ... 6.00

MARVEL: NOW WHAT?!
Marvel Comics: Dec, 2013 ($3.99, one-shot)

1-Short story spoofs; Doc Octopus, X-Men, Avengers; s/a by various; Skottie Young-c ... 4.00

MARVELOUS ADVENTURES OF GUS BEEZER
Marvel Comics: May, 2003; Feb, 2004 ($2.99, one-shots)

...: Gus Beezer & Spider-Man 1 - (5/03) Gurihiru-a ... 3.00
...: Hulk 1 - (5/03) Simone-s/Lethcoe-a; She-Hulk app. ... 3.00
...: Spider-Man 1 - (5/03) Simone-s/Lethcoe-a; The Lizard & Dr. Doom app. ... 3.00
...: X-Men 1 - (5/03) Simone-s/Lethcoe-a ... 3.00

MARVELOUS LAND OF OZ (Sequel to Wonderful Wizard of Oz)
Marvel Comics: Jan, 2010 - No. 8, Sept, 2010 ($3.99, limited series)

1-8-Eric Shanower-a/Skottie Young-a/c. 1-Two covers by Young ... 4.00
1-Variant Pumpkinhead/Saw-Horse cover by McGuinness ... 6.00

MARVEL PETS HANDBOOK (Also see "Lockjaw and the Pet Avengers")
Marvel Comics: 2009 ($3.99, one-shot)

1-Official Handbook-style profile pages of animal characters ... 4.00

MARVEL PREMIERE
Marvel Comics Group: April, 1972 - No. 61, Aug, 1981 (A tryout book for new characters)

1-Origin Warlock (pre-#1) by Gil Kane/Adkins; origin Counter-Earth; Hulk & Thor cameo (#1-14 are 20¢-c) | 23 | 46 | 69 | 161 | 356 | 550
2-Warlock ends; Kirby Yellow Claw-r | 6 | 12 | 18 | 38 | 69 | 100
3-Dr. Strange series begins (pre #1, 7/72), Stan Lee-s/B. Smith-c/a(p) | 10 | 20 | 30 | 69 | 147 | 225
4-Barry Smith-a; Roy Thomas brings the world of Robert E. Howard into the Marvel Universe (via serpent people) | 5 | 10 | 15 | 34 | 60 | 85
5-9: 5-1st app. Sligguth; 1st mention of Shuma-Gorath. 6-Brunner-a; 1st N'Gabthoth (Shambler from the sea). 7-1st Dagoth; P. Craig Russell-a. 8-Starlin-(p). 9-Englehart-s; Brunner-a(p) begin | 3 | 6 | 9 | 19 | 30 | 40
10-Death of the Ancient One; 1st app. Shuma-Gorath | 12 | 24 | 36 | 83 | 182 | 280
11-14: 11-Three pages of original material; mostly reprint of origin from Strange Tales #115 with Ditko-a. 13-Baron Mordo app; 1st app. Cagliostro & Sise-Neg. 14-Sise-Neg & Shuma-Gorath app.14-Last Dr. Strange (3/74), gets own title 3 months later | 3 | 6 | 9 | 16 | 23 | 30
15-Origin/1st app. Iron Fist (5/74), ends #25 | 23 | 46 | 69 | 161 | 356 | 550
16,25: 16-2nd app. Iron Fist; origin cont'd from #15; Hama's 1st Marvel-a. 25-1st Byrne Iron Fist (moves to own title next) | 6 | 12 | 18 | 37 | 66 | 95
17,18,20,22-24: Iron Fist in all | 4 | 8 | 12 | 23 | 37 | 50
19-1st app. Colleen Wing; Iron Fist app. | 10 | 20 | 30 | 64 | 132 | 200
21-1st app. Misty Knight; Iron Fist app. | 7 | 14 | 21 | 46 | 86 | 125
26-Hercules. | 3 | 6 | 9 | 14 | 19 | 24
27-Satana | 5 | 10 | 15 | 35 | 63 | 90
28-Legion of Monsters (Ghost Rider, Man-Thing, Morbius, Werewolf) | 16 | 32 | 48 | 110 | 243 | 375
29-46: 29,30-The Liberty Legion. 29-1st modern app. Patriot. 31-1st app. Woodgod; last 25¢ issue. 32-1st app. Monark Starstalker. 33,34-1st color app. Solomon Kane (Robert E. Howard adaptation "Red Shadows".) 35-Origin/1st app. 3-D Man. 36,37-3-D Man. 38-1st Weirdworld. 39,40-Torpedo. 41-1st Seeker 3000! 42-Tigra. 43-Paladin. 44-Jack of Hearts (1st solo book, 10/78). 45,46-Man-Wolf | 1 | 3 | 4 | 6 | 8 | 10
29-31-(30¢-c variants, limited distribution) | 5 | 10 | 15 | 33 | 57 | 80
36-38-(35¢-c variants, limited distribution)(6,8,10/77) | 6 | 12 | 18 | 41 | 76 | 110
47-Origin/1st app. new Ant-Man (Scott Lang); Byrne-a | 10 | 20 | 30 | 68 | 138 | 210
48-Ant-Man; Byrne-a | 4 | 8 | 12 | 25 | 40 | 55
49-The Falcon (1st solo book, 8/79) | 3 | 6 | 9 | 17 | 25 | 34
50-1st app. Alice Cooper; co-plotted by Alice | 5 | 10 | 15 | 33 | 57 | 80
51-53-Black Panther vs. KKK | 4 | 8 | 12 | 23 | 37 | 50
54-56: 54-1st Caleb Hammer. 55-Wonder Man. 56-1st color app. Dominic Fortune | 1 | 3 | 4 | 6 | 8 | 10
57-Dr. Who (2nd U.S. app.-see Movie Classics) | 4 | 8 | 12 | 25 | 40 | 55
58-60-Dr. Who | 2 | 4 | 6 | 10 | 11 | 12
61-Star Lord | 2 | 4 | 6 | 11 | 16 | 20

NOTE: *N. Adams* (Crusty Bunkers) part inks-10, 12, 13. *Austin* a-50i, 56i; c-46i, 50i, 56i, 58. *Brunner* a-5/6, 9-14p; c-9-14. *Byrne* a-47p, 48p. *Chaykin* a-32-34; c-32, 33, 56. *Giffen* a-31p, 44p; c-44. *Gil Kane* a(p)-1, 2, 15; c(p)-1, 2, 15, 16, 22-24, 27, 36, 37. *Kirby* c-26, 29-31, 35. *Layton* a-47i, 48i; c-47. *McWilliams* a-25i. *Miller* c-49p, 53p, 58p. *Nebres* a-44i; c-38i. *Nino* a-38i. *Perez* c/a-38p, 45p, 46p. *Ploog* a-38; c-5-7. *Russell* a-7p. *Simonson* a-60(2pgs.); c-57. *Starlin* a-8p; c-8. *Sutton* a-41, 43, 50p, 61; c-50p, 61. #57-60 publ'd w/two different prices on-c.

MARVEL PRESENTS
Marvel Comics: October, 1975 - No. 12, Aug, 1977 (#1-6 are 25¢ issues)

1-Origin & 1st app. Bloodstone | 6 | 12 | 18 | 42 | 79 | 115
2-Origin Bloodstone continued; Buckler-c | 2 | 4 | 6 | 11 | 16 | 20
3-Guardians of the Galaxy (1st solo book, 2/76) begins, ends #12 | 6 | 12 | 18 | 38 | 69 | 100
4-7,9-12: 9,10-Origin Starhawk | 2 | 4 | 6 | 8 | 11 | 14
4-6-(30¢-c variants, limited distribution)(4-8/76) | 5 | 10 | 15 | 30 | 50 | 70
8-r/story from Silver Surfer #2 plus 4 pgs. new-a | 3 | 6 | 9 | 14 | 20 | 26
11,12-(35¢-c variants, limited distribution)(6,8/77) | 8 | 16 | 24 | 54 | 102 | 150

NOTE: *Austin* a-6i. *Buscema* r-8p. *Chaykin* a-5p. *Kane* c-1p. *Starlin* layouts-10.

MARVEL PREVIEW (Magazine) (Bizarre Adventures #25 on)
Marvel Comics: Feb (no month), 1975 - No. 24, Winter, 1980 (B&W) ($1.00)

1-Man-Gods From Beyond the Stars; Crusty Bunkers (Neal Adams)-a(i) & cover; Nino-a | 4 | 8 | 12 | 23 | 37 | 50
2-1st origin The Punisher (see Amaz. Spider-Man #129 & Classic Punisher); 1st app. Dominic Fortune; Morrow-c | 17 | 34 | 51 | 117 | 259 | 400
3,8,10: 3-Blade the Vampire Slayer. 8-Legion of Monsters; Morbius app. 10-Thor the Mighty; Starlin frontispiece | 4 | 8 | 12 | 25 | 40 | 55
4-Star-Lord & Sword in the Star (origins & 1st app.); Morrow-c | 20 | 40 | 60 | 138 | 307 | 475
5-Sherlock Holmes | 3 | 6 | 9 | 17 | 26 | 35
6,9: 6-Sherlock Holmes; N. Adams frontispiece. 9-Man-God; origin Star Hawk, ends #20 | 3 | 6 | 9 | 14 | 19 | 24
7-(Summer/76) Debut of Rocket Raccoon (called Rocky Raccoon) in Sword in the Star story (see Incredible Hulk #271 (5/82) for next app.); Satana on cover | 33 | 66 | 99 | 238 | 532 | 825
11,14,15,18-Star-Lord. 11-Byrne-a; Starlin frontispiece; 2 versions: with and w/o white Heinlein text at lower right corner of front-c; 1st app. Spartax. 14-Starlin painted-c. 18-Sienkiewicz-a; Veitch & Bissette-a | 5 | 10 | 15 | 33 | 57 | 80
12-Haunt of Horror | 5 | 10 | 15 | 37 | 66 | 95
13,17,20,22,24: 17-Blackmark by G. Kane (see Savage Sword of Conan #3-3). 20-Bizarre Advs.-13. 22-King Kull. 24-Detect Flexible | 3 | 4 | 6 | 8 | 9 | 10
16,19,21,23: 16-Masters of Terror. 19-Kull. 21-Moon Knight (Spr/80)- Predates Moon Knight #1; The Shroud by Ditko. 23-Bizarre Advs.; Miller-a | 2 | 4 | 6 | 8 | 11 | 14

NOTE: *N. Adams* (C. Bunkers) r-20i. *Buscema* a-22, 23. *Byrne* a-11. *Chaykin* a-20r; c-20 (new). *Colan* a-8, 16p(3), 18p, 23p; c-16p. *Elias* a-18. *Giffen* a-7. *Infantino* a-14p. *Kaluta* a-12; c-15. *Miller* a-23. *Morrow* a-8i; c-2-4. *Perez* a-20p. *Ploog* a-8. *Starlin* c-13, 14. Nudity in some issues.

MARVEL RIOT
Marvel Comics: Dec, 1995 ($1.95, one-shot)

1-"Age of Apocalypse" spoof; Lobdell script ... 4.00

MARVEL RISING
Marvel Comics: Jun, 2018 - Nov, 2018; May, 2019 - No. 5, Sept, 2019 ($5.99/$4.99, lim. series)

0-(6/18, free) Grayson-s/Failla-a; preview of Marvel Super Hero Adventures titles ... 3.00
1-5: 1-(5/19, $3.99) Capt. Marvel, Ms. Marvel, Squirrel Girl, America & Spider-Gwen app. ... 4.00
...: Alpha 1 (8/18, $4.99) Part 1; Squirrel Girl & Ms. Marvel team-up; Grayson-s/Duarte-a ... 5.00
...: Ms. Marvel/Squirrel Girl 1 (10/18, $5.99) Part 3; America Chavez app. ... 6.00
...: Omega 1 (11/18, $4.99) Part 4 conclusion; Arcade app. ... 5.00
...: Squirrel Girl/Ms. Marvel 1 (9/18, $5.99) Part 2; battle Emulator ... 6.00

MARVEL ROMANCE
Marvel Comics: 2006 ($19.99, TPB)

nn-Reprints romance stories from 1960-1972; art by Kirby, Buscema, Colan, Romita ... 20.00

MARVEL ROMANCE REDUX (Humor stories using art reprinted from Marvel romance comics)
Marvel Comics: Apr, 2006 - Aug, 2006 ($2.99, one-shots)

...: But I Thought He Loved Me Too (4/06) art by Kirby, Colan, Buscema & Romita; Giffen-c ... 3.00
...: Guys & Dolls (5/06) art by Starlin, Heck, Colan & Buscema; Conner-c ... 3.00
...: I Should Have Been a Blonde (7/06) art by Brodsky Colletta & Colan; Cho-c ... 3.00
...: Love is a Four Letter Word (8/06) art by Kirby, Buscema, Colan & Heck; Land-c ... 3.00
...: Restraining Orders are for Other Girls (6/06) art by Giordano, Kirby; Kyle Baker-c ... 3.00
...: Another Kind of Love TPB (2007, $13.99) r/one-shots ... 14.00

MARVELS (Also see Marvels: Eye of the Camera)
Marvel Comics: Jan, 1994 - No. 4, Apr, 1994 ($5.95, painted lim. series)
No. 1 (2nd Printing), Apr, 1996 - No. 4 (2nd Printing), July, 1996 ($2.95)

1-4: Kurt Busiek scripts & Alex Ross painted-c/a in all; double-c w/acetate overlay | 2 | 4 | 6 | 8 | 10 | 12
Marvel Classic Collectors Pack ($11.90)-Issues #1 & 2 boxed (1st printings) | 2 | 4 | 6 | 9 | 13 | 16
0-(8/94, $2.95)-no acetate overlay. | | | | | | 5.00
1-4-(2nd printing)-limited series w/o acetate overlay | | | | | | 3.00
... Annotated 1-4 (4/19 - No. 4, 8/19, $7.99) reprints with original script, commentary, sketch and unlettered painted art; additional extras | | | | | | 8.00
... Epilogue 1 (9/19, $4.99) Phil Sheldon & family during events of X-Men #98; Busiek-s/Ross-a; new interview with creators; MAD-style spoof (2 pgs.); sketch deign pages | | | | | | 5.00

	GD 2.0	VG 4.0	FN 6.0	VF 8.0	VF/NM 9.0	NM- 9.2

Hardcover (1994, $59.95)-r/#0-4; w/intros by Stan Lee, John Romita, Sr., Kurt Busiek & Scott McCloud. ... 60.00

...: 10th Anniversary Edition (2004, $49.99, hardcover w/dustjacket) r/#0-4; scripts and commentaries; Ross sketch pages, cover gallery, behind the scenes art ... 50.00

Trade paperback ($19.95) ... 20.00

MARVELS, THE
Marvel Comics: Jun, 2021 - No. 12, Sept, 2022 ($4.99/$3.99, limited series)

1-($4.99) Kurt Busiek-s/Yildiray Cinar-a/Alex Ross-c; intro. Kevin Schumer ... 5.00
2-12-($3.99) 3-Winter Soldier app. 4-Spider-Man app. 5-Intro Warbird ... 4.00

MARVEL SAGA, THE
Marvel Comics Group: Dec, 1985 - No. 25, Dec, 1987

1-25 ... 4.00
NOTE: Williamson a(i)-9, 10; c(i)-7, 10-12, 14, 16.

MARVEL'S ANT-MAN AND THE WASP PRELUDE (For the 2018 movie)
Marvel Comics: May, 2018 - No. 2, Jun, 2018 ($3.99, limited series)

1,2-Will Corona Pilgrim-s/Chris Allen-a; adaptation of Ant-Man movie ... 4.00

MARVEL'S ANT-MAN PRELUDE (For the 2015 movie)
Marvel Comics: Apr, 2015 - No. 2, May, 2015 ($2.99, limited series)

1,2-Will Corona Pilgrim-s/Sepulveda-a; photo-c on both; Agent Carter app. ... 3.00

MARVEL'S AVENGERS (Based on the Marvel's Avengers video game)
Marvel Comics: Feb, 2020 - May, 2020 ($3.99, series of one-shots)

...: Black Widow 1 (5/20) Gage-s/Bandini-a; Taskmaster app. ... 4.00
...: Captain America 1 (5/20) Allor-s/Jeanty-a; Batroc app. ... 4.00
...: Hulk 1 (4/20) Jim Zub-s/Ariel Olivetti-a ... 4.00
...: Iron Man 1 (4/20) Zub-s/Paco Diaz-a; Avengers & Titania app. ... 4.00
...: Thor 1 (4/20) Zub-s/Robert Gill-a; Loki app. ... 4.00

MARVEL'S AVENGERS: INFINITY WAR PRELUDE (For the 2018 movie)
Marvel Comics: Mar, 2018 - No. 2, Apr, 2018 ($3.99, limited series)

1,2-Will Corona Pilgrim-s; photo-c on both. 1-Tigh Walker-a. 2-Jorge Fornés-a ... 4.00

MARVEL'S AVENGERS: UNTITLED PRELUDE (Issue #1 released before final title revealed)
MARVEL'S AVENGERS: ENDGAME PRELUDE (Adaptation of Avengers: Inifinity War)
Marvel Comics: Feb, 2019 - No. 3, Apr, 2019 ($3.99, limited series)

1-3-Will Corona Pilgrim-s/Paco Diaz-a; photo-c on each ... 4.00

MARVEL'S BLACK PANTHER PRELUDE (For the 2018 movie)
Marvel Comics: Dec, 2017 - No. 2, Jan, 2018 ($3.99, limited series)

1,2-Will Corona Pilgrim-s/Annapaola Martello-a; photo-c on both ... 4.00

MARVEL'S BLACK WIDOW PRELUDE (For the 2021 movie)
Marvel Comics: Dec, 2017 - No. 2, Jan, 2018 ($3.99, limited series)

1,2-Peter David-s/C.F. Villa-a; photo-c on both; recaps her history with the Avengers ... 4.00

MARVEL'S CAPTAIN AMERICA: CIVIL WAR PRELUDE (For the 2016 movie)
Marvel Comics: Feb, 2016 - No. 4, Mar, 2016 ($3.99, limited series)

1-4: 1,2-Adaptation of Iron Man 3 movie; Pilgrim-s/Kudranski-a. 3,4-Adapts Captain America: The Winter Soldier movie; Ferguson-a ... 3.00

MARVEL'S CAPTAIN MARVEL PRELUDE (For the 2019 movie)
Marvel Comics: Jan, 2019 ($3.99, one-shot)

1-Will Corona Pilgrim-s/Andrea Di Vito-a; Fury & Hill's events during Capt. A. Civil War ... 4.00

MARVELS COMICS: ... (Marvel-type comics read in the Marvel Universe)
Marvel Comics: Jul, 2000 ($2.25, one-shots)

...Captain America #1 -Frenz & Sinnott-a; ...Daredevil #1 -Isabella-s/Newell-a; ...Fantastic Four #1 -Kesel-s/Paul Smith-a; Spider-Man #1 -Oliff-a; ...Thor #1 -Templeton/Aucoin-a ... 3.00
...X-Men #1 -Millar-s/ Sean Phillips & Duncan Fegredo-a ... 3.00
The History of Marvels Comics (no cover price)-Faux history; previews titles ...

MARVEL'S DOCTOR STRANGE PRELUDE (2016 movie)
Marvel Comics: Sept, 2016 - No. 2, Oct, 2016 ($3.99, limited series)

1,2-Corona Pilgrim-s/Fornés-a; photo-c ... 4.00

MARVEL SELECT FLIP MAGAZINE
Marvel Comics: Aug, 2005 - No. 24 ($3.99/$4.99)

1-11-Reprints Astonishing X-Men and New X-Men: Academy X in flip format ... 4.00
12-24-($4.99) Reprints recent X-Men mini-series in flip format ... 5.00

MARVEL SELECTS:
Marvel Comics: Jan, 2000 - No. 6, June, 2000 ($2.75/$2.99, reprints)

...Fantastic Four 1-6: Reprints F.F. #107-112; new Davis-c ... 3.00
...Spider-Man 1,2,4-6: Reprints AS-M #100,101,103,104,93; Wieringo-c ... 3.00
...Spider-Man 3 ($2.99): Reprints AS-M #102; new Wieringo-c ... 3.00

MARVEL 75TH ANNIVERSARY CELEBRATION
Marvel Comics: Dec, 2014 ($5.99, one-shot)

1-Short stories by various incl. Stan Lee, Timm, Bendis, Stan Goldberg, Rivera-c ... 6.00

MARVELS: EYE OF THE CAMERA (Sequel to Marvels)
Marvel Comics: Feb, 2009 - No. 6, Apr, 2010 ($3.99, limited series)

1-6-Kurt Busiek-s/Jay Anacleto-a; continuing story of photographer Phil Sheldon ... 4.00
1-6-B&W edition ... 4.00

MARVEL'S GREATEST COMICS (Marvel Collectors' Item Classics #1-22)
Marvel Comics Group: No. 23, Oct, 1969 - No. 96, Jan, 1981

	GD 2.0	VG 4.0	FN 6.0	VF 8.0	VF/NM 9.0	NM- 9.2
23-34 (Giants). Begin Fantastic Four-r/#30s?-116	3	6	9	17	26	35
35-37-Silver Surfer-r/Fantastic Four #48-50	2	4	6	11	16	20
38-50: 42-Silver Surfer-r/F.F.(others?)	2	4	6	9	13	16
51-70: 63,64-(25¢ editions)	2	4	6	8	10	12
63,64-(30¢-c variants, limited distribution)(5,7/76)	5	10	15	30	50	70
71-96: 71-73-(30¢ editions)	1	2	3	5	6	8
71-73-(35¢-c variants, limited distribution)(7,9-10/77)	7	14	21	49	92	135

...: Fantastic Four #52 (2006, $2.99) reprints entire comic with ads and letter column ... 6.00
NOTE: Dr. Strange, Fantastic Four, Iron Man, Watcher-#23, 24. Capt. America, Dr. Strange, Fantastic Four-#25-28. Buscema r-85-92; c-87-92r. Ditko r-23-28. Kirby r-23-82; c-75, 77p, 80p. #81 reprints Fantastic Four #100.

MARVEL'S GREATEST CREATORS...

Marvel Comics: Jul, 2019 ($1.00, one-shot reprints)

... Avengers – The Origin of Mantis 1 – Reprints Avengers #123; Englehart-s/Brown-a ... 3.00
... Hulk – The Wedding of Rick Jones 1 – Reprints Inc. Hulk #418; David-s/Frank-a ... 3.00
... Invaders 1 – Reprints Invaders #1; Roy Thomas-s/Frank Robbins-a ... 3.00
... Iron Fist – Colleen Wing 1 – Reprints Marvel Premiere #19; Moench-s/Hama-a ... 3.00
... Iron Fist – Misty Knight 1 – Reprints Marvel Premiere #21; Isabella-s/Arvell Jones-a ... 3.00
... Luke Cage, Power Man – Piranha 1 – Reprints Power Man #30; McGregor-s ... 3.00
... Power Pack 1 – Reprints Power Pack #1; Louise Simonson-s/June Brigman-a ... 3.00
... Silver Surfer – Rude Awakening 1 – Reprints Silver Surfer #51; Marz-s/Lim-a ... 3.00
... Spider-Man – Kraven's Last Hunt 1 – Reprints Web of Spider-Man #31; Zeck-a ... 3.00
... What If? – Spider-Girl 1 – Reprints What If? #105; DeFalco-s/Frenz-a ... 3.00

MARVEL'S GREATEST SUPERHERO BATTLES (See Fireside Book Series)

MARVEL: SHADOWS AND LIGHT
Marvel Comics: Feb, 1997 ($2.95, B&W, one-shot)

1-Tony Daniel-c ... 4.00

MARVEL 1602
Marvel Comics: Nov, 2003 - No. 8, June, 2004 ($3.50/$3.99, limited series)

1-7-Neil Gaiman-s; Andy Kubert & Richard Isanove-a ... 3.50
8-($3.99) ... 4.00
... MGC #1 (7/10, $1.00) r/#1 with "Marvel's Greatest Comics" logo on cover ... 3.00
HC (2004, $24.99) r/series; script pages for #1, sketch pages and Gaiman afterword ... 25.00
SC (2005, $19.99) ... 20.00

MARVEL 1602: FANTASTICK FOUR
Marvel Comics: Nov, 2006 - No. 5, Mar, 2007s ($3.50, limited series)

1-5-Peter David-s/Pascal Alixe-a/Leinil Yu-c ... 3.50
TPB (2007, $14.99) r/#1-5; sketch page ... 15.00

MARVEL 1602: NEW WORLD
Marvel Comics: Oct, 2005 - No. 5, Jan, 2006 ($3.50, limited series)

1-5-Greg Pak-s/Greg Tocchini-a; "Hulk" and "Iron Man" app. ... 3.50
TPB (2006, $14.99) r/#1-5 ... 15.00

MARVEL 65TH ANNIVERSARY SPECIAL
Marvel Comics: 2004 ($4.99, one-shot)

1-Reprints Sub-Mariner & Human Torch battle from Marvel Mystery Comics #8-10 ... 6.00

MARVELS OF SCIENCE
Charlton Comics: March, 1946 - No. 4, June, 1946

	GD 2.0	VG 4.0	FN 6.0	VF 8.0	VF/NM 9.0	NM- 9.2
1-A-Bomb story	31	62	93	182	296	410
2-4	17	34	51	100	158	215

MARVEL SPECIAL EDITION FEATURING... (Also see Special Collectors' Ed.)
Marvel Comics Group: 1975 - 1978 (84 pgs.) (Oversized)

	GD 2.0	VG 4.0	FN 6.0	VF 8.0	VF/NM 9.0	NM- 9.2
1-The Spectacular Spider-Man ($1.50); r/Amazing Spider-Man #6,35, Annual 1; Ditko-a	3	6	9	19	30	40
1,2-Star Wars ('77,'78) r/Star Wars #1-3 & #4-6; regular edition	3	6	9	14	20	25
1,2-Star Wars ('77,'78) Whitman variant	3	6	9	19	30	40
3-Star Wars ('78, $2.50, 116 pgs.); r/S. Wars #1-6; regular edition and Whitman variant exist	3	6	9	14	20	26
3-Close Encounters of the Third Kind (1978, $1.50, 56 pgs.)-Movie adaptation; Simonson-a(p)	2	4	6	10	14	18
V2#2(Spring, 1980, $2.00, oversized)- "Star Wars: The Empire Strikes Back"; r/Marvel Comics Super Special #16	3	6	9	17	26	35

NOTE: Chaykin c/a(r)-1(1977), 2, 3. Stevens a(r)-2i, 3i. Williamson a(r)-V2#2.

MARVEL SPECTACULAR
Marvel Comics Group: Aug, 1973 - No. 19, Nov, 1975

	GD 2.0	VG 4.0	FN 6.0	VF 8.0	VF/NM 9.0	NM- 9.2
1-Thor-r from mid-sixties begin by Kirby	3	6	9	17	25	34
2-19	2	4	6	8	10	12

MARVELS: PORTRAITS
Marvel Comics: Mar, 1995 - No. 4, June, 1995 ($2.95, limited series)

1-4: Different artists renditions of Marvel characters ... 4.00

MARVEL SPOTLIGHT (...& Son of Satan #19, 20, 23, 24)
Marvel Comics Group: Nov, 1971 - No. 33, Apr, 1977; V2#1, July, 1979 - V2#11, Mar, 1981
(A try-out book for new characters)

	GD 2.0	VG 4.0	FN 6.0	VF 8.0	VF/NM 9.0	NM- 9.2
1-Origin Red Wolf (western hero)(1st solo book, pre#1); Wood inks; Neal Adams-c; only 15¢ issue	9	18	27	57	111	165
2-(25¢, 52 pgs.)-Venus-r by Everett; origin/1st app. Werewolf By Night (begins) by Ploog; N. Adams-c	71	142	213	568	1284	2000
3-Werewolf By Night	13	26	39	86	188	290
4-1st app. of the Darkhold book; Werewolf By Night ends (6/72); gets own title 9/72	17	34	51	117	259	400
5-Origin/1st app. Ghost Rider (8/72) & begins	300	600	900	2550	5775	9000
6-8: 6-Origin G.R. retold. 8-Last Ploog issue	9	18	27	57	111	165
9-11-Last Ghost Rider (gets own title next mo.)	6	12	18	41	76	110
12-Origin & 2nd full app. The Son of Satan (10/73); story cont'd from Ghost Rider #2 & into #3; series begins, ends #24	9	18	27	62	126	190
13-24: 13-Partial origin Son of Satan. 14-Last 20¢ issue. 22-Ghost Rider-c & cameo (5 panels). 24-Last Son of Satan (10/75); gets own title 12/75	2	4	6	11	16	20
25,27,30,31: 27-(Regular 25¢-c), Sub-Mariner app. 30-The Warriors Three. 31-Nick Fury	3	6	9	10		12
26-Scarecrow	3	6	9	15	22	28
27-(30¢-c variant, limited distribution	5	10	15	33	57	80
28-(Regular 25¢-c) 1st solo Moon Knight app.	21	42	63	147	324	500
28-(30¢-c variant, limited distribution	36	72	108	259	580	900
29-(Regular 25¢-c) (8/76) Moon Knight app.; last 25¢ issue	6	12	18	42	79	115
29-(30¢-c variant, limited distribution	8	16	24	56	108	160
32-1st app./partial origin Spider-Woman (2/77); Nick Fury app.	14	28	42	96	211	325
33-Deathlok; 1st app. Devil-Slayer (see Demon-Hunter #1)	3	6	9	19	30	40
V2#1-Captain Marvel & Drax app.	2	4	6	10	14	18

Marvel 1602 #4 © MAR

Marvel Spotlight: Captain America © MAR

Marvel Super Action #18 © MAR

	GD 2.0	VG 4.0	FN 6.0	VF 8.0	VF/NM 9.0	NM- 9.2

1-Variant copy missing issue #1 on cover — 4 8 12 28 47 65
2-5,9-11: 2-4-Captain Marvel. 2-Drax app. 4-Ditko-c/a. 5-Dragon Lord. 9-11-Captain Universe (see Micronauts #8) — 1 3 4 6 8 10
6-Star-Lord origin — 6 12 18 38 69 100
7-Star-Lord; Miller-c — 4 8 12 23 37 50
8-Capt. Marvel; Miller-c/a(p) — 2 4 6 10 14 18

NOTE: *Austin* c-V2#2i, 8. *J. Buscema* c/a-30p. *Chaykin* a-31; c-26, 31. *Colan* a-18p, 19p. *Ditko* a-V2#4, 5, 9-11; c-V2#4, 9-11. *Kane* c-21p, 32p. *Kirby* c-29p. *McWilliams* a-20i. *Miller* a-V2#8p; c(p)-V2#2, 5, 7, 8. *Mooney* a-8i, 10i, 14p, 15, 16p, 17p, 24p, 27, 32i. *Nasser* a-33p. *Ploog* a-2-5, 6-8p; c-3-9. *Romita* c-13. *Sutton* a-9-11p, V2#6, 7. #29-25¢ & 30¢ issues exist.

MARVEL SPOTLIGHT (Most issues spotlight one Marvel artist and one Marvel writer)
Marvel Comics: 2005 - Apr, 2010 ($2.99/$3.99)

...Brian Bendis/Mark Bagley; Daniel Way/Olivier Coipel; David Finch/Roberto Aguirre-Sacasa; Ed Brubaker/Billy Tan; John Cassaday/Sean McKeever; Joss Whedon/Michael Lark; Laurell K. Hamilton/George R.R. Martin; Neil Gaiman/Salvador Larroca; Greg Land; Stan Lee/Jack Kirby; Warren Ellis/Jim Cheung   each... 3.00
...Steve McNiven/Mark Millar - Civil War 10.00
...: Captain America (2009) interviews with Brubaker & Hitch; Reborn preview 3.00
...: Captain America Remembered (2007) character features; creator interviews 3.00
...: Civil War Aftermath (2007) Top 10 Moments, casualty list, previews of upcoming series 3.00
...: Dark Reign (2009) features on the Avengers, Fury and others; creator interview 4.00
...: Dark Tower (2007) previews the Stephen King adaptation; creator interviews 5.00
...: Deadpool (2009) character features; interviews with Kelly, Way, Medina & Benson 3.00
...: Fantastic Four and Silver Surfer (2007) character features; creator interviews 3.00
...: Ghost Rider (2007) character and movie features; creator interviews 3.00
...: Halo (2007) a World of Halo feature; Bendis & Maleev interviews 3.00
...: Heroes Reborn/Onslaught Reborn (2006) 3.00
...: Hulk Movie (2008) character and movie features; comic & movie creator interviews 3.00
...: Iron Man Movie (2008) character and movie features; Terrence Howard interview 3.00
...: Iron Man 2 (4/10) movie preview; Granov, Fraction interviews; Whiplash profile 4.00
...: Marvel Knights 10th Anniversary (2008) Quesada interview; series synopsis 3.00
...: Marvel Zombies/Mystic Arcana (2008) character features; creator interviews 3.00
...: Marvel Zombies Return (2009) character features; creator interviews 3.00
...: New Mutants (2009) character features; Claremont & McLeod interviews 3.00
...: Punisher Movie (2008) character and movie features; creator interviews 3.00
...: Secret Invasion (2008) features on the Skrulls; Bendis, Reed & Yu interviews 3.00
...: Secret Invasion Aftermath (2008) Skrull profiles; Bendis, Reed & Diggle interviews 4.00
...: Spider-Man (2007) character features; creator interviews; Ditko art showcase 3.00
...: Spider-Man - Brand New Day (2008) storyline features; Romitas interviews 3.00
...: Spider-Man One More Day/Brand New Day (2008) storyline features; interviews 3.00
...: Summer Events (2009, $3.99) 2009 title previews; creator interviews 4.00
...: Thor (2007) character features; Straczynski interview; Romita Jr. art showcase 3.00
...: Ultimates 3 (2008) character features; Loeb & Madureira interviews 3.00
...: Ultimatum (2008) previews the limited series; Loeb & Bendis interviews 3.00
...: Uncanny X-Men 500 Issues Celebration (2008) creator interviews; timeline 3.00
...: War of Kings (2009) character features; Abnett, Lanning, Pelletier interviews 4.00
...: Wolverine (2009, $3.99) preview of 2009 Wolverine stories; creator interviews 4.00
...: World War Hulk (2007) character features; creator interviews; early art showcase 3.00
...: X-Men: Messiah Complex (2008) X-Men crossover features; creator interviews 3.00

MARVELS PROJECT, THE
Marvel Comics: Oct, 2009 - No. 8, July, 2010 ($3.99, limited series)
1-8-Emergence of Marvel heroes in 1939-40; Brubaker-s/Epting-a; Epting & McNiven-c 4.00
1-8-Variant covers by Parel 5.00

MARVELS SNAPSHOTS (See Sub-Mariner: ...)

MARVEL'S SPIDER-MAN: CITY AT WAR (Based on the 2018 videogame)
Marvel Comics (Gamerverse): May, 2019 - No. 6, Oct, 2019 ($3.99, limited series)
1-6: Hallum-s/Bandini-a/Crain-c; gets the new costume; Mr. Negative app. 4.00

MARVEL'S SPIDER-MAN: HOMECOMING PRELUDE
Marvel Comics: May, 2017 - No. 2, Jun, 2017 ($3.99, limited series)
1,2-Adaptation from Captain America: Civil War movie; Pilgrim-s/Nauck-a; photo covers 4.00

MARVEL'S SPIDER-MAN: THE BLACK CAT STRIKES (Based on the 2018 videogame)
Marvel Comics (Gamerverse): Mar, 2020 - No. 5, Nov, 2020 ($3.99, limited series)
1-5: Hallum-s/Maresca-a/Takeda-c 4.00

MARVEL'S SPIDER-MAN: VELOCITY (Titled Gamerverse Spider-Man: Velocity for #1)
Marvel Comics (Gamerverse): Oct, 2020 - No. 5, Feb, 2020 ($3.99, limited series)
1-5-Hallum-s/Laiso-a/Skan-c 4.00

MARVEL'S THE AVENGERS
Marvel Comics: Feb, 2015 - No. 2, Mar, 2015 ($2.99, limited series)
1,2-Adaptation of 2012 movie; Pilgrim-s/Bennett-a; photo covers 3.00

MARVEL'S THE AVENGERS: BLACK WIDOW STRIKES

	GD 2.0	VG 4.0	FN 6.0	VF 8.0	VF/NM 9.0	NM- 9.2

Marvel Comics: Jul, 2012 - No. 3, Aug, 2012 ($2.99, limited series)
1-3-Prelude to 2012 movie; Van Lente-s. 1,3-Photo-c. 2-Granov-c 3.00

MARVEL'S THE AVENGERS PRELUDE
Marvel Comics: May, 2012 - No. 4, Jun, 2012 ($2.99, limited series)
1-4: 1-Prelude to 2012 movie; Luke Ross & Daniel HDR-a 3.00

MARVEL'S THE AVENGERS: THE AVENGERS INITIATIVE
Marvel Comics: Jul, 2012 ($2.99, one-shot)
1-Prelude to 2012 movie; Van Lente-s/Lim-a 3.00

MARVEL'S THOR: RAGNAROK PRELUDE
Marvel Comics: Sept, 2017 - No. 4, Oct, 2017 ($3.99, limited series)
1-4: 1,2-Adapts Thor: Ragnarok movie. 3,4-Adapts Thor: The Dark World movie 4.00

MARVEL SUPER ACTION (Magazine)
Marvel Comics Group: Jan, 1976 (B&W, 76 pgs.)
1-2nd app. Dominic Fortune (see Marvel Preview); early Punisher app.; Weird World & The Huntress; Evans, Ploog-a — 9 18 27 58 114 170

MARVEL SUPER ACTION
Marvel Comics: May, 1977 - No. 37, Nov, 1981
1-Reprints Capt. America #100 by Kirby — 3 6 9 21 33 45
2-13: 2,3,5-13 reprint Capt. America #101,102,103-111. 4-Marvel Boy(origin)/M. Boy #1. 11-Origin-r. 12,13-Classic Steranko-c/a(r). — 2 4 6 9 13 16
2,3-(35¢ variants, limited distribution)(6,8/77) — 12 24 36 79 170 260
14-20: r/Avengers #55,56, Annual 2, others — 2 4 6 8 10 12
21-37: 30-r/Hulk #6 from U.K. — 1 3 4 6 8 10

NOTE: *Buscema* a(r)-14p, 15p; c-18-20, 22, 35r-37. *Everett* a-4r. *Heath* a-4r. *Kirby* r-1-3, 5-11. *B. Smith* a-27r, 28r. *Steranko* a(r)-12p, 13p; c-12r, 13r.

MARVEL SUPER HERO ADVENTURES (All ages title)
Marvel Comics: Jun, 2018 - Jun, 2019 ($3.99, series of one-shots)
...: Captain Marvel - First Day of School 1 (11/18) Spider-Man and Capt. Marvel team-up 4.00
...: Captain Marvel - Frost Giants Among Us! 1 (2/19) Avengers & Squirrel Girl app. 4.00
...: Captain Marvel - Halloween Spooktacular 1 (12/18) Spider-Man app. 4.00
...: Captain Marvel - Mealtime Mayhem 1 (1/19) Spider-Gwen & Venom app. 4.00
...: Inferno 1 (10/18) Spider-Man and Inferno team-up; Venom & Medusa app. 4.00
...: Ms. Marvel and the Teleporting Dog 1 (9/18) Lockjaw and The Serpent Society app. 4.00
...: Spider-Man - Across the Super-Verse 1 (3/19) Grandmaster and other Spiders app. 4.00
...: Spider-Man and the Stolen Vibranium 1 (6/18) Spider-Man & Black Panther team-up 4.00
...: Spider-Man - Spider-Sense of Adventure 1 (5/19) Ghost-Spider and Arcade app. 4.00
...: Spider-Man - Web Designers 1 (6/19) Mysterio app. 4.00
...: Spider-Man - Web Head 1 (3/19) Miles, Gwen & Sinister Six app. 4.00
...: The Spider-Doctor 1 (7/18) Spider-Man and Doctor Strange team-up; Hela app. 4.00
...: Webs and Arrows and Ants, Oh My! 1 (4/18) Kate Bishop & Ant-Man app. 4.00

MARVEL SUPER HERO CONTEST OF CHAMPIONS
Marvel Comics Group: June, 1982 - No. 3, Aug, 1982 (Limited series)
1-Features nearly all Marvel characters currently appearing in their comics; 1st Marvel limited series — 4 8 12 25 40 55
2,3 — 3 6 9 15 22 28

MARVEL SUPER HEROES
Marvel Comics Group: October, 1966 (25¢, 68 pgs.) (1st Marvel one-shot)
1-r/origin Daredevil from D.D. #1; r/Avengers #2; G.A. Sub-Mariner-r/Marvel Mystery #8 (Human Torch app.). Kirby-a — 10 20 30 67 141 215

MARVEL SUPER-HEROES (Formerly Fantasy Masterpieces #1-11)
(Also see Giant-Size Super Heroes) (#12-20: 25¢, 68 pgs.)
Marvel Comics: No. 12, 12/67 - No. 31, 11/71; No. 32, 9/72 - No. 105, 1/82
12-Origin & 1st app. Capt. Marvel of the Kree; G.A. Human Torch, Destroyer, Capt. America, Black Knight, Sub-Mariner-r (#12-20 all contain new stories and reprints) — 29 58 87 209 467 725
13-2nd app. Capt. Marvel; 1st app. of Carol Danvers (later becomes Ms. Marvel); Golden Age Black Knight, Human Torch, Vision, Capt. America, Sub-Mariner-r — 79 158 237 632 1416 2200
14-Amazing Spider-Man (5/68, new-a by Andru/Everett); G.A. Sub-Mariner, Torch, Mercury (1st Kirby-a at Marvel), Black Knight, Capt. America reprints — 10 20 30 66 138 210
15-Black Bolt cameo in Medusa (new-a); Black Knight, Sub-Mariner, Black Marvel, Capt. America-r — 8 16 24 52 99 145
16-Origin & 1st app. S. A. Phantom Eagle; G.A. Torch, Capt. America, Black Knight, Patriot, Sub-Mariner-r — 5 10 15 35 63 90
17-Origin Black Knight (new-a); G.A. Torch, Sub-Mariner-r; reprint from All-Winners Squad #21 (cover & story) — 21 41 147 324 500
18-Origin/1st app. Guardians of the Galaxy (1/69); G.A. Sub-Mariner, All-Winners Squad-r — 68 136 204 544 1222 1900

	GD 2.0	VG 4.0	FN 6.0	VF 8.0	VF/NM 9.0	NM- 9.2

19-Ka-Zar (new-a); G.A. Torch, Marvel Boy, Black Knight, Sub-Mariner reprints; Smith-c(p);
Tuska-a(r) — 5 10 15 31 53 75
20-Doctor Doom (5/69); r/Young Men #24 w-c — 40 80 120 296 673 1050
21-31: All-r issues. 21-X-Men, Daredevil, Iron Man-r begin, end #31. 31-Last Giant issue
— 3 6 9 19 30 40
32-50: 32-Hulk/Sub-Mariner-r begin from TTA. — 2 4 6 8 11 14
51-70,100: 56-r/origin Hulk/Inc. Hulk #102; Hulk-r begin
— 2 4 6 8 10 12
57,58-(30¢-c variants, limited distribution)(5,7/76) — 5 10 15 35 63 90
65,66-(35¢-c variants, limited distribution)(7,9/77) — 8 16 24 56 108 160
71-99,101-105 — 1 3 4 6 8 10
NOTE: Austin a-104. Colan a(p)-12, 13, 15, 18; c-12, 13, 15, 18. Everett a-14i(new); r-14, 15i, 18, 19, 33; c-85(r).
New Kirby c-22, 27, 54. Maneely r-14, 15, 19. Severin r-83-85i, 100-102; c-100-102i. Starlin c-47. Tuska a-19p.
Black Knight-r by Maneely in 12-16, 19. Sub-Mariner-r by Everett in 12-20.

MARVEL SUPER-HEROES
Marvel Comics: May, 1990 - V2#15, Oct, 1993 ($2.95/$2.50, quart., 68-84 pgs.)

1-Moon Knight, Hercules, Black Panther, Magik, Brother Voodoo, Speedball (by Ditko)
& Hellcat; Hembeck-a — 2 4 6 8 10 12
2,4,5,V2#3,6,7,9,13-15: 2-Summer Special(7/90); Rogue, Speedball (by Ditko), Iron Man,
Falcon, Tigra & Daredevil. 4-Spider-Man/Nick Fury, Daredevil,Speedball, Wonder Man,
Spitfire & Black Knight; Byrne-a. 5-Thor, Dr. Strange, Thing & She-Hulk; Speedball by
Ditko(p). V2#3-Retells origin Capt. America w/new facts; Blue Shield, Capt. Marvel,
Speedball, Wasp; Hulk by Ditko/Rogers V2#6-9: 6,7-($2.25-c) X-Men, Cloak & Dagger,
The Shroud (by Ditko) & Marvel Boy in each. 9-West Coast Avengers, Iron Man app.;
Kieth-c(p). V2#13-15 ($2.75, $4.95); 13-All Iron Man 30th anniversary.
15-Iron Man/Thor/Volstagg/Dr. Druid — — — — — 5.00
V2#8-1st app. Squirrel Girl; X-Men, Namor & Iron Man (by Ditko); Larsen-c
— 6 12 18 38 69 100
V2#10-Ms. Marvel/Sabretooth-c/story (intended for Ms. Marvel #24); shows-c to #24);
Namor, Vision, Scarlet Witch stories; $2.25-c — 2 4 6 8 10 12
V2#11-Original Ghost Rider-c/story; Giant-Man, Ms. Marvel stories
— 3 6 9 14 19 24
V2#12-Dr. Strange, Falcon, Iron Man — — — — — 5.00

MARVEL SUPER-HEROES MEGAZINE
Marvel Comics: Oct, 1994 - No. 6, Mar, 1995 ($2.95, 100 pgs.)

1-6: 1-r/FF #232, DD #159, Iron Man #115, Incred. Hulk #314 — — — — — 6.00

MARVEL SUPER-HEROES SECRET WARS (See Secret Wars II)
Marvel Comics Group: May, 1984 - No. 12, Apr, 1985 (limited series)

1 — 5 10 15 35 63 90
1-3-(2nd printings, sold in multi-packs) — — — — — 4.00
2 — 2 4 6 9 13 16
3-6,9-11: 6-The Wasp dies — 1 3 4 6 8 10
7,12: 7-Intro. new Spider-Woman. 12-($1.00, 52 pgs.)2 — 4 6 11 16 20
8-Spider-Man's new black costume explained as alien costume (1st app. Venom as
alien costume) — 10 20 30 67 141 215
10-Doctor Doom cover — 3 6 9 21 33 45
No. 1 Facsimile Edition (3/24, $4.99) Reprints #1 with original ads — — — — — 5.00
No. 2 Facsimile Edition (4/24, $4.99) Reprints #1 with original ads — — — — — 5.00
Secret Wars Omnibus HC (2008, $99.99, dustjacket) r/#1-12, Thor #383, She-Hulk (2004) #10
and What If? (1989) #4 & #114; photo gallery of sealed toys; pencil-a from #1 — — 100.00
NOTE: Zeck a-1-3,6-12; c-1,3,8-12. Additional artists (Romita Sr., Art Adams and others) had uncredited art in #12.

MARVEL SUPER-HEROES SECRET WARS: BATTLEWORLD
Marvel Comics: Jan, 2024 - No. 4, Apr, 2024 $4.99/$3.99, limited series)

1-($4.99) DeFalco-s/Olliffe-a; black-costume Spider-Man and Human Torch app. — — 5.00
2-4-($3.99) Daredevil, Falcon & Iceman app. — — — — — 4.00

MARVEL SUPER HERO SPECTACULAR (All ages)
Marvel Comics: Dec, 2015 ($3.99, one-shot)

1-Avengers, Guardians of the Galaxy and Spider-Man app.; bonus puzzle pages — — 4.00

MARVEL SUPER HERO SQUAD (All ages)
Marvel Comics: Mar, 2009; Nov, 2009 - No. 4, Feb, 2010 ($3.99/$2.99)

1-4-Based on the animated series; back-up humor strips and pin-ups — — — — — 3.00
...Hero Up! (3/09, $3.99) Collects humor strips from MarvelKids.com; 2 covers — — 4.00

MARVEL SUPER HERO SQUAD (All ages)
Marvel Comics: Mar, 2010 - No. 12, Feb, 2011 ($2.99)

1-12-Based on the animated series. 1-Wraparound-c — — — — — 3.00
Super Hero Squad Spectacular 1 (4/11, $3.99) The Beyonder app. — — — — — 4.00

MARVEL SUPER SPECIAL, A (See Marvel Comics Super...)

MARVEL'S VOICES (Inspired by the Marvel's Voices podcast)
Marvel Comics: Apr, 2020 - Present ($4.99/$5.99/$9.99)

1-(4/20) Short essays & stories from various creators of color; intro. by Angélique Roché 5.00
1-(1/21) Expanded version of first edition; Miles Morales mask-c — — — — — 5.00
... Avengers 1 (2/24, $6.99) Short stories intro by David Betancourt — — — — — 7.00
... Comunidades 1 (11/22, $5.99) Short stories celebrating Latin & Latinx heritage — — 6.00
... Identity 1 (11/22, $5.99) Short stories celebrating Asian/Pacific Islander heroes — — 6.00
... Indigenous Voices 1 (1/21, $4.99) Short stories by Native American creators — — — 5.00
...: Legacy 1 (4/21, $4.99) Short stories by African American creators; afterword by Roché 6.00
...: Legacy 1 (4/22, $5.99) Short stories by African American creators; Crisscross-c — 6.00
...: Legends 1 (3/24, $5.99) Short stories celebrating African American heroes — — 6.00
...: Pride 1 (8/21, $9.99) Short stories celebrating LGBTQIA+ heroes; bonus Handbook bios 10.00
...: Pride 1 (8/23, $9.99) Short stories celebrating LGBTQIA+ heroes; bonus interviews 10.00
...: Wakanda Forever (4/23, $5.99) Spotlight on Wakandan characters by Black creators — 6.00
...: X-Men 1 (10/23, $6.99) Short stories; intro by Vita Ayala — — — — — 7.00

MARVEL SWIMSUIT SPECIAL (Also see Marvel Illustrated...)
Marvel Comics: 1992 - No. 4, 1995 ($3.95/$4.50, magazine, 52 pgs.)

1,3,4: 1-Silvestri-c; pin-ups by diff. artists. 3-Hughes-c 2 — 4 6 10 14 18
2-Rogue-c by Jusko — 3 6 9 14 20 25

MARVELS X (Prequel to Earth X, Paradise X and Universe X series)
Marvel Comics: Mar, 2020 - No. 6, Dec, 2020 ($4.99)

1-6-Jim Krueger & Alex Ross/Well-Bee-a; covers by Ross and others — — — — — 5.00

MARVEL TAILS STARRING PETER PORKER THE SPECTACULAR SPIDER-HAM

(Also see Peter Porker... and Spider-Ham)(Appears in Spider-Man: Into the Spider-Verse movie)
Marvel Comics Group: Nov, 1983 (one-shot)

1-1st app. Peter Porker, the Spectacular Spider-Ham; Captain Americat, Goose Rider,
Hulk Bunny app. — 5 10 15 31 53 75

MARVEL TALES (Formerly Marvel Mystery Comics #1-92)
Marvel/Atlas Comics (MCI): No. 93, Aug, 1949 - No. 159, Aug, 1957

93-Horror/weird stories begin — 300 600 900 2070 3635 5200
94-Everett-a — 194 388 582 1242 2121 3000
95-New logo; classic Sci-Fi cover — 343 686 1029 2400 4200 6000
96,99,101,103,105 — 100 200 300 635 1093 1550
97-Sun Girl, 2 pgs.; Kirbyish-a; one story used in N.Y. State Legislative document
— 116 232 348 742 1271 1800
98,100: 98-Krigstein-a — 84 168 252 538 919 1300
102-Wolverton-a "The End of the World", (6 pgs.) — 100 200 300 635 1093 1550
104-Wolverton-a "Gateway to Horror", (6 pgs.) — 123 246 369 787 1344 1900
106,107-Krigstein-a. 106-Decapitation story — 71 142 213 454 777 1100
108-120: 116-(7/53) Werewolf By Night story. 118-Hypo-c/panels in End of World story.
120-Jack Katz-a — 58 116 174 371 636 900
121,123-131: 128-Flying Saucer-c. 131-Last precode (2/55)
— 53 106 159 334 567 800
122-Kubert-a — 55 110 165 352 601 850
132,133,135-141,143,145 — 41 82 123 256 428 600
134-Krigstein, Kubert-a; flying saucer-c — 48 96 144 302 514 725
142-Krigstein-a — 41 82 123 256 428 600
144-Williamson/Krenkel-a, 3 pgs. — 42 84 126 265 445 625
146,148-151,154-156,158: 150-1st S.A. issue. 156-Torres-a
— 37 74 111 222 361 500
147,152: 147-Ditko-a. 152-Wood, Morrow-a — 40 80 120 246 411 575
153-Everett End of World c/story — 47 94 141 296 498 700
157,159-Krigstein-a — 39 78 117 231 378 525
NOTE: Andru a-103. Briefer a-118. Check a-147. Colan a-102, 105, 107, 118, 120, 121, 127, 131. Drucker
a-127, 135, 141, 146, 150. Everett a-98, 104, 106(2), 108(2), 131, 148, 151, 153, 155; c-107, 109, 111, 112, 114,
117, 127, 143, 147-151, 153, 155, 156. Forte a-119, 125, 130, 158. Heath a-110, 113, 130, 132, 159; c-104-106, 110,
130. Gil Kane a-117. Lawrence a-130. Maneely a-111, 126, 129; c-108, 116, 120, 129, 152. Mooney a-114.
Morisi a-153. Morrow a-152, 159. Orlando a-149, 151, 157. Pakula a-119, 121, 133, 135, 144, 150, 152,
156. Powell a-136, 137, 150, 154. Ravielli a-117, 123. Rico a-97, 99. Romita a-108. Sekowsky a-96-98. Shores
a-110; c-96. Sinnott a-105, 116, 144. Tuska a-114. Whitney a-107. Wildey a-126, 138.

MARVEL TALES (...Annual #1,2; ...Starring Spider-Man #123 on)
Marvel Comics Group (NPP earlier issues): 1964 - No. 291, Nov, 1994 (No. 1-32: 72 pgs.)
(#1-3 have Canadian variants; back & inside-c are blank, same value)

1-Reprints origins of Spider-Man/Amazing Fantasy #15, Hulk/Inc. Hulk#1, Ant-Man/T.T.A. #35,
Giant Man/T.T.A. #49, Iron Man/T.O.S. #39,48, Thor/J.I.M. #83 & r/Sgt. Fury #1
— 57 114 171 456 1028 1600
2 ('65)-r/X-Men #1(origin), Avengers #1(origin), origin Dr. Strange-r/Strange Tales #115 &
origin Hulk(Hulk #3) — 12 24 36 81 176 270
3 (7/66)-Spider-Man, Strange Tales (H. Torch), Journey into Mystery (Thor), Tales to Astonish
(Ant-Man)-r begin. r/Strange Tales #101 — 7 14 21 48 89 130
4,5 — 5 10 15 34 60 85
6-8,10: 10-Reprints 1st Kraven/Amaz. S-M #15 — 4 8 12 25 37 50
9-r/Amazing Spider-Man #14 w/cover — 5 10 15 30 50 70
11-33: 11-Spider-Man battles Daredevil-r/Amaz. Spider-Man #16. 13-Origin Marvel Boy-r from
M. Boy #1. 22-Green Goblin-c/story-r/Amaz. Spider-Man #27. 30-New Angel story (x-over
w/Ka-Zar #2,3). 32-Last 72 pg. iss. 33-(52 pgs.) Kraven-r
— 6 9 17 25 34
34-50: 34-Begin regular size issues — 2 4 6 8 10 12
51-65 — 1 3 4 6 8 10
66-70-(Regular 25¢ editions)(4-8/76) — 1 3 4 6 8 10
66-70-(30¢-c variants, limited distribution) — 5 10 15 34 60 85
71-105: 75-Origin Spider-Man-r. 77-79-Drug issues-r/Amaz. Spider-Man #96-98. 98-Death of
Gwen Stacy-r/Amaz. Spider-Man #121. 99-Death Green Goblin-r/Amaz.
Spider-Man #122. 100-(52 pgs.)-New Hawkeye/Two Gun Kid story.
101-105-All Spider-Man-r — 1 2 3 5 6 8
80-84-(35¢-c variants, limited distribution)(6-10/77) — 7 14 21 44 82 120
106-r/1st Punisher-Amazing Spider-Man #129 — 7 14 21 44 82 120
107-136: 107-133-All Spider-Man-r. 111,112-r/Spider-Man #134,135 (Punisher).
113,114-r/Spider-Man #136,137(Green Goblin). 126-128-r/clone story from Amazing
Spider-Man #149-151. 134-136-Dr. Strange-r begin; SpM stories continue.
134-Dr. Strange-r/Strange Tales #110 — — — — — 6.00
137-Origin-r Dr. Strange; shows original unprinted-c & origin Spider-Man/Amazing Fantasy #15
— 3 6 9 19 30 40
137-Nabisco giveaway — 3 6 9 14 20 25
138-Reprints all Amazing Spider-Man #1; begin reprints of Spider-Man with covers similar to
originals — 3 6 9 15 22 28
139-144: r/Amazing Spider-Man #2-7 — 1 2 3 5 6 8
145-149,151-190,193-199: Spider-Man-r continue w/#8 on. 149-Contains skin "Tattooz" decals.
153-r/1st Kraven/Amaz. Spider-Man #15. 155-r/2nd Green Goblin/Spider-Man #17.
161,164,165-Gr. Goblin-c/stories-r/Spider-Man #23,26,27. 178,179-Green Goblin-c/story-r/
Spider-Man #39,40. 187,189-Kraven-r. 193-Byrne-r/Marvel Team-Up begin w/scripts — 4.00
150,191,192,200: 150-($1.00, 52pgs.)-r/Spider-Man Annual #1(Kraven app.). 191-($1.50, 68
pgs.)-r/Spider-Man #96-98. 192-($1.25, 52 pgs.)-r/Spider-Man #121,122. 200-Double size
($1.25)-Miller-c & r/Annual #14 — 1 2 3 5 6 8
201-249,251,252,254-257: 208-Last Byrne-r. 210,211-r/Spidey #134,135. 212,213-r/Giant-Size
Spidey #4. 213-r/1st solo Silver Surfer story/F.F. Annual #5. 214,215-r/Spidey #161,162.
222-Reprints origin Punisher/Spect. Spider-Man #83; last Punisher reprint. 209-Reprints
1st app. The Punisher/Amazing Spider-Man #129; Punisher reprints begin, end #222.
223-McFarlane-c begins, end #239. 233-Spider-Man/X-Men team-ups begin; r/X-Men #35.
234-r/Marvel Team-Up #4. 235-r/Marvel Team-Up Annual #1. 237,238-r/M. Team-Up #150.
239,240-r/M. Team-Up #38,90(Beast). 242-r/M.Team-Up #89. 243-r/M. Team-Up #117
(Wolverine). 251-r/Spider-Man #100 (Green Goblin). 252-257-r/1st app. Morbius/Amaz.
Spider-Man #101. 254-r/M. Team-Up #15(Ghost Rider); new painted-c. 255,256-Spider-Man
& Ghost Rider-r/Marvel Team-Up #58,91. 257-Hobgoblin-r begin (r/ASM #238) — 4.00
250,253: 250-($1.50, 52 pgs.)-r/1st Karma/M. Team-Up #100. 253-($1.50, 52 pgs.) -r/Amaz.
S-M #102 — 1 2 3 5 6 8
258-291: 258-261-r/A. Spider-Man #239,249-251(Hobgoblin). 262,263-r/Marv. Team-Up #53,54.
262-New X-Men vs. Sunstroke story. 263-New Woodgod origin story. 264,265-r/Amazing
Spider-Man Annual 5. 266-273-Reprints alien costume stories/A. S-M 252-259. 277-r/1st

Marvel's Voices: Pride #1 © MAR

Marvel Tales #112 © MAR

Marvel Team-Up #9 © MAR

MA

	GD 2.0	VG 4.0	FN 6.0	VF 8.0	VF/NM 9.0	NM- 9.2

Silver Sable/A. S-M 265. 283-r/A. S-M 275 (Hobgoblin). 284-r/A. S-M 276 (Hobgoblin) 5.00
285-variant w/Wonder-Con logo on c-no price-giveaway 5.00
286-($2.95)-p/bagged w/16 page insert & animation print 1 2 3 5 6 8

NOTE: All contain reprints; some have new art. #89-97-r/Amazing Spider-Man #110-118; #98-136-r/#121-159; #137-150-r/Amazing Fantasy #15, #1-12 & Annual 1; #151-167-r/#13-28 & Annual 2; #168-186-r/#29-46. **Austin** a-100i; c-272i, 273i. **Byrne** a(r)-193-198p, 201-208p. **Ditko** a-1-30, 83, 100, 137-155. **G. Kane** a-71, 81, 98-101p, 249r; c-125-127p, 130p, 137-155. **Sam Kieth** c-255, 262, 263. **Ron Lim** c-266p-281p, 283p-285p. **McFarlane** c-223-239. **Mooney** a-63, 95-97i, 103(i). **Nasser** a-100p. **Nebres** a-242i. **Perez** c-259-261. **Rogers** c-240, 241, 243-252.

MARVEL TALES
Marvel Comics: Mar, 2019 - Nov, 2020 ($7.99)

...: Annihilation 1 (2/20) reprints Marvel Two-In-One #53, Daredevil #105 and Darkhawk #6; Inhyuk Lee-c; intro. by Macchio; features Quasar, Moondragon & Darkhawk 8.00
...: Avengers 1 (7/19) reprints Avengers #16,57,264; Bartel-c; intro. by Macchio 8.00
...: Black Panther 1 (11/19) reprints notable appearances; Bartel-c; intro. by Macchio 8.00
...: Black Widow 1 (4/19) reprints notable appearances; Bartel-c; intro. by Macchio 8.00
...: Captain America 1 (9/19) reprints notable appearances; Bartel-c; intro. by Macchio 8.00
...: Captain Britain 1 (11/20) reprints Captain Britain #1-2, Marvel Team-up #65-66, and Excalibur #1; Inhyuk Lee-c; intro. by Macchio 8.00
...: Doctor Strange 1 (1/20) reprints notable appearances; Bartel-c; intro. by Macchio 8.00
...: Fantastic Four 1 (3/19) reprints FF #4, Annual #6; #245; Bartel-c; intro. by Macchio 8.00
...: Ghost Rider 1 (12/19) reprints notable appearances; Inhyuk Lee-c; intro. by Macchio 8.00
...: Hulk 1 (9/19) reprints notable appearances; Bartel-c; intro. by Macchio 8.00
...: Iron Man 1 (7/19) reprints TOS #39,45 & Iron Man #150; Bartel-c; intro. by Macchio 8.00
...: Ravencroft 1 (3/20) reprints notable appearances; Inhyuk Lee-c; intro. by Macchio 8.00
...: Silver Surfer 1 (12/19) r/Thor #193 & Sub-Mariner #34,35; Lee-c; intro. by Macchio 8.00
...: Spider-Man 1 (8/19) reprints ASM #66, Marvel Spotlight #32 & Peter Parker #90 8.00
...: Thanos 1 (6/19) reprints Warlock #10, Silver Surfer #45, Warlock & Infinity Watch #8 8.00
...: Thor 1 (5/19) reprints JIM #85 & notable appearances; Bartel-c; intro. by Macchio 8.00
...: Venom 1 (4/19) reprints ASM #316, 361 and Peter Parker Spec. S-M #119; Bartel-c; intro. by Macchio 8.00
...: Wolverine 1 (4/20) reprints notable appearances; Inhyuk Lee-c; intro. by Macchio 8.00
...: X-Men 1 (10/19) reprints notable stories; Bartel-c; intro. by Macchio 8.00

MARVEL TALES FLIP MAGAZINE
Marvel Comics: Sept, 2005 - No. 25, Sept, 2007 ($3.99/$4.99)

1-6-Reprints Amazing Spider-Man #30-up and Amazing Fantasy (2004) in flip format 4.00
7-10-Reprints Amazing Spider-Man #36-up and Runaways Vol. 2 in flip format 4.00
11-25-($4.99) Reprints Amazing Spider-Man #36-up and Runaways Vol. 2 in flip format 5.00

MARVEL TAROT, THE
Marvel Comics: 2007 ($3.99, one-shot)

1-Marvel characters featured in Tarot deck images; Djurdjevic-c 4.00

MARVEL TEAM-UP (See Marvel Treasury Edition #18 & Official Marvel Index To...) (Replaced by Web of Spider-Man)
Marvel Comics Group: March, 1972 - No. 150, Feb, 1985
NOTE: Spider-Man team-ups in all but Nos. 18, 23, 26, 29, 32, 35, 97, 104, 105, 137.

1-Human Torch 22 44 66 154 340 525
2-Human Torch 7 14 21 44 82 120
3-Spider-Man/Human Torch vs. Morbius (part 1); 3rd app. of Morbius (7/72) 8 14 24 56 108 160
4-Spider-Man/X-Men vs. Morbius (part 2 of story); 4th app of Morbius 8 16 24 52 99 145
5-10: 5-Vision. 6-Thing. 7-Thor. 8-The Cat (4/73, came out between The Cat #3 & 4). 9-Iron Man. 10-Human Torch. 4 8 12 22 35 48
11-Inhumans 4 8 12 23 37 50
12-Werewolf (By Night) (8/73) 5 10 15 31 53 75
13,14,16-20: 13-Capt. America. 14-Sub-Mariner. 16-Capt. Marvel. 17-Mr. Fantastic. 18-Human Torch/Hulk. 19-Ka-Zar. 20-Black Panther; last 20c issue 3 6 9 14 20 25
15-1st Spider-Man/Ghost Rider team-up (11/73) 10 20 30 64 132 200
21,23-30: 21-Dr. Strange. 23-H-T/Iceman (X-Men cameo). 24-Brother Voodoo. 25-Daredevil. 26-H-T/Thor. 27-Hulk. 28-Hercules. 29-H-T/Iron Man. 30-Falcon 2 4 6 8 11 14
22-Hawkeye 3 6 9 17 26 35
31-45,47-50: 31-Iron Fist. 32-H-T/Son of Satan. 33-Nighthawk. 34-Valkyrie. 35-H-T/Dr. Strange. 36-Frankenstein. 37-Man-Wolf. 38-Beast. 39-H-T. 40-Sons of the Tiger/H-T. 41-Scarlet Witch. 42-The Vision. 43-Dr. Doom; retells origin. 44-Moondragon. 45-Killraven. 47-Thing. 48-Iron Man; last 25c issue. 49-Dr. Strange; Iron Man app. 50-Iron Man; Dr. Strange app. 2 4 6 8 10 12
44-48-(30c-c variants, limited distribution)(4-8/76) 7 14 21 48 89 130
46-Spider-Man/Deathlok team-up 4 6 11 16 20
51,52,56,57: 51-Iron Man; Dr. Strange app. 52-Capt. America. 56-Daredevil. 57-Black Widow; 2nd app. Silver Samurai 2 4 6 8 10 12
53-Hulk; Woodgod & X-Men app., 1st Byrne on X-Men (1/77) 5 10 15 30 50 70

54,55,58-60: 54,59,60: 54-Hulk; Woodgod app. 59-Yellowjacket/The Wasp. 60-The Wasp (Byrne-a in all). 55-Warlock-c/story; Byrne-a. 58-Ghost Rider 2 4 6 8 11 14
58-62-(35c-c variants, limited distribution)(6-10/77) 10 20 30 67 141 215
61-64,67-70: All Byrne-a; 61-H-T. 62-Ms. Marvel; last 30c issue. 63-Iron Fist. 64-Daughters of the Dragon. 67-Tigra; Kraven the Hunter app. 68-Man-Thing. 69-Havok (from X-Men). 70-Thor 2 4 6 8 11 14
65-Capt. Britain (1st U.S. app.) 8 16 24 54 102 150
66-Capt. Britain; 1st app. Arcade 3 6 9 18 28 38
71-74,76-78,80: 71-Falcon. 72-Iron Man. 73-Daredevil. 74-Not Ready for Prime Time Players (Belushi). 76-Dr. Strange. 77-Ms. Marvel. 78-Wonder Man. 80-Dr. Strange/Clea; last 35c issue 1 3 4 6 8 10
75,79,81: Byrne-a(p). 75-Power Man; Cage app. 79-Mary Jane Watson as Red Sonja; Clark Kent cameo (1 panel, 3/79). 81-Death of Satana 2 4 6 8 11 14
82-85,87-94,96-99: 82-Black Widow. 83-Nick Fury. 84-Shang-Chi. 89-Nightcrawler (X-Men). 91-Ghost Rider. 92-Hawkeye. 93-Werewolf by Night. 94-Spider-Man vs. The Shroud. 96-Howard the Duck; last app. issue. 97-Spider-Woman/ Hulk. 98-Black Widow. 99-Machine Man. 85-Shang-Chi/Black Widow/Nick Fury. 87-Black Panther. 88-Invisible Girl.
90-Beast 1 2 3 5 6 8
86-Guardians of the Galaxy 2 4 6 11 16 20
95-Mockingbird (intro.); Nick Fury app. 6 12 18 37 66 95
100-(Double-size)-Spider-Man & Fantastic Four story with origin/1st app. Karma, one of the New Mutants; X-Men & Professor X cameo; Miller-c/a(p); Storm & Black Panther story; brief origins; Byrne-a(p) 3 6 9 18 27 36
101,102,104-116,118-140,142-149: 101-Nighthawk(Ditko-a). 102-Doc Samson. 104-Ka-Zar. 105-Hulk/Power Man/Iron Fist. 106-Capt. America. 107-She-Hulk. 108-Paladin; Dazzler cameo. 109-Dazzler; Paladin app. 110-Iron Man. 111-Devil-Slayer. 112-King Kull; last 50c issue. 113-Quasar. 114-Falcon. 115-Thor. 116-Valkyrie. 118-Professor X; Wolverine app. (4 pgs.); X-Men cameo. 119-Gargoyle. 120-Dominic Fortune. 121-Human Torch. 122-Man-Thing. 123-Daredevil. 124-The Beast. 125-Tigra. 126-Hulk & Powerman/Son of Satan. 127-The Watcher. 128-Capt. America; Spider-Man/ Capt. America photo-c. 129-Vision. 130-Scarlet Witch. 131-Frogman. 132-Mr. Fantastic. 133-Fantastic Four. 134-Jack of Hearts. 135-Kitty Pryde; X-Men cameo. 136-Wonder Man. 137-Aunt May/Franklin Richards. 138-Sandman. 139-Nick Fury. 140-Black Widow. 142-Capt. Marvel. 143-Starfox. 144-Moon Knight. 145-Iron Man. 146-Nomad. 147-Human Torch; Spider-Man back to old costume. 148-Thor. 149-Cannonball 6.00
103-Ant-Man 3 6 9 14 20 25
117-Wolverine-c/story 3 6 9 17 26 35
141-Daredevil; SpM/Black Widow app. (Spidey in new black costume; ties w/ Amazing Spider-Man #252 for 1st black costume) 8 16 24 54 102 150
150-X-Men ($1.00, double-size); Byrne-a 3 6 9 14 19 24
Annual 1 (1976)-Spider-Man/X-Men (early app.) 5 10 15 35 63 90
Annual 2 (1979)-Spider-Man/Hulk 2 4 6 10 14 18
Annual 3,4: 3 (1980)-Hulk/Power Man/Machine Man/Iron Fist; Miller-c(p). 4 (1981)-Spider-Man /Daredevil/Moon Knight/Power Man/Iron Fist; brief origins of each; Miller-c; Miller scripts on Daredevil 1 3 4 6 8 10
Annuals 5-7: 5 (1982)-SpM/The Thing/Scarlet Witch/Dr. Strange/Quasar. 6 (1983)-Spider-Man/ New Mutants (early app.), Cloak & Dagger. 7 (1984)-Alpha Flight; Byrne-c(i) 1 2 3 5 6 8

NOTE: **Art Adams** c-141p. **Austin** a-7i; c-76i, 79i, 96i, 101i, 112i, 130i. **Bolle** a-9i. **Byrne** a(p)-53-55, 59-70, 75, 79, 100; c-68p, 70p, 72p, 75, 76p, 79p, 129i, 133i. **Colan** a-87p. **Ditko** a-101. **Kane** a(p)-4-6, 13, 14, 16-19, 23; c(p)-4, 13, 14, 17-19, 23-25, 28, 33, 37, 41, 44, 45, 47, 53, 54. **Miller** a-100p; c-95p, 99p, 100p, 102p, 106. **Mooney** a-2i, 7i, 8, 10p, 11p, 16i, 24-31p, 72, 93i, Annual 5i. **Nasser** a-89p; c-101p. **Simonson** c-99i, 148. **Paul Smith** c-131, 132. **Starlin** c-27. **Sutton** a-93p. "H-T" means Human Torch; "SpM" means Spider-Man; "S-M" means Sub-Mariner.

MARVEL TEAM-UP (2nd Series)
Marvel Comics: Sept, 1997 - No. 11, July, 1998 ($1.99)

1-11: 1-Spider-Man team-ups begin, Generation x-app. 2-Hercules-c/app.; two covers. 3-Sandman. 4-Man-Thing. 7-Blade. 8-Namor team-ups begin, Dr. Strange app. 9-Capt. America. 10-Thing. 11-Iron Man 4.00

MARVEL TEAM-UP
Marvel Comics: Jan, 2005 - No. 25, Dec, 2006 ($2.25/$2.99)

1-7,9: 1,2-Spider-Man & Wolverine; Kirkman-s/Kolins-a. 5,6-X-23 app. 3.00
8,10-25 ($2.99-c) 10-Spider-Man & Daredevil. 12-Origin of Titannus. 14-Invincible app. 15-2nd app. of 2nd Sleepwalker 3.00
... Vol. 1: The Golden Child TPB (2005, $12.99) r/#1-6 13.00
... Vol. 2: Master of the Ring TPB (2005, $17.99) r/#7-13 18.00
... Vol. 3: League of Losers TPB (2005, $13.99) r/#14-18 14.00
... Vol. 4: Freedom Ring TPB (2007, $17.99) r/#19-25 18.00

MARVEL TEAM-UP (Ms. Marvel Team-Up in indicia for #1)
Marvel Comics: Jun, 2019 - No. 6, Nov, 2019 ($3.99, limited series)

1-6: 1-3-Ms. Marvel & Spider-Man team-up. -Flip book. 4-6-Ms. Marvel/Captain Marvel 4.00

MARVEL: THE LOST GENERATION

	GD 2.0	VG 4.0	FN 6.0	VF 8.0	VF/NM 9.0	NM- 9.2

Marvel Comics: No. 12, Mar, 2000 - No. 1, Feb, 2001 ($2.99, issue #s go in reverse)

1-12-Stern-s/Byrne-s/a; untold story of The First Line. 5-Thor app. ... 3.00

MARVEL/ TOP COW CROSSOVERS
Image Comics (Top Cow): Nov, 2005 ($24.99, TPB)

Vol. 1-Reprints crossovers with Wolverine, Witchblade, Hulk, Darkness; Devil's Reign ... 25.00

MARVEL TREASURY EDITION
Marvel Comics Group/Whitman #17,18: 1974; #2, Dec, 1974 - #28, 1981 ($1.50/$2.50, 100 pgs., oversized, new-a & -r)(Also see Amazing Spider-Man, The, Marvel Spec. Ed. Feat.--, Savage Fists of Kung Fu, Superman Vs. , and 2001, A Space Odyssey)

1-Spectacular Spider-Man; story-r/Marvel Super-Heroes #14; Romita-c/a(r); G. Kane, Ditko-r; Green Goblin/Hulk-r	6	12	18	42	79	115
1-1,000 numbered copies signed by Stan Lee & John Romita on front-c & sold thru mail for $5.00; these were the 1st 1,000 copies off the press	14	28	42	96	211	325
2-10,12: 2-Fantastic Four-r/F.F. 6,11,48-50(Silver Surfer). 3-The Mighty Thor-r/Thor #125-130. 4-Conan the Barbarian; Barry Smith-c/a(r)/Conan #11. 5-The Hulk (origin-r/Hulk #3). 6-Dr. Strange. 7-Mighty Avengers. 8-Giant Superhero Holiday Grab-Bag; Spider-Man, Hulk, Nick Fury. 9-Giant; Super-hero Team-up. 10-Thor; r/Thor #154-157. 12-Howard the Duck (r/#H. the Duck #1 & G.S. Man-Thing #4,5) plus new Defenders story.	3	6	9	21	33	45

11,13-20: 11-Fantastic Four. 13-Giant Super-Hero Holiday Grab-Bag. 14-The Sensational Spider-Man; r/1st Morbius from Amazing S-M #101,102 plus #100 & r/Not Brand Echh #6. 15-Conan; B. Smith, Neal Adams-r; r/Conan #24. 16-The Defenders (origin) & Valkyrie; r/Defenders #1,4,13,14. 17-Incredible Hulk; Blob, Havok, Rhino and The Leader app. 18-The Astonishing Spider-Man; r/Spider-Man's 1st team-ups with Iron Fist, The X-Men, Ghost Rider & Werewolf by Night; inside back-c has photos from 1978 Spider-Man TV show. 19-Conan the Barbarian. 20-Hulk

	3	6	9	17	26	35
21-24,27: 21-Fantastic Four. 22-Spider-Man. 23-Conan. 24-Rampaging Hulk. 27-Spider-Man	3	6	9	17	26	35
25-Spider-Man vs. The Hulk new story	4	8	12	27	44	60
26-The Hulk; 6 pg. new Wolverine/Hercules-s	3	6	9	17	26	35
28-Spider-Man/Superman; (origin of each)	5	10	15	35	63	90

NOTE: Reprints-2, 3, 5, 7-9, 13, 14, 16, 17. Neal Adams a(i)-6, 15. Brunner a-6, 12; c-28. Colan a-6r; c-12p. Ditko a-1, 6. Gil Kane c-16p. Kirby a-1-3, 5, 7, 9-11; c-7. Perez a-26. Romita c-1, 5. B. Smith a-4, 15, 19; c-4, 19.

MARVEL TREASURY OF OZ FEATURING THE MARVELOUS LAND OF OZ
Marvel Comics Group: 1975 ($1.50, oversized) (See MGM's Marvelous…)

1-Roy Thomas/Alfredo Alcala-a; Romita-c & bk-c	4	8	12	23	37	50

MARVEL TREASURY SPECIAL (Also see 2001: A Space Odyssey)
Marvel Comics Group: 1974; 1976 ($1.50, oversized, 84 pgs.)

Vol. 1-Spider-Man, Torch, Sub-Mariner, Avengers "Giant Superhero Holiday Grab-Bag"; Wood, Colan/Everett, plus 2 Kirby-r; reprints Hulk vs. Thing from Fantastic Four #25,26

	3	6	9	19	30	40
Vol. 1-… Featuring Captain America's Bicentennial Battles (6/76)-Kirby-a; B. Smith inks, 11 pgs.	3	6	9	21	33	45

MARVEL TRIPLE ACTION (See Giant-Size…)
Marvel Comics Group: Feb, 1972 - No. 24, Mar, 1975; No. 25, Aug, 1975 - No. 47, Apr, 1979

1-(25¢ giant, 52 pgs.)-Dr. Doom, Silver Surfer, The Thing begin, and #4 ('66 reprints from Fantastic Four)	5	10	15	31	53	75
2-5	2	4	6	11	16	20
6-10	2	4	6	8	11	14
11-47: 45-r/X-Men #45. 46-r/Avengers #53(X-Men	2	4	6	8	10	12
29,30-(30¢-c variants, limited distribution)(5,7/76)	5	10	15	35	63	90
36,37-(35¢-c variants, limited distribution)(7,9/77)	9	18	27	58	114	175

NOTE: #5-44, 46, 47 reprint Avengers #11 thru ?. #40-r/Avengers #48(1st Black Knight). Buscema a(r)-35p, 36p, 38p, 39p, 41, 42, 43p, 44p, 46p, 47p. Ditko a-2r; c-47. Kirby a(r)-1-4p; c-9-19, 22, 24, 29. Starlin c-7. Tuska a(r)-40p, 43, 46i, 47. #2 through #17 are 20¢-c.

MARVEL TRIPLE ACTION
Marvel Comics: May, 2009 - No. 2, Jun, 2009 ($5.99, limited series)

1,2-Reprints stories from Wolverine First Class, Marvel Adventures Avengers & Marvel Super Heroes ... 6.00

MARVEL TSUM TSUM
Marvel Comics: Oct, 2016 - No. 4, Jan, 2017 ($3.99, limited series)

1-4-Based on Japanese stackable plush toys. 1-Spider-Man and the Avengers app. ... 4.00

MARVEL TV: GALACTUS - THE REAL STORY
Marvel Comics: Apr, 2009 ($3.99, one-shot)

1-The "hoax" of Galactus, Tieri-s/Santacruz-a; r/Fantastic Four #50 ... 4.00

MARVEL TWO-IN-ONE (…Featuring … #82 on; also see The Thing)
Marvel Comics Group: January, 1974 - No. 100, June, 1983

1-Thing team-ups begin; Man-Thing	7	14	21	48	89	130
2,3: 2-Sub-Mariner; last 20¢ issue. 3-Daredevil	3	6	9	21	33	45
4,6: 4-Capt. America. 6-Dr. Strange (11/74)	3	6	9	16	23	30
5-Guardians of the Galaxy (9/74, 2nd app.)	5	10	15	30	50	70
7,9,10	2	4	6	11	16	20
8-Early Ghost Rider app. (3/75)	3	6	9	17	26	35
11-14,19,20: 13-Power Man. 14-Son of Satan (early app.)	2	4	6	8	10	12
15-18-(Regular 25¢ editions)(5-7/76) 17-Spider-Man	2	4	6	8	10	12
15-18-(30¢-c variants, limited distribution)	4	8	12	27	44	60
21-29: 27-Deathlok. 29-Master of Kung Fu; Spider-Woman cameo	1	3	4	6	8	10
28,29,31-(35¢-c variants, limited distribution)	4	8	12	25	43	60
30-2nd full app. Spider-Woman (see Marvel Spotlight #32 for 1st app.)	3	6	9	17	26	35
30-(35¢-c variant, limited distribution)(8/77)	9	18	27	62	126	190
31-33-Spider-Woman app.	2	4	6	8	10	12
34-40: 39-Vision	1	2	3	5	6	8
41,42,44,45,47-49: 42-Capt. America. 45-Capt. Marvel	1	2	3	4	5	7
43,50,53,55-Byrne-a(p). 53-Quasar(7/79, 2nd app.)	1	3	4	6	8	10
46-Thing battles Hulk-c/story	2	4	6	10	14	18
51-The Beast, Nick Fury, Ms. Marvel; Miller-a/c	1	3	4	6	8	10
52-Moon Knight; 1st app. Crossfire	2	4	6	19	30	40

54-Death of Deathlok; Byrne-a	4	8	12	25	40	55

56-60,64-68,70-74,76-79,81,82: 60-Intro. Impossible Woman. 68-Angel. 71-1st app. Maelstrom. 76-Iceman ... 5.00

61-63: 61-Starhawk (from Guardians); "The Coming of Her" storyline begins, ends #63; cover similar to F.F. #67 (Him-c). 62-Moondragon; Thanos & Warlock cameo in flashback; Starhawk app. 63-Warlock revived shortly; Starhawk & Moondragon app.

	2	4	6	8	10	12
69-Guardians of the Galaxy	2	4	6	9	12	15
75-Avengers (52 pgs.)						6.00
80,90,100: 80-Ghost Rider. 90-Spider-Man. 100-Double size, Byrne-s						6.00
83-89,91-99: 83-Sasquatch. 84-Alpha Flight app. 93-Jocasta dies. 96-X-Men-c & cameo						5.00
Annual 1 (1976, 52 pgs.)-Thing/Liberty Legion; Kirby-c	3	6	9	15	22	28
Annual 2 (1977, 52 pgs.)-Thing/Spider-Man; 2nd death of Thanos; end of Thanos saga; Warlock app.; Starlin-c/a	6	12	18	47	79	115
Annual 3,4 (1978-79, 52 pgs.): 3-Nova. 4-Black Bolt	1	2	3	5	6	8
Annual 5-7 (1980-82, 52 pgs.): 5-Hulk. 6-1st app. American Eagle. 7-The Thing/Champion; Sasquatch, Colossus app.; X-Men cameo (1 pg.)						6.00

NOTE: Austin c(i)-42, 54, 56, 58, 61, 63, 66. John Buscema a-30p, 45; c-30p. Byrne p-43, 50, 53-55; c-43, 53p, 56p, 98i, 99i. Gil Kane a-1p, 2p; c(p)-1-3, 9-11, 14, 28. Kirby c-12, 19p, 20, 25, 27. Mooney a-18i, 38i, 90i. Nasser a-70p. Perez a(p)-56-58, 60, 64, 65; c(p)-32, 43, 50-52, 54, 55, 57, 58, 61-66, 70. Roussos a-Annual 1i. Simonson c-43i, 97p, Annual 6i. Starlin c-6, Annual 1. Tuska a-6p.

MARVEL TWO-IN-ONE
Marvel Comics: Sept, 2007 - No. 17, Jan, 2009 ($4.99, 64 pgs.)

1-8,13-16-Reprints Marvel Adventures Avengers and X-Men: First Class stories ... 5.00
9-12,17-Reprints Marvel Adventures Iron Man and Avengers stories ... 5.00

MARVEL 2-IN-ONE
Marvel Comics: Feb, 2018 - No. 12, Jan, 2019 ($3.99)

1-12: 1-Human Torch & The Thing team-up; Zdarsky-s/Cheung-a; Doctor Doom app. ... 4.00
Annual 1 (8/18, $4.99) Spotlight on Infamous Iron Man; Zdarsky-s/Shalvey-a ... 5.00

MARVEL UNIVERSE (See Official Handbook Of The…)

MARVEL UNIVERSE (Title on variant covers for newsstand editions of some 2001 Marvel titles. See indicia for actual titles and issue numbers)

MARVEL UNIVERSE
Marvel Comics: June, 1998 - No. 7, Dec, 1998 ($2.99/$1.99)

1-($2.99)-Invaders stories from WW2; Stern-s ... 5.00
2-7-($1.99): 2-Two covers. 4-7-Monster Hunters; Manley-a/Stern-s ... 4.00

MARVEL UNIVERSE AVENGERS AND ULTIMATE SPIDER-MAN
Marvel Comics: 2012 (no price, Halloween giveaway)

1-Reprints from Marvel Universe Ultimate Spider-Man #1 & Avengers E.M.H #1 ... 4.00

MARVEL UNIVERSE AVENGERS ASSEMBLE (Based on the Disney XD animated series)
(Titled Avengers Assemble for #1,2)
Marvel Comics: Dec, 2013 - No. 12, Nov, 2014 ($3.99/$2.99)

1-($3.99) Red Skull app.; bonus Lego-style story ... 4.00
2-12-($2.99) 5-Dracula app. 7-Hyperion app. 12-Impossible Man app. ... 3.00

MARVEL UNIVERSE AVENGERS ASSEMBLE: CIVIL WAR
Marvel Comics: May, 2016 - No. 4, Aug, 2016 ($2.99)

1-4: 1,2,4-Ultron app. ... 3.00

MARVEL UNIVERSE AVENGERS ASSEMBLE SEASON TWO
Marvel Comics: Jan, 2015 - No. 16, Apr, 2016 ($3.99/$2.99)

1-($3.99) Red Skull & Thanos app. ... 4.00
2-16-($2.99) 2-Thanos & The Watcher app. 4-Winter Soldier app. 9-Ant-Man joins ... 3.00

MARVEL UNIVERSE AVENGERS: ULTRON REVOLUTION
Marvel Comics: Sept, 2016 - No. 12, Oct, 2017 ($2.99)

1-12-Ultron returns; A.I.M. app. 11-Ms. Marvel joins. 12-Captain Marvel app. ... 3.00

MARVEL UNIVERSE GUARDIANS OF THE GALAXY (Disney XD animated series)
Marvel Comics: Apr, 2015 - No. 4, Jul, 2015 ($2.99)

1-4: 1-Back-up story with Star-Lord origin ... 3.00

MARVEL UNIVERSE GUARDIANS OF THE GALAXY (Disney XD animated series)
Marvel Comics: Dec, 2015 - No. 23, Oct, 2017 ($3.99/$2.99)

1-($3.99) Cosmo & Korath app.; bonus Lego story ... 4.00
2-23-($2.99) 3-Fin Fang Foom app. 4-Grandmaster app. 13-Loki app. 20-Thanos app. 3.00

MARVEL UNIVERSE HULK: AGENTS OF S.M.A.S.H. (Disney XD animated series)
Marvel Comics: Dec, 2013 - No. 4, Mar, 2014 ($2.99)

1-4: 1-Hulk, A-Bomb, She-Hulk, Red Hulk and Skaar team-up ... 3.00

MARVEL UNIVERSE: MILLENNIAL VISIONS
Marvel Comics: Feb, 2002 ($3.99, one-shot)

1-Pin-ups by various; wraparound-c by JH Williams & Gray ... 4.00

MARVEL UNIVERSE: THE END (Also see Infinity Abyss)
Marvel Comics: May, 2003 - No. 6, Aug, 2003 ($3.50/$2.99, limited series)

1-($3.50)-Thanos, X-Men, F.F, Avengers, Spider-Man, Daredevil app.; Starlin-s/a(p) ... 4.00
2-6-($2.99) Akhenaten, Eternity, Living Tribunal app. ... 3.00
Thanos Vol. 3: Marvel Universe - The End (2003, $16.99) r/#1-6 ... 17.00

MARVEL UNIVERSE ULTIMATE SPIDER-MAN (Based on the animated series)
Marvel Comics: Jun, 2012 - No. 31, Dec, 2014 ($2.99)

1-31: 1-Agent Coulson app. 13-Iron Man app. 16,19-Venom app. 29-Spider-Ham app. ... 3.00

MARVEL UNIVERSE ULTIMATE SPIDER-MAN: CONTEST OF CHAMPIONS
Marvel Comics: May, 2016 - No. 4, Aug, 2016 ($2.99, limited series)

1-4-The Collector & Grandmaster app. 1-Iron Man, Hulk & Kraven app. ... 3.00

MARVEL UNIVERSE ULTIMATE SPIDER-MAN: SPIDER-VERSE
Marvel Comics: Jan, 2016 - No. 4, Apr, 2016 ($3.99/$2.99)

1-($3.99) 1-Spider-Man 2099 and Spider-Girl app. ... 4.00
2-4-($2.99) 3,4-Miles Morales app. ... 3.00

MARVEL UNIVERSE ULTIMATE SPIDER-MAN VS. THE SINISTER SIX
Marvel Comics: Sept, 2016 - No. 11, Sept, 2017 ($2.99)

1-11: 1,2-Doctor Octopus & Scarlet Spider app. 3-Dr. Strange app. 6-Venom app. ... 3.00

Marvel Tsum Tsum #1 © MAR

Marvel Voices: Community #1 © MAR

Marvel Zombies #1 © MAR

	GD	VG	FN	VF	VF/NM	NM-		GD	VG	FN	VF	VF/NM	NM-
	2.0	4.0	6.0	8.0	9.0	9.2		2.0	4.0	6.0	8.0	9.0	9.2

MARVEL UNIVERSE ULTIMATE SPIDER-MAN: WEB WARRIORS
Marvel Comics: Jan, 2015 - No. 12, Dec, 2015 ($3.99/$2.99)

1-($3.99) Captain America & Doctor Doom app.; back-up with Iron Spider — 4.00
2-12-($2.99) 2-Hawkeye app. 3-Iron Man app. 8-Deadpool app. 12-Howling Commandos 3.00
.../Avengers Assemble Halloween ComicFest 2015 #1 (giveaway) reprints — 3.00

MARVEL UNIVERSE VS. THE AVENGERS
Marvel Comics: Dec, 2012 - No. 4, Mar, 2013 ($3.99, limited series)

1-4-Avengers vs. Marvel Zombies; Maberry-s/Fernandez-a/Kuder-c — 4.00

MARVEL UNIVERSE VS. THE PUNISHER
Marvel Comics: Oct, 2010 - No. 4, Nov, 2010 ($3.99, limited series)

1-4-Punisher vs. Marvel Zombies; Maberry-s/Parlov-a/c — 4.00

MARVEL UNIVERSE VS. WOLVERINE
Marvel Comics: Aug, 2011 - No. 4, Nov, 2011 ($3.99, limited series)

1-4-Wolverine vs. Marvel Zombies; Maberry-s/Laurence Campbell-a/c — 4.00

MARVEL UNLEASHED
Marvel Comics: Oct, 2023 - No. 4, Jan, 2024 ($4.99, limited series)

1-4-Animal heroes team-up; Redwing, Lockjaw, Chewie and Throg app. — 4.00

MARVEL UNLIMITED (Title on variant covers for newsstand editions of some 2001 Daredevil issues. See indicia for actual titles and issue numbers)

MARVEL VALENTINE SPECIAL
Marvel Comics: Mar, 1997 ($2.99, one-shot)

1-Valentine stories w/Spider-Man, Daredevil, Cyclops, Phoenix — 2 — 4 — 6 — 10 — 14 — 18

MARVEL VERSUS DC (See DC Versus Marvel) (Also see Amazon, Assassins, Bruce Wayne: Agent of S.H.I.E.L.D., Bullets & Bracelets, Doctor Strangefate, JLX, Legend of the Dark Claw, Magneto & The Magnetic Men, Speed Demon, Spider-Boy, Super Soldier, & X-Patrol)
Marvel Comics: No. 2, 1996 - No. 3, 1996 ($3.95, limited series)

2,3: 2-Peter David script. 3-Ron Marz script; Dan Jurgens-a(p). 1st app. of Super Soldier, Spider-Boy, Dr. Doomsday, Doctor Strangefate, The Dark Claw, Nightcreeper, Amazon, Wraith & others. Storyline continues in Amalgam books. — 5.00

MARVEL VISIONARIES
Marvel Comics: 2002 - 2007 (various prices, HC and TPB)

...: Chris Claremont (2005, $29.99) r/X-Men #137, Uncanny X-Men #153,205,268 & Ann. #12, Iron Fist #14, Wolverine #3, New Mutants #21 and other highlights — 30.00
...: Gil Kane (8/02, $24.95) r/Amazing Spider-Man #99, Marvel Premiere #1,#15, TOA #76 & others; plus sketch pages and a cover gallery — 25.00
...: Jack Kirby HC (2004, $29.99) r/career highlights- Red Raven Comics #1 (1st work), Captain America Comics #1, Avengers #4, Fantastic Four #48-50 and more — 30.00
...: Jack Kirby Vol. 2 HC (2006, $34.99) r/career highlights- Captain America, Two-Gun Kid, Fantastic Four, Thor, Fin Fang Foom, Devil Dinosaur, romance and more — 35.00
...: Jim Steranko (9/02, $14.95) r/Captain America #110,111,113; X-Men #50,51 and stories from Tower of Shadows #1 and Our Love Story #5; plus a cover gallery — 15.00
...: John Buscema (2007, $34.99) r/career highlights-Avengers, Silver Surfer, Thor, FF, Hulk, Wolverine and others; Roy Thomas intro.; sketch pages and pin-up art — 35.00
...: John Romita Jr. (2005, $29.99) r/various stories 1977-2002; debut in AS-M Ann. #11; Iron Man #128, AS-M V2 #36, issues of Hulk, Daredevil: The Man Without Fear, Punisher; sketch pages; intro. by John Romita Sr. — 30.00
...: John Romita Sr. (2005, $29.99) r/various stories 1951-1997 including Young Men #24&26, Daredevil #16, ASM #39,42,50; sketch pages; intro. by John Romita Jr. — 30.00
...: Roy Thomas (2006, $34.99) r/career highlights; intro. by Stan Lee — 35.00
...: Steve Ditko (2005, $29.99) r/various stories 1961-1992; intro. by Blake Bell — 30.00
...: Stan Lee HC (2005, $29.99) r/career highlights- Captain America Comics #3 (1st work), and various Spider-Man, FF, Thor, Daredevil stories; 1940-1995; Roy Thomas intro. — 30.00

MARVEL VOICES (Also see Marvel's Voices:...)
Marvel Comics: Aug, 2021 - Present (series of one-shots)

...: Community 1 (12/21, $9.99) Stories celebrating Latin & Latinx characters & creators — 10.00
...: Heritage (3/22, $4.99) Spotlight on Indigenous characters & creators — 5.00
...: Identity (10/21, $5.99) Spotlight on Asian American & Pacific Islander characters & creators — 6.00
...: Pride (8/21, $9.99) Spotlight on LGBTQ+ characters & creators — 5.00

MARVEL WEDDINGS
Marvel Comics: 2005 ($19.99, TPB)

TPB-Reprints weddings of Peter & Mary Jane, Reed & Sue, Scott & Jean, and others — 20.00

MARVEL WESTERNS: ...
Marvel Comics: 2006 ($3.99, one-shots)

... Kid Colt and the Arizona Girl 1 (9/06) 2 short stories & 3 Kirby/Ayers reps.; Powell-c — 4.00
... Outlaw Files-Profiles and essays about Marvel western characters — 4.00
... Strange Westerns Starring The Black Rider 1 (10/06) Englehart-s/Rogers-a & 2 Kirby Rawhide Kid reprints; Rogers-c — 4.00

... The Two-Gun Kid 1 (8/06) 2 short stories & a Kirby/Ayers reprint; Powell-c — 4.00
... Western Legends 1 (9/06) 2 short stories & r/Rawhide Kid origin by Kirby; Powell-c — 4.00
HC (2006, $20.99, dustjacket) r/one-shots — 21.00

MARVEL X-MEN COLLECTION, THE
Marvel Comics: Jan, 1994 - No. 3, Mar, 1994 ($2.95, limited series)

1-3-r/X-Men trading cards by Jim Lee — 4.00

MARVEL - YEAR IN REVIEW (Magazine)
Marvel Comics: 1989 - No. 3, 1991 (52 pgs.)

1-3: 1-Spider-Man-c by McFarlane. 2-Capt. America-c. 3-X-Men/Wolverine-c — 6.00

MARVEL: YOUR UNIVERSE
Marvel Comics: May, 2009 - No. 3, July, 2009 ($5.99)

1-3-Reprints of 5 recent comics (Ms. Marvel, Nova, Immortal Iron Fist & others) — 6.00
...Saga (2008, no cover price) - Re-caps of crossovers (Secret War thru Secret Invasion) — 3.00

MARVEL ZERO (Collects Marvel's Gold 2023 Free Comic Book Day titles)
Marvel Comics: Sept, 2023 ($6.99, one-shot)

1-Previews upcoming Marvel storylines; X-Men, Uncanny Avengers, Spider-Man, Venom — 7.00

MARVEL ZOMBIE (Simon Garth)
Marvel Comics: Dec, 2018 ($4.99, one-shot)

1-Prince-s/Raffaele-a; Spider-Man, Moon Girl, Daredevil, others in zombie apocalypse — 5.00

MARVEL ZOMBIES (See Ultimate Fantastic Four #21-23, 30-32)
Marvel Comics: Feb, 2006 - No. 5, June, 2006 ($2.99, limited series)

1-Zombies vs. Magneto; Kirkman-s/Phillips-a/Suydam-c swipe of A.F. #15 — 4 — 8 — 12 — 23 — 37 — 50
1-(2nd printing) Variant Suydam-c swipe of Spider-Man #1 — 2 — 4 — 6 — 11 — 16 — 20
1-(3rd-4th printings) Variant Suydam-c swipes of Amazing Spider-Man #50 and Incredible Hulk #1 — 6.00
2-Avengers #4 cover swipe by Suydam — 2 — 4 — 6 — 9 — 12 — 15
3-Inc. Hulk #340 c-swipe — 3 — 6 — 9 — 16 — 23 — 30
3-5-(2nd printings) 3-Daredevil #179 c-swipe. 4-AS-M #39 c-swipe. 5-Silver Surfer #1 — 4.00
4,5: 4-X-Men #1 c-swipe. 5-AS-M Ann. #21 c-swipe — 1 — 2 — 3 — 5 — 6 — 8
...: Dead Days (7/07, $3.99) Early days of the plague; Kirkman-s/Phillips-a/Suydam-c — 5.00
...: Dead Days HC (2008, $29.99, oversized) r/Dead Days one-shot, Ultimate Fantastic Four #21-23, 30-32, and Black Panther #28-30 — 30.00
...: Evil Evolution (1/10, $4.99) Apes vs. Zombies; Marcos Martin-c — 1 — 2 — 3 — 5 — 6 — 8
... Halloween (12/12, $3.99) Van Lente-s/Vitti-a/Francavilla-c — 6.00
... MGC #1 (7/10, $1.00) r/#1 with "Marvel's Greatest Comics" logo on cover — 3.00
...: The Book of Angels, Demons and Various Monstrosities (2007, $3.99) profile pages — 5.00
...: The Covers (2007, $19.99, d.j.) Suydam's covers with originals and commentary — 20.00
HC (2006, $19.99) r/#1-5; Kirkman foreword; cover gallery with variants — 20.00

MARVEL ZOMBIES 2
Marvel Comics: Dec, 2007 - No. 5, Apr, 2008 ($2.99, limited series)

1-5-Kirkman-s/Phillips-a/Suydam zombie-fied cover swipes — 5.00
HC (2008, $19.99) r/#1-5; cover swipe gallery — 20.00

MARVEL ZOMBIES 3
Marvel Comics: Dec, 2008 - No. 4, Mar, 2009 ($3.99, limited series)

1-4-Van Lente-s/Walker-a/Land-c; Machine Man, Jocasta and Morbius app. — 5.00

MARVEL ZOMBIES 4
Marvel Comics: Jun, 2009 - No. 4, Sept, 2009 ($3.99, limited series)

1-4-Van Lente-s/Walker-a/Land-c; Zombie Deadpool head app. — 4.00

MARVEL ZOMBIES 5
Marvel Comics: Jun, 2010 - No. 5, Sept, 2010 ($3.99, limited series)

1-5-Van Lente-s; Machine Man and Howard the Duck app. 3-Kaluta-a — 4.00

MARVEL ZOMBIES (Secret Wars tie-in)
Marvel Comics: Aug, 2015 - No. 4, Dec, 2015 ($3.99, limited series)

1-4-Spurrier-s/Walker-a; Elsa Bloodstone vs. zombies. 2,3-Deadpool app. — 4.00

MARVEL ZOMBIES / ARMY OF DARKNESS
Marvel Comics/Dynamite Entertainment: May, 2007 - No. 5, Aug, 2007($2.99, limited series)

1-Zombies vs. Ash during the start of the plague; Layman-s/Neves-a/Suydam-c — 7.00
1-Second printing with Suydam zombie-fied Captain America Comics #1 cover swipe — 4.00
2-5-Suydam zombie-fied cover swipes on all — 5.00
HC (2007, $19.99) r/#1-5; cover gallery with variants and non-zombied original covers — 20.00

MARVEL ZOMBIES: BLACK, WHITE & BLOOD
Marvel Comics: Dec, 2023 - No. 4, Mar, 2024 ($5.99, limited series, B&W&Red)

1-4-Anthology of short stories by various. 2-Simone-s. 3-Momoko-s/a. 4-Skroce-s/a — 4.00

	GD 2.0	VG 4.0	FN 6.0	VF 8.0	VF/NM 9.0	NM- 9.2

MARVEL ZOMBIES CHRISTMAS CAROL ("Zombies Christmas Carol" on cover)
Marvel Comics: Aug, 2011 - No. 5, Oct, 2011 ($3.99, limited series)

1-5-Adaptation of the Dickens classic with zombies; Kaluta-c/Baldeon-a ... 4.00

MARVEL ZOMBIES DESTROY!
Marvel Comics: Jul, 2012 - No. 5, Sept, 2012 ($3.99, limited series)

1-5-Howard the Duck, Dum Dum Dugan vs. zombies; Del Mundo-c ... 4.00

MARVEL ZOMBIES: RESURRECTION
Marvel Comics: Dec, 2019; Nov, 2020 - No. 4, Jan, 2021 ($5.99/$3.99)

1-(12/19, $4.99) Phillip Kennedy Johnson-s/Leonard Kirk-a/Inhyuk Lee-c ... 5.00
1-(11/20, $5.99) Johnson-s/Kirk-a/Inhyuk Lee-c; story continues; Blade app. ... 6.00
2-4-($3.99) 2-Viv Vision app. 3-Logan & Silver Surfer app. ... 5.00

MARVEL ZOMBIES RETURN
Marvel Comics: Nov, 2009 - No. 5, Nov, 2009, weekly limited series)

1-5-Suydam-c. 1-Zombie Spider-Man eats the Earth-Z Sinister Six; Dragotta-a ... 4.00

MARVEL ZOMBIES SUPREME
Marvel Comics: May, 2011 - No. 5, Aug, 2011 ($3.99, limited series)

1-5-Zombies in Squadron Supreme dimension; Blanco-a/Komarck-c; Jack of Hearts app. 4.00

MARVILLE
Marvel Comics: Nov, 2002 - No. 7, Jul, 2003 ($2.25, limited series)

1-6-Satire on DC/AOL-Time-Warner; Jemas-a/Bright-a/Horn-c ... 3.00
1-($3.95) Variant foil cover by Udon Studios; bonus sketch pages and Jemas afterword ... 4.00
7-($2.99) Intro. to Epic Comics line with submission guidelines ... 3.00

MARVIN MOUSE
Atlas Comics (BPC): September, 1957

1-Everett-c/a; Maneely-a ... 20 40 60 117 189 260

MARY JANE (Spider-Man) (Also see Amazing Mary Jane and Spider-Man Loves Mary Jane)
Marvel Comics: Aug, 2004 - No. 4, Nov, 2004 ($2.25, limited series)

1-4-Marvel Age series with teen-age MJ Watson; Miyazawa-c/a; McKeever-s ... 3.00
... Vol. 1: Circle of Friends (2004, $5.99, digest-size) r/#1-4 ... 6.00

MARY JANE & BLACK CAT (Dark Web tie-in)
Marvel Comics: Feb, 2023 - No. 5, Jun, 2023 ($4.99/$3.99)

1-($4.99) MacKay-s/Carratu-a; Belasco app. ... 5.00
2-5-($3.99) ... 4.00

MARY JANE & BLACK CAT: BEYOND (Spider-Man)
Marvel Comics: Mar, 2022 ($4.99, one-shot)

1-MacKay-s/Villa-a; The Hood, Count Nefaria, & Tombstone app. ... 5.00

MARY JANE & SNIFFLES (See Looney Tunes)
Dell Publishing Co.: No. 402, June, 1952 - No. 474, June, 1953

Four Color 402 (#1) ... 10 20 30 69 147 225
Four Color 474 ... 8 16 24 55 105 155

MARY JANE: HOMECOMING (Spider-Man)
Marvel Comics: May, 2005 - No. 4, Aug, 2005 ($2.99, limited series)

1-4-Teen-age MJ Watson in high school; Miyazawa-c/a; McKeever-s ... 3.00
... Vol. 2 (2005, $6.99, digest-size) r/#1-4 ... 7.00

MARY MARVEL COMICS (Monte Hale #29 on) (Also see Captain Marvel #18, Marvel Family, Shazam, & Wow Comics)
Fawcett Publications: Dec, 1945 - No. 28, Sept, 1948

1-Captain Marvel introduces Mary on-c; intro/origin Georgia Sivana ... 200 400 600 1280 2190 3100
2 ... 87 174 261 553 952 1350
3,4- 3-New logo ... 55 110 165 352 601 850
5-8- 8-Bulletgirl x-over; classic Christmas-c ... 45 90 135 284 480 675
9,10 ... 41 82 123 256 428 600
11-20 ... 30 60 90 177 289 400
21-28- 28-Western-c ... 27 54 81 156 266 370

MARY POPPINS (See Movie Comics & Walt Disney Showcase No. 17)

MARY SHELLEY MONSTER HUNTER
AfterShock Comics: Apr, 2019 - No. 5, Aug, 2019 ($3.99, limited series)

1-5-Adam Glass & Olivia Cuartero-Briggs-s/Hayden Sherman-a ... 4.00

MARY SHELLEY'S FRANKENSTEIN
Topps Comics: Oct, 1994 - Jan, 1995 ($2.95, limited series)

1-4-polybagged w/3 trading cards ... 5.00
1-4 ($2.50)-Newstand ed. ... 4.00

MARY WORTH (See Harvey Comics Hits #55 & Love Stories of...)
Argo: March, 1956 (Also see Romantic Picture Novelettes)

1-Senator's mistress makes wife jealous-s ... 10 20 30 58 79 100

MASK (TV)
DC Comics: Dec, 1985 - No. 4, Mar, 1986; Feb, 1987 - No. 9, Oct, 1987

1-Saturday morning TV show ... 3 6 9 19 30 40
2-4 ... 1 3 4 6 8 10
1-9 (2nd series) ... 5.00

MASK, THE (Also see Mayhem)
Dark Horse Comics: Aug, 1991 - No. 4, Oct, 1991; No. 0, Dec, 1991 ($2.50, 36 pgs., limited series)

1-1st app. Lt. Kellaway as The Mask (see Dark Horse Presents #10 for 1st app.) ... 4 8 12 23 37 50
2-4 ... 1 3 4 6 8 10
0-(12/91, B&W, 56 pgs.)-r/Mayhem #1-4 ... 1 3 4 6 8 10
...Omnibus Vol. 1 (8/08, $24.95) r/#1-4, Mask Returns and Mask Strikes Back series ... 50.00
...Omnibus Vol. 2 (4/09, $24.95) r/#1-4, The Hunt For Green October, World Tour, Southern Discomfort, Toys in the Attic series and short stories from DHP ... 40.00

...: HUNT FOR GREEN OCTOBER July, 1995 - Oct, 1995 ($2.50, lim. series)

1-4-Evan Dorkin scripts ... 4.00

...: I PLEDGE ALLEGIANCE TO THE MASK Oct, 2019 - No. 4, Jan, 2020 ($3.99, lim. series)

1-4-Christopher Cantwell-s/Patric Reynolds-a ... 4.00

.../ MARSHAL LAW Feb, 1998 - No. 2, Mar, 1998 ($2.95, lim. series)

1,2-Mills-s/O'Neill-a ... 2 4 6 11 16 20

...: OFFICIAL MOVIE ADAPTATION July, 1994 - Aug, 1994 ($2.50, lim. series)

1,2 ... 6.00

... RETURNS Oct, 1992 - No. 4, Mar, 1993 ($2.50, limited series)

1-4 ... 4.00

... SOUTHERN DISCOMFORT Mar, 1996 - No. 4, July, 1996 ($2.50, limited series)

1-4 ... 4.00

... STRIKES BACK Feb, 1995 - No. 5, Jun, 1995 ($2.50, limited series)

1-5 ... 4.00

... SUMMER VACATION July, 1995 ($10.95, one shot, hard-c)

1-nn-Rick Geary c/a ... 11.00

... TOYS IN THE ATTIC Aug, 1998 - No. 4, Nov, 1998 ($2.95, lim. series)

1-4-Fingerman-s ... 4.00

... VIRTUAL SURREALITY July, 1997 ($2.95, one shot)

nn-Mignola, Aragonés, and others-s/a ... 4.00

... WORLD TOUR Dec, 1995 - No. 4, Mar, 1996 ($2.50, limited series)

1-4- 3-X & Ghost-c/app. ... 4.00

MASK COMICS
Rural Home Publ.: Feb-Mar, 1945 - No. 2, Apr-May, 1945; No. 2, Fall, 1945

1-Classic L. B. Cole Satan-c/a; Palais-a ... 3500 7000 10,500 26,600 48,300 70,000
2-(Scarce)-Classic L. B. Cole Satan-c; Black Rider, The Boy Magician, & The Collector app. ... 1250 2500 3750 9500 17,250 25,000
2-(Fall, 1945)-No publ.-same as regular #2; L. B. Cole-c ... 1050 2100 3150 7980 14,490 21,000

MASKED BANDIT, THE
Avon Periodicals: 1952

nn-Kinstler-a ... 24 48 72 144 237 330

MASKED MAN, THE
Eclipse Comics: 12/84 - #10, 4/86; #11, 10/87; #12, 4/88 ($1.75/$2.00, color/B&W #9 on, Baxter paper)

1-12: 1-Origin retold. 3-Origin Aphid-Man; begin $2.00-c ... 3.00

MASKED MARVEL (See Keen Detective Funnies)
Centaur Publications: Sept, 1940 - No. 3, Dec, 1940

1-The Masked Marvel begins ... 226 452 678 1446 2473 3500
2,3- 2-Gustavson, Tarpe Mills-a ... 168 336 504 1075 1838 2600

MASKED RAIDER, THE (Billy The Kid #9 on; Frontier Scout, Daniel Boone #10-13) (Also see Blue Bird)
Charlton Comics: June, 1955 - No. 8, July, 1957; No. 14, Aug, 1958 - No. 30, June, 1961

1-Masked Raider & Talon the Golden Eagle begin; painted-c ... 22 44 66 132 216 300
2 ... 11 22 33 62 86 110
3-8,15: 8-Billy The Kid app. 15-Williamson-a, 7 pgs. ... 8 16 24 44 57 70
14,16-30: 22-Rocky Lane app. ... 7 14 21 37 46 55

MASKED RANGER
Premier Magazines: Apr, 1954 - No. 9, Aug, 1955

1-The Masked Ranger, his horse Streak, & The Crimson Avenger (origin) begin, end #9; Woodbridge/Frazetta-a ... 52 104 156 328 552 775
2,3 ... 20 40 60 117 189 260
4-8-All Woodbridge-a. 5-Jesse James by Woodbridge. 6-Billy The Kid by Woodbridge. 7-Wild Bill Hickok by Woodbridge. 8-Jim Bowie's Life Story ... 20 40 60 120 195 270
9-Torres-a; Wyatt Earp by Woodbridge; Says Death of Masked Ranger on-c ... 22 44 66 128 209 290

NOTE: **Check** a-1. Woodbridge c/a-1, 4-9.

MASKERADE
Dark Horse Comics (Secret Stash Press): Sept, 2022 - No. 8, Sept, 2023 ($3.99)

1-8-Kevin Smith & Andy McElfresh-s/John Sprengelmeyer-a ... 4.00

M.A.S.K.: MOBILE ARMORED STRIKE KOMMAND (Hasbro toy)
IDW Publishing: Nov, 2016 - No. 10, Aug, 2017 ($3.99)

1-10: 1,2-Easton-s/Vargas-a. 3,6,7-Samu-a ... 4.00
Annual 2017 (2/17, $7.99, squarebound) Griffith-a; bonus character profiles ... 8.00
M.A.S.K. First Strike 1 (10/17, $3.99) G.I. Joe & Cobra app.; 3 covers; Kyriazis-a ... 4.00
...: Revolution 1 (9/16, $3.99) Easton-s/Vargas-a ... 4.00

MASK OF DR. FU MANCHU, THE (See Dr. Fu Manchu)
Avon Periodicals: 1951

1-Sax Rohmer adapt.; Wood-c/a (26 pgs.); Hollingsworth-a ... 148 296 444 947 1624 2300

MASK OF ZORRO, THE
Image Comics: Aug, 1998 - No. 4, Dec, 1998 ($2.95, limited series)

1-4-Movie adapt. Photo variant-c ... 4.00

MASKS
Dynamite Entertainment: 2012 - No. 8, 2013 ($3.99)

1-Team-up of the Shadow, Green Hornet, Spider; Alex Ross-a; multiple covers ... 5.00
2-8: 2-Miss Fury and Green Lama app.; Calero-a. 3-Black Terror app. ... 4.00

MASKS 2
Dynamite Entertainment: 2015 - No. 8, 2015 ($3.99)

1-8-Pulp hero team-up; Bunn-s/Casallos-a; multiple covers on each ... 4.00

MASKS: TOO HOT FOR TV!
DC Comics (WildStorm): Feb, 2004 ($4.95)

1-Short stories by various incl. Thompson, Brubaker, Mahnke, Conner; Fabry-c ... 5.00

MASQUE OF THE RED DEATH (See Movie Classics)

MASQUERADE (See Project Superpowers)
Dynamite Entertainment: 2009 - No. 4, 2009 ($3.50, limited series)

Mary Jane & Black Cat #4 © MAR

Mary Marvel #4 © FAW

Master Comics #26 © FAW

	GD	VG	FN	VF	VF/NM	NM-
	2.0	4.0	6.0	8.0	9.0	9.2

1-4-Alex Ross & Phil Hester-s/Carlos Paul-a; covers by Ross & others 3.50

MASS EFFECT: DISCOVERY (Based on the EA video game)
Dark Horse Comics: May, 2017 - No. 4, Oct, 2017 ($3.99, limited series)
1-4-Barlow-s/Guzmán-a 4.00

MASS EFFECT: EVOLUTION (2nd series based on the EA video game)
Dark Horse Comics: Jan, 2011 - No. 4, Apr, 2011 ($3.50, limited series)
1-4-Walters & Jackson Miller-s/Carnevale-c 3.50

MASS EFFECT: FOUNDATION (Based on the EA video game)
Dark Horse Comics: Mar, 2013 - No. 13, Jul, 2014 ($3.99, limited series)
1-13: 1-Walters-s/Francia-a. 2-4-Parker-a 4.00

MASS EFFECT: HOMEWORLDS (Based on the EA video game)
Dark Horse Comics: Apr, 2012 - No. 4, Aug, 2012 ($3.50, limited series)
1-4: 1-Walters-s/Francisco-a 3.50

MASS EFFECT: INVASION (3rd series based on the EA video game)
Dark Horse Comics: Oct, 2011 - No. 4, Jan, 2012 ($3.50, limited series)
1-4-Walters & Jackson Miller-s/Carnevale-c 3.50

MASS EFFECT: REDEMPTION (Based on the EA video game)
Dark Horse Comics: Jan, 2010 - No. 4, Apr, 2010 ($3.50, limited series)
1-4-Walters & Jackson Miller-s/Francia-a 3.50

MASSIVE, THE
Dark Horse Comics: Jun, 2012 - No. 30, Dec, 2014 ($3.50)
1-30: 1-Brian Wood-s/Kristian Donaldson-a. 4-9,25-30-Brown-a. 10-Erskine-a 3.50
...: Ninth Wave 1-6 ($3.99, 12/15 - No. 6, 5/16) Prequel to series; Wood-s/Brown-a 4.00

MASTER COMICS (Combined with Slam Bang Comics #7 on)
Fawcett Publications: Mar, 1940 - No. 133, Apr, 1953 (No. 1-6: oversized issues) (#1-3: 15¢, 52 pgs.; #4-6: 10¢, 36 pgs.; #7-Begin 68 pg. issues)

1-Origin & 1st app. Master Man; The Devil's Dagger, El Carim, Master of Magic, Rick O'Say, Morton Murch, White Rajah, Shipwreck Roberts, Frontier Marshal, Streak Sloan, Mr. Clue begin (all features end #6)
1025 2050 3075 7800 14,150 20,500
2 (Rare) 314 628 942 2198 3849 5500
3-6-Last Master Man (Rare) 271 542 813 1734 2967 4200
NOTE: #1-6 rarely found in near mint or very fine condition due to large-size format.

7-(10/40)-Bulletman, Zoro, the Mystery Man (ends #22), Lee Granger, Jungle King & Buck Jones begin; only app. The War Bird & Mark Swift & the Time Retarder; Zoro, Lee Granger, Jungle King & Mark Swift all continue from Slam Bang; Bulletman moves from Nickel
300 600 900 2010 3505 5000

8-The Red Gaucho (ends #13), Captain Venture (ends #22) & The Planet Princess begin
181 362 543 1158 1979 2800

9,10: 10-Lee Granger ends 155 310 465 992 1696 2400
11-Origin & 1st app. Minute-Man (2/41) 300 600 900 1920 3310 4700
12 142 284 426 909 1555 2200
13-Origin & 1st app. Bulletgirl; Hitler-c 290 580 870 1856 3178 4500
14-16: 14-Companions Three begins, ends #31 129 258 387 826 1413 2000
17-20: 17-Raboy-a on Bulletman begins. 20-Captain Marvel cameo app. in Bulletman
123 246 369 787 1344 1900

21-(12/41; Scarce)-Captain Marvel & Bulletman team up against Capt. Nazi; origin & 1st app. Capt. Marvel Jr.'s most famous nemesis Captain Nazi who will cause creation of Capt. Marvel Jr. 1st Mac Raboy-c for Fawcett; Capt. Nazi-c
1050 2100 3150 8400 14,500 21,000

22-(1/42)-Captain Marvel Jr. moves over from Whiz #25 & teams up with Bulletman against Captain Nazi; part III of trilogy origin of Capt. Marvel Jr. & his 1st cover and adventure
865 1730 2595 6315 11,158 16,000

23-Capt. Marvel Jr. c/stories begin (1st solo story); fights Capt. Nazi by himself.
326 652 978 2282 3991 5700

24,25 152 304 456 965 1658 2350
26,28,30-Captain Marvel Jr. vs. Capt. Nazi. 28-Liberty Bell-c. 30-Flag-c
148 296 444 947 1624 2300

27-Captain Marvel Jr. "V For Victory"-c; Capt. Nazi app.
290 580 870 1856 3178 4500
29-Hitler & Hirohito-c 400 800 1200 2800 4900 7000

31,32,35: 31-Captain Marvel & Spy Smasher Comix Cards on back-c. 32-Last El Carim & Buck Jones; intro Balbo, the Boy Magician in El Carim story; classic Eagle-c by Raboy
123 246 369 787 1344 1900

33-Capt. Marvel Jr. smashing swastika-c; Balbo, the Boy Magician (ends #47), Hopalong Cassidy (ends #49) begins
219 438 657 1402 2401 3400

34-Capt. Marvel Jr. vs. Capt. Nazi-c/story; 1st mention of Capt. Nippon
206 412 618 1318 2259 3200

36-Statue of Liberty-c 129 258 387 826 1413 2000
37-39 93 186 279 591 1021 1450
40-Classic flag-c 174 348 522 1114 1907 2700

41-(8/43)-Bulletman, Capt. Marvel Jr. & Bulletgirl x-over in Minute-Man; only app. Crime Crusaders Club (Capt. Marvel Jr., Minute-Man, Bulletman & Bulletgirl)
106 212 318 673 1162 1650

42-46,49: 46-Hitler story. 49-Last Minute-Man 61 122 183 390 670 950
47-Hitler becomes Corpl. Hitler Jr. 71 142 213 454 777 1100
48-Intro. Bulletboy; Capt. Marvel cameo in Minute-Man
71 142 213 454 777 1100

50-Intro Radar & Nyoka the Jungle Girl & begin series (5/44); Radar also intro in Captain Marvel #35 (same date); Capt. Marvel x-over in Radar; origin Radar; Capt. Marvel & Capt. Marvel, Jr. introduce Radar on-c
55 110 165 352 601 850
51-58 36 72 108 211 343 475

59-62: Nyoka serial "Terrible Tiara" in all; 61-Capt. Marvel Jr. 1st meets Uncle Marvel
37 74 111 222 361 500
63-80 27 54 81 162 266 370

81,83-87,89-91,95-99: 88-Hopalong Cassidy begins (ends #94). 95-Tom Mix begins (cover only in #123, ends #133)
24 48 72 142 234 325
82,88,92-94-Krigstein-a 25 50 75 150 245 340
100 28 56 84 168 274 380
101-106-Last Bulletman (not in #104) 24 48 72 140 230 320
107-120: 118-Mary Marvel 22 44 66 132 216 300
121-131-(lower print run): 123-Tom Mix-c only 24 48 72 144 237 330
132-B&W and color illos in POP; last Nyoka 26 52 78 154 252 350
133-Bill Battle app. 34 68 102 199 325 450
NOTE: *Mac Raboy* a-15-39, 40(part), 42, 58. c-21-49, 51, 52, 54, 56, 58, 68(part), 69(part). *Bulletman* c-7-11, 13(half), 15, 18(part), 19, 20, 21(w/Capt. Marvel & Capt. Nazi), 22(w/Capt. Marvel, Jr.). Capt. Marvel, Jr. c-23-133. *Master Man* c-1-6. *Minute Man* c-12, 13(half), 14, 16, 17, 18(part).

MASTER DARQUE
Acclaim Comics (Valiant): Feb, 1998 ($3.95)
1-Manco-a/Christina Z.-s 4.00

MASTER DETECTIVE
Super Comics: 1964 (Reprints)
17-r/Criminals on the Loose V4 #2; r/Young King Cole #?; McWilliams-r
2 4 6 11 16 20

MASTER OF KUNG FU (Formerly Special Marvel Edition; see Deadly Hands of Kung Fu & Giant-Size...)
Marvel Comics Group: No. 17, April, 1974 - No. 125, June, 1983
17-Starlin-a; intro Black Jack Tarr; 3rd Shang-Chi (ties w/Deadly Hands #1)
7 14 21 44 82 120
18,20 3 6 9 17 25 34
19-Man-Thing-c/story 4 8 12 23 37 50
21-23,25-30 2 4 6 11 16 20
24-Starlin, Simonson-a 2 4 6 13 18 22
31-50: 33-1st Leiko Wu. 43-Last 25¢ issue 2 4 6 8 10 12
39-43-(30¢-c variants, limited distribution)(5-7/76) 7 14 21 44 82 120
51-75 1 2 3 5 6 8
53-57-(35¢-c variants, limited distribution)(6-10/77) 8 16 24 52 99 145
76-99 .... 6.00
100,118,125-Double size 1 2 3 5 6 8
101-117,119-124 .... 5.00
Annual 1(4/76)-Iron Fist app. 5 10 15 31 53 75
NOTE: *Austin* c-63i, 74i. *Buscema* c-44p. *Gulacy* a(p)-18-20, 22, 25, 29-31, 33-35, 38, 39, 40(p&i), 42-50, 53r(#20). c-51, 55, 64, 67. *Gil Kane* c(p)-20, 38, 39, 42, 45, 59, 63. *Nebres* c-73i. *Starlin* a-17p, 24; c-54. *Sutton* a-42i. #53 reprints #20.

MASTER OF KUNG FU (Secret Wars tie-in)
Marvel Comics: Jul, 2015 - No. 4, Oct, 2015 ($3.99, limited series)
1-4-Blackman; Talajic-a/Francavilla-c; Shang-Chi & Iron Fist app. 4.00

MASTER OF KUNG FU (Marvel Legacy)
Marvel Comics: No. 126, Jan, 2018 ($3.99, one-shot)
126-CM Punk-s/Talajic-a 4.00

MASTER OF KUNG-FU: BLEEDING BLACK
Marvel Comics: Feb, 1991 ($2.95, 84 pgs., one-shot)
1-The Return of Shang-Chi 4.00

MASTER OF KUNG-FU, SHANG-CHI:... (2002 series, see Shang Chi:...)

MASTER OF THE WORLD
Dell Publishing Co.: No. 1157, July, 1961
Four Color 1157-Movie based on Jules Verne's "Master of the World" and "Robur the Conqueror" novels; with Vincent Price & Charles Bronson 8 16 24 55 105 155

MASTERPIECE
Dark Horse Comics: Dec, 2023 - Present ($3.99, limited series)
1-3-Bendis-s/Maleev-a 4.00

	GD	VG	FN	VF	VF/NM	NM-
	2.0	4.0	6.0	8.0	9.0	9.2

MASTERS OF TERROR (Magazine)
Marvel Comics Group: July, 1975 - No. 2, Sept, 1975 (B&W) (All reprints)

		GD	VG	FN	VF	VF/NM	NM-
1-Brunner, Barry Smith-a; Morrow/Steranko-c; Starlin-a(p); Gil Kane-a		4	8	12	25	40	55
2-Reese, Kane, Mayerik-a; Adkins/Steranko-c		3	6	9	16	23	30

MASTERS OF THE UNIVERSE (See DC Comics Presents #47 for 1st app.)
DC Comics: Dec, 1982 - No. 3, Feb, 1983 (Mini-series)

	GD	VG	FN	VF	VF/NM	NM-
1	6	12	18	37	66	95
2,3: 2-Origin He-Man & Ceril	3	6	9	14	20	26

NOTE: *Alcala a-1i, 2i. Tuska a-1-3p; c-1-3p. #2 has 75 & 95 cent cover price.*

MASTERS OF THE UNIVERSE (Comic Album)
Western Publishing Co.: 1984 (8-1/2x11", $2.95, 64 pgs.)

	GD	VG	FN	VF	VF/NM	NM-
11362-Based on Mattel toy & cartoon	3	6	9	18	28	38

MASTERS OF THE UNIVERSE
Star Comics/Marvel #7 on: May, 1986 - No. 13, May, 1988 (75c/$1.00)

	GD	VG	FN	VF	VF/NM	NM-
1	5	10	15	33	57	80
2-9,11: 8-Begin $1.00-c	2	4	6	8	10	12
10	3	6	9	14	20	25
12-Death of He-Man (1st Marvel app.)	6	12	18	37	66	95
13-Return of He-Man & death of Skeletor	5	10	15	35	63	90
The Motion Picture (11/87, $2.00)-Tuska-p	3	6	9	21	33	45

MASTERS OF THE UNIVERSE
Image Comics: Nov, 2002 - No. 4, March, 2003 ($2.95, limited series)

	GD	VG	FN	VF	VF/NM	NM-
1-($2.95) Two covers by Santalucia and Campbell; Santalucia-a	2	4	6	10	14	18
1-($5.95) Variant-c by Norem w/gold foil logo	2	4	6	9	12	15
2-4($2.95) 2-Two covers by Santalucia and Manapul. 3,4-Two covers						6.00
TPB (CrossGen, 2003, $9.95, 8-1/4" x 5-1/2") digest-sized reprints #1-4						10.00

MASTERS OF THE UNIVERSE (Volume 2)
Image Comics: March, 2003 - No. 6, Aug, 2003

	GD	VG	FN	VF	VF/NM	NM-
1-6($2.95) 1-Santalucia-c. 2-Two covers by Santalucia & JJ Kirby	1	3	4	6	8	10
1-($5.95) Wraparound variant-c by Struzan w/silver foil logo	2	4	6	8	10	12
3,4-($5.95) Wraparound variant holofoil-c. 3-By Edwards 4-By Boris Vallejo & Julie Bell						6.00
Volume 2 Dark Reflections TPB (2004, $18.95) r/#1-6						19.00

MASTERS OF THE UNIVERSE (Volume 3)
MVCreations: Apr, 2004 - No. 8, Dec, 2004 ($2.95)

	GD	VG	FN	VF	VF/NM	NM-
1-Santalucia-c	1	2	3	5	6	8
2-8						4.00

MASTERS OF THE UNIVERSE...
CrossGen Comics

...Rise of the Snake-Men (Nov, 2003 - No. 3, $2.95) Meyers-a						6.00
...The Power of Fear (12/03, $2.95, one-shot) Santalucia-a						6.00

MASTERS OF THE UNIVERSE: FORGE OF DESTINY
Dark Horse Comics: Sept, 2023 - No. 4, Dec, 2023 ($3.99, limited series)

1-4-Seeley-s/Nunez-a						4.00

MASTERS OF THE UNIVERSE, ICONS OF EVIL
Image Comics/CrossGen Comics: 2003 ($4.95, one-shots)

...Beastman -(Image) Origin of Beast Man; Tony Moore-a						5.00
...Mer-Man -(CrossGen)						5.00
...Trapjaw -(CrossGen)						5.00
...Tri-Klops -(CrossGen) Walker-c						5.00
TPB (3/04, $18.95, MVCreations) r/one-shots; sketch pages						19.00

MASTERS OF THE UNIVERSE: ...
DC Comics: Dec, 2012; Mar, 2013; Jul, 2013 ($2.99, one-shots)

... Origin Of He-Man (3/13) Fialkov-s; Ben Oliver-a/c; Prince Adam finds the sword						3.00
... Origin Of Hordak (7/13) Giffen & Keene-s/Giffen-a/c						3.00
... The Origin Of Skeletor (12/12) Fialkov-s; Fraser Irving-a/c; Keldor becomes Skeletor						3.00

MASTERS OF THE UNIVERSE: MASTERVERSE
Dark Horse Comics: Feb, 2023 - No. 4, May, 2023 ($3.99, limited series)

1-4-Anthology of multiverse stories by various incl. Kelley Jones, Aragonés, Seeley						4.00

MASTERS OF THE UNIVERSE: REVELATION
Dark Horse Comics: Jul, 2021 - No. 4, Oct, 2021 ($3.99, limited series)

1-4-Prequel to the Netflix animated series; Kevin Smith & Rob David-s/Mindy Lee-a						4.00

MASTERWORKS SERIES OF GREAT COMIC BOOK ARTISTS, THE
Sea Gate Dist./DC Comics: May, 1983 - No. 3, Dec, 1983 (Baxter paper)

1-3: 1,2-Shining Knight by Frazetta r-/Adventure. 2-Tomahawk by Frazetta r.						
3-Wrightson-c/a(r)						6.00

MATADOR
DC Comics (WildStorm): July, 2005 - No. 6, May, 2006 ($2.99, limited series)

1-6-Devin Grayson-s/Brian Stelfreeze-a/c						3.00

MATA HARI
Dark Horse Comics (Berger Books): Feb, 2018 - No. 5, Sept, 2018 ($3.99, limited series)

1-5-Beeby-s/Kristantina-a/c; story of the World War 1 spy						4.00

MATRIX COMICS, THE (Movie)
Burlyman Entertainment: 2003; 2004 ($21.95, trade paperback)

nn-Short stories by various incl. Wachowskis, Darrow, Gaiman, Sienkiewicz, Bagge						22.00
...Volume One Preview (7/03, no cover price) bios of creators; Chadwick-s/a						3.00
Volume 2-(2004) Short stories by various incl. Wachowskis, Sale, McKeever, Dorman						22.00

MATT SLADE GUNFIGHTER (Kid Slade Gunfighter #5 on; See Western Gunfighters)
Atlas Comics (SPI): May, 1956 - No. 4, Nov, 1956

	GD	VG	FN	VF	VF/NM	NM-
1-Intro Matt & horse Eagle; Williamson/Torres-a	34	68	102	199	325	450
2-Williamson-a	17	34	51	105	165	225
3	14	28	42	82	121	160

NOTE: *Maneely a-1, 3, 4; c-1, 2, 4. Roth a-2-4. Severin a-1, 3, 4. Maneely c/a-1. Issue #s stamped on cover*

---

after printing.

MAUS: A SURVIVOR'S TALE (First graphic novel to win a Pulitzer Prize)
Pantheon Books: 1986, 1991 (B&W)

Vol. 1-(...: My Father Bleeds History)(1986) Art Spiegelman-s/a; recounts stories of Spiegelman's father in 1930s-40s Nazi-occupied Poland; collects first six stories serialized in Raw Magazine from 1980-1985	30.00
Vol. 2-(...: And Here My Troubles Began)(1991)	25.00
Complete Maus Survivor's Tale -HC Vols. 1 & 2 w/slipcase	35.00
Hardcover Vol. 1 (1991)	30.00
Hardcover Vol. 2 (1991)	30.00
TPB (1992, $14.00) Vols. 1 & 2	18.00

MAVERICK (TV)
Dell Publishing Co.: No. 892, 4/58 - No. 19, 4-6/62 (All have photo-c)

	GD	VG	FN	VF	VF/NM	NM-
Four Color 892 (#1)-James Garner photo-c begin	21	42	63	147	324	500
Four Color 930,945,962,980,1005 (6-8/59): 945-James Garner/Jack Kelly photo-c begin	11	22	33	73	157	240
7 (10-12/59) - 14: 11-Variant edition has "Time For Change" comic strip on back-c.	8	16	24	56	108	160
14-Last Garner/Kelly-c	7	14	21	44	82	120
15-18: Jack Kelly/Roger Moore photo-c	7	14	21	46	86	125
19-Jack Kelly photo-c (last issue)						

MAVERICK (See X-Men)
Marvel Comics: Jan, 1997 ($2.95, one-shot)

1-Hama-s						5.00

MAVERICK (See X-Men)
Marvel Comics: Sept, 1997 - No. 12, Aug, 1998 ($2.99/$1.99)

1,12: 1-($2.99)-Wraparound-c. 12-($2.99) Battles Omega Red						5.00
2-11: 2-Two covers. 4-Wolverine app. 6,7-Sabretooth app.						4.00

MAVERICK MARSHAL
Charlton Comics: Nov, 1958 - No. 7, May, 1960

	GD	VG	FN	VF	VF/NM	NM-
1	7	14	21	37	46	55
2-7	5	10	15	24	30	35

MAW
BOOM! Studios: Sept, 2021 - No. 5, Jan, 2022 ($3.99, limited series)

1-5-Jude Ellison S. Doyle-s/A.L. Kaplan-a						4.00

MAX BRAND (See Silvertip)

MAX HAMM FAIRY TALE DETECTIVE
Nite Owl Comix: 2002 - 2004 ($4.95, B&W, 6 1/2" x 8")

1-(2002) Frank Cammuso-s/a						5.00
Vol. 2 #1-3 (2003-2004) Frank Cammuso-s/a						5.00

MAXIMAGE
Image Comics (Extreme Studios): Dec, 1995 - No. 7, June 1996 ($2.50)

1-7: 1-Liefeld-c. 2-Extreme Destroyer Pt. 2; polybagged w/card. 4-Angela & Glory-c/app.						4.00

MAXIMO
Dreamwave Prods.: Jan, 2004 ($3.95, one-shot)

1-Based on the Capcom video game						4.00

MAXIMUM SECURITY (Crossover)
Marvel Comics: Oct, 2000 - No. 3, Jan, 2001 ($2.99)

1-3-Busiek-s/Ordway-a; Ronan the Accuser, Avengers app.						3.00
...Dangerous Planet 1: Busiek-s/Ordway-a; Ego, the Living Planet						3.00
Thor vs. Ego (11/00, $2.99) Reprints Thor #133,160,161; Kirby-a						3.00

MAX RIDE: FINAL FLIGHT (Based on the James Patterson novel Maximum Ride)
Marvel Comics: Nov, 2016 - No. 5, Mar, 2017 ($3.99, limited series)

1-5-Jody Houser-s/Marco Failla-a. 1-Two covers (Nakamura & Oum)						4.00

MAX RIDE: FIRST FLIGHT (Based on the James Patterson novel Maximum Ride)
Marvel Comics: Jun, 2015 - No. 5, Oct, 2015 ($3.99, limited series)

1-5-Marguerite Bennett-s/Alex Sanchez-a. 1-Three covers						4.00

MAX RIDE: ULTIMATE FLIGHT (Based on the James Patterson novel Maximum Ride)
Marvel Comics: Jan, 2016 - No. 5, May, 2016 ($3.99, limited series)

1-5-Jody Houser-s/RB Silva-a. 1-Two covers						4.00

MAXX (Also see Darker Image, Primer #5, & Friends of Maxx)
Image Comics (I Before E): Mar, 1993 - No. 35, Feb, 1998 ($1.95)

	GD	VG	FN	VF	VF/NM	NM-
1/2	2	4	6	8	11	14
1/2 (Gold)						20.00
1-Sam Kieth-c/a/scripts						5.00
1-Glow-in-the-dark variant	2	4	6	11	16	20
1-"3-D Edition" (1/98, $4.95) plus new back-up story						5.00
2-12: 6-Savage Dragon cameo(1 pg.). 7,8-Pitt-c & story						3.00
13-16						3.00
17-35: 21-Alan Moore-s						3.00
Volume 1 TPB (DC/WildStorm, 2003, $17.95) r/#1-6						18.00
Volume 2 TPB (DC/WildStorm, 2004, $17.95) r/#7-13						18.00
Volume 3 TPB (DC/WildStorm, 2004, $17.95) r/#14-20						18.00
Volume 4 TPB (DC/WildStorm, 2005, $17.95) r/#21-27						18.00
Volume 5 TPB (DC/WildStorm, 2005, $19.99) r/#28-35						20.00
Volume 6 TPB (DC/WildStorm, 2006, $19.99) r/Friends of Maxx #1-3 & The Maxx 3-D						20.00

MAXX: MAXXIMIZED
IDW Publishing: Nov, 2013 - No. 35, Sept, 2016 ($3.99)

1-35-Remastered, recolored reprint of the original Maxx issues						4.00

MAYA (See Movie Classics)
Gold Key: Mar, 1968

	GD	VG	FN	VF	VF/NM	NM-
1 (10218-803)(TV) Photo-c	3	6	9	16	24	32

MAYHEM
Dark Horse Comics: May, 1989 - No. 4, Sept, 1989 ($2.50, B&W, 52 pgs.)

	GD	VG	FN	VF	VF/NM	NM-
1-Four part Stanley Ipkiss/Mask story begins; Mask-c	4	8	12	27	44	60

Maverick #9 © DELL

The Maxx: Maxximized #14 © Sam Kieth

Mech Cadets #1 © Pak & Miyazawa

	GD 2.0	VG 4.0	FN 6.0	VF 8.0	VF/NM 9.0	NM- 9.2
2-4: 2-Mask 1/2 back-c. 4-Mask-c	1	3	4	6	8	10

MAYHEM (Tyrese Gibson's...)
Image Comics: Aug, 2009 - No. 3, Oct, 2009 ($2.99, limited series)

1-3-Tyrese Gibson co-writer; Tone Rodriguez-a/c						3.00

MAZE AGENCY, THE
Comico/Innovation Publ. #8 on: Dec, 1988 - No. 23, Aug, 1991 ($1.95-$2.50, color)

1-23: 1-5,8,9,12-Adam Hughes-c/a. 9-Ellery Queen app. 7 ($2.50)-Last Comico issue						4.00
Annual 1 (1990, $2.75)-Ploog-c; Spirit tribute ish						5.00
Special 1 (1989, $2.75)-Staton-p (Innovation)						5.00
TPB (IDW Publ., 11/05, $24.99) r/#1-5						25.00

MAZE AGENCY, THE (Vol. 2)
Caliber Comics: July, 1997 - No. 3, 1998 ($2.95, B&W)

1-3: 1-Barr-s/Gonzales-a(p). 3-Hughes-c						4.00

MAZE AGENCY, THE
IDW Publishing: Nov, 2005 - No. 3, Jan, 2006 ($3.99, limited series)

1-3-Barr-s/Padilla-a(p)/c						4.00

MAZEBOOK
Dark Horse Comics: Sept, 2021 - No. 5, Jan, 2022 ($5.99, limited series)

1-5-Jeff Lemire-s/a/c						6.00

MAZE RUNNER: THE SCORCH TRIALS (Based on the Maze Runner movies)
BOOM! Studios: Jun, 2015 ($14.99, squarebound SC)

...Official Graphic Novel Prelude - Short stories about the characters; s/a by various						15.00

MAZIE (...& Her Friends) (See Flat-Top, Mortie, Stevie & Tastee-Freez)
Mazie Comics(Magazine Publ.)/Harvey Publ. No. 13-on: 1953 - #12, 1954; #13, 12/54 - #22, 9/56; #23, 9/57 - #28, 8/58

1-(Teen-age)-Stevie's girlfriend	18	36	54	103	162	220
2	11	22	33	62	86	110
3-10	9	18	27	50	65	80
11-28	8	16	24	44	57	70

MAZIE
Nation Wide Publishers: 1950 - No. 7, 1951 (5¢) (5x7-1/4"-miniature)(52 pgs.)

1-Teen-age	23	46	69	138	227	315
2-7	16	32	48	92	144	195

MAZINGER (See First Comics Graphic Novel #17)

'MAZING MAN
DC Comics: Jan, 1986 - No. 12, Dec, 1986

1-11: 7,8-Hembeck-a						4.00
12-Dark Knight part-c by Miller						5.00
Special 1 ('87), 2 (4/88), 3 ('90)-All $2.00, 52pgs.						5.00

McCANDLESS & COMPANY
Mandalay Books/American Mythology

...: Dead Razor (2001, $7.95) J.C. Vaughn-s/Busch & Sheehan-a; 3 covers						8.00
...: Insecuritues (American Myth., 10/16, $4.99) Vaughn-s/Gonzales-a/Oeming-c						5.00
Crime Scenes: A McCandless & Company Reader TPB (Spring 2006, $17.95) Vaughn-s						18.00

McHALE'S NAVY (TV) (See Movie Classics)
Dell Publ. Co.: May-July, 1963 - No. 3, Nov-Jan, 1963-64 (All have photo-c)

1	9	18	27	59	117	175
2,3	5	10	15	35	63	90

McKEEVER & THE COLONEL (TV)
Dell Publishing Co.: Feb-Apr, 1963 - No. 3, Aug-Oct, 1963

1-Photo-c	5	10	15	34	60	85
2,3-Photo-c	4	8	12	28	47	65

McLINTOCK (See Movie Comics)

MD
E. C. Comics: Apr-May, 1955 - No. 5, Dec-Jan, 1955-56

1-Not approved by code; Craig-c	26	52	78	208	329	450
2-5	15	30	45	120	195	270

NOTE: *Crandall, Evans, Ingels, Orlando art in all issues; Craig c-1-5.*

MD
Russ Cochran/Gemstone Publishing: Sept, 1999 - No. 5, Jan, 2000 ($2.50)

1-5-Reprints original EC series						4.00
Annual 1 (1999, $13.50) r/#1-5						14.00

MEASLES
Fantagraphics Books: Christmas 1998 - No. 8 ($2.95, B&W, quarterly)

1-8-Anthology: 1-Venus-s by Hernandez						4.00

MECHA (Also see Mayhem)
Dark Horse Comics: June, 1987 - No. 6, 1988 ($1.50/$1.95, color/B&W)

1-6: 1,2 ($1.95, color), 3,4-($1.75, B&W), 5,6-($1.50, B&W)						4.00

MECHANIC, THE
Image Comics: 1998 ($5.95, one-shot, squarebound)

1-Chiodo-painted art; Peterson-s						6.00
1-($10.00) DF Alternate Cover Ed.						10.00

MECHANISM
Image Comics (Top Cow): Jul, 2016 - No. 5, Nov, 2016 ($3.99)

1-5-Raffaele Ienco-s/a						4.00

MECHA SPECIAL
Dark Horse Comics: May, 1995 ($2.95, one-shot)

1						4.00

MECH CADETS (Netflix animated series)
BOOM! Studios: Aug, 2023 - No. 6, Feb, 2024 ($4.99)

1-6-Greg Pak-s/Takeshi Miyazawa-a						5.00

MECH CADET YU
BOOM! Studios: Aug, 2017 - No. 12, Sept, 2018 ($3.99)

1-12-Greg Pak-s/Takeshi Miyazawa-a						4.00

MECH DESTROYER
Image Comics: Apr, 2001 - No. 4, Sept, 2001 ($2.95, limited series)

1-4-Jae Kim-c/a; Robert Chong-s						3.00

MECH STRIKE: MONSTER HUNTERS (Follow up to Avengers Mech Strike)
Marvel Comics: Aug, 2022 - No. 5, Dec, 2022 ($3.99, limited series)

1-5-Christos Gage-s/Paco Diaz-a; Doctor Doom, Loki, Venom and Green Goblin app.						4.00

MEDAL FOR BOWZER, A (See Promotional Comics section)

MEDAL OF HONOR COMICS
A. S. Curtis: Spring, 1946

1-War stories	21	42	63	122	199	275

MEDAL OF HONOR SPECIAL
Dark Horse Comics: 1994 ($2.50, one-shot)

1-Kubert-c/a (first story)						4.00

MEDIA STARR
Innovation Publ.: July, 1989 - No. 3, Sept, 1989 ($1.95, mini-series, 28 pgs.)

1-3: Deluxe format						4.00

MEDIEVAL SPAWN/WITCHBLADE
Image Comics (Top Cow Productions): May, 1996 - No. 3, June, 1996 ($2.95, limited series)

1-Garth Ennis scripts	2	4	6	8	10	12
1-Platinum foil-c (500 copies from Pittsburgh Con)						35.00
1-Gold	2	4	6	9	12	15
1-ETM Exclusive Edition; gold foil logo	2	4	6	8	10	12
2-3-Garth Ennis scripts in all						6.00
TPB ($9.95) r/#1-3						10.00

MEDIEVAL SPAWN & WITCHBLADE
Image Comics: May, 2018 - No. 4, Aug, 2018 ($2.99, limited series)

1-4-Haberlin & Holguin-s/Haberlin-a						3.00

MEET ANGEL (Formerly Angel & the Ape)
National Periodical Publications: No. 7, Nov-Dec, 1969

7-Wood-a(i)	4	8	12	27	44	60

MEET CORLISS ARCHER (Radio/Movie)(My Life #4 on)
Fox Feature Syndicate: Mar, 1948 - No. 3, July, 1948

1-(Teen-age)-Feldstein-c/a; headlight-c	161	322	483	1030	1765	2500
2-Feldstein-c/a	77	154	231	493	847	1200
3-Feldstein-c/a	65	130	195	416	708	1000

NOTE: *No. 1-3 used in Seduction of the Innocent, pg. 39.*

MEET HERCULES (See Three Stooges)

MEET MERTON
Toby Press: Dec, 1953 - No. 4, June, 1954

1-(Teen-age)-Dave Berg-c/a	25	50	75	150	245	340
2-Dave Berg-c/a	15	30	45	88	137	185
3,4-Dave Berg-c/a	15	30	45	83	124	165
I.W. Reprint #9, Super Reprint #11('63), 18	3	6	9	14	19	24

MEET MISS BLISS (Becomes Stories Of Romance #5 on)
Atlas Comics (LMC): May, 1955 - No. 4, Nov, 1955

	GD 2.0	VG 4.0	FN 6.0	VF 8.0	VF/NM 9.0	NM- 9.2
1-Al Hartley-c/a	84	168	252	538	919	1300
2-4	37	74	111	222	361	500

MEET MISS PEPPER (Formerly Lucy, The Real Gone Gal)
St. John Publishing Co.: No. 5, April, 1954 - No. 6, June, 1954

5-Kubert/Maurer-a	45	90	135	284	480	675
6-Kubert/Maurer-a; Kubert-c	37	74	111	222	361	500

MEET THE SKRULLS
Marvel Comics: May, 2019 - No. 5, Aug, 2019 ($3.99, limited series)

1-5-Robbie Thompson-s/Niko Henrichon-a						4.00

MEGAGHOST
Albatross Funnybooks: 2018 - No. 5, 2019 ($3.99)

1-5-Gabe Soria-s/Gideon Kendall-a						4.00

MEGALITH (Megalith Deathwatch 2000 #1,2 of second series)
Continuity: 1989 - No. 9, Mar, 1992; No. 0, Apr, 1993 - No. 7, Jan, 1994

	1	2	3	5	6	8
1-($2.00-c) Neal Adams & Mark Texiera-c/Texiera & Nebres-a						
2-9-($2.00-c)						4.00
2nd series: 0-(4/93)-Foil-c; no c-price, giveaway; Adams plot						4.00
1-7: 1-Bagged w/card: 1-Gatefold-c by Nebres; Adams plot. 2-Fold-out-c; Adams plot. 3-Indestructible-c. 4-7-Embossed-c: 4-Adams/Nebres-c; Adams part-i. 5-Sienkiewicz-i. 6-Adams part-i. 7-Adams-c(p); Adams plot						4.00

MEGAMAN
Dreamwave Productions: Sept, 2003 - No. 4, Dec, 2003 ($2.95)

1-4-Brian Augustyn-s/Mic Fong-a						3.00
1-($5.95) Chromium wraparound variant-c						6.00

MEGA MAN (Based on the Capcom video game character)
Archie Comics Publications: Jul, 2011 - No. 55, Feb, 2016 ($2.99/$3.99)

1-39 1-Spaziante-a. 20-39-Multiple covers. 24-Worlds Collide x-over begins						3.00
40-49,51-55 ($3.99) Two covers on most. 51,52-Three covers						4.00
50-($4.99) Six covers; "Worlds Unite" Sonic/Mega Man x-over pt. 4						5.00
Free Comic Book Day Edition (2012, giveaway) Origin re-told						3.00
...: Worlds Unite Battles 1 (8/15, $3.99) Sonic/Mega Man x-over; 3 wraparound covers						4.00

MEGA MAN: FULLY CHARGED (Capcom video game character)
BOOM! Studios: Aug, 2020 - No. 6, Jan, 2021 ($4.99)

1-6-Marchisello & Rinehart-s/Simeone-a						5.00

MEGAMIND: BAD. BLUE. BRILLIANT (DreamWorks'...) (Based on the 2010 movie)
Ape Entertainment: 2010 - No. 4, 2011 ($3.95, limited series)

1-4: 1-High school flashback						4.00
nn-($6.95, 9x6") Prequel to the movie; Joe Kelly-s						7.00

MEGA MORPHS
Marvel Comics: Oct, 2005 - No. 4, Dec, 2005 ($2.99, limited series)

1-4-Giant robots based on action figures; McKeever-s; Kang-a						3.00
Digest (2006, $7.99) r/#1-4 plus mini-comics						8.00

MEGATON (A super hero)
Megaton Publ.: Nov, 1983; No. 2, Oct, 1985 - No. 8, Aug, 1987 (B&W)

1-($2.00, 68 pgs.)-Erik Larsen's 1st pro work; Vanguard by Larsen begins (1st app.), ends #4; 1st app. Megaton, Berzerker, & Ethrian; Guice-c/a(p); Gustovich-a(p) in #1,2	5	10	15	34	60	85
2-($2.00, 68 pgs.)-1st brief app. The Dragon (1 pg.) by Larsen (later The Savage Dragon in Image Comics); Guice-c/a(p)	3	6	9	14	19	24
3-(44 pgs.)-1st full app. Savage Dragon-c/story by Larsen; (earlier apps. were in the 1982 fanzine Graphic Fantasy); 1st comic book work by Angel Medina (pin-up)	5	10	15	31	53	75
4-(52 pgs.)-2nd full app. Savage Dragon by Larsen; 4,5-Wildman by Grass Green	2	4	6	8	11	14
5-1st Liefeld published-a (inside f/c, 6/86)	1	3	4	6	8	10
6,7: 6-Larsen-c	1	3	4	6	8	10
8-1st Liefeld story-a (7 pg. super hero story) plus 1 pg. Youngblood ad	3	6	9	14	19	24
...Explosion (6/87, 16 pg. color giveaway)-1st app. Youngblood by Rob Liefeld (2 pg. spread); shows Megaton heroes	5	10	15	35	63	90
...Holiday Special 1 (1994, $2.95, color, 40 pgs., publ. by Entity Comics)-Gold foil logo; bagged w/Kelley Jones card; Vanguard, Megaton plus shows unpublished-c to 1987 Youngblood #1 by Liefeld/Ordway	1	2	3	5	6	8

NOTE: Copies of Megaton Explosion were also released in early 1992 all signed by Rob Liefeld and were made available to retailers.

MEGATON MAN (See Don Simpson's Bizarre Heroes)
Kitchen Sink Enterprises: Nov, 1984 - No. 10, 1986

1-10, 1-2nd printing (1989)						4.00
...Meets The Uncategorizable X-Thems 1 (4/89, $2.00)						4.00

MEGATON MAN: BOMB SHELL
Image Comics: Jul, 1999 - No. 2 ($2.95, B&W, mini-series)

1-Reprints stories from Megaton Man internet site						4.00

MEGATON MAN: HARD COPY
Image Comics: Feb, 1999 - No. 2, Apr, 1999 ($2.95, B&W, mini-series)

1,2-Reprints stories from Megaton Man internet site						4.00

MEGATON MAN VS. FORBIDDEN FRANKENSTEIN (Double titled as Don Simpson's Bizarre Heroes #16)
Fiasco Comics: Apr, 1996 ($2.95, B&W, one-shot)

1-Intro The Tomb Team (Forbidden Frankenstein, Drekula, Bride of the Monster, & Moon Wolf)	1	3	4	6	8	10

MEK (See Reload/Mek flipbook for TPB reprint)
DC Comics (Homage): Jan, 2003 - No. 3, Mar, 2003 ($2.95, limited series)

1-3-Warren Ellis-s/Steve Rolston-a						4.00

MEKANIX (See X-Men titles) (See X-Treme X-Men Vol. 4 for TPB)
Marvel Comics: Dec, 2002 - No. 6, May, 2003 ($2.99, limited series)

1-6-Kitty Pryde in college; Claremont-s/Bobillo & Sosa-a						4.00

MEL ALLEN SPORTS COMICS (The Voice of the Yankees)
Standard Comics: No. 5, Nov, 1949; No. 6, June, 1950

5-(#1 on inside)-Tuska-a	24	48	72	142	234	325
6-(#2)-Lou Gehrig story	17	34	51	100	158	215

MELVIN MONSTER
Dell Publishing Co.: Apr-June, 1965 - No. 10, Oct, 1969

1-By John Stanley	6	12	18	40	73	105
2-10-All by Stanley. #10-r/#1	5	10	15	30	50	70

MELVIN THE MONSTER (See Peter, the Little Pest & Dexter The Demon #7)
Atlas Comics (HPC): July, 1956 - No. 6, July, 1957

1-Maneely-c/a	21	42	63	122	199	275
2-6: 4-Maneely-c/a	14	28	42	81	118	155

MENACE
Atlas Comics (HPC): Mar, 1953 - No. 11, May, 1954

1-Horror & sci/fi stories begin; Everett-c/a	300	600	900	1950	3375	4800
2-Post-atom bomb disaster by Everett; anti-Communist propaganda/torture scenes; Sinnott sci/fi story "Rocket to the Moon"	194	388	582	1212	2121	3000
3,4,6-Everett-a. 4-Sci/fi story "Escape to the Moon". 6-Romita sci/fi story "Science Fiction"	135	270	405	864	1482	2100
5-Origin & 1st app. The Zombie by Everett (reprinted in Tales of the Zombie #1)(7/53); 5-Sci/fi story "Rocket Ship"	476	952	1428	3475	6138	8800
7,8,10,11: 7-Frankenstein story. 8-End of world story; Heath 3-D art(3 pgs.). 10-H-Bomb panels	116	232	348	742	1271	1800
9-Everett-a r-in Vampire Tales #1	300	600	900	1920	3310	4700

NOTE: Brodsky c-7, 8, 11. Colan a-6; c-9. Everett a-1-6, 9; c-1-6. Heath a-1,6; c-10. Katz a-11. Maneely a-3-5, 7-9. Powell a-11. Romita a-3, 6, 8, 11. Shelly a-10. Shores a-7. Sinnott a-2, 7. Tuska a-1, 2, 5.

MENACE
Awesome-Hyperwerks: Nov, 1998 ($2.50)

1-Jada Pinkett Smith-s/Fraga-a						4.00

MEN AGAINST CRIME (Formerly Mr. Risk; Hand of Fate #8 on)
Ace Magazines: No. 3, Feb, 1951 - No. 7, Oct, 1951

3-Mr. Risk app.	18	36	54	105	165	225
4-7: 4-Colan-a; entire book-r as Trapped! #4. 5-Meskin-a	14	28	42	76	108	140

MEN, GUNS, & CATTLE (See Classics Illustrated Special Issue)

MEN IN ACTION (Battle Brady #10 on)
Atlas Comics (IPS): April, 1952 - No. 9, Dec, 1952 (War stories)

1-Berg, Reinman-a	41	82	123	256	428	600
2,3: 3-Heath-c/a	22	44	66	132	216	300
4-6,8,9	20	40	60	117	189	260
7-Krigstein-a; Heath-c	22	44	66	132	216	300

NOTE: Brodsky a-3; c-1, 4-6. Maneely a-4; c-5. Pakula a-1, 6. Robinson a-5. Shores c-9. Sinnott a-6.

MEN IN ACTION
Ajax/Farrell Publications: Apr, 1957 - No. 6, Jun, 1958

1	15	30	45	85	130	175
2	9	18	27	52	69	85
3-6	9	18	27	47	61	75

MEN IN BLACK, THE (1st series)
Aircel Comics (Malibu): Jan, 1990 - No. 3 Mar, 1990 ($2.25, B&W, lim. series)

1-Cunningham-s/a in all	7	14	21	49	92	135
2,3	3	6	9	21	33	45
Graphic Novel (Jan, 1991) r/#1-3	3	6	9	17	26	35

MEN IN BLACK (2nd series)
Aircel Comics (Malibu): May, 1991 - No. 3, Jul, 1991 ($2.50, B&W, lim. series)

1-Cunningham-s/a in all	3	6	9	20	31	42
2,3	2	4	6	13	18	22

MEN IN BLACK: FAR CRY
Marvel Comics: Aug, 1997 ($3.99, color, one-shot)

1-Cunningham-s	1	3	4	6	8	10

MEN IN BLACK: RETRIBUTION
Marvel Comics: Dec, 1997 ($3.99, color, one-shot)

1-Cunningham-s; continuation of the movie	1	3	4	6	8	10

MEN IN BLACK: THE MOVIE
Marvel Comics: Oct, 1997 ($3.99, one-shot, movie adaptation)

1-Cunningham-s	2	4	6	8	10	12

MEN INTO SPACE
Dell Publishing Co.: No. 1083, Feb-Apr, 1960

Four Color 1083-Anderson-a, photo-c	6	12	18	41	76	110

MEN OF BATTLE (Also see New Men of Battle)
Catechetical Guild: V1#5, March, 1943 (Hardcover)

V1#5-Topix reprints	8	16	24	47	61	75

MEN OF WAR
DC Comics, Inc.: August, 1977 - No. 26, March, 1980 (#9,10: 44 pgs.)

1-Enemy Ace, Gravedigger (origin 1,2) begin	3	6	9	21	33	45
2-4,8-10,12-14,19,20: All Enemy Ace stories. 4-1st Dateline Frontline. 9-Unknown Soldier app.	2	4	6	11	16	20
5-7,11,15-18,21-25: 17-1st app. Rosa	2	4	6	9	13	16
26-Sgt. Rock & Easy Co.-c/s	3	6	9	14	20	26

NOTE: Chaykin a-9, 18,19, 20. Evans c-25. Kubert c-2-23, 24p, 26.

MEN OF WAR (DC New 52)
DC Comics: Nov, 2011 - No. 8, Jun, 2012 ($3.99)

1-8: 1-Sgt. Rock's grandson in modern times; Derenick-a; Navy Seals back-up; Winslade-a. 6-Back-up w/Corben-a. 8-Frankenstein & G.I. Robot app.						4.00

MEN OF WRATH
Marvel Comics (ICON): Oct, 2014 - No. 5, Feb, 2015 ($3.50, limited series)

1-5-Jason Aaron-s/Ron Garney-a; two covers on each. 5-Alex Ross var-c						3.50

Meet the Skrulls #1 © MAR

Mercy #3 © Mirko Andolfo

Metal Men #44 © DC

	GD	VG	FN	VF	VF/NM	NM-		GD	VG	FN	VF	VF/NM	NM-
	2.0	4.0	6.0	8.0	9.0	9.2		2.0	4.0	6.0	8.0	9.0	9.2

MEN'S ADVENTURES (Formerly True Adventures)
Marvel/Atlas Comics (CCC): No. 4, Aug, 1950 - No. 28, July, 1954

	GD	VG	FN	VF	VF/NM	NM-
4(#1)(52 pgs.)	48	96	144	302	514	725
5-Flying Saucer story	32	64	96	188	307	425
6-8: 7-Buried alive story. 8-Sci/fic story	28	56	84	165	270	375
9-20: All war format	21	42	63	122	199	275
21,22,24,26: All horror format	50	100	150	315	533	750
23-Crandall-a; Fox-a(i); horror format	53	106	159	334	567	800
25-Shrunken head-c	123	246	369	787	1344	1900
27,28-Human Torch & Toro-c/stories; Captain America & Sub-Mariner stories in each						
(also see Young Men #24-28)	187	374	561	1197	2049	2900

NOTE: **Ayers** a-20, 27(H. Torch). **Berg** a-15, 16. **Brodsky** c-4-9, 11, 12, 16-18, 24. **Burgos** c-27, 28 (Human Torch). **Colan** a-13, 14, 19. **Everett** a-10, 14, 22, 25, 28; c-11, 21-23. **Hartley** a-12. **Heath** a-8, 11, 16, 26. **Katz** c-13, 20, 26. **Lawrence** a-23; 27(Captain America). **Maneely** a-24; c-10, 15. **Mac Pakula** a-15, 25. **Post** a-23. **Powell** a-27(Sub-Mariner). **Reinman** a-10-12, 16. **Robinson** c-19. **Romita** a-22. **Sale** a-12-14. **Shores** c-25. **Sinnott** a-13, 21. **Tuska** a-24. Adventure-#4-8; War-#9-20; Weird/Horror-#21-26.

MENZ INSANA
DC Comics (Vertigo): 1997 ($7.95, one-shot)

nn-Fowler-s/Bolton painted art	1	2	3	5	6	8

MEPHISTO VS... (See Silver Surfer #3)
Marvel Comics Group: Apr, 1987 - No. 4, July, 1987 ($1.50, mini-series)

1-4: 1-Fantastic Four; Austin-i. 2-X-Factor. 3-X-Men. 4-Avengers						4.00

MERA: QUEEN OF ATLANTIS (Leads into Aquaman #38)
DC Comics: Apr, 2018 - No. 6, Sept, 2018 ($3.99, limited series)

1-6: 1-Abnett-s/Medina-a; origin retold; Ocean Master app.						4.00

MERC (See Mark Hazzard: Merc)

MERCENARIES (Based on the Pandemic video game)
Dynamite Entertainment: 2007 - No. 3, 2008 ($3.99, limited series)

1-3-Michael Turner-c; Brian Reed-s/Edgar Salazar-a						4.00

MERCHANTS OF DEATH
Acme Press (Eclipse): Jul, 1988 - No. 4, Nov, 1988 ($3.50, B&W/16 pgs. color, 44 pg. mag.)

1-4: 4-Toth-c						4.00

MERCILESS: THE RISE OF MING (Also see Flash Gordon: Zeitgeist)
Dynamite Entertainment: 2012 - No. 4, 2012 ($3.99, limited series)

1-4 Ming the Merciless' rise to power; Alex Ross-c; Beatty-c/Adrian-a						4.00

MERCY (Mirka Andolfo's...)
Image Comics: Mar, 2020 - No. 6, Sept, 2020 ($3.99, limited series)

1-6-Mirka Andolfo-s/a. 1-Five covers						4.00

MERCY THOMPSON (Patricia Briggs'...)
Dynamite Entertainment: 2014 - No. 6, 2015 ($3.99, limited series)

1-6-Patricia Briggs & Rik Hoskin-s/Tom Garcia-a						4.00

MERIDIAN
CrossGeneration Comics: Jul, 2000 - No. 44, Apr, 2004 ($2.95)

1-44: Barbara Kesel-s						3.00
Flying Solo Vol. 1 TPB (2001, $19.95) r/#1-7; cover by Steve Rude						20.00
Going to Ground Vol. 2 TPB (2002, $19.95) r/#8-14						20.00
Taking the Skies Vol. 3 TPB (2002, $15.95) r/#15-20						16.00
Vol. 4: Coming Home (12/02, $15.95) r/#21-26						16.00
Vol. 5: Minister of Cadador (7/03, $15.95) r/#27-32						16.00
Vol. 6: Changing Course (1/04, $15.95) r/#33-38						16.00
Traveler Vol. 1-4 ($9.95): Digest-size reprints of TPBs						10.00

MERLIN JONES AS THE MONKEY'S UNCLE (See Movie Comics and The Misadventures of... under Movie Comics)

MERRILL'S MARAUDERS (See Movie Classics)

MERRY CHRISTMAS (See A Christmas Adventure, Donald Duck..., Dell Giant #39, & March of Comics #153 in the Promotional Comics section)

MERRY COMICS
Carlton Publishing Co.: Dec, 1945 (10¢)

nn-Boogeyman app.	32	64	96	188	307	425

MERRY COMICS: Four Star Publications: 1947 (Advertised, not published)

MERRY-GO-ROUND COMICS
LaSalle Publ. Co./Croyden Publ./Rotary Litho.: 1944 (25¢, 132 pgs.); 1946; 9-10/47 - No. 2, 1948

nn(1944)(LaSalle)-Funny animal; 29 new features	27	54	81	158	259	360
21 (Publisher?)	14	28	42	80	115	150
1(1946)(Croyden)-Al Fago-c; funny animal	15	30	45	88	137	185
V1#1,2(1947-48; 52 pgs.)(Rotary Litho. Co. Ltd., Canada); Ken Hultgren-a						
	13	26	39	74	105	135

MERRY MAILMAN (See Fawcett's Funny Animals #87-89)

MERRY MOUSE (Also see Funny Tunes & Space Comics)
Avon Periodicals: June, 1953 - No. 4, Jan-Feb, 1954

1-1st app.; funny animal; Frank Carin-c/a	15	30	45	85	130	175
2-4	9	18	27	52	69	85

MERRY X-MEN HOLIDAY SPECIAL
Marvel Comics: Feb, 2019 ($4.99, one-shot)

1-Holiday short stories by various; Nakayama-c						4.00

MERV PUMPKINHEAD, AGENT OF D.R.E.A.M. (See The Sandman)
DC Comics (Vertigo): 2000 ($5.95, one-shot)

1-Buckingham-a(p); Nowlan painted-c						6.00

META-4
First Comics: Feb, 1991 - No. 4, 1991 ($2.25)

1-($3.95, 52pgs.)						5.00
2-4						4.00

METAL GEAR SOLID (Based on the video game)
IDW Publ.: Sept, 2004 - No. 12, Aug, 2005 ($3.99)

1-12: 1-Two covers; Ashley Wood-a/Kris Oprisko-s						4.00
1-Retailer edition with foil cover						20.00

METAL GEAR SOLID: SONS OF LIBERTY
IDW Publ.: Sept, 2005 - No. 12, Sept, 2007 ($3.99)

#0 (9/05) profile pages on characters; Ashley Wood-a						4.00
1-12: 1-Two covers; Ashley Wood-a/Alex Garner-s						4.00

METALLIX
Future Comics: Dec, 2002 - No. 6, June, 2003 ($3.50)

0-6-Ron Lim-a. 0-(6/03) Origin. 1-Layton-c						3.50
1-Collector's Edition with variant cover by Lim						3.50
1-Free Comic Book Day Edition (4/03) Layton-c						3.00

METAL MEN (See Brave & the Bold, DC Comics Presents, and Showcase #37-40)
National Periodical/DC Comics: 4-5/63 - No. 41, 12-1/69-70; No. 42, 2-3/73 - No. 44, 7-8/73; No. 45, 4/5/76 - No. 56, 2-3/78

1-(4-5/63)-5th app. Metal Men	59	118	177	472	1061	1650
2	20	40	60	144	317	490
3-5	13	26	39	89	195	300
6-10	9	18	27	59	117	175
11-20: 12-Beatles cameo (2-3/65)	7	14	21	46	86	125
21-Batman, Robin & Flash x-over	6	12	18	41	76	110
22-26,28-30	5	10	15	34	60	85
27-Origin Metal Men retold	6	12	18	42	79	115
31-41(1968-70): 38-Last 12¢ issue. 41-Last 15¢	5	10	15	31	53	75
42-44(1973)-Reprints	2	4	6	10	14	18
45('76)-49-Simonson-a in all: 48,49-Re-intro Eclipso	2	4	6	10	14	18
50-56: 50-Part-r. 54,55-Green Lantern x-over	2	4	6	9	12	15

NOTE: **Andru/Esposito** c-1-30. **Aparo** c-53-56. **Giordano** c-45, 46. **Kane/Esposito** a-30, 31; c-31. **Simonson** a-45-49; c-47-52. **Staton** a-50-56.

METAL MEN (Also see Tangent Comics/ Metal Men)
DC Comics: Oct, 1993 - No. 4, Jan, 1994 ($1.25, mini-series)

1-($2.50)-Multi-colored foil-c						5.00
2-4: 2-Origin						4.00

METAL MEN (Also see 52)
DC Comics: Oct, 2007 - No. 8, Jul, 2008 ($2.99, limited series)

1-8-Duncan Rouleau-s/a; origin re-told. 3-Chemo returns						3.00
HC (2008, $24.99, dustjacket) r/#1-8; cover gallery and sketch pages						25.00
SC (2009, $14.99) r/#1-8; cover gallery and sketch pages						15.00

METAL MEN
DC Comics: Dec, 2019 - No. 12, Feb, 2021 ($3.99, limited series)

1-12-Dan DiDio-s/Shane Davis-a. 1-Intro. Nth Metal Man. 3-Devil Ray monster returns. 7-Intro. Animal Gas Gang. 7-9-Chemo app. 10-Origin of Nth Metal Man						4.00

METAL SOCIETY
Image Comics (Top Cow): May, 2022 - No. 5, Sept, 2022 ($3.99, limited series)

1-5-Zack Kaplan-s/Guilherme Balbi-a						4.00

METAMORPHO (See Action Comics #413, Brave & the Bold #57,58, 1st Issue Special, & World's Finest #217)
National Periodical Publications: July-Aug, 1965 - No. 17, Mar-Apr, 1968 (All 12¢ issues)

1-(7-8/65)-3rd app. Metamorpho	18	36	48	111	246	380
2,3	7	14	21	49	92	135
4-6,10: 10-Origin & 1st app. Element Girl (1-2/67)	6	12	18	38	69	100

	GD 2.0	VG 4.0	FN 6.0	VF 8.0	VF/NM 9.0	NM- 9.2

7-9 | 5 | 10 | 15 | 33 | 57 | 80

11-17: 17-Sparling-c/a | 5 | 10 | 15 | 30 | 50 | 70

NOTE: *Ramona Fradon* a-B&B 57, 58, 1-4, **Orlando** a-5, 6; c-5-9, 11. **Trapani** a(p)-7-16; i-16.

METAMORPHO
DC Comics: Aug, 1993 - No. 4, Nov, 1993 ($1.50, mini-series)
1-4 — 4.00

METAMORPHO: YEAR ONE
DC Comics: Early Dec, 2007 - No. 6, Late Feb, 2008 ($2.99, limited series)
1-6-Origin re-told; Jurgens-s/Jurgens & Delperdang-a/Nowlan-c. 6-Justice League app. — 3.00
TPB ('08, $14.99) r/#1-6 — 15.00

METAPHYSIQUE
Malibu Comics (Bravura): Apr, 1995 - No. 6, Oct, 1995 ($2.95, limited series)
1-6: Norm Breyfogle-c/a/scripts — 4.00

METEOR COMICS
L. L. Baird (Croyden): Nov, 1945
1-Captain Wizard, Impossible Man, Race Wilkins app.; origin Baldy Bean, Capt. Wizard's sidekick; bare-breasted mermaids story | 65 | 130 | 195 | 416 | 708 | 1000

METEOR MAN
Marvel Comics: Aug, 1993 - No. 6, Jan, 1994 ($1.25, limited series)
1-6: 1-Regular unbagged. 4-Night Thrasher-c/story. 6-Terry Austin-c(i) — 4.00
1-Polybagged w/button & rap newspaper — 5.00
...: The Movie (4/93 [7/93 on cover], $2.25) movie adaptation — 4.00

METROPOL (See Ted McKeever's...)
METROPOL A.D. (See Ted McKeever's...)
METROPOLIS S.C.U. (Also see Showcase '96 #1)
DC Comics: Nov, 1995 - No. 4, Feb, 1996 ($1.50, limited series)
1-4: 1-Superman-c & app. — 4.00

ME YOU LOVE IN THE DARK, THE
Image Comics: Aug, 2021 - No. 5, Dec, 2021 ($3.99, limited series)
1-5-Skottie Young-s/Jorge Corona-a — 4.00

MEZZ: GALACTIC TOUR 2494 (Also See Nexus)
Dark Horse Comics: May, 1994 ($2.50, one-shot)
1 — 4.00

MGM'S MARVELOUS WIZARD OF OZ (See Marvel Treasury of Oz)
Marvel Comics Group/National Periodical Publications: 1975 ($1.50, 84 pgs.; oversize)
1-Adaptation of MGM's movie; J. Buscema-a | 4 | 8 | 12 | 28 | 47 | 65

M.G.M'S MOUSE MUSKETEERS (Formerly M.G.M.'s The Two Mouseketeers)
Dell Publishing Co.: No. 670, Jan, 1956 - No. 1290, Mar-May, 1962

	GD 2.0	VG 4.0	FN 6.0	VF 8.0	VF/NM 9.0	NM- 9.2
Four Color 670 (#4)	6	12	18	41	76	110
Four Color 711,728,764	5	10	15	31	53	75
8 (4-6/57) - 21 (3-5/60)	4	8	12	27	44	60
Four Color 1135,1175,1290	4	8	12	28	47	65

M.G.M.'S SPIKE AND TYKE (also see Tom & Jerry #79)
Dell Publishing Co.: No. 499, Sept, 1953 - No. 1266, Dec-Feb, 1961-62

	GD 2.0	VG 4.0	FN 6.0	VF 8.0	VF/NM 9.0	NM- 9.2
Four Color 499 (#1)	9	18	27	58	114	170
Four Color 577,638	6	12	18	41	76	110
4(12-2/55-56)-10	4	8	12	28	47	65
11-24(12-2/60-61)	4	8	12	23	37	50
Four Color 1266	5	10	15	30	50	70

M.G.M.'S THE TWO MOUSEKETEERS
Dell Publishing Co.: No. 475, June, 1953 - No. 642, July, 1955

	GD 2.0	VG 4.0	FN 6.0	VF 8.0	VF/NM 9.0	NM- 9.2
Four Color 475 (#1)	9	18	27	61	123	185
Four Color 603 (11/54), 642	7	14	21	44	82	120

MIAMI VICE REMIX
IDW Publishing (Lion Forge): Mar, 2015 - No. 5, Jul, 2015 ($3.99, limited series)
1-5-Joe Casey/Jim Mahfood-a; re-imagined Crockett & Tubbs — 4.00

MICE TEMPLAR, THE
Image Comics: Sept, 2007 - No. 6, Oct, 2008 ($3.99/$2.99)
1-($3.99)-Bryan Glass-s/Michael Avon Oeming-a/c — 4.00
2-6-($2.99) — 3.00

MICE TEMPLAR, THE , VOLUME 2: DESTINY
Image Comics: July, 2009 - No. 9, May, 2010 ($3.99/$2.99/$4.99)
1,2-($3.99) 1-Bryan Glass-s/Oeming & Santos-a; 2 covers. 2-Santos-a — 4.00
3-8-($2.99)-Santos-a; 2 covers by Oeming & Santos — 3.00
9-($4.99) — 5.00

MICE TEMPLAR, THE , VOLUME 3: A MIDWINTER NIGHT'S DREAM
Image Comics: Dec, 2010 - No. 8, Mar, 2012 ($3.99/$2.99)
1,8-($3.99) 1-Bryan Glass/Oeming & Santos-a; 2 covers — 4.00
2-7-($2.99)-Santos-a; 2 covers by Oeming & Santos — 3.00

MICE TEMPLAR, THE , VOLUME 4: LEGEND
Image Comics: Mar, 2013 - No. 14, Oct, 2014 ($3.99/$2.99/$4.99)
1-($3.99)-Bryan Glass/Victor Santos-a; 2 covers — 4.00
2-7-($2.99)-Santos-a; 2 covers by Oeming & Santos — 3.00
8-($4.99) — 5.00
9-13-($3.99) — 4.00
14-($5.99) Bonus back-up Hammer of the Gods by Oeming & Wheatley — 6.00

MICE TEMPLAR, THE , VOLUME 5: NIGHT'S END
Image Comics: Mar, 2015 - No. 5, Sept, 2015 ($3.99/$5.99)
1,3,5-($3.99)-Bryan Glass/Victor Santos-a; 2 covers by Oeming & Santos — 4.00
2,4-($5.99)-Bonus back-up Hammer of the Gods — 6.00

MICHAELANGELO CHRISTMAS SPECIAL (See Teenage Mutant Ninja Turtles Christmas Special)
MICHAELANGELO, TEENAGE MUTANT NINJA TURTLE
Mirage Studios: 1986 (One shot) ($1.50, B&W)

	GD 2.0	VG 4.0	FN 6.0	VF 8.0	VF/NM 9.0	NM- 9.2
1-Christmas-c/story	4	8	12	28	47	65
1-2nd printing ('89, $1.75)-Reprint plus new-a						6.00

MICHAEL CHABON PRESENTS THE AMAZING ADVENTURES OF THE ESCAPIST
Dark Horse Comics: Feb, 2004 - No. 8, Nov, 2005 ($8.95, squarebound)
1-5,7,8-Short stories by Chabon and various incl. Chaykin, Starlin, Brereton, Bake. — 9.00
6-Includes 6 pg. Spirit & Escapist story (Will Eisner's last work); Spirit on cover — 9.00
... Vol. 1 (5/04, $17.95, digest-size) r/#1&2; wraparound-c by Chris Ware — 18.00
... Vol. 2 (11/04, $17.95, digest-size) r/#3&4; wraparound-c by Matt Kindt — 18.00
... Vol. 3 (4/06, $14.95, digest-size) r/#5&6; Tim Sale-c — 15.00

MICHAEL MOORCOCK'S ELRIC: THE MAKING OF A SORCEROR
DC Comics: 2004 - No. 4, 2006 ($5.95, prestige format, limited series)
1-4-Moorcock-s/Simonson-a — 6.00
TPB (2007, $19.99) r/#1-4 — 20.00

MICHAEL MOORCOCK'S MULTIVERSE
DC Comics (Helix): Nov, 1997 - No. 12, Oct, 1998 ($2.50, limited series)
1-12: Simonson, Reeve & Ridgway-a — 4.00
TPB (1999, $19.95) r/#1-12 — 20.00

MICHAEL TURNER, A TRIBUTE TO...
Aspen MLT: 2008 ($8.99, squarebound)
nn-Pin-ups and tributes from Turner's colleagues and friends; Turner & Ross-c — 9.00
Michael Turner Legacy Vol. 1 #1 (6/18, $5.99) Pin-ups and tributes — 6.00

MICHAEL TURNER PRESENTS: ASPEN (See Aspen)

MICKEY AND DONALD (See Walt Disney's...)

MICKEY AND DONALD CHRISTMAS PARADE
IDW Publishing: Dec, 2015 - No. 5, Nov, 2019 ($5.99/$6.99, squarebound, annual)
1,2-($5.99) English translations of Dutch, Italian and Swedish Disney Christmas stories — 6.00
3-5-($6.99) English translations of Dutch and Italian Christmas stories. 3-r/Four Color #62 — 7.00

MICKEY AND DONALD IN VACATIONLAND (See Dell Giant No. 47)

MICKEY & THE BEANSTALK (See Story Hour Series)

MICKEY & THE SLEUTH (See Walt Disney Showcase #38, 39, 42)

MICKEY FINN (Also see Big Shot Comics #74 & Feature Funnies)
Eastern Color 1-4/McNaught Synd. #5 on (Columbia)/Headline V3#2:
Nov?, 1942 - V3#2, May, 1952

	GD 2.0	VG 4.0	FN 6.0	VF 8.0	VF/NM 9.0	NM- 9.2
1	39	78	117	231	378	525
2	19	38	57	112	179	240
3-Charlie Chan story	15	30	45	83	124	165
4	13	26	39	72	101	130
5-10	10	20	30	56	76	95
11-15(1949): 12-Sparky Watts app.	9	18	27	50	65	80
V3#1,2(1952)	8	16	24	42	54	65

MICKEY MALONE
Hale Nass Corp.: 1936 (Color, punchout-c) (B&W-a on back)

	GD 2.0	VG 4.0	FN 6.0	VF 8.0	VF/NM 9.0	NM- 9.2
nn - 1pg. of comics	450	900	1800	--	--	--

MICKEY MANTLE (See Baseball's Greatest Heroes #1)

MICKEY MOUSE (See Adventures of Mickey Mouse, The Best of Walt Disney Comics, Cheerios giveaways, Donald and ..., Dynabrite Comics, 40 Big Pages..., Gladstone Comic Album, Merry Christmas From..., Walt Disney's Mickey and Donald, Walt Disney's Comics & Stories, Walt Disney's..., & Wheaties)

MICKEY MOUSE (...Secret Agent #107-109; Walt Disney's... #148-205?)
(See Dell Giants for annuals) (#204 exists from code & Whitman)
Dell Publ. Co./Gold Key #85-204/Whitman #204-218/Gladstone #219 on:
#16, 1941 - #84, 7-9/62; #85, 11/62 - #218, 6/84; #219, 10/86 - #256, 4/90

	GD 2.0	VG 4.0	FN 6.0	VF 8.0	VF/NM 9.0	NM- 9.2
Four Color 16(1941)-1st Mickey Mouse comic book; "...vs. the Phantom Blot" by Gottfredson	1550	3100	4650	20,150	--	--
Four Color 27(1943)- "7 Colored Terror"	82	164	246	656	1478	2300
Four Color 79(1945)-By Carl Barks (1 story)	104	208	312	832	1866	2900
Four Color 116(1946)	27	54	81	194	435	675
Four Color 141,157(1947)	26	52	78	182	404	625
Four Color 170,181,194('48)	22	44	66	154	340	525
Four Color 214('49),231,248,261	17	34	51	119	265	410
Four Color 268-Reprints/WDC&S #22-24 by Gottfredson ("Surprise Visitor")	17	34	51	117	259	400
Four Color 279,286,296	13	26	39	89	195	300
Four Color 304,313(#1),325(#2),334	12	24	36	82	179	275
Four Color 343,352,362,371,387	10	20	30	70	150	230
Four Color 401,411,427(10-11/52)	9	18	27	62	126	190
Four Color 819-Mickey Mouse in Magicland	8	16	24	54	102	150
Four Color 1057,1151,1246(1959-61)-Album; #1057 has 10c & 12c editions; back covers are different	7	14	21	46	86	125
28(12-1/52-53)-32,34	7	14	21	49	92	135
33-(Exists with 2 dates, 10-11/53 & 12-1/54)	7	14	21	46	86	125
35-50	6	12	18	37	66	95
51-73,75-80	5	10	15	33	57	80
74-Story swipe "The Rare Stamp Search" from 4-Color #422- "The Gilded Man"	6	12	18	40	73	105
81-105: 93,95-titled "Mickey Mouse Club Album". 100-105: Reprint 4-Color #427,194,279, 170,343,214 in that order	4	8	12	25	40	55
106-120	3	6	9	19	30	40
121-130	3	6	9	16	23	30
131-146	3	6	9	14	20	25
147,148: 147-Reprints "The Phantom Fires" from WDC&S #200-202.148-Reprints "The Mystery of Lonely Valley" from WDC&S #208-210	3	6	9	14	20	25
149-158	2	4	6	10	14	18
159-Reprints "The Sunken City" from WDC&S #205-207						
160-178: 162-165,167-170-r	2	4	6	10	14	18
167-Whitman edition	2	4	6	10	14	18
179-(52 pgs.)	2	4	6	11	16	20
180-203: 200-r/Four Color #371	2	4	6	8	10	12
204-(Whitman or G.K.), 205,206	2	4	6	9	13	16
207(8/80), 209(pre-pack?)	6	12	18	38	69	100

Miami Vice Remix #1 © Universal Studios

Mickey Mouse #41 © DIS

Mickey Mouse and Friends #296 © DIS

	GD 2.0	VG 4.0	FN 6.0	VF 8.0	VF/NM 9.0	NM- 9.2
208-(8-12/80)-Only distr. in Whitman 3-pack	10	20	30	69	147	225
210(2/81),211-214	2	4	6	9	13	16
215-218: 215(2/82), 216(4/82), 217(3/84), 218(misdated 8/82; actual date 7/84)	2	4	6	10	14	18
219-1st Gladstone issue; The Seven Ghosts serial-r begins by Gottfredson	2	4	6	11	16	20
220,221	2	3	4	6	8	10
222-225: 222-Editor-in Grief strip-r						5.00
226-230						5.00
231-243,246-254: 240-r/March of Comics #27. 245-r/F.C. #279. 250-r/F.C. #248						4.00
244 (1/89, $2.95, 100 pgs.)-Squarebound 60th anniversary issue; gives history of Mickey						5.00
245,255,256: 245-r/F.C. #279. 255,256-($1.95, 68 pgs.)						5.00

NOTE: Reprints #195-197, 198(2/3), 199(1/3), 200-208, 211(1/2), 212, 213, 215(1/3), 216-on. *Gottfredson Mickey Mouse serials in #219-239, 241-244, 246-249, 251-253, 255.*

	GD 2.0	VG 4.0	FN 6.0	VF 8.0	VF/NM 9.0	NM- 9.2
Album 01-518-210(Dell), 1(10082-309)(9/63-Gold Key)	3	6	9	21	33	45
...Club 1(1/64-Gold Key)(TV)	4	8	12	22	35	48
Mini Comic 1(1976)(3-1/4x6-1/2)-Reprints 158	1	2	3	5	6	8
Surprise Party 1(30037-901, G.K.)(1/69)-40th Anniversary (see Walt Disney Showcase #47)	3	6	9	20	31	42
Surprise Party 1(1979)-r/1969 issue	1	2	3	5	6	8

MICKEY MOUSE (Continued from Mickey Mouse and Friends)
BOOM! Studios: No. 304, Jan, 2011 - No. 309, Jun, 2011 ($3.99)

	NM- 9.2
304-309: 304-Peg-Leg Pete app. 309-Continues in Walt Disney's C&S #720	4.00

MICKEY MOUSE
IDW Publishing: Jun, 2015 - No. 21, Jun, 2017 ($3.99)

	NM- 9.2
1-Legacy numbered (#310); art by Cavazzano and others; multiple covers	4.00
2-21-Classic Disney and foreign reprints; multiple covers on each. 21-(Legacy #330)	4.00

MICKEY MOUSE ADVENTURES
Disney Comics: June, 1990 - No. 18, Nov, 1991 ($1.50)

	NM- 9.2
1,8,9: 1-Bradbury, Murry-r/M.M. #45,73 plus new-a. 8-Byrne-c. 9-Fantasia 50th ann. issue w/new adapt. of movie	5.00
2-7,10-18: 2-Begin all new stories. 10-r/F.C. #214	4.00

MICKEY MOUSE AND FRIENDS (Continued from Walt Disney's Mickey Mouse #304-on)
(Title continues as Mickey Mouse #304-on)
BOOM! Studios: No. 296, Sept, 2009 - No. 303, Dec, 2010 $2.99/$3.99)

	NM- 9.2
296-299,301-303: 296-299-Wizards of Mickey stories. 301-Conclusion to story in #300	3.00
300($3.99, 56 pgs.) Petrucha-a/Pelaez-a; back-up Tanglefoot story w/Gottfredson-a	4.00
300 Deluxe Edition ($6.99) Variant cover by Daan Jippes	7.00

MICKEY MOUSE CLUB FUN BOOK
Golden Press: 1977 (1.95, 228 pgs.)(square bound)

	GD 2.0	VG 4.0	FN 6.0	VF 8.0	VF/NM 9.0	NM- 9.2
11190-1950s-r; 20,000 Leagues, M. Mouse Silly Symphonys, The Reluctant Dragon, etc.	5	10	15	30	50	70

MICKEY MOUSE CLUB MAGAZINE (See Walt Disney…)

MICKEY MOUSE COMICS DIGEST
Gladstone: 1986 - No. 5, 1987 (96 pgs.)

	GD 2.0	VG 4.0	FN 6.0	VF 8.0	VF/NM 9.0	NM- 9.2
1 ($1.25-c)	1	2	3	5	6	8
2-5: 3-5 ($1.50-c)						5.00

MICKEY MOUSE IN COLOR
Another Rainbow/Pantheon: 1988 (Deluxe, 13"x17", hard-c, $250.00)
(Trade, 9-7/8"x11-1/2", hard-c, $39.95)

	GD 2.0	VG 4.0	FN 6.0	VF 8.0	VF/NM 9.0	NM- 9.2
Deluxe limited edition of 3,000 copies signed by Floyd Gottfredson and Carl Barks, designated as the "Official Mickey Mouse 60th Anniversary" book. Mickey Sunday and daily reprints, plus Barks "Riddle of the Red Hat" from Four Color #79. Comes with 45 r.p.m. record interview with Gottfredson and Barks. 240 pgs.	12	24	36	82	179	275
Deluxe, limited to 100 copies, as above, but with a unique colored pencil original drawing of Mickey Mouse by Carl Barks.						900.00
Pantheon trade edition, edited down & without Barks, 192 pgs.	3	6	9	19	30	40

MICKEY MOUSE MAGAZINE (Becomes Walt Disney's Comics & Stories)(Also see 40 Big Pages of Mickey Mouse)
K. K. Publ./Western Publishing Co.: Summer, 1935 (June-Aug, indicia) - V5#12, Sept, 1940; V1#1-5, V3#11,12, V4#1-3 are 44 pgs; V2#3-100 pgs; V5#12-68 pgs; rest are 36 pgs.(No V3#1, V4#6)

	GD 2.0	VG 4.0	FN 6.0	VF 8.0	VF/NM 9.0	NM- 9.2
V1#1 (Large size, 13-1/4x10-1/4", 25c)-Contains puzzles, games, cels, stories & comics of Disney characters. Promotional magazine for Disney cartoon movies and paraphernalia	1575	3150	4725	10,150	21,000	--

Note: Some copies were autographed by the editors & given away with all early one year subscriptions.

2 (Size change, 11-1/2x8-1/2") 10/35, 10c)-High quality paper begins; Messmer-a

	GD 2.0	VG 4.0	FN 6.0	VF 8.0	VF/NM 9.0	NM- 9.2
	376	752	1128	3200	--	--
3,4: 3-Messmer-a	235	470	705	2000	--	--
5-1st Donald Duck solo-c; 2nd cover app. ever; last 44 pg. & high quality paper issue	447	894	1341	3800	--	--
6-9: 6-36 pg. issues begin; Donald becomes editor. 8-2nd Donald solo-c.	188	376	564	1600	--	--
9-1st Mickey/Minnie-c	176	352	528	1500	--	--
10-12, V2#1,2: 11-1st Pluto/Mickey-c; Donald fires himself and appoints Mickey as editor						
V2#3-Special 100 pg. Christmas issue (25c); Messmer-a; Donald becomes editor of Wise Quacks	518	1038	1554	4400	--	--
4-Mickey Mouse Comics & Roy Ranger (adventure strip) begin; both end V2#9; Messmer-a	153	306	459	1300	--	--
5-9: 5-Ted True (adventure strip, ends V2#9) & Silly Symphony Comics (ends V3#3) begin. 6-1st solo Minnie-c. 6-9-Mickey Mouse Movies cut-out in each	71	142	213	454	777	1100
6-Variant (3/37) Rare; distributed with "Mickey Mouse Birthday Party March 6th 1937" invitation outer cover attached to book. Only one example is known. Value will be based on future recorded sales						
10-1st full color issue; Mickey Mouse (by Gottfredson; ends V3#12) & Silly Symphony (ends V3#3) full color Sunday-r, Peter The Farm Detective (ends V5#8) & Ole The North (ends V3#9) begins	129	258	387	826	1413	2000
11-13: 12-Hiawatha-c & feature story	63	126	189	403	689	975
V3#2-Big Bad Wolf Halloween-c		162	243	518	884	1250
3 (12/37)-1st app. Snow White & The Seven Dwarfs (before release of movie) (possibly 1st in print); Mickey X-Mas-c	161	322	483	1030	1765	2500
4 (1/38)-Snow White & The Seven Dwarfs serial begins (on stands before release of movie); Ducky Symphony (ends V3#11) begins	106	212	318	682	1166	1650
5-1st Snow White & Seven Dwarfs-c (St. Valentine's Day)	138	276	414	876	1513	2150
6-Snow White serial ends; Lonesome Ghosts app. (2 pp.)	84	168	252	538	919	1300
7-Seven Dwarfs Easter-c	77	154	231	493	847	1200
8-10: 9-Dopey-c. 10-1st solo Goofy-c	55	110	165	352	601	850
11,12 (44 pgs; 8 more pgs. color added). 11-Mickey the Sheriff serial (ends V4#3) & Donald Duck strip-r (ends V3#12) begin. Color feature on Snow White's Forest Friends	63	126	189	403	689	975
V4#1 (10/38; 44 pgs.)-Brave Little Tailor-c/feature story, nominated for Academy Award; Bobby & Chip by Otto Messmer (ends V4#2) & The Practical Pig (ends V4#3) begin	63	126	189	403	689	975
2 (44 pgs.)-1st Huey, Dewey & Louie-c	74	148	222	470	810	1150
3 (12/38, 44 pgs.)-Ferdinand The Bull-c/feature story, Academy Award winner; Mickey & The Whalers serial begins, ends V4#12	63	126	189	403	689	975
4-Spotty, Mother Pluto strip-r, end V4#8	61	122	183	390	670	950
5-St. Valentine's day-c. 1st Pluto solo-c	58	116	174	371	636	900
7 (3/39)-The Ugly Duckling-c/feature story, Academy Award winner	71	142	213	454	777	1100
7 (4/39)-Goofy & Wilbur The Grasshopper classic-c/feature story from 1st Goofy solo cartoon movie; Timid Elmer begins, ends V5#5	57	114	171	362	619	875
8-Big Bad Wolf-c from Practical Pig movie poster; Practical Pig feature story	60	120	180	381	653	925
9-Donald Duck & Mickey Mouse Sunday-r begin; The Pointer feature story, nominated for Academy Award	58	116	174	371	636	900
10-Classic July 4th drum & fife-c; last Donald Sunday-r	60	120	180	381	653	925
11-1st slick-c; last over-sized issue	142	284	426	909	1555	2200
12 (9/39; format change, 10-1/4x8-1/4")-1st full color, cover to cover issue; Donald's Penguin-c/feature story	61	122	183	390	670	950
V5#1-Black Pete-c; Officer Duck-c/feature story, Autograph Hound feature story; Robinson Crusoe serial begins	63	126	189	403	689	975
2-Goofy-c; 1st brief app. Pinocchio	97	194	291	621	1061	1500
3 (12/39)-Pinocchio Christmas-c (Before movie release). 1st app. Jiminy Cricket; Pinocchio serial begins	110	220	304	704	1202	1700
4,5: 5-Jiminy Cricket-c; Pinocchio serial ends; Donald's Dog Laundry feature story	135	270	405	864	1482	2100
6,7: 6-Tugboat Mickey feature story; Rip Van Winkle feature story, ends V5#8.	65	130	195	416	708	1000
7-2nd Huey, Dewey & Louie-c	61	122	183	390	670	950
8-Last magazine size issue; 2nd solo Pluto-c; Figaro & Cleo feature story	68	136	204	435	743	1050
9-11: 9 (6/40; change to comic book size)-Jiminy Cricket feature story; Donald-c & Sunday-r begin. 10-Special Independence Day issue. 11-Hawaiian Holiday & Mickey's Trailer feature stories; last 36 pg. issue	74	148	222	470	810	1150

12 (Format change)-The transition issue (68 pgs.) becoming a comic book.

	GD 2.0	VG 4.0	FN 6.0	VF 8.0	VF/NM 9.0	NM- 9.2

With only a title change to follow, becomes Walt Disney's Comics & Stories #1 with the next issue — 486 972 1456 3550 6275 9000

NOTE: *Otto Messmer-a* is in many issues of the first two-three years. The following story titles and issues have gags created by *Carl Barks*: V4#3(12/38)-'Donald's Better Self' & 'Donald's Golf Game;' V4#4(1/39)-'Donald's Lucky Day;' V4#7(3/39)-'Hockey Champ;' V4#8(4/39)-'Donald's Cousin Gus;' V4#9(5/39)-'Sea Scouts;' V4#12(9/39)-'Donald's Penguin;' V5#9 (6/40)-'Donald's Vacation;' V5#10(7/40)-'Bone Trouble;' V5#12(9/40)-'Window Cleaners.'

MICKEY MOUSE MAGAZINE (Russian Version)
May 16, 1991 (1st Russian printing of a modern comic book)
1-Bagged w/gold label commemoration in English — 2 4 6 10 14 18

MICKEY MOUSE MARCH OF COMICS (See March of Comics #8,27,45,60,74)

MICKEY MOUSE SHORTS: SEASON ONE
IDW Publishing: Jul, 2016 - No. 4, Oct, 2016 ($3.99, limited series)
1-4-Adaptations of new Disney cartoon shorts — 4.00

MICKEY MOUSE'S SUMMER VACATION (See Story Hour Series)

MICKEY MOUSE SUMMER FUN (See Dell Giants)

MICKEY SPILLANE'S MIKE DANGER
Tekno Comix: Sept, 1995 - No. 11, May, 1996 ($1.95)
1-11: 1-Frank Miller-c. 7-polybagged; Simonson-c. 8,9-Simonson-c — 4.00

MICKEY SPILLANE'S MIKE DANGER
Big Entertainment: V2#1, June, 1996 - No. 10, Apr, 1997 ($2.25)
V2#1-10: Max Allan Collins scripts — 4.00

MICKEY SPILLANE'S MIKE HAMMER
Titan Comics: Jul, 2018 - No. 4, Oct, 2018 ($3.99, limited series)
1-4-Max Allan Collins-s/Marcelo Salaza & Marcio Freire-a — 4.00

MICKEY'S TWICE UPON A CHRISTMAS (Disney)
Gemstone Publishing: 2004 ($3.95, square-bound, one-shot)
nn-Christmas short stories with Mickey, Minnie, Donald, Uncle Scrooge, Goofy and others 4.00

MICROBOTS, THE
Gold Key: Dec, 1971 (one-shot)
1 (10271-112) Painted-c — 3 6 9 15 22 28

MICRONAUTS (Toys)
Marvel Comics Group: Jan, 1979 - No. 59, Aug, 1984 (Mando paper #53 on)
1-Intro/1st app. Baron Karza — 3 6 9 20 31 42
2-7,9,10,35,37,57: 7-Man-Thing app.9-1st app. Cilicia. 35-Double size; origin Microverse; intro Death Squad; Dr. Strange app. 37-Nightcrawler app.; X-Men cameo (2 pgs.).
57-(52 pgs.) — 1 2 3 5 6 8
8-1st app. Capt. Universe (8/79) — 4 8 12 25 40 55
11-34,36,38-56,58,59: 13-1st app. Jasmine. 15-Death of Microtron. 15-17-Fantastic Four app. 17-Death of Jasmine. 20-Ant-Man app. 21-Microverse series begins. 25-Origin Baron Karza. 25-29-Nick Fury app. 27-Death of Biotron. 34-Dr. Strange app. 38-First direct sale. 40-Fantastic Four app. 48-Early Guice-a begins. 59-Golden painted-c — 5.00
Annual 1,2 (12/79,10/80)-Ditko-c/a — 6.00
... No. 1 Facsimile Edition (11/23, $4.99) Reprints first issue with original ads — 5.00
NOTE: *#38-on distributed only through comic shops. N. Adams c-7i. Chaykin a-13-18p. Ditko a-39p. Giffen a-36p, 37p(part). Golden a-1-12p; c-2-7p, 8-23, 24p, 38, 39, 59. Guice a-48-58p; c-49-58. Gil Kane a-38, 40-45p; c-40-45. Layton c-33-37. Miller c-31.*

MICRONAUTS (Micronauts: The New Voyages on cover)
Marvel Comics Group: Oct, 1984 - No. 20, May, 1986
V2#1-20 — 4.00
NOTE: *Kelley Jones a-1; c-1, 6. Guice a-20p; c-2p.*

MICRONAUTS
Image Comics: 2002 - No. 11, Sept, 2003 ($2.95)
2002 Convention Special (no cover price, B&W) previews series — 3.00
1-11: 1-3-Hanson-a; Dave Johnson-c. 2 covers by Linsner & Hanson — 3.00
...Vol. 1: Revolution (2003, $12.95, digest size) r/#1-5 — 13.00

MICRONAUTS (Volume 2)
Devil's Due Publishing: Mar, 2004 - No. 3, May, 2004 ($2.95)
1-3-Jolley-s/Broderick-a — 3.00

MICRONAUTS
IDW Publishing: Apr, 2016 - No. 11, Mar, 2017 ($4.99/$3.99)
1-($4.99) Cullen Bunn-s/David Baldeón-a; multiple covers; Baron Karza app. — 5.00
2-11-($3.99) Max Dunbar-a. 5-Revolution tie-in — 4.00
Annual #1 (1/17, $7.99) Bunn-s/Ferreira-a; future Micronauts app. — 8.00
...: Revolution 1 (9/16, $3.99) Tie-in w/Transformers, G.I. Joe, M.A.S.K.,Action Man, Rom — 4.00

MICRONAUTS: KARZA
Image Comics: Feb, 2003 - No. 4, May, 2003 ($2.95)
1-4-Krueger-s/Kurth-a — 3.00

MICRONAUTS SPECIAL EDITION
Marvel Comics Group: Dec, 1983 - No. 5, Apr, 1984 ($2.00, limited series, Baxter paper)
1-5: r/original series 1-12; Guice-c(p)-all — 4.00

MICRONAUTS: WRATH OF KARZA (Leads into First Strike #1)
IDW Publishing: Apr, 2017 - No. 5, Aug, 2017 ($3.99)
1-5-Cullen Bunn & Jimmy Johnston-s/Andrew Griffith-a; multiple covers — 4.00

MIDDLEWEST
Image Comics: Nov, 2018 - No. 18 ($3.99)
1-18-Skottie Young-s/Jorge Corona-a. 1-Three covers — 4.00

MIDGET COMICS (Fighting Indian Stories)
St. John Publishng Co.: Feb, 1950 - No. 2, Apr, 1950 (5-3/8x7-3/8", 68 pgs.)
1-Fighting Indian Stories; Matt Baker-c — 40 80 120 246 411 575
2-Tex West, Cowboy Marshal (also in #1) — 19 38 57 111 176 240

MIDLIFE (OR HOW TO HERO AT FIFTY)
Image Comics: Oct, 2023 - Present ($3.99)
1-5-Buccellato-s/Simeone-a — 4.00

MIDNIGHT (See Smash Comics #18)

MIDNIGHT
Ajax/Farrell Publ. (Four Star Comic Corp.): Apr, 1957 - No. 6, June, 1958
1-Reprints from Voodoo & Strange Fantasy with some changes — 22 44 66 132 216 300
2-6 — 15 30 45 84 127 170

MIDNIGHTER (See The Authority)
DC Comics (WildStorm): Jan, 2007 - No. 20, Aug, 2008 ($2.99)
1-20: 1-Ennis-s/Sprouse-a/c. 6-Fabry-a. 7-Vaughan-s. 8-Gage-s. 9-Stelfreeze-a — 3.00
1-4-Variant covers. 1-Michael Golden. 2-Art Adams 3-Jason Pearson. 4-Glenn Fabry — 4.00
...: Anthem TPB (2008, $14.99) r/#7,10-15 — 15.00
...: Armageddon (12/07, $2.99) Gage-s/Coleby-a/McKone-c — 3.00
...: Assassin8 TPB (2009, $14.99) r/#16-20 — 15.00
...: Killing Machine TPB (2008, $14.99) r/#1-6 — 15.00

MIDNIGHTER (See The Authority)
DC Comics: Aug, 2015 - No. 12, Jul, 2016 ($2.99)
1-12: 1-Orlando-s/Aco-a. 3-5-Grayson app. 9-12-Harley Quinn & Suicide Squad app. — 3.00
2021 Annual 1 (10/21, $5.99) Cloonan & Conrad-s/Oeming-a; Mister Miracle app. — 6.00

MIDNIGHTER AND APOLLO (The Authority)
DC Comics: Dec, 2016 - No. 6, May, 2017 ($3.99)
1-6-Orlando-s/Blanco-a. 1,2-Henry Bendix app. 2-6-Neron app. — 4.00

MIDNIGHT MASS
DC Comics (Vertigo): Jun, 2002 - No. 8, Jan, 2003 ($2.50)
1-8-Rozum-s/Saiz & Palmiotti-a — 3.00

MIDNIGHT MASS: HERE THERE BE MONSTERS
DC Comics (Vertigo): March, 2004 - No. 6, Aug, 2004 ($2.95, limited series)
1-6-Rozum-s/Paul Lee-a — 3.00

MIDNIGHT MEN
Marvel Comics (Epic Comics/Heavy Hitters): June, 1993 - No. 4, Sept, 1993 ($2.50/$1.95, limited series)
1-($2.50)-Embossed-c; Chaykin-c/a & scripts in all — 5.00
2-4 — 4.00

MIDNIGHT MYSTERY
American Comics Group: Jan-Feb, 1961 - No. 7, Oct, 1961
1-Sci/Fi story — 10 20 30 68 144 220
2-7: 7-Gustavson-a — 6 12 18 37 66 95
NOTE: *Reinman a-1, 3. Whitney a-1, 4-6; c-1-3, 5, 7.*

MIDNIGHT NATION
Image Comics (Top Cow): Oct, 2000 - No. 12, July, 2002 ($2.50/$2.95)
1-Straczynski-s/Frank-a; 2 covers — 3.50
2-11: 9-Twin Towers cover — 3.00
12-($2.95) Last issue — 3.00
Wizard #1/2 (2001) Michael Zulli-a; two covers by Frank — 3.00
Vol. 1 ('03, $29.99, TPB) r/#1-12 & Wizard #1/2; cover gallery; afterword by Straczynski — 30.00

MIDNIGHT OF THE SOUL
Image Comics: Jun, 2016 - No. 5, Oct, 2016 ($3.50, limited series)
1-5-Howard Chaykin-s/a/c; set in 1950s New York City — 3.50

MIDNIGHT SOCIETY: THE BLACK LAKE
Dark Horse Comics: Jun, 2015 - No. 4, Oct, 2015 ($3.99)
1-4-Drew Johnson-s/a/c — 4.00

MIDNIGHT SONS UNLIMITED
Marvel Comics (Midnight Sons imprint #4 on): Apr, 1993 - No. 9, May, 1995 ($3.95, 68 pgs.)
1-9: Blaze, Darkhold (by Quesada #1), Ghost Rider, Morbius & Nightstalkers in all. 1-Painted-c. 3-Spider-Man app. 4-Siege of Darkness part 17; new Dr. Strange & new Ghost Rider app.; spot varnish-c — 4.00
NOTE: *Sears a-2.*

MIDNIGHT SUNS
Marvel Comics: Nov, 2022 - No. 5, Mar, 2023 ($3.99, limited series)
1-5-Wolverine, Magik, Blade, Spirit Rider, Agatha Harkness app. — 4.00

MIDNIGHT TALES
Charlton Press: Dec, 1972 - No. 18, May, 1976
V1#1 — 3 6 9 21 33 45
2-10 — 2 4 6 10 14 18
11-18: 11-14-Newton-a(p) — 2 4 6 8 11 14
12,17(Modern Comics reprint, 1977) — 6.00
NOTE: *Adkins a-12i, 13i. Ditko a-12. Howard (Wood imitator) a-1-15, 17, 18; c-1-18. Don Newton a-11-14p. Staton a-1, 3-11, 13. Sutton a-3-10.*

MIDNIGHT VISTA
AfterShock Comics: Sept, 2019 - No. 5, Jan, 2020 ($3.99)
1-5-Eliot Rahal-s/Clara Meath-a/Juan Doe-c — 4.00

MIDNITE SHOW, THE
Dark Horse Comics: Oct, 2023 - No. 4, Jan, 2024 ($3.99, limited series)
1-4-Cullen Bunn-s/Brian Hurtt-a — 4.00

MIGHTY, THE
DC Comics: Apr, 2009 - No. 12, Mar, 2010 ($2.99)
1-12: Tomasi & Champagne-s/Dave Johnson-c. 1-4-Snejbjerg-a. 5-12-Samnee-a — 3.00
...: Volume 1 TPB (2009, $17.99) r/#1-6 — 18.00
...: Volume 2 TPB (2010, $17.99) r/#7-12 — 18.00

MIGHTY ATOM, THE (...& the Pixies #6) (Formerly The Pixies #1-5)
Magazine Enterprises: No. 6, 1949; Nov, 1957 - No. 6, Aug-Sept, 1958
6(1949-M.E.)-no month (1st Series) — 8 16 24 44 57 70
1-6(2nd Series)-Pixies-r — 5 10 15 24 29 34
I.W. Reprint #1(nd) — 2 4 6 11 16 20

MIGHTY AVENGERS
Marvel Comics: May, 2007 - No. 36, Jun, 2010 ($3.99/$2.99)

Micronauts #12 © Mego

Midnighter #7 © DC

Mighty Avengers #30 © MAR

	GD 2.0	VG 4.0	FN 6.0	VF 8.0	VF/NM 9.0	NM- 9.2
1-($3.99) Iron Man, Ms. Marvel select new team; Bendis-s/Cho-a/c; Mole Man app.						5.00
2-20: 2-6-($2.99) Ultron returns. 7-15: 7-Bagley-a begins; Venom on-c. 9-11-Dr. Doom app. 12-20-Secret Invasion. 12,13-Maleev-a. 15-Romita Jr.-a. 16-Elektra. 20-Wasp funeral						3.00
21-($3.99) Dark Reign; Scarlet Witch returns; new team assembled; Pham-a						4.00
22-36: 25,26-Fantastic Four app. 35,36-Siege; Ultron returns						3.00
...: Most Wanted Files (2007, $3.99) profiles of members, accomplices & adversaries						4.00
... Vol. 1: The Ultron Initiative HC (2008, $19.99) r/#1-6; variant covers and sketch art						20.00
... Vol. 2: Venom Bomb HC (2008, $19.99) r/#7-11; B&W cover art						20.00

MIGHTY AVENGERS (Continues in Captain America and the Mighty Avengers)
Marvel Comics: Nov, 2013 - No. 14, Nov, 2014 ($3.99)

1-14: 1-Luke Cage, White Tiger, Power Man, Spectrum & Superior Spider-Man team; Land-a. 4-Falcon app. 5-She-Hulk app. 6-8-Schiti-a. 9-Ronin unmasked. 10-12-Original Sin						4.00

MIGHTY BARBARIANS, THE
Ablaze Publishing: 2023 - No. 6, 2023 ($3.99)

1-6-Moreci-s/Cafaro-a						4.00

MIGHTY BEAR (Formerly Fun Comics; becomes Unsane #15)
Star Publ. No. 13,14/Ajax-Farrell (Four Star): No. 13, Jan, 1954 - No. 14, Mar, 1954; 9/57 - No. 3, 2/58

13,14-L. B. Cole-c	20	40	60	120	195	270
1-3('57-58)Four Star; becomes Mighty Ghost #4	8	16	24	44	57	70

MIGHTY CAPTAIN MARVEL, THE (Follows Civil War II)(Continues in Captain Marvel #125)
Marvel Comics: No. 0, Feb, 2017 - No. 9, Nov, 2017 ($3.99)

0-Stohl-s/Laiso-a; Alpha Flight app.						4.00
1-9: 1-(3/17) Stohl-s/Rosanas-a. 5-8-Secret Empire tie-ins						4.00

MIGHTY COMICS (...Presents) (Formerly Flyman)
Radio Comics (Archie): No. 40, Nov, 1966 - No. 50, Oct, 1967 (All 12¢ issues)

40-Web	5	10	15	30	50	70
41-50: 41-Shield, Black Hood. 42-Black Hood. 43-Shield, Web & Black Hood. 44-Black Hood, Steel Sterling & The Shield. 45-Shield & Hangman; origin Web retold. 46-Steel Sterling, Web & Black Hood. 47-Black Hood & Mr. Justice. 48-Shield & Hangman; Wizard x-over in Shield. 49-Steel Sterling & Fox; Black Hood x-over in Steel Sterling. 50-Black Hood & Web; Inferno x-over in Web	4	8	12	28	47	65

NOTE: *Paul Reinman a-40-50.*

MIGHTY CRUSADERS, THE (Also see Adventures of the Fly, The Crusaders & Fly Man)
Mighty Comics Group (Radio Comics): Nov, 1965 - No. 7, Oct, 1966 (12¢)

1-Origin The Shield	8	16	24	52	99	145
2-Origin Comet	4	8	12	28	47	65
3,5-7: 3-Origin Fly-Man. 5-Intro. Ultra-Men (Fox, Web, Capt. Flag) & Terrific Three (Jaguar, Mr. Justice, Steel Sterling). 7-Steel Sterling feature; origin Fly-Girl	4	8	12	27	44	60
4-1st S.A. app. Fireball, Inferno & Fox; Firefly, Web, Bob Phantom, Blackjack, Hangman, Zambini, Kardak, Steel Justice, Mr. Justice, Wizard, Capt. Flag, Jaguar x-over	5	10	15	30	50	70
Volume 1: Origin of a Super Team TPB (2003, $12.95) r/#1 & Fly Man #31-33						13.00

NOTE: *Reinman a-6.*

MIGHTY CRUSADERS, THE (All New Advs. of...#2)
Red Circle Prod./Archie Ent. No. 6 on: Mar, 1983 - No. 13, Sept, 1985 ($1.00, 36 pgs, Mando paper)

1-Origin Black Hood, The Fly, Fly Girl, The Shield, The Wizard, The Jaguar, Pvt. Strong & The Web; return of MLJ heroes	1	2	3	4	5	7
2-10: 2-Mister Midnight begins. 4-Darkling replaces Shield. 5-Origin Jaguar, Shield begins. 7-Untold origin Jaguar. 10-Veitch-a						5.00
11-13-Lower print run						6.00

NOTE: *Buckler a-1-3, 4i, 5p, 7p, 8i, 9i; c-1-10p.*

MIGHTY CRUSADERS, THE (Also see The Shield, The Web and The Red Circle)
DC Comics: Sept, 2010 - No. 6, Feb, 2011 ($3.99, limited series)

1-6-The Shield, The Web, Fly-Girl, Inferno, War Eagle & The Comet team-up						4.00
... Special 1 (7/10, $4.99) Prequel to series; Pina-a/Lau-a						5.00

MIGHTY CRUSADERS, THE (Volume 3)
Archie Comic Publications (Dark Circle): Jan, 2018 - No. 4, May, 2018 ($3.99)

1-4-The Shield, Jaguar, Firefly, Darkling, Steel Sterling, The Comet & The Web team-up						4.00
...: The Shield 1 (8/21, $3.99) Rob Liefeld-s/a; multiple covers						4.00

MIGHTY GHOST (Formerly Mighty Bear #1-3)
Ajax/Farrell Publ.: No. 4, June, 1958

4	8	16	24	44	57	70

MIGHTY HERCULES, THE (TV)
Gold Key: July, 1963 - No. 2, Nov, 1963

1 (10072-307)	13	26	39	89	195	300

	GD 2.0	VG 4.0	FN 6.0	VF 8.0	VF/NM 9.0	NM- 9.2
2 (10072-311)	12	24	36	79	170	260

MIGHTY HEROES, THE (TV) (Funny)
Dell Publishing Co.: Mar, 1967 - No. 4, July, 1967

1-Also has a 1957 Heckle & Jeckle-r	11	22	33	73	157	240
2-4: 4-Has two 1958 Mighty Mouse-r	8	16	24	51	95	140

MIGHTY HEROES
Spotlight Comics: 1987 (B&W, one-shot)

1-Heckle & Jeckle backup						5.00

MIGHTY HEROES
Marvel Comics: Jan, 1998 ($2.99, one-shot)

1-Origin of the Mighty Heroes						4.00

MIGHTY LOVE
DC Comics: 2003 ($24.99/$17.95, graphic novel)

HC-($24.95) Howard Chaykin-s/a; intro. Skylark and the Iron Angel						25.00
SC-($17.95)						18.00

MIGHTY MAN (From Savage Dragon titles)
Image Comics: Dec, 2004 ($7.95, one-shot)

1-Reprints the serialized back-ups from Savage Dragon #109-118						8.00

MIGHTY MAN (From Savage Dragon)
Image Comics: Apr, 2017 ($3.99, one-shot)

1-Larsen-s/Koutsis-a; Superpatriot, Malcolm Dragon, Horridus, Barbaric, Ricochet app.						4.00

MIGHTY MARVEL TEAM-UP THRILLERS
Marvel Comics: 1983 ($5.95, trade paperback)

1-Reprints team-up stories	3	6	9	21	33	45

MIGHTY MARVEL WESTERN, THE
Marvel Comics Group (LMC earlier issues): Oct, 1968 - No. 46, Sept, 1976 (#1-14: 68 pgs.; #15,16: 52 pgs.)

1-Begin Kid Colt, Rawhide Kid, Two-Gun Kid-r	8	16	24	51	96	140
2-5: (2-14 are 68 pgs.)	4	8	12	28	47	65
6-16: (15,16 are 52 pgs.)	4	8	12	22	35	48
17-20	3	6	9	14	19	24
21-30,32,37: 24-Kid Colt-r end. 25-Matt Slade-r begin. 32-Origin-r/Rawhide Kid #23; Williamson-r/Kid Slade #7. 37-Williamson, Kirby-r/Two-Gun Kid 51	2	4	6	10	14	18
31,33-36,38-46: 31-Baker-r.	2	4	6	9	13	16
45-(30¢-c variant, limited distribution)(6/76)	9	18	27	63	129	195

NOTE: *Jack Davis a(r)-21-24. Keller r-1-13, Jack Kirby a(r)-1-3, 6, 9, 12-14, 16, 25-29, 32-38, 40, 41, 43-46; c-29. Maneely a(r)-22. Severin c-3i, 9. No Matt Slade-r #43.*

MIGHTY MIDGET COMICS, THE (Miniature)
Samuel E. Lowe & Co.: No date; circa 1942-1943 (Sold 2 for 5¢, B&W and red, 36 pgs, approx. 5x4")

Bulletman #11(1943)-r/cover/Bulletman #3	16	32	48	94	147	200
Captain Marvel Adventures #11	19	38	57	111	176	240
Captain Marvel #11 (Same as above except for full color ad on back cover; this issue was glued to cover of Captain Marvel #20 and is not found in fine-mint condition)	345	690	1035	--	--	--
Captain Marvel Jr. #11 (Same-c as Master #27)	18	36	54	103	162	220
Captain Marvel Jr. #11 (Same as above except for full color ad on back-c; this issue was glued to cover of Captain Marvel #21 and is not found in fine-mint condition)	345	690	1035	--	--	--
Golden Arrow #11	15	30	45	90	140	190
Golden Arrow #11 (Same as above except for full color ad on back-c; this issue was glued to cover of Captain Marvel #21 and is not found in fine-mint condition)	285	570	855	--	--	--
Ibis the Invincible #11(1942)-Origin; reprints cover to Ibis #1 (Predates Fawcett's Ibis the Invincible #1).	18	36	54	105	165	225
Spy Smasher #11(1942)	16	32	48	94	147	200

NOTE: *The above books came in a box called "box full of books" and was distributed with other Samuel Lowe puzzles, paper dolls, coloring books, etc. They are not titled Mighty Midget Comics. All have a war bond seal on back cover which is otherwise blank. These books came in a "Mighty Midget" flat cardboard counter display rack.*

Balbo, the Boy Magician #12 (1943)-1st book devoted entirely to character.	10	20	30	58	79	100
Bulletman #12	12	24	36	69	97	125
Commando Yank #12 (1943)-Only comic devoted entirely to character.	10	20	30	56	76	95
Dr. Voltz the Human Generator (1943)-Only comic devoted entirely to character.	10	20	30	54	72	90
Lance O'Casey #12 (1943)-1st comic devoted entirely to character (Predates Fawcett's Lance O'Casey #1).	10	20	30	54	72	90
Leatherneck the Marine (1943)-Only comic devoted entirely to character.						

	GD 2.0	VG 4.0	FN 6.0	VF 8.0	VF/NM 9.0	NM- 9.2

	GD 2.0	VG 4.0	FN 6.0	VF 8.0	VF/NM 9.0	NM- 9.2
	10	20	30	54	72	90
Minute Man #12	12	24	36	67	94	120
Mister "Q" (1943)-Only comic devoted entirely to character.						
	10	20	30	54	72	90
Mr. Scarlet and Pinky #12 (1943)-Only comic devoted entirely to character.						
	10	20	30	58	79	100
Pat Wilton and His Flying Fortress (1943)-1st comic devoted entirely to character.						
	10	20	30	54	72	90
The Phantom Eagle #12 (1943)-Only comic devoted entirely to character.						
	10	20	30	58	79	100
State Trooper Stops Crime (1943)-Only comic devoted entirely to character.						
	10	20	30	54	72	90
Tornado Tom (1943)-Origin, r/from Cyclone #1-3; only comic devoted entirely to character.						
	10	20	30	54	72	90

MIGHTY MORPHIN (Mighty Morphin' Power Rangers)
BOOM! Studios: Nov. 2020 - No. 22, Aug, 2022 ($4.99)

1-($4.99) Parrott-s/Renna-a; multiple covers						5.00
2-22-($3.99) 4-Green Ranger unmasks						4.00

MIGHTY MORPHIN POWER RANGERS (Also see Saban's Mighty Morphin' Power Rangers)
BOOM! Studios: No. 0, Jan, 2016; Mar, 2016 - No. 55, Oct, 2020; (title skips #56-#99) No. 100, Sept, 2022 - Present ($3.99)

0-Higgins-s/Prasetya-a; Rita Repulsa & Scorpina app.; multiple covers						4.00
1-24,26-49,51-55: 1-4,6-9,11-Higgins-s/Prasetya-a. 5-Silas-a. 10-Lam-a						4.00
25,50-($4.99) 25-Sold in black polybag; Tommy dies						5.00
100-(9/22, $9.99) Legacy issue #100; Death Rangers app.; art by various						10.00
101-110: 101-Rita Repulsa returns						4.00
111-FCBD ($4.99) Darkest Hour						5.00
2016 Annual 1 (8/16, $7.99) Short stories; art by Guillory, Terry Moore, Kochalka						8.00
2017 Annual 1 (5/17, $7.99) Short stories; art by Mora, Irving, Montes; 3 covers						8.00
2018 Annual 1 (4/18, $7.99) Shattered Grid; short stories; 3 covers						8.00
... FCBD 2018 Special (5/18, giveaway) Shattered Grid; Galindo-a						3.00
.. Shattered Grid 1 (8/18, $7.99) Di Nicuolo & Galindo-a						8.00
.. 25th Anniversary Special 1 (6/18, $7.99) Short stories; art by Quinones & others						8.00
.. 30th Anniversary Special 1 (8/23, $9.99) Short stories by various; Dan Mora-c						10.00

MIGHTY MORPHIN POWER RANGERS: PINK
BOOM! Studios: Jun, 2016 - No. 6, Jan, 2017 ($3.99, limited series)

1-6-Fletcher & Thompson-s/DiNicuolo-a; multiple covers						4.00

MIGHTY MORPHIN POWER RANGERS / TEENAGE MUTANT NINJA TURTLES
BOOM! Studios: Dec, 2019 - No. 5, Jun, 2020 ($4.99/$3.99, limited series)

1-($4.99) Ryan Parrott-s/Simone di Meo-a; Shredder app.; multiple covers						5.00
2-5-($3.99) Rita Repulsa, BeBop & Rocksteady app.						4.00

MIGHTY MORPHIN POWER RANGERS / TEENAGE MUTANT NINJA TURTLES II
BOOM! Studios: Dec, 2022 - No. 5, May, 2023 ($4.99, limited series)

1-5-Parrott-s/Mora-a; multiple covers						5.00
... Black & White Edition 1 (12/23, $4.99) Reprints #1 in B&W						5.00

MIGHTY MORPHIN POWER RANGERS: THE MOVIE (Also see Saban's Mighty Morphin' Power Rangers)
Marvel Comics: Sept, 1995 ($3.95, one-shot)

	GD 2.0	VG 4.0	FN 6.0	VF 8.0	VF/NM 9.0	NM- 9.2
nn-Adaptation of movie	3	6	9	15	22	28

MIGHTY MORPHIN POWER RANGERS: THE RETURN
BOOM! Studios: Feb, 2024 - Present ($4.99, limited series)

1-Kimberly 22 years later; Amy Jo Johnson & Matt Hotson-s/Nico Leon-a						5.00

MIGHTY MOUSE (See Adventures of..., Dell Giant #43, Giant Comics Edition, March of Comics #205, 237, 247, 257, 447, 459, 471, 483, Oxydol-Dreft, Paul Terry's, & Terry-Toons Comics)

MIGHTY MOUSE (1st Series)
Timely/Marvel Comics (20th Century Fox): Fall, 1946 - No. 4, Summer, 1947

	GD 2.0	VG 4.0	FN 6.0	VF 8.0	VF/NM 9.0	NM- 9.2
1	219	438	657	1402	2401	3400
2	77	154	231	493	847	1200
3,4	52	104	156	328	552	775

MIGHTY MOUSE (2nd Series) (Paul Terry's... #62-71)
St. John Publishing Co./Pines No. 68 (3/56) on (TV issues #72 on): Aug, 1947 - No. 67, 11/55; No. 68, 3/56 - No. 83, 6/59

	GD 2.0	VG 4.0	FN 6.0	VF 8.0	VF/NM 9.0	NM- 9.2
5(#1)	77	154	231	493	847	1200
6-10: 10-Over-sized issue	27	54	81	162	266	370
11-19	16	32	48	94	147	200
20 (11/50) - 25-(52 pg. editions)	14	28	42	80	115	150
20-25-(36 pg. editions)	13	26	39	72	101	130
26-37: 35-Flying saucer-c	12	24	36	67	94	120
38-45-(100 pgs.)	22	44	66	128	209	290
46-83: 62-64,67-Painted-c. 82-Infinity-c	11	22	33	62	86	110
Album nn (nd, 1952/53?, St. John)(100 pgs.)(Rebound issues w/new cover)						
	32	64	96	188	307	425
Album 1(10/52, 25¢, 100 pgs., St. John)-Gandy Goose app.						
	37	74	111	222	361	500
Album 2,3(11/52 & 12/52, St. John) (100 pgs.)	28	56	84	165	270	375
Fun Club Magazine 1(Fall, 1957-Pines, 25¢, 100 pgs.) (CBS TV)-Tom Terrific, Heckle & Jeckle, Dinky Duck, Gandy Goose	22	44	66	128	209	290
Fun Club Magazine 2-6(Winter, 1958-Pines)	12	24	36	67	94	120
3-D 1-(1st printing-9/53, 25¢)(St. John)-Came w/glasses; stiff covers; says World's First! on-c; 1st 3-D comic	29	58	87	170	278	385
3-D 1-(2nd printing-10/53, 25¢)-Came w/glasses; slick, glossy covers, slightly smaller	20	40	60	114	182	250
3-D 2,3(11/53, 12/53, 25¢)-(St. John)-With glasses	20	40	60	114	182	250

MIGHTY MOUSE (TV)(3rd Series)(Formerly Adventures of Mighty Mouse)
Gold Key/Dell Publ. Co. No. 166-on: No. 161, Oct, 1964 - No. 172, Oct, 1968

	GD 2.0	VG 4.0	FN 6.0	VF 8.0	VF/NM 9.0	NM- 9.2
161(10/64)-165(9/65)-(Becomes Adventures of... No. 166 on)						
	4	8	12	28	47	65
166(3/66), 167(6/66)-172	3	6	9	20	31	42

MIGHTY MOUSE (TV)
Spotlight Comics: 1987 - No. 2, 1987 ($1.50, color)

	GD 2.0	VG 4.0	FN 6.0	VF 8.0	VF/NM 9.0	NM- 9.2
1,2-New stories						5.00
...And Friends Holiday Special (11/87, $1.75)						5.00

MIGHTY MOUSE (TV)
Marvel Comics: Oct, 1990 - No. 10, July, 1991 ($1.00)(Based on Sat. cartoon)

1-10: 1-Dark Knight-c parody. 2-10: 3-Intro Bat-Bat; Byrne-c. 4,5-Crisis-c/story parodies w/Perez-c. 6-Spider-Man-c parody. 7-Origin Bat-Bat						4.00

MIGHTY MOUSE (TV)
Dynamite Entertainment: 2017 - No. 5, 2017 ($3.99)

1-5: 1-Multiple covers incl. Alex Ross & Neal Adams; Mighty Mouse in the real world						4.00

MIGHTY MOUSE ADVENTURE MAGAZINE
Spotlight Comics: 1987 ($2.00, B&W, 52 pgs., magazine size, one-shot)

1-Deputy Dawg, Heckle & Jeckle backup stories						5.00

MIGHTY MOUSE ADVENTURES (Adventures of... #2 on)
St. John Publishing Co.: November, 1951

	GD 2.0	VG 4.0	FN 6.0	VF 8.0	VF/NM 9.0	NM- 9.2
1	47	94	141	296	498	700

MIGHTY MOUSE ADVENTURE STORIES (Paul Terry's... on-c only)
St. John Publishing Co.: 1953 (50¢, 384 pgs.)

	GD 2.0	VG 4.0	FN 6.0	VF 8.0	VF/NM 9.0	NM- 9.2
nn-Rebound issues	63	126	189	403	689	975

MIGHTY MUTANIMALS (See Teenage Mutant Ninja Turtles Adventures #19)
Archie Comics: Apr, 1992 - No. 3, July, 1991 ($1.00, limited series)

	GD 2.0	VG 4.0	FN 6.0	VF 8.0	VF/NM 9.0	NM- 9.2
1-3: 1-Story cont'd from TMNT Advs. #19.	1	2	3	5	6	8
1-4 (1992)	1	2	3	5	6	8
5-9: 7-1st app. Merdude	2	4	6	8	10	12

MIGHTY SAMSON (Also see Gold Key Champion)
Gold Key/Whitman #32: July, 1964 - No. 20, Nov, 1969; No. 21, Aug, 1972; No. 22, Dec, 1973 - No. 31, Mar, 1976; No. 32, Aug, 1982 (Painted-c #1-31)

	GD 2.0	VG 4.0	FN 6.0	VF 8.0	VF/NM 9.0	NM- 9.2
1-Origin/1st app.; Thorne-a begins	10	20	30	66	138	210
2-5	5	10	15	31	53	75
6-10: 7-Tom Morrow begins, ends #20	3	6	9	21	33	45
11-20	3	6	9	17	25	34
21-31: 21,22-r	2	4	6	13	18	22
32(Whitman, 8/82)-r	2	4	6	8	11	14

MIGHTY SAMSON
Dark Horse Comics: Dec, 2010 - No. 4, Oct, 2011 ($3.50)

1-4: 1-Origin retold; Shooter & Vaughn-s/Olliffe-a/Swanland-c; r/1st app. from 1964						3.50
1-Variant-c by Olliffe						4.00

MIGHTY THOR, THE (Continues in Thor: God of Thunder)
Marvel Comics: Jun, 2011 - No. 22, Dec, 2012 ($3.99)

1-Fraction-s/Coipel-a; Silver Surfer app.; bonus concept art from the movie						4.00
1-Variant-c by Charest						6.00
1-Variant-c by Simonson						10.00
2-22: 3-6-Galactus app. 7-Fear Itself tie-in; Odin's 1st battle vs. the Serpent. 8-Tanarus. 13-17-Simonson-c. 18-21-Alan Davis-a						4.00
12.1 (6/12, $2.99) Kitson-a/Coipel-c; flashbacks from Volstagg & Sif						3.00
Annual 1 (8/12, $4.99) Silver Surfer & Galactus app.; DeMatteis-s/Elson-a						5.00

MIGHTY THOR (Jane Foster as Thor)
Marvel Comics: Jan, 2016 - No. 23, Nov, 2017; No. 700, Dec, 2017 - No. 706, Jun, 2018 ($4.99/$3.99)

1-($4.99) Tri-fold cover; Aaron-s/Dauterman-a; Loki app.						5.00
2-23-($3.99) 3-Multiple Lokis app. 12-Origin of Mjolnir; Frazer Irving-a. 14-Epting-a. 20-Volstagg becomes the War Thor						4.00
[Title switches to legacy numbering after #23 (11/17)]						
700-(12/17, $5.99) Aaron-s; art by various incl. Dauterman, Simonson, Acuna, Coipel						6.00
701-706: 701-Mangog vs. War Thor; Harren-a. 703-706-Dauterman-a						4.00
...: At the Gates of Valhalla 1 (7/18, $4.99) Intro Goddesses of Thunder; Bartel-a						5.00
.. 3D #1 (6/19, $7.99, polybagged with 3D glasses) r/#1 in 3D; wraparound-c						8.00

MIGHTY VALKYRIES, THE
Marvel Comics: Jun, 2021 - No. 5, Nov, 2021 ($4.99/$3.99, limited series)

1-($4.99) Aaron & Gronbekk-s/De Iulis & D'Urso-a; Jane Foster, Loki and Hela app.						5.00
2-5-($3.99) Kraven the Hunter app.						4.00

MIGUEL O'HARA - SPIDER-MAN: 2099
Marvel Comics: Mar, 2024 - No. 5, Mar, 2024 ($4.99/$3.99, weekly limited series)

1-($4.99) Orlando-s/Pramanik-a; The Zombie of 2099 app.						5.00
2-5-($3.99) 2-Dracula app. 3-Werewolf By Night of 2099 app.. 5-Man-Thing						4.00

MIKE BARNETT, MAN AGAINST CRIME (TV)
Fawcett Publications: Dec, 1951 - No. 6, Oct, 1952

	GD 2.0	VG 4.0	FN 6.0	VF 8.0	VF/NM 9.0	NM- 9.2
1	27	54	81	158	259	360
2	16	32	48	94	147	200
3,4,6	15	30	45	83	124	165
5- "Market for Morphine" cover/story	20	40	60	117	189	260

MIKE DANGER (See Mickey Spillane's...)

MIKE DEODATO'S...
Caliber Comics: 1996, ($2.95, B&W)

...FALLOUT 3000 #1, ...JONAS (mag. size) #1,...PRIME CUTS (mag. size) #1, ...PROTHEUS #1,2, ...RAMTHAR #1,...RAZOR NIGHTS #1						4.00

MIKE GRELL'S SABLE (Also see Jon Sable & Sable)
First Comics: Mar, 1990 - No. 10, Dec, 1990 ($1.75)

1-10: r/Jon Sable Freelance #1-10 by Grell						4.00

MIKE MIST MINUTE MIST-ERIES (See Ms. Tree/Mike Mist in 3-D)
Eclipse Comics: April, 1981 ($1.25, B&W, one-shot)

1						4.00

MIKE SHAYNE PRIVATE EYE
Dell Publishing Co.: Nov-Jan, 1962 - No. 3, Sept-Nov, 1962

	GD 2.0	VG 4.0	FN 6.0	VF 8.0	VF/NM 9.0	NM- 9.2
1	4	8	12	28	47	65

Mighty Mouse (2017 series) #3 © CBS

Miles Morales: Spider-Man #19 © MAR

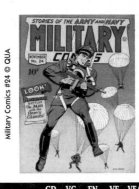

Military Comics #24 © QUA

	GD 2.0	VG 4.0	FN 6.0	VF 8.0	VF/NM 9.0	NM- 9.2

2,3 — 3 6 9 16 24 32

MILES MORALES & MOON GIRL (Continues in Avengers & Moon Girl)
Marvel Comics: Aug, 2022 ($4.99, one-shot)
1-Mashigo-s/Guara-a; Devil Dinosaur goes missing; Taskmaster app. — 5.00

MILES MORALES: SPIDER-MAN
Marvel Comics: Feb, 2019 - No. 42, Nov, 2022 ($3.99)
1-Ahmed-s/Garrón-a; Rhino app. — 4 8 12 28 47 65
2,4,8,9,11,12,14-24,26-29: 20,21-Captain America app. 23-"King in Black" tie-in. 26-29-Clone Saga. 29-New costume on last page — 4.00
3-1st Snatcher; Captain America app. — 2 4 6 11 16 20
5-Starling cameo — 3 6 9 14 21 26
6-Starling 1st full app. — 4 8 12 23 37 50
7-1st Quantum — 3 6 9 17 25 34
10-1st Ultimatum — 3 4 6 11 16 20
13-Rhino app.; Billie Morales born — 3 6 9 19 30 40
25-($4.99) The Clone Saga begins; Peter Parker app.; back-up with Bustos-a — 5.00
30-($4.99) New costume; Taskmaster app.; back-up by Lord & Miller-s/Pichelli-a — 5.00
31-41: 31,32-Taskmaster app. 36-Spider-Ham app. — 4.00
42-($4.99) Rhino app. — 5.00
Miles Morales: The End (3/20, $4.99) Damian Scott-a; future Miles' last adventure — 5.00

MILES MORALES: SPIDER-MAN
Marvel Comics: Present ($3.99)
1-($4.99) Ziglar-s/Vincentini-a — 5.00
2-17-($3.99) 2-Scorpion app. 6,7-Carnage Reigns parts 2 & 7. 8,9-Hobgoblin app. 10-12-Blade app. 13-16-Gang War tie-in — 4.00

MILES MORALES: ULTIMATE SPIDER-MAN
Marvel Comics: Jul, 2014 - No. 12, Jun, 2015 ($3.99)
1-Bendis-s/Marquez-a; Peter Parker & Norman Osborn return — 4 8 12 23 37 50
2-11: 11-Dr. Doom app. — 6.00
12-Doctor Doom and the Ultimates app.; leads into Secret Wars #1 — 1 2 3 5 6 8

MILES TO GO
AfterShock Comics: Sept, 2020 - No. 5, Sept, 2021 ($3.99)
1-5-B. Clay Moore-s/Stephen Molnar-a — 4.00

MILESTONE FOREVER
DC Comics: Apr, 2010 - No. 2, May, 2010 ($5.99, squarebound, limited series)
1-McDuffie-s/Leon & Bright-a; Icon, Blood Syndicate, Hardware and Static app. — 2 4 6 9 12 15
2-McDuffie-s/Leon & Bright-a — 6.00

MILESTONE RETURNS: INFINITE EDITION
DC Comics: No. 0, Jul, 2021 ($4.99, one-shot)
0-Hudlin-s/Cowan & ChrisCross-a; Cowan-c — 5.00

MILESTONES IN HISTORY
DC Comics: Aug, 2022 ($9.99, one-shot)
1-Short stories highlighting black achievements in history; s/a by various — 10.00

MILESTONE 30TH ANNIVERSARY SPECIAL
DC Comics: May, 2023 ($9.99, one-shot)
1-Short stories by various; Static, Blood Syndicate, Icon, Batman Beyond; Cowan-c — 10.00

MILITARY COMICS (Becomes Modern Comics #44 on)
Quality Comics Group: Aug, 1941 - No. 43, Oct, 1945
1-Origin/1st app. Blackhawk (Eisner scripts); Miss America, The Death Patrol by Jack Cole (also #2-7,27-30), & The Blue Tracer by Guardineer; X of the Underground, The Yankee Eagle, Q-Boat & Shot & Shell, Archie Atkins, Loops & Banks by Bud Ernest (Bob Powell)(ends #13) begin — 541 1082 1623 3950 6975 10,000
2-Secret War News begins (by McWilliams #2-16); Cole-a; new uniform with yellow circle & hawk's head for Blackhawk — 168 336 504 1075 1838 2600
3-Origin/1st app. Chop Chop (9/41) — 135 270 405 864 1482 2100
4 — 110 220 330 704 1202 1700
5-The Sniper begins; Miss America in costume #4-7 — 103 206 309 659 1130 1600
6-9: 8-X of the Underground begins (ends #13). 9-The Phantom Clipper begins (ends #16) — 77 154 231 493 847 1200
10-Classic Eisner-c — 110 220 330 704 1202 1700
11-Flag-c — 81 162 243 518 884 1250
12-Blackhawk by Crandall begins, ends #22 — 81 162 243 518 884 1250
13-15: 14-Private Dogtag begins (ends #83) — 61 122 183 390 670 950
16-20: 16-Blue Tracer ends. 17-P.T. Boat begins — 55 110 165 352 601 850

21-31: 22-Last Crandall Blackhawk. 23-Shrunken head-c. 27-Death Patrol revived. 28-True story of Mussolini — 50 100 150 315 533 750
32-43 — 43 86 129 271 461 650
NOTE: *Berg* a-6. *Al Bryant* c-31-34, 38, 40-43. *J. Cole* a-1-3, 27-32. *Crandall* a-12-22; c-13-20. *Cuidera* c-2-9. *Eisner* c-1, 2(part), 9, 10. *Kotsky* c-21-29, 35, 37, 39. *McWilliams* a-2-16. *Powell* a-1-13. *Ward* Blackhawk-30, 31(15 pgs. each); c-30.

MILK AND CHEESE (Also see Cerebus Bi-Weekly #20)
Slave Labor: 1991 - No. 7, Jan, 1997 ($2.50, B&W)
1-Evan Dorkin story & art in all — 5 10 15 35 63 90
1-2nd-6th printings — 5.00
2-"Other #1" — 3 6 9 16 24 32
2-reprint — 3.00
3-"Third #1" — 2 4 6 11 16 20
4-"Fourth #1", 5-"First Second Issue" — 1 3 4 6 8 10
6,7: 6-"#666" — 5.00
NOTE: *Multiple printings of all issues exist and are worth cover price unless listed here.*

MILKMAN MURDERS, THE
Dark Horse Comics: Jun, 2004 - No. 4, Aug, 2004 ($2.99, limited series)
1-4-Casey-s/Parkhouse-a — 3.00

MILLARWORLD (Mark Millar characters)
Image Comics: Jul, 2016; Sept, 2017 ($2.99)
...Annual 2016 1 (7/16) Short stories of Kick-Ass, Hit-Girl, Chrononauts and others — 3.00
...Annual 2017 1 (9/17) Short stories of Kick-Ass, Superior, Huck, Nemesis and others — 3.00

MILLENNIUM
DC Comics: Jan, 1988 - No. 8, Feb, 1988 (Weekly limited series)
1-Englehart-s/Staton c/a(p) — 5.00
2-8 — 4.00
TPB (2008, $19.99) r/#1-8 — 20.00

MILLENNIUM (TV, spin-off from The X-Files)
IDW Publishing: Jan, 2015 - No. 5, May, 2015 ($3.99, limited series)
1-5: 1-Frank Black & Agent Mulder app.; Joe Harris-s/Colin Lorimer-a; three covers — 4.00

MILLENNIUM EDITION:... (Reprints of classic DC issues, plus some WildStorm and non-DC issues with characters now published by DC)
DC Comics: Feb, 2000 - Feb, 2001 (gold foil cover stamps)
Action Comics #1, Adventure Comics #61, All Star Comics #3, All Star Comics #8, Batman #1, Detective Comics #1, Detective Comics #27, Detective Comics #38, Flash Comics #1, Military Comics #1, More Fun Comics #73, Police Comics #1, Sensation Comics #1, Superman #1, Whiz Comics #2, Wonder Woman #1 -($3.95-c) — 5.00
Action Comics #252, Adventure Comics #247, Brave and the Bold #28, Brave and the Bold #85, Crisis on Infinite Earths #1, Detective #225, Detective #327, Detective #359, Detective #395, Flash #123, Gen13 #1, Green Lantern #76, House of Mystery #1, House of Secrets #92, JLA #1, Justice League #1, Mad #1, Man of Steel #1, Mysterious Suspense #1, New Gods, #1, New Teen Titans #1, Our Army at War #81, Plop! #1, Saga of the Swamp Thing #21, Shadow #1, Showcase #4, Showcase #9, Showcase #22, Showcase #233, Superman (2nd) #75, Superman's Pal Jimmy Olsen #1, Watchmen #1, WildC.A.T.s #1, Wonder Woman #1, World's Finest #1 -($2.50-c) — 4.00
All-Star Western #10, Hellblazer #1, More Fun Comics #101, Preacher #1, Sandman #1, Spirit #1, Superboy #1, Superman #76, Young Romance #1-($2.95-c) — 4.00
Batman: The Dark Knight Returns #1, Kingdom Come #1 -($5.95-c) — 6.00
All Star Comics #3, Batman #1, Justice League #1: Chromium cover — 12.00
Crisis on Infinite Earths #1 Chromium cover — 20.00

MILLENNIUM FEVER
DC Comics (Vertigo): Oct, 1995 - No.4, Jan, 1996 ($2.50, limited series)
1-4: Duncan Fegredo-c/a — 4.00

MILLENNIUM: THE GIRL WHO DANCED WITH DEATH
Titan Comics: Sept, 2018 - No. 3, Nov, 2018 ($5.99, limited series)
1-3-Adaptation of the Stieg Larsson novel; Runberg-s/Ortega-a — 6.00

MILLENNIUM: THE GIRL WHO KICKED THE HORNET'S NEST
Titan Comics: Jan, 2018 - No. 2, Feb, 2018 ($5.99, limited series)
1,2-Adaptation of the Stieg Larsson novel; Runberg-s. 1-Homs-a. 2-Carot-a — 6.00

MILLENNIUM: THE GIRL WHO PLAYED WITH FIRE
Titan Comics: Oct, 2017 - No. 2, Nov, 2017 ($5.99, limited series)
1,2-Adaptation of the Stieg Larsson novel; Runberg-s. 1-Gonzalez-a. 2-Carot-a — 6.00

MILLENNIUM: THE GIRL WITH THE DRAGON TATTOO
Titan Comics: Jul, 2017 - No. 2, Aug, 2017 ($5.99, limited series)
1,2-Adaptation of the Stieg Larsson novel; Runberg-s/Homs-a — 6.00

MILLENNIUM 2.5 A.D.
ACG Comics: No. 1, 2000 ($2.95)

	GD 2.0	VG 4.0	FN 6.0	VF 8.0	VF/NM 9.0	NM- 9.2

1-Reprints 1934 Buck Rogers daily strips #1-48 — 3.00

MILLIE, THE LOVABLE MONSTER
Dell Publishing Co.: Sept-Nov, 1962 - No. 6, Jan, 1973

	GD	VG	FN	VF	VF/NM	NM-
12-523-211-Bill Woggon c/a in all	5	10	15	33	57	80
2(8-10/63)	4	8	12	28	47	65
3(8-10/64)	4	8	12	25	40	55
4(7/72), 5(10/72), 6(1/73)	3	6	9	14	19	24

NOTE: *Woggon a-3-6; c-3-6. 4 reprints 1; 5 reprints 2; 6 reprints 3.*

MILLIE THE MODEL (See Comedy Comics, A Date With…, Joker Comics #28, Life With…, Mad About…, Marvel Mini-Books, Misty & Modeling With…)
Marvel/Atlas/Marvel Comics(CnPC #1)(SPI/Male/VPI):1945 - No. 207, Dec, 1973

	GD	VG	FN	VF	VF/NM	NM-
1-Origin	394	788	1182	2758	4829	6900
2 (10/46)-Millie becomes The Blonde Phantom to sell Blonde Phantom perfume; a pre-Blonde Phantom app. (see All-Select #11, Fall, 1946)	194	388	582	1242	2121	3000
3-8,10: 4-7-Willie app. 7-Willie smokes extra strong tobacco. 8,10-Kurtzman's "Hey Look".						
8-Willie & Rusty app.	63	126	189	463	689	975
9-Powerhouse Pepper by Wolverton, 4 pgs.	90	180	270	576	988	1400
11-Kurtzman-a, "Giggles 'n' Grins"	47	94	141	296	498	700
12,15,17,19,20: 12-Rusty & Hedy Devine app.	43	86	129	271	461	650
13,14,16,18: 13,14,16-Kurtzman's "Hey Look". 13-Hedy Devine app. 18-Dan DeCarlo-a begins	.37	74	111	222	361	500
21-30	34	68	102	204	332	460
31-40	19	38	57	131	291	450
41-60: 47-Millie's 3-D poses	18	36	54	122	271	420
61-80	16	32	48	111	246	380
81-99: 93-Last DeCarlo issue?	12	24	36	83	182	280
100	14	28	42	96	211	325
101-106,108-130	8	16	24	51	105	155
107-Jack Kirby app. in story	9	18	27	58	114	170
131-134,136,138-153: 141-Groovy Gears-c/s	6	12	18	38	69	100
135-(2/66) 1st app. Groovy Gears	8	16	24	51	96	140
137-2nd app. Groovy Gears	6	12	18	41	76	110
154-New Millie begins (10/67)	8	16	24	52	99	145
155-190	6	12	18	37	66	95
191,193-199,201-206	5	10	15	34	60	85
192-(52 pgs.)	6	12	18	37	66	95
200,207(Last issue)	6	12	18	37	66	95

(Beware: cut-up pages are common in all Annuals)

	GD	VG	FN	VF	VF/NM	NM-
Annual 1(1962)-Early Marvel annual (2nd?)	46	92	138	340	770	1200
Annual 2(1963)	22	44	66	154	340	525
Annual 3-5 (1964-1966)	10	20	30	64	132	200
Annual 6-10(1967-11/71)	8	16	24	54	102	150
Queen-Size 11(9/74), 12(1975)	7	14	21	48	89	130

NOTE: *Dan DeCarlo a-18-93.*

MILLION DOLLAR DIGEST (Richie Rich… #23 on; also see Richie Rich…)
Harvey Publications: 11/86 - No. 7, 11/87; No. 8, 4/88 - No. 34, Nov, 1994 ($1.25/$1.75, digest size)

	GD	VG	FN	VF	VF/NM	NM-
1	1	2	3	5	6	8
2-8: 8-(68 pgs.)						6.00
9-20: 9-Begin $1.75-c. 14-May not exist	1	2	3	4	5	7
21-34	1	3	4	6	8	10

MILT GROSS FUNNIES (Also see Picture News #1)
Milt Gross, Inc. (ACG?): Aug, 1947 - No. 2, Sept, 1947

	GD	VG	FN	VF	VF/NM	NM-
1	34	68	102	199	325	450
2	22	44	66	128	209	290

MILTON THE MONSTER & FEARLESS FLY (TV)
Gold Key: May, 1966

	GD	VG	FN	VF	VF/NM	NM-
1 (10175-605)	9	18	27	60	120	180

MINDFIELD
Aspen MLT: No. 0, May, 2010 - No. 6, Sept, 2011 ($2.50/$2.99)

0-($2.50) Krul-s/Konat-a; 3 covers — 3.00
1-6-($2.99) Multiples covers on each — 3.00

MIND MGMT
Dark Horse Comics: May, 2012 - No. 35, Jul, 2015 ($3.99)

1-Matt Kindt-s/a/c — 30.00
2-6 — 10.00
7-35 — 4.00
#0 (11/12, $2.99) Prints background stories from Mind MGMT Secret Files digital site — 3.00
New MGMT#1/Mind Mgmt #36 (8/15, $3.99) Series conclusion — 4.00

MIND MGMT: BOOTLEG
Dark Horse Comics: Jul, 2022 - No. 4, Oct, 2022 ($3.99)

1-4-Matt Kindt-s. 1-Dalrymple-a. 2-Lesniewski-a. 3-Dave Rubin-a. 4-Jill Thompson-a — 4.00

MIND THE GAP
Image Comics: May, 2012 - No. 17, May, 2014 ($2.99)

1-17: 1-8,10-McCann-s/Esquejo-a/c. 9-McDaid-a. 11,12-Basri-a — 3.00

MINIMUM CARNAGE
Marvel Comics: Dec, 2012 - Jan, 2013 ($3.99, limited series)

…: Alpha (12/12) Venom, Carnage and Scarlet Spider app.; Medina-a/Crain-a — 4.00
…: Omega (1/13) The Enigma Force in the Microverse app. — 4.00

MINIMUM WAGE
Fantagraphics Books: V1#1, July, 1995 ($9.95, B&W, graphic novel, mature)
V2#1, 1995 - 1997 ($2.95, B&W, mature)

	GD	VG	FN	VF	VF/NM	NM-
V1#1-Bob Fingerman story & art	1	3	4	6	8	10
V2#1-9($2.95): Bob Fingerman story & art. 2-Kevin Nowlan back-c. 4-w/pin-ups. 5-Mignola back-c						4.00
Book Two TPB ('97, $12.95) r/V2#1-5						13.00

MINIMUM WAGE
Image Comics: Jan, 2014 - No. 6, Jun, 2014 ($3.50, B&W&Green, mature)

1-6-Bob Fingerman story & art; story resumes in May 2000 — 3.50

MINIMUM WAGE: SO MANY BAD DECISIONS
Image Comics: May, 2015 - No. 6, Oct, 2015 ($3.99, B&W&Green/color pages, mature)

1-6-Bob Fingerman story & art. 3-Marc Maron app. — 4.00

MINIONS (From Despicable Me movies)
Titan Comics: Jul, 2015 - No. 2, Aug, 2015 ($3.99, limited series)

1,2-Short stories and one-page gags; Ah-Koon-s/Collin-a — 4.00

MINIONS: MINI BOSS (From Despicable Me movies)
Titan Comics: May, 2022 - No. 2, Jun, 2022 ($3.99, limited series)

1,2-Minions and young Gru; short stories and one-page gags; Lapuss-s/Collin-a — 4.00

MINIONS PAELLA! (From Despicable Me movies)
Titan Comics: Nov, 2019 - No. 2, Dec, 2019 ($3.99, limited series)

1,2-Short stories and one-page gags; Lapuss-s/Collin-a — 4.00

MINIONS SPORTS! (From Despicable Me movies)
Titan Comics: Apr, 2020 - No. 2, May, 2021 ($3.99, limited series)

1,2-Short stories and one-page gags; Lapuss-s/Collin-a — 4.00

MINIONS VIVA LE BOSS! (From Despicable Me movies)
Titan Comics: Nov, 2018 - No. 2, Jan, 2018 ($3.99, limited series)

1,2-Short stories and one-page gags; Lapuss-s/Collin-a — 4.00

MINISTRY OF COMPLIANCE, THE
IDW Publishing: Nov, 2023 - Present ($5.99/$4.99, limited series)

1-($5.99) John Ridley-s/Stefano Raffaele-a — 6.00
2,3-($4.99) — 5.00

MINISTRY OF SPACE
Image Comics: Apr, 2001 - No. 3, Apr, 2004 ($2.95, limited series)

1-3-Warren Ellis-s/Chris Weston-a — 3.00
…Vol. 1 Omnibus (3/04, $4.95) r/1&2 — 5.00
TPB (12/04, $12.95) r/series; sketch & design pages; intro by Mark Millar — 13.00

MINKY WOODCOCK: THE GIRL WHO ELECTRIFIED TESLA
Titan Comics: May, 2021 - No. 4, Aug, 2021 ($3.99, limited series)

1-4-Cynthia Von Buhler-s/a; multiple covers on each — 4.00

MINKY WOODCOCK: THE GIRL WHO HANDCUFFED HOUDINI
Titan Comics: Nov, 2017 - No. 4, May, 2018 ($3.99, limited series)

1-4-Cynthia Von Buhler-s/a. 1-Covers by Mack, McGinnis, Von Buhler & photo — 4.00

MINOR MIRACLES
DC Comics: 2000 ($12.95, B&W, squarebound)

nn-Will Eisner-s/a — 13.00

MINOR THREATS
Dark Horse Comics: Aug, 2022 - No. 4, Feb, 2023 ($4.99, limited series)

1-4-Patton Oswalt & Jordan Blum-s/Scott Hepburn-a — 5.00

MINUTE MAN (See Master Comics & Mighty Midget Comics)
Fawcett Publications: Summer, 1941 - No. 3, Spring, 1942 (68 pgs.)

	GD	VG	FN	VF	VF/NM	NM-
1	252	504	756	1613	2757	3900
2-Japanese invade NYC Statue of Liberty WWII-c	181	362	543	1158	1979	2800
3-Bondage & torture-c	155	310	465	992	1696	2400

MINX, THE
DC Comics (Vertigo): Oct, 1998 - No. 8, May, 1999 ($2.50, limited series)

1-8-Milligan-s/Phillips-c/a — 4.00

MIRACLE COMICS
Hillman Periodicals: Feb, 1940 - No. 4, Mar, 1941

	GD	VG	FN	VF	VF/NM	NM-
1-Sky Wizard Master of Space, Dash Dixon, Man of Might, Pinkie Parker, Dusty Doyle, The Kid Cop, K-7, Secret Agent, The Scorpion, & Blandu, Jungle Queen begin; Masked Angel only app. (all 1st app.)	371	742	1113	2600	4550	6500
2-Classic Sky Wizard-c	258	516	774	1651	2826	4000
3,4: 3-Devil-c; Bill Colt, the Ghost Rider begins. 4-The Veiled Prophet & Bullet Bob (by Burnley) app.	181	362	543	1158	1979	2800

MIRACLEMAN
Eclipse Comics: Aug, 1985 - No. 15, Nov, 1988; No. 16, Dec, 1989 - No. 24, Aug, 1993

	GD	VG	FN	VF	VF/NM	NM-
1-r/British Marvelman series; Alan Moore scripts in #1-16	3	6	9	19	30	40
1-Gold variant (edition of 400, same as regular comic, but signed by Alan Moore, came with signed & #'d gold certificate of authenticity)	38	76	114	285	641	1000
1-Blue variant (edition of 600, comic came with signed blue certificate of authenticity)	34	68	102	245	548	850
2-8,10: 8-Airboy preview. 6,9,10-Origin Miracleman. 10-Snyder-c	1	2	3	5	6	8
9-Shows graphic scenes of childbirth	2	4	6	8	10	12
11-14(5/87-4/88) Totleben-a	2	4	6	11	16	20
15-($1.75-c, low print) death of Kid Miracleman	7	14	21	44	82	120
16-Last Alan Moore-s; self $1.95-c (low print)	3	6	9	17	25	34
17-22: 17-"The Golden Age" begins, ends #22. Dave McKean-c begins, end #22; Neil Gaiman scripts in #17-24	2	4	6	11	16	20
23-"The Silver Age" begins; Barry W. Smith-c	3	6	9	19	30	40
24-Last issue; Smith-c	3	6	9	19	30	40
3-D #1 (12/85)	2	4	6	10	12	
3-D #1 Blue variant (edition of 99)	3	6	9	21	33	45
3-D #1 Gold variant (edition of 199)	3	6	9	16	23	30

NOTE: *Miracleman 3-D #1 (12/85) (2D edition) Interior is the same as the 3-D version except in non 3-D format. Indicia are for both versions of the book with only the non 3-D art distinguishing this book from the standard 3-D version. Standard 3-D edition has house ad mentioning the non 3-D edition. Two known copies exist, one in the Michigan State University Special Collection Department. (No known sales)*

Book One: A Dream of Flying (1988, $9.95, TPB) r/#1-5; Leach-c			25.00
Book One: A Dream of Flying-Hardcover (1988, $29.95) r/#1-5			70.00
Book Two: The Red King Syndrome (1990, $12.95, TPB) r/#6-10; Bolton-a			30.00
Book Two: The Red King Syndrome-Hardcover (1990, $30.95) r/#6-10			85.00
Book Three: Olympus (1990, $12.95, TPB) r/#11-16			130.00
Book Three: Olympus-Hardcover (1990, $30.95) r/#11-16			250.00

Mind Mgmt #23 © Matt Kindt

Miracleman (2016 series) #16 © MAR

Miss Fury Comics #8 © MAR

	GD	VG	FN	VF	VF/NM	NM-
	2.0	4.0	6.0	8.0	9.0	9.2

Book Four: The Golden Age (1992, $15.95, TPB) r/#17-22 — 30.00
Book Four: The Golden Age Hardcover (1992, $33.95) r/#17-22 — 50.00
Book Four: The Golden Age (1993, $12.99, TPB) new McKean-c — 15.00
NOTE: Eclipse archive copies exist for #4,5,8,17,23. Each has a small Miracleman image foil-stamped on the cover. Chaykin c-3. Gulacy c-7. McKean c-17-22. B. Smith c-23, 24. Starlin c-4. Totleben a-11-13; c-9, 11-13. Truman c-6.

MIRACLEMAN
Marvel Comics: Mar, 2014 - No. 16, May, 2015 ($5.99/$4.99)
1-($5.99) Remastered reprints of Miracleman #1 and stories from Warrior #1&2; interview with Mick Anglo; reprints of 1950s Marvelman stories; Quesada-c — 6.00
2-15: 2-($4.99) R/Warrior #3-5 and Kid Marvelman debut (1955) — 5.00
16-($5.99) End of Book Three; bonus pencil art and design sketches — 6.00
All-New Miracleman Annual 1 (2/15, $4.99) New stories; Morrison-s/Quesada-a and Milligan-s/Allred-a; bonus script and art pages — 5.00
...: Marvel Tales 1 (6/23, $9.99) Reprints #1-4; Alan Davis-c — 10.00

MIRACLEMAN
Marvel Comics: No. 0, Dec, 2022 ($5.99)
0-($5.99) Short stories by Gaiman/Buckingham, Stegman, Momoko, Aaron/Yu — 6.00

MIRACLEMAN: APOCRYPHA
Eclipse Comics: Nov, 1991 - No. 3, Feb, 1992 ($2.50, limited series)
1-3: 1-Stories by Neil Gaiman, Mark Buckingham, Alex Ross & others. 3-Stories by James Robinson, Kelley Jones, Matt Wagner, Neil Gaiman, Mark Buckingham & others

	1	2	3	4	5	7
TPB (12/92, $15.95) Buckingham-c						20.00

MIRACLEMAN BY GAIMAN & BUCKINGHAM (The Golden Age)
Marvel Comics: Nov, 2015 - No. 6, Mar, 2016 ($4.99)
1-6-Remastered reprints of Miracleman #17-22 with bonus script and art pages — 5.00

MIRACLEMAN BY GAIMAN & BUCKINGHAM: THE SILVER AGE
Marvel Comics: Dec, 2022 - Present ($4.99)
1-7: 1-Remastered Miracleman #23 with bonus script and art pages. 2-Remastered #24. 3-7-New continuation of story — 5.00

MIRACLEMAN FAMILY
Eclipse Comics: May, 1988 - No. 2, Sept, 1988 ($1.95, lim. series, Baxter paper)
1,2: 2-Gulacy-c — 5.00

MIRACLE OF THE WHITE STALLIONS, THE (See Movie Comics)

MIRROR'S EDGE (Based on the EA video game)
DC Comics (WildStorm): Dec, 2008 - No. 6, Jun, 2009 ($3.99, limited series)
1-6: 1-Origin of Faith; Rhianna Pratchett-s/Matthew Dow Smith-a — 4.00
TPB (2009, $19.99) r/#1-6 — 20.00

MIRROR'S EDGE: EXORDIUM (Based on the EA video game)
Dark Horse Comics: Sept, 2015 - No. 6, Feb, 2016 ($3.99, limited series)
1-6: 1-Emgård-s/Häggström-a & Sammelin-a — 4.00

MISADVENTURES OF ADAM WEST, THE
Bluewater Comics: Jul, 2011 - Feb, 2012 ($3.99)
1-4: 1-Two covers; co-created by Adam West — 4.00
Second series 1-3 (1/12 - No. 3, 2/12) — 4.00

MISADVENTURES OF MERLIN JONES, THE (See Movie Comics & Merlin Jones as the Monkey's Uncle under Movie Comics)

MISFIT CITY
BOOM! Studios (BOOM! Box): May, 2017 - No. 8, Dec, 2017 ($3.99)
1-8-Kirsten Smith & Kurt Lustgarten-s/Naomi Franquiz-a — 4.00

MISPLACED
Image Comics: May, 2003 - No. 4, Dec, 2004 ($2.95)
1-4: 1-Three covers by Blaylock, Green and Clugston-Major; Blaylock-s/a — 3.00
...@17 (12/04, $4.95) Nara from "Dead @17" app.; Blaylock-s/a — 5.00

MISS AMERICA COMICS (Miss America Magazine #2 on; also see Blonde Phantom & Marvel Mystery Comics)
Marvel Comics (20CC): 1944 (one-shot)

	GD	VG	FN	VF	VF/NM	NM-
1-2 pgs. pin-up	428	856	1284	3124	5512	7900

MISS AMERICA COMICS 70th ANNIVERARY SPECIAL
Marvel Comics: Aug, 2009 ($3.99, one-shot)
1-Eaglesham-c; new Miss America & Whizzer story; reps. from All Winners #9-11 — 5.00

MISS AMERICA MAGAZINE (Formerly Miss America; Miss America #51 on)
Miss America Publ. Corp./Marvel/Atlas (MAP): V1#2, Nov, 1944 - No. 93, Nov, 1958
V1#2-Photo-c of teenage girl in Miss America costume; Miss America, Patsy Walker (intro.) comic stories plus movie reviews & stories; intro. Buzz Baxter & Hedy Wolfe;

	GD	VG	FN	VF	VF/NM	NM-
	2.0	4.0	6.0	8.0	9.0	9.2
1 pg. origin Miss America	389	778	1167	2723	4762	6800
3-5-Miss America & Patsy Walker stories	129	258	387	826	1413	2000
6-Patsy Walker only	77	154	231	493	847	1200
V2#1(4/45)-6(9/45)-Patsy Walker continues	31	62	93	182	296	410
V3#1(10/45)-6(4/46)	25	50	75	150	245	340
V4#1(5/46),2,5(9/46)	21	42	63	122	199	275
V4#3(7/46)-Liz Taylor photo-c	57	114	171	362	619	875
V4#4 (8/46; 68 pgs.), V4#6 (10/46; 92 pgs.)	27	54	81	158	259	360
V5#1(11/46)-6(4/47), V6#1(5/47)-3(7/47)	19	38	57	111	176	240
V7#1(8/47)-23(#56, 6/49)	19	38	57	109	172	235
V7#24(#57, 7/49)-Kamen-a (becomes Best Western #58 on?)						
	19	38	57	111	176	240
V7#25(8/49), 27-44(3/52), VII,nn(5/52)	18	36	54	103	162	220
V7#26(9/49)-All comics	19	38	57	111	176	240
V1,nn(7/52)-V1,nn(1/53)(#46-49), V7#50(Spring '53), V1#51-V7?#54(7/53),						
55-93	17	34	51	98	154	210
NOTE: Photo-c #1, 4, V2#1, 4, 5, V3#5, V4#3, 4, 6, V7#15, 16, 24, 26, 34, 37, 38. Powell a-V7#31.

MISS BEVERLY HILLS OF HOLLYWOOD (See Adventures of Bob Hope)
National Periodical Publ.: Mar-Apr, 1949 - No. 9, July-Aug, 1950 (52 pgs.)

	GD	VG	FN	VF	VF/NM	NM-
1 (Meets Alan Ladd)	84	168	252	538	919	1300
2-William Holden photo on-c	55	110	165	352	601	850
3-5: 2-9-Part photo-c. 5-Bob Hope photo on-c	47	94	141	296	498	700
6,7,9: 6-Lucille Ball photo-c	41	82	123	256	428	600
8-Reagan photo on-c	48	96	144	302	514	725
NOTE: Beverly meets Alan Ladd in #1, Eve Arden #2, Betty Hutton #4, Bob Hope #5.

MISS CAIRO JONES
Croyden Publishers: 1945

	GD	VG	FN	VF	VF/NM	NM-
1-Bob Oksner daily newspaper-r (1st strip story); lingerie panels						
	45	90	135	284	480	675

MISS FURY
Adventure Comics: 1991 - No. 4, 1991 ($2.50, limited series)
1-4: 1-Origin; granddaughter of original Miss Fury — 5.00
1-Limited ed. ($4.95) — 6.00

MISS FURY
Dynamite Entertainment: 2013 - No. 11, 2014 ($3.99)
1-11: 1-Multiple covers on all; Herbert-a; origin — 4.00

MISS FURY (VOLUME 2)
Dynamite Entertainment: 2016 - No. 5, 2016 ($3.99, limited series)
1-5-Corinna Bechko-s/Jonathan Lau-a; covers by Lotay & Lau — 4.00

MISS FURY COMICS (Newspaper strip reprints)
Timely Comics (NPI 1/CmPI 2/MPC 3-8): Winter, 1942-43 - No. 8, Winter, 1946 (Published twice a year)

	GD	VG	FN	VF	VF/NM	NM-
1-Origin Miss Fury by Tarpe' Mills (68 pgs.) in costume w/paper dolls with cut-out costumes						
	649	1298	1947	4738	8369	12,000
2-(60 pgs.)-In costume w/paper dolls; hooded Nazi-c						
	337	674	1011	2359	4130	5900
3-(60 pgs.)-In costume w/paper dolls; Hitler-c	300	600	900	1950	3375	4800
4-(52 pgs.)-Classic Nazi WWII-c with giant swastika, Tojo, Mussolini & Hitler photo on wall; in costume, 2 pgs. w/paper dolls						
	245	490	735	1568	2684	3800
5-(52 pgs.)-In costume w/paper dolls; Japanese WWII-c						
	200	400	600	1280	2190	3100
6-(52 pgs.)-Not in costume in inside stories, w/paper dolls						
	161	322	483	1030	1765	2500
7,8-(36 pgs.)-In costume 1 pg. each; no paper dolls	129	258	387	826	1413	2000
NOTE: Schomburg c-1, 5, 6.

MISS FURY DIGITAL FIRST
Dynamite Entertainment: 2013 - No. 2, 2013 ($3.99, limited series)
1,2-Prints online stories. 1-Reis, Desjardins, Casas-a. 2-Casas-a — 4.00

MISSION IMPOSSIBLE (TV) (Also see Wild!)
Dell Publ. Co.: May, 1967 - No. 4, Oct, 1968; No. 5, Oct, 1969 (All have photo-c)

	GD	VG	FN	VF	VF/NM	NM-
1	9	18	27	61	123	185
2-5: 5-Reprints #1	5	10	15	35	63	90

MISSION IMPOSSIBLE (Movie) (1st Paramount Comics book)
Marvel Comics (Paramount Comics): May, 1996 ($2.95, one-shot)
1-Liefeld-c & back-up story — 4.00

MISS LIBERTY (Becomes Liberty Comics)
Burten Publishing Co.: 1945 (MLJ reprints)

	GD	VG	FN	VF	VF/NM	NM-
1-The Shield & Dusty, The Wizard, & Roy, the Super Boy app.; r/Shield-Wizard #13						
	47	94	141	296	498	700

	GD 2.0	VG 4.0	FN 6.0	VF 8.0	VF/NM 9.0	NM- 9.2

MISS MELODY LANE OF BROADWAY (See The Adventures of Bob Hope)
National Periodical Publ.: Feb-Mar, 1950 - No. 3, June-July, 1950 (52 pgs.)

	GD	VG	FN	VF	VF/NM	NM-
1-Movie stars photos app. on all-c.	100	200	300	635	1093	1550
2,3: 3-Ed Sullivan photo on-c.	48	96	144	302	514	725

MISS PEACH
Dell Publishing Co.: Oct-Dec, 1963; 1969

1-Jack Mendelsohn-s/script	7	14	21	44	82	120
…Tells You How to Grow (1969; 25¢)-Mel Lazarus-a; also given away (36 pgs.)	5	10	15	30	50	70

MISS PEPPER (See Meet Miss Pepper)

MISS SUNBEAM (See Little Miss…)

MISS TRUESDALE AND THE FALL OF HYPERBOREA (From the world of Hellboy)
Dark Horse Comics: May, 2023 - No. 4, Aug, 2023 ($3.99)

1-4-Mike Mignola-s/Jesse Lonergan-a						4.00

MISS VICTORY (See Captain Fearless #1,2, Holyoke One-Shot #3, Veri Best Sure Fire & Veri Best Sure Shot Comics)

MR. & MRS. BEANS
United Features Syndicate: No. 11, 1939

Single Series 11	40	80	120	246	411	575

MR. & MRS. J. EVIL SCIENTIST (TV)(See The Flintstones & Hanna-Barbera Band Wagon #3)
Gold Key: Nov, 1963 - No. 4, Sept, 1966 (Hanna-Barbera, all 12¢)

1	8	16	24	52	99	145
2-4	4	8	12	25	40	55

MR. AND MRS. X (Gambit and Rogue)
Marvel Comics: Sept, 2018 - No. 12, Aug, 2019 ($3.99)

1-12: 1-Thompson-s/Bazaldua-a; the wedding. 2,3-Deadpool app. 4-Starjammers app.						4.00

MR. ANTHONY'S LOVE CLINIC (Based on radio show)
Hillman Periodicals: Nov, 1949 - No. 5, Apr-May, 1950 (52 pgs.)

1-Photo-c on all	30	60	90	177	289	400
2	19	36	54	105	165	225
3-5	15	30	45	85	130	175

MISTER BLANK
Amaze Ink: No. 0, Jan, 1996 - No. 14, May, 2000 ($1.75/$2.95, B&W)

0-($1.75, 16 pgs.) Origin of Mr. Blank						4.00
1-14-($2.95) Chris Hicks-s/a						4.00

MR. DISTRICT ATTORNEY (Radio/TV)
National Per. Publ.: Jan-Feb, 1948 - No. 67, Jan-Feb, 1959 (1-23: 52 pgs.)

1-Howard Purcell c-5-23 (most)	135	270	405	864	1482	2100
2	48	96	144	302	514	725
3-5	34	68	102	204	332	460
6-10: 8-Rise & fall of Lucky Lynn	27	54	81	162	266	370
11-20	20	40	60	118	192	265
21-43: 43-Lcast pre-code (1-2/55)	15	30	45	88	137	185
44-67: 55-UFO story	14	28	42	81	118	155

MR. DISTRICT ATTORNEY (See The Funnies #35)
Dell Publishing Co.: No. 13, 1942

Four Color 13-See The Funnies #35 for 1st app.	38	76	114	281	628	975

MISTER E (Also see Books of Magic limited series)
DC Comics: Jun, 1991- No. 4, Sept, 1991($1.75, limited series)

1-4-Snyder III-c/a; follow-up to Books of Magic limited series						4.00

MISTER ED, THE TALKING HORSE (TV)
Dell Publishing Co./Gold Key: Mar-May, 1962 - No. 6, Feb, 1964 (All photo-c; photo back-c: 1-6)

Four Color 1295	15	30	45	100	220	340
1(11/62) (Gold Key)-Photo-c	10	20	30	66	138	210
2-6: Photo-c	5	10	15	35	63	90

(See March of Comics #244, 260, 282, 290)

MR. GUM (From The Atomics)
Oni Press: April, 2003 ($2.99, one-shot)

1-Mike Allred-s/J. Bone-a; Madman & The Atomics app.						3.00

MR. HERO, THE NEWMATIC MAN (See Neil Gaiman's…)

MR. MAGOO (TV) (The Nearsighted…, …& Gerald McBoing Boing 1954 issues; formerly Gerald McBoing-Boing and …)
Dell Publishing Co.: No. 6, Nov-Jan, 1953-54; 5/54 - 3-5/62; 9-11/63 - 3-5/65

6	9	18	27	62	126	190
Four Color 561(5/54),602(11/54)	9	18	27	62	126	190
Four Color 1235(#1, 12-2/62),1305(#2, 3-5/62)	7	14	21	48	89	130
3(9-11/63) - 5	6	12	18	42	79	115
Four Color 1235(12-536-505)(3-5/65)-2nd Printing	5	10	15	35	63	90

MR. MAJESTIC (See WildC.A.T.S.)
DC Comics (WildStorm): Sept, 1999 - No. 9, May, 2000 ($2.50)

1-9: 1-McGuinness-a/Casey & Holguin-s. 2-Two covers						4.00
TPB (2002, $14.95) r/#1-6 & Wildstorm Spotlight #1						15.00

MISTER MIRACLE (1st series) (See Cancelled Comic Cavalcade)
National Periodical Publications/DC Comics: 3-4/71 - V4#18, 2-3/74; V5#19, 9/77 - V6#25, 8-9/78; 1987 (Fourth World)

1-1st app. Mr. Miracle (#1-3 are 15¢)	16	32	48	111	246	380
2,3: 2-Intro. Granny Goodness. 3-Last 15¢ issue	6	12	18	37	66	95
4-Intro. Barda; Boy Commandos-r begin; (52 pgs.)	15	30	45	103	227	350
5-8: All 15¢	5	10	15	33	57	80
9-18: 9-Origin Mr. Miracle; Darkseid cameo. 15-Intro/1st app. Shilo Norman. 18-Barda & Scott Free wed; New Gods app. & Darkseid cameo; Last Kirby issue.	3	6	9	17	26	35
19-25 (1977-78)	2	4	6	8	11	14
Special 1(1987, $1.25, 52 pgs.)	1	3	4	6	8	10

Jack Kirby's Fourth World TPB ('01, $12.95) B&W&Grey-toned reprint of #11-18; Mark Evanier intro. ... 13.00

Jack Kirby's Mister Miracle TPB ('98, $12.95) B&W&Grey-toned reprint of #1-10; David Copperfield intro. ... 13.00

NOTE: *Austin* a-19i. *Ditko* a-6r. *Golden* a-23-25p; c-25p. *Heath* a-24i, 25i; c-25i. *Kirby* a(p)/c-1-18. *Nasser* a-19i. *Rogers* a-19-22p; c-19, 20p, 21p, 22-24. 4-8 contain *Simon & Kirby* Boy Commandos reprints from Detective 82,76, Boy Commandos 1, 3 & Detective 64 in that order.

MISTER MIRACLE (2nd Series) (See Justice League)
DC Comics: Jan, 1989 - No. 28, June, 1991 ($1.00/$1.25)

1-28: 13,14-Lobo app. 22-1st new Mr. Miracle w/new costume						4.00

MISTER MIRACLE (3rd Series)
DC Comics: Apr, 1996 - No. 7, Oct, 1996 ($1.95)

1-7: 2-Vs. JLA. 6-Simonson-c						4.00

MISTER MIRACLE (4th Series)
DC Comics: Oct, 2017 - No. 12, Jan, 2019 ($3.99, limited series)

1-Tom King-s/Mitch Gerads-a; covers by Derington & Gerads						15.00
1-Director's Cut (4/18, $5.99) r/#1 B&W art; bonus script						
	1	2	3	5	6	8
2-12-King-s/Gerads-a. 7-Jacob born						5.00

MR. MIRACLE (See Capt. Fearless #1 & Holyoke One-Shot #4)

MISTER MIRACLE: THE SOURCE OF FREEDOM
DC Comics: Jul, 2021 - No. 6, Jan, 2022 ($3.99, limited series)

1-6-Shilo Norman as Mister Miracle; Easton-s/Ossio-a. 1-Intro N'Vir Free. 6-Orion app.						4.00

MR. MONSTER (1st Series)(Doc Stearn… #7 on; See Airboy-Mr. Monster Special, Dark Horse Presents, Super Duper Comics & Vanguard Illustrated #7)
Eclipse Comics: Jan, 1985 - No. 10, June, 1987 ($1.75, Baxter paper)

1,3: 1-1st story-r from Vanguard III. #7(1st app.). 3-Alan Moore scripts; Wolverton-r/Weird Mysteries #5.						5.00
2-Dave Stevens-a	2	4	6	8	11	14
4-10: 6-Ditko-r/Fantastic Fears #5 plus new Giffen-a. 10- "6-D" issue						4.00

MR. MONSTER
Dark Horse Comics: Feb, 1988 - No. 8, July, 1991 ($1.75, B&W)

1-7						4.00
8-($4.95, 60 pgs.)-Origins conclusion						5.00

MR. MONSTER ATTACKS! (Doc Stearn…)
Tundra Publ.: Aug, 1992 - No. 3, Oct, 1992 ($3.95, limited series, 32 pgs.)

1-3: Michael T. Gilbert-a/scripts; Gilbert/Dorman painted-c						4.00

MR. MONSTER PRESENTS (CRACK-A-BOOM!)
Caliber Comics: 1997 - No. 3, 1997 ($2.95, B&W&Red, limited series)

1-3: Michael T. Gilbert-a/scripts: 1-Wraparound-c						4.00

MR. MONSTER'S GAL FRIDAY…KELLY!
Image Comics: Jan, 2000 - No. 3, May, 2004 ($3.50, B&W)

1-3-Michael T. Gilbert-c; story & art by various. 3-Alan Moore-s						3.50

MR. MONSTER'S SUPER-DUPER SPECIAL
Eclipse Comics: May, 1986 - No. 8, June, 1987

1-(5/86)…3-D High Octane Horror #1						5.00
1-(5/86)…2-D version, 100 copies	2	4	6	11	16	20
2-(8/86)…High Octane Horror #3, 3-(9/86)…True Crime #1, 4-(11/86)…True Crime #2, 5-(1/87)…Hi-Voltage Super Science #1, 6-(3/87)…High Shock Schlock #1, 7-(5/87)…High Shock Schlock #2, 8-(7/87)…Weird Tales Of The Future #1						4.00

NOTE: *Jack Cole* r-3, 4. *Evans* a-2r. *Kubert* a-1r. *Powell* a-5r. *Wolverton* a-2r, 7r, 8r.

MR. MONSTER VS. GORZILLA
Image Comics: July, 1998 ($2.95, one-shot)

1-Michael T. Gilbert-a						4.00

MR. MONSTER: WORLDS WAR TWO
Atomeka Press: 2004 ($6.99, one-shot)

nn-Michael T. Gilbert-s/George Freeman-a; two covers by Horley & Dorman						7.00

MR. MUSCLES (Formerly Blue Beetle #18-21)
Charlton Comics: No. 22, Mar, 1956; No. 23, Aug, 1956

22,23	14	28	42	80	115	150

MR. MXYZPTLK (VILLAINS)
DC Comics: Feb, 1998 ($1.95, one-shot)

1-Grant-s/Morgan-a/Pearson-c						4.00

MISTER MYSTERY (Tales of Horror and Suspense)
Mr. Publ. (Media Publ.) No. 1-3/SPM Publ./Stanmore (Aragon): Sept, 1951 - No. 19, Oct, 1954

1-Kurtzman-*esque* horror story	277	554	831	1759	3030	4300
2,3-Kurtzman-*esque* story. 3-Anti-Wertham edit.	97	194	291	621	1061	1500
4-Bondage-c	148	296	444	947	1624	2300
5,8,10	93	186	279	591	1021	1450
6-Classic torture-c	423	846	1269	3088	5444	7800
7- "The Brain Bats of Venus" by Wolverton; partially re-used in Weird Tales of the Future #7	423	846	1269	3000	5250	7500
9-Nostrand-a	142	284	426	909	1555	2200
11-(5-6/53) Wolverton "Robot Woman" story/Weird Mysteries #2, cut up, rewritten, retitled "Beauty & the Beast"" & partially redrawn; girl in "Beauty & the Beast", splash pg. redrawn from cover of Weird Tales of the Future #4 (11/52); woman on pg. 6 taken from cover of Weird Tales of the Future #.2 (6/52)	703	1406	2109	5132	9066	13,000
12-Classic injury to eye-c	1000	2000	3000	7600	13,800	20,000
13-16,19: 15- "Living Dead" junkie story. 16-Bondage-c. 19-Reprints	77	154	231	493	847	1200
17-Severed heads-c	155	310	465	992	1696	2400
18- "Robot Woman" by Wolverton reprinted from Weird Mysteries #2; decapitation, bondage-c	232	464	696	1485	2543	3600

NOTE: *Andru* a-1, 2p, 3p. *Andru/Esposito* c-1-3. *Baily* c-10-18(most). *Mortellaro* c-5-7. Bondage c-7, 16. Some issues have graphic dismemberment scenes.

MR. PEABODY AND SHERMAN (Based on the 2014 Dreamworks movie)
IDW Publishing: Nov, 2013 - No. 4, Jan, 2014 ($3.99)

Mister Miracle #11 © DC

Mockingbird #1 © MAR

Modern Comics #45 © QUA

	GD	VG	FN	VF	VF/NM	NM-
	2.0	4.0	6.0	8.0	9.0	9.2

1-4: 1-Fisch-s/Monlongo-a; 3 covers. 2-Three covers. 3,4-Two covers 4.00

MR. PUNCH
DC Comics (Vertigo): 1994 ($24.95, one-shot)
nn (Hard-c)-Gaiman scripts; McKean-c/a 40.00
nn (Soft-c) 18.00

MISTER Q (See Mighty Midget Comics & Our Flag Comics #5)

MR. RISK (Formerly All Romances; Men Against Crime #3 on)(Also see Our Flag Comics & Super-Mystery Comics)
Ace Magazines: No. 7, Oct, 1950; No. 2, Dec, 1950
7,2 | 21 | 42 | 63 | 122 | 199 | 275

MR. SCARLET & PINKY (See Mighty Midget Comics)

MR. T
APComics: May, 2005 ($3.50)
1-Chris Bunting-s/Neil Edwards-a 3.50

MR. T AND THE T-FORCE
Now Comics: June, 1993 - No. 10, May, 1994 ($1.95, color)
1-10-Newsstand editions: 1-7-polybagged with photo trading card in each.
1,2-Neal Adams-c/a(p). 3-Dave Dorman painted-c 5.00
1-10-Direct Sale editions polybagged w/line drawn trading cards. 1-Contains gold foil trading card by Neal Adams 6.00

MISTER TERRIFIC (DC New 52)(Leads into Earth 2 series)
DC Comics: Nov, 2011 - No. 8, Jun, 2012 ($2.99)
1-8: 1-Wallace-s/Gugliotta-a/JG Jones-c; origin re-told. 2-Intro. Brainstorm 3.00

MISTER UNIVERSE (Professional wrestler)
Mr. Publications Media Publ. (Stanmor, Aragon): July, 1951; No. 2, Oct, 1951 - No. 5, April, 1952
1 | 34 | 68 | 102 | 199 | 325 | 450
2- "Jungle That Time Forgot", (24 pg. story); Andru/Esposito-a
| 19 | 38 | 57 | 111 | 176 | 240
3-Marijuana story | 20 | 40 | 60 | 114 | 182 | 250
4,5-"Goes to War" cover/stories (Korean War) | 15 | 30 | 45 | 85 | 130 | 175

MISTER X (See Vortex)
Mr. Publications/Vortex Comics/Caliber V3#1 on: 6/84 - No. 14, 8/88 $1.50/$2.25, direct sales, coated paper);V2#1, Apr, 1989 - V2#12, Mar, 1990 ($2.00/$2.50, B&W, newsprint) V3#1, 1996 - No. 4, 1996 ($2.95, B&W)
1-14: 11-Dave McKean story & art (6 pgs.) 4.00
V2 #1-12: 1-11 (Second Coming, B&W): 1-Four diff.-c. 10-Photo-c 4.00
V3 #1-4 4.00
Return of... ($11.95, graphic novel)-r/V1#1-4 12.00
Return of... ($34.95, hardcover limited edition)-r/1-4 35.00
Special (no date, 1990?) 4.00

MISTER X
Dark Horse Comics: Mar, 2013 ($2.99, one-shot)
...: Hard Candy (3/13) Dean Motter-s/a 3.00

MISTER X: CONDEMNED
Dark Horse Comics: Dec, 2008 - No. 4, Mar, 2009 ($3.50, limited series)
1-4-Dean Motter-s/a 3.50

MISTER X: EVICTION
Dark Horse Comics: May, 2013 - No. 3, Jul, 2013 ($3.99, limited series)
1-3-Dean Motter-s/a 4.00

MISTER X: RAZED
Dark Horse Comics: Feb, 2015 - No. 4, May, 2015 ($3.99, limited series)
1-4-Dean Motter-s/a 4.00

MISTY
Marvel Comics (Star Comics): Dec, 1985 - No. 6, May, 1986 (Limited series)
1-6: Millie The Model's niece 4.00

MITZI COMICS (Becomes Mitzi's Boy Friend #2-7)(See All Teen)
Timely Comics: Spring, 1948 (one-shot)
1-Kurtzman's "Hey Look" plus 3 pgs. "Giggles 'n' Grins"
| 81 | 162 | 243 | 518 | 884 | 1250

MITZI'S BOY FRIEND (Formerly Mitzi Comics; becomes Mitzi's Romances)
Marvel Comics (TCI): No. 2, June, 1948 - No. 7, April, 1949
2 | 34 | 68 | 102 | 199 | 325 | 450
3-7 | 24 | 48 | 72 | 140 | 230 | 320

MITZI'S ROMANCES (Formerly Mitzi's Boy Friend)
Timely/Marvel Comics (TCI): No. 8, June, 1949 - No. 10, Dec, 1949

8-Becomes True Life Tales #8 (10/49) on? | 24 | 48 | 72 | 144 | 237 | 330
9,10: 10-Painted-c | 20 | 40 | 60 | 120 | 195 | 270

MNEMOVORE
DC Comics (Vertigo): Jun, 2005 - No. 6, Nov, 2005 ($2.99, limited series)
1-6-Rodionoff & Fawkes-s/Huddleston-a/c 3.00

MOBY DICK (See Feature Presentations #6, King Classics, and Classic Comics #5)
Dell Publishing Co.: No. 717, Aug, 1956
Four Color 717-Movie, Gregory Peck photo-c | 9 | 18 | 27 | 62 | 126 | 190

MOBY DUCK (See Donald Duck #112 & Walt Disney Showcase #2,11)
Gold Key (Disney): Oct, 1967 - No. 11, Oct, 1970; No. 12, Jan, 1974 - No. 30, Feb, 1978
1-Three Little Pigs app. | 4 | 8 | 12 | 25 | 40 | 55
2-5: 2-Beagle Boys app. 5-Captain Hook app. | 2 | 4 | 6 | 11 | 16 | 20
6-11: 6-Huey, Dewey & Louie app. | 2 | 4 | 6 | 9 | 13 | 16
12-30: 21,30-r | 1 | 3 | 4 | 6 | 8 | 10

MOCKINGBIRD (From S.H.I.E.L.D.)
Marvel Comics: May, 2016 - No. 8, Dec, 2016 ($3.99)
1-8: 1-4-Chelsea Cain-s/Kate Niemczyk-a/Joëlle Jones-c. 5-Moustafa-a. 6-Civil War II tie-in 4.00
... S.H.I.E.L.D. 50th Anniversary (11/15, $3.99) Joëlle Jones-a; back-up with Red Widow 4.00

MOCKING DEAD, THE
Dynamite Entertainment: 2013 - No. 5, 2014 ($3.99, B&W, limited series)
1-5: 1-Fred Van Lente/Max Dunbar-a 4.00

MODEL FUN (With Bobby Benson)
Harle Publications: No. 2, Fall, 1954 - No. 5, July, 1955
2-Bobby Benson | 8 | 16 | 24 | 42 | 54 | 65
3-5-Bobby Benson | 5 | 10 | 15 | 25 | 31 | 36

MODELING WITH MILLIE (Formerly Life With Millie)
Atlas/Marvel Comics (Male Publ.): No. 21, Feb, 1963 - No. 54, June, 1967
21 | 10 | 20 | 30 | 70 | 150 | 230
22-30 | 7 | 14 | 21 | 48 | 89 | 130
31-53 | 6 | 12 | 18 | 38 | 69 | 100
54-Last issue; Gears-c & 6 pg. story; Beatles swipe imitators; FF #63 comic appears in story; "Millie the Marvel" 6 pg. story as super-hero | 6 | 12 | 18 | 41 | 76 | 110

MODELS, INC.
Marvel Comics: Oct, 2009 - No. 4, Jan, 2010 ($3.99, limited series)
1-4-Millie the Model, Patsy Walker, Mary Jane Watson app.; Land-c. 1-Tim Gunn app. 4.00

MODERN COMICS (Formerly Military Comics #1-43)
Quality Comics Group: No. 44, Nov, 1945 - No. 102, Oct, 1950
44-Blackhawk continues | 60 | 120 | 180 | 381 | 653 | 925
45-52: 49-1st app. Fear, Lady Adventuress | 39 | 78 | 117 | 240 | 395 | 550
53-Torchy by Ward begins (9/46) | 50 | 100 | 150 | 315 | 533 | 750
54-60: 55-J. Cole-a | 36 | 72 | 108 | 211 | 343 | 475
61-Classic-c | 42 | 84 | 126 | 265 | 445 | 625
62-64,66-77,79,80: 73-J. Cole-a | 32 | 64 | 96 | 188 | 307 | 425
65-Classic Grim Reaper Skull-c | 71 | 142 | 213 | 454 | 777 | 1100
78-1st app. Madame Butterfly | 39 | 78 | 117 | 231 | 378 | 525
81-99,101: 82,83-One pg. J. Cole-a. 83-Last 52 pg. issue | 32 | 64 | 96 | 188 | 307 | 425
99-Blackhawks on the moon-c/story | 37 | 74 | 111 | 218 | 354 | 490
100 | 42 | 84 | 126 | 265 | 445 | 625
102-(Scarce)-J. Cole-a; Spirit by Eisner app.
NOTE: Al Bryant c-44-51, 54, 55, 66, 69. Jack Cole a-55, 73. Crandall Blackhawk-#46, 47, 50, 51, 54, 56, 58-60, 64, 67-70, 73, 74, 76-78, 80-83; c-60-65, 67, 68, 70-95. Crandall/Cuidera c-56-59, 96-102. Gustavson a-47, 49. Ward Blackhawk-#52, 53, 55 (15 pgs. each). Torchy in #53-102; by Ward only in #53-89(9/49); by Gil Fox #92, 93, 102.

MODERN FANTASY
Dark Horse Comics: Jun, 2018 - No. 4, Sept, 2018 ($3.99, limited series)
1-4-Rafer Roberts-s/Kristen Gudsnuk-a 4.00

MODERN LOVE
E. C. Comics: June-July, 1949 - No. 8, Aug-Sept, 1950
1-Feldstein, Ingels-a | 174 | 348 | 522 | 1114 | 1907 | 2700
2-Craig/Feldstein-c/s | 110 | 220 | 330 | 704 | 1202 | 1700
3 | 84 | 168 | 252 | 538 | 919 | 1300
4-6 (Scarce): 4-Bra/panties panels | 106 | 212 | 318 | 673 | 1162 | 1650
7 | 84 | 168 | 252 | 538 | 919 | 1300
8-Bill Gaines/Al Feldstein app. in comic industry parody sty. | 103 | 206 | 309 | 659 | 1130 | 1600
NOTE: Craig a-3. Feldstein a-in most issues; c-1, 2i, 3-8. Harrison a-4. Iger a-6-8. Ingels a-1, 2, 4-7. Palais a-5. Wood a-7. Wood/Harrison a-5-7. (Canadian reprints known; see Table of Contents.)

	GD 2.0	VG 4.0	FN 6.0	VF 8.0	VF/NM 9.0	NM- 9.2

MODERN WARFARE 2: GHOST (Based on the videogame)
DC Comics (WildStorm): Jan. 2010 - No. 6, Sept. 2010 ($3.99, limited series)

	GD	VG	FN	VF	VF/NM	NM-
1-6: 1-Two covers; Lapham-s/West-a						4.00
TPB (2010, $17.99) r/#1-6; cover sketches and sketch art						18.00

MOD LOVE
Western Publishing Co.: 1967 (50¢, 36 pgs.)

	GD	VG	FN	VF	VF/NM	NM-
1-(Low print)	10	20	30	67	141	215

MODNIKS, THE
Gold Key: Aug, 1967 - No. 2, Aug, 1970

	GD	VG	FN	VF	VF/NM	NM-
10206-708(#1)	4	8	12	23	37	50
2	3	6	9	15	22	28

M.O.D.O.K. ASSASSIN (Secret Wars tie-in)
Marvel Comics: Jul, 2015 - No. 5, Nov, 2015 ($3.99, limited series)

	GD	VG	FN	VF	VF/NM	NM-
1-5-Yost-s/Pinna-a; Angela app. 1-Bullseye, Baron Mordo & Clea app.						4.00

M.O.D.O.K.: HEAD GAMES
Marvel Comics: Feb, 2021 - No. 4, Jun, 2021 ($3.99, limited series)

	GD	VG	FN	VF	VF/NM	NM-
1-4-Blum & Oswalt-s/Hepburn-a; Monica Rappaccini app. 2-Tony Stark app. 3-Gwenpool app. 4-TV family cameos						4.00

M.O.D.O.K.: REIGN DELAY
Marvel Comics: Nov, 2009 ($3.99, one-shot)

	GD	VG	FN	VF	VF/NM	NM-
1-M.O.D.O.K. cartoony humor stories from Marvel Digital Comics; Ryan Dunlavey-s/a						4.00

MOD SQUAD (TV)
Dell Publishing Co.: Jan, 1969 - No. 3, Oct, 1969 - No. 8, April, 1971

	GD	VG	FN	VF	VF/NM	NM-
1-Photo-c	9	18	27	57	111	165
2-4: 2-4-Photo-c	4	8	12	28	47	65
5-8: 8-Photo-c; Reprints #2	4	8	12	23	37	50

MOD WHEELS
Gold Key: Mar, 1971 - No. 19, Jan, 1976

	GD	VG	FN	VF	VF/NM	NM-
1	4	8	12	25	40	55
2-9	3	6	9	16	23	30
10-19: 11,15-Extra 16 pgs. ads	3	6	9	14	19	24

MOE & SHMOE COMICS
O. S. Publ. Co.: Spring, 1948 - No. 2, Summer, 1948

	GD	VG	FN	VF	VF/NM	NM-
1	14	28	42	80	115	150
2	9	18	27	47	61	75

MOEBIUS (Graphic novel)
Marvel Comics (Epic Comics): Oct, 1987 - No. 6, 1988; No. 7, 1990; No. 8, 1991; No. 9, 1994 ($9.95, 8x11", mature)

	GD	VG	FN	VF	VF/NM	NM-
1	4	8	12	28	47	65
2	5	10	15	34	60	85
3-(1st & 2nd printings, $12.95)	7	14	21	46	86	125
4-6,8	4	8	12	23	37	50
7,0 (1990, $12.95)	4	8	12	28	47	65
9-(1994) Printed 3 years after #8	8	16	24	51	96	140
Moebius I-Signed & #'d hard-c ($45.95, Graphitti Designs, 1,500 copies printed)-r/#1-3	10	20	30	67	141	215

MOEBIUS COMICS
Caliber: May, 1996 - No. 6 ($2.95, B&W)

	GD	VG	FN	VF	VF/NM	NM-
1,5,6-Moebius-c/a on all; William Stout-a	3	6	9	15	22	28
2-4-Moebius-c/a	2	4	6	10	14	18

MOEBIUS: THE MAN FROM CIGURI
Dark Horse Comics: 1996 ($7.95, digest-size)

	GD	VG	FN	VF	VF/NM	NM-
nn-Moebius-c/a	4	8	12	25	40	55

MOLLY MANTON'S ROMANCES (Romantic Affairs #3)
Marvel Comics (SePI): Sept, 1949 - No. 2, Dec, 1949 (52 pgs.)

	GD	VG	FN	VF	VF/NM	NM-
1-Photo-c (becomes Blaze the Wonder Collie #2 (10/49) on? & Molly Manton's Romances #2	30	60	90	177	289	400
2-Titled "Romances of..."; photo-c	20	40	60	117	189	260

MOLLY O'DAY (Super Sleuth)
Avon Periodicals: February, 1945 (1st Avon comic)

	GD	VG	FN	VF	VF/NM	NM-
1-Molly O'Day, The Enchanted Dagger by Tuska (r/Yankee #1), Capt'n Courage, Corporal Grant app.	100	200	300	640	1095	1550

MOMENT OF SILENCE
Marvel Comics: Feb, 2002 ($3.50, one-shot)

	GD	VG	FN	VF	VF/NM	NM-
1-Tributes to the heroes and victims of Sept. 11; s/a by various						3.50

M.O.M. MOTHER OF MADNESS
Image Comics: Jul, 2021 - No. 3, Oct, 2021 ($5.99/$4.99, limited series)

	GD	VG	FN	VF	VF/NM	NM-
1-($5.99) Emilia Clarke & Marguerite Bennett-s/Leila Leiz-a						6.00
2,3-($4.99)						5.00

MONARCH
Image Comics: Feb, 2023 - No. 6, Sept, 2023 ($3.99)

	GD	VG	FN	VF	VF/NM	NM-
1-6-Rodney Barnes-s/Alex Lins-a						4.00

MONARCHY, THE (Also see The Authority and StormWatch)
DC Comics (WildStorm): Apr, 2001 - No. 12, May, 2002 ($2.50)

	GD	VG	FN	VF	VF/NM	NM-
1-12: 1-McCrea & Leach-a/Young-s						3.00
Bullets Over Babylon TPB (2001, $12.95) r/#1-4, Authority #21						13.00

MONICA RAMBEAU: PHOTON
Marvel Comics: Feb, 2023 - No. 5, Jun, 2023 ($3.99)

	GD	VG	FN	VF	VF/NM	NM-
1-5-Eve Ewing-s/Luca Maresca-a; Doctor Strange and Spider-Man app.						4.00

MONKEES, THE (TV)(Also see Circus Boy, Groovy, Not Brand Echh #3, Teen-Age Talk, Teen Beam & Teen Beat)
Dell Publishing Co.: March, 1967 - No. 17, Oct, 1969

	GD	VG	FN	VF	VF/NM	NM-
1-Photo-c	15	30	45	105	233	360
2-17: All photo-c. 17-Reprints #1	7	14	21	48	89	130

MONKEY AND THE BEAR, THE
Atlas Comics (ZPC): Sept, 1953 - No. 3, Jan, 1954

	GD	VG	FN	VF	VF/NM	NM-
1-Howie Post-c/a in all; funny animal	15	30	45	90	140	190
2,3	11	22	33	62	86	110

MONKEYMAN AND O'BRIEN (Also see Dark Horse Presents #80, 100-5, Gen13/..., Hellboy: Seed of Destruction, & San Diego Comic Con #2)
Dark Horse Comics (Legend): Jul, 1996 - No. 3, Sept, 1996 ($2.95, lim. series)

	GD	VG	FN	VF	VF/NM	NM-
1-3: New stories; Art Adams-c/a						4.00
nn-(2/96, $2.95)-r/back-up stories from Hellboy: Seed of Destruction; Adams-c/a/scripts						4.00

MONKEY PRINCE
DC Comics: Apr, 2022 - Present ($3.99)

	GD	VG	FN	VF	VF/NM	NM-
1-12-Gene Luen Yang-s/Bernard Chang-a. 1-4-Batman & Robin app. 7,8-Aquaman app. 9,10-Supergirl and the Ultra-Humanite app. 10,11-Lazarus Planet tie-ins						4.00

MONKEYSHINES COMICS
Ace Periodicals/Publishers Specialists/Current Books/Unity Publ.: Summer, 1944 - No. 27, July, 1949

	GD	VG	FN	VF	VF/NM	NM-
1-Funny animal	21	42	63	124	202	280
2-(Aut/44)	14	28	42	82	121	160
3-10: 3-(Win/44)	12	24	36	69	97	125
11-18,20-27: 23,24-Fago-c/a	10	20	30	56	76	95
19-Frazetta-a	13	26	39	74	105	155

MONKEY'S UNCLE, THE (See Merlin Jones As... under Movie Comics)

MONOLITH, THE
DC Comics: Apr, 2004 - No. 12, Mar, 2005 ($3.50/$2.95)

	GD	VG	FN	VF	VF/NM	NM-
1-($3.50) Palmiotti & Gray-s/Winslade-a						3.50
2-12-($2.95): 6-8-Batman app.; Coker-a						3.00
...: Volume One HC (Image Comics, 2012, $17.99) r/#1-4; intro. by Jim Steranko						18.00

MONROES, THE (TV)
Dell Publishing Co.: Apr, 1967

	GD	VG	FN	VF	VF/NM	NM-
1-Photo-c	3	6	9	17	26	35

MONSTER
Fiction House Magazines: 1953 - No. 2, 1953

	GD	VG	FN	VF	VF/NM	NM-
1-Dr. Drew by Grandenetti; reprint from Rangers Comics #48; Whitman-c	100	200	300	640	1095	1550
2-Whitman-c	84	168	252	538	919	1300

MONSTER CRIME COMICS (Also see Crime Must Stop)
Hillman Periodicals: Oct, 1952 (15¢, 52 pgs.)

	GD	VG	FN	VF	VF/NM	NM-
1 (Scarce)	290	580	870	1875	3178	4500

MONSTER HOUSE (Companion to the 2006 movie)
IDW Publishing: June, 2006 ($7.99, one-shot)

	GD	VG	FN	VF	VF/NM	NM-
nn-Two stories about Bones and Skull by Joshua Dysart and Simeon Wilkins						8.00

MONSTER HOWLS (Magazine)
Humor-Vision: December, 1966 (Satire) (35¢, 68 pgs.)

	GD	VG	FN	VF	VF/NM	NM-
1-John Severin-a	5	10	15	34	60	85

MONSTER HUNTERS
Charlton Comics: Aug, 1975 - No. 9, Jan, 1977; No. 10, Oct, 1977 - No. 18, Feb, 1979

	GD	VG	FN	VF	VF/NM	NM-
1-Howard-a; Newton-c; 1st Countess Von Bludd and Colonel Whiteshroud	3	6	9	19	30	40
2-Sutton-c/a; Ditko-a	3	6	9	14	19	24
3,4,5,7: 4-Sutton-c/a	2	4	6	9	12	15
6,8,10: 6,8,10-Ditko-a	2	4	6	10	14	18
9,11,12	1	3	4	6	8	10
13,15,18-Ditko-c/a. 18-Sutton-a	2	4	6	10	14	18
14-Special all-Ditko issue	3	6	9	16	24	32
16,17-Sutton-a	2	3	4	6	8	10
1,2 (Modern Comics reprints, 1977)						6.00

NOTE: Ditko-a 2, 6, 8, 10, 13-15r, 18r; c-13-15, 18. Howard a-1, 3, 17; r-13. Morisi a-1. Staton a-1, 13. Sutton a-2, 4; c-2, 4; r-16-18. Zeck a-4-9. Reprints in #12-18.

MONSTER KILL SQUAD
Bad Idea: Sept, 2021 - No. 4, Dec, 2021 ($6.99, limited series)

	GD	VG	FN	VF	VF/NM	NM-
1-4-Lead story with Christos Gage-s/Tomas Giorello-a; back-ups by various						7.00

MONSTER MADNESS (Magazine)
Marvel Comics: 1972 - No. 3, 1973 (60¢, B&W)

	GD	VG	FN	VF	VF/NM	NM-
1-3: Stories by "Sinister" Stan Lee. 1-Frankenstein photo-c. 2-Son of Frankenstein photo-c. 3-Bride of Frankenstein photo-c	4	8	12	27	44	60

MONSTER MAN
Image Comics (Action Planet): Sept, 1997 ($2.95, B&W)

	GD	VG	FN	VF	VF/NM	NM-
1-Mike Manley-c/s/a						4.00

MONSTER MASTERWORKS
Marvel Comics: 1989 ($12.95, TPB)

	GD	VG	FN	VF	VF/NM	NM-
nn-Reprints 1960's monster stories; art by Kirby, Ditko, Ayers, Everett						20.00

MONSTER MATINEE
Chaos! Comics: Oct, 1997 - No. 3, 1997 ($2.50, limited series)

	GD	VG	FN	VF	VF/NM	NM-
1-3: pin-ups						4.00

MONSTER MENACE
Marvel Comics: Dec, 1993 - No. 4, Mar, 1994 ($1.25, limited series)

	GD	VG	FN	VF	VF/NM	NM-
1-4: Pre-code Atlas horror reprints.						6.00

NOTE: Ditko-r & Kirby-r in all.

MONSTER OF FRANKENSTEIN (See Frankenstein and Essential Monster of Frankenstein)

MONSTER PILE-UP
Image Comics: Aug, 2008 ($1.99)

	GD	VG	FN	VF	VF/NM	NM-
1-New short stories of Astounding Wolf-Man, Firebreather, Perhapanauts, Proof						3.00

MONSTERS ATTACK (Magazine)
Globe Communications Corpse: Sept, 1989 - No. 5, Dec, 1990 (B&W)

M.O.D.O.K.: Head Games #2 © MAR

Monster World #1 © AGP

Moon Girl and Devil Dinosaur #4 © MAR

	GD	VG	FN	VF	VF/NM	NM-
	2.0	4.0	6.0	8.0	9.0	9.2

1-5-Ditko, Morrow, J. Severin-a. 5-Toth, Morrow-a | 1 | 2 | 3 | 4 | 5 | 7

MONSTERS, INC. (Based on the Disney/Pixar movie)
BOOM! Studios: Jun, 2009 - No. 4, Nov, 2009 ($2.99, limited series)
...: Laugh Factory 1-4. 1,3-Three covers. 2,4-Two covers | | | | | | 3.00

MONSTERS, INC. (Based on the Disney/Pixar movie)
Marvel Worldwide Inc.: Feb, 2013 - No. 2 ($2.99, limited series)
1,2-Movie adaptation | | | | | | 3.00
...: A Perfect Date (2013, $2.99) | | | | | | 3.00
...: The Humanween Party (4/13, $2.99) | | | | | | 3.00

MONSTERS ON THE PROWL (Chamber of Darkness #1-8)
Marvel Comics Group (No. 13,14: 52 pgs.): No. 9, 2/71 - No. 27, 11/73; No. 28, 6/74 - No. 30, 10/74
9-Barry Smith inks | 6 | 12 | 18 | 37 | 66 | 95
10-12,15: 12-Last 15¢ issue | 4 | 8 | 12 | 25 | 40 | 55
13,14-(52 pgs.) | 4 | 8 | 12 | 27 | 44 | 60
16-(4/72)-King Kull 4th app.; Severin-c | 4 | 8 | 12 | 28 | 47 | 65
17-30 | 3 | 6 | 9 | 18 | 28 | 38
NOTE: *Ditko r-9, 14, 16. Kirby r-10-17, 21, 23, 25, 27, 28, 30; c-9, 25. Kirby/Ditko r-14, 17-20, 22, 24, 26, 29. Marie/John Severin a-16(Kull). 9-13, 15 contain one new story. Woodish art by Reese-11. King Kull created by Robert E. Howard.*

MONSTERS TO LAUGH WITH (Magazine) (Becomes Monsters Unlimited #4)
Marvel Comics Group: 1964 - No. 3, 1965 (B&W)
1-Humor by Stan Lee | 9 | 18 | 27 | 57 | 111 | 165
2,3: 3-Frankenstein photo-c | 5 | 10 | 15 | 34 | 60 | 85

MONSTERS UNLEASHED (Magazine)
Marvel Comics Group: July, 1973 - No. 11, Apr, 1975; Summer, 1975 (B&W)
1-Soloman Kane sty; Werewolf app. | 7 | 14 | 21 | 49 | 92 | 135
2-4: 2-The Frankenstein Monster begins, ends #10. 3-Neal Adams-c/a; The Man-Thing begins (origin-r). Son of Satan preview. 4-Werewolf app. | 4 | 8 | 12 | 28 | 47 | 65
5-7: Werewolf in all. 5-Man-Thing. 7-Williamson-a | 3 | 6 | 9 | 21 | 33 | 45
8-11: 8-Man-Thing; N. Adams-r. 9-Man-Thing; Wendigo app. 10-Origin Tigra | 3 | 6 | 9 | 21 | 33 | 45
Annual 1 (Summer,1975, 92 pgs.)-Kane-a | 4 | 8 | 12 | 25 | 40 | 55
NOTE: *Boris c-2, 6. Brunner a-2; c-11. J. Buscema a-2p, 4p, 5p. Colan a-1, 4r. Davis a-3r. Everett a-3, c-3. G. Kane a-3. Krigstein r-4. Morrow a-3; c-1. Perez a-8. Ploog a-6. Reese a-1, 2. Tuska a-3p. Wildey a-1r.*

MONSTERS UNLEASHED
Marvel Comics: Mar, 2017 - No. 5, May, 2017 ($4.99, limited series with tie-ins)
1-5: 1-Cullen Bunn-s/Steve McNiven-a; Avengers, X-Men, Guardians of the Galaxy, Inhumans & Champions app. 2-Land-a. 3-Leinil Yu-a. 4-Larroca-a. 5-Adam Kubert-a | | | | | | 5.00

MONSTERS UNLEASHED (Ongoing series)
Marvel Comics: Jun, 2017 - No. 12, May, 2018 ($3.99)
1-12: 1-Bunn-s/Baldeón-a; Elsa Bloodstone & Mole Man app. 7,8-Fin Fang Foom app. | | | | | | 4.00

MONSTERS UNLIMITED (Magazine) (Formerly Monsters To Laugh With)
Marvel Comics Group: No. 4, 1965 - No. 7, 1966 (B&W)
4-7: 4,7-Frankenstein photo-c | 5 | 10 | 15 | 34 | 60 | 85

MONSTER WORLD
DC Comics (WildStorm): Jul, 2001 - No. 4, Oct, 2001 ($2.50, limited series)
1-4-Lobdell-s/Meglia-c/a | | | | | | 3.00

MONSTER WORLD
American Gothic Press: Dec, 2015 - No. 4, May, 2016 ($3.99)
1-4-Philip Kim & Steve Niles-s/Piotr Kowalski-a | | | | | | 4.00

MONSTRESS
Image Comics: Nov, 2015 - Present ($4.99/$3.99)
1-($4.99) Marjorie Liu-s/Sana Takeda-a | 3 | 6 | 9 | 21 | 33 | 45
2 | 2 | 4 | 6 | 9 | 12 | 15
3,4 | | | | | | 6.00
5-48-($3.99) | | | | | | 4.00

MONSTRESS: TALK-STORIES
Image Comics: Nov, 2020 - No. 2, Dec, 2020 ($3.99)
1,2-Marjorie Liu-s/Sana Takeda-a; spotlight on Kippa | | | | | | 4.00

MONSTRO MECHANICA
AfterShock Comics: Dec, 2017 - No. 5, Apr, 2018 ($3.99)
1-5-Paul Allor-s/Chris Evenhuis-a; Leonardo Da Vinci and his robot in 1472 | | | | | | 4.00

MONTANA KID, THE (See Kid Montana)

MONTE HALE WESTERN (Movie star; Formerly Mary Marvel #1-28; also see Fawcett Movie Comic, Motion Picture Comics, Picture News #8, Real Western Hero, Six-Gun Heroes, Western Hero & XMas Comics)

Fawcett Publ./Charlton No. 83 on: No. 29, Oct, 1948 - No. 88, Jan, 1956
29-(#1, 52 pgs.)-Photo-c begin, end #82; Monte Hale & his horse Pardner begin | 26 | 52 | 78 | 154 | 252 | 350
30-(52 pgs.)-Big Bow and Little Arrow begin, end #34; Captain Tootsie by Beck | 14 | 28 | 42 | 80 | 115 | 150
31-36,38-40-(52 pgs.): 34-Gabby Hayes begins, ends #80. 39-Captain Tootsie by Beck | 12 | 24 | 36 | 67 | 94 | 120
37,41,45,49-(36 pgs.) | 10 | 20 | 30 | 54 | 72 | 90
42-44,46-48,50-(52 pgs.): 47-Big Bow & Little Arrow app. | 10 | 20 | 30 | 58 | 79 | 100
51,52,54-56,58,59-(52 pgs.) | 9 | 18 | 27 | 52 | 69 | 85
53,57-(36 pgs.): 53-Slim Pickens app. | 8 | 16 | 24 | 44 | 57 | 70
60-81: 36 pgs. #60-on. 80-Gabby Hayes ends | 8 | 16 | 24 | 42 | 54 | 65
82-Last Fawcett issue (6/53) | 9 | 18 | 27 | 52 | 69 | 85
83-1st Charlton issue (2/55); B&W photo back-c begin. Gabby Hayes returns, ends #86 | 10 | 20 | 30 | 58 | 79 | 100
84 (4/55) | 8 | 16 | 24 | 44 | 57 | 70
85-86 | 8 | 16 | 24 | 42 | 54 | 65
87,88: 87-Wolverton-r, 1/2 pg. 88-Last issue | 8 | 16 | 24 | 44 | 57 | 70
NOTE: *Gil Kane a-33?, 34? Rocky Lane -1 pg. (Carnation ad)-38, 40, 41, 43, 44, 46, 55.*

MONTY HALL OF THE U.S. MARINES (See With the Marines...)
Toby Press: Aug, 1951 - No. 11, Apr, 1953
1 | 19 | 38 | 57 | 111 | 176 | 240
2 | 12 | 24 | 36 | 67 | 94 | 120
3-5 | 10 | 20 | 30 | 54 | 72 | 90
6-11 | 9 | 18 | 27 | 50 | 65 | 80
NOTE: *Full page pin-ups (Pin-Up Pete) by Jack Sparling in #1-9.*

MOON, A GIRL...ROMANCE, A (Becomes Weird Fantasy #13 on; formerly Moon Girl #1-8)
E. C. Comics: No. 9, Sept-Oct, 1949 - No. 12, Mar-Apr, 1950
9-Moon Girl cameo | 181 | 362 | 543 | 1158 | 1979 | 2800
10,11 | 148 | 296 | 444 | 947 | 1624 | 2300
12-(Scarce) | 232 | 464 | 696 | 1485 | 2543 | 3600
NOTE: *Feldstein, Ingels art in all. Feldstein c-9-12. Wood/Harrison a-10-12. Canadian reprints known; see Table of Contents.*

MOON GIRL AND DEVIL DINOSAUR
Marvel Comics: Jan, 2016 - No. 47, Nov, 2019 ($3.99)
1-47: 1-Reeder & Montclare-s/Bustos-a; intro. Lunella Lafayette. 4-Hulk app. 9-11-Ms. Marvel app. 14-Thing & Hulk (Cho) app. 15-Ironheart app. 19-Intro. Girl-Moon. 22,23-Ego the Living Planet app. 25-30-The Thing and Human Torch app. | | | | | | 4.00

MOON GIRL AND DEVIL DINOSAUR
Marvel Comics: Feb, 2023 - No. 5, Jun, 2023 ($3.99, limited series)
1-5: 1-Jordan Ifueko-s/Alba Glez-a | | | | | | 4.00

MOON GIRL AND THE PRINCE (#1) (Moon Girl #2-6; Moon Girl Fights Crime #7, 8; becomes A Moon, A Girl, Romance #9 on)(Also see Animal Fables #7, Int. Crime Patrol #6, Happy Houlihans & Tales From The Crypt #22)
E. C. Comics: Fall, 1947 - No. 8, Summer, 1949
1-Origin Moon Girl (see Happy Houlihans #1). Intro Santana, Queen of the Underworld | 284 | 568 | 852 | 1818 | 3109 | 4400
2-Moon Girl battles Futureman | 142 | 284 | 426 | 909 | 1555 | 2200
3,4: 3-Santana, Queen of the Underworld returns. 4-Moon Girl vs. a vampire | 110 | 220 | 330 | 704 | 1202 | 1700
5-E.C.'s 1st horror story, "Zombie Terror" | 331 | 662 | 993 | 2317 | 4059 | 5800
6-8 (Scarce): 7-Origin Star (Moongirl's sidekick) | 129 | 258 | 387 | 826 | 1413 | 2000
NOTE: *Craig a-2, 5; c-1, 2. Moldoff a-3; c-3-8 (Shelly). Wheelan's Fat and Slat app. in #3, 4, 6. #2 & #3 are 52 pgs., #4 on, 36 pgs. Canadian reprints known; (see Table of Contents).*

MOON KNIGHT (Also see The Hulk, Marc Spector..., Marvel Preview #21, Marvel Spotlight & Werewolf by Night #32)
Marvel Comics Group: Nov, 1980 - No. 38, Jul, 1984 (Mando paper #33 on)
1-Origin resumed in #4; Moench-s/Sienkiewicz-a | 5 | 10 | 15 | 33 | 57 | 80
2 | 4 | 6 | 11 | 16 | 20
3-1st Midnight Man | 3 | 6 | 9 | 19 | 30 | 40
4-Werewolf By Night app. | 3 | 6 | 9 | 14 | 20 | 25
5-15,25,35: 25-Double size. 35-($1.00, 52 pgs.)-X-Men app.; F.F. cameo | 1 | 2 | 3 | 5 | 6 | 8
16-22: 16-The Thing app. | | | | | | 6.00
23,24,26-28,31-34,36-38 | 2 | 4 | 6 | 11 | 16 | 20
29-Werewolf By Night app. | 3 | 6 | 9 | 21 | 33 | 45
30-Werewolf By Night app. | 3 | 6 | 9 | 14 | 20 | 25
... No. 1 Facsimile Edition (7/22, $3.99) Reprints #1 with original 1980 ads | | | | | | 4.00
... vs. Werewolf By Night: Marvel Tales 1 (12/23, $7.99). Reps. #29,30, Solo Avengers #3 and Marc Spector: Moon Knight #52,53; intro by Ralph Macchio | | | | | | 8.00
NOTE: *Austin c-27!, 31!. Cowan a-16; c-16, 17. Kaluta c-36-38; back c-35. Miller c-9, 12p, 13p, 15p, 27p. Ploog*

	GD	VG	FN	VF	VF/NM	NM-
	2.0	4.0	6.0	8.0	9.0	9.2

back c-35. **Sienkiewicz** *a-1-15, 17-20, 22-26, 28-30, 33i, 36(4), 37; c-1-5, 7, 8, 10, 11, 14-16, 18-26, 28-30, 31p, 33, 34.*

MOON KNIGHT
Marvel Comics Group: June, 1985 - V2#6, Dec, 1985

V2#1-Double size; new costume	2	4	6	11	16	20
V2#2-Khonshu & Harrow app.	4	8	12	23	37	50
V2#3-6: 6-Sienkiewicz painted-c	1	2	3	5	6	8

MOON KNIGHT
Marvel Comics: Jan, 1998 - No. 4, Apr, 1998 ($2.50, limited series)

1-Moench-s/Edwards-c/a	1	3	4	6	8	10
2-4-Moench-s/Edwards-c/a						5.00

MOON KNIGHT (Volume 3)
Marvel Comics: Jan, 1999 - No. 4, Feb, 1999 ($2.99, limited series)

1-Moench-s/Texeira-a(p)	1	3	4	6	8	10
2-4						5.00

MOON KNIGHT (Fourth series) (Leads into Vengeance of the Moon Knight)
Marvel Comics: June, 2006 - No. 30, Jul, 2009 ($2.99)

1-Finch-a/c; Huston-s	2	4	6	10	14	18
1-B&W sketch variant-c	3	6	9	14	19	24
2-19,21-26: 7-Spider-Man app. 9,10-Punisher app. 23-25-Bullseye						3.00
20-($3.99) Deodato-a; back-up r/1st app. in Werewolf By Night #32,33						
	2	4	6	13	18	22
Annual 1 (1/08, $3.99) Swierczynski-a/Palo-a						6.00
... Saga (2009, free) synopsis of origin and major storylines						4.00
...: Silent Knight 1 (1/09, $3.99) Milligan-s/Laurence Campbell-a/Crain-c						
	3	6	9	17	26	35

MOON KNIGHT (Fifth series)
Marvel Comics: Jul, 2011 - No. 12, Jun, 2012 ($3.99, limited series)

1-Bendis-s/Maleev-a/c; Wolverine, Spider-Man and Capt. America "app."						
	1	2	3	5	6	8
2-12: 2-Echo returns. 3-Bullseye-c						4.00

MOON KNIGHT (Sixth series)
Marvel Comics: May, 2014 - No. 17, Sept, 2015 ($3.99)

1-Ellis-s/Shalvey-a	2	4	6	8	10	12
2-17: 2-6-Ellis-s/Shalvey-a. 7-12-Wood-s/Smallwood-a. 13-17-Bunn						4.00

MOON KNIGHT (Seventh series)
Marvel Comics: Jun, 2016 - No. 14, Jul, 2017 ($4.99/$3.99)

1-($4.99)-Lemire-s/Smallwood-a	2	4	6	11	16	20
2-($3.99)-Lemire-s/Smallwood-a	1	2	3	5	6	8
3-14-($3.99) 5-9-Art by Smallwood, Stokoe, Torres, and Francavilla						4.00

MOON KNIGHT (Marvel Legacy, Eighth series)
Marvel Comics: No. 188, Jan, 2018 - No. 200, Dec, 2018 ($3.99)

188-Intro. Sun King; Bemis-s/Burrows-a	2	4	6	8	10	12
189-Intro. The Truth	1	2	3	5	6	8
190-199						4.00
200-($4.99) Davidson-a						5.00
Annual 1 (11/19, $4.99) Acts of Evil; Moustafa & Horak-a; Kang the Conqueror app.						5.00

MOON KNIGHT (Ninth series)
Marvel Comics: Sept, 2021 - No. 30, Feb, 2024 ($4.99/$3.99)

1-($4.99) MacKay-s/Cappuccio-a						5.00
2-19,21-24,26-29-($3.99) 4,6,7,22-Tigra app. 23-Venom app.						4.00
20,30-($4.99) 20-Back-up story with Blade. 30-Leads into Vengeance of the Moon Knight						5.00
25-($9.99) 8-Ball and Black Spectre app.						10.00
Annual 1 (12/22, $4.99) Werewolf By Night app.; MacKay-s/Sabbatini-a						5.00
Annual 1 (10/23, $4.99) Taegukgi (Tiger Division) app.; MacKay-s/Creees Lee-a						5.00

MOON KNIGHT: BLACK, WHITE & BLOOD
Marvel Comics: Jul, 2022 - No. 4, Oct, 2022 ($4.99, B&W&red, limited series)

1-4: Short stories by various. 1-Hickman/Bachalo-a. 3-Frank Cho-c						5.00

MOON KNIGHT: CITY OF THE DEAD
Marvel Comics: Sept, 2023 - Present ($4.99/$3.99, limited series)

1-Pepose-s/Ferreira-a; Scarlet Scarab app.						5.00
2-5-($3.99)						4.00

MOON KNIGHT: DIVIDED WE FALL
Marvel Comics: 1992 ($4.95, 52 pgs.)

nn-Denys Cowan-c/a(p)	1	3	4	6	8	10

MOON KNIGHT SPECIAL
Marvel Comics: Oct, 1992 ($2.50, 52 pgs.)

1-Shang Chi, Master of Kung Fu-c/story						6.00

MOON KNIGHT SPECIAL EDITION
Marvel Comics: Nov, 1983 - No. 3, Jan, 1984 ($2.00, limited series, Baxter paper)

1-Reprints from Hulk mag. by Sienkiewicz in all	3	6	9	14	19	24
2-3	1	3	4	6	8	10

MOON MAN (Kid Cudi Presents...)
Image Comics: Jan, 2024 - Present ($3.99)

1-Mescudi & Higgins-s/Locati-a; bonus sketch art						4.00

MOON MULLINS (See Popular Comics, Super Book #3 & Super Comics)
Dell Publishing Co.: 1941 - 1945

Four Color 14(1941)	58	116	174	371	636	900
Large Feature Comic 29(1942)	39	78	117	240	395	550
Four Color 31(1943)	18	36	54	125	276	430
Four Color 81(1945)	12	24	36	81	176	270

MOON MULLINS
Michel Publ. (American Comics Group)#1-6/St. John #7,8: Dec-Jan, 1947-48 - No. 8, Mar-May, 1949 (52 pgs.)

1-Alternating Sunday & daily strip-r	31	62	93	182	296	410
2	18	36	54	105	165	225

3-8: 7,8-St. John Publ. 7,8-...Featuring Kayo on-c	17	34	51	98	154	210

NOTE: *Milt Gross a-2-6, 8. Frank Willard r-all.*

MOON PILOT
Dell Publishing Co.: No. 1313, Mar-May, 1962

Four Color 1313-Movie, photo-c	7	14	21	44	82	120

MOONSHADOW (Also see Farewell, Moonshadow)
Marvel Comics (Epic Comics): 5/85 - #12, 2/87 ($1.50/$1.75, mature)
(1st fully painted comic book)

1-Origin; J. M. DeMatteis scripts & Jon J. Muth painted-c.						6.00
2-12: 11-Origin						4.00
Trade paperback (1987?)-r/#1-12						14.00
Signed & #ed HC ($39.95, 1,200 copies)-r/#1-12	4	8	12	27	44	60

MOONSHADOW
DC Comics (Vertigo): Oct, 1994 - No. 12, Aug, 1995 ($2.25/$2.95)

1-11: Reprints Epic series.						4.00
12 ($2.95)-w/expanded ending						5.00
The Complete Moonshadow TPB ('98, $39.95) r/#1-12 and Farewell Moonshadow; new Muth painted-c						40.00

MOONSHINE
Image Comics: Oct, 2016 - No. 28, Nov, 2021 ($2.99/$3.99)

1-6-Brian Azzarello-s/Eduardo Risso-a. 1-Covers by Risso & Frank Miller						3.00
7-28-($3.99) Azzarello-s/Risso-a						4.00

MOON-SPINNERS, THE (See Movie Comics)

MOONSTONE MONSTERS
Moonstone: 2003 - 2005 ($2.95, B&W)

...: Demons ($2.95) - Short stories by various; Frenz-c						3.00
...: Ghosts ($2.95) - Short stories by various; Frenz-c						3.00
...: Sea Creatures ($2.95) - Short stories by various; Frenz-c						3.00
...: Witches ($2.95) - Short stories by various; Frenz-c						3.00
...: Zombies ($2.95) - Short stories by various; Frenz-c						3.00
Volume 1 (2004, $16.95, TPB) r/short stories from series; Wolak-c						17.00

MOONSTONE NOIR
Moonstone: 2003 - 2004 ($2.95/$4.95/$5.50, B&W)

...: Bulldog Drummond (2004, $4.95) - Messner-Loebs-s/Barkley-a						5.00
...: Johnny Dollar ($4.95) - Gallaher-s/Theriault-a						5.00
...: Mr. Keen, Tracer of Lost Persons 1,2 ($4.95, limited series) - Ferguson-s						3.00
...: Mysterious Traveler (2003, $5.50) - Trevor Von Eeden-a/Joe Gentile-s						5.50
...: Mysterious Traveler Returns (2004, $4.95) - Trevor Von Eeden-a/Joe Gentile-s						5.00
...: The Lone Wolf ($4.95) - Jolley-s/Croall-a						5.00

MOPSY (See Pageant of Comics & TV Teens)
St. John Publ. Co.: Feb, 1948 - No. 19, Sept, 1953

1-Part-r; reprints "Some Punkins" by Neher	54	108	162	343	574	825
2	22	44	66	128	209	290
3-10(1953): 8-Lingerie panels	19	38	57	111	176	240
11-19: 19-Lingerie-c	18	36	54	103	162	220

NOTE: *#1-7, 13, 18, 19 have paper dolls.*

MORBIUS
Marvel Comics: Jan, 2020 - No. 5, May, 2020 ($3.99)

1-5-Ayala-s/Ferreira-a. 1-Intro. Elizabeth; the Melter app. 2-5-Spider-Man app.						4.00

MORBIUS: BOND OF BLOOD
Marvel Comics: Apr, 2021 ($3.99, one-shot)

1-Ralph Macchio-s/Tom Reilly-a; origin told in flashback; Mister Hyde app.						4.00

MORBIUS REVISITED
Marvel Comics: Aug, 1993 - No. 5, Dec, 1993 ($1.95, mini-series)

1-5-Reprints Fear #27-31						4.00

MORBIUS: THE LIVING VAMPIRE (Also see Amazing Spider-Man #101,102, Fear #20, Marvel Team-Up #3, 4, Midnight Sons Unl. & Vampire Tales)
Marvel Comics (Midnight Sons imprint #16 on): Sep, 1992 - No. 32, Apr, 1995 ($1.75/$1.95)

1-($2.75, 52 pgs.)-Polybagged w/poster; Ghost Rider & Johnny Blaze x-over (part 3 of Rise of the Midnight Sons)	2	4	6	10	14	18
2	2	4	6	8	10	12
3-11,13-24,26-32: 3,4-Vs. Spider-Man-c/s.15-Ghost Rider app. 16-Spot varnish-c. 16,17-Siege of Darkness, parts 5 &13. 18-Deathlok app. 21-Bound-in Spider-Man trading card sheet; Spider-Man app.						5.00
12-($2.25)-Outer-c is a Darkhold envelope made of black parchment w/gold ink; Midnight Massacre x-over	1	3	4	6	8	10
25-($2.50, 52 pgs.)-Gold foil logo						6.00

MORBIUS: THE LIVING VAMPIRE (Marvel NOW!)
Marvel Comics: Mar, 2013 - No. 9, Nov, 2013 ($2.99)

1-9: 1-Keatinge-s/Elson-a/Dell'Otto-c. 6,7-Superior Spider-Man app.						4.00

MORE FUN COMICS (Formerly New Fun Comics #1-6)
National Periodical Publs: No. 7, Jan, 1936 - No. 127, Nov-Dec, 1947 (No. 7,9-11: paper-c)

7(1/36)-Oversized, paper-c; 1 pg. Kelly-a	1188	2376	3564	9500	--	--
8(2/36)-Oversized (10x12"), paper-c; 1 pg. Kelly-a; Sullivan-c	1163	2326	3489	9300	--	--
9(3-4/36)-(Very rare, 1st standard-sized comic book with original material)-Last multiple panel-c	1625	3250	4875	13,000	--	--
10,11(7/36): 10-Last Henri Duval by Siegel & Shuster. 11-1st "Calling All Cars" by Siegel & Shuster; new classic logo begins	825	1650	2475	6600	--	--
12(8/36)-Slick-c begin	673	1226	1839	4900	--	--
V2#1(9/36, #13) 1 pg. Fred Astaire photo/bio	563	1126	1689	4500	--	--
2(10/36, #14)-Dr. Occult in costume (1st in color)(Superman prototype; 1st DC appearance) continues from The Comics Magazine, ends #17	2125	4250	6375	17,000	--	--
V2#3(11/36, #15), 17(V2#5)	850	1700	2550	6800	--	--
16(V2#4)-Cover numbering begins; ties with New Comics #11 as 1st DC Christmas-c; last Superman tryout issue	975	1950	2925	7800	--	--
18-20(V2#8, 5/37)	413	826	1239	3300	--	--

Moon Knight (2021 series) #13 © MAR

Morbius: Bond of Blood #1 © MAR

More Fun Comics #66 © DC

	GD	VG	FN	VF	VF/NM	NM-
	2.0	4.0	6.0	8.0	9.0	9.2
21(V2#9)-24(V2#12, 9/37)	271	542	813	1734	2967	4200
25(V3#1, 10/37)-27(V3#3, 12/37): 27-Xmas-c	271	542	813	1734	2967	4200
28-30: 30-1st non-funny cover	265	530	795	1694	2897	4100
31-Has ad for Action Comics #1	343	686	1029	2400	4200	6000
32-35: 32-Last Dr. Occult	245	490	735	1568	2684	3800
36-40: 36-(10/38)-The Masked Ranger & sidekick Pedro begins; Ginger Snap by Bob Kane (2 pgs.; 1st-a?). 39-Xmas-c	232	464	696	1485	2543	3600
41-50: 41-Last Masked Ranger. 43-Beany (1 pg.) and Ginger Snap centerfold by Bob Kane	219	438	657	1402	2401	3400
51-The Spectre app. (in costume) in one panel ad at end of Buccaneer story	649	1298	1947	4738	8369	12,000
52-(2/40)-Origin/1st app. The Spectre (in costume splash panel only), part 1 by Bernard Baily (parts 1 & 2 written by Jerry Siegel; Spectre's costume changes color from purple & blue to green & grey; last Wing Brady; Spectre-c 17,800	35,600	53,400	124,600	222,300	320,000	
53-Origin The Spectre (in costume at end of story) part 2; Capt. Desmo begins; Spectre-c	3600	7200	10,800	25,200	59,600	94,000
54-The Spectre in costume; last King Carter; class c-Spectre-c	3400	6800	10,200	23,800	46,900	70,000
55-(Scarce, 5/40)-Dr. Fate begins (1st app.); last Bulldog Martin; Spectre-c	3400	6800	10,200	23,800	46,900	70,000
56-1st Dr. Fate-c (classic), origin continues. Congo Bill begins (6/40), 1st app.;	1300	2600	3900	9750	17,875	26,000
57-60-All Spectre-c	541	1082	1623	3950	6975	10,000
61,65: 61-Classic Dr. Fate-c. 65-Classic Spectre-c	514	1028	1542	3750	6625	9500
62-64,66: 63-Last Lt. Bob Neal. 64-Lance Larkin begins; all Spectre-c	400	800	1200	2800	4900	7000
67-(5/41)-Origin (1st) Dr. Fate; last Congo Bill & Bif Bronson (Congo Bill continues in Action Comics #37, 6/41)-Spectre-c	1050	2100	3150	8000	14,500	21,000
68-70: 68-Clip Carson begins. 70-Last Dr. Fate-c	360	720	1080	2520	4410	6300
71-Origin & 1st app. Johnny Quick by Mort Weisinger (9/41); classic sci/fi Dr. Fate-c	508	1015	1524	3708	6554	9400
72-Dr. Fate's new helmet; last Sgt. Carey, Sgt. O'Malley & Captain Desmo; German submarine-c (Nazi war-c)	326	652	978	2282	3991	5700
73-Origin & 1st app. Aquaman (11/41) by Paul Norris; intro. Green Arrow & Speedy; Dr. Fate-c	15,650	31,300	46,950	101,700	140,850	180,000
74-2nd Aquaman; 1st Percival Popp, Supercop; Dr. Fate-c	975	1950	2925	7100	12,550	18,000
75,76: 75-New origin Spectre; Nazi spy ring cover w/Hitler's photo. 76-Last Dr. Fate-c; Johnny Quick (by Meskin #76-97) begins, ends #107; last Clip Carson	550	2100	3150	8000	14,500	21,000
77-Green Arrow-c begin	314	628	942	2198	3849	5500
78-80	300	600	900	1920	3310	4700
81-83,85,88,90: 81-Last large logo. 82-1st small logo.	206	412	618	1318	2259	3200
84-Green Arrow Japanese war-c	142	284	426	909	1555	2200
86,87-Johnny Quick-c. 87-Last Radio Squad	181	362	543	1158	1979	2800
89-Origin Green Arrow & Speedy Team-up	142	284	426	909	1555	2200
91-97,99: 91-1st bi-monthly issue. 93-Dover & Clover begins (1st app., 9-10/43).	168	336	504	1075	1838	2600
97-Kubert-a	103	206	309	659	1130	1600
98-Last Dr. Fate (scarce)	123	246	369	787	1344	1900
100 (11-12/44)-Johnny Quick-c	110	220	330	704	1202	1700
101-Origin & 1st app. Superboy (1-2/45)(not by Siegel & Shuster) issue; Green Arrow-c	1050	2100	3150	8000	14,500	21,000
102-2nd Superboy app; 1st Dover & Clover-c	181	362	543	1158	1979	2800
103-3rd Superboy app; last Green Arrow-c	129	258	387	826	1413	2000
104-1st Superboy-c w/Dover & Clover	155	310	465	992	1676	2400
105,106-Superboy-c	129	258	387	826	1413	2000
107-Last Johnny Quick & Superboy	97	194	291	621	1061	1500
108-120: 108-Genius Jones begins; 1st c-app. (3-4/46; cont'd from Adventure Comics #102)	33	66	99	194	317	440
121-124,126: 121-123,126-Post funny animal (Jiminy & the Magic Book)-c	30	60	90	177	289	400
125-Superman c-app.w/Jimminy	110	220	330	704	1202	1700
127-(Scarce)-Post-c/a	54	108	162	343	574	825

NOTE: All issues are scarce to rare. Cover features: The Spectre-#52-55, 57-60, 62-67. Dr. Fate-#56, 61, 68-76. The Green Arrow & Speedy-#77-85, 88-99, 101 (w/Dover & Clover-#98, 103). Johnny Quick-#86, 87, 100. Dover & Clover-#102, (104, 106 w/Superboy), 107, 103(w/Genius Jones), 104, 112, 114, 117, 119. Genius Jones-#109, 111, 113, 115, 116, 118, 120. Baily-a-45, 52-o?, c-52-55, 57-60, 62-67. Al Capp a-45(signed Koppy). Ellsworth c-7. Creig Flessel c-30, 31, 35-48(most). Guardineer c-47, 49, 50. Kiefer a-20, 35-48(most). Meskin c-86, 87, 100? Moldoff c-51. George Papp c-77-85. Post c-121-127. Vincent Sullivan c-8-28, 32-34.

MORE FUND COMICS (Benefit book for the Comic Book Legal Defense Fund) (Also see Even More Fund Comics)
Sky Dog Press: Sept, 2003 ($10.00, B&W, trade paperback)

nn-Anthology of short stories and pin-ups by various; Hulk-c by Pèrez						10.00

MORE SEYMOUR (See Seymour My Son)
Archie Publications: Oct, 1963

	GD	VG	FN	VF	VF/NM	NM-
	2.0	4.0	6.0	8.0	9.0	9.2
1-DeCarlo-a?	3	6	9	21	33	45

MORE THAN MORTAL (Also see Lady Pendragon/...)
Liar Comics: June, 1997 - No. 4, Apr, 1998 ($2.95, limited series)
Image Comics: No. 5, Dec, 1999 - No. 6, Mar, 2000 ($2.95)

1-Blue forest background-c, 1-Variant-c	5.00
1-White-c	6.00
1-2nd printing; purple sky cover	4.00
2-4: 3-Silvestri-c, 4-Two-c, one by Randy Queen	4.00
5,6: 5-1st Image Comics issue	4.00

MORE THAN MORTAL: OTHERWORLDS
Image Comics: July, 1999 - No. 4, Dec, 1999 ($2.95, limited series)

1-4-Firchow-a. 1-Two covers	4.00

MORE THAN MORTAL SAGAS
Liar Comics: Jun, 1998 - No. 3, Dec, 1998 ($2.95, limited series)

1,2-Painted art by Romano. 2-Two-c, one by Firchow	4.00
1-Variant-c by Linsner	5.00

MORE THAN MORTAL TRUTHS AND LEGENDS
Liar Comics: Aug, 1998 - No. 6, Apr, 1999 ($2.95)

1-6-Firchow-a(p)	4.00
1-Variant-c by Dan Norton	5.00

MORE TRASH FROM MAD (Annual)
E. C. Comics: 1958 - No. 12, 1969
(Note: Bonus missing = half price)

	GD	VG	FN	VF	VF/NM	NM-
nn(1958)-8 pgs. color Mad reprint from #20	19	38	57	131	291	450
2(1959)-Market Product Labels	12	24	36	82	179	275
3(1960)-Text book covers	10	20	30	69	147	225
4(1961)-Sing Along with Mad booklet	10	20	30	69	147	225
5(1962)-Window Stickers; r/from Mad #39	8	16	24	54	102	150
6(1963)-TV Guise booklet	8	16	24	54	102	150
7(1964)-Alfred E. Neuman commemorative stamps	7	14	21	44	82	120
8(1965)-Life size poster-Alfred E. Neuman	5	10	15	35	63	90
9-12: 9,10(1966-67)-Mischief Sticker. 11(1968)-Campaign poster & bumper sticker.						
12(1969)-Pocket medals	5	10	15	35	63	90

NOTE: Kelly Freas c-1, 2, 4. Mingo c-3, 5-9, 12.

MORGAN THE PIRATE (Movie)
Dell Publishing Co.: No. 1227, Sept-Nov, 1961

	GD	VG	FN	VF	VF/NM	NM-
Four Color 1227-Photo-c	8	16	24	51	96	140

MORLOCKS
Marvel Comics: June, 2002 - No. 4, Sept, 2002 ($2.50, limited series)

1-4-Johns-s/Martinbrough-c/a. 1-1st app. Angel Dust	3.00

MORLOCK 2001
Atlas/Seaboard Publ.: Feb, 1975 - No. 3, July, 1975

	GD	VG	FN	VF	VF/NM	NM-
1,2: 1-(Super-hero)-Origin & 1st app.; Milgrom-c	2	4	6	11	16	20
3-Ditko/Wrightson-a; origin The Midnight Man & The Mystery Men	3	6	9	15	22	28

MORNING GLORIES
Image Comics: Aug, 2010 - Present ($3.99/$3.50/$2.99)

1-($3.99) Nick Spencer-s/Joe Eisma-a/Rodin Esquejo-c; group cover	12.00
1-Second-Fourth printings	4.00
2-($3.50) Regular cover and white background 2nd printing	5.00
3-6-Regular covers and white background 2nd printings	4.00
7-23-($2.99)	3.00
24,25,27,28-($3.99)	4.00
26-($1.00) Start of Season Two	3.00
29-48-($3.50)	3.50
49-($4.99) Spencer-s/Eisma-a	5.00
50-(7/16, $5.99)	6.00
...Vol. 1 TPB (2/11, $9.99) r/#1-6	10.00

MORNINGSTAR SPECIAL
Comico: Apr, 1990 ($2.50)

1-From the Elementals; Willingham-c/a/scripts	4.00

MORTAL KOMBAT
Malibu Comics: July, 1994 - No. 6, Dec, 1994 ($2.95)

	GD	VG	FN	VF	VF/NM	NM-
1-Two diff. covers exist	2	4	6	10	14	18
1-Limited edition gold foil embossed-c	3	6	9	17	26	35
2-6						6.00

MO

753

	GD 2.0	VG 4.0	FN 6.0	VF 8.0	VF/NM 9.0	NM- 9.2

0 (12/94), Special Edition 1 (11/94) — 3, 6, 9, 16, 23, 30
Tournament Edition I12/94, $3.95), ('95)($3.95) — 2, 4, 6, 13, 18, 22
...: BARAKA ,June, 1995 ($2.95, one-shot) #1; ...BATTLEWAVE ,2/95 - No. 6, 7/95 , #1-6;
...GORO, PRINCE OF PAIN ,9/94 - No. 3, 11/94, #1-3; ...KITANA AND MILEENA ,8/95 ,
...KUNG LAO ,7/95 , #1; ... RAYDON & KANO ,3/95 - No. 3, 5/95, #1-3: ...(all $2.95-c)
— 2, 4, 6, 9, 12, 15
...: U.S. SPECIAL FORCES (1/95 - No. 2, $3.50), 1,2 — 2, 4, 6, 9, 12, 15

MORTAL KOMBAT X
DC Comics: Mar, 2015 - No. 12, Jan. 2016 ($3.99, printings of digital-first stories)
1-Kittelsen-s/Soy-a/Reis-c — 2, 4, 6, 9, 12, 15
2-6 — 1, 2, 3, 5, 6, 8
7-12: 9-12-Jae Lee-c — 5.00

MORTAL TERROR
Dark Horse Comics: Nov, 2023 - Present ($4.99)
1-Golden-s/Lebbon-a; Dracula app. — 5.00

MORTIE (Mazie's Friend; also see Flat-Top)
Magazine Publishers: Dec, 1952 - No. 4, June, 1953?
1 — 15, 30, 45, 85, 130, 175
2-4 — 9, 18, 27, 47, 61, 75

MORTIGAN GOTH: IMMORTALIS (See Marvel Frontier Comics Unlimited)
Marvel Comics: Sept, 1993 - No. 4, Mar, 1994 ($1.95, mini-series)
1-($2.95)-Foil-c — 5.00
2-4 — 4.00

MORT THE DEAD TEENAGER
Marvel Comics: Nov, 1993 - No. 4, Mar, 1994 ($1.75, mini-series)
1-4 — 4.00

MORTY MEEKLE
Dell Publishing Co.: No. 793, May, 1957
Four Color 793 — 5, 10, 15, 31, 53, 75

MOSAIC
Marvel Comics: Dec, 2016 - No. 8, Jul, 2017 ($4.99/$3.99)
1-($4.99) Geoffrey Thorne-s/Khary Randolph-a; intro. Morris Sackett — 5.00
2-8-($3.99) 3,4-Spider-Man app. 6-Inhumans app. 8-Diablo app. — 4.00

MOSES & THE TEN COMMANDMENTS (See Dell Giants)

MOSTLY WANTED
DC Comics (WildStorm): Jul, 2000 - No. 4, Nov, 2000 ($2.50, limited series)
1-4-Lobdell-s/Flores-a — 3.00

MOTEL HELL (Based on the 1980 movie)
IDW Publishing: Oct, 2010 - No. 3, Dec, 2010 ($3.99, limited series)
1-3-Matt Nixon-s/Chris Moreno-a. 1,2-Bradstreet-c. 3-Moreno-c — 4.00

MOTH, THE
Dark Horse Comics: Apr, 2004 - No. 4, Aug, 2004 ($2.99)
1-4-Steve Rude-c/a; Gary Martin-s — 3.00
... Special (3/04, $4.95) — 5.00
TPB (5/05, $12.95) r/#1-4 and Special; gallery of extras — 13.00

MOTH, THE
Rude Dude Productions: May 2008 (Free Comic Book Day giveaway)
... Special Edition - Steve Rude-s/a; sketch pages — 3.00

MOTH & WHISPER
AfterShock Comics: Sept, 2018 - No. 5, Jan, 2019 ($3.99, limited series)
1-5-Ted Anderson-s/Jen Hickman-a — 4.00

MOTHER GOOSE AND NURSERY RHYME COMICS (See Christmas With Mother Goose)
Dell Publishing Co.: No. 41, 1944 - No. 862, Nov, 1957
Four Color 41-Walt Kelly-c/a — 27, 54, 81, 189, 420, 650
Four Color 59, 68-Kelly c/a — 20, 40, 60, 140, 310, 480
Four Color 862-The Truth About..., Movie (Disney) — 8, 16, 24, 51, 96, 140

MOTHERLANDS
DC Comics (Vertigo): Mar, 2018 - No. 6, Aug, 2018 ($3.99, limited series)
1-6-Spurrier-s/Stott-a/Canete-c — 4.00

MOTHER PANIC
DC Comics (Young Animal): Jan, 2017 - No. 12, Dec, 2017 ($3.99)
1-12: 1-Houser-s/Edwards-a; Batman cameo. 3-Batman & Batwoman app. 7-9-Leon-a — 4.00
.../ Batman Special 1 (4/18, $4.99) Part 2 of Milk Wars crossover; Templeton-a/Quitely-a — 5.00

MOTHER PANIC: GOTHAM A.D.
DC Comics (Young Animal): May, 2018 - No. 6, Oct, 2018 ($3.99)
1-6: 1-Houser-s/Moustafa-a/Edwards-c. 1-Joker cameo. 2-Catwoman app. — 4.00

MOTHER TERESA OF CALCUTTA
Marvel Comics Group: 1984
1-(52 pgs.) No ads — 2, 4, 6, 9, 12, 15

MOTHS (Also see The Resistance)
Artists, Writers & Artisans, Inc.: Jun, 2021 - No. 6, Nov, 2021 ($3.99, limited series)
1-6-J. Michael Straczynski-s/Mike Choi-a — 4.00

MOTION PICTURE COMICS (See Fawcett Movie Comics)
Fawcett Publications: No. 101, 1950 - No. 114, Jan, 1953 (All-photo-c)
101- "Vanishing Westerner"; Monte Hale (1950) — 18, 36, 54, 105, 165, 225
102- "Code of the Silver Sage"; Rocky Lane (1/51) — 15, 30, 45, 85, 130, 175
103- "Covered Wagon Raid"; Rocky Lane (3/51) — 15, 30, 45, 85, 130, 175
104- "Vigilante Hideout"; Rocky Lane (5/51)-Book length Powell-a
— 15, 30, 45, 85, 130, 175
105- "Red Badge of Courage"; Audie Murphy; Bob Powell-a (7/51)
— 20, 40, 60, 120, 195, 270
106- "The Texas Rangers"; George Montgomery (9/51)
— 15, 30, 45, 85, 130, 175
107- "Frisco Tornado"; Rocky Lane (11/51) — 14, 28, 42, 82, 121, 160

108- "Mask of the Avenger"; John Derek — 13, 26, 39, 74, 105, 135
109- "Rough Rider of Durango"; Rocky Lane — 14, 28, 42, 82, 121, 160
110- "When Worlds Collide"; George Evans-a (5/52); Williamson & Evans drew themselves in
story; (also see Famous Funnies No. 72-88) — 84, 168, 252, 538, 919, 1300
111- "The Vanishing Outpost"; Lash LaRue — 16, 32, 48, 94, 147, 200
112- "Brave Warrior"; Jon Hall & Jay Silverheels — 13, 26, 39, 72, 101, 130
113- "Walk East on Beacon"; George Murphy; Schaffenberger-a
— 10, 20, 30, 58, 79, 100
114- "Cripple Creek"; George Montgomery (1/53) — 11, 22, 33, 62, 86, 110

MOTION PICTURE FUNNIES WEEKLY (See Promotional Comics section)

MOTOR CRUSH
Image Comics: Dec, 2016 - No. 11, Apr, 2018 ($3.99)
1-11-Fletcher & Stewart/Tarr-a; covers by Tarr & Stewart. 6-Stewart-a — 4.00

MOTOR GIRL
Abstract Studio: 2016 - No. 10, 2017 ($3.99, B&W)
1-10-Terry Moore-s/a/c — 4.00

MOTORHEAD (See Comic's Greatest World)
Dark Horse Comics: Aug, 1995 - No. 6, Jan, 1996 ($2.50)
1-6: Bisley-c on all. 1-Predator app. — 4.00
Special 1 (3/94, $3.95, 62pgs.)-Jae Lee-c; Barb Wire, The Machine & Wolf Gang app. — 5.00

MOTORMOUTH (... & Killpower #7? on)
Marvel Comics UK: June, 1992 - No. 12, May, 1993 ($1.75)
1-13: 1,2-Nick Fury app. 3-Punisher-c/story. 5,6-Nick Fury & Punisher app. 6-Cable cameo.
7-9-Cable app. — 4.00

MOUNTAIN MEN (See Ben Bowie)

MOUSE MUSKETEERS (See M.G.M.'s...)

MOUSE ON THE MOON, THE (See Movie Classics)

MOVEMENT, THE
DC Comics: Jul, 2013 - No. 12, Jul. 2014 ($2.99)
1-12: 1-Gail Simone-s/Freddie Williams-a/Amanda Conner-c. 2-4-Rainmaker app.
9,10-Batgirl app. — 3.00

MOVIE CARTOONS
DC Comics: Dec, 1944 (cover only ashcan)
nn-Ashcan comic, not distributed to newsstands, only for in house use. Covers were produced,
but not the rest of the book. A copy sold in 2006 for $500.

MOVIE CLASSICS
Dell Publishing Co.: Apr, 1956; May-Jul, 1962 - Dec, 1969
(Before 1963, most movie adaptations were part of the 4-Color series)
(Disney movie adaptations after 1970 are in Walt Disney Showcase)
Around the World Under the Sea 12-030-612 (12/66) — 4, 8, 12, 23, 37, 50
Bambi 3(4/56)-Disney; r/4-Color #186 — 5, 10, 15, 33, 57, 80
Battle of the Bulge 12-056-606 (6/66) — 3, 6, 9, 20, 31, 42
Beach Blanket Bingo 12-058-509 — 7, 14, 21, 49, 92, 135
Bon Voyage 01-068-212 (12/62)-Disney; photo-c — 3, 6, 9, 21, 33, 45
Castilian, The 12-110-401 — 3, 6, 9, 19, 30, 40
Cat, The 12-109-612 (12/66) — 3, 6, 9, 20, 31, 42
Cheyenne Autumn 12-112-506 (4-6/65) — 5, 10, 15, 31, 53, 75
Circus World, Samuel Bronston's 12-115-411; John Wayne app.; John Wayne photo-c
— 9, 18, 27, 58, 114, 170
Countdown 12-150-710 (10/67)-James Caan photo-c — 3, 6, 9, 20, 31, 42
Creature, The 1 (12-142-302) (12-2/62-63) — 30, 60, 90, 216, 483, 750
Creature, The 12-142-410 (10/64) — 7, 14, 21, 49, 92, 135
David Ladd's Life Story 12-173-212 (10-12/62)-Photo-c
— 6, 12, 18, 40, 73, 105
Die, Monster, Die 12-175-603 (3/66)-Photo-c — 6, 12, 18, 38, 69, 100
Dirty Dozen 12-180-710 (10/67) — 5, 10, 15, 37, 66, 95
Dr. Who & the Daleks 12-190-612 (12/66)-Peter Cushing photo-c; 1st U.S. app. of Dr. Who
— 26, 52, 78, 182, 404, 625
Dracula 12-231-212 (10/12/62) — 11, 22, 33, 73, 157, 240
El Dorado 12-240-710 (10/67)-John Wayne; photo-c 13 — 26, 39, 89, 195, 300
Ensign Pulver 12-257-410 (8-10/64) — 3, 6, 9, 18, 28, 38
Frankenstein 12-283-305 (3-5/63)(see Frankenstein 8-10/64 for 2nd printing)
— 11, 22, 33, 73, 157, 240
Great Race, The 12-299-603 (3/66)-Natallie Wood, Tony Curtis photo-c
— 6, 12, 18, 38, 69, 100
Hallelujah Trail, The 12-307-602 (2/66) (Shows 1/66 inside); Burt Lancaster, Lee Remick
photo-c — 5, 10, 15, 30, 50, 70
Hatari 12-340-301 (1/63)-John Wayne — 8, 16, 24, 51, 96, 140
Horizontal Lieutenant, The 12-348-210 (10/62) — 3, 6, 9, 18, 28, 38
Incredible Mr. Limpet, The 12-370-408; Don Knotts photo-c
— 5, 10, 15, 38, 57, 80
Jack the Giant Killer 12-374-301 (1/63) — 7, 14, 21, 48, 89, 130
Jason and the Argonauts 12-376-310 (8-10/63)-Photo-c
— 10, 20, 30, 64, 132, 200
Lancelot & Guinevere 12-416-310 (10/63) — 5, 10, 15, 30, 50, 70
Lawrence of Arabia 12-426-308 (4/63)-Story of Lawrence of Arabia; movie ad on back-c;
not exactly like movie — 5, 10, 15, 30, 50, 70
Lion of Sparta 12-439-301 (1/63) — 4, 8, 12, 23, 37, 50
Mad Monster Party 12-460-801 (9/67)-Based on Kurtzman's screenplay
— 10, 20, 30, 66, 138, 210
Magic Sword, The 01-496-209 (9/62) — 5, 10, 15, 35, 63, 90
Masque of the Red Death 12-490-410 (8-10/64)-Vincent Price photo-c
— 7, 14, 21, 44, 82, 120
Maya 12-495-612 (12/66)-Clint Walker & Jay North part photo-c
— 4, 8, 12, 25, 40, 55
McHale's Navy 12-500-412 (10-12/64) — 4, 8, 12, 27, 44, 60
Merrill's Marauders 12-510-301 (4/63)-Photo-c — 3, 6, 9, 18, 28, 38
Mouse on the Moon, The 12-530-312 (10/12/63)-Photo-c
— 3, 6, 9, 21, 33, 45
Mummy, The 12-537-211 (9-11/62) 2 versions with different back-c
— 21, 42, 63, 147, 324, 500

Motel Hell #1 © MGM

Motor Girl #3 © Terry Moore

Movie Comics #1 © FH

	GD 2.0	VG 4.0	FN 6.0	VF 8.0	VF/NM 9.0	NM- 9.2

Music Man, The 12-538-301 (1/63) 3 6 9 19 30 40
Naked Prey, The 12-545-612 (12/66)-Photo-c 5 10 15 33 57 80
Night of the Grizzly, The 12-558-612 (12/66)-Photo-c 4 8 12 23 37 50
None But the Brave 12-565-506 (4-6/65) 5 10 15 31 53 75
Operation Bikini 12-597-310 (10/63)-Photo-c 4 8 12 23 37 50
Operation Crossbow 12-590-512 (10-12/65) 3 6 9 19 30 40
Prince & the Pauper, The 01-654-207 (5-7/62)-Disney
  4 8 12 23 37 50
Raven, The 12-680-309 (9/63)-Vincent Price photo-c 6 12 18 42 79 115
Ring of Bright Water 01-701-910 (10/69) (inside shows #12-701-909)
  3 6 9 21 33 45
Runaway, The 12-707-412 (10-12/64) 3 6 9 18 28 38
Santa Claus Conquers the Martians #? (1964)-Photo-c
  13 26 39 86 188 290
Santa Claus Conquers the Martians 12-725-603 (3/66, 12c)-Reprints 1964 issue; photo-c
  8 16 24 54 102 150
Another version given away with a Golden Record SLP 170, nn, no price (3/66)-Complete with record
  12 24 36 79 170 260
Six Black Horses 12-750-301 (1/63)-Photo-c 3 6 9 19 30 40
Ski Party 12-743-511 (9-11/65)-Frankie Avalon photo-c; photo inside-c; Adkins-a
  4 8 12 28 47 65
Smoky 12-746-702 (2/67) 3 6 9 18 28 38
Sons of Katie Elder 12-748-511 (9-11/65); John Wayne app.; photo-c
  10 20 30 68 144 220
Tales of Terror 12-793-302 (2/63)-Evans-a 5 10 15 35 63 90
Three Stooges Meet Hercules 01-828-208 (8/62)-Photo-c
  10 20 30 66 138 210
Tomb of Ligeia 12-803-506 (4-6/65) 5 10 15 31 53 75
Treasure Island 01-845-211 (7-9/62)-Disney; r/4-Color #624
  3 6 9 19 30 40
Twice Told Tales (Nathaniel Hawthorne) 12-840-401 (11-1/63-64);
  Vincent Price photo-c 5 10 15 34 60 85
Two on a Guillotine 12-850-506 (4-6/65) 3 6 9 21 33 45
Valley of Gwangi 01-880-912 (12/69) 9 18 27 57 111 165
War Gods of the Deep 12-900-509 (7-9/65) 3 6 9 19 30 40
War Wagon, The 12-533-709 (9/67); John Wayne app.
  8 16 24 54 102 150
Who's Minding the Mint? 12-924-708 (8/67) 3 6 9 18 28 38
Wolfman, The 12-922-308 (6-8/63) 10 20 30 70 150 230
Wolfman, The 12-922-410)(8-10/64)-2nd printing; r/#12-922-308
  5 10 15 33 57 80
Zulu 12-950-410 (8-10/64)-Photo-c 7 14 21 44 82 120

MOVIE COMICS (See Cinema Comics Herald & Fawcett Movie Comics)

MOVIE COMICS
National Periodical Publications/Picture Comics: April, 1939 - No. 6, Sept-Oct, 1939 (Most all photo-c)
1- "Gunga Din", "Son of Frankenstein", "The Great Man Votes", "Fisherman's Wharf", & "Scouts to the Rescue" part 1; Wheelan "Minute Movies" begin
  366 732 1098 2562 4481 6400
2- "Stagecoach", "The Saint Strikes Back", "King of the Turf", "Scouts to the Rescue" part 2, "Arizona Legion", Andy Devine photo-c
  274 548 822 1754 3027 4300
3- "East Side of Heaven", "Mystery in the White Room", "Four Feathers", "Mexican Rose" with Gene Autry, "Spirit of Culver", "Many Secrets", "The Mikado" (1st Gene Autry photo cover)
  206 412 618 1318 2259 3200
4- "Captain Fury", Gene Autry in "Blue Montana Skies", "Streets of N.Y." with Jackie Cooper, "Oregon Trail" part 1 with Johnny Mack Brown, "Big Town Czar" with Barton MacLane, & "Star Reporter" with Warren Hull
  152 304 456 965 1658 2350
5- "The Man in the Iron Mask", "Five Came Back", "Wolf Call", "The Girl & the Gambler", "The House of Fear", "The Family Next Door", "Oregon Trail" part 2
  165 330 495 1056 1803 2550
6- "The Phantom Creeps", "Chumps at Oxford", & "The Oregon Trail" part 3; 2nd Robot-c
  290 580 870 1856 3178 4500

NOTE: Above books contain many original movie stills with dialogue from movie scripts. All issues are scarce.

MOVIE COMICS
Fiction House Magazines: Dec, 1946 - No. 4, 1947
1-Big Town (by Lubbers), Johnny Danger begins; Celardo-a; Mitzi of the Movies by Fran Hopper
  47 94 141 296 498 700
2-(2/47)- "White Tie & Tails" with William Bendix; Mitzi of the Movies begins; Matt Baker-a
  37 74 111 222 361 500
3-(6/47)-Andy Hardy starring Mickey Rooney
  37 74 111 222 361 500
4-Mitzi in Hollywood by Matt Baker; Merton of the Movies with Red Skelton; Yvonne DeCarlo & George Brent in "Slave Girl"
  41 82 123 256 428 600

MOVIE COMICS

Gold Key/Whitman: Oct, 1962 - 1984
Alice in Wonderland 10144-503 (3/65)-Disney; partial reprint of 4-Color #331
  4 8 12 27 44 60
Alice In Wonderland #1 (Whitman pre-pack, 3/84) 3 6 9 14 20 25
Aristocats, The 1 (30045-103)(3/71)-Disney; with pull-out poster (25c)
  6 12 18 40 73 105
  (No poster = half price)
Bambi 1 (10087-309)(9/63)-Disney; r/4-Color #186 5 10 15 30 50 70
Bambi 2 (10087-607)(7/66)-Disney; r/4-Color #186 4 8 12 23 37 50
Beneath the Planet of the Apes 30044-012 (12/70)-with pull-out poster; photo-c
  10 20 30 68 144 220
  (No poster = half price) 10 20 30 68 144 220
Big Red 10026-211 (11/62)-Disney; photo-c 3 6 9 19 30 40
Big Red 10026-503 (3/65)-Disney; reprints 10026-211; photo-c
  3 6 9 16 23 30
Blackbeard's Ghost 10222-806 (6/68)-Disney 3 6 9 20 31 42
Bullwhip Griffin 10181-706 (6/67)-Disney; Spiegle-a; photo-c
  3 6 9 21 33 45
Captain Sindbad 10077-309 (9/63)-Manning-a; photo-c
  5 10 15 35 63 90
Chitty Chitty Bang Bang 1 (30038-902)(2/69)-with pull-out poster; Disney; photo-c
  8 16 24 51 96 140
  (No poster = half price)
Cinderella 10152-508 (8/65)-Disney; r/4-C #786 5 10 15 31 53 75
Darby O'Gill & the Little People 10251-001(1/70)-Disney; reprints 4-Color #1024 (Toth-a); photo-c
  4 8 12 28 47 65
Dumbo 1 (10090-310)(10/63)-Disney; r/4-C #668 4 8 12 25 40 55
Emil & the Detectives 10120-502 (11/64)-Disney; photo-c & back-c photo pin-up
  3 6 9 19 30 40
Escapade in Florence 1 (10043-301)(1/63)-Disney; starring Annette Funicello
  8 16 24 57 96 140
Fall of the Roman Empire 10118-407 (7/64); Sophia Loren photo-c
  4 8 12 23 37 50
Fantastic Voyage 10178-702 (2/67)-Wood/Adkins-a; photo-c
  6 12 18 40 73 105
55 Days at Peking 10081-309 (9/63)-Photo-c 3 6 9 19 30 40
Fighting Prince of Donegal, The 10193-701 (1/67)-Disney
  3 6 9 18 28 38
First Men in the Moon 10132-503 (3/65)-Fred Fredericks-a; photo-c
  4 8 12 27 44 60
Gay Purr-ee 30017-301(1/63, 84 pgs.) 5 10 15 31 53 75
Gnome Mobile, The 10207-710 (10/67)-Disney; Walter Brennan photo-c & back-c photo pin-up
  4 8 12 23 37 50
Goodbye, Mr. Chips 10246-006 (6/70)-Peter O'Toole photo-c
  3 6 9 19 30 40
Happiest Millionaire, The 10221-804 (4/68)-Disney 3 6 9 21 33 45
Hey There, It's Yogi Bear 10122-409 (9/64)-Hanna-Barbera
  6 12 18 37 66 95
Horse Without a Head, The 10109-401 (1/64)-Disney 3 6 9 18 28 38
How the West Was Won 10074-307 (7/63)-Based on the L'Amour novel; Tufts-a
  4 8 12 27 44 60
In Search of the Castaways 10048-303 (3/63)-Disney; Hayley Mills photo-c
  6 12 18 37 66 95
Jungle Book, The 1 (6022-801)(1/68-Whitman)-Disney; large size (10x13-1/2"); 59c
  6 12 18 69 100
Jungle Book, The 1 (30033-803)(3/68, 68 pgs.)-Disney; same contents as Whitman #1
  4 8 12 23 37 50
Jungle Book, The 1 (6/78, $1.00 tabloid) 3 6 9 16 23 30
Jungle Book (7/84)-r/Giant; Whitman pre-pack 2 4 6 10 14 18
Kidnapped 10080-306 (6/63)-Disney; reprints 4-Color #1101
  4 8 12 23 37 50
King Kong 30036-809(9/68-68 pgs.)-painted-c 4 8 12 57 111 165
King Kong nn-Whitman Treasury($1.00, 68 pgs.,1968), same cover as Gold Key issue
  7 14 21 48 89 130
King Kong 11299(#1-786, 10x13-1/4" 68 pgs, $1.00, 1978)
  4 8 12 22 35 48
Lady and the Tramp 10042-301 (1/63)-Disney; r/4-Color #629
  7 14 21 46 86 125
Lady and the Tramp 1 (1967-Giant; 25c)-Disney; reprints part of Dell #1
  6 12 18 37 66 95
Lady and the Tramp 2 (10042-203)(3/72)-Disney; r/4-Color #629
  3 6 9 21 33 45
Legend of Lobo, The 1 (10059-303)(3/63)-Disney; photo-c
  3 6 9 16 23 30
Lt. Robin Crusoe, U.S.N. 10191-610 (10/66)-Disney; Dick Van Dyke photo-c & back-c photo pin-up
  3 6 9 17 26 35
Lion, The 10035-301 (1/63)-Photo-c 3 6 9 16 24 32
Lord Jim 10156-509 (9/65)-Photo-c 3 6 9 16 24 32

	GD	VG	FN	VF	VF/NM	NM-
	2.0	4.0	6.0	8.0	9.0	9.2

Love Bug, The 10237-906 (6/69)-Disney; Buddy Hackett photo-c

| | 4 | 8 | 12 | 27 | 44 | 60 |

Mary Poppins 10136-501 (1/65)-Disney; photo-c

| | 5 | 10 | 15 | 34 | 60 | 85 |

Mary Poppins 30023-501 (1/65-68 pg.)-Disney; photo-c

| | 8 | 16 | 24 | 51 | 96 | 140 |

McLintock 10110-403 (3/64); John Wayne app.; John Wayne & Maureen O'Hara photo-c

| | 11 | 22 | 33 | 73 | 157 | 240 |

Merlin Jones as the Monkey's Uncle 10115-510 (10/65)-Disney; Annette Funicello front/back photo-c

| | 5 | 10 | 15 | 34 | 60 | 85 |

Miracle of the White Stallions, The 10065-306 (6/63)-Disney

| | 3 | 6 | 9 | 18 | 28 | 38 |

Misadventures of Merlin Jones, The 10115-405 (5/64)-Disney; Annette Funicello photo front/back-c

| | 5 | 10 | 15 | 34 | 60 | 85 |

Moon-Spinners, The 10124-410 (10/64)-Disney; Hayley Mills photo-c

| | 6 | 12 | 18 | 37 | 66 | 95 |

Mutiny on the Bounty 1 (10040-302) (2/63)-Marlon Brando photo-c

| | 3 | 6 | 9 | 21 | 33 | 45 |

Nikki, Wild Dog of the North 10141-412 (12/64)-Disney; reprints 4-Color #1226

| | 3 | 6 | 9 | 16 | 23 | 30 |

Old Yeller 10168-601 (1/66)-Disney; reprints 4-Color #869; photo-c

| | 3 | 6 | 9 | 16 | 23 | 30 |

One Hundred & One Dalmations 1 (10247-002) (2/70)-Disney; reprints Four Color #1183

| | 3 | 6 | 9 | 21 | 33 | 45 |

Peter Pan 1 (10086-309)(9/63)-Disney; reprints Four Color #442

| | 4 | 8 | 12 | 25 | 40 | 55 |

Peter Pan 2 (10086-909)(9/69)-Disney; reprints Four Color #442

| | 3 | 6 | 9 | 19 | 30 | 40 |

Peter Pan 1 (3/84)-r/4-Color #442; Whitman pre-pack

| | 3 | 6 | 9 | 14 | 19 | 24 |

P.T. 109 10123-409 (9/64)-John F. Kennedy

| | 5 | 10 | 15 | 33 | 57 | 80 |

Rio Conchos 1143-503 (3/65)

| | 3 | 6 | 9 | 21 | 33 | 45 |

Robin Hood 10163-506 (6/65)-Disney; reprints Four Color #413

| | 3 | 6 | 9 | 16 | 23 | 32 |

Shaggy Dog & the Absent-Minded Professor 30032-708 (8/67-Giant, 68 pgs.) Disney; reprints 4-Color #985,1199

| | 5 | 10 | 15 | 30 | 50 | 70 |

Sleeping Beauty 1 (30042-009)(9/70)-Disney; reprints Four Color #973; with pull-out poster (No poster = half price)

| | 7 | 14 | 21 | 48 | 89 | 130 |

Snow White & the Seven Dwarfs 1 (10091-310)(10/63)-Disney; reprints Four Color #382

| | 4 | 8 | 12 | 28 | 47 | 65 |

Snow White & the Seven Dwarfs 10091-709 (9/67)-Disney; reprints Four Color #382

| | 4 | 8 | 12 | 23 | 37 | 50 |

Snow White & the Seven Dwarfs 90091-204 (2/84)-Reprints Four Color #382; Whitman pre-pack

| | 2 | 4 | 6 | 11 | 16 | 20 |

Son of Flubber 1 (10057-304)(4/63)-Disney; sequel to "The Absent-Minded Professor"

| | 3 | 6 | 9 | 21 | 33 | 45 |

Summer Magic 10076-309 (9/63)-Disney; Hayley Mills photo-c; Manning-a

| | 6 | 12 | 18 | 38 | 69 | 100 |

Swiss Family Robinson 10236-904 (4/69)-Disney; reprints Four Color #1156; photo-c

| | 4 | 8 | 12 | 27 | 44 | 60 |

Sword in the Stone, The 30019-402 (2/64-Giant, 68 pgs.)-Disney (see March of Comics #258 & Wart and the Wizard

| | 6 | 12 | 18 | 42 | 79 | 115 |

That Darn Cat 10171-602 (2/66)-Disney; Hayley Mills photo-c

| | 6 | 12 | 18 | 38 | 69 | 100 |

Those Magnificent Men in Their Flying Machines 10162-510 (10/65); photo-c

| | 3 | 6 | 9 | 19 | 30 | 40 |

Three Stooges in Orbit 30016-211 (11/62-Giant, 32 pgs.)-All photos from movie; stiff-photo-c

| | 9 | 18 | 27 | 60 | 120 | 180 |

Tiger Walks, A 10117-406 (6/64)-Disney; Torres?, Tufts-a; photo-c

| | 4 | 8 | 12 | 23 | 37 | 50 |

Toby Tyler 10142-502 (2/65)-Disney; reprints Four Color #1092; photo-c

| | 3 | 6 | 9 | 17 | 26 | 35 |

Treasure Island 1 (10200-703)(3/67)-Disney; reprints Four Color #624; photo-c

| | 3 | 6 | 9 | 16 | 23 | 30 |

20,000 Leagues Under the Sea 1 (10095-312)(12/63)-Disney; reprints Four Color #614

| | 3 | 6 | 9 | 19 | 30 | 40 |

Wonderful Adventures of Pinocchio, The 1 (10089-310)(10/63)-Disney; reprints Four Color #545 (see Wonderful Advs. of…)

| | 4 | 8 | 12 | 28 | 47 | 65 |

Wonderful Adventures of Pinocchio, The 10089-109 (9/71)-Disney; reprints Four Color #545

| | 3 | 6 | 9 | 16 | 24 | 32 |

Wonderful World of the Brothers Grimm 1 (10008-210)(10/62)

| | 5 | 10 | 15 | 31 | 53 | 75 |

X, the Man with the X-Ray Eyes 10083-309 (9/63)-Ray Milland photo on-c

| | 7 | 14 | 21 | 48 | 89 | 130 |

Yellow Submarine 35000-902 (2/69-Giant, 68 pgs.)-With pull-out poster; The Beatles cartoon movie; Paul S. Newman-s

| | 28 | 56 | 84 | 202 | 451 | 700 |

Without poster

| | 10 | 20 | 30 | 64 | 132 | 200 |

MOVIE FABLES
DC Comics: Dec, 1944 (cover only ashcan)

nn-Ashcan comic, not distributed to newsstands, only for in house use. Covers were produced, but not the rest of the book. A copy sold in 2006 for $500.

MOVIE GEMS
DC Comics: Dec, 1944 (cover only ashcan)

nn-Ashcan comic, not distributed to newsstands, only for in house use. Covers were produced, but not the rest of the book. A copy sold in 2006 for $500.

MOVIE LOVE (Also see Personal Love)
Famous Funnies: Feb, 1950 - No. 22, Aug, 1953 (All photo-c)

1-Dick Powell, Evelyn Keyes, & Mickey Rooney photo-c

| | 27 | 54 | 81 | 158 | 259 | 360 |

2-Myrna Loy photo-c

| | 16 | 32 | 48 | 94 | 147 | 200 |

3-7,9: 6-Ricardo Montalban photo-c. 9-Gene Tierney, John Lund, Glenn Ford, & Rhonda Fleming photo-c

| | 14 | 28 | 42 | 81 | 118 | 155 |

8-Williamson/Frazetta-a, 6 pgs.

| | 63 | 126 | 189 | 403 | 689 | 975 |

10-Frazetta-a, 6 pgs.

| | 61 | 122 | 183 | 390 | 670 | 950 |

11,14-16: 14-Janet Leigh photo-c

| | 14 | 28 | 42 | 80 | 115 | 150 |

12-Dean Martin & Jerry Lewis photo-c (12/51, pre-dates Advs. of Dean Martin & Jerry Lewis comic)

| | 33 | 66 | 99 | 194 | 317 | 440 |

13-Ronald Reagan photo-c with 1 pg. biog.

| | 39 | 78 | 117 | 231 | 378 | 525 |

17-Leslie Caron & Ralph Meeker photo-c; 1 pg. Frazetta ad

| | 14 | 28 | 42 | 78 | 112 | 145 |

18-22: 19-John Derek photo-c. 20-Donald O'Connor & Debbie Reynolds photo-c. 21-Paul Henreid & Patricia Medina photo-c. 22-John Payne & Coleen Gray photo-c

| | 13 | 26 | 39 | 74 | 105 | 135 |

NOTE: Each issue has a full-length movie adaptation with photo covers.

MOVIE MONSTERS (Magazine)
Atlas/Seaboard: Dec, 1974 - No. 4, Aug, 1975 (B&W; Film, photo & article magazine)

1-(84 pages) Planet of the Apes, King Kong, Sindbad & Harryhausen, Christopher Lee Dracula, Star Trek, Werewolf, Creature from the Black Lagoon, Hammer's Mummy, Gorgo, & Exorcist

| | 8 | 16 | 24 | 47 | 65 |

2-(2/1975) 2001: Planet of the Apes-c; 2001: A Space Odyssey, Doc Savage; Frankenstein; Rodan; One Million Years BC; (lower print run)

| | 8 | 16 | 24 | 47 | 65 |

3-(4/1975) Phantom of the Opera-c; Wolfman, Godzilla, Boris Karloff, Batman, Forbidden Planet, Jack the Giant Killer

| | 8 | 16 | 24 | 44 | 60 |

4-(6/1975) Thing, Flash Gordon, Lon Chaney Jr., Lost Worlds, Loch Ness Monster, Day the Earth Stood Still, Star Trek

| | 8 | 16 | 24 | 44 | 60 |

MOVIE THRILLERS (Movie)
Magazine Enterprises: 1949

1-Adaptation of "Rope of Sand" w/Burt Lancaster; Burt Lancaster photo-c

| | 30 | 60 | 90 | 177 | 289 | 400 |

MOVIE TOWN ANIMAL ANTICS (Formerly Animal Antics; becomes Raccoon Kids #52 on)
National Periodical Publ.: No. 24, Jan-Feb, 1950 - No. 51, July-Aug, 1954

24-Raccoon Kids continue

| | 13 | 26 | 39 | 72 | 101 | 130 |

25-51

| | 10 | 20 | 30 | 56 | 76 | 95 |

NOTE: Sheldon Mayer a-28-33, 35, 37-41, 43, 44, 47, 49-51.

MOVIE TUNES COMICS (Formerly Animated…; Frankie No. 4 on)
Marvel Comics (MgPC): No. 3, Fall, 1946

3-Super Rabbit, Krazy Krow, Silly Seal & Ziggy Pig

| | 21 | 42 | 63 | 124 | 202 | 280 |

MOWGLI JUNGLE BOOK (Rudyard Kipling's...)
Dell Publ. Co.: No. 487, Aug-Oct, 1953 - No. 620, Apr, 1955

Four Color 487 (#1)

| | 8 | 16 | 24 | 55 | 105 | 155 |

Four Color 582 (8/54), 620

| | 5 | 10 | 15 | 34 | 60 | 85 |

MPH
Image Comics: May, 2014 - No. 5, Feb, 2015 ($2.99/$4.99)

1-4-($2.99) Mark Millar-s/Duncan Fegredo-a; multiple covers on each

| | | | | | 3.00 |

5-($4.99) Two covers

| | | | | | 5.00 |

MR. (See Mister)

MRS. DEADPOOL AND THE HOWLING COMMANDOS (Secret Wars tie-in)
Marvel Comics: Aug, 2015 - No. 4, Nov, 2015 ($3.99, limited series)

1-4-Duggan-s/Espin-a; Dracula and Ghost Deadpool app.

| | | | | | 4.00 |

M. REX
Image Comics: July, 1999 - No. 2, Dec, 1999 ($2.95)

Preview ($5.00) B&W pages and sketchbook; Rouleau-a

| | | | | | 5.00 |

1,2-($2.95) 1-Joe Kelly-s/Rouleau-a/Anacleto-c. 2-Rouleau-a

| | | | | | 4.00 |

MS. MARVEL (Also see The Avengers #183)
Marvel Comics Group: Jan, 1977 - No. 23, Apr, 1979

1-1st app. Ms. Marvel; Scorpion app. in #1,2

| | 8 | 16 | 24 | 54 | 102 | 150 |

2-Origin

| | 4 | 8 | 12 | 23 | 37 | 50 |

3-10: 5-Vision app. 6-10(.30c-c). 9-1st Deathbird. 10-1st 30c issue

| | 3 | 6 | 9 | 14 | 19 | 24 |

6-10-(35¢-c variants, limited dist.)(6/77)

| | 15 | 30 | 45 | 103 | 227 | 350 |

11-15,19-22: 19-Capt. Marvel app. 20-New costume

| | 2 | 4 | 6 | 11 | 16 | 20 |

16-1st brief app. Mystique (Raven Darkholme)

| | 6 | 12 | 18 | 41 | 76 | 110 |

17-Brief app. Mystique, disguised as Nick Fury

| | 5 | 10 | 15 | 31 | 53 | 75 |

18-1st full app. Mystique; Avengers x-over

| | 14 | 28 | 42 | 96 | 211 | 325 |

23-Vance Astro (leader of the Guardians) app.

| | 3 | 6 | 9 | 18 | 27 | 36 |

NOTE: Austin c-14i, 16i, 17i, 22i. Buscema a-1-3p; c(p)-2, 4, 6, 7, 15. Infantino a-14p, 19p. Gil Kane c-8. Mooney a-4-8p, 13p, 15-18p. Starlin c-12.

MS. MARVEL (Also see New Avengers)
Marvel Comics: May, 2006 - No. 50, Apr, 2010 ($2.99)

1-Cho-c/Reed-s/De La Torre-a; Stilt-Man app.

| | 3 | 6 | 9 | 17 | 25 | 34 |

1-Variant cover by Michael Turner

| | 3 | 6 | 9 | 19 | 30 | 40 |

2-24: 4,5-Dr. Strange app. 6,7-Araña app.

| | | | | | 4.00 |

25-($3.99) Two covers by Horn and Dodson; Secret Invasion

| | | | | | 5.00 |

26-49: 26-31-Secret Invasion. 34-Spider-Man app. 35-Dark Reign. 37-Carol explodes. 39,40,46,48,49-Takeda-a. 40-Deadpool app. 41-Carol returns. 47-Spider-Man app.

| | | | | | 3.00 |

50-($3.99) Mystique and Captain Marvel app.; Takeda & Oliver-a

| | | | | | 5.00 |

... Annual 1 (11/08, $3.99) Spider-Man app.; Horn-c

| | | | | | 4.00 |

... Special (3/07, $2.99) Reed-s/Camuncoli-a/c

| | | | | | 3.00 |

... Storyteller (1/09, $2.99) Reed-s/Camuncoli-a/c

| | | | | | 3.00 |

... Vol. 1: Best of the Best HC (2006, $19.99) r/#1-5 & Giant-Size Ms. Marvel #1

| | | | | | 20.00 |

... Vol. 1: Best of the Best SC (2007, $14.99) r/#1-5 & Giant-Size Ms. Marvel #1

| | | | | | 15.00 |

... Vol. 2: Civil War HC (2007, $19.99) r/#6-10 & Ms. Marvel Special #1

| | | | | | 20.00 |

... Vol. 2: Civil War SC (2007, $14.99) r/#6-10 & Ms. Marvel Special #1

| | | | | | 15.00 |

... Vol. 3: Operation Lightning Storm HC (2007, $19.99) r/#11-17

| | | | | | 20.00 |

... Vol. 4: Monster Smash HC (2008, $19.99) r/#18-24

| | | | | | 20.00 |

MS. MARVEL (Kamala Khan)(See Captain Marvel [2012-2014] #14&17 for cameo 1st apps.)
Marvel Comics: Apr, 2014 - No. 19, Dec, 2015 ($2.99)

1-Intro. Kamala Khan; G. Willow Wilson-s/Adrian Alphona-a; Pichelli-c

| | 3 | 6 | 9 | 21 | 33 | 45 |

2-McKelvie-c

| | 1 | 3 | 4 | 6 | 8 | 10 |

3-7: 3-5-Alphona-a. 3-McKelvie-c. 6,7-Wolverine app.; Wyatt-a

| | | | | | 5.00 |

8-15: 8-11-Alphona-a. 9-Medusa app. 12-Loki app.; Bondoc-a. 13-15-Miyazawa-a.

| | | | | | 3.00 |

16-19-Secret Wars tie-ins. 19-Captain Marvel app.; Takeda-a

| | | | | | 3.00 |

...: Marvel Tales 1 (12/21, $7.99) Reprints early app. in Captain Marvel #17, All-New Marvel Now! Point One #1 and Ms. Marvel #1,2

| | | | | | 8.00 |

MS. MARVEL (Kamala Khan)(Follows events of Secret Wars)
Marvel Comics: Jan, 2016 - No. 38, Apr, 2019 ($4.99/$3.99)

Ms. Marvel (2016 series) #1 © MAR

Mulan: Revelations #2 © Project Mulan

Muppet Sherlock Holmes #2 © Muppet Studios

	GD	VG	FN	VF	VF/NM	NM-
	2.0	4.0	6.0	8.0	9.0	9.2

1-($4.99) Wilson/Miyazawa & Alphona-a; Chiang-c   1   2   3   5   6   8
2-11,13-30,32-38-($3.99) 2,3-Dr. Faustus app. 4-6 Nico Leon-a. 8-11-Civil War II tie-in.   4.00
12-($4.99) Andolfo-a; back-up Red Widow story   5.00
31-($4.99) 50th issue special; Wilson, Ahmed, Minhaj & Rowell-s; art by Leon & various   5.00
... & Moon Knight 1 (10/22, $4.99) Part 2; Houser-s Roberson-a; Hunter's Moon app.   5.00
... & Venom 1 (11/22, $4.99) Part 3 of story; Houser-s/Wachter-a; Wolverine app.   5.00
... & Wolverine 1 (11/22, $4.99) Part 1 of story; Houser-s/Carlos-a; X-Men app.   5.00

MS. MARVEL: BEYOND THE LIMIT (Kamala Khan)
Marvel Comics: Feb, 2022 - No. 5, Jun, 2022 ($3.99, limited series)
1-5-Samira Ahmed-s/Andrés Genolet-a   4.00

MS. MARVEL: THE NEW MUTANT (Kamala Khan)
Marvel Comics: Oct, 2023 - No. 4, Jan, 2024 ($4.99/$3.99)
1-($4.99) Iman Vellani & Sabir Pirzada-s   5.00
2-4-($3.99) X-Men app.   4.00

MS. MYSTIC
Pacific Comics: Oct, 1982 - No. 2, Feb, 1984 ($1.00/$1.50)
1,2: Neal Adams-c/a/script. 1-Origin; intro Erth, Aye, Fyre & Watr   5.00

MS. MYSTIC
Continuity Comics: 1988 - No. 9, May, 1992 ($2.00)
1-9: 1,2-Reprint Pacific Comics issues   4.00

MS. MYSTIC
Continuity Comics: V2#1, Oct, 1993 - V2#4, Jan, 1994 ($2.50)
V2#1-4: 1-Adams-c(i)/part-i. 2-4-Embossed-c. 2-Nebres part-i. 3-Adams-c(i)/plot.
4-Adams-c(p)/plot   4.00

MS. MYSTIC DEATHWATCH 2000 (Ms. Mystic #3)
Continuity: May, 1993 - No. 3, Aug, 1993 ($2.50)
1-3-Bagged w/card; Adams plots   4.00

MS. TREE QUARTERLY / SPECIAL
DC Comics: Summer, 1990 -No. 10, 1992 ($3.95/$3.50, 84 pgs, mature)
1-10: 1-Midnight story; Batman text story, Grell-a. 2,3-Midnight stories; The Butcher
text stories   4.00
NOTE: **Cowan** c-2. **Grell** c-1, 6. **Infantino** a-8.

MS. TREE'S THRILLING DETECTIVE ADVENTURES (Ms. Tree #4 on; also see The Best of
Ms. Tree)(Baxter paper #4-9) (See Eclipse Magazine #1 for 1st app.)
Eclipse Comics/Aardvark-Vanaheim 10-18/Renegade Press 19 on:
2/83 - #9, 7/84; #10, 8/84 - #18, 5/85; #19, 6/85 - #50, 6/89
1   5.00
2-49: 2-Scythe begins. 9-Last Eclipse & last color issue. 10,11-two-tone   4.00
50-Contains flexi-disc ($3.95, 52 pgs.)   5.00
Ms. Tree 3-D 1 (Renegade, 8/85)-With glasses; Mike Mist app.   4.00
Summer Special 1 (8/86)   4.00
1950s Three-Dimensional Crime (7/87, no glasses)-Johnny Dynamite in 3-D   4.00
NOTE: **Miller** pin-up 1-4. Johnny Dynamite r begin #36 by **Morisi.**

MS. VICTORY SPECIAL(Also see Capt. Paragon & Femforce)
Americomics: Jan, 1985 (nd)
1   4.00

MUCHA LUCHA (Based on Kids WB animated TV show)
DC Comics: Jun, 2003 - No. 3, Aug, 2003 ($2.25, limited series)
1-3-Rikochet, Buena Girl and The Flea app.   4.00

MUDMAN
Image Comics: Nov, 2011 - No. 6 ($3.50)
1-6-Paul Grist-s/a   3.50

MUGGSY MOUSE (Also see Tick Tock Tales)
Magazine Enterprises: 1951 - No. 3, 1951; No. 4, 1954 - No. 5, 1954; 1963
1(A-1 #33)	16	32	48	92	144	195
2(A-1 #36)-Racist-c	25	50	75	150	245	340
3(A-1 #39), 4(A-1 #95), 5(A-1 #99)	10	20	30	58	79	100
Super Reprint #14(1963), I.W. Reprint #1,2 (nd)	3	6	9	15	22	28

MUGGY-DOO, BOY CAT
Stanhall Publ.: July, 1953 - No. 4, Jan, 1954
1-Funny animal; Irving Spector-a	14	28	42	82	121	160
2-4	8	16	24	42	54	65
Super Reprint #12('63), 16('64)	2	4	6	11	16	20

MULAN: REVELATIONS
Dark Horse Comics: Jun, 2015 - No. 4, Nov, 2015 ($3.99)
1-4-Andreyko-s/Kaneshiro-a; Mulan in 2125 Shanghai   4.00

MULTIPLE MAN (Jamie Madrox from X-Factor)
Marvel Comics: Aug, 2018 - No. 5, Dec, 2018 ($3.99, limited series)
1-5: 1-Rosenberg-s/MacDonald-a; New Mutants & Beast app.   4.00

MULTIVERSITY, THE
DC Comics: Oct, 2014 - No. 2, Jun, 2015 ($4.99/$5.99)
1-($4.99) Morrison-s/Reis-a; Earth-23 Superman, Capt. Carrot, alternate Earth heroes gather   5.00
2-($5.99) Morrison-s/Reis-a/c   6.00
...1&2 Director's Cut (2/16, $7.99, squarebound) reprints #1&2 with original B&W pencil art
plus Morrison's original story proposals   8.00
...: Guidebook (3/15, $7.99) Legion of Sivanas, Kamandi app.; Multiverse map   8.00
...: Mastermen (4/15, $4.99) Earth-10 Overman & The Freedom Fighters; Jim Lee-a   5.00
...: Pax Americana 1 (1/15, $4.99) Earth-4 Charlton heroes; Quitely-a   5.00
... Pax Americana Director's Cut 1 (7/15, $9.99) Quitely pencil art and Morrison's script
excerpts; polybagged with large folded Multiverse map   10.00
...: The Just 1 (12/14, $4.99) Earth-16 Super-Sons and Justice League offspring; Oliver-a   5.00
...: The Society of Super-Heroes: Conquerors of the Counter-World 1 (11/14, $4.99) Earth-40
Dr. Fate, Green Lantern, Blackhawks, The Atom vs. Vandal Savage; Sprouse-a   5.00
...: Thunderworld Adventures 1 (2/15, $4.99) Earth-5 Shazam Family; Cam Stewart-c   5.00
...: Ultra Comics 1 (5/15, $4.99) Earth-33 Ultra; Mahnke-a   5.00

MULTIVERSITY: HARLEY SCREWS UP THE DCU
DC Comics: May, 2023 - No. 6, Oct, 2023 ($4.99, limited series)
1-6-Tieri-s/Faerber-a/Conner-c; Harley & Old Harley vs. Starro   5.00

MULTIVERSITY: TEEN JUSTICE
DC Comics: Aug, 2022 - No. 6, Jan, 2023 ($3.99, limited series)
1-6-Gender-swapped team from Earth-11; Cohen & Lore-s/Failla-a   4.00

MUMMY, THE (See Universal Presents... under Dell Giants & Movie Classics)

MUMMY, THE: PALIMPSEST
Titan Comics (Hammer Comics): Dec, 2016 - No. 5, May, 2017 ($3.99)
1-5-Peter Milligan-s/Ronilson Freire-a   4.00

MUMMY, THE: THE RISE AND FALL OF XANGO'S AX (Based on the Brendan Fraser movies)
IDW Publishing: Apr, 2008 - No. 4, July, 2008 ($3.99, limited series)
1-4-Prequel to '08 movie The Mummy: Tomb of the Dragon Emperor; Stephen Mooney-a   4.00

MUNCHKIN
BOOM! Studios (BOOM! Box): Jan, 2015 - No. 25, Jan, 2017 ($3.99)
1-24-Short stories of characters from the card game; each issue contains a card   4.00
25-($4.99) Covers by McGinty & Fridolfs   5.00
...: Deck the Dungeons (12/15, $4.99) Katie Cook-s/Mike Luckas-a; 2 covers   5.00

MUNDEN'S BAR ANNUAL
First Comics: Apr, 1988; 1989 ($2.95/$5.95)
1-($2.95)-r/from Grimjack; Fish Police story; Ordway-c   4.00
| 2-($5.95)-Teenage Mutant Ninja Turtles app. | 2 | 4 | 6 | 10 | 14 | 18 |

MUNSTERS, THE (TV)
Gold Key: Jan, 1965 - No. 16, Jan, 1968 (All photo-c)
1 (10134-501)	32	64	96	230	515	800
2	13	26	39	91	201	310
3-5	10	20	30	67	141	215
6-16	9	18	27	63	129	195

MUNSTERS, THE (TV)
TV Comics!: Aug, 1997 - No. 4 ($2.95, B&W)
1-4-All have photo-c	1	3	4	6	8	10
1,4-($7.95)-Variant-c	2	4	6	10	14	18
2-Variant-c w/Beverly Owens as Marilyn	1	3	4	6	8	10
Special Comic Con Ed. (7/97, $9.95)   10.00

MUPPET... (TV)
BOOM! Studios
... King Arthur 1-4 (12/09 - No. 4, 3/10, $2.99) Benjamin & Storck-s/Alvarez-a; 2 covers   3.00
... Peter Pan 1-4 (8/09 - No. 4, 11/09, $2.99) Randolph-s/Mebberson-a; multiple covers   3.00
... Robin Hood 1-4 (4/09 - No. 4, 7/09, $2.99) Beedle-s/Villavert Jr.-a; multiple covers   3.00
... Sherlock Holmes 1-4 (8/10 - No. 4, 11/10, $2.99) Storck-s/Mebberson-a/c   3.00
... Snow White 1-4 (4/10 - No. 4, 7/10, $2.99) Snider & Storck-s/Paroline-a; 2 covers   3.00

MUPPET BABIES, THE (TV)(See Star Comics Magazine)
Marvel Comics (Star Comics)/Marvel #18 on: Aug, 1985 - No. 26, July, 1989
(Children's book)
1	3	6	9	17	26	35
2-10	1	3	4	6	8	10
11-26						5.00

	GD 2.0	VG 4.0	FN 6.0	VF 8.0	VF/NM 9.0	NM- 9.2

MUPPETS (The Four Seasons)
Marvel Worldwide: Sept, 2012 - No. 4, Dec, 2012 ($2.99, limited series)
1-4-Roger Landridge-s/a — 3.00

MUPPET SHOW, THE (TV)
BOOM! Studios: Mar, 2009 - No. 4, Jun, 2009 ($2.99, limited series)
1-4-Roger Landridge-s/a; multiple covers — 3.00
...: The Treasure of Peg Leg Wilson (7/09 - No. 4, 10/09) 1-4-Landridge-s/a; multiple-c — 3.00

MUPPET SHOW COMIC BOOK, THE (TV)
BOOM! Studios: No. 0, Nov, 2009 - No. 11, Oct, 2010 ($2.99)
0-11: 0-3-Roger Landridge-s/a; multiple covers. 0-Paroline-a; Pigs in Space — 3.00

MUPPETS TAKE MANHATTAN, THE
Marvel Comics (Star Comics): Nov, 1984 - No. 3, Jan, 1985
1-3-Movie adapt. r-/Marvel Super Special — 5.00

MURCIELAGA, SHE-BAT
Heroic Publishing: Jan, 1993 - No. 2, 1993 (B&W)
1-($1.50, 28 pgs.) — 4.00
2-($2.95, 36 pgs.)-Coated-c — 4.00

MURDER CAN BE FUN
Slave Labor Graphics: Feb, 1996 - No. 12 ($2.95, B&W)
1-12: 1-Dorkin-c. 2-Vasquez-c — 4.00

MURDER INC.: JAGGER ROSE
Dark Horse Comics: May, 2023 - No. 6, Oct, 2023 ($3.99)
1-6-Bendis-s/Oeming-a — 4.00

MURDER INCORPORATED (My Private Life #16 on)
Fox Feature Syndicate: 1/48 - No. 15, 12/49; (2 No.9's); 6/50 - No. 3, 8/51

	GD 2.0	VG 4.0	FN 6.0	VF 8.0	VF/NM 9.0	NM- 9.2
1 (1st Series); 1,2 have 'For Adults Only' on-c	206	412	618	1318	2259	3200
2-Electrocution story	68	136	204	435	743	1050
3,5-7,9(4/49),10(5/49),11-15	41	82	123	256	428	600
4-Classic lingerie-c	271	542	813	1734	2967	4200
8-Used in SOTI, pg. 160	58	116	174	371	636	900
9(3/49)-Possible use in SOTI, pg. 145; r/Blue Beetle #56('48)	77	154	231	493	847	1200
5(#1, 6/50)(2nd Series)-Formerly My Desire #4; bondage-c.	32	64	96	188	307	425
2(8/50)-Morisi-a	28	56	84	168	274	380
3(8/51)-Used in POP, pg. 81; Rico-a; lingerie-c/panels	37	74	111	222	361	500

MURDERLAND
Image Comics: Aug, 2010 - No. 3, Nov, 2010 ($2.99)
1-3-Stephen Scott-s/David Haun-a — 3.00

MURDER ME DEAD
El Capitán Books: July, 2000 - No. 9, Oct, 2001 ($2.95/$4.95, B&W)
1-8-David Lapham-s/a — 3.00
9-($4.95) — 5.00

MURDEROUS GANGSTERS
Avon Periodical/Realistic No. 3 on: Jul, 1951; No. 2, Dec, 1951 - No. 4, Jun, 1952

	GD 2.0	VG 4.0	FN 6.0	VF 8.0	VF/NM 9.0	NM- 9.2
1-Pretty Boy Floyd, Leggs Diamond; 1 pg. Wood-a	161	322	483	1030	1765	2500
2-Baby-Face Nelson; 1 pg. Wood-a; classic painted-c	142	284	426	909	1555	2200
3-Painted-c	58	116	174	371	636	900
4- "Murder by Needle" drug story; Mort Lawrence-a; Kinstler-c	71	142	213	454	777	1100

MURDER MYSTERIES (Neil Gaiman's...)
Dark Horse Comics: 2002 ($13.95, HC, one-shot)
HC-Adapts Gaiman story; P. Craig Russell-script/art — 14.00

MURDER TALES (Magazine)
World Famous Publications: V1#10, Nov, 1970 - V1#11, Jan, 1971 (52 pgs.)

	GD 2.0	VG 4.0	FN 6.0	VF 8.0	VF/NM 9.0	NM- 9.2
V1#10-One pg. Frazetta ad	8	16	24	52	99	145
11-Guardineer-r; bondage-c	5	10	15	35	63	90

MURDERWORLD
Marvel Comics: Jan, 2023 - May, 2023 ($3.99, series of one-shots)
...: Avengers (1/23) Part 1; Arcane app.; Jim Zub & Ray Fawkes-s/Jethro Morales-a — 4.00
...: Game Over (5/23) Part 5; Jim Zub & Ray Fawkes-s/Tammetta-a — 4.00
...: Moon Knight (4/23) Part 4; Jim Zub & Ray Fawkes-s/Pizzari-a — 4.00
...: Spider-Man (2/23) Part 2; Jim Zub & Ray Fawkes-s/Karami-a — 4.00
...: Wolverine (3/23) Part 5; Jim Zub & Ray Fawkes-s/Nieto-a — 4.00

MUSHMOUSE AND PUNKIN PUSS (TV)
Gold Key: September, 1965 (Hanna-Barbera)

	GD 2.0	VG 4.0	FN 6.0	VF 8.0	VF/NM 9.0	NM- 9.2
1 (10153-509)	8	16	24	55	105	155

MUSIC BOX (Jennifer Love Hewitt's...)
IDW Publishing: Nov, 2009 - No. 5, Apr, 2010 ($3.99, lim. series)
1-5-Anthology; Scott Lobdell-s/art by various. 1-Gaydos-a. 3-Archer-a — 4.00

MUSIC MAN, THE (See Movie Classics)

MUTANT CHRONICLES (Video game)
Acclaim Comics (Armada): May, 1996 - No. 4, Aug, 1996 ($2.95, lim. series)
1-4: Simon Bisley-c on all, Sourcebook (#5) — 4.00

MUTANT EARTH (Stan Winston's...)
Image Comics: April, 2002 - No. 4, Jan, 2003 ($2.95)
1-4-Flip book w/Realm of the Claw — 3.00
Trakk...His Adventures in Mutant Earth TPB (2003, $16.95) r/#1-4; Winston interview — 17.00

MUTANT MISADVENTURES OF CLOAK AND DAGGER, THE
(Becomes Cloak and Dagger #14 on)
Marvel Comics: Oct, 1988 - No. 19, Aug, 1991 ($1.25/$1.50)
1-8,10-15: 1-X-Factor app. 10-Painted-c. 12-Dr. Doom app. 14-Begin new direction — 4.00

9,16-19: 9-(52 pgs.) The Avengers x-over; painted-c. 16-18-Spider-Man x-over. 18-Infinity Gauntlet x-over; Thanos cameo; Ghost Rider app. 19-(52 pgs.) Origin Cloak & Dagger — 5.00
NOTE: Austin a-12i; c(i)-4, 12, 13; scripts-all. Russell a-2i. Williamson a-14i-16i; c-15i.

MUTANTS & MISFITS
Silverline Comics (Solson): 1987 - No. 3, 1987 ($1.95)
1-3 — 4.00

MUTANTS VS. ULTRAS
Malibu Comics (Ultraverse): Nov, 1995 ($6.95, one-shot)
1-r/Exiles vs. X-Men, Night Man vs. Wolverine, Prime vs. Hulk — 7.00

MUTANT, TEXAS: TALES OF SHERIFF IDA RED (Also see Jingle Belle)
Oni Press: May, 2002 - No. 4, Nov, 2002 ($2.95, B&W, limited series)
1-4-Paul Dini-s/J. Bone-c/a — 3.00
TPB (2003, $11.95) r/#1-4; intro. by Joe Lansdale — 12.00

MUTANT 2099
Marvel Comics (Marvel Knights): Nov, 2004 ($2.99, one-shot)
1-Kirkman-s/Pat Lee-c — 3.00

MUTANT X (See X-Factor)
Marvel Comics: Nov, 1998 - No. 32, June, 2001 ($2.99/$1.99/$2.25)
1-($2.99) Alex Summers with alternate world's X-Men — 5.00
2-11,13-19-($1.99): 2-Two covers. 5-Man-Spider-c/app. — 4.00
12,25-($2.99): 12-Pin-up gallery by Kaluta, Romita, Byrne — 5.00
20-24,26-32: 20-Begin $2.25-c. 28-31-Logan-c/app. 32-Last issue — 4.00
Annual '99, '00 (5/99,'00, $3.50) '00-Doran-a(p) — 5.00
Annual 2001 ($2.99) Story occurs between #31 & #32; Dracula app. — 5.00

MUTANT X (Based on TV show)
Marvel Comics: May, 2002; June, 2002 ($3.50)
...: Dangerous Decisions (6/02) -Kuder-s/Immonen-a — 3.50
...: Origin (5/02) -Tischman & Chaykin-s/Ferguson-a — 3.50

MUTATIS
Marvel Comics (Epic Comics): 1992 - No. 3, 1992 ($2.25, mini-series)
1-3: Painted-c — 4.00

MUTIES
Marvel Comics: Apr, 2002 - No. 6, Sept, 2002 ($2.50)
1-6: 1-Bollars-s/Ferguson-a. 2-Spaziante-a. 3-Haspiel-a. 4-Kanuiga-a — 3.00

MUTINY (Stormy Tales of the Seven Seas)
Aragon Magazines: Oct, 1954 - No. 3, Feb, 1955

	GD 2.0	VG 4.0	FN 6.0	VF 8.0	VF/NM 9.0	NM- 9.2
1-Backlash torture bondage-c	22	44	66	128	209	290
2,3: 2-Capt. Mutiny. 3-Lashing torture bondage-c	16	32	48	92	144	195

MUTINY ON THE BOUNTY (See Classics Illustrated #100 & Movie Comics)

MUTOPIA X (Also see House of M and related titles)
Marvel Comics: Sept, 2005 - No. 5, Jan, 2006 ($2.99, limited series)
1-5-Medina-a/Hine-a — 3.00
House of M: Mutopia X (2006, $13.99, TPB) r/series — 14.00

MUTT AND JEFF (See All-American, All-Flash #18, Cicero's Cat, Comic Cavalcade, Famous Feature Stories, The Funnies, Popular & Xmas Comics)
All American/National 1-103(6/58)/Dell 104(10/58)-115 (10-12/59)/Harvey 116(2/60)-148: Summer, 1939 (No.1) - No. 148, Nov, 1965

	GD 2.0	VG 4.0	FN 6.0	VF 8.0	VF/NM 9.0	NM- 9.2
1(nn)-Lost Wheels	213	426	639	1363	2332	3300
2(nn)-Charging Bull (Summer, 1940, nd; on sale 6/20/40)	97	194	291	621	1061	1500
3(nn)-Bucking Broncos (Summer, 1941, nd)	61	122	183	390	670	950
4(Winter, '41), 5(Summer, '42)	55	110	165	352	601	850
6-10: 6-Includes Minute Man Answers the Call	32	64	96	188	307	425
11-20: 20-X-Mas-c	21	42	63	126	206	285
21-30	16	32	48	94	147	200
31-50: 32-X-Mas-c	14	28	42	82	121	160
51-75-Last Fisher issue. 53-Last 52 pgs.	12	24	36	67	94	120
76-99,101-103: 76-Last pre-code issue(1/55)	5	10	15	35	63	90
100	6	12	18	37	66	95
104-115,132-148	5	10	15	30	48	65
116-131-Richie Rich app.	5	10	15	32	51	70
...Jokes 1-3(8/60-61, Harvey)-84 pgs.; Richie Rich in all; Little Dot in #2,3; Lotta in #2						65
...New Jokes 1-4(10/63-11/65, Harvey)-68 pgs.; Richie Rich in #1-3; Stumbo in #1	4	8	12	24	37	50

NOTE: Most all issues by Al Smith. Issues from 1963 on have Fisher reprints. Clarification: early issues signed by Fisher are mostly drawn by Smith.

MY BAD
AHOY Comics: 2021 - No. 5, 2022 ($3.99)
1-5-Mark Russell-s/Bryce Ingman-a; intro The Chandelier, Emperor King, Rush Hour — 4.00

MY BAD (Volume 2)
AHOY Comics: 2022 - No. 5, 2023 ($3.99)
1-5-Mark Russell-s/Bryce Ingman-a — 4.00

MY BROTHERS' KEEPER
Spire Christian Comics (Fleming H. Revell Co.): 1973 (35/49¢, 36 pgs.)

	GD 2.0	VG 4.0	FN 6.0	VF 8.0	VF/NM 9.0	NM- 9.2
nn	2	4	6	13	18	22

MY CONFESSIONS (My Confession #7&8; formerly Western True Crime; A Spectacular Feature Magazine #11)
Fox Feature Syndicate: No. 7, Aug, 1949 - No. 10, Jan-Feb, 1950

	GD 2.0	VG 4.0	FN 6.0	VF 8.0	VF/NM 9.0	NM- 9.2
7-Wood-a (10 pgs.)	97	194	291	621	1061	1500
8,9: 8-Harrison/Wood-a (19 pgs.). 9-Wood-a	43	86	129	271	461	650
10	28	56	84	165	270	375

MYCROFT HOLMES AND THE APOCALYPSE HANDBOOK
Titan Comics: Sept, 2016 - No. 5, Mar, 2017 ($3.99)
1-5-Sherlock Holmes' older brother; Kareem Abdul-Jabbar & Raymond Obstfeld-s — 4.00

MY DATE COMICS (Teen-age)

	GD 2.0	VG 4.0	FN 6.0	VF 8.0	VF/NM 9.0	NM- 9.2
Hillman Periodicals: July, 1947 - V1#4, Jan, 1948				2nd Romance comic; see Young Romance)		
1-S&K-c/a	74	148	222	470	810	1150
2-4-S&K-c/a; Dan Barry-a	39	78	117	231	376	525
MY DATE WITH MONSTERS						
AfterShock Comics: Nov, 2021 - No. 5, Mar, 2022 ($4.99/$3.99, limited series)						
1-($4.99) Paul Tobin-s/Andy MacDonald-a						5.00
2,3-($3.99)						4.00
MY DESIRE (Formerly Jo-Jo Comics; becomes Murder, Inc. #5 on)						
Fox Feature Syndicate: No. 30, Aug, 1949 - No. 4, April, 1950						
30 (#1)	36	72	108	214	347	480
31 (#2, 10/49),3(2/50),4	24	48	72	142	234	325
31 (Canadian edition)	15	30	45	86	133	180
32(12/49)-Wood-a	39	78	117	240	395	550
MY DIARY (Becomes My Friend Irma #3 on?)						
Marvel Comics (A Lovers Mag.): Dec, 1949 - No. 2, Mar, 1950						
1,2-Photo-c	27	54	81	158	259	360
MY EXPERIENCE (Formerly All Top; becomes Judy Canova #23 on)						
Fox Feature Syndicate: No. 19, Sept, 1949 - No. 2, Mar, 1950						
19,21: 19-Wood-a. 21-Wood-a(2)	41	82	123	256	428	600
20	23	46	69	136	223	310
22-Wood-a (9 pgs.)	39	78	117	231	378	525
MY FAITH IN FRANKIE						
DC Comics (Vertigo): March, 2004 - No. 4, June, 2004 ($2.95, limited series)						
1-4-Mike Carey-s/Sonny Liew & Marc Hempel-a						3.00
TPB (2004, $6.95, digest-size) r/series in B&W; Dead Boy Detectives preview						7.00
MY FAVORITE MARTIAN (TV)						
Gold Key: 1/64; No.2, 7/64 - No. 9, 10/66 (No. 1,3,9 have photo-c)						
1-Russ Manning-a	12	24	36	82	179	275
2	6	12	18	42	79	115
3-9	5	10	15	35	63	90
MY FRIEND IRMA (Radio/TV) (Formerly My Diary, and/or Western Life Romances?)						
Marvel/Atlas Comics (BFP): No. 3, June, 1950 - No. 47, Dec, 1954; No. 48, Feb, 1955						
3-Dan DeCarlo-a in all; 52 pgs. begin, end ?	103	206	309	659	1130	1600
4-Kurtzman-a (10 pgs.)	43	86	129	271	461	650
5- "Egghead Doodle" by Kurtzman (4 pgs.)	28	56	84	168	274	380
6,8-10: 9-Paper dolls, 1 pg. Millie app. (5 pgs.)	22	44	66	128	209	290
7-One pg. Kurtzman-a	23	46	69	136	223	310
11-23: 23-One pg. Frazetta-a	17	34	51	100	158	215
24-48: 41,48-Stan Lee & Dan DeCarlo app.	16	32	48	94	147	200
MY GIRL PEARL						
Atlas Comics: 4/55 - #4, 10/55; #5, 7/57 - #6, 9/57; #7, 8/60 - #11, ?/61						
1-Dan DeCarlo-c/a in #1-6	110	220	330	704	1202	1700
2	48	96	144	302	514	775
3-6	39	78	117	231	378	525
7-11	17	34	51	114	252	390
MY GREATEST ADVENTURE (Doom Patrol #86 on)						
National Periodical Publications: Jan-Feb, 1955 - No. 85, Feb, 1964						
1-Before CCA	159	318	477	1312	2956	4600
2	64	128	192	512	1156	1800
3-5	46	92	138	340	770	1200
6-10: 6-Science fiction format begins	35	70	105	252	564	875
11-14: 12-1st S.A. issue	27	54	81	189	420	650
15-17: Kirby-a in all	29	58	87	209	467	725
18-Kirby-c/a	31	62	93	203	499	775
19,23-25	23	46	69	156	348	540
20,21,28-Kirby-a	24	54	81	189	420	650
22-Space Ranger prototype (7-8/58)(see Showcase #15 for Space Ranger debut)	26	52	78	182	404	625
26,27,29,30	18	36	54	128	284	440
31-40	15	30	45	105	233	360
41,42,44-57,59	14	28	42	94	207	320
43-Kirby-a	15	30	45	100	220	340
58,60,61-Toth-a; Last 10¢ issue	14	28	42	97	214	330
62-76,78,79: 79-Promotes "Legion of the Strange" for next issue; renamed Doom Patrol for #80	12	24	36	79	170	260
77-Toth-a; Robotman prototype	13	26	39	86	188	290
80-(6/63)-Intro/origin Doom Patrol and begin series; origin & 1st app. Negative Man, Elasti-Girl & S.A. Robotman	155	310	465	1279	2890	4500
80 (Facsimile Edition)(9/23, $3.99) Reprints issue with original ads and letter column						6.00
81,85-Toth-a	26	52	78	182	404	625
82-84	23	46	69	156	348	540
NOTE: **Anderson** a-42. **Cameron** a-24. **Colan** a-77. **Meskin** a-25, 26, 32, 39, 45, 50, 56, 57, 61, 64, 70, 73, 74, 76, 79; c-76. **Moreira** a-11, 12, 15, 17, 20, 23, 25, 27, 37, 40-43, 46, 48, 55-57, 59, 60, 62-65, 67, 69, 70; c-1-4, 7-10. **Roussos** c/a-71-73. **Wildey** a-32.						
MY GREATEST ADVENTURE (Also see 2011 Weird Worlds series)						
DC Comics: Dec, 2011 - No. 6, May, 2012 ($3.99, limited series)						
1-6-Short stories of Tanga, Robotman, and Garbage Man; Lopresti-s/a, Maguire-s/a						4.00
MY GREAT LOVE (Becomes Will Rogers Western #5)						
Fox Feature Syndicate: Oct, 1949 - No. 4, Apr, 1950						
1	34	68	102	199	325	450
2-4	19	38	57	111	176	240
MY INTIMATE AFFAIR (Inside Crime #3)						
Fox Feature Syndicate: Mar, 1950 - No. 2, May, 1950						
1	47	94	141	296	498	700
2	20	40	60	117	189	260
MY LIFE (Formerly Meet Corliss Archer)						
Fox Feature Syndicate: No. 4, Sept, 1948 - No. 15, July, 1950						
4-Used in **SOTI**, pg. 39; Kamen/Feldstein-a	84	168	252	538	919	1300
5-Kamen-a	43	86	129	271	461	650
6-Kamen/Feldstein-a	48	96	144	302	514	725
7-Wood-a; wash cover	50	100	150	315	533	750
8,9,11-15	26	52	78	154	252	350
10-Wood-a	39	78	117	231	378	525
MY LITTLE MARGIE (TV)						
Charlton Comics: July, 1954 - No. 54, Nov, 1964						
1-Photo front/back-c	43	86	129	271	461	650
2-Photo front/back-c	22	44	66	128	209	290
3-7,10	14	28	42	82	121	160
8,9-Infinity-c	14	28	42	82	121	160
11-14: Part-photo-c (#13, 8/56). 14-UFO cover	13	26	39	72	101	130
15-19	12	24	36	67	94	120
20-(25¢, 100 pg. issue)	17	34	51	100	158	215
21-40: 40-Last 10¢ issue	5	10	15	35	63	90
41-53	5	10	15	33	57	80
54-(11/64) Beatles on cover; lead story spoofs the Beatle haircut craze of the 1960's; Beatles app. (scarce)	21	42	63	147	324	500
NOTE: Doll cut-outs in 32, 33, 40, 45, 50.						
MY LITTLE MARGIE'S BOY FRIENDS (TV) (Freddy V2#12 on)						
Charlton Comics: Aug, 1955 - No. 11, Apr?, 1958						
1-Has several Archie swipes	20	40	60	117	189	260
2	12	24	36	67	94	120
3-11	10	20	30	54	72	90
MY LITTLE MARGIE'S FASHIONS (TV)						
Charlton Comics: Feb, 1959 - No. 5, Nov, 1959						
1	22	44	66	132	216	300
2-5	10	20	30	58	79	100
MY LITTLE PHONY: A BRONY ADVENTURE						
Dynamite Entertainment: 2014 ($5.99, one-shot)						
1-My Little Pony fandom parody; Moreci & Seeley-a/Haeser & Baal-a; 2 covers						6.00
MY LITTLE PONY						
IDW Publishing						
... Annual #1: Equestria Girls (10/13, $7.99) Price & Fleecs-a; multiple covers						10.00
... Annual 2014 (9/14, $7.99) Anderson-s/Bates-a; two covers						8.00
... Annual 2017 (2/17, $7.99) Short stories by Whitley, Rice, Price & others; two covers						8.00
... Art Gallery (11/13, $3.99) Pin-ups by Sara Richard & others						4.00
... Best of Applejack (10/23, $6.99) Character highlights from MLP:FIM #72,85 and others						7.00
... Best of Pinkie Pie (8/23, $6.99) Character highlights from MLP:FIM #86,94,95						7.00
... Best of Rarity (2/24, $7.99) Character highlights from MLP:FIM #42 and others						8.00
... Black, White & Blue (10/23, $5.99) Tee Franklin-s/Agnes Garbowska-a						7.00
... Cover Gallery (8/13, $3.99) Gallery of regular and variant covers						4.00
... 40th Anniversary (7/23, $8.99) Main story with Maggs-s/Okafor-a						12.00
... Halloween Comicfest 2016 (10/16, giveaway) reprints Friends Forever #4						3.00
... Holiday Special (12/15, $3.99) Whitley, Fleecs, Garbowska, Price, Cook-a; 3 covers						6.00
... Holiday Special 2017 (12/17, $4.99) Asmus-s/Hickey-a; 3 covers						5.00
... Holiday Special (11/19, $4.99) Asmus-s/Price & Forstner-a; 3 covers						5.00
... Valentine's Day Special, Romeo & Juliet (2/24, $4.99) Megan Brown-s						5.00
MY LITTLE PONY						
IDW Publishing: May, 2022 - No. 20, Dec, 2024 ($3.99)						

	GD 2.0	VG 4.0	FN 6.0	VF 8.0	VF/NM 9.0	NM- 9.2

1-20: 1-Bronfman-s/Mebberson-a ... 4.00

MY LITTLE PONY: CAMP BIGHOOF
IDW Publishing: Jul, 2023 - No. 5, Dec, 2023 ($3.99, limited series)
1-5-Stephanie Cooke-s/Kate Sherron-a ... 4.00

MY LITTLE PONY: CLASSICS REIMAGINED - LITTLE FILLIES
IDW Publishing: Nov, 2022 - No. 4, Feb, 2023 ($3.99, limited series)
1-4-Megan Brown-s/Jenna Ayoub-a ... 4.00

MY LITTLE PONY: CLASSICS REIMAGINED - THE UNICORN OF ODD
IDW Publishing: Aug, 2023 - No. 4, Dec, 2023 ($3.99, limited series)
1-4-Jeremy Whitley-s/Jenna Ayoub-a ... 4.00

MY LITTLE PONY: FEATS OF FRIENDSHIP
IDW Publishing: Aug, 2019 - No. 3, Oct, 2019 ($3.99, limited series)
1-3-Ian Flynn-s/Tony Fleecs-a ... 4.00

MY LITTLE PONY: FIENDS FOREVER
IDW Publishing: Apr, 2015 - No. 5, May, 2015 ($3.99, weekly mini-series)
1-5-Spotlight on Equestria's villains. 1-Whitley-s/Hickey-a. 3-Garbowska-a ... 4.00

MY LITTLE PONY: FRIENDS FOREVER
IDW Publishing: Jan, 2014 - No. 38, Mar, 2017 ($3.99)
1-38: 1-de Campi-s/McNeil-a; multiple covers. 3,6,10,13,14,21,27,30,34,37-Garbowska-a. 8-Katie Cook-s ... 4.00
... - Halloween Fest 2014 (10/14, giveaway) reprints #2 ... 3.00

MY LITTLE PONY: FRIENDSHIP IS MAGIC
IDW Publishing: Nov, 2012 - No. 102, Sept, 2021 ($3.99)
1-Katie Cook-s/Andy Price-a; 7 covers ... 10.00
1-Subscription variant cover by Jill Thompson ... 10.00
2-49,51-74,76-99,101-Multiple covers on each. 18,19-Interlocking covers ... 4.00
50-($5.99) Anderson-s/Price-a; Whitley-s/Fosgitt-a ... 6.00
75-($7.99) Katie Cook-s/Andy Price-s/a; four covers ... 8.00
100-($7.99) Jeremy Whitley-s/Andy Price-s/a; four covers; bonus pin-ups ... 8.00
102-($5.99) Jeremy Whitley-s/Andy Price-s/a; last issue; three covers; bonus pin-ups ... 6.00
... #1 Greatest Hits (8/16, $1.00) reprints #1 ... 3.00
... #1 Hundred Penny Press (2/14, $1.00) reprints #1 ... 3.00
... Deviations 1 (3/17, $4.99) Cook-s/Garbowska-a; 3 covers; Prince Blueblood app. ... 5.00
... 10th Anniversary Edition (12/22, $7.99) Reprints #1 ... 8.00
... 20/20 (1/19, $4.99) Ponies meet their future selves; Anderson-s/Kuusisto-a ... 5.00

MY LITTLE PONY: GENERATIONS
IDW Publishing: Oct, 2021 - No. 5, Feb, 2022 ($3.99)
1-5-Gilly-s/Cacciatore-a ... 4.00

MY LITTLE PONY: KENBUCKY ROLLER DERBY
IDW Publishing: Jan, 2024 - Present ($3.99)
1,2-Gilly-s/Haines-a ... 4.00

MY LITTLE PONY: LEGENDS OF MAGIC
IDW Publishing: Apr, 2017 - No. 12, Mar, 2018 ($3.99)
1-12: 1-6-Whitley-s/Hickey-a. 7-12-Fleecs-a ... 4.00
Annual 2018 (4/18, $7.99) Whitley-s/Hickey-a ... 8.00

MY LITTLE PONY MICRO-SERIES
IDW Publishing: Feb, 2013 - No. 10, Dec, 2013 ($3.99)
1-Twilight Sparkle - Zahler-s/a ... 5.00
2-10: 2-Rainbow Dash. 3-Rarity. 4-Fluttershy ... 4.00

MY LITTLE PONY: NIGHTMARE KNIGHTS
IDW Publishing: Oct, 2018 - No. 5, Feb, 2019 ($3.99, limited series)
1-5-Whitley-s/Fleecs-a ... 4.00

MY LITTLE PONY: PONYVILLE MYSTERIES
IDW Publishing: May, 2018 - Aug, 2018 ($3.99, limited series)
1-4-Christina Rice-s/Agnes Garbowska-a ... 4.00

MY LITTLE PONY: SPIRIT OF THE FOREST
IDW Publishing: May, 2019 - No. 3, Jul, 2019 ($3.99, limited series)
1-3-Whitley-s/Hickey-a ... 4.00

MY LITTLE PONY: THE MOVIE PREQUEL
IDW Publishing: Jun, 2017 - No. 4, Sept, 2017 ($3.99, limited series)
1-4-Ted Anderson-s/Andy Price-a; The Storm King app. ... 4.00

MY LITTLE PONY / TRANSFORMERS
IDW Publishing: Apr, 2021 - No. 4, Jul, 2021 ($3.99, limited series)
1-4-Anthology of short stories by various ... 4.00

MY LOVE (Becomes Two Gun Western #5 (11/50) on?)
Marvel Comics (CLDS): July, 1949 - No. 4, Apr, 1950 (All photo-c)

	GD 2.0	VG 4.0	FN 6.0	VF 8.0	VF/NM 9.0	NM- 9.2
1	31	62	93	186	303	420
2,3	20	40	60	114	182	250
4-Bettie Page photo-c (see Cupid #2)	61	122	183	390	670	950

MY LOVE
Marvel Comics Group: Sept, 1969 - No. 39, Mar, 1976

	GD 2.0	VG 4.0	FN 6.0	VF 8.0	VF/NM 9.0	NM- 9.2
1	11	22	33	72	154	235
2-9: 4-6-Colan-a	6	12	18	37	66	95
10-Williamson-r/My Own Romance #71; Kirby-a	6	12	18	38	69	100
11-13,15-19	5	10	15	31	53	75
14-(52 pgs.)-Woodstock-s/sty; Morrow-c/a; Kirby/Colletta-r	12	24	36	79	170	260
20-Starlin-a	5	10	15	31	53	75
21,22,24-27,29-38: 38-Reprints	4	8	12	27	44	60
23-Steranko-r/Our Love Story #5	5	10	15	30	50	70
28-Kirby-a	4	8	12	28	47	65
39-Last issue; reprints	5	10	15	30	50	70
Special 1 (12/71)(52 pgs.)	6	12	18	41	76	110

NOTE: *John Buscema* a-1-7, 10, 18-21, 22r(2), 24r, 25r, 29r, 34r, 36r, 37r, Spec. (r)(4); c-13, 15, 25, 27, Spec. *Colan* a-4, 5, 6, 8, 9, 16, 17, 20, 21, 22, 24r, 27r, 30r, 35r, 39r. *Colan/Everett* a-13, 15, 16, 27(r/#13). *Kirby* a-(r-)

10, 14, 26, 28. *Romita* a-1-3, 19, 20, 25, 34, 38; c-1-3, 15.

MY LOVE AFFAIR (March of Crime #7 on)
Fox Feature Syndicate: July, 1949 - No. 6, May, 1950

	GD 2.0	VG 4.0	FN 6.0	VF 8.0	VF/NM 9.0	NM- 9.2
1	43	86	129	271	461	650
2	20	40	60	120	195	270
3-6-Wood-a. 5-(3/50)-Becomes Love Stories #6	36	72	108	211	343	475

MY LOVE LIFE (Formerly Zegra)
Fox Feature Synd.: No. 6, June, 1949 - No. 13, Aug, 1950; No. 13, Sept, 1951

	GD 2.0	VG 4.0	FN 6.0	VF 8.0	VF/NM 9.0	NM- 9.2
6-Kamenish-a	39	78	117	231	378	525
7-13	21	42	63	122	199	275
13 (9/51)(Formerly My Story #12)	19	38	57	111	176	240

MY LOVE MEMOIRS (Formerly Women Outlaws; Hunted #13 on)
Fox Feature Syndicate: No. 9, Nov, 1949 - No. 12, May, 1950

	GD 2.0	VG 4.0	FN 6.0	VF 8.0	VF/NM 9.0	NM- 9.2
9,11,12-Wood-a	39	78	117	231	378	525
10	20	40	60	117	189	260

MY LOVE SECRET (Formerly Phantom Lady; Animal Crackers #31)
Fox Feature Syndicate/M. S. Distr.: No. 24, June, 1949 - No. 30, June, 1950; No. 53, 1954

	GD 2.0	VG 4.0	FN 6.0	VF 8.0	VF/NM 9.0	NM- 9.2
24-Kamen/Feldstein-a	39	78	117	231	378	525
25-Possible caricature of Wood on-c?	23	46	69	136	223	310
26,28-Wood-a	35	70	105	208	339	470
27,29,30: 30-Photo-c	22	44	66	128	209	290
53-(Reprint, M.S. Distr.) 1954? nd given; formerly Western Thrillers; becomes Crimes by Women #54; photo-c	14	28	42	76	108	140

MY LOVE STORY (Hoot Gibson Western #5 on)
Fox Feature Syndicate: Sept, 1949 - No. 4, Mar, 1950

	GD 2.0	VG 4.0	FN 6.0	VF 8.0	VF/NM 9.0	NM- 9.2
1	36	72	108	211	343	475
2	20	40	60	117	189	260
3,4-Wood-a	37	74	111	218	354	490

MY LOVE STORY
Atlas Comics (GPS): April, 1956 - No. 9, Aug, 1957

	GD 2.0	VG 4.0	FN 6.0	VF 8.0	VF/NM 9.0	NM- 9.2
1	24	48	72	142	234	325
2	15	30	45	86	133	180
3,7: Matt Baker-a. 7-Toth-a	20	40	60	114	182	250
4-6,8,9	15	30	45	84	127	170

NOTE: *Brewster* a-3. *Colletta* a-1(2), 3, 4(2), 5; c-3.

MYLO XYLOTO COMICS
Bongo Comics: 2013 - No. 6, 2013 ($3.99, limited series)
1-6-Mark Osborne & Coldplay-s/Fuentes-a ... 4.00

MY NAME IS BRUCE
Dark Horse Comics: Sept, 2008 ($3.50, one-shot)
nn-Adaptation of the Bruce Campbell movie; Cliff Richards-a/Bart Sears-c ... 3.50

MY NAME IS HOLOCAUST
DC Comics: May, 1995 - No. 5, Sept, 1995 ($2.50, limited series)

	GD 2.0	VG 4.0	FN 6.0	VF 8.0	VF/NM 9.0	NM- 9.2
1-5	1	2	3	4	5	7

MY ONLY LOVE
Charlton Comics: July, 1975 - No. 9, Nov, 1976

	GD 2.0	VG 4.0	FN 6.0	VF 8.0	VF/NM 9.0	NM- 9.2
1	3	6	9	16	24	32
2,4-9	2	4	6	9	13	16
3-Toth-a	2	4	6	11	16	20

MY OWN ROMANCE (Formerly My Romance; Teen-Age Romance #77 on)
Marvel/Atlas (MjPC/RCM No. 4-59/ZPC No. 60-76): No. 4, Mar, 1949 - No. 76, July, 1960

	GD 2.0	VG 4.0	FN 6.0	VF 8.0	VF/NM 9.0	NM- 9.2
4-Photo-c	30	60	90	177	289	400
5-10: 5,6,8-10-Photo-c	19	38	57	111	176	240
11-20: 14-Powell-a	16	32	48	94	147	200
21-42,55: 42-Last precode (2/55). 55-Toth-a	15	30	45	90	140	190
43-54,56-60	9	18	27	59	117	175
61-70,72,73,75,76	9	18	27	57	111	165
71-Williamson-a	9	18	27	60	120	180
74-Kirby-a	9	18	27	60	120	180

NOTE: *Brewster* a-59. *Colletta* a-45(2), 48, 50, 55, 57(2), 59; c-58i, 59, 61. *Everett* a-25; c-58p. *Kirby* c-71, 75, 76. *Maneely* c-18. *Morisi* a-18. *Orlando* a-61. *Romita* a-36. *Tuska* a-10.

MY PAL DIZZY (See Color Books, Series I)

MY PAST (...Confessions) (Formerly Western Thrillers)
Fox Feature Syndicate: No. 7, Aug, 1949 - No. 11, Apr, 1950 (Crimes Inc. #12)

	GD 2.0	VG 4.0	FN 6.0	VF 8.0	VF/NM 9.0	NM- 9.2
7	34	68	102	204	332	460
8-10	20	40	60	117	189	260
11-Wood-a	34	68	102	204	332	460

MY PERSONAL PROBLEM
Ajax/Farrell/Steinway Comic: 11/55, No. 2, 2/56; No. 3, 9/56 - No. 4, 11/56; 10/57 - No. 3, 5/58

	GD 2.0	VG 4.0	FN 6.0	VF 8.0	VF/NM 9.0	NM- 9.2
1	16	32	48	94	147	200
2-4	10	20	30	54	72	90
1-3('57-'58)-Steinway	8	16	24	44	57	70

MY PRIVATE LIFE (Formerly Murder, Inc.; becomes Pedro #18)
Fox Feature Syndicate: No. 16, Feb, 1950 - No. 17, April, 1950

	GD 2.0	VG 4.0	FN 6.0	VF 8.0	VF/NM 9.0	NM- 9.2
16,17	25	50	75	150	245	340

MYRA NORTH (See The Comics, Crackajack Funnies & Red Ryder)
Dell Publishing Co.: No. 3, Jan, 1940

	GD 2.0	VG 4.0	FN 6.0	VF 8.0	VF/NM 9.0	NM- 9.2
Four Color 3	135	270	405	864	1482	2100

MY REAL LOVE
Standard Comics: No. 5, June, 1952 (Photo-c)

	GD 2.0	VG 4.0	FN 6.0	VF 8.0	VF/NM 9.0	NM- 9.2
5-Toth-a, 3 pgs.; Tuska, Cardy, Vern Greene-a	20	40	60	117	189	260

MY ROMANCE (Becomes My Own Romance #4 on)
Marvel Comics (RCM): Sept, 1948 - No. 3, Jan, 1949

	GD 2.0	VG 4.0	FN 6.0	VF 8.0	VF/NM 9.0	NM- 9.2
1	34	68	102	199	325	450
2,3: 2-Anti-Wertham editorial (11/48)	21	42	63	124	202	280

My Little Pony: Friends Forever #1 © Hasbro

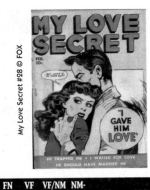

My Love Secret #28 © FOX

Mysterious Adventures #12 © Story

	GD 2.0	VG 4.0	FN 6.0	VF 8.0	VF/NM 9.0	NM- 9.2		GD 2.0	VG 4.0	FN 6.0	VF 8.0	VF/NM 9.0	NM- 9.2

MY ROMANTIC ADVENTURES (Formerly Romantic Adventures)
American Comics Group: No. 72, 12/56 - No. 115, 12/60; No. 116, 7/61 - No. 138, 3/64

72	14	28	42	76	108	140
73-85	8	16	24	44	57	70
86-Three pg. Williamson-a (2/58)	10	20	30	54	72	90
87-100	4	8	12	27	44	60
101-138	3	6	9	21	33	45

NOTE: *Whitney* art in most issues.

MY SECRET (Becomes Our Secret #4 on)
Superior Comics, Ltd.: Aug, 1949 - No. 3, Oct, 1949

1	28	56	84	165	270	375
2,3	19	38	57	112	179	240

MY SECRET AFFAIR (Becomes Martin Kane #4)
Hero Book (Fox Feature Syndicate): Dec, 1949 No. 3, April, 1950

1-Harrison/Wood-a (10 pgs.)	42	84	126	265	445	625
2,3-Wood-a	36	72	108	214	347	480

MY SECRET CONFESSION
Sterling Comics: September, 1955

1-Sekowsky-a	15	30	45	86	133	180

MY SECRET LIFE (Formerly Western Outlaws; Romeo Tubbs #26 on)
Fox Feature Syndicate: No. 22, July, 1949 - No. 27, July, 1950; No. 27, 9/51

22	27	54	81	162	266	370
23,26-Wood-a, 6 pgs.	37	74	111	218	354	490
24,25,27	20	40	60	120	195	270
27 (9/51)	19	38	57	111	176	240

NOTE: *The title was changed to Romeo Tubbs after #25 even though #26 & 27 did come out.*

MY SECRET LIFE (Formerly Young Lovers; Sue & Sally Smith #48)
Charlton Comics: No. 19, Aug, 1957 - No. 47, Sept, 1962

19	5	10	15	31	53	75
20-35	3	6	9	19	30	40
36-47: 44-Last 10¢ issue. 47-1st app. Sue & Sally Smith						
	3	6	9	17	26	35

MY SECRET MARRIAGE
Superior Comics, Ltd.: May, 1953 - No. 24, July, 1956 (Canadian)

1	26	52	78	154	252	350
2	15	30	45	84	127	170
3-24	14	28	42	78	112	145
I.W. Reprint #9	3	6	9	15	22	28

NOTE: *Many issues contain Kamen-ish art.*

MY SECRET ROMANCE (Becomes A Star Presentation #3)
Hero Book (Fox Feature Syndicate): Jan, 1950 - No. 2, March, 1950

1	34	68	102	199	325	450
2-Wood-a	36	72	108	214	347	480

MY SECRETS (Magazine) (Also see Gothic Romances)
Atlas/Seaboard: Feb, 1975 (50¢, B&W, 68 pgs.)

Vol. 1 #1	17	34	51	117	259	400

MY SECRET STORY (Formerly Captain Kidd #25; Sabu #30 on)
Fox Feature Syndicate: No. 26, Oct, 1949 - No. 29, April, 1950

26	28	56	84	168	274	380
27-29	19	38	57	111	176	240

MYSPACE DARK HORSE PRESENTS
Dark Horse Books: Sept, 2008 - Feb, 2011 ($19.95/$19.99, TPB)

Vol. 1 - Short stories previously appearing on Dark Horse's MySpace.com webpage; s/a by various incl. Whedon, Bá, Bagge, Mignola, Moon, Nord, Trimpe, Warren, Way	20.00
Vol. 2 - Collects stories from online #7-12; s/a by Way, Niles, Dorkin, Hotz & others	20.00
Vol. 3 - Collects stories from online #13-19; s/a by Mignola, Cloonan & others	20.00
Vol. 4 - Collects stories from online #20-24; s/a by Whedon, Chen & others	20.00
Vol. 5 - Collects stories from online #25-30; s/a by Thompson, Aragonés & others	20.00
Vol. 6 - Collects stories from online #31-36; s/a by Sakai, Dorkin & others	20.00

MYSTERIES (...Weird & Strange)
Superior/Dynamic Publ. (Randall Publ. Ltd.): May, 1953 - No. 11, Jan, 1955

1-All horror stories	142	284	426	909	1555	2200
2-A-Bomb blast story	77	154	231	493	847	1200
3-11: 10-Kamenish-c/a reprinted from Strange Mysteries #2; cover is from a panel in Strange Mysteries #2	47	94	141	296	498	700

MYSTERIES IN SPACE (See Fireside Book Series)

MYSTERIES OF LOVE IN SPACE
DC Comics: Mar, 2019 ($9.99, square-bound, one shot)

1-Anthology by various; Superman, Lois, Darkseid, Bizarro, Space Cabbie, Crush app. 10.00	

MYSTERIES OF SCOTLAND YARD (Also see A-1 Comics)
Magazine Enterprises: No. 121, 1954 (one shot)

A-1 121-Reprinted from Manhunt (5 stories)	21	42	63	124	202	280

MYSTERIES OF UNEXPLORED WORLDS (See Blue Bird)(Becomes Son of Vulcan V2#49 on)
Charlton Comics: Aug, 1956; No. 2, Jan, 1957 - No. 48, Sept, 1965

1	42	84	126	265	445	625
2-No Ditko	22	44	66	128	209	290
3,4,8,9 Ditko-a. 3-Diko c/a (4). 4-Ditko c/a (2).	36	72	108	214	347	480
5,6,10,11: 5,6-Ditko-c/a (all). 10-Ditko-c/a(4). 11-Ditko-c/a(3); signed J. Kotdi						
	37	74	111	222	361	500
7-(2/58, 68 pgs.) 4 stories w/Ditko-a	40	80	120	244	402	560
12-Ditko sty (3); Baker story "The Charm Bracelet"	36	72	108	211	343	475
13-18,20	14	28	42	78	112	145
19,21-24,26-Ditko-a	27	54	81	158	259	360
25,27-30: 28-Communist A-bomb story w/Khrushchev						
	6	12	18	37	66	95
31-45: 43-Atomic bomb panel	5	10	15	31	53	75
46(5/65)-Son of Vulcan begins (origin/1st app.)	5	10	15	33	57	80
47,48	4	8	12	28	47	65

NOTE: *Ditko c-3-6, 10, 11, 19, 21-24. Covers to #19, 21-24 reprint story panels.*

MYSTERIOUS ADVENTURES
Story Comics: Mar, 1951 - No. 24, Mar, 1955; No. 25, Aug, 1955

1-All horror stories	123	246	369	787	1344	1900
2-(6/51)	65	130	195	416	708	1000
3,4,6,10	58	116	174	371	636	900
5-Severed heads/bondage-c	226	452	678	1446	2473	3500
7-Dagger in eye panel; dismemberment stories	148	296	444	947	1624	2300
8-Eyeball story	97	194	291	621	1061	1500
9-Extreme violence (8/52)	77	154	231	493	847	1200
11-(12/52)-Used in SOTI, pg. 84	65	130	195	416	708	1000
12,14: 14-E.C. Old Witch swipe	63	126	189	403	689	975
13-Classic skull-c	784	1568	2352	5723	10,112	14,500
15-21: 18-Used in Senate Investigative report, pgs. 5,6; E.C. swipe/TFTC #35; The Coffin-Keeper & Corpse (hosts). 20-Electric chair-c; used by Wertham in the Senate hearings. 21-Bondage/beheading-c; extreme violence						
	110	220	330	704	1202	1700
22- "Cinderella" parody	63	126	189	403	689	975
23-Disbrow-a (6 pgs.); E.C. swipe "The Mystery Keeper's Tale" (host) and "Mother Ghoul's Nursery Tale"	60	120	180	381	653	925
24,25	52	104	156	328	552	775

NOTE: *Tothish art by Ross Andru-#22, 23. Bache a-8. Cameron a-5-7. Harrison a-12. Hollingsworth a-3-8, 12. Schaffenberger a-24, 25. Wildey a-15, 17.*

MYSTERIOUS ISLAND (Also see Classic Comics #34)
Dell Publishing Co.: No. 1213, July-Sept, 1961

Four Color 1213-Movie, photo-c	9	18	27	61	123	185

MYSTERIOUS ISLE
Dell Publishing Co.: Nov-Jan, 1963/64 (Jules Verne)

1-Painted-c	3	6	9	21	33	45

MYSTERIOUS RIDER, THE (See Zane Grey, 4-Color 301)

MYSTERIOUS STORIES (Formerly Horror From the Tomb #1)
Premier Magazines: No. 2, Dec-Jan, 1954-1955 - No. 7, Dec, 1955

2-Woodbridge-c; last pre-code issue	65	130	195	416	708	1000
3-Woodbridge-c	45	90	135	284	480	675
4-7: 5-Cinderella parody. 6-Woodbridge-c	41	82	123	256	428	600

NOTE: *Hollingsworth a-2, 4.*

MYSTERIOUS STRANGER
DC Comics: Aug/Sept, 1952

nn-Ashcan comic, not distributed to newsstands, only for in-house use. Cover art is All Star Western #60 with interior being Sensation Comics #100. A FN/VF copy sold for $2,357.50 in 2002.

MYSTERIOUS SUSPENSE (Also see Blue Beetle #1 (1967))
Charlton Comics: Oct, 1968 (12¢)

1-Return of the Question by Ditko (c/a)	11	22	33	73	157	240

MYSTERIOUS TRAVELER (See Tales of the...)

MYSTERIOUS TRAVELER COMICS (Radio)
Trans-World Publications: Nov, 1948

1-Powell-c/a(2); Poe adaptation, "Tell Tale Heart"	97	194	291	621	1061	1500

	GD 2.0	VG 4.0	FN 6.0	VF 8.0	VF/NM 9.0	NM- 9.2

MYSTERIUS
DC Comics (WildStorm): Mar, 2009 - No. 6, Aug, 2009 ($2.99, limited series)

| 1-6-Jeff Parker-a/Tom Fowler-a | | | | | | 3.00 |
| TPB (2010, $17.99) r/#1-6 | | | | | | 18.00 |

MYSTERY COMICS
William H. Wise & Co.: 1944 - No. 4, 1944 (No months given)

1-The Magnet, The Silver Knight, Brad Spencer, Wonderman, Dick Devins, King of Futuria, & Zudo the Jungle Boy begin (all 1st app.); Schomburg-c on all	245	490	735	1568	2684	3800
2-Bondage-c	155	310	465	992	1696	2400
3,4: 3-Lance Lewis, Space Detective begins (1st app.); Robot-c. 4-(V2#1 inside); KKK-c	142	284	426	909	1555	2200

MYSTERY COMICS DIGEST
Gold Key/Whitman?: Mar, 1972 - No. 26, Oct, 1975

1-Ripley's Believe It or Not; reprint of Ripley's #1 origin Ra-Ka-Tep the Mummy; Wood-a	4	8	12	26	41	55
2-9: 2-Boris Karloff Tales of Mystery; Wood-a; 1st app. Werewolf Count Wulfstein. 3-Twilight Zone (TV); Crandall, Toth & George Evans-a; 1st app. Tragg & Simbar the Lion Lord; (2) Crandall/Frazetta-r/Twilight Zone #1 4-Ripley's Believe It or Not; 1st app. Baron Tibor, the Vampire. 5-Boris Karloff Tales of Mystery; 1st app. Dr. Spektor. 6-Twilight Zone (TV); 1st app. U.S. Marshal Reid & Sir Duane; Evans-r. 7-Ripley's Believe It or Not; origin The Lurker in the Swamp; 1st app. Duroc. 8-Boris Karloff Tales of Mystery; McWilliams-r; Orlando-r. 9-Twilight Zone (TV); Williamson, Crandall, McWilliams-a; 2nd Tragg app.;Torres, Evans, Heck/Tuska-a	3	6	9	20	30	40
10-26: 10,13-Ripley's Believe It or Not: 13-Orlando-r. 11,14-Boris Karloff Tales of Mystery. 14-1st app. Xorkon. 12,15-Twilight Zone (TV). 16,19,22,25-Ripley's Believe It or Not. 17-Boris Karloff Tales of Mystery; Williamson-r; Orlando-r. 18,21,24-Twilight Zone (TV). 20,23,26-Boris Karloff Tales of Mystery	3	6	9	16	23	30

NOTE: Dr. Spektor app.-#5, 10-12, 21. Durak app.-#15. Duroc app.-#14 (later called Durak). King George 1st app.-#8.

MYSTERY GIRL
Dark Horse Comics: Dec, 2015 - No. 4, Mar, 2016 ($3.99)

| 1-4-Tobin-s/Albuquerque-a | | | | | | 4.00 |

MYSTERY IN SPACE (Also see Fireside Book Series and Pulp Fiction Library: ...)
National Periodical Pub.: 4-5/51 - No. 110, 9/66; No. 111, 9/80 - No. 117, 3/81 (#1-3: 52 pgs.)

1-Frazetta-a. 8 pgs.; Knights of the Galaxy begins, ends #8	287	574	861	2440	5520	8600
2	111	222	333	888	1994	3100
3	64	128	192	512	1156	1800
4,5	57	114	171	456	1028	1600
6-10: 7-Toth-a	46	92	138	359	805	1250
11-15	36	72	108	266	596	925
16-18,20-25: Interplanetary Insurance feature by Infantino in all. 21-1st app. Space Cabbie. 24-Last pre-code issue	33	66	99	238	532	825
19-Virgil Finlay-a	40	80	120	296	673	1050
26-40: 26-Space Cabbie feature begins. 34-1st S.A. issue. 36,40-Grey-tone-c	26	52	78	182	404	625
41-52: 45,46-Grey-tone-c. 47-Space Cabbie ends	19	38	57	133	297	460
53-Adam Strange begins (8/59, 10pg. sty); robot-c	159	318	477	1312	2956	4600
54	46	92	138	340	770	1200
55-Grey tone-c	46	92	138	359	805	1250
56-60: 59-Kane/Anderson-a	26	52	78	182	404	625
61-71: 61-1st app. Adam Strange foe Ulthoon. 62-1st app. A.S. foe Mortan. 63-Origin Vandor. 66-Star Rovers begin (1st app.). 68-1st app. Dust Devils (6/61). 69-1st Mailbag. 70-2nd app. Dust Devils. 71-Last 10¢ issue	20	40	60	142	316	490
72-74,76-80	14	28	42	93	204	315
75-JLA x-over in Adam Strange (5/62)(sequel to J.L.A. #3, 2nd app. of Kanjar Ro)	22	44	66	152	336	520
75-(Facsimile Edition) (2020, $3.99) Reprints #75 with original 1962 ads & letter column						6.00
81-86	10	20	30	68	144	220
87-(11/63)-Adam Strange/Hawkman double feat begins; 3rd Hawkman tryout starts	17	34	51	119	265	410
88-Adam Strange & Hawkman stories	15	30	45	105	233	360
89-Adam Strange & Hawkman stories	14	28	42	96	211	325
90-Book-length Adam Strange & Hawkman story; 1st team-up (3/64); Hawkman moves to own title next month; classic-c	16	32	48	110	243	375
91-102: 91-End Infantino art on Adam Strange; double-length Adam Strange story. 92-Space Ranger begins (6/64), ends #103. 92-94,96,98-Space Ranger-c. 94,98-Adam Strange/Space Ranger team-up. 102-Adam Strange ends (no Space Ranger)	8	16	24	51	96	140
103-Origin Ultra, the Multi-Alien; last Space Ranger	7	14	21	44	82	120
104-110: 110-Space Cabbie-a (3 pgs.)	5	10	15	31	53	75
V17#111(9/80)-117: 117-Newton-a(3 pgs.)	2	4	6	9	13	16

NOTE: Anderson-a-2, 4, 8-10, 12-17, 19, 45-48, 51, 57, 59i, 61-64, 70, 76, 87-91; c-9, 10, 15-25, 87, 89, 105-108, 110. Aparo-a-111. Austin-a-112i. Bolland-a-115. Craig-a-114, 116. Ditko-a-111, 114-116. Drucker-a-13, 14. Elias a-98, 102, 103. Golden-a-113p. Gil Greene-a-78, 91. Infantino a-18, 11, 14-25, 27-46, 48, 49, 51, 53-91, 103, 117; c-60-86, 88, 90, 91, 105, 107. Gil Kane-a-14p, 15p, 18p, 19p, 26p, 29-59p(most), 100-102; c-52, 101. Kubert a-113; c-111-115. Moreira-c-27, 28. Rogers a-111. Sekowsky a-52. Simon & Kirby a-4(2 pgs.). Spiegle a-111, 114. Starlin-c-116. Sutton a-112. Tuska a-115p, 117p.

MYSTERY IN SPACE
DC Comics: Nov, 2006 - No. 8, Jul, 2007 ($3.99, limited series)

1-8: 1-Captain Comet's rebirth; Starlin-s/Shane Davis-a; The Weird by Starlin						4.00
1-Variant cover by Neal Adams						10.00
Volume One TPB (2007, $17.99) r/#1-5						18.00
Volume Two TPB (2007, $17.99) r/#6-8 and The Weird from #1-4						18.00

MYSTERY IN SPACE
DC Comics (Vertigo): Jul, 2012 ($7.99, one-shot)

| 1-Short sci-fi stories by various incl. Kaluta, Allred, Baker, Diggle, Gianfelice, Sook-c | | | | | | 8.00 |

MYSTERY MEN
Marvel Comics: Aug, 2011 - No. 5, Nov, 2011 ($2.99, limited series)

| 1-5-Zircher-a/c; Liss-s; Pulp-era characters in 1932 | | | | | | 3.00 |

MYSTERY MEN COMICS
Fox Feature Syndicate: Aug, 1939 - No. 31, Feb, 1942

1-Intro. & 1st app. The Blue Beetle, The Green Mask, Rex Dexter of Mars by Briefer, Zanzibar by Tuska, Lt. Drake, D-13-Secret Agent by Powell, Chen Chang, Wing Turner, & Captain Denny Scott	2430	4860	7290	18,200	31,600	45,000
2-Robot & sci-fi-c (2nd Robot-c w/Movie #6)	544	1082	1623	3950	6975	10,000
3 (10/39)-Classic Lou Fine-c	1250	2500	3750	9500	17,250	25,000
4,5: 4-Capt. Savage begins (11/39)	420	840	1260	2940	5170	7400
6-Tuska-c	377	754	1131	2639	4620	6600
7-1st Blue Beetle-c app.	423	846	1269	3088	5444	7800
8-Lou Fine bondage-c	383	766	1149	2691	4691	6700
9-The Moth begins; Lou Fine-c	300	600	900	1920	3310	4700
10-Wing Turner by Kirby; Simon bondage-c	300	600	900	1920	3410	4900
11,12: Both Joe Simon-c. 11-Intro. Domino	290	580	870	1856	3178	4500
13-Intro. Lynx & sidekick Blackie (8/40)	226	452	678	1446	2473	3500
14-18: 16-Bondage/Hypo needle-c	194	388	582	1242	2121	3000
19-Intro. & 1st app. Miss X (ends #21)	226	452	678	1446	2473	3500
20-31: 26-The Wraith begins	181	362	543	1158	1979	2800

NOTE: Briefer a-1-15, 20, 24; c-9. Cuidera a-22. Lou Fine c-1-5,8,9. Powell a-1-15, 24. Simon c-10-12. Tuska a-1-16, 22, 24, 27; c-6. Bondage-c 1, 3, 7, 8, 10, 16, 25, 27-29, 31. Blue Beetle c-7, 8, 10-31. D-13 Secret Agent c-6. Green Mask c-1, 3-5. Rex Dexter of Mars c-2, 9.

MYSTERY MEN MOVIE ADAPTION
Dark Horse Comics: July, 1999 - No. 2, Aug, 1999 ($2.95, mini-series)

| 1,2-Fingerman-s; photo-c | | | | | | 4.00 |

MYSTERY PLAY, THE
DC Comics (Vertigo): 1994 ($19.95, one-shot)

| nn-Hardcover-Morrison-s/Muth-painted art | | | | | | 25.00 |
| Softcover ($9.95)-New Muth cover | | | | | | 10.00 |

MYSTERY SCIENCE THEATER 3000: THE COMIC
Dark Horse Comics: Sept, 2018 - No. 6, May, 2019 ($3.99)

| 1-6-Hodgson and others-s. 1-Nauck & Manley-a. 5,6-Black Cat app. | | | | | | 4.00 |

MYSTERY SOCIETY
IDW Publishing: May, 2010 - No. 5, Oct, 2010 ($3.99, limited series)

| 1-5-Niles-s/Staples-a | | | | | | 4.00 |
| ... Special (3/13, $3.99) Niles-s/Ritchie-a/c | | | | | | 4.00 |

MYSTERY TALES
Atlas Comics (20CC): Mar, 1952 - No. 54, Aug, 1957

1-Horror/weird stories in all	245	490	735	1568	2684	3800
2-Krigstein-a	135	270	405	864	1482	2100
3-10: 6-A-Bomb panel. 10-Story similar to "The Assassin" from Shock SuspenStories	113	226	339	718	1234	1750
11,13-21: 14-Maneely s/f story. 20-Electric chair issue. 21-Matt Fox-a; decapitation story	74	148	222	470	810	1150
12,22: 12-Matt Fox-a. 22-Forte/Matt Fox-c; a(i)	77	154	231	493	847	1200
23-26 (2/55)-Last precode issue	61	122	183	390	670	950
27,29-35,37,38,41-43,48,49- 43-Morisi story contains Frazetta art swipes from Untamed Love	63	126	189	403	689	975
28,36,39,40,45- 28-Jack Katz-a. 36,39-Krigstein-a. 40,45-Ditko-a (#45 is 3 pgs. only)	50	100	150	315	533	750
44-Labyrinth c/s; Williamson/Krenkel-a	61	122	183	390	670	950
46,51-Williamson/Krenkel-a. 46-Crandall text illos	53	106	159	334	567	800
47-Crandall, Ditko, Powell-a	53	106	159	334	567	800
50,52,53: 50-Torres, Morrow-a	52	104	156	328	552	775
54-Crandall, Morrow-a	50	100	150	315	533	750

NOTE: Ayers a-18, 49, 52. Berg a-17, 51. Colan a-1, 3, 18, 35, 43. Colletta a-18. Drucker a-41. Everett a-2, 29, 33, 35, 41; c-8-11, 14, 38, 39, 43. Heath a-3; c-3, 15, 17, 26. Heck a-25. Kinstler a-15. Mort Lawrence a-26, 32, 34. Maneely a-1, 9, 14, 22; c-12, 23, 24, 27. Mooney a-3, 40. Morisi a-43, 50. Morrow a-50. Orlando a-51. Pakula a-16. Powell a-25, 29, 37, 38, 47. Reinman a-1, 14, 17. Robinson a-7p, 42. Romita a-37. Roussos a-4, 44. R.Q. Sale a-45, 46, 49. Severin c-52. Shores a-17, 45. Tuska a-10, 12, 14. Whitney a-37. Wildey a-37.

MYSTERY TALES
Super Comics: 1964

| Super Reprint #16,17('64): 16-r/Tales of Horror #2. 17-r/Eerie #14(Avon), 18-Kubert-r/Strange Terrors #4 | 3 | 6 | 9 | 16 | 24 | 32 |

MYSTERY TRAIL
DC Comics: Feb/Mar 1950

nn - Ashcan comic, not distributed to newsstands, only for in-house use. Cover art is Danger Trail #3 with interior being Star Spangled Comics #109. A FN/VF copy sold for $2,357.50 in 2002.

MYSTIC (3rd Series)
Marvel/Atlas Comics (CLDS 1/CSI 2-21/OMC 22-35/CSI 35-61): March, 1951 - No. 61, Aug, 1957

1-Atom bomb panels; horror/weird stories in all	168	336	504	1075	1838	2600
2	84	168	252	538	919	1300
3-Eyes torn out	81	162	248	518	884	1250
4- "The Devil Birds" by Wolverton (6 pgs.)	126	252	378	806	1378	1950
5,7-10	57	114	171	362	619	875
6- "The Eye of Doom" by Wolverton (7 pgs.)	116	232	346	742	1271	1800
11-17,19,20: 16-Bondage/torture c/story	52	104	156	328	552	775
18-Classic Everett skeleton-c	297	594	891	1901	3251	4600
21-25,27-36-Last precode (3/55). 25-E.C. swipe	43	86	129	271	461	650
26-Atomic War story; severed head story/cover	60	120	180	381	653	925
37-51,53-56,61	39	78	117	240	395	550
52-Wood-a; Crandall-a?	41	82	123	256	428	600
57-Story "Trapped in the Ant-Hill" (1957) is very similar to "The Man in the Ant Hill" in TTA #27	58	116	174	371	636	900
58,59-Krigstein-a	39	78	117	231	378	525
60-Williamson/Mayo-a (4 pgs.)	40	80	120	246	411	575

NOTE: Andru a-23, 25. Ayers a-35, 53; c-38. Berg a-49. Cameron a-49, 51. Check a-51, 60. Colan a-3, 7, 12, 21, 37, 60. Colletta a-29. Drucker a-46, 52, 56. Everett a-8, 9, 17, 40, 44, 57; c-13, 18, 21, 42, 47, 49, 51-55, 57-59, 61. Forte a-35, 52, 58. Fox a-24i. Al Hartley a-35. Heath a-10; c-10, 20, 22, 23, 35, 60. Infantino a-12. Kane a-8, 24p. Jack Katz a-31, 33. Mort Law.rence a-19, 37. Maneely a-22, 24, 58; c-7, 15, 28, 29, 31. Moldoff a-29. Morisi a-48, 49, 52. Morrow a-51. Orlando a-57, 61. Pakula a-52, 57, 59. Powell a-52, 54-56. Robinson a-5. Romita a-11, 15. R.Q. Sale a-35, 53, 58. Sekowsky a-1, 2, 4, 5. Severin c-56, 60. Tuska a-15. Whitney a-33. Wildey a-28, 30. Ed Win a-17, 20. Canadian reprints known-title 'Startling.'

MYSTIC (Also see CrossGen Chronicles)

Mystery Girl #3 © Tobin & Alburquerque

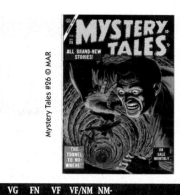

Mystery Tales #26 © MAR

Mystik U #1 © DC

	GD	VG	FN	VF	VF/NM	NM-
	2.0	4.0	6.0	8.0	9.0	9.2

CrossGeneration Comics: Jul, 2000 - No. 43, Jan 2004 ($2.95)

1-43: 1-Marz-s/Peterson & Dell-a. 15-Cameos by DC & Marvel characters ... 3.00

MYSTIC (CrossGen characters)
Marvel Comics: Oct, 2011 - No. 4, Jan, 2012 ($2.99, limited series)

1-4-G. Willow Wilson-s/David López-a/Amanda Conner-c ... 3.00

MYSTICAL TALES
Atlas Comics (CCC 1/EPI 2-8): June, 1956 - No. 8, Aug, 1957

1-Everett-c/a	90	180	270	576	988	1400
2-4: 2-Berg-a. 3,4-Crandall-a.	42	84	126	265	445	625
5-Williamson-a (4 pgs.)	47	94	141	296	498	700
6-Torres, Krigstein-a	42	84	126	265	445	625
7-Bolle, Forte, Torres, Orlando-a	39	78	117	231	378	525
8-Krigstein, Check-a	39	78	117	240	395	550

NOTE: Ayers a-6. Everett a-1; c-1-4, 6, 7. Orlando a-1, 2, 7. Pakula a-3. Powell a-1, 4. Sale a-5. Sinnott a-6.

MYSTIC ARCANA
Marvel Comics: Aug, 2007 - Jan, 2008 ($2.99)

1-Magik on-c; art by Scott and Nguyen; Ian McNee and Dani Moonstar app. ... 3.00
(#2)...: Black Knight 1 (9/07, $2.99) Djurdjevic-c/Grummett & Hanna-a; origin retold ... 3.00
3-("Scarlet Witch" on cover)(10/07, $2.99) Djurdjevic-c/Santacruz-a; childhood ... 3.00
(#4)...: Sister Grimm 1 (1/08, $2.99) Nico Minoru from Runaways; Djurdjevic-c/Noto-a ... 3.00
...: The Book of Marvel Magic ('07, $3.99) Official Handbook profiles of the magic-related ... 4.00
HC (2007, $24.99, d.j.) r/series and ...: The Book of Marvel Magic ... 25.00

MYSTIC COMICS (1st Series)
Timely Comics (TPI 1-5/TCI 8-10): March, 1940 - No. 10, Aug, 1942

1-Origin The Blue Blaze, The Dynamic Man, & Flexo the Rubber Robot; Zephyr Jones, 3X's
& Deep Sea Demon app.; The Magician begins (all 1st app.);
c-from Spider pulp V18#1, 6/39 ... 1880 3760 5640 15,000 32,000 49,000
2-The Invisible Man & Master Mind Excello begin; Space Rangers, Zara of the Jungle,
Taxi Taylor app. (scarce) ... 1000 2000 3000 7400 13,200 19,000
3-Origin Hercules; last appears in #4 ... 530 1060 1590 3869 6835 9800
4-Origin The Thin Man & The Black Widow; Merzah the Mystic app.; last Flexo, Dynamic
Man, Invisible Man & Blue Blaze (some issues have date sticker on cover; others have July
w/August overprint in silver color); Roosevelt assassination-c ... 100 2200 3300 8360 15,180 22,000
5-(3/41)-Origin The Black Marvel, The Blazing Skull, The Sub-Earth Man, Super Slave &
The Terror; The Moon Man & Black Widow app. 5-German war-c begin, end #10 ...
508 1016 1524 3708 6554 9400
6-(10/41)-Origin The Challenger & The Destroyer 1st app.?; also see All-Winners #2,
Fall, 1941) ... 1400 2800 4200 10,600 19,300 28,000
7-The Witness begins (12/41, origin & 1st app.); origin Davey & the Demon; last Black
Widow; Hitler opens his trunk of terror-c by Simon & Kirby (classic-c) ...
100 2200 3300 8360 15,180 22,000
8,10: 8-Classic Destroyer WWII Nazi bondage/torture-c. 10-Father Time, World of Wonder,
& Red Skeleton app.; last Challenger & Terror ... 838 1676 2514 6117 10,809 15,500
9-Gary Gaunt app.; last Black Marvel, Mystic & Blazing Skull; Hitler-c ...
... 600 1200 1800 4200 7600 13,800 20,000

NOTE: Gabrielle c-8-10. Rico a-9(2). Schomburg a-1-4; c-4, 6. Sekowsky a-9. Sekowsky/Klein a-8 (Challenger). Bondage c-1, 2, 9.

MYSTIC COMICS (2nd Series)
Timely Comics (ANC): Oct, 1944 - No. 3, Win, 1944-45; No. 4, Mar, 1945

1-The Angel, The Destroyer, The Human Torch, Terry Vance the Schoolboy Sleuth,
& Tommy Tyme begin ... 394 788 1182 2758 4829 6900
2-(Fall/44)-Last Human Torch & Terry Vance; bondage/hypo-c ...
... 284 568 852 1818 3109 4400
3-Last Angel (two stories) & Tommy Tyme ... 206 412 618 1318 2259 3200
4-The Young Allies-c & app.; Schomburg-c ... 194 388 582 1242 2121 3000

MYSTIC COMICS 70th ANNIVERARY SPECIAL
Marvel Comics: 2009 ($3.99, one-shot)

1-New story of The Vision; r/G.A. Vision app. from Marvel Myst. Comics #13 & 16 ... 5.00

MYSTIC HANDS OF DR. STRANGE
Marvel Comics: May, 2010 ($3.99, B&W, one-shot)

1-Short stories; art by Irving, Brunner, McKeever & Marcos Martin; Parrillo-c ... 4.00

MYSTIK U
DC Comics: Jan, 2018 - No. 3, Mar 2018 ($5.99, limited series)

1-3: 1-Teenage Zatanna, Enchantress at magic college; intro. Plop; Kwitney-s/Norton-a ... 6.00

MYSTIQUE (See X-Men titles)
Marvel Comics: June, 2003 - No. 24, Apr, 2005 ($2.99)

1-24: 1-6-Linsner-c/Vaughan-s/Lucas-a. 7-Ryan-a begins. 8-Horn-c. 9-24-Mayhew-a.
23-Wolverine & Rogue app. ... 3.00

... Vol. 1: Drop Dead Gorgeous TPB (2004, $14.99) r/#1-6 ... 15.00
... Vol. 2: Tinker, Tailor, Mutant, Spy TPB (2004, $17.99) r/#7-13 ... 18.00
... Vol. 3: Unnatural TPB (2004, $13.99) r/#14-18 ... 14.00

MYSTIQUE & SABRETOOTH (Sabretooth and Mystique on-c)
Marvel Comics: Dec, 1996 - No. 4, Mar, 1997 ($1.95, limited series)

1-4: Characters from X-Men ... 4.00

MY STORY (...True Romances in Pictures #5,6; becomes My Love Life #13) (Formerly Zago)
Hero Books (Fox Feature Syndicate): No. 5, May, 1949 - No. 12, Aug, 1950

5-Kamen/Feldstein-a	58	116	174	371	636	900
6-8,11,12: 12-Photo-c	25	50	75	150	245	340
9,10-Wood-a	37	74	111	222	361	500

MYTHIC
Image Comics: May, 2015 - No. 8, 2016 ($1.99/$2.99/$3.99)

1-3: 1-($1.99) Phil Hester-s/John McCrea-a. 2,3-($2.99) ... 3.00
4-8-($3.99) ... 4.00

MYTHOS
Marvel Comics: Mar, 2006 - Dec, 2007 ($3.99)

1-Retelling of X-Men #1 with painted-a by Paolo Rivera; Paul Jenkins-s ... 4.00
...: Captain America 1 (8/08) Retelling of origin; painted-a by Rivera; Jenkins-s ... 4.00
...: Fantastic Four 1 (12/07) Retelling of Fantastic Four #1; painted-a by Rivera, Jenkins-s ... 4.00
...: Ghost Rider 1 (3/07) Retelling of Marvel Spotlight #5; painted-a by Rivera; Jenkins-s ... 4.00
...: Hulk 1 (10/06) Retelling of Incredible Hulk #1; painted-a by Rivera; Jenkins-s ... 4.00
...: Spider-Man 1 (8/07) Retelling of Amazing Fantasy #15; painted-a by Rivera; Jenkins-s ... 4.00

MYTHOS: THE FINAL TOUR
DC Comics/Vertigo: Dec, 1996 - No. 3, Feb, 1997 ($5.95, limited series)

1-3: 1-Ney Rieber-s/Amaro-a. 2-Snejberg-a; Constantine-app. 3-Kristiansen-a;
Black Orchid-app. ... 6.00

MYTHSTALKERS
Image Comics: Mar, 2003 - No. 8, Mar, 2004 ($2.95)

1-8-Jiro-a ... 3.00

MY TRUE LOVE (Formerly Western Killers #64; Frank Buck #70 on)
Fox Feature Syndicate: No. 65, July, 1949 - No. 69, March, 1950

65	34	68	102	204	332	460
66,68,69: 69-Morisi-a	23	46	69	196	223	310
67-Wood-a	34	68	102	204	332	460

NAIL, THE
Dark Horse Comics: June, 2004 - No. 4, Oct, 2004 ($2.99, limited series)

1-4-Rob Zombie & Steve Niles-s/Nat Jones-a/Simon Bisley-c ... 3.00
TPB (2005, $12.95) r/series ... 13.00

NAILBITER
Image Comics: May, 2014 - No. 30, Mar, 2017 ($2.99)

1-29: 1-Williamson-s/Henderson-a. 7-Brian Bendis appears as a character. 13-Archie style
cover ... 3.00
30-($3.99) Final issue ... 4.00
.../ Hack/Slash 1 (3/15, $4.99) Flip book with Hack/Slash / Nailbiter 1 ... 5.00

NAILBITER RETURNS
Image Comics: Apr, 2020 - No. 10, Feb, 2021 ($3.99)

1-10-Williamson-s/Henderson-a ... 4.00

NAKED BRAIN (Marc Hempel's...)
Insight Studios Group: 2002 - No. 3, 2002 ($2.95, B&W, limited series)

1-3-Marc Hempel cartoons and sketches; Tug & Buster app. ... 3.00

NAKED PREY, THE (See Movie Classics)

'NAM, THE (See Savage Tales #1, 2nd series & Punisher Invades...)
Marvel Comics Group: Dec, 1986 - No. 84, Sept, 1993

| 1-Golden a(p/c begins, ends #13 | 2 | 4 | 6 | 10 | 14 | 18 |
| 1 (2nd printing) | | | | | | 4.00 |

2-7,9-25,27-66,70-74: 7-Golden-a (2 pgs.). 32-Death R. Kennedy. 52,53-Frank Castle
(The Punisher) app. 52,53-Gold 2nd printings. 58-Silver logo. 65-Heath-c/a.
70-Lomax scripts begin ... 4.00
| 8-1st app. Fudd Verzyl, Tunnel Rat | 1 | 3 | 4 | 6 | 8 | 10 |
26-2nd app. Fudd Verzyl, Tunnel Rat ... 4.00
67-69-Punisher 3 part story ... 4.00
75-($2.25, 52 pgs.) ... 6.00
76-84 ... 4.00
| Trade Paperback 1,2: 1-r/#1-4. 2-r/#5-8 | 1 | 2 | 3 | 5 | 6 | 8 |
TPB ('99, $14.95) r/#1-4; recolored ... 15.00

	GD 2.0	VG 4.0	FN 6.0	VF 8.0	VF/NM 9.0	NM- 9.2

'NAM MAGAZINE, THE
Marvel Comics: Aug, 1988 - No. 10, May, 1989 ($2.00, B&W, 52pgs.)

1-10: Each issue reprints 2 issues of the comic						5.00

NAMELESS
Image Comics: Feb, 2015 - No. 6, Dec, 2015 ($2.99)

1-6-Morrison-s/Burnham-a						3.00

NAMELESS, THE
Image Comics: May, 1997 - No. 5, Sept, 1997 ($2.95, B&W)

1-5: Pruett/Hester-s/a						4.00
...: The Director's Cut TPB (2006, $15.99) r/#1-5; original proposal by Pruett						16.00

NAMES, THE
DC Comics (Vertigo): Nov, 2014 - No. 9, Jul, 2015 ($2.99, limited series)

1-9-Peter Milligan-s/Leandro Fernandez-a						3.00

NAMESAKE
BOOM! Studios: Nov, 2016 - No. 4, Feb, 2017 ($3.99, limited series)

1-4-Orlando-s/Rebelka-a						4.00

NAMES OF MAGIC, THE (Also see Books of Magic)
DC Comics (Vertigo): Feb, 2001 - No. 5, June, 2001 ($2.50, limited series)

1-5: Bolton painted-c on all; Case-a; leads into Hunter: The Age of Magic						3.00
TPB (2002, $14.95) r/#1-5						15.00

NAME OF THE GAME, THE
DC Comics: 2001 ($29.95, graphic novel)

Hardcover ($29.95) Will Eisner-s/a						30.00

NAMOR (Volume 2)
Marvel Comics: June, 2003 - No. 12, May, 2004 (25¢/$2.25/$2.99)

1-(25¢-c)Young Namor in the 1920s; Larroca-c/a						3.00
2-6-($2.25) Larroca-a						3.00
7-12-($2.99); 7-Olliffe begins						3.00

NAMORA (See Marvel Mystery Comics #82 & Sub-Mariner Comics)
Marvel Comics (PrPl): Fall, 1948 - No. 3, Dec, 1948

1-Sub-Mariner x-over in Namora; Namora by Everett(2), Sub-Mariner by Rico (10 pgs.)	423	846	1269	3000	5250	7500
2-The Blonde Phantom & Sub-Mariner story; Everett-a	271	542	813	1734	2967	4200
3-(Scarce)-Sub-Mariner app.; Everett-a	309	618	927	2163	3782	5400

NAMORA (See Agents of Atlas)
Marvel Comics: Aug, 2010 ($3.99, one-shot)

1-Parker-s/Pichelli-a						4.00

NAMOR: CONQUERED SHORES
Marvel Comics: Dec, 2022 - No. 4, Apr, 2023 ($4.99, limited series)

1-5- Cantwell-s/Ferry-a; post-apocalyptic future; Luke Cage app.						5.00

NAMOR: THE BEST DEFENSE (Also see Immortal Hulk, Doctor Strange, Silver Surfer)
Marvel Comics: Feb, 2019 ($4.99, one-shot)

1-Chip Zdarsky-s/Carlos Magno-a; Ron Garney-c						5.00

NAMOR: THE FIRST MUTANT (Curse of the Mutants x-over with X-Men titles)
Marvel Comics: Oct, 2010 - No. 11, Aug, 2011 ($3.99/$2.99)

1-($3.99) Olivetti-a/Stuart Moore-s/Jae Lee-c; back-up retelling of origin and history						4.00
2-11-($2.99) 2-Emma Frost app. 5-Mayhew-c. 6-10-Noto-c						3.00
...Annual 1 (7/11, $3.99) Part 3 of "Escape From the Negative Zone" x-over; Fiumara-a						4.00

NAMOR, THE SUB-MARINER (See Prince Namor & Sub-Mariner)
Marvel Comics: Apr, 1990 - No. 62, May, 1995 ($1.00/$1.25/$1.50)

1-Byrne-c/a/scripts in 1-25 (scripts only #26-32)	2	4	6	10	14	18
2-5: 5-Iron Man app.						5.00
6-11,13-23,25,27-36,38-49,51-62: 16-Re-intro Iron Fist (8-cameo only). 18-Punisher cameo (1 panel); 21-23,25-Wolverine cameos. 22,23-Iron Fist app. 28-Iron Fist-c/story. 31-Dr. Doom-c/story. 33,34-Iron Fist cameo. 35-New Tiger Shark-c/story. 48-The Thing story.						4.00
12,24: 12-(52pgs.)-Re-intro. The Invaders. 24-Namor vs. Wolverine						5.00
26-Namor w/new costume; 1st Jae Lee-c/a this title (5/92) & begins	1	3	4	6	8	10
37-Aqua holografx foil-c						5.00
50-($1.75, 52 pgs.)-Newsstand ed.; w/bound-in S-M trading card sheet (both versions)						5.00
50-($2.95, 52 pgs.)-Collector edition w/foil-c						5.00
Annual 1-4 ('91-94, 68 pgs.): 1-3 pg. origin recap. 2-Return/Defenders. 3-Bagged w/card. 4-Painted-c						5.00

NOTE: *Jae Lee a-26-30p, 31-37, 38p, 39, 40; c-26-40.*

'NAMWOLF
Albatross Funnybooks: 2017 - No. 4, 2017 ($3.99, limited series)

1-4-Fabian Rangel Jr.-s/Logan Faerber-a; werewolf in 1970 Viet Nam						4.00

NANCY AND SLUGGO (See Comics On Parade & Sparkle Comics)
United Features Syndicate: No. 16, 1949 - No. 23, 1954

16(#1)	13	26	39	74	105	135
17-23	8	16	24	44	57	70

NANCY & SLUGGO (Nancy #146-173; formerly Sparkler Comics)
St. John/Dell #146-187/Gold Key #188 on: No. 121, Apr, 1955-No. 192, Oct, 1963

121(4/55)(St. John)	10	20	30	56	76	95
122-145(7/57)(St. John)	9	18	27	47	61	75
146(9/57)-Peanuts begins, ends #192 (Dell)	9	18	27	59	117	175
147-161 (Dell) Peanuts in all	7	14	21	48	89	130
162-165,177-180-John Stanley-a	7	14	21	48	89	130
166-176-Oona & Her Haunted House series; Stanley-a	8	16	24	52	99	145
181-187(3-5/62)(Dell)	5	10	15	35	63	90
188(10/62)-192 (Gold Key)	5	10	15	35	63	90
Four Color 1034(9-11/59)-Summer Camp	5	10	15	30	50	70

(See Dell Giant #34, 45 & Dell Giants)

NANCY DREW
Dynamite Entertainment: 2018 - No. 5, 2018 ($3.99, limited series)

1-5-Kelly Thompson-s/Jenn St-Onge-a; Hardy Boys app.						4.00

NANCY DREW AND THE HARDY BOYS: THE BIG LIE
Dynamite Entertainment: 2017 - No. 6, 2017 ($3.99, limited series)

1-6-Anthony Del Col-s/Werther Dell'Edera-a; multiple-c on each; Bobbsey twins app.						4.00

NANCY DREW: THE DEATH OF NANCY DREW
Dynamite Entertainment: 2020 - No. 6, 2020 ($3.99, limited series)

1-6-Anthony Del Col-s/Joe Eisma-a; Hardy Boys app.						4.00

NANNY AND THE PROFESSOR (TV)
Dell Publishing Co.: Aug, 1970 - No. 2, Oct, 1970 (Photo-c)

1-(01-546-008)	5	10	15	30	50	70
2	4	8	12	25	40	55

NAOMI
DC Comics (Wonder Comics): Mar, 2019 - No. 6, Sept, 2019 ($3.99)

1-6-Brian Bendis & David F. Walker-s/Jamal Campbell-a. 1-Superman app. 3-6-Origin						4.00

NAOMI: SEASON TWO
DC Comics: May, 2022 - No. 6, Oct, 2022 ($3.99)

1-6-Brian Bendis & David F. Walker-s/Jamal Campbell-a. 3,5-Cyborg app.						4.00

NAPOLEON
Dell Publishing Co.: No. 526, Dec, 1953

Four Color 526	7	14	21	46	86	125

NAPOLEON & SAMANTHA (See Walt Disney Showcase No. 10)

NAPOLEON & UNCLE ELBY (See Clifford McBride's...)
Eastern Color Printing Co.: July, 1942 (68 pgs.) (One Shot)

1	50	100	150	315	533	750
1945-American Book-Strafford Press (128 pgs.) (8x10-1/2"; B&W reprints; hardcover)	16	32	48	94	147	200

NAPOLEON DYNAMITE (Based on the 2004 movie)
IDW Publishing: Sept, 2019 - No. 4, Dec, 2019 ($3.99, limited series)

1-4-Sequel to movie; Monlongo-a; multiple covers on each						4.00
... Valentine's Day Special (2/20, $3.99) Megan Brown-s/Christine Larsen-a; 3 covers						4.00

NARCOS (Based on the 2015-2017 TV series)
IDW Publishing: Dec, 2019 - Present ($3.99)

1,2-Ferrier-s/Malhotra-a. 1-Three covers. 2-Two covers						4.00

NARRATIVE ILLUSTRATION, THE STORY OF THE COMICS (Also see Good Triumphs Over Evil!)
M.C. Gaines: Summer, 1942 (32 pgs., 7-1/4"x10", B&W w/color inserts)

nn-16 pgs. text with illustrations of ancient art, strips and comic covers; 4 pg. WWII War Bond promo, "The Minute Man Answers the Call" color comic drawn by Shelly and a special 8-page color comic insert of "The Story of Saul" (from *Picture Stories from the Bible* #10 or soon to appear in PS #10) or "Noah and His Ark" or "The Story of Ruth". Insert has special title page indicating it was part of a Sunday newspaper supplement insert series that had already run in a New England "Sunday Herald." Another version exists with insert from *Picture Stories from the Bible* #7.						
(very rare)				Estimated value...		2000.00

NOTE: *Print, A Quarterly Journal of the Graphic Arts Vol. 3 No. 2 (88 pg., square bound) features the 1st printing of Narrative Illustration, The Story of The Comics. A VG+ copy sold for $750 in 2005.*

NASCAR HEROES
Starbridge Media: 2007 - No. 3 ($3.95)

1-3: 1-Origin of fictional racer Jimmy Dash. 3-Origin of the Daytona 500; DeStefano-s						4.00
nn-(2008, Free Comic Book Day giveaway) The Mystery of Driver Z						3.00

NASH (WCW Wrestling)
Image Comics: July, 1999 - No. 2, July, 1999 ($2.95)

1,2-Regular and photo-c						4.00
1-($6.95) Photo-split-cover Edition						7.00

NATHANIEL DUSK
DC Comics: Feb, 1984 - No. 4, May, 1984 ($1.25, mini-series, direct sales, Baxter paper)

1-4: 1-Intro/origin; Gene Colan-c/a in all						4.00

NATHANIEL DUSK II
DC Comics: Oct, 1985 - No. 4, Jan, 1986 ($2.00, mini-series, Baxter paper)

1-4: Gene Colan-c/a in all						4.00

NATIONAL COMICS
Quality Comics Group: July, 1940 - No. 75, Nov, 1949

1-Uncle Sam begins (1st app.); origin sidekick Buddy by Eisner; origin Wonder Boy & Kid Dixon; Merlin the Magician (ends #45); Cyclone, Kid Patrol, Sally O'Neil Policewoman, Pen Miller (by Klaus Nordling; ends #22), Prop Powers (ends #26), & Paul Bunyan (ends #22) begin	946	1892	2838	6906	12,203	17,500
2	300	600	900	2010	3505	5000
3-Last Eisner Uncle Sam	245	490	735	1568	2684	3800
4-Last Cyclone	187	374	561	1197	2049	2900
5-(11/40)-Quicksilver begins (1st app.; 3rd w/lightning speed?; re-intro'd by DC in 1993 as Max Mercury in Flash #76, 2nd series); origin Uncle Sam; bondage-c	366	732	1098	2562	4481	6400
6,8-11: 8-Jack & Jill begins (ends #22). 9-Flag-c	181	362	543	1158	1979	2800
7-Classic Lou Fine-c	541	1082	1623	3950	6975	10,000
12-15-Lou Fine-a	148	296	444	947	1624	2300
16-Classic skeleton-c; Lou Fine-a	476	952	1428	3475	6138	8800
17,19-22: 21-Classic Nazi swastika cover. 22-Last Pen Miller (moves to Crack #23)	234	351	743	1297	1850	
18-(12/41)-Shows Asians attacking Pearl Harbor; on stands one month before actual event	309	618	927	2163	3782	5400
23-The Unknown & Destroyer 171 begin	113	226	339	718	1234	1750
24-Japanese War-c	129	258	387	824	1413	2000
25-30: 25-Nazi drug usage/hypodermic needle in story. 26-Wonder Boy ends. 27- G-2 the Unknown begins (ends #46). 29-Origin The Unknown	84	168	252	538	919	1300

Namor: Conquered Shores #5 © MAR

Naomi #1 © DC

Navy Action #1 © MAR

	GD 2.0	VG 4.0	FN 6.0	VF 8.0	VF/NM 9.0	NM- 9.2
31-33: 33-Chic Carter begins (ends #47)	74	148	222	470	810	1150
34-37,40: 35-Last Kid Patrol	63	126	189	403	689	975
38-Hitler, Tojo, Mussolini-c	129	258	387	826	1413	2000
39-Hitler-c	148	296	444	947	1624	2300
41-Classic Uncle Sam American Eagle WWII-c	81	162	243	518	884	1250
42-The Barker begins (1st app?, 5/44); The Barker covers begin	45	90	135	284	480	675
43-50: 48-Origin The Whistler	32	64	96	188	307	425
51-Sally O'Neil by Ward, 8 pgs. (12/45)	34	68	102	204	332	460
52-60	23	46	69	136	223	310
61-67: 67-Format change; Quicksilver app.	18	36	54	105	165	225
68-75: The Barker ends	16	32	48	94	147	200

NOTE: Cole Quicksilver-43; c-43, 46, 47, 49-51. Crandall Uncle Sam-11-13 (with Fine), 25, 26; c-24-26, 30-33, 43. Crandall Paul Bunyan-10-13. Fine Uncle Sam-13 (w/Crandall), 17, 18; c-1-14, 16, 18, 21. Gill Fox c-69-74. Guardineer Quicksilver-27, 35. Gustavson Quicksilver-14-26. McWilliams a-23-28, 55, 57. Uncle Sam c-1-41. Barker c-42-75.

NATIONAL COMICS (Also see All Star Comics 1999 crossover titles)
DC Comics: May, 1999 ($1.99, one-shot)

1-Golden Age Flash and Mr. Terrific; Waid-s/Lopresti-a						4.00

NATIONAL COMICS
DC Comics: Sept, 2012 ($3.99, one-shots)

... Eternity 1 (9/12) Re-intro of Kid Eternity; Lemire-s/Hamner-a/c						4.00
... Looker 1 (10/12) Vampire supermodel; Edginton-s/Mike S. Miller-a/March-c						4.00
... Madame X 1 (12/12) Rob Williams-s/Trevor Hasine-a/Fiona Staples-c						4.00
... Rose & Thorn 1 (11/12) Taylor-s/Googe-a/Sook-c						4.00

NATIONAL CRUMB, THE (Magazine-Size)
Mayfair Publications: August, 1975 (52 pgs., B&N) (Satire)

1-Grandenetti-c/a, Ayers-a	2	4	6	11	16	20

NATIONAL VELVET (TV)
Dell Publishing Co./Gold Key: May-July, 1961 - No. 2, Mar, 1963 (All photo-c)

Four Color 1195 (#1)	6	12	18	41	76	110
Four Color 1312, 01-556-207, 12-556-210 (Dell)	4	8	12	27	44	60
1,2: 1(12/62) (Gold Key). 2(3/63)	4	8	12	27	44	60

NATION OF SNITCHES
Piranha Press (DC): 1990 ($4.95, color, 52 pgs.)

nn						5.00

NATION X (X-Men on the Utopia island)
Marvel Comics: Feb, 2010 - No. 4, May, 2010 ($3.99, limited series)

1-4-Short stories by various. 1,4-Allred-a. 2-Choi, Cloonan-a. 4-Doop app.						4.00
...: X-Factor (3/10, $3.99) David-s/DeLandro-a						4.00

NATURE BOY (Formerly Danny Blaze; Li'l Rascal Twins #6 on)
Charlton Comics: No. 3, March, 1956 - No. 5, Feb, 1957

3-1st app./origin; Blue Beetle story (last Golden Age app.); Buscema-c/a	30	60	90	177	289	400
4,5	20	40	60	117	189	260

NOTE: John Buscema a-3, 4p, 5; c-3. Powell a-4.

NATURE OF THINGS (Disney, TV/Movie)
Dell Publishing Co.: No. 727, Sept, 1956 - No. 842, Sept, 1957

Four Color 727 (#1), 842-Jesse Marsh-a	5	10	15	33	57	80

NAUGHTY LIST
AfterShock Comics: Apr, 2022 - No. 4, Jul, 2022 ($4.99, limited series)

1-4-Retelling the legend of Santa Claus; Santoro-s/Ferguson-a						5.00

NAUSICAA OF THE VALLEY OF WIND
Viz Comics: 1988 - No. 7, 1989; 1989 - No. 4, 1990 ($2.50, B&W, 68pgs.)

Book 1-Contains Moebius poster	3	6	9	14	20	25
Book 2-7						7.00
Part II, Book 1-4 ($2.95)						5.00

NAVY ACTION (Sailor Sweeney #12-14)
Atlas Comics (CDS): Aug, 1954 - No. 11, Apr, 1956; No. 15, 1/57 - No. 18, 8/57

1-Powell-a	52	104	156	328	552	775
2-Lawrence-a; RQ Sale-a	31	62	93	182	296	410
3-11: 4-Last precode (2/55)	24	48	72	142	234	325
15-18	22	44	66	128	209	290

NOTE: Berg a-7, 9. Colan a-8. Drucker a-7, 17. Everett c-3, 7, 16; c-16, 17. Heath c-1, 2, 5, 6. Maneely a-5, 7, 8, 18; c-9, 11. Pakula a-2, 3, 9. Reinman a-17.

NAVY COMBAT
Atlas Comics (MPI): June, 1955 - No. 20, Oct, 1958

1-Torpedo Taylor begins by Don Heck; Heath-c	50	100	150	315	533	750

	GD 2.0	VG 4.0	FN 6.0	VF 8.0	VF/NM 9.0	NM- 9.2
2	30	60	90	177	289	400
3-10	23	46	69	136	223	310
11,13-16,18-20: 14-Torres-a	21	42	63	124	202	280
12-Crandall-a	22	44	66	132	216	300
17-Williamson-a, 4 pgs.; Torres-a	22	44	66	132	216	300

NOTE: Ayers a-15. Berg a-10, 11. Colan a-11. Drucker a-7. Everett a-3, 20; c-8 & 9 w/Tuska, 10, 13-16. Forte a-15, 18. Heck a-11(2), 15, 19. Maneely c-1, 5, 6, 11, 17. Morisi a-8. Pakula a-7, 18. Powell a-20. Reinman a-18.

NAVY HEROES
Almanac Publishing Co.: 1945

1-Heavy in propaganda	30	60	90	177	289	400

NAVY PATROL
Key Publications: May, 1955 - No. 4, Nov, 1955

1	14	28	42	82	121	160
2-4	9	18	27	50	65	80

NAVY TALES
Atlas Comics (CDS): Jan, 1957 - No. 4, July, 1957

1-Everett-c; Berg, Powell-a	42	84	126	265	445	625
2-Williamson/Mayo-a(5 pgs); Crandall-a	28	56	84	168	274	380
3,4-Reinman-a; Severin-c. 4-Crandall-a	21	42	63	124	202	280

NOTE: Colan a-4. Maneely c-2. Reinman a-2-4. Sinnott a-4.

NAVY TASK FORCE
Stanmor Publications/Aragon Mag. No. 4-8: Feb, 1954 - No. 8, April, 1956

1	17	34	51	98	154	210
2	10	20	30	56	76	95
3-8: 8-r/Navy Patrol #1; defeat of the Japanese Navy	9	18	27	47	61	75

NAVY WAR HEROES
Charlton Comics: Jan, 1964 - No. 7, Mar-Apr, 1965

1	4	8	12	27	44	60
2-7	3	6	9	16	23	30

NAZA (Stone Age Warrior)
Dell Publishing Co.: Nov-Jan, 1963-64 - No. 9, March, 1966

12-555-401 (#1)-Painted-c	6	12	18	37	66	95
2-9: 2-4-Painted-c	4	8	12	27	44	60

NEBBS, THE (Also see Crackajack Funnies)
Dell Publishing Co./Croydon Publishing Co.: 1941; 1945

Large Feature Comic 23(1941)	28	56	84	168	274	380
1(1945, 36 pgs.)-Reprints	15	30	45	85	130	175

NEBULA (Guardians of the Galaxy)
Marvel Comics: Apr, 2020 - Present ($3.99)

1,2-Vita Ayala-s/Claire Roe-a						4.00

NECESSARY EVIL
Desperado Publishing: Oct, 2007 - No. 9, Nov, 2008 ($3.99)

1-9: 1-Joshua Williamson-s/Marcus Harris-a/Dustin Nguyen-c						4.00

NECROMANCER
Image Comics (Top Cow): Sept, 2005 - No. 6, July 2006 ($2.99)

1-6: 1-Manapul-a/Ortega-s; three covers by Manapul, Horn & Bachalo						3.00
... Pilot Season Vol. 1 #1 (11/07, $2.99) Ortega-s/Meyers-a/Manapul-c						3.00

NECROMANCER: THE GRAPHIC NOVEL
Marvel Comics (Epic Comics): 1989 ($8.95)

nn						9.00

NECROWAR
Dreamwave Productions: July, 2003 - No. 3, Sept, 2003 ($2.95)

1-3-Furman-s/Granov-digital art						3.00

NEGAN LIVES! (The Walking Dead)
Image Comics: Jul, 2020 ($4.99, one-shot)

1-Kirkman-s/Adlard-a; takes place between Walking Dead #174-193						8.00
1-2nd printing with blue title logo						5.00
1-Variant with Gold foil title logo						55.00
1-Variant with Silver foil title logo						30.00
1-2nd printing with Bronze foil title logo						8.00

NEGATION
CrossGeneration Comics: Dec, 2001 - No. 27, Mar, 2004 ($2.95)

Prequel (12/01)						3.00
1-27: 1-(1/02) Pelletier-a/Bedard & Waid-s						3.00
... Lawbringer (11/02, $2.95) Nebres-a						3.00

	GD 2.0	VG 4.0	FN 6.0	VF 8.0	VF/NM 9.0	NM- 9.2

Vol. 1: Bohica! (10/02, $19.95, TPB) r/ Prequel & #1-6 20.00
Vol. 2: Baptism of Fire (5/03, $15.95, TPB) r/#7-12 16.00
Vol. 3: Hounded (12/03, $15.95, TPB) r/#13-18 16.00

NEGATION WAR
CrossGeneration Comics: Apr, 2004 - No. 6 ($2.95)
1-4-Bedard-s/Pelletier-a 3.00

NEGATIVE BURN
Caliber: 1993 - No. 50, 1997 ($2.95, B&W, anthology)
1,2,4-12,14-29,31-47: Anthology by various including Bolland, Burden, Doran, Gaiman,
Moebius, Moore, & Pope 4.00
3,13: 3-Bone story. 13-Strangers in Paradise story 2 4 6 8 10 12
30-Budd Root, Frankenstein, Cavewoman 2 4 6 11 16 20
48,49-($4.95) 5.00
50-($6.95, 96 pgs.)-Gaiman, Robinson, Bolland 7.00
...Summer Special 2005 (Image, 2005, $9.99) new short stories by various 10.00
...: The Best From 1993-1998 (Image, 1/05, $19.95) r/short stories by various 20.00
...Winter Special 2005 (Image, 2005, $9.95) new short stories by various 10.00

NEGATIVE BURN
Image Comics (Desperado): May, 2006 - No. 21 ($5.99, B&W, anthology)
1-21: 1-Art by Bolland, Powell, Luna, Smith, Hester. 2-Milk & Cheese by Dorkin 6.00

NEGRO (See All-Negro)

NEGRO HEROES (Calling All Girls, Real Heroes, & True Comics reprints)
Parents' Magazine Institute: Spring, 1947 - No. 2, Summer, 1948
1 206 412 618 1318 2259 3200
2-Jackie Robinson-c/story 181 362 543 1158 1979 2800

NEGRO ROMANCE (Negro Romances #4)
Fawcett Publications: June, 1950 - No. 3, Oct, 1950 (All photo-c)
1-Evans-a (scarce) 284 568 852 1818 3109 4400
2,3 (scarce) 232 464 696 1485 2543 3600

NEGRO ROMANCES (Formerly Negro Romance; Romantic Secrets #5 on)
Charlton Comics: No. 4, May, 1955
4-Reprints Fawcett #2 (scarce) 265 530 795 1694 2897 4100

NEIGHBORS, THE
BOOM! Studios: Mar, 2023 - No. 5, Jul, 2023 ($4.99, limited series)
1-5-Jude Ellison S. Doyle-s/Letizia Cadonici-a 5.00

NEIL GAIMAN AND CHARLES VESS' STARDUST
DC Comics (Vertigo): 1997 - No. 4, 1998 ($5.95/$6.95, square-bound, lim. series)
1-4: Gaiman text with Vess paintings in all 7.00
Hardcover (1998, $29.95) r/series with new sketches 35.00
Softcover (1999, $19.95) oversized; new Vess-c 20.00

NEIL GAIMAN'S LADY JUSTICE
Tekno Comix: Sept, 1995 - No. 11, May, 1996 ($1.95/$2.25)
1-11: 1-Sienkiewicz-c; pin-ups. 1-5-Brereton-c. 7-Polybagged. 11-The Big Bang Pt. 7 4.00
Free Comic Book Day (Super Genius, 2015, giveaway) r/#1 4.00

NEIL GAIMAN'S LADY JUSTICE
BIG Entertainment: V2#1, June, 1996 - No. 9, Feb, 1997 ($2.25)
V2#1-9: Dan Brereton-c on all. 6-8-Dan Brereton script 4.00

NEIL GAIMAN'S MIDNIGHT DAYS
DC Comics (Vertigo): 1999 ($17.95, trade paperback)
nn-Reprints Gaiman's short stories; new Swamp Thing w/ Bissette-a 18.00

NEIL GAIMAN'S MR. HERO-THE NEWMATIC MAN
Tekno Comix: Mar, 1995 - No. 17, May, 1996 ($1.95/$2.25)
1-17: 1-Intro Mr. Hero & Teknophage; bound-in game piece and trading card. 4-w/Steel
edition Neil Gaiman's Teknophage #1 coupon. 13-Polybagged 4.00

NEIL GAIMAN'S MR. HERO-THE NEWMATIC MAN
BIG Entertainment: V2#1, June, 1996 ($2.25)
V2#1-Teknophage destroys Mr. Hero; includes The Big Bang Pt. 10 4.00

NEIL GAIMAN'S NEVERWHERE
DC Comics (Vertigo): Aug, 2005 - No. 9, Sept, 2006 ($2.99, limited series)
1-9-Adaptation of Gaiman novel; Carey-s/Fabry-a/c 3.00
TPB (2007, $19.99) r/series; intro. by Carey 20.00

NEIL GAIMAN'S PHAGE-SHADOWDEATH
BIG Entertainment: June, 1996 - No. 6, Nov, 1996 ($2.25, limited series)
1-6: Bryan Talbot-c & scripts in all. 1-st app. Orlando Holmes 4.00

NEIL GAIMAN'S TEKNOPHAGE
Tekno Comix: Aug, 1995 - No. 10, Mar, 1996 ($1.95/$2.25)
1-6-Rick Veitch scripts & Bryan Talbot-c/a. 4.00
1-Steel Edition 5.00
7-10: Paul Jenkins scripts in all. 8-polybagged 4.00

NEIL GAIMAN'S WHEEL OF WORLDS
Tekno Comix: Apr, 1995 - No. 1, May, 1996 ($2.95/$3.25)
0-1st app. Lady Justice; 48 pgs.; bound-in poster 5.00
0-Regular edition 4.00
1 ($3.25, 5/96)-Bruce Jones scripts; Lady Justice & Teknophage app.; CGI photo-c 4.00

NEIL THE HORSE (See Charlton Bullseye #2)
Aardvark-Vanaheim #1-10/Renegade Press #11 on: 2/83 - No. 10, 12/84; No. 11, 4/85 - #15, 1985 (B&W)
1 ($1.40) 5.00
1-2nd print 4.00
2-12: 11-w/paperdolls 4.00
13-15: Double size ($3.00). 13-w/paperdolls. 15 is a flip book(2-c) 5.00

NEIL YOUNG'S GREENDALE
DC Comics (Vertigo): 2010 ($19.99, hardcover graphic novel)
HC-Story based on the Neil Young album; Dysart-s/Chiang-a; intro. by Neil Young 20.00

NELLIE THE NURSE (Also see Gay Comics & Joker Comics)
Marvel/Atlas Comics (SPI/LMC): 1945 - No. 36, Oct, 1952; 1957
1-(1945) 168 336 504 1075 1838 2600
2-(Spring/46) 48 96 144 302 514 725
3,4: 3-New logo (9/46) 39 78 117 231 378 525
5-Kurtzman's "Hey Look" (3); Georgie app. 37 74 111 222 361 500
6-8,10: 7,8-Georgie app. 10-Millie app. 32 64 96 190 310 430
9-Wolverton-a (1 pg.); Mille the Model app. 36 72 108 214 347 480
11,14-16,18-Kurtzman's "Hey Look" 33 66 99 194 317 440
12- "Giggles 'n' Grins" by Kurtzman 32 64 96 190 310 430
13,17,19,20: 17-Annie Oakley app. 27 54 81 158 259 360
21-30: 28-Mr. Nexdoor-r (3 pgs.) by Kurtzman/Rusty #22 23 46 69 136 223 310
31-36: 36-Post-c 22 44 66 128 209 290
1('57)-Leading Mag. (Atlas)-Everett-a, 20 pgs 42 84 126 265 445 625

NELLIE THE NURSE
Dell Publishing Co.: No. 1304, Mar-May, 1962
Four Color 1304-Stanley-a 10 20 30 67 141 215

NEMESIS (Millar & McNiven's...)
Marvel Comics (Icon): May, 2010 - No. 4, Feb, 2011 ($2.99)
1-4-Millar-s/McNiven-a 3.00
1,2-Variant covers: 1-Yu. 2-Cassaday 8.00

NEMESIS ARCHIVES (Listed with Adventures Into the Unknown)

NEMESIS RELOADED (Reboot of the Millar & McNiven series)
Image Comics: Jan, 2023 - No. 5, May, 2023 ($3.99, limited series)
1-4-Millar-s/Jiménez-a 4.00
5-($5.99) Characters from Wanted app.; leads into Big Game series 6.00

NEMESIS: THE IMPOSTERS
DC Comics: May, 2010 - No. 4, Aug, 2010 ($2.99, limited series)
1-4-Richards-a/Luvisi-a. 1-Joker app. 2-4-Batman app. 3.00

NEMESIS THE WARLOCK (Also see Spellbinders)
Eagle Comics: Sept, 1984 - No. 7, Mar, 1985 (limited series, Baxter paper)
1-7: 2000 A.D. reprints 4.00

NEMESIS THE WARLOCK
Quality Comics/Fleetway Quality #2 on: 1989 - No. 19, 1991 ($1.95, B&W)
1-19 4.00

NEMO (The League of Extraordinary Gentlemen)
Top Shelf Productions: ($14.95, hardcover, one-shots)
...: Heart of Ice HC (2/13) Alan Moore-s/Kevin O'Neill-a 15.00
...: River of Ghosts HC (2015) Alan Moore-s/Kevin O'Neill-a 15.00
...: Roses of Berlin HC (3/14) Alan Moore-s/Kevin O'Neill-a 15.00

NEON FUTURE (Steve Aoki Presents...)
Impact Theory, LLC: Oct, 2018 - No. 6, Aug, 2019 ($3.99)
1-6: 1-Neil Edwards & Jheremy Raapack-a 4.00

NEON JOE, WEREWOLF HUNTER (Based on Adult Swim TV series)
DC Comics: 2015 (no price, one-shot)
nn - Origin of Neon Joe; Glaser-s/Mandrake-a & Duursema-a/Panosian-c 3.00

NEUTRO
Dell Publishing Co.: Jan, 1967
1-Jack Sparling-c/a (super hero); UFO-s 5 10 15 33 55 80

NEVADA (See Zane Grey's Four Color 412, 996 & Zane Grey's Stories of the West #1)

NEVADA (Also see Vertigo Winter's Edge #1)
DC Comics (Vertigo): May, 1998 - No. 6, Oct, 1998 ($2.50, limited series)
1-6-Gerber-s/Winslade-c/a 4.00
TPB-(1999, $14.95) r/#1-6 & Vertigo Winter's Edge preview 15.00

NEVER AGAIN (War stories; becomes Soldier & Marine V2#9)
Charlton Comics: Aug, 1955; No. 8, July, 1956 (No #2-7)
1-WWII 15 30 45 84 127 170
8-(Formerly Foxhole?) 10 20 30 54 72 90

NEVERBOY
Dark Horse Comics: Mar, 2015 - No. 6, Aug, 2015 ($3.99)
1-6-Shaun Simon-s/Tyler Jenkins-a 4.00

NEVERMEN, THE (See Dark Horse Presents #148-150)
Dark Horse Comics: May, 2000 - No. 4, Aug, 2000 ($2.95, limited series)
1-4-Phil Amara-s/Guy Davis-a 3.00

NEVERMEN, THE: STREETS OF BLOOD
Dark Horse Comics: Jan, 2003 - No. 3, Apr, 2003 ($2.99, limited series)
1-3-Phil Amara-s/Guy Davis-a 3.00
TPB (7/03, $9.95) r/#1-3; Paul Jenkins intro.; Davis sketch pages 10.00

NEW ADVENTURE COMICS (Formerly New Comics; becomes Adventure Comics #32 on; V1#12 indicia says NEW COMICS #12)
National Periodical Publications: V1#12, Jan, 1937 - No. 31, Oct, 1938
V1#12-Federal Men by Siegel & Shuster continues; Jor-L mentioned;
Whitney Ellsworth-c begin, end #14 775 1550 2325 6200 – –
V2#1(2/37, #13)-(Rare) 775 1550 2325 6200 – –
V2#2 (#14) 650 1300 1950 5200 – –
15(V2#3)-20(V2#8): 15-1st Adventure logo; Creig Flessel-c begin, end #31.
16-1st non-funny cover. 17-Nadir, Master of Magic begins, ends #30 485 970 1455 2670 4485 6300
21(V2#9),22(V2#10, 2/37): 22-X-Mas-c 405 810 1215 2230 3765 5300
23-25,28-31 375 750 1125 2060 3480 4900
26(5/38) (rare) has house ad for Action Comics #1 showing B&W image of cover
(early published image of Superman)(prices vary widely on this book) 5300 10,600 15,900 38,500 – –
27(6/38) has house ad for Action Comics #1 showing B&W image of cover (rare)

Nemesis #3 © Millarworld & Recluse Ent.

Neverboy #5 © Shaun Simon

New Avengers #17 © MAR

	GD 2.0	VG 4.0	FN 6.0	VF 8.0	VF/NM 9.0	NM- 9.2

(early published image of Superman) 2630 5260 7890 15,000 22,500 30,000

NEW ADVENTURES OF ABRAHAM LINCOLN, THE
Image Comics (Homage): 1998 ($19.95, one-shot)

- 1-Scott McCloud-s/computer art ... 20.00

NEW ADVENTURES OF CHARLIE CHAN, THE (TV)
National Periodical Publications: May-June, 1958 - No. 6, Mar-Apr, 1959

1 (Scarce)-John Broome-s/Sid Greene-a in all	97	194	291	621	1061	1500
2 (Scarce)	65	130	195	416	708	1000
3-6 (Scarce)-Greene/Giella-a	57	114	171	362	619	875

NEW ADVENTURES OF CHOLLY AND FLYTRAP, THE
Epic Comics: Dec, 1990 - No. 3, Feb, 1991 ($4.95, limited series)

- 1-3-Arthur Suydam-s/a/c; painted covers ... 5.00

NEW ADVENTURES OF HUCK FINN, THE (TV)
Gold Key: December, 1968 (Hanna-Barbera)

1- "The Curse of Thut"; part photo-c	3	6	9	21	33	45

NEW ADVENTURES OF PINOCCHIO (TV)
Dell Publishing Co.: Oct-Dec, 1962 - No. 3, Sept-Nov, 1963

12-562-212(#1)	7	14	21	48	89	130
2,3	6	12	18	38	69	100

NEW ADVENTURES OF ROBIN HOOD (See Robin Hood)

NEW ADVENTURES OF SHERLOCK HOLMES (Also see Sherlock Holmes)
Dell Publishing Co.: No. 1169, Mar-May, 1961 - No. 1245, Nov-Jan, 1961/62

Four Color 1169(#1)	13	26	39	89	195	300
Four Color 1245	11	22	33	75	160	245

NEW ADVENTURES OF SPEED RACER
Now Comics: Dec, 1993 - No. 7, 1994? ($1.95)

- 1-7 ... 4.00
- 0-(Premiere)-3-D cover ... 4.00

NEW ADVENTURES OF SUPERBOY, THE (Also see Superboy)
DC Comics: Jan, 1980 - No. 54, June, 1984

1		2	4	6	9	13	16
2-6,8-10						5.00

- 11-49,51-54: 11-Superboy gets new power. 14-Lex Luthor app. 15-Superboy gets new parents. 28-Dial "H" For Hero begins, ends #49. 45-47-1st app. Sunburst. 48-Begin 75¢-c. ... 4.00

1,2,5,6,8 (Whitman variants; low print run; no issue # shown on cover)	3	6	9	16	23	30

- 7,50: 7-Has extra story "The Computers That Saved Metropolis" by Starlin (Radio Shack giveaway w/indicia). 50-Legion app. ... 5.00
NOTE: *Buckler* a-9p; c-36p. *Giffen* a-50; c-50. 40i. *Gil Kane* c-32p, 33p, 35, 39, 41-49. *Miller* c-51. *Starlin* a-7. Krypto back-ups in 17, 22. Superboy in 11, 14, 19, 24.

NEW AMERICA
Eclipse Comics: Nov, 1987 - No. 4, Feb, 1988 ($1.75, Baxter paper)

- 1-4: Scout limited series ... 4.00

NEW ARCHIES, THE (TV)
Archie Comic Publications: Oct, 1987 - No. 22, May, 1990 (75¢)

- 1 ... 5.00
- 2-10: 3-Xmas issue ... 4.00
- 11-22: 17-22 (95¢-$1.00): 21-Xmas issue ... 4.00

NEW ARCHIES DIGEST (TV)(...Comics Digest Magazine #4?-10; ...Digest Magazine #11 on)
Archie Comics: May, 1988 - No. 14, July, 1991 ($1.35/$1.50, quarterly)

- 1 ... 6.00
- 2-14: 6-Begin $1.50-c ... 4.00

NEW AVENGERS, THE (Also see Promotional section for military giveaway)
Marvel Comics: Jan, 2005 - No. 64, Jun, 2010 ($2.25/$2.50/$2.99/$3.99)

- 1-Bendis-s/Finch-a; Spider-Man app.; re-intro The Sentry; 4 covers by McNiven, Quesada & Finch; variants from #1-6 combine for one team image

		1	3	4	6	8	10

- 1-Director's Cut ($3.99) includes alternate covers, script, villain gallery ... 6.00
- 1-MGC (6/10 $1.00) r/#1 with "Marvel's Greatest Comics" cover logo ... 3.00
- 2-6,8-20: 2-6-Finch-a. 4-1st app. Maria Hill. 5-Wolverine app. 8-10-Origin of the Sentry; McNiven-a. 11-Debut of Ronin. 14,15-Cho-c/a. 17-20-Deodato-a. ... 3.00
- 7-1st app. The Illuminati; origin of the Sentry begins; McNiven-a

		3	6	9	21	33	45

- 21-48: 21-26-Civil War. 21-Chaykin-a/c. 26-Maleev-a. 27-31-Yu-a; Echo & "Elektra" app. 33-37-The Hood app. 38-Gaydos-a. 39-Mack-a. 40-47-Secret Invasion ... 3.00

	GD 2.0	VG 4.0	FN 6.0	VF 8.0	VF/NM 9.0	NM- 9.2

49-($3.99) Dark Reign		4.00
50-($4.99) Dark Reign; Tan, Hitch, McNiven, Yu, Horn & others-a; Tan wraparound-c		5.00
50-($4.99) Adam Kubert variant-c		6.00

- 51-64-($3.99) Dark Reign. 51,52-Tan & Bachalo-a. 54-Brother Voodoo becomes Sorcerer Supreme. 56-Wrecking Crew app. 61-64-Siege; Steve Rogers app. ... 4.00
- 51-54-Variant covers by Bachalo ... 7.00
- 56,57-Variant covers. 56-70th Anniversary frame. 57-Super Hero Squad ... 6.00
- Annual 1 (6/06, $3.99) Wedding of Luke Cage and Jessica Jones; Bendis-s/Coipel-a ... 4.00
- Annual 2 (2/08, $3.99) Avengers vs. The Hood's gang; Bendis-s/Pagulayan-a ... 4.00
- Annual 3 (2/10, $4.99) Mayhew-c/a; Dark Avengers app.; Siege preview ... 5.00
- ... Finale (6/10, $4.99) Follows Siege #4; Bendis-s/Hitch-a/c; Count Nefaria app. ... 5.00
- ...: Illuminati (5/06, $3.99) Bendis-s/Maleev-a; leads into Planet Hulk; Civil War preview ... 4.00
- ... Most Wanted Files (2006, $3.99) profile pages of Avenger villains ... 4.00
- ... Volume 1 HC (2007, $29.99) oversized r/#1-10, ... Most Wanted Files, and ... Guest Starring the Fantastic Four (militiary giveaway); new intro. by Bendis; script & sketch pages ... 30.00
- ... Volume 2 HC (2008, $29.99) oversized r/#11-20, ... Annual #1, and story from Giant-Size Spider-Woman; variant covers & sketch pages ... 30.00

NEW AVENGERS (The Heroic Age)
Marvel Comics: Aug, 2010 - No. 34, Jan, 2013 ($3.99)

- 1-Bendis-s/Immonen-a/c; Luke Cage forms new team; back-up text Avengers history ... 4.00
- 1-Variant-c by Djurdjevic ... 6.00
- 2-16: Hellstrom & Doctor Voodoo app.; back-up text Avengers history. 6-Doctor Voodoo killed. 9-13-Nick Fury flashback w/Chaykin-a. 10-Intro. Avengers 1959. 14-16-Fear Itself. 16-Daredevil joins ... 4.00
- 16.1 (11/11, $2.99) Neal Adams-a/c; Bendis-s; Norman Osborn app. ... 3.00
- 17-23-($3.99) 17-Norman Osborn attacks; Deodato-a. 6-Doctor Voodoo killed. ... 4.00
- 24-33: 24-30-Avengers vs. X-Men tie-in. 26,27-DaVinci app. 31-Gaydos-a. 32-Pacheco-a ... 4.00
- 34-($4.99) Dr. Strange become Sorcerer Supreme again; Deodato-a; gallery of Bendis-era Avengers covers ... 5.00
- Annual 1 (11/11, $4.99) Dell'Otto-a; Wonder Man app.; continues in Avengers Annual #1 ... 5.00

NEW AVENGERS (Marvel NOW!)
Marvel Comics: Mar, 2013 - No. 33, Jun, 2015 ($3.99)

- 1-7: 1-Hickman-s/Epting-a; Black Panther and the Illuminati. 4-Galactus app. ... 4.00
- 8-23: 8-12-Infinity tie-in; Deodato-a. 13-Inhumanity; Bianchi-a. 17-21-Great Society app. ... 4.00
- 24-($4.99) Doctor Doom, Thanos and the Cabal app. ... 5.00
- 25-32: 27-Kudranski-a. 28,32-Deodato-a ... 4.00
- 33-($4.99) Doctor Doom & Molecule Man app.; leads into Secret Wars x-over; Deodato-a ... 5.00
- Annual 1 (8/14, $4.99) Spotlight on Doctor Strange; Marco Rudy-a ... 5.00

NEW AVENGERS (Follows events of Secret Wars)(See U.S.Avengers)
Marvel Comics: Dec, 2015 - No. 18, Jan, 2017 ($3.99)

- 1-18: 1-Ewing-s/Sandoval-a; Squirrel Girl app. 5,6-Avengers of 20XX app. 8-10-Standoff tie-in; Marcus To-a. 12-17-Civil War II tie-in. 12-16-Interlocking covers ... 4.00

NEW AVENGERS: ILLUMINATI (Also see Civil War and Secret Invasion)
Marvel Comics: Feb, 2007 - No. 5, Jan, 2008 ($2.99, limited series)

- 1-5-Bendis & Reed-s/Cheung-a. 3-Origin of The Beyonder. 5-Secret Invasion ... 3.00
- HC (2008, $19.99, dustjacket) r/#1-5; cover sketch art ... 20.00
- SC (2008, $14.99) r/#1-5; cover sketch art ... 15.00

NEW AVENGERS: LUKE CAGE
Marvel Comics: Jun, 2010 - No. 3, Aug, 2010 ($3.99, limited series)

- 1-3-Arcudi-s/Canete-a; Spider-Man & Ronin app. ... 4.00

NEW AVENGERS: THE REUNION
Marvel Comics: May, 2009 - No. 4, Aug, 2009 ($3.99, limited series)

- 1-4-Mockingbird and Ronin (Hawkeye); McCann-s/López-a/Jo Chen-c ... 4.00

NEW AVENGERS/TRANSFORMERS
Marvel Comics: Sept, 2007 - No. 4, Dec, 2007 ($2.99, limited series)

- 1-4-Kirkham-a; Capt. America app. 1-Cheung-c. 2-Pearson-c ... 3.00
- TPB (2008, $10.99) r/#1-4 ... 11.00

NEW AVENGERS: ULTRON FOREVER
Marvel Comics: Jun, 2015 ($4.99)(Continues in Uncanny Avengers: Ultron Forever)

- 1-Part 2 of 3-part crossover with Avengers and Uncanny Avengers; Ewing-s/Alan Davis-a; team-up of past, present and future Avengers vs. Ultron ... 5.00

NEW BOOK OF COMICS (Also see Big Book Of Fun)
National Periodical Publ.: 1937; No. 2, Spring, 1938 (100 pgs. each) (Reprints)

1(Rare)-1st regular size comic annual; 2nd DC annual; contains r/New Comics #1-4 & More Fun #9; r/Federal Men (8 pgs.), Henri Duval (1 pg.), & Dr. Occult in costume (1 pg.) by Siegel & Shuster; Moldoff, Sheldon Mayer (15 pgs.)-a	2000	4000	6000	13,000	22,750	32,500
2-Contains-r/More Fun #15 & 16; r/Dr. Occult in costume (a Superman prototype), & Calling All Cars (4 pgs.) by Siegel & Shuster	1046	2092	3138	6800	11,900	17,000

	GD	VG	FN	VF	VF/NM	NM-
	2.0	4.0	6.0	8.0	9.0	9.2

NEWBURN
Image Comics: Nov, 2021 - No. 8, Jun, 2022 ($3.99)

1-15-Chip Zdarsky-s/Jacob Phillips-a					4.00

NEW CHALLENGERS (Challengers of the Unknown)(Follows events of Dark Nights: Metal)
DC Comics: Jul, 2018 - No. 6, Dec, 2018 ($2.99)

1-5: 1-New team recruited; Snyder & Gillespie-s/Andy Kubert-a/c. 2-Original team returns.
4-6-Marion-a 3.00

NEW CHAMPION OF SHAZAM!, THE (Continues in Lazarus Planet: We Once Were Gods)
DC Comics: Oct, 2022 - No. 4, Mar, 2023 ($3.99, limited series)

1-4-Mary receives all the power of Shazam!; Hoppy app.; Josie Campbell-s/Doc Shaner-a 4.00

NEW COMICS (New Adventure #12 on)
National Periodical Publ.: 12/35 - No. 11, 12/36 (No. 1-6: paper cover) (No. 1-5: 84 pgs.)

V1#1-Billy the Kid, Sagebrush 'n' Cactus, Jibby Jones, Needles, The Vikings, Sir Loin of Beef,
Now-When I Was a Boy, & other 1-2 pg. strips; 2 pgs. Kelly art(1st)-(Gulliver's Travels);
Sheldon Mayer-a(1st)(2 pgg. strips); Vincent Sullivan-c(1st)
| | 2540 | 5080 | 7620 | 16,000 | – | – |
2-1st app. Federal Men by Siegel & Shuster & begins (also see The Comics Magazine #2);
Mayer, Kelly-a (Rare)(1/36) | | 1460 | 2920 | 4380 | 9200 | – | – |
3-6: 3,4-Sheldon Mayer-a which continues in The Comics Magazine #1. 3-Vincent Sullivan-a.
4-Dickens' "A Tale of Two Cities" adaptation begins. 5-Junior Federal Men Club; Kiefer-a.
6- "She" adaptation begins | | 1000 | 2000 | 3000 | 6300 | – | – |
7-10 | | 650 | 1300 | 1950 | 4100 | – | – |
11-Ties with More Fun #16 as DC's 1st Christmas-c | | 733 | 1466 | 2199 | 4600 | – | – |
NOTE: #1-6 rarely occur in mint condition. **Whitney Ellsworth** c-4-11.

NEW CRUSADERS (Rise of the Heroes)
Archie Comics (Red Circle Comics): Oct, 2012 - No. 6, Mar, 2013 ($2.99)

1-6-The Shield and the offspring of the Mighty Crusaders 3.00

NEW DEADWARDIANS, THE
DC Comics (Vertigo): May, 2012 - No. 8, Dec, 2012 ($2.99, limited series)

1-8-Abnett-s/Culbard-a 3.00

NEW DEFENDERS (See Defenders)

NEW DNAGENTS, THE (Formerly DNAgents)
Eclipse Comics: V2#1, Oct, 1985 - V2#17, Mar, 1987 (Whole #s 25-40; Mando paper)

V2#1-17: 1-Origin recap. 7-Begin 95 cent-c. 9,10-Airboy preview 4.00
3-D 1 (1/86, $2.25) 4.00
2-D 1 (1/86)-Limited ed. (100 copies) 10.00

NEW DYNAMIX
DC Comics (WildStorm): May, 2008 - No. 5, Sept, 2008 ($2.99, limited series)

1-5-Warner-s/J.J. Kirby-a/c. 1-Variant-c by Jim Lee. 1-Convention Ed. with Lee-c 3.00

NEW ETERNALS: APOCALYPSE NOW (Also see Eternals, The)
Marvel Comics: Feb, 2000 ($3.99, one-shot)

1-Bennett & Hanna-a; Ladronn-c 4.00

NEW EXCALIBUR
Marvel Comics: Jan, 2006 - No. 24, Dec, 2007 ($2.99)

1-24: 1-Claremont-s/Ryan-a. 3-Juggernaut app. 4-Lionheart app. 3.00
... Vol. 1: Defenders of the Realm TPB (2006, $17.99) r/#1-7 .... 18.00
... Vol. 2: Last Days of Camelot TPB (2007, $19.99) r/#8-15 .... 20.00
... Vol. 3: Battle for Eternity TPB (2007, $24.99) r/#16-24; sketch pages 25.00

NEW EXILES (Continued from Exiles #100 and Exiles - Days of Then and Now)
Marvel Comics: Mar, 2008 - No. 18, Apr, 2009 ($2.99)

1-18: 1-Claremont-s/Grummett-a; 2 covers by Land & Golden; new team 3.00
1-2nd printing with Grummett-c 3.00
Annual 1 (2/09, $3.99) Claremont-s/Grummett-a 4.00

NEW FANTASTIC FOUR
Marvel Comics: Aug, 2022 - No. 5, Dec, 2022 ($4.99/$3.99)

1-($4.99)-Spider-Man, Wolverine, Ghost Rider & Joe Fixit team; David-s/Robinson-a 5.00
2-5-($3.99) Regular Fantastic Four app. 4.00
... Marvel Tales 1 (8/22, $7.99) Reprints Fantastic Four #347-349; bonus art 8.00

NEW 52: FUTURE'S END
DC Comics: No 0, Jun, 2014 - No. 48, Jun, 2015 ($2.99, weekly limited series)

FCBD Special Edition #0 (6/14, giveaway) Part 1; 35 years in the future 3.00
1-36: 1-Set 5 years in the future; Azzarello, Lemire, Jurgens & Giffen-s. 29-New Firestorm.
33-Kid Deathstroke-a. 44-Brainiac steals New York (Convergence) 3.00

NEWFORCE (Also see Newmen)
Image Comics (Extreme Studios): Jan, 1996-No.4, Apr, 1996 ($2.50, lim. series)

1-4: 1-"Extreme Destroyer" Pt. 8; polybagged w/gaming card. 4-Newforce disbands 4.00

NEW FUN COMICS (More Fun #7 on; see Big Book of Fun Comics)
National Periodical Publications: Feb, 1935 - No. 6, Oct, 1935 (10x15", No. 1-4,: slick-c
(No. 1-5: 36 pgs; 40 pgs. No. 6)

V1#1 (1st DC comic): 1st app. Oswald The Rabbit; Jack Woods (cowboy) begins
| | 9000 | 18,000 | 27,000 | 63,000 | – | – |
2(3/35)-(Very Rare) | | 4575 | 9151 | 13,725 | 32,000 | – | – |
3-5(8/35): 3-Don Drake on the Planet Soro-c/story (sci/fi, 4/35); early (maybe 1st) DC letter
column. 5-Soft-c | | 2930 | 5860 | 8790 | 20,500 | – | – |
6(10/35)-1st Dr. Occult by Siegel & Shuster (Leger & Reuths); last "New Fun" title.
"New Comics" #1 begins in Dec. which is reason for title change to More Fun;
Henri Duval (ends #10) by Siegel & Shuster begins; paper-c
| | 4700 | 9400 | 14,100 | 33,000 | – | – |

NEW FUNNIES (The Funnies #1-64; Walter Lantz...#109 on; New TV... #259, 260, 272, 273;
TV Funnies #261-271)
Dell Publishing Co.: No. 65, July, 1942 - No. 288, Mar-Apr, 1962

65(#1)-Andy Panda in a world of real people, Raggedy Ann & Andy, Oswald the Rabbit
(with Woody Woodpecker x-overs), Li'l Eight Ball & Peter Rabbit begins;
Bugs Bunny and Elmer app. | | 107 | 214 | 321 | 856 | 1928 | 3000 |
66-70: 66-Felix the Cat begins. 67-Billy & Bonny Bee by Frank Thomas begins. 69-Kelly-a
(2 pgs.); The Brownies begin (not by Kelly); Halloween-c

| | 35 | 70 | 105 | 252 | 564 | 875 |
71-75: 71-Christmas-c. 72-Kelly illos. 75-Brownies by Kelly? | | 22 | 44 | 66 | 154 | 340 | 525 |
76-Andy Panda (Carl Barks & Pabian-a); Woody Woodpecker x-over in Oswald ends
| | 54 | 108 | 162 | 432 | 966 | 1500 |
77,78: 77-Kelly-c. 78-Andy Panda in a world with real people ends
| | 16 | 32 | 48 | 110 | 243 | 375 |
79-81 | | 10 | 20 | 30 | 69 | 147 | 225 |
82-Brownies by Kelly begins | | 12 | 24 | 36 | 82 | 179 | 275 |
83-85-Brownies by Kelly in ea. 83-X-mas-c; Homer Pigeon begins. 85-Woody Woodpecker,
1 pg. strip begins | | 11 | 22 | 33 | 72 | 154 | 235 |
86-90: 87-Woody Woodcock stories begin | | 9 | 18 | 27 | 57 | 111 | 165 |
91-99 | | 8 | 16 | 24 | 51 | 96 | 140 |
100 (6/45) | | 8 | 16 | 24 | 54 | 102 | 150 |
101-120: 119-X-Mas-c | | 7 | 14 | 21 | 46 | 86 | 125 |
121-150: 131,143-X-Mas-c | | 6 | 12 | 18 | 40 | 73 | 105 |
151-200: 155-X-Mas-c. 167-X-Mas-c. 182-Origin & 1st app. Knothead & Splinter.
191-X-Mas-c | | 5 | 10 | 15 | 35 | 63 | 90 |
201-240 | | 5 | 10 | 15 | 35 | 57 | 80 |
241-288: 270,271-Walter Lantz c-app. 281-1st story swipes/WDC&S #100
| | 5 | 10 | 15 | 30 | 50 | 70 |
NOTE: Early issues written by **John Stanley.**

NEW GODS, THE (1st Series)(New Gods #12 on)(See Adventure #459, DC Graphic Novel #4,
1st Issue Special #13 & Super-Team Family)
National Periodical Publications/DC Comics: 2-3/71 - V2#11, 10-11/72; V3#12, 7/77 - V3#19,
7-8/78 (Fourth World)

1-Intro/1st app. Orion; 4th app. Darkseid (cameo; 3 weeks after Forever People #1)
(#1-3 are 15¢ issues) | | 10 | 20 | 30 | 69 | 147 | 225 |
2-Darkseid-c/story (2nd full app., 4-5/71) | | 7 | 14 | 21 | 44 | 82 | 120 |
3-1st app. Black Racer; last 15¢ issue | | 6 | 12 | 18 | 46 | 76 | 110 |
4-6,8,9: (25¢, 52 pg. giants): 4-Darkseid cameo; origin Manhunter-r. 5,8-Young Gods feature.
9-1st app. Forager | | 4 | 8 | 12 | 27 | 44 | 60 |
7-1st app. Steppenwolf (2-3/72); Darkseid app.; origin Orion; 1st origin of all New Gods as
a group; Young Gods feature | | 9 | 18 | 27 | 59 | 117 | 175 |
10,11: 11-Last Kirby issue. | | 8 | 12 | 23 | 37 | 50 | |
12-19: Darkseid storyline w/minor apps. 12-New costume Orion (see 1st Issue Special #13 for
1st new costume). 19-Story continued in Adventure Comics #459,460
| | 2 | 4 | 6 | 8 | 11 | 14 |
Jack Kirby's New Gods TPB ('98, $11.95, B&W&Grey) r/#1-11 plus cover gallery of original
series and '84 reprints | | | | | | 12.00 |
NOTE: #4-9(25¢, 52 pgs.) contain Manhunter-r by **Simon & Kirby** from Adventure #73, 74, 75, 76, 77, 78 with
covers in that order. **Adkins** i-12-14, 17-19. **Buckler** a(p)-15. **Kirby** c/a-1-11,p. **Newton** a(p)-12-14, 16-19. **Starlin**
c-17. **Staton** c-19,p.

NEW GODS (Also see DC Graphic Novel #4)
DC Comics: June, 1984 - No. 6, Nov, 1984 ($2.00, Baxter paper)

1-New Kirby-c; r/New Gods #1,2 | | 1 | 3 | 4 | 6 | 8 | 10 |
2-5: New Kirby-c; r/New Gods #3-10. | | | | | | | 5.00 |
6-Reprints New Gods #11 w/48 pgs of new Kirby story & art; leads into DC Graphic Novel #4
| | 2 | 4 | 6 | 8 | 10 | 12 |

NEW GODS (2nd Series)
DC Comics: Feb, 1989 - No. 28, Aug, 1991 ($1.50)

1-28: 1,5-28-Evanier-s. 2-4-Starlin-s. 13-History of New Gods 20th anniv.
.... 4.00

NEW GODS (3rd Series) (Becomes Jack Kirby's Fourth World) (Also see Showcase '94 #1 &
Showcase '95 #7)
DC Comics: Oct, 1995 - No. 15, Feb, 1997 ($1.95)

1-11,13-15: 9-Giffen-a(p). 10,11-Superman app. 13-Takion, Mr. Miracle & Big Barda app.
13-15-Byrne-a(p)/scripts & Simonson-c. 15-Apokolips merged w/ New Genesis; story cont'd
in Jack Kirby's Fourth World 4.00
12-(11/96, 99¢)-Byrne-a(p)/scripts & Simonson-c begin; Takion cameo; indicia reads
October 1996 .... 4.00
...Secret Files 1 (9/98, $4.95) Origin-s 5.00

NEW GODS SPECIAL, THE (Jack Kirby's 100th Birthday tribute)
DC Comics: Oct, 2017 ($4.99, one-shot)

1-Spotlight on Orion; Shane Davis-s/a; back-up by Walt Simonson-s/a; short reprints 5.00

NEW GOLDEN AGE, THE (Leads into Justice Society of America 2023 series)
DC Comics: Jan, 2023 ($4.99, one-shot)

1-Per Degaton vs. various eras of the JSA & Huntress; Johns-s; profile pgs of missing 13 .... 5.00
... Special Edition 1 (12/23, $4.99) r/#1 with previews of Wesley Dodds, Jay Garrick, Alan Scott
mini-series 5.00

NEW GUARDIANS, THE
DC Comics: Sept, 1988 - No. 12, Sept, 1989 ($1.25)

1-($2.00, 52 pgs)-Staton-c/a in #1-9 .... 5.00
2-12 .... 4.00

NEW HEROIC (See Heroic)

NEW INVADERS (Titled Invaders for #0 & #1) (See Avengers V3#83,84)
Marvel Comics: No. 0, Aug, 2004 - No. 9, June, 2005 ($2.99)

0-9-Roster of U.S. Agent, Sub-Mariner, Blazing Skull and others. 0-Avengers app. 3.00

NEW JUSTICE MACHINE, THE (Also see The Justice Machine)
Innovation Publishing: 1989 - No. 3, 1989 ($1.95, limited series)

1-3 .... 4.00

NEW KIDS ON THE BLOCK, THE (Also see Richie Rich and...)
Harvey Comics: Dec, 1990 - No. 8, Dec, 1991 ($1.25)

1-8 .... 5.00
...Back Stage Pass 1(12/90) - 7 (11/91) Chillin' 1(12/90) - 7(12/91): 1-Photo-c
...Comic Tour '90/91 1 (12/90) - 7 (12/91) Digest 1(1/91) - 5(1/92) Hanging Tough 1 (2/91)
Magic Summer Tour 1 (Fall/90) Magic Summer Tour nn (Fall/90, sold at concerts)
Step By Step 1 (Fall/90, one-shot) Valentine Girl 1 (Fall/90, one-shot)-Photo-c 5.00

NEW LINE CINEMA'S TALES OF HORROR (Anthology)
DC Comics (WildStorm): Nov, 2007 ($2.99, one-shot)

1-Freddy Krueger and Leatherface app.; Darick Robertson-c 3.00

New 52: Future's End #45 © DC

New Exiles #17 © MAR

New Mutants #21 © MAR

	GD	VG	FN	VF	VF/NM	NM-		GD	VG	FN	VF	VF/NM	NM-
	2.0	4.0	6.0	8.0	9.0	9.2		2.0	4.0	6.0	8.0	9.0	9.2

NEW LOVE (See Love & Rockets)
Fantagraphics Books: Aug, 1996 - No. 6, Dec, 1997 ($2.95, B&W, lim. series)

1-6: Gilbert Hernandez-s/a 4.00

NEWMAN
Image Comics (Extreme Studios): Jan, 1996 - No. 4, Apr, 1996 ($2.50, lim. series)

1-4: 1-Extreme Destroyer Pt. 3; polybagged w/card. 4-Shadowhunt tie-in;
Eddie Collins becomes new Shadowhawk 4.00

NEW MANGVERSE (Also see Marvel Mangaverse)
Marvel Comics: Mar, 2006 - No. 5, July, 2006 ($2.99, lim. series)

1-5: Cebulski-s/Ohtsuka-a; The Hand and Elektra app. 3.00
...: The Rings of Fate (2006, $7.99, digest) r/#1-5 .... 8.00

NEWMEN (becomes The Adventures of The...#2?)
Image Comics (Extreme Studios): Apr, 1994 - No. 20, Nov, 1995; No. 21, Nov, 1996
($1.95/$2.50)

1-21: 1-5: Matsuda-c/a. 10-Polybagged w/trading card. 11-Polybagged.
20-Has a variant-c; Babewatch! x-over. 21-(11/96)-Series relaunch; Chris Sprouse-a begins;
pin-up. 16-Has a variant-c by Quesada & Palmiotti 4.00
TPB-(1996, $12.95) r/#1-4 w/pin-ups 13.00

NEW MEN OF BATTLE, THE
Catechetical Guild: 1949 (nn) (Carboard-c)

nn(V8#1-3,5,6)-192 pgs.; contains 6 issues of Topix rebound	13	26	39	74	105	135
nn(V8#7-V8#11)-160 pgs.; contains 5 iss. of Topix	10	20	30	58	79	100

NEW MGMT (See Mind MGMT)

NEW MUTANTS, THE (See Marvel Graphic Novel #4 for 1st app.)(Also see X-Force &
Uncanny X-Men #167)
Marvel Comics Group: Mar, 1983 - No. 100, Apr, 1991

	GD	VG	FN	VF	VF/NM	NM-
1-Claremont-s/McLeod-a	3	6	9	21	33	45
2-,8,10: 3;4-Ties into X-Men #167. 10-1st app. Magma						
	1	3	4	6	8	10
9-1st app. Selene, the Black Queen	2	4	6	11	16	20
11-15,17,19,20: 13-Kitty Pryde app.						5.00
16-1st app. Warpath (w/out costume); see Uncanny X-Men #193						
	3	6	9	15	22	28
18-Intro. new Warlock	3	6	9	14	20	25
21-Double size; origin new Warlock; newsstand version has cover price written in by Sienkiewicz	2	4	6	11	16	20
22-24,27-30: 23-25-Cloak & Dagger app.						5.00
25-1st brief app. Legion (David Haller)	3	6	9	17	25	34
26-1st full Legion app.	3	6	9	19	30	40
31-49,51-58: 35-Magneto intro'd as new headmaster. 43-Portacio-i. 58-Contains pull-out mutant registration form						5.00
50,73: 50-Double size. 73-(52 pgs.).						6.00
59-61: Fall of The Mutants series. 60-(52 pgs.)						6.00
62-72,74-85: 68-Intro Spyder. 63-X-Men & Wolverine clones app. 76-X-Factor & X-Terminator app. 85-Liefeld-c begin						5.00
86-Rob Liefeld begins; McFarlane-c(i) swiped from Ditko splash pg.; 1st brief app. Cable (last page teaser)	3	6	9	17	26	35
87-1st full app. Cable (3/90)	9	18	27	59	117	175
87-2nd printing; gold metallic ink-c ($1.00)	3	6	9	16	23	30
88-2nd app. Cable	2	4	6	10	14	18
92-No variant-c; Liefeld-c						5.00
89,90,91,93-97,99: 89-3rd app. Cable. 90-New costumes. 90,91-Sabretooth app.						
93,94-Cable vs. Wolverine. 95-97-X-Tinction Agenda x-over. 95-Death of new Warlock. 97-Wolverine & Cable-c. app. 99-1st app. of Feral (of X-Force); 2nd app. Shatterstar (cameo); Byrne-c/swipe (X-Men, 1st Series #138)						6.00
95,100-Gold 2nd printing. 100-Silver ink 3rd printing						6.00
98-1st app. Deadpool, Gideon & Domino (2/91); Liefeld-c/a						
	16	32	48	110	243	375
100-(52 pgs.)-1st brief app. X-Force; 1st full app. of Shatterstar						
	3	6	9	16	23	30
Annual 1 (1984)	3	6	9	14	19	24
Annual 2 (1985, $1.25)-1st Psylocke	6	12	18	38	69	100
Annual 3,4,6,7 ('87, '88,'90,'91, 68 pgs.): 4-Evolutionary War x-over. 6-1st new costumes by Liefeld (3 pgs.); 1st brief app. Shatterstar (1 pg.). 7-Liefeld-a/co-plot						5.00
Annual 5 (1989, $2.00, 68 pgs.)-Atlantis Attacks; 1st Liefeld-a on New Mutants						5.00
... Classic Vol. 1 TPB (2006, $24.99) r/#1-7, Marvel Graphic Novel #4, Uncanny X-Men #167						25.00
... Classic Vol. 2 TPB (2007, $24.99) r/#8-17						25.00
... Classic Vol. 3 TPB (2008, $24.99) r/#18-25 & Annual 1						25.00
... No. 98 Facsimile Edition (9/19, $3.99) Reprints #98 with original 1991 ads and letters						4.00

... No. 98 Facsimile Edition (1/23, $3.99) Reprints #98 with original 1991 ads and letters 4.00

Special 1-Special Edition ('85, 68 pgs.)-Ties in w/X-Men Alpha Flight limited series; cont'd in X-Men Annual #9; Art Adams/Austin-a	2	4	6	10	14	18
Summer Special 1(Sum/90, $2.95, 84 pgs.)						5.00

NOTE: **Art Adams** c-38, 39. **Austin** c-57i. **Byrne** c/a-75p. **Liefeld** a-86-91p, 93-96p, 98-100, Annual 5p, 6(3 pgs.); c-85-91p, 92, 93p, 94, 95, 96p, 97-100, Annual 5, 6p. **McFarlane** c-85-89i, 93i. **Russell** a-48i. **Portacio** a(i)-43. **Sienkiewicz** a-18-31, 35-38i; c-17-31, 35i, 37i, Annual 1. **Simonson** c-11p. **B. Smith** c-36, 40-48. **Williamson** a(i)-69, 71-73, 78-80, 82, 83; c(i)-69, 72, 73, 78i.

NEW MUTANTS (Continues as New X-Men (Academy X))
Marvel Comics: July, 2003 - No. 13, June, 2004 ($2.50/$2.99)

1-13: 1-6-Josh Middleton-c. 7-11-Bachalo-c. 8-Begin $2.99 ...... 3.00
... Vol. 1: Back To School TPB (2005, $16.99) r/#1-6; new Middleton-c 17.00

NEW MUTANTS
Marvel Comics: July, 2009 - No. 50, Dec, 2012 ($3.99/$2.99)

1-($3.99) Neves-a; Legion app.; covers by Ross, Adam Kubert, McLeod, Benjamin .. 4.00
2-24-($2.99) 2-10-Adam Kubert-c. 11-Siege; Dodson-c. 12-14-Second Coming .. 3.00
25-($3.99) Fernandez-a; wraparound-c by Djurdjevic; Nate Grey returns .. 4.00
26-50: 29-32-Fear Itself tie-in. 33-Regenesis. 34-Blink returns. 42,43-Exiled x-over with
Exiled #1 & Journey Into Mystery #637,638 .... 3.00
... Saga (2009, giveaway) New Mutants character profiles and story synopses; Neves-c .. 3.00

NEW MUTANTS
Marvel Comics: Jan, 2020 - No. 33, Feb, 2023 ($4.99/$3.99)

1-($4.99) Brisson & Hickman-s/Rod Reis-a; Starjammers app. 5.00
2-24,26-29,31-33-($3.99) 13- "X of Swords" tie-in 4.00
25-($4.99) Reis-a; flashback art by Jan Duursema 5.00
30-($5.99) Celebration of 40 years; short stories by various; Deadpool app. .. 6.00
...: War Children 1 (11/19, $4.99) Claremont-s/Sienkiewicz-a/c .. 5.00

NEW MUTANTS: DEAD SOULS
Marvel Comics: May, 2018 - No. 6, Oct, 2018 ($3.99, limited series)

1-6-Rosenberg-s/Gorham-a; Rictor, Boom Boom, Magik, Strong Guy & Wolfsbane app. .. 4.00

NEW MUTANTS FOREVER
Marvel Comics: Oct, 2010 - No. 5, Feb, 2011 ($3.99, limited series)

1-5-Claremont-s/Rio & McLeod-a; Red Skull app. 1-Back-up history of New Mutants .. 4.00

NEW MUTANTS: LETHAL LEGION
Marvel Comics: May, 2023 - No. 5, Sept, 2023 ($3.99, limited series)

1-5-Charlie Jane Anders-s/Enid Balám-a; Count Nefaria app. 4.00

NEW MUTANTS, THE: TRUTH OR DEATH
Marvel Comics: Nov, 1997 - No. 3, Jan, 1998 ($2.50, limited series)

1-3-Raab-s/Chang-a(p) 4.00

NEW PEOPLE, THE (TV)
Dell Publishing Co.: Jan, 1970 - No. 2, May, 1970

	GD	VG	FN	VF	VF/NM	NM-
1	3	6	9	17	25	34
2-Photo-c	3	6	9	15	21	26

NEW ROMANCER
DC Comics (Vertigo): Feb, 2016 - No. 6, Jul, 2016 ($3.99, limited series)

1-6-Milligan-s/Parson-a; Lord Byron & Casanova in present day .. 4.00

NEW ROMANCES
Standard Comics: No. 5, May, 1951 - No. 21, May, 1954

	GD	VG	FN	VF	VF/NM	NM-
5-Photo-c	24	48	72	144	237	330
6-9: 6-Barbara Bel Geddes, Richard Basehart "Fourteen Hours" photo-c. 7-Ray Milland & Joan Fontaine photo-c. 9-Photo-c from '50s movie						
	16	32	48	94	147	200
10,14,16,17-Toth-a	17	34	51	100	158	215
11-Toth-a; Liz Taylor, Montgomery Clift photo-c	42	84	126	265	445	625
12,13,15,18-21	15	30	45	85	130	175

NOTE: **Celardo** a-9. **Moreira** a-6. **Tuska** a-7, 20. Photo c-5-16.

NEWSBOY LEGION AND THE BOY COMMANDOS SPECIAL, THE (Jack Kirby's 100th Birthday tribute)
DC Comics: Oct, 2017 ($4.99, one-shot)

1-Howard Chaykin-s/a/c; reprint from Star Spangled Comics #29; Simon-s/Kirby-a .. 5.00

NEWSBOY LEGION BY JOE SIMON AND JACK KIRBY, THE
DC Comics: 2010 ($49.99, hardcover with dustjacket)

Vol. 1 - Reprints apps. in Star Spangled Comics #7-32; new intro. by Joe Simon .. 50.00

NEW SHADOWHAWK, THE (Also see Shadowhawk & Shadowhunt)
Image Comics (Shadowline Ink): June, 1995 - No. 7, Mar, 1996 ($2.50)

1-7: Kurt Busiek scripts in all 4.00

NEWSTRALIA

	GD 2.0	VG 4.0	FN 6.0	VF 8.0	VF/NM 9.0	NM- 9.2

Innovation Publ.: July, 1989 - No. 5, 1989 ($1.75, color)(#2 on, $2.25, B&W)

1-5: 1,2: Timothy Truman-c/a; Gustovich-i — 4.00

NEW SUICIDE SQUAD (DC New 52)
DC Comics: Sept, 2014 - No. 22, Sept, 2016 ($2.99)

1-New team of Harley Quinn, Joker's Daughter, Black Manta, Deathstroke, Deadshot — 2 4 6 11 16 20
2,3 — 5.00
4-10 — 4.00
11-22: 22-Cliquet-a — 3.00
Annual 1 (11/15, $4.99) Continues story from #12; Briones-a — 5.00
...: Futures End 1 (11/14, $2.99, regular-c) Five years later; Coelho-a — 3.00
...: Futures End 1 (11/14, $3.99, 3-D cover) — 4.00

NEW SUPER-MAN (DC Rebirth)(See Batman/Superman #32 for 1st app.)
DC Comics: Sept, 2016 - No. 19, Mar, 2018 ($2.99/$3.99)

1-9: 1-Kong Kenan as China's Superman; origin; Gene Luen Yang-s/Bogdanovic-a.
7-9-Master I-Ching app. 8-Ching Lung (from Detective Comics #1) app. 9-Luthor app. — 3.00
10-19-($3.99) 10-Superman app. 15-Suicide Squad app. 17,18-Justice League app.

NEW SUPER-MAN & THE JUSTICE LEAGUE OF CHINA
DC Comics: No. 20, Apr, 2018 - No. 24, Aug, 2018 ($3.99)

20-24-Yang-s/Peeples-a — 4.00

NEW TALENT SHOWCASE (Talent Showcase #16 on)
DC Comics: Jan, 1984 - No. 19, Oct, 1985 (Direct sales only)

1-19: Features new strips & artists. 18-Williamson-c(i) — 4.00

NEW TALENT SHOWCASE
DC Comics: Jan, 2017 ($7.99, one-shot)

1-Janson-c; short stories by various; Wonder Woman, Harley Quinn, Deadman app. — 8.00
... 2017 #1 (1/18, $7.99) Short stories by various; Wonder Woman, Red Hood, Duke, Katana, Deadshot, Poison Ivy and Dr. Fate app. — 8.00
... 2018 #1 (2/19, $7.99) Short stories by various; Batman, Catwoman, Wonder Woman, Constantine, John Stewart and Zatanna app. — 8.00
...: The Milestone Initiative 1 (7/23, $3.99) Short stories by Black and diverse creators — 4.00

NEW TEEN TITANS, THE (See DC Comics Presents #26, Marvel and DC Present & Teen Titans; Tales of the Teen Titans #41 on)
DC Comics: Nov, 1980 - No. 40, Mar, 1984

1-Robin, Kid Flash, Wonder Girl, The Changeling (1st app.), Starfire, The Raven, Cyborg begin; original origin — 5 10 15 31 53 75
2-1st app. Deathstroke the Terminator — 9 18 27 58 114 170
3,4: 3-Origin Starfire; Intro The Fearsome Five. 4-Origin continues; J.L.A. app. — 3 6 9 15 22 28
5-9: 6-Origin Raven. 7-Cyborg origin. 8-Origin Kid Flash retold. 9-Minor app. Deathstroke on last pg. — 2 4 6 11 14 18
10-2nd app. Deathstroke the Terminator (see Marvel & DC Present for 3rd app.); origin Changeling retold — 3 6 9 14 19 25
11-20: 13-Return of Madame Rouge & Capt. Zahl; Robotman revived. 14-Return of Mento; origin Doom Patrol. 15-Death of Madame Rouge & Capt. Zahl; intro. new Brotherhood of Evil. 16-1st app. Captain Carrot (free 16 pg. preview). 18-Return of Starfire. 19-Hawkman teams-up — 1 3 4 6 8 10
21,22: 21-Intro Night Force in free 16 pg. insert; intro Brother Blood. 22-1st app. Bethany Snow — 2 4 6 13 18 22
23-25,27-33,35-40: 23-1st app. Vigilante (not in costume) & Blackfire; bondage-c. 24-Omega Men app. 25-Omega Men cameo; free 16 pg. preview Masters of the Universe. 27-Free 16 pg. preview Atari Force. 29-The New Brotherhood of Evil & Speedy app. 30-Terra joins the Titans. 37-Batman & The Outsiders x-over. 38-Origin Wonder Girl. 39-Last Dick Grayson as Robin; Kid Flash quits — 1 2 3 5 6 8
26-1st app. Terra — 2 4 6 10 14 18
34-4th app. Deathstroke the Terminator — 2 4 6 9 13 16
Annual 1(11/82)-Omega Men app. — 2 4 6 9 13 16
Annual V2#2(9/83)-1st app. Vigilante in costume; 1st app. Lyla — 4 8 12 23 37 50
Annual 3 (See Tales of the Teen Titans Annual #3)
... #1 (Facsimile Edition) (2/24, $3.99) reprints #1 with original ads — 4.00
... Games GN (2011, $24.99, HC) Wolfman-s/Pérez-a/c; original GN started in 1988, finished in 2011; '80s NTT roster; afterword by Pérez; Wolfman's original plot — 25.00
... Games GN (2011, $16.99, SC) same contents as HC — 17.00
... Terra Incognito TPB (2006, $19.99) r/#26,28-34 & Annual #2 — 20.00
... The Judas Contract TPB (2003, $19.95) r/#39,40 plus Tales of the Teen Titans #41-44 & Annual #3 — 20.00
...: Who is Donna Troy? TPB (2005, $19.99) r/#38,Tales of the Teen Titans #50, New Titans #50-55 and Teen Titans/Outsiders Secret Files 2003 — 20.00
NOTE: Pérez a-1-4, 6-34p; 37-40p, Annual 1p; 2p; c-1-12, 13-17p, 18-21, 22p, 23p, 24-37, 38, 39(painted), 40, Annual 1, 2.

NEW TEEN TITANS, THE (Becomes The New Titans #50 on)
DC Comics: Aug, 1984 - No. 49, Nov, 1988 ($1.25/$1.75; deluxe format)

1-New storyline; Pérez-c/a begins — 2 4 6 10 14 18
2,3: 2-Re-intro Lilith — 6.00
4-10: 5-Death of Trigon. 7-9-Origin Lilith. 8-Intro Kole. 10-Kole joins — 5.00
11-49: 13,14-Crisis x-over. 20-Robin (Jason Todd) joins; original Teen Titans return. 38-Infinity, Inc. x-over. 47-Origin of all Titans; Titans (East & West) pin-up by Pérez — 4.00
Annual 1-4 (9/85-'88): 1-Intro. Vanguard. 2-Byrne & Pérez-a. 3-Intro. Danny Chase. 4-Pérez-c — 4.00
...: The Terror of Trigon TPB (2003, $17.95) r/#1-5; new cover by Phil Jimenez — 18.00
NOTE: Buckler c-10. Kelley Jones a-47, Annual 4. Erik Larsen a-33. Orlando c-33p. Pérez a-1-5; c-1-7, 19-23, 3. Steacy a-47.

NEW TERRYTOONS (TV)
Dell Publishing Co./Gold Key: 6-8/60 - No. 8, 3-5/62; 10/62 - No. 54, 1/79

1(1960-Dell)-Deputy Dawg, Dinky Duck & Hashimoto-San begin (1st app. of each) — 10 20 30 68 144 220
2-8(1962) — 6 12 18 41 76 110
1(30010-210)(10/62-Gold Key, 84 pgs.)-Heckle & Jeckle begins — 9 18 27 58 114 170
2(30010-301)-84 pgs. — 7 14 21 49 92 135
3-5 — 4 8 12 27 44 60
6-10 — 4 8 12 21 33 45
11-20 — 3 6 9 15 22 28
21-30 — 2 4 6 9 13 16
31-43 — 1 3 4 6 8 10
44-54: Mighty Mouse-c/s in all — 2 4 6 8 11 14
NOTE: Reprints: #4-12, 38, 40, 47. (See March of Comics #379, 393, 412, 435).

NEW TESTAMENT STORIES VISUALIZED
Standard Publishing Co.: 1946 - 1947

"New Testament Heroes–Acts of Apostles Visualized, Book I"
"New Testament Heroes–Acts of Apostles Visualized, Book II"
"Parables Jesus Told" Set.... — 18 36 54 105 165 225
NOTE: All three are contained in a cardboard case, illustrated on front and info about the set.

NEWTHINK
AWA Studios: Jun, 2022 - No. 5, Oct, 2022 ($3.99)

1-5-Hurwitz-s. 1-Deodato Jr.-a. 2-Rosanas-a. 3-Keron Grant-a. 4-Mike Choi-a. 5-Conrad-a — 4.00

NEW THUNDERBOLTS (Continues in Thunderbolts #100)
Marvel Comics: Jan, 2005 - No. 18, Apr, 2006 ($2.99)

1-18: 1-Grummett-a/Nicieza-s. 1-Captain Marvel app. 2-Namor app. 4-Wolverine app. — 3.00
... Vol. 1: One Step Forward (2005, $14.99) r/#1-6 — 15.00
... Vol. 2: Modern Marvels (2005, $14.99) r/#7-12 — 15.00
... Vol. 3: Right of Power (2006, $17.99) r/#13-18 & Thunderbolts #100 — 18.00

NEW TITANS, THE (Formerly The New Teen Titans)
DC Comics: No. 50, Dec, 1988 - No. 130, Feb, 1996 ($1.75/$2.25)

50-Perez-c/a begins; new origin Wonder Girl — 6.00
51-59: 50-55-Painted-c. 55-Nightwing (Dick Grayson) forces Danny Chase to resign; Batman app. in flashback, Wonder Girl becomes Troia — 5.00
60,61: 60-A Lonely Place of Dying Part 2 continues from Batman #440; new Robin tie-in; Timothy Drake app. 61-A Lonely Place of Dying Part 4 — 5.00
62-70,72-99,101-124,126-130: 62-65: Deathstroke the Terminator app. 65-Tim Drake (Robin) app. 70-1st Deathstroke solo cover/sty. 72-79-Deathstroke in all: 74-Intro. Pantha. 79-Terra brought back to life; 1 panel cameo Team Titans (1st app.). Deathstroke in #80-84,86. 80-2nd full app. Team Titans. 83,84-Deathstroke kills his son, Jericho. 85-Team Titans app. 86-Deathstroke vs. Nightwing-c/story; last Deathstroke app. 87-New costume Nightwing. 90-92-Parts 2,5,8 Total Chaos (Team Titans). 99-1st app. Arsenal. 115-(11/94) — 4.00
71-(44 pgs.)-10th anniversary issue; Deathstroke cameo — 5.00
100-($3.50, 52 pgs.)-Holo-grafx foil-c — 5.00
125 (3.50)-wraparound-c — 4.00
#0-(10/94) Zero Hour, released between #114 & 115 — 4.00
Annual 5-10 ('89-'94, 68 pgs.)-7-Armaggedon 2001 x-over; 1st full app. Teen (Team) Titans (new group). 8-Deathstroke app.; Eclipso app. (minor). 10-Elseworlds story — 5.00
Annual 11 (1995, $3.95)-Year One story — 5.00
NOTE: Perez a-50-55p, 57,60p, 58,59,61(layouts); c-50-61, 62-67i, Annual 5i; co-plots-66.

NEW TV FUNNIES (See New Funnies)

NEW TWO-FISTED TALES, THE
Dark Horse Comics/Byron Preiss: 1993 ($4.95, limited series, 52 pgs.)

1-Kurtzman-r & new-a — 5.00
NOTE: Eisner c-1i. Kurtzman c-1p, 2.

NEWUNIVERSAL
Marvel Comics: Feb, 2007 - No. 6, July, 2007 ($2.99)

1-6-Warren Ellis-s/Salvador Larroca-a. 1,2-Variant covers by Ribic — 3.00
...: 1959 (9/08, $3.99) Aftermath of the White Event of 1953; Tony Stark app. — 4.00
...: Conqueror (10/08, $3.99) The White Event of 2689 B.C.; Eric Nguyen-a — 4.00
...: Everything Went White HC (2007, $19.99) r/#1-6; sketch pages — 20.00
...: Everything Went White SC (2008, $14.99) r/#1-6; sketch pages — 15.00

NEWUNIVERSAL: SHOCKFRONT
Marvel Comics: Jul, 2008 - No. 2 ($2.99)

1,2-Warren Ellis-s/Steve Kurth-a — 3.00

NEW WARRIORS, THE (See Thor #411,412)
Marvel Comics: July, 1990 - No. 75, 1996 ($1.00/$1.25/$1.50)

1-Williamson-i; Bagley-c/a(p) in #1-13, (1st printing has red cover) — 3 6 9 16 23 32
1-Gold 2nd printing (7/91) — 1 2 3 5 6 8
2-5: 1,3-Guice-c(i). 3-Williamson-c/a(i). — 5.00
6-24,26-49,51-75: 7-Punisher cameo (last pg.). 8,9-Punisher app. 14-Darkhawk & Namor x-over. 17-Fantastic Four & Silver Surfer x-over. 19-Gideon (of X-Force) app. 28-Intro Turbo & Cardinal. 31-Cannonball & Warpath app. 42-Nova & Firelord. 46-Photo-c. 47-Bound-in S-M trading card sheet. 52-12 pg. ad insert. 62-Scarlet Spider-c/app. 70-Spider-Man-c/app. 72-Avengers-c/app. — 4.00
25-($2.50, 52 pgs.)-Die-cut cover — 5.00
40,60: 40-($2.25)-Gold foil collector's edition — 5.00
50-($2.95, 52 pgs.)-Glow in the dark-c — 5.00
Annual 1-4('91-'94,68 pgs.)-1-Origins all members; 3rd app. X-Force (cont'd from New Mutants Ann. #7 & cont'd in X-Men Ann. #15); x-over before X-Force #1; Bagley-c/a(p); Williamson-i. 3-Bagged w/card — 5.00

NEW WARRIORS, THE
Marvel Comics: Oct, 1999 - No. 10, July, 2000 ($2.99/$2.50)

0-Wizard supplement; short story and preview sketchbook — 4.00
1-($2.99) — 5.00
2-10: 2-Two covers. 5-Generation X app. 9-Iron Man-c — 4.00

NEW WARRIORS (See Civil War #1)
Marvel Comics: Aug, 2005 - No. 6, Feb, 2006 ($2.99, limited series)

1-6-Scottie Young-a — 3.00
...: Reality Check TPB (2006, $14.99) r/#1-6 — 15.00

NEW WARRIORS (The Initiative)
Marvel Comics: Aug, 2007 - No. 20, Mar, 2009 ($2.99)

1-19: 1-Medina-a; new team is formed. 2-Jubilee app. 14-16-Secret Invasion — 3.00
20-($3.99) — 4.00
...: Defiant TPB (2008, $14.99) r/#1-6 — 15.00

NEW WARRIORS (All-New Marvel Now)

New Teen Titans #32 © DC

New Warriors #9 © MAR

Nexus #43 © Rude Dude Prods.

	GD	VG	FN	VF	VF/NM	NM-
	2.0	4.0	6.0	8.0	9.0	9.2

Marvel Comics: Apr, 2014 - No. 12, Jan, 2015 ($3.99)
1-12: 1-Nova, Speedball, Justice, Sun Girl, Scarlet Spider team; Yost-s/To-a ... 4.00

NEW WAVE, THE
Eclipse Comics: 6/10/86 - No. 13, 3/87 (#1-8: bi-weekly, 20pgs; #9-13: monthly)
1-13:1-Origin, concludes #5. 6-Origin Megabyte. 8,9-The Heap returns. 13-Snyder-c ... 3.00
...Versus the Volunteers 3-D #1,2(4/87): 1-Snyder c ... 3.00

NEW WEST, THE
Black Bull Comics: Mar, 2005 - No. 2, Jun, 2005 ($4.99, limited series)
1,2-Phil Noto-a/c; Jimmy Palmiotti-s ... 5.00

NEW WORLD (See Comic Books, series I)

NEW WORLD, THE
Image Comics: Jul, 2018 - No. 5, Nov, 2018 ($4.99/$3.99, limited series)
1-($4.99) Ales Kot-s/Tradd Moore-a ... 5.00
2-5-($3.99) ... 4.00

NEW WORLDS
Caliber: 1996 - No. 6 ($2.95/$3.95, 80 pgs., B&W, anthology)
1-6: 1-Mister X & other stories ... 5.00

NEW X-MEN (See X-Men 2nd series #114-156)

NEW X-MEN (Academy X) (Continued from New Mutants)
Marvel Comics: July, 2004 - No. 46, Mar, 2008 ($2.99)
1-46: 1,2-Green-c/a. 16-19-House of M. 20,21-Decimation. 40-Endangered Species back-ups begin. 44-46-Messiah Complex x-over; Ramos-a ... 3.00
Yearbook 1 (12/05, $3.99) new story and profile pages ... 4.00
...: Childhood's End Vol. 1 TPB (2006, $10.99) r/#20-23 ... 11.00
...: Childhood's End Vol. 2 TPB (2006, $10.99) r/#24-27 ... 11.00
...: Childhood's End Vol. 3 TPB (2006, $10.99) r/#28-32 ... 11.00
...: Childhood's End Vol. 4 TPB (2006, $10.99) r/#33-36 ... 11.00
...: Childhood's End Vol. 5 TPB (2007, $17.99) r/#37-43 ... 18.00
House of M: New X-Men TPB (2006, $13.99) r/#16-19 and selections from Secrets Of The House Of M one-shot ... 14.00
... Vol. 1: Choosing Sides TPB (2004, $14.99) r/#1-6 ... 15.00
... Vol. 2: Haunted TPB (2005, $14.99) r/#7-12 ... 15.00
... Vol. 3: X-Posed TPB (2006, $14.99) r/#12-15 & Yearbook Special ... 15.00

NEW X-MEN: HELLIONS
Marvel Comics: July, 2005 - No. 4, Oct, 2005 ($2.99, limited series)
1-4-Henry-a/Weir & DeFilippis-s ... 3.00
TPB (2006, $9.99) r/#1-4 ... 10.00

NEW YEAR'S EVIL
DC Comics: Feb, 2020 ($9.99, squarebound one-shot)
1-Short Holiday stories featuring DC villains; Harley Quinn app.; Cheung-c ... 10.00

NEW YORK FIVE, THE
DC Comics (Vertigo): Mar, 2011 - No. 4, Jun, 2011 ($2.99, B&W, limited series)
1-4-Brian Wood-s/Ryan Kelly-a ... 3.00

NEW YORK GIANTS (See Thrilling True Story of the Baseball Giants)

NEW YORK STATE JOINT LEGISLATIVE COMMITTEE TO STUDY THE PUBLICATION OF COMICS, THE
N.Y. State Legislative Document: 1951, 1955
This document was referenced by Wertham for Seduction of the Innocent. Contains numerous repros from comics showing violence, sadism, torture, and sex. 1955 version (196p, no. 37, 2/23/55) - Sold for $180 in 1986.

NEW YORK, THE BIG CITY
Kitchen Sink Press: 1986 ($10.95, B&W); DC Comics: July, 2000 ($12.95, B&W)
nn-(1986, $10.95) Will Eisner-s/a ... 25.00
nn-(2000, $12.95) new printing ... 13.00

NEW YORK WORLD'S FAIR (Also see Big Book of Fun & New Book of Fun)
National Periodical Publ.: 1939, 1940 (100 pgs.; cardboard covers) (DC's 4th & 5th annuals)

1939-Scoop Scanlon, Superman (blond haired Superman on-c), Sandman, Zatara, Slam Bradley, Ginger Snap by Bob Kane begin; 1st published app. The Sandman (see Adventure #40 for his 1st drawn story); Vincent Sullivan-c; cover background by Guardineer
1950 3900 5850 14,625 33,500 —
1940-Batman, Hourman, Johnny Thunderbolt, Red, White & Blue & Hanko (by Creig Flessel) app.; Superman, Batman & Robin-c (1st time they all appear together); early Robin app.; 1st Burnley-c/a (per Burnley)
1125 2250 3375 8325 19,575 —
NOTE: The 1939 edition was published 4/29/39 and released 4/30/39, the day the fair opened, at 25c, and was first sold only at the fair. Since all other comics were 10c, it didn't sell. Remaining copies were advertised beginning in the August issues of most DC comics for 25c, but soon the price was dropped to 15c. Everyone that sent a quarter through the mail for it received a free Superman #1 or a #2 to make up the dime difference. 15c stickers were placed

over the 25c price. Four variations on the 15c stickers are known. The 1940 edition was published 5/11/40 and was priced at 15c. It was a precursor to World's Best #1.

NEW YORK: YEAR ZERO
Eclipse Comics: July, 1988 - No. 4, Oct, 1988 ($2.00, B&W, limited series)
1-4 ... 4.00

NEXT, THE
DC Comics: Sept, 2006 - No. 6, Feb, 2007 ($2.99, limited series)
1-6-Tad Williams-s/Dietrich Smith-a; Superman app. ... 3.00

NEXT BATMAN, THE : SECOND SON (From Future State: The Next Batman)
DC Comics: Jun, 2021 - No. 4, Sept, 2021 ($4.99, limited series)
1-4-Ridley-s; Tim Fox as Batman; Grifter app. 4-Katana app. ... 5.00

NEXT MEN (See John Byrne's)

NEXT MEN: AFTERMATH (Continued from John Byrne's Next Men 2010-2011 series)
IDW Publishing: No. 40, Feb, 2012 - No. 44, Jun, 2012 ($3.99)
40-44-John Byrne-s/a/c ... 4.00

NEXT NEXUS, THE
First Comics: Jan, 1989 - No. 4, April, 1989 ($1.95, limited series, Baxter paper)
1-4: Mike Baron scripts & Steve Rude-c/a. ... 4.00
TPB (10/89, $9.95) r/series ... 10.00

NEXTWAVE: AGENTS OF H.A.T.E
Marvel Comics: Mar, 2006 - No. 12, Mar, 2007 ($2.99)
1-12-Warren Ellis-s/Stuart Immonen-a. 2-Fin Fang Foom app. 12-Devil Dinosaur app. ... 3.00
Vol. 1 - This Is What They Want HC (2006, $19.99) r/#1-6; Ellis original pitch ... 20.00
Vol. 1 - This Is What They Want SC (2007, $14.99) r/#1-6; Ellis original pitch ... 15.00
Vol. 2 - I Kick Your Face HC (2007, $19.99) r/#7-12 ... 20.00
Vol. 2 - I Kick Your Face SC (2008, $14.99) r/#7-12 ... 15.00

NEXUS (See First Comics Graphic Novel #4, 19 & The Next Nexus)
Capital Comics/First Comics No. 7 on: June, 1981 - No. 6, Mar, 1984; No. 7, Apr, 1985 - No. 80?, May, 1991 (Direct sales only, 36 pgs.; V2#1('83)-printed on Baxter paper)

	GD 2.0	VG 4.0	FN 6.0	VF 8.0	VF/NM 9.0	NM- 9.2
1-B&W version; mag. size; w/double size poster	4	8	12	23	37	50
1-B&W 1981 limited edition; 500 copies printed and signed; same as above except this version has a 2-pg. poster & a pencil sketch on paperboard by Steve Rude	7	14	21	48	89	130
2-B&W, magazine size	3	6	9	14	20	25
3-B&W, magazine size; Brunner back-c; contains 33-1/3 rpm record ($2.95 price)	2	4	6	9	13	16
V2#1-Color version	2	4	6	9	12	15

2-49,51-80: 2-Nexus' origin begins. 67-Snyder-c/a ... 3.00
50-($3.50, 52 pgs.) ... 4.00
Hardcover Volume One (Dark Horse Books, 11/05, $49.95) r/#1-3 & V2 #1-4; creator bios ... 50.00
HC Volume Two (Dark Horse Books, 3/06, $49.95) r/V2 #5-11; creator bios ... 50.00
HC Volume Three (Dark Horse Books, 5/06, $49.95) r/V2 #12-18; Marz forward ... 50.00
HC Volume Four (Dark Horse Books, 8/06, $49.95) r/V2 #19-25; Powell forward ... 50.00
HC Volume Five (Dark Horse Books, 2/07, $49.95) r/V2 #26-32; Brubaker forward ... 50.00
HC Volume Six (Dark Horse Books, 2/07, $49.95) r/V2 #33-39; Evanier forward ... 50.00
HC Volume Seven (Dark Horse Books, 2/08, $49.95) r/V2 #40-46; Brunning forward ... 50.00
HC Volume Eight (Dark Horse Books, 1/09, $49.95) r/V2 #47-52 and The Next Nexus #1; interview with original publishers John Davis and Milton Griepp ... 50.00
HC Volume Nine (Dark Horse Books, 8/09, $49.95) r/V2 #53-57 & The Next Nexus #2-4 ... 50.00
NOTE: **Bissette** c-V2#29. **Giffen** c/a-V2#23. **Gulacy** c-1 (B&W), 2(B&W). **Mignola** c/a-V2#28. **Rude** c-3(B&W), V2#1-22, 24-27, 33-36, 39-42, 45-48, 50, 58-60, 75; a-1-3, V2#1-7, 8-16p, 18-22p, 24-27p, 33-36p, 39-42p, 45-48p, 50, 58, 59p, 60. **Paul Smith** a-V2#37, 38, 43, 44, 51-55p; c-V2#37, 38, 43, 44, 51-55.

NEXUS
Rude Dude Productions: No. 99, July, 2007 - No. 102, Jun, 2009 ($2.99)
99-Mike Baron scripts & Steve Rude-c/a ... 3.00
100-($4.99) Part 2 of Space Opera; back-up feature: History of Nexus ... 5.00
101/102-(6/09, $4.95) Combined issue ... 5.00
...., Free Comic Book Day 2007 - Excerpts from previous issues and preview of #99 ... 3.00
... Greatest Hits (8/07, $1.99) same content as Free Comic Book Day 2007 ... 3.00
...: The Origin (11/07, $3.99) reprints the 7/96 one-shot ... 4.00

NEXUS: ALIEN JUSTICE
Dark Horse Comics: Dec, 1992 - No. 3, Feb, 1993 ($3.95, limited series)
1-3-Mike Baron scripts & Steve Rude-c/a ... 4.00

NEXUS: EXECUTIONER'S SONG (Also labeled as Nexus #89-92 in the indicia)
Dark Horse Comics: June, 1996 - No. 4, Sept, 1996 ($2.95, limited series)
1-4: Mike Baron scripts & Steve Rude-c/a ... 4.00

NEXUS FILES
First Comics: 1989 ($4.50, color/16pgs. B&W, one-shot, squarebound, 52 pgs.)

	GD 2.0	VG 4.0	FN 6.0	VF 8.0	VF/NM 9.0	NM- 9.2

1-New Rude-a; info on Nexus ... 5.00

NEXUS: GOD CON (Also labeled as Nexus #93,94 in the indicia)
Dark Horse Comics: Apr, 1997 - No. 2, May, 1997 ($2.95, limited series)
1,2-Baron-s/Rude-c/a ... 4.00

NEXUS LEGENDS
First Comics: May, 1989 - No. 23, Mar, 1991 ($1.50, Baxter paper)
1-23: R/1-3(Capital) & early First Comics issues w/new Rude covers #1-6,9,10 ... 4.00

NEXUS MEETS MADMAN (...Special)
Dark Horse Comics: May, 1996 ($2.95, one-shot)
nn-Mike Baron & Mike Allred scripts, Steve Rude-c/a. ... 4.00

NEXUS: NIGHTMARE IN BLUE (Also labeled as Nexus #95-98 in the indicia)
Dark Horse Comics: July, 1997 - No. 4, Oct, 1997 ($2.95, limited series)
1-4: Steve Rude-c/a ... 4.00

NEXUS: THE LIBERATOR
Dark Horse Comics: Aug, 1992 - No. 4, Nov, 1992 ($2.95, limited series)
1-4: 1,2,4-Adam Hughes-c. 3-Portacio-c. ... 4.00

NEXUS: THE ORIGIN
Dark Horse Comics: July, 1996 ($3.95, one-shot)
nn-Mike Baron- scripts, Steve Rude-c/a. ... 4.00

NEXUS: THE WAGES OF SIN
Dark Horse Comics: Mar, 1995 - No. 4, June, 1995 ($2.95, limited series)
1-4 ... 4.00

NFL RUSH ZONE: SEASON OF THE GUARDIANS
Action Lab Comics: Feb, 2013 - No. 4 ($3.99)
'1-4: 1-Matt Ryan & Roddy White app. ... 4.00
Free Comic Book Day edition (2013, giveaway) ... 3.00

NFL SUPERPRO
Marvel Comics: Oct, 1991 - No. 12, Sept, 1992 ($1.00)
1-12: 1-Spider-Man-c/app. ... 4.00
Special Edition (9/91, $2.00) Jusko painted-c ... 5.00
Super Bowl Edition (3/91, squarebound) Jusko painted-c ... 5.00

NICE HOUSE ON THE LAKE, THE
DC Comics (Black Label): Aug, 2021 - No. 12, Feb, 2023 ($3.99)
1-12-James Tynion IV-s/Álvaro Martínez Bueno ... 4.00

NICK CALM, AGENT OF C.O.D.P.I.E.C.E. (Reprints from Cerebus in Hell)
Aardvark-Vanaheim: Aug, 2018 ($4.00, B&W)
1-Cerebus figures placed over original Gustave Doré artwork; Nick Fury #4-c swipe ... 4.00

NICKEL COMICS
Dell Publishing Co.: 1938 (Pocket size - 7-1/2x5-1/2")(68 pgs.)

1- "Bobby & Chip" by Otto Messmer, Felix the Cat artist. Contains some English reprints	93	186	279	591	1021	1450

NICKEL COMICS
Fawcett Publications: Feb 1940
nn - Ashcan comic, not distributed to newsstands, only for in-house use. A CGC certified 9.6 copy sold for $7,200 in 2003. In 2008, a CGC certified 8.5 sold for $2,390 and an uncertified Near Mint copy sold for $3,100.

NICKEL COMICS
Fawcett Publications: May, 1940 - No. 8, Aug, 1940 (36 pgs.; Bi-Weekly; 5¢)

	GD 2.0	VG 4.0	FN 6.0	VF 8.0	VF/NM 9.0	NM- 9.2
1-Origin/1st app. Bulletman	423	846	1269	3046	5323	7600
2	148	296	444	947	1624	2300
3	115	230	348	742	1271	1800
4-The Red Gaucho begins	93	186	279	591	1021	1450
5-7	87	174	261	553	952	1350
8-World's Fair-c; Bulletman moved to Master Comics #7 in October (scarce)	113	226	339	718	1234	1750

NOTE: **Beck** c-5-8. **Jack Binder** c-1-4. Bondage c-5. Bulletman c-1-8.

NICK FURY
Marvel Comics: Jun, 2017 - No. 6, Nov, 2017 ($3.99, limited series)
1-6-James Robinson-s/Aco-a; Nick Fury Jr. vs. Hydra; Frankie Noble app. ... 4.00

NICK FURY, AGENT OF SHIELD (See Fury, Marvel Spotlight #31 & Shield)
Marvel Comics Group: 6/68 - No. 15, 11/69; No. 16, 11/70 - No. 18, 3/71

	GD 2.0	VG 4.0	FN 6.0	VF 8.0	VF/NM 9.0	NM- 9.2
1	21	42	63	147	324	500
2,3	8	16	24	55	105	155
4-Origin retold	14	28	42	97	214	330
5-Classic-c	9	18	27	62	126	190
6,7: 7-Salvador Dali painting swipe	8	16	24	51	96	140
8-11,13: 9-Hate Monger begins, ends #11. 10-Smith layouts/pencil. 11-Smith-c. 13-1st app. Super-Patriot; last 12¢ issue	5	10	15	30	50	70
12-Smith-c/a	5	10	15	31	53	75
14-Begin 15¢ issues	4	8	12	27	44	60
15-1st app. & death of Bullseye-c/story(11/69); Nick Fury shot & killed; last 15¢ issue	8	16	24	52	99	145
16-18-(25¢, 52 pgs.)-r/Str. Tales #135-143	3	6	9	21	33	45
TPB (May 2000, $19.95) r/ Strange Tales #150-168						20.00
...: Who is Scorpio? TPB (11/00, $12.95) r/#1-3,5; Steranko-c						13.00

NOTE: **Adkins** a-3i. **Craig** a-10i. **Sid Greene** a-12i. **Kirby** a-16-18r. **Springer** a-4, 6, 7, 8p, 9, 10p, 11; c-8, 9. **Steranko** a(p)-1-3, 5; c-1-7.

NICK FURY AGENT OF SHIELD (Also see Strange Tales #135)
Marvel Comics: Dec, 1983 - No. 2, Jan, 1984 (2.00, 52 pgs., Baxter paper)

	GD 2.0	VG 4.0	FN 6.0	VF 8.0	VF/NM 9.0	NM- 9.2
1,2-r/Nick Fury #1-4; new Steranko-c	1	3	4	6	8	10

NICK FURY, AGENT OF S.H.I.E.L.D.
Marvel Comics: Sept, 1989 - No. 47, May, 1993 ($1.50/$1.75)
V2#1 ... 5.00
2-26,30-47: 10-Capt. America app. 13-Return of The Yellow Claw. 15-Fantastic Four app. 30,31-Deathlok app. 36-Cage app. 37-Woodgod c/story. 38-41-Flashes back to pre-Shield

days after WWII. 44-Capt. America-c/s. 45-Viper-c/s. 46-Gideon x-over ... 4.00
27-29-Wolverine-c/stories ... 4.00
NOTE: **Alan Grant** scripts-11. **Guice** a(p)-20-23, 25, 26; c-20-28.

NICK FURY'S HOWLING COMMANDOS
Marvel Comics: Dec, 2005 - No. 6, May, 2006 ($2.99)
1-6: 1-Giffen-s/Francisco-a ... 3.00
1-Director's Cut ($3.99) r/#1 with original script and sketch design pages ... 4.00

NICK FURY VS. S.H.I.E.L.D.
Marvel Comics: June, 1988 - No. 6, Nov, 1988 ($3.50, 52 pgs, deluxe format)
1,2: 1-Steranko-a. 2-(Low print run) Sienkiewicz-c ... 6.00
3-6 ... 5.00

NICK HALIDAY (Thrill of the Sea)
Argo: May, 1956

	GD 2.0	VG 4.0	FN 6.0	VF 8.0	VF/NM 9.0	NM- 9.2
1-Daily & Sunday strip-r by Petree	13	26	39	74	105	135

NIGHT AND THE ENEMY (Graphic Novel)
Comico: 1988 (8-1/2x11") ($11.95, color, 80 pgs.)
1-Harlan Ellison scripts/Ken Steacy-c/a; r/Epic Illustrated & new-a (1st & 2nd printings) ... 12.00
1-Limited edition ($39.95) ... 40.00

NIGHT BEFORE CHRISTMAS, THE (See March of Comics No. 152 in the Promotional Comics section)

NIGHT BEFORE CHRISTMASK, THE
Dark Horse Comics: Nov, 1994 ($9.95, one-shot)
nn-Hardcover book; The Mask; Rick Geary-c/a ... 10.00

NIGHTBREED (See Clive Barker's Nightbreed)

NIGHT CLUB
Image Comics: Apr, 2005 - No. 4, Dec, 2006 ($2.95/$2.99, limited series)
1-4: 1-Mike Baron-s/Mike Norton-a ... 3.00

NIGHT CLUB
Image Comics: Dec, 2022 - No. 6 ($1.99, limited series)
1-5-Vampire story; Mark Millar-s/Juanan Ramírez-a ... 3.00
6-($3.99) ... 4.00

NIGHTCRAWLER (X-Men)
Marvel Comics Group: Nov, 1985 - No. 4, Feb, 1986 (Mini-series from X-Men)
1-4: 1-Cockrum-c/a ... 6.00

NIGHTCRAWLER (Volume 2)
Marvel Comics: Feb, 2002 - No. 4, May, 2002 ($2.50, limited series)
1-4-Matt Smith-a ... 3.00

NIGHTCRAWLER
Marvel Comics: Nov, 2004 - No. 12, Jan, 2006 ($2.99)
1-12: 1-6-Robertson-a/Land-c. 2-Magik app. 8-Wolverine app. 10-Man-Thing app. ... 3.00
...: The Devil Inside TPB (2005, $14.99) r/#1-6 ... 15.00
...: The Winding Way TPB (2006, $14.99) r/#7-12 ... 15.00

NIGHTCRAWLER
Marvel Comics: Jun, 2014 - No. 12, May, 2015 ($3.99)
1-12: 1-Claremont-s/Nauck-a. 7-Death of Wolverine tie-in ... 4.00

NIGHTCRAWLERS (Tie-in series to the Sins of Sinister event)
Marvel Comics: Apr, 2023 - No. 3, Jun, 2023 ($3.99, limited series)
1-3: 1-Spurrier-s/Medina-a. 2-Di Vito-a. 3-Tammetta-a ... 4.00

NIGHTFALL: THE BLACK CHRONICLES
DC Comics (Homage): Dec, 1999 - No. 3, Feb, 2000 ($2.95, limited series)
1-3-Coker-a/Gilmore-s ... 4.00

NIGHT FEVER
Image Comics: Jun, 2023 ($24.99, HC graphic novel)
HC - Ed Brubaker-s/Sean Phillips-a ... 25.00

NIGHT FORCE, THE (See New Teen Titans #21)
DC Comics: Aug, 1982 - No. 14, Sept, 1983 (60¢)
1 ... 5.00
2-14: 13-Origin Baron Winter. 14-Nudity panels ... 4.00
NOTE: **Colan** c/a-1-14p. **Giordano** c-1i, 2i, 4i, 5i, 7i, 12i.

NIGHT FORCE
DC Comics: Dec, 1996 - No. 12, Nov, 1997 ($2.25)
1-12: 1-3-Wolfman-s/Anderson-a(p). 8-"Convergence" part 2 ... 4.00

NIGHT FORCE
DC Comics: May, 2012 - No. 7, Nov, 2012 ($2.99, limited series)
1-7-Wolfman-s/Mandrake-a/Manco-c ... 3.00

NIGHT GLIDER
Topps Comics (Kirbyverse): April, 1993 ($2.95, one-shot)
1-Kirby c-1, Heck-a; polybagged w/Kirbychrome trading card ... 5.00

NIGHTHAWK
Marvel Comics: Sept, 1998 - No. 3, Nov, 1998 ($2.99, mini-series)
1-3-Krueger-s; Daredevil app. ... 4.00

NIGHTHAWK (From Squadron Supreme)
Marvel Comics: Jul, 2016 - No. 6, Dec, 2016 ($3.99)
1-6: 1-Walker-s/Villalobos-a/Cowan-c. 3-Morazzo-a ... 4.00

NIGHTINGALE, THE
Henry H. Stansbury Once-Upon-A-Time Press, Inc.: 1948 (10¢, 7-1/4x10-1/4", 14 pgs., 1/2 B&W)
(Very Rare)-Low distribution; distributed to Westchester County & Bronx, N.Y. only; used in **Seduction of the Innocent**, pg. 312,313 as the 1st and only "good" comic book ever published. Ill. by Dong Kingman; 1,500 words of text, printed on high quality paper & no word balloons. Copyright registered 10/22/48, distributed week of 12/5/48. Only 5000 copies printed, 6 currently known to still exist. (By Hans Christian Andersen)
Estimated value ... 475.00

NIGHT MAN, THE (See Sludge #1)
Malibu Comics (Ultraverse): Oct, 1993 - No. 23, Aug, 1995 ($1.95/$2.50)
1-($2.50, 48 pgs.)-Rune flip-c/story by B. Smith (3 pgs.) ... 5.00

Nickel Comics #2 © FAW

Night Club #1 © Netflix

Nightmare #14 © Skywald

	GD	VG	FN	VF	VF/NM	NM-
	2.0	4.0	6.0	8.0	9.0	9.2

	GD	VG	FN	VF	VF/NM	NM-
	2.0	4.0	6.0	8.0	9.0	9.2

1-Ultra-Limited silver foil-c 1 3 4 6 8 10
2-15, 17: 3-Break-Thru x-over; Freex app. 4-Origin Firearm (2 pgs.) by Chaykin. 6-TNTNT app. 8-1st app. Teknight 4.00
16 ($3.50)-flip book (Ultraverse Premiere #11) 5.00
...The Pilgrim Conundrum Saga (1/95, $3.95, 68 pgs.)-Strangers app. 5.00
18-23: 22-Loki-c/app. 4.00
Infinity ($1.50) 4.00
...Vs. Wolverine #0-Kelley Jones-c; mail in offer 1 3 4 6 8 10
NOTE: *Zeck* a-16.

NIGHT MAN, THE
Malibu Comics (Ultraverse): Sept, 1995 - No.4, Dec, 1995 ($1.50, lim. series)
1-4: Post Black September storyline 4.00

NIGHT MAN, THE /GAMBIT
Malibu Comics (Ultraverse): Mar, 1996 - No. 3, May, 1996 ($1.95, lim. series)
0-Limited Premium Edition 5.00
1-3: David Quinn scripts in all. 3-Rhiannon discovered to be The Night Man's mother 4.00

NIGHTMARE
Ziff-Davis (Approved Comics)/St. John No. 3: Summer, 1952 - No. 3, Winter, 1952, 53 (Painted-c)
1-1 pg. Kinstler-a; Tuska-a(2) 87 174 261 553 952 1350
2-Kinstler-a-Poe's "Pit & the Pendulum" 68 136 204 435 743 1050
3-Kinstler-a 61 122 183 390 670 950

NIGHTMARE (Weird Horrors #1-9) (Amazing Ghost Stories #14 on)
St. John Publishing Co.: No. 10, Dec, 1953 - No. 13, Aug, 1954
10-Reprints Ziff-Davis Weird Thrillers #2 w/new Kubert-c plus 2 pgs. Kinstler-a; Anderson, Colan & Toth-a 84 168 252 538 919 1300
11-Krigstein-a; painted-c; Poe adapt., "Hop Frog" 60 120 180 381 653 925
12-Kubert bondage-c; adaptation of Poe's "The Black Cat"; Cannibalism story 58 116 174 371 636 900
13-Reprints Z-D Weird Thrillers #3 with new cover; Powell-a(2), Tuska-a; Baker-c 277 554 831 1759 3030 4300

NIGHTMARE (Magazine) (Also see Psycho)
Skywald Publishing Corp.: Dec, 1970 - No. 23, Feb, 1975 (B&W, 68 pgs.)
1-Everett-a; Heck-a; Shores-a 12 24 36 79 170 260
2-5,8,9: 2,4-Decapitation story. 5-Nazis-a; Boris Karloff 4 pg. photo/text-a. 8-Features E.C. movie "Tales From the Crypt"; reprints some EC comics panels. 9-Wrightson-a; bondage-c; 1st Lovecraft Saggoth Chronicles/Cthulhu 6 12 18 38 69 100
6-Kaluta-a; Jeff Jones-c, photo & interview; 1st Living Gargoyle; Love Witch-a w/nudity; Boris Karloff-s 8 16 24 51 96 140
7 ..... 5 10 15 34 60 85
10-Wrightson-a (1 pg.); Princess of Earth-c/s; Edward & Mina Sartyros, the Human Gargoyles series continues from Psycho #8 ..... 6 12 18 44 76 110
11-19: 12-Excessive gore, severed heads. 13-Lovecraft-a. 15-Dracula-c/s. 17-Vampires issue; Autobiography of a Vampire story begins 4 8 12 28 47 65
20-John Byrne's 1st artwork (2 pgs.)(8/74); severed head-c; Hitler app. 8 18 27 62 126 190
21-23: 21-(1974 Summer Special)-Kaluta-a. 22-Tomb of Horror issue. 23-(1975 Winter Special) 5 10 15 31 53 75
Annual 1(1972)-Squarebound; B. Jones-a 5 10 15 34 60 85
Winter Special 1(1973)-All new material 4 8 12 28 47 65
Yearbook nn(1974)-B. Jones, Reese, Wildey-a 4 8 12 28 47 65
NOTE: *Adkins* a-5. *Boris* c-2, 3, 5 (#4 is not by Boris). *Buckler* a-3, 15. *Byrne* a-20p. *Everett* a-1, 2, 4, 5, 12. *Jeff Jones* a-6, 21r(Psycho #6); c-6. *Katz* a-3, 5, 21. *Rees* a-4, 5. *Wildey* a-4, 5, 6, 21, '74 Yearbook. *Wrightson* a-9, 10.

NIGHTMARE (Alex Nino's)
Innovation Publishing: 1989 ($1.95)
1-Alex Nino-a 4.00

NIGHTMARE
Marvel Comics: Dec, 1994 - No. 4, Mar, 1995 ($1.95, limited series)
1-4 ..... 4.00

NIGHTMARE & CASPER (See Harvey Hits #71) (Casper & Nightmare #6 on)
(See Casper The Friendly Ghost #19)
Harvey Publications: Aug, 1963 - No. 5, Aug, 1964 (25¢)
1-All reprints? 8 16 24 52 99 145
2-5: All reprints 5 10 15 31 53 75

NIGHTMARE ON ELM STREET, A (Also see Freddy Krueger's...)
DC Comics (WildStorm): Dec, 2006 - No. 8, Aug, 2007 ($2.99)
1-Two covers by Harris & Bradstreet; Dixon-s 2 4 6 11 16 20
2-8 ..... 1 3 4 6 8 10

NIGHTMARES (See Do You Believe in Nightmares)

NIGHTMARES
Eclipse Comics: May, 1985 - No. 2, May, 1985 ($1.75, Baxter paper)
1,2 ..... 5.00

NIGHTMARE THEATER
Chaos! Comics: Nov, 1997 - No. 4, Nov, 1997 ($2.50, mini-series)
1-4-Horror stories by various; Wrightson-a 4.00

NIGHTMASK
Marvel Comics Group: Nov, 1986 - No. 12, Oct, 1987
1-12 ..... 4.00

NIGHT MASTER
Silverwolf: Feb, 1987 ($1.50, B&W)
1-Tim Vigil-c/a 2 4 6 9 12 15

NIGHTMASTER (See Shadowpact)
DC Comics: Jan, 2011 ($2.99, one-shot)
1-Wrightson-c/Beechen-s/Dwyer-a; Shadowpact app. 3.00

NIGHT MUSIC (See Eclipse Graphic Album Series; The Magic Flute)
Eclipse Comics: Dec, 1984 - No. 11, 1990 ($1.75/$3.95/$4.95, Baxter paper)
1-7: 3-Russell's Jungle Book adapt. 4,5-Pelleas And Melisande (double titled) 4.00
6-Salomé (double titled). 7-Red Dog #1 ..... 4.00
8-($3.95) Ariane and Bluebeard 5.00
9-11-($4.95) The Magic Flute; Russell adapt. 5.00

NIGHT NURSE (Also see Linda Carter, Student Nurse)
Marvel Comics Group: Nov, 1972 - No. 4, May, 1973
1 ..... 38 76 111 274 612 975
2-4 ..... 12 24 36 81 176 270

NIGHT NURSE
Marvel Comics: Jul, 2015 ($7.99, one-shot)
1-Reprints 1972 series #1-4 and Daredevil V2 #80; Siya Oum-c 2 4 6 11 16 20

NIGHT OF MYSTERY
Avon Periodicals: 1953 (no month) (one-shot)
nn-1 pg. Kinstler-a, Hollingsworth-c 97 194 291 621 1061 1500

NIGHT OF THE GHOUL
Dark Horse Comics: Oct, 2022 - No. 3, Dec, 2022 ($4.99, limited series)
1-3-Scott Snyder-s/Francesco Francavilla-a 5.00

NIGHT OF THE GRIZZLY, THE (See Movie Classics)

NIGHT OF THE LIVING DEADPOOL
Marvel Comics: Mar, 2014 - No. 4, May, 2014 ($3.99, limited series)
1-4-Bunn-s/Rosanas-a; Deadpool in a zombie apocalypse 4.00

NIGHT OF THE LIVING DEAD: REVENANCE
American Mythology Prods.: 2022 - No. 4, 2023 ($3.99)
1-4-S.A. Check & James Kuhoric-s/Giancarlo Caracuzo-a 4.00

NIGHTRAVEN (See Marvel Graphic Novel)

NIGHT RIDER (Western)
Marvel Comics Group: Oct, 1974 - No. 6, Aug, 1975
1: 1-6 reprint Ghost Rider #1-6 (#1-origin) 6 12 18 38 69 100
2-6 ..... 3 6 9 14 20 26

NIGHT'S CHILDREN: THE VAMPIRE
Millenium: July, 1995 - No. 2, Aug, 1995 ($2.95, B&W)
1,2: Wendy Snow-Lang story & art 3.00

NIGHTSIDE
Marvel Comics: Dec, 2001 - No. 4, Mar, 2002 ($2.99)
1-4: 1-Weinberg-s/Derenick-a; intro Sydney Taine 3.00

NIGHTS INTO DREAMS (Based on video game)
Archie Comics: Feb, 1998 -No. 6, Oct, 1998 ($1.75, limited series)
1-6 ..... 4.00

NIGHTSTALKERS (Also see Midnight Sons Unlimited)
Marvel Comics (Midnight Sons #14 on): Nov, 1992 - No. 18, Apr, 1994 ($1.75)
1-($2.75, 52 pgs.)-Polybagged w/poster; part 5 of Rise of the Midnight Sons storyline; Garney/Palmer-c/a begins; Hannibal King, Blade & Frank Drake begin 4 6 9 13 16
2-9,11-18: 5-Punisher app. 7-Ghost Rider app. 8,9-Morbius app. 14-Spot varnish-c 4.00

	GD	VG	FN	VF	VF/NM	NM-
	2.0	4.0	6.0	8.0	9.0	9.2

14,15-Siege of Darkness Pts 1 & 9 — 4.00
10-($2.25)-Outer-c is a Darkhold envelope made of black parchment w/gold ink; Midnight Massacre part 1 — 6.00

NIGHT TERRORS,THE
Chanting Monks Studios: 2000 ($2.75, B&W)
1-Bernie Wrightson-c; short stories, one by Wrightson-s/a — 6.00

NIGHT THRASHER (Also see The New Warriors)
Marvel Comics: Aug, 1993 - No. 21, Apr, 1995 ($1.75/$1.95)
1-($2.95, 52 pgs.)-Red holo-grafx foil-c; origin — 5.00
2-21: 2-Intro Tantrum. 3-Gideon (of X-Force) app. 10-Bound-in trading card sheet; Iron Man app. 15-Hulk app. — 4.00

NIGHT THRASHER: FOUR CONTROL
Marvel Comics: Oct, 1992 - No. 4, Jan, 1993 ($2.00, limited series)
1-4: 2-Intro Tantrum. 3-Gideon (of X-Force) app. — 5.00

NIGHT TRIBES
DC Comics (WildStorm): July, 1999 ($4.95, one-shot)
1-Golden & Sniegoski-s/Chin-a — 5.00

NIGHTVEIL (Also see Femforce)
Americomics/AC Comics: Nov, 1984 - No. 7, 1987 ($1.75)
1-7 — 4.00
...'s Cauldron Of Horror 1 (1989, B&W)-Kubert, Powell, Wood-r plus new Nightveil story — 4.00
...'s Cauldron Of Horror 2 (1990, $2.95, B&W)-Pre-code horror-r by Kubert & Powell — 4.00
...'s Cauldron Of Horror 3 (1991) — 4.00
Special 1 ('88, $1.95)-Kaluta-c — 4.00
One Shot ('96, $5.95)-Flip book w/ Colt — 6.00

NIGHTWATCH
Marvel Comics: Apr, 1994 - No. 12, Mar, 1995 ($1.50)
1-($2.95)-Collectors edition; foil-c; Ron Lim-c/a begins; Spider-Man app. — 6.00
1-12-Regular edition. 2-Bound-in S-M trading card sheet; 5,6-Venom-c & app. — 4.00
7,11-Cardiac app. — 4.00

NIGHTWING (Also see New Teen Titans, New Titans, Showcase '93 #11,12, Tales of the New Teen Titans & Teen Titans Spotlight)
DC Comics: Sept, 1995 - No. 4, Dec, 1995 ($2.25, limited series)

1-Dennis O'Neil story/Greg Land-a in all	2	4	6	11	16	20
2-4						5.00
...: Alfred's Return (7/95, $3.50) Giordano-a						6.00
...Ties That Bind (1997, $12.95, TPB) r/mini-series & Alfred's Return						13.00

NIGHTWING
DC Comics: Oct, 1996 - No. 153, Apr, 2009 ($1.95/$1.99/$2.25/$2.50/$2.99)

1-Chuck Dixon scripts & Scott McDaniel-c/a	4	8	12	23	37	50
2,3		1	3	4	6	8	10
4-10: 6-Robin-c/app.						5.00
11-20: 13-15-Batman app. 19,20-Cataclysm pts. 2,11						4.00
21-49,51-64: 23-Green Arrow app. 26-29-Huntress-c/app. 30-Superman-c/app. 35-39-No Man's Land. 41-Land/Geraci-a begins. 46-Begin $2.25-c. 47-Texiera-c. 52-Catwoman-c/app. 54-Shrike app.						3.00
65-74,76-99: 65,66-Bruce Wayne: Murderer x-over pt. 3,9. 68,69: B.W.: Fugitive pt. 6,9. 70-Last Dixon-s. 71-Devin Grayson-s begin. 81-Batgirl vs. Deathstroke. 93-Blockbuster killed. 94-Copperhead app. 96-Bagged w/#12-War Games						3.00
75-(1/03, $2.95) Intro. Tarantula						4.00
100-(2/05, $2.95) Tarantula app.						4.00
101-117: 101-Year One begins. 103-Jason Todd & Deadman app. 107-110-Hester-a. 109-Begin $2.50-c. 109,110-Villains United tie-ins. 112-Deathstroke app.						3.00
118-One Year Later; Jason Todd as 2nd Nightwing	2	4	6	8	10	12
119-149,151-153: 120-Begin $2.99-c. 138,139-Resurrection of Ra's al Ghul x-over. 138-2nd printing. 147-Two-Face app.						3.00
150-($3.99) Batman R.I.P. x-over; Nightwing vs. Two-Face; Tan-c						4.00
#1,000,000 (11/98) teams with future Batman						3.00
Annual 1(1997, $3.95) Pulp Heroes						4.00
Annual 2 (6/07, $3.99) Dick Grayson and Barbara Gordon's shared history						4.00
...Eighty Page Giant 1 (12/00, $5.95) Intro. of Hella; Dixon-s/Haley-a						6.00
...: Big Guns (2004, $14.95, TPB) r/#47-50; Secret Files 1, Eighty Page Giant 1						15.00
...: Brothers in Blood (2007, $14.99, TPB) r/#118-124						15.00
...: A Darker Shade of Justice (2001, $19.95, TPB) r/#30-39, Secret Files #1						20.00
...: Freefall (2008, $17.99, TPB) r/#140-146						18.00
...: A Knight in Blüdhaven (1998, $14.95, TPB) r/#1-8						15.00
...: Love and Bullets (2000, $17.95, TPB) r/#1/2, 19,21,22,24-29						18.00
...: Love and War (2007, $14.99, TPB) r/#125-132						15.00
...: On the Razor's Edge (2005, $14.99, TPB) r/#52,54-60						15.00
...: Our Worlds at War (9/01, $2.95) Jae Lee-c						3.00
...: Renegade TPB (2006, $17.95) r/#112-117						18.00
...: Rough Justice (1999, $17.95, TPB) r/#9-18						18.00
Secret Files 1 (10/99, $4.95) Origin-s and pin-ups						5.00
...: The Great Leap (2009, $19.99) r/#147-153						20.00
...: The Hunt for Oracle (2003, $14.95, TPB) r/#41-46 & Birds of Prey #20,21						15.00
...: The Lost Year (2008, $14.99) r/#133-137 & Annual #2						15.00
...: The Target (2001, $5.95) McDaniel-c/a						6.00
Wizard 1/2 (Mail offer)						5.00
...: Year One (2005, $14.99) r/#101-106						15.00

NIGHTWING (DC New 52)(Leads into Grayson series)
DC Comics: Nov, 2011 - No. 30, Jul, 2014 ($2.99)

1-Dick Grayson in black/red costume; Higgins-s/Barrows-a/c						20.00
1-2nd printing with red background-c						10.00
2,3			1	2	3	5	6	8
4-7,10-14: 2-4-Batgirl app. 13,14-Lady Shiva app. 14-Joker cameo						4.00
8,9: 8-Night of the Owls prelude. 9-Night of the Owls x-over						5.00
5-Die-cut cover with Joker mask; Death of the Family tie-in						5.00
16-18: 16-Death of the Family tie-in. 18-Requiem; Tony Zucco returns						4.00
19-24,26-29: 19-24-Prankster app. 26,27-Mad Hatter app. 28,29-Mr. Zsasz app.						3.00
25-($3.99) Zero Year flashback to Haly's Circus days; Higgins-s/Conrad & Richards-a						4.00

30-($3.99) Aftermath of Forever Evil series; Grayson joins Spyral						4.00
#0-(11/12, $2.99) Origin re-told/updated; Lady Shiva app.; DeFalco-s/Barrows-a						4.00
Annual #1 (12/13, $4.99) Batgirl Wanted! tie-in; Firefly app.						5.00

NIGHTWING (DC Rebirth)
DC Comics: Sept, 2016 - Present ($2.99/$3.99)

1-Seeley-s/Fernandez-a; intro. Raptor	2	4	6	8	10	12
2-24: 5,6-Night of the Monster Men x-over. 17-20-Deathwing & Prof. Pyg app.						
21-Flash (Wally) app. 22-24-Blockbuster app.						3.00
25-($3.99) Blockbuster & Tiger Shark app.						4.00
26-43: 26-28-Huntress app. 29-Dark Nights: Metal tie-in						3.00
44-49: 44-($3.99) Mooneyham-a. 49-Silencer app.						4.00
50-($4.99) Follows Grayson's shooting in Batman #55; flashback art by Janson						5.00
51-74,76,77: 51-Foil-c. 53-56-Scarecrow app. 57,58-Joker's Daughter app. 62-69-Talon app.						4.00
70,71-Joker app. 72-74-Punchline app. 73,74-Joker War tie-in						4.00
75-($5.99) Joker War tie-in; Nightwing regains real memory; KGBeast app.						6.00
78-Infinite Frontier; Taylor-s begins; intro. Bitewing the dog						12.00
79-99: 79,80-Heartless app. 84-86-Fear State tie-ins. 88-Titans app. 90,91-Flash app.						4.00
100-(3/23, $6.99) Titans app.; art by various						7.00
101-111: 93-($4.99) 101-104-Neron and the Titans app. 110-Jon Kent & Damian app.						5.00
Annual 1 (10/18, $4.99) Percy-s/Schmidt-a; Vicki Vale app.						5.00
Annual 2 (12/19, $4.99) Jurgens/Moore-a; follows shooting in Batman #55						5.00
Annual 3 (8/20, $4.99) Jurgens-s/Miranda-a; Condor Red app.; takes place after #68						5.00
2021 Annual (1/22, $5.99) Red Hood app.; Taylor-s/Tormey & HDR-a						6.00
2022 Annual (1/23, $4.99) Origin of Heartless; Bitewing Year One						6.00
.../Magilla Gorilla Special 1 (12/18, $4.99) Grape Ape app.; Secret Squirrel back-up						5.00
...: Rebirth (9/16, $2.99) Seeley-s/Paquette-a; Damian app.; back in Nightwing costume						3.00

NIGHTWING (See Tangent Comics/ Nightwing)

NIGHTWING AND HUNTRESS
DC Comics: May, 1998 - No. 4, Aug, 1998 ($1.95, limited series)

1-4-Grayson-s/Land & Sienkiewicz-a						4.00
TPB (2003, $9.95) r/#1/4; cover gallery						10.00

NIGHTWINGS (See DC Science Fiction Graphic Novel)

NIGHTWING: THE NEW ORDER
DC Comics: Oct, 2017 - No. 6, Mar, 2018 ($3.99, limited series)
1-6-Higgins-s/McCarthy-a; future Nightwing in 2040. 4,5-Titans app. 5-Superman app. — 4.00

NIGHTWORLD
Image Comics: Aug, 2014 - No. 4, Nov, 2014 ($3.99, limited series)
1-4-McGovern-s/Leandri-a/c — 4.00

NIKKI, WILD DOG OF THE NORTH (Disney, see Movie Comics)
Dell Publishing Co.: No. 1226, Sept, 1961

Four Color 1226-Movie, photo-c		5	10	15	33	57	80

9-11 - ARTISTS RESPOND
Dark Horse Comics: 2002 ($9.95, TPB, proceeds donated to charities)
Volume 1-Short stories about the September 11 tragedies by various Dark Horse, Chaos! and Image writers and artists; Eric Drooker-c — 10.00

9-11: EMERGENCY RELIEF
Alternative Comics: 2002 ($14.95, TPB, proceeds donated to the Red Cross)
nn-Short stories by various inc. Pekar, Eisner, Hester, Oeming, Noto; Cho-c — 15.00

9-11 - THE WORLD'S FINEST COMIC BOOK WRITERS AND ARTISTS TELL STORIES TO REMEMBER
DC Comics: 2002 ($9.95, TPB, proceeds donated to charities)
Volume 2-Short stories about the September 11 tragedies by various DC, MAD, and WildStorm writers and artists; Alex Ross-c — 10.00

NINE RINGS OF WU-TANG
Image Comics: July, 1999 - No. 5, July, 2000 ($2.95)

Preview (7/99, $5.00, B&W)						5.00
1-5: 1-(11/99, $2.95) Clayton Henry-a						4.00
Tower Records Variant-c						5.00
Wizard #0 Prelude						4.00
TPB (1/01, $19.95) r/#1-5, Preview & Prelude; sketchbook & cover gallery						20.00

1963
Image Comics (Shadowline Ink): Apr, 1993 - No. 6, Oct, 1993 ($1.95, lim. series)

1-6: Alan Moore scripts; Veitch, Bissette & Gibbons-a(p)						4.00
1-Gold						5.00

NOTE: *Bissette* a-2-4; *Gibbons* a-1; 2i, 6i; c-2.

1984 (Magazine) (1994 #11 on)
Warren Publishing Co.: June, 1978 - No. 10, Jan, 1980 ($1.50, B&W with color inserts, mature content with nudity; 84 pgs. except #4 has 92 pgs.)

1-Nino-a in all; Mutant World begins by Corben	3	6	9	16	23	30
2-10: 4-Rex Havoc begins. 7-1st Ghita of Alizarr by Thorne. 9-1st Starfire	2	4	6	10	14	18

NOTE: *Alcala* a-1-3,5,7i. *Corben* a-1-8; c-1,2. *Nebres* a-1-8,10. *Thorne* a-7,8,10. *Wood* a-1,2,5i.

1994 (Formerly 1984) (Magazine)
Warren Publishing Co.: No. 11, Feb, 1980 - No. 29, Feb, 1983 (B&W with color; mature; #11-(84 pgs.); #12-16,18-21,24-(76 pgs.); #17,22,23,25-29-(68 pgs.)

11,17,18,20,22,23,29: 11,17-8 pgs. color app. 20-1st Diana Jacklighter Manhuntress by Maroto. 22-1st Sigmund Pavlov by Nino; 1st Ariel Hart by Hsu. 23-All Nino issue	2	4	6	8	11	14
12-16,19,21,24-28: 21-1st app. Angel by Nebres. 27-The Warhawks return	1	3	4	6	8	10

NOTE: *Corben* c-26. *Maroto* a-20, 21, 24-28. *Nebres* a-11-13, 15, 16, 18, 21, 22, 25, 28. *Nino* a-11-19, 20(2), 21, 25, 26, 28; c-21. *Redondo* c-20. *Thorne* a-11-14, 17-21, 24-26, 28, 29.

NINJA BOY
DC Comics (WildStorm): Oct, 2001 - No. 6, Mar, 2002 ($3.50/$2.95)

1-($3.50) Ale Garza-a/c						3.50
2-6-($2.95)						3.00
...: Faded Dreams TPB (2003, $14.95) r/#1-6; sketch pages						15.00

NINJA HIGH SCHOOL (1st series)

Nightwing #119 © DC

Ninjak (2015 series) #27 © VAL

Nocterra #10 © Snyder & Daniel

	GD 2.0	VG 4.0	FN 6.0	VF 8.0	VF/NM 9.0	NM- 9.2

Antarctic Press: 1986 - No. 3, Aug, 1987 (B&W)
| 1-Ben Dunn-s/c/a; early Manga series | 2 | 4 | 6 | 11 | 16 | 20 |
| 2,3 | 2 | 4 | 6 | 8 | 10 | 12 |

NINJAK (See Bloodshot #6, 7 & Deathmate)
Valiant/Acclaim Comics (Valiant) No. 16 on: Feb, 1994 - No. 26, Nov. 1995 ($2.25/$2.50)
1 ($3.50)-Chromium-c; Quesada-c/a(p) in #1-3						6.00
1-Gold	3	6	9	19	30	40
2-13: 3-Batman, Spawn & Random (from X-Factor) app. as costumes at party (cameo).						4.00
4-w/bound-in trading card. 5,6-X-O app.						4.00
0,00,14-26: 14-(4/95)-Begin $2.50-c. 0-(6/95, $2.50). 00-(6/95, $2.50)						4.00
... Black Water HC (2013, $24.99) r/#1-6, #0, #00; bonus Quesada sketch-a						25.00
Yearbook 1 (1994, $3.95)						5.00

NINJAK
Acclaim Comics (Valiant Heroes): V2#1, Mar, 1997 - No. 12, Feb, 1998 ($2.50)
| V2#1-Intro new Ninjak; 1st app. Brutakon; Kurt Busiek scripts begin; painted variant-c exists | 2 | 4 | 6 | 9 | 12 | 15 |
| V2#2-12: 2-1st app. Karnivor & Zeer. 3-1st app. Gigantik, Shurikai, & Nixie. 4-Origin; 1st app. Yasuiti Motomiya; intro The Dark Dozen; Colin King cameo. 9-Copycat-c | | | | | | 3.00 |

NINJAK (See Rapture)
Valiant Entertainment: Mar, 2015 - No. 27, May, 2017 ($3.99)
| 1-27-Multiple covers on each: 1-Kindt-s/Guice and Mann-a. 4-Origin of Roku; Ryp-a | | | | | | 4.00 |

NINJAK
Valiant Entertainment: Jul, 2021 - No. 4, Oct, 2021 ($3.99)
| 1-4-Jeff Parker-s/Javier Pulido-a | | | | | | 4.00 |

NINJA-K
Valiant Entertainment: No. 0, Sept, 2017; No. 1, Nov, 2017 - No. 14, Dec, 2018 ($3.99)
0-Kindt-s/Portela-a; recaps origin						4.00
1-14: 1-5-Gage-s/Giorello-a. 1-History of Ninja-A in 1917. 6-9-Ryp-a						4.00
... One Dollar Debut (5/19, $1.00) r/#1						3.00

NINJAK: SUPERKILLERS
Valiant Entertainment: Dec, 2023 - No. 2, Jan, 2024 ($9.99, squarebound)
| 1,2-Jeff Parker-s/Mike Norton-a | | | | | | 10.00 |

NINJAK VS. THE VALIANT UNIVERSE
Valiant Entertainment: Jan, 2018 - No. 4, Apr, 2018 ($3.99, limited series)
| 1-4-Rahal-s/Bennett-a | | | | | | 4.00 |

NINJA SCROLL
DC Comics (WildStorm): Nov, 2006 - No. 12, Oct, 2007 ($2.99)
1-12: 1-J. Torres-s/Michael Chang Ting Yu-a/c. 1-Puckett-s/Meyers-a						3.00
1-3-Variant covers by Jim Lee						5.00
TPB (2007, $19.99) r/#1-3,5-7						20.00

NINJETTES (See Jennifer Blood #4)
Dynamite Entertainment: 2012 - No. 6, 2012 ($3.99, limited series)
| 1-6-Origin of the team; Ewing-s/Casallos-a. 6-Jennifer Blood app. | | | | | | 4.00 |

NINJETTES (See Jennifer Blood #4)
Dynamite Entertainment: 2022 - No. 5, 2022 ($3.99, limited series)
| 1-5-Training camp for the recruits; Van Lente-s/Cooper-a | | | | | | 4.00 |

NINTENDO COMICS SYSTEM (Also see Adv. of Super Mario Brothers)
Valiant Comics: Feb, 1990 - No. 9, Oct, 1991 ($1.95, card stock-c, 68 pgs.)
1-Featuring Game Boy, Super Mario, Clappwall	5	10	15	31	53	75
2	3	6	9	18	28	35
3-9: 3-Layton-c. 5-8-Super Mario Bros. 9-Dr. Mario 1st app.	2	4	6	9	13	16

(Ninth) **IXTH GENERATION** (See Aphrodite IX & Poseidon IX)
Image Comics (Top Cow): Jan, 2015 - No. 8, Mar, 2016 ($3.99)
| 1-8: 1-4-Hawkins-s/Sejic-a; Aphrodite IX app. 5-7-Atilio Rojo-a | | | | | | 4.00 |
| ... Hidden Files 1 (4/15, $3.99) Short story and guide to the cities; Hawkins-s/Rojo-a | | | | | | 4.00 |

NITA HAWES' NIGHTMARE BLOG
Image Comics: Oct, 2021 - No. 12, Feb, 2023 ($3.99)
| 1-12: 1-Rodney Barnes-s/Jason Shawn Alexander-a. 4-12-Kudranski-a | | | | | | 4.00 |

NOAH (Adaptation of the 2014 movie)
Image Comics: Mar, 2014 (HC, $29.99, 8-3/4" x 11-1/2")
| HC-Darren Aronofsky & Ari Handel-s/Niko Henrichon-a | | | | | | 30.00 |

NOAH'S ARK
Spire Christian Comics/Fleming H. Revell Co.: 1973,1975 (35/49¢)
| nn-By Al Hartley | 2 | 4 | 6 | 11 | 16 | 20 |

NOBLE CAUSES
Image Comics: July, 2001; Jan, 2002 - No. 4, May, 2002 ($2.95)
...First Impressions (7/01) Intro. the Noble family; Faerber-s						3.00
1-4: 1-(1/02) Back-up-s with Conner-a. 2-Igle back-up-a. 2-4-Two covers						3.00
...: Extended Family (5/03, $6.95) short stories by various						7.00
...: Extended Family 2 (6/04, $7.95) short stories by various						8.00
Vol. 1: In Sickness and in Health (2003, $12.95) r/#1-4 & ...First Impressions						13.00

NOBLE CAUSES (Volume 3)
Image Comics: July, 2004 - No. 40, Mar, 2009 ($3.50)
1-24,26-40-Faerber-s. 1-Two covers. 2-Venture app. 5-Invincible app.						3.50
25-($4.99) Art by various; Randolph-a						5.00
Vol. 4: Blood and Water (2005, $14.95) r/#1-6						15.00
Vol. 5: Betrayals (2006, $14.99) r/#7-12 & The Pact V2 #2						15.00
Vol. 6: Hidden Agendas (2006, $15.99) r/#13-18 and Image Holiday Spec. 2005 story						16.00
Vol. 7: Powerless (2007, $15.99) r/#19-25; Wieringo sketch page						16.00

NOBLE CAUSES: DISTANT RELATIVES
Image Comics: Jul, 2003 - No. 4, Oct, 2003 ($2.95, B&W, limited series)
| 1-4-Faerber-s/Richardson & Ponce-a | | | | | | 3.00 |
| Vol. 3: Distant Relatives (1/05, $12.95) r/#1-4; intro. by Joe Casey | | | | | | 13.00 |

NOBLE CAUSES: FAMILY SECRETS
Image Comics: Oct, 2002 - No. 4, Jan, 2003 ($2.95, limited series)
1,2,4-Faerber-s/Oeming-a. 1-Variant cover by Walker. 2-Valentino var-c. 4-Hester var-c						3.00
3-1st app. of Invincible (cameo & Valentino var-c)	5	10	15	35	63	90
3-1st app. of Invincible (cameo); regular Oeming-c	3	6	9	16	24	30
Vol. 2: Family Secrets (2004, $12.95) r/#1-4; sketch pages						13.00

NOBODY (Amado, Cho & Adlard's...)
Oni Press: Nov, 1998 - No. 4, Feb, 1999 ($2.95, B&W, mini-series)
| 1-4 | | | | | | 4.00 |

NOCTERRA
Image Comics: Mar, 2021 - No. 16, Sept, 2023 ($3.99)
1-16-Scott Snyder-s/Tony S. Daniel-a						4.00
... Blacktop Bill Special 1 (1/22, $3.99) Snyder & Daniel-s/Denys Cowan-a						4.00
... Nemesis Special 1 (7/23, $3.99) Snyder & Daniel-s/Liam Sharp-a						4.00
... Val Special 2 (12/22, $3.99) Snyder & Daniel-s/Manapul-a						4.00

NOCTURNALS, THE
Malibu Comics (Bravura): Jan, 1995 - No. 6, Aug, 1995 ($2.95, limited series)
| 1-6: Dan Brereton painted-c/a & scripts | | | | | | 4.00 |
| 1-Glow-in-the-Dark premium edition | | | | | | 5.00 |

NOCTURNALS, THE
Dark Horse Comics/Image Comics/Oni Press: one-shots and trade paperbacks
Black Planet TPB (Oni Press, 1998, $19.95) r/#1-6 (Malibu Comics series)						20.00
Black Planet and Other Stories HC (Olympian Publ.; 7/07, $39.95) r/Black Planet & Witching Hour contents; cover & sketch gallery with Brereton interviews						40.00
Carnival of Beasts (Image, 7/08, $6.99) short stories; Brereton-s/Brereton & others-a						7.00
Sinister Path (Big Wow! Art, 2017) original GN; Brereton-s/a						16.00
Troll Bridge (Oni Press, 2000, $4.95, B&W & orange) Brereton-s/painted-c; art by Brereton, Chin, Art Adams, Sakai, Timm, Warren, Thompson, Purcell, Stephens and others						5.00
Unhallowed Eve TPB (Oni Press, 10/02, $9.95) r/Witching Hour & Troll Bridge one-shots						10.00
Witching Hour (Dark Horse, 5/98, $4.95) Brereton-s/a; reprints DHP stories + 8 new pgs.						5.00

NOCTURNALS: THE DARK FOREVER
Oni Press: Jul, 2001 - No. 3, Feb, 2002 ($2.95, limited series)
| 1-3-Brereton-s/painted-a/c | | | | | | 3.00 |
| TPB (5/02, $9.95) r/#1-3; afterword & pin-ups by Alex Ross | | | | | | 10.00 |

NOCTURNE
Marvel Comics: June, 1995 - No. 4, Sept. 1995 ($1.50, limited series)
| 1-4 | | | | | | 4.00 |

NO ESCAPE (Movie)
Marvel Comics: June, 1994 - No. 3, Aug, 1994 ($1.50)
| 1-3: Based on movie | | | | | | 4.00 |

NO HONOR
Image Comics (Top Cow): Feb, 2001 - No. 4, July, 2001 ($2.50)
Preview (12/00, B&W) Silvestri-c						3.00
1-4-Avery-c/Crain-a						3.00
TPB (8/03, $12.99) r/#1-4; intro. by Straczynski						13.00

NOIR
Dynamite Entertainment: 2013 - No. 5, 2014 ($3.99, limited series)
| 1-5: 1-Miss Fury, Black Sparrow & The Shadow app.; Gischler-s/Mutti-a | | | | | | 5.00 |

	GD 2.0	VG 4.0	FN 6.0	VF 8.0	VF/NM 9.0	NM- 9.2

NOMAD (See Captain America #180)
Marvel Comics: Nov, 1990 - No. 4, Feb, 1991 ($1.50, limited series)

1-4: 1,4-Captain America app.   4.00

NOMAD
Marvel Comics: V2#1, May, 1992 - No. 25, May, 1994 ($1.75)

V2#1-25: 1-Has gatefold-c w/map/wanted poster. 4-Deadpool x-over. 5-Punisher vs. Nomad-c/story. 6-Punisher & Daredevil-c/story cont'd in Punisher War Journal #48. 7-Gambit-c/story. 10-Red Wolf app. 21-Man-Thing-c/story. 25-Bound-in trading card sheet   4.00

NOMAD: GIRL WITHOUT A WORLD (Rikki Barnes from Captain America V2 Heroes Reborn)
Marvel Comics: Nov, 2009 - No. 4, Feb, 2010 ($3.99, limited series)

1-4-McKeever-s. 2-Falcon app. 4-Young Avengers app.   5.00

NOMAN (See Thunder Agents)
Tower Comics: Nov, 1966 - No. 2, March, 1967 (25¢, 68 pgs.)

1-Wood/Williamson-c; Lightning begins; Dynamo cameo; Kane-a(p) & Whitney-a

| | 9 | 18 | 27 | 57 | 111 | 165 |

2-Wood-c only; Dynamo x-over; Whitney-a

| | 5 | 10 | 15 | 35 | 63 | 90 |

NOMEN OMEN
Image Comics: Oct, 2019 - No. 15, May, 2021 ($3.99)

1-15-Bucci-s/Camagni-a; 3 covers   4.00

NO MERCY
Image Comics: Apr, 2015 - No. 14, Mar, 2017 ($2.99/$3.99)

1-4-Alex de Campi-s/Carla Speed McNeil-a   3.00
5-14-($3.99) 6-EC-style cover   4.00

NONE BUT THE BRAVE (See Movie Classics)

NON-HUMANS
Image Comics: Oct, 2012 - No. 4, Jul, 2013 ($2.99)

1-4-Brunswick-s/Portacio-a/c   3.00

NON-STOP SPIDER-MAN (Leads into Savage Spider-Man series)
Marvel Comics: May, 2021 - No. 5, Nov, 2021 ($4.99/$3.99)

1-($4.99) Joe Kelly-s/Chris Bachalo-a; back-up story with Baron Zemo   5.00
2-5-($3.99) Baron Zemo app.   4.00

NOODNIK COMICS (See Pinky the Egghead)
Comic Media/Mystery/Biltmore: Dec, 1953; No. 2, Feb, 1954 - No. 5, Aug, 1954

3-D(1953, 25¢; Comic Media) (#1)-Came w/glasses

| | 37 | 74 | 111 | 222 | 361 | 500 |

2-5

| | 14 | 28 | 42 | 78 | 112 | 145 |

NO/ONE
Image Comics: Mar, 2023 - No. 10 ($3.99)

1-7-Higgins & Buccellato-s/Borges-a   4.00

NO ONE LEFT TO FIGHT
Dark Horse Comics: Jul, 2019 - No. 5, Nov, 2019 ($3.99)

1-5-Aubrey Sitterson-s/Fico Ossio-a   4.00

NO ONE LEFT TO FIGHT II
Dark Horse Comics: Oct, 2021 - No. 5, Feb, 2022 ($3.99)

1-5-Aubrey Sitterson-s/Fico Ossio-a   4.00

NORMALMAN (See Cerebus the Aardvark #55, 56)
Aardvark-Vanaheim/Renegade Press #6 on: Jan, 1984 - No. 12, Dec, 1985 ($1.70/$2.00)

1-12: 1-Jim Valentino-c/a in all. 6-12 ($2.00, B&W): 10-Cerebus cameo; Sim-a (2 pgs.)   4.00
...- Megaton Man Special 1 (Image Comics, 8/94, $2.50)   4.00
...-3-D 1 (Annual, 1986, $2.25)   4.00
...Twentieth Anniversary Special (7/04, $2.95)   3.00

NORMALS
AfterShock Comics: May, 2017 - No. 6, Oct, 2017 ($3.99, limited series)

1-6-Adam Glass-s/Dennis Calero-a   4.00

NORSE MYTHOLOGY
Dark Horse Comics: Oct, 2020 - No. 6, Mar, 2021 ($3.99, limited series)

1-6-Neil Gaiman & P. Craig Russell-s. 1-Art by Russell, Mignola, & Ordway. 2-Ordway-a   4.00

NORSE MYTHOLOGY II
Dark Horse Comics: Jun, 2021 - No. 6, Nov, 2021 ($3.99, limited series)

1-6-Gaiman & Russell-s. 1,2-Horak-a. 3,4-Buckingham-a. 5,6-Walta-a   4.00

NORSE MYTHOLOGY III
Dark Horse Comics: Feb, 2022 - No. 6, Jul, 2022 ($3.99, limited series)

1-6-Gaiman & Russell-s. 1,2-Rubin-a. 2,3-Doran-a. 3-6-Showman-a   4.00

NORTHANGER ABBEY (Adaptation of the Jane Austen novel)
Marvel Comics: Jan, 2012 - No. 5, May, 2012 ($3.99, mini-series)

1-5-Nancy Butler-s/Janet K. Lee-a/Julian Tedesco-c   4.00

NORTH AVENUE IRREGULARS (See Walt Disney Showcase #49)

NORTH FORCE
Image Comics: No. 0, Jun, 2021 ($3.99, one-shot)

0-Canada's Premier Super-Team; Savage Dragon app.; Erik Larsen-s/a   4.00

NORTH 40
DC Comics (WildStorm): Sept, 2009 - No. 6, Feb, 2010 ($2.99)

1-6-Aaron Williams-s/Fiona Staples-a   3.00
TPB (2010, $17.99) r/#1-6   18.00

NORTHLANDERS
DC Comics (Vertigo): Feb, 2008 - No. 50, Jun, 2012 ($2.99)

1-50: 1-Vikings in 980 A.D.; Wood-s/Gianfelice-a; covers by Carnivale. 35-Cloonan-a   3.00
1-3-Variant covers. 1-Adam Kubert. 2-Andy Kubert. 3-Dave Gibbons   5.00
...: Blood in the Snow TPB (2010, $14.99) r/#9,10,17-20   15.00
...: Metal and Other Stories TPB (2011, $17.99) r/#29-36   18.00
...: Sven the Returned TPB (2008, $9.99) r/#1-8; cover gallery   10.00
...: The Cross + The Hammer TPB (2009, $14.99) r/#11-16   15.00
...: The Plague Widow TPB (2010, $16.99) r/#21-28   17.00

NORTHSTAR
Marvel Comics: Apr, 1994 - No. 4, July, 1994 ($1.75, mini-series)

1-4: Character from Alpha Flight   4.00

NORTH TO ALASKA
Dell Publishing Co.: No. 1155, Dec, 1960

Four Color 1155-Movie, John Wayne photo-c

| | 15 | 30 | 45 | 105 | 233 | 360 |

NORTHWEST MOUNTIES (Also see Approved Comics #12)
Jubilee Publications/St. John: Oct, 1948 - No. 4, July, 1949

1-Rose of the Yukon by Matt Baker; Walter Johnson-a; Lubbers-c

| | 60 | 120 | 180 | 381 | 653 | 925 |

2-Baker-a; Lubbers-c. Ventrilo app.

| | 47 | 94 | 141 | 296 | 498 | 700 |

3-Bondage-c, Baker-a; Sky Chief, K-9 app.

| | 50 | 100 | 150 | 315 | 533 | 750 |

4-Baker-c/a(2 pgs.); Blue Monk & The Desperado app.

| | 61 | 122 | 183 | 390 | 670 | 950 |

NOSFERATU WARS
Dark Horse Comics: Mar, 2014 ($3.99, one-shot)

1-Reprints serial story from Dark Horse Presents #26-29; Niles-s/Menton3-a   4.00

NO SLEEP 'TIL DAWN
Dell Publishing Co.: No. 831, Aug, 1957

Four Color 831-Movie, Karl Malden photo-c

| | 8 | 16 | 24 | 54 | 102 | 150 |

NOSTALGIA ILLUSTRATED
Marvel Comics: Nov, 1974 - V2#8, Aug, 1975 (B&W, 76 pgs.)

V1#1

| | 4 | 8 | 12 | 23 | 37 | 50 |

V1#2, V2#1-8

| | 3 | 6 | 9 | 16 | 23 | 32 |

NOT ALL ROBOTS
Artists, Writers & Artisans, Inc.: Aug, 2021 - No. 5, Dec, 2021 ($3.99, limited series)

1-5-Russell-s/Deodato, Jr-a   4.00

NOT BRAND ECHH (Brand Echh #1-4; See Crazy, 1973)
Marvel Comics Group (LMC): Aug, 1967 - No. 13, May, 1969; No. 14, Jan, 2018
(1st Marvel parody book)

1: 1-8 are 12¢ issues

| | 9 | 18 | 27 | 59 | 117 | 175 |

2-8: 2-Origin Thor, Hulk & Capt. America; Monkees, Alfred E. Neuman cameo. 4-X-Men app. 5-Origin/intro. Forbush Man. 7-Origin Fantastical-4 & Stuporman. 8-Beatles cameo; X-Men satire; last 12¢-c

| | 5 | 10 | 15 | 35 | 63 | 90 |

9-13 (25¢, 68 pgs., all Giants) 9-Beatles cameo. 10-All-r; The Old Witch, Crypt Keeper & Vault Keeper cameos. 12,13-Beatles cameo

| | 5 | 10 | 15 | 33 | 57 | 80 |

14-(1/18, $3.99) Forbush Man app.; s/a by Zdarsky, Spencer & others; Nakamura-c   4.00

NOTE: **Colan** a(p)-4, 5, 8, 9. **Everett** a-1i. **Kirby** a(p)-1, 3, 5-7, 10r; c-1p. **J. Severin** a-1; c-3, 6-8, 11. **M. Severin** a-1-13; c-2, 9, 10, 12, 13. **Sutton** a-3, 4, 5i, 6i, 8, 9, 10r, 11-13; c-5. Archie satire in #9. Avengers satire in #8, 12.

NOTHING CAN STOP THE JUGGERNAUT
Marvel Comics: 1989 ($3.95)

1-r/Amazing Spider-Man #229 & 230

| | 1 | 3 | 4 | 6 | 8 | 10 |

NO TIME FOR SERGEANTS (TV)
Dell Publ. Co.: No. 914, July, 1958; Feb-Apr, 1965 - No. 3, Aug-Oct, 1965

Four Color 914 (Movie)-Toth-a; Andy Griffith photo-c

| | 10 | 20 | 30 | 66 | 138 | 210 |

1(2-4/65) (TV): Photo-c

| | 5 | 10 | 15 | 35 | 63 | 90 |

2,3 (TV): Photo-c

| | 4 | 8 | 12 | 28 | 47 | 65 |

NOVA (The Man Called... No. 22-25)(See New Warriors)
Marvel Comics Group: Sept, 1976 - No. 25, May, 1979

1-Origin/1st app. Nova (Richard Rider) Marv Wolfman-s; John Buscema-a

| | 8 | 16 | 24 | 54 | 102 | 150 |

2,3: 2-1st app. Condor & Powerhouse. 3-1st app. Diamondhead; Sal Buscema-a begin

| | 3 | 6 | 9 | 19 | 30 | 40 |

4,12: 4-Thor x-over; 1st app. The Corrupter; Kirby-c. 12-Spider-Man x-over w/Amazing Spider-Man #171

| | 3 | 6 | 9 | 21 | 33 | 45 |

5-11: 5-Nova vs. Tyrannus; Kirby-c; Marvel Bullpen app (incl. Stan Lee)-1st app. The Sphinx & Megaman. 7-Sphinx, Condor, Powerhouse & Diamondhead app. 8-Origin Megaman. 9-Megaman app. 10-Sphinx, Condor, Powerhouse & Diamondhead app. 11-vs. Sphinx

| | 3 | 5 | 8 | 11 | 14 | |

10,11-(35¢-c variants, limited distribution)(6,7/77)

| | 10 | 20 | 30 | 66 | 138 | 210 |

12-(35¢-c variant, limited distribution)(8/77)

| | 12 | 24 | 36 | 81 | 176 | 270 |

13,14-(Regular 30¢ editions)(9/77) 13-Intro Crime-Buster; Sandman app. 14-vs. Sandman

| | 2 | 4 | 6 | 9 | 13 | 16 |

13,14-(35¢-c variants, limited distribution)

| | 10 | 20 | 30 | 68 | 144 | 220 |

15-24: 15-Infantino-a begins. 16-18-vs. Yellow Claw; Nick Fury and SHIELD app. 19-Wally West (Kid Flash) cameo; 1st app Blackout. 20-1st Project X (Sherlock Holmes robot). 21-Richard reveals his Nova I.D to parents; vs Corrupter. 22-1st app the Comet (in costume). 23-Dr. Sun app. (origin) from Tomb of Dracula; Sphinx cameo. 24-Origin Powerhouse, Diamondhead, Crime-Buster, Comet Man, Sphinx & Dr. Sun app.

| | 1 | 3 | 4 | 6 | 8 | 10 |

25-Last issue; Powerhouse, Diamondhead, Crime-Buster, Comet Man, Sphinx & Dr. Sun app. story continues in Fantastic Four #204-214

| | 3 | 6 | 9 | 14 | 20 | 26 |

NOTE: **Austin** c-21i, 23i. **John Buscema** a(p)-1-3, 8, 21; c-1p, 2, 15. **Infantino** a(p)-15-20, 22-25; c-17-20, 21p, 23p, 24p. **Kirby** c-4p, 5, 7. **Nebres** c-25i. **Simonson** a-23i.

NOVA
Marvel Comics: Jan, 1994 - June, 1995 ($1.75/$1.95) (Started as 4-part mini-series)

1-($2.95, 52 pgs.)-Collector's Edition w/gold foil-c; new Nova costume; Nicieza-s/Marrinan-a; continued from New Warriors #42; re-intro Richard Rider's supporting cast – Ginger Jaye, Bernie Dillon & Roger 'Caps' Cooper; origin & history recap; vs. Gladiator of the Shi'ar Imperial Guard; Queen Adora app.

| | 3 | 6 | 9 | 15 | 22 | 28 |

1-($2.25, 52 pgs.)-Newsstand Edition w/o foil-c   5.00
2-5: 2-1st app. Tailhook; Speedball app. 3-vs. Spider-Man; Corrupter app; 1st app Nova 00. 4-Vs. Nova 00; contains Rock Video Monthly insert (centerfold). 5-Re-intro Condor; Sphinx cameo; leads into New Warriors #47; contains centerfold insert for Marvel 'Masterprints'   3.00
6,7: 6-'Time and Time Again', pt.3; story continued from Night Thrasher #11; Rage & Firestar solo stories; continues in New Warriors #48. 7- 'Time and Time Again' pt.6; continued from Night Thrasher #12; Rage & Firestar solo stories; Cloak and Dagger app; continues in New Warriors #49; last Nicieza-s   4.00

Non-Stop Spider-Man #4 © MAR

Nova (2013 series) #29 © MAR

Nukla #1 © DELL

	GD	VG	FN	VF	VF/NM	NM-		GD	VG	FN	VF	VF/NM	NM-
	2.0	4.0	6.0	8.0	9.0	9.2		2.0	4.0	6.0	8.0	9.0	9.2

8-12: 8-1st app. Shatterforce. 9-Vs. Shatterforce. 10-Vs. Diamondhead & Rhino; New Warriors and Corrupter app. 11-She-Hulk, the Thing & Ant-Man guest star; Nick Fury cameo; contains two inserts – a Marvel Subscription offer and a centerfold insert for a personalized X-Men/Captain Universe comic. 12-Vs. Nova 00; Nick Fury, Black Bolt & the Inhumans app. 13-'Deathstorm' T-Minus 3; Firestar, Night Thrasher & Nick Fury app. 14-'Deathstorm' T-Minus 2; Nova 00, Darkhawk & the New Warriors app. 15-'Deathstorm' T-Minus 1; 1st app. Kraa (brother of Zorr from Nova #1, 1976)   3.00

16-18: 16-'Deathstorm' conclusion; vs. Kraa; Nova Corps app; death of Nova 00.
17-vs. Supernova (Garthan Saal); Richard is stripped of his rank; Queen Adora app.
18-Last issue; Richard Rider de-powered; Supernova becomes Nova-Prime; Dire Wraith Queen app; story continues in New Warriors #10   6.00

NOVA
Marvel Comics: May, 1999 - No. 7, Nov, 1999 ($2.99/$1.99)
1-($2.99, 38 pgs.) –Larsen-s/Bennett-a; wraparound-c by Larsen; origin retold; Nebula app; reveals her father to be Zorr (from issue #1, 1976); She-Hulk, Spider-Man, Speedball, Namorita app.   5.00
2-6: 2-Two covers; vs. Diamondhead; Captain America app.; Namorita's skin returns to normal. 3-Savage Dragon app.; (as a Skrull); New Warriors, Thor, Fantastic Four & the Condor app.; restoration of the Sphinx. 4-vs. Condor; Fantastic Four app; Red Raven cameo. 5-Spider-Man app. 6-vs. the Sphinx; Venom cameo   4.00
7-Last issue; Red Raven & Bi-Beast app. vs. Venom   5.00

NOVA (See Secret Avengers and The Thanos Imperative)
Marvel Comics: June, 2007 - No. 36, Jun, 2010 ($2.99)
1-Abnett/Lanning-s; Chen-a; Granov-c; continued from Annihilation #6; brief Iron Man app.
    3   6   9   16   24   32
2-The Initiative x-over; Nova returns to Earth; vs Diamondhead; Iron Man & the Thunderbolts (Penance, Radioactive Man, Venom & Moonstone) app.
    2   4   6   8   10
3-The Initiative x-over; vs. the Thunderbolts; Iron Man app.; Nova leaves Earth
    1   2   3   5   6   8
4-7,9: Annihilation Conquest x-overs. 4-Phalanx and Gamora app. 5-Nova infected with the Phalanx virus; Gamora app. 6-Gamora-c by Granov; Drax app. 7-Gamora and Drax app; last Chen-a. 9-Cosmo, Gamora and Drax app   7.00
8-1st app. Cosmo - the Russian telepathic dog; 1st app. Knowhere – a space station formed out of the severed head of a Celestial (as seen in the GOTG movie); 1st app. of the Luminals; 1st app Wellington Alves-a; brief Peter Quill (Star-Lord) app.
    4   8   12   23   37   50
10-14: 10-Nova and Gamora solo story; Drax app.; leads into Nova Annual #1. 11-Gamora, Drax & Warlock of the New Mutants app; Pelletier-a begins. 12-Warlock of the New Mutants app. Gamora & Drax cured of the Phalanx virus; leads into Annihilation Conquest #6. 13-Galactus & Silver Surfer app; contains 5-pg preview of the new Eternals series; Alves-a. 14-Galactus app.; Nova vs. Silver Surfer. 15-Galactus & Silver Surfer app.   6.00
16-18: Secret Invasion x-over. 16-Super-Skrull app.; Nova returns to Earth. 17-Team up w/Darkhawk at Project Pegasus w/the Skrulls; Quasar (Wendell Vaughn) returns. 18-Quasar & Darkhawk app; vs. the Skrulls; return of the Nova Corps   5.00 / 6.00
18-Zombie 1:10 variant-c by Wellington Alves
19-Darkhawk app.; Robbie Rider joins the Nova Corps; Serpent Society app.
20-New Warriors flashback; Darkhawk app; Ego the Living Planet app. 21-Fantastic Four app; Ego the Living Planet becomes new base for the Nova Corps; Nova's powers are taken away. 22-Quasar app.; Andrea Divito-a begins   4.00
20-Villain 'Sphinx' variant-c by Mike Deodato Jr.   1   2   3   5   6   8
23-28: War of Kings x-over. 23-Richard Rider dons the Quantum Bands – becomes the new Quasar. 24-Gladiator & the Shi'ar Imperial Guard app. 25-Richard regains his Nova powers; Wendell Vaughn (Quasar) regains the Quantum Bands; Emperor Vulcan app. 26-Lord Ravenous app. 27-Blastaar & Lord Ravenous app. 28-War of Kings ends; Robbie Rider officially joins the Nova Corps. Quasar app.   6.00
25-'Dirty Dancing' 1980s decade 1:10 variant by Alina Urusov   5.00
28-Marvel Comics 70th Anniversary frame variant   6.00
29,30: 'Starstalker' parts 1-2. 29-1st Marvel Universe app. of Monark Starstalker (previously from Marvel Premiere #32). 30-vs. Ego the Living Planet   3.00 / 5.00
31-Darkhawk app.
32-34: Realm of Kings x-over; 32,33-Reed Richards, Black Bolt, Darkhawk, Namorita & the Sphinx app. 33-Moonstone, Man-Wolf, Bloodstone, Basilisk app. 34-'Death' of Black Bolt; Nova vs. Moonstone, Reed Richards vs. Bloodstone, Namorita vs. Man-Wolf, Darkhawk vs. Gyre the Raptor; contains 6 pg. preview of the New Ultimates series
    1   2   3   5   6   8
34-Deadpool variant-c   2   4   6   8   12   15
35-Realm of Kings x-over; Reed Richards, Darkhawk, Namorita vs. Sphinx; Namorita brought back to current continuity   1   3   4   6   8   10
36-Last issue; Darkhawk & Quasar app.; leads into Thanos Imperative Ignition
    2   4   6   10   14   18
Annual #1 (4/08, $3.99); Slightly altered origin retold; Annihilation Conquest tie-in; Quasar app.; takes place between Nova issues #10-11   1   1   2   3   5   6   8

...: Origin of Richard Rider (2009, $4.99) origin retold from Nova #1 & 4 ('76)   5.00
... Vol. 1: Annihilation - Conquest TPB (2007, $17.99) r/#1-7; cover sketches   18.00

NOVA (Marvel NOW!)
Marvel Comics: Apr, 2013 - No. 31, Jul, 2015 ($3.99)
1-Loeb-s/McGuinness-a/c; Rocket Raccoon & Gamora app.; multiple variant covers   6.00
2-9: 2,3-Rocket Raccoon & Gamora app. 7-Superior Spider-Man app. 8,9-Infinity tie-in   4.00
10-($4.99) "Issue #100"; Speedball & Justice app.; cover gallery   5.00
11-24,26-31: 12-16-Beta Ray Bill app. 18-20-Original Sin tie-in. 19,20-Rocket Raccoon app.   4.00
23,24-Axis tie-in. 28-Black Vortex crossover   5.00
25-($4.99) Axis tie-in; Sam joins the Avengers   5.00
Annual 1 (5/15, $4.99) The Hulk app.; Duggan-s/Baldeon-a   5.00
... Special 1 (10/14, $4.99) Part 3 of x-over with Iron Man & Uncanny X-Men   5.00

NOVA
Marvel Comics: Jan, 2016 - No. 11, Nov, 2016 ($3.99)
1,2,5-11: 1-Sean Ryan-s/Cory Smith-a. 8,9-Civil War II tie-in. 10,11-Richard Rider returns   4.00
3,4-Ms. Marvel & Spider-Man (Miles) app.   1   2   3   5   6   8

NOVA
Marvel Comics: Feb, 2017 - No. 7, Aug, 2017 ($3.99)
1-7: 1-Ramón Pérez-a; Richard Rider & Ego app. 4-Gamora app.   4.00

NOW AGE ILLUSTRATED (See Pendulum Illustrated Classics)
NOW AGE BOOKS ILLUSTRATED (See Pendulum Illustrated Classics)

NOWHERE MAN
Dynamite Entertainment: 2011 - No. 4, 2011 ($3.99)
1-4-Marc Guggenheim-s/Jeevan J. Kang-a   4.00

NOWHERE MEN
Image Comics: Nov, 2012 - No. 11, Sept, 2016 ($2.99)
1-Stephenson-s/Bellegarde-a   15.00
1-2nd thru 5th printings   4.00
2   6.00
3-11   4.00

NO WORLD
Aspen MLT: Apr, 2017 - No. 6, Oct, 2017 ($3.99, limited series)
1-6-Lobdell-s/Gunderson-a; multiple covers on each   4.00

NTH MAN THE ULTIMATE NINJA (See Marvel Comics Presents #25)
Marvel Comics: Aug, 1989 - No. 16, Sept, 1990 ($1.50)
1-16-Ninja mercenary. 8-Dale Keown's 1st Marvel work (1/90, pencils)   4.00

NUBIA & THE AMAZONS (From Wonder Woman)
DC Comics: Dec, 2021 - No. 6, May, 2022 ($3.99, limited series)
1-6-Stephanie Williams/Alitha Martinez-a   5.00

NUBIA & THE JUSTICE LEAGUE SPECIAL (From Wonder Woman)
DC Comics: Jan, 2023 ($5.99, limited series)
1-Firefly and Parasite app.; takes place before Justice League #75   6.00

NUBIA: CORONATION SPECIAL (Prelude to Nubia: Queen of the Amazons series)
DC Comics: Jul, 2022 ($5.99, one-shot)
1-Stephanie Williams & Vita Ayala-s; art by Sauvage, Doran, Thompson, Banks, Martinez   6.00

NUBIA: QUEEN OF THE AMAZONS (From Wonder Woman)
DC Comics: Aug, 2022 - No. 4, Nov, 2022 ($3.99, limited series)
1-4-Stephanie Williams-s/Alitha Martinez-a. 1-Justice League app.   4.00

NUCLEAR FAMILY (Based on the short story Breakfast at Twilight by Philip K. Dick)
AfterShock Comics: Feb, 2021 - No. 5, Jun, 2021 ($4.99/$3.99, limited series)
1-($4.99) Stephanie Phillips-s/Tony Shasteen-a   5.00
2-5-($3.99)   4.00

NUCLEUS (Also see Cerebus)
Heiro-Graphic Publications: May, 1979 ($1.50, B&W, adult fanzine)
1-Contains "Demonhorn" by Dave Sim; early app. of Cerebus The Aardvark (4 pg. story)   5   10   15   34   60   85

NUKLA
Dell Publishing Co.: Oct-Dec, 1965 - No. 4, Sept, 1966
1-Origin & 1st app. Nukla (super hero)   5   10   15   33   57   80
2,3   3   6   9   21   33   45
4-Ditko-a (3)   4   8   12   25   40   55

NUMBER OF THE BEAST
DC Comics (WildStorm): June, 2008 - No. 8, Sept, 2008 ($2.99, limited series)
1-8-Beatty-s/Sprouse-a/c. 1-Variant-c by Mahnke. 6-The Authority app.   3.00

	GD	VG	FN	VF	VF/NM	NM-
	2.0	4.0	6.0	8.0	9.0	9.2

TPB (2008, $19.99) r/#1-8; character dossiers — 20.00

NURSE BETSY CRANE (Formerly Teen Secret Diary) (Also see Registered Nurse for reprints)
Charlton Comics: V2#12, Aug, 1961 - V2#27, Mar, 1964 (See Soap Opera Romances)

	GD	VG	FN	VF	VF/NM	NM-
V2#12-27	6	12	18	37	66	95

NURSE HELEN GRANT (See The Romances of...)

NURSE LINDA LARK (See Linda Lark)

NURSERY RHYMES
Ziff-Davis Publ. Co. (Approved Comics): No. 10, July-Aug, 1951 - No. 2, Winter, 1951 (Painted-c)

10 (#1), 2: 10-Howie Post-a	22	44	66	132	216	300

NURSES, THE (TV)
Gold Key: April, 1963 - No. 3, Oct, 1963 (Photo-c: #1,2)

1	5	10	15	35	63	90
2,3	3	6	9	21	33	45

NUTS! (Satire)
Premiere Comics Group: March, 1954 - No. 5, Nov, 1954

1-Hollingsworth-a	40	80	120	246	411	575
2,4,5: 5-Capt. Marvel parody	27	54	81	162	266	370
3-Drug "reefers" mentioned; Marilyn Monroe & Joe DiMaggio parody-c	30	60	90	177	289	400

NUTS (Magazine) (Satire)
Health Knowledge: Feb, 1958 - No. 2, April, 1958

1	10	20	30	58	79	100
2	8	16	24	40	50	60

NUTS & JOLTS
Dell Publishing Co.: No. 22, 1941

Large Feature Comic 22	24	48	72	142	234	330

NUTSY SQUIRREL (Formerly Hollywood Funny Folks)(See Comic Cavalcade)
National Periodical Publications: #61, 9-10/54 - #69, 1-2/56; #70, 8-9/56 - #71, 10-11/56; #72, 11/57

61-Mayer-a; Grossman-a in all	15	30	45	90	140	190
62-72: Mayer a-62,65,67-72	12	24	36	67	94	120

NUTTY COMICS
Fawcett Publications: Winter, 1946

1-Capt. Kidd story; 1 pg. Wolverton-a	16	32	48	92	144	195

NUTTY COMICS
Home Comics (Harvey Publications): 1945; No. 4, May-June, 1946 - No. 8, June-July, 1947 (No #2,3)

nn-Helpful Hank, Bozo Bear & others (funny animal)	10	20	30	56	76	95
4	8	16	24	42	54	65
5-Rags Rabbit begins(1st app.); infinity-c	9	18	27	50	65	80
6-8	7	14	21	37	46	55

NUTTY LIFE (Formerly Krazy Life #1; becomes Wotalife Comics #3 on)
Fox Feature Syndicate: No. 2, Summer, 1946

2	27	54	81	158	259	360

NU WAY
Aspen MLT: Jul, 2018 - No. 5, Jan, 2019 ($3.99, limited series)

1-5-Krul-s/Konat-a; multiple covers on each						4.00

NYOKA, THE JUNGLE GIRL (Formerly Jungle Girl; see The Further Adventures of..., Master Comics #50 & XMas Comics)
Fawcett Publications: No. 2, Winter, 1945 - No. 77, June, 1953 (Movie serial)

2	68	136	204	435	743	1050
3	40	80	120	246	411	575
4,5-Bondage covers	36	72	108	214	347	480
6-11,13,14,16-18-Krigstein-a: 17-Sam Spade ad by Lou Fine	22	44	66	128	209	290
12,15,19,20	20	40	60	115	185	255
21-30: 25-Clayton Moore photo-c?	14	28	42	81	118	155
31-40	12	24	36	69	97	125
41-50	11	22	33	62	86	110
51-60	10	20	30	54	72	90
61-77	9	18	27	50	65	80

NOTE: *Photo-c from movies 25, 30-70, 72, 75-77. Bondage c-4, 5, 7, 8, 14, 24.*

NYOKA, THE JUNGLE GIRL (Formerly Zoo Funnies; Space Adventures #23 on)
Charlton Comics: No. 14, Nov, 1955 - No. 22, Nov, 1957

14	14	28	42	76	108	140
15-22	10	20	30	58	79	100

NYX (Also see X-23 title)
Marvel Comics: Nov, 2003 - No. 7, Oct, 2005 ($2.99)

1-Quesada-s/Middleton-a/c; intro. Kiden Nixon	3	6	9	16	23	30
2	2	4	6	11	16	20
3-1st app. X-23	24	48	72	168	372	575
4-2nd app X-23	6	12	18	38	69	100
5,6-Teranishi-a	2	4	6	9	13	16
7-($3.99) Teranishi-a	2	4	6	8	10	12
NYX X-23 (2005, $34.99, oversized with d.j.) r/X-23 #1-6 & NYX #1-7; intro by Craig Kyle; sketch pages, development art and unused covers						45.00
...: Wannabe TPB (2006, $19.99) r/#1-7; development art and unused covers						20.00

NYX: NO WAY HOME
Marvel Comics: Oct, 2008 - No. 6, Apr, 2009 ($3.99)

1-6: 1-Andrasofszky-s/Liu-s/Urusov-c; sketch pages, character and cover design art						5.00

NYX, VOLUME 1
Dynamite Entertainment: 2021 - No. 10, 2022 ($3.99)

1-10-Christos Gage-s/Marc Borstel-a; multiple covers on each. 3,8-Vampirella app.						4.00

OAKLAND PRESS FUNNYBOOK, THE

The Oakland Press: 9/17/78 - 4/13/80 (16 pgs.) (Weekly)
Full color in comic book form; changes to tabloid size 4/20/80-on

Contains Tarzan by Manning, Marmaduke, Bugs Bunny, etc. (low distribution); 9/23/79 - 4/13/80 contain Buck Rogers by Gray Morrow & Jim Lawrence						5.00

OAKY DOAKS (See Famous Funnies #190)
Eastern Color Printing Co.: July, 1942 (One Shot)

1	39	78	117	240	395	550

OBERGEIST: RAGNAROK HIGHWAY
Image Comics (Top Cow/Minotaur): May, 2001 - No. 6, Nov, 2001 ($2.95, limited series)

Preview ('01, B&W, 16 pgs.) Harris painted-c						3.00
1-6-Harris-c/a/Jolley-s. 1-Three covers						3.00
... :The Directors' Cut (2002, $19.95, TPB) r/#1-6; Bruce Campbell intro.						20.00
... :The Empty Locket (3/02, $2.95, B&W) Harris & Snyder-a						3.00

OBERON
AfterShock Comics: Feb, 2019 - No. 5, Jul, 2019 ($3.99)

1-5-Ryan Parrott-s/Milos Slavkovic-a						4.00

OBIE
Store Comics: 1953 (6¢)

1	10	20	30	56	76	95

OBI-WAN AND ANAKIN (Star Wars)
Marvel Comics: Mar, 2016 - No. 5, Jul, 2016 ($3.99)

1-5-Takes place a few years after Episode One; Soule-s/Checchetto-a/c						4.00

OBJECTIVE FIVE
Image Comics: July, 2000 - No. 6, Jan, 2001 ($2.95)

1-6-Lizalde-a						3.00

OBLIVION
Comico: Aug, 1995 - No. 3, May, 1996 ($2.50)

1-3: 1-Art Adams-c. 2-(1/96)-Bagged w/gaming card. 3-(5/96)-Darrow-c						4.00

OBLIVION SONG
Image Comics: Mar, 2018 - No. 36, Jun, 2022 ($3.99)

1-24,26-35-Kirkman-s/De Felici-a						4.00
25-($4.99) Flip book with Science Dog #25 - Kirkman-s/Cory Walker-a						5.00
36-($5.99) Last issue						6.00

OBNOXIO THE CLOWN (Character from Crazy Magazine)
Marvel Comics Group: April, 1983 (one-shot)

1-Vs. the X-Men						5.00

OCCULT CRIMES TASKFORCE
Image Comics: July, 2006 - No. 4, May, 2007 ($2.99, limited series)

1-4-Rosario Dawson & David Atchison-s/Tony Shasteen-a						3.00
... Vol. 1 TPB (2007, $14.99) r/#1-4; sketch and cover development art						15.00

OCCULTIST, THE
Dark Horse Comics: Dec, 2010 ($3.50, one-shot)

1-Richardson & Seeley-s/Drujiniu/Morris-c						3.50

OCCULTIST, THE
Dark Horse Comics: Nov, 2011 - No. 3, Jan, 2012 ($3.50, limited series)

1-3-Seeley-s/Drujiniu-a/Morris-c. 1-Variant-c by Frison						3.50

OCCULTIST, THE
Dark Horse Comics: Oct, 2013 - No. 5, Feb, 2014 ($3.50, limited series)

1-5-Seeley-s/Norton-a/Morris-c. 1-Variant-c by Rivera						3.50

OCCULT FILES OF DR. SPEKTOR, THE
Gold Key/Whitman No. 25: Apr, 1973 - No. 24, Feb, 1977; No. 25, May, 1982 (Painted-c #1-24)

1-1st app. Lakota; Baron Tibor begins	6	12	18	38	69	100
2-5: 3-Mummy-c/s. 5-Jekyll & Hyde-c/s	4	8	12	23	37	50
6-10: 6,9-Frankenstein. 8,9-Dracula c/s. 9.-Jekyll & Hyde c/s. 9,10-Mummy-c/s	3	6	9	16	23	30
11-13,15-17,19-22,24: 11-1st app. Spektor as Werewolf. 11-13-Werewolf-c/s. 12,16-Frankenstein c/s. 17-Zombie/Voodoo-c. 19-Sea monster-c/s. 20-Mummy-c						
21-Swamp monster-c/s. 24-Dragon-c/s	2	4	6	11	16	20
14-Dr. Solar app.	3	6	9	16	24	32
18,23-Dr. Solar cameo	2	4	6	13	18	22
22-Return of the Owl-c/s	2	4	6	14	20	25
25(Whitman, 5/82)-r/#1 with line drawn-c	2	4	6	9	13	16

NOTE: *Also see Dan Curtis, Golden Comics Digest 33, Gold Key Spotlight, Mystery Comics Digest 5, & Spine Tingling Tales.*

OCCUPY AVENGERS (Follows Civil War II)
Marvel Comics: Jan, 2017 - No. 9, Sept, 2017 ($3.99)

1-4-Hawkeye and Red Wolf team; Pacheco-a. 3,4-Nighthawk & Nick Fury LMD app. 8,9-Secret Empire tie-ins. 9-Leads into Secret Empire #7						4.00

OCCUPY COMICS
Black Mask Studios: 2013 - No. 3, 2013 ($3.50)

1-3-Short stories and essays about the Occupy movement; s/a by various. 1-Allred-c						3.50

OCEAN
DC Comics (WildStorm): Dec, 2005 - No. 6, Sept, 2006 ($2.95/$2.99/$3.99, limited series)

1-5-Warren Ellis-s/Chris Sprouse-a						3.00
6-($3.99) Conclusion						4.00

OCEAN MASTER: YEAR OF THE VILLAIN
DC Comics: 2019 ($4.99, one-shot)

1-Watters-s/Mendonca-a; Apex Lex and Marine Marauder app.						5.00

OCTOBER FACTION, THE
IDW Publishing: Oct, 2014 - No. 18, Jul, 2016 ($3.99)

1-18-Steve Niles-s/Damien Worm-a/c						4.00
...#1 Special Edition (9/19, $3.99) r/#1 with added Netflix logo on cover						4.00

OCTOBER FACTION, THE: DEADLY SEASON
IDW Publishing: Oct, 2016 - No. 5, Feb, 2017 ($3.99, limited series)

NYX (2021 series) #3 © DYN

Obi-Wan and Anakin #4 © Lucasfilm

Odyssey of the Amazons #2 © DC

	GD 2.0	VG 4.0	FN 6.0	VF 8.0	VF/NM 9.0	NM- 9.2

1-5-Steve Niles-s/Damien Worm-a/c ... 4.00

OCTOBER FACTION: SUPERNATURAL DREAMS
IDW Publishing: Mar, 2018 - No. 5, Jul, 2018 ($3.99, limited series)

1-5-Steve Niles-s/Damien Worm-a/c ... 4.00

ODDLY NORMAL
Image Comics: Sept, 2014 - No. 10, Sept, 2015 ($2.99)

1-10-Otis Frampton-s/a ... 3.00

ODDLY PEDESTRIAN LIFE OF CHRISTOPHER CHAOS, THE
Dark Horse Comics: Jun, 2023 - Present ($4.99)

1-7-Tynion IV & Brombal-s/Goodhart-a ... 5.00

ODELL'S ADVENTURES IN 3-D (See Adventures in 3-D)

ODIN'S EYE
Bad Idea: Dec, 2021 - No. 5, Dec, 2021 ($9.99/$7.99, weekly limited series)

	GD 2.0	VG 4.0	FN 6.0	VF 8.0	VF/NM 9.0	NM- 9.2
1-($9.99) Dysart-s/Giorello-a	2	4	6	11	16	20
2-5	1	2	3	5	6	8

ODY-C
Image Comics: Nov, 2014 - No. 12, Oct, 2016 ($3.99)

1-12: 1-Matt Fraction-s/Christian Ward-a; 8-page gatefold ... 4.00

ODYSSEY, THE (See Marvel Illustrated: The Odyssey)

ODYSSEY OF THE AMAZONS
DC Comics: Mar, 2017 - No. 6, Aug, 2017 ($3.99 limited series)

1-6-Early history of the Amazons; Kevin Grevioux-s/Ryan Benjamin-a ... 4.00

OFFCASTES
Marvel Comics (Epic Comics/Heavy Hitters): July, 1993 - No. 3, Sept, 1993 ($1.95, limited series)

1-3: Mike Vosburg-c/a/scripts in all ... 4.00

OFFICIAL CRISIS ON INFINITE EARTHS INDEX, THE
Independent Comics Group (Eclipse): Mar, 1986 ($1.75)

1 ... 5.00

OFFICIAL CRISIS ON INFINITE EARTHS CROSSOVER INDEX, THE
Independent Comics Group (Eclipse): July, 1986 ($1.75)

1-Pérez-c ... 5.00

OFFICIAL DOOM PATROL INDEX, THE
Independent Comics Group (Eclipse): Feb, 1986 - No. 2, Mar, 1986 ($1.50, limited series)

1,2: Byrne-c ... 4.00

OFFICIAL HANDBOOK OF THE CONAN UNIVERSE ANNIVERSARY EDITION
Marvel Comics: Dec, 2020 ($5.99, one-shot)

1-Reprints The Handbook of the Conan Universe ('85,'86); Kaluta wraparound-c ... 6.00

OFFICIAL HANDBOOK OF THE MARVEL UNIVERSE, THE
Marvel Comics Group: Jan, 1983 - No. 15, May 1984 (Limited series)

1-Lists Marvel heroes & villains (letter A) ... 6.00
2-15: 2 (B-C), 3-(C-D). 4-(D-G). 5-(H-J), 6-(K-L). 7-(M). 8-(N-P); Punisher-c. 9-(Q-S), 10-(S). 11-(S-U). 12-(V-Z); Wolverine-c. 13,14-Book of the Dead. 15-Weaponry catalogue ... 5.00
NOTE: Bolland a-8. Byrne c/a(p)-1-14; c-15p. Grell a-6, 1. Kirby a-1, 3. Layton a-2, 5, 7. Mignola a-3, 4, 5, 6, 8, 12. Miller a-4-6, 8, 10. Nebres a-3, 4, 8. Redondo a-3, 4, 3, 13, 14. Simonson a-1, 4, 6-13. Paul Smith a-1-12. Starlin a-5, 7, 8, 10, 13, 14. Steranko a-8p. Zeck-2-14.

OFFICIAL HANDBOOK OF THE MARVEL UNIVERSE, THE
Marvel Comics Group: Dec, 1985 - No. 20, Feb, 1988 ($1.50, maxi-series)

V2#1-Byrne-c ... 5.00
2-20: 2,3-Byrne-c ... 4.00

	GD 2.0	VG 4.0	FN 6.0	VF 8.0	VF/NM 9.0	NM- 9.2
Trade paperback Vol. 1-10 ($6.95)	1	3	4	6	8	10

NOTE: Art Adams a-7, 8, 11, 12, 14. Bolland a-8, 10, 13. Buckler a-1, 3, 5, 10. Buscema a-1, 5, 8, 9, 10, 13, 14. Byrne a-1-14; c-1-11. Ditko a-1, 2, 4, 6, 7, 11. Mignola a-2, 4, 9, 11, 13. Miller a-2, 4, 12. Simonson a-1, 2, 4-13, 15. Paul Smith a-1-5, 7-12, 14. Starlin a-6, 1, 9, 12, 16. Zeck a-1-4, 6, 7, 9-14, 16.

OFFICIAL HANDBOOK OF THE MARVEL UNIVERSE, THE
Marvel Comics: July, 1989 - No. 8, Mid-Dec, 1990 ($1.50, lim. series, 52 pgs.)

V3#1-8: 1-McFarlane-a (2 pgs.) ... 5.00

OFFICIAL HANDBOOK OF THE MARVEL UNIVERSE, THE (Also see Spider-Man)
Marvel Comics: 2004 - 2005 ($3.99, one-shots)

...: Alternate Universes 2005 - Profile pages of 1602, MC2, 2099, Earth X, Mangaverse, Days of Future Past, Squadron Supreme, Spider-Ham's Larval Earth and others ... 4.00
...: Avengers 2004 - Profile pages; art by various; lists of character origins and 1st apps. ... 4.00
...: Avengers 2005 - Profile pages and info for New Avengers, Young Avengers & others ... 4.00
...: Book of the Dead 2004 - Profile pages of deceased Marvel characters; art by various ... 4.00
...: Daredevil 2004 - Profile pages; art by various; lists of character origins and 1st apps. ... 4.00

...: Fantastic Four 2005 - Profile pages of members, friends & enemies ... 4.00
...: Golden Age 2005 - Profile pages; art by various; lists of character origins and 1st apps. ... 4.00
...: Horror 2005 - Profile pages; art by various; lists of character origins and 1st apps. ... 4.00
...: Hulk 2004 - Profile pages; art by various; lists of character origins and 1st apps. ... 4.00
...: Marvel Knights 2005 - Profile pages of characters from Marvel Knights line ... 4.00
...: Spider-Man 2004 - Profile pages; art by various; lists of character origins and 1st apps. ... 4.00
...: Spider-Man 2005 - Profile pages of Spidey's friends and foes, emphasizing the recent ... 4.00
...: Wolverine 2004 - Profile pages; art by various; lists of character origins and 1st apps. ... 4.00
...: Teams 2005 - Profile pages of Avengers, X-Men and other teams ... 4.00
...: Women of Marvel 2005 - Profile pages; art by various; Greg Land-c ... 4.00
...: X-Men 2004 - Profile pages; art by various; lists of character origins and 1st apps. ... 4.00
...: X-Men 2005 - Profile pages; art by various; lists of character origins and 1st apps. ... 4.00
...: X-Men - The Age of Apocalypse 2005 - Profile pages of characters plus Exiles ... 4.00

OFFICIAL HANDBOOK OF THE MARVEL UNIVERSE A-Z UPDATE
Marvel Comics: Apr, 2010 - No. 5, 2010 ($3.99, one-shots)

1-5-Profile pages; Andrasofszky-c ... 4.00

OFFICIAL HANDBOOK OF THE ULTIMATE MARVEL UNIVERSE, THE
Marvel Comics: 2005 (one-shots)

... 2005: The Fantastic Four and Spider-Man - Profile pages; art by various ... 4.00
... The Ultimates and X-Men 2005 - Profile pages; art by various; Bagley-c ... 4.00

OFFICIAL HAWKMAN INDEX, THE
Independent Comics Group: Nov, 1986 - No. 2, Dec, 1986 ($2.00)

1,2 ... 4.00

OFFICIAL IMAGE COMICS TIMELINE, THE
Image Comics: Feb, 2022 ($7.99, squarebound, one-shot)

1-History of Image Comics; lists of awards, crossovers, photo gallery of creators ... 8.00

OFFICIAL INDEX TO THE MARVEL UNIVERSE (Also see "Avengers, Thor...")
Marvel Comics: 2009 - No. 14, April, 2010 ($3.99)

1-14-Each issue has chronological synopses, creator credits, character lists for 40-50 issues of apps. for Iron Man, Spider-Man and the X-Men starting with 1st apps. in issue #1 ... 4.00

OFFICIAL JUSTICE LEAGUE OF AMERICA INDEX, THE
Independent Comics Group (Eclipse): April, 1986 - No. 8, Mar, 1987 ($2.00, Baxter paper)

1-8: 1,2-Perez-c. ... 6.00

OFFICIAL LEGION OF SUPER-HEROES INDEX, THE
Independent Comics Group (Eclipse): Dec, 1986 - No. 5, 1987 ($2.00, limited series) (No Official in Title #2 on)

1-5: 4-Mooney-c ... 6.00

OFFICIAL MARVEL INDEX TO MARVEL TEAM-UP
Marvel Comics Group: Jan, 1986 - No. 6, 1987 ($1.25, limited series)

1-6 ... 4.00

OFFICIAL MARVEL INDEX TO THE AMAZING SPIDER-MAN
Marvel Comics Group: Apr, 1985 - No. 9, Dec, 1985 ($1.25, limited series)

1 ($1.00)-Byrne-c. ... 5.00
2-9: 5,6,8,9-Punisher-c. ... 4.00

OFFICIAL MARVEL INDEX TO THE AVENGERS, THE
Marvel Comics: Jun, 1987 - No. 7, Aug, 1988 ($2.95, limited series)

1-7 ... 5.00

OFFICIAL MARVEL INDEX TO THE AVENGERS, THE
Marvel Comics: V2#1, Oct, 1994 - V2#6, 1995 ($1.95, limited series)

V2#1-#6 ... 4.00

OFFICIAL MARVEL INDEX TO THE FANTASTIC FOUR
Marvel Comics Group: Dec, 1985 - No. 12, Jan, 1987 ($1.25, limited series)

1-12: 1-Byrne-c. 1,2-Kirby back-c (unpub. art) ... 4.00

OFFICIAL MARVEL INDEX TO THE X-MEN, THE
Marvel Comics: May, 1987 - No. 7, July, 1988 ($2.95, limited series)

1-7 ... 5.00

OFFICIAL MARVEL INDEX TO THE X-MEN, THE
Marvel Comics: V2#1, Apr, 1994 - V2#5, 1994 ($1.95, limited series)

V2#1-5: 1-Covers X-Men #1-51. 2-Covers #52-122, Special #1,2, Giant-Size #1,2. 3-Byrne-c; covers #123-177, Annuals 3-7, Spec. Ed. #1. 4-Covers Uncanny X-Men #178-234, Annuals 8-12. 5-Covers #235-287, Annuals 13-15 ... 4.00

OFFICIAL SOUPY SALES COMIC (See Soupy Sales)

OFFICIAL TEEN TITANS INDEX, THE
Indep. Comics Group (Eclipse): Aug, 1985 - No. 5, 1986 ($1.50, lim. series)

1-5 ... 4.00

	GD 2.0	VG 4.0	FN 6.0	VF 8.0	VF/NM 9.0	NM- 9.2

OFFICIAL TRUE CRIME CASES (Formerly Sub-Mariner #23; All-True Crime Cases #26 on)
Marvel Comics (OCI): No. 24, Fall, 1947 - No. 25, Winter, 1947-48

	GD 2.0	VG 4.0	FN 6.0	VF 8.0	VF/NM 9.0	NM- 9.2
24(#1)-Burgos-a; Syd Shores-c	39	78	117	240	395	550
25-Syd Shores-c; Kurtzman's "Hey Look"	25	50	75	150	245	340

OF SUCH IS THE KINGDOM
George A. Pflaum: 1955 (15¢, 36 pgs.)

nn-Reprints from 1951 Treasure Chest	5	10	14	20	24	28

O.G. WHIZ (See Gold Key Spotlight #10)
Gold Key: 2/71 - No. 6, 5/72; No. 7, 5/78 - No. 11, 1/79 (No. 7: 52 pgs.)

1-John Stanley script	5	10	15	31	53	75
2-John Stanley script	4	8	12	23	37	50
3-6(1972)	3	6	9	17	26	35
7-11(1978-79)-Part-r: 9-Tubby issue	2	4	6	9	12	15

OH, BROTHER! (Teen Comedy)
Stanhall Publ.: Jan, 1953 - No. 5, Oct, 1953

1-By Bill Williams	20	40	60	120	195	270
2-5	15	30	45	83	124	165

OH MY GODDESS! (Manga)
Dark Horse Comics: Aug, 1994 - No. 112 ($2.50-$3.99, B&W)

1-6-Kosuke Fujishima-s/a in all						3.00
... PART II 2/95 - No. 9, 9/95 ($2.50, B&W, lim.series) #1-9						3.00
... PART III 11/95 - No. 11, 9/96 ($2.95, B&W, lim. series) #1-11						3.00
... PART IV 12/96 - No. 8, 7/97 ($2.95, B&W, lim. series) #1-8						3.00
... PART V 9/97 - No. 12, 8/98 ($2.95, B&W, lim. series)						
1,2,5,8: 5-Ninja Master pt. 1						3.00
3,4,6,7,10-12-($3.95, 48 pgs.) 10-Fallen Angel. 11-Play The Game						4.00
9-($3.50) "It's Lonely At The Top"						3.50
... PART VI 10/98 - No. 3, 3/99 ($3.50-$2.95, B&W, lim. series)						
1-($3.50)						3.50
2-6-($2.95)-6-Super Urd one-shot						3.00
... PART VII 5/99 - No. 8, 12/99 ($2.95, B&W, lim. series) #1-3						3.50
4-8-($3.50)						3.50
... PART VIII 1/00 - No. 6, 6/00 ($3.50, B&W, lim. series) #1-3,5,7						3.50
4-($2.95) "Hail To The Chief" begins						3.00
... PART IX 7/00 - No. 7, 1/01 ($3.50/$2.99) #1-4: 3-Queen Sayoko						3.50
5-7-($2.99)						3.00
... PART X 2/01 - No. 5, 6/01 ($3.50) #1-5						3.50
... PART XI 10/01 - No. 10, 3/02 ($3.50) #1,2,7,8						3.50
3-6,9-($2.99) Mystery Child						3.00
10-($3.99)						4.00
(Series adapts new numbering) 88-90-($3.50) Learning to Love						3.50
91-94,96-103,105,107-110: 91-94 ($2.99) Traveler. 96-98-The Phantom Racer						3.00
95,104,106-($3.50) 95-Traveler pt. 5						3.50
111,112-($3.99)						4.00

OH SUSANNA (TV)
Dell Publishing Co.: No. 1105, June-Aug, 1960 (Gale Storm)

Four Color 1105-Toth-a, photo-c	10	20	30	69	147	225

OKAY COMICS
United Features Syndicate: July, 1940

1-Captain & the Kids & Hawkshaw the Detective reprints						
	58	116	174	371	636	900

O.K. COMICS
Hit Publications: May, 1940 (ashcan)

nn-Ashcan comic, not distributed to newsstands, only for in house use. A CGC certified 8.0 copy sold in 2003 for $1,000.

O.K. COMICS
United Features Syndicate/Hit Publications: July, 1940 - No. 2, Oct, 1940

1-Little Giant (w/super powers), Phantom Knight, Sunset Smith, & The Teller Twins begin	87	174	261	553	952	1350
2 (Rare)-Origin Mister Mist by Chas. Quinlan	97	194	291	621	1061	1500

OKLAHOMA KID
Ajax/Farrell Publ.: June, 1957 - No. 4, 1958

1	11	22	33	62	86	110
2-4	7	14	21	37	46	55

OKLAHOMAN, THE
Dell Publishing Co.: No. 820, July, 1957

Four Color 820-Movie, photo-c	9	18	27	60	120	180

OKTANE
Dark Horse Comics: Aug, 1995 - Nov, 1995 ($2.50, color, limited series)

1-4-Gene Ha-a						4.00

OKTOBERFEST COMICS
Now & Then Publ.: Fall 1976 (75¢, Canadian, B&W, one-shot)

1-Dave Sim-s/a; Gene Day-a; 1st app. Uncle Hans & Natter P. Bombast; The Beavers sty; 1st Cap'n Riverrat, Sim-s/Day-a	3	6	9	16	23	30

OLD GLORY COMICS
DC Comics: 1941

nn - Ashcan comic, not distributed to newsstands, only for in-house use. Cover art is
Flash Comics #12 with interior being Action Comics #37 (no known sales)

OLD GUARD, THE (Inspired the 2020 Netflix movie)
Image Comics: Feb, 2017 - No. 5, Jun, 2017 ($3.99)

1-5-Greg Rucka-s/Leandro Fernández-a						4.00

OLD GUARD, THE: FORCE MULTIPLIED
Image Comics: Dec, 2019 - No. 5, Jul, 2020 ($3.99)

1-5-Greg Rucka-s/Leandro Fernández-a						4.00

OLD GUARD, THE: TALES THROUGH TIME
Image Comics: Apr, 2021 - No. 6, Sept, 2021 ($3.99)

1-6-Short stories by various creators: 1,6-Rucka-s/Fernández-a. 2-Bendis-s/Oeming-a						4.00

OLD HAUNTS
AWA Studios: Jun, 2020 - No. 5 ($3.99)

1-5-Ollie Masters & Rob Williams-s/Laurence Campbell-a						4.00

OLD IRONSIDES (Disney)
Dell Publishing Co.: No. 874, Jan, 1958

Four Color 874-Movie w/Johnny Tremain	8	16	24	51	96	140

OLD LADY HARLEY (See Harley Quinn #42)
DC Comics: Dec, 2018 - No. 5, Apr, 2019 ($3.99, limited series)

1-5-Tieri-s/Miranda-a/Conner-c; future Harley, Joker, Red Tool and Catwoman app.						4.00

OLD MAN HAWKEYE
Marvel Comics: Mar, 2018 - No. 12, Feb, 2019 ($3.99)

1-12-Sacks-s/Checchetto-a; takes place 5 years before the original Old Man Logan						4.00

OLD MAN LOGAN (Secret Wars tie-in)
Marvel Comics: Jul, 2015 - No. 5, Dec, 2015 ($4.99/$3.99, limited series)

1-($4.99) Bendis-s/Sorrentino-a; future Logan from Wolverine V3 #66; Emma Frost app.						5.00
2-5-($3.99) 2-Sabretooth app. 3-Apocalypse app. 5-X-Men app.						4.00

OLD MAN LOGAN (Follows Secret Wars)(Continues in Dead Man Logan)
Marvel Comics: Mar, 2016 - No. 50, Dec, 2018 ($4.99/$3.99)

1-($4.99) Lemire-s/Sorrentino-a; future Logan in current Marvel Universe						5.00
2-49-($3.99) 2-Amadeus Cho Hulk app. 4-Steve Rogers app. 7-Lady Deathstrike app. 14,15-Dracula app. 21-24-Past Lives. 25-30-Maestro app. 25-32-Deodato-a 31-35-Scarlet Samurai. 36-38,43-45-Bullseye app. 41,42-Kraven app.						4.00
50-($4.99) Brisson-s/Roberson & Edwards-a; Maestro app.						5.00
Annual 1 (1/18, $4.99) Frank Castle app.; Brisson-s/Di Meo-a/Shane Davis-c						5.00

OLD MAN QUILL
Marvel Comics: Apr, 2019 - No. 12, Feb, 2020 ($3.99)

1-12: 1-Sacks-s/Gill-a; Star-Lord with Guardians of the Galaxy 45+ years in the future. 6,11,12-Galactus app.						4.00

OLD YELLER (Disney, see Movie Comics, and Walt Disney Showcase #25)
Dell Publishing Co.: No. 869, Jan, 1958

Four Color 869-Movie, photo-c	6	12	18	42	73	115

OLIVER
Image Comics: Jan, 2019 - Present ($3.99)

1-4-Gary Whitta-s/Darick Robertson-a. 1-Covers by Robertson & Fabry						4.00

OLIVIA TWIST
Dark Horse Comics (Berger Books): Sept, 2018 - No. 4, Jan, 2019 ($4.99, limited series)

1-4-Darin Strauss & Adam Dalva-s/Emma Vieceli-a. 3-Tula Lotay-c. 4-Sana Takeda-c						5.00

OLYMPUS: REBIRTH
DC Comics: Oct, 2022 ($5.99, one-shot)

1-Hippolyta joins the Olympian gods; Conrad & Cloonan-s/Yarsky-a						6.00

OMAC (One Man Army; ...Corps. #4 on; also see Kamandi #59 & Warlord)
(See Cancelled Comic Cavalcade)
National Periodical Publications: Sept-Oct, 1974 - No. 8, Nov-Dec, 1975

1-Origin	5	10	15	34	60	85
2-8: 8-2 pg. Neal Adams ad	3	6	9	17	26	35
Jack Kirby's Omac: One Man Army Corps HC (2008, $24.99, d.j.) r/#1-8; Evanier intro.						25.00

NOTE: *Kirby* a-1-8p; c-1-7p. *Kubert* c-8.

OMAC (See DCU Brave New World)
DC Comics: Sept, 2006 - No. 8, Apr, 2007 ($2.99, limited series)

1-8: 1-Bruce Jones-s/Renato Guedes-a. 1-3-Firestorm & Cyborg app. 8-Superman app.						3.00

O.M.A.C. (DC New 52)
DC Comics: Nov, 2011 - No. 8, Jun, 2012 ($2.99)

1-8: 1-DiDio-s/Giffen-a/c; Dubbilex and Brother Eye app. 2-Max Lord & Sarge Steel app. 5-Crossover with Frankenstein, Agent of SHADE #5. 6-Kolins-a						3.00

OMAC: ONE MAN ARMY CORPS
DC Comics: 1991 - No. 4, 1991 ($3.95, B&W, mini-series, mature, 52 pgs.)

Book One - Four: John Byrne-c/a & scripts						5.00

OMAC PROJECT, THE
DC Comics: June, 2005 - No. 6, Nov, 2005 ($2.50, limited series)

1-6-Prelude to Infinite Crisis x-over; Rucka-s/Saiz-a						3.00
...: Infinite Crisis Special 1 (5/06, $4.99) Rucka-s/Saiz-a; follows destruction of satellite						5.00
TPB (2005, $14.99) r/#1-6, Countdown to Infinite Crisis, Wonder Woman #219						15.00

O'MALLEY AND THE ALLEY CATS
Gold Key: April, 1971 - No. 9, Jan, 1974 (Disney)

1	3	6	9	16	23	30
2-9	2	4	6	9	13	16

OMEGA ELITE
Blackthorne Publishing: 1987 ($1.25)

1-Starlin-c						4.00

OMEGA FLIGHT
Marvel Comics: Jun, 2007 - No. 5, Oct, 2007 ($2.99, limited series)

1-Oeming-s/Kolins-a; Wrecking Crew app.						4.00
1-Second printing with Sasquatch variant-c						3.00
2-5: 5-Beta Ray Bill app.						3.00
...: Alpha to Omega TPB ('07, $13.99) r/#1-5, USAgent story/Civil War: Choosing Sides						14.00

OMEGA MEN, THE (See Green Lantern #141)
DC Comics: Dec, 1982 - No. 38, May, 1986 ($1.00/$1.25/$1.50; Baxter paper)

1-Giffen-c/a	2	4	6	8	10	12
2,4-9,11-19,21-25,28-30,32,33,36,38: 2-Origin Broot. 5,9-2nd & 3rd app. Lobo (cameo, 2 pgs. each). 7-Origin The Citadel. 19-Lobo cameo. 30-Intro new Primus						4.00
3-1st app. Lobo (5 pgs.)(6/83); Lobo-c	5	10	15	35	63	90
3 (Facsimile Edition)(2023, $3.99) Reprints issue with original 1983 ads						4.00
10-1st full Lobo story	2	4	6	11	16	20

Old Lady Harley #1 © DC

Omega Men #6 © DC

100 Bullets #100 © Azzarello & Risso & DC

	GD	VG	FN	VF	VF/NM	NM-
	2.0	4.0	6.0	8.0	9.0	9.2

20: 20-2nd full Lobo story ... 5.00
26,27,31,34,35: 26,27-Alan Moore scripts. 31-Crisis x-over. 34,35-Teen Titans x-over ... 4.00
37-1st solo Lobo story (8 pg. back-up by Giffen) ... 6.00
Annual 1(11/84, 52 pgs.), 2(11/85) ... 5.00
NOTE: *Giffen* c/a-1-6p. *Morrow* a-24r. *Nino* c/a-16, 21; a-Annual 1i.

OMEGA MEN, THE
DC Comics: Dec, 2006 - No. 6, May, 2007 ($2.99 limited series)
1-6: 1-Superman, Wonder Girl, Green Lantern app.; Flint-a/Gabrych-s ... 3.00

OMEGA MEN, THE
DC Comics: Aug, 2015 - No. 12, Jul, 2016 ($2.99
1-12: 1-Tom King-s/Barnaby Bagenda-a; Kyle Rayner app. 4-Cypress-a ... 3.00

OMEGA THE UNKNOWN
Marvel Comics Group: March, 1976 - No. 10, Oct, 1977
1-1st app. Omega	3	6	9	21	33	45
2,3-(Regular 25¢ editions). 2-Hulk-c/story. 3-Electro-c/story.	2	4	6	9	12	15
2,3-(30¢-c variants, limited distribution)	5	10	15	30	50	70
4-10: 8-1st brief app. 2nd Foolkiller (Greg Salinger), 1 panel only. 9,10-(Reg. 30¢ editions). 9-1st full app. 2nd Foolkiller	1	3	4	6	8	10
9,10-(35¢-c variants, limited distribution)	7	14	21	48	89	130
... Classic TPB (2005, $29.99) r/#1-10						30.00

NOTE: *Kane* c(p)-3, 5, 8, 9. *Mooney* a-1-3, 4p, 5, 6p, 7, 8i, 9, 10.

OMEGA: THE UNKNOWN
Marvel Comics: Dec, 2007 - No. 10, Sept, 2008 ($2.99, limited series)
1-10-Jonathan Lethem-s/Farel Dalrymple-a ... 3.00

OMEN
Northstar Publishing: 1989 - No. 3, 1989 ($2.00 B&W, mature)
1-Tim Vigil-c/a in all	1	2	3	5	7	9
1, (2nd printing)						4.00
2,3						6.00

OMEN, THE
Chaos! Comics: May, 1998 - No. 5, Sept, 1998 ($2.95, limited series)
1-5: 1-Six covers, ...: Vexed (10/98, $2.95) Chaos! characters appear ... 4.00

OMNI MEN
Blackthorne Publishing: 1987 - No. 3, 1987 ($1.25)
1-3 ... 4.00
Graphic Novel (1989, $3.50) ... 5.00

ONCE & FUTURE
BOOM! Studios: Aug, 2019 - No. 30, Oct, 2022 ($3.99)
1-Kieron Gillen-s/Dan Mora-a in all	2	4	6	11	16	20
2	1	3	4	6	8	10
3-8						5.00
9-24,26-29: 9-12-Beowulf and Grendel app.						4.00
25,30: 25-($4.99) Bonus preview of Grim #1. 30-Last issue						5.00

ONCE UPON A TIME: OUT OF THE PAST (TV)
Marvel Comics: 2015 ($24.99, hardcover with dustjacket)
HC-Sequel to Shadow of the Queen HC; Bechko & Vazquez-s; Stacy Lee-c ... 25.00

ONCE UPON A TIME: SHADOW OF THE QUEEN (TV)
Marvel Comics: 2013 ($19.99, hardcover with dustjacket)
HC-Regina and the Huntsman; Bechko-s; art by Del Mundo, Lolos, Henderson, & Kaluta ... 20.00

ONE, THE
Marvel Comics (Epic Comics): July, 1985 - No. 6, Feb, 1986 (Limited series, mature)
1-6: Post nuclear holocaust super-hero. 2-Intro The Other ... 4.00

ONE-ARM SWORDSMAN, THE
Victory Prod./Lueng's Publ. #4 on: 1987 - No. 12, 1990 ($2.75/$1.80, 52 pgs.)
1-3 ($2.75) ... 5.00
4-12: 4-6-$1.80-c. 7-12-$2.00-c ... 5.00

ONE-HIT WONDER
Image Comics: Feb, 2014 - No. 5, Apr, 2015 ($3.50)
1-5: 1-4-Sapolsky-s/Olivetti-a/c. 5-Thompson & Fiorelli-a/Roux-a ... 3.50

ONE HUNDRED AND ONE DALMATIANS (Disney, see Cartoon Tales, Movie Comics, and Walt Disney Showcase #9, 51)
Dell Publishing Co.: No. 1183, Mar, 1961
Four Color 1183-Movie	12	24	36	79	170	260

101 DALMATIONS (Movie)
Disney Comics: 1991 (52 pgs., graphic novel)

---

nn-($4.95, direct sales)-r/movie adaptation & more ... 1 ... 2 ... 3 ... 5 ... 6 ... 8
1-($2.95, newsstand edition) ... 5.00

101 WAYS TO END THE CLONE SAGA (See Spider-Man)
Marvel Comics: Jan, 1997 ($2.50, one-shot)
1 ... 4.00

100 BULLETS
DC Comics (Vertigo): Aug, 1999 - No. 100, Jun, 2009 ($2.50/$2.75/$2.99)
1-Azzarello-s/Risso-a/Dave Johnson-c	4	8	12	23	37	50
2-5						6.00
6-49,51-61: 26-Series summary; art by various. 45-Preview of Losers						4.00
50-($3.50) History of the Trust						5.00
62-71: 62-Begin $2.75-c. 64-Preview of Loveless						3.00
72-99: 72-Begin $2.99-c						3.00
100-($4.99) Final issue	1	3	4	6	8	10
...#1/Crime Line Sampler Flip-Book (9/09, 1.00) r/#1 with previews of upcoming GNs						3.00
... A Foregone Tomorrow TPB (2002, $17.95) r/#20-30						18.00
... Decayed TPB (2006, $14.99) r/#68-75; Darwyn Cooke intro.						15.00
... First Shot, Last Call TPB (2000, $9.95) r/#1-5, Vertigo Winter's Edge #3						10.00
... Hang Up on the Hang Low TPB (2001, $9.95) r/#15-19; Jim Lee intro.						10.00
... Once Upon a Crime TPB (2007, $12.99) r/#76-83						13.00
... Samurai TPB (2003, $12.95) r/#43-49						13.00
... Six Feet Under the Gun TPB (2003, $12.95) r/#37-42						13.00
... Split Second Chance TPB (2001, $14.95) r/#6-14						15.00
... Strychnine Lives TPB (2006, $14.99) r/#59-67; Manuel Ramos intro.						15.00
... The Counterfifth Detective TPB (2003, $12.95) r/#31-36						13.00
... The Hard Way TPB (2005, $14.99) r/#50-58						15.00
... Wilt TPB (2009, $19.99) r/#89-100; Azzarello intro.						20.00

100 BULLETS: BROTHER LONO
DC Comics (Vertigo): Aug, 2013 - No. 8, Apr, 2014 ($3.99/$2.99, limited series)
1-($3.99) Azzarello-s/Risso-a/Dave Johnson-c ... 4.00
2-8-($2.99) Azzarello-s/Risso-a/Dave Johnson-c on all ... 3.00

100 GREATEST MARVELS OF ALL TIME
Marvel Comics: Dec, 2001 ($7.50/$3.50, limited series)
1-5-Reprints top #6-#25 stories voted by poll for Marvel's 40th ann. ... 7.50
6-($3.50) Reprints X-Men (2nd series) #1 ... 4.00
7-($3.50) #4 on-c) Reprints Giant-Size X-Men #1 ... 4.00
8-($3.50) #3 on-c) Reprints (Uncanny) X-Men #137 (Death of Jean Grey) ... 4.00
9-($3.50) #2 on-c) Reprints Fantastic Four #1 ... 4.00
10-($3.50) #1 on-c) Reprints Amazing Fantasy #15 (1st app. Spider-Man) ... 4.00

100 PAGES OF COMICS
Dell Publishing Co.: 1937 (Stiff covers, square binding)
101(Found on back cover)-Alley Oop, Wash Tubbs, Capt. Easy, Og Son of Fire, Apple Mary, Tom Mix, Dan Dunn, Tailspin Tommy, Doctor Doom		174	348	522	1114	1907	2700

100 PAGE SUPER SPECTACULAR (See DC 100 Page Super Spectacular)

100%
DC Comics (Vertigo): Aug, 2002 - No. 5, July, 2003 ($5.95, B&W, limited series)
1-5-Paul Pope-s/a ... 6.00
HC (2009, $39.99, dustjacket) r/#1-5; sketch pages and background info ... 40.00
TPB (2005, $24.99) r/#1-5; sketch pages and background info ... 25.00
TPB (2009, $29.99) r/#1-5; sketch pages and background info ... 30.00

100% TRUE?
DC Comics (Paradox Press): Summer 1996 - No. 2 ($4.95, B&W)
1,2-Reprints stories from various Paradox Press books. ... 5.00

$1,000,000 DUCK (See Walt Disney Showcase #5)

ONE MILLION YEARS AGO (Tor #2 on)
St. John Publishing Co.: Sept, 1953
1-Origin & 1st app. Tor; Kubert-c/a; Kubert photo inside front cover		27	54	81	158	259	360

ONE MONTH TO LIVE ("Heroic Age: ..." in indicia)
Marvel Comics: Nov, 2010 - No. 5, Nov, 2010 ($2.99, weekly limited series)
1-5-Remender-s; Spider-Man and the Fantastic Four app. ... 3.00

ONES, THE
Dark Horse Comics: Nov, 2022 - No. 4, Feb, 2023 ($4.99, limited series)
1-4-Brian Michael Bendis-s/Jacob Edgar-a ... 5.00

ONE SHOT (See Four Color...)

ONE-STAR SQUADRON

	GD	VG	FN	VF	VF/NM	NM-
	2.0	4.0	6.0	8.0	9.0	9.2

DC Comics: Feb, 2022 - No. 6, Jul, 2022 ($3.99, limited series)
1-6-Mark Russell-s/Steve Lieber-a; Red Tornado, Power Girl, The Heckler app. ... 4.00

1001 HOURS OF FUN
Dell Publishing Co.: No. 13, 1943
Large Feature Comic 13 (nn)-Puzzles & games; by A.W. Nugent. This book was bound as #13
w/Large Feature Comics in publisher's files ... 39 | 78 | 117 | 240 | 395 | 550

ONE TRICK RIP OFF, THE (See Dark Horse Presents)

ONI (Adaption of video game)
Dark Horse Comics: Feb, 2001 - No. 3, Apr, 2001 ($2.99, limited series)
1-3-Sunny Lee-a(p) ... 3.00

ONIBA: SWORDS OF THE DEMON
Aspen MLT: No. 0, Oct, 2015 ($2.50)
0-Hernandez-s/Pantalena-a; two covers ... 3.00

ONI DOUBLE FEATURE (See Clerks: The Comic Book and Jay & Silent Bob)
Oni Press: Jan, 1998 - No. 13, Sept, 1999 ($2.95, B&W)
1-Jay & Silent Bob; Kevin Smith-s/Matt Wagner-a ... 1 | 3 | 4 | 6 | 8 | 10
1-2nd printing ... 3.00
2-11,13: 2,3-Paul Pope-s/a. 3,4-Nixey-s/a. 4,5-Sienkewicz-s/a. 6,7-Gaiman-s. 9-Bagge-c.
13-All Paul Dini-s; Jingle Belle ... 3.00
12-Jay & Silent Bob as Bluntman & Chronic; Smith-s/Allred-a ... 5.00

ONI PRESS COLOR SPECIAL
Oni Press: Jun, 2001; Jul, 2002 ($5.95, annual)
...2001-Oeming "Who Killed Madman?" cover; stories & art by various ... 6.00
...2002-Allred wraparound-c; stories & art by various ... 6.00

ONSLAUGHT: EPILOGUE
Marvel Comics: Feb, 1997 ($2.95, one-shot)
1-Hama-s/Green-a; Xavier-c; Bastion-app. ... 4.00

ONSLAUGHT: MARVEL
Marvel Comics: Oct, 1996 ($3.95, one-shot)
1-Conclusion to Onslaught x-over; wraparound-c ... 6.00

ONSLAUGHT REBORN
Marvel Comics: Jan, 2007 - No. 5, Feb, 2008 ($2.99, limited series)
1-5-Loeb-s/Liefeld-a; female Bucky app. 2-Variant-c by Joe Madureira. 3-McGuiness var-c.
4-Campbell var-c. 5-Bianchi var-c; female Bucky goes to regular Marvel Universe ... 3.00
1-Variant-c by Michael Turner ... 4.00
HC (2008, $19.99) r/#1-5; sketch pages; foreword by Liefeld ... 20.00

ONSLAUGHT UNLEASHED
Marvel Comics: Apr, 2011 - No. 4, Jul, 2011 ($3.99, limited series)
1-4-McKeever-s/Andrade-a/Ramos-c; Secret Avengers & Young Allies app. ... 4.00

ONSLAUGHT: X-MEN
Marvel Comics: Aug, 1996 ($3.95, one-shot)
1-Waid & Lobdell script; Fantastic Four & Avengers app.; Xavier as Onslaught
| | 1 | 3 | 4 | 6 | 8 | 10
1-Variant-c | | 3 | 6 | 8 | 11 | 13 | 15
1-Gold Edition | | 6 | 12 | 18 | 38 | 69 | 100

ON STAGE
Dell Publishing Co.: No. 1336, Apr-June, 1962
Four Color 1336-Not by Leonard Starr ... 5 | 10 | 15 | 34 | 60 | 85

ON THE DOUBLE (Movie)
Dell Publishing Co.: No. 1232, Sept-Nov, 1961
Four Color 1232 ... 6 | 12 | 18 | 37 | 66 | 95

ON THE ROAD TO PERDITION (Movie)
DC Comics (Paradox Press): 2003 - Book 3, 2004 ($7.95, 8"x5 1/2", B&W, limited series)
...: Oasis, Book 1-Max Allan Collins-a/José Luis García-López-a/David Beck-c ... 8.00
...: Sanctuary, Book 2-Max Allan Collins-s/Steve Lieber-a/José Luis García-López-c ... 8.00
...: Detour, Book 3-Max Allan Collins-s/José Luis García-López-a/Steve Lieber-c/a(i) ... 8.00
Road to Perdition 2: On the Road (2004, $14.95) r/series; Collins intro. ... 15.00

ON THE ROAD WITH ANDRAE CROUCH
Spire Christian Comics (Fleming H. Revell): 1973, 1974 (39¢)
nn-1973 Edition ... 2 | 4 | 6 | 13 | 18 | 22
nn-1974 Edition ... 2 | 4 | 6 | 9 | 13 | 16

ON THE SCENE PRESENTS:...
Warren Publishing Co.: Oct, 1966 - No. 2, 1967 (B&W magazine, two #1 issues)
#1 "Super Heroes" (68 pgs.) Batman 1966 movie photo-c/s; has articles/photos/comic art from
serials on Superman, Flash Gordon, Capt. America, Capt. Marvel and The Phantom
| | 10 | 15 | 33 | 57 | 80
#1 "Freak Out, USA" (Fall/1966, 60 pgs.) (lower print run) articles on musicians like Zappa,
Jefferson Airplane, etc. ... 5 | 10 | 15 | 34 | 60 | 85
#2 "Freak Out, USA" (2/67, 52 pgs.) Beatles, Country Joe, Doors/Jim Morrison, Bee Gees
| | 5 | 10 | 15 | 34 | 60 | 85

ON THE SPOT (Pretty Boy Floyd...)
Fawcett Publications: Fall, 1948
nn-Pretty Boy Floyd photo on-c; bondage-c ... 48 | 96 | 144 | 302 | 514 | 725

ONYX
IDW Publishing: Jul, 2015 - No. 4, Oct, 2015 ($3.99)
1-4-Gabriel Rodriguez & Chris Ryall-s&a. 1-Three covers ... 4.00

ONYX OVERLORD
Marvel Comics (Epic): Oct, 1992 - No. 4, Jan, 1993 ($2.75, mini-series)
1-4: Moebius scripts ... 4.00

OPEN SPACE
Marvel Comics: Mid-Dec, 1989 - No. 4, Aug, 1990 ($4.95, bi-monthly, 68 pgs.)
1-4: 1-Bill Wray-a; Freas-c ... 5.00
0-(1999) Wizard supplement; unpubl. early Alex Ross-a; new Ross-c ... 4.00

OPERATION BIKINI (See Movie Classics)

OPERATION: BROKEN WINGS, 1936
BOOM! Studios: Nov, 2011 - No. 3, Jan, 2012 ($3.99, limited series)
1-3-Hanna-s/Hairsine-a; English translation of French comic ... 4.00

OPERATION BUCHAREST (See The Crusaders)

OPERATION CROSSBOW (See Movie Classics)

OPERATION: KNIGHTSTRIKE (See Knightstrike)
Image Comics (Extreme Studios): May, 1995 - No.3, July, 1995 ($2.50)
1-3 ... 4.00

OPERATION PERIL
American Comics Group (Michel Publ.): Oct-Nov, 1950 - No. 16, Apr-May, 1953 (#1-5: 52 pgs.)
1-Time Travelers, Danny Danger (by Leonard Starr) & Typhoon Tyler
(by Ogden Whitney) begin | 52 | 104 | 156 | 328 | 552 | 775
2-War-c | 30 | 60 | 90 | 177 | 289 | 400
3-War-c; horror story | 29 | 58 | 87 | 172 | 281 | 390
4,5-Sci/fi-c/story | 58 | 116 | 174 | 371 | 636 | 900
6-10: 6,8,9,10-Sci/fi-c. 6-Tank vs. T-Rex-c. 7-Sabretooth-c
| 25 | 50 | 75 | 150 | 245 | 340
11,12-War-c; last Time Travelers | 16 | 32 | 48 | 92 | 144 | 195
13-16: All war format | 13 | 26 | 39 | 74 | 105 | 135
NOTE: *Starr* a-2, 5. *Whitney* a-1, 2, 5-10, 12; c-1, 3, 5, 8, 9.

OPERATION: S.I.N.
Marvel Comics: Mar, 2015 - No. 5, Jul, 2015 ($3.99, limited series)
1-5-Peggy Carter & Howard Stark in 1952; Kathryn Immonen-s/Rich Ellis-a ... 4.00

OPERATION: STORMBREAKER
Acclaim Comics (Valiant Heroes): Aug, 1997 ($3.95, one-shot)
1-Waid/Augustyn-s, Braithwaite-a; Nazi-c ... 5.00

OPTIC NERVE
Drawn and Quarterly: Apr, 1995 - Present ($2.95-$3.95, bi-annual)
1-7: Adrian Tomine-c/a/scripts in all ... 4.00
8-11: 8-($3.50). 9-11-($3.95) ... 5.00
12,13-($5.95) Half front-c. 12-Amber Sweet story ... 6.00
14-($6.95) Half front-c ... 7.00
32 Stories-($9.95, trade paperback)-r/Optic Nerve mini-comics ... 10.00
32 Stories-($29.95, hardcover)-r/Optic Nerve mini-comics; signed & numbered ... 30.00

OPTIMUS PRIME (Transformers)
IDW Publishing: Nov, 2016 - No. 18, Oct, 2018 ($3.99)
1-Follows Revolution x-over; Barber-s/Zama-a; multiple covers
| | 1 | 2 | 3 | 5 | 6 | 8
2-25-Multiple covers on each. 2,3-Barber-s/Zama-a. 4-Milne-a ... 4.00
Annual 2018 (2/18, $7.99) Barber-s/Tramontano & Griffith-a ... 8.00
... First Strike 1 (9/17, $3.99) Barber-s/Guidi & Wycough-a; part of Hasbro x-over ... 4.00

ORACLE: THE CURE
DC Comics: May, 2009 - No. 3, Jul, 2009 ($2.99, limited series)
1-3-Guillem March-c; Calculator app. ... 3.00
TPB (2010, $17.99) r/#1-3 and Birds of Prey #126,127 ... 18.00

ORAL ROBERTS' TRUE STORIES (Junior Partners #120 on)
TelePix Publ. (Oral Roberts' Evangelistic Assoc./Healing Waters): 1956 (no month) - No.
119, 7/59 (15¢)(No. 120: 25¢)
V1#1(1956)-(Not code approved)- "The Miracle Touch"
| 20 | 40 | 60 | 120 | 195 | 270
102-(Only issue approved by code, 10/56) "Now I See"
| 14 | 28 | 42 | 78 | 112 | 145
103-119: 115-(114 on inside) | 10 | 20 | 30 | 56 | 79 | 95
NOTE: Also see Happiness & Healing For You.

ORANGE BIRD, THE
Walt Disney Educational Media Co.: No date (1980) (36 pgs.; in color; slick cover)
nn-Included with educational kit on foods, ...in Nutrition Adventures nn (1980)
...and the Nutrition Know-How Revue nn (1983) ... 4.00

ORB (Magazine)
Orb Publishing: 1974 - No. 6, Mar/Apr 1976 (B&W/color)
1-1st app. Northern Light & Kadaver, both series begin
| 5 | 10 | 15 | 30 | 50 | 70
2,3 (72 pgs.) | 3 | 6 | 9 | 16 | 23 | 30
4-6 (60 pgs.) | 4,5-origin Northern Light | 2 | 4 | 6 | 10 | 14 | 18
NOTE: *Allison* a-1-3. *Gene Day* a-1-6. *P. Hsu* a-4-6. *Steacy* s/a-3,4.

ORBIT
Eclipse Books: 1990 - No. 3, 1990 ($4.95, 52 pgs., squarebound)
1-3: Reprints from Isaac Asimov's Science Fiction Magazine; 1-Dave Stevens-c, Bolton-a.
3-Bolton-c/a, Yeates-a ... 5.00

ORBITER
DC Comics (Vertigo): 2003 ($24.95, hardcover with dust jacket)
HC-Warren Ellis-s/Colleen Doran-a ... 25.00
SC-(2004, $17.95) Warren Ellis-s/Colleen Doran-a ... 18.00

ORCHID
Dark Horse Comics: Oct, 2011 - No. 12, Jan, 2013 ($1.00/$3.50)
1-Tom Morello-s/Scott Hepburn-a; covers by Carnevale & Fairey ... 3.00
2-12-($3.50) Carnevale-c ... 3.50

ORCS!
BOOM! Studios (kaboom!): Feb, 2021 - No. 6, Jul, 2021 ($4.99)
1-6-Christine Larsen-s/a ... 5.00

ORCS IN SPACE (Issues #9-on released digitally)
Oni Press: Apr, 2021 - No. 8, Feb, 2022 ($6.99/$4.99)
#1 & #2: 2 in 1 ($6.99) Justin Roiland co-writer/Vigneault-a ... 7.00
3-8-($3.99) ... 4.00

ORCS!: THE CURSE

Onslaught Reborn #5 © MAR

Orcs! #1 © Christine Larsen

Origin II #5 © MAR

	GD	VG	FN	VF	VF/NM	NM-
	2.0	4.0	6.0	8.0	9.0	9.2

BOOM! Studios (kaboom!): Jun, 2022 - No. 4, Nov, 2022 ($5.99, limited series)

1-4-Christine Larsen-s/a — 6.00

ORCS!: THE GIFT
BOOM! Studios (kaboom!): Nov, 2023 - No. 4 ($3.99, limited series)

1-3-Christine Larsen-s/a — 6.00

ORDER, THE (cont'd from Defenders V2#12)
Marvel Comics: Apr, 2002 - No. 6, Sept, 2002 ($2.25, limited series)

1-6: 1-Haley-a/Duffy & Busiek-s. 3-Avengers-c/app. 4-Jurgens-a — 3.00

ORDER, THE (The Initiative following Civil War)
Marvel Comics: Sept, 2007 - No. 10, Jun, 2008 ($2.99)

1-10-California's Initiative team; Fraction/Kitson-a/c — 3.00
... Vol. 1: The Next Right Thing TPB (2008, $14.99) r/#1-7 — 15.00

ORDER & OUTRAGE
Dark Horse Comics: Mar, 2023 - No. 4, Aug, 2023 ($4.99, limited series)

1-4-Jim Starlin-s/a; Rags Morales-a/c — 5.00

ORDINARY GODS
Image Comics: Jul, 2021 - No. 12, May, 2023 ($3.99)

1-12: 1-8-Higgins-s/Watanabe-a. 9-12-Daniel HDR-a — 4.00

ORIENTAL HEROES
Jademan Comics: Aug, 1988 - No. 55, Feb, 1993 ($1.50/$1.95, 68 pgs.)

1,55 — 5.00
2-54 — 4.00

ORIGINAL ADVENTURES OF CHOLLY & FLYTRAP, THE
Image Comics: Feb, 2006 - No. 2, June, 2006 ($5.99, limited series)

1,2-Arthur Suydam-s/a; interview with Suydam and art pages — 6.00

ORIGINAL ASTRO BOY, THE
Now Comics: Sept, 1987 - No. 20, Jun, 1989 ($1.50/$1.75)

1-All have Ken Steacy painted-c/a	1	3	4	6	8	10
2-20						5.00

ORIGINAL BLACK CAT, THE
Recollections: Oct. 6, 1988 - No. 9, 1992 ($2.00, limited series)

1-9: Elias-r; 1-Bondage-c. 2-Murphy Anderson-c — 5.00

ORIGINAL DICK TRACY, THE
Gladstone Publishing: Sept, 1990 - No. 5, 1991 ($1.95, bi-monthly, 68pgs.)

1-5: 1-Vs. Pruneface. 2-& the Evil influence; begin $2.00-c — 5.00
NOTE: #1 reprints strips 7/16/43 - 9/30/43. #2 reprints strips 12/1/46 - 2/2/47. #3 reprints 8/31/46 - 11/14/46. #4 reprints 9/17/45 - 12/23/45. #5 reprints 6/10/46 - 8/28/46.

ORIGINAL DOCTOR SOLAR, MAN OF THE ATOM, THE
Valiant: Apr, 1995 ($2.95, one-shot)

1-Reprints Doctor Solar, Man of the Atom #1,5; Bob Fugitani-r; Paul Smith-c; afterword by Seaborn Adamson — 4.00

ORIGINAL E-MAN AND MICHAEL MAUSER, THE
First Comics: Oct, 1985 - No. 7, April, 1986 ($1.75/$2.00, Baxter paper)

1-6: 1-Has r-/Charlton's E-Man, Vengeance Squad. 2-Shows #4 in indicia by mistake — 4.00
7-($2.00, 44 pgs.)-Staton-a — 5.00

ORIGINAL GHOST RIDER, THE
Marvel Comics: July, 1992 - No. 20, Feb, 1994 ($1.75)

1-20: 1-7-r/Marvel Spotlight #5-11 by Ploog w/new-c. 3-New Phantom Rider (former Night Rider) back-ups begin by Ayers. 4-Quesada-c (p). 8-Ploog-c. 8,9-r/Ghost Rider #1,2. 10-r/Marvel Spotlight #12. 11-18,20-r/Ghost Rider #3-12. 19-r/Marvel Two-in-One #8 — 4.00

ORIGINAL GHOST RIDER RIDES AGAIN, THE
Marvel Comics: July, 1991 - No. 7, Jan, 1992 ($1.50, limited series, 52 pgs.)

1-7: 1-r/Ghost Rider #68(origin),69 w/covers. 2- ?: R/ G.R. #70-81 w/covers — 5.00

ORIGINAL MAGNUS ROBOT FIGHTER, THE
Valiant: Apr, 1995 ($2.95, one-shot)

1-Reprints Magnus, Robot Fighter 4000 #2; Russ Manning-r; Rick Leonardi-c; afterword by Seaborn Adamson — 5.00

ORIGINAL MARVEL ZOMBIES, THE: MARVEL TALES
Marvel Comics: Dec, 2020 ($7.99, one-shot)

1-Reprints Ultimate Fantastic Four #21-23 and Marvel Zombies #1; Macchio foreword — 8.00

ORIGINAL NEXUS GRAPHIC NOVEL (See First Comics Graphic Novel #19)

ORIGINALS, THE
DC Comics (Vertigo): 2004 ($24.95/$17.99, B&W graphic novel)

HC (2004, $24.95) Dave Gibbons-s/a — 25.00
SC (2005, $17.99) — 18.00

ORIGINAL SHIELD, THE
Archie Enterprises, Inc.: Apr, 1984 - No. 4, Oct, 1984

1-4: 1,2-Origin Shield; Ayers p-1-4, Nebres c-1,2 — 5.00

ORIGINAL SIN
Marvel Comics: No. 0, Jun, 2014 - No. 8, Nov, 2014 ($4.99/$3.99, limited series)

0-($4.99) Origin of the Watcher re-told; Nova (Sam Alexander) app.; Waid-s/Cheung-a — 5.00
1-($4.99) The Watcher is murdered; Aaron-s/Deodato-a — 5.00
2-7-($3.99) 5-Nick Fury's origin. 7-Thor loses use of his hammer — 4.00
8-($4.99) Murderer revealed; new Watcher begins — 5.00
Annual 1 (12/14, $4.99) Fury and Howard Stark in 1958; Cisic-a/Tedesco-c — 5.00
#3.1 - #3.4 (Hulk vs. Iron Man) ($3.99, 8/14 - 10/14) Flashback to the Gamma bomb — 4.00
#5.1 - #5.5 (Thor & Loki: The Tenth Realm) ($3.99, 9/14 - 11/14) Angela revealed as Thor's sister; Aaron & Ewing-s — 4.00

ORIGINAL SINS (Secrets from the Watcher's Eyes unleashed in Original Sin #3)
Marvel Comics: Aug, 2014 - No. 5, Oct, 2014 ($3.99, limited series)

1-5-Short stories; Young Avengers in all issue; The Hood apps. 1-Deathlok prelude. 5-Secret of Dum Dum Dugan — 4.00

ORIGINAL SWAMP THING SAGA, THE (See DC Special Series #2, 14, 17, 20)

ORIGINAL TUROK, SON OF STONE, THE
Valiant: Apr, 1995 - No. 2, May, 1995 ($2.95, limited series)

1,2: 1-Reprints Turok, Son of Stone #24,25,42; Alberto Gioletti-r; Rags Morales-c; afterword by Seaborn Adamson. 2-Reprints Turok, Son of Stone #24,33; Gioletti-r; McKone-c — 4.00

ORIGINAL X-MEN
Marvel Comics: Feb, 2024 ($5.99, one-shot)

1-Gage-s/Land-a; the original teen team vs. Onslaught — 6.00

ORIGIN OF GALACTUS (See Fantastic Four #48-50)
Marvel Comics: Feb, 1996 ($2.50, one-shot)

1-Lee & Kirby reprints w/pin-ups	1	3	4	6	8	10

ORIGIN OF THE DEFIANT UNIVERSE, THE
Defiant Comics: Feb, 1994 ($1.50, 20 pgs., one-shot)

1-David Lapham, Adam Pollina & Alan Weiss-a; Weiss-c — 5.00
NOTE: The comic was originally published as Defiant Genesis and was distributed at the 1994 Philadelphia ComicCon.

ORIGINS
BOOM! Studios: Nov, 2020 - No. 6, Apr, 2021 ($3.99, limited series)

1-6-Clay McLeod Chapman-s/Jakub Rebelka-a — 4.00

ORIGINS OF MARVEL COMICS (Also see Fireside Book Series)
Marvel Comics: July, 2010 ($3.99, one-shot)

1-Single page origins of prominent Marvel characters; text and art by various — 4.00
...: Marvel Tales 1 (2/23, $7.99) Reprints Fantastic Four #1, Amazing Fantasy #15, X-Men #1 and Avengers #1; intro by Ralph Macchio — 8.00
...: X-Men (11/10, $3.99) single page origins of X-Men and other mutants; s/a-various — 4.00

ORIGIN II (Sequel to Wolverine: The Origin)
Marvel Comics: Feb, 2014 - No. 5, Jun, 2014 ($4.99/$3.99, limited series)

1-($4.99) Gillen-s/Adam Kubert-a/c; acetate overlay on cover; set in 1907 — 5.00
2-5-($3.99) Sabretooth app. — 4.00

ORION (Manga)
Dark Horse Comics: Sept, 1992 - No. 6, July, 1993 ($2.95/$3.95, B&W, bimonthly, lim. series)

1-6: 1,2,6-Squarebound- 1-Masamune Shirow-c/a/s in all — 4.00

ORION (See New Gods)
DC Comics: June, 2000 - No. 25, June, 2002 ($2.50)

1-14-Simonson-s/a. 3-Back-up story w/Miller-a. 4-Gibbons-a back-up. 7-Chaykin back-up. 8-Loeb/Liefeld back-up. 10-A. Adams back-up-a 12-Jim Lee back-up-a. 13-JLA/c/app.; Byrne-a — 3.00
15-($3.95) Black Racer app.; back-up story w/J.P. Leon-a — 4.00
16-24-Simonson-s/a. 19-Joker: Last Laugh x-over — 3.00
25-($3.95) Last issue; Mister Miracle-c/app. — 4.00
The Gates of Apocalypse (2001, $12.95, TPB) r/#1-5 & various short-s — 13.00

ORORO: BEFORE THE STORM (Storm from X-Men)
Marvel Comics: Aug, 2005 - No. 4, Nov, 2005 ($2.99, limited series)

1-4-Barberi-a/Sumerak-s; young Storm in Egypt — 3.00
... Digest (2006, $6.99) r/#1-4 — 7.00

ORPHAN AGE
AfterShock Comics: Apr, 2019 - No. 5, Aug, 2019 ($3.99)

	GD 2.0	VG 4.0	FN 6.0	VF 8.0	VF/NM 9.0	NM- 9.2

1-5-Ted Anderson-s/Nuno Plati-a ... 4.00

ORPHAN AND THE FIVE BEASTS
Dark Horse Comics: Mar, 2021 - No. 4 ($3.99, limited series)

1-4-James Stokoe-s/a/c ... 4.00

ORPHAN BLACK (Based on the BBC TV show)
IDW Publishing: Feb, 2015 - No. 5, Jun, 2015 ($3.99)

1-6: Multiple covers on all. 1-Kudranski-a; spotlight on Sarah. 2-Spotlight on Helena.
  3-Alison. 4-Cosima. 5-Rachel ... 4.00
... #1: IDW's Greatest Hits (6/18, $1.00) r/#1 ... 3.00

ORPHAN BLACK: CRAZY SCIENCE
IDW Publishing: Jun, 2018 ($3.99, unfinished limited series)

1-Heli Kennedy-s/Fico Ossio-a; 3 covers ... 4.00

ORPHAN BLACK: DEVIATIONS
IDW Publishing: Mar, 2017 - No. 6, Aug, 2017 ($4.99/$3.99)

1-($4.99) Kennedy-s/Nichols-a; what if Beth wasn't hit by the train; multiple covers ... 5.00
2-6-($3.99) Kennedy-s/Nichols-a ... 4.00

ORPHAN BLACK: HELSINKI
IDW Publishing: Nov, 2015 - No. 5, Mar, 2016 ($3.99)

1-5: Multiple covers on all. 1-Alan Quah-a ... 4.00

ORVILLE, THE (Based on the 2017 sci-fi TV show)
Dark Horse Comics: Jul, 2019 - No. 4, Oct, 2019 ($3.99, limited series)

1-4: 1,2-New Beginnings; Goodman-s/Cabeza-a. 3,4-The Word of Avis; the Krill app. ... 4.00

ORVILLE, THE (Based on the 2017 sci-fi TV show)
Dark Horse Comics: Sept, 2020 - No. 4, Dec, 2020 ($3.99, limited series)

1-4: 1,2-Launch Day; Goodman-s/Cabeza-a; the Krill app. 3,4-Heroes ... 4.00

ORVILLE, THE: ARTIFACTS
Dark Horse Comics: Oct, 2021 - No. 2, Nov, 2021 ($3.99, limited series)

1,2-Goodman-s/Cabeza-a ... 4.00

ORVILLE, THE: DIGRESSIONS
Dark Horse Comics: May, 2021 - No. 2, Jun, 2021 ($3.99, limited series)

1,2-Goodman-s/Cabeza-a; takes place in Kelly Grayson's alternate timeline ... 4.00

OSBORN (Green Goblin)
Marvel Comics: Jan, 2011 - No. 5, Jun, 2011 ($3.99, limited series)

1-5-Deconnick-s/Rios-a/Oliver-c ... 4.00

OSBORN JOURNALS (See Spider-Man titles)
Marvel Comics: Feb, 1997 ($2.95, one-shot)

1-Hotz-c/a ... 4.00

OSCAR COMICS (Formerly Funny Tunes; Awful...#11 & 12) (Also see Cindy Comics)
Marvel Comics: No. 24, Spring, 1947 - No. 10, Apr, 1949; No. 13, Oct, 1949

24(#1, Spring, 1947)	34	68	102	204	332	460
25(#2, Sum, 1947)-Wolverton-a plus Kurtzman's "Hey Look"						
	36	72	108	214	347	480
26(#3)-Same as regular #3 except #26 was printed over in black ink with #3 appearing on-c below the over print	24	48	72	142	234	325
3-9,13: 8-Margie app.	24	48	72	142	234	325
10-Kurtzman's "Hey Look"	25	50	75	150	245	340

OSWALD THE RABBIT (Also see New Fun Comics #1)
Dell Publishing Co.: No. 21, 1943 - No. 1268, 12-2/61-62 (Walter Lantz)

Four Color 21(1943)	46	92	138	359	805	1250
Four Color 39(1943)	29	58	87	209	467	725
Four Color 67(1944)	16	32	48	112	249	385
Four Color 102(1946)-Kelly-a, 1 pg.	15	30	45	100	220	340
Four Color 143,183	9	18	27	59	117	175
Four Color 225,273	7	14	21	46	86	125
Four Color 315,388	6	12	18	40	73	105
Four Color 458,507,549,593	5	10	15	35	63	90
Four Color 623,697,792,894,979,1268	5	10	15	33	57	80

OSWALD THE RABBIT (See The Funnies, March of Comics #7, 38, 53, 67, 81, 95, 111, 126, 141, 156, 171, 186, New Funnies & Super Book #9)

OTHER DEAD, THE
IDW Publishing: Sept, 2013 - No. 6, Feb, 2014 ($3.99)

1-6-Zombie animals; Ortega-s/Mui-a. 1-Variant-c by Dorman. 2-6-Pres. Obama app. ... 4.00

OTHER HISTORY OF THE DC UNIVERSE, THE
DC Comics (Black Label): Jan, 2021 - No. 5, Sept, 2021 ($6.99, 10-3/4" x 8-1/2", lim. series)

1-5-Ridley-s/Camuncoli & Cucchi-a; two covers by Camuncoli & Jamal Campbell. 1-Black Lightning origin & history. 2-Mal Duncan & Bumblebee. 3-Katana. 4-Renee Montoya ... 7.00

OTHER SIDE, THE
DC Comics (Vertigo): Dec, 2006 - No. 5, Apr, 2007 ($2.99, limited series)

1-5-Soldiers from both sides of the Vietnam War; Aaron-s/Stewart-a/c ... 3.00
TPB (2007, $12.99) r/#1-5; sketch pages, Stewart's travelogue to Saigon ... 13.00

OTHERWORLD
DC Comics (Vertigo): May, 2005 - No. 7, Nov, 2005 ($2.99)

1-7-Phil Jimenez-s/a(p) ... 3.00
...: Book One TPB (2006, $19.99) r/#1-7; cover gallery ... 20.00

OUR ARMY AT WAR (Becomes Sgt. Rock #302 on; also see Army At War)
National Periodical Publications: Aug, 1952 - No. 301, Feb, 1977

1	300	600	900	2475	5588	8700
2	125	250	375	1000	2250	3500
3,4: 4-Krigstein-a	86	172	258	688	1544	2400
5-7	62	124	186	496	1123	1750
8-11,14-Krigstein-a	59	118	177	472	1061	1650
12,15-20	50	100	150	400	900	1400
13-Krigstein-c/a; flag-c	64	128	192	512	1156	1800
21-31: Last precode (2/55)	36	72	108	259	580	900
32-40	32	64	96	230	515	800

41-60: 51-1st S.A. issue. 57,60-Grey tone-c	28	56	84	202	451	700
61-70: 61-(8/57) Pre-Sgt. Rock Easy Co.-c/s. 67-Minor Sgt. Rock prototype						
	26	52	78	182	404	625
71-80	24	48	72	168	377	585
81-(4/59) "The Rock of Easy" - Sgt. Rock prototype. Part of lead-up trio to 1st definitive Sgt. Rock. Story features a character named "Sgt. Rocky" as a "4th grade rate" sergeant (three stripes/chevrons) who is referred to as "The Rock of Easy". Editor also promises more stories of "...Rock-like Sergeant". Andru & Esposito-a/Haney's-a.						
	367	734	1100	3100	7050	11,000
82-(5/59) "Hold up Easy"- 1st app. of a Sgt. Rock. Part of lead-up trio to 1st definitive Sgt. Rock. Character named Sgt. Rock appears in a supporting "motivator" role as a "4th grade rate" sergeant (three stripes/chevrons) in six panels in six page story; Haney's/Drucker-a						
	141	282	423	1128	2614	4100
83-(6/59) "The Rock and Wall" - 1st true appearance of Sgt. Rock. Sgt. Rock finally introduced as a Master Sergeant (three chevrons and three rockers) and is main character of story. 1st specific narration that defines the "Rock of Easy" as Sgt. Rock. 1st actual "Sgt. Rock" collaboration between creators Robert Kanigher and Joe Kubert						
	1080	2160	3240	9200	21,100	33,000
84-(7/59) "Laughter on Snakehead Hill" - 2nd appearance of Sgt. Rock. Story advances true Sgt. Rock continuity in 13-page title story featuring Sgt. Rock and Easy Co.; Kanigher-s/Novick-a/Kubert-c	100	200	300	800	1800	2800
85-Origin & 1st app. Ice Cream Soldier	75	150	225	600	1350	2100
86,87-Early Sgt. Rock; Kubert-a	55	110	165	444	997	1550
88-1st app. Rock; Kubert-c/a	71	142	213	568	1084	2000
89-"No Shot From Easy!" story; Heath-c	46	92	138	359	805	1250
90-Kubert-c/a; How Rock got his stripes	80	160	240	648	1399	2150
91-All-Sgt. Rock issue; Grandenetti-c/Kubert-a	123	246	369	984	2217	3450
92,94,96-99: 97-Regular Kubert-c begin	35	70	105	252	564	875
93-1st Zack Nolan	40	80	120	296	673	1050
95-1st app. Bulldozer	46	92	138	359	805	1250
100	50	100	150	400	900	1400
101,108,113: 101-1st app. Buster. 113-1st app. Wildman & Jackie Johnson						
	28	56	84	202	451	700
102-104,106,107,109,110,114,116-120: 104-Nurse Jane-c/s. 109-Pre Sgt. Co. Sgt. Rock-s. 118-Sunny injured	26	52	78	182	404	625
105-1st app. Junior	34	68	102	245	548	850
111-1st app. Wee Willie & Sunny	36	72	108	266	596	925
112-Classic Easy Co. roster-c	79	158	237	632	1416	2200
115-Rock revealed as orphan; 1st x-over Mlle. Marie. 1st Sgt. Rock's battle family						
	34	68	102	245	548	850
121-125	18	36	54	122	271	420
126-1st app. Canary; grey tone-c	27	54	81	194	435	675
127-2nd all-Sgt. Rock issue; 1st app. Little Sure Shot	32	64	96	230	515	800
128-Training & origin Sgt. Rock; 1st Sgt. Krupp	42	84	126	311	706	1100
129-139: 138-1st Sparrow. 141-1st Shaker	16	32	48	110	243	375
140-3rd all-Sgt. Rock issue	18	36	54	128	284	440
141-150: 147,148-Rock becomes a General	12	24	36	82	179	275
151-Intro. Enemy Ace by Kubert (2/65), black-c	50	100	150	400	900	1400
152-4th all-Sgt. Rock issue	16	32	48	111	246	380
153-2nd app. Enemy Ace	21	42	63	147	324	500
154,156,157,159-161,165-167: 157-2 pg. centerfold spread pin-up as part of story. 159-1st Nurse Wendy Winston-c/s. 165-2nd Iron Major	10	20	30	69	147	225
155-3rd app. Enemy Ace (6/65)(see Showcase)	11	22	33	76	220	340
158-Book-length Rock story; origin & 1st app. Iron Major(9/65), formerly Iron Captain; flashback to death of Rock's brother Josh	12	24	36	82	179	275
162,163-Viking Prince x-over in Sgt. Rock	11	22	33	75	160	245
164-Giant G-19	16	32	48	107	236	365
168-1st Unknown Soldier app.; referenced in Star-Spangled War Stories #157; (Sgt. Rock x-over) (6/66)	35	70	105	252	564	875
169,170	8	16	24	56	108	160
171-176,178-181: 171-1st Mad Emperor	8	16	24	54	102	150
177-(80 pg. Giant G-32)	10	20	30	64	132	200
182,183,186-Neal Adams-a. 186-Origin retold	8	16	27	59	117	175
184-Wee Willie dies	9	18	27	63	129	195
185,187,188,193-195,197-199	7	14	21	44	82	120
189,191,192,196: 189-Intro. The Teen-age Underground Fighters of Unit 3. 196-Hitler cameo	7	14	21	46	86	125
190-(80 pg. Giant G-44)	9	18	27	58	114	170
200-12 pg. Rock story told in verse; Evans-a	7	14	21	48	89	130
201,202,204-207: 201-Krigstein-r/#14. 204,205-All reprints; no Sgt. Rock. 207-Last 12¢ cover	5	10	15	35	63	90
203-(80 pg. Giant G-56)-All-r, Sgt. Rock story	8	16	24	54	102	150
208-215	4	8	12	27	44	60
216,229-(80 pg. Giants G-68, G-80): 216-Has G-58 on-c by mistake						
	6	12	18	41	76	110
217-219: 218-1st U.S.S. Stevens	4	8	12	27	44	60
220-Classic dinosaur/Sgt. Rock-c/s	5	10	15	33	57	80
221-228,230-234: 231-Intro/death Rock's brother. 234-Last 15¢ issue						
	4	8	12	23	37	50
235-239,241: 52 pg. Giants	4	8	12	28	47	65
240-Neal Adams-a; 52 pg. Giant	5	10	15	33	57	80
242-Also listed as DC 100 Page Super Spectacular #9						
	10	20	30	64	132	200
243-246: (All 52 pgs.) 244-No Adams-a	4	8	12	27	44	60
247-250,254-268,270: 247-Joan of Arc	3	6	9	16	23	30
251-253-Return of Iron Major	3	6	9	17	25	34
269,275-(100 pgs.)	5	10	15	33	57	80
271,272,274,276-279	3	6	9	14	19	24
273-Crucifixion-c	3	6	9	16	24	32
280-(68 pgs.)-200th app. Sgt. Rock; reprints Our Army at War #81,83						
	4	8	12	22	35	48
281-299,301: 295-Bicentennial cover	2	4	6	13	18	22
300-Sgt. Rock-s by Kubert (2/77)	4	8	12	25	40	55

NOTE: **Alcala** a-251. **Drucker** a-27, 67, 68, 79, 82, 83, 96, 164, 177, 203, 212, 243r, 244, 269r, 275r, 280r. **Evans** a-165-175, 200, 266, 269, 277, 278, 280. **Glanzman** a-218, 220, 222, 223, 225, 227, 230-232, 238-241, 244, 247, 248, 256-259, 261, 265-267, 271, 282, 283, 298. **Grandenetti** c-91,120. **Grell** a-287. **Heath** a-44, 50, 164, & most 176-281. **Kubert** a-38, 59, 67, 68 & most issues from 83-165, 171, 233, 236, 267, 275, 300; c-84, 280. **Maurer** a-233, 237, 239, 240, 45, 280, 284, 288, 290, 291, 295. **Severin** a-236, 252, 265, 267, 269r, 272. **Toth**

The Orville #1 © 20Fox

Our Army at War #88 © DC

Our Fighting Forces #71 © DC

	GD	VG	FN	VF	VF/NM	NM-
	2.0	4.0	6.0	8.0	9.0	9.2

a-235, 241, 254. **Wildey** a-283-285, 287p. **Wood** a-249.

OUR ARMY AT WAR
DC Comics: Nov, 2010 ($3.99, one-shot)

	GD	VG	FN	VF	VF/NM	NM-
1-Joe Kubert-c; Mike Marts-s/Victor Ibáñez-a						4.00

TPB (2011, $14.99) r/#1 and other 2010 war one-shots Weird War Tales #1, Our Fighting
Forces #1, G.I. Combat #1 and Star-Spangled War Stories #1 ... 15.00

OUR FIGHTING FORCES
National Per. Publ./DC Comics: Oct-Nov, 1954 - No. 181, Sept-Oct, 1978

	GD	VG	FN	VF	VF/NM	NM-
1-Grandenetti-c/a	152	304	456	1254	2827	4400
2	64	128	183	488	1094	1800
3-Kubert-c; last precode issue (3/55)	46	92	138	368	834	1300
4,5	38	76	114	285	641	1000
6-9: 7-1st S.A. issue	32	64	96	230	515	800
10-Wood-a	35	70	105	252	564	875
11-19	27	54	81	189	420	650
20-Grey tone-c (4/57)	37	74	111	274	612	950
21-30	22	44	66	154	340	525
31-40	19	38	57	131	291	450
41-Unknown Soldier tryout	27	54	81	189	420	650
42-44	18	36	54	128	284	440
45-1st app. of Gunner & Sarge, app. thru #94	64	128	192	512	1156	1800
46	28	56	84	202	451	700
47	20	40	60	138	307	475
48,50	16	32	48	110	243	375
49-1st Pooch	31	62	93	223	499	775
51-Grey tone-c	30	60	90	216	483	750
52-64: 64-Last 10¢ issue	13	26	39	89	195	300
65-70: 66-Panel inspired a famous Roy Lichtenstein painting	10	20	30	68	144	220
71-Classic grey tone-c; Pooch fires machine gun; panel inspired a famous Roy Lichtenstein painting	27	54	81	194	435	675
72-80	9	18	27	60	120	180
81-90	8	16	24	51	96	140
91-98: 95-Devil-Dog begins, ends #98.	6	12	18	41	76	110
99-Capt. Hunter begins, ends #106	8	16	24	54	102	150
100	6	12	18	41	76	110
101-105,107-120: 116-Mlle. Marie app. 120-Last 12¢ issue	5	10	15	31	53	75
106-Hunters Hellcats begin	5	10	15	33	57	80
121,122: 121-Intro. Heller	4	8	12	28	47	65
123-The Losers (Capt. Storm, Gunner & Sarge, Johnny Cloud) begin	10	20	30	68	144	220
124-132: 132-Last 15¢ issue	4	8	12	25	40	55
133-137 (Giants). 134-Toth-a	4	8	12	28	47	65
138-145,147-150: 149-Frank Thorne-c	3	6	9	17	25	34
146-Classic "Burma Sky" story; Toth-a/Goodwin-s	3	6	9	20	31	42
151-162-Kirby a(p)	3	6	9	14	20	26
163-180	3	6	9	17	25	34
181-Last issue	3	6	9	17	25	34
...(War One-Shot) 1 (11/10, $3.99) The Losers app.; B. Clay Moore-s/Chad Hardin-a						4.00

NOTE: **N. Adams** c-147. **Drucker** a-28, 37, 39, 42-44, 49, 53, 133r. **Evans** a-149, 164-174, 177-181. **Glanzman** a-125-128, 132, 134, 138-141, 143, 144. **Heath** a-2, 16, 18, 28, 41, 44, 49, 51, 104, 114, 135-138r; c-51. **Kirby** a-151-162p; c-152-159. **Kubert** c/a in many issues. **Maurer** a-135. **Redondo** a-166. **Severin** a-123-130, 131l, 132-150.

OUR FIGHTING FORCES GIANT
DC Comics: 2020 ($4.99, one-shot, 100 pgs., squarebound, Mass Market & Direct Market editions exist with different covers)

	GD	VG	FN	VF	VF/NM	NM-
1-New stories of The Unknown Soldier, Batwoman, and Batman w/Jim Lee-a and reprints from Men of War #4-7; art by Corben, Winslade, Kolins and others						5.00

OUR FIGHTING MEN IN ACTION (See Men In Action)

OUR FLAG COMICS
Ace Magazines: Aug, 1941 - No. 5, April, 1942

	GD	VG	FN	VF	VF/NM	NM-
1-Captain Victory, The Unknown Soldier (intro) & The Three Cheers begin	432	864	1296	3154	5577	8000
2-Origin The Flag (patriotic hero); 1st app?	290	580	870	1856	3178	4500
3-5: 5-Intro & 1st app. Mr. Risk	219	438	657	1402	2401	3400

NOTE: **Anderson** a-1, 4. **Mooney** a-1, 2; c-2.

OUR GANG COMICS (With Tom & Jerry #39-58; becomes Tom & Jerry #60 on; based on film characters)
Dell Publishing Co.: Sept-Oct, 1942 - No. 59, June, 1949

	GD	VG	FN	VF	VF/NM	NM-
1-Our Gang & Barney Bear by Kelly, Tom & Jerry, Pete Smith, Flip & Dip, The Milky Way begin (all 1st app.)	121	242	363	968	2184	3400

	GD	VG	FN	VF	VF/NM	NM-
2-Benny Burro begins (#2 by Kelly)	50	100	150	400	900	1400
3-5	26	52	78	182	404	625
6-Bumbazine & Albert only app. by Kelly	32	64	96	230	515	800
7-No Kelly story	18	36	54	128	284	440
8-Benny Burro begins by Barks	42	84	126	311	706	1100
9-Barks-a(2): Benny Burro & Happy Hound; no Kelly story	38	76	114	285	641	1000
10-Benny Burro by Barks	27	54	81	189	420	650
11-1st Barney Bear & Benny Burro by Barks (5-6/44); Happy Hound by Barks	34	68	102	242	541	840
12-20	16	32	48	110	243	375
21-30: 30-X-Mas-c	11	22	33	77	166	255
31-36-Last Barks issue	9	18	27	63	129	195
37-40	7	14	21	44	82	120
41-50	6	12	18	38	69	100
51-57	6	12	18	37	66	95
58,59-No Kelly art or Our Gang stories	5	10	15	35	63	90

Our Gang Volume 1 (Fantagraphics Books, 2006, $12.95, TPB) r/Our Gang stories written and by Walt Kelly from #1-8; Leonard Maltin intro.; Jeff Smith-c ... 13.00
Our Gang Volume 2 (Fantagraphics Books, 2007, $12.95, TPB) r/Our Gang stories written and by Walt Kelly from #9-15; Steve Thompson intro.; Jeff Smith-c ... 13.00
Our Gang Volume 3 (Fantagraphics Books, 2008, $14.99, TPB) r/Our Gang stories written and by Walt Kelly from #16-23; Steve Thompson intro.; Jeff Smith-c ... 15.00
NOTE: **Barks** art in part only. **Barks** did not write Barney Bear stories #30-34. (See March of Comics #3, 26). Early issues have photo back-c.

OUR LADY OF FATIMA (Also see Fatima...)
Catechetical Guild Educational Society: 3/11/55 (15¢) (36 pgs.)

	GD	VG	FN	VF	VF/NM	NM-
395	7	14	21	35	43	50

OUR LOVE (True Secrets #3 on? or Romantic Affairs #3 on?)
Marvel Comics (SPC): Sept, 1949 - No. 2, Jan, 1950

	GD	VG	FN	VF	VF/NM	NM-
1-Photo-c	34	68	102	204	332	450
2-Photo-c	20	40	60	117	189	260

OUR LOVE STORY
Marvel Comics Group: Oct, 1969 - No. 38, Feb, 1976

	GD	VG	FN	VF	VF/NM	NM-
1	13	26	39	86	188	290
2	7	14	21	49	92	135
3,4,6-8,10,11	6	12	18	38	69	100
5-Steranko-a	12	24	36	80	173	265
9,12-Kirby-a	6	12	18	38	69	100
13-(10/71, 52 pgs.)	6	12	18	38	69	100
14-New story by Gary Fredrich & Tarpe' Mills	4	8	10	15	34	60	85
15-20,27: 27-Colan/Everett-a(r?); Kirby/Colletta-r	4	8	12	27	44	60
21-26,28-37	4	8	12	25	40	55
38-Last issue	4	8	12	28	47	65

NOTE: **J. Buscema** a-1-3, 5-7, 9, 13r, 16r, 19r(2), 21r, 22r(2), 23r, 34r, 35r; c-11, 13, 16, 22, 23, 24, 27, 35. **Colan** a-3-6, 21r(#6), 22r, 23r(#3), 24r(#4), 27; c-19. **Katz** a-17. **Maneely** a-13r. **Romita** a-13r; c-1, 2, 4-6. **Weiss** a-17, 29r(#17).

OUR MEN AT WAR
DC Comics: Aug/Sept 1952

nn - Ashcan comic, not distributed to newsstands, only for in-house use. Cover art is All Star Western #60, interior being Detective Comics #181 (a FN/VF copy sold for $1195 in 2012)

OUR MISS BROOKS
Dell Publishing Co.: No. 751, Nov, 1956

	GD	VG	FN	VF	VF/NM	NM-
Four Color 751-Photo-c	9	18	27	59	117	175

OUR SECRET (Exciting Love Stories)(Formerly My Secret)
Superior Comics Ltd.: No. 4, Nov, 1949 - No. 8, Jan, 1950

	GD	VG	FN	VF	VF/NM	NM-
4-Kamen-a; spanking scene	44	88	123	256	428	600
5,6,8	19	38	57	141	176	240
7-Contains 9 pg. story intended for unpublished Ellery Queen #5; lingerie panels	21	42	63	122	199	275

OUT
Artists, Writers & Artisans, Inc.: Oct, 2021 - No. 5, Feb, 2022 ($3.99, limited series)

	GD	VG	FN	VF	VF/NM	NM-
1-Rob Williams-s/Will Conrad-a; vampire in a Nazi POW fortress						4.00

OUTCAST, THE
Valiant: Dec, 1995 ($2.50, one-shot)

	GD	VG	FN	VF	VF/NM	NM-
1-Breyfogle-a						4.00

OUTCAST BY KIRKMAN & AZACETA
Image Comics: Jun, 2014 - No. 48, Apr, 2021 ($2.99/$3.99)

	GD	VG	FN	VF	VF/NM	NM-
1-Kirkman-s/Azaceta-a/c						10.00
2						5.00

	GD 2.0	VG 4.0	FN 6.0	VF 8.0	VF/NM 9.0	NM- 9.2

3-47: 25-(25¢-c) — — — — — 4.00
48-($4.99) Last issue — — — — — 5.00

OUTCASTS
DC Comics: Oct, 1987 - No. 12, Sept, 1988 ($1.75, limited series)

1-12: John Wagner & Alan Grant scripts in all — — — — — 4.00

OUTER DARKNESS
Image Comics (Skybound): Nov, 2018 - Present ($3.99)

1-12-John Layman-s/Afu Chan-a — — — — — 4.00
.../ Chew (3/20 - Present, $3.99) 1-3-Tony Chu brought to the future — — — — — 4.00

OUTER LIMITS, THE (TV)
Dell Publishing Co.: Jan-Mar, 1964 - No. 18, Oct, 1969 (Most painted-c)

1 — 14 — 28 — 42 — 97 — 214 — 330
2-5 — 8 — 16 — 24 — 52 — 99 — 145
6-10 — 6 — 12 — 18 — 42 — 79 — 115
11-18: 17-Reprints #1. 18-r/#2 — 5 — 10 — 15 — 35 — 63 — 90

OUTER SPACE (Formerly This Magazine Is Haunted, 2nd Series)
Charlton Comics: No. 17, May, 1958 - No. 25, Dec, 1959; Nov, 1968

17-Williamson/Wood-a — 17 — 34 — 51 — 98 — 154 — 210
18-20-Ditko-a — 30 — 60 — 90 — 177 — 289 — 400
21-Ditko-c — 23 — 46 — 69 — 136 — 223 — 310
22-25 — 16 — 32 — 48 — 92 — 144 — 195
V2#1(11/68)-Ditko-a, Boyette-c — 6 — 12 — 18 — 37 — 66 — 95

OUT FOR BLOOD
Dark Horse: Sept, 1999 - No. 4, Dec, 1999 ($2.95, B&W, limited series)

1-4-Kelley Jones-c; Erskine-a — — — — — 4.00

OUTLANDERS (Manga)
Dark Horse Comics: Dec, 1988 - No. 33, Sept,1991 ($2.00-$2.50, B&W, 44 pgs.)

1-33: Japanese Sci-fi manga — — — — — 5.00

OUTLAW (See Return of the...)

OUTLAWED
Marvel Comics: May, 2020 ($4.99, one-shot)

1-Eve L. Ewing-s/Kim Jacinto-a; teen heroes banned; leads into Champions #1 (2020) — 1 — 3 — 4 — 6 — 8 — 10

OUTLAW FIGHTERS
Atlas Comics (IPC): Aug, 1954 - No. 5, Apr, 1955

1-Tuska-a — 20 — 40 — 60 — 117 — 189 — 260
2-5: 5-Heath-c/a, 7 pgs. — 15 — 30 — 45 — 83 — 124 — 165
NOTE: Colan a-4. Hartley a-3. Heath c/a-5. Maneely c/a-2, 4. Pakula a-2. Reinman a-2, 4. Tuska a-1-3.

OUTLAW KID, THE (1st Series; see Wild Western)
Atlas Comics (CCC No. 1-11/EPI No. 12-29): Sept, 1954 - No. 19, Sept, 1957

1-Origin; The Outlaw Kid & his horse Thunder begin; Black Rider app. — 43 — 86 — 129 — 271 — 461 — 650
2-Black Rider app. — 20 — 40 — 60 — 117 — 189 — 260
3-7,9: 3-Wildey-a(3) — 15 — 30 — 45 — 88 — 137 — 185
8-Williamson/Woodbridge-a, 4 pgs. — 15 — 30 — 45 — 90 — 140 — 190
10-Williamson-a — 15 — 30 — 45 — 90 — 140 — 190
11-17,19: 13-Baker text illo. 15-Williamson text illo (unsigned) — 13 — 26 — 39 — 72 — 101 — 130
18-Williamson/Mayo-a — 14 — 28 — 42 — 76 — 108 — 140
NOTE: Berg a-4, 7, 13. Maneely c-1-3, 5-8, 11-13, 15, 16, 18. Pakula a-3. Severin c-10, 17, 19. Shores a-1. Wildey a-1(3), 2-8, 10, 11, 12(4), 13(4), 15-19(4 each); c-4.

OUTLAW KID, THE (2nd Series)
Marvel Comics Group: Aug, 1970 - No. 30, Oct, 1975

1-Reprints; 1-Orlando-r, Wildey-r(3) — 5 — 10 — 15 — 30 — 50 — 70
2,3,9: 2-Reprints. 3,9-Williamson-a(r) — 2 — 4 — 6 — 13 — 18 — 22
4-7: 7-Last 15¢ issue — 2 — 4 — 6 — 11 — 16 — 20
8-Double size (52 pgs.); Crandall-r — 3 — 6 — 9 — 18 — 27 — 36
10-Origin — 3 — 6 — 9 — 19 — 30 — 40
11-20: new-a in #10-16 — 2 — 4 — 6 — 13 — 18 — 22
21-30: 27-Origin-r/#10 — 2 — 4 — 6 — 9 — 13 — 16
NOTE: Ayers a-10, 27r, Berg a-7, 25r. Everett a-2(2 pgs.) Gil Kane c-10, 11, 15, 27r, 28. Roussos a-10i, 27i(r). Severin c-1, 9, 20, 25. Wildey r-1-4, 6-9, 19-22, 25, 26. Williamson a-28r. Woodbridge/Williamson a-9r.

OUTLAW NATION
DC Comics (Vertigo): Nov, 2000 - No. 19, May, 2002 ($2.50)

1-19-Fabry painted-c/Delano-s/Sudzuka-a — — — — — 3.00
TPB (Image Comics, 11/06, $15.99) B&W reprint of #1-19; Delano intro. — — — — — 16.00

OUTLAW PRINCE, THE
Dark Horse Books: 2011 ($12.99, SC, 80 pgs.)

SC-Adaptation of ERB's The Outlaw of Torn; Rob Hughes-s/Thomas Yeates painted-a; origin/1st app. Norman of Torn; intro. & death of Lady Maud — — — — — 13.00
Deluxe HC Limited Edition ($49.99, 112 pgs.) Bonus 2 articles (approx. 200 signed) — — — — — 50.00

OUTLAWS
D. S. Publishing Co.: Feb-Mar, 1948 - No. 9, June-July, 1949

1-Violent & suggestive stories — 41 — 82 — 123 — 256 — 428 — 600
2-Ingels-a; Baker-a — 45 — 90 — 135 — 284 — 480 — 675
3,5,6: 3-Not Frazetta. 5-Sky Sheriff by Good app. 6-McWilliams-a — 21 — 42 — 63 — 124 — 202 — 280
4-Orlando-a — 22 — 44 — 66 — 132 — 216 — 300
7,8-Ingels-a in each — 31 — 62 — 93 — 184 — 300 — 415
9-(Scarce)-Frazetta-a (7 pgs.) — 65 — 130 — 195 — 416 — 708 — 1000
NOTE: Another #3 was printed in Canada with Frazetta art "Prairie Jinx", 7 pgs.

OUTLAWS, THE (Formerly Western Crime Cases)
Star Publishing Co.: No. 10, May, 1952 - No. 13, Sep, 1953; No. 14, Apr, 1954

10-L.B. Cole-c — 32 — 64 — 96 — 188 — 307 — 425
11-14-L.B. Cole-c. 14-Reprints Western Thrillers #4 (Fox) w/new L.B. Cole-c; Kamen, Feldstein-a — 22 — 44 — 66 — 132 — 216 — 300

OUTLAWS
DC Comics: Sept, 1991 - No. 8, Apr, 1992 ($1.95, limited series)

1-8: Post-apocalyptic Robin Hood. — — — — — 4.00

OUTLAWS OF THE WEST (Formerly Cody of the Pony Express #10)
Charlton Comics: No. 11, 7/57 - No. 81, 5/70; No. 82, 7/79 - No. 88, 4/80

11 — 9 — 18 — 27 — 50 — 65 — 80
12,13,15-17,19,20 — 6 — 12 — 18 — 31 — 38 — 45
14-(68 pgs.), 2/58) — 10 — 20 — 30 — 54 — 72 — 90
18-Ditko-a — 11 — 22 — 33 — 62 — 86 — 110
21-30 — 3 — 6 — 9 — 16 — 23 — 30
31-50: 34-Gunmaster app. — 2 — 4 — 6 — 13 — 18 — 22
51-63,65,67-70: 54-Kid Montana app. — 2 — 4 — 6 — 10 — 14 — 18
64,66: 64-Captain Doom begins (1st app.). 68-Kid Montana series begins — 2 — 4 — 6 — 13 — 18 — 22
71-79: 73-Origin & 1st app. The Sharp Shooter, last app. #74. 75-Last Capt. Doom — 2 — 4 — 6 — 9 — 12 — 15
80,81-Ditko-a — 2 — 4 — 6 — 13 — 18 — 22
82-88 — — — — — 6.00
64,79(Modern Comics-r, 1977, '78) — — — — — 6.00

OUTLAWS OF THE WILD WEST
Avon Periodicals: 1952 (25¢, 132 pgs.) (4 rebound comics)

1-Wood back-c; Kubert-a (3 Jesse James-r) — 45 — 90 — 135 — 284 — 480 — 675

OUTLAW TRAIL (See Zane Grey 4-Color 511)

OUT OF BODY
AfterShock Comics: Jun, 2021 - No. 5, Oct, 2021 ($4.99/$3.99)

1-($4.99) Peter Milligan-s/Inaki Miranda-a — — — — — 5.00
2-5-($3.99) — — — — — 4.00

OUT OF SANTA'S BAG (See March of Comics #10 in the Promotional Comics section)

OUT OF THE NIGHT (The Hooded Horseman #18 on)
Amer. Comics Group (Creston/Scope): Feb-Mar, 1952 - No. 17, Oct-Nov, 1954

1-Williamson/LeDoux-a (9 pgs.); ACG's 1st editor's page — 245 — 490 — 735 — 1568 — 2684 — 3800
2-Williamson-a (5 pgs.) — 68 — 136 — 204 — 435 — 743 — 1050
3,5-10: 9-Sci/Fic story — 42 — 84 — 126 — 265 — 445 — 625
4-Williamson-a (7 pgs.) — 60 — 120 — 180 — 381 — 653 — 925
11-17: 13-Nostrand-a? 17-E.C. Wood swipe — 37 — 74 — 111 — 218 — 354 — 490
NOTE: Landau a-14, 17. Shelly a-12.

OUT OF THE SHADOWS
Standard Comics/Visual Editions: No. 5, July, 1952 - No. 14, Aug, 1954

5-Toth-p; Moreira, Tuska-a; Roussos-a — 110 — 220 — 330 — 704 — 1202 — 1700
6-Toth/Celardo-a; Katz-a(2) — 57 — 114 — 171 — 362 — 619 — 875
7,9: 7-Jack Katz-c/a(2). 9-Crandall-a(2) — 50 — 100 — 150 — 315 — 533 — 750
8-Katz shrunken head-c — 219 — 438 — 657 — 1402 — 2401 — 3400
10-Spider-c; Sekowsky-a — 142 — 284 — 426 — 909 — 1555 — 2200
11-Toth-a, 2 pgs.; Katz-a; Andru-a — 52 — 104 — 156 — 328 — 552 — 775
12-Toth/Peppe-a(2) — 65 — 130 — 195 — 416 — 708 — 1000
13-Cannabalism story; Sekowsky-a; Roussos-a — 71 — 142 — 213 — 454 — 777 — 1100
14-Toth-a — 53 — 106 — 159 — 334 — 567 — 800

OUT OF THE VORTEX (Comics' Greatest World:... #1-4)
Dark Horse Comics: Oct., 1993 - No. 12, Oct, 1994 ($2.00, limited series)

1-12: 1-Foil logo. 6-Hero Zero x-over. 12-$2.50-c — — — — — 4.00
NOTE: Art Adams c-7. Golden c-8. Mignola c-2. Simonson c-3. Zeck c-10.

OUT OF THIS WORLD
Charlton Comics: Aug, 1956 - No. 16, Dec, 1959

1 — 48 — 96 — 144 — 302 — 514 — 725
2 — 21 — 42 — 63 — 124 — 202 — 280
3-6-Ditko-c/a (3) each — 39 — 78 — 117 — 231 — 378 — 525
7-(2/58, 15¢, 68 pgs.)-Ditko-c/a(4) — 43 — 86 — 129 — 271 — 461 — 650
8-(5/58, 15¢, 68 pgs.)-Ditko-a(2) — 40 — 80 — 120 — 246 — 411 — 575
9,10,12,16-Ditko-a — 29 — 58 — 87 — 172 — 281 — 390
11-Ditko c/a (3) — 39 — 78 — 117 — 231 — 378 — 525
13,15 — 15 — 30 — 45 — 88 — 137 — 185
14-Matt Baker-a, 7 pg. story — 18 — 36 — 54 — 105 — 165 — 225
NOTE: Ditko c-3-12, 16. Reinman a-10.

OUT OF THIS WORLD
Avon Periodicals: June, 1950; Aug, 1950

1-Kubert-a(2) (one reprinted/Eerie #1, 1947) plus Crom the Barbarian by Gardner Fox & John Giunta art; Fawcette-c — 194 — 388 — 582 — 1242 — 2121 — 3000
1-(8/50) Reprint; no month on cover — 87 — 174 — 261 — 533 — 952 — 1350

OUT OF THIS WORLD ADVENTURES
Avon Periodicals: July, 1950 - No. 2, Apr, 1951 (25¢ sci-fi pulp magazine with 32-page color comic insert)

1-Kubert-a(2); Crom the Barbarian by Fox & Giunta; text stories by Cummings, Van Vogt, del Rey, Chandler — 116 — 232 — 348 — 742 — 1271 — 1800
2-Kubert-a plus The Spider God of Akka by Gardner Fox & John Giunta pulp magazine w/comic insert; Wood-a (5 pgs.); mentioned in SOTI, page 120 — 68 — 136 — 204 — 435 — 743 — 1050

OUT OUR WAY WITH WORRY WART
Dell Publishing Co.: No. 680, Feb, 1956

Four Color 680 — 5 — 10 — 15 — 35 — 63 — 90

OUTPOSTS
Blackthorne Publishing: June, 1987 - No. 4, 1987 ($1.25)

1-4: 1-Kaluta-c(p) — — — — — 4.00

OUTSIDERS, THE
DC Comics: Nov, 1985 - No. 28, Feb, 1988

1 — — — — — 5.00
2-28: 18-26-Batman returns. 21-Intro. Strike Force Kobra; 1st app. Clayface IV. 22-E.C. parody; Orlando-a. 21- 25-Atomic Knight app. 27,28-Millennium tie-ins — — — — — 4.00
Annual 1 (12/86, $2.50), Special 1 (7/87, $1.50) — — — — — 5.00
NOTE: Aparo a-1-7, 9-14, 17-22, 25, 26; c-1-7, 9-14, 17, 19-26. Byrne a-11. Bolland a-6, 18; c-16. Ditko a-13p. Erik Larsen a-24, 27 28; c-27, 28. Morrow a-12.

Outer Darkness #1 © Skybound

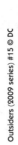
Outsiders (2009 series) #15 © DC

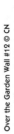
Over the Garden Wall #12 © CN

	GD	VG	FN	VF	VF/NM	NM-
	2.0	4.0	6.0	8.0	9.0	9.2

OUTSIDERS
DC Comics: Nov, 1993 - No. 24, Nov, 1995 ($1.75/$1.95/$2.25)

1-11,0,12-24: 1-Alpha; Travis Charest-c. 1-Omega; Travis Charest-c. 5-Atomic Knight app.
  8-New Batman-c/story. 11-(9/94)-Zero Hour. 0 (10/94).12-(11/94). 21-Darkseid cameo.
  22-New Gods app. 4.00

OUTSIDERS (See Titans/Young Justice: Graduation Day)(Leads into Batman and the Outsiders)
DC Comics: Aug, 2003 - No. 50, Nov, 2007 ($2.50/$2.99)

1-Nightwing, Arsenal, Metamorpho app.; Winick s/Raney-a 5.00
2-Joker and Grodd app. 4.00
3-33: 3-Joker-c. 5,6-ChrisCross-a. 8-Huntress app. 9,10-Capt. Marvel Jr. app.
  24,25-X-over with Teen Titans. 26,27-Batman & old Outsiders 3.00
34-50: 34-One Year Later. 36-Begin $2.99-c. 37-Superman app. 44-Red Hood app. .. 3.00
Annual 1 (6/07, $3.99) McDaniel-a; Black Lightning app. 4.00
...Checkmate: Checkout TPB (2008, $14.99) r/#47-49 & Checkmate #13-15 .... 15.00
... Double Feature (10/03, $4.95) r/#1,2 .... 5.00
...: Crisis Intervention TPB (2006, $12.99) r/#29-33 .... 13.00
...: Looking For Trouble TPB (2004, $12.95) r/#1-7 & Teen Titans/Outsiders Secret Files &
  Origins 2003; intro. by Winick 13.00
... Pay As You Go TPB (2007, $14.99) r/#42-46 & Annual #1 .... 15.00
...: Sum of All Evil TPB (2004, $14.95) r/#8-15 .... 15.00
...: The Good Fight TPB (2006, $14.99) r/#34-41 .... 15.00
...: Wanted TPB (2005, $14.99) r/#16-23 .... 15.00

OUTSIDERS, THE (See Batman and the Outsiders for #1-14 and #40)
DC Comics: No. 15, Apr, 2009 - No. 39, Jun, 2011 ($2.99)

15-23,26-39: 15-Alfred assembles a new team; Garbett-a. 17-19-Deathstroke app. .. 3.00
24,25-($3.99) Blackest Night; Terra rises as a Black Lantern 4.00
...: The Deep TPB (2009, $14.99) r/#15-20 & Batman and the Outsiders Special #1 . 15.00
...: The Great Divide TPB (2011, $17.99) r/#32-40; cover gallery 18.00
...: The Hunt TPB (2010, $14.99) r/#21-25 .... 15.00
...: The Road to Hell TPB (2010, $14.99) r/#26-31 .... 15.00

OUTSIDERS (Dawn of DC)
DC Comics: Jan, 2024 - Present ($4.99)

1-5-Team of Batwoman, Batwing, Drummer, Jenny Crisis 5.00

OUTSIDERS: FIVE OF A KIND (Bridges Outsiders #49 & 50)
DC Comics: Oct, 2007 ($2.99, weekly limited series)

...Katana/Shazam! (part 2 of 5) - Barr-s/Sharpe-a 3.00
...Metamorpho/Aquaman (part 4 of 5) - Wilson-s/Middleton-a 3.00
...Nightwing/Captain Boomerang (part 1 of 5) - DeFilippis & Weir-s/Williams-a ... 3.00
...Thunder/Martian Manhunter (part 3 of 5) - Beechen-s/Turnbull-a; Grayven app. . 3.00
...Wonder Woman/Grace (part 5 of 5) - Andreyko-s/Richards-a 3.00
TPB (2008, $14.99) r/series & Outsiders #50 .... 15.00

OUT THERE
DC Comics(Cliffhanger): July, 2001 - No. 18, Aug, 2003 ($2.50/$2.95)

1-Humberto Ramos-c/a; Brian Augustyn-s 3.00
1-Variant-c by Carlos Meglia 4.00
2-18: 3-Variant-c by Bruce Timm. 9-Begin $2.95-c 3.00
...: The Evil Within TPB (2002, $12.95) r/#1-6; Ramos sketch pages 13.00

OVERKILL: WITCHBLADE/ ALIENS/ DARKNESS/ PREDATOR
Image Comics/Dark Horse Comics: Dec, 2000 - No. 2, 2001 ($5.95)

1,2-Jenkins-s/Lansing, Ching & Benitez-a 6.00

OVERTAKEN
Aspen/MLT: Aug, 2013 - No. 5, Jan, 2018 ($1.00/$3.99)

1-5-Mastromauro-s/Lorenzana-a; multiple covers on each. 1-($1.00-c). 2-(3/16) . 4.00

OVER THE EDGE
Marvel Comics: Nov, 1995 - No. 10, Aug, 1996 (99¢)

1-10: 1,6,10-Daredevil-c/story. 2,7-Dr. Strange c/story. 3-Hulk-c/story. 4,9-Ghost Rider-c/story.
  5-Punisher-c/story. 8-Elektra-c/story 4.00

OVER THE GARDEN WALL (Based on the Cartoon Network mini-series)
Boom Entertainment (KaBOOM!): Aug, 2015 - No. 4, Nov, 2015 ($3.99, limited series)

1-4-Pat McHale-s/Jim Campbell-a; multiple covers on each 4.00
Special 1 (11/14, $4.99)-Prequel to the Cartoon Network mini-series; McHale-s/Campbell-a . 5.00

OVER THE GARDEN WALL: HOLLOW TOWN (Cartoon Network)
Boom Entertainment (KaBOOM!): Sept, 2018 - No. 5, Jan, 2019 ($3.99, limited series)

1-5-Celia Lowenthal-s/Jorge Monlongo-a; multiple covers on each 4.00

OVER THE GARDEN WALL ONGOING (Cartoon Network)
Boom Entertainment (KaBOOM!): Apr, 2016 - No. 20, Nov, 2018 ($3.99, limited series)

1-20: 1-4-Two stories in each; Campbell-s/Burgos-a & Levari-s/McGee-a; multiple covers 4.00

... 2017 Special 1 (9/17, $7.99) Three stories; covers by Mercado & Derek Kim .. 8.00

OVER THE GARDEN WALL: SOULFUL SYMPHONIES (Cartoon Network)
Boom Entertainment (KaBOOM!): Aug, 2019 - No. 5, Dec, 2019 ($3.99, limited series)

1-5-Birdie Willis-s/Rowan MacColl-a; multiple covers on each 4.00

OVERWATCH: NEW BLOOD (Based on the video game)
Dark Horse Comics: Jul, 2022 - No. 5, Nov, 2022 ($3.99, limited series)

1-5-Ray Fawkes-s/Irene Koh-a 4.00

OVERWATCH: TRACER – LONDON CALLING (Based on the video game)
Dark Horse Comics: Dec, 2020 - No. 5, Apr, 2021 ($3.99, limited series)

1-5-Mariko Tamaki-s/Babs Tarr-a 4.00

OWL, THE (See Crackajack Funnies #25, Popular Comics #72 and Occult Files of
Dr. Spektor #22)
Gold Key: April, 1967; No. 2, April, 1968

	GD	VG	FN	VF	VF/NM	NM-
1-Written by Jerry Siegel; '40s super hero	5	10	15	34	60	85
2	4	8	12	28	47	65

OWL, THE (See Project Superpowers)
Dynamite Entertainment: 2013 - No. 4, 2013 ($3.99, limited series)

1-4-Golden Age hero in modern times; Krul-s/H.K. Michael-a; covers by Ross & Syaf . 4.00

OZ (See First Comics Graphic Novel, Marvel Treaury Of Oz & MGM's Marvelous...)
OZ
Caliber Press: 1994 - 1997 ($2.95, B&W)

	GD	VG	FN	VF	VF/NM	NM-
0,1: 0-Released between #10 & #11	1	2	3	5	6	8
1 ($5.95)-Limited Edition; double-c	1	3	4	6	8	10
2-20						3.00
...Specials: Freedom Fighters. Lion. Scarecrow. Tin Man						5.00

OZARK IKE
Dell Publishing Co./Standard Comics B11 on: Feb, 1948; Nov, 1948 - No. 24, Dec, 1951;
No. 25, Sept, 1952

	GD	VG	FN	VF	VF/NM	NM-
Four Color 180(1948-Dell)	13	26	39	89	195	300
B11, B12, 13-15	15	30	45	85	130	175
16-25	14	28	42	80	115	150

OZ: DAEMONSTORM
Caliber Press: 1997 ($3.95, B&W, one-shot)

1 .... 4.00

OZMA OF OZ (Dorothy Gale from Wonderful Wizard of Oz)
Marvel Comics: Jan, 2011 - No. 8, Sept, 2011 ($3.99, limited series)

1-6-Eric Shanower/Skottie Young-a/c 4.00
Oz Primer (5/11, $3.99) creator interviews and character profiles 4.00

OZ: ROMANCE IN RAGS
Caliber Press: 1996 ($2.95, B&W, limited series)

1-3, ..Special 4.00

OZ SQUAD
Brave New Worlds/Patchwork Press: 1992 - No. 4, 1994 ($2.50/$2.75, B&W)

1-4-Patchwork Press 4.00

OZ SQUAD
Patchwork Press: Dec, 1995 - No. 10, 1996 ($3.95/$2.95, B&W)

1-($3.95) 5.00
2-10 .... 4.00

OZ: STRAW AND SORCERY
Caliber Press: 1997 ($2.95, B&W, limited series)

1-3 .... 4.00

OZ-WONDERLAND WARS, THE
DC Comics: Jan, 1986 - No. 3, March, 1986 (Mini-series)(Giants)

1-3-Capt. Carrot app.; funny animals 6.00

OZZIE & BABS (TV Teens #14 on)
Fawcett Publications: Dec, 1947 - No. 13, Fall, 1949

	GD	VG	FN	VF	VF/NM	NM-
1-Teen-age	18	36	54	107	169	230
2	12	24	36	67	94	120
3-13	10	20	30	56	76	95

OZZIE AND HARRIET (The Adventures of... on cover) (Radio)
National Periodical Publications: Oct-Nov, 1949 - No. 5, June-July, 1950

	GD	VG	FN	VF	VF/NM	NM-
1-Photo-c	123	246	369	787	1344	1900
2	55	110	165	352	601	850
3-5	47	94	141	296	498	700

	GD 2.0	VG 4.0	FN 6.0	VF 8.0	VF/NM 9.0	NM- 9.2

OZZY OSBOURNE (Todd McFarlane Presents)
Image Comics (Todd McFarlane Prod.): June, 1999 ($4.95, magazine-sized)

1-Bio, interview and comic story; Ormston painted-a; Ashley Wood-c	1	2	3	5	6	8

PACIFIC COMICS GRAPHIC NOVEL (See Image Graphic Novel)

PACIFIC PRESENTS (Also see Starslayer #2, 3)
Pacific Comics: Oct, 1982 - No. 2, Apr, 1983; No. 3, Mar, 1984 - No. 4, Jun, 1984

1-Chapter 3 of The Rocketeer; Stevens-c/a; Bettie Page model	3	6	9	16	23	30
2-Chapter 4 of The Rocketeer (4th app.); nudity; Stevens-c/a	2	4	6	13	18	22
3,4: 3-1st app. Vanity						4.00

NOTE: **Conrad** a-3, 4; c-3. **Ditko** a-1-3; c-1(1/2). **Dave Stevens** a-1, 2; c-1(1/2), 2.

PACIFIC RIM: AFTERMATH
Legendary Comics: Jan, 2018 - No. 5, May, 2018 ($3.99)

1-5-Cavan Scott-s						4.00

PACIFIC RIM: TALES FROM THE DRIFT
Legendary Comics: Nov, 2015 - No. 4, Apr, 2016 ($3.99)

1-4-Beachum & Fialkov-s/Marz-a						4.00

PACIFIC RIM: TALES FROM YEAR ZERO
Legendary Comics: Jun, 2013 ($24.99, HC graphic novel)

HC - Prequel to the 2013 movie; Beacham-s/Alex Ross-c; art by various						25.00

PACT, THE
Image Comics: Feb, 1994 - No. 3, June, 1994 ($1.95, limited series)

1-3: Valentino co-scripts & layouts						4.00

PACT, THE
Image Comics: Apr, 2005 - No. 4, Jan, 2006 ($2.99/$2.95)

1-4: Invincible, Shadowhawk, Firebreather & Zephyr team-up. 1-Valentino-s/a						3.00

PAGEANT OF COMICS (See Jane Arden & Mopsy)
Archer St. John: Sept, 1947 - No. 2, Oct, 1947

1-Mopsy strip-r	27	54	81	160	263	365
2-Jane Arden strip-r	16	32	48	94	147	200

PAINKILLER JANE
Event Comics: June, 1997 - No. 5, Nov, 1997 ($3.95/$2.95)

1-Augustyn/Waid-s/Leonardi/Palmiotti-a, variant-c						5.00
2-5: Two covers (Quesada, Leonardi)						4.00
0-(1/99, $3.95) Retells origin; two covers						5.00
Essential Painkiller Jane TPB (2007, $19.99) r/#0-5; cover gallery and pin-ups						20.00

PAINKILLER JANE
Dynamite Entertainment: 2006 - No. 3, 2006 ($2.99)

1-3-Quesada & Palmiotti-s/Moder-a. 1-Four covers by Q&P, Moder, Tan and Conner						3.00
Volume #1 TPB (2007, $9.99) r/#1-3; cover gallery and Palmiotti interview						10.00

PAINKILLER JANE
Dynamite Entertainment: No. 0, 2007 - No. 5, 2007 ($3.50)

0-(25¢) Quesada & Palmiotti-s/Moder-a						3.00
1-5-($3.50) 1-Continued from #0; 5 covers. 4,5-Crossover with Terminator 2 #6,7						3.50
Volume #2 TPB (2007, $11.99) r/#0-3; cover gallery						12.00

PAINKILLER JANE / DARKCHYLDE
Event Comics: Oct, 1998 ($2.95, one-shot)

Preview-($6.95) DF Edition, 1-($6.95) DF Edition						7.00
1-Three covers; J.G. Jones-a						4.00

PAINKILLER JANE / HELLBOY
Event Comics: Aug, 1998 ($2.95, one-shot)

1-Leonardi & Palmiotti-a						5.00

PAINKILLER JANE: THE PRICE OF FREEDOM
Marvel Comics (ICON): Nov, 2013 - No. 4, Jan, 2014 ($3.99/$2.99, limited series)

1-($3.99) Palmiotti-s/Santacruz & Lotfi-a; covers by Amanda Conner & Dave Johnson						4.00
2-4-($2.99) Santacruz-a/Conner-c						3.00

PAINKILLER JANE: THE 22 BRIDES
Marvel Comics (ICON): May, 2014 - No. 3, Oct, 2014 ($4.99/$3.99, limited series)

1-($4.99) Palmiotti-s/Santacruz & Fernandez-a; covers by Christian & Conner						5.00
2,3-($3.99) Santacruz-a2-Photo-c. 3-Conner-c						4.00

PAINKILLER JANE VS. THE DARKNESS
Event Comics: Apr, 1997 ($2.95, one-shot)

1-Ennis-s; four variant-c (Conner, Hildebrandts, Quesada, Silvestri)						4.00

PAKLIS
Image Comics: May, 2017 - Present ($5.99/$3.99/$4.99)

1,2,5-($5.99) Serialized anthology by Dustin Weaver-s/a/c						6.00
3-($3.99) Dustin Weaver-s/a/c						4.00
4-($4.99) Dustin Weaver-s/a/c						5.00

PANCHO VILLA
Avon Periodicals: 1950

nn-Kinstler-c	36	72	108	211	343	475

PANDEMICA
IDW Publishing: Sept, 2019 - No. 5, Jan, 2020 ($3.99)

1-5-Jonathan Maberry-s/Alex Sanchez-a						4.00

PANHANDLE PETE AND JENNIFER (TV) (See Gene Autry #20)
J. Charles Laue Publishing Co.: July, 1951 - No. 3, Nov, 1951

1	15	30	45	84	127	170
2,3: 2-Interior photo-cvrs	10	20	30	56	76	95

PANIC (Companion to Mad)
E. C. Comics (Tiny Tot Comics): Feb-Mar, 1954 - No. 12, Dec-Jan, 1955-56

1-Used in Senate Investigation hearings; Elder draws entire E. C. staff; Santa Claus &						

	GD 2.0	VG 4.0	FN 6.0	VF 8.0	VF/NM 9.0	NM- 9.2

Mickey Spillane parody	54	108	162	432	691	950
2-Atomic bomb-c	33	66	99	264	420	575
3,4: 3-Senate Subcommittee parody; Davis draws Gaines, Feldstein & Kelly, 1 pg.; Old King Cole smokes marijuana. 4-Infinity-c; John Wayne parody	21	42	63	168	272	375
5-11: 8-Last pre-code issue (5/55). 9-Superman, Smilin' Jack & Dick Tracy app. on-c; has photo of Walter Winchell on-c. 11-Wheedies cereal box-c	19	38	57	152	241	330
12 (Low distribution; thousands were destroyed)	27	54	81	216	348	480

NOTE: **Davis** a-1-12; c-12. **Elder** a-1-12. **Feldstein** c-1-3, 5. **Kamen** a-1. **Orlando** a-1-9. **Wolverton** c-4, panel-3. **Wood** a-2-9, 11, 12.

PANiC (Magazine) (Satire)
Panic Publ.: July, 1958 - No. 6, July, 1959; V2#10, Dec, 1965 - V2#12, 1966

1	14	28	42	82	121	160
2-6	9	18	27	50	65	80
V2#10-12: Reprints earlier issues	3	6	9	17	26	35

NOTE: **Davis** a-3(2 pgs.), 4, 5, 10; c-10. **Elder** a-5. **Powell** a-V2#10, 11. **Torres** a-1-5. **Tuska** a-V2#1.

PANIC
Gemstone Publishing: March, 1997 - No. 12, Dec, 1999 ($2.50, quarterly)

1-12: E.C. reprints						4.00

PANTHA (See Vampirella-The New Monthly #16,17)

PANTHA (Also see Prophecy)
Dynamite Entertainment: 2012 - No. 6, 2013 ($3.99)

1-6: 1-Jerwa-s/Rodrix-a; covers by Sean Chen & Texiera. 2-6-Texiera-c						4.00

PANTHA: HAUNTED PASSION (Also see Vampirella Monthly #0)
Harris Comics: May, 1997 ($2.95, B&W, one-shot)

1-r/Vampirella #30,31						4.00

PANTHA: VOLUME 2
Dynamite Entertainment: 2022 - Present ($3.99)

1-5-Sniegoski & Acheson-s/Lima-a						4.00

PANTHEON
IDW Publishing: Apr, 2010 - No. 5, Aug, 2010 ($3.99)

1-5-Andreyko-s/Molnar-a; co-created by Michael Chiklis						4.00

PANYA: THE MUMMY'S CURSE (World of Hellboy)
Dark Horse Comics: Jul, 2023 - No. 4, Nov, 2023 ($3.99, limited series)

1-4-Roberson-s/Mitten-a						4.00

PAPA MIDNITE (See John Constantine - Hellblazer Special:...)

PAPER GIRLS
Image Comics: Oct, 2015 - No. 30, Jul, 2019 ($2.99/$3.99)

1-20-Brian K. Vaughn-s/Cliff Chiang-a						3.00
21-29-($3.99)						4.00
30-($4.99) Last issue						5.00

PARADE (See Hanna-Barbera...)

PARADE COMICS (See Frisky Animals on Parade)

PARADE OF PLEASURE
Derric Verschoyle Ltd., London, England: 1954 (192 pgs.) (Hardback book)

By Geoffrey Wagner. Contains section devoted to the censorship of American comic books with illustrations in color and black and white. (Also see *Seduction of the Innocent*). Distributed in USA by Library Publishers, N. Y.	163	326	489	652	814	975
with dust jacket....	333	666	1000	1332	1666	2000

PARADISE TOO!
Abstract Studios: 2000 - No. 14, 2003 ($2.95, B&W)

1-14-Terry Moore's unpublished newspaper strips and sketches						3.00
Complete Paradise Too TPB (2010, $29.95) r/#1-14 with bonus material						30.00
...: Checking For Weirdos TPB (4/03, $14.95) r/#8-12						15.00
...: Drunk Ducks! TPB (7/02, $15.95) r/#1-7						16.00

PARADISE X (Also see Earth X and Universe X)
Marvel Comics: Apr, 2002 - No. 12, Aug, 2003 ($4.50/$2.99)

0-Ross-c; Braithwaite-a						4.50
1-12-($2.99) Ross-c; Braithwaite-a. 7-Punisher on-c. 10-Kingpin on-c						3.00
...:A (10/03, $2.99) Braithwaite-a; Ross-c						3.00
...:Devils (11/02, $4.50) Sadowski-a; Ross-c						4.50
...:Ragnarok 1,2 (3/02, 4/03; $2.99) Yeates-a; Ross-c						3.00
...:X (11/03, $2.99) Braithwaite-a; Ross-c; conclusion of story						3.00
...:Xen (7/02, $4.50) Yeowell & Sienkiewicz-a; Ross-c						4.50
Earth X Vol. 4: Paradise X Book 1 (2003, $29.99, TPB) r/#0,1-5, ...: Xen; Heralds #1-3						30.00
Vol. 5: Paradise X Book 2 (2004, $29.99, TPB) r/#6-12, Ragnarok #1&2; Devils, A & X						30.00

PARADISE X: HERALDS (Also see Earth X and Universe X)
Marvel Comics: Dec, 2001 - No. 3, Feb, 2002 ($3.50)

1-3-Prelude to Paradise X series; Ross-c; Pugh-a						3.50
Special Edition (Wizard preview) Ross-c						3.00

PARADOX
Dark Visions Publ.: June, 1994 - No. 2, Aug, 1994 ($2.95, B&W, mature)

1,2: 1-Linsner-c. 2-Boris-c.						4.00

PARALLAX: EMERALD NIGHT (See Final Night)
DC Comics: Nov, 1996 ($2.95, one-shot, 48 pgs.)

1-Final Night tie-in; Green Lantern (Kyle Rayner) app.						5.00

PARAMOUNT ANIMATED COMICS (See Harvey Comics Hits #60, 62)
Harvey Publications: No. 3, Jun, 1953 - No. 22, Jul, 1956

3-Baby Huey, Herman & Katnip, Buzzy the Crow begin	37	74	111	222	361	500
4-6	17	34	51	98	154	210
7-Baby Huey becomes permanent cover feature; cover title becomes Baby Huey with #9	31	62	93	182	296	410
8-10: 9-Infinity-c	15	30	45	85	130	175
11-22	13	26	39	72	101	130

Painkiller Jane (2006 series) #1 © Q&P

Parker Girls #5 © Terry Moore

Patsy and Hedy #14 © MAR

	GD 2.0	VG 4.0	FN 6.0	VF 8.0	VF/NM 9.0	NM- 9.2

PARASOMNIA
Dark Horse Comics: Jun, 2021 - No. 4, Sept, 2021 ($3.99, limited series)
1-4-Cullen Bunn-s/Andrea Mutti-a ... 4.00

PARASOMNIA: THE DREAMING GOD
Dark Horse Comics: Aug, 2022 - No. 4, Nov, 2022 ($3.99, limited series)
1-4-Cullen Bunn-s/Andrea Mutti-a ... 4.00

PARENT TRAP, THE (Disney)
Dell Publishing Co.: No. 1210, Oct-Dec, 1961

Four Color 1210-Movie, Hayley Mills photo-c	10	20	30	67	141	215

PARIAH (Aron Warner's...)
Dark Horse Comics: Feb, 2014 - No. 8, Sept, 2014 ($3.99)
1-8-Aron Warner & Philip Gelatt-s/Brett Weldele-a ... 4.00

PARKER GIRLS (Characters from Strangers in Paradise)
Abstract Studio: 2022 - No. 10, 2023 ($3.99, limited series)
1-10-Terry Moore-s/a; Katchoo & Tambi app. ... 4.00

PARLIAMENT OF JUSTICE
Image Comics: Mar, 2003 ($5.95, B&W, one-shot, square-bound)
1-Michael Avon Oeming-c/s; Neil Vokes-a ... 6.00

PARODY
Armour Publishing: Mar, 1977 - No. 3, Aug, 1977 (B&W humor magazine)

1	3	6	9	21	33	45
2,3: 2-King Kong, Happy Days. 3-Charlie's Angels, Rocky	2	4	6	11	16	20

PAROLE BREAKERS
Avon Periodicals/Realistic #2 on: Dec, 1951 - No. 3, July, 1952

1(#2 on inside)-r-c/Avon paperback #283 (painted-c)	71	142	213	454	777	1100
2-Kubert-a; r-c/Avon paperback #114 (photo-c)	53	106	154	334	567	800
3-Kinstler-c	43	86	129	271	461	650

PARTRIDGE FAMILY, THE (TV)(Also see David Cassidy)
Charlton Comics: Mar, 1971 - No. 21, Dec, 1973

1-(2 versions: B&W photo-c & tinted color photo-c)	9	18	27	59	117	175
2-4,6-10	5	10	15	33	57	80
5-Partridge Family Summer Special (52 pgs.): The Shadow, Lone Ranger, Charlie McCarthy, Flash Gordon, Hopalong Cassidy, Gene Autry & others app.	9	18	27	59	117	175
11-21	4	8	12	27	44	60

PARTS OF A HOLE
Caliber Press: 1991 ($2.50, B&W)
1-Short stories & cartoons by Brian Michael Bendis ... 4.00

PARTS UNKNOWN
Eclipse Comics/FX: July, 1992 - No. 4, Oct, 1992 ($2.50, B&W, mature)
1-4: All contain FX gaming cards ... 4.00

PARTS UNKNOWN
Image Comics: May, 2000 - Sept, 2000 ($2.95, B&W)
...: Killing Attractions 1 (5/00) Beau Smith-s/Brad Gorby-a ... 3.00
...: Hostile Takeover 1-4 (6-9/00) ... 3.00

PASSION, THE
Catechetical Guild: No. 394, 1955

394	10	20	30	56	76	95

PASSOVER (See Avengelyne)
Maximum Press: Dec, 1996 ($2.99, one-shot)
1 ... 4.00

PAST AWAYS
Dark Horse Comics: Mar, 2015 - No. 9, Mar, 2016 ($3.99)
1-9: 1-Matt Kindt-s/Scott Kolins-a; two covers by Kolins & Kindt ... 4.00

PAT BOONE (TV)(Also see Superman's Girlfriend Lois Lane #9)
National Per. Publ.: Sept-Oct, 1959 - No. 5, May-Jun, 1960 (All have photo-c)

1	43	86	129	271	461	650
2-5: 3-Fabian, Connie Francis & Paul Anka photos on-c. 4-Previews "Journey To The Center Of The Earth". 4-Johnny Mathis & Bobby Darin photos on-c. 5-Dick Clark & Frankie Avalon photos on-c	35	70	105	208	339	470

PATCHES
Rural Home/Patches Publ. (Orbit): Mar-Apr, 1945 - No. 11, Nov, 1947

1-L. B. Cole-c	58	116	174	371	636	900
2	26	52	78	154	252	350
3,4,6,8-11: 6-Henry Aldrich story. 8-Smiley Burnette-c/s (6/47); pre-dates Smiley Burnette #1. 9-Mr. District Attorney story (radio). Leav/Keigstein-a (16 pgs.). 9-11-Leav-c. 10-Jack Carson (radio) c/story; Leav-c. 11-Red Skelton story	20	40	60	117	189	260
5-Danny Kaye-c/story; L.B. Cole-c.	26	52	78	154	252	350
7-Hopalong Cassidy-c/story	24	48	72	140	230	320

PATH, THE (Also see Negation War)
CrossGeneration Comics: Apr, 2002 - No. 23, Apr, 2004 ($2.95)
1-23: 1-Ron Marz-s/Bart Sears-a. 13-Matthew Smith-a begins ... 3.00

PATHFINDER (Based on the Pathfinder roleplaying game)
Dynamite Entertainment: 2012 - No. 12, 2013 ($3.99)
1-12: 1-Jim Zub-s/Andrew Huerta-a; four covers. 2-12-Multiple covers on each ... 4.00
... Special 2013 ($4.99, 40 pgs.) Jim Zub-s/Kevin Stokes-a ... 5.00

PATHFINDER: CITY OF SECRETS (Based on the Pathfinder roleplaying game)
Dynamite Entertainment: 2014 - No. 6, 2014 ($4.99)
1-6-Zub-s/Oliveira-a; Bound-in poster; multiple covers on each ... 5.00

PATHFINDER: GOBLINS! (Based on the Pathfinder roleplaying game)
Dynamite Entertainment: 2013 - No. 5, 2013 ($3.99)
1-5: Short stories by various; multiple covers on each ... 4.00

PATHFINDER: HOLLOW MOUNTAIN (Based on the Pathfinder roleplaying game)
Dynamite Entertainment: 2015 - No. 6, 2016 ($4.99)
1-6: 1-Sutter-s/Garcia-a; multiple covers ... 5.00

PATHFINDER: ORIGINS (Based on the Pathfinder roleplaying game)
Dynamite Entertainment: 2015 - No. 6, 2015 ($4.99)
1-6: 1-Spotlight on Valeros; multiple-c. 2-Kyra. 3-Seoni. 4-Merisiel. 5-Harsk. 6-Ezren ... 5.00

PATHFINDER: RUNESCARS (Based on the Pathfinder roleplaying game)
Dynamite Entertainment: 2017 - No. 5, 2017 ($3.99/$4.99)
1-($3.99) Schneider-s/Silva-a; multiple covers ... 4.00
2-5-($4.99) 2,4,5-Sutter-s. 3,5-Schneider-s ... 5.00

PATHFINDER: SPIRAL OF BONES (Based on the Pathfinder roleplaying game)
Dynamite Entertainment: 2018 - No. 5, 2018 ($3.99)
1-5: 1-Frasier-s/Garcia-a; multiple covers; encounter map included in each ... 5.00

PATHFINDER: WAKE THE DEAD (Based on the Pathfinder roleplaying game)
Dynamite Entertainment: 2023 - No. 5, 2024 ($4.99)
1-5-Van Lente-s/Casallos-a ... 5.00

PATHFINDER: WORLDSCAPE (Based on the Pathfinder roleplaying game)
Dynamite Entertainment: 2016 - No. 6, 2017 ($4.99)
1-6-Red Sonja, John Carter and Tarzan app.; Jonathan Lau-a ... 5.00

PATHWAYS TO FANTASY
Pacific Comics: July, 1984
1-Barry Smith-c/a; Jeff Jones-a (4 pgs.) ... 4.00

PATORUZU (See Adventures of...)

PATRIOTS, THE
DC Comics (WildStorm): Jan, 2000 - No. 10, Oct, 2000 ($2.50)
1-10-Choi and Peterson-s/Ryan-a ... 3.00

PATSY & HEDY (Teenage)(Also see Hedy Wolfe)
Atlas Comics/Marvel (GPI/Male): Feb, 1952 - No. 110, Feb, 1967

1-Patsy Walker & Hedy Wolfe; Al Jaffee-c	110	220	330	704	1202	1700
2	28	56	84	168	274	380
3-10: 3,7,8,9-Al Jaffee-c	24	48	72	142	234	325
11-20: 17,19,20-Al Jaffee-c	20	40	60	117	189	260
21-40	18	36	54	105	165	225
41-50	9	18	27	60	120	180
51-60	9	18	27	58	114	170
61-80,100: 88-Lingerie panel	8	16	24	54	102	150
81-87,89-99,101-110	8	16	24	51	96	140
Annual 1(1963)-Early Marvel annual	13	26	39	91	201	310

PATSY & HER PALS (Teenage)
Atlas Comics (PPI): May, 1953 - No. 29, Aug, 1957

1-Patsy Walker	45	90	135	284	480	675
2	23	46	69	136	223	310
3-10	20	40	60	118	192	265
11-29: 24-Everett-c	17	34	51	98	154	210

PATSY WALKER (See All Teen, A Date With Patsy, Girls' Life, Miss America Magazine, Patsy

	GD 2.0	VG 4.0	FN 6.0	VF 8.0	VF/NM 9.0	NM- 9.2

& Hedy, Patsy & Her Pals & Teen Comics)
Marvel/Atlas Comics (BPC): 1945 (no month) - No. 124, Dec, 1965

	GD 2.0	VG 4.0	FN 6.0	VF 8.0	VF/NM 9.0	NM- 9.2
1-Teenage	454	908	1362	3632	6016	8400
2	58	116	174	371	636	900
3,4,6-10	41	82	.123	256	428	600
5-Injury-to-eye-c	52	104	156	328	552	775
11,12,15,16,18	29	58	87	172	281	390
13,14,17,19-22-Kurtzman's "Hey Look"	31	62	93	182	296	410
23,24	24	48	72	140	230	320
25-Rusty by Kurtzman; painted-c	34	68	102	199	325	450
26-29,31: 26-31: 52 pgs.	21	42	63	124	202	280
30(52 pgs.)-Egghead Doodle by Kurtzman (1 pg.)	22	44	66	132	216	300
32-57: Last precode (3/55)	20	40	60	114	182	250
58-80,100	10	20	30	66	138	210
81-98: 92,98-Millie x-over	9	18	27	61	123	185
.99-Linda Carter x-over	15	30	45	103	227	350
101-124	8	16	24	54	102	150
Fashion Parade 1(1966, 68 pgs.) (Beware cut-out & marked pages)						
	13	26	39	89	195	300

NOTE: Painted c-25-28. Anti-Wertham editorial in #21. Georgie app. in #8, 11, 17. Millie app. in #10, 92, 98. Mitzi app. in #11. Rusty app. in #12, 25. Willie app. in #12. *Al Jaffee* c-44, 47, 49, 51, 57, 58.

PATSY WALKER, A.K.A. HELLCAT
Marvel Comics: Feb, 2016 - No. 17, Jun, 2017 ($3.99)

1-17: 1-Kate Leth-s/Brittney Williams-a; She-Hulk and Tom Hale app. 2-Hedy Wolfe app. 6-Natasha Allegri-a. 6,7-Jessica Jones app. 8-Civil War II tie-in   4.00

PATSY WALKER: HELLCAT
Marvel Comics: Sept, 2008 - No. 5, Feb, 2009 ($2.99, limited series)

1-5-Lafuente-a/Kathryn Immonen-s/Stuart Immonen-c; Hellcat joins The Initiative   3.00

PAT THE BRAT (Adventures of Pipsqueak #34 on)
Archie Publications (Radio): June, 1953; Summer, 1955 - No. 4, 5/56; No. 15, 7/56 - No. 33, 7/59

	GD 2.0	VG 4.0	FN 6.0	VF 8.0	VF/NM 9.0	NM- 9.2
nn(6/53)	22	44	66	132	216	300
1(Summer, 1955)	20	40	60	115	185	255
2-4-(5/56) (#5-14 not published). 3-Early Bolling-a	11	22	33	62	86	110
15-(7/56)-33: 18-Early Bolling-a	5	10	15	35	63	90

PAT THE BRAT COMICS DIGEST MAGAZINE
Archie Publications: October, 1980 (95¢)

	GD 2.0	VG 4.0	FN 6.0	VF 8.0	VF/NM 9.0	NM- 9.2
1-Li'l Jinx & Super Duck app.	2	4	6	11	16	20

PATTY CAKE
Permanent Press: Mar, 1995 - No. 9, Jul, 1996 ($2.95, B&W)

1-9: Scott Roberts-s/a   4.00

PATTY CAKE
Caliber Press (Tapestry): Oct, 1996 - No. 3, Apr, 1997 ($2.95, B&W)

1-3: Scott Roberts-s/a, ...Christmas (12/96)   4.00

PATTY CAKE & FRIENDS
Slave Labor Graphics: Nov, 1997 - Nov, 2000 ($2.95, B&W)

Here There Be Monsters (10/97), 1-14: Scott Roberts-s/a   4.00
Volume 2 #1 (11/00, $4.95)   5.00

PATTY POWERS (Formerly Della Vision #3)
Atlas Comics: No. 4, Oct, 1955 - No. 7, Oct, 1956

	GD 2.0	VG 4.0	FN 6.0	VF 8.0	VF/NM 9.0	NM- 9.2
4	23	46	69	136	223	310
5-7	18	36	54	105	165	225

PAT WILTON (See Mighty Midget Comics)

PAUL
Spire Christian Comics (Fleming H. Revell Co.): 1978 (49¢)

	GD 2.0	VG 4.0	FN 6.0	VF 8.0	VF/NM 9.0	NM- 9.2
nn	2	4	6	10	14	18

PAULINE PERIL (See The Close Shaves of...)

PAUL IS DEAD (The Beatles)
Image Comics: Apr, 2020 ($16.99, graphic novel)

nn-Speculative fiction about the legend of Paul McCartney's 1966 death   17.00

PAUL REVERE'S RIDE (TV, Disney, see Walt Disney Showcase #34)
Dell Publishing Co.: No. 822, July, 1957

	GD 2.0	VG 4.0	FN 6.0	VF 8.0	VF/NM 9.0	NM- 9.2
Four Color 822-w/Johnny Tremain, Toth-a	9	18	27	57	111	165

PAUL TERRY (See Heckle and Jeckle)

PAUL TERRY'S ADVENTURES OF MIGHTY MOUSE (See Adventures of...)

PAUL TERRY'S COMICS (Formerly Terry-Toons Comics; becomes Adventures of Mighty Mouse No. 126 on)
St. John Publishing Co.: No. 85, Mar, 1951 - No. 125, May, 1955

	GD 2.0	VG 4.0	FN 6.0	VF 8.0	VF/NM 9.0	NM- 9.2
85,86-Same as Terry-Toons #85, & 86 with only a title change; published at same time?; Mighty Mouse, Heckle & Jeckle & Gandy Goose continue from Terry-Toons						
	15	30	45	83	124	165
87-99	10	20	30	58	79	100
100	12	24	36	67	94	120
101-104,107-125: 121,122,125-Painted-c	10	20	30	56	76	95
105,106-Giant Comics Edition (25¢, 100 pgs.) (9/53 & ?). 105-Little Roquefort-c/story						
	21	42	63	124	202	280

PAUL TERRY'S MIGHTY MOUSE (See Mighty Mouse)

PAUL TERRY'S MIGHTY MOUSE ADVENTURE STORIES (See Mighty Mouse Adventure Stories)

PAUL THE SAMURAI (See The Tick #4)
New England Comics: July, 1992 - No. 6, July, 1993 ($2.75, B&W)

1-6   4.00

PAWNEE BILL
Story Comics (Youthful Magazines?): Feb, 1951 - No. 3, July, 1951

	GD 2.0	VG 4.0	FN 6.0	VF 8.0	VF/NM 9.0	NM- 9.2
1-Bat Masterson, Wyatt Earp app.	18	36	54	107	169	230
2,3: 3-Origin Golden Warrior; Cameron-a	11	22	33	62	86	110

PAYBACKS, THE
Dark Horse Comics: Sept, 2015 - No. 4, Dec, 2015 ($3.99)

1-4: 1-Cates & Rahal-s/Shaw-a   4.00

PAY-OFF (This is the..., ...Crime, ...Detective Stories)
D. S. Publishing Co.: July-Aug, 1948 - No. 5, Mar-Apr, 1949 (52 pgs.)

	GD 2.0	VG 4.0	FN 6.0	VF 8.0	VF/NM 9.0	NM- 9.2
1-True Crime Cases #1,2	48	96	144	302	514	725
2	26	52	78	154	252	350
3-5-Thrilling Detective Stories	19	38	57	111	176	240

PEACEMAKER, THE (Also see Fightin' Five)
Charlton Comics: V3#1, Mar, 1967 - No. 5, Nov, 1967 (All 12¢ cover price)

	GD 2.0	VG 4.0	FN 6.0	VF 8.0	VF/NM 9.0	NM- 9.2
1-Fightin' Five begins	50	100	150	400	900	1400
2,3,5	6	12	18	37	66	95
4-Origin The Peacemaker	5	10	15	31	53	75
1,2(Modern Comics reprint, 1978)	2	4	6	8	10	12

PEACEMAKER (Also see Crisis On Infinite Earths & Showcase '93 #7,9,10)
DC Comics: Jan, 1988 - No. 4, Apr, 1988 ($1.25, limited series)

	GD 2.0	VG 4.0	FN 6.0	VF 8.0	VF/NM 9.0	NM- 9.2
1-Paul Kupperberg-s/Tod Smith-a	3	6	9	16	23	30
2-4						6.00

PEACEMAKER: DISTURBING THE PEACE (Suicide Squad)
DC Comics (Black Label): Mar, 2022 ($5.99, one-shot)

1-Garth Ennis-s/Garry Brown-a; revisits childhood and past missions   6.00

PEACEMAKER TRIES HARD (Suicide Squad)
DC Comics (Black Label): Jul, 2023 - No. 6, Dec, 2023 ($4.99, limited series)

1-6-Kyle Starks-s/Steve Pugh-a. 4-Snowflame app.   5.00

PEANUTS (Charlie Brown) (See Tip Top #173 and United Comics #21 for Peanuts 1st comic book app.)(Also see Fritzi Ritz, Nancy & Sluggo, Sparkle & Sparkler, Tip Top, Tip Topper & United Comics)
United Features Syndicate/Dell Publishing Co./Gold Key: 1953-54; No. 878, 2/58 - No. 13, 5-7/62; 5/63 - No. 4, 2/64

	GD 2.0	VG 4.0	FN 6.0	VF 8.0	VF/NM 9.0	NM- 9.2
1(U.F.S.)(1953-54)-Reprints United Features' Strange As It Seems, Willie, Ferdnand (scarce)	1250	2500	3750	9500	17,250	25,000
Four Color 878(#1) (Dell) Schulz-s/a, with assistance from Dale Hale and Jim Sasseville thru #4	162	324	486	1337	3019	4700
Four Color 969,1015('59)	36	72	108	259	580	900
4(2-4/60) Schulz-s/a; one story by Anthony Pocrnich, Schulz's assistant cartoonist						
	20	40	60	138	307	475
5-13-Schulz-c only; s/a by Pocrnich	17	34	51	114	252	390
1(Gold Key, 5/63)	36	72	108	259	580	900
2-4	15	30	45	100	220	340

PEANUTS (Charlie Brown)
BOOM! Entertainment: No. 0, Nov, 2011 - No. 4, Apr, 2012; V2 No. 1, Aug, 2012 - No. 32, Apr, 2016 ($1.00/$3.99)

0-(11/11, $1.00) New short stories and Sunday page reprints   3.00
1-4: 1-(1/12, $3.99) New short stories and Sunday page reprints; Snoopy sled cover   4.00
1-4-Variant-c with first appearance image. 1-Charlie Brown. 2-Lucy. 3-Linus. 4-Snoopy   6.00
(Volume 2)
1-32: 1-(8/12, "#1 of 4" on-c)   4.00
1-12-Variant-c with first appearance image. 1-Schroeder. 2-Pig-Pen. 4-Woodstock   10.00
... Free Comic Book Day Edition (5/12) Giveaway flip book with Adventure Time   3.00
...: Friends Forever 2016 Special (7/16, $7.99) New and classic short stories   8.00
Happiness is a Warm Blanket, Charlie Brown HC (Boom Entertainment, 3/11, $19.99) adaptation of new animated special   20.00
It's Tokyo, Charlie Brown (10/12, $13.99, squarebound GN) Vicki Scott-s/a; bonus art   14.00
...: Scotland Bound, Charlie Brown (4/21, $9.99, squarebound GN) adapted from a Schulz story meant for an unproduced animated special; bonus storyboards & art   10.00
...: The Snoopy Special 1 (11/15, $4.99) New and classic Snoopy short stories   5.00
...: Where Beagles Dare! GN (9/15, $9.99, SC) Jason Cooper-s/Vicki Scott-a   10.00

PEANUTS HALLOWEEN
Fantagraphics Books: Sept, 2008 (8-1/2" x 5-3/8" ashcan giveaway)

nn-Halloween themed reprints in color and B&W   3.00

PEARL
DC Comics (Jinxworld): Oct, 2018 - No. 12, Oct, 2019 ($3.99)

1-12-Bendis-s/Gaydos-a. 1-Bonus reprint of 1st Bendis Batman-s (Batman Chrons. #21)   4.00

PEARL
Dark Horse Comics: May, 2022 - No. 6, Oct, 2022 ($3.99)

1-6-Bendis-s/Gaydos-a   4.00

PEBBLES & BAMM BAMM (TV) (See Cave Kids #7, 12)
Charlton Comics: Jan, 1972 - No. 36, Dec, 1976 (Hanna-Barbera)

	GD 2.0	VG 4.0	FN 6.0	VF 8.0	VF/NM 9.0	NM- 9.2
1-From the Flintstones; "Teen Age..." on cover	5	10	15	35	63	90
2-10	3	6	9	16	24	32
11-20	2	4	6	13	18	22
21-36	2	4	6	9	13	16
nn (1973, digest, 100 pgs.) B&W one page gags	3	6	9	21	33	45

PEBBLES & BAMM BAMM (TV)
Harvey Comics: Nov, 1993 - No. 3, Mar, 1994 ($1.50) (Hanna-Barbera)

V2#1-3   4.00
...Giant Size 1 (10/93, $2.25, 68 pgs.)("Summer Special" on-c)   5.00

PEBBLES FLINTSTONE (TV) (See The Flintstones #11)
Gold Key: Sept, 1963 (Hanna-Barbera)

	GD 2.0	VG 4.0	FN 6.0	VF 8.0	VF/NM 9.0	NM- 9.2
1 (10088-309)-Early Pebbles app.	9	18	27	63	129	195

PEDRO (Formerly My Private Life #17; also see Romeo Tubbs)
Fox Feature Syndicate: No. 18, June, 1950 - No. 2, Aug, 1950?

	GD 2.0	VG 4.0	FN 6.0	VF 8.0	VF/NM 9.0	NM- 9.2
18(#1)-Wood-c/a(p)	29	58	87	172	281	390
2-Wood-a?	19	38	57	112	179	240

PEE-WEE PIXIES (See The Pixies)

PELLEAS AND MELISANDE (See Night Music #4, 5)

Patsy Walker: Hellcat #1 © MAR

Pearl #2 © Jinxworld

Pep Comics #49 © ACP

	GD 2.0	VG 4.0	FN 6.0	VF 8.0	VF/NM 9.0	NM- 9.2

PENALTY (See Crime Must Pay the...)

PENANCE: RELENTLESS (See Civil War, Thunderbolts and related titles)
Marvel Comics: Nov, 2007 - No. 5 ($2.99)

1-5-Speedball/Penance; Jenkins-s/Gulacy-a. 3-Wolverine app.   3.00
TPB (2008, $13.99) r/#1-5   14.00

PENDRAGON (Knights of... #5 on; also see Knights of...)
Marvel Comics UK, Ltd.: July, 1992 - No. 15, Sept, 1993 ($1.75)

1-15: 1-4-Iron Man app. 6-8-Spider-Man app.   4.00

PENDULUM ILLUSTRATED BIOGRAPHIES
Pendulum Press: 1979 (B&W)

19-355x-George Washington/Thomas Jefferson, 19-3495-Charles Lindbergh/Amelia Earhart, 19-3509-Harry Houdini/Walt Disney, 19-3517-Davy Crockett/Daniel Boone-Redondo-a, 19-3525-Elvis Presley/Beatles, 19-3533-Benjamin Franklin/Martin Luther King Jr, 19-3541-Abraham Lincoln/Franklin D. Roosevelt, 19-3568-Marie Curie/Albert Einstein-Redondo-a, 19-3576-Thomas Edison/Alexander Graham Bell-Redondo-a, 19-3592-Babe Ruth/Jackie Robinson, 19-3606-Jim Thorpe/Althea Gibson

Softback					5.00
Hardback	1	2	3	4	5	7

PENDULUM ILLUSTRATED CLASSICS (Now Age Illustrated)
Pendulum Press: 1973 - 1978 (75¢, 62pp, B&W, 5-3/8x8")
(Also see Marvel Classics)

64-100x(1973)-Dracula-Redondo art, 64-131x-The Invisible Man-Nino art, 64-0968-Dr. Jekyll and Mr. Hyde-Redondo art, 64-1005-Black Beauty, 64-1010-Call of the Wild, 64-1020-Frankenstein, 64-1025-Huckleburn Finn, 64-1030-Moby Dick-Nino-a, 64-1040-Red Badge of Courage, 64-1045-The Time Machine-Nino-a, 64-1050-Tom Sawyer, 64-1055-Twenty Thousand Leagues Under the Sea, 64-1069-Treasure Island, 64-1328(1974)-Kidnapped, 64-1336-Three Musketeers-Nino art, 64-1344-A Tale of Two Cities, 64-1352-Journey to the Center of the Earth, 64-1360-The War of the Worlds-Nino-a, 64-1379-The Greatest Advs. of Sherlock Holmes-Redondo art, 64-1387-Mysterious Island, 64-1395-Hunchback of Notre Dame, 64-1409-Helen Keller-story of my life, 64-1417-Scarlet Letter, 64-1425-Gulliver's Travels, 64-2318(1977)-Around the World in Eighty Days, 64-2626-Captains Courageous, 64-2634-Connecticut Yankee, 64-2642-The Hound of the Baskervilles, 64-2650-The House of Seven Gables, 64-2669-Jane Eyre, 64-2677-The Last of the Mohicans, 64-2685-The Best of O'Henry, 64-2693-The Best of Poe-Redondo-a, 64-2707-Two Years Before the Mast, 64-2715-White Fang, 64-2723-Wuthering Heights, 64-3126(1978)-Ben Hur-Redondo art, 64-3134-A Christmas Carol, 64-3142-The Food of the Gods, 64-3150-Ivanhoe, 64-3169-The Man in the Iron Mask, 64-3177-The Prince and the Pauper, 64-3185-The Prisoner of Zenda, 64-3193-The Return of the Native, 64-3207-Robinson Crusoe, 64-3215-The Scarlet Pimpernel, 64-3223-The Sea Wolf, 64-3231-The Swiss Family Robinson, 64-3851-Billy Budd, 64-386x-Crime and Punishment, 64-3878-Don Quixote, 64-3886-Great Expectations, 64-389x-Heidi, 64-3908-The Iliad, 64-3916-Lord Jim, 64-3924-The Mutiny on Board H.M.S. Bounty, 64-3932-The Odyssey, 64-3940-Oliver Twist, 64-3959-Pride and Prejudice, 64-3967-The Turn of the Screw

Softback					6.00
Hardback	1	2	3	5	6	8

NOTE: All of the above books can be ordered from the publisher; some were reprinted as Marvel Classic Comics #1-12. In 1972 there was another brief series of 12 titles which contained Classics III. artwork. They were entitled *Now Age Books* Illustrated, but can be easily distinguished from later series by the small Classics Illustrated logo at the top of the front cover. The format is the same as the later series. The 48 pg. C.I. art was stretched out to make 62 pgs. After Twin Circle Publ. terminated the Classics III. series in 1971, they made a one year contract with Pendulum Press to rent these twelve titles of C.I. art. Pendulum was unhappy with the contract, and at the end of 1972 began their own art series, utilizing the talents of the Filipino art group. One detail which makes this rather confusing is that when they redid the art in 1973, they gave it the same identifying no. as the 1972 series. All 12 of the 1972 C.I. editions have new covers, taken from internal art panels. In spite of their recent age, all of the 1972 C.I. series are very rare. Mint copies would fetch at least $50. Here is a list of the 1972 series, with C.I. title no. counterpart:

64-1005 (CI#60-A2) 64-1010 (CI#91) 64-1015 (CI-Jr #505) 64-1020 (CI#26)
64-1025 (CI#19-A2) 64-1030 (CI#5-A2) 64-1035 (CI#169) 64-1040 (CI#98)
64-1045 (CI#133) 64-1050 (CI#50-A2) 64-1055 (CI#47) 64-1060 (CI-Jr#35)

PENDULUM ILLUSTRATED ORIGINALS
Pendulum Press: 1979 (In color)

94-4254-Solarman: The Beginning (See Solarman)   6.00

PENDULUM'S ILLUSTRATED STORIES
Pendulum Press: 1990 - No. 72, 1990? (No cover price ($4.95), squarebound, 68 pgs.)

1-72: Reprints Pendulum III. Classics series   5.00

PENGUIN (Dawn of DC)
DC Comics: No. 0, Oct, 2023 - Present ($3.99, limited series)

0-7: 0-Zdarsky-s/Ortega-a; Catwoman app. 1-7-Tom King-s   4.00

PENGUIN: PAIN & PREJUDICE (Batman)
DC Comics: Dec, 2011 - No. 5, Apr, 2012 ($2.99, limited series)

1-5-Hurwitz-s/Kudranski-a/c; Penguin's childhood and rise to power   3.00

PENGUINS OF MADAGASCAR (Based on the DreamWorks movie and TV series)
Ape Entertainment: 2010 - No. 4, 2011 ($3.95, limited series)

1-4-Skipper, Kowalski, Private and Rico app.   4.00

PENGUINS OF MADAGASCAR (Based on the DreamWorks movie and TV series)
Titan Comics: Dec, 2014 - No. 4, Mar, 2015 ($3.99, limited series)

1-4-Skipper, Kowalski, Private and Rico app.   4.00

PENNY

	GD 2.0	VG 4.0	FN 6.0	VF 8.0	VF/NM 9.0	NM- 9.2

Avon Comics: 1947 - No. 6, Sept-Oct, 1949 (Newspaper reprints)

1-Photo & biography of creator	40	80	120	246	411	575
2-5	20	40	60	117	189	260
6-Perry Como photo on-c	20	40	60	120	195	270

PENNY CENTURY (See Love and Rockets)
Fantagraphics Books: Dec, 1997 - No. 7, Jul, 2000 ($2.95, B&W, mini-series)

1-7-Jaime Hernandez-s/a   3.00

PENNY DORA AND THE WISHING BOX
Image Comics: Nov, 2014 - No. 5, Jun, 2015 ($2.99)

1-5-Michael Stock-s/Sina Grace-a   3.00

PENNY DREADFUL (Based on the Showtime TV series)
Titan Comics: Jun, 2016 - No. 5, Nov, 2016 ($3.99)

1-5: 1-Wilson-Cairns-s/De Martinis-a; multiple covers   4.00

PENNYWORTH (Alfred from Batman)
DC Comics: Oct, 2021 - No. 7, Apr, 2022 ($3.99)

1-7-Alfred's past in British Intelligence; Scott Bryan Wilson-s/Juan Gedeon-a   4.00

PENULTIMAN (See Steel Cage #1 for debut)
AHOY Comics: 2020 - No. 5, 2021 ($3.99)

1-5-Tom Peyer-s/Alan Robinson-a   4.00

PEP COMICS (See Archie Giant Series #576, 589, 601, 614, 624)
MLJ Magazines/Archie Publications No. 56 (3/46) on: Jan, 1940 - No. 411, Mar, 1987

	GD 2.0	VG 4.0	FN 6.0	VF 8.0	VF/NM 9.0	NM- 9.2
1-Intro. The Shield (1st patriotic hero) by Irving Novick; origin & 1st app. The Comet by Jack Cole, The Queen of Diamonds & Kayo Ward; The Rocket, The Press Guardian (The Falcon #1 only), Sergeant Boyle, Fu Chang, & Bentley of of Scotland Yard; Robot-c; Shield-c begin	1750	3500	5250	13,300	24,150	35,000
2-Origin The Rocket	389	778	1167	2723	4762	6800
3-Nazi WWII-c	314	628	942	2198	3849	5500
4-WWII brought to U.S. Capitol building; Wizard cameo; early robot-c	400	800	1200	2800	4900	7000
5-Wizard cameo in Shield story	300	600	900	1950	3375	4800
6,7,9,10: 7-Bondage-c	239	478	717	1530	2615	3700
8-Last Jack Cole Comet; no Cole-a in #6,7; torture by branding-c	371	742	1113	2600	4550	6500
11-Dusty, Shield's sidekick begins (1st app.); last Press Guardian, Fu Chang	300	600	900	2010	3505	5000
12-Origin & 1st app. Fireball (2/41); last Rocket & Queen of Diamonds; Danny in Wonderland begins; bondage-c	290	580	871	1856	3178	4500
13-15: All bondage/torture covers	219	438	657	1402	2401	3400
16-Origin Madam Satan; blood drainage-c	486	972	1458	3550	6275	9000
17-Origin/1st app. The Hangman (7/41); death of The Comet; Comet is revealed as Hangman's brother	975	1950	2919	7100	12,550	18,000
18,19,21: 18,21-Bondage/torture-c. 19-WWII Nazi-c. 21-Last Madam Satan	232	464	698	1485	2543	3600
20-Classic Nazi swastika-c; last Fireball	1900	3800	5700	14,400	26,200	38,000
22-Intro. & 1st app. Archie, Betty, & Jughead (12/41); (on sale 10/41)(also see Jackpot)	35,000	70,000	105,000	233,500	344,250	455,000
23-Statue of Liberty-c & Nazi-c (1/42; on sale 11/41)	3000	6000	9000	18,000	25,500	33,000
24-Coach Kleats app. (unnamed until Archie #94); bondage/torture-c	1000	2000	3000	7400	13,200	19,000
25-1st app. Archie's jalopy; 1st skinny Mr. Weatherbee prototype	703	1406	2109	5132	9066	13,000
26-1st app. Veronica Lodge (4/42); "Remember Pearl Harbor!" cover caption	2100	4200	6300	16,000	28,000	40,000
27-Bill of Rights & sunburst swastika-c	703	1406	2109	5132	9066	13,000
28-Classic swastika/Hangman-c	497	994	1491	3628	6414	9200
29,30: 29-Origin Shield retold; 30-Capt. Commando begins; bondage/torture-c; 1st Miss Grundy (definitive version); see Jackpot #4	486	972	1458	3550	6275	9000
31-MLJ offices & artists are visited in Sgt. Boyle story; 1st app. Mr. Lodge; cover has woman steam-broiled alive, Nazi bondage-c	703	1406	2109	5132	9066	13,000
32,33,35: 32-Shield dons new costume; bondage/brain drilling/Nazi-c. 33-Pre-Moose tryout (see Jughead #1); Nazi Viking-c. 35-WWII nurse bondage/torture-c	371	742	1113	2600	4550	6500
34-Classic Bondage/Hypo-c	3225	6450	9675	20,150	31,075	42,000
36-1st full Archie-c in Pep (2/43) w/Shield & Hangman (see Jackpot #4 where Archie's face appears in a small circle)	2120	4240	6360	14,800	24,900	35,000
37-40: 37-WWII Japanese firing squad-c. 38-Nazi WWII-c. 39-Bondage-c. 40-Bondage/ Japanese WWII-c	300	600	900	2010	3505	5000
41-Archie-c begin	377	754	1131	2639	4620	6600
42-45	245	490	735	1568	2684	3800
46,47,49,50: 47-Last Hangman issue; infinity-c	213	426	639	1363	2332	3300

	GD 2.0	VG 4.0	FN 6.0	VF 8.0	VF/NM 9.0	NM- 9.2
48-Black Hood begins (5/44); ends #51,59,60; Archie fish-c						
	284	568	852	1818	3109	4400
51-60: 52-Suzie begins; 1st Mr Weatherbee-c. 56-Last Capt. Commando. 59-Black Hood not in costume; lingerie panels; Archie dresses as his aunt; Suzie ends. 60-Katy Keene begins(3/47), ends #154						
	110	220	330	704	1202	1700
61-65-Last Shield. 62-1st app. Li'l Jinx (7/47)	84	168	252	538	919	1300
66-80: 66-G-Man Club becomes Archie Club (2/48); Nevada Jones by Bill Woggon. 76-Katy Keene story. 78-1st app. Dilton						
	47	94	141	296	498	700
81-99	31	62	93	182	296	410
100	37	74	111	222	361	500
101-130	21	42	63	122	199	275
131(2/59)-137	9	18	27	59	117	175
138-140-Neal Adams-a (1 pg.) in each	9	18	27	60	120	180
141-149(9/61)	8	16	24	52	99	145
150-160-Super-heroes app. in each (see note). 150 (10/61?)-2nd or 3rd app. The Jaguar?						
151-154,156-158-Horror/Sci/Fi-c. 157-Li'l Jinx. 159-Both 12¢ and 15¢ covers exist	10	20	30	64	120	200
161(3/63) 3rd Josie app.; early Josie stories w/DeCarlo-a begin (see Note for others)						
	9	18	27	57	111	165
162-167,169-180	6	12	18	37	66	95
168,200: 168-(1/64)-Jaguar app. 200-(12/66)	6	12	18	38	69	100
181(7/65)-199: 187-Pureheart try-out story. 192-UFO-c. 198-Giantman-c(only)						
	5	10	15	30	50	70
201-217,219-226,228-240(4/70): 224-(12/68) 1st app. Archie's pet, Hot Dog (later becomes Jughead's pet)						
	3	6	9	18	28	38
218,227-Archies Band-c only	3	6	9	20	31	42
241-270(10/72)	3	6	9	15	22	28
271-297,299	2	4	6	11	16	20
298, 300: 298-Josie and the Pussycats-c. 300(4/75)	3	6	9	15	22	28
301-340(8/78)	2	4	6	8	11	14
341-382	1	3	4	6	8	10
383(4/82),393(3/84): 383-Marvelous Maureen begins (Sci/fi). 393-Thunderbunny begins						
	2	4	6	8	10	12
384-392,394,395,397-399,401-410						6.00
396-Early Cheryl Blossom-c	2	4	6	11	14	20
400(5/85),411: 400-Story featuring Archie staff (DeCarlo-a)						
	1	2	3	5	6	8

NOTE: *Biro* a-2, 4, 5. *Jack Cole* a-1-5, 8. *Al Fagaly* c-55-72. *Fuje* a-39, 45, 47; c-34. *Meskin* a-2, 4, 5, 11(2). *Montana* c-30, 32, 33, 36, 73-87(most). *Novick* c-1-28, 29(w/Schomburg), 31i. *Harry Sahle* c-35, 39-50. *Schomburg* c-38. *Bob Wood* a-2, 4-6, 11. The Fly app. in 151, 154, 160. Flygirl app. in 153, 155, 156, 158. Jaguar app. in 150, 152, 157, 159, 168. Josie app. by DeCarlo in 161-166, 168-171, 173, 175-177, 179, 181. Katy Keene app. by *Bill Woggon* in 73-126. Bondage c-7, 12, 13, 15, 18, 21, 31, 32. Cover features: Shield #1-16; Shield/Hangman #17-27, 29-41; Hangman #28. Archie #36, 41-on.

PEP COMICS FEATURING BETTY AND VERONICA
Archie Comic Publications: May, 2011 (Giveaway)

Free Comic Book Day Edition - Little Archie flashback						5.00

PEPE
Dell Publishing Co.: No. 1194, Apr, 1961

Four Color 1194-Movie, photo-c	5	10	15	33	57	80

PERFECT CRIME, THE
Cross Publications: Oct, 1949 - No. 33, May, 1953 (#2-14, 52 pgs.)

1-Powell-a(2)	60	120	180	381	653	925
2 (4/50)	34	68	102	199	325	450
3-10: 7-Steve Duncan begins, ends #30. 10-Flag-c	27	54	81	162	266	370
11-used in **SOTI**, pg. 159	32	64	96	188	307	425
12-14	25	50	75	150	245	340
15- "The Most Terrible Menace" 2 pg. drug editorial (8/51)						
	32	64	96	188	307	425
16,17,19-25,27-29,31-33	22	44	66	128	209	290
18-Drug cover, heroin drug propaganda story, plus 2 pg. anti-drug editorial (11/51)						
	48	96	144	302	514	725
26-Drug-c with hypodermic needle; drug propaganda story (7/52)						
	50	100	150	315	533	750
30-Strangulation cover (11/52)	58	116	174	371	636	900

NOTE: *Powell* a-No. 1, 2, 4. *Wildey* a-1, 5. Bondage c-11.

PERFECT LOVE
Ziff-Davis(Approved Comics)/St. John No. 9 on: #10, 8-9/51 (cover date; 5-6/51 indicia date); #2, 10-11/51 - #10, 12/53

10(#1)(8-9/51)-Painted-c	36	72	108	211	343	475
2(10-11/51)	22	44	66	132	216	300
3,5-7: 3-Painted-c. 5-Photo-c	20	40	60	114	182	250
4,8 (Fall, 1952)-Kinstler-a; last Ziff-Davis issue	20	40	60	114	182	250
9,10 (10/53, 12/53, St. John): 9-Painted-c. 10-Photo-c						
	19	38	57	109	172	235

PERHAPANAUTS, THE
Dark Horse Comics: Nov, 2005 - No. 4, Feb, 2006 ($2.99, limited series)

1-4-Todd Dezago-s/Craig Rousseau-a/c						3.00
... Annual #1 (2/08, $3.50) Two covers by Rousseau and Allred						3.50
... Danger Down Under! 1-5 (11/12 - No. 5, 6/13, $3.50) Two covers on each						3.50
... Halloween Spooktacular 1 (10/09, $3.50) Hembeck, Rousseau and others-a						3.50
,,, - Molly's Story (2/10, $3.50) Copland-a						3.50
(2nd series) 1-6 (2/08, $3.50) 1-6: 1-Two covers by Art Adams and Rousseau						3.50

PERHAPANAUTS: SECOND CHANCES, THE
Dark Horse Comics: Oct, 2006 - No. 4, Jan, 2007 ($2.99, limited series)

1-4-Todd Dezago-s/Craig Rousseau-a/c						3.00

PERRI (Disney)
Dell Publishing Co.: No. 847, Jan, 1958

Four Color 847-Movie, w/2 diff-c publ.	6	12	18	42	79	115

PERRY MASON
David McKay Publications: No. 49, 1946 - No. 50, 1946

Feature Books 49, 50-Based on Gardner novels	42	84	126	265	445	625

PERRY MASON MYSTERY MAGAZINE (TV)

Dell Publishing Co.: June-Aug, 1964 - No. 2, Oct-Dec, 1964

1-Raymond Burr painted-c	10	20	30	64	132	200
2-Raymond Burr photo-c	6	12	18	41	76	110

PERSONAL LOVE (Also see Movie Love)
Famous Funnies: Jan, 1950 - No. 33, June, 1955

1-Photo-c	31	62	93	182	296	410
2-Kathryn Grayson & Mario Lanza photo-c	18	36	54	105	165	225
3-7,10: 7-Robert Walker & Joanne Dru photo-c. 10-Loretta Young & Joseph Cotton photo-c						
	16	32	48	94	147	200
8,9: 8-Esther Williams & Howard Keel photo-c. 9-Debra Paget & Louis Jourdan photo-c						
	17	34	51	98	154	210
11-Toth-a; Glenn Ford & Gene Tierney photo-c	20	40	60	114	182	250
12,16,17-One pg. Frazetta each. 17-Rock Hudson & Yvonne DeCarlo photo-c						
	17	34	51	98	154	210
13-15,18-23: 12-Jane Greer & William Lundigan photo-c. 14-Kirk Douglas photo-c. 15-Dale Robertson & Joanne Dru photo-c. 18-Gregory Peck & Susan Hayworth photo-c. 19-Anthony Quinn & Suzan Ball photo-c. 20-Robert Wagner & Kathleen Crowley photo-c. 21-Roberts Peters & Byron Palmer photo-c. 22-Dale Robertson photo-c. 23-Rhonda Fleming-c						
	15	30	45	90	140	190
24,27,28-Frazetta-a in each (8,8&6 pgs.). 27-Rhonda Fleming & Fernando Lamas photo-c. 28-Mitzi Gaynor photo-c						
	58	116	174	371	636	900
25-Frazetta-a (tribute to Bettie Page, 7 pg. story); Tyrone Power/Terry Moore photo-c from "King of the Khyber Rifles"	100	200	300	638	1093	1550
26,29,30,33: 26-Constance Smith & Byron Palmer photo-c. 29-Charlton Heston & Nicol Morey photo-c. 30-Johnny Ray & Mitzi Gaynor photo-c. 33-Dana Andrews & Piper Laurie photo-c						
	15	30	45	86	133	180
31-Marlon Brando & Jean Simmons photo-c; last pre-code (2/55)						
	20	40	60	114	182	250
32-Classic Frazetta-a (8 pgs.); Kirk Douglas & Bella Darvi photo-c						
	97	194	291	621	1061	1500

NOTE: All have photo-c. Many feature movie stars. *Everett* a-5, 9, 10. 24.

PERSONAL LOVE (Going Steady V3#3 on)
Prize Publ. (Headline): V1#1, Sept, 1957 - V3#2, Nov-Dec, 1959

V1#1	16	32	48	94	147	200
2	11	22	33	62	86	110
3-6(7-8/58)	9	18	27	50	65	80
V2#1(9-10/58)-V2#6(7-8/59)	8	16	24	42	54	65
V3#1-Wood?/Orlando-a	8	16	24	44	57	70
2	8	16	24	40	50	60

PESTILENCE
AfterShock Comics: May, 2017 - No. 6, Jan, 2018 ($3.99)

1-6-Tieri-s/Okunev-a/Bradstreet-c; Crusaders and zombies in the year 1347						4.00

PESTILENCE: A STORY OF SATAN
AfterShock Comics: May, 2018 - No. 5, Nov, 2018 ($3.99)

1-5-Tieri-s/Okunev-a/Bradstreet-c						4.00

PETER CANNON - THUNDERBOLT (See Crisis on Infinite Earths)(Also see Thunderbolt)
DC Comics: Sept, 1992 - No. 12, Aug, 1993 ($1.25)

1-12						4.00

PETER CANNON: THUNDERBOLT
Dynamite Entertainment: 2012 - No. 13, 2013 ($3.99)

1-10: 1-Darnell & Ross-s/Lau-a; back-up unpublished '80s Thunderbolt story; Pete Morisi-s/a. 1-3-Four covers on each. 4-7-Covers by Ross & Segovia						4.00

PETER CANNON: THUNDERBOLT, VOLUME 1
Dynamite Entertainment: 2019 - No. 5, 2019 ($3.99)

1-5-Gillen-s/Wijngaard-a						4.00

PETER COTTONTAIL
Key Publications: Jan, 1954; Feb, 1954 - No. 2, Mar, 1954 (Says 3/53 in error)

1(1/54)-Not 3-D	14	28	42	76	108	140
1(2/54)-(3-D, 25¢)-Came w/glasses; written by Bruce Hamilton						
	26	52	78	154	252	350
2-Reprints 3-D #1 but not in 3-D	8	16	24	40	50	60

PETER GUNN (TV)
Dell Publishing Co.: No. 1087, Apr-June, 1960

Four Color 1087-Photo-c	8	16	24	52	99	145

PETE ROSE: HIS INCREDIBLE BASEBALL CAREER
Masstar Creations Inc.: 1995

1-John Tartaglione-a						4.00

PETER PAN (Disney) (See Hook, Movie Classics & Comics, New Adventures of... & Walt Disney Showcase #36)
Dell Publishing Co.: No. 442, Dec, 1952 - No. 926, Aug, 1958

Four Color 442 (#1)-Movie	12	24	36	83	182	280
Four Color 926-Reprint of 442	6	12	18	42	79	115

PETER PAN
Disney Comics: 1991 ($5.95, graphic novel, 68 pgs.)(Celebrates video release)

nn-r/Peter Pan Treasure Chest from 1953						7.00

PETER PANDA
National Periodical Publications: Aug-Sept, 1953 - No. 31, Aug-Sept, 1958

1-Grossman-c/a in all	97	194	291	621	1061	1500
2	39	78	117	231	378	525
3,4,6-8,10	31	62	93	182	296	410
5-Classic-c (scarce)	126	252	378	806	1378	1950
9-Robot-c	43	86	129	271	461	650
11-31	23	46	69	136	223	310

PETER PAN RECORDS (See Power Records)

PETER PAN TREASURE CHEST (See Dell Giants)

PETER PANZERFAUST
Image Comics (Shadowline): Feb, 2012 - No. 25, Dec, 2016 ($3.50/$3.99)

Peter Cannon: Thunderbolt #3 © DYN

Peter Parker #1 © MAR

Peter Rabbit #3 © AVON

	GD 2.0	VG 4.0	FN 6.0	VF 8.0	VF/NM 9.0	NM- 9.2
1-Kurtis Wiebe-s/Tyler Jenkins-a/c; Peter Pan-type character in WWII Europe	3	6	9	17	26	35
1-Second printing	1	3	4	6	8	10
2,3	1	2	3	5	6	8
4-8						5.00
9-1st full app. Kapitan Haken						6.00
10-24						4.00
25-Last issue; bonus preview of Rat Queens v2						5.00

PETER PARKER (See The Spectacular Spider-Man)

PETER PARKER
Marvel Comics: May, 2010 - No. 5, Sept, 2010 ($3.99/$2.99)

1-($3.99) Prints material from Marvel Digital Comics; Olliffe-a; back-up w/Hembeck-s/a						4.00
2-5-($2.99): 2-4-Olliffe-a. 3-Braithwaite-c. 5-Nauck-a; Thing app.						3.00

PETER PARKER & MILES MORALES: SPIDER-MEN DOUBLE TROUBLE (All ages)
Marvel Comics: No. 1 - No. 4, Apr, 2023 ($3.99, limited series)

1-4-Tamaki & Ayala-s/Gurihiru-a; Mysterio & Thanos app.						4.00

PETER PARKER: SPIDER-MAN
Marvel Comics: Jan, 1999 - No. 57, Aug, 2003 ($2.99/$1.99/$2.25)

1-Mackie-s/Romita Jr.-a; wraparound-c	2	4	6	8	10	12
1-($6.95) DF Edition w/variant-c by the Romitas	2	4	6	11	16	20
2,3,5-11,13-17-($1.99): 2-Two covers; Thor app. 3-Iceman-c/app. 5-Spider-Woman app.						4.00
7,8-Blade app. 9,10-Venom app. 11-Iron Man & Thor-c/app.						4.00
4-1st Hunger; Marrow-c/app.	2	4	6	9	11	14
12-($2.99) Sinister Six and Venom app.						5.00
18-24,26-43: 18-Begin $2.25-c. 20-Jenkins-s/Buckingham-a start. 23-Intro Typeface. 24-Maximum Security x-over. 29-Rescue of MJ. 30-Ramos-c. 42,43-Mahfood-a						4.00
25-($2.99) Two covers; Spider-Man & Green Goblin						5.00
44-47-Humberto Ramos-c/a; Green Goblin-c/app.						4.00
48,49,51-57: 48,49-Buckingham-c/a. 51,52-Herrera-a. 56,57-Kieth-a; Sandman returns						4.00
50-($3.50) Buckingham-c/a						5.00
#156.1 (10/12, $2.99, 50th Anniversary one-shot) Stern-s/De La Torre-a/Romita Jr.-c						4.00
...'99 Annual (8/99, $3.50) Man-Thing app.						5.00
...'00 Annual ($3.50) Bounty app.; Joe Bennett-a; Black Cat back-up story						5.00
...'01 Annual ($2.99) Avery-s						5.00
...: A Day in the Life TPB (5/01, $14.95) r/#20-22, 26; Webspinners #10-12						15.00
...: One Small Break TPB (2002, $16.95) r/#27,23,30-34; Andrews-c						17.00
Spider-Man: Return of the Goblin TPB (2002, $6.99) r/#44-47; Ramos-c						9.00
...Vol. 4: Trials & Tribulations TPB (2003, $11.99) r/#35,37,48-50; Cho-c						12.00

PETER PARKER: THE SPECTACULAR SPIDER-MAN
Marvel Comics: Aug, 2017 - No. 6, Jan, 2018; No. 297, Feb, 2018 - No. 313, Feb, 2019 ($4.99/$3.99)

1-($4.99) Zdarsky-s/Adam Kubert-a; Johnny Storm app.; back-up w/Black Widow app.						5.00
2-6-($3.99) 3,4-Kingpin app. 6-Walsh-a						4.00
[Title switches to legacy numbering after #6 (1/18)]						
297-299-Kubert-a. 298,299-Black Panther app.						4.00
300-($5.99) Black Panther, Human Torch, Ironheart app.; bonus cover gallery						6.00
301-313: 301-303-Spider-Man teams with younger version; Quinones-a. 310-Zdarsky-a. 311-313-Spider-Geddon tie-in; Morlun app.						4.00
Annual 1 (8/18, $4.99) Zdarsky-s/Allred-a/c; spotlight on J. Jonah Jameson; Bachalo-a						5.00

PETER PAT
United Features Syndicate: No. 8, 1939

Single Series 8	41	82	123	258	428	600

PETER PAUL'S 4 IN 1 JUMBO COMIC BOOK
Capitol Stories (Charlton): No date (1953)

1-Contains 4 comics bound; Space Adventures, Space Western, Crime & Justice, Racket Squad in Action	48	96	144	302	514	725

PETER PIG
Standard Comics: No. 5, May, 1953 - No. 6, Aug, 1953

5,6	9	18	27	50	65	80

PETER PORKCHOPS (See Leading Comics #23) (Also see Capt. Carrot)
National Periodical Publications: 11-12/49 - No. 61, 9-11/59; No. 62, 10-12/60 (1-11: 52 pgs.)

1	41	82	123	256	428	600
2	20	40	60	114	182	250
3-10: 6- "Peter Rockets to Mars!" c/story	14	28	42	82	121	160
11-30	11	22	33	62	86	110
31-62	9	18	27	52	69	85

NOTE: *Otto Feuer a-all. Rube Grossman-a most issues. Sheldon Mayer a-30-38, 40-44, 46-52, 61.*

PETER PORKER, THE SPECTACULAR SPIDER-HAM
Star Comics (Marvel): May, 1985 - No. 17, Sept, 1987 (Also see Marvel Tails)

	GD 2.0	VG 4.0	FN 6.0	VF 8.0	VF/NM 9.0	NM- 9.2
1-Michael Golden-c	3	6	9	17	26	35
2-17: 12-Origin/1st app. Bizarro Phil. 13-Halloween issue						5.00

NOTE: *Back-up features: 2-X-Bugs. 3-Iron Mouse. 4-Croctor Strange. 5-Thrr, Dog of Thunder.*

PETER POTAMUS (TV)
Gold Key: Jan, 1965 (Hanna-Barbera)

1-1st app. Peter Potamus & So-So, Breezly & Sneezly	9	18	27	63	129	195

PETER RABBIT (See New Funnies #65 & Space Comics)
Dell Publishing Co.: No. 1, 1942

Large Feature Comic 1	90	180	270	576	988	1400

PETER RABBIT (Adventures of...; New Advs. of...; #9 on)(Also see Funny Tunes & Space Comics)
Avon Periodicals: 1947 - No. 34, Aug-Sept, 1956

1(1947)-Reprints 1943-44 Sunday strips; contains a biography & drawing of Cady	43	86	129	271	461	650
2 (4/48)	29	58	87	172	281	390
3 ('48) - 6(7/49)-Last Cady issue	25	50	75	150	245	340
7-10(1950-8/51): 9-New logo	14	28	42	78	112	145
11(11/51)-34('56)-Avon's character	11	22	33	62	86	110
...Easter Parade (1952, 25¢, 132 pgs.)	26	52	78	154	252	350
...Jumbo Book (1954-Giant Size, 25¢)-Jesse James by Kinstler (6 pgs.); space ship-c	29	58	87	172	281	390

PETER RABBIT 3-D
Eternity Comics: April, 1990 ($2.95, with glasses; sealed in plastic bag)

1-By Harrison Cady (reprints)						5.00

PETER, THE LITTLE PEST (#4 titled Petey)
Marvel Comics Group: Nov, 1969 - No. 4, May, 1970

1	9	18	27	57	111	165
2-4-r-Dexter the Demon & Melvin the Monster	5	10	15	33	57	80

PETE'S DRAGON (See Walt Disney Showcase #43)

PETE THE PANIC
Stanmor Publications: November, 1955

nn-Code approved	10	20	30	58	79	100

PETEY (See Peter, the Little Pest)

PETTICOAT JUNCTION (TV, inspired Green Acres)
Dell Publ. Co.: Oct-Dec, 1964 - No. 5, Oct-Dec, 1965 (#1-3, 5 have photo-c)

1	7	14	21	49	92	135
2-5	5	10	15	34	60	85

PETUNIA (Also see Looney Tunes and Porky Pig)
Dell Publishing Co.: No. 463, Apr, 1953

Four Color 463	6	12	18	40	73	105

PHAGE (See Neil Gaiman's Teknophage & Neil Gaiman's Phage-Shadowdeath)

PHALANX, THE
Image Comics: Jun, 2022 ($3.99, one-shot)

1-Jonathan Luna-s/a						4.00

PHANTACEA
McPherson Publishing Co.: Sept, 1977 - No. 6, Summer, 1980 (B&W)

1-Early Dave Sim-a (32 pgs.)	4	8	12	28	47	65
2-Dave Sim-a(10 pgs.)	3	6	9	14	19	24
3-6: 3-Flip-c w/Damnation Bridge. 4-Gene Day-a	2	4	6	10	14	18

PHANTASMO (See The Funnies #45)
Dell Publishing Co.: No. 18, 1941

Large Feature Comic 18	52	104	156	328	552	775

PHANTOM, THE
David McKay Publishing Co.: 1939 - 1949

Feature Books 20	314	628	942	2198	3849	5500
Feature Books 22	116	232	348	742	1271	1800
Feature Books 39	90	180	270	576	988	1400
Feature Books 53,56,57	136	136	204	435	743	1050

PHANTOM, THE (See Ace Comics, Defenders Of The Earth, Eat Right to Work and Win, Future Comics, Harvey Comics Hits #51,56, Harvey Hits #1, 6, 12, 15, 26, 36, 44, 48, & King Comics)

PHANTOM, THE (nn (#29)-Published overseas only) (Also see Comics Reading Libraries in the Promotional Comics section)
Gold Key(#1-17)/King(#18-28)/Charlton(#30 on): Nov, 1962 - No. 17, Jul, 1966; No. 18, Sept, 1966 - No. 28, Dec, 1967; No. 30, Feb, 1969 - No. 74, Jan, 1977

	GD 2.0	VG 4.0	FN 6.0	VF 8.0	VF/NM 9.0	NM- 9.2

	GD 2.0	VG 4.0	FN 6.0	VF 8.0	VF/NM 9.0	NM- 9.2
1-Origin revealed on inside-c & back-c	34	68	102	245	548	850
2-King, Queen & Jack begins, ends #11	11	22	33	72	154	235
3-5	9	18	27	58	114	170
6-10	7	14	21	46	86	125
11-17: 12-Track Hunter begins	6	12	18	38	69	100
18-Flash Gordon begins; Wood-a	5	10	15	31	53	75
19-24: 20-Flash Gordon ends (both by Gil Kane). 21-Mandrake begins. 20,24- Girl Phantom app.	4	8	12	28	47	65
25-28: 25-Jeff Jones-a(4 pgs.); 1 pg. Williamson ad. 26-Brick Bradford app. 28-Brick Bradford app.	4	8	12	23	37	50
30-33: 33-Last 12¢ issue	3	6	9	17	25	
34						
34-40: 36,39-Ditko-a	3	6	9	16	24	32
41-66,72: 46-Intro. The Piranha. 51-Grey tone-c. 62-Bolle-c	3	6	9	14	20	26
67-Origin retold; Newton-c/a; Humphrey Bogart, Lauren Bacall & Peter Lorre app.	3	6	9	17	25	34
68,70,71,73-Newton-c/a	3	6	9	14	19	24
69-Newton-c only	3	6	9	14	19	24
74-Classic flag-c by Newton; Newton-a;	3	6	9	18	28	38

NOTE: Aparo a-31-34, 36-38; c-31-38, 60, 61. Painted c-1-17.

PHANTOM, THE
DC Comics: May, 1988 - No. 4, Aug, 1988 ($1.25, mini-series)

1-4: Orlando-c/a in all						4.00

PHANTOM, THE
DC Comics: Mar, 1989 - No. 13, Mar, 1990 ($1.50)

1-13: 1-Brief origin						4.00

PHANTOM, THE
Wolf Publishing: 1992 - No. 8, 1993 ($2.25)

1-8						4.00

PHANTOM, THE
Moonstone: 2003 - No. 26, Dec, 2008 ($3.50/$3.99)

1-26: 1-Cassaday-c/Raab-s/Quinn-a						4.00
... Annual #1 (2007, $6.50) Blevins-c; stroy and art by various incl. Nolan						6.50
... - Captain Action 1 (2010, $3.99) covers by Thibert, Sparacio, and Gilbert						4.00

PHANTOM, THE
Hermes Press: 2014 - No. 6, 2016 ($3.99)

1-6: 1-Peter David-s/Sal Velluto-a; four covers						4.00

PHANTOM BLOT, THE (#1 titled New Adventures of,..)
Gold Key: Oct, 1964 - No. 7, Nov, 1966 (Disney)

1 (Meets The Mysterious Mr. X)	9	18	27	58	114	170
2-1st Super Goof	6	12	18	38	69	100
3-7	3	6	9	21	33	45

PHANTOM EAGLE (See Mighty Midget, Marvel Super Heroes #16 & Wow #6)

PHANTOM FORCE
Image Comics/Genesis West #0, 3-7: 12/93 - #2, 1994; #0, 3/94; #3, 5/94 - #8, 10/94 ($2.50/$3.50, limited series)

0 (3/94, $2.50)-Kirby/Jim Lee-c; Kirby-p pgs. 1,5,24-29.						
1 (12/93, $2.50)-Polybagged w/trading card; Kirby/Liefeld-c; Kirby plots/pencils w/inks by Liefeld, McFarlane, Jim Lee, Silvestri, Larsen, Williams, Ordway & Miki						4.00
2 ($3.50)-Kirby-a(p); Kirby/Larson-a						5.00
3-8: 3 (5/94, $2.50)-Kirby/McFarlane-c 4-(5/94)-Kirby(p). 5-(6/94)						4.00

PHANTOM GUARD
Image Comics (WildStorm Productions): Oct, 1997 - No. 6, Mar, 1998 ($2.50)

1-6: 1-Two covers						4.00
1-($3.50)-Voyager Pack w/Wildcore preview						5.00

PHANTOM JACK
Image Comics: Mar, 2004 - No. 5, July, 2004 ($2.95)

1-5-Mike San Giacomo-s/Mitchell Breitweiser-a. 4-Initial printings with errors exist						3.00
The Collected Edition (Speakeasy Comics, 2005, $17.99) r/series; Bendis intro						18.00

PHANTOM LADY (1st Series) (My Love Secret #24 on) (Also see All Top, Daring Adventures, Freedom Fighters, Jungle Thrills, & Wonder Boy)
Fox Feature Syndicate: No. 13, Aug, 1947 - No. 23, Apr, 1949

13(#1)-Phantom Lady by Matt Baker begins (see Police Comics #1 for 1st app.); Blue Beetle story	622	1244	1866	4541	8021	11,500
14-16: 14(#2)-Not Baker-c. 15-P.L. injected with experimental drug. 16-Negligee-c, panels; true crime stories begin	331	662	993	2317	4059	5800
17-Classic bondage cover; used in SOTI, illo "Sexual stimulation by combining 'headlights' with the sadist's dream of tying up a woman"	2925	5850	8775	22,400	41,200	60,000
18,19	320	640	960	2240	3920	5600
20-22	290	580	870	1856	3178	4500
23-Classic bondage-c	1300	2600	3900	9900	17,950	26,000

NOTE: Matt Baker a-in all; c-13, 15-21. Kamen a-22, 23.

PHANTOM LADY (2nd Series) (See Terrific Comics) (Formerly Linda)
Ajax/Farrell Publ.: V1#5, Dec-Jan, 1954/1955 - No. 4, June, 1955

V1#5(#1)-By Matt Baker	232	464	696	1485	2543	3600
V1#2-Last pre-code	155	310	465	992	1696	2400
3,4-Red Rocket. 3-Heroin story	116	232	348	742	1271	1800

PHANTOM LADY
Verotik Publications: 1994 ($9.95)

1-Reprints G. A. stories from Phantom Lady and All Top Comics; Adam Hughes-c	4	8	12	23	37	50

PHANTOM LADY
DC Comics: Oct, 2012 - No. 4, Jan, 2013 ($2.99, limited series)

1-4-Gray and Palmiotti-s/Staggs-a. 1-Re-intro with Doll Man; Conner-c						3.00

PHANTOM ON THE SCAN
AfterShock Comics: Apr, 2021 - No. 5, Sept, 2021 ($4.99/$3.99, limited series)

1-($4.99) Cullen Bunn-s/Mark Torres-a						5.00

	GD 2.0	VG 4.0	FN 6.0	VF 8.0	VF/NM 9.0	NM- 9.2
2-5-($3.99)						4.00

PHANTOM PLANET, THE
Dell Publishing Co.: No. 1234, 1961

Four Color 1234-Movie	9	18	27	57	111	165

PHANTOM ROAD
Image Comics: Mar, 2023 - Present ($3.99)

1-9-Lemire-s/Walta-a						4.00

PHANTOM STRANGER, THE (1st Series) (See Saga of Swamp Thing)
National Periodical Publications: Aug-Sept, 1952 - No. 6, June-July, 1953

1(Scarce)-1st app.	541	1082	1623	3950	6975	10,000
2 (Scarce)	300	600	900	2010	3505	5000
3-6 (Scarce)	290	580	870	1856	3178	4500
Ashcan (8,9/52) Not distributed to newsstands, only for in house use (no known sales)						

PHANTOM STRANGER, THE (2nd Series) (See Showcase #80) (See Showcase Presents for B&W reprints)
National Periodical Publs.: May-June, 1969 - No. 41, Feb-Mar, 1976; No. 42, Mar, 2010

1-2nd S.A. app. P. Stranger; only 12¢ issue	12	24	36	83	182	280
2,3	6	12	18	41	76	110
4-1st new look Phantom Stranger; N. Adams-a	7	14	21	46	86	125
5-7	5	10	15	33	57	80
8-14: 14-Last 15¢ issue	4	8	12	25	40	55
15-19: All 25¢ giants (52 pgs.)	4	8	12	27	44	60
20-Dark Circle begins, ends #24.	3	6	9	16	24	32
21,22	3	6	9	14	20	25
23-Spawn of Frankenstein begins by Kaluta	4	8	12	27	44	60
24,25,27-30-Last Spawn of Frankenstein	3	6	9	21	33	45
26- Book-length story featuring Phantom Stranger, Dr. 13 & Spawn of Frankenstein	4	8	12	23	37	50
31-The Black Orchid begins (6-7/74)	3	6	9	20	31	42
32,34-38: 34-Last 20¢ issue (#35 on are 25¢)	2	4	6	13	18	22
33,39-41: 33-Deadman-c/story. 39-41-Deadman app.	3	6	9	14	20	25
42-(3/10, $2.99) Blackest Night one-shot; Syaf-a; Spectre, Deadman and Blue Devil app.						3.00

NOTE: N. Adams a-4; c-3-19. Anderson a-4, 5i. Aparo a-7-17, 19-26; c-20-24, 33-41. B. Bailey a-27-30. DeZuniga a-12-16, 18, 19, 21, 22, 31, 34. Grell a-33. Kaluta c-23; c-26. Meskin r-15, 16, 18, 19. Redondo a-32, 35, 36. Sparling a-20. Starr a-17t. Toth a-15r. Black Orchid by Carrillo-38-41. Dr. 13 solo in-13, 18, 19, 20, 21, 34. Frankenstein by Kaluta-23-25; by Baily-27-30. No Black Orchid-33, 34, 37.

PHANTOM STRANGER (See Justice League of America #103)
DC Comics: Oct, 1987 - No. 4, Jan, 1988 (75¢, limited series)

1-4-Mignola-c/a & Eclipso app. in all. 3,4-Eclipso-c						5.00

PHANTOM STRANGER (See intro. in DC Comics - The New 52 FCBD Special Edition)
(Title changes to Trinity of Sin: The Phantom Stranger with #9 (Aug, 2013))
DC Comics: No. 0, Nov, 2012 - No. 22, Oct, 2015 ($2.99)

0-22: 0-Origin retold; Spectre app.; DiDio-s/Anderson-a. 2-Pandora app. 4,5-Jae Lee-c; Justice League Dark app. 6,7-Gene Ha-a/c. 8-The Question app. 11-Trinity War. 12-17-Forever Evil tie-in. 18-Superman app. 20-The Spectre app.						3.00
... Future's End (11/14, $3.99) 3-D lenticular cover; five years later; Winslade-a						4.00
... Future's End (11/14, $2.99) regular cover; five years later						3.00

PHANTOM STRANGER (See Vertigo Visions-The Phantom Stranger)

PHANTOM: THE GHOST WHO WALKS
Marvel Comics: Feb, 1995 - No. 3, April, 1995 ($2.95, limited series)

1-3						4.00

PHANTOM: THE GHOST WHO WALKS
Moonstone: 2003 ($16.95, TPB)

nn-Three new stories by Raab, Goulart, Collins, Blanco and others; Klauba painted-c						17.00

PHANTOM 2040 (TV cartoon)
Marvel Comics: May, 1995 - No. 4, Aug, 1995 ($1.50)

1-4-Based on animated series; Ditko-a(p) in all						4.00

PHANTOM WITCH DOCTOR (Also see Durango Kid #8 & Eerie #8)
Avon Periodicals: 1952

1-Kinstler-c/a (7 pgs.)	123	246	369	787	1344	1900

PHANTOM ZONE, THE (See Adventure #283 & Superboy #100, 104)
DC Comics: January, 1982 - No. 4, April, 1982

1-4-Superman app. in all. 2-4: Batman, Green Lantern, Supergirl, Wonder Woman app.						4.00

NOTE: Colan a-1-4p; c-1-4p. Giordano c-1-4i.

PHAZE
Eclipse Comics: Apr, 1988 - No. 2, Oct, 1988 ($2.25)

1,2: 1-Sienkiewicz-c. 2-Gulacy painted-c						4.00

PHENOMX
Image Comics: Oct, 2021 - No. 4, Jan, 2022 ($6.99/$3.99)

1-($6.99) John Leguizamo co-plotter/Batista-a						7.00
2-4-($3.99)						4.00

PHIL RIZZUTO (Baseball Hero) (See Sport Thrills, Accepted reprint)
Fawcett Publications: 1951 New York Yankees

nn-Photo-c	74	148	222	470	810	1150

PHOENIX
Atlas/Seaboard Publ.: Jan, 1975 - No. 4, Oct, 1975

1-Origin; Rovin-s/Amendola-a	3	6	9	14	19	24
2-4: 3-Origin & only app. The Dark Avenger. 4-New origin/costume The Protector (formerly Phoenix)	2	4	6	9	13	16

NOTE: Infantino appears in #1, 2. Austin a-3i. Thorne c-3.

PHOENIX
Ardden Entertainment (Atlas Comics): Mar, 2011 - No. 6, May, 2012 ($2.99)

1-6-Krueger & Deneen-s/Zachary-a; origin re-told						3.00
... Issue Zero - NY Comicon Edtion (10/10, $2.99) Dorien-a; origin prequel to #1						3.00

PHOENIX (...The Untold Story)
Marvel Comics Group: April, 1984 ($2.00, one-shot)

Phantom Lady #22 © FOX

Phantom Stranger (2012 series) #2 © DC

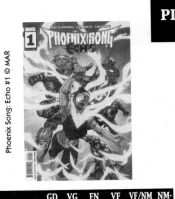

Phoenix Song: Echo #1 © MAR

	GD	VG	FN	VF	VF/NM	NM-
	2.0	4.0	6.0	8.0	9.0	9.2

1-Byrne/Austin-r/X-Men #137 with original unpublished ending

| | | 2 | 4 | 6 | 11 | 16 | 20 |

PHOENIX RESURRECTION, THE
Malibu Comics (Ultraverse): 1995 - 1996 ($3.95

Genesis #1 (12/95)-X-Men app; wraparound-c, Revelations #1 (12/95)-X-Men app;
wraparound-c, Aftermath #1 (1/96)-X-Men app ... 5.00
0-($1.95)-r/series ... 4.00
0-American Entertainment Ed. ... 5.00

PHOENIX RESURRECTION: THE RETURN OF JEAN GREY
Marvel Comics: Feb, 2018 - No. 5 ($4.99/$3.99, limited series)

1,5-($4.99) Yu-a. 5-Leads into Jean Grey #1 and X-Men Red #1 ... 5.00
2-4-($3.99) 2-Pacheco-a. 3-Bennett-a. 4-Rosanas-a ... 4.00

PHOENIX SONG: ECHO
Marvel Comics: Dec, 2021 - No. 5, Apr, 2022 ($4.99/$3.99, limited series)

1-($4.99) Maya Lopez gets the Phoenix Force; Boanhorse-s/Maresca-a ... 5.00
2-5-($3.99) ... 4.00

PHOENIX WITHOUT ASHES
IDW Publishing: Aug, 2010 - No. 4, Nov, 2010 ($3.99, limited series)

1-4-Harlan Ellison-s/Alan Robinson-a ... 4.00

PHONOGRAM
Image Comics: Aug, 2006 - No. 6, May, 2007 ($3.50, limited series)

1-Gillen-s/McKelvie-a ... 15.00
2-6 ... 5.00

PHONOGRAM: THE SINGLES CLUB (Volume 2)
Image Comics: Dec, 2008 - No. 7, Feb, 2010 ($3.50, limited series)

1-7-Gillen-s/McKelvie-a. 5-Recalled for bar-code error ... 4.00

PHONOGRAM (Volume 3)(The Immaterial Girl)
Image Comics: Aug, 2015 - No. 6, Jan, 2016 ($3.99, limited series)

1-6-Gillen-s/McKelvie-a ... 4.00

PICNIC PARTY (See Dell Giants)

PICTORIAL CONFESSIONS (Pictorial Romance #4 on)
St. John Publishing Co.: Sept, 1949 - No. 3, Dec, 1949

	GD	VG	FN	VF	VF/NM	NM-
1-Baker-c/a(3)	129	258	387	826	1413	2000
2-Baker-a; photo-c	47	94	141	296	498	700
3-Kubert, Baker-a; part Kubert-c	52	104	156	328	552	775

PICTORIAL LOVE STORIES (Formerly Tim McCoy)
Charlton Comics: No. 22, Oct, 1949 - No. 26, July, 1950 (all photo-c)

	GD	VG	FN	VF	VF/NM	NM-
22-26: All have "Me-Dan Cupid". 25-Fred Astaire-c	24	48	72	142	234	325

PICTORIAL LOVE STORIES
St. John Publishing Co.: October, 1952

	GD	VG	FN	VF	VF/NM	NM-
1-Baker-c	129	258	387	826	1413	2000

PICTORIAL ROMANCES (Formerly Pictorial Confessions)
St. John Publ. Co.: No. 4, Jan, 1950; No. 5, Jan, 1951 - No. 24, Mar, 1954

	GD	VG	FN	VF	VF/NM	NM-
4-Baker-a; photo-c	61	122	183	390	670	950
5,10-All Matt Baker issues. 5-Reprints all stories from #4 w/new Baker-c	74	148	222	470	810	1150
6-9,12,13,15,16-Baker-c, 2-3 stories	65	130	195	416	708	1000
11-Baker-c/a(3); Kubert-r/Hollywood Confessions #1	74	148	222	470	810	1150
14,21-24: Baker-c/a each. 21,24-Each has signed story by Estrada	81	162	243	518	884	1250
17-20(7/53, 25¢, 100 pgs.): Baker-c/a; each has two signed stories by Estrada	135	270	405	864	1482	2100

NOTE: *Matt Baker* art in most issues. *Estrada* a-17-20(2) 21, 24.

PICTURE CRIMES
David McKay Publ.: June, 1937

1-Story in photo panels (a GD+ copy sold in 2012 for $478, a certified 5.5 copy sold for $2051 in 2017 and an 8.0 copy sold for $780 in Sept. 2022)

PICTURE NEWS
Lafayette Street Corp.: Jan, 1946 - No. 10, Jan/Feb, 1947

	GD	VG	FN	VF	VF/NM	NM-
1-Milt Gross begins, ends No. 6; 4 pg. Kirby-a; A-Bomb-c/story	53	106	159	334	567	800
2-Atomic explosion panels; Frank Sinatra/Perry Como story	28	56	84	168	274	380
3-Atomic explosion panels; Frank Sinatra, June Allyson, Benny Goodman stories	24	48	72	144	237	330

	GD	VG	FN	VF	VF/NM	NM-
	2.0	4.0	6.0	8.0	9.0	9.2

4-Atomic explosion panels; "Caesar and Cleopatra" movie adapt. w/Claude Raines & Vivian Leigh; Jackie Robinson story	28	56	84	165	270	375
5-7: 5-Hank Greenberg story; Atomic explosion panel. 6-Joe Louis-c/story	20	40	60	117	189	260
8,10: 8-Monte Hale story (9-10/46; 1st?). 10-Dick Quick; A-Bomb story; Krigstein, Gross-a	20	40	60	120	195	270
9-A-Bomb story; "Crooked Mile" movie adaptation; Joe DiMaggio story.	27	54	81	158	259	360

PICTURE PARADE (Picture Progress #5 on)
Gilberton Company (Also see A Christmas Adventure): Sept, 1953 - V1#4, Dec, 1953 (28 pgs.)

	GD	VG	FN	VF	VF/NM	NM-
V1#1-Andy's Atomic Adventures; A-bomb blast-c; (Teachers version distributed to schools exists)	47	94	141	296	498	700
2-Around the World with the United Nations	15	30	45	85	130	175
3-Adventures of the Lost One(The American Indian), 4-A Christmas Adventure (r-under same title in 1969)	15	30	45	85	130	175

PICTURE PROGRESS (Formerly Picture Parade)
Gilberton Corp.: V1#5, Jan, 1954 - V3#2, Oct, 1955 (28-36 pgs.)

V1#5-9, V2#1-9: 5-News in Review 1953. 6-The Birth of America. 7-The Four Seasons. 8-Paul Revere's Ride. 9-The Hawaiian Islands(5/54). V2#1-The Story of Flight(9/54). 2-Vote for Crazy River (The Meaning of Elections). 3-Louis Pasteur. 4-The Star Spangled Banner. 5-News in Review 1954. 6-Alaska: The Great Land. 7-Life in the Circus. 8-The Time of the Cave Man. 9-Summer Fun(5/55).

| | | 9 | 18 | 27 | 50 | 65 | 80 |

V3#1,2: 1-The Man Who Discovered America. 2-The Lewis & Clark Expedition

| | | 9 | 18 | 27 | 47 | 61 | 75 |

PICTURE SCOPE JUNGLE ADVENTURES (See Jungle Thrills)

PICTURE STORIES FROM AMERICAN HISTORY
National/All-American/E. C. Comics: 1945 - No. 4, Sum, 1947 (#1,2: 10¢, 56 pgs.; #3,4: 15¢, 52 pgs.)

	GD	VG	FN	VF	VF/NM	NM-
1	32	64	96	188	307	425
2-4	24	48	72	140	230	320

PICTURE STORIES FROM SCIENCE
E.C. Comics: Spring, 1947 - No. 2, Fall, 1947

	GD	VG	FN	VF	VF/NM	NM-
1-(15¢)	34	68	102	204	332	460
2-(10¢)	27	54	81	162	266	370

PICTURE STORIES FROM THE BIBLE (See Narrative Illustration, the Story of the Comics by M.C. Gaines)
National/All-American/E.C. Comics: 1942 - No. 4, Fall, 1943; 1944-46

	GD	VG	FN	VF	VF/NM	NM-
1-4('42-Fall, '43)-Old Testament (DC)	28	56	84	165	270	375

Complete Old Testament Edition, (12/43-DC, 50¢, 232 pgs.):-1st printing; contains #1-4; 2nd - 8th (1/47) printings exist; later printings by E.C. some with 65¢-c

| | 37 | 74 | 111 | 222 | 361 | 500 |

Complete Old Testament Edition (1945-publ. by Bible Pictures Ltd.)-232 pgs., hardbound, in color with dust jacket

| | 37 | 74 | 111 | 222 | 361 | 500 |

NOTE: *Both Old and New Testaments published in England by Bible Pictures Ltd. in hardback, 1943, in color, pgs. (2 vols.): O.T. 232 pgs. & N.T. 144 pgs.), and were also published by Scarf Press in 1979 (Old Test., $9.95) and in 1980 (New Test., $7.95)*

1-3(New Test.): 1944-46, DC)-52 pgs. ea.

| | 22 | 44 | 66 | 128 | 209 | 290 |

The Complete Life of Christ Edition (1945, 25¢, 96 pgs.)-Contains #1&2 of the New Testament Edition

| | 37 | 74 | 111 | 222 | 361 | 500 |

1,2(Old Testament-r in comic book form)(E.C., 1946; 52 pgs.)

| | 22 | 44 | 66 | 128 | 209 | 290 |

1(DC),2(AA),3(EC)(New Testament-r in comic book form)(E.C., 1946; 52 pgs.)

| | 22 | 44 | 66 | 128 | 209 | 290 |

Complete New Testament Edition (1945-E.C., 40¢, 144 pgs.)-Contains #1-3 1946 printing has 50¢-c

| | 37 | 74 | 111 | 222 | 361 | 500 |

NOTE: *Another British series entitled The Bible Illustrated from 1947 has recently been discovered, with the same internal artwork. This eight edition series (5-OT, 3-NT) is of particular interest to Classics Ill. collectors because it exactly copied the C.I. logo format. The British publisher was Thorpe & Porter, who in 1951 began publishing the British Classics Ill. series. All editions of The Bible Ill. have new British painted covers. While this market is still new, and not all editions have as yet been found, current market value is about the same as the first U.S. editions of Picture Stories From The Bible.*

PICTURE STORIES FROM WORLD HISTORY
E.C. Comics: Spring, 1947 - No. 2, Summer, 1947 (52, 48 pgs.)

	GD	VG	FN	VF	VF/NM	NM-
1-(15¢)	34	68	102	199	325	450
2-(10¢)	24	48	72	140	230	320

PIECEMEAL
AfterShock Comics: Dec, 2020 ($6.99, oversized 8-1/2" x 10-7/8", one shot)

1-Cullen Bunn-s/Szymon Kudranski-a ... 7.00

PIGS

	GD	VG	FN	VF	VF/NM	NM-
	2.0	4.0	6.0	8.0	9.0	9.2

Image Comics: Sept, 2011 - No. 8, Aug, 2012 ($2.99)

1-8: 1-Cosby & McCool-s/Tamura-a/Jock-c. 3-Conner-c. 5-Gibbons-c. 7-Ramos-c						3.00

PILGRIM, THE
IDW Publishing: Apr, 2010 - No. 2, Jun, 2010 ($3.99, limited series)

1,2-Mike Grell-a/ Mark Ryan-s						4.00

PILOT SEASON...
Image Comics (Top Cow): 2008 - 2011 ($1.00/$2.99/$3.99, one-shots)

...: Asset (9/10, $3.99) Sablik-s/Marquez-a/Frison-c						4.00
...: City of Refuge (10/11, $3.99) Foehl-s/Calero-a/c						4.00
...: Crosshair (10/10, $3.99) Katz-s/Jefferson-a/Silvestri-c						4.00
...: Declassified (10/09, $1.00) Preview of one-shots with covers, script and sketch pgs.						3.00
...: Demonic (1/10, $2.99) Kirkman-s/Benitez-a; two covers by Silvestri						3.00
...: Fleshdigger (10/11, $3.99) Denton & Keene-s; Sanchez-a; Francavilla-c						4.00
...: Forever (10/10, $3.99) Inglesby-s/Nachlik-a/Hutomo-c						4.00
...: Murdered (11/09, $2.99) Kirkman-s/Blake-a; two covers by Silvestri						3.00
...: 7 Days From Hell (10/10, $3.99) Noto-a/Hill & Levin-s/Stelfreeze-c						4.00
...: Stellar (7/10, $2.99) Kirkman-s/Chang-a/Silvestri-c						4.00
...: The Beauty (10/11, $3.99) Haun & Hurley-s/Haun-a/c (becomes a 2015 series)						10.00
...: The Test (10/10, $3.99) Fialkov-s/Ekedal-a/Hutomo-c						4.00
...: 39 Minutes (9/10, $3.99) Harms-s/Lando-a/Albuquerque-c						4.00
...: Twilight Guardian (5/08, $3.99) Hickman-s						4.00

PINE & MERRIMAC
BOOM! Studios: Jan, 2024 - Present ($4.99)

1,2-Starks-s/Galán-a						5.00

PINHEAD
Marvel Comics (Epic Comics): Dec, 1993 - No. 6, May, 1994 ($2.50)

1-($2.95)-Embossed foil-c by Kelley Jones; Intro Pinhead & Disciples (Snakeoil, Hangman, Fan Dancer & Dixie)						5.00
2-6						4.00

PINHEAD & FOODINI (TV)(Also see Foodini & Jingle Dingle Christmas...)
Fawcett Publications: July, 1951 - No. 4, Jan, 1952 (Early TV comic)

1-(52 pgs.)-Photo-c; based on TV puppet show	37	74	111	218	354	490
2,3-Photo-c	20	40	60	117	189	260
4	16	32	48	92	144	195

PINHEAD VS. MARSHALL LAW (Law in Hell)
Marvel Comics (Epic): Nov, 1993 - No. 2, Dec, 1993 ($2.95, lim. series)

1,2: 1-Embossed red foil-c. 2-Embossed silver foil-c						4.00

PINK DUST
Kitchen Sink Press: 1998 ($3.50, B&W, mature)

1-J. O'Barr-s/a						4.00

PINK PANTHER, THE (TV)(See The Inspector & Kite Fun Book)
Gold Key #1-70/Whitman #71-87: April, 1971 - No. 87, Mar, 1984

1-The Inspector begins	10	20	30	64	132	200
2-5	3	6	9	19	30	40
6-10	3	6	9	14	19	24
11-30: Warren Tufts-a #16-on	2	4	6	9	13	16
31-60	2	4	6	8	11	14
61-70	1	2	3	5	7	9
71-74,81-83: 81(2/82), 82(3/82), 83(4/82)	2	4	6	8	10	12
75(8/80)-77 (Whitman pre-pack) (scarce)	4	8	12	27	44	60
78(1/81)-80 (Whitman pre-pack) (not as scarce)	2	4	6	11	16	20
78 (1/81, 40c-c) Cover price error variant	3	6	9	15	22	28
84-87(All #90266 on-c, no date or date code): 84(6/83), 85(8/83), 87(3/84)						
			9	14	20	26
Mini-comic No. 1(1976)(3-1/4x6-1/2")	2	4	6	8	10	12

NOTE: Pink Panther began as a movie cartoon. (See Golden Comics Digest #38, 45 and March of Comics #376, 384, 390, 409, 418, 429, 441, 449, 461, 473, 486); #37, 72, 80-85 contain reprints.

PINK PANTHER SUPER SPECIAL (TV)
Harvey Comics: Oct, 1993 ($2.25, 68 pgs.)

V2#1-The Inspector & Wendy Witch stories also						5.00

PINK PANTHER, THE
Harvey Comics: Nov, 1993 - No. 9, July, 1994 ($1.50)

V2#1-9						4.00

PINK PANTHER, THE (Volume 3)
American Mythology Productions: 2016 - Present ($3.99)

1-4-New and classic short stories by various; multiple covers on each. 4-Trick or Pink						4.00
... Anniversary Special 1 (2017, $3.99) New short stories and reprints; 3 covers						4.00
...: Cartoon Hour Special 1,2 (2017, $4.99) Short stories by various; 3 covers						5.00
...: Classic Christmas 1 (2018, $3.99) Reprint from Pink Panther #60 (1979)						4.00
... 55th Anniversary Special 1 (2019, $3.99) New short stories and reprints; 3 covers						4.00
...: Presents the Ant and the Aardvark 1 (2018, $3.99) New short stories and reprints						4.00
...: Snow Day (2017, $3.99) New short stories by S.A. Check and reprint; 3 covers						4.00
...: Super-Pink Special 1 (2017, $3.99) New short stories and reprints; 3 covers						4.00
...: Surfside Special 1 (2018, $3.99) New short stories and reprints; 2 covers						4.00
... Vs. The Inspector 1 (2018, $3.99) New short stories and reprints; 2 covers						4.00
... Winter Special 1 (2018, $3.99) New short stories and reprints; 2 covers						4.00

PINKY & THE BRAIN (See Animaniacs)
DC Comics: July, 1996 - No. 27, Nov, 1998 ($1.75/$1.95/$1.99)

1-27, ...Christmas Special (1/96, $1.50)						4.00

PINKY LEE (See Adventures of...)

PINKY THE EGGHEAD
I.W./Super Comics: 1963 (Reprints from Noodnik)

I.W. Reprint #1,2(nd)	2	4	6	10	14	18
Super Reprint #14-r/Noodnik Comics #4	2	4	6	10	14	18

PINOCCHIO (See 4-Color #92, 252, 545, 1203, Mickey Mouse Mag. V5#3, Movie Comics under Wonderful Advs. of..., New Advs. of..., Thrilling Comics #2, Walt Disney Showcase, Walt Disney's..., Wonderful Advs. of..., & World's Greatest Stories #2)
Dell Publishing Co.: No. 92, 1945 - No. 1203, Mar, 1962 (Disney)

Four Color 92-The Wonderful Adventures of...; 16 pg. Donald Duck story ;						
entire book by Kelly	54	108	162	432	966	1500
Four Color 252 (10/49)-Origin, not by Kelly	15	30	45	103	227	350
Four Color 545 (3/54)-The Wonderful Advs. of...; part-r of 4-Color #92; Disney-movie						
	10	20	30	64	132	200
Four Color 1203 (3/62)	8	16	24	54	102	150

PINOCCHIO AND THE EMPEROR OF THE NIGHT
Marvel Comics: Mar, 1988 ($1.25, 52 pgs.)

1-Adapts film						5.00

PINOCCHIO LEARNS ABOUT KITES (See Kite Fun Book)

PIN-UP PETE (Also see Great Lover Romances & Monty Hall...)
Toby Press: 1952

1-Jack Sparling pin-ups	34	68	102	199	325	450

PIONEER MARSHAL (See Fawcett Movie Comics)

PIONEER PICTURE STORIES
Street & Smith Publications: Dec, 1941 - No. 9, Dec, 1943

1-The Legless Air Ace begins; WWII-c	55	110	165	352	601	850
2 -True life story of Errol Flynn	28	56	84	168	274	380
3-5,7-9	24	48	72	140	230	320
6-Classic Japanese WWII "Remember Pearl Harbor"-c						
	206	412	618	1318	2259	3200

PIONEER WEST ROMANCES (Firehair #1,2,7-11)
Fiction House Magazines: No. 3, Spring, 1950 - No. 6, Winter, 1950-51

3-(52 pgs.)-Firehair continues	24	48	72	140	230	320
4-6	25	50	75	150	245	340

PIPSQUEAK (See The Adventures of...)

PIRACY
E. C. Comics: Oct-Nov, 1954 - No. 7, Oct-Nov, 1955

1-Williamson/Torres-a; has full page subscription ad for unpublished Crypt of Terror #1						
	44	88	132	352	564	775
2-Williamson/Torres-a	24	48	72	192	309	425
3-7: 5-7-Comics Code symbol on cover	19	38	57	152	241	330

NOTE: Crandall a-in all; c-2-4. Davis a-1, 2, 6. Evans a-3-7; c-7. Ingels a-3-7. Krigstein a-3-5, 7; c-5, 6. Wood a-1, 2; c-1.

PIRACY
Gemstone Publishing: March, 1998 - No. 7, Sept, 1998 ($2.50)

1-7: E.C. reprints						4.00
Annual 1 ($10.95) Collects #1-4						11.00
Annual 2 ($7.95) Collects #5-7						8.00

PIRANA (See The Phantom #46 & Thrill-O-Rama #2, 3)

PIRATE CORPS, THE (See Hectic Planet)
Eternity Comics/Slave Labor Graphics: 1987 - No. 4, 1988 ($1.95)

1-4: 1,2-Color. 3,4-B&W						4.00
Special 1 ('89, B&W)-Slave Labor Publ.						4.00

PIRATE CORPS, THE (Volume 2)
Slave Labor Graphics: 1989 - No. 6, 1992 ($1.95)

1-6-Dorkin-s/a						4.00

PIRATE OF THE GULF, THE (See Superior Stories #2)

PIRATES COMICS
Hillman Periodicals: Feb-Mar, 1950 - No. 4, Aug-Sept, 1950 (All 52 pgs.)

1	37	74	111	222	361	500
2-Dave Berg-a	21	42	63	122	199	275
3,4-Berg-a	20	40	60	114	182	250

PIRATES OF CONEY ISLAND, THE
Image Comics: Oct, 2006 - No. 8 ($2.99)

1-6-Rick Spears-s/Vasilis Lolos-a; two covers. 2-Cloonan var-c						3.00

PIRATES OF DARK WATER, THE (Hanna Barbera)
Marvel Comics: Nov, 1991 - No. 9, Aug, 1992 ($1.95)

1-9: 9-Vess-c						4.00

PISCES
Image Comics: Apr, 2015 - No. 3, Jul, 2015 ($3.50/$3.99, unfinished series)

1-3-Kurtis Wiebe-s/Johnnie Christmas-a						4.00

P.I.'S: MICHAEL MAUSER AND MS. TREE, THE
First Comics: Jan, 1985 - No. 3, May, 1985 ($1.25, limited series)

1-3: Staton-c/a(p)						4.00

PITT, THE (Also see The Draft & The War)
Marvel Comics: Mar, 1988 ($3.25, 52 pgs., one-shot)

1-Ties into Starbrand, D.P.7						5.00

PITT (See Youngblood #4 & Gen 13 #3,#4)
Image Comics #1-9/Full Bleed #1/2,10-on: Jan, 1993 - No. 20 ($1.95, intended as a four part limited series)

1/2-(12/95)-1st Full Bleed issue						5.00
1-Dale Keown-c/a. 1-1st app. The Pitt						5.00
2-13: All Dale Keown-c/a. 3 (Low distribution). 10 (1/96)-Indicia reads "January 1995"						4.00
14-20: 14-Begin $2.50-c, pullout poster						4.00
TPB-(1997, $9.95) r/#1/2, 1-4						12.00
TPB 2-(1999, $11.95) r/#5-9						12.00

PITT CREW
Full Bleed Studios: Aug, 1998 - No. 5, Dec, 1999 ($2.50)

1-5: 1-Richard Pace-s/Ken Lashley-a. 2-4-Scott Lee-a						4.00

PITT IN THE BLOOD
Full Bleed Studios: Aug, 1996 ($2.50, one-shot)

nn-Richard Pace-a/script						4.00

PIXIE & DIXIE & MR. JINKS (TV)(See Jinks, Pixie, and Dixie & Whitman Comic Books)

Piracy #6 © WMG

Planetary #13 © WSP

Planet of the Apes (2023 series) #1 © 20th Century Studios

	GD 2.0	VG 4.0	FN 6.0	VF 8.0	VF/NM 9.0	NM- 9.2

Dell Publishing Co./Gold Key: July-Sept, 1960 - Feb, 1963 (Hanna-Barbera)

	GD	VG	FN	VF	VF/NM	NM-
Four Color 1112	8	16	24	54	102	150
Four Color 1196,1264, 01-631-207 (Dell, 7/62)	5	10	15	35	63	90
1(2/63-Gold Key)	6	12	18	37	66	95

PIXIE PUZZLE ROCKET TO ADVENTURELAND
Avon Periodicals: Nov, 1952

	GD	VG	FN	VF	VF/NM	NM-
1	27	54	81	158	259	360

PIXIES, THE (Advs. of...)(The Mighty Atom and .. #6 on)(See A-1 Comics #16)
Magazine Enterprises: Winter, 1946 - No. 4, Fall ?, 1947; No. 5, 1948

	GD	VG	FN	VF	VF/NM	NM-
1-Mighty Atom	15	30	45	90	140	190
2-5-Mighty Atom	10	20	30	54	72	90
I.W. Reprint #1(1958), 8-(Pee-Wee Pixies), 10-I.W. on cover, Super on inside	3	6	9	15	22	28

PIZZAZZ
Marvel Comics: Oct, 1977 - No. 16, Jan, 1979 (slick-color kids mag. w/puzzles, games, comics)

	GD	VG	FN	VF	VF/NM	NM-
1-Star Wars photo-c/article; origin Tarzan; KISS photos/article; Iron-On bonus; 2 pg. pin-up calendars thru #8	5	10	15	31	53	75
2-Spider-Man-c; Beatles pin-up calendar	3	6	9	13	18	22
3-8: 3-Close Encounters-s; Bradbury-s. 4-Alice Cooper, Travolta; Charlie's Angels/Fonz/Hulk/Spider-Man-c. 5-Star Trek quiz. 6-Asimov-s. 7-James Bond; Spock/Darth Vader-c.	4	6	9	11	16	20
8-TV Spider-Man photo-c/article	3	6	9	13	18	22
9-14: 9-Shaun Cassidy-c. 10-Sgt. Pepper-c/s. 12-Battlestar Galactica-c; Spider-Man app. 13-TV Hulk-c/s. 14-Meatloaf-c/s	2	4	6	10	14	18
15,16: 15-Battlestar Galactica-c. 16-Movie Superman photo-c/s, Hulk.	2	4	6	11	16	20

NOTE: *Star Wars* comics in all (1-6:Chaykin-a, 7-9: DeZuniga-a, 10-13:Simonson/Janson-a. 14-16:Cockrum-a). *Tarzan* comics, 1pg.-#1-8. *Spider-Man* by Kurtzman #1?-16.

PLANETARY (See Preview in flip book Gen13 #3)
DC Comics (WildStorm Prod.): Apr, 1999 - No. 27, Dec, 2009 ($2.50/$2.95/$2.99)

	GD	VG	FN	VF	VF/NM	NM-
1-Ellis-s/Cassaday-a/c	2	4	6	9	14	18
1-Special Edition (6/09, $1.00) r/#1 with "After Watchmen" cover frame						3.00
2-5						6.00
6-10						5.00
11-15: 12-Fourth Man revealed						4.00
16-26: 16-Begin $2.95-c. 23-Origin of The Drummer						3.00
27-($3.99) Wraparound gatefold-c						4.00
... All Over the World and Other Stories (2000, $14.95) r/#1-6 & Preview						15.00
... All Over the World and Other Stories-Hardcover (2000, $24.95) r/#1-6 & Preview; with dustjacket						25.00
...Batman: Night on Earth 1 (8/03, $5.95) Ellis-s/Cassaday-a						6.00
... : Crossing Worlds (2004, $14.95) r/Batman, JLA, and The Authority x-overs						15.00
...JLA: Terra Occulta (11/02, $5.95) Elseworlds; Ellis-s/Ordway-a						6.00
... : Leaving the 20th Century -HC (2004, $24.95) r/#13-18						25.00
... : Leaving the 20th Century -SC (2004, $14.99) r/#13-18						15.00
... : Spacetime Archaeology -HC (2010, $24.99) r/#19-27						25.00
... : Spacetime Archaeology -SC (2010, $17.99) r/#19-27						18.00
.../The Authority: Ruling the World (8/00, $5.95) Ellis-s/Phil Jimenez-a						6.00
... : The Fourth Man -Hardcover (2001, $24.95) r/#7-12						25.00
... : The Planetary Reader (8/03, $5.95) r/#13-15						6.00

PLANETARY BRIGADE (Also see Hero Squared)
BOOM! Studios: Feb, 2006 - No. 2, Mar, 2006 ($2.99)

	GD	VG	FN	VF	VF/NM	NM-
1-3-Giffen & DeMatteis-s/art by various; Haley-c						3.00
... Origins 1-3 (10/06-4/07, $3.99) Giffen & DeMatteis-s/Julia Bax-a						4.00

PLANET COMICS
Fiction House Magazines: 1/40 - No. 62, 9/49; No. 63, Wint, 1949-50; No. 64, Spring, 1950; No. 65, 1951(nd); No. 66-68, 1952(nd); No. 69, Wint, 1952(nd); No. 70-72, 1953(nd); No. 73, Winter, 1953-54

	GD	VG	FN	VF	VF/NM	NM-
1-Origin Auro, Lord of Jupiter by Briefer (ends #31); Flint Baker & The Red Comet begin; Eisner/Fine-c	2150	4300	6450	16,100	30,550	45,000
2-Lou Fine-c (Scarce)	1000	2000	3000	7400	13,200	19,000
3-Eisner-c	427	854	1281	3117	5509	7900
4-Gale Allen and the Girl Squadron begins	389	778	1167	2723	4762	6800
5,6-5-Eisner/Fine-c	423	846	1269	3000	5250	7500
7-12: 8-Robot-c. 12-The Star Pirate begins	320	640	960	2240	3920	5600
13,14-13-Reff Ryan begins	300	600	900	2070	3635	5200
15-(Scarce)-Mars, God of War begins (11/41); see Jumbo Comics #31 for 1st app.	1500	3000	4500	11,400	20,700	30,000
16-20,22	232	464	696	1485	2543	3600
21-The Lost World & Hunt Bowman begin	265	530	795	1694	2897	4100
23-26: 26-Space Rangers begin (9/43), end #71	206	412	618	1318	2259	3200
27-30	161	322	483	1030	1765	2500
31-35: 33-Origin Star Pirates Wonder Boots, reprinted in #52. 35-Mysta of the Moon begins, ends #62	155	310	465	992	1696	2400
36-45: 38-1st Mysta of the Moon-c. 41-New origin of "Auro, Lord of Jupiter". 42-Last Gale Allen. 43-Futura begins	126	252	378	806	1378	1950
46-60: 48-Robot-c. 53-Used in SOTI, pg. 32	106	212	318	673	1162	1650
61-68,70: 64,70-Robot-c. 65-70-All partial-r of earlier issues. 70-r/stories from #41	87	174	261	553	952	1350
69-Used in POP, pgs. 101,102	103	206	309	659	1130	1600
71-73-No series stories. 71-Space Rangers strip	81	162	243	518	884	1250
I.W. Reprint 1,8,9: 1(nd)-r/#70; cover-r from Attack on Planet Mars. 8 (r/#72), 9-r/#73	10	20	30	69	147	225

NOTE: **Anderson** a-33-38, 40-51 (Star Pirate), 58. **Matt Baker** a-53-59 (Mysta of the Moon). **Celardo** c-12. **Bill Discount** a-71 (Space Rangers). **Elias** c-70. **Evans** a-46-49 (Auro, Lord of Jupiter), 50-64 (Lost World). **Fine** c-2, 5. **Hopper** a-31, 35 (Gale Allen), 41, 42, 48, 49 (Mysta of the Moon). **Ingels** a-24-31 (Lost World), 56-61 (Auro, Lord of Jupiter). **Lubbers** a-44-47 (Space Rangers); c-40, 41. **Moreira** a-43, 44 (Mysta of the Moon). **Renee** a-40-49 (Lost World); c-33, 35, 39. **Tuska** a-30 (Star Pirate). **M. Whitman** a-50-52 (Mysta of the Moon), 53-58 (Star Pirate); c-71-73. **Starr** a-59. **Zolnerwich** c-10. 13-25. Bondage c-53.

PLANET COMICS
Pacific Comics: 1984 ($5.95)

	GD	VG	FN	VF	VF/NM	NM-
1-Reprints Planet Comics #1(1940)	1	2	3	5	6	8

PLANET COMICS
Blackthorne Publishing: Apr, 1988 - No. 3 ($2.00, color/B&W #3)

	GD	VG	FN	VF	VF/NM	NM-
1-New stories; Dave Stevens-c	8	16	24	56	108	160
2,3: New stories	1	2	3	5	6	8

PLANET HULK (See Incredible Hulk and Giant-Size Hulk #1 (2006))

PLANET HULK (Secret Wars tie-in)
Marvel Comics: Jul, 2015 - No. 5, Nov, 2015 ($4.99/$3.99, limited series)

	GD	VG	FN	VF	VF/NM	NM-
1-($4.99) Humphries-s/Laming-a; Steve Rogers app.; back-up Pak-s/Miyazawa-a						5.00
2-5-($3.99) Doc Green & Devil Dinosaur app.						4.00

PLANET HULK: WORLDBREAKER
Marvel Comics: Jan, 2023 - No. 5, May, 2023 ($4.99/$3.99, limited series)

	GD	VG	FN	VF	VF/NM	NM-
1-($4.99) Pak-s/Garcia-a; a thousand years later on Sakaar; back-up story with Skaar						5.00
2-5-($3.99)						4.00

PLANET OF THE APES (Magazine) (Also see Adventures on the... & Power Record Comics)
Marvel Comics Group: Aug, 1974 - No. 29, Feb, 1977 (B&W) (Based on movies)

	GD	VG	FN	VF	VF/NM	NM-
1-Ploog-a	5	10	15	35	63	90
2-Ploog-a	3	6	9	16	24	32
3-10	3	6	9	14	20	26
11-20	3	6	9	15	22	28
21-28 (low distribution)	3	6	9	21	33	45
29 (low distribution)	6	12	18	37	66	95

NOTE: **Alcala** a-7-11, 17-22, 24. **Ploog** a-1-6, 8, 11, 13, 14, 19. **Sutton** a-11, 12, 15, 17, 19, 20, 23, 24. **Tuska** a-1-6.

PLANET OF THE APES
Adventure Comics: Apr, 1990 - No. 24, 1992 ($2.50, B&W)

	GD	VG	FN	VF	VF/NM	NM-
1-New movie tie-in; comes w/outer-c (3 colors)						5.00
1-Limited serial numbered edition ($5.00)	1	3	4	6	8	10
1-2nd printing (no outer-c, 2.50)						4.00
2-24						4.00
Annual 1 ($3.50)						5.00
...Urchak's Folly 1-4 ($2.50, mini-series)						4.00

PLANET OF THE APES (The Human War)
Dark Horse Comics: Jun, 2001 - No. 3, Aug, 2001 ($2.99, limited series)

	GD	VG	FN	VF	VF/NM	NM-
1-3-Follows the 2001 movie; Edginton-s						3.00

PLANET OF THE APES
Dark Horse Comics: Sept, 2001 - No. 6, Feb, 2002 ($2.99, ongoing series)

	GD	VG	FN	VF	VF/NM	NM-
1-6: 1-3-Edginton-s. 1-Photo & Wagner covers. 2-Plunkett & photo-c						3.00

PLANET OF THE APES
BOOM! Studios: Apr, 2011 - No. 15, Jun, 2012 ($3.99)

	GD	VG	FN	VF	VF/NM	NM-
1-4,6-15-Takes place 1200 years before Taylor's arrival; Magno-a; three covers						4.00
5-($1.00) Three covers						3.00
Annual 1 (8/12, $4.99) Short stories by various; six covers						5.00
Giant 1 (9/13, $4.99) Gregory-s/Barreto-a						5.00
Special 1 (2/13, $4.99) Continued from #15; Diego Barreto-a						5.00
Spectacular 1 (7/13, $4.99) Gregory-s/Barreto-a						5.00
... : The Simian Age 1 (12/18, $7.99) Short stories by various; 2 covers						8.00
... : The Time of Man 1 (10/18, $7.99) Short stories by various incl. Magno; 2 covers						8.00

PLANET OF THE APES (Based on the 2001 movie)
Marvel Comics: Jun, 2023 - No. 5, Oct, 2023 ($4.99)

	GD	VG	FN	VF	VF/NM	NM-
	2.0	4.0	6.0	8.0	9.0	9.2

1-5-David F. Walker-s/Dave Wachter-a ... 5.00

PLANET OF THE APES: CATACLYSM
BOOM! Studios: Sept, 2012 - No. 12, Aug, 2013 ($3.99)
1-12-Takes place 8 years before Taylor's arrival; Couceiro-a. 1-Multiple covers ... 4.00

PLANET OF THE APES/ GREEN LANTERN
BOOM! Studios: Feb, 2017 - No. 6, Jul, 2017 ($3.99, limited series)
1-6-Bagenda-a; Hal Jordan & Sinestro on the POTA; Cornelius app.; multiple covers ... 4.00

PLANET OF THE APES: URSUS
BOOM! Studios: Jan, 2018 - No. 6, Jun, 2018 ($3.99, limited series)
1-6-Spotlight on General Ursus; Walker-s/Mooneyham-a ... 4.00

PLANET OF THE APES VISIONARIES
BOOM! Studios: Aug, 2018 ($19.99, hardcover graphic novel)
HC-Alternate version in an adaptation of Rod Serling's original screenplay; Dana Gould-s/ Chad Lewis-a/Paolo Rivera-c; bonus character design art ... 20.00

PLANET OF THE NERDS
AHOY Comics: 2019 - No. 5, 2019 ($3.99, limited series)
1-5-Paul Constant-s/Alan Robinson-a. 1,2-Nakayama-c ... 4.00

PLANET OF VAMPIRES
Seaboard Publications (Atlas): Feb, 1975 - No. 3, July, 1975

	GD	VG	FN	VF	VF/NM	NM-
1-Neal Adams-c(i); 1st Brodrek-c/a(p); Hama-s	3	6	9	19	30	40
2,3: 2-Neal Adams-c. 3-Heath-c/a	3	6	9	14	19	24

PLANET-SIZE X-MEN
Marvel Comics: Aug, 2021 ($4.99, one-shot)
1-X-Men terraform Mars to create the Planet Arakko for mutants; Duggan-s/Larraz-a ... 5.00

PLANET TERRY
Marvel Comics (Star Comics)/Marvel: April, 1985 - No. 12, March, 1986 (Children's comic)
1-12 ... 5.00
1-Variant with "Star Chase" game on last page & inside back-c ... 15.00

PLANTS VS. ZOMBIES (Based on the Electronic Arts game)
Dark Horse Comics: Jun, 2015 - No. 12, Jun, 2016 ($2.99)
1-12: 1-3-Bully For You; Tobin-s/Chan-a. 4-6-Grown Sweet Home. 7-9-Petal to the Metal ... 3.00
...: Garden Warfare 1-3 (10/15 - No. 3, 12/15, $2.99) Tobin-s/Chabot-a ... 3.00

PLASM (See Warriors of Plasm)
Defiant: June, 1993

	GD	VG	FN	VF	VF/NM	NM-
0-Came bound into Diamond Previews V3#6 (6/93); price is for complete Previews with comic still attached	3	6	9	17	26	35
0-Comic only removed from Previews	3	6	9	14	20	25
0-One staple variant	11	22	33	73	157	240

PLASMER
Marvel Comics UK: Nov, 1993 - No. 4, Feb, 1994 ($1.95, limited series)
1-($2.50)-Polybagged w/4 trading cards ... 5.00
2-4: 4-Capt. America & Silver Surfer app. ... 4.00

PLASTIC FORKS
Marvel Comis (Epic Comics): 1990 - No. 5, 1990 ($4.95, 68 pgs., limited series, mature)
Book 1-5: Squarebound ... 5.00

PLASTIC MAN (Also see Police Comics & Smash Comics #17)
Vital Publ. No. 1,2/Quality Comics No. 3 on: Sum, 1943 - No. 64, Nov, 1956
nn(#1)- "In The Game of Death"; Skull-c; Jack Cole-c/a begins; ends-#64?

	GD	VG	FN	VF	VF/NM	NM-
	595	1190	1785	4350	7675	11,000
nn(#2, 2/44)- "The Gay Nineties Nightmare"	187	374	561	1197	2049	2900
3 (Spr, '46)	118	236	354	749	1287	1825
4 (Sum, '46)	89	178	267	565	970	1375
5 (Aut, '46)	73	146	219	467	796	1125
6-10	60	120	180	381	653	925
11-15,17-20	53	106	159	334	567	800
16-Classic-c	63	130	195	416	708	1000
21-30: 26-Last non-r issue?	41	82	123	256	428	600
31-40: 40-Used in POP, pg. 91	34	68	102	199	325	450
41-53,55-63: 53-Last precode issue	28	56	84	165	270	375
54-Robot-c	53	106	159	334	567	800
64-Sci-fi-c	41	82	123	256	428	600
Super Reprint 11,16,18: 11('63)-r/#16. 16-r/#18 & #21; Cole-a. 18('64)-Spirit-r by Eisner from Police #95	4	8	12	27	44	60

NOTE: Cole r-44, 49, 56, 58, 59 at least. Cuidera c-32-64i.

PLASTIC MAN (See DC Special #15 & House of Mystery #160)
National Periodical Publications/DC Comics: 11-12/66 - No. 10, 5-6/68; V4#11, 2-3/76 - No. 20, 10-11/77

	GD	VG	FN	VF	VF/NM	NM-
1-Real 1st app. Silver Age Plastic Man (House of Mystery #160 is actually tryout); Gil Kane-c/a; 12c issues begin	15	30	45	103	227	350
2-5: 4-Infantino-c; Mortimer-a	5	10	15	34	60	85
6-10('68): 7-G.A. Plastic Man & Woozy Winks (1st S.A. app.); origin retold. 10-Sparling-a; last 12c issue	4	8	12	27	44	60
V4#11('76)-20: 11-20-Fradon-p. 17-Origin retold	2	4	6	8	11	14
...80-Page Giant (2003, $6.95) reprints origin and other stories in 80-Pg. Giant format						7.00
...Special 1 (8/99, $3.95)						6.00

PLASTIC MAN
DC Comics: Nov, 1988 - No. 4, Feb, 1989 ($1.00, mini-series)
1-4: 1-Origin; Woozy Winks app. ... 4.00

PLASTIC MAN
DC Comics: Feb, 2004 - No. 20, Mar, 2006 ($2.95/$2.99)
1-20-Kyle Baker-s/a in most. 1-Retells origin. 7,12-Scott Morse-s/a. 8-JLA cameo ... 3.00
...: On the Lam TPB (2004, $14.95) r/#1-6 ... 15.00
...: Rubber Bandits TPB (2005, $14.99) r/#8-11,13,14 ... 15.00

PLASTIC MAN
DC Comics: Aug, 2018 - No. 6, Jan, 2019 ($3.99, limited series)
1-6-Gail Simone-s/Adriana Melo-a. 1-Origin re-told. 2,3-Man-Bat app. 3-Ross-c ... 4.00

PLASTRON CAFE
Mirage Studios: Dec, 1992 - No. 4, July, 1993 ($2.25, B&W)
1-4: 1-Teenage Mutant Ninja Turtles app.; Kelly Freas-c. 2-Hildebrandt painted-c. 4-Spaced & Alien Fire stories ... 4.00

PLAYFUL LITTLE AUDREY (TV)(Also see Little Audrey #25)
Harvey Publications: 6/57 - No. 110, 11/73; No. 111, 8/74 - No. 121, 4/76

	GD	VG	FN	VF	VF/NM	NM-
1	36	72	108	259	580	900
2	14	28	42	94	207	320
3-5	8	16	24	58	108	160
6-10	6	12	18	40	73	105
11-20	5	10	15	31	53	75
21-40	4	8	12	25	40	55
41-60	3	6	9	19	30	40
61-84: 84-Last 12c issue	3	6	9	15	22	28
85-99	2	4	6	11	16	20
100-52 pg. Giant	3	6	9	16	23	30
101-103: 52 pg. Giants	3	6	9	14	20	25
104-121	1	3	4	6	8	10
...In 3-D (Spring, 1988, $2.25, Blackthorne #66)						6.00

PLOP! (Also see The Best of DC #60,63 digests)
National Periodical Publications: Sept-Oct, 1973 - No. 24, Nov-Dec, 1976

	GD	VG	FN	VF	VF/NM	NM-
1-Sergio Aragonés-a begins; Wrightson-a	4	8	12	28	47	65
2-4,6-20	3	6	9	14	20	26
5-Wrightson-a	3	6	9	15	22	28
21-24 (52 pgs.). 23-No Aragonés-a; Lord of the Rings parody with Wally Wood-s/a	3	6	9	16	23	30

NOTE: **Alcala** a-1-3. **Anderson** a-5. **Aragonés** a-1-22, 24. **Ditko** a-16p. **Evans** a-1. **Mayer** a-1. **Orlando** a-21, 22; c-21. **Sekowsky** a-5, 6p. **Toth** a-11. **Wolverton** r-4, 22-24(1 pg.ea.); c-1-12, 14, 17, 18. **Wood** a-14, 16i, 18-24; c-13, 15, 16, 19.

PLOT HOLES, THE
Massive Publishing: Aug, 2023 - No. 5, Dec, 2023 ($3.99)
1-5-Sean Murphy-s/a ... 4.00

PLUNGE
DC Comics (Black Label/Hill House Comics): Apr, 2020 - No. 6, Oct, 2020 ($3.99)
1-6-Joe Hill-s/Stuart Immonen-a; back-up Sea Dogs serial in #1-5 ... 4.00

PLUTO (See Cheerios Premiums, Four Color #537, Mickey Mouse Magazine, Walt Disney Showcase #4, 7, 13, 20, 23, 33 & Wheaties)
Dell Publ. Co.: No. 7, 1942; No. 429, 10/52 - No. 1248, 11-1/61-62 (Disney)

	GD	VG	FN	VF	VF/NM	NM-
Large Feature Comic 7(1942)-Written by Carl Barks, Jack Hannah & Nick George (Barks' 1st comic book work)	265	530	795	1694	2897	4100
Four Color 429 (#1)	12	24	36	83	182	280
Four Color 509	8	16	24	52	99	145
Four Color 595,654,736,853	7	14	21	46	86	125
Four Color 941,1039,1143,1248	5	10	15	35	63	90

PLUTONA
Image Comics: Sept, 2015 - No. 5, Jun, 2016 ($2.99)
1-5-Lemire-s/Lenox-a ... 3.00

POCKET CLASSICS
Academic Inc. Publications: 1984 (B&W, 4 1/4" x 6 3/4", 68 pages)
C1(Black Beauty. C2(The Call of the Wild). C3(Dr. Jekyll and Mr. Hyde). C4(Dracula). C5(Frankenstein). C6(Huckleberry Finn). C7(Moby Dick). C8(The Red Badge of Courage). C9(The Time Machine). C10(Tom Sawyer). C11(Treasure Island). C12(20,000 Leagues Under the Sea). C13(The Great Adventures of Sherlock Holmes). C14(Gulliver's Travels). C15(The Hunchback of Notre Dame). C16(The Invisible Man). C17(Journey to the Center of the Earth). C18(Kidnapped). C19(The Mysterious Island). C20(The Scarlet Letter). C21(The Story of My Life). C22(A Tale of Two Cities). C23(The Three Musketeers). C24(The War of the Worlds). C25(Around the World in Eighty Days). C26(Captains Courageous). C27(A Connecticut Yankee in King Arthur's Court). C28(Sherlock Holmes - The Hound of the Baskervilles). C29(The House of the Seven Gables). C30(Jane Eyre). C31(The Last of the Mohicans). C32(The Best of O. Henry). C33(The Best of Poe). C34(Two Years Before the Mast). C35(White Fang). C36(Wuthering Heights). C37(Ben Hur). C38(A Christmas Carol). C39(The Food of the Gods). C40(Ivanhoe). C41(The Man in the Iron Mask). C42(The Prince and the Pauper). C43(The Prisoner of Zenda). C44(The Return of the Native). C45(Robinson Crusoe). C46(The Scarlet Pimpernel). C47(The Sea Wolf). C48(The Swiss Family Robinson). C49(Billy Budd). C50(Crime and Punishment). C51(Don Quixote). C52(Great Expectations). C53(Heidi). C54(The Illiad). C55(Lord Jim). C56(The Mutiny on Board H.M.S. Bounty). C57(The Odyssey). C58(Oliver Twist). C59(Pride and Prejudice). C60(The Turn of the Screw) each... 8.00

Shakespeare Series:
S1(As You Like It). S2(Hamlet). S3(Julius Caesar). S4(King Lear). S5(Macbeth). S6(The Merchant of Venice). S7(A Midsummer Night's Dream). S8(Othello). S9(Romeo and Juliet). S10(The Taming of the Shrew). S11(The Tempest). S12(Twelfth Night) each... 9.00

POCKET COMICS (Also see Double Up)
Harvey Publications: Aug, 1941 - No. 4, Jan, 1942 (Pocket size; 100 pgs.)

	GD	VG	FN	VF	VF/NM	NM-
1-Origin & 1st app. The Black Cat, Cadet Blakey the Spirit of '76, The Red Blazer, The Phantom, Sphinx, & The Zebra; Phantom Ranger, British Agent #99, Spin Hawkins, Satan, Lord of Evil begin (1st app. of each); classic Simon horror cover showing an army battling a gigantic monster with the Statue of Liberty in its claws; Simon-c/a in #1-3	377	754	1131	2639	4620	6600
2 (9/41)-Black Cat & Nazi WWII-c by Simon	300	600	900	2010	3505	5000
3,4-Black Cat & Nazi WWII-c. 3-Simon-c	245	490	735	1568	2684	3800

POE DAMERON (Star Wars) (Title changes to Star Wars: Poe Dameron with #13)
Marvel Comics: Jun, 2016 - No. 12, May, 2017 ($4.99/$3.99)
1-($4.99) Soule-s/Noto-a/c; prelude to The Force Awakens; back-up w/Eliopoulos-a ... 5.00
2-6,8-12-($3.99) Black Squadron app. ... 4.00
7-($4.99) Anzueta-a; Leia cameo ... 5.00

POGO PARADE (See Dell Giants)

POGO POSSUM (Also see Animal Comics & Special Delivery)
Dell Publishing Co.: No. 105, 4/46 - No. 148, 5/47; 10-12/49 - No. 16, 4-6/54

Planet-Size X-Men #1 © MAR

Poe Dameron #3 © Lucasfilm

Poison Elves #80 © Sirius

	GD	VG	FN	VF	VF/NM	NM-
	2.0	4.0	6.0	8.0	9.0	9.2
Four Color 105(1946)-Kelly-c/a	68	136	204	544	1222	1900
Four Color 148-Kelly-c/a	44	88	132	326	738	1150
1-(10-12/49)-Kelly-c/a in all	38	76	114	285	641	1000
2	23	46	69	161	356	550
3-5	15	30	45	105	233	360
6-10: 10-Infinity-c	13	26	39	91	201	310
11-16: 11-X-Mas-c	10	20	30	69	147	225

NOTE: #1-4, 9-13: 52 pgs.; #5-8, 14-16: 36 pgs.

POINT BLANK (See Wildcats)
DC Comics (WildStorm): Oct, 2002 - No. 5, Feb, 2003 ($2.95, limited series)
1-5-Brubaker-s/Wilson-a/Bisley-c. 1-Variant-c by Wilson; Grifter and John Lynch app. 3.00
TPB (2003, $14.95), (2009, $14.99) r/#1-5; afterword by Brubaker 15.00

POINT ONE
Marvel Comics: Jan, 2012 ($5.99, one-shot)
1-Short story preludes to Marvel's event storylines for 2012; s/a by various 6.00

POISON ELVES (Formerly I, Lusiphur)
Mulehide Graphics: No. 8, 1993- No. 20, 1995 (B&W, magazine/comic size, mature readers)

	GD	VG	FN	VF	VF/NM	NM-
8-Drew Hayes-c/a/scripts.	2	4	6	8	10	12
9-11: 11-1st comic size issue	2	4	6	8	10	12
12,14,16	1	2	3	5	6	8
13,15-(low print)	2	4	6	8	11	14
15-2nd print						4.00
17-20	1	2	3	5	6	8

...Desert of the Third Sin-(1997, $14.95, TPB)-r/#' 3-18 15.00
...Patrons-($4.95, TPB)-r/#19,20 5.00
...Traumatic Dogs-(1996, $14.95,TPB)-Reprints I, Lusiphur 7, Poison Elves #8-12 15.00

POISON ELVES (See I, Lusiphur)
Sirius Entertainment: June, 1995 - No. 79, Sept 2004 ; No. 80, Nov, 2007 ($2.50/$2.95, B&W, mature readers)
1-Linsner-c; Drew Hayes-a/scripts in all. 6.00
1-2nd print 3.00
2-25: 12-Purple Marauder-c/app. 3.00
26-45, 47-49 3.00
46,50-79: 61-Fillbäch Brothers-s/a. 74-Art by Crilley (3 pgs.) 3.00

	GD	VG	FN	VF	VF/NM	NM-
80-($3.50) Tribute issue to Drew Hayes; sketchbook and notebook art with commentary	2	4	6	11	16	20

... Baptism By Fire-(2003, $19.95, TPB)-r/#48-59 20.00
... Color Special #1 (12/98, $2.95) 5.00
... Companion (12/02, $3.50) Back-story and character bios 3.50
... : Dark Wars TPB Vol. 1 (2005, $15.95) r/#60,62-68 16.00

	GD	VG	FN	VF	VF/NM	NM-
... FAN Edition #1 mail-in offer; Drew Hayes-c/s/a	1	2	3	5	6	8

... Rogues-(2002, $15.95, TPB)-r/#40-47 16.00
...Salvation-(2001, $19.95, TPB)-r/#26-39 20.00
...Sanctuary-(1999, $14.95, TPB)-r/#1-12 15.00

POISON ELVES
Ape Entertainment: 2013 - No. 3 ($2.99, B&W)
1-3: 1-Horan-s/Montos-a; Davidsen-s/Ritchie-a; 3 covers by Robertson, Montos & Moore 3.00

POISON ELVES: DOMINION
Sirius Entertainment: Sept, 2005 - No. 6, 2006 ($3.50, B&W, limited series)
1-6-Keith Davidsen-s/Scott Lewis-a 3.50

POISON ELVES: HYENA
Sirius Entertainment: Sept, 2004 - No. 4, Feb, 2005 ($2.95, limited series)
1-4-Keith Davidsen-s/Scott Lewis-a 3.00
Ventures TPB Vol. 1: The Hyena Collection (2006, $14.95) r/#1-4 & 2 short stories 15.00

POISON ELVES: LOST TALES
Sirius Entertainment: Jan, 2006 - No. 11 ($2.95 B&W, limited series)
1-11-Aaron Bordner-a; Bordner & Davidsen-s 3.00

POISON ELVES: LUSIPHUR & LIRILITH
Sirius Entertainment: 2001 - No. 4, 2001 ($2.95 B&W, limited series)
1-4-Drew Hayes-s/Jason Alexander-a 3.00
TPB (2002, $11.95) r/#1-4 12.00

POISON ELVES: PARINTACHIN
Sirius Entertainment: 2001 - No. 3, 2002 ($2.95 B&W, limited series)
1-3-Drew Hayes-s/Fillbäch Brothers-s/a 3.00
TPB (2003, $8.95) r/#1-3 9.00

POISON ELVES VENTURES
Sirius Entertainment: May, 2005 - No. 4, Apr, 2006 ($3.50, B&W, limited series)
... #1: Cassanova; ...#2: Lynn; ...#3: The Purple Marauder; ...#4: Jace - Bordner-a 3.50

POISON IVY
DC Comics: Aug, 2022 - Present ($3.99)
1-21: 1-G. Willow Wilson-s/Marcio Takara-a. 5,6-Jason Woodrue app. 9,12,13-Harley Quinn app. 13-Art by Takara, March, Kelley Jones, Kaplan. 19-21-Origin retold 4.00

POISON IVY: CYCLE OF LIFE AND DEATH
DC Comics: Mar, 2016 - No. 6 ($2.99, limited series)
1-6: 1-Amy Chu-s/Clay Mann-a; covers by Mann & Dodson; Harley Quinn app. 3.00

POKÉMON (TV) (Also see Magical Pokémon Journey)
Viz Comics: Nov, 1998 - 2000 ($3.25/$3.50, B&W)

...Part 1: The Electric Tale of Pikachu

	GD	VG	FN	VF	VF/NM	NM-
1-Toshiro Ono-s/a	3	6	9	17	26	35
1-4 (2nd through current printings)						4.00
2	2	4	6	8	10	12
3,4	1	3	4	6	8	10
TPB ($12.95)	2	4	6	9	13	16

...Part 2: Pikachu Strikes Back

	GD	VG	FN	VF	VF/NM	NM-
1	2	4	6	8	11	14
2-4						5.00
TPB						13.00

...Part 3: Electric Pikachu Boogaloo

	GD	VG	FN	VF	VF/NM	NM-
1	2	4	6	8	11	14
2-4 ($2.95-c)						5.00
TPB						13.00

...Part 4: Surf's Up Pikachu

	GD	VG	FN	VF	VF/NM	NM-
1	2	4	6	8	11	14
2 ($2.95-c), 3,4						5.00
TPB						13.00

NOTE: Multiple printings exist for most issues

POKÉMON ADVENTURES
Viz Comics: Sept, 1999 - No. 4 ($5.95, B&W, magazine-size)
1-4-Includes stickers bound in 6.00

POKÉMON ADVENTURES
Viz Comics: 2000 - 2002 ($2.95/$4.95, B&W)
Part 2 (2/00-7/00) 1-6-Includes stickers bound in 5.00
Part 3 (8/00-2/01) 1-7 5.00
Part 4 (3/00-6/01) 1-7 5.00
Part 5 (7/01-10/01) 1-4 5.00
Part 6: 1-4, Part 7 1-5 5.00

POKÉMON: THE FIRST MOVIE
Viz Comics: 1999 ($3.95)

	GD	VG	FN	VF	VF/NM	NM-
Mewtwo Strikes Back 1	2	4	6	9	12	15
2-4						5.00
Pikachu's Vacation						5.00

POKÉMON: THE MOVIE 2000
Viz Comics: 2000 ($3.95)
1-Official movie adaption 5.00
Pikachu's Rescue Adventure 5.00
...:The Power of One (mini-series) 1-3 5.00

POLARITY
BOOM! Studios: Apr, 2013 - No. 4 ($3.99, limited series)
1-4: 1-Bemis-s/Coelho-a; 3 covers 4.00

POLICE ACADEMY (TV)
Marvel Comics: Nov, 1989 - No. 6, Feb, 1990 ($1.00)
1-6: Based on TV cartoon; Post-c/a(p) in all 4.00

POLICE ACTION
Atlas News Co.: Jan, 1954 - No. 7, Nov, 1954

	GD	VG	FN	VF	VF/NM	NM-
1-Violent-a by Robert Q. Sale	39	78	117	240	395	550
2	20	40	60	117	189	260
3-7: 7-Powell-a	18	36	54	107	169	230

NOTE: Ayers a-4, 5. Colan a-1. Forte a-1, 2. Mort Lawrence a-5. Maneely a-5; c-1, 5. Reinman a-6, 7.

POLICE ACTION
Atlas/Seaboard Publ.: Feb, 1975 - No. 3, June, 1975

	GD	VG	FN	VF	VF/NM	NM-
1-3: 1-Lomax, N.Y.P.D., Luke Malone begin; McWilliams-a. 2-Origin Luke Malone, Manhunter; Ploog-a	2	4	6	11	16	20

NOTE: Ploog art in all. Sekowsky/McWilliams a-1-3. Thorne c-3.

POLICE AGAINST CRIME
Premiere Magazines: April, 1954 - No. 9, Aug, 1955

	GD 2.0	VG 4.0	FN 6.0	VF 8.0	VF/NM 9.0	NM- 9.2

1-Disbrow-a; extreme violence (man's face slashed with knife); Hollingsworth-a

| | | 50 | 100 | 150 | 315 | 533 | 750 |

2-Hollingsworth-a

| | 28 | 56 | 84 | 165 | 270 | 375 |

3-9

| | 23 | 46 | 69 | 136 | 223 | 310 |

POLICE BADGE #479 (Formerly Spy Thrillers #1-4)
Atlas Comics (PrPI): No. 5, Sept, 1955

5-Maneely-c/a (6 pgs.); Heck-a

| | 18 | 36 | 54 | 103 | 162 | 220 |

POLICE CASE BOOK (See Giant Comics Editions)

POLICE CASES (See Authentic... & Record Book of...)

POLICE COMICS
Quality Comics Group (Comic Magazines): Aug, 1941 - No. 127, Oct, 1953

1-Origin/1st app. Plastic Man by Jack Cole (r-in DC Special #15), The Human Bomb by Gustavson, & No. 711; intro. The Firebrand by Reed Crandall, The Mouthpiece by Guardineer, Phantom Lady, & The Sword; Chic Carter by Eisner app.; Firebrand-c 1-4

| | 1750 | 3500 | 5250 | 13,300 | 24,150 | 35,000 |

2-Plastic Man smuggles opium

| | 331 | 662 | 993 | 2317 | 4059 | 5800 |

3

| | 337 | 674 | 1011 | 2339 | 3130 | 3900 |

4

| | 226 | 452 | 678 | 1446 | 2473 | 3500 |

5-Plastic Man covers begin, end #102; Plastic Man forced to smoke marijuana

| | 389 | 778 | 1167 | 2723 | 4762 | 6800 |

6,7

| | 187 | 374 | 561 | 1197 | 2049 | 2900 |

8-Manhunter begins (origin/1st app.) (3/42)

| | 219 | 438 | 657 | 1402 | 2401 | 3400 |

9,10

| | 155 | 310 | 465 | 992 | 1696 | 2400 |

11-The Spirit strip reprints begin by Eisner (origin-strip #1); 1st comic book app. The Spirit & 1st cover app. (9/42)

| | 420 | 840 | 1260 | 2940 | 5170 | 7400 |

12-Intro. Ebony

| | 194 | 388 | 582 | 1242 | 2121 | 3000 |

13-Intro. Woozy Winks; last Firebrand

| | 194 | 388 | 582 | 1242 | 2121 | 3000 |

14-19: 15-Last No. 711; Destiny begins

| | 81 | 162 | 243 | 518 | 884 | 1250 |

20-The Raven x-over in Phantom Lady; features Jack Cole himself

| | 90 | 180 | 270 | 576 | 988 | 1400 |

21,22: 21-Raven & Spider Widow x-over in Phantom Lady (cameo in #22)

| | 71 | 142 | 213 | 454 | 777 | 1100 |

23-30: 23-Last Phantom Lady. 24-26-Flatfoot Burns by Kurtzman in all

| | 61 | 122 | 183 | 390 | 670 | 950 |

31-41: 37-1st app. Candy by Sahle & begins (12/44). 41-Last Spirit-r by Eisner

| | 52 | 104 | 156 | 328 | 552 | 775 |

42,43-Spirit-r by Eisner/Fine

| | 45 | 90 | 135 | 284 | 480 | 675 |

44-Fine Spirit-r begin, end #88,90,92

| | 55 | 110 | 165 | 352 | 601 | 650 |

45-50: 50-(#50 on-c, #49 on inside, 1/46)

| | 37 | 74 | 111 | 222 | 361 | 500 |

51-60: 58-Last Human Bomb

| | 31 | 62 | 93 | 186 | 303 | 420 |

61-88,90,92: 63-(Some issues have #65 printed on cover, but #63 on inside) Kurtzman, 6 pgs. 90,92-Spirit by Fine

| | 27 | 54 | 81 | 158 | 259 | 360 |

89,91,93-No Spirit stories

| | 24 | 48 | 72 | 142 | 234 | 325 |

94-99,101,102: Spirit by Eisner in all; 101-Last Manhunter. 102-Last Spirit & Plastic Man by Jack Cole

| | 34 | 68 | 102 | 199 | 325 | 450 |

100

| | 40 | 80 | 120 | 246 | 411 | 575 |

103-Content change to crime; Ken Shannon & T-man begin (1st app. of each, 12/50)

| | 40 | 80 | 120 | 246 | 411 | 575 |

104-112,114-127: Crandall-a most issues (not in 104,105,122,125-127). 109-Atomic bomb story. 112-Crandall-a

| | 25 | 50 | 75 | 150 | 245 | 340 |

113-Crandall-a(2), 9 pgs. each

| | 29 | 58 | 87 | 172 | 281 | 390 |

NOTE: Most Spirit stories signed by Eisner are not by him; all are reprints. Crandall Firebrand-1-8. Spirit by Eisner 1-41, 99(r). by Eisner/Fine-42, 43; by Fine-44-88, 90, 92. 103, 109. Al Bryant c-33, 34. Cole c-17-32, 35-102(most). Crandall c-13, 14. Crandall/Cuidera c-105-127. Eisner c-4i. Gill Fox c-1-3, 4p, 5-12, 15. Bondage c-103, 109, 125.

POLICE LINE-UP
Avon Periodicals/Realistic Comics #3,4: Aug, 1951 - No. 4, July, 1952 (Painted-c #1-3)

1-Wood-a, 1 pg. plus part-c; spanking panel-r/Saint #5

| | 57 | 114 | 171 | 362 | 619 | 875 |

2-Classic story "The Religious Murder Cult", drugs, torture; r/Saint #5; c-r/Avon paperback #329

| | 42 | 84 | 126 | 265 | 445 | 625 |

3,4: 3-Kubert-a(r?)/part-c; Kinstler-a (inside-c only) 33

| | 33 | 66 | 99 | 194 | 317 | 440 |

POLICE TRAP (Public Defender in Action #7 on)
Mainline #1-4/Charlton #5,6: 8-9/54 - No. 4, 2-3/55; No. 5, 7/55 - No. 6, 9/55

1-S&K covers-all issues; Meskin-a; Kirby scripts

| | 47 | 94 | 141 | 296 | 498 | 700 |

2-4

| | 28 | 56 | 84 | 158 | 274 | 380 |

5,6-S&K-c/a

| | 36 | 72 | 108 | 211 | 343 | 475 |

POLICE TRAP
Super Comics: No. 11, 1963; No. 16-18, 1964

Reprint #11,16-18: 11-r/Police Trap #3. 16-r/Justice Traps the Guilty #? 17-r/Inside Crime #3 & r/Justice Traps The Guilty #83; 18-r/Inside Crime #3

| | 3 | 6 | 9 | 14 | 19 | 24 |

POLLY & HER PALS (See Comic Monthly #1)

POLLY & THE PIRATES
Oni Press: Sept, 2005 - No. 6, June, 2006 ($2.99, B&W, limited series)

1-6-Ted Naifeh-s/a; Polly is shanghaied by the pirate ship Titania

| | | | | | | 3.00 |

TPB (7/06, $11.95, digest) r/#1-6

| | | | | | | 12.00 |

POLLYANNA (Disney)
Dell Publishing Co.: No. 1129, Aug-Oct, 1960

Four Color 1129-Movie, Hayley Mills photo-c

| | 8 | 16 | 24 | 52 | 99 | 145 |

POLLY PIGTAILS (Girls' Fun & Fashion Magazine #44 on)
Parents' Magazine Institute/Polly Pigtails: Jan, 1946 - V4#43, Oct-Nov, 1949

1-Infinity-c; photo-c

| | 27 | 54 | 81 | 158 | 259 | 360 |

2-Photo-c

| | 15 | 30 | 45 | 90 | 140 | 190 |

3-5: 3,4-Photo-c

| | 14 | 28 | 42 | 76 | 108 | 140 |

6-10: 7-Photo-c

| | 10 | 20 | 30 | 56 | 76 | 95 |

11-30: 22-Photo-c

| | 9 | 18 | 27 | 50 | 65 | 80 |

31-43: 38-Natalie Wood photo-c

| | 8 | 16 | 24 | 42 | 54 | 65 |

PONY EXPRESS (See Tales of the...)

PONYTAIL (Teen-age)
Dell Publishing Co./Charlton No. 13 on: 7-9/62 - No. 12, 10-12/65; No. 13, 11/69 - No. 20,

---

1/71

12-641-209(#1)

| | 4 | 8 | 12 | 23 | 37 | 50 |

2-12

| | 3 | 6 | 9 | 17 | 26 | 35 |

13-20

| | 3 | 6 | 9 | 14 | 19 | 24 |

POP
Dark Horse Comics: Aug, 2014 - No. 4, Nov, 2014 ($3.99, limited series)

1-4-Curt Pires-s/Jason Copland-a

| | | | | | | 4.00 |

POP COMICS
Modern Comics Publ.: 1955 (36 pgs.; 5x7"; in color) (7¢)

1-Funny animal

| | 10 | 20 | 30 | 54 | 72 | 90 |

POPEYE (See Comic Album #7, 11, 15, Comics Reading Libraries in the Promotional Comics section, Eat Right to Work and Win, Giant Comic Album, King Comics, Kite Fun Book, Magic Comics, March of Comics #37,52, 66, 80, 96, 117, 134, 148, 157, 169, 194, 246, 264, 274, 294, 453, 465, 477 & Wow Comics 1st series)

POPEYE
David McKay Publications: 1937 - 1939 (All by Segar)

Feature Books nn (100 pgs.) (Very Rare)

| | 1300 | 2600 | 3900 | 9900 | 17,950 | 26,000 |

Feature Books 2 (52 pgs.)

| | 168 | 336 | 504 | 1075 | 1838 | 2600 |

Feature Books 3 (100 pgs.)-r/nn issue with new-c

| | 123 | 246 | 369 | 787 | 1344 | 1900 |

Feature Books 5,10 (76 pgs.)

| | 110 | 220 | 330 | 704 | 1202 | 1700 |

Feature Books 14 (76 pgs.) (Scarce)

| | 129 | 258 | 387 | 826 | 1413 | 2000 |

POPEYE (Strip reprints through 4-Color #70)
Dell #1-65/Gold Key #66-80/King #81-92/Charlton #94-138/Gold Key #139-155/Whitman #156 on: 1941 - 1947; #1, 2-4/48 - #65, 7-9/62; #66, 10/62 - #80, 5/66; #81, 8/66 - #92, 12/67; #94, 2/69 - #138, 1/77; #139, 5/78 - #171, 6/84 (no #93,160,161)

Large Feature Comic 24('41)-Half by Segar

| | 110 | 220 | 330 | 704 | 1202 | 1700 |

Four Color 25('41)-by Segar

| | 123 | 246 | 369 | 787 | 1344 | 1900 |

Large Feature Comic 10('43)

| | 81 | 162 | 243 | 518 | 884 | 1250 |

Four Color 17('43),26('43)-by Segar

| | 54 | 108 | 162 | 432 | 966 | 1500 |

Four Color 43('44)

| | 30 | 60 | 90 | 216 | 483 | 750 |

Four Color 70('45)-Title: ...& Wimpy

| | 25 | 50 | 75 | 175 | 388 | 600 |

Four Color 113('46-original strips begin),127,145('47),168

| | 15 | 30 | 45 | 105 | 233 | 360 |

1(2-4/48)(Dell)-All new stories continue

| | 42 | 84 | 126 | 311 | 706 | 1100 |

2

| | 18 | 36 | 54 | 128 | 284 | 440 |

3-10: 5-Popeye on moon w/rocket-c

| | 13 | 26 | 39 | 91 | 201 | 310 |

11-20

| | 10 | 20 | 30 | 64 | 132 | 200 |

21-40,46: 46-Origin Swee' Pee

| | 8 | 16 | 24 | 54 | 102 | 150 |

41-45,47-50

| | 6 | 12 | 18 | 42 | 79 | 115 |

51-60

| | 5 | 10 | 15 | 35 | 63 | 90 |

61-65 (Last Dell issue)

| | 5 | 10 | 15 | 31 | 53 | 75 |

66(10/62),67-Both 84 pgs. (Gold Key)

| | 6 | 12 | 18 | 40 | 73 | 105 |

68-80

| | 4 | 8 | 12 | 25 | 40 | 55 |

81-92,94-97 (no #93): 97-Last 12¢ issue

| | 3 | 6 | 9 | 20 | 31 | 42 |

98,99,101-107,123: 123-Wimpy beats Neil Armstrong to the moon. 130-1st app. Superstuff

| | 3 | 6 | 9 | 14 | 19 | 24 |

100

| | 3 | 6 | 9 | 17 | 26 | 35 |

108-Traces Popeye's origin from 1929

| | 3 | 6 | 9 | 15 | 22 | 28 |

139-155: 144-50th Anniversary issue

| | 2 | 4 | 6 | 8 | 10 | 12 |

156,157,162-167(Whitman)(no #160,161).167(3/82)

| | 2 | 4 | 6 | 10 | 14 | 18 |

158(9/80),159(11/80)-pre-pack only

| | 5 | 10 | 15 | 34 | 60 | 85 |

168-171:(All #90069 on-c; pre-pack) 168(6/83). 169(#168 on-c)(8/83). 170(3/84). 171(6/84)

| | 3 | 6 | 9 | 17 | 26 | 35 |

NOTE: Reprints-#145, 147, 149, 151, 153, 155, 157, 163-168(1/3), 170.

POPEYE
Harvey Comics: Nov, 1993 - No. 7, Aug, 1994 ($1.50)

V2#1-7

| | | | | | | 4.00 |

...Summer Special V2#1-(10/93, $2.25, 68 pgs.)-Sagendorf-r & others

| | | | | | | 5.00 |

POPEYE
IDW Publishing: Apr, 2012 - No. 12, Apr, 2013 ($3.99)

1-12-New stories in classic style; Langridge-s. 1-Action #1 cover swipe. 12-Barney Google and Spark Plug app.

| | | | | | | 4.00 |

POPEYE (CLASSIC...)
IDW Publishing: Aug, 2012 - No. 65, Dec, 2017 ($3.99/$4.99)

1-43-Reprints of Bud Sagendorf's classic stories

| | | | | | | 4.00 |

44-65-($4.99)

| | | | | | | 5.00 |

POPEYE SPECIAL
Ocean Comics: Summer, 1987 - No. 2, Sept, 1988 ($1.75/$2.00)

1,2: 1-Origin

| | | | | | | 4.00 |

POPPLES (TV, movie)
Star Comics (Marvel): Dec, 1986 - No. 4, Jun, 1987

1-4-Based on toys

| | | | | | | 5.00 |

POPPO OF THE POPCORN THEATRE
Fuller Publishing Co. (Publishers Weekly): 10/29/55 - No. 13, 1956 (weekly)

1

| | 10 | 20 | 30 | 58 | 79 | 100 |

2-5

| | 7 | 14 | 21 | 37 | 46 | 55 |

6-13

| | 6 | 12 | 18 | 31 | 38 | 45 |

NOTE: By Charles Biro. 10¢ cover, given away by supermarkets such as IGA.

POP-POP COMICS
R. B. Leffingwell Co.: No date (Circa 1945) (52 pgs.)

1-Funny animal

| | 20 | 40 | 60 | 117 | 189 | 260 |

POPULAR COMICS
Dell Publishing Co.: Feb, 1936 - No. 145, July-Sept, 1948

1-Dick Tracy (1st comic book app.), Little Orphan Annie, Terry & the Pirates, Gasoline Alley, Don Winslow (1st app.), Harold Teen, Little Joe, Skippy, Moon Mullins, Mutt & Jeff, Tailspin Tommy, Smitty, Smokey Stover, Winnie Winkle & The Gumps begin (all strip-r)

| | 1143 | 2286 | 3429 | 8000 | -- | -- |

2

| | 343 | 686 | 1029 | 2400 | -- | -- |

3

| | 257 | 514 | 771 | 1800 | -- | -- |

4-6(7/36): 5-Tom Mix begins. 6-1st app. Scribbly 193

| | 193 | 386 | 579 | 1350 | -- | -- |

Police Comics #18 © QUA

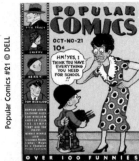

Popular Comics #21 © DELL

Porcelain #1 © Maria Llovet

	GD 2.0	VG 4.0	FN 6.0	VF 8.0	VF/NM 9.0	NM- 9.2
7-10: 8,9-Scribbly & Reglar Fellers app.	157	314	471	1100	--	--
11-20: 12-X-Mas-c	92	184	322	529	840	1150
21-27: 27-Last Terry & the Pirates, Little Orphan Annie, & Dick Tracy	66	132	231	380	603	825
28-37: 28-Gene Autry app. 31,32-Tim McCoy app. 35-Christmas-c; Tex Ritter app.	52	104	182	299	475	650
38-43: Tarzan in text only. 38-(4/39)-Gang Busters (Radio, 2nd app.) & Zane Grey's Tex Thorne begins? 43-The Masked Pilot app.; 1st non-funny-c?	48	96	168	276	438	600
44,45: 45-Hurricane Kid-c	44	88	154	253	402	550
46-Origin/1st app. Martan, the Marvel Man(12/39)	60	120	210	334	459	750
47-49-Martan, the Marvel Man-c	48	96	168	276	438	600
50-Gang Busters-c	40	80	140	230	365	500
51-Origin The Voice (The Invisible Detective) strip begins (5/40)	44	88	154	253	402	550
52-Classic Martan blasting robots-c/sty	78	156	273	449	712	975
53-56: 55-End of World story	38	76	133	219	350	480
57-59-Martan, the Marvel Man-c	48	96	168	276	438	600
60-Origin/1st app. Professor Supermind and Son (2/41)	45	90	158	259	410	560
61-64,66-Professor Supermind-c. 63-Smilin' Jack begins	36	72	126	207	329	450
65-Classic Professor Supermind WWII-c	52	104	182	299	475	650
67-71	26	52	91	150	238	325
72-The Owl & Terry & the Pirates begin (2/42); Smokey Stover reprints begin	42	84	126	242	371	500
73-75	30	60	105	173	272	370
76-78-Capt. Midnight in all (see The Funnies #57)	40	80	120	230	358	485
79-85-Last Owl	27	54	81	155	238	320
86-Gremlins take down a Japanese WWII plane	50	100	150	315	533	750
87-99: 98-Felix the Cat, Smokey Stover-r begin	18	36	54	104	157	210
100	20	40	60	115	175	235
101-130	10	20	30	58	89	120
131-145: 142-Last Terry & the Pirates	9	18	27	52	79	105

NOTE: Martan, the Marvel Man c-47-49, 52, 57-59. Professor Supermind c-60-63, 64(1/2), 65, 66. The Voice c-53.

POPULAR FAIRY TALES (See March of Comics #6, 18)

POPULAR ROMANCE
Better-Standard Publications: No. 5, Dec. 1949 - No. 29, July, 1954

5	23	46	69	136	223	310
6-9: 7-Palais-c; lingerie panels	16	32	48	94	147	200
10-Wood-a (2 pgs.)	19	38	57	109	172	235
11,12,14-16,18-21,28,29	15	30	45	84	127	170
13,17-Severin/Elder-a (3&8 pgs.)	15	30	45	86	133	180
22-27-Toth-a	16	32	48	92	144	195

NOTE: All have photo-c. Tuska art in most issues.

POPULAR TEEN-AGERS (Secrets of Love) (School Day Romances #1-4)
Star Publications: No. 5, Sept. 1950 - No. 23, Nov, 1954

5-Toni Gay, Midge Martin & Eve Adams continue from School Day Romances; Ginger Bunn (formerly Ginger Snapp) becomes Honey Bunn (#6 on) begins; all features end #8	57	114	171	362	619	875
6-8 (7/51)-Honey Bunn begins; all have L. B. Cole-c; 6-Negligee panels	45	90	135	284	480	675
9-(...Romances; 1st romance issue, 10/51)	77	154	231	493	847	1200
10-(...Secrets of Love thru #23)	77	154	231	493	847	1200
11,16,18,19,22,23	40	80	120	246	411	575
12,13,17,20,21-Disbrow-a	42	84	126	265	445	625
14-Harrison/Wood-a	53	106	159	334	567	800
15-Wood?, Disbrow-a	45	90	135	284	480	675
Accepted Reprint 5,6 (nd); L.B. Cole-c	13	26	39	74	105	135

NOTE: All have L. B. Cole covers.

PORCELAIN
Ablaze Publishing: 2021 - No. 5, 2021 ($3.99, limited series)

1-5-Maria Llovet-s/a; multiple covers on each						4.00

PORKY PIG (See Bugs Bunny &..., Kite Fun Book, Looney Tunes, March of Comics #42, 57, 71, 89, 99, 113, 130, 143, 164, 175, 192, 209, 218, 367, and Super Book #6, 18, 30)

PORKY PIG (...& Bugs Bunny #40-69)
Dell Publishing Co./Gold Key No. 1-93/Whitman No. 94 on: No. 16, 1942 - No. 81, Mar-Apr, 1962; Jan, 1965 - No. 109, June, 1984

Four Color 16(#1)	107	214	321	856	1928	3000
Four Color 48(1944)-Carl Barks-a	107	214	321	856	1928	3000
Four Color 78(1945)	32	64	96	230	515	800
Four Color 112(7/46)	18	36	54	128	284	440

Four Color 156,182,191('49)	12	24	36	81	176	270
Four Color 226,241('49),260,271,277,284,295	9	18	27	63	129	195
Four Color 303,311,322,330: 322-Sci/fi-c/story	8	16	24	54	102	150
Four Color 342,351,360,370,385,399,410,426	6	12	18	54	102	115
25 (11-12/52)-30	5	10	15	34	60	85
31-40	5	10	15	30	50	70
41-60	4	8	12	25	40	55
61-81(3-4/62)	3	6	9	21	33	45
1 (1/65-Gold Key)(2nd Series)	5	10	15	31	53	75
2,4,5-r/4-Color 226,284 & 271 in that order	3	6	9	19	30	40
3,6-10: 3-r/Four Color #342	3	6	9	16	24	32
11-30	3	6	9	14	19	24
31-54	2	4	6	10	14	18
55-70	2	4	6	8	11	14
71-93(Gold Key)	2	3	4	6	8	10
94-96	2	4	6	8	10	12
97(9/80),98-pre-pack only (99 known not to exist)	4	8	12	27	44	60
100	2	4	6	10	14	18
101-105: 104(2/82). 105(4/82)	2	4	6	8	11	14
106-109 (All #90140 on-c, no date or date code): 106(7/83), 107(8/83), 108(2/84), 109(6/84) low print run	3	6	9	14	20	26

NOTE: Reprints-#1-8, 9-35(2/3); 36-46(1/4-1/2), 58, 67, 69-74, 76, 78, 102-109(1/3-1/2).

PORKY PIG'S DUCK HUNT
Saalfield Publishing Co.: 1938 (12pgs.)(large size)(heavy linen-like paper)

2178-1st app. Porky Pig & Daffy Duck by Leon Schlesinger. Illustrated text story book written in verse. 1st book ever devoted to these characters. (see Looney Tunes #1 for their 1st comic book app.)	93	186	279	591	1021	1450

PORTAL BOUND
Aspen MLT: No. 0, Feb, 2018 - No. 5, Aug, 2018 ($1.50/$3.99)

0-($1.50) Roslan & Carrasco-s/Arizmendi-a; 2 covers; bonus character sketches						3.00
1-5-($3.99) Roslan & Carrasco-s/Arizmendi-a						4.00

PORTENT, THE
Image Comics: Feb, 2006 - No. 4, Aug, 2006 ($2.99)

1-4-Peter Bergting-s/a						3.00
Vol. 1: Duende TPB (2006, 12.99) r/#1-4; pin-up art; intro. by Kaluta						13.00

PORTIA PRINZ OF THE GLAMAZONS
Eclipse Comics: Dec, 1986 - No. 6, Oct, 1987 ($2.00, B&W, Baxter paper)

1-6						4.00

POSEIDON IX (Also see Aphrodite IX and (Ninth) IX Generation)
Image Comics (Top Cow): Sept, 2015 ($3.99, one-shot)

1-Howard-s/Sevy-a; story continues in IX Generation #5						4.00

POSSESSED, THE
DC Comics (Cliffhanger): Sept, 2003 - No. 6, March, 2004 ($2.95, limited series)

1-6-Johns & Grimminger-s/Sharp-a						3.00
TPB (2004, $14.95) r/#1-6; promo art and sketch pages						15.00

POSTAL (Also see Eden's Fall)
Image Comics (Top Cow): Feb, 2015 - Present ($3.99)

1-24: 1-Matt Hawkins & Bryan Hill-s/Issac Goodheart-a						4.00
25-($5.99) Matt Hawkins & Bryan Hill-s/Issac Goodheart-a						6.00
...: Dossier 1 (11/15, $3.99) Ryan Cady-a; background on Eden and character profiles						4.00
...: Mark 1 (2/18, $3.99) Spotlight on Mark; Ienco-a						4.00
...: Night Shift 1 (12/20, $3.99) Spotlights on Roy Magnus & Molly; Goodheart-c						4.00

POSTAL: DELIVERANCE
Image Comics (Top Cow): Jul, 2019 - Present ($3.99)

1-8-Bryan Hill-s/Raffaele Ienco-a						4.00

POST AMERICANA
Image Comics: Dec, 2020 - No. 7, Dec, 2021 ($3.99)

1-7-Steve Skroce-s/a						4.00

POST GAZETTE (See Meet the New... in the Promotional Comics section)

POWDER RIVER RUSTLERS (See Fawcett Movie Comics)

POWER & GLORY (See American Flagg! & Howard Chaykin's American Flagg!
Malibu Comics (Bravura): Feb, 1994 - No. 4, May, 1994 ($2.50, limited series, mature)

1A, 1B-By Howard Chaykin; w/Bravura stamp						4.00
1-Newsstand ed. (polybagged w/children's warning on bag), Gold ed., Silver-foil ed., Blue-foil ed.(print run of 10,000), Serigraph ed. (print run of 3,000)($2.95)-Howard Chaykin-c/a begin						5.00
2-4-Contains Bravura stamp						4.00
Holiday Special (Win '94, $2.95)						4.00

	GD 2.0	VG 4.0	FN 6.0	VF 8.0	VF/NM 9.0	NM- 9.2

POWER COMICS
Holyoke Publ. Co./Narrative Publ.: 1944 - No. 4, 1945

	GD 2.0	VG 4.0	FN 6.0	VF 8.0	VF/NM 9.0	NM- 9.2
1-L.B. Cole-c	271	542	813	1734	2967	4200
2-Hitler, Hirohito-c (scarce)	1000	2000	3000	7400	13,200	19,000
3-Classic L.B. Cole-c; Dr. Mephisto begins?	1000	2000	3000	7500	13,500	19,500
4-L.B. Cole-c; Miss Espionage app. #3,4; Leav-a	465	930	1395	3395	5998	8600

POWER COMICS
Power Comics Co.: 1977 - No. 5, Dec, 1977 (B&W)

	GD 2.0	VG 4.0	FN 6.0	VF 8.0	VF/NM 9.0	NM- 9.2
1- "A Boy And His Aardvark" by Dave Sim; first Dave Sim aardvark (not Cerebus)	3	6	9	21	33	45
1-Reprint (3/77, black-c)	1	2	3	5	6	8
2-Cobalt Blue by Gustovich	1	3	4	6	8	10
3-5: 3-Nightwitch. 4-Northern Light. 5-Bluebird	1	3	4	6	8	10

POWER COMICS
Eclipse Comics (Acme Press): Mar, 1988 - No. 4, Sept, 1988 ($2.00, B&W, mini-series)
1-4: Bolland, Gibbons-r in all — 4.00

POWER COMPANY, THE
DC Comics: Apr, 2002 - No. 18, Sep, 2003 ($2.50/$2.75)
1-6-Busiek-s/Grummett-a. 6-Green Arrow & Black Canary-c/app. — 3.00
7-18: 7-Begin $2.75-c. 8,9-Green Arrow app. 11-Firestorm joins. 15-Batman app. — 3.00
...Bork (3/02) Busiek-s/Dwyer-a; Batman & Flash (Barry Allen) app. — 3.00
...Josiah Power (3/02) Busiek-s/Giffen-a; Superman app. — 3.00
...Manhunter (3/02) Busiek-s/Jurgens-a; Nightwing app. — 3.00
...Sapphire (3/02) Busiek-s/Bagley-a; JLA & Kobra app. — 3.00
...Skyrocket (3/02) Busiek-s/Staton-a; Green Lantern (Hal Jordan) app. — 3.00
...Striker Z (3/02) Busiek-s/Bachs-a; Superboy app. — 3.00
...Witchfire (3/02) Busiek-s/Haley-a; Wonder Woman app. — 3.00

POWER CUBED
Dark Horse Comics: Sept, 2015 - No. 4, Jan, 2016 ($3.99, limited series)
1-4-Aaron Lopresti-s/a — 4.00

POWER FACTOR
Wonder Color Comics #1/Pied Piper #2: May, 1987 - No. 2, 1987 ($1.95)
1,2: Super team. 2-Infantino-c — 4.00

POWER FACTOR
Innovation Publishing: Oct, 1990 - No. 3, 1991 ($1.95/$2.25)
1-3: 1-R-/1st story + new-a, 2-r/2nd story + new-a. 3-Infantino-a — 4.00

POWER GIRL (See All-Star #58, Infinity, Inc., JSA Classified, Showcase #97-99)
DC Comics: June, 1988 - No. 4, Sept, 1988 ($1.00, color, limited series)

	GD 2.0	VG 4.0	FN 6.0	VF 8.0	VF/NM 9.0	NM- 9.2
1	3	6	9	16	23	30
2-4	1	2	3	5	6	8

TPB (2006, $14.99) r/Showcase #97-99; Secret Origins #11; JSA Classified #1-4 and pages from JSA #32,39; cover gallery — 15.00

POWER GIRL
DC Comics: Jul, 2009 - No. 27, Oct, 2011 ($2.99)

	GD 2.0	VG 4.0	FN 6.0	VF 8.0	VF/NM 9.0	NM- 9.2
1-Amanda Conner-a; covers by Conner and Hughes; Ultra-Humanite app.	3	6	9	19	30	40
2-Conner-a; covers by Conner and Hughes	3	6	9	14	20	26
3-10: 3-6-Covers by Conner and March						5.00

11-26: 13-23-Winick-s/Basri-a. 20,21-Crossover with Justice League: Generation Lost #18-22 23-Zatanna app. 24,25-Batman app.; Prasetya-a

	GD 2.0	VG 4.0	FN 6.0	VF 8.0	VF/NM 9.0	NM- 9.2
27-Ample cleavage cover; Cyclone app.	6	12	18	41	76	110

...Aliens and Apes SC (2010, $17.99) r/#7-12 — 18.00
...A New Beginning SC (2010, $17.99) r/#1-6; gallery of variant covers — 18.00
...Bomb Squad SC (2011, $14.99) r/#13-18 — 15.00
... Special 1 (7/23, $5.99) Johnny Sorrow app.; back-up with Fire, Ice & Guy Gardner — 6.00

POWER GIRL
DC Comics: Nov, 2023 - Present ($3.99)
1-6: 1-4-Leah Williams-s/Eduardo Pansica-a — 4.00
...Uncovered 1 (#24, $5.99) Gallery of classic Power Girl covers and variant covers — 6.00

POWERHOUSE PEPPER COMICS (See Gay Comics, Joker Comics & Tessie the Typist)
Marvel Comics (20CC): No. 1, 1943; No. 2, May, 1948 - No. 5, Nov, 1948

	GD 2.0	VG 4.0	FN 6.0	VF 8.0	VF/NM 9.0	NM- 9.2
1-(60 pgs.)-Wolverton-a in all; c-2,3	252	504	756	1613	2757	3900
2	119	238	357	762	1306	1850
3,4	103	206	309	659	1130	1600
5-(Scarce)	126	252	378	806	1378	1950

POWERLESS
Marvel Comics: Aug, 2004 - No. 6, Jan, 2005 ($2.99, limited series)
1-6-Peter Parker, Matt Murdock and Logan without powers; Gaydos-a — 3.00
TPB (2005, $14.99) r/series; sketch page by Gaydos — 15.00

POWER LINE
Marvel Comics (Epic Comics): May, 1988 - No. 8, Sept, 1989 ($1.25/$1.50)
1-8: 2-Williamson-i. 3-Dr. Zero app. 4-7-Morrow-a. 8-Williamson-i — 4.00

POWER LINES
Image Comics: Mar, 2016 - No. 3 ($3.50/$3.99)
1-3-Jimmie Robinson-s/a. 1-($3.50-c). 2-Begin $3.99-c — 4.00

POWER LORDS
DC Comics: Dec, 1983 - No. 3, Feb, 1984 (Limited series, Mando paper)
1-3: Based on Revell toys — 4.00

POWER MAN (Formerly Hero for Hire; ...& Iron Fist #50 on; see Cage & Giant-Size...)
Marvel Comics Group: No. 17, Feb, 1974 - No. 125, Sept, 1986

	GD 2.0	VG 4.0	FN 6.0	VF 8.0	VF/NM 9.0	NM- 9.2
17-Luke Cage continues; Iron Man app.	5	10	15	34	60	85
18,20: 18-Last 20¢ issue; intro. Wrecking Crew	3	6	9	16	23	30
19-1st app. Cottonmouth	5	10	15	30	50	70
21-23,25-30	2	4	6	9	12	15
24-Intro. Black Goliath	9	18	27	57	111	165
30-(30¢-c variant, limited distribution)(4/76)	5	10	15	33	57	80
31-46: 31-Part Neal Adams-i. 34-Last 25¢ issue. 36-r/Hero For Fist #12.						
41-1st app. Thunderbolt. 45-Starlin-c.	2	4	6	8	10	12
31-34-(30¢-c variants, limited distribution)(5-8/76)	5	10	15	31	53	75
44-46-(35¢-c variants, limited distribution)(6-8/77)	10	20	30	67	141	215
47-Barry Smith-a	2	4	6	8	11	14
47-(35¢-c variant, limited distribution)(10/77)	9	18	27	58	114	170
48-Power Man/Iron Fist 1st meet; Byrne-a(p)	6	12	18	37	66	95
49-Byrne-a(p)	3	6	9	16	23	30
50-Iron Fist joins Cage; Byrne-a(p)	5	10	15	34	60	85
51-56,58-65,67-77: 58-Intro El Aguila. 75-Double size. 77-Daredevil app.	1	3	4	6	8	10
57-New X-Men app. (6/79)	3	8	12	25	40	55
66-2nd app. Sabretooth (see Iron Fist #14)	6	12	18	37	66	95
78,84: 78-3rd app. Sabretooth (cameo under cloak). 84-4th app. Sabretooth	4	8	12	25	40	55
79-83,85-99,101-124: 87-Moon Knight app. 109-The Reaper app.						6.00
100-Double size; Origin K'un Lun	2	4	6	8	10	12
125-Double size; Death of Iron Fist	2	4	6	9	12	15
Annual 1(1976)-Punisher cameo in flashback	3	6	9	18	28	38

NOTE: **Austin** c-102i. **Byrne** a-48-50; c-102, 104, 106, 107, 112-116. **Kane** c(p)-24, 25, 28, 48. **Miller** a-68, 76(2 pgs.); c-66-68, 70-74, 80i. **Mooney** a-38i, 53i, 55i. **Nebres** a-76i. **Nino** a-42i, 43i. **Perez** a-27. **B. Smith** a-47i. **Tuska** c(p)-17, 20, 24, 26, 28, 29, 36, 47. Painted c-75, 100.

POWER MAN AND IRON FIST
Marvel Comics: Apr, 2011 - No. 5, Jul, 2011 ($2.99, limited series)
1-5-Van Lente-s/Alves-a; Victor Alvarez as Power Man — 3.00

POWER MAN AND IRON FIST
Marvel Comics: Apr, 2016 - No. 15, Jun, 2017 ($3.99)
1-15: 1-Luke Cage and Danny Rand; David Walker-s/Sanford Greene-a; Tombstone app. — 4.00
6-9-Civil War II tie-in — 4.00
...: Sweet Christmas Annual 1 (2/17, $4.99) Walker-s/Hepburn-a; Daimon Hellstrom app. — 5.00

POWER OF PRIME
Malibu Comics (Ultraverse): July, 1995 - No. 4, Nov, 1995 ($2.50, lim. series)
1-4 — 4.00

POWER OF SHAZAM!, THE (See SHAZAM!)
DC Comics: 1994 (Painted graphic novel) (Prequel to new series)

	GD 2.0	VG 4.0	FN 6.0	VF 8.0	VF/NM 9.0	NM- 9.2
Hardcover-($19.95)-New origin of Shazam!; Ordway painted-c/a & script	3	6	9	16	23	30
Softcover-($7.50), Softcover-($9.95)-New-c	2	4	6	8	10	12

POWER OF SHAZAM!, THE
DC Comics: Mar, 1995 - No. 47, Mar, 1999; No. 48, Mar, 2010 ($1.50/$1.75/$1.95/$2.50)

	GD 2.0	VG 4.0	FN 6.0	VF 8.0	VF/NM 9.0	NM- 9.2
1-Jerry Ordway scripts begin	2	4	6	8	10	12

2-20: 4-Begin $1.75-c. 6-Re-intro of Capt. Nazi. 8-Re-intro of Spy Smasher, Bulletman & Minuteman; Swan-a (7 pgs.). 11-Re-intro of Ibis, Swan-a(2 pgs.). 14-Gil Kane-a(p). 20-Superman-c/app.; "Final Night" — 4.00
21-45,47: 21-Plastic Man-c/app. 22-Batman-c/app. 24-Spy Smasher WWII story. 35,36-X-over w/Starman #39,40. 38-41-Mr. Mind. 43-Bulletman app. 45-JLA-c/app. — 4.00

	GD 2.0	VG 4.0	FN 6.0	VF 8.0	VF/NM 9.0	NM- 9.2
46-Superman vs. Shazam	1	3	4	6	8	10

48-(3/10, $2.99) Blackest Night one-shot; Osiris rises as a Black Lantern; Kramer-a — 4.00
#1,000,000 (11/98) 853rd Century x-over; Ordway-c/s/a — 4.00
Annual 1 (1996, $2.95)-Legends of the Dead Earth story; Jerry Ordway; Mike Manley-a — 4.00

POWER OF STRONGMAN, THE (Also see Strongman)
AC Comics: 1989 ($2.95)
1-Powell G.A.-r — 4.00

POWER OF THE ATOM (See Secret Origins #29)
DC Comics: Aug, 1988 - No. 18, Nov, 1989 ($1.00)
1-18: 6-Chronos returns; Byrne-p. 9-JLI app. — 4.00

POWER OF THE DARK CRYSTAL (Jim Henson)
BOOM! Studios (Archaia): Feb, 2017 - No. 12, Mar, 2018 ($3.99)
1-12-Simon Spurrier-s/Kelly & Nichole Matthews-a; multiple covers — 4.00

POWER PACHYDERMS
Marvel Comics: Sept, 1989 ($1.25, one-shot)
1-Elephant super-heroes; parody of X-Men, Elektra, & 3 Stooges — 4.00

POWER PACK
Marvel Comics Group: Aug, 1984 - No. 62, Feb, 1991

	GD 2.0	VG 4.0	FN 6.0	VF 8.0	VF/NM 9.0	NM- 9.2
1-($1.00, 52 pgs.)-Origin & 1st app. Power Pack	3	6	9	16	23	30
2-18,20-26,28,30-45,47-62						4.00
19-(52 pgs.)-Cloak & Dagger, Wolverine app.						5.00
27-Mutant massacre; Wolverine & Sabretooth app.	1	2	3	5	6	8
29,46: 29-Spider-Man & Hobgoblin app. 46-Punisher app.						5.00

Graphic Novel: Power Pack & Cloak & Dagger: Shelter From the Storm ('89, SC, $7.95) Velluto/Farmer-a — 12.00

	GD 2.0	VG 4.0	FN 6.0	VF 8.0	VF/NM 9.0	NM- 9.2
...Holiday Special 1 (2/92, $2.25, 68 pgs.)	1	3	4	6	8	10

NOTE: **Austin** scripts-53. **Mignola** c-20. **Morrow** a-51. **Spiegle** a-55i. **Williamson** a(i)-43, 50, 52.

POWER PACK (Volume 2)
Marvel Comics: Aug, 2000 - No. 4, Nov, 2000 ($2.99, limited series)
1-4-Doran & Austin-c/a — 3.00

POWER PACK
Marvel Comics: June, 2005 - No. 4, Aug, 2005 ($2.99, limited series)
1-4-Sumerak-s/Gurihiru-a; back-up Franklin Richards story. 3-Fantastic Four app. — 3.00
... Digest (2006, $6.99) r/#1-4 — 7.00

POWER PACK (Marvel Legacy)
Marvel Comics: No. 63, Jan, 2018 ($3.99, one-shot)
63-Devin Grayson-s/Marika Cresta-a — 4.00

POWER PACK (Also see Outlawed #1 and Champions)
Marvel Comics: Jun, 2020 - No. 5, Jun, 2021 ($3.99, limited series)
1-5-Ryan North-s/Nico Leon-a. 1-Origin retold. 2-The Wizard app. 3-Taskmaster app. — 4.00

POWER PACK: DAY ONE
Marvel Comics: May, 2008 - No. 4, Aug, 2008($2.99, limited series)
1-4-Van Lente-s/Gurihiru-a; origin retold; Coover-a back-ups. 1-Fantastic Four cameo — 3.00

Power Girl (2009 series) #8 © DC

Powerpuff Girls (2013 series) #3 © CN

Powers V2 #26 © jinxworld

	GD 2.0	VG 4.0	FN 6.0	VF 8.0	VF/NM 9.0	NM- 9.2

POWER PACK: GROW-UP
Marvel Comics: Oct, 2019 ($4.99, one-shot)
1-Louise Simonson-s/June Brigman-a; back-up w/art by Gurihiru; Kofi & Wolverine app.   5.00

POWER PACK: INTO THE STORM
Marvel Comics: Mar, 2024 - Present ($3.99, limited series)
1,2-Louise Simonson-s/June Brigman-a   4.00

POWERPUFF GIRLS, THE (Also see Cartoon Network Starring... #1)
DC Comics: May, 2000 - No. 70, Mar, 2006 ($1.99/$2.25)

1	3	6	9	15	22	28
2-10						6.00
11-55,57-70: 25-Pin-ups by Allred, Byrne, Baker, Mignola, Hernandez, Warren						4.00
56-($2.95) Bonus pages; Mojo Jojo-c						5.00
...Double Whammy (12/00, $3.95) r/#1,2 & a Dexter's Lab story						
	2	4	6	10	14	18
...Movie: The Comic (9/02, $2.95) Movie adaptation; Phil Moy & Chris Cook-a						
	2	4	6	9	12	15

POWERPUFF GIRLS
IDW Publishing: Sept, 2013 - No. 10, Jun, 2014 ($3.99)

1-Five covers; Troy Little-s/a; Mojo Jojo app.	1	3	4	6	8	10
2-10-Multiple covers on each						4.00

POWERPUFF GIRLS (Based on the 2016 TV reboot)
IDW Publishing: Jul, 2016 - No. 6, Dec, 2016 ($3.99)
1-6: 1-4 Derek Charm-a; multiple covers on each. 1-Mojo Jojo app.   4.00

POWERPUFF GIRLS: BUREAU OF BAD
IDW Publishing: Nov, 2017 - No. 3, Jan, 2018 ($3.99, limited series)
1-3-Mancini & Goldman-s/Murphy-a; multiple covers on each   4.00

POWERPUFF GIRLS: SUPER SMASH-UP!
IDW Publishing: Jan, 2015 - No. 5, May, 2015 ($3.99, limited series)
1-5-Dexter's Laboratory's Dexter & Dee-Dee app.; multiple covers on each   4.00

POWERPUFF GIRLS: THE TIME TIE
IDW Publishing: May, 2017 - No. 3, Jul, 2017 ($3.99, limited series)
1-3-Mancini & Goldman-s/Murphy-a; multiple covers on each   4.00

POWER RANGERS (Mighty Morphin Power Rangers)
BOOM! Studios: Nov, 2020 - Present ($3.99/$3.99)
1-($4.99) Parrott-s/Mortarino-a; multiple covers; Omega Rangers app.   5.00
2-22-($3.99): 13-16-The Eltarian War   4.00
... Unlimited: Edge of Darkness 1 (6/22, $7.99) Silver Ranger app.   8.00
... Unlimited: Countdown to Ruin 1 (6/22, $7.99) Silver Ranger app.   8.00
... Unlimited: Heir to Darkness 1 (3/21, $7.99) Origin of Astronema   8.00
... Unlimited: Hyperforce 1 (7/23, $7.99) Santa Claus app.   8.00
... Unlimited: The Coinless 1 (6/23, $7.99) Hildago-a   8.00
... Unlimited: The Death Ranger 1 (8/22, $7.99) Sister Supernova app.   8.00

POWER RANGERS: DRAKKON NEW DAWN (Mighty Morphin Power Rangers)
BOOM! Studios: Aug, 2020 - No. 3, Oct, 2020 ($4.99, limited series)
1-3-Burch-s/Ragazzoni-a; multiple covers   5.00

POWER RANGERS: RANGER SLAYER (Mighty Morphin Power Rangers)
BOOM! Studios: Jul, 2020 ($7.99, one-shot)
1-Parrott-s/Mora-a; multiple covers   8.00

POWER RANGERS UNIVERSE (Mighty Morphin Power Rangers)
BOOM! Studios: 2021 - No. 6, May, 2022 ($4.99)
1-6-($4.99) Andelfinger-s/Ragazzoni-a; multiple covers   5.00

POWER RANGERS ZEO (TV)(Saban's...)(Also see Saban's Mighty Morphin Power Rangers)
Image Comics (Extreme Studios): Aug, 1996 ($2.50)

1-Based on TV show	2	4	6	8	10	12

POWER RECORD COMICS (Named Peter Pan Record Comics for #33-47)
Marvel Comics/Power Records: 1974 - 1978 ($1.49, 7x10" comics, 20 pgs. with 45 R.P.M. record) (Clipped corners - reduce value 20%) (Comic alone - 50% / record alone - 50%) (Some copies significantly warped by shrinkwrapping - reduce value 20%) (PR22, PR23, PR38, PR43, PR44 do not exist)
PR10-Spider-Man-r/from #124,125; Man-Wolf app. PR18-Planet of the Apes-r. PR19-Escape From the Planet of the Apes-r. PR20-Beneath the Planet of the Apes-r. PR21-Battle for the Planet of the Apes-r. PR24-Spider-Man II-New-a begins. PR27-Batman "Stacked Cards"; N. Adams-a(p). PR30-Batman "Robin Meets Man-Bat"; N. Adams-r/Det.(7 pgs.).

With record; each...	5	10	15	35	63	90

PR11-Incredible Hulk-r/#171. PR12-Captain America-r/#168. PR13-Fantastic Four-r/#126. PR14-Frankenstein-Ploog-r/#1. PR15-Tomb of Dracula-Colan-r/#2. PR16-Man-Thing-

Ploog-r/#5. PR17-Werewolf By Night-Ploog-r/Marvel Spotlight #2. PR28-Superman "Alien Creatures". PR29-Space: 1999 "Breakaway". PR31-Conan-N. Adams-a; reprinted in Conan #116. PR32-Space: 1999 "Return to the Beginning". PR33-Superman-G.A. origin, Buckler-a(p). PR34-Superman. PR35-Wonder Woman-Buckler-a(p)

With record; each...	5	10	15	31	53	75

PR11, PR24-(1981 Peter Pan records re-issues) PR11-New Abomination & Rhino-c

With record; each...	5	10	15	33	57	80

PR25-Star Trek "Passage to Moauv". PR26-Star Trek "Crier in Emptiness." PR36-Holo-Man. PR37-Robin Hood. PR39-Huckleberry Finn. PR40-Davy Crockett. PR41-Robinson Crusoe. PR42-20,000 Leagues Under the Sea. PR47-Little Women

With record; each...	4	8	12	28	47	65

PR25, PR26 (Peter Pan records re-issues with photo covers). PR45-Star Trek "Dinosaur Planet". PR46-Star Trek "The Robot Masters"

	4	8	12	28	47	65

NOTE: Peter Pan re-issues exist for #25-32 and are valued the same.

POWERS
Image Comics: 2000 - No. 37, Feb, 2004 ($2.95)

1-Bendis-s/Oeming-a; murder of Retro Girl	2	4	6	9	11	14
2-6: 6-End of Retro Girl arc.						6.00
7-14: 7-Warren Ellis app. 12-14-Death of Olympia						4.00
15-37: 31-36-Origin of the Powers						3.00
Annual 1 (2001, $3.95)						4.00
...: Anarchy TPB (11/03, $14.95) r/#21-24; interviews, sketchbook, cover gallery						15.00
...Coloring/Activity Book (2001, $1.50, B&W, 8 x 10.5") Oeming-a						3.00
...: Firsts 1 (6/15, $1.00) r/#1						3.00
...: Forever TPB (2005, $19.95) r/#31-37; script for #31, sketchbook, cover gallery						20.00
...: Little Deaths TPB (2002, $19.95) r/#7,12-14, Ann. #1, Coloring/Activity Book; sketch pages, cover gallery						20.00
...: Roleplay TPB (2001, $13.95) r/#8-11; sketchbook, cover gallery						14.00
...: Scriptbook (2001, $19.95) scripts for #1-11; Oeming sketches						20.00
...: Supergroup TPB (2003, $19.95) r/#15-20; sketchbook, cover gallery						20.00
...: The Definitive Collection Vol. 1 HC (2006, $29.99, dust jacket) r/#1-11 & Coloring/Activity Book, script for #1, sketch pages and covers, interviews, letter column highlights						30.00
...: The Definitive Collection Vol. 2 HC (2009, $29.99, dust jacket) r/#12-24 & Annual #1; cover gallery; 1st Bendis/Oeming Jinx story; interviews, letter column highlights						30.00
...: Who Killed Retro Girl TPB (2000, $21.95) r/#1-6; sketchbook, cover gallery, and promotional strips from Comic Shop News						22.00

POWERS
Marvel Comics (Icon): Jul, 2004 - No. 30, Sept, 2008 ($2.95/$3.95)

1-11,13-24-Bendis-s/Oeming-a. 14-Cover price error						3.00
12-($3.95, 64 pages) 2 covers; Bendis & Oeming interview						4.00
25-30-($3.95, 40 pages) 25-Two covers; Bendis interview						4.00
Annual 2008 (5/08, $4.95) Bendis-s/Oeming-a; interview with Brubaker, Simone, others						5.00
...: Legends TPB (2005, $17.95) r/#1-6; sketchbook, cover gallery						18.00
...: Psychotic TPB (1/06, $19.95) r/#7-12; Bendis & Oeming interview, cover gallery						20.00
...: Cosmic TPB (10/07, $19.95) r/#13-18; script and sketch pages						20.00
...: Secret Identity TPB (12/07, $19.95) r/#19-24; script pages						20.00

POWERS (Volume 3)
Marvel Comics (Icon): Nov, 2009 - No. 11, Jul, 2012 ($3.95)
1-11-Bendis-s/Oeming-a   4.00

POWERS (Volume 5)
Marvel Comics (Icon): Jan, 2015 - No. 8, Apr, 2017 ($3.99)
1-8-Bendis-s/Oeming-a. 1-Bonus photo spread of TV show cast   4.00

POWERS: BUREAU (Follows Volume 3)
Marvel Comics (Icon): Feb, 2013 - No. 12, Nov, 2014 ($3.95)
1-12-Bendis-s/Oeming-a   4.00

POWERS OF X (Weekly series alternating with House of X #1-6)
Marvel Comics: Sept, 2019 - No. 6, Dec, 2019 ($5.99/$4.99)
1-($5.99) Hickman-s/Silva-a   6.00
2-6-($4.99) 4-Mr. Sinister app.   5.00

POWERS THAT BE (Becomes Star Seed on)
Broadway Comics: Nov, 1995 - No. 6, June, 1996 ($2.50)
1-6: 1-Intro of Fatale & Star Seed. 6-Begin $2.95-c.   4.00
Preview Editions 1-3 (9/95 - 11/95, B&W)   4.00

POWER UP
BOOM! Studios: Jul, 2015 - No. 6, Dec, 2015 ($3.99)
1-6-Katie Leth-s/Matt Cummings-a. 1-Multiple covers   4.00

POW MAGAZINE (Bob Sproul's) (Satire Magazine)
Humor-Vision: Aug, 1966 - No. 3, Feb, 1967 (30¢)

	GD	VG	FN	VF	VF/NM	NM-
	2.0	4.0	6.0	8.0	9.0	9.2

	GD	VG	FN	VF	VF/NM	NM-
	2.0	4.0	6.0	8.0	9.0	9.2

	GD 2.0	VG 4.0	FN 6.0	VF 8.0	VF/NM 9.0	NM- 9.2
1,2: 2-Jones-a	5	10	15	30	50	70
3-Wrightson-a	5	10	15	35	63	90

PREACHER
DC Comics (Vertigo): Apr, 1995 - No. 66, Oct, 2000 ($2.50, mature)

	GD 2.0	VG 4.0	FN 6.0	VF 8.0	VF/NM 9.0	NM- 9.2
nn-Preview	6	12	18	38	69	100
1 ($2.95)-Ennis scripts, Dillon-a & Fabry-c in all; 1st app. Jesse, Tulip, & Cassidy	6	12	18	42	79	115
1-Retailer Incentive Edition (5/16, $3.99) r/#1 with new cover by Steve Dillon						4.00
1-Special Edition (6/09, $1.00) r/#1 with "After Watchmen" cover frame						4.00
2-1st app. Saint of Killers.	3	6	9	19	30	40
3	3	6	9	16	23	30
4,5	3	6	9	14	20	25
6-10	2	4	6	10	14	18
11,12,14,15: 12-Polybagged w/videogame w/Ennis text	1	3	4	6	8	10
13-Hunters storyline begins; ends #17; 1st app. Herr Starr	3	6	9	21	33	45
16-20: 19-Saint of Killers app.; begin "Crusaders", ends #24						6.00
21-25: 21-24-Saint of Killers app. 25-Origin of Cassidy.						4.00
26-49,52-64: 52-Tulip origin						3.00
50-($3.75) Pin-ups by Jim Lee, Bradstreet, Quesada and Palmiotti						4.00
51-Includes preview of 100 Bullets; Tulip origin	2	4	6	8	10	12
65,66-($3.75) 65-Almost everyone dies. 66-Final issue	1	3	4	6	8	10
Alamo (2001, $17.95, TPB) r/#59-66; Fabry-c						18.00
All Hell's a-Coming (2000, $17.95, TPB)-r/#51-58, ...Tall in the Saddle						18.00
... Book One HC (2009, $39.99, d.j.) r/#1-12; new Ennis intro.; pin-ups from #50,66						40.00
... Book Two HC (2010, $39.99, d.j.) r/#13-26; new Stuart Moore intro.						40.00
... Book Three HC (2010, $39.99, d.j.) r/#27-33, ...Special: Saint of Killers #1-4 & ...Special: Cassidy: Blood & Whiskey #1; new Ennis intro.						40.00
... Book Four HC (2011, $39.99, d.j.) r/#34-40, ...Special: One Man's War, ...Special: The Story of You-Know-Who, & ...Special: The Good Old Boys; new Dillon intro.						40.00
...: Dead or Alive HC (2000, $29.95) Gallery of Glenn Fabry's cover paintings for every Preacher issue; commentary by Fabry & Ennis						30.00
...: Dead or Alive SC (2003, $19.95)						20.00
Dixie Fried (1998, $14.95, TPB)-r/#27-33, Special: Cassidy						15.00
Gone To Texas (1996, $14.95, TPB)-r/#1-7; Fabry-c						15.00
Proud Americans (1997, $14.95, TPB)-r/#18-26; Fabry-c						15.00
Salvation (1999, $14.95, TPB)-r/#41-50; Fabry-c						15.00
Until the End of the World (1996, $14.95, TPB)-r/#8-17; Fabry-c						15.00
War in the Sun (1999, $14.95, TPB)-r/#34-40						15.00

PREACHER SPECIAL: CASSIDY: BLOOD & WHISKEY
DC Comics (Vertigo): 1998 ($5.95, one-shot)

1-Ennis-scripts/Dillon-a						6.00

PREACHER SPECIAL: ONE MAN'S WAR
DC Comics (Vertigo): Mar, 1998 ($4.95, one-shot)

1-Ennis-scripts/Fabry-c /Snejbjerg-a						5.00

PREACHER SPECIAL: SAINT OF KILLERS
DC Comics (Vertigo): Aug, 1996 - No. 4, Nov, 1996 ($2.50, lim. series, mature)

1-4: Ennis-scripts/Fabry-c. 1,2-Pugh-a. 3,4-Ezquerra-a						4.00
1-Signed & numbered						20.00

PREACHER SPECIAL: THE GOOD OLD BOYS
DC Comics (Vertigo): Aug, 1997 ($4.95, one-shot, mature)

1-Ennis-scripts/Fabry-c /Esquerra-a						5.00

PREACHER SPECIAL: THE STORY OF YOU-KNOW-WHO
DC Comics (Vertigo): Dec, 1997 ($4.95, one-shot, mature)

1-Ennis-scripts/Fabry-c/Case-a						5.00

PREACHER: TALL IN THE SADDLE
DC Comics (Vertigo): 2000 ($5.95, one-shot)

1-Ennis-scripts/Fabry-c/Dillon-a; early romance of Tulip and Jesse						6.00

PRECINCT, THE
Dynamite Entertainment: 2015 - No. 5, 2016 ($3.99)

1-5-Barbarie-s/Zamora-a. 1-Covers by Benitez & Robertson						4.00

PREDATOR (Also see Aliens Vs. ..., Batman vs. ..., Dark Horse Comics, & Dark Horse Presents)
Dark Horse Comics: June, 1989 - No. 4, Mar, 1990 ($2.25, limited series)

	GD 2.0	VG 4.0	FN 6.0	VF 8.0	VF/NM 9.0	NM- 9.2
1-Based on movie; 1st app. Predator	6	12	18	37	66	95
1-2nd printing	3	6	9	16	23	30
2	3	6	9	15	33	28
3,4	2	4	6	9	12	15
Trade paperback (1990, $12.95)-r/#1-4						15.00
... Omnibus Volume 1 (8/07, $24.95, 6" x 9") r/#1-4, ... Cold War, ... Dark River, ...Bloody Sands of Time mini-series and stories from Dark Horse Comics #1,2,4-7,10-12						50.00
... Omnibus Volume 2 (2/08, $24.95, 6" x 9") r/ ... Big Game, ... Race War, ...Invaders From The Fourth Dimension mini-series and stories from Dark Horse Comics #16-18,20,21; Dark Horse Presents #46 and A Decade of Dark Horse						50.00
... Omnibus Volume 3 (6/08, $24.95, 6" x 9") r/ ... Bad Blood, ... Kindred, ...Hell and Hot Water, ... Strange Roux mini-series and stories from Dark Horse Comics #12-14 and Dark Horse Presents #119 & 124						50.00

PREDATOR
Dark Horse Comics: June, 2009 - No. 4, Jan, 2010 ($3.50, limited series)

1-4-Arcudi-s/Saltares-a/Swanland-c; variant-c by Warner						5.00

PREDATOR
Marvel Comics: Oct, 2022 - No. 6, Mar, 2023 ($4.99/$3.99, limited series)

1-($4.99) Set in 2056; Ed Brisson-s/Kev Walker-a						5.00
2-6-($3.99)						4.00

PREDATOR
Marvel Comics: May, 2023 - No. 5, Sept, 2023 ($4.99/$3.99, limited series)

1-($4.99) Set in 2062; Ed Brisson-s/Netho Diaz-a						5.00
2-5-($3.99)						4.00

PREDATOR: (title series) **Dark Horse Comics**

	GD 2.0	VG 4.0	FN 6.0	VF 8.0	VF/NM 9.0	NM- 9.2
--BAD BLOOD, 12/93 - No. 4, 1994 ($2.50) 1-4						5.00
--BIG GAME, 3/91 - No. 4, 6/91 ($2.50) 1-4: 1-3-Contain 2 Dark Horse trading cards						5.00
--BLOODY SANDS OF TIME, 2/92 - No. 2, 2/92 ($2.50) 1,2-Dan Barry-c/a(p)/scripts						5.00
--CAPTIVE, 4/98 ($2.95, one-shot) 1	1	3	4	6	8	10
--COLD WAR, 9/91 - No. 4, 12/91 ($2.50) 1-4: All have painted-c						5.00
--DARK RIVER, 7/96 - No. 4, 10/96 ($2.95) 1-Miran Kim-c	2	4	6	8	10	12
2-4-Miran Kim-c						6.00
--HELL & HOT WATER, 4/97 - No. 3, 6/97 ($2.95) 1-3						5.00
--HELL COME A WALKIN', 2/98 - No. 2, 3/98 ($2.95) 1,2-In the Civil War	2	4	6	8	12	15
--HOMEWORLD, 3/99 - No. 4, 6/99 ($2.95) 1-4						5.00
--HUNTERS, 5/17 - No. 5, 8/17 ($3.99) 1-5-Warner-s/Velasco-a/Doug Wheatley-c						5.00
--HUNTERS II, 8/18 - No. 4, 1/19 ($3.99) 1-4-Warner-s/Padilla-a						4.00
--HUNTERS III, 2/20 - No. 4, ($3.99) 1,2-Warner-s/Thies-a						4.00
--INVADERS FROM THE FOURTH DIMENSION, 7/94 ($3.95, one-shot, 52 pgs.) 1						5.00
--JUNGLE TALES, 3/95 ($2.95) 1-r/Dark Horse Comics						5.00
--KINDRED, 12/96 - No. 4, 3/97 ($2.50) 1	2	4	6	9	12	15
2-4						5.00
--NEMESIS, 12/97 - No. 2, 1/98 ($2.95) 1,2-Predator in Victorian England; Taggart-c						5.00
--PRIMAL, 7/97 - No. 2, 8/97 ($2.95) 1,2						5.00
--RACE WAR (See Dark Horse Presents #67), 2/93 - No. 4,10/93 ($2.50, color) 1-4,0: 1-4-Dorman painted-c #1-4, 0(4/93)						5.00
--STRANGE ROUX, 11/96 ($2.95, one-shot) 1						5.00
--XENOGENESIS (Also see Aliens Xenogenesis), 8/99 - No. 4, 11/99 ($2.95) 1,2-Edginton-s						5.00

PREDATOR: FIRE AND STONE (Crossover with Aliens, AvP, and Prometheus)
Dark Horse Comics: Sep, 2014 - No. 4, Jan, 2015 ($3.50, limited series)

1-4-Williamson-s/Mooneyham-a						3.50

PREDATOR: LIFE AND DEATH (Continues in Prometheus: Life and Death)
Dark Horse Comics: Mar, 2016 - No. 4, Jun, 2016 ($3.99, limited series)

1-4-Abnett-s/Thies-a						4.00

PREDATORS (Based on the 2010 movie)
Dark Horse Comics: Jun, 2010 - No. 4, Jun, 2010 ($2.99, weekly limited series)

1-4-Prequel to the 2010 movie; stories by Andreyko and Lapham; Paul Lee-c						3.00
... Film Adaptation (7/10, $6.99) Tobin-s/Drujiniu-s/photo-c						7.00
...: Preserve the Game (7/10, $3.50) Sequel to the movie; Lapham-s/Jefferson-a						3.50

PREDATOR: THE LAST HUNT
Marvel Comics: Apr, 2024 - Present ($4.99, limited series)

1-Brisson-s/Manna-a						5.00

PREDATOR 2
Dark Horse Comics: Feb, 1991 - No. 2, June, 1991 ($2.50, limited series)

1,2: 1-Adapts movie; both w/trading cards & photo-c						5.00

PREDATOR VS. JUDGE DREDD
Dark Horse Comics: Oct, 1997 - No. 3 ($2.50, limited series)

	GD 2.0	VG 4.0	FN 6.0	VF 8.0	VF/NM 9.0	NM- 9.2
1-Wagner-s/Alcatena-a/Bolland-c	2	4	6	9	12	15
2,3						5.00

PREDATOR VS. JUDGE DREDD VS. ALIENS
Dark Horse Comics/IDW: Jul, 2016 - No. 4, Jun, 2017 ($3.99, limited series)

	GD 2.0	VG 4.0	FN 6.0	VF 8.0	VF/NM 9.0	NM- 9.2
1-4-Layman-s/Mooneyham-a/Fabry-c	2	4	6	9	12	15

PREDATOR VS. MAGNUS ROBOT FIGHTER
Dark Horse/Valiant: Oct, 1992 - No. 2, 1993 ($2.95, limited series)
(1st Dark Horse/Valiant x-over)

1,2: (Reg.)-Barry Smith-c; Lee Weeks-a. 2-w/trading cards						5.00
1 (Platinum edition, 11/92)-Barry Smith-c						10.00

PREDATOR VS. WOLVERINE
Marvel Comics: Nov, 2023 - No. 4, Feb, 2024 ($7.99/$5.99, limited series)

1-($7.99) Percy-s/Lashley & Land-a; flashback to 1900 in Alaska						8.00
2-4-($5.99) 2-Team X app.; Di Vito-a. 3-Weapon X flashback; Sherman-a						6.00

PREHISTORIC WORLD (See Classics Illustrated Special Issue)

PRELUDE TO DEADPOOL CORPS (Leads into Deadpool Corps #1)
Marvel Comics: May, 2010 - No. 5, May, 2010 ($3.99/$2.99, weekly limited series)

1-($3.99) Deadpool & Lady Deadpool vs. alternate dimension Capt. America; Liefeld-a						4.00
2-5-($2.99) Alternate reality Deadpools team-up; Dave Johnson interlocking covers						3.00

PRELUDE TO INFINITE CRISIS
DC Comics: 2005 ($5.99, squarebound)

nn-Reprints stories and panels with commentary leading into Infinite Crisis series						6.00

PREMIERE (See Charlton Premiere)

PRESIDENTIAL MATERIAL
IDW Publishing: Oct, 2008 ($3.99/$7.99)

...: Barack Obama - Biography of the candidate; Mariotte-s/Morgan-a/Campbell-c						4.00
...: John McCain - Biography of the candidate; Helfer-s/Thompson-a/Campbell-c						4.00
Flipbook ($7.99) Both issues in flipbook format						8.00

PRESTO KID, THE (See Red Mask)

PRETTY BOY FLOYD (See On the Spot)

PRETTY DEADLY
Image Comics: Oct, 2013 - No. 10, Jun, 2016 ($3.50)

1-10-DeConnick-s/Rios-a/c						3.50

PRETTY DEADLY: THE RAT

Predator (2023 series) #2 © 20th Century Studios

Primer #2 © Comico

Princess Leia #5 © Lucasfilm

	GD	VG	FN	VF	VF/NM	NM-
	2.0	4.0	6.0	8.0	9.0	9.2

Image Comics: Sept, 2019 - No. 5, Jan, 2020 ($3.99, limited series)
1-5-DeConnick-s/Rios-a/c ... 4.00

PRETTY VIOLENT
Image Comics: Aug, 2019 - No. 11, Nov, 2020 ($3.99)
1-11-Derek Hunter-a; Hunter & Jason Young-s ... 4.00

PREZ (See Cancelled Comic Cavalcade, Sandman #54 & Supergirl #10)
National Periodical Publications: Aug-Sept, 1973 - No. 4, Feb-Mar, 1974

1-Origin; Joe Simon scripts	3	6	9	17	26	35
2-4	2	4	6	13	18	22

PREZ
DC Comics: Aug, 2015 - No. 6, Feb, 2016 ($2.99)
1-6; 1-Intro. Beth Ross; Mark Russell-s/Ben Caldwell-a ... 3.00

PRICE, THE (See Eclipse Graphic Album Series)

PRIDE & JOY
DC Comics (Vertigo): July, 1997 - No. 4, Oct, 1997 ($2.50, limited series)
1-4-Ennis-s ... 4.00
TPB (2004, $14.95) r/#1-4 ... 15.00

PRIDE & PREJUDICE
Marvel Comics: June, 2009 - No. 5, Oct, 2009 ($3.99, limited series)
1-5-Adaptation of the Jane Austen novel; Nancy Butler-s/Hugo Petrus-a ... 4.00

PRIDE AND THE PASSION, THE
Dell Publishing Co.: No. 824, Aug, 1957

Four Color 824-Movie, Frank Sinatra & Cary Grant photo-c	10	20	30	66	138	210

PRIDE OF BAGHDAD
DC Comics (Vertigo): 2006 ($19.99, hardcover with dustjacket)
HC-A pride of lions escaping from the Baghdad zoo in 2003; Vaughan-s/Henrichon-a ... 20.00
SC-(2007, $12.99) ... 13.00

PRIDE OF THE YANKEES, THE (See Real Heroes & Sport Comics)
Magazine Enterprises: 1949 (The Life of Lou Gehrig)

nn-Photo-c; Ogden Whitney-a	100	200	300	635	1093	1550

PRIEST (Also see Asylum)
Maximum Press: Aug, 1996 - No. 2, Oct, 1996 ($2.99)
1,2 ... 4.00

PRIMAL FORCE
DC Comics: No. 0, Oct, 1994 - No. 14, Dec, 1995 ($1.95/$2.25)
0-14: 0- Teams Red Tornado, Golem, Jack O'Lantern, Meridian & Silver Dragon.
9-begin $2.25-c ... 4.00

PRIMAL MAN (See The Crusaders)

PRIMAL RAGE
Sirius Entertainment: 1996 ($2.95)
1-Dark One-c; based of video game ... 4.00

PRIME (See Break-Thru, Flood Relief & Ultraforce)
Malibu Comics (Ultraverse): June, 1993 - No. 26, Aug, 1995 ($1.95/$2.50)
1-1st app. Prime; has coupon for Ultraverse Premiere #0 ... 4.00
1-With coupon missing ... 2.00
1-Full cover holographic edition; 1st of kind w/Hardcase #1 & Strangers #1 ... 10.00
1-Ultra 5,000 edition w/silver ink-c ... 6.00
2-4,6-11,14-26: 2-Polybagged w/card & coupon for U. Premiere #0. 3,4-Prototype app.
 4-Direct sale w/o card.4-($2.50)-Newsstand ed. polybagged w/card.
 6-Bill & Chelsea Clinton app.115-Intro Papa Verite; Pérez-c/a. 16-Intro Turbo Charge ... 4.00
5-($2.50, 48 pgs.)-Rune flip-c/story part B by Barry Smith; see Sludge #1 for 1st app. Rune;
 3-pg. Night Man preview ... 5.00
12-($3.50, 68 pgs.)-Flip book w/Ultraverse Premiere #3; silver foil logo ... 5.00
13-($2.95, 52 pgs.)-Variant covers ... 5.00
... Gross and Disgusting 1 (10/94, $3.95)-Boris-c; "Annual" on cover, published monthly
 in indicia ... 5.00
...Month "Ashcan" (8/94, 75¢)-Boris-c ... 4.00
...Time: A Prime Collection (1994, $9.95)-r/1-4 ... 10.00
...Vs. The Incredible Hulk (1995)-mail away limited edition ... 10.00
...Vs. The Incredible Hulk Premium edition ... 10.00
...Vs. The Incredible Hulk Super Premium edition ... 15.00
NOTE: *Perez a-15; c-15, 16.*

PRIME (Also see Black September)
Malibu Comics (Ultraverse): Infinity, Sept, 1995 - V2#15, Dec, 1996 ($1.50)
Infinity, V2#1-15: Post Black September storyline. 6-8-Solitaire app. 9-Breyfogle-c/a.

10-12-Ramos-c. 15-Lord Pumpkin app.						4.00
Infinity Signed Edition (2,000 printed)	1	2	3	5	6	8

PRIME/CAPTAIN AMERICA
Malibu Comics: Mar, 1996 ($3.95, one-shot)
1-Norm Breyfogle-a ... 5.00

PRIME8: CREATION
Two Morrows Publishing: July, 2001 ($3.95, B&W)
1-Neal Adams-c ... 4.00

PRIMER (Comico...)
Comico: Oct (no month), 1982 - No. 6, Feb, 1984 (B&W)

1 (52 pgs.)	3	6	9	17	26	35
2-1st app. Grendel & Argent by Wagner	31	62	93	223	499	775
3,4	2	4	6	10	14	18
5-1st Sam Kieth art in comics ('83) & 1st The Maxx	7	14	21	49	92	135
6-Intro & 1st app. Evangeline	3	6	9	14	19	24

PRIMORDIAL
Image Comics: Sept, 2021 - No. 6, Feb, 2022 ($3.99)
1-6-Jeff Lemire-s/Andrea Sorrentino-a ... 4.00

PRIMORTALS (Leonard Nimoy's...)

PRIMOS
AWA Studios: Feb, 2022 - No. 4, Jun, 2022 ($3.99, limited series)
1-4-Al Madrigal-s/Carlo Barberi-a ... 4.00

PRIMUS (TV)
Charlton Comics: Feb, 1972 - No. 7, Oct, 1972

1-Staton-a in all	2	4	6	11	16	20
2-7: 6-Drug propaganda story	2	4	6	8	11	14

PRINCE NAMOR, THE SUB-MARINER (Also see Namor ...)
Marvel Comics Group: Sept, 1984 - No. 4, Dec, 1984 (Limited-series)
1-4 ... 5.00

PRINCE OF PERSIA: BEFORE THE SANDSTORM (Based on the 2010 movie)
Dynamite Entertainment: 2010 - No. 4, 2010 ($3.99, limited series)
1-4-Art by Fowler and various. 1-Chang-a. 2-Lopez-a. 3-Edwards-a ... 5.00

PRINCESS LEIA (Star Wars)
Marvel Comics: May, 2015 - No. 5, Sept, 2015 ($3.99)
1-5-Mark Waid-s/Terry Dodson-a; story follows the ending of Episode IV ... 4.00

PRINCESS SALLY (Video game)
Archie Publications: Apr, 1995 - No. 3, June, 1995 ($1.50, limited series)
1-3: Spin-off from Sonic the Hedgehog ... 4.00

PRINCESS UGG
Oni Press: Jun, 2014 - No. 8, Mar, 2015 ($3.99)
1-8-Ted Naifeh-s/a ... 4.00

PRINCE VALIANT (See Ace Comics, Comics Reading Libraries *in the Promotional Comics section,* & King Comics #146, 147)
David McKay Publ./Dell: No. 26, 1941; No. 67, June, 1954 - No. 900, May, 1958
Feature Books 26 ('41)-Harold Foster-c/a; newspaper strips reprinted, pgs. 1-28,30-63; color & 68 pgs; Foster cover is only original comic book artwork by him

	174	348	522	1114	1907	2700
Four Color 567 (6/54)(#1)-By Bob Fuje-Movie, photo-c						
	11	22	33	73	157	240
Four Color 650 (9/55), 699 (4/56), 719 (8/56),-Fuje-a	8	16	24	55	105	155
Four Color 788 (4/57), 849 (1/58), 900-Fuje-a	7	14	21	44	82	120

PRINCE VALIANT
Marvel Comics: Dec, 1994 - No. 4, Mar, 1995 ($3.95, limited series)
1-4: Kaluta-c in all ... 4.00

PRINCE VANDAL
Triumphant Comics: Nov, 1993 - Apr?, 1994 ($2.50)
1-6: 1,2-Triumphant Unleashed x-over ... 4.00

PRIORITY: WHITE HEAT
AC Comics: 1986 - No. 2, 1986 ($1.75, mini-series)
1,2-Bill Black-a ... 4.00

PRISCILLA'S POP
Dell Publishing Co.: No. 569, June, 1954 - No. 799, May, 1957

Four Color 569 (#1), 630 (5/55), 704 (5/56),799	7	14	21	46	86	125

PRISON BARS (See Behind...)

	GD 2.0	VG 4.0	FN 6.0	VF 8.0	VF/NM 9.0	NM- 9.2

PRISON BREAK!
Avon Per./Realistic No. 3 on: Sept, 1951 - No. 5, Sept, 1952 (Painted c-3)

1-Wood-c & 1 pg.; has-r/Saint #7 retitled Michael Strong Private Eye	181	362	543	1158	1979	2800
2-Wood-c; Kubert-a; Kinstler inside front-c	63	126	189	403	689	975
3-Orlando, Check-a; c-/Avon paperback #179	45	90	135	284	480	675
4,5: 4-Kinstler-c & inside f/c; Lawrence, Lazarus-a. 5-Kinstler-c; Infantino-a	42	84	126	265	445	625

PRISONER, THE (TV)
DC Comics: 1988 - No. 4, 1989 ($3.50, squarebound, mini-series)

1-4 (Books a-d)						5.00

PRISONER, THE: THE UNCERTAINTY MACHINE (TV)
Titan Comics: Jun, 2018 - No. 4, Sept, 2018 ($3.99, limited series)

1-4-Milligan-s/Lorimer-a						4.00

PRISON RIOT
Avon Periodicals: 1952

1-Marijuana Murders-1 pg text; Kinstler-c; 2 Kubert illos on text pages	57	114	171	362	619	875

PRISON TO PRAISE
Logos International: 1974 (35¢) (Religious, Christian)

nn-True Story of Merlin R. Carothers	3	6	9	14	20	25

PRIVATE BUCK
Dell Publishing Co./Rand McNally: No. 21, 1941 - No. 12, 1942 (4-1/2" x 5-1/2", 1942)

Large Feature Comic 21 (#1)(1941)(Series I), 22 (1941)(Series I), 12 (1942)(Series II)

	24	48	72	142	234	325
382-Rand McNally, one panel per page; small size	14	28	42	80	115	150

PRIVATE EYE (Cover title: Rocky Jorden...#6-8)
Atlas Comics (MCI): Jan, 1951 - No. 8, March, 1952

1-Cover title: Crime Cases... #1-5	36	72	108	211	343	475
2,3-Tuska c/a(3)	19	38	57	111	176	240
4-8	15	30	45	90	140	190

NOTE: *Henkel a-6(3), 7; c-7. Sinnott a-6.*

PRIVATE EYE (See Mike Shayne...)

PRIVATE SECRETARY
Dell Publishing Co.: Dec-Feb, 1962-63 - No. 2, Mar-May, 1963

1	5	10	15	33	57	80
2	4	8	12	23	37	50

PRIVATE STRONG (See The Double Life of...)

PRIZE COMICS (...Western #69 on) (Also see Treasure Comics)
Prize Publications: March, 1940 - No. 68, Feb-Mar, 1948

1-Origin Power Nelson, The Futureman & Jupiter, Master Magician; Ted O'Neil, Secret Agent M-11, Jaxon of the Jungle, Bucky Brady & Storm Curtis begin (1st app. of each)	423	846	1269	3088	5444	7800
2-The Black Owl begins (1st app.)	277	554	831	1759	3030	4300
3-Classic sci-fi-c	300	600	900	1920	3310	4700
4-Classic robot-c	326	652	978	2282	3991	5700
5-Dr. Dekkar, Master of Monsters app.	232	464	696	1485	2543	3600
6-Classic sci-fi-c; Dr. Dekkar app.	258	516	774	1651	2826	4000
7-(Scarce)-1st app. The Green Lama (12/40); Black Owl by S&K; origin/1st app. Dr. Frost & Frankenstein; Capt. Gallant, The Great Voodini & Twist Turner begin;	1200	2400	3600	9100	16,550	24,000
8,9-Black Owl & Ted O'Neil by S&K	232	464	696	1485	2543	3600
10-12,14,15: 11-Origin Bulldog Denny. 14-War-c	168	336	504	1075	1838	2600
13-Yank & Doodle begin (8/41, origin/1st app.)	213	426	639	1363	2332	3300
16-19: 16-Spike Mason begins	155	310	465	992	1696	2400
20-(Rare) Frankenstein, Black Owl, Green Lama, Yank and Doodle WWII parade-c	649	1298	1947	4738	8369	12,000
21,25,27,28,31-All WWII covers	155	310	465	992	1696	2400
22-24,26: 22-Statue of Liberty Japanese attack war-c. 23-Uncle Sam patriotic war-c. 24-Lincoln statue patriotic-c. 26-Liberty Bell-c	174	348	522	1114	1907	2700
29,30,32	129	258	387	826	1413	2000
33-Classic bondage/torture-c	284	568	852	1818	3109	4400
34-Origin Airmale, Yank & Doodle; The Black Owl joins army, Yank & Doodle's father assumes Black Owl's role	123	246	369	787	1344	1900
35-36,38-39: 35-Flying Fist & Bingo begin	81	162	243	518	884	1250
37-Intro. Stampy, Airmale's sidekick; Hitler-c	1000	2000	3000	7600	13,800	20,000
40-Nazi WWII-c	174	348	522	1114	1907	2700
41-45,47-50: 45-Yank & Doodle learn Black Owl's I.D. (their father). 48-Prince Ra begins	60	120	180	381	653	925
46-Classic Zombie Horror-c/story	194	388	582	1242	2121	3000
51-62,64,67,68: 53-Transvestism story. 55-No Frankenstein. 57-X-Mas-c. 64-Black Owl retires	42	84	126	265	445	625
63-Simon & Kirby begin	53	106	159	334	567	800
65,66-Frankenstein-c by Briefer	77	154	231	493	847	1200

NOTE: *Briefer a-7-on; c-65, 66. J. Binder a-16; c-21-29. Guardineer a-62. Kiefer c-62. Palais c-68. Simon & Kirby c-63, 75, 83.*

PRIZE COMICS WESTERN (Formerly Prize Comics #1-68)
Prize Publications (Feature): No. 69(V7#2), Apr-May, 1948 - No. 119, Nov-Dec, 1956 (No. 69-84: 52 pgs.)

69(V7#2)	25	50	75	150	245	340
70-75: 74-Kurtzman-a (8 pgs.)	19	38	57	111	176	240
76-Randolph Scott photo-c; "Canadian Pacific" movie adaptation	18	36	54	103	162	220
77-Photo-c; Severin/Elder, Mart Bailey-a; "Streets of Laredo" movie adaptation	16	32	48	94	147	200
78-Photo-c; S&K-a, 10 pgs.; Severin, Mart Bailey-a; "Bullet Code", & "Roughshod" movie adaptations	18	36	54	107	169	230
79-Photo-c; Kurtzman-a, 8 pgs.; Severin/Elder, Severin, Mart Bailey-a; "Stage To Chino" movie adaptation w/George O'Brien	18	36	54	103	169	230
80-82-Photo-c; 80,81-Severin/Elder-a(2). 82-1st app. The Preacher by Mart Bailey;						

Severin/Elder-a(3)	15	30	45	84	127	170
83,84	13	26	39	74	105	135
85-1st app. American Eagle by John Severin & begins (V9#6, 1-2/51)	25	50	75	150	245	340
86,101-105, 109-Severin/Williamson-a	14	28	42	78	112	145
87-99,110,111-Severin/Elder-a(2-3) each	14	28	42	81	110	155
100	15	30	45	85	124	165
106-108,112	10	20	30	56	76	95
113-Williamson/Severin-a(2)/Frazetta?	15	30	45	84	127	170
114-119: Drifter series in all; by Mort Meskin #114-118	9	18	27	52	69	85

NOTE: *Fass a-81. Severin & Elder c-84-99. Severin a-72, 75, 77-79, 83-86, 96, 97, 100-105; c-92,100-109(most), 110-119. Simon & Kirby c-75, 83.*

PRIZE MYSTERY
Key Publications: May, 1955 - No. 3, Sept, 1955

1	42	84	126	265	445	625
2,3	14	28	42	82	121	160

PRO, THE
Image Comics: July, 2002 ($5.95, squarebound, one-shot)

1-Ennis/Conner & Palmiotti-a; prostitute gets super-powers						8.00
1-Second printing with different cover						6.00
Hardcover Edition (10/04, $14.95) oversized reprint plus new 8 pg. story; sketch pages						15.00

PROCTOR VALLEY ROAD
BOOM! Studios: Mar, 2021 - No. 5, Jul, 2021 ($3.99, limited series)

1-5-Grant Morrison & Alex Child-s/Naomi Franquiz-a						4.00

PRODIGY
Image Comics: Dec, 2018 - No. 6, Jun, 2019 ($3.99)

1-6-Mark Millar-s/Rafael Albuquerque-a						4.00

PRODIGY: THE ICARUS SOCIETY
Image Comics: Jul, 2022 - No. 5, Nov, 2022 ($3.99, limited series)

1-5-Mark Millar-s/Matteo Buffagni-a						4.00

PROFESSIONAL FOOTBALL (See Charlton Sport Library)

PROFESSOR COFFIN
Charlton Comics: No. 19, Oct, 1985 - No. 21, Feb, 1986

19-21: Wayne Howard-a(r); low print run	1	2	3	5	6	8

PROFESSOR OM
Innovation Publishing: May, 1990 - No. 2, 1990 ($2.50, limited series)

1,2-East Meets West spin-off						4.00

PROFESSOR XAVIER AND THE X-MEN (Also see X-Men, 1st series)
Marvel Comics: Nov, 1995 - No. 18 (99¢)

1-18: Stories featuring the Original X-Men. 2-vs. The Blob. 5-Vs. the Original Brotherhood of Evil Mutants. 10-Vs. The Avengers						4.00

PROGRAMME, THE
DC Comics (WildStorm): Sept, 2007 - No. 12, Aug, 2008 ($2.99, limited series)

1-12: 1-Milligan-s/C.P. Smith-a; covers by Smith & Van Sciver						3.00
Book One TPB (2008, $17.99) r/#1-6; cover sketches						18.00
Book Two TPB (2008, $17.99) r/#7-12; cover sketches						18.00

PROJECT A-KO (Manga)
Malibu Comics: Mar, 1994 - No. 4, June, 1994 ($2.95)

1-4-Based on anime film						4.00

PROJECT A-KO 2 (Manga)
CPM Comics: May, 1995 - No. 3, Aug, 1995 ($2.95, limited series)

1-3						4.00

PROJECT A-KO VERSUS THE UNIVERSE (Manga)
CPM Comics: Oct, 1995 - No. 5, June, 1996 ($2.95, limited series, bi-monthly)

1-5						4.00

PROJECT BLACK SKY
Dark Horse Comics

... Sampler (10/14, $4.99) 1-Reprints The Occultist (2013) #1, Brain Boy (2013) #0, Ghost (2013) #1, Blackout #1						5.00
Free Comic Book Day: Project Black Sky (5/14, giveaway) Capt. Midnight & Brain Boy app.						3.00

PROJECT: PATRON
AfterShock Comics: Apr, 2021 - No. 5, Aug, 2021 ($4.99/$3.99, limited series)

1-($4.99) Steve Orlando-s/Patrick Piazzalunga-a						5.00
2-5-($3.99)						4.00

PROJECT SUPERPOWERS
Dynamite Entertainment: 2008 - No. 7, 2008 ($1.00/$3.50/$2.99)

0-($1.00) Two connecting covers by Alex Ross; re-intro of Golden Age heroes						3.00
0-($1.00) Variant cover by Michael Turner						5.00
1-($3.50) Covers by Ross and Turner; Jim Krueger-s/Carlos Paul-a						3.50
2-7-($2.99)						3.00
... Chapter One HC (2008, $29.99, dustjacket) r/#0-7; Ross sketch pages; layout art						30.00

PROJECT SUPERPOWERS: BLACKCROSS
Dynamite Entertainment: 2015 - No. 6, 2015 ($3.99)

1-6-Warren Ellis-s/Colton Worley-a; multiple covers on each						4.00

PROJECT SUPERPOWERS: CHAPTER TWO
Dynamite Entertainment: 2009 - No. 12, 2010 ($1.00/$2.99)

... Chapter Two Prelude (2008, $1.00) Ross sketch pages and mini-series previews						3.00
0-($1.00) Three connecting covers by Alex Ross; The Inheritors assemble						3.00
1-12-($2.99) 1-Krueger & Ross-s/Salazar-a; Ross sketch pages; 2 Ross covers						3.00
... X-Mas Carol (2010, $5.99) Benkentotter-a/Ross-c						6.00

PROJECT SUPERPOWERS: CHAPTER THREE
Dynamite Entertainment: 2018 - No. 6, 2018 ($1.00/$2.99)

0-(10¢) Six covers; Rob Williams-s/Sergio Davila-a						3.00
1-6-($3.99)-Rob Williams-s/Sergio Davila-a; multiple covers on each						4.00

Prize Comics #8 © Prize

Promethea #5 © ABC

Prophet (2014 series) #45 © Rob Liefeld

	GD	VG	FN	VF	VF/NM	NM-
	2.0	4.0	6.0	8.0	9.0	9.2

PROJECT SUPERPOWERS: FRACTURED STATES
Dynamite Entertainment: 2022 - No. 5, 2022 ($3.99, limited series)

1-5-Marz & Lanning-s/Utrera-a 4.00

PROJECT SUPERPOWERS: HERO KILLERS
Dynamite Entertainment: 2017 - No. 5, 2017 ($3.99)

1-5-Browne-s/Woods-a. 1-Black Terror killed 4.00

PROJECT SUPERPOWERS: MEET THE BAD GUYS
Dynamite Entertainment: 2009 - No. 4, 2009 ($2.99)

1-4: Ross & Casey-s. 1-Bloodlust. 2-The Revolutionary. 3-Dagon. 4-Supremacy 3.00

PROMETHEA
America's Best Comics: Aug, 1999 - No. 32, Apr, 2005 ($3.50/$2.95)

	1	3	4	6	8	10
1-Alan Moore-s/Williams III & Gray-a; Alex Ross painted-c						
1-Variant-c by Williams III & Gray	2	4	6	8	10	12

2-31-($2.95): 7-Villarrubia photo-c. 10-"Sex, Stars & Serpents". 26-28-Tom Strong app. 27-Cover swipe of Superman vs. Spider-Man treasury ed. 4.00

32-($3.95) Final issue; pages can be cut & assembled into a 2-sided poster

	3	6	9	15	22	28

32-Limited edition of 1000; variant issue printed as 2-sided poster, signed by Moore and Williams; each came with a 48 page book of Promethea covers 120.00

Book 1 Hardcover ($24.95, dust jacket) r/#1-6 .... 25.00
Book 1 TPB ($14.95) r/#1-6 .... 15.00
Book 2 Hardcover ($24.95, dust jacket) r/#7-12 .... 25.00
Book 2 TPB ($14.95) r/#7-12 .... 15.00
Book 3 Hardcover ($24.95, dust jacket) r/#13-18 .... 25.00
Book 3 TPB ($14.95) r/#13-18 .... 15.00
Book 4 Hardcover ($24.95, dust jacket) r/#19-25 .... 25.00
Book 4 TPB ($14.99) r/#19-25 .... 15.00
Book 5 Hardcover ($24.95, d.j.) r/#26-32; includes 2-sided poster image from #32 ..... 25.00
Book 5 TPB ($14.99) r/#26-32; includes 2-sided poster image from #32 ...... 15.00

PROMETHEE 13:13
Ablaze Publishing: 2022 - No. 4, 2022 ($3.99, limited series)

1-4-Andy Diggle-s/Shawn Martinbrough-a 4.00

PROMETHEUS: FIRE AND STONE (Crossover with Aliens, AvP, and Predator)
Dark Horse Comics: Sept, 2014 - No. 4, Dec, 2014 ($3.50, limited series)

1-4-Tobin-s/Ferreyra-a 3.50
... — Omega (2/15, $4.99) DeConnick-s/Alessio-a; finale to the crossover 4.00

PROMETHEUS: LIFE AND DEATH (Continues in Aliens: Life and Death)
Dark Horse Comics: Jun, 2016 - No. 4, Sept, 2016 ($3.99, limited series)

1-4-Abnett-s/Mutti-a 4.00
... — Final Conflict (4/17, $5.99) Abnett-s/Thies-a; finale of Life and Death x-over 6.00

PROMETHEUS (VILLAINS) (Leads into JLA #16,17)
DC Comics: Feb, 1998 ($1.95, one-shot)

1-Origin & 1st app.; Morrison-s/Pearson-c 4.00

PROPELLERMAN
Dark Horse Comics: Jan, 1993 - No. 8, Mar, 1994 ($2.95, limited series)

1-8: 2,4,8-Contain 2 trading cards 4.00

PROPHECY
Dynamite Entertainment: 2012 - No. 7, 2013 ($3.99, limited series)

1-7: 1-Marz-s/Geovani-a; Vampirella,Red Sonja, Dracula & Pantha app. 4-Ash app. 4.00

PROPHET (See Youngblood #2)
Image Comics (Extreme Studios): Oct, 1993 - No. 10, 1995 ($1.95)

1-($2.50)-Liefeld/Panosian-c/a; 1st app. Mary McCormick; Liefeld scripts in 1-4; #1-3 contain coupons for Prophet #0 .... 5.00
1-Gold foil embossed-c edition rationed to dealers 6.00
2-10: 2-Liefeld-c(p). 3-1st app. Judas. 4-1st app. Omen; Black and White Pt. 3 by Thibert. 4-Alternate-c by Stephen Platt. 5,6-Platt-c/a. 7-(9/94, $2.50)-Platt-c/a. 8-Bloodstrike app. 10-Polybagged w/trading card; Platt-c. 3.00
0-(7/94, $2.50)-San Diego Comic Con ed. (2200 copies) 5.00
... Facsimile Edition #1 (2/22, $3.99) Reprint of #1 .... 4.00
... Remastered Edition #1 (7/22, $3.99) Issue #1 with pages re-drawn by modern artists 4.00

PROPHET
Image Comics (Extreme Studios): V2#1, Aug, 1995 - No. 8 ($3.50)

V2#1-8: Dixon scripts in all. 1-4-Platt-a. 1-Boris-c. 4-Newmen app. 5,6-Wraparound-c 4.00
Annual 1 (9/95, $2.50)-Bagged w/Youngblood gaming card; Quesada-c 4.00
Babewatch Special 1 (12/95, $2.50)-Babewatch tie-in 4.00

1995 San Diego Edition-B&W preview of V2#1. .... 4.00
TPB-(1996, $12.95) r/#1-7 .... 13.00

PROPHET (Volume 3)
Awesome Comics: Mar, 2000 ($2.99)

1-Flip-c by Jim Lee and Liefeld 3.00

PROPHET
Image Comics: No. 21, Jan, 2012 - No. 45, Jul, 2014 ($2.99/$3.99)

21-27-($2.99): 21-Two covers; Graham-s 3.00
28-45-($3.99): 29-Dalrymple-a 4.00

PROPHET/CABLE
Image Comics (Extreme): Jan, 1997 - No. 2, Mar, 1997 ($3.50, limited series)

1,2-Liefeld-c/a: 2-#1 listed on cover 4.00

PROPHET/CHAPEL: SUPER SOLDIERS
Image Comics (Extreme): May, 1996 - No. 2, June, 1996 ($2.50, limited series)

1,2: 1-Two covers exist 4.00
1-San Diego Edition; B&W-c 4.00

PROPHET EARTHWAR
Image Comics: Jan, 2016 - No. 6, Nov, 2016 ($3.99)

1-6: 1-Graham & Roy-s/Milonogiannis & Roy-a 4.00

PROPHET: STRIKEFILE
Image Comics: Sept, 2014 - No. 2, Nov, 2015 ($3.99)

1,2-Short stories and profile pages by various 4.00

PROPOSITION PLAYER
DC Comics (Vertigo): Dec, 1999 - No. 6, May, 2000 ($2.50, limited series)

1-6-Willingham-s/Guinan-a/Bolton-c 4.00
TPB (2003, $14.95) r/#1-6; intro. by James McManus 15.00

PROTECTORS (Also see The Ferret)
Malibu Comics: Sept, 1992 - No. 20, May, 1994 ($1.95-$2.95)

1-20 ($2.50, direct sale)-With poster & diff-c: 1-Origin; has 3/4 outer-c. 3-Polybagged w/Skycap 4.00
1-12 ($1.95, newsstand)-Without poster 4.00

PROTECTORS, INC.
Image Comics: Nov, 2013 - No. 10, Nov, 2014 ($2.99)

1-10-Straczynski-s/Purcell-a; multiple covers on #1-7 .... 3.00

PROTOTYPE (Also see Flood Relief & Ultraforce)
Malibu Comics (Ultraverse): Aug, 1993 - No. 18, Feb, 1995 ($1.95-$2.50)

	1	2	3	5	6	8
1-Holo-c						6.00

1-Ultra Limited silver foil-c 6.00
1,3: 3-($2.50, 48 pgs.)-Rune flip-c/story by B. Smith (3 pgs.) 4.00
2,4-12,14-18: 4-Intro Wrath. 5-Break-Thru & Strangers x-over. 6-Arena cameo. 7,8-Arena-c/story. 12-(7/94). 14 (10/94) 3.00
13 (8/94, $3.50)-Flip book (Ultraverse Premiere #6) 4.00
#0-(8/94, $2.50, 44 pgs.) 4.00
Giant Size 1 (10/94, $2.50, 44 pgs.) 4.00

PROTOTYPE (Based on the Activision video game)
DC Comics (WildStorm): Jun, 2009 - No. 6, Nov, 2009 ($3.99, limited series)

1-6-Darick Robertson-c/a 4.00
TPB (2010, $19.99) r/#1-6 .... 20.00

PROWLER (Also see Clone Conspiracy and Amazing Spider-Man)
Marvel Comics: Dec, 2016 - May, 2017 ($3.99)

1-6-Sean Ryan-s/Javier Saltares-a. 6-Spider-Man app. 4.00

PRUDENCE & CAUTION (See Dogs of War & Warriors of Plasm)
Defiant: May, 1994 - No. 2, June, 1994 ($3.50/$2.50)(Spanish versions exist)

1-($3.50, 52 pgs.)-Chris Claremont scripts in all 5.00
2-($2.50) 4.00

PRYDE AND WISDOM (Also see Excalibur)
Marvel Comics: Sept, 1996 - No. 3, Nov, 1996 ($1.95, limited series)

1-3: Warren Ellis scripts; Terry Dodson & Karl Story-c/a 4.00

PSI-FORCE
Marvel Comics Group: Nov, 1986 - No. 32, June, 1989 (75¢/$1.50)

1-25: 11-13-Williamson-i 4.00
26-32 .... 4.00
Annual 1 (10/87) 5.00
... Classic Vol. 1 TPB (2008, $24.99) r/#1-9 .... 25.00

PSI-JUDGE ANDERSON

	GD	VG	FN	VF	VF/NM	NM-
	2.0	4.0	6.0	8.0	9.0	9.2

Fleetway Publications (Quality): 1989 - No. 15, 1990 ($1.95, B&W)

	GD	VG	FN	VF	VF/NM	NM-
1-15						4.00

PSI-LORDS
Valiant: Sept, 1994 - No. 10, June, 1995 ($2.25)

	GD	VG	FN	VF	VF/NM	NM-
1-($3.50)-Chromium wraparound-c						5.00
1-Gold						8.00
2-10: 3-Chaos Effect Epsilon Pt. 2						4.00

PSI-LORDS
Valiant Entertainment: Jun, 2019 - No. 8, Jan, 2020 ($3.99)

	GD	VG	FN	VF	VF/NM	NM-
1-8-Fred Van Lente-s/Renato Guedes-a. 7-X-O Manowar app.						4.00

PSYBA-RATS (Also see Showcase '94 (3,4))
DC Comics: Apr, 1995-No. 3, June, 1995 ($2.50, limited series)

	GD	VG	FN	VF	VF/NM	NM-
1-3						4.00

PSYCHO (Magazine) (Also see Nightmare)
Skywald Publ. Corp.: Jan, 1971 - No. 24, Mar, 1975 (68 pgs.; B&W)

	GD	VG	FN	VF	VF/NM	NM-
1-All reprints	9	18	27	61	123	185
2-Origin & 1st app. The Heap, series begins	7	14	21	44	82	120
3-Frankenstein series by Adkins begins	6	12	18	41	76	110
4-7,9,10: 4-7-Squarebound. 4-1st Out of Chaos/Satan-c/s						
	5	10	15	35	63	90
8-(Squarebound)1st app. Edward & Mina Sartyros, the Human Gargoyles						
	6	12	18	38	69	100
11-17: 13-Cannabalism; 3 pgs of Christopher Lee as Dracula photos						
	4	8	12	28	47	65
18-Injury to eye-c	5	10	15	35	63	90
19-Origin Dracula.	5	10	15	31	53	75
20-Severed Head-c	6	12	18	37	66	95
21-24: 22-1974 Fall Special; Reese, Wildey-a(r). 24-1975 Winter Special;						
Dave Sim scripts (1st work)	5	10	15	31	53	75
Annual 1 (1972)(68 pgs.) Dracula & the Heap app.	5	10	15	31	53	75
Yearbook (1974-nn)-Everett, Reese-a	4	8	12	27	44	60

NOTE: *Boris c-3, 5. Buckler a-2, 4, 5. Gene Day a-21, 23, 24. Everett a-3-6. B. Jones a-4. Jeff Jones a-6, 7, 9; c-12. Kaluta a-13. Katz/Buckler a-3. Kim a-24. Morrow a-1. Reese a-5. Dave Sim s-24. Sutton a-3. Wildey a-5.*

PSYCHO, THE
DC Comics: 1991 - No. 3, 1991 ($4.95, squarebound, limited series)

	GD	VG	FN	VF	VF/NM	NM-
1-3-Hudnall-s/Brereton painted-a/c						5.00
TPB (Image Comics, 2006, $17.99) r/series; Brereton sketch pages; Hudnall afterword						18.00

PSYCHOANALYSIS
E. C. Comics: Mar-Apr, 1955 - No. 4, Sept-Oct, 1955

	GD	VG	FN	VF	VF/NM	NM-
1-All Kamen-c/a; not approved by code	33	66	99	264	420	575
2-4-Kamen-c/a in all	20	40	60	160	255	350

PSYCHOANALYSIS
Gemstone Publishing: Oct, 1999 - No. 4, Jan, 2000 ($2.50)

	GD	VG	FN	VF	VF/NM	NM-
1-4-Reprints E.C. series						4.00
Annual 1 (2000, $10.95) r/#1-4						11.00

PSYCHO BONKERS
Aspen MLT: May, 2015 - No. 4, Sept, 2015 ($3.99)

	GD	VG	FN	VF	VF/NM	NM-
1-4-Vince Hernandez-s/Adam Archer-a						4.00

PSYCHONAUTS
Marvel Comics (Epic Comics): Oct, 1993 - No. 4, Jan, 1994 ($4.95, lim. series)

	GD	VG	FN	VF	VF/NM	NM-
1-4: American/Japanese co-produced comic						5.00

PSYLOCKE
Marvel Comics: Jan, 2010 - No. 4, Apr, 2010 ($3.99, limited series)

	GD	VG	FN	VF	VF/NM	NM-
1-Finch-c/Yost-s/Tolibao-a in all	5	10	15	34	60	85
2	3	6	9	17	26	35
3,4-Wolverine app.	2	4	6	9	13	16

PSYLOCKE & ARCHANGEL CRIMSON DAWN
Marvel Comics: Aug, 1997 - No. 4, Nov, 1997 ($2.50, limited series)

	GD	VG	FN	VF	VF/NM	NM-
1-4-Raab-s/Larroca-a(p)						4.00

PTOLUS: CITY BY THE SPIRE
Dabel Brothers Productions/Marvel Comics (Dabel Brothers) #2 on: June, 2006 - No. 6, Mar, 2007 ($2.99)

	GD	VG	FN	VF	VF/NM	NM-
1-(1st printing, Dabel) Adaptation of the Monte Cook novel; Cook-s						4.00
1-(2nd printing, Marvel), 2-6						3.00
Monte Cooke's Ptolus: City By the Spire TPB (2007, $14.99) r/#1-6						15.00

P.T. 109 (See Movie Comics)

PUBLIC DEFENDER IN ACTION (Formerly Police Trap)
Charlton Comics: No. 7, Mar, 1956 - No. 12, Oct, 1957

	GD	VG	FN	VF	VF/NM	NM-
7	16	32	48	94	147	200
8-12	11	22	33	64	90	115

PUBLIC DOMAIN
Image Comics: Jun, 2022 - No. 5, Oct, 2022 ($3.99, limited series)

	GD	VG	FN	VF	VF/NM	NM-
1-5-Chip Zdarsky-s/a						4.00

PUBLIC ENEMIES
D. S. Publishing Co.: 1948 - No. 9, June-July, 1949

	GD	VG	FN	VF	VF/NM	NM-
1-True Crime Stories	53	106	159	334	567	800
2-Used in SOTI, pg. 95	43	86	129	271	461	650
3-5: 5-Arrival date of 10/1/48	26	52	78	154	252	350
6,8,9	22	44	66	132	216	300
7-McWilliams-a; injury to eye panel	24	48	72	140	230	320

PUBLIC RELATIONS
Devil's Due/1First Comics: 2015 - No. 13, Nov, 2016 ($3.99)

	GD	VG	FN	VF	VF/NM	NM-
1-13: 1-3-Sturges & Justus/Hahn-a; Annie Wu-c						4.00

PUBO
Dark Horse Comics: Dec, 2002 - No. 3, Mar, 2003 ($3.50, B&W, limited series)

	GD	VG	FN	VF	VF/NM	NM-
1-3-Leland Purvis-s/a						3.50

PUDGY PIG
Charlton Comics: Sept, 1958 - No. 2, Nov, 1958

	GD	VG	FN	VF	VF/NM	NM-
1,2	5	10	15	30	50	70

PUFFED
Image Comics: Jul, 2003 - No. 3, Sept, 2003 ($2.95, B&W)

	GD	VG	FN	VF	VF/NM	NM-
1-3-Layman-s/Crosland-a. 1-Two covers by Crosland & Quitely						3.00

PULP
Image Comics: Jul, 2020 ($16.95, HC graphic novel)

	GD	VG	FN	VF	VF/NM	NM-
HC - Ed Brubaker-s/Sean Phillips-a/c						17.00

PULP FANTASTIC (Vertigo V2K)
DC Comics (Vertigo): Feb, 2000 - No. 3, Apr, 2000 ($2.50, limited series)

	GD	VG	FN	VF	VF/NM	NM-
1-3-Chaykin & Tischman/Burchett-a						3.00

PULP FICTION LIBRARY: MYSTERY IN SPACE
DC Comics: 1999 ($19.95, TPB)

	GD	VG	FN	VF	VF/NM	NM-
nn-Reprints classic sci-fi stories from Mystery in Space, Strange Adventures, Real Fact Comics and My Greatest Adventure						20.00

PULSE, THE (Also see Alias and Deadline)
Marvel Comics: Apr, 2004 - No. 14, May, 2006 ($2.99)

	GD	VG	FN	VF	VF/NM	NM-
1-Jessica Jones, Ben Urich, Kat Farrell app.; Bendis-s/Bagley-a						5.00
2-14: 2-5-Bendis-s/Bagley-a. 3-5-Green Goblin app. 6,7-Brent Anderson-a 9-Wolverine app.						
10-House of M. 11-14-Gaydos-a						3.00
...: House of M Special (9/05, 50¢) tabloid newspaper format; Mayhew- "photos"						3.00
Vol. 1: Thin Air (2004, $13.99) r/#1-5, gallery of cover layouts and sketches						14.00
Vol. 2: Secret War (2005, $11.99) r/#6-9						12.00
Vol. 3: Fear (2006, $14.99) r/#11-14 and New Avengers Annual #1						15.00

PUMA BLUES
Aardvark One International/Mirage Studios #21 on: 1986 - No. 26, 1990 ($1.70-$1.75, B&W)

	GD	VG	FN	VF	VF/NM	NM-
1-19, 21-26: 1-1st & 2nd printings. 25,26-$1.75-c						4.00
20 ($2.25)-By Alan Moore, Miller, Grell, others						5.00
Trade Paperback (12/88, $14.95)						15.00

PUMPKINHEAD (Movie)
Dynamite Entertainment: 2018 - No. 5, 2018 ($3.99, limited series)

	GD	VG	FN	VF	VF/NM	NM-
1-5-Cullen Bunn-s/Blacky Shepherd-a. 1-Three covers. 2-5-Two covers						4.00

PUMPKINHEAD: THE RITES OF EXORCISM (Movie)
Dark Horse Comics: 1993 - No. 2, 1993 ($2.50, limited series)

	GD	VG	FN	VF	VF/NM	NM-
1,2: Based on movie; painted-c by McManus						4.00

PUNCH & JUDY COMICS
Hillman Per.: 1944; No. 2, Fall, 1944 - V3#2, 12/47; V3#3, 6/51 - V3#9, 12/51

	GD	VG	FN	VF	VF/NM	NM-
V1#1-(60 pgs.)	39	78	117	240	395	550
2	19	38	57	111	176	240
3-12(7/46)	15	30	45	90	140	190
V2#1(8/49),3-9	14	28	42	80	115	150
V2#2,10-12, V3#1-Kirby-a(2) each	27	54	81	158	259	360
V3#2-Kirby-a	24	48	72	140	230	320
3-9	12	24	36	67	94	120

PUNCH COMICS
Harry 'A' Chesler: 12/41; #2, 2/42; #9, 7/44 - #19, 10/46; #20, 7/47 - #23, 1/48

	GD	VG	FN	VF	VF/NM	NM-
1-Mr. E, The Sky Chief, Hale the Magician, Kitty Kelly begin						
	326	652	978	2282	3991	5700
2-Captain Glory app.	168	336	504	1075	1838	2600
9-Rocketman & Rocket Girl & The Master Key begin; classic-c						
	975	1950	2919	7100	12,550	18,000
10-Sky Chief app.; J. Cole-a; Master Key-r/Scoop #3						
	181	362	543	1158	1979	2800
11-Origin Master Key-r/Scoop #1; Sky Chief, Little Nemo app.; Jack Cole-a; Fine-*ish* art by Sultan						
	284	568	852	1818	3109	4400
12-Rocket Boy & Capt. Glory app; classic Skull-c	2800	12,800	19,200	35,200	52,600	70,000
13-Cover has list of 4 Chesler artists' names on tombstone						
	181	362	543	1158	1979	2800
14,15,21: 21-Hypo needle story	110	220	330	704	1202	1700
16,17-Gag-c	53	106	159	334	567	800
18-Bondage-c; hypodermic panels	116	232	348	742	1271	1800
19-Giant bloody hands-c	226	452	678	1446	2473	3500
20-Unique cover with bare-breasted women. Rocket Girl-c						
	300	600	900	1950	3375	4800
22,23-Little Nemo-not by McCay. 22-Intro Baxter (teenage)(68 pgs.)						
	37	74	111	222	361	500

PUNCHLINE
DC Comics: Jan, 2021 ($4.99, one-shot)

	GD	VG	FN	VF	VF/NM	NM-
1-Origin revealed; Tynion IV & Sam Johns-s/Mirka Andolfo-a						5.00

PUNCHLINE: THE GOTHAM GAME
DC Comics: Dec, 2022 - No. 6, May, 2023 ($3.99, limited series)

	GD	VG	FN	VF	VF/NM	NM-
1-6: Tini & Blake Howard-s/Gleb Melnikov-a; Batman app. 6-Joker app.						4.00

PUNCHY AND THE BLACK CROW
Charlton Comics: No. 10, Oct, 1985 - No. 12, Feb, 1986

	GD	VG	FN	VF	VF/NM	NM-
10-12: Al Fago funny animal-r; low print run						6.00

PUNISHER (See Amazing Spider-Man #129, Blood and Glory, Born, Captain America #241, Classic Punisher, Daredevil #182-184, 257, Daredevil and the..., Ghost Rider V2#5, 6, Marvel Super Action #8 & 9, Marvel Preview #2, Marvel Super Action, Marvel Tales, Power Pack #46, Spectacular Spider-Man #81-83, 140, 141, 143 & newsstand Strange Tales #13 & 14)

PUNISHER (The...)
Marvel Comics Group: Jan, 1986 - No. 5, May, 1986 (Limited series)

	GD	VG	FN	VF	VF/NM	NM-
1-Double size; Grant-s/Zeck-a; Jigsaw app.	6	12	18	37	66	95
2	3	6	9	17	26	35
3-5	2	4	6	13	18	22
Trade Paperback (1988)-r/#1-5						16.00

The Pulse #14 © MAR

Punch Comics #31 © CHES

Punisher (2009 series) #11 © MAR

	GD	VG	FN	VF	VF/NM	NM-		GD	VG	FN	VF	VF/NM	NM-
	2.0	4.0	6.0	8.0	9.0	9.2		2.0	4.0	6.0	8.0	9.0	9.2

Circle of Blood TPB (8/01, $15.95) Zeck-c   16.00
Circle of Blood HC (2008, $19.99) two covers   20.00
NOTE: **Zeck** a-1-4; c-1-5.

PUNISHER (The…) (Volume 2)
Marvel Comics: July, 1987 - No. 104, July, 1995
1   4   8   12   27   44   60
2-9: 8-Portacio/Williams-c/a begins, ends #18. 9-Scarcer, low dist.   6.00
10-Daredevil app; ties in w/Daredevil #257   3   6   9   16   23   30
11-25,50: 13-18-Kingpin app. 19-Stroman-c/a. 20-Portacio(c). 24-1st app. Shadowmasters.
    25,50:($1.50,52 pgs.). 25-Shadowmasters app.   4.00
26-49,51-74,76-85,87-89: 57-Photo-c; came w/outer-c. (newsstand ed. has no outer-c).
    59-Punisher is severely cut & has skin grafts (has black skin). 60-62-Luke Cage app.
    62-Punisher back to white skin. 68-Tarantula-c/story. 85-Prequel to Suicide Run Pt. 0.
    87,88-Suicide Run Pt. 6 & 9   4.00
75-($2.75, 52 pgs.)-Embossed silver foil-c   5.00
86-($2.95, 52 pgs.)-Embossed & foil stamped-c; Suicide Run part 3   5.00
90-99: 90-bound-in cards. 99-Cringe app.   4.00
100,104: 100-($2.95, 68 pgs.). 104-Last issue   5.00
100-($3.95, 68 pgs.)-Foil cover   6.00
101-103: 102-Bullseye   4.00
"Ashcan" edition (75¢)-Joe Kubert-c   4.00
Annual 1-7 ('88-'94, 68 pgs.) 1-Evolutionary War x-over. 2-Atlantis Attacks x-over; Jim Lee-c(p)
    (back-up story, 6 pgs.). Moon Knight app. 4-Golden-c(p). 6-Bagged w/card.   7.00
…: A Man Named Frank (1994, $6.95, TPB)   6.00
…and Wolverine in African Saga nn (1989, $5.95, 52 pgs.)-Reprints Punisher War Journal
    #6 & 7; Jim Lee-c/a(r)   6.00
…Assassin Guild ('88, $6.95, graphic novel)   10.00
Back to School Special 1-3 (11/92-10/94, $2.95, 68 pgs.)   5.00
…/Batman: Deadly Knights (10/94, $4.95)   6.00
…/Black Widow: Spinning Doomsday's Web (1992, $9.95, graphic novel)   12.00
…Bloodlines nn (1991, $5.95, 68 pgs.)   6.00
… Die Hard in the Big Easy nn ('92, $4.95, 52 pgs.)   7.00
…: Empty Quarter nn ('94, $6.95)   6.00
…G-Force nn (1992, $4.95, 52 pgs.)-Painted-c   5.00
…Holiday Special 1-3 (1/93-1/95, 52 pgs.,68pgs.)-1-Foil-c   6.00
…Intruder Graphic Novel (1989, $14.95, hardcover)   20.00
…Intruder Graphic Novel (1991, $9.95, softcover)   12.00
…Invades the 'Nam: Final Invasion nn (2/94, $6.95)-J. Kubert-c & chapter break art; reprints
    The 'Nam #84 & unpublished #85,86   10.00
…Kingdom Gone Graphic Novel (1990, $16.95, hardcover)   20.00
…Meets Archie (8/94, $3.95, 52 pgs.)-Die cut-c; no ads; same contents as
    Archie Meets The Punisher   6.00
…Movie Special 1 (6/90, $5.95, squarebound, 68 pgs.) painted-c; Brent Anderson-a;
    contents intended for a 3 issue series which was advertised but not published   6.00
…: No Escape nn (1990, $4.95, 52 pgs.)-New-a   6.00
…Return to Big Nothing Graphic Novel (Epic, 1989, $16.95, hardcover)   25.00
…Return to Big Nothing Graphic Novel (Marvel, 1989, $12.95, softcover)   15.00
…The Prize nn (1990, $4.95, 68 pgs.)-New-a   6.00
Summer Special 1-4(8/91-7/94, 52 pgs.):1-No ads. 2-Bisley-c; Austin-a(i). 3-No ads   4.00
NOTE: **Austin** c(i)-47, 48. **Cowan** c-50, 85, 86, 100. **Heath** a-26, 27, 89, 90, 91; c-26, 27. **Quesada**
c-56p, 62p. **Sienkiewicz** c-Back to School 1.**Stroman** a-76p(9 pgs.). **Williamson** a(i)-25, 60-62i, 64-70, 74, Annual
5; c(i)-62, 65-68.

PUNISHER (Also see Double Edge)
Marvel Comics: Nov, 1995 - No. 18, Apr, 1997 ($2.95/$1.95/$1.50)
1 ($2.95)-Ostrander scripts begin; foil-c.   5.00
2-18: 7-Vs. S.H.I.E.L.D. 11-"Onslaught." 12-17-X-Cutioner-c/app. 17-Daredevil,
    Spider-Man-c/app.   4.00

PUNISHER (Marvel Knights)
Marvel Comics: Nov, 1998 - No. 4, Feb, 1999 ($2.99, limited series)
1-4: 1-Wrightson-a; Wrightson & Jusko-c   4.00
1-($6.95) DF Edition; Jae Lee variant-c   7.00

PUNISHER (Marvel Knights) (Volume 3)
Marvel Comics: Apr, 2000 - No. 12, Mar, 2001 ($2.99, limited series)
1-Ennis-s/Dillon & Palmiotti-a/Bradstreet-c   2   4   6   9   12   15
1-Bradstreet white variant-c   2   4   6   9   12   15
1-($6.95) DF Edition; Jurgens & Ordway variant-c   2   4   6   10   14   18
2-Two covers by Bradstreet & Dillon   3.00
3-($3.99) Bagged with Marvel Knights Genesis Edition; Daredevil app.   4.00
4-12: 9-11-The Russian app.   3.00
HC (6/02, $34.95) r/#1-12, Punisher Kills the Marvel Universe, and Marvel Knights
    Double Shot #1   35.00
… By Garth Ennis Omnibus (2008, $99.99) oversized r/#1-12, #1-7 & #13-37 of 2001 series,
    Punisher Kills the Marvel Universe, and Marvel Knights Double Shot #1; extras   100.00

…/Painkiller Jane (1/01, $3.50) Jusko-c; Ennis-s/Jusko and Dave Ross-a(p)   3.50
…: Welcome Back Frank TPB (4/01, $19.95) r/#1-12   20.00

PUNISHER (Marvel Knights) (Volume 4)
Marvel Comics: Aug, 2001 - No. 37, Feb, 2004 ($2.99)
1-Ennis-s/Dillon & Palmiotti-a/Bradstreet-c; The Russian app.   4.00
2-Two covers (Dillon & Bradstreet) Spider-Man-c/app.   3.00
3-37: 3-7-Ennis-s/Dillon-a. 9-12-Peyer-s/Gutierrez-a. 13,14-Ennis-s/Dillon-a.
    16,17-Wolverine app.; Robertson-a. 18-23,32-Dillon-a. 24-27-Mandrake-a. 27-Elektra app.
    33-37-Spider-Man, Daredevil, & Wolverine app. 36,37-Hulk app.   3.00
Vol. 2 HC (2003, $29.95) r/#1-7,13-18; intro. by Mike Millar   30.00
Vol. 2 HC (2004, $29.95) r/#19-27; script pages for #19   30.00
Vol. 3: Business as Usual TPB (2003, $14.99) r/#13-18; Bradstreet-c   15.00
Vol. 4: Full Auto TPB (2003, $17.99) r/#20-26; Bradstreet-c   18.00
Vol. 5: Streets of Laredo TPB (2003, $17.99) r/#19,27-32   18.00
Vol. 6: Confederacy of Dunces TPB (2004, $13.99) r/#33-37   14.00

PUNISHER (Marvel MAX)(Title becomes "Punisher: Frank Castle MAX" with #66)
Marvel Comics: Mar, 2004 - No. 75, Dec, 2009 ($2.99/$3.99)
1-49,51-60: 1-Ennis-s/LaRosa-a/Bradstreet-c; flashback to his family's murder; Micro app.
    6-Micro killed. 7-12,19-25-Fernandez-a. 13-18-Braithwaite-a. 31-36-Barracuda.
    43-49-Medina-a. 51-54-Barracuda app. 60-Last Ennis-s/Bradstreet-c   3.00
50-($3.99) Barracuda returns; Chaykin-a   4.00
61-65-Gregg Hurwitz-s/Dave Johnson-c/Laurence Campbell-a   3.00
66-73-($3.99) 66-70-Six Hours to Kill; Swiercczynski-s. 71-73-Parlov-a   4.00
74,75-($4.99) 74-Parlov-a. 75-Short stories; art by Lashley, Coker, Parlov & others   5.00
Annual (11/07, $3.99) Mike Benson-s/Laurence Campbell-a   4.00
…: Bloody Valentine (4/06, $3.99) Palmiotti & Gray-s/Gulacy & Palmiotti-a; Gulacy-c   4.00
…: Force of Nature (4/08, $4.99) Swierczynski-s/Lacombe-a/Deodato-c   5.00
…: MAX: Naked Kill (8/09, $3.99) Campbell-a/Bradstreet-c   4.00
… MAX MGC #1 (5/10, $1.00) reprints #1 with "Marvel's Greatest Comics" cover logo   4.00
…: MAX Special: Little Black Book (8/08, $3.99) Gischler-s/Palo-a/Johnson-c   4.00
…: MAX X-Mas Special (2/09, $3.99) Aaron-s/Boschi-a/Bachalo-c   4.00
…: Red X-Mas (2/05, $3.99) Palmiotti & Gray-s/Texeira & Palmiotti-a; Texeira-c   4.00
…: Silent Night (2/06, $3.99) Diggle-s/Hotz-a/Deodato-c   4.00
…: The Cell (7/05, $4.99) Ennis-s/LaRosa-a/Bradstreet-c; Castle's childhood   5.00
…: The Tyger (2/06, $4.99) Ennis-s/Severin-a/Bradstreet-c   5.00
…: Very Special Holidays TPB ('06, $12.99) r/Red X-Mas, Bloody Valentine and Silent Night   13.00
…: X-Mas Special (1/07, $3.99) Stuart Moore-s/CP Smith-a   4.00
…: MAX: From First to Last HC (2009, $19.99) r/The Tyger, The Cell and The End 1-shots   20.00
… MAX Vol. 1 (2005, $29.99) oversized r/#1-12; gallery of Fernandez art from #7 shown from
    layout to completed pages   30.00
… MAX Vol. 2 (2006, $29.99) oversized r/#13-24; gallery of Fernandez pencil art   30.00
… MAX Vol. 3 (2007, $29.99) oversized r/#25-36; gallery of Fernandez & Parlov art   30.00
… MAX Vol. 4 (2008, $29.99) oversized r/#37-49; gallery of Fernandez & Medina art   30.00
Vol. 1: In the Beginning TPB (2004, $14.99) r/#1-6   15.00
Vol. 2: Kitchen Irish TPB (2004, $14.99) r/#7-12   15.00
Vol. 3: Mother Russia TPB (2005, $14.99) r/#13-18   15.00
Vol. 4: Up is Down and Black is White TPB (2005, $14.99) r/#19-24   15.00
Vol. 5: The Slavers TPB (2006, $15.99) r/#25-30; Fernandez pencil pages   16.00
Vol. 6: Barracuda TPB (2006, $15.99) r/#31-36; Parlov sketch page   16.00
Vol. 7: Man of Stone TPB (2007, $15.99) r/#37-42   16.00
Vol. 8: Widowmaker TPB (2007, $15.99) r/#43-49   18.00
Vol. 9: Long Cold Dark TPB (2008, $15.99) r/#50-54   16.00

PUNISHER (Frank Castle in the Marvel Universe after Secret Invasion)
(Title changes to Franken-Castle for #17-21)
Marvel Comics: Mar, 2009 - No. 21, Jan, 2010 ($3.99/$2.99)
1-($3.99) Dark Reign; Sentry app.; Remender-s/Opena-a; character history; 2 covers   4.00
2-5,7-10($2.99) 2-7-The Hood app. 4-Microchip returns. 5-Daredevil #183 cover swipe   3.00
6-($3.99) Huat-a/McKone-c; profile pages of resurrected villains   4.00
11-Follows Dark Reign: The List - Punisher; Franken-Castle begins; Tony Moore-a   3.00
12-16-Franken-Castle continues; Legion of Monsters app. 14-Brereton & Moore-a   3.00
Franken-Castle 17-20: 19, 20-Wolverine & Daken app.   4.00
Franken-Castle 21-($3.99) Brereton-a/c; Legion of Monsters app.; Frank gets body back   4.00
Annual 1 (11/09, $3.99) Pearson-a/c; Juggernaut app.   4.00
…: Franken-Castle - The Birth of the Monster 1 (7/10, $4.99) r/#11 & Dark Reign: The List   5.00

PUNISHER (Frank Castle in the Marvel Universe)(Continues in Punisher: War Zone [2012])
Marvel Comics: Oct, 2011 - No. 16, Dec, 2012 ($3.99/$2.99)
1-($3.99) Rucka-s/Checchetto-a/Hitch-c   4.00
1-Variant-c by Sal Buscema   6.00
1-Variant-c by Neal Adams   10.00
2-16-($2.99): 2,3-Vulture app. 10-Spider-Man & Daredevil app.   3.00
…, Moon Knight & Daredevil: The Big Shots (10/11, $3.99) Previews new series for

	GD	VG	FN	VF	VF/NM	NM-
	2.0	4.0	6.0	8.0	9.0	9.2

Punisher, Moon Knight & Daredevil; creator interviews and production art   **4.00**

PUNISHER, THE
Marvel Comics: Apr, 2014 - No. 20, Sept, 2015 ($3.99)

1-20: 1-Edmonson-s/Gerads-a; Howling Commandos app. 2-6-Electro app. 16,17-Captain America (Falcon) app. 19,20-Secret Wars tie-ins   **4.00**

PUNISHER, THE
Marvel Comics: Jul, 2016 - No. 17, Dec, 2017; No. 218, Jan, 2018 - No. 228, Sept, 2018 ($3.99)

1-17: 1-Becky Cloonan-s/Steve Dillon-a. 7-Steve Dillon's last work. 8-12-Horak-a. 13-Anka-a 14-17-Horak-a   **4.00**

[Title switches to legacy numbering after #11 (11/17)]
218-228-Castle gets the War Machine armor. 218-223-Vilanova-a   **4.00**
Annual 1 (12/16, $4.99) Gerry Conway-s/Felix Ruiz-a   **5.00**

PUNISHER, THE
Marvel Comics: Oct, 2018 - No. 16, Dec, 2019 ($4.99/$3.99)

1-($4.99) Rosenberg-s/Kudranski-a; Baron Zemo & The Mandarin app.   **5.00**
2-16-($3.99) 2-Luke Cage, Iron Fist & Daredevil app. 3-Daredevil app. 13-Thunderbolts   **4.00**
Annual 1 (9/19, $4.99) Acts of Evil; Karla Pacheco-s/Gorham-a; J. Jonah Jameson app.   **5.00**

PUNISHER
Marvel Comics: May, 2022 - No. 12, Jul, 2023 ($5.99/$4.99)

1-($5.99) Aaron-s/Saiz-a; Frank Castle joins The Hand   **6.00**
2-12-($4.99) 2-Maria Castle returns; Ares app. 6,7-Daredevil app.   **5.00**
... War Journal: Base 1 (4/23, $4.99) Castle before becoming the Punisher   **5.00**

PUNISHER
Marvel Comics: Jan, 2024 - No. 4, Apr, 2024 ($5.99/$4.99)

1-($5.99) Pepose-s/Wachter-a; Joe Garrison as the new Punisher   **6.00**
2-4-($4.99) 3,4-Jigsaw app.   **5.00**

PUNISHER AND WOLVERINE: DAMAGING EVIDENCE (See Wolverine and...)

PUNISHER ARMORY, THE
Marvel Comics: 7/90 ($1.50); No. 2, 6/91; No. 3, 4/92 - 10/94($1.75/$2.00)

1-10: 1-r/weapons pgs. from War Journal. 1,2-Jim Lee-c. 3-10-All new material. 3-Jusko painted-c   **4.00**

PUNISHER: IN THE BLOOD (Marvel Universe Frank Castle)
Marvel Comics: Jan, 2011 - No. 5, May, 2011 ($3.99, limited series)

1-5-Remender-s/Boschi-a; Jigsaw & Microchip app.   **4.00**

PUNISHER KILL KREW (Follows War of the Realms series)
Marvel Comics: Oct, 2019 - No. 5, Jan, 2020 ($3.99, limited series)

1-5-Duggan-s/Ferreyra-a; Juggernaut & The Black Knight app.   **4.00**

PUNISHER KILLS THE MARVEL UNIVERSE
Marvel Comics: Nov, 1995 ($5.95, one-shot)

1-Garth Ennis script/Doug Braithwaite-a	4	8	12	18	37	50
2-2nd printing (3/00) Steve Dillon-c						**6.00**
1-3rd printing (2008, $4.99) original 1995 cover						**5.00**

PUNISHER MAGAZINE, THE
Marvel Comics: Oct, 1989 - No. 16, Nov, 1990 ($2.25, B&W, Magazine, 52 pgs.)

1-16: 1-r/Punisher #1('86). 2,3-r/Punisher 2-5. 4-16: 4-7-r/Punisher V2#1-8. 4-Chiodo-c. 8-r/Punisher #10 & Daredevil #257; Portacio & Lee-r. 14-r/Punisher War Journal 1,2 w/new Lee-c. 16-r/Punisher W. J. #3,8   **4.00**
NOTE: Chiodo painted c-4, 7, 16. Jusko painted c-6, 8. Jim Lee r-8, 14-16; c-14. Portacio/Williams r-7-12.

PUNISHERMAX
Marvel Comics (MAX): Jan, 2010 - No. 22, Apr, 2012 ($3.99)

1-22-Aaron-s/Dillon-a/Johnson-c. 1-5-Rise of the Kingpin. 6-11-Bullseye. 17-20-Elektra app. 21-Castle dies. 22-Afterword by Aaron   **4.00**
...: Butterfly (5/10, $4.99) Valerie D'Orazio-s/Laurence Campbell-a/c   **5.00**
...: Get Castle (3/10, $4.99) Rob Williams-s/Laurence Campbell-a/Bradstreet-c   **5.00**
...: Happy Ending (10/10, $3.99) Milligan-s/Ryp-a/c   **4.00**
...: Hot Rods of Death (11/10, $4.99) Huston/Martinbrough-a/Bradstreet-c   **5.00**
...: Tiny Ugly World (12/10, $4.99) Lapham-s/Talajic-a/Bradstreet-c   **4.00**

PUNISHER MAX: THE PLATOON (Titled Punisher: The Platoon for #3-6)
Marvel Comics: Dec, 2017 - No. 6, Apr, 2018 ($3.99, limited series)

1-6-Ennis-s/Parlov-a; Castle's first tour of Vietnam   **4.00**

PUNISHER: NIGHTMARE
Marvel Comics: Mar, 2013 - No. 5, Mar, 2013 ($3.99, weekly limited series)

1-5-Texeira-a/c; Gimple-s   **4.00**

PUNISHER NOIR
Marvel Comics: Oct, 2009 - No. 4, Jan, 2010 ($3.99)

1-4-Pulp-style set in 1935; Tieri-s/Azaceta-a   **4.00**

PUNISHER: OFFICIAL MOVIE ADAPTATION
Marvel Comics: May, 2004 - No. 3, May, 2004 ($2.99, limited series)

1-3-Photo-c of Thomas Jane; Milligan-s/Olliffe-a   **3.00**

PUNISHER: ORIGIN OF MICRO CHIP, THE
Marvel Comics: July, 1993 - No. 2, Aug, 1993 ($1.75)

1,2   **4.00**

PUNISHER: P.O.V.
Marvel Comics: 1991 - No. 4, 1991 ($4.95, painted, limited series, 52 pgs.)

1-4: Starlin scripts & Wrightson painted-c/a in all. 2-Nick Fury app.   **6.00**

PUNISHER PRESENTS: BARRACUDA MAX
Marvel Comics (MAX): Apr, 2007 - No. 5, Aug, 2007 ($3.99, limited series)

1-5-Ennis-s/Parlov-a/c   **4.00**
SC (2007, $17.99) r/series; sketch pages   **18.00**

PUNISHER: SOVIET
Marvel Comics (MAX): Jan, 2020 - No. 6, May, 2020 ($3.99)

1-6-Ennis-s/Burrows-a   **4.00**

PUNISHER: THE END
Marvel Comics: June, 2004 ($4.50, one-shot)

1-Ennis-s/Corben-a/c   **4.50**

PUNISHER: THE GHOSTS OF INNOCENTS
Marvel Comics: Jan, 1993 - No. 2, Jan, 1993 ($5.95, 52 pgs.)

1,2-Starlin scripts   **6.00**

PUNISHER: THE MOVIE
Marvel Comics: 2004 ($12.99,TPB)

nn-Reprints Amazing Spider-Man #129; Official Movie Adaptation and Punisher V3 #1   **13.00**

PUNISHER: THE PLATOON (See Punisher MAX: The Platoon)

PUNISHER: THE TRIAL OF THE PUNISHER
Marvel Comics: Nov, 2013 - No. 2, Dec, 2013 ($3.99, limited series)

1-Guggenheim-s/Yu-a/c. 2-Suayan-a; Matt Murdock app.   **4.00**

PUNISHER 2099 (See Punisher War Journal #50)
Marvel Comics: Feb, 1993 - No. 34, Nov, 1995 ($1.25/$1.50/$1.95)

1-Foil stamped-c   **6.00**
1-(Second printing)   **4.00**
2-24,26-34: 13-Spider-Man 2099 x-over; Ron Lim-c(p). 16-bound-in card sheet   **4.00**
25-($2.95, 52 pgs.)-Deluxe edition; embossed foil-cover   **6.00**
25-($2.25, 52 pgs.)   **5.00**
(Marvel Knights) #1 (11/04, $2.99) Kirkman-s/Mhan-a/Pat Lee-c   **4.00**
... No. 1 (1/20, $4.99) Matt Horak-a   **5.00**

PUNISHER VS. BULLSEYE
Marvel Comics: Jan, 2006 - No. 5, May, 2006 ($2.99, limited series)

1-5-Daniel Way-s/Steve Dillon-a   **3.00**
TPB (2006, $13.99) r/#1-5; cover sketch pages   **14.00**

PUNISHER VS. DAREDEVIL
Marvel Comics: Jun, 2000 ($3.50, one-shot)

1-Reprints Daredevil #183,#184 & #257   **4.00**

PUNISHER WAR JOURNAL, THE
Marvel Comics: Nov, 1988 - No. 80, July, 1995 ($1.50/$1.75/$1.95)

1-Origin The Punisher; Matt Murdock cameo; Jim Lee inks begin						
		3	6	9	18	27	36

2-7: 2,3-Daredevil x-over. 3-Jim Lee-c(i). 4-Jim Lee c/a begins. 6-Two part Wolverine story begins. 7-Wolverine-c, story ends   **5.00**
8-49,51-60,62,63,65: 13-16,20-22: No. 8-Jim Lee-a. 13-Jim Lee-c only. 13-15-Heath-i. 14,15-Spider-Man x-over. 19-Last Jim Lee-c/a.29,30-Ghost Rider app. 31-Andy & Joe Kubert art. 36-Photo-c. 47,48-Nomad/Daredevil-c/stories; see Nomad. 57,58-Daredevil & Ghost Rider-c/stories. 62,63-Suicide Run Pt. 4 & 7   **5.00**
50,61,64($2.95, 52 pgs.): 50-Preview of Punisher 2099 (1st app.); embossed-c. 61-Embossed foil cover; Suicide Run Pt. 1. 64-Die-cut-c; Suicide Run Pt. 10   **5.00**
64-($2.25, 52 pgs.)-Regular cover edition   **5.00**
66-74,76-80: 66-Bound-in card sheet   **5.00**
75 ($2.50, 52 pgs.)   **5.00**
NOTE: Golden c-25-30, 40, 61, 62. Jusko painted c-31, 32. Jim Lee a-1i-3i, 4p-13p, 17p-19p; c-2i, 3i, 4p-15p, 17p, 18p, 19p. Painted c-40.

PUNISHER WAR JOURNAL (Frank Castle back in the regular Marvel Universe)
Marvel Comics: Jan, 2007 - No. 26, Feb, 2009 ($2.99)

1-Civil War tie-in; Spider-Man app; Fraction-s/Olivetti-a   **5.00**
1-B&W edition (11/06)   **5.00**
2-5: 2,3-Civil War tie-in. 4-Deodato-a   **4.00**
6-11,13-24,26: 6-10-Punisher dons Captain America-esque outfit. 7-Two covers. 11-Winter Soldier app. 16-23-Chaykin-a. 18-23-Jigsaw app. 24-Secret Invasion   **3.00**
12,25-($3.99) 12-World War Hulk x-over; Fraction-s/Olivetti-a. 25-Secret Invasion   **4.00**
... Annual 1 (1/09, $3.99) Spurrier-s/Dell'edera-a   **4.00**
... Vol. 1: Civil War HC (2007, $19.99) r/#1-4 and #1 B&W edition; Olivetti sketch pages   **20.00**
... Vol. 1: Civil War SC (2007, $14.99) r/#1-4 and #1 B&W edition; Olivetti sketch pages   **15.00**
... Vol. 2: Goin' Out West HC (2007, $24.99) r/#5-11; Olivetti sketch page   **25.00**
... Vol. 2: Goin' Out West SC (2008, $17.99) r/#5-11; Olivetti sketch page   **18.00**
... Vol. 3: Hunter Hunted HC (2008, $19.99) r/#12-17   **20.00**

PUNISHER WAR JOURNAL
Marvel Comics: Aug, 2022 - Present ($4.99, series of one-shots)

...: Blitz 1 (8/22, $4.99) Frank Castle with the Hand; Gronbekk-s/Medina-a   **5.00**
...: Brother 1 (12/22, $4.99) Jigsaw app.; Gronbekk-s/Pimentel-a   **5.00**

PUNISHER: WAR ZONE, THE
Marvel Comics: Mar, 1992 - No. 41, July, 1995 ($1.75/$1.95)

1-($2.25, 40 pgs.)-Die cut-c; Romita, Jr.-c/a begins   **6.00**
2-22,24,26,27-41: 8-Last Romita, Jr.-c/a. 19-Wolverine app. 24-Suicide Run Pt. 5. 27-Bound-in card sheet. 31-36-Joe Kubert-a   **4.00**
23-($2.95, 52 pgs.)-Embossed foil-c; Suicide Run part 2; Buscema-a(part)   **5.00**
25-($2.25, 52 pgs.)-Suicide Run part 8; painted-c   **5.00**
Annual 1,2 ('93, 94, $2.95, 68 pgs.)-1-Bagged w/card; John Buscema-a   **5.00**
...: River of Blood TPB (2006, $15.99) r/#31-36; Joe Kubert-a   **16.00**
NOTE: Golden c-23. Romita, Jr. c/a-1-8.

PUNISHER: WAR ZONE
Marvel Comics: Feb, 2009 - No. 6, Mar, 2009 ($3.99, weekly limited series)

1-6-Ennis-s/Dillon-a/c; return of Ma Gnucci   **4.00**
1-Variant cover by John Romita, Jr.   **6.00**

PUNISHER: WAR ZONE (Follows Punisher 2011-2012 series)
Marvel Comics: Dec, 2012 - No. 5, Apr, 2013 ($3.99, limited series)

1-5: Rucka-s; Spider-Man and The Avengers app.   **4.00**

PUNISHER: YEAR ONE
Marvel Comics: Dec, 1994 - No. 4, Apr, 1995 ($2.50, limited series)

1-4   **4.00**

PUNK MAMBO
Valiant Entertainment: No. 0, Nov, 2014; Apr, 2019 - No. 5, Aug, 2019 ($3.99, limited series)

0-(11/14) Milligan-s/Gill-a; bonus preview of The Valiant #1   **4.00**
1-5-Cullen Bunn-s/Adam Gorham-a/ Dan Brereton-c   **4.00**

PUNK ROCK JESUS

Punisher: War Zone (2009 series) #1 © MAR

Purgatori Must Die #1 © DYN

PvP V2 #25 © Scott R. Kurtz

	GD	VG	FN	VF	VF/NM	NM-			GD	VG	FN	VF	VF/NM	NM-
	2.0	4.0	6.0	8.0	9.0	9.2			2.0	4.0	6.0	8.0	9.0	9.2

DC Comics (Vertigo): Sept, 2012 - No. 6, Feb, 2013 ($2.99, B&W, limited series)
1-6-Sean Murphy-s/a/c; cloning of Jesus — 3.00

PUNKS NOT DEAD
IDW Publishing (Black Crown): Feb, 2018 - No. 6, Jul, 2018 ($3.99)
1-6-Barnett-s/Simmonds-a; 3 covers — 4.00

PUNKS NOT DEAD: LONDON CALLING
IDW Publishing (Black Crown): Feb, 2019 - No. 5, Jun, 2019 ($3.99)
1-5-Barnett-s/Simmonds-a — 4.00

PUNX
Acclaim (Valiant): Nov, 1995 - No. 3, Jan, 1996 ($2.50, unfinished lim. series)
1-3: Giffen story & art in all. 2-Satirizes Scott McCloud's Understanding Comics — 4.00
(Manga) Special 1 (3/96, $2.50)-Giffen scripts — 4.00

PUPPET COMICS
George W. Dougherty Co.: Spring, 1946 - No. 2, Summer, 1946
| 1-Funny animal in both | 30 | 60 | 90 | 177 | 289 | 400 |
| 2 | 18 | 36 | 54 | 105 | 165 | 225 |

PUPPETOONS (See George Pal's...)

PUREHEART (See Archie as...)

PURGATORI
Chaos! Comics: Prelude #-1, 5/96 ($1.50, 16 pgs.); 1996 - No. 3 Dec, 1996 (limited series)
Prelude #-1-Pulido story; Balent-c/a; contains sketches & interviews — 4.00
0-(2/01, $2.99) Prelude to "Love Bites"; Rio-c/a — 4.00
1/2 (12/00, $2.95) Al Rio-c/a — 4.00
1-($3.50)-Wraparound cover; red foil embossed-c; Jim Balent-a — 5.00
1-($19.95)-Premium Edition (1000 print run) — 20.00
2-($3.00)-Wraparound-c — 4.00
2-Variant-c — 5.00
...: Heartbreaker 1 (3/02, $2.99) Jolley-s — 3.00
...: Love Bites 1 (3/01, $2.99) Turnbull-a/Kaminski-s — 3.00
...: Mischief Night 1 (11/01, $2.99) — 3.00
...: Re-imagined 1 (7/02, $2.99) Jolley-s/Neves-a — 3.00
...The Dracula Gambit-($2.95) — 3.00
...The Dracula Gambit Sketchbook-($2.95) — 3.00
...The Vampire's Myth 1-($19.95) Premium Ed. (10,000) — 20.00
...Vs. Chastity (7/00, $2.95) Two versions (Alpha and Omega) with different endings; Rio-a — 3.00
...Vs. Lady Death (1/01, $2.95) Kaminski-s — 3.00
...Vs. Vampirella (4/00, $2.95) Zanier-a; Chastity app. — 3.00

PURGATORI
Chaos! Comics: Oct, 1998 - No. 7, Apr, 1999 ($2.95)
1-7-Quinn-s/Rio-c/a. 2-Lady Death-c — 4.00

PURGATORI
Dynamite Entertainment: 2014 - No. 5, 2015 ($3.99)
1-5-Gillespie-s; multiple covers. 2-4-Jade app. — 4.00

PURGATORI: DARKEST HOUR
Chaos! Comics: Sept, 2001 - No. 2, Oct, 2001 ($2.99, limited series)
1,2 — 3.00

PURGATORI: EMPIRE
Chaos! Comics: May, 2000 - No. 3, July, 2000 ($2.95, limited series)
1-3-Cleavenger-c — 3.00

PURGATORI: GODDESS RISING
Chaos! Comics: July, 1999 - No. 4, Oct, 1999 ($2.95, limited series)
1-4-Deodato-c/a — 4.00

PURGATORI: GOD HUNTER
Chaos! Comics: Apr, 2002 - No. 2, May, 2002 ($2.99, limited series)
1,2-Molenaar-a/Jolley-s — 3.00

PURGATORI: GOD KILLER
Chaos! Comics: Jun, 2002 - No. 2, July, 2002 ($2.99, limited series)
1,2-Molenaar-a/Jolley-s — 3.00

PURGATORI MUST DIE
Dynamite Entertainment: 2022 - No. 5, 2023 ($3.99, limited series)
1-5-Ray Fawkes-s/Salvatore Aiala-a — 4.00

PURGATORI: THE HUNTED
Chaos! Comics: Jun, 2001 - No. 2, Aug, 2001 ($2.99, limited series)
1,2 — 3.00

PURGATORI, VOLUME 2
Dynamite Entertainment: 2021 - No. 5, 2021 ($3.99)
1-5-Ray Fawkes-s/Alvaro Sarraseca-a; multiple covers on all — 4.00

PURPLE CLAW, THE (Also see Tales of Horror)
Minoan Publishing Co./Toby Press: Jan, 1953 - No. 3, May, 1953
1-Origin; horror/weird stories in all	60	120	180	381	653	925
2,3: 1-3 r-in Tales of Horror #9-11	43	86	129	271	461	650
I.W. Reprint #8-Reprints #1	4	8	12	28	47	65

PURR EVIL
Image Comics: Jul, 2023 - No. 6 ($3.99, limited series)
1-Mirka Andolfo-s/Laura Braga-a — 4.00

PUSH (Based on the 2009 movie)
DC Comics (WildStorm): Early Jan, 2009 - No. 6, Apr, 2009 ($3.50, limited series)
1-6-Movie prequel; Bruno Redondo-a. 1-Jock-c — 3.50
TPB (2009, $19.99) r/#1-6 — 20.00

PUSSYCAT (Magazine)
Marvel Comics Group: Oct, 1968 (B&W reprints from Men's magazines)
| 1-(Scarce)-Ward, Everett, Wood-a; Everett-c | 87 | 174 | 261 | 553 | 952 | 1350 |

PUZZLE FUN COMICS (Also see Jingle Jangle)
George W. Dougherty Co.: Spring, 1946 - No. 2, Summer, 1946 (52 pgs.)
| 1-Gustavson-a | 34 | 69 | 102 | 199 | 325 | 450 |
| 2 | 21 | 42 | 63 | 122 | 199 | 275 |
NOTE: #1 & 2('46) each contain a **George Carlson** cover plus a 6 pg. story "Alec in Fumbleland"; also many puzzles in each.

PvP (Player vs. Player)
Image Comics: Mar, 2003 - No. 45, Mar, 2010 ($2.95/$2.99/$3.50, B&W, reads sideways)
1-34,36-Scott Kurtz-s/a in all. 1,16-Frank Cho-c. 11-Savage Dragon-c/app. 14-Invincible app. —
19-Jonathan Luna-c. 25-Cho-a (2 pgs.) — 3.00
35,37-45 ($3.50)-Brandy from Liberty Meadows app. — 3.50
#0 (7/05, 50¢) Secret Origin of Skull — 3.00
...: At Large TPB (7/04, $11.95) r/#1-6 — 12.00
...: Vol. 2: Reloaded TPB (12/04, $11.95) r/#7-12 — 12.00
...: Vol. 3: Rides Again TPB (2005, $11.99) r/#13-18 — 12.00
...: Vol. 4: PVP Goes Bananas TPB (2007, $12.99) r/#19-24 — 13.00
...: Vol. 5: PVP Treks On TPB (2008, $14.99) r/#25-31 — 15.00
...: The Dork Ages TPB (2/04, $11.95) r/#1-6 from Dork Storm Press — 12.00

PYRATE QUEEN
Bad Idea: Sept, 2021 - No. 4, Dec, 2021 ($7.99, limited series)
1-4-Lead story with Peter Milligan-s/Adam Pollina-a; back-ups by Kindt-s/Foreman-a — 8.00

Q2: THE RETURN OF QUANTUM & WOODY
Valiant Entertainment: Oct, 2014 - No. 5, Feb, 2015 ($3.99, limited series)
1-5: 1-Priest-s/Bright-a; multiple covers — 4.00

QUACK!
Star Reach Productions: July, 1976 - No. 6, 1977? ($1.25, B&W)
| 1-Brunner-a on Duckaneer (Howard the Duck clone); Dave Stevens, Gilbert, Shaw-a | | | 3 | 6 | 9 | 14 | 19 | 24 |
1-2nd printing (10/76) — 5.00
2-6: 2-Newton the Rabbit Wonder by Aragonés/Leialoha; Gilbert, Shaw-a; Leialoha-c.								
3-The Beavers by Dave Sim begin, end #5; Gilbert, Shaw-a; Sim/Leialoha-a. 6-Brunner-a								
(Duckeneer); Gilbert-a	2	4	6	8	10	12

QUADRANT
Quadrant Publications: 1983 - No. 8, 1986 (B&W, nudity, adults)
| 1-Peter Hsu-c/a in all | 3 | 6 | 9 | 17 | 25 | 34 |
| 2-8 | 2 | 4 | 6 | 8 | 10 | 12 |

QUAKE: S.H.I.E.L.D. 50TH ANNIVERSARY
Marvel Comics: Nov, 2015 ($3.99, one-shot)
1-Spotlight on Daisy Johnson; Daniel Johnson-a/Nakayama-c; Avengers app. — 4.00

QUANTUM AGE, THE (Also see Black Hammer)
Dark Horse Comics: Jul, 2018 - No. 6, Jan, 2019 ($3.99, limited series)
1-6-Lemire-s/Torres-a. 4-6-Colonel Weird app. — 4.00

QUANTUM & WOODY
Acclaim Comics: June, 1997 - No. 17, No. 32 (9/99), No. 18 - No. 21, Feb, 2000 ($2.50)
1-1st app.; drawn cover	1	2	3	5	6	8
1-Painted cover	2	4	6	9	12	15
2,4-17: 6-Copycat-c. 9-Troublemakers app.						4.00
3-1st Vincent Van Goat	2	4	6	11	16	20

	GD	VG	FN	VF	VF/NM	NM-
	2.0	4.0	6.0	8.0	9.0	9.2

32-(9/99); 18-(10/99),19-21							4.00
The Director's Cut TPB ('97, $7.95) r/#1-4 plus extra pages							12.00

QUANTUM & WOODY
Valiant Entertainment: Jul, 2013 - No. 12, Jul, 2014 ($3.99)

1-12: 1-Asmus-s/Fowler-a; covers by Ryan Sook & Marcos Martin; origin re-told	4.00
#0 -(3/14, $3.99) Story of the goat; Asmus-s/Fowler-a/c	4.00
... Valiant-Sized #1 (12/14, $4.99) Thomas Edison app.	5.00

QUANTUM AND WOODY!
Valiant Entertainment: Dec, 2017 - No. 12, Nov, 2018 ($3.99)

1-3: 1-Daniel Kibblesmith-s/Kano-a. 3,6,7,12-Portela-a. 8-11-Eisma-a	4.00

QUANTUM AND WOODY
Valiant Entertainment: Jan, 2020 - Present ($3.99)

1-4-Hastings-s/Browne-a	4.00

QUANTUM AND WOODY MUST DIE
Valiant Entertainment: Jan, 2015 - No. 4, Apr, 2015 ($3.99, limited series)

1-4: 1-James Asmus-s/Steve Lieber-a; multiple covers on each	4.00

QUANTUM LEAP (TV) (See A Nightmare on Elm Street)
Innovation Publishing: Sept, 1991 - No. 12, Jun, 1993 ($2.50, painted-c)

1-Based on TV show; all have painted-c	2	4	6	11	16	20
2-12: 8-Has photo gallery						4.00
Special Edition 1 (10/92)-r/#1 w/8 extra pgs. of photos & articles		1	3	4	6	8	10
Time and Space Special 1 (#13) ($2.95)-Foil logo	1	3	4	6	8	10

QUANTUM TUNNELER, THE
Revolution Studio: Oct, 2001 (no cover price, one-shot)

1-Prequel to "The One" movie; Clayton Henry-a	3.00

QUARANTINE ZONE
DC Comics: Apr, 2016 ($22.99, HC graphic novel)

HC - Daniel Wilson-s/Fernando Pasarin-a	23.00

QUASAR (See Avengers #302, Captain America #217, Incredible Hulk #234, Marvel Team-Up #113 & Marvel Two-in-One #53)
Marvel Comics: Oct, 1989 - No. 60, Jul, 1994 ($1.00/$1.25, Direct sales #17 on)

1-Gruenwald-s/Paul Ryan-c/a begin; Origin of Wendell Vaughn from Marvel Man to Quasar; Marvel Boy & Fantastic Four app.	6.00
2-6: 2-Origin of the Quantum-Bands; Deathurge & Eon app; Quasar becomes 'Protector of the Universe'. 3-Human Torch app. 4-Aquarian app. 5,6-Acts of Vengeance tie-in. 5-Absorbing Man & Loki app. 6-Red Ghost, Living Laser, Uatu the Watcher app; Venom cameo (2pgs); last Ryan-a(p)	4.00
7-Spider-Man & Quasar vs. Terminus	5.00
8-14,18: 8-Secret Wars cameo; Mike Manley-a begins. 9-Modam (female Modok) app. 10-Dr. Minerva app. 11-Excalibur & Mordred app; first Moondragon as 'H.D Steckley'. 12-Eternals app.; death of Quasar's father (Gilbert). 13-Squadron Supreme & Overmind app. 14-McFarlane-c; Squadron Supreme, Overmind app. 18-1st app. Origin & Unbeing; new Quasar costume; 1st Greg Capullo-a	4.00
15,16: 15-Mignola-c; Squadron Supreme, Overmind, the Stranger & the Watchers app. 16-($1.50, 52 pgs.) Squadron Supreme, Overmind, Stranger & the Watchers app.	5.00
17-Features Marvel's speedsters: Quicksilver, Makkari, Captain Marvel (Monica Rambeau), Speed Demon, Black Racer, Super Sabre & the Runner; Flash parody 'Buried Alien'	5.00
19-(2/91)-Re-intro Jack of Hearts & Maelstrom (both seen since 1984); Dr. Strange app.	6.00
20,21: 20-Fantastic Four & the Presence app. 21-Maelstrom revealed as the 'Cosmic Assassin'	5.00
22,23,27,29: 22-Quasar dies; Deathurge app. 'H.D Steckley' revealed to be Moondragon. 23-Ghost Rider app. 27-Original Marvel Boy app. 29-Kismet (Her) app; Vanity Fair Demi Moore pregnancy parody-c	4.00
24-Brief Infinity Gauntlet reference; Thanos & Mephisto app.; vs. Maelstrom; 1st app. Infinity (the female aspect of Eternity)	2	4	6	9	12	15
25-($1.50)-New costume Quasar (returns to life); Eternity, Infinity, Oblivion, Death, Celestials, Galactus, Watchers app.; 'death' of Maelstrom	5.00
26-Infinity Gauntlet tie-in; Thanos & Moondragon app.	5.00
28,30-33: 28-Kismet (Her) app.; Avengers; Warlock, Moondragon, Jack of Hearts app. 30-What If..? smear app; Watcher, Thanos, Moondragon. 31-Quasar in the New Universe; gains the power of the Starbrand. 32-Operation Galactic Storm Pt. 3; continued from Avengers West Coast #80; Shi'ar Imperial Guard app.; 1st app. Korath the Pursuer. 33-Operation Galactic Storm.10; continued from Avengers West Coast #81; story continues in Wonder Man #8 (#32-34 same as Special #1-3)	5.00
34-39,41-49,51-53: 34-Opertation Galactic Storm Pt. 17; continued from Captain America #400; continued in Avengers West Coast #82. 35-Operation Galactic Storm aftermath; Quasar quits the Avengers. 38-Infinity War x-over; Quasar & the Avengers vs. Warlock, Thanos & the Infinity Watch; last Capullo-a. 39-Infinity War x-over; Thanos & Deathurge app. 41-Avengers app. 42-Punisher app. 43-Quasar returns to life. 47,48-Thunderstrike app. 49-Kismet app. 51,52: 52-Squadron Supreme app. 53-Warlock & the Infinity Watch app.	4.00
40,50: 40-Infinity War x-over; Quasar uses the Ultimate Nullifier and dies; Thanos app. 50-($2.95, 52 pgs.)-Holo-grafix foil-c/ Silver Surfer, Man-Thing, Ren & Stimpy app.	5.00
54,55: 53-Warlock & the Infinity Watch app. 54-Starblast tie-in; continued from Starblast #1; Hyperion vs. Gladiator. 55-Starblast tie-in; continued from Starblast #2; Black Bolt app; continued in Starblast #3	5.00
56-57: 56-Starblast tie-in; continued from Starblast #4; New Universe app.; continued in Starblast #4. 57-Living Tribunal & the New Universe app.	5.00
58,59: 58-w/bound-in card sheet; Makkari wins the Galactic Race; DC Comics Flash (as Fastforward) app. 59-Thanos & Starfox app.	6.00
60-Last issue; Avengers, New Warriors & Fantastic Four app; Quasar leaves Earth	1	2	3	5	6	8
Special #1-3 ($1.25, newsstand)-Same as #32-34						4.00

QUEEN & COUNTRY (See Whiteout)
Oni Press: Mar, 2001 - No. 32, Dec, 2007 ($2.95/$2.99, B&W)

1-Rucka-s in all. Rolston/Sale-c	1	2	3	4	5	7
2-5: 2-4-Rolston-a/Sale-c. 5-Snyder-c/Hurtt-a						4.00
6-24,26-32: 6,7-Snyder-c/Hurtt-a. 13-15-Alexander-a. 16-20-McNeil-a. 21-24-Hawthorne-a. 26-28-Norton-a						3.00

25-($5.99) Rolston-a	6.00
Free Comic Book Day giveaway (5/02) r/#1 with "Free Comic Book Day" banner on-c	3.00
Operation: Blackwall (10/03, $8.95, TPB) r/#13-15; John Rogers intro.	9.00
Operation: Broken Ground (2002, $11.95, TPB) r/#1-4; Ellis intro.	12.00
Operation: Crystal Ball (1/03, $14.95, TPB) r/#8-12; Judd Winick intro.	15.00
Operation: Dandelion HC (8/04, $25.00) r/#21-24; Jamie S. Rich intro.	25.00
Operation: Dandelion (8/04, $11.95, TPB) r/#21-24; Jamie S. Rich intro.	12.00
Operation: Morningstar (9/02, $8.95, TPB) r/#5-7; Stuart Moore intro.	9.00
Operation: Storm Front (3/04, $14.95, TPB) r/#16-20; Geoff Johns intro.	15.00

QUEEN & COUNTRY: DECLASSIFIED
Oni Press: Nov, 2002 - No. 3, Jan, 2003 ($2.95, B&W, limited series)

1-3-Rucka-s/Hurtt-a/Morse-c	3.00
TPB (7/03, $8.95) r/#1-3; intro. by Micah Wright	9.00

QUEEN & COUNTRY: DECLASSIFIED (Volume 2)
Oni Press: Jan, 2005 - No. 3, Feb, 2006 ($2.95/$2.99, B&W, limited series)

1-3-Rucka-s/Burchett-a/c	3.00
TPB (3/06, $8.95) r/#1-3	9.00

QUEEN & COUNTRY: DECLASSIFIED (Volume 3)
Oni Press: Jun, 2005 - No. 3, Aug, 2005 ($2.95, B&W, limited series)

1-3- "Sons & Daughters;" Johnston-s/Mitten-a/c	3.00
TPB (3/06, $8.95) r/#1-3	9.00

QUEEN OF THE WEST, DALE EVANS (TV)(See Dale Evans Comics, Roy Rogers & Western Roundup under Dell Giants)
Dell Publ. Co.: No. 479, 7/53 - No. 22, 1-3/59 (All photo-c; photo back c-4-8,15)

Four Color 479(#1, '53)	17	34	51	114	252	390
Four Color 528(#2, '54)	9	18	27	62	126	190
3,4: 3(4-6/54)-Toth-a. 4- Toth, Manning-a	7	14	21	46	86	125
5-10-Manning-a. 5-Marsh-a	6	12	18	40	73	105
11,19,21-No Manning 21-Tufts-a	5	10	15	31	53	75
12-18,20,22-Manning-a	5	10	15	34	60	85

QUEEN SONJA (See Red Sonja)
Dynamite Entertainment: 2009 - No. 35, 2013 ($2.99/$3.99)

1-10: 1-Rubi-a/Ortega-s; 3 covers; back-up r/Marvel Feature #1	4.00
11-35-($3.99) 16-Thulsa Doom returns	4.00

QUENTIN DURWARD
Dell Publishing Co.: No. 672, Jan, 1956

Four Color 672-Movie, photo-c	6	12	18	42	79	115

QUEST
Image Comics: Aug, 2023 - No. 5, Jan, 2024 ($3.99)

1-5-Jonathan Luna & Crystal Wood-s/Luna-a	4.00

QUESTAR ILLUSTRATED SCIENCE FICTION CLASSICS
Golden Press: 1977 (226 pgs.) ($1.95)

11197-Stories by Asimov, Sturgeon, Silverberg & Niven; Starstream-r						
	3	6	9	20	30	40

QUEST FOR CAMELOT
DC Comics: July, 1998 ($4.95)

1-Movie adaption	5.00

QUEST FOR DREAMS LOST (Also see Word Warriors)
Literacy Volunteers of Chicago: July 4, 1987 ($2.00, B&W, 52 pgs.)(Proceeds donated to help fight illiteracy)

1-Teenage Mutant Ninja Turtles by Eastman/Laird, Trollords, Silent Invasion, The Realm, Wordsmith, Reacto Man, Eb'nn, Aniverse	5.00

QUESTION, THE (See Americomics, Blue Beetle (1967), Charlton Bullseye & Mysterious Suspense)
QUESTION, THE (Also see Showcase '95 #3)
DC Comics: Feb, 1987 - No. 36, Mar, 1990; No. 37, Mar, 2010 ($1.50)

1-36: 1-Denny O'Neil scripts in all. 17-Rorshach app.	4.00
37-(3/10, $2.99) Blackest Night one-shot; Victor Sage rises; Shiva app.; Cowan-a	4.00
Annual 1 (1988, $2.50)	5.00
Annual 2 (1989, $3.50)	5.00
...: Epitaph For a Hero TPB (2008, $19.99) r/#13-18	20.00
...: Peacemaker TPB (2010, $19.99) r/#31-36	20.00
...: Pipeline TPB (2011, $14.99) r/stories from Detective Comics #854-865; sketch-a	15.00
...: Poisoned Ground TPB (2008, $19.99) r/#7-12	20.00
...: Riddles TPB (2009, $19.99) r/#25-30	20.00
...: Welcome to Oz TPB (2009, $19.99) r/#19-24	20.00
...: Zen and Violence TPB (2007, $19.99) r/#1-6	20.00

QUESTION, THE (Also see Crime Bible and 52)
DC Comics: Jan, 2005 - No. 6, Jun, 2005 ($2.99, limited series)

1-6-Rick Veitch-s/Tommy Lee Edwards-a. 4,6-Superman app.	3.00

QUESTION QUARTERLY, THE
DC Comics: Summer, 1990 - No. 5, Spring, 1992 ($2.50/$2.95, 52pgs.)

1-5	5.00

NOTE: Cowan a-1, 2, 4, 5; c-1-3, 5. Mignola a-5i. Quesada a-3-5.

QUESTION RETURNS, THE
DC Comics: Feb, 1997 ($3.50, one-shot)

1-Brereton-c	4.00

QUESTION, THE : THE DEATHS OF VIC SAGE
DC Comics (Black Label): Jan, 2020 - No. 4, Oct, 2020 ($6.99, over-sized 10-7/8" x 8-1/2", limited series)

1-4-Jeff Lemire-s/Denys Cowan & Bill Sienkiewicz-a; two covers on each	7.00

QUESTPROBE
Marvel Comics: 8/84 - No. 2, 1/85; No. 3, 11/85 (lim. series)

1-3: 1-The Hulk app. by Romita. 2-Spider-Man; Mooney-a(i). 3-Human Torch & Thing	4.00

QUICK DRAW McGRAW (TV) (Hanna-Barbera)(See Whitman Comic Books)
Dell Publishing Co./Gold Key No. 12 on: No. 1040, 12-2/59-60 - No. 11, 7-9/62; No. 12, 11/62; No. 13, 2/63; No. 14, 4/63; No. 15, 6/69 (1st show aired 9/29/59)

Queen Sonja #1 © DYN

Quick Stops #1 © Secret Stash Press

Rachel Rising #1 © Terry Moore

	GD	VG	FN	VF	VF/NM	NM-		GD	VG	FN	VF	VF/NM	NM-
	2.0	4.0	6.0	8.0	9.0	9.2		2.0	4.0	6.0	8.0	9.0	9.2

Four Color 1040(#1) 1st app. Quick Draw & Baba Looey, Augie Doggie & Doggie
Daddy and Snooper & Blabber
2(4-6/60)-4,6: 2-Augie Doggie & Snooper & Blabber stories (8 pgs. each); pre-dates both of
their #1 issues. 4-Augie Doggie & Snooper & Blabber stories.

		6	12	18	37	66	95

5-1st Snagglepuss app.; last 10¢ issue   8   16   24   51   102   150
7-11   5   10   15   30   50   70
12,13-Title change to …Fun-Type Roundup (84pgs.) 6   12   18   38   69   100
14,15: 15-Reprints   4   8   12   27   44   60

QUICK DRAW McGRAW (TV)(See Spotlight #2)
Charlton Comics: Nov. 1970 - No. 8, Jan, 1972 (Hanna-Barbera)
1   5   10   15   31   53   75
2-8   3   6   9   18   28   38

QUICKSILVER (See Avengers)
Marvel Comics: Nov, 1997 - No. 13, Nov, 1998 ($2.99/$1.99)
1-($2.99)-Peyer-s/Casey Jones-a; wraparound-c   5.00
2-11: 2-Two covers-variant by Golden. 4-6-Inhumans app.   4.00
12-($2.99) Siege of Wundagore pt. 4   5.00
13-Magneto-c/app.; last issue   4.00

QUICKSILVER: NO SURRENDER (Avengers)
Marvel Comics: Jul, 2018 - No. 5, Nov, 2018 ($3.99, limited series)
1-5-Saladin Ahmed-s/Eric Nguyen-a; Scarlet Witch app.   4.00

QUICK STOP (Set in the universe of Kevin Smith's Jay and Silent Bob)
Dark Horse Comics: Nov, 2022 - No. 4, Feb, 2023 ($3.99, B&W, limited series)
1-4-Kevin Smith-s. 2-Phil Hester-a   4.00

QUICK STOPS II (Set in the universe of Kevin Smith's Jay and Silent Bob)
Dark Horse Comics: Dec, 2023 - Present ($3.99, B&W, limited series)
1,2-Kevin Smith-s/Ahmed Raafat-a   4.00

QUICK-TRIGGER WESTERN (…Action #12; Cowboy Action #5-11)
Atlas Comics (ACI #12/WPI #13-19): No. 12, May, 1956 - No. 19, Sept, 1957
12-Baker-a   25   50   75   150   245   340
13-Williamson-a, 5 pgs.   20   40   60   114   182   250
14-Everett, Crandall, Torres-a; Heath-c   18   36   54   103   162   220
15,16: 15-Torres, Crandall-a. 16-Orlando, Kirby-a   15   30   45   86   133   180
17,18: 18-Baker-a   15   30   45   85   130   175
19   14   28   42   78   112   145
NOTE: *Ayers* a-17. *Colan* a-16. *Maneely* a-15, 17; c-15, 18. *Morrow* a-18. *Powell* a-14. *Severin* a-19; c-12, 13,
16, 17, 19. *Shores* a-16. *Tuska* a-17.

QUINCY (See Comics Reading Libraries in the Promotional Comics section)

QUITTER, THE
DC Comics (Vertigo): 2005 ($19.99, B&W graphic novel)
HC ($19.99) Autobiography of Harvey Pekar; Pekar-s/Daen Haspiel-a   20.00
SC (2006, $12.99)   13.00

RACCOON KIDS, THE (Formerly Movietown Animal Antics)
National Periodical Publications (Arleigh No. 63,64): No. 52, Sept-Oct, 1954 - No. 62,
Oct-Nov, 1956; No. 63, Sept, 1957; No. 64, Nov, 1957
52-Doodles Duck by Mayer   15   30   45   90   140   190
53-64: 53-62-Doodles Duck by Mayer   12   24   36   67   94   120
NOTE: *Otto Feuer*-a most issues. *Rube Grossman*-a most issues.

RACE FOR THE MOON
Harvey Publications: Mar, 1958 - No. 3, Nov, 1958
1-Powell-a(5); 1/2-pg. S&K-a; cover redrawn from Galaxy Science Fiction pulp (5/53)
   26   52   78   154   252   350
2-Kirby/Williamson-c/a(3); Kirby-p 6 more stys   32   64   96   188   307   425
3-Kirby/Williamson-c/a(4); Kirby-p 6 more stys   37   74   111   218   354   490

RACER-X
Now Comics: 8/88 - No. 11, 8/89; V2#1, 9/89 - V2#10, 1990 ($1.75)
0-Deluxe ($3.50)   5.00
1 (9/88) - 11, V2#1-10   4.00

RACER X (See Speed Racer)
DC Comics (WildStorm): Oct, 2000 - No. 3, Dec, 2000 ($2.95, limited series)
1-3: 1-Tommy Yune-s/Jo Chen/-a; 2 covers by Yune. 2,3-Kabala app.   4.00

RACHEL RISING
Abstract Studio: 2011 - No. 42, 2016 ($3.99, B&W)
1-Terry Moore-s/a/c; back cover by Fabio Moon; green background on cover   50.00
1-(2nd printing) Red background on cover   35.00
1-(3rd printing) Red background on cover   35.00

2   35.00
3-6   10.00
7-42: 42-Final issue   4.00
Halloween ComicFest Edition (2014, giveaway) Reprints #1 with orange bkgd on cover
   1   2   3   5   6   8

RACING PETTYS
STP Corp.: 1980 ($2.50, 68 pgs., 10 1/8" x 13 1/4")
1-Bob Kane-a. Kane bio on inside back-c   2   4   6   9   13   16

RACK & PAIN
Dark Horse Comics: Mar, 1994 - No. 4, June, 1994 ($2.50, limited series)
1-4: Brian Pulido scripts in all. 1-Greg Capullo-c   4.00

RACK & PAIN: KILLERS
Chaos! Comics: Sept, 1996 - No. 4, Jan, 1997 ($2.95, limited series)
1-4: Reprints Dark Horse series; Jae Lee-c   4.00

RACKET SQUAD IN ACTION
Capitol Stories/Charlton Comics: May-June, 1952 - No. 29, Mar, 1958
1   41   82   123   256   428   600
2-4,6: 3,4,6-Dr. Neff, Ghost Breaker app.   21   42   63   124   202   280
5-Dr. Neff, Ghost Breaker app; headlights-c   61   122   183   390   670   950
7-10: 10-Explosion-c   19   38   57   111   176   240
11-Ditko-c/a   41   82   123   256   428   600
12-Ditko explosion-c (classic); Shuster-a(2)   81   162   243   518   884   1250
13-Shuster-c(p)/a; "Acid in Face story" titled "Your Money or Your Face"
   17   34   51   98   154   210
14-Marijuana story "Shakedown"; Giordano-c   24   48   72   140   230   320
15-28: 15,20,22,23-Giordano-a   15   30   45   88   137   185
29-(15¢, 68 pgs.)   19   38   57   111   176   240

RADIANT BLACK
Image Comics: Feb, 2021 - Present ($3.99)
1-28: 1-5-Kyle Higgins-s/Marcelo Costa-a. 6-Lafuente-a   4.00

RADIANT LOVE (Formerly Daring Love #1)
Gilmor Magazines: No. 2, Dec, 1953 - No. 6, Aug, 1954
2   28   56   84   165   270   375
3-6   19   38   57   111   176   240

RADIANT PINK
Image Comics: Dec, 2022 - No. 5, May, 2023 ($3.99)
1-5-Meghan Camarena & Melissa Flores-s/Emma Kubert-a   4.00

RADIANT RED
Image Comics: Mar, 2022 - No. 5, Jul, 2022 ($3.99)
1-5-Cherish Chen-s/David Lafuente-a   4.00

RADICAL DREAMER
Blackball Comics: No. 0, May, 1994 - No. 4, Nov, 1994 ($1.99, bi-monthly)
(1st poster format comic)
0-4: 0-2-($1.99, poster format): 0-1st app. Max Wrighter. 3,4-($2.50-c)   4.00

RADICAL DREAMER
Mark's Giant Economy Size Comics: V2#1, June, 1995 - V2#6, Feb, 1996 ($2.95, B&W,
limited series)
V2#1-6   4.00
Prime (5/96, $2.95)   4.00
Dreams Cannot Die!-(1996, $20.00, softcover)-Collects V1#0-4 & V2#1-6; intro by Kurt Busiek;
afterward by Mark Waid   20.00
Dreams Cannot Die!-(1996, $60.00, hardcover)-Signed & limited edition; collects
V1#0-4 & V2#1-6; intro by Kurt Busiek; afterward by Mark Waid   60.00

RADICALLY REARRANGED RONIN RAGDOLLS
Kevin Eastman Studios, Inc.: 2019 ($3.99)
1-TMNT pastiche with cats; Kevin Eastman & Troy Little-a; David Avallone-s   4.00

RADIOACTIVE MAN (Simpsons TV show)
Bongo Comics: 1993 - No. 6, 1994 ($1.95/$2.25, limited series)
1-($2.95)-Glow-in-the-dark-c; bound-in jumbo poster; origin Radioactive Man;
(cover dated Nov. 1952)   4   8   12   27   44   60
2-6: 2-Says #88 on-c & inside & dated May 1962; cover parody of Atlas Kirby monster-c;
Superior Squad app.; origin Fallout Boy. 3-($1.95)-Cover "dated" Aug 1972 #216.
4-($2.25)-Cover "dated" Oct 1980 #412; w/trading card. 5-Cover "dated" Jan 1986 #679;
w/trading card. 6-(Jan 1995 #1000)   5.00
Colossal #1-($4.95)   2   4   6   8   10   12
#4 (2001, $2.50) Faux 1953 issue; Murphy Anderson-i (6 pgs.)   5.00
#100 (2000, $2.50) Comic Book Guy-c/app.; faux 1963 issue inside   5.00

	GD 2.0	VG 4.0	FN 6.0	VF 8.0	VF/NM 9.0	NM- 9.2

#136 (2001, $2.50) Dan DeCarlo-c/a ... 5.00
#222 (2001, $2.50) Batton Lash-s; Radioactive Man in 1972-style ... 5.00
#575 (2002, $2.50) Chaykin-c; Radioactive Man in 1984-style ... 5.00
1963-106 (2002, $2.50) Radioactive Man in 1960s Gold Key-style; Groening-c ... 5.00
#7 Bongo Super Heroes Starring... (2003, $2.50) Marvel Silver Age-style Superior Squad ... 5.00
#8 Official Movie Adaptation (2004, $2.99) starring Rainier Wolfcastle and Milhouse ... 5.00
#9 (#197 on-c) (2004, $2.50) Kirby-esque New Gods spoof; Golden Age Radio Man app. ... 5.00

RADIO FUNNIES
DC Comics: Mar. 1939; undated variant

nn-(3/39) Ashcan comic, not distributed to newsstands, only for in-house use. Cover art is Adventure Comics #39 with interior being Detective Comics #19 (no known sales)
nn - Ashcan comic. No date. Cover art is Detective #26 with interior from Detective #17; one copy, graded at GD/VG, sold at auction for $4481.25 in Nov, 2009. Another copy graded at GD/VG sold at auction for $3346 in Feb, 2010.

RADIO SPACEMAN
Dark Horse Comics: Mar, 2022 - No. 2, Apr, 2022 ($3.99, limited series)

1,2-Mike Mignola-s/Greg Hinkle-a ... 4.00

RAGAMUFFINS
Eclipse Comics: Jan, 1985 ($1.75, one shot)

1-Eclipse Magazine-r, w/color; Colan-a ... 4.00

RAGE (Based on the id video game)
Dark Horse Comics: Jun, 2011 - No. 3, Aug, 2011 ($3.50, limited series)

1-3-Nelson-s/Mutti-a/Fabry-c. 1-Variant-c by Martiniere ... 3.50

RAGEMOOR
Dark Horse Comics: Mar, 2012 - No. 4, Jun, 2012 ($3.50, B&W, limited series)

1-4-Richard Corben-a/c; Jan Strnad-s ... 3.50

RAGGEDY ANN AND ANDY (See Dell Giants, March of Comics #23 & New Funnies)
Dell Publishing Co.: No. 5, 1942 - No. 533, 2/54; 10-12/64 - No. 4, 3/66

	GD 2.0	VG 4.0	FN 6.0	VF 8.0	VF/NM 9.0	NM- 9.2
Four Color 5(1942)	52	104	156	416	933	1450
Four Color 23(1943)	35	70	105	252	564	875
Four Color 45(1943)	26	52	78	182	404	625
Four Color 72(1945)	21	42	63	147	324	500
1(6/46)-Billy & Bonnie Bee by Frank Thomas	30	60	90	216	483	750
2,3- 3-Egbert Elephant by Dan Noonan begins	15	30	45	100	220	340
4-Kelly-a, 16 pgs.	15	30	45	105	233	360
5,6,8-10	12	24	36	80	173	265
7-Little Black Sambo, Black Mumbo & Black Jumbo only app; Christmas-c	14	28	42	97	214	330
11-20	10	20	30	64	132	200
21-Alice In Wonderland cover/story	12	24	36	80	173	265
22-27,29-39(8/49), Four Color 262 (1/50): 34-"...In Candyland"	9	18	27	57	111	165
28-Kelly-a	9	18	27	59	117	175
Four Color 306,354,380,452,533	7	14	21	46	86	125
1(10-12/64-Dell)	4	8	12	23	37	50
2,3(10-12/65), 4(3/66)	3	6	9	15	21	26

NOTE: Kelly art "Animal Mother Goose"-#1-34, 36, 37; c-28. Peterkin Pottle by John Stanley in 32-38.

RAGGEDY ANN AND ANDY
Gold Key: Dec, 1971 - No. 6, Sept, 1973

	GD 2.0	VG 4.0	FN 6.0	VF 8.0	VF/NM 9.0	NM- 9.2
1	3	6	9	18	28	38
2-6	3	6	9	15	21	26

RAGGEDY ANN & THE CAMEL WITH THE WRINKLED KNEES (See Dell Jr. Treasury #8)

RAGMAN (See Batman Family #20, The Brave & The Bold #196 & Cancelled Comic Cavalcade)
National Per. Publ./DC Comics No. 5: Aug-Sept, 1976 - No. 5, Jun-Jul, 1977

	GD 2.0	VG 4.0	FN 6.0	VF 8.0	VF/NM 9.0	NM- 9.2
1-Origin & 1st app.	4	8	12	25	40	55
2-5: 2-Origin ends; Kubert-c. 4-Drug use story	2	4	6	8	11	14

NOTE: Kubert a-4, 5; c-1-5. Redondo studios a-1-4.

RAGMAN (2nd Series)
DC Comics: Oct, 1991 - No. 8, May, 1992 ($1.50, limited series)

1-8: 1-Giffen plots/breakdowns. 3-Origin. 8-Batman-c/story ... 4.00

RAGMAN (3rd Series)
DC Comics: Dec, 2017 - No. 6, May, 2018 ($2.99, limited series)

1-6-Ray Fawkes-s/Inaki Miranda-a/Guillem March-c; new origin. 3-6-Etrigan app. ... 3.00

RAGMAN: CRY OF THE DEAD
DC Comics: Aug, 1993 - No. 6, Jan, 1994 ($1.75, limited series)

1-6: Joe Kubert-c ... 4.00

RAGMAN: SUIT OF SOULS
DC Comics: Dec, 2010 ($3.99, one-shot)

1-Gage-s/Segovia-a/Saiz-c; origin retold ... 4.00

RAGNAROK
IDW Publishing: Jul, 2014 - No. 12, Feb, 2017 ($3.99/$4.99)

1-7-Walt Simonson-s/a; two covers on each ... 4.00
8-12-($4.99) ... 5.00

RAGNAROK: THE BREAKING OF HELHEIM
IDW Publishing: Jul, 2019 - Present ($4.99)

1-4-Walt Simonson-s/a; multiple covers on each ... 4.00

RAGS RABBIT (Formerly Babe Ruth Sports #10 or Little Max #10?; also see Harvey Hits #2, Harvey Wiseguys & Tastee Freez)
Harvey Publications: No. 11, June, 1951 - No. 18, March, 1954 (Written & drawn for little folks)

	GD 2.0	VG 4.0	FN 6.0	VF 8.0	VF/NM 9.0	NM- 9.2
11-(See Nutty Comics #5 for 1st app.)	9	18	27	50	65	80
12-18	7	14	21	35	43	50

RAI (Rai and the Future Force #9-23) (See Magnus #5-8)
Valiant: Mar, 1992 - No. 0, Oct, 1992; No. 9, May, 1993 - No. 33, Jun, 1995 ($1.95/$2.25)

	GD 2.0	VG 4.0	FN 6.0	VF 8.0	VF/NM 9.0	NM- 9.2
1-Valiant's 1st original character	3	6	9	14	19	24
2-5: 4-Low print run	2	4	6	11	16	20
0,6: 6,7-Unity x-overs. 7-Death of Rai. 9-($2.50)-Gatefold-c; story cont'd from Magnus #24;						

Magnus, Eternal Warrior & X-O app. ... 6.00
11-33: 15-Manowar Armor app. 17-19-Magnus x-over. 21-1st app. The Starwatchers (cameo); trading card. 22-Death of Rai. 26-Chaos Effect Epsilon Pt. 3 ... 4.00
#0-(11/92) Origin/1st app. new Rai (Rising Spirit) & 1st full app. & partial origin Bloodshot; also see Eternal Warrior #4; tells future of all characters

	GD 2.0	VG 4.0	FN 6.0	VF 8.0	VF/NM 9.0	NM- 9.2
	3	6	9	14	20	25

NOTE: Layton c-2i, 9i. Miller c-6. Simonson c-7.

RAI
Valiant Entertainment: May, 2014 - No. 16, Aug, 2016 ($3.99)

1-16: 1-Kindt-s/Crain-a; Rai in Japan in the year 4001. 15,16-4001 AD tie-ins ... 4.00
...: The History of the Valiant Universe 1 (6/17, $3.99) Roberts-s/Portela-a; 2 covers ... 4.00

RAI
Valiant Entertainment: Nov, 2019 - Present ($3.99)

1-10: 1-Abnett-s/Ryp-a ... 4.00

RAIDERS OF THE LOST ARK (Movie)
Marvel Comics Group: Sept, 1981 - No. 3, Nov, 1981 (Movie adaptation)

	GD 2.0	VG 4.0	FN 6.0	VF 8.0	VF/NM 9.0	NM- 9.2
1-r/Marvel Comics Super Special #18	3	6	9	16	23	30
2,3	2	4	6	8	10	12

NOTE: Buscema a(p)-1-3; c(p)-1. Simonson a-3i; scripts-1-3.

RAINBOW BRITE
Dynamite Entertainment: 2018 - No. 5, 2019 ($3.99, limited series)

1-5-Origin story; Jeremy Whitley-s/Brittney Williams-a; multiple covers on each ... 4.00

RAINBOW BRITE AND THE STAR STEALER
DC Comics: 1985

	GD 2.0	VG 4.0	FN 6.0	VF 8.0	VF/NM 9.0	NM- 9.2
nn-Movie adaptation	3	6	9	16	23	30

RAISE THE DEAD
Dynamite Entertainment: 2007 - No. 4, Aug, 2007 ($3.50)

1-4-Arthur Suydam-c/Leah Moore & John Reppion-s/Petrus-a; Phillips var-c on all ... 4.00
... Vol. 1 HC (2007, $19.99) r/#1-4; script, interview & sketch pages; cover gallery ... 20.00

RAISE THE DEAD 2
Dynamite Entertainment: 2010 - No. 4, 2011 ($3.99)

1-4-Leah Moore & John Reppion-s/Vilanova-a ... 4.00

RALPH KINER, HOME RUN KING
Fawcett Publications: 1950 (Pittsburgh Pirates)

	GD 2.0	VG 4.0	FN 6.0	VF 8.0	VF/NM 9.0	NM- 9.2
nn-Photo-c; life story	60	120	180	381	658	935

RALPH SNART ADVENTURES
Now Comics: June, 1986 - V2#9, 1987; V3#1 - #26, Feb, 1991; V4#1, 1992 - #4, 1992

1-3, V2#1-7,V3#1-23,25,26:1-($1.00, B&W)-1(B&W),V2#1(11/86), 8,9-color. V3#1(9/88)-Color begins ... 4.00
V3#24-($2.50)-3-D issue, V4#1-3-Direct sale versions w/cards ... 4.00
V4#1-3-Newsstand versions w/random cards ... 4.00

	GD 2.0	VG 4.0	FN 6.0	VF 8.0	VF/NM 9.0	NM- 9.2
Book 1	1	2	3	5	6	8
3-D Special (11/92, $3.50)-Complete 12-card set w/3-D glasses						5.00

RAMAR OF THE JUNGLE (TV)
Toby Press No. 1/Charlton No. 2 on: 1954 (no month); No. 2, Sept, 1955 - No. 5, Sept, 1956

	GD 2.0	VG 4.0	FN 6.0	VF 8.0	VF/NM 9.0	NM- 9.2
1-Jon Hall photo-c; last pre-code issue	28	56	84	168	274	380
2-5-Jon Hall photo-c	19	38	57	112	179	245

RAMAYAN 3392 A.D.
Virgin Comics: Sept, 2006 - No. 8, Aug, 2008 ($2.99)

1-8: 1-Alex Ross-c; re-imagining of the Indian myth of Ramayana; poster of cover inside ... 3.00
... Reloaded (8/07 - No. 7, 7/08, $2.99) 1-7: 1-Two covers by Kang and Oeming ... 3.00
... Reloaded Guidebook (4/08, $2.99) Profiles of characters and weapons ... 3.00

RAMM
Megaton Comics: May, 1987 - No. 2, Sept, 1987 ($1.50, B&W)

1,2-Both have 1 pg. Youngblood by Liefeld ... 4.00

RAMPAGING HULK (The Hulk #10 on; also see Marvel Treasury Edition)
Marvel Comics Group: Jan, 1977 - No. 9, June, 1978 ($1.00, B&W magazine)

	GD 2.0	VG 4.0	FN 6.0	VF 8.0	VF/NM 9.0	NM- 9.2
1-Bloodstone story w/Buscema & Nebres-a. Origin re-cap w/Simonson-a; Gargoyle, UFO story; Ken Barr-c	3	6	9	15	31	63	75
2-Old X-Men app; origin old w/Simonson-a & new X-Men in text w/Cockrum illos; Bloodstone story w/Brown & Nebres-a	3	6	9	19	30	40
3-9: 3-Iron Man app.; Norem-c. 4-Gallery of villains w/Giffen-a. 5,6-Hulk vs. Sub-Mariner. 7-Man-Thing story. 8-Original Avengers app. 9-Thor vs. Hulk battle; Shanna the She-Devil story w/DeZuniga-a	3	6	9	15	22	28

NOTE: Alcala a-1-3i, 5i, 8i. Buscema a-1. Giffen a-4. Nino a-4i. Simonson a-1-3p. Starlin a-4(w/Nino), 7; c-4, 5, 7.

RAMPAGING HULK
Marvel Comics: Aug, 1998 - No. 6, Jan, 1999 ($2.99/$1.99)

1-($2.99) Flashback stories of Savage Hulk; Leonardi-a ... 5.00
2-6-($1.99): 2-Two covers ... 4.00

RAMPAGING WOLVERINE
Marvel Comics: June, 2009 ($3.99, B&W, one-shot)

1-Short stories by Fialkov, Luque, Ted McKeever, Yost, Santolouco, Firth, Nelson ... 4.00

RANDOLPH SCOTT (Movie star)(See Crack Western #67, Prize Comics Western #76, Western Hearts #8, Western Love #1 & Western Winners #7)

RANGE BUSTERS
Fox Feature Syndicate: Sept, 1950 (10¢, one shot)

	GD 2.0	VG 4.0	FN 6.0	VF 8.0	VF/NM 9.0	NM- 9.2
1-Saga of John Wesley Hardin	24	48	72	142	234	325

RANGE BUSTERS (Formerly Cowboy Love?; Wyatt Earp, Frontier Marshall #11 on)
Charlton Comics: No. 8, May, 1955 - No. 10, Sept, 1955

	GD 2.0	VG 4.0	FN 6.0	VF 8.0	VF/NM 9.0	NM- 9.2
8	10	20	30	54	72	90
9,10	7	14	21	37	46	55

RANGELAND LOVE
Atlas Comics (CDS): Dec, 1949 - No. 2, Mar, 1950 (52 pgs.)

	GD 2.0	VG 4.0	FN 6.0	VF 8.0	VF/NM 9.0	NM- 9.2
1-Robert Taylor & Arlene Dahl photo-c	30	60	90	177	289	400

Ragman (2017 series) #1 © DC

Rainbow Brite #3 © Hallmark

Rat God #4 © Richard Corben

	GD	VG	FN	VF	VF/NM	NM-
	2.0	4.0	6.0	8.0	9.0	9.2

	GD	VG	FN	VF	VF/NM	NM-
	2.0	4.0	6.0	8.0	9.0	9.2

2-Photo-c	20	40	60	120	195	270

RANGER, THE (See Zane Grey, Four Color #255)
RANGER ACADEMY (Mighty Morphin Power Rangers)
BOOM! Studios: Oct, 2023 - No. 4, Jan, 2024 ($3.99, limited series)

1-4-Maria Mora-s/Jo Mi-Gyeong-a						4.00

RANGE RIDER, THE (TV)(See Flying A's...)
RANGE ROMANCES
Comic Magazines (Quality Comics): Dec, 1949 - No. 5, Aug, 1950 (#5: 52 pg)

1-Gustavson-c/a	34	68	102	199	325	450
2-Crandall-c/a	32	64	96	190	310	430
3-Crandall, Gustavson-a; photo-c	27	54	81	158	259	360
4-Crandall-a; photo-c	24	48	72	140	230	320
5-Gustavson-a; Crandall-a(p); photo-c	24	48	72	140	230	320

RANGERS COMICS (...of Freedom #1-7)
Fiction House Magazines: 10/41 - No. 67, 10/52; No. 68, Fall, 1952; No. 69, Winter, 1952-53
(Flying stories)

1-Intro. Ranger Girl & The Rangers of Freedom; ends #7, cover app. only #5						
	622	1244	1866	4541	8021	11,500
2-WWII-c	300	600	900	2010	3505	5000
3-Good Girl bondage/torture-c	290	580	870	1856	3178	4500
4,5	142	284	426	909	1555	2200
6-10-All Japanese war covers. 8-U.S. Rangers begin						
	106	212	318	673	1162	1650
11,12-Commando Rangers app.	97	194	291	621	1061	1500
13-Commando Ranger begins-not same as Commando Rangers; Nazi war-c						
	110	220	330	704	1202	1700
14-Classic Japanese bondage/torture WWII-c	219	438	657	1402	2401	3400
15-20: 15,17,19-Japanese war-c. 18-Nazi war-c	90	180	270	576	988	1400
21-Intro/origin Firehair (begins, 2/45)	371	742	1113	2600	4550	6500
22-25,27,29-Japanese war-c. 23-Kazanda begins, ends #28						
	68	136	204	435	743	1050
26-Classic Japanese WWII good girl-c	371	742	1113	2600	4550	6500
28,30: 28-Tiger Man begins (origin/1st app., 4/46), ends #46. 30-Crusoe Island begins,						
ends #40	55	110	165	352	601	850
31-40: 33-Hypodermic panels	42	84	126	265	445	625
41-46: 41-Last Werewolf Hunter	32	64	96	188	307	425
47-56- "Eisnerish" Dr. Drew by Grandenetti. 48-Last Glory Forbes. 53-Last 52 pg. issue.						
55-Last Sky Rangers	28	56	84	168	274	380
57-60-Straight run of Dr. Drew by Grandenetti	22	44	66	128	209	290
61-69: 64-Suicide Smith begins. 63-Used in **POP**, pgs. 85, 99. 67-Space Rangers begin,						
end #69	20	40	60	117	189	260

NOTE: Bondage, discipline covers, lingerie panels are common. Crusoe Island by **Larsen**-#30-36. Firehair by **Lubbers**-#30-49. Glory Forbes by **Baker**-#36-45, 47; by **Whitman**-#34, 35. I Confess in #41-53. Jan of the Jungle in #42-58. King of the Congo in #49-53. Tiger Man by Celardo-#30-39. **M. Anderson**-a-30? Baker a-36-38, 42, 44. John Celardo a-34, 36-39. Lee Elias a-21-28. Evans a-19, 38-46, 48-52. Hopper a-25, 26. Ingels a-13-16. Larsen a-34. Bob Lubbers a-30-38, 40-44; c-40-45. Moreira a-41-47. Tuska a-16, 17, 19, 22. M. Whitman c-11-66. Zolnerwich c-1-17.

RANGERS OF THE DIVIDE
Dark Horse Comics: May, 2021 - No. 4, Aug, 2021 ($3.99, limited series)

1-4-Megan Huang-s/a/c						4.00

RANGO (TV)
Dell Publishing Co.: Aug, 1967

1-Photo-c of comedian Tim Conway	4	8	12	28	47	65

RANN-THANAGAR HOLY WAR (Also see Hawkman Special #1)
DC Comics: July, 2008 - No. 8, Feb, 2009 ($3.50, limited series)

1-8-Adam Strange & Hawkman app.; Starlin-s/Lim-a. 1-Two covers by Starlin & Lim						3.50
Volume One TPB (2009, $19.99) r/#1-4 & Hawkman Special #1						20.00
Volume Two TPB (2009, $19.99) r/#5-8 & Adam Strange Special #1						20.00

RANN-THANAGAR WAR (See Adam Strange 2004 mini-series)(Prelude to Infinite Crisis)
DC Comics: July, 2005 - No. 6, Dec, 2005 ($2.50, limited series)

1-6-Adam Strange, Hawkman and Green Lantern (Kyle Rayner) app.; Gibbons-s/Reis-a						3.00
...: Infinite Crisis Special (4/06, $4.99) Kyle Rayner becomes Ion again; Jade dies						5.00
TPB (2005, $12.99) r/#1-6; cover gallery; new Bolland-c						13.00

RAPHAEL (See Teenage Mutant Ninja Turtles)
Mirage Studios: 1985 ($1.50, 7-1/2x11", B&W w/2 color cover, one-shot)

1-1st Turtles one-shot spin-off; contains 1st drawing of the Turtles as a group from 1983;						
1st app. Casey Jones	25	50	75	175	388	600
1-2nd printing (11/87); new-c & 8 pgs. art	5	10	15	33	57	80

RAPHAEL BAD MOON RISING (See Teenage Mutant Ninja Turtles)
Mirage Publishing: July, 2007 - No. 4, Oct, 2007 ($3.25, B&W, limited series)

1-Continued from Tales of the TMNT #7; Lawson-a	3	6	9	19	30	40
2-4	2	4	6	11	16	20

RAPTURE
Dark Horse Comics: May, 2009 - No. 6, Jan, 2010 ($2.99, limited series)

1-6-Taki Soma & Michael Avon Oeming-s/a/c. 1-Maleev var-c. 2-Mack var-c						3.00

RAPTURE
Valiant Entertainment: May, 2017 - No. 4, Aug, 2017 ($3.99)

1-4-Kindt-s/Cafu-a; Ninjak, Shadowman & Punk Mambo app. 4-Ryp-a; preview of Eternity						4.00

RASCALS IN PARADISE
Dark Horse Comics: Aug, 1994 - No. 3, Dec, 1994 ($3.95, magazine size)

1-3-Jim Silke-a/story						4.00
Trade paperback-($16.95)-r/#1-3						17.00

RASL
Cartoon Books: Mar, 2008 - No. 15, Jul, 2012 ($3.50/$4.99, B&W)

1-14-Jeff Smith-s/a/c						3.50
15-($4.99) Conclusion						5.00

RASPUTIN: VOICE OF THE DRAGON
Dark Horse Comics: Nov, 2017 - No. 5, Mar, 2018 ($3.99, limited series)

1-5-Mignola & Roberson-s/Mittens-a; Rasputin in 1941 Nazi Germany						4.00

RATCHET & CLANK (Based on the Sony videogame)
DC Comics (WildStorm thru #4): Nov, 2010 - No. 6, Apr, 2011 ($3.99/$2.99, limited series)

1-4-Fixman-c/Archer-a						4.00
5,6-($2.99)						3.00
TPB (2011, $17.99) r/#1-6						18.00

RATFINK (See Frantic and Zany)
Canrom, Inc.: Oct, 1964

1-Woodbridge-a	10	20	30	64	132	200

RAT GOD
Dark Horse Comics: Feb, 2015 - No. 5, Jun, 2015 ($3.99, limited series)

1-5-Richard Corben-s/a/c						5.00

RAT PATROL, THE (TV) (Also see Wild!)
Dell Publishing Co.: Mar, 1967 - No. 5, Nov, 1967; No. 6, Oct, 1969

1-Christopher George photo-c	7	14	21	44	82	120
2-6: 3-6-Photo-c	4	8	12	28	47	65

RAT QUEENS
Image Comics (Shadowline): Sept, 2013 - No. 16, May, 2016 ($3.50/$3.99)

1-Kurtis Wiebe-s/Roc Upchurch-a	1	3	4	6	8	10
1-Variant-c by Fiona Staples						40.00
2-10: 2-8-Two covers on each. 9,10-Sejic-a. 9-Frison-c						3.50
11-16-($3.99) Fowler-a						4.00
... Special: Braga #1 (1/15, $3.50) Wiebe-s/Tess Fowler-a; origin of Braga the Orc						3.50

RAT QUEENS (Volume 2)
Image Comics (Shadowline): Mar, 2017 - No. 25, Mar, 2021 ($3.99)

1-25: 1-15-Kurtis Wiebe-s/Owen Gieni-a/c. 16-19-Ferrier-s/Petraites-a. 22-25-Moritat-a						4.00
... Special: Neon Static 1 (7/18, $3.99) Wiebe/Kirkby-a/c; set in future city						4.00
... Special: Orc Dave 1 (9/17, $3.99) Staples-c; Dave's 1st meeting with the Queens						4.00
... Special: Swamp Romp 1 (4/19, $3.99) Ferrier-s/Petraites-a						4.00

RAVAGERS, THE (See Teen Titans and Superboy New 52 series)
DC Comics: Jul, 2012 - No. 12, Jul, 2013 ($2.99)

1-12: 1-Fairchild, Beast Boy, Terra, Thunder, Lightning, Ridge team; Churchill-a						3.00
#0 (11/12, $2.99) Churchill-a; origin of Beast Boy & Terra						3.00

RAVAGE 2099 (See Marvel Comics Presents #117)
Marvel Comics: Dec, 1992 - No. 33, Aug, 1995 ($1.25/$1.50)

1-($1.75)-Gold foil stamped-c; Stan Lee scripts						5.00
1-($1.75)-2nd printing						4.00
2-24,26-33: 5-Last Ryan-c. 6-Last Ryan-a. 14-Punisher 2099 x-over. 15-Ron Lim-c(p).						
18-Bound-in card sheet						4.00
25 ($2.25, 52 pgs.)						5.00
25 ($2.95, 52 pgs.)-Silver foil embossed-c						6.00

RAVEN (See DC Special: Raven and Teen Titans titles)

RAVEN (From Teen Titans)
DC Comics: Nov, 2016 - No. 6, Apr, 2017 ($2.99, limited series)

1-6: 1-3-Wolfman-s/Borges-a. 4-6-Neves-a						3.00

RAVEN, THE (See Movie Classics)
RAVEN CHRONICLES

	GD 2.0	VG 4.0	FN 6.0	VF 8.0	VF/NM 9.0	NM- 9.2

Caliber (New Worlds): 1995 - No. 16 ($2.95, B&W)

1-16: 10-Flip book w/Wordsmith #6. 15-Flip book w/High Caliber #4 — 4.00

RAVENCROFT (Also see Ruins of Ravencroft)(Leads into King in Black series)
Marvel Comics: Mar, 2020 - No. 5, Nov, 2020 ($3.99, limited series)

1-5-Tieri-s/Unzueta-a; Misty Knight app. — 4.00

RAVEN: DAUGHTER OF DARKNESS (From Teen Titans)
DC Comics: Mar, 2018 - No. 12, Mar, 2019 ($3.99, limited series)

1-12-Wolfman-s/Mhan-a; Baron Winters app. — 4.00

RAVENS AND RAINBOWS
Pacific Comics: Dec, 1983 (Baxter paper)(Reprints fanzine work in color)

1-Jeff Jones-c/a(r); nudity scenes — 4.00

RAWHIDE (TV)
Dell Publishing Co./Gold Key: Sept-Nov, 1959 - June-Aug, 1962; July, 1963 - No. 2, Jan, 1964

Four Color 1028 (#1)	26	52	78	182	404	625
Four Color 1097,1160,1202,1261,1269	13	26	39	91	201	310
01-684-208 (8/62, Dell)	12	24	36	79	170	260
1(10071-307) (7/63, Gold Key)	11	22	33	73	157	240
2-(12¢)	10	20	30	66	138	210

NOTE: All have Clint Eastwood photo-c. Tufts-1028.

RAWHIDE KID
Atlas/Marvel Comics (CnPC No. 1-16/AMI No. 17-30): Mar, 1955 - No. 16, Sept, 1957; No. 17, Aug, 1960 - No. 151, May, 1979

1-Rawhide Kid, his horse Apache & sidekick Randy begin; Wyatt Earp app.; #1 was not code approved; Maneely splash pg.	300	600	900	1920	3310	4700
2	74	148	222	470	810	1150
3-5	47	94	141	296	498	700
6-10: 7-Williamson-a (4 pgs.)	37	74	111	222	361	500
11-16: 16-Torres-a	32	64	96	188	307	425
17-Origin by Jack Kirby; Kirby-a begins	366	732	1098	2562	4481	6400
18-21,24-30	27	54	81	194	435	675
22-Monster-c/story by Kirby/Ayers	40	80	120	296	673	1050
23-Origin retold by Jack Kirby	57	114	171	456	1028	1600
31-35,40: 31,32-Kirby-a. 33-35-Davis-a. 34-Kirby-a. 35-Intro & death of The Raven. 40-Two-Gun Kid x-over.	15	30	45	103	227	350
36,37,39,41,42-No Kirby. 42-1st Larry Lieber issue	12	24	36	79	170	260
38-Red Raven-c/story; Kirby-c (2/64); Colan-a	18	36	54	128	284	440
43-Kirby-a (beware: pin-up often missing)	15	30	45	105	233	360
44,46: 46-Toth-a. 46-Doc Holliday-c/s	10	20	30	69	147	225
45-Origin retold, 17 pgs.	14	28	42	97	214	330
47-49,51-60	7	14	21	49	92	135
50-Kid Colt x-over; vs. Rawhide Kid	8	16	24	52	99	145
61-70: 64-Kid Colt story. 66-Two-Gun Kid story. 67-Kid Colt story. 70-Last 12¢ issue	5	10	15	35	63	90
71-78,80-83,85	4	8	12	23	44	65
79,84,86,95: 79-Williamson-a(r). 84,86: Kirby-a. 86-Origin-r; Williamson-r/Ringo Kid #13 (4 pgs.)	4	8	12	24	42	60
87-91: 90-Kid Colt app. 91-Last 15¢ issue	3	6	9	19	30	40
92,93 (52 pg.Giants). 92-Kirby-a	4	8	12	27	44	60
94,96-99	3	6	9	17	26	35
100 (6/72)-origin retold & expanded	4	8	12	23	37	50
101-120: 115-Last new story	3	6	9	15	22	28
121-151	2	4	6	11	16	20
133,134-(30¢-c variants, limited distribution)(5,7/76)	9	18	27	63	129	195
140,141-(35¢-c variants, limited distribution)(7,9/77)	19	38	57	131	291	450
Special 1(9/71, 25¢, 68 pgs.)-All Kirby/Ayers-r	6	12	18	37	66	95

NOTE: Ayers a-13, 14, 16, 29, 37-39, 61. Colan a-5, 35, 37, 38; c-145p, 148p, 149p. Davis a-125r. Everett a-54i, 65, 66, 88, 96i, 148i(r). Gulacy c-147. Heath c-4. G. Kane c-101, 144. Keller a-5, 39, 41, 144r. Kirby a-17-32, 34, 42, 43, 84, 86, 92, 100r, 112r, 116r, 117r, 137r. Spec 1; c-17-35, 37, 38, 40, 41, 43-47, 137r. Maneely c-1-3, 5, 6, 14. Morisi a-13. Morrow/Williamson r-111. Roussos c-146i, 147i, 149-151i. Severin a-16; c-8, 13. Sutton a-61, 93. Torres a-99r. Tuska a-3. Wildey r-146-151(Outlaw Kid). Williamson r-79, 86, 95.

RAWHIDE KID
Marvel Comics Group: Aug, 1985 - No. 4, Nov, 1985 (Mini-series)

1-4 — 5.00

RAWHIDE KID
Marvel Comics (MAX): Apr, 2003 - No. 5, June, 2003 ($2.99, limited series)

1-John Severin-a/Ron Zimmerman-s; Dave Johnson-c — 3.00
2-5: 3-Dodson-a. 4-Darwyn Cooke-c. 5-J. Scott Campbell-c — 3.00
Vol. 1: Slap Leather TPB (2003, $12.99) r/#1-5 — 13.00

RAWHIDE KID (The Sensational Seven)
Marvel Comics: Aug, 2010 - No. 4, Nov, 2010 ($3.99, limited series)

1-4-Chaykin-a/Zimmerman-s. 1-Cassaday-c. 2-Dave Johnson-c. 4-Suydam-c — 4.00

RAY, THE (See Freedom Fighters & Smash Comics #14)
DC Comics: Feb, 1992 - No. 6, July, 1992 ($1.00, mini-series)

1-Sienkiewicz-c; Joe Quesada-a(p) in 1-5 — 5.00
2-6: 3-6-Quesada-c(p). 6-Quesada layouts only — 4.00
...In a Blaze of Power (1994, $12.95)-r/#1-6 w/new Quesada-c — 13.00

RAY, THE
DC Comics: May, 1994 - No. 28, Oct, 1996 ($1.75/$1.95/$2.25)

1-Quesada-c(p); Superboy app. — 4.00
1-($2.95)-Collectors Edition w/diff. Quesada-c; embossed foil-c — 5.00
2-24,26-28: 2-Quesada-c(p); Superboy app. 5-(9/94); leads into issue #0 — 4.00
25-($3.50)-Future Flash (Bart Allen)-c/app; double size — 5.00
#0-(10/94) Zero Hour; published between #5 & #6 — 4.00
Annual 1 ($3.95, 68 pgs.)-Superman app. — 5.00

RAY, THE
DC Comics: Feb, 2012 - No. 4, May, 2012 ($2.99, limited series)

1-4: 1-Igle-a/Palmiotti & Gray-s; origin of the new Ray; intro. Lucien Gates — 3.00

RAY BRADBURY COMICS
Topps Comics: Feb, 1993 - V4#1, June, 1994 ($2.95)

1-5-Polybagged w/3 trading cards each. 1-All dinosaur issue; Corben-a; Williamson/Torres/

Krenkel-r/Weird Science-Fantasy #25. 3-All dinosaur issue; Steacy painted-c; Stout-a						4.00
Special Edition 1 (1994, $2.95)-The Illustrated Man						4.00

...Special: Tales of Horror #1 ($2.50), ... Trilogy of Terror V3#1 (5/94, $2.50), ...Martian Chronicles V4#1 (6/94, $2.50)-Steranko-c — 4.00

NOTE: Kelley Jones a-Trilogy of Terror V3#1. Kaluta a-Martian Chronicles V4#1. Kurtzman/Matt Wagner c-2. McKean c-4. Mignola a-4. Wood c-Trilogy of Terror V3#1r.

RAZORLINE
Marvel Comics: Sept, 1993 (75¢, one-shot)

1-Clive Barker super-heroes: Ectokid, Hokum & Hex, Hyperkind & Saint Sinner — 4.00

RAZOR'S EDGE, THE
DC Comics (WildStorm): Dec, 2004 - No. 5, Apr, 2005 ($2.95)

1-5-Warblade; Bisley-c/a; Ridley-s — 3.00

REAL ADVENTURE COMICS (Action Adventure #2 on)
Gillmor Magazines: Apr, 1955

1	15	30	45	84	127	170

REAL ADVENTURES OF JONNY QUEST, THE
Dark Horse Comics: Sept, 1996 - No. 12, Sept, 1997 ($2.95)

1-12 — 3.00

REAL CLUE CRIME STORIES (Formerly Clue Comics)
Hillman Periodicals: V2#4, June, 1947 - V8#3, May, 1953

V2#4(#1)-S&K c/a(3); Dan Barry-a	57	114	171	362	619	875
5-7-S&K-c/a(3-4). 7-Iron Lady app.	43	86	129	271	461	650
8-12	16	32	48	94	147	200
V3#1-8,10-12, V4#1-3,5-8,11,12	15	30	45	84	127	170
V3#9-Used in SOTI, pg. 102	18	36	54	103	162	220
V4#4-S&K-a	18	36	54	107	169	230
V4#9,10-Krigstein-a	15	30	45	85	130	175
V5#1-5,7,8,10,12	13	26	39	72	101	130
6,9,11(1/54)-Krigstein-a	14	28	42	76	108	140
V6#1-5,8,9,11	11	22	33	62	86	110
6,7,10,12-Krigstein-a. 10-Bondage-c	14	28	42	76	108	140
V7#1-3,5-11, V8#1-3: V7#6-1 pg. Frazetta ad "Prayer" - 1st app.?	13	26	39	72	101	130
4,12-Krigstein-a	14	28	42	80	115	150

NOTE: Barry a-9, 10; c-V2#8. Briefer a-V6#6. Fuje a- V2#7(2), 8, 11. Infantino a-V2#8; c-V2#11. Lawrence a-V3#8, V5#7. Powell a-V4#11, 12. V5#4, 5, 7 are 68 pgs.

REAL EXPERIENCES (Formerly Tiny Tessie)
Atlas Comics (20CC): No. 25, Jan, 1950

25-Virginia Mayo photo-c from movie "Red Light"	19	38	57	111	176	240

REAL FACT COMICS
National Periodical Publications: Mar-Apr, 1946 - No. 21, July-Aug, 1949

1-S&K-c/a; Harry Houdini story; Just Imagine begins (not by Finlay); Fred Ray-a	53	106	159	334	567	800
2-S&K-a; Rin-Tin-Tin & P. T. Barnum stories	18	36	54	103	162	220
3-H.G. Wells, Lon Chaney stories; early DC letter column (New Fun Comics #3 from 1935 may be the 1st)	27	54	81	162	266	370
4-Virgil Finlay-a on 'Just Imagine' begins, ends #12 (2 pgs. each); Jimmy Stewart & Jack London stories; Joe DiMaggio 1 pg. biography	31	62	93	182	296	410
5-Batman/Robin-c taken from cover of Batman #9; 5 pg. story about creation of Batman & Robin; Tom Mix story	158	316	474	1011	1731	2450
6-Origin & 1st app. Tommy Tomorrow by Weisinger and Sherman (1-2/47); Flag-c; 1st writing by Harlan Ellison (letter column, non-professional); "First Man to Reach Mars" epic-c/story	90	180	270	576	988	1400
7-(No. 6 on inside)-Roussos-a; D. Fairbanks sty.	18	36	54	103	162	220
8-2nd app. Tommy Tomorrow by Finlay (5-6/47)	50	100	150	315	533	750
9-S&K-a; Glenn Miller, Indianapolis 500 stories	22	44	66	128	209	290
10-Vigilante by Meskin (based on movie serial); 4 pg. Finlay s/f story	22	44	66	128	209	290
11,12: 11-Annie Oakley, G-Men stories; Kinstler-a	15	30	45	85	130	175
13-Dale Evans and Tommy Tomorrow-c/stories	39	78	117	231	378	525
14,17,18: 14-Will Rogers story	14	28	42	82	121	160
15-Nuclear explosion part-c ("Last War on Earth" story); Clyde Beatty story	18	36	54	107	169	230
16-Tommy Tomorrow app.; 1st Planeteers?	37	74	111	222	361	500
19-Sir Arthur Conan Doyle story	15	30	45	88	137	185
20-Kubert-a, 4 pgs; Daniel Boone story	16	32	48	92	144	195
21-Kubert-a, 2 pgs; Kit Carson story	14	28	42	82	121	160

Ashcan (2/46) nn-Not distributed to newsstands, only for in house use. Covers were produced, but not the rest of the issue. A copy sold in 2008 for $500.

NOTE: Barry c-16. Virgil Finlay c-6, 8. Meskin c-10. Roussos a-1-4, 6.

REAL FUNNIES
Nedor Publishing Co.: Jan, 1943 - No. 3, June, 1943

1-Funny animal, humor; Black Terrier app. (clone of The Black Terror)	39	78	117	240	395	550
2,3	20	40	60	117	189	260

REAL GHOSTBUSTERS, THE (Also see Slimer)
Now Comics: Aug, 1988 - No. 28, Feb, 1991 ($1.75/$1.95)

1-Based on Ghostbusters movie	4	8	12	25	40	55
2	2	4	6	9	12	15
3-28						5.00

REAL HEROES
Image Comics: Mar, 2014 - No. 4, Nov, 2014 ($3.99)

1-3-Bryan Hitch-s/a — 4.00
4-($4.99) — 5.00

REAL HEROES COMICS
Parents' Magazine Institute: Sept, 1941 - No. 16, Oct, 1946

1-Roosevelt-c/story	36	72	108	211	343	475
2-J. Edgar Hoover-c/story	15	30	45	83	124	185
3-5,7-10: 4-Churchill, Roosevelt stories	14	28	42	78	112	145
6-Lou Gehrig-c/story	20	40	60	115	190	260

The Ray (2012 series) #4 © DC

Real Fact Comics #13 © DC

Realm of Kings: Inhumans #3 © MAR

	GD	VG	FN	VF	VF/NM	NM-
	2.0	4.0	6.0	8.0	9.0	9.2

11-16: 13-Kiefer-a — 10 · 20 · 30 · 54 · 72 · 90

REALISTIC ROMANCES
Realistic Comics/Avon Periodicals: July-Aug, 1951 - No. 17, Aug-Sept, 1954 (No #9-14)

	GD	VG	FN	VF	VF/NM	NM-
1-Kinstler-a; c-/Avon paperback #211	50	100	150	315	533	750
2	27	54	81	162	266	370
3,4	25	50	75	150	245	340
5,8-Kinstler-a	25	50	75	150	245	340
6-c-/Diversey Prize Novels #6; Kinstler-a	26	52	78	154	252	350
7-Evans-a?; c-/Avon paperback #360	28	56	84	168	274	380
15,17: 17-Kinstler-c	24	48	72	140	230	320
16-Kinstler marijuana story-r/Romantic Love #6	26	52	78	154	252	350
I.W. Reprint #1,8,9: #1-r/Realistic Romances #4; Astarita-a. 9-r/Women To Love #1	3	6	9	19	30	40

NOTE: *Astarita* a-2-4, 7, 8, 17. Photo c-1, 2. Painted c-3, 4.

REALITY CHECK
Image Comics: Sept, 2013 - No. 4, Dec, 2013 ($2.99)

	NM-
1-4-Brunswick-s/Bogdanovic-a	3.00

REAL LIFE COMICS
Nedor/Better/Standard Publ./Pictorial Magazine No. 13: Sept, 1941 - No. 59, Sept, 1952

	GD	VG	FN	VF	VF/NM	NM-
1-Uncle Sam-c/story; Daniel Boone story	90	180	270	576	988	1400
2-Woodrow Wilson-c/story	43	86	129	271	461	650
3-Classic Schomburg Hitler-c with "Emperor of Hate" emblazoned in blood behind him. Cover shows world at war, concentration camps and Nazis killing civilians; Hitler 10 pg. bio	1700	3400	5100	12,900	23,450	34,000
4,5: 4-Story of American flag "Old Glory"	39	78	117	231	378	525
6-10: 6-Wild Bill Hickok story	33	66	99	194	317	440
11-14,16-20: 17-Albert Einstein story	27	54	81	158	259	360
15-Japanese WWII-c by Schomburg	37	74	111	222	361	500
21-23,25,26,29,30: 29-A-Bomb story. 28-Japanese WWII-c	22	44	66	132	216	300
24-Story of Baseball (Babe Ruth); Japanese WWII-c	34	68	102	199	325	450
27,28: 27-Schomburg A-Bomb-c; story of A-Bomb	32	64	96	188	307	425
31-33,35,36,42-44,48,49: 32-Frank Sinatra story. 49-Baseball issue	19	38	57	111	176	240
34,37-41,45-47: 34-Jimmy Stewart story. 37-Story of motion pictures; Bing Crosby story. 38-Jane Froman story. 39- "1,000,000 A.D." story. 40-Bob Feller. 41-Jimmie Foxx story ("Jimmy" on-c); "Home Run" Baker story. 45-Story of Olympic games; Burl Ives & Kit Carson story. 46-Douglas Fairbanks Jr. & Sr. story. 47-George Gershwin story	20	40	60	117	189	260
50-Frazetta-a (5 pgs.)	34	68	102	204	332	460
51-Jules Verne "Journey to the Moon" by Evans; Severin/Elder-a	25	50	75	150	245	340
52-Frazetta-a (4 pgs.); Severin/Elder-a(2); Evans-a	37	74	111	222	361	500
53-57-Severin/Elder-a. 54-Bat Masterson-c/story	20	40	60	117	189	260
58-Severin/Elder-a(2)	20	40	60	120	195	270
59-1 pg. Frazetta; Severin/Elder-a	20	40	60	120	195	270

NOTE: *Guardineer* a-40(2), 44. *Meskin* a-52. *Roussos* a-50. *Schomburg* c-1-5, 7, 11, 13-21, 23, 24, 26-28, 30-32-40, 42, 44-50, 54, 55. *Tuska* a-53. Photo-c 5, 6.

REAL LIFE SECRETS (Real Secrets #2 on)
Ace Periodicals: Sept, 1949 (one-shot)

	GD	VG	FN	VF	VF/NM	NM-
1-Painted-c	24	48	72	140	230	320

REAL LIFE STORY OF FESS PARKER (Magazine)
Dell Publishing Co.: 1955

	GD	VG	FN	VF	VF/NM	NM-
1	9	18	27	59	117	175

REAL LIFE TALES OF SUSPENSE (See Suspense)

REAL LOVE (Formerly Hap Hazard)
Ace Periodicals (A. A. Wyn): No. 25, April, 1949 - No. 76, Nov, 1956

	GD	VG	FN	VF	VF/NM	NM-
25	26	52	78	154	232	350
26	18	36	54	107	169	230
27-L. B. Cole-a	17	34	51	98	154	210
28-35	15	30	45	90	140	190
36-66: 66-Last pre-code (2/55)	15	30	45	86	133	180
67-76	14	28	42	82	121	160

NOTE: Photo c-50-76. Painted c-46.

REALM, THE
Arrow Comics/WeeBee Comics #13/Caliber Press #14 on: Feb, 1986 - No. 21, 1991 (B&W)

	NM-
1-3	4.00
4-1st app. Deadworld (9/86)	5.00
5-21	3.00
Book 1 ($4.95, B&W)	5.00

REALM, THE
Image Comics: Sept, 2017 - Present ($3.99)

	NM-
1-15-Seth Peck & Jeremy Haun-s/a. 1-Covers by Haun & Tony Moore	4.00

REAL McCOYS, THE (TV)
Dell Publ. Co.: No. 1071, 1-3/60 - 5-7/1962 (All have Walter Brennan photo-c)

	GD	VG	FN	VF	VF/NM	NM-
Four Color 1071,1134-Toth-a in both	10	20	30	64	132	200
Four Color 1193,1265	7	14	21	48	89	130
01-689-207 (5-7/62)	6	12	18	42	79	115

REALM OF KINGS (Also see Guardians of the Galaxy and Nova)
Marvel Comics: Jan, 2010, one-shot)

	GD	VG	FN	VF	VF/NM	NM-
1-Abnett & Lanning-s/Manco & Asrar-a; Guardians of the Galaxy app.	1	3	4	6	8	10

REALM OF KINGS: IMPERIAL GUARD
Marvel Comics: Jan, 2010 - No. 5, May, 2010 ($3.99, limited series)

	NM-
1-5-Abnett & Lanning-s/Walker-a; Starjammers app.	4.00

REALM OF KINGS: INHUMANS
Marvel Comics: Jan, 2010 - No. 5, May, 2010 ($3.99, limited series)

	NM-
1-5-Abnett & Lanning-s/Raimondi-a; Mighty Avengers app.	4.00

REALM OF KINGS: SON OF HULK
Marvel Comics: Apr, 2010 - No. 4, July, 2010 ($3.99, limited series)

	GD	VG	FN	VF	VF/NM	NM-
1-4-Reed-s/Munera-a; leads into Incredible Hulk #609	1	3	4	6	8	10

REALM OF THE CLAW (Also see Mutant Earth as part of a flipbook)
Image Comics: Oct, 2003 - No. 2 ($2.95)

	NM-
0-(7/03, $5.95) Convention Special; cover has gold-foil title logo	6.00
1,2-Two covers by Yardin	3.00
Vol. 1 TPB (2006, $16.99) r/series; concept art & sketch pages	17.00

REALM OF X (X-Men)
Marvel Comics: Oct, 2023 - No. 4, Jan, 2024 ($4.99/$3.99, limited series)

	NM-
1-($4.99) Gronbekk-s/Neves-a; Majik app.	5.00
2-4-($3.99)	4.00

REAL SCREEN COMICS (#1 titled Real Screen Funnies; TV Screen Cartoons #129-138)
National Periodical Publications: Spring, 1945 - No. 128, May-June, 1959 (#1-40: 52 pgs.)

	GD	VG	FN	VF	VF/NM	NM-
1-The Fox & the Crow, Flippity & Flop, Tito & His Burrito begin	129	258	387	826	1413	2000
2	50	100	150	315	533	750
3-5	32	64	96	188	307	425
6-10 (2-3/47)	21	42	63	122	199	275
11-20 (10-11/48): 13-The Crow x-over in Flippity & Flop	16	32	48	94	147	200
21-30 (6-7/50)	14	28	42	76	108	140
31-50	11	22	33	60	83	105
51-99	10	20	30	54	72	90
100	10	20	30	56	76	95
101-128	8	16	24	44	57	70

REAL SCREEN FUNNIES
DC Comics: Spring 1945

1-Ashcan comic, not distributed to newsstands, only for in-house use. Cover art is Real Screen Funnies #1 with interior being Detective Comics #92. Only ashcan cover to be produced using the regular production first issue art and only using the color yellow. A copy sold in 2008 for $3,000. A FN/VF copy sold for $1314.50 in 2012. A CGC 6.5 copy sold for $1050 in 2018.

REAL SECRETS (Formerly Real Life Secrets)
Ace Periodicals: No. 2, Nov, 1950 - No. 5, May, 1950

	GD	VG	FN	VF	VF/NM	NM-
2-Painted-c	19	38	57	111	176	240
3-5: 3-Photo-c	15	30	45	83	124	165

REAL SPORTS COMICS (All Sports Comics #2 on)
Hillman Periodicals: Oct-Nov, 1948 (52 pgs.)

	GD	VG	FN	VF	VF/NM	NM-
1-Powell-a (12 pgs.)	47	94	141	296	498	700

REAL WAR STORIES
Eclipse Comics: July, 1987; No. 2, Jan, 1991 ($2.00, 52 pgs.)

	NM-
1-Bolland-a(p), Bissette-a, Totleben-a(i); Alan Moore scripts (2nd printing exists, 2/88)	5.00
2-($4.95)	5.00

REAL WESTERN HERO (Formerly Wow #1-69; Western Hero #76 on)
Fawcett Publications: No. 70, Sept, 1948 - No. 75, Feb, 1949 (All 52 pgs.)

70(#1)-Tom Mix, Monte Hale, Hopalong Cassidy, Young Falcon begin

	GD 2.0	VG 4.0	FN 6.0	VF 8.0	VF/NM 9.0	NM- 9.2

	GD 2.0	VG 4.0	FN 6.0	VF 8.0	VF/NM 9.0	NM- 9.2
	24	48	72	142	234	325
71-75: 71-Gabby Hayes begins. 71,72-Captain Tootsie by Beck. 75-Big Bow and Little Arrow app.	15	30	45	90	140	190

NOTE: Painted/photo c-70-73; painted c-74, 75.

REAL WEST ROMANCES
Crestwood Publishing Co./Prize Publ.: 4-5/49 - V1#6, 3/50; V2#1, Apr-May, 1950 (All 52 pgs. & photo-c)

	GD 2.0	VG 4.0	FN 6.0	VF 8.0	VF/NM 9.0	NM- 9.2
V1#1-S&K-a(p)	34	68	102	199	325	450
2-Gail Davis and Rocky Shahan photo-c	18	36	54	103	162	220
3-Kirby-a(p) only	18	36	54	107	169	230
4-S&K-a; Whip Wilson, Reno Browne photo-c	22	44	66	132	216	300
5-Audie Murphy, Gale Storm photo-c; S&K-a	20	40	60	120	195	270
6-Produced by S&K, no S&K-a; Robert Preston & Cathy Downs photo-c	15	30	45	83	124	165
V2#1-Kirby-a(p)	15	30	45	83	124	165

NOTE: Meskin a-V1#5, 6. Severin/Elder a-V1#3-6, V2#1. Meskin a-V1#6. Leonard Starr a-1-3. Photo-c V1#1-6, V2#1.

REALWORLDS :...
DC Comics: 2000 ($5.95, one-shots, prestige format)

Batman - Marshall Rogers-a/Golden & Sniegoski-s; Justice League of America -Dematteis-s/Barr-painted art; Superman - Vance-s/García-López & Rubenstein-a; Wonder Woman - Hanson & Neuwirth-s/Sam-a ... 6.00

REANIMATOR (Based on the 1985 horror movie)
Dynamite Entertainment: 2015 - No. 4, 2015 ($3.99, mini-series)

1-4-Further exploits of Herbert West; Davidsen-s/Valiente-a; four covers on each ... 4.00

RE-ANIMATOR IN FULL COLOR
Adventure Comics: Oct, 1991 - No. 3, 1992 ($2.95, mini-series)

1-3: Adapts horror movie. 1-Dorman painted-c ... 4.00

REAP THE WILD WIND (See Cinema Comics Herald)

REAVER
Image Comics (Skybound): Jul, 2019 - No. 11, Sept, 2020 ($3.99)

1-11: 1-Justin Jordan-s/Rebekah Isaacs-a. 7-11-Henrichon-a ... 4.00

REBEL, THE (TV)(Nick Adams as Johnny Yuma)
Dell Publishing Co.: No. 1076, Feb-Apr, 1960 - No. 1262, Dec-Feb, 1961-62

	GD 2.0	VG 4.0	FN 6.0	VF 8.0	VF/NM 9.0	NM- 9.2
Four Color 1076 (#1)-Sekowsky-a	10	20	30	68	144	220
Four Color 1138 (9-11/60), 1207 (9-11/61), 1262-Photo-c	8	16	24	55	105	155

REBEL MOON: HOUSE OF THE BLOODAXE (From the 2023 Netflix movie Rebel Moon)
Titan Comics: Feb, 2024 - Present ($3.99)

1-Visaggio-s/Bint-a ... 4.00

REBELS (Also see Rebels: These Free And Independent States)
Dark Horse Comics: Apr, 2015 - No. 10, Jan, 2016 ($3.99)

1-Set in Revolutionary War 1775 Vermont; Brian Wood-s/Andrea Mutti-a/Tula Lotay-c ... 5.00
2-10: 4-General Washington app. ... 4.00

R.E.B.E.L.S.
DC Comics: Apr, 2009 - No. 28, Jul, 2011 ($2.99)

1-9,12-28: 1-Bedard-s/Clarke-a; Vril Dox returns; Supergirl app.; 2 covers. 15-Starfire app. 19-28-Lobo app. ... 3.00
10,11-($3.99) Blackest Night x-over; Vril Dox joins the Sinestro Corps ... 4.00
Annual 1 (12/09, $4.99) Origin of Starro the Conqueror; Despero app. ... 5.00
...: Sons of Brainiac TPB (2011, $14.99) r/#15-20 ... 15.00
...: Strange Companions TPB (2010, $14.99) r/#7-9 & Annual #1 ... 15.00
...: The Coming of Starro TPB (2010, $17.99) r/#1-6 ... 18.00
...: The Son and the Stars TPB (2010, $17.99) r/#10-14 ... 18.00

R.E.B.E.L.S. '94 (Becomes R.E.B.E.L.S. '95 & R.E.B.E.L.S. '96)
DC Comics: No. 0, Oct, 1994 - No. 17, Mar, 1996 ($1.95/$2.25)

0-17: 8-$2.25-c begins. 15-R.E.B.E.L.S. '96 begins. ... 4.00

REBELS: THESE FREE AND INDEPENDENT STATES
Dark Horse Comics: Mar, 2017 - No. 8, Oct, 2017 ($3.99)

1-8: 1-Birth of the U.S. Navy in 1794; Brian Wood-s/Andrea Mutti-a ... 4.00

REBORN
Image Comics: Oct, 2016 - No. 6, Jun, 2017 ($3.99)

1-Mark Millar-s/Greg Capullo-a ... 5.00
2-5 ... 4.00
6-($5.99) Bonus sketch pages and creator interview ... 6.00

RECKLESS (Also see Destroy All Monsters, Follow Me Down, Friend of the Devil & The Ghost in You)
Image Comics: Dec, 2020 ($24.99, HC graphic novel)

HC - Ed Brubaker-s/Sean Phillips-a; 1st book in the Reckless series ... 25.00

RECKONING WAR: TRIAL OF THE WATCHER
Marvel Comics: May, 2022 ($4.99, one-shot)

1-What if the Watcher never interfered in Fantastic Four #48-50; Slott-s/Rodríguez-a ... 5.00

RECORD BOOK OF FAMOUS POLICE CASES
St. John Publishing Co.: 1949 (25¢, 132 pgs.)

	GD 2.0	VG 4.0	FN 6.0	VF 8.0	VF/NM 9.0	NM- 9.2
nn-Kubert-a(3); r/Son of Sinbad; Baker-c	129	258	387	826	1413	2000

RED (Inspired the 2010 Bruce Willis movie)
DC Comics (Homage): Sept, 2003 - No. 3, Feb, 2004 ($2.95, limited series)

1-3-Warren Ellis-s/Cully Hamner-a/c ... 5.00
Red/Tokyo Storm Warning TPB (2004, $14.95) Flip book r/both series ... 15.00
Red: Eyes Only (2/11, $4.99) comic prequel; Hamner-s/a/c ... 5.00
Red: Frank (11/10, $3.99) movie prequel; Noveck-s/Masters-a/Hamner & photo-c ... 4.00
Red: Joe (11/10, $3.99) movie prequel; Wagner-s/Redondo-a/Hamner & photo-c ... 4.00
Red: Marvin (11/10, $3.99) movie prequel; Hoeber-s/Olmos-a/Hamner & photo-c ... 4.00
Red: Victoria (11/10, $3.99) movie prequel; Hoeber-s/Hahn-a/Hamner & photo-c ... 4.00
...: Better R.E.D. Than Dead TPB (2011, $14.99) r/movie prequel issues; sketch-a ... 15.00

RED ARROW

P. L. Publishing Co.: May-June, 1951 - No. 3, Oct, 1951

	GD 2.0	VG 4.0	FN 6.0	VF 8.0	VF/NM 9.0	NM- 9.2
1-Bondage-c	20	40	60	118	192	265
2,3	14	28	42	81	118	155

RED ATLANTIS
AfterShock Comics: Nov, 2020 - No. 5, Mar, 2021 ($4.99, limited series)

1-5-Stephanie Phillips-s/Robert Carey-a ... 5.00

RED BAND COMICS
Enwil Associates: Nov, 1944, No. 2, Jan, 1945 - No. 4, May, 1945

	GD 2.0	VG 4.0	FN 6.0	VF 8.0	VF/NM 9.0	NM- 9.2
1-Bogeyman-c/intro. (The Spirit swipe)	60	120	180	381	653	925
2-Origin Bogeyman & Santanas; c-reprint/#1	39	78	117	240	395	550
3,4-Captain Wizard app. in both (1st app.); each has identical contents/cover	39	78	117	231	378	525

REDBLADE
Dark Horse Comics: Apr, 1993 - No. 3, July, 1993 ($2.50, mini-series)

1-3: 1-Double gatefold-c ... 4.00

RED BORDER
AWA Studios: Mar, 2020 - No. 4, Aug, 2020 ($3.99, limited series)

1-4-Jason Starr-s/Will Conrad-a ... 4.00

RED CIRCLE, THE (Re-introduction of characters from MLJ/Archie publications)
DC Comics: Oct, 2009 ($2.99, series of one-shots)

...Inferno 1 - Hangman app.; Straczynski-s/Greg Scott-a ... 5.00
...The Hangman 1 - (origin retold); Straczynski-s/Derenick & Sienkiewicz-a ... 5.00
...The Shield 1 - Origin retold; Straczynski-s/McDaniel-a ... 5.00
...The Web 1 - Straczynski-s/Robinson-a ... 5.00

RED CIRCLE COMICS (Also see Blazing Comics & Blue Circle Comics)
Rural Home Publications (Enwil): Jan, 1945 - No. 4, April, 1945

	GD 2.0	VG 4.0	FN 6.0	VF 8.0	VF/NM 9.0	NM- 9.2
1-The Prankster & Red Riot begin	93	186	279	591	1021	1450
2-Starr-a; The Judge (costumed hero) app.	41	82	123	256	428	600
3,4-Starr-c/a. 3-The Prankster not in costume	36	72	108	214	347	480
4-(Dated 4/45)-Leftover covers to #4 were later restapled over early 1950s coverless comics; variations in the coverless comics used are endless; Woman Outlaws, Dorothy Lamour, Crime Does Not Pay, Sabu, Diary Loves, Love Confessions & Young Love V3#3 known	26	52	78	154	252	350

RED CIRCLE SORCERY (Chilling Adventures in Sorcery #1-5)
Red Circle Prod. (Archie): No. 6, Apr, 1974 - No. 11, Feb, 1975 (All 25¢ iss.)

	GD 2.0	VG 4.0	FN 6.0	VF 8.0	VF/NM 9.0	NM- 9.2
6,8,9,11: 6-Early Chaykin-a. 7-Pino-a. 8-Only app. The Cobra	2	4	6	9	13	16
7-Bruce Jones-a with Wrightson, Kaluta, Jeff Jones	3	6	9	14	19	24
10-Wood-a(i)	2	4	6	10	14	18

NOTE: Chaykin a-6, 10. McWilliams a-10(2 & 3 pgs.). Mooney a-11p. Morrow a-6-8, 9(text illos), 10, 11i; c-6-11. Thorne a-8, 10. Toth a-8, 9.

RED DOG (See Night Music #7)

RED DRAGON
Comico: June, 1996 ($2.95)

1-Bisley-c ... 4.00

RED DRAGON COMICS (1st Series) (Formerly Trail Blazers; see Super Magician V5#7, 8)
Street & Smith Publications: No. 5, Jan, 1943 - No. 9, Jan, 1944

	GD 2.0	VG 4.0	FN 6.0	VF 8.0	VF/NM 9.0	NM- 9.2
5-Origin Red Rover, the Crimson Crimebuster; Rex King, Man of Adventure, Captain Jack Commando, & The Minute Man begin; text origin Red Dragon; Binder-c	129	258	387	826	1413	2000
6-Origin The Black Crusader & Red Dragon (3/43); 1st story app. Red Dragon & 1st cover (classic-c)	265	530	795	1694	2897	4100
7-Classic Japanese exploding soldier WWII-c	454	908	1362	3314	5857	8400
8-The Red Knight app.	87	174	261	553	952	1350
9-Origin Chuck Magnon, Immortal Man	90	180	270	576	988	1400

RED DRAGON COMICS (2nd Series) (See Super Magician V2#8)
Street & Smith Publications: Nov, 1947 - No. 6, Jan, 1949; No. 7, July, 1949

	GD 2.0	VG 4.0	FN 6.0	VF 8.0	VF/NM 9.0	NM- 9.2
1-Red Dragon begins; Elliman, Nigel app.; Edd Cartier-c/a	142	284	426	909	1555	2200
2-Cartier-c	71	142	213	454	777	1100
3-1st app. Dr. Neff Ghost Breaker by Powell; Elliman, Nigel app.	63	126	189	403	689	975
4-Cartier c/a	77	154	231	493	847	1200
5-7	41	82	123	256	428	650

NOTE: Maneely a-5, 7. Powell a-2-7; c-3, 5, 7.

RED EAGLE
David McKay Publications: No. 16, Aug, 1938

	GD 2.0	VG 4.0	FN 6.0	VF 8.0	VF/NM 9.0	NM- 9.2
Feature Books 16	40	80	120	246	411	575

REDEMPTION
AWA Studios: Feb, 2021 - No. 5, Jun, 2021 ($3.99, limited series)

1-5-Christa Faust-s/Mike Deodato Jr.-a; 1-Bonus afterwords from the creators ... 4.00

REDEYE (See Comics Reading Libraries in the Promotional Comics section)

RED FOX (Formerly Manhunt! #1-14; also see Extra Comics)
Magazine Enterprises: No. 15, 1954

	GD 2.0	VG 4.0	FN 6.0	VF 8.0	VF/NM 9.0	NM- 9.2
15-(A-1 #108)-Undercover girl story; L.B. Cole-c/a (Red Fox); r-from Manhunt; Powell-a	23	46	69	136	223	310

RED GOBLIN
Marvel Comics: Apr, 2023 - No. 10, Jan, 2024 ($4.99/$3.99)

1-($4.99) Paknadel-s/Bazaldua-a Norman Osborn app. ... 5.00
2-10-($3.99) 4-Gold Goblin app. 5-Carnage Reigns part 4 ... 4.00

RED GOBLIN: RED DEATH (See Absolute Carnage series)
Marvel Comics: Dec, 2019 ($4.99)

1-Norman Osborn and the Carnage symbiote ... 5.00

RED GOOSE COMIC SELECTIONS (See Comic Selections)

RED HAWK (See A-1 Comics, Bobby Benson's ..#14-16 & Straight Arrow #2)
Magazine Enterprises: No. 90, 1953

Reborn #1 © MillarWorld & Cappulo

Red Goblin #1 © MAR

Red Lanterns #21 © DC

	GD	VG	FN	VF	VF/NM	NM-
	2.0	4.0	6.0	8.0	9.0	9.2

11-(A-1 Comics #90)-Powell-c/a   15 30 45 85 130 175

RED HERRING
DC Comics (WildStorm): Oct, 2009 - No. 6, Mar, 2010 ($2.99, limited series)
1-6-Tischman-s/Bond-a 3.00

RED HOOD (Title changed from Red Hood: Outlaw #50)
DC Comics: No. 51, Jan, 2021 - Present ($3.99)
51,52-Shawn Martinbrough-s/Tony Akins-a 4.00

RED HOOD AND THE OUTLAWS (DC New 52)
DC Comics: Nov, 2011 - No. 40, May, 2015 ($2.99)
1-Jason Todd, Starfire, Roy Harper team; Lobdell-s/Rocafort-a/c   2   4   6   9   13   16
2-4 .... 6.00
5-8 .... 4.00
9-Night of the Owls tie-in; Mr. Freeze vs. Talon 5.00
10-14 .... 3.00
15-(2/13) Death of the Family tie-in; die-cut cover; Joker app. 5.00
16-18: 16,17-Death of the Family tie-in 4.00
19-24,26-40: 24,26,27-Ra's al Ghul app. 30,31-Lobo app. 37-Arsenal's origin 3.00
25-($3.99) Zero Year tie-in; Talia and the Red Hood Gang app.; Haun-a 4.00
#0-(11/12, $2.99) Jason Todd's origin re-told; Joker app. 6.00
Annual 1 (7/13, $4.99) Takes place between #20 & 21; Green Arrow app.; Barrionuevo-a 5.00
Annual 2 (2/15, $4.99) Christmas-themed; Derenick-a 5.00
...: Futures End 1 (11/14, $2.99, regular-c) Five years later; Lobdell-s/Kolins-a 3.00
...: Futures End 1 (11/14, $3.99, 3-D cover) 4.00

RED HOOD AND THE OUTLAWS (DC Rebirth)(Title changes to Red Hood: Outlaw with #27)
DC Comics: Oct, 2016 - No. 26, Nov, 2018 ($2.99/$3.99)
1-8: 1-Jason Todd, Artemis & Bizarro team; Lobdell-s/Soy-a; Blask Mask app. 3.00
9-24,26-($3.99) 12-Solomon Grundy app. 13-Lex Luthor app. 16,17-Harley Quinn app. 4.00
18-The Creeper app. 5.00
25-($4.99) Art by Soy & Hairsine; back-up with Hester-a; leads into Annual 2 .... 5.00
Annual 1 (10/17, $4.99) Nightwing & KGBeast app.; Kirkham-a/c 5.00
Annual 2 (10/18, $4.99) Arsenal app.; Lobdell-s/Henry-a/Rocafort-c 5.00
Annual 3 (9/19, $4.99) Lobdell-s/Pollina-a/Soy-c; leads into Red Hood: Outlaw #37 .... 5.00
...: Rebirth (9/16, $2.99) Jason Todd origin re-told; Batman app. 3.00

RED HOOD / ARSENAL
DC Comics: Aug, 2015 - No. 13, Aug, 2016 ($2.99)
1-13: 1-Jason Todd & Roy Harper team; Lobdell-s/Medri. 3-5-Batman (Gordon) app.
6-13-Joker's Daughter app. 7-"Robin War" tie-in. 13-Bonus flashback 1st meeting 3.00

RED HOOD: OUTLAW (Title changed from Red Hood and the Outlaws)(Becomes Red Hood #51)
DC Comics: No. 27, Dec, 2018 - No. 50, Dec, 2020 ($3.99)
27-49: 27-31,33,34-Lobdell-s/Woods-a. 28,29-Batwoman app. 32-Segovia-a. 48-Joker War tie-in; Punchline app. 4.00
50-($5.99) Duela Dent (Joker's Daughter) app.; Pantalena-a 6.00

RED HOOD: THE HILL
DC Comics: No. 0, Apr, 2024 - Present ($3.99, limited series)
0-2-Martinbrough-s 4.00

RED HOOD: THE LOST DAYS
DC Comics: Aug, 2010 - No. 6, Jan, 2011 ($2.99, limited series)
1-6-The Return of Jason Todd; Winick-s/Raimondi-a/Tucci-c. 6-Joker & Hush app. 4.00
TPB (2011, $14.99) r/#1-6 .... 15.00

RED LANTERNS (DC New 52)
DC Comics: Nov, 2011 - No. 40, May, 2015 ($2.99)
1-34: 1-Milligan-s/Benes-a/c; Atrocitus, Dex-Starr & Bleez app. 6-8,11-Guy Gardner app.
10-Stormwatch app. 13-15-Rise of the Third Army. 17-First Lantern app. 24-Lights Out pt. 4. 28-Flipbook with Green Lantern #28; Supergirl app. 29-Superman app. 3.00
35-40: 35-37-Godhead x-over; Simon Baz app. 3.00
#0-(11/12, $2.99) Origin of Atrocitus, the 1st Red Lantern; Syaf-a 3.00
Annual 1 (9/14, $4.99) Story occurs between #33 & 34; Batman cameo 5.00
...: Futures End 1 (11/14, $2.99, regular-c) Five years later; Soule-s/Calafiore-a 3.00
...: Futures End 1 (11/14, $3.99, 3-D cover) 4.00

RED LIGHT
Artists, Writers & Artisans, Inc.: Nov, 2023 - Present ($3.99, limited series)
1,2-Sarah Cho-s/Priscilla Petraites-a 4.00

RED MASK (Formerly Tim Holt; see Best Comics, Blazing Six-Guns)
Magazine Enterprises No. 42-53/Sussex No. 54 (M.E. on-c): No. 42, June-July, 1954 - No. 53, May, 1956; No. 54, Sept, 1957
42-Ghost Rider by Ayers continues, ends #50; Black Phantom continues; 3-D effect c/stories begin   23 46 69 136 223 310

43- 3-D effect-c/stories   20 40 60 120 195 270
44-52: 3-D effect stories only. 47-Last pre-code issue. 50-Last Ghost Rider. 51-The Presto Kid begins by Ayers (1st app.); Presto Kid-c begins; last 3-D effect story.
52-Origin The Presto Kid   19 38 57 111 176 240
53,54-Last Black Phantom; last Presto Kid-c   15 30 45 88 137 185
I.W. Reprint #1 (r-/#52). 2 (nd, r/#51 w/diff.-c). 3, 8 (nd; Kinstler-c); 8-r/Red Mask #52   3   6   9   17   26   35

NOTE: *Ayers* art on Ghost Rider & Presto Kid. *Bolle* art in all (Red Mask); c-43, 44, 49. *Guardineer* a-52. Black Phantom in #42-44, 47-50, 53, 54.

REDMASK OF THE RIO GRANDE
AC Comics: 1990 ($2.50, 28 pgs.)(Has photos of movie posters)
1-Bolle-c/a(r); photo inside-c 4.00

RED MENACE
DC Comics (WildStorm): Jan, 2007 - No. 6, Jun, 2007 ($2.99, limited series)
1-6-Ordway-a/c; Bilson, DeMeo & Brody-s 3.00
TPB (2007, $17.99) r/series, sketch pages & variant covers 18.00

RED MOTHER, THE
BOOM! Studios: Dec, 2019 - No. 12, Jan, 2021 ($3.99)
1-12-Jeremy Haun-s/Danny Luckert-a 4.00

RED MOUNTAIN FEATURING QUANTRELL'S RAIDERS (Movie)(Also see Jesse James #28)
Avon Periodicals: 1952
nn-Alan Ladd; Kinstler-c   36 72 108 211 343 475

REDNECK
Image Comics (Skybound): Apr, 2017 - Present ($3.99)
1-Donny Cates-s/Lisandro Estherren-a 5.00
2-32 .... 4.00

RED ONE
Image Comics: Mar, 2015 - No. 4, Oct, 2016 ($2.99)
1-4-Xavier Dorison-s/Terry Dodson-a/c 3.00

RED PROPHET: THE TALES OF ALVIN MAKER
Dabel Brothers Prods./Marvel Comics (Dabel Brothers): Mar, 2006 - No. 12, Mar, 2008 ($2.99)
1-12-Adaptation of Orson Scott Card novel. 1-Miguel Montenegro-a 3.00
... Vol. 1 HC (2007, $19.99, dustjacket) r/#1-6 .... 20.00
... Vol. 1 SC (2007, $15.99) r/#1-6 .... 16.00
... Vol. 2 HC (2008, $19.99, dustjacket) r/#7-12 .... 20.00

"RED" RABBIT COMICS
Dearfield Comic/J. Charles Laue Publ. Co.: Jan, 1947 - No. 22, Aug-Sep, 1951
1   20 40 60 114 182 250
2   14 28 42 76 108 140
3-10   11 22 33 62 86 110
11-17,19-22   10 20 30 54 72 90
18-Flying Saucer-c (1/51)   13 26 39 72 101 130

RED RAVEN COMICS (Human Torch #2 on)(See X-Men #44 & Sub-Mariner #26, 2nd series)
Timely Comics: August, 1940
1-Jack Kirby-a (his 1st signed work); origin & 1st app. Red Raven; Comet Pierce & Mercury by Kirby, The Human Top & The Eternal Brain; intro. Magar, the Mystic & only app.
3000 6000 9000 22,800 41,400 60,000

RED ROBIN (Batman: Reborn)
DC Comics: Aug, 2009 - No. 26, Oct, 2011 ($2.99)
1-26-Tim (Drake) Wayne in the Kingdom Come costume; Bachs-a. 1-Two covers 3.00

RED ROCKET 7
Dark Horse Comics: Aug, 1997 - No. 7, June, 1998 ($3.95, square format, limited series)
1-7-Mike Allred-c/s/a 4.00

RED RYDER COMICS (Hi Spot #2)(Movies, radio)(See Crackajack Funnies & Super Book of Comics)
Hawley Publ. No. 1/Dell Publishing Co.(K.K.) No. 3 on: 9/40; No. 3, 8/41 - No. 5, 12/41; No. 4/42 - No. 151, 4-6/57 (Beware of almost identical reprints of #1 made in the late 1980s)
1-Red Ryder, his horse Thunder, Little Beaver & his horse Papoose strip reprints begin by Fred Harman; 1st meeting of Red & Little Beaver; Harman line-drawn-c #1-85
265 530 795 1694 2897 4100
3-(Scarce)-Alley Oop, Capt. Easy, Dan Dunn, Freckles & His Friends, King of the Royal Mtd., Myra North strip-r begin   57 114 171 456 1028 1600
4-6: 6-1st Dell issue (4/42)   27 54 81 194 435 675
7-10   23 46 69 161 356 550
11-20   16 32 48 108 239 370
21-32-Last Alley Oop, Dan Dunn, Capt. Easy, Freckles

	GD 2.0	VG 4.0	FN 6.0	VF 8.0	VF/NM 9.0	NM- 9.2
	10	20	30	69	147	225
33-40 (52 pgs.): 40-Photo back-c begin, end #57	9	18	27	58	114	170
41 (52 pgs.)-Rocky Lane photo back-c	9	18	27	60	120	180
42-46 (52 pgs.): 46-Last Red Ryder strip-r	7	14	21	49	92	135
47-53 (52 pgs.): 47-New stories on Red Ryder begin. 49,52-Harmon photo back-c	6	11	18	41	76	110

54-92: 54-73 (36 pgs.). 59-Harmon photo back-c. 73-Last King of the Royal Mtd; strip-r by Jim Gary. 74-85 (52 pgs.)-Harman line-drawn-c. 86-92 (52 pgs.)-Harman painted-c

	6	12	18	37	66	95

93-99,101-106: 94-96 (36 pgs.)-Harman painted-c. 97,98,(36 pgs.)-Harman line-drawn-c.

99,101-106 (36 pgs.)-Jim Bannon Photo-c	5	10	15	33	57	80
100 (52 pgs.)-Bannon photo-c	5	10	15	34	60	85
107-118 (52 pgs.)-Harman line-drawn-c	5	10	15	31	53	75
119-129 (52 pgs.): 119-Painted-c begin, not by Harman, end #151	5	10	15	30	50	70
130-151 (36 pgs.): 145-Title change to Red Ryder Ranch Magazine	4	8	12	28	47	65
149-Title change to Red Ryder Ranch Comics						
Four Color 916 (7/58)	4	8	12	28	47	65

NOTE: *Fred Harman a-1-99; c-1-98, 107-118. Don Barry, Allan Rocky Lane; Wild Bill Elliott & Jim Bannon starred as Red Ryder in the movies. Robert Blake starred as Little Beaver.*

RED RYDER PAINT BOOK
Whitman Publishing Co.: 1941 (8-1/2x11-1/2", 148 pgs.)

nn-Reprints 1940 daily strips	77	154	231	493	847	1200

RED SEAL COMICS (Formerly Carnival Comics, and/or Spotlight Comics?)
Harry 'A' Chesler/Superior Publ. No. 19 on: No. 14, 10/45 - No. 18, 10/46; No. 19, 6/47 - No. 22, 12/47

14-The Black Dwarf begins (continued from Spotlight?); Little Nemo app; bondage/hypo-c; Tuska-a	155	310	465	992	1696	2400
15-Torture story; funny-c	50	100	150	315	533	750
16-Used in SOTI, pg. 181, illo "Outside the forbidden pages of de Sade, you find draining a girl's blood only in children's comics"; drug club story r-later in Crime Reporter #1; Veiled Avenger & Barry Kuda app; Tuska-a; funny-c	77	154	231	493	847	1200
17,18,20: Lady Satan, Yankee Girl & Sky Chief app; 17-Tuska-a	77	154	231	493	847	1200
19-No Black Dwarf (on-c only); Zor, El Tigre app.	81	162	243	518	884	1250
21-Lady Satan & Black Dwarf app.	45	90	135	284	480	675
22-Zor, Rocketman app. (68 pgs.)	45	90	135	284	480	675

RED SHE-HULK (Title continues from Hulk (2008 series) #57)
Marvel Comics: No. 58, Dec, 2012 - No. 67, Sept, 2013 ($2.99)
58-67-Betty Ross character; Pagulayan-a/c. 59,60-Avengers app. 66-Man-Thing app.   3.00

RED SITHA (From Red Sonja)
Dynamite Entertainment: 2022 - No. 4, 2022 ($3.99)
1-4-Andolfo & Blengino-a/Pinti-a; multiple covers   4.00

REDSKIN (Thrilling Indian Stories)(Famous Western Badmen #13 on)
Youthful Magazines: Sept, 1950 - No. 12, Oct, 1952

1-Walter Johnson-a (7 pgs.)	26	52	78	154	252	330
2	15	30	45	90	140	190
3-12: 3-Daniel Boone story. 6-Geronimo story	14	28	42	81	118	155

NOTE: *Walter Johnson c-3, 4. Palais a-11. Wildey a-5, 11. Bondage c-6, 12.*

RED SKULL
Marvel Comics: Sept, 2011 - No. 5, Jan, 2012 ($2.99, limited series)
1-5-Pak-s/Colak-a/Aja-c; Red Skull's childhood and origin   5.00

RED SKULL (Secret Wars Battleworld tie-in)
Marvel Comics: Sept, 2015 - No. 3, Nov, 2015 ($3.99, limited series)
1-3-Joshua Williamson-s/Luca Pizzari-a; Crossbones, Magneto & Bucky app.   4.00

RED SONJA (Also see Conan #23, Kull & The Barbarians, Marvel Feature & Savage Sword Of Conan #1)
Marvel Comics Group: 1/77 - No. 15, 5/79; V1#1, 2/83 - V2#2, 3/83; V3#1, 8/83 - V3#4, 2/84; V3#5, 1/85 - V3#13, 5/86

1-Created by Robert E. Howard	5	10	15	31	53	75
2-10: 5-Last 30¢ issue	2	4	6	8	11	14
4,5-(35¢ variants, limited distribution)(7,9/77)	10	20	30	67	141	215
11-15, V2#1,V2#2: 14-Last 35¢ issue	1	3	4	6	8	10
V3#1 ($1.00, 52 pgs.)	1	3	4	6	8	10
V3#2-#4 ($1.00, 52 pgs.)						5.00

...Special Edition (2021, $3.99) Facsimile reprinting of #1   4.00
NOTE: *Brunner c-12-14. J. Buscema a(p)-12, 13, 15; c-V#1. Nebres a-V3#3i(part). N. Redondo a-8i, V3#2i, 3i. Simonson a-V3#1. Thorne c/a-1-11.*

RED SONJA (Continues in Queen Sonja) (Also see Classic Red Sonja)
Dynamite Entertainment: No. 0, Apr, 2005 - No. 80, 2013 (25¢/$2.99/$3.99)
0-(4/05, 25¢) Greg Land-a/Mel Rubi-a/Oeming & Carey-s   4.00
1-(6/05, $2.99) Five covers by Ross, Linsner, Cassaday, Turner, Rivera; Rubi-a   10.00
2-46-Multiple covers on all. 29-Sonja dies. 34-Sonja reborn   3.00
5-RRP Edition with Red Foil logo and Isanove-a   15.00
50-('10, $4.99) new stories and reprints; Marcos, Chin, Desjardins-a; 4 covers   5.00
51-79-($3.99)- 51-56-Geovani-a; multiple covers on each   4.00
80-($4.99) Red Sonja vs. Dracula; bonus interview with Gail Simone   5.00
Annual #1 (2007, $3.50) Oeming-s/Sadowski-a; Red Sonja Comics Chronology   4.00
Annual #2 (2009, $3.99) Gage-s/Marcos-a; wraparound Prado-c & Marcos-c   4.00
Annual #3 (2010, $5.99) Brereton-s/c/a; Batista-a   5.00
Annual #4 (2013, $4.99) Beatty-s/Mena-a   6.00
... Blue (2011, $4.99) Brett-s/Geovani-a; covers by Geovani & Rubi   5.00
... Break the Skin (2011, $4.99) Winslade-c/Van Meter-s/Salazar-a   5.00
... Cover Showcase Vol. 1 (2007, $5.99) gallery of variant covers; Cho sketches   6.00
... Deluge (2011, $4.99) Brereton-s/c; Bolson-a/var-c; reprint from Conan #48 ('74)   5.00
Giant Size Red Sonja #1 (2007, $4.99) Chaykin-c; new story and reprints and pin-ups   5.00
Giant Size Red Sonja #2 (2008, $4.99) Segovia-c; new story and reprints and pin-ups   5.00
... Goes East ($4.99) three covers; Joe Ng-a   5.00
... Monster Isle ($4.99) two covers; Pablo Marcos-a/Roy Thomas-s   5.00
... One More Day ($4.99) two covers; Liam Sharp-a   5.00
... Raven ('12, $4.99) Antonio-a/Martin-c; bonus pin-up gallery   5.00

...: Revenge of the Gods 1-5 (2011 - No. 5, 2011, $3.99) Sampere-a/Lieberman-s   4.00
... Vacant Shell ($4.99) two covers; Remender-s/Renaud-a   5.00
...: Wrath of the Gods 1-5 (2010 - No. 5, 2010, $3.99) Geovani-a   4.00
The Adventures of Red Sonja TPB (2005, $19.99) r/Marvel Feature #1-7   20.00
The Adventures of Red Sonja Vol. 2 TPB (2007, $19.99) r/#1-7 of '77 Marvel series   20.00
... Vol. 1 TPB (2006, $19.99) r/#0-6; gallery of covers and variants; creators interview   20.00
... Vol. 2 Arrowsmith TPB (2007, $19.99) r/#7-12; gallery of covers and variants   20.00
... Vol. 3 The Rise of Gath TPB (2007, $19.99) r/#13-18; gallery of covers and variants   20.00
... Vol. 4 Animals & More TPB (2007, $24.99) r/#19-24; gallery of covers and variants   25.00

RED SONJA (Volume 2)
Dynamite Entertainment: 2013 - No. 18, 2015 ($3.99)
1-18: 1-Gail Simone-s/Walter Geovani-a; six covers. 2-18-Multiple covers   4.00
#0 (2014, $3.99) Simone-s/Salonga-a/Hardman-a   4.00
#100 (2015, $7.99) Five short stories by various incl. Simone, Oeming, Marcos; 5 covers   8.00
#1973 (2015, $7.99) Five short stories by various incl. Simone, Bunn, Thomas & others   8.00
... and Cub (2014, $4.99) Nancy Collins-s/Fritz Casas-a/J.M. Linsner-c   5.00
... Berserker (2014, $4.99) Jim Zub-s/Jonathan Lau-a/Jeffrey Cruz-c   5.00
...: Dynamite Edition (2022, $4.99) Reprints #1 (2013)   4.00
...: Sanctuary (2014, $4.99) Mason-s/Salonga-a/Davila-c; includes full script   5.00

RED SONJA (Volume 3)
Dynamite Entertainment: 2016 - No. 6, 2016 ($3.99)
1-6: 1-Marguerite Bennett-s/Aneke-a; multiple covers   4.00

RED SONJA (Volume 4)
Dynamite Entertainment: No. 0, 2016 - No. 25, 2019 ($3.99)
0-(25¢) Sonja transported to present day New York City; Amy Chu-s/Carlos Gomez-a   3.00
1-25-($3.99) Chu-s/Gomez-a in most; multiple covers. 17-HDR-a. 23-Castro-a   4.00
... Halloween Special One-Shot (2018, $4.99) Burnham-s/Garcia-a; Reilly Brown-c   5.00
... Holiday Special One-Shot (2018, $4.99) Chu & Burnham-s/Jamie-a; Romero-c   5.00

RED SONJA (Volume 5) (Also see Killing Red Sonja)
Dynamite Entertainment: 2019 - No. 28, 2021 ($3.99)
1-28: 1-6-Mark Russell-s/Mirko Colak-a; multiple covers. 7-9,13-Bob Q-a. 10-12-Colak-a   4.00
... Lord of Fools One-Shot (2019, $4.99) Russell-s/Bob Q-a; takes place around #6   5.00
... 1982 (2021, $4.99) Amy Chu-s/Eric Blake-a   5.00
... Valentine's Special (2021, $4.99) Willingham-s/Cafaro-a   5.00

RED SONJA
Dynamite Entertainment: 2021 - No. 12, 2022 ($3.99)
1-12-Andolfo & Blengino-s/Cafaro-a; multiple covers   4.00
... Fairy Tales ($4.99) Sonja climbs Jack's beanstalk   5.00
... Holiday Special 2021 ($3.99) Andolfo & Blengino-s   4.00
... Valentine's Day Special (2022, $4.99) Chuck Brown-s; Sozomaika main-c   5.00

RED SONJA
Dynamite Entertainment: 2023 - Present ($3.99)
1-8-Grønbekk-s/Geovani-a; multiple covers   4.00

RED SONJA: AGE OF CHAOS
Dynamite Entertainment: 2020 - No. 6, 2020 ($3.99, limited series)
1-6-Erik Burnham-s/Jonathan Lau-a; Evil Ernie, Purgatori app.; multiple covers   4.00

RED SONJA AND VAMPIRELLA MEET BETTY AND VERONICA
Dynamite Entertainment: 2019 - No. 12, 2020 ($3.99)
1-12: 1-8,10,11-Amy Chu-s/Maria Sanapo-a; multiple covers. 6-11-Draculina app. 9-Parent-a   4.00

RED SONJA: ATLANTIS RISES
Dynamite Entertainment: 2012 - No. 4, 2012 ($3.99, limited series)
1-4-Lieberman-s/Dunbar-a/Parrillo-c   4.00

RED SONJA: BIRTH OF THE SHE-DEVIL
Dynamite Entertainment: 2019 - No. 4, 2019 ($3.99, limited series)
1-4-Luke Lieberman-s/Sergio Davila-a   4.00

RED SONJA BLACK WHITE RED
Dynamite Entertainment: 2021 - No. 8, 2022 ($3.99, B&W&Red)
1-8-Short story anthology by various; multiple covers   4.00

RED SONJA/CLAW: THE DEVIL'S HANDS (See Claw the Unconquered)
DC Comics (WildStorm)/Dynamite Ent.: May, 2006 - No. 4, Aug, 2006 ($2.99, limited series)
1-4-Covers by Jim Lee & Dell'Otto; Andy Smith-a 1-Alex Ross var-c. 2-Dell'Otto var-c.   3.00
3-Bermejo var-c; Andy Smith var-c   3.00
TPB (2007, $12.99) r/#1-4; cover gallery   13.00

RED SONJA/ CONAN
Dynamite Entertainment: 2015 - No. 4, 2015 ($3.99)
1-4-Gischler-s/Castro-a; multiple covers   4.00

RED SONJA HELL SONJA
Dynamite Entertainment: 2022 - No. 4, 2023 ($3.99)
1-4-Jordan Clark-s/Miriana Piglia-a; multiple covers   4.00

RED SONJA: SCAVENGER HUNT
Marvel Comics: Dec, 1995 ($2.95, one-shot)

RED SONJA/ TARZAN
Dynamite Entertainment: 2018 - No. 6, 2018 ($3.99)
1-6-Simone-s/Geovani-a; multiple covers   4.00

RED SONJA: THE BLACK TOWER
Dynamite Entertainment: 2014 - No. 4, 2015 ($3.99)
1-4-Tieri-s/Razek-a/Conner-c   4.00

RED SONJA: THE MOVIE
Marvel Comics Group: Nov, 1985 - No. 2, Dec, 1985 (Limited series)
1,2-Movie adapt-r/Marvel Super Spec. #38   4.00

RED SONJA: THE PRICE OF BLOOD
Dynamite Entertainment: 2020 - No. 3, 2021 ($3.99, limited series)

Red She-Hulk #66 © MAR

Red Sonja (2021 series) #12 © RS LLC

Reggie and Me #55 © ACP

	GD 2.0	VG 4.0	FN 6.0	VF 8.0	VF/NM 9.0	NM- 9.2

1-3-Lieberman-s/Geovani-a; multiple covers — 4.00

RED SONJA: THE SUPERPOWERS
Dynamite Entertainment: 2020 - No. 5, 2021 ($3.99, limited series)
1-5-Abnett-s/Lau-a; multiple covers; Captain Future, Vana, Mr. Raven & The Sword app. 4.00

RED SONJA: UNCHAINED
Dynamite Entertainment: 2013 - No. 4, 2013 ($3.99, limited series)
1-4-Follows the Red Sonja: Blue one-shot; Jadsen-a 4.00

RED SONJA: VULTURE'S CIRCLE
Dynamite Entertainment: 2015 - No. 5, 2015 ($3.99, limited series)
1-5-Collins & Lieberman-s/Casas-a; three covers on each 4.00

RED SONJA VS. THULSA DOOM
Dynamite Entertainment: 2005 - No. 4, 2006 ($3.50)
1-4-Conrad-a; Conrad & Dell'Otto covers 3.50
..., Volume 1 TPB (2006, $14.99) r/series; cover gallery 15.00

RED STAR, THE
Image Comics/Archangel Studios: June, 2000 - No. 9, June, 2002 ($2.95)
1-Christian Gossett-s/a(p) 4.00
2-9: 9-Beck-c 3.00
#(7.5) Reprints Wizard #1/2 story with new pages 3.00
Annual 1 (Archangel Studios, 11/02, $3.50) "Run Makita Run" 4.00
TPB (4/01, $24.95, 9x12") oversized r/#1-4; intro. by Bendis 25.00
Nokgorka TPB (8/02, $24.95, 9x12") oversized r/#6-9; w/sketch pages 25.00
Wizard 1/2 (mail order) 10.00

RED STAR, THE (Volume 2)
CrossGen #1,2/Archangel Studios #3 on: Feb, 2003 - No. 5, July, 2004 ($2.95/$2.99)
1-5-Christian Gossett-s/a(p) 3.00
Prison of Souls TPB (8/04, $24.95, 9x12") oversized r/#1-5; w/sketch pages 25.00

RED STAR, THE: SWORD OF LIES
Archangel Studios: Aug, 2006 ($4.50)
1-Christian Gossett-s/a(p); origin of the Red Star team 4.50

RED TEAM
Dynamite Entertainment: 2013 - No. 7, 2014 ($3.99)
1-7: 1-Ennis-s/Cermak-a; covers by Chaykin & Sook 4.00

RED TEAM, VOLUME 2: DOUBLE TAP, CENTER MASS
Dynamite Entertainment: 2016 - No. 9, 2017 ($3.99)
1-8: 1-Ennis-s/Cermak-a/Panosian-c 4.00
9-($4.99) 5.00

RED THORN
DC Comics (Vertigo): Jan, 2016 - No. 13, Feb, 2017 ($3.99)
1-13: 1-6-David Baillie-s/Meghan Hetrick-a. 7-Steve Pugh-a 4.00

RED TORNADO (See All-American #20 & Justice League of America #64)
DC Comics: June, 1985 - No. 4, Oct, 1985 (Limited series)
1-4: Kurt Busiek scripts in all. 1-3-Superman & Batman cameos 4.00

RED TORNADO
DC Comics: Nov, 2009 - No. 6, Apr, 2010 ($2.99, limited series)
1-6: 1-3-Benes-c. 5,6-Vixen app. 3.00
...: Family Reunion TPB (2010, $17.99) r/#1-6 18.00

RED WARRIOR
Marvel/Atlas Comics (TCI): Jan, 1951 - No. 6, Dec, 1951

	GD 2.0	VG 4.0	FN 6.0	VF 8.0	VF/NM 9.0	NM- 9.2	
1-Red Warrior & his horse White Wing; Tuska-a	24	48	72	142	234	325	
2-Tuska-c	14	28	42	78	112	145	
3-6: 4-Origin White Wing. 6-Maneely-c	12	24	36	67	94	120	

RED, WHITE & BLUE COMICS
DC Comics: 1941
nn - Ashcan comic, not distributed to newsstands, only for in-house use. Cover art is All-American Comics #20 with interior being Flash Comics #17 (no known sales)

RED WING
Image Comics: Jul, 2011 - No. 4, Oct, 2011 ($3.50, limited series)
1-4-Hickman-s/Pitarra-a 3.50

RED WOLF (See Avengers #80 & Marvel Spotlight #1)
Marvel Comics Group: May, 1972 - No. 9, Sept, 1973

	GD 2.0	VG 4.0	FN 6.0	VF 8.0	VF/NM 9.0	NM- 9.2
1-(Western hero); Gil Kane/Severin-c; Shores-a	5	10	15	35	63	90
2-9: 2-Kane-c. 6-Tuska-r in back-up. 7-Red Wolf as super hero begins.						
9-Origin sidekick, Lobo (wolf)	3	6	9	17	26	35

RED WOLF (From the Secret Wars tie-in series 1872)
Marvel Comics: Feb, 2016 - No. 6, Jul, 2016 ($3.99)
1-6: 1-Edmondson-s/Talajic-a. 2-Red Wolf in the present 4.00

RED ZONE
Artists, Writers & Artisans: Mar, 2023 - No. 4, Jun, 2023 ($3.99, limited series)
1-4-Cullen Bunn-s/Mike Deodato Jr.-a 4.00

REESE'S PIECES
Eclipse Comics: Oct, 1985 - No.2, Oct, 1985 ($1.75, Baxter paper)
1,2-B&W-r in color 4.00

REFORM SCHOOL GIRL!
Realistic Comics: 1951

	GD 2.0	VG 4.0	FN 6.0	VF 8.0	VF/NM 9.0	NM- 9.2
nn-Used in SOTI, pg. 358, & cover ill. with caption "Comic books are supposed to be like fairy tales"; classic photo-c	1600	3200	4800	12,200	22,100	32,000

(Prices vary widely on this book)
NOTE: The cover and title originated from a digest-sized book published by Diversey Publishing Co. of Chicago in 1948. The original book "House of Fury", Doubleday, came out in 1941. The girl's real name which appears on the cover of the digest and comic is Marty Collins, Canadian model and ice skating star who posed for this special color photograph for the Diversey novel.

REFRIGERATOR FULL OF HEADS (Also see Basketful of Heads)
DC Comics (Black Label)(Hill House Comics): Dec, 2021 - No. 6, Jun, 2022 ($3.99)
1-6-Rio Youers-s/Tow Fowler-a 4.00

REFUSE X LAST RESORTS
Bad Idea: Nov, 2021 ($9.99, one-shot)

	GD 2.0	VG 4.0	FN 6.0	VF 8.0	VF/NM 9.0	NM- 9.2
1-Kindt-s/Sauvage-a; Russell-s/Pollina-a	1	3	4	6	8	10

REGARDING THE MATTER OF OSWALD'S BODY
BOOM! Studios: Nov, 2021 - No. 5, Mar, 2022 ($3.99, limited series)
1-5-Cantwell-s/Casalanguida-a 4.00

REGENTS ILLUSTRATED CLASSICS
Prentice Hall Regents, Englewood Cliffs, NJ 07632: 1981 (Plus more recent reprintings)
(48 pgs., B&W-a with 14 pgs. of teaching helps)
NOTE: This series contains Classics Ill. art, and was produced from the same illegal source as Cassette Books. But when Twin Circle sued to stop the sale of the Cassette Books, they decided to permit this series to continue. This series was produced as a teaching aid. The 20 title series is divided into four levels based upon number of basic words used therein. There is also a teacher's manual for each level. All of the titles are still available from the publisher for about $5 each retail. The number to call for mail order purchases is (201)767-5937. Almost all of the issues have new covers taken from some interior art panel. Here is a list of the series by Regents ident. no. and the Classics Ill. counterpart.

16770(CI#24-A2)18333(CI#3-A2)21668(CI#13-A2)32224(CI#21)33051(CI#26)35788(CI#84)37153(CI#16)44460 (CI#19-A2)44808(CI#18-A2)52395(CI#4-A2)58627(CI#5-A2)60067(CI#30)68405(CI#23A1)70302(CI#29)78192 (CI#7-A2)78193(CI#10-A2)79679(CI#85)92046(CI#1-A2)93062(CI#64)93512(CI#25)

RE: GEX
Awesome-Hyperwerks: Jul, 1998 - No. 0, Dec, 1998; ($2.50)
Preview (7/98) Wizard Con Edition 4.00
0-(12/98) Loeb-s/Liefeld-a/Pat Lee-c, 1-(9/98) Loeb-s/Liefeld-a/c 4.00

REGGIE (Formerly Archie's Rival...; Reggie & Me #19 on)
Archie Publications: No. 15, Sept, 1963 - No. 18, Nov, 1965

	GD 2.0	VG 4.0	FN 6.0	VF 8.0	VF/NM 9.0	NM- 9.2
15(9/63), 16(10/64), 17(8/65), 18(11/65)	6	12	18	40	73	105

NOTE: Cover title No. 15 & 16 is Archie's Rival Reggie.

REGGIE AND ME (Formerly Reggie)
Archie Publ.: No. 19, Aug, 1966 - No. 126, Sept, 1980 (No. 50-68: 52 pgs.)

	GD 2.0	VG 4.0	FN 6.0	VF 8.0	VF/NM 9.0	NM- 9.2
19-Evilheart app.	4	8	12	28	47	65
20-23-Evilheart app.; with Pureheart #22	3	6	9	21	33	45
24-40(3/70)	3	6	9	16	23	30
41-49(7/71)	2	4	6	13	18	22
50(9/71)-68 (1/74, 52 pgs.)	3	6	9	14	20	26
69-99	2	4	6	8	10	12
100(10/77)	2	4	6	9	12	15
101-126	1	2	3	5	7	9

REGGIE AND ME (Volume 2)
Archie Comic Publications: Jan, 2017 - No. 5, ($3.99)
1-5-Multiple covers and classic back-up reprints in#1,2. Tom DeFalco-s/Sandy Jarrell-a 4.00

REGGIE'S JOKES (See Reggie's Wise Guy Jokes)

REGGIE'S REVENGE!
Archie Comic Publications, Inc.: Spring, 1994 - No. 3 ($2.00, 52 pgs.) (Published semi-annually)

	GD 2.0	VG 4.0	FN 6.0	VF 8.0	VF/NM 9.0	NM- 9.2
1-Bound-in pull-out poster	2	4	6	8	10	12
2,3						5.00

REGGIE'S WISE GUY JOKES
Archie Publications: Aug, 1968 - No. 55, 1980 (#5-28 are Giants)

	GD 2.0	VG 4.0	FN 6.0	VF 8.0	VF/NM 9.0	NM- 9.2
1	6	12	18	38	69	100
2-4	3	6	9	16	23	30
5-16 (1/71)(68 pg. Giants)	3	6	9	16	23	30
17-28 (52 pg. Giants)	2	4	6	13	18	22
29-40(1/77)	1	3	4	6	8	10
41-55	1	2	3	5	6	8

REGISTERED NURSE
Charlton Comics: Summer, 1963

1-r/Nurse Betsy Crane & Cynthia Doyle	5	10	15	35	63	90

REG'LAR FELLERS
Visual Editions (Standard): No. 5, Nov, 1947 - No. 6, Mar, 1948

5,6	12	24	36	69	97	125

REG'LAR FELLERS HEROIC (See Heroic Comics)

REGRESSION
Image Comics: May, 2017 - No. 15, Jan, 2019 ($3.99)

1-15-Bunn-s/Luckert-a						4.00

REGULAR SHOW (Based on Cartoon Network series)
Boom Entertainment (kaBOOM!): Apr, 2013 - No. 40, Oct, 2016 ($3.99)

1-40-Multiple covers on all						4.00
2014 Annual 1 (6/14, $4.99) Four short stories by various; three covers						5.00
2015 Special 1 (3/15, $4.99) Four short stories by various; two covers						5.00
2017 Special 1 (4/17, $7.99) Six short stories by various; two covers						8.00
2018 Special 1 (2/18, $7.99) Four short stories; McCreery-s; art by various						8.00

REGULAR SHOW: SKIPS (Based on Cartoon Network series)
Boom Entertainment (kaBOOM!): Nov, 2013 - No. 6, Apr, 2014 ($3.99)

1-6-Mad Rupert-s/a; multiple covers on all						4.00

REGULAR SHOW: 25 YEARS LATER (Based on Cartoon Network series)
Boom Entertainment (kaBOOM!): Jun, 2018 - No. 6, Nov, 2018 ($3.99)

1-6-Christopher Hastings-s/Anna Johnstone-a; multiple covers on all						4.00

REID FLEMING, WORLD'S TOUGHEST MILKMAN
Eclipse Comics/ Deep Sea Comics: 1980; 8/86; V2#1, 12/86 - V2#3, 12/88; V2#4, 11/89; V2#5, 11/90 - V2#9, 4/98 (B&W)

1-(1980, self-published) David Boswell-s/a						5.00
1-2nd, 4th & 5th printings ($2.50); (3rd print, large size, 8/86, $2.50)						4.00
V2#1 (10/86, regular size, $2.00), 1-2nd print, 3rd print ($2.00, 2/89)						4.00
2-9 -New stories						
7-9-New stories						4.00

(2-9-2nd & 3rd printings, V2#4-2nd printing, V2#5 ($2.00), V2#6 (Deep Sea, r/V2#5))

REIGN IN HELL
DC Comics: Sept, 2008 - No. 8, Apr, 2009 ($3.50, limited series)

1-8-Neron, Shadowpact app.; Giffen-s; Dr. Occult back-up w/Segovia-a. 1-Two covers						3.50
TPB (2009, $19.99) r/#1-8						20.00

REIGN OF THE ZODIAC
DC Comics: Oct, 2003 - No. 8, May, 2004 ($2.75)

1-8: 1-6,8-Giffen-s/Doran-a/Harris-c. 7-Byrd-a						3.00

RELATIVE HEROES
DC Comics: Mar, 2000 - No. 6, Aug, 2000 ($2.50, limited series)

1-6-Grayson-s/Guichet & Sowd-a. 6-Superman-c/app.						3.00

RELAY
AfterShock Comics: Jul, 2018 - No. 5, Apr, 2019 ($3.99, limited series)

1-5-Zac Thompson-s/Andy Clarke-a						4.00
#0 (Free Comic Book Day, 5/18, giveaway) Thompson-s/Clarke-a						3.00

RELOAD
DC Comics (Homage): May, 2003 - No. 3, Sept, 2003 ($2.95, limited series)

1-3-Warren Ellis-s/Paul Gulacy & Jimmy Palmiotti-a						3.00
.../Mek TPB (2004, $14.95, flip book) r/Reload #1-3 & Mek #1-3						15.00

RELUCTANT DRAGON, THE (Walt Disney's...)
Dell Publishing Co.: No. 13, 1940

Four Color 13-Contains 2 pgs. of photos from film; 2 pg. foreword to Fantasia by Leopold Stokowski; Donald Duck, Goofy, Baby Weems & Mickey Mouse (as the Sorcerer's Apprentice) app.

	239	478	717	1530	2615	3700

REMAINS
IDW Publishing: May, 2004 - No. 5, Sept, 2004 ($3.99)

1-5-Steve Niles-s/Kieron Dwyer-a						4.00

REMARKABLE WORLDS OF PROFESSOR PHINEAS B. FUDDLE, THE
DC Comics (Paradox Press): 2000 - No. 4, 2000 ($5.95, limited series)

1-4-Boaz Yakin-s/Erez Yakin-a						6.00
TPB (2001, $19.95) r/series						20.00

REMEMBER PEARL HARBOR
Street & Smith Publications: 1942 (68 pgs.) (Illustrated story of the battle)

nn-Uncle Sam-c; Jack Binder-a	119	238	357	762	1306	1850

REN & STIMPY SHOW, THE (TV) (Nickelodeon cartoon characters)
Marvel Comics: Dec, 1992 - No. 44, July, 1996 ($1.75/$1.95)

1-($2.25)-Polybagged w/scratch & sniff Ren or Stimpy air fowler (equal numbers of each were made)	3	6	9	14	20	25
1-2nd & 3rd printing; different dialogue on-c						4.00
2-6: 4-Muddy Mudskipper back-up. 5-Bill Wray painted-c. 6-Spider-Man vs. Powdered Toast						5.00
7-17: 12-1st solo back-up story w/Tank & Brenner						4.00
18-44: 18-Powered Toast Man app.						4.00
25 ($2.95) Deluxe edition w/die cut cover						5.00
...Don't Try This at Home (3/94, $12.95, TPB)-r/#9-12						13.00
...Eenteractive Special ('95, $2.95)						6.00
...Holiday Special 1994 (2/95, $2.95, 52 pgs.)	1	2	3	5	6	8
...Mini Comic (1995)	1	2	3	5	6	8
...Pick of the Litter nn (1993, $12.95, TPB)-r/#1-4						13.00

...Radio Daze (11/95, $1.95)						6.00
...Running Joke nn (1993, $12.95, TPB)-r/#1-4 plus new-a						13.00
...Seeck Little Monkeys (1/95, $12.95)-r/#17-20						13.00
...Special 2 (7/94, $2.95, 52 pgs.), ...Special 3 (10/94, $2.95, 52 pgs.)-Choose adventure,						
...Special: Around the World in a Daze ($2.95), ...Special: Four Swerks (1/95, $2.95, 52 pgs.)-FF #1 cover swipe; cover reads "Four Swerks w/5 pg. coloring book.", ...Special: Powdered Toast Man 1 (4/94, $2.95, 52 pgs.), ...Special: Powdered Toast Man's Cereal Serial (4/95, $2.95), ...Special: Sports (10/95, $2.95)						6.00
...Tastes Like Chicken nn (11/93,$12.95,TPB)-r/#5-8						13.00
...Your Pals (1994, $12.95, TPB)-r/#13-16						13.00

RENATO JONES: THE ONE %
Image Comics: May, 2016 - No. 5, Oct, 2016 ($3.99)

1-5-Kaare Andrews-s/a/c						4.00
Renato Jones, Season 2: Freelancer (5/17 - No. 5, 11/17, $3.99) 1-5-Andrews-s/a/c						4.00

RENFIELD
Caliber Press: 1994 - No. 3, 1995 ($2.95, B&W, limited series)

1-3						4.00

RENO BROWNE, HOLLYWOOD'S GREATEST COWGIRL (Formerly Margie Comics; Apache Kid #53 on; also see Western Hearts, Western Life Romances & Western Love)
Marvel Comics (MPC): No. 50, April, 1950 - No. 52, Sept, 1950 (52 pgs.)

50-Reno Browne photo-c on all	37	74	111	222	361	500
51,52	32	64	96	188	307	425

REPLACER, THE
AfterShock Comics: Apr, 2019 ($7.99, one-shot)

1-Zac Thompson-s/Arjuna Susini-a						8.00

REPLICA
AfterShock Comics: Dec, 2015 - No. 5, Apr, 2016 ($3.99)

1-5-Paul Jenkins-s/Andy Clarke-a						4.00

REPRESENT!
DC Comics: Aug, 2021 ($9.99, squarebound, one-shot, printing of digital first stories)

1-Short stories of social change and personal histories; Christian Cooper-s						10.00

REPTIL
Marvel Comics: Jul, 2021 - No. 4, Nov, 2021 ($3.99)

1-4-Terry Blas-s/Enid Balám/Paco Medina-c; variant-c on each						4.00

REPTILICUS (Becomes Reptisaurus #3 on)
Charlton Comics: Aug, 1961 - No. 2, Oct, 1961

1 (Movie)	24	48	72	168	372	575
2	12	24	36	81	176	270

REPTISAURUS (Reptilicus #1,2)
Charlton Comics: V2#3, Jan, 1962 - No. 8, Dec, 1962; Summer, 1963

V2#3-8: 3-Flying saucer-c/s. 8-Montes/Bache-c/a	6	12	18	41	76	110
Special Edition 1 (Summer, 1963)	6	12	18	38	69	100

REQUIEM FOR DRACULA
Marvel Comics: Feb, 1993 ($2.00, 52 pgs.)

nn-r/Tomb of Dracula #69,70 by Gene Colan						5.00

RESCUE (Pepper Potts in Iron Man armor)
Marvel Comics: July, 2010 ($3.99, one-shot)

1-DeConnick-s/Mutti-a/Foreman-c						4.00

RESCUERS, THE (See Walt Disney Showcase #40)

RESIDENT ALIEN
Dark Horse Comics: No. 0, Apr, 2012 - No. 3, Jul, 2012 ($3.50, limited series)

0-3-Hogan-s/Parkhouse-a: 0-Reprints chapters from Dark Horse Presents #4-6						3.50

RESIDENT ALIEN: AN ALIEN IN NEW YORK
Dark Horse Comics: Apr, 2018 - No. 4, Jul, 2018 ($3.99, limited series)

1-4-Hogan-s/Parkhouse-a						4.00

RESIDENT ALIEN: THE BOOK OF LOVE
Dark Horse Comics: Nov, 2022 - No. 4, Feb, 2023 ($3.99, limited series)

1-4-Hogan-s/Parkhouse-a						4.00

RESIDENT ALIEN: THE MAN WITH NO NAME
Dark Horse Comics: Sept, 2016 - No. 4, Dec, 2016 ($3.99, limited series)

1-4-Hogan-s/Parkhouse-a						4.00

RESIDENT ALIEN: THE SAM HAIN MYSTERY
Dark Horse Comics: No. 0, Apr, 2015 - No. 3, Jul, 2015 ($3.99, limited series)

0-3-Hogan-s/Parkhouse-a: 0-Reprints chapters from Dark Horse Presents V3 #1-3						4.00

RESIDENT ALIEN: THE SUICIDE BLONDE
Dark Horse Comics: No. 0, Aug, 2013 - No. 3, Nov, 2013 ($3.99, limited series)

0-3-Hogan-s/Parkhouse-a: 0-Reprints chapters from Dark Horse Presents #18-20						4.00

RESIDENT ALIEN: YOUR RIDE'S HERE
Dark Horse Comics: Nov, 2020 - No. 6, May, 2021 ($3.99, limited series)

1-6-Hogan-s/Parkhouse-a						4.00

RESIDENT EVIL (Based on video game)
Image Comics (WildStorm): Mar, 1998 - No. 5 ($4.95, quarterly magazine)

1	6	12	18	41	76	110
2-5	4	8	12	23	370	50
...Code: Veronica 1-4 (2002, $14.95) English reprint of Japanese comics	3	6	9	19	30	40
...Collection One ('99, $14.95, TPB) r/#1-4	5	10	15	31	53	75

RESIDENT EVIL (Volume 2)
DC Comics (WildStorm): May, 2009 - No. 6, Feb, 2011 ($3.99)

1-6: 1,2-Liam Sharpe-a. 1-Two covers	1	3	4	6	8	10
...Volume 2 TPB (2011, $19.99) r/#1-6	3	6	9	19	30	40

RESIDENT EVIL: FIRE AND ICE
DC Comics (WildStorm): Dec, 2000 - No. 4, May, 2001 ($2.50, limited series)

Regular Show #24 © CN

Rescue #1 © MAR

The Resistance #3 © AWA

	GD	VG	FN	VF	VF/NM	NM-
	2.0	4.0	6.0	8.0	9.0	9.2

1-Bermejo-c ... 2 · 4 · 6 · 8 · 10 · 12
2-4-Bermejo-c ... 6.00
TPB (2009, $24.99) r/#1-4 plus short stories from Resident Evil magazine
... 3 · 6 · 9 · 19 · 30 · 40

RESISTANCE (Based on the video game)
DC Comics (WildStorm): Early Mar, 2009 - No. 6, Jul, 2009 ($3.99, limited series)
1-6-Ramón Pérez-a/C.P. Smith-c ... 4.00
TPB (2010, $19.99) r/#1-6 ... 20.00

RESISTANCE, THE
DC Comics (WildStorm): Nov, 2002 - No. 8, June, 2003 ($2.95)
1-8-Palmiotti & Gray-s/Santacruz-a ... 3.00

RESISTANCE, THE
AWA Studios: Mar, 2020 - No. 6, Sept, 2020 ($3.99, limited series)
1-6-Straczynski-s/Deodato Jr.-a ... 4.00
...: Reborns (1/21, $3.99) Straczynski-s/C.P. Smith-a ... 4.00

RESISTANCE, THE: UPRISING (Also see Moths)
AWA Studios: Apr, 2021 - No. 6, Sept, 2021 ($3.99, limited series)
1-6-Straczynski-s/C.P. Smith-a ... 4.00

REST (Milo Ventimiglia Presents...)
Devil's Due Publ.: No. 0, Aug, 2008 - No. 2 (99¢/$3.50)
0-(99¢) Prelude to series; Powers-s/McManus-a ... 3.00
1,2-($3.50) 1-Two covers (Tim Sale art & Milo Ventimiglia photo) ... 3.50

RESTAURANT AT THE END OF THE UNIVERSE, THE (See Hitchhiker's Guide to the Galaxy & Life, the Universe & Everything)
DC Comics: 1994 - No. 3, 1994 ($6.95, limited series)
1-3 ... 7.00

RESTLESS GUN (TV)
Dell Publishing Co.: No. 934, Sept, 1958 - No. 1146, Nov-Jan, 1960-61
Four Color 934 (#1)-Photo-c ... 10 · 20 · 30 · 64 · 132 · 200
Four Color 986 (5/59), 1045 (11-1/60), 1089 (3/60), 1146-Wildey-a; all photo-c
... 7 · 14 · 21 · 49 · 92 · 135

RESURRECTIONISTS
Dark Horse Comics: Nov, 2014 - No. 4, Feb, 2015 ($3.50)
1-4-Van Lente-s/Rosenzweig-a ... 3.50

RESURRECTION MAN
DC Comics: May, 1997 - No. 27, Aug, 1999 ($2.50)
1-Lenticular disc on cover ... 6.00
2-5: 2-JLA app. ... 4.00
6-27: 6-Genesis-x-over. 7-Batman app. 10-Hitman-c/app. 16,17-Supergirl x-over. 18-Deadman & Phantom Stranger-c/app. 21-JLA-c/app. ... 4.00
#1,000,000 (11/98) 853rd Century x-over ... 4.00

RESURRECTION MAN (DC New 52)
DC Comics: Nov, 2011 - No. 12, Oct, 2012; No. 0, Nov, 2012 ($2.99)
1-12: 1-Abnett & Lanning-s/Dagnino-a/Reis-c; Body Doubles app. 9-Suicide Squad app. ... 3.00
#0 (11/12) Origin of Mitch Shelley and the Body Doubles; Bachs-a/Francavilla-a ... 3.00

RESURRECTION OF MAGNETO (X-Men)
Marvel Comics: Mar, 2024 - Present ($5.99, limited series)
1-Ewing-s/Vecchio-a; Storm app. ... 6.00

RETIEF (Keith Laumer's)
Adventure Comics (Malibu): Dec, 1989 - Vol. 2, No.6, ($2.25, B&W)
1-6,Vol. 2, #1-6,Vol. 3 (...of The CDT) #1-6 ... 4.00
...and The Warlords #1-6, ...: Diplomatic Immunity #1 (4/91), ...: Giant Killer #1 (9/91), ...: Crime & Punishment #1 (11/91) ... 4.00

RETROVIRUS
Image Comics: Nov, 2012 ($12.99, hardcover GN)
HC-Gray & Palmiotti-s/Fernandez-a/Conner-c ... 13.00

RETURN FROM WITCH MOUNTAIN (See Walt Disney Showcase #44)

RETURNING, THE
BOOM! Studios: Mar, 2014 - No. 4, Jun, 2014 ($3.99, limited series)
1-4-Jason Starr-s/Andrea Mutti-a/Frazer Irving-c ... 4.00

RETURN OF ALISON DARE: LITTLE MISS ADVENTURES, THE (Also see Alison Dare: Little Miss Adventures)
Oni Press: Apr, 2001 - No. 3, Sept, 2001 ($2.95, B&W, limited series)
1-3-J. Torres-s/J.Bone-c/a ... 3.00

RETURN OF CHILLING ADVENTURES IN SORCERY, THE
Archie Comic Publications: Dec, 2022 ($3.99)
1-Short horror stories, Madam Satan, Sabrina & Veronica app.; art by various ... 4.00

RETURN OF GORGO, THE (Formerly Gorgo's Revenge)
Charlton Comics: No. 2, Aug, 1963; No. 3, Fall, 1964 (12¢)
2,3-Ditko-c/a; based on M.G.M. movie ... 8 · 16 · 24 · 55 · 105 · 155

RETURN OF KONGA, THE (Konga's Revenge #2 on)
Charlton Comics: 1962
nn ... 8 · 16 · 24 · 56 · 108 · 160

RETURN OF MEGATON MAN
Kitchen Sink Press: July, 1988 - No. 3, 1988 ($2.00, limited series)
1-3: Simpson-c/a ... 4.00

RETURN OF SUPERMAN 30TH ANNIVERSARY SPECIAL, THE
DC Comics: Dec, 2023 ($9.99, squarebound, one-shot)
1-New stories set after the death of Superman by the original creative teams incl. Jurgens, Kesel, Ordway, Louise Simonson, Bogdanove, Guice, Grummett; bonus promo art ... 10.00

RETURN OF THE GREMLINS (The Roald Dahl characters)
Dark Horse Comics: Mar, 2008 - No. 3, May, 2008 ($2.99, limited series)
1-3-Richardson-s/Yeagle-a. 1-Back-up reprint of intro. from 1943. 2-Back-up reprints of three Gremlin Gus 2-pagers from 1943. 3-Back-up reprints ... 3.00

RETURN OF THE LIVING DEADPOOL
Marvel Comics: Apr, 2015 - No. 4, Jul, 2015 ($3.99, limited series)
1-4-Cullen Bunn-s/Nik Virella-a ... 6.00

RETURN OF THE OUTLAW
Toby Press (Minoan): Feb, 1953 - No. 11, 1955
1-Billy the Kid ... 14 · 28 · 42 · 82 · 121 · 160
2 ... 9 · 18 · 27 · 47 · 61 · 75
3-11 ... 8 · 16 · 24 · 44 · 57 · 70

RETURN OF WOLVERINE (Continued in Wolverine: Infinity Watch)
Marvel Comics: Nov, 2018 - No. 5, Apr, 2019 ($4.99/$3.99, limited series)
1,5-($4.99) Soule-s/McNiven-a ... 5.00
2-4-($3.99) Shalvey-a ... 4.00

RETURN TO JURASSIC PARK
Topps Comics: Apr, 1995 - No. 9, Feb, 1996 ($2.50/$2.95)
1 ... 2 · 4 · 6 · 9 · 12 · 15
2-9: 3-Begin $2.95-c. 9-Artists' Jam issue ... 5.00

RETURN TO THE AMALGAM AGE OF COMICS: THE MARVEL COMICS COLLECTION
Marvel Comics: 1997 ($12.95, TPB)
nn-Reprints Amalgam one-shots: Challengers of the Fantastic #1, The Exciting X-Patrol #1, Iron Lantern #1, The Magnetic Men Featuring Magneto #1, Spider-Boy Team-Up #1 & Thorion of the New Asgods #1 ... 13.00

REVEAL
Dark Horse Comics: Nov, 2002 ($6.95, squarebound)
1-Short stories of Dark Horse characters by various; Lone Wolf 2100, Buffy, Spyboy app. 7.00

REVEALING LOVE STORIES (See Fox Giants)

REVEALING ROMANCES
Ace Magazines: Sept, 1949 - No. 6, Aug, 1950
1 ... 30 · 60 · 90 · 177 · 289 · 400
2 ... 15 · 30 · 45 · 88 · 137 · 185
3-6 ... 14 · 28 · 42 · 82 · 121 · 160

REVELATIONS
Dark Horse Comics: Aug, 2005 - No. 6, Jan, 2006 ($2.99)
1-6-Paul Jenkins-s/Humberto Ramos-a/c ... 3.00
1-6-(BOOM! Studios, 1/14 - No. 6, 6/14, $3.99) reprints original series ... 4.00

REVENGE
Image Comics: Feb, 2014 - No. 4, Jun, 2014 ($2.99)
1-4-Jonathan Ross-s/Ian Churchill-a ... 3.00

REVENGE OF THE COSMIC GHOST RIDER (Also see Cosmic Ghost Rider)
Marvel Comics: Feb, 2020 - No. 5, Oct, 2020 ($4.99/$3.99, limited series)
1-($4.99) Hallum-s/Hepburn-a; back-up w/Gates-s/Shaw-a; present-day Frank Castle app. ... 5.00
2-5-($3.99) 3-5-Mephisto app. ... 4.00

REVENGE OF THE PROWLER (Also see The Prowler)
Eclipse Comics: Feb, 1988 - No. 4, June, 1988 ($1.75/$1.95)
1,3,4: 1-$1.75. 3,4-$1.95-c; Snyder III-a(p) ... 4.00

	GD	VG	FN	VF	VF/NM	NM-
	2.0	4.0	6.0	8.0	9.0	9.2

2 ($2.50)-Contains flexi-disc ... 5.00

REVISIONIST, THE
AfterShock Comics: Jun, 2016 - No. 6, Nov, 2016 ($3.99)
1-6: 1-Frank Barbiere-s/Garry Brown-a ... 4.00

REVIVAL
Image Comics: Jul, 2012 - No. 47, Feb, 2017 ($2.99/$3.99)
1-Tim Seeley-s/Mike Norton-a/Jenny Frison-c ... 12.00
1-Variant-c by Craig Thompson ... 18.00
1-Second-fourth printings ... 4.00
2-26 ... 3.00
27-47-($3.99) ... 4.00

REVOLUTION
IDW Publishing: Sept, 2016 - No. 5, Nov, 2016 ($3.99, limited series)
1-5-Barber & Bunn-s/Ossio-a; multiple covers on each; G.I. Joe, Transformers, Rom, Micronauts, and M.A.S.K. app. 2-5-Bonus character profile pages ... 4.00

REVOLUTIONARIES (Follows the Revolution x-over)
IDW Publishing: Dec, 2016 - No. 8, Jul, 2017 ($3.99)
1-7: 1,2-Barber-s/Ossio-a; multiple covers on each; G.I. Joe, Transformers, Rom app. ... 4.00
8-($4.99) Barber-s/Ossio & Joseph-a ... 5.00

REVOLUTIONARY WAR
Marvel Comics: Mar, 2014 - May, 2014 ($3.99)
...: Alpha 1 (3/14) Part 1; Lanning & Cowsill-s/Elson-a; Capt. Britain & Pete Wisdom app. ... 4.00
...: Dark Angel 1 (3/14) Part 2; Gillen-s/Dietrich Smith-a; Mephisto app. ... 4.00
...: Death's Head II 1 (4/14) Part 4; Lanning & Cowsill-s/Roche-a ... 4.00
...: Knights of Pendragon 1 (3/14) Part 3; Williams-s/Sliney-a; Union Jack app. ... 4.00
...: Motormouth 1 (5/14) Part 6; Dakin-s/Cliquet-a; Killpower app. ... 4.00
...: Omega 1 (5/14) Part 8; conclusion; Lanning & Cowsill-s/Elson-a ... 4.00
...: Supersoldiers 1 (4/14) Part 5; Williams-s/Brent Anderson-a ... 4.00
...: Warheads 1 (5/14) Part 7; Lanning & Cowsill-s/Erskine-a ... 4.00

REVOLUTION: AW YEAH!
IDW Publishing: Feb, 2017 - No. 3, Jul, 2017 ($3.99, limited series)
1-3-All ages x-over of Rom, Transformers, G.I. Joe, Micronauts; Art Baltazar-s/a ... 4.00

REVOLUTION ON THE PLANET OF THE APES
Mr. Comics: Dec, 2005 - No. 6, Aug, 2006 ($3.95)
1-6: 1,2-Salgood Sam-a ... 4.00

REX ALLEN COMICS (Movie star)(Also see Four Color #877 & Western Roundup under Dell Giants)
Dell Publ. Co.: No. 316, Feb, 1951 - No. 31, Dec-Feb, 1958-59 (All-photo-c)

	GD	VG	FN	VF	VF/NM	NM-
	2.0	4.0	6.0	8.0	9.0	9.2

Four Color 316(#1)(52 pgs.)-Rex Allen & his horse Koko begin; Marsh-a | 14 | 28 | 42 | 94 | 207 | 320
2 (9-11/51, 36 pgs.) | 8 | 16 | 24 | 55 | 105 | 150
3-10 | 6 | 12 | 18 | 38 | 69 | 100
11-20 | 5 | 10 | 15 | 34 | 60 | 85
21-23,25-31 | 5 | 10 | 15 | 31 | 53 | 75
24-Toth-a | 5 | 10 | 15 | 34 | 60 | 85

NOTE: Manning a-20, 27-30. Photo back-c F.C. #316, 2-12, 20, 21.

REX DEXTER OF MARS (See Mystery Men Comics)
Fox Feature Syndicate: Fall, 1940 (68 pgs.)
1-Rex Dexter, Patty O'Day, & Zanzibar (Tuska-a) app.; Briefer-c/a
... | 300 | 600 | 900 | 2010 | 3505 | 5000

REX HART (Formerly Blaze Carson; Whip Wilson #9 on)
Timely/Marvel Comics (USA): No. 6, Aug, 1949 - No. 8, Feb, 1950 (All photo-c)
6-Rex Hart & his horse Warrior begin; Black Rider app; Captain Tootsie by Beck; Heath-a
... | 29 | 58 | 87 | 172 | 281 | 390
7,8: 18 pg. Thriller in each. 7-Heath-a. 8-Blaze the Wonder Collie app. in text | 20 | 40 | 60 | 1148 | 192 | 265

REX MORGAN, M.D. (Also see Harvey Comics Library)
Argo Publ.: Dec, 1955 - No. 3, Apr?, 1956
1-r/Rex Morgan daily newspaper strips & daily panel-r of "These Women" by D'Alessio & "Timeout" by Jeff Keate | 18 | 36 | 54 | 107 | 169 | 230
2,3 | 14 | 28 | 42 | 80 | 115 | 150

REX MUNDI (Latin for "King of the World")
Image Comics: No. 0, Aug, 2002 - No. 18, Apr, 2006 ($2.95/$2.99)
0-18-Arvid Nelson-s. 0-13-Eric Johnson-a. 14,15-Jim DiBartolo-a. 18-Ramos-c ... 3.00
Vol. 1: The Guardian of the Temple TPB (1/04, $14.95) r/#0-5 ... 15.00
Book 1: The Guardian of the Temple TPB (Dark Horse, 11/06, $16.95) r/#0-5 & Brother Matthew web comic; Dysart intro. ... 17.00
Vol. 2: The River Underground TPB (4/05, $14.95) r/#6-11 ... 15.00
Book 2: The River Underground (Dark Horse, 2006, $16.95) r/#6-11 ... 17.00
Vol. 3: The Lost Kings TPB (Dark Horse, 9/06, $16.95) r/#12-17 ... 17.00
Book Four: Crowd and Sword TPB (Dark Horse, 12/07, $16.95) r/#18 plus V2 #1-5 and story from Dark Horse Book of Monsters ... 17.00

REX MUNDI (Volume 2)
Dark Horse Comics: July, 2006 - No. 19, Aug, 2009 ($2.99)
1-19-Arvid Nelson-s. 1-JH Williams-c. 16-Chen-c. 18-Linsner-c ... 3.00
Book Five: The Valley at the End of the World TPB (11/08, $17.95) r/#6-12 ... 18.00

REX THE WONDER DOG (See The Adventures of...)

REYN
Image Comics: Jan, 2015 - No. 10, Nov, 2015 ($2.99)
1-10-Symons-s/Stockman-a ... 3.00

RHUBARB, THE MILLIONAIRE CAT
Dell Publishing Co.: No. 423, Sept-Oct, 1952 - No. 563, June, 1954
Four Color 423 (#1) | 8 | 16 | 24 | 52 | 99 | 145
Four Color 466(5/53),563 | 6 | 12 | 18 | 38 | 69 | 100

RIB
Dilemma Productions: Oct, 1995 - April, 1996 ($1.95, B&W)

Ashcan, 1 ... 4.00

RIB
Bookmark Productions: 1996 ($2.95, B&W)
1-Sakai-c; Andrew Ford-s/a ... 4.00

RIB
Caliber Comics: May, 1997 - No. 5, 1998 ($2.95, B&W)
1-5: 1-"Beginnings" pts. 1 & 2 ... 4.00

RIBBON QUEEN
Artists, Writers & Artisans: Jul, 2023 - No. 8, Feb, 2024 ($3.99, limited series)
1-8-Garth Ennis-s/Jacen Burrows-a ... 4.00

RIBIT! (Red Sonja imitation)
Comico: Jan, 1989 - No. 4, Apr, 1989 ($1.95, limited series)
1-4: Frank Thorne-c/a/scripts ... 4.00

RIBTICKLER (Also see Fox Giants)
Fox Feature Synd./Green Publ. (1957)/Norlen (1959): 1945, No. 2, 1946, No. 3, Jul-Aug, 1946 - No. 9, Jul-Aug, 1947; 1957; 1959

	GD	VG	FN	VF	VF/NM	NM-
	2.0	4.0	6.0	8.0	9.0	9.2

1-Funny animal | 29 | 58 | 87 | 172 | 281 | 390
2-(1946) | 15 | 30 | 45 | 85 | 130 | 175
3-9: 3,5,7-Cosmo Cat app. | 14 | 28 | 42 | 76 | 108 | 140
3,7,8 (Green Publ.-1957), 7,8 (Norlen Mag.-1959) 3 | 6 | 9 | 19 | 30 | 40

RICHARD DRAGON
DC Comics: July, 2004 - No. 12, Jun, 2005 ($2.50)
1-12: 1-Dixon-s/McDaniel-a/c; Ben Turner app. 2,3-Nightwing app. 4-6,11,12-Lady Shiva ... 3.00

RICHARD DRAGON, KUNG-FU FIGHTER (See The Batman Chronicles #5, Brave & the Bold, & The Question)
National Periodical Publ./DC Comics: Apr-May, 1975 - No. 18, Nov-Dec, 1977
1-Intro Richard Dragon, Ben Stanley (later Ben Turner) & O-Sensei; 1st app. Barney Ling; adaptation of Jim Dennis (Denny O'Neil) novel "Dragon's Fists" begins, ends #4 | 5 | 10 | 15 | 33 | 57 | 80
2,3: 2-Intro Carolyn Woosan; Starlin/Weiss-c/a; bondage-c. 3-Kirby-a(p); Giordano bondage-c | 3 | 6 | 10 | 14 | 18
4,6-8-Wood inks. 4-Carolyn Woosan dies | 2 | 4 | 6 | 8 | 11 | 14
5-1st app. Lady Shiva; Wood inks | 8 | 16 | 24 | 56 | 108 | 160
9-13,15-17: 9-Ben Stanley becomes Ben Turner; intro Preying Mantis. 16-1st app. Prof Ojo. | 1 | 3 | 4 | 6 | 8 | 12
14-"Spirit of Bruce Lee" | 3 | 6 | 9 | 17 | 26 | 35
18-1st app. Ben Turner as The Bronze Tiger | 3 | 6 | 9 | 14 | 19 | 24
NOTE: Buckler a-14, c-15, 18. Chua c-13, 18. Estrada a-9, 13-18. Estrada/Abel a-10-12. Estrada/Wood a-4-8. Giordano c-1, 3-11. Weiss a-2(partial) c-2i.

RICHARD THE LION-HEARTED (See Ideal a Classical Comic)

RICHIE RICH (See Harvey Collectors Comics, Harvey Hits, Little Dot, Little Lotta, Little Sad Sack, Million Dollar Digest, Mutt & Jeff, Super Richie & 3-D Dolly; also Tastee-Freez Comics in the Promotional Comics section)

RICHIE RICH (...the Poor Little Rich Boy) (See Harvey Hits #3, 9)
Harvey Publ.: Nov, 1960 - #218, Oct, 1982; #219, Nov, 1986 - #254, Jan, 1991
1-(See Little Dot #1 for 1st app.) | 433 | 866 | 1299 | 3681 | 8336 | 13,000
2 | 96 | 192 | 288 | 768 | 1734 | 2700
3-5 | 48 | 96 | 144 | 374 | 862 | 1350
6-10: 8-Christmas-c | 27 | 54 | 81 | 194 | 435 | 675
11-20 | 17 | 34 | 51 | 117 | 259 | 400
21-30 | 12 | 24 | 36 | 81 | 176 | 270
31-40 | 9 | 18 | 27 | 63 | 129 | 195
41-50: 42(2/66)-X-mas-c | 8 | 16 | 24 | 52 | 99 | 145
51-55,57-60: 59-Buck, prototype of Dollar the Dog | 6 | 12 | 18 | 37 | 66 | 95
56-1st app. Super Richie | 7 | 14 | 21 | 44 | 82 | 120
61-64,66-80: 71-Nixon & Robert Kennedy caricatures; outer space-c | 5 | 10 | 15 | 30 | 50 | 70
65-Buck the Dog (Dollar prototype) on cover | 6 | 12 | 18 | 42 | 79 | 115
81-99 | 4 | 8 | 12 | 25 | 40 | 55
100(12/70)-1st app. Irona the robot maid | 4 | 8 | 12 | 25 | 40 | 55
101-111,117-120 | 3 | 6 | 9 | 14 | 20 | 26
112-116: All 52 pg. Giants | 3 | 6 | 9 | 16 | 24 | 32
121-140: 137-1st app. Mr. Cheepers and Professor Keenbean | 2 | 4 | 6 | 9 | 13 | 16
141-160: 145-Infinity-c. 155-3rd app. The Money Monster | 2 | 4 | 6 | 8 | 10 | 12
161-180 | 1 | 3 | 4 | 6 | 8 | 10
181-199 | 1 | 2 | 3 | 5 | 6 | 8
200 | 1 | 3 | 4 | 6 | 8 | 10
201-218: 210-Stone-Age Riches app | 1 | 2 | 3 | 4 | 5 | 7
219-254: 237-Last original material | | | | | | 6.00
Harvey Comics Classics Vol. 2 TPB (Dark Horse Books, 10/07, $19.95) Reprints Richie Rich's early appearances in this title, Little Dot and Richie Rich Success Stories, mostly B&W with some color stories; history and interview with Ernie Colón ... 20.00

RICHIE RICH
Harvey Comics: Mar, 1991 - No. 28, Nov, 1994 ($1.00, bi-monthly)
1-28: Reprints best of Richie Rich ... 4.00
Giant Size 1-4 (10/91-10/93, $2.25, 68 pgs.) ... 5.00

RICHIE RICH ADVENTURE DIGEST MAGAZINE
Harvey Comics: 1992 - No. 7, Sept, 1994 ($1.25, quarterly, digest-size)
1-7 ... 4.00

RICHIE RICH AND...
Harvey Comics: Oct, 1987 - No. 11, May, 1990 ($1.00)
1-Professor Keenbean ... 5.00
2-11: 2-Casper. 3-Dollar the Dog. 4-Cadbury. 5 Mayda Munny. 6-Irona. 7-Little Dot. 8-Professor Keenbean. 9-Little Audrey. 10-Mayda Munny. 11-Cadbury ... 4.00

RICHIE RICH AND BILLY BELLHOPS
Harvey Publications: Oct, 1977 (52 pgs., one-shot)
1 | 3 | 6 | 9 | 14 | 20 | 25

RICHIE RICH AND CADBURY

Revolutionaries #5 © Hasbro

Ribbon Queen #1 © AWA

Richie Rich Billions #30 © HARV

(continued) Harvey Publ.: 10/77; #2, 9/78 - #23, 7/82; #24, 7/90 - #29, 1/91 (1-10: 52pgs.)

	GD 2.0	VG 4.0	FN 6.0	VF 8.0	VF/NM 9.0	NM- 9.2
1-(52 pg. Giant)	3	6	9	14	20	25
2-10-(52 pg. Giant)	2	4	6	8	10	12
11-23						6.00
24-29: 24-Begin $1.00-c						4.00

RICHIE RICH AND CASPER
Harvey Publications: Aug, 1974 - No. 45, Sept, 1982

	GD 2.0	VG 4.0	FN 6.0	VF 8.0	VF/NM 9.0	NM- 9.2
1	3	6	9	21	33	45
2-5	2	4	6	13	18	22
6-10: 10-Xmas-c	2	4	6	9	13	16
11-20	1	3	4	6	8	10
21-45: 22-Xmas-c						6.00

RICHIE RICH AND DOLLAR THE DOG (See Richie Rich #65)
Harvey Publications: Sept, 1977 - No. 24, Aug, 1982 (#1-10: 52 pgs.)

	GD 2.0	VG 4.0	FN 6.0	VF 8.0	VF/NM 9.0	NM- 9.2
1-(52 pg. Giant)	3	6	9	14	20	25
2-10-(52 pg. Giant)	2	4	6	8	10	12
11-24						6.00

RICHIE RICH AND DOT
Harvey Publications: Oct, 1974 (one-shot)

	GD 2.0	VG 4.0	FN 6.0	VF 8.0	VF/NM 9.0	NM- 9.2
1	3	6	9	16	23	30

RICHIE RICH AND GLORIA
Harvey Publications: Sept, 1977 - No. 25, Sept, 1982 (#1-11: 52 pgs.)

	GD 2.0	VG 4.0	FN 6.0	VF 8.0	VF/NM 9.0	NM- 9.2
1-(52 pg. Giant)	3	6	9	14	20	25
2-11-(52 pg. Giant)	2	4	6	8	10	12
12-25						6.00

RICHIE RICH AND HIS GIRLFRIENDS
Harvey Publications: April, 1979 - No. 16, Dec, 1982

	GD 2.0	VG 4.0	FN 6.0	VF 8.0	VF/NM 9.0	NM- 9.2
1-(52 pg. Giant)	2	4	6	11	16	20
2-(52 pg. Giant)	1	3	4	6	8	10
3-10	1	2	3	5	6	8
11-16						6.00

RICHIE RICH AND HIS MEAN COUSIN REGGIE
Harvey Publications: April, 1979 - No. 3, 1980 (50¢) (#1,2: 52 pgs.)

	GD 2.0	VG 4.0	FN 6.0	VF 8.0	VF/NM 9.0	NM- 9.2
1	2	4	6	11	16	20
2-3:	1	3	4	6	8	10

NOTE: No. 4 was advertised, but never released.

RICHIE RICH AND JACKIE JOKERS (Also see Jackie Jokers)
Harvey Publications: Nov, 1973 - No. 48, Dec, 1982

	GD 2.0	VG 4.0	FN 6.0	VF 8.0	VF/NM 9.0	NM- 9.2
1: 52 pg. Giant; contains material from unpublished Jackie Jokers #5	4	8	12	23	37	50
2,3-(52 pg. Giants). 2-R.R. & Jackie 1st meet	3	6	9	15	22	28
4,5	2	4	6	13	18	22
6-10	2	4	6	9	13	16
11-20,26: 11-1st app. Kool Katz. 26-Star Wars parody	1	3	4	6	8	10
21-25,27-40	1	2	3	4	5	7
41-48						6.00

RICHIE RICH AND PROFESSOR KEENBEAN
Harvey Comics: Sept, 1990 - No. 2, Nov, 1990 ($1.00)

	GD 2.0	VG 4.0	FN 6.0	VF 8.0	VF/NM 9.0	NM- 9.2
1,2						4.00

RICHIE RICH AND THE NEW KIDS ON THE BLOCK
Harvey Publications: Feb, 1991 - No. 3, June, 1991 ($1.25, bi-monthly)

	GD 2.0	VG 4.0	FN 6.0	VF 8.0	VF/NM 9.0	NM- 9.2
1-3: 1,2-New Richie Rich stories						4.00

RICHIE RICH AND TIMMY TIME
Harvey Publications: Sept, 1977 (50¢, 52 pgs, one-shot)

	GD 2.0	VG 4.0	FN 6.0	VF 8.0	VF/NM 9.0	NM- 9.2
1	2	4	6	11	16	20

RICHIE RICH BANK BOOK
Harvey Publications: Oct, 1972 - No. 59, Sept, 1982

	GD 2.0	VG 4.0	FN 6.0	VF 8.0	VF/NM 9.0	NM- 9.2
1	5	10	15	33	57	80
2-5: 2-2nd app. The Money Monster	3	6	9	16	23	30
6-10	2	4	6	11	16	20
11-20: 18-Super Richie app.	2	4	6	8	10	12
21-30	1	2	3	4	5	7
31-40	1	2	3	4	5	
41-59						6.00

RICHIE RICH BEST OF THE YEARS
Harvey Publications: Oct, 1977 - No. 6, June, 1980 (128 pgs., digest-size)

	GD 2.0	VG 4.0	FN 6.0	VF 8.0	VF/NM 9.0	NM- 9.2
1(10/77)-Reprints	2	4	6	9	12	15
2-6(11/79-6/80, 95¢). #2(10/78)-Rep. #3(6/79, 75¢)	1	2	3	5	7	9

RICHIE RICH BIG BOOK
Harvey Publications: Nov, 1992 - No. 2, May, 1993 ($1.50, 52 pgs.)

	GD 2.0	VG 4.0	FN 6.0	VF 8.0	VF/NM 9.0	NM- 9.2
1,2						5.00

RICHIE RICH BIG BUCKS
Harvey Publications: Apr, 1991 - No. 8, July, 1992 ($1.00, bi-monthly)

	GD 2.0	VG 4.0	FN 6.0	VF 8.0	VF/NM 9.0	NM- 9.2
1-8						4.00

RICHIE RICH BILLIONS
Harvey Publications: Oct, 1974 - No. 48, Oct, 1982 (#1-33: 52 pgs.)

	GD 2.0	VG 4.0	FN 6.0	VF 8.0	VF/NM 9.0	NM- 9.2
1	4	8	12	23	37	50
2-5: 2-Christmas issue	3	6	9	14	20	25
6-10	2	4	6	10	14	18
11-20	2	4	6	8	10	12
21-33	1	2	3	5	6	8
34-48: 35-Onion app.						6.00

RICHIE RICH CASH
Harvey Publications: Sept, 1974 - No. 47, Aug, 1982

	GD 2.0	VG 4.0	FN 6.0	VF 8.0	VF/NM 9.0	NM- 9.2
1-1st app. Dr. N-R-Gee	3	6	9	21	33	45
2-5	2	4	6	13	18	22
6-10	2	4	6	9	13	16
11-20	1	3	4	6	8	10
21-30	1	2	3	4	5	7
31-47: 33-Dr. Blemish app.						6.00

RICHIE RICH CASH MONEY
Harvey Comics: May, 1992 - No. 2, Aug, 1992 ($1.25)

	GD 2.0	VG 4.0	FN 6.0	VF 8.0	VF/NM 9.0	NM- 9.2
1,2						4.00

RICHIE RICH, CASPER AND WENDY - NATIONAL LEAGUE
Harvey Comics: June, 1976 (50¢)

	GD 2.0	VG 4.0	FN 6.0	VF 8.0	VF/NM 9.0	NM- 9.2
1-Newsstand version of the baseball giveaway	2	4	6	13	18	22

RICHIE RICH COLLECTORS COMICS (See Harvey Collectors Comics)

RICHIE RICH DIAMONDS
Harvey Publications: Aug, 1972 - No. 59, Aug, 1982 (#1, 23-45: 52 pgs.)

	GD 2.0	VG 4.0	FN 6.0	VF 8.0	VF/NM 9.0	NM- 9.2
1-(52 pg. Giant)	5	10	15	33	57	80
2-5	3	6	9	17	26	35
6-10	2	4	6	11	16	20
11-22	2	4	6	8	10	12
23-30-(52 pg. Giants)	2	4	6	8	11	14
31-45: 39-r/Origin Little Dot	1	2	3	5	7	9
46-50	1	2	3	4	5	7
51-59						6.00

RICHIE RICH DIGEST MAGAZINE
Harvey Publications: Oct, 1986 - No. 42, Oct, 1994 ($1.25/$1.75, digest-size)

	GD 2.0	VG 4.0	FN 6.0	VF 8.0	VF/NM 9.0	NM- 9.2
1	1	2	3	5	6	8
2-10						5.00
11-20						4.00
21-42						4.00

RICHIE RICH DIGEST STORIES (...Magazine #?-on)
Harvey Publications: Oct, 1977 - No., 17, Oct, 1982 (75¢/95¢, digest-size)

	GD 2.0	VG 4.0	FN 6.0	VF 8.0	VF/NM 9.0	NM- 9.2
1-Reprints	2	4	6	10	14	18
2-10: Reprints	1	2	3	5	7	9
11-17: Reprints						6.00

RICHIE RICH DIGEST WINNERS
Harvey Publications: Dec, 1977 - No. 16, Sept, 1982 (75¢/95¢, 132 pgs., digest-size)

	GD 2.0	VG 4.0	FN 6.0	VF 8.0	VF/NM 9.0	NM- 9.2
1	2	4	6	9	12	15
2-5	1	2	3	5	7	9
6-16						6.00

RICHIE RICH DOLLARS & CENTS
Harvey Publications: Aug, 1963 - No. 109, Aug, 1982 (#1-43: 68 pgs.; 44-60, 71-94: 52 pgs.)

	GD 2.0	VG 4.0	FN 6.0	VF 8.0	VF/NM 9.0	NM- 9.2
1: (#1-64 are all reprint issues)	22	44	66	154	340	525
2	12	24	36	79	170	260
3-5: 5-r/1st app. of R.R. from Little Dot #1	8	16	24	56	108	160
6-10	6	12	18	40	73	105
11-20	4	8	12	28	47	65
21-30: 25-r/1st app. Nurse Jenny (Little Lotta #62)	3	6	9	21	33	45
31-43: 43-Last 68 pg. issue	3	6	9	17	26	35
44-60: All 52 pgs.	3	6	9	14	19	25
61-71	1	3	4	6	8	10
72-94: All 52 pgs.	2	4	6	8	10	12

	GD 2.0	VG 4.0	FN 6.0	VF 8.0	VF/NM 9.0	NM- 9.2
95-99,101-109						6.00
100-Anniversary issue	1	2	3	5	7	9

RICHIE RICH FORTUNES
Harvey Publications: Sept, 1971 - No. 63, July, 1982 (#1-15: 52 pgs.)

	GD 2.0	VG 4.0	FN 6.0	VF 8.0	VF/NM 9.0	NM- 9.2
1	5	10	15	35	63	90
2-5	3	6	9	19	30	45
6-10	2	4	6	13	18	22
11-15: 11-r/1st app. The Onion	2	4	6	9	12	15
16-30	1	2	3	5	7	.9
31-40	1	2	3	4	5	7
41-63: 62-Onion app.						6.00

RICHIE RICH GEMS
Harvey Publications: Sept, 1974 - No. 43, Sept, 1982

	GD 2.0	VG 4.0	FN 6.0	VF 8.0	VF/NM 9.0	NM- 9.2
1	3	6	9	21	33	45
2-5	2	4	6	13	18	22
6-10	2	4	6	9	13	16
11-20	1	3	4	6	8	10
21-30	1	2	3	4	5	7
31-43: 36-Dr. Blemish, Onion app. 38-1st app. Stone-Age Riches						6.00
44-48: Ape Entertainment, 2011-2012, $3.99) new stories w/Colon-a & reprints						4.00
... Special Collection (Ape Entertainment, 2012, $6.99) r/Valentine & Winter Specials						7.00
... Valentines Special (Ape Entertainment, 2012, $3.99) new story w/Colon-a & reprints						4.00
... Winter Special (Ape Entertainment, 2011, $3.99) new story w/Colon-a & reprints						4.00

RICHIE RICH GOLD AND SILVER
Harvey Publications: Sept, 1975 - No. 42, Oct, 1982 (#1-27: 52 pgs.)

	GD 2.0	VG 4.0	FN 6.0	VF 8.0	VF/NM 9.0	NM- 9.2
1	3	6	9	21	33	45
2-5	2	4	6	11	16	20
6-10	2	4	6	8	11	14
11-27	1	2	3	5	7	9
28-42: 34-Stone-Age Riches app.						6.00

RICHIE RICH GOLD NUGGETS DIGEST
Harvey Publications: Dec., 1990 - No. 4, June, 1991 ($1.75, digest-size)

	GD 2.0	VG 4.0	FN 6.0	VF 8.0	VF/NM 9.0	NM- 9.2
1-4						4.00

RICHIE RICH HOLIDAY DIGEST MAGAZINE (...Digest #4)
Harvey Publications: Jan, 1980 - #3, Jan, 1982; #4, 3/88; #5, 2/89 (annual)

	GD 2.0	VG 4.0	FN 6.0	VF 8.0	VF/NM 9.0	NM- 9.2
1-X-Mas-c	1	3	4	6	8	10
2-5: 2,3: All X-Mas-c. 4-(3/88, $1.25), 5-(2/89, $1.75)	1	2	3	4	5	7

RICHIE RICH INVENTIONS
Harvey Publications: Oct, 1977 - No. 26, Oct, 1982 (#1-11: 52 pgs.)

	GD 2.0	VG 4.0	FN 6.0	VF 8.0	VF/NM 9.0	NM- 9.2
1	3	6	9	14	19	24
2-5	2	4	6	8	10	12
6-11	1	2	3	5	6	8
12-26						6.00

RICHIE RICH JACKPOTS
Harvey Publications: Oct, 1972 - No. 58, Aug, 1982 (#41-43: 52 pgs.)

	GD 2.0	VG 4.0	FN 6.0	VF 8.0	VF/NM 9.0	NM- 9.2
1-Debut of Cousin Jackpots	5	10	15	31	53	75
2-5	3	6	9	17	26	35
6-10	2	4	6	11	16	20
11-15,17-20	2	4	6	8	10	12
16-Super Richie app.	2	4	6	9	12	15
21-30	1	2	3	5	7	9
31-40,44-50: 37-Caricatures of Frank Sinatra, Dean Martin, Sammy Davis, Jr.						
45-Dr. Blemish app.	1	2	3	4	5	7
41-43 (52 pgs.)	2	4	6	8	10	
51-58						6.00

RICHIE RICH MILLION DOLLAR DIGEST (...Magazine #?-on)(See Million Dollar Digest)
Harvey Publications: Oct, 1980 - No. 10, Oct, 1982 ($1.50)

	GD 2.0	VG 4.0	FN 6.0	VF 8.0	VF/NM 9.0	NM- 9.2
1	2	3	4	6	8	10
2-10						7.00

RICHIE RICH MILLIONS
Harvey Publ.: 9/61; #2, 9/62 - #113, 10/82 (#1-48: 68 pgs.; 49-64, 85-97: 52 pgs.)

	GD 2.0	VG 4.0	FN 6.0	VF 8.0	VF/NM 9.0	NM- 9.2
1: (#1-3 are all reprint issues)	27	54	81	194	435	675
2	12	24	36	83	182	280
3-5: All other giants are new & reprints. 5-1st 15 pg. Richie Rich story	9	18	27	61	123	185
6-10	8	16	24	52	99	145
11-20	6	12	18	37	66	95
21-30	4	8	12	27	44	60
31-48: 31-1st app. The Onion. 48-Last 68 pg. Giant	3	6	9	19	30	40
49-64: 52 pg. Giants	3	6	9	14	20	25
65-67,69-73,75-84	2	4	6	8	10	12
68-1st Super Richie-c (11/74)	2	4	6	13	18	22
74-1st app. Mr. Woody; Super Richie app.	2	4	6	8	11	14
85-97: 52 pg. Giants	2	4	6	8	11	14
98,99	1	2	3	4	5	7
100						
101-113						6.00

RICHIE RICH MONEY WORLD
Harvey Publications: Sept, 1972 - No. 59, Sept, 1982

	GD 2.0	VG 4.0	FN 6.0	VF 8.0	VF/NM 9.0	NM- 9.2
1-(52 pg. Giant)-1st app. Mayda Munny	5	10	15	34	60	85
2-Super Richie app.	3	6	9	19	30	40
3-5	3	6	9	16	23	30
6-10: 9,10-Richie Rich mistakenly named Little Lotta on covers	2	4	6	11	16	20
11-20: 16,20-Dr. N-R-Gee	2	4	6	8	10	12
21-30	1	2	3	5	7	9
31-50	1	2	3	4	5	7
51-59						6.00
Digest 1 (2/91, $1.75)						5.00
2-8 (12/93, $1.75)						3.00

RICHIE RICH PROFITS
Harvey Publications: Oct, 1974 - No. 47, Sept, 1982

	GD 2.0	VG 4.0	FN 6.0	VF 8.0	VF/NM 9.0	NM- 9.2
1	3	6	9	21	33	45
2-5	2	4	6	13	18	22
6-10: 10-Origin of Dr. N-R-Gee	2	4	6	9	13	16
11-20: 15-Christmas-c	1	3	4	6	8	10
21-30	1	2	3	4	5	7
31-47						6.00

RICHIE RICH RELICS
Harvey Comics: Jan, 1988 - No.4, Feb, 1989 (75¢/$1.00, reprints)

	GD 2.0	VG 4.0	FN 6.0	VF 8.0	VF/NM 9.0	NM- 9.2
1-4						4.00

RICHIE RICH RICHES
Harvey Publications: July, 1972 - No. 59, Aug, 1982 (#1, 2, 41-45: 52 pgs.)

	GD 2.0	VG 4.0	FN 6.0	VF 8.0	VF/NM 9.0	NM- 9.2
1-(52 pg. Giant)-1st app. The Money Monster	5	10	15	35	63	90
2-(52 pg. Giant)	3	6	9	21	33	45
3-5	3	6	9	16	23	30
6-10: 7-1st app. Aunt Novo	2	4	6	11	16	20
11-20: 17-Super Richie app. (3/75)	2	4	6	8	10	12
21-40	1	2	3	5	6	8
41-45: 52 pg. Giants	1	3	4	6	8	10
46-59: 56-Dr. Blemish app.						6.00

RICHIE RICH: RICH RESCUE
Ape Entertainment: 2011 - No. 4, 2011 ($3.95, limited series)

	GD 2.0	VG 4.0	FN 6.0	VF 8.0	VF/NM 9.0	NM- 9.2
1-6-New short stories by various incl. Ernie Colon; Jack Lawrence-c						4.00
FCBD Edition (2011, giveaway) Flip book with Kung Fu Panda						3.00

RICHIE RICH SUCCESS STORIES
Harvey Publications: Nov, 1964 - No. 105, Sept, 1982 (#1-38: 68 pgs., 39-55, 67-90: 52 pgs.)

	GD 2.0	VG 4.0	FN 6.0	VF 8.0	VF/NM 9.0	NM- 9.2
1	23	46	69	161	356	550
2	9	18	27	60	120	150
3-5	8	16	24	54	102	150
6-10	5	10	15	35	63	90
11-20	5	10	15	31	53	75
21-30: 27-1st Penny Van Dough (8/69)	4	8	12	23	37	50
31-38: 38-Last 68 pg. Giant	3	6	9	19	30	40
39-55-(52 pgs.): 44-Super Richie app.	3	6	9	14	20	25
56-66	2	4	6	8	10	12
67-90: 52 pgs.	2	4	6	8	11	14
91-99,101-105: 91-Onion app. 101-Dr. Blemish app.						6.00
100	1	2	3	5	7	9

RICHIE RICH SUMMER BONANZA
Harvey Comics: Oct, 1991 ($1.95, one-shot, 68 pgs.)

	GD 2.0	VG 4.0	FN 6.0	VF 8.0	VF/NM 9.0	NM- 9.2
1-Richie Rich, Little Dot, Little Lotta						5.00

RICHIE RICH TREASURE CHEST DIGEST (...Magazine #3)
Harvey Publications: Apr, 1982 - No. 3, Aug, 1982 (95¢, Digest Mag.)
(#4 advertised but not publ.)

	GD 2.0	VG 4.0	FN 6.0	VF 8.0	VF/NM 9.0	NM- 9.2
1	1	3	4	6	8	10
2,3	1	2	3	4	5	7

RICHIE RICH VACATION DIGEST
Harvey Comics: Oct, 1991; Oct, 1992; Oct, 1993 ($1.75, digest-size)

	GD 2.0	VG 4.0	FN 6.0	VF 8.0	VF/NM 9.0	NM- 9.2
1-(10/91), 2-(10/92), 1-(10/93)						4.00

RICHIE RICH VACATIONS DIGEST
Harvey Publ.: 11/77; No. 2, 10/78 - No. 7, 10/81; No. 8, 8/82; No. 9, 10/82 (Digest, 132 pgs.)

	GD 2.0	VG 4.0	FN 6.0	VF 8.0	VF/NM 9.0	NM- 9.2
1-Reprints	2	4	6	9	12	15
2-6	1	2	3	5		
7-9						6.00

RICHIE RICH VAULT OF MYSTERY
Harvey Publications: Nov, 1974 - No. 47, Sept, 1982

	GD 2.0	VG 4.0	FN 6.0	VF 8.0	VF/NM 9.0	NM- 9.2
1	4	8	12	25	40	55
2-5: 5-The Condor app.	3	6	9	14	20	25
6-10	2	4	6	9	13	16
11-20	1	3	4	6	8	10
21-30	1	2	3	4	5	7
31-47						6.00

RICHIE RICH ZILLIONZ
Harvey Publ.: Oct, 1976 - No. 33, Sept, 1982 (#1-4: 68 pgs.; #5-18: 52 pgs.)

	GD 2.0	VG 4.0	FN 6.0	VF 8.0	VF/NM 9.0	NM- 9.2
1	3	6	9	19	30	40
2-4: 4-Last 68 pg. Giant	2	4	6	11	16	20
5-10	2	4	6	8	10	12
11-18: 18-Last 52 pg. Giant	1	2	3	4	5	7
19-33						6.00

RICH JOHNSTON'S... (Parody of the Avengers movie characters)
BOOM! Studios: Apr, 2012 ($3.99, series of one-shots)

	GD 2.0	VG 4.0	FN 6.0	VF 8.0	VF/NM 9.0	NM- 9.2
... Captain American Idol 1 - Rich Johnston-s/Chris Haley-a						4.00
... Iron Muslim 1 - Rich Johnston-s/Bryan Turner-a; Demon in a Bottle cover swipe						4.00
... Scienthorlogy 1 - Rich Johnston-s/Michael Netzer-a						4.00
... The Avengefuls 1 - Rich Johnston-s/Joshua Covey; two printings						4.00

RICK AND MORTY (Based on the Adult Swim animated series)
Oni Press: Apr, 2015 - No. 60, Mar, 2020 ($3.99)

	GD 2.0	VG 4.0	FN 6.0	VF 8.0	VF/NM 9.0	NM- 9.2
1-Zac Gorman-s/CJ Cannon-a; multiple covers	10	20	30	68	144	220
2,3	3	6	9	19	30	40
4-49,51-60: 44-The Vindicators app.						4.00
50-($6.99) Morty's Mind Blowers						7.00
..#1 50th Issue Celebration Reprint (5/19, $3.99) r/#1						4.00
..#100 (10/22, $4.99) Reprints issues from various mini-series						3.00
... Free Comic Book Day 2017 (5/17, giveaway) r/#1; preview of Pocket Like You Stole It						3.00
... : Mr. Nimbus 1 (10/21, $4.99) Retells 1st meeting with Rick; Time Lord Jessica app.						5.00
Oni 25th Anniversary: Rick and Morty #1 (8/22, $9.99) Reprints #1; silver foil trade logo						10.00
... Presents: Big, Dumb, Summer Vacation 1 (7/22, $4.99) Griggs-s						5.00
... Presents: Birdperson 1 (7/20, $4.99) Origin & 1st meeting with Rick						5.00

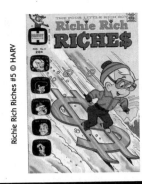

Richie Rich Riches #5 © HARV

Rick and Morty (2023 series) #6 © CN

Riddler: Year One #4 © DC

	GD	VG	FN	VF	VF/NM	NM-
	2.0	4.0	6.0	8.0	9.0	9.2

... Presents: Council of Ricks 1 (6/20, $4.99) Goldman-s/Ellerby & Murphy-a — 5.00
... Presents: Death Stalkers 1 (1/21, $4.99) Phillips-s/Ryan Lee-a; Hemorrhage app. — 5.00
... Presents: Fricky Friday 1 (10/23, $5.99) Moreci-s — 6.00
... Presents: HeRickttics of Rick 1 (1/22, $4.99) Homage to Dune — 5.00
... Presents: Jaguar 1 (11/20, $4.99) Ellerby-s/a — 5.00
... Presents: Jerry 1 (3/19, $4.99) Ferrier-s/Cannon-a — 5.00
... Presents: Jerryboree 1 (3/21, $4.99) Grace Thomas-s/Gina Allnatt-a — 5.00
... Presents: Krombopulos Michael 1 (6/18, $4.99) Ortberg-s/Cannon-a — 5.00
... Presents: Maximum Crescendo 1 (1/24, $5.99) Sequel to Maximum Overture — 6.00
... Presents: Maximum Overture 1 (5/23, $5.99) Concerto app. — 6.00
... Presents: Morty's Run 1 (3/22, $4.99) — 5.00
... Presents: Mr. Meeseeks 1 (6/19, $4.99) Asmus & Festante-s/Cannon-a — 5.00
... Presents: Pickle Rick 1 (11/18, $4.99) Delilah S. Dawson-s/CJ Cannon-a; Jaguar app. — 6.00
... Presents: Rick in a Box 1 (12/23, $5.99) Cannon-a — 6.00
... Presents: Sleepy Gary 1 (9/18, $4.99) Visaggio-s/Cannon-a — 5.00
... Presents: Snuffles Goes to War 1 (10/21, $4.99) Snowball app. — 5.00
... Presents: The Flesh Curtains 1 (9/19, $4.99) Sturges-s/Cannon-a; Birdman app. — 5.00
... Presents: The Science of Summer 1 (8/23, $5.99) Visaggio-s/Ellerby-a — 6.00
... Presents: The Hotel Immortal 1 (7/21, $4.99) Arbony-s/Ellerby-a — 5.00
... Presents: The Vindicators 1 (3/18, $4.99) Cannon-a; Pickle Rick app. — 5.00
... Presents: Time Zoo 1 (2/23, $4.99) Goldman-s/Murphy-a — 5.00
... Presents: Unity 1 (11/19, $4.99) Tini Howard-s/Marco Mazzarello-a — 5.00

RICK AND MORTY (Volume 2)
Oni Press: Jan, 2023 - No. 12, Dec, 2023 ($3.99/$4.99)
1-6: 1-3-The Multiverse of Goldenfolds app.; multiple covers — 4.00
7-12-($4.99, 40 pgs) — 5.00

RICK AND MORTY: CORPORATE ASSETS (Adult Swim)
Oni Press: Nov, 2021 - No. 4, Feb, 2022 ($3.99, limited series)
1-4-James Asmus-s/Jarrett Williams-a; multiple covers — 4.00

RICK AND MORTY: CRISIS ON EARTH C-137 (Adult Swim)
Oni Press: Aug, 2022 - No. 4, Nov, 2022 ($3.99, limited series)
1-4-Supernova & Noob Noob app.; multiple covers — 4.00

RICK AND MORTY EVER AFTER (Adult Swim)
Oni Press: Oct, 2020 - No. 4, Jan, 2021 ($3.99, limited series)
1-4-Sam Maggs-s/Sarah Stern-a; multiple covers — 4.00

RICK AND MORTY GO TO HELL (Adult Swim)
Oni Press: Jun, 2020 - No. 5, Oct, 2020 ($3.99, limited series)
1-5-Ferrier-s/Oroza-a; multiple covers — 4.00

RICK AND MORTY: HEART OF RICKNESS (Adult Swim)
Oni Press: Jun, 2023 - No. 4, Oct, 2024 ($4.99, limited series)
1-4-Moreci-s/Tramontano-a; multiple covers — 5.00

RICK AND MORTY INFINITY HOUR (Adult Swim)
Oni Press: Mar, 2022 - No. 4, Jun, 2023 ($3.99, limited series)
1-4-Visaggio-s/Ellerby-a; multiple covers — 4.00

RICK AND MORTY: LIL' POOPY SUPERSTAR (Adult Swim)
Oni Press: Jul, 2016 - No. 5, Nov, 2016 ($3.99, limited series)
1-5-Sarah Graley-s/a; multiple covers — 4.00

RICK AND MORTY: MEESEEKS P.I. (Adult Swim)
Oni Press: Nov, 2023 - No. 4, Feb, 2024 ($4.99, limited series)
1-4-Stresing-s/Casey-a; multiple covers — 5.00

RICK AND MORTY: POCKET LIKE YOU STOLE IT (Adult Swim)
Oni Press: Jul, 2017 - No. 5, Nov, 2017 ($3.99, limited series)
1-5-Tim Howard-s/Marc Ellerby-a; multiple covers — 4.00

RICK AND MORTY: RICK'S NEW HAT (Adult Swim)
Oni Press: Jun, 2021 - No. 5, Dec, 2021 ($3.99, limited series)
1-5-Alex Firer-s/Fred C. Stresing-a — 4.00

RICK AND MORTY VS. CTHULHU (Adult Swim)
Oni Press: Dec, 2022 - No. 4, Mar, 2023 ($3.99, limited series)
1-4-Jim Zub-s/Troy Little-a — 4.00

RICK AND MORTY VS. DUNGEONS & DRAGONS (Adult Swim)
Oni Press/IDW Publishing: Aug, 2018 - No. 4, Dec, 2018 ($3.99, limited series)
1-4-Patrick Rothfuss & Jim Zub-s/Troy Little-a — 4.00
1: Director's Cut Edition (2/19, $4.99) r/#1 with some script pages and B&W art — 5.00
...: The Meeseeks Adventure 1 (2/22, $5.99) Jim Zub-s/Troy Little-a — 6.00

RICK AND MORTY VS. DUNGEONS & DRAGONS II: PAINSCAPE (Adult Swim)
Oni Press/IDW Publishing: Aug, 2019 - No. 4, Dec, 2019 ($3.99, limited series)

1-4-Jim Zub-s/Troy Little-a — 4.00

RICK AND MORTY WORLDS APART (Adult Swim)
Oni Press: Feb, 2021 - No. 4, May, 2021 ($3.99, limited series)
1-4-Trujillo-s/Fleecs-a; the dragon Balthrowmaw app. — 4.00

RICKY
Standard Comics (Visual Editions): No. 5, Sept, 1953

	GD	VG	FN	VF	VF/NM	NM-
5-Teenage humor	13	26	39	72	101	130

RICKY NELSON (TV)(See Sweethearts V2#42)
Dell Publishing Co.: No. 956, Dec, 1958 - No. 1192, June, 1961 (All photo-c)

	GD	VG	FN	VF	VF/NM	NM-
Four Color 956,998	17	34	51	119	265	410
Four Color 1115,1192: 1192-Manning-a	12	24	36	82	179	275

RIDDLER, THE : YEAR OF THE VILLAIN
DC Comics: 2019 ($4.99, one-shot)
1-King Tut and Apex Lex app.; origin re-told; Russell-s/Godlewski-a/Janin-c — 5.00

RIDDLER, THE : YEAR ONE (Based on the 2022 Batman movie)
DC Comics (Black Label): Jun, 2022 - No. 6, Sept, 2023 ($4.99, limited series)
1-6-Origin of the Riddler from the 2022 Batman movie; Paul Dano-s/Stevan Subic-a — 5.00

RIDE, THE (Also see Gun Candy flip-book)
Image Comics: June, 2004 - No. 2, July, 2004 ($2.95, B&W, anthology)
1,2: Hughes-c/Wagner-s. 1-Hamner & Stelfreeze-a. 2-Jeanty & Pearson-a — 3.00
... Burning Desire 1-5 (6/19 - No. 5, 10/19, $3.99) 1-Hughes-c/a(6 pgs.) 4-Coker-a — 4.00
... Die Valkyrie 1-3 (6/07 - No. 3, 2/08, $2.99) Stelfreeze-a/Wagner-a/Pearson-c — 3.00
... Foreign Parts 1 (1/05, $2.95) Dixon-s/Haynes-a; Marz-s/Brunner-a; Pearson-c — 3.00
... Halloween Special: The Key to Survival (10/07, $3.50) Tomm Coker-s/a — 3.50
... Savannah 1 (4/07, $4.99) s/a by students of Savannah College of Art — 5.00
... 2 For the Road 1 (10/04, $2.95) Dixon-s/Hamner & Gregory-a/Johnson-c — 3.00
Vol. 1 TPB (2005, $9.99) r/#1,2, Foreign Parts, 2 For the Road; Chaykin intro. — 10.00
Vol. 2 TPB (2005, $15.99) r/Gun Candy #1,2 & Die Valkyrie #1-3; sketch pages — 16.00

RIDER, THE (Frontier Trail #6; also see Blazing Sixguns I.W. Reprint #10, 11)
Ajax/Farrell Publ. (Four Star Comic Corp.): Mar, 1957 - No. 5, 1958

	GD	VG	FN	VF	VF/NM	NM-
1-Swift Arrow, Lone Rider begin	15	30	45	83	124	165
2-5	9	18	27	47	61	75

RIDERS OF THE PURPLE SAGE (See Zane Grey & Four Color #372)

RIFLEMAN, THE (TV)
Dell Publ. Co/Gold Key No. 13 on: No. 1009, 7-9/59 - No. 12, 7-9/62; No. 13, 11/62 - No. 20, 10/64

	GD	VG	FN	VF	VF/NM	NM-
Four Color 1009 (#1)	24	48	72	168	372	575
2 (1-3/60)	10	20	30	67	141	215
3-Toth-a (4 pgs.); variant edition has back-c with "Something Special" comic strip	10	20	30	65	135	205
4-9: 6-Toth-a (4 pgs.)	9	18	27	59	117	175
10-Classic-c	50	100	150	400	900	1400
11-20	7	14	21	46	86	125

NOTE: *Warren Tufts* a-2-9. All have Chuck Connors & Johnny Crawford photo-c. Photo back c-13-15.

RIFTWAR
Marvel Comics: July, 2009 - No. 5, Dec, 2009 ($3.99, limited series)
1-5-Adaptation of Raymond E. Feist novel; Glass-s/Stegman-a — 4.00

RIGHTEOUS THIRST FOR VENGEANCE, A
Image Comics: Oct, 2021 - Present ($3.99, limited series)
1-11-Remender-s/Araújo-a — 4.00

RIMA, THE JUNGLE GIRL
National Periodical Publications: Apr-May, 1974 - No. 7, Apr-May, 1975

	GD	VG	FN	VF	VF/NM	NM-
1-Origin, part 1 (#1-5: 20¢; 6,7: 25¢)	3	6	9	19	30	40
2-7: 2-4-Origin, parts 2-4. 7-Origin & only app. Space Marshal	2	4	6	8	10	12

NOTE: *Kubert* c-1-7. *Nino* a-1-7. *Redondo* a-1-7.

RING OF BRIGHT WATER (See Movie Classics)

RING OF THE NIBELUNG, THE
DC Comics: 1989 - No. 4, 1990 ($4.95, squarebound, 52 pgs., mature readers)
1-4: Adapts Wagner cycle of operas, Gil Kane-c/a — 5.00

RING OF THE NIBELUNG, THE
Dark Horse Comics: Feb, 2000 - Sept, 2001 ($2.95/$2.99/$5.99, limited series)
Vol. 1 (The Rhinegold) 1-4: Adapts Wagner; P. Craig Russell-s/a — 3.00
Vol. 2,3: Vol. 2 (The Valkyrie) 1-3 -(8/00). Vol. 3 (Siegfried) 1-3 -(12/00) — 3.00
Vol. 4 (The Twilight of the Gods) 1-3: 1-(6/01) — 3.00
4-(9/01, $5.99, 64 pgs.) Conclusion with sketch pages — 3.00

	GD 2.0	VG 4.0	FN 6.0	VF 8.0	VF/NM 9.0	NM- 9.2

RINGO KID, THE (2nd Series)
Marvel Comics Group: Jan, 1970 - No. 23, Nov, 1973; No. 24, Nov, 1975 - No. 30, Nov, 1976

1-Williamson-a r-from #10, 1956.	5	10	15	33	57	80
2-11: 2-Severin-c. 11-Last 15¢ issue	2	4	6	11	16	20
12 (52 pg. Giant)	3	6	9	16	24	32
13-20: 13-Wildey-r. 20-Williamson-r/#1	2	4	6	9	13	16
21-30	2	4	6	8	10	12
27,28-(30¢-c variant, limited distribution)(5,7/76)	15	30	45	100	220	340

RINGO KID WESTERN, THE (1st Series) (See Wild Western & Western Trails)
Atlas Comics (HPC)/Marvel Comics: Aug, 1954 - No. 21, Sept, 1957

1-Origin; The Ringo Kid begins	43	86	129	271	461	650
2-Black Rider app.; origin/1st app. Ringo's Horse Arab	24	48	72	142	234	325
3-5	16	32	48	92	144	195
6-8-Severin-a(3) each	17	34	51	98	154	210
9,11,12,14-21: 12-Orlando-a (4 pgs.)	14	28	42	81	118	155
10,13-Williamson-a (4 pgs.)	15	30	45	83	124	165

NOTE: *Berg* a-8. *Maneely* a-1-5, 15, 16(text illos only), 17(4), 18, 20, 21; c-1-6, 8, 13, 15-18, 20. *J. Severin* c-10, 11. *Sinnott* a-1. *Wildey* a-16-18.

RINGSIDE
Image Comics: Nov, 2015 - No. 15, Apr, 2018 ($3.99)

| 1-15-Keatinge-s/Barber-a | | | | | | 4.00 |

RINSE, THE
BOOM! Studios: Sept, 2011 - No. 4, Dec, 2011 ($1.00/$3.99)

| 1-($1.00)-Phillips-s/Laming-a | | | | | | 3.00 |
| 2-4-($3.99) | | | | | | 4.00 |

RIN TIN TIN (See March of Comics #163,180,195)

RIN TIN TIN (TV) (....& Rusty #21 on; see Western Roundup under Dell Giants)
Dell Publishing Co./Gold Key: Nov, 1952 - No. 38, May-July, 1961; Nov, 1963 (All Photo-c)

Four Color 434 (#1)	17	34	51	117	259	400
Four Color 476,523	10	20	30	64	132	200
4(3-5/54)-10	6	12	18	40	73	105
11-17,19,20	6	12	18	37	66	95
18-(4-5/57) 1st app. of Rusty and the Cavalry of Fort Apache, photo-c	7	14	21	46	86	125
21-38: 36-Toth-a (4 pgs.)	5	10	15	31	53	75
... & Rusty 1 (11/63-Gold Key)	5	10	15	33	57	80

RIO (Also see Eclipse Monthly)
Comico: June, 1987 ($8.95, 64 pgs.)

| 1-Wildey-c/a | | | | | | 9.00 |

RIO AT BAY
Dark Horse Comics: July, 1992 - No. 2, Aug, 1992 ($2.95, limited series)

| 1,2-Wildey-c/a | | | | | | 4.00 |

RIO BRAVO (Movie) (See 4-Color #1018)
Dell Publishing Co.: 1959

| Four Color 1018-Toth-a; John Wayne, Dean Martin, & Ricky Nelson photo-c. | 30 | 60 | 90 | 216 | 483 | 750 |

RIO CONCHOS (See Movie Comics)

RIOT (Satire)
Atlas Comics (ACI No. 1-5/WPI No. 6): Apr, 1954 - No. 3, Sept, 1954; No. 4, Feb, 1956 - No. 6, June, 1956

1-Russ Heath-a	55	110	165	352	601	850
2-Li'l Abner satire by Post	34	68	102	204	332	460
3-Last precode (8/54)	31	62	93	182	296	410
4-Infinity-c; Marilyn Monroe "7 Year Itch" movie satire; Mad Rip-off ads	39	78	117	231	378	525
5-Marilyn Monroe, John Wayne parody; part photo-c	39	78	117	236	388	540
6-Lorna of the Jungle satire by Everett; Dennis the Menace satire-c/story; part photo-c	31	62	93	182	296	410

NOTE: *Berg* a-3. *Burgos* c-1, 2. *Colan* a-1. *Everett* a-4, 6. *Heath* a-1. *Maneely* a-1, 2, 4-6; c-3, 4, 6. *Post* a-1-4. *Reinman* a-3. *Severin* a-3.

RIOT GEAR
Triumphant Comics: Sept, 1993 - No. 11, July, 1994 ($2.50, serially numbered)

1-8: 1-2nd app. Riot Gear. 2-1st app. Rabin. 3,4-Triumphant Unleashed x-over. 3-1st app. Surzar. 4-Death of Captain Tich						4.00
9-11 (May not exist)	1	3	4	6	8	10
Violent Past 1,2: 1-(2/94, $2.50)						4.00

R.I.P.
TSR, Inc.: 1990 - No. 8, 1991 ($2.95, 44 pgs.)

| 1-8-Based on TSR game | | | | | | 5.00 |

RIPCLAW (See Cyberforce)
Image Comics (Top Cow Prod.): Apr, 1995 - No. 3, June, 1995 (Limited series)

1/2-Gold, 1/2-San Diego ed., 1/2-Chicago ed.	1	3	4	6	8	10
1-3: Brandon Peterson-a(p)						4.00
Special 1 (10/95, $2.50)						4.00

RIPCLAW
Image Comics (Top Cow Prod.): V2#1, Dec, 1995 - No. 6, June, 1996 ($2.50)

| V2#1-6: 5-Medieval Spawn/Witchblade Preview | | | | | | 4.00 |
| ...: Pilot Season 1 (2007, $2.99) Jason Aaron-s/Jorge Lucas-a/Tony Moore-a | | | | | | 4.00 |

RIPCORD (TV)
Dell Publishing Co.: Mar-May, 1962

| Four Color 1294 | 7 | 14 | 21 | 46 | 86 | 125 |

R.I.P.D.
Dark Horse Comics: Oct, 1999 - No. 4, Jan, 2000 ($2.95, limited series)

| 1-4 | | | | | | 4.00 |
| TPB (2003, $12.95) r/#1-4 | | | | | | 13.00 |

R.I.P.D.: CITY OF THE DAMNED
Dark Horse Comics: Nov, 2012 - No. 4, Mar, 2013 ($3.50, limited series)

| 1-4-Barlow-s/Parker-a/Wilkins-c | | | | | | 3.50 |

RIP HUNTER TIME MASTER (See Showcase #20, 21, 25, 26 & Time Masters)
National Periodical Publications: Mar-Apr, 1961 - No. 29, Nov-Dec, 1965

1-(3-4/61)	71	142	213	568	1284	2000
2	25	50	75	175	388	600
3-5: 5-Last 10¢ issue	18	30	45	105	232	360
6,7-Toth-a in each	11	22	33	73	157	240
8-15	8	16	24	54	102	150
16-19	6	12	18	41	76	110
20-Hitler-c/s	11	22	33	73	157	240
21-28	6	12	18	37	66	95
29-Gil Kane-c	8	16	24	52	99	145

RIP IN TIME (Also see Teenage Mutant Ninja Turtles #5-7)
Fantagor Press: Aug, 1986 - No.5, 1987 ($1.50, B&W)

| 1-5: Corben-c/a in all | | | | | | 4.00 |

RIP KIRBY (Also see Harvey Comics Hits #57, & Street Comix)
David McKay Publications: 1948

| Feature Books 51,54: Raymond-c; 51-Origin | 42 | 84 | 126 | 265 | 445 | 625 |

RIPLEY'S BELIEVE IT OR NOT! (See Ace Comics, All-American Comics, Mystery Comics Digest #1, 4, 7, 10, 13, 16, 19, 22, 25)

RIPLEY'S BELIEVE IT OR NOT!
Harvey Publications: Sept, 1953 - No. 4, March, 1954

| 1-Powell-a | 22 | 44 | 66 | 132 | 216 | 300 |
| 2-4 | 12 | 24 | 36 | 67 | 94 | 120 |

RIPLEY'S BELIEVE IT OR NOT! (Continuation of Ripleys'...True Ghost Stories & Ripley's...True War Stories)
Gold Key: No. 4, April, 1967 - No. 94, Feb, 1980

4-Shrunken head photo-c; McWilliams-a	5	10	15	30	50	70
5-Subtitled "True War Stories"; Evans-a; 1st Jeff Jones in comics? (2 pgs.)	4	8	12	28	47	65
6-10: 6-McWilliams-a. 10-Evans-a(2)	3	6	9	19	30	40
11-20: 15-Evans-a	3	6	9	16	23	30
21-30	2	4	6	13	18	22
31-38,40-60	2	4	6	10	14	18
39-Crandall-a	2	4	6	10	14	18
61-73	1	3	4	6	8	10
74,77-83-(52 pgs.)	2	4	6	9	13	16
75,76,84-94	1	2	3	5	6	8
Story Digest Mag. 1(6/70)-4-3/4x6-1/2", 148pp.	5	10	15	31	53	75

NOTE: *Evanish* art by Luiz Dominguez #22-25, 27, 30, 31, 40. *Jeff Jones* a-5(2 pgs.). *McWilliams* a-65, 66, 70, 89. *Orlando* a-8. *Sparling* c-68. Reprints-74, 77-84, 87 (part), 91, 93 (all). *Williamson, Wood* a-80r/#1.

RIPLEY'S BELIEVE IT OR NOT!
Dark Horse Comics: May, 2002 - No. 3, Oct, 2002 ($2.99, B&W, unfinished limited series)

| 1-3-Nord-c/a. 1-Stories of Amelia Earhart & D.B. Cooper | | | | | | 3.00 |

RIPLEY'S BELIEVE IT OR NOT! TRUE GHOST STORIES (Along with Ripley's...True War Stories, the three issues together precede the 1967 series that starts its numbering with #4) (Also see Dan Curtis)
Gold Key: June, 1965 - No. 2, Oct, 1966

1-Williamson, Wood & Evans-a; photo-c	9	18	27	59	117	175
2-Orlando, McWilliams-a; photo-c	5	10	15	34	60	85
Mini-Comic 1(1976-3-1/4x6-1/2")	2	4	6	8	11	14
11186(1977)-Golden Press; ($1.95, 224 pgs.)-All-r	5	10	15	30	50	70
11401(3/79)-Golden Press; ($1.00, 96 pgs.)-All-r	3	6	9	17	26	35

RIPLEY'S BELIEVE IT OR NOT! TRUE WAR STORIES (Along with Ripley's...True Ghost Stories, the three issues together precede the 1967 series that starts its numbering with #4)
Gold Key: Nov, 1965 (Aug, 1965 in indicia)

| 1-No Williamson-a | 5 | 10 | 15 | 33 | 57 | 80 |

RIPLEY'S BELIEVE IT OR NOT! TRUE WEIRD
Ripley Enterprises: June, 1966 - No. 2, Aug, 1966 (B&W Magazine)

| 1,2-Comic stories & text | 4 | 8 | 12 | 27 | 44 | 60 |

RISE OF APOCALYPSE
Marvel Comics: Oct, 1996 - No. 4, Jan, 1997 ($1.95, limited series)

| 1-Adam Pollina-c/a in all | 1 | 3 | 4 | 6 | 8 | 10 |
| 2-4 | | | | | | 5.00 |

RISE OF THE BLACK FLAME
Dark Horse Comics: Sept, 2016 - No. 5, Jan, 2017 ($3.99, limited series)

| 1-5-Mignola & Roberson-s/Mitten-a/Laurence Campbell-c | | | | | | 4.00 |

RISE OF THE BLACK PANTHER
Marvel Comics: Mar, 2018 - No. 6, Aug, 2018 ($3.99, limited series)

| 1-6: 1-Origin of T'Challa; Narcisse-s/Renaud-a/Stelfreeze-c; Klaw app. 2-Namor app. | | | | | | 4.00 |

RISE OF THE MAGI
Image Comics (Top Cow): No. 0, May, 2014 - No. 5 ($3.50)

| 0 (5/14, Free Comic Book Day giveaway) Silvestri-s/c; bonus character and concept art | | | | | | 3.00 |
| 1-5: 1-(6/14) Silvestri-s/Kesgin-a; four covers | | | | | | 3.50 |

RISE OF THE POWERS OF X (X-Men)
Marvel Comics: Mar, 2024 - Present ($5.99/$4.99)

| 1-($5.99) Gillen-s/Silva-a | | | | | | 6.00 |
| 2-($4.99) | | | | | | 5.00 |

RISE OF THE TEENAGE MUTANT NINJA TURTLES
Image Comics (Top Cow): No. 0, Jul, 2018 - No. 5, Jan, 2019 ($3.99)

| 0-5-Based on the Nickelodeon animated series; Matthew K. Manning-s/Chad Thomas-a | | | | | | 4.00 |

RISE OF THE TEENAGE MUTANT NINJA TURTLES: SOUND OFF!
Image Comics (Top Cow): Jul, 2019 - No. 3, Sept, 2019 ($3.99)

| 1-3-Matthew K. Manning-s/Chad Thomas-a | | | | | | 4.00 |

Rise of the Black Flame #4 © Mike Mignola

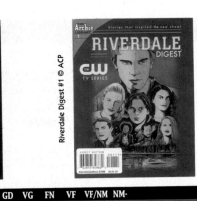
Riverdale Digest #1 © ACP

Robin #7 © DC

	GD	VG	FN	VF	VF/NM	NM-		GD	VG	FN	VF	VF/NM	NM-
	2.0	4.0	6.0	8.0	9.0	9.2		2.0	4.0	6.0	8.0	9.0	9.2

RISE OF ULTRAMAN, THE (Also see The Trials of Ultraman)
Marvel Comics: Nov, 2020 - No. 5, Mar, 2021 ($5.99/$3.99, limited series)

1-($5.99) Intro. Shin Hayata; Higgins & Groom-s/Manna-a; main cover by Alex Ross — 6.00
2-5-($3.99) Origin of Ultraman — 4.00

RISING STARS
Image Comics (Top Cow): Mar, 1999 - No. 24, Mar, 2005 ($2.50/$2.99)

Preview-(3/99, $5.00) Straczynski-s — 6.00
0-(6/00), $2.50) Gary Frank-a/c — 3.00
1/2-(8/01, $2.95) Anderson-c; art & sketch pages by Zanier — 3.00
1-Four covers; Keu Cha-c/a — 5.00
1-($10.00) Gold Editions-four covers — 10.00
1-($50.00) Holofoil-c — 50.00
2-7: 5-7-Zanier & Lashley-a(p) — 4.00
8-23: 8-13-Zanier & Lashley-a(p). 14-Immonen-a. 15-Flip book B&W preview of Universe. — 3.00
15-23-Brent Anderson-a — 4.00
24-($3.99) Series finale; Anderson-a — 3.00
Born In Fire TPB (11/00, $19.95) r/#1-8; foreword by Neil Gaiman — 20.00
Power TPB (2002, $19.95) r/#9-16 — 20.00
Prelude-(10/00, $2.95) Cha-a/Lashley-c — 3.00
...: Visitations (2002, $8.99) r/#0, 1/2, Preview; new Anderson-c; cover gallery — 9.00
Vol. 3: Fire and Ash TPB (2005, $19.99) r/#17-24; design pages & cover gallery — 20.00
Vol. 4 TPB (2006, $19.99) r/Rising Stars Bright #1-3 and Voices of the Dead #1-6 — 20.00
Vol. 5 TPB (2007, $16.99) r/Rising Stars: Untouchable #1-5 and ...: Visitations — 17.00
Wizard #0-(3/99) Wizard supplement; Straczynski-s — 3.00
Wizard #1/2 — 5.00

RISING STARS BRIGHT
Image Comics (Top Cow): Mar, 2003 - No. 3, May, 2003 ($2.99, limited series)

1-3-Avery-s/Jurgens & Gorder-a/Beck-c — 3.00

RISING STARS: UNTOUCHABLE
Image Comics (Top Cow): Mar, 2006 - No. 5, July, 2006 ($2.99, limited series)

1-5-Avery-s/Anderson-a — 3.00

RISING STARS: VOICES OF THE DEAD
Image Comics (Top Cow): June, 2005 - No. 6, Dec, 2005 ($2.99, limited series)

1-6-Avery-s/Staz Johnson-a — 3.00

RISING SUN (Based on the CMON board game)
IDW Publishing: Nov, 2019 - Present ($4.99)

1,2-Ron Marz & David Rodriguez-s/Martin Coccolo-a — 5.00

RIVERDALE (Based on the 2017 TV series)
Archie Comic Publications: Apr, 2017; May, 2017 - No. 12, Jul, 2018 ($3.99)

1-12: 1-4-Eisma-a. 5-12-Pitilli-a. 6-History of Pop's — 4.00
... FCBD Edition (5/18, giveaway) r/#6 — 3.00
... One-Shot (4/17, $4.99) Short story prologues to the TV series; multiple covers — 4.00

RIVERDALE (Volume 2)(Season 3 on cover)
Archie Comic Publications: May, 2019 - No. 5, Sept, 2019 ($3.99)

1-5-Short stories; Ostow-s; art by Pitilli & Eisma — 4.00
... FCBD Edition (5/19, giveaway) new story; Ostow-s/Pitilli-a — 3.00

RIVERDALE DIGEST (Tie-in to 2017 TV series)
Archie Comic Publications: Jun, 2017 - No. 7, May, 2018 ($5.99/$6.99)

1,2-($5.99) 1-Reprints of first issues of recent 2015-2017 Archie series; Francavilla TV cast-c. 2-Reprints of early 2015-2017 issues and classic reprints — 6.00
3-7-($6.99)-Reprints of early 2015-2017 issues and classic reprints — 7.00

RIVERDALE HIGH (Archie's... #7,8)
Archie Comics: Aug, 1990 - No. 8, Oct, 1991 ($1.00, bi-monthly)

1 — 5.00
2-8 — 4.00

RIVER FEUD (See Zane Grey & Four Color #484)

RIVETS
Dell Publishing Co.: No. 518, Nov, 1953

Four Color 518 — 5 | 10 | 15 | 35 | 63 | 90

RIVETS (A dog)
Argo Publ.: Jan, 1956 - No. 3, May, 1956

1-Reprints Sunday & daily newspaper strips — 8 | 16 | 24 | 40 | 50 | 60
2,3 — 5 | 10 | 15 | 22 | 26 | 30

ROACHMILL
Blackthorne Publ.: Dec, 1986 - No. 6, Oct, 1987 ($1.75, B&W)

1-6 — 4.00

ROACHMILL
Dark Horse Comics: May, 1988 - No. 10, Dec, 1990 ($1.75, B&W)

1-10: 10-Contains trading cards — 4.00

ROADIE, THE
Dark Horse Comics: Sept, 2022 - No. 4, Dec, 2022 ($3.99, limited series)

1-4-Tim Seeley-s/Fran Galán-a — 4.00

ROAD OF THE DEAD: HIGHWAY TO HELL
IDW Publishing: Oct, 2018 - No. 3, Dec, 2018 ($4.99, limited series)

1-3-Jonathan Maberry-s/Drew Moss-a — 5.00

ROAD RUNNER (See Beep Beep, the...)

ROAD TO EMPYRE: THE KREE/SKRULL WAR (Leads into Empyre series)
Marvel Comics: May, 2020 ($4.99, one-shot)

1-Thompson-s/De Iulis & Rodriguez-a; origin of Hulkling & Kree/Skrull history re-told — 4.00

ROAD TO OZ (Adaptation of the L. Frank Baum book)
Marvel Comics: Nov, 2012 - No. 6, May, 2013 ($3.99, limited series)

1-6-Eric Shanower-s/Skottie Young-a/c — 4.00

ROAD TO PERDITION (Inspired the 2002 Tom Hanks/Paul Newman movie)
(Also see On the Road to Perdition)
DC Comics/Paradox Press: 1998, 2002 ($13.95, B&W paperback graphic novel)

nn-(1st printing) Max Allan Collins-s/Richard Piers Rayner-a — 30.00
2nd & 3rd printings (2002, $13.95) — 14.00
Movie photo cover edition (2002) — 14.00

ROADTRIP
Oni Press: Aug, 2000 ($2.95, B&W, one-shot)

1-Reprints Judd Winick's back-up stories from Oni Double Feature #9,10 — 3.00

ROADWAYS
Cult Press: May, 1994 ($2.75, B&W, limited series)

1 — 4.00

ROARIN' RICK'S RARE BIT FIENDS
King Hell Press: July, 1994 - No. 21, Aug, 1996 ($2.95, B&W, mature)

1-21: Rick Veitch-c/a/scripts in all. 20-(5/96). 21-(8/96)-Reads Subtleman #1 on cover — 4.00
Rabid Eye: The Dream Art of Rick Veitch ($14.95, B&W, TPB)-r/#1-8 & the appendix from #12 — 15.00
Pocket Universe (6/96, $14.95, B&W, TPB)-Reprints — 15.00

ROBERT E. HOWARD'S CONAN THE BARBARIAN
Marvel Comics: 1983 ($2.50, 68 pgs., Baxter paper)

1-r/Savage Tales #2,3 by Smith, c-r/Conan #21 by Smith. — 5.00

ROBERT LOUIS STEVENSON'S KIDNAPPED (See Kidnapped)

ROBIN (See Aurora, Birds of Prey, Detective Comics #38, New Teen Titans, Robin II, Robin III, Robin 3000, Star Spangled Comics #65, Teen Titans & Young Justice)

ROBIN (See Batman #457)
DC Comics: Jan, 1991 - No. 5, May, 1991 ($1.00, limited series)

1-Free poster by N. Adams; Bolland-c on all — 6.00
1-2nd & 3rd printings (without poster) — 4.00
2-5 — 4.00
2-2nd printing — 4.00
Annual 1,2 (1992-93, $2.50, 68 pgs.): 1-Grant/Wagner scripts; Sam Kieth-c.
2-Intro Razorsharp; Jim Balent-c(p) — 5.00

ROBIN (See Detective #668) (Also see Red Robin and Tim Drake: Robin)
DC Comics: Nov, 1993 - No. 183, Apr, 2009 ($1.50/$1.95/$1.99/$2.25/$2.50/$2.99)

1-($2.95)-Collector's edition w/foil embossed-c; 1st app. Robin's car, The Redbird; Azrael as Batman app. — 6.00
1-Newsstand ed. — 4.00
2-49,51-66-Regular editions: 3-5-The Spoiler app. 6-The Huntress-c/story cont'd from Showcase '94 #5. 7-Knightquest: The Conclusion w/new Batman (Azrael) vs. Bruce Wayne. 8-KnightsEnd Pt. 5. 9-KnightsEnd Aftermath; Batman-c & app. 10-(9/94)-Zero Hour. 11-(11/94). 25-Green Arrow-c/app. 26-Batman app. 27-Contagion Pt. 3; Catwoman-c/app; Penguin app. 28-Contagion Pt. 11. 29-Penguin app. 31-Wildcat-c/app. 32-Legacy Pt. 3. 33-Legacy Pt. 7. 35-Final Night. 46-Genesis. 52,53-Cataclysm pt. 7, conclusion. 55-Green Arrow app. 62-64-Flash-c/app.
14 ($2.50)-Embossed-c; Troika Pt. 4 — 4.00
50-($2.95)-Lady Shiva & King Snake app. — 5.00
67-74,76-97: 67-72-No Man's Land. 79-Green Arrow app. 86-Pander Bros.-a — 5.00
75-($2.95) — 4.00
98,99-Bruce Wayne: Murderer x-over pt. 6, 11 — 3.00
100-($3.50) Last Dixon-s. — 4.00
101-174: 101-Young Justice x-over. 106-Kevin Lau-c. 121,122-Willingham-s/Mays-a. 125-Tim

	GD	VG	FN	VF	VF/NM	NM-
	2.0	4.0	6.0	8.0	9.0	9.2

Drake quits. 126-Spoiler becomes the new Robin. 129-131-War Games. 132-Robin moves to Bludhaven, Batgirl app. 138-Begin $2.50-c. 139-McDaniel-a begins. 146-147-Teen Titans app. 148-One Year Later; new costume. 150-Begin $2.99-c. 152,153-Boomerang app.

168,169-Resurrection of Ra's al Ghul x-over. 174 Spoiler unmasked						3.00
175-183: 175,176-Batman R.I.P. x-over. 180-Robin vs. Red Robin						3.00
#0-(10/94) Zero Hour; released betwen #10 & #11						4.00
#1,000,000 (11/98) 853rd Century x-over						4.00

Annual 3-5: 3-(1994, $2.95)-Elseworlds story. 4-(1995, $2.95)-Year One story.

5-(1996, $2.95)-Legends of the Dead Earth story						5.00
Annual 6 (1997, $3.95)-Pulp Heroes story						5.00
Annual 7 (12/07, $3.99)-Pearson-c/a; prelude to Resurrection of Ra's al Ghul x-over						4.00
.../Argent 1 (2/98, $1.95) Argent (Teen Titans) app.						4.00
.../Batgirl: Fresh Blood TPB (2005, $12.99) r/#132,133 & Batgirl #58,59						13.00
...: Days of Fire and Madness (2006, $12.99, TPB) r/#140-145						13.00
...-Eighty-Page Giant 1 (9/00, $5.95) Chuck Dixon-s/Diego Barreto-a						6.00
...: Flying Solo (2000, $12.95, TPB) r/#1-6, Showcase '94 #5,6						13.00
...Plus 1 (12/96, $2.95) Impulse-c/app.; Waid-s						4.00
...Plus 2 (12/97, $2.95) Fang (Scare Tactics) app.						4.00
...: Search For a Hero (2009, $19.99, TPB) r/#175-183; cover gallery						20.00
.../Spoiler Special 1 (8/08, $3.99) Follows Spoiler's return in Robin #174; Dixon-s						4.00
...: Teenage Wasteland (2007, $17.99, TPB) r/#154-162						18.00
...: The Big Leagues (2008, $12.99, TPB) r/#163-167						13.00
...: Unmasked (2004, $12.95, TPB) r/#121-125; Pearson-c						13.00
...: Violent Tendencies (2008, $17.99, TPB) r/#170-174 & Robin/Spoiler Special 1						18.00
...: Wanted (2007, $12.99, TPB) r/#148-153						13.00

ROBIN (Damian Wayne)
DC Comics: Jun, 2021 - No. 17, Oct, 2022 ($3.99)

1-17: 1-Williamson-s/Melnikov-a; intro Flatline; Connor Hawke app. 13,14-Shadow War. 16,17-Lord Death Man app.						4.00
... 2021 Annual 1 (1/22, $5.99) Takes place before Robin #6; origin of Flatline						6.00

ROBIN: A HERO REBORN
DC Comics: 1991 ($4.95, squarebound, trade paperback)

nn-r/Batman #455-457 & Robin #1-5; Bolland-c	2	4	6	8	10	12

ROBIN & BATMAN (Dick Grayson)
DC Comics: Jan, 2022 - No. 3, Mar, 2022 ($5.99, squarebound limited series)

1-3-Dick Grayson's early days as Robin; Lemire-s/Nguyen-a. 2-Teen Titans app.						6.00

ROBIN 80TH ANNIVERSARY 100-PAGE SUPER SPECTACULAR
DC Comics: May, 2020 ($9.99, squarebound, one-shot)

1-Short stories and pin-ups of the various Robins; s/a by various; multiple covers						10.00

ROBIN HOOD (See The Advs. of..., Brave and the Bold, Classic Comics #7, Classics Giveaways (12/44), Four Color #413, #69, King Classics, Movie Comics & Power Record Comics) (...& His Merry Men, The Illustrated Story of...)

ROBIN HOOD (Disney)
Dell Publishing Co.: No. 413, Aug, 1952; No. 669, Dec, 1955

Four Color 413-(1st Disney movie Four Color book)(8/52)-Photo-c

		10	20	30	64	132	200
Four Color 669 (12/55)-Reprints #413 plus photo-c	6	12	18	42	79	115

ROBIN HOOD (Adventures of... #6-8)
Magazine Enterprises (Sussex Pub. Co.): No. 52, Nov, 1955 - No. 5, Mar, 1957

52 (#1)-Origin Robin Hood & Sir Gallant of the Round Table

	19	38	57	111	176	240
53 (#2), 3-5	13	26	39	74	105	135
I.W. Reprint #1,2,9: 1-r/#3. 2-r/#4. 9-r/#52 (1963)	2	4	6	9	13	16
Super Reprint #10,15: 10-r/#53. 15-r/#5	2	4	6	9	13	16

NOTE: *Bolle* a-in all; c-52.

ROBIN HOOD (Not Disney)
Dell Publishing Co.: May-July, 1963 (one-shot)

1	3	6	9	16	23	30

ROBIN HOOD (Disney) (Also see Best of Walt Disney)
Western Publishing Co.: 1973 ($1.50, 8-1/2x11", 52 pgs., cardboard-c)

96151- "Robin Hood", based on movie, 96152- "The Mystery of Sherwood Forest", 96153- "In King Richard's Service", 96154- "The Wizard's Ring"

each....		3	6	9	15	22	28

ROBIN HOOD
Eclipse Comics: July, 1991 - No. 3, Dec, 1991 ($2.50, limited series)

1-3-Timothy Truman layouts						4.00

ROBIN HOOD AND HIS MERRY MEN (Formerly Danger & Adventure)
Charlton Comics: No. 28, Apr, 1956 - No. 38, Aug, 1958

28	11	22	33	64	90	115
29-37	9	18	27	47	61	75
38-Ditko-a (5 pgs.); Rocke-a	15	30	45	86	133	180

ROBIN HOOD TALES (Published by National Periodical #7 on)
Quality Comics Group (Comic Magazines): Feb, 1956 - No. 6, Nov-Dec, 1956

1-All have Baker/Cuidera-c	39	78	117	231	376	525
2-6-Matt Baker-a	37	74	111	218	354	490

ROBIN HOOD TALES (Cont'd from Quality series)(See Brave & the Bold #5)
National Periodical Pub.: No. 7, Jan-Feb, 1957 - No. 14, Mar-Apr, 1958

7-All have Andru/Esposito-a	39	78	117	231	378	525
8-14	33	66	99	194	317	440

ROBIN RISES: OMEGA (See Batman & Robin #33-37)
DC Comics: Sept, 2014; Feb, 2015 ($4.99, one-shots)

Alpha 1 (2/15)-Tomasi-s/Andy Kubert-a/c; Damien returns; Talia app.						5.00
Omega 1 (9/14)-Tomasi-s/Andy Kubert-a/c; Ra's al Ghul and Justice League app.						5.00

ROBINS
DC Comics: Jan, 2022 - No. 6, Jun, 2022 ($3.99, limited series)

1-6-Nightwing, Red Hood and the Robins app.; Seeley-s/Rivas-a						4.00

ROBINSON CRUSOE (See King Classics & Power Record Comics)

Dell Publishing Co.: Nov-Jan, 1963-64

1	3	6	9	15	21	26

ROBIN: SON OF BATMAN (Damian Wayne)
DC Comics: Aug, 2015 - No. 13, Aug, 2016 ($3.99)

1-13: 1-Gleason-s/a. 4-Deathstroke app. 5-Damian vs. Talia. 7-"Robin War" tie-in						4.00

ROBIN II (The Joker's Wild)
DC Comics: Oct, 1991 - No. 4, Dec, 1991 ($1.50, mini-series)

1-(Direct sales, $1.50)-With 4 diff.-c; same hologram on each						6.00
1-(Newsstand, $1.00)-No hologram; 1 version						4.00
1-Collector's set ($10.00)-Contains all 5 versions bagged with hologram trading card inside						18.00
2-(Direct sales, $1.50)-With 3 different-c						5.00
2-4-(Newsstand, $1.00)-1 version of each						4.00
2-Collector's set ($8.00)-Contains all 4 versions bagged with hologram trading card inside						12.00
3-(Direct sale, $1.50)-With 2 different-c						4.00
3-Collector's set ($6.00)-Contains all 3 versions bagged with hologram trading card inside						10.00
4-(Direct sales, $1.50)-Only one version						4.00
4-Collector's set ($4.00)-Contains both versions bagged with Bat-Signal hologram trading card						6.00
Multi-pack (All four issues w/hologram sticker)						14.00
Deluxe Complete Set ($30.00)-Contains all 14 versions of #1-4 plus a new hologram trading card; numbered & limited to 25,000; comes with slipcase & 2 acid free backing boards						45.00

ROBIN III: CRY OF THE HUNTRESS
DC Comics: Dec, 1992 - No. 6, Mar, 1993 (Limited series)

1-6 ($2.50, collector's ed.)-Polybagged w/movement enhanced-c plus mini-poster of newsstand-c by Zeck						5.00
1-6 ($1.25, newsstand ed.): All have Zeck-c						4.00

ROBIN 3000
DC Comics (Elseworlds): 1992 - No. 2, 1992 ($4.95, mini-series, 52 pgs.)

1,2-Foil logo; Russell-c/a						6.00

ROBIN WAR (Crossover with Grayson, Robin: Son of Batman, and We Are Robin)
DC Comics: Feb, 2016 - No. 2, Mar, 2016 ($4.99)

1,2-Tom King-s; art by various; The Court of Owls app.						5.00

ROBIN: YEAR ONE
DC Comics: 2000 - No. 4, 2001 ($4.95, square-bound, limited series)

1-4: Earliest days of Robin's career; Javier Pulido-c/a. 2,4-Two-Face app.						6.00
TPB (2002, 2008, $14.95/$14.99, 2 printings) r/#1-4						15.00

ROBOCOP
Marvel Comics: Oct, 1987 ($2.00, B&W, magazine, one-shot)

1-Movie adaptation	11	22	33	76	163	250

ROBOCOP (Also see Dark Horse Comics)
Marvel Comics: Mar, 1990 - No. 23, Jan, 1992 ($1.50)

1-Based on movie	2	4	6	10	14	18
2-23						4.00
nn (7/90, $4.95, 52 pgs.)-r/B&W magazine in color; adapts 1st movie						5.00

ROBOCOP
Dynamite Entertainment: 2010 - No. 6, 2010 ($3.50, limited series)

1-6-Follows the events of the first film; Neves-a						4.00

ROBOCOP
BOOM! Studios: Jul, 2014 - No. 12, Jun, 2015 ($3.99)

1-12: 1-8-Williamson-s/Magno-a. 1-Multiple covers. 9,10-Aragon-a						4.00

ROBOCOP (FRANK MILLER'S...)
Avatar Press: July, 2003 - No. 9, Jan, 2006 ($3.50/$3.99, limited series)

1-9-Frank Miller-s/Juan Ryp-a. 1-Three covers by Miller, Ryp, and Barrows. 2-Two covers						4.00
Free Comic Book Day Edition (4/03) Previews Robocop & Stargate SG•1; Busch-c						3.00

ROBOCOP (Tie-ins to the 2014 movie)
BOOM! Studios: Feb, 2014 ($3.99)

...: Beta (2/14) Brisson-s/Laiso-a						4.00
...: Hominem Ex Machina (2/14) Moreci-s/Copland-a						4.00
...: Memento Mori (2/14) Barbiere-s/Vieira-a						4.00
...: To Live and Die in Detroit (2/14) Joe Harris-s/Piotr Kowalski-a						4.00

ROBOCOP: CITIZENS ARREST
BOOM! Studios: Apr, 2018 - No. 5, Aug, 2018 ($3.99, limited series)

1-5-Brian Wood-s/Jorge Coelho-a						4.00

ROBOCOP: LAST STAND
BOOM! Studios: Aug, 2013 - No. 8, Mar, 2014 ($3.99, limited series)

1-8: 1-Miller & Grant-s/Oztekin-a						4.00

ROBOCOP: MORTAL COILS
Dark Horse Comics: Sept, 1993 - No. 4, Dec, 1993 ($2.50, limited series)

1-4: 1,2-Cago painted-a						4.00

ROBOCOP: PRIME SUSPECT
Dark Horse Comics: Oct, 1992 - No. 4, Jan, 1993 ($2.50, limited series)

1-4: 1,3-Nelson painted-c. 2,4-Bolton painted-c						4.00

ROBOCOP: ROAD TRIP
Dynamite Entertainment: 2012 - No. 4, 2012 ($3.99, limited series)

1-4-De Zarate-a						4.00

ROBOCOP: ROULETTE
Dark Horse Comics: Dec, 1993 - No. 4, 1994 ($2.50, limited series)

1-4: 1,3-Nelson painted-c. 2,4-Bolton painted-c						4.00

ROBOCOP 2
Marvel Comics: Aug, 1990 ($2.25, B&W, magazine, 68 pgs.)

Robin & Batman #1 © DC

Robocop (2010 series) #4 © Orion

Robotech (2017 series) #9 © Harmony Gold

	GD 2.0	VG 4.0	FN 6.0	VF 8.0	VF/NM 9.0	NM- 9.2

1-Adapts movie sequel scripted by Frank Miller; Bagley-a ... 5.00

ROBOCOP 2
Marvel Comics: Aug, 1990; Late Aug, 1990 - #3, Late Sept, 1990 ($1.00, limited series)
nn-(8/90, $4.95, 68 pgs., color)-Same contents as B&W magazine ... 5.00
1: #1-3 reprint no number issue ... 4.00
2,3: 2-Guice-c(i) ... 4.00

ROBOCOP 3
Dark Horse Comics: July, 1993 - No. 3, Nov, 1993 ($2.50, limited series)
1-3: Nelson painted-c; Nguyen-a(p) ... 4.00

ROBOCOP VERSUS THE TERMINATOR
Dark Horse Comics: Sept, 1992 - No. 4, 1992 (Dec.) ($2.50, limited series)
1-4: Miller scripts & Simonson-c/a in all ... 5.00
1-Platinum Edition ... 10.00
NOTE: All contain a different Robocop cardboard cut-out stand-up.

ROBO DOJO
DC Comics (WildStorm): Apr, 2002 - No. 6, Sept, 2002 ($2.95, limited series)
1-6-Wolfman-s ... 3.00

ROBO-HUNTER (Also see Sam Slade…)
Eagle Comics: Apr, 1984 - No. 5, 1984 ($1.00)
1-5-2000 A.D. ... 4.00

ROBONIC STOOGES (Three Stooges)
American Mythology: 2021 - No. 3, 2021 ($3.99)
1-3-The Stooges as robot heroes. 2-Fantastic Four #1 cover swipe. 3-X-Men #141 swipe ... 4.00

R.O.B.O.T. BATTALION 2050
Eclipse Comics: Mar, 1988 ($2.00, B&W, one-shot)
1 ... 4.00

ROBOT COMICS
Renegade Press: No. 0, June, 1987 ($2.00, B&W, one-shot)
0-Bob Burden story & art ... 4.00

ROBOTECH
Antarctic Press: Mar, 1997 - No. 11, Nov, 1998 ($2.95)
1-11, Annual 1 (4/98, $2.95) ... 4.00
...Class Reunion (12/98, $3.95, B&W) ... 4.00
...Escape (5/98, $2.95, B&W), ...Final Fire (12/98, $2.95, B&W) ... 4.00

ROBOTECH
DC Comics (WildStorm): No. 0, Feb, 2003 - No. 6, Jul, 2003 ($2.50/$2.95, limited series)
0-Tommy Yune-s; art by Jim Lee, Garza, Bermejo and others; pin-up pages by various ... 3.00
1-6 ($2.95)-Long Vo-a ... 3.00
...: From the Stars (2003, $9.95, digest-size) r/#0-6 & Sourcebook ... 10.00
... Sourcebook (3/03, $2.95) pin-ups and info on characters and mecha; art by various ... 3.00

ROBOTECH
Titan Comics: Aug, 2017 - No. 24, Oct, 2019 ($3.99)
1-24: 1-11-Brian Wood-s/Marco Turini-a; multiple covers on each. 12-14-Prasetya-a ... 4.00
... Free Comic Book Day 2019 - Furman-s/Prasetya-a ... 3.00

ROBOTECH: COVERT-OPS
Antarctic Press: Aug, 1998 - No. 2, Sept, 1998 ($2.95, B&W, limited series)
1,2-Gregory Lane-s/a ... 4.00

ROBOTECH DEFENDERS
DC Comics: Mar, 1985 - No. 2, Apr, 1985 (Mini-series)
1,2 ... 4.00

ROBOTECH IN 3-D (TV)
Comico: Aug, 1987 ($2.50)
1-Steacy painted-c ... 5.00

ROBOTECH: INVASION
DC Comics (WildStorm): Feb, 2004 - No. 5, July, 2004 ($2.95, limited series)
1-5-Faerber & Yune-s/Miyazawa & Dogan-a ... 3.00

ROBOTECH: LOVE AND WAR
DC Comics (WildStorm): Aug, 2003 - No. 6, Jan, 2004 ($2.95, limited series)
1-6-Long Vo & Charles Park-a/Faerber & Yune-s. 2-Variant-c by Warren ... 3.00

ROBOTECH MASTERS (TV)
Comico: July, 1985 - No. 23, Apr, 1988 ($1.50)
1 ... 6.00
2-23 ... 4.00

ROBOTECH: PRELUDE TO THE SHADOW CHRONICLES

DC Comics (WildStorm): Dec, 2005 - No. 5, Mar, 2006 ($3.50, limited series)
1-5-Yune-s/Dogan & Udon Studios-a ... 3.50
TPB (2010, $17.99) r/#1-5; production art ... 18.00

ROBOTECH: REMIX
Titan Comics: Nov, 2019 - No. 4 ($3.99)
1-4-Continues from Robotech 2017-19 series; Fletcher-s/Damaso-a ... 4.00

ROBOTECH: RICK HUNTER
Titan Comics: Sept, 2023 - Present ($3.99)
1-3-Easton-s/Ragazzoni-a ... 4.00

ROBOTECH: SENTINELS - RUBICON
Antarctic Press: July, 1998 ($2.95, B&W)
1 ... 4.00

ROBOTECH SPECIAL
Comico: May, 1988 ($2.50, one-shot, 44 pgs.)
1-Steacy wraparound-c; partial photo-c ... 5.00

ROBOTECH THE GRAPHIC NOVEL
Comico: Aug, 1986 ($5.95, 8-1/2x11", 52 pgs.)
1-Origin SDF-1; intro T.R. Edwards, Steacy-c/a ... 15.00
1-Second printing (12/86) ... 10.00

ROBOTECH: THE MACROSS SAGA (TV)(Formerly Macross)
Comico: No. 2, Feb, 1985 - No. 36, Feb, 1989 ($1.50)

	GD 2.0	VG 4.0	FN 6.0	VF 8.0	VF/NM 9.0	NM- 9.2
2	1	2	3	5	6	8
3-10						5.00
11-36: 12,17-Ken Steacy painted-c. 26-Begin $1.75-c. 35,36-($1.95)						4.00

Volume 1-4 TPB (WildStorm, 2003, $14.95, 5-3/4" x 8-1/4")1-Reprints #2-6 & Macross #1.
2- r/#7-12. 3-r/#13-18. 4-r/#19-24 ... 15.00

ROBOTECH: THE NEW GENERATION
Comico: July, 1985 - No. 25, July, 1988
1 ... 6.00
2-25 ... 4.00

ROBOTECH: VERMILION
Antarctic Press: Mar, 1997 - No. 4, ($2.95, B&W, limited series)
1-4 ... 4.00

ROBOTECH / VOLTRON
Dynamite Entertainment: 2013 - No. 5, 2014 ($3.99, limited series)
1-5-Tommy Yune-s ... 4.00

ROBOTECH: WINGS OF GIBRALTAR
Antarctic Press: Aug, 1998 - No. 2, Sept, 1998 ($2.95, B&W, limited series)
1,2-Lee Duhig-s/a ... 4.00

ROBOTIX
Marvel Comics: Feb, 1986 (75¢, one-shot)
1-Based on toy ... 4.00

ROBOTMEN OF THE LOST PLANET (Also see Space Thrillers)
Avon Periodicals: 1952 (Also see Strange Worlds #19)

	GD 2.0	VG 4.0	FN 6.0	VF 8.0	VF/NM 9.0	NM- 9.2
1-McCann-a (3 pgs.); Fawcette-a	213	426	639	1363	2332	3300

ROB ROY
Dell Publishing Co.: 1954 (Disney-Movie)

	GD 2.0	VG 4.0	FN 6.0	VF 8.0	VF/NM 9.0	NM- 9.2
Four Color 544-Manning-a, photo-c	9	18	27	60	120	180

ROCK, THE (WWF Wrestling)
Chaos! Comics: June, 2001 ($2.99, one-shot)
1-Photo-c; Grant-s/Neves-a ... 4.00

ROCK & ROLL HIGH SCHOOL
Roger Corman's Cosmic Comics: Oct, 1995 ($2.50)
1-Bob Fingerman scripts ... 4.00

ROCK AND ROLLO (Formerly TV Teens)
Charlton Comics: V2#14, Oct, 1957 - No. 19, Sept, 1958

	GD 2.0	VG 4.0	FN 6.0	VF 8.0	VF/NM 9.0	NM- 9.2
V2#14-19	7	14	21	37	46	55

ROCK COMICS
Landgraphic Publ.: Jul/Aug, 1979 ($1.25, tabloid size, 28 pgs.)

	GD 2.0	VG 4.0	FN 6.0	VF 8.0	VF/NM 9.0	NM- 9.2
1-N. Adams-c; Thor (not Marvel's) story by Adams	3	6	9	14	20	25

ROCKET (Rocket Raccoon from Guardians of the Galaxy)
Marvel Comics: Jul, 2017 - No. 6, Dec, 2017 ($3.99, limited series)
1-6: 1-Ewing-s/Gorham-a/Mayhew-c. 4-Deadpool app. ... 4.00

	GD 2.0	VG 4.0	FN 6.0	VF 8.0	VF/NM 9.0	NM- 9.2

ROCKET COMICS
Hillman Periodicals: Mar, 1940 - No. 3, May, 1940

1-Rocket Riley, Red Roberts the Electro Man (origin), The Phantom Ranger, The Steel Shark, The Defender, Buzzard Barnes and his Sky Devils, Lefty Larson, & The Defender, the Man with a Thousand Faces begin (1st app. of each); all have Rocket Riley-c

	366	732	1098	2562	4481	6400
2,3: 2-Jack Cole-a	271	542	813	1734	2967	4200

ROCKET COMICS: IGNITE
Dark Horse Comics: Apr, 2003 (Free Comic Book Day giveaway)

1-Previews Dark Horse series Syn, Lone, and Go Boy 7 ... 3.00

ROCKETEER, THE (See Eclipse Graphic Album Series, Pacific Presents & Starslayer)

ROCKETEER ADVENTURE MAGAZINE, THE
Comico/Dark Horse Comics No. 3: July, 1988 ($2.00); No. 2, July, 1989 ($2.75); No. 3, Jan, 1995 ($2.95)

1-(7/88, $2.00)-Dave Stevens-c/a in all; Kaluta back-up-a; 1st app. Jonas (character based on The Shadow)

	3	6	9	14	20	25
2-(7/89, $2.75)-Stevens/Dorman painted-c	2	4	6	8	10	12

3-(1/95, $2.95)-Includes pinups by Stevens, Gulacy, Plunkett, & Mignola ... 5.00
Volume 2-(9/96, $9.95, magazine size TPB)-Reprints #1-3 ... 10.00

ROCKETEER ADVENTURES
IDW Publishing: May, 2011 - No. 4, Aug, 2011 ($3.99, limited series)

1-4-Anthology by various; covers by Alex Ross and Dave Stevens ... 4.00
The Rocketeer: The Best of Rocketeer Adventures-Funko Edition 1 (1/18, $4.99) r/stories from series; art by Cassaday, Ha, Kaluta, Sakai, & Weston; Funko fig cover ... 5.00

ROCKETEER ADVENTURES VOLUME 2
IDW Publishing: Mar, 2012 - No. 4, Jun, 2012 ($3.99, limited series)

1-4-Anthology by various; covers by Darwyn Cooke and Stevens. 1-Sakai-a. 4-Simonson & Byrne-a ... 4.00

ROCKETEER AT WAR, THE
IDW Publishing: Dec, 2015 - No. 4, Apr, 2016 ($4.99, limited series)

1-4-Guggenheim-s; covers by Bullock & Bradshaw. 1,2-Bullock-a. 3,4-J. Bone-a ... 5.00

ROCKETEER: CARGO OF DOOM
IDW Publishing: Aug, 2012 - No. 4, Nov, 2012 ($3.99, limited series)

1-4-Waid-s/Samnee-a/c; variant-c by Stevens on all ... 4.00

ROCKETEER: HOLLYWOOD HORROR
IDW Publishing: Feb, 2013 - No. 4, May, 2013 ($3.99, limited series)

1-Langridge-s/Bone-a/Simonson-c; variant-c on all ... 4.00

ROCKETEER: IN THE DEN OF THIEVES
IDW Publishing: Jul, 2023 - No. 4, Nov, 2023 ($4.99, limited series)

1-4-Mooney-s/Messina-a; variant-c on all ... 5.00

ROCKETEER JETPACK TREASURY EDITION
IDW Publishing: Nov, 2011 ($9.99, oversized 13" x 9-3/4" format)

1-Recolored r/Starslayer #1-3, Pacific Presents #1,2 & Rocketeer Special Edition ... 10.00

ROCKETEER ONE-SHOT, THE
IDW Publishing: May 2023 ($4.99)

1-Short stories; Bilson & De Meo-s/Hughes-a; Mao-s/Cermak-a' Windom-s/Jae Lee-a ... 5.00

ROCKETEER SPECIAL EDITION, THE
Eclipse Comics: Nov, 1984 ($1.50, Baxter paper)(Chapter 5 of Rocketeer serial)

1-Stevens-c/a; Kaluta back-c; pin-ups inside

	3	6	9	16	23	30

NOTE: *Originally intended to be published in Pacific Presents.*

ROCKETEER, THE: THE COMPLETE ADVENTURES
IDW Publishing: Oct, 2009 ($29.99/$75.00, hardcover)

HC-Reprints of Dave Stevens' Rocketeer stories in Starslayer #1-3, Pacific Presents #1,2, Rocketeer Special Edition and Rocketeer Adventure Magazine #1-3; all re-colored ... 30.00
... Deluxe Edition ($75.00, 8"x12" slipcased HC) larger size reprints of HC content plus 100 bonus pages of sketch art, layouts, design work; intro. by Thomas Jane ... 110.00
... Deluxe Edition 2nd printing ($75.00, oversized slipcased HC) ... 75.00

ROCKETEER, THE: THE OFFICIAL MOVIE ADAPTATION
W. D. Publications (Disney): 1991

nn-($5.95, 68 pgs.)-Squarebound deluxe edition ... 6.00
nn-($2.95, 68 pgs.)-Stapled regular edition ... 5.00
3-D Comic Book (1991, $7.98, 52 pgs.) ... 8.00

ROCKETEER: THE GREAT RACE
IDW Publishing: Apr, 2022 - No. 4, Jul, 2022 ($3.99, limited series)

1-4-Stephen Mooney-s/a; back-up history of Dave Stevens and the Rocketeer ... 5.00

ROCKETEER/THE SPIRIT: PULP FRICTION
IDW Publishing: Jul, 2013 - No. 4, Dec, 2013 ($3.99, limited series)

1-4: 1-Waid-s/Paul Smith-a; covers by Smith & Darwyn Cooke. 2-Wallace-a. 3,4-Bone-a ... 4.00

ROCKET GIRL
Image Comics: Oct, 2013 - No. 10, Oct, 2017 ($3.50/$3.99)

1-10-Brandon Montclare-a/Amy Reeder-a/c. 6-Begin $3.99-c ... 4.00

ROCKET KELLY (See The Bouncer, Green Mask #10); becomes Li'l Pan #6)
Fox Feature Syndicate: 1944; Fall, 1945 - No. 5, Oct-Nov, 1946

nn (1944), 1 (Fall, 1945)	50	100	150	315	533	750
2-The Puppeteer app. (costumed hero)	39	78	117	231	378	525
3-5: 5-(#5 on cover, #4 inside)	34	68	102	199	325	450

ROCKETMAN (Strange Fantasy #2 on) (See Hello Pal & Scoop Comics)
Ajax/Farrell Publications: June, 1952 (Strange Stories of the Future)

1-Rocketman & Cosmo	74	148	222	470	810	1150

ROCKETMAN & ROCKETGIRL
Dynamite Entertainment: 2023 ($4.99, one-shot)

1-Jacob Edgar-s/Jordi Perez-a ... 5.00

ROCKET RACCOON (Also see Marvel Preview #7 and Incredible Hulk #271)
Marvel Comics: May, 1985 - No. 4, Aug, 1985 (color, limited series)

1-Mignola-a/Mantlo-s in all	4	8	12	28	47	65
2-4	2	4	6	11	16	20

...: Marvel Tales (6/23, $7.99) r/#1-4; new cover by Bradshaw; intro by Macchio ... 8.00
...: Tales From Half-World 1 (10/13, $7.99) r/#1-4; new cover by McNiven ... 8.00

ROCKET RACCOON (Guardians of the Galaxy)
Marvel Comics: Sept, 2014 - No. 11, Jul, 2015 ($3.99)

1-Skottie Young-s/a; Groot app. ... 5.00
2-11-Skottie Young-s. 7,8-Andrade-a ... 4.00
Free Comic Book Day 2014 (5/14, giveaway) Archer-a; Groot and Wal-rus app. ... 3.00

ROCKET RACCOON (Guardians of the Galaxy)
Marvel Comics: Feb, 2017 - No. 5, Jun, 2017 ($3.99)

1-5-Rosenberg-s/Coelho-a. 1-Johnny Storm app. 2-5-Kraven app. ... 4.00

ROCKET RACCOON & GROOT (Guardians of the Galaxy)
Marvel Comics: Nov, 2016 - No. 10, Nov, 2016 ($3.99)

1-10: 1-6-Skottie Young-s. 1-3-Filipe Andrade-a. 8-10-Gwenpool app. ... 4.00

ROCKET SHIP X
Fox Feature Syndicate: September, 1951; 1952

1	97	194	291	621	1061	1500
1952 (nn, nd, no publ.)-Edited 1951-c (exist?)	50	100	150	315	533	750

ROCKET TO ADVENTURE LAND (See Pixie Puzzle...)

ROCKET TO THE MOON
Avon Periodicals: 1951

nn-Orlando-c/a; adapts Otis Adelbert Kline's "Maza of the Moon"

	219	438	657	1402	2401	3400

ROCK FANTASY COMICS
Rock Fantasy Comics: Dec, 1989 - No. 16?, 1991 ($2.25/$3.00, B&W)(No cover price)

1-Pink Floyd part 1 ... 5.00
1-2nd printing ($3.00-c) ... 4.00
2,3: 2-Rolling Stones #1. 3-Led Zeppelin #1 ... 4.00
2,3: 2nd printings ($3.00-c, 1/90 & 2/90) ... 4.00
4-Stevie Nicks Not published
5-Monstrosities of Rock #1; photo back-c ... 5.00
5-2nd printing (3/90 indicia, 2/90) ... 4.00
6-9,11-15,17,18: 6-Guns n' Roses #1 (1st & 2nd printings, 3/90)-Begin $3.00-c. 7-Sex Pistols #1. 8-Alice Cooper; not published. 9-Van Halen #1; photo back-c. 11-Jimi Hendrix #1; wraparound-c ... 4.00

10-Kiss #1; photo back-c	2	4	6	8	10	12

16-($5.00, 68 pgs.)-The Great Gig in the Sky(Floyd) ... 5.00

ROCK HAPPENING (See Bunny and Harvey Pop Comics:...)

ROCK N' ROLL COMICS
DC Comics: Dec./Jan 1956 (ashcan)

nn-Ashcan comic, not distributed to newsstands, only for in house use   (no known sales)

ROCK N' ROLL COMICS
Revolutionary Comics: Jun, 1989 - No. 65 ($1.50/$1.95/$2.50, B&W/col. #15 on)

1-Guns N' Roses	2	4	6	8	10	12
1-2nd thru 7th printings. 7th printing (full color w/new-c/a)						4.00
2-Metallica	2	4	6	8	10	12
2-2nd thru 6th printings (6th in color)						4.00
3-Bon Jovi (no reprints)	1	2	3	5	6	8

4-8,10-20,22-29,31-65: 4-Motley Crue(2nd printing only, 1st destroyed). 5-Def Leppard (2 printings). 6-Rolling Stones(4 printings). 7-The Who (3 printings). 8-Skid Row; not publ'd. 10-Warrant/Whitesnake (2 printings; 1st has 2 diff.-c). 11-Aerosmith (2 printings?). 12-New Kids on the Block(2 printings). 12-3rd printing; rewritten & titled NKOTB Hate Book. 13-Led Zeppelin. 14-Sex Pistols. 15-Poison; 1st color issue. 16-Van Halen. 17-Madonna. 18-Alice Cooper. 19-Public Enemy/2 Live Crew. 20-Queensryche/Tesla. 22-AC/DC; begin $2.50-c. 23-Living Colour. 26-Michael Jackson. 29-Ozzy. 45,46-Grateful Dead. 49-Rush. 50,51-Bob Dylan. 56-David Bowie ... 6.00

9-Kiss	2	4	6	8	10	12
9-2nd & 3rd printings						3.00
21,30: 21-Prince. 30-The Cure	3	6	9	14	20	25

NOTE: *Most issues were reprinted except #3. Later reprints are in color. #8 was not released.*

ROCKO'S MODERN AFTERLIFE (TV)
BOOM! Studios (kaboom!): Apr, 2019 - No. 4, Jul, 2019 ($3.99, limited series)

1-4-Burch-s/Di Meo-a; multiple covers; the undead attach O-Town ... 4.00

ROCKO'S MODERN LIFE (TV) (Nickelodeon cartoon)
Marvel Comics: June, 1994 - No. 7, Dec, 1994 ($1.95)

1-7 ... 4.00

ROCKO'S MODERN LIFE (TV) (Nickelodeon cartoon)
BOOM! Studios (kaboom!): Dec, 2017 - No. 8, Sept, 2018 ($3.99)

1-8-Ferrier-s/McGinty-a; multiple covers ... 4.00

ROCKSTARS
Image Comics: Dec, 2016 - No. 8 ($3.99)

1-8-Joe Harris-s/Megan Hutchison-a ... 4.00

ROCKY AND BULLWINKLE (TV)
IDW Publishing: Mar, 2014 - No. 4, Jun, 2014 ($3.99)

1-4-Evanier-s/Langridge-a; bonus Dudley Do-Right short story in each; two covers ... 4.00

ROCKY AND BULLWINKLE SHOW, THE (TV)
American Mythology: 2017 - No. 3, 2018 ($3.99, limited series)

1-3: 1-New short stories and reprints from Bullwinkle #1&2; three covers ... 4.00

ROCKY AND BULLWINKLE (TV)
American Mythology: 2019 - 2020 ($3.99, one-shots)

... As Seen on TV 1-3 (2019-2020, $3.99) new story & reprints; Peabody & Sherman app. ... 4.00
... Present: The Best of Boris & Natasha 1 (2019, $3.99) reprints from 1973-1976 ... 4.00
... Present: The Best of Dudley Do-Right of the Mounties 1 (2019, $3.99) reps. from 1973 ... 4.00
... Present: The Best of Mr. Peabody & Sherman 1 (2019, $3.99) reprints from 1963-1974 ... 4.00

Rocket Girl #2 © Montclare & Reeder

Rocky and Bullwinkle #1 © Ward Prods.

Rogue & Gambit #4 © MAR

	GD	VG	FN	VF	VF/NM	NM-
	2.0	4.0	6.0	8.0	9.0	9.2

ROCKY AND HIS FIENDISH FRIENDS (TV)(Bullwinkle)
Gold Key: Oct, 1962 - No. 5, Sept, 1963 (Jay Ward)

	GD	VG	FN	VF	VF/NM	NM-
1 (25¢, 80 pgs.)	14	28	42	97	214	330
2,3 (25¢, 80 pgs.)	10	20	30	64	132	200
4,5 (Regular size, 12¢)	7	14	21	49	92	135

ROCKY AND HIS FRIENDS (See Kite Fun Book & March of Comics #216 in the Promotional Comics section)

ROCKY AND HIS FRIENDS (TV)
Dell Publishing Co.: No. 1128, 8-10/60 - No.1311,1962 (Jay Ward)

	GD	VG	FN	VF	VF/NM	NM-
Four Color 1128 (#1) (8-10/60)	28	56	84	202	451	700
Four Color 1152 (12-2/61), 1166, 1208, 1275, 1311('62)	17	34	51	114	252	390

ROCKY HORROR PICTURE SHOW THE COMIC BOOK, THE
Caliber Press: Jul, 1990 - No. 3, Jan, 1991 ($2.95, mini-series, 52 pgs.)

	GD	VG	FN	VF	VF/NM	NM-
1-Adapts cult film plus photos, etc.	3	6	9	14	20	25
1-2nd printing, 2,3	2	4	6	9	13	16
...Collection ($4.95)	2	4	6	10	14	18

ROCKY JONES SPACE RANGER (See Space Adventures #15-18)

ROCKY JORDEN PRIVATE EYE (See Private Eye)

ROCKY LANE WESTERN (Allan Rocky Lane starred in Republic movies & TV for a short time as Allan Lane, Red Ryder & Rocky Lane) (See Black Jack Fawcett Movie Comics, Motion Picture Comics & Six-Gun Heroes)
Fawcett Publications/Charlton No. 56 on: May, 1949 - No. 87, Nov, 1959

	GD	VG	FN	VF	VF/NM	NM-
1 (36 pgs.)-Rocky, his stallion Black Jack, & Slim Pickens begin; photo back-c begin, end #57; photo back-c	55	110	165	352	601	850
2 (36 pgs.)-Last photo back-c	22	44	66	132	216	300
3-5 (36 pgs.): 4-Captain Tootsie by Beck	17	34	51	98	154	210
6,10 (36 pgs.): 10-Complete western novelette "Badman's Reward"	14	28	42	76	108	140
7-9 (52 pgs.)	14	28	42	82	121	160
11-13,15-17,19,20 (52 pgs.): 15-Black Jack's Hitching Post begins, ends #25.						
20-Last Slim Pickens	12	24	36	67	94	120
14,18 (36 pgs.)	10	20	30	58	79	100
21,23,24 (52 pgs.): 21-Dee Dickens begins, ends #55,57,65-68	10	20	30	58	79	100
22,25-28,30 (36 pgs. begin)	10	20	30	54	72	90
29-Classic complete novel "The Land of Missing Men" with hidden land of ancient temple ruins (r-in #65)	14	28	42	76	108	140
31-40	9	18	27	52	69	85
41-54	9	18	27	47	61	75
55-Last Fawcett issue (1/54)	9	18	27	52	69	85
56-1st Charlton issue (2/54)-Photo-c	14	28	42	82	121	160
57,60-Photo-c	10	20	30	54	72	90
58,59,61-64,66-78,80-86: 59-61-Young Falcon app. 64-Slim Pickens app.						
66-68: Reprints #30,31,32	8	16	24	44	57	70
65-r/#29, "The Land of Missing Men"	9	18	27	50	65	80
79-Giant Edition (68 pgs.)	10	20	30	58	79	100
87-Last issue	9	18	27	52	69	85

NOTE: Complete novels in #10, 14, 18, 22, 25, 30-32, 36, 38, 39, 49. Captain Tootsie in #4, 12, 20. Big Bow and Little Arrow in #11, 28, 63. Black Jack's Hitching Post in #15-25, 64, 73.

ROCKY LANE WESTERN
AC Comics: 1989 ($2.50, B&W, one-shot?)

					NM-
1-Photo-c; Giordano reprints					4.00
Annual 1 (1991, $2.95, B&W, 44 pgs.)-photo front/back & inside-c; reprints					5.00

ROD CAMERON WESTERN (Movie star)
Fawcett Publications: Feb, 1950 - No. 20, Apr, 1953

	GD	VG	FN	VF	VF/NM	NM-
1-Rod Cameron, his horse War Paint, & Sam The Sheriff begin; photo front/back-c begin	34	68	102	199	325	450
2	17	34	51	98	154	210
3-Novel length story "The Mystery of the Seven Cities of Cibola"	14	28	42	82	121	160
4-10: 9-Last photo back-c	12	24	36	69	97	125
11-19	10	20	30	58	79	100
20-Last issue & photo-c	11	22	33	62	86	110

NOTE: Novel length stories in No. 1-8, 12-14.

RODEO RYAN (See A-1 Comics #8)

ROGAN GOSH
DC Comics (Vertigo): 1994 ($6.95, one-shot)

					NM-
nn-Peter Milligan scripts					7.00

ROGER DODGER (Also in Exciting Comics #57 on)
Standard Comics: No. 5, Aug, 1952

	GD	VG	FN	VF	VF/NM	NM-
5-Teen-age	26	52	78	154	252	350

ROGER RABBIT (Also see Marvel Graphic Novel)
Disney Comics: June, 1990 - No. 18, Nov, 1991 ($1.50)

	GD	VG	FN	VF	VF/NM	NM-
1-All new stories	3	6	9	14	20	25
2-5-All new stories	1	2	3	5	6	7
6-18-All new stories						4.00
In 3-D 1 (1992, $2.50)-Sold at Wal-Mart?; w/glasses	1	3	4	6	8	10

ROGER RABBIT'S TOONTOWN
Disney Comics: Aug, 1991 - No. 5, Dec, 1991 ($1.50)

	GD	VG	FN	VF	VF/NM	NM-
1	2	4	6	9	12	15
2-5						6.00

ROGER ZELAZNY'S AMBER: THE GUNS OF AVALON
DC Comics: 1996 - No. 3, 1996 ($6.95, limited series)

					NM-
1-3: Based on novel					7.00

ROG 2000
Pacific Comics: June, 1982 ($2.95, 44 pgs., B&W, one-shot, magazine)

	GD	VG	FN	VF	VF/NM	NM-
nn-Byrne-c/a (r)	2	4	6	9	13	16
2nd printing (7/82)	1	2	3	4	5	7

ROGUE (From X-Men)
Marvel Comics: Jan, 1995 - No. 4, Apr, 1995 ($2.95, limited series)

					NM-
1-4: Gold foil logo					4.00
TPB-($12.95) r/#1-4					13.00

ROGUE (Volume 2)
Marvel Comics: Sept, 2001 - No. 4, Dec, 2001 ($2.50, limited series)

					NM-
1-4-Julie Bell painted-c/Lopresti-a; Rogue's early days with X-Men					3.00

ROGUE (From X-Men)
Marvel Comics: Sept, 2004 - No. 12, Aug, 2005 ($2.99)

					NM-
1-12: 1-Richards-a. 4-Gambit app. 11-Sunfire dies, Rogue absorbs his powers					3.00
...: Going Rogue TPB (2005, $14.99) r/#1-6					15.00
...: Forget-Me-Not TPB (2006, $14.99) r/#7-12					15.00

ROGUE & GAMBIT
Marvel Comics: Mar, 2018 - No. 5, Jul, 2018 ($3.99, limited series)

					NM-
1-5-Kelly Thompson-s/Pere Pérez-a					4.00

ROGUE & GAMBIT
Marvel Comics: May, 2023 - No. 5, Sept, 2023 ($3.99, limited series)

					NM-
1-5-Phillips-s/Gômez-a; Destiny app.					4.00

ROGUE ANGEL: TELLER OF TALL TALES (Based on the Alex Archer novels)
IDW Publishing: Feb, 2008 - No. 5, Jun, 2008 ($3.99)

					NM-
1-5-Annja Creed adventures; Barbara-Kesel-s/Renae De Liz-a					4.00

ROGUES
DC Comics (Black Label): May, 2022 - No. 4, Dec, 2022 ($6.99, oversized 8-1/2" x 10-3/4", lim. series)

					NM-
1-4-Captain Cold reunites the Rogues after 10 years; Williamson-s/Leomacs-a					7.00

ROGUES GALLERY
DC Comics: 1996 ($3.50, one-shot)

					NM-
1-Pinups of DC villains by various artists					4.00

ROGUES' GALLERY
Image Comics: Jul, 2022 - No. 4, Oct, 2022 ($3.99, limited series)

					NM-
1-4-Hannah Rose May-s/Justin Mason-a					4.00

ROGUE SUN
Image Comics: Mar, 2022 - Present ($3.99)

					NM-
1-18: 1-Ryan Parrott-s/Abel-a					4.00

ROGUE TROOPER
IDW Publishing: Feb, 2014 - No. 4, May, 2014 ($3.99)

					NM-
1-4-Ruckley-s/Ponticelli-a/Fabry-c					4.00

ROGUE TROOPER CLASSICS
IDW Publishing: May, 2014 - No. 8, Dec, 2014 ($3.99)

					NM-
1-8-Newly colored reprints of strips from 2000 AD magazine. 1-4-Gibbons-a					4.00

ROGUES, THE (VILLAINS) (See The Flash)
DC Comics: Feb, 1998 ($1.95, one-shot)

					NM-
1-Augustyn-s/Pearson-c					4.00

ROKKIN
DC Comics (WildStorm): Sept, 2006 - No. 6, Feb, 2007 ($2.99, limited series)

	GD 2.0	VG 4.0	FN 6.0	VF 8.0	VF/NM 9.0	NM- 9.2

1-6-Hartnell-s/Bradshaw-a ... 3.00

ROKU
Valiant Entertainment: Oct, 2019 - No. 4, Jan, 2020 ($3.99, limited series)

1-4-Cullen Bunn-s/Ramón Bachs-a; multiple covers on each ... 4.00

ROLLING STONES: VOODOO LOUNGE
Marvel Comics: 1995 ($6.95, Prestige format, one-shot)

nn-Dave McKean-script/design/art ... 7.00

ROLY POLY COMIC BOOK
Green Publishing Co.: 1945 - No. 15, 1946 (MLJ reprints)

	GD 2.0	VG 4.0	FN 6.0	VF 8.0	VF/NM 9.0	NM- 9.2
1-(No number on cover or indicia, "1945 issue" on cover) Red Rube & Steel Sterling begin; Sahle-c	40	80	120	246	411	575
6-The Blue Circle & The Steel Fist app.	28	56	84	168	274	380
10-Origin Red Rube retold; Steel Sterling story (Zip #41)	34	68	102	199	325	450
11,12: The Black Hood app. in both	39	78	117	231	378	525
14-Classic decapitation-c; the Black Hood app.	400	800	1200	2800	4900	7000
15-The Blue Circle & The Steel Fist app.; cover exact swipe from Fox Blue Beetle #1	41	82	123	256	428	600

ROM (Based on the Parker Brothers toy)
Marvel Comics Group: Dec, 1979 - No. 75, Feb, 1986

	GD 2.0	VG 4.0	FN 6.0	VF 8.0	VF/NM 9.0	NM- 9.2
1-Origin/1st app.	4	8	12	25	40	55
2-16,19-23,28-30: 5-Dr. Strange. 13-Saga of the Space Knights begins. 19-X-Men cameo.	1	2	3	5	6	8
23-Powerman & Iron Fist app.	1	2	3	5	6	8
17,18-X-Men app.	2	4	6	10	14	18
24-27: 24-F.F. cameo; Skrulls, Nova & The New Champions app. 25-Double size.						
26,27-Galactus app.	1	2	3	5	7	9
31-49,51-60: 31,32-Brotherhood of Evil Mutants app. 32-X-Men cameo. 34,35-Sub-Mariner app. 41,42-Dr. Strange app. 56,57-Alpha Flight app. 58,59-Ant-Man app.						6.00
50-Skrulls app. (52 pgs.) Pin-ups by Konkle, Austin	1	2	3	4	5	7
61-74: 65-West Coast Avengers & Beta Ray Bill app. 65,66-X-Men app.	2	4	6	9	12	15
75-Last issue						6.00
Annual 1-4: (1982-85, 52 pgs.)						6.00
... And the X-Men: Marvel Tales (2/24, $7.99) Reprints Rom #17,18,31,32						8.00
... No. 1 Facsimile Edition (2/24, $4.99) Reprints #1 with original ads						5.00

NOTE: *Austin* a-31, 18i, 61i. *Byrne* a-74i; c-56, 57, 74. *Ditko* a-59-75p. Annual 4. *Golden* c-7-12, 19. *Guice* a-61i; c-55, 58, 60p, 70p. *Layton* a-59i, 72i; c-15, 59i, 69. *Miller* c-2p?, 3p, 17p, 18p. *Russell* a(i)-64, 65, 67, 69, 71, 75; c-64, 65i, 66, 71i, 75. *Severin* a-41p. *Sienkiewicz* a-53i; c-46, 47, 52-54, 68, 71p, Annual 2. *Simonson* c-18. *P. Smith* c-59p. *Starlin* c-67. *Zeck* c-50.

ROM (Based on the Parker Brothers toy) (Also see Rom & The Micronauts)
IDW Publishing: Jul, 2016 - No. 14, Aug, 2017 ($4.99/$3.99)

	GD 2.0	VG 4.0	FN 6.0	VF 8.0	VF/NM 9.0	NM- 9.2
1-($4.99) Ryall & Gage-s/Messina-a						5.00
2-14-($3.99) 2-4-Revolution tie-in. 2-G.I. Joe app. 5-Transformers app.						4.00
Annual 2017 (1/17, $7.99) Origin of Rom; Ryall & Gage-s/Messina-a						8.00
... First Strike 1 (10/17, $3.99) Part of the Hasbro character x-over; Gage-s/Panda-a						4.00
FCBD 2016 Edition #0 - (5/16, giveaway) Prelude to series; Action Man flip book						3.00
...: Revolution (9/16, $3.99) Revolution x-over; Ryall-s/Gage-a; multiple covers						4.00
...: Tales of the Solstar Order (3/18, $3.99) Ryall & Gage-s/Dorian-a						5.00

ROMANCE (See True Stories of...)

ROMANCE AND CONFESSION STORIES (See Giant Comics Edition)
St. John Publishing Co.: No date (1949) (25¢, 100 pgs.)

	GD 2.0	VG 4.0	FN 6.0	VF 8.0	VF/NM 9.0	NM- 9.2
1-Baker-c/a; remaindered St. John love comics	258	516	774	1651	2826	4000

ROMANCE DIARY
Marvel Comics (CDS)(CLDS): Dec, 1949 - No. 2, Mar, 1950

	GD 2.0	VG 4.0	FN 6.0	VF 8.0	VF/NM 9.0	NM- 9.2
1,2-Photo-c	25	50	75	150	245	340

ROMANCE OF FLYING, THE
David McKay Publications: 1942

	GD 2.0	VG 4.0	FN 6.0	VF 8.0	VF/NM 9.0	NM- 9.2
Feature Books 33 (nn)-WW II photos	22	44	66	132	216	300

ROMANCES OF MOLLY MANTON (See Molly Manton)

ROMANCES OF NURSE HELEN GRANT, THE
Atlas Comics (VPI): Aug, 1957

	GD 2.0	VG 4.0	FN 6.0	VF 8.0	VF/NM 9.0	NM- 9.2
1	41	82	123	256	428	600

ROMANCES OF THE WEST (Becomes Romantic Affairs #3?)
Marvel Comics (SPC): Nov, 1949 - No. 2, Mar, 1950

	GD 2.0	VG 4.0	FN 6.0	VF 8.0	VF/NM 9.0	NM- 9.2
1-Movie photo-c of Yvonne DeCarlo & Howard Duff (Calamity Jane & Sam Bass)	34	68	102	199	325	450
2-Photo-c	20	40	60	117	189	260

ROMANCE STORIES OF TRUE LOVE (Formerly True Love Problems & Advice Illustrated)
Harvey Publications: No. 45, 5/57 - No. 50, 3/58; No. 51, 9/58 - No. 52, 11/58

	GD 2.0	VG 4.0	FN 6.0	VF 8.0	VF/NM 9.0	NM- 9.2
45-51: 45,46,48-50-Powell-a	8	16	24	44	57	70
52-Matt Baker-a	12	24	36	67	94	120

ROMANCE TALES (Formerly Western Winners #6?)
Marvel Comics (CDS): No. 7, Oct, 1949 - No. 9, April, 1950 (7-9: photo-c)

	GD 2.0	VG 4.0	FN 6.0	VF 8.0	VF/NM 9.0	NM- 9.2
7	22	44	66	128	209	290
8,9: 8-Everett-a	15	30	45	86	133	180

ROMANCE TRAIL
National Periodical Publications: July-Aug, 1949 - No. 6, May-June, 1950
(All photo-c & 52 pgs.)

	GD 2.0	VG 4.0	FN 6.0	VF 8.0	VF/NM 9.0	NM- 9.2
1-Kinstler, Toth-a; Jimmy Wakely photo-c	65	130	195	416	708	1000
2-Kinstler-a; Jim Bannon photo-c	36	72	108	214	347	480
3-Tex Williams photo-c; Kinstler, Toth-a	39	78	117	231	378	525
4-Jim Bannon as Red Ryder photo-c; Toth-a	28	56	84	168	274	380
5,6: Photo-c on both. 5-Kinstler-a	27	54	81	158	259	360

ROM & THE MICRONAUTS (Based on the Parker Brothers toys)
IDW Publishing: Dec, 2017 - No. 5, Apr, 2018 ($3.99, limited series)

	GD 2.0	VG 4.0	FN 6.0	VF 8.0	VF/NM 9.0	NM- 9.2
1-5-Gage-s/Villanelli-a; multiple covers; Baron Karza app.						4.00

ROMAN HOLIDAYS, THE (TV)
Gold Key: Feb, 1973 - No. 4, Nov, 1973 (Hanna-Barbera)

	GD 2.0	VG 4.0	FN 6.0	VF 8.0	VF/NM 9.0	NM- 9.2
1	4	8	12	27	44	60
2-4	3	6	9	17	26	35

ROMANTIC ADVENTURES (My... #49-67, covers only)
American Comics Group (B&I Publ. Co.): Mar-Apr, 1949 - No. 71, Nov, 1956 (Becomes My... #72 on)

	GD 2.0	VG 4.0	FN 6.0	VF 8.0	VF/NM 9.0	NM- 9.2
1	28	56	84	165	270	375
2	16	32	48	94	147	200
3-10	14	28	42	78	112	145
11-20 (4/52)	12	24	36	69	97	125
21-45,51,52: 52-Last Pre-code (2/55)	11	22	33	62	86	110
46-49-3-D effect-c/stories (TrueVision)	18	36	54	103	162	220
50-Classic cover/story "Love of A Lunatic"	161	322	483	1030	1765	2500
53-71	11	22	33	62	86	110

NOTE: #1-23, 52 pgs. *Shelly* a-40. *Whitney* c/art in many issues.

ROMANTIC AFFAIRS (Formerly Molly Manton's Romances #2 and/or Romances of the West #2 and/or Our Love #2?)
Marvel Comics (SPC): No. 3, Mar, 1950

	GD 2.0	VG 4.0	FN 6.0	VF 8.0	VF/NM 9.0	NM- 9.2
3-Photo-c from Molly Manton's Romances #2	19	38	57	111	176	240

ROMANTIC CONFESSIONS
Hillman Periodicals: Oct, 1949 - V3#1, Apr-May, 1953

	GD 2.0	VG 4.0	FN 6.0	VF 8.0	VF/NM 9.0	NM- 9.2
V1#1-McWilliams-a	28	56	84	168	274	380
2-Briefer-a; negligee panels	18	36	54	107	169	220
3-12	15	30	45	83	124	165
V2#1,2,4-8,10-12: 2-McWilliams-a	14	28	42	80	115	150
3-Krigstein-a	15	30	45	83	124	165
9-One pg. Frazetta ad	14	28	42	80	115	150
V3#1	14	28	42	80	115	150

ROMANTIC HEARTS
Story Comics/Master/Merit Pubs.: Mar, 1951 - No. 10, Oct, 1952; July, 1953 - No. 12, July, 1955

	GD 2.0	VG 4.0	FN 6.0	VF 8.0	VF/NM 9.0	NM- 9.2
1(3/51) (1st Series)	24	48	72	142	234	325
2	15	30	45	86	133	180
3-10: Cameron-a	15	30	45	83	124	165
1(7/53) (2nd Series)-Some say #11 on-c	18	36	54	105	165	225
2	15	30	45	83	124	165
3-12	14	28	42	78	112	145

ROMANTIC LOVE
Avon Periodicals/Realistic (No #14-19): 9-10/49 - #3, 1-2/50; #4, 2-3/51 - #13, 10/52; #20, 3-4/54 - #23, 9-10/54

	GD 2.0	VG 4.0	FN 6.0	VF 8.0	VF/NM 9.0	NM- 9.2
1-c-/Avon paperback #252	53	106	159	334	567	800
2-5: 3-c/paperback Novel Library #12. 4-c/paperback Diversey Prize Novel #5.						
5-c-/paperback Novel Library #34	33	66	99	194	317	440
6- "Thrill Crazy" marijuana story; c-/Avon paperback #207; Kinstler-c	43	86	129	271	461	650
7,8: 8-Astarita-a(2)	32	64	96	188	307	425
9-c-/Avon paperback #41; Kinstler-a; headlights-c	43	86	129	271	461	650
10-12: 10-c-/Avon paperback #212. 11-c-/paperback Novel Library #17; Kinstler-a.						
12-c-/paperback Novel Library #13	34	68	102	204	332	460
13,21-23: 22,23-Kinstler-c	32	64	96	188	307	425
20-Kinstler-c	33	66	99	194	317	440
nn(1-3/53)(Realistic-r)	20	40	60	120	195	270

NOTE: *Astarita* a-7, 10, 11, 21. Painted c-1-3, 5, 7-11, 13. Photo c-4, 6.

ROMANTIC LOVE
Quality Comics Group: 1963-1964

	GD 2.0	VG 4.0	FN 6.0	VF 8.0	VF/NM 9.0	NM- 9.2
I.W. Reprint #2,3,8,11: 2-r/Romantic Love #2	3	6	9	19	30	40

ROMANTIC MARRIAGE (Cinderella Love #25 on)
Ziff-Davis/St. John No. 18 on (#1-8: 52 pgs.): #1-3 (1950, no months); #4, 5-6/51 - #17, 9/52; #18, 9/53 - #24, 9/54

	GD 2.0	VG 4.0	FN 6.0	VF 8.0	VF/NM 9.0	NM- 9.2
1-Photo-c; Cary Grant/Betsy Drake photo back-c	36	72	108	211	343	475
2-Painted-c; Anderson-a (also #15)	23	46	69	136	223	310
3-9: 3,4,8,9-Painted-c; 5-7-Photo-c	21	42	63	122	199	275
10-Unusual format; front-c is a painted-c; back-c is a photo-c complete with logo, price, etc.	34	68	102	204	332	460
11-17 13-Photo-c. 15-Signed story by Anderson. 17-(9/52)-Last Z-D issue	20	40	60	115	185	255
18-22: 20-Photo-c	20	40	60	115	185	255
23-Baker-c; all stories are reprinted from #15	63	126	189	403	689	975
24-Baker-c	116	232	348	742	1271	1800

ROMANTIC PICTURE NOVELETTES
Magazine Enterprises: 1946

	GD 2.0	VG 4.0	FN 6.0	VF 8.0	VF/NM 9.0	NM- 9.2
1-Mary Worth-r; Creig Flessel-c	25	50	75	150	245	340

ROMANTIC SECRETS (Becomes Time For Love)
Fawcett/Charlton Comics No. 5 (10/55) on: Sept, 1949 - No. 39, 4/53; No. 5, 10/55 - No. 52, 11/64 (#1-39: photo-c)

	GD 2.0	VG 4.0	FN 6.0	VF 8.0	VF/NM 9.0	NM- 9.2
1-(52 pg. issues begin, end #?)	22	44	66	132	216	300
2,3	14	28	42	82	121	160
4,9-Evans-a	15	30	45	84	127	170
5-8,10(9/50)	11	22	33	62	86	110
11-23	10	20	30	54	72	90
24-Evans-a	10	20	30	58	79	100
25-39('53)	9	18	27	52	69	85
5 (Charlton, 2nd Series)(10/55, formerly Negro Romances #4)	14	28	42	76	108	140
6-10	9	18	27	52	69	85
11-20	8	16	24	47	61	75
21-35	4	8	12	23	37	50
36-52('64)	4	8	12	20	30	40

NOTE: *Bailey* a-20. *Powell* a(1st series)-5, 7, 10, 12, 16, 17, 20, 26, 29, 33, 34, 36, 37. *Sekowsky* a-26. *Swayze* a(1st series)-16, 18, 19, 23, 26-28, 31, 32, 39.

ROMANTIC STORY (Cowboy Love #28 on)
Fawcett/Charlton Comics No. 23 on: 11/49 - #22, Sum, 1953; #23, 5/54 - #27, 12/54; #28,

Rom (2016 series) #4 © Hasbro

Romantic Secrets #8 © FAW

Ronald McDonald #1 © McDonald's

	GD	VG	FN	VF	VF/NM	NM-
	2.0	4.0	6.0	8.0	9.0	9.2

8/55 - #130, 11/73

1-Photo-c begin, end #24; 52 pgs. begins	21	42	63	126	206	285
2	14	28	42	80	115	150
3-5	11	22	33	62	86	110
6-14	10	20	30	56	76	95
15-Evans-a	12	24	36	67	94	120
16-22(Sum, '53; last Fawcett issue). 21-Toth-a?	9	18	27	47	61	75
23-39: 26,29-Wood swipes	8	16	24	42	54	65
40-(100 pgs.)	14	28	42	78	112	145
41-50	4	8	12	23	37	50
51-80: 57-Hypo needle story	3	6	9	17	26	35
81-99	3	6	9	14	19	24
100	3	6	9	14	20	26
101-130: 120-Bobby Sherman pin-up	2	4	6	11	16	20

NOTE: *Jim Aparo* a-94. *Powell* a-7, 8, 16, 20, 30. *Marcus Swayze* a-2, 12, 20, 32.

ROMANTIC THRILLS (See Fox Giants)

ROMANTIC WESTERN
Fawcett Publications: Winter, 1949 - No. 3, June, 1950 (All Photo-c)

1	25	50	75	147	241	335
2-(Spr/50)-Williamson, McWilliams-a	21	42	63	126	206	285
3	16	32	48	98	154	210

ROM: DIRE WRAITHS
IDW Publishing: Oct, 2019 - No. 3, Oct, 2020 ($4.99, limited series)

1-3: 1-Ryall-s/Pizzari & Dorian Sr.-a ... 5.00

ROMEO TUBBS (...That Lovable Teenager; formerly My Secret Life)
Fox Features Syndicate/Green Publ. Co. No. 27: No. 26, 5/50 - No. 28, 7/50; No. 1, 1950; No. 27, 12/52

26-Teen-age	19	38	57	111	176	240
28 (7/50)	18	36	54	103	162	220
27 (12/52)-Contains Pedro on inside; Wood-a	20	40	60	117	189	260

ROMULUS
Image Comics: Oct, 2016 - No. 4, May, 2017 ($3.99)

1-4-Bryan Hill-s/Nelson Blake II-a ... 4.00

ROM VS. TRANSFORMERS: SHINING ARMOR
IDW Publishing: Jul, 2017 - No. 5, Nov, 2017 ($3.99, limited series)

1-5-Barber & Gage-s/Milne-a ... 4.00

RONALD McDONALD (TV)
Charlton Press: Sept, 1970 - No. 4, March, 1971

1-Bill Yates-a in all	10	20	30	66	138	210
2-4: 2 & 3 both dated Jan, 1971	6	12	18	37	66	95
V2#1-4-Special reprint for McDonald systems; new cover art on each; "Not for resale" on cover	7	14	21	49	92	135

RONIN
DC Comics: July, 1983 - No. 6, June, 1984 ($2.50, limited series, 52 pgs.)

1-Frank Miller-c/a/scripts in all	2	4	6	11	16	20
2-5	2	4	6	8	11	14
6-Scarcer; has fold-out poster.	3	6	9	14	19	24

Trade paperback (1987, $12.95)-Reprints #1-6 ... 18.00

RONIN BOOK II
Frank Miller Presents: 2022 - No. 6, 2023 ($7.99, B&W, limited series)

1-6-Frank Miller-s/Philip Tan-a ... 8.00

RONIN ISLAND
BOOM! Studios: Mar, 2019 - No. 12, July, 2020 ($3.99, limited series)

1-12-Greg Pak-s/Giannis Milonogiannis-a ... 4.00

RONNA
Knight Press: Apr, 1997 ($2.95, B&W, one-shot)

1-Beau Smith-s ... 4.00

ROOK (See Eerie Magazine & Warren Presents: The Rook)
Warren Publications: Oct, 1979 - No. 14, April, 1982 (B&W magazine)

1-Nino-a/Corben-c; with 8 pg. color insert	3	6	9	16	23	30
2-4,6,7: 2-Voltar by Alcala begins. 3,4-Toth-a	2	4	6	9	13	16
5,8-14: 11-Zorro-s. 12-14-Eagle by Severin	2	4	6	9	13	16

ROOK
Harris Comics: No. 0, Jun, 1995 - No. 4, 1995 ($2.95)

0-4: 0-short stories (3) w/preview. 4-Brereton-c. ... 4.00

ROOK, THE

Dark Horse Comics: Oct, 2015 - No. 4, Jan, 2016 ($3.99)

1-4-Steven Grant-s/Paul Gulacy-a/c ... 4.00

ROOKIE COP (Formerly Crime and Justice?)
Charlton Comics: No. 27, Nov, 1955 - No. 33, Aug, 1957

27	14	28	42	82	121	160
28-33	9	18	27	59	65	80

ROOM 222 (TV)
Dell Publishing Co.: Jan, 1970; No. 2, May, 1970 - No. 4, Jan, 1971

1	6	12	18	38	69	100
2-4-Photo-c. 3-Marijuana story. 4 r/#1	4	8	12	25	40	55

ROOTIE KAZOOTIE (TV)(See 3-D-ell)
Dell Publishing Co.: No. 415, Aug, 1952 - No. 6, Oct-Dec, 1954

Four Color 415 (#1)	11	22	33	73	157	240
Four Color 459,502(#2,3), 4(4-6/54)-6	7	14	21	46	86	125

ROOTS OF THE SWAMP THING
DC Comics: July, 1986 - No.5, Nov, 1986 ($2.00, Baxter paper, 52 pgs.)

1-5: r/Swamp Thing #1-10 by Wrightson & House of Mystery-r. 1-new Wrightson-c (2-5 reprinted covers). ... 5.00

RORSCHACH
DC Comics (Black Label): Dec, 2020 - No. 12, Nov, 2021 ($4.99, limited series)

1-12-Tom King-s/Jorge Fornés-a ... 5.00

ROSE (See Bone)
Cartoon Books: Nov, 2000 - No. 3, Feb, 2002 ($5.95, lim. series, square-bound)

1-3-Prequel to Bone; Jeff Smith-s/Charles Vess painted-a/c		6.00
HC (2001, $29.95) r/#1-3; new Vess cover painting		30.00
SC (2002, $19.95) r/#1-3; new Vess cover painting		20.00
1-($6.00)-Blood & Glory Edition		6.00

ROSE
Image Comics: Apr, 2017 - No. 17, Feb, 2019 ($3.99)

1-17-Meredith Finch-s/Ig Guara-a ... 4.00

ROSE AND THORN
DC Comics: Feb, 2004 - No. 6, July, 2004 ($2.95, limited series)

1-6-Simone-s/Melo-a/Hughes-c ... 3.00

ROSWELL: LITTLE GREEN MAN (See Simpsons Comics #19-22)
Bongo Comics: 1996 - No. 6 ($2.95, quarterly)

1-6		4.00
...Walks Among Us ('97, $12.95, TPB) r/ #1-3 & Simpsons flip books		13.00

ROUGH RIDERS
AfterShock Comics: Apr, 2016 - No. 7, Nov, 2016 ($3.99)

1-7: 1-Teddy Roosevelt, Annie Oakley, Houdini, Jack Johnson, Thomas Edison team		4.00
... Nation 1 (11/16, $3.99) Dossier of other Rough Rider teams; art by various		4.00

ROUGH RIDERS: RIDE OR DIE
AfterShock Comics: Feb, 2018 - No. 4, May, 2018 ($3.99)

1-4-Glass-s/Olliffe-a; H.P. Lovecraft app. ... 4.00

ROUGH RIDERS: RIDERS ON THE STORM
AfterShock Comics: Feb, 2017 - No. 6, Sept, 2017 ($3.99)

1-6-Glass-s/Olliffe-a; Monk Eastman joins team ... 4.00

ROUND TABLE OF AMERICA: PERSONALITY CRISIS (See Big Bang Comics)
Image Comics: Aug, 2005 ($3.50, one-shot)

1-Carlos Rodriguez-a/Pedro Angosto-s ... 3.50

ROUNDUP (...Western Crime Stories)
D. S. Publishing Co.: July-Aug, 1948 - No. 5, Mar-Apr, 1949 (All 52 pgs.)

1-Kiefer-a	24	48	72	142	234	325
2-5: 2-Marijuana drug mention story	17	34	51	98	154	210

ROUTE 666
CrossGeneration Comics: July, 2002 - No. 22, Jun, 2004 ($2.95)

1-22-Bedard-s/Moline-a in most. 5-Richards-a. 15-McCrea-a ... 3.00

ROWANS RUIN
BOOM! Studios: Oct, 2015 - No. 4, Jan, 2016 ($3.99, limited series)

1-4-Mike Carey-s/Mike Perkins-a. 1-Multiple covers ... 4.00

ROYAL CITY
Image Comics: Mar, 2017 - No. 14, Aug, 2018 ($4.99/$3.99)

1-($4.99) Jeff Lemire-s/a ... 5.00

	GD 2.0	VG 4.0	FN 6.0	VF 8.0	VF/NM 9.0	NM- 9.2

2-14-($3.99) — — — — — 4.00

ROYAL ROY
Marvel Comics (Star Comics): May, 1985 - No. 6, Mar, 1986 (Children's book)
1-6 — — — — — 4.00

ROYALS (The Inhumans) (Leads into Inhumans: Judgment Day)
Marvel Comics: Jun, 2017 - No. 12, Feb, 2018 ($3.99)
1-12: 1-Ewing-s/Meyers-a; Marvel Boy app. 2-Maximus returns. 4,5-Ronan app. — 4.00

ROYALS, THE: MASTERS OF WAR
DC Comics (Vertigo): Apr, 2014 - No. 6, Sept, 2014 ($2.99, limited series)
1-6-Rob Williams-s/Simon Coleby-a/c; super-powered Royal families during WWII — 3.00

ROY CAMPANELLA, BASEBALL HERO
Fawcett Publications: 1950 (Brooklyn Dodgers)
nn-Photo-c; life story — 65 — 130 — 195 — 416 — 708 — 1000

ROY ROGERS (See March of Comics #17, 35, 47, 62, 68, 73, 77, 86, 91, 100, 105, 116, 121, 131, 136, 146, 151, 161, 167, 176, 191, 206, 221, 236, 250)

ROY ROGERS AND TRIGGER
Gold Key: Apr, 1967
1-Photo-c; reprints — 5 — 10 — 15 — 33 — 57 — 80

ROY ROGERS ANNUAL
Wilson Publ. Co., Toronto/Dell: 1947 ("Giant Edition" on-c)(132 pgs., 50¢)
nn-Seven known copies. Front and back cover art are from Roy Rogers #2. Stories reprinted from Roy Rogers #2, Four Color #137 and Four Color #153. (A copy in VG/FN was sold in 1986 for $400, in 1996 for $1200 and in 2000 for $1500; a FN+ sold for $1,650; a GD sold for $448 in 2008, a FN sold for $717 in 2009 and a FR sold for $156 in 2015.)

ROY ROGERS COMICS (See Western Roundup under Dell Giants)
Dell Publishing Co.: No. 38, 4/44 - No. 177, 12/47 (#38-166: 52 pgs.)

	2.0	4.0	6.0	8.0	9.0	9.2
Four Color 38 (1944)-49 pg. story; photo front/back-c on all 4-Color issues (1st western comic with photo-c)	155	310	465	1279	2890	4500
Four Color 63 (1945)-Color photos on all four-c	40	80	120	296	673	1050
Four Color 86,95 (1945)	29	58	87	209	467	725
Four Color 109 (1946)	22	44	66	154	340	525
Four Color 117,124,137,144	17	34	51	119	265	410
Four Color 153,160,166: 166-48 pg. story	15	30	45	105	233	360
Four Color 177 (36 pgs.)-32 pg. story	15	30	45	100	220	340
HC (Dark Horse Books, 8/08, $49.95) r/Four Color #38,63,86,95,109; Roy Rogers Jr intro.						50.00

ROY ROGERS COMICS (...& Trigger #92(8/55)-on)(Roy starred in Republic movies, radio & TV) (Singing cowboy) (Also see Dale Evans, It Really Happened #8, Queen of the West Dale Evans, & Roy Rogers' Trigger)
Dell Publishing Co.: Jan, 1948 - No. 145, Sept-Oct, 1961 (#1-19: 36 pgs.)

	2.0	4.0	6.0	8.0	9.0	9.2
1-Roy, his horse Trigger, & Chuck Wagon Charley's Tales begin; photo-c begin, end #145	68	136	204	544	1222	1900
2	22	44	66	154	340	525
3-5	15	30	45	100	220	340
6-10	12	24	36	80	173	265
11-19: 19-Chuckwagon Charley's Tales ends	10	20	30	68	144	220
20 (52 pgs.)-Trigger feature begins, ends #46	10	20	30	69	147	225
21-30 (52 pgs.)	9	18	27	60	120	180
31-46 (52 pgs.): 37-X-Mas-c	8	16	24	51	96	140
47-56 (36 pgs.): 47-Chuck Wagon Charley's Tales returns, ends #133. 49-X-mas-c. 55-Last photo back-c	6	12	18	40	73	105
57 (52 pgs.)-Heroin drug propaganda story	7	14	21	48	89	130
58-70 (52 pgs.): 58-Heroin drug use/dealing story. 61-X-Mas-c	6	12	18	40	73	105
71-80 (52 pgs.): 73-X-Mas-c	5	10	15	35	63	90
81-91 (36 pgs. #81-on): 85-X-Mas-c	5	10	15	34	60	85
92-99,101-110,112-118: 92-Title changed to Roy Rogers and Trigger (8/55)	5	10	15	33	57	80
100-Trigger feature returns, ends #131	6	12	18	37	66	95
111,119-124: 73-X-Mas-c	6	12	18	38	69	100
125-131: 125-Totha-a (1 pg.)	5	10	15	31	53	75
132-144-Manning-a. 132-1st Dale Evans-sty by Russ Manning. 138,144-Dale Evans featured	5	10	15	34	60	85
145-Last issue	6	12	18	42	79	115

NOTE: *Buscema* a-74-108(2 stories each). *Manning* a-123, 124, 132-144. *Marsh* a-110. *Photo back-c* 1-9, 11-35, 38-55.

ROY ROGERS' TRIGGER
Dell Publishing Co.: No. 329, May, 1951 - No. 17, June-Aug, 1955

	2.0	4.0	6.0	8.0	9.0	9.2
Four Color 329 (#1)-Painted-c	14	28	42	97	214	330
2 (9-11/51)-Photo-c	10	20	30	64	132	200
3-5: 3-Painted-c begin, end #17, most by S. Savitt	6	12	18	38	69	100
6-17: Title merges with Roy Rogers after #17	5	10	15	31	53	75

ROY ROGERS WESTERN CLASSICS
AC Comics: 1989 -No. 4 ($2.95/$3.95, 44pgs.) (24 pgs. color, 16 pgs. B&W)
1-4: 1-Dale Evans-r by Manning, Trigger-r by Buscema; photo covers & interior photos by Roy & Dale. 2-Buscema-r (3); photo-c & B&W photos inside. 3-Dale Evans-r by Manning; Trigger-r by Buscema plus other Buscema-r; photo-c — 4.00

RUBY FALLS
Dark Horse Comics (Berger Books): Oct, 2019 - No. 4, Jan, 2020 ($3.99, limited series)
1-4-Ann Nocenti-s/Flavia Biondi-a — 4.00

RUDOLPH, THE RED-NOSED REINDEER
National Per. Publ.: 1950 - No. 13, Winter, 1962-63 (Issues are not numbered)

	2.0	4.0	6.0	8.0	9.0	9.2
1950 issue (#1); Grossman-c/a in all	48	96	144	302	514	725
1951-53 issues (3 total)	28	56	84	168	274	380
1954/55, 55/56, 56/57	23	46	69	136	223	310
1957/58, 58/59, 59/60, 60/61, 61/62	12	24	36	79	170	260
1962/63 (rare)(84 pgs.)(shows "Annual" in indicia)	23	46	69	161	358	550

NOTE: *13 total issues have been published. Has games & puzzles also.*

RUDOLPH, THE RED-NOSED REINDEER (Also see Limited Collectors' Edition C-20, C-24, C-33, C-42, C-50; and All-New Collectors' Edition C-53 & C-60)

National Per. Publ.: Christmas 1972 (Treasury-size)
nn-Precursor to Limited Collectors' Edition title (scarce) (implied to be Lim. Coll .Ed. C-20) — 20 — 40 — 60 — 140 — 310 — 480

RUFF AND REDDY (TV)
Dell Publ. Co.: No. 937, 9/58 - No. 12, 1-3/62 (Hanna-Barbera)(#9 on: 15¢)

	2.0	4.0	6.0	8.0	9.0	9.2
Four Color 937(#1)(1st Hanna-Barbera comic book)	12	24	36	82	179	275
Four Color 981,1038	8	16	24	52	99	145
4(1-3/60)-12: 8-Last 10¢ issue	6	12	18	41	76	110

RUFF & REDDY SHOW, THE
DC Comics: Dec, 2017 - No. 6, May, 2018 ($3.99, limited series)
1-6-Ruff & Ready in the real world; Chaykin-s/Mac Rey-a; 2 covers (Chaykin & Rey) — 4.00

RUGGED ACTION (Strange Stories of Suspense #5 on)
Atlas Comics (CSI): Dec, 1954 - No. 4, June, 1955

	2.0	4.0	6.0	8.0	9.0	9.2
1-Brodsky-c	20	40	60	122	199	275
2-4: 2-Last precode (2/55)	15	30	45	86	133	180

NOTE: *Ayers a-2, 3. Maneely c-2, 3. Severin a-2.*

RUGRATS (TV) (Nickelodeon cartoon)
BOOM! Studios (kaboom!): Oct, 2017 - No. 8, May, 2018 ($3.99)
1-8: 1-3,5-Box Brown-s/Lisa DuBois-a; multiple covers — 4.00
...: C Is For Chanukah 2018 Special 1 (11/18, $7.99) Kibblesmith & Crawford-s/Sherron-a — 8.00
...: R Is For Reptar 2018 Special 1 (4/18, $7.99) Short stories by various — 8.00

RUINS
Marvel Comics (Alterniverse): July, 1995 - No. 2, Sept, 1995 ($5.00, painted, limited series)
1,2: Phil Sheldon from Marvels; Warren Ellis scripts; acetate-c — 6.00
Reprint (2009, $4.99) r/#1,2; cover gallery — 5.00

RUINS OF RAVENCROFT
Marvel Comics: Mar, 2020 ($4.99, series of one-shots)
...: Carnage - Tieri/Unzueta-a; Set in the early 1400s New York — 5.00
...: Dracula - Tieri-s/Unzueta-a; Dracula vs. Golden Age Captain America — 5.00
...: Sabretooth - Tieri-s/Unzueta-a; Wolverine vs. Sabretooth in 1909 — 5.00

RULAH JUNGLE GODDESS (Formerly Zoot; I Loved #28 on) (Also see All Top Comics & Terrors of the Jungle)
Fox Feature Syndicate: No. 17, Aug, 1948 - No. 27, June, 1949

	2.0	4.0	6.0	8.0	9.0	9.2
17	168	336	504	1075	1838	2600
18-Classic girl-fight interior splash	110	220	330	704	1202	1700
19,20	106	212	318	673	1162	1650
21-Used in SOTI, pg. 388,389	155	310	465	992	1696	2400
22-Used in SOTI, pg. 22,23	113	226	339	718	1234	1750
23-27	81	162	243	518	884	1250

NOTE: *Kamen c-17-19, 21. 22.*

RUMPUS ROOM
Artists, Writers & Artisans: Sept, 2023 - No. 5, Jan, 2024 ($3.99, limited series)
1-5-Mark Russell-s/Ramon Rosanas-a/Tony Harris-c — 4.00

RUNAWAY, THE (See Movie Classics)

RUNAWAYS
Marvel Comics: July, 2003 - No. 18, Nov, 2004 ($2.95/$2.25/$2.99)
1-($2.95) Vaughan-s/Alphona-a/Jo Chen-c — 4.00
2-9-($2.50) — 3.00
10-18-($2.99) 11,12-Miyazawa-a; Cloak and Dagger app. 16-The mole revealed — 3.00
Hardcover (2005, $34.99) oversized r/#1-18; proposal & sketch pages; Vaughan intro. — 35.00
Marvel Age Runaways Vol. 1: Pride and Joy (2004, $7.99, digest size) r/#1-6 — 8.00
...Vol. 2: Teenage Wasteland (2004, $7.99, digest size) r/#7-12 — 8.00
...Vol. 3: The Good Die Young (2004, $7.99, digest size) r/#13-18 — 8.00

RUNAWAYS (Also see X-Men/Runaways 2006 FCBD Edition)
Marvel Comics: Apr, 2005 - No. 30, Aug, 2008 ($2.99)
1-24: 1-6-Vaughan-s/Alphona-a/Jo Chen-c. 7,8-Miyazawa-a/Bachalo-a. 11-Spider-Man app. 12-New Avengers app. 18-Gert killed — 3.00
25-30-Joss Whedon-s/Michael Ryan-a. 25-Punisher app. — 3.00
...: Dead End Kids HC (2008, $19.99) r/#25-30 — 20.00
...: Saga (2007, $3.99) re-caps the 2 series thru #24; 4 new pages w/Ramos-a; Ramos-c — 4.00
Hardcover (2006, $24.99) oversized r/#1-12 & X-Men/Runaways; script & sketch pages — 25.00
Hardcover Vol. 3 (2007, $24.99) oversized r/#13-24; sketch pages — 25.00
...Vol. 4: True Believers (2006, $7.99, digest size) r/#1-6 — 8.00
...Vol. 5: Escape To New York (2006, $7.99, digest size) r/#7-12 — 8.00
...Vol. 6: Parental Guidance (2006, $7.99, digest size) r/#13-18 — 8.00

RUNAWAYS (3rd series)
Marvel Comics: Oct, 2008 - No. 14, Nov, 2009 ($2.99/$3.99)
1-9,11-14: 1-6-Terry Moore-s/Humberto Ramos-a/c. 7-9-Miyazawa-a — 3.00
10-($3.99) Wolverine & the X-men app.; Yost & Asmus-s; Pichelli & Rios-a; Lafuente-c — 4.00

RUNAWAYS (Secret Wars Battleworld tie-in)
Marvel Comics: Aug, 2015 - No. 4, Nov, 2015 ($3.99, limited series)
1-4-Noelle Stevenson-s/Sanford Greene-a — 4.00

RUNAWAYS
Marvel Comics: Nov, 2017 - No. 38 Oct, 2021 ($3.99)
1-37: 1-Gert revived; Rowell-s/Anka-a. 8-Julie Power app. 33-35-Wolverine app. — 4.00
38-($4.99) Legacy issue #100 — 5.00
... Halloween Comic Fest 2017 1 (12/17, giveaway) r/#1 (2003) first app. — 3.00

RUN BABY RUN
Logos International: 1974 (39¢, Christian religious)
nn-By Tony Tallarico from Nicky Cruz's book — 2 — 4 — 6 — 11 — 16 — 20

RUN, BUDDY, RUN (TV)
Gold Key: June, 1967 (Photo-c)
1 (10204-706) — 3 — 6 — 9 — 17 — 26 — 35

RUNE (See Curse of Rune, Sludge & all other Ultraverse titles for previews)
Malibu Comics (Ultraverse): 1994 - No. 9, Apr, 1995 ($1.95)
0-Obtained by sending coupons from 11 comics; came w/Solution #0, poster,

Roy Rogers Comics #33 © RR

Runaways (2017 series) #13 © MAR

Saban's Go Go Power Rangers #16 © Saban

	GD 2.0	VG 4.0	FN 6.0	VF 8.0	VF/NM 9.0	NM- 9.2
temporary tattoo, card	1	3	4	6	8	10

1,2,4-9: 1-Barry Windsor-Smith-c/a/stories begin, ends #6. 5-1st app. of Gemini.
6-Prime & Mantra app. ... 4.00
1-(1/94)-"Ashcan" edition flip book w/Wrath #1 ... 4.00
1-Ultra 5000 Limited silver foil edition ... 6.00
3-(3/94, $3.50, 68 pgs.)-Flip book w/Ultraverse Premiere #1 ... 5.00
Giant Size 1 ($2.50, 44 pgs.)-B.Smith story & art. ... 5.00

RUNE (2nd Series)(Formerly Curse of Rune)(See Ultraverse Unlimited #1)
Malibu Comics (Ultraverse): Infinity, Sept, 1995 - V2#7, Apr, 1996 ($1.50)
Infinity, V2#1-7: Infinity-Black September tie-in; black-c & painted-c exist. 1,3-7-Marvel's Adam
Warlock app; regular & painted-c exist. 2-Flip book w/ "Phoenix Resurrection" Pt. 6 ... 4.00
...Vs. Venom 1 (12/95, $3.95) ... 5.00

RUNE: HEARTS OF DARKNESS
Malibu Comics (Ultraverse): Sept, 1996 - No. 3, Nov, 1996 ($1.50, lim. series)
1-3: Moench scripts & Kyle Hotz-c/a; flip books w/6 pg. Rune story by the Pander Bros. ... 4.00

RUNE/SILVER SURFER
Marvel Comics/Malibu Comics (Ultraverse): Apr, 1995 ($5.95/$2.95, one-shot)
1 ($5.95, direct market)-BWS-c ... 6.00
1 ($2.95, newsstand)-BWS-c ... 4.00
1-Collector's limited edition ... 6.00

RUNLOVEKILL
Image Comics: Apr, 2015 - No. 8 ($2.99, limited series)
1-4: 1-Tsuei-s/Canete-a ... 3.00

RUSE (Also see Archard's Agents)
CrossGeneration Comics: Nov, 2001 - No. 26, Jan, 2004 ($2.95)
1-Waid-s/Guice & Perkins-a ... 5.00
2-26: 6-Jeff Johnson-a. 11,15-Paul Ryan-a. 12-Last Waid-s ... 3.00
Enter the Detective Vol. 1 TPB (2002, $15.95, TPB) r/#1-6; Guice-c ... 16.00
...: The Silent Partner Vol. 2 (3/03, $15.95, TPB) r/#7-12 ... 16.00
...: Criminal Intent Vol. 3 ('03, $15.95, TPB) r/#13-18 ... 16.00
Traveler 1,2 ($9.95): Digest-size editions of the TPBs ... 10.00

RUSE
Marvel Comics: May, 2011 - No. 4 ($2.99, limited series)
1-4-Waid-s/Guice-c. 1,3,4-Pierfederici-a ... 3.00

RUSH CITY
DC Comics: Sept, 2006 - No. 6, May, 2007 ($2.99, limited series)
1-6: 1-Dixon-s/Green-a/Jock-c. 2,3-Black Canary app. ... 3.00

RUSTLERS, THE (See Zane Grey Four Color 532)

RUSTY, BOY DETECTIVE
Good Comics/Lev Gleason: Mar-April, 1955 - No. 5, Nov, 1955

	GD 2.0	VG 4.0	FN 6.0	VF 8.0	VF/NM 9.0	NM- 9.2
1-Bob Wood, Carl Hubbell-a begins	14	28	42	78	112	145
2-5	10	20	30	54	72	90

RUSTY COMICS (Formerly Kid Movie Comics; Rusty and Her Family #21, 22;
The Kelleys #23 on; see Millie The Model)
Marvel Comics (HPC): No. 12, Apr, 1947 - No. 22, Sept, 1949

	GD 2.0	VG 4.0	FN 6.0	VF 8.0	VF/NM 9.0	NM- 9.2
12-Mitzi app.	39	78	117	231	378	525
13	23	46	69	136	223	310
14-Wolverton's Powerhouse Pepper (4 pgs.) plus Kurtzman's "Hey Look"	42	84	126	265	445	625
15-17-Kurtzman's "Hey Look"	25	50	75	150	245	340
18,19	21	42	63	122	199	275
20-Kurtzman-a (5 pgs.)	27	54	81	158	259	360
21,22-Kurtzman-a (17 & 22 pgs.)	33	66	99	194	317	440

RUSTY DUGAN (See Holyoke One-Shot #2)

RUSTY RILEY
Dell Publishing Co.: No. 418, Aug, 1952 - No. 554, April, 1954 (Frank Godwin strip reprints)

	GD 2.0	VG 4.0	FN 6.0	VF 8.0	VF/NM 9.0	NM- 9.2
Four Color 418 (...a Boy, a Horse, and a Dog #1)	9	18	27	57	111	165
Four Color 451(2/53), 486 ('53), 554	5	10	15	35	63	90

RUULE
Beckett Comics: Dec, 2003 - No. 5, Apr, 2004 ($2.99)
1-5-David Mack-c/Mike Hawthorne-a ... 3.00

RUULE: KISS & TELL
Beckett Comics: Jun, 2004 - No. 8 ($1.99)
1-8: 1-Amano-s/c; Rousseau-a. 4-Maleev-c ... 3.00
TPB (2005, $19.99) r/#1-8 ... 20.00

RWBY (Based on the online series from Rooster Teeth)(Issue #7 printing cancelled, digital only)

	GD 2.0	VG 4.0	FN 6.0	VF 8.0	VF/NM 9.0	NM- 9.2

DC Comics: Dec, 2019 - No. 6, May, 2020 ($3.99)
1-6-Marguerite Bennett-s; two covers on each. 1-3,6-Mirka Andolfo-a. 4,5-Hetrick-a ... 4.00

RWBY / JUSTICE LEAGUE
DC Comics: Jun, 2021 - No. 7, Dec, 2021 ($3.99, limited series)
1-7-Marguerite Bennett-s; two covers on each. 1,4-Aneke-a. 2,5-Pepper-a ... 4.00

RYDER OF THE STORM
Radical Comics: Oct, 2010 - No. 3, Apr, 2011 ($4.99, limited series)
1-3-David Hine-s/Wayne Nichols-a ... 5.00

SAARI ("The Jungle Goddess")
P. L. Publishing Co.: November, 1951

	GD 2.0	VG 4.0	FN 6.0	VF 8.0	VF/NM 9.0	NM- 9.2
1	71	142	213	454	777	1100

SABAN POWERHOUSE (TV)
Acclaim Books: 1997 ($4.50, digest size)

	GD 2.0	VG 4.0	FN 6.0	VF 8.0	VF/NM 9.0	NM- 9.2
1,2-Power Rangers, BeetleBorgs, and others	2	4	6	11	16	20

SABAN PRESENTS POWER RANGERS TURBO VS. BEETLEBORGS METALLIX (TV)
Acclaim Books: 1997 ($4.50, digest size, one-shot)

	GD 2.0	VG 4.0	FN 6.0	VF 8.0	VF/NM 9.0	NM- 9.2
nn	3	6	9	14	20	25

SABAN'S GO GO POWER RANGERS
BOOM! Studios: Jul, 2017 - No. 32, Jun, 2020 ($3.99)
1-32: 1-Parrott-s/Mora-a; multiple covers; retells 1st meeting with Rita Repulsa ... 4.00
...: Back To School 1 (9/18, $7.99) Rangers separately on Spring Break; art by various ... 8.00
...: Forever Rangers 1 (6/19, $7.99) Parrott-s/Carlini & Mortarino-a; origin of Zordon ... 8.00

SABAN'S MIGHTY MORPHIN POWER RANGERS
Hamilton Comics: Dec, 1994 - No. 6, May, 1995 ($1.95, limited series)

	GD 2.0	VG 4.0	FN 6.0	VF 8.0	VF/NM 9.0	NM- 9.2
1-w/bound-in Power Ranger Barcode Card	3	6	9	16	23	30
2-6						6.00

SABAN'S MIGHTY MORPHIN POWER RANGERS (TV)
Marvel Comics: 1995 - No. 8, 1996 ($1.75)

	GD 2.0	VG 4.0	FN 6.0	VF 8.0	VF/NM 9.0	NM- 9.2
1	2	4	6	11	16	20
2-8						5.00

SABAN'S POWER RANGERS: AFTERSHOCK
BOOM! Studios: Mar, 2017 ($14.99, SC)
SC - Sequel to the 2017 movie; Parrott-s/Werneck-a; movie photo-c ... 15.00

SABLE (Formerly Jon Sable, Freelance; also see Mike Grell's...)
First Comics: Mar, 1988 - No. 27, May, 1990 ($1.75/$1.95)
1-27: 10-Begin $1.95-c ... 4.00

SABLE & FORTUNE (Also see Silver Sable and the Wild Pack)
Marvel Comics: Mar, 2006 - No. 4, June, 2006 ($2.99, limited series)
1-4-John Burns-a/Brendan Cahill-s ... 3.00

SABRE (See Eclipse Graphic Album Series)
Eclipse Comics: Aug, 1982 - No. 14, Aug, 1985 (Baxter paper #4 on)
1-14: 1-Sabre & Morrigan Tales begin. 4-6-Incredible Seven origin ... 4.00

SABRETOOTH (See Iron Fist, Power Man, X-Factor #10 & X-Men)
Marvel Comics: Aug, 1993 - No. 4, Nov, 1993 ($2.95, lim. series, coated paper)
1-4: 1-Die-cut-c. 3-Wolverine app. ... 5.00
...Special 1 "In the Red Zone" (1995, $4.95) Chromium wraparound-c ... 6.00
V2 #1 (1/98, $5.95, one-shot) Wildchild app. ... 6.00
Trade paperback (12/94, $12.95) r/#1-4 ... 13.00

SABRETOOTH
Marvel Comics: Dec, 2004 - No. 4, Feb, 2005 ($2.99, limited series)
1-4-Sears-a. 3,4-Wendigo app. ... 3.00
...: Open Season TPB (2005, $9.99) r/#1-4 ... 10.00

SABRETOOTH
Marvel Comics: Apr, 2022 - No. 5, Sept, 2022 ($3.99, limited series)
1-($4.99)-LaValle-s/Kirk-a ... 5.00
2-5-($3.99) ... 4.00

SABRETOOTH AND MYSTIQUE (See Mystique and Sabretooth)

SABRETOOTH & THE EXILES
Marvel Comics: Jan, 2023 - No. 5, May, 2023 ($4.99/$3.99, limited series)
1-($4.99)-LaValle-s/Kirk-a; Toad app. ... 5.00
2-5-($3.99) ... 4.00

SABRETOOTH CLASSIC
Marvel Comics: May, 1994 - No. 15, July, 1995 ($1.50)

	GD 2.0	VG 4.0	FN 6.0	VF 8.0	VF/NM 9.0	NM- 9.2

1-15: 1-3-r/Power Man & Iron Fist #66,78,84. 4-r/Spec. S-M #116. 9-Uncanny X-Men #212, 10-r/Uncanny X-Men #213. 11-r/ Daredevil #238. 12-r/Classic X-Men #10 — 4.00

SABRETOOTH: MARY SHELLEY OVERDRIVE
Marvel Comics: Aug, 2002 - No. 4, Nov, 2002 ($2.99, limited series)
1-4-Jolley-s; Harris-c — 3.00

SABRINA (Volume 2) (Based on animated series)
Archie Publications: Jan, 2000 - No. 104, Sept, 2009 ($1.79/$1.99/$2.19/$2.25/$2.50)

	GD	VG	FN	VF	VF/NM	NM-
1-Teen-age Witch magically reverted to 12 years old	2	4	6	8	10	12
2-10: 4-Begin $1.99-c						4.00

11-104: 38-Sabrina aged back to 16 years old. 39-Begin $2.19-c. 58-Manga-style begins; Tania Del Rio-a. 67-Josie and the Pussycats app. 101-Young Salem; begin $2.50-c — 3.00
... And The Archies (2004, 8 1/2"x 5 1/2", Diamond Comic Dist. Halloween giveaway) - Tania Del Rio-s/a; manga-style; Josie and the Pussycats app. — 3.00

SABRINA (one-shots)
Archie Comic Publications: Oct, 2022; Oct, 2023 ($2.99/$3.99, one-shots)
... Anniversary Special 1 (10/22, $2.99) Intro. Amber Nightstone in new story; Parent-s/a — 3.00
... Annual Spectacular 1 (10/23, $3.99) Amber Nightstone, Jade, and Sapphire app. — 4.00

SABRINA'S CHRISTMAS MAGIC (See Archie Giant Series Magazine #196, 207, 220, 231, 243, 455, 467, 479, 491, 503, 515)

SABRINA'S HALLOWEEN SPOOOKTACULAR
Archie Publications: 1993 - 1995 ($2.00, 52 pgs.)

	GD	VG	FN	VF	VF/NM	NM-
1-Neon orange ink-c; bound-in poster	2	4	6	8	10	12
2,3-Titled "Sabrina's Holiday Spectacular"						6.00

SABRINA, THE TEEN-AGE WITCH (TV)(See Archie Giant Series, Archie's Madhouse 22, Archie's TV…, Chilling Advs. In Sorcery, Little Archie #59)
Archie Publications: April, 1971 - No. 77, Jan, 1983 (52 pg.Giants No. 1-17)

	GD	VG	FN	VF	VF/NM	NM-
1-52 pgs. begin, end #17	28	56	84	202	451	700
2-Archie's group x-over	10	20	30	64	132	200
3-5: 3,4-Archie's Group x-over	7	14	21	46	86	125
6-10	6	12	18	38	69	100
11-17(2/74)	4	8	12	28	47	65
18-30	3	6	9	21	33	45
31-40(8/77)	3	6	9	16	23	30
41-60(6/80)	2	4	6	11	16	20
61-70	2	4	6	9	13	16
71-76-low print run	3	6	9	14	19	24
77-Last issue; low print run	3	6	9	16	23	30

SABRINA, THE TEEN-AGE WITCH
Archie Publications: 1996 ($1.50, 32 pgs., one-shot)

	GD	VG	FN	VF	VF/NM	NM-
1-Updated origin	2	4	6	9	12	15

SABRINA, THE TEEN-AGE WITCH (Continues in Sabrina, Vol. 2)
Archie Publications: May, 1997 - No. 32, Dec, 1999 ($1.50/$1.75/$1.79)

	GD	VG	FN	VF	VF/NM	NM-
1-Photo-c with Melissa Joan Hart	2	4	6	8	10	12
2-10: 9-Begin $1.75-c						6.00
11-20						5.00
21-32: 24-Begin $1.79-c. 28-Sonic the Hedgehog-c/app.						4.00

SABRINA THE TEEN-AGE WITCH (Volume 3)
Archie Comic Publications: May, 2019 - No. 5, Nov, 2019 ($3.99)
1-5-Kelly Thompson-s/Veronica & Andy Fish-a; multiple covers — 4.00

SABRINA THE TEEN-AGE WITCH (Volume 4)
Archie Comic Publications: May, 2020 - No. 5, Apr, 2021 ($3.99)
1-5-Kelly Thompson-s/Veronica & Andy Fish-a; multiple covers — 4.00
... Holiday Special 1 (2/24, $3.99) Stories for the Winter Solstice; covers by Fish & Braga — 5.00

SABU, "ELEPHANT BOY" (Movie; formerly My Secret Story)
Fox Feature Syndicate: No. 30, June, 1950 - No. 2, Aug, 1950

	GD	VG	FN	VF	VF/NM	NM-
30(#1)-Wood-a; photo-c from movie	27	54	81	158	259	360
2-Photo-c from movie; Kamen-a	20	40	60	114	182	250

SACHS & VIOLENS
Marvel Comics (Epic Comics): Nov, 1993 - No. 4, July, 1994 ($2.25, limited series, mature)
1-($2.75)-Embossed-c w/bound-in trading card — 4.00
1-($3.50)-Platinum edition (1 for each 10 ordered) — 5.00
2-4: Perez-c/a; bound-in trading card: 2-(5/94) — 4.00
TPB (DC, 2006, $14.99) r/series; intro. by Peter David; creator bios. — 15.00

SACRAMENT
AWA Inc.: Aug, 2022 - No. 5, Dec, 2022 ($3.99, limited series)
1-5-Milligan-s/Frusin-a — 4.00

SACRAMENTS, THE
Catechetical Guild Educational Society: Oct, 1955 (35¢)

	GD	VG	FN	VF	VF/NM	NM-
30304	8	16	24	44	57	70

SACRED AND THE PROFANE, THE (See Eclipse Graphic Album Series #9 & Epic Illustrated #20)

SACRED CREATURES
Image Comics: Jul, 2017 - No. 6, May, 2018 ($4.99/$3.99)
1,4-6-($4.99) Pablo Raimondi & Klaus Janson-s/Raimondi-a. 4-6-Janson partial-a — 5.00
2,3-($3.99) — 4.00

SACRED SIX
Dynamite Entertainment: 2020 - No. 12, 2021 ($3.99)
1-12-Vampirella, Draculina, Pantha, Nyx, Chastity & Lilith app. 1-Jae Lee & Gabriel Ibarra-a — 4.00

SACRIFICERS, THE
Image Comics: Aug, 2023 - Present ($3.99)
1-6-Remender-s/Fiumara-a — 4.00

SADDLE JUSTICE (Happy Houlihans #1,2) (Saddle Romances #9 on)
E. C. Comics: No. 3, Spring, 1948 - No. 8, Fall, 1949

	GD	VG	FN	VF	VF/NM	NM-
3-The 1st E.C. by Bill Gaines to break away from M. C. Gaines' old Educational Comics format. Craig, Feldstein, H. C. Kiefer, & Stan Asch-a; mentioned in Love and Death	97	194	291	621	1061	1500
4-1st Graham Ingels-a for E.C.	71	142	213	454	777	1100
5-8-Ingels-a in all	60	120	180	381	653	925

NOTE: *Craig* and *Feldstein* art in most issues. Canadian reprints known; see Table of Contents. *Craig* c-3, 4. *Ingels* c-5-8. #4 contains a biography of *Craig*.

SADDLE ROMANCES (Saddle Justice #3-8; Weird Science #12 on)
E. C. Comics: No. 9, Nov-Dec, 1949 - No. 11, Mar-Apr, 1950

	GD	VG	FN	VF	VF/NM	NM-
9,11: 9-Ingels-c/a. 11-Ingels-a; Feldstein-c	71	142	213	454	777	1100
10-Wally Wood's 1st work at E. C.; Ingels-a; Feldstein-c	103	206	309	659	1130	1600

NOTE: Canadian reprints known; see Table of Contents. *Wood/Harrison* a-10, 11.

SADIE SACK (See Harvey Hits #93)

SAD SACK AND THE SARGE
Harvey Publications: Sept, 1957 - No. 155, June, 1982

	GD	VG	FN	VF	VF/NM	NM-
1	12	24	36	82	179	275
2	7	14	21	46	86	125
3-10	5	10	15	35	63	90
11-20	5	10	15	30	50	70
21-30	3	6	9	19	30	40
31-50	3	6	9	14	20	25
51-70	2	4	6	9	13	16
71-90,97-99	1	3	4	6	8	10
91-96: All 52 pg. Giants	2	4	6	9	13	16
100	2	4	6	8	10	12
101-120	1	2	3	4	5	7
121-155						5.00

NOTE: *George Baker* covers on numerous issues.

SAD SACK COMICS (See Harvey Collector's Comics #16, Little Sad Sack, Tastee Freez Comics #4 & True Comics #55 for 1st app.)
Harvey Publications/Lorne-Harvey Publications (Recollections) #288 On: Sept, 1949 - No. 287, Oct, 1982; No. 288, 1992 - No. 291, 1993

	GD	VG	FN	VF	VF/NM	NM-
1-Infinity-c; Little Dot begins (1st app.); civilian issues begin, end #21; based on comic strip (first app. in True Comics #55)	139	278	417	1112	2506	3900
2-Flying Fool by Powell	31	62	93	223	499	775
3	17	34	51	117	259	400
4-10	12	24	36	79	170	260
11-21	8	16	24	54	102	150
22-("Back In The Army Again" on covers #22-36); "The Specialist" story about Sad Sack's return to Army	9	18	27	59	117	175
23-30	5	10	15	34	60	85
31-50	3	6	8	28	47	65
51-80,100: 62-"The Specialist" reprinted	3	6	9	21	33	45
81-99	3	6	9	16	23	30
101-140	3	6	9	14	19	24
141-170,200	2	4	6	11	16	20
171-199	2	4	6	9	13	16
201-207: 207-Last 12¢ issue	2	4	6	8	11	14
208-222	1	3	4	6	8	10
223-228 (25¢ Giants, 52 pgs.)	2	4	6	8	11	14
229-250	1	3	4	6	8	10
251-285						6.00
286,287-Limited distribution	1	2	3	5	7	9
288,289 ($2.75, 1992): 289-50th anniversary issue						6.00
290,291 ($1.00, 1993, B&W)						4.00
3-D 1 (1/54, 25¢)-Came with 2 pairs of glasses; titled "Harvey 3-D Hits"	14	28	42	93	204	315
…At Home for the Holidays 1 (1993, no-c price)-Publ. by Lorne-Harvey' X-mas issue						4.00

NOTE: The Sad Sack Comics comic book was a spin-off from a Sunday Newspaper strip launched through John Wheeler's Bell Syndicate. The previous Sunday page and the first 21 comics depicted the Sad Sack in civvies. Unpopularity caused the Sunday page to be discontinued in the early '50s. Meanwhile Sad Sack returned to the Army, by popular demand, in issue No. 22, remaining there ever since. Incidentally, relatively few of the first 21 issues were ever collected and remain scarce due to this. *George Baker* covers on numerous issues.

SAD SACK FUN AROUND THE WORLD
Harvey Publications: 1974 (no month)

	GD	VG	FN	VF	VF/NM	NM-
1-About Great Britain	2	4	6	11	16	20

SAD SACK GOES HOME
Harvey Publications: 1951 (16 pgs. in color, no cover price)

	GD	VG	FN	VF	VF/NM	NM-
nn-By George Baker	5	10	15	33	57	80

SAD SACK LAUGH SPECIAL
Harvey Publications: Winter, 1958-59 - No. 93, Feb, 1977 (#1-9: 84 pgs.; #10-60: 68 pgs.; #61-76: 52 pgs.)

	GD	VG	FN	VF	VF/NM	NM-
1-Giant 25¢ issues begin	9	18	27	60	120	180
2	5	10	15	35	63	90
3-10	5	10	15	30	50	70
11-30	4	8	12	25	40	55
31-60: 31-Hi-Fi Tweeter app. 60-Last 68 pg. Giant	3	6	9	16	23	30
61-76-(All 52 pg. issues)	2	4	6	10	14	18
77-93	1	2	3	6	6	8

SAD SACK NAVY, GOBS 'N' GALS
Harvey Publications: Aug, 1972 - No. 8, Oct, 1973

	GD	VG	FN	VF	VF/NM	NM-
1: 52 pg. Giant	3	6	9	16	23	30
2-8	2	4	6	9	12	15

SAD SACK'S ARMY LIFE (See Harvey Hits #8, 17, 22, 28, 32, 39, 43, 47, 51, 55, 58, 61, 64, 67, 70)

SAD SACK'S ARMY LIFE (…Parade #1-57, …Today #58 on)
Harvey Publications: Oct, 1963 - No. 60, Nov, 1975; No. 61, May, 1976

	GD	VG	FN	VF	VF/NM	NM-
1-(68 pg. issues begin)	7	14	21	44	82	120
2-10	4	8	12	27	44	60
11-20	3	6	9	19	30	40
21-34: Last 68 pg. issue	3	6	9	16	23	30
35-51: All 52 pgs.	2	4	6	10	14	18
52-61	2	4	6	9	12	15

SAD SACK'S FUNNY FRIENDS (See Harvey Hits #75)
Harvey Publications: Dec, 1955 - No. 75, Oct, 1969

Sabrina the Teenage Witch V4 #2 © ACP

Sad Sack Comics #14 © HARV

Saga #20 © Vaughan & Staples

	GD 2.0	VG 4.0	FN 6.0	VF 8.0	VF/NM 9.0	NM- 9.2
1	9	18	27	60	120	180
2-10	5	10	15	35	63	90
11-20	4	8	12	23	37	50
21-30	3	6	9	17	26	35
31-50	3	6	9	14	20	25
51-75	2	4	6	9	13	16

SAD SACK'S MUTTSY (See Harvey Hits #74, 77, 80, 82, 84, 87, 89, 92, 96, 99, 102, 105, 108, 111, 113, 115, 117, 119, 121)

SAD SACK USA (...Vacation #8)
Harvey Publications: Nov, 1972 - No. 7, Nov, 1973; No. 8, Oct, 1974

	GD	VG	FN	VF	VF/NM	NM-
1	3	6	9	14	20	25
2-8	2	4	6	8	10	12

SAD SACK WITH SARGE & SADIE
Harvey Publications: Sept, 1972 - No. 8, Nov 1973

	GD	VG	FN	VF	VF/NM	NM-
1-(52 pg. Giant)	3	6	9	14	20	25
2-8	2	4	6	8	10	12

SAD SAD SACK WORLD
Harvey Publ.: Oct, 1964 - No. 46, Dec, 1973 (#1-31: 68 pgs.; #32-38: 52 pgs.)

	GD	VG	FN	VF	VF/NM	NM-
1	6	12	18	41	76	110
2-10	4	8	12	25	40	55
11-20	3	6	9	19	30	40
21-31: 31-Last 68 pg. issue	3	6	9	16	23	30
32-39-(All 52 pgs)	2	4	6	10	14	18
40-46	1	3	4	6	8	10

SAFEST PLACE IN THE WORLD, THE
Dark Horse Comics: 1993 ($2.50, one-shot)
1-Steve Ditko-c/a/scripts — 4.00

SAFETY-BELT MAN
Sirius Entertainment: June, 1994 - No. 6, 1995 ($2.50, B&W)
1-6: 1-Horan-a/Dark One-a/Sprouse-c. 2,3-Warren-c. 4-Linsner back-up story.
5,6-Crilley-a — 4.00

SAFETY-BELT MAN ALL HELL
Sirius Entertainment: June, 1996 - No. 6, Mar, 1997 ($2.95, color)
1-6-Horan-s/Fillbach Bros.-a — 4.00

SAGA
Image Comics: Mar, 2012 - Present ($2.99/$3.99)

	GD	VG	FN	VF	VF/NM	NM-
1-Brian K. Vaughan-s/Fiona Staples-a/c; 1st app. Alana, Marko, Hazel, The Will, and Lying Cat	9	18	27	59	117	175
1-Second printing	3	6	9	15	22	28
2-1st app. The Stalk	3	6	9	17	26	35
3-5: 3-1st app. Izabel	3	6	9	14	20	25
6,7,9-12						6.00
8-1st app. Gwendolyn	3	6	9	14	19	24

13-53: 19-Intro. Ginny. 24-Lying Cat returns. 25,37-Wraparound-c. 43-(25c-c). 51-Doff killed.
53-Prince Robot killed — 4.00
54-(7/18) Marko dies — 4.00
55-60: 55-(1/22) Jumps to 3 years later; intro Bombazine — 3.00
61-66-($3.99) — 4.00

SAGA OF BIG RED, THE
Omaha World-Herald: Sept, 1976 ($1.25) (In color)
nn-by Win Mumma; story of the Nebraska Cornhuskers (sports) — 6.00

SAGA OF CRYSTAR, CRYSTAL WARRIOR, THE
Marvel Comics: May, 1983 - No. 11, Feb, 1985 (Remco toy tie-in)
1,6: 1-(Baxter paper). 6-Nightcrawler; Golden-c — 5.00
2-5,7-11: 3-Dr. Strange app. 3-11-Golden-c (painted-4,5). 11-Alpha Flight app. — 4.00

SAGA OF RA'S AL GHUL, THE
DC Comics: Jan, 1988 - No. 4, Apr, 1988 ($2.50, limited series)
1-4-r/N. Adams Batman — 6.00

SAGA OF SABAN'S MIGHTY MORPHIN POWER RANGERS (Also see Saban's Mighty Morphin Power Rangers)
Hamilton Comics: 1995 - No. 4, 1995 ($1.95, limited series)
1-4 — 6.00

SAGA OF SEVEN SUNS, THE : VEILED ALLIANCES
DC Comics (WildStorm): 2004 ($24.95, hardcover graphic novel with dustjacket)
HC-Kevin J. Anderson-s/Robert Teranishi-a — 25.00
SC-(2004, $17.95) — 18.00

SAGA OF THE ORIGINAL HUMAN TORCH
Marvel Comics: Apr, 1990 - No. 4, July, 1990 ($1.50, limited series)
1-4: 1-Origin; Buckler-c/a(p). 3-Hitler-c — 4.00

SAGA OF THE SUB-MARINER, THE
Marvel Comics: Nov, 1988 - No. 12, Oct, 1989 ($1.25/$1.50 #5 on, maxi-series)
1-12: 9-Original X-Men app. — 4.00

SAGA OF THE SWAMP THING, THE (See Swamp Thing)

SAILOR MOON (Manga)
Mixx Entertainment Inc.: 1998 - No. 25 ($2.95)

	GD	VG	FN	VF	VF/NM	NM-
1	5	10	15	31	53	75
1-(San Diego edition)	12	24	36	80	173	265
2-5	2	4	6	11	16	20
6-10	1	3	4	6	8	10
11-25	1	2	3	4	5	7
26-35						5.00
...Rini's Moon Stick 1						15.00

SAILOR ON THE SEA OF FATE (See First Comics Graphic Novel #11)

SAILOR SWEENEY (Navy Action #1-11, 15 on)
Atlas Comics (CDS): No. 12, July, 1956 - No. 14, Nov, 1956

	GD	VG	FN	VF	VF/NM	NM-
12-14: 12-Shores-a. 13,14-Severin-c	40	80	120	246	411	575

SAINT, THE (Also see Movie Comics(DC) #2 & Silver Streak #18)
Avon Periodicals: Aug, 1947 - No. 12, Mar, 1952

	GD	VG	FN	VF	VF/NM	NM-
1-Kamen bondage-c/a	194	388	582	1242	2121	3000
2	74	148	222	470	810	1150
3,5	58	116	174	371	636	900
4-Lingerie panels, black background, Good Girl art-c	90	180	270	576	988	1400
6-Miss Fury app. by Tarpe Mills (14 pgs.)	93	186	279	591	1021	1450
7-c-/Avon paperback #118	52	104	156	328	552	775
8,9(12/50): Saint strip-r in #8-12; 9-Kinstler-c	43	86	129	271	461	650
10-Wood-a, 1 pg; c-/Avon paperback #289	43	86	129	271	461	650
11	40	80	120	246	411	575
12-c-/Avon paperback #123	41	82	123	256	428	600

NOTE: *Lucky Dale, Girl Detective in #1,2,4,6.* **Hollingsworth** *a-4, 6. Painted-c 7, 8, 10-12.*

SAINT ANGEL
Image Comics: Mar, 2000 - No. 4, Mar, 2001 ($2.95/$3.95)
0-Altstaetter & Napton-s/Altstaetter-a — 3.00
1-4-($3.95) Flip book w/Deity. 1-(6/00). 2-(10/00) — 4.00

ST. GEORGE
Marvel Comics (Epic Comics): June, 1988 - No.8, Oct, 1989 ($1.25,/$1.50)
1-8: Sienkiewicz-c. 3-begin $1.50-c — 4.00

SAINT GERMAINE
Caliber Comics: 1997 - No. 8, 1998 ($2.95)
1-8: 1,5-Alternate covers — 4.00

SAINT JOHN (Portland Gear Presents)
Dark Horse Comics: Sept, 2023 - Present ($4.99, limited series)
1,2-Dan Schkade & Brennan Wagner-s/Schkade-a — 5.00

ST. MERCY
Image Comics (Top Cow): Aug, 2021 - No. 4, Nov, 2021 ($3.99, limited series)
1-4-Platten-s/Rojo-a — 4.00

ST. SWITHIN'S DAY
Trident Comics: Apr, 1990 ($2.50, one-shot)
1-Grant Morrison scripts — 4.00

ST. SWITHIN'S DAY
Oni Press: Mar, 1998 ($2.95, B&W, one-shot)
1-Grant Morrison-s/Paul Grist-a — 4.00

SALOMÉ (See Night Music #6)

SALVATION RUN
DC Comics: Jan, 2008 - No. 7, Jul, 2008 ($2.99/$3.50, limited series)
1-6-DC villains banished to an alien planet; Willingham-s/Chen-a/c. 1-Var-c by Corroney — 3.00
7-($3.50) Luthor cover by Chen — 3.50

	GD	VG	FN	VF	VF/NM	NM-
7-($3.50) Variant Joker cover by Neal Adams	4	8	12	25	40	

SAM AND MAX, FREELANCE POLICE SPECIAL
Fishwrap Prod./Comico: 1987 ($1.75, B&W); Jan, 1989 ($2.75, 44 pgs.)
1 ($1.75, B&W, Fishwrap) — 5.00
2 ($2.75, color, Comico) — 5.00

	GD 2.0	VG 4.0	FN 6.0	VF 8.0	VF/NM 9.0	NM- 9.2

SAM AND TWITCH (See Spawn and Case Files:...)
Image Comics (Todd McFarlane Prod.): Aug, 1999 - No. 26, Feb, 2004 ($2.50)

1-26: 1-19-Bendis-s. 1-14-Medina-a. 15-19-Maleev-a. 20-24-McFarlane-s/Maleev-a						4.00
Book One: Udaku (2000, $21.95, TPB) B&W reprint of #1-8						22.00
...: The Brian Michael Bendis Collection Vol. 1 (2/06, $24.95) r/#1-9 in color; sketch pages						25.00
...: The Brian Michael Bendis Collection Vol. 2 (6/07, $24.95) r/#10-19; cover gallery						25.00

SAM AND TWITCH: THE WRITER
Image Comics (Todd McFarlane Prod.): May, 2010 - No. 4, Jun, 2010 ($2.99)

1-4-Blengino-s/Erbetta-a/c						3.00

SAMARITAN VERITAS
Image Comics: Mar, 2017 - No. 3, Jul, 2017 ($3.99)

1-3-Hawkins-s/Rojo-a						4.00

SAM HILL PRIVATE EYE
Close-Up (Archie): 1950 - No. 7, 1951

1	27	54	81	158	259	360
2	15	30	45	88	137	185
3-7	13	26	39	72	101	130

SAMSON (1st Series) (Captain Aero #7 on; see Big 3 Comics)
Fox Feature Syndicate: Fall, 1940 - No. 6, Sept, 1941 (See Fantastic Comics)

1-Samson begins, ends #6; Powell-a, signed 'Rensie'; Wing Turner by Tuska app; Fine-c?	239	478	717	1530	2615	3700
2-Dr. Fung by Powell; Fine-c?	116	232	348	742	1271	1800
3-Navy Jones app.; Joe Simon-c	84	168	252	538	919	1300
4-Yarko the Great, Master Magician begins	87	174	261	553	952	1350
5,6: 5-WWII Nazi-c. 6-Origin The Topper	77	154	231	493	847	1200

SAMSON (2nd Series) (Formerly Fantastic Comics #10, 11)
Ajax/Farrell Publications (Four Star): No. 12, April, 1955 - No. 14, Aug, 1955

12-Wonder Boy	41	82	123	256	428	600
13,14: 13-Wonder Boy, Rocket Man	36	72	108	214	347	480

SAMSON (See Mighty Samson)

SAMSON & DELILAH (See A Spectacular Feature Magazine)

SAMUEL BRONSTON'S CIRCUS WORLD (See Circus World under Movie Classics)

SAMURAI (Also see Eclipse Graphic Album Series #14)
Aircel Publications: 1985 - No. 23, 1987 ($1.70, B&W)

1, 14-16-Dale Keown-a						4.00
1-(reprinted),2-12,17-23: 2 (reprinted issue exists)						4.00
13-Dale Keown's 1st published artwork (1987)						6.00

SAMURAI
Warp Graphics: May, 1997 ($2.95, B&W)

1						4.00

SAMURAI: BROTHERS IN ARMS
Titan Comics: Oct, 2016 - No. 6 ($3.99)

1-6-Genet-a/DiGiorgio-s; English version of French comic						4.00

SAMURAI CAT
Marvel Comics (Epic Comics): June, 1991 - No. 3, Sept, 1991 ($2.25, limited series)

1-3: 3-Darth Vader-c/story parody						4.00

SAMURAI: HEAVEN & EARTH
Dark Horse Comics: Dec, 2004 - No. 5, Dec, 2005 ($2.99)

1-5-Luke Ross-a/Ron Marz-s						3.00
TPB (4/06, $14.95) r/#1-5; sketch pages and cover and pin-up gallery						15.00

SAMURAI: HEAVEN & EARTH (Volume 2)
Dark Horse Comics: Nov, 2006 - No. 5, June, 2007 ($2.99)

1-5-Luke Ross-a/Ron Marz-s						3.00
TPB (10/07, $14.95) r/#1-5; sketch pages and cover and pin-up gallery						15.00

SAMURAI JACK (TV)
IDW Publishing: Oct, 2013 - No. 20, May, 2015 ($3.99)

1-20: 1-5-Jim Zub-s/Andy Suriano-a; multiple covers on each						4.00
... Special - Director's Cut (#4, $7.99) Reprints '02 DC issue; commentary by Bill Wray						8.00

SAMURAI JACK: LOST WORLDS (TV)
IDW Publishing: Apr, 2019 - No. 4, Jul, 2019 ($3.99, limited series)

1-4-Paul Allor-s/Adam Bryce Thomas-a; multiple covers on each						4.00

SAMURAI JACK: QUANTUM JACK (TV)
IDW Publishing: Sept, 2017 - No. 5, Jan, 2018 ($3.99, limited series)

1-5-Rangel, Jr.-s/Johnson-Cadwell-a; multiple covers						4.00

SAMURAI JACK SPECIAL (TV)
DC Comics: Sept, 2002 ($3.95, one-shot)

1-Adaptation of pilot episode with origin story; Tartakovsky-s/Naylor & Wray-a						4.00

SAMURAI: LEGEND
Marvel Comics (Soleil): 2008 - No. 4, 2009 ($5.99)

1-4-Genet-a/DiGiorgio-s; English version of French comic; preview of other titles						6.00

SAMURAI SONJA
Dynamite Entertainment: 2022 - No. 5, 2022 ($3.99, limited series)

1-5-Red Sonja-like warrior in ancient Japan						4.00

SAMUREE
Continuity Comics: May, 1987 - No. 9, Jan, 1991

1						6.00
2-9						4.00

SAMUREE
Continuity Comics: V2#1, May, 1993 - V2#4, Jan,1994 ($2.50)

V2#1-4-Embossed-c: 2,4-Adams plot, Nebres-i. 3-Nino-c(i)						4.00

SAMUREE
Acclaim Comics (Windjammer): Oct, 1995 - No. 2, Nov,1995 ($2.50, lim. series)

	GD 2.0	VG 4.0	FN 6.0	VF 8.0	VF/NM 9.0	NM- 9.2
1,2						4.00

SAN DIEGO COMIC CON COMICS
Dark Horse Comics: 1992 - No.4, 1995 (B&W, promo comic for the San Diego Comic Con)

1-(1992)-Includes various characters published from Dark Horse including Concrete, The Mask, RoboCop and others; 1st app. of Sprint from John Byrne's Next Men; art by Quesada, Byrne, Rude, Burden, Moebius & others; pin-ups by Rude, Dorkin, Allred & others; Chadwick-c				9	13	16
2-(1993)-Intro of Legend imprint; 1st app. of John Byrne's Danger Unlimited, Mike Mignola's Hellboy (also see John Byrne's Next Men #21), Art Adams' Monkeyman & O'Brien; contains stories featuring Concrete, Sin City, Martha Washington & others; Grendel, Madman, & Big Guy pin-ups; Don Martin-c	9	18	27	61	123	185
3-(1994)-Contains stories featuring Barb Wire, The Mask, The Dirty Pair, & Grendel by Matt Wagner; contains pin-ups of Ghost, Predator & Rascals In Paradise; The Mask-c	1	2	3	5	6	8
4-(1995)-Contains Sin City story by Miller (3pg.), Star Wars, The Mask, Tarzan, Foot Soldiers; Sin City & Star Wars flip-c	1	3	4	6	8	10

SANDMAN, THE (1st Series) (Also see Adventure Comics #40, New York World's Fair, Sandman Special (2017) and World's Finest #3)
National Periodical Publ.: Winter, 1974; No. 2, Apr-May, 1975 - No. 6, Dec-Jan, 1975-76

1-1st app. Bronze Age Sandman by Simon & Kirby (last S&K collaboration)		6	12	18	41	76	110
2-6: 6-Kirby/Wood-c/a		3	6	9	21	33	45
The Sandman By Joe Simon & Jack Kirby HC (2009, $39.99, d.j.) r/Sandman app. from World's Finest #6,7, Adventure Comics #72-102 and Sandman #1; Morrow intro.						40.00

NOTE: Kirby a-1p, 4-6p; c-1-5, 6p.

SANDMAN (2nd Series) (See Books of Magic, Vertigo Jam & Vertigo Preview)
DC Comics (Vertigo imprint #47 on): Jan, 1989 - No. 75, Mar, 1996 ($1.50-$2.50, mature)

1 ($2.00, 52 pgs.)-1st app. Modern Age Sandman (Morpheus); Neil Gaiman scripts begin; Sam Kieth-a(p) in #1-5; Wesley Dodds (G.A. Sandman) cameo.	10	20	30	61	132	200
1 (Facsimile Edition) (2022, $3.99) r/1 with original 1989 ads						4.00
2-Cain & Abel app. (from HOM & HOS)	3	6	9	19	30	40
3,5: 3-John Constantine app.	3	6	9	16	23	30
4-1st app. Lucifer Morningstar; The Demon app.	5	10	15	35	63	90
6,7	2	4	6	10	14	18
8-Death-c/story (1st app.)-Regular ed. has Jeanette Kahn publishorial & American Cancer Society ad w/no indicia on inside front-c	8	16	24	54	102	150
8-Limited ed. (600+ copies?); has Karen Berger editorial and next issue teaser on inside covers (has indicia)	27	54	81	194	435	675
9-14: 10-Has explanation about #8 mixup; has bound-in Shocker movie poster.	2	4	6	11	14	18
14-(52 pgs.)-Bound-in Nightbreed fold-out	3	6	8	11	14
15-20: 16-Photo-c. 17,18-Kelley Jones-a. 19-Vess-a	1	3	4	6	8	10
18-Error version w/1st 3 panels on pg. 1 in blue ink	17	34	51	117	259	400
19-Error version w/pages 18 & 20 facing each other	3	6	9	14	19	24
21,23-27: Seasons of Mist storyline. 22-World Without End preview. 24-Kelley Jones/Russell-a						6.00
22-1st Daniel (Later becomes new Sandman)	3	6	9	23	30
28-30						5.00
31-49,51-74: 36-(52 pgs.). 41,44-48-Metallic ink on-c. 48-Cerebus appears as a doll. 54-Re-intro Prez; Death app.; Belushi, Nixon & Wildcat cameos. 57-Metallic ink on c. 65-w/bound-in trading card. 69-Death of Sandman. 70-73-Zulli-a. 74-Jon J. Muth-a.						4.00
50-($2.95, 52 pgs.)-Black-c w/metallic ink by McKean; Russell-a; McFarlane pin-up	1	3	4	6	8	10
50-($2.95)-Signed & limited (5,000) Treasury Edition with sketch of Neil Gaiman	3	6	9	16	23	30
50-Platinum	3	6	9	21	33	45
75-($3.95)-Vess-a.						5.00
Special 1 (1991, $3.50, 68 pgs.)-Glow-in-the-dark-c						5.00
Absolute Sandman Special Edition #1 (2006, 50c) sampling from HC; recolored r/#1						3.00
Absolute Sandman Volume One (2006, $99.00, slipcased hardcover) recolored r/#1-20; Gaiman's original proposal; script and pencils from #19; character sketch gallery						100.00
Absolute Sandman Volume Two (2007, $99.00, slipcased hardcover) recolored r/#21-39; r/A Gallery of Dreams one-shot; bonus stories, scripts and pencil art						100.00
Absolute Sandman Volume Three (2008, $99.00, slipcased hardcover) recolored r/#40-56; & Special #1; bonus galleries, scripts and pencil art; Jill Thompson intro.						100.00
Absolute Sandman Volume Four (2008, $99.00, slipcased hardcover) recolored r/#57-75; scripts & sketch pages for #57 & 75; gallery of Dreaming memorabilia; Berger intro.						100.00
...: A Gallery of Dreams ($2.95)-Intro by N. Gaiman						4.00
...: Preludes & Nocturnes ($29.95, HC)-r/#1-8.						30.00
...: The Doll's House (1990, $29.95, HC)-r/#8-16.						30.00
...: Dream Country ($29.95, HC)-r/#17-20.						30.00
...: Season of Mists ($29.95, HC)-r/#21-28.						50.00
...: A Game of You ($29.95, HC)-r/32-37, ...: Fables and Reflections ($29.95, HC)-r/Vertigo Preview #1, Sandman Special #1, #29-31, #38-40 & #50. ...: Brief Lives ($29.95, HC)-r/#41-49. ...: World's End ($29.95, HC)-r/#51-56						30.00
...: The Kindly Ones (1996, $34.95, HC)-r/#57-69 & Vertigo Jam #1						35.00
...: The Wake ($29.95, HC)-r/#70-75.						30.00

NOTE: A new set of hardcover printings with new covers was introduced in 1998-99. Multiple printings exist of softcover collections. Recolored (from the Absolute HC) softcover editions were released in 2010. Bachalo a-12; Kelley Jones a-17, 18, 22, 23, 26, 27. Vess a-19, 75.

SANDMAN: ENDLESS NIGHTS
DC Comics (Vertigo): 2003 ($24.95, hardcover, with dust jacket)

HC-Neil Gaiman stories of Morpheus and the Endless illustrated by Fabry, Manara, Prado, Quitely, Russell, Sienkiewicz, and Storey; McKean-c						25.00
...Special (11/03, $2.95) Previews hardcover; Dream story w/Prado-a; McKean-c						4.00
SC (2004, $17.95)						18.00

SANDMAN MIDNIGHT THEATRE
DC Comics (Vertigo): Sept, 1995 ($6.95, squarebound, one-shot)

nn-Modern Age Sandman (Morpheus) meets G.A. Sandman; Gaiman & Wagner story; McKean-c; Kristiansen-a						7.00

SANDMAN MYSTERY THEATRE (Also see Sandman (2nd Series) #1)
DC Comics (Vertigo): Apr, 1993 - No. 70, Feb, 1999 ($1.95/$2.25/$2.50)

1-G.A. Sandman advs. begin; Matt Wagner scripts begin						5.00
2-49,51-70: 5-Neon ink logo. 29-32-Hourman app. 38-Ted Knight (G.A. Starman) app.						

Samurai Sonja #3 © RS LLC

The Sandman #45 © DC

Sandman Universe: Nightmare Country #3 © DC

	GD 2.0	VG 4.0	FN 6.0	VF 8.0	VF/NM 9.0	NM- 9.2
42-Jim Corrigan (Spectre) app. 45-48-Blackhawk app.						4.00
50-($3.50, 48 pgs.) w/bonus story of S.A. Sandman, Torres-a						5.00
Annual 1 (10/94, $3.95, 68 pgs.)-Alex Ross, Bolton & others-a						5.00
...: Dr. Death and the Night of the Butcher (2007, $19.99) r/#21-28						20.00
...: The Blackhawk and The Return of the Scarlet Ghost (2010, $19.99) r/#45-52						20.00
...: The Face and the Brute (2004, $19.95) r/#5-12						20.00
...: The Hourman and The Python (2008, $19.99) r/#29-36						20.00
...: The Mist and The Phantom of the Fair (2009, $19.99) r/#37-44						20.00
...: The Scorpion (2006, $12.99) r/#17-20						13.00
...: The Tarantula (1995, $14.95) r/#1-4						15.00
...: The Vamp (2005, $12.99) r/#13-16						13.00

SANDMAN MYSTERY THEATRE (2nd Series)
DC Comics (Vertigo): Feb, 2007 - No. 5, Jun, 2007 ($2.99, limited series)

1-5-Wesley Dodds and Dian in 1997; Rieber-s/Nguyen-a						4.00

SANDMAN: OVERTURE
DC Comics (Vertigo): Dec, 2013 - No. 6, Nov, 2015 ($4.99/$3.99, limited series)

1-($4.99) Prelude to Sandman #1 ('89); Gaiman-s/JH Williams III-a/c; var-c by McKean						5.00
2-6-($3.99) Gaiman-s/JH Williams III-a/c						4.00
... Special Edition 1 (1/14, $5.99) B&W version of #1 with creator interviews; bonus info						6.00
... Special Edition 2-6 ($4.99) B&W versions with creator interviews; bonus info. 6-(12/15)						5.00

SANDMAN PRESENTS...
DC Comics (Vertigo)

Taller Tales TPB (2003, $19.95) r/S.P.: The Thessaliad #1-4; Merv Pumpkinhead, Agent...; The Dreaming #55; S.P. Everything You Always...; new McKean-c; intro by Willingham						20.00

SANDMAN PRESENTS: BAST
DC Comics (Vertigo): Mar, 2003 - No. 3, May, 2003 ($2.95, limited series)

1-3-Kiernan-s/Bennett-a/McKean-c						3.00

SANDMAN PRESENTS: DEADBOY DETECTIVES (See Sandman #21-28)
DC Comics (Vertigo): Aug, 2001 - No. 4, Nov, 2001 ($2.50, limited series)

1-4-Talbot-a/McKean-c/Brubaker-s						3.00
TPB (2008, $12.99) r/#1-4						13.00

SANDMAN PRESENTS: EVERYTHING YOU ALWAYS WANTED TO KNOW ABOUT DREAMS...BUT WERE AFRAID TO ASK
DC Comics (Vertigo): Jul, 2001 ($3.95, one-shot)

1-Short stories by Willingham; art by various; McKean-c						4.00

SANDMAN PRESENTS: LOVE STREET
DC Comics (Vertigo): Jul, 1999 - No. 3, Sept, 1999 ($2.95, limited series)

1-3: Teenage Hellblazer in 1968 London; Zulli-a						4.00

SANDMAN PRESENTS: LUCIFER
DC Comics (Vertigo): Mar, 1999 - No. 3, May, 1999 ($2.95, limited series)

	GD	VG	FN	VF	VF/NM	NM-
1-Scott Hampton painted-c/a in all	1	2	3	5	6	8
2,3						4.00

SANDMAN PRESENTS: PETREFAX
DC Comics (Vertigo): Mar, 2000 - No. 4, Jun, 2000 ($2.95, limited series)

1-4-Carey-s/Leialoha-a						3.00

SANDMAN PRESENTS: THE CORINTHIAN
DC Comics (Vertigo): Dec, 2001 - No. 3, Feb, 2002 ($2.95, limited series)

1-3-Macan-s/Zezelj-a/McKean-c						3.00

SANDMAN PRESENTS, THE: THE FURIES
DC Comics (Vertigo): 2002 ($24.95, one-shot)

Hardcover-Mike Carey-s/John Bolton-painted art; Lyta Hall's reunion with Daniel						30.00
Softcover-(2003, $17.95)						18.00

SANDMAN PRESENTS, THE: THESSALY: WITCH FOR HIRE
DC Comics (Vertigo): Apr, 2004 - No. 4, July, 2004 ($2.95, limited series)

1-4-Willingham-s/McManus-a/McPherson-c						3.00
TPB-(2005, $12.99) r/#1-4						13.00

SANDMAN PRESENTS, THE: THE THESSALIAD
DC Comics (Vertigo): Mar, 2002 - No. 4, Jun, 2002 ($2.95, limited series)

1-4-Willingham-s/McManus-a/McKean-c						3.00

SANDMAN SPECIAL, THE (Jack Kirby 100th Birthday tribute)
DC Comics: Oct, 2017 ($4.99, one-shot)

1-Jurgens-s/Bogdanove-a and Orlando-s/Leonardi-a; Brute & Glob app.; Paul Pope-c						5.00

SANDMAN, THE: THE DREAM HUNTERS
DC Comics: Oct, 1999 ($29.95/$19.95, one-shot graphic novel)

Hardcover-Neil Gaiman-s/Yoshitaka Amano-painted art						30.00

Softcover-(2000, $19.95) new Amano-c						20.00

SANDMAN, THE: THE DREAM HUNTERS
DC Comics (Vertigo): Jan, 2009 - No. 4, Apr, 2009 ($2.99, limited series)

1-4-Adaptation of the Gaiman/Amano GN by P. Craig Russell-s/a; 2 covers on each						3.00
HC (2009, $24.99) afterwords by Gaiman, Russell, Berger; cover gallery & sketch art						25.00
SC (2010, $19.99) afterwords by Gaiman, Russell, Berger; cover gallery & sketch art						20.00

SANDMAN UNIVERSE, THE
DC Comics: Oct, 2018 ($4.99, one-shot)

1-Intro to 4 new related series (The Dreaming, Books of Magic, House of Whispers & Lucifer); stories by Gaiman & others; Jae Lee-c; Cain, Abel & Lucien app.						5.00
...Special: Thessaly 1(10/23, $4.99) Tynion IV-s/Llovet-a; part of Nightmare Country saga						5.00

SANDMAN UNIVERSE: DEAD BOY DETECTIVES
DC Comics (Black Label): Feb, 2023 - No. 6, Jul, 2023 ($3.99)

1-6: 1-Pichetshote-s/Stokely-a; Thessaly app.						4.00

SANDMAN UNIVERSE: NIGHTMARE COUNTRY, THE
DC Comics (Black Label): Jun, 2022 - No. 6, Nov, 2022 ($3.99)

1-6: 1-Tynion IV-s/Esthrenen-a; The Corinthian app. 6-Llovet-a						4.00

SANDMAN UNIVERSE: NIGHTMARE COUNTRY - THE GLASS HOUSE
DC Comics (Black Label): Jun, 2023 - No. 6, Feb, 2024 ($3.99)

1-5: 1-Tynion IV-s/Esthrenen-a. 2-Delpeche-a						4.00

SANDMAN UNIVERSE PRESENTS HELLBLAZER, THE
DC Comics (Black Label): 2019 ($4.99)

1-Spurrier-s/Takara-a; two covers						5.00

SANDS OF THE SOUTH PACIFIC
Toby Press: Jan, 1953

	GD	VG	FN	VF	VF/NM	NM-
1-Good Girl Art-c	71	142	213	454	777	1100

SANJULIAN'S QUEENS OF THE LOST WORLD
OPUS: May, 2023 - Present ($4.99)

1,2-Moore & Reppion-s/Califano-a; story of The Huntress						5.00

SANTA AND HIS REINDEER (See March of Comics #166)

SANTA AND THE ANGEL (See Dell Junior Treasury #7)
Dell Publishing Co.: Dec, 1949 (Combined w/Santa at the Zoo) (Gollub-a condensed from FC#128)

	GD	VG	FN	VF	VF/NM	NM-
Four Color 259	9	18	27	62	126	190

SANTA AT THE ZOO (See Santa And The Angel)

SANTA CLAUS AROUND THE WORLD (See March of Comics #241 in Promotional Comics section)

SANTA CLAUS CONQUERS THE MARTIANS (See Movie Classics)

SANTA CLAUS FUNNIES (Also see Dell Giants)
Dell Publishing Co.: Dec?, 1942 - No. 1274, Dec, 1961

	GD	VG	FN	VF	VF/NM	NM-
nn(#1)(1942)-Kelly-a	40	80	120	296	673	1050
2(12/43)-Kelly-a	28	56	84	202	451	700
Four Color 61(1944)-Kelly-a	27	54	81	189	420	650
Four Color 91(1945)-Kelly-a	18	36	54	128	284	440
Four Color 128('46),175('47)-Kelly-a	16	32	48	108	239	370
Four Color 205,254-Kelly-a	13	26	39	89	195	300
Four Color 302,361,525,607,666,756,867	8	16	24	54	102	150
Four Color 958,1063,1154,1274	7	14	21	44	82	120

NOTE: *Most issues contain only one Kelly story.*

SANTA CLAUS PARADE
Ziff-Davis (Approved Comics)/St. John Publishing Co.: 1951; No. 2, Dec, 1952; No. 3, Jan, 1955 (25¢)

	GD	VG	FN	VF	VF/NM	NM-
nn(1951-Ziff-Davis)-116 pgs. (Xmas Special 1,2)	39	78	117	240	395	550
2(12/52-Ziff-Davis)-100 pgs.; Dave Berg-a	33	66	99	194	317	440
V1#3(1/55-St. John)-100 pgs.; reprints-c/#1	25	50	75	150	245	340

SANTA CLAUS' WORKSHOP (See March of Comics #50,168 in Promotional Comics section)

SANTA IS COMING (See March of Comics #197 in Promotional Comics section)

SANTA IS HERE (See March of Comics #49 in Promotional Comics section)

SANTA'S BUSY CORNER (See March of Comics #31 in Promotional Comics section)

SANTA'S CANDY KITCHEN (See March of Comics #14 in Promotional Comics section)

SANTA'S CHRISTMAS BOOK (See March of Comics #123 in Promotional Comics section)

SANTA'S CHRISTMAS COMICS
Standard Comics (Best Books): Dec, 1952 (100 pgs.)

	GD	VG	FN	VF	VF/NM	NM-
nn-Supermouse, Dizzy Duck, Happy Rabbit, etc.	27	54	81	158	259	360

SANTA'S CHRISTMAS LIST (See March of Comics #255 in Promotional Comics section)

	GD	VG	FN	VF	VF/NM	NM-
	2.0	4.0	6.0	8.0	9.0	9.2

SANTA'S HELPERS (See March of Comics #64, 106, 198 in Promotional Comics section)

SANTA'S LITTLE HELPERS (See March of Comics #270 in Promotional Comics section)

SANTA'S SHOW (See March of Comics #311 in Promotional Comics section)

SANTA'S SLEIGH (See March of Comics #298 in Promotional Comics section)

SANTA'S SURPRISE (See March of Comics #13 in Promotional Comics section)

SANTA'S TINKER TOTS
Charlton Comics: 1958

| 1-Based on "The Tinker Tots Keep Christmas" | 7 | 14 | 21 | 46 | 86 | 125 |

SANTA'S TOYLAND (See March of Comics #242 in Promotional Comics section)

SANTA'S TOYS (See March of Comics #12 in Promotional Comics section)

SANTA'S VISIT (See March of Comics #283 in Promotional Comics section)

SANTA THE BARBARIAN
Maximum Press: Dec, 1996 ($2.99, one-shot)

| 1-Fraga/Mhan-s/a | | | | | | 4.00 |

SANTERIA: THE GODDESS KISS
Aspen MLT: Mar, 2016 - No. 5, Nov, 2017 ($3.99, limited series)

| 1-5-Wohl-s/Cafaro-a | | | | | | 4.00 |

SANTIAGO (Movie)
Dell Publishing Co.: Sept, 1956 (Alan Ladd photo-c)

| Four Color 723-Kinstler-a | 10 | 20 | 30 | 64 | 132 | 200 |

SARGE SNORKEL (Beetle Bailey)
Charlton Comics: Oct, 1973 - No. 17, Dec, 1976

1	2	4	6	11	16	20
2-10	2	4	6	8	10	12
11-17	1	2	3	5	7	9

SARGE STEEL (Becomes Secret Agent #9 on; also see Judomaster)
Charlton Comics: Dec, 1964 - No. 8, Mar-Apr, 1966 (All 12¢ issues)

1-Origin & 1st app.	5	10	15	30	50	70
2-5,7,8	3	6	9	17	26	35
6-2nd app. Judomaster	4	8	12	25	40	55

SASQUATCH DETECTIVE SPECIAL
DC Comics: Feb, 2019 ($7.99, one-shot)

| 1-New origin story; Stilwell-s/Randall-a; also reprints back-ups from Exit Stage Left: The Snagglepus Chronicles; bonus sketch art | | | | | | 8.00 |

SATAN'S SIX
Topps Comics (Kirbyverse): Apr, 1993 - No. 4, July, 1993 ($2.95, lim. series)

| 1-3: 1-Polybagged w/Kirbychrome trading card; Kirby/McFarlane-c plus 8 pgs. Kirby-a(p); has coupon for Kirbychrome ed. of Secret City Saga #0. 2,3-Polybagged w/3 cards. | | | | | | 4.00 |
| 4-Teenagents preview; polybagged w/3 cards | 2 | 4 | 6 | 8 | 10 | 12 |

NOTE: *Ditko* a-1. *Miller* a-1.

SATAN'S SIX: HELLSPAWN
Topps Comics (Kirbyverse): June, 1994 - No. 3, July, 1994 ($2.50, limited series)

| 1-3: 1-(6/94)-Indicia incorrectly shows "Vol 1 #2". 2-(6/94) | | | | | | 4.00 |

SATELLITE FALLING
IDW Publishing: May, 2016 - No. 5, May, 2017 ($3.99)

| 1-5-Steve Horton-s/Stephen Thompson-a | | | | | | 4.00 |

SATELLITE SAM
Image Comics: Jul, 2013 - No. 15, Jul, 2015 ($3.50, B&W, mature)

| 1-15-Matt Fraction-s/Howard Chaykin-a/c | | | | | | 3.50 |

SAUCER COUNTRY
DC Comics (Vertigo): May, 2012 - No. 14, Jun, 2013 ($2.99)

| 1-14: 1-Cornell-s/Kelly-a. 6-Broxton-a. 11-Colak-a | | | | | | 3.00 |
| ...: The Finale One-Shot (Image Comics, 2/24, $3.99) Concludes story; Cornell-s/Kelly-a | | | | | | 4.00 |

SAUCER STATE (Sequel to Saucer Country)
IDW Publishing: May, 2017 - No. 6, Oct, 2017 ($3.99)

| 1-6-Cornell-s/Kelly-a | | | | | | 4.00 |

SAURIANS: UNNATURAL SELECTION (See Sigil)
CrossGeneration Comics: Feb, 2002 - No. 2, Mar, 2002 ($2.95, limited series)

| 1,2-Waid-s/DiVito-a | | | | | | 3.00 |

SAVAGE
Image Comics (Shadowline): Oct, 2008 - No. 4, Jan, 2009 ($3.50, limited series)

| 1-4-Mayhew-c/a; Niles and Frank-s | | | | | | 3.50 |

SAVAGE
Valiant Entertainment: Nov, 2016 - No. 4, Feb, 2017 ($3.99, limited series)

| 1-4-B. Clay Moore-s/Larosa & Henry-a | | | | | | 4.00 |

SAVAGE
Valiant Entertainment: Feb, 2021 - No. 4, May, 2021 ($3.99, limited series)

| 1-4-Max Bemis-s/Nathan Stockman-a | | | | | | 4.00 |

SAVAGE AVENGERS
Marvel Comics: Jul, 2019 - No. 28, Mar, 2022 ($4.99/$3.99)

1-($4.99) Team of Conan, Wolverine, Punisher, Doctor Voodoo; Duggan-s/Deodato-a						5.00
2-28-($3.99) 2-5-Kulan Gath & Venom app. 6-Jacinto-a. 13-16-Zircher-a. 14,16-Juggernaut & Black Knight app. 17-19-King In Black tie-in; Deadpool app. 25,26,28-Kang app.						4.00
#0 (4/20, $4.99) Reprints Uncanny X-Men #190 & 191 with Kulan Gath, new framing story						5.00
Annual 1 (12/19, $4.99) Garney-a; Conan, Black Widow & Hellstrom app.						5.00

SAVAGE AVENGERS
Marvel Comics: Jun, 2022 - No. 10, Apr, 2023 ($3.99)

| 1-10: 1-Team of Conan, Deathlok, Black Knight, Elektra, Anti-Venom, Cloak & Dagger | | | | | | 4.00 |

SAVAGE AXE OF ARES
Marvel Comics: June, 2010 ($3.99, B&W, one-shot)

| 1-B&W short stories by Hurwitz, Palo, McKeever, Swierczynski, Manco and others | | | | | | 4.00 |

SAVAGE COMBAT TALES
Atlas/Seaboard Publ.: Feb, 1975 - No. 3, July, 1975

| 1,3: 1-Sgt. Stryker's Death Squad begins (origin); Goodwin-s | 3 | 6 | 9 | 14 | 19 | 24 |
| 2-Toth-a; only app. War Hawk; Goodwin-s | 3 | 6 | 9 | 15 | 22 | 28 |

NOTE: *Buckler* c-3. *McWilliams* a-1-3; c-1. *Sparling* a-1, 3.

SAVAGE DRAGON, THE (See Megaton #3 & 4)
Image Comics (Highbrow Entertainment): July, 1992 - No. 3, Dec, 1992 ($1.95, lim. series)

1-Erik Larsen-c/a/scripts & bound-in poster in all; 4 cover color variations w/4 different posters; 1st Highbrow Entertainment title	1	3	4	6	8	10
2-Intro SuperPatriot-c/story (10/92)						5.00
3-Contains coupon for Image Comics #0						4.00
3-With coupon missing						2.00
...Vs. Savage Megaton Man 1 (3/93, $1.95)-Larsen & Simpson-c/a.						4.00
TPB ('93, $9.95) r/#1-3						10.00

SAVAGE DRAGON, THE
Image Comics (Highbrow Entertainment): June, 1993 - Present ($1.95/$2.50/$2.99/$3.50)

1-Erik Larsen-c/a/scripts	1	2	3	5	6	8
2-($2.95, 52 pgs.)-Teenage Mutant Ninja Turtles-c/story; flip book features Vanguard #0 (See Megaton for 1st app.); 1st app. Supreme						6.00
3-30: 3-7: Erik Larsen-c/a/scripts. 3-Mighty Man back-up story w/Austin(i). 4-Flip book w/Ricochet. 5-Mighty Man flip-c & back-up plus poster. 6-Jae Lee poster. 7-Vanguard poster. 8-Deadly Duo poster by Larsen. 13A (10/94)-Jim Lee-c/a; 1st app. Max Cash (Condition Red). 13B (6/95)-Larsen story. 15-Dragon poster by Larsen. 22-TMNT-c/a; Bisley pin-up. 27-"Wondercon Exclusive" new-c. 28-Maxx-c/app. 29-Wildstar-c/app. 30-Spawn app.						4.00
25 ($3.95)-variant-c exists.						6.00
31-49,51-71: 31-God vs. The Devil; alternate version exists w/o expletives (has "God Is Good" inside Image logo) 33-Birth of Dragon/Rapture's baby. 34,35-Hellboy-c/app. 51-Origin of She-Dragon. 70-Ann Stevens killed						4.00
50-($5.95, 100 pgs.) Kaboom and Mighty Man app.; Matsuda back-c; pin-ups by McFarlane, Simonson, Capullo and others						6.00
72-74: 72-Begin $2.95-c						6.00
75-($5.95)						6.00
76-99,101-106,108-114,116-124,126-127,129-131,133-136,138: 76-New direction starts. 83,84-Madman-c/app. 84-Atomics app. 97-Dragon returns home; Mighty Man app. 134-Bomb Queen app.						4.00
100-($8.95) Larsen-s/a; inked by various incl. Sienkiewicz, Timm, Austin, Simonson, Royer; plus pin-ups by Turner, Silvestri, Miller, Cho, Art Adams, Pacheco						9.00
107-($3.95) Firebreather, Invincible, Mighty Man back-up w/Major Damage						5.00
115-($7.95, 100 pgs.) Wraparound-c; Freak Force app.; Larsen & Englert-a						8.00
125-($4.99, 64 pgs.) new story, The Fly, & various Mr. Glum reprints						5.00
128-Wesley and the villains from Wanted app.; J.G. Jones-c						5.00
132-($6.99, 80 pgs.) new story with Larsen-a; back-up story with Fosco-a						7.00
137-(8/08) Madman & Amazing Joy Buzzards-c/app.	1	2	3	5	6	8
137-(8/08) Variant cover with Barack Obama endorsed by Savage Dragon; yellow bkgrd	7	14	21	48	89	130
137-(8/08) 2nd printing of variant cover with Barack Obama and red background	1	3	4	6	8	10
137-3rd & 4th printings: 3rd-Blue background. 4th-Purple background						6.00
139-144,146-149,151-174,176-183: 139-Start $3.50-c. 140,141-Witchblade, Spawn app. 148-Also a FCBD edition.155-160-Dragon War. 160-163-Flip book						3.50
145-Obama-c/app.	1	3	4	5	6	8
150-($5.99, 100 pgs.) back up r/Daredevil's origin from Daredevil #18 (1943)						6.00
175-($3.99, 48 pgs.) Darklord app.; Vanguard back-c and back-up story						5.00
184-199,201-224 ($3.99) 184,186-188-The Claw app. 190-Regular & digest-size versions. 209-Malcolm's wedding. 217-Spawn app.						4.00
200-(12/14, $8.99, 100 pgs., squarebound) Back-up story w/Trimpe-a; Burnham-a						9.00
225-(7/17, $9.99, 100 pgs., squarebound) Death of Savage Dragon; back-up by various						10.00
226-249,251-268: 226-Donald Trump on cover. 227-Malcolm & family move to Toronto. 252-Salutes the Funnies; newspaper comics homages. 259-North Force app.						4.00
250-(11/19, $9.99, 100 pgs., squarebound) Savage Dragon returns; back-up by various						10.00
#0-(7/06, $1.95) reprints origin story from 2005 Image Comics Hardcover						4.00
...Archives Vol. 1 (12/06, $19.99) B&W rep. 1st mini-series #1-3 & #1-21						20.00
...Archives Vol. 2 (2007, $19.99) B&W rep. #22-50; roster pages of Dragon's fellow cops						20.00
...Companion (7/02, $2.95) guide to issues #1-100, character backgrounds						3.50
...Endgame (2/04, $15.95, TPB) r/#47-52						16.00
The Fallen (11/97, $12.95, TPB) r/#47-52, ...Possessed (9/98, $12.95, TPB) r/#12-16, ...Revenge (1998, $12.95, TPB) r/#17-21						13.00
...Gang War (4/00, $16.95, TPB) r/#22-26						17.00
...Hellboy (10/02, $5.95) r/#34 & #35; Mignola-c						6.00
Image Firsts: Savage Dragon #1 (4/10, $1.00) reprints #1						3.00
...Legacy FCBD 1 (5/15, giveaway) Story later re-worked for issue #211						3.00
...Team-Ups (10/98, $19.95, TPB) r/team-ups						20.00
...: Terminated TPB (2/03, $28.95) r/#34-40 & #1/2						29.00
...: This Savage World HC (2002, $24.95) r/#76-81; intro. by Larsen						25.00
...: This Savage World SC (2003, $15.95) r/#76-81; intro. by Larsen						16.00
...: Worlds at War SC (2004, $16.95) r/#41-46; intro. by Larsen; sketch pages						17.00

SAVAGE DRAGON ARCHIVES (Also see Dragon Archives, The)

SAVAGE DRAGONBERT: FULL FRONTAL NERDITY
Image Comics: Oct, 2002 ($5.95, B&W, one-shot)

| 1-Reprints of the Savage Dragon/Dilbert spoof strips | | | | | | 6.00 |

SAVAGE DRAGON/DESTROYER DUCK, THE
Image Comics/ Highbrow Entertainment: Nov, 1996 ($3.95, one-shot)

| 1 | | | | | | 4.00 |

SAVAGE DRAGON: GOD WAR
Image Comics: July, 2004 - No. 4, Oct, 2005 ($2.95, limited series)

| 1-4-Kirkman-s/Englert-a | | | | | | 3.50 |

SAVAGE DRAGON/MARSHALL LAW
Image Comics: July, 1997 - No. 2, Aug, 1997 ($2.95, limited series)

| 1,2-Pat Mills-s, Kevin O'Neill-a | | | | | | 4.00 |

SAVAGE DRAGON: SEX & VIOLENCE

Savage Dragon #172 © Erik Larsen

Savage Hulk (2014 series) #1 © MAR

Savage Sword of Conan #2 © CPI

SA

	GD	VG	FN	VF	VF/NM	NM-
	2.0	4.0	6.0	8.0	9.0	9.2

Image Comics: Aug, 1997 - No. 2, Sept, 1997 ($2.50, limited series)

1,2-T&M Bierbaum-s; Mays, Lupka, Adam Hughes-a 4.00

SAVAGE DRAGON/TEENAGE MUTANT NINJA TURTLES CROSSOVER
Mirage Studios: Sept, 1993 ($2.75, one-shot)

1-Erik Larsen-c(i) only 5.00

SAVAGE DRAGON: THE RED HORIZON
Image Comics/ Highbrow Entertainment: Feb, 1997 - No. 3 ($2.50, lim. series)

1-3 ..... 4.00

SAVAGE FISTS OF KUNG FU
Marvel Comics Group: 1975 (Marvel Treasury)

1-Iron Fist, Shang Chi, Sons of Tiger; Adams, Starlin-a

| | 4 | 8 | 12 | 27 | 44 | 60 |

SAVAGE HAWKMAN, THE (DC New 52)
DC Comics: Nov, 2011 - No. 20, Jun, 2013 ($2.99)

1-20: 1-Tony Daniel-s/Philip Tan-a/c; Carter Hall bonds with the Nth metal 3.00
#0-(11/12, $2.99) Origin story of Katar Hol on Thanagar; Bennett-a/c 3.00

SAVAGE HEARTS
Dark Horse Comics: Jul, 2021 - No. 5, Nov, 2021 ($3.99, limited series)

1-5-Sitterson-s/Dougherty-a 4.00

SAVAGE HULK, THE (Also see Incredible Hulk)
Marvel Comics: Jan, 1996 ($6.95, one-shot)

1-Bisley-c; David, Lobdell, Wagner, Loeb, Gibbons, Messner-Loebs scripts; McKone, Kieth, Ramos & Sale-a 7.00

SAVAGE HULK
Marvel Comics: Aug, 2014 - No. 6, Jan, 2015 ($3.99)

1-6: 1-Alan Davis-s/a; includes story from X-Men #66 ('70) Silver Age X-Men & The Leader app. 2-Abomination app. 5,6-Bechko-s/Hardman-a; Dr. Strange app. 4.00

SAVAGE RAIDS OF GERONIMO (See Geronimo #4)

SAVAGE RANGE (See Luke Short, Four Color 807)

SAVAGE RED SONJA
Dynamite Entertainment: 2023 - No. 5, 2024 ($3.99, limited series)

1-5-Panosian-s/Petillo-a; multiple covers on each 4.00

SAVAGE RED SONJA: QUEEN OF THE FROZEN WASTES
Dynamite Entertainment: 2006 - No. 4, 2006 ($3.50, limited series)

1-4: 1-Three covers by Cho, Texeira & Homs; Cho & Murray-s/Homs-a 3.50
TPB (2007, $14.99) r/series; cover gallery and sketch pages 15.00

SAVAGE RETURN OF DRACULA
Marvel Comics: 1992 ($2.00, 52 pgs.)

1-r/Tomb of Dracula #1,2 by Gene Colan 5.00

SAVAGE SHE-HULK, THE (See The Avengers, Marvel Graphic Novel #18 & The Sensational She-Hulk)
Marvel Comics Group: Feb, 1980 - No. 25, Feb, 1982

1-Origin & 1st app. She-Hulk	7	14	21	44	82	120
2	3	6	9	18	23	30
3-5,25: 25-(52 pgs.)	2	4	6	8	11	14
6,7,10-24: 6-She-Hulk vs. Iron Man.	1	3	4	6	8	10
8-Vs. Man-Thing	2	4	6	10	14	18
9-1st app Ultiman	3	6	9	14	19	24

...No. 1 Facsimile Edition (2/23, $3.99) Reprints 1980 issue with original ads 4.00
NOTE: *Austin* a-25i; c-23i-25i. *J. Buscema* a-1p; c-1, 2p. *Golden* c-8-11.

SAVAGE SHE-HULK (Titled All New Savage She Hulk for #3,4)
Marvel Comics: Jun, 2009 - No. 4, Sept, 2009 ($3.99, limited series)

1-4-Lyra, daughter of the Hulk; She-Hulk & Dark Avengers app. 2-Campbell-c 4.00

SAVAGE SKULLKICKERS (See Skullkickers #20)

SAVAGE SPIDER-MAN (Story continues from Non-Stop Spider-Man series)
Marvel Comics: Apr, 2022 - No. 5, Sept. 2022 ($3.99, limited series)

1-5-Joe Kelly-s/Gerardo Sandoval-a; Baron Zemo app. 4.00

SAVAGE SQUAD 6
Dark Horse Comics: Jun, 2023 - No. 4, Oct, 2023 ($3.99)

1-4-Venditti & McKinney-s/Dalton-a 4.00

SAVAGE SWORD (ROBERT E. HOWARD'S...)
Dark Horse Comics: Dec, 2010 - No. 9 ($7.99, squarebound)

1-9-Short stories by various incl. Roy Thomas, Barry-Windsor-Smith; Conan app. 8.00

SAVAGE SWORD OF CONAN (The... #41 on; ...The Barbarian #175 on)

Marvel Comics Group: Aug, 1974 - No. 235, July, 1995 ($1.00/$1.25/$2.25, B&W magazine, mature)

1-Smith-r; J. Buscema/N. Adams/Krenkel-a; origin Blackmark by Gil Kane (part 1, ends #3); Blackmark's 1st app. in magazine form-r/from paperback) & Red Sonja (3rd app.)

	10	20	30	69	147	225
2-Neal Adams-c; Chaykin/N. Adams-a	5	10	15	35	63	90
3-Severin/B. Smith-a; N. Adams-a	4	8	12	28	47	65
4-Neal Adams/Kane-a(r)	3	6	9	21	33	45
5-10: 5-Jeff Jones frontispiece (r)	3	6	9	17	26	35
11-20	2	4	6	13	18	22
21-30	2	4	6	10	14	18

31-50: 34-3 pg. preview of Conan newspaper strip. 35-Cover similar to Savage Tales #1.
45-Red Sonja returns; begin $1.25-c 2 4 6 8 11 14
51-99: 63-Toth frontispiece. 65-Kane-a w/Chaykin/Miller/Simonson/Sherman finishes. 70-Article on movie. 83-Red Sonja-r by Neal Adams from #1

| | 1 | 2 | 3 | 5 | 7 | 9 |
| 100 | 1 | 3 | 4 | 6 | 8 | 10 |

101-176: 163-Begin $2.25-c. 169-King Kull story. 171-Soloman Kane by Williamson (i).
172-Red Sonja story 6.00
177-199: 179,187,192-Red Sonja app. 190-193-4 part King Kull story. 196-King Kull story 5.00
200-220: 200-New Buscema-a; Robert E. Howard app. with Conan in story. 202-King Kull story. 204-60th anniversary (1932-92). 211-Rafael Kayanan's 1st Conan-a. 214-Sequel to Red Nails by Howard 6.00

221-230	2	4	6	8	10	12
231-234	2	4	6	11	16	20
235-Last issue	4	8	12	27	44	60
Special 1(1975, B&W)-B. Smith-r/Conan #10,13	3	6	9	18	27	36

Volume 1 TPB (Dark Horse Books, 12/07, $17.95, B&W) r/#1-10 and selected stories from Savage Tales #1-5 with covers 18.00
Volume 2 TPB (Dark Horse Books, 3/08, $17.95, B&W) r/#11-24 ..... 18.00
Volume 3 TPB (Dark Horse Books, 5/08, $19.95, B&W) r/#25-36 and selected pin-ups 20.00
Volume 4 TPB (Dark Horse Books, 9/08, $19.95, B&W) r/#37-48 and selected pin-ups 20.00
Volume 5 TPB (Dark Horse Books, $19.95, B&W) r/#49-60 and selected pin-ups 20.00
NOTE: *N. Adams* a-14p, 60, 83p(r). *Alcala* a-2, 4, 7, 12, 15-20, 23, 24, 28, 59, 67, 69, 75, 76i, 80i, 82i, 83i, 89, 180i, 184i, 187i, 189i, 216p. *Austin* a-78i. *Boris* painted c-1, 4, 5, 7, 9, 10, 12, 15. *Brunner* a-30; c-8, 30. *Buscema* a-1-5, 7, 10-12, 15-24, 26-28, 31, 32, 36-43, 45, 47-58p, 60-67p, 70, 71-74p, 76-81p, 87-96p, 98, 99-101p, 190-204p; painted c-40. *Chaykin* c-31. *Chiodo* painted c-71, 76, 79, 81, 84, 85, 178. *Conrad* c-215, 217. *Corben* a-4, 16, 29. *Finlay* a-16. *Golden* a-98, 101; c-98, 101, 105, 106, 117, 124, 150. *Kaluta* a-11, 18; c-3, 91, 93. *Gil Kane* a-2, 3, 8, 13r, 29, 47, 64, 65, 67, 85p, 86p. *Rafael Kayanan* a-211-213, 215, 217. *Krenkel* a-9, 11, 14, 16, 24. *Morrow* a-7. *Nebres* a-93i, 101i, 107, 114. *Newton* a-6. *Nino* c/a-6. *Redondo* painted c-48-50, 52, 56, 57, 85i, 90, 96i. *Marie & John Severin* a-Special 1. *Simonson* a-7, 8, 12, 15-17. *Barry Smith* a-7, 16, 24, 82r, Special 1r. *Starlin* c-26. *Toth* a-64. *Williamson* a(i)-162, 171, 186. No. 8, 12 & 16 contain a Robert E. Howard Conan adaptation.

SAVAGE SWORD OF CONAN
Marvel Comics: Apr, 2019 - No. 12, Feb, 2020 ($4.99/$3.99)

1-($4.99) Duggan-s/Garney-a; main cover by Alex Ross; bonus text story 5.00
2-5-($3.99) Duggan-s/Garney-a; main cover by Alex Ross; bonus text story 4.00
6-12: 6-Meredith Finch-s/Luke Ross-a; main cover by David Finch. 10,11-Alan Davis-a 4.00

SAVAGE SWORD OF CONAN
Titan Comics: Mar, 2024 - Present ($6.99, B&W, magazine size)

1,2-Short stories and pin-ups by various. 1-Intro by Roy Thomas 7.00

SAVAGE TALES (...Featuring Conan #4 on)(Magazine)
Marvel Comics Group: May, 1971; No. 2, 10/73; No. 3, 2/74 - No. 12, Summer, 1975 (B&W)

1-Origin/1st app. The Man-Thing by Morrow; Conan the Barbarian by Barry Smith (1st Conan x-over outside his own title); Femizons by Romita-r/in #3; Ka-Zar story by Buscema

	57	114	171	456	1028	1600
2-B. Smith, Brunner, Morrow, Williamson-a; Wrightson King Kull reprint/ Creatures on the Loose #10	6	12	18	37	66	95
3-B. Smith, Brunner, Steranko, Williamson-a	5	10	15	31	53	75

4,5-N. Adams-c; last Conan (Smith-r/#4) plus Kane/N. Adams-a. 5-Brak the Barbarian begins, ends #8

	4	8	12	28	47	65
6-Ka-Zar begins; Williamson-r; N. Adams-c	3	6	9	21	33	45
7-N. Adams-i	3	6	9	16	23	30

8,9,11: 8-Shanna, the She-Devil app. thru #10; Williamson-r

| | 3 | 6 | 9 | 15 | 22 | 28 |
| 10-Neal Adams-a(i), Williamson-r | 3 | 6 | 9 | 17 | 26 | 35 |

...Featuring Ka-Zar Annual 1 (Summer, '75, B&W)(#12 on inside)-Ka-Zar origin by Gil Kane; B. Smith-r/Astonishing Tales 3 6 9 18 28 38
NOTE: *Boris* c-7, 10. *Buscema* a-5r, 6p, 8p; c-2. *Colan* a-1, 4; c-1. *Heath* a-10p, 11p. *Kaluta* c-9. *Maneely* c/a-2,4(The Crusader in both). *Morrow* a-1, 2, Annual 1. *Reese* a-2. *Severin* a-1-7. *Starlin* a-1-5. Robert E. Howard adaptations 1-4.

SAVAGE TALES (Volume 2)
Marvel Comics Group: Oct, 1985 - No. 8, Dec, 1986 ($1.50, B&W, magazine, mature)

1-1st app. The Nam; Golden, Morrow-a (indicia incorrectly lists this as Volume 1) 6.00

	GD	VG	FN	VF	VF/NM	NM-
	2.0	4.0	6.0	8.0	9.0	9.2

	GD	VG	FN	VF	VF/NM	NM-
	2.0	4.0	6.0	8.0	9.0	9.2

2-8: 2,7-Morrow-a. 4-2nd Nam story; Golden-a ... 4.00

SAVAGE TALES
Dynamite Entertainment: 2007 - No. 10, 2008 ($4.99)

1-10: 1-Anthology; Red Sonja app.; three covers ... 5.00
... One-Shot (2022, $4.99) Short stories with Vampirella, Red Sonja, Allan Quartermane ... 5.00
... Red Sonja One-Shot (2019, $4.99) Russell-s; Sorcerers of Wigur-Nomadene app. ... 5.00
... Vampirella One-Shot (2018, $4.99) Burnham-s; back-up Valaka story; Robert Hack-c ... 5.00
... Winter Special One-Shot (2022, $4.99) Short stories with Vampirella, Draculina, John Carter & Dejah Thoris, Captain Gullivar Jones ... 5.00

SAVAGE THINGS
DC Comics (Vertigo): May, 2017 - No. 8, Dec, 2018 ($3.99)

1-8-Justin Jordan-s/Ibrahim Moustafa-a/J.P. Leon-c ... 4.00

SAVAGE WOLVERINE
Marvel Comics: Mar, 2013 - No. 23, Nov, 2014 ($3.99)

1-5-Frank Cho-s/a/c; Shanna & Amadeus Cho app. ... 4.00
1-Variant-c by Skottie Young ... 8.00
6-23: 6-8-Wells-s/Madureira-a/c; Elektra, Kingpin & Spider-Man app. 9-11-Jock-s/a. 14-17-Isanove-s/a. 19-Simone-s. 21,22-WWI; Quinones-a/Nowlan-c ... 4.00

SAVANT GARDE (Also see WildC.A.T.S...)
Image Comics/WildStorm Productions: Mar, 1997 - No. 7, Sept, 1997 ($2.50)

1-7 ... 4.00

SAVED BY THE BELL (TV)
Harvey Comics: Mar, 1992 - No. 5, May, 1993 ($1.25, limited series)

1		2	4	6	9	12	15
2-5, Holiday Special (3/92), Special 1 (9/92, $1.50)-photo-c, Summer Break 1 (10/92)						6.00

SAVE YOURSELF
BOOM! Studios (BOOM! Box): Jun, 2021 - No. 4, Sept, 2021 ($4.99, limited series)

1-4-Bones Leopard-s/Kelly & Nichole Matthews-a ... 5.00

SAVIOR
Image Comics/Todd McFarlane Productions: Apr, 2015 - No. 8, Nov, 2015 ($2.99)

1-8-Todd McFarlane & Brian Holguin-s/Clayton Crain-a/c ... 3.00

SAW: REBIRTH (Based on 2004 movie Saw)
IDW Publ.: Oct, 2005 ($3.99, one-shot)

1-Guedes-a ... 4.00

SCALPED
DC Comics (Vertigo): Mar, 2007 - No. 60, Oct, 2012 ($2.99, limited series)

	GD	VG	FN	VF	VF/NM	NM-
1-Aaron-s/Guera-a/Jock-c	5	10	15	30	50	70
1-Special Edition (7/10, $1.00) r/#1 with "What's Next?" cover frame						3.00
2-5		1	2	3	5	6	8
6-20: 12-Leon-a						4.00
21-60: 50-Bonus pin-ups by various						3.00
... : Casino Blood TPB (2008, $14.99) r/#6-11; intro. by Garth Ennis ... 15.00
... : Dead Mothers TPB (2008, $17.99) r/#12-18 ... 18.00
... : High Lonesome TPB (2009, $14.99) r/#25-29; intro. by Jason Starr ... 15.00
... : Indian Country TPB (2007, $9.99) r/#1-5; intro. by Brian K. Vaughan ... 10.00
... : Rez Blues (2011, $17.99) r/#35-42 ... 18.00
... : The Gnawing (2010, $14.99) r/#30-34; intro. by Matt Fraction ... 15.00
... : The Gravel in Your Guts (2009, $14.99) r/#19-24; intro. by Ed Brubaker ... 15.00

SCAMP (Walt Disney)(See Walt Disney's Comics & Stories #204)
Dell Publ. Co./Gold Key: No. 703, 5/56 - No. 1204, 8-10/61; 11/67 - No. 45, 1/79

	GD	VG	FN	VF	VF/NM	NM-
Four Color 703(#1)	11	22	33	73	157	240
Four Color 777,806('57),833	7	14	21	48	89	130
5(3-5/58)-10(6-8/59)	5	10	15	31	53	75
11-16(12-2/60-61), Four Color 1204(1961)	4	8	12	27	44	60
1(12/67-Gold Key)-Reprints begin	4	8	12	25	40	55
2(3/69)-10	2	4	6	13	18	22
11-20	2	4	6	11	14	14
21-45	1	2	3	4	5	7

NOTE: New stories-#20(in part), 22-25, 29-31, 34, 36-40, 42-45. New covers-#11, 12, 14, 15, 17-25, 27, 29-31, 34, 36-38.

SCARAB
DC Comics (Vertigo): Nov, 1993 - No. 8, June, 1994 ($1.95, limited series)

1-8-Glenn Fabry painted-c: 1-Silver ink-c. 2-Phantom Stranger app. ... 4.00

SCARECROW OF ROMNEY MARSH, THE (See W. Disney Showcase #53)
Gold Key: April, 1964 - No. 3, Oct, 1965 (Disney TV Show)

	GD	VG	FN	VF	VF/NM	NM-
10112-404 (#1)	10	20	30	69	147	225
2,3	6	12	18	38	69	100

SCARECROW (VILLAINS) (See Batman)
DC Comics: Feb, 1998 ($1.95, one-shot)

1-Fegredo-a/Milligan-s/Pearson-c ... 4.00

SCARE TACTICS
DC Comics: Dec, 1996 - No. 12, Mar, 1998 ($2.25)

1-12: 1-1st app. ... 4.00

SCAR FACE (See The Crusaders)

SCARFACE: SCARRED FOR LIFE (Based on the 1983 movie)
IDW Publishing: Dec, 2006 - No. 5, Apr, 2007 ($3.99, limited series)

1-5-Tony Montana survives his shooting; Layman-s/Crosland-a ... 4.00
Scarface: Devil in Disguise (7/07 - No. 4, 10/07, $3.99) Alberto Dose-a ... 4.00

SCARLET
Marvel Comics (ICON): July, 2010 - No. 10, Aug, 2016 ($3.95)

1-10-Bendis-s/Maleev-a. 1-Second printing exists. 8-(5/16) ... 4.00
1-5-Variant covers. 1-Deodato & Lafuente. 2-Oeming & Mack. 3,4-Oeming. 5-Bendis ... 6.00

SCARLET
DC Comics (Jinxworld): Oct, 2018 - No. 5, Mar, 2019 ($3.99)

1-5-Bendis-s/Maleev-a ... 4.00

SCARLET O'NEIL (See Harvey Comics Hits #59 & Invisible...)

SCARLET SISTERS (From Project Superpowers)
Dynamite Entertainment: 2022 ($4.99, one-shot)

1-Alex Segura-s/Emiliana Pinna-a ... 5.00

SCARLET SPIDER
Marvel Comics: Nov, 1995 - No. 2, Jan, 1996 ($1.95, limited series)

1,2: Replaces Spider-Man title ... 4.00

SCARLET SPIDER
Marvel Comics: Mar, 2012 - No. 25, Feb, 2014 ($3.99/$2.99)

1-Kaine following "Spider Island"; Yost-s/Stegman-a; 2 covers by Stegman ... 4.00
2-12, 12.1, 13-24-($2.99) 10,11-Carnage & Venom app. 17-19-Wolverine app. ... 3.00
25-($3.99) Last issue; Yost/Baldeon-a ... 4.00

SCARLET SPIDERS (Tie-in for Spider-Verse in Amazing Spider-Man [2014] #9-15)
Marvel Comics: Jan, 2015 - No. 3, Mar, 2015 ($3.99, limited series)

1-3-Kaine, Ben Reilly and Jessica Drew app.; Costa-s/Diaz-a ... 4.00

SCARLET SPIDER UNLIMITED
Marvel Comics: Nov, 1995 ($3.95, one-shot)

1-Replaces Spider-Man Unlimited title ... 4.00

SCARLETT COUTURE
Titan Comics: May, 2015 - No. 4, Aug, 2015 ($3.99)

1-4-Des Taylor-s/a ... 4.00

SCARLETT COUTURE: THE MUNICH FILE
Titan Comics: Sept, 2023 - No. 5, Jan, 2024 ($3.99)

1-5-Des Taylor-s/a ... 4.00

SCARLET WITCH (See Avengers #16, Vision &... & X-Men #4)
Marvel Comics: Jan, 1994 - No. 4, Apr, 1994 ($1.75, limited series)

	GD	VG	FN	VF	VF/NM	NM-
1-Abnett & Lanning-s; Agatha Harkness app.	2	4	6	9	13	16
2-1st Lore	3	6	9	14	20	26
3,4						5.00

SCARLET WITCH
Marvel Comics: Feb, 2016 - No. 15, Apr, 2017 ($3.99)

1-15: 1-3: 1-Robinson-s/Del Rey-a/Wu-a. 3-Dillon-a. 7-Wu-a. 9-Civil War II tie-in; Quicksilver app.; Joelle Jones-a ... 4.00

SCARLET WITCH
Marvel Comics: Mar, 2023 - No. 10, Jan, 2024 ($4.99/$3.99)

1,2,9-($4.99)-Orlando-s/Pichelli-a; Viv Vision & Darcy app. ... 5.00
3-8,10-($3.99) 3-Polaris app. 8-Loki app. ... 4.00
Annual 1 (8/23, $4.99) Prelude to Contest of Chaos; Orlando-s/Nieto-a ... 5.00

SCARY GODMOTHER (Hardcover story books)
Sirius: 1997 - 2002 ($19.95, HC with dust jackets, one-shots)

Volume 1 (9/97) Jill Thompson-s/a; first app. of Scary Godmother ... 20.00
Vol. 2 - The Revenge of Jimmy (9/98, $19.95) ... 20.00
Vol. 3 - The Mystery Date (10/99, $19.95) ... 20.00
Vol. 4 - The Boo Flu (9/02, $19.95) ... 20.00

SCARY GODMOTHER
Sirius: 2001 - No. 6, 2002 ($2.95, B&W, limited series)

1-6-Jill Thompson-s/a ... 3.00
... : Activity Book (12/00, $2.95, B&W) Jill Thompson-s/a ... 3.00
... : Bloody Valentine Special (2/98, $3.95, B&W) Jill Thompson-s/a; pin-ups by Ross, Mignola, Russell ... 4.00
... : Ghoul's Out For Summer (2002,$14.95, B&W) r/#1-6 ... 15.00
... : Holiday Spooktakular (11/98, $2.95, B&W) Jill Thompson-s/a; pin-ups by Brereton, LaBan, Dorkin, Fingerman ... 4.00

SCARY GODMOTHER: WILD ABOUT HARRY
Sirius: 2000 - No. 3 ($2.95, B&W, limited series)

1-3-Jill Thompson-s/a ... 3.00
TPB (2001; $9.95) r/series ... 10.00

SCARY TALES
Charlton Comics: 8/75 - #9, 1/77; #10, 9/77 - #20, 6/79; #21, 8/80 - #46, 10/84

	GD	VG	FN	VF	VF/NM	NM-
1-Origin/1st app. Countess Von Bludd, not in #2	4	8	12	28	47	65
2,4,6,9,10: 4,9-Sutton-c/a. 4-Man-Thing copy	3	6	9	14	19	24
3-Sutton painted-c; Ditko-a	3	6	9	15	22	28
5,11-Ditko-c/a.	3	6	9	17	26	35
7,8-Ditko-a	3	6	9	16	25	34
12,15,16,19,21,39-Ditko-a	2	4	6	11	16	20
13,17,20	2	4	6	9	12	15
14,18,30,32-Ditko-c/a	2	4	6	14	20	25
22-29,33-37,39,40: 37,38,40-New-a. 39-All Ditko reprints and cover	2	4	6	8	10	12
31,38: 31-Newton-c/a. 38-Mr. Jigsaw app.	2	4	6	8	10	12
41-45-New-a. 41-Ditko-a(3). 42-45-(Low print)	2	4	6	9	12	15
46-Reprints (Low print)	2	4	6	11	16	20
1(Modern Comics reprint, 1977)	1	3	4	6	8	10

NOTE: Adkins a-31i; c-31i. Ditko a-3, 5, 7, 8(2), 11, 12, 14-16r, 18(3)r, 19r, 21r, 30r, 32, 39r, 41(3); c-5, 11, 14, 18, 30, 32. Newton a-31r; c-31r. Powell a-18r. Staton a-1(2 pgs.), 4, 20r; c-1, 20. Sutton a-4, 9; c-4, 9. Zeck a-9.

SCATTERBRAIN
Dark Horse Comics: Jun, 1998 - No. 4, Sept, 1998 ($2.95, limited series)

1-4-Humor anthology by Aragonés, Dorkin, Stevens and others ... 4.00

SCAVENGERS
Triumphant Comics: 1993(nd, July) - No. 11, May, 1994 ($2.50, serially numbered)

1-9,0,10,11: 5,6-Triumphant Unleashed x-over. 9-(3/94). 0-Retail ed. (3/94, $2.50, 36 pgs.). 0-Giveaway edition (3/94, 20 pgs.). 0-Coupon redemption edition. 10-(4/94) ... 4.00

SCENE OF THE CRIME (Also see Vertigo: Winter's Edge #2)

Savage Wolverine #6 © MAR

Scarlet Witch (2023 series) #3 © MAR

Scooby Doo #144 © H-B

	GD	VG	FN	VF	VF/NM	NM-		GD	VG	FN	VF	VF/NM	NM-
	2.0	4.0	6.0	8.0	9.0	9.2		2.0	4.0	6.0	8.0	9.0	9.2

DC Comics (Vertigo): May, 1999 - No. 4, Aug, 1999 ($2.50, limited series)

1-4-Brubaker-s/Lark-a						4.00
...: A Little Piece of Goodnight TPB ('00, $12.95) r/#1-4; Winter's Edge #2						13.00

SCHOOL DAY ROMANCES (...of Teen-Agers #4; Popular Teen-Agers #5 on)
Star Publications: Nov-Dec, 1949 - No. 4, May-June, 1950 (Teenage)

	GD	VG	FN	VF	VF/NM	NM-
1-Toni Gayle (later Toni Gay), Ginger Snapp, Midge Martin & Eve Adams begin	48	96	144	302	514	725
2,3; 3-Jane Powell photo on-c & true life story	39	78	117	231	378	525
4-Ronald Reagan photo on-c; L.B. Cole-c	54	108	162	343	574	825

NOTE: All have **L. B. Cole** covers.

SCHWINN BICYCLE BOOK (...Bike Thrills, 1959)
Schwinn Bicycle Co.: 1949; 1952; 1959 (10¢)

	GD	VG	FN	VF	VF/NM	NM-
1949	9	18	27	47	61	75
1952-Believe It or Not facts; comic format; 36 pgs.	6	12	18	28	34	40
1959	5	10	15	33	26	30

SCIENCE COMICS (1st Series)
Fox Feature Syndicate: Feb, 1940 - No. 8, Sept, 1940

	GD	VG	FN	VF	VF/NM	NM-
1-Origin Dynamo (1st app., called Electro in #1), The Eagle (1st app.), & Navy Jones; Marga, The Panther Woman (1st app.), Cosmic Carson & Perisphere Payne, Dr. Doom begin; bondage/hypo-c; Electro-c	1300	2600	3900	9900	17,950	26,000
2-Classic Lou Fine Dynamo-c	1400	2800	4200	10,600	19,300	28,000
3-Classic Lou Fine Dynamo-c	476	952	1428	3475	6138	8800
4-Kirby-a; Cosmic Carson-c by Joe Simon	975	1950	2919	7100	12,550	18,000
5-8: 5,8-Eagle-c. 6,7-Dynamo-c	331	662	993	2317	4033	5800

NOTE: Cosmic Carson by Tuska-#1-3; by Kirby-#4. Lou Fine c-1-3 only.

SCIENCE COMICS (2nd Series)
Humor Publications (Ace Magazines?): Jan, 1946 - No. 5, 1946

	GD	VG	FN	VF	VF/NM	NM-
1-Palais-c/a in #1-3; A-Bomb-c	34	68	102	199	325	450
2	19	38	57	111	176	240
3-Feldstein-a (6 pgs.); Palais-c	24	48	72	142	234	325
4,5: 4-Palais-c	15	30	45	85	130	175

SCIENCE COMICS
Ziff-Davis Publ. Co.: May, 1947 (8 pgs. in color)

	GD	VG	FN	VF	VF/NM	NM-
nn-Could be ordered by mail for 10¢; like the nn Amazing Adventures (1950) & Boy Cowboy (1950); used to test the market	60	120	180	381	653	925

SCIENCE COMICS (True Science Illustrated)
Export Publication Ent., Toronto, Canada: Mar, 1951 (Distr. in U.S. by Kable News Co.)

	GD	VG	FN	VF	VF/NM	NM-
1-Science Adventure stories plus some true science features; man on moon story	26	52	78	154	252	350

SCIENCE DOG SPECIAL (Also see Invincible)
Image Comics: Aug, 2010; No. 2, May, 2011 ($3.50)

1,2: 1-Kirkman-s/Walker-a/c; leads into Invincible #75						3.50

SCIENCE FICTION SPACE ADVENTURES (See Space Adventures)

SCION (Also see CrossGen Chronicles)
CrossGeneration Comics: July, 2000 - No. 43, Apr, 2004 ($2.95)

1-43: 1-Marz-s/Cheung-a						3.00

SCI-SPY
DC Comics (Vertigo): Apr, 2002 - No. 6, Sept, 2002 ($2.50, limited series)

1-6-Moench-s/Gulacy-c/a						3.00

SCI-TECH
DC Comics (WildStorm): Sept, 1999 - No. 4, Dec, 1999 ($2.50, limited series)

1-4-Benes-a/Choi & Peterson-s						4.00

SCOOBY APOCALYPSE (Scooby Doo)
DC Comics: Jul, 2016 - No. 36, Jun, 2019 ($3.99)

1-36: 1-Giffen & DeMatteis-s/Porter-a; covers by Jim Lee and various; team's 1st meeting 4-Intro. Scrappy-Doo. 6-Velma's origin. 7-Eaglesham-a. 9-18-Scrappy-Doo app. 16-29-Secret Squirrel back-up. 25-Fred killed. 30-36-Atom Ant back-up; JLA app.						4.00
.../Hanna-Barbera Halloween Comics Fest Special Edition 1 (12/16, giveaway) previews Scooby Apocalypse, Future Quest, The Flintstones, and Wacky Races						3.00

SCOOBY DOO (TV)(...Where are you? #1-16,26; ...Mystery Comics #17-25, 27 on)
(See March Of Comics #356, 368, 382, 391 in the Promotional Comics section)
Gold Key: Mar, 1970 - No. 30, Feb, 1975 (Hanna-Barbera)

	GD	VG	FN	VF	VF/NM	NM-
1-First comic book app.	314	628	942	2198	3849	5500
2	23	46	69	161	356	500
3-5	20	40	60	138	307	475
6-10	13	26	39	91	201	310
11-20: 11-Tufts-a	10	20	30	67	141	215

	GD	VG	FN	VF	VF/NM	NM-
21-30: 28-Whitman edition	9	18	27	59	117	175

SCOOBY DOO (TV)
Charlton Comics: Apr, 1975 - No. 11, Dec, 1976 (Hanna-Barbera)

	GD	VG	FN	VF	VF/NM	NM-
1	12	24	36	83	182	280
2-5	9	18	27	57	111	165
6-11	6	12	18	41	76	110
nn-(1976, digest, 68 pgs., B&W)	5	10	15	35	63	90

SCOOBY-DOO (TV) (Newsstand sales only) (See Dynamutt & Laff-A-Lympics)
Marvel Comics Group: Oct, 1977 - No. 9, Feb, 1979 (Hanna-Barbera)

	GD	VG	FN	VF	VF/NM	NM-
1-Dyno-Mutt begins	7	14	21	49	92	135
1-(35¢-c variant, limited distribution)(10/77)	15	30	45	100	220	340
2-5	4	8	12	23	37	50
6-9	4	8	12	27	44	60

SCOOBY-DOO (TV)
Harvey Comics: Sept, 1992 - No. 3, May, 1993 ($1.25)

	GD	VG	FN	VF	VF/NM	NM-
V2#1-3: 3-(Low print and scarce)	3	6	9	14	19	24
Big Book 1,2 (11/92, 4/93, $1.95, 52 pgs.)	2	4	6	9	11	14
Giant Size 1,2 (10/92, 3/93, $2.25, 68 pgs.)	2	4	6	9	11	14

SCOOBY DOO (TV)
Archie Comics: Oct, 1995 -No. 21, June, 1997 ($1.50)

	GD	VG	FN	VF	VF/NM	NM-
1	3	6	9	16	24	32
2	1	3	4	6	8	10
3-21: 12-Cover by Scooby Doo creative designer Iwao Takamoto						6.00

SCOOBY DOO (TV)
DC Comics: Aug, 1997 - No. 159, Oct, 2010 ($1.75/$1.95/$1.99/$2.25/$2.50/$2.99)

	GD	VG	FN	VF	VF/NM	NM-
1	2	4	6	10	14	18
2-10: 5-Begin-$1.95-c						6.00
11-25,28-45: 14-Begin $1.99-c						5.00
26-Alien encounter cover	1	3	4	6	8	10
27-UFO abduction cover	1	3	6	9	12	15
46-89,91-157: 63-Begin $2.25-c. 75-With 2 Garbage Pail Kids stickers. 100-Wray-a						4.00
90,158,159: 90-($2.95) Bonus stories. 158,159-($2.99-c)						5.00
...Spooky Spectacular 1 (10/99, $3.95) Comic Convention story						
	1	3	4	6	8	10
...Spooky Spectacular 2000 (10/00, $3.95)	1	3	4	6	8	10
...Spooky Summer Special 2001 (8/01, $3.95) Staton-a						5.00
...Super Scarefest (8/02, $3.95) r/#20,25,30-32						5.00

SCOOBY-DOO 50TH ANNIVERSARY GIANT (TV)
DC Comics: 2019 ($4.99, squarebound one-shot)

1-Three new stories plus reprints from Scooby-Doo: Where Are You?; Brizuela-a						5.00

SCOOBY-DOO TEAM-UP (TV)
DC Comics: Jan, 2014 - No. 50, Nov, 2019 ($2.99)

	GD	VG	FN	VF	VF/NM	NM-
1-11,13-20,22-26,28-50: 1-Batman & Robin app.; Man-Bat app. 2-Ace the Bat-Hound app. 3-Bat-Mite app. 4-Teen Titans Go! 6-Super Friends & Legion of Doom app. 7-Flintstones. 8-Jetsons. 10-Jonny Quest. 13-Spectre, Deadman & Phantom Stranger. 28-Jonah Hex app. 31-The Atom. 33-Legion of Super-Heroes. 34-Birds of Prey. 43-Doom Patrol. 45-Mr. Miracle & Big Barda. 46-Black Lightning. 50-Bat-Mite, Scooby-Mite, cartoon & movie versions and Scooby Apocalypse characters						3.00
12-Harley Quinn, Poison Ivy, Catwoman & Batgirl app.	2	4	6	8	10	12
21-Harley Quinn, Joker, Batman, Robin & Batgirl app.						6.00
27-Plastic Man	1	3	4	6	8	10
... FCBD Special Edition 1 (6/15, giveaway) flipbook with Teen Titans Go!						4.00
... Halloween Special Edition (12/14, giveaway) r/#1						4.00

SCOOBY-DOO: WHERE ARE YOU? (TV)
DC Comics: Nov, 2010 - Present ($2.99)

	GD	VG	FN	VF	VF/NM	NM-
1	3	6	9	14	20	25
2-Alien encounter cover	2	4	6	9	12	15
3-5	1	3	4	6	8	10
6-20						6.00
21-31,33-50						4.00
32-KISS spoof	3	6	9	14	20	25
51-126						3.00

SCOOP COMICS (Becomes Yankee Comics #4-7, a digest sized cartoon book; then after #8 it becomes Snap #9)
Harry 'A' Chesler (Holyoke): November, 1941 - No. 3, Mar, 1943; No. 8, 1944

	GD	VG	FN	VF	VF/NM	NM-
1-Intro. Rocketman & Rocketgirl & begins; origin The Master Key & begins; Dan Hastings begins; Charles Sultan-c/a	161	322	483	1030	1765	2500
2-Rocket Boy begins; injury to eye story (reprinted in Spotlight #3); classic-c	486	972	1458	3550	6275	9000

	GD 2.0	VG 4.0	FN 6.0	VF 8.0	VF/NM 9.0	NM- 9.2

3-Injury to eye story-r from #2; Rocket Boy — 129 258 387 826 1413 2000
8-Formerly Yankee Comics; becomes Snap — 181 362 543 1158 1979 2800

SCOOTER (See Swing With...)

SCOOTER COMICS
Rucker Publ. Ltd. (Canadian): Apr, 1946

1-Teen-age/funny animal — 26 52 78 154 252 350

SCOOTER GIRL
Oni Press: May, 2003 - No. 6, Feb, 2004 ($2.99, B&W, limited series)

1-6-Chynna Clugston-Major-s/a — 3.00
TPB (5/04, $14.95, digest size) r/series; sketch pages — 15.00

SCORCHED, THE
Image Comics (Todd McFarlane Prods.): Jan, 2022 - Present ($5.99/$2.99)

1-Spawn, Medieval Spawn, She-Spawn, Gunslinger Spawn app.; Segovia-a — 6.00
2-26-($2.99) — 3.00

SCORPION
Atlas/Seaboard Publ.: Feb, 1975 - No. 3, July, 1975

1-Intro.; bondage-c by Chaykin — 3 6 9 18 27 36
2-Chaykin-a w/Wrightson, Kaluta, Simonson assists(p) — 3 6 9 15 22 28
3-Jim Craig-c/a — 2 4 6 11 16 20
NOTE: *Chaykin a-1, 2; c-1. Colon c-2. Craig c/a-3.*

SCORPION KING, THE (Movie)
Dark Horse Comics: March, 2002 - No. 2, Apr, 2002 ($2.99, limited series)

1,2-Photo-c of the Rock; Richards-a — 3.00

SCORPIO ROSE
Eclipse Comics: Jan, 1983 - No. 2, Oct, 1983 ($1.25, Baxter paper)

1,2: Dr. Orient back-up story begins. 2-origin. — 4.00

SCOTLAND YARD (Inspector Farnsworth of)(Texas Rangers in Action #5 on?)
Charlton Comics Group: June, 1955 - No. 4, Mar, 1956

1-Tothish-a — 17 34 51 98 154 210
2-4-Tothish-a — 10 20 30 58 79 100

SCOTT PILGRIM, ... (Inspired the 2010 movie)
Oni Press: Jul, 2004 - Vol. 6, Jul, 2010 ($11.99, B&W, 7-1/2" x 5", multiple printings exist)

Scott Pilgrim's Precious Little Life (Vol. 1) Bryan Lee O'Malley-s/a in all — 12.00
Scott Pilgrim Vs. The World (Vol. 2), S.P. & The Infinite Sadness (Vol. 3), S.P. Gets it Together (Vol. 4), S.P. Vs. The Universe (Vol. 5), Scott Pilgrim's Finest Hour (Vol. 6) each — 12.00
Free Scott Pilgrim #1 (Free Comic Book Day Edition, 2006) — 15.00
Full-Colour Odds & Ends 2008 — 12.00

SCOURGE, THE
Aspen MLT: No. 0, Aug, 2010 - No. 6, Dec, 2011 ($2.50/$2.99)

0-($2.50) Lobdell-s/Battle-a; multiple covers — 3.00
1-6-($2.99) Lobdell-s/Battle-a; multiple covers — 3.00

SCOURGE OF THE GODS
Marvel Comics (Soleil): 2009 - No. 3, 2009 ($5.99, limited series)

1-3-Mangin-s/Gajic-a; English version of French comic — 6.00
...: The Fall 1-3 (2009 - No. 3, 2009) — 6.00

SCOUT (See Eclipse Graphic Album #16, New America & Swords of Texas)
(Becomes Scout: War Shaman)
Eclipse Comics: Dec, 1985 - No. 24, Oct, 1987($1.75/$1.25, Baxter paper)

1-15,17,18,20-24: 19-Airboy preview. 10-Bissette-a. 11-Monday, the Eliminator begins. 15-Swords of Texas — 4.00
16,19: 16-Scout 3-D Special ($2.50), 16-Scout 2-D Limited Edition, 19-contains flexidisk ($2.50) — 5.00
...Handbook 1 (8/87, $1.75, B&W) — 4.00
Mount Fire (1989, $14.95, TPB) r/#8-14 — 15.00

SCOUT'S HONOR
AfterShock Comics: Jan, 2021 - No. 5, May, 2021 ($4.99/$3.99)

1-($4.99) David Pepose-s/Luca Casalanguida-a — 5.00
2-5-($3.99) — 4.00

SCOUT: WAR SHAMAN (Formerly Scout)
Eclipse Comics: Mar, 1988 - No. 16, Dec, 1989 ($1.95)

1-16 — 4.00

SCRAPPER
Image Comics: Jul, 2023 - No. 6, Dec, 2023 ($3.99, limited series)

1-6-Bleszinski & De Campi-s. 1-Jarrell-a. 2,3-Kelly-a — 4.00

SCRATCH
DC Comics: Aug, 2004 - No. 5, Dec, 2004 ($2.50, limited series)

1-5-Sam Kieth-s/a/c; Batman app. — 3.00

SCREAM (...Comics) (Andy Comics #20 on)
Humor Publications/Current Books(Ace Magazines): Autumn, 1944 - No. 19, Apr, 1948

1-Teenage humor — 24 48 72 142 234 325
2 — 15 30 45 88 137 185
3-16: 11-Racist humor (Indians). 16-Intro. Lily-Belle — 14 28 42 78 112 145
17,19 — 13 26 39 72 101 130
18-Hypo needle story — 14 28 42 80 115 150

SCREAM (Magazine)
Skywald Publ. Corp.: Aug, 1973 - No. 11, Feb, 1975 (68 pgs., B&W) (Painted-c on all)

1-Nosferatu-c/1st app. (series thru #11); Morrow-a. Cthulhu/Necronomicon-s — 10 20 30 64 132 200
2,3: 2-(10/73) Lady Satan 1st app. & series begins; Edgar Allan Poe adaptations begin (thru #11); Phantom of the Opera-s. 3-(12/73) Origin Lady Satan — 5 10 15 34 60 85
4-1st Cannibal Werewolf and 1st Lunatic Mummy — 5 10 15 35 63 90
5,7,8: 5,7-Frankenstein app. 8-Buckler-a; Werewolf-s; Slither-Slime Man-s — 5 10 15 31 53 75
6, 9,10: 6-(6/74) Saga of The Victims/ I Am Horror, classic GGA Hewetson series begins

(thru #11); Frankenstein 2073-s. 9-Severed head-c; Marcos-a. 9,10-Werewolf-s. 10-Dracula-c/s — 5 10 15 33 57 80
11- (1975 Winter Special) "Mr. Poe and the Raven" story — 5 10 15 34 60 85
NOTE: *Buckler a-8. Hewetson s-1-11. Marcos a-9. Miralles c-2. Morrow a-1. Poe s-2-11. Segrelles a-7; c-1.*

SCREAM: CURSE OF CARNAGE (Follows the Absolute Carnage series)
Marvel Comics: Jan, 2020 - No. 5 ($4.99/$3.99, limited series)

1-($4.99) Andi Benton with the Scream symbiote; Chapman-s/Mooneyham-a — 5.00
2-5-($3.99) Brown & Mooneyham-a. 4,5-Thor app. — 4.00

SCREEN CARTOONS
DC Comics: Dec, 1944 (cover only ashcan)

nn-Ashcan comic, not distributed to newsstands, only for in house use. Covers were produced, but not the rest of the book. A copy sold in 2006 for $400 and in 2008 for $500.

SCREEN COMICS
DC Comics: Dec, 1944 (cover only ashcan)

nn-Ashcan comic, not distributed to newsstands, only for in house use. Covers were produced, but not the rest of the book. A copy sold in 2006 for $400, in 2008 for $500 and in 2013 for $500.

SCREEN FABLES
DC Comics: Dec, 1944 (cover only ashcan)

nn-Ashcan comic, not distributed to newsstands, only for in house use. Covers were produced, but not the rest of the book. A copy sold in 2006 for $400 and in 2008 for $500.

SCREEN FUNNIES
DC Comics: Dec, 1944 (cover only ashcan)

nn-Ashcan comic, not distributed to newsstands, only for in house use. Covers were produced, but not the rest of the book. A copy sold in 2006 for $400 and in 2008 for $500.

SCREEN GEMS
DC Comics: Dec, 1944 (cover only ashcan)

nn-Ashcan comic, not distributed to newsstands, only for in house use. Covers were produced, but not the rest of the book. A copy sold in 2010 for $891 and a VF copy sold for $775.

SCREWBALL SQUIRREL
Dark Horse Comics: July, 1995 - No. 3, Sept, 1995 ($2.50, limited series)

1-3: Characters created by Tex Avery — 4.00

SCRIBBLENAUTS UNMASKED: A CRISIS OF IMAGINATION (Based on the video game)
DC Comics: Mar, 2014 - No. 7, Sept, 2014 ($2.99)

1-7: 1-The Bat Family, the Joker and Phantom Stranger app. 3-The Anti-Monitor app. — 3.00

SCRIBBLY (See All-American Comics, Buzzy, The Funnies, Leave It To Binky & Popular Comics)
National Periodical Publ.: 8-9/48 - No. 13, 8-9/50; No. 14, 10-11/51 - No. 15, 12-1/51-52

1-Sheldon Mayer-c/a in all; 52 pgs. begin — 116 232 348 742 1271 1800
2 — 71 142 213 454 777 1100
3-5 — 55 110 165 352 601 850
6-10 — 42 84 126 265 445 625
11-15: 13-Last 52 pgs. — 37 74 111 222 361 500

SCUD: TALES FROM THE VENDING MACHINE
Fireman Press: 1998 - No. 5 ($2.50, B&W)

1-5: 1-Kaniuga-a. 2-Ruben Martinez-a — 4.00

SCUD: THE DISPOSABLE ASSASSIN
Fireman Press: Feb, 1994 - No. 20, 1997 ($2.95, B&W)
Image Comics: No. 21, Feb, 2008 - No. 24, May, 2008 ($3.50, B&W)

1 — 7 14 21 46 86 125
1-2nd printing in color — 1 3 4 6 8 10
2 — 2 4 6 10 14 18
3 — 6.00
4-20 — 3.00
21-24: 21-(2/08, $3.50) Ashley Wood-c. 22-Mahfood-c — 3.50
Heavy 3PO ($12.95, TPB) r/#1-4 — 13.00
Programmed For Damage ($14.95, TPB) r/#5-9 — 15.00
Solid Gold Bomb ($17.95, TPB) r/#10-15 — 18.00

SCUMBAG, THE
Image Comics: Oct, 2020 - No. 14, Aug, 2022 ($3.99)

1-14: 1-Remender-s/Larosa-a; intro. Ernie Ray Clementine. 2-Robinson-a. 3-Powell-a — 4.00

SEA DEVILS (See Showcase #27-29)
National Periodical Publications: Sept-Oct, 1961 - No. 35, May-June, 1967

1-(9-10/61) — 61 122 183 488 1094 1700
2-Last 10¢ issue; grey-tone-c — 27 54 81 194 435 675
3-Begin 12¢ issues thru #35; grey-tone-c — 19 38 57 133 297 460
4,5-Grey-tone-c — 16 32 48 110 243 375
6-10 — 10 20 30 69 147 225
11,12,14-20: 12-Grey-tone-c — 8 16 24 54 102 150
13-Kubert, Colan-a; Joe Kubert app. in story — 9 18 27 57 114 165
21-35: 22-Intro. International Sea Devils; origin & 1st app. Capt. X & Man Fish. 33,35-Grey-tone-c — 7 14 21 40 73 105
NOTE: *Heath a-Showcase 27-29, 1-10; c-Showcase 27-29, 1-10, 14-16. Moldoff a-16i.*

SEA DEVILS (See Tangent Comics/ Sea Devils)

SEADRAGON (Also see the Epsilion Wave)
Elite Comics: May, 1986 - No. 8, 1987 ($1.75)

1-8: 1st & 2nd printings exist — 4.00

SEAGUY
DC Comics (Vertigo): July, 2004 - No. 3, Sept, 2004 ($2.95, limited series)

1-3-Grant Morrison-s/Cameron Stewart-a/c — 3.00
TPB (2005, $9.95) r/#1-3 — 10.00

SEAGUY: THE SLAVES OF MICKEY EYE
DC Comics (Vertigo): Jun, 2009 - No. 3, Aug, 2009 ($3.99, limited series)

1-3-Grant Morrison-s/Cameron Stewart-a/c — 4.00

SEA HOUND, THE (Captain Silver's Log Of The...)

Scout #1 © Timothy Truman

Sea Devils #35 © DC

Secret Avengers (2013 series) #3 © MAR

	GD 2.0	VG 4.0	FN 6.0	VF 8.0	VF/NM 9.0	NM- 9.2

Avon Periodicals: 1945 (no month) - No. 2, Sept-Oct, 1945
nn (#1)-29 pg. novel length sty-"The Esmeralda's Treasure"

	GD 2.0	VG 4.0	FN 6.0	VF 8.0	VF/NM 9.0	NM- 9.2
	21	42	63	122	199	275
2	15	30	45	83	124	165

SEA HOUND, THE (Radio)
Capt. Silver Syndicate: No. 3, July, 1949 - No. 4, Sept, 1949

3,4	11	22	33	64	90	115

SEA HUNT (TV)
Dell Publishing Co.: No. 928, 8/58 - No. 1041, 10-12/59; No. 4, 1-3/60 - No. 13, 4-6/62 (All have Lloyd Bridges photo-c)

Four Color 928(#1)	12	24	36	83	182	280
Four Color 994(#2), 4-13: Manning-a #4-6,8-11,13	9	18	27	59	117	175
Four Color 1041(#3)-Toth-a	9	18	27	59	117	175

SEA OF RED
Image Comics: Mar, 2005 - No. 13, Nov, 2006 ($2.95/$2.99/$3.50)

1-12-Vampirates at sea; Remender & Dwyer-s/Dwyer & Sam-a		3.00
13-($3.50)		3.50
Vol. 1: No Grave But The Sea (9/05, $8.95) r/#1-4		9.00
Vol. 2: No Quarter (2006, $11.99) r/#5-8		12.00
Vol. 3: The Deadlights (2006, $14.99) r/#9-13		15.00

SEA OF STARS
Image Comics: Jul, 2019 - No. 11, Nov, 2021 ($3.99, limited series)

1-11-Jason Aaron & Dennis Hallum-s/Stephen Green-a	4.00

SEA OF THIEVES (Based on the Microsoft computer game)
Titan Comics: Apr, 2018 - No. 4, Jul, 2018 ($3.99)

1-4-Jeremy Whitley-s/Rhoald Marcellius-a; multiple covers; bonus character profiles	4.00

SEAQUEST (TV)
Nemesis Comics: Mar, 1994 ($2.25)

1-Has 2 diff-c stocks (slick & cardboard); Alcala-i	4.00

SEARCHERS, THE (Movie)
Dell Publishing Co.: No. 709, 1956

Four Color 709-John Wayne photo-c	29	58	87	209	467	725

SEARCHERS, THE
Caliber Comics: 1996 - No. 4, 1996 ($2.95, B&W)

1-4	4.00

SEARCHERS, THE : APOSTLE OF MERCY
Caliber Comics: 1997 - No. 2, 1997 ($2.95/$3.95, B&W)

1-($2.95)	4.00
2-($3.95)	5.00

SEARCH FOR HU
AfterShock Comics: Sept, 2021 - No. 5, Jan, 2022 ($4.99/$3.99, limited series)

1-($4.99) Tsuei & Orlando-s/Rubine-a	5.00
2-4-($3.99)	4.00

SEARCH FOR LOVE
American Comics Group: Feb-Mar, 1950 - No. 2, Apr-May, 1950 (52 pgs.)

1-Ken Bald-c	24	48	72	142	234	325
2	16	32	48	94	147	200

SEARS (See Merry Christmas From...)

SEASON'S BEATINGS
Marvel Comics: Feb, 2019 ($4.99, one-shot)

1-Christmas-themed short stories; Deadpool, X-Force, Spider-Man, Squirrel Girl app.	5.00

SEASON'S GREETINGS
Hallmark (King Features): 1935 (6-1/4x5-1/4", 24 pgs. in color)
nn-Cover features Mickey Mouse, Popeye, Jiggs & Skippy. "The Night Before Christmas" told one panel per page, each panel by a famous artist featuring their character. Art by Alex Raymond, Gottfredson, Swinnerton, Segar, Chic Young, Milt Gross, Sullivan (Messmer), Herriman, McManus, Percy Crosby & others (22 artists in all)

Estimated value...	1000.00

SEASONS HAVE TEETH, THE
BOOM! Studios: Apr, 2023 - No. 4, Jul, 2023 ($4.99, limited series)

1-4-Dan Watters-s/Sebastián Cabrol-a	5.00

SEBASTIAN O
DC Comics (Vertigo): May, 1993 - No. 3, July, 1993 ($1.95, limited series)

1-3-Grant Morrison scripts; Steve Yeowell-a	4.00

TPB (2004, $9.95) r/#1-3; intro. chronology by Morrison		10.00

SECOND CHANCES
Image Comics: Aug, 2021 - Present ($3.99, B&W)

1-3-Mammone-s/Bertolini-a	4.00

SECOND COMING
AHOY Comics: 2019 - No. 6, 2020 ($3.99, limited series)

1-6-Russell-s/Pace & Kirk-a/Conner-c; Jesus meets Sunstar. 1-3-Variant-c by Pace	4.00

SECOND COMING: ONLY BEGOTTEN SON
AHOY Comics: 2020 - No. 6, 2021 ($3.99, limited series)

1-6-Russell-s/Pace & Kirk-a/Pace-c. 1-Origin of Sunstar	4.00

SECOND COMING: TRINITY
AHOY Comics: 2023 - No. 6, 2023 ($4.99, limited series)

1-6-Russell-s/Pace & Kirk-a/Pace-c	5.00

SECOND LIFE OF DOCTOR MIRAGE, THE (See Shadowman #16)
Valiant: Nov, 1993 - No. 18, May, 1995 ($2.50)

1-18: 1-With bound-in poster. 5-Shadowman x-over. 7-Bound-in trading card						4.00
1-Gold ink logo edition; no price on-c	2	4	6	9	12	15

SECOND SIGHT
AfterShock Comics: Feb, 2016 - No. 6, Jul, 2016 ($3.99)

1-6-David Hine-s/Alberto Ponticelli-a	4.00

SECRET AGENT (Formerly Sarge Steel)
Charlton Comics: V2#9, Oct, 1966; V2#10, Oct, 1967

V2#9-Sarge Steel part-r begins	3	6	9	17	26	35
10-Tiffany Sinn, CIA app. (from Career Girl Romances #39); Aparo-a	3	6	9	14	20	26

SECRET AGENT (TV) (See Four Color #1231)
Gold Key: Nov, 1966; No. 2, Jan, 1968

1-John Drake photo-c	9	18	27	57	111	165
2-Photo-c	6	12	18	37	66	95

SECRET AGENT X-9 (See Flash Gordon #4 by King)
David McKay Publ.: 1934 (Book 1: 84 pgs.; Book 2: 124 pgs.) (8x7-1/2")
Book 1-Contains reprints of the first 13 weeks of the strip by Alex Raymond; complete except for 2 dailies

	57	114	171	362	619	875

Book 2-Contains reprints immediately following contents of Book 1, for 20 weeks by Alex Raymond; complete except for two dailies. Note: Raymond mis-dated the last five strips from 6/34, and while the dating sequence is confusing, the continuity is correct

	47	94	141	296	498	700

SECRET AGENT X-9 (See Magic Comics)
Dell Publishing Co.: Dec, 1937 (Not by Raymond)

Feature Books 8	65	130	195	416	708	1000

SECRET AGENT Z-2 (See Holyoke One-Shot No. 7)

SECRET AVENGERS (The Heroic Age)
Marvel Comics: Jul, 2010 - No. 37, Mar, 2013 ($3.99)

1-Bendis-s/Deodato-a/Djurdjevic-c; Steve Rogers assembles covert squad	2	4	6	8	10	12
1-Variant-c by Yardin	2	4	6	9	12	15
2-12: Two covers. 2-4-Deodato-a. 5-Nick Fury app.; Aja-a						4.00
12.1 ($2.99) Spencer-s/Eaton-a/Deodato-c						3.00
13-18,20, 21: 13-15-Fear Itself tie-in; Granov-c. 15-Aftermath of Bucky's demise. 16-21-Warren Ellis-s						4.00
19-1st Mr. Knight	3	6	9	14	19	24
21.2-($2.99) Remender-s/Zircher-a; intro. new Masters of Evil						3.00
22,24-37: 22-25-Remender-s/Hardman-a/Art Adams-c. 26-28-A vs. X						4.00
23-1st Agent Venom, joins team	3	6	9	17	26	35

SECRET AVENGERS (Marvel NOW!)
Marvel Comics: Apr, 2013 - No. 16, Apr, 2014 ($3.99)

1-16: 1-5-Spencer-s/Luke Ross-a/Coker-c; Agent Coulson app. 5,7-Hulk app. 7,9-Guice-a 9,16-Winter Soldier app.	4.00

SECRET AVENGERS (All-New Marvel NOW!)
Marvel Comics: May, 2014 - No. 15, Jun, 2015 ($3.99)

1-15: 1-Ales Kot-s/Michael Walsh-a; M.O.D.O.K. app. 7-Deadpool app.	4.00

SECRET CITY SAGA (See Jack Kirby's Secret City Saga)

SECRET DEFENDERS (Also see The Defenders & Fantastic Four #374)
Marvel Comics: Mar, 1993 - No. 25, Mar, 1995 ($1.75/$1.95)

1-($2.50)-Red foil stamped-c; Dr. Strange, Nomad, Wolverine, Spider Woman	

	GD	VG	FN	VF	VF/NM	NM-
	2.0	4.0	6.0	8.0	9.0	9.2

& Darkhawk begin ... 5.00
2-11,13-24: 9-New team w/Silver Surfer, Thunderstrike, Dr. Strange & War Machine. 13-Thanos replaces Dr. Strange as leader; leads into Cosmic Powers limited series; 14-Dr. Druid. 15-Bound in card sheet. 15-17-Deadpool app. 18-Giant Man & Iron Fist app. ... 4.00
12,25: 12-($2.50)-Prismatic foil-c. 25 ($2.50, 52 pgs.) ... 5.00

SECRET DIARY OF EERIE ADVENTURES
Avon Periodicals: 1953 (25¢ giant, 100 pgs., one-shot)
nn-(Rare)-Kubert-a; Hollingsworth-c; Sid Check back-c

	486	972	1458	3550	6275	9000

SECRET EMPIRE (Also see Free Comic Book Day 2017 Secret Empire)
Marvel Comics: No. 0, Jun, 2017 - No. 10, Oct, 2017 ($4.99/$3.99, limited series)
0-2-($4.99): 0-Spencer-s/Acuña-a. Steve Rogers and Hydra take over. 1-McNiven-a ... 5.00
3-5,7-($3.99) 3,5-Sorrentino-a. 4-Yu-a. 5-Bruce Banner returns ... 5.00
6,8-10-($4.99): 6,9-Yu-a. 7-Black Widow killed. 8-Acuña-a. 10-McNiven-a ... 5.00
... Omega 1 (11/17, $4.99) Epilogue to series; Sorrentino & Bennett-a ... 5.00
...: Underground 1 (8/17, $4.99) Whitley-s/Koda-a; takes place after #4; Sauron app. ... 5.00
...: United 1 (8/17, $4.99) X-Men & Deadpool app.; Anindito-a ... 5.00
...: Uprising 1 (7/17, $4.99) The Champions & Black Widow app.; Landy-s/Cassara-a ... 5.00

SECRET EMPIRE: BRAVE NEW WORLD
Marvel Comics: Aug, 2017 - No. 5, Oct, 2017 ($3.99, limited series)
1-5: Namor/Invaders and back-up short stories of various heroes under Hydra rule ... 5.00

SECRET FILES & ORIGINS GUIDE TO THE DC UNIVERSE
DC Comics: Mar, 2000; Feb, 2002 ($6.95/$4.95)
2000 (3/00, $6.95)-Overview of DC characters; profile pages by various ... 7.00
2001-2002 (2/02, $4.95) Olivetti-c ... 5.00

SECRET FILES PRESIDENT LUTHOR
DC Comics: Mar, 2001 ($4.95, one-shot)
1-Short stories & profile pages by various; Harris-c ... 5.00

SECRET HEARTS
National Periodical Publications (Beverly)(Arleigh No. 50-113):
9-10/49 - No. 6, 7-8/50; No. 7, 12-1/51-52 - No. 153, 7/11

1-Kinstler-a; photo-c begin, end #6	84	168	252	538	919	1300
2-Toth-a (1 pg.); Kinstler-a	40	80	120	246	411	575
3,6 (1950)	36	72	108	211	343	475
4,5-Toth-a	37	74	111	218	354	490
7(12-1/51-52) (Rare)	50	100	150	315	533	750
8-10 (1952)	28	56	84	165	270	375
11-20	20	40	60	118	192	265
21-26: 26-Last precode (2-3/55)	18	36	54	105	165	225
27-40	8	16	24	56	108	160
41-50	7	14	21	46	86	125
51-60	6	12	18	38	69	100
61-75,100: 75-Last 10¢ issue	5	10	15	34	60	85

76-99,101-109: 83,88-Each has panel which inspired a famous Roy Lichtenstein painting

	4	8	12	27	44	60
110- "Reach for Happiness" serial begins, ends #138	4	8	12	28	47	65
111-119,121-126: 114-Colan-a/c	3	6	9	19	30	40
120,134-Neal Adams-c/a	4	8	12	28	47	65
127 (4/68)-Beatles cameo	5	10	15	30	50	70

128-133,135-142: 141,142- "20 Miles to Heartbreak", Chapter 2 & 3 (see Young Love for Chapters 1 & 4); Toth, Colletta-a

	3	6	9	18	28	38
143-148,150-152: 144-Morrow-a	3	6	9	16	23	30
149,153: 149-Toth-a. 153-Kirby-i	3	6	9	17	26	35

SECRET HISTORY OF THE AUTHORITY: HAWKSMOOR
DC Comics (WildStorm): May, 2008 - No. 6, Oct, 2008 ($2.99, limited series)
1-6-Costa-s/Staples-a/Hamner-c ... 3.00
TPB (2009, $19.99) r/#1-6 ... 20.00

SECRET HISTORY OF THE WAR ON WEED
Image Comics: Apr, 2022 ($4.99, one-shot)
1-Scotch McTiernan vs. marijuana; Duggan & Posehn-s/Koblish-a ... 5.00

SECRET IDENTITIES
Image Comics: Feb, 2015 - No. 7, Sept, 2015 ($3.50/$3.99)
1-6-Faerber & Joines-s/Kyriazis-a ... 3.50
7-($3.99) ... 4.00

SECRET INVASION (Also see Mighty Avengers, New Avengers, and Skrulls!)
Marvel Comics: June, 2008 - No. 8, Jan, 2009 ($3.99, limited series)

1-Skrull invasion; Bendis-s/Yu-a/Dell'Otto-c	2	4	6	10	14	18
1-Variant cover with blank area for sketches	1	3	4	6	8	10

1-McNiven variant-c ... 12.00
1-Yu variant-c ... 30.00
1-2nd printing with old Avengers variant-c by Yu ... 4.00
1 Director's Cut (2008, $4.99) r/#1 with script; concept and promo art; cover gallery ... 5.00
2-8-Dell'Otto-c. 8-Wasp killed ... 4.00
2-4-McNiven variant-c. 2-Avengers. 3-Nick Fury. 4-Tony Stark, Spider-Woman, Black Widow ... 6.00
2-8-Yu variant-c. 2-Hawkeye & Mockingbird. 3-Spider-Woman. 4-Nick Fury ... 10.00
5-Rubi variant-c ... 5.00
6-Cho Spider-Woman variant-c ... 8.00
...: Aftermath: Beta Ray Bill - The Green of Eden (6/09, $3.99) Brereton-a ... 4.00
...: Chronicles 1,2 (4/09,6/09, $5.99) reprints from New Avengers & Illuminati issues ... 6.00
...: Dark Reign (2/09, $3.99) villain meeting after #8; previews new series; Maleev-a/c ... 4.00
...: Dark Reign (2/09, $3.99) Variant Green Goblin cover by Bryan Hitch ... 8.00
...: Requiem (2009, $3.99) Hank Pym becomes The Wasp; r/TTA #44 & Avengers #215 ... 4.00
...: Saga (2008, giveaway) history of the Skrulls told through reprint panels and text ... 3.00
...: The Infiltration TPB (2008, $19.99) r/FF #2; New Avengers #31,32,38,39; New Avengers: Illuminati #1,5; Mighty Avengers #7; and Avengers: The Initiative Annual #1 ... 20.00
...: War of Kings (2/09, $3.99) Black Bolt and the Inhumans; Pelletier & Dazo-a ... 4.00
...: Who Do You Trust? (8/08, $3.99) short tie-in stories by various; Jimenez-a ... 4.00
SECRET INVASION

Marvel Comics: Jan, 2023 - No. 5, May, 2023 ($4.99/$3.99, limited series)
1-($4.99) North-s/Mobili-a; Nick Fury & Maria Hill app. ... 5.00
2-5-($3.99) 2-Avengers app. ... 4.00

SECRET INVASION: AMAZING SPIDER-MAN
Marvel Comics: Oct, 2008 - No. 3, Dec, 2008 ($2.99, limited series)
1-3-Jackpot battles a Super-Skrull; Santucci-a. 2-Menace app. ... 3.00

SECRET INVASION: FANTASTIC FOUR
Marvel Comics: July, 2008 - No. 3, Sept, 2008 ($2.99, limited series)
1-3-Skrulls and Lyja invade; Kitson-a/Davis-c ... 3.00
1-Variant Skrull cover by McKone ... 5.00

SECRET INVASION: FRONT LINE
Marvel Comics: Sept, 2008 - No. 5, Jan, 2009 ($2.99, limited series)
1-5-Ben Urich covering the Skrull invasion; Reed-s/Castiello-a ... 3.00

SECRET INVASION: INHUMANS
Marvel Comics: Oct, 2008 - No. 4, Jan, 2009 ($2.99, limited series)
1-4-Raney-s/Sejic-c/Pokasky-s; search for Black Bolt ... 3.00

SECRET INVASION: RUNAWAYS/YOUNG AVENGERS (Follows Runaways #30)
Marvel Comics: Aug, 2008 - No. 3, Nov, 2008 ($2.99, limited series)
1-3-Miyazawa-a/Ryan-c ... 3.00

SECRET INVASION: THOR
Marvel Comics: Oct, 2008 - No. 3, Dec, 2008 ($2.99, limited series)
1-3-Fraction-s/Braithwaite-a; Skrulls invade Asgard; Beta Ray Bill app. ... 3.00
1-2nd printing with Beta Ray Bill cover ... 3.00

SECRET INVASION: X-MEN
Marvel Comics: Oct, 2008 - No. 4, Jan, 2009 ($2.99, limited series)
1-4-Carey-s/Nord-a/Dodson-c; Skrulls invade San Francisco ... 3.00
1-2nd printing with variant Nord-c ... 3.00

SECRET ISLAND OF OZ, THE (See First Comics Graphic Novel)

SECRET LAND, THE
Dark Horse Comics: Jun, 2021 - No. 4, Oct, 2021 ($3.99, limited series)
1-4-Christofer Emgård-s/Tomás Aira-a ... 4.00

SECRET LIFE OF PETS, THE (Based on the 2016 animated movie)
Titan Comics: Jun, 2019 - Dec, 2019 ($3.99)
1,2-Lapuss-s/Goum-a ... 4.00
...Volume 2 (11/19 - No. 2, 12/19) 1,2-Lapuss-s/Goum-a ... 4.00

SECRET LOVE (See Fox Giants & Sinister House of...)

SECRET LOVE
Ajax-Farrell/Four Star Comic Corp. No. 2 on: 12/55 - No. 3, 8/56; 4/57 - No. 5, 2/58; No. 6, 6/58

1(12/55-Ajax, 1st series)	18	36	54	105	165	225
2,3	13	26	39	74	105	135
1(4/57-Ajax, 2nd series)	15	30	45	83	124	165
2-6: 5-Bakerish-a	11	22	33	62	88	110

SECRET LOVES
Comic Magazines/Quality Comics Group: Nov, 1949 - No. 6, Sept, 1950

1-Ward-c	39	78	117	240	395	550
2-Ward-c	34	68	102	199	325	450
3-Crandall-a	21	42	63	124	202	280
4,6	18	36	54	107	169	230
5-Suggestive art "Boom Town Babe"; photo-c	25	50	75	150	245	340

SECRET LOVE STORIES (See Fox Giants)

SECRET MISSIONS (Admiral Zacharia's...)
St. John Publishing Co.: February, 1950
1-Joe Kubert-c; stories of U.S. foreign agents

	37	74	111	222	361	500

SECRET MYSTERIES (Formerly Crime Mysteries & Crime Smashers)
Ribage/Merit Publications No. 17 on: No. 16, Nov, 1954 - No. 19, July, 1955

16-Horror, Palais-a; Myron Fass-c	52	104	156	328	552	775
17-19-Horror. 17-Fass-c; mis-dated 3/54?	37	74	111	222	361	500

SECRET ORIGINS (1st Series) (See 80 Page Giant #8)
National Periodical Publications: Aug-Oct, 1961 (Annual) (Reprints)
1-Origin Adam Strange (Showcase #17), Green Lantern (Green Lantern #1), Challengers (partial-r/Showcase #6, 6 pgs. Kirby-a), J'onn J'onzz (Det. #225), The Flash (Showcase #4), Green Arrow (1 pg. text), Superman-Batman team (World's Finest #94), Wonder Woman (Wonder Woman #105)

	46	92	138	368	834	1300

Replica Edition (1998, $4.95) r/entire book and house ads ... 5.00
Even More Secret Origins (2003, $6.95) reprints origins of Hawkman, Eclipso, Kid Flash, Blackhawks, Green Lantern's oath, and Jimmy Olsen-Robin team in 80 pg. Giant style ... 7.00

SECRET ORIGINS (2nd Series)
National Periodical Publications: Feb-Mar, 1973 - No. 6, Jan-Feb, 1974; No. 7, Oct-Nov, 1974 (All 20¢ issues) (All origin reprints)

1-Superman(r/1 pg. origin/Action #1, 1st time since G.A.), Batman(Detective #33), Ghost(Flash #88), The Flash(Showcase #4)	7	14	21	50	115	180
2-7: 2-Green Lantern & The Atom(Showcase #22 & 34), Supergirl(Action #252).	5	10	15	35	63	90

3-Wonder Woman (W.W. #1), Wildcat (Sensation #1). 4-Vigilante (Action #42) by Meskin, Kid Eternity(Hit #25). 5-The Spectre by Baily (More Fun #52,53). 6-Blackhawk(Military #1) & Legion of Super-Heroes(Superboy #147). 7-Robin (Detective #38), Aquaman (More Fun #73)

	3	6	9	19	30	40

NOTE: *Infantino a-1. Kane a-2. Kubert a-1.*

SECRET ORIGINS (3rd Series)
DC Comics: Apr, 1986 - No. 50, Aug, 1990 (All origins)(52 pgs. #6 on)(#27 on: $1.50)

1,3: 1-Origin Superman. 3-Shazam	2	4	6	8		10
2,4-6: 2-Blue Beetle. 4-Firestorm. 5-Crimson Avenger. 6-Halo/G.A. Batman	1	3	4	6		10

7-9,11,12,15-20,22-26: 7-Green Lantern (Guy Gardner)/G.A. Sandman. 8-Shadow Lass/Doll Man. 9-G.A. Flash/Skyman.11-G.A. Hawkman/Power Girl. 12-Challengers of Unknown/ G.A. Fury (2nd modern app.). 15-Spectre/Deadman. 16-G.A. Hourman/Warlord. 17-Adam Strange story by Carmine Infantino; Dr. Occult. 18-G.A. Gr. Lantern/The Creeper.

Secret Invasion #6 © MAR

Secret Origins (2014 series) #4 © DC

Secret Romance #20 © CC

	GD	VG	FN	VF	VF/NM	NM-
	2.0	4.0	6.0	8.0	9.0	9.2

19-Uncle Sam/The Guardian. 20-Batgirl/G.A. Dr. Mid-Nite. 22-Manhunters. 23-Floronic Man/Guardians of the Universe. 24-Blue Devil/Dr. Fate. 25-LSH/Atom. 26-Black Lightning/Miss America ... 5.00

10-Phantom Stranger w/Alan Moore scripts; Legends spin-off ... 5.00

13-Origin Nightwing; Johnny Thunder app. ... 5.00

14-Suicide Squad; Legends spin-off ... 1 3 4 6 8 10

21-Jonah Hex/Black Condor ... 5.00

27-30,36-38,40-49: 27-Zatara/Zatanna. 28-Midnight/Nightshade. 29-Power of the Atom/Mr. America; new 3 pg. Red Tornado story by Mayer (last app. of Scribbly, 8/88). 30-Plastic Man/Elongated Man. 36-Poison Ivy by Neil Gaiman & Mark Buckingham/Green Lantern. 37-Legion Of Substitute Heroes/Doctor Light. 38-Green Arrow/Speedy; Grell scripts. 40-All Ape issue. 41-Rogues Gallery of Flash. 42-Phantom Girl/GrimGhost. 43-Original Hawk & Dove/Cave Carson/Chris KL-99. 44-Batman app.; story based on Det. #40. 45-Blackhawk/El Diablo. 46-JLA/LSH/New Titans. 47-LSH. 48-Ambush Bug/Stanley & His Monster/Rex the Wonder Dog/Trigger Twins. 49-Newsboy Legion/Silent Knight/Bouncing Boy ... 4.00

31-35,39: 31-JSA. 32-JLA. 33-35-JLI. 39-Animal Man-c/story continued in Animal Man #10; Grant Morrison scripts; Batman app. ... 4.00

50-($3.95, 100 pgs.)-Batman & Robin in text, Flash of Two Worlds, Johnny Thunder, Dolphin, Black Canary & Space Museum ... 5.00

Annual 1 (8/87)-Capt. Comet/Doom Patrol ... 5.00

Annual 2 ('88, $2.00)-Origin Flash II & Flash III ... 5.00

Annual 3 ('89, $2.95, 84 pgs.)-Teen Titans; 1st app. new Flamebird who replaces original Bat-Girl ... 5.00

Special 1 (10/89, $2.00)-Batman villains: Penguin, Riddler, & Two-Face; Bolland-c; Sam Kieth-a; Neil Gaiman scripts(2) ... 5.00

NOTE: Art Adams a-33i(part). M. Anderson 8, 19, 21, 25i; c-19(part). Aparo c-a10. Bissette c-23. Bolland c-7. Byrne c/a-Annual 1. Colan c/a-5p. Forte a-37. Giffen a-18p, 44p, 48. Infantino a-17, 50p. Kaluta c-39. Gil Kane a-2, 28; c-2p. Kirby c-19(part). Erik Larsen a-13. Mayer a-29. Morrow a-21, Orlando a-10. Perez a-50i, Annual 3i; c- Annual 3. Rogers a-6p. Russell a-27i. Simonson c-22. Staton a-36, 50p. Steacy a-35. Tuska a-4p, 9p.

SECRET ORIGINS (4th Series)(DC New 52)
DC Comics: Jun, 2014 - No. 11, May, 2015 ($4.99)

1-3,5-9,11: 1-Origin Superman, Robin. 2-Batman. 6-Wonder Woman ... 5.00

4-Harley Quinn ... 2 4 6 8 10 12

10-Batgirl; Stewart & Fletcher-s/Koh-a; Firestorm & Poison Ivy ... 6.00

SECRET ORIGINS 80 PAGE GIANT (Young Justice)
DC Comics: Dec, 1998 ($4.95, one-shot)

1-Origin-s of Young Justice members; Ramos-a (Impulse) ... 5.00

SECRET ORIGINS FEATURING THE JLA
DC Comics: 1999 ($14.95, TPB)

1-Reprints recent origin-s of JLA members; Cassaday-c ... 15.00

SECRET ORIGINS OF SUPER-HEROES (See DC Special Series #10, 19)

SECRET ORIGINS OF SUPER-VILLAINS 80 PAGE GIANT
DC Comics: Dec, 1999 ($4.95, one-shot)

1-Origin-s of Sinestro, Amazo and others; Gibbons-c ... 5.00

SECRET ORIGINS OF THE WORLD'S GREATEST SUPER-HEROES
DC Comics: 1989 ($4.95, 148 pgs.)

nn-Reprints Superman, JLA origins; new Batman origin-s; Bolland-c ... 2 4 6 8 10 12

SECRET ROMANCE
Charlton Comics: Oct, 1968 - No. 41, Nov, 1976; No. 42, Mar, 1979 - No. 48, Feb, 1980

	GD	VG	FN	VF	VF/NM	NM-
1-Begin 12c issues, ends #?	4	8	12	22	35	48
2-10: 9-Reese-a	2	4	6	11	16	20
11-16,18,19,21-30	2	4	6	9	13	16
17,20: 17-Susan Dey poster. 20-David Cassidy pin-up2	4	6	11	16	20	
31-48	2	4	6	8	10	12

NOTE: Beyond the Stars app.-No. 9, 11, 12, 14.

SECRET ROMANCES (Exciting Love Stories)
Superior Publications Ltd.: Apr, 1951 - No. 27, July, 1955

	GD	VG	FN	VF	VF/NM	NM-
1	28	56	84	165	270	375
2	19	38	57	11	176	240
3-10	15	30	45	90	140	190
11-13,15-18,20-27	15	30	45	83	121	165
14,19-Lingerie panels	15	30	45	84	127	170

SECRET SERVICE (See Kent Blake of the...)

SECRET SERVICE (Inspired the 2015 movie Kingsmen: The Secret Service)(Also see Kingsmen: The Red Diamond)
Marvel Comics (Icon): Jun, 2012 - No. 6, Jun, 2013 ($2.99/$4.99, limited series)

1-5-Mark Millar-s/Dave Gibbons-a/c ... 3.00

6-($4.99) ... 5.00

SECRET SIX (See Action Comics Weekly)

National Periodical Publications: Apr-May, 1968 - No. 7, Apr-May, 1969 (12c)

	GD	VG	FN	VF	VF/NM	NM-
1-Origin/1st app.	10	20	30	64	132	200
2-7	4	8	12	28	47	65

SECRET SIX (See Tangent Comics/ Secret Six)

SECRET SIX (See Villains United)

SECRET SIX
DC Comics: Jul, 2006 - No. 6, Jan, 2007 ($2.99, limited series)

1-6-Gail Simone-s/Brad Walker-a. 4-Doom Patrol app. ... 3.00

...: Six Degrees of Devastation TPB (2007, $14.99) r/#1-6 ... 15.00

SECRET SIX
DC Comics: Nov, 2008 - No. 36, Oct, 2011 ($2.99)

1-36: 1-Gail Simone-s/Nicola Scott-a. 2-Batman app. 8-Rodriguez-a. 11-13-Wonder Woman & Artemis app. 16-Black Alice app. 17,18-Blackest Night ... 3.00

...: Cats in the Cradle TPB (2011, $14.99) r/#19-24 ... 15.00

...: Danse Macabre TPB (2010, $14.99) r/#15-18 & Suicide Squad #67 (Blackest Night) ... 15.00

...: Depths TPB (2010, $14.99) r/#8-14 ... 15.00

...: The Reptile Brain TPB (2011, $14.99) r/#25-29 ... 15.00

...: Unhinged TPB (2009, $14.99) r/#1-7; intro. by Paul Cornell ... 15.00

SECRET SIX
DC Comics: Feb, 2015 - No. 14, Jul, 2016 ($2.99)

1-14: 1-Simone-s/Lashley-a; Catman & Black Alice app. 10-Superman app. 12-14-Shiva app.; Elongated Man returns ... 3.00

SECRET SOCIETY OF SUPER-VILLAINS
National Per. Publ.: May-June, 1976 - No. 15, June-July, 1978

	GD	VG	FN	VF	VF/NM	NM-
1-Origin; JLA cameo & Capt. Cold app.	3	6	9	21	33	45
2-5,15: 2-Re-intro/origin Capt. Comet; Green Lantern x-over. 5-Green Lantern, Hawkman x-over; Darkseid app. 15-G.A. Atom, Dr. Midnite, & JSA app.	2	4	6	8	11	14
6-14: 9,10-Creeper x-over. 11-Capt. Comet; Orlando-i2	3	4	6	8	10	14

SECRET SOCIETY OF SUPER-VILLAINS SPECIAL (See DC Special Series #6)

SECRETS OF HAUNTED HOUSE
National Periodical Publications/DC Comics: 4-5/75 - #5, 12-1/75-76; #6, 6-7/77 - #14, 10-11/78; #15, 8/79 - #46, 3/82

	GD	VG	FN	VF	VF/NM	NM-
1	6	12	18	37	66	95
2-4	3	6	9	21	33	45
5-Wrightson-c	10	20	30	64	132	200
6-14	3	6	9	14	19	24
15-30	2	4	6	9	13	16
31,44: 31-(12/80) Mr. E begins (1st app.), ends #41. 44-Wrightson-c	2	4	6	10	14	18
32-1(8/1) Origin of Mr. E	2	4	6	8	11	14
33-43,45,46: 34,35-Frankenstein Monster app.	2	4	6	8	10	10

NOTE: Aparo c-7. Aragones a-1. B. Bailey a-46. Bissette a-46. Buckler c-32-40p. Ditko a-9, 12, 41, 45. Golden a-10. Howard a-13i. Kaluta c-8, 10, 11, 14, 16, 29. Kubert c-41, 42. Sheldon Mayer a-43p. McWilliams a-35. Nasser a-24. Newton a-30p. Nino a-1, 13, 19. Orlando c-13, 30, 43, 45i. N. Redondo a-4, 5, 29. Rogers c-26. Spiegle a-31-41. Wrightson c-5, 44.

SECRETS OF HAUNTED HOUSE SPECIAL (See DC Special Series #12)

SECRETS OF LIFE (Movie)
Dell Publishing Co.: 1956 (Disney)

	GD	VG	FN	VF	VF/NM	NM-
Four Color 749-Photo-c	5	10	15	31	53	75

SECRETS OF LOVE (See Popular Teen-Agers...)

SECRETS OF LOVE AND MARRIAGE
Charlton Comics: V2#1, Aug, 1956 - V2#25, June, 1961

	GD	VG	FN	VF	VF/NM	NM-
V2#1-Matt Baker-c?	17	34	51	117	259	400
V2#2-6	5	10	15	34	60	85
V2#7-9-(All 68 pgs.)	8	16	24	51	96	140
10-25	5	10	15	30	50	70

SECRETS OF MAGIC (See Wisco)

SECRETS OF SINISTER HOUSE (Sinister House of Secret Love #1-4)
National Periodical Publ.: No. 5, June-July, 1972 - No. 18, June-July, 1974

	GD	VG	FN	VF	VF/NM	NM-
5-(52 pgs.).	9	18	27	58	114	170
6-9: 7-Redondo-a	4	8	12	25	40	55
10-Neal Adams-a(i)	4	8	12	27	44	60
11-18: 15-Redondo-a. 17-Barry-a; early Chaykin 1 pg. strip	3	6	9	17	26	35

NOTE: Alcala a-6, 13, 14. Glanzman a-7. Kaluta c-6, 7. Nino a-8, 11-13. Ambrose Bierce adapt-#14.

SECRETS OF SINISTER HOUSE
DC Comics: Dec, 2019 ($9.99, square-bound oneshot, 80 pgs.)

1-Short stores of horror by various incl. Dini, Hester, Layman, Raney; Romita Jr.-c ... 10.00

	GD	VG	FN	VF	VF/NM	NM-
	2.0	4.0	6.0	8.0	9.0	9.2

SECRETS OF THE LEGION OF SUPER-HEROES
DC Comics: Jan, 1981 - No. 3, Mar, 1981 (Limited series)

1-3: 1-Origin of the Legion. 2-Retells origins of Brainiac 5, Shrinking Violet, Sun-Boy, Bouncing Boy, Ultra-Boy, Matter-Eater Lad, Mon-El, Karate Kid & Dream Girl ... 5.00

SECRETS OF TRUE LOVE
St. John Publishing Co.: Feb, 1958

1-Matt Baker-c	39	78	117	240	395	550

SECRETS OF YOUNG BRIDES
Charlton Comics: No. 5, Sept, 1957 - No. 44, Oct, 1964; July, 1975 - No. 9, Nov, 1976

	GD	VG	FN	VF	VF/NM	NM-
5	6	12	18	37	66	95
6-10: 8-Negligee panel	4	8	12	28	47	65
11-20	4	8	12	25	40	55
21-30: Last 10¢ issue?	4	8	12	23	37	50
31-44(10/64)	3	6	9	17	26	35
1-(2nd series) (7/75)	4	8	12	23	37	50
2-9	2	4	6	9	12	15

SECRET SQUIRREL (TV)(See Kite Fun Book)
Gold Key: Oct, 1966 (12¢) (Hanna-Barbera)

1-1st Secret Squirrel and Morocco Mole, Squiddly Diddly, Winsome Witch	14	28	42	96	211	325

SECRET STORY ROMANCES (Becomes True Tales of Love)
Atlas Comics (TCI): Nov, 1953 - No. 21, Mar, 1956

1-Everett-a; Jay Scott Pike-c	37	74	111	222	361	500
2	20	40	60	114	182	250
3-11: 11-Last pre-code (2/55)	16	32	48	94	147	200
12-21	15	30	45	82	124	165

NOTE: *Colletta* a-10, 14, 15, 17, 21; c-10, 14, 17.

SECRET VOICE, THE (See Great American Comics Presents...)

SECRET WAR
Marvel Comics: Apr, 2004 - No. 5, Dec, 2005 ($3.99, limited series)

1-Bendis-s/Dell'Otto painted-a/c; ... 6.00
1-2nd printing with gold logo on white cover and full-color Spider-Man ... 4.00
1-3rd printing with white cover and B&W sketched Spider-Man ... 4.00
2-Wolverine-c; intro. Daisy Johnson (Quake) ... 14.00
2-2nd printing with white cover and B&W sketched Wolverine ... 12.00
3-5: 3-Capt. America-c. 4-Black Widow-c. 5-Daredevil-c ... 4.00
...: From the Files of Nick Fury (2005, $3.99) Fury's journal entries; profiles of characters ... 4.00
HC (2005, $29.99, dust jacket) r/#1-5 & ...From the Files of Nick Fury; additional art ... 30.00
SC (2006, $24.99) r/#1-5 & ...From the Files of Nick Fury; additional art ... 25.00

SECRET WARPS (Characters merging within the Soul Stone)
Marvel Comics: Sept, 2019 ($4.99, weekly series of one-shots)

...: Arachknight Annual 1 - Part 4; Spider-Man/Moon Knight vs Supreme Seven ... 5.00
...: Ghost Panther Annual 1 - Part 3; Ghost Rider/Black Panther ... 5.00
...: Iron Hammer Annual 1 - Part 5; Iron Man/Thor ... 5.00
...: Soldier Supreme Annual 1 - Part 1; Captain America/Doctor Strange vs. Madame Hel ... 5.00
...: Weapon Hex Annual 1 - Part 2; X-23/Scarlet Witch ... 5.00

SECRET WARRIORS (Also see 2009 Dark Reign titles)
Marvel Comics: Apr, 2009 - No. 28, Sept, 2011 ($3.99/$2.99)

1-Bendis & Hickman-s/Caselli-a/Cheung-c; Nick Fury app.; Hydra dossier; sketch pages ... 4.00
2-24,26-28-($2.99) 8-Dark Avengers app. 17-19-Howling Commandos return ... 3.00
25-($3.99) Baron Strucker app.; Vitti-a ... 4.00

SECRET WARRIORS (Tie-in to Secret Empire)
Marvel Comics: Jul, 2017 - No. 12, Mar, 2018 ($3.99)

1-12: 1-Rosenberg-s/Garrón-a; Ms. Marvel, Moon Girl, Karnak app. 7-Deadpool app. ... 4.00

SECRET WARS
Marvel Comics: 2014 (Giveaway)

... No. 1 Halloween Comic Fest 2014 - Reprints Marvel Super Heroes Secret Wars #1 ... 3.00

SECRET WARS (See Free Comic Book Day 2015 for prelude)
Marvel Comics: Jul, 2015 - No. 9, Mar, 2016 ($4.99/$3.99, limited series, originally planned as 8 issues)

1,2-($4.99) Hickman/s/Ribic-a; end of the Marvel 616 and Ultimate universes ... 5.00
3-8-($3.99): 3-Miles Morales app. ... 4.00
9-($4.99) End of Battleworld, beginning of the Prime Earth ... 5.00
...: Agents of Atlas (12/15, $4.99) Taylor-s/Pugh-a/Kirk-c; Baron Zemo app. ... 5.00
...: Official Guide to the Marvel Multiverse 1 (12/15, $4.99) Handbook-style info on characters, events and realities tied-in with the Secret Wars series ... 5.00
...: Secret Love 1 (10/15, $4.99) Romance stories by various; Ms. Marvel, Squirrel Girl, Daredevil, Ghost Rider, Iron Fist & Misty Knight app.; 2 covers ... 5.00
..., Too 1 (1/16, $4.99) Humor short stories by various incl. Powell, Guillory, Leth ... 5.00

SECRET WARS: BATTLEWORLD
Marvel Comics: Jul, 2015 - No. 4, Oct, 2015 ($3.99, limited series)

1-4-Short stories by various. 2-Howard the Duck app. 4-Silver Surfer app.; Francavilla-c ... 4.00

SECRET WARS: JOURNAL
Marvel Comics: Jul, 2015 - No. 5, Nov, 2015 ($3.99, limited series)

1-5-Short stories by various. 1-Leads into Siege #1. 3-Isanove-a. 4-Lashley-a ... 4.00

SECRET WARS 2099
Marvel Comics: Jul, 2015 - No. 5, Nov, 2015 ($3.99, limited series)

1-5-Peter David-s/Will Sliney-a; Avengers vs. Defenders; Baron Mordo app. ... 4.00

SECRET WARS II (Also see Marvel Super Heroes...)
Marvel Comics Group: July, 1985 - No. 9, Mar, 1986 (Maxi-series)

1,9: 9-(52 pgs.) X-Men app., Spider-Man app. ... 6.00
2-8: 2,8-X-Men app. 5-1st app. Boom Boom. 5,8-Spider-Man app. ... 4.00

SECRET WEAPONS
Valiant: Sept, 1993 - No. 21, May, 1995 ($2.25)

1-10,12-21: 3-Reese-a(i). 5-Ninjak app. 9-Bound-in trading card. 12-Bloodshot app. ... 4.00
11-(Sept. on envelope, Aug on-c, $2.50)-Enclosed in manilla envelope; Bloodshot app;

---

intro new team. ... 5.00

SECRET WEAPONS
Valiant Entertainment: Jun, 2017 - No. 4, Sept, 2017 ($3.99)

1-4-Heisserer-s/Allén-a ... 4.00
#0-(1/18, $3.99) Heisserer-s/Pollina-a; origin of Nikki Finch ... 4.00
...: Owen's Story #0 (3/18, $3.99) Heisserer-s/Allén-a ... 4.00

SECRET X-MEN, THE
Marvel Comics: Apr, 2022 ($4.99, one-shot)

1-Howard-s/Mobili-a ... 5.00

SECTAURS
Marvel Comics: June, 1985 - No. 8, Sept, 1986 (75¢) (Based on Coleco Toys)

1-8, 1-Giveaway; same-c with "Coleco 1985 Toy Fair Collectors' Edition" ... 4.00

SECTION ZERO
Image Comics (Gorilla): June, 2000 - No. 3, Sept, 2000 (2.50)

1-3-Kesel-s/Grummett-a ... 3.00

SECTION ZERO
Image Comics (Gorilla): Apr, 2019 - No. 6, Sept, 2019 ($3.99)

1-6-Kesel-s/Grummett-a; 3 covers on each ... 4.00

SEDUCTION OF THE INNOCENT (Also see New York State Joint Legislative Committee to Study...)
Rinehart & Co., Inc., N. Y.: 1953, 1954 (400 pgs.) (Hardback, $4.00)(Written by Fredric Wertham, M.D.)(Also printed in Canada by Clarke, Irwin & Co. Ltd.)

	GD	VG	FN	VF	VF/NM	NM-
(1st Version)-with bibliographical note intact (pages 399 & 400)(several copies got out before the comic publishers forced the removal of this page)						
	283	566	849	1217	1459	1700
Dust jacket only	45	90	135	284	467	675
(1st Version)-without bibliographical note	129	258	387	555	665	775
Dust jacket only	26	52	78	151	251	350
(2nd Version)-Published in England by Rinehart, 1954, 399 pgs. no bibliographical page; "Second print" listed on inside flap of the dust jacket; publication page has no "R" colophon; unlike 1st version	20	40	60	117	189	260
1972 r-/of 2nd version; 400 pgs. w/bibliography page; Kennikat Press	7	14	21	48	89	130
2004 r/with new intro. by Wertham scholar James E. Reibman, 424 pg.; 6" x 9"; limited to 220 copies	7	14	21	46	86	125

NOTE: *Material from this book appeared in the November, 1953 (Vol.70, pp50-53,214) issue of the* **Ladies' Home Journal** *under the title "What Parents Don't Know About Comic Books". With the release of this book, Dr. Wertham reveals seven years of research attempting to link juvenile delinquency to comic books. Many illustrations showing excessive violence, sex, sadism, and torture are shown. This book was used at the Kefauver Senate hearings which led to the Comics Code Authority. Because of the influence this book had on the comic industry and the collector's interest in it, we feel this listing is justified. Modern printings exist in limited editions. Also see* **Parade of Pleasure.**

SEDUCTION OF THE INNOCENT! (Also see Halloween Horror)
Eclipse Comics: Nov, 1985 - 3-D#2, Apr, 1986 ($1.75)

	GD	VG	FN	VF	VF/NM	NM-
1-6: Double listed under cover title from #7 on	1	2	3	5	6	8
3-D 1 (10/85, $2.25, 36 pgs.)-contains unpublished Advs. Into Darkness #15 (pre-code); Dave Stevens-c	2	4	6	11	16	20
2-D 1 (100 copy limited signed & #ed edition)(B&W)	4	8	12	28	47	65
3-D 2 (4/86)-Baker, Toth, Wrightson-c	1	3	4	6	8	10
2-D 2 (100 copy limited signed & #ed edition)(B&W)	3	6	9	19	30	40

NOTE: *Anderson r-2, 3. Crandall c/a(r)-1. Meskin c/a(r)-3, 3-D 1. Moreira r-2. Toth a-1-6r; c4r. Tuska r-6.*

SEDUCTION OF THE INNOCENT
Dynamite Entertainment: 2015 - No. 4, 2016 ($3.99, limited series)

1-4-Ande Parks-s/Esteve Polls-a/Francesco Francavilla-c ... 4.00

SEEDS, THE
Dark Horse Comics (Berger Books): Aug, 2018 - No. 4 ($3.99, limited series)

1,2-Ann Nocenti-s/David Aja-a ... 4.00

SEEKERS INTO THE MYSTERY
DC Comics (Vertigo): Jan, 1996 - No. 15, Apr, 1997 ($2.50)

1-14: J.M. DeMatteis scripts in all. 1-4-Glenn Barr-a. 5,10-Muth-c/a. 6-9-Zulli-c/a. 11-14-Bolton-c; Jill Thompson-a ... 4.00
15-($2.95)-Muth-c/a ... 4.00

SEEKER 3000 (See Marvel Premiere #41)
Marvel Comics: Jun, 1998 - No. 4, Sept, 1998 ($2.99/$2.50, limited series)

1-($2.99)-Set 25 years after 1st app.; wraparound-c ... 5.00
2-4-($2.50) ... 4.00
...Premiere 1 (6/98, $1.50) Reprints 1st app. from Marvel Premiere #41; wraparound-c ... 5.00

SELECT DETECTIVE (Exciting New Mystery Cases)
D. S. Publishing Co.: Aug-Sept, 1948 - No. 3, Dec-Jan, 1948-49

1-Matt Baker-a	48	96	144	302	514	725
2-Baker, McWilliams-a	39	78	117	240	395	550
3	24	48	72	142	234	325

SELF / MADE
Image Comics: Dec, 2018 - No. 6, May, 2019 ($3.99)

1-6-Mat Groom-s/Eduardo Ferigato-a ... 4.00

SEMPER FI (Tales of the Marine Corp)
Marvel Comics: Dec, 1988- No. 9, Aug, 1989 (75¢)

1-9: Severin-c/a ... 4.00

SENSATIONAL POLICE CASES (Becomes Captain Steve Savage, 2nd Series)
Avon Periodicals: 1952; No. 2, 1954 - No. 4, July-Aug, 1954

nn-(1952, 25¢, 100 pgs.)-Kubert-a?; Check, Larsen, Lawrence & McCann-a; Kinstler-c	71	142	213	454	777	1100
2-4: 2-Kirbyish-a (3-4/54). 4-Reprint/Saint #5	26	52	78	154	252	350
I.W. Reprint #5-(1963?, nd)-Reprints Prison Break #5(1952-Realistic). Infantino-a	4	8	12	23	37	50

SENSATIONAL SHE-HULK, THE (She-Hulk #21-23) (See Savage She-Hulk)
Marvel Comics: V2#1, 5/89 - No. 60, Feb, 1994 ($1.50/$1.75, deluxe format)

V2#1-Byrne-c/a(p)/scripts begin, end #8	3	6	9	19	30	40

Secret Wars (2015 series) #1 © MAR

Sensational She-Hulk #26 © MAR

Sensation Comics #2 © DC

	GD 2.0	VG 4.0	FN 6.0	VF 8.0	VF/NM 9.0	NM- 9.2

2,3: 3-Spider-Man app. — 2 4 6 8 10 12
4-8,14-17,21-23: 4-Reintro G.A. Blonde Phantom. 14-17-Howard the Duck app. 21-23-Return of the Blonde Phantom. 22-All Winners Squad app. — 6.00
9-13,18-20,24-33,35-38,41,42,44-49,55-60: 25-Thor app. 26-Excalibur app.; Guice-c. 29-Wolverine app. (3 pgs.). 30-Hobgoblin-c/a cameo. 31-Byrne-c/a/scripts begin again. 35-Last $1.50-c. 37-Wolverine/Punisher/Spidey-c, but no app. 39-Thing app. 56-War Zone app.; Hulk cameo. 57-Vs. Hulk-c/story. 58-Electro-c/story. 59-Jack O'Lantern app. — 5.00

#	GD 2.0	VG 4.0	FN 6.0	VF 8.0	VF/NM 9.0	NM- 9.2
34-Classic swimsuit/beachball-c by Byrne	5	10	15	31	53	75
39-Swimsuit-c	3	6	9	21	33	45
40-Classic CCA logo/jump rope-c by Byrne	10	20	30	69	147	225
43-Byrne Good Girl/purple bra-c	3	6	9	17	26	35
50-($2.95, 52 pgs.)-Embossed green foil-c; Byrne app.; last Byrne-c/a; Austin, Chaykin, Simonson-a; Miller-a(2 pgs.)	2	4	6	9	12	15
51-Pink elephants, cat fight-c	2	4	6	10	14	18
52-Death-c by Adam Hughes	3	6	9	16	23	30
53-Cover swipe of Amazing Spider-Man #39	2	4	6	11	16	20
54-Headlights-c	3	6	9	14	20	25
60-Last issue	5	10	15	30	50	70

NOTE: *Dale Keown* a(p)-13, 15-22.

SENSATIONAL SHE-HULK
Marvel Comics: Dec, 2023 - Present ($4.99/$3.99)
1,2-($4.99) Rowell-s/Genolet-a; Jack of Hearts and Hulk app. — 5.00
3-5-($3.99) 4,5-Patsy Walker and Carol Danvers app. — 4.00

SENSATIONAL SHE-HULK IN CEREMONY, THE
Marvel Comics: 1989 - No. 2, 1989 ($3.95, squarebound, 52 pgs.)
nn-Part 1, nn-Part 2 — 6.00

SENSATIONAL SPIDER-MAN
Marvel Comics: Apr, 1989 ($5.95, squarebound, 80 pgs.)
1-r/Amazing Spider-Man Annual #14,15 by Miller & Annual #8 by Kirby & Ditko — 6.00

SENSATIONAL SPIDER-MAN, THE
Marvel Comics: Jan, 1996 - No. 33, Nov, 1998 ($1.95/$1.99)

#	GD 2.0	VG 4.0	FN 6.0	VF 8.0	VF/NM 9.0	NM- 9.2
0 ($4.95)-Lenticular-c; Jurgens-a/scripts	2	4	6	9	12	15
1	1	2	3	5	6	8
1-($2.95) variant-c; polybagged w/cassette	4	8	12	25	40	55

2-5: 2-Kaine & Rhino app. 3-Giant-Man app. — 5.00
6-18: 9-Onslaught tie-in; revealed that Peter & Mary Jane's unborn baby is a girl. 11-Revelations. 13-15-Ka-Zar app. 14,15-Hulk app. — 4.00
19-24: Living Pharoah app. 22,23-Dr. Strange app. — 4.00
25-($2.99) Spiderhunt pt. 1; Normie Osborne kidnapped — 5.00

#	GD 2.0	VG 4.0	FN 6.0	VF 8.0	VF/NM 9.0	NM- 9.2
25-Variant-c			1	2	3	5.00

26-33: 26-Nauck-a. 27-Double-c with "The Sensational Hornet #1"; Vulture app. 28-Hornet vs. Vulture. 29,30-Black Cat-c/app. 33-Last issue; Gathering of Five concludes — 4.00
33.1, 33.2 (10/12, $2.99) DeFalco-s/Barberi-a/Bianchi-c — 4.00
#(-1) Flashback(7/97) Dezago-s/Wieringo-a — 4.00
'96 Annual ($2.95) — 5.00

SENSATIONAL SPIDER-MAN, THE (Previously Marvel Knights Spider-Man #1-22)
Marvel Comics: No. 23, Apr, 2006 - No. 41, Dec, 2007 ($2.99)
23-40: 23-25-Aguirre-Sacasa-s/Medina-a. 23-Wraparound-c. 24,34,37-Black Cat app. 26-New costume. 28-Unmasked; Dr. Octopus app.; Crain-a. 35-Black costume resumes — 3.00
41-($3.99) One More Day pt. 3; Straczynski-s/Quesada-a/c — 4.00
... Annual 1 (2007, $3.99) Flashbacks of Peter & MJ's relationship; Larroca-a/Fraction-s — 4.00
... Feral HC (2006, $19.99, dustjacket) r/#23-27; sketch pages — 20.00
Civil War: Peter Parker, Spider-Man TPB (2007, $17.99) r/#28-34; Crain cover concepts — 18.00
...: Self Improvement 1(10/19, $4.99) Unpublished story of Spidey's 1st black costume — 5.00

SENSATIONAL WONDER WOMAN (Printing of a digital first series)
DC Comics: May, 2021 - No. 7, Nov, 2021 ($3.99, limited series)
1-7: 1-Doctor Psycho & Hawkgirl app. 3-Colleen Doran-s/a — 4.00
... Special 1 (5/22, $9.99) Short stories by various — 10.00

SENSATION COMICS (Sensation Mystery #110 on)
National Per. Publ./All-American: Jan, 1942 - No. 109, May-June, 1952

#	GD 2.0	VG 4.0	FN 6.0	VF 8.0	VF/NM 9.0	NM- 9.2
1-Origin Mr. Terrific (1st app.), Wildcat (1st app.), The Gay Ghost, & Little Boy Blue; Wonder Woman (cont'd from All Star #8), The Black Pirate begin; intro. Justice & Fair Play Club	15,000	30,000	45,000	100,000	175,000	250,000

1-Reprint, Oversize 13-1/2x10". WARNING: This comic is an exact duplicate copy of the original except for its size. DC published it in 1974 with a second cover titling it as a Famous First Edition. There have been many reported cases of the outer cover being removed and the interior sold as the original edition. The reprint with the new outer cover removed is practically worthless. See Famous First Edition for value.

#	GD 2.0	VG 4.0	FN 6.0	VF 8.0	VF/NM 9.0	NM- 9.2
2-Etta Candy begins	1000	2000	3000	7400	13,200	19,000
3-W. Woman gets secretary's job	530	1060	1590	3869	6835	9800
4-1st app. Stretch Skinner in Wildcat	343	686	1029	2400	4200	6000
5-Intro. Justin, Black Pirate's son	300	600	900	2010	3635	5200
6-Origin/1st app. Wonder Woman's magic lasso	865	1730	2595	6315	11,158	16,000
7-10	265	530	795	1694	2897	4100
11,12,14-20	187	374	561	1197	2049	2900
13-Hitler, Tojo, Mussolini-c (as bowling pins)	481	962	1443	3511	6206	8900
21-30: 22-Cheetah app. (2nd cover)	142	284	426	909	1555	2200
31-33	119	238	357	762	1306	1850
34-Sargon, the Sorcerer begins (10/44), ends #36; begins again #52	135	270	405	864	1482	2100
35-40: 36-2nd app. Giganta/1st cover; Cheetah app. 38-Christmas-c	119	238	357	762	1306	1850
41-50: 43-The Whip app.	110	220	330	704	1202	1700
51-60: 51-Last Black Pirate. 56,57-Sargon by Kubert	106	212	318	673	1162	1650
61-67,70-80: 63-Last Mr. Terrific. 66-Wildcat by Kubert	97	194	291	621	1061	1500
68-Origin & 1st app. Huntress (8/47)	300	600	900	2040	3570	5100
69-2nd app. Huntress	113	226	339	718	1234	1750
81-Used in SOTI, pg. 33,34; Krigstein-a	110	220	330	704	1202	1700
82-93: 83-Last Sargon. 86-The Atom app. 90-Last Wildcat. 91-Streak begins by Alex Toth. 92-Toth-a (2 pgs.)	93	186	279	591	1021	1450
94-1st all girl issue	155	310	465	992	1696	2400
95-99,101-106: 95-Unmasking of Wonder Woman-c/story. 99-1st app. Astra, Girl of the Future, ends #106. 103-Robot-c. 105-Last 52 pgs. 106-Wonder Woman ends	123	246	369	787	1344	1900
100-(11-12/50)	168	336	504	1075	1838	2600
107-(Scarce, 1-2/52)-1st mystery issue; Johnny Peril by Toth(p), 8 pgs. & begins; continues from Danger Trail #5 (3-4/51)(see Comic Cavalcade #15 for 1st app.)	129	258	387	826	1413	2000
108-(Scarce)-Johnny Peril by Toth(p)	113	232	348	742	1271	1800
109-(Scarce)-Johnny Peril by Toth(p)	123	246	369	787	1344	1900

NOTE: *Krigstein* a-(Wildcat)-81, 83, 84. *Moldoff* Black Pirate-1-25; Black Pirate not in 34-36, 43-48. *Oskner* c(i)-89-91, 94-106. *Wonder Woman* by H. G. Peter, all issues except #8, 17-19, 21; c-4-7, 9-18, 20-88, 92, 93. *Toth* a-91, 98; c-107. *Wonder Woman* c-1-106.

SENSATION COMICS (Also see All Star Comics 1999 crossover titles)
DC Comics: May, 1999 ($1.99, one-shot)
1-Golden Age Wonder Woman and Hawkgirl; Robinson-s — 4.00

SENSATION COMICS FEATURING WONDER WOMAN
DC Comics: Oct, 2014 - No. 17, Feb, 2016 ($3.99, printing of digital-first comics)
1-17-Short story anthology. 1-Simone-s/Van Sciver-a. 2-Gene Ha-c. 5-Darkseid app. 8-Noelle Stevenson-a; Jae Lee-c. 10-Francavilla-c. 12-Poison Ivy app. 13-Superwoman app. 15-Garcia-López-a; Cheetah app.; McNeil-s/a. 16-Scott Hampton-a; Harley Quinn app. — 4.00

SENSATION MYSTERY (Formerly Sensation Comics #1-109)
National Periodical Publ.: No. 110, July-Aug, 1952 - No. 116, July-Aug, 1953

#	GD 2.0	VG 4.0	FN 6.0	VF 8.0	VF/NM 9.0	NM- 9.2
110-Johnny Peril continues	84	168	252	538	919	1300
111-116-Johnny Peril in all. 116-M. Anderson-a	84	168	252	538	919	1300

NOTE: *M. Anderson* c-110. *Colan* a-114p; *Giunta* a-112. *G. Kane* c(p)-108, 109, 111-115.

SENSE & SENSABILITY
Marvel Comics: July, 2010 - No. 5, Nov, 2010 ($3.99, limited series)
1-5-Adaptation of the Jane Austen novel; Nancy Butler-s/Sonny Liew-a/c — 4.00

SENTENCES: THE LIFE OF M.F. GRIMM
DC Comics (Vertigo): 2007 ($19.99, B&W graphic novel)
HC-Autobiography of Percy Carey (M.F. Grimm); Ronald Wimberly-a — 20.00
SC (2008, $14.99) — 15.00

SENTINEL
Marvel Comics: June, 2003 - No. 12, April, 2004 ($2.99/$2.50)
1-Sean McKeever-s/Udon Studios-a — 3.00
2-12 — 3.00
Marvel Age Sentinel Vol. 1: Salvage (2004, $7.99, digest size) r/#1-6 — 8.00
Vol. 2: No Hero (2004, $7.99, digest size) r/#7-12; sketch pages — 8.00

SENTINEL (2nd series)
Marvel Comics: Jan, 2006 - No. 5, May, 2006 ($2.99, limited series)
1-5-Sean McKeever-s/Joe Vriens-a — 3.00
Vol. 3: Past Imperfect (2006, $7.99, digest size) r/#1-5 — 8.00

SENTINELS OF JUSTICE, THE (See Americomics & Captain Paragon &...)

SENTINEL SQUAD O*N*E
Marvel Comics: Mar, 2006 - No. 5, July, 2006 ($2.99, limited series)
1-5-Lopresti-a/Layman-s — 3.00
Decimation: Sentinel Squad O*N*E (2006, $13.99, TPB) r/series; sketch pg. by Caliafore — 14.00

SENTRY (Also see New Avengers and Siege)

	GD	VG	FN	VF	VF/NM	NM-
	2.0	4.0	6.0	8.0	9.0	9.2

Marvel Comics: Sept, 2000 - No. 5, Jan, 2001 ($2.99, limited series)

1-5-Paul Jenkins-s/Jae Lee-a. 3-Spider-Man-c/app. 4-X-Men, FF app.	3.00
.../Fantastic Four (2/01, $2.99) Continues story from #5; Winslade-a	3.00
.../Hulk (2/01, $2.99) Sienkiewicz-c/a	3.00
.../Spider-Man (2/01, $2.99) back story of the Sentry; Leonardi-a	3.00
.../The Void (2/01, $2.99) Conclusion of story; Jae Lee-a	3.00
.../X-Men (2/01, $2.99) Sentry and Archangel; Texeira-a	3.00
TPB (10/01, $24.95) r/#1-5 & all one-shots; Stan Lee interview	25.00
TPB (2nd edition, 2005, $24.99)	25.00

SENTRY (Follows return in New Avengers #10)
Marvel Comics: Nov, 2005 - No. 8, Jun, 2006 ($2.99, limited series)

1-8-Paul Jenkins-s/John Romita Jr.-a. 1-New Avengers app. 3-Hulk app.	3.00
1-(Rough Cut) (12/05, $3.99) Romita sketch art and Jenkins script; cover sketches	4.00
...: Fallen Sun (7/10, $3.99) Siege epilogue; Jenkins-s/Raney-a/Yu-c	4.00
...: Reborn TPB (2006, $21.99) r/#1-8	22.00

SENTRY
Marvel Comics: Aug, 2018 - No. 5, Dec, 2018 ($3.99)

1-5: 1-Lemire-s/Jacinto-a/Hitch-c; Misty Knight app.	4.00

SENTRY
Marvel Comics: Feb, 2024 - Present ($4.99/$3.99)

1-($4.99) Jason Loo-s/Luigi Zagaria-a; Misty Knight app.	5.00
2,3-($3.99) 3-Avengers app.	4.00

SEPTEMBER MOURNING
Image Comics (Top Cow): Feb, 2017 ($4.99)

1-Marc Silvestri-c; Lazar & McCourt-a	5.00

SERENITY (Based on 2005 movie Serenity and 2003 TV series Firefly)
Dark Horse Comics: July, 2005 - No. 3, Sept, 2005 ($2.99, limited series)

1-3: Whedon & Matthews-s/Conrad-a. Three covers for each issue by various	4.00
...: Float Out (6/10, $3.50) Story of Wash; Patton Oswalt-s; covers by Jo Chen & Stockton	3.50
...: One For One (9/10, $1.00) reprints #1, Cassaday-c with red cover frame	3.00
...: Those Left Behind HC (11/07, $19.95, dustjacket) r/series; intro. by Nathan Fillion; pre-production art for the movie; Hughes-c	20.00
...: Those Left Behind TPB (1/06, $9.95) r/series; intro. by Nathan Fillion; Hughes-c	10.00

SERENITY BETTER DAYS (Firefly)
Dark Horse Comics: Mar, 2008 - No. 3, May, 2008 ($2.99, limited series)

1-3: Whedon & Matthews-s/Conrad-a; Adam Hughes-c	3.00

SERENITY: FIREFLY CLASS 03-K64 - LEAVES ON THE WIND (Follows movie)
Dark Horse Comics: Jan, 2014 - No. 6, Jun, 2014 ($3.50, limited series)

1-6: Zack Whedon-s/Georges Jeanty-a; covers by Dos Santos & Jeanty	3.50

SERENITY: FIREFLY CLASS 03-K64 - NO POWER IN THE 'VERSE (Follows movie)
Dark Horse Comics: Oct, 2016 - No. 6, Mar, 2017 ($3.99, limited series)

1-6: Chris Roberson-s/Georges Jeanty-a; covers by Dos Santos & Jeanty	4.00

SERGEANT BARNEY BARKER (Becomes G. I. Tales #4 on)
Atlas Comics (MCI): Aug, 1956 - No. 3, Dec, 1956

1-Severin-c/a(4)	34	68	102	199	325	450
2,3: 2-Severin-c/a(4). 3-Severin-c/a(5)	20	40	60	120	195	270

SERGEANT BILKO (Phil Silvers Starring as...) (TV)
National Periodical Publications: May-June, 1957 - No. 18, Mar-Apr, 1960

1-All have Bob Oskner-c	68	136	204	435	743	1050
2	37	74	111	218	354	490
3-5	30	60	90	177	289	400
6-18: 11,12,15-17-Photo-c	24	48	72	140	230	320

SGT. BILKO'S PVT. DOBERMAN (TV)
National Periodical Publications: June-July, 1958 - No. 11, Feb-Mar, 1960

1-Bob Oskner c-1-4,7,11	28	56	84	202	451	700
2	13	26	39	89	195	300
3-5: 5-Photo-c	19	18	27	60	120	180
6-11: 6,9-Photo-c	7	14	21	44	82	120

SGT. DICK CARTER OF THE U.S. BORDER PATROL (See Holyoke One-Shot)

SGT. FURY (& His Howling Commandos)(See Fury & Special Marvel Edition)
Marvel Comics Group (BPC earlier issues)**:** May, 1963 - No. 167, Dec, 1981

1-1st app. Sgt. Nick Fury (becomes agent of Shield in Strange Tales #135); Kirby/Ayers-c/a; 1st Dum-Dum Dugan & the Howlers	1025	2050	3075	9000	22,000	35,000
2-Kirby-a	71	142	213	568	1284	2000
3-5: 3-Reed Richards x-over. 4-Death of Junior Juniper. 5-1st Baron Strucker app.; Kirby-a	33	66	99	238	532	825
6-10: 8-Baron Zemo, 1st Percival Pinkerton app. 9-Hitler-c & app. 10-1st app. Capt. Savage (the Skipper)(9/64)	18	36	54	124	275	425
11,12,14-20: 14-1st Blitz Squad. 18-Death of Pamela Hawley	10	20	30	66	138	210
13-Captain America & Bucky app.(12/64); 2nd solo Capt. America x-over outside The Avengers; Kirby-a	54	108	162	432	966	1500
13-2nd printing (1994)	3	6	9	17	26	35
21-24,26,28-30	5	10	15	31	42	79	115
25,27: 25-Red Skull app. 27-1st app. Eric Koenig; origin Fury's eye patch	8	16	24	54	102	150
31-33,35-50: 35-Eric Koenig joins Howlers. 43-Bob Hope, Glen Miller app. 44-Flashback on Howlers' 1st mission	4	8	12	28	47	65
34-Origin Howling Commandos	6	12	18	40	73	105
51-60	4	8	12	25	40	55
61-67: 64-Capt. Savage & Raiders x-over; peace symbol-c. 67-Last 12¢ issue; flag-c	3	6	9	21	33	45
68-80: 76-Fury's Father app. in WWI story	3	6	9	17	26	35
81-91: 91-Last 15¢ issue	3	6	9	14	20	26
92-(52 pgs.)	3	6	9	16	24	32
93-99: 98-Deadly Dozen x-over	3	6	9	14	19	24
100-Capt. America, Fantastic 4 cameos; Stan Lee, Martin Goodman & others app.	6	12	18	23	37	50

101-120: 101-Origin retold	2	4	6	10	14	18
121-130: 121-123-r/#19-21	2	4	6	8	11	14
131-167: 167-Reprints (from 1963)	2	4	6	8	10	12
133,134-(30¢-c variants, limited dist.)(5,7/76)	9	18	27	62	126	190
141,142-(35¢-c variants, limited dist.)(7,9/77)	23	46	69	161	356	550
Annual 1(1965, 25¢, 72 pgs.)-r/#4,5 & new-a	14	28	42	96	211	325
Special 2(1966)	7	14	21	46	86	125
Special 3(1967) All new material	5	10	15	30	50	70
Special 4(1968)	3	6	9	21	33	45
Special 5-7(1969-11/71)	3	6	9	17	26	35

NOTE: *Ayers* a-8, Annual 1. *Ditko* a-15i. *Gil Kane* c-37, 96. *Kirby* a-1-7, 13p, 167p(r). Special 5; c-1-8, 10-20, 25, 167p. *Severin* a-44-46, 48, 162, 164; inks-49-79, Special 4, 6; c-4i, 5, 6, 44, 46, 110, 149i, 155i, 162-166. *Sutton* a-57p. Reprints in #80, 82, 85, 87, 89, 91, 93, 95, 99, 101, 103, 105, 107, 109, 111, 121-123, 145-155, 167.

SGT. FURY AND HIS HOWLING COMMANDOS
Marvel Comics: July, 2009 ($3.99, one-shot)

1-John Paul Leon-a/c; WWII tale set in 1942; Baron Strucker app.	4.00

SGT. FURY AND HIS HOWLING DEFENDERS (See The Defenders #147)

SERGEANT PRESTON OF THE YUKON (TV)
Dell Publishing Co.: No. 344, Aug, 1951 - No. 29, Nov-Jan, 1958-59

Four Color 344(#1)-Sergeant Preston & his dog Yukon King begin; painted-c begin, end #18	15	30	45	103	227	350
Four Color 373,397,419('52)	9	18	27	61	123	185
5(11-1/52-53)-10(2-4/54): 6-Bondage-c	6	12	18	38	69	100
11,12,14-17	5	10	15	34	60	85
13-Origin Sgt. Preston	6	12	18	37	66	95
18-Origin Yukon King; last painted-c	6	12	18	37	66	95
19-29: All photo-c	6	12	18	41	76	110

SGT. ROCK (Formerly Our Army at War; see Brave & the Bold #52 & Showcase #45)
National Periodical Publications/DC Comics: No. 302, Mar, 1977 - No. 422, July, 1988

302	5	10	15	31	53	75
303-310	3	6	9	17	25	34
311-320: 318-Reprints	2	4	6	10	16	20
321-350	2	4	6	8	11	14
329-Whitman variant	3	6	9	14	19	24
351-399,401-421: 412-Mlle Marie & Haunted Tank	1	2	3	5	7	9
400-(6/85) Anniversary issue	2	4	6	8	11	14
422-1st Joe, Adam, Andy Kubert-a team; last issue	2	4	6	11	16	20
Annual 2-4: 2(1982)-Formerly Sgt. Rock's Prize Battle Tales #1. 3(1983). 4(1984)	2	4	6	8	11	14

NOTE: *Estrada* a-322, 327, 331, 336, 337, 341, 342i. *Glanzman* a-384, 421. *Kubert* a-302, 303, 305r, 306, 328, 351, 356, 368, 373, 422; c-317, 318r, 319-323, 325-333-on, Annual 2, 3. *Severin* a-347. *Spiegle* a-382, Annual 2, 3. *Thorne* a-384. *Toth* a-385r. *Wildey* c-307, 311, 313, 314.

SGT. ROCK: BETWEEN HELL AND A HARD PLACE
DC Comics (Vertigo): 2003 ($24.95, hardcover one-shot)

HC-Joe Kubert-a/c; Brian Azzarello-s	25.00
SC (2004, $17.95)	18.00

SGT. ROCK'S COMBAT TALES
DC Comics: 2005 ($9.99, digest)

Vol. 1-Reprints early app. in Our Army at War, G.I. Combat, Star Spangled War Stories	10.00

SGT. ROCK SPECIAL (Sgt. Rock #14 on; see DC Special Series #3)
DC Comics: Oct, 1988 - No. 21, Feb, 1992; No. 1, 1992; No. 2, 1994
($2.00, quarterly/monthly, 52 pgs)

1-Reprint begin	2	4	6	8	11	14
2-21: All-r; 5-r/early Sgt. Rock/Our Army at War #81. 7-Tomahawk-r by Thorne. 9-Enemy Ace-r by Kubert. 10-All Rock issue. 11-r/1st Haunted Tank story. 12-All Kubert issue; begins monthly. 13-Dinosaur story by Heath(r). 14-Enemy Ace-r (22 pgs.) by Adams/Kubert. 15-Enemy Ace (22 pgs.) by Kubert. 16-Iron Major-c/story. 16,17-Enemy Ace-r. 19-r/Batman/Sgt. Rock team-up/B&B #108 by Aparo	2	4	6	8	11	14

	1	2	3	4	6	8
1 (1992, $2.95, 68 pg.)-Simonson-c; unpubbed Kubert-a; Glanzman, Russell, Pratt, & Wagner-a						6.00
2 (1994, $2.95) Brereton painted-c						4.00

NOTE: *Neal Adams* r-1, 8, 14p. *Chaykin* r-2; r-3, 9(2pgs.); c-3. *Drucker* r-6. *Glanzman* r-20. *Golden* a-1. *Heath* a-2; r-5, 9-13, 16, 19, 21. *Krigstein* r-8. *Kubert* r-1-17, 20, 21; c-1p, 2, 8, 14-21. *Miller* r-6p. *Severin* r-3, 6, 10. *Simonson* r-2, 14p. *Thorne* r-7. *Toth* r-2, 8, 11. *Wood* r-1.

SGT. ROCK SPECTACULAR (See DC Special Series #13)

SGT. ROCK'S PRIZE BATTLE TALES (Becomes Sgt. Rock Annual #2 on; see DC Special Series #18 & 80 Page Giant #7)
National Periodical Publications: Winter, 1964 (Giant - 80 pgs., one-shot)

1-Kubert, Heath-r; new Kubert-c	36	72	108	266	596	925
... Replica Edition (2000, $5.95) Reprints entire issue						6.00

SGT. ROCK: THE LOST BATTALION
DC Comics: Jan, 2009 - No. 6, Jun, 2009 ($2.99, limited series)

1-6-Billy Tucci-s/a. 1-Tucci & Sparacio-c	3.00
HC (2009, $24.99, d.j.) r/#1-6; production art; cover art gallery	25.00
SC (2010, $17.99) r/#1-6; production art; cover art gallery	18.00

SGT. ROCK: THE PROPHECY
DC Comics: Mar, 2006 - No. 6, Aug, 2006 ($2.99, limited series)

1-6-Joe Kubert-s/a/c. 1-Variant covers by Andy and Adam Kubert	3.00
TPB (2007, $17.99) r/#1-6	18.00

SGT. ROCK VS. THE ARMY OF THE DEAD (See DC Horror Presents:...)

SGT. STRYKER'S DEATH SQUAD (See Savage Combat Tales)

SERGIO ARAGONÉS' ACTIONS SPEAK
Dark Horse Comics: Jan, 2001 - No. 6, Jun, 2001 ($2.99, B&W, limited series)

1-6-Aragonés-c/a; wordless one-page cartoons	3.00

SERGIO ARAGONÉS' BLAIR WHICH?
Dark Horse Comics: Dec, 1999 ($2.95, B&W, one-shot)

nn-Aragonés-c/a; Evanier-s. Parody of "Blair Witch Project" movie	4.00

SERGIO ARAGONÉS' BOOGEYMAN

The Sentry (2018 series) #1 © MAR

Sgt. Rock #315 © DC

Serial #6 © Terry Moore

	GD	VG	FN	VF	VF/NM	NM-
	2.0	4.0	6.0	8.0	9.0	9.2

Dark Horse Comics: June, 1998 - No. 4, Sept, 1998 ($2.95, B&W, lim. series)
1-4-Aragonés-c/a — 4.00

SERGIO ARAGONÉS DESTROYS DC
DC Comics: June, 1996 ($3.50, one-shot)
1-DC Superhero parody book; Aragonés-c/a; Evanier scripts — 4.00

SERGIO ARAGONÉS' DIA DE LOS MUERTOS
Dark Horse Comics: Oct, 1998 ($2.95, one-shot)
1-Aragonés-c/a; Evanier scripts — 4.00

SERGIO ARAGONÉS FUNNIES
Bongo Comics: 2011 - No. 12, 2014 ($3.50)
1-12-Color and B&W humor strips by Aragonés — 3.50

SERGIO ARAGONÉS' GROO & RUFFERTO
Dark Horse Comics: Dec, 1998 - No. 4, Mar, 1999 ($2.95, lim. series)
1-3-Aragonés-c/a — 4.00

SERGIO ARAGONÉS' GROO: DEATH AND TAXES
Dark Horse Comics: Dec, 2001 - No. 4, Apr, 2002 ($2.99, lim. series)
1-4-Aragonés-c/a; Evanier-s — 3.00

SERGIO ARAGONÉS' GROO: HELL ON EARTH
Dark Horse Comics: Nov, 2007 - No. 4, Apr, 2008 ($2.99, lim. series)
1-4-Aragonés-c/a; Evanier-s — 3.00

SERGIO ARAGONÉS' GROO: MIGHTIER THAN THE SWORD
Dark Horse Comics: Jan, 2000 - No. 4, Apr, 2000 ($2.95, lim. series)
1-4-Aragonés-c/a; Evanier-s — 3.00

SERGIO ARAGONÉS' GROO: THE HOGS OF HORDER
Dark Horse Comics: Oct, 2009 - No. 4, Mar, 2010 ($3.99, lim. series)
1-4-Aragonés-c/a; Evanier-s — 4.00

SERGIO ARAGONÉS' GROO THE WANDERER (See Groo...)

SERGIO ARAGONÉS' GROO: 25TH ANNIVERSARY SPECIAL
Dark Horse Comics: Aug, 2007 ($5.99, one-shot)
nn-Aragonés-c/a; Evanier scripts; wraparound cover — 6.00

SERGIO ARAGONÉS' LOUDER THAN WORDS
Dark Horse Comics: July, 1997 - No. 6, Dec, 1997 ($2.95, B&W, limited series)
1-6-Aragonés-c/a — 4.00

SERGIO ARAGONÉS MASSACRES MARVEL
Marvel Comics: June, 1996 ($3.50, one-shot)
1-Marvel Superhero parody book; Aragonés-c/a; Evanier scripts — 4.00

SERGIO ARAGONÉS STOMPS STAR WARS
Marvel Comics: Jan, 2000 ($2.95, one-shot)
1-Star Wars parody; Aragonés-c/a; Evanier scripts — 4.00

SERIAL (See Rachel Rising and Five Years)
Abstract Studios: 2021 - No. 10, 2021 ($3.99)
1-10-Zoe from Rachel Rising app.; Terry Moore-s/a/c — 4.00

SESAME STREET
Ape Entertainment: 2013 ($3.99)
1-Short stories by various; multiple covers — 4.00
Free Comic Book Day edition (2013) Flip book with Strawberry Shortcake — 3.00

SEVEN
Intrinsic Comics: July, 2007 ($3.00)
1-Jim Shooter-s/Paul Creddick-a — 3.00

SEVEN BLOCK
Marvel Comics (Epic Comics): 1990 ($4.50, one-shot, 52 pgs.)
1-Dixon-s/Zaffino-a — 6.00
nn-(IDW Publ., 2004, $5.99) reprints #1 — 6.00

SEVEN BROTHERS (John Woo's...)
Virgin Comics: Oct, 2006 - No. 5, Feb, 2007 ($2.99)
1-5-Garth Ennis-s/Jeevan Kang-a. 1-Two covers by Amano & Horn. 2-Kang var-c — 3.00
TPB (6/07, $14.99) r/#1-5; cover gallery, deleted scenes and concept art — 15.00
Volume 2 (9/07 - No. 5, 2/08) 1-Edison George-a. 4,5-David Mack-c — 3.00

SEVEN DEAD MEN (See Complete Mystery #1)

SEVEN DWARFS (Also see Snow White)
Dell Publishing Co.: No. 227, 1949 (Disney-Movie)
Four Color 227 — 16 | 32 | 48 | 110 | 243 | 375

SEVEN MILES A SECOND
DC Comics (Vertigo Verité): 1996 ($7.95, one-shot)
nn-Wojnarowicz-s/Romberg-a — 8.00

SEVEN-PER-CENT SOLUTION
IDW Publishing: Aug, 2015 - No. 5 ($3.99)
1-4-Sherlock Holmes/Sigmund Freud team-up; David & Scott Tipton-s/Joseph-a/Jones-c — 4.00

SEVEN SAMUROID, THE (See Image Graphic Novel)

SEVEN SEAS COMICS
Universal Phoenix Features/Leader No. 6: Apr, 1946 - No. 6, 1947(no month)
1-South Sea Girl by Matt Baker, Capt. Cutlass begin; Tugboat Tessie by Baker app.

	GD 2.0	VG 4.0	FN 6.0	VF 8.0	VF/NM 9.0	NM- 9.2
1	113	226	339	718	1234	1750
2-Swashbuckler-c	77	154	231	493	847	1200
3-Six pg. Feldstein-a	411	822	1233	2877	5039	7200
4-Classic Baker-c	1000	2000	3000	7600	13,800	20,000
5-Baker Headlights Good Girl-c	300	600	900	1930	3375	4800
6-Baker Good Girl-c	757	1514	2271	5526	9763	14,000

NOTE: *Baker a-1-6; c-3-6.*

SEVEN SECRETS
BOOM! Studios: Aug, 2020 - No. 18, Jun, 2022 ($3.99)
1-18-Tom Taylor-s/Danielle Di Nicuolo-a — 4.00

SEVEN SOLDIERS OF VICTORY (Book-ends for seven related mini-series)
DC Comics: No. 0, Apr, 2005; No. 1; Dec, 2006 ($2.95/$3.99)
0-Grant Morrison-s/J.H. Williams-a — 3.00
1-($3.99) Series conclusion; Grant Morrison-s/J.H. Williams-a — 4.00
... Volume One (2006, $14.99) r/#0, Shining Knight #1,2; Zatanna #1,2; Guardian #1,2; and Klarion the Witch Boy #1; intro. by Morrison; character design sketches — 15.00
... Volume Two (2006, $14.99) r/Shining Knight #3,4; Zatanna #3; Guardian #3,4; and Klarion the Witch Boy #2,3 — 15.00
... Volume Three ('06, $14.99) r/Zatanna #4; Mister Miracle #1,2; Bulleteer #1,2; Frankenstein #1 and Klarion the Witch Boy #4; — 15.00
... Volume Four ('07, $14.99) r/Mister Miracle #3,4; Bulleteer #3,4; Frankenstein #2-4 and Seven Soldiers of Victory #1; script pages — 15.00

SEVEN SOLDIERS: BULLETEER
DC Comics: Jan, 2006 - No. 4, May, 2006 ($2.99, limited series)
1-4-Grant Morrison-s/Yanick Paquette-a/c — 3.00

SEVEN SOLDIERS: FRANKENSTEIN
DC Comics: Jan, 2006 - No. 4, May, 2006 ($2.99, limited series)
1-4-Grant Morrison-s/Doug Mahnke-a/c — 3.00

SEVEN SOLDIERS: GUARDIAN
DC Comics: May, 2005 - No. 4, Nov, 2005 ($2.99, limited series)
1-4-Grant Morrison-s/Cameron Stewart-a; Newsboy Army app. — 3.00

SEVEN SOLDIERS: KLARION THE WITCH BOY
DC Comics: Jun, 2005 - No. 4, Dec, 2005 ($2.99, limited series)
1-4-Grant Morrison-s/Frazer Irving-a — 3.00

SEVEN SOLDIERS: MISTER MIRACLE
DC Comics: Nov, 2005 - No. 4, May, 2006 ($2.99, limited series)
1-4: 1-Grant Morrison-s/Pasqual Ferry-a/c. 3,4-Freddie Williams II-a/c — 3.00

SEVEN SOLDIERS: SHINING KNIGHT
DC Comics: May, 2005 - No. 4, Oct, 2005 ($2.99, limited series)
1-4-Grant Morrison-s/Simone Bianchi-a — 3.00

SEVEN SOLDIERS: ZATANNA
DC Comics: Jun, 2005 - No. 4, Dec, 2005 ($2.99, limited series)
1-4-Grant Morrison-s/Ryan Sook-a — 3.00

SEVEN SONS
Image Comics: Jun, 2022 - No. 7, Dec, 2022 ($3.99, limited series)
1-7-Robert Windom & Kelvin Mao-s/Jae Lee-a/c — 4.00

SEVEN SWORDS
AfterShock Comics: Jun, 2021 - No. 5, Jan, 2022 ($4.99/$3.99, limited series)
1-($4.99) Evan Daugherty-s/Riccardo Latina-a; D'Artagnan & Cardinal Richelieu app. — 5.00
2-5-($3.99) — 4.00

1776 (See Charlton Classic Library)

7TH SWORD, THE
IDW Publishing (Darby Pop): Apr, 2014 - No. 6 ($3.99)
1-6: 1-John Raffo-s/Nelson Blake II-a. 3-6-Nur Iman-a — 4.00

7TH VOYAGE OF SINBAD, THE (Movie)

	GD 2.0	VG 4.0	FN 6.0	VF 8.0	VF/NM 9.0	NM- 9.2

Dell Publishing Co.: Sept, 1958 (photo-c)
Four Color 944-Buscema-a — 12 24 36 84 185 285

SEVEN TO ETERNITY
Image Comics: Sept, 2016 - No. 17, Aug, 2021 ($3.99)
1-Rick Remender-s/Jerome Opeña-a — 3 6 9 14 20 25
2 — 1 3 4 6 8 10
3-17: 7,8-James Harren-a — 4.00

77 SUNSET STRIP (TV)
Dell Publ. Co./Gold Key: No. 1066, Jan-Mar, 1960 - No. 2, Feb, 1963 (All photo-c)
Four Color 1066-Toth-a — 9 18 27 63 129 195
Four Color 1106,1159-Toth-a — 7 14 21 49 92 135
Four Color 1211,1263,1291, 01-742-209(7-9/62)-Manning-a in all — 7 14 21 46 86 125
1,2: Manning-a. 1(11/62-G.K.) — 7 14 21 46 86 125

77TH BENGAL LANCERS, THE (TV)
Dell Publishing Co.: May, 1957
Four Color 791-Photo-c — 7 14 21 44 82 120

SEVERED
Image Comics: Aug, 2011 - No. 7, Feb, 2012 ($2.99)
1-7-Scott Snyder & Scott Tuft-s/Attila Futaki-a/c — 3.00

SEX
Image Comics: Mar, 2013 - No. 34, Dec, 2016 ($2.99/$3.99)
1-26-Joe Casey-s/Piotr Kowalski-a/c — 3.00
27-34-($3.99) — 4.00

SEX CRIMINALS
Image Comics: Sept, 2013 - No. 30, Aug, 2020; No. 69, Oct, 2020 ($3.50/$3.99)
1-Matt Fraction-s/Chip Zdarsky-a/c — 3 6 9 16 24 32
1-Variant-c by Shimizu — 3 6 9 14 20 25
2 — 1 3 4 6 8 10
3-10 — 5.00
11-24,26-30 — 4.00
11-24,26-30,69-($4.69) Variant cover in pink polybag — 5.00
25-($4.99) — 5.00
25-($5.69) Variant cover by Skottie Young, in pink polybag — 6.00
69-($3.99) Final issue; numbering skips from 30 to 69 — 4.00
...: Sexual Gary Special (9/20, $4.99) Matt Fraction-s/Rachael Stott-a — 5.00

SEYMOUR, MY SON (See More Seymour)
Archie Publications (Radio Comics): Sept, 1963
1-DeCarlo-c/a — 5 10 15 35 63 90

SFSX
Image Comics: Sept, 2019 - Present ($3.99)
1-7-Tina Horn-s. 1,2,4-Michael Dowling-a. 6,7-Jen Hickman-a — 4.00

SHADE, THE (See Starman)
DC Comics: Apr, 1997 - No. 4, July, 1997 ($2.25, limited series)
1-4-Robinson-s/Harris-c: 1-Gene Ha-a. 2-Williams/Gray-a 3-Blevins-a. 4-Zulli-a — 4.00

SHADE, THE (From Starman)
DC Comics: Dec, 2011 - No. 12, Nov, 2012 ($2.99, limited series)
1-12: 1-Robinson-s/Hamner-a/Harris-c; Deathstroke app. 4-Cooke-a. 8-Thompson-a — 3.00
12-Origin of the Shade; Gene Ha-a — 4.00
1-12-Variant covers. 1-3-Hamner. 4-Darwyn Cooke. 5-7-Pulido. 11-Irving — 4.00

SHADECRAFT
Image Comics: Mar, 2021 - Present ($3.99)
1-5-Joe Henderson-s/Lee Garbett-a — 4.00

SHADE, THE CHANGING GIRL (Continues as Shade, The Changing Woman)
DC Comics (Young Animal): Dec, 2016 - No. 12, Nov, 2017 ($3.99)
1-12: 1-Castellucci-s/Zarcone-a; intro. Megan Boyer/Loma Shade. 4-Element Girl back-up. 7-Sauvage-a — 4.00
.../ Wonder Woman Special 1 (4/18, $4.99) Part 3 of Milk Wars crossover; Quitely-c — 5.00

SHADE, THE CHANGING MAN (See Cancelled Comic Cavalcade)
National Per. Publ./DC Comics: June-July, 1977 - No. 8, Aug-Sept, 1978
1-1st app. Shade; Ditko-c/a in all — 3 6 9 17 25 34
2-8 — 2 3 4 6 8 10

SHADE, THE CHANGING MAN (2nd series) (Also see Suicide Squad #16)
DC Comics (Vertigo imprint #33 on): July, 1990 - No. 70, Apr, 1996 ($1.50-$2.25, mature)
1-($2.50, 52 pgs.)-Peter Milligan scripts in all — 5.00
2-41,45-49,51-59: 6-Preview of World Without End. 17-Begin $1.75-c. 33-Metallic ink on-c — 4.00
41-Begin $1.95-c — 4.00
42-44-John Constantine app. — 4.00
50-($2.95, 52 pgs.) — 5.00
60-70: 60-begin $2.25-c — 4.00
...: Edge of Vision TPB (2009, $19.99) r/#7-13 — 20.00
...: Scream Time TPB (2010, $19.99) r/#14-19 — 20.00
...: The American Scream TPB (2003, 2009, $17.95/$17.99) r/#1-6 — 18.00
NOTE: Bachalo a-1-9, 11-13, 15-21, 23-26, 33-39, 42-45, 47, 49, 50; c-30, 33-41.

SHADE, THE CHANGING WOMAN (Continues from Shade, The Changing Girl)
DC Comics (Young Animal): May, 2018 - No. 6, Oct, 2018 ($3.99)
1-6-Castellucci-s/Zarcone-a — 4.00

SHADO: SONG OF THE DRAGON (See Green Arrow #63-66)
DC Comics: 1992 - No. 4, 1992 ($4.95, limited series, 52 pgs.)
Book One - Four: Grell scripts; Morrow-a(i) — 6.00

SHADOW, THE (See Batman #253, 259 & Marvel Graphic Novel #35)

SHADOW, THE (Pulp, radio)
Archie Comics (Radio Comics): Aug, 1964 - No. 8, Sept, 1965 (All 12c)
1-Jerry Siegel scripts in all; Shadow-c. — 9 18 27 63 129 195

2-8: 2-App. in super-hero costume on-c only; Reinman-a(backup). 3-Superhero begins; Reinman-a (book-length novel). 3,4,6,7-The Fly 1 pg. strips. 4-8-Reinman-a. 5-8-Siegel scripts. 7-Shield app. — 5 10 15 34 60 85

SHADOW, THE
National Periodical Publications: Oct-Nov, 1973 - No. 12, Sept-Oct, 1975
1-Kaluta-a begins — 6 12 18 38 69 100
2 — 3 6 9 21 33 45
3-Kaluta/Wrightson-a — 4 8 12 23 37 50
4,6-Kaluta-a ends. 4-Chaykin, Wrightson part-i — 3 6 9 18 28 38
5,7-12: 11-The Avenger (pulp character) x-over — 2 4 6 13 18 22
NOTE: Craig a-10. Cruz a-10-12. Kaluta a-1, 2, 3p, 4, 6; c-1-4, 6, 10-12. Kubert c-9. Robbins a-5, 7-9; c-5, 7, 8.

SHADOW, THE
DC Comics: May, 1986 - No. 4, Aug, 1986 (limited series)
1-4: Howard Chaykin art in all — 4.00
Blood & Judgement ($12.95)-r/1-4 — 13.00

SHADOW, THE
DC Comics: Aug, 1987 - No. 19, Jan, 1989 ($1.50)
1-19: Andrew Helfer scripts in all. — 4.00
Annual 1,2 (12/87, '88,)-2-The Shadow dies; origin retold (story inspired by the movie "Citizen Kane"). — 5.00
NOTE: Kyle Baker a-7i, 8-19, Annual 2. Chaykin c-Annual 1. Helfer scripts in all. Orlando a-Annual 1. Rogers c/a-7. Sienkiewicz c/a-1-6.

SHADOW, THE (Movie)
Dark Horse Comics: June, 1994 - No. 2, July, 1994 ($2.50, limited series)
1,2-Adaptation from Universal Pictures film — 4.00
NOTE: Kaluta c/a-1, 2.

SHADOW, THE
Dynamite Entertainment: 2012 - No. 25, 2014 ($3.99)
1-25: 1-Ennis-s/Campbell-a; multiple covers on all. 7-10-Gischler-s — 4.00
#0-(2014, $3.99) Cullen Bunn-s/Colton Worley-a/Gabriel Hardman-c — 4.00
#100-(2014, $7.99, squarebound) Short stories by various incl. Francavilla, Chaykin, Wagner, Uslan; 2 covers by Wagner & Hack — 8.00
Annual 1 (2012, $4.99) Sniegoski-s/Calero-a/Alex Ross-c — 5.00
Annual 2013 ($4.99) Parks-s/Evely-a/Worley-c — 5.00
One Shot 2014: Agents of the Shadow ($7.99, squarebound) Robert Hack-c — 8.00
... Over Innsmouth (2014, $4.99) Ron Marz-s/Ivan Rodriguez-a — 5.00
Special 1 (2012, $4.99) Beatty-s/Cliquet-a/Alex Ross-c — 5.00
Special 2014: Death Factory ($7.99, squarebound) Phil Hester-s/c; Ivan Rodriguez-a — 8.00

SHADOW, THE (Volume 2)
Dynamite Entertainment: 2014 - No. 5, 2015 ($1.00/$3.99, limited series)
1-($1.00) Bunn-s/Timpano-a/Guice-c — 3.00
2-5-($3.99) Bunn-s/Timpano-a/Guice-c — 4.00

SHADOW, THE (Volume 3)
Dynamite Entertainment: 2017 - No. 6, 2018 ($3.99, limited series)
1-6: 1-Spurrier & Watters-s/Daniel HDR-a; multiple covers on all. 4-Jaime-a — 4.00

SHADOW AND DOC SAVAGE, THE
Dark Horse Comics: July, 1995 - No. 2, Aug, 1995 ($2.95, limited series)
1,2 — 4.00

SHADOW AND THE MYSTERIOUS 3, THE
Dark Horse Comics: Sept, 1994 ($2.95, one-shot)
1-Kaluta co-scripts. — 4.00
NOTE: Stevens c-1.

SHADOW, THE / BATMAN
Dynamite Entertainment: 2017 - No. 6, 2018 ($3.99, limited series)
1-6-Orlando-s/Timpano-a; multiple covers on each; Ra's al Ghul & Shiwan Khan app. — 4.00

SHADOW CABINET (See Heroes)
DC Comics (Milestone): No. 0, Jan, 1994 - No. 17, Oct, 1995 ($1.75/$2.50)
0-(1/94, $2.50, 52 pgs.)-Silver ink-c; Simonson-c — 1 2 3 5 6 8
1-(6/94) Byrne-c — 5.00
2-17 — 4.00

SHADOW COMICS (Pulp, radio)
Street & Smith Publications: Mar, 1940 - V9#5, Aug-Sept, 1949
NOTE: The Shadow first appeared on radio in 1929 and was featured in pulps beginning in April, 1931, written by Walter Gibson. The early covers of this series were reprinted from the pulp covers.
V1#1-Shadow, Doc Savage, Bill Barnes, Nick Carter (radio), Frank Merriwell, Iron Munro, the Astonishing Man begin — 1000 2000 3000 7600 13,800 20,000
2-The Avenger begins, ends #6; Capt. Fury only app. — 277 554 831 1579 3030 4300
3(nn-5/40)-Norgil the Magician app.; cover is exact swipe of Shadow pulp from 1/33 — 200 400 600 1280 2190 3100
4-The Three Musketeers begins, ends #8; classic painted decapitation-c — 400 800 1200 2800 4900 7000
5-Doc Savage ends — 155 310 465 992 1696 2400
6,8,9: 9-Norgil the Magician app. — 123 246 369 787 1344 1900
7-Origin/1st app. The Hooded Wasp & Wasplet (11/40); series ends V3#8; Hooded Wasp/Wasplet app. on-c thru #9 — 129 258 387 826 1413 2000
10-Origin The Iron Ghost, ends #11; The Dead End Kids begins, ends #14 — 110 220 330 704 1202 1700
11-Origin Hooded Wasp & Wasplet retold — 113 226 339 718 1234 1750
12-Dead End Kids app. — 106 212 318 673 1162 1650
V2#1(11/41, Vol. II#2 in indicia) Dead End Kids -s — 103 206 309 659 1130 1600
2-(Rare, 1/42, Vol. II#3 in indicia) Giant ant-c — 200 400 600 1280 2190 3100
3-Origin & 1st app. Supersnipe (3/42); series begins; Little Nemo story (Vol.II#4 in indicia) — 168 336 504 1075 1838 2600
4,5: 4,8-Little Nemo story — 97 194 291 621 1061 1500
6-9-Blackstone the Magician story — 90 180 270 576 988 1400
10,12: 10-Supersnipe app. Skull-c — 90 180 270 576 988 1400
11-Classic Devil Kyoti World War 2 sunburst-c — 116 232 348 742 1271 1800
V3#1,2,5,7-12: 10-Doc Savage begins, not in V5#5, V6#10-12, V8#4 — 87 174 261 553 952 1350

Shadecraft #3 © Henderson & Garbett

The Shadow #2 © AMP

Shadowland: Elektra #1 © MAR

	GD 2.0	VG 4.0	FN 6.0	VF 8.0	VF/NM 9.0	NM- 9.2
3-1st Monstrodamus-c/sty	123	246	369	787	1344	1900
4-2nd Monstrodamus; classic-c of giant salamander getting shot in the head						
	123	246	369	787	1344	1900
6-Classic underwater-c	135	270	405	864	1482	2100
V4#1,3-12	58	116	174	371	636	900
2-Classic severed head-c	187	374	561	1197	2049	2900
V5#1-12: 1-(4/45). 12-(3/46)	54	108	162	343	574	825
V6#1-11: 9-Intro. Shadow, Jr. (12/46)	52	104	156	328	552	775
12-Powell-c/a; atom bomb panels	55	110	165	352	601	850
V7#1,2,5,7-9,12: 2,5-Shadow, Jr. app.; Powell-a	48	96	144	302	514	725
3,6,11-Powell-c/a	54	108	162	343	574	825
4-Powell-c/a; Atom bomb panels	55	110	165	352	601	850
10(1/48)-Flying Saucer-c/story (2nd of this theme; see The Spirit 9/28/47); Powell-c/a						
	93	186	279	591	1021	1450
V8#1,2,4-12-Powell-a.	54	108	162	343	574	825
3-Powell Spider-c/a	58	116	174	371	636	900
V9#1,5-Powell-a.	54	108	162	343	574	825
2-4-Powell-c/a	53	106	159	334	567	800

NOTE: *Binder c-V3#1. Powell art in most issues beginning V6#12. Painted c-1-6.*

SHADOW DOCTOR
AfterShock Comics: Feb, 2021 - No. 5, Jul, 2021 ($3.99, limited series)

1-5-Peter Calloway-s/Georges Jeanty-a; covers by Chiarello & Jeanty						4.00

SHADOWDRAGON
DC Comics: 1995 ($3.50, annual)

Annual 1-Year One story						4.00

SHADOW EMPIRES: FAITH CONQUERS
Dark Horse Comics: Aug, 1994 - No. 4, Nov, 1994 ($2.95, limited series)

1-4						4.00

SHADOW/GREEN HORNET: DARK NIGHTS (Pulp characters)
Dynamite Entertainment: 2013 - No. 5, 2013 ($3.99)

1-5-Lamont Cranston & Britt Reid team-up in 1939; Uslan-s; multiple covers on each						4.00

SHADOWHAWK (See Images of Shadowhawk, New Shadowhawk, Shadowhawk II, Shadowhawk III & Youngblood #2)
Image Comics (Shadowline Ink): Aug, 1992 - No. 4, Mar, 1993; No. 12, Aug, 1994 - No. 18, May, 1995 ($1.95/$2.50)

1-($2.50)-Embossed silver foil stamped-c; Valentino/Liefeld-c; Valentino-c/a/ scripts in all; has coupon for Image #0; 1st Shadowline Ink title						5.00
1-With coupon missing						2.00
1-($1.95)-Newsstand version w/o foil stamp						4.00
2-13,0,1418: 2-Shadowhawk poster w/McFarlane-i; brief Spawn app.; wraparound-c w/silver ink highlights. 3-($2.50)-Glow-in-the-dark-c. 4-Savage Dragon-c/story; Valentino/Larsen-c. 5-11-(See Shadowhawk II and III). 12-Cont'd from Shadowhawk III; pull-out poster by Texeira.13-w/ShadowBone poster; WildC.A.T.s app. 0 (10/94)-Liefeld c/a/story: ShadowBart poster. 14-(10/94, $2.50)-The Others app. 16-Supreme app. 17-Spawn app.; story cont'd from Badrock & Co. #6. 18-Shadowhawk dies; Savage Dragon & Brigade app.						4.00
Special 1(12/94, $3.50, 52 pgs.)-Silver Age Shadowhawk flip book						5.00
Gallery (4/94, $1.95)						4.00
Out of the Shadows ($19.95)-r/Youngblood #2, Shadowhawk #1-4, Image Zero #0, Operation: Urban Storm (Never published)						20.00
.../Vampirella (2/95, $4.95)-Pt.2 of x-over (See Vampirella/Shadowhawk for Pt. 1)						5.00

NOTE: *Shadowhawk was originally a four issue limited series. The story continued in Shadowhawk II, Shadowhawk III & then became Shadowhawk again with issue #12.*

SHADOWHAWK II (Follows Shadowhawk #4)
Image Comics (Shadowline Ink): V2#1, May, 1993 - V2#3, Aug, 1993 ($3.50/$1.95/$2.95, limited series)

V2#1 ($3.50)-Cont'd from Shadowhawk #4; die-cut mirricard-c						4.00
2 ($1.95)-Foil embossed logo; reveals identity; gold-c variant exists						4.00
3 ($2.95)-Pop-up-c w/Pact ashcan insert						4.00

SHADOWHAWK III (Follows Shadowhawk II #3)
Image Comics (Shadowline Ink): V3#1, Nov, 1993 - V3#4, Mar, 1994 ($1.95, limited series);

V3#1-4: 1-Cont'd from Shadowhawk II; intro Valentine; gold foil & red foil stamped-c variations. 2-(52 pgs.)-Shadowhawk contracts HIV virus; U.S. Male by M. Anderson (p) in free 16 pg.insert. 4-Continues in Shadowhawk #12						4.00

SHADOWHAWK (Volume 2) (Also see New Man #4)
Image Comics: May, 2005 - No. 15, Sept, 2006 ($2.99/$3.50)

1-4-Eddie Collins as Shadowhawk; Rodriguez-a; Valentino-co-plotter						3.50
5-15-($3.50) 5-Cover swipe of Superman Vs. Spider-Man treasury edition						3.50
...One Shot #1 (7/06, $1.99) r/Return of Shadowhawk						3.00
Return of Shadowhawk (12/04, $2.99) Valentino-s/a/c; Eddie Collins origin retold						3.00

SHADOWHAWK (Volume 3)

Image Comics: May, 2010 - No. 5, Dec, 2010 ($3.50)						
1-5-Rodríguez-a. 1-Back-up with Valentino-a/Niles-s						3.50

SHADOWHAWKS OF LEGEND
Image Comics (Shadowline Ink): Nov, 1995 ($4.95, one-shot)

nn-Stories of past Shadowhawks by Kurt Busiek, Beau Smith & Alan Moore						5.00

SHADOW, THE: HELL'S HEAT WAVE (Movie, pulp, radio)
Dark Horse Comics: Apr, 1995 - No. 3, June, 1995 ($2.95, limited series)

1-3: Kaluta story						4.00

SHADOW HUNTER (Jenna Jameson's...)
Virgin Comics: No. 0, Dec, 2007 - No. 3 ($2.99)

0-Preview issue; creator interviews; gallery of covers for upcoming issues; Greg Horn-c						3.00
1-3: 1-Two covers by Horn & Land; Jameson & Christina Z-s/Singh-a. 2-Three covers						3.00

SHADOWHUNT SPECIAL
Image Comics (Extreme Studios): Apr, 1996 ($2.50)

1-Retells origin of past Shadowhawks; Valentino script; Chapel app.						4.00

SHADOW, THE: IN THE COILS OF THE LEVIATHAN (Movie, pulp, radio)
Dark Horse Comics: Oct, 1993 - No. 4, Apr, 1994 ($2.95, limited series)

1-4-Kaluta-c & co-scripter						4.00
Trade paperback (10/94, $13.95)-r/1-4						14.00

SHADOWLAND (Also see Daredevil #508-512 & Black Panther: The Man Without Fear #513)
Marvel Comics: Sept, 2010 - No. 5, Jan, 2011 ($3.99, limited series)

1-5: 1-Diggle-s/Tan-a; Bullseye killed; Cassaday-c. 2-Ghost Rider app.						4.00
1-Variant-c by Tan						6.00
... After the Fall 1 (2/11, $3.99) Finch-c; Black Panther app.						4.00
...: Bullseye 1 (10/10, $3.99) Chen-a; Bullseye's funeral						4.00
...: Elektra 1 (11/10, $3.99) Wells-s/Rios-a/Takeda-c						4.00
...: Ghost Rider 1 (11/10, $3.99) Williams-s/Crain-a/c						4.00
...: Spider-Man 1 (11/10, $3.99) Shang-Chi & Mr. Negative app.; Siqueira-a						4.00

SHADOWLAND: BLOOD IN THE STREETS (Leads into Heroes For Hire)
Marvel Comics: Oct, 2010 - No. 4, Jan, 2011 ($3.99, limited series)

1-4-Johnston-s/Alves-a; Misty Knight, Silver Sable, Paladin, Shroud app.						4.00

SHADOWLAND: DAUGHTERS OF THE SHADOW
Marvel Comics: Oct, 2010 - No. 3, Dec, 2010 ($3.99, limited series)

1-3-Henderson-s/Rodriguez-a; Colleen Wing app. 3-Preview of Black Panther #513						4.00

SHADOWLAND: MOON KNIGHT
Marvel Comics: Oct, 2010 - No. 3, Dec, 2010 ($3.99, limited series)

1-3-Hurwitz-s/Dazo-a						4.00

SHADOWLAND: POWER MAN
Marvel Comics: Oct, 2010 - No. 4, Jan, 2011 ($3.99, limited series)

1-4-Van Lente-s/Asrar-a. 1-New Power Man debut; Iron Fist app.						4.00

SHADOWLINE SAGA: CRITICAL MASS, A
Marvel Comics (Epic): Jan, 1990 - No. 7, July, 1990 ($4.95, lim. series, 68 pgs)

1-6: Dr. Zero, Powerline, St. George						5.00
7 ($5.95, 84 pgs.)-Morrow-a, Williamson-c(i)						6.00

SHADOWMAN (See X-O Manowar #4)
Valiant/Acclaim Comics (Valiant): May, 1992 - No. 43, Dec, 1995 ($2.50)

1-Partial origin	3	6	9	16	23	30
2-5: 3-1st app. Sousa the Soul Eater						5.00
6,7,9-42: 15-Minor Turok app. 16-1st app. Dr. Mirage (8/93). 17,18-Archer & Armstrong x-over. 19-Aerosmith-c/story. 23-Dr. Mirage x-over. 24-(4/94). 25-Bound-in trading card. 29-Chaos Effect.						4.00
8-1st app. Master Darque	2	4	6	8	11	14
43-Shadowman jumps to his death	1	3	4	6	8	10
0-($2.50, 4/94)-Regular edition						6.00
0-($3.50)-Wraparound chromium-c edition	1	2	3	5	6	8
0-Gold						20.00
Yearbook 1 (12/94, $3.95)						5.00

SHADOWMAN (Volume 2)
Acclaim Comics (Valiant Heroes): Mar, 1997 - No. 20, Jun, 1998 ($2.50, mature)

1-1st app. Zero; Garth Ennis scripts begin, end #4	1	2	3	5	6	8
2-20: 2-Zero becomes new Shadowman. 4-Origin; Jack Boniface (original Shadowman) rises from the grave. 5-Jamie Delano scripts begin. 9-Copycat-c						3.00
1-Variant painted cover	1	2	3	5	6	8

SHADOWMAN (Volume 3)
Acclaim Comics: July, 1999 - No. 5, Nov, 1999 ($3.95/$2.50)

	GD 2.0	VG 4.0	FN 6.0	VF 8.0	VF/NM 9.0	NM- 9.2

1-($3.95)-Abnett & Lanning-s/Broome & Benjamin-a 2 4 6 8 10 12
2-5-($2.50): 3,4-Flip book with Unity 2000 — — — — — 3.00

SHADOWMAN
Valiant Entertainment: Nov, 2012 - No. 16, Mar, 2014 ($3.99)

1-Jordan-s/Zircher-a; two covers by Zircher (regular & pullbox) — 5.00
1-Variant-c by Dave Johnson — 8.00
1-Variant-c by Bill Sienkiewicz — 20.00
2-16: 2-6-Jordan-s/Zircher-a — 4.00
2-4-Pullbox variants — 6.00
5-16-Pullbox variants — 4.00
11-Variant-c with detachable Halloween mask — 4.00
13X-(10/13, bagged with Bleeding Cool Magazine #7) prelude to #13; Milligan-s — 3.00
#0-(5/13, $3.99) Origin of Master Darque — 4.00

SHADOWMAN
Valiant Entertainment: Mar, 2018 - No. 11, Jan, 2019 ($3.99)

1-11: 1-Diggle-s/Segovia-a. 4-Martinbrough & Segovia-a. 6-11-Guedes-a — 4.00

SHADOWMAN
Valiant Entertainment: Apr, 2021 - No. 8, Apr, 2022 ($3.99)

1-8: 1-Cullen Bunn-s/Jon Davis-Hunt-a. 5-8-Pedro Andreo-a — 4.00

SHADOWMAN END TIMES
Valiant Entertainment: Apr, 2014 - No. 3, Jun, 2014 ($3.99, limited series)

1-3-Milligan-s/De Landro-a — 4.00

SHADOWMAN / RAE SREMMURD
Valiant Entertainment: Oct, 2017 ($3.99, one-shot)

1-Rahal-s/Guedes-a; bonus preview of Ninja•K #1 — 4.00

SHADOWMASTERS
Marvel Comics: Oct, 1989 - No.4, Jan, 1990 ($3.95, squarebound, 52 pgs.)

1-4: Heath-a(i). 1-Jim Lee-c; story cont'd from Punisher — 5.00

SHADOW, THE: MIDNIGHT IN MOSCOW (Pulp character)
Dynamite Entertainment: 2014 - No. 6, 2014 ($3.99, limited series)

1-6:-Howard Chaykin-s/a/c — 4.00

SHADOW NOW, THE (Pulp character)
Dynamite Entertainment: 2013 - No. 6, 2014 ($3.99, limited series)

1-6: 1-David Liss-s/ColtonWorley-a; The Shadow in present day New York — 4.00

SHADOW OF THE BATMAN
DC Comics: Dec, 1985 - No. 5, Apr, 1986 ($1.75, limited series)

1-Detective-r (all have wraparound-c) 2 4 6 8 10 12
2,3,5: 3-Penguin-c & cameo. 5-Clayface app. — — — — — 6.00
4-Joker-c/story 1 2 3 4 6 8
NOTE: *Austin a(new)-2i, 3i; r-2-4i. Rogers a(new)-1, 2p, 3p, 4, 5; r-1-5p; c-1-5. Simonson a-1r.*

SHADOW ON THE TRAIL (See Zane Grey & Four Color #604)

SHADOWPACT (See Day of Vengeance)
DC Comics: Jul, 2006 - No. 25, Jul, 2008 ($2.99)

1-25: 1-Bill Willingham-s; Detective Chimp, Ragman, Blue Devil, Nightshade, Enchantress
and Nightmaster app. 13-Zauriel app. S. Hampton-a — 3.00
...: Cursed TPB (2007, $14.99) r/#4,9-13 — 15.00
...: Darkness and Light TPB (2008, $14.99) r/#14-19 — 15.00
...: The Burning Age TPB (2008, $17.99) r/#20-25 — 18.00
...: The Pentacle Plot TPB (2007, $14.99) r/#1-3,5-8 — 15.00

SHADOW PLAY (Tales of the Supernatural)
Whitman Publications: June, 1982

1-Painted-c 1 2 3 5 6 8

SHADOWPLAY
IDW Publ.: Sept, 2005 - No. 4, Dec, 2005 ($3.99)

1-4-Benson-s/Templesmith-a; Christina Z-s/Wood-a; 2 covers by Templesmith & Wood — 6.00
TPB (3/06, $17.99) r/series; flip book format — 18.00

SHADOW REAVERS
Black Bull Ent.: Oct, 2001 - No. 5, Mar, 2002 ($2.99)

1-5-Nelson-a; two covers for each issue — 3.00
Limited Preview Edition (5/01, no cover price) — 3.00

SHADOW RIDERS
Marvel Comics UK, Ltd.: June, 1993 - No. 4, Sept, 1993 ($1.75, limited series)

1-($2.50)-Embossed-c; Cable-c/story — 5.00
2-4-Cable app. 2-Ghost Rider app. — 4.00

SHADOWS
Image Comics: Feb, 2003 - No. 4, Nov, 2003 ($2.95)

1-4-Jade Dodge-s/Matt Camp-a/c — 3.00

SHADOWS & LIGHT
Marvel Comics: Feb, 1998 - No. 3, July, 1998 ($2.99, B&W, quarterly)

1-3: 1-B&W anthology of Marvel characters; Black Widow art by Gene Ha, Hulk
by Wrightson, Iron Man by Ditko & Daredevil by Stelfreeze; Stelfreeze painted-c. 2-Weeks,
Sharp, Starlin, Thompson-a. 3-Buscema, Grindberg, Giffen, Layton-a — 4.00

SHADOW'S FALL
DC Comics (Vertigo): Nov, 1994 - No. 6, Apr, 1995 ($2.95, limited series)

1-6: Van Fleet-c/a in all. — 4.00

SHADOWS FROM BEYOND (Formerly Unusual Tales)
Charlton Comics: V2#50, October, 1966

V2#50-Ditko-c/a 5 10 15 33 57 80

SHADOWS ON THE GRAVE
Dark Horse Comics: Dec, 2016 - No. 8, Sept, 2017 ($3.99, B&W, limited series)

1-8-Horror story anthology; Richard Corben-s/a/c — 4.00

SHADOW STATE
Broadway Comics: Dec, 1995 - No. 5, Apr, 1996 ($2.50)

1-5: 1,2-Fatale back-up story; Cockrum-a(p) — 4.00

Preview Edition 1,2 (10-11/95, $2.50, B&W) — 4.00

SHADOW STRIKES!, THE (Pulp, radio)
DC Comics: Sept, 1989 - No.31, May, 1992 ($1.75)

1-4,7-31: 31-Mignola-c — 4.00
5,6-Doc Savage x-over — 5.00
Annual 1 (1989, $3.50, 68 pgs.)-Spiegle a; Kaluta-c — 5.00

SHADOW, THE : THE DEATH OF MARGO LANE (Pulp characters)
Dynamite Entertainment: 2016 - No. 5, 2016 ($3.99, limited series)

1-5-Matt Wagner-s/a/c. 4-The Red Empress app. — 4.00

SHADOW WALK
Legendary Comics: Nov, 2013 ($24.99, graphic novel)

HC - Mark Waid-s/Shane Davis-a — 25.00

SHADOW WAR
DC Comics: May, 2022 - Jul, 2022 (limited series)

... Alpha (5/22, $5.99) Assassination of Ra's al Ghul; Deathstroke app. — 6.00
... Omega (7/22, $5.99) Conclusion of x-over; Geo-Force app.; leads into Dark Crisis #1 — 6.00
Shadow War Zone (7/22, $5.99) Tales from the War Zone — 6.00

SHADOW WAR OF HAWKMAN
DC Comics: May, 1985 - No. 4, Aug, 1985 (limited series)

1-4 — 4.00

SHADOW, THE: YEAR ONE
Dynamite Entertainment: 2012 - No. 10, 2014 ($3.99)

1-9: 1-Matt Wagner-s/Wilfredo Torres-a; multiple covers — 4.00
10-($4.99) — 5.00

SHAFT (Based on the movie character)
Dynamite Entertainment: 2014 - No. 6, 2015 ($3.99, limited series)

1-6-David F. Walker-s/Bilquis Evely-a; multiple covers on each — 4.00

SHAFT: IMITATION OF LIFE (Based on the movie character)
Dynamite Entertainment: 2016 - No. 4, 2016 ($3.99, limited series)

1-4-David F. Walker-s/Dietrich Smith-a/Matthew Clark-c — 4.00

SHAGGY DOG & THE ABSENT-MINDED PROFESSOR (See Movie Comics &
Walt Disney Showcase #46)(Disney-Movie)
Dell Publ. Co.: No. 985, Apr-Jun, 1959; No. 1199, Apr, 1961; Aug, 1967

Four Color 985 9 18 27 57 111 165
Four Color 1199 (4/61) Movie, photo-c; variant "Double Feature" edition; has a "Fabulous
Formula" strip on back-c 8 16 24 54 102 150
Four Color 1199-(8/67) Movie, photo-c 8 16 24 54 102 150

SHAHRAZAD
Big Dog Ink: No. 0, Apr, 2013 - No. 5, Apr, 2014 ($1.99/$3.99)

0-($1.99) Hutchison-s/Krome-a; multiple covers — 3.00
1-3 ($3.99) Hutchison & Castor-s/Krome-a; multiple covers on each — 4.00

SHAHRAZAD
Aspen MLT: Apr, 2015 - No. 5, Aug, 2015 ($2.99/$3.99)

1,2-($2.99) Remastered reprints of 2013 series; multiple covers on each — 3.00
3-5-($3.99) Hutchison & Castor-s/Krome-a; multiple covers on each — 4.00

SHALOMAN (Jewish-themed stories and history)
Al Wiesner/ Mark 1 Comics: 1988 - 2012 (B&W)

V1#1-Al Wiesner-s/a in all — 5.00
2-9 — 4.00
V2 #1(The New Adventures)-4,6-10, V3 (The Legend of...) #1-12 — 3.00
V2 #5 (Color)-Shows Vol 2, No. 4 in indicia — 3.00
V4 (The Saga of ...) #1(2004), 2-8: 8-Chanukah & The Holocaust — 3.00
...: The Sequel (2010) "11-9" , ...: The Sequel 2 (2011) Genesis #2 Jews in Space — 3.00
...: The Sequel 3 (2012) Purim and the X-Suit — 3.00
The Saga of Shaloman (20th Anniversary Edition) TPB (10/08, $15.99) r/V4 #1-8 — 16.00

SHAMAN'S TEARS (Also see Maggie the Cat)
Image Comics (Creative Fire Studio): 5/93 - No. 2, 8/93; No. 3, 11/94 - No. 0, 1/96
($2.50/$1.95)

0-2: 0-(DEC-c, 1/96)-Last Issue. 1-(5/93)-Embossed red foil-c; Grell-c/a & scripts in all.
2-Cover unfolds into poster (8/93-c, 7/93 inside) — 5.00
3-12: 3-Begin $1.95-c. 5-Re-intro Jon Sable. 12-Re-intro Maggie the Cat (1 pg.) — 4.00

SHAME ITSELF
Marvel Comics: Jan, 2012 ($3.99, one-shot)

1-Spoof of "Fear Itself" x-over event; short stories by various incl. Cenac & Kupperman — 4.00

SHANG-CHI
Marvel Comics: Nov, 2020 - No. 5, Mar, 2021 ($3.99)

1-5-Gene Luen Yang-s/Dike Ruan & Philip Tan-a. 1-Fin Fang Foom cameo — 4.00

SHANG-CHI
Marvel Comics: Jul, 2021 - No. 12, Jul, 2022 ($3.99)

1-12: 1-8-Gene Luen Yang-s/Dike Ruan-a. 1-Spider-Man app. 9-12-Marcus To-a — 4.00
...: Master of the Ten Rings 1 (3/23, $4.99) Gene Luen Yang-s/Michael Yg-a — 5.00

SHANG-CHI AND THE TEN RINGS
Marvel Comics: Sept, 2022 - No. 6, Feb, 2023 ($3.99)

1-6-Gene Luen Yang-s/Marcus To-a — 4.00

SHANG-CHI: MASTER OF KUNG-FU ("Master of Kung Fu" on cover for #1&2)
Marvel Comics: Nov, 2002 - No. 6, Apr, 2003 ($2.99, limited series)

1-6-Moench-s/Gulacy-c/a — 3.00
...One-Shot 1 (11/09, $3.99, B&W) Deadpool app. — 4.00
...: Vol. 1: The Hellfire Apocalypse TPB (2003, $14.99) r/#1-6 — 15.00

SHANNA, THE SHE-DEVIL (See Savage Tales #8)
Marvel Comics Group: Dec, 1972 - No. 5, Aug, 1973 (All are 20¢ issues)

1-1st app. Shanna; Steranko-c; Tuska-a(p) 11 22 33 76 163 250
2-Steranko-c; heroin drug story 5 10 15 33 57 80
3-5 3 6 9 16 23 30

Shadows on the Grave #6 © Richard Corben

Shang-Chi (2021 series) #11 © MAR

Shazam! (2023 series) #1 © DC

	GD 2.0	VG 4.0	FN 6.0	VF 8.0	VF/NM 9.0	NM- 9.2		GD 2.0	VG 4.0	FN 6.0	VF 8.0	VF/NM 9.0	NM- 9.2

SHANNA, THE SHE-DEVIL
Marvel Comics: Apr, 2005 - No. 7, Oct, 2005 ($3.50, limited series)

1-7-Reintro of Shanna; Frank Cho-s/a/c in all					3.50
HC (2005, $24.99, dust jacket) r/#1-7					25.00
SC (2006, $16.99) r/#1-7					17.00

SHANNA, THE SHE-DEVIL: SURVIVAL OF THE FITTEST
Marvel Comics: Oct, 2007 - No. 4, Jan, 2008 ($2.99, limited series)

1-4-Khari Evans-a/c; Gray & Palmiotti-s					3.00
SC (2008, $10.99) r/#1-4					11.00

SHAOLIN COWBOY
Burlyman Entertainment: Dec, 2004 - No. 7, May, 2007 ($3.50)

1-7-Geof Darrow-s/a. 3-Moebius-c					3.50

SHAOLIN COWBOY
Dark Horse Comics: Oct, 2013 - No. 4, Feb, 2014 ($3.99)

1-4-Geof Darrow-s/a. 1-Variant-c by Simonson					4.00

SHAOLIN COWBOY: CRUEL TO BE KIN
Dark Horse Comics: May, 2022 - No. 7, Nov, 2022 ($4.99)

1-7-Geof Darrow-s/a. 1-Variant-c by Mignola					5.00

SHAOLIN COWBOY: WHO'LL STOP THE REIGN?
Dark Horse Comics: Apr, 2017 - No. 4, 2017 ($3.99)

1-4-Geof Darrow-s/a. 1-Variant-c by Frank Miller					4.00

SHAPER
Dark Horse Comics: Mar, 2015 - No. 5, Jul, 2015 ($3.99)

1-5: 1-Heisserer-s/Massafera-a. 2-5-Continuado-a					4.00

SHARKEY THE BOUNTY HUNTER
Image Comics: Feb, 2019 - No. 6, Oct, 2019 ($3.99, limited series)

1-6-Mark Millar-s/Simone Bianchi-a/c					4.00

SHARK FIGHTERS, THE (Movie)
Dell Publishing Co.: Jan, 1957

Four Color 762 - Buscema-a; photo-c	9	18	27	62	126	190

SHARK-MAN
Thrill House/Image Comics: Jul, 2006; Jul, 2007; Jan, 2008 - No. 3, Jun, 2008 ($3.99/$3.50)

1,2: 1-(Thrill House, 7/06, $3.99)-Steve Pugh-s/a. 2-(Image Comics, 7/07)					4.00
1-3: 1-(Image, 1/08, $3.50) reprints Thrill House #1					3.50

SHARKY
Image Comics: Feb, 1998 - No. 4, 1998 ($2.50, bi-monthly)

1-4: 1-Mask app.; Elliot-s/a. Horley painted-c. 3-Three covers by Horley, Bisley, & Horley/Elliot. 4-Two covers (swipe of Avengers #4 and wraparound)					4.00
1-($2.95) "$1,000,000" variant					4.00
2-($2.50) Savage Dragon variant-c					4.00

SHARP COMICS (Slightly large size)
H. C. Blackerby: Winter, 1945-46 - V1#2, Spring, 1946 (52 pgs.)

V1#1-Origin Dick Royce Planetarian	68	136	204	435	743	1050
2-Origin The Pioneer; Michael Morgan, Dick Royce, Sir Gallagher, Planetarian, Steve Hagen, Weeny and Pop app.	68	136	204	435	743	1050

SHARPY FOX (See Comic Capers & Funny Frolics)
I. W. Enterprises/Super Comics: 1958; 1963

1,2-I.W. Reprint (1958)- 2-r/Kiddie Kapers #1	2	4	6	11	16	20
14-Super Reprint (1963)	2	4	6	10	14	18

SHATTER (See Jon Sable #25-30)
First Comics: June, 1985; Dec, 1985 - No. 14, Apr, 1988 ($1.75, Baxter paper/deluxe paper)

1 (6/85)-1st computer generated-a in a comic book (1st printing)					5.00
1-(2nd print.); 1(12/85)-14: computer generated-a & lettering in all					4.00
Special 1 (1988)					4.00

SHATTERED IMAGE
Image Comics (WildStorm Productions): Aug, 1996 - No. 4, Dec, 1996 ($2.50, lim. series)

1-4: 1st Image company-wide x-over; Kurt Busiek scripts in all. 1-Tony Daniel-c/a(p). 2-Alex Ross-c/swipe (Kingdom Come) by Ryan Benjamin & Travis Charest					4.00

SHATTERSTAR (From X-Force)
Marvel Comics: Dec, 2018 - No. 5, Apr, 2019 ($3.99, limited series)

1-Tim Seeley-s/Carlos Villa-a; Grandmaster app.					4.00

SHAUN OF THE DEAD (Movie)
IDW Publishing: June, 2005 - No. 4, Sept, 2005 ($3.99, limited series)

1-4-Adaptation of 2004 movie; Zach Howard-a					4.00

TPB (12/05, $17.99) r/series; sketch pages and cover gallery 18.00

SHAZAM (See Billy Batson and the Magic of Shazam!, Giant Comics to Color, Limited Collectors' Edition, Power Of Shazam! and Trials of Shazam!)

SHAZAM! (TV)(See World's Finest #253 for story from unpublished #36)
National Periodical Publ./DC Comics: Feb, 1973 - No. 35, May-June, 1978

1-1st revival of original Captain Marvel since G.A. (origin retold), by C.C. Beck; Mary Marvel & Captain Marvel Jr. app.; Superman-c	8	16	24	52	99	145
2-5: 2-Infinity photo-c.; re-intro Mr. Mind & Tawny. 3-Capt. Marvel-r. (10/46). 4-Origin retold; Capt. Marvel-r. (1949). 5-Capt. Marvel Jr. origin retold; Capt. Marvel-r. (1948, 7 pgs.)	3	6	9	19	30	40
6,7,9-11: 6-photo-c; Capt. Marvel-r (1950, 6 pgs.). 9-Mr. Mind app. 10-Last C.C. Beck issue. 11-Schaffenberger-a begins.	3	6	9	16	23	30
8-(100 pgs.) 8-r/1st Black Adam app. from Marvel Family #1; r/Capt. Marvel Jr. by Raboy; origin/C.M. #80; origin Mary Marvel/C.M.A. #18; origin Mr. Tawny/C.M.A. #79	10	20	30	64	132	200
12-17-(All 100 pgs.). 15-vs. Lex Luthor & Mr. Mind	5	10	15	33	57	80
18-24,26,27,29,30: 21-24-All reprints. 26-Sivana app. (10/76). 27-Kid Eternity teams up w/Capt. Marvel. 30-1st DC app. 3 Lt. Marvels	3	6	9	14	20	25
25-1st app. Isis	9	18	27	51	111	165
28-(3-4/77) 1st Bronze Age app. of Black Adam	10	20	30	64	132	200
31-35: 31-1st DC app. Minuteman. 34-Origin Capt. Marvel Jr. retold	3	6	9	16	23	30

...: The Greatest Stories Ever Told TPB (2008, $24.99) reprints; Alex Ross-c 25.00
NOTE: Reprints in #1-8, 10, 12-17, 21-24. Beck a-1-10, 12-17r, 21-24r; c-1, 3-9. Nasser c-35p. Newton a-35p. Raboy a-5r, 8r, 17r. Schaffenberger a-11, 14-20, 25, 26, 27p, 28, 29-31p, 33i, 35i; c-20, 22, 23, 25, 26i, 27i, 28-33.

SHAZAM!
DC Comics: March, 2011 ($2.99, one-shot)

1-Richards-a/Chiang-c; Blaze app.; story continues in Titans #32					3.00

SHAZAM! (See back-up stories in Justice League [2011 series] #0,7-11,14-16,18-21)
DC Comics: Feb, 2019 - No. 15, Nov, 2020 ($4.99/$3.99)

1-($4.99) Johns-s/Eaglesham-a; back-up origin of Hoppy w/Naito-a					5.00
2-13,15-($3.99): 2-Johns-s/Santucci-a; Sivana & Mr. Mind app.; intro. King Kid. 4-6,8-11-Black Adam app. 8-Billy's father gains the power. 11,13-Monster Society app. 12-Batman & Scarecrow app.; Loveness-s/Peterson-a. 13-Eaglesham-a. 15-Peterson-a					4.00
14-($4.99) Superboy Prime app.; Eaglesham-a					5.00

SHAZAM!
DC Comics: Sept, 2021 - No. 4, Dec, 2021 ($3.99, limited series)

1-4-Sheridan-s/Henry-a. 1-Teen Titans app. 3,4-Black Adam app.					4.00

SHAZAM! (Dawn of DC)
DC Comics: Jul, 2023 - Present ($3.99)

1-9: 1-6-Waid-s/Mora-a. 2-Psycho Pirate app. 4,5-Queen Bee app. 6,7-Black Adam app.					4.00

SHAZAM! AND THE SHAZAM FAMILY! ANNUAL
DC Comics: 2002 ($5.95, squarebound, one-shot)

1-Reprints Golden Age stories including 1st Mary Marvel and 1st Black Adam	1	2	3	4	6	8	10

SHAZAM! FURY OF THE GODS SPECIAL: SHAZAMILY MATTERS
DC Comics: Apr, 2023 ($9.99, one-shot)

1-Short stories of the Shazam Family characters, some written by their movie actors					10.00

SHAZAM!: POWER OF HOPE
DC Comics: Nov, 2000 ($9.95, treasury size, one-shot)

nn-Painted art by Alex Ross; story by Alex Ross and Paul Dini					10.00

SHAZAM!: THE MONSTER SOCIETY OF EVIL
DC Comics: 2007 - No. 4, 2007 ($5.99, square-bound, limited series)

1-4: Jeff Smith-s/a/c in all. 1-Retelling of origin. 2-Mary Marvel & Dr. Sivana app.					6.00
HC (2007, $29.99, over-sized with dust jacket that unfolds to a poster) r/#1-4; Alex Ross Smith afterword; sketch pages, script pages and production notes					30.00
SC (2009, $19.99) r/#1-4; Alex Ross intro.					20.00

SHAZAM: THE NEW BEGINNING
DC Comics: Apr, 1987 - No. 4, July, 1987 (Legends spin-off) (Limited series)

1-4: 1-New origin & 1st modern app. Captain Marvel; Marvel Family cameo. 2-4-Sivana & Black Adam app.					4.00

SHEA THEATRE COMICS
Shea Theatre: No date (1940's) (32 pgs.)

nn-Contains Rocket Comics; MLJ cover in one color	34	68	102	199	325	450

SHE-BAT (See Murcielaga, She-Bat & Valeria the She-Bat)

SHE COULD FLY
Dark Horse Comics (Berger Books): Jul, 2018 - No. 4, Oct, 2018 ($4.99, limited series)

	GD 2.0	VG 4.0	FN 6.0	VF 8.0	VF/NM 9.0	NM- 9.2

1-4-Christopher Cantwell-s/Martín Morazzo-a … 5.00

SHE COULD FLY: THE LOST PILOT
Dark Horse Comics (Berger Books): Apr, 2019 - No. 5, Aug, 2019 ($3.99, limited series)
1-5-Christopher Cantwell-s/Martín Morazzo-a … 4.00

SHE-DRAGON (See Savage Dragon #117)
Image Comics: July, 2006 ($5.99, one-shot)
nn- She-Dragon in Dimension-X; origin retold; Francesco-s/Larsen-s; sketch pages … 6.00

SHEENA (Movie)
Marvel Comics: Dec, 1984 - No. 2, Feb, 1985 (limited series)
1,2-r/Marvel Comics Super Special #34; Tanya Roberts movie … 5.00

SHEENA, QUEEN OF THE JUNGLE (See Jerry Iger's Classic…, Jumbo Comics, & 3-D Sheena)
Fiction House Magazines: Spr, 1942; No. 2, Wint, 1942-43; No. 3, Spr, 1943; No. 4, Fall, 1948; No. 5, Sum, 1949; No. 6, Spr, 1950; No. 7-10, 1950(nd); No. 11, Spr, 1951 - No. 18, Wint, 1952-53 (#1-3: 68 pgs.; #4-7: 52 pgs.)

	GD 2.0	VG 4.0	FN 6.0	VF 8.0	VF/NM 9.0	NM- 9.2
1-Sheena begins	300	600	900	2070	3635	5200
2 (Winter, 1942-43)	174	348	522	1114	1907	2700
3 (Spring, 1943) Classic Giant Ape-c	194	388	582	1242	2121	3000
4,5 (Fall, 1948, Sum, 1949): 4-New logo; cover swipe from Jumbo #20	68	136	204	435	743	1050
6,7 (Spring, 1950, 1950)	54	108	162	343	574	825
8-10(1950 - Win/50, 36 pgs.)	48	96	144	302	514	725
11-17: 15-Cover swipe from Jumbo #43	43	86	129	271	461	650
18-Used in POP, pg. 98	47	94	141	296	498	700
I.W. Reprint #9-r/#18; c-r/White Princess #3	5	10	15	31	53	75

NOTE: *Baker* c-5-10? *Whitman* c-11-18(most). *Zolnerowich* c-1-3.

SHEENA, QUEEN OF THE JUNGLE
Devil's Due Publishing: Mar, 2007; Jun, 2007 - No. 5, Jan, 2008 (99¢/$3.50)
1-5: 1-Rodi-s/Merhoff-a; 5 covers … 3.50
… 99¢ Special (3/07) Revival of the character; Rodi-s/Cummings-a; sketch pages; history … 3.00
…: Dark Rising (10/08 - No. 3, 12/08) 1-3 … 3.50
… Trail of the Mapinguari (4/08, $5.50) Two covers … 5.50

SHEENA, QUEEN OF THE JUNGLE
Dynamite Entertainment: No. 0, 2017 - No. 10, 2018 (25¢/$3.99)
0-(25¢) Marguerite Bennett & Christina Trujillo-s/Moritat-a; multiple covers … 3.00
1-10-($3.99) 1-Bennett & Trujillo-s/Moritat-a. 4-10-Sanapo-a … 4.00

SHEENA, QUEEN OF THE JUNGLE: FATAL EXAMS, VOLUME 3
Dynamite Entertainment: 2023 - No. 5, 2024 ($3.99)
1-5-Wes Clark Jr. & Steven E. de Souza-s/Ediano Silva-a … 4.00

SHEENA, QUEEN OF THE JUNGLE, VOLUME 2
Dynamite Entertainment: 2021 - No. 10, 2022 ($3.99)
1-10: 1-Stephen Mooney-s/Jethro Morales-a; multiple covers. 6-10-Steven E. de Souza-s … 4.00

SHEENA 3-D SPECIAL (Also see Blackthorne 3-D Series #1)
Eclipse Comics: Jan, 1985 ($2.00)

	GD 2.0	VG 4.0	FN 6.0	VF 8.0	VF/NM 9.0	NM- 9.2
1-Dave Stevens-a	3	6	9	17	26	35

SHE-HULK (Also see The Savage She-Hulk & The Sensational She-Hulk)
Marvel Comics: May, 2004 - No. 12, Apr, 2005 ($2.99)

	GD 2.0	VG 4.0	FN 6.0	VF 8.0	VF/NM 9.0	NM- 9.2
1-Bobillo-a/Slott-s/Granov-c; Avengers app.	2	4	6	9	12	15
2-4-Bobillo-a/Slott-s/Granov-c. 4-Spider-Man/app.						5.00
5-12- Mayhew-a. 9-12-Pelletier-a. 10-Origin of Titania						5.00
Vol. 1: Single Green Female TPB (2004, $14.99) r/#1-6						15.00
Vol. 2: Superhuman Law TPB (2005, $14.99) r/#7-12						15.00

SHE-HULK (2nd series)
Marvel Comics: Dec, 2005 - No. 38, Apr, 2009 ($2.99)

	GD 2.0	VG 4.0	FN 6.0	VF 8.0	VF/NM 9.0	NM- 9.2
1-Bobillo-a/Slott-s/Horn-c; New Avengers app.	2	4	6	10	14	18
2,4,5,7,9,11-21,24: 2-Hawkeye-c/app. 9-Jen marries John Jameson. 12-Thanos app. 16-Wolverine app.						5.00
3-($3.99) 100th She-Hulk issue; new story w/art by various incl. Bobillo, Conner, Mayhew & Powell; r/Savage She-Hulk #1 and r/Sensational She-Hulk #1	3	6	9	14	20	25
6-Starfox sexual assault trial	3	6	9	16	23	30
8-Civil War	2	4	6	9	12	15
8-2nd printing with variant Bobillo-c	1	3	4	6	8	10
10- "I Married a Man-Wolf!!"-c	2	4	6	10	14	18
22-1st Jazinda	2	4	6	10	14	18
23-1st full app. Jazinda	2	4	6	13	18	22
25-($3.99) Intro. the Behemoth; Juggernaut cameo; Handbook bio pages of She-Hulk						5.00
26-28,30-37: 27-Iron Man app. 30-Hercules app. 31-X-Factor app. 32,33-Secret Invasion	2	4	6	11	16	20
29-Sexy-c by Deodato	2	4	6	10	14	18
38-($3.99) Thundra, Valkyrie & Invisible Woman app.	2	4	6	9	12	15
…: Cosmic Collision 1 (2/09, $3.99) Lady Liberators app.; David-s/Asrar-a/Sejic-c	1	3	4	6	8	10
… Sensational 1 (5/10, $4.99) 30th Anniversary celebration; Stan Lee app.; Frank-c	3	6	9	17	26	35
Vol. 3: Time Trials (2006, $14.99) r/#1-5; Bobillo sketch page						15.00
Vol. 4: Laws of Attraction (2007, $19.99) r/#6-12; Paul Smith sketch page						30.00
Vol. 5: Planet Without a Hulk (2007, $19.99) r/#14-21; Slott's original series pitch						20.00
…: Jaded HC (2008, $19.99) r/#22-27; cover gallery						20.00

SHE-HULK (3rd series)
Marvel Comics: Apr, 2014 - No. 12, Apr, 2015 ($2.99)

	GD 2.0	VG 4.0	FN 6.0	VF 8.0	VF/NM 9.0	NM- 9.2
1-Soule-s/Pulido-a/Wada-c; Tony Stark app.	3	6	9	14	20	25
2-12-Hellcat app.						4.00

SHE-HULK (Marvel Legacy)
Marvel Comics: No. 159, Jan, 2018 - No. 163, May, 2018 ($3.99)
159-163: 159-Tamaki-s/Lindsay-a. 159-161-The Leader app. … 4.00
Annual 1(10/19, $4.99) Acts of Evil; Bullseye-c/app.; Andolfo-a … 5.00

SHE-HULK (5th series)
Marvel Comics: Mar, 2022 - No. 15, Sept, 2023 ($3.99)

	GD 2.0	VG 4.0	FN 6.0	VF 8.0	VF/NM 9.0	NM- 9.2

1-11,13-15: 1-Rowell-s/Antonio-a; multiple covers; Titania app.; Jack of Hearts returns … 4.00
12-($4.99) Legacy 175th issue; back-up story with Quinones-a … 5.00

SHE-HULKS
Marvel Comics: Jan, 2011 - No. 4, Apr, 2011 ($3.99/$2.99, limited series)
1-($3.99) She-Hulk & Lyra team-up; Stegman-a/McGuinness-c; character profile pages … 6.00
2-4-($2.99) McGuinness-c … 4.00

SHELTERED
Image Comics: Jul, 2013 - No. 15, Mar, 2015 ($2.99)
1-15-Brisson-s/Christmas-a … 3.00

SHERIFF BOB DIXON'S CHUCK WAGON (TV) (See Wild Bill Hickok #22)
Avon Periodicals: Nov, 1950

	GD 2.0	VG 4.0	FN 6.0	VF 8.0	VF/NM 9.0	NM- 9.2
1-Kinstler-c/a(3)	16	32	48	98	154	210

SHERIFF OF BABYLON, THE
DC Comics (Vertigo): Feb, 2016 - No. 12, Jan, 2017 ($3.99)
1-12-Tom King-s/Mitch Gerads/John Paul Leon-c … 4.00

SHERIFF OF TOMBSTONE
Charlton Comics: Nov, 1958 - No. 17, Sept, 1961

	GD 2.0	VG 4.0	FN 6.0	VF 8.0	VF/NM 9.0	NM- 9.2
V1#1-Giordano-c; Severin-a	6	12	18	41	76	110
2	4	8	12	25	40	55
3-10	3	6	9	17	25	32
11-17	3	6	9	14	20	25

SHERLOCK: A SCANDAL IN BELGRAVIA (Adaptation of episode from the BBC TV series)
Titan Comics: Jan, 2020 - No. 5, May, 2020 ($4.99/$3.99, B&W, reads back to front, right to left)
1-5-($4.99) English version of original Japanese manga; art by Jay.; multiple covers … 5.00
… Part 2 1-4 (9/22 - No. 4, 12/22) Art by Jay.; multiple covers … 5.00

SHERLOCK: A STUDY IN PINK (Adaptation of episode from the BBC TV series)
Titan Comics: Jul, 2016 - No. 6, Dec, 2016 ($4.99/$3.99, B&W, reads back to front, right to left)
1-($4.99) English version of original Japanese manga; art by Jay.; multiple covers … 5.00
2-6-($3.99) … 4.00

SHERLOCK FRANKENSTEIN AND THE LEGION OF EVIL (Also see Black Hammer)
Dark Horse Comics: Oct, 2017 - No. 4, Jan, 2018 ($3.99, limited series)
1-4-Lemire-s/Rubín-a … 4.00

SHERLOCK HOLMES (See Classic Comics #33, Marvel Preview, New Adventures of…, & Spectacular Stories)

SHERLOCK HOLMES (All New Baffling Adventures of…)(Young Eagle #3 on?)
Charlton Comics: Oct, 1955 - No. 2, Mar, 1956

	GD 2.0	VG 4.0	FN 6.0	VF 8.0	VF/NM 9.0	NM- 9.2
1-Dr. Neff, Ghost Breaker app.	50	100	150	315	533	750
2	41	82	123	256	428	600

SHERLOCK HOLMES (Also see The Joker)
National Periodical Publications: Sept-Oct, 1975

	GD 2.0	VG 4.0	FN 6.0	VF 8.0	VF/NM 9.0	NM- 9.2
1-Cruz-a; Simonson-c	3	6	9	19	30	40

SHERLOCK HOLMES
Dynamite Entertainment: 2009 - No. 5, 2009 ($3.50, limited series)
1-5-Cassaday-c/Moore & Reppion-s/Aaron Campbell-a … 3.50

SHERLOCK HOLMES: MORIARTY LIVES
Dynamite Entertainment: 2014 - No. 5, 2014 ($3.99, limited series)
1-5-Liss-s/Indro-a/Francavilla-c … 4.00

SHERLOCK HOLMES: THE LIVERPOOL DEMON
Dynamite Entertainment: 2012 - No. 5, 2013 ($3.99, limited series)
1-5-Moore & Reppion-s/Triano-a/Francavilla-c … 4.00

SHERLOCK HOLMES: THE VANISHING MAN
Dynamite Entertainment: 2018 - No. 4, 2018 ($3.99)
1-4-Moore & Reppion-s/Ohta-a/Cassaday-c … 4.00

SHERLOCK HOLMES VS. HARRY HOUDINI
Dynamite Entertainment: 2014 - No. 5, 2015 ($3.99)
1-5-Del Col & McCreery-s/Furuzono-a; multiple covers on each … 4.00

SHERLOCK HOLMES: YEAR ONE
Dynamite Entertainment: 2011 - No. 6, 2011 ($3.99, limited series)
1-6-Beatty-s; multiple covers on each … 4.00

SHERLOCK: THE BLIND BANKER (Adaptation of episode from the BBC TV series)
Titan Comics: Feb, 2017 - No. 6, Jul, 2017 ($4.99/$3.99, B&W, reads back to front, right to left)
1-6-English version of original Japanese manga; art by Jay.; multiple covers … 5.00

SHERLOCK: THE GREAT GAME (Adaptation of episode from the BBC TV series)
Titan Comics: Sept, 2017 - No. 6, Feb, 2018 ($4.99, B&W, reads back to front, right to left)
1-6-English version of original Japanese manga; art by Jay.; multiple covers … 5.00

SHERRY THE SHOWGIRL (Showgirls #4)
Atlas Comics: July, 1956 - No. 3, Dec, 1956; No. 5, Apr, 1957 - No. 7, Aug, 1957

	GD 2.0	VG 4.0	FN 6.0	VF 8.0	VF/NM 9.0	NM- 9.2
1-Dan DeCarlo-c/a in all	326	652	978	2282	3991	5700
2	148	296	444	947	1624	2300
3,5-7	84	168	252	538	919	1300

SHE'S JOSIE (See Josie)

SHEVA'S WAR
DC Comics (Helix): Oct, 1998 - No. 5, Feb, 1999 ($2.95, mini-series)
1-5-Christopher Moeller-s/painted-a/c … 4.00

SHI (one-shots and TPBs)
Crusade Comics
…: Akai (2001, $2.99)-Intro. Victoria Cross; Tucci-a/c; J.C. Vaughn-s … 3.00
…: Akai Victoria Cross Ed. ($5.95, edition of 2000) variant Tucci-c … 6.00
…: C.G.I. (2001, $4.99) preview of unpublished series … 5.00
…/ Cyblade: The Battle for the Independents (9/95, $2.95) Tucci-c; Hellboy, Bone app. … 4.00
…/ Cyblade: The Battle for the Independents (9/95, $2.95) Silvestri variant-c … 4.00

She-Hulk (2008 series) #26 © MAR

Sherlock Holmes: Moriarty Lives #1 © DYN

Shi: Ju-Nen #2 © Billy Tucci

	GD 2.0	VG 4.0	FN 6.0	VF 8.0	VF/NM 9.0	NM- 9.2

.../ Daredevil: Honor Thy Mother (1/97, $2.95) Flip book 4.00
...- Judgment Night (2000, $3.99) Wolverine app.; Battlebook card and pages; Tucci-a 4.00
.... Kaidan (10/96, $2.95) Two covers; Tucci-; Jae Lee wraparound-c 4.00
.... Masquerade (3/98, $3.50) Painted art by Lago, Texeira, and others 4.00
.... Nightstalkers (9/97, $3.50) Painted art by Val Mayerik 4.00
.... Rekishi (1/97, $2.95) Character bios and story summaries of Shi: The Way of the Warrior
   told in Detective Joe Labianca's point of view; Christopher Golden script; Tucci-c;
   J.G. Jones-a; flip book w/Shi: East Wind Rain preview 4.00
... The Art of War Tourbook (1998, $4.95) Blank cover for sketches; early Tucci inside 5.00
.../ Vampirella (10/97, $2.95) Ellis-s/Lau-a 4.00
... Vs. Tomoe (8/96, $3.95) Tucci-a/scripts; wraparound foil-c 5.00
... Vs. Tomoe (6/96, $5.00, B&W)-Preview Ed.; sold at San Diego Comic Con 5.00
The Definitive Shi Vol. 1 (2006-2007, $24.99, TPB) B&W r/Way of the Warrior, Tomoe, Rekishi,
   and Senryaku series; cover gallery with sketches; Tucci & Sparacio-c 25.00

SHI: BLACK, WHITE AND RED
Crusade Comics: Mar, 1998 - No. 2, May, 1998 ($2.95, B&W&Red, mini-series)
1,2-J.G. Jones-painted art 4.00
...- Year of the Dragon Collected Edition (2000, $5.95) r/#1&2 6.00

SHIDIMA
Image Comics: Jan, 2001 - No. 7, Nov, 2002 ($2.95, limited series)
1-7-Prequel to Warlands 3.00
#0-(10/01, $2.25) Short story and sketch pages 3.00

SHI: EAST WIND RAIN
Crusade Comics: Nov, 1997 - No. 2, Feb, 1998 ($3.50, limited series)
1,2-Shi at WW2 Pearl Harbor 4.00

S.H.I.E.L.D. (Nick Fury & His Agents of...) (Also see Nick Fury)
Marvel Comics Group: Feb, 1973 - No. 5, Oct, 1973 (All 20¢ issues)

	GD 2.0	VG 4.0	FN 6.0	VF 8.0	VF/NM 9.0	NM- 9.2
1-All contain reprint stories from Strange Tales #146-155; new Steranko-c	5	10	15	31	53	75
2-New Steranko flag-c	3	6	9	17	26	35
3-5: 3-Kirby/Steranko-c(r). 4-Steranko-c(r)	2	4	6	10	14	18

NOTE: Buscema a-3p(r). Kirby layouts 1-5; c-3 (w/Steranko). Steranko a-3r, 4r(2).

S.H.I.E.L.D.
Marvel Comics: Jun, 2010 - No. 6, Apr, 2011 ($3.99/$2.99)
1-($3.99) Leonardo DaVinci app.; Weaver-a/Hickman-s/Parel-c; 4 printings 4.00
1-Variant-c by Weaver 6.00
1-Director's Cut (9/10, $4.99) r/#1 with character sketch and bios; design-a 5.00
2-6-($2.99) 2-Three printings. 3-Galactus app. 3.00
Infinity (6/11, $4.99) DaVinci, Nostradamus, Newton & Tesla app.; Parel-c 5.00
... Origins (1/14, $7.99) r/Battle Scars #6, Secret Avengers #1, Strange Tales #135 8.00

S.H.I.E.L.D. (2nd series; title becomes S.H.I.E.L.D. by Hickman & Weaver with #5)
Marvel Comics: Aug, 2011 - No. 4, Feb, 2012; No. 5, Jul, 2018 - No. 6, Aug, 2018 ($3.99/$2.99)
1-($3.99) Weaver-a/Hickman-s/Parel-c; profile pgs of main characters 4.00
2-4-($2.99) 3.00
5,6- 5-(7/18, $3.99) Continuation after 6-year hiatus 4.00
... By Hickman & Weaver: The Rebirth 1 (7/18, $5.99) r/#1-4; Parel-c 6.00

S.H.I.E.L.D. (Based on the TV series)
Marvel Comics: Feb, 2015 - No. 12, Jan, 2016 ($4.99/$3.99)
1-($4.99) Waid-s/Pacheco-a/Tedesco-c; Avengers app. 5.00
2-8-($3.99) 2-Ms. Marvel (Kamala Khan) app.; Ramos-a. 3-Spider-Man app.; Davis-a 4.00
9-(5/99) 50th Anniversary issue; Howling Commandos app.; r/Strange Tales #135 6.00
10-12: 10-Howard the Duck app. 11-Dominic Fortune app.; Chaykin-a 4.00

SHIELD, THE (Becomes Shield-Steel Sterling #3; #1 titled Lancelot Strong; also see Advs. of
the Fly, Double Life of Private Strong, Fly Man, Mighty Comics, The Mighty Crusaders,
The Original... & Pep Comics #1)
Archie Enterprises, Inc.: June, 1983 - No. 2, Aug, 1983
1,2: Steel Sterling app. 1-Weiss-c/a. 2-Kaniger-s/Buckler-c/Nebres-a 5.00
America's 1st Patriotic Comic Book Hero, The Shield (2002, $12.95, TPB) r/Pep Comics #1-5,
   Shield-Wizard Comics #1; foreward by Robert M. Overstreet 13.00

SHIELD, THE (Archie Ent. character) (Continued from The Red Circle)
DC Comics: Nov, 2009 - No. 10, Aug, 2010 ($3.99)
1-10: 1-Magog app.; Inferno back-up feature thru #6; Green Arrow app. 2,3-Grodd app.
   4,5-The Great Ten app. 7-10-The Fox back-up feature; Oeming-a 4.00
... Kicking Down the Door TPB ('10, $19.99) r/#1-6, Red Circle: The Web & RC: The Shield 20.00

SHIELD, THE
Archie Comic Publications: Dec, 2015 - No. 4, Jan, 2017 ($3.99)
1-4-Christopher & Wendig-s/Drew Johnson-a; a new Shield recruited; multiple covers 4.00

SHIELD, THE: SPOTLIGHT (TV)

IDW Publishing: Jan, 2004 - No. 5, May, 2004 ($3.99)
1-5-Jeff Marriote-s/Jean Diaz-a/Tommy Lee Edwards-c 4.00
TPB (7/04, $19.99) r/#1-5; Michael Chiklis photo-c 20.00

SHIELD-STEEL STERLING (Formerly The Shield)
Archie Enterprises, Inc.: No. 3, Dec, 1983 (Becomes Steel Sterling No. 4)
3-Nino-a; Steel Sterling by Kaniger & Barreto 5.00

SHIELD WIZARD COMICS (Also see Pep Comics & Top-Notch Comics)
MLJ Magazines: Summer, 1940 - No. 13, Spring, 1944

	GD 2.0	VG 4.0	FN 6.0	VF 8.0	VF/NM 9.0	NM- 9.2
1-(V1#5 on inside)-Origin The Shield by Irving Novick & The Wizard by Ed Ashe, Jr; Flag-c	520	1040	1560	3800	7650	11,500
2-(Winter/40)-Origin The Shield retold; Wizard's sidekick, Roy the Super Boy begins (see Top-Notch #8 for 1st app.)	300	600	900	1950	3375	4800
3,4	232	464	696	1485	2543	3600
5-Dusty, the Boy Detective begins; Nazi bondage-c	206	412	618	1318	2259	3200
6,7: 6-Roy the Super Boy app. 7-Shield dons new costume (Summer, 1942); S & K-c?	181	362	543	1158	1979	2800
8-Nazi bondage-c; Hitler photo on-c	389	778	1167	2723	4762	6800
9-Japanese WWII bondage-c	245	490	735	1568	2684	3800
10-Nazi swastika-c	300	600	900	1920	3310	4700
11	168	336	504	1075	1838	2600
12-Nazi bondage-c	400	800	1200	2800	4900	7000
13-Japanese WWII bondage-c/torture-c (scarce)	300	600	900	1950	3375	4800

NOTE: Bob Montana c-13. Novick c-1,3-6,8-11. Harry Sahle c-12.

SHI: FAN EDITIONS
Crusade Comics: 1997
1-3-Two covers polybagged in FAN #19-21 4.00
1-3-Gold editions 5.00

SHIFT
Image Comics: Dec, 2023 ($5.99, one-shot)
1-Short stories from the Massive-verse (Radiant Black, Radiant Red) 6.00

SHI: HAIKYO (Follows story in Shi: Return of the Warrior)
Crusade Fine Arts: Apr, 2021 (no price shown, crowdfunded graphic novel)
nn-Steven Peros-s/Billy Tucci-a; multiple variant covers 25.00
Variant covers by Maria Sanapo, Cupliny Valentina and Gatecrasher edition 30.00
Cosplay variant-c 35.00
HC 50.00

SHI: HEAVEN AND EARTH
Crusade Comics: June, 1997 - No. 4, Apr, 1998 ($2.95)
1-4 4.00
4-($4.95) Pencil-c variant 5.00
Rising Sun Edition-signed by Tucci in FanClub Starter Pack 5.00
"Tora No Shi" variant-c 4.00

SHI: JU-NEN
Dark Horse Comics: July, 2004 - No. 4, May, 2005 ($2.99, mini-series)
1-4-Tucci-a/Tucci & Vaughn-s; origin retold 3.00
TPB (2/06, $13.99) r/#1-4; Tucci and Sparacio-c 13.00

SHINING KNIGHT (See Adventure Comics #66)

SHINKU
Image Comics: Jun, 2011 - No. 5, Oct, 2012 ($2.99)
1-5-Marz-s/Moder-a 3.00

SHINOBI (Based on Sega video game)
Dark Horse Comics: Aug, 2002 ($2.99, one-shot)
1-Medina-a/c 3.00

SHIP AHOY
Spotlight Publishers: Nov, 1944 (52 pgs.)

	GD 2.0	VG 4.0	FN 6.0	VF 8.0	VF/NM 9.0	NM- 9.2
1-L. B. Cole-c	33	66	99	194	317	440

SHIP OF FOOLS
Image Comics: Aug, 1997 - No. 3 ($2.95, B&W)
0-3-Glass-s/Oeming-a 4.00

SHI: POISONED PARADISE
Avatar Press: July, 2002 - No. 2, Aug, 2002 ($3.50, limited series)
1,2-Vaughn and Tucci-s/Waller-a; 1-Four covers 3.50

SHIPWRECK
AfterShock Comics: Oct, 2016 - No. 6, Jun, 2018 ($3.99)
1-6-Warren Ellis-s/Phil Hester-a 3.00

SHIPWRECKED! (Disney-Movie)

Grade columns: **GD 2.0 · VG 4.0 · FN 6.0 · VF 8.0 · VF/NM 9.0 · NM- 9.2**

Disney Comics: 1990 ($5.95, graphic novel, 68 pgs.)
nn-adaptation; Spiegle-a ... 6.00

SHI: RETURN OF THE WARRIOR
Crusade Fine Arts: July, 2020 (no price shown, crowdfunded graphic novel)
nn-Billy Tucci and Steven Peros-s/Tucci-a; multiple variant covers ... 25.00
Variant-c by Amanda Conner ... 35.00
Variant-c by George Pérez ... 45.00
HC ... 50.00

SHIRTLESS BEAR FIGHTER
Image Comics: Jun, 2017 - No. 5, Oct, 2017 ($3.99, limited series)
1-5-Leheup & Girner-s/Vendrell-a; multiple covers on each ... 4.00

SHIRTLESS BEAR FIGHTER 2
Image Comics: Aug, 2022 - No. 7, Feb, 2023 ($3.99, limited series)
1-7-Leheup-s/Vendrell-a; multiple covers on each ... 4.00

SHI: SAKURA (Follows story in Shi: Haikyo)
Crusade Fine Arts: Sept, 2022 (no price shown, crowdfunded graphic novel)
nn-Steven Peros-s/Billy Tucci-a; multiple variant covers ... 25.00
Variant covers by Gardenio Lima, Asha Kishna ... 30.00
Variant covers by Kenneth Rocafort, Jeff Chapman ... 35.00
HC by Tucci ... 50.00

SHI: SEMPO
Avatar Press: Aug, 2003 - No. 2, ($3.50, B&W, limited series)
1,2-Vaughn and Tucci-s/Alves-a; -Four covers ... 3.50

SHI: SENRYAKU
Crusade Comics: Aug, 1995 - No. 3, Nov, 1995 ($2.95, limited series)
1-3: 1-Tucci-c; Quesada, Darrow, Sim, Lee, Smith-a. 2-Tucci-c; Silvestri, Balent, Perez, Mack-a. 3-Jusko-c; Hughes, Ramos, Bell, Moore-a ... 4.00
1-variant-c (no logo) ... 5.00
Hardcover ($24.95)-r/#1-3; Frazetta-c. ... 25.00
Trade Paperback ($13.95)-r/#1-3; Frazetta-c. ... 14.00

SHI: THE ILLUSTRATED WARRIOR
Crusade Comics: 2002 - No. 7, 2003 ($2.99, B&W)
1-7-Story text with Tucci full page art ... 3.00

SHI: THE SERIES
Crusade Comics: Aug, 1997 - No. 13 ($2.95, color #1-10, B&W #11)
1-10 ... 4.00
11-13: 11-B&W. 12-Color; Lau-a ... 4.00
#0 Convention Edition ... 5.00

SHI: THE WAY OF THE WARRIOR
Crusade Comics: Mar, 1994 - No. 12, Apr, 1997 ($2.50/$2.95)

Issue	GD	VG	FN	VF	VF/NM	NM-
1/2						5.00
1	2	4	6	9	12	15
1-Commemorative ed., B&W, new-c; given out at 1994 San Diego Comic Con	2	4	6	10	16	20
1-Fan appreciation edition -r/#1	1	3	4	6	8	10
1-Fan appreciation edition (variant)	1	3	4	6	8	10
1- 10th Anniversary Edition (2004, $2.99)						4.00
2						5.00
2-Commemorative edition (3,000)	2	4	6	9	13	16
2-Fan appreciation edition						6.00
3						4.00
4-7: 4-Silvestri poster. 7-Tomoe app.						4.00
5,6: 5-Silvestri variant-c. 6-Tomoe #1 variant-c						4.00
5-Gold edition						12.00
6,8-12: 6-Fan appreciation edition						4.00
8-Combo Gold edition						6.00
8-Signed Edition-(5000)						5.00
Trade paperback (1995, $12.95)-r/#1-4						15.00
Trade paperback (1995, $14.95)-r/#1-4 revised; Julie Bell-c						15.00

SHI: YEAR OF THE DRAGON
Crusade Comics: 2000 - No. 3, 2000 ($2.99, limited series)
1-3: 1-Two covers; Tucci-a/c; flashback to teen-aged Ana ... 3.00

SHMOO (See Al Capp's... & Washable Jones &...)

SHOCK (Magazine)
Stanley Publ.: May, 1969 - V3#4, Sept, 1971 (B&W reprints from horror comics, including some pre-code) (No V2#1,3)

Issue	GD	VG	FN	VF	VF/NM	NM-
V1#1-Cover-r/Weird Tales of the Future #7 by Bernard Baily; r/Weird Chills #1	8	16	24	54	102	150
2-Wolverton-r/Weird Mysteries 5; r-Weird Mysteries #7 used in SOTI; cover reprints cover to Weird Chills #1	6	12	18	41	76	110
3,5,6	4	8	12	28	47	65
4-Harrison/Williamson-r/Forbid. Worlds #6	5	10	15	30	50	70
V2#2(5/70), V1#8(7/70), V2#4(9/70)-6(1/71), V3#1-4: V2#4-Cover swipe from Weird Mysteries #6	4	8	12	27	44	60

NOTE: Disbrow-r-V2#4; Bondage c-V1#4, V2#6, V3#1.

SHOCK DETECTIVE CASES (Formerly Crime Fighting Detective) (Becomes Spook Detective Cases No. 22)
Star Publications: No. 20, Sept, 1952 - No. 21, Nov, 1952

Issue	GD	VG	FN	VF	VF/NM	NM-
20,21-L.B. Cole-c; based on true crime cases	148	296	444	947	1624	2300

NOTE: Palais a-20. 21-Fox-r.

SHOCK ILLUSTRATED (...Adult Crime Stories, Magazine format)
E. C. Comics: Sept-Oct, 1955 - No. 3, Spring, 1956 (Adult Entertainment on-c #1,2)(All 25¢)

Issue	GD	VG	FN	VF	VF/NM	NM-
1-All by Kamen; drugs, prostitution, wife swapping	37	74	111	222	361	500
2-Williamson-a redrawn from Crime SuspenStories #13 plus Ingels, Crandall, Evans & part Torres-i; painted-c	28	56	84	168	274	380
3-Only 100 known copies bound & given away at E.C. office; Crandall, Evans-a; painted-c; shows May, 1956 on-c	300	600	900	2010	3505	5000

SHOCKING MYSTERY CASES (Formerly Thrilling Crime Cases)

Star Publications: No. 50, Sept, 1952 - No. 60, Oct, 1954 (All crime reprints?)

Issue	GD	VG	FN	VF	VF/NM	NM-
50-Disbrow "Frankenstein" story	239	478	717	1530	2615	3700
51-Disbrow-a	174	348	522	1114	1907	2700
52-60: 56-Drug use story	110	220	330	704	1202	1700

NOTE: L. B. Cole covers on all; a-60(2 pgs.). Hollingsworth a-52. Morisi a-55.

SHOCKING TALES DIGEST MAGAZINE
Harvey Publications: Oct, 1981 (95¢)

Issue	GD	VG	FN	VF	VF/NM	NM-
1-1957-58-r; Powell, Kirby, Nostrand-a	2	4	6	9	13	16

SHOCK ROCKETS
Image Comics (Gorilla): Apr, 2000.- No. 6, Oct, 2000 ($2.50)
1-6-Busiek-s/Immonen & Grawbadger-a. 6-Flip book w/Superstar preview ... 3.00
...: We Have Ignition TPB (Dark Horse, 8/04, $14.95, 6" x 9") r/#1-6 ... 15.00

SHOCK SHOP
Dark Horse Comics: Sept, 2022 - No. 4, Dec, 2022 ($3.99)
1-4-Cullen Bunn-s/Leila Leiz & Danny Luckert-a; flip cover on each ... 4.00

SHOCK SUSPENSTORIES (Also see EC Archives • Shock SuspenStories)
E. C. Comics: Feb-Mar, 1952 - No. 18, Dec-Jan, 1954-55

Issue	GD	VG	FN	VF	VF/NM	NM-
1-Classic Feldstein electrocution-c	149	298	447	1192	1896	2600
2	77	154	231	616	983	1350
3,4: 3-Classic decapitation splash. 4-Used in SOTI, pg. 387,388	63	126	189	504	802	1100
5-Hanging-c	131	262	393	1048	1674	2300
6-Classic hooded vigilante bondage-c	263	526	789	2104	3352	4600
7-Classic face melting-c	103	206	309	824	1312	1800
8-Williamson-a	77	154	231	616	983	1350
9-11: 9-Injury to eye panel. 10-Junkie story	46	92	138	368	584	800
12- "The Monkey" classic junkie cover/story; anti-drug propaganda issue	166	332	498	1328	2114	2900
13-Frazetta's only solo story for E.C., 7 pgs, draws himself as main male character	80	160	240	640	1020	1400
14-Used in Senate Investigation hearings	154	308	462	1232	1966	2700
15-Used in 1954 Reader's Digest article, "For the Kiddies to Read"	103	206	309	824	1312	1800
16-18: 16- "Red Dupe" editorial; rape story	43	86	129	344	547	750

NOTE: Ray Bradbury adaptations-1, 7, 9. Craig a-11; c-11. Crandall a-9-13, 15-18. Davis a-1-5. Evans a-7, 8, 14-18; c-16-18. Feldstein c-1, 7-9, 12. Ingels a-1-5, 14. Kamen a-in all; c-10, 13, 15. Krigstein a-14, 18. Orlando a-1, 3-7, 9, 10, 12, 16, 17. Wood a-2-15; c-2-6, 14.

SHOCK SUSPENSTORIES (Also see EC Archives • Shock SuspenStories)
Russ Cochran/Gemstone Publishing: Sept, 1992 - No. 18, Dec, 1996 ($1.50/$2.00/$2.50, quarterly)
1-18: 1-3: Reprints with original-c. 17-r/HOF #17 ... 4.00

SHOGUN WARRIORS
Marvel Comics Group: Feb, 1979 - No. 20, Sept, 1980 (Based on Mattel toys of the classic Japanese animation characters) (1-3: 35¢; 4-19: 40¢; 20: 50¢)

Issue	GD	VG	FN	VF	VF/NM	NM-
1-Raydeen, Combatra, & Dangard Ace begin; Trimpe-a	3	6	9	19	30	40
2-20: 2-Lord Maurkon & Elementals of Evil app.; Rok-Korr app. 6-Shogun vs. Shogun. 7,8-Cerberus. 9-Starchild. 11-Austin-i. 12-Simonson-a. 14-16-Doctor Demonicus. 17-Juggernaut. 19,20-FF x-over	2	4	6	8	10	12

SHOOK UP (Magazine) (Satire)
Dodsworth Publ. Co.: Nov, 1958

Issue	GD	VG	FN	VF	VF/NM	NM-
V1#1	5	10	15	33	57	80

SHOPLIFTERS WILL BE LIQUIDATED
AfterShock Comics: Oct, 2019 - No. 5, Mar, 2020 ($3.99, limited series)
1-5-Patrick Kindlon-s/Stefano Simeone-a ... 4.00

SHORT RIBS
Dell Publishing Co.: No. 1333, Apr - June, 1962

Issue	GD	VG	FN	VF	VF/NM	NM-
Four Color 1333	6	12	18	42	79	115

SHORTSTOP SQUAD (Baseball)
Ultimate Sports Ent. Inc.: 1999 ($3.95, one-shot)
1-Ripken Jr., Larkin, Jeter, Rodriguez app.; Edwards-c/a ... 4.00

SHORT STORY COMICS (See Hello Pal...)

SHORTY SHINER (The Five-Foot Fighter in the Ten Gallon Hat)
Dandy Magazine (Charles Biro): June, 1956 - No. 3, Oct, 1956

Issue	GD	VG	FN	VF	VF/NM	NM-
1	10	20	30	56	76	95
2,3	8	16	24	42	54	65

SHOTGUN SLADE (TV)
Dell Publishing Co.: No. 1111, July-Sept, 1960

Issue	GD	VG	FN	VF	VF/NM	NM-
Four Color 1111-Photo-c	6	12	18	40	73	105

SHOWCASE (See Cancelled Comic Cavalcade & New Talent...)
National Per. Publ./DC Comics: 3-4/56 - No. 93, 9/70; No. 94, 8-9/77 - No. 104, 9/78

Issue	GD	VG	FN	VF	VF/NM	NM-
1-Fire Fighters; w/Fireman Farrell	333	666	1000	2831	6416	10,000
2-Kings of the Wild; Kubert-a (animal stories)	145	290	435	1196	2698	4200
3-The Frogmen by Russ Heath; Heath greytone-c (early DC example, 7-8/56)	129	258	387	1032	2316	3600
4-Origin/1st app. The Flash (1st DC Silver Age hero, Sept-Oct, 1956); Kanigher-s; Infantino & Kubert-a; 1st app. Iris West and The Turtle; r/in Secret Origins #1 ('61 & '73); Flash shown reading G.A. Flash Comics #13; back-up story w/Broome-s/Infantino & Kubert-a	8000	16,000	32,000	72,000	128,500	185,000
5-Manhunters; Meskin-a	111	222	333	888	1994	3100
6-Origin/1st app. Challengers of the Unknown by Kirby, partly r/in Secret Origins #1 & Challengers #64,65 (1st S.A. hero team & 1st original concept S.A. series)(1-2/57)	467	934	1400	3970	8985	14,000
7-Challengers of the Unknown by Kirby (2nd app.) reprinted in Challengers of the Unknown #75	176	352	528	1452	3276	5100
8-The Flash (5-6/57, 2nd app.); origin & 1st app. Captain Cold	1060	2120	3180	9540	18,020	26,500

9-Lois Lane (Pre-#1, 7-8/57) (1st Showcase character to win own series)

Shock SuspenStories #10 © WMG

Showcase #25 © DC

Showcase '96 #5 © DC

Issue	GD 2.0	VG 4.0	FN 6.0	VF 8.0	VF/NM 9.0	NM- 9.2
Superman app. on-c	715	1430	2145	5700	10,350	15,000
10-Lois Lane; Jor-El cameo; Superman app. on-c	220	440	660	1815	4108	6400
11-Challengers of the Unknown by Kirby (3rd)	141	282	429	1163	2632	4100
12-Challengers of the Unknown by Kirby (4th)	141	282	429	1163	2632	4100
13-The Flash (3rd app.); origin Mr. Element	450	900	1350	3825	8660	13,500
14-The Flash (4th app.); origin Dr. Alchemy, former Mr. Element (rare in NM)	450	900	1350	3825	8660	13,500
15-Space Ranger (7-8/58, 1st app., also see My Greatest Aventure #22)	183	366	549	1510	3405	5300
16-Space Ranger (9-10/58, 2nd app.)	100	200	300	800	1800	2800
17-(11-12/58)-Adventures on Other Worlds; origin/1st app. Adam Strange by Gardner Fox & Mike Sekowsky	580	1160	1740	4930	11,215	17,500
18-Adventures on Other Worlds (2nd A. Strange)	100	200	300	800	1800	2800
19-Adam Strange; 1st Adam Strange logo	107	214	321	856	1928	3000
20-Rip Hunter; origin & 1st app. (5-6/59); Moreira-a	155	310	465	1279	2890	4500
21-Rip Hunter (7-8/59, 2nd app.); Sekowsky-c/a	68	136	204	544	1222	1900
22-Origin & 1st app. Silver Age Green Lantern by Gil Kane and John Broome (9-10/59); reprinted in Secret Origins #2	1750	3500	7000	21,400	45,700	70,000
23-Green Lantern (11-12/59, 2nd app.); nuclear explosion-c	217	434	651	1790	4045	6300
24-Green Lantern (1-2/60, 3rd app.)	179	358	537	1477	3339	5200
25,26-Rip Hunter by Kubert. 25-Grey tone-c	49	98	147	382	866	1350
27-Sea Devils (7-8/60, 1st app.); Heath-c/a; Grey tone-c	82	164	246	656	1478	2300
28-Sea Devils (9-10/60, 2nd app.); Heath-c/a; Grey tone-c	44	88	132	326	738	1150
29-Sea Devils; Heath-c/a; grey tone c-27-29	44	88	132	326	738	1150
30-Origin Silver Age Aquaman (1-2/61) (see Adventure #260 for 1st S.A. origin)	282	564	846	2327	5264	8200
31-Aquaman	61	122	183	488	1094	1700
32,33-Aquaman	44	88	132	326	738	1150
34-Origin & 1st app. Silver Age Atom by Gil Kane & Murphy Anderson (9-10/61); reprinted in Secret Origins #2	193	386	579	1592	3596	5600
35-The Atom by Gil Kane (2nd); last 10¢ issue	52	104	156	413	932	1450
36-The Atom by Gil Kane (1-2/62, 3rd app.)	40	80	120	296	673	1050
37-Metal Men (3-4/62, 1st app.)	214	428	642	1766	3983	6200
38-Metal Men (5-6/62, 2nd app.)	34	68	102	245	548	850
39-Metal Men (7-8/62, 3rd app.)	26	52	78	182	404	625
40-Metal Men (9-10/62, 4th app.)	26	52	78	182	404	625
41,42-Tommy Tomorrow (parts 1 & 2). 42-Origin	14	28	42	96	211	325
43-Dr. No (James Bond); Nodel-a; originally published as British Classics Illustrated #158A & as #6 in a European Detective series, all with diff. painted-c. This Showcase #43 version is actually censored, deleting all racial skin color and dialogue thought to be racially demeaning (1st DC S.A. movie adaptation)(based on Ian Fleming novel & movie)	61	122	183	488	1094	1700
44-Tommy Tomorrow	10	20	30	68	144	220
45-Sgt. Rock (7-8/63); pre-dates B&B #52; origin retold; Heath-c	36	72	108	259	580	900
46,47-Tommy Tomorrow	9	18	27	61	123	185
48,49-Cave Carson (3rd tryout series; see B&B)	8	16	24	56	108	160
50,51-I Spy (Danger Trail-r by Infantino), King Faraday story (#50 has new 4 pg. story)	8	16	24	51	96	140
52-Cave Carson	8	16	24	52	99	145
53,54-G.I. Joe (11-12/64, 1-2/65); Heath-a	12	24	36	84	185	285
55-Dr. Fate & Hourman (3-4/65); origin of each in text; 1st solo app. G.A. Green Lantern in Silver Age (pre-dates Gr. Lantern #40); 1st S.A. app. Solomon Grundy	54	108	162	432	966	1500
56-Dr. Fate & Hourman	15	30	45	110	220	340
57-Enemy Ace by Kubert (7-8/65, 4th app. after Our Army at War #155)	20	40	60	143	317	490
58-Enemy Ace by Kubert (5th app.)	16	32	48	107	236	365
59-Teen Titans (11-12/65, 3rd app.)	19	38	57	133	297	460
60-1st S.A. app. The Spectre; Anderson-a (1-2/66); origin in text	30	60	90	216	483	750
61-The Spectre by Anderson (2nd app.)	13	26	39	89	195	300
62-Origin & 1st app. Inferior Five (5-6/66)	10	20	30	70	150	230
63,65-Inferior Five. 63-Hulk parody. 65-X-Men parody (11-12/66)	6	12	18	42	79	115
64-The Spectre by Anderson (5th app.)	12	24	36	82	179	275
66,67-B'wana Beast	6	12	18	58	69	100
68-Maniaks (1st app., spoof of The Monkees)	5	10	15	34	60	85
69,71-Maniaks. 71-Woody Allen-c/app.	5	10	15	30	50	70
70-Binky (9-10/67)-Tryout issue; 1950's Leave It To Binky reprints with art changes	6	12	18	38	69	100
72-Top Gun (Johnny Thunder-r)-Toth-a	5	10	15	31	53	75

Issue	GD 2.0	VG 4.0	FN 6.0	VF 8.0	VF/NM 9.0	NM- 9.2
73-Origin/1st app. Creeper; Ditko-c/a (3-4/68)	15	30	45	100	220	340
74-Intro/1st app. Anthro; Post-c/a (5/68)	7	14	21	49	92	135
75-Origin/1st app. Hawk & the Dove; Ditko-c/a	14	28	42	96	211	325
76-1st app. Bat Lash (8/68)	8	16	24	55	105	155
77-1st app. Angel & The Ape (9/68)	8	16	24	51	96	140
78-1st app. Jonny Double (11/68)	5	10	15	30	50	70
79-1st app. Dolphin (12/68); Aqualad origin-r	35	70	105	252	564	875
80-1st S.A. app. Phantom Stranger (1/69); Neal Adams-c	17	34	51	117	259	400
81-Windy & Willy; r/Many Loves of Dobie Gillis #26 with art changes	5	10	15	35	63	90
82-1st app. Nightmaster (5/69) by Grandenetti & Giordano; Kubert-c	7	14	21	44	82	120
83,84-Nightmaster by Wrightson w/Jones/Kaluta ink assist in each; Kubert-c 83-Last 12¢ issue 84-Origin retold; begin 15¢	6	12	18	41	76	110
85-87-Firehair; Kubert-a	3	6	9	16	23	30
88-90-Jason's Quest: 90-Manhunter 2070 app.	3	6	9	14	20	25
91-93-Manhunter 2070: 92-Origin. 93-(9/70) Last 15¢ issue	3	6	9	14	20	25
94-Intro/origin new Doom Patrol & Robotman(8-9/77)	3	6	9	14	20	25
95,96-The Doom Patrol. 95-Origin Celsius	2	4	6	8	10	12
97-Power Girl; JSA cameos	4	8	12	25	40	55
98,99-Power Girl; origin in #98; JSA cameos	2	4	6	11	16	20
100-(52 pgs.)-Most Showcase characters featured	3	6	9	14	20	25
101-103-Hawkman; Adam Strange x-over	3	6	9	10	12	15
104-(52 pgs.)-O.S.S. Spies at War	3	6	9	12	16	20

NOTE: **Anderson** a-22-24i, 34-36i, 55, 56, 60, 61, 64, 101-103i; c-50i, 51i, 55, 56, 60, 61, 64. **Aparo** a-94. **Boring** c-10. **Estrada** a-104. **Fraden** c(p)-30, 31, 33. **Heath** c-3, 27-29. **Infantino** c/a(p)-4, 8, 13, 14; c-50p, 51p. **Gil Kane** a-22-24p, 34-36p; c-17-19, 22-24p(w/Giella), 31. **Kane/Anderson** c-34-36. **Kirby** c-11, 12. **Kirby/Stein** c-6, 7. **Kubert** a-2, 4i, 25, 26, 45, 53, 54, 57, 58, 82-87, 101-104; c-2, 4i. **Moreira** a-20, 21. **Orlando** a-62p, 63p, 97i; c-62, 63, 97i. **Sekowsky** a-65p. **Sparling** a-78. **Staton** a-94, 95-99p, 100; c-97-100p.

SHOWCASE '93
DC Comics: Jan, 1993 - No. 12, Dec, 1993 ($1.95, limited series, 52 pgs.)

1-12: 1-Begin 4 part Catwoman story & 6 part Blue Devil story; begin Cyborg story; Art Adams/Austin-a. 3-Flash by Charest (p). 6-Azrael in Bat-costume (2 pgs.). 7,8-Knightfall parts 13 & 14. 6-10-Deathstroke app. (6,10-cameo). 9,10-Austin-i. 10-Azrael as Batman in new costume app.; Gulacy-c. 11-Perez-c. 12-Creeper app.; Alan Grant scripts   5.00

NOTE: **Chaykin** c-9. **Fabry** c-8. **Giffen** a-12. **Golden** i-5. **Zeck** c-6.

SHOWCASE '94
DC Comics: Jan, 1994 - No. 12, Dec, 1994 ($1.95, limited series, 52 pgs.)

1-12: 1,2-Joker & Gunfire stories. 1-New Gods. 4-Riddler story. 5-Huntress-c/story w/app. new Batman. 6-Huntress-c/story w/app. Robin; Atom story. 7-Penguin story by Peter David, P. Craig Russell, & Michael T. Gilbert; Penguin-c by Jae Lee. 8,9-Scarface origin story by Alan Grant, John Wagner,& Teddy Kristiansen; Prelude to Zero Hour. 10-Zero Hour tie-in story. 11-Man-Bat.   5.00

NOTE: **Alan Grant** scripts-3, 4. **Kelley Jones** c-12. **Mignola** c-3. **Nebres** a(i)-2. **Quesada** c-10. **Russell** a-7p. **Simonson** c-11.

SHOWCASE '95
DC Comics: Jan, 1995 - No. 12, Dec, 1995 ($2.50/$2.95, limited series)

1-4-Supergirl story. 3-Eradicator-c; The Question story. 4-Thorn-c/story   4.00
5-12: 5-Thorn-c/story; begin $2.95-c. 8-Spectre story. 12-The Shade story by James Robinson & Wade Von Grawbadger; Maitresse story by Claremont & Alan Davis   4.00

SHOWCASE '96
DC Comics: Jan, 1996 - No. 12, Dec, 1996 ($2.95, limited series)

1-12: 1-Steve Geppi cameo. 3-Black Canary & Lois Lane-c/story; Deadman story by Jamie Delano & Wade Von Grawbadger, Gary Frank-c. 4-Firebrand & Guardian-c/story; The Shade & Dr. Fate "Times Past" story by James Robinson & Matt Smith begins, ends #5. 6-Superboy-c/app.; Atom app.; Capt. Marvel (Mary Marvel)-c/app. 8-Supergirl by David & Dodson. 10-Scare Tactics app. 11,12-Legion of Super-Heroes vs. Brainiac. 12-Jesse Quick app.   4.00

SHOWCASE PRESENTS... (B&W archive reprints of DC Silver Age stories)
DC Comics: 2005 - 2011 ($9.99/$16.99/$17.99/$19.99, B&W, over 500 pgs., squarebound)

Adam Strange Vol. 1 (2007, $16.99) r/Showcase #17-19 & Mystery in Space #53-84   17.00
Ambush Bug (2009, $16.99) r/first app. in DC Comics Presents #52 other early app.   17.00
Aquaman Vol. 1 (2007, $16.99) r/Aquaman #1-6 & other early app.   17.00
Aquaman Vol. 2 (2008, $16.99) r/Aquaman #7-23 & other early app.   17.00
Aquaman Vol. 3 (2008, $16.99) r/Aquaman #24-39 & other early app.   17.00
The Atom Vol. 1 (2007, $16.99) r/Showcase #34-36 & The Atom #1-17   17.00
The Atom Vol. 2 (2008, $16.99) r/The Atom #18-38   17.00
Batgirl Vol. 1 (2007, $16.99) r/early apps. from Detective #359 (1967) thru 1975   17.00
Bat Lash Vol. 1 (2009, $9.99) r/#1-7, Showcase #76, DC Special Series #16, and Jonah Hex #49,51,52   10.00
Batman Vol. 1 (2006, $16.99) r/"new look" from Detective #327-342, Batman #164-174   17.00

	GD	VG	FN	VF	VF/NM	NM-
	2.0	4.0	6.0	8.0	9.0	9.2

Batman Vol. 2 (2007, $16.99) r/"new look" from Detective #343-358, Batman #175-188 ... 17.00
Batman Vol. 3 (2008, $16.99) r/"new look" from Detective #359-375, Batman #189, 190-192,194-197,199-202 ... 17.00
Blackhawk Vol. 1 (2008, $16.99) r/#108-127 ... 17.00
Booster Gold Vol. 1 (2008, $16.99) r/#1-25 & Action Comics #594 ... 17.00
The Brave and the Bold Batman Team-ups Vol. 1 (2007, $16.99) r/#59,64,67-71,74-87 ... 17.00
The Brave and the Bold Batman Team-ups Vol. 2 (2007, $16.99) r/#88-108 ... 17.00
The Brave and the Bold Batman Team-ups Vol. 3 (2008, $16.99) r/#109-134 ... 17.00
Challengers of the Unknown Vol. 1 (2006, $16.99) r/#1-17 & Showcase #6,7,11,12 ... 17.00
Challengers of the Unknown Vol. 2 (2008, $16.99) r/#18-37 ... 17.00
DC Comics Presents: The Superman Team-ups Vol. 1 (2009, $17.99) r/#1-26 ... 18.00
Dial H For Hero ('10, $9.99) r/early apps. in House of Mystery #156-173 ... 10.00
Doc Savage ('11, $19.99) r/Doc Savage #1-8 (1975-77 Marvel B&W magazine) ... 20.00
The Doom Patrol Vol. 1 (2009, $16.99) r/#86-101 and My Greatest Adventure #80-85 ... 17.00
The Doom Patrol Vol. 2 (2010, $19.99) r/#102-121 ... 20.00
The Elongated Man Vol. 1 ('06, $16.99) r/early apps. in Flash & Detective ('60-'68) ... 17.00
Eclipso Vol. 1 (2009, $9.99) r/stories from House of Secrets #61-80 ... 10.00
Enemy Ace Vol. 1 (2008, $16.99) r/Our Army at War #151 & other early app. ... 17.00
The Flash Vol. 1 (2007, $16.99) r/Flash Comics #104 (last G.A. issue), Showcase #4,8,13,14 & The Flash #105-119 ... 17.00
The Flash Vol. 2 (2008, $16.99) r/The Flash #120-140 ... 17.00
The Flash Vol. 3 (2009, $16.99) r/The Flash #141-161 ... 17.00
The Flash, The Trial of ... (2011, $19.99) r/The Flash #323-327,329-336,340-350 ... 20.00
The Great Disaster Featuring The Atomic Knights and Hercules Vol. 1 (2007, $16.99) ... 17.00
Green Arrow Vol. 1 (2006, $16.99) r/Adventure #250-269, Brave and the Bold #50,71,85; Justice League of America #4; World's Finest #95-134,136,138,140 ... 17.00
Green Lantern Vol. 1 (2005, $16.99) r/Showcase #22-24 & Green Lantern #1-17 ... 20.00
Green Lantern Vol. 1 (2010, $19.99) r/Showcase #22-24 & Green Lantern #1-17 ... 20.00
Green Lantern Vol. 2 (2007, $16.99) r/Green Lantern #18-38 ... 17.00
Green Lantern Vol. 3 (2008, $16.99) r/Green Lantern #39-59 ... 17.00
Green Lantern Vol. 4 (2009, $16.99) r/Green Lantern #60-75 ... 17.00
Green Lantern Vol. 5 (2011, $19.99) r/Green Lantern #76-87,89 and back up stories from Flash #217-246 ... 20.00
Haunted Tank Vol. 1 ('06, $16.99) r/G.I. Combat #87-119, Brave & The Bold #52 and Our Army at War #155; Russ Heath-c ... 17.00
Haunted Tank Vol. 2 ('08, $16.99) r/G.I. Combat #120-156 ... 17.00
Hawkman Vol. 1 ('07, $16.99) r/Brave & The Bold #34-36,42-44, Mystery in Space #87-90, Hawkman #11-11, and The Atom #7 ... 17.00
Hawkman Vol. 2 ('08, $16.99) r/Brave & The Bold #70, Hawkman #12-27, The Atom #31, & The Atom and Hawkman #39-45 ... 17.00
The House of Mystery Vol. 1 ('06, $16.99) r/House of Mystery #174-194 ('68-'71) ... 17.00
The House of Mystery Vol. 2 ('07, $16.99) r/House of Mystery #195-211 ('71-'73) ... 17.00
The House of Mystery Vol. 3 ('09, $16.99) r/House of Mystery #212-226 ('73-'74) ... 17.00
The House of Secrets Vol. 1 ('08, $16.99) r/House of Secrets #81-98 ('69-'72) ... 17.00
The House of Secrets Vol. 2 ('09, $17.99) r/House of Secrets #99-119 ('72-'74) ... 18.00
Jonah Hex Vol. 1 (2005, $16.99) r/All Star Western #10-12, Weird Western Tales #13,14, 16-33; plus the continued adventures of Outlaw from All Star Western #2-8 ... 17.00
Justice League of America Vol. 1 ('05, $16.99) r/Brave & the Bold #28-30, J.L. of A. #1-16 and Mystery in Space #75 ... 17.00
Justice League of America Vol. 2 ('07, $16.99) r/Justice League of America #17-36 ... 17.00
Justice League of America Vol. 3 ('08, $16.99) r/Justice League of America #37-60 ... 17.00
Justice League of America Vol. 4 ('09, $16.99) r/Justice League of America #61-83 ... 17.00
Justice League of America Vol. 5 ('11, $19.99) r/Justice League of America #84-106 ... 20.00
Legion of Super-Heroes Vol. 1 ('07, $16.99) r/Adventure #247 & early app. thru 1964 ... 17.00
Legion of Super-Heroes Vol. 2 ('08, $16.99) r/app. in Adventure & Superboy 1964-66 ... 17.00
Legion of Super-Heroes Vol. 3 ('09, $16.99) r/Adventure #349-368 & S.P. Jimmy Olsen #106 ... 17.00
Legion of Super-Heroes Vol. 4 ('10, $19.99) r/app. in Adv., Action & Superboy 1968-72 ... 17.00
Martian Manhunter Vol. 1 (2007, $16.99) r/Detective #225-304 & Batman #78 (prototype) ... 17.00
Martian Manhunter Vol. 2 ('09, $16.99) r/Detective #305-326 & House of Myst. #143-173 ... 17.00
Metal Men Vol. 1 (2007, $16.99) r/#1-16; Brave & Bold #55, Showcase #37-40 ... 17.00
Metamorpho Vol. 1 ('05, $16.99) r/Brave&Bold #57,58,66,68; Metamorpho #1-17;JLA #42 ... 17.00
Our Army at War Vol. 1 ('10, $19.99) r/#1-20 ... 20.00
Phantom Stranger Vol. 1 (2006, $16.99) r/#1-21 (2nd series) & Showcase #80 ... 17.00
Phantom Stranger Vol. 2 (2008, $16.99) r/#22-41 and various 1970-1978 appearances ... 17.00
Robin The Boy Wonder Vol. 1 (2007, $16.99) r/back-ups from Batman, Detective, WF ... 17.00
Secrets of Sinister House ('10, $17.99) r/#5-18 and Sinister House of Secret Love #1-4 ... 18.00
Sgt. Rock Vol. 1 ('07, $16.99) r/G.I. Combat #68, Our Army at War #81-117 ... 17.00
Sgt. Rock Vol. 2 ('08, $16.99) r/Our Army at War #118-148 ... 17.00
Sgt. Rock Vol. 3 ('10, $19.99) r/Our Army at War #149-163,165-172,174-176,178-180 ... 20.00
Shazam! Vol. 1 ('06, $16.99) r/#1-33 ... 17.00
Strange Adventures Vol. 1 ('08, $16.99) r/#54-73 ... 17.00
Supergirl Vol. 1 ('07, $16.99) r/prototype from Superman #123 (8/58); 1st app. Action #252 (5/59) and early appearances thru Nov. 1961 ... 17.00
Supergirl Vol. 2 ('08, $16.99) r/appearances in Action Comics #283-321 (1961-1965) ... 17.00
Superman Vol. 1 ('05, $9.99) r/Action #241-257 & Superman #122-134 (1958-59) ... 20.00
Superman Vol. 1 ('10, $19.99) r/Action #241-257 & Superman #122-134 (1958-59) ... 20.00
Superman Vol. 2 ('06, $16.99) r/Action #258-275 & Superman #134-145 (1959-61) ... 17.00
Superman Vol. 3 ('07, $16.99) r/Action #279-292 & Superman #146-156 & Annual 3,4 ... 17.00
Superman Vol. 4 ('08, $16.99) r/Action #293-309 & Superman #157-166 (1962-64) ... 17.00
Superman Family Vol. 1 ('06, $16.99) r/Superman's Pal, Jimmy Olsen #1-22; Showcase #9 and Superman #22 ... 17.00
Superman Family Vol. 2 ('08, $16.99) r/Superman's Pal, Jimmy Olsen #23-34; Showcase #10 and Superman's Girl Friend, Lois Lane #1-7 ... 17.00
Superman Family Vol. 3 ('09, $16.99) r/Superman's Pal, Jimmy Olsen #35-44 and Superman's Girl Friend, Lois Lane #8-16 ... 17.00
Teen Titans Vol. 1 ('06, $16.99) r/#1-18; Brave & the Bold #54,60; Showcase #59 ... 17.00
Teen Titans Vol. 2 ('07, $16.99) r/#19-37, World's Finest #205 and Brave & Bold #83,94 ... 17.00
The Unknown Soldier Vol. 1 ('06, $16.99) r/Star Spangled War Stories #158-188 ... 17.00
The War That Time Forgot Vol. 1 ('07, $16.99) r/S.S.W.S. #90,92,94-125,127,128 ... 17.00
Warlord Vol. 1 ('09, $16.99) r/#1-28 and debut in 1st Issue Special #1 ... 17.00
The Witching Hour Vol. 1 ('11, $19.99) r/#1-19 ... 20.00
Wonder Woman Vol. 1 ('07, $16.99) r/#98-117 ... 17.00
Wonder Woman Vol. 2 ('08, $16.99) r/#118-137 ... 17.00
World's Finest Vol. 1 ('07, $16.99) r/#71-111 & Superman #76 ... 17.00

World's Finest Vol. 2 ('08, $16.99) r/#112-145 ... 17.00
World's Finest Vol. 3 ('10, $17.99) r/#146-160,162-169,171-173 ('64-'68) ... 18.00

SHOWGIRLS (Formerly Sherry the Showgirl #3)
Atlas Comics (MPC No. 2): No. 4, 2/57; June, 1957 - No. 2, Aug, 1957

	GD	VG	FN	VF	VF/NM	NM-
	2.0	4.0	6.0	8.0	9.0	9.2
4-(2/57) Dan DeCarlo-c/a begins	194	388	582	1242	2121	3000
1-(6/57) Millie, Sherry, Chili, Pearl & Hazel begin	232	464	696	1485	2543	3600
2	84	168	252	538	919	1300

SHREK (Movie)
Dark Horse Comics: Sept, 2003 - No. 3, Dec, 2003 ($2.99, limited series)
1-3-Takes place after 1st movie; Evanier/Bachs-a; CGI cover ... 4.00

SHREK (Movie)
Ape Entertainment: 2010 - No. 4, 2011 ($3.95, limited series)
1-3-Short stories by various ... 4.00

SHROUD, THE (See Super-Villain Team-Up #5)
Marvel Comics: Mar, 1994 - No. 4, June, 1994 ($1.75, mini-series)
1-4: 1,2,4-Spider-Man & Scorpion app. ... 4.00

SHROUD OF MYSTERY
Whitman Publications: June, 1982

	GD	VG	FN	VF	VF/NM	NM-
1	1	2	3	4	5	7

SHRUGGED
Aspen MLT, Inc.: No. 0, June, 2006 - No. 8, Feb, 2009 ($2.50/$2.99)
0-($2.50) Turner & Mastromauro-s/Gunnell-a; intro. story and character profiles ... 3.00
1-8-($2.99)-Six covers. 2-Three covers ... 3.00
... : Beginnings (5/06, $1.99) Prequel intro. to Ange and Dev; Gunnell-a; development art ... 3.00
Volume 2 (3/13, $1.00) 1-Marks & Gunnell-a; multiple covers ... 3.00
V2 #2-6-($3.99) Mastromauro-s/Marks-a. 6-(2/18) ... 4.00
Volume 3 (2/18, $3.99) 1-4-Mastromauro-s/André Risso-a; multiple covers ... 4.00

SHURI (From Black Panther)
Marvel Comics: Dec, 2018 - No. 10, Sept, 2019 ($3.99)

	GD	VG	FN	VF	VF/NM	NM-
1-Nnedi Okorafor-s/Leonardo Romero-a	3	6	9	14	19	24
2-Rocket & Groot app.; Okorafor-s/Romero-a	2	4	6	9	12	15
3-10: 3-5-Okorafor-s/Romero-a. 3-Rocket & Groot app. 6,7-Miles Morales app.; Ayala-s/Davidson-a. 8-10-Shuri in the Black Panther costume						6.00

SHUTTER
Image Comics: Apr, 2014 - No. 30, Jul, 2017 ($3.50/$3.99)
1-11-Keatinge-s/Del Duca-a ... 3.50
12-30-($3.99) ... 4.00

SHUT UP AND DIE
Image Comics/Halloween: 1998 - No. 3, 1998 ($2.95,B&W, bi-monthly)
1-3: Hudnall-s ... 3.00

SICK (Sick Special #131) (Magazine) (Satire)
Feature Publ./Headline Publ./Crestwood Publ. Co./Hewfred Publ./ Pyramid Comm./ Charlton Publ. No. 109 (4/76) on: Aug, 1960 - No. 134, Fall, 1980

	GD	VG	FN	VF	VF/NM	NM-
V1#1-Jack Paar photo on-c; Torres-a; Untouchables-s; Ben Hur movie photo-s	17	34	51	117	259	400
2-Torres-a; Elvis app.; Lenny Bruce app.	10	20	30	67	141	215
3-5-Torres-a in all. 3-Khruschev-c; Hitler-a. 4-Newhart-s; Castro-s; John Wayne.						
5-JFK/Castro-c; Elvis pin-up; Hitler.	8	16	24	56	108	160
6-Photo of Ricky Nelson & Marilyn Monroe; JFK	9	18	27	59	117	175
V2#1,2,4-8 (#7,8,10-14): 1-(#7) Hitler-s; Brando photo-s. 2-(#8) Dick Clark-s. 4-(#10) Untouchables-c; Candid Camera-s. 5-(#11) Nixon-c; Lone Ranger-s; JFK-s. 6-(#12) Beatnik-c/s. 8-(#14) Liz Taylor pin-up, JFK-s; Dobie Gillis-s; Sinatra & Dean Martin photo-s	8	16	24	51	96	140
3-(#9) Marilyn Monroe/JFK-c; Kingston Trio-s	9	18	27	57	111	165
V3#1-7(#15-21): 1-(#15) JFK app.; Liz Taylor/Richard Burton-s. 2-(#16) Ben Casey/ Frankenstein-c/s; Hitler photo-s. 5-(#19) Nixon back-c/s; Sinatra photo-s. 6-(#20) 1st Huckleberry Fink-c	5	10	15	33	57	80
8-(#22) Cassius Clay vs. Liston-s; 1st Civil War Blackouts-/Pvt. Bo Reargard w/ Jack Davis-a	5	10	15	35	63	90
V4#1-5 (#23-27): Civil War Blackouts-/Pvt. Bo Reargard w/ Jack Davis-a in all. 1-(#23) Smokey Bear-c; Tarzan-s. 2-(#24) Goldwater & Paar-s; Castro-s. 3-(#25) Frankenstein-c; Cleopatra/Liz Taylor-s; Steve Reeves photo-s. 4-(#26) James Bond-s; Hitler-s. 5-(#27) Taylor/Burton pin-up; Sinatra, Martin, Andress, Ekberg photo-s	4	8	12	27	44	60
28,31,36,39: 31-Pink Panther movie photo-s; Burke's Law-s. 39-Westerns; Elizabeth Montgomery photo-s; Beat mag-s	4	8	12	23	37	50
29,34,37,38: 29-Beatles-c by Jack Davis. 34-Two pg. Beatles-s & photo pin-up. 37-Playboy parody issue. 38-Addams Family-s	4	8	12	27	44	60
30,32,35,40: 30-Beatles photo pin-up; James Bond photo-s. 32-Ian Fleming-s; LBJ-s; Tarzan-s. 35-Beatles cameo; Three Stooges parody. 40-Tarzan-s; Crosby/Hope-s; Beatles parody	4	8	12	28	47	65
33-Ringo Starr photo-c & spoof on "A Hard Day's Night"; inside-c has Beatles photos	5	10	15	35	63	90
41,50,51,53,54,60: 41-Beatles Illustrated parody-c/s. 50-Mod issue; flip-c w/1967 calendar w/Bob Taylor-s. 51-Get Smart-s. 53-Beatles cameo; nudity panels. 54-Monkees-c. 60-TV Daniel Boone-s	3	6	9	19	30	40
42-Fighting American-c revised from Simon/Kirby/-s; "Good girl" art by Sparling; profile on Bob Powell; superhero parodies	5	10	15	33	57	80
43,49,52,55-59: 43-Sneaker set begins by Sparling. 45-Has #44 on-c & #45 on inside; TV Westerns-s. 46-Hell's Angels-s; NY Mets-s. 47-UFO/Space-c. 49-Men's Adventure mag. parody issue; nudity. 52-LBJ-s. 55-Underground culture special. 56-Alfred E. Neuman-c; inventors issue. 58-Hippie issue-c/s. 59-Hippie-s	3	6	9	16	24	32
61-64,66-69,71,73,75-80: 63-Tiny Tim-c & poster; Monkees-s. 64-Flip-c. 66-Flip-c; Mod Squad-s. 69-Beatles cameo; Peter Sellers photo-s. 71-Flip-c; Clint Eastwood-s. 76-Nixon-s; Marcus Welby-s. 78-Ma Barker-s; Courtship of Eddie's Father-s; Abbie Hoffman-s	3	6	9	15	22	28
65,70,74: 65-Cassius Clay/Brando/J. Wayne-s; Johnny Carson-s. 70-(9/69) John & Yoko-c, 1/2 pg. story. 74-Clay, Agnew, Namath & others as superheroes-c/s; Easy Rider-s;						

Shuri #8 © MAR

Sif #1 © MAR

Sigil (2011 series) #1 © MAR

	GD	VG	FN	VF	VF/NM	NM-
	2.0	4.0	6.0	8.0	9.0	9.2

Ghost and Mrs. Muir-s ... 3 6 9 16 24 32
72-(84 pgs.) Xmas issue w/2 pg. slick color poster; Tarzan-s; 2 pg. Superman & superheroes-s ... 3 6 9 21 33 45
81-85,87-95,98,99: 81-(2/71) Woody Allen photo-s. 85 Monster Mag. parody-s; Nixon-s w/Ringo & John cameo. 88-Klute photo-s; Nixon paper dolls page. 92-Lily Tomlin; Archie Bunker pin-up. 93-Woody Allen ... 2 4 6 13 18 22
86,96,97,100: 86-John & Yoko, Tiny Tim-c; Love Story movie photo-s. 96-Kung Fu-c; Mummy-s, Dracula & Frankenstein app. 97-Superman-s; 1974 Calendar; Charlie Brown & Snoopy pin-up. 100-Serpico-s; Cosell; Jacques Cousteau-s ... 3 6 9 14 19 24
101-103,105-114,116,119,120: 101-Three Musketeers-s; Dick Tracy-s. 102-Young Frankenstein-s. 103-Kojak-s; Evel Knievel-s. 105-Towering Inferno-s; Peanuts/Snoopy-s. 106-Cher-c/s. 10 7-Jaws-c/s. 108-Pink Panther-c/s; Archie-s. 109-Adam & Eve-s(nudity). 110-Welcome Back Kotter-s. 111-Sonny & Cher-s. 112-King Kong-c/s. 120-Star Trek-s ... 2 4 6 9 13 16
104,115,117,118: 104-Muhammad Ali-c/s. 115-Charlie's Angels-c/s. 117-Bionic Woman & Six Million $ Man-c/s; Cher D'Flower begins by Sparling (nudity). 118-Star Wars-s; Popeye-s ... 2 4 6 11 16 20
121-125,128-130: 122-Darth Vader-c/s. 123-Jaws II-s. 128-Superman-c/movie parody. 130-Alien movie-s ... 2 4 6 10 14 18
126,127: 126-(68 pgs.) Battlestar Galactica-c/s; Star Wars-s; Wonder Woman-s. 127-Mork & Mindy-s; Lord of the Rings-s ... 2 4 6 13 18 22
131-(1980 Special) Star Wars/Star Trek/Flash Gordon wraparound-c/s; Superman parody; Battlestar Galactica-s ... 3 6 9 14 19 24
132,133: 132-1980 Election-c/s; Apocalypse Now-s. 133-Star Trek-s; Chips-s; Superheroes page ... 3 6 9 14 19 24
134 (scarce)(68 pg. Giant)-Star Wars-c/s; Alien-s; WKRP-s; Mork & Mindy-s; Taxi-s; MASH-s ... 4 8 12 19 30 40
Annual 1- Birthday Annual (1966)-3 pg. Huckleberry Fink fold out ... 4 8 12 23 37 50
Annual 2- 7th Annual Yearbook (1967)-Davis-c, 2 pg. glossy poster insert ... 4 8 12 23 37 50
Annual 3 (1968) "Big Sick Laff-in" on-c (84 pgs.)-w/psychedelic posters; Frankenstein poster ... 3 6 9 17 26 35
Annual 1969 "Great Big Fat Annual Sick", 1969 "9th Year Annual Sick", 1970, 1971 ... 3 6 9 16 24 32
Annual 12,13-(1972,1973, 84 pgs.) 13-Monster-c ... 3 6 9 16 24 32
Annual 14,15-(1974,1975, 84 pgs.) 14-Hitler photo-s ... 3 6 9 16 24 32
Annual 2-4 (1980) ... 2 4 6 9 13 16
Special 1 (1980) Buck Rogers-c/s; MASH-s ... 3 6 9 14 19 24
Special 2 (1980) Wraparound Star Wars: Empire Strikes Back-c; Charlie's Angels/Farrah-s; Rocky-s; plus reprints ... 3 6 9 14 19 24
Yearbook 15(1975, 84 pgs.) Paul Revere-c ... 3 6 9 16 23 30
NOTE: Davis a-42, 87; c-22, 23, 25, 29, 31, 32. Powell a-7, 31, 57. Simon a-1-3, 10, 41, 42, 87, 99; c-1, 47, 57, 59, 69, 91, 95-97, 99, 100, 102, 107, 112. Torres a-1-3, 29, 31, 47, 49. Tuska a-14, 41-43. Civil War Blackouts-23, 24. #42 has biography of Bob Powell.

SIDEKICK (Paul Jenkins'...)
Image Comics (Desperado): June, 2006 - No. 5, May, 2007 ($3.50, limited series)
1-5-Paul Jenkins-s/Chris Moreno-a ... 3.50
... Super Summer Sidekick Spectacular 1 (7/07, $2.99) ... 3.50
... Super Summer Sidekick Spectacular 2 (9/07, $2.99) ... 3.50

SIDEKICK
Image Comics (Joe's Comics): Aug, 2013 - No. 12, Dec, 2015 ($2.99)
1-7,9-12: 1-Straczynski-a/Mandrake-a; intro. The Cowl and Flyboy; 6 covers. 4-6-Two covers ... 3.00
8-($3.99) Chrome-c ... 4.00

SIDEKICKS
Fanboy Ent., Inc.: Jun, 2000 - No. 3, Apr, 2001 ($2.75, B&W, lim. series)
1-3-J.Torres-s/Takeshi Miyazawa-a. 3-Variant-c by Wieringo ... 3.00
... Super Fun Summer Special (Oni Press, 7/03, $2.99) art by various incl. Wieringo ... 3.00
... The Substitute (Oni Press, 7/02, $2.95) ... 3.00
... The Transfer Student TPB (Oni Press, 6/02, $8.95, 9" x 6") r/#1-3 ... 9.00
... The Transfer Student TPB 2nd Ed. (10/03, $11.95, 9" x 6") r/#1-3; The Substitute ... 12.00

SIDESHOW
Avon Periodicals: 1949 (one-shot)
1-(Rare)-Similar to Bachelor's Diary ... 181 362 543 1158 1979 2800

SIDEWAYS (Follows events from Dark Nights: Metal)
DC Comics: Apr, 2018 - No. 13, Apr, 2019 ($2.99)
1-13: 1-Didio-s/Rocafort-a; intro Derek James ... 4.00
Annual 1 (1/19, $4.99) Takes place after #9; New 52 Superman & Seven Soldiers app. ... 5.00

SIEGE
Marvel Comics: Mar, 2010 - No. 4, Jun, 2010 ($3.99, limited series)

1-4-Asgard is invaded; Bendis-s/Coipel-a. 4-End of The Sentry ... 4.00
1-4-Variant covers by Dell'Otto ... 8.00
...: Captain America (6/10, $2.99) Gage-s/Dallocchio-a/Djurdjevic-c; both Caps app. ... 4.00
...: Loki (6/10, $2.99) Gillen-s/McKelvie-a/Djurdjevic-c; Hela & Mephisto app. ... 4.00
...: Secret Warriors (6/10, $2.99) Hickman-s/Vitti-a/Djurdjevic-c; Phobos attacks ... 4.00
...: Spider-Man (6/10, $2.99) Reed-s/Santucci-a/Djurdjevic-c; Venom & Ms. Marvel app. ... 4.00
...: Storming Asgard - Heroes & Villains (3/10, $3.99) Dossiers on participants; Land-c ... 4.00
...: The Cabal (2/10, $3.99) series prelude; Bendis-s/Lark-a; covers by Finch & Davis ... 4.00
...: Young Avengers (6/10, $2.99) McKeever-s/Santucci-a/Djurdjevic-c; Wrecking Crew app. ... 4.00

SIEGE (Secret Wars tie-in) (Continued from Secret Wars: Journal #1)
Marvel Comics: Sept, 2015 - No. 4, Dec, 2015 ($3.99, limited series)
1-4-Gillen-s/Andrade-a; Abigail Brand, Kate Bishop & Ms. America app. ... 4.00

SIEGE: EMBEDDED
Marvel Comics: Mar, 2010 - No. 4, Jul, 2010 ($3.99, limited series)
1-4-Reed-s/Samnee-a/Granov-c; Ben Urich & Volstagg cover the invasion ... 4.00

SIEGEL AND SHUSTER: DATELINE 1930s
Eclipse Comics: Nov, 1984 - No. 2, Sept, 1985 ($1.50/$1.75, Baxter paper #1)
1,2: 1-Unpublished samples of strips from the '30s; includes 'Interplanetary Police'; Shuster-c. 2 ($1.75, B&W)-unpublished strips; Shuster-c ... 4.00

SIF (See Thor titles)
Marvel Comics: Jun, 2010 ($3.99, one shot)
1-Deconnick-s/Stegman-a/Foreman-c; Beta Ray Bill app. ... 4.00

SIGIL (Also see CrossGen Chronicles)
CrossGeneration Comics: Jul, 2000 - No. 42, Dec, 2003 ($2.95)
1-42: 1-Barbara Kesel-s/Ben & Ray Lai-a. 12-Waid-s begin. 21-Chuck Dixon-s begin ... 3.00

SIGIL
Marvel Comics: May, 2011 - No. 4, Aug, 2011 ($2.99)
1-4-Carey-s/Kirk-a ... 3.00
1-Variant-c by McGuinness ... 5.00

SIGMA
Image Comics (WildStorm): March, 1996 - No. 3, June, 1996 ($2.50, limited series)
1-3: 1-"Fire From Heaven" prelude #2; Coker-a. 2-"Fire From Heaven" pt. 6. 3-"Fire From Heaven" pt. 14. ... 4.00

SILENCER, THE
DC Comics: Mar, 2018 - No. 18, Aug, 2019 ($2.99/$3.99)
1-12: 1-Abnett-s/Romita Jr.-a; intro. Honor Guest; Talia al Ghul app. 3-6-Deathstroke app. 4-8-Bogdanovic-a ... 3.00
13-18-($3.99): 13-Origin of Silencer; Talia al Ghul app.; Marion-a/Kirkham-c ... 4.00

SILENT DRAGON
DC Comics (WildStorm): Sept, 2005 - No. 6, Feb, 2006 ($2.99, limited series)
1-6-Tokyo 2066 A.D.; Leinil Yu-a/c; Andy Diggle-s ... 3.00
TPB (2006, $19.99) r/series; sketch page ... 20.00

SILENT HILL: DEAD/ALIVE
IDW Publishing: Dec, 2005 - No. 5, Apr, 2006 ($3.99, limited series)
1-5-Stakal-a/Ciencin-s. 1-Four covers. 2-5-Two covers ... 4.00

SILENT HILL DOWNPOUR: ANNE'S STORY
IDW Publishing: Aug, 2014 - No. 4, Nov, 2014 ($3.99, limited series)
1-4-Tom Waltz-s/Tristan Jones-a; two covers on each ... 4.00

SILENT HILL: DYING INSIDE
IDW Publishing: Feb, 2004 - No. 5, June, 2004 ($3.99, limited series)
1-5-Based on the Konami computer game. 1-Templesmith-a; Ashley Wood-c ... 4.00
... Paint It Black (2/05, $7.49) Ciencin-s/Thomas-a ... 7.50
...: The Grinning Man 5/05, $7.49) Ciencin-s/Stakal-a ... 7.50
TPB (8/04, $19.99) r/#1-5; Ashley Wood-c ... 20.00

SILENT HILL: PAST LIFE
IDW Publishing: Oct, 2010 - No. 4, Jan, 2011 ($3.99, limited series)
1-4-Waltz-s; two covers on each ... 4.00

SILENT HILL: SINNER'S REWARD
IDW Publishing: Feb, 2008 - No. 4, Apr, 2008 ($3.99, limited series)
1-4-Waltz-s/Stamb-a ... 4.00

SILENT INVASION, THE
Renegade Press: Apr, 1986 - No.12, Mar, 1988 ($1.70/$2.00, B&W)
1-12-UFO sightings of the '50's ... 4.00
Book 1- reprints ($7.95) ... 8.00

SILENT MOBIUS

	GD	VG	FN	VF	VF/NM	NM-		GD	VG	FN	VF	VF/NM	NM-
	2.0	4.0	6.0	8.0	9.0	9.2		2.0	4.0	6.0	8.0	9.0	9.2

Viz Select Comics: 1991 - No. 5, 1992 ($4.95, color, squarebound, 44 pgs.)
1-5: Japanese stories translated to English — 5.00

SILENT NIGHT DEADLY NIGHT
American Mythology Productions: 2022 - No. 4, 2023 ($3.99)
1-4-Kuhoric & Check-s/Calzada-a — 4.00

SILENT SCREAMERS (Based on the Aztech Toys figures)
Image Comics: Oct, 2000 ($4.95)
Nosferatu Issue - Alex Ross front & back-c — 5.00

SILENT WAR
Marvel Comics: Mar, 2007 - No. 6, Aug, 2007 ($2.99, limited series)
1-6-Inhumans, Black Bolt and Fantastic Four app.; Hine-s/Irving-a/Watson-c — 3.00
TPB (2007, $14.99) r/series — 15.00

SILK (See Amazing Spider-Man 2014 series #1 & #4 for debut)
Marvel Comics: Apr, 2015 - No. 7, Nov, 2015 ($3.99)
1-Robbie Thompson-s/Stacey Lee-a/Dave Johnson-c; Spider-Man app.

	2	4	6	11	16	20

2-7: 3-6-Black Cat app. 4-Fantastic Four app. 7-Secret Wars tie-in — 4.00

SILK (Spider-Man)
Marvel Comics: Jan, 2016 - No. 19, Jun, 2017 ($3.99)
1-Robbie Thompson-s/Stacey Lee-a; Black Cat & Mockingbird app.

	1	2	3	5	6	8

2-19: 4,5-Fish-a. 7,8-"Spider-Women" tie-in; Spider-Woman & Spider-Gwen app. — 4.00
14-17-Clone Conspiracy

SILK (Spider-Man)
Marvel Comics: May, 2021 - No. 5, Oct, 2021 ($3.99)
1-5: 1-Maurene Goo-s/Takeshi Miyazawa-a. 3-Silvermane app. — 4.00

SILK (Spider-Man)
Marvel Comics: Mar, 2022 - No. 5, Jul, 2022 ($3.99, limited series)
1-5-Emily Kim-s/Takeshi Miyazawa-a — 4.00

SILK (Spider-Man)
Marvel Comics: Jul, 2023 - No. 5, Nov, 2023 ($3.99, limited series)
1-5-Emily Kim-s/Ig Guara-a/Dave Johnson-c — 4.00

SILKE
Dark Horse Comics: Jan, 2001 - No. 4, Sept, 2001 ($2.95)
1-4-Tony Daniel-s/a — 3.00

SILKEN GHOST
CrossGen Comics: June, 2003 - No. 5, Oct, 2003 ($2.95, limited series)
1-5-Dixon-s/Rosado-a — 3.00
Traveler Vol. 1 (2003, $9.95) digest-sized reprint #1-5 — 10.00

SILLY PILLY (See Frank Luther's...)

SILLY SYMPHONIES (See Dell Giants)

SILLY TUNES
Timely Comics: Fall, 1945 - No. 7, June, 1947

1-Silly Seal, Ziggy Pig begin	36	72	108	211	343	475
2-(2/46)	20	40	60	117	189	260
3-7: 6-New logo	17	34	51	98	154	210

SILVER (See Lone Ranger's Famous Horse...)

SILVER AGE
DC Comics: July, 2000 ($3.95, limited series)
1-Waid-s/Dodson-a; "Silver Age" style x-over; JLA & villains switch bodies — 4.00
....: Challengers of the Unknown ($2.50) Joe Kubert-c; vs. Chronos — 3.00
....: Dial H For Hero ($2.50) Jim Mooney-c; Waid-s/Kitson-a; vs. Martian Manhunter — 3.00
....: Doom Patrol ($2.50) Ramona Fradon-c/Peyer-s — 3.00
....: Flash ($2.50) Carmine Infantino-c; Kid Flash and Elongated Man app. — 3.00
....: Green Lantern ($2.50) Gil Kane-c/Busiek-s/Anderson-a; vs. Sinestro — 3.00
....: Justice League of America ($2.50) Ty Templeton-c; Millar-s/Kolins-a — 3.00
....: Showcase ($2.50) Dick Giordano-c/a; Johns-s; Batgirl, Adam Strange app. — 3.00
....: Secret Files ($4.95) Intro. Agamemno; short stories & profile pages — 5.00
....: Teen Titans ($2.50) Nick Cardy-c; vs. Penguin, Mr. Element, Black Manta — 3.00
... The Brave and the Bold ($2.50) Jim Aparo-c; Batman & Metal Men — 3.00
... 80-Page Giant ($5.95) Conclusion of x-over; "lost" Silver Age stories — 6.00

SILVERBACK
Comico: 1989 - No. 3, 1990 ($2.50, color, limited series, mature readers)
1-3: Character from Grendel: Matt Wagner-a — 4.00

SILVERBLADE
DC Comics: Sept, 1987 - No. 12, Sept, 1988
1-12-Colan-c/a in all — 4.00

SILVER CEREBUS
Aardvark-Vanaheim: Feb, 2020 ($4.00, B&W, one-shot)
1-Cerebus figures placed over outer space backgrounds; Silver Surfer #1-c swipe — 4.00

SILVER CITY
AfterShock Comics: May, 2021 - No. 5, Sept, 2021 ($4.99/$3.99, limited series)
1-($4.99)-Olivia Cuartero-Briggs-s/Luca Merli-a — 5.00
2-5-($3.99) — 4.00

SILVER COIN, THE
Image Comics: May, 2021 - Present ($3.99, anthology)
1-15: 1-Zdarsky-s/Walsh-a. 2-Kelly Thompson-s. 3-Ed Brisson-s. 4-Jeff Lemire-s — 4.00

SILVERHAWKS
Star Comics/Marvel Comics#6: Aug, 1987 - No. 6, June, 1988 ($1.00)
1-6 — 4.00

SILVERHEELS
Pacific Comics: Dec, 1983 - No. 3, May, 1984 ($1.50)
1-3-Bruce Jones-s, Scott Hampton-c/a; Steacy-a in back-up stories — 4.00

SILVER KID WESTERN
Key/Stanmor Publications: Oct, 1954 - No. 5, July, 1955

1	13	26	39	74	105	135
2-Hanging cover	8	16	24	40	50	60
3-5	6	12	18	31	38	60
I.W. Reprint #1,2-Severin-c: 1-r/#? 2-r/#1	2	4	6	9	13	16

SILVER SABLE AND THE WILD PACK (See Amazing Spider-Man #265 and Sable & Fortune)
Marvel Comics: June, 1992 - No. 35, Apr, 1995; No. 36, Jan, 2018 ($1.25/$1.50)
1-($2.00)-Embossed & foil stamped-c; Spider-Man app. — 5.00
2-24,26-35: 4,5-Dr. Doom-c/story. 6,7-Deathlok-c/story. 9-Origin Silver Sable.
10-Punisher-c/s. 15-Capt. America-c/s. 16,17-Intruders app. 18,19-Venom-c/s. 19-Siege
of Darkness x-over. 23-Daredevil (in new costume) & Deadpool app. 24-Bound-in card
sheet. Li'l Sylvie backup story — 4.00
25-($2.00, 52 pgs.)-Li'l Sylvie backup story — 5.00
36-(1/18, $3.99) Marvel Legacy one-shot; Faust-s/Siqueira-a — 5.00

SILVER STAR (Also see Jack Kirby's...)
Pacific Comics: Feb, 1983 - No. 6, Jan, 1984 ($1.00)
1-6: 1-1st app. Last of the Viking Heroes. 1-5-Kirby-c/a. 2-Ditko-a — 5.00
...: Graphite Edition TPB (TwoMorrows Publ., 3/06, $19.95) r/series in B&W including Kirby's
original pencils; sketch pages; original screenplay — 20.00
Jack Kirby's Silver Star, Volume 1 HC (Image Comics, 2007, $34.99) r/series in color;
sketch pages; original screenplay — 35.00

SILVER STREAK COMICS (Crime Does Not Pay #22 on)
**Your Guide Publs. No. 1-7/New Friday Publs. No. 8-17/Comic House Publ./
Newsbook Publ.:** Dec, 1939 - No. 21, May, 1942; No. 23, 1946; nn, Feb, 1946
(Silver logo-#1-5)

1-(Scarce)-Intro the Claw by Cole (r-in Daredevil #21), Red Reeves Boy Magician (ends #2),
Captain Fearless (ends #2), The Wasp (ends #2), Mister Midnight (ends #2) begin;
Spirit Man only app. Calling The Duke begins (ends #2). Barry Lane only app. Silver
Metallic-c begin, end #5; Claw-c 1,2,6-8

	1250	2500	3750	9500	18,250	27,000

2-The Claw ends (by Cole); makes pact w/Hitler; Simon-c/a (The Claw); ad for Marvel
Mystery Comics #2 (12/39). Lance Hale begins (receives super powers). Solar Patrol app.

	486	972	1458	3550	6275	9000

3-1st app. & origin Silver Streak (2nd with Lightning speed); Dickie Dean the Boy Inventor,
Lance Hale, Ace Powers (ends #6), Bill Wayne The Texas Terror (ends #6) & The Planet
Patrol (ends #6) begin. Detective Snoop, Sergeant Drake only app.

	432	864	1296	3154	5577	8000

4-Sky Wolf begins (ends #6); Silver Streak by Jack Cole (new costume); 1st app. Jackie,
Lance Hale's sidekick. Lance Hale gains immortality

	219	438	657	1402	2401	3400

5-Cole c/a(2); back-c ad for Claw app. in #6

	252	504	756	1613	2757	3900

6-(Scarce, 9/40)-Origin & 1st app. Daredevil (blue & yellow costume) by Jack Binder;
The Claw returns as the Green Claw; classic Cole Claw-c

	3550	7100	10,650	24,800	44,400	64,000

7-Claw vs. Daredevil serial begins c/sty, ends #11. Daredevil new costume-blue & red
by Jack Cole & 3 other Cole stories (38 pgs.). Origin Whiz, S. S.'s Falcon 2nd app.
Daredevil & 1st Daredevil-c (by Cole). Cloud Curtis, Presto Martin begins. Dynamo Hill
& Zongar The Miracleman only app.

	1300	2600	3900	9900	17,950	26,000

8-Classic Claw vs. Daredevil by Cole c/sty; last Cole Silver streak. Dan Dearborn begins
(ends #12). Secret Agent X-101 begins, (ends #9)

	1000	2000	3000	7600	13,800	20,000

9-Claw vs. Daredevil by Cole. Silver Streak-c by Bob Wood

	290	580	870	1856	3178	4500

10-Origin & 1st app. Captain Battle (5/41) by Binder; Claw vs. Daredevil by Cole;
Silver Streak/robot-c by Bob Wood

	290	580	870	1856	3178	4500

11-Intro./origin Mercury by Bob Wood, Silver Streak's sidekick; conclusion Claw vs. Daredevil
by Rico; in 'Presto Martin,' 2nd pg., newspaper says 'Roussos does it again'

	206	412	618	1318	2259	3200

12-Daredevil-c by Rico; Lance Hale finds lost valley w/cave men, battles dinosaurs,
sabre-toothed cats; his last app.

	187	374	561	1197	2049	2900

13-Origin Thun-Dohr; Scarlet Skull (a Red Skull swipe) vs. Daredevil; Bingham Boys app.

	187	374	561	1197	2049	2900

14-Classic Nazi skull men-c/sty	300	600	900	2010	3505	5000
15-Classic Mummy horror-c	300	600	900	2070	3635	5200

16-(1/41) Hitler-c; Silver Streak battles Hitler sty w/classic splash page. Capt. Battle fights
walking corpses

	595	1190	1785	4350	7675	11,000

17-Last Daredevil issue.	206	412	618	1318	2259	3200

18-The Saint begins (2/42, 1st app.) by Leslie Charteris (see Movie Comics #2 by DC);
The Saint-c

	181	362	543	1158	1979	2800

19,20 (1942)-Ned of the Navy app. 19-Silver Streak-c by Bob Wood. 20-Japanese WWII-c/sty; last
Captain Battle, Dickie Dean, Cloud Curtis; Red Reed, Alonzo Appleseed only app.;
Wolverton's Scoop Scuttle app.

	93	186	279	591	1021	1450

21-(5/42)-Hitler app. in strip on cover; Wolverton's Scoop Scuttle app.

	123	246	387	818	1413	2000

nn(#22, 2/46, 60 pgs.)(Newsbook Publ.)-R-/S.S. story from #4-7 by Jack Cole plus 2 Captain
Fearless stories-r from #1&2, all in color; bondage/torture-c by Dick Briefer w/torture meter

	423	846	1269	3088	5444	7800

23 (nd, 11/1946?, 52 pgs.)(An Atomic Comic) bondage-c, Silver Streak c/sty

	135	270	405	864	1482	2100

NOTE: *Jack Binder* a-8-12, 15; c-3, 4, 13-15, 17. *Dick Briefer* a-9-50; c-nn(#22). *Jack Cole*-a-(Claw)-#2, 3,
6-10, nn(#22). (Daredevil)-#6-10, (Dickie Dean)-#3-10, (Pirate Prince)-#7, (Silver Streak)-#4-8, nn; c-5 (Silver
Streak), 6 (Claw), 7, 8 (Daredevil). *Bill Everett* Red Reed begins #20. *Fred Guardineer* a-#8-12. *Don Rico*
a-11-17 (Daredevil), 15, 19 (Silver Streak); c-11, 12, 16. *Joe Simon* a-2 (Solar Patrol), 3 (Silver Streak); c-2. *Basil
Wolverton* a-20, 21. *Bob Wood* a-8-15 (Presto Martin), 9 (Silver Streak); c-9, 10. Captain Battle c-11, 13-15, 17.
Claw c-#1, 2, 6-8. Daredevil c-7, 8, 12. Dickie Dean c-19. Ned of the Navy c-20 (war). The Saint c-18. Silver Streak
c-5, 10, 16, nn(#22), 23.

SILVER STREAK COMICS (Homage with Golden Age size and Golden Age art styles)
Image Comics: No. 24, Dec, 2009 ($3.99, one-shot)
24-New Daredevil, Claw, Silver Streak & Captain Battle stories; Larsen, Grist, Gilbert-a — 5.00

SILVER SURFER (See Fantastic Four, Fantasy Masterpieces V2#1, Fireside Book Series, Marvel Graphic
Novel, Marvel Presents #8, Marvel's Greatest Comics & Tales To Astonish #92)

SILVER SURFER, THE (Also see Essential Silver Surfer)
Marvel Comics Group: Aug, 1968 - No. 18, Sept, 1970; June, 1982
1-More detailed origin by John Buscema (p); The Watcher back-up stories begin (origin),

Silk #5 © MAR

Silver Streak Comics #13 © LEV

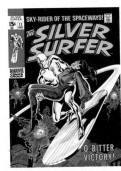

Silver Surfer #11 © MAR

	GD	VG	FN	VF	VF/NM	NM-
	2.0	4.0	6.0	8.0	9.0	9.2

	GD 2.0	VG 4.0	FN 6.0	VF 8.0	VF/NM 9.0	NM- 9.2
end #7; (No. 1-7: 25¢, 68 pgs.)	221	442	663	1823	4112	6400
2-1st app. Badoon	21	42	63	147	324	500
3-1st app. Mephisto	111	222	333	888	1994	3100
4-Lower distribution; Thor & Loki app.	172	344	516	1419	3210	5000
5-7-Last giant size. 5-The Stranger app.; Fantastic Four app. 6-Brunner inks. 7-(8/69)-Early cameo Frankenstein's monster (see X-Men #40)	15	30	45	110	227	350
8-10: 8-18-(15c issues)	12	24	36	79	170	260
11-13,15,18: 15-Silver Surfer vs. Human Torch; Fantastic Four app. 17-Nick Fury app. 18-Vs. The Inhumans; Kirby-a; Trimpe-c	10	20	30	70	150	230
14-Spider-Man x-over	23	46	69	161	356	550
14 Facsimile Edition (3/2019, $3.99) reprints #14 with original ads and letter column	2	4	6	9	12	15
...Omnibus Vol. 1 Hardcover (2007, $74.99, dustjacket) r/#1-18 re-colored with original letter pages, Fantastic Four Annual #5 & Not Brand Echh #13; Lee and Buscema bios						80.00
V2#1 (6/82, 52 pgs.)-Byrne-c/a	2	4	6	9	13	16

NOTE: *Adkins* a-8-15i. *Brunner* a-6i. *J. Buscema* a-1-17p. *Colan* a-1-3p. *Reinman* a-1-4i. #1-14 were reprinted in *Fantasy Masterpieces* V2#1-14.

SILVER SURFER (Volume 3) (See Marvel Graphic Novel #38)
Marvel Comics Group: V3#1, July, 1987 - No. 146, Nov. 1998

	GD 2.0	VG 4.0	FN 6.0	VF 8.0	VF/NM 9.0	NM- 9.2
1-Double-size ($1.25)-Englehart & Rogers-s/a begins; vs. the Champion; Fantastic Four app. w/She-Hulk; Nova (Frankie Raye) & Galactus app; Surfers exile on Earth ends	3	6	9	17	26	35
2-9: 2-Surfer returns to Zenn-La; Shalla-Bal app. as Empress of Zenn-La; Skrulls app.; Surfer story next in West Coast Avengers Annual #2 and Avengers Annual #16. 3-Collector & Champion app.; Surfer vs. the Runner (not seen since 1975). 4-Elders of the Universe app.; Collector, Champion, Runner, Gardener, Contemplator, Grandmaster & Possessor; 1st app. of Astronomer, Obliterator & Trader; Ego revealed as an Elder; origin Mantis. 5-vs. the Obliterator. 6-Origin of the Obliterator. 7-Supreme Intelligence & the Elders app. 8-Supreme Intelligence app.; Surfer gains the Soul Gem. 9-Elders vs. Galactus; six Soul Gems app.	1	2	3	5	6	8
10-Galactus absorbs Elders; Eternity app.	2	4	6	10	14	18
11-14: 11-1st app. Reptyl, Clumsy Foulup & the fake Surfer; Nova (Frankie Raye) app. 12-Death of fake Contemplator; Reptyl & Nova (Frankie Raye) app.; last Rogers-a. 13-Ronan the Accuser vs. Surfer and Nova (Frankie Raye); fake Surfer app.; last Rogers-a. 14-Origin & death of the fake Surfer; Ronan app.; Nova (Frankie Raye) app.; story continues in Surfer Ann. #1						6.00
15,16: 15-Ron Lim-c/a begins (9/88); Soul Gems app.; Reed, Sue and Franklin of the Fantastic Four app.; Galactus & Nova (Frankie Raye) app.; Elders of the Universe app.; Astronomer, Possessor & Trader. 16-Astronomer, Trader & In-Betweener app.; brief x-over w/Fantastic Four #319	1	2	3	5	6	8
17,18: 17-Elders of the Universe, In-Betweener, Death & Galactus app. 18-Galactus vs. the In-Betweener; Elders of the Universe, the Soul Gems & Lord Order & Master Chaos app.	1	2	3	5	6	8
19,20-Firelord & Starfox app.						6.00
21-24,26-30,32,33,39-43: 21-vs. the Obliterator. 22-Ego the Living Planet app. 26-Super-Skrull app. 27-Stranger & Super-Skrull app. 28-Death of Super-Skrull; Reptyl app. 29-Midnight Sun app; death of Reptyl. 30-Midnight Sun & the Stranger app. 32,33-Jim Valentino-s; 33-Impossible Man app. 39-Alan Grant scripts. 40-43-Surfer in Dynamo City						5.00
25,31-($1.50, 52 pgs.) 25-New Kree/Skrull war; Badoon app; Skrulls regain their shape-shifting ability. 31-Conclusion of Kree/Skrull war; Stranger & the Living Tribunal app.						6.00
34-Thanos-series begins.; Starlin scripts begin:	3	6	9	19	30	40
35-38: 35-1st full Thanos in Silver Surfer (3/90); return Drax the Destroyer on last pg. (cameo). 36-Recaps history of Thanos, Captain Marvel & Warlock app. in recap. 37-Full reintro Drax the Destroyer; Drax-c. 38-Silver Surfer battles Thanos, Nebula app; Thanos story continues in Thanos Quest #1-2	3	4	6	8		10
44-Classic Thanos-c; 1st app. of the Infinity Gauntlet; Thanos defeats the Surfer & Drax; Mephisto cameo	5	10	15	35	63	90
45-Thanos-c; Mephisto app.; origin of the Infinity Gems	3	6	9	17	26	35
46-Return of Adam Warlock (2/91); reintro Gamora & Pip the Troll (within Soul World)	3	6	9	16	23	30
47-49: 47-Warlock vs. Drax. 48-Galactus app; last Starlin scripts (also #50). 49-Thanos & Mephisto app.; Ron Marz scripts begin	1	3	4	6	8	10
50-($1.50, 52 pgs.)-Embossed & silver foil-c; Silver Surfer has brief battle w/Thanos; story cont'd in Infinity Gauntlet #1; extended origin flashback to the Silver Surfer's life on Zenn-La	3	6	9	16	23	30
50-2nd & 3rd printings						5.00
51-59-Infinity Gauntlet x-overs; 51-Galactus and Nova (Frankie Raye) app. 52-Firelord vs. Drax; continued in Infinity Gauntlet #2. 53-Death of Clumsy Foulup. 54-vs the Rhino; Hulk cameo. 55,56-Thanos kills everyone (Surfer dream sequence); Warlock app; continued in Infinity Gauntlet #4. 57-x-over w/Infinity Gauntlet #5. 58-Defenders app. (dream sequence); Warlock app. 59-Warlock, Dr. Strange, Dr. Doom, Firelord, Drax & Thanos app; concluded in Infinity Gauntlet #6						6.00

	GD 2.0	VG 4.0	FN 6.0	VF 8.0	VF/NM 9.0	NM- 9.2
60-69,71-73: 60-vs. Midnight Sun; Warlock & Dr. Strange cameo; Black Bolt, Gorgon & Karnak of the Inhumans app. 61-Collector app. 63-Captain Marvel app. 64-Collector app. 65-Reptyl returns. 66-Mistress Love & Master Hate app. 67-69-Infinity War x-overs. 67-Continued from Infinity War #1; x-over w/Dr. Strange #42; Nebula, Galactus, Nova (Frankie Raye) & Dr. Strange app; Magus cameo; continued in Infinity War #2. 68,69-Galactus, Nova & Dr. Strange app. 69-Magus cameo; continues in Infinity War #3. 71-Herald Ordeal Pt. 2; Nebula, Firelord & Galactus app; Surfer vs. Morg. 72-Herald Ordeal Pt. 3; 1st app. Cyborg Nebula (from the GOTG movie); Firelord, Nova, Galactus & Morg app. 73-Herald Ordeal Pt. 4; reintro Gabriel the Airwalker; Firelord, Galactus, Nova, Morg app; Terrax cameo						4.00
70,74: Herald Ordeal Pts.1,5. 70-1st app. Morg (becomes the new Herald of Galactus), Nova released of her duties; Nebula app. 74-Terrax, Firelord, Airwalker, Nova, Nebula app.						5.00
75-($2.50, 52 pgs.)-Embossed foil-c; Lim-c/a; Herald Ordeal Pt. 6; Surfer, Firelord, Airwalker, Terrax & Nova vs. Morg; death of Nova; Morg stripped of the power cosmic; Firelord & Airwalker resume Herald duties						5.00
76-81,83-87,90-97: 76-Origin Jack of Hearts retold; Galactus, Airwalker, Firelord & Nebula app.; Morg cameo. 77-Jack of Hearts & Nebula app; return of Morg. 78-New Jack of Hearts costume; Nebula, Morg & Galactus app. 79-Captain Atlas & Dr. Minerva app.; Morg vs. Terrax; Gladiator & Beta Ray Bill cameo. 80-1st app. Ganymede (named in issue #81); Morg vs. Terrax. 81-1st cameo app. Tyrant; Morg, Terrax, Gladiator, Beta Ray Bill cameos. 83-85-Infinity Crusade x-overs. 83-Surfer vs. Firelord; x-over w/Infinity Crusade #3; Thanos cameo; cont'd in Infinity Crusade #4. 84-Thanos app. 85-Wonder Man & Storm vs. Surfer; concluded in Infinity Crusade #6. 86-Blood & Thunder Pt. 2; cont'd from Thor #468; Surfer & Beta Ray Bill vs. insane Thor; Pip the Troll & Warlock cameo; cont'd in Warlock Chronicles #6. 87-Blood & Thunder Pt. 6; cont'd from Thor #469; Dr. Strange, Warlock & the Infinity Watch app; cont'd in Warlock Chronicles #7. 89-Colleen Doran-a(p). 90-Legacy (son of Capt. Marvel) app. 92-Marvel Masterprints card insert; last Lim-a. 93-Fantastic Four app; Thing, Human Torch & Ant-Man (Scott Lang); Spider-Man cameo. 94-Fantastic Four & Warlock and the Infinity Watch app. 95-Fantastic Four app.; Hulk cameo. 97-Terrax app. Champion cameo						4.00
82-($1.75. 52 pgs.)-Surfer, Morg, Terrax, Gladiator, Beta Ray Bill, Jack of Hearts & Ganymede vs. Tyrant; Galactus app.						5.00
88,99: 88-Blood & Thunder Pt. 10-cont'd from Thor #470; Thanos vs. insane Thor; Dr. Strange, Warlock & the Infinity Watch app; cont'd in Warlock Chronicles #7; 'Kay-bee Toys' coupon insert for Ghost Rider 'Hot Pursuit' comic; 7-pg. Punisher 'Suicide Run' advertisement; 7-pg. 'Juice' magazine insert featuring interviews with the New Warriors. 99-Mephisto cameo						5.00
98-vs. Champion; Drax & Thanos app.						6.00
100-($2.25. 52 pgs.)-Wraparound-c; vs. Mephisto						5.00
100-($3.95, 52 pgs.)-Enhanced-silver holofoil-c						5.00
101-108,110: 101-Tyrant cameo; Surfer returns to Zenn-La; Shalla-Bal app. 102-Galactus & Morg app; Tyrant cameo. 104-Morg app. Galactus, Morg & Legacy app; Surfer vs. Super-Skrull; 4-pg Rune/Silver Surfer preview. 106-Galactus, Morg & Tyrant app. 108-Tyrant vs. Galactus; Morg & Legacy app. 110-Legacy & Nebula app; John Buscema-a.						4.00
109-Tyrant vs. Galactus; Legacy app.; Morg no longer Herald.						4.00
111-121: 111-New direction; Pérez scripts begin. 112-1st app. Uni-Lord. 114-Watcher app. 120-vs. Uni-Lord. 121-End of the Uni-Lord saga; Beta Ray Bill & Quasar cameo						5.00
122-Legacy & Beta Ray Bill app.						4.00
123-124,126-127,129-130: 123-1st Dematteis script; Surfer returns to Earth; Alicia Masters app. 124-Kymaera (Namorita) app. 126-Dr. Strange app. 127-Alicia Masters & the Puppet Master app. 130-Surfer learns that Zenn-La has been destroyed; Galactus app.						4.00
125 ($2.95)-Wraparound-c; Hulk-c/app.						5.00
128-Spider-Man & Daredevil-c/app.	1	3	4	6	8	10
131-134: 131-Galactus app. 133-Puppet Master app. 134-Scrier & The Other app.						6.00
135-140: 135-Agatha Harkness, Scrier & the Thing app. 136,137-Scrier & Mephisto app. 138-Thing app. 140-Jon J. Muth-a begins						6.00
141-144: 143,144-Psycho-Man app.	1	2	3	4	6	7
145-Alicia Masters; Surfer returns to Earth	2	4	6	9	12	15
146-Firelord app; last issue.	3	6	9	19	30	40
#(-1) Flashback (7/97)-Stan Lee app.; 1st app. The Other; Galactus app.						6.00
Annual 1 (1988, $1.75)-Evolutionary War Pt. 3; continued in Punisher Annual #1; 1st Ron Lim-a on Silver Surfer (20 pg. back-up story & pin-ups); Eternals app. & Super-Skrull team-up; Mantis app.; story continues in West Coast Avengers #37; Evolutionary War continues in New Mutants Annual #4						6.00
Annual 2 (1989, $2.00)-Atlantis Attacks Pt. 3; Ghaur the Deviant cameo; Dr. Strange cameo; story continues in Iron Man Annual #10						5.00
Annual 3-6: 3-(1990, $2.00)-Lifeform Pt. 4; continued from Punisher Annual #3. 4-(1991, $2.00)-The Korvac Quest Pt. 3; continued from Thor Annual #16; 3-pg. origin story; Silver Surfer battles the Guardians of the Galaxy (30th Century version); continued in Guardians of the Galaxy Annual #1. 5-(1992, $2.25)- Return of the Defenders Pt. 3; continued from Namor the Sub-Mariner Annual #2; Hulk & Dr. Strange app.; continued in Dr. Strange Annual #2; Nebula app. in Firelord & Starfox back-up story. 6-(1993, $2.95)-Polybagged w/trading card; 1st app. Legacy; card is by Lim/Austin; Surfer & Legacy vs. Ronan the Accuser; Terrax, Jack of Hearts & Ganymede back up features						5.00

	GD	VG	FN	VF	VF/NM	NM-		GD	VG	FN	VF	VF/NM	NM-
	2.0	4.0	6.0	8.0	9.0	9.2		2.0	4.0	6.0	8.0	9.0	9.2

Annual 7-(1994, $2.95)-Morg resumes being Herald to Galactus; Firelord leaves; Legacy app. in back-up ... 5.00

Annual '97-($2.95)-Scrier app. Annual '98-($2.95)..& Thor; vs. Millennius; Avengers app. ... 5.00

...Dangerous Artifacts-(1996, 48 pgs.)-Marz scripts w/Claudio Castellini-a; Galactus & Thanos app; 1st app. White Raven ... 1 3 4 6 9

Graphic Novel (1988, HC, $14.95)-Judgment Day; Lee-s/Buscema-a; Galactus vs. Mephisto ... 30.00

Graphic Novel (1988, SC, $10.95)-Judgment Day; Jusko-c ... 20.00

Graphic Novel (1990, HC, $16.95)-The Enslavers; Stan Lee-s & Pollard-a; non-canon Marvel universe story ... 25.00

Graphic Novel (1991, HC, $12.95)-Homecoming; Starlin-s/ death of Shalla-Bal ... 15.00

Inner Demons TPB (4/98, $3.50)/r#123,125,126 ... 5.00

...: Rebirth of Thanos TPB (2006, $24.99) r/#34-38, Thanos Quest #1,2; Logan's Run #6 ... 25.00

...: The First Coming of Galactus nn (11/92, $5.95, 68 pgs.)-Reprints Fantastic Four #48-50 with new Lim-c ... 6.00

Wizard 1/2 ... 2 4 6 9 12 15

NOTE: *Austin* c(i)-7, 8, 71, 73, 74, 76, 79. *Cowan* a-143,146. *Cully Hamner* a-83p. *Ron Lim* a(p)-15-31, 33-38, 40-55, (56, 57-part-p), 60-65, 73-82, Annual 2, 4; c(p)-15-31, 32-38, 40-84, 86-92, Annual 2, 4-6. *Muth* c/a-140-142,144,145. *M. Rogers* a-1-10, 12, 19, 21; c-1-9, 11, 12, 21.

SILVER SURFER (Volume 4)
Marvel Comics: Sept, 2003 - No. 14, Dec, 2004 ($2.25/$2.99)

1-6: 1-Milx-a; Jusko/a. 2-Jae Lee-c ... 4.00
7-14-($2.99) ... 4.00
...Vol. 1: Communion (2004, $14.99) r/#1-6 ... 15.00

SILVER SURFER (Volume 5)
Marvel Comics: Apr, 2011 - No. 5, Aug, 2011 ($2.99, limited series)

1-5-Pagulayan-a. 1-Segovia-a. 4,5-Fantastic Four app. ... 4.00

SILVER SURFER (6th series)
Marvel Comics: May, 2014 - No. 15, Jan, 2016 ($3.99)

1-10: 1-Dan Slott-s/Michael Allred-a/c. 3-Guardians of the Galaxy app. 8-10-Galactus app. ... 4.00
11-($4.99) Story runs upside down on top or bottom halves of the pages ... 5.00
12-15: 13-15-Secret Wars tie-in ... 4.00

SILVER SURFER (7th series)
Marvel Comics: Mar, 2016 - No. 14, Dec, 2017 ($3.99)

1-5,7-14-Slott-s/Allred-a. 1-4-The Thing app. 3-50th Anniversary issue; Shalla Bal app. ... 4.00
6-(10/16, $4.99) 200th issue; Spider-Man app.; cover gallery ... 5.00
Annual 1 (1/18, $4.99) Ethan Sacks-s/André Lima Araujo-a; Galactus app. ... 5.00
...: The Prodigal Sun 1 (10/19, $4.99) Peter David-s/Francesco Manna-a; Prah'd'gul app. ... 5.00

SILVER SURFER, THE (Epic): Dec, 1988 - No. 2, Jan, 1989 ($1.00, lim. series)

1-By Stan Lee scripts & Moebius-c/a ... 2 4 6 11 16 20
2 ... 2 4 6 8 10 12
HC (1988, $19.95, dust jacket) r/#1,2; "Making Of" text section and sketch pages ... 30.00
... By Stan Lee & Moebius (3/13, $7.99) r/#1&2; bonus production diary from Moebius ... 3 6 9 19 30 40
...: Parable ('98, $5.99) r/#1&2 ... 3 6 9 16 23 30

SILVER SURFER: BLACK
Marvel Comics: Aug, 2019 - No. 5, Dec, 2019 ($3.99, limited series)

1-5-Donny Cates-s/Tradd Moore-a; Ego & Knull app. ... 4.00

SILVER SURFER: GHOST LIGHT
Marvel Comics: Apr, 2023 - No. 5, Aug, 2023 ($4.99/$3.99, limited series)

1-($4.99) Jennings-s/De Landro-a; the return of Al Harper ... 5.00
2-5-($3.99) ... 4.00

SILVER SURFER: IN THY NAME
Marvel Comics: Jan, 2008 - No. 4, Apr, 2008 ($2.99, limited series)

1-4-Spurrier-s/Huat-a. 1-Turner-c. 2-Dell'Otto-c. 3-Paul Pope-c. 4-Galactus app. ... 4.00

SILVER SURFER: LOFTIER THAN MORTALS
Marvel Comics: Oct, 1999 - No. 2, Oct, 1999 ($2.50, limited series)

1,2-Remix of Fantastic Four #57-60; Velluto-a ... 5.00

SILVER SURFER REBIRTH
Marvel Comics: Mar, 2022 - No. 5, Jul, 2022 ($3.99, limited series)

1-5-Ron Marz-s/Ron Lim-a; Mar-Vell and Thanos app. ... 4.00

SILVER SURFER REBIRTH: LEGACY
Marvel Comics: Nov, 2023 - No. 5, Mar, 2024 ($3.99, limited series)

1-5-Ron Marz-s/Ron Lim-a ... 4.00

SILVER SURFER: REQUIEM
Marvel Comics: July, 2007 - No. 4, Oct, 2007 ($3.99, limited series)

1-4-Straczynski-s/Ribic-a. 1-Origin retold; Fantastic Four app. ... 4.00
HC (2007, $19.99) r/#1-4, Ribic cover sketches ... 20.00

SILVER SURFER/SUPERMAN
Marvel Comics: 1996 ($5.95,one-shot)

1-Perez-s/Lim-c/a(p) ... 2 4 6 8 11 14

SILVER SURFER: THE BEST DEFENSE (Also see Immortal Hulk, Doctor Strange, Namor)
Marvel Comics: Feb, 2019 ($4.99, one-shot)

1-Jason Latour-s/a; Ron Garney-c; Galactus app. ... 5.00

SILVER SURFER VS. DRACULA
Marvel Comics: Feb, 1994 ($1.75, one-shot)

1-r/Tomb of Dracula #50; Everett Vampire/Venus #19; Howard the Duck back-up by Brunner; Lim-c(p) ... 1 3 4 6 8 10

SILVER SURFER/WARLOCK: RESURRECTION
Marvel Comics: Mar, 1993 - No. 4, June, 1993 ($2.50, limited series)

1-4-Starlin-s/a & scripts. 1-Surfer joins Warlock & the Infinity Watch to rescue Shalla-Bal; story continued from the 'Homecoming' GN. 2-Death app.; Mephisto cameo. 3-Surfer vs. Mephisto. 4-Warlock vs. Mephisto; Shalla-Bal revived. ... 4.00

SILVER SURFER/WEAPON ZERO

Marvel Comics: Apr, 1997 ($2.95, one-shot)

1-"Devil's Reign" pt. 8 ... 3.00

SILVERTIP (Max Brand)
Dell Publishing Co.: No. 491, Aug, 1953 - No. 898, May, 1958

Four Color 491 (#1); all painted-c ... 9 18 27 59 117 175
Four Color 572,608,637,667,731,789,898-Kinstler-a ... 5 10 15 34 60 85
Four Color 835 ... 5 10 15 34 60 85

SIM CITY
Aardvark-Vanaheim: ($4.00, B&W, with cover swipes from Sin City)

...: A Dave To Kill For 1 (2/19) Cerebus figures in Frank Miller style backgrounds ... 4.00
... - That Issue After 1 (3/19) Cerebus figures with Gustave Doré artwork of Hell ... 4.00

SIMON DARK
DC Comics: Dec, 2007 - No. 18, May, 2009 ($2.99)

1-Intro. Simon Dark; Steve Niles-s/Scott Hampton-a/c ... 4.00
1-Second printing with full face variant cover ... 3.00
2-18 ... 3.00
...: Ashes TPB (2009, $17.99) r/#7-12 ... 18.00
...: The Game of Life TPB (2009, $17.99) r/#13-18 ... 18.00
...: What Simon Does TPB (2008, $14.99) r/#1-6 ... 18.00

SIMPSONS COMICS (See Bartman, Futurama, Itchy & Scratchy & Radioactive Man)
Bongo Comics Group: 1993 - No. 245, 2018 ($1.95/$2.50/$2.99/$3.99)

1-($2.25)-FF#1-c swipe; pull-out poster; flip book ... 4 8 12 23 37 50
2-5: 2-Patty & Selma flip-c/sty. 3-Krusty, Agent of K.L.O.W.N. flip-c/story. 4-Infinity-c; flip-c of Busman #1; w/trading card. 5-Wraparound-c w/trading card ... 1 3 4 6 8 10
6-40: All Flip books. 6-w/"Chief Wiggum's "Crime Comics". 7-w/"McBain Comics". 8-w/"Edna, Queen of the Congo". 9-w/"Barney Gumble". 10-w/"Apu". 11-w/"Homer". 12-w/"White Knuckled War Stories". 13-w/"Jimbo Jones' Wedgie Comics". 14-w/"Grampa". 15-w/"Itchy & Scratchy". 16-w/"Bongo Grab Bag". 17-w/"Headlight Comics". 18-w/"Milhouse". 19,20-w/"Roswell." 21,22-w/"Roswell". 23-w/"Hellfire Comics". 24-w/"Lil' Homey".
36-39-Flip book w/Radioactive Man ... 6.00
41-49,51-99: 43-Flip book w/Poochie. 52-Dini-s. 77-Dixon-s. 85-Begin $2.99-c ... 5.00
50-($5.95) Wraparound-c; 80 pgs.; square-bound ... 1 2 3 5 6 8
100-($6.99) 100 pgs.; square-bound; clip issue of past highlights ... 1 3 4 6 8 10
101-182,184-199,201-224: 102-Barks Ducks homage. 117-Hank Scorpio app. 122-Archie spoof. 132-Movie poster enclosed. 132-133-Two-parter. 144-Flying Hellfish flashback. 150-w/Poster. 163-Aragonés-s/a. 218-Guardians of the Galaxy spoof ... 3.00
183-Archie homage with Stan Goldberg-a ... 3.00
200-(2013, $4.99) Wraparound-c; short stories incl. Dorkin-s/a; Matt Groening cameo ... 5.00
225-244-($3.99) 225-Bonus back-up 1970s Eddie & Lou story. 237-Bartman app. ... 4.00
245-($3.99) Last issue; Bongo the rabbit app.; bonus cover gallery of #1-245 ... 4.00
... A Go-Go (1999, $11.95)-r/#32-35; ...Big Bonanza (1998, $11.95)-r/#28-31, ...Extravaganza (1994, $10.00)-r/#1-4; infinity-c, ...On Parade (1998, $11.95)-r/#24-27, ...Simpsorama (1996, $10.95)-r/#11-14 ... 12.00
Simpsons Classics 1-30 (2004 - 2011, $3.99, magazine-size, quarterly) reprints ... 4.00
Simpsons Comics Barn Burner ('04, $14.95) r/#57-61,63 ... 15.00
Simpsons Comics Beach Blanket Bongo ('07, $14.95) r/#71-75,77 ... 15.00
Simpsons Comics Belly Buster ('04, $14.95) r/#49,51,53-56 ... 15.00
Simpsons Comics Hit the Road! ('08, $15.95) r/#85,86,88,89,90 ... 16.00
Simpsons Comics Jam-Packed Jamboree ('06, $14.95) r/#64-69 ... 15.00
Simpsons Comics Madness ('03, $14.95) r/#43-48 ... 15.00
Simpsons Comics Royale ('01, $14.95) r/various Bongo issues ... 15.00
Simpsons Comics Treasure Trove 1-4 ('08-'09, $3.99, 6" x 8") r/various Bongo issues ... 4.00
Simpsons Summer Shindig ('07-'15, $4.99) 1-9-Anthology. 1-Batman/Ripken insert ... 5.00
Simpsons Winter Wing Ding ('06-'14, $4.99) 1-10-Holiday anthology. 1-Dini-s ... 5.00

SIMPSONS COMICS AND STORIES
Welsh Publishing Group: 1993 ($2.95, one-shot)

1-(Direct Sale)-Polybagged w/Bartman poster ... 4 8 12 23 37 50
1-(Newsstand Edition)-Without poster ... 4 8 12 28 47 65

SIMPSONS COMICS PRESENTS BART SIMPSON
Bongo Comics Group: 2000 - No. 100; 2016 ($2.50/$2.99)

1-Bill Morrison-c ... 2 4 6 11 16 20
2-40: 7-9-Dan DeCarlo-layouts. 13-Begin $2.99-c. 17,37-Bartman app. ... 5.00
41-99: 50-Aragonés-s/a ... 3.00
100-($4.99) 100-year old Bart, Mrs. Krabappel, Fruit Bat Man app. ... 5.00
The Big Book of Bart Simpson TPB (2002, $12.95) r/#1-4 ... 15.00
The Big Bad Book of Bart Simpson TPB (2003, $12.95) r/#5-8 ... 15.00
The Big Bratty Book of Bart Simpson TPB (2004, $12.95) r/#9-12 ... 15.00
The Big Beefy Book of Bart Simpson TPB (2005, $13.95) r/#13-16 ... 15.00
The Big Bouncy Book of Bart Simpson TPB (2006, $13.95) r/#17-20 ... 15.00
The Big Beastly Book of Bart Simpson TPB (2007, $14.95) r/#21-24 ... 15.00
The Big Brilliant Book of Bart Simpson TPB (2008, $14.95) r/#25-28 ... 15.00

SIMPSONS FUTURAMA CROSSOVER CRISIS II (TV) (Also see Futurama/Simpsons Infinitely Secret Crossover Crisis)
Bongo Comics: 2005 - No. 2, 2005 ($3.00, limited series)

1,2-The Professor brings the Simpsons' Springfield crew to the 31st century ... 2 4 6 9 12 15

SIMPSONS ILLUSTRATED (TV)
Bongo Comics: 2012 - No. 27, 2017 ($3.99, quarterly)

1-Reprints in all ... 2 4 6 8 10 12
2-20 ... 4.00
21-27-($4.99) 25-All-monster issue ... 5.00

SIMPSONS ONE-SHOT WONDERS (TV)
Bongo Comics: 2012 - 2018 ($2.99/$3.99)

...: Bart Simpson's Pal Milhouse 1 - Short stories; centerfold with decal ... 1 3 4 6 8 10
...: Chief Wiggum's Felonius Funnies 1 ($3.99) - Future Cop app. ... 5.00
...: Duffman 1 ($3.99) - Green Lantern spoof; centerfold with die-cut Duffman mask ... 2 4 6 9 12 15

Simpsons Comics #183 © Bongo

Sin City: Silent Night #1 © Frank Miller

Sinestro #15 © DC

	GD	VG	FN	VF	VF/NM	NM-
	2.0	4.0	6.0	8.0	9.0	9.2

	GD	VG	FN	VF	VF/NM	NM-
	2.0	4.0	6.0	8.0	9.0	9.2

...: Grampa 1 ($3.99) - "Choose Your Adventure" format; wraparound-c

	1	3	4	6	8	10

...: Jimbo 1 ($3.99) - Short stories; centerfold with die-cut skull sticker   4.00

...: Kang & Kodos 1 ($3.99) - Short stories; centerfold with bumper stickers

	1	3	4	6	8	10

...: Krusty 1 ($3.99) - Krusty's backstory; back-c swipe of Uncanny X-Men #141   6.00

...: Li'l Homer 1 - Short stories of Homer's childhood; centerfold with cut-outs

	1	2	3	5	6	8

...: Lisa 1 ($3.99) - Short stories by Matsumoto and others; sticker page centerfold   6.00

...: Maggie 1 - Short stories by Aragonés and others; paperdoll centerfold; Aragonés-c   6.00

...: McBain 1 ($3.99) - Entire issue unfolds to a poster on the back

	1	3	4	6	8	10

...: Mr. Burns 1 ($3.99) - Short stories incl. Richie Rich spoof; Fruit Bat Man mask

	1	2	3	5	6	8

...: Professor Frink 1 ($3.99) - Short stories; 3-D glasses insert; 3-D story and back-c

	1	3	4	6	8	10

...: Ralph Wiggums Comics 1 - Short stories by Aragonés and others

	3	6	9	14	20	25

...: The Mighty Moe Szyslak 1 - Short stories by various; Flintstones homage back-c

	2	4	6	9	12	15

SIMPSONS SUPER SPECTACULAR (TV)
Bongo Comics: 2006 - No. 16, 2013 ($2.99)

1	1	3	4	6	8	10
2-16: 2-Bartman, Stretch Dude and The Cupcake Kid team up; back-up story Brereton-a.
5-Fradona on Metamorpho spoof. 8-Spirit spoof. 9,10,14-16-Radioactive Man app.   4.00

SINBAD, JR (TV Cartoon)
Dell Publishing Co.: Sept-Nov, 1965 - No. 3, May, 1966

1	4	8	12	25	40	55
2,3	3	6	9	17	26	35

SIN BOLDLY
Image Comics: Dec, 2013 ($3.50, B&W, one-shot)
1-J.M. Linsner-s/a/c; short stories with Sinful Suzi and Obsidian Stone   3.50

SIN CITY (See Dark Horse Presents, A Decade of Dark Horse, & San Diego Comic Con Comics #2,4)
Dark Horse Comics (Legend)
TPB ($15.00) Reprints early DHP stories   15.00
Booze, Broads & Bullets TPB ($15.00)   15.00
Frank Miller's Sin City: One For One (8/10, $1.00) reprints debut story from DHP #51   3.00

SIN CITY (FRANK MILLER'S...) (Reissued TPBs to coincide with the April 2005 movie)
Dark Horse Books: Feb, 2005 ($17.00/$19.00, 6" x 9" format with new Miller covers)
Volume 1: The Hard Goodbye ($17.00) reprints stories from Dark Horse Presents #51-62 and
DHP Fifth Anniv. Special; covers and publicity pieces   17.00
Volume 2: A Dame to Kill For ($17.00) r/Sin City: A Dame to Kill For #1-6   17.00
Volume 3: The Big Fat Kill ($17.00) r/Sin City: The Big Fat Kill #1-5; pin-up gallery   17.00
Volume 4: That Yellow Bastard ($19.00) r/Sin City: That Yellow Bastard #1-6; pin-up gallery by
Mike Allred, Kyle Baker, Jeff Smith and Bruce Timm; cover gallery   19.00
Volume 5: Family Values ($12.00) r/Sin City: Family Values GN   12.00
Volume 6: Booze, Broads & Bullets ($15.00) r/Sin City: The Babe Wore Red and Other Stories;
Silent Night; story from A Decade of Dark Horse; Lost Lonely & Lethal; Sex & Violence; and
Just Another Saturday Night   15.00
Volume 7: Hell and Back ($28.00) r/Sin City: Hell and Back #1-9; pin-up gallery   28.00

SIN CITY: A DAME TO KILL FOR
Dark Horse Comics (Legend): Nov, 1993 - No. 6, May, 1994 ($2.95, B&W, limited series)
1-6: Frank Miller-c/a & story in all. 1-1st app. Dwight.   6.00
1-3-Second printing   4.00
Limited Edition Hardcover   85.00
Hardcover   25.00
TPB ($15.00)   15.00

SIN CITY: FAMILY VALUES
Dark Horse Comics (Legend): Oct, 1997 ($10.00, B&W, squarebound, one-shot)
nn-Miller-c/a & story   10.00
Limited Edition Hardcover   75.00

SIN CITY: HELL AND BACK
Dark Horse (Maverick): Jul, 1999 - No. 9 ($2.95/$4.95, B&W, limited series)
1-8-Miller-c/a & story. 7-Color   5.00
9-($4.95)   6.00

SIN CITY: JUST ANOTHER SATURDAY NIGHT
Dark Horse Comics (Legend): Aug, 1997 (Wizard 1/2 offer, B&W, one-shot)

1/2-Miller-c/a & story	1	2	3	5	6	8

nn (10/98, $2.50) r/#1/2   4.00

SIN CITY: LOST, LONELY & LETHAL
Dark Horse Comics (Legend): Dec, 1996 ($2.95, B&W and blue, one-shot)
nn-Miller-c/s/a; w/pin-ups   5.00

SIN CITY: SEX AND VIOLENCE
Dark Horse Comics (Legend): Mar, 1997 ($2.95, B&W and blue, one-shot)
nn-Miller-c/a & story   5.00

SIN CITY: SILENT NIGHT
Dark Horse Comics (Legend): Dec, 1995 ($2.95, B&W, one-shot)
1-Miller-c/a & story; Marv app.   6.00

SIN CITY: THAT YELLOW BASTARD (Second Ed. TPB listed under Sin City (Frank Miller's...))
Dark Horse Comics (Legend): Feb, 1996 - No. 6, July, 1996 ($2.95/$3.50, B&W and yellow, limited series)
1-5: Miller-c/a & story in all. 1-1st app. Hartigan.   6.00
6-($3.50) Error & corrected   6.00
Limited Edition Hardcover   25.00
TPB ($15.00)   15.00

SIN CITY: THE BABE WORE RED AND OTHER STORIES
Dark Horse Comics (Legend): Nov, 1994 ($2.95, B&W and red, one-shot)
1-r/serial run in Previews as well as other stories; Miller-c/a & scripts; Dwight app.   6.00

SIN CITY: THE BIG FAT KILL (Second Edition TPB listed under Sin City (Frank Miller's...))
Dark Horse Comics (Legend): Nov, 1994 - No. 5, Mar, 1995 ($2.95, B&W, limited series)
1-5-Miller story & art in all; Dwight app.   6.00
Hardcover   25.00
TPB ($15.00)   15.00

SIN CITY: THE FRANK MILLER LIBRARY
Dark Horse Books: Set 1, Nov, 2005; Set 2, Mar, 2006 ($150, slipcased hardcover, 8" x 12")
Set 1 - Individual hardcovers for Volume 1: The Hard Goodbye, Volume 2: A Dame to Kill For,
Volume 3: The Big Fat Kill, Volume 4: That Yellow Bastard; new red foil stamped covers;
slipcase box is black with red foil graphics   150.00
Set 2 - Individual hardcovers for Volume 5: Family Values, Volume 6: Booze, Broads & Bullets,
Volume 7: Hell and Back, new red foil stamped covers; The Art of Sin City red hardcover;
slipcase box is black with red foil graphics   150.00

SINDBAD (See Capt. Sinbad under Movie Comics, and Fantastic Voyages of Sindbad)

SINERGY
Image Comics (Shadowline): Nov, 2014 - No. 5, Mar, 2015 ($3.50)
1-5: 1-Oeming & Soma-s/Oeming-a/c   3.50

SINESTRO
DC Comics: Jun, 2014 - No. 23, Jul, 2016 ($2.99)
1-23: 1-Bunn-s/Eaglesham-a; Lyssa Drak & Arkillo app. 6-8-Godhead x-over; New Gods app.
7-Van Sciver-a. 9-11-Mongul app. 15-Lobo app. 16-20-Black Adam app.
17-20-Wonder Woman app. 19,20-Harley Quinn & Superman app.   3.00
Annual 1 (6/15, $4.99) Bunn-s/Eaglesham-a; art by various   5.00
...: Futures End 1 (11/14, $2.99, regular-c) Five years later; Bunn-s/Lima-a/Nowlan-c   3.00
...: Futures End 1 (11/14, $3.99, 3-D cover)   4.00
...: Year of the Villain 1 (10/19, $4.99) Russell-s/Cinar-a; Apex Lex Luthor app.   5.00

SINGING GUNS (See Fawcett Movie Comics)

SINGLE SERIES (Comics on Parade #30 on)(Also see John Hix...)
United Features Syndicate: 1938 - No. 28, 1942 (All 68 pgs.)

Note: See Individual Alphabetical Listings for prices

1-Captain and the Kids (#1)   2-Broncho Bill (1939) (#1)
3-Ella Cinders (1939)   4-Li'l Abner (1939) (#1)
5-Fritzi Ritz (#1)   6-Jim Hardy by Dick Moores (#1)
7-Frankie Doodle   8-Peter Pat (On sale 7/14/39)
9-Strange As It Seems   10-Little Mary Mixup
11-Mr. and Mrs. Beans   12-Joe Jinks
13-Looy Dot Dope   14-Billy Make Believe
15-How It Began (1939)   16-Illustrated Gags (1940)-Has ad
17-Danny Dingle   for Captain and the Kids #1
18-Li'l Abner (#2 on-c)   reprint listed below
19-Broncho Bill (#2 on-c)   20-Tarzan by Hal Foster
21-Ella Cinders (#2 on-c; on sale 3/19/40)   22-Iron Vic
23-Tailspin Tommy by Hal Forrest (#1)   24-Alice in Wonderland (#1)
25-Abbie and Slats   26-Little Mary Mixup (#2 on-c, 1940)
27-Jim Hardy by Dick Moores (1942)   28-Ella Cinders & Abbie and Slats (1942)
1-Captain and the Kids (1939 reprint)-2nd   1-Fritzi Ritz (1939 reprint)-2nd ed.
Edition

NOTE: Some issues given away at the 1939-40 New York World's Fair (#6).

	GD 2.0	VG 4.0	FN 6.0	VF 8.0	VF/NM 9.0	NM- 9.2

SINISTER DEXTER
IDW Publishing: Dec, 2013 - No. 7, Jun, 2014 ($3.99)
1-7: 1-Dan Abnett-s/Andy Clarke-a; two covers by Clarke and Fuso   4.00

SINISTER HOUSE OF SECRET LOVE, THE (Becomes Secrets of Sinister House No. 5 on)
National Periodical Publ.: Oct-Nov, 1971 - No. 4, Apr-May, 1972

1 (All 52 pgs.) -Grey-tone-c	14	28	42	96	211	325
2,4	8	16	24	51	96	140
3-Toth-a; Grey-tone-c	8	16	24	55	105	155

SINISTER SONS
DC Comics: Apr, 2024 - Present ($3.99)
1-3: 1-Sons of General Zod and Sinestro; Tomasi-s/Lafuente-a   4.00

SINISTER WAR
Marvel Comics: Sept, 2021 - No. 4, Nov, 2021 ($4.99, limited series)
1-4-Spider-Man vs. Sinister Six & others; Doctor Strange & Mephisto app.; Bagley-a   5.00

SINS OF SINISTER
Marvel Comics: Mar, 2023 ($5.99, one-shot)
1-Mister Sinister from X-Men; Gillen-s/Werneck-a; part 1 of crossover saga   6.00
... Dominion 1 (6/23, $5.99) Part 11 of crossover saga   6.00

SINS OF THE BLACK FLAMINGO
Image Comics: Jun, 2022 - No. 5, Oct, 2022 ($3.99, limited series)
1-5-Andrew Wheeler-s/Travis Moore-a   4.00

SINS OF THE SALTON SEA
Artists, Writers & Artisans, Inc.: Jun, 2023 - No. 5, Oct, 2023 ($3.99, limited series)
1-5-Ed Brisson-s/C.P. Smith-a/Tim Bradstreet-c   4.00

SINS OF YOUTH... (Also see Young Justice: Sins of Youth)
DC Comics: May 2000 ($4.95/$2.50, limited crossover series)
Secret Files 1 ($4.95) Short stories and profile pages; Nauck-a   5.00
...Aquaboy/Lagoon Man; Batboy and Robin; JLA Jr.; Kid Flash/Impulse; Starwoman and the
   JSA, Superman, Jr./Superboy, Sr.; The Secret/ Deadboy, Wonder Girls ($2.50-c)
   Old and young heroes switch ages   3.00

SIP KIDS (Strangers in Paradise)
Abstract Studio: 2014 - No. 4, 2015 ($4.99, color)
1-4-Strangers in Paradise characters as young kids; Terry Moore-s/a/c   5.00

SIR CHARLES BARKLEY AND THE REFEREE MURDERS
Hamilton Comics: 1993 ($9.95, 8-1/2" x 11", 52 pgs.)

nn-Photo-c; Sports fantasy comic book fiction (uses real names of NBA superstars). Script by Alan Dean Foster, art by Joe Staton. Comes with bound-in sheet of 35 gummed "Moods of Charles Barkley" stamps. Photo/story on Barkley	2	4	6	9	12	15
Special Edition of 100 copies for charity signed on an affixed book plate by Barkley, Foster & Staton						175.00
Ashcan edition given away to dealers, distributors & promoters (low distribution). Four pages in color, balance of story in b&w	2	4	6	9	12	15

SIR EDWARD GREY: ACHERON (From Hellboy)
Dark Horse Comics: Dec, 2021 ($3.99, one-shot)
1-Mike Mignola-a   4.00

SIR EDWARD GREY, WITCHFINDER: IN THE SERVICE OF ANGELS (From Hellboy)
Dark Horse Comics: July, 2009 - No. 5, Nov, 2009 ($2.99, limited series)
1-5-Mignola-s/c; Stenbeck-a   3.00

SIR EDWARD GREY, WITCHFINDER: THE MYSTERIES OF UNLAND (From Hellboy)
Dark Horse Comics: Jun, 2014 - No. 5, Oct, 2014 ($3.50, limited series)
1-5-Newman & McHugh-s/Crook-a/Tedesco-c   3.50

SIREN (Also see Eliminator & Ultraforce)
Malibu Comics (Ultraverse): Sept, 1995 - No. 3, Dec, 1995 ($1.50)
Infinity, 1-3: Infinity-Black-c & painted-c exists. 1-Regular-c & painted-c; War Machine app.
   2-Flip book w/Phoenix Resurrection Pt. 3   4.00
Special 1-(2/96, $1.95, 28 pgs.)-Origin Siren; Marvel Comic's Juggernaut/app.   4.00

SIRENS (See George Pérez's Sirens)

SIRENS GATE
Dynamite Entertainment: 2022 - No. 5, 2023 ($3.99, limited series)
1-5-Shannon Maer-s/a   4.00

SIRENS OF THE CITY
BOOM! Studios: Jul, 2023 - No. 6, Jan, 2024 ($3.99, limited series)
1-6-Joanne Starer-s/Khary Randolph-a   4.00

SIR LANCELOT (TV)
Dell Publishing Co.: No. 606, Dec, 1954 - No. 775, Mar, 1957

Four Color 606 (not TV)	7	14	21	46	86	125
Four Color 775(...and Brian)-Buscema-a; photo-c	9	18	27	59	117	175

SIR WALTER RALEIGH (Movie)
Dell Publishing Co.: May, 1955 (Based on movie "The Virgin Queen")

Four Color 644-Photo-c	6	12	18	42	79	115

SISTERHOOD OF STEEL (See Eclipse Graphic Adventure Novel #13)
Marvel Comics (Epic Comics): Dec, 1984 - No. 8, Feb, 1986 ($1.50, Baxter paper, mature)
1-8   4.00

SISTERS OF SORROW
BOOM! Studios: Jul, 2017 - No. 4, Oct, 2017 ($3.99, limited series)
1-4-Kurt Sutter & Courtney Alameda-s/Hyeonjin Kim-a. 1-Jae Lee-c   4.00

SITUATION, THE (TV's Jersey Shore)
Wizard World: July, 2012 (no cover price)
1-Jenkins-s/Caldwell-a; two covers by Horn & Caldwell

6 BLACK HORSES (See Movie Classics)

SIX FROM SIRIUS
Marvel Comics (Epic Comics): July, 1984 - No. 4, Oct, 1984 ($1.50, limited series, mature)
1-4: Moench scripts; Gulacy-c/a in all   4.00

SIX FROM SIRIUS II
Marvel Comics (Epic Comics): Feb, 1986 - No. 4, May, 1986 ($1.50, limited series, mature)
1-4: Moench scripts; Gulacy-c/a in all   4.00

SIX-GUN GORILLA
BOOM! Studios: Jun, 2013 - No. 6, Nov, 2013 ($3.99, limited series)
1-6: 1-Spurrier-s/Stokely-a   4.00

SIX-GUN HEROES
Fawcett Publications: March, 1950 - No. 23, Nov, 1953 (Photo-c #1-23)

1-Rocky Lane, Hopalong Cassidy, Smiley Burnette begin (same date as Smiley Burnette #1)						
	34	68	102	199	325	450
2	17	34	51	100	158	215
3-5: 5-Lash LaRue begins	14	28	42	76	108	140
6-15	11	22	33	62	86 –	110
16-22: 17-Last Smiley Burnette. 18-Monte Hale begins						
	10	20	30	54	72	90
23-Last Fawcett issue	10	20	30	58	79	100

NOTE: Hopalong Cassidy photo c-1-3. Monte Hale photo c-18. Rocky Lane photo c-4, 5, 9, 11, 13, 15, 17, 20, 21, 23. Lash LaRue photo c-6, 8, 10, 12, 14, 16, 19, 22.

SIX-GUN HEROES (Cont'd from Fawcett; Gunmasters #84 on) (See Blue Bird)
Charlton Comics: No. 24, Jan, 1954 - No. 83, Mar-Apr, 1965 (All Vol. 4)

24-Lash LaRue, Hopalong Cassidy, Rocky Lane & Tex Ritter begin; photo-c						
	14	28	42	80	115	150
25	10	20	30	54	72	90
26-30: 26-Rod Cameron story. 28-Tom Mix begins?	9	18	27	47	61	75
31-40: 38-40-Jingles & Wild Bill Hickok (TV)	8	16	24	42	54	65
41-46,48,50: 41-43-Wild Bill Hickok (TV)	8	16	24	40	50	60
47-Williamson-a, 2 pgs.; Torres-a	8	16	24	42	54	65
49-Williamson-a (5 pgs.)	9	18	27	50	65	80
51-56,58-60: 58-Gunmaster app.	3	6	9	19	30	40
57-Origin & 1st app. Gunmaster	4	8	12	25	40	55
61-70	3	6	9	16	23	30
71-75,77,78,80-83	3	6	9	14	18	22
76,79: 76-Gunmaster begins. 79-1st app. & origin of Bullet, the Gun-Boy						
	3	6	9	14	19	24

SIXGUN RANCH (See Luke Short & Four Color #580)

SIX GUNS
Marvel Comics: Jan, 2012 - No. 5, Apr, 2012 ($2.99, limited series)
1-5-Diggle-s/Gianfelice-a; Tarantula and Tex Dawson app.   3.00

SIX-GUN WESTERN
Atlas Comics (CDS): Jan, 1957 - No. 4, July, 1957

1-Crandall-a; two Williamson text illos	25	50	75	150	245	340
2,3-Williamson-a in both	17	34	51	100	158	215
4-Woodbridge-a	15	30	45	83	124	165

NOTE: Ayers a-2, 3. Maneely a-1; c-2, 3. Orlando a-2. Pakula a-3. Powell a-3. Romita c-1, 4. Severin c-1, 4. Shores a-2.

SIX MILLION DOLLAR MAN, THE (TV) (Also see The Bionic Man)
Charlton Comics: 6/76 - No. 4, 12/76; No. 5, 10/77; No. 6, 2/78 - No. 9, 6/78

1-Staton c/a; Lee Majors photo on-c	6	12	18	42	79	115
2-Neal Adams-c; Staton-a	4	8	12	28	47	65
3-9	3	6	9	15	22	28

SIX MILLION DOLLAR MAN, THE (TV)(Magazine)
Charlton Comics: July, 1976 - No. 7, Nov, 1977 (B&W)

1-Neal Adams-c/a	5	10	15	34	60	85
2-Neal Adams-c	3	6	9	17	25	34
3-N. Adams part inks; Chaykin-a	3	6	9	14	19	24
4-7	2	4	6	11	16	20

SIX MILLION DOLLAR MAN, THE: FALL OF MAN (TV)
Dynamite Entertainment: 2016 - No. 5, 2016 ($3.99)
1-5: 1-Van Jensen-s/Ron Salas-a; three covers   4.00

SIX MILLION DOLLAR MAN, THE: SEASON 6 (TV)
Dynamite Entertainment: 2014 - No. 6, 2014 ($3.99)
1-Jim Kuhoric-s/Juan Antonio Ramirez-a; covers by Alex Ross & Ken Haeser & photo-c   4.00
2-6-Two covers by Ross & Haeser on each. 2-Maskatron returns   4.00

SIX MILLION DOLLAR MAN, THE: VOLUME 1 (TV)
Dynamite Entertainment: 2019 - No. 5, 2019 ($3.99, limited series)
1-5-Christopher Hastings-s/David Hahn-a; set in 1974   4.00

SIXPACK AND DOGWELDER: HARD TRAVELIN' HEROZ (See All-Star Section Eight)
DC Comics: Oct, 2016 - No. 6, Mar, 2017 ($3.99)
1-6-Ennis-s/Braun-a/Dillon-c. 1-Power Girl, Catwoman, & Starfire app. 2-6-Constantine app.
   2-The Spectre app.   4.00

SIX STRING SAMURAI
Awesome-Hyperwerks: Sept, 1998 ($2.95)
1-Stinsman & Fraga-a; Liefeld-c   4.00

1602 WITCH HUNTER ANGELA (Secret Wars tie-in)
Marvel Comics: Aug, 2015 - No. 4, Dec, 2015 ($3.99, limited series)
1-4-Marguerite Bennett-s; Hans & Sauvage-a; The Enchantress app.   4.00

67 SECONDS
Marvel Comics (Epic Comics): 1992 ($15.95, 54 pgs., graphic novel)

nn-James Robinson scripts; Steve Yeowell-c/a	2	4	6	11	14	18

SKAAR: KING OF THE SAVAGE LAND
Marvel Comics: Jun, 2011 - No. 5 ($2.99, limited series)
1-5-Shanna & Ka-Zar app.; Ching-a. 1-Komarck-c. 2-McGuinness-c   3.00

SKAAR: SON OF HULK (Title continues in Son of Hulk #13)(Also see World War Hulk x-over)
Marvel Comics: Aug, 2008 - No. 12, Aug, 2009 ($2.99)
1-Garney-a/Pak-s; 2 covers by Pagulayan and Julie Bell; origin   4.00

SIP Kids #1 © Terry Moore

Six-Gun Gorilla #2 © BOOM!

Skullkickers #31 © Jim Zub

	GD	VG	FN	VF	VF/NM	NM-		GD	VG	FN	VF	VF/NM	NM-
	2.0	4.0	6.0	8.0	9.0	9.2		2.0	4.0	6.0	8.0	9.0	9.2

1-Second printing - 2 covers by Garney and Hulk movie image		3.00
1-Third printing - Garney sketch variant-c		3.00
2-12: 2-6-Back-up story with Guice-a. 7-12-Silver Surfer app.		3.00
Planet Skaar Prologue 1 (7/09, $3.99) Panosian-a; Fantastic Four & She-Hulk app.		4.00
... Presents - Savage World of Sakaar (11/08, $3.99) Pak-s/art by various; Garney-c		4.00

SKATEMAN
Pacific Comics: Nov, 1983 (Baxter paper, one-shot)

1-Adams-c/a		4.00

SKELETON HAND (...In Secrets of the Supernatural)
American Comics Gr. (B&M Dist. Co.): Sept-Oct, 1952 - No. 6, Jul-Aug, 1953

1	100	200	300	635	1093	1550
2	53	106	159	334	567	800
3-6	42	84	126	265	445	625

SKELETON KEY
Amaze Ink: July, 1995 - No. 30, Jan, 1998 ($1.25/$1.50/$1.75, B&W)

1-30		4.00
Special #1 (2/98, $4.95) Unpublished short stories		5.00
Sugar Kat Special (10/98, $2.95) Halloween stories		4.00
Beyond The Threshold TPB (6/96, $11.95)-r/#1-6		12.00
Cats and Dogs TPB ($12.95)-r/#25-30		13.00
The Celestial Calendar TPB ($19.95)-r/#7-18		20.00
Telling Tales TPB ($12.95)-r/#19-24		13.00

SKELETON KEY (Volume 2)
Amaze Ink: 1999 - No. 4, 1999 ($2.95, B&W)

1-4-Andrew Watson-s/a		4.00

SKELETON WARRIORS
Marvel Comics: Apr, 1995 - No. 4, July, 1995 ($1.50)

1-4: Based on animated series.		4.00

SKIN GRAFT: THE ADVENTURES OF A TATTOOED MAN
DC Comics (Vertigo): July, 1993 - No. 4, Oct, 1993 ($2.50, lim. series, mature)

1-4		4.00

SKINWALKER
Oni Press: May, 2002 - No. 4, Sept, 2002 ($2.95, limited series)

1-4-Hurtt & Dela Cruz-a; Talon-c		3.00
1-(5/05) Free Comic Book Day Edition		3.00

SKI PARTY (See Movie Classics)

SKREEMER
DC Comics: May, 1989 - No. 6, Oct, 1989 ($2.00, limited series, mature)

1-6: Contains graphic violence; Milligan-s		4.00
TPB (2002, $19.95) r/#1-6		20.00

SKRULL KILL KREW
Marvel Comics: Sept, 1995 - No. 5, Dec, 1995 ($2.95, limited series)

1-5: Grant Morrison & Mark Millar scripts; Steve Yeowell-a. 2,3-Cap America app.		5.00
TPB (8/16, $16.99) r/#1-5		17.00

SKRULL KILL KREW
Marvel Comics: Jun, 2009 - No. 5, Dec, 2009 ($3.99, limited series)

1-5-Felber-s/Robinson-a		4.00

SKRULLS! (Tie-in to Secret Invasion crossover)
Marvel Comics: 2008 ($4.99, one-shot)

1-Skrull history, profiles of Skrulls, their allies & foes; checklist of appearances; Horn-c		5.00

SKRULLS VS. POWER PACK (Tie-in to Secret Invasion crossover)
Marvel Comics: Sept, 2008 - No. 4 ($2.99, limited series)

1-4-Van Lente-s/Hamscher-a; Franklin Richards app.		3.00

SKUL, THE
Virtual Comics (Byron Preiss Multimedia): Oct, 1996 - No. 3, Dec, 1996 ($2.50, lim. series)

1-3: Ron Lim & Jimmy Palmiotti-a		4.00

SKULL & BONES
DC Comics: 1992 - No. 3, 1992 ($4.95, limited series, 52 pgs.)

Book 1-3: 1-1st app.		5.00

SKULL AND BONES (Based on the Ubisoft videogame)
Dark Horse Comics: Mar, 2023 - No. 3, May, 2023 ($3.99, limited series)

1-3-John Jackson Miller-s & James Mishler/Christian Rosado		4.00

SKULLDIGGER AND SKELETON BOY (From Black Hammer)
Dark Horse Comics: Dec, 2019 - No. 6, Feb, 2021 ($3.99)

1-6-Lemire-s/Zonjic-a; origin of Skeleton Boy		5.00

SKULLKICKERS
Image Comics: Sept, 2010 - No. 33, Jul, 2015; No. 100, Aug, 2015 ($2.99/$3.50)

1-Jim Zubkavich-s/Edwin Huang-a; two covers		4.00
1-(2nd & 3rd printings), 2-18		3.00
24-29,31-33: 24-($3.50) "Before Watchmen" cover swipe (no issues #34-99)		3.50
30-($3.99) Multi-dimensional variant Skullkickers		4.00
#100 ($3.99, 8/15) Last issue; conclusion of Infinite Icons of the Endless Epic		4.00
All-New Secret Skullkickers 1 (6/13, $3.50) issue #22; cover swipe of X-Men #125 ('79)		3.50
Dark Skullkickers Dark 1 (7/13, $3.50) issue #23; cover swipe of Green Lantern #85 ('71)		3.50
Savage Skullkickers 1 (3/13, $3.50) issue #20; cover swipe of Savage Wolverine #1		3.50
The Mighty Skullkickers 1 (4/13, $3.50) issue #21; cover swipe of Thor #337		3.50
... Super Special 1 (11/22, $3.99) 10th Anniversary Special		4.00
Uncanny Skullkickers 1 (2/13, $3.50) issue #19		3.50

SKULL, THE SLAYER
Marvel Comics Group: Aug, 1975 - No. 8, Nov, 1976 (20¢/25¢)

1-Origin & 1st app.; Gil Kane-c	3	6	9	19	30	40
2-8: 2-Gil Kane-c. 5,6-(Regular 25¢-c). 8-Kirby-c	2	4	6	8	10	12
5,6-(30¢-c variants, limited distribution)(5,7/76)	5	10	15	30	50	70

SKY BLAZERS (CBS Radio)
Hawley Publications: Sept, 1940 - No. 2, Nov, 1940

1-Sky Pirates, Ace Archer, Flying Aces begin	93	186	279	591	1021	1450
2-WWII air battle grey-tone-c	47	94	141	296	498	700

SKYBOUND PRESENTS AFTERSCHOOL
Image Comics (Skybound): Jun, 2022 - No. 4, Nov, 2022 ($4.99, horror anthology series)

1-4: 1-Hinkle-a. 2-Leila Leiz-a. 3-Zarcone & Sterle-a. 4-Zadwadzki-a		5.00

SKYBOUND X
Image Comics (Skybound): Jul, 2021 - No. 5, Aug, 2021 ($4.99, square-bound, weekly limited anthology series)(Issues #6-24 don't exist)

1-5-Rick Grimes 2000 (Walking Dead) w/Kirkman-s/Ottley-a in all. 1-1st comic app. of Clementine. 2-Stillwater & Birthright. 3-5-Negan app. 4-Excellence & Redneck		5.00
25-(7/22, $4.99) Battle Beast, Dark Ride, Kroma & Scurry		5.00

SKYBOURNE
BOOM! Studios: Sept, 2016 - No. 5, Feb, 2018 ($3.99)

1-5-Frank Cho-s/a		4.00

SKY DOLL
Marvel Comics (Soleil): 2008 - No. 3, 2008 ($5.99, mature)

1-3-Barbucci & Canepa-s/a; English version of French comic; preview of other titles		6.00
...: Doll's Factory 1,2 (2009 - No. 2, 2009, $5.99) Barbucci & Canepa-s/a		6.00
...: Lacrima Christi 1,2 (9/10 - No. 2, 10/10, $5.99) Barbucci & Canepa and others-s/a		6.00
...: Space Ship 1,2 (7/10 - No. 2, 8/10, $5.99) Barbucci & Canepa and others-s/a		6.00

SKY DOLL: SUDRA
Titan Comics: Apr, 2017 - No. 2, May, 2017 ($3.99, mature)

1,2-Barbucci & Canepa-s/a; English version of French comic		4.00

SKYE RUNNER
DC Comics (WildStorm): June, 2006 - No. 6, Mar, 2007 ($2.99)

1-6: 1-Three covers; Warner-s/Garza-a. 2-Three covers, incl. Campbell		3.00

SKYLANDERS (Based on the Activision video game)
IDW Publishing: No. 0, Jul, 2014 - No. 12, Aug, 2015 ($3.99)

0-(no cover price) Lord Kaos app.; Bowden-a; character bios		3.00
1-12: 1-Marz & Rodriguez-s/Baldeón-a		4.00
... Quarterly - Spyro & Friends: Biting Back (3/18, $4.99) Marz & Rodriguez-s		5.00
... Quarterly - Spyro & Friends: Full Blast (7/17, $4.99) Marz & Rodriguez-s		5.00
... Quarterly - Spyro & Friends: Goldslinger (11/17, $4.99) Marz & Rodriguez-s		5.00
... Superchargers 1-6 (10/15 - No. 6, 3/16, $3.99) Marz & Rodriguez-s		4.00

SKYMAN (See Big Shot Comics & Sparky Watts)
Columbia Comics Gr.: Fall?, 1941 - No. 2, Fall?, 1942; No. 3, 1948 - No. 4, 1948

1-Origin Skyman, The Face, Sparky Watts app.; Whitney-c/a; 3rd story-r from Big Shot #1; Whitney c-1-4	142	284	426	909	1555	2200
2 (1942)-Yankee Doodle	81	162	243	518	884	1250
3,4 (1948)	47	94	141	296	498	700

SKYMAN (Also see Captain Midnight 2013 series #4)
Dark Horse Comics: Jan, 2014 - No. 4, Apr, 2014 ($2.99)

1-4: 1-Fialkov-s/Garcia-a; origin of a new Skyman. 3,4-Captain Midnight app.		3.00
... One-Shot (11/14, $2.99) Garcia-a		3.00

SKYPILOT
Ziff-Davis Publ. Co.: No. 10, 1950(nd) - No. 11, Apr-May, 1951

	GD 2.0	VG 4.0	FN 6.0	VF 8.0	VF/NM 9.0	NM- 9.2

10,11-Frank Borth-a; Saunders painted-c ... 22 44 66 132 216 300

SKY RANGER (See Johnny Law...)

SKYROCKET
Harry 'A' Chesler: 1944
nn-Alias the Dragon, Dr. Vampire, Skyrocket & The Desperado app.; WWII Japan zero-c
    71 142 213 454 777 1100

SKY SHERIFF (Breeze Lawson...) (Also see Exposed & Outlaws)
D. S. Publishing Co.: Summer, 1948
1-Edmond Good-c/a ... 22 44 66 132 216 300

SKYWARD
Image Comics: Apr, 2018 - No. 15, Jul, 2019 ($3.99)
1-15: 1-Joe Henderson-s/Lee Garbett-a ... 4.00

SKY WOLF (Also see Airboy)
Eclipse Comics: Mar, 1988 - No. 3, Oct, 1988 ($1.25/$1.50/$1.95, lim. series)
1-3 ... 4.00

SLAINE, THE BERSERKER (Slaine the King #21 on)
Quality: July, 1987 - No. 28, 1989 ($1.25/$1.50)
1-28 ... 4.00

SLAINE, THE HORNED GOD
Fleetway: 1998 - No. 3 ($6.99)
1-3-Reprints series from 2000 A.D.; Bisley-a ... 7.00

SLAM!
BOOM! Studios (Boom! Box): Nov, 2016 - No. 4, Feb, 2017 ($3.99)
1-4-Roller derby; Pamela Ribon-s/Veronica Fish-a ... 4.00

SLAM BANG COMICS (Western Desperado #8)
Fawcett Publications: Mar, 1940 - No. 7, Sept, 1940 (Combined with Master Comics #7)
1-Diamond Jack, Mark Swift & The Time Retarder, Lee Granger, Jungle King begin & continue in Master ... 295 590 885 1888 3244 4600
2 ... 135 270 405 864 1462 2100
3-Classic monster-c (scarce) ... 343 686 1029 2400 4200 6000
4,6,7: 6-Intro Zoro, the Mystery Man (also in #7) ... 116 232 348 742 1271 1800
5-Classic Dragon-c ... 129 258 387 826 1413 2000
(ashcan)(1940) Not distributed to newsstands, only for in house use. A copy sold in 2006 for ... ,500.

SLAM! THE NEXT JAM
BOOM! Studios (Boom! Box): Sept, 2017 - No. 4, Dec, 2017 ($3.99)
1-4-Roller derby; Pamela Ribon-s/Marina Julia-a ... 4.00

SLAPSTICK
Marvel Comics: Nov, 1992 - No. 4, Feb, 1993 ($1.25, limited series)
1-4: Fry/Austin-c/a. 4-Ghost Rider, D.D., F.F. app. ... 4.00

SLAPSTICK
Marvel Comics: Feb, 2017 - No. 6, Jul, 2017 ($3.99, limited series)
1-6-Brown & Van Lente-s/Olortegui-a ... 4.00

SLAPSTICK COMICS
Comic Magazines Distributors: nd (1946?) (36 pgs.)
Firetop feature; Post-a(2); Munson Paddock-c ... 45 90 135 284 480 675

SLASH & BURN
... Comics (Vertigo): Jan, 2016 - No. 6, Jun, 2016 ($3.99/$4.99)
1-5-Si Spencer-s/Max Dunbar-a ... 4.00
6-($4.99) ... 5.00

SLASH-D DOUBLECROSS
St. John Publishing Co.: 1950 (Pocket-size, 132 pgs.)
nn-Western comics ... 28 56 84 165 270 375

SLASH MARAUD
DC Comics: Nov, 1987 - No. 6, Apr, 1988 ($1.75, limited series)
1-6-Moench-s/Gulacy-a/c ... 4.00

SLAVE GIRL COMICS (See Malu... & White Princess of the Jungle #2)
Avon Periodicals/Eternity Comics (1989): Feb, 1949 - No. 2, 1949 (52 pgs.); Mar, 1989 (B&W, 44 pgs)
1-Larsen-c/a ... 200 400 600 1280 2190 3100
2-Larsen-a (no month listed) ... 161 322 483 1030 1765 2500
1(3/89, $2.25, B&W, 44 pgs.)-r/#1 ... 2 4 6 10 14 18

SLAVE LABOR STORIES
Slave Labor Publishing: May, 2003 (Giveaway, B&W)
nn-Free Comic Book Day Edition; short stories by various; Dorkin Milk & Cheese-c ... 3.00

SLAY BELLS
Idea: Jul, 2021 ($7.99, one-shot)
nn-Wells-s/Lafuente-a; Rahal-s/Pollina-a ... 1 2 3 5 6 8

SLAYER: REPENTLESS (Based on the band Slayer)
Dark Horse Comics: Jan, 2017 - No. 3, Jun, 2017 ($4.99, limited series)
1-3-Jon Schnepp-s/Guiu Villanova-a/Glenn Fabry-c; Slayer app. ... 5.00

SLEDGE HAMMER (TV)
Marvel Comics: Feb, 1988 - No. 2, Mar,1988 ($1.00, limited series)
1-2 ... 4.00

SLEDGEHAMMER 44
Dark Horse Comics: Mar, 2013 - No. 2, Apr, 2013 ($3.50, limited series)
1,2-Mignola & Arcudi-s/Latour-a; Mignola-c ... 3.50

SLEDGEHAMMER 44: THE LIGHTNING WAR
Dark Horse Comics: Nov, 2013 - No. 3, Jan, 2014 ($3.50, limited series)
1-3-Mignola & Arcudi-s/Laurence Campbell-a. 1-Mignola-c. 2,3-Campbell-c ... 3.50

SLEEPER
... Comics (WildStorm): Mar, 2003 - No. 12, Mar, 2004 ($2.95)

1-12-Brubaker-s/Phillips-c/a. 3-Back-up preview of The Authority: High Stakes pt. 2 ... 3.00
...: All False Moves TPB (2004, $17.95) r/#7-12 ... 18.00
...: Out in the Cold TPB (2004, $17.95) r/#1-6 ... 18.00

SLEEPER: SEASON TWO
DC Comics (WildStorm): Aug, 2004 - No. 12, July, 2005 ($2.95/$2.99)
1-12-Brubaker-s/Phillips-c/a. ... 3.00
TPB (2009, $24.99) r/#1-12 ... 25.00
....: A Crooked Line TPB (2005, $17.99) r/#1-6 ... 18.00
...: The Long Way Home TPB (2005, $14.99) r/#7-12 ... 15.00

SLEEPING BEAUTY (See Dell Giants & Movie Comics)
Dell Publishing Co.: No. 973, May, 1959 - No. 984, June, 1959 (Disney)
Four Color 973 (...and the Prince) ... 13 26 39 86 188 290
Four Color 984 (...Fairy Godmother's) ... 10 20 30 69 147 225

SLEEPLESS
Image Comics: Dec, 2017 - No. 11, Jan, 2019 ($3.99)
1-11-Sarah Vaughn-s/Leila Del Duca-a ... 4.00

SLEEPWALKER (Also see Infinity Wars: Sleepwalker)
Marvel Comics: June, 1991 - No. 33, Feb, 1994 ($1.00/$1.25)
1-1st app. Sleepwalker ... 5.00
2-33: 4-Williamson-i. 5-Spider-Man-c/story. 7-Infinity Gauntlet x-over. 8-Vs. Deathlok-c/story. 11-Ghost Rider-c/story. 12-Quesada-c/a(p) 14-Intro Spectra. 15-F.F.-c/story. 17-Darkhawk & Spider-Man x-over. 18-Infinity War x-over; Quesada/Williamson-c. 21,22-Hobgoblin app. 19-($2.00)-Die-cut Sleepwalker mask-c ... 4.00
25-($2.95, 52 pgs.)-Holo-grafx foil-c; origin ... 5.00
Holiday Special 1 (1/93, $2.00, 52 pgs.)-Quesada-c(p) ... 5.00

SLEEPWALKING
Hall of Heroes: Jan, 1996 ($2.50, B&W)
1-Kelley Jones-c ... 4.00

SLEEPY HOLLOW (Movie Adaption)
DC Comics (Vertigo): 2000 ($7.95, one-shot)
1-Kelley Jones-a/Seagle-s ... 8.00

SLEEPY HOLLOW (Based on the Fox TV show)
BOOM! Studios: Oct, 2014 - No. 4, Jan, 2015 ($3.99, limited series)
1-4-Marguerite Bennett-s/Jorge Coelho-a/Phil Noto-c ... 4.00
...: Origins 1 (4/15, $4.99) Mike Johnson-s/Matias Bergara-a; Quinones-c ... 5.00
...: Providence 1-4 (8/15 - No. 4 11/15, $3.99) Carrasco-s/Santos-a ... 4.00

SLEEZE BROTHERS, THE
Marvel Comics (Epic Comics): Aug, 1989 - No. 6, Jan, 1990 ($1.75, mature)
1-6: 4-6 (9/89 - 11/89 indicia dates) ... 4.00
nn-(1991, $3.95, 52 pgs.) ... 5.00

SLICK CHICK COMICS
Leader Enterprises: 1947(nd) - No. 3, 1947(nd)
1-Teenage humor ... 52 104 156 328 552 725
2,3 ... 32 64 96 188 307 425

SLIDERS (TV)
Acclaim Comics (Armada): June, 1996 - No. 2, July, 1996 ($2.50, lim. series)
1,2: D.G. Chichester scripts; Dick Giordano-a. ... 4.00

SLIDERS: DARKEST HOUR (TV)
Acclaim Comics (Armada): Oct, 1996 - No. 3, Dec, 1996 ($2.50, limited series)
1-3 ... 4.00

SLIDERS SPECIAL
Acclaim Comics (Armada): Nov, 1996 - No 3, Mar, 1997 ($3.95, limited series)
1-3: 1-Narcotica-Jerry O'Connell-s. 2-Blood and Splendor. 3-Deadly Secrets ... 4.00

SLIDERS: ULTIMATUM (TV)
Acclaim Comics (Armada): Sept, 1996 - No. 2, Sept, 1996 ($2.50, lim. series)
1,2 ... 4.00

SLIMER! (TV cartoon) (Also see the Real Ghostbusters)
Now Comics: 1989 - No. 19, Nov, 1990 ($1.75)
1-19: Based on animated cartoon ... 4.00

SLIM MORGAN (See Wisco)

SLINGERS (See Spider-Man: Identity Crisis issues)
Marvel Comics: Dec, 1998 - No. 12, Nov, 1999 ($2.99/$1.99)
0-(Wizard #88 supplement) Prelude story ... 4.00
1-($2.99) Four editions w/different covers for each hero, 16 pages common to all, the other pages from each hero's perspective ... 5.00
2-12: 2-Two-c. 12-Saltares-a ... 4.00

SLITHISS ATTACKS! (Also see Very Weird Tales)
Oceanspray Comics Group: Dec, 2001 - No. 4, Aug, 2004 ($3.00/$4.00)
1-($3.00) Origin and 1st app. of the monster Slithiss; 1st app. Overconfident Man ... 15.00
2-($4.00) 2nd app. Overconfident Man; "Chris Lamo" Newport, OR murder parody ... 12.00
3-($3.00) Rutland Vermont Halloween x-over; 3rd app. Overconfident Man ... 12.00
4-($3.00) 4th app. Overconfident Man ... 10.00
Special Edition 1($20.00) reprints #1-2 without letter column ... 20.00
Special Edition 1($20.00) second printing ... 20.00
NOTE: Created in prevention classes taught by Jon McClure at the Oceanspray Family Center in Newport, OR and paid for by the Housing Authority of Lincoln County, all books are b&w with color covers. Bob Overstreet and other comics' professionals wrote letters of encouragement that were published in issues #2-4. Issues #1-2 penciled and inked by various artists; #3-4 penciled by James Gilmer. All comics feature characters created by students, signed and numbered by Jon McClure. Issue #1 had a 200 issue print run, while issues #2-4 have print runs of 100 each. Special Edition #1 had a print run of 26 issues, while the second printing had a 10 issue print run. Ties in with live action movie Face Eater released in 2007 and card game FaceEater released in 2010.

SLOTS
Image Comics: Oct, 2017 - No. 6, Mar, 2018 ($3.99)
1-6-Dan Panosian-s/a/c ... 4.00

SLOW BURN
BOOM! Studios: Oct, 2023 - No. 5, Feb, 2024 ($4.99, limited series)

Slave Girl Comics #2 © AVON

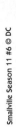

Smallville Season 11 #6 © DC

Smiley #1 © Chaos!

	GD 2.0	VG 4.0	FN 6.0	VF 8.0	VF/NM 9.0	NM- 9.2

1-5-Ollie Masters-s/Pierluigi Monotti-a ... 5.00

SLUDGE
Malibu Comics (Ultraverse): Oct, 1993 - No. 12, Dec, 1994 ($2.50/$1.95)
1-($2.50, 48 pgs.)-Intro/1st app. Sludge; Rune flip-c/story Pt. 1 (1st app., 3 pgs.) by Barry Smith; The Night Man app. (3 pg. preview); The Mighty Magnor 1 pg strip begins by Aragonés (cont. in other titles) ... 5.00
1-Ultra 5000 Limited silver foil ... 8.00
2-11: 3-Break-Thru x-over. 4-2 pg. Mantra origin. 8-Bloodstorm app. ... 4.00
12 ($3.50)-Ultraverse Premiere #8 flip book; Alex Ross poster ... 5.00
...:Red Xmas (12/94, $2.50, 44 pgs.) ... 5.00

SLUGGER (Little Wise Guys Starring…)(Also see Daredevil Comics)
Lev Gleason Publications: April, 1956
1-Biro-c ... 11 22 33 64 90 115

SMALLVILLE (Based on TV series)
DC Comics: May, 2003 - No. 11, Jan, 2005 ($3.50/$3.95, bi-monthly)
1-6-Photo-c. 1-Plunkett-a; interviews with cast; season 1 episode guide begins ... 4.00
7-11-($3.95) 7-Chloe Chronicles begin; season 2 episode guide begins ... 4.00
Vol. 1 TPB (2004, $9.95) r/#1-4 & Smallville: The Comic; photo-c ... 10.00

SMALLVILLE: ALIEN (Based on TV series)
DC Comics: Feb, 2014 - No. 4, May, 2014 ($3.99, printings of previously released digital comics)
1-4: 1-The Monitor lands on Earth; Staggs-a. 2-Batman app. ... 4.00

SMALLVILLE: CHAOS (Based on TV series)(Season 11)
DC Comics: Oct, 2014 - No. 4, Jan, 2015 ($3.99, printings of previously released digital comics)
1-4: 1-Eclipso app; Padilla-a. 3-Darkseid app. 3,4-Supergirl & Superboy app. ... 4.00

SMALLVILLE: LANTERN (Based on TV series)
DC Comics: Jun, 2014 - No. 4, Sept, 2014 ($3.99, printings of previously released digital comics)
1-4: 1-Kal-El joins the Green Lantern Corps; Takara-a. 2-4-Parallax app. ... 4.00

SMALLVILLE SEASON 11 (Based on TV series)
DC Comics: Jul, 2012 - No. 19, Jan, 2014 ($3.99, printings of previously released digital comics)
1-19: 1-Two covers by Gary Frank & Cat Staggs; Pere Perez-a. 5-8-Batman app. 13-15-Legion app. 15-Doomsday app. 16-19-Diana of Themyscira app. ... 4.00
... Special 1 (7/13, $4.99) Batman, Nightwing and Martian Manhunter app. ... 5.00
... Special 2 (9/13, $4.99) Lana Lang and John Corben app. ... 5.00
... Special 3 (12/13, $4.99) Spotlight on Luthor and Tess; Lobel-a ... 5.00
... Special 4 (3/14, $4.99) Superboy, Jay Garrick, Blue Beetle, Wonder Twins app. ... 5.00
... Special 5 (9/14, $4.99) Zatanna and John Constantine app. ... 5.00

SMALLVILLE SEASON 11: CONTINUITY (Based on TV series)
DC Comics: Feb, 2015 - No. 4, May, 2015 ($3.99, printings of previously released digital comics)
1-4-The Crisis vs. the Monitors; Legion of Super-Heroes app.; Guara-a ... 4.00

SMALLVILLE: THE COMIC (Based on TV series)
DC Comics: Nov, 2002 ($3.95, 64 pages, one-shot)
1-Photo-c; art by Martinez and Leon; interviews with cast; season 2 preview ... 5.00

SMASH COMICS (Becomes Lady Luck #86 on)
Quality Comics Group: Aug, 1939 - No. 85, Oct, 1949
1-Origin Hugh Hazard & His Iron Man, Bozo the Robot, Espionage, Starring Black X by Eisner, & Hooded Justice (Invisible Justice #2 on); Chic Carter & Wings Wendall begin; 1st Robot on the cover of a comic book (Bozo) ... 389 778 1167 2723 4762 6800
2-The Lone Star Rider app; Invisible Hood gains power of invisibility; bondage/torture-c ... 174 348 522 1114 1907 2700
3-Captain Cook & Eisner's John Law begin ... 110 220 330 704 1202 1700
4,5-4-Flash Fulton begins ... 103 206 309 659 1130 1600
6-12: 12-One pg. Fine-a ... 97 194 291 621 1061 1500
13-Magno begins (8/40); last Eisner issue; The Ray app. in full page ad; The Purple Trio begins ... 97 194 291 621 1061 1500
14-Intro. The Ray (9/40) by Lou Fine & others ... 383 766 1149 2681 4691 6700
15-1st Ray-c, 2nd app. ... 198 374 561 1197 2049 2900
16-The Scarlet Seal begins ... 148 296 444 947 1624 2300
17-Wun Cloo becomes plastic super-hero by Jack Cole (9-months before Plastic Man); Ray-c ... 161 322 483 1030 1765 2500
18-Midnight by Jack Cole begins (origin & 1st app., 1/41) ... 194 388 582 1242 2121 3000
19-22: Last Ray by Fine; The Jester begins-#22. 19,21-Ray-c ... 103 206 309 659 1130 1600
23,24: 23-Ray-c. 24-The Sword app.; last Chic Carter; Wings Wendall dons new costume #24,25 ... 87 174 261 553 952 1350
25-Origin/1st app. Wildfire; Rookie Rankin begins; Ray-c ... 97 194 291 621 1061 1500
26-30: 28-Midnight-c begin, end #85 ... 74 148 222 470 810 1150

31,32,34: The Ray by Rudy Palais; also #33 ... 68 136 204 435 743 1050
33-Origin The Marksman ... 74 148 222 470 810 1150
35-37 ... 54 108 162 343 574 825
38-The Yankee Eagle begins; last Midnight by Jack Cole; classic-c by Cole ... 103 206 309 621 1061 1600
39,40-Last Ray issue ... 52 104 156 328 552 775
41,44-50 ... 42 84 126 265 445 625
42-Lady Luck begins by Klaus Nordling ... 148 296 444 947 1624 2300
43-Lady Luck-c (1st & only in Smash) ... 97 194 291 621 1061 1500
51-60 ... 33 66 99 194 317 440
61-70 ... 25 50 75 150 245 340
71-85: 79-Midnight battles the Men from Mars-c/s ... 21 42 63 126 206 285

NOTE: Al Bryant c-54, 63-68. Cole a-17-38, 68, 69, 72, 73, 78, 80, 83, 85; c-38, 60-62, 69-84. Crandall a-(Ray)-23-29, 35-38; c-36, 39, 40, 42-44, 46. Fine a-(Ray)-14, 15, 16(w/Tuska), 17-22. Fox c-24-35. Fuje (Ray)-30. Gil Fox a-6-7, 9, 11-13. Guardineer a-(The Marksman)-39-7, 49, 52. Gustavson a-4-7, 9, 11-13 (The Jester)-22-46; (Magno)-13-21; (Midnight)-39(Cole inks), 49, 52, 63-65. Kotzky a-(Espionage)-33-38; c-45, 47-53. Nordling a-49, 52, 63-65. Powell a-11, 12, (Abdul the Arab)-13-24. Black X c-2, 6, 9, 11, 13, 16. Bozo the Robot c-1, 3, 5, 8, 10, 12, 14, 18, 20, 22, 24, 26. Midnight c-28-85. The Ray c-15, 17, 19, 21, 23, 25, 27. Wings Wendall c-4, 7.

SMASH COMICS (Also see All Star Comics 1999 crossover titles)
DC Comics: May, 1999 ($1.99, one-shot)
1-Golden Age Doctor Mid-nite and Hourman ... 4.00

SMASH HIT SPORTS COMICS
Essankay Publications: V2#1, Jan, 1949
V2#1-L.B. Cole-c/a ... 42 84 126 265 445 625

SMAX (Also see Top Ten)
America's Best Comics: Oct, 2003 - No. 5, May, 2004 ($2.95, limited series)
1-5-Alan Moore-s/Zander Cannon-a ... 3.00
... Collected Edition (2004, $19.95, HC with dustjacket) r/#1-5 ... 20.00
... Collected Edition SC (2005, $12.99) r/#1-5 ... 13.00

SMILE COMICS (Also see Gay Comics, Tickle, & Whee)
Modern Store Publ.: 1955 (52 pgs.; 5x7-1/4") (7c)
1 ... 12 24 36 69 97 125

SMILEY BURNETTE WESTERN (Also see Patches #8 & Six-Gun Heroes)
Fawcett Publ.: March, 1950 - No. 4, Oct, 1950 (All photo front & back-c)
1-Red Eagle begins ... 26 52 78 154 252 350
2-4 ... 17 34 51 98 154 210

SMILEY (THE PSYCHOTIC BUTTON) (See Evil Ernie)
Chaos! Comics: July, 1998 - May, 1999 ($2.95, one-shots)
1-Ivan Reis-a ... 4.00
... Holiday Special (1/99), ...'s Spring Break (4/99), ...Wrestling Special (5/99) ... 4.00

SMILIN' JACK (See Famous Feature Stories and Popular Comics) (Also see Super Book of Comics #1&2 and Super-Book of Comics #7&19 in the Promotional Comics section)
Dell Publishing Co.: No. 5, 1940 - No. 8, Oct-Dec, 1949
Four Color 5 (1940) ... 103 206 309 659 1130 1600
Four Color 36 (1940) ... 84 168 252 538 919 1300
Large Feature Comic 12,14,25 (1941) ... 81 162 243 518 884 1250
Four Color 4 (1942) ... 81 162 243 518 884 1250
Four Color 14 (1943) ... 35 70 105 252 564 875
Four Color 36,58 (1943-44) ... 23 46 69 164 362 560
Four Color 80 (1945) ... 14 28 42 93 204 315
Four Color 149 (1947) ... 10 20 30 66 138 210
1 (1-3/48) ... 12 24 36 83 182 280
2 ... 7 14 21 44 82 120
3-8 (10-12/49) ... 6 12 18 37 66 95

SMILING SPOOK SPUNKY (See Spunky)

SMITTY (See Popular Comics, Super Book #2, 4 & Super Comics)
Dell Publishing Co.: No. 11, 1940 - No. 7, Aug-Oct, 1949; No. 909, Apr, 1958
Four Color 11 (1940) ... 65 130 195 416 708 1000
Large Feature Comic 26 (1941) ... 48 96 144 302 514 725
Four Color 6 (1942) ... 36 72 108 259 580 900
Four Color 32 (1943) ... 18 36 54 128 284 440
Four Color 65 (1945) ... 15 30 45 100 220 340
Four Color 99 (1946) ... 12 24 36 79 170 260
Four Color 138 (1947) ... 10 20 30 67 141 215
1 (2-4/48) ... 10 20 36 68 132 200
2-(5/48) ... 5 10 15 34 60 85
3,4: 3-(8-10/48), 4-(11-1/48-49) ... 5 10 15 30 50 70
5-7, Four Color 909 (4/58) ... 4 8 12 27 44 60

SMOKEY BEAR (TV) (See March Of Comics #234, 362, 372, 383, 407)

	GD 2.0	VG 4.0	FN 6.0	VF 8.0	VF/NM 9.0	NM- 9.2

Gold Key: Feb, 1970 - No. 13, Mar, 1973

	GD 2.0	VG 4.0	FN 6.0	VF 8.0	VF/NM 9.0	NM- 9.2
1	3	6	9	18	28	38
2-5	2	4	6	10	14	18
6-13				8	10	12

SMOKEY STOVER (See Popular Comics, Super Book #5,17,29 & Super Comics)
Dell Publishing Co.: No. 7, 1942 - No. 827, Aug, 1957

	GD 2.0	VG 4.0	FN 6.0	VF 8.0	VF/NM 9.0	NM- 9.2
Four Color 7 (1942)-Reprints	27	54	81	194	435	675
Four Color 35 (1943)	17	34	51	119	265	410
Four Color 64 (1944)	13	26	39	89	195	300
Four Color 229 (1949)	7	14	21	46	86	125
Four Color 730,827	5	10	15	35	63	90

SMOKEY THE BEAR (See Forest Fire for 1st app.)
Dell Publ. Co.: No. 653, 10/55 - No. 1214, 8/61 (See March of Comics #234)

	GD 2.0	VG 4.0	FN 6.0	VF 8.0	VF/NM 9.0	NM- 9.2
Four Color 653 (#1)	10	20	30	67	141	215
Four Color 708,754,818,932	6	12	18	40	73	105
Four Color 1016,1119,1214	5	10	15	31	53	75

SMOKY (See Movie Classics)

SMOOTH CRIMINALS
BOOM! Studios (BOOM! Box): Nov, 2018 - No. 8, Aug, 2019 ($3.99)
1-8-Kurt Lustgarten & Kirsten Smith-s/Leisha Riddel-a 4.00

SMOSH
Dynamite Entertainment: 2016 - No. 6, 2016 ($3.99)
1-6: 1-3-McDermott-s/Viglino/a; back-up with Yale Stewart-s/a. 4-Boxman origin 4.00

SMURFS (TV)
Marvel Comics: 1982 (Dec) - No. 3, 1983

	GD 2.0	VG 4.0	FN 6.0	VF 8.0	VF/NM 9.0	NM- 9.2
1-3	3	6	9	16	23	30
Treasury Edition 1 (64 pgs.)-r/#1-3	3	6	9	21	33	45

SNAFU (Magazine)
... Comics (RCM): Nov, 1955 - V2#2, Mar, 1956 (B&W)

	GD 2.0	VG 4.0	FN 6.0	VF 8.0	VF/NM 9.0	NM- 9.2
1#1-Heath/Severin-a; Everett, Maneely-a	19	38	57	111	176	240
1#1,2-Severin-a	15	30	45	83	124	165

SNAGGLEPUSS (TV)(See Hanna-Barbera Band Wagon, Quick Draw McGraw #5 & ...tlight #4)
...ld Key: Oct, 1962 - No. 4, Sept, 1963 (Hanna-Barbera)

	GD 2.0	VG 4.0	FN 6.0	VF 8.0	VF/NM 9.0	NM- 9.2
	9	18	27	62	126	190
...4	6	12	18	38	69	100

SNAGGLEPUSS CHRONICLES (See Exit Stage Left: The Snagglepuss Chronicles)

SNAKE EYES (G.I. Joe)
...vil's Due Publ.: Aug, 2005 - No. 6, Jan, 2006 ($2.95)
...6-Santalucia-a 5.00
...Declassified TPB (4/06, $18.95) r/series; source guide 19.00
... and Storm Shadow #13-on)(Cont. from G.I. Joe: Snake Eyes, Volume 2 #7)
...V Publishing: No. 8, Dec, 2011 - No. 21, Nov, 2011 ($3.99)
...21: 13-Title change to Snake Eyes and Storm Shadow 4.00

SNAKE EYES: DEADGAME
...V Publishing: Jul, 2020 - No. 5, Jul, 2021 ($4.99, limited series)
...5-Rob Liefeld-s/a; multiple covers; Joseph Colton app. 5.00
...Declassified 1 (10/21, $6.99) B&W artwork inked by various w/commentary by Liefeld 7.00

SNAKE PLISSKEN CHRONICLES, (John Carpenter's...)
...rricane Entertainment: June, 2003 - No. 4, Feb, 2004 ($2.99)
...view Issue (8/02, no cover price) B&W preview; John Carpenter interview 3.00
...1: 1-Three covers; Rodriguez-a 3.00

SNAKES AND LADDERS
...ie Campbell Comics: 2001 ($5.95, B&W, one-shot)
...Alan Moore-s/Eddie Campbell-a 6.00

SNAKES ON A PLANE (Adaptation of the 2006 movie)
...in Comics: Oct, 2006 - No. 2, Nov, 2006 ($2.99, limited series)
...: 1-Dixon-s/Purcell-a. JG Jones and photo-c. 2-Klebs, Jr.-a; Moore & photo-c 3.00

SNAKE WOMAN (Shekhar Kapur's...)
...in Comics: July, 2006 - No. 10, Apr, 2007 ($2.99)
...0: 1-6-Michael Gaydos/Zeb Wells-s. 1-Two covers by Gaydos & Singh 3.00
...5/07, 99c) reprint of the Snake Goddess; background info; Gaydos-a/c 3.00
...urse of the 68 (3/08 - No. 4, 5/08, $2.99) 1-4: 1-Ingale-a. 2-Manu-a 3.00
...ale of the Snake Charmer 1-6 (6/07-12/07, $2.99) Vivek Shinde-a 3.00
...ol. 1 TPB (6/07, $14.99) r/#1-5; Gaydos sketch pages; creator commentary 15.00
...ol. 2 TPB (9/07, $14.99) r/#6-10; Cebulski intro. 15.00

...P (Formerly Scoop #8; becomes Jest #10,11 & Komik Pages #10)
...y 'A' Chesler: No. 9, 1944

	GD 2.0	VG 4.0	FN 6.0	VF 8.0	VF/NM 9.0	NM- 9.2
...anhunter, The Voice; WWII gag-c	42	84	126	265	445	625

...PPY COMICS
...a Publ. Co. (Prize Publ.): 1945

	GD 2.0	VG 4.0	FN 6.0	VF 8.0	VF/NM 9.0	NM- 9.2
...rmale app.; 9 pg. Sorcerer's Apprentice adapt; Kiefer-a	42	84	126	265	445	625

...PSHOT
...ie Comics: Feb, 2013 - No. 4, May, 2013 ($2.99, B&W, limited series)
...Andy Diggle-s/Jock-a/c 3.00

...RKED
...n Entertainment (Kaboom!): No. 0, Aug, 2011 - No. 12, Sept, 2012 ($1.00/$3.99)
...1.00) Roger Langridge-s/a; sketch gallery, bonus content and games 3.00
...: 1-($3.99) Covers by Langridge & Samnee 4.00

...KY PARKER (See Life With...)

...SON: COMEDY IS DYING
... Comics: 2021 - No. 5, 2021 ($3.99, limited series)

1-5-Paul Constant-s/Fred Harper-a; back-up prose stories by various 4.00

SNIFFY THE PUP
Standard Publ. (Animated Cartoons): No. 5, Nov, 1949 - No. 18, Sept, 1953

	GD 2.0	VG 4.0	FN 6.0	VF 8.0	VF/NM 9.0	NM- 9.2
5-Two Frazetta text illos	16	32	48	94	147	200
6-10	10	20	30	56	76	95
11-18	9	18	27	47	61	75

SNOOPER AND BLABBER DETECTIVES (TV)(See Whitman Comic Books)
Gold Key: Nov, 1962 - No. 3, May, 1963 (Hanna-Barbera)

	GD 2.0	VG 4.0	FN 6.0	VF 8.0	VF/NM 9.0	NM- 9.2
1	7	14	21	46	86	125
2,3	5	10	15	34	60	85

SNOTGIRL
Image Comics: Jul, 2016 - Present ($2.99/$3.99)
1-10-Bryan O'Malley-s/Leslie Hung-a; two covers by O'Malley & Hung on each 3.00
11-15-($3.99) 4.00

SNOW BLIND
BOOM! Studios: Dec, 2015 - No. 4, Mar, 2016 ($3.99)
1-4-Ollie Masters-s/Tyler Jenkins-a 4.00

SNOWFALL
Image Comics: Feb, 2016 - No. 9, Jun, 2017 ($3.99)
1-9-Joe Harris-s/Martín Morazzo-a 4.00

SNOW WHITE (See Christmas With… (in Promotional Comics section), Mickey Mouse Magazine, Movie Comics & Seven Dwarfs)
Dell Publishing Co.: No. 49, July, 1944 - No. 382, Mar, 1952 (Disney-Movie)

	GD 2.0	VG 4.0	FN 6.0	VF 8.0	VF/NM 9.0	NM- 9.2
Four Color 49 (...& the Seven Dwarfs)	52	104	156	413	932	1450
Four Color 382 (1952)-origin; partial reprint of Four Color 49	13	26	39	86	188	290

SNOW WHITE
Marvel Comics: Jan, 1995 ($1.95, one-shot)
1-r/1937 Sunday newspaper pages 4.00

SNOW WHITE AND THE SEVEN DWARFS
Whitman Publications: April, 1982 (60¢)

	GD 2.0	VG 4.0	FN 6.0	VF 8.0	VF/NM 9.0	NM- 9.2
nn-r/Four Color 49	2	4	6	10	12	15

SNOW WHITE AND THE SEVEN DWARFS
Dark Horse Comics: Jun, 2019 - No. 3, Aug, 2019 ($3.99, limited series)
1-3-Cecil Castellucci-s/Gabriele Bagnoli-a 4.00

SNOW WHITE AND THE SEVEN DWARFS GOLDEN ANNIVERSARY
Gladstone: Fall, 1987 ($2.95, magazine size, 52 pgs.)

	GD 2.0	VG 4.0	FN 6.0	VF 8.0	VF/NM 9.0	NM- 9.2
1-Contains poster	2	4	6	9	13	16

SOAP OPERA LOVE
Charlton Comics: Feb, 1983 - No. 3, June, 1983

	GD 2.0	VG 4.0	FN 6.0	VF 8.0	VF/NM 9.0	NM- 9.2
1-3-Low print run	3	6	9	19	30	40

SOAP OPERA ROMANCES
Charlton Comics: July, 1982 - No. 5, March, 1983

	GD 2.0	VG 4.0	FN 6.0	VF 8.0	VF/NM 9.0	NM- 9.2
1-5-Nurse Betsy Crane-r; low print run	3	6	9	19	30	40

SOCK MONKEY
Dark Horse Comics: Sept, 1998 - No. 2, Oct, 1998 ($2.95/$2.99, B&W)

	GD 2.0	VG 4.0	FN 6.0	VF 8.0	VF/NM 9.0	NM- 9.2
1,2-Tony Millionaire-s/a	1	2	3	5	6	8

Vol. 2 -(Tony Millionaire's Sock Monkey) July, 1999 - No. 2, Aug, 1999
1,2 .... 4.00
Vol. 3 -(Tony Millionaire's Sock Monkey) Nov, 2000 - No. 2, Dec, 2000
1,2 .... 3.00
Vol. 4 -(Tony Millionaire's Sock Monkey) May, 2003 - No. 2, Aug, 2003
1,2 .... 3.00
...The Inches Incident (Sept, 2006 - No. 4, Apr, 2007) 1-4-Tony Millionaire-s/a 3.00

SOJOURN
White Cliffs Publ. Co.: Sept, 1977 - No. 2, 1978 ($1.50, B&W & color, tabloid size)

	GD 2.0	VG 4.0	FN 6.0	VF 8.0	VF/NM 9.0	NM- 9.2
1,2: 1-Tor by Kubert, Eagle by Severin, E. V. Race, Private Investigator by Doug Wildey, T. C. Mars by Aragonés begin plus other strips	2	4	6	8	10	12

NOTE: Most copies came folded. Unfolded copies are worth 50% more.

SOJOURN
CrossGeneration Comics: July, 2001 - No. 34, May, 2004 ($2.95)
Prequel -Ron Marz-s/Greg Land-c/a; preview pages 3.00
1-Ron Marz-s/Greg Land-c/a in most 6.00
2,3 .... 5.00
4-24: 7-Immonen-a. 12-Brigman-a. 17-Lopresti-a. 21-Luke Ross-a 3.00
25-34: 25-$1.00-c. 34-Cariello-a 3.00
...: From the Ashes TPB (2001, $19.95) r/#1-6; Land painted-c 20.00
...: The Dragon's Tale TPB (2002, $15.95) r/#7-12; Jusko painted-c 16.00
...: The Warrior's Tale TPB (2003, $15.95) r/#13-18 .... 16.00
Vol. 4: The Thief's Tale (2003, $15.95) r/#19-24 .... 16.00
Vol. 5: The Sorcerer's Tale (Checker Book Publ.,2007, $17.95) r/#25-30 .... 18.00
Vol. 6: The Berzerker's Tale (Checker Book Publ.,2007, $17.95) r/#31-34, Prequel 18.00
Traveler 1,2 ($9.95) digest-sized reprints of TPBs 10.00

SOLAR (...Man of the Atom) (Also see Doctor Solar)
Valiant/Acclaim Comics (Valiant): Sept, 1991 - No. 60, Apr, 1996 ($1.75-$2.50, 44 pgs.)

	GD 2.0	VG 4.0	FN 6.0	VF 8.0	VF/NM 9.0	NM- 9.2
1-Layton-a(i) on Solar; Barry Windsor-Smith-a/c	3	6	9	14	20	25
2,4-9: 2-Layton-a(i) on Solar, B. Smith-a. 7-vs. X-O Armor	1	3	4	6	8	10
3-1st app. Harada (11/91); intro. Harbinger	4	8	12	23	37	50
10-(6/92, $3.95)-1st app. Eternal Warrior (6 pgs.); black embossed-c; origin & 1st app. Geoff McHenry (Geomancer)	4	8	12	25	40	55

10-($3.95)-2nd printing 6.00
11-15: 11-1st full app. Eternal Warrior. 12,13-Unity x-overs. 14-1st app. Fred Bender (becomes Dr. Eclipse). 15-2nd Dr. Eclipse 5.00
16-60: 17-X-O Manowar app. 25-Solar splits. 29-1st Valiant Vision book. 33-Valiant Vision; bound-in trading card. 38-Chaos Effect Epsilon Pt.1. 46-52-Dan Jurgens-a(p)/scripts w/Giordano-i. 53,54-Jurgens scripts only. 60-Giffen scripts; Jeff Johnson-a(p) 4.00

Snake Eyes: Deadgame #3 © Hasbro

Soldier and Marine Comics #11 © CC

Soldier Zero #8 © BOOM!

	GD	VG	FN	VF	VF/NM	NM-
	2.0	4.0	6.0	8.0	9.0	9.2

0-($9.95, trade paperback)-r/Alpha and Omega origin story; polybagged w/poster ... 15.00
...: Second Death (1994, $9.95)-r/-issues #1-4. 20.00
NOTE: #1-10 all have free 8 pg. insert "Alpha and Omega" which is a 10 chapter Solar origin story. All 10 centerfolds can pieced together to show climax of story. Ditko a-11p, 14p. Giordano a-46, 47, 48, 49, 50, 51, 52i. Johnson a-60p. Jurgens a-46, 47, 48, 49, 50 , 51, 52p. Layton a-1-3i; c-2i, 11i, 17i, 25i. Miller a-c12. Quesada c-17p, 20-23p, 29p. Simonson c-13. B. Smith a-1-10; c-1, 3, 5, 7, 19i. Thibert c-22i, 23i.

SOLARMAN (See Pendulum III. Originals)
Marvel Comics: Jan, 1989 - No. 2, May, 1990 ($1.00, limited series)
1,2 4.00

SOLAR, MAN OF THE ATOM (Man of the Atom on cover)
Acclaim Comics (Valiant Heroes): Vol. 2, May, 1997 ($3.95, one-shot, 46 pgs)
(1st Valiant Heroes Special Event)
Vol. 2-Reintro Solar; Ninjak cameo; Warren Ellis scripts; Darick Robertson-a 5.00

SOLAR: MAN OF THE ATOM
Dynamite Entertainment: 2014 - No. 12, 2015 ($3.99)
1-12: 1-Barbiere-s/Bennett-a; 5 covers. 3-Female Solar in costume. 5-White costume 4.00

SOLAR, MAN OF THE ATOM: HELL ON EARTH
Acclaim Comics (Valiant Heroes): Jan, 1998 - No. 4 ($2.50, limited series)
1-4-Priest-s/ Zircher-a(p) 4.00

SOLAR, MAN OF THE ATOM: REVELATIONS
Acclaim Comics (Valiant Heroes): Nov, 1997 ($3.95, one-shot, 46 pgs.)
1-Krueger-s/ Zircher-a(p) 5.00

SOLDIER & MARINE COMICS (Fightin' Army #16 on)
Charlton Comics (Toby Press of Conn. V1#11): No. 11, Dec, 1954 - No. 15, Aug, 1955; V2#9, Dec, 1956

V1#11 (12/54)-Bob Powell-a	15	30	45	83	124	165
V1#12(2/55)-15: 12-Photo-c. 14-Photo-c; Colan-a	11	22	33	64	90	115
V2#9(Formerly Never Again; Jerry Drummer V2#10 on)	10	20	30	56	76	95

SOLDIER COMICS
Fawcett Publications: Jan, 1952 - No. 11, Sept, 1953

1	19	38	57	111	176	240
2	11	22	33	61	90	115
3-5: 4-What Happened in Taewah	10	20	30	56	76	95
6-11: 8-Illo. in POP	9	18	27	52	69	.85

SOLDIERS OF FORTUNE
American Comics Group (Creston Publ. Corp.): Mar-Apr, 1951 - No. 13, Feb-Mar, 1953

1-Capt. Crossbones by Shelly, Ace Carter, Lance Larson begin	32	64	96	188	307	425
2-(52 pgs.)	18	36	54	103	162	220
3-10: 6-Bondage-c	15	30	45	86	133	180
11-13 (War format)	11	22	33	62	86	110

NOTE: Shelly a-1-3, 5. Whitney a-6, 8-11, 13; c-1-3, 5, 6.

SOLDIERS OF FREEDOM
Americomics: 1987 - No. 2, 1987 ($1.75)
1,2 4.00

SOLDIER STORIES
Image Comics: Nov, 2022 ($5.99, one-shot)
1-Military-themed stories by various; Tucci-c 6.00

SOLDIER X (Continued from Cable)
Marvel Comics: Sept, 2002 - No. 12, Aug, 2003 ($2.99/$2.25)
1,10,11,12-($2.99) 1-Kordey-a/Macan-s. 10-Bollers-s/Ranson-a 3.00
2-9-($2.25) 3.00

SOLDIER ZERO (From Stan Lee)
BOOM! Studios: Oct, 2010 - No. 12, Sept, 2011 ($3.99)
1-12: 1-4-Cornell-s/Pina-a 4.00

SOLID BLOOD
Image Comics: No. 17, Dec, 2020 ($3.99, one-shot, newsprint paper)
17-Robert Kirkman-s/Ryan Ottley-a; homage to 1990s Image comics; Michonne cameo 4.00

SOLITAIRE (Also See Prime V2#6-8)
Malibu Comics (Ultraverse): Nov, 1993 - No. 12, Dec, 1994 ($1.95)
1-($2.50)Collector's edition bagged w/playing card 5.00
1-12: 1-Regular edition w/o playing card. 2,4-Break-Thru x-over. 3-2 pg. origin The Night Man. 4-Gatefold-c. 5-Two pg. origin the Strangers 4.00

SOLO
Marvel Comics: Sept, 1994 - No. 4, Dec, 1994 ($1.75 limited series)

1-4: Spider-Man app. 4.00

SOLO (Movie)
Dark Horse Comics: July, 1996 - No. 2, Aug, 1996 ($2.50, limited series)
1,2: Adaptation of film; photo-c 4.00

SOLO (Anthology showcasing individual artists)
DC Comics: Dec, 2004 - No. 12, Oct, 2006 ($4.95/$4.99)
1-12: 1-Tim Sale-a; stories by Sale and various. 2-Richard Corben-a; stories by Corben and Arcudi. 3-Paul Pope. 4-Howard Chaykin. 5-Darwyn Cooke. 6-Jordi Bernet. 7-Michael Allred; Teen Titans & Doom Patrol app. 8-Teddy Kristiansen. 9-Scott Hampton. 10-Damion Scott. 11-Sergio Aragonés. 12-Brendan McCarthy

| | 1 | 2 | 3 | 5 | 6 | 8 |

SOLO
Marvel Comics: Dec, 2016 - No. 5, Apr, 2017 ($3.99)
1-5: 1-Thorne & Duggan-s/Diaz-a; Dum Dum Dugan app. 4.00

SOLO: A STAR WARS STORY ADAPTATION (Titled Star Wars: Solo Adaptation for #1)
Marvel Comics: Dec, 2018 - No. 7, Jun, 2019 ($4.99/$3.99, limited series)

1-($4.99) Thompson-s/Sliney-a; 1st Qi'ra	3	6	9	19	30	40
2-5,7-($3.99) Noto-c						4.00
6-1st Darth Maul Crime Syndicate	2	4	6	9	12	15

SOLO AVENGERS (Becomes Avenger Spotlight #21 on)
Marvel Comics: Dec, 1987 - No. 20, July, 1989 (75c/$1.00)

1-Jim Lee-a on back-up story	1	3	4	6	8	10
2-20: 11-Intro Bobcat						4.00

SOLOMON AND SHEBA (Movie)
Dell Publishing Co.: No. 1070, Jan-Mar, 1960
Four Color 1070-Sekowsky-a; photo-c 10 20 30 64 132 200

SOLOMON GRUNDY
DC Comics: May, 2009 - No. 7, Nov, 2009 ($2.99)
1-7-Scott Kolins-s/a. 2-Bizarro app. 7-Blackest Night prelude 3.00
TPB (2010, $19.99) r/#1-7 20.00

SOLOMON KANE (Based on the Robert E. Howard character. Also see Blackthorne 3-D Series #60 & Marvel Premiere)
Marvel Comics: Sept, 1985 - No. 6, July, 1986 (Limited series)
1-Double size 5.00
2-6: 3-6-Williamson-a(i) 4.00

SOLOMON KANE
Dark Horse Comics: Sept, 2008 - No. 5, Feb, 2009 ($2.99)
1-5: 1-Two covers by Cassaday and Joe Kubert; Guevara-a 3.00
...: Death's Black Riders 1-4 (1/10 - No. 4, 6/10, $3.50) Robertson-c 3.50
...: Red Shadows 1-4 (4/11 - No. 4, 7/11, $3.50) Bruce Jones-s/Rahsan Ekedal-a; two covers by Davis & Manchess on each 3.50

SOLUS
CG Entertainment, Inc.: Apr, 2003 - No. 8, Jan, 2004 ($2.95)
1-8: 1-4,6,7-George Pérez-a/c; Barbara Kesel-s. 5-Ryan-a. 8-Kirk-a 3.00

SOLUTION, THE
Malibu Comics (Ultraverse): Sept, 1993 - No. 17, Feb, 1995 ($1.95)
1,3-15: 1-Intro Meathook, Deathdance, Black Tiger, Tech. 4-Break-Thru x-over; gatefold-c. 5-2 pg. origin The Strangers. 11-Brereton-c 4.00
1-($2.50)-Newsstand ed. polybagged w/trading card 5.00
1-Ultra 5000 Limited silver foil 8.00
0-Obtained w/Rune #0 by sending coupons from 11 comics 5.00
2-($2.50, 48 pgs.)-Rune flip-c/story by B. Smith; The Mighty Magnor 1 pg. strip by Aragonés 5.00
16 ($3.50)-Flip-c Ultraverse Premiere #10 5.00
17 ($2.50) 4.00

SOMERSET HOLMES (See Eclipse Graphic Novel Series)
Pacific Comics/ Eclipse Comics No. 5, 6: Sept, 1983 - No. 6, Dec, 1984 ($1.50, Baxter paper)
1-6: 1-Brent Anderson-c/a. Cliff Hanger by Williamson in all 4.00

SOMETHING EPIC
Image Comics: May, 2023 - Present ($3.99)
1-7-Szymon Kudranski-s/a 4.00

SOMETHING IS KILLING THE CHILDREN (Also see Enter the House of Slaughter)
BOOM! Studios: Sept, 2019 - Present ($3.99)

1-Tynion IV-s/Dell'edera-a	11	22	33	76	163	250
2	3	6	9	21	33	45
3	3	6	9	17	26	35

	GD 2.0	VG 4.0	FN 6.0	VF 8.0	VF/NM 9.0	NM- 9.2
4-8	2	4	6	9	12	15
9-1st Jessica (cameo)	3	6	9	14	20	25
10-20: 16-19-Origin of Erica						6.00
21-24,26-35						4.00
25-($4.99)						5.00
...: Pen & Ink #1 (6/23, $6.99) Issue #1's original B&W ink art with artist commentary						7.00

SOMNA
DSTLRY: Nov, 2023 - No. 3, Mar, 2024 ($8.99, oversized 10-7/8 x 8-1/2")

	GD 2.0	VG 4.0	FN 6.0	VF 8.0	VF/NM 9.0	NM- 9.2
1-3-Becky Cloonan & Tula Lotay-s/a						9.00

SONATA
Image Comics: Jun, 2019 - No. 12 ($3.99)

	GD 2.0	VG 4.0	FN 6.0	VF 8.0	VF/NM 9.0	NM- 9.2
1-12-David Hine/Brian Haberlin-s/a. 12-Flashback to the 1st meeting of Sonata and Treen						4.00
12-(3D Edition, $7.99) Polybagged with 3D glasses; bonus cover gallery in 3D						8.00

SONG OF THE SOUTH (See Brer Rabbit)

SONIC & KNUCKLES
Archie Comics: Aug, 1995 ($2.00)

	GD 2.0	VG 4.0	FN 6.0	VF 8.0	VF/NM 9.0	NM- 9.2
1	2	4	6	9	13	16

SONIC BOOM
Archie Comic Publications: Dec, 2014 - No. 11, Oct, 2015 ($3.99)

	GD 2.0	VG 4.0	FN 6.0	VF 8.0	VF/NM 9.0	NM- 9.2
1-11: 1-Regular-c and 4 interlocking variant covers. 2-7,11-Two covers on each. 8-10-"Worlds Unite" Sonic/Mega Man x-over; 3 covers						4.00

SONIC COMIC ORIGINS AND MEGA MAN X
Archie Comic Publications: Jun/Jul 2014 (giveaway)

	GD 2.0	VG 4.0	FN 6.0	VF 8.0	VF/NM 9.0	NM- 9.2
... Free Comic Book Day Edition - Flipbook; Freedom Fighters app.						3.00

SONIC DISRUPTORS
DC Comics: Dec, 1987 - No. 7, July, 1988 ($1.75, unfinished limited series)

	GD 2.0	VG 4.0	FN 6.0	VF 8.0	VF/NM 9.0	NM- 9.2
1-7	1	3	4	6	8	10

SONIC MEGA DRIVE
Archie Comic Publications: Aug, 2016 ($3.99, limited series)

	GD 2.0	VG 4.0	FN 6.0	VF 8.0	VF/NM 9.0	NM- 9.2
1-25th Anniversary celebration; Flynn-s/Hesse-a						4.00
... - The Next Level (12/16, $4.99) Flynn-s/Hesse-a; Metal Sonic app.						5.00

SONIC'S FRIENDLY NEMESIS KNUCKLES
Archie Publications: July, 1996 - No. 3, Sept, 1996 ($1.50, limited series)

	GD 2.0	VG 4.0	FN 6.0	VF 8.0	VF/NM 9.0	NM- 9.2
1-3	1	3	4	6	8	10

SONIC SUPER DIGEST
Archie Publications: Dec, 2012 - No. 17 ($3.99/$4.99)

	GD 2.0	VG 4.0	FN 6.0	VF 8.0	VF/NM 9.0	NM- 9.2
1-7-($3.99)	1	2	3	5	6	8
8-17-($4.99)	1	3	4	6	8	10

SONIC SUPER SPECIAL
Archie Publications: 1997 - No. 15, Feb, 2001 ($2.00/$2.25/$2.29, 48 pgs)

	GD 2.0	VG 4.0	FN 6.0	VF 8.0	VF/NM 9.0	NM- 9.2
1	2	4	6	11	16	20
2,3	1	2	3	5	6	8
4-6,8-12: 10-Sabrina-c/app.						5.00
7-(w/Image) Spawn, Maxx, Savage Dragon-c/app.; Valentino-a	3	6	9	14	19	24
13-Epic story conclusion	3	6	9	16	23	30
14,15-Low print run. 15-Sin City spoof	2	4	6	11	16	20

SONIC THE HEDGEHOG (TV, video game)
Archie Comics: No. 0, Feb, 1993 - No. 3, May, 1993 ($1.25, mini-series)

	GD 2.0	VG 4.0	FN 6.0	VF 8.0	VF/NM 9.0	NM- 9.2
0(2/93),1: Shaw-a(p) & covers on all	5	10	15	30	50	70
2,3	3	6	9	16	23	30
Beginnings TPB (2003, $10.95) r/#0-3						15.00
...: The Beginning TPB (2006, $10.95) r/#0-3						11.00

SONIC THE HEDGEHOG (TV, video game)
Archie Comics: July, 1993 - No. 290, Feb, 2017 ($1.25-$2.99)

	GD 2.0	VG 4.0	FN 6.0	VF 8.0	VF/NM 9.0	NM- 9.2
1	6	12	18	38	69	100
2	4	8	12	23	37	50
3	3	6	9	16	23	30
4-10: 8-Neon ink-c	2	4	6	11	16	20
11-20	2	4	6	9	13	16
21-30 ($1.50): 25-Silver ink-c	2	4	6	8	10	12
31-50	1	2	3	5	6	8
51-55,57-92						4.00
56-Super Sonic and Hyper Knuckles app.	2	4	6	9	12	15
93-Shadow Knuckles	3	6	9	14	20	25
94-97,99-145,147-212: 117-Begin $2.19-c. 152-Begin $2.25-c. 157-Shadow app. 198-Begin $2.50						4.00
98-1st Shadow the Hedgehog	10	20	30	64	132	200
146-Shadow the Hedgehog-c	3	6	9	14	20	25
213-249,252-263: 213-Begin $2.99-c. 248-263-Two covers						3.00
250-($3.99) Wraparound-c; part 9 of Worlds Collide x-over with Mega Man	1	2	3	5	6	8
251-Worlds Collide conclusion	2	4	6	9	12	15
264-274,276-290-($3.99) Two covers on most. 273,274-"Worlds Unite" Sonic/Mega Man x-over; 3 covers on each. 288-290-Genesis of a Hero						4.00
275-($4.99) "Worlds Unite" Sonic/Mega Man x-over; six covers	1	2	3	5	6	8
Free Comic Book Day Edition 1 (2007)- Leads into Sonic the Hedgehog #175	2	4	6	9	12	15
Free Comic Book Day Edition 2009 - Reprints Sonic the Hedgehog #1 from July 1993	2	4	6	9	12	15
Free Comic Book Day Edition 2010 - 2012: 2010-New story						4.00
Free Comic Book Day Edition 2021-Previews "Battle For the Empire" story						3.00
Sonic and Mega Man: World's Collide Prelude, FCBD Edition (6-7/13)	1	2	3	5	6	8
Sonic and Mega Man: Worlds Unite FCBD Edition (6-7/15) Prelude to crossover						4.00
Sonic Sampler: Free Comic Book Day Edition (5/16) Sonic & Sonic Universe stories	1	2	3	5	6	8
Sonic: Worlds Unite Battles (9/15, $3.99) Sonic/Mega Man x-over; 3 wraparound covers						4.00

	GD 2.0	VG 4.0	FN 6.0	VF 8.0	VF/NM 9.0	NM- 9.2
Triple Trouble Special (10/95, $2.00, 48 pgs.)	1	3	4	6	8	10

SONIC THE HEDGEHOG (TV, video game)
IDW Publishing: Apr, 2018 - Present ($3.99, #1-4 weekly, #5-on monthly)

	GD 2.0	VG 4.0	FN 6.0	VF 8.0	VF/NM 9.0	NM- 9.2
1-Flynn-s/Yardley-a	3	6	9	14	20	25
2-5: 3-Knuckles app. 4-Intro. Tangle the Lemur	1	3	4	6	8	10
6-12,14-24,26-49,51-68						4.00
13,25-($4.99) 13-Tails, Rough & Tumble app.; four covers. 25-The Deadly Six app.						6.00
50-($7.99) Sonic vs. Surge the Tenrec	1	3	4	6	8	10
Annual 2022 (8/22, $7.99) Short stories by various						8.00
... Amy's 30th Anniversary Special (9/23, $5.99) Flynn-s/Hammerstrom-a						6.00
... 5th Anniversary Special (4/23, $7.99) Eight covers						8.00
... Halloween Comicfest 1 (10/19, free giveaway) r/#1						3.00
... Halloween Special One-Shot 1 (10/23, $4.99) Bouchard-s/Lawrence-a						5.00
... 900th Adventure (9/23, $7.99) Story and art by various						8.00
... 30th Anniversary Special (6/21, $8.99) Five covers; Knuckles app.						9.00
... 2: The Official Movie Pre-Quill (3/22, $6.99) Short stories; Knuckles app.						7.00
... Winter Jam 1 (12/23, $4.99) Ata-s/Kim-a; Orbot & Cubot app.						5.00

SONIC THE HEDGEHOG: BAD GUYS
IDW Publishing: Sept, 2020 - No. 4, Dec, 2020 ($3.99, limited series)

	GD 2.0	VG 4.0	FN 6.0	VF 8.0	VF/NM 9.0	NM- 9.2
1-4-Ian Flynn-s/Jack Lawrence-a. 1-Five covers. 2-4-Three covers						4.00

SONIC THE HEDGEHOG: FANG THE HUNTER
IDW Publishing: Jan, 2024 - Present ($3.99, limited series)

	GD 2.0	VG 4.0	FN 6.0	VF 8.0	VF/NM 9.0	NM- 9.2
1,2-Ian Flynn-s/Mauro Fonseca-a; the hunt for the Eighth Emerald						4.00

SONIC THE HEDGEHOG: IMPOSTER SYNDROME
IDW Publishing: Nov, 2020 - No. 4, May, 2021 ($3.99, limited series)

	GD 2.0	VG 4.0	FN 6.0	VF 8.0	VF/NM 9.0	NM- 9.2
1-4-Ian Flynn-s/Thomas Rothlisberger-a. 1,4-Four covers. 2,3-Three covers						4.00

SONIC THE HEDGEHOG: SCRAPNIK ISLAND
IDW Publishing: Oct, 2022 - No. 4, Jan, 2023 ($3.99, limited series)

	GD 2.0	VG 4.0	FN 6.0	VF 8.0	VF/NM 9.0	NM- 9.2
1-4-Daniel Barnes-s/Jack Lawrence-a						4.00

SONIC THE HEDGEHOG: TANGLE & WHISPER
IDW Publishing: No. 0, Apr, 2019 - No. 4, Oct, 2019 ($3.99, limited series)

	GD 2.0	VG 4.0	FN 6.0	VF 8.0	VF/NM 9.0	NM- 9.2
0-(4/19, no price) Ian Flynn-s/Evan Stanley-a; previews series and Sonic storyline						3.00
1-4-($3.99) Ian Flynn-s/Evan Stanley-a; Mimic app.; multiple covers on each						4.00

SONIC UNIVERSE (Sonic the Hedgehog)
Archie Publications: Apr, 2009 - No. 94, Mar, 2017 ($2.50/$2.99/$3.99)

	GD 2.0	VG 4.0	FN 6.0	VF 8.0	VF/NM 9.0	NM- 9.2
1-15						3.00
16-66: 16-Begin $2.99-c. 51-66-Two covers						3.00
67-94-($3.99) Two covers on most. 75-"Worlds Unite" Sonic/Mega Man x-over prelude with nine covers. 76-78-"Worlds Unite" x-over; 3 covers on each. 87-90-Shattered						4.00

SONIC VS. KNUCKLES "BATTLE ROYAL" SPECIAL
Archie Publications: 1997 ($2.00, one-shot)

	GD 2.0	VG 4.0	FN 6.0	VF 8.0	VF/NM 9.0	NM- 9.2
1	2	4	6	9	12	15

SONIC X (Sonic the Hedgehog)
Archie Publications: Nov, 2005 - No. 40, Feb, 2009 ($2.25)

	GD 2.0	VG 4.0	FN 6.0	VF 8.0	VF/NM 9.0	NM- 9.2
1-Sam Speed app.	2	4	6	8	10	12
2-40						4.00

SONJAVERSAL (Red Sonja) (Leads into Hell Sonja #1)
Dynamite Entertainment: 2021 - No. 10, 2021 ($3.99)

	GD 2.0	VG 4.0	FN 6.0	VF 8.0	VF/NM 9.0	NM- 9.2
1-10: 1-Hastings-s/Qualano & Perez-a; alternate Sonjas meet						4.00

SON OF AMBUSH BUG (See Ambush Bug)
DC Comics: July, 1986 - No. 6, Dec, 1986 (75¢)

	GD 2.0	VG 4.0	FN 6.0	VF 8.0	VF/NM 9.0	NM- 9.2
1-6: Giffen-c/a in all. 5-Bissette-a.						4.00

SON OF BLACK BEAUTY (Also see Black Beauty)
Dell Publishing Co.: No. 510, Oct, 1953 - No. 566, June, 1954

	GD 2.0	VG 4.0	FN 6.0	VF 8.0	VF/NM 9.0	NM- 9.2
Four Color 510,566	5	10	15	31	53	75

SON OF FLUBBER (See Movie Comics)

SON OF HULK (Continues from Skaar: Son of Hulk #12) (See Realm of Kings)
Marvel Comics: No. 13, Sept, 2009 - No. 17, Jan, 2010 ($2.99)

	GD 2.0	VG 4.0	FN 6.0	VF 8.0	VF/NM 9.0	NM- 9.2
13-17: 13,15-17-Galactus app.						3.00

SON OF M (Also see House of M series)
Marvel Comics: Feb, 2006 - No. 6, July, 2006 ($2.99, limited series)

	GD 2.0	VG 4.0	FN 6.0	VF 8.0	VF/NM 9.0	NM- 9.2
1-6: 1-Powerless Quicksilver; Martinez-a. 2-Quicksilver regains powers; Inhumans app.						3.00
Decimation: Son of M (2006, $13.99, TPB) r/series; Martinez sketch pages						14.00

SON OF MERLIN
Image Comics (Top Cow): Feb, 2013 - No. 5, Jun, 2013 ($1.00/$2.99, limited series)

	GD 2.0	VG 4.0	FN 6.0	VF 8.0	VF/NM 9.0	NM- 9.2
1-5: 1-($1.00-c); Napton-s/Zid-a; covers by Zid & Sejic. 2-($2.99)						3.00

SON OF MUTANT WORLD
Fantagor Press: 1990 - No. 5, 1990? ($2.00, bi-monthly)

	GD 2.0	VG 4.0	FN 6.0	VF 8.0	VF/NM 9.0	NM- 9.2
1-5: 1-3: Corben-c/a. 4,5 ($1.75, B&W)						4.00

SON OF ORIGINS OF MARVEL COMICS (See Fireside Book Series)

SON OF ORIGINS OF MARVEL COMICS: MARVEL TALES
Marvel Comics: Aug, 2023 (squarebound, one-shot)

	GD 2.0	VG 4.0	FN 6.0	VF 8.0	VF/NM 9.0	NM- 9.2
1-Reprints origins of Hulk, Thor, Iron Man, Daredevil and Doctor Strange						8.00

SON OF SATAN (Also see Ghost Rider #1 & Marvel Spotlight #12)
Marvel Comics Group: Dec, 1975 - No. 8, Feb, 1977 (25¢)

	GD 2.0	VG 4.0	FN 6.0	VF 8.0	VF/NM 9.0	NM- 9.2
1-Mooney-a; Kane-c(p), Starlin splash(p)	5	10	15	33	57	80
2,6-8: 2-Origin The Possessor. 8-Heath-a	3	6	9	14	19	24
3-5-(Regular 25¢ editions)(4-8/76): 5-Russell-p	3	6	9	14	19	24
3-5-(30¢-c variants, limited distribution)	5	10	15	30	50	70
...: Marvel Spotlight #12 Facsimile Edition (11/19, $3.99) r/issue with original 1973 ads						5.00

SON OF SINBAD (Also see Abbott & Costello & Daring Adventures)
St. John Publishing Co.: Feb, 1950

	GD 2.0	VG 4.0	FN 6.0	VF 8.0	VF/NM 9.0	NM- 9.2
1-Kubert-c/a	68	136	204	435	743	1050

Something is Killing the Children #17
© Tynion IV & Dell'edera

Sonic the Hedgehog #33 © SEGA

Soulfire V4 #7 © AspenMLT

	GD 2.0	VG 4.0	FN 6.0	VF 8.0	VF/NM 9.0	NM- 9.2

SON OF SUPERMAN (Elseworlds)
DC Comics: 1999 ($14.95, prestige format, one-shot)
nn-Chaykin & Tischman-s/Williams III & Gray-a ... 15.00

SON OF TOMAHAWK (See Tomahawk)

SON OF VULCAN (Formerly Mysteries of Unexplored Worlds #1-48; Thunderbolt V3#51 on)
Charlton Comics: V2#49, Nov, 1965 - V2#50, Jan, 1966

V2#49,50: 50-Roy Thomas scripts (1st pro work)	3	6	9	19	30	40

SONS OF ANARCHY (Based on the TV series)
BOOM! Studios: Sept, 2013 - No. 25, Sept, 2015 ($3.99, originally a 6-issue limited series)
1-24: 1-6-Christopher Golden-s/Damian Couceiro-a; multiple covers on each ... 4.00
25-($4.99) Last issue; Ferrier-s/Bergara-a; three covers ... 5.00

SONS OF ANARCHY REDWOOD ORIGINAL (TV series)
BOOM! Studios: June - No. 12, Jul, 2017

1-12: 1-Prequel with 18-year-old Jax Teller. 1-4-Masters-s/Pizzari-a; multiple covers ... 4.00

SONS OF KATIE ELDER (See Movie Classics)

SONS OF THE DEVIL
Image Comics: May, 2015 - No. 14, Jul, 2017 ($2.99/$3.99)
1-5: 1-Brian Buccellato-s/Toni Infante-a ... 3.00
6-14-($3.99) ... 4.00

SORCERY (See Chilling Adventures in... & Red Circle...)

SORORITY SECRETS
Toby Press: July, 1954

1		47	94	141	296	498	700

SOULFIRE (MICHAEL TURNER PRESENTS:...) (Also see Eternal Soulfire)
Aspen MLT, Inc.: No. 0, 2004 - No. 10, Jul, 2009 ($2.50/$2.99)
0-($2.50) Turner-a/c; Loeb-s; intro. to characters & development sketches ... 3.00
1-($2.99) Two covers ... 3.00
1-Diamond Previews Exclusive ... 5.00
1 Special Edition (4/22, $1.99) R/#1; preview of Soulfire: The Core ... 3.00
2-9: 2,3-Two covers. 4-Four covers ... 3.00
10-($3.99) Benitez-a ... 4.00
... Sourcebook 1 (3/15, $4.99) Character profiles; two covers by Turner ... 5.00
...: The Collected Edition Vol. 1 (5/05, $6.99) r/#1,2; cover gallery ... 7.00
Hardcover Volume 1 (12/05, $24.99) r/#0-5 & preview from Wizard Mag.; Johns intro. ... 25.00

SOULFIRE (MICHAEL TURNER PRESENTS:...) (Volume 2)
Aspen MLT, Inc.: No. 0, Oct, 2009 - No. 9, Jan, 2011 ($2.50/$2.99)
0-($2.50) Marcus To-a ... 3.00
1-9-($3.99) 1-Five covers. 9-Covers by To and Linsner ... 3.00

SOULFIRE (MICHAEL TURNER'S...) (Volume 3)
Aspen MLT, Inc.: No. 0, Apr, 2011 - No. 8, May, 2012 ($1.99/$2.99)
0-($1.99) Krul-s/Fabok-a; 4 covers ... 3.00
1-8-($2.99) 1-Four covers ... 3.00
... Despair (7/12, $3.99) Schwartz-s/Marks-a; 3 covers ... 4.00
... Faith (7/12, $3.99) McMurray-s/Oum-a; 3 covers ... 4.00
... Hope (7/12, $3.99) Krul-s/Varese-a; 3 covers ... 4.00
... Power (7/12, $3.99) Wohl-s/Randolph-a; 3 covers ... 4.00
... Primer (6/12, $1.00) Reprints and story summaries ... 3.00

SOULFIRE (MICHAEL TURNER'S...) (Volume 4)
Aspen MLT, Inc.: Aug, 2012 - No. 8, Oct, 2013 ($3.99)
1-8-Krul-s/DeBalfo-a; multiple covers on each ... 4.00

SOULFIRE (MICHAEL TURNER'S...) (Volume 5)
Aspen MLT, Inc.: Nov, 2013 - No. 8, Oct, 2014 ($1.00/$3.99)
1-($1.00) Krul-s/Marion-a; multiple covers ... 3.00
2-8-($3.99) Multiple covers on each ... 4.00
Annual 1 2014 (7/14, $5.99) Art by Garbowska, Hanson, Turner, Cafaro ... 6.00

SOULFIRE (ALL NEW MICHAEL TURNER'S...) (Volume 6)
Aspen MLT, Inc.: Mar, 2017 - No. 8, Oct, 2017 ($3.99)
1-8-($3.99) Multiple covers on each. 1-Krul-s/Cafaro-a ... 4.00

SOULFIRE (MICHAEL TURNER'S...) (Volume 7)
Aspen MLT, Inc.: Jul, 2018 - No. 8, Feb, 2019 ($3.99)
1-8: 1-Krul-s/Ladjouze-a; multiple covers ... 4.00
... Primer 1 (7/18, 25¢) Series intro. and bonus text recaps of previous volumes ... 3.00

SOULFIRE (MICHAEL TURNER'S...) (Volume 8)
Aspen MLT, Inc.: Jun, 2019 - No. 6, Nov, 2019 ($3.99)

1-6: 1-Krul-s/Forté-a; multiple covers ... 4.00

SOULFIRE: CHAOS REIGN
Aspen MLT, Inc.: No. 0, June, 2006 - No. 3, Jan, 2007 ($2.50/$2.99)
0-($2.50) Three covers; Marcus To-a; J.T. Krul-s ... 3.00
1-3-($2.99) 1-Three covers ... 3.00
...: Beginnings (7/06, $1.99) Marcus To-a; J.T. Krul-s ... 3.00
...: Beginnings 1 (7/07, $1.99) Francisco Herrera-a; J.T. Krul-s ... 3.00

SOULFIRE: DYING OF THE LIGHT
Aspen MLT, Inc.: No. 0, 2004 - No. 5, Feb, 2006 ($2.50/$2.99)
0-($2.50) Three covers; Gunnell-a; Krul-s; back-story to the Soulfire universe ... 3.00
1-5-($2.99) 1-Five covers ... 3.00
... Vol. 1 TPB (2007, $14.99) r/#0-5; Gunnell sketch pages, cover gallery ... 15.00

SOULFIRE: NEW WORLD ORDER
Aspen MLT, Inc.: No. 0, Jul, 2007; May, 2009 - No. 5, Dec, 2009 ($2.50/$2.99)
0 (7/07, $2.50) Two covers; Herrera-a/Krul-s ... 3.00
1-5-($2.99) 1-Four covers ... 3.00

SOULFIRE: SHADOW MAGIC
Aspen MLT, Inc.: No. 0, Nov, 2008 - No. 5, May, 2009 ($2.50/$2.99)
0-($2.50) Two covers; Sana Takeda-a ... 3.00
1-5-($2.99) 1-Two covers ... 3.00

SOULFIRE: THE CORE
Aspen MLT, Inc.: Oct, 2022 - Present ($3.99)
1,2-Krul-s/Konat-a; multiple covers on each ... 4.00

SOUL SAGA
Image Comics (Top Cow): Feb, 2000 - No. 5, Apr, 2001 ($2.50)
1-5: 1-Madureira-c; Platt & Batt-a ... 3.00

SOULSEARCHERS AND COMPANY
Claypool Comics: June, 1995 - No. 82, Jan, 2007 ($2.50, B&W)
1-10: Peter David scripts ... 5.00
11-82 ... 4.00

SOULWIND
Image Comics: Mar, 1997 - No. 8 ($2.95, B&W, limited series)
1-8: 5-"The Day I Tried To Live" pt. 1 ... 4.00
Book Five; The August Ones (Oni Press, 3/01, $8.50) ... 8.50
... The Kid From Planet Earth (1997, $9.95, TPB) ... 10.00
... The Kid From Planet Earth (Oni Press, 1/00, $8.50, TPB) ... 8.50
... The Day I Tried to Live (Oni Press, 4/00, $8.50, TPB) ... 8.50
The Complete Soulwind TPB ($29.95, 11/03, 8" x 5 1/2") r/Oni Books #1-5 ... 30.00

SOUPY SALES COMIC BOOK (TV)(The Official...)
Archie Publications: 1965

1-(Teen-age)		8	16	24	56	108	160

SOUTHERN BASTARDS
Image Comics: Apr, 2014 - No. 20, May, 2018 ($3.50/$3.99)
1-Jason Aaron-s/Jason Latour-a ... 8.00
2-20: 18-Chris Brunner-a ... 4.00

SOUTHERN CROSS
Image Comics: Mar, 2014 - No. 14, Mar, 2018 ($2.99/$3.99)
1-6-Becky Cloonan-s/c; Andy Belanger-a ... 3.00
7-14-($3.99) Cloonan-s/c; Belanger-a ... 4.00

SOUTHERN KNIGHTS, THE (See Crusaders #1)
Guild Publ/Fictioneer Books: No. 2, 1983 - No. 41, 1993 (B&W)

2-Magazine size	1	2	3	5	6	8
3-35, 37-41						4.00
36-($3.50-c)						5.00
Dread Halloween Special 1, Primer Special 1 (Spring, 1989, $2.25)						4.00
Graphic Novels #1-4						4.00

SOUTH SIDE SERPENTS (Based on the Riverdale TV series)
Archie Comic Publications: Mar, 2021 ($3.99, one-shot)
1-Jughead, FP Jones & Toni Topaz app.; David Barnett-s/Richard Ortiz-a ... 4.00

SOVEREIGNS
Dynamite Entertainment: No. 0, 2017 - No. 5, 2017 ($1.00/$3.99)
0-($1.00) Short stories of Magnus, Turok, Solar and Doctor Spektor ... 3.00
1-5-($3.99) Fawkes-s/Desjardins-a; back-up stories on each ... 4.00

SOVEREIGN SEVEN (Also see Showcase '95 #12)
DC Comics: July, 1995 - No. 36, July, 1998 ($1.95) (1st creator-owned mainstream DC comic)

	GD	VG	FN	VF	VF/NM	NM-
	2.0	4.0	6.0	8.0	9.0	9.2

1-1st app. Sovereign Seven (Reflex, Indigo, Cascade, Finale, Cruiser, Network & Rampart); 1st app. Maitresse; Darkseid app.; Chris Claremont-s & Dwayne Turner-c/a begins ... 5.00
1-Gold ... 8.00
1-Platinum ... 40.00
2-36: 2-Wolverine cameo. 4-Neil Gaiman cameo. 5,8-Batman app. 7-Ramirez cameo (from the movie Highlander). 9-Humphrey Bogart cameo from Casablanca. 10-Impulse app; Manoli Wetherell & Neal Conan cameo from Uncanny X-Men #226. 11-Robin app. 16-Final Night. 24-Superman app. 25-Power Girl app. 28-Impulse-c/app. ... 4.00
Annual 1 (1995, $3.95)-Year One story; Big Barda & Lobo app.; Jeff Johnson-c/a ... 5.00
Annual 2 (1996, $2.95)-Legends of the Dead Earth; Leonardi-a ... 5.00
...Plus 1(2/97, $2.95)-Legion-c/app. ... 5.00
TPB-($12.95) r/#1-5, Annual #1 & Showcase '95 #12 ... 13.00

SPACE: ABOVE AND BEYOND (TV)
Topps Comics: Jan., 1996 - No. 3, Mar, 1996 ($2.95, limited series)

1-3: Adaptation of pilot episode; Steacy-c. ... 4.00

SPACE: ABOVE AND BEYOND—THE GAUNTLET (TV)
Topps Comics: May, 1996 -No. 2, June, 1996 ($2.95, limited series)

1,2 ... 4.00

SPACE ACE (Also see Manhunt!)
Magazine Enterprises: No. 5, 1952

5(A-1 #61)-Guardineer-a	90	180	270	576	988	1400

SPACE ACE: DEFENDER OF THE UNIVERSE (Based on the Don Bluth video game)
CrossGen Comics: Oct., 2003 - No. 6 ($2.95, limited series)

1,2-Kirkman-s/Borges-a ... 3.00

SPACE ACTION
Ace Magazines (Junior Books): June, 1952 - No. 3, Oct, 1952

1-Cameron-a in all (1 story)	116	232	348	742	1271	1800
2,3	74	148	222	470	810	1150

SPACE ADVENTURES (War At Sea #22 on)
Capitol Stories/Charlton Comics: 7/52 - No. 21, 8/56; No. 23, 5/58 - No. 59, 11/64; V3#60, 10/67; V1#2, 7/68 - V1#4, 7/69; No. 9, 5/78 - No. 13, 3/79

1-Fago/Morales world on fire-c	103	206	309	659	1130	1600
2	40	80	120	246	441	575
3-5: 4,6-Flying saucer-c/stories	34	68	102	204	332	460
6,8,9: 8-Robot-c. 9-A-Bomb panel	29	58	87	172	281	390
7-Sex change story "Transformation"	123	246	369	787	1344	1900
10,11-Ditko-c/a. 10-Robot-c. 11-Two Ditko stories	90	180	270	576	988	1400
12-Ditko-c (classic)	432	864	1296	3154	5577	8000
13-(Fox-r, 10-11/54); Blue Beetle-c/story	21	42	63	124	202	280
14,15,17,18: 14-Blue Beetle-c/story; Fox-r (12-1/54-55, last pre-code)						
15,17,18-Rocky Jones-c/s.(TV); 15-Part photo-c	25	50	75	150	245	340
16-Krigstein-a; Rocky Jones-c/story (TV)	28	56	84	168	274	380
19-Robot-c by Giordano	41	82	123	256	428	600
20-Reprints Fawcett's "Destination Moon"	30	60	90	177	289	400
21-(8/56) (no #22)(Becomes War At Sea)	20	40	60	118	192	265
23-(5/58; formerly Nyoka, The Jungle Girl)-Reprints Fawcett's "Destination Moon"						
	25	50	75	150	245	340
24,25,31,32-Ditko-a. 24-Severin-a(signed "LePoer")	25	50	75	150	245	340
26,27-Ditko-a(4) each. 26,28-Flying saucer-c	27	54	81	158	259	360
28-30	15	30	45	83	124	165
33-Origin/1st app. Capt. Atom by Ditko (3/60)	284	568	852	1818	3109	4400
34-40,42-All Captain Atom by Ditko	34	68	102	199	325	450
41,43,45-59: 43-Alan Shephard strory, 2nd man in space. 45-Mercury Man app.						
	6	12	18	38	69	100
44-1st app. Mercury Man	7	14	21	46	86	125
V3#60(#1, 10/67)-Presents UFO origin & 1st app. Paul Mann & The Saucers From the Future						
	6	12	18	37	66	95
2,5,6,8 (1968-69)-Ditko-a: 2-Aparo-c/a	4	8	12	23	37	50
3,4,7: 4-Aparo-c/a	3	6	9	19	30	40
9-13(1978-79)-Capt. Atom-r/Space Adventures by Ditko; 9-Reprints origin/1st app. Capt. Atom from #33						6.00

NOTE: Aparo a-V3#60. c-V3#8. Ditko c-2, 31-42. Giordano c-3, 4, 7-9, 18p, 19 Krigstein a-15. Shuster a-11.
Issues 13 & 14 have Blue Beetle logos; #15-18 have Rocky Jones logos.

SPACE BANDITS
Image Comics: Jul, 2019 - No. 5, Nov, 2019 ($3.99/$5.99, limited series)

1-4-($3.99) Mark Millar-s/Matteo Scalera-a ... 4.00
5-($5.99) ... 6.00

SPACE BASTARDS
Humanoids Inc.: 2021 - Present ($5.99/$4.99)

1-($5.99) Darick Robertson-a/Eric Peterson & Joe Aubrey-s ... 6.00
2-6,8,9-($4.99) ... 5.00
7-($5.99) "Giant-Size Manny issue"; Bisley-a; back-up w/Langley-a ... 6.00
... Special Delivery (2022, $7.99) Short stories; art by Bisley, Gabo & Boo Cook ... 8.00

SPACE BUSTERS
Ziff-Davis Publ. Co.: Spring, 1952 - No. 2, Fall, 1952

1-Krigstein-a(3); Painted-c by Norman Saunders	106	212	318	673	1162	1650
2-Kinstler-a(2 pgs.); Saunders painted-c	87	174	261	553	952	1350

NOTE: Anderson a-2. Bondage c-2.

SPACE CADET (See Tom Corbett,...)

SPACE CIRCUS
Dark Horse Comics: July, 2000 - No. 4, Oct, 2000 ($2.95, limited series)

1-4-Aragonés-a/Evanier-s ... 3.00

SPACE COMICS (Formerly Funny Tunes)
Avon Periodicals: No. 4, Mar-Apr, 1954 - No. 5, May-June, 1954

4,5-Space Mouse, Peter Rabbit, Super Pup (formerly Spotty the Pup) & Merry Mouse continue from Funny Tunes	14	28	42	76	108	140
I.W. Reprint #8 (nd)-Space Mouse-r	3	6	9	14	20	25

SPACE DETECTIVE
Avon Periodicals: July, 1951 - No. 4, July, 1952

1-Rod Hathway, Space Detective begins, ends #4; Wood-c/a(3)-23 pgs.; "Opium Smugglers of Venus" drug story; Lucky Dale-r/Saint #4

	194	388	582	1242	2121	3000
2-Tales from the Shadow Squad story; Wood/Orlando-c; Wood inside layouts; "Slave Ship of Saturn" story	142	284	426	909	1555	2200
3-Classic Kinstler-c	142	284	426	909	1555	2200
4-Kinstlerish-a by McCann	68	136	204	435	743	1050
I.W. Reprint #1(Reprints #2), 8(Reprints cover #1 & part Famous Funnies #191)						
	5	10	15	30	50	70

SPACE EXPLORER (See March of Comics #202)

SPACE FAMILY ROBINSON (TV)(...Lost in Space #15-37, ...Lost in Space On Space Station One #38 on)(See Gold Key Champion)
Gold Key: Dec, 1962 - No. 36, Oct, 1969; No. 37, 10/73 - No. 54, 11/78; No. 55, 3/81 - No. 59, 5/82 (All painted covers)

1-(Low distribution); Spiegle-a in all	40	80	120	296	673	1050
2(3/63)-Family becomes lost in space	13	26	39	87	195	300
3-5	8	16	24	54	102	150
6-10: 6-Captain Venture back-up stories begin	6	12	18	41	76	110
11-20: 14-(10/65). 15-Title change (1/66)	5	10	15	31	53	75
21-36: 28-Last 12c issue. 36-Captain Venture ends	4	8	12	25	40	55
37-48: 37-Origin retold	3	6	9	14	19	24
49-59: Reprints #49,50,55-59	2	4	6	8	11	14

NOTE: The TV show first aired on 9/15/65. Title changed after TV show debuted.

SPACE FAMILY ROBINSON (See March of Comics #320, 328, 352, 404, 414)

SPACE GHOST (TV) (Also see Golden Comics Digest #2 & Hanna-Barbera Super TV Heroes #3-7)
Gold Key: March, 1967 (Hanna-Barbera) (TV debut was 9/10/66)

1 (10199-703)-Spiegle-a	37	74	111	274	612	950

SPACE GHOST (TV cartoon)
Comico: Mar, 1987 ($3.50, deluxe format, one-shot) (Hanna-Barbera)

1-Steve Rude-c/a; Evanier-s; Steacy painted-a	3	6	9	16	23	30

SPACE GHOST (TV cartoon)
DC Comics: Jan, 2005 - No. 6, June, 2005 ($2.95/$2.99, limited series)

1-6-Alex Ross-c/Ariel Olivetti-a/Joe Kelly-s; origin of Space Ghost ... 3.00
TPB (2005, $14.99) r/series; cover gallery ... 15.00

SPACE GIANTS, THE (TV cartoon)
FBN Publications: 1979 ($1.00, B&W, one-shots)

1-Based on Japanese TV series	3	6	9	15	22	28

SPACEHAWK
Dark Horse Comics: 1989 - No. 3, 1990 ($2.00, B&W)

1-3-Wolverton-c/a(r) plus new stories by others. ... 5.00

SPACE JAM
DC Comics: 1996 ($5.95, one-shot, movie adaption)

1-Wraparound photo cover of Michael Jordan	3	6	9	19	30	40

SPACE JOB
Dark Horse Comics: Feb, 2023 - No. 4, Jun, 2023 ($3.99, limited series)

1-4-Goodman-s/Sarrasaca-a ... 4.00

SPACE KAT-ETS (...in 3-D)
Power Publishing Co.: Dec, 1953 (25¢, came w/glasses)

1	40	80	120	246	411	575

SPACEKNIGHTS
Marvel Comics: Oct, 2000 - No. 5, Feb, 2001 ($2.99, limited series)

1-5-Starlin-s/Batista-a ... 3.00

SPACEKNIGHTS
Marvel Comics: Dec, 2012 - No. 3, Feb, 2013 ($3.99, limited series)

1-3-Reprints the 2000-2001 series & Annihilation: Conquest Prologue ... 4.00

SPACEMAN (Speed Carter...)
Atlas Comics (CnPC): Sept, 1953 - No. 6, July, 1954

1-Grey tone-c	135	270	405	864	1482	2100
2	65	130	195	416	708	1000
3-6: 4-A-Bomb explosion-c	58	116	174	371	636	900

NOTE: Everett c-1, 3. Heath a-1. Maneely a-1(3), 2(4), 3(3), 4-6; c-5, 6. Romita a-1. Sekowsky c-4. Sekowsky/Abel a-4(3). Tuska a-5(3).

SPACE MAN
Dell Publ. Co.: No. 1253, 1-3/62 - No. 8, 3/5-64; No. 9, 7/72 - No. 10, 10/72

Four Color 1253 (#1)-3/62)(15c-c)	9	18	27	62	126	190
2,3: 2-(15c-c). 3-(12c-c)	5	10	15	30	50	70
4-8-(12c-c)	3	6	9	21	33	45
9,10-(15c-c): 9-Reprints #1253. 10-Reprints #2	2	4	6	9	12	15

SPACEMAN (From the Atomics)
Oni Press: July, 2002 ($2.95, one-shot)

1-Mike Allred-s/a; Lawrence Marvit additional art ... 3.00

SPACEMAN
DC Comics (Vertigo): Dec, 2011 - No. 9, Oct, 2012 ($1.00/$2.99, limited series)

1-($1.00) Azzarello-s/Risso-a/Johnson-c ... 4.00
2-9-($2.99) ... 3.00

SPACE MOUSE (Also see Funny Tunes & Space Comics)
Avon Periodicals: April, 1953 - No. 5, Apr-May, 1954

1	24	48	72	142	234	325
2	10	20	30	56	76	95
3-5	8	16	24	44	57	70

SPACE MOUSE (Walter Lantz...#1; see Comic Album #17)
Dell Publishing Co./Gold Key: No. 1132, Aug-Oct, 1960 - No. 5, Nov, 1963 (Walter Lantz)

Four Color 1132,1244, 1(11/62)(G.K.)	6	12	18	37	66	95
2-5	4	8	12	27	44	60

SPACE MYSTERIES
I.W. Enterprises: 1964 (Reprints)

Space Detective #2 © AVON

Spaceman #5 © Azzarello & Risso

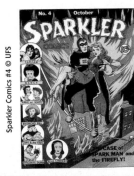

Sparkler Comics #4 © UFS

	GD 2.0	VG 4.0	FN 6.0	VF 8.0	VF/NM 9.0	NM- 9.2
1-r/Journey Into Unknown Worlds #4 w/new-c	3	6	9	19	30	40
8,9: 9-r/Planet Comics #73	3	6	9	19	30	40

SPACE: 1999 (TV) (Also see Power Record Comics)
Charlton Comics: Nov, 1975 - No. 7, Nov, 1976

1-Origin Moonbase Alpha; Staton-c/a	4	8	12	25	40	55
2,7: 2-Staton-a	3	6	9	17	26	35
3-6: All Byrne-a; c-3,5,6	3	6	9	16	23	30
nn (Charlton Press, digest, 100 pgs., B&W, no cover price) new stories & art	5	10	15	30	50	70

SPACE: 1999 (TV)(Magazine)
Charlton Comics: Nov, 1975 - No. 8, Nov, 1976 (B&W) (#7 shows #6 inside)

1-Origin Moonbase Alpha; Morrow-c/a	3	6	9	18	28	38
2-8: 2,3-Morrow-c/a. 5,8-Morrow-a	2	4	6	11	16	20

SPACE PATROL (TV)
Ziff-Davis Publishing Co. (Approved Comics): Summer, 1952 - No. 2, Oct-Nov, 1952
(Painted-c by Norman Saunders)

1-Krigstein-a	103	206	309	659	1130	1600
2-Krigstein-a(3)	74	148	222	470	810	1150

SPACE PIRATES (See Archie Giant Series #533)

SPACE: PUNISHER
Marvel Comics: Sept, 2012 - No. 4, Dec, 2012 ($3.99, limited series)

1-4-Outer space sci-fi pulp version of the Punisher; Tieri-s/Texeira-a/c						4.00

SPACE RANGER (See Mystery in Space #92, Showcase #15 & Tales of the Unexpected)

SPACE SQUADRON (In the Days of the Rockets)(Becomes Space Worlds #6)
Marvel/Atlas Comics (ACI): June, 1951 - No. 5, Feb, 1952

1-Space team; Brodsky c-1,5	116	232	348	742	1271	1800
2: Tuska c-2-4	84	168	252	538	919	1300
3-5: 3-Capt. Jet Dixon by Tuska(3); Maneely-a. 4-Weird advs. begin	74	148	222	470	810	1150

SPACE THRILLERS
Avon Periodicals: 1954 (25¢ Giant)

nn-(Scarce)-Robotmen of the Lost Planet; contains 3 rebound comics of The Saint & Strange Worlds. Contents could vary	174	348	522	1114	1907	2700

SPACE TRIP TO THE MOON (See Space Adventures #23)

SPACE TRUCKIN'
Opus Comics: 2023 - Present ($5.99)

1-Hedrick-s/Beltramo-a						6.00

SPACE USAGI
Mirage Studios: June, 1992 - No. 3, 1992 ($2.00, B&W, mini-series)
V2#1, Nov, 1993 - V2#3, Jan, 1994 ($2.75)

1-Stan Sakai-c/a/scripts	3	6	9	21	33	45
2,3, V2#1-3	2	4	6	9	12	15

SPACE USAGI
Dark Horse Comics: Jan, 1996 - No. 3, Mar, 1996 ($2.95, B&W, limited series)

1-Stan Sakai-c/a/scripts	2	4	6	9	12	15
2,3						6.00

SPACE USAGI: DEATH AND HONOR
Dark Horse Comics: Nov, 2023 - No. 3 ($4.99, limited series)

1,2-Reprints the 1992 Space Usagi series with new color; Stan Sakai-s/a						5.00

SPACE USAGI: YOKAI HUNTER
Dark Horse Comics: Oct, 2023 ($4.99, one-shot)

1-Stan Sakai-s/a						5.00

SPACE WAR (Fightin' Five #28 on)
Charlton Comics: Oct, 1959 - No. 27, Mar, 1964; No. 28, Mar, 1978 - No. 34, 3/79

V1#1-Giordano-c begin, end #3	16	32	48	110	243	375
2,3	9	18	27	62	126	190
4-6,8,10-Ditko-c/a	14	28	42	97	214	330
7,9,11-15 (3/62): Last 10¢ issue	7	14	21	48	89	130
16 (6/62)-27 (3/64): 18,19-Robot-c	6	12	18	37	66	95
28 (3/78),29-31,33,34-Ditko-c/a(r): 30-Staton, Sutton/Wood-a. 31-Ditko-c/a(3); same-c as Strange Suspense Stories #2 (1968); atom blast-c	2	4	6	8	11	14
32-r/Charlton Premiere V2#2; Sutton-a	1	3	4	6	8	10

SPACE WARPED
Boom Entertainment (Kaboom!): Jun, 2011 - No. 6, Dec, 2011 ($3.99, limited series)

	GD 2.0	VG 4.0	FN 6.0	VF 8.0	VF/NM 9.0	NM- 9.2
1-6-Star Wars spoof; Bourhis-s/Spjessert-a						4.00

SPACE WESTERN (Formerly Cowboy Western Comics; becomes Cowboy Western Comics #46 on)
Charlton Comics (Capitol Stories): No. 40, Oct, 1952 - No. 45, Aug, 1953

40-Intro Spurs Jackson & His Space Vigilantes; flying saucer story	148	296	444	947	1624	2300
41,43: 41-Flying saucer-c	68	136	204	435	743	1050
42-Atom bomb explosion-c	81	162	243	518	884	1250
44-Cowboys battle Nazis on Mars	129	258	387	826	1413	2000
45-"The Valley That Time Forgot", a pre-Turok story with dinosaurs & a bow-hunting Indian; Hitler app.	84	168	252	538	919	1300

SPACE WORLDS (Formerly Space Squadron #1-5)
Atlas Comics (Male): No. 6, April, 1952

6-Sol Brodsky-c	63	126	189	403	689	975

SPANKY & ALFALFA & THE LITTLE RASCALS (See The Little Rascals)

SPARKIE, RADIO PIXIE (Radio)(Becomes Big Jon & Sparkie #4)
Ziff-Davis Publ. Co.: Winter, 1951 - No. 3, July-Aug, 1952 (Painted-c)(Sparkie #2,3; #1?)

1-Based on children's radio program	34	68	102	199	325	450
2,3: 3-Big Jon and Sparkie on-c only	22	44	66	128	209	290

SPARKLE COMICS
United Features Synd.: Oct-Nov, 1948 - No. 33, Dec-Jan, 1953-54

1-Li'l Abner, Nancy, Captain & the Kids, Ella Cinders (#1-3: 52 pgs.)	20	40	60	120	195	270
2	13	26	39	72	101	130
3-10	9	18	27	52	69	85
11-20	9	18	27	47	61	75
21-32	8	16	24	42	54	65
33-(2-3/54) 2 pgs. early Peanuts by Schulz	17	34	51	98	154	210

SPARKLE PLENTY (See Harvey Comics Library #2 & Dick Tracy)
Dell Publishing Co.: 1949

Four Color 215 - Dick Tracy reprint by Gould	12	24	36	82	179	275

SPARKLER COMICS (1st series)
United Feature Comic Group: July, 1940 - No. 2, 1940

1-Jim Hardy	47	94	141	296	498	700
2-Frankie Doodle	39	78	117	231	378	525

SPARKLER COMICS (2nd series)(Nancy & Sluggo #121 on)(Cover title becomes Nancy and Sluggo #101? on)
United Features Syndicate: July, 1941 - No. 120, Jan, 1955

1-Origin 1st app. Sparkman; Tarzan (by Hogarth in all issues); Captain & the Kids, Ella Cinders, Danny Dingle, Dynamite Dunn, Nancy, Abbie & Slats, Broncho Bill, Frankie Doodle, begin; Spark Man c-1-9,11,12; Hap Hopper c-10,13	200	400	600	1280	2190	3100
2	74	148	222	470	810	1150
3,4	54	108	162	343	574	825
5-9: 9-Spark Man's new costume	47	94	141	296	498	700
10-Spark Man's secret ID revealed	50	100	150	315	533	750
11,12-Spark Man war-c. 12-Spark Man's new costume (color change)	43	86	129	271	461	650
13-Hap Hopper war-c	36	72	108	211	343	475
14-Tarzan-c by Hogarth	74	148	222	470	810	1150
15,17: 15-Capt & Kids-c. 17-Nancy & Sluggo-c	29	58	87	172	281	390
16,18-Spark Man-c. 16-Japanese WWII-c. 18-Nazi WWII-c	45	90	135	284	480	675
19-1st Race Riley and the Commandos-c/s	42	84	126	265	445	625
20-Nancy war-c	34	68	102	199	325	450
21,25,28,31,34,37-Tarzan-c by Hogarth	55	110	165	352	601	850
22-24,26,27,29,30: 22-Race Riley & the Commandos strips begin, ends #44	26	52	78	154	252	350
32,33,35,36,38,40	15	30	45	88	137	185
39-Classic Tarzan shooting an arrow into a dinosaur's eye on cover by Hogarth	97	194	291	621	1061	1500
41,43,45,46,48,49	13	26	39	74	105	135
42,44,47,50-Tarzan-c (42,47,50 by Hogarth)	32	64	96	188	307	425
51,52,54-68,70: 57-Li'l Abner begins (not in #58); Fearless Fosdick app. in #58	13	26	39	72	101	130
53-Tarzan-c by Hogarth	29	58	87	172	281	390
69-Wolverton-esque Horror-c	14	28	42	81	118	155
71-80	10	20	30	54	72	90
81,82,84-86: 86 Last Tarzan; lingerie panels	9	18	27	47	61	75
83-Tarzan-c; Li'l Abner ends	14	28	42	80	115	150

Grade columns: **GD 2.0 · VG 4.0 · FN 6.0 · VF 8.0 · VF/NM 9.0 · NM- 9.2**

	GD 2.0	VG 4.0	FN 6.0	VF 8.0	VF/NM 9.0	NM- 9.2
87-96,98-99	8	16	24	42	54	65
97-Origin Casey Ruggles by Warren Tufts	9	18	27	47	61	75
100	9	18	27	52	69	85
101-107,109-112,114-119	7	14	21	37	46	55
108,113-Toth-a	8	16	24	42	54	65
120-(10-11/54) 2 pgs. early Peanuts by Schulz	15	30	45	90	140	190

SPARKLING LOVE
Avon Periodicals/Realistic (1953): June, 1950; 1953

	GD 2.0	VG 4.0	FN 6.0	VF 8.0	VF/NM 9.0	NM- 9.2
1(Avon)-Kubert-a; photo-c	39	78	117	240	395	550
nn(1953)-Reprint; Kubert-a	16	32	48	94	147	200

SPARKLING STARS
Holyoke Publishing Co.: June, 1944 - No. 33, March, 1948

	GD 2.0	VG 4.0	FN 6.0	VF 8.0	VF/NM 9.0	NM- 9.2
1-Hell's Angels, FBI, Boxie Weaver, Petey & Pop, & Ali Baba begin	30	60	90	177	289	400
2-Speed Spaulding story	18	36	54	103	162	220
3-Actual FBI case photos & war photos	14	28	42	82	121	160
4-10: 7-X-Mas-c	13	26	39	72	101	130
11-19: 13-Origin/1st app. Jungo the Man-Beast-c/s	11	22	33	62	86	110
20-Intro Fangs the Wolf Boy	13	26	39	72	101	130
21-33: 29-Bondage-c. 31-Sid Greene-a	10	20	30	58	79	100

SPARK MAN (See Sparkler Comics)
Frances M. McQueeny: 1945 (36 pgs., one-shot)

	GD 2.0	VG 4.0	FN 6.0	VF 8.0	VF/NM 9.0	NM- 9.2
1-Origin Spark Man r/Sparkler #1-3; female torture story; cover redrawn from Sparkler #1	57	114	171	362	619	875

SPARKY WATTS (Also see Big Shot Comics & Columbia Comics)
Columbia Comic Corp.: Nov?, 1942 - No. 10, 1949

	GD 2.0	VG 4.0	FN 6.0	VF 8.0	VF/NM 9.0	NM- 9.2
1(1942)-Skyman & The Face app; Hitler/Goering story/c	155	310	465	992	1696	2400
2(1943)	41	82	123	256	428	600
3(1944) "6000 Lbs. Block Buster to Bust Adolf"-c	32	64	96	188	307	425
4(1944)-Origin	22	44	66	132	216	300
5(1947)-Skyman app.; Boody Rogers-c/a	20	40	60	114	182	250
6,7,9,10: 6(1947). 9-Haunted House-c. 10(1949)	14	28	42	82	121	160
8(1948)-Surrealistic-c	15	30	45	90	140	190

NOTE: *Boody Rogers c-1-8.*

SPARROWHAWK
BOOM! Studios: Oct, 2018 - No. 5, Mar, 2019 ($3.99, limited series)

						NM- 9.2
1-5-Delilah S. Dawson-s/Matias Basla-a						4.00

SPARTACUS (Movie)
Dell Publishing Co.: No. 1139, Nov, 1960 (Kirk Douglas photo-c)

	GD 2.0	VG 4.0	FN 6.0	VF 8.0	VF/NM 9.0	NM- 9.2
Four Color 1139-Buscema-a	11	22	33	77	166	255

SPARTACUS (Television series)
Devil's Due Publishing: Oct, 2009 - No. 2 ($3.99)

						NM- 9.2
1,2: 1-DeKnight-s. 2-Palmiotti-s						4.00

SPARTAN: WARRIOR SPIRIT (Also see WildC.A.T.S: Covert Action Teams)
Image Comics (WildStorm Productions): July, 1995 - No. 4, Nov, 1995 ($2.50, lim. series)

						NM- 9.2
1-4: Kurt Busiek scripts; Mike McKone-c/a						4.00

SPARTA: USA
DC Comics (WildStorm): May, 2010 - No. 6, Oct, 2010 ($2.99, limited series)

						NM- 9.2
1-6: 1-Lapham-s/Timmons-a; covers by Timmons and Lapham						3.00

SPAWN (Also see Curse of the Spawn and Sam & Twitch)
Image Comics (Todd McFarlane Prods.): May, 1992 - Present ($1.95/$2.50/$2.99)

	GD 2.0	VG 4.0	FN 6.0	VF 8.0	VF/NM 9.0	NM- 9.2
1-1st app. Spawn; McFarlane-c/a begins; McFarlane/Steacy-c; 1st Todd McFarlane Productions title.	5	10	15	30	50	70
1-Newsstand edition	7	14	21	46	86	125
1-Black & white edition	25	50	75	175	388	600
2,3: 2-1st app. Violator; McFarlane/Steacy-c	3	6	9	13	30	40
4-Contains coupon for Image Comics #0	3	6	9	14	19	24
4-With coupon missing						4.00
4-Newsstand edition w/o poster or coupon	2	4	6	9	12	15
5-Cerebus cameo (1 pg.) as stuffed animal; Spawn mobile poster #1	3	6	9	14	20	25
6-8,10: 7-Spawn Mobile poster #2. 8-Alan Moore scripts; Miller poster. 10-Cerebus app.; Dave Sim scripts; 1 pg. cameo app. by Superman	2	4	6	9	12	15
9-Neil Gaiman scripts; Jim Lee poster; 1st Angela	3	6	9	19	30	40
11-17,19,20,22-30: 11-Miller script; Darrow poster. 12-Bloodwulf poster by Liefeld. 14,15-Violator app. 16,17-Grant Morrison scripts; Capullo-c/a(p). 23,24-McFarlane-a/stories. 25-(10/94). 19-(10/94). 20-(11/94)	1	2	3	5	6	8
18-Grant Morrison script, Capullo-c/a(p); low distr.	2	4	6	8	10	12
21-low distribution	2	4	6	8	10	12
31-49: 31-1st app. The Redeemer; new costume (brief). 32-1st full app. new costume. 38-40,42,44,46,48-Tony Daniel-c/a(p). 38-1st app. Cy-Gor. 40,41-Cy-Gor & Curse app.						
50-($3.95, 48 pgs.)	2	4	6	9	12	15
51-87,89,90,92,93,95,96: 52-Savage Dragon app. 56-w/ Darkchylde preview. 57-Cy-Gor-c/app. 64-Polybagged w/McFarlane Toys catalog. 65-Photo-c of movie Spawn and McFarlane. 81-Billy Kincaid returns	1	2	3	5	6	8
88-Halloween-c	3	6	9	14	20	25
91,94-Low print run	2	4	6	9	12	15
97-Angela-c/app.	3	6	9	19	30	40
98,99-Angela app.	3	6	9	14	19	24
100-($4.95) Angela dies; 6 total covers; the 3 variants by McFarlane, Miller, and Mignola	3	6	9	16	24	32
100-($4.95) 3 variant covers by Ross, Capullo, and Wood						
101-111,114,116,118,123,124,134,152,158,159,164,169,170,172,173,176,177,201-208,210,212-219-Low print run: 101-Begin $2.50-c. 210-215-Michael Golden-c	2	4	6	9	14	20
112,113,115,117,120,121,125-130,132,136-138,144,146,148,155,157,161,163,166-168,171,178,180-182,186-188,190-192,198-Lower print run: 167-Clown app.	2	4	6	11	16	20
119-Gunslinger Spawn cameo	7	14	21	46	86	125
122-1st Nyx She-Spawn	6	12	18	38	69	100
131,199,209-Low print run	4	8	12	25	40	55
133,135,140,142,145,147,149,153,156,160,162,184,189,194-197,211-Low print run: 184-2nd app. Morana. 211-Michael Golden-c	3	6	9	16	23	30
139-Nyx She-Spawn app.	5	10	15	35	63	90
141-She-Spawn-c	8	16	24	54	102	150
143,151,193-Low print run: 151-Begin $2.95-c; wraparound-c by Tan	3	6	9	21	33	45
150-($4.95) 4 covers by McFarlane, Capullo, Tan, Jim Lee	4	8	12	23	37	50
154-1st app. Zera	3	6	9	17	26	35
165-1st Mandarin Spawn	6	12	18	42	79	115
174-Origin/1st full app. of Gunslinger Spawn	16	32	48	107	236	365
175-Origin of Gunslinger Spawn continues	11	22	33	76	163	250
179-1st War Spawn; Mayhew-a	5	10	15	31	53	75
183-1st Morena Spawn-c	5	10	15	31	53	75
185-1st Jim Downing and death of Al Simmons; McFarlane & Holguin-s; Portacio-a begins	6	12	18	49	89	100
200-(1/11, $3.99) 7 covers by McFarlane, Capullo, Finch, Jim Lee, Liefeld, Silvestri, Wood	3	6	9	16	23	30
220-(6/12, $3.99) 20th Anniversary issue; McFarlane-s/Kudranski-a; bonus interview, timeline and cover gallery	2	4	6	11	16	20
220: 20th Anniversary Collector's Special-(6/12, $4.99) B&W version of #220 w/bonuses	4	8	12	23	37	50
221-Cover swipe of Amazing Fantasy #15	4	8	12	21	46	86
222-226,229,231-237,239-241,244-249,251-299: 222-231-Cover swipes of classic covers. 225-Election special with 2 covers (Obama & Romney). 231-Spider-Man #1 ('90) c-swipe. 234-Haunt app. 251-Follows Spawn Resurrection #1. 258-Erik Larsen & McFarlane-a begin. 265-Ant app. 266-Savage Dragon app. '267-275,291,292-Kudranski-a. 276-282-Darragh Savage-s/Alexander-a	1	3	4	6	8	10
227-Cover swipe of Amazing Spider-Man #300	5	10	15	35	63	90
228-Cover swipe of Action Comics #1	5	10	15	34	60	85
230-Cover swipe of Batman #423	7	14	21	49	92	135
238-Low print run	4	8	12	22	35	48
242,243-Low print run	5	10	15	31	53	75
250-($5.99) McFarlane-s/Kudranski-a; Al Simmons returns; multiple covers						
300-(9/19, $7.99) McFarlane-s; art by Capullo, McFarlane, JS Campbell, Alexander & Opeña; intro. She-Spawn, bonus cover gallery; multiple covers	2	4	6	8	10	12
301-($4.99) McFarlane-s; art by Capullo, McFarlane, Crain, Alexander & Opeña	3	6	9	14	20	25
302-326: 302-305-Alexander-a; She-Spawn app. 306-Tan-a; intro. Raptor. 309,311-313-Gunslinger Spawn returns	1	2	3	5	6	8
309-Gunslinger Spawn variant-c by McFarlane						10.00
327-349						3.00
350-($4.99) McConville-s/Booth & Barberi-a						5.00
Annual 1-Blood & Shadows ('99, $4.95) Ashley Wood-c/a; Jenkins-s						6.00
... #1 Director's Cut (5/17, $4.99) 25th Anniversary edition; r/#1 B&W inked art with McFarlane commentary; bonus promotional art; 3 covers (McFarlane, Crain, Ashley Wood)	3	6	9	14	19	24
... #1 Free Comic Book Day 2019 (giveaway) r/#1; new cover by Francesco Mattina						3.00
...: Architects of Fear (2/11, $6.99, squarebound GN) Briclot-a	2	4	6	11	16	20
...: Armageddon Complete Collection TPB ('07, $29.95) r/#150-163	7	14	21	46	86	125
...: Armageddon, Part 1 TPB (10/06, $14.99) r/#150-155	5	10	15	31	53	75
...: Armageddon, Part 2 TPB (2/07, $15.95) r/#156-164	5	10	15	31	53	75
...: Bible-(8/96, $1.95)-Character bios	2	4	6	11	14	18
Book 1 TPB($9.95) r/#1-5; Book 2- r/#6-9,11; Book 3 -r/#12-15, Book 4-r/#16-20; Book 5-r/#21-25; Book 6- r/#26-30; Book 7-r/#31-34; Book 8-r/#35-38; Book 9-r/#39-42; Book 10-r/#43-47						11.00
Book 11 TPB ($10.95) r/#48-50; Book 12-r/#51-54						11.00
... Collection Vol. 1 (10/05, $19.95) r/#1-8,11,12; intro. by Frank Miller						20.00
... Collection Vol. 2 HC (7/07, $49.95) r/#13-33						50.00
... Collection Vol. 2 SC (9/06, $29.95) r/#13-33						30.00
... Collection Vol. 3 (3/07, $29.95) r/#34-54						30.00
... Collection Vol. 4 (9/07, $29.95) r/#55-75						30.00
... Collection Vol. 5 ('08, $29.95) r/#76-95						30.00
... Collection Vol. 6 (8/08, $29.95) r/#96-116; cover gallery						30.00
Image Firsts: Spawn #1 (4/10, $1.00) reprints #1	1	3	4	6	8	10
Godslayer Vol. 1 (9/06, $6.99) Anacleto-c/a; Holguin-s; sketch pages	1	3	4	6	8	10
... Kills Everyone! 1 (8/16, $2.99) McFarlane-s/JJ Kirby-a; mini Spawn vs. cosplayers			4	6	8	10
...: Neonoir TPB (11/08, $14.95) r/#170-175						15.00
...: New Flesh TPB ('07, $14.95) r/#166-169						15.00
...: Resurrection 1 (3/15, $2.99) Follows issue #250; Jenkins-s/Jonboy-a	2	4	6	8	10	12
...Simony (5/04, $7.95) English translation of French Spawn story; Briclot-a	2	4	6	8	10	12

NOTE: *Capullo a-16p-18p; c-16p-18p. Daniel a-38-40, 42, 44, 46. McFarlane a-1-15; c-1-15p. Thibert a-16i(part). Posters come with issues 1, 4, 7-9, 11, 12. #25 was released before #19 & 20.*

SPAWN-BATMAN (Also see Batman/Spawn: War Devil under Batman: One-Shots)
Image Comics (Todd McFarlane Productions): 1994 ($3.95, one-shot)

	GD 2.0	VG 4.0	FN 6.0	VF 8.0	VF/NM 9.0	NM- 9.2
1-Miller scripts; McFarlane-a	3	6	9	17	26	35

SPAWN: BLOOD FEUD
Image Comics (Todd McFarlane Prods.): June, 1995 - No. 4, Sept, 1995 ($2.25, lim. series)

						NM- 9.2
1-4-Alan Moore scripts; Tony Daniel-a						6.00

SPAWN FAN EDITION
Image Comics (Todd McFarlane Productions): Aug, 1996 - No. 3, Oct, 1996 (Giveaway, 12 pgs.) (Polybagged w/Overstreet's FAN)

Spawn #156 © TMP

Spawn's Universe #1 © TMP

Special Marvel Edition #10 © MAR

	GD	VG	FN	VF	VF/NM	NM-		GD	VG	FN	VF	VF/NM	NM-
	2.0	4.0	6.0	8.0	9.0	9.2		2.0	4.0	6.0	8.0	9.0	9.2

1-3: Beau Smith scripts; Brad Gorby-a(p). 1-1st app. Nordik, the Norse Hellspawn.

	GD	VG	FN	VF	VF/NM	NM-
2-1st app. McFallon. 3-1st app. Mercy	1	2	3	5	6	8
1-3-(Gold): All retailer incentives						16.00
1-3-Variant-c	1	2	3	5	6	8
2-(Platinum)-Retailer incentive						25.00

SPAWN GODSLAYER
Image Comics (Todd McFarlane Prods.): May, 2007 - No. 8, Apr, 2008 ($2.99)

1-8: 1-Holguin-s/Tan-a/Anacleto-c	1	2	3	5	6	8

SPAWN KILLS EVERYONE TOO (Also titled Spawn Kills Everyone 2)
Image Comics (Todd McFarlane Prod.): Dec, 2018 - No. 4, Mar, 2019 ($3.99, limited series)

1-4-McFarlane-s/Robson-a; Baby Spawn having babies. 3,4-Infinity Gauntlet spoof						4.00

SPAWN'S UNIVERSE (Leads into King Spawn #1, Gunslinger Spawn #1 & The Scorched #1)
Image Comics (Todd McFarlane Productions): Jun, 2021 ($5.99, one-shot)

1-Gunslinger Spawn, Medieval Spawn, She-Spawn & Cy-Gor app.; Cheung-a						6.00

SPAWN: THE DARK AGES
Image Comics (Todd McFarlane Productions): Mar, 1999 - No. 28, Oct, 2001 ($2.50)

1-Fabry-c; Holguin-s/Sharp-a; variant-c by McFarlane	1	3	4	6	8	10
2-28						4.00

SPAWN THE IMPALER
Image Comics (Todd McFarlane Prods.): Oct, 1996 - No. 3, Dec, 1996 ($2.95, limited series)

1-3-Mike Grell scripts, painted-a						5.00

SPAWN: THE UNDEAD
Image Comics (Todd McFarlane Prod.): Jun, 1999 - No. 9, Feb, 2000 ($1.95/$2.25)

1-9-Dwayne Turner-c/a; Jenkins-s. 7-9-($2.25-c)						5.00
TPB (6/08, $24.99) r/#1-9						25.00

SPAWN: UNWANTED VIOLENCE
Image Comics (Todd McFarlane Prod): Jan, 2023 - No. 2, Feb, 2023 ($4.99, limited series)

1,2-McFarlane-s/Del Mundo-a						5.00

SPAWN/WILDC.A.T.S
Image Comics (WildStorm): Jan, 1996 - No. 4, Apr, 1996 ($2.50, lim. series)

1-4: Alan Moore scripts in all.						5.00

SPEAKER FOR THE DEAD (ORSON SCOTT CARD'S...) (Ender's Game)
Marvel Comics: Mar, 2011 - No. 5, Jul, 2011 ($3.99, limited series)

1-3-Johnston-s/Mhan-a/Camuncoli-c						4.00

SPECIAL AGENT (Steve Saunders...)(Also see True Comics #68)
Parents' Magazine Institute (Commended Comics No. 2): Dec, 1947 - No. 8, Sept, 1949
(Based on true FBI cases)

1-J. Edgar Hoover photo on-c	19	38	57	111	176	240
2	14	28	42	76	108	140
3-8	10	20	30	58	79	100

SPECIAL COLLECTORS' EDITION (See Savage Fists of Kung-Fu)

SPECIAL COMICS (Becomes Hangman #2 on)
MLJ Magazines: Winter, 1941-42

1-Origin The Boy Buddies (Shield & Wizard x-over); death of The Comet retold (see Pep #17); origin The Hangman retold; Hangman-c	443	886	1329	7234	7717	8200

SPECIAL EDITION (See Gorgo and Reptisaurus)

SPECIAL EDITION COMICS (See Promotional Section)

SPECIAL EDITION COMICS
Fawcett Publications: 1940 (August) (68 pgs., one-shot)

1-1st book devoted entirely to Captain Marvel; C.C. Beck-c/a; only app. of Captain Marvel with belt buckle; Capt. Marvel appears with button-down flap; 1st story (came out before Captain Marvel #1.)	1000	2000	3000	7600	13,800	20,000

NOTE: Prices vary widely on this book. Since this book is all Captain Marvel stories, it is actually a pre-Captain Marvel #1. There is speculation that this book almost became *Captain Marvel #1*. It was published early in 1941. This book was followed by a 2nd book several months later. This 2nd book was advertised as a #3 (making *Special Edition* the #1, & the nn issue the #2). However, the 2nd book did come out as a #2.

SPECIAL EDITION: SPIDER-MAN VS. THE HULK (See listing under The Amazing Spider-Man)

SPECIAL EDITION X-MEN
Marvel Comics Group: Feb, 1983 ($2.00, one-shot, Baxter paper)

1-r/Giant-Size X-Men #1 plus one new story	3	6	9	16	23	30

SPECIAL FORCES
Image Comics: Oct, 2007 - No. 4, Mar, 2009 ($2.99)

1-4-Iraq war combat; Kyle Baker-s/a/c						3.00

SPECIAL MARVEL EDITION (Master of Kung Fu #17 on)

Marvel Comics Group: Jan, 1971 - No. 16, Feb, 1974 (#1-3: 25¢, 68 pgs.; #4: 52 pgs.; #5-16: 20¢, regular ed.)

	GD	VG	FN	VF	VF/NM	NM-
1-Thor-r by Kirby; 68 pgs.	5	10	15	33	57	80
2-4: Thor-r by Kirby; 2,3-68 pg. Giant. 4-(52 pgs.)	3	6	9	17	26	35
5-14: Sgt. Fury-r; 11-r/Sgt. Fury #13 (Capt. America)	2	4	6	10	14	18
15-Master of Kung Fu (Shang-Chi) begins (1st app., 12/73); Starlin-a; origin/1st app. Nayland Smith & Dr. Petrie	24	48	72	168	372	575
16-1st app. Midnight; Starlin-a (2nd Shang-Chi)	9	18	27	59	117	175

NOTE: Kirby c-10-14.

SPECIAL MISSIONS (See G.I. Joe...)

SPECIAL WAR SERIES (Attack V4#3 on?)
Charlton Comics: Aug, 1965 - No. 4, Nov, 1965

V4#1-D-Day (also see D-Day listing)	5	10	15	31	53	75
2-Attack!	3	6	9	16	23	30
3-War & Attack (also see War & Attack)	3	6	9	14	20	25
4-Judomaster (intro/1st app.; see Sarge Steel)	15	30	45	103	227	350

SPECIES (Movie)
Dark Horse Comics: June, 1995 - No. 4, Sept, 1995 ($2.50, limited series)

1-4: Adaptation of film						4.00

SPECIES: HUMAN RACE (Movie)
Dark Horse Comics: Nov, 1996 - No. 4, Feb, 1997 ($2.95, limited series)

1-4						4.00

SPECS
BOOM! Studios: Nov, 2022 - No. 4, Feb, 2023 ($3.99, limited series)

1-4-Booher-s/Shehan-a						4.00

SPECTACULAR ADVENTURES (See Adventures)

SPECTACULAR FEATURE MAGAZINE, A (Formerly My Confession)
(Spectacular Features Magazine #12)
Fox Feature Syndicate: No. 11, April, 1950

11 (#1)-Samson and Delilah	34	68	102	204	332	460

SPECTACULAR FEATURES MAGAZINE (Formerly A Spectacular Feature Magazine)
Fox Feature Syndicate: No. 12, June, 1950 - No. 3, Aug, 1950

12 (#2)-Iwo Jima; photo flag-c	33	66	99	194	317	440
3-True Crime Cases From Police Files	26	52	78	154	252	350

SPECTACULAR SCARLET SPIDER
Marvel Comics: Nov, 1995 - No. 2, Dec, 1995 ($1.95, limited series)

1,2: Replaces Spectacular Spider-Man						4.00

SPECTACULAR SPIDER-GIRL
Marvel Comics: Jul, 2010 - No. 4, Oct, 2010 ($3.99, limited series)

1-4-Frenz-a; Frank Castle and the Hobgoblin app.						4.00

SPECTACULAR SPIDER-MAN, THE (See Marvel Special Edition and Marvel Treasury Edition)

SPECTACULAR SPIDER-MAN, THE (Magazine)
Marvel Comics Group: July, 1968 - No. 2, Nov, 1968 (35¢)

1-(B&W)-Romita/Mooney 52 pg. story plus updated origin story with Everett-a(i)	13	26	39	87	191	295
1-Variation w/single c-price of 40¢	12	24	36	84	185	285
2-(Color)-Green Goblin-c & 58 pg. story; Romita painted-c (story reprinted in King Size Spider-Man #9); Romita/Mooney-a	12	24	36	81	178	270

SPECTACULAR SPIDER-MAN, THE (Peter Parker...#54-132, 134)
Marvel Comics Group: Dec, 1976 - No. 263, Nov, 1998

1-Origin recap in text; return of Tarantula	6	12	18	37	66	95
2-Kraven the Hunter app.	4	8	12	23	37	50
3-5: 3-Intro Lightmaster. 4-Vulture app.	3	6	9	16	23	30
6-8-Morbius app.; 6-r/Marvel Team-Up #3 w/Morbius	3	6	9	17	26	35
7,8-(35¢-c variants, limited distribution)(6,7/77)	9	18	27	63	129	195
9-20: 9,10-White Tiger app. 11-Last 30¢-c. 17,18-Angel & Iceman app. (from Champions); Ghost Rider cameo. 18-Gil Kane-c	2	4	6	10	14	18
9-11-(35¢-c variants, limited distribution)(8-10/77)	9	18	27	63	129	195
21,24-26: 21-Scorpion app. 26-Daredevil app.	2	4	6	8	11	14
22-Moon Knight app.	4	8	12	28	47	65
23-Moon Knight app.	3	6	9	21	33	45
27-Miller's 1st art on Daredevil (2/79); also see Captain America #235	5	10	15	35	63	90
28-Miller Daredevil (p)	3	6	9	19	30	40
29-55,57,59: 33-Origin Iguana. 38-Morbius app.	1	2	3	5	6	8
56-2nd app. Jack O'Lantern (Macendale) & 1st Spidey/Jack O'Lantern battle (7/81)						

	GD 2.0	VG 4.0	FN 6.0	VF 8.0	VF/NM 9.0	NM- 9.2
58-Byrne-a(p)	2	4	6	11	16	20
60-Double size; origin retold with new facts revealed	2	4	6	8	10	12
61-63,65-68,71-74: 65-Kraven the Hunter app.	1	2	3	5	6	8
64-1st app. Cloak & Dagger (3/82)	5	10	15	31	53	75
69,70-Cloak & Dagger app. (origin retold in #69). 70-1st app. of Silvermane in cyborg form	2	4	6	9	12	15
75-Double size	1	2	3	5	6	8
76-80: 78,79-Punisher cameo						6.00
81,82-Punisher, Cloak & Dagger app.	1	3	4	6	8	10
83-Origin Punisher retold (10/83)	2	4	6	10	14	18
84,86-89,91-99: 94-96-Cloak & Dagger app. 98-Intro The Spot						6.00
85-Hobgoblin (Ned Leeds) app. (12/83); gains powers of original Green Goblin (see Amazing Spider-Man #238)	2	4	6	9	13	16
90-Spider-Man's new black costume, last panel (ties w/Amazing Spider-Man #252 & Marvel Team-Up #141 for 1st app.)	5	10	15	30	50	70
100-(3/85)-Double size	1	3	4	6	8	10
101-115,117,118,120-129: 107-110-Death of Jean DeWolff. 111-Secret Wars II tie-in.						5.00
128-Black Cat new costume						5.00
116,119-Sabretooth-c/story	2	4	6	9	12	15
130-132: 130-Hobgoblin app. 131-Six part Kraven tie-in. 132-Kraven tie-in	2	3	4	6	8	10
133-137,139,140: 140-Punisher cameo						5.00
138-1st full app. Tombstone (origin #139)	2	4	6	8	10	12
141-143-Punisher app.	1	2	3	4	5	7
144-146,148-157: 151-Tombstone returns						4.00
147-1st brief app. Hobgoblin (Macendale), 1 page; continued in Web of Spider-Man #48	2	4	6	11	16	20
158-Spider-Man gets new powers (1st Cosmic Spidey, cont'd in Web of Spider-Man #59)	3	6	9	16	23	30
159-Cosmic Spider-Man app.	1	2	3	4	5	7
160-175,177-188,190-199: 161-163-Hobgoblin app. 168-170-Avengers x-over. 169-1st app. The Outlaws. 180-184-Green Goblin app. 197-199-Original X-men/c/story						4.00
176-1st Corona (Dagny Forrester)	2	4	6	10	14	18
189-($2.95, 52 pgs.)-Silver hologram on-c; battles Green Goblin; origin Spidey retold; Vess poster w/Spidey & Hobgoblin						6.00
189-(2nd printing)-Gold hologram on-c						4.00
195-(Deluxe ed.)-Polybagged w/"Dirt" magazine #2 & Beastie Boys/Smithereens music cassette	2	4	6	8	10	12
200-($2.95)-Holo-grafx foil-c; Green Goblin-c/story						6.00
201-219,221,222,224,226-228,230-247: 212-w/card sheet. 203-Maximum Carnage x-over. 204-Begin 4 part death of Tombstone story. 207,208-The Shroud-c/story. 208-Siege of Darkness x-over (#207 is a tie-in). 209-Black Cat back-up. 215,216-Scorpion app. 217-Power & Responsibility Pt. 4. 231-Return of Kaine; Spider-Man corpse discovered. 232-New Doc Octopus app. 233-Carnage-c/app. 235-Dragon Man cameo. 236-Dragon Man-c/app; Lizard app.; Peter Parker regains powers. 238,239-Lizard app. 239-w/card insert. 240-Revelations storyline begins. 241-Flashback						5.00
213-Collectors ed. polybagged w/16 pg. preview & animation cel; foil-c; 1st meeting Spidey & Typhoid Mary						5.00
213-Version polybagged w/Gamepro #7; no-c date, price						4.00
217,219 ($2.95)-Deluxe edition foil-c: flip book						5.00
220 ($2.25, 52 pgs.)-Flip book, Mary Jane reveals pregnancy						5.00
223,229·($2.95) 229-Spidey quits						5.00
223,225: ($2.95)-223-Die Cut-c. 225-Newsstand ed.						5.00
225,229: ($3.95) 225-Direct Market Holodisk-c (Green Goblin). 229-Acetate-c, Spidey quits						5.00
240-Variant-c						5.00
248,249,251-254,256: 249-Return of Norman Osborn 256-1st app. Prodigy						4.00
250-($3.25) Double gatefold-c						5.00
255-($2.99) Spiderhunt pt. 4						5.00
257-262: 257-Double cover with "Spectacular Prodigy #1"; battles Jack O'Lantern. 258-Spidey is cleared. 259,260-Green Goblin & Hobgoblin app. 262-Byrne-s						4.00
263-Final issue; Byrne-c; Aunt May returns						4.00
#(-1) Flashback (7/97)						4.00
#1000 ($6.11, $4.99) Punisher app.; Nauck & Ryan-a/Rivera-c; r/ASM #129						5.00
Annual 1 (1979)-Doc Octopus-c & 46 pg. story	3	6	9	14	20	25
Annual 2 (1980)-Origin/1st app. Rapier	1	3	4	6	8	10
Annual 3: ('81-'83) 3-Last Man-Wolf						6.00
Annual 6-14: 8 ('88,$ 1.75)-Evolutionary War x-over; Daydreamer returns Gwen Stacy "clone" back to real self (not Gwen Stacy). 9 ('89, $2.00, 68 pgs.)-Atlantis Attacks. 10 ('90, $2.00, 68 pgs.)-McFarlane-a. 11 ('91, $2.00, 68 pgs.)-Iron Man app. 12 ('92, $2.25, 68 pgs.)-Venom solo story cont'd from Amazing Spider-Man Annual #26. 13 ('93, $2.95, 68 pgs.)-Polybagged w/trading card; John Romita, Sr. back-up-a						6.00
... No. 1 Facsimile Edition (6/22, $3.99) Reprints #1 with original 1976 ads						5.00
Special 1 (1995, $3.95)-Flip book	1	2	3	5	6	8

NOTE: Austin c-21i, Annual 11i. Buckler a-103, 107-111, 116, 117, 119, 122 Annual 1, Annual 10; c-103, 107-111, 113, 116-119, 122, Annual 1. Buscema a-121. Byrne c(p)-17, 43, 58, 101, 102. Giffen a-120p. Hembeck c/a-86p. Larsen c-Annual 11i. Miller c-46p, 48p, 50, 51p, 52p, 54p, 55, 56p, 57, 60. Mooney a-7i, 11i, 21p, 23p, 25p, 26p, 29-34p, 36p, 37p, 39i, 41, 42i, 49p, 50i, 51i, 53p, 54-57i, 59-66i, 68i, 71i, 73-79i, 81-83i, 85i, 87-99i, 102i, 125p, Annual 1i, 2p. Nasser c-37p. Perez c-10. Simonson c-54i. Zeck a-22, 118, 131, 132; c-131, 132.

SPECTACULAR SPIDER-MAN (2nd series)
Marvel Comics: Sept, 2003 - No. 27, June, 2005 ($2.25/$2.99)

	GD 2.0	VG 4.0	FN 6.0	VF 8.0	VF/NM 9.0	NM- 9.2
1-Jenkins-s/Ramos-a/c; Venom-c/app.						4.00
2-26: 2-5-Venom app. 6-9-Dr. Octopus app. 11-13-The Lizard app. 14-Rivera painted-a. 15,16-Capt. America app. 17,18-Ramos-a. 20-Spider-Man gets organic webshooters 21,22-Caldwell-a. 23-26-Sarah & Gabriel app.; Land-c						3.00
27-($2.99) Last issue; Uncle Ben app. in flashback; Buckingham-a						4.00
... Vol. 1: The Hunger TPB (2003, $11.99) r/#1-5						12.00
... Vol. 2: Countdown TPB (2004, $11.99) r/#6-10						12.00
... Vol. 3: Here There Be Monsters TPB (2004, $9.99) r/#11-14						10.00
... Vol. 4: Disassembled TPB (2004, $14.99) r/#15-20						15.00
... Vol. 5: Sins Remembered (2005, $9.99) r/#23-26						10.00
... Vol. 6: The Final Curtain (2005, $14.99) r/#21,22,27 & Peter Parker: Spider-Man #39-41						15.00

SPECTACULAR STORIES MAGAZINE (Formerly A Star Presentation)
Fox Feature Syndicate (Hero Books): No. 4, July, 1950 - No. 3, Sept, 1950

	GD 2.0	VG 4.0	FN 6.0	VF 8.0	VF/NM 9.0	NM- 9.2
4-Sherlock Holmes (true crime stories)	42	84	126	265	445	625
3-The St. Valentine's Day Massacre (true crime)	31	62	93	182	296	410

SPECTER INSPECTORS
BOOM! Studios (BOOM! Box): Feb, 2021 - No. 5, Jun, 2021 ($4.99)

	GD 2.0	VG 4.0	FN 6.0	VF 8.0	VF/NM 9.0	NM- 9.2
1-5-Bowen McCurdy & Kaityn Musto-s/Musto-a						5.00

SPECTRE, THE (1st Series) (See Adventure Comics #431-440, More Fun & Showcase)
National Periodical Publ.: Nov-Dec, 1967 - No. 10, May-June, 1969 (All 12¢)

	GD 2.0	VG 4.0	FN 6.0	VF 8.0	VF/NM 9.0	NM- 9.2
1-(11-12/67)-Anderson-c/a	17	34	51	119	265	410
2-5-Neal Adams-c/a; 3-Wildcat x-over	9	18	27	61	123	185
6-8,10: 6-8-Anderson inks. 7-Hourman app.	7	14	21	48	89	130
9-Wrightson-a	8	16	24	55	105	155

SPECTRE, THE (2nd Series) (See Saga of the Swamp Thing #58, Showcase '95 #8 & Wrath of the...)
DC Comics: Apr, 1987 - No. 31, Oct, 1989 ($1.00, new format)

	GD 2.0	VG 4.0	FN 6.0	VF 8.0	VF/NM 9.0	NM- 9.2
1-Colan-a begins	1	2	3	5	6	8
2-32: 9-Nudity panels. 10-Batman cameo. 10,11-Millennium tie-ins						4.00
Annual 1 (1988, $2.00)-Deadman app.						4.00

NOTE: Art Adams c-Annual 1. Colan a-1-6. Kaluta c-1-3. Mignola c-7-9. Morrow a-9-15. Sears c/a-22. Vess c-13-15.

SPECTRE, THE (3rd Series) (Also see Brave and the Bold #72, 75, 116, 180 & 199 & Showcase '95 #8)
DC Comics: Dec, 1992 - No. 62, Feb, 1998 ($1.75/$1.95/$2.25/$2.50)

	GD 2.0	VG 4.0	FN 6.0	VF 8.0	VF/NM 9.0	NM- 9.2
1-($1.95)-Glow-in-the-dark-c; Mandrake-a begins	1	3	4	6	8	10
2,3						5.00
4-7,9-12,14-20: 10-Kaluta-c. 11-Hildebrandt painted-c. 16-Aparo/K. Jones-a. 19-Snyder III-c. 20-Sienkiewicz-c						4.00
8,13-($2.50)-Glow-in-the-dark-c						6.00
21-62: 22-(9/94)-Superman-c & app. 23-(11/94). 43-Kent Williams-c. 44-Kaluta-c. 47-Final Night x-over. 49-Begin Bolton-c. 51-Batman-c/app. 52-Gianni-c. 54-1st app. Michael Holt (Mr. Terrific); Corben-c. 60-Harris-c.						4.00
#0 (10/94) Released between #22 & #23						4.00
Annual 1 (1995, $3.95)-Year One story						5.00

NOTE: Bisley c-21. Fabry c-2. Kelley Jones c-31. Vess c-5.

SPECTRE, THE (4th Series) (Hal Jordan; also see Day of Judgment #5 and Legends of the DC Universe #33-36)
DC Comics: Mar, 2001 - No. 27, May, 2003 ($2.50/$2.75)

	GD 2.0	VG 4.0	FN 6.0	VF 8.0	VF/NM 9.0	NM- 9.2
1-DeMatteis-s/Ryan Sook-c/a						4.00
2-27: 3,4-Superman & Batman-c/app. 5-Two-Face-c/app. 20-Begin $2.75-c. 21-Sinestro returns. 24-JLA app.						3.00

SPECTRE, THE (See Crisis Aftermath: The Spectre)

SPECTRO
AfterShock Comics: May, 2022 ($7.99, oversized 8-1/2" x 10-7/8", one shot)

	GD 2.0	VG 4.0	FN 6.0	VF 8.0	VF/NM 9.0	NM- 9.2
1-Juan Doe-s/a						8.00

SPEEDBALL (See Amazing Spider-Man Annual #22, Marvel Super-Heroes & The New Warriors)
Marvel Comics: Sept, 1988(10/88-inside) - No. 10, Jun, 1989 (75¢)

	GD 2.0	VG 4.0	FN 6.0	VF 8.0	VF/NM 9.0	NM- 9.2
1-Ditko/Guice-a/c	2	4	6	10	14	18
2-10: Ditko/Guice-a-2-4; Ditko a-2-10; c-2-10p						4.00

SPEED BUGGY (TV)(Also see Fun-In #12, 15)
Charlton Comics: July, 1975 - No. 9, Nov, 1976 (Hanna-Barbera)

	GD 2.0	VG 4.0	FN 6.0	VF 8.0	VF/NM 9.0	NM- 9.2
1	3	6	9	18	26	35
2-9	2	4	6	11	16	20

SPEED CARTER SPACEMAN (See Spaceman)

SPEED COMICS (New Speed)(Also see Double Up)
Brookwood Publ./Speed Publ./Harvey Publications No. 14 on:
10/39 - #11, 8/40; #12, 3/41 - #44, 1-2/47 (#14-16: pocket size, 100 pgs.)

	GD 2.0	VG 4.0	FN 6.0	VF 8.0	VF/NM 9.0	NM- 9.2
1-Origin & 1st app. Shock Gibson; Ted Parrish, the Man with 1000 Faces begins; Powell-a; becomes Champion #2 on?; has earliest? full page panel in comics; classic war-c	508	1016	1524	3708	6554	9400
2-Powell-a	245	490	735	1568	2684	3800
3-War-c	181	362	543	1158	1979	2800
4,5: 4-Powell-a. 5-Dinosaur-c	161	322	483	1030	1765	2500
6-9,11: 7-Mars Mason begins, ends #11. 9,11-War-c	148	296	444	947	1624	2300
10-Classic Giant Moth Monster-c	219	438	657	1402	2401	3400
12 (3/41; shows #11 in indicia)-The Wasp begins; Major Colt app. (Capt. Colt #12)	188	376	582	1242	2121	3000
13-Intro. Captain Freedom & Young Defenders; Girl Commandos; Pat Parker (costumed heroine), War Nurse begins; Major Colt app.	300	600	900	1856	3178	4500
14,15-(100 pg. pocket size, 1941): 14-2nd Harvey comic (See Pocket); Shock Gibson dons new costume; Nazi war-c. 15-Pat Parker dons costume, last in costume #23; no Girl Commandos; Nazi monsters war-c	343	686	1029	2400	4200	6000
16-(100 pg. pocket size, 1941) Cover with Hitler leading an army of Nazi ghouls to the White House	389	778	1167	2723	4762	6800
17-Classic Simon & Kirby WWII Nazi bondage/torture-c; Black Cat begins (4/42, early app.; see Pocket #1); origin Black Cat-r/Pocket #1; not in #40,41	389	778	1167	2723	4762	6800
18-20-S&K-c. 18-Bondage/torture-c. 19,20-Japanese war-c	290	580	870	1856	3178	4500
21-Hitler, Tojo-c; Kirby-c	389	778	1167	2723	4762	6800
22-Nazi WWII-c by Kirby	290	580	870	1856	3178	4500
23-Origin Girl Commandos; war-c by Kirby	290	580	870	1856	3178	4500
24-Pat Parker team-up with Girl Commandos; Hitler, Tojo, & Mussolini-c	331	662	993	2317	4059	5800
25,27,29: 25-War-c. 27 Nazi WWII-c. 29-Nazi WWII bondage-c	219	438	657	1402	2401	3400
26-Flag-c	300	600	900	1920	3310	4700
28-Classic Nazi monster WWII-c	757	1514	2271	5526	9763	14,000
30-Nazi WWII Death Chamber bondage-c	300	600	900	1950	3375	4800
31-Classic Schomburg Hitler & Tojo-c	486	972	1458	3550	6275	9000
32-35-Schomburg. 32,34-Nazi war-c. 33,35-Japanese war-c	219	438	657	1402	2401	3400
36-Schomburg Japanese war-c	148	296	444	947	1624	2300

Spectacular Spider-Man #89 © MAR

Speed Comics #2 © HARV

Spider-Boy #1 © MAR

	GD	VG	FN	VF	VF/NM	NM-		GD	VG	FN	VF	VF/NM	NM-
	2.0	4.0	6.0	8.0	9.0	9.2		2.0	4.0	6.0	8.0	9.0	9.2

	GD 2.0	VG 4.0	FN 6.0	VF 8.0	VF/NM 9.0	NM- 9.2
37,39-42,44: 37-Japanese war-c. 41-War-c	55	110	165	352	601	850
38-Iwo-Jima Flag-c	74	148	222	470	810	1150
43-Robot-c	65	130	195	416	708	1000

NOTE: *Al Avison* c-14-16, 30, 43. *Briefer* a-6, 7. *Jon Henri* (Kirbyesque) c-17-20. *Kubert* a-37, 38, 42-44. *Kirby/Caseneuve* c-21-23. *Cecelia Munson* a-7-11(Mars Mason). *Palais* c-37, 39-42. *Powell* a-1, 2, 4-7, 28, 31, 44. *Schomburg* c-31-36. *Tuska* a-3, 6, 7. *Bondage* c-18, 35. *Captain Freedom* c-16-24, 25(part), 26-44(w/Black Cat #27, 29, 31, 32-40). *Shock Gibson* c-1-15.

SPEED DEMON (Also see Marvel Versus DC #3 & DC Versus Marvel #4)
Marvel Comics (Amalgam): Apr, 1996 ($1.95, one-shot)

1						4.00

SPEED DEMONS (Formerly Frank Merriwell at Yale #1-4?; Submarine Attack #11 on)
Charlton Comics: No. 5, Feb, 1957 - No. 10, 1958

5-10	8	16	24	44	57	70

SPEED FORCE (See The Flash 2nd Series #143-Cobalt Blue)
DC Comics: Nov, 1997 ($3.95, one-shot)

1-Flash & Kid Flash vs. Cobalt Blue; Waid-s/Aparo & Sienkiewicz-a; Flash family stories and pin-ups by various						4.00

SPEED FORCE
DC Comics: Jan, 2024 - No. 6, Jun, 2024 ($3.99, limited series)

1-6-Kid Flash and The Flash of China vs. Music Meister						4.00

SPEED RACER (Also see The New Adventures of...)
Now Comics: July, 1987 - No. 38, Nov, 1990 ($1.75)

1						5.00
2-38, 1-2nd printing						4.00
Special 1 (1988, $2.00), Special 2 (1988, $3.50)						5.00

SPEED RACER (Also see Racer X)
DC Comics (WildStorm): Oct, 1999 - No. 3, Dec, 1999 ($2.50, limited series)

1-3-Tommy Yune-s/a; origin of Racer X; debut of the Mach 5						4.00
...: Born To Race (2000, $9.95, TPB) r/series & conceptual art						10.00
...: The Original Manga Vol. 1 ('00, $9.95, TPB) r/1950s B&W manga						10.00

SPEED RACER: CHRONICLES OF THE RACER
IDW Publishing: 2007 - No. 4, Apr, 2008 ($3.99)

1-4-Multiple covers for each						4.00

SPEED RACER FEATURING NINJA HIGH SCHOOL
Now Comics: Aug, 1993 - No. 2, 1993 ($2.50, mini-series)

1,2: 1-Polybagged w/card. 2-Exists?						4.00

SPEED RACER: RETURN OF THE GRX
Now Comics: Mar, 1994 - No. 2, Apr, 1994 ($1.95, limited series)

1,2						4.00

SPEED SMITH-THE HOT ROD KING (Also see Hot Rod King)
Ziff-Davis Publishing Co.: Spring, 1952

1-Saunders painted-c	31	62	93	182	296	410

SPEEDY GONZALES
Dell Publishing Co.: No. 1084, Mar, 1960

Four Color 1084	8	16	24	51	96	140

SPEEDY RABBIT (See Television Puppet Show)
Realistic/I. W. Enterprises/Super Comics: nd (1953); 1963

nn (1953)-Realistic Reprint?	3	6	9	17	26	35
I.W. Reprint #1 (2 versions w/diff. c/stories exist)-Peter Cottontail #?						
Super Reprint #14(1963)	3	6	9	14	19	24

SPELLBINDERS
Quality: Dec, 1986 - No. 12, Jan, 1988 ($1.25)

1-12: Nemesis the Warlock, Amadeus Wolf						4.00

SPELLBINDERS
Marvel Comics: May, 2005 - No. 6, Oct, 2005 ($2.99, limited series)

1-6-Carey-s/Perkins-a						3.00
...: Signs and Wonders TPB (2006, $7.99, digest) r/#1-6						8.00

SPELLBOUND (Tales to Hold You... #1, Stories to Hold You...)
Atlas Comics (ACI 1-15/Male 16-23/BPC 24-34): Mar, 1952 - #23, June, 1954; #24, Oct, 1955 - #34, June, 1957

1-Horror/weird stories in all	148	296	444	947	1624	2300
2-Edgar A. Poe app.	129	258	387	826	1413	2000
3-Whitney-a; cannibalism story; classic Heath-c	194	388	582	1242	2121	3000
4,5	68	136	204	436	743	1050

	GD 2.0	VG 4.0	FN 6.0	VF 8.0	VF/NM 9.0	NM- 9.2
6-Krigstein-a	71	142	213	454	777	1100
7-10: 7,8-Ayers-a	58	116	174	371	636	900
11-13,15,16,18-20	54	108	162	343	574	825
14-Ed Win-a; classic Everett-c	290	580	870	1856	3178	4500
17-Krigstein-a; classic Everett skeleton-c	181	362	543	1158	1979	2800
21-23: 23-Last precode (6/54)	47	94	141	296	498	700
24-28,30,31,34: 25-Orlando-a	39	78	117	231	378	525
29-Ditko-a (4 pgs.)	41	82	123	256	428	600
32,33-Torres-a	39	78	117	231	378	525

NOTE: *Brodsky* a-5; c-1. *Check* a-5, 7, 10, 11, 13, 15, 25-27, 32. *Colan* a-17. *Everett* a-2, 5, 7, 10, 16, 28, 31; c-2, 8, 9, 14, 17-19, 28, 33. *Forgione/Abel* a-29. *Forte/Fox* a-16. *Al Hartley* a-2. *Heath* a-2, 4, 8, 9, 12, 14, 16; c-3, 4, 12, 16, 20, 21. *Infantino* a-15. *Keller* a-5. *Kida* a-2, 14. *Maneely* a-7, 14, 27; c-24, 29, 31. *Mooney* a-5, 13, 18. *Mac Pakula* a-22, 32. *Post* a-8. *Powell* a-19, 20, 32. *Robinson* a-1. *Romita* a-24, 26, 27. *R.Q. Sale* a-29. *Sekowsky* a-5. *Severin* c-29. *Sinnott* a-8, 16, 17.

SPELLBOUND
Marvel Comics: Jan, 1988 - Apr, 1988 ($1.50, bi-weekly, Baxter paper)

1-5						4.00
6 ($2.25, 52 pgs.)						5.00

SPELLJAMMER (Also see TSR Worlds Comics Annual)
DC Comics: Sept, 1990 - No. 15, Nov, 1991 ($1.75)

1-15: Based on TSR game. 11-Heck-a.						4.00

SPELL ON WHEELS
Dark Horse Comics: Oct, 2016 - No. 5, Feb, 2017 ($3.99)

1-5-Kate Leth-s/Megan Levens-a. 1-Ming Doyle-c						4.00

SPENCER SPOOK (Formerly Giggle Comics)
American Comics Group: No. 100, Mar-Apr, 1955 - No. 101, May-June, 1955

100,101	10	20	30	56	76	95

SPIDER, THE
Eclipse Books: 1991 - Book 3, 1991 ($4.95, 52 pgs., limited series)

Book 1-3-Truman-c/a						5.00

SPIDER, THE
Dynamite Entertainment: 2012 - No. 18, 2014 ($3.99)

1-18: 1-Revival of the pulp character; Liss-s/Worley-a; 4 covers. 2-18-Multiple covers						4.00
Annual 1 (2013, $4.99) Denton-s/Vitorino-a/c						5.00

SPIDER-BOY (Also see Marvel Versus DC #3)
Marvel Comics (Amalgam): Apr, 1996 ($1.95)

1-Mike Wieringo-c/a; Karl Kesel story; 1st app. of Bizarnage, Insect Queen, Challengers of the Fantastic, Sue Storm: Agent of S.H.I.E.L.D. & King Lizard						4.00
... Team-Up 1 (6/97, $1.95) Karl Kesel & Roger Stern-s/Jo Ladronn-a(p)						4.00

SPIDER-BOY (Bailey Briggs)(see debut in Spider-Man #7 2022 series)
Marvel Comics: Jan, 2024 - Present ($5.99/$3.99)

1-($5.99) Slott-s/Medina-a; back-up story with Squirrel Girl, Templeton-a						6.00
2-4-($3.99) Captain America & Taskmaster app.						5.00

SPIDER-FORCE (Tie-in to Spider-Geddon)
Marvel Comics: Dec, 2018 - No. 3, Feb, 2019 ($3.99, limited series)

1-3: 1-Priest-s/Siqueira-a; Spider-Woman, Spider-Kid, Scarlet Spider app.						4.00

SPIDER-GEDDON (Also see Edge of Spider-Geddon, Spider-Girls and Superior Octopus)
Marvel Comics: No. 0, Nov, 2018 - No. 5, Feb, 2019 ($4.99/$3.99)

0,5-($4.99) 0-Clayton Crain-a; app. Spider-Man from PS4 videogame						5.00
1-4-($3.99) 1-Gage-s/Molina-a; multiverse of Spider-Mans app.; Morlun returns						4.00
... Handbook 1 (2/19, $4.99) Profiles of various Spider-Men of the Multiverse						5.00

SPIDER-GIRL (See What If... #105)
Marvel Comics: Oct, 1998 - No. 100, Sept, 2006 ($1.99/$2.25/$2.99)

0-($2.99)-r/1st app. Peter Parker's daughter from What If #105; previews regular series, Avengers-Next and J2	2	4	6	8	11	14
1-DeFalco-s/Olliffe & Williamson-s	2	4	6	10	14	18
2-Two covers						5.00
3-16,18-20: 3-Fantastic Five-c/app. 10,11-Spider-Girl time-travels to meet teenaged Spider-Man						4.00
17-($2.99) Peter Parker suits up						5.00
21-24,26-49,51-59: 21-Begin $2.25-c. 31-Avengers app.						4.00
25-($2.99) Spider-Girl vs. the Savage Six						5.00
50-($3.50)						5.00
59-69-($2.99) 59-Avengers app.; Ben Parker born. 75-May in Black costume. 82-84-Venom bonds with Normie Osborn. 93-Venom-c. 95-Tony Stark app.						3.00
100-($3.99) Last issue; story plus Rogues Gallery, profile pages; r/#27,53						4.00
1999 Annual ($3.99)						4.00
...: The End! (10/10, $3.99) Frenz & Buscema-a; Mayhem app.						4.00
Wizard #1/2 (1999)						4.00

	GD 2.0	VG 4.0	FN 6.0	VF 8.0	VF/NM 9.0	NM- 9.2		GD 2.0	VG 4.0	FN 6.0	VF 8.0	VF/NM 9.0	NM- 9.2

... A Fresh Start (1/99,$5.99, TPB) r/#1&2 6.00

... Presents The Buzz and Darkdevil (2007, $7.99, digest) r/mini-series 8.00

SPIDER-GIRL (Araña Corazon from Arana Heart of the Spider)
Marvel Comics: Jan, 2011 - No. 8, Sept, 2011 ($3.99/$2.99)

1-($3.99) Tobin-s/Henry-a/Kitson-c; back-up w/Haspiel-a; Fantastic Four app. 4.00
1-Variant-c by Del Mundo 5.00
2-8-($2.99) 2,3-Red Hulk app. 4,5-Ana Kravenoff app. 6-Hobgoblin app. 8-Powers return 3.00

SPIDER-GIRLS (Spider-Geddon tie-in)
Marvel Comics: Dec, 2018 - No. 3, Feb, 2019 ($3.99, limited series)

1-3-Houser-s/Genolet-a; Mayday Parker, Anya Corazon & Annie Parker app. 4.00

SPIDER-GWEN (See debut in Edge of Spider-Verse #2)
Marvel Comics: Apr, 2015 - No. 5, Aug, 2015 ($3.99)

1-Latour-s/Robbi Rodriguez-a/c; The Vulture app. 3 6 9 14 20 25
2-5- 2-Spider-Ham app. 3-The Vulture & The Punisher app. 5.00

SPIDER-GWEN
Marvel Comics: Dec, 2015 - No. 34, Sept, 2018 ($3.99)

1-Latour-s/Robbi Rodriguez-a/c; The Lizard & female Capt. America app.
 2 4 6 9 12 15
2-18,20-23,25-34: 7,8-"Spider-Women" tie-in; Silk & Spider-Woman app. 10-Kraven app.
 16-18-Miles app.; x-over with Spider-Man #12-14. 25-32-Gwenom app. 4.00
19-Elsa Brock creates the Venom symbiote 2 4 6 11 16 20
24-1st app. Gwenom 6 12 18 38 69 100
#0 (1/16, $4.99) Reprints #1 (4/15) plus script of Edge of Spider-Verse #2
 2 4 6 9 12 15
Annual 1 (8/16, $4.99) Short stories; Latour-s; art by various
 1 3 4 6 8 10
Annual 1 (11/23, $4.99) "Contest of Chaos" x-over part 5; White Fox app. 5.00

SPIDER-GWEN: GHOST-SPIDER (Spider-Geddon tie-in)(Also see Ghost-Spider series)
Marvel Comics: Dec, 2018 - No. 10, Sept, 2019 ($3.99)

1-Spider-Ham app. 1 3 4 6 8 10
2-10: 4-10-Miyazawa-a. 10-Adopts Ghost-Spider name 4.00

SPIDER-GWEN: GWENVERSE
Marvel Comics: May, 2022 - No. 5, Oct, 2022 ($4.99/$3.99, limited series)

1-($4.99) Seeley-s/Nishijima-a; Multiverse Gwens app.; ThorGwen & Nightbird app. 5.00
2-5-($3.99) Iron Gwen and Gwen versions of Capt. America, Wolverine, Capt Marvel app. 4.00

SPIDER-GWEN: SHADOW CLONES
Marvel Comics: May, 2023 - No. 5, Sept, 2023 ($4.99/$3.99, limited series)

1-($4.99) Emily Kim-s/Kei Zama-a; Gwen versions of Sinister Six villains app. 5.00
2-5-($3.99) 4.00

SPIDER-GWEN: SMASH
Marvel Comics: Feb, 2024 - Present ($4.99/$3.99, limited series)

1-($4.99) Melissa Flores-s/Enid Balám-a; Dazzler app. 5.00
2,3-($3.99) 2,3-Dazzler app. 4.00

SPIDER-HAM (Peter Porker, The Spectacular...)(See Marvel Tails & Spider-Geddon)
Marvel Comics: Dec, 2019 - No. 5, Jun, 2020 ($3.99)

1-5: 1-Origin re-told; Sca-vengers and the Unhumanati app. 2-5-Spider-Man app. 4.00

SPIDER-HAM 25TH ANNIVERSARY SPECIAL
Marvel Comics: Aug, 2010 ($3.99, one-shot)

1-Jusko-c/DeFalco/Chabot-a; Peter Porker vs. the Swinester Six 4.00

SPIDER ISLAND... (one-shots) (See Amazing Spider-Man #666-673)
Marvel Comics

...: Deadly Foes 1 (10/11, $4.99) Hobgoblin & Jackal stories; Caselli-c 5.00
...: Emergence of Evil - Jackal & Hobgoblin 1 (10/11, $4.99) Hobgoblin & Jackal reprints 5.00
...: Heroes For Hire 1 (12/11, $2.99) Misty Knight & Paladin; Hotz-a/Yardin-c 3.00
... I Love New York City 1 (11/11, $3.99) Short stories by various; Punisher app. 4.00
...: Spider-Woman 1 (11/11, $2.99) Van Lente-s/Camuncoli-a; Alicia Masters app. 3.00
... Spotlight 1 ('11, $3.99) Creator interviews and story previews 3.00
...: The Avengers 1 (11/11, $2.99) McKone-a/Yu-c; Frog-Man app. 3.00

SPIDER-ISLAND (Secret Wars tie-in)(Back-up MC2 Spider-Girl story in each issue)
Marvel Comics: Sept, 2015 - No. 5, Dec, 2015 ($4.99/$3.99, limited series)

1-($4.99) Gage-s/Diaz-a/Ramos-c; Venom and Werewolf By Night app. 5.00
2-5-($3.99) Tony Stark as the Green Goblin. 3-5-Peter Parker returns 4.00

SPIDER ISLAND: CLOAK & DAGGER (See Amazing Spider-Man #666-673)
Marvel Comics: Oct, 2011 - No. 3, Dec, 2011 ($2.99, limited series)

1-3-Spencer-s/Rios-a/Choi-c; Mr. Negative app. 3.00

SPIDER ISLAND: DEADLY HANDS OF KUNG FU (See Amazing Spider-Man #666-673)
Marvel Comics: Oct, 2011 - No. 3, Dec, 2011 ($2.99, limited series)

1-3-Johnston-s/Fiumara-a; Madame Web & Iron Fist app. 3.00

SPIDER ISLAND: THE AMAZING SPIDER-GIRL (Continued from Spider-Girl #8)
Marvel Comics: Oct, 2011 - No. 3, Dec, 2011 ($2.99, limited series)

1-3-Hobgoblin & Kingpin app.; Tobin-s/Larraz-a 3.00

SPIDER-MAN (Peter Parker Spider-Man on cover but not indicia #75-on)
(See Amazing..., Friendly Neighborhood..., Giant-Size..., Marvel Age..., Marvel Knights...,
Marvel Tales, Marvel Team-Up, Spectacular..., Spidey Super Stories, Marvel Team-Up, Ultimate...,
Venom, & Web Of...)
Marvel Comics: Aug, 1990 - No. 98, Nov, 1998 ($1.75/$1.95/ $1.99)

1-Silver edition, direct sale only (unbagged) 3 6 9 14 19 24
1-Silver bagged edition; direct sale, no price on comic, but $2.00 on plastic bag
 (125,000 print run) 3 6 9 18 28 38
1-Regular edition w/Spidey face in UPC area (unbagged); green-c
 2 4 6 13 18 22
1-Regular bagged edition w/Spidey face in UPC area; green cover (125,000) 14.00
1-Newsstand bagged w/UPC code 3 6 9 16 23 30
1-Gold edition, 2nd printing (unbagged) with Spider-Man in box (400,000-450,000)
 3 6 9 21 33 45
1-Gold 2nd printing w/UPC code; (less than 10,000 print run) intended for Wal-Mart;

much scarcer than originally believed 13 26 39 91 201 310
1-Platinum ed. mailed to retailers only (10,000 print run); has new McFarlane & editorial
 material instead of ads; stiff-c, no cover price 17 34 51 119 265 410
1-Facsimile Edition (10/20, $3.99) reprints #1 with original ads and letter page
 2 4 6 8 10 12
2-10: 2-McFarlane-c/a/scripts cont.; Lizard origin retold in brief. 3-Spider-Man origin retold in
 brief. 6,7-Ghost Rider & Hobgoblin app. 8-Wolverine cameo; Wolverine storyline begins
 1 2 3 5 6 8
11-25: 12-Wolverine storyline ends. 13-Spidey's black costume returns; Morbius app.
 14-Morbius app. 15-Erik Larsen-c/a; Beast c/s. 16-X-Force-c/story w/Liefeld assists;
 continues in X-Force #4; reads sideways; last McFarlane issue. 17-Thanos-c/story;
 Leonardi/Williamson-c/a. 18-Ghost Rider-c/story. 18-23-Sinister Six storyline w/Erik
 Larsen-c/a/scripts. 19-Hulk & Hobgoblin app. 20-22-Deathlok app. 22,23-Ghost Rider,
 Hulk, Hobgoblin app. 23-Wrap-around gatefold-c. 24-Infinity War x-over w/Demogoblin &
 Hobgoblin-c/story. 24-Demogoblin dons new costume & battles Hobgoblin-c/story 5.00
26-($3.50, 52 pgs.)-Silver hologram on-c w/gatefold poster by Ron Lim; origin retold
 1 2 3 5 6 8
26-2nd printing; gold hologram on-c 5.00
27-45: 32-34-Punisher-c/story. 37-Maximum Carnage x-over. 39,40-Electro-c/s (cameo #38).
 41-43-Iron Fist-c/stories w/Jae Lee-c/a. 42-Intro Platoon. 44-Hobgoblin app. 4.00
46-49,51-53, 55, 56,58-74,76-81: 46-Begin $1.95-c; bound-in card sheet. 51-Power &
 Responsibility Pt. 3. 52,53-Venom app. 60-Kaine revealed. 61-Origin Kaine. 65-Mysterio
 app. 66-Kaine-c/app.; Peter Parker app. 67-Carnage-c/app. 68,69-Hobgoblin-c/app.
 72-Onslaught x-over; Spidey vs. Sentinels. 74-Daredevil-c/app. 77-80-Morbius-c/app. 4.00
46-($2.95)-Polybagged; silver ink-c w/16 pg. preview of cartoon series & animation style
 print; bound-in trading card sheet 5.00
50-($2.50)-Newsstand edition 5.00
50-($3.95)-Collectors edition w/holographic-c 5.00
51-($2.95)-Deluxe edition foil-c; flip book 5.00
54-($2.75, 52 pgs.)-Flip book 5.00
57-($2.50) 5.00
57-($2.95)-Die cut-c 5.00
65-($2.95)-Variant-c; polybagged w/cassette 5.00
75-($2.95)-Wraparound-c; Green Goblin returns; death of Ben Reilly (who was the clone) 5.00
82-97: 84-Juggernaut app. 91-Double cover with "Dusk #1"; battles the Shocker.
 93-Ghost Rider app. 4.00
98-Double cover; final issue 4.00
#(-1) Flashback (7/97) 4.00
Annual '97 ($2.99), '98 ($2.99)-Devil Dinosaur-c/app. 5.00
NOTE: **Erik Larsen** c/a-15, 18-23. **M. Rogers/Keith Williams** c/a-27, 28.

SPIDER-MAN (Miles Morales in regular Marvel Universe)
Marvel Comics: Apr, 2016 - No. 21, Dec, 2017; No. 234, Jan, 2018 - No. 240, Jul, 2018 ($3.99)

1-19,21: 1,2-Bendis-s/Pichelli-a; Avengers & Peter Parker app. 1-Ms. Marvel app.
 6-10-Civil War II tie-in. 12,13-Crossover with Spider-Gwen #16-18. 16,18-Black Cat app.
 21-Nico Leon-a 4.00
20-Miles Morales pinned down by police officer-c; Nico Leon-a
 2 4 6 11 16 20
[Title switches to legacy numbering after #21 (12/17)]
234-240: 234-239-Hobgoblin, Sandman, Electro, The Spot, Bombshell, Iron Spider app. 4.00
Annual 1 (10/18, $4.99) Morbius app. 5.00

SPIDER-MAN
Marvel Comics: Nov, 2019 - No. 5, Feb, 2021 ($3.99)

1-($4.99) J.J. & Henry Abrams-s/Pichelli-a; intro Cadaverous and future Ben Parker 5.00
2-5-($3.99) Ben becomes the new Spider-Man. 3-5-Tony Stark and Riri Williams app. 4.00

SPIDER-MAN (Peter Parker)
Marvel Comics: Dec, 2022 - No. 11, Oct, 2023 ($4.99/$3.99)

1-($4.99) Slott-s/Bagley-a; Morlun returns; multiverse Spiders app. 5.00
2-4,6-10-($3.99) 7-Debut of Spider-Boy. 8-10-Electro app. 10-Spider-Boy app. 4.00
5-($4.99) Back-up story with Monica Rambeau 5.00
11-($4.99) Origin of Spider-Boy revealed; Daredevil app. 5.00
Annual 1 (10/23, $4.99) "Contest of Chaos" x-over part 1; Wolverine app. 5.00

SPIDER-MAN (one-shots, hardcovers and TPBs)

...& Arana Special: The Hunter Revealed (5/06, $3.99) Del Rio-s; art by Del Rio & various 4.00
...and Batman ('95, $5.95) DeMatteis-s; Joker, Carnage app.
 3 6 9 16 23 30
...and Daredevil ('84, $2.00) 1-r/Spectacular Spider-Man #26-28 by Miller
 3 4 6 8 10
...and The Human Torch in...Bahia de Los Muertos! 1 (5/09, $3.99) Beland-s/Juan Doe-a;
 Diablo app.; printed in two versions (English and Spanish language)
 3 6 9 14 19 24
... Annual 1 (8/19, $4.99) Spider-Ham spotlight; back-up by Phil Lord & Christopher Miller
 2 4 6 9 12 15
...: Back in Black HC (2007, $34.99, dustjacket) oversized r/Amaz. S-M #539-543, Friendly
 Neighborhood S-M #17-23 & Annual #1; cover pencils and sketch pages 55.00
...: Back in Black SC (2008, $24.99) same contents as HC 25.00
...: Back in Black Handbook (2007, $3.99) Official Handbook format; Lizard app. 10.00
...: Back in Quack (11/10, $3.99) Howard the Duck, Beverly and Man-Thing app.
 2 4 6 9 12 15
...: Birth of Venom TPB (2007, $29.99) r/Secret Wars #8, AS-M #252-259,298-300,315-317,
 AS-M Annual #25, Fantastic Four #274 and Web of Spider-Man #1 30.00
...: Brand New Day TPB (2008, $24.99, dustjacket) r/Amaz. S-M #344,345,359-363; Spider-Man: Swing
 Shift and story from Venom Super-Special 25.00
...: Carnage nn (6/93, $6.95, TPB)-r/Amazing S-M #344,345,359-363; spot varnish-c 15.00
...: Curse of the Man-Thing 1 (6/21, $4.99) Orlando-s/Failla-a (Also see Avengers: Curse
 of the Man-Thing and X-Men: Curse of the Man-Thing) 5.00
.../Daredevil (10/02, $2.99) Vatche Mavlian-c/a; Brett Matthews-s 3.00
...: Dead Man's Hand 1 (4/97, $2.99) 1 2 3 5 6 8
...: Death of the Stacys HC (2007, $19.99, dustjacket) r/Amazing Spider-Man #88-92 and
 #121,122; intro. by Gerry Conway; afterword by Romita; cover gallery incl. reprints 20.00
.../Dr. Strange: "The Way to Dusty Death" nn (1992, $6.95, 68 pgs.) 8.00
...: Election Day HC (2009, $29.99) r/#584-588; includes Barack Obama app from #583 30.00
.../Elektra '98 ($2.99) vs. The Silencer 4.00
...: Family (2005, $4.99, 100 pgs.) new story and reprints; Spider-Ham app. 5.00
... Fear Itself (3/09, $3.99) Spider-Man and Man-Thing; Stuart Moore-s/Joe Suitor-a
 1 3 4 6 8 10

Spider-Gwen #17 © MAR

Spider-Man (2016 series) #1 © MAR

Spider-Man and the X-Men #1 © MAR

	GD 2.0	VG 4.0	FN 6.0	VF 8.0	VF/NM 9.0	NM- 9.2
... Fear Itself Graphic Novel (2/92, $12.95)						20.00
Free Comic Book Day 2012 (Spider-Man: Season One) #1 (Giveaway) Previews the GN						3.00
Giant-Sized Spider-Man (12/98, $3.99) r/team-ups						5.00
...: Grim Hunt - The Kraven Saga (5/10, free) prelude to Grim Hunt arc; Kraven history						3.00
Holiday Special 1995 ($2.95)						10.00
...: Hot Shots nn (1/96, $2.95) fold out posters by various, inc. Vess and Ross						6.00
Identity Crisis (9/98, $19.95, TPB)						20.00
...: Kraven's Last Hunt HC (2006, $19.99) r/Amaz. S-M #293,294; Web of S-M #31,32 and Spect. S-M #131-132; intro. by DeMatteis; Zeck-a; cover pencils and interior pencils						20.00
...: Legacy of Evil 1 (6/96, $3.95) Kurt Busiek script & Mark Texeira-c/a						6.00
...Legends Vol. 1: Todd McFarlane ('03, $19.95, TPB)-r/Amaz. S-M #298-305						20.00
...Legends Vol. 2: Todd McFarlane ('03, $19.99, TPB)-r/Amaz. S-M #306-314, & Spec. Spider-Man Annual #10						20.00
...Legends Vol. 3: Todd McFarlane ('04, $24.99, TPB)-r/Amaz. S-M #315-323,325,328						25.00
...Legends Vol. 4: Spider-Man & Wolverine ('03, $13.95, TPB) r/Spider-Man & Wolverine #1-4 and Spider-Man/Daredevil #1						14.00
...Marrow (2/01, $2.99) Garza-a						5.00
...Marvels Snapshots 1 (12/20, $4.99) Howard Chaykin-s/a; Alex Ross-c						5.00
...Mary Jane: ... You Just Hit the Jackpot TPB (2009, $24.99) early apps. & key stories						25.00
...: Master Plan 1 (9/17, $3.99) Thompson-s/Stockman-a; bonus r/ASM #2						4.00
100th Anniversary Special: Spider-Man 1 (9/14, $3.99) In-Hyk Lee-a/c; Venom app.						4.00
	1	3	4	6	8	10
...: One More Day HC (2008. $24.99, dustjacket) r/Amaz. S-M #544-545, Friendly N.S-M #24, Sensational S-M #41 and Marvel Spotlight: Spider-Man-One More Day						25.00
...: Origin of the Hunter (6/10, $3.99) r/Kraven apps. in ASM #15 & 34; new Mayhew-a						
	1	3	4	6	8	10
..., Peter Parker: Back in Black HC (2007, $34.99) oversized r/Sensational Spider-Man #35-40 & Annual #1, Spider-Man Family #1,2; Marvel Spotlight: Spider-Man and Spider-Man Back in Black Handbook; cover sketches						35.00
...: Punisher, Sabretooth: Designer Genes (1993, $8.95)						10.00
...: Reptilian Rage 1 (8/19, $3.99) Macchio-s/Chris Allen-a; The Lizard app.						4.00
...: Return of the Goblin TPB (see Peter Parker: Spider-Man)						
...: Revelations ('97, $14.99, TPB) r/end of Clone Saga plus 14 new pages by Romita Jr.						40.00
...: Saga of the Sandman TPB (2007, $19.99) r/1st app. Amazing S-M #4 and other app.						20.00
...: Season One HC (2012, $24.99) Origin and early days; Bunn-s/Neil Edwards-a						25.00
...: Son of the Goblin (2004, $15.99, TPB) r/AS-M#136-137,312 & Spec. S-M #189,200						30.00
...: Special: Black and Blue and Read All Over 1 (11/06, $3.99) new story and r/ASM #12						4.00
Special Edition 1 (12/92-c, 11/92 inside)-The Trial of Venom; ordered thru mail with $5.00 donation or more to UNICEF; embossed metallic ink; came bagged w/bound-in poster; Daredevil app.	3	6	9	14	20	25
... Spectacular 1 (8/14, $4.99) Reprints all-ages tales; Green Goblin, Kraven app.						5.00
Super Special (7/95, $3.95)-Planet of the Symbiotes	2	4	6	11	16	20
The Best of Spider-Man Vol 1 (2003, $29.99, HC with dust jacket) r/AS-M V2 #37-45, Peter Parker: S-M #44-47, and S-M's Tangled Web #10,11; Pearson-c						30.00
The Best of Spider-Man Vol. 3 (2004, $29.99, HC with d.j.) r/AS-M V2 #46-58, 500						30.00
The Best of Spider-Man Vol. 4 (2005, $29.99, HC with d.j.) r/#501-514; sketch pages						30.00
The Best of Spider-Man Vol. 5 (2006, $29.99, HC with d.j.) r/#515-524; sketch pages						30.00
The Complete Frank Miller Spider-Man (2002, $29.95, HC) r/Miller-s/a						30.00
The Death of Captain Stacy (2000, $3.50) r/AS-M#88-90						
	1	2	3	5	6	8
The Death of Gwen Stacy ($14.95) r/AS-M#96-98,121,122						15.00
...: The Movie ($12.95) adaptation by Stan Lee-s/Alan Davis-a; plus r/Ultimate Spider-Man #8, Peter Parker #35, Tangled Web #10; photo-c						13.00
...: The Official Movie Adaptation (2002, $5.95) Stan Lee-s/Alan Davis-a						6.00
...: The Other HC (2006, $29.99, dust jacket) r/Amazing S-M #525-528, Friendly Neighborhood S-M #1-4 and Marvel Knights S-M #19-22; gallery of variant covers						30.00
...: The Other SC (2006, $24.99) r/crossover; gallery of variant covers						25.00
...: The Other Sketchbook (2005, $2.99) sketch page preview of 2005-6 x-over						3.00
Torment TPB (5/01$15.95) r/#1-5, Spec. S-M #10						16.00
...: Unforgiven (5/23, $4.99) Seeley-s/Kotian-a; leads into X-Men: Unforgiven						5.00
...: Vs. Doctor Octopus ($17.95) reprints early battles; Sean Chen-c						18.00
...: Vs. Punisher (7/00, $2.99) Michael Lopez-c/a	1	2	3	5	6	8
...: Vs. Silver Sable (2006, $15.99, TPB)-r/Amazing Spider-Man #265,279-281 & Peter Parker, The Spectacular Spider-Man #128,129						16.00
...Vs. The Black Cat (2005, $14.99, TPB)-r/Amaz. S-M #194,195,204,205,226,227						15.00
...Vs. Vampires (12/10, $3.99) Blade app.; Castro-a/Grevioux-s						4.00
...Vs. Venom (1990, $8.95, TPB)-r/Amaz. S-M #300,315-317 w/new McFarlane-c						15.00
...Visionaries (10/01, $19.95, TPB)-r/Amaz. S-M #298-305; McFarlane-a						20.00
...Visionaries: John Romita (8/01, $19.95, TPB)-r/Amaz. S-M #39-42, 50,68,69,108,109; new Romita-c/a						20.00
...Visionaries: Kurt Busiek (2006, $19.99, TPB)-r/Untold Tales of Spider-Man #1-8						20.00
...Visionaries: Roger Stern (2007, $24.99, TPB)-r/Amazing Spider-Man #206 & Spectacular Spider-Man #43-52,54; Stern interview						25.00
Wizard 1/2 ($10.00) Leonardi-a; Green Goblin app.						10.00

SPIDER-MAN ADVENTURES
Marvel Comics: Dec, 1994 - No. 15, Mar, 1996 ($1.50)

	GD 2.0	VG 4.0	FN 6.0	VF 8.0	VF/NM 9.0	NM- 9.2
1-($1.50)-Yellow cover; based on animated series	1	2	3	5	6	8
1-($2.95)-Foil embossed-c						12.00
2-15						4.00

SPIDER-MAN AND HIS AMAZING FRIENDS (See Marvel Action Universe)
Marvel Comics Group: Dec, 1981 (one-shot)

	GD 2.0	VG 4.0	FN 6.0	VF 8.0	VF/NM 9.0	NM- 9.2
1-Adapted from NBC TV cartoon show; Green Goblin-c/story; 1st Spidey, Firestar, Iceman team-up; Spiegle-p	6	12	18	37	66	95

SPIDER-MAN AND POWER PACK
Marvel Comics: Jan, 2007 - No. 4, Apr, 2007 ($2.99, limited series)

	NM- 9.2
1-4-Sumerak-s/Gurihiru-a; Sandman app. 3,4-Venom app.	3.00
...: Big City Heroes (2007, $6.99, digest) r/#1-4	7.00

SPIDER-MAN AND THE FANTASTIC FOUR
Marvel Comics: Jun, 2007 - No. 4, Sept, 2007 ($2.99, limited series)

	NM- 9.2
1-4-Mike Wieringo-a/c; Jeff Parker-s. 1,4-Impossible Man app.	3.00
...: Silver Rage TPB (2007, $10.99) r/#1-4; series outline and cover sketches	11.00

SPIDER-MAN AND THE LEAGUE OF REALMS (War of the Realms tie-in)
Marvel Comics: Jul, 2019 - No. 3, Aug, 2019 ($3.99, limited series)

	NM- 9.2
1-3-Sean Ryan-s/Nico Leon-a	4.00

SPIDER-MAN AND THE SECRET WARS
Marvel Comics: Feb, 2010 - No. 4, May, 2010 ($2.99, limited series)

	NM- 9.2
1-4-Tobin-s/Scherberger-a. 3-Black costume app.	3.00

SPIDER-MAN AND THE INCREDIBLE HULK (See listing under Amazing...)

SPIDER-MAN AND THE UNCANNY X-MEN
Marvel Comics: Mar, 1996 ($16.95, trade paperback)

	NM- 9.2
nn-r/Uncanny X-Men #27, Uncanny X-men #35, Amazing Spider-Man #92, Marvel Team-Up Annual #1, Marvel Team-Up #150, & Spectacular Spider-Man #197-199	17.00

SPIDER-MAN & THE X-MEN
Marvel Comics: Feb, 2015 - No. 6, Jub, 2015 ($3.99)

	NM- 9.2
1-3: Spider-Man teaching at the Jean Grey School; Kalan-s/Failla-a. 2,3-Mojo app.	4.00

SPIDER-MAN & VENOM: DOUBLE TROUBLE (All-ages)
Marvel Comics: Jan, 2020 - No. 4, Apr, 2020 ($3.99, limited series)

	NM- 9.2
1-4-Spider-Man & Venom as roommates; Tamaki-s/Gurihiru-a; Ghost-Spider app.	4.00

SPIDER-MAN & WOLVERINE (See Spider-Man Legends Vol. 4 for TPB reprint)
Marvel Comics: Aug, 2003 - No. 4, Nov, 2003 ($2.99, limited series)

	NM- 9.2
1-4-Matthews/Mavlian-a	3.00

SPIDER-MAN AND X-FACTOR
Marvel Comics: May, 1994 - No. 3, July, 1994 ($1.95, limited series)

	NM- 9.2
1-3	4.00

SPIDER-MAN /BADROCK
Maximum Press: Mar, 1997 ($2.99, mini-series)

	NM- 9.2
1A, 1B(#2)-Jurgens-s	5.00

SPIDER-MAN/BLACK CAT: THE EVIL THAT MEN DO (Also see Marvel Must Haves)
Marvel Comics: Aug, 2002 - No. 6, Mar, 2006 ($2.99, limited series)

	NM- 9.2
1-6-Kevin Smith-s/Terry Dodson-c/a	3.00
HC (2006, $19.99, dust jacket) r/#1-6; script to #6 with sketches	20.00

SPIDER-MAN: BLUE
Marvel Comics: July, 2002 - No. 6, Apr, 2003 ($3.50, limited series)

	NM- 9.2
1-6: Jeph Loeb-s/Tim Sale-a/c; flashback to early MJ and Gwen Stacy	3.50
HC (2003, $21.99, with dust jacket) over-sized r/#1-6; intro. by John Romita	22.00
SC (2004, $14.99) r/#1-6; cover gallery	15.00

SPIDER-MAN: BRAND NEW DAY (See Amazing Spider-Man Vol. 2)

SPIDER-MAN: BREAKOUT (See New Avengers #1)
Marvel Comics: June, 2005 - No. 5, Oct, 2005 ($2.99, limited series)

	NM- 9.2
1-5-Bedard-s/Garcia-a. 1-U-Foes app. 5-New Avengers app.	3.00
TPB (2006, $13.99) r/#1-5	14.00

SPIDER-MAN: CHAPTER ONE
Marvel Comics: Dec, 1998 - No. 12, Oct, 1999 ($2.50, limited series)

	NM- 9.2
1-Retelling/updating of origin; John Byrne-s/c/a	4.00
1-($6.95) DF Edition w/variant-c by Jae Lee	7.00
2-11: 2-Two covers (one is swipe of ASM #1); Fantastic Four app. 9-Daredevil. 11-Giant-Man-c/app.	4.00
12-($3.50) Battles the Sandman	5.00
0-(5/99) Origins of Vulture, Lizard and Sandman	4.00

SPIDER-MAN CLASSICS

	GD	VG	FN	VF	VF/NM	NM-		GD	VG	FN	VF	VF/NM	NM-
	2.0	4.0	6.0	8.0	9.0	9.2		2.0	4.0	6.0	8.0	9.0	9.2

Marvel Comics: Apr, 1993 - No. 16, July, 1994 ($1.25)

1-14,16: 1-r/Amaz. Fantasy #15 & Strange Tales #115. 2-16-r/Amaz. Spider-Man #1-15.
  6-Austin-c(i) 4.00
15-($2.95)-Polybagged w/16 pg. insert & animation style print; r/Amazing Spider-Man #14
  (1st Green Goblin) 5.00

SPIDER-MAN COLLECTOR'S PREVIEW
Marvel Comics: Dec, 1994 ($1.50, 100 pgs., one-shot)

1-wraparound-c; no comics 6.00

SPIDER-MAN COMICS MAGAZINE
Marvel Comics Group: Jan, 1987 - No. 13, 1988 ($1.50, digest-size)

1-13-Reprints 1   3   4   6   8   10

SPIDER-MAN/DEADPOOL
Marvel Comics: Mar, 2016 - No. 50, Jul, 2019 ($3.99)

1-49: 1-Joe Kelly-s/Ed McGuinness-a; back-up reprint of Vision #1. 6-Aukerman-s.
  7-Art in 1968 Ditko-style by Koblish. 8-New black Spidey suit. 11-Penn Jillette-s.
  16-Dracula app. 17,18-McGuinness-a. 19,20-Slapstick app. 23-25,27,28-Bachalo-a.
  48,49-Gwenpool app. 4.00
50-($4.99) Last issue; Gwenpool app. 5.00
#1.MU (3/17, $4.99) Corin-s/Walker-a/Dave Johnson-c 5.00

SPIDER-MAN: DEATH AND DESTINY
Marvel Comics: Aug, 2000 - No. 3, Oct, 2000 ($2.99, limited series)

1-3-Aftermath of the death of Capt. Stacy 3.00

SPIDER-MAN/ DOCTOR OCTOPUS: OUT OF REACH
Marvel Comics: Jan, 2004 - No. 5, May, 2004 ($2.99, limited series)

1-5: 1-Keron Grant-a/Colin Mitchell-s 3.00
Marvel Age.... TPB (2004, $5.99, digest size) r/#1-5 .... 6.00

SPIDER-MAN/ DOCTOR OCTOPUS: YEAR ONE
Marvel Comics: Aug, 2004 - No. 5, Dec, 2004 ($2.99, limited series)

1-5-Kaare Andrews-a/Zeb Wells-s 3.00

SPIDER-MAN: ENTER THE SPIDER-VERSE
Marvel Comics: Jan, 2019 ($4.99, one-shot)

1-Web-Warriors and Sinister Six app.; Macchio-s/Flaviano-a; r/Spider-Man #1 (2016) 5.00

SPIDER-MAN FAIRY TALES
Marvel Comics: July, 2007 - No. 4, Oct, 2007 ($2.99, limited series)

1-4: 1-Cebulski-s/Tercio-a. 2-Henrichon-a. 3-Kobayashi-a. 4-Dragotta-p/Allred-i 3.00
TPB (2007, $10.99) r/#1-4 .... 11.00

SPIDER-MAN FAMILY (Also see Amazing Spider-Man Family)
Marvel Comics: Apr, 2007 - No. 9, Aug, 2008 ($4.99, anthology)

1-9-New tales and reprints. 1-Black costume, Sandman, Black Cat app. 4-Agents of Atlas
  app., Kirk-a; Puppet Master by Eliopoulos. 8-Iron Man app. 9-Hulk app. 5.00
... Featuring Spider-Clan 1 (1/07, $4.99) new Spider-Clan story; reprints w/Spider-Man
  2099 and Amazing Spider-Man #252 (black costume) 5.00
... Featuring Spider-Man's Amazing Friends 1 (10/06, $4.99) new story with Iceman
  and Firestar; Mini Marvels w/Giarrusso-a; reprints w/Spider-Man 2099 .... 5.00
... Back In Black ($7.99, digest) r/new content from #1-3 .... 8.00
....: Untold Team-Ups (2008, $9.99, digest) r/new content from #4-6 .... 10.00

SPIDER-MAN/FANTASTIC FOUR (Spider-Man and the Fantastic Four on cover)
Marvel Comics: Sept, 2010 - No. 4, Dec, 2010 ($3.99, limited series)

1-4-Gage-s/Alberti-a; Dr. Doom app. 4.00

SPIDER-MAN: FAR FROM HOME PRELUDE
Marvel Comics: May, 2019 - No. 2, Jun, 2019 ($3.99, limited series)

1,2-Adaptation of Spider-Man: Homecoming movie; Pilgrim-s/Maresca-a; photo-c 4.00

SPIDER-MAN: FEVER
Marvel Comics: Jun, 2010 - No. 3, Aug, 2010 ($3.99, limited series)

1-3-Brendan McCarthy-s/a; Dr. Strange app. 4.00

SPIDER-MAN: FRIENDS AND ENEMIES
Marvel Comics: Jan, 1995 - No. 4, Apr, 1995 ($1.95, limited series)

1-4-Darkhawk, Nova & Speedball app. 4.00

SPIDER-MAN: FUNERAL FOR AN OCTOPUS
Marvel Comics: Mar, 1995 - No. 3, May, 1995 ($1.50, limited series)

1-3 .... 4.00

SPIDER-MAN/ GEN 13
Marvel Comics: Nov, 1996 ($4.95, one-shot)

nn-Peter David-s/Stuart Immonen-a 5.00

SPIDER-MAN: GET KRAVEN
Marvel Comics: Aug, 2002 - No. 6, Jan, 2003 ($2.99/$2.25, limited series)

1-($2.99) McCrea-a/Quesada-c; back-up story w/Rio-a 4.00
2-6-($2.25) 2-Sub-Mariner app. 3.00

SPIDER-MAN: HOBGOBLIN LIVES
Marvel Comics: Jan, 1997 - No. 3, Mar, 1997 ($2.50, limited series)

1-3-Wraparound-c 4.00
TPB (1/98, $14.99) r/#1-3 plus timeline 15.00

SPIDER-MAN: HOUSE OF M (Also see House of M and related x-overs)
Marvel Comics: Aug, 2005 - No. 5, Dec, 2005 ($2.99, limited series)

1-5-Waid & Peyer-s/Larroca-a; rich and famous Peter Parker in mutant-ruled world 3.00
House of M: Spider-Man TPB (2006, $13.99) r/series 14.00

SPIDER-MAN/ HUMAN TORCH
Marvel Comics: Mar, 2005 - No. 5, July, 2005 ($2.99, limited series)

1-5-Ty Templeton-a/Dan Slott-s; team-ups from early days to the present 3.00
... I'm With Stupid (2006, $7.99, digest) r/#1-5 .... 8.00

SPIDER-MAN: INDIA
Marvel Comics: Jan, 2005 - No. 4, Apr, 2005 ($2.99, limited series)

1-4-Pavitr Prabhakar gains spider powers; Kang-a/Seetharaman-s 3.00

SPIDER-MAN: INDIA
Marvel Comics: Aug, 2023 - No. 5, Dec, 2023 ($3.99, limited series)

1-5: 1-Pavitr Prabhakar in the 616 universe; Peter and Miles app. 5-New costume 4.00

SPIDER-MAN: LEGEND OF THE SPIDER-CLAN (See Marvel Mangaverse for TPB)
Marvel Comics: Dec, 2002 - No. 5, Apr, 2003 ($2.25, limited series)

1-5-Marvel Mangaverse Spider-Man; Kaare Andrews-s/Skottie Young-c/a 3.00

SPIDER-MAN: LIFELINE
Marvel Comics: Apr, 2001 - No. 3, June, 2001 ($2.99, limited series)

1-3-Nicieza-s/Rude-c/a; The Lizard app. 3.00

SPIDER-MAN: LIFE STORY
Marvel Comics: May, 2019 - No. 6, Oct, 2019 ($4.99, limited series)

1-6-The 1962 Spider-Man ages in real time; Zdarsky-s/Bagley-a. 2-The '70s. 3-The '80s;
  Venom app. 5-Morlun app.; Civil War. 6-The 2010s; Venom/Kraven & Miles app. 5.00
Annual 1 (10/21, $4.99) Zdarsky-s/Bagley-a; spotlight on Jameson; Scorpion app. 5.00

SPIDER-MAN LOVES MARY JANE (Also see Mary Jane limited series)
Marvel Comics: Feb, 2006 - No. 20, Sept, 2007 ($2.99)

1-20-Mary Jane & Peter in high school; McKeever-s/Miyazawa-a/c. 5-Gwen Stacy app.
  16-18,20-Firestar app. 17-Felicia Hardy app. 3.00
... Vol. 1: Super Crush (2006, $7.99, digest) r/#1-5; cover concepts page 8.00
... Vol. 2: The New Girl (2006, $7.99, digest) r/#6-10; sketch pages 8.00
... Vol. 3: My Secret Life (2007, $7.99, digest) r/#11-15; sketch pages 8.00
... Vol. 4: Still Friends (2007, $7.99, digest) r/#16-20 .... 8.00
Hardcover Vol. 1 (2007, $24.99) oversized reprints of #1-5, Mary Jane #1-4 and Mary Jane:
  Homecoming #1-4; series proposals, sketch pages and covers; coloring process 25.00
Hardcover Vol. 2 (2008, $39.99) oversized reprints of #6-20, sketch & layout pages 40.00

SPIDER-MAN LOVES MARY JANE SEASON 2
Marvel Comics: Oct, 2008 - No. 5, Feb, 2009 ($2.99, limited series)

1-5-Terry Moore-s/c; Craig Rousseau-a 3.00
1-Variant-c by Alphona 8.00

SPIDER-MAN: MADE MEN
Marvel Comics: Aug, 1998 ($5.99, one-shot)

1-Spider-Man & Daredevil vs. Kingpin 6.00

SPIDER-MAN MAGAZINE
Marvel Comics: 1994 - No. 3, 1994 ($1.95, magazine)

1-3: 1-Contains 4 S-M promo cards & 4 X-Men Ultra Fleer cards; Spider-Man story by
  Romita, Sr.; X-Men story; puzzles & games. 2-Doc Octopus & X-Men stories 4.00

SPIDER-MAN: MAXIMUM CLONAGE
Marvel Comics: 1995 ($4.95)

Alpha #1-Acetate-c, Omega #1-Chromium-c. 6.00

SPIDER-MAN MAGAZINE
Marvel Comics: Oct, 1994 - No. 6, Mar, 1995 ($2.95, 100 pgs.)

1-6: 1-r/ASM #16,224,225, Marvel Team-Up #1 .... 5.00

SPIDER-MAN NOIR
Marvel Comics: Dec, 2008 - No. 4, May, 2009 ($3.99, limited series)

1-Pulp-style Spider-Man in 1933; DiGiandomenico-a; covers by Zircher & Calero

	7	14	21	44	82	120
2	2	4	6	8	10	12
3	2	4	6	8	8	10
4	2	4	6	9	12	15

...: Eyes Without a Face 1-4 (2/10 - No. 4, 5/10) DiGiandomenico-a; Zircher & Calero-c

| | 1 | 3 | 4 | 6 | 8 | 10 |

SPIDER-MAN NOIR
Marvel Comics: May, 2020 - No. 5, Dec, 2020 ($3.99, limited series)

1-5-Pulp-style Spider-Man in 1939; Stohl-s/Ferreyra-a 5.00

SPIDER-MAN: POWER OF TERROR
Marvel Comics: Jan, 1995 - No. 4, Apr, 1995 ($1.95, limited series)

1-4-Silvermane & Deathlok app. 4.00

SPIDER-MAN/PUNISHER: FAMILY PLOT
Marvel Comics: Feb, 1996 - No. 2, Mar, 1996 ($2.95, limited series)

1,2 .... 4.00

SPIDER-MAN: QUALITY OF LIFE
Marvel Comics: Jul, 2002 - No. 4, Oct, 2002 ($2.99, limited series)

1-4-All CGI art by Scott Sava; Rucka-s; Lizard app. 3.00
TPB (2002, $12.99) r/#1-4; a "Making of..." section detailing the CGI process 13.00

SPIDER-MAN: REDEMPTION
Marvel Comics: Sept, 1996 - No. 4, Dec, 1996 ($1.50, limited series)

1-4: DeMatteis scripts; Zeck-a 4.00

SPIDER-MAN/ RED SONJA
Marvel Comics: Oct, 2007 - No. 5, Feb, 2008 ($2.99, limited series)

1-5-Rubi-a/Oeming-s/Turner-c; Venom & Kulan Gath app. 3.00
HC (2008, $19.99, dustjacket) r/#1-5 and Marvel Team-Up #79; sketch pages 20.00

SPIDER-MAN: REIGN
Marvel Comics: Feb, 2007 - No. 4, May, 2007 ($3.99, limited series)

1-Kaare Andrews-s/a; red costume on cover 4.00
1-Variant cover with black costume 10.00
2-4 .... 4.00
HC (2007, $19.99, dustjacket) r/#1-4; sketch pages and cover variant gallery 20.00
HC 2nd printing (2007, $19.99, dustjacket) with variant black cover 20.00
SC (2018, $14.99) r/#1-4; sketch pages and cover variant gallery 15.00

SPIDER-MAN: REVENGE OF THE GREEN GOBLIN
Marvel Comics: Oct, 2000 - No. 3, Dec, 2000 ($2.99, limited series)

1-3-Frenz & Olliffe-a; continues in AS-M #25 & PP:S-M #25 .... 3.00

SPIDER-MAN SAGA
Marvel Comics: Nov, 1991 - No. 4, Feb, 1992 ($2.95, limited series)

Spider-Man Family #8 © MAR

Spider-Man Noir #1 © MAR

Spider-Man 2099 #21 © MAR

	GD	VG	FN	VF	VF/NM	NM-			GD	VG	FN	VF	VF/NM	NM-
	2.0	4.0	6.0	8.0	9.0	9.2			2.0	4.0	6.0	8.0	9.0	9.2

1-4: Gives history of Spider-Man: text & illustrations — 4.00

SPIDER-MAN 1602
Marvel Comics: Dec, 2009 - No. 5, Apr, 2010 ($3.99, limited series)
1-5- Peter Parquagh from Marvel 1602; Parker-s/Rosanas-a — 4.00

SPIDER-MAN: SPIDER'S SHADOW (See Spider-Man: The Spider's Shadow)

SPIDER-MAN: SWEET CHARITY
Marvel Comics: Aug, 2002 ($4.95, one-shot)
1-The Scorpion-c/app.; Campbell-c/Zimmerman-s/Robertson-a — 5.00

SPIDER-MAN'S TANGLED WEB (Titled "Tangled Web" in indicia for #1-4)
Marvel Comics: Jun, 2001 - No. 22, Mar, 2003 ($2.99)
1-3: "The Thousand" on-c; Ennis-s/McCrea-a/Fabry-c — 4.00
4-"Severance Package" on-c; Rucka-s/Risso-a; Kingpin-c/app. — 5.00
5,6-Flowers for Rhino; Milligan-s/Fegredo-a — 3.00
7-10,12,15-20,22: 7-9-Gentlemen's Agreement; Bruce Jones-s/Lee Weeks-a. 10-Andrews-s/a.
12-Fegredo-a. 15-Paul Pope-s/a. 18-Ted McKeever-s/a. 19-Mahfood-a. 20-Haspiel-a — 3.00
11,13,21-($3.50) 11-Darwyn Cooke-s/a. 13-Phillips-a. 21-Christmas-s by Cooke & Bone — 4.00
14-Azzarello & Scott Levy (WWE's Raven)-s about Crusher Hogan — 4.00
TPB (10/01, $15.95) r/#1-6 — 16.00
Volume 2 TPB (4/02, $14.95) r/#7-11 — 15.00
Volume 3 TPB (2002, $15.99) r/#12-17; Jason Pearson-c — 16.00
Volume 4 TPB (2003, $15.99) r/#18-22; Frank Cho-c — 16.00

SPIDER-MAN TEAM-UP
Marvel Comics: Dec, 1995 - No. 7, June, 1996 ($2.95)
1-7: 1-w/ X-Men. 2-w/Silver Surfer. 3-w/Fantastic Four. 4-w/Avengers.
5-Gambit & Howard the Duck-c/app. 7-Thunderbolts-c/app. — 4.00
... Special 1 (5/05, $2.99) Fantastic Four app.; Todd Dezago-s/Shane Davis-a — 4.00

SPIDER-MAN: THE ARACHNIS PROJECT
Marvel Comics: Aug, 1994 - No. 6, Jan, 1995 ($1.75, limited series)
1-6-Venom, Styx, Stone & Jury app. — 4.00

SPIDER-MAN: THE CLONE JOURNAL
Marvel Comics: Mar, 1995 ($2.95, one-shot)
1 — 4.00

SPIDER-MAN: THE CLONE SAGA
Marvel Comics: Nov, 2009 - No. 6, Apr, 2010 ($3.99, limited series)
1-6-Retelling of the saga with different ending; DeFalco & Mackie-s/Nauck-a — 4.00

SPIDER-MAN: THE FINAL ADVENTURE
Marvel Comics: Nov, 1995 - No. 4, Feb, 1996 ($2.95, limited series)
1-4: 1-Nicieza scripts; foil-c — 4.00

SPIDER-MAN: THE JACKAL FILES
Marvel Comics: Aug, 1995 ($1.95, one-shot)
1 — 4.00

SPIDER-MAN: THE LOST HUNT
Marvel Comics: Jan, 2023 - No. 5, May, 2023 ($4.99/$3.99)
1-($4.99) DeMatteis-s/Messias-a — 5.00
2-5-($3.99) 4-Origin of Gregor the Hunter — 4.00

SPIDER-MAN: THE LOST YEARS
Marvel Comics: Aug, 1995-No. 3, Oct, 1995; No. 0, 1996 ($2.95/$3.95,lim. series)
0-(1/96, $3.95)-Reprints. — 5.00
1-3-DeMatteis scripts, Romita, Jr.-c/a — 4.00
NOTE: Romita c-0i. Romita, Jr. a-0r, 1-3p. c-0-3p. Sharp a-0r.

SPIDER-MAN: THE MANGA
Marvel Comics: Dec, 1997 - No. 31, June, 1999 ($3.99/$2.99, B&W, bi-weekly)
1-($3.99)-English translation of Japanese Spider-Man — 5.00
2-31-($2.99) — 4.00

SPIDER-MAN: THE MUTANT AGENDA
Marvel Comics: No. 0, Feb, 1994; No. 1, Mar, 1994 - No. 3, May, 1994 ($1.75, limited series)
0-(2/94, $1.25, 52 pgs.)-Crosses over w/newspaper strip; has empty pages to paste
in newspaper strips; gives origin of Spidey — 5.00
1-3: Beast & Hobgoblin app. 1-X-Men app. — 4.00

SPIDER-MAN: THE MYSTERIO MANIFESTO (Listed as "Spider-Man and Mysterio" in indicia)
Marvel Comics: Jan, 2001 - No. 3, Mar, 2001 ($2.99, limited series)
1-3-Daredevil-c/app.; Weeks & McLeod-a — 3.00

SPIDER-MAN: THE PARKER YEARS
Marvel Comics: Nov, 1995 ($2.50, one-shot)

1 — 4.00

SPIDER-MAN: THE SPIDER'S SHADOW
Marvel Comics: Jun, 2021 - No. 5, Oct, 2021 ($4.99/$3.99, limited series)
1-($4.99) What If..Spider-Man kept the Venom suit; Zdarsky-s/Ferry-a — 5.00
2-5-($3.99) 2-Sinister Six & Eddie Brock app. 4,5-Avengers & FF app. — 4.00

SPIDER-MAN 2: THE MOVIE
Marvel Comics: Aug, 2004 ($3.50/$12.99, one-shot)
1-($3.50) Movie adaptation; Johnson, Lim & Olliffe-a — 4.00
TPB-($12.99) Movie adaptation; r/Amazing Spider-Man #50, Ultimate Spider-Man #14,15 — 13.00

SPIDER-MAN 2099 (See Amazing Spider-Man #365)
Marvel Comics: Nov, 1992 - No. 46, Aug, 1996 ($1.25/$1.50/$1.95)

											2.0	4.0	6.0	8.0	9.0	9.2

1-(stiff-c)-Red foil stamped-c; begins origin of Miguel O'Hara (Spider-Man 2099);
Leonardi/Williamson-c/a begins — 1 3 4 6 8 — 10
1-2nd printing, 2-12,14-24,26-34,39,40: 2-Origin continued, ends #3. 4-Doom 2099 app.
19-Bound-in trading cards. — 4.00
13-Extra 16 pg. insert on Midnight Sons — 5.00
25-($2.25, 52 pgs.)-Newsstand edition — 5.00
25-($2.95, 52 pgs.)-Deluxe edition w/embossed foil-c — 5.00
35-38-Venom app. 35-Variant-c. 36-Two-c; Jae Lee-a. 37,38-Two-c — 5.00
41-46: 46-The Vulture app; Mike McKone-a(p) — 4.00
Annual 1 (1994, $2.95, 68 pgs.) — 5.00
Special 1 (1995, $3.95) — 5.00
NOTE: Chaykin c-37. Ron Lim a(p)-18; c(p)-13, 16, 18. Kelley Jones c/a-9. Leonardi/Williamson a-1-8, 10-13, 15-17, 19, 20, 22-25; c-1-13, 15, 17-19, 20, 22-25, 35.

SPIDER-MAN 2099
Marvel Comics: Sept, 2014 - No. 12, July, 2015 ($3.99)
1-12: 1-Miguel O'Hara in 2014; Peter David-s/Will Sliney-a. 5-8-Spider-Verse tie-in — 4.00

SPIDER-MAN 2099
Marvel Comics: Dec, 2015 - No. 25, Sept, 2017 ($3.99)
1-24: 1-Miguel O'Hara still in the present; David-s/Sliney-a. 2-New costume. 13-16-Civil
War II tie-ins. 14-16-Power Pack app. 17-19-Elektra app. — 4.00
25-($4.99) David-s/Sliney-a — 5.00

SPIDER-MAN 2099 (Tie-in to 2099 Alpha & 2099 Omega crossover)
Marvel Comics: Feb, 2020 ($4.99)
1-Spencer-s/Carlos-a — 5.00

SPIDER-MAN 2099: DARK GENESIS
Marvel Comics: Jul, 2023 - No. 5, Jul, 2023 ($3.99, weekly limited series)
1-5-Orlando-s/Mason-a; Carnage app. 2-Intro Blade 2099 — 4.00

SPIDER-MAN 2099: EXODUS
Marvel Comics: Jul, 2022 - Oct, 2022 ($4.99/$3.99, limited series)
Alpha 1-($4.99) Ghost Rider 2099 app. — 5.00
1-5-($3.99) 1-Winter Soldier 2099 app. 2-Loki 2099 app. 4-Black Widow 2099 app. — 4.00
Omega 1-($4.99) Conclusion to series; Avengers app. — 5.00

SPIDER-MAN 2099 MEETS SPIDER-MAN
Marvel Comics: 1995 ($5.95, one-shot)
nn-Peter David script; Leonardi/Williamson-c/a. — 6.00

SPIDER-MAN UNIVERSE
Marvel Comics: Mar, 2000 - No. 7, Oct, 2000 ($4.95/$3.99, reprints)
1-5-Reprints recent issues from the various Spider-Man titles — 5.00
6,7-($3.99) — 4.00

SPIDER-MAN UNLIMITED
Marvel Comics: May, 1993 - No. 22, Nov, 1998 ($3.95, #1-12 were quarterly, 68 pgs.)
1-Begin Maximum Carnage storyline, ends; Carnage-c/story —
2 4 6 9 12 — 15
2-12: 2-Venom & Carnage-c/story; Lim-c/a(p) in #2-6. 10-Vulture app. — 4.00
13-22: 13-Begin $2.99-c; Scorpion-c/app. 15-Daniel-c; Puma-c/app. 19-Lizard-c/app.
20-Hannibal King and Lilith app. 21,22-Deodato-a — 4.00

SPIDER-MAN UNLIMITED (Based on the TV animated series)
Marvel Comics: Dec, 1999 - No. 5, Apr, 2000 ($2.99/$1.99)
1-($2.99) Venom and Carnage app. — 5.00
2-5: 2-($1.99) Green Goblin app. — 4.00

SPIDER-MAN UNLIMITED (3rd series)
Marvel Comics: Mar, 2004 - No. 15, July, 2006 ($2.99)
1-16: 1-Short stories by various incl. Miyazawa & Chen-a. 2-Mays-a. 6-Allred-c. 14-Finch-c/a;
Black Cat app. — 3.00

SPIDER-MAN UNMASKED

	GD 2.0	VG 4.0	FN 6.0	VF 8.0	VF/NM 9.0	NM- 9.2

Marvel Comics: Nov, 1996 ($5.95, one-shot)

nn-Art w/text ... 6.00

SPIDER-MAN: VENOM AGENDA
Marvel Comics: Jan, 1998 ($2.99, one-shot)

1-Hama-s/Lyle-c/a ... 5.00

SPIDER-MAN VS. DRACULA
Marvel Comics: Jan, 1994 ($1.75, 52 pgs., one-shot)

1-r/Giant-Size Spider-Man #1 plus new Matt Fox-a ... 4.00

SPIDER-MAN VS. WOLVERINE
Marvel Comics Group: Feb, 1987; V2#1, 1990 (68 pgs.)

1-Williamson-c/a(i); intro Charlemagne; death of Ned Leeds (old Hobgoblin)

| | | 3 | 6 | 9 | 21 | 33 | 45 |
V2#1 (1990, $4.95)-Reprints #1 (2/87) ... 6.00

SPIDER-MAN: WEB OF DOOM
Marvel Comics: Aug, 1994 - No. 3, Oct, 1994 ($1.75, limited series)

1-3 ... 4.00

SPIDER-MAN: WITH GREAT POWER...
Marvel Comics: Mar, 2008 - No. 5, Sept, 2008 ($3.99, limited series)

1-5-Origin and early days re-told; Lapham-s/Harris-a/c ... 4.00

SPIDER-MAN: WITH GREAT POWER COMES GREAT RESPONSIBILITY
Marvel Comics: Jun, 2011 - No. 7, Dec, 2011 ($3.99, limited series)

1-7: Reprints of noteworthy Spider-Man stories. 1-R/Ultimate Spider-Man #33,97, and Ultimate Comics Spider-Man #1. 4-R/ Amazing Spider-Man #1,11,20 ... 4.00

SPIDER-MAN: YEAR IN REVIEW
Marvel Comics: Feb, 2000 ($2.99)

1-Text recaps of 1999 issues ... 3.00

SPIDER-MEN
Marvel Comics: Aug, 2012 - No. 5, Nov, 2012 ($3.99, limited series)

1-5-Peter Parker goes to Ultimate Universe; teams with Miles Morales; Pichelli-a ... 4.00

SPIDER-MEN II
Marvel Comics: Sept, 2017 - No. 5, Feb, 2018 ($3.99, limited series)

1-5-Peter Parker teams with Miles Morales; Bendis-s/Pichelli-a ... 4.00

SPIDER-PUNK (Hobie Brown)
Marvel Comics: Jun, 2022 - No. 5, Nov, 2022 ($3.99, limited series)

1-5-Cody Ziglar-s/Justin Mason-a ... 4.00

SPIDER-PUNK: ARMS RACE (Hobie Brown)
Marvel Comics: Apr, 2024 - Present ($4.99, limited series)

1-Cody Ziglar-s/Justin Mason-a ... 5.00

SPIDER REIGN OF THE VAMPIRE KING, THE (Also see The Spider)
Eclipse Books: 1992 - No. 3, 1992 ($4.95, limited series, coated stock, 52 pgs.)

Book One - Three: Truman scripts & painted-c ... 5.00

SPIDER'S WEB, THE (See G-8 and His Battle Aces)

SPIDER-VARK
Aardvark-Vanaheim: Aug, 2020 ($8.00, B&W, one-shot)

1-Cerebus figures w/Doré artwork of Hell; cover swipe of Amazing Spider-Man Annual #21 ... 8.00

SPIDER-VERSE (See Amazing Spider-Man 2014 series #7-14)
Marvel Comics: Jan, 2015 - No. 2, Mar, 2015 ($4.99, limited series)

1,2-Short stories of alternate Spider-Men; s/a by various. 2-Anarchic Spider-Man ... 5.00

SPIDER-VERSE (Secret Wars tie-in)
Marvel Comics: Jul, 2015 - No. 5, Nov, 2015 ($4.99/$3.99, limited series)

1-($4.99) Costa-s/Araujo-a; Spider-Gwen, Spider-Ham & Norman Osborn app. ... 5.00
2-5-($3.99) Alternate Spider-Men vs. Sinister Six ... 4.00

SPIDER-VERSE (Secret Wars tie-in)
Marvel Comics: Dec, 2019 - No. 6, May, 2020 ($3.99, limited series)

1-6: Miles teams up with Spider-heroes. 4-Killam-s/Gedeon-a. 5-Spider-Man Noir app. ... 4.00

SPIDER-VERSE TEAM-UP (See Amazing Spider-Man 2014 series #7-14)
Marvel Comics: Jan, 2015 - No. 3, Mar, 2015 ($3.99, limited series)

1-3-Short stories of alternate Spider-Men team-ups; s/a by various. 2-Spider-Gwen, Miles Morales and '67 animated Spider-Man app. ... 4.00

SPIDER-WHORE
Aardvark-Vanaheim: Nov, 2020 ($4.00, B&W, one-shot)

1-Cerebus figures with Gustave Doré artwork of Hell; cover swipe of What If #105

| | | 1 | 3 | 4 | 6 | 8 | 10 |

SPIDER-WOMAN (Also see The Avengers #240, Marvel Spotlight #32, Marvel Super Heroes Secret Wars #7, Marvel Two-In-One #29 and New Avengers)
Marvel Comics Group: April, 1978 - No. 50, June, 1983 (New logo #47 on)

1-New complete origin & mask added | 5 | 10 | 15 | 34 | 60 | 85 |
2-5,7-18: 2-Excalibur app. 3,11,12-Brother Grimm app. 13,15-The Shroud-c/app. 16-Sienkiewicz-a | 1 | 2 | 3 | 5 | 6 | 8 |
6,19,20,28,29,32: 6-Morgan LeFay app. 6,19,32-Werewolf by Night-c/s. 20,28,29-Spider-Man app. 32-Universal Monsters photo/Miller-c | 1 | 3 | 4 | 6 | 8 | 10 |
1-27,30,31,33-36 | 1 | 2 | 3 | 5 | 6 | 8 |
37-1st app. Siryn of X-Force; X-Men x-over; origin retold | 4 | 8 | 12 | 25 | 40 | 55 |
38-X-Men x-over | 2 | 4 | 6 | 11 | 16 | 20 |
39-49: 46-Kingpin app. 49-Tigra-c/story | | | | | | 6.00 |
50-(52 pgs.)-Death of Spider-Woman; photo-c | 2 | 4 | 6 | 11 | 16 | 20 |
NOTE: Austin a-37i. Byrne a-26p. Infantino a-1-19. Layton c-19. Miller c-32p. | | | | | | 6.00 |
1 Facsimile Edition (11/19, $3.99) Reprints #1 with original 1978 ads ... 6.00

SPIDER-WOMAN
Marvel Comics: Nov, 1993 - No. 4, Feb, 1994 ($1.75, mini-series)

1-#1-Origin; U.S. Agent app. | 2 | 4 | 6 | 8 | 10 | 12 |
2-#2-4: 2-Origin continues; U.S. Agent app. | | | | | | 4.00 |

SPIDER-WOMAN
Marvel Comics: July, 1999 - No. 18, Dec, 2000 ($2.99/$1.99/$2.25)

1-($2.99) Byrne-s/Sears-a | 1 | 3 | 4 | 6 | 8 | 10 |
2-18: 2-11-($1.99). 2-Two covers. 12-Begin $2.25-c. 15-Capt. America-c/app. ... 4.00

SPIDER-WOMAN (Printed version of the motion comic for computers)
Marvel Comics: Nov, 2009 - No. 7, May, 2010 $3.99/$2.99)

1-($3.99) Bendis-s/Maleev-a; covers by Maleev & Alex Ross; Jessica joins S.W.O.R.D.
| | | 1 | 3 | 4 | 6 | 8 | 10 |
2-6-($2.99) 2-4-Madame Hydra app. 6-Thunderbolts app. ... 3.00
7-($3.99) New Avengers app. ... 4.00

SPIDER-WOMAN (Also see Spider-Verse event in Amazing Spider-Man 2014 series #7-14)
Marvel Comics: Jan, 2015 - No. 10, Oct, 2015 ($3.99)

1-4-Spider-Verse tie-ins; Silk app.; Hopeless-s/Land-a/c. 4-Avengers app. ... 4.00
5-10: 5-New costume; Javier Rodriguez-a/c. 10-Black Widow app. ... 4.00

SPIDER-WOMAN
Marvel Comics: Jan, 2016 - No. 17, May, 2017 ($3.99)

1-17: 1-5-Hopeless-s/Javier Rodriguez-a. 4-Jessica's baby is born. 6,7-"Spider-Women x-over; Spider-Gwen & Silk app.; Joelle Jones-a. 9-11-Civil War II tie-in. 13-16-Hobgoblin app. ... 4.00

SPIDER-WOMAN
Marvel Comics: May, 2020 - No. 21, May, 2022 ($4.99/$3.99)

1-($4.99) Karla Pacheco-s/Pere Pérez-a; new costume debuts; Siqueira-a ... 5.00
2-4,6-21-($3.99) 2-Night Nurse & Rhino app. 6-Capt. Marvel app. 7,8-King in Black tie-in. 11-Back to classic costume. 18,19-Devil's Reign ... 4.00
5-($4.99) Legacy issue #100; back-up story with Captain Marvel app. ... 5.00

SPIDER-WOMAN (Tie-in to the Gang War x-over in Amazing Spider-Man and Spider-titles)
Marvel Comics: Jan, 2024 - Present ($4.99/$3.99)

1-($4.99) Foxe-s/Borelli-a; Madame Web, Captain Marvel & Armadillo app. ... 5.00
2-4-($3.99) ... 4.00

SPIDER-WOMAN: ORIGIN (Also see New Avengers)
Marvel Comics: Feb, 2006 - No. 5, June, 2006 ($2.99, limited series)

1-5-Bendis & Reed-s/Jonathan & Joshua Luna-a/c ... 3.00
1-Variant cover by Olivier Coipel ... 3.00
HC (2006, $19.99) r/series ... 20.00
SC (2007, $13.99) r/series ... 14.00

SPIDER-WOMEN (Crossover with Silk, Spider-Gwen and Spider-Woman)
Marvel Comics: Alpha, Jun, 2016 - Omega, Aug, 2016 ($4.99, limited series)

... Alpha 1 - Thompson-s/Del Rey-a/Putri-c; part 1 of x-over; intro. Earth-65 Cindy Moon ... 5.00
... Omega 1 - Hopeless-s/Leon-a/Putri-c; part 8 conclusion of x-over ... 5.00

SPIDEY (Spider-Man)
Marvel Comics: Feb, 2016 - No. 12, Jan, 2017 ($3.99)

1-12-High school-era Spider-Man. 1-3-Bradshaw-a. 1-Doc Ock app. 7-Black Panther app. 4.00
... No. 1 Halloween Comic Fest 2016 (12/16, giveaway) r/#1 ... 3.00

SPIDEY SUPER STORIES (Spider-Man) (Also see Fireside Books)
Marvel/Children's TV Workshop: Oct, 1974 - No. 57, Mar, 1982 (35¢, no ads)

1-Origin (stories simplified for younger readers) | 7 | 14 | 21 | 49 | 92 | 135 |
2-Kraven | 3 | 6 | 9 | 21 | 33 | 45 |
3-10,15: 6-Iceman. 15-Storm-c/sty | 3 | 6 | 9 | 14 | 20 | 26 |
11-14,16-20: 19,20-Kirby-c | 3 | 6 | 9 | 14 | 19 | 24 |
21-30: 22-Early Ms. Marvel app. | 2 | 4 | 6 | 13 | 18 | 22 |
31-53: 31-Moondragon-c/app.; Dr. Doom app. 33-Hulk. 34-Sub-Mariner. 38-F.F. 39-Thanos-c/story. 44-Vision. 45-Silver Surfer & Dr. Doom app. | 2 | 4 | 6 | 11 | 16 | 20 |
54-57: 56-Battles Jack O'Lantern-c/sty (exactly one year after 1st app. in Machine Man #19) | | | | | | |
| | 3 | 6 | 9 | 14 | 20 | 26 |

SPIKE AND TYKE (See M.G.M.'s...)

SPIKE... (Also see Buffy the Vampire Slayer and related titles)
IDW Publ.: Aug, 2005; Jan, 2006; Apr, 2006 ($7.49, squarebound, one-shots)

...: Lost & Found (4/06, $7.49) Scott Tipton-s/Fernando Goni-a ... 8.00
...: Old Times (8/05, $7.49) Peter David-s/Fernando Goni-a; Cecily/Halfrek app. ... 8.00
...: Old Wounds (1/06, $7.49) Tipton-s/Goni-a; flashback to Black Dahlia murder case ... 8.00
TPB (7/06, $19.99) r/one-shots ... 20.00

SPIKE (Buffy the Vampire Slayer)
IDW Publ.: Oct, 2010 - No. 8, May, 2011 ($3.99, limited series)

1-8-Lynch-s; multiple covers on each. 1,2-Urru-a. 5-7-Willow app. ... 4.00
... 100 Page Spectacular (6/11, $7.99) reprints of four IDW Spike stories; Frison-c ... 8.00

SPIKE (A Dark Place) (From Buffy the Vampire Slayer)
Dark Horse Comics: Aug, 2012 - No. 5, Dec, 2012 ($2.99, limited series)

1-5-Paul Lee-a; 2 covers by Frison & Morris on each ... 3.00

SPIKE: AFTER THE FALL (Also see Angel: After the Fall) (Follows the last Angel TV episode)
IDW Publ.: July, 2008 - No. 4, Oct, 2008 ($3.99, limited series)

1-4-Lynch-s/Urru-a; multiple covers on each ... 4.00

SPIKE: ASYLUM (Buffy the Vampire Slayer)
IDW Publ.: Sept, 2006 - No. 5, Jan, 2007 ($3.99, limited series)

1-5-Lynch-s/Urru-a; multiple covers on each ... 4.00

SPIKE: SHADOW PUPPETS (Buffy the Vampire Slayer)
IDW Publ.: June, 2007 - No. 4, Sept, 2007 ($3.99, limited series)

1-4-Lynch-s/Urru-a; multiple covers on each ... 4.00

SPIKE: THE DEVIL YOU KNOW (Buffy the Vampire Slayer)
IDW Publ.: Jun, 2010 - No. 4, Sept, 2010 ($3.99, limited series)

1-4-Bill Williams-s/Chris Cross-a/Urru-c ... 4.00

SPIKE VS. DRACULA (Buffy the Vampire Slayer)
IDW Publ.: Feb, 2006 - No. 5, Mar, 2006 ($3.99, limited series)

1-5: 1-Peter David-s/Joe Corroney-a; Dru and Bela Lugosi app. ... 4.00

SPIN & MARTY (TV) (Walt Disney's)(See Walt Disney Showcase #32)
Dell Publishing Co. (Mickey Mouse Club): No. 714, June, 1956 - No. 1082, Mar-May, 1960 (All photo-c)

Spider-Man: With Great Power #1 © MAR

Spider-Woman (2020 series) #11 © MAR

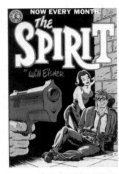

The Spirit (1983 series) #12 © Will Eisner

	GD	VG	FN	VF	VF/NM	NM-		GD	VG	FN	VF	VF/NM	NM-
	2.0	4.0	6.0	8.0	9.0	9.2		2.0	4.0	6.0	8.0	9.0	9.2

	GD 2.0	VG 4.0	FN 6.0	VF 8.0	VF/NM 9.0	NM- 9.2
Four Color 714 (#1)	12	24	36	79	170	260
Four Color 767,808 (#2,3)	9	18	27	61	123	185
Four Color 826 (#4)-Annette Funicello photo-c	18	36	54	126	281	435
5(3-5/58) - 9(6-8/59)	7	14	21	44	82	120
Four Color 1026,1082	7	14	21	44	82	120

SPIN ANGELS
Marvel Comics (Soleil): 2009 - No. 4, 2009 ($5.99)

1-4-English version of French comics; Jean-Luc Sala-s/Pierre-Mony Chan-a						6.00

SPINE-TINGLING SPIDER-MAN
Marvel Comics: No. 0, Nov, 2023 - No. 4, Mar, 2024 ($9.99/$4.99/$3.99)

	GD 2.0	VG 4.0	FN 6.0	VF 8.0		NM- 9.2
0-(11/23, $9.99) Saladin Ahmed-s/Juan Ferreyra-a	1	3	4	6	8	10
1-(12/23, $4.99)						5.00
2-4-($3.99) 3,4-Mysterio app.						4.00

SPINE-TINGLING TALES (Doctor Spektor Presents...)
Gold Key: May, 1975 - No. 4, Jan, 1976 (All 25¢ issues)

	GD 2.0	VG 4.0	FN 6.0	VF 8.0	VF/NM 9.0	NM- 9.2
1-1st Tragg-r/Mystery Comics Digest #3	3	6	9	14	19	24
2-4: 2-Origin Ra-Ka-Tep-r/Mystery Comics Digest #1; Dr. Spektor #12. 3-All Durak-r issue;						
4-Baron Tibor's 1st app.-r/Mystery Comics Digest #4; painted-c	1	2	3	5	7	9

SPINWORLD
Amaze Ink (Slave Labor Graphics): July, 1997 - No. 4, Jan, 1998 ($2.95/$3.95, B&W, mini-series)

1-3-Brent Anderson-a(p)						4.00
4-($3.95)						5.00

SPIRAL ZONE
DC Comics: Feb, 1988 - No. 4, May, 1988 ($1.00, mini-series)

1-4-Based on Tonka toys						4.00

SPIRIT, THE (Newspaper comics - see Promotional Comics section)

SPIRIT, THE (1st Series)(Also see Police Comics #11 and The Best of the Spirit TPB)
Quality Comics Group (Vital): 1944 - No. 22, Aug, 1950

	GD 2.0	VG 4.0	FN 6.0	VF 8.0	VF/NM 9.0	NM- 9.2
nn(#1)- "Wanted Dead or Alive"	168	336	504	1075	1838	2600
nn(#2)- "Crime Doesn't Pay"	61	122	183	390	670	950
nn(#3)- "Murder Runs Wild"	55	110	165	352	601	850
4,5: 4-Flatfoot Burns begins, ends #22. 5-Wertham app.	47	94	141	296	498	700
6-10	39	78	117	240	395	550
11-Crandall-c	39	78	117	240	395	550
12-17-Eisner-c. 19-Honeybun app.	53	106	159	334	567	800
18,19-Strip-r by Eisner; Eisner-c	77	154	231	493	847	1200
20,21-Eisner good girl covers; strip-r by Eisner	135	270	405	864	1482	2100
22-Used by N.Y. Legis. Comm; classic Eisner-c	919	1838	2757	6709	11,855	17,000
Super Reprint #11-r/Quality Spirit #19 by Eisner	3	6	9	19	30	40
Super Reprint #12-r/Spirit #17 by Fine; Sol Brodsky-c	3	6	9	19	30	40

SPIRIT, THE (2nd Series)
Fiction House Magazines: Spring, 1952 - No. 5, 1954

	GD 2.0	VG 4.0	FN 6.0	VF 8.0	VF/NM 9.0	NM- 9.2
1-Not Eisner	71	142	213	454	777	1100
2-Eisner-c/a(2)	63	126	189	403	689	975
3-Eisner/Grandenetti-c	65	130	195	416	708	1000
4-Eisner/Grandenetti-c; Eisner-a	68	136	204	435	743	1050
5-Eisner-c/a(4)	71	142	213	454	777	1100

SPIRIT, THE
Harvey Publications: Oct, 1966 - No. 2, Mar, 1967 (Giant Size, 25¢, 68 pgs.)

	GD 2.0	VG 4.0	FN 6.0	VF 8.0	VF/NM 9.0	NM- 9.2
1-Eisner-r plus 9 new pgs.(origin Denny Colt, Take 3, plus 2 filler pgs.)						
(#3 was advertised, but never published)	8	16	24	56	108	160
2-Eisner-r plus 9 new pgs.(origin of the Octopus)	7	14	21	44	82	120

SPIRIT, THE (Underground)
Kitchen Sink Enterprises (Krupp Comics): Jan, 1973 - No. 2, Sept, 1973 (Black & White)

	GD 2.0	VG 4.0	FN 6.0	VF 8.0	VF/NM 9.0	NM- 9.2
1-New Eisner-c & 4 pgs. new Eisner-a plus-r (titled Crime Convention)						
	4	8	12	23	37	50
2-New Eisner-c & 4 pgs. new Eisner-a plus-r (titled Meets P'Gell)						
	4	8	12	25	40	55

SPIRIT, THE (Magazine)
Warren Publ. Co./Krupp Comic Works No. 17 on: 4/74 - No. 16, 10/76; No. 17, Winter, 1977 - No. 41, 6/83 (B&W w/color) (#6-14,16 are squarebound)

	GD 2.0	VG 4.0	FN 6.0	VF 8.0	VF/NM 9.0	NM- 9.2
1-Eisner-r begin; 8 pg. color insert	6	12	18	41	76	110
2-5: 2-Powder Pouf-s; UFOs. 4-Silk Satin-s	4	8	12	27	44	60
6-9,11-15: 7-All Ebony issue. 8-Female Foes issue. 8,12-Sand Seref-s.						
9-P'Gell & Octopus-s. 12-X-Mas issue	4	8	12	25	40	55
10-Giant Summer Special ($1.50)-Origin	4	8	12	27	44	60

	GD 2.0	VG 4.0	FN 6.0	VF 8.0	VF/NM 9.0	NM- 9.2
16-Giant Summer Special ($1.50)-Olga Bustle-c/s	4	8	12	25	40	55
17,18(8/78): 17-Lady Luck-r	3	6	9	17	26	35
19-21-New Eisner-a. 20,21-Wood-r (#21-r/A DP on the Moon by Wood). 20-Outer Space-r						
	3	6	9	17	26	35
22-41: 22,23-Wood-r (#22-r/Mission the Moon by Wood). 28-r/last story (10/5/52).						
30-(7/81)-Special Spirit Jam issue w/Caniff, Corben, Bolland, Byrne, Miller, Kurtzman, Rogers, Sienkiewicz-a & 40 others. 36-Begin Spirit Section-r; r/1st story (6/2/40) in color; new Eisner-c/a(18 pgs.)($2.95). 37-r/2nd story in color plus 18 pgs. new Eisner-a.						
38-41: r/3rd - 6th stories in color. 41-Lady Luck Mr. Mystic in color						
	3	6	9	15	22	28
Special 1(1975)-All Eisner-a (mail only, 1500 printed, full color)						
	13	26	39	89	195	300

NOTE: Covers pencilled/inked by **Eisner** only #1-9,12-16; painted by Eisner & Ken Kelly #10 & 11; painted by Eisner #17-up; one color story reprinted in #1-10. Austin a-30i. Byrne a-30p. Miller a-30p.

SPIRIT, THE
Kitchen Sink Enterprises: Oct, 1983 - No. 87, Jan, 1992 ($2.00, Baxter paper)

1-60: 1-Origin-r/12/23/45 Spirit Section. 2-r/ 1/20/46-2/10/46. 3-r/2/17/46-3/10/46. 4-r/3/17/46-4/7/46. 11-Last color issue. 54-r/section 2/19/50						4.00
61-87: 85-87-Reprint the Outer Space Spirit stories by Wood. 86-r/A DP on the Moon by Wood from 1952						4.00

SPIRIT, THE (Also see Batman/The Spirit in Batman one-shots)
DC Comics: Feb, 2007 - No. 32, Oct, 2009 ($2.99)

1-32: 1-6,8-12-Darwyn Cooke-s/a/c. 3-P'Gell app. 3-Origin re-told. 7-Short stories by Baker, Bernet, Palmiotti, Simonson & Sprouse; Cooke-c. 13-Short stories by various						3.00
... Femme Fatales TPB (2008, $19.99) r/1940s stories focusing on the Spirit's female adversaries like Silk Satin, P'gell, Powder Pouf and Silken Floss; Michael Uslan intro.						20.00
... Special 1 (2008, $2.99) r/stories from '47, '49, '50 newspaper strips; the Octopus app.						3.00

SPIRIT, THE (First Wave)
DC Comics: Jun, 2010 - No. 17, Oct, 2011 ($3.99/$2.99)(B&W back-up stories by various)

1-10: 1-Schultz-s/Moritat-a; covers by Ladronn and Schultz; back-up by O'Neil & Sienkiewicz. 2-Back-up by Ellison & Baker. 7-Corben-a back-up. 8-Ploog-a back-up						4.00
11-17-($2.99) 11-16-Hine-s/Moritat-a; no back-up story. 17-B&W; Bolland, Russell-a						3.00
...: Angel Smerti TPB (2011, $17.99) r/#1-7						18.00

SPIRIT, (WILL EISNER'S THE...)
Dynamite Entertainment: 2015 - No. 12, 2016 ($3.99)

1-12: 1-Wagner-s/Schkade-a; multiple covers. 2-12-Powell-c						4.00

SPIRIT, (WILL EISNER'S THE...): CORPSE MAKERS (Volume 2)
Dynamite Entertainment: 2017 - No. 5, 2018 ($3.99)

1-5-Francesco Francavilla-s/a/c						4.00

SPIRIT JAM
Kitchen Sink Press: Aug, 1998 ($5.95, B&W, oversized, square-bound)

nn-Reprints Spirit (Magazine) #30 by Eisner & 50 others; and "Cerebus Vs. The Spirit" from Cerebus Jam #1						6.00

SPIRITMAN (Also see Three Comics)
No publisher listed: No date (1944) (10¢)(Triangle Sales Co. ad on back cover)

	GD 2.0	VG 4.0	FN 6.0	VF 8.0	VF/NM 9.0	NM- 9.2
1-Three 16pg. Spirit sections bound together, (1944, 10¢, 52 pgs.)						
	39	78	117	240	395	550
2-Two Spirit sections (3/26/44, 4/2/44) bound together; by Lou Fine						
	34	68	102	199	325	450

SPIRIT OF THE BORDER (See Zane Grey & Four Color #197)

SPIRIT OF THE TAO
Image Comics (Top Cow): Jun, 1998 - No. 15, May, 2000 ($2.50)

Preview						5.00
1-14: 1-D-Tron-s/Tan & D-Tron-a						4.00
15-($4.95)						5.00

SPIRIT, THE: THE NEW ADVENTURES
Kitchen Sink Press: 1997 - No. 8, Nov, 1998 ($3.50, anthology)

1-Moore-s/Gibbons-c/a						5.00
2-8: 2-Gaiman-s/Eisner-c. 3-Moore-s/Bolland-c/Moebius back-c. 4-Allred-s/a; Busiek-s/Anderson-a. 5-Chadwick-s/c/a(p); Nyberg-i. 6-S.Hampton & Mandrake-c						4.00
Will Eisner's The Spirit Archives Volume 27 (Dark Horse, 2009, $49.95) r/#1-8						50.00

SPIRIT: THE ORIGIN YEARS
Kitchen Sink Press: May, 1992 - No. 10, Dec, 1993 ($2.95, B&W)

1-10: 1-r/sections 6/2/40-6/23/40 (all 1940s)						4.00

SPIRITS OF GHOST RIDER: MOTHER OF DEMONS (Story continues in Ghost Rider #5)
Marvel Comics: Apr, 2020 ($3.99, one-shot)

1-Story of Lilith; Jack O'Lantern app.; Brisson-s/Boschi-a						4.00

	GD	VG	FN	VF	VF/NM	NM-
	2.0	4.0	6.0	8.0	9.0	9.2

SPIRITS OF VENGEANCE (Marvel Legacy)
Marvel Comics: Dec, 2017 - No. 5, Apr, 2018 ($3.99)

	GD	VG	FN	VF	VF/NM	NM-
1-5-Gischler-s/Baldeón-a; Blade, Ghost Rider, Daimon Hellstrom, Satana app.						4.00
.... Spirit Rider 1 (10/21, $4.99) Kushala and Johnny Blaze app.; Davidson-a						5.00

SPIRIT WORLD (Magazine)
Hampshire Distributors Ltd.: Fall, 1971 (B&W)

1-New Kirby-a; Neal Adams-c; poster inside	8	16	24	51	96	140
(1/2 price without poster)						

SPIRIT WORLD
DC Comics: Jul, 2023 - No. 6, Dec, 2023 ($3.99)

1-6-Alyssa Wong-s/Haining-a; John Constantine and Batgirl (Cassandra Cain) app.						4.00

SPITFIRE (Female undercover agent)
Malverne Herald (Elliot)(J. R. Mahon): No. 132, 1944 (Aug) - No. 133, 1945
Both have Classics Gift Box ads on back-c with checklist to #20

132-British spitfire WWII-c	53	106	159	334	567	800
133-Female agent/Nazi WWII-c	320	640	960	2240	3920	5600

SPITFIRE (WW2 speedster from MI:13)
Marvel Comics: Oct, 2010 ($3.99, one-shot)

1-Cornell-s/Casagrande-a; Blade app.						4.00

SPITFIRE AND THE TROUBLESHOOTERS
Marvel Comics: Oct, 1986 - No. 9, June, 1987 (Codename: Spitfire #10 on)

1-3,5-9						4.00
4-McFarlane-a						6.00

SPITFIRE COMICS (Also see Double Up) (Tied with Pocket Comics #1 for earliest Harvey)
Harvey Publications: Aug, 1941 - No. 2, Oct, 1941 (Pocket size; 100 pgs.)

1-Origin The Clown, The Fly-Man, The Spitfire & The Magician From Bagdad; British spitfire, Nazi bomber WWII-c	129	258	387	826	1413	2000
2-(Rare) Fly-Man-c	116	232	348	742	1271	1800

SPLITTING IMAGE
Image Comics: Mar, 1993 - No. 2, 1993 ($1.95)

1,2-Simpson-c/a; parody comic						4.00
...80-Page Giant 1 (4/17, $7.99) r/#1,2 plus Normalman - Megaton Man Special						8.00

SPONGEBOB COMICS (TV's Spongebob Squarepants)
United Plankton Pictures: 2011 - No. 85, 2018 ($2.99/$3.99)

1-51-Short stories by various. 1-Kochalka back-c. 3-Aquaman homage w/Fradon-c. 32-36-Showdown at the Shady Shoals; Mermaid Man app; Ordway-a						3.00
52-85-($3.99) 53,59,60,68-Chuck Dixon-s. 63,64-Mermaid Girl spotlight. 66-70-Ordway-a						4.00
Annual-Size Super-Giant Swimtacular 1 (2013, $4.99) art by Fradon, Ordway, Kochalka						5.00
Annual-Size Super-Giant Swimtacular 2 (2014, $4.99) Mermaid Man app.						5.00
Annual-Size Super-Giant Swimtacular 3 (2015, $4.99) art by Barta, Kochalka, Chabot						5.00
Annual-Size Super-Giant Swimtacular 4 (2016, $4.99) Neal Adams & others-a; Ordway-c						5.00
Annual-Size Super-Giant Swimtacular 2017 (2017, $4.99) Mayerik & others-a; Chabot-c						5.00
Annual-Size Super-Giant Swimtacular 2018 (2018, $4.99) Ordway & others-a; Gianni-c						5.00
SpongeBob Freestyle Funnies 1 (2014, Free Comic Book Day giveaway) Short stories						3.00
SpongeBob Freestyle Funnies 2014 (Free Comic Book Day giveaway) Short stories						3.00
SpongeBob Freestyle Funnies 2015 (Free Comic Book Day giveaway) Short stories						3.00
SpongeBob Freestyle Funnies 2016 (FCBD giveaway) Short stories						3.00
SpongeBob Freestyle Funnies 2017 (FCBD giveaway) Short stories; Kochalka-a						3.00
SpongeBob Freestyle Funnies 2018 (FCBD giveaway) Short stories; Mermaid Man app.						3.00

SPOOF
Marvel Comics Group: Oct, 1970; No. 2, Nov, 1972 - No. 5, May, 1973

1-Infinity-c; Dark Shadows-c & parody	4	8	12	25	40	55
2-5: 2-All in the Family. 3-Beatles, Osmonds, Jackson 5, David Cassidy, Nixon & Agnew-c. 5-Rod Serling, Woody Allen, Ted Kennedy-c	3	6	9	16	24	32

SPOOK (Formerly Shock Detective Cases)
Star Publications: No. 22, Jan, 1953 - No. 30, Oct, 1954

22-Sgt. Spook-r; acid in face story; hanging-c	300	600	900	1950	3375	4800
23,25,27: 25-Jungle Lil-r. 27-Two Sgt. Spook-r	84	168	252	538	919	1300
24-Used in SOTI, pgs. 182,183-r/Inside Crime #2; Transvestism story	110	22	330	704	1202	1700
26,28-30: 26-Disbrow-a. 28,29-Rulah app. 29-Jo-Jo app. 30-Disbrow-c/a(2); only Star-c	90	180	270	576	988	1400

NOTE: **L. B. Cole** covers-all issues except #30; a-28(1 pg.) Disbrow a-26(2), 28, 29(2), 30(2); No. 30 r/Blue Bolt Weird Tales #114.

SPOOK COMICS
Baily Publications/Star: 1946

1-Mr. Lucifer story	90	180	270	576	988	1400

SPOOK HOUSE
Albatross Funnybooks: 2016 - No. 5, 2017 ($3.99)

1-5-Horror anthology by Eric Powell and others; Powell-c						4.00
... 2019 Halloween Special (2019, $3.99) Short stories by Eric Powell & others; Powell-c						4.00

SPOOK HOUSE 2
Albatross Funnybooks: 2018 - No. 4, 2018 ($3.99)

1-4-Horror anthology by Eric Powell and others; Powell-c. 2-Lula app.						4.00

SPOOKY (The Tuff Little Ghost; see Casper The Friendly Ghost)
Harvey Publications: 11/55 - 139, 11/73; No. 140, 7/74 - No. 155, 3/77; No. 156, 12/77 - No. 158, 4/78; No. 159, 9/78; No. 160, 10/79; No. 161, 9/80

1-Nightmare begins (see Casper #19)	93	186	279	744	1672	2600
2	25	50	75	175	388	600
3-10(1956-57)	12	24	36	82	179	275
11-20(1957-58)	7	14	21	44	82	120
21-40(1958-59)	5	10	15	33	57	80
41-60	3	6	8	12	27	44	60
61-80,100	3	6	9	19	30	40
81-99	3	6	9	16	24	32
101-120	2	4	6	11	16	20
121-126,133-140	2	4	6	11	16	20
127-132: All 52 pg. Giants	2	4	6	11	16	20

141-161	1	2	3	5	7	9

SPOOKY
Harvey Comics: Nov, 1991 - No. 4, Sept, 1992 ($1.00/$1.25)

1						5.00
2-4: 3-Begin $1.25-c						4.00
...Digest 1-3 (10/92, 6/93, 10/93, $1.75, 100 pgs.)-Casper, Wendy, etc.						5.00

SPOOKY HAUNTED HOUSE
Harvey Publications: Oct, 1972 - No. 15, Feb, 1975

1	3	6	9	19	30	40
2-5	2	4	6	10	14	18
6-10	2	4	6	8	10	12
11-15	1	2	3	5	7	9

SPOOKY MYSTERIES
Your Guide Publ. Co.: No date (1946) (10¢)

1-Mr. Spooky, Super Snooper, Pinky, Girl Detective app.	37	74	111	222	361	500

SPOOKY SPOOKTOWN
Harvey Publ.: 9/61; No. 2, 9/62 - No. 52, 12/73; No. 53, 10/74 - No. 66, 12/76

1-Casper, Spooky; 68 pgs. begin	14	28	42	94	207	320
2	8	16	24	54	102	150
3-5	6	12	18	38	69	100
6-10	5	10	15	31	53	75
11-20	4	8	12	23	37	50
21-39: 39-Last 68 pg. issue	3	6	9	19	30	40
40-45: All 52 pgs.	2	4	6	11	16	20
46-66: 61-Hot Stuff/Spooky team-up story	1	2	3	5	7	9

SPORT COMICS (Becomes True Sport Picture Stories #5 on)
Street & Smith Publications: Oct, 1940 (No mo.) - No. 4, Nov, 1941

1-Life story of Lou Gehrig	74	148	222	470	810	1150
2	37	74	111	222	361	500
3,4: 4-Story of Notre Dame coach Frank Leahy	30	60	90	177	289	400

SPORT LIBRARY (See Charlton Sport Library)

SPORTS ACTION (Formerly Sport Stars)
Marvel/Atlas Comics (ACI No. 2,3/SAI No. 4-14): No. 2, Feb, 1950 - No. 14, Sept, 1952

2-Powell-a; George Gipp life story	43	86	129	269	455	640
1-(nd,no price, no publ., 52pgs, #1 on-c; has same-c as #2; blank inside-c (giveaway?)	22	44	66	132	216	300
3-Everett-a	24	48	72	142	234	325
4-11,14: Weiss-a	22	44	66	128	209	290
12,13: 12-Everett-c. 13-Krigstein-a	23	46	69	136	223	310

NOTE: Title may have changed after No. 3, to Crime Must Lose No. 4 on, due to publisher change. **Sol Brodsky** c-4-7, 13, 14. **Maneely** c-3, 8-11.

SPORT STARS
Parents' Magazine Institute (Sport Stars): Feb-Mar, 1946 - No. 4, Aug-Sept, 1946 (Half comic, half photo magazine)

1- "How Tarzan Got That Way" story of Johnny Weissmuller	40	80	120	243	402	560
2-Baseball greats	26	52	78	154	252	350
3,4	23	46	69	136	223	310

SPORT STARS (Becomes Sports Action #2 on)
Marvel Comics (ACI): Nov, 1949 (52 pgs.)

1-Knute Rockne; painted-c	47	94	141	296	498	700

SPORT THRILLS (Formerly Dick Cole; becomes Jungle Thrills #16)
Star Publications: No. 11, Nov, 1950 - No. 15, Nov, 1951

11-Dick Cole begins; Ted Williams & Ty Cobb life stories	37	74	111	222	361	500
12-Joe DiMaggio, Phil Rizzuto stories & photos on-c; L.B. Cole-c/a	28	56	84	165	270	375
13-15-All L. B. Cole-c. 13-Jackie Robinson, Pee Wee Reese stories & photo on-c.	28	56	84	165	270	375
14-Johnny Weissmuler life story	28	56	84	165	270	375
Accepted Reprint #11 (#15 on-c, nd); L.B. Cole-c	10	20	30	54	72	90
Accepted Reprint #12 (nd); L.B. Cole-c; Joe DiMaggio & Phil Rizzuto life stories-r/#12	10	20	30	54	72	90

SPOTLIGHT (TV) (newsstand sales only)
Marvel Comics Group: Sept, 1978 - No. 4, Mar, 1979 (Hanna-Barbera)

1-Huckleberry Hound, Yogi Bear; Shaw-a	9	18	27	43	59	75
2,4: 2-Quick Draw McGraw, Augie Doggie, Snooper & Blabber. 4-Magilla Gorilla, Snagglepuss	3	6	9	16	23	30
3-The Jetsons; Yakky Doodle	3	6	9	19	30	40

SPOTLIGHT COMICS
Country Press Inc.: Sept, 1940

nn-Ashcan, not distributed to newsstands, only for in house use. A NM copy sold in 2009 for $1015.

SPOTLIGHT COMICS (Becomes Red Seal Comics #14 on?)
Harry 'A' Chesler (Our Army, Inc.): Nov, 1944, No. 2, Jan, 1945 - No. 3, 1945

1-The Black Dwarf (cont'd in Red Seal?), The Veiled Avenger, & Barry Kuda begin; Tuska-c	155	310	465	992	1696	2400
2-Puppet Master-c	103	206	309	659	1130	1600
3-Injury to eye story (reprinted from Scoop #3)	100	200	300	635	1093	1550

SPOTTY THE PUP (Becomes Super Pup #4, see Television Puppet Show)
Avon Periodicals/Realistic Comics: No. 2, Oct-Nov, 1953 - No. 3, Dec-Jan, 1953-54 (Also see Funny Tunes)

2,3	10	20	30	56	76	95
nn (1953, Realistic-r)	7	14	21	35	43	50

SPUNKY (...Junior Cowboy)(...Comics #2 on)
Standard Comics: April, 1949 - No. 7, Nov, 1951

1-Text illos by Frazetta	20	40	60	114	182	250
2-Text illos by Frazetta	14	28	42	81	118	155
3-7	10	20	30	58	79	100

Spongebob Comics #23 © UPP

Spook House #5 © Eric Powell

Squadron Supreme (2006 series) #1 © MAR

	GD	VG	FN	VF	VF/NM	NM-
	2.0	4.0	6.0	8.0	9.0	9.2

SPUNKY THE SMILING SPOOK
Ajax/Farrell (World Famous Comics/Four Star Comic Corp.): Aug, 1957 - No. 4, May, 1958

1-Reprints from Frisky Fables	14	28	42	81	118	155
2-4	8	16	24	44	57	70

SPY AND COUNTERSPY (Becomes Spy Hunters #3 on)
American Comics Group: Aug-Sept, 1949 - No. 2, Oct-Nov, 1949 (52 pgs.)

1-Origin, 1st app. Jonathan Kent, Counterspy	37	74	111	222	361	500
2	22	44	66	128	209	290

SPYBOY
Dark Horse Comics: Oct, 1999 - No. 17, May, 2001 ($2.50/$2.95/$2.99)

1-17: 1-6-Peter David-s/Pop Mhan-a. 7,8-Meglia-a. 9-17-Mhan-a	4.00
13.1-13.3 (4/03-8/03, $2.99), 13.2,13.3-Mhan-a	4.00
... Special (5/02, $4.99) David-s/Mhan-a	5.00

SPYBOY: FINAL EXAM
Dark Horse Comics: May, 2004 - No. 4, Aug, 2004 ($2.99, limited series)

1-4-Peter David-s/Pop Mhan-a/c	3.00
TPB (2005, $12.95) r/series	13.00

SPYBOY: YOUNG JUSTICE
Dark Horse Comics: Feb, 2002 - No. 3, Apr, 2002 ($2.99, limited series)

1-3: 1-Peter David-s/Todd Nauck-a/Pop Mhan-c. 2-Mhan-a	3.00

SPY CASES (Formerly The Kellys)
Marvel/Atlas Comics (Hercules Publ.): No. 26, Sept, 1950 - No. 19, Oct, 1953

26 (#1)	40	80	120	246	411	575
27(#2),28(#3, 2/51): 27-Everett-a; bondage-c	22	44	66	132	216	300
4(4/51) - 7,9,10: 4-Heath-a	20	40	60	117	189	260
8-A-Bomb-c/story	22	44	66	132	216	300
11-19: 10-14-War format	19	38	57	111	176	240

NOTE: Sol Brodsky c-1-5, 8, 9, 11-14, 17, 18. Maneely a-8; c-7, 10. Tuska a-7.

SPY FIGHTERS
Marvel/Atlas Comics (CSI): March, 1951 - No. 15, July, 1953
(Cases from official records)

1-Clark Mason begins; Tuska-a; Brodsky-c	41	82	123	256	428	600
2-Tuska-a	22	44	66	128	209	290
3-13: 3-5-Brodsky-c. 7-Heath-c	19	38	57	111	176	240
14,15-Pakula-a(3), 15-Brodsky-c	20	40	60	117	189	260

SPY-HUNTERS (Formerly Spy & Counterspy)
American Comics Group: No. 3, Dec-Jan, 1949-50 - No. 24, June-July, 1953 (#3-14: 52 pgs.)

3-Jonathan Kent continues, ends #10	30	60	90	177	289	400
4-10: 4,8,10-Starr-a	16	32	48	92	144	195
11-15,17-22,24: 18-War-c begin. 21-War-c/stories begin	13	26	39	72	101	130
16-Williamson-a (9 pgs.)	18	36	54	107	169	230
23-Graphic torture, injury to eye panel	24	48	72	142	234	325

NOTE: Drucker a-12. Whitney a-many issues; c-7, 8, 10-12, 15, 16.

SPY ISLAND
Dark Horse Comics: Apr, 2020 - No. 4, Dec, 2020 ($3.99, limited series)

1-4-Chelsea Cain-s/Elise McCall-a	4.00

SPYMAN (Top Secret Adventures on cover)
Harvey Publications (Illustrated Humor): Sept, 1966 - No. 3, Feb, 1967 (12¢)

1-Origin and 1st app. of Spyman. Steranko-a(p)-1st pro work; 1 pg. Neal Adams ad; Tuska-c/a, Crandall-a(i)	17	34	51	117	259	400
2-Simon-c; Steranko-a(i)	5	10	15	35	63	90
3-Simon-c	5	10	15	31	53	75

SPY SMASHER (See Mighty Midget, Whiz & Xmas Comics) (Also see Crime Smasher)
Fawcett Publications: Fall, 1941 - No. 11, Feb, 1943

1-Spy Smasher begins; silver metallic-c	354	708	1062	2478	4339	6200
2-Raboy-c	174	348	522	1114	1907	2700
3,4: 3-Bondage-c. 4-Irvin Steinberg-c	129	258	387	826	1413	2000
5-7: Raboy-a; 6-Raboy-c/a. 7-Part photo-c (movie) Japanese dragon-c	103	206	309	659	1130	1600
8,11: War-c	90	180	270	576	988	1400
9-Hitler, Tojo, Mussolini-c	194	388	582	1242	2121	3000
10-Hitler-c	187	374	561	1197	2049	2900

SPY THRILLERS (Police Badge No. 479 #5)
Atlas Comics (PrPI): Nov, 1954 - No. 4, May, 1955

1-Brodsky c-1,2	36	72	108	211	343	475
2-Last precode (1/55)	20	40	60	117	189	260
3,4	17	34	51	98	154	210

SQUADRON SINISTER (Secret Wars tie-in)
Marvel Comics: Aug, 2015 - No. 4, Jan, 2016 ($3.99, limited series)

1-4-Guggenheim-s/Pacheco-a/c. 1-Squadron Supreme app. 2-Frightful Four app.	4.00

SQUADRON SUPREME (Also see Marvel Graphic Novel - ...: Death of a Universe)
Marvel Comics Group: Aug, 1985 - No. 12, Aug, 1986 (Maxi-series)

1-Double size	5.00
2-12	4.00
TPB ($24.99) r/#1-12; Alex Ross painted-c; printing inks contain some of the cremated remains of late writer Mark Gruenwald	50.00
TPB-2nd printing ($24.99): Inks contain no ashes	25.00
...Death of a Universe TPB (2006, $24.99) r/Marvel Graphic Novel, Thor #280, Avengers #5,6; Avengers/Squadron Supreme Annual and Squadron Supreme: New World Order	25.00

SQUADRON SUPREME (Also see Supreme Power)
Marvel Comics: May, 2006 - No. 7, Nov, 2006 ($2.99)

1-7-Straczynski-s/Frank-a/c	3.00
Saga of Squadron Supreme (2006, $3.99) summary of Supreme Power #1-18; plus Hyperion and Nighthawk limited series; wraparound-c; preview of Squadron Supreme #1	4.00
... Vol. 1: The Pre-War Years (2006, $20.99, dustjacket) r/#1-5 & Saga of S.S.	21.00

SQUADRON SUPREME
Marvel Comics: Sept, 2008 - No. 12, Aug, 2009 ($2.99)

1-12: 1-Set 5 years after Ultimate Power; Nick Fury app.; Chaykin-a/Turini-a/Land-c	3.00

SQUADRON SUPREME
Marvel Comics: Feb, 2016 - No. 15, Mar, 2017 ($3.99)

1-15-Robinson-s; main covers by Alex Ross thru #4. 1-Kirk-a; Namor killed. 3-Avengers app. 9-12-Civil War II tie-in. 10-Thundra & Blue Marvel app. 11,12-Spider-Man app.	4.00

SQUADRON SUPREME: HYPERION VS. NIGHTHAWK
Marvel Comics: Mar, 2007 - No. 4, June, 2007 ($2.99, limited series)

1-4-Hyperion and Nighthawk in Darfur; Gulacy-a/c; Guggenheim-s	3.00
TPB (2007, $10.99) r/#1-4	11.00

SQUADRON SUPREME: MARVEL TALES
Marvel Comics: June, 2021 ($7.99, one-shot)

1-Reprints Avengers #69,70,85,86; foreward by Ralph Macchio	8.00

SQUADRON SUPREME: NEW WORLD ORDER
Marvel Comics: Sept, 1998 ($5.99, one-shot)

1-Wraparound-c; Kaminski-s	6.00

SQUALOR
First Comics: Dec, 1989 - Aug, 1990 ($2.75, limited series)

1-4: Sutton-a	4.00

SQUEE (Also see Johnny The Homicidal Maniac)
Slave Labor Graphics: Apr, 1997 - No. 4, May, 1998 ($2.95, B&W)

1-4: Jhonen Vasquez-s/a in all	4.00

SQUEEKS (Also see Boy Comics)
Lev Gleason Publications: Oct, 1953 - No. 5, June, 1954

1-Funny animal; Biro-c; Crimebuster's pet monkey "Squeeks" begins	14	28	42	81	118	155
2-Biro-c	9	18	27	50	65	80
3-5: 3-Biro-c	8	16	24	44	57	70

S.R. BISSETTE'S SPIDERBABY COMIX
SpiderBaby Grafix: Aug, 1996 - No. 2 ($3.95, B&W, magazine size)

Preview-(8/96, $3.95)-Graphic violence & nudity; Laurel & Hardy app.	4.00
1,2	4.00

S.R. BISSETTE'S TYRANT
SpiderBaby Grafix: Sept, 1994 - No. 4 ($2.95, B&W)

1-4	4.00

STALKER (Also see All Star Comics 1999 and crossover issues)
National Periodical Publications: June-July, 1975 - No. 4, Dec-Jan, 1975-76

1-Origin & 1st app; Ditko/Wood-c/a	3	6	9	14	19	24
2-4-Ditko/Wood-a	2	3	4	6	8	10

STALKERS
Marvel Comics (Epic Comics): Apr, 1990 - No. 12, Mar, 1991 ($1.50)

1-12: 1-Chadwick-a	4.00

STAMP COMICS (Stamps... on-c; Thrilling Adventures In...#8)
Youthful Magazines/Stamp Comics, Inc.: Oct, 1951 - No. 7, Oct, 1952

1-(15¢) ('Stamps' on indicia No. 1-3,5,7)	31	62	93	182	296	410
2	18	36	54	103	162	220

	GD 2.0	VG 4.0	FN 6.0	VF 8.0	VF/NM 9.0	NM- 9.2

3-6: 3,4-Kiefer, Wildey-a | 15 | 30 | 45 | 90 | 140 | 190
7-Roy Krenkel (4 pgs.) | 20 | 40 | 60 | 117 | 189 | 260

NOTE: Promotes stamp collecting; gives stories behind various commemorative stamps. No. 2, 10¢ printed over 15¢ c-price. Kiefer a-1-7. Kirkel a-1-6. Napoli a-2-7. Palais a-2-4, 7.

STAND, THE ... (Based on the Stephen King novel)
Marvel Comics: 2008 - 2012 ($3.99, limited series)

...: American Nightmares 1-5 (5/09 - No. 5, 10/09, $3.99) Aguirre-Sacasa-s/Perkins-a | | | | | | 4.00
...: Captain Trips 1-5 (12/08 - No. 5, 3/09, $3.99) Aguirre-Sacasa-s/Perkins-a | | | | | | 4.00
...: Hardcases 1-5 (8/10 - No. 5, 1/11, $3.99) Aguirre-Sacasa-s/Perkins-a | | | | | | 4.00
...: No Man's Land 1-5 (4/11 - No. 5, 8/11, $3.99) Aguirre-Sacasa-s/Perkins-a | | | | | | 4.00
...: Soul Survivors 1-5 (12/09 - No. 5, 5/10, $3.99) Aguirre-Sacasa-s/Perkins-a | | | | | | 4.00
...: The Night Has Come 1-6 (10/11 - No. 6, 3/12, $3.99) Aguirre-Sacasa-s/Perkins-a | | | | | | 4.00

STAN LEE MEETS...
Marvel Comics: Nov, 2006 - Jan, 2007 ($3.99, series of one-shots)

Doctor Doom 1 (12/06) Lee-s/Larroca-a/c; Loeb-s/McGuinness-a; r/Fantastic Four #87 | | | | | | 4.00
Doctor Strange 1 (11/06) Lee-s/Bendis-s/Bagley-a; r/Marvel Premiere #3 | | | | | | 4.00
Silver Surfer 1 (1/07) Lee-s/Wieringo-a/c; Jenkins-s/Buckingham-a; r/S.S. #14 | | | | | | 4.00
Spider-Man 1 (11/06) Lee-s/Coipel-a/c; Whedon-s/Gaydos-a; r/AS-M #87 | | | | | | 4.00
The Thing 1 (12/06) Lee-s/Weeks-a/c; Thomas-s/Kolins-a; r/FF #79; FF #51 cover swipe | | | | | | 4.00
HC (2007, $24.99, dustjacket) r/one-shots; interviews and features | | | | | | 25.00

STAN LEE'S MIGHTY 7
Archie Comics (Stan Lee Comics): May, 2012 - No. 3, Sept, 2012 ($2.99, limited series)

1-3-Co-written by Stan Lee; Alex Saviuk-a; multiple covers on each | | | | | | 3.00

STANLEY & HIS MONSTER (Formerly The Fox & the Crow)
National Periodical Publ.: No. 109, Apr-May, 1968 - No. 112, Oct-Nov, 1968

109-112 | | 3 | 6 | 9 | 21 | 33 | 45

STANLEY & HIS MONSTER
DC Comics: Feb, 1993 - No. 4, May, 1993 ($1.50, limited series)

1-4 | | | | | | 4.00

STAN SHAW'S BEAUTY & THE BEAST
Dark Horse Comics: Nov, 1993 ($4.95, one-shot)

1 | | | | | | 5.00

STAR (See Captain Marvel 2019 series #8)
Marvel Comics: Mar, 2020 - No. 5, Nov, 2020 ($3.99)

1-5: 1-Loki, Jessica Jones and Scarlet Witch app. 2-5-The Black Order app. 3-5-Captain Marvel. 3,5-Scarlet Witch app. | | | | | | 4.00

STARBLAST
Marvel Comics: Jan, 1994 - No. 4, Apr, 1994 ($1.75, limited series)

1-($2.00, 52 pgs.)-Nova, Quasar, Black Bolt; painted-c | | | | | | 5.00
2-4 | | | | | | 4.00

STAR BLAZERS
Comico: Apr, 1987 - No. 4, July, 1987 ($1.75, limited series)

1-4 | | | | | | 4.00

STAR BLAZERS
Comico: 1989 ($1.95/$2.50, limited series)

1-5- Steacy wraparound painted-c on all | | | | | | 4.00

STAR BLAZERS (The Magazine of Space Battleship Yamato)
Argo Press: No. 0, Aug, 1995 - No. 3 Dec, 1995 ($2.95)

0-3 | | | | | | 4.00

STARBORN (From Stan Lee)
BOOM! Studios: Dec, 2010 - No. 12, Nov, 2011 ($3.99)

1-12: 1-9,11-Roberson-s/Randolph-a. 1-7-Three covers on each. 10-Scalera-a | | | | | | 4.00

STAR BRAND
Marvel Comics (New Universe): Oct, 1986 - No. 19, May, 1989 (75¢/$1.25)

1-15: 14-begin $1.25-c | | | | | | 4.00
16-19-Byrne story & art; low print run | | | | | | 5.00
Annual 1 (10/87) | | | | | | 4.00
... Classic Vol. 1 TPB (2006, $19.99) r/#1-7 | | | | | | 20.00

STARBRAND & NIGHTMASK
Marvel Comics: Feb, 2016 - No. 6, Jul, 2016 ($3.99)

1-6: 1-Weisman-s/Broccardo-a; Kevin and Adam go to college; Nitro & Graviton app. | | | | | | 4.00

STARCADIA QUEST (Based on the tabletop game)
IDW Publishing: Aug, 2019 - No. 3, Oct, 2019 ($4.99, limited series)

1-3-James Roberts-s/Aurelio Mazzara-a | | | | | | 5.00

STARCHILD
Tailspin Press: 1992 - No. 12 ($2.25/$2.50, B&W)

1,2-('92),0(4/93),3-12: 0-Illos by Chadwick, Eisner, Sim, M. Wagner. 3-(7/93). 4-(11/93). 6-(2/94) | | | | | | 4.00

STARCHILD: MYTHOPOLIS
Image Comics: No. 0, July, 1997 - No. 4, Apr, 1998 ($2.95, B&W, limited series)

0-4-James Owen-s/a | | | | | | 4.00

STAR COMICS
Ultem Publ. (Harry `A' Chesler)/Centaur Publications: Feb, 1937 - V2#7 (No. 23), Aug, 1939 (#1-6: large size)

V1#1-Dan Hastings (s/f) begins | 465 | 930 | 1395 | 3395 | 5998 | 8600
2-(4/37) | 290 | 580 | 870 | 1856 | 3178 | 4500
3-Classic Black Americana cover (rare) | 465 | 930 | 1395 | 3395 | 5998 | 8600
4,5-Classic Winsor McCay Little Nemo-c/stories (rare) | 300 | 600 | 900 | 2010 | 3505 | 5000
6-(9/37) | 271 | 542 | 813 | 1734 | 2967 | 4200
7-9: 8-Severed head centerspread; Impy & Little Nemo by Winsor McCay Jr, Popeye app. by Bob Wood; Mickey Mouse & Popeye app. as toys in Santa's bag on-c; X-Mas-c | 187 | 374 | 561 | 1197 | 2049 | 2900
10 (1st Centaur; 3/38)-Impy by Winsor McCay Jr; Don Marlow by Guardineer begins | 232 | 464 | 696 | 1485 | 2543 | 3600

11-1st Jack Cole comic-a, 1 pg. (4/38) | 297 | 594 | 891 | 1901 | 3251 | 4600
12-15: 12-Riders of the Golden West begins; Little Nemo app. 15-Speed Silvers by Gustavson & The Last Pirate by Burgos begins | 135 | 270 | 405 | 864 | 1482 | 2100
16 (12/38)-The Phantom Rider & his horse Thunder begins, ends V2#6 | 168 | 336 | 504 | 1075 | 1838 | 2600
V2#1(#17, 2/39)-Phantom Rider-c (only non-funny-c) | 206 | 412 | 618 | 1318 | 2259 | 3200
2-7(#18-23): 2-Diana Deane by Tarpe Mills app. 3-Drama of Hollywood by Mills begins. | 116 | 232 | 348 | 742 | 1271 | 1800

NOTE: Biro c-6, 9, 10. Burgos a-15, 16, V2#1-7. Ken Ernst a-10, 12, 14. Filchock c-15, 18, 22. Gill Fox c-14, 19. Guardineer a-6, 8-14. Gustavson a-13-16, V2#1-7. Winsor McCay c-4, 5. Tarpe Mills a-15, V2#1-7. Schwab c-20, 23. Bob Wood a-10, 12, 13; c-7, 8.

STAR COMICS MAGAZINE
Marvel Comics (Star Comics): Dec, 1986 - No. 13, 1988 ($1.50, digest-size)

1,9-Spider-Man-c/s | 2 | 4 | 6 | 8 | 11 | 14
2-8-Heathcliff, Ewoks, Top Dog, Madballs-r in #1-13 | 1 | 2 | 3 | 5 | 7 | 9
10-13 | 2 | 4 | 6 | 8 | 10 | 12

S.T.A.R. CORPS
DC Comics: Nov, 1993 - No. 6, Apr, 1994 ($1.50, limited series)

1-6: 1,2-Austin-c(i). 1-Superman app. | | | | | | 4.00

STARCRAFT (Based on the video game)
DC Comics (WildStorm): Jul, 2009 - No. 7, Jan, 2010 ($2.99)

1-7-Furman-s; two covers on each | | | | | | 3.00
HC (2010, $19.99, dustjacket) r/#1-7 | | | | | | 20.00
SC (2011, $14.99) r/#1-7 | | | | | | 15.00

STARCRAFT: SCAVENGERS (Based on the Blizzard Ent. video game)
Dark Horse Comics: Jul, 2018 - No. 4, Oct, 2018 ($3.99, limited series)

1-4-Jody Houser-s/Gabriel Guzmán-a | | | | | | 4.00

STARCRAFT: SOLDIERS (Based on the Blizzard Ent. video game)
Dark Horse Comics: Jan, 2019 - No. 4, Apr, 2019 ($3.99, limited series)

1-4-Jody Houser & Andrew Robinson-s/Miguel Sepulveda-a | | | | | | 4.00

STARCRAFT: SURVIVORS (Based on the Blizzard Ent. video game)
Dark Horse Comics: Jul, 2019 - No. 4, Apr, 2019 ($3.99, limited series)

1-4-Jody Houser-s/Gabriel Guzmán-a | | | | | | 4.00

STAR CROSSED
DC Comics (Helix): June, 1997 - No. 3, Aug, 1997 ($2.50, limited series)

1-3-Matt Howarth-s/a | | | | | | 4.00

STARDUST (See Neil Gaiman and Charles Vess' Stardust)

STARDUST KID, THE
Image Comics/Boom! Studios #4-on: May, 2005 - No. 4 ($3.50)

1-4-J.M. DeMatteis-s/Mike Ploog-a | | | | | | 3.50

STAR FEATURE COMICS
I. W. Enterprises: 1963

Reprint #9-Stunt-Man Stetson-r/Feat. Comics #141 | 3 | 6 | 9 | 14 | 19 | 24

STARFINDER: ANGELS OF THE DRIFT (Based on the role-playing game)
Dynamite Entertainment: 2023 - No. 5, 2024 ($4.99, limited series)

1-5-James L. Sutter-s/Edu Menna-a | | | | | | 5.00

STARFIRE (Not the Teen Titans character)
National Periodical Publ./DC Comics: Aug-Sept, 1976 - No. 8, Oct-Nov, 1977

1-Origin (CCA stamp fell off cover art; so it was approved by code) | | 3 | 6 | 9 | 14 | 20 | 25
2-8 | | 1 | 3 | 4 | 6 | 8 | 10

STARFIRE (Teen Titans character)(Also see Red Hood and the Outlaws)
DC Comics: Aug, 2015 - No. 12, Jul, 2016 ($2.99)

1-12: 1-Conner & Palmiotti-s/Lupacchino-a; Conner-c. 3-Intro. Atlee. 7,8-Grayson app. 9-Charretier begins; intro. Syl'khee | | | | | | 3.00

STARGATE
Dynamite Entertainment

...: Daniel Jackson 1-4 (2010 - No. 4, 2010, $3.99) Watson-a/Murray-s | | | | | | 4.00
...: Vala Mal Doran 1-5 (2010 - No. 5, 2010, $3.99) Razek-a/Jerwa-s | | | | | | 4.00

STARGATE ATLANTIS (Based on the TV series)
American Mythology Prods.: 2016 - No. 6 ($3.99)

1-6: 1-Haynes-s/LaRocque-a; covers by Wheatley & LaRocque. 4-6-Gateways #1-3 on cover; Watson-a | | | | | | 4.00

STARGATE ATLANTIS HEARTS & MINDS
American Mythology Prods.: 2017 - No. 3, 2017 ($3.99)

1-3-Haynes & Vaughn-s/LaRocque-a | | | | | | 4.00

STARGATE ATLANTIS SINGULARITY
American Mythology Prods.: 2018 - No. 3, 2018 ($3.99)

1-3: 1-Haynes & Vaughn-s/Purcell & LaRocque-a. 2,3-Purcell-a | | | | | | 4.00

STARGATE ATLANTIS / STARGATE UNIVERSE ANTHOLOGY
American Mythology Prods.: 2018 ($3.99)

1-Haynes & Vaughn-s/LaRocque & Purcell-a; 3 covers | | | | | | 4.00

STARGATE ATLANTIS / STARGATE UNIVERSE ANTHOLOGY ONGOING
American Mythology Prods.: 2018 - No. 3, 2018 ($3.99)

1-3: 1-Haynes & Vaughn-s/Hilinski-a; Check-s/Gouveia-a; 3 covers. 3-Purcell-a | | | | | | 4.00

STARGATE UNIVERSE (Based on the TV series)
American Mythology Prods.: 2017 - No. 6, 2018 ($3.99)

1-6: 1-Haynes & Vaughn-s/Caracuzzo-a. 2,3-Gouveia-a. 4-6-Hilinski-a | | | | | | 4.00

STARGIRL SPRING BREAK SPECIAL
DC Comics: Jul, 2021 ($5.99, one-shot)

1-Seven Soldiers of Victory & Clock King app.; Johns-s/Nauck-a; Hitch-a | | | | | | 6.00

STARGIRL: THE LOST CHILDREN (See Flashpoint Beyond)

Starborn #1 © BOOM!

Stargirl: The Lost Children #6 © DC

Starman #81 © DC

	GD	VG	FN	VF	VF/NM	NM-
	2.0	4.0	6.0	8.0	9.0	9.2

DC Comics: Jan, 2023 - No. 6, Jul, 2023 ($3.99)

1-6-The search for the forgotten Golden Age sidekicks; Johns-s/Nauck-a   4.00

STARHENGE, BOOK ONE: THE DRAGON & THE BOAR
Image Comics: Jul, 2022 - No. 6, Dec, 2022 ($3.99, limited series)

1-6-Liam Sharp-s/a   4.00

STAR HUNTERS (See DC Super Stars #16)
National Periodical Publ./DC Comics: Oct-Nov, 1977 - No. 7, Oct-Nov, 1978

1,7: 1-Newton-a(p). 7-44 pgs.	2	4	6	8	10	12
2-6		1	2	3	4	5	7

NOTE: *Buckler* a-4-7p; c-1-7p. *Layton* a-1-5i; c-1-6i. *Nasser* a-3p. *Sutton* a-6i.

STARJAMMERS (See X-Men Spotlight on Starjammers)

STARJAMMERS (Also see Uncanny X-Men)
Marvel Comics: Oct, 1995 - No. 4, Jan, 1996 ($2.95, limited series)

1-4: Foil-c; Ellis scripts   4.00

STARJAMMERS
Marvel Comics: Sept, 2004 - No. 6, Jan, 2005 ($2.99, limited series)

1-6-Kevin J. Anderson-s. 1-Garza-a. 2-6-Lucas-a   3.00

STARK TERROR
Stanley Publications: Dec, 1970 - No. 5, Aug, 1971 (B&W, magazine, 52 pgs.)
(1950s Horror reprints, including pre-code)

1-Bondage, torture-c	10	20	30	64	132	200
2-4 (Gillmor/Aragon-r)	5	10	15	35	63	90
5 (ACG-r)	5	10	15	31	53	75

STARLET O'HARA IN HOLLYWOOD (Teen-age) (Also see Cookie)
Standard Comics: Dec, 1948 - No. 4, Sept, 1949

1-Owen Fitzgerald-a in all	61	122	183	390	670	950
2	43	86	129	271	461	650
3,4	39	78	117	231	378	525

STARLIGHT
Image Comics: Mar, 2014 - No. 6, Oct, 2014 ($2.99)

1-5-Mark Millar-s/Goran Parlov-a. 1-Covers by Cassaday & Parlov. 2-Sienkiewicz var-c   3.00
6-($4.99) Two covers by Cassaday and Chiang   5.00

STARLORD
Marvel Comics: Dec, 1996 - No. 3, Feb, 1997 ($2.50, limited series)

1-3-Timothy Zahn-s   4.00

STAR-LORD (Guardians of the Galaxy)
Marvel Comics: Aug, 2013; 2014 ($7.99, series of reprints)

...: Annihilation - Conquest 1 (2014) r/Annihilation: Conquest - Starlord 1-4; design art   8.00
...: Tears For Heaven 1 (2014) r/Marvel Preview #18, Marvel Spotlight #6,7, and
     Marvel Premiere #61; bonus art; new cover by Pichelli   8.00
...: The Hollow Crown 1 (8/13) r/Marvel Preview #4,11 and Star-Lord Special Edition   8.00

STAR-LORD
Marvel Comics: Jan, 2016 - No. 8, Aug, 2016 ($3.99)

1-8: 1-Humphries-s/Garron-a; 18-year-old Peter Quill's 1st meeting with Yondu   4.00

STAR-LORD
Marvel Comics: Feb, 2017 - No. 8, 2017 ($3.99)

1-6-Zdarsky-s/Anka-a. 1,5,6-Old Man Logan app. 3-5-Daredevil app.   4.00
Annual 1 (7/17, $4.99) Zdarsky-s/Morissette-a/Anka-c   5.00

STAR-LORD & KITTY PRYDE (Secret Wars tie-in)
Marvel Comics: Sept, 2015 - No. 3, Nov, 2015 ($3.99, limited series)

1-3-Humphries-s/Firmansyah-a; Gambit app.   4.00

STARLORD MAGAZINE
Marvel Comics: Nov, 1996 ($2.95, one-shot)

1-Reprints w/preview of new series   6.00

STAR-LORD THE SPECIAL EDITION (Also see Marvel Comics Super Special #10, Marvel Premiere & Preview & Marvel Spotlight V2#6,7)
Marvel Comics Group: Feb, 1982 (one-shot, direct sales) (1st Baxter paper comic)

1-Byrne/Austin-a; Austin-c; 8 pgs. of new-a by Golden (p); Dr. Who story by Dave Gibbons; 1st deluxe format comic	3	6	9	16	23	30

STAR MAGE
IDW Publishing: Apr, 2014 - No. 6, Sept, 2014 ($3.99, limited series)

1-6: 1-JC De La Torre-s/Ray Dillon-a. 2-6-Franco Cespedes-a   4.00

STARMAN (1st Series) (Also see Justice League & War of the Gods)
DC Comics: Oct, 1988 - No. 45, Apr, 1992 ($1.00)

1-Origin	1	2	3	5	6	8
2-25,29-45: 4-Intro The Power Elite. 9,10,34-Batman app. 14-Superman app.						
17-Power Girl app. 38-War of the Gods x-over. 42-45-Eclipso-c/stories						4.00
26-1st app. David Knight (G.A.Starman's son).						6.00
27,28: 27-Starman (David Knight) app. 28-Starman disguised as Superman; leads into						
Superman #50						4.00

STARMAN (2nd Series) (Also see The Golden Age, Showcase 95 #12, Showcase 96 #4,5)
DC Comics: No. 0, Oct, 1994 - No. 80, Aug, 2001; No. 81, Mar, 2010 ($1.95/$2.25/$2.50)

0,1: 0-James Robinson scripts, Tony Harris-c/a(p) & Wade Von Grawbadger-a(i) begins;
   Sins of the Father storyline begins, ends #3; 1st app. new Starman (Jack Knight); reintro of
   the G.A. Mist & G.A. Shade; 1st app. Nash; David Knight dies					

	2	4	6	8	10	12

2-7: 2-Reintro Charity from Forbidden Tales of Dark Mansion. 3-Reintro/2nd app. "Blue"
   Starman (1st app. in 1st Issue Special #12); Will Payton app. (both cameos). 5-David
   Knight app. 6-The Shade "Times Past" story; Kristiansen-a. 7-The Black Pirate cameo
						5.00

8-17: 8-Begin $2.25-c. 10-1st app. new Mist (Nash). 11-JSA "Times Past" story; Matt Smith-a. 12-16-Sins of the Child. 17-The Black Pirate app.						4.00

18-37: 18-G.A. Starman "Times Past" story; Watkiss-a. 19-David Knight app.
   20-23-G.A. Sandman app. 24-26-Demon Quest; all 3 covers make-up triptych.
   33-36-Batman-c/app. 37-David Knight and deceased JSA members app.
						4.00

38-49,51-56: 38-Nash vs. Justice League Europe. 39,40-Crossover w/ Power of
   Shazam! #35,36; Bulletman app. 42-Demon-c/app. 43-JLA-c/app. 44-Phantom Lady-c/app.
   46-Gene Ha-a. 51-Jor-El app. 52,53-Adam Strange-c/app.
						4.00

50-($3.95) Gold foil logo on-c; Star Boy (LSH) app.						5.00
57-79: 57-62-Painted covers by Harris and Alex Ross. 72-Death of Ted Knight						3.00
80-($3.95) Final issue; cover by Harris & Robinson						4.00
81-(3/10, $2.99) Blackest Night one-shot; The Shade vs. David Knight; Harris-c						3.00
#1,000,000 (11/98) 853rd Century x-over; Snejbjerg-a						4.00
Annual 1 (1996, $3.50)-Legends of the Dead Earth story; Prince Gavyn & G.A. Starman stories; J.H. Williams III, Bret Blevins, Craig Hamilton-c/a(p)						5.00
Annual 2 (1997, $3.95)-Pulp Heroes story;						5.00
...80 Page Giant (1/99, $4.95) Harris-c						5.00
...Secret Files 1 (4/98, $4.95)-Origin stories and profile pages						5.00
...The Mist (6/98, $1.95) Girlfrenzy; Mary Marvel app.						4.00
A Starry Knight-($17.95, TPB) r/#47-53						18.00
Grand Guignol-(2004, $19.95, TPB)-r/#61-73						20.00
Infernal Devices-($17.95, TPB) r/#29-35,37,38						18.00
Night and Day-($14.95, TPB) r/#7-10,12-16						15.00
Sins of the Father-($12.95, TPB)-r/#0-5						13.00
Sons of the Father-($14.99, TPB)-r/#75-80						15.00
Stars My Destination-(2003, $14.95, TPB)-r/#55-60						15.00
Times Past-($17.95, TPB)-r/stories of other Starmen						18.00
The Starman Omnibus Vol. One (2008, $49.99, HC with dj) r/#0,1-16; James Robinson intro.						50.00
The Starman Omnibus Vol. Two (2009, $49.99, HC with dj) r/#17-29, Annual #1, Showcase '95 #12, Showcase '96 #4,5; Harris intro.; merchandise gallery						50.00
The Starman Omnibus Vol. Three (2009, $49.99, HC with dj) r/#30-38, Annual #2, Starman Secret Files #1 and The Shade #1-4						50.00
The Starman Omnibus Vol. Four (2010, $49.99, HC with dj) r/#39-46, 80 Page Giant #1, Power of Shazam! #35,36; Starman: The Mist #1 and Batman/Hellboy/Starman #1,2						50.00
The Starman Omnibus Vol. Five (2010, $49.99, HC with dj) r/#47-60, #1,000,000; Stars and S.T.R.I.P.E. #0; All Star Comics 80 Page Giant #1; JSA: All Stars #4						50.00
The Starman Omnibus Vol. Six (2011, $49.99, HC with dj) r/#61-81, Johns intro.						50.00

STARMAN/CONGORILLA (See Justice League: Cry For Justice)
DC Comics: Mar, 2011 ($2.99, one-shot)

1-Animal Man and Rex the Wonder Dog app.; Robinson-s/Booth-a/Ha-c   3.00

STARMASTERS
Marvel Comics: Dec, 1995 - No. 3, Feb, 1996 ($1.95, limited series)

1-3-Continues in Cosmic Powers Unlimited #4   4.00

STAR PIG
IDW Publishing: Jul, 2019 - No. 4, Oct, 2019 ($3.99, limited series)

1-4-Delilah S. Dawson-s/Francesco Gaston-a; two covers on each   4.00

STAR PRESENTATION, A (Formerly My Secret Romance #1,2; Spectacular Stories #4 on)
(Also see This Is Suspense)
Fox Feature Syndicate (Hero Books): No. 3, May, 1950

3-Dr. Jekyll & Mr. Hyde by Wood & Harrison (reprinted in Startling Terror Tales #10); "The Repulsing Dwarf" by Wood; Wood-c	87	174	261	553	952	1350

STAR QUEST COMIX (Warren Presents... on cover)
Warren Publications: Oct, 1978 ($1.50, B&W magazine, 84 pgs., square-bound)

1-Corben, Maroto, Neary-a; Ken Kelly-c; Star Wars	2	4	6	9	12	15

STAR RAIDERS (See DC Graphic Novel #1)

	GD 2.0	VG 4.0	FN 6.0	VF 8.0	VF/NM 9.0	NM- 9.2

STAR RANGER (Cowboy Comics #13 on)
Chesler Publ./Centaur Publ.: Feb, 1937 - No. 12, May, 1938 (Large size: No. 1-6)

1-(1st Western comic)-Ace & Deuce, Air Plunder; Creig Flessel-a

	GD	VG	FN	VF	VF/NM	NM-
1	354	708	1062	2478	4339	6200
2	194	388	582	1242	2121	3000
3-6	74	348	522	1114	1907	2700

7-9: 8(12/37)-Christmas-c; Air Patrol, Gold coast app.; Guardineer centerfold

	GD	VG	FN	VF	VF/NM	NM-
7-9	142	284	426	909	1555	2200
V2#10 (1st Centaur; 3/38)	155	310	465	992	1696	2400
11,12	135	270	405	864	1482	2100

NOTE: *J. Cole* a-10, 12; c-12. *Ken Ernst* a-11. *Gill Fox* a-8(illo), 9, 10. *Guardineer* a-1-3, 5-7, 8(illos), 9, 10, 12. *Gustavson* a-10, 12. *Fred Schwab* c-2-11. *Bob Wood* a-8-10.

STAR RANGER FUNNIES (Formerly Cowboy Comics)
Centaur Publications: V1#15, Oct, 1938 - V2#5, Oct, 1939

V1#15-Lyin Lou, Ermine, Wild West Junior, The Law of Caribou County by Eisner, Cowboy Jake, The Plugged Dummy, Spurs by Gustavson, Red Coat, Two Buckaroos & Trouble Hunters begin

	GD	VG	FN	VF	VF/NM	NM-
V1#15	161	322	483	1030	1765	2500
V2#1 (1/39)	129	258	387	826	1413	2000

2-5: 2-Night Hawk by Gustavson. 4-Kit Carson app.

	GD	VG	FN	VF	VF/NM	NM-
2-5	110	220	330	704	1202	1700

NOTE: *Jack Cole* a-V2#1, 3; c-V#1. *Filchock* c-V2#2, 3. *Guardineer* a-V2#3. *Gustavson* a-V2#2. *Pinajian* c/a-V2#5.

STAR REACH (Mature content)
Star Reach Publ.: Apr, 1974 - No. 18, Oct, 1979 (B&W, #12-15 w/color)

1-(75¢, 52 pgs.) Art by Starlin, Simonson. Chaykin-c/a; origin Death. Cody Starbuck-sty

	GD	VG	FN	VF	VF/NM	NM-
1	3	6	9	17	26	35

1-2nd, 3th, and 4th printings ($1.00-$1.50-c) — 6.00
2-11: 2-Adams, Giordano-a; 1st Stephanie Starr-c/s. 3-1st Linda Lovecraft. 4-1st Sherlock Duck. 5-1st Gideon Faust by Chaykin. 6-Elric-c. 7-BWS-c. 9-14-Sacred & Profane-c/s by Steacy. 11-Samurai

	GD	VG	FN	VF	VF/NM	NM-
2-11	2	4	6	8	11	14

2-2nd printing — 4.00

	GD	VG	FN	VF	VF/NM	NM-
12-15 (44 pgs.): 12-Zelazny-s. Nasser-a, Brunner-c	2	4	6	9	13	16
16-18-Magazine size: 17-Poe's Raven-c/s	2	4	6	9	13	16

NOTE: *Adams* c-2. *Bonivert* a-17. *Brunner* a-3,5; c-3,10,12. *Chaykin* a-1,4,5; c-1(1st ed),4,5; back-c-1(2nd,3rd,4th ed). *Gene Day* a-6,8,9,11,15. *Friedrich* c-2,3,8,10. *Gasbarri* a-7. *Gilbert* a-9,12. *Giordano* a-2. *Gould* a-6. *Hirota/Mukaide* a/a-7. *Jones* c-6. *Konz* a-17. *Leialoha* a-3,4,6-, 13,15; c-13,15. *Lyda* a-6,12-15. *Marrs* a-2-5,7,10,14,15,16,18; c-18. *Mayerick* c-7. *Mukaide* a-8. *Nasser* a-12. *Nino* a-6; *Russell* a-8,10; c-8. *Dave Sim* s-7; lettering-9. *Simonson* a-1. *Skeates* a-1,2. *Starlin* a-1(x2), 2(x2); back-c-1(1st ed); c-1(2nd,3rd,4th ed). *Barry Smith* c-7. *Staton* a-5,6,7. *Steacy* a-5-14,16. *Vosburg* a-2-5,7,10. *Workman* a-2-5,8. Nudity panels in most. Wraparound-c-3-5,7-11,13-16,18.

STAR REACH CLASSICS
Eclipse Comics: Mar, 1984 - No. 6, Aug, 1984 ($1.50, Baxter paper)

1-6: 1-Neal Adams-r/Star Reach #1; Sim & Starlin-a — 4.00

STARR FLAGG, UNDERCOVER GIRL (See Undercover...)

STARRIORS
Marvel Comics: Aug, 1984 - Feb, 1985 (Limited series) (Based on Tomy toys)

1-4 — 4.00

STARR THE SLAYER
Marvel Comics (MAX): Nov, 2009 - No. 4, Feb, 2010 ($3.99, limited series)

1-4: Richard Corben-c/a; Daniel Way-s — 4.00

STARS AND S.T.R.I.P.E. (Also see JSA)
DC Comics: July, 1999 - No. 14, Sept, 2000 ($2.95/$2.50)

0-($2.95) 1st app. Courtney Whitmore; Moder and Weston-a; Starman app. — 4.00
1-Johns and Robinson-s/Moder-a; origin new Star Spangled Kid — 4.00
2-14: 4-Marvel Family app. 9-Seven Soldiers of Victory-c/app. — 4.00
JSA Presents: Stars and S.T.R.I.P.E. Vol. 1 TPB (2007, $17.99) r/#1-8; Johns intro. — 18.00
JSA Presents: Stars and S.T.R.I.P.E. Vol. 2 TPB (2008, $17.99) r/#0,9-14 — 18.00

STARS AND STRIPES COMICS
Centaur Publications: No. 2, May, 1941 - No. 6, Dec, 1941

2(#1)-The Shark, The Iron Skull, A-Man, The Amazing Man, Mighty Man, Minimidget begin; The Voice & Dash Dartwell, the Human Meteor, Reef Kinkaid app.; Gustavson Flag-c

	GD	VG	FN	VF	VF/NM	NM-
2(#1)	300	600	900	2010	3505	5000
3-Origin Dr. Synthe; The Black Panther app.	284	568	852	1818	3109	4400

4-Origin/1st app. The Stars and Stripes; injury to eye-c

	GD	VG	FN	VF	VF/NM	NM-
4	187	374	561	1197	2049	2900
5(#5 on cover & inside)	142	284	426	909	1555	2200
5(#6)-(#5 on cover, #6 on inside)	142	284	426	909	1555	2200

NOTE: *Gustavson* ca-3. *Myron Strauss* c-4, 5(#5), 5(#6).

STAR SEED (Formerly Powers That Be)
Broadway Comics: No. 7, 1996 - No. 9 ($2.95)

7-9 — 4.00

STARSHIP DOWN
Dark Horse Comics: Mar, 2020 - Present ($3.99)

1-Justin Giampaoli-s/Andrea Mutti-a — 4.00

STARSHIP TROOPERS
Dark Horse Comics: 1997 - No. 2, 1997 (limited series)

	GD	VG	FN	VF	VF/NM	NM-
1-Movie adaptation	2	4	6	9	12	15

2 — 6.00

STARSHIP TROOPERS: BRUTE CREATIONS
Dark Horse Comics: 1997 ($2.95, one-shot)

	GD	VG	FN	VF	VF/NM	NM-
1	2	4	6	8	10	12

STARSHIP TROOPERS: DOMINANT SPECIES
Dark Horse Comics: Aug, 1998 - No. 4, Nov, 1998 ($2.95, limited series)

1-4-Strnad-s/Bolton-c — 5.00

STARSHIP TROOPERS: INSECT TOUCH
Dark Horse Comics: 1997 - No. 3, 1997 ($2.95, limited series)

1-3 — 5.00

STAR SLAMMERS (See Marvel Graphic Novel #6)
Malibu Comics (Bravura): May, 1994 - No. 4, Aug, 1994 ($2.50, unfinished limited series)

1-4: W. Simonson-a/stories; contain Bravura stamps — 4.00

STAR SLAMMERS
IDW Publishing: Mar, 2014 - No. 8, Oct, 2014 ($3.99)

1-8-Recolored reprint of 1994 series; Walt Simonson-s/a. 1-4-Two covers by Simonson — 4.00

STAR SLAMMERS SPECIAL
Dark Horse Comics (Legend): June, 1996 ($2.95, one-shot)

nn-Simonson-c/a/scripts; concludes Bravura limited series. — 4.00

STARSLAYER
Pacific Comics/First Comics No. 7 on: Feb, 1982 - No. 6, Apr, 1983; No. 7, Aug, 1983 - No. 34, Nov, 1985

1-Origin & 1st app., 1 pg. Rocketeer brief app. which continues in #2

	GD	VG	FN	VF	VF/NM	NM-
1	3	6	9	14	19	24

2-Origin/1st full app. the Rocketeer (4/82) by Dave Stevens (Chapter 1 of Rocketeer saga; see Pacific Presents #1,2)

	GD	VG	FN	VF	VF/NM	NM-
2	3	6	9	19	30	40
3-Chapter 2 of Rocketeer saga by Stevens	2	4	6	13	18	22

4,6,7: 7-Grell-a ends — 5.00

	GD	VG	FN	VF	VF/NM	NM-
5-2nd app. Groo the Wanderer by Aragonés	2	4	6	9	13	16

8,9,11-34: 18-Starslayer meets Grimjack. 20-The Black Flame begins (9/84, 1st app.), ends #33. 27-Book length Black Flame story — 5.00

	GD	VG	FN	VF	VF/NM	NM-
10-1st app. Grimjack (11/83, ends #17)	2	4	6	9	12	15

NOTE: *Grell* a-1-7; c-1-8. *Stevens* back c-2, 3. *Sutton* a-17p, 20-22p, 24-27p, 29-33p.

STARSLAYER (The Director's Cut)
Acclaim Comics (Windjammer): June, 1994 - No. 8, Dec, 1995 ($2.50)

1-8: Mike Grell-c/a/scripts — 4.00

STAR SPANGLED COMICS (Star Spangled War Stories #131 on)
National Periodical Publications: Oct, 1941 - No. 130, July, 1952

1-Origin/1st app. Tarantula; Captain X of the R.A.F., Star Spangled Kid (see Action #40), Armstrong of the Army begin; Robot-c

	GD	VG	FN	VF	VF/NM	NM-
1	649	1298	1947	4738	8369	12,000
2	194	388	582	1242	2121	3000
3-5	123	246	369	787	1344	1900
6-Last Armstrong/Army; Penniless Palmer begins	81	162	243	518	884	1250

7-(4/42)-Origin/1st app. The Guardian by S&K & Robotman (by Paul Cassidy & created by Siegel);The Newsboy Legion (1st app.), Robotman & TNT begin; last Captain X

	GD	VG	FN	VF	VF/NM	NM-
7	892	1784	2676	6512	11,506	16,500
8-Origin TNT & Dan the Dyna-Mite	258	516	774	1651	2826	4000
9,10	174	348	522	1114	1907	2700
11-17	123	246	369	787	1344	1900
18-Origin Star Spangled Kid	155	310	465	992	1696	2400
19-Last Tarantula	123	246	369	787	1344	1900
20-Liberty Belle begins (5/43)	155	310	465	992	1696	2400

21-29-Last S&K issue; 23-Last TNT. 25-Robotman by Jimmy Thompson begins. 29-Intro Robbie the Robotdog

	GD	VG	FN	VF	VF/NM	NM-
21-29	103	206	309	659	1130	1600
30-40: 31-S&K-c	63	126	189	403	689	975
41-51: 41,49-Kirby-c. 51-Robot-c by Kirby	57	114	171	362	619	875
52-64: 53 by S&K. 64-Last Newsboy Legion & The Guardian	52	104	156	328	552	775
65-Robin begins with c/app. (2/47); Robin-c begins, end #95	219	438	657	1402	2401	3400
66-Batman cameo in Robin story	100	200	300	635	1093	1550
67,68,70-80: 68-Last Liberty Belle	74	148	222	470	810	1150

69-Origin/1st app. Tomahawk by F. Ray; atom bomb story & splash (6/47); black-c (rare in high grade)

	GD	VG	FN	VF	VF/NM	NM-
69	271	542	813	1734	2967	4200
81-Origin Merry, Girl of 1000 Gimmicks in Star Spangled Kid story	68	136	204	435	743	1050
82,85: 82-Last Robotman? 85-Last Star Spangled Kid?	58	116	174	371	636	900

83-Tomahawk enters the lost valley, a land of dinosaurs; Capt. Compass begins, ends #130

	GD	VG	FN	VF	VF/NM	NM-
83	61	122	183	390	670	950
84,87: (Rare): 87-Batman cameo in Robin	90	180	270	576	988	1400
86-Batman cameo in Robin story	68	136	204	435	743	1050

88(1/49)-94: Batman-c/stories in all. 91-Federal Men begin, end #121. 94-Manhunters Around the World begin, end #121

	GD	VG	FN	VF	VF/NM	NM-
88-94	84	168	252	538	919	1300
95-Batman story; last Robin-c	65	130	195	416	708	1000
96,98-Batman cameo in Robin stories. 96-1st Tomahawk-c (also #97-121)	43	86	129	271	461	650
97,99	39	78	117	231	378	525
100 (1/50)-Pre-Bat-Hound tryout in Robin story (pre-dates Batman #92).	48	96	144	302	514	725
101-109,118,119,121: 121-Last Tomahawk-c	35	70	105	208	339	470
110,111,120-Batman cameo in Robin stories. 120-Last 52 pg. issue	37	74	111	222	361	500
112-Batman & Robin story	40	80	120	246	411	575
113-Frazetta-a (10 pgs.)	45	90	135	284	480	675
114-Retells Robin's origin (3/51); Batman & Robin story	48	96	144	302	514	725
115,117-Batman in Robin stories	39	78	117	240	395	550
116-Flag-c	41	82	123	256	428	600

122-(11/51)-Ghost Breaker-c/stories begin (origin/1st app.), ends #130 (Ghost Breaker covers #122-130)

	GD	VG	FN	VF	VF/NM	NM-
122	68	136	204	435	743	1050
123-126,128,129	40	80	120	246	411	575
127-Batman app.	45	90	135	284	480	675
130-Batman cameo in Robin story	50	100	150	315	533	750

NOTE: Most all issues after #29 signed by Simon & Kirby but none by them. *Bill Ely* c-122-130. *Mortimer* c-65-74(most), 96-95(most). *Fred Ray* c-96-106, 109, 110, 112, 113, 115-120. *S&K* c-7-31, 33, 34, 36, 37, 39, 40, 48, 49, 50-54, 56-58. *Hal Sherman* c-1-6. *Dick Sprang* c-75.

STAR SPANGLED COMICS (Also see All Star Comics 1999 crossover titles)
DC Comics: May, 1999 ($1.99, one-shot)

1-Golden Age Sandman and the Star Spangled Kid — 4.00

STAR SPANGLED KID (See Action #40, Leading Comics & Star Spangled Comics)

STAR SPANGLED WAR STORIES
DC Comics: Aug/Sept 1952

Starr The Slayer #3 © MAR

Star Spangled Comics #8 © DC

Star Spangled War Stories #90 © DC

	GD	VG	FN	VF	VF/NM	NM-		GD	VG	FN	VF	VF/NM	NM-
	2.0	4.0	6.0	8.0	9.0	9.2		2.0	4.0	6.0	8.0	9.0	9.2

nn - Ashcan comic, not distributed to newsstands, only for in-house use. Cover art is Western Comics #28 with interior being Western Comics #13 (a VG- copy sold for $2151 in 2012)

STAR SPANGLED WAR STORIES (Formerly Star Spangled Comics #1-130; Becomes The Unknown Soldier #205 on) (See Showcase)
National Periodical Publ.: No. 131, 8/52 - No. 133, 10/52; No. 3, 11/52 - No. 204, 2-3/77

131(#1)	226	452	678	1446	2473	3500
132	135	270	405	864	1482	2100
133-Used in POP, pg. 94	106	212	318	673	1162	1650
3,5,6: 6-Evans-a	74	148	222	470	810	1150
4-Devil Dog Dugan app.	77	154	231	493	847	1200
7-10	35	70	105	252	564	875
11-20	28	56	84	202	451	700
21-30: 30-Last precode (2/55)	25	50	75	175	388	600
31-33,35-40	21	42	63	147	324	500
34-Krigstein-a	22	44	66	154	340	525
41-44,46-50: 50-1st S.A. issue	19	38	57	131	291	450
45-1st DC grey tone war-c (5/56)	52	104	156	411	931	1450
51,52,54-63,65,66, 68-83	17	34	51	114	252	390
53-"Rock Sergeant," 3rd Sgt. Rock prototype; inspired "P.I. & The Sand Fleas" in G.I. Combat #56 (1/57)	30	60	90	216	483	750
64-Pre-Sgt. Rock Easy Co. story (12/57)	21	42	63	147	324	500
67-Two Easy Co. stories without Sgt. Rock	23	46	69	161	356	550
84-Origin Mlle. Marie	145	290	435	1196	2698	4200
85-89-Mlle. Marie in all	35	70	105	252	584	875
90-1st app. "War That Time Forgot" series; dinosaur issue-c/story (4-5/60) (also see Weird War Tales #94 & #99)	111	222	333	888	1994	3100
91,93-No dinosaur stories	18	36	54	124	275	425
92-2nd dinosaur-c/s	35	70	105	252	564	875
94 (12/60)- "Ghost Ace" story; Baron Von Richter as The Enemy Ace (predates Our Army at War #151)	37	74	111	274	612	950
95-99: Dinosaur-c/s	25	50	75	175	388	600
100-Dinosaur-c/story.	25	50	75	175	388	600
101-115: All dinosaur issues. 102-Panel inspired a famous Roy Lichtenstein painting	18	36	54	124	275	425
116-125,127-133,135-137: 120-1st app. Caveboy and Dino. 137-Last dinosaur story; Heath Birdman-#129,131	14	28	42	94	207	320
126-No dinosaur story	11	22	33	73	157	240
134-Dinosaur story; Neal Adams-a	18	36	54	124	275	425
138-New Enemy Ace-c/stories begin by Joe Kubert (4-5/68), end #150 (also see Our Army at War #151 and Showcase #57)	19	38	57	131	291	450
139-Origin Enemy Ace (7/68)	10	20	30	69	147	225
140-143,145: 145-Last 12c issue (6-7/69)	8	16	24	54	102	150
144-Neal Adams/Kubert-a	9	18	27	60	120	180
146-Enemy Ace-c/app.	6	12	18	41	76	110
147,148-New Enemy Ace stories	7	14	21	48	89	130
149,150-Last new Enemy Ace by Kubert. Viking Prince by Kubert	7	14	21	44	82	120
151-1st solo app. Unknown Soldier (6-7/70); Enemy Ace-r begin (from Our Army at War, Showcase & SSWS); end #161	18	36	54	128	284	440
152-Reprints 2nd Enemy Ace app.	6	12	18	38	69	100
153,155-Enemy Ace reprints; early Unknown Soldier stories	5	10	15	34	60	85
154-Origin Unknown Soldier	13	26	39	87	191	295
156-1st Battle Album; Unknown Soldier story; Kubert-c/a	5	10	15	31	53	75
157-Sgt. Rock x-over in Unknown Soldier story.	8	12	18	28	47	65
158-163-(52 pgs.): New Unknown Soldier stories; Kubert-c/a. 161-Last Enemy Ace-r	4	8	12	25	40	55
164-183,200: 181-183-Enemy Ace vs. Balloon Buster serial app; Frank Thorne-a. 200-Enemy Ace back-up	3	6	9	15	22	28
184-199,201-204	2	4	6	13	18	22

NOTE: *Anderson* a-28. *Chaykin* a-167. *Drucker* a-59, 61, 64, 66, 67, 73-84. *Estrada* a-149. *John Giunta* a-72. *Glanzman* a-167, 171, 172, 174. *Heath* a-42,122, 132, 133; c-67, 122, 132-134. *Kaluta* a-197i; c-167. *G. Kane* a-169. *Kubert* a-6-163(most later issues). 200. *Maurer* a-160, 165. *Severin* a-65, 162. *S&K* c-7-31, 33, 34, 37, 40. *Simonson* a-170, 172, 174, 180. *Sutton* a-168. *Thorne* a-183. *Toth* a-164. *Wildey* a-161. *Suicide Squad* in 110, 116-118, 120, 121, 127.

STAR SPANGLED WAR STORIES (Featuring Mademoiselle Marie)
DC Comics: Nov, 2010 ($3.99, one-shot)

1-Mademoiselle Marie in 1944 France; Tucci-s/Justiniano-a/Bolland-c						4.00

STAR SPANGLED WAR STORIES (Featuring G.I. Zombie)
DC Comics: Sept, 2014 - No. 8, May, 2015 ($2.99)

1-8-Palmiotti & Gray-s/Scott Hampton-a. 1-6-Darwyn Cooke-c. 7-Dave Johnson-c						3.00
...: Futures End 1 (11/14, $2.99, regular-c) Five years later; Dave Johnson-c						3.00
...: Futures End 1 (11/14, $3.99, 3-D cover)						4.00

STARSTREAM (Adventures in Science Fiction)(See Questar illustrated)
Whitman/Western Publishing Co.: 1976 (79¢, 68 pgs, cardboard-c)

1-4: 1-Bolle-a. 2-4-McWilliams & Bolle-a	2	4	6	10	14	18

STARSTRUCK
Marvel Comics (Epic Comics): Feb, 1985 - No. 6, Feb, 1986 ($1.50, mature)

1-6: Kaluta-a						6.00

STARSTRUCK
Dark Horse Comics: Aug, 1990 - No. 4, Nov?, 1990 ($2.95, B&W, 52pgs.)

1-3: Kaluta-r/Epic series plus new-c/a in all						4.00
4 (68 pgs.)-contains 2 trading cards						5.00
Reprint 1-13 (IDW, 8/09 - No. 13, Sept, 2010, $3.99) newly colored; Galactic Girl Guides						4.00

STARSTRUCK: OLD PROLDIERS NEVER DIE
IDW Publishing: Feb, 2017 - No. 6, Jul, 2017 ($4.99)

1-Expanded version of old stories with new art; Elaine Lee-s/Michael Kaluta-a						5.00

STAR STUDDED
Cambridge House/Superior Publishers: 1945 (25¢, 132 pgs.); 1945 (196 pgs.)

nn-Captain Combat by Giunta, Ghost Woman, Commandette, & Red Rogue app.; Infantino-a	55	110	165	352	601	850
nn-The Cadet, Edison Bell, Hoot Gibson, Jungle Lil (196 pgs.); copies vary; Blue Beetle in some	61	122	183	390	670	950

STARTLING COMICS
Better Publications (Nedor): June, 1940 - No. 53, Sept, 1948

1-Origin Captain Future-Man Of Tomorrow, Mystico (By Sansone), The Wonder Man; The Masked Rider & his horse Pinto begins; Masked Rider formerly in pulps; drug use story	400	800	1200	2800	4900	7000
2 -Don Davis, Espionage Ace begins	206	412	618	1318	2259	3200
3	174	348	522	1114	1907	2700
4	142	284	426	909	1555	2200
5,6,9	123	246	369	787	1344	1900
7,8-Nazi WWII-c	181	362	543	1158	1979	2800
10-The Fighting Yank begins (9/41, origin/1st app.); Nazi WWII-c	1200	2400	3600	9100	16,550	24,000
11-2nd app. Fighting Yank; Nazi WWII-c	300	600	900	2010	3505	5000
12-Hitler, Tojo, Mussolini-c	394	788	1182	2758	4829	6900
13-15	142	284	426	909	1555	2200
16-Origin The Four Comrades; not in #32,35	168	336	504	1075	11838	2600
17-Last Masked Rider & Mystico	155	310	465	992	1696	2400
18-Pyroman begins (12/42, origin)(also see America's Best Comics #3 for 1st app., 11/42)	226	452	678	1446	2473	3500
19-Nazi WWII-c	300	600	900	2010	3505	5000
20-Classic hooded Nazi giant snake bondage/torture-c (scarce); The Oracle begins (3/43); not in issues 26,28,33,34	514	1028	1542	3750	6625	9500
21-Origin The Ape, Oracle's enemy; Schomburg hypo-c	245	490	735	1568	2684	3800
22-34: All have Schomburg WWII-c. 34-Origin The Scarab & only app.	168	336	504	1075	1838	2600
35-Hypodermic syringe attacks Fighting Yank in drug story; Schomburg WWII-c	172	374	561	1197	2049	2900
36-43: 36-Last Four Comrades. 38-Bondage/torture-c. 40-Last Capt. Future & Oracle. 41-Front Page Peggy begins; A-Bomb-c. 43-Last Pyroman	84	168	252	538	919	1300
44,45: 44-Lance Lewis, Space Detective begins; Ingels-c; sci/fi-c begin. 45-Tygra begins (intro/origin, 5/47); Ingels-c/a (splash pg. & inside f/c B&W ad)	142	284	426	909	1555	2200
46-Classic Ingels-c; Ingels-a	297	594	891	1901	3251	4600
47,48,50-53: 50,51-Sea-Eagle app.	148	296	444	947	1624	2300
49-Classic Schomburg Robot-c; last Fighting Yank	1630	3260	4890	12,100	21,550	31,000

NOTE: *Ingels* a-44, 45; c-44, 45, 46(wash). *Schomburg (Xela)* c-21-43; 47-53 (airbrush). *Tuska* c-45? Bondage c-16, 21, 37, 46-49. *Captain Future* c-1-9, 13, 14. *Fighting Yank* c-10-12, 15-17, 21, 22, 24, 26, 28, 30, 32, 34, 36, 38, 40, 42. *Pyroman* c-18-20, 23, 25, 27, 29, 31, 33, 35, 37, 39, 41, 43.

STARTLING STORIES: BANNER
Marvel Comics: July, 2001 - No. 4, Oct, 2001 (limited series)

1-4-Hulk story by Azzarello; Corben-c/a						3.00
TPB (11/01, $12.95) r/1-4						13.00

STARTLING STORIES: FANTASTIC FOUR - UNSTABLE MOLECULES (See Fantastic Four - ...)

STARTLING STORIES: THE MEGALOMANIACAL SPIDER-MAN
Marvel Comics: Jun, 2002 ($2.99, one-shot)

1-Spider-Man spoof; Peter Bagge-s/a	3	4	6	9	12	15

STARTLING STORIES: THE THING
Marvel Comics: 2003 ($3.50, one-shot)

	GD	VG	FN	VF	VF/NM	NM-
	2.0	4.0	6.0	8.0	9.0	9.2

1-Zimmerman-s/Kramer-a; Inhumans and the Hulk app.   3.50

STARTLING STORIES: THE THING - NIGHT FALLS ON YANCY STREET
Marvel Comics: Jun, 2003 - No. 4, Sept, 2003 ($3.50, limited series)

1-4-Dorkin-s/Haspiel-a. 2,3-Frightful Four app.   3.50

STARTLING TERROR TALES
Star Publications: No. 10, May, 1952 - No. 14, Feb, 1953; No. 4, Apr, 1953 - No. 11, 1954

10-(1st Series)-Wood/Harrison-a (r/A Star Presentation #3) Disbrow/Cole-c; becomes 4
different titles after #10; becomes Confessions of Love #11 on, The Horrors #11 on,
Terrifying Tales #11 on, Terrors of the Jungle #11 on & continues w/Startling Terror #11

	142	284	426	909	1555	2200

11-(8/52)- L.B. Cole Spider-c; r-Fox's "A Feature Presentation" #5 (blue-c)

	811	1622	2433	5920	10,460	15,000

11-Black-c (variant; believed to be a pressrun change) (Unique)

	865	1230	2595	6315	11,158	16,000
12,14	77	154	231	493	847	1200
13-Jo-Jo-r; Disbrow-a	74	148	222	470	810	1150
4-9,11(1953-54) (2nd Series): 11-New logo	53	106	159	334	567	800
10-Disbrow-a	58	116	174	371	636	900

NOTE: *L. B. Cole covers-all issues. Palais a-V2#8r, V2#11r.*

STAR TREK (TV) (See Dan Curtis Giveaways, Dynabrite Comics & Power Record Comics)
Gold Key: 7/67; No. 2, 6/68; No. 3, 12/68; No. 4, 6/69 - No. 61, 3/79

1-Photo-c begin, end #9; photo back-c is on all copies,
no variant exists with an ad on the back-c

	148	296	444	1221	2761	4300
2-Regular version has an ad on back-c	30	60	90	216	483	750
2 (rare variation w/photo back-c)	61	122	183	488	1094	1700
3-5-All have back-c ads	18	36	54	128	284	440
3 (rare variation w/photo back-c)	35	70	105	252	564	875
6-9	12	24	36	81	176	275
10-20	6	12	18	38	69	100
21-30	5	10	15	31	53	80
31-40	4	8	12	27	44	60
41-61: 52-Drug propaganda story	3	6	9	21	33	45

... Gold Key 100-Page Spectacular (IDW, 2/17, $7.99) r/#1,8,14; cover & pin-up gallery 8.00
... the Enterprise Logs nn (8/76)-Golden Press, ($1.95, 224 pgs.)-r/#1-8 plus 7 pgs. by
McWilliams (#11185)-Photo-c

	7	14	21	48	89	130

... the Enterprise Logs Vol. 2 ('76)-r/#9-17 (#11187)-Photo-c

	5	10	15	34	60	85

... the Enterprise Logs Vol. 3 ('77)-r/#18-26 (#11188); McWilliams-a (4 pgs.)-Photo-c

	5	10	15	33	57	80

Star Trek Vol. 4 (Winter '77)-Reprints #27,28,30-34,36,38 (#11189) plus 3 pgs.
new art

	5	10	15	31	53	75

... : The Key Collection (Checker Book Publ. Group, 2004, $22.95) r/#1-8   23.00
... : The Key Collection Volume 2 (Checker, 2004, $22.95) r/#9-16   23.00
... : The Key Collection Volume 3 (Checker, 2005, $22.95) r/#17-24   23.00
... : The Key Collection Volume 4 (Checker, 2005, $22.95) r/#25-33   23.00
... : The Key Collection Volume 5 (Checker, 2005, $22.95) r/#34,36,38,39,40-43   23.00
NOTE: *McWilliams a-38, 40-44, 46-61. #29 reprints #1; #35 reprints #4; #37 reprints #5; #45 reprints #7. The tabloids all have photo back covers and blank inside covers. Painted covers #10-44, 46-59.*

STAR TREK
Marvel Comics Group: April, 1980 - No. 18, Feb, 1982

	GD	VG	FN	VF	VF/NM	NM-
1: 1-3-r/Marvel Super Special; movie adapt.	3	6	9	17	26	35
2-16: 5-Miller-c	2	4	6	8	10	12
17-Low print run	2	4	6	10	14	18
18-Last issue; low print run	2	4	6	11	16	20

NOTE: *Austin c-18i. Buscema a-13. Gil Kane a-15. Nasser c/a-7. Simonson c-17.*

STAR TREK (Also see Who's Who In Star Trek)
DC Comics: Feb, 1984 - No. 56, Nov, 1988 (75¢, Mando paper)

1-Sutton-a(p) begins	2	4	6	13	18	22
2-5						6.00
6-10: 7-Origin Saavik						5.00
11-32,34-49,51-56: 19-Walter Koenig story. 37-Painted-c						4.00
33-($1.25, 52 pgs.)-20th anniversary issue						5.00
50-($1.50, 52 pgs.)						5.00
Annual 1-3: 1(1985). 2(1986). 3(1988, $1.50)						5.00

... : To Boldly Go TPB (Titan Books, 7/05, $19.95) r/#1-6; Koenig foreward; cast interviews   20.00
... : The Trial of James T. Kirk TPB (Titan Books, 6/06, $19.95) r/#7-12; cast interviews   20.00
... : The Return of the Worthy TPB (Titan Books, 12/06, $19.95) r/#13-18; cast interviews   20.00
NOTE: *Morrow a-28, 35, 36, 56. Orlando c-8i. Perez c-1-3. Spiegle a-19. Starlin c-24, 25. Sutton a-1-6p, 8-18p, 20-27p, 29p, 31-34p, 39-52p, 55p; c-4-6p, 8-22p, 46p.*

STAR TREK
DC Comics: Oct, 1989 - No. 80, Jan, 1996 ($1.50/$1.75/$1.95/$2.50)

1-Capt. Kirk and crew	2	4	6	8	10	12
2,3						5.00
4-23,25-30: 10-12-The Trial of James T. Kirk. 21-Begin $1.75-c						3.00
24-($2.95, 68 pgs.)-40 pg. epic w/pin-ups						4.00
31-49,51-74,76-80						3.00
50-($3.50, 68 pgs.)-Painted-c						4.00
75 ($3.95)						4.00
Annual 1-6('90-'95, 68 pgs.): 1-Morrow-a. 3-Painted-c						4.00
Special 1-3 ('9-'95, 68 pgs.)-1-Sutton-a.						4.00

... : The Ashes of Eden (1995, $14.95, 100 pgs.)-Shatner story   18.00
... Generations (1994, $3.95, 68 pgs.)-Movie adaptation

		1	3	4	6	8	10

... Generations (1994, $5.95, 68 pgs.)-Squarebound

	1	3	4	6	8	10

STAR TREK... (TV)
DC Comics (WildStorm): one-shots

All of Me (4/00, $5.95, prestige format) Lopresti-a   6.00
Enemy Unseen TPB (2001, $17.95) r/Perchance to Dream, Embrace the Wolf,
The Killing Shadows; Struzan-c   18.00
Enter the Wolves (2001, $5.95) Crispin & Weinstein-s; Mota-a/c   6.00
New Frontier – Double Time (11/00, $5.95)-Captain Calhoun's USS Excalibur; Peter David-s;
Stelfreeze-c   6.00
Other Realities TPB (2001, $14.95) r/All of Me, New Frontier - Double Time, and DS9-N-Vector;

Van Fleet-c   15.00
Special (2001, $6.95) Stories from all 4 series by various; Van Fleet-c   7.00

STAR TREK (Further adventures of the crew from the 2009 movie)
IDW Publishing: Sept, 2011 - No. 60, Aug, 2016 ($3.99)

1-49: 1,2-Gary Mitchell app.; Molnar-a. 11,12-Tribbles. 15,16-Mirror Universe. 21-Follows
the 2013 movie; Klingons & Section 31 app. 35-40-The Q Gambit; DS9 crew app.   4.00
50-($4.99) Mirror Universe; Khan app.; bonus history of Star Trek comics, aliens   5.00
51-60: 51,52-Mirror Universe. 52-Variant Archie Comics cover. 55-58-Legacy of Spock   4.00
Annual (2012/13, $7.99) "Strange New Worlds" on cover; photonovel by John Byrne   8.00
... #1: Greatest Hits (3/16, $1.00) reprints #1   3.00
... #1: Hundred Penny Press (8/13, $1.00) reprints #1   3.00
... : Deviations 1 (3/17, $4.99) Timeline where Romulans, not Vulcans made 1st Contact   5.00
... : Ferengi 1 (4/22, $7.99) Quark, Rom and Moogie app; Christina Rice-s/Andy Price-a   8.00
... : 50th Anniversary Cover Celebration (8/16, $7.99) Gallery of IDW Star Trek covers   8.00
... : Flesh and Stone (7/14, $3.99) Doctors Bashir, Crusher, Pulaski, McCoy app.   4.00
... : IDW 20/20 (1/19, $4.99) Picard on the Stargazer 20 years before TNG; Woodward-a   5.00
... : Klingons 1 (2/22, $7.99) Story of Kahless; Timothy Green II-a   8.00
... : Space Spanning Treasury Edition (3/19, $9.99, 13" x 8.5") Reprints #9,10,13   10.00

STAR TREK (400th issue published by IDW)
IDW Publishing: No. 400, Sept, 2022 ($7.99, one-shot)

400-IDW Legacy issue; short story anthology spanning all the crews by various   8.00

STAR TREK (Also see Star Trek: Defiant)
IDW Publishing: Oct, 2022 - Present ($4.99)

1-17-Crew of Sisko, Dr. Crusher, Tom Paris and Worf. 11,12-Day of Blood x-over   5.00
... Annual 2023 (5/23, $5.99) Stott-a; holographic James T. Kirk app.   6.00
... : Day of Blood 1 (7/23, $5.99) Crossover with Star Trek #11,12 & Star Trek: Defiant #6,7   6.00
... : Day of Blood Director's Cut 1 (10/23, $6.99) Reprint in B&W; original story pitch   7.00
... : Day of Blood – Shax's Best Day 1 (9/23, $5.99) Ryan North-s/Derek Charm-a   6.00
... : Trill 1 (11/22, $7.99) Houser-s/Prasetya-a   8.00

STAR TREK: ALIEN SPOTLIGHT
IDW Publishing: Sept, 2007 - Feb, 2008 ($3.99, series of one-shots)

... Andorians (11/07) Storrie-s/O'Grady-a; Counselor Troi app.; two art & one photo-c   4.00
... Borg (1/08) Harris-s/Murphy-a; Janeway & Next Gen crew app.; two art & one photo-c   4.00
... Cardassians (12/09) Padilla-a; Garak & Kira app.   4.00
... The Gorn (9/07) Messina-a; Chekov app.; two art & one photo-c   4.00
... Orions (12/07) Casagrande-a; Capt. Pike app.; two art & one photo-c   4.00
... Q (8/09) Casagrande-a; takes place after Star Trek 8 movie; two art & one photo-c   4.00
... Romulans (2/08) John Byrne-s/a; Kirk era; two art & one photo-c   4.00
... Romulans (5/09) Wagner Reis-a; David Williams-c   4.00
... Tribbles (3/09) Hawthorne-a; first encounter with Klingons; one art & one photo-c   4.00
... Vulcans (10/07) Spock's early Enterprise days with Capt. Pike; two art & one photo-c   4.00

STAR TREK: ASSIGNMENT EARTH
IDW Publishing: May, 2008 - No. 5, Sept, 2008 ($3.99, limited series)

1-5-Further adventures of Gary Seven and Roberta; John Byrne-s/a/c. 5-Nixon app.   4.00

STAR TREK: BOLDLY GO (Takes place after the 2016 movie Star Trek Beyond)
IDW Publishing: Oct, 2016 - No. 18, Mar, 2018 ($3.99)

1-18-The 2009 movie crew; Mike Johnson-s/Shasteen-a; The Borg app.; multiple covers   4.00

STAR TREK: BURDEN OF KNOWLEDGE
IDW Publishing: Jun, 2010 - No. 4, Sept, 2010 ($3.99, limited series)

1-4-Original series Kirk and crew; Manfredi-a   4.00

STAR TREK: CAPTAIN'S LOG
IDW Publishing: one-shots

... : Harriman (4/10, $3.99) Captain of the Enterprise-B following Kirk's "demise"; Currie-a   4.00
... : Jellico (10/10, $3.99) Woodward-a   4.00
... : Pike (9/10, $3.99) Events that put Pike in the chair; Woodward-a   4.00
... : Sulu (1/10, $3.99) Manfredi-a   4.00

STAR TREK: COUNTDOWN (Prequel to the 2009 movie)
IDW Publishing: Jan, 2009 - No. 4, Apr, 2009 ($3.99, limited series)

1-4: 1-Ambassador Spock on Romulus; intro. Nero; Messina-a   4.00
Hundred Penny Press: Star Trek: Countdown 1 (4/11, $1.00) r/#1 w/new cover frame   3.00

STAR TREK: COUNTDOWN TO DARKNESS (Prequel to the 2013 movie)
IDW Publishing: Jan, 2013 - No. 4, Apr, 2013 ($3.99, limited series)

1-4-Captain April app.; Messina-a; regular & photo covers on each   4.00

STAR TREK: CREW
IDW Publishing: Mar, 2009 - No. 5, Jul, 2009 ($3.99, limited series)

1-5: John Byrne-s/a; Captain Pike era   4.00

STAR TREK: DEBT OF HONOR
DC Comics: 1992 ($24.95/$14.95, graphic novel)

Hardcover ($24.95) Claremont-s/Hughes-a(p)   25.00
Softcover ($14.95)   15.00

STAR TREK: DEEP SPACE NINE (TV)
Malibu Comics: Aug, 1993 - No. 32, Nov, 1996 ($2.50)

1-Direct Sale Edition w/line drawn-c	1	2	3	5	6	8
1-Newsstand Edition with photo-c						6.00
0-(1/95, $2.95)-Terok Nor						6.00
2-30: 2-Polybagged w/trading card. 9-4 pg. prelude to Hearts & Minds						4.00
31-($3.95)						5.00
32-($3.50)						5.00
Annual 1 (1/95, $3.95, 68 pgs.)						5.00
Special 1 (1995, $3.50)						5.00
Ultimate Annual 1 (12/95, $5.95)						6.00
... : Lightstorm (12/94, $3.50)						5.00

STAR TREK: DEEP SPACE NINE (TV)
Marvel Comics (Paramount Comics): Nov, 1996 - No. 15, Mar, 1998 ($1.95/$1.99)

1-15: 12,13-"Telepathy War" pt.2,3   4.00

STAR TREK: DEEP SPACE NINE: FOOL'S GOLD
IDW Publishing: Dec, 2009 - No. 4, Mar, 2010 ($3.99)

Star Trek #8 © Paramount

Star Trek: Boldly Go #7 © CBS

Star Trek: Mirror Images #4 © CBS

	GD 2.0	VG 4.0	FN 6.0	VF 8.0	VF/NM 9.0	NM- 9.2
1-4-Mantovani-a						4.00

STAR TREK: DEEP SPACE NINE – N-VECTOR (TV)
DC Comics (WildStorm): Aug, 2000 - No. 4, Nov, 2000 ($2.50, limited series)

	GD 2.0	VG 4.0	FN 6.0	VF 8.0	VF/NM 9.0	NM- 9.2
1-4-Cypress-a						3.00

STAR TREK DEEP SPACE NINE-THE CELEBRITY SERIES
Malibu Comics: May, 1995 ($2.95)

1-Blood and Honor; Mark Lenard script						4.00
1-Rules of Diplomacy; Aron Eisenberg script						4.00

STAR TREK: DEEP SPACE NINE HEARTS AND MINDS
Malibu Comics: June, 1994 - No. 4, Sept, 1994 ($2.50, limited series)

1-4						4.00
1-Holographic-c						5.00

STAR TREK: DEEP SPACE NINE, THE MAQUIS
Malibu Comics: Feb, 1995 - No. 3, Apr, 1995 ($2.50, limited series)

1-3-Newsstand-c, 1-Photo-c						4.00

STAR TREK: DEEP SPACE NINE/THE NEXT GENERATION
Malibu Comics: Oct, 1994 - No. 2, Nov, 1994 ($2.50, limited series)

1,2: Parts 2 & 4 of x-over with Star Trek: TNG/DS9 from DC Comics						4.00

STAR TREK: DEEP SPACE NINE – THE DOG OF WAR
IDW Publishing: Apr, 2023 - No. 5, Aug, 2023 ($4.99, limited series)

1-5-Multiple covers on each						5.00

STAR TREK: DEEP SPACE NINE – TOO LONG A SACRIFICE
IDW Publishing: Mar, 2020 - No. 4, Oct, 2020 ($3.99, limited series)

1-4-Steve & David Tipton-s/Greg Scott-a						4.00

STAR TREK: DEEP SPACE NINE WORF SPECIAL
Malibu Comics: Dec, 1995 ($3.95, one-shot)

1-Includes pinups						6.00

STAR TREK: DEFIANT
IDW Publishing: Mar, 2023 - Present ($4.99, limited series)

1-12: 1-Cantwell-s/Unzueta-s; Worf, Spock, Lore, B'Elanna and Ro Laren app.						5.00
Annual (1/24, $5.99) Spotlight on Sela; Cantwell-s/Rosanas-a						6.00

STAR TREK: DISCOVERY (Based on the 2017 TV series)
IDW Publishing: Mar, 2018 ($7.99)

Annual 2018 (3/18, $7.99)-Beyer & Johnson-s/Hernandez-a; spotlight on Lt. Stamets						8.00
...: Captain Saru (2/19, $7.99) Beyer & Johnson-s/Hernandez-a; two covers						8.00

STAR TREK: DISCOVERY: ADVENTURES IN THE 32ND CENTURY (2017 TV series)
IDW Publishing: Mar, 2022 - No. 4, Jun, 2022 ($3.99, limited series)

1-4-Johnson-s/Hernandez-a						4.00

STAR TREK: DISCOVERY – AFTERMATH (Based on the 2017 TV series)
IDW Publishing: Aug, 2019 - No. 3, Oct, 2019 ($3.99, limited series)

1-3-Beyer & Johnson-s/Shasteen-a; takes place before Spock joins the Enterprise						4.00

STAR TREK: DISCOVERY: SUCCESSION (Based on the 2017 TV series)
IDW Publishing: Apr, 2018 - No. 4, Jul, 2018 ($3.99, limited series)

1-4-Beyer & Johnson-s/Hernandez-a; takes place in the Mirror Universe						4.00

STAR TREK: DISCOVERY: THE LIGHT OF KAHLESS (Based on the 2017 TV series)
IDW Publishing: Oct, 2017 - No. 4, Jan, 2018 ($3.99, limited series)

1-4-Beyer & Johnson-s/Shasteen-a						4.00

STAR TREK: DIVIDED WE FALL
DC Comics (WildStorm): July, 2001 - No. 4, Oct, 2001 ($2.95, limited series)

1-4: Ordover & Mack-s; Lenara Kahn, Verad and Odan app.						3.00

STAR TREK EARLY VOYAGES (TV)
Marvel Comics (Paramount Comics): Feb, 1997 - No. 17, Jun, 1998 ($2.95/$1.95/$1.99)

1-($2.95)						6.00
2-17						4.00

STAR TREK: ENTERPRISE EXPERIMENT
IDW Publishing: Apr, 2008 - No. 5, Aug, 2008 ($3.99, limited series)

1-5-Year Four story; D.C. Fontana & Derek Chester-s; Purcell-a						4.00

STAR TREK: FIRST CONTACT (Movie)
Marvel Comics (Paramount Comics): Nov, 1996 ($5.95, one-shot)

nn-Movie adaptation						6.00

STAR TREK/ GREEN LANTERN (The Spectrum War)
IDW Publishing: Jul, 2015 - No. 6, Dec, 2015 ($3.99, limited series)

	GD 2.0	VG 4.0	FN 6.0	VF 8.0	VF/NM 9.0	NM- 9.2
1-6-Crew from 2009 movie and Hal Jordan; Sinestro & Nekron app.; multiple covers						4.00

STAR TREK/ GREEN LANTERN (Stranger Worlds)
IDW Publishing: Dec, 2016 - No. 6, May, 2017 ($3.99, limited series)

1-6-Sinestro & The Manhunters app.; multiple covers. 2-6-Khan app.						4.00

STAR TREK: HARLAN ELLISON'S ORIGINAL CITY ON THE EDGE OF FOREVER TELEPLAY
IDW Publishing: Jun, 2014 - No. 5, Oct, 2014 ($3.99, limited series)

1-5-Adaptation of Ellison's teleplay; J.K. Woodward-a; two covers on each						4.00

STAR TREK: HOLO-WEEN
IDW Publishing: Oct, 2023 - No. 4, Oct, 2023 ($3.99, weekly limited series)

1-4-Sequeira-s/Eisma-a; classic horror characters emerge from the holodeck						4.00

STAR TREK: INFESTATION (Crossover with G.I. Joe, Transformers & Ghostbusters)
IDW Publishing: Feb, 2011 - No. 2, Feb, 2011 ($3.99, limited series)

1,2-Zombies in the Kirk era; Maloney & Erskine-a; two covers on each						4.00

STAR TREK: KHAN
IDW Publishing: Oct, 2013 - No. 5, Feb, 2014 ($3.99, limited series)

1-5-Follows the 2013 movie; Khan's origin; Messina & Balboni-a						4.00

STAR TREK: KHAN RULING IN HELL
IDW Publishing: Oct, 2010 - No. 4, Jan, 2011 ($3.99, limited series)

1-4-Khan and the Botany Bay crew after banishment on Ceti Alpha V; Mantovani-a						4.00

STAR TREK: KLINGONS: BLOOD WILL TELL
IDW Publishing: Apr, 2007 - No. 5 ($3.99, limited series)

1-5-Star Trek TOS episodes from the Klingon viewpoint; Messina-a. 2-Tribbles						4.00
1-($4.99) Klingon Language Variant; comic with Kliingon text; English script						5.00

STAR TREK/ LEGION OF SUPER-HEROES
IDW Publishing: Oct, 2011 - No. 6, Mar, 2012 ($3.99, limited series)

1-6-Jeff Moy-a/Jimenez-c 1-Giffen var-c. 2-Lightle var-c. 3-Grell var-c. 5-Allred var-c						4.00

STAR TREK: LEONARD McCOY, FRONTIER DOCTOR
IDW Publishing: Apr, 2010 - No. 4, Jul, 2010 ($3.99, limited series)

1-4-Dr. McCoy right before Star Trek: TMP; John Byrne-s/a						4.00

STAR TREK: LOWER DECKS (Based on the animated TV series)
IDW Publishing: Sept, 2022 - No. 3, Nov, 2022 ($6.99, limited series)

1-3-Ryan North-s/Chris Fenoglio-a						7.00

STAR TREK: MANIFEST DESTINY
IDW Publishing: Apr, 2016 - No. 4, May, 2016 ($4.99/$3.99, limited series)

1-The 2009 movie crew vs. Klingons; Angel Hernandez-a						5.00
2-4-($3.99)						4.00

STAR TREK: MIRROR BROKEN (Series previewed in Star Trek: The Next Generation: Mirror Broken #0 FCBD giveaway)
IDW Publishing: May, 2017 - No. 5, Oct, 2017 ($3.99, limited series)

1-5-The Mirror Universe Next Generation crew; David & Scott Tipton-s/Woodward-a						4.00

STAR TREK: MIRROR IMAGES
IDW Publishing: June, 2008 - No. 5, Nov, 2008 ($3.99, limited series)

1-5-Further adventures in the Mirror Universe. 3-Mirror-Picard app.						4.00

STAR TREK: MIRROR MIRROR
Marvel Comics (Paramount Comics): Feb, 1997 ($3.95, one-shot)

1-DeFalco-s						4.00

STAR TREK: MISSION'S END
IDW Publishing: Mar, 2009 - No. 5, July, 2009 ($3.99, limited series)

1-5-Kirk, Spock, Bones crew, their last mission on the pre-movie Enterprise						4.00

STAR TREK MOVIE ADAPTATION
IDW Publishing: Feb, 2010 - No. 6, Aug, 2010 ($3.99, limited series)

1-6-Adaptation of 2009 movie; Messina-a; regular & photo-c on each						4.00

STAR TREK MOVIE SPECIAL
DC Comics: 1984 (June) - No. 2, 1987 ($1.50); No. 1, 1989 ($2.00, 52 pgs)

nn-(#1)-Adapts Star Trek III; Sutton-p (68 pgs.)						5.00
2-Adapts Star Trek IV; Sutton-a; Chaykin-c. (68 pgs.)						5.00
1 (1989)-Adapts Star Trek V; painted-c						5.00

STAR TREK: NERO
IDW Publishing: Aug, 2009 - No. 4, Nov, 2009 ($3.99, limited series)

1-4-Nero's ship after the attack on the Kelvin to the arrival of Spock						4.00

STAR TREK: NEW FRONTIER
IDW Publishing: Mar, 2008 - No. 5, July, 2008 ($3.99, limited series)

	GD 2.0	VG 4.0	FN 6.0	VF 8.0	VF/NM 9.0	NM- 9.2

1-5-Capt. Calhoun & Adm. Shelby app.; Peter David-s — 4.00

STAR TREK: NEW VISIONS
IDW Publishing: May, 2014 - No. 22, Jun, 2018 ($7.99, squarebound)
1-22-Photonovels of original crew by John Byrne. 1-Mirror Universe — 8.00
... Special: More Of The Serpent Than The Dove (9/16, Humble Bundle) Gorn app. — 20.00
... Special: The Cage (7/16, $7.99) — 8.00

STAR TREK 100 PAGE...
IDW Publishing: Nov, 2011 - 2012 ($7.99)
...Spectacular #1 (11/11) Reprints stories of the original crew; s/a by Byrne and others — 8.00
...Spectacular 2012 (2/12) Reprints; Khan, Q, Capt. Pike, the Gorn app. — 8.00
...Spectacular Summer 2012 (8/12) Reprints of TNG and Voyager stories — 8.00
...Spectacular Winter 2012 - Reprints; Capt. Harriman, Mirror Universe — 8.00

STAR TREK: OPERATION ASSIMILATION
Marvel Comics (Paramount Comics): Dec, 1996 ($2.95, one-shot)
1 — 4.00

STAR TREK: PICARD COUNTDOWN (Prelude to the 2020 TV series)
IDW Publishing: Nov, 2019 - No. 3, Jan, 2020 ($3.99, limited series)
1-3-Beyer & Johnson-s/Hernandez-a; intro. Raffi Musiker, Laris & Zhaban — 4.00

STAR TREK: PICARD'S ACADEMY
IDW Publishing: Sept, 2023 - No. 6, Feb, 2024 ($3.99, limited series)
1-6-Sam Maggs-s/Ornella Greco-a; Picard's 2nd year at the Academy — 4.00

STAR TREK: PICARD STARGAZER (Follows season 2 of the TV series)
IDW Publishing: Aug, 2022 - No. 3, Nov, 2022 ($4.99, limited series)
1-3-Beyer & Johnson-s/Hernandez-a; Seven app. — 5.00

STAR TREK/PLANET OF THE APES: THE PRIMATE DIRECTIVE
IDW Publishing: Dec, 2014 - No. 5, Apr, 2015 ($3.99, limited series)
1-5-Classic crew on the Planet of the Apes; Klingons app. 2-Kirk meets Taylor — 8.00

STAR TREK: RESURGENCE (Prequel to the video game)
IDW Publishing: Nov, 2022 - No. 5, Mar, 2023 ($3.99, limited series)
1-5-Leah Brahms app.; Josh Hood-a — 4.00

STAR TREK: ROMULANS SCHISMS
IDW Publishing: Sept, 2009 - No. 3, Nov, 2009 ($3.99, limited series)
1-3-John Byrne-s/a/c — 4.00

STAR TREK: ROMULANS THE HOLLOW CROWN
IDW Publishing: Sept, 2008 - No. 2, Oct, 2008 ($3.99, limited series)
1,2-John Byrne-s/a/c — 4.00

STAR TREK VI: THE UNDISCOVERED COUNTRY (Movie)
DC Comics: 1992

	GD 2.0	VG 4.0	FN 6.0	VF 8.0	VF/NM 9.0	NM- 9.2
1-($2.95, regular edition, 68 pgs.)-Adaptation of film		2	3	5	6	8
nn-($5.95, prestige edition)-Has photos of movie not included in regular edition; painted-c by Palmer; photo back-c	1	3	4	6	8	10

STAR TREK: SPOCK: REFLECTIONS
IDW Publishing: July, 2009 - No. 4, Oct, 2009 ($3.99, limited series)
1-4-Flashbacks of Spock's childhood and career; Messina & Manfredi-a — 4.00

STAR TREK: STARFLEET ACADEMY
Marvel Comics (Paramount Comics): Dec, 1996 - No. 19, Jun, 1998 ($1.95/$1.99)
1-19-Begin new series. 12-"Telepathy War" pt. 1. 18-English & Klingon editions — 4.00

STAR TREK: STARFLEET ACADEMY
IDW Publishing: Dec, 2015 - No. 5, Apr, 2016 ($3.99, limited series)
1-5-Crew of the 2009 movie at the academy; Charm-a — 4.00

STAR TREK: STRANGE NEW WORLDS - THE ILLYRIAN ENIGMA
IDW Publishing: Dec, 2022 - No. 4, Mar, 2023 ($3.99, limited series)
1-4-Beyer & Johnson-s/Levens-a — 4.00

STAR TREK: STRANGE NEW WORLDS - THE SCORPIUS RUN
IDW Publishing: Aug, 2023 - No. 5, Jan, 2024 ($3.99, limited series)
1-5-Johnson & Parrott-s/Hernandez-a — 4.00

STAR TREK: TELEPATHY WAR
Marvel Comics (Paramount Comics): Nov, 1997 ($2.99, 48 pgs., one-shot)
1-"Telepathy War" x-over pt. 6 — 5.00

STAR TREK: THE MIRROR WAR
IDW Publishing: No. 0, Aug, 2021 - No. 8, Aug, 2022 ($3.99)
0-8-Mirror Universe Enterprise crew. 1-5-Scott & David Tipton-s/Gavin Smith-a — 4.00
...: Data 1 (12/21, $3.99) Bronfman-s/Ingranata-a; Barclay app. — 4.00
...: La Forge 1 (3/22, $3.99) Holtham-s/Rodriguez-a — 4.00
...: Sisko 1 (6/22, $3.99) Lore-s/Prasetya-a — 4.00
...: Troi 1 (9/22, $3.99) Nijkamp-s/Levens-a — 4.00

STAR TREK - THE MODALA IMPERATIVE
DC Comics: Late July, 1991 - No. 4, Late Sept, 1991 ($1.75, limited series)
1-4 — 4.00
TPB ($19.95) r/series and ST:TNG - The Modala Imperative — 20.00

STAR TREK: THE MOTION PICTURE - ECHOES
IDW Publishing: May, 2023 - No. 5, Sept, 2023 ($4.99, limited series)
1-5-Guggenheim-s/Chudakov-a; takes place after the first movie — 5.00

STAR TREK: THE NEXT GENERATION (TV)
DC Comics: Feb, 1988 - No. 6, July, 1988 (limited series)

	GD 2.0	VG 4.0	FN 6.0	VF 8.0	VF/NM 9.0	NM- 9.2
1 ($1.50, 52 pgs.)-Sienkiewicz painted-c		2	4	6	9	13	16
2-6 ($1.00)						5.00

STAR TREK: THE NEXT GENERATION (TV)
DC Comics: Oct, 1989 -No. 80, 1995 ($1.50/$1.75/$1.95)

	GD 2.0	VG 4.0	FN 6.0	VF 8.0	VF/NM 9.0	NM- 9.2
1-Capt. Picard and crew from TV show		2	4	6	9	13	16
2,3						6.00
4-10						5.00

11-23,25-49,51-60 — 4.00
24,50: 24-($2.50, 52 pgs.). 50-($3.50, 68 pgs.)-Painted-c — 6.00
61-74,76-80 — 4.00
75-($3.95, 50 pgs.) — 5.00
Annual 1-6 ('90-'95, 68 pgs.) — 5.00
Special 1 -3('93-'95, 68 pgs.)-1-Contains 3 stories — 5.00
...-The Series Finale (1994, $3.95, 68 pgs.) — 5.00

STAR TREK: THE NEXT GENERATION (TV)
DC Comics (WildStorm): one-shots
Embrace the Wolf (6/00, $5.95, prestige format) Golden & Sniegoski-s — 6.00
Forgiveness (2001, $24.95, HC) David Brin-s/Scott Hampton painted-a; dust jacket-c — 30.00
Forgiveness (2002, $17.95, SC) — 18.00
The Gorn Crisis (1/01, $29.95, HC) Kordey painted-a/dust jacket-c — 30.00
The Gorn Crisis (1/01, $17.95, SC) Kordey painted-a — 18.00

STAR TREK: THE NEXT GENERATION – BEST OF PICARD
IDW Publishing: Jan, 2022 ($6.99, one-shot)
1-Reprints ST:TNG #1 (1989) and 3 recent stories; Mirror Universe Picard & Q app. — 7.00

STAR TREK: THE NEXT GENERATION/DEEP SPACE NINE (TV)
DC Comics: Dec, 1994 - No. 2, Jan, 1995 ($2.50, limited series)
1,2-Parts 1 & 3 of x-over with Star Trek: DS9/TNG from Malibu Comics — 4.00

STAR TREK: THE NEXT GENERATION / DOCTOR WHO: ASSIMILATION²
IDW Publishing: May, 2012 - No. 8, Dec, 2012 ($3.99, limited series)
1-8-The Borg and Cybermen team-up; Tipton-s/Woodward-a; multiple covers on each — 4.00

STAR TREK: THE NEXT GENERATION: GHOSTS
IDW Publishing: Nov, 2009 - No. 5, Mar, 2010 ($3.99)
1-5-Cannon-s/Aranda-a — 4.00

STAR TREK: THE NEXT GENERATION - ILL WIND
DC Comics: Nov, 1995 - No. 4, Feb, 1996 ($2.50, limited series)
1-4- Hugh Fleming painted-c on all — 4.00

STAR TREK: THE NEXT GENERATION: INTELLIGENCE GATHERING
IDW Publishing: Jan, 2008 - No. 5, May, 2008 ($3.99, limited series)
1-5-Messina-a/Scott & David Tipton-s; two covers on each — 4.00

STAR TREK: THE NEXT GENERATION: MIRROR BROKEN (See Star Trek: Mirror Broken)
IDW Publishing: May, 2017 (free giveaway)
0-(5/17, FCBD giveaway) Mirror Universe crew, prelude to series; J.K. Woodward-a/c; bonus design art — 3.00

STAR TREK: THE NEXT GENERATION - PERCHANCE TO DREAM
DC Comics/WildStorm: Feb, 2000 - No. 4, May, 2000 ($2.50, limited series)
1-4-Bradstreet-c — 3.00

STAR TREK: THE NEXT GENERATION - RIKER
Marvel Comics (Paramount Comics): July, 1998 ($3.50, one-shot)
1-Riker joins the Maquis — 4.00

STAR TREK: THE NEXT GENERATION - SHADOWHEART
DC Comics: Dec, 1994 - No. 4, Mar, 1995 ($1.95, limited series)
1-4 — 4.00

STAR TREK: THE NEXT GENERATION: TERRA INCOGNITA
IDW Publishing: Jul, 2018 - No. 6, Dec, 2018 ($3.99)
1-6: 1-Shasteen-a; Mirror Universe Barclay app. — 4.00

STAR TREK: THE NEXT GENERATION: THE GIFT FACSIMILE EDITION
IDW Publishing: Feb, 2021 ($5.99, one-shot)
1-Reprints ST:TNG Annual #1 (1990); John de Lancie-s/Gordon Purcell-a; Q app. — 6.00

STAR TREK: THE NEXT GENERATION - THE KILLING SHADOWS
DC Comics/WildStorm: Nov, 2000 - No. 4, Feb, 2001 ($2.50, limited series)
1-4-Scott Ciencin-s; Sela app. — 3.00

STAR TREK: THE NEXT GENERATION: THE LAST GENERATION
IDW Publishing: Nov, 2008 - No. 5, Mar, 2009 ($3.99, limited series)
1-5-Purcell-a; alternate timeline with Klingon war; Sulu app. — 4.00

STAR TREK: THE NEXT GENERATION - THE MODALA IMPERATIVE
DC Comics: Early Sept, 1991 - No. 4, Late Oct, 1991 ($1.75, limited series)
1-4 — 4.00

STAR TREK: THE NEXT GENERATION: THE SPACE BETWEEN
IDW Publishing: Jan, 2007 - No. 6, June, 2007 ($3.99)
1-6-Single issue stories from various seasons; photo & art covers — 4.00

STAR TREK: THE NEXT GENERATION: THROUGH THE MIRROR
IDW Publishing: May, 2018 - No. 5, May, 2018 ($3.99, weekly limited series)
1-5-David & Scott Tipton-s; Mirror Universe crew crosses over — 4.00

STAR TREK: THE Q CONFLICT
IDW Publishing: Jan, 2019 - No. 6, Jun, 2019 ($3.99, limited series)
1-6-Crews of Kirk, Picard, Sisko, Janeway vs. Q, Metron, Ayelborne & Trelane; Messina-a — 4.00

STAR TREK: THE WRATH OF KHAN
IDW Publishing: Jun, 2009 - No. 3, Jul, 2009 ($3.99, limited series)
1-3-Movie adaptation; Chee Yang Ong-a — 4.00

STAR TREK: TNG: HIVE
IDW Publishing: Sept, 2012 - No. 4, Feb, 2013 ($3.99, limited series)
1-4-Brannon Braga-s/Joe Corroney-a; Next Generation crew vs. the Borg — 4.00

STAR TREK UNLIMITED
Marvel Comics (Paramount Comics): Nov, 1996 - No. 10, July, 1998 ($2.95/$2.99)
1,2-Stories from original series and Next Generation — 5.00
3-10: 3-Begin $2.99-c. 6- "Telepathy War" pt. 4. 7-Q & Trelane swap Kirk & Picard — 4.00

STAR TREK UNTOLD VOYAGES
Marvel Comics (Paramount Comics): May, 1998 - No. 5, July, 1998 ($2.50)
1-5-Kirk's crew after the 1st movie — 4.00

Star Trek: TNG: The Space Between #1 © CBS

Star Trek: Year Four #4 © CBS

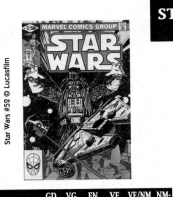

Star Wars #52 © Lucasfilm

	GD	VG	FN	VF	VF/NM	NM-
	2.0	4.0	6.0	8.0	9.0	9.2

STAR TREK: VOYAGER
Marvel Comics (Paramount Comics): Nov, 1996 - No. 15, Mar, 1998 ($1.95/$1.99)

1-15: 13-"Telepathy War" pt. 5. 14-Seven of Nine joins crew — 4.00

STAR TREK: VOYAGER
DC Comics/WildStorm/IDW: one-shots and trade paperbacks

- Elite Force (7/00, $5.95) The Borg app.; Abnett & Lanning-s — 6.00
... Encounters With the Unknown TPB (2001, $19.95) reprints — 20.00
- False Colors (1/00, $5.95) Photo-c and Jim Lee-c; Jeff Moy-a — 6.00
...: Mirrors and Smoke (IDW, 10/19, $4.99) Mirror Universe Janeway's crew; Woodward-a — 5.00

STAR TREK: VOYAGER – SEVEN'S RECKONING
IDW Publishing: Nov, 2020 - No. 4, Feb, 2021 ($3.99, limited series)

1-4-Dave Baker-s/Angel Hernandez-a — 4.00

STAR TREK: VOYAGER-- THE PLANET KILLER
DC Comics/WildStorm: Mar, 2001 - No. 3, May, 2001 ($2.95, limited series)

1-3-Voyager vs. the Planet Killer from the ST:TOS episode; Teranishi-a — 3.00

STAR TREK: VOYAGER SPLASHDOWN
Marvel Comics (Paramount Comics): Apr, 1998 - No. 4, July, 1998 ($2.50, limited series)

1-4-Voyager crashes on a water planet — 4.00

STAR TREK VS. TRANSFORMERS
IDW Publishing: Sept, 2018 - No. 5, Jan, 2019 ($3.99, limited series)

1-5-Crew from Star Trek animated series meets Transformers; multiple covers — 4.00

STAR TREK: WAYPOINT
IDW Publishing: Sept, 2016 - No. 6, Jul, 2017 ($4.99/$3.99)

1-($4.99) Short story anthology; future Next Gen Data & Geordi; multiple covers — 5.00
2-6-($3.99) 2-Gold Key style story. 3-Voyager & DS9 crews — 4.00
... Special 1 (11/18, $7.99) Ezri Dax, Q, Will Decker & Ilia app.; Sonny Liew-a — 8.00
... Special 2 (3/19, $7.99) Short stories by various; Mooney-c — 8.00

STAR TREK/ X-MEN
Marvel Comics (Paramount Comics): Dec, 1996 ($4.99, one-shot)

1-Kirk's crew & X-Men; art by Silvestri, Tan, Winn & Finch; Lobdell-s — 6.00

STAR TREK/ X-MEN: 2ND CONTACT
Marvel Comics (Paramount Comics): May, 1998 ($4.99, 64 pgs., one-shot)

1-Next Gen crew & X-Men battle Kang, Sentinels & Borg following First Contact movie — 6.00
1-Painted wraparound variant cover — 6.00

STAR TREK: YEAR FIVE
IDW Publishing: Apr, 2019 - No. 25, Jul, 2021 ($3.99)

1-24-Original series crew; multiple covers on each. 7-Intro. Ayal. 10-Lt. Arex app.
17-Origin of Gary Seven & Isis; Woodward painted-a — 4.00
25-($4.99) Epilogue to the Five Year Mission; leads into the 1979 movie — 5.00
...: Valentine's Day Special (2/20, $3.99) Paul Cornell-s/Christopher Jones-a; 3 covers — 4.00

STAR TREK: YEAR FOUR (Also see Star Trek: Enterprise Experiment)
IDW Publishing: July, 2007 - No. 5, Nov, 2007 ($3.99, limited series)

1-5: 1-Original series crew; Tischman-s/Conley-a; three covers on each — 4.00

STARVE
Image Comics: Jun, 2015 - No. 10, Jun, 2016 ($3.99)

1-10-Brian Wood-s/Danijel Zezelj-a — 4.00

STAR WARS (Movie) (See Classic…, Contemporary Motivators, Dark Horse Comics, The Droids, The Ewoks, Marvel Movie Showcase, Marvel Special Ed.)
Marvel Comics Group: July, 1977 - No. 107, Sept, 1986

	GD	VG	FN	VF	VF/NM	NM-
1-(Regular 30¢ edition)-Price in square box w/UPC code; #1-6 adapt first movie; first issue on sale before movie debuted	21	42	63	147	324	500
1-(35¢-c; limited distribution - 1500 copies?)- Price in square w/UPC code (Prices vary widely on this book. In 2005 a CGC certified 9.4 sold for $6,500, a CGC certified 9.2 sold for $3,403, and a CGC certified 6.0 sold for $610)	530	1060	1590	4500	10,250	16,000

NOTE: The rare 35¢ edition has the cover price in a square box, and the UPC box in the lower left hand corner has the UPC code lines running through it.

	GD	VG	FN	VF	VF/NM	NM-
1-Reprint; has "reprint" in upper lefthand corner of cover or on inside or price and number inside a diamond with no date or UPC on cover; 30¢ and 35¢ issues published	7	14	21	48	86	125
2-9: Reprints; has "reprint" in upper lefthand corner of cover or on inside or price and number inside a diamond with no date or UPC on cover; 30¢ and 35¢ issues published	2	4	6	8	10	12
2-(30¢ cover)	11	22	33	76	163	250
2-(35¢ with UPC code; not reprint)	82	164	246	656	1478	2300
3,4-(30¢ issues). 4-Battle with Darth Vader	6	12	18	38	69	100
3,4-(35¢ with UPC code; not reprints)	79	158	237	632	1416	2200

	GD	VG	FN	VF	VF/NM	NM-
	2.0	4.0	6.0	8.0	9.0	9.2
5,6: 5-Begin 35¢-c on all editions. 6-Stevens-a(i)	4	8	12	27	44	60
7-20	3	6	9	15	22	28
21-38,45-67,69,70: 50-Giant	2	4	6	11	16	20
39-41,43,44-The Empire Strikes Back-r by Al Williamson in all	2	4	6	10	14	18
42-Reprints 1st Boba Fett app. in comics	13	26	39	89	195	300
68-Reintro Boba Fett	12	24	36	82	179	275
71-80	2	4	6	8	11	14
81-Boba Fett app.	7	14	21	46	86	125
82-90	2	4	6	10	14	18
91,93-99: 98-Williamson-a	3	6	9	14	19	24
92,100-106: 92,100-($1.00, 52 pgs.)	3	6	9	15	22	28
107 (low dist.)-Portacio-a(i)	7	14	21	44	82	120
Annual 1 (12/79, 52 pgs.)-Simonson-c	3	6	9	17	26	35
Annual 2 (11/82, 52 pgs.), 3(12/83, 52 pgs.)	2	4	6	11	16	20
... A Long Time Ago...Vol. 1 TPB (Dark Horse Comics, 6/02, $29.95) r/#1-14						30.00
... A Long Time Ago...Vol. 2 TPB (Dark Horse Comics, 7/02, $29.95) r/#15-28						30.00
... A Long Time Ago...Vol. 3 TPB (Dark Horse Comics, 11/02, $29.95) r/#39-53						30.00
... A Long Time Ago...Vol. 4 TPB (Dark Horse Comics, 1/03, $29.95) r/#54-67 & Ann. 2						30.00
... A Long Time Ago...Vol. 5 TPB (Dark Horse Comics, 3/03, $29.95) r/#68-81 & Ann. 3						30.00
... A Long Time Ago...Vol. 6 TPB (Dark Horse Comics, 5/03, $29.95) r/#82-93						30.00
... A Long Time Ago...Vol. 7 TPB (Dark Horse Comics, 6/03, $29.95) r/#96-107						30.00
... No. 1 Facsimile Edition (2/20, $3.99) Reprints #1 with original 1977 ads						4.00

Austin a-11-15i, 21i, 38; c-12-15i, 21i. Byrne c-13p. Chaykin a-1-10p; c-1. Golden c/a-38. Miller c-47p; pin-up-43. Nebres c/a-Annual 2i. Portacio a-107i. Sienkiewicz c-92i, 98. Simonson a-16p, 49p, 51-63p, 65p, 66p; c-16, 49-51, 52p, 53-62, Annual 1. Steacy painted a-105i, 106i; c-105. Williamson a-39-44p, 50p, 98; c-39, 40, 41-44p. Painted c-81, 87, 92, 95, 98, 100, 105.

STAR WARS (Modern continuation from 1986's Star Wars #107)
Marvel Comics: No. 108, Jul, 2019 ($5.99, one-shot)

108-Valence the Hunter, Jaxon & Amaiza app.; Rosenberg-s; art by various; Simonson-c — 6.00

STAR WARS (Monthly series) (Becomes Star Wars Republic #46-on)
Dark Horse Comics: Dec, 1998 - No. 45, Aug, 2005 ($2.50/$2.95/$2.99)

	GD	VG	FN	VF	VF/NM	NM-
1-Prelude To Rebellion; Strnad-s	1	3	4	6	8	10
2-6,8,9,11-45: 2-6-Prelude To Rebellion; Strnad-s. 4-Brereton-c. 8-12-Outlander. 13,17-18-($2.95). 13-18-Emissaries to Malastare; Truman-s. 14-16-($2.50) Schultz-s. 19-22-Twilight; Duursema-a. 23-26-Infinity's End. 42-45-Rite of Passage						5.00
5,6 (Holochrome-c variants)	1	2	3	5	6	8
7-1st app. Aurra Sing; Outlander story arc begins	4	8	12	27	44	60
10-1st A'shared Hett (later becomes Darth Krayt)	6	12	18	38	69	100
#0 Another Universe.com Ed.($10.00) r/serialized pages from Pizzazz Magazine; new Dorman painted-c						12.00
... A Valentine Story (2/03, $3.50) Leia & Han Solo on Hoth; Winick-s/Chadwick-a/c						3.50
...: Rite of Passage (2004, $12.95) r/#42-45						13.00
...: The Stark Hyperspace War (903, $12.95) r/#36-39						13.00

STAR WARS (Monthly series)
Dark Horse Comics: Jan, 2013 - No. 20, Aug, 2014 ($2.99)

	GD	VG	FN	VF	VF/NM	NM-
1-Takes place after Episode IV; Brian Wood-s/Carlos D'Anda-a/Alex Ross-c						8.00
2-Ross-c						5.00
3-20: 3,4-Ross-c. 5-7-Migliari-c						3.00

STAR WARS
Dark Horse Comics (Free Comic Book Day giveaways)

	GD	VG	FN	VF	VF/NM	NM-
...: and Starkiller (5/13) flip book with new Captain Midnight story & Avatar						3.00
...: Clone Wars #0 (5/09) flip book with short stories of Usagi Yojimbo, Emily the Strange						3.00
...: Clone Wars Adventures (7/04) based on Cartoon Network series; Fillbach Bros. -a	1	3	4	6	8	10
...: FCBD 2005 Special (5/05) Anakin & Obi-Wan during Clone Wars						3.00
...: FCBD 2006 Special (5/06) Clone Wars story; flip book with Conan FCBD Special						3.00
...: Tales - A Jedi's Weapon (5/02, 16 pgs.) Anakin Skywalker Episode 2 photo-c						3.00
Free Comic Book Day and Star Wars: The Clone Wars (5/11) flip book with Avatar: The Last Airbender						3.00

STAR WARS (Also see Darth Vader and Star Wars: Vader Down)
Marvel Comics: Mar, 2015 - No. 75, Jan, 2020 ($4.99/$3.99)

	GD	VG	FN	VF	VF/NM	NM-
1-($4.99) Takes place after Episode IV; Aaron-s/Cassaday-a; multiple covers	1	3	4	6	8	10
2-6-($3.99) Darth Vader app.; Cassaday-a. 4-6-Boba Fett app. 6-Intro Sana Solo						4.00
7-24,26-36: 7-Bianchi-a; Obi-Wan flashback. 8-12-Immonen-a. 13,14-Vader Down pts. 3,5; Deodato-a. 15,20-Obi-Wan flashback. 16-19-Yu-a. 26-35-Yoda app.						4.00
31,32-Doctor Aphra app.						
25-($4.99) Darth Vader app.; Molina-a; back-up Droids story by Eliopoulos						5.00
37-($4.99) SCAR Squadron app.; back-up Tusken Raiders story; Sorrentino-a						5.00
38-49,51-55-Larroca-a. 45-Wedge app. 55-Leia promoted to General						4.00
50-(9/18, $5.99) Larroca; back-up with Camuncoli-a; bonus cover gallery						6.00

	GD 2.0	VG 4.0	FN 6.0	VF 8.0	VF/NM 9.0	NM- 9.2

56-74: 56,61,62-Broccardo-a. 57-60,63-67-Unzueta-a. 57-Intro Thane Markona & Tula
75-($4.99) Luke & Chewbacca vs. Vader; Noto-a ... 5.00
Annual 1 (2/16, $4.99) Gillen-s/Unzueta-a/Cassaday-c; Emperor Palpatine app. ... 5.00
Annual 2 (1/17, $4.99) Kelly Thompson-s/Emilio Laiso-a; intro. Pash Davane ... 5.00
Annual 3 (11/17, $4.99) Latour-s/Walsh-a ... 5.00
Annual 4 (7/18, $4.99) Bunn-s/Anindito, Boschi & Laming-a; Sana Starros app. ... 5.00
...: Empire Ascendant 1 (2/20, $5.99) Short stories following #75; the Rebels reach Hoth; Beilert Valance app.; leads into events of Empire Strikes Back ... 6.00
Saga 1 (2/20, $3.99) Synopsis of the 2015-2020 series; panels and summaries ... 4.00
... Special: C-3PO 1 (6/16, $4.99) Robinson-s/Harris-a/c; story of C-3PO's red arm ... 5.00

STAR WARS (Also see Star Wars: Darth Vader 2020 series)
Marvel Comics: Mar, 2020 - Present ($4.99/$3.99)
1-($4.99) Takes place after Empire Strikes Back; Soule-s/Saiz-a; multiple covers
2-36-($3.99) 2-Jabba the Hutt app. 3,4-Return to Cloud City; Lobot app. 13-18-Tie in to "War of the Bounty Hunters." 22-24-Crimson Reign ... 4.00
37-42: 37-43-($4.99) Dark Droids tie-in; Lando & Lobot app. ... 5.00
...: Revelations 1 (1/23, $5.99) Short stories with framing scenes of Vader; Noto-c ... 6.00

STAR WARS, THE
Dark Horse Comics: Sept, 2013 - No. 8, May, 2014 ($3.99)
1-Adaptation of George Lucas' original rough-draft screenplay; Mayhew-a/Runge-c
  1 — 2 — 3 — 6 — — 8
2-8 ... 4.00
#0-(1/14, $3.99) Design work of characters, settings, vehicles
  1 — 2 — 3 — 5 — — 8

STAR WARS ADVENTURES (Anthology of All-ages stories)
IDW Publishing: Sept, 2017 - No. 32, Mar, 2020 ($3.99)
1 ... 1 — 3 — 4 — 6 — 8 — 10
2-5,8-13,15,17-32: 2-Charretier-a. 3-Tudyk-s. 5-Porgs app. 10,11-Lando app. 30-Kylo Ren-c ... 4.00
6-1st Rose Tico ... 2 — 4 — 6 — 9 — 12 — 15
7-Hondo Ohnaka-c ... 3 — 6 — 9 — 17 — 26 — 35
14-Full app. Fulcrum Agent Kallus ... 3 — 6 — 9 — 16 — 23 — 30
16-Embo & Kaz Xiono ... 2 — 4 — 6 — 9 — 12 — 15
Annual 2018 (4/18, $7.99) John Jackson Miller-s; Jaxxon app.; Sommariva-c ... 8.00
Annual 2019 (5/19, $7.99) Lando & Jaxxon app.; Stan Sakai-c
  2 — 4 — 6 — 9 — 12 — 15
...: Flight of the Falcon (1/19, $4.99) Moreci-s/Florean-a; Chewbacca app. ... 5.00
... Free Comic Book Day 2018 (5/18, giveaway) Derek Charm-a/c; Han & Chewie app. ... 6.00
... Free Comic Book Day 2019 (5/19, giveaway) Derek Charm-a/c; Han & Chewie app. ... 6.00
... Greatest Hits (12/19, $1.00) Reprints #1; Scott-s/Charm-a; Rey on Jakku ... 3.00

STAR WARS ADVENTURES (Anthology of All-ages stories)
IDW Publishing: Sept, 2020 - No. 14, Jan, 2022 ($3.99)
1-14-Francavilla-c. 3-Darth Maul app. ... 4.00
Annual 2020 (8/20, $5.99) Jaxxon app.; Scott-s/Gaston-a; IG-88 app.; Brokenshire-s/a ... 6.00
Annual 2021 (11/21, $7.99) Jaxxon app.; Scott-s/Florean-a; Lando app.; Zdarsky & Loo-s ... 8.00

STAR WARS ADVENTURES: DESTROYER DOWN (All-ages stories)
IDW Publishing: Nov, 2018 - No. 3, Jan, 2019 ($3.99, limited series)
1-3: Rey app.; Beatty-s/Charm-a; back-up with Beatty-s/Sommariva-a ... 5.00

STAR WARS ADVENTURES: GHOSTS OF VADER'S CASTLE (All-ages stories)
IDW Publishing: Sept, 2021 - No. 5, Oct, 2021 ($3.99, weekly limited series)
1-5-Francavilla-c on all. 2,5-Jaxxon app. 3-Robert Hack-a. 5-Francavilla-c ... 4.00

STAR WARS ADVENTURES: RETURN TO VADER'S CASTLE (All-ages stories)
IDW Publishing: Oct, 2019 - No. 5, Oct, 2019 ($3.99, weekly limited series)
1-5-Francavilla-c on all. 1-Darth Maul app. 2-Kelley Jones-a. 5-Darth Vader spotlight ... 5.00

STAR WARS ADVENTURES: SMUGGLER'S RUN (All-ages stories)
IDW Publishing: Dec, 2020 - No. 2, Jan, 2021 ($5.99, limited series)
1,2-Adaptation of the Greg Rucka novel; Han Solo & Chewbacca app.; Römling-a ... 6.00

STAR WARS ADVENTURES: TALES FROM VADER'S CASTLE (All-ages stories)
IDW Publishing: Oct, 2018 - No. 5, Oct, 2018 ($3.99, limited series)
1-5-Francavilla-c on all. 2-Count Dooku app.; Kelley Jones-a. 4-Hack-a ... 5.00

STAR WARS ADVENTURES: THE WEAPON OF A JEDI (Based on the novel by Jason Fry)
IDW Publishing: May, 2021 - No. 2, Jun, 2021 ($5.99, limited series)
1,2-Luke Skywalker during the original trilogy; Worley-s/Coleman-a ... 6.00

STAR WARS: AGENT OF THE EMPIRE - HARD TARGETS
Dark Horse Comics: Oct, 2012 - No. 5, Feb, 2013 ($2.99, limited series)
1-5: 1-Ostrander-s/Fabbri-a; Boba Fett app. ... 5.00

STAR WARS: AGENT OF THE EMPIRE - IRON ECLIPSE
Dark Horse Comics: Dec, 2011 - No. 5, Apr, 2012 ($3.50, limited series)
1-5: 1-Ostrander-s/Roux-a; Han Solo & Chewbacca app. ... 4.00

STAR WARS: AGE OF REBELLION ...
Marvel Comics: Jun, 2019 - Aug, 2019 ($3.99, series of one-shots)
- Boba Fett 1 (7/19) Pak-s/Laming-a/Dodson-c ... 2 — 4 — 6 — 8 — 10 — 12
- Darth Vader 1 (8/19) Greg Pak-s/Ramon Bachs-a ... 1 — 3 — 4 — 6 — 8 — 10
- Grand Moff Tarkin 1 (6/19) Pak-s/Laming-a/Dodson-c; Princess Leia app. ... 4.00
- Han Solo 1 (7/19) Pak-s/Sprouse-a/Dodson-c; Luke and Chewbacca app. ... 4.00
- Jabba The Hutt 1 (7/19) Pak-s/Laiso, Boschi & Turini-a/Dodson-c ... 4.00
- Lando Calrissian 1 (7/19) Pak-s/Buffagni-a/Dodson-c; Lobot app. ... 4.00
- Luke Skywalker 1 (8/19) Pak-s/Sprouse-a/Dodson-c; Vader & The Emperor app. ... 4.00
- Princess Leia 1 (6/19) Pak-s/Sprouse-a/Dodson-c; Lando & Chewbacca app. ... 4.00
... Special 1 (6/19, $4.99) Short stories of Yoda, IG-88, Biggs and Porkins ... 5.00

STAR WARS: AGE OF REPUBLIC ...
Marvel Comics: Feb, 2019 - Aug, 2019 ($3.99, series of one-shots)
- Anakin Skywalker 1 (4/19) Houser-s/Smith & Santos-a; Obi-Wan Kenobi app. ... 4.00
- Count Dooku 1 (4/19) Houser-s/Luke Ross-a ... 4.00
- Darth Maul 1 (2/19) Houser-s/Smith & Santos-a; Darth Sidious app.
  2 — 4 — 6 — 9 — 12 — 15
- General Grievous 1 (5/19) Houser-s/Luke Ross-a ... 4.00
- Jango Fett 1 (3/19) Houser-s/Luke Ross-a; young Boba Fett app. ... 6.00

- Obi-Wan Kenobi 1 (3/19) Houser-s/Smith & Santos-a; early days of Anakin's training
  1 — 3 — 4 — 6 — 8 — 10
- Padmé Amidala 1 (5/19) Houser-s/Smith & Santos-a; takes place during Clone Wars ... 4.00
- Qui-Gon Jinn 1 (3/19) Houser-s/Cory Smith-a; Yoda app. ... 4.00
- Special 1 (3/19, $3.99) Short stories of Mace Windu, Asajj Ventress, Jar Jar Binks
  2 — 4 — 6 — 9 — 12 — 15

STAR WARS: AGE OF RESISTANCE ... (Each has a bonus character essay)
Marvel Comics: Sept, 2019 - Nov, 2019 ($3.99, series of one-shots)
- Captain Phasma 1 (9/19) Taylor-s/Kirk-a/Noto-c ... 4.00
- Finn 1 (9/19) Taylor-s/Rosanas/Noto-c; FN-2187's custodian days ... 4.00
- General Hux 1 (109/19) Taylor-s/Kirk-a/Noto-c; Kylo Ren app. ... 4.00
- Kylo Ren 1 (11/19) Taylor-s/Kirk-a/Noto-c ... 4.00
- Poe Dameron 1 (10/19) Taylor-s/Rosanas-a/Noto-c ... 4.00
- Rey 1 (9/19) Taylor-s/Rosanas/Noto-c; takes place after Han Solo's death; Leia app. ... 4.00
- Rose Tico 1 (11/19) Taylor-s/Rosanas/Noto-c; Paige and Leia app. ... 4.00
... Special 1 (9/19, $4.99) Short stories of Maz Kanata, Adm. Holdo, BB-8 by various ... 5.00
- Supreme Leader Snoke 1 (11/19) Taylor-s/Rosanas-a/Noto-c; training Kylo Ren ... 4.00

STAR WARS: A NEW HOPE - THE SPECIAL EDITION
Dark Horse Comics: Jan, 1997 - No. 4, Apr, 1997 ($2.95, limited series)
1-4-Dorman-c ... 5.00

STAR WARS BECKETT (From Solo: A Star Wars Story movie)
Marvel Comics: Oct, 2018 ($4.99, one-shot)
1-Prelude to Star Wars: Solo Adaptation; Duggan-s; art by Salazar, Laming, Sliney ... 5.00

STAR WARS: BLOOD TIES - BOBA FETT IS DEAD
Dark Horse Comics: Apr, 2012 - No. 4, Jul, 2012 ($3.50, limited series)
1-Scalf painted-a/c on all ... 3 — 6 — 9 — 14 — 20 — 25
2-4 ... 1 — 3 — 4 — 6 — 8 — 10

STAR WARS: BLOOD TIES: JANGO AND BOBA FETT
Dark Horse Comics: Aug, 2010 - No. 4, Nov, 2010 ($3.50, limited series)
1,4-Scalf painted-a/c on all ... 2 — 4 — 6 — 11 — 16 — 20
2,3 ... 1 — 2 — 3 — 5 — 6 — 8

STAR WARS: BOBA FETT
Dark Horse Comics: Dec, 1995 - No. 3, Aug, 1997 ($3.95) (Originally intended as a one-shot)
1-Kennedy-c/a ... 2 — 4 — 6 — 9 — 12 — 15
2,3 ... 5.00
Death, Lies, & Treachery TPB (1/98, $12.95) r/#1-3 ... 13.00
... - Agent of Doom (11/00, $2.99) Ostrander-s/Cam Kennedy-a
  2 — 4 — 6 — 9 — 12 — 15
... - Overkill (3/06, $2.99) Hughes-c/Velasco-a ... 2 — 4 — 6 — 9 — 12 — 15
Twin Engines of Destruction (1/97, $2.95) ... 2 — 4 — 6 — 8 — 10 — 12

STAR WARS: BOBA FETT: ENEMY OF THE EMPIRE
Dark Horse Comics: Jan, 1999 - No. 4, Apr, 1999 ($2.95, limited series)
1-Recalls 1st meeting of Fett and Vader ... 3 — 6 — 9 — 16 — 23 — 30
2-4 ... 1 — 3 — 4 — 6 — 8 — 10

STAR WARS: BOUNTY HUNTERS
Marvel Comics: May, 2020 - No. 42, Mar, 2024 ($3.99/$4.99)
1-36: 1-Valance, Bossk, Boba Fett, Doctor Aphra app.; Sacks-s/Villanelli-a ... 4.00
37-41-($4.99) Dark Droids tie-in ... 5.00
42-($5.99) Jabba the Hutt & Boba Fett app. ... 6.00

STAR WARS: CHEWBACCA
Dark Horse Comics: Jan, 2000 - No. 4, Apr, 2000 ($2.95, limited series)
1-4-Macan-s/art by various incl. Anderson, Kordey, Gibbons; Phillips-c ... 5.00

STAR WARS: CLONE WARS ADVENTURES
Dark Horse Comics: 2004 - No. 10, 2007 ($6.95, digest-sized)
1-10-Short stories inspired by Clone Wars animated series ... 7.00

STAR WARS: CRIMSON EMPIRE
Dark Horse Comics: 1997 - No. 6, May, 1998 ($2.95, limited series)
1-Richardson/Gulacy-a ... 3 — 6 — 9 — 19 — 30 — 40
2-6 ... 1 — 2 — 3 — 5 — 6 — 8

STAR WARS: CRIMSON EMPIRE II: COUNCIL OF BLOOD
Dark Horse Comics: Nov, 1998 - No. 6, Apr, 1999 ($2.95, limited series)
1-Richardson & Stradley-s/Gulacy-a in all ... 1 — 2 — 3 — 5 — 6 — 8
2-6 ... 5.00

STAR WARS: CRIMSON EMPIRE III: EMPIRE LOST
Dark Horse Comics: Oct, 2011 - No. 6, Apr, 2012 ($3.50, limited series)
1-6: 1-Richardson-s/Gulacy-a/Dorman-c ... 6.00

STAR WARS: CRIMSON REIGN
Marvel Comics: Feb, 2022 - No. 5. Aug, 2022 ($4.99/$3.99)
1-($4.99) Soule-s/Cummings-a; Qi'ra, Deathstick, The Knights of Ren app. ... 5.00
2-5-($3.99) 4,5-Darth Vader app. ... 4.00

STAR WARS: DARK DROIDS
Marvel Comics: Oct, 2023 - No. 5, Feb, 2024 ($5.99/$4.99)
1-($5.99) Soule-s/Luke Ross-a; part 1 of the crossover event ... 6.00
2-5-($4.99) ... 5.00

STAR WARS: DARK DROIDS – D-SQUAD
Marvel Comics: Nov, 2023 - No. 4, Feb, 2024 ($5.99/$4.99)
1-($5.99) Guggenheim-s; Espin & Messina-a; spotlight on R2-D2 ... 6.00
2-4-($4.99) ... 5.00

STAR WARS: DARK EMPIRE
Dark Horse Comics: Dec, 1991 - No. 6, Oct, 1992 ($2.95, limited series)
Preview-(99¢) ... 6.00
1-All have Dorman painted-c ... 2 — 4 — 6 — 10 — 14 — 18
1-3-2nd printing ... 4.00
2-Low print run ... 2 — 4 — 6 — 9 — 12 — 15
3 ... 1 — 3 — 4 — 6 — 8 — 10
4-6 ... 5.00

Star Wars Adventures #12 © Lucasfilm

Star Wars: Crimson Reign #5 © Lucasfilm

Star Wars: Darth Vader (2020 series) #22 © Lucasfilm

	GD 2.0	VG 4.0	FN 6.0	VF 8.0	VF/NM 9.0	NM- 9.2

Gold Embossed Set (#1-6)-With gold embossed foil logo (price is for set) — 150.00
Platinum Embossed Set (#1-6) — 175.00
Trade paperback (4/93, $16.95) — 24.00
Dark Empire 1 - TPB 3rd printing (2003, $16.95) — 17.00
Ltd. Ed. Hardcover ($99.95) Signed & numbered — 100.00

STAR WARS: DARK EMPIRE II
Dark Horse Comics: Dec, 1994 - No. 6, May, 1995 ($2.95, limited series)

	GD 2.0	VG 4.0	FN 6.0	VF 8.0	VF/NM 9.0	NM- 9.2
1-Dave Dorman painted-c	2	4	6	9	12	15
2-6: Dorman-c in all.						4.00
Platinum Embossed Set (#1-6)						45.00
Trade paperback ($17.95)						18.00
TPB Second Edition (9/06, $19.95) r/#1-6 and Star Wars: Empire's End.#1,2						20.00

STAR WARS: DARK FORCE RISING
Dark Horse Comics: May, 1997 - No. 6, Oct, 1997 ($2.95, limited series)

	GD 2.0	VG 4.0	FN 6.0	VF 8.0	VF/NM 9.0	NM- 9.2
1-6	1	3	4	6	8	10
TPB (2/98, $17.95) r/#1-6						25.00

STAR WARS: DARK TIMES (Continued from Star Wars Republic #83)(Storyline continues in Star Wars: Rebellion #15)
Dark Horse Comics: Oct, 2006 - No. 17, Jun, 2010 ($2.99)

	GD 2.0	VG 4.0	FN 6.0	VF 8.0	VF/NM 9.0	NM- 9.2
1-17-Nineteen years before Episode IV; Doug Wheatley-a. 11-Celeste Morne awakens 13-17-Blue Harvest						4.00
#0-(7/09, $2.99) Prologue to Blue Harvest						5.00

STAR WARS: DARK TIMES - A SPARK REMAINS
Dark Horse Comics: Jul, 2013 - No. 5, Dec, 2013 ($3.50, limited series)
1-5-Stradley-s/Wheatley-a; Darth Vader app. — 4.00

STAR WARS: DARK TIMES - FIRE CARRIER
Dark Horse Comics: Feb, 2013 - No. 5, Jun, 2013 ($2.99, limited series)
1-5-Stradley-s/Guzman-a; Darth Vader app. — 4.00

STAR WARS: DARK TIMES - OUT OF THE WILDERNESS
Dark Horse Comics: Aug, 2011 - No. 5, Apr, 2012 ($2.99, limited series)
1-5-Doug Wheatley-a — 4.00

STAR WARS: DARTH MAUL
Dark Horse Comics: Sept, 2000 - No. 4, Dec, 2000 ($2.95, limited series)

	GD 2.0	VG 4.0	FN 6.0	VF 8.0	VF/NM 9.0	NM- 9.2
1-Photo-c and Struzan painted-c; takes place 6 months before Ep. 1	2	4	6	11	16	20
2-4-Photo-c and Struzan painted-c	1	3	4	6	8	10

STAR WARS: DARTH MAUL (Issue #1 titled Darth Maul)
Marvel Comics: Apr, 2017 - No. 5, Sept, 2017 ($4.99, limited series)

	GD 2.0	VG 4.0	FN 6.0	VF 8.0	VF/NM 9.0	NM- 9.2
1-($4.99) Cullen Bunn-s/Luke Ross-a; back-up by Eliopoulos-s/a	2	4	6	9	12	15
2-1st Cad Bane	3	6	9	16	23	30
3-5-($3.99) Aurra Sing & Cad Bane app.						4.00
... Halloween Comic Fest 2017 1 (12/17, giveaway) r/#1 without Eliopoulos back-up						5.00

STAR WARS: DARTH MAUL - DEATH SENTENCE
Dark Horse Comics: Jul, 2012 - No. 4, Oct, 2012 ($2.99, limited series)

	GD 2.0	VG 4.0	FN 6.0	VF 8.0	VF/NM 9.0	NM- 9.2
1-Tom Taylor-s/Bruno Redondo-a/Dave Dorman-c	2	4	6	9	12	15
2-4	1	3	4	6	8	10

STAR WARS: DARTH MAUL - SON OF DATHOMIR
Dark Horse Comics: May, 2014 - No. 4, Aug, 2014 ($3.50, limited series)

	GD 2.0	VG 4.0	FN 6.0	VF 8.0	VF/NM 9.0	NM- 9.2
1-Barlow-s/Frigeri-a/Scalf-c	6	12	18	41	76	110
2-4	3	6	9	16	23	30

STAR WARS: DARTH VADER (Also see Star Wars 2020 series)
Marvel Comics: Apr, 2020 - Present ($4.99/$3.99)

	GD 2.0	VG 4.0	FN 6.0	VF 8.0	VF/NM 9.0	NM- 9.2
1-($4.99) Takes place after Empire Strikes Back; Pak-s/Ienco-a; multiple covers	3	6	9	17	26	35
2-5,7-36-($3.99) 2-Intro. Sabé. 12-17-War of the Bounty Hunters tie-ins						4.00
6-1st Ochi	2	4	6	9	12	15
37-42: 37-43-($4.99) Dark Droids tie-in						5.00

STAR WARS: DARTH VADER AND THE CRY OF SHADOWS
Dark Horse Comics: Dec, 2013 - No. 5, Apr, 2014 ($3.50, limited series)
1-5-Siedell-s/Guzman-a/Massaferra-c — 5.00

STAR WARS: DARTH VADER AND THE GHOST PRISON
Dark Horse Comics: May, 2012 - No. 5, Sept, 2012 ($3.50, limited series)

	GD 2.0	VG 4.0	FN 6.0	VF 8.0	VF/NM 9.0	NM- 9.2
1-Blackman-s/Alessio-a/Wilkins-c; variant-c by Sanda	1	2	3	5	6	8
2-5-Blackman-s/Alessio-a/Wilkins-c						4.00

STAR WARS: DARTH VADER AND THE LOST COMMAND

	GD 2.0	VG 4.0	FN 6.0	VF 8.0	VF/NM 9.0	NM- 9.2

Dark Horse Comics: Jan, 2011 - No. 5, May, 2011 ($3.50, limited series)

	GD 2.0	VG 4.0	FN 6.0	VF 8.0	VF/NM 9.0	NM- 9.2
1-Blackman-s/Leonardi-a/Sanda-c; variant-c by Wheatley	1	3	4	6	8	10
2-5-Blackman-s/Leonardi-a/Sanda-c						4.00

STAR WARS: DARTH VADER AND THE NINTH ASSASSIN
Dark Horse Comics: Apr, 2013 - No. 5, Aug, 2013 ($3.50, limited series)
1-5-Siedell-s. 1,2,4-Thompson-a. 3,5-Fernandez-a — 4.00

STAR WARS: DARTH VADER - BLACK, WHITE & RED
Marvel Comics: Jun, 2023 - No. 4, Sept, 2023 ($4.99, limited series, B&W&Red)
1-4-Anthology by various; serialized story Aaron-s/Kirk-a — 5.00

STAR WARS: DAWN OF THE JEDI
Dark Horse Comics: No. 0, Feb, 2012 ($3.50, one-shot)

	GD 2.0	VG 4.0	FN 6.0	VF 8.0	VF/NM 9.0	NM- 9.2
0-Guide to the worlds, characters, sites, vehicles; Migliari-c	3	6	9	14	19	24

STAR WARS: DAWN OF THE JEDI - FORCE STORM
Dark Horse Comics: Feb, 2012 - No. 5, Jun, 2012 ($3.50, limited series)

	GD 2.0	VG 4.0	FN 6.0	VF 8.0	VF/NM 9.0	NM- 9.2
1-Ostrander-s/Duursema-a/c	4	8	12	23	37	60
2-5	1	3	4	6	8	10

STAR WARS: DAWN OF THE JEDI - FORCE WAR
Dark Horse Comics: Nov, 2013 - No. 5, Mar, 2014 ($3.50, limited series)

	GD 2.0	VG 4.0	FN 6.0	VF 8.0	VF/NM 9.0	NM- 9.2
1-Ostrander-s/Duursema-a/c	2	4	6	11	16	20
2-5	1	3	4	6	8	10

STAR WARS: DAWN OF THE JEDI - PRISONER OF BOGAN
Dark Horse Comics: Nov, 2012 - No. 5, May, 2013 ($2.99, limted series)

	GD 2.0	VG 4.0	FN 6.0	VF 8.0	VF/NM 9.0	NM- 9.2
1-5-Ostrander-s/Duursema-a/c	1	3	4	6	8	10

STAR WARS: DOCTOR APHRA (See Doctor Aphra for #1-6)(See Darth Vader #3 for debut)
Marvel Comics: No. 7, Jul, 2017 - No. 40, Feb, 2020 ($3.99)

	GD 2.0	VG 4.0	FN 6.0	VF 8.0	VF/NM 9.0	NM- 9.2
7-24: 7,8-Luke, Han, Leia & Sana app. 12,13-Darth Vader app. 20-24-Sana Starros app.						4.00
25-($4.99) Darth Vader & Sana Starros app.						5.00
26-40: 26-31-Laiso-a. 40-Darth Vader app.						4.00
Annual 1 (10/17, $4.99) Gillen-s/Laming & Sliney-a	1	3	4	6	8	10
Annual 2 (11/18, $4.99) Spurrier-s/Wijngaard-a	2	4	6	9	12	15
Annual 3 (12/19, $4.99) Spurrier-s/Charretier-a						5.00

STAR WARS: DOCTOR APHRA (Star Wars)(2nd series)(First issue titled Doctor Aphra)
Marvel Comics: Jun, 2020 - Present ($3.99)

	GD 2.0	VG 4.0	FN 6.0	VF 8.0	VF/NM 9.0	NM- 9.2
1-Alyssa Wong-s/Marika Cresta-a	2	4	6	9	12	15
2-34: 2-5-Alyssa Wong-s/Marika Cresta-a. 5-Lady Domina app. 7-18-Sana Starros app. 12-15-War of the Bounty Hunters tie-ins. 19-21-Crimson Reign						4.00
35-40-($4.99): 35-39-Dark Droids tie-in						5.00

STAR WARS: DROIDS (See Dark Horse Comics #17-19)
Dark Horse Comics: Apr, 1994 - #6, Sept, 1994; V2#1, Apr, 1995 - V2#8, Dec, 1995 ($2.50, limited series)

	GD 2.0	VG 4.0	FN 6.0	VF 8.0	VF/NM 9.0	NM- 9.2
1-($2.95)-Embossed-c	1	3	4	6	8	10
2-6, Special 1 (1/95, $2.50), V2#1-8						4.00
Star Wars Omnibus: Droids One TPB (6/08, $24.95) r/#1-6, Special 1, V2#1-8, Star Wars: The Protocol Offensive and "Artoo's Day Out" story from Star Wars Galaxy Magazine #1						25.00

STAR WARS: DROIDS UNPLUGGED
Marvel Comics: Aug, 2017 ($4.99, one-shot)
1-Chris Eliopoulos-s/a; short stories with R2-D2, BB-8 and a probe droid — 5.00

STAR WARS: EMPIRE
Dark Horse Comics: Sept, 2002 - No. 40, Feb, 2006 ($2.99)

	GD 2.0	VG 4.0	FN 6.0	VF 8.0	VF/NM 9.0	NM- 9.2
1-Benjamin-a; takes place weeks before SW: A New Hope	1	3	4	6	8	10
2-40: 7,28-Boba Fett-c. 14-Vader after the destruction of the Death Star. 15-Death of Biggs; Wheatley-a						4.00
... Volume 1 (2003, $12.95, TPB) r/#1-4						13.00
... Volume 2 (2004, $17.95, TPB) r/#8-12,15						18.00
... Volume 3: The Imperial Perspective (2004, $17.95, TPB) r/#13,14,16-19						18.00
... Volume 4: The Heart of the Rebellion (2005, $17.95, TPB) r/#5,6,20-22 & Star Wars: A Valentine Story						18.00
... Volume 5 (2006, $14.95, TPB) r/#23-27						15.00
... Volume 6: In the Shadows of Their Fathers (10/06, $17.95, TPB) r/#29-34						18.00
... Volume 7: The Wrong Side of the War (1/07, $17.95, TPB) r/#34-40						18.00

STAR WARS: EMPIRE'S END
Dark Horse Comics: Oct, 1995 - No. 2, Nov, 1995 ($2.95, limited series)

	GD 2.0	VG 4.0	FN 6.0	VF 8.0	VF/NM 9.0	NM- 9.2
1,2-Dorman-c	1	3	4	6	8	10

	GD 2.0	VG 4.0	FN 6.0	VF 8.0	VF/NM 9.0	NM- 9.2

STAR WARS: EPISODE 1 THE PHANTOM MENACE
Dark Horse Comics: May, 1999 - No. 4, May, 1999 ($2.95, movie adaptation)

	GD	VG	FN	VF	VF/NM	NM-
1-Damaggio & Williamson-a; full cast painted-c	2	4	6	11	16	20
1-Qui-Gon & Obi-Wan photo variant-c	2	4	6	8	10	12
2-Darth Maul app.; painted pod race-c	3	6	9	21	33	45
2-Anakin photo variant-c	3	6	9	14	20	25
3-Painted Darth Maul-c by Fleming	5	10	15	33	57	80
3-Darth Maul photo variant-c	3	6	9	14	20	25
4-Fleming painted lightsaber battle-c						6.00
4-Padmé photo variant-c	1	2	3	5	6	8
TPB ($12.95) r/#1-4						13.00
...Anakin Skywalker-Photo-c & Bradstreet-c, ...Obi-Wan Kenobi-Photo-c & Egeland-c, ...Queen Amidala-Photo-c & Bradstreet-c, ...Qui-Gon Jinn-Photo-c & Bradstreet-c	1	3	4	6	8	10
Wizard 1/2	3	6	9	17	26	35
Gold Wizard 1/2	5	10	15	35	63	90

STAR WARS: EPISODE II - ATTACK OF THE CLONES
Dark Horse Comics: Apr, 2002 - No. 4, May, 2002 ($3.99, movie adaptation)

	GD	VG	FN	VF	VF/NM	NM-
1-4-Regular and photo-c; Duursema-a	1	3	4	6	8	10
TPB ($17.95) r/#1-4; Struzan-a						18.00

STAR WARS: EPISODE III - REVENGE OF THE SITH
Dark Horse Comics: May, 2005 - No. 4, May, 2005 ($2.99, movie adaptation)

	GD	VG	FN	VF	VF/NM	NM-
1-4-Wheatley-a/Dorman-a						6.00
TPB ($12.95) r/#1-4; Dorman-c						13.00

STAR WARS FORCES OF DESTINY (All-ages anthology spotlighting female characters)
IDW Publishing: Jan, 2018 ($3.99, series of one-shots)

	GD	VG	FN	VF	VF/NM	NM-
... - Ahsoka & Padme - Revis-s/Pinto-a	2	4	6	11	16	20
... - Hera - Grayson-s/Widermann-a	1	2	3	5	6	8
... - Leia - Charretier-a; Leia on planet Hoth before the events of Empire	1	2	3	5	6	8
... - Rey - Houser-s/Florean-a; Rey meets BB-8 on Jakku	1	2	3	5	6	8
... - Rose & Paige - Dawson-s/Baldari-a; the sisters before the events of The Last Jedi	1	2	3	5	6	8

STAR WARS: GALAXY'S EDGE
Marvel Comics: Jun, 2019 - No. 5, Oct, 2019 ($3.99, limited series)

1-5: 1-Han Solo & Chewbacca app.; Sacks-s/Sliney-a. 2-Greedo app. 4-Dr. Aphra app. — 4.00

STAR WARS: GENERAL GRIEVOUS
Dark Horse Comics: Mar, 2005 - No. 4, June, 2005 ($2.99, limited series)

1-4-Leonardi-a/Dixon-s — 5.00
TPB (2005, $12.95) r/#1-4 — 13.00

STAR WARS HANDBOOK
Dark Horse Comics: July, 1998 - Mar, 2000 ($2.95, one-shots)

	GD	VG	FN	VF	VF/NM	NM-
... X-Wing Rogue Squadron (7/98)-Guidebook to characters and spacecraft	1	3	4	6	8	10
... Crimson Empire (7/99) Dorman-c	1	3	4	6	8	10
... Dark Empire (3/00) Dorman-c	1	3	4	6	8	10

STAR WARS: HAN SOLO & CHEWBACCA
Marvel Comics: May, 2022 - No. 10, May, 2023 ($4.99/$3.99)

1-($4.99) Guggenheim-s/Messina-a; takes place before Episode 4; Greedo app. — 5.00
2-10-($3.99) 3,4-Krrsantan app. — 4.00

STAR WARS: HAN SOLO - IMPERIAL CADET
Marvel Comics: Jan, 2019 - No. 5, May 2019 ($3.99)

1-5-Robbie Thompson-s/Leonard Kirk-a; Han's early days in Imperial Navy; Qi'Ra app. — 4.00

STAR WARS: HEIR TO THE EMPIRE (Adaptation of Timothy Zahn novel)
Dark Horse Comics: Oct, 1995 - No. 6, Apr, 1996 ($2.95, limited series)

	GD	VG	FN	VF	VF/NM	NM-
1-1st app. Grand Admiral Thrawn & Mara Jade	8	16	24	54	102	150
2-2nd app. of Admiral Thrawn	3	6	9	17	25	34
3,5,6	1	3	4	6	8	10
4-1st cover app. of Mara Jade	3	6	9	21	33	45

STAR WARS: HIDDEN EMPIRE
Marvel Comics: Jan, 2023 - No. 5, Jun, 2023 ($4.99/$3.99)

1-($4.99) Soule-s/Cummings-a; Lady Qi'ra app. — 5.00
2-5-($3.99) Darth Vader app. — 4.00

STAR WARS HYPERSPACE STORIES
Dark Horse Comics: Aug, 2022 - No. 12, Dec, 2023 ($3.99, anthology, limited series)

1-12: 1-Set before Episode 2; General Grievous app. 12-Battle of Endor — 4.00

STAR WARS: INFINITIES - A NEW HOPE
Dark Horse Comics: May, 2001 - No. 4, Oct, 2001 ($2.99, limited series)

	GD	VG	FN	VF	VF/NM	NM-
1- "What If..." the Death Star wasn't destroyed in Episode 4	1	3	4	6	8	10
2-4						5.00
TPB (2002, $12.95) r/ #1-4						13.00

STAR WARS: INFINITIES - THE EMPIRE STRIKES BACK
Dark Horse Comics: July, 2002 - No. 4, Oct, 2002 ($2.95, limited series)

	GD	VG	FN	VF	VF/NM	NM-
1-4: "What If..." Luke died on the ice planet Hoth; Bachalo-a	1	2	3	5	6	8
TPB (2/03, $12.95) r/ #1-4						13.00

STAR WARS: INFINITIES - RETURN OF THE JEDI
Dark Horse Comics: Nov, 2003 - No. 4, Mar, 2004 ($2.99, limited series)

	GD	VG	FN	VF	VF/NM	NM-
1-4:"What If..." ; Benjamin-a	1	3	4	6	8	10

STAR WARS: INVASION
Dark Horse Comics: July, 2009 - No. 5, Nov, 2009 ($2.99)

	GD	VG	FN	VF	VF/NM	NM-
1-5-Jo Chen-c						5.00
0-(10/09, $3.50) Dorman-c; Han Solo and Chewbacca app.	1	2	3	5	6	8

	GD	VG	FN	VF	VF/NM	NM-
... - Rescues 1-6 (5/10 - No. 6, 12/10) Chen-c						5.00
... - Revelations 1-5 (7/11 - No. 5, 11/11, $3.50) Luke Skywalker app.; Scalf-c						5.00

STAR WARS: JABBA THE HUTT
Dark Horse Comics: Apr, 1995 ($2.50, one-shots)

	GD	VG	FN	VF	VF/NM	NM-
nn, ...The Betrayal, ...The Dynasty Trap, ...The Hunger of Princess Nampi	1	3	4	6	8	10

STAR WARS: JANGO FETT - OPEN SEASONS
Dark Horse Comics: Apr, 2002 - No. 4, July, 2002 ($2.99, limited series)

	GD	VG	FN	VF	VF/NM	NM-
1-Bachs & Fernandez-a	4	8	12	23	37	50
2	3	6	9	14	20	25
3,4	2	4	6	9	12	15

STAR WARS: JEDI
Dark Horse Comics: Feb, 2003 - Jun, 2004 ($4.99, one-shots)

	GD	VG	FN	VF	VF/NM	NM-
... - Aayla Secura (8/03) Ostrander-s/Duursema-a	2	4	6	11	16	20
... - Count Dooku (11/03) Duursema-a	2	4	6	8	10	12
... - Mace Windu (2/03) Duursema-a; 1st app. Asajj Ventress	6	12	18	42	79	115
... - Shaak Ti (5/03) Ostrander-s/Duursema-a	2	4	6	11	16	20
... - Yoda (6/04) Barlow-s/Hoon-a; 1st app. Cal Kestis	4	8	12	23	37	50

STAR WARS: JEDI ACADEMY - LEVIATHAN
Dark Horse Comics: Oct, 1998 - No. 4, Jan, 1999 ($2.95, limited series)

	GD	VG	FN	VF	VF/NM	NM-
1-1st app. Kyp Durron; Lago-c	3	6	9	16	23	30
2-4-Chadwick-c						5.00

STAR WARS: JEDI COUNCIL: ACTS OF WAR
Dark Horse Comics: Jun, 2000 - No. 4, Sept, 2000 ($2.95, limited series)

	GD	VG	FN	VF	VF/NM	NM-
1-4-Stradley-s; set one year before Episode 1	1	2	3	5	6	8

STAR WARS: JEDI FALLEN ORDER – DARK TEMPLE (Based on video game)
Marvel Comics: Nov, 2019 - No. 5, Feb, 2020 ($3.99, limited series)

	GD	VG	FN	VF	VF/NM	NM-
1-Rosenburg-s/Villanelli-a/Checchetto-c; Trilla Suduri app. (see Darth Vader #19 [10/18] for debut)	3	6	9	16	23	30
2-4						5.00
5-Cal Kestis app. (see Star Wars: Jedi - Yoda for debut)	2	4	6	9	12	15

STAR WARS: JEDI QUEST
Dark Horse Comics: Sept, 2001 - No. 4, Dec, 2001 ($2.99, limited series)

1-4-Anakin's Jedi training; Windham-s/Mhan-a — 5.00

STAR WARS: JEDI - THE DARK SIDE
Dark Horse Comics: May, 2011 - No. 5, Sept, 2011 ($2.99, limited series)

1-5: 1-Qui-Gon Jinn 21 years befor Episode 1; Asrar-a — 5.00

STAR WARS: JEDI VS. SITH
Dark Horse Comics: Apr, 2001 - No. 6, Sept, 2001 ($2.99, limited series)

	GD	VG	FN	VF	VF/NM	NM-
1-Macan-s/Bachs/Robinson-c	6	12	18	38	69	100
2,4-6	1	2	3	5	6	8
3-Darth Bane-c	3	6	9	21	33	45

STAR WARS: KNIGHT ERRANT
Dark Horse Comics: Oct, 2010 - No. 5, Feb, 2011 ($2.99)

1-5: 1-John Jackson Miller-s/Federico Dallocchio-a — 5.00
... - Deluge 1-5 (8/11 - No. 5 12/11, $3.50) 1-Miller-s/Rodriguez-a/Quinones-c — 5.00
... - Escape 1-5 (6/12 - No. 5 10/12, $3.50) 1-Miller-s/Castiello-a/Carré-c — 5.00

STAR WARS: KNIGHTS OF THE OLD REPUBLIC
Dark Horse Comics: Jan, 2006 - No. 50, Feb, 2010 ($2.99)

	GD	VG	FN	VF	VF/NM	NM-
1-Takes place 3,964 years before Episode IV, Brian Ching-a/Charest-c in #1-6	3	6	9	19	30	40
2,4,5,10-15	1	2	3	5	6	8
3-1st Jaarael	2	4	6	14	20	25
6-Cameo Rohlan Dyre	2	4	6	11	16	20
7-1st full app. Rohlan Dyre	3	6	9	17	25	34
8-1st Carth Onasi	2	4	6	11	16	20
9-1st full app. of Revan	12	24	36	82	179	275
16-41,43-50						4.00
42-Origin Darth Malak	8	16	24	54	102	150
... Handbook (11/07, $2.99) profiles of characters, ships, locales	1	2	3	5	6	8
.../Rebellion #0 (3/06, 25¢) flip book preview of both series	1	3	4	6	8	10
... - War 1-5 (1/12 - No. 5, 5/12, $3.50) J.J. Miller-s/Mutti-a						5.00
... - Vol. 1 Commencement TPB (11/06, $18.95) r/#0-6						19.00
... - Vol. 2 Flashpoint TPB (5/07, $18.95) r/#17-12						19.00
... - Vol. 3 Days of Fear, Nights of Anger TPB (1/08, $18.95) r/#13-18						19.00

STAR WARS: LANDO - DOUBLE OR NOTHING
Marvel Comics: Jul, 2018 - No. 5, Nov, 2018 ($3.99, limited series)

1-5: 1-Barnes-s/Villanelli-a; young Lando & L3-37 before Solo movie — 4.00

STAR WARS: LEGACY
Dark Horse Comics: No. 0, June, 2006 - No. 50, Aug, 2010 ($2.99)
Volume 2, Mar, 2013 - No. 18, Aug, 2014 ($2.99)

	GD	VG	FN	VF	VF/NM	NM-
0-(25¢) Dossier of characters, settings, ships and weapons; 1st app. Cade Skywalker and Darth Talon; Duursema-c	3	6	9	14	20	25
0 1/2-(1/08, $2.99) Updated dossier of characters, settings, ships, and history						4.00
1-Takes place 130 years after Episode IV; Darth Krayt app.; see Star Wars #7 (6/99) for debut; Hughes-c/Duursema-a	4	8	12	23	37	50
2-1st Darth Ruyn	3	6	9	21	33	45
3-Hughes-c	2	4	6	11	16	20
4-50: 4-Duursema-c. 7,39-Luke Skywalker app. 16-Obi-Wan Kenobi app. 50-Wraparound-c						4.00
...: Broken Vol. 1 TPB (4/07, $17.95) r/#1-3,5,6						18.00
...: One for One (9/10, $1.00) reprints #1 with red cover frame	2	4	6	11	16	20
... Volume Two 1 (3/13 - No. 18, 8/14, $2.99) 1-18: 1-Bechko-s/Hardman-a/Wilkins-c						4.00

Star Wars: Han Solo & Chewbacca #1 © Lucasfilm

Star Wars: Legacy #39 © Lucasfilm

Star Wars: Sana Starros #5 © Lucasfilm

	GD 2.0	VG 4.0	FN 6.0	VF 8.0	VF/NM 9.0	NM- 9.2
... War 1-6 (12/10 - No. 6, 5/11, $3.50) 1-Ostrander-s/Duursema-a; Darth Krayt app.						4.00

STAR WARS: LIFE DAY
Marvel Comics: Jan, 2022 ($4.99, one-shot)
1-Three short stories from the Wookiee holiday; Han Solo and Chewbacca app. ... 5.00

STAR WARS: LOST TRIBE OF THE SITH - SPIRAL
Dark Horse Comics: Aug, 2012 - No. 5, Dec, 2012 ($2.99, limited series)

	GD	VG	FN	VF	VF/NM	NM-
1-J.J. Miller-s/Mutti-a/Renaud-c	2	4	6	9	12	15
2-5						6.00

STAR WARS: MACE WINDU
Marvel Comics: Oct, 2017 - No. 5, Feb, 2018 ($3.99, limited series)

	GD	VG	FN	VF	VF/NM	NM-
1-Matt Owens-s/Denys Cowan-a; follows after the Battle of Geonosis	1	3	4	6	8	10
2-4						4.00
5-Ahsoka Tano app.	3	6	9	14	20	25

STAR WARS: MACE WINDU
Marvel Comics: Apr, 2024 - Present ($4.99, limited series)
1-Bernardin-s/Jeanty-a; takes place before Episode 1 ... 5.00

STAR WARS: MARA JADE
Dark Horse Comics: Aug, 1998 - No. 6, Jan, 1999 ($2.95, limited series)

	GD	VG	FN	VF	VF/NM	NM-
1-Ezquerra-a in all	3	6	9	16	23	30
2-6						6.00

STAR WARS: OBI-WAN (Titled STAR WARS: OBI-WAN KENOBI in Indicia for issue #1)
Marvel Comics: Jul, 2022 - No. 5, Nov, 2022 ($3.99, limited series)
1-5-Flashback stories from various times before Episode 4 ... 4.00

STAR WARS: OBI-WAN KENOBI
Marvel Comics: Nov, 2023 - Present ($4.99)
1-5-Adaptation of the TV series 1st season; Houser-s/Larroca-a ... 5.00

STAR WARS: OBSESSION (Clone Wars)
Dark Horse Comics: Nov, 2004 - No. 5, Apr, 2005 ($2.99, limited series)

	GD	VG	FN	VF	VF/NM	NM-
1-Blackman-s/Ching-a/c; Anakin & Obi-Wan 5 months before Episode III	2	4	6	11	16	20
2-5						5.00
...: Clone Wars Vol. 7 (2005, $17.95) r/#1-5 and 2005 Free Comic Book Day edition						18.00

STAR WARS: POE DAMERON (Titled Poe Dameron for #1-12)
Marvel Comics: No. 13, Jun, 2017 - No. 31, Nov, 2018 ($3.99)
13-31: 13-Soule-s/Noto-a. 14-22-Unzueta-a. 20-25-Lor San Tekka app. 26-28-Recounts
events from Episode VII & VIII ... 4.00
Annual 1 (8/17, $4.99) Thompson-s/Virella-a; General Organa app. ... 5.00
Annual 2 (10/18, $4.99) Houser-s/Broccardo-a; Leia, Han Solo & Chewbacca app. ... 5.00

STAR WARS: PURGE
Dark Horse Comics: Dec, 2005 ($2.99, one-shot)

	GD	VG	FN	VF	VF/NM	NM-
nn-Vader vs. remaining Jedi one month after Episode III; Hughes-c/Wheatley-a	1	3	4	6	8	10
... - Seconds To Die (11/09, $3.50) Vader app.; Charest-c/Ostrander-s	1	3	4	6	8	10
... - The Hidden Blade (4/10, $3.50) Vader app.; Scalf-c/a; Blackman-s	1	3	4	6	8	10
... - The Tyrant's Fist 1,2 (12/12 - No, 2, 1/13, $3.50) Vader app.; Freed-s/Dan Scott-c						5.00

STAR WARS: QUI-GON & OBI-WAN - LAST STAND ON ORD MANTELL
Dark Horse Comics: Dec, 2000 - No. 3, Mar, 2001 ($2.99, limited series)
1-3: 1-Three covers (photo, Tony Daniel, Bachs) Windham-s ... 3.00

STAR WARS: QUI-GON & OBI-WAN - THE AURORIENT EXPRESS
Dark Horse Comics: Feb, 2002 - No. 2, Mar, 2002 ($2.99, limited series)
1,2-Six years prior to Phantom Menace; Marangon-a ... 3.00

STAR WARS: REBEL HEIST
Dark Horse Comics: Apr, 2014 - No. 4, Jul, 2014 ($3.50)
1-4-Kindt-s/Castiello-a; two covers by Kindt and Adam Hughes on each ... 5.00

STAR WARS: REBELLION (Also see Star Wars: Knights of the Old Republic flip book)
Dark Horse Comics: Apr, 2006 - No. 16, Aug, 2008 ($2.99)
1-16-Takes place 9 months after Episode IV; Luke Skywalker app. 1-Badeaux-a/c ... 3.00
Vol. 1 TPB (2/07, $14.95) r/#0 (flip book) & r/#1-5 ... 15.00

STAR WARS: REPUBLIC (Formerly Star Wars monthly series)
Dark Horse Comics: No. 46, Sept, 2002 - No. 83, Feb, 2006 ($2.99)
46-83-Events of the Clone Wars ... 3.00
...: Clone Wars Vol. 1 (2003, $14.95) r/#46-50 ... 15.00

	GD 2.0	VG 4.0	FN 6.0	VF 8.0	VF/NM 9.0	NM- 9.2
...: Clone Wars Vol. 2 (2003, $14.95) r/#51-53 & Star Wars: Jedi - Shaak Ti						15.00
...: Clone Wars Vol. 3 (2004, $14.95) r/#55-59						15.00
...: Clone Wars Vol. 4 (2004, $16.95) r/#54, 63 & Star Wars: Jedi - Aayla Secura & Dooku						17.00
...: Clone Wars Vol. 5 (2004, $17.95) r/#60-62, 64 & Star Wars: Jedi - Yoda						18.00
...: Clone Wars Vol. 6 (2005, $17.95) r/#65-71						18.00
(Clone Wars Vol. 7 - see Star Wars: Obsession)						
...: Clone Wars Vol. 8 (2006, $17.95) r/#72-78						18.00
...: Clone Wars Vol. 9 (2006, $17.95) r/#79-83 & Star Wars: Purge						18.00
...: Honor and Duty TPB (5/06, $12.95) r/#46-48,78						13.00

STAR WARS: RETURN OF THE JEDI (Movie)
Marvel Comics: Oct, 1983 - No. 4, Jan, 1984 (limited series)

	GD	VG	FN	VF	VF/NM	NM-
1-Williamson-p in all; r/Marvel Super Special #27	3	6	9	14	20	25
2-4-Continues r/Marvel Super Special #27	2	4	6	9	12	15
Oversized issue (1983, $2.95, 10-3/4x8-1/4", 68 pgs., cardboard-c)-r/#1-4	2	4	6	10	13	16

STAR WARS: RETURN OF THE JEDI (40th Anniversary Celebration)
Marvel Comics: Apr, 2023 - Jan, 2024 ($4.99)
... – Ewoks (6/23) Alyssa Wong-s; art by various; campfire stories without dialogue ... 5.00
... – Jabba's Palace (5/23) Guggenheim-s/Miracolo-a ... 5.00
... – Lando (7/23) Phillips-s/Lopez-a; prelude to the movie ... 5.00
... – Max Rebo (10/23) Older-s/Fry-a ... 5.00
... – The Empire (8/23) Houser-s/Morales-a ... 5.00
... – The 40th Anniversary Covers By Chris Sprouse 1 (1/24, $6.99) Gallery of variant covers ... 7.00
... – The Rebellion (9/23) Segura-s/Horak-a ... 5.00

STAR WARS: REVELATIONS
Marvel Comics: Feb, 2024 ($6.99, one-shot)
1-Seven short story preludes to various 2024 Star Wars series ... 7.00

STAR WARS: RIVER OF CHAOS
Dark Horse Comics: June, 1995 - No. 4, Sept, 1995 ($2.95, limited series)
1-4: Louise Simonson scripts ... 4.00

STAR WARS: ROGUE ONE ADAPTATION
Marvel Comics: Jun, 2017 - No. 6, Nov, 2017 ($4.99/$3.99, limited series)

	GD	VG	FN	VF	VF/NM	NM-
1-($4.99) Houser-s/Laiso & Bazaldua-a; Noto-c; afterword by director Gareth Edwards	3	6	9	14	20	25
2-6-($3.99) 3-Villanelli-a. 4-6-Laiso-a						4.00
Star Wars: Rogue One - Cassian & K2-SO Special 1 (10/17, $4.99) Swierczynski-s	1	3	4	6	8	10

STAR WARS: SANA STARROS
Marvel Comics: Apr, 2023 - No. 5, Aug, 2023 ($4.99/$3.99)
1-($4.99) Justina Ireland-s/Pere Pérez-a ... 5.00
2-5-($3.99) ... 4.00

STAR WARS: SHADOWS OF THE EMPIRE
Dark Horse Comics: May, 1996 - No. 6, Oct, 1996 ($2.95, limited series)

	GD	VG	FN	VF	VF/NM	NM-
1-Story details events between The Empire Strikes Back & Return of the Jedi; Russell-a(i)	3	6	9	17	26	35
2,3	2	4	6	11	16	20
4-6						5.00

STAR WARS: SHADOWS OF THE EMPIRE - EVOLUTION
Dark Horse Comics: Feb, 1998 - No. 5, June, 1998 ($2.95, limited series)
1-5: Perry-s/Fegredo-c ... 5.00

STAR WARS: SHADOW STALKER
Dark Horse Comics: Sept, 1997 ($2.95, one-shot)
nn-Windham-a. ... 4.00

STAR WARS: SOLO ADAPTATION (See Solo: A Star Wars Story Adaptation)

STAR WARS: SPLINTER OF THE MIND'S EYE
Dark Horse Comics: Dec, 1995 - No. 4, June, 1996 ($2.50, limited series)
1-4: Adaption of Alan Dean Foster novel ... 5.00

STAR WARS: STARFIGHTER
Dark Horse Comics: Jan, 2002 - No. 3, March, 2002 ($2.99, limited series)
1-3-Williams & Gray-c ... 4.00

STAR WARS: TAG & BINK ARE DEAD
Dark Horse Comics: Oct, 2001 - No. 2, Nov, 2001($2.99, limited series)
1,2-Rubio-s ... 5.00
Star Wars: Tag & Bink Were Here TPB (11/06, $14.95) r/both SW: Tag & Bink series ... 15.00
Star Wars: Tag & Bink Were Here (Marvel, 7/18, $7.99) r/both SW: Tag & Bink series ... 8.00

STAR WARS: TAG & BINK II

	GD 2.0	VG 4.0	FN 6.0	VF 8.0	VF/NM 9.0	NM- 9.2

Dark Horse Comics: Mar, 2006 - No. 2, Apr, 2006($2.99, limited series)

1-Tag & Bink invade Return of the Jedi; Rubio-s						5.00
2-1st app. Darth Plagueis; Tag & Bink as Jedi younglings during Ep II						
	2	4	6	9	12	15

STAR WARS TALES
Dark Horse Comics: Sept, 1999 - No. 24, Jun, 2005 ($4.95/$5.95/$5.99, anthology)

1-Short stories by various in all	2	4	6	9	12	15
2,3,5,8,11,12,14-17,20,23: 5-Begin art and photo-c on all thru #24						6.00
4-1st Dark Troopers	2	4	6	9	12	15
6-Darth Vader, Boba Fett, Yoda app.	3	6	9	16	23	30
7-1st Ailyn Vel (daughter of Boba Fett)	3	6	9	21	33	45
9-Darth Vader vs. Darth Maul	3	6	9	19	30	40
10-A'Sharad Hett app. (becomes Darth Krayt)	6	12	18	38	69	100
13-1st app. Yoda-like infant (similar to Grogu)	3	6	9	17	26	35
18-Boba Fett-c	3	6	9	14	20	25
19-1st Ben Skywalker	4	8	12	23	37	50
24-1st Darth Nihilus & Darth Traya	6	12	18	38	69	100
Volume 1-6 ($19.95) 1-(1/02) r/#1-4. 2-('02) r/#5-8. 3-(1/03) r/#9-12. 4-(1/04) r/#13-16						
5-(1/05) r/#17-20; introduction pages from #1-20. 6-(1/06) r/#21-24						20.00

STAR WARS: TALES FROM MOS EISLEY
Dark Horse Comics: Mar, 1996 ($2.95, one-shot)

nn-Bret Blevins-a.						4.00

STAR WARS: TALES OF THE JEDI (See Dark Horse Comics #7)
Dark Horse Comics: Oct, 1993 - No. 5, Feb, 1994 ($2.50, limited series)

1-Dave Dorman painted-c	2	4	6	11	16	20
1-5-Gold foil embossed logo; limited # printed-7500 (set)						
	10	20	30	64	132	200
2-5: All have Dave Dorman painted-c. 3-r/Dark Horse Comics #7-9 w/new coloring & some panels redrawn						5.00
Star Wars Omnibus: Tales of the Jedi Volume One TPB (11/07, $24.95) r/#1-5, ... The Golden Age of the Sith #0-5 and ... The Fall of the Sith Empire #1-5						
	4	8	12	23	37	50

STAR WARS: TALES OF THE JEDI-DARK LORDS OF THE SITH
Dark Horse Comics: Oct, 1994 - No. 6, Mar, 1995 ($2.50, limited series)

1-6: 1-Polybagged w/trading card	1	2	3	5	6	8

STAR WARS: TALES OF THE JEDI-REDEMPTION
Dark Horse Comics: July, 1998 - No. 5, Nov, 1998 ($2.50, limited series)

1-5: 1-Kevin J. Anderson-s/Kordey-c	1	3	4	6	8	10

STAR WARS: TALES OF THE JEDI-THE FALL OF THE SITH EMPIRE
Dark Horse Comics: June, 1997 - No. 5, Oct, 1997 ($2.95, limited series)

1-5						5.00

STAR WARS: TALES OF THE JEDI-THE FREEDON NADD UPRISING
Dark Horse Comics: Aug, 1994 - No. 2, Nov, 1994 ($2.50, limited series)

1,2	1	3	4	6	8	10

STAR WARS: TALES OF THE JEDI-THE GOLDEN AGE OF THE SITH
Dark Horse Comics: July, 1996 - No. 5, Feb, 1997 (99c/$2.95, limited series)

0-(99c)-Anderson-s						5.00
1-5-Anderson-s	1	2	3	5	6	8

STAR WARS: TALES OF THE JEDI-THE SITH WAR
Dark Horse Comics: Aug, 1995 - No. 6, Jan, 1996 ($2.50, limited series)

1-6: Anderson scripts	1	3	4	6	8	10

STAR WARS: TARGET VADER
Marvel Comics: Sept, 2019 - No. 6, Feb, 2020 ($3.99, limited series)

1-6-Robbie Thompson-s; Valance app.						5.00

STAR WARS: THE BOUNTY HUNTERS
Dark Horse Comics: July, 1999 - Oct, 1999 ($2.95, one-shots)

...Aurra Sing (7/99), ...Kenix Kil (10/99), ...Scoundrel's Wages (8/99) Lando Calrissian app.						5.00

STAR WARS: THE CLONE WARS (Based on the Cartoon Network series)
Dark Horse Comics: Sept, 2008 - No. 12, Jan, 2010 ($2.99)

1-1st comic app. of Ahsoka Tano	27	54	81	189	420	650
2-Gilroy-s/Hepburn-a/Filoni-c	5	10	15	34	60	85
3,4-Gilroy-s/Hepburn-a/Filoni-c	3	6	9	16	23	30
5,8-12: 5-Gilroy-s/Hepburn-a/Filoni-c	2	4	6	10	14	18
6-Ahsoka Tano-c by Filoni	4	8	12	28	47	65
7-Cameo of Clone Commander	3	6	9	17	26	35

STAR WARS: THE FORCE AWAKENS ADAPTATION (Episode VII movie)
Marvel Comics: Aug, 2016 - No. 6, Jan, 2017 ($4.99, limited series)

1-Chuck Wendig-s/Luke Ross-a/Esad Ribic-c	1	3	4	6	8	10
2,3,5,6: 3-Marc Laming-a						5.00
4-1st Knights of Ren	2	4	6	8	10	12

STAR WARS: THE FORCE UNLEASHED (Based on the LucasArts video game)
Dark Horse Comics: Aug, 2008 ($15.95, one-shot graphic novel)

GN-Intro. Starkiller, Vader's apprentice; takes place 2 years before Battle of Yavin						
	3	6	9	14	20	25

STAR WARS: THE HALCYON LEGACY
Marvel Comics: Apr, 2022 - No. 5, Oct, 2022 ($4.99/$3.99)

1-($4.99) Sacks-s/Sliney-a						5.00
2-5-($3.99) 2-Aurra Sing app. 3-Anakin, Padmé & Asajj Ventress app. 4-Lando app.						4.00

STAR WARS: THE HIGH REPUBLIC (Takes place before Phantom Menace)
Marvel Comics: Mar, 2021 - No. 15, May, 2022 ($3.99)

1-15: 1-Cavan Scott-s/Ario Anindito-a; intro Keeve Trennis; Yoda app.						4.00

STAR WARS: THE HIGH REPUBLIC
Marvel Comics: Dec, 2022 - No. 10, Jul, 2023 ($4.99/$3.99)

1-($4.99) Cavan Scott-s/Ario Anindito-a						5.00
2-10-($3.99)						4.00

STAR WARS: THE HIGH REPUBLIC
Marvel Comics: Jan, 2024 - Present ($5.99/$4.99)

1-($5.99) Cavan Scott-s/Ario Anindito & Jim Towe-a						6.00
2,3-($4.99)						5.00

STAR WARS: THE HIGH REPUBLIC ADVENTURES (Takes place before Phantom Menace)
IDW Publishing: Feb, 2021 - No. 13, Feb, 2022 ($3.99)

1-13: 1-7,11,12-Older-s/Talibao-a. 8-10-Bruno-a						4.00
Annual 2021 (12/21, $7.99) Five short stories by various incl. Soule, Gray & Scott						8.00
... Free Comic Book Day 2021 (8/21, giveaway) Art by Tolibao & Brokenshire						3.00
... Galactic Bake-Off Special (1/22, $5.99) Older & Ayala-s/Geyong & Bruno-a						6.00

STAR WARS: THE HIGH REPUBLIC ADVENTURES
Dark Horse Comics: Nov, 2022 - No. 8, Jun, 2023 ($3.99)

1-8: 5-Tolibao-a						4.00
... Quest of the Jedi One Shot (4/23, $5.99)						6.00

STAR WARS: THE HIGH REPUBLIC ADVENTURES (Phase III)
Dark Horse Comics: Dec, 2023 - Present ($3.99)

1,2-Older-s/Talibao-a						4.00

STAR WARS: THE HIGH REPUBLIC – SHADOWS OF STARLIGHT
Marvel Comics: Dec, 2023 - No. 4, Mar, 2024 ($5.99, limited series)

1-($5.99) Charles Soule-s/Ibraim Roberson-a						6.00
2-4-($4.99)						5.00

STAR WARS: THE HIGH REPUBLIC – EYE OF THE STORM
Marvel Comics: Mar, 2022 - No. 2, May, 2022 ($4.99, limited series)

1,2-Charles Soule-s/Guillermo Sanna-a						5.00

STAR WARS: THE HIGH REPUBLIC – THE BLADE
Marvel Comics: Feb, 2023 - No. 4, May, 2023($4.99, limited series)

1-4-Charles Soule-s/Marco Castiello-a						5.00

STAR WARS: THE HIGH REPUBLIC – THE MONSTER OF TEMPLE PEAK
IDW Publishing: Aug, 2021 - No. 4, Nov, 2021 ($4.99, limited series)

1-4-Cavan Scott-s/Rachael Stott-a						5.00

STAR WARS: THE HIGH REPUBLIC – THE NAMELESS TERROR
IDW Publishing: Feb, 2023 - No. 4, May, 2023 ($4.99, limited series)

1-4-George Mann-s/Eduardo Mello-a						5.00

STAR WARS: THE HIGH REPUBLIC – TRAIL OF SHADOWS
Marvel Comics: Dec, 2021 - No. 5, Apr, 2022 ($3.99, limited series)

1-5-Older-s/Wachter-a						4.00

STAR WARS: THE JABBA TAPE
Dark Horse Comics: Dec, 1998 ($2.95, one-shot)

nn-Wagner-s/Plunkett-a						6.00

STAR WARS: THE LAST COMMAND
Dark Horse Comics: Nov, 1997 - No. 6, July, 1998 ($2.95, limited series)

1-6: Based on the Timothy Zaun novel						6.00

STAR WARS: THE LAST JEDI ADAPTATION
Marvel Comics: Jul, 2018 - No. 6, Nov, 2018 ($4.99/$3.99)

1,6-($4.99) Whitta-s/Walsh-a. 1-Del Mundo-c						5.00
2-5-($3.99) 2-Shirahama-c. 3-Noto-c. 4-Rahzzah-c. 5-Rivera-c						4.00

STAR WARS: THE LAST JEDI - DJ - MOST WANTED
Marvel Comics: Mar, 2018 ($4.99, one-shot)

1-Acker & Blacker-s/Walker-a						5.00

STAR WARS: THE MANDALORIAN
Marvel Comics: Sept, 2022 - No. 8, May, 2023 ($4.99)

1-8-Adaptation of the TV series 1st season; Barnes-s/Jeanty-a						5.00

STAR WARS: THE MANDALORIAN SEASON 2
Marvel Comics: Aug, 2023 - No. 8, Mar, 2024 ($6.99/$4.99)

1-($6.99)-Adaptation of the TV series 2nd season; Barnes-s/Jeanty-a; intro. Cobb Vanth						7.00
2-8-($4.99) 5-Ahsoka Tano app.; Simonson-c						5.00

STAR WARS: THE OLD REPUBLIC (Based on the video game)
Dark Horse Comics: July, 2010 - No. 6, Dec, 2010 ($2.99, limited series)

1-(Threat of Peace)-Sanchez-a; two covers	3	6	9	14	20	25
2-3 (Threat of Peace)-Chestny-s/Sanchez-a						5.00
4-(Blood of the Empire) 1st Darth Marr	3	6	9	16	23	30
5,6 (Blood of the Empire)-Freed-s/Dave Ross-a						5.00

STAR WARS: THE OLD REPUBLIC - THE LOST SUNS (Based on the video game)
Dark Horse Comics: Jun, 2011 - No. 5, Oct, 2011 ($3.50, limited series)

1-5-Freed-s/Carré-c/Freeman-c						3.50

STAR WARS: THE PROTOCOL OFFENSIVE
Dark Horse Comics: Sept, 1997 $4.95, one-shot)

nn-Anthony Daniels & Ryder Windham-s						5.00

STAR WARS: THE RISE OF KYLO REN
Marvel Comics: Feb, 2020 - No. 4, May, 2020 ($4.99/$3.99, limited series)

1-($4.99)-Soule-s/Sliney-a; Ben Solo after the burning of the temple						5.00
2-4-($3.99) 2-Young Ben meets the Knights of Ren; Snoke app.						4.00

STAR WARS: THRAWN
Marvel Comics: Apr, 2018 - No. 6, Sept, 2018 ($3.99, limited series)

1-6-Houser-s/Luke Ross-a; Thrawn's intro to the Empire; Palpatine app.						4.00

STAR WARS: THRAWN ALLIANCES
Marvel Comics: Mar, 2024 - Present ($5.99/$4.99, limited series)

1-($5.99) Zahn & Houser-s/Olliffe & Di Vito-a; Palpatine & Vader app. Anakin flashback						6.00
2-($4.99)						5.00

STAR WARS: TIE FIGHTER (Tie-in to Alphabet Squadron novel)
Marvel Comics: Jun, 2019 - No. 5, Oct, 2019 ($3.99, limited series)

1-5-Houser-s/Antonio-a; spotlight on Shadow Wing squad						4.00

Star Wars: Thrawn #4 © Lucasfilm

Star Wars: Yoda #8 © Lucasfilm

Static: Season One #5 © DC

	GD	VG	FN	VF	VF/NM	NM-
	2.0	4.0	6.0	8.0	9.0	9.2

STAR WARS: UNDERWORLD - THE YAVIN VASSILIKA
Dark Horse Comics: Dec, 2000 - No. 5, June, 2001 ($2.99, limited series)

1-5-(Photo and Robinson covers)	1	3	4	6	8	10

STAR WARS: UNION
Dark Horse Comics: Nov, 1999 - No. 4, Feb, 2000 ($2.95, limited series)

1-4-Wedding of Luke and Mara Jade; Teranishi-a/Stackpole-s						6.00

STAR WARS: VADER - DARK VISIONS
Marvel Comics: May, 2019 - No. 5, Aug, 2019 ($4.99/$3.99, limited series)

1-($4.99)-Hallum-s/Villanelli-a/Smallwood-c	1	3	4	6	8	10
2-5-($3.99)-Hallum-s/Smallwood-c. 2-Level-a. 3-David Lopez-a. 4-Mooney-a. 5-Borges-a						4.00

STAR WARS: VADER DOWN
Marvel Comics: Jan, 2016 (one-shot)

1-Part 1 of x-over with Star Wars (2015) #13,14 and Darth Vader #13-15; Deodato-a	1	3	4	6	8	10

STAR WARS: VADER'S QUEST
Dark Horse Comics: Feb, 1999 - No. 4, May, 1999 ($2.95, limited series)

1-Follows destruction of 1st Death Star; Gibbons-a	1	3	4	6	8	10
2-4						4.00

STAR WARS: VISIONS
Marvel Comics: Dec, 2022; Jan, 2024 ($4.99/$5.99, one-shots)

1-($4.99) Samurai version of Mace Windu in manga-style; Takashi Okazaki-s/a						5.00
... − Peach Momoko 1 (1/24, $5.99) Peach Momoko-s/a						6.00

STAR WARS: VISIONARIES
Dark Horse Comics: Apr, 2005 ($17.95, TPB)

nn-Short stories from the concept artists for Revenge of the Sith movie						18.00

STAR WARS: WAR OF THE BOUNTY HUNTERS
Marvel Comics: Jul, 2021 - No. 5, Dec, 2021 ($3.99/$4.99)

... Alpha (7/21, $3.99) Boba Fett with Han Solo frozen in carbonite; Soule-s/McNiven-a						4.00
... Alpha Director's Cut (7/21, $5.99) Reprints #1 with bonus B&W art and cover gallery						6.00
1-(8/21, $4.99) Part 2; Luke Ross-a; Qi'ra app.						5.00
2-4-($3.99) 2-Boba Fett, Bossk, Aphra, Sana & Darth Vader app.						4.00
5-($4.99) Conclusion; leads into Star Wars: Crimson Reign series						5.00
... − Boussh 1 (11/21, $4.99) Alyssa Wong-s/David Baldeón-a						5.00
... − 4-Lom & Zuckuss 1 (10/21, $4.99) Daniel José Older-s/Kei Zama-a						5.00
... − IG-88 1 (12/21, $4.99) Rodney Barnes/Guiu Vilanova-a; Boba Fett-a						5.00
... − Jabba the Hutt 1 (9/21, $4.99) Ireland-s/Roberson & Pizzari-a; Boba Fett-a						5.00

STAR WARS: X-WING ROGUE SQUADRON (Star Wars: X-Wing Rogue Squadron-The Phantom Affair #5-8 appears on cover only)
Dark Horse Comics: July, 1995 - No. 35, Nov, 1998 ($2.95)

1/2						8.00
1-Baron script	2	4	6	8	10	12
2-24,26-35: 2-4-Baron scripts. 5-20-Stackpole scripts						4.00
25-($3.95)						5.00
The Phantom Affair TPB ($12.95) r/#5-8						13.00

STAR WARS: X-WING ROGUE SQUADRON: ROGUE LEADER
Dark Horse Comics: Sept, 2005 - No. 3, Nov, 2005 ($2.99)

1-3-Takes place one week after the Batttle of Endor						3.00

STAR WARS: YODA
Marvel Comics: Jan, 2023 - No. 10, Oct, 2023 ($4.99/$3.99)

1,10-($4.99) 1-Cavan Scott-s/Nico Leon-a. 12-Roberson-a						5.00
2-9-($3.99) 4-Dooku app.						4.00

STATIC (See Charlton Action: Featuring "Static")

STATIC (See Heroes)
DC Comics (Milestone): June, 1993 - No. 45, Mar, 1997 ($1.50/$1.75/$2.50)

1-($2.95)-Collector's Edition; Static on red background; polybagged w/poster & trading card & backing board (direct sales only)	3	6	9	21	33	45
1-Platinum Edition with red background cover	10	20	30	64	132	200
1-Intro. Virgil Hawkins; blue background cover	4	8	12	25	40	55
1-Facsimile Edition (2023, $9.99) reprints Collector's Edition with polybag & extras						10
2-13,15-24,26-44: 2-Origin. 8-Shadow War; Simonson silver ink-c. 24-Kent Williams-c						4.00
14-($2.50, 52 pgs.)-Worlds Collide Pt. 14						6.00
25 ($3.95)						5.00
45-Last issue; cover by Moebius	13	26	39	89	195	300
...: Trial by Fire (2000, $9.95) r/#1-4; Leon-c	2	4	6	11	16	20

STATIC: SEASON ONE (Milestone Returns)
DC Comics: Aug, 2021 - No. 6, May, 2022 ($3.99, limited series)

1-6: 1-Vita Ayala-s/ChrisCross-a						4.00

STATIC: SHADOWS OF DAKOTA (Season Two)
DC Comics: Apr, 2023 - No. 7, Jan, 2024 ($3.99, limited series)

1-7-Nikolas Draper-Ivey & Vita Ayala-s/Draper-Ivey-a						4.00

STATIC SHOCK (DC New 52)
DC Comics: Nov, 2011 - No. 8, Jun, 2012 ($2.99)

1-McDaniel & Rozum-s/McDaniel-a/c	2	4	6	11	16	20
1-2nd printing	1	3	4	6	8	10
2-8: 6-Hardware & Technique app. 8-Origin retold						4.00

STATIC SHOCK!: REBIRTH OF THE COOL (TV)
DC Comics: Jan, 2001 - No. 4, Sept, 2001 ($2.50, limited series)

1-McDuffie-s/Leon-c/a	5	10	15	34	60	85
2	4	8	12	27	44	60
3,4	3	6	9	19	30	40

STATIC SHOCK SPECIAL
DC Comics: Aug, 2011 ($2.99, one-shot)

1-Cowan-a/Williams III-c; pin-ups by various; tribute to Dwayne McDuffie	2	4	6	9	13	16

STATIC TEAM-UP: ANANSI
DC Comics: Aug, 2023 ($3.99, one-shot)

1-Evan Narcisse-s/Charles Stewart III-a						4.00

STATIC-X
Chaos! Comics: Aug, 2002 ($5.99)

1-Polybagged with music CD; metal band as super-heroes; Pulido-s	2	4	6	11	16	20

STEALTH (Pilot Season: ...)
Image Comics (Top Cow): May, 2010; Mar, 2020 - No. 6, Oct, 2020 ($2.99/$3.99)

1-(5/10) Kirkman-s/Mitchell-a/Silvestri-c						3.00
1-6: 1-(3/20, $3.99) Costa-s/Bellegarde-a						4.00

STEAM MAN, THE
Dark Horse Comics: Oct, 2015 - No. 5, Feb, 2016 ($3.99)

1-5-Kowalski-a; Steam robot and crew in 1899						4.00

STEAMPUNK
DC/WildStorm (Cliffhanger): Apr, 2000 - No. 12, Aug, 2002 ($2.50/$3.50)

Catechism (1/00) Prologue -Kelly-s/Bachalo-a						3.00
1-4,6-11: 4-Four covers by Bachalo, Madureira, Ramos, Campbell						3.00
5,12-($3.50)						4.00
...: Drama Obscura ('03, $14.95) r/#6-12						15.00
...: Manimatron ('01, $14.95) r/#1-5, Catechism, Idiosincratica						15.00

STEAMPUNK BATTLESTAR GALACTICA 1880 (See Battlestar Galactica 1880)

STEED AND MRS. PEEL (TV)(Also see The Avengers)
Eclipse Books/ ACME Press: 1990 - No. 3, 1991 ($4.95, limited series)

Books One - Three: Grant Morrison scripts/Ian Gibson-a						5.00
1-6: 1-(BOOM! Studios, 1/12 - No. 6, 6/12, $3.99) r/Books One - Three						4.00

STEED AND MRS. PEEL (TV)(The Avengers)
BOOM! Studios: No. 0, Aug, 2012 - No. 11, Jul, 2013 ($3.99)

0-11: 0-Mark Waid-s/Steve Bryant-a; eight covers. 1-3-Sliney-a; five covers						4.00

STEED AND MRS. PEEL: WE'RE NEEDED (TV)(The Avengers)
BOOM! Studios: Jul, 2014 - No. 3, Sept, 2014 ($3.99)(Issue #1 says "1 of 6")

1-3-Edginton-s/Cosentino-a. 1-Two covers						4.00

STEEL (Also see JLA)
DC Comics: Feb, 1994 - No. 52, July, 1998 ($1.50/$1.95/$2.50)

1-8,0,9-52: 1-From Reign of the Supermen storyline. 6,7-Worlds Collide Pt. 5 &12. 8-(9/94). 9-(10/94). 9-(11/94). 46-Superboy-c/app. 50-Millennium Giants x-over						4.00
1-(3/11, $2.99, one-shot) Benes-a/Garner-c; Reign of Doomsday x-over						5.00
Annual 1 (1994, $2.95)-Elseworlds story						5.00
Annual 2 (1995, $3.95)-Year One story						5.00
...Forging of a Hero TPB (1997, $19.95) reprints early app.						20.00

STEEL: THE OFFICIAL COMIC ADAPTATION OF THE WARNER BROS. MOTION PICTURE
DC Comics: 1997 ($4.95, Prestige format, one-shot)

nn-Adaptation of the Shaquille O'Neal movie; Bogdanove & Giordano-a						5.00

STEEL CAGE (Also see Penultiman)
AHOY Comics: 2019 ($3.99)

1-Series try-outs for Bright Boy, Noah Zark and Penultiman; Elsa Charretier-c						4.00

	GD 2.0	VG 4.0	FN 6.0	VF 8.0	VF/NM 9.0	NM- 9.2

STEELGRIP STARKEY
Marvel Comics (Epic): June, 1986 - No. 6, July, 1987 ($1.50, lim. series, Baxter paper)

1-6						4.00

STEEL STERLING (Formerly Shield-Steel Sterling; see Blue Ribbon, Jackpot, Mighty Comics, Mighty Crusaders, Roly Poly & Zip Comics)
Archie Enterprises, Inc.: No. 4, Jan, 1984 - No. 7, July, 1984

4-7: 4-6-Kanigher-s; Barreto-a. 5,6-Infantino-a. 6-McWilliams-a						5.00

STEEL, THE INDESTRUCTIBLE MAN (See All-Star Squadron #8 and J.L. of A. Annual #2)
DC Comics: Mar, 1978 - No. 5, Oct-Nov, 1978

	GD	VG	FN	VF	VF/NM	NM-
1	3	6	9	17	26	35
2-5: 5-44 pgs.	1	3	4	6	8	10

STEELTOWN ROCKERS
Marvel Comics: Apr, 1990 - No. 6, Sept, 1990 ($1.00, limited series)

1-6: Small town teens form rock band						4.00

STEELWORKS (John Henry Irons)
DC Comics: Aug, 2023 - No. 6, Jan, 2024 ($3.99)

1-6-Michael Dorn-s/Sami Basri-a. 3,5,6-Superwoman app.						4.00

STEEPLE
Dark Horse Comics: Sept, 2019 - No. 5, Jan, 2020 ($3.99, limited series)

1-5-John Allison-s/a/c; variant-c for each by various						4.00

STELLAR
Image Comics (Skybound): Jun, 2018 - No. 6, Nov, 2018 ($3.99, limited series)

1-6-Joseph Keatinge-s/Bret Blevins-a						4.00

STEPHEN COLBERT'S TEK JANSEN (From the animated shorts on The Colbert Report)
Oni Press: July, 2007 - No. 5, Jan, 2009 ($3.99, limited series)

1-Chantier-a/Layman & Peyer-s; back-up story by Massey-s/Rodriguez-a; Chantier-c						4.00
1-Variant-c by John Cassaday						6.00
1-Second printing with flip book of Cassaday & Chantier covers						4.00
2-5: 2-(6/08) Flip book with covers by Rodriguez & Wagner. 3-Flip-c by Darwyn Cooke						4.00

STEPHEN KING'S N. THE COMIC SERIES
Marvel Comics: May, 2010 - No. 4, Aug, 2010 ($3.99, limited series)

1-4-Guggenheim-s/Maleev-a/c						4.00

STEVE AUSTIN (See Stone Cold Steve Austin)

STEVE CANYON (See Harvey Comics Hits #52)
Dell Publishing Co.: No. 519, 11/53 - No. 1033, 9/59 (All Milton Caniff-a except #519, 939, 1033)

	GD	VG	FN	VF	VF/NM	NM-
Four Color 519 (1, 1953)	9	18	27	59	117	175
Four Color 578 (8/54), 641 (7/55), 737 (10/56), 804 (5/57), 939 (10/58), 1033 (9/59) (photo-c)	5	10	15	35	63	90

STEVE CANYON
Grosset & Dunlap: 1959 (6-3/4x9", 96 pgs., B&W, no text, hardcover)

	GD	VG	FN	VF	VF/NM	NM-
100100-Reprints 2 stories from strip (1953, 1957)	6	12	18	31	38	45
100100 (softcover edition)	5	10	15	24	30	35

STEVE CANYON COMICS
Harvey Publ.: Feb, 1948 - No. 6, Dec, 1948 (Strip reprints, No. 4,5: 52pgs.)

	GD	VG	FN	VF	VF/NM	NM-
1-Origin; has biography of Milton Caniff; Powell-a, 2 pgs.; Caniff-a	20	40	60	120	195	270
2-Caniff, Powell-a in #2-6	14	28	42	80	115	150
3-6: 6-Intro Madame Lynx-c/story	14	28	42	76	108	140

STEVE CANYON IN 3-D
Kitchen Sink Press: June, 1986 ($2.25, one-shot)

1-Contains unpublished story from 1954						5.00

STEVE DITKO'S STRANGE AVENGING TALES
Fantagraphics Books: Feb, 1997 ($2.95, B&W)

1-Ditko-c/s/a						5.00

STEVE DONOVAN, WESTERN MARSHAL (TV)
Dell Publishing Co.: No. 675, Feb, 1956 - No. 880, Feb, 1958 (All photo-c)

	GD	VG	FN	VF	VF/NM	NM-
Four Color 675-Kinstler-a	8	16	24	55	105	155
Four Color 768-Kinstler-a	6	12	18	42	79	115
Four Color 880	5	10	15	33	57	80

STEVEN UNIVERSE (TV)
BOOM! Studios (kaBOOM): Aug, 2014 - No. 8, Mar, 2015 ($3.99)

1-8: 1-Four covers; Uncle Grandpa preview. 2-8-Three covers						4.00
...: Anti-Gravity OGN (11/17, $14.99), 9" x 6") Perper-s/Chan & Ayoub-a						15.00
...: Greg Universe Special 1 (4/15, $4.99) Short stories by various; two covers						5.00
...: 2016 Special 1 (12/16, $7.99) Short donut-themed stories by various; two covers						8.00

STEVEN UNIVERSE (Ongoing) (TV)
BOOM! Studios (kaBOOM): Feb, 2017 - No. 36, Jan, 2020 ($3.99)

1-24,26-36: 1-Four covers; Lapis & Peridot app. 19-Sugilite app.						4.00
25-($4.99) Captain Lars and his crew vs. Emerald						5.00
...: Fusion Frenzy 1 (3/19, $7.99) Short stories by various; 3 covers						8.00

STEVEN UNIVERSE AND THE CRYSTAL GEMS (TV)
BOOM! Studios (kaBOOM): Mar, 2016 - No. 4, Jun, 2016 ($3.99)

1-4-Fenton-s/Garland-a; multiple covers on each. 1-Preview of Over the Garden Wall						4.00

STEVEN UNIVERSE: HARMONY (TV)
BOOM! Studios (kaBOOM): Aug, 2018 - No. 5, Dec, 2018 ($3.99, 8" x 8" square size)

1-5-S.M. Vidaurri-s/Mollie Rose-a; Aquamarine, Topaz & Sugilite app.						4.00

STEVE ROGERS: SUPER-SOLDIER (Captain America - The Heroic Age)
Marvel Comics: Sept, 2010 - No. 4, Dec, 2010 ($3.99, limited series)

1-4-Brubaker-s/Eaglesham-a/Pacheco-c. 1-Back-up rep. of origin from CA #1 ('41)						4.00
Annual 1 (6/11, $3.99) Continued from Uncanny X-Men Annual #3; Roberson-a						4.00

STEVE ROPER
Famous Funnies: Apr, 1948 - No. 5, Dec, 1948

	GD	VG	FN	VF	VF/NM	NM-
1-Contains 1944 daily newspaper-r	15	30	45	90	140	190
2	10	20	30	58	79	100
3-5	9	18	27	50	65	80

STEVE SAUNDERS SPECIAL AGENT (See Special Agent)

STEVE SAVAGE (See Captain...)

STEVE ZODIAC & THE FIRE BALL XL-5 (TV)
Gold Key: Jan, 1964

	GD	VG	FN	VF	VF/NM	NM-
10108-401 (#1)	8	16	24	56	108	160

STEVIE (Mazie's boy friend)(Also see Flat-Top, Mazie & Mortie)
Mazie (Magazine Publ.): Nov, 1952 - No. 6, Apr, 1954

	GD	VG	FN	VF	VF/NM	NM-
1-Teenage humor; Stevie, Mortie & Mazie begin	18	36	54	107	169	230
2-6	10	20	30	58	79	100

STEVIE MAZIE'S BOY FRIEND (See Harvey Hits #5)

STEWART THE RAT (See Eclipse Graphic Album Series)

ST. GEORGE (See listing under Saint...)

STIG'S INFERNO
Vortex/Eclipse: 1985 - No. 7, Mar, 1987 ($1.95, B&W)

1-7 ($1.95)						4.00
Graphic Album (1988, $6.95, B&W, 100 pgs.)						7.00

STILLWATER
Image Comics (Skybound): Sept, 2020 - No. 18, Apr, 2023 ($3.99)

1-17-Chip Zdarsky-s/Ramón Perez-a						4.00
18-($4.99) Last issue						5.00
... The Escape (3/22, $4.99) Four short stories by Zdarsky-s/Perez-a and others						5.00

STING OF THE GREEN HORNET (See The Green Hornet)
Now Comics: June, 1992 - No. 4, 1992 ($2.50, limited series)

1-4: Butler-a						4.00
1-4 ($2.75)-Collectors Ed.; polybagged w/poster						5.00

STOKER'S DRACULA (Reprints unfinished Dracula story from 1974-75 with new ending)
Marvel Comics: 2004 - No. 4, May, 2005 ($3.99, B&W)

1-4: 1-Reprints from Dracula Lives! #5-8; Roy Thomas-s/Dick Giordano-a. 2-R/#10,11 & Legion of Monsters #1. 3,4-New story/artwork to finish story. 4-Giordano afterword						4.00
HC (2005, $24.99) r/#1-4; foreword by Thomas; Giordano afterword; bonus art & covers						25.00

STONE
Avalon Studios: Aug, 1998 - No. 4, Apr, 1999 ($2.50, limited series)

1-4-Portacio-a/Haberlin-s						4.00
1-Alternate-c						5.00
2-($14.95) DF Stonechrome Edition						15.00

STONE (Volume 2)
Avalon Studios: Aug, 1999 - No. 4, May, 2000 ($2.50)

1-4-Portacio-a/Haberlin-s						4.00
1-Chrome-c						5.00

STONE COLD STEVE AUSTIN (WWF Wrestling)
Chaos! Comics: Oct, 1999 - No. 4, Feb, 2000 ($2.95)

	GD	VG	FN	VF	VF/NM	NM-
1-Reg. & photo-c; Steven Grant-s	1	3	4	6	8	10
1-Premium Ed. ($10.00)	2	4	6	9	12	15
2-4-Reg. & photo-c						4.00
Preview ($5.00)						5.00

STONEHEART
Image Comics: Mar, 2023 - Present ($3.99)

1-6-Emma Kubert-s/a						4.00

STONE PROTECTORS
Harvey Pubications: May, 1994 - No. 3, Sept, 1994

nn (1993, giveaway)(limited distribution, scarce)						6.00
1-3-Ace Novelty action figures						4.00

STONEY BURKE (TV Western)
Dell Publishing Co.: June-Aug, 1963 - No. 2, Sept-Nov, 1963

	GD	VG	FN	VF	VF/NM	NM-
1,2-Jack Lord photo-c on both	3	6	9	16	24	32

STONY CRAIG
Pentagon Publishing Co.: 1946 (No #)

	GD	VG	FN	VF	VF/NM	NM-
nn-Reprints Bell Syndicate's "Sgt. Stony Craig" newspaper strips; story of the Japanese soldier who wouldn't surrender	14	28	42	81	118	155

STOOGE WARS (Three Stooges)
American Mythology Prods.: 2022 ($3.99)

1-S.A. Check-s/Diego Tapie-a; Robonic Stooges app.						4.00

STORIES BY FAMOUS AUTHORS ILLUSTRATED (Fast Fiction #1-5)
Seaboard Publ./Famous Authors Ill.: No. 6, Aug, 1950 - No. 13, Mar, 1951

	GD	VG	FN	VF	VF/NM	NM-
1-Scarlet Pimpernel-Baroness Orczy	27	54	81	160	263	365
2-Capt. Blood-Raphael Sabatini	26	52	78	154	252	350
3-She, by Haggard	30	60	90	177	289	400
4-The 39 Steps-John Buchan	18	36	54	107	169	230
5-Beau Geste-P. C. Wren	18	36	54	107	169	230

NOTE: The above five issues are exact reprints of Fast Fiction #1-5 except for the title change and new Kiefer covers on #1 and 2. Kiefer c(r)-3-5. The above 5 issues were released before Famous Authors #6.

	GD	VG	FN	VF	VF/NM	NM-
6-Macbeth, by Shakespeare; Kiefer art (8/50); used in SOTI, pg. 22,143; Kiefer-c; 36 pgs.	24	48	72	142	234	325
7-The Window; Kiefer-c/a; 52 pgs.	18	36	54	107	169	230
8-Hamlet, by Shakespeare; Kiefer-c/a; 36 pgs.	21	42	63	126	206	285
9,10: 9-Nicholas Nickleby, by Dickens; G. Schrotter-a; 52 pgs. 10-Romeo & Juliet, by Shakespeare; Kiefer-c/a; 36 pgs.	18	36	54	107	169	230
11-13: 11-Ben-Hur; Schrotter-a; 52 pgs. 12-La Svengali; Schrotter-a; 36 pgs.						
13-Scaramouche; Kiefer-c/a; 36 pgs.	18	36	54	103	162	220

NOTE: Artwork was prepared/advertised for #14, The Red Badge of Courage. Gilberton bought out Famous Authors, Ltd. and used that story as C.I. #98. Famous Authors, Ltd. then published the Classics Junior series. The Famous Authors titles were published as part of the regular Classics Ill. Series in Brazil starting in 1952.

STORIES FROM THE TWILIGHT ZONE

Stellar #1 © Kirkman & TCOW

Steven Universe #22 © CN

Storm (2023 series) #1 © MAR

	GD	VG	FN	VF	VF/NM	NM-
	2.0	4.0	6.0	8.0	9.0	9.2

Skylark Pub: Mar, 1979, 68 pgs. (B&W comic digest, 5-1/4x7-5/8")

| 15405-2: Pfevfer-a, 56 pgs, new comics | 3 | 6 | 9 | 17 | 26 | 35 |

STORIES OF ROMANCE (Formerly Meet Miss Bliss)
Atlas Comics (LMC): No. 5, Mar, 1956 - No. 13, Aug, 1957

5-Baker-a?	22	44	66	132	216	300
6-10,12,13	15	30	45	90	140	190
11-Baker, Romita-a; Colletta-c/a	22	44	66	132	216	300

NOTE: Ann Brewster a-13. Colletta a-9(2), 11; c-5, 11.

STORM (X-Men)
Marvel Comics: Feb, 1996 - No. 4, May, 1996 ($2.95, limited series)

| 1-Foil-c on all; Dodson-a(p)/Ellis-s | 2 | 4 | 6 | 10 | 14 | 18 |
| 2-4-Callisto app. | | | | | | 4.00 |

STORM (X-Men)
Marvel Comics: Apr, 2006 - No. 6, Sept, 2006 ($2.99, limited series)

1-6: Ororo and T'Challa meet as teens; Eric Jerome Dickey-s						3.00
HC (2007, $19.99, dustjacket) r/#1-6						20.00
SC (2008, $14.99) r/#1-6						15.00

STORM (X-Men)
Marvel Comics: Sept, 2014 - No. 11, Jul, 2015 ($3.99)

| 1-11: 1-Greg Pak-s/Victor Ibañez-a. 9-Gambit app. | | | | | | 4.00 |

STORM (X-Men)
Marvel Comics: Jul, 2023 - No. 5, Nov, 2023 ($4.99/$3.99)

| 1-($4.99) Nocenti-s/Kotian-a; takes place around Uncanny X-Men #176 | | | | | | 5.00 |
| 2-5-($3.99) 3-5-Borges-a | | | | | | 4.00 |

STORM & THE BROTHERHOOD OF MUTANTS (Sins of Sinister tie-ins)
Marvel Comics: Apr, 2023 - No. 3, Jun, 2023 ($3.99, limited series)

| 1-3-Ewing-s. 1-Medina-a. 2-Di Vito-a. 3-Vitti-a | | | | | | 4.00 |

STORMBREAKER: THE SAGA OF BETA RAY BILL (Also see Thor)
Marvel Comics: Mar, 2005 - No. 6, Aug, 2005 ($2.99, limited series)

| 1-6-Oeming & Berman-s/DiVito-a; Galactus app. 6-Spider-Man app. | | | | | | 3.00 |
| TPB (2006, $16.99) r/#1-6 | | | | | | 17.00 |

STORMING PARADISE
DC Comics (WildStorm): Sept, 2008 - No. 6, Aug, 2009 ($2.99, limited series)

| 1-6-WWII invasion of Japan; Dixon-s/Guice-a/c | | | | | | 3.00 |
| TPB (2009, $19.99) r/#1-6 | | | | | | 20.00 |

STORM SHADOW (G.I. Joe character)
Devil's Due Publishing: May, 2007 - No. 7, Nov, 2007 ($3.50)

| 1-7-Larry Hama-s | | | | | | 3.50 |

STORMWATCH (Also see The Authority)
Image Comics (WildStorm Prod.): May, 1993 - No. 50, Jul, 1997 ($1.95/$2.50)

1-8,0,9-36: 1-Intro StormWatch (Battalion, Diva, Winter, Fuji, & Hellstrike); 1st app. Weatherman; Jim Lee-c & part scripts; Lee plots in all. 1-Gold edition.1-3-Includes coupon for limited edition StormWatch trading card #00 by Lee. 3-1st brief app. Backlash. 0-($2.50)-Polybagged w/card; 1st full app. Backlash. 9-(4/94, $2.50)-Intro Defile. 10-(6/94),11,12-Both (8/94). 13,14-(9/94). 15-(10/94). 21-Reads in on-c. 22-Direct Market; Wildstorm Rising Pt. 9, bound-in card. 23-Spartan joins team. 25-(6/94, June 1995 on-c, $2.50). 35-Fire From Heaven Pt. 5. 36-Fire From Heaven Pt. 12						4.00
10-Alternate Portacio-c, see Deathblow #5						4.00
22-($1.95)-Newsstand, Wildstorm Rising Pt. 9						4.00
37-(7/96, $2.50, 38 pgs.)-Weatherman forms new team; 1st app. Jenny Sparks, Jack Hawksmoor & Rose Tattoo; Warren Ellis scripts begin; Justice League #1-c/swipe						5.00
38-49: 44-Three covers.						5.00
50-($4.50)						5.00
Special 1 ,2(1/94, 5/95, $3.50, 52 pgs.)						5.00
Sourcebook 1 (1/94, $2.50)						4.00

STORMWATCH (Also see The Authority)
Image Comics (WildStorm): Oct, 1997 - No. 11, Sept, 1998 ($2.50)

1-Ellis-s/Jimenez-a(p); two covers by Bennett						4.00
1-($3.50)-Voyager Pack bagged w/Gen 13 preview						5.00
2-11: 4-1st app. Midnighter and Apollo. 7,8-Freefall app. 9-Gen13 & DV8 app.						4.00
A Finer Walk ('99, $14.95, TPB) r/V2 #4-9						15.00
Change or Die ('99, $14.95, TPB) r/V1 #48-50 & V2 #1-3						15.00
Final Orbit ('01, $9.95, TPB) r/V2 #10,11 & WildC.A.T.S./Aliens; Hitch-c						10.00

STORMWATCH (DC New 52)
DC Comics: Nov, 2011 - No. 30, Jun, 2014 ($2.99)

| 1-Cornell-s/Sepulveda-a; Martian Manhunter app.; blue bkgrd cover | | | | | | 4.00 |
| 1-(2nd printing, cover has red bkgrd), 2-8: 7,8-Jenkins-s. 12-Martian Manhunter leaves | | | | | | 3.00 |

| 13-30: 13,14-Etrigan returns. 18-Team re-booted; Starlin-s/c. 20-Lobo origin | | | | | | 3.00 |
| #0-(11/12, $2.99) Flashback to Demon Knights; Milligan-s/Conrad-a | | | | | | 3.00 |

STORMWATCH: P.H.D. (Post Human Division)
DC Comics (WildStorm): Jan, 2007 - No. 24, Jan, 2010 ($2.99)

1-24: 1-Two covers by Mahnke & Hairsine; Gage-s/Mahnke-a. 2-Var-c by Dell'Otto						3.00
...: Armageddon 1 (2/08, $2.99) Gage-s/Fernández-a/McKone-c						3.00
TPB (2007, $17.99) r/#1-4,6,7 & story from Worldstorm #1						18.00
... Book Two TPB (2008, $17.99) r/#5,8-12; sketch pages and concept art						18.00
... Book Three TPB (2009, $17.99) r/#13-19						18.00

STORMWATCH: TEAM ACHILLES
DC Comics (WildStorm): Sept, 2002 - No. 23, Aug, 2004 ($2.95)

1-8: 1-Two covers by Portacio; Portacio-a/Wright-s. 5,6-The Authority app.						3.00
9-23: 9-Back-up preview of The Authority: High Stakes pt. 1						3.00
TPB (2003, $14.95) r/Wizard Preview and #1-6; Portacio art pages						15.00
Book 2 (2004, $14.95) r/#7-11 & short story from Eye of the Storm Annual						15.00

STORMY (Disney) (Movie)
Dell Publishing Co.: No. 537, Feb, 1954

| Four Color 537 (...the Thoroughbred)-on top 2/3 of each page; Pluto story on bottom 1/3 | 6 | 12 | 18 | 42 | 79 | 115 |

STORY OF JESUS (See Classics Illustrated Special Issue)

STORY OF MANKIND, THE (Movie)
Dell Publishing Co.: No. 851, Jan, 1958

| Four Color 851-Vincent Price/Hedy Lamarr photo-c | 8 | 16 | 24 | 54 | 102 | 150 |

STORY OF MARTHA WAYNE, THE
Argo Publ.: April, 1956

| 1-Newspaper strip-r | 8 | 16 | 24 | 40 | 50 | 60 |

STORY OF RUTH, THE
Dell Publishing Co.: No. 1144, Nov-Jan, 1961 (Movie)

| Four Color 1144-Photo-c | 9 | 18 | 27 | 57 | 111 | 165 |

STORY OF THE COMMANDOS, THE (Combined Operations)
Long Island Independent: 1943 (15c, B&W, 68 pgs.) (Distr. by Gilberton)

| nn-All text (no comics); photos & illustrations; ad for Classic Comics on back cover (Rare) | 52 | 104 | 156 | 328 | 552 | 775 |

STORY OF THE GLOOMY BUNNY, THE (See March of Comics #9)

STORYTELLER, THE: FAIRIES (Jim Henson's)
BOOM! Studios (Archaia): Dec, 2017 - No. 4, Mar, 2018 ($3.99, limited series)

| 1-4: 1-Matt Smith-s/a. 2-Benjamin Schipper-s/a. 3-Tyler Jenkins-s/a. 4-Celia Lowenthal-s/a | | | | | | 4.00 |

STORYTELLER, THE: GIANTS (Also see Jim Henson's The Storyteller)
BOOM! Studios (Archaia): Dec, 2016 - No. 4, Mar, 2017 ($3.99, limited series)

| 1-4: 1-Conor Nolan-s/a. 2-Benjamin Dayton-s/a. 3-Jared Cullum-s/a. 4-Feifei Ruan-s/a | | | | | | 4.00 |

STORYTELLER, THE: SIRENS (Jim Henson's)
BOOM! Studios (Archaia): Apr, 2019 - No. 4 ($3.99, limited series)

| 1-4: 1-Rebelka-a. 2-Chan Chau-s/a. 3-Sarah Webb-s/a. 4-Aud Koch-s/a | | | | | | 4.00 |

STRAIGHT ARROW (Radio)(See Best of the West & Great Western)
Magazine Enterprises: Feb-Mar, 1950 - No. 55, Mar, 1956 (All 36 pgs.)

1-Straight Arrow (alias Steve Adams) & his palomino Fury begin; 1st mention of Sundown Valley & the Secret Cave	50	100	150	315	533	750
2-Red Hawk begins (1st app?) by Powell (origin), ends #55	26	52	78	154	252	350
3-Frazetta-c	60	120	180	381	653	925
4,5: 4-Secret Cave-c	22	44	66	132	216	300
6-10	17	34	51	100	158	215
11-Classic story "The Valley of Time", with an ancient civilization made of gold	25	50	75	150	245	340
12-19	14	28	42	82	121	160
20-Origin Straight Arrow's Shield	16	32	48	92	144	195
21-Origin Fury	19	38	57	109	172	235
22-Frazetta-c	39	78	117	231	378	525
23,25-30: 25-Secret Cave-c. 28-Red Hawk meets The Vikings	11	22	33	62	86	110
24-Classic story "The Dragons of Doom!" with prehistoric pteradactyls	15	30	45	88	137	185
31-38: 36-Red Hawk drug story by Powell	10	20	30	54	72	90
39-Classic story "The Canyon Beast", with a dinosaur egg hatching a Tyranosaurus Rex	14	28	42	81	118	155
40-Classic story "Secret of The Spanish Specters", with Conquistadors' lost treasure	13	26	39	72	101	130

	GD 2.0	VG 4.0	FN 6.0	VF 8.0	VF/NM 9.0	NM- 9.2

41,42,44-54: 45-Secret Cave-c 9 18 27 50 65 80
43-Intro & 1st app. Blaze, S. Arrow's Warrior dog 10 20 30 58 79 100
55-Last issue 11 22 33 62 86 110
NOTE: *Fred Meagher* a 1-55; c-1, 2, 4-21, 23-55. *Powell* a-2-55. *Whitney* a-1. Many issues advertise the radio premiums associated with Straight Arrow.

STRAIGHT ARROW'S FURY (Also see A-1 Comics)
Magazine Enterprises: No. 119, 1954 (one-shot)
A-1 119-Origin; Fred Meagher-c/a 20 40 60 117 189 260

STRAIN, THE (Adaptation of novels by Guillermo del Toro and Chuck Hogan)
Dark Horse Comics: Dec, 2011 - No. 11, Feb, 2013 ($1.00/$3.50)
1-($1.00) Lapham, Hogan & del Toro-s/Huddleston-a/c; variant-c by Morris 3.50
2-11-($3.50) Lapham-s/Huddleston-a/c 3.50

STRAIN, THE: MISTER QUINLAN - VAMPIRE HUNTER
Dark Horse Comics: Sept, 2016 - No. 5 ($3.99)
1-5: 1-Lapham, Hogan & del Toro-s/Salazar-a; origin of Mister Quinlan in ancient Rome 4.00

STRAIN, THE: THE FALL (Guillermo del Toro and Chuck Hogan)
Dark Horse Comics: Jul, 2013 - No. 9, Mar, 2014 ($3.99)
1-9-Lapham, Hogan & del Toro-s/Huddleston-a/Gist-c 4.00

STRAIN, THE: THE NIGHT ETERNAL (Guillermo del Toro and Chuck Hogan)
Dark Horse Comics: Aug, 2014 - No. 12, Aug, 2015 ($3.99)
1-12-Lapham, Hogan & del Toro-s/Huddleston-a/Gist-c 4.00

STRANGE (Tales You'll Never Forget)
Ajax-Farrell Publ. (Four Star Comic Corp.): March, 1957 - No. 6, May, 1958
1 34 68 102 204 332 460
2-Censored r/Haunted Thrills 19 38 57 111 176 240
3-6 15 30 45 90 140 190

STRANGE (Dr. Strange)
Marvel Comics (Marvel Knights): Nov, 2004 - No. 6, July, 2005 ($3.50)
1-6-Straczynski & Barnes-s/Peterson-a; Dr. Strange's origin retold 3.50
...: Beginnings and Endings TPB (2006, $17.99) r/#1-6 18.00

STRANGE (Dr. Strange)
Marvel Comics: Jan, 2010 - No. 4, Apr, 2010 ($3.99, limited series)
1-4-Waid-s/Rios-a/Coker-c 4.00

STRANGE (Clea as the Sorceror Supreme)
Marvel Comics: May, 2022 - No. 10, Mar, 2023 ($4.99/$3.99, limited series)
1-($4.99) MacKay-s/Ferreira-a; Doctor Doom app. 5.00
2-10-($3.99) 2-Clea vs. The Harvestman. 5-Moon Knight app. 4.00

STRANGE ACADEMY
Marvel Comics: May, 2020 - No. 18, Jun, 2022 ($4.99/$3.99)
1-($4.99) Skottie Young-s/Humberto Ramos-a; Dr. Strange, Doctor Voodoo, Loki app.
5 10 15 31 53 75
2-($3.99) Ancient One, Man-Thing app. 3 6 9 14 20 25
3-18: 10-Field trip to Asgard; The Enchantress app. 11-Howard the Duck app. 4.00
...: Amazing Spider-Man 1 (12/23, $4.99) "Solve For X" part 3; Georgiev-a 5.00
...: Miles Morales 1 (10/23, $4.99) "Solve For X" part 1 5.00
...: Moon Knight 1 (11/23, $4.99) "Solve For X" part 2 5.00
... Presents: The Death of Doctor Strange 1 (12/21, $4.99) Young-s/Del Mundo-a 5.00

STRANGE ACADEMY: FINALS
Marvel Comics: Dec, 2022 - No. 6, Jun, 2023 ($3.99, limited series)
1-6-Skottie Young-s/Humberto Ramos-a 4.00

STRANGE ADVENTURE MAGAZINE
CJH Publications: Dec, 1936 (10¢)
1-Flash Gordon, The Master of Mars, text stories w/some full pg. panels of art by Fred Meagher (a FN+ copy sold for $1075 in 2012)

STRANGE ADVENTURES
DC Comics: July/Aug 1950
nn - Ashcan comic, not distributed to newsstands, only for in-house use. Cover art is All Star Comics #47 with interior being Detective Comics #140. A second example has the interior of Detective Comics #146. A third example has an unidentified issue of Detective Comics as the interior. This is the only ashcan with multiple interiors. A FN+ copy sold for $1,000 in 2007.

STRANGE ADVENTURES
National Periodical Publ.: Aug-Sept, 1950 - No. 244, Oct-Nov, 1973 (No. 1-12: 52 pgs.)
1-Adaptation of "Destination Moon"; preview of movie w/photo-c from movie (also see Fawcett Movie Comic #2); adapt. of Edmond Hamilton's "Chris KL-99" in #1-3; Darwin Jones begins 186 372 558 1535 3468 5400
2 86 172 258 888 1544 2400
3,4 61 122 183 448 1094 1700
5-8,10: 7-Origin Kris KL-99 48 96 144 374 862 1350
9-(6/51)-Origin/1st app. Captain Comet (c/story) 121 242 363 968 2184 3400
11-20: 12,13,17,18-Toth-a. 14-Robot-c 34 68 102 245 548 850
21-30: 28-Atomic explosion panel. 30-Robot-c 32 64 96 230 515 800
31,34-38 29 58 87 209 467 725
32,33-Krigstein-a 31 62 93 223 499 775
39-Ill. in SOTI "Treating police contemptuously" (top right)
40 80 120 296 673 1050
40-49-Last Capt. Comet; not in 45,47,48 28 56 84 202 451 700
50-53-Last precode issue (2/55) 25 50 75 175 388 600
54-70 20 40 60 144 317 490
71-79,81-99 17 34 51 114 252 390
80-Grey-tone-c 32 64 96 230 515 800
100 19 38 57 131 291 450
101-110: 104-Space Museum begins by Sekowsky 13 26 39 89 195 300
111-116,118,119: 114-Star Hawkins begins, ends #185; Heath-a in Wood E.C. style
13 26 39 86 188 290
117-(6/60)-Origin/1st app. Atomic Knights. 52 104 156 411 931 1450
120-2nd app. Atomic Knights 23 46 69 161 356 550
121,122,125,127,128,130,131,133,134: 134-Last 10c issue
11 22 33 76 163 250

123,126-3rd & 4th app. Atomic Knights 15 30 45 100 220 340
124-Intro/origin Faceless Creature 17 34 51 119 265 410
129,132,135,138,141,147-Atomic Knights app. 12 24 36 82 179 275
136,137,139,140,143,145,146,148,149,151,152,154,155,157-159: 136-Robot cover.
159-Star Rovers app.; Gil Kane/Anderson-a. 9 18 27 63 129 195
142-2nd app. Faceless Creature 12 24 36 82 179 275
144-Only Atomic Knights-c (by M. Anderson) 15 30 45 105 233 360
150,153,156,160: Atomic Knights in each. 150-Greytone-c. 153-(6/63)-3rd app. Faceless Creature; atomic explosion-c. 160-Last Atomic Knights
11 22 33 73 157 240
161-179: 161-Last Space Museum. 163-Star Rovers app. 170-Infinity-c.
177-Intro/origin Immortal Man 8 16 24 52 99 145
180-Origin/1st app. Animal Man 71 142 213 568 1284 2000
181-183,185,186,188,189 6 12 18 41 76 110
184-2nd app. Animal Man by Gil Kane 12 24 36 80 173 265
187-Intro/origin The Enchantress 40 80 120 296 673 1050
190-1st app. Animal Man in costume 16 32 48 111 246 380
191-194,196-200,202-204 6 12 18 37 66 95
195-1st full app. Animal Man 9 18 27 59 117 175
201-Last Animal Man; 2nd full app. 7 14 21 46 86 125
205-(10/67)-Intro/origin Deadman by Infantino & begin Deadman series, ends #216
93 186 279 744 1672 2600
206-Neal Adams-a begins 17 34 51 114 252 390
207-210 10 20 30 69 147 225
211-216: 211-Space Museum-r. 215-1st app. League of Assassins. 216-(1-2/69)-Deadman story finally concludes in Brave & the Bold #86 (10-11/69); secret message panel by Neal Adams (pg. 13); tribute to Steranko 9 18 27 62 126 190
217-r/origin & 1st app. Adam Strange from Showcase #17, begin & Atomic Knights-r begin
4 8 12 23 37 50
218-221,223-225: 218-Last 12¢ issue. 225-Last 15¢ issue
3 6 9 16 23 30
222-New Adam Strange story; Kane/Anderson-a 4 8 12 23 37 50
226,227,230-236-(68-52 pgs.): 226, 227-New Adam Strange text story w/illos by Anderson (8,6 pgs.) 231-Last Atomic Knights-r. 235-JLA-c/s 3 6 9 16 23 30
228,229 (68 pgs.) 3 6 9 17 26 35
237-243 2 4 6 11 16 20
244-Last issue 3 6 9 14 20 25
NOTE: *Neal Adams* a-206-216; c-207-218, 228, 235. *Anderson* a-8-52, 94, 96, 99, 115, 117, 119-163, 217r, 218r, 222, 223-225r; 226, 229r, 242i(r); c-18, 19, 21, 23, 24, 27, 30, 32-44(most); c/r-157i, 190i, 217-224, 228-231, 233, 235-239, 241-243. *Ditko* a-188, 189. *Drucker* a-42, 43, 45. *Elias* a-212. *Finlay* a-2, 3, 6, 7, 210r, 229r. *Giunta* a-237r. *Heath* a-116. *Infantino* a-10-101, 106-151, 154, 157-163, 180, 190, 218-221r, 223-244p(r); c-50; c/r-190p, 197, 199-211, 218-221, 223-244. *Kaluta* c-238, 240. *Gil Kane* a-8-116, 124, 125, 130, 138, 146-157, 173-186, 204r, 222r; 227-231r; c(p)-11-17, 25, 154, 157. *Kubert* a-55(2 pgs.); 226; c-219, 220, 225-227, 232, 234. *Moreira* c-26, 28, 29, 71. *Morrow* c-230. *Mortimer* c-8. *Powell* a-4. *Sekowsky* a-71p, 97-162p, 217p(r); 218p(r); c-206, 217-219. *Simon & Kirby* a-25. *Sparling* a-201. *Toth* a-8, 12, 13, 17-19. *Wood* a-154i. Atomic Knights in #117, 120, 123, 126, 129, 132, 135, 138, 141, 144, 147, 150, 153, 156, 160. Atomic Knights reprints by *Anderson* 217-223, 231, 233-231. Chris KL99 in 1-3, 5, 7, 9, 11, 15. Capt. Comet covers-9-14, 17-19, 24, 26, 27, 32-44.

STRANGE ADVENTURES
DC Comics (Vertigo): Nov, 1999 - No. 4, Feb, 2000 ($2.50, limited series)
1-4: 1-Bolland-c; art by Bolland, Gibbons, Quitely 4.00

STRANGE ADVENTURES
DC Comics: May, 2009 - No. 8, Dec, 2009 ($3.99, limited series)
1-8: 1-Starlin-s/a; Adam Strange, Capt. Comet, Bizarro & Prince Gavyn app. 4.00
TPB (2010, $19.99) r/#1-8; cover gallery 20.00

STRANGE ADVENTURES
DC Comics (Vertigo): Jul, 2011 ($7.99, one-shot)
1-Short story anthology; s/a by Azzarello, Risso, Milligan and others; Paul Pope-c 8.00

STRANGE ADVENTURES
DC Comics (Black Label): May, 2020 - No. 12, Dec, 2021 ($4.99, limited series)
1-12-Adam Strange's book tour; Tom King-s/Mitch Gerads & Evan Shaner-a; 2 covers on each. 2-12-Mister Terrific & Batman app. in most 5.00
1-Director's Cut (1/21, $5.99) Original script with black & white art 6.00

STRANGE AS IT SEEMS (See Famous Funnies-A Carnival of Comics, Feature Funnies #1, The John Hix Scrap Book & Peanuts)

STRANGE AS IT SEEMS
United Features Syndicate: 1939
Single Series 9, 1, 2 42 84 126 265 445 625

STRANGE CEREBUS (Reprints from Cerebus in Hell)
Aardvark-Vanaheim: Oct, 2017 ($4.00, B&W)
1-Cerebus figures placed over original Doré artwork of Hell; Dr. Strange #180-c swipe 4.00

STRANGE COMBAT TALES
Marvel Comics (Epic Comics): Oct, 1993 - No. 4, Jan, 1994 ($2.50, limited series)
1-4 4.00

STRANGE CONFESSIONS
Ziff-Davis Publ. Co.: Jan-Mar (Spring on-c), 1952 - No. 4, Fall, 1952 (All have photo-c)
1(Scarce)-Kinstler-a 97 194 291 621 1061 1500
2(Scarce) 7-8/52) 63 126 189 403 689 975
3(Scarce, 9-10/52)-#3 on-c, #2 on inside; Reformatory girl story; photo-c
58 116 174 371 636 900
4(Scarce) 55 110 165 352 601 850

STRANGE DAYS
Eclipse Comics: Oct, 1984 - No. 3, Apr, 1985 ($1.75, Baxter paper)
1-3: Freakwave, Johnny Nemo, & Paradax from Vanguard Illustrated; nudity, violence & strong language 6.00

STRANGE DAYS (Movie)
Marvel Comics: Dec, 1995 ($5.95, squarebound, one-shot)
1-Adaptation of film 6.00

STRANGE FANTASY (Eerie Tales of Suspense!)(Formerly Rocketman #1)
Ajax-Farrell: Aug, 1952 - No. 14, Oct-Nov, 1954
2(#1, 8/52)-Jungle Princess story; Kamenish-a; reprinted from Ellery Queen #1
100 200 300 635 1093 1550

Strange Academy #14 © MAR

Strange Adventures #231 © DC

Strangers in Paradise V2 #13 © Terry Moore

	GD 2.0	VG 4.0	FN 6.0	VF 8.0	VF/NM 9.0	NM- 9.2
2(10/52)-No Black Cat or Rulah; Bakerish, Kamenish-a; hypo/meathook-c	87	174	261	553	952	1350
3-Rulah story, called Pulah	58	116	174	371	636	900
4-Rocket Man app. (2/53)	57	114	171	362	619	875
5,6,8,10,12,14	48	96	144	302	514	725
7-Madam Satan/Slave story	103	206	309	659	1130	1600
9(w/Black Cat), 9(w/Boy's Ranch; S&K-a), 9(w/War)(A rebinding of Harvey interiors; not publ. by Ajax)	116	232	348	742	1271	1800
9-Regular issue; Steve Ditko's 3rd published work (tied with Captain 3D)	103	206	309	659	1130	1600
11-Jungle story	57	114	171	362	619	875
13-Bondage-c; Rulah (Kolah) story	61	122	183	390	670	950

STRANGE FRUIT
BOOM! Studios: Jul, 2015 - No. 4, Nov, 2016 ($3.99, limited series)

1-4-J.G. Jones-a; Jones & Mark Waid-s						4.00

STRANGE GALAXY
Eerie Publications: V1#8, Feb, 1971 - No. 11, Aug, 1971 (B&W, magazine)

V1#8-Reprints-c/Fantastic V19#3 (2/70) (a pulp)	4	8	12	25	40	55
9-11	3	6	9	19	30	40

STRANGE GIRL
Image Comics: June, 2005 - No. 18, Sept, 2007 ($2.95/$2.99/$3.50)

1-18: 1-Rick Remender-s/Eric Nguyen-a. 13-18-($3.50)						3.50
... Vol. 1: Girl Afraid TPB (2005, $12.99) r/#1-4; sketch pages and pin-ups						13.00

STRANGE JOURNEY
America's Best (Steinway Publ.) (Ajax/Farrell): Sept, 1957 - No. 4, Jun, 1958 (Farrell reprints)

1-The Phantom Express	28	56	84	168	274	380
2-4: 2-Flying saucer-c. 3-Titanic-c	20	40	60	117	189	260

STRANGE LOVE (See Fox Giants)

STRANGE LOVE ADVENTURES
DC Comics: Apr, 2022 ($9.99, squarebound, one-shot)

1-Short story romance anthology: Harley Quinn, Sgt. Rock, Peacemaker app.; Paquette-c						10.00

STRANGE MYSTERIES
Superior/Dynamic Publications: Sept, 1951 - No. 21, Jan, 1955

1-Kamenish-a & horror stories begin	116	232	348	742	1271	1800
2	65	130	195	416	708	1000
3-5	55	110	165	352	601	850
6-8	50	100	150	315	533	750
9-Bondage 3-D effect-c	135	270	405	864	1482	2100
10-Used in SOTI, pg. 181	103	206	309	659	1130	1600
11-18: 13-Eyeball-c	54	108	162	343	574	825
19-r/Journey Into Fear #1; cover is a splash from one story; Baker-c(2)	50	100	150	315	533	750
20,21-Reprints; 20-r/#1 with new-c (The Devil)	37	74	111	222	361	500

STRANGE MYSTERIES
I. W. Enterprises/Super Comics: 1963 - 1964

I.W. Reprint #9; Rulah-r/Spook #28; Disbrow-a	4	8	12	23	37	50
Super Reprint #10-12,15-17(1963-64): 10,11-r/Strange #2,1. 12-r/Tales of Horror #5 (3/53) less-c. 15-r/Dark Mysteries #23. 16-r/The Dead Who Walk. 17-r/Dark Mysteries #22	4	8	12	23	37	50
Super Reprint #18-r/Witchcraft #1; Kubert-a	4	8	12	23	37	50

STRANGE PLANETS
I. W. Enterprises/Super Comics: 1958; 1963-64

I.W. Reprint #1(nd)-Reprints E. C. Incredible S/F #30 plus-c/Strange Worlds #3	7	14	21	46	86	125
I.W. Reprint #9-Orlando/Wood-r/Strange Worlds #4; cover-r from Flying Saucers #1	8	16	24	55	105	155
Super Reprint #10-Wood-r (22 pg.) from Space Detective #1; cover-r/Attack on Planet Mars	8	16	24	55	105	155
Super Reprint #11-Wood-r (25 pg.) from An Earthman on Venus	8	16	24	55	105	155
Super Reprint #12-Orlando-r/Rocket to the Moon	9	18	27	57	111	165
Super Reprint #15-Reprints Journey Into Unknown Worlds #8; Heath, Colan-r	5	10	15	33	57	80
Super Reprint #16-Reprints Avon's Strange Worlds #6; Kinstler, Check-a	5	10	15	34	60	85
Super Reprint #18-r/Great Exploits #1 (Daring Adventures #6); Space Busters, Explorer Joe, The Son of Robin Hood; Krigstein-a	5	10	15	30	50	70

STRANGERS
Image Comics: Mar, 2003 - No. 6, Sept, 2003 ($2.95)

	GD 2.0	VG 4.0	FN 6.0	VF 8.0	VF/NM 9.0	NM- 9.2
1-6-Randy & Jean-Marc Lofficier-s; two covers. 2-Nexus back-up story						3.00

STRANGERS, THE
Malibu Comics (Ultraverse): June, 1993 - No. 24, May, 1995 ($1.95/$2.50)

1-4,6-12,14-20: 1-1st app. The Strangers; has coupon for Ultraverse Premiere #0; 1st app. the Night Man (not in costume). 2-Polybagged w/trading card. 7-Break-Thru x-over. 8-2 pg. origin Solution. 12-Silver foil logo; wraparound-c. 17-Rafferty app.						4.00
1-With coupon missing						3.00
1-Full cover holographic edition, 1st of kind w/Hardcase #1 & Prime #1	1	3	4	6	8	10
1-Ultra 5000 limited silver foil						6.00
4-($2.50)-Variant Newsstand edition bagged w/card						5.00
5-($2.50, 52 pgs.)-Rune flip-c/story by B. Smith (3 pgs.); The Mighty Magnor 1 pg. strip by Aragones; 3-pg. Night Man preview						5.00
13-($3.50, 68 pgs.)-Mantra app.; flip book w/Ultraverse Premiere #4						5.00
21-24 ($2.50)						4.00
...:The Pilgrim Conundrum Saga (1/95, $3.95, 68pgs.)						5.00

STRANGERS IN CEREBUS (Strangers in Paradise: I Dream of You cover parody)
Aardvark-Vanaheim: June, 2021 ($4.00, B&W)

1-Cerebus figures placed over original Gustave Doré artwork of Hell						4.00

STRANGERS IN PARADISE (Also see SIP Kids)
Antarctic Press: Nov, 1993 - No. 3, Feb, 1994 ($2.75, B&W, limited series)

1	14	28	42	96	211	325
1-2nd/3rd prints	2	4	6	11	16	20
2 (2300 printed)	5	10	15	34	60	85
3	3	6	9	21	33	45
Trade paperback (Antarctic Press, $6.95) (5000 print run)						10.00
Trade paperback (Abstract Studios, $6.95)-Red-c (2000 print run)						15.00
Trade paperback (Abstract Studios, $6.95, 1st-4th printing)-Blue-c						7.00
Hardcover ('98, $29.95) includes first draft pages						30.00
Gold Reprint Series ($2.75) 1-3-r/#1-3						4.00

STRANGERS IN PARADISE
Abstract Studios: Sept, 1994 - No. 14, July, 1996 ($2.75, B&W)

1	2	4	6	11	16	20
1,3- 2nd printings						4.00
2,3- 2-Color dream sequence	1	3	4	6	8	10
4-10						5.00
4-6-2nd printings						4.00
11-14: 14-The Letters of Molly & Poo						4.00
Gold Reprint Series ($2.75) 1-13-r/#1-13						4.00
I Dream Of You ($16.95, TPB) r/#1-9						17.00
It's a Good Life ($8.95, TPB) r/#10-13						9.00

STRANGERS IN PARADISE (Volume Three)
Homage Comics #1-8/Abstract Studios #9-on: Oct, 1996 - No. 90, May, 2007 ($2.75-$2.99, color #1-5, B&W #6-on)

1-Terry Moore-c/s/a in all; dream seq. by Jim Lee-a	1	2	3	5	6	8
1-Jim Lee variant-c	2	4	6	8	10	12
2-5						5.00
6-16: 6-Return to B&W. 13-15-High school flashback. 16-Xena Warrior Princess parody; two covers						4.00
17-89: 33-Color issue. 46-Molly Lane. 49-Molly & Poo. 86-David dies						5.00
90-Last issue; 3 covers of Katchoo, Francine and David forming a triptych						4.00
...Lyrics and Poems (2/99)						4.00
...Source Book (2003, $2.95) Background on characters & story arcs, checklists						9.00
Brave New World ('02, $8.95, TPB) r/#44,45,47,48						16.00
Child of Rage ('04, $8.95, TPB) r/#31-38						9.00
David's Story (6/04, $8.95, TPB) r/#61-63						16.00
Ever After ('07, $15.95, TPB) r/#83-90						16.00
Flower to Flame ('03, $15.95, TPB) r/#55-60						13.00
Heart in Hand ('03, $12.95, TPB) r/#50-54						9.00
High School ('98, $8.95, TPB) r/#13-16						15.00
Immortal Enemies ('98, $14.95, TPB) r/#6-12						15.00
Love & Lies (2006, $14.95, TPB)r/#77-82						13.00
Love Me Tender ($12.95, TPB) r/#1-5 in B&W w/ color Lee seq.						15.00
Molly & Poo (2005, $8.95, TPB)r/#46,49,73						15.00
My Other Life ($14.95, TPB) r/#25-30						
Pocket Books 1-5 ($17.95, 5 1/2" x 8", TPB) 1-r/Vol.1 & 2. 2-r/#17-17 in B&W. 3-r/#18-24,26-32,34-38. 4-r/#41-45,47,48,50-60. 5-r/#46,49,61-76						18.00
Sanctuary ($15.95, TPB) r/#17-24						16.00
Tattoo ($14.95, TPB) r/#70-76; sketch pages and fan tattoo photos						15.00
Tomorrow Now (11/04, $14.95, TPB) r/#64-69						15.00
Tropic of Desire ($12.95, TPB) r/#39-43						13.00
The Complete... : Volume 3 Part 1 HC ($49.95) r/#1-12						50.00

	GD 2.0	VG 4.0	FN 6.0	VF 8.0	VF/NM 9.0	NM- 9.2

The Complete... : Volume 3 Part 2 HC ($49.95) r/#13-15,17-25 — 50.00
The Complete... : Volume 3 Part 3 HC ('01, $49.95) r/#26-38 — 50.00
The Complete... : Volume 3 Part 4 HC ('02, $39.95) r/#39-46,49 — 40.00
The Complete... : Volume 3 Part 5 HC ('03, $49.95) r/#47,48,50-57 — 50.00
The Complete... : Volume 3 Part 6 HC ('04, $49.95) r/#58-69 — 50.00
The Complete... : Volume 3 Part 7 HC ('06, $49.95) r/#70-80 — 50.00

STRANGERS IN PARADISE XXV
Abstract Studio: 2018 - No. 10, 2019 ($3.99, B&W)
1-10-Terry Moore-c/s/a; Rachel, Zoe & Lilith app. — 4.00
1-Free Comic Book Day edition (2018, giveaway) r/#1 — 3.00

STRANGER THINGS (Based on the Netflix TV series)
Dark Horse Comics: Sept, 2018 - No. 4, Jan 2019 ($3.99, limited series)
1-4-Will Byers time in the Upside Down; Houser-s/Martino-a; multiple covers — 4.00
...: Halloween Special One Shot (10/20, $3.99) Moreci-s/Hristov-a/Francavilla-c — 4.00
...: Summer Special One Shot (7/22, $3.99) Officers Powell & Callahan during season 3 — 6.00
...: Winter Special One Shot (11/21, $6.99) Powell & ABEL-a/ABEL-a; 2 covers — 7.00

STRANGER THINGS / D&D CROSSOVER (Based on the Netflix TV series)
Dark Horse Comics: Nov, 2020 - No. 4 Feb 2021 ($3.99, limited series)
1-4-Houser & Zub-s/Galindo-a/multiple covers — 4.00

STRANGER THINGS: INTO THE FIRE (Based on the Netflix TV series)
Dark Horse Comics: Jan, 2020 - No. 4, Jul, 2020 ($3.99, limited series)
1-4-The search for subject Eight; Houser-s/Kelly-a/Kalvachev-c — 4.00

STRANGER THINGS: KAMCHATKA (Based on the Netflix TV series)
Dark Horse Comics: Mar, 2022 - No. 4, Aug 2022 ($3.99, limited series)
1-4-The demogorgon in Russia; Moreci-s/Hristov-a — 4.00

STRANGER THINGS: SCIENCE CAMP (Based on the Netflix TV series)
Dark Horse Comics: Sept, 2020 - No. 4, Dec, 2020 ($3.99, limited series)
1-4-Houser-s/Salazar-a/Kalvachev-c — 4.00

STRANGER THINGS SIX (Based on the Netflix TV series)
Dark Horse Comics: May, 2019 - No. 4, Aug 2019 ($3.99, limited series)
1-4-Prequel focusing on subject Six, Francine; Houser-s/Salazar-a — 4.00

STRANGER THINGS: TALES FROM HAWKINS (Based on the Netflix TV series)
Dark Horse Comics: Feb, 2023 - No. 4, Sept, 2023 ($3.99, limited series)
1-4: 1-Houser-s/Filipe-a. 3-Spotlight on Robin — 4.00

STRANGER THINGS: THE VOYAGE (Based on the Netflix TV series)
Dark Horse Comics: Nov, 2023 - No. 4, June, 2024 ($3.99, limited series)
1-3-The demogorgon on a ship from Russia; Moreci-s/Hristov-a — 4.00

STRANGER THINGS TOMB OF YBWEN (Based on the Netflix TV series)
Dark Horse Comics: Sept, 2021 - No. 4, Dec, 2021 ($3.99, limited series)
1-4-Bob Newby's treasure map to the Tomb of Ybwen; Pak-s/Galindo-a — 4.00

STRANGE SKIES OVER EAST BERLIN
BOOM! Studios: Oct, 2019 - No. 4, Jan, 2020 ($3.99, limited series)
1-4-Jeff Loveness-s/Lisandro Estherren-a — 4.00

STRANGE SPORTS STORIES (See Brave & the Bold #45-49, DC Special, and DC Super Stars #10)
National Periodical Publications: Sept-Oct, 1973 - No. 6, July-Aug, 1974
1-Devil-c — 3 / 6 / 9 / 18 / 27 / 36
2-6: 2-Swan/Anderson-a — 2 / 4 / 6 / 10 / 14 / 18

STRANGE SPORTS STORIES
DC Comics (Vertigo): May, 2015 - No. 4, Aug, 2015 ($4.99, limited series)
1-4-Anthology of short stories by various. 1-Paul Pope-c. 4-Pope-s/a — 5.00

STRANGE STORIES FROM ANOTHER WORLD (Unknown World #1)
Fawcett Publications: No. 2, Aug, 1952 - No. 5, Feb, 1953
2-Saunders painted-c — 68 / 136 / 204 / 435 / 743 / 1050
3-5-Saunders painted-c — 54 / 108 / 162 / 343 / 574 / 825

STRANGE STORIES OF SUSPENSE (Rugged Action #1-4)
Atlas Comics (CSI): No. 5, Oct, 1955 - No. 16, Aug, 1957
5(#1) — 58 / 116 / 174 / 371 / 636 / 900
6,7,9 — 41 / 82 / 123 / 256 / 428 / 600
8-Morrow/Williamson-a; Pakula-a — 43 / 86 / 129 / 271 / 461 / 650
10-Crandall, Torres, Meskin-a — 39 / 78 / 117 / 240 / 395 / 550
11-13: 12-Torres, Pakula-a. 13-E.C. art swipes — 36 / 72 / 108 / 211 / 343 / 475
14-16: 14-Williamson/Mayo-a. 15-Krigstein-a. 16-Fox, Powell-a — 37 / 74 / 111 / 222 / 361 / 500
NOTE: *Everett* a-6, 7, 13; c-8, 9, 11-14. *Forte* a-12, 16. *Heath* a-5. *Maneely* c-5. *Morisi* a-11. *Morrow* a-13. *Powell* a-8. *Sale* a-11. *Severin* c-7. *Wildey* a-14.

STRANGE STORY (Also see Front Page)
Harvey Publications: June-July, 1946 (52 pgs.)
1-The Man in Black Called Fate by Powell — 48 / 96 / 144 / 302 / 514 / 725

STRANGE SUSPENSE STORIES (Lawbreakers Suspense Stories #10-15; This Is Suspense #23-26; Captain Atom V1#78 on)
Fawcett Publications/Charlton Comics No. 16 on: 6/52 - No. 5, 2/53; No. 16, 1/54 - No. 22, 11/54; No. 27, 10/55 - No. 77, 10/65; V3#1, 10/67 - V1#9, 9/69
1-(Fawcett)-Powell, Sekowsky-a — 106 / 212 / 318 / 673 / 1162 / 1650
2-George Evans horror story — 58 / 116 / 174 / 371 / 636 / 900
3-5 (2/53)-George Evans horror stories — 48 / 96 / 114 / 302 / 514 / 725
16(1-2/54)-Formerly Lawbreakers S.S. — 41 / 82 / 123 / 256 / 428 / 600
17 — 34 / 68 / 102 / 199 / 325 / 450
18-E.C. swipe/HOF 7; Ditko-c/a(2) — 61 / 122 / 183 / 390 / 670 / 950
19-Ditko electric chair-c; Ditko-a — 703 / 1406 / 2109 / 5132 / 9066 / 13,000
20-Ditko-c/a(2) — 46 / 92 / 115 / 362 / 601 / 850
21-Shuster-a; a woman dangling over an alligator pit while a madman smashes her fingers with a hammer — 57 / 114 / 171 / 362 / 619 / 875
22(11/54)-Ditko-c, Shuster-a; last pre-code issue; becomes This Is Suspense — 54 / 108 / 162 / 343 / 574 / 825
27(10/55)-(Formerly This Is Suspense #26) — 20 / 40 / 60 / 120 / 195 / 270

28-30,38 — 15 / 30 / 45 / 88 / 137 / 185
31-33,35,37,40-Ditko-c/a(2-3 each) — 25 / 50 / 75 / 150 / 245 / 340
34-Story of ruthless business man, Wm. B. Gaines; Ditko-c/a — 65 / 130 / 195 / 416 / 708 / 1000
36-(15¢, 68 pgs.); Ditko-a(4) — 30 / 60 / 90 / 177 / 289 / 400
39,41,52,53-Ditko-a — 22 / 44 / 66 / 128 / 209 / 290
42-44,46,49,54-60 — 6 / 12 / 18 / 41 / 66 / 110
45,47,48,50,51-Ditko-c/a — 14 / 28 / 42 / 94 / 207 / 320
61-74: 72-Has panel which inspired a famous Roy Lichtenstein painting — 5 / 10 / 15 / 34 / 60 / 85
75(6/65)-Reprints origin/1st app. Captain Atom by Ditko from Space Advs. #33; r/Severin-a/Space Advs. #24 (75-77: 12¢ issues) — 10 / 20 / 30 / 70 / 150 / 230
76,77-Captain Atom-r by Ditko/Space Advs. — 7 / 14 / 21 / 46 / 86 / 125
V3#1(10/67): 12¢ issues begin — 3 / 6 / 9 / 20 / 31 / 42
V1#2-Ditko-c/a; atom bomb-c — 3 / 6 / 9 / 20 / 31 / 42
V1#3-9: 3-8-All 12¢ issues. 9-15¢ issue — 3 / 6 / 9 / 14 / 19 / 24
NOTE: *Alascia* a-19. *Aparo* a-60, V3#1, 2, 4; c-V1#4, 8, 9. *Baily* a-1-3; c-2, 5. *Evans* c-3, 4. *Giordano* c-16, 17p, 24p, 25p. *Montes/Bache* c-60. *Powell* a-4. *Shuster* a-19, 21. *Marcus Swayze* a-7.

STRANGE TALENT OF LUTHER STRODE, THE (Also see The Legend of Luther Strode)
Image Comics: Oct, 2011 - No. 6, Mar, 2012 ($2.99, limited series)
1-6: Justin Jordan-s/Tradd Moore-a — 3.00

STRANGE TALES (...Featuring Warlock #178-181; Doctor Strange #169 on)
Atlas (CCPC #1-67/ZPC #68-79/VPI #80-85)/Marvel #86(7/61) on:
June, 1951 - No. 168, May, 1968; No. 169, Sept, 1973 - No. 188, Nov, 1976
1-Horror/weird stories begin — 1000 / 2000 / 3000 / 7300 / 12,900 / 18,500
2 — 232 / 464 / 696 / 1485 / 2543 / 3600
3,5: 3-Atom bomb panels — 174 / 348 / 522 / 1114 / 1907 / 2700
4-Cosmic eyeball story "The Evil Eye" — 187 / 374 / 561 / 1197 / 2049 / 2900
6-9: 6-Heath-c/a. 7-Colan-a — 135 / 270 / 405 / 864 / 1482 / 2100
10-Krigstein-a — 148 / 296 / 444 / 947 / 1624 / 2300
11-14,16-20 — 110 / 220 / 330 / 704 / 1202 / 1700
15-Krigstein-a; detached head-c — 123 / 246 / 369 / 787 / 1344 / 1900
21,23-27,29-34: 27-Atom bomb panels. 33-Davis-a. 34-Last pre-code issue (2/55) — 97 / 194 / 291 / 621 / 1061 / 1500
22-Krigstein, Forte/Fox-a — 110 / 220 / 330 / 704 / 1202 / 1700
28-Jack Katz story used in Senate Investigation report, pgs. 7 & 169; classic skull-c — 676 / 1372 / 2028 / 4935 / 8718 / 12,500
35-41,43,44: 37-Vampire story by Colan — 48 / 96 / 144 / 374 / 862 / 1350
42,45,59,61-Krigstein-a; #61 (2/58) — 54 / 108 / 162 / 432 / 966 / 1500
46-57,60: 51-(10/56) 1st S.A. issue. 53,56-Crandall-a. 60-(8/57) — 46 / 92 / 138 / 359 / 805 / 1250
58,64-Williamson-a in each, with Mayo-a/#58 — 46 / 92 / 138 / 368 / 834 / 1300
62,63,65,66: 62-Torres-a. 66-Crandall-a — 46 / 92 / 138 / 359 / 805 / 1250
67-Prototype ish. (Quicksilver) — 57 / 114 / 171 / 456 / 1028 / 1600
68,71,72,74,77,80: Ditko/Kirby-a in #67-80 — 46 / 92 / 138 / 359 / 805 / 1250
69,70,73,75,76,78,79: 69-Prototype ish. (Prof. X). 70-Prototype ish. (Giant Man). 73-Prototype ish. (Ant-Man). 75-Prototype ish. (Iron Man). 76-Prototype ish. (Human Torch). 78-Prototype ish. (Ant-Man). 79-Prototype ish. (Dr. Strange) (12/60) — 52 / 104 / 156 / 416 / 933 / 1450
81-83,85-88,90,91-Ditko/Kirby-a in all: 86-Robot-c. 90-(11/61)-Atom bomb blast panel — 46 / 92 / 138 / 340 / 770 / 1200
84-Prototype ish. (Magneto)(5/61); has powers like Magneto of X-Men, but two years earlier; Ditko/Kirby-a — 64 / 128 / 192 / 512 / 1156 / 1800
89-1st app. Fin Fang Foom (10/61) by Kirby — 367 / 734 / 1101 / 3120 / 7060 / 11,000
92-Prototype ish. (Ancient One & Ant-Man); last 10¢ issue — 46 / 92 / 138 / 368 / 834 / 1300
93,95,96,98-100: Kirby-a — 38 / 76 / 114 / 285 / 641 / 1000
94-Creature similar to The Thing; Kirby-a — 46 / 92 / 138 / 359 / 805 / 1250
97-1st app. of an Aunt May & Uncle Ben by Ditko (6/62), before Amazing Fantasy #15; (see Tales Of Suspense #7); Kirby-a — 136 / 272 / 408 / 1088 / 2444 / 3800
101-Human Torch begins by Kirby (10/62); origin recap Fantastic Four & Human Torch; Human Torch-c begin — 183 / 366 / 549 / 1510 / 3405 / 5300
102-1st app. Wizard; robot-c — 54 / 108 / 162 / 432 / 966 / 1500
103-105: 104-1st app. Trapster (as Paste-Pot Pete). 105-2nd Wizard — 46 / 92 / 138 / 340 / 770 / 1200
106,108,109: 106-Fantastic Four guests (3/63) — 36 / 72 / 108 / 266 / 596 / 925
107-(4/63)-Human Torch/Sub-Mariner battle; 4th S.A. Sub-Mariner app. & 1st x-over outside of Fantastic Four — 82 / 164 / 246 / 656 / 1478 / 2300
110-(7/63)-Intro Doctor Strange, Ancient One & Wong by Ditko — 1500 / 3000 / 6000 / 11,400 / 21,200 / 31,000
111-2nd Dr. Strange; intro. Baron Mordo — 118 / 236 / 354 / 944 / 2122 / 3300
112-1st Eel — 35 / 70 / 105 / 252 / 564 / 875
113-Origin/1st app. Plantman — 31 / 62 / 93 / 223 / 499 / 775
114-Acrobat disguised as Captain America, 1st app. since the G.A.; intro. & 1st app. Victoria Bentley; 3rd Dr. Strange app. & begin series (11/63) — 64 / 128 / 192 / 512 / 1156 / 1800
115-Origin Dr. Strange; Human Torch vs. Sandman (Spidey villain; 2nd app. & brief origin); early Spider-Man x-over, 12/63 — 132 / 264 / 396 / 1056 / 2378 / 3700
116-(1/64)-Human Torch battles The Thing; 1st Thing x-over — 28 / 56 / 84 / 202 / 451 / 700
117,118,120: 118-1st cover app. of Dr. Strange. 120-1st Iceman x-over (from X-Men) — 19 / 36 / 54 / 122 / 271 / 420
119-Spider-Man x-over (2 panel cameo) — 21 / 42 / 63 / 147 / 324 / 500
121,122,124,127-134: Thing/Torch team-up in 121-134. 128-Quicksilver & Scarlet Witch app. (1/65). 130-The Beatles cameo. 134-Last Human Torch; The Watcher-c/story; Wood-a(i) — 14 / 28 / 42 / 96 / 211 / 325
123-1st app. The Beetle (see Amazing Spider-Man #21 for next app.); 1st Thor x-over (8/64); Loki app. — 25 / 50 / 75 / 175 / 388 / 600
125-Torch & Thing battle Sub-Mariner (10/64) — 21 / 42 / 63 / 147 / 324 / 500
126-Intro Clea and Dormammu (cont'd in #127) — 89 / 178 / 267 / 712 / 1606 / 2500
135-Col. (formerly Sgt.) Nick Fury becomes Nick Fury Agent of Shield (origin/1st app.) by Kirby (8/65); series begins — 75 / 150 / 225 / 600 / 1350 / 2100
136,137,139,140 — 9 / 18 / 27 / 57 / 111 / 165
138-Intro Eternity — 29 / 58 / 87 / 209 / 467 / 725
141-147,149: 145-Begins alternating-c features w/Nick Fury (odd #'s) & Dr. Strange (even #'s). 146-Last Ditko Dr. Strange who is in consecutive stories since #113; only full Ditko

Strange Suspense Stories #18 © CC

Strange Tales #180 © MAR

Strange Worlds #1 © AVON

	GD 2.0	VG 4.0	FN 6.0	VF 8.0	VF/NM 9.0	NM- 9.2
Dr. Strange-c this title. 147-Dr. Strange (by Everett #147-152) continues thru #168, then						
Dr. Strange #169	7	14	21	46	86	125
148-Origin Ancient One	9	18	27	62	126	190
150(11/66)-John Buscema's 1st work at Marvel	12	24	36	82	179	275
151-Kirby/Steranko-c/a; 1st Marvel work by Steranko	11	22	33	73	157	240
152,153-Kirby/Steranko-a	7	14	21	49	92	135
154-158-Steranko-a/script. 157,158-Debut of The Living Tribunal	7	14	21	49	92	135
159-Origin Nick Fury retold; Intro Val; Captain America-c/story; Steranko-a	33	66	99	238	532	825
160-162-Steranko-a/scripts; Capt. America app.	7	14	21	49	92	135
163-166,168-Steranko(p). 168-Last Nick Fury (gets own book next month) & last						
Dr. Strange who also gets own book	7	14	21	46	86	125
167-Steranko pen/script; classic flag-c	12	24	36	82	179	275
169-1st app. Brother Voodoo(origin in #169,170) & begin series, ends #173	38	76	114	285	641	1000
170-174: 174-Origin Golem	6	12	18	38	69	100
175-177: 177-Brunner-c	3	6	9	15	22	28
178-(2/75)-Warlock by Starlin begins; origin Warlock & Him retold; 1st app. Magus;						
Starlin-c/a/scripts in #178-181 (all before Warlock #9)	12	24	36	82	179	275
179-Intro/1st app. Pip the Troll; Warlock app.	10	20	30	69	147	225
180-(6/75) Intro. Gamora (Guardians of the Galaxy) (5 panels); Warlock by Starlin	13	26	39	89	195	300
181-(8/75)-Warlock story continued in Warlock #9; 1st full app. of Gamora	6	12	18	42	79	115
182-188: 185,186-(Regular 25¢ editions)	2	4	6	10	14	18
185,186-(30¢-c variants, limited distribution)(5,7/76)	6	12	18	42	79	115
Annual 1(1962)-Reprints from Strange Tales #73,76,78, Tales of Suspense #7,9, Tales to Astonish #1,6,7, & Journey Into Mystery #53,55,59; (1st Marvel annual)	93	186	279	744	1672	2600
Annual 2(7/63)-New Human Torch vs. Spider-Man story by Kirby/Ditko (1st Spidey x-over; 4th app.); reprints from Strange Tales #67, Strange Worlds #1-3, World of Fantasy #16; Kirby-c	148	296	444	1221	2761	4300

NOTE: **Briefer** a-17. **Burgos** a-123p. **J. Buscema** a-174p. **Colan** a-7, 11, 20, 37, 53, 169-173p, 188p. **Davis** c-71. **Ditko** a-46, 50, 67-122, 123-125p, 126-146, 175r, 182-188r; c-51, 93, 115, 121, 146. **Everett** a-4, 21, 40-42, 73, 147-152, 164i; c-8, 10, 11, 13, 15, 24, 45, 49-54, 56, 58, 60, 61, 63, 148, 150, 152, 158i. **Forte** a-27, 43, 50, 53, 54, 60. **Heath** a-2, 6; c-6, 18-20. **Kamen** a-45. **G. Kane** c-170-173, 182p. **Kirby** Human Torch-101-105, 108, 109, 114, 120; Nick Fury-135p, 141-143p; (Layouts)-135-153; 138-145, 147, 149, 151p. **Kirby/Ayers** c-101-106, 108-110. **Kirby/Ditko** a-80d, 88, 121; c-75, 93, 97, 100, 139. **Lawrence** a-29. **Leiber/Fox** a-110-113. **Maneely** a-1, 50, 74, 80, 88, 95, 104, 106, 112, 124-127i. **Robinson** a-7. **Romita** c-169. **Roussos** a-201i. **R.Q. Sale** a-56; c-16. **Sekowski** a-3. **Severin** a(i)-136-138; c-137. **Starlin** a-178, 179, 180p, 181p; c-178-180, 181p. **Steranko** a-151-161, 162-168p; c-151i, 153, 155, 157, 159, 161, 163, 165, 167. **Torres** a-53, 62. **Tuska** a-14, 166p. **Whitney** a-149. **Wildey** a-3. **Woodbridge** a-59. Fantastic Four cameos #101-134. Jack Katz app.-26.

STRANGE TALES
Marvel Comics Group: Apr, 1987 - No. 19, Oct, 1988

V2#1-19						5.00

STRANGE TALES
Marvel Comics: Nov, 1994 ($6.95, one-shot)

V3#1-acetate-c	1	2	3	5	6	8

STRANGE TALES (Anthology; continues stories from Man-Thing #8 and Werewolf By Night #6)
Marvel Comics: Sept, 1998 - No. 2, Oct, 1998 ($4.99)

1,2: 1-Silver Surfer app. 2-Two covers						5.00

STRANGE TALES (Humor anthology)
Marvel Comics: Nov, 2009 - No. 3, Jan, 2010 ($4.99, limited series)

1-3: 1-Paul Pope, Kochalka, Bagge and others-s/a. 2-Bagge-c/a. 3-Sakai-c/a						5.00

STRANGE TALES II (Humor anthology)
Marvel Comics: Dec, 2010 - No. 3, Feb, 2011 ($4.99, limited series)

1-3: 2-Jaime Hernandez-a. 3-Terry Moore-s/a; Pekar-s/Templeton-a						5.00

STRANGE TALES: DARK CORNERS
Marvel Comics: May, 1998 ($3.99, one-shot)

1-Anthology; stories by Baron & Maleev, McGregor & Dringenberg, DeMatteis & Badger; Estes painted-a						4.00

STRANGE TALES OF THE UNUSUAL
Atlas Comics (ACI No. 1-4/WPI No. 5-11): Dec, 1955 - No. 11, Aug, 1957

	GD 2.0	VG 4.0	FN 6.0	VF 8.0	VF/NM 9.0	NM- 9.2
1-Powell-a	68	136	204	435	743	1050
2	41	82	123	256	428	600
3-Williamson-a (4 pgs.)	42	84	126	265	445	625
4,6,8,11: 4-UFO-c	33	66	99	194	317	440
5-Crandall, Ditko-a	39	78	117	240	395	550

	GD 2.0	VG 4.0	FN 6.0	VF 8.0	VF/NM 9.0	NM- 9.2
7,9: 7-Kirby, Orlando-a. 9-Krigstein-a	37	74	111	222	361	500
10-Torres, Morrow-a	34	68	102	204	332	460

NOTE: **Baily** a-6. **Brodsky** c-2-4. **Everett** a-2; c-6, 9, 11. **Heck** a-1. **Maneely** c-1. **Orlando** a-7. **Pakula** a-10. **Romita** a-1. **R.Q. Sale** a-3. **Wildey** a-3.

STRANGE TERRORS
St. John Publishing Co.: June, 1952 - No. 7, Mar, 1953

	GD 2.0	VG 4.0	FN 6.0	VF 8.0	VF/NM 9.0	NM- 9.2
1-Bondage-c; Zombies spelled Zoombies on-c; Fine-esque -a	103	206	309	659	1130	1600
2	48	96	144	302	514	725
3-Kubert-a; painted-c	60	120	180	381	653	925
4-Kubert-a (reprinted in Mystery Tales #18); Ekgren painted-c; Fine-esque -a; Jerry Iger caricature	119	238	357	762	1306	1850
5-Kubert-a; painted-c	58	116	174	371	636	900
6-Giant (25¢, 100 pgs.)(1/53); Tyler classic bondage/skull-c	97	194	291	621	1061	1500
7-Giant (25¢, 100 pgs.); Kubert-c/a	84	168	252	538	919	1300

NOTE: **Cameron** a-6. **Morisi** a-6.

STRANGE WORLD OF YOUR DREAMS
Prize Publications: Aug, 1952 - No. 4, Jan-Feb, 1953

	GD 2.0	VG 4.0	FN 6.0	VF 8.0	VF/NM 9.0	NM- 9.2
1-Simon & Kirby-a	93	186	279	591	1021	1450
2,3-Simon & Kirby-c/a. 2-Meskin-a	65	130	195	416	708	1000
4-S&K-c; Meskin-a	53	106	159	334	567	800

STRANGE WORLDS
Avon Periodicals: 11/50 - No. 9, 11/52; No. 18, 10-11/54, No. 22, 9-10/55
(No #11-17)

	GD 2.0	VG 4.0	FN 6.0	VF 8.0	VF/NM 9.0	NM- 9.2
1-Kenton of the Star Patrol by Kubert (r/Eerie #1 from 1947); Crom the Barbarian by John Giunta	194	388	582	1242	2121	3000
2-Wood-a; Crom the Barbarian by Giunta; Dara of the Vikings app.; used in SOTI, pg. 112; injury to eye panel	187	374	561	1197	2049	2900
3-Wood/Orlando-a (Kenton), Wood/Williamson/Frazetta/Krenkel/Orlando-a (7 pgs.); Malu Slave Girl Princess app.; Kinstler-c	271	542	813	1734	2967	4200
4-Wood-a (Kenton); Orlando-a; origin The Enchanted Daggar; Sultan-a; classic cover	300	600	900	2010	3505	5000
5-Orlando/Wood-a (Kenton); Wood-c	226	452	678	1446	2473	3500
6-Kinstler-a(2); Orlando/Wood-c; Check-a	174	348	522	1114	1907	2700
7-Fawcette & Becker/Alascia-a	84	168	252	538	919	1300
8-Kubert, Kinstler, Hollingsworth & Lazarus-a; Lazarus Robot-c	87	174	261	553	952	1350
9-Kinstler, Fawcette, Alascia, Kubert-a	81	162	243	518	884	1250
18-(Formerly Eerie #17)-Reprints "Attack on Planet Mars" by Kubert	57	114	171	362	619	875
19-r/Avon's "Robotmen of the Lost Planet"; last pre-code issue; Robot-c	58	116	174	371	636	900
20-War-c/story; Wood-c(r)/U.S. Paratroops #1	20	40	60	117	189	260
21,22-War-c/stories. 22-New logo	15	30	45	88	137	185
I.W. Reprint #5-Kinstler-a(r)/Avon's #9	5	10	15	34	60	85

STRANGE WORLDS
Marvel Comics (MPI No. 1,2/Male No. 3,5): Dec, 1958 - No. 5, Aug, 1959

	GD 2.0	VG 4.0	FN 6.0	VF 8.0	VF/NM 9.0	NM- 9.2
1-Kirby & Ditko-a; flying saucer issue	135	270	405	864	1482	2100
2-Ditko-c/a	74	148	222	470	810	1150
3-Kirby-a(2)	65	130	195	416	708	1000
4-Williamson-a	58	116	174	371	636	900
5-Ditko-a	55	110	165	352	601	850

NOTE: **Buscema** a-3, 4. **Ditko** a-1-5; c-2-. **Heck** a-2. **Kirby** a-1, 3. **Kirby/Brodsky** c-1, 3-5.

STRAWBERRY SHORTCAKE
Marvel Comics (Star Comics): Jun, 1985 - No. 6, Feb, 1986 (Children's comic)

	GD 2.0	VG 4.0	FN 6.0	VF 8.0	VF/NM 9.0	NM- 9.2
1-Howie Post-a in all	3	6	9	14	19	24
2-6	2	4	6	8	10	12

STRAWBERRY SHORTCAKE
Ape Entertainment: 2011 - No. 4, 2011 ($3.95, limited series)

1-4: 1-Scratch 'n' sniff cover						5.00
Volume 2 (2012, $3.99) 1,2						5.00

STRAWBERRY SHORTCAKE
IDW Publishing: Apr, 2016 - No. 8, Nov, 2016 ($3.99)

1-8: Multiple covers on each. 1-Georgia Ball-s/Amy Mebberson-a						4.00
... Funko Universe One-Shot (5/17, $4.99) Ball-s; art in Funko Pop! style						5.00

STRAY
DC Comics (Homage Comics): 2001 ($5.95, prestige format, one-shot)

1-Pollina-c/a; Lobdell & Palmiotti-s						6.00

STRAY

	GD 2.0	VG 4.0	FN 6.0	VF 8.0	VF/NM 9.0	NM- 9.2

Dark Horse Comics: 2004 (8 1/2"x 5 1/2", Diamond Comic Dist. Halloween giveaway)
nn-Reprint from The Dark Horse Book of Hauntings; Evan Dorkin-s/Jill Thompson-a ... 3.00

STRAY BULLETS
El Capitan Books/Image Comics: 1995 - No. 41, Mar, 2014 ($2.95/$3.50, B&W, mature)

1-David Lapham-c/a/scripts	2	4	6	11	16	20
2,3						6.00
4-8						4.00
9-21,31,32-($2.95)						3.50
22-30,33-41-($3.50) 22-Includes preview to Murder Me Dead. 40-(10/05). 41-(3/14)						3.50

Free Comic Book Day giveaway (5/02) Reprints #2 with "Free Comic Book Day" banner on-c;
  flip book with The Matrix (printing of internet comic) ... 3.00
Innocence of Nihilism Volume 1 HC ($29.95, hardcover) r/#1-7 ... 30.00
Somewhere Out West Volume 2 HC ($34.95, hardcover) r/#8-14 ... 35.00
Other People Volume 3 HC ($34.95, hardcover) r/#15-22 ... 35.00
Volume 1-3 TPB ($11.95, softcover) 1-r/#1-4. 2-r/#5-8. 3-r/ #9-12 ... 12.00
Volume 4-7 TPB ($14.95) 4- r/#13-16. 5- r/#17-20. 6- r/#21-24. 7-r/#25-28 ... 15.00
NOTE: Multiple printings of most issues exist & are worth cover price.

STRAY BULLETS: KILLERS
Image Comics (El Capitan Books): Mar, 2014 - No. 8, Oct, 2014 ($3.50, B&W)
1-8-David Lapham-c/a/scripts; set in 1978 ... 3.50

STRAY BULLETS: SUNSHINE AND ROSES
Image Comics (El Capitan Books): Feb, 2015 - No. 41, Jun, 2019 ($3.50/$3.99, B&W)
1-10-David Lapham-c/a/scripts; set in 1979 Baltimore ... 3.50
11-36,41-($3.99) 20-Amy Racecar app. ... 4.00
37-40-($4.99) ... 5.00

STRAY DOGS
Image Comics: Feb, 2021 - No. 5, Jun, 2021 ($3.99, limited series)

1-Tony Fleecs-s/Trish Forstner-a; two covers	3	6	9	19	30	40
2-4-Two covers on each	1	3	4	6	8	10
5-Two covers						4.00

STRAY DOGS: DOG DAYS
Image Comics: Dec, 2021 - Present ($4.99, limited series)
1,2-Tony Fleecs-s/Trish Forstner-a ... 6.00
1-Creepshow homage variant-c ... 5.00

STRAYER
AfterShock Comics: Jan, 2016 - No. 5 ($3.99)
1-5-Justin Jordan-s/Juan Gedeon-a ... 4.00

STRAY TOASTERS
Marvel Comics (Epic Comics): Jan, 1988 - No. 4, April, 1989 ($3.50, squarebound, limited series)
1-4: Sienkiewicz-c/a/scripts ... 4.00

STREET COMIX
Street Enterprises/King Features: 1973 (50¢, B&W, 36 pgs.)(20,000 print run)

1-Rip Kirby	2	4	6	8	11	14
2-Flash Gordon	2	4	6	10	14	18

STREETFIGHTER
Ocean Comics: Aug, 1986 - No. 4, Spr, 1987 ($1.75, limited series)
1-4: 2-Origin begins ... 5.00

STREET FIGHTER
Malibu Comics: Sept, 1993 - No. 3, Nov, 1993 ($2.95)

1	1	3	4	6	8	10
2,3: 3-Includes poster; Ferret x-over						4.00

STREET FIGHTER
Image Comics: Sept, 2003 - No. 14, Feb, 2005 ($2.95)

1-Back-up story w/Madureira-a; covers by Madureira and Tsang	1	2	3	5	6	8
2-6,8-14: 2-Two covers by Campbell and Warren; back-up story w/Warren-a						3.00
7-($4.50) Larocca-c						4.50
... Vol. 1 (3/04, $9.99, digest-size) r/main stories from #1-6						10.00

STREET FIGHTER: THE BATTLE FOR SHADALOO
DC Comics/CAP Co. Ltd.: 1995 ($3.95, one-shot)

1-Polybagged w/trading card & Tattoo	1	3	4	6	8	10

STREET FIGHTER II
Tokuma Comics (Viz): Apr, 1994 - No. 8, Nov, 1994 ($2.95, limited series)
1-8 ... 4.00

STREET FIGHTER II
UDON Comics: No. 0, Oct, 2005 - No. 6, Nov, 2006 ($1.99/$3.95/$2.95)
0-(10/05, $1.99) prelude to series; Alvin Lee-a ... 3.00
1-($3.95) Two covers by Alvin Lee & Ed McGuinness ... 4.00
2-6-($2.95) ... 3.00
... Legends 1 (8/06, $3.95) Spotlight on Sakura; two covers ... 4.00

STREET FIGHTER X G.I. JOE
IDW Publishing: Feb, 2016 - No. 6, Jul, 2016 ($4.99)
1-Sitterson-s/Laiso-a; multiple covers; Destro, Snake Eyes, Baroness, Ryu app. ... 5.00
2-6-($3.99) Multiple covers on each ... 4.00

STREET SHARKS
Archie Publications: Jan, 1996 - No. 3, Mar, 1996 ($1.50, limited series)

1	3	6	9	16	23	30
2,3	1	3	4	6	8	10

STREET SHARKS
Archie Publications: May, 1996 - No. 6 ($1.50)

1	3	6	9	14	20	25
2-6						6.00

STRETCH ARMSTRONG AND THE FLEX FIGHTERS (Based on the Netflix animated series)
IDW Publishing: Jan, 2018 - No. 3, Mar, 2018 ($3.99, limited series)

1-3-Burke & Wyatt-s/Koutsis-a; 3 covers ... 4.00

STRICTLY PRIVATE (You're in the Army Now)
Eastern Color Printing Co.: July, 1942 (#1 on sale 6/15/42)

1,2: Private Peter Plink. 2-Says 128 pgs. on-c	39	78	117	240	395	550

STRIKE!
Eclipse Comics: Aug, 1987 - No. 6, Jan, 1988 ($1.75)
1-6, ...Vs. Sgt. Strike Special 1 (5/88, $1.95) ... 4.00

STRIKEBACK! (The Hunt For Nikita)
Malibu Comics (Bravura): Oct, 1994 - No. 3, Jan, 1995 ($2.95, unfinished limited series)
1-3: Jonathon Peterson script, Kevin Maguire-c/a ... 4.00
1-Gold foil embossed-c ... 5.00

STRIKEBACK!
Image Comics (WildStorm Productions): Jan, 1996 - No. 5, May, 1996 ($2.50, lim. series)
1-5: Reprints original Bravura series w/additional story & art by Kevin Maguire
  & Jonathon Peterson; new Maguire-c in all. 4,5-New story & art ... 4.00

STRIKEFORCE
Marvel Comics: Nov, 2019 - No. 9, Oct 2020 ($3.99)
1-9: 1-Team of Blade, Angela, Spectrum, Winter Soldier, Spider-Woman, Wiccan and
  Hellstrom; Howard-s/Peralta-a. 7-9-Deadpool app. ... 4.00

STRIKEFORCE: AMERICA
Comico: Dec, 1995 ($2.95)
V2#1-Polybagged w/gaming card; S. Clark-a(p) ... 5.00

STRIKEFORCE: MORITURI
Marvel Comics Group: Dec, 1986 - No. 31, July, 1989
1,13: 13-Double size ... 5.00
2-12,14-31: 14-Williamson-i. 25-Heath-c ... 4.00
... – We Who Are About To Die 1 (3/12, $0.99) r/#1 with profile pages and cover gallery ... 3.00

STRIKEFORCE MORITURI: ELECTRIC UNDERTOW
Marvel Comics: Dec, 1989 - No. 5, Mar, 1990 ($3.95, 52 pgs., limited series)
1-5 Squarebound ... 5.00

STRONG GUY REBORN (See X-Factor)
Marvel Comics: Sept, 1997 ($2.99, one-shot)
1-Dezago-s/Andy Smith, Art Thibert-a ... 4.00

STRONGHOLD
AfterShock Comics: Feb, 2019 - No. 5, Aug, 2019 ($3.99)
1-5-Phil Hester-s/Ryan Kelly-a ... 4.00

STRONG MAN (Also see Complimentary Comics & Power of...)
Magazine Enterprises: Mar-Apr, 1955 - No. 4, Sept-Oct, 1955

1(A-1 #130)-Powell-c/a	28	56	84	168	274	380
2-4: (A-1 #132,134,139)-Powell-a. 2-Powell-c	21	42	63	122	199	275

STRONTIUM DOG
Eagle Comics: Dec, 1985 - No. 4, Mar, 1986 ($1.25, limited series)
1-4, Special 1: 4-Moore script. Special 1 (1986)-Moore script ... 4.00

STRYFE'S STRIKE FILE
Marvel Comics: Jan, 1993 ($1.75, one-shot, no ads)
1-Stroman, Capullo, Andy Kubert, Brandon Peterson-a; silver metallic ink-c;
  X-Men tie-in to X-Cutioner's Song ... 5.00
1-Gold metallic ink 2nd printing ... 4.00

STRYKEFORCE
Image Comics (Top Cow): May, 2004 - No. 5, Oct, 2004 ($2.99)
1-5-Faerber-s/Kirkham-a. 4,5-Preview of HumanKind ... 3.00
Vol. 1 TPB (2005, $16.99) r/#1-5 & Codename: Strykeforce #0-3; sketch pages ... 17.00

STUFF OF NIGHTMARES
BOOM! Studios: Sept, 2022 - No. 4, Dec, 2022 ($4.99, limited series)
1-4-R.L. Stine-s/A.L. Kaplan-a ... 4.00
...: Red Murder 1 (9/23, $7.99) R.L. Stine-s/Adam Gorham-a/Francavilla-c ... 8.00
...: Slay Ride 1 (12/23, $7.99) R.L. Stine-s/Pius Bak-a/Francavilla-c ... 8.00

STUMBO THE GIANT (See Harvey Hits #49,54,57,60,63,66,69,72,78,88 & Hot Stuff #2)

STUMBO TINYTOWN
Harvey Publications: Oct, 1963 - No. 13, Nov, 1966 (All 25¢ giants)

1-Stumbo, Hot Stuff & others begin	15	30	45	103	227	350
2	8	16	24	54	102	150
3-5	6	12	18	38	69	100
6-13	5	10	15	33	57	80

STUNTMAN COMICS (Also see Thrills Of Tomorrow)
Harvey Publ.: Apr-May, 1946 - No. 2, June-July, 1946; No. 3, Oct-Nov, 1946

1-Origin Stuntman by S&K reprinted in Black Cat #9; S&K-c	123	246	369	787	1344	1900
2-S&K-c/a; The Duke of Broadway story	77	154	231	493	847	1200
3-Small size (5-1/2x8-1/2"; B&W; 32 pgs.); distributed to mail subscribers only; S&K-a; Kid Adonis by S&K reprinted in Green Hornet #37	129	258	387	826	1413	2000

(Also see All-New #15, Boy Explorers #2, Flash Gordon #5 & Thrills of Tomorrow)

STUPID COMICS (Also see 40 oz. Collected)
Oni Press/Image Comics: July, 2000; Sept, 2002 - No. 3, Aug, 2005 ($2.95, B&W)
1-(Oni Press, 7/00) Jim Mahfood 1 page satire strips reprinted from JAVA magazine ... 3.00
1-3-(Image Comics, 9/02; 10/03) Jim Mahfood 1 page and 2 page satire strips ... 3.00
TPB (4/06, $12.99) r/#1(Oni) and #1-3(Image); Phoenix New Times strips ... 13.00

STUPID HEROES
Mirage Studios: Sept, 1993 - No. 3, Dec, 1994 ($2.75, unfinished limited series)
1-3-Laird-c/a & scripts; 2 trading cards bound in ... 4.00

STUPID, STUPID RAT TAILS (See Bone)
Cartoon Books: Dec, 1999 - No. 3, Feb, 2000 ($2.95, limited series)

Strayer #4 © Jordan & Gedeon

Stuff of Nightmares #1 © RL Stine

Sub-Mariner #6 © MAR

	GD 2.0	VG 4.0	FN 6.0	VF 8.0	VF/NM 9.0	NM- 9.2

1-3-Jeff Smith-a/Tom Sniegoski-s ... 4.00

SUBGENRE
Dark Horse Comics: Oct, 2023 - Present ($7.99, over-sized 8" x 10-7/8")
1-3-Matt Kindt-s/Wilfredo Torres-a ... 8.00

SUBMARINE ATTACK (Formerly Speed Demons)
Charlton Comics: No. 11, May, 1958 - No. 54, Feb-Mar, 1966
11 ... 5 10 15 33 57 80
12-20: 16-Atomic bomb panels ... 4 8 12 23 37 50
21-30 ... 3 6 9 19 30 40
31-54: 43-Cuban missile crisis story. 47-Atomic bomb panels
... 3 6 9 17 26 35
NOTE: Glanzman c/a-25. **Montes/Bache** a-38, 40, 41.

SUB-MARINER (See All-Select, All-Winners, Blonde Phantom, Daring, The Defenders, Fantastic Four #4, Human Torch, The Invaders, Iron Man &... Marvel Mystery, Marvel Spotlight #27, Men's Adventures, Motion Picture Funnies Weekly, Namora, Namor, The..., Prince Namor, The Sub-Mariner, Saga Of The..., Tales to Astonish #70 & 2nd series, USA & Young Men)

SUB-MARINER, THE (2nd Series)(Sub-Mariner #31 on)
Marvel Comics Group: May, 1968 - No. 72, Sept, 1974 (No. 43: 52 pgs.)
1-Origin Sub-Mariner; story continued from Iron Man & Sub-Mariner #1
... 61 122 183 488 1094 1700
2-Triton app. ... 11 22 33 73 157 240
3,4 ... 8 16 24 55 105 155
5-1st Tiger Shark (9/68) ... 27 54 81 189 420 650
6,7,9,10: 6-Tiger Shark-c & 2nd app., cont'd from #5. 7-Photo-c. (1968).
9-1st app. Serpent Crown (origin in #10 & 12) ... 6 12 18 38 69 100
8-Sub-Mariner vs. Thing ... 27 54 81 194 435 675
8-2nd printing (1994) ... 2 4 6 11 16 20
11-13,15: 15-Last 12¢ issue ... 5 10 15 33 57 80
14-Sub-Mariner vs. G.A. Toro, who assumes identity of G. A. Human Torch; death of Toro (1st modern app. & only app. Toro, 6/69) ... 7 14 21 46 86 125
16-20: 19-1st Sting Ray (11/69); Stan Lee, Romita, Heck, Thomas, Everett & Kirby cameos.
... 4 8 12 23 37 50
20-Dr. Doom app.
21,23-33,37-42: 25-Origin Atlantis. 30-Capt. Marvel x-over. 37-Death of Lady Dorma.
38-Origin retold. 40-Spider-Man x-over. 42-Last 12¢ issue
... 3 6 9 17 26 35
22-Dr. Strange x-over ... 7 14 21 48 89 130
34-Prelude (w/#35) to 1st Defenders story; Hulk & Silver Surfer x-over
... 13 26 39 86 188 290
35-Namor/Hulk/Silver Surfer team-up to battle The Avengers-c/story (3/71); hints at teaming up again ... 10 20 30 68 144 220
36-Wrightson-a(i) ... 3 6 9 20 31 42
43-King Size Special (52 pgs.) ... 4 8 12 25 40 55
44,45-Sub-Mariner vs. Human Torch ... 4 8 12 23 37 50
46-49,56,62,64-72: 47,48-Dr. Doom app. 49-Cosmic Cube story. 52-1st app. Dragon-Lord. 52,53-Sunfire app. 62-1st Tales of Atlantis, Chaykin-s/a; ends #66. 64-Hitler cameo. 67-New costume; F.F. x-over. 69-Spider-Man x-over (6 panels)
... 2 4 6 10 14 18
50-1st app. Nita, Namor's niece (later Namorita in New Warriors)
... 16 32 48 89 195 300
51-55,57,58,60,61,63-Everett issues: 57-Venus app. (1st since 4/52); anti-Vietnam War panels. 61-Last artwork by Everett; 1st 4 pgs. completed by Mortimer; pgs. 5-20 by Mooney
... 2 4 6 11 16 20
59-1st battle with Thor; Everett-a ... 8 16 24 51 96 140
Special 1 (1/71)-r/Tales to Astonish #70-73 ... 5 10 15 34 60 85
Special 2 (1/72)-(52 pgs.)-r/T.T.A. #74-76; Everett-a ... 4 8 12 23 37 50
NOTE: **Bolle** a-67i. **Buscema** a(p)-1-8, 20, 24. **Colan** a(p)-10, 11, 40, 43, 46-49, Special 1, 2; c(p)-10, 11, 40. **Craig** a-17i, 19-23i. **Everett** a-45r, 50-55, 57, 58, 59-61(p), 63(plot); c-47, 48i, 55, 57, 58-59i, 61, Spec. 2. **G. Kane** c(p)-42-52, 58, 66, 70, 71. **Mooney** a-24i, 25i, 32-35i, 39i, 42i, 44i, 45i, 60i, 61i, 65p, 66p, 68i. **John Severin** c/a-38i. **Marie Severin** c/a 14p. **Starlin** c-59p. **Tuska** a-41p, 42p, 69-71p. **Wrightson** a-36i. #53, 54-r/stories Sub-Mariner Comics #41 & 39.

SUB-MARINER (The Initiative, follows Civil War series)
Marvel Comics: Aug, 2007 - No. 6, Jan, 2008 ($2.99, limited series)
1-6: 1-Turner-c/Briones-a/Cherniss & Johnson-s; Iron Man app. 3-Yu-c; Venom app. ... 4.00
...: Revolution TPB (2008, $14.99) r/#1-6 ... 15.00

SUB-MARINER COMICS (1st Series) (The Sub-Mariner #1, 33-42)(Official True Crime Cases #24 on; Amazing Mysteries #32 on; Best Love #33 on)
Timely/Marvel Comics (TCI 1-7/SePI 8/MPI 9-32/Atlas Comics (CCC 33-42)):
Spring, 1941 - No. 23, Sum, 1947; No. 24, Wint, 1947 - No. 31, 4/49; No. 32, 7/49; No. 33, 4/54 - No. 42, 10/55
1-The Sub-Mariner by Everett & The Angel begin; Nazi WWII-c
... 7600 15,200 26,600 57,000 123,500 190,000
2-Everett-a; Nazi WWII-c ... 1000 2000 3000 7400 13,200 19,000
3-Churchill assassination-c; 40 pg. S-M story ... 892 1784 2676 6512 11,506 16,500

	GD 2.0	VG 4.0	FN 6.0	VF 8.0	VF/NM 9.0	NM- 9.2

4-Everett, 40 pgs.; 1 pg. Wolverton-a; Nazi WWII-c
... 811 1622 2433 5920 10,460 15,000
5-Gabrielle/Klein-c; Japanese WWII-c ... 465 930 1395 3395 5998 8600
6-8,10-Japanese WWII-c ... 423 846 1269 3088 5444 7800
9-Classic Japanese WWII flag-c (Spr. 1943); Wolverton-a, 3 pgs.
... 508 1016 1524 3708 6554 9400
11-Classic Schomburg-c ... 865 1730 2595 6315 11,158 16,000
12,14-Nazi WWII-c ... 394 788 1182 2758 4829 6900
13-Classic Schomburg hooded Japanese WWII bondage-c
... 649 1298 1947 4738 8369 12,000
15-Schomburg Japanese WWII-c ... 389 778 1167 2723 4762 6800
16,17-Japanese WWII-c ... 331 662 993 2317 4059 5800
18-20 ... 300 600 900 1920 3310 4700
21-Last Angel; Everett-a ... 226 452 678 1446 2473 3500
22-Young Allies app. ... 226 452 678 1446 2473 3500
23-The Human Torch, Namora x-over (Sum/47); 2nd app. Namora after
Marvel Mystery #82 ... 252 504 756 1613 2757 3900
24-Namora x-over (3rd app.) ... 258 516 774 1651 2826 4000
25-The Blonde Phantom begins (Spr/48), ends No. 31; Kurtzman-a; Namora x-over;
last quarterly issue ... 245 490 735 1568 2684 3800
26,27: 26-Namora c/app. ... 206 412 618 1318 2259 3200
28-Namora cover; Everett-a ... 252 504 756 1613 2757 3900
29-31 (4/49): 29-The Human Torch app. 31-Capt. America app.
... 226 452 678 1446 2473 3500
32 (7/49, Scarce)-Origin Sub-Mariner ... 486 972 1458 3550 6275 9000
33 (4/54)-Origin Sub-Mariner; The Human Torch app.; Namora x-over in Sub-Mariner #33-42
... 206 412 618 1318 2259 3200
34,35-Human Torch in ea. 34-Namora bondage-c ... 155 310 465 992 1696 2400
36,37,39-41: 36,39-41-Namora app. ... 135 270 405 864 1482 2100
38-Origin Sub-Mariner's wings; Namora app.; last pre-code (2/55)
... 168 336 504 1075 1838 2600
42-Last issue ... 181 362 543 1158 1979 2800
NOTE: Angel by **Gustavson**-#1, 8. **Brodsky** c-34-36, 42. **Everett** a-1-4, 22-24, 26-42; c-32, 33, 40. **Maneely** a-38; c-37, 39-41. **Rico** c-27-31. **Schomburg** c-1-4, 6, 8-18, 20. **Sekowsky** c-24. 25, 26(w/Rico). **Shores** c-21-23, 38. Bondage c-13, 22, 24, 25, 34.

SUB-MARINER COMICS 70th ANNIVERARY SPECIAL
Marvel Comics: June, 2009 ($3.99, one-shot)
1-New WWII story, Breitweiser-a; Williamson-a; r/debut app. from Sub-Mariner Comics #1 ... 5.00

SUB-MARINER: MARVELS SNAPSHOTS
Marvel Comics: May, 2020 ($4.99, one-shot)
1-Alan Brennert-s/Jerry Ordway-a; set in Spring 1946; All-Winners Squad app. ... 5.00

SUB-MARINER: THE DEPTHS
Marvel Comics: Nov, 2008 - No. 5, May, 2009 ($3.99, limited series)
1-5-Peter Milligan-s/Esad Ribic-a/c ... 4.00

SUBSPECIES
Eternity Comics: May, 1991 - No. 4, Aug, 1991 ($2.50, limited series)
1-4: New stories based on horror movie ... 4.00

SUBTLE VIOLENTS
CFD Productions: 1991 ($2.50, B&W, mature)
1-Linsner-c & story ... 1 3 4 8 10 12
San Diego Limited Edition ... 5 10 15 30 50 70

SUE & SALLY SMITH (Formerly My Secret Life)
Charlton Comics: V2#48, Nov, 1962 - No. 54, Nov, 1963 (Flying Nurses)
V2#48-2nd app. ... 3 6 9 21 33 45
49-54 ... 3 6 9 14 20 26

SUGAR & SPIKE (Also see The Best of DC, DC Silver Age Classics and Legends of Tomorrow)
National Periodical Publications: Apr-May, 1956 - No. 98, Oct-Nov, 1971
1 (Scarce) ... 514 1028 1542 3750 6625 9500
2 ... 174 348 522 1114 1907 2700
3-5: 3-Letter column begins ... 97 194 291 621 1061 1500
6-10 ... 55 110 165 352 601 850
11-20 ... 41 82 123 256 428 600
21-29: 26-Christmas-c ... 28 56 84 168 274 380
30-Scribbly & Scribbly, Jr. x-over ... 29 58 87 172 281 390
31-40 ... 22 44 66 128 209 290
41-60 ... 9 18 27 60 120 170
61-80: 69-1st app. Tornado-Tot-c/story. 72-Origin & 1st app. Bernie the Brain
... 8 16 24 52 99 140
81-84,86-93,95: 84-Bernie the Brain apps. as Superman in 1 panel (9/69)
... 6 12 18 38 69 100
85 (68 pgs.)-r/#72 ... 7 14 21 44 82 120

	GD 2.0	VG 4.0	FN 6.0	VF 8.0	VF/NM 9.0	NM- 9.2

94-1st app. Raymond, African-American child

94-1st app. Raymond, African-American child	7	14	21	44	82	120
96 (68 pgs.)	7	14	21	48	89	130
97,98 (52 pgs.)	7	14	21	44	82	120

No. 1 Replica Edition (2002, $2.95) reprint of #1 .... 5.00
NOTE: All written and drawn by **Sheldon Mayer**. Issues with Paper Doll pages cut or missing are common.

SUGAR BOWL COMICS (Teen-age)
Famous Funnies: May, 1948 - No. 5, Jan, 1949

1-Toth-c/a	20	40	60	117	189	260
2,4,5	13	26	39	74	105	150
3-Toth-a	14	28	42	80	115	150

SUGARFOOT (TV)
Dell Publishing Co.: No. 907, May, 1958 - No. 1209, Oct-Dec, 1961

Four Color 907 (#1)-Toth-a, photo-c	12	24	36	79	170	260
Four Color 992 (5-7/59), Toth-a, photo-c	10	20	30	66	138	210
Four Color 1059 (11-1/60), 1098 (5-7/60), 1147 (11-1/61), 1209-all photo-c. 1059,1098,1147-all						
have variant edition, back-c comic strip	7	14	21	49	92	135

SUGARSHOCK (Also see MySpace Dark Horse Presents)
Dark Horse Comics: Oct, 2009 ($3.50, one-shot)

1-Joss Whedon-s/Fabio Moon-a/c; story from online comic; Moon sketch pgs. 3.50

SUICIDE RISK
BOOM! Studios: May, 2013 - No. 25, May, 2015 ($3.99)

1-25: 1-Carey-s/Casagrande-a. 5-Joëlle Jones-a. 10-Coelho-a 4.00

SUICIDERS
DC Comics (Vertigo): Apr, 2015 - No. 6, Nov, 2015 ($3.99)

1-6-Lee Bermejo-s/a/c 4.00

SUICIDERS: KINGS OF HELL.A.
DC Comics (Vertigo): May, 2016 - No. 6 ($3.99)

1-6-Lee Bermejo-s/c. 1-5-Alessandro Vitti-a. 6-Gerardo Zaffino-a; Bermejo-a (2 pgs.) 4.00

SUICIDE SQUAD (See Brave & the Bold, Doom Patrol & Suicide Squad Spec.,
Legends #3 & note under Star Spangled War stories)
DC Comics: May, 1987 - No. 66, June, 1992; No. 67, Mar, 2010 (Direct sales only #32 on)

1-Chaykin-c	5	10	15	30		70
2-10: 9-Millennium x-over. 10-Batman-c/story						6.00
11-22,24-47,50-66: 13-JLI app. (Batman). 16-Re-intro Shade The Changing Man. 27-34,36,37-Snyder-a. 38-Origin Bronze Tiger. 40-43-"The Phoenix Gambit" Batman storyline. 40-Free Batman/Suicide Squad poster						4.00
23-1st Oracle	4	8	12	23	37	50
48-Joker/Batgirl-c/s	3	6	9	20	31	42
49-Joker/Batgirl-c/s	2	4	6	11	16	20
67-(3/10, $2.99) Blackest Night one-shot; Fiddler rises as a Black Lantern; Califiore-a						4.00
Annual 1 (1988, $1.50)-Manhunter x-over						5.00
...: Trial By Fire TPB (2011, $19.99) r/#1-8 & Secret Origins #14						20.00

SUICIDE SQUAD (2nd series)
DC Comics: Nov, 2001 - No. 12, Oct, 2002 ($2.50)

1-Giffen-s/Medina-a; Sgt. Rock app.						5.00
2-9: 4-Heath-a						4.00
10-12-Suicide Squad vs. Antiphon: 10-J. Severin-a. 12-JSA app.						
	1	3	4	6	8	10

SUICIDE SQUAD (3rd series)
DC Comics: Nov, 2007 - No. 8, Jun, 2008 ($2.99, limited series)

1-8-Ostrander-s/Pina-a/Snyder III-c 4.00
...: From the Ashes TPB (2008, $19.99) r/#1-8 .... 20.00

SUICIDE SQUAD (DC New 52)(Also see New Suicide Squad)
DC Comics: Nov, 2011 - No. 30, Jul, 2014 ($2.99)

1-Harley Quinn, Deadshot, King Shark, El Diablo, Voltaic, Black Spider team up						
	4	8	12	23	37	50
1-(2nd printing)	2	4	6	13	28	22
1 Special Edition (5/16, FCBD giveaway)						3.00
2-5	1	2	3	5	6	8
6-Origin Harley Quinn part 1	2	4	6	11	16	20
6,7-(2nd printing)	1	2	3	5	6	8
7-Origin Harley Quinn part 2	2	4	6	9	12	15
8-13,16-20,22-30: 19-Unknown Soldier joins. 24-29-Forever Evil tie-in. 24-Omac returns						4.00
14,15-Death of the Family tie-in; Joker app.						5.00
14-Variant die-cut mask-c; Death of the Family tie-in						6.00
21-Harley Quinn-c/s	1	3	4	6	8	10
30-($3.99) Forever Evil tie-in; Coelho-a/Mahnke-c						4.00
#0 (11/12, $2.99) Amanda Waller pre-Suicide Squad; Dagnino-a						4.00
...: Amanda Waller (5/14, $4.99) Jim Zub-s/Coelho-a						5.00

SUICIDE SQUAD (DC Rebirth)
DC Comics: Oct, 2016 - No. 50, Mar, 2019 ($2.99)

1-Harley Quinn, Deadshot, Killer Croc, Katana, Boomerang team up; Jim Lee-a; back-up origin of Deadshot retold; Fabok-a 3.00
1-Director's Cut (5/17, $5.99) r/#1,2 with pencil-a; bonus original script for #1 .... 6.00
2-7: 2,3-Zod app. 2-Back-up Boomerang origin w/Reis-a. 3-Back-up Katana origin 3.00
8-24: 8-Killer Frost joins; Justice League vs. Suicide Squad prelude; Lee-a. 9,10-JL vs. SS tie-ins. 11-15-Romita Jr.-a. 16-18-Daniel-a. 20-Sejic-a. 23,24-Batman app. 3.00
25-($3.99) Batman app.; Cafaro-a; cameo app. Rick Flag & Karin Grace 4.00
26-49: 26-Dark Nights: Metal tie-in. 27-32-Secret History of Task Force X. 41-44-Batman app. 5.00
50-($4.99) Williams-s/Peralta, Schoonover & Conrad-a 5.00
Annual 1 (10/18, $4.99) New team with Merlyn vs. Swamp Thing; Cliquet-a 5.00
.../Banana Splits Special 1 (5/17, $4.99) Caldwell-a; Snagglepuss back-up; Porter-a 5.00
...: Rebirth (10/16, $2.99) Rick Flag joins; Harley Quinn, Boomerang app. 3.00
..: Special: War Crimes 1 (10/16, $4.99) Ostrander-s/Gus Vazquez-a; Shado app. 5.00

SUICIDE SQUAD
DC Comics: Feb, 2020 - No. 11, Jan, 2021 ($4.99/$3.99)

1-($4.99) Harley Quinn, Deadshot, The Shark, Zebra-Man; intro The Revolutionaries 5.00
2-11-($3.99) 6-Batman app. 4.00

SUICIDE SQUAD
DC Comics: May, 2021 - No. 15, Jul, 2022 ($3.99)

1-15: 1-Rick Flag, Peacemaker, Shrike, Talon team. 5,6-Crime Syndicate app. 7-Ambush Bug joins. 13-War for Earth-3 tie-in 4.00
2021 Annual 1 (11/21, $5.99) Superboy app.; follows Suicide Squad #6 .... 6.00
... Special Edition (FCBD) 1 (10/21, giveaway) Previews Suicide Squad: King Shark & Suicide Squad: Get Joker series 3.00

SUICIDE SQUAD BLACK FILES
DC Comics: Jan, 2019 - No. 6, Jun, 2019 ($4.99, limited series)

1-6-New squad incl. Gentleman Ghost, El Diablo, Klarion, Enchantress; Eaton-a 5.00

SUICIDE SQUAD: BLAZE
DC Comics (Black Label): Apr, 2022 - No. 3 ($6.99, oversized 8-1/2" x 10-3/4", lim. series)

1,2-Simon Spurrier-s/Aaron Campbell-a; Harley Quinn & Peacemaker app. 7.00

SUICIDE SQUAD: DREAM TEAM
DC Comics: May, 2024 - No. 4 ($3.99, limited series)

1-Maines-s/Barrows-a; Dreamer, Harley Quinn, Clock King, Bizarro app. 4.00

SUICIDE SQUAD: GET JOKER
DC Comics (Black Label): Oct, 2021 - No. 3, Jul, 2022 ($6.99, over-sized squarebound, limited series)

1-3-Azzarello-s/Maleev-a; Jason Todd & Harley Quinn app. 7.00

SUICIDE SQUAD: KILL ARKHAM ASYLUM
DC Comics: Apr, 2024 - No. 5 ($4.99, limited series, polybagged)

1,2-Prequel to the Suicide Squad: Kill the Justice League video game; Layman-s/Hervas-a 5.00

SUICIDE SQUAD: KING SHARK (Printing of a digital first series)
DC Comics: Nov, 2021 - No. 6, Apr, 2022 ($3.99, limited series)

1-6-Seeley-s/Kolins-a; Defacer & B'Wana Beast app. 3,4-The Demon app. 4.00

SUICIDE SQUAD MOST WANTED: DEADSHOT & KATANA
DC Comics: Mar, 2016 - No. 6, Aug, 2016 ($4.99, limited series)

1-6-Deadshot by Buccellato-s/Bogdanovic-a; Katana by Barr-s/Neves-a; Nord-c 5.00

SUICIDE SQUAD MOST WANTED: EL DIABLO & BOOMERANG (Title changes to Suicide Squad Most Wanted: El Diablo & Amanda Waller for #5,6)
DC Comics: Oct, 2016 - No. 6, Mar, 2017 ($4.99, limited series)

1-4-El Diablo by Nitz-s/Richards-a; Boomerang by Moreci-s/Bazaldua-a; Huddleston-c 5.00
5,6-Amanda Waller by Ayala-s/Merhoff-a; El Diablo by Nitz-s/Richards-a 5.00

SUMMER FUN (See Dell Giants)

SUMMER FUN (Formerly Li'l Genius; Holiday Surprise #55)
Charlton Comics: No. 54, Oct, 1966 (Giant)

54	4	8	12	23	37	50

SUMMER FUN (Walt Disney's...)
Disney Comics: Summer, 1991 ($2.95, annual, 68 pgs.)

1-D. Duck, M. Mouse, Brer Rabbit, Chip 'n' Dale & Pluto, Li'l Bad Wolf, Super Goof, Scamp stories 5.00

SUMMER LOVE (Formerly Brides in Love?)
Charlton Comics: V2#46, Oct, 1965; V2#47, Oct, 1966; V2#48, Nov, 1968

V2#46-Beatles-c & 8 pg. story	15	30	45	103	227	350
47-(68 pgs.) Beatles-c & 12 pg. story	12	24	36	79	170	260
48	6	12	18	38	69	100

SUMMER MAGIC (See Movie Comics)

SUMMONERS WAR: AWAKENING (Based on the online mobile game)
Image Comics (Skybound): Apr, 2023 - No. 6, Sept, 2023 ($3.99)

1-6-Justin Jordan-s/Luca Claretti-a 4.00

SUMMONER'S WAR: LEGACY (Based on the online mobile game)
Image Comics (Skybound): Apr, 2021 - No. 6, Sept, 2021 ($3.99)

1-6-Justin Jordan-s/Luca Claretti-a 4.00

SUNDANCE (See Hotel Deparee...)

SUNDANCE KID (Also see Blazing Six-Guns)
Skywald Publications: June, 1971 - No. 3, Sept, 1971 (52 pgs.)(Pre-code reprints & new-s)

1-Durango Kid; Two Kirby Bullseye-r	3	6	9	16	23	30
2,3: 2-Swift Arrow, Durango Kid, Bullseye by S&K; Meskin plus 1 pg. origin.						
3-Durango Kid, Billy the Kid, Red Hawk-r	2	4	6	11	16	20

SUNDAY PIX (Christian religious)
David C. Cook Pub/USA Weekly Newsprint Color Comics: V1#1, Mar,1949 - V16#26, July 19, 1964 (7x10", 12 pgs., mail subscription only)

V1#1	10	20	30	54	72	90
V1#2-35	6	12	18	31	38	45
V2#1-52 (1950)	5	10	15	23	28	32
V3-V6 (1951-1953)	4	9	13	18	22	26
V7-V11#1-7,23-52 (1954-1959)	4	8	12	18	18	22
V11#8-22 (2/22-5/31/59) H.G. Wells First Men in the Moon serial						
	5	9	14	19	24	
V12#1-19,21-52; V13-V15#1,2,9-52; V16#1-26(7/19/64)						
	2	4	6	10	14	18
V12#20 (5/15/60) 2 page interview with Peanuts' Charles Schulz						
	4	8	12	25	40	55
V15#3-8 (2/24/63) John Glenn, Christian astronaut	3	6	9	16	23	30

SUN DEVILS
DC Comics: July, 1984 - No. 12, June, 1985 ($1.25, maxi series)

1-12: 6-Death of Sun Devil 4.00

SUNDIATA: A LEGEND OF AFRICA
NBM Publishing Inc.: 2002 ($15.95, hardcover with dustjacket)

nn-Will Eisner-s/a; adaptation of an African folk tale 16.00

SUNDOWNERS
Dark Horse Comics: Aug, 2014 - No. 6, Jan, 2015 ($3.50)

1-6: 1-Tim Seeley-s/Jim Terry-a 3.50

Suicide Squad (2020 series) #1 © DC

Super Angry Birds #4 © Rovio

Superboy #199 © DC

	GD	VG	FN	VF	VF/NM	NM-
	2.0	4.0	6.0	8.0	9.0	9.2

SUN FUN KOMIKS
Sun Publications: 1939 (15¢, B&W & red)

	GD	VG	FN	VF	VF/NM	NM-

1-Satire on comics (rare); 1st Hitler app. in comics?

	865	1730	2595	6315	11,158	16,000

NOTE: Hitler, Stalin and Mussolini featured gag in 1-page story written in Hebrew and English. Nazi swastika and Nazi flag app. in a different 1-page "Gussie the Gob" story.

SUNFIRE & BIG HERO SIX (See Alpha Flight)
Marvel Comics: Sept, 1998 - No. 3, Nov, 1998 ($2.50, limited series)

1-Lobdell-s	5	10	15	31	63	75
2,3	3	6	9	14	19	24

SUN GIRL (See The Human Torch & Marvel Mystery Comics #88)
Marvel Comics (CCC): Aug, 1948 - No. 3, Dec, 1948

1-1st app. Sun Girl; Miss America app.	394	788	1182	2758	4829	6900
2,3: 2-The Blonde Phantom begins	290	580	870	1856	3178	4500

SUNNY, AMERICA'S SWEETHEART (Formerly Cosmo Cat #1-10)
Fox Feature Syndicate: No. 11, Dec, 1947 - No. 14, June, 1948

11-Feldstein-c/a	226	452	678	1446	2473	3500
12-14: 12,13-Feldstein-a; 13,14-Lingerie panels. 13-L.B. Cole-a						
	135	270	405	864	1482	2100
I.W. Reprint #8-Feldstein-a; r/Fox issue	12	24	36	79	170	260

SUN-RUNNERS (Also see Tales of the...)
Pacific Comics/Eclipse Comics/Amazing Comics: 2/84 - No. 3, 5/84; No. 4, 11/84 - No. 7, 1986 (Baxter paper)

1-7: P. Smith-a in #2-4						4.00
Christmas Special 1 (1987, $1.95)-By Amazing						4.00

SUNSET CARSON (Also see Cowboy Western)
Charlton Comics: Feb, 1951 - No. 4, 1951 (No month) (Photo-c on each)

1-Photo/retouched-c (Scarce, all issues)	68	136	204	435	743	1050
2-Kit Carson story; adapts "Kansas Raiders" w/Brian Donlevy, Audie Murphy & Margaret Chapman	47	94	141	296	408	700
3,4	37	74	111	222	361	500

SUNSET PASS (See Zane Grey & 4-Color #230)

SUPER ANGRY BIRDS (Based on Rovio videogame Angry Birds)
IDW Publishing: Sept, 2015 - No. 4, Dec, 2015 ($3.99, limited series)

1-4: 1-The Eagle's Eye - Jeff Parker-s/Ron Randall-a; two covers						4.00

SUPER ANIMALS PRESENTS PIDGY & THE MAGIC GLASSES
Star Publications: Dec, 1953 (25¢, came w/glasses)

1-(3-D Comics)-L. B. Cole-c	50	100	150	315	533	750

SUPER BAD JAMES DYNOMITE
5-D Comics: Dec, 2005 - No. 5, Feb, 2007 ($3.99)

1-5-Created by the Wayans brothers						4.00

SUPERBOY
DC Comics: Jan, 1942

nn-Ashcan comic, not distributed to newsstands, only for in house use. Covers were produced, but not the rest of the book. A CGC certified 9.2 copy sold in 2003 for $6,600.

SUPERBOY (See Adventure, Aurora, DC Comics Presents, DC 100 Page Super Spectacular #15, DC Super Stars, 80 Page Giant #10, More Fun Comics, The New Adv... & Superman Family #191, Young Justice)

SUPERBOY (1st Series)(...& the Legion of Super-Heroes with #231)
(Becomes The Legion of Super-Heroes No. 259 on)
National Periodical Publ./DC Comics: Mar-Apr, 1949 - No. 258, Dec, 1979 (#1-16: 52 pgs.)

1-Superman cover; intro in More Fun #101 (1-2/45)	1275	2550	3825	9700	17,600	25,500
2-Used in SOTI, pgs. 35-36,226	290	580	870	1856	3178	4500
3	206	412	618	1318	2259	3200
4	161	322	483	1030	1765	2500
5-1st pre-Supergirl tryout (c/story, 11-12/49)	187	374	561	1197	2049	2900
6-9: 8-1st Superbaby	135	270	405	864	1482	2100
10-1st app. Lana Lang	187	374	561	1197	2049	2900
11-15: 11-2nd Lana Lang app.; 1st Lana cover	97	194	291	621	1061	1500
16-20: 20-2nd Jor-El cover	68	136	204	435	743	1050
21-26,28-30: 21-Lana Lang app.	57	114	171	362	619	875
27-Low distribution	71	142	213	454	777	1100
31-38: 38-Last pre-code issue (1/55)	50	100	150	315	533	750
39-48,50 (7/56)	45	90	135	284	480	675
49 (6/56)-1st app. Metallo (this one's Jor-El's robot)	93	186	279	591	1021	1450
51-60: 51-Krypto app. 52-1st S.A. issue. 56-Krypto-c	37	74	111	218	354	490
61-67	31	62	93	182	296	410
68-Origin/1st app. original Bizarro (10-11/58)	530	1060	1590	4000	7750	11,500

69-77,79: 76-1st Supermonkey	27	54	81	158	259	360
78-Origin Mr. Mxyzptlk & Superboy's costume	37	74	111	222	361	500
80-1st meeting Superboy/Supergirl (4/60)	45	90	135	284	480	675
81,83-85,87,88: 83-Origin/1st app. Kryptonite Kid	14	28	42	94	207	320
82-1st Bizarro Krypto	18	36	54	128	284	440
86-(1/61)-4th Legion app.; Intro Pete Ross	30	60	90	216	483	750
89-(6/61)-1st app. Mon -El; 2nd Phantom Zone	46	92	138	340	770	1200
90-92: 90-Pete Ross learns Superboy's I.D. 92-Last 10¢ issue						
	12	24	36	82	179	275
93-10th Legion app.(12/61); Chameleon Boy app.	13	26	39	91	201	310
94-97,99: 94-1st app. Superboy Revenge Squad	11	22	33	72	154	235
98-(7/62) Legion app; origin & 1st app. Ultra Boy; Pete Ross joins Legion						
	18	36	54	124	275	425
100-(10/62)-Ultra Boy app; 1st app. Phantom Zone villains, Dr. Xadu & Erndine. 2 pg. map of Krypton; origin Superboy retold; r-cover of Superman #1						
	18	36	54	124	275	425
101-120: 104-Origin Phantom Zone. 115-Atomic bomb-c. 117-Legion app.						
	9	18	27	59	117	175
121-128: 124-(10/65)-1st app. Insect Queen (Lana Lang). 125-Legion cameo. 126-Origin Krypto the Super Dog retold with new facts	8	16	24	52	99	145
129-(80-pg. Giant G-22)-Reprints origin Mon-El	9	18	27	59	117	175
130-137,139,140: 131-Legion statues cameo in Dog Legionnaires story. 132-1st app. Supremo. 133-Superboy meets Robin	7	14	21	44	82	120
138 (80-pg. Giant G-35)	7	14	21	49	92	135
141-146,148-155,157: 145-Superboy's parents regain their youth. 148-Legion app. 157-Last 12¢ issue	6	12	18	37	66	95
147(6/68)-Giant G-47; 1st origin of L.S.H. (Saturn Girl, Lightning Lad, Cosmic Boy); origin Legion of Super-Pets-r/Adv. #293	9	18	27	58	114	170
147 Replica Edition (2003, $6.95) reprints entire issue; cover recreation by Ordway						10.00
156-(Giant G-59)	6	12	18	42	79	115
158-164,166-171,175: 171-1st app. Aquaboy	3	6	9	19	30	40
165,174 (Giant G-71,G-83): 165-r/1st app. Krypto the Superdog from Adventure Comics #210	5	10	15	35	63	90
172,173,176-Legion app.: 172-1st app. & origin Yango (The Super Ape). 176-Partial photo-c; last 15¢ issue	3	6	9	20	31	42
177-184,186,187 (All 52 pgs.): 182-All new origin of the classic World's Finest team (Superman & Batman) as teenagers (2/72, 22pgs). 184-Origin Dial H for Hero-r	3	6	9	15	22	28
185-Also listed as DC 100 Pg. Super Spectacular #12; Legion-c/story; Teen Titans, Kid Eternity(r/Hit #46), Star Spangled Kid-r(S.S. #55)	3	6	9	13	17	45
188-190,192,194,196: 188-Origin Karkan. 196-Last Superboy solo story	8	16	24	56	108	160
191,193,195: 191-Origin Sunboy retold; Legion app. 193-Chameleon Boy & Shrinking Violet get new costumes. 195-1st app. Erg-1/Wildfire; Phantom Girl gets new costume	3	6	9	14	20	26
197-Legion series begins; Lightning Lad's new costume	3	6	9	15	22	28
198,199: 198-Element Lad & Princess Projectra get new costumes	5	10	15	33	57	80
200-Bouncing Boy & Duo Damsel marry; J'onn J'onzz cameo	3	6	9	15	22	28
201,204,206,207,209: 201-Re-intro Erg-1 as Wildfire. 204-Supergirl resigns from Legion. 206-Ferro Lad & Invisible Kid app. 209-Karate Kid gets new costume	3	6	9	21	33	45
202,205-(100 pgs.): 202-Light Lass gets new costume; Mike Grell's 1st comic work-i (5-6/74)	3	6	9	14	20	26
203-Invisible Kid killed by Validus	5	10	15	35	63	90
208,210: 208-(68 pgs.). 208-Legion of Super-Villains app. 210-Origin Karate Kid	3	6	9	13	18	45
211-220: 212-Matter-Eater Lad resigns. 216-1st app. Tyroc, who joins the Legion in #218	3	6	9	15	22	28
221-230,246-249: 226-Intro. Dawnstar. 228-Death of Chemical King	2	4	6	8	11	14
231-245: (Giants) 240-Origin Dawnstar; Chaykin-a. 242-(52 pgs.). 243-Legion of Substitute Heroes app. 243-245-(44 pgs.).	2	4	6	10	14	18
244,245-(Whitman variants; low print run, no issue# shown on cover)						
	3	6	9	17	26	35
246-248-(Whitman variants; low ...)	3	6	9	15	22	28
250-258: 253-Intro Blok. 257-Return of Bouncing Boy & Duo Damsel by Ditko	2	4	6	8	10	12
251-258-(Whitman variants; low print run)	2	4	6	11	16	24
Annual 1 (Sum/64, 84 pgs.)-Origin Krypto-r	17	34	51	117	259	400
Spectacular 1 (1980, Giant)-1st comic distributed only through comic stores; mostly-r	2	4	6	9	13	16

	GD 2.0	VG 4.0	FN 6.0	VF 8.0	VF/NM 9.0	NM- 9.2

...: The Greatest Team-Up Stories Ever Told TPB (2010, $19.99) r/team-ups with Robin, Supergirl, young versions of Aquaman, Green Arrow, Bruce Wayne; Davis-c 20.00
NOTE: *Neal Adams* c-143, 145, 146, 148-155, 157-161, 163, 164, 166-168, 172, 173, 175, 176, 178. *M. Anderson* a-178,179, 245i. *Ditko* a-257p. *Grell* a-202i, 203-219, 220-224p, 225p; c-207-232, 235, 236p, 237, 239p, 240p, 243p, 246, 258. *Nasser* a(p)-222, 225, 226, 230, 231, 233, 236. *Simonson* a-237p. *Starlin* a(p)-239, 250, 251; c-238. *Staton* a-243-249p, 252-258p; c-247-251p. *Swan/Moldoff* c-109. *Tuska* a-172, 173, 176, 183, 235p. *Wood* inks-153-155, 157-161. Legion app.-172, 173, 176, 177, 183, 184, 188, 190, 191, 193, 195, 197-258.

SUPERBOY (TV)(2nd Series)(The Adventures of...#19 on)
DC Comics: Feb, 1990 - No. 22, Dec, 1991 ($1.00/$1.25)

1-Photo-c from TV show; Mooney-a(p) 6.00
2-22: Mooney-a in 2-8,18-20; 8-Bizarro-c/story; Arthur Adams-a(i). 9-12,14-17-Swan-a 4.00
...Special 1 (1992, $1.75) Swan-a 5.00

SUPERBOY (3rd Series)
DC Comics: Feb, 1994 - No. 100, Jul, 2002 ($1.50/$1.95/$1.99/$2.25)

1-Metropolis Kid from Reign of the Supermen	2	4	6	8	10	12

2-8,10-24,26-76: 6,7-Worlds Collide Pts. 3 & 8. 6-(9/94)-Zero Hour x-over. 21-Legion app.
28-Supergirl-c/app. 33-Final Night. 38-41-"Meltdown". 45-Legion-c/app. 47-Green Lantern app.
50-Last Boy on Earth begins. 60-Crosses Hypertime. 68-Demon-c/app. 4.00

9-(11/94)-1st full app. King Shark	5	10	15	30	50	70

25-($2.95)-New Gods & Female Furies app.; w/pin-ups 5.00
77-99: 77-Begin $2.25-c. 79-Superboy's powers return. 80,81-Titans app. 83-New costume.
85-Batgirl app. 90,91-Our Worlds at War x-over 4.00
100-($3.50) Sienkiewicz-c; Grummett & McCrea-a; Superman cameo 5.00

#0-(10/94) Zero Hour issue released between #8 & #9; cameo of King Shark	2	4	6	9	12	15

#1,000,000 (11/98) 853rd Century x-over 4.00
Annual 1 (1994, $2.95, 68 pgs.)-Elseworlds story, Pt. 2 of The Super Seven
  (see Adventures Of Superman Annual #6) 6.00
Annual 2 (1995, $3.95)-Year One story 5.00
Annual 3 (1996, $2.95)-Legends of the Dead Earth 5.00
Annual 4 (1997, $3.95)-Pulp Heroes story 5.00
...Plus 1 (Jan, 1997, $2.95) w/Capt. Marvel Jr. 4.00
...Plus 2 (Fall, 1997, $2.95) w/Slither (Scare Tactics) 4.00
...Risk Double-Shot 1 (Feb, 1998, $1.95) w/Risk (Teen Titans) 4.00

SUPERBOY (4th Series)
DC Comics: Jan, 2011 - No. 11, Early Oct, 2011 ($2.99)

1-11: 1-Lemire-s/Gallo-a/Albuquerque-c; Parasite & Poison Ivy app. 2,3-Noto-c 3.00
1-5: 1-Variant-c by Cassaday. 2-March-var-c. 3-Nguyen var-c. 4-Lau var-c. 5-Manapul 4.00

SUPERBOY (DC New 52)
DC Comics: Nov, 2011 - No. 34, Oct, 2014 ($2.99)

1-34: 1-New origin; Lobdell-s/Silva-a/Canete-c; Caitlin Fairchild app. 6-Supergirl app.
8-Grunge, Beast Boy & Terra app. from Teen Titans Annual #1;
  Teen Titans and the Legion app. 14-17-H'El on Earth tie-in; Batman app. 3.00
#0-(11/12, $2.99) Origin of Kryptonian clones; Silva-a 3.00
Annual 1 (3/13, $4.99) H'El on Earth tie-in between Superboy #16 & Superman #16 .... 5.00
...: Futures End 1 (11/14, $2.99, regular) Five years later, Freefall app.; Caldwell-a 3.00
...: Futures End 1 (11/14, $3.99, 3-D cover) 4.00

SUPERBOY AND THE LEGION OF SUPER-HEROES
DC Comics: 2011 ($14.99, TPB)

SC-Reprints stories from Adventure Comics #515-520 .... 15.00

SUPERBOY & THE RAVERS
DC Comics: Sept, 1996 - No. 19, March, 1998 ($1.95)

1-19: 4-Adam Strange app. 7-Impulse-c/app. 9-Superman-c/app. 4.00

SUPERBOY COMICS
DC Comics: Jan. 1942

nn - Ashcan comic, not distributed to newsstands, only for in-house use. Cover art is Detective Comics #57 with interior being Action Comics #38. A CGC certified 9.2 copy sold for $6,600 in 2003 and for $15,750 in 2008.

SUPERBOY/ROBIN: WORLD'S FINEST THREE
DC Comics: 1996 - No. 2, 1996 ($4.95 squarebound, limited series)

1,2: Superboy & Robin vs. Metallo & Poison Ivy; Karl Kesel & Chuck Dixon scripts;
  Tom Grummett-c(p)/a(p) 5.00

SUPERBOY'S LEGION (Elseworlds)
DC Comics: 2001 - No. 2, 2001 ($5.95, squarebound, limited series)

1,2- 31st century Superboy forms Legion; Farmer-s/i; Davis-a(p)/c 6.00

SUPERBOY: THE BOY OF STEEL
DC Comics: 2010 ($19.99, hardcover with dustjacket)

HC-Reprints stories from Adventure Comics #0-3,5,6 & Superman Secret Files 2009 .... 20.00
SC-(2011, $14.99) Same contents as HC 15.00

SUPERBOY: THE MAN OF TOMORROW (Dawn of DC)
DC Comics: Jun, 2023 - No. 6, Dec, 2023 ($3.99)

1-6: 1-Kenny Porter-s/Jahnoy Lindsay-a 4.00

SUPER BRAT (Li'l Genius #6 on)
Toby Press: Jan, 1954 - No. 4, July, 1954

1	14	28	42	82	121	160
2-4: 4-Li'l Teevy by Mel Lazarus	8	16	24	42	54	65
I.W. Reprint #1,2,3,7,8('58): 1-r/#1	2	4	6	11	16	20
I.W. (Super) Reprint #10('63)	2	4	6	10	14	18

SUPERCAR (TV)
Gold Key: Nov, 1962 - No. 4, Aug, 1963 (All painted-c)

1	12	24	36	83	182	280
2,3	8	16	24	52	99	145
4-Last issue	9	18	27	58	114	170

SUPER CAT (Formerly Frisky Animals; also see Animal Crackers)
Star Publications (#56-58/Ajax/Farrell Publ. (Four Star Comic Corp.):
No. 56, Nov, 1953 - No. 58, May, 1954; Aug, 1957 - No. 4, May, 1958

56-58-L.B. Cole-c on all	24	48	72	142	234	325
1(1957-Ajax)- "The Adventures of..." c-only	13	26	39	72	101	130

2-4	8	16	24	44	57	70

SUPER CEREBUS ANNUAL
Aardvark-Vanaheim: Apr, 2019 ($8.00, B&W)

1-Cerebus figures with original Gustave Doré artwork; Superman Annual #1-c swipe 8.00

SUPER CEREBUS VS. COVID-19
Aardvark-Vanaheim: Oct, 2021 ($4.00, B&W)

1-Cerebus figures with Doré artwork; Superman vs. Muhammad Ali-c swipe 4.00

SUPER CIRCUS (TV)
Cross Publishing Co.: Jan, 1951 - No. 5, Sept, 1951 (Mary Hartline)

1-(52 pgs.)-Cast photos on-c	22	44	66	132	216	300
2-Cast photos on-c	15	30	45	83	124	165
3-5	13	26	39	74	105	135

SUPER CIRCUS (TV)
Dell Publ. Co.: No. 542, Mar, 1954 - No. 694, Mar, 1956 (Mary Hartline)

Four Color 542: Mary Hartline photo-c	9	18	27	59	117	175
Four Color 592,694: Mary Hartline photo-c	7	14	21	44	82	120

SUPER COMICS
Dell Publishing Co.: May, 1938 - No. 121, Feb-Mar, 1949

1-Terry & The Pirates, The Gumps, Dick Tracy, Little Orphan Annie, Little Joe, Gasoline Alley,
  Smilin' Jack, Smokey Stover, Smitty, Tiny Tim, Moon Mullins, Harold Teen, Winnie Winkle

begin	258	516	774	1651	2826	4000
2	103	206	309	659	1130	1600
3	87	174	261	553	952	1350
4,5: 4-Dick Tracy-c; also #8-10,17,26(part),31	65	130	195	416	708	1000
6-10	53	106	159	334	567	800
11-20: 20-Smilin' Jack-c (also #29,32)	42	84	126	205	445	625
21-29: 21-Magic Morro begins (origin & 1st app., 2/40). 22,27-Ken Ernst-c (also #25?);						
Magic Morro c-22,25,27,34	37	74	111	222	361	500
30- "Sea Hawk" movie adaptation-c/story with Errol Flynn						
	37	74	111	222	361	500
31-40: 34-Ken Ernst-c	30	60	90	177	289	400
41-50: 41-Intro Lightning Jim. 43-Terry & The Pirates ends						
	25	50	75	150	245	340
51-60	20	40	60	117	189	260
61-70: 62-Flag-c. 65-Brenda Starr-r begin? 67-X-Mas-c						
	19	38	57	109	172	235
71-80	15	30	45	85	130	175
81-99	14	28	42	81	118	155
100	15	30	45	83	124	165
101-115-Last Dick Tracy (moves to own title)	14	22	33	62	86	110
116-121: 116,118-All Smokey Stover. 117-All Gasoline Alley. 119-121-Terry & The Pirates						
app. in all	10	20	30	54	72	90

SUPER COPS, THE
Red Circle Productions (Archie): July, 1974 (one-shot)

1-Morrow-c/a; art by Pino, Hack, Thorne	2	4	6	8	11	14

SUPER COPS
Now Comics: Sept, 1990 - No. 4, Dec?, 1990 ($1.75)

1-($2.75, 52 pgs.)-Dave Dorman painted-c (both printings) 5.00
2-4 .... 4.00

SUPER CRACKED (See Cracked)

SUPERCROOKS
Marvel Comics (Icon): May, 2012 - No. 4, Aug, 2012 ($2.99/$4.99)

1-3-($2.99) Millar-s/Yu-a. 1-Covers by Yu & Gibbons. 2-Covers by Yu & Hitch 3.00
4-($4.99) Bonus preview of Jupiter's Children (later re-titled Jupiter's Legacy) 5.00

SUPER DC GIANT (25-50c, all 68-52 pg. Giants)
National Per. Publ.: No. 13, 9-10/70 - No. 26, 7-8/71; V3#27, Summer, 1976 (No #1-12)

S-13-Binky	10	20	30	69	147	225
S-14-Top Guns of the West; Kubert-c; Trigger Twins, Johnny Thunder, Wyoming Kid-r;						
Moreira-r (9-10/70)	5	10	15	33	57	80
S-15-Western Comics; Kubert-c; Pow Wow Smith, Vigilante, Buffalo Bill-r; new Gil Kane-a						
(9-10/70)	5	10	15	33	57	80
S-16-Best of the Brave & the Bold; Batman-r & Metamorpho origin-r from Brave & the Bold;						
Spectre pin-up	4	8	12	27	44	60
S-17-Love 1970 (scarce)	9	18	27	57	111	165
S-18-Three Mouseketeers: Dizzy Dog, Doodles Duck, Bo Bunny-r; Sheldon Mayer-a						
	27	54	81	189	420	650
S-19-Jerry Lewis; Neal Adams pin-up	9	18	27	57	111	165
S-20-House of Mystery; N. Adams-c; Kirby-r(3)	7	14	21	48	89	130
S-21-Love 1971 (scarce)	29	58	87	209	467	725
S-22-Top Guns of the West; Kubert-c	4	8	12	25	40	55
S-23-The Unexpected	4	8	12	28	47	65
S-24-Supergirl	4	8	12	27	44	60
S-25-Challengers of the Unknown; all Kirby/Wood-r	4	8	12	27	44	60
S-26-Aquaman (1971)-r/S.A. Aquaman origin story from Showcase #30						
	4	8	12	27	44	60
27-Strange Flying Saucers Adventures (Sum, 1976)	3	6	9	18	28	38

NOTE: *Sid Greene* r-27p(2), *Heath* r-27. *G. Kane* a-14r(2), 15, 27r(p). *Kubert* r-16.

SUPER DINOSAUR
Image Comics: Apr, 2011 - No. 23, Dec, 2014 ($2.99)

1-23: 1-Robert Kirkman-s/Jason Howard-a; origin story and character profiles 3.00
... Origin Special #1 FCBD Edition (5/11, giveaway) r/#1 .... 3.00

SUPER-DOOPER COMICS
Able Mfg. Co./Harvey: 1946 - No. 7, May, 1946; No. 8, 1946 (10c, 32 pgs., paper-c)

1-The Clock, Gangbuster app. (scarce)	110	220	330	704	1202	1700
2	22	44	66	128	209	290
3-6	20	40	60	117	189	260
7,8-Shock Gibson. 7-Where's Theres A Will by Ed Wheelan, Steve Case Crime Rover,						
Penny & Ullysses Jr. 8-Sam Hill app.	24	48	72	140	230	350

SUPER DUCK

Supercar #4 © GK

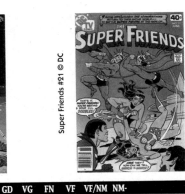

Super Friends #21 © DC

Supergirl (2016 series) #25 © DC

	GD	VG	FN	VF	VF/NM	NM-		GD	VG	FN	VF	VF/NM	NM-
	2.0	4.0	6.0	8.0	9.0	9.2		2.0	4.0	6.0	8.0	9.0	9.2

Archie Comics Publications: May, 2020 - No. 4 ($3.99, limited series)

1-Frank Tieri & Ian Flynn-s/Ryan Jampole-a; revival of Golden Age character   4.00

SUPER DUCK COMICS (The Cockeyed Wonder) (See Jolly Jingles)
MLJ Mag. No. 1-4(9/45)/Close-Up No. 5 on (Archie): Fall, 1944 - No. 94, Dec, 1960 (Also see Laugh #24)(#1-5 are quarterly)

1-Origin; Hitler & Hirohito-c	194	388	582	1242	2121	3000
2-Bill Vigoda-c	40	80	120	246	411	575
3-5: 4-20-Al Fagaly-c (most)	29	58	87	172	281	390
6-10	16	32	48	94	147	200
11-20(6/48)	14	28	42	78	112	145
21,23-40 (10/51)	12	24	36	67	94	120
22-Used in SOTI, pg. 35,307,308	15	30	45	90	140	190
41-60 (2/55)	10	20	30	56	76	95
61-94	9	18	27	47	61	75

SUPER DUPER (Formerly Pocket Comics #1-4?)
Harvey Publications: No. 5, 1941 - No. 11, 1941

5-Captain Freedom & Shock Gibson app.	87	174	261	553	952	1350
8,11	57	114	171	362	619	875

SUPER DUPER COMICS (Formerly Latest Comics?)
F. E. Howard Publ.: No. 3, May-June, 1947

3-1st app. Mr. Monster	300	600	900	2010	3505	5000

SUPER FREAKS (See Savage Dragon titles)
Image Comics: Jun, 2022 ($4.99, one-shot)

1-Fan-made tribute comic to the Savage Dragon; s/a by various; Larsen-c   5.00

SUPER FRIENDS (TV) (Also see Best of DC & Limited Collectors' Edition)
National Periodical Publications/DC Comics: Nov, 1976 - No. 47, Aug, 1981 (#14 is 44 pgs.)

1-Superman, Batman, Robin, Wonder Woman, Aquaman, Atom, Wendy, Marvin & Wonder Dog begin (1st Super Friends)	7	14	21	46	86	125
2-Penguin-c/sty	3	6	9	16	23	30
3-5	3	6	9	14	20	26
6,8-10,14: 8-1st app. Jack O'Lantern. 9-1st app. Icemaiden. 14-Origin Wonder Twins						
	2	4	6	13	18	22
7-1st app. Wonder Twins & The Seraph	11	22	33	73	157	240
11-13,15-30: 13-1st app. Dr. Mist. 25-1st app. Fire as Green Fury. 28-Bizarro app.						
	2	4	6	9	13	16
13-16,20-23,25,32-(Whitman variants; low print run, no issue# on cover)						
	2	4	6	11	16	20
31,47: 31-Black Orchid app. 47-Origin Fire & Green Fury						
	2	4	6	10	14	18
32-46: 36,43-Plastic Man app.	2	4	6	8	11	14
TBP (2001, $14.95) r/#1,6-9,14,21,27 & Limited Collectors' Edition C-41; Alex Ross-c						15.00
...: Truth, Justice and Peace TPB (2003, $14.95) r/#10,12,13,25,28,29,31,36,37						15.00

NOTE: Estrada a-1p, 2p. Orlando a-1p. Staton a-43, 45.

SUPER FRIENDS (All ages stories with puzzles and games)(Based on Mattel toy line)
DC Comics: May, 2008 - No. 29, Sept, 2010 ($2.25/$2.99)

1-29-Superman, Batman, Wonder Woman, Aquaman, Flash & Green Lantern. 29-Begin $2.99-c; Bat-Mite & Mr. Mxyzptlk app.	3.00
...: Calling All Super Friends TPB (2009, $12.99) r/#8-14; puzzles and games	13.00
...: For Justice TPB (2009, $12.99) r/#1-7; puzzles and games	13.00
...: Head of the Class TPB (2010, $12.99) r/#15-21; puzzles and games	13.00
...: Mystery in Space TPB (2011, $12.99) r/#22-28; puzzles and games	13.00

SUPER FUN
Gillmor Magazines: Jan, 1956 (By A.W. Nugent)

1-Comics, puzzles, cut-outs by A.W. Nugent	11	22	33	64	90	115

SUPER FUNNIES (...Western Funnies #3,4)
Superior Comics Publishers Ltd. (Canada): Dec, 1953 - No. 4, Sept, 1954

1-(3-D, 10c)-...Presents Dopey Duck; make your own 3-D glasses cut-out						
inside front-c; did not come w/glasses	43	86	129	271	461	650
2-Horror & crime satire	19	38	57	111	176	240
3-Phantom Ranger-c/s; Geronimo, Billy the Kid app.	13	26	39	72	101	130
4-Phantom Ranger-c/story	13	26	39	72	101	130

SUPERGIRL
DC Comics: Feb. 1944

nn - Ashcan comic, not distributed to newsstands, only for in-house use. Cover art is Boy Commandos #1 with interior being Action Comics #80. A copy sold for $15,750 in 2008.

SUPERGIRL (See Action, Adventure #281, Brave & the Bold, Crisis on Infinite Earths #7, Daring New Advs. of..., Super DC Giant, Superman Family, & Super-Team Family)

SUPERGIRL

National Periodical Publ.: Nov, 1972 - No. 9, Dec-Jan, 1973-74; No. 10, Sept-Oct, 1974 (1st solo title)(20¢)

1-Zatanna back-up stories begin, end #5	12	24	36	81	176	270
2-4,6,7,9: 7-Zatanna battles Supergirl	4	8	12	27	44	60
5,8,10: 5-Zatanna origin-r. 8-JLA x-over. 10-Prez app.						
	4	8	12	28	47	65

NOTE: Zatanna in #1-5, 7(Guest); Prez app. in #10. #1-10 are 20¢ issues.

SUPERGIRL (Formerly Daring New Adventures of...)
DC Comics: No. 14, Dec, 1983 - No. 23, Sept, 1984

14-23: 16-Ambush Bug app. 20-JLA & New Teen Titans app.	5.00
...Movie Special (1985)-Adapts movie; Morrow-a; photo back-c	5.00

SUPERGIRL
DC Comics: Feb, 1994 - No. 4, May, 1994 ($1.50, limited series)

1-Matrix clone Supergirl; Stern-s/Brigman-a	2	4	6	8	10	12
2-4: Guice-a(i)						5.00

SUPERGIRL (See Showcase '96 #8)
DC Comics: Sept, 1996 - No. 80, May, 2003 ($1.95/$1.99/$2.25/$2.50)

1-Peter David scripts & Gary Frank-c/a	2	4	6	11	16	20
1-2nd printing						4.00
2,4-9: 4-Gorilla Grodd-c/app. 6-Superman-c/app. 9-Last Frank-a						5.00
3						6.00
10-19: 14-Genesis x-over. 16-Power Girl app.						4.00
20-35: 20-Millennium Giants x-over; Superman app. 23-Steel-c/app. 24-Resurrection Man x-over. 25-Comet ID revealed; begin $1.99-c						4.00
36-46: 36,37-Young Justice x-over						4.00
47-49,51-74: 47-Begin $2.25-c. 51-Adopts costume from animated series. 54-Green Lantern app. 59-61-Our Worlds at War x-over. 62-Two-Face-c/app. 66,67-Demon-c/app.						4.00
68-74-Mary Marvel app. 70-Nauck-a. 73-Begin $2.50-c						5.00
50-($3.95) Supergirl's final battle with the Carnivore						
75-80: 75-Re-intro. Kara Zor-El; cover swipe of Action Comics #252 by Haynes; Benes-a.						4.00
78-Spectre app. 80-Last issue; Romita-c						4.00
#1,000,000 (11/98) 853rd Century x-over						6.00
Annual 1 (1996, $2.95)-Legends of the Dead Earth						5.00
Annual 2 (1997, $3.95)-Pulp Heroes; LSH app.; Chiodo-c						5.00
...: Many Happy Returns TPB (2003, $14.95) r/#75-80; intro. by Peter David						15.00
...Plus (2/97, $2.95) Capt.(Mary) Marvel-c/app.; David-s/Frank-a						4.00
.../Prysm Double-Shot 1 (Feb, 1998, $1.95) w/Prysm (Teen Titans)						4.00
...: Wings (2001, $5.95) Elseworlds; DeMatteis-s/Tolagson-a						6.00
TPB-('98, $14.95) r/Showcase '96 #8 & Supergirl #1-9						15.00

SUPERGIRL (See Superman/Batman #8 & #19)
DC Comics: No. 0, Oct, 2005 - No. 67, Oct, 2011 ($2.99)

0-Reprints Superman/Batman #19 with white variant of that cover						4.00
1-Loeb-s/Churchill-a; two covers by Churchill & Turner; Power Girl app.	1	3	4	6	8	10
1-2nd printing with B&W sketch variant of Turner-c						3.00
1-3rd printing with variant-c homage to Action Comics #252 by Churchill						3.00
2-4: 2-Teen Titans app. 3-Outsiders app.; covers by Turner & Churchill						3.00
5-($3.99) Supergirl vs. Supergirl; Churchill & Turner-c						4.00
6-49: 6-9-One Year Later; Power Girl app. 11-Intro. Powerboy. 12-Terra debut; Conner-a						
20-Amazons Attack x-over. 28-31-Resurrection Man app. 35,36-New Krypton x-over; Argo City story re-told; Superwoman app. 35-Ross-c. 36-Zor-El dies						3.00
50-($4.99) Lana Lang Insect Queen app.; Superwoman returns; back-up story co-written by Helen Slater with Chiang-a; Turner-c						5.00
50-Variant cover by Middleton						6.00
51-67: 51-52-New Krypton. 52-Brainiac 5 app. 53-57-Bizarro-Girl app. 55-63-Reeder-c						3.00
58-DC 75th Anniversary variant cover by Conner						6.00
Annual 1 (11/09, $3.99) Origin of Superwoman						4.00
Annual 2 (12/10, $4.99) Silver Age Legion of Super-Heroes app.; Reeder-c						5.00
...: Beyond Good and Evil TPB (2009, $17.99) r/#27 and Action Comics #850						18.00
...: Bizarrogirl TPB (2011, $19.99) r/#53-59 & Annual #2						20.00
...: Candor TPB (2007, $14.99) r/#6-9; and pages from JSA Classified #2, Superman #223, Superman/Batman #27 and JLA #122,123						15.00
...: Death & The Family TPB (2010, $17.99) r/#48-50 & Annual #1						18.00
...: Friends & Fugitives TPB (2010, $17.99) r/#43,45-47; Action Comics #881,882						18.00
...: Identity TPB (2007, $19.99) r/#10-16 and story from DCU Infinite Holiday Special						20.00
...: Power TPB (2006, $14.99) r/#1-5 and Superman/Batman #19; variant-c gallery						15.00
...: Way of the World TPB (2009, $17.99) r/#28-33						18.00
...: Who is Superwoman TPB (2009, $17.99) r/#34,37-42						18.00

SUPERGIRL (DC New 52)
DC Comics: Nov, 2011 - No. 40, May, 2015 ($2.99)

1-New origin; Green & Johnson-s/Asrar-a/c; Superman app.

	GD 2.0	VG 4.0	FN 6.0	VF 8.0	VF/NM 9.0	NM- 9.2

2-40: 2,3-Superman app. 8-Pérez-a. 14-17-H'El on Earth tie-in. 17-Wonder Woman app. 19,20-Power Girl app. 19-Power Girl gets classic costume. 23,24-Cyborg Superman app. 26-28-Lobo app. 28-33-Kara joins Red Lanterns. 33-Gen13 app. 36-40-Maxima app. — 1 / 3 / 4 / 6 / 8 / 10 · 3.00
#0-(11/12, $2.99) Kara's escape from Krypton · 3.00
...: Futures End 1 (11/14, $2.99, regular-c) Five years later; Cyborg Superman app. · 3.00
...: Futures End 1 (11/14, $3.99, 3-D cover) · 4.00
... Special Edition 1 (12/15, $1.00) reprints #1 with Supergirl TV banner at top of cover · 3.00

SUPERGIRL (DC Rebirth)(Issues #41 & #42 were only released digitally)
DC Comics: Nov, 2016 - No. 40, May, 2020 ($2.99/$3.99)
1-Orlando-s/Ching-a; Cyborg Superman app. — 1 / 2 / 3 / 5 / 6 / 8
2-7 · 3.00
8-24,26-40-($3.99) 8-Superman & Emerald Empress app. 9-11-Batgirl app. 12-Fatal Five. 12-20-Variant covers by Stanley "Artgerm" Lau. 20-The Unexpected app. 26-Omega Men app. 31-33-Maguire-a. 33-Legion of Super-Heroes app. 36-40-The Infected
25-($4.99) Lupacchino-a · 4.00
· 5.00
Annual 1 (10/17, $4.99) The new Fatal Five app.; takes place between #11,12 · 5.00
Annual 2 (1/20, $4.99) Venditti-s/Braga-a; follows #36; The Batman Who Laughs app. · 5.00
...: Rebirth 1 (10/16, $2.99) Orlando-s/Lupacchino-a; gets the Kara Danvers identity · 3.00

SUPERGIRL AND THE LEGION OF SUPER-HEROES (Continues from Legion of Super-Heroes #15, Apr, 2006)(Continues as Legion of Super-Heroes #37)
DC Comics: No. 16, May, 2006 - No. 36, Jan, 2008 ($2.99)
16-Supergirl appears in the 31st century · 4.00
16-2nd printing · 3.00
17-22,24-36: 24,25-Mon-El returns · 3.00
23-Regular-c; Mon-El cameo — 1 / 3 / 4 / 6 / 8 / 10
23-Variant-c by Adam Hughes — 13 / 26 / 39 / 89 / 195 / 300
...: Adult Education TPB (2007, $14.99) r/#20-25 & LSH #6,9,13-15 · 15.00
...: Dominator War TPB (2007, $14.99) r/#26-30 · 15.00
...: Strange Visitor From Another Century TPB (2006, $14.99) r/#16-19 & LSH #11,12,15 · 15.00
...: The Quest For Cosmic Boy TPB (2008, $14.99) r/#31-36 · 15.00

SUPERGIRL: BEING SUPER
DC Comics: Feb, 2017 - No. 4, Aug, 2017 ($5.99, limited series)
1-4-Mariko Tamaki-s/Joëlle Jones-a · 6.00

SUPERGIRL: COSMIC ADVENTURES IN THE 8TH GRADE (Cartoony all-ages title)
DC Comics: Feb, 2008 - No. 6, Jul, 2009 ($2.50, limited series)
1-6: 1-Supergirl lands on Earth; Eric Jones-a. 5,6-Comet & Streaky app. · 3.00

SUPERGIRL/LEX LUTHOR SPECIAL (Supergirl and Team Luthor on-c)
DC Comics: 1993 ($2.50, 68 pgs., one-shot)
1-Pin-ups by Byrne & Thibert · 6.00

SUPERGIRL SPECIAL
DC Comics: Dec, 2023 ($5.99, one-shot)
1-Tamaki-s/Patridge-a; Power Girl app. · 6.00

SUPERGIRL: WOMAN OF TOMORROW
DC Comics: Aug, 2021 - No. 8, Apr, 2022 ($4.99, limited series)
1-8-Tom King-s/Bilquis Evely-a · 5.00

SUPERGOD (Warren Ellis'...)
Avatar Press: Oct, 2009 - No. 5, Nov, 2010 ($3.99, limited series)
1-5-Warren Ellis-s/Garrie Gastony-a; multiple covers on each · 4.00

SUPER GOOF (Walt Disney) (See Dynabrite & The Phantom Blot)
Gold Key No. 1-57/Whitman No. 58 on: Oct, 1965 - No. 74, July, 1984
1 — 6 / 12 / 18 / 38 / 69 / 100
2-5 — 3 / 6 / 9 / 17 / 26 / 35
6-10 — 3 / 6 / 9 / 14 / 19 / 24
11-20 — 2 / 4 / 6 / 8 / 11 / 14
21-30 — 1 / 3 / 4 / 6 / 8 / 10
31-50 — 1 / 2 / 3 / 4 / 5 / 7
51-57 · 6.00
58,59 (Whitman) — 1 / 2 / 3 / 5 / 6 / 8
60(8/80), 62(11/80) 3-pack only (scarce) — 6 / 12 / 18 / 41 / 76 / 110
61(9-10/80) 3-pack only (rare) — 10 / 20 / 30 / 66 / 138 / 210
63-66('81) — 1 / 2 / 3 / 5 / 6 / 8
63 (1/81, 40¢-c) Cover price error variant (scarce) — 3 / 6 / 9 / 14 / 19 / 24
67-69: 67(2/82), 68(2-3/82), 69(3/82) · 6.00
70-74 (#90180 on-c; pre-pack, nd, nd code): 70(5/83), 71(8/83), 72(5/84), 73(6/84), 74(7/84) — 3 / 6 / 9 / 15 / 22 / 28
NOTE: Reprints in #16, 24, 28, 29, 37, 38, 43, 45, 46, 54(1/2), 56-58, 65(1/2), 72(r-#2).

SUPER GREEN BERET (Tod Holton...)
Lightning Comics (Milson Publ. Co.): Apr, 1967 - No. 2, Jun, 1967
1-(25¢, 68 pgs) — 5 / 10 / 15 / 30 / 50 / 70
2-(25¢, 68 pgs) — 3 / 6 / 9 / 21 / 33 / 45

SUPER HEROES (See Giant-Size... & Marvel...)

SUPER HEROES
Dell Publishing Co.: Jan, 1967 - No. 4, June, 1967
1-Origin & 1st app. Fab 4 — 5 / 10 / 15 / 35 / 63 / 90
2-4 — 3 / 6 / 9 / 17 / 26 / 35

SUPER-HEROES BATTLE SUPER-GORILLAS (See DC Special #16)
National Periodical Publications: Winter, 1976 (52 pgs., all reprints, one-shot)
1-Superman, Batman, Flash stories; Infantino-a(p) — 3 / 6 / 9 / 14 / 19 / 24

SUPER HEROES VERSUS SUPER VILLAINS
Archie Publications (Radio Comics): July, 1966 (no month given)(68 pgs.)
1-Flyman, Black Hood, Web, Shield-r; Reinman-a — 6 / 12 / 18 / 37 / 66 / 95

SUPER HERO SQUAD (See Marvel Super Hero Squad)

SUPERHERO WOMEN, THE - FEATURING THE FABULOUS FEMALES OF MARVEL COMICS (See Fireside Book Series)

SUPERICHIE (Formerly Super Richie)
Harvey Publications: No. 5, Oct, 1976 - No. 18, Jan, 1979 (52 pgs. giants)

5-Origin/1st app. new costumes for Rippy & Crashman — 2 / 4 / 6 / 11 / 16 / 20
6-18 — 2 / 4 / 6 / 9 / 12 / 15

SUPERIOR
Marvel Comics (ICON): Dec, 2010 - No. 7, Mar, 2012 ($2.99/$4.99)
1-6-Mark Millar-s/Leinil Yu-a. 1-1st & 2nd printings · 3.00
7-($4.99) Bonus preview of Supercrooks #1 · 5.00
... World Record Special 1 (12/11, $2.99, B&W) Comic created in less than 12 hours · 3.00

SUPERIOR CARNAGE
Marvel Comics: Sept, 2013 - No. 5, Jan, 2014 ($3.99)
1-5: 1-Shinick-s/Segovia-a; covers by Crain & Checchetto. 2-5-Superior Spider-Man app. · 4.00
Annual 1 (4/14, $4.99) Bunn-s/Jacinto & Henderson-a; follows #5; Kasady in prison · 5.00

SUPERIOR FOES OF SPIDER-MAN (Superior Spider-Man)
Marvel Comics: Sept, 2013 - No. 17, Jan, 2015 ($3.99)
1-17: 1-Boomerang, Shocker, Overdrive, Speed Demon & Beetle team; Spencer-s · 4.00

SUPERIOR IRON MAN (Follows events of the Avengers & X-Men: Axis series)
Marvel Comics: Jan, 2015 - No. 9, Aug, 2015 ($3.99)
1-9: 1-Tom Taylor-s/Yildiray Cinar-a. 1-4-Daredevil app. · 4.00

SUPERIOR OCTOPUS (Tie-in to Spider-Geddon event)
Marvel Comics: Dec, 2018 ($3.99)
1-Cloned Otto Octavius; Arnim Zola & The Gorgon app.; Gage-s/Hawthorne-a · 4.00

SUPERIOR SPIDER-MAN (Follows Amazing Spider-Man #700)
Marvel Comics: Mar, 2013 - No. 31, Jun, 2014; No. 32, Oct, 2014 - No. 33, Nov, 2014 ($3.99)
1-Doc Ock as Spider-Man; new Sinister Six app.; Slott-s/Stegman-a · 8.00
1-Variant baby-c by Skottie Young · 10.00
2-6: 4,5-Camuncoli-a. 4-Green Goblin cameo. 6-Ramos-a. · 5.00
6AU (5/13, $3.99) Alternate timeline Age of Ultron tie-in; Gage-s/Soy-a · 4.00
7-24: 7,8-Ramos-a; Avengers app. 9-Peter's memories removed. 14-New costume. 17-19-Spider-Man 2099 app. 20-Black Cat app. 22-24-Venom app. · 4.00
25-($4.99) Superior Venom vs. the Avengers; Ramos-a · 5.00
26-30: 27-Goblin Nation begins. 29-Spider-Man 2099 app. · 4.00
31-($5.99) Goblin Nation finale; covers by Camuncoli & Campbell; Silver Surfer bonus · 5.00
32,33-($4.99) Edge of Spider-Verse tie-ins; takes place during issue #19 · 5.00
Annual 1 (1/14, $4.99) Blackout app.; Gage-s/Rodriguez-a · 5.00
Annual 2 (5/14, $4.99) Leads into Superior Spider-Man #30; Gage-s/Rodriguez-a · 5.00

SUPERIOR SPIDER-MAN (Otto Octavius)(See Spider-Geddon)
Marvel Comics: Feb, 2019 - No. 12, Dec, 2019 ($3.99)
1-6-Gage-s/Hawthorne-a. 1-Stilt-Man app. 1-3-Terrax app. 5,6-Doctor Strange app. · 4.00
7-12: 7,8-War of the Realms tie-ins. 11-Doctor Octopus returns; Mephisto app. · 4.00

SUPERIOR SPIDER-MAN
Marvel Comics: Jan, 2024 - Present ($5.99/$4.99)
1-($5.99) Spider-Boy, Doctor Octopus app.; Slott-s/Bagley-a; back-up Spider-Boy story · 6.00
2-4-($4.99) · 5.00
... Returns 1 (12/23, $6.99) Prelude to series; origin of Supernova · 7.00

SUPERIOR SPIDER-MAN TEAM UP
Marvel Comics: Sept, 2013 - No. 12, Jun, 2014 ($3.99)
1-10: 1-Avengers app. 8-Namor app. 9,10-Daredevil & The Punisher app. · 4.00
... Special 1 (12/13, $4.99) Hulk & the original X-Men app.; Dialynas/Lozano-a · 5.00

SUPERIOR STORIES
Nesbit Publishers, Inc.: May-June, 1955 - No. 4, Nov-Dec, 1955
1-The Invisible Man by H.G. Wells — 32 / 64 / 96 / 188 / 307 / 425
2-4: 2-The Pirate of the Gulf by J.H. Ingrahams. 3-Wreck of the Grosvenor by William Clark Russell. 4-The Texas Rangers by O'Henry — 15 / 30 / 45 / 83 / 124 / 165
NOTE: Morisi c/a in all. Kiwanis stories in #3 & 4. #4 has photo of Gene Autry on-c.

SUPER MAGIC (Super Magician Comics #2 on)
Street & Smith Publications: May, 1941
V1#1-Blackstone the Magician-c/story; origin/1st app. Rex King (Black Fury); Charles Sultan-c; Blackstone-c begin — 219 / 438 / 657 / 1402 / 2401 / 3400

SUPER MAGICIAN COMICS (Super Magic #1)
Street & Smith Publications: No. 2, Sept, 1941 - V5#8, Feb-Mar, 1947
V1#2-Blackstone the Magician continues; Rex King, Man of Adventure app. — 103 / 206 / 309 / 659 / 1130 / 1600
3-Tao-Anwar, Boy Magician begins — 58 / 116 / 174 / 371 / 636 / 900
4-7,9-12: 4-Origin Transo. 11-Supersnipe app. — 54 / 108 / 162 / 343 / 574 / 825
8-Abbott & Costello story (1st app?, 11/42) — 57 / 114 / 171 / 362 / 619 / 875
V2#1-The Shadow app. — 53 / 106 / 159 / 334 / 567 / 800
2-12: 5-Origin Tigerman. 8-Red Dragon begins — 33 / 66 / 99 / 194 / 317 / 440
V3#1-12: 5-Origin Mr. Twilight — 32 / 64 / 96 / 188 / 307 / 425
V4#1-4,6-12: 11-Nigel Elliman Ace of Magic begins (3/46) — 27 / 54 / 81 / 158 / 259 / 360
5-KKK-c/sty — 60 / 120 / 180 / 381 / 653 / 925
V5#1-6 — 25 / 50 / 75 / 150 / 245 / 340
7,8-Red Dragon by Edd Cartier-c/a — 48 / 96 / 144 / 302 / 514 / 725
NOTE: Jack Binder c-1-14(most). Red Dragon c-V5#7, 8.

SUPERMAN (See Action Comics, Advs. of..., All-New Coll. Ed., All-Star Comics, Best of DC, Brave & the Bold, Cosmic Odyssey, DC Comics Presents, Heroes Against Hunger, JLA, The Kents, Krypton Chronicles, Limited Coll. Ed., Man of Steel, Phantom Zone, Power Record Comics, Special Edition, Steel, Super Friends, Superman: The Man of Steel, Superman: The Man of Tomorrow, Superman's Christmas Tabloid, Three-Dimension Advs., World Of Krypton, World Of Metropolis, World Of Smallville & World's Finest)

SUPERMAN (Becomes Adventures of...#424 on)
National Periodical Publ./DC Comics: Summer, 1939 - No. 423, Sept, 1986
(#1-5 are quarterly)
1(nn)-1st four Action stories reprinted; origin Superman by Siegel & Shuster; has a new 2 pg. origin plus 4 pgs. omitted in Action story; see The Comics Magazine #1 & More Fun #14-17 for Superman prototype app.; cover r/splash page from Action #10; 1st pin-up Superman on back-c - 1st pin-up in comics — 200,000 / 400,000 / 800,000 / 1,500,000 / 2,250,000 / 3,000,000
1-Reprint, Oversize 13-1/2x10". WARNING: This comic is an exact duplicate reprint of the original except for its size. DC published it in 1978 with a second cover titling it as a Famous First Edition. There have been many reported cases of the outer cover being removed and the interior sold as the original edition. The reprint with the new outer cover removed is practically worthless. See Famous First Edition for value.

Super Goof #20 © DIS

Superior Spider-Man #20 © MAR

Superman #1 © DC

Description	GD 2.0	VG 4.0	FN 6.0	VF 8.0	VF/NM 9.0	NM- 9.2
2-All daily strip-r; full pg. ad for N.Y. World's Fair	4167	8334	12,500	31,250	65,625	100,000
3-2nd story-r from Action #5; 3rd story-r from Action #6	2100	4200	6300	15,300	31,150	50,000
4-2nd mention of Daily Planet (Spr/40); also see Action #23; 2nd & 3rd app. Luthor (red-headed; also see Action #23); first issue of title to feature original stories	1400	2800	4200	10,600	19,300	28,000
5-4th Luthor app. (grey hair)	975	1950	2919	7100	12,550	18,000
6,7: 6-1st splash pg. in a Superman comic. 7-1st Perry White? (11-12/40)	595	1190	1785	4350	7675	11,000
8-10: 10-5th app. Luthor (1st bald Luthor, 5-6/41)	481	962	1443	3511	6206	8900
11-13,15: 13-Jimmy Olsen & Luthor app.	406	812	1218	2842	4971	7100
14-Patriotic Shield-c classic by Fred Ray	1600	3200	4800	12,200	22,100	32,000
16,19,20: 16-1st Lois Lane-c this title (5-6/42); 2nd Lois-c after Action #29	343	686	1029	2400	4200	6000
17-Hitler, Hirohito-c	1500	3000	4500	11,400	20,700	30,000
18-Classic WWII-c	427	854	1281	3117	5509	7900
21,22,25: 25-Clark Kent's only military service; Fred Ray's only super-hero story	290	580	871	1856	3178	4500
23-Classic periscope-c	427	854	1281	3117	5509	7900
24-Classic Jack Burnley flag-c	919	1838	2757	6709	11,855	17,000
26-Classic war-c	465	930	1395	3395	5998	8600
27-29: 27,29-Lois Lane-c. 28-Lois Lane Girl Reporter series begins, ends #40,42	226	452	678	1446	2473	3500
28-Overseas edition for Armed Forces; same as reg. #28	226	452	678	1446	2473	3500
30-Origin & 1st app. Mr. Mxyztplk (9-10/44)(pronounced "Mix-it-plk" in comic books; name later became Mxyzptlk ("Mix-yez-pit-l-ick"); the character was inspired by a combination of the name of Al Capp's Joe Blyfstyk (the little man with the black cloud over his head) & the devilish antics of Bugs Bunny; he first app. in newspapers 3/7/44; Superman flies for the first time	459	918	1377	3350	5925	8500
31-40: 33-(3-4/45)-3rd app. Mxyztplk. 35,36-Lois Lane-c. 38-Atomic bomb story (1-2/46); delayed because of gov't censorship; Superman shown reading Batman #32 on cover. 40-Mxyztplk-c	181	362	543	1158	1979	2800
41-50: 42-Lois Lane-c. 45-Lois Lane as Superwoman (see Action #60 for 1st app.). 46-(5-6/47)-1st app. Superboy this title. 48-1st time Superman travels thru space	155	310	465	982	1696	2400
51,52: 51-Lois Lane-c	142	284	426	909	1555	2200
53-Third telling of Superman origin; 10th anniversary issue ('48); classic origin-c by Boring	459	918	1377	3350	5925	8500
54,56-60: 57-Lois Lane as Superwoman-c. 58-Intro Tiny Trix. 59-Early use of heat vision (possibly first time)	135	270	405	864	1482	2100
55-Used in SOTI, pg. 33	148	296	444	947	1624	2300
61-Origin Superman retold; origin Green Kryptonite (1st Kryptonite story); Superman returns to Krypton for 1st time & sees his parents for 1st time since infancy, discovers he's not an Earth man	284	568	852	1818	3109	4400
62-70: 62-Orson Welles-c/story. 65-1st Krypton Foes: Mala, Kizo, & U-Ban. 66-2nd Superbaby story. 67-Perry Como-c/story. 68-1st Luthor-c this title (see Action Comics)	135	270	405	864	1482	2100
71-75: 74-2nd Luthor-c this title. 75-Some have #74 on-c	129	258	387	826	1413	2000
76-Batman x-over; Superman & Batman learn each other's I.D. for the 1st time (5-6/52) (also see World's Finest #71)	423	846	1269	3088	5444	7800
77-81: 78-Last 52 pg. issue; 1st meeting of Lois Lane & Lana Lang. 81-Used in POP, pg. 88.	116	232	348	742	1271	1800
81-"Superwoman From Space" story	103	206	309	659	1130	1600
82-87,89,90: 89-1st Curt Swan-c in title	116	232	348	742	1271	1800
88-Prankster, Toyman & Luthor team-up	97	194	291	621	1061	1500
91-95: 95-Last precode issue (2/55)	90	180	270	576	988	1400
96-99: 96-Mr. Mxyztplk-c/story	284	568	852	1818	3109	4400
100 (9-10/55)-Shows cover to #1 on-c	284	568	852	1818	3109	4400
101-105,107-110: 109-1st S.A. issue	63	126	189	400	850	1300
106 (7/56)-Retells origin	68	136	204	430	915	1400
111-120	56	112	168	350	750	1150
121,122,124-127,129: 127-Origin/1st app. Titano.	49	98	147	308	654	1000
123-Pre-Supergirl tryout-c/story (8/58)	183	366	732	1700	3900	6100
128-(4/59)-Red Kryptonite used. Bruce Wayne x-over who protects Superman's i.d. (3rd story)	51	102	153	320	675	1050
130-(7/59)-2nd app. Krypto, the Superdog with Superman (see Sup.'s Pal Jimmy Olsen #29) (all other previous app. w/Superboy)	58	116	174	370	785	1200
131-139: 135-2nd Lori Lemaris app. 139-Lori Lemaris app.:	42	84	168	252	526	800
140-1st Blue Kryptonite & Bizarro Supergirl; origin Bizarro Jr. #1	43	86	129	258	542	825
141-145,148: 142-2nd Batman x-over	36	72	108	216	446	675
146-(7/61)-Superman's life story; back-up hints at Earth II. Classic-c						

Description	GD 2.0	VG 4.0	FN 6.0	VF 8.0	VF/NM 9.0	NM- 9.2
	58	116	174	348	724	1100
147(8/61)-7th Legion app.; 1st app. Legion of Super-Villains; 1st app. Adult Legion; swipes-c to Adv. #247	47	94	141	282	591	900
149(11/61)-8th Legion app. (cameo); "The Death of Superman" imaginary story; last 10c issue	45	90	135	270	560	850
150,151,153,154,157,159,160: 157-Gold Kryptonite used (see Adv. #299); Mon-El app.; Lightning Lad cameo (11/62)	16	32	48	110	243	375
152,155,156,158,162: 152(4/62)-15th Legion app. 155-(8/62)-Legion app; Lightning Man & Cosmic Man, & Adult Legion app. 156,162-Legion app. 158-1st app. Superman as Nightwing & Jimmy Olsen as Flamebird & Nor-Kann of Kandor (12/62)	16	32	48	108	239	370
161-1st told death of Ma and Pa Kent	17	34	51	117	259	400
161-2nd printing (1987, $1.25)-New DC logo; sold thru So Much Fun Toy Stores (cover title: Superman Classic)	1	2	3	5	6	8
163-166,168-180: 166-XMas-c. 168-All Luthor issue; JFK tribute/memorial. 169-Bizarro Invasion of Earth-c/story; last Jolly Selwyn. 170-Pres. Kennedy story is finally published after delay from #168 due to assassination. 172,173-Legion cameos. 174-Super-Mxyztplk; Bizarro app. 176-Legion of Super-Pets	12	24	36	82	179	275
167-New origin Braniac, text reference of Brainiac 5 descending from adopted human son Braniac II; intro Tharla (later Luthor's wife)	19	38	57	131	291	450
181,182,184-186,188-192,194-196,198,200: 181-1st 2965 story/series. 182-1st S.A. app. of The Toyman (1/66). 189-Origin/destruction of Krypton II.	10	20	30	64	132	200
183 (Giant G-18)	12	24	36	82	179	275
187,193,197 (Giants G-23,G-31,G-36)	10	20	30	65	135	205
199-1st Superman/Flash race (8/67); also see Flash #175 & World's Finest #198,199 (r-in Limited Coll. Ed. C-48)	56	112	168	448	999	1550
201,203-206,208-211,213-216: 213-Brainiac-5 app. 216-Last 12c issue	6	12	18	41	76	110
202 (80-pg. Giant G-42)-All Bizarro issue	8	16	24	55	105	155
207,212,217 (Giants G-48,G-54,G-60): 207-30th anniversary Superman (6/68)	7	14	21	46	86	125
218-221,223-226,228-231	6	12	18	37	66	95
222,229(Giants, G-66,G-84)	7	14	21	44	82	120
227,232(Giants, G-72,G-78): 232-All Krypton issue	7	14	21	44	82	120
233-2nd app. Morgan Edge; Clark Kent switches from newspaper reporter to TV newscaster; all Kryptonite on Earth destroyed; classic Neal Adams-c; 1st Fabulous World of Krypton story; Superman pin-up by Swan	36	72	108	259	580	900
234-238	5	10	15	34	60	85
240-Kaluta-a; last 15c issue	5	10	15	33	57	80
241-244 (All 52 pgs.): 241-New Wonder Woman app. 243-G.A.-r/#38	5	10	15	31	53	75
245-Also listed as DC 100 Pg. Super Spectacular #7; Air Wave, Kid Eternity, Hawkman-r; Atom-r/Atom #3	10	20	30	68	144	220
246-248,250,251,253 (All 52 pgs.): 246-G.A.-r/#40. 248-World of Krypton story. 251-G.A.-r/#45. 253-Finlay-a, 2 pgs., G.A.-r/#1	5	10	15	31	53	75
249,254-Neal Adams-a. 249-(52 pgs.); 1st app. Terra-Man (Swan-a) & origin-s by Dick Dillin (r) & Neal Adams (inks)	4	8	18	40	73	105
252-Also listed as DC 100 Pg. Super Spectacular #13; Ray(r/Smash #17), Black Condor, (r/Crack #18), Hawkman(r/Flash #24); Starman-r/Adv. #67; Dr. Fate & Spectre-r/More Fun #57; N. Adams-c	11	22	33	76	163	250
255-271,273-277,279-283: 263-Photo-c. 264-1st app. Steve Lombard. 276-Intro Capt. Thunder. 279-Batman, Batgirl app. 282-Luthor battlesuit	3	6	9	15	22	28
272,278,284-All 100 pgs. G.A.-r in all. 272-r/2nd app. Mr. Mxyztplk from Action #80	5	10	15	31	53	75
285-299: 289-Partial photo-c. 292-Origin Lex Luthor retold	2	4	6	13	19	24
300-(6/76) Superman in the year 2001	4	8	12	28	47	65
301-316,318-350: 301,320-Solomon Grundy app. 323-Intro. Atomic Skull. 327-329-(44 pgs.). 327-Kobra app. 330-More facts revealed about I.D. 331,332-1st/2nd app. Master Jailer. 335-Mxyzptlk marries Ms. Bgbznz. 336-Rose & Thorn app. 338-(8/79) 40th Anniv. issue; the bottled city of Kandor enlarged. 344-Frankenstein & Dracula app.	2	4	6	8	11	14
317-Classic Neal Adams kryptonite cover	5	10	15	31	53	75
321-323,325-327,329-332,335-345,348,350 (Whitman variants; low print run; no issue # on cover)	2	4	6	11	16	20
351-399: 353-Brief origin. 354,355,357-Superman 2020 stories (354-Debut of Superman III). 356-World of Krypton story (also #360,367,375). 366-Fan letter by Todd McFarlane. 369-Christmas-c. 372-Superman 2021 story. 376-Free 6 pg. preview Daring New Advs. of Supergirl. 377-Terra-Man-c/app.; free 16 pg. preview Masters of the Universe. 378-Origin & 1st app. Colonel Future. 379-Bizarro World app.	2	4	6	8	10	12
400 (10/84, $1.50, 68 pgs.)-Many top artists featured; Chaykin painted cover, Miller back-c; Steranko-s/a (10 pages)	2	4	6	11	16	20
401-422: 405-Super-Batman story. 408-Nuclear Holocaust-c/story. 411-Special Julius Schwartz tribute issue. 414,415-Crisis x-over. 422-Horror-c by Bolland						

	GD 2.0	VG 4.0	FN 6.0	VF 8.0	VF/NM 9.0	NM- 9.2

	GD 2.0	VG 4.0	FN 6.0	VF 8.0	VF/NM 9.0	NM- 9.2
	1	3	4	6	8	10
409-(7/85) Var-c with Superman/Superhombre logo	17	34	51	114	252	390
423-Alan Moore scripts; Curt Swan-a/George Pérez-a(i); "Whatever Happened to the Man of Tomorrow?" story, cont'd in Action #583	3	6	9	14	20	25
Annual 1 (10/60, 84 pgs.)-Reprints 1st Supergirl story/Action #252; r/Lois Lane #1; Krypto-r (1st Silver Age DC annual)	100	200	300	800	1800	2800
Annual 2 (Win, 1960-61)-Super-villain issue; Brainiac, Titano, Metallo, Bizarro origin-r	37	74	111	274	612	950
Annual 3 (Sum, 1961)-Strange Lives of Superman	27	54	81	189	420	650
Annual 4(Win, 1961-62)-11th Legion app.; 1st Legion origins (text & pictures); advs. in time, space & on alien worlds	22	44	66	154	340	525
Annual 5 (Sum, 1962)-All Krypton issue	17	34	51	117	259	400
Annual 6 (Win, 1962-63)-Legion-r/Adv. #247; Superman Family portrait on back-c	16	32	48	107	236	365
Annual 7 (Sum, 1963)-Silver Anniversary Issue; origin-r/Superman-Batman team/Adv. #275; cover gallery of Annuals	12	24	36	82	179	275
Annual 8 (Win, 1963-64)-All origins issue	12	24	36	80	173	265
Annual 9 (8/64)-Was advertised but came out as 80 Page Giant #1 instead						
Annual 9 (1983)-Toth/Austin-a	1	2	4	6	8	10
Annuals 10,12: 10(1984, $1.25)-M. Anderson-i. 12(1986)-Bolland-a	1	2	3	5	6	8
Annual 11 (1985) "For the Man Who Has Everything" story; Alan Moore-s/Dave Gibbons-a; Mongul, and the Black Mercy app.; Wonder Woman, Batman & Robin app. (adapted for a Justice League Unlimited animated episode)	5	10	15	30	50	70
... 1 (Facsimile Edition) (2022, $6.99) Reprints #1 with original 1939 ads						7.00
Special 1-3 ('83-'85): 1-G. Kane-c/a; contains German-r						6.00
The Amazing World of Superman "Official Metropolis Edition" (1973, $2.00, treasury-size)- Origin retold; Wood-r(i) from Superboy #153,161; poster incl. (half price if poster missing)	4	8	12	27	44	60
11195 (2/79, $1.95, 224 pgs.)-Golden Press	4	8	12	23	37	50

NOTE: **N. Adams**-a249; *254p*; c-204-206, 210, 212-215, 219, 233-237, 240-243, 249-252, 254, 263, 307, 308, 313, 314, 317. **Adkins**-a323i. **Austin**-c368i. **Wayne Boring** art-late 1940's to early 1960's. **Buckler** a(p)-352, 363, 364, 369; c(p)-324-327, 356, 363, 368, 369, 373, 376, 378. **Burnley** a-252r; c-19-25, 30, 33, 34, 35p, 38p, 39p, 45p. **Fine** a-252r. **Kaluta**-a-400. **Gil Kane** a-272r, 367, 372, 375, c-374p, 375p, 377, 381, 382, 384-390, 392. Annual 9. Special 2. **Joe Kubert** c-216. **Morrow** a-238. **Mortimer** a-250r. **Perez** c-366r. **Fred Ray** a-25; c-6, 8-18. **Starlin** c-355. **Staton** a-354i, 355i. **Swan/Moldoff** c-149. **Williamson** a(i)-408-410, 412-416; c(i)-408i, 409i. **Wrightson** a-400, 416.

SUPERMAN (2nd Series) (Title continues numbering from Adventures of Superman #649)
DC Comics: Jan, 1987 - No. 226, Apr, 2006; No. 650, May, 2006 - No. 714, Oct, 2011

	GD 2.0	VG 4.0	FN 6.0	VF 8.0	VF/NM 9.0	NM- 9.2
0-(10/94) Zero Hour; released between #93 & #94	1	3	4	6	8	10
1-Byrne-c/a begins; intro new Metallo	2	4	6	11	16	20
2,3,5,6,8,10: 3-Legends x-over; Darkseid-c & app. 8-Legion app.						6.00
4-1st Bloodsport	3	6	9	14	20	25
7-Origin/1st app. Rampage	1	3	4	6	8	10
9-Joker-c	1	2	3	5	6	8
11-15,17-20,22-49,51,52,54-56,58-67: 11-1st new Mr. Mxyzptlk. 12-Lori Lemaris revived. 13-1st app. new Toyman. 13,14-Millennium x-over. 20-Doom Patrol app.; Supergirl cameo. 31-Mr. Mxyzptlk app. 37-Newsboy Legion app. 41-Lobo app. 44-Batman storyline, part 1. 45-Free extra 8 pgs. 54-Newsboy Legion story. 63-Aquaman x-over. 67-Last $1.00-c						5.00
16,21: 16-1st app. new Supergirl (4/88). 21-Supergirl-c/story; 1st app. Matrix who becomes new Supergirl						6.00
50-($1.50, 52 pgs.)-Clark Kent proposes to Lois						6.00
50-2nd printing						4.00
53-Clark reveals i.d. to Lois (Cont'd from Action #662)						5.00
53-2nd printing						4.00
57-($1.75, 52 pgs.)						5.00
68-72: 65,66,68-Deathstroke-c/stories. 70-Superman & Robin team-up						5.00
73-Doomsday cameo	1	3	4	6	8	10
74-Doomsday Pt. 2 (Cont'd from Justice League #69); Superman battles Doomsday	2	4	6	9	12	15
73,74-2nd printings						4.00
75-(1/93, $2.50)-Collector's Ed.; Doomsday Pt. 6; Superman dies; polybagged w/poster of funeral, obituary from Daily Planet, postage stamp & armband premiums (direct sales only)	3	6	9	21	33	45
75-Direct sales copy (no upc code, 1st print)	2	4	6	10	14	18
75-Direct sales copy (no upc code, 2nd-4th prints)						4.00
75-Newsstand copy w/upc code	4	8	12	23	37	50
75-Platinum Edition; given away to retailers	8	16	24	56	108	160
75-Special Edition (2022, $3.99) 30th Anniversary reprint; creators interview						4.00
76,77-Funeral For a Friend parts 4 & 8						6.00
78-($1.95)-Collector's Edition with die-cut outer-c & mini poster; Doomsday cameo						6.00
78-($1.50)-Newsstand Edition w/poster and different-c; Doomsday-c & cameo						6.00
79-81,83-89: 83-Funeral For a Friend epilogue; new Batman (Azrael) cameo. 87,88-Bizarro-c/story						4.00
82-($2.00, 44 pgs.)-Collector's Edition w/all chromium-c; real Superman revealed; Green Lantern x-over from G.L. #46; no ads	1	3	4	6	8	10
82-($2.00, 44 pgs.)-Regular Edition w/different-c						6.00
90-99: 93-(9/94)-Zero Hour. 94-(11/94). 95-Atom app. 96-Brainiac returns	1	2	3	5	6	8
100-Death of Clark Kent foil-c	1	2	3	5	6	8
100-Newsstand						4.00
101-122: 101-Begin $1.95-c; Black Adam app. 105-Green Lantern app. 110-Plastic Man-c/app. 114-Brainiac app; Dwyer-c. 115-Lois leaves Metropolis. 116-(10/96)-1st app. Teen Titans by Jurgens & Perez in 8 pg. preview. 117-Final Night. 118-Wonder Woman app. 119-Legion app. 120-New powers						4.00
123-Collector's Edition w/glow in the dark-c, new costume						
	1	3	4	6	8	10
123-Standard ed., new costume						5.00
124-149: 126-Cyborg-c/app. 131-Birth of Lena Luthor. 132-Superman Red/Superman Blue. 134-Millennium Giants. 136,137-Superman 2999. 139-Starlin-a. 140-Grindberg-a						4.00
150-($2.95) Standard Ed.; Brainiac 2.0 app.; Jurgens-s						5.00
150-($3.95) Collector's Ed.; hi-holo-foil enhanced variant-c						6.00
151-158: 151-Loeb-s begins; Daily Planet reopens						4.00
159-174: 159-$2.25-c begin. 161-JLA app. 162-Aquaman-c/app. 163-Young Justice app. 165-JLA app.; Ramos, Madureira, Liefeld, A. Adams, Wieringo, Churchill-a. 166-Collector's and reg. editions. 167-Return to Krypton. 168-Batman-c/app.(cont'd in Detective #756). 171-173-Our Worlds at War. 173-Sienkiewicz-a (2 pgs.). 174-Adopts black & red "S" logo						4.00

	GD 2.0	VG 4.0	FN 6.0	VF 8.0	VF/NM 9.0	NM- 9.2
175-($3.50) Joker: Last Laugh x-over; Doomsday-c/app.						5.00
176-189,191-199: 176,180-Churchill-a. 180-Dracula app. 181-Bizarro-c/app. 184-Return to Krypton II. 189-Van Fleet-c. 192,193,195,197-199-New Supergirl app.						3.00
190-($2.25) Regular edition						3.00
190-($3.50) Double-Feature Issue; included reprint of Superman: The 10¢ Adventure						4.00
200-($3.50) Gene Ha-c/art by various; preview art by Yu & Bermejo						4.00
201-Mr Majestic-c/app.; cover swipe of Action #1						3.00
202,203-Godfall parts 3,6; Turner-c; Caldwell-a/c. 203-Jim Lee sketch pages						3.00
204-Jim Lee-c/a begins; Azzarello-s	3	6	9	14	19	24
204-Diamond Retailer Summit edition with sketch-c	6	12	18	41	76	110
205-214: 205-Two covers by Jim Lee and Michael Turner. 208-JLA app. 211-Battles Wonder Woman						3.00
215-($2.99) Conclusion to Azzarello/Lee arc						4.00
216-218,220-226: 216-Captain Marvel app. 221-Bizarro & Zoom app. 226-Earth-2 Superman story; Chaykin,Sale, Benes, Ordway-a						3.00
219-Omac/Sacrifice pt. 1; JLA app.						4.00
219-2nd printing with red background variant-c						3.00

(Title continues numbering from Adventures of Superman #649)

	GD 2.0	VG 4.0	FN 6.0	VF 8.0	VF/NM 9.0	NM- 9.2
650-(5/06) One Year Later; Clark powerless after Infinite Crisis						4.00
651-665,667-669,671-674,676-680: 652-Begin $2.99-c. 654-658,662-664,667-Pacheco-a. 665-Origin of Jimmy Olsen. 671-673-Insect Queen. 676-680-Ross-c						3.00
666, 670,675-($3.99) 666-Simonson-a. 670-The Third Kryptonian. 675-Ross-c						4.00
681-699: 681-683-New Krypton x-over; Ross-c. 685-Mon-El freed from Phantom Zone. 694-Mon-El new costume. 698,699-Last Stand of New Krypton x-over						3.00
700-(6/10, $4.99) Cover by Gary Frank; Robinson-s; Straczynski-s begin						5.00
700-Variant-c by Risso						8.00
701-714: 701-"Grounded" begins; Straczynski-s/Cassaday-c. 704,706-Wilson-s						3.00
701-DC 75th Variant-c by Cassaday (Superman #1 swipe)						8.00
#1,000,000 (11/98) 853rd Century x-over; Gene Ha-c						4.00
Annual 1,2: 1 (1987)-No Byrne-a. 2 (1988)-Byrne-a; Newsboy Legion; Guardian returns						4.00
Annual 3-6 ('91-'94 68 pgs.): 1-Armageddon 2001 x-over; Batman app.; Austin-c(i) & part inks. 4-Eclipso app. 6-Elseworlds sty						5.00
Annual 2-2nd & 3rd printings; 3rd has silver ink						5.00
Annual 7 (1995, $3.95, 69 pgs.)-Year One story						5.00
Annual 8 (1996, $2.95)-Legends of the Dead Earth story						5.00
Annual 9 (1997, $3.95)-Pulp Heroes story						5.00
Annual 10 (1998, $2.95)-Ghosts; Wrightson-c						4.00
Annual 11 (1999, $2.95)-JLApe; Art Adams-c						5.00
Annual 12 (2000, $3.50)-Planet DC						5.00
Annual 13 (1/08, $3.99) Finale of Camelot Falls						4.00
Annual 14 (10/09, $3.99) Origin of Mon-El re-told; Pina-a/Guedes-a						4.00
...: 80 Page Giant (2/99, $4.95) Jurgens-c						6.00
...: 80 Page Giant 1 (5/10, $5.99) Lopresti-c; short stories by various						6.00
...: 80 Page Giant 2 (6/99, $4.95) Harris-c						6.00
...: 80 Page Giant 3 (8/99, $5.95) Nowlan-c; art by various						6.00
...: 80 Page Giant 2011 (4/11, $5.99) Nguyen-c; art by various; Bizarros app.						6.00
Special 1 (1992, $3.50, 68 pgs.)-Simonson-c/a						5.00

SUPERMAN (DC New 52)
DC Comics: Nov, 2011 - No. 52, Jul, 2016 ($2.99/$3.99)

	GD 2.0	VG 4.0	FN 6.0	VF 8.0	VF/NM 9.0	NM- 9.2
1-Pérez-s/c; Merino-a	2	4	6	11	16	20
1-Variant-c by Jim Lee	2	4	6	11	16	20
2-23: 3-6-Nicola Scott-a. 6-Supergirl app. 13-Clark quits job. 14-17-H'El on Earth x-over with Superboy & Supergirl. 17-H'El on Earth conclusion. 19,20-Orion app.						3.00
23.1, 23.2, 23.3, 23.4 (11/13, $2.99, regular covers)						3.00
23.1 (11/13, $3.99, 3-D cover) "Bizarro #1" on cover; Fisch-s/Kuder-a/Jeff Johnson-a						5.00
23.2 (11/13, $3.99, 3-D cover) "Brainiac #1" on cover; origin; Bedard-s/Alixe-a						5.00
23.3 (11/13, $3.99, 3-D cover) "H'El #1" on cover; Jor-El app.; Lobdell-s/Jurgens-a						5.00
23.4 (11/13, $3.99, 3-D cover) "Parasite #1" on cover; origin; Kuder-a						5.00
24-31: 25-Krypton Returns pt. 4. 26,27-Parasite app. 28,29-Starfire app.						3.00
32-($3.99) Romita Jr.-a/Johns-s begin; intro. Ulysses; wraparound-c by Romita Jr.						4.00
33-49: 33-39-Romita Jr.-a/Johns-s. 41-Yang-s begin. 45-48-Porter-a. 49-Vandal Savage						4.00
50-($4.99) Conclusion vs. Vandal Savage; Romita Jr. -c						4.00
51,52-Final Days of Superman x-over. 52-Superman dies; pre-Flashpoint Superman app.						4.00
#0-(11/12, $2.99) Jor-El & Lara flashback on Krypton; Rocafort-a/c						3.00
Annual 1 (10/12, $4.99) Alixe-a/Rocafort-c; Helspont app.						5.00
Annual 2 (9/13, $4.99) Jurgens-a/Andy Kubert-c; Brainiac app.						5.00
Annual 3 (2/16, $4.99) Origin/history of Vandal Savage; art by Sienkiewicz & others						5.00
... By Geoff Johns and John Romita Jr. Director's Cut 1 (11/14, $4.99) r/#32 B&W pencil art and full script						5.00
...: Futures End 1 (11/14, $2.99, regular-c) Five years later; Jurgens-s/Weeks-a						3.00
...: Futures End 1 (11/14, $3.99, 3-D cover)						4.00

SUPERMAN (DC Rebirth)
DC Comics: Aug, 2016 - No. 45, Jun, 2018 ($2.99)

	GD 2.0	VG 4.0	FN 6.0	VF 8.0	VF/NM 9.0	NM- 9.2
1-24-Tomasi & Gleason-s. 2-The Eradicator returns. 8,9-Dinosaur Island. 10,11-Batman & Robin (Damian) app. 14-16-Multiplicity; alternate Earth Supermans & Capt. Carrot app. 18,19-Superman Reborn. 23,24-Manchester Black app.						3.00
25-($3.99) Manchester Black & Batman app.; Mahnke & Gleason-a						4.00
26-45: 29,30-Parallax & Sinestro app. 31,32-Deathstroke app. 38-Teen Titans app.						3.00
Annual 1 (1/17, $4.99) Swamp Thing app.; Tomasi & Gleason-s/Jimenez-a						5.00
...: Rebirth (8/16, $2.99) Pre-Flashpoint Superman and Lana Lang app.; Tomasi/Mahnke-a						5.00
... Special 1 (7/18, $4.99) Dinosaur Island; Capt. Storm app.; bonus short stories						5.00

SUPERMAN
DC Comics: Sept, 2018 - No. 32, Aug, 2021 ($3.99/$4.99)

	GD 2.0	VG 4.0	FN 6.0	VF 8.0	VF/NM 9.0	NM- 9.2
1-17: 1-Bendis-s/Reis-a; Martian Manhunter app. 2-6,12-Rogol Zaar app. 7-Lobo app. 8-10-Crime Syndicate app. 14,15-Legion of Super-Heroes app.						4.00
13-($4.99) Variant "Year of the Villain" Lois Lane-c by Adam Hughes						5.00
18-24,26-28: 18-Superman reveals his Clark Kent ID to the world. 19-22-Mongul app. 22-24-Maguire-a. 23,24-Dr. Fate app.						4.00
25-($5.99) Intro. Synmar						4.00
29-32-($4.99) Tales of Metropolis back-up stories is all. 30-32-Godlewski-a						5.00

SUPERMAN (Dawn of DC)
DC Comics: Apr, 2023 - Present ($4.99)

	GD 2.0	VG 4.0	FN 6.0	VF 8.0	VF/NM 9.0	NM- 9.2
1-6,8-11: 1-Williamson-s/Campbell-a; LexCorp becomes SuperCorp; Livewire app. 2,3-Parasite app. 4,5-Silver Banshee app. 10-Terra-Man app.						5.00

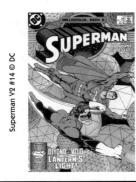

Superman V2 #14 © DC

Superman (2011 series) #20 © DC

Superman (2023 series) #1 © DC

	GD 2.0	VG 4.0	FN 6.0	VF 8.0	VF/NM 9.0	NM- 9.2

7-($5.99) Legacy issue #850; Melnikov & Jurgens-a; Brainiac returns   6.00
2023 Annual (10/23, $5.99) Takes place between #5 & #6; Lobo app.   6.00

SUPERMAN (Hardcovers and Trade Paperbacks)
... and the Legion of Super-Heroes HC (2008, $24.99) r/Action Comics #858-863, covers
   and variants; intro. by Giffen; Gary Frank design sketch pages   25.00
... and the Legion of Super-Heroes SC (2009, $14.99) same contents as HC   15.00
...: Back in Action TPB (2007, $14.99) r/Action Comics #841-843 and DC Comics Presents
   #4,17,24; commentary by Busiek   15.00
.../Batman: Saga of the Super Sons TPB (2007, $19.99) r/Super Sons stories from '70s World's
   Finest #215,216,221,222,224,228,230,231,233,242,263 & Elseworlds 80-Page Giant   20.00
...: Brainiac HC (2009, $19.99, dustjacket) r/Action Comics #866-870 & Superman: New
   Krypton Special #1   20.00
...: Brainiac SC (2010, $12.99) r/Action #866-870 & Superman: New Krypton Spec. #1   13.00
...: Camelot Falls HC (2007, $19.99, dustjacket) r/Superman #654-658   20.00
...: Camelot Falls SC (2008, $12.99) r/Superman #654-658   13.00
...: Camelot Falls Vol. 2 HC (2008, $19.99, dj) r/Superman #662-664,667 & Ann. #13   20.00
...: Camelot Falls Vol. 2 The Weight of the World SC (2008, $12.99) r/Superman #662-664,667
   & Ann. #13   13.00
...: Chronicles Vol. 1 ('06, $14.99, TPB) r/early Superman app. in Action Comics #1-13, New
   York World's Fair 1939 and Superman #1
...: Chronicles Vol. 2 ('07, $14.99, TPB) r/early Superman app. in Action Comics #14-20 and
   Superman #2,3   15.00
...: Chronicles Vol. 3 ('07, $14.99, TPB) r/early Superman app. in Action Comics #21-25,
   Superman #3,4 and New York World's Fair 1940   15.00
...: Chronicles Vol. 4 ('08, $14.99, TPB) r/early Superman app. in Action Comics #26-31,
   Superman #6,7   15.00
...: Chronicles Vol. 5 ('08, $14.99, TPB) r/early Superman app. in Action Comics #32-36,
   Superman #8,9 and World's Best Comics #1   15.00
...: Chronicles Vol. 6 ('09, $14.99, TPB) r/early Superman app. in Action Comics #37-40,
   Superman #10,11 and World's Finest Comics #2,3   15.00
...: Chronicles Vol. 7 ('09, $14.99, TPB) r/early Superman app. in Action Comics #41-43,
   Superman #12,13 and World's Finest Comics #4   15.00
...: Chronicles Vol. 8 ('10, $14.99, TPB) r/early Superman app. in Action Comics #44-47,
   and Superman #14,15   15.00
...: Chronicles Vol. 9 ('11, $17.99, TPB) r/early Superman app. in Action Comics #48-52,
   and Superman #16,17 and World's Finest Comics #6   18.00
...: Codename: Patriot HC ('10, $24.99, d.j.) r/partial New Krypton storyline   25.00
...: Codename: Patriot SC ('11, $14.99) r/partial New Krypton storyline   15.00
...: Critical Condition ('03, $14.95, TPB) r/2000 Kryptonite poisoning storyline   15.00
.../ Doomsday: The Collection (2006, $19.99) r/Superman/Doomsday: Hunter/Prey #1-3,
   Doomsday Ann. #1, Superman: The Doomsday Wars #1-3, Advs. of Superman #594
   and Superman #175; intro. by Dan Jurgens   20.00
...: Daily Planet (2006, $19.99, TPB)-Reprints stories of Daily Planet staff   20.00
...: Earth One HC (2010, $19.99)-Updated re-imagining of Superman's debut in Metropolis;
   Straczynski-s/Shane Davis-a; sketch pages by Davis   20.00
...: Earth One Volume Two HC (2012, $22.99)-Straczynski/Davis-a; sketch pages   23.00
...: Earth One Volume Three HC (2015, $22.99)-Straczynski-s/Syaf-a; sketch pages   23.00
...: Emperor Joker TPB (2007, $14.99) reprints 2000 x-over from Superman titles   15.00
...: Endgame (2000, $14.95, TPB)-Reprints Y2K and Brainiac story line   15.00
...: Ending Battle (2009, $14.99, TPB) r/crossover from Superman titles from 2002   15.00
...: Eradication! The Origin of the Eradicator (1996, $12.95, TPB)   15.00
...: Escape From Bizarro World HC (2008, $24.99, dustjacket) r/Action #855-857; early apps.
   in Superman #140, DC Comics Presents #71 and Man of Steel #5; Vaughan intro.   25.00
...: Escape From Bizarro World SC (2009, $14.99) same contents as hardcover   15.00
...: Exile (1998, $14.95, TPB)-Reprints space exile following execution of Kryptonian criminals;
   1st Eradicator   15.00
...: For Tomorrow Volume 1 HC (2005, $24.99, dustjacket) r/#204-209; intro by Azzarello;
   new cover and sketch section by Lee   25.00
...: For Tomorrow Volume 1 SC (2005, $14.99) r/#204-209; foil-stamped S emblem-c   15.00
...: For Tomorrow Volume 2 HC (2005, $24.99, dustjacket) r/#210-215; afterword and sketch
   section by Lee; new Lee-c with foil-stamped S emblem   25.00
...: For Tomorrow Volume 2 SC (2005, $14.99) r/#210-215; foil-stamped S emblem-c   15.00
...: Godfall HC (2004, $19.95, dustjacket) r/Action #812-813, & Advs. of Superman #625-626,
   Superman #202-203; Caldwell sketch pages; Turner cover gallery; new Turner-c   20.00
...: Godfall SC (2004, $9.99) r/Action #812-813, Advs. of Superman #625-626,
   Superman #202-203; Caldwell sketch pages; Turner cover gallery; new Turner-c   10.00
...: Infinite Crisis TPB (2006, $12.99) r/Infinite Crisis #5, I.C. Secret Files and Origins 2006,
   Action Comics #836, Superman #226 and Advs. of Superman #649   13.00
...: In the Forties ('05, $19.99, TPB) Intro. by Bob Hughes   20.00
...: In the Fifties ('02, $19.99, TPB) Intro. by Mark Waid   20.00
...: In the Sixties ('01, $19.95, TPB) Intro. by Mark Waid   20.00
...: In the Seventies ('00, $19.99, TPB) Intro. by Christopher Reeve   20.00
...: In the Eighties ('06, $19.99, TPB) Intro. by Jerry Ordway   20.00
...: In the Name of Gog ('05, $17.99, TPB) r/Action Comics #820-825   18.00
...: Kryptonite HC ('08, $24.99) r/Superman Confidential #1-5,11; Darwyn Cooke intro. 25.00

...: Last Son HC (2008, $19.99) r/Action Comics #844-846,851 and Annual #11; sketch pages
   and variant covers; Marc McClure intro.   20.00
...: Mon-El HC ('10, $24.99) r/Superman #684-690, Action #874 & Annual #1, Superman: Secret
   Files 2009 #1   25.00
...: Mon-El SC ('11, $17.99) r/Superman #684-690, Action #874 & Annual #1, Superman: Secret
   Files 2009 #1   18.00
...: Mon-El - Man of Valor HC ('10, $24.99) r/Superman #692-697 & Annual #14, Adventure #11,
   Superman: Secret Files 2009 #1   25.00
...: New Krypton Vol. 1 HC ('09, $24.99, d.j.) r/Superman #681, Action #871 & one-shots 25.00
...: New Krypton Vol. 1 SC ('10, $17.99) r/Superman #681, Action #871 & one-shots   18.00
...: New Krypton Vol. 2 HC ('09, $24.99, d.j.) r/Superman #682,683, Action #872,873 &
   Supergirl #35,36; gallery of covers and variants   25.00
...: New Krypton Vol. 2 SC ('10, $17.99) same contents as HC   18.00
...: New Krypton Vol. 3 HC ('10, $24.99, d.j.) r/Superman: World of New Krypton #1-5 &
   Action Comics Annual #10; gallery of covers and variants   25.00
...: New Krypton Vol. 3 SC ('11, $17.99) same contents as HC   18.00
...: New Krypton Vol. 4 HC ('10, $24.99, d.j.) r/Superman: World of New Krypton #6-12;
   gallery of covers and variants; sketch and design art   25.00
...: New Krypton Vol. 4 SC ('11, $17.99) same contents as HC   18.00
...: Nightwing and Flamebird HC ('10, $24.99, d.j.) r/Action #875-879 & Annual #12   25.00
...: Nightwing and Flamebird SC ('11, $17.99) r/Action #875-879 & Annual #12   18.00
...: Nightwing and Flamebird 2 HC ('10, $24.99, d.j.) r/Action #883-889, Superman #696
   & Adventure Comics #8-10   25.00
...: No Limits ('00, $14.95, TPB) Reprints early 2000 stories   15.00
...: Our Worlds at War Book 1 ('02, $19.95, TPB) r/1st half of x-over   20.00
...: Our Worlds at War Book 2 ('02, $19.95, TPB) r/2nd half of x-over   20.00
...: Our Worlds at War - The Complete Collection ('06, $24.99, TPB) r/entire x-over   25.00
...: Past and Future (2008, $19.99, TPB) r/time travel stories 1947-1983   20.00
...: President Lex TPB (2003, $17.95) r/Luthor's run for the White House; Harris-c   18.00
...: Redemption TPB (2007, $12.99) r/Superman #659,666 & Action Comics #848,849   13.00
...: Return to Krypton (2004, $17.95, TPB) r/2001-2002 x-over   18.00
...: Sacrifice (2005, $14.99, TPB) prelude x-over to Infinite Crisis; r/Superman #218-220,
   Advs. of Superman #642,643; Action #829, Wonder Woman #219,220   15.00
...: Shadows Linger (2008, $14.99, TPB) r/Superman #671-675   15.00
...: Strange Attractors (2008, $14.99, TPB) r/Action Comics #827,828,830-835   15.00
...: Tales From the Phantom Zone ('09, $19.99, TPB) r/Phantom Zone stories 1961-68   20.00
...: That Healing Touch TPB (2005, $14.99) r/Advs. of Superman #633-638 & Superman
   Secret Files 2004   15.00
...: The Adventures of Nightwing and Flamebird TPB (2009, $19.99)-reprints appearances
   in Superman Family #173,183-194   20.00
...: The Black Ring Volume One HC (2011, $19.99, d.j.) r/Action Comics #890-895   20.00
...: The Bottle City of Kandor TPB (2007, $14.99)-Reprints 1st app. in Action #242 and other
   stories; Nightwing and Flamebird app.   15.00
...: The Coming of Atlas HC (2009, $19.99, dustjacket)-r/Superman #677-680 & Atlas' debut in
   First Issue Special #1 (1975); intro by James Robinson 20.00
...: The Coming of Atlas SC (2010, $14.99) same contents as HC   15.00
The Death of Clark Kent (1997, $19.95, TPB)-Reprints Man of Steel #43 (1 page),
   Superman #99 (1 page),#100-102, Action #709 (1 page), #710,711, Advs. of Superman
   #523-525, Superman:The Man of Tomorrow #1   20.00
The Death of Superman (1993, $4.95, TPB)-Reprints Man of Steel #17-19, Superman #73-75,
   Advs. of Superman #496,497, Action #683,684, & Justice League #69

		2	4	6	9	12	15
The Death of Superman, 2nd & 3rd printings		1	3	4	6	8	10
The Death of Superman Platinum Edition		3	6	9	14	20	25

...: The Greatest Stories Ever Told ('04, $19.95, TPB) Ross-c, Uslan intro.   20.00
...: The Greatest Stories Ever Told 2 ('06, $19.99, TPB) Ross-c, Greenberger intro. 20.00
...: The Journey ('06, $14.99, TPB) r/Action Comics #831 & Superman #217,221-225   15.00
...: The Man of Steel Vol. 2 ('03, $19.95, TPB) r/Superman #1-3, Action #584-586, Advs. of
   Superman #424-426 & Who's Who Update '87   20.00
...: The Man of Steel Vol. 3 ('04, $19.95, TPB) r/Superman #4-6, Action #587-589, Advs. of
   Superman #427-429; intro. by Ordway; new Ordway-c   20.00
...: The Man of Steel Vol. 4 ('05, $19.99, TPB) r/Superman #7,8; Action #590,591; Advs. of
   Superman #430,431; Legion of Super-Heroes #37,38; new Ordway-c   20.00
...: The Man of Steel Vol. 5 ('06, $19.99, TPB) r/Superman #9-11, Action #592-593, Advs. of
   Superman #432-435; intro. by Mike Carlin; new Ordway-c   20.00
...: The Man of Steel Vol. 6 ('08, $19.99, TPB) r/Superman #12 & Ann. #1, Action #594-595 &
   Ann. #1, Advs. of Superman Ann.#1; Booster Gold #23; new Ordway-c   20.00
The Third Kryptonian ('08, $14.99, TPB) r/Action #847, Superman #668-670 & Ann. #13 15.00
The Trial of Superman ('97, $14.95, TPB) reprints story arc   15.00
The World of Krypton ('08, $14.99, TPB) r/World of Krypton Vol 2 #1-4 and various tales
   of Krypton and its history; Kupperberg intro.   15.00
The Wrath of Gog ('05, $14.99, TPB) reprints Action Comics #812-819   15.00
...: They Saved Luthor's Brain ('00, $14.95) r/ "death" and return of Luthor   15.00
...: 3-2-1 Action! ('08, $14.99) Jimmy Olsen super-powered stories; Steve Rude-c   15.00
...: 'Til Death Do Us Part ('01, $17.95) reprints; Mahnke-c   18.00

	GD	VG	FN	VF	VF/NM	NM-			GD	VG	FN	VF	VF/NM	NM-
	2.0	4.0	6.0	8.0	9.0	9.2			2.0	4.0	6.0	8.0	9.0	9.2

...: Time and Time Again (1994, $7.50, TPB)-Reprints — 10.00
...: Transformed ('98, $12.95, TPB) r/post Final Night powerless Superman to Electric Superman — 13.00
...: Unconventional Warfare (2005, $14.95, TPB) r/Adventures of Superman #625-632 and pages from Superman Secret Files 2004 — 15.00
... Up, Up and Away! (2006, $14.99, TPB) r/Superman #650-653 and Action #837-840 — 15.00
... Vs. Brainiac (2008, $19.99, TPB) reprints 1st meeting in Action #242 and other duels — 20.00
... Vs. Lex Luthor (2006, $19.99, TPB) reprints 1st meeting in Action #23 and 11 other classic duels 1940-2001 — 20.00
... Vs. The Flash (2005, $19.99, TPB) reprints their races from Superman #199, Flash #175, World's Finest #198, DC Comics Presents #1&2, Advs. of Superman #463 & DC First: Flash/Superman; new Alex Ross-c — 20.00
... Vs. The Revenge Squad (1999, $12.95, TPB) — 13.00
...: Whatever Happened to the Man of Tomorrow? TPB (1/97, $5.99) r/Superman #423 & Action Comics #583, intro. by Paul Kupperberg — 8.00
...: Whatever Happened to the Man of Tomorrow? Deluxe Edition HC (2009, $24.99, d.j.) r/Superman #423, Action #583, DC Comics Presents #85, Superman Ann #11 — 25.00
...: Whatever Happened to the Man of Tomorrow? SC (2010, $14.99) r/same as HC — 15.00
NOTE: Austin a(i)-1-3. Byrne a-1-16p, 17, 19-21p, 22; c-1-17, 20-22. Guice a-64. Kirby c-37p. Joe Quesada a-Annual 4. Russell c/a-23i. Simonson c-69i. #19-21 2nd printings sold in multi-packs.

SUPERMAN (one-shots)
Daily News Magazine Presents DC Comics' Superman nn-(1987, 8 pgs.)-Supplement to New York Daily News; Perez-c/a — 5.00
...: A Nation Divided (1999, $4.95)-Elseworlds Civil War story — 5.00
... & Robin Special (2022, $5.99) Jon Kent & Damian Wayne; Bogdanovic-a — 6.00
... & Savage Dragon: Chicago (2002, $5.95) Larsen-a; Bogdanove-a — 5.00
... & Savage Dragon: Metropolis (11/99, $4.95) Bogdanove-a — 5.00
...: At Earth's End (1995, $4.95)-Elseworlds story — 6.00
...Beyond #0 (10/11, $3.99) The Batman Beyond future; Frenz-a/Nguyen-c — 4.00
...: Blood of My Ancestors (2003, $6.95)-Gil Kane & John Buscema-a — 7.00
... Distant Fires (1998, $5.95)-Elseworlds; Chaykin-s — 4.00
...: Emperor Joker (10/00, $3.50)-Follows Action #769 — 6.00
...: Endless Winter Special 1 (2/21, $3.99) Part 3 of crossover event; Hester-a — 5.00
... End of the Century (2/00, $24.95, HC)-Immonen-s/a — 25.00
... End of the Century (2003, $17.95, SC)-Immonen-s/a — 18.00
... For Earth (1991, $4.95, 52 pgs, printed on recycled paper)-Ordway wraparound-c — 6.00
...IV Movie Special (1987, $2.00)-Movie adaptation; Heck-a — 4.00
...Gallery, The 1 (1993, $2.95)-Poster-a — 3.00
...: Heroes (4/20, $5.99) Aftermath of revealing Clark Kent ID to world; art by various — 6.00
..., Inc. (1999, $6.95)-Elseworlds Clark as a sports hero; Garcia-Lopez-a — 7.00
...: Infinite City HC (2005, $24.99, dustjacket) Mike Kennedy-s/Carlos Meglia-a — 25.00
...: Infinite City SC (2006, $17.99) Mike Kennedy-s/Carlos Meglia-a — 18.00
...: Kal (1995, $5.95)-Elseworlds story — 5.00
...Kal-El Returns Special 1 (1/23, $5.99) Short stories from after Superman's return from Warworld; s/a by Waid, Grace, Wolfman, Segura, Henry, Haspiel, Herbert & others — 6.00
...: Leviathan Rising Special 1 (7/19, $9.99) Leads into Event Leviathan series — 10.00
...: Lex 2000 (1/01, $3.50) Election night for the Luthor Presidency — 4.00
...: Lois Lane 1 (4/14, $4.99) Marguerite Bennett-s; Rocafort-c — 5.00
...: Monster (1999, $5.95)-Elseworlds story; Anthony Williams-a — 6.00
...: Movie Special-(9/83)-Adaptation of Superman III; other versions exist with store logos on bottom 1/3 of-c — 4.00
...: New Krypton Special 1 (12/08, $3.99) Funeral of Pa Kent; newly enlarged Kandor — 4.00
... Our Worlds at War Secret Files 1-(8/01, $5.95)-Stories & profile pages — 6.00
... Plus 1(2/97, $2.95)-Legion of Super-Heroes-c/app. — 4.00
...'s Metropolis-(1996, $5.95, prestige format)-Elseworlds; McKeever-c/s — 6.00
...: Speeding Bullets-(1993, $4.95, 52 pgs.)-Elseworlds — 6.00
.../Spider-Man-(1995, $3.95)-r/DC and Marvel Presents... — 6.00
...: 10-Cent Adventure 1 (3/02, 10c) McDaniel-a; intro. Cir-El Supergirl — 3.00
...: The Earth Stealers 1-(1988, $2.95, 52 pgs, prestige format) Byrne script; painted-c — 4.00
...: The Earth Stealers 1-2nd printing — 3.00
...: The Legacy of Superman #1 (3/93, $2.50, 68 pgs.)-Art Adams-c; Simonson-a — 5.00
...: The Last God of Krypton ('99,$4.95) Hildebrandt Bros.-a/Simonson-s — 5.00
...: The Last Son of Krypton FCBD Special Edition (7/13) r/Action #844; Jim Lee-c — 3.00
...: The Odyssey ('99, $4.95) Clark Kent's post-Smallville journey — 4.00
...: 3-D (12/98, $3.95)-with glasses — 4.00
...Thundercats (1/04, $5.95) Winick-s/Garza-a; two covers by Garza & McGuinness — 5.00
.../Through the Ages (2006, $3.99) r/Action #1, Superman ('87) #7; origins and pin-ups — 4.00
.../Top Cat Special 1 (12/18, $4.99) Amazo app.; Shane Davis-a; Secret Squirrel back-up — 5.00
...Toyman-(1996, $1.95) — 3.00
...: True Brit (2004, $24.95, HC w/dust jacket) Elseworlds; Kal-El's rocket lands in England; co-written by John Cleese and Kim Howard Johnson; John Byrne-a — 25.00
...: True Brit (2005, $17.99, TPB) Elseworlds; Kal-El's rocket lands in England — 18.00
...: Under A Yellow Sun (1994, $5.95, 68 pgs.)-A Novel by Clark Kent; embossed-c — 6.00
...: Vs. Darkseid: Apokolips Now! 1 (3/03, $2.95) McKone-a; Kara (Supergirl #75) app. — 4.00
...: Villains 1 (5/20, $5.99) Aftermath of revealing Clark Kent ID to world; art by various — 6.00
... War of the Worlds (1999, $5.95)-Battles Martians — 6.00
...Warworld Apocalypse 1 (10/22, $6.99) Conclusion of Warworld Saga — 7.00
...: Where is thy Sting? (2001, $6.95)-McCormack-Sharp-c/a — 7.00
...: Y2K (2/00, $4.95)-1st Brainiac 13 app.; Guice-c/a — 5.00

SUPERMAN ADVENTURES, THE (Based on animated series)
DC Comics: Oct, 1996 - No. 66, Apr, 2002 ($1.75/$1.95/$1.99)

1-Rick Burchett-c/a begins; Paul Dini script; Lex Luthor app.; 1st app. Mercy Graves in comics; silver ink, wraparound-c — 5.00
2-20,22: 2-McCloud scripts begin; Metallo/c/app. 3-Brainiac-c/app. 5-1st app. Livewire in comics. 6-Mxyzptlk-c/app. — 4.00
21-($3.95) 1st animated Supergirl — 5.00
23-66: 23-Begin $1.99-c; Livewire app. 25-Batgirl-c/app. 28-Manley-a. 54-Retells Superman #233 "Kryptonite Nevermore" 58-Ross-c — 4.00
Annual 1 (1997, $3.95)-Zatanna and Bruce Wayne app. — 5.00
Special 1 (2/98, $2.95) Superman vs. Lobo — 5.00
TPB (1998, $7.95) r/#1-6 — 8.00
... Vol 1: Up, Up and Away (2004, $6.95, digest) r/#16,19,22-24; Amancio-a — 7.00
... Vol 2: The Never-Ending Battle (2004, $6.95) r/#25-29 — 7.00
... Vol 3: Last Son of Krypton (2006, $6.99) r/#30-34 — 7.00
... Vol 4: The Man of Steel (2006, $6.99) r/#35-39 — 7.00

SUPERMAN ALIENS 2: GOD WAR (Also see Superman Vs. Aliens)

DC Comics/Dark Horse Comics: May, 2002 - No. 4, Nov, 2002 ($2.99, limited series)

1-4-Bogdanove & Nowlan-a; Darkseid & New Gods app. — 3.00
TPB (6/03, $12.95) r/#1-4 — 13.00

SUPERMAN: AMERICAN ALIEN
DC Comics: Jan, 2016 - No. 7, Jul, 2016 ($3.99, limited series)

1-7-Flashbacks to Clark Kent's upbringing; Max Landis-s in all. 1-Dragotta-a. 4-Jae Lee-a; Batman app. 7-Lobo app.; Jock-a — 4.00

SUPERMAN & BATMAN: GENERATIONS (Elseworlds)
DC Comics: 1999 - No. 4, 1999 ($4.95, limited series)

1-4-Superman & Batman team-up from 1939 to the future; Byrne-c/s/a — 5.00
TPB (2000, $14.95) r/series — 15.00

SUPERMAN & BATMAN: GENERATIONS II (Elseworlds)
DC Comics: 2001 - No. 4, 2001 ($5.95, limited series)

1-4-Superman, Batman & others team-up from 1942-future; Byrne-c/s/a — 6.00
TPB (2003, $19.95) r/series — 20.00

SUPERMAN & BATMAN: GENERATIONS III (Elseworlds)
DC Comics: Mar, 2003 - No. 12, Feb, 2004 ($2.95, limited series)

1-12-Superman & Batman through the centuries; Byrne-c/s/a — 3.00

SUPERMAN AND BATMAN VS. ALIENS AND PREDATOR
DC Comics: 2007 - No. 2, 2007 ($5.99, squarebound, limited series)

	GD	VG	FN	VF	VF/NM	NM-
1,2-Schultz-s/Olivetti-a	1	3	4	6	8	10

TPB (2007, $12.99) r/#1,2; pencil breakdown pages — 13.00

SUPERMAN AND BATMAN VS. VAMPIRES AND WEREWOLVES
DC Comics: Early Dec, 2008 - No. 6, Late Feb, 2009 ($2.99, limited series)

1-6-Van Hook-s/Mandrake-a/c. 1-Wonder Woman app. 5-Demon-c/app. — 3.00
TPB (2009, $14.99) r/#1-6; intro. by John Landis — 15.00

SUPERMAN & BATMAN: WORLD'S FUNNEST (Elseworlds)
DC Comics: 2000 ($6.95, square-bound, one-shot)

nn-Mr. Mxyzptlk and Bat-Mite destroy each DC Universe; Dorkin-s; art by various incl. Ross, Timm, Miller, Allred, Moldoff, Gibbons, Cho, Jimenez — 7.00

SUPERMAN & BUGS BUNNY
DC Comics: Jul, 2000 - No. 4, Oct, 2000 ($2.50, limited series)

1-4-JLA & Looney Tunes characters meet — 5.00

SUPERMAN/BATMAN
DC Comics: Oct, 2003 - No. 87, Oct, 2011 ($2.95/$2.99)

	GD	VG	FN	VF	VF/NM	NM-
1-Two covers (Superman or Batman in foreground) Loeb-s/McGuinness-a; Metallo app.						
	1	2	3	6	8	10

1-2nd printing (Batman cover) — 3.00
1-3rd printing; new McGuinness cover — 3.00

	GD	VG	FN	VF	VF/NM	NM-
1-Diamond/Alliance Retailer Summit Edition-variant	7	14	21	46	86	125

1-(6/06, Free Comic Book Day giveaway) reprints #1 — 3.00
2-6: 2,5-Future Superman app. 6-Luthor in battlesuit — 3.00
7-Pat Lee-c/a; Superboy & Robin app. — 3.00
8-Michael Turner-c/a; intro. new Kara Zor-El — 5.00
8-Second printing with sketch cover — 3.00
8-Third printing with new Turner cover — 3.00
9-13-Michael Turner-c/a; Wonder Woman app. 10,13-Variant-c by Jim Lee — 4.00
14-25: 14-18-Pacheco-a; Lightning Lord, Saturn Queen & Cosmic King app. 19-Supergirl app.; leads into Supergirl #1. 21-25-Bizarro app. 25-Superman & Batman covers; 2nd printing with white bkgrd cover — 3.00
26-($3.99) Sam Loeb tribute issue; 2 covers by Turner; story & art by 26 various; back-up by Loeb & Sale — 5.00
27-49: 27-Flashback to Earth-2 Power Girl & Huntress; Maguire-a. 34-36-Metal Men app. — 3.00
50-($3.99) Thomas Wayne meets Jor-El; Justice League app. — 4.00
51-74: 51,52-Mr. Mxyzptlk app. 66,67-Blackest Night; Man-Bat and Bizarro app. — 3.00
75-(Quitely-c; Legion of Super-Heroes app.; Ordway-a; 2-pg. features by various — 5.00
76-87: 76-Aftermath of Batman's "death". 77-Supergirl/Damian team-up — 3.00
Annual #1 (12/06, $3.99) Re-imaging of 1st meeting from World's Finest #71 — 4.00
Annual #2 (5/08, $3.99) Kolins-a; re-imaging of Superman as Supernova story — 4.00
Annual #3 (3/09, $3.99) Composite Superman-c by Wrightson; Batista-a — 4.00
Annual #4 (8/10, $4.99) Batman Beyond; Levitz-s/Guedes-a/Lau-c — 8.00
Annual #5 (6/11, $4.99) Reign of Doomsday x-over, Cyborg Superman app.; Sepulveda-a — 5.00
...Absolute Power HC (2009, $19.99) r/#14-18 — 20.00
...Absolute Power SC (2006, $12.99) r/#14-18 — 13.00
..."Batman V Superman: Dawn of Justice Day" Special Edition 1 (4/16, free) r/#1 — 3.00
...Big Noise SC (2010, $14.99) r/#64,68-71 — 15.00
...Enemies Among Us SC (2009, $12.99) r/#28-33 — 13.00
...Finest Worlds SC (2010, $14.99) r/#50-56 — 15.00
...Night and Day HC (2010, $19.99) r/#60-63,65-67 — 20.00
...Public Enemies HC (2004, $19.95) r/#1-6 & Secret Files 2003; sketch art pages — 20.00
...Public Enemies SC (2005, $12.99) r/#1-6 & Secret Files 2003; sketch art pages — 15.00
...Public Enemies SC (2009, $14.99) r/#1-6 & Secret Files 2003; sketch art pages — 15.00
...Secret Files 2003 (11/03, $4.95) Reis-a; pin-ups by various; Loeb/Sale short-s — 5.00
...: Supergirl HC (2006, $19.95) r/#8-13; intro by Loeb, cover gallery, sketch pages — 20.00
...: Supergirl SC (2005, $12.99) r/#8-13; intro by Loeb, cover gallery, sketch pages — 13.00
...: The Search For Kryptonite HC (2008, $19.99) r/#44-49; Davis sketch pages — 20.00
...: The Search For Kryptonite SC (2009, $12.99) r/#44-49; Davis sketch pages — 13.00
...: Torment HC (2008, $19.99) r/#37-42; cover gallery, Nguyen sketch pages — 20.00
...: Vengeance HC (2006, $19.99) r/#20-25; sketch pages — 20.00
...: Vengeance SC (2008, $12.99) r/#20-25; sketch pages — 13.00
...: Worship SC (2011, $17.99) r/#72-75 & Annual #4 — 18.00

SUPERMAN/BATMAN: ALTERNATE HISTORIES
DC Comics: 1996 ($14.95, trade paperback)

nn-Reprints Detective Comics Annual #7, Action Comics Annual #6, Steel Annual #1, Legends of the Dark Knight Annual #4 — 15.00

SUPERMAN: BIRTHRIGHT
DC Comics: Sept, 2003 - No. 12, Sept, 2004 ($2.95, limited series)

1-12-Waid-s/Leinil Yu-a; retelling of origin and early Superman years — 3.00
HC (2004, $29.95, dustjacket) r/series; cover gallery; Waid proposal with Yu concept art — 30.00

Superman/Batman Annual #1 © DC

Superman Confidential #1 © DC

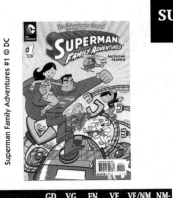

Superman Family Adventures #1 © DC

	GD 2.0	VG 4.0	FN 6.0	VF 8.0	VF/NM 9.0	NM- 9.2

SC (2005, $19.99) r/series; cover gallery; Waid proposal with Yu concept art 20.00

SUPERMAN COMICS
DC Comics: 1939

nn - Ashcan comic, not distributed to newsstands, only for in-house use. Cover art is Action Comics #7 with interior being Action Comics #8. A CGC certified 9.0 copy sold for $90,000 in 2007 and for $83,000 in Sept. 2018. A CGC 8.5 sold for $288,000 in Apr. 2022.

SUPERMAN CONFIDENTIAL (See Superman Hardcovers and TPBs listings for reprint)
DC Comics: Jan, 2007 - No. 14, Jun, 2008 ($2.99)

1-14: 1-5,9-Darwyn Cooke-s/Tim Sale-a/c; origin of Kryptonite re-told. 8-10-New Gods and Darkside app. 3.00
...: Kryptonite TPB (2009, $14.99) r/#1-5,11; intro. by Darwyn Cooke; Tim Sale sketch-a 15.00

SUPERMAN: DAY OF DOOM
DC Comics: Jan, 2003 - No. 4, Feb, 2003 ($2.95, weekly limited series)

1-4-Jurgens-s/Jurgens & Sienkiewicz-a 3.00
TPB (2003, $9.95) r/#1-4 .... 10.00

SUPERMAN DOOMED (DC New 52) (See Action Comics #31-34 and Superman/Wonder Woman)
DC Comics: Jul, 2014 - No. 2, Nov, 2014 ($4.99, bookends for crossover)

1,2: 1-Lashley-a; Wonder Woman & Steel app. 2-Superman vs. Braniac 6.00

SUPERMAN/DOOMSDAY: HUNTER/PREY
DC Comics: 1994 - No. 3, 1994 ($4.95, limited series, 52 pgs.)

1-3 .... 6.00

SUPERMAN FAMILY, THE (Formerly Superman's Pal Jimmy Olsen)
National Per. Publ./DC Comics: No. 164, Apr-May, 1974 - No. 222, Sept, 1982

164-(100 pgs.) Jimmy Olsen, Supergirl, Lois Lane begin

164-(100 pgs.)		4	8	12	28	47	65
165-169 (100 pgs.)	3	6	9	18	28	38
170-176 (68 pgs.)	3	6	9	14	19	24
177-190 (52 pgs.): 177-181-52 pgs. 182-Marshall Rogers-a; $1.00 issues begin;						
Krypto begins, ends #192. 183-Nightwing-Flamebird begins, ends #194.						
189-Braniac 5, Mon -El app.	2	4	6	9	13	16
191-193,195-199: 191-Superboy begins, ends #198	2	3	4	6	8	10
194,200: 194-Rogers-a. 200-Book length sty	2	4	6	8	10	12
201-210,212-222	1	2	3	5	6	8
211-Earth II Batman & Catwoman marry	2	4	6	8	11	14

NOTE: *N. Adams* c-182-185. *Anderson* a-186i. *Buckler* c(p)-190, 191, 209, 210, 215, 217, 220. *Jones* a-191-193. *Gil Kane* c(p)-221, 222. *Mortimer* a(p)-191-193, 199, 201-222. *Orlando* a(i)-186, 187. *Rogers* a-182, 194. *Staton* a-191-194, 196p. *Tuska* a(p)-203, 207-209.

SUPERMAN FAMILY ADVENTURES
DC Comics: Jul, 2012 - No. 12, Jun, 2013 ($2.99)

1-12-Young-reader stories, games and DC Nation character profiles; Baltazar-a 3.00

SUPERMAN/FANTASTIC FOUR
DC Comics/Marvel Comics: 1999 ($9.95, tabloid size, one-shot)

1-Battle Galactus and the Cyborg Superman; wraparound-c by Alex Ross and Dan Jurgens; Jurgens-s/a; Thibert-a 10.00

SUPERMAN FOR ALL SEASONS
DC Comics: 1998 - No. 4, 1998 ($4.95, limited series, prestige format)

1-Loeb-s/Sale-a/c; Superman's first year in Metropolis 6.00
2-4 .... 5.00
Hardcover (1999, $24.95) r/#1-4 .... 25.00

SUPERMAN FOR EARTH (See Superman one-shots)

SUPERMAN FOREVER
DC Comics: Jun, 1998 ($5.95, one-shot)

1-($5.95)-Collector's Edition with a 7-image lenticular-c by Alex Ross; Superman returns to normal; s/a by various	1	3	4	6	8	10
1-($4.95) Standard Edition with single image Ross-c 5.00

SUPERMAN/GEN13
DC Comics (WildStorm): Jun, 2000 - No. 3, Aug, 2000 ($2.50, limited series)

1-3-Hughes-s/ Bermejo-a; Campbell variant-c for each 3.00
TPB (2001, $9.95) new Bermejo-c; cover gallery 10.00

SUPERMAN GIANT (See reprint of new stories in Superman: Up In The Sky)
DC Comics: 2018 - No. 16, 2019 ($4.99, 100 pgs., squarebound, Walmart exclusive)

1-New story Palmiotti-s/Derenick-a; reprints from Superman/Batman, Green Lantern ('05), and The Terrifics in all 8.00
2-6,8-16: 2-Palmiotti-s/Derenick-a. 3-Tom King-s/Andy Kubert-a begins plus reprints 5.00
7-Many deaths of Lois Lane 10.00

SUPERMAN GIANT
DC Comics: Dec, 2019 - No. 3, 2020 ($4.99, 100 pgs., squarebound, Mass Market & Direct

Market editions exist for each issue, with different covers)
1-3: 1-New story w/Parasite; plus reprints. 2,3-New story w/Pelletier-a 5.00

SUPERMAN: KING OF THE WORLD
DC Comics: June, 1999 ($3.95/$4.95, one-shot)

1-($3.95) Regular Ed. 4.00
1-($4.95) Collectors' Ed. with gold foil enhanced-c 5.00

SUPERMAN: LAST SON OF EARTH
DC Comics: 2000 - No. 2, 2000 ($5.95, limited series, prestige format)

1,2-Elseworlds; baby Clark rockets to Krypton; Gerber-s/Wheatley-a 6.00

SUPERMAN: LAST STAND OF NEW KRYPTON
DC Comics: May, 2010 - No. 3, Late June, 2010 ($3.99, limited series)

1-3-Robinson & Gates-s/Woods-a. 2-Pérez-c. 3-Sook-c 4.00
HC (2010, $24.99, DJ) r/#1,2, Adventure Comics #8,9, Supergirl #51 & Superman #698 .... 25.00
Vol. 2 HC (2010, $19.99, DJ) r/#3, Adventure #10,11, Supergirl #52 & Superman #699 .... 20.00

SUPERMAN: LAST STAND ON KRYPTON
DC Comics: 2003 ($6.95, one-shot, prestige format)

1-Sequel to Superman: Last Son of Earth; Gerber-s/Wheatley-a 7.00

SUPERMAN: LOIS & CLARK (See Convergence Superman #1 & 2)
DC Comics: Dec, 2015 - No. 8, Jul, 2016 ($3.99)

1-8: 1-Pre-Flashpoint Superman & Lois on New 52 Earth; Jurgens-s/Weeks-a 4.00

SUPERMAN: LOIS LANE (Girlfrenzy)
DC Comics: Jun, 1998 ($1.95, one shot)

1-Connor & Palmiotti-a 4.00

SUPERMAN: LOST
DC Comics: May, 2023 - No. 10, Mar, 2024 ($4.99, limited series)

1-7: 1-Priest-s/Pagulayan-a; Justice League app. 5.00

SUPERMAN/MADMAN HULLABALOO!
Dark Horse Comics: June, 1997 - No. 3, Aug, 1997 ($2.95, limited series)

1-3-Mike Allred-c/s/a 4.00
TPB (1997, $8.95) 9.00

SUPERMAN: METROPOLIS
DC Comics: Apr, 2003 - No. 12, Mar, 2004 ($2.95, limited series)

1-12-Focus on Jimmy Olsen; Austen-s. 1-6-Zezelj-a. 7-12-Kristiansen-a. 8,9-Creeper app. 3.00

SUPERMAN METROPOLIS SECRET FILES
DC Comics: Jun, 2000 ($4.95, one shot)

1-Short stories, pin-ups and profile pages; Hitch and Neary-c 5.00

SUPERMAN: PEACE ON EARTH
DC Comics: Jan, 1999 ($9.95, Treasury-sized, one-shot)

1-Alex Ross painted-c/a; Paul Dini-s		3	6	9	17	26	35

SUPERMAN: RED AND BLUE
DC Comics: May, 2021 - No. 6, Oct, 2021 ($5.95, limited series, squarebound)

1-6-Short story anthology; art in B&W with red & blue coloring; three covers on each 6.00

SUPERMAN: RED SON
DC Comics: 2003 - No. 3, 2003 ($5.95, limited series, prestige format)

1-Elseworlds; Superman's rocket lands in Russia; Mark Millar-s/Dave Johnson-c/a 28.00
2,3 .... 15.00
TPB (2004, $17.95) r/#1-3; intro. by Tom DeSanto; sketch pages 18.00
... - The Deluxe Edition HC (2009, $24.99, d.j.) r/#1-3; sketch art by various 45.00

SUPERMAN RED/ SUPERMAN BLUE
DC Comics: Feb, 1998 ($4.95, one-shot)

1-Polybagged w/3-D glasses and reprint of Superman 3-D (1955); Jurgens-plot/3-D cover; script and art by various 5.00
1-($3.95)-Standard Ed.; comic only, non 3-D cover 4.00

SUPERMAN RETURNS... (2006 movie)
DC Comics: Aug, 2006 ($3.99, movie tie-in stories by Singer, Dougherty and Harris)

Prequel 1 - Krypton to Earth; Olivetti-a/Hughes-c; retells Jor-El's story 6.00
Prequel 2 - Ma Kent; Kerschl-a/Hughes-c; Ma Kent during Clark childhood and absence 4.00
Prequel 3 - Lex Luthor; Leonardi-a/Hughes-c; Luthor's 5 years in prison 4.00
Prequel 4 - Lois Lane; Dias-a/Hughes-c; Lois during Superman's absence 4.00
The Movie and Other Tales of the Man of Steel (2006, $12.99, TPB) adaptation; origin from Amazing World of Superman; Action #810, Superman #185; Advs. of Superman #575 .... 13.00
The Official Movie Adaptation (2006, $6.99) Pasko-s/Haley-a; photo-c 7.00
...: The Prequels TPB (2006, $12.99) r/the 4 prequels 13.00

SUPERMAN: SAVE THE PLANET

	GD	VG	FN	VF	VF/NM	NM-
	2.0	4.0	6.0	8.0	9.0	9.2

DC Comics: Oct, 1998 ($2.95, one-shot)
1-($2.95) Regular Ed.; Luthor buys the Daily Planet						4.00
1-($3.95) Collector's Ed. with acetate cover						5.00

SUPERMAN SCRAPBOOK (Has blank pages; contains no comics)

SUPERMAN: SECRET FILES
DC Comics: Jan, 1998; May 1999 ($4.95)
1,2: 1-Retold origin story, "lost" pages & pin-ups						5.00
... & Origins 2004 (8/04) pin-ups by Lee, Turner and others						5.00
... & Origins 2005 (1/06) short stories and pin-ups by various						5.00
... 2009 (10/09, $4.99) short stories and pin-ups about New Krypton x-over						5.00

SUPERMAN: SECRET IDENTITY
DC Comics: 2004 - No. 4, 2004 ($5.95, squarebound, limited series)
1-4-Busiek-s/Immonen-a/c						6.00

SUPERMAN: SECRET ORIGIN
DC Comics: Nov, 2009 - No. 6, Oct, 2010 ($3.99, limited series)
1-6-Geoff Johns-s/Gary Frank-a/c; origin mythos re-told. 2-Legion app. 5-Metallo app.						4.00
1-6-Variant covers by Frank						6.00
HC (2011, $29.99) r/#1-6; intro. by David Goyer; variant covers						30.00

SUPERMAN '78 (Based on the Christopher Reeve movie version)
DC Comics: Oct, 2021 - No. 6, Mar, 2022 ($3.99, limited series)
1-6-Venditti-s/Torres-a; Brainiac app.						4.00
1-6-($4.99) Cardstock variant covers						5.00

SUPERMAN '78: THE METAL CURTAIN (Based on the Christopher Reeve movie version)
DC Comics: Jan, 2024 - No. 6, Jun, 2024 ($3.99, limited series)
1-6-Venditti-s/Guidry-a; Metallo and Lex Luthor app.						4.00

SUPERMAN'S GIRLFRIEND LOIS LANE (See Action Comics #1, 80 Page Giant #3, 14, Lois Lane, Showcase #9, 10, Superman #28 & Superman Family)

SUPERMAN'S GIRLFRIEND LOIS LANE (See Showcase #9,10)
National Periodical Publ.: Mar-Apr, 1958 - No. 136, Jan-Feb, 1974; No. 137, Sept-Oct, 1974
	GD 2.0	VG 4.0	FN 6.0	VF 8.0	VF/NM 9.0	NM- 9.2
1-(3-4/58)	415	830	1660	4560	10,530	16,500
2	114	228	342	912	2056	3200
3	75	150	225	600	1350	2100
4,5	52	104	156	416	933	1450
6,7	42	84	126	311	706	1100
8-10: 9-Pat Boone-c/story	35	70	105	252	564	875
11-13,15-19: 12-(10/59)-Aquaman app. 17-(5/60) 2nd app. Brainiac.						
	22	44	66	154	340	525
14-Supergirl x-over; Batman app. on-c only	27	54	81	189	420	650
20-Supergirl-c/sty	25	50	75	175	388	600
21-28: 23-1st app. Lena Thorul, Lex Luthor's sister; 1st Lois as Elastic Lass.						
27-Bizarro-c/story	15	30	45	105	233	360
29-Aquaman, Batman, Green Arrow cover app. and cameo; last 10¢ issue						
	17	34	51	119	265	410
30-32,34-46,48,49	9	18	27	61	123	185
33(5/62)-Mon -El app.	11	22	33	73	157	240
47-Legion app.	10	20	30	69	147	225
50(7/64)-Triplicate Girl, Phantom Girl & Shrinking Violet app.						
	10	20	30	66	138	210
51-55,57-67,69: 59-Jor -El app.; Batman back-up sty	7	14	21	44	82	120
56-Saturn Girl app.	8	16	24	55	105	155
68-(Giant G-26)	9	18	27	59	117	175
70-Penguin & Catwoman app. (1st S.A. Catwoman, 11/66; also see Detective #369 for 3rd						
app.); Batman & Robin cameo	64	128	192	512	1156	1800
71-Batman & Robin cameo (3 panels); Catwoman story cont'd from #70 (2nd app.); see						
Detective #369 for 3rd app.	12	24	36	79	170	260
72,73,75,76,78	5	10	15	34	60	85
74-1st Bizarro Flash (5/67); JLA cameo	7	14	21	44	82	120
77-(Giant G-39)	7	14	21	48	89	130
79-Neal Adams c or c(i) begin, end #95,108	7	14	21	44	82	120
80-85,87,88,90-92: 92-Last 12¢ issue	8	16	24	47	65	—
86,95 (Giants G-51, G-63)-Both have Neal Adams-c	7	14	21	44	82	120
89,93: 89-Batman x-over; all N. Adams-c. 93-Wonder Woman-c/story						
	5	10	15	33	57	80
94,96-99,101-103,107-110	4	8	12	23	37	50
100	4	8	12	25	40	55
104-(Giant G-75)	5	10	15	35	63	90
105-Origin/1st app. The Rose & the Thorn.	11	22	33	73	157	240
106-"I Am Curious (Black)" story; Lois changes her skin color to black (11/70)						
	42	84	126	311	706	1100
111-Justice League-c/s; Morrow-a; last 15¢ issue	6	12	18	38	69	100
112,114-123 (52 pgs.): 115-Black Racer app. 116,119-Darkseid app. 122-G.A. Lois Lane-r/						
Superman #30. 123-G.A.Batman-r/Batman #35 (w/Catwoman)						
	4	8	12	23	37	50
113-(Giant G-87) Kubert-a (previously unpublished G.A. story)(scarce in NM)						
	6	12	18	41	76	110
124-135: 130-Last Rose & the Thorn. 132-New Zatanna story						
	3	6	9	16	23	30
136,137: 136-Wonder Woman x-over	3	6	9	21	33	45
Annual 1(Sum, 1962)-r/L. Lane #12; Aquaman app.	23	46	69	161	356	550
Annual 2(Sum, 1963)	15	30	45	100	220	340

NOTE: **Buckler** a-117-121p. Curt Swan or Kurt Schaffenberger a-1-81(most); c(p)-1-15.

SUPERMAN/SHAZAM: FIRST THUNDER
DC Comics: Nov, 2005 - No. 4, Feb, 2006 ($3.50, limited series)
1-4-Retells first meeting. Winick-s/Middleton-a. Dr. Sivana app.						6.00

SUPERMAN: SILVER BANSHEE
DC Comics: Dec, 1998 - No. 2, Jan, 1999 ($2.25, mini-series)
1,2-Brereton-s/c; Chin-a						4.00

SUPERMANSION (Based on the animated series)
Titan Comics: May, 2018 - No. 2, Jun, 2018 ($5.99, series)
1,2-Hutchinson-s/Elphick-a; multiple covers						6.00

SUPERMAN SMASHES THE KLAN (Inspired by the 1940s Superman radio show)
DC Comics: Oct, 2019 - No. 3, Feb, 2020 ($7.99, 6" x 9" squarebound, limited series)
1-3-Gene Luen Yang-s/Gurihiru-a/c; set in 1946. 1-Variant-c by Kyle Baker						8.00

SUPERMAN'S NEMESIS: LEX LUTHOR
DC Comics: Mar, 1999 - No. 4, Jun, 1999 ($2.50, mini-series)
1-4-Semeiks-a						4.00

SUPERMAN: SON OF KAL-EL (Leads into Adventures of Superman: Jon Kent series)
DC Comics: Sept, 2021 - No. 18, Feb, 2023 ($3.99)
1-Jon Kent as Superman; Taylor-s/Timms-a; birth re-told; Damian app.						4.00
2-18: 2-Intro. Jay Nakamura; Henry Bendix app. 9-Nightwing app.						4.00
... 2021 Annual 1 (2/22, $5.99) Lex Luthor app.; Pugh & Henry-a						6.00

SUPERMAN: SPACE AGE
DC Comics: Sept, 2022 - No. 3, ($9.99, limited series)
1-3-Mark Russell-s/Mike Allred-a. 1-Set in the 1960s. 3-Events of Crisis on Infinite Earths						10.00

SUPERMAN'S PAL JIMMY OLSEN (Superman Family #164 on)
(See Action Comics #6 for 1st app. & 80 Page Giant)
National Periodical Publ.: Sept-Oct, 1954 - No. 163, Feb-Mar, 1974 (Fourth World #133-148)
	GD 2.0	VG 4.0	FN 6.0	VF 8.0	VF/NM 9.0	NM- 9.2
1	550	1100	1925	5500	12,750	20,000
2	190	380	570	1568	3534	5500
3-Last pre-code issue	125	250	375	1000	2250	3500
4,5	79	158	237	632	1416	2200
6-10	48	96	144	374	862	1350
11-20: 15-1st S.A. issue	36	72	108	259	580	900
21-28,30	25	50	75	175	388	600
29-(6/58) 1st app. Krypto with Superman	28	56	84	202	451	700
31-Origin & 1st app. Elastic Lad (Jimmy Olsen)	27	54	81	189	420	650
32-40: 33-One pg. biography of Jack Larson (TV Jimmy Olsen). 36-Intro Lucy Lane.						
37-2nd app. Elastic Lad & 1st cover app.	15	30	45	105	233	360
41-50: 41-1st J.O. Robot. 48-Intro/origin Superman Emergency Squad						
	12	24	36	81	176	270
51-56: 56-Last 10¢ issue	10	20	30	60	120	180
57-62,64-70: 57-Olsen marries Supergirl. 62-Mon-El & Elastic Lad app. but not as						
Legionnaires. 70-Element Boy (Lad) app.	7	14	21	48	89	130
63 (9/62)-Legion of Super-Villains app.	8	16	24	56	108	160
71,74,75,78,80-84,86,89,90: 86-Jimmy Olsen Robot becomes Congorilla						
	6	12	18	37	66	95
72,73,76,77,79,85,87,88: 72(10/63)-Legion app; Elastic Lad (Olsen) joins. 73-Ultra Boy app.						
76,85-Legion app. 76-Legion app. 77-Olsen with Colossal Boy's powers & costume; origin						
Titano retold. 79-(9/64)-Titled The Red-headed Beatle of 1000 B.C. 85-Legion app.						
87-Legion of Super-Villains app. 88-Star Boy app.	6	12	18	38	69	100
91-94,96-98	5	10	15	33	57	80
95 (Giant G-25)	5	10	15	35	63	90
99-Olsen w/powers & costumes of Lightning Lad, Sun Boy & Element Lad						
	5	10	15	35	63	90
100-Legion cameo	5	10	15	35	63	90
101-103,105-112,114-120: 106-Legion app. 110-Infinity-c. 117-Batman & Legion cameo.						
120-Last 12¢ issue	4	8	12	27	44	60
104 (Giant G-38)	6	12	18	37	66	95
113,122,131,140 (Giants G-50,G-62,G-74,G-86)	5	10	15	34	60	85
121,123-130,132	4	8	12	25	40	55
133-(10/70)-Jack Kirby story & art begins; re-intro Newsboy Legion; 1st app. Morgan Edge						
	16	32	48	108	160	—
134-1st app. Darkseid (1 panel, 12/70)	62	124	186	434	742	1050
135-2nd app. Darkseid (11 pg. cameo; see New Gods & Forever People)						
G.A. Guardian app.	10	20	30	66	138	210
136-139: 136-Origin new Guardian. 138-Partial photo-c. 139-Last 15¢ issue						
	4	8	12	27	44	60
141-150: (25¢,52 pgs.). 141-Photo-c with Don Rickles; Newsboy Legion-r by S&K begin;						
full pg. self-portrait of Jack Kirby; Don Rickles cameo. 149,150-G.A. Plastic Man-r in both;						
150-Newsboy Legion app.	4	8	12	25	40	55
151-161	3	6	9	16	24	34
... Special 1 (12/08, $4.99) New Krypton tie-in; The Guardian and Dubbilex app.						5.00
... Special 2 (10/09, $4.99) New Krypton tie-in; Mon-El app.; Chang-a						5.00

Superman: The Amazing Transformations of Jimmy Olsen TPB (2007, $14.99) reprints Olsen's transformations in Wolf-Man, Elastic Lad, Turtle Boy and others; new Bolland-c

NOTE: Issues #141-148 contain **Simon & Kirby** Newsboy Legion reprints from Star Spangled #7, 8, 9, 10, 11, 12, 13, 14 in that order. **N. Adams** c-109-112, 115, 117, 118, 120. **Kirby** a/133-139p, 141-148p; c-133, 137, 139, 142, 145p. **Kirby/N. Adams** c-137, 138, 141-144, 146. **Curt Swan** c-1-14(most)., 140.

SUPERMAN'S PAL JIMMY OLSEN
DC Comics: Sept, 2019 - No. 12, Sept, 2020 ($3.99)
1-12-Matt Fraction-s/Steve Lieber-a. 5,6-Batman app.						4.00

SUPERMAN'S PAL JIMMY OLSEN'S BOSS PERRY WHITE
DC Comics: Aug, 2022 ($4.99, one-shot)
1-New story with Matt Fraction-s/Steve Lieber-a; 5 reprint stories; Lieber-c						5.00

SUPERMAN SPECTACULAR (Also see DC Special Series #5)
DC Comics: 1982 (Magazine size, 52 pgs., square binding)
	GD 2.0	VG 4.0	FN 6.0	VF 8.0	VF/NM 9.0	NM- 9.2
1-Saga of Superman Red/ Superman Blue; Luthor and Terra-Man app.; Gonzales & Colletta-a	2	4	6	9	13	16

SUPERMAN: STRENGTH
DC Comics: 2005 - No. 3, 2005 ($5.95, limited series)
1-3-Alex Ross-c/Scott McCloud-s/Aluir Amancio-a						6.00

SUPERMAN / SUPERGIRL: MAELSTROM
DC Comics: Early Jan, 2009 - No. 5, Mar, 2009 ($2.99, limited series)
1-5: Palmiotti & Gray-s/Noto-c/a; Darkseid app.						3.00
TPB (2009, $12.99) r/#1-5						13.00

SUPERMAN / SUPERHOMBRE
DC Comics: Apr, 1945
nn - Ashcan comic, not distributed to newsstands					(no known sales)	

SUPERMAN / TARZAN: SONS OF THE JUNGLE
Dark Horse Comics: Oct, 2001 - No. 3, May, 2002 ($2.99, limited series)

Superman '78 #5 © DC

Superman: Space Age #2 © DC

Superman: Up in the Sky #1 © DC

	GD	VG	FN	VF	VF/NM	NM-
	2.0	4.0	6.0	8.0	9.0	9.2

	GD	VG	FN	VF	VF/NM	NM-
	2.0	4.0	6.0	8.0	9.0	9.2

1-3-Elseworlds; Kal-El lands in the jungle; Dixon-s/Meglia-a/Ramos-c — 3.00

SUPERMAN: THE COMING OF THE SUPERMEN
DC Comics: Apr, 2016 - No. 6, Sept, 2016 ($3.99, limited series)

1-6: 1-Neal Adams-s/a/c in all; Kalibak app. 3,4-Orion app. 3-6-Darkseid app. — 4.00

SUPERMAN: THE DARK SIDE
DC Comics: 1998 - No. 3, 1998 ($4.95, squarebound, mini-series)

1-3: Elseworlds; Kal-El lands on Apokolips	1	2	3	5	6	8

SUPERMAN: THE DOOMSDAY WARS
DC Comics: 1998 - No. 3, 1999 ($4.95, squarebound, mini-series)

1-3: Superman & JLA vs. Doomsday; Jurgens-s/a(p) — 5.00

SUPERMAN: THE KANSAS SIGHTING
DC Comics: 2003 - No. 2, 2003 ($6.95, squarebound, mini-series)

1,2-DeMatteis-s/Tolagson-a — 7.00

SUPERMAN: THE LAST DAYS OF LEX LUTHOR
DC Comics (Black Label): Sept, 2023 - Present ($6.99, squarebound, oversized, lim. series)

1-Mark Waid-s/Bryan Hitch-a — 7.00

SUPERMAN: THE LAST FAMILY OF KRYPTON
DC Comics: Oct, 2010 - No. 3, Dec, 2010 ($4.99, limited series)

1-3-Elseworlds; the El family lands on Earth; Bates-s/Arlem-a/Massafera-c — 5.00

SUPERMAN: THE MAN OF STEEL (Also see Man of Steel, The)
DC Comics: July, 1991 - No. 134, Mar, 2003 ($1.00/$1.25/$1.50/$1.95/$2.25)

0-(10/94) Zero Hour; released between #37 & #38	1	3	4	6	8	10
1-($1.75, 52 pgs.)-Painted-c	1	3	4	6	8	10
2-16: 3-War of the Gods x-over. 5-Reads sideways. 10-Last $1.00-c.						
14-Superman & Robin team-up						4.00
17-1st brief app. Doomsday	3	6	9	16	23	30
17-(2nd printing)	3	6	9	15	22	28
18-1st full app. Doomsday	3	6	9	19	30	40
18-(2nd-4th printings)	2	4	6	11	16	20
18-(5th printing)	4	8	12	28	47	65
19-Doomsday battle issue (c/story)	2	4	6	8	11	14
19-(2nd & 3rd printings)	3	6	9	16	23	30
20-22: 20,21-Funeral for a Friend. 22-($1.95)-Collector's Edition w/die-cut outer-c &						
bound-in poster; Steel-c/story						5.00
22-($1.50)-Newsstand Ed. w/poster & different-c						5.00
23-49,51-99: 30-Regular edition. 32-Bizarro-c/app. 35,36-Worlds Collide Pt. 1 & 10.						
37-(9/94)-Zero Hour x-over. 38-(11/94). 48-Aquaman app. 54-Spectre-c/app; Lex Luthor app.						
56-Mxyzptlk-c/app. 57-G.A. Flash app. 59-Parasite-c/app.; Steel app.						
60-Reintro Bottled City of Kandor. 62-Final Night. 64-New Gods app. 67-New powers.						
75-"Death" of Mxyzptlk. 78,79-Millennium Giants. 80-Golden Age style. 92-JLA app.						
98-Metal Men app.						4.00
30-($2.50)-Collector's Edition; polybagged with Superman & Lobo vinyl clings						
that stick to wraparound-c; Lobo-c/story						5.00
50 ($2.95)-The Trial of Superman						4.00
100-($2.99) New Fortress of Solitude revealed						3.00
100-($3.99) Special edition with fold out cardboard-c						4.00
101,102-101-Batman app.						3.00
103-133: 103-Begin $2.25. 105-Batman-c/app. 111-Return to Krypton. 115-117-Our Worlds						
at War. 117-Maxima killed. 121-Royal Flush Gang app. 128-Return to Krypton II.						3.00
134-($2.75) Last issue; Bogdanove-c						3.00
#1,000,000 (11/98) 853rd Century x-over; Gene Ha-c						4.00
Annual 1-5 ('92-'96,68 pgs.): 1-Eclipso app.						
Mignola-c; Batman app. 4-Year One story. 5-Legends of the Dead Earth story						5.00
Annual 6 (1997, $3.95)-Pulp Heroes story						5.00
...Gallery (1995, $3.50) Pin-ups by various						4.00

SUPERMAN: THE MAN OF TOMORROW
DC Comics: 1995 - No. 15, Fall, 1999 ($1.95-$2.95, quarterly)

1-15: 1-Lex Luthor app. 3-Lex Luthor-c/app; Joker app. 4-Shazam! app.						
5-Wedding of Lex Luthor. 10-Maxima-c/app. 13-JLA-c/app.						4.00
#1,000,000 (11/98) 853rd Century x-over; Gene Ha-c						4.00

SUPERMAN: THE SECRET YEARS
DC Comics: Feb, 1985 - No. 4, May, 1985 (limited series)

1-4-Miller-c on all — 5.00

SUPERMAN: THE WEDDING ALBUM
DC Comics: Dec, 1996 ($4.95, 96 pgs, one-shot)

1-Standard Edition-Story & art by past and present Superman creators; gatefold back-c.
Byrne-c — 5.00
1-Collector's Edition-Embossed cardstock variant-c w/ metallic silver ink and matte and —

gloss varnishes — 8.00
Retailer Rep. Program Edition (#'d to 250, signed by Bob Rozakis on back-c) — 55.00
TPB ('97, $14.95) r/Wedding and honeymoon stories — 15.00

SUPERMAN 3-D (See Three-Dimension Adventures)

SUPERMAN-TIM (See Promotional Comics section)

SUPERMAN UNCHAINED (DC New 52)
DC Comics: Aug, 2013 - No. 9, Jan, 2015 ($4.99/$3.99)

1-($4.99) Snyder-s/Jim Lee-a/c; back-up with Nguyen-a; bonus creator interviews — 5.00
1-Director's Cut (9/13, $5.99) Lee's pencil art and Scott Snyder's scripts; cover gallery — 6.00
2-8-($3.99) 2,6,7-Batman app. — 4.00
9-($4.99) Wraparound-c by Jim Lee — 5.00

SUPERMAN: UP IN THE SKY (Reprints serialized story in Walmart exclusive Superman Giant)
DC Comics: Sept, 2019 - No. 6, Feb, 2020 ($4.99, limited series)

1-6:1-Reprints Superman Giant #3,4; Andy Kubert-a. 2-R/#5,6. 3-R/#7,8; Sgt. Rock app.
4-R/#9,10; Flash app. 5-R/#12,13; Darkseid app. 6-R/#15,16 — 5.00

SUPERMAN VILLAINS SECRET FILES
DC Comics: Jun, 1998 ($4.95, one shot)

1-Origin stories, "lost" pages & pin-ups — 5.00

SUPERMAN VS. ALIENS (Also see Superman Aliens 2: God War)
DC Comics/Dark Horse Comics: July, 1995 - No. 3, Sept, 1995 ($4.95, limited series)

1-3: Jurgens/Nowlan-a — 5.00

SUPERMAN VS. LOBO
DC Comics (Black Label): Oct, 2021 - No. 3, May, 2022 ($6.99, oversized 8-1/2" x 10-3/4", lim. series)

1-3-Seeley & Beattie-s/Andolfo-a. 2-Lobo goes to Krypton, Superman to Czarnia — 7.00

SUPERMAN VS. MUHAMMAD ALI (See All-New Collectors' Edition C-56 for original 1978 printing)
DC Comics: 2010

... Deluxe Edition (2010, $19.99, HC w/dustjacket) recolored reprint in comic size; new intro.
by Neal Adams; afterword by Jenette Kahn; sketch pages, key to cover celebs — 40.00
... Facsimile Edition (2010, $39.99, HC no dustjacket) recolored reprint in original Treasury
size; new intro. by Neal Adams; key to cover celebs — 60.00

SUPERMAN VS. PREDATOR
DC Comics/Dark Horse Comics: 2000 - No. 3, 2000 ($4.95, limited series)

1-3-Micheline-s/Maleev-a — 5.00
TPB (2001, $14.95) r/series — 15.00

SUPERMAN VS. THE AMAZING SPIDER-MAN (Also see Marvel Treasury Edition No. 28)
National Periodical Publications/Marvel Comics Group: 1976
($2.00, Treasury sized, 100 pgs.)

1-Superman and Spider-Man battle Lex Luthor and Dr. Octopus; Andru/Giordano-a;						
1st Marvel/DC x-over.	10	20	30	67	141	215
1-2nd printing; 2000 numbered copies signed by Stan Lee on front cover & sold through mail	19	38	57	131	291	450
nn-(1995, $5.95)-r/#1	3	6	9	21	33	45

SUPERMAN VS. THE TERMINATOR: DEATH TO THE FUTURE
Dark Horse/DC Comics: Dec, 1999 - No. 4, Mar, 2000 ($2.95, limited series)

1-4-Grant-s/Pugh-a/c; Steel and Supergirl app. — 5.00

SUPERMAN: WAR OF THE SUPERMEN
DC Comics: No. 0, Jun, 2010 - No. 4, Jul, 2010 ($2.99, limited series)

0-Free Comic Book Day issue; Barrows-c — 3.00
1-4: 1-New Krypton destroyed — 3.00
HC (2011, $19.99) r/#0-4 & Superman #700 — 20.00

SUPERMAN/WONDER WOMAN (DC New 52)
DC Comics: Dec, 2013 - No. 29, Jul, 2016 ($3.99)

1-Soule-s/Daniel-a; wraparound gatefold-c; Doomsday app. — 5.00
2-29: 2-6-Zod app. 4-6-Faora app. 7-Doomsday app. 8-12-Doomed x-over. 14-17-Magog
app. 18,19-Suicide Squad app. 26,27-Vandal Savage app. 28,29-Supergirl app. — 4.00
Annual 1 (9/14, $4.99) Doomsday Superman vs. Cyborg Superman — 5.00
Annual 2 (2/16, $4.99) Short stories by various; Paquette-a — 5.00
...: Futures End 1 (11/14, $2.99, regular-c) Cont'd from Wonder Woman: FE #1 — 3.00
...: Futures End 1 (11/14, $3.99, 3-D cover) — 4.00

SUPERMAN/WONDER WOMAN: WHOM GODS DESTROY
DC Comics: 1997 ($4.95, prestige format, limited series)

1-4-Elseworlds; Claremont-s — 5.00

SUPERMAN WORKBOOK
National Periodical Publ./Juvenile Group Foundation: 1945 (B&W, reprints, 68 pgs)

nn-Cover-r/Superman #14	300	600	900	2070	3635	5200

	GD	VG	FN	VF	VF/NM	NM-
	2.0	4.0	6.0	8.0	9.0	9.2

SUPERMAN: WORLD OF NEW KRYPTON
DC Comics: May, 2009 - No. 12,Apr, 2010 ($2.99, limited series)

1-12: Robinson & Rucka-s/Woods-a; Frank-c and variant for each. 4-Green Lantern app. 3.00						

SUPERMAN YEAR ONE
DC Comics (Black Label): Aug, 2019 - No. 3, Dec, 2019 ($7.99, 10-7/8" x 8-1/2", lim. series)

1-3-Frank Miller-s/John Romita Jr.-a; two covers on each; origin re-told					8.00	

SUPER MARIO BROS. (Also see Adventures of the…, Blip, Gameboy, and Nintendo Comics System)
Valiant Comics: 1990 - No. 6, 1991 ($1.95, slick-c) V2#1, 1991 - No. 5, 1991

	GD	VG	FN	VF	VF/NM	NM-
1-Wildman-a	13	26	39	89	195	300
2	5	10	15	31	53	75
3-6, V2#1-5-($1.50)	2	4	6	10	14	18
Special Edition 1 (1990, $1.95)-Wildman-a; 1st Valiant comic	8	16	24	54	102	150

SUPER MARKET COMICS
Fawcett Publications: No date (1950s)

nn - Ashcan comic, not distributed to newsstands, only for in-house use   (no known sales)

SUPER MARKET VARIETIES
Fawcett Publications: No date (1950s)

nn - Ashcan comic, not distributed to newsstands, only for in-house use   (no known sales)

SUPERMASSIVE
Image Comics: Feb, 2022 ($5.99, one-shots)

1-Crossover of Radiant Black, Radiant Red, Rogue Sun & Inferno Girl Red					6.00	
... 2023 (5/23)					6.00	

SUPERMEN OF AMERICA
DC Comics: Mar, 1999 ($3.95/$4.95, one-shot)

1-($3.95) Regular Ed.; Immonen-s/art by various					4.00	
1-($4.95) Collectors' Ed. with membership kit					5.00	

SUPERMEN OF AMERICA (Mini-series)
DC Comics: Mar, 2000 - No. 6, Aug, 2000 ($2.50)

1-6-Nicieza-s/Braithwaite-a					3.00	

SUPERMOUSE (…the Big Cheese; see Coo Coo Comics)
Standard Comics/Pines No. 35 on (Literary Ent.): Dec, 1948 - No. 34, Sept, 1955; No. 35, Apr, 1956 - No. 45, Fall, 1958

	GD	VG	FN	VF	VF/NM	NM-
1-Frazetta text illos (3)	43	86	129	271	461	650
2-Frazetta text illos	21	42	63	126	206	285
3,5,6-Text illos by Frazetta in all	16	32	48	92	144	195
4-Two pg. text illos by Frazetta	17	34	51	98	154	210
7-10	10	20	30	58	79	100
11-20: 13-Racist humor (Indians)	9	18	27	50	65	80
21-45	8	16	24	42	54	65
1-Summer Holiday issue (Summer, 1957, 25¢, 100 pgs.)-Pines		17	34	51	98	154	210
2-Giant Summer issue (Summer, 1958, 25¢, 100 pgs.)-Pines; has games, puzzles & stories	13	26	39	74	105	135

SUPER-MYSTERY COMICS
Ace Magazines (Periodical House): July, 1940 - V8#6, July, 1949

	GD	VG	FN	VF	VF/NM	NM-
V1#1-Magno, the Magnetic Man & Vulcan begins (1st app.); Q-13, Corp. Flint, & Sky Smith begin	530	1060	1590	3869	6835	9800
2	258	516	774	1651	2826	4000
3-The Black Spider begins (1st app.)	290	580	870	1856	3178	4500
4-Origin Davy	148	296	444	947	1624	2300
5-Intro. The Clown & begin series (12/40)	161	322	483	1030	1765	2500
6(2/41)	129	258	387	826	1413	2000
V2#1(4/41)-Origin Buckskin	123	246	369	787	1344	1900
2-6(2/42): 3-Hitler & Mussolini app. 4-WWII Nazi-c. 6-Vulcan begins again; bondage/torture-c	123	246	369	787	1344	1900
V3#1(4/42),2: 1-Black Ace begins	142	284	426	909	1555	2200
3-Classic Kurtzman Japanese WWII giant robot bondage-c; intro. The Lancer; Dr. Nemesis & The Sword begin; Kurtzman-a(2)(Mr. Risk & Paul Revere Jr.)	194	388	582	1242	2121	3000
4-Kurtzman-c/a; classic-c	290	580	870	1856	3178	4500
5-Kurtzman-a(2); L.B. Cole-a; Mr. Risk app.	194	388	582	1242	2121	3000
6(10/43)-Mr. Risk app.; Kurtzman's Paul Revere Jr.; L.B. Cole-a	135	270	405	864	1482	2100
V4#1(1/44)-L.B. Cole-a; Hitler app.	93	186	279	591	1021	1450
2-6(4/45): 2,5,6-Mr. Risk app.	65	130	195	416	708	1000
V5#1(7/45)-6	61	122	183	390	670	950
V6#1,2,4,5,6: 4-Last Magno. Mr. Risk app. in #2,4-6. 6-New logo	58	116	174	371	636	900
3-Classic torture c/story	1400	2800	4200	10,600	19,300	28,000
V7#1-6, V8#1-4,6	55	110	165	352	601	850
V8#5-Meskin, Tuska, Sid Greene-a	57	114	171	362	619	875

NOTE: Sid Greene a-V7#4. Mooney c-V1#5, 6, V2#1-6. Palais a-V5#3, 4; c-V4#6-V5#4, V6#2, V8#4. Bondage c-V2#5, 6, V3#2, 5. Magno c-V1#1-6. Mr. Risk a-V4#4. Steranko 1-2. Sutton a-15. Tuska a-6p.

SUPERNATURAL (Volume 4) (Based on the CW television series)
DC Comics: Dec, 2011 - No. 6, May, 2012 ($2.99, limited series)

1-6: 1-Sam in Scotland; Brian Wood-s/Grant Bond-a					3.00	

SUPERNATURAL: BEGINNING'S END (Based on the CW television series)
DC Comics (WildStorm): Mar, 2010 - No. 6, Aug, 2010 ($2.99, limited series)

1-6-Prequel to the series; Dabb & Loflin-s/Olmos-a. 1-Olmos and photo-c					3.00	
TPB (2010, $14.99) r/#1-6; character sketch pages					15.00	

SUPERNATURAL FREAK MACHINE: A CAL MCDONALD MYSTERY
IDW Publishing: Mar, 2005 - No. 3 ($3.99)

1-3-Steve Niles/Kelley Jones-a					4.00	

SUPERNATURAL LAW (Formerly Wolff & Byrd, Counselors of the Macabre)
Exhibit A Press: No. 24, Oct, 1999 - No. 45, 2008 ($2.50/$2.95/$3.50, B&W)

24-35-Batton Lash-s/a. 29-Marie Severin-c. 33-Cerebus spoof					4.00	

36-40-($2.95). 37-Frank Cho pin-up and story panels						3.00
(#41) ...First Amendment Issue (2005, $3.50) anti-censorship story; CBLDF info						3.50
(#42) With a Silver Bullet (2006, $3.50) new stories and pin-ups						3.50
(#43) At the Box Office (2006, $3.50) new stories and pin-ups						3.50
(#44) Wolff & Byrd: The Movie (2007, $3.50) new stories and pin-ups						3.50
45-($3.50) Toxic Avenger and Lloyd Kaufman app.						3.50
#1 (2005, $2.95) r/Wolff & Byrd with redrawn and re-toned art; relettered						3.00

SUPERNATURAL LAW SECRETARY MAVIS
Exhibit A Press: 2001 - No. 5, 2008 ($2.95/$3.50, B&W)

1-3: 3-DeCarlo-c						3.00
4,5-($3.50) Jaime Hernandez-c						3.50

SUPERNATURAL: ORIGINS (Based on the CW television series)
DC Comics (WildStorm): July, 2007 - No. 6, Dec, 2007 ($2.99, limited series)

1-6: 1-Bradstreet-c; Johnson-s/Smith-a; back-up w/Johns-s/Hester-a						3.00
TPB (2008, $14.99) r/#1-6; sketch pages						15.00

SUPERNATURAL: RISING SON (Based on the CW television series)
DC Comics (WildStorm): Jun, 2008 - No. 6, Nov, 2008 ($2.99, limited series)

1-6-Johnson & Dessertine-s/Olmos-a. 1-Oliver-c						3.00
1-Variant-c by Nguyen						6.00
TPB (2009, $14.99) r/#1-6						15.00

SUPERNATURALS
Marvel Comics: Dec, 1998 - No. 4, Dec, 1998 ($3.99, weekly limited series)

1-4-Pulido-s/Balent-c; bound-in Halloween masks						4.00
1-4-With bound-in Ghost Rider mask (1 in 10)						4.00
... Preview Tour Book (10/98, $2.99) Reis-c						4.00

SUPERNATURAL THRILLERS
Marvel Comics Group: Dec, 1972 - No. 6, Nov, 1973; No. 7, Jun, 1974 - No. 15, Oct, 1975

	GD	VG	FN	VF	VF/NM	NM-
1-It!; Sturgeon adap. (see Astonishing Tales #21)	6	12	18	38	69	100
2-4,6: 2-The Invisible Man; H.G. Wells adapt. 3-The Valley of the Worm; R.E. Howard adapt. 4-Dr. Jekyll & Mr. Hyde; R.L. Stevenson adapt.. 6-The Headless Horseman; last 20¢ issue	5	10	15	30	53	75
5-1st app. The Living Mummy	3	6	9	16	23	30
7-15: 7-The Living Mummy begins. 8-1st app. The Elementals	10	20	30	66	138	210
	3	6	9	19	30	40

NOTE: Brunner c-11. Buckler a-5p. Ditko a-8r, 9r. G. Kane a-3p; c-3, 9p, 15p. Mayerik a-2p, 7, 8, 9p, 10p, 11. McWilliams a-14i. Mortimer a-4. Steranko 1-2. Sutton a-15. Tuska a-6p.

SUPERPATRIOT (Also see Freak Force & Savage Dragon #2)
Image Comics (Highbrow Entertainment): July, 1993 - No. 4, Dec, 1993 ($1.95, lim. series)

1-4: Dave Johnson-c/a; Larsen scripts; Giffen plots						4.00

SUPERPATRIOT: AMERICA'S FIGHTING FORCE
Image Comics: July, 2002 - No. 4, Oct, 2002 ($2.95, limited series)

1-4-Cory Walker-a/c; Savage Dragon app.						3.00

SUPERPATRIOT: LIBERTY & JUSTICE
Image Comics (Highbrow Entertainment): July, 1995 - No. 4, Oct, 1995 ($2.50, lim. series)

1-4: Dave Johnson-a. 1-1st app. Liberty & Justice						4.00
TPB (2002, $12.95) r/#1-4; new cover by Dave Johnson; sketch pages						13.00

SUPERPATRIOT: WAR ON TERROR
Image Comics: June, 2004 - No. 4, May, 2007 ($2.95/$2.99, limited series)

1-4-Kirkman-s/Su-a						3.00

SUPER POWERS (1st Series)
DC Comics: July, 1984 - No. 5, Nov, 1984

1-5: 1-Joker/Penguin-c/story; Batman app.; all Kirby-c. 5-Kirby c/a						6.00

SUPER POWERS (2nd Series)
DC Comics: Sept, 1985 - No. 6, Feb, 1986

1-6: Kirby-c/a; Capt. Marvel & Firestorm join; Batman cameo; Darkseid storyline in all. 4-Batman cameo. 5,6-Batman app.						5.00

SUPER POWERS (3rd Series)
DC Comics: Sept, 1986 - No. 4, Dec, 1986

1-4: 1-Cyborg joins; 1st app. Samurai from Super Friends TV show. 1-4-Batman cameos; Darkseid storyline in #1-4						4.00

SUPER POWERS (All ages series)
DC Comics: Jan, 2017 - No. 6, Jun, 2017 ($2.99, limited series)

1-6-Franco & Baltazar-s/Baltazar-a/c; Superman, Batman & Wonder Woman vs. Brainiac 3.00						

SUPER PUP (Formerly Spotty The Pup) (See Space Comics)
Avon Periodicals: No. 2, Mar-Apr, 1954 - No. 5, 1954

	GD	VG	FN	VF	VF/NM	NM-
4,5: 4-Atom bomb-c. 5-Robot-c	11	22	33	64	90	115

SUPER RABBIT (See All Surprise, Animated Movie Tunes, Comedy Comics, Comic Capers, Ideal Comics, It's A Duck's Life, Li'l Pals, Movie Tunes & Wisco)
Timely Comics (CmPI): Fall, 1944 - No. 14, Nov, 1948

	GD	VG	FN	VF	VF/NM	NM-
1-Hitler & Hirohito-c; war effort paper recycling PSA by S&K; Ziggy Pig & Silly Seal begin	314	628	942	2198	3849	5500
2	58	116	174	371	636	900
3-5	37	74	111	222	361	500
6-Origin	40	80	120	246	411	575
7-10: 9-Infinity-c	27	54	81	158	259	360
11-Kurtzman's "Hey Look"	30	60	90	177	289	400
12-14	27	54	81	158	259	360
I.W. Reprint #1,2('58),7,10('63): 1-r/#13. 2-r/#10.	3	6	9	19	30	40

SUPER RICHIE (Superichie #5 on) (See Richie Rich Millions #68)
Harvey Publications: Sept, 1975 - No. 4, Mar, 1976 (All 52 pg. Giants)

	GD	VG	FN	VF	VF/NM	NM-
1	3	6	9	17	26	35
2-4	2	4	6	11	16	20

SUPER SECRET CRISIS WAR! (Crossover of Cartoon Network characters)
IDW Publishing: Jun, 2014 - No. 6, Nov, 2014 ($3.99, limited series)

1-6-Powerpuff Girls, Samurai Jack, Dexter, Ben 10 vs. Aku, Mojo Jojo, Mandark						4.00
... Codename: Kids Next Door One-Shot (11/14 $3.99) 3 covers; Jampole-a						4.00

Supermouse #1 © STD

Supersnipe Comics #11 © S&S

Superwoman #1 © DC

	GD	VG	FN	VF	VF/NM	NM-		GD	VG	FN	VF	VF/NM	NM-
	2.0	4.0	6.0	8.0	9.0	9.2		2.0	4.0	6.0	8.0	9.0	9.2

... Cow and Chicken One-Shot (10/14 $3.99) 3 covers; Jim Zub-s   4.00
... Foster's Home For Imaginary Friends One-Shot (9/14 $3.99) 3 covers; Ganucheau-a   4.00
... Johnny Bravo One-Shot (7/14 $3.99) 3 covers; Erica Henderson-a   4.00
... The Grimm Adventures of Billy and Mandy One-Shot (7/14 $3.99) 3 covers; Leth-s   4.00

SUPER SLUGGERS (Baseball)
Ultimate Sports Ent. Inc.: 1999 ($3.95, one-shot)
1-Bonds, Piazza, Caminiti, Griffey Jr. app.; Martinbrough-c/a   4.00

SUPERSNIPE COMICS (Formerly Army & Navy #1-5)
Street & Smith Publications: V1#6, Oct, 1942 - V5#1, Aug-Sept, 1949
(See Shadow Comics V2#3)

V1#6-Rex King - Man of Adventure (costumed hero, see Super Magic/Magician) by Jack							
Binder begins; Supersnipe by George Marcoux continues from Army & Navy #5;							
Bill Ward-a	103	206	309	659	1130	1600	
7,10-12: 10,11-Little Nemo app.	58	116	174	371	636	900	
8-Hitler, Tojo, Mussolini in Hell with Devil-c	486	972	1458	3550	6275	9000	
9-Doc Savage x-over in Supersnipe; Hitler-c	432	864	1296	3154	5577	8000	
V2 #1: Both V2#1(2/44) & V2#2(4/44) have V2#1 on outside-c; Huck Finn by Clare Dwiggins							
begins, ends V3#5 (rare)	63	126	189	403	689	975	
V2#2 (4/44) has V2#1 on outside-c; classic shark-c	50	100	150	315	533	750	
3-12: 12-Statue of Liberty-c	27	54	81	158	259	360	
V3#1-12: 8-Bobby Crusoe by Dwiggins begins, ends V3#12. 9-X-Mas-c							
	23	46	69	136	223	310	
V4#1-12, V5#1: V4#10-X-Mas-c	20	40	60	117	189	260	

NOTE: *George Marcoux c-V1#6-V3#4. Doc Savage app. in some issues.*

SUPER SOLDIER (See Marvel Versus DC #3)
DC Comics (Amalgam): Apr, 1996 ($1.95, one-shot)
1-Mark Waid script & Dave Gibbons-c/a.   4.00

SUPER SOLDIER: MAN OF WAR
DC Comics (Amalgam): June, 1997 ($1.95, one-shot)
1-Waid & Gibbons-s/Gibbons & Palmiotti-c/a.   4.00

SUPER SOLDIERS
Marvel Comics UK: Apr, 1993 - No. 8, Nov, 1993 ($1.75)
1-($2.50)-Embossed silver foil logo   5.00
2-8: 5-Capt. America app. 6-Origin; Nick Fury app.; neon ink-c   4.00

SUPER SONS
DC Comics: Apr, 2017 - No. 16, Jul, 2018 ($2.99/$3.99)
1,2: 1-Damian Wayne (Robin) & Jon Kent (Superboy) team-up; Tomasi-s/Jimenez-a   3.00
3-16-($3.99) 3,4-Battle Kid Amazo. 6,7-Teen Titans app. 11,12-Future adult Superboy
(Conner), Wonder Girl (Cassie) and Kid Flash (Bart) app. 13,14-Talia app.   4.00
Annual 1 (1/18, $4.99) Tomasi-s/Pelletier-a; Krypto, Titus & the Super-Pets app.   5.00
... / Dynomutt Special 1 (7/18, $4.99) Blue Falcon and Red Vulture app.; Pasarin-a   5.00

SUPERSPOOK (Formerly Frisky Animals on Parade)
Ajax/Farrell Publications: No. 4, June, 1958

4	10	20	30	58	79	100	

SUPER SPY (See Wham Comics)
Centaur Publications: Oct, 1940 - No. 2, Nov, 1940 (Reprints)

1-Origin The Sparkler	126	252	378	806	1378	1950	
2-The Inner Circle, Dean Denton, Tim Blain, The Drew Ghost, The Night Hawk							
by Gustavson, & S.S. Swanson by Glanz begin	297	594	891	1901	3251	4600	

SUPERSTAR: AS SEEN ON TV
Image Comics (Gorilla): 2001 ($5.95)
1-Busiek-s/Immonen-a   6.00

SUPER STAR HOLIDAY SPECIAL (See DC Special Series #21)

SUPER-TEAM FAMILY
National Periodical Publ./DC Comics: Oct-Nov, 1975 - No. 15, Mar-Apr, 1978

1-Reprints by Neal Adams & Kane/Wood; 68 pgs. begin, ends #4. New Gods app.							
	4	8	12	25	40	55	
2,3: New stories	3	6	9	15	22	28	
4-7: Reprints. 4-G.A. JSA-r & Superman/Batman/Robin-r from World's Finest.							
5-52 pgs. begin	2	4	6	10	14	18	
8-14: 8-10-New Challengers of the Unknown stories. 9-Kirby-a. 11-14: New stories							
	3	6	9	14	19	24	
15-New Gods app. New stories	3	6	9	14	20	26	

NOTE: *Neal Adams r-1-3. Brunner c-3. Buckler c-8p. Tuska a-7r. Wood a-1i(r), 3.*

SUPER TV HEROES (See Hanna-Barbera...)

SUPER-VILLAIN CLASSICS
Marvel Comics Group: May, 1983

1-Galactus -The Origin; Kirby-a

4	8	12	23	37	50	

SUPER-VILLAIN TEAM-UP (See Fantastic Four #6 & Giant-Size...)
Marvel Comics Group: 8/75 - No. 14, 10/77; No. 15, 11/78; No. 16, 5/79; No. 17, 6/80

1-Continued from Giant-Size Super-Villain Team-Up #2; Sub-Mariner & Dr. Doom begin,							
end #10	6	12	18	38	69	100	
2-5: 5-1st app. The Shroud	3	6	9	16	23	30	
5-(30¢-c variant, limited distribution)(4/76)	7	14	21	46	86	125	
6,7-(25¢ editions) 6-(6/76)-F.F., Shroud app. 7-Origin Shroud							
	2	4	6	11	16	20	
6,7-(30¢-c, limited distribution)(6,8/76)	6	12	18	38	69	110	
8,9,11-17: 9-Avengers app. 11-15-Dr. Doom & Red Skull app.							
	2	4	6	9	13	16	
10-Classic Dr. Doom, Red Skull, Captain America battle-c							
	3	6	9	17	26	35	
12-14-(35¢-c variants, limited distribution)(6,8,10/77)							
	13	26	39	89	195	300	

NOTE: *Buckler c-4p, 5p, 7p. Buscema c-1. Byrne/Austin a-13. Evans a-1p, 3p. Everett a-1p. Giffen a-8p, 13p;
c-13p. Kane c-2p, 9p. Mooney a-4i. Starlin c-6. Tuska a-1p, 15p. Wood r-15p.*

SUPER-VILLAIN TEAM-UP/ MODOK'S 11
Marvel Comics: Sept, 2007 - No. 5, Jan, 2008 ($2.99, limited series)
1-5: 1-MODOK's origin re-told; Portela-a/Powell-c; Purple Man & Mentallo app.   3.00
... TPB (2008, $13.99) r/#1-5   14.00

SUPER WESTERN COMICS (Also see Buffalo Bill)
Youthful Magazines: Aug, 1950 (One shot)

1-Buffalo Bill begins; Wyatt Earp, Calamity Jane & Sam Slade app; Powell-c/a							
	21	42	63	122	199	275	

SUPER WESTERN FUNNIES (See Super Funnies)

SUPERWOMAN
DC Comics: Jan 1942
nn - Ashcan comic, not distributed to newsstands, only for in-house use. Cover art is More Fun
Comics #73 with interior being Action Comics #38   (no known sales)

SUPERWOMAN (DC Rebirth)
DC Comics: Oct, 2016 - No. 18, Mar, 2018 ($2.99/$3.99)
1-8: 1-Phil Jimenez-s; Lois and Lana with powers. 2-8-Lena Luthor app.   3.00
9-18-($3.99): 9,10-Segovia-a. 13-15-Supergirl app. 14-18-Maxima app.   4.00

SUPERWORLD COMICS
Hugo Gernsback Publ.): Apr, 1940 - No. 3, Aug, 1940 (68 pgs.)

1-Origin & 1st app. Hip Knox, Super Hypnotist; Mitey Powers & Buzz Allen,							
the Invisible Avenger, Little Nemo begin; cover by Frank R. Paul (all have sci/fi-c)							
(Scarce)	1180	2360	3540	8600	18,300	28,000	
2-Marvo 1-2 Go+, the Super Boy of the Year 2680 (7/40 app.); Paul-c (Scarce)							
	919	1838	2757	6709	11,855	17,000	
3 (Scarce)	568	1136	1704	4146	7323	10,500	

SUPERZERO
AfterShock Comics: Dec, 2015 - No. 6, Jun, 2016 ($3.99)
1-6-Conner & Palmiotti-s/De Latorre-a. 1-Covers by Conner, Cooke & Hester   4.00

SUPER ZOMBIES
Dynamite Entertainment: 2009 - No. 5, 2009 ($3.50)
1-5-Mel Rubi-a; Guggenheim & Gonzales-s; two covers for each by Rubi & Neves   3.50

SUPREME (Becomes ...The New Adventures #43-48)(See Youngblood #3)
(Also see Bloodwulf Special, Legend of Supreme, & Trencher #3)
Image Comics (Extreme Studios)/ Awesome Entertainment #49 on:
V2#1, Nov, 1992 - V2#42, Sept, 1996; V3#49 - No. 56, Feb, 1998

V2#1-Liefeld-a(i) & scripts; embossed foil logo						5.00	
1-Gold Edition	1	2	3	5	6	7	
2-(3/93)-Liefeld co-plots & inks; 1st app. Grizlock						4.00	
3-42: 3-Intro Bloodstrike; 1st app. Khrome. 5-1st app. Thor. 6-1st brief app. The Starguard.							
7-1st full app. The Starguard. 10-Black and White Pt 1 (1st app.) by Art Thibert (2 pgs.							
ea. installment). 25-(5/94)-Platt-c. 11-Coupon #4 for Extreme Prejudice #0; Black and							
White Pt. 7 by Thibert. 12-(4/94)-Platt-c. 13,14-(6/94). 15 (7/94). 16 (7/94)-Stormwatch							
app. 18-Kid Supreme Sneak Preview; Pitt app.19,20-Polybagged w/trading card.							
20-1st app. Woden & Loki (as a dog); Overtkill app. 21-1st app. Loki (in true form).							
21-23-Poly-bagged trading card. 32-Lady Supreme cameo. 33-Origin & 1st full app.							
Lady Supreme (Probe from the Starguard); Babewatch! tie-in. 37-Intro Loki; Fraga-c.							
40-Retells Supreme's past advs. 41-Alan Moore scripts begin; Supreme revised;							
intro The Supremacy; Jerry Ordway-c (Joe Bennett variant-c exists). 42-New origin							
w/Rick Veitch-a; intro Radar, The Hound Supreme & The League of Infinity						4.00	
28-Variant-c by Quesada & Palmiotti						4.00	

(#43-48-**See Supreme: The New Adventures**)

	GD 2.0	VG 4.0	FN 6.0	VF 8.0	VF/NM 9.0	NM- 9.2

V3#49,51: 49-Begin $2.99-c | | | | | | 4.00
50-($3.95)-Double sized, 2 covers, pin-up gallery | | | | | | 5.00
52a,52b-($3.50) | | | | | | 5.00
53-56: 53-Sprouse-a begins. 56-McGuinness-c | | | | | | 4.00
Annual 1-(1995, $4.95) | | | | | | 5.00
...: Supreme Sacrifice (3/06, $3.99) Flip book with Suprema; Kirkman-s/Malin-a | | | | | | 5.00
...: The Return TPB (Checker Book Publ., 2003, $24.95) r/#53-56 & Supreme; The Return #1-6; Ross-c; additional sketch pages by Ross | | | | | | 25.00
...: The Story of the Year TPB (Checker Book Publ., 2002, $26.95) r/#41-52; Ross-c | | | | | | 27.00
NOTE: *Rob Liefeld* a(i)-1, 2; co-plots-2-4; scripts-1, 5, 6. *Ordway* c-41. *Platt* c-12, 25. *Thibert* c(i)-7-9.

SUPREME
Image Comics: No. 63, Apr, 2012 - No. 68, Jan, 2013 ($2.99)
63-66: 63-Moore-s; two covers by Larsen & Hamscher; Larsen-a in all | | | | | | 3.00
67,68-($3.99) 67-Omni-Man (from Invincible) app.; Larsen-a | | | | | | 4.00

SUPREME BLUE ROSE
Image Comics: Jul, 2014 - No. 7, Mar, 2015 ($2.99)
1-7-Warren Ellis-s/Tula Lotay-a | | | | | | 3.00

SUPREME: GLORY DAYS
Image Comics (Extreme Studios): Oct, 1994 - No. 2, Dec, 1994 ($2.95/$2.50, limited series)
1,2: 2-Diehard, Roman, Superpatriot, & Glory app. | | | | | | 4.00

SUPREME POWER (Also see Squadron Supreme 2006 series)
Marvel Comics (MAX): Oct, 2003 - No. 18, Oct, 2005 ($2.99)
1-($2.99) Straczynski-s/Frank-a; Frank-c | | | | | | 3.00
1-($4.99) Special Edition with variant Quesada-c; includes r/early Squadron Supreme apps. | | | | | | 5.00
2-18: 4-Intro. Nighthawk. 6-The Blur debuts. 10-Princess Zarda returns. 17-Hyperion revealed as alien. 18-Continues in mini-series | | | | | | 3.00
... MGC #1 (7/11, $1.00) r/#1 with "Marvel's Greatest Comics" banner on cover | | | | | | 3.00
Vol. 1: Contact TPB (2004, $14.99) r/#1-6 | | | | | | 15.00
Vol. 2: Powers & Principalities TPB (2004, $14.99) r/#7-12 | | | | | | 15.00
Vol. 3: High Command TPB (2005, $14.99) r/#13-18 | | | | | | 15.00
Vol. 1 HC (2005, $29.99, 7 1/2" x 11" with dustjacket) r/#1-12; Avengers #85 & 86, Straczynski intro., Frank cover sketches and character design pages | | | | | | 30.00
Vol. 2 HC (2006, $29.99, 7 1/2" x 11" with dustjacket) r/#13-18; ...: Hyperion #1-5; character design pages | | | | | | 30.00

SUPREME POWER
Marvel Comics (MAX): Aug, 2011 - No. 4, Nov, 2011 ($3.99, limited series)
1-4-Higgins-s/Garcia-a/Fiumara-c; Doctor Spectrum app. | | | | | | 4.00

SUPREME POWER: HYPERION
Marvel Comics (MAX): Nov, 2005 - No. 5, Mar, 2006 ($2.99, limited series)
1-5: 1-Straczynski-s/Jurgens-a/Dodson-c | | | | | | 3.00
TPB (2006, $14.99) r/#1-5 | | | | | | 15.00

SUPREME POWER: NIGHTHAWK
Marvel Comics (MAX): Nov, 2005 - No. 6, Apr, 2006 ($2.99, limited series)
1-6-Daniel Way-s/Steve Dillon-a; origin of Whiteface | | | | | | 3.00
TPB (2006, $16.99) r/#1-6; cover concept art | | | | | | 17.00

SUPREME: THE NEW ADVENTURES (Formerly Supreme)
Maximum Press: V3#43, Oct, 1996 - V3#48, May, 1997 ($2.50)
V3#43-48: 43-Alan Moore scripts in all; Joe Bennett-a; Rick Veitch-a (8 pgs.); Dan Jurgens-a (1 pg.); intro Citadel Supreme & Suprematons; 1st Allied Supermen of America | | | | | | 4.00

SUPREME: THE RETURN
Awesome Entertainment: May, 1999 - No. 6, June, 2000 ($2.99)
1-6: Alan Moore-s. 1,2-Sprouse & Gordon-a/c. 2,4-Liefeld-c. 6-Kirby app. | | | | | | 4.00

SUPURBIA (GRACE RANDOLPH'S...)
BOOM! Studios: Mar, 2012 - No. 4, Jun, 2012 ($3.99, limited series)
1-4-Grace Randolph-s/Dauterman-a. 1-Garza-c | | | | | | 4.00

SUPURBIA (GRACE RANDOLPH'S...) (Volume 2)
BOOM! Studios: Nov, 2012 - No. 12, Oct, 2013 ($3.99, limited series)
1-12-Grace Randolph-s/Dauterman-a; multiple covers on #1-5 | | | | | | 4.00

SURE-FIRE COMICS (Lightning Comics #4 on)
Ace Magazines: June, 1940 - No. 4, Oct, 1940 (Two No. 3's)
V1#1-Origin Flash Lightning & begins; X-The Phantom Fed, Ace McCoy, Buck Steele, Marvo the Magician, The Raven, Whiz Wilson (Time Traveler) begin (all 1st app.); Flash Lightning c-1-4 | 300 | 600 | 900 | 2070 | 3635 | 5200
2 | 219 | 438 | 657 | 1402 | 2401 | 3400
3(9/40), 3(#4)(10/40)-nn on-c, #3 on inside | 161 | 322 | 483 | 1030 | 1765 | 2500

SURFACE TENSION
Titan Comics: Jun, 2015 - No. 5, Oct, 2015 ($3.99, limited series)
1-5-Jay Gunn-s/a. 1,2-Two covers | | | | | | 4.00

SURF 'N' WHEELS
Charlton Comics: Nov, 1969 - No. 6, Sept, 1970
1 | 3 | 6 | 9 | 21 | 33 | 45
2-6 | 3 | 6 | 9 | 14 | 19 | 24

SURGE
Eclipse Comics: July, 1984 - No. 4, Jan, 1985 ($1.50, lim. series, Baxter paper)
1-4-Ties into DNAgents series | | | | | | 4.00

SURGEON X
Image Comics: Sept, 2016 - No. 6, Feb, 2017 ($3.99)
1-6: 1-Sara Kenney-s/John Watkiss-a. 6-Watkiss & Pleece-a | | | | | | 4.00

SURPRISE ADVENTURES (Formerly Tormented)
Sterling Comic Group: No. 3, Mar, 1955 - No. 5, July, 1955
3-5: 3,5-Sekowsky-a | 14 | 28 | 42 | 82 | 121 | 160

SURVIVAL STREET
Dark Horse Comics: Aug, 2022 - No. 4, Nov, 2022 ($3.99, limited series)
1-4-Asmus & Festante-s/Kussainov-a | | | | | | 4.00

SURVIVE (Follows Cataclysm: The Ultimates Last Stand)

Marvel Comics: May, 2014 ($3.99, one-shot)
1-Bendis-s/Quinones-a; the new Ultimates team is formed | | | | | | 4.00

SURVIVORS' CLUB
DC Comics (Vertigo): Dec, 2015 - No. 9, Aug, 2016 ($3.99)
1-9-Beukes & Halvorsen-s/Ryan Kelly-a/Sienkiewicz-c | | | | | | 4.00

SUSIE Q. SMITH
Dell Publishing Co.: No. 323, Mar, 1951 - No. 553, Apr, 1954
Four Color 323 (#1) | 8 | 16 | 24 | 55 | 105 | 155
Four Color 377, 453 (2/53), 553 | 6 | 12 | 18 | 37 | 66 | 95

SUSPENSE (Radio/TV issues #1-11; Real Life Tales of... #1-4) (Amazing Detective Cases #3 on?)
Marvel/Atlas Comics (CnPC No. 1-10/BFP No. 11-29): Dec, 1949 - No. 29, Apr, 1953 (#1-8, 17-23: 52 pgs.)
1-Powell-a; Peter Lorre, Sidney Greenstreet photo-c from Hammett's "The Verdict" | 123 | 246 | 369 | 787 | 1344 | 1900
2-Crime stories; Dennis O'Keefe & Gale Storm photo-c from Universal movie "Abandoned" | 53 | 106 | 159 | 334 | 567 | 800
3-Change to horror | 68 | 136 | 204 | 435 | 743 | 1050
4,7-10: 7-Dracula-sty | 55 | 110 | 165 | 352 | 601 | 850
5-Krigstein, Tuska, Everett-a | 58 | 116 | 174 | 371 | 636 | 900
6-Tuska, Everett, Morisi-a | 52 | 104 | 156 | 378 | 552 | 775
11-13,15-17,19,20 | 47 | 94 | 141 | 296 | 408 | 700
14-Classic Heath Hypo-c; A-Bomb panels | 135 | 270 | 405 | 864 | 1482 | 2100
18,22-Krigstein-a | 47 | 94 | 141 | 296 | 498 | 700
21,23,24,26-29: 24-Tuska-a | 42 | 84 | 126 | 265 | 445 | 625
25-Electric chair-c/story | 60 | 120 | 180 | 381 | 653 | 925
NOTE: *Ayers* a-20. *Briefer* a-5, 7, 27. *Brodsky* c-4, 6-9, 11, 16, 17, 26. *Colan* a-8(2), 9. *Everett* a-5, 6(2), 19, 23, 28; c-21-23, 26. *Fuje* a-29. *Heath* a-5, 6, 8, 10, 12, 14; c-14, 19, 24. *Maneely* a-11, 12, 23, 24, 28, 29; c-5, 6p, 10, 13, 15, 18. *Mooney* a-24, 28. *Morisi* a-12. *Palais* a-10. *Rico* a-7-9. *Robinson* a-29. *Romita* a-20(2), 25. *Sekowsky* a-11, 13, 14. *Sinnott* a-23, 25. *Tuska* a-5, 6(2), 12; c-12. *Whitney* a-15, 16, 22. *Ed Win* a-27.

SUSPENSE COMICS
Continental Magazines: Dec, 1943 - No. 12, Sept, 1946
1-The Grey Mask begins; bondage/torture-c; L. B. Cole-a (7 pgs.) | 1000 | 2000 | 3000 | 7600 | 13,800 | 20,000
2-Intro. The Mask; Rico, Giunta, L. B. Cole-a (7 pgs.) | 423 | 846 | 1269 | 3046 | 5323 | 7600
3-L.B. Cole-a; classic Schomburg-c (Scarce) | 12,950 | 25,900 | 38,850 | 77,700 | 133,850 | 190,000
4-L. B. Cole-c begin | 343 | 686 | 1029 | 2400 | 4200 | 6000
5,6 | 300 | 600 | 900 | 1950 | 3375 | 4800
7,9,10,12: 9-L.B. Cole eyeball-c | 245 | 490 | 735 | 1568 | 2684 | 3800
8-Classic L. B. Cole spider-c | 975 | 1950 | 2919 | 7100 | 12,550 | 18,000
11-Classic Devil-c | 486 | 972 | 1458 | 3550 | 6275 | 9000
NOTE: *L. B. Cole* c-4-12. *Fuje* a-8. *Larsen* a-11. *Palais* a-10, 11. *Bondage* c-1, 3, 4.

SUSPENSE DETECTIVE
Fawcett Publications: June, 1952 - No. 5, Mar, 1953
1-Evans-a (11 pgs); Baily-c/a | 63 | 126 | 189 | 403 | 689 | 975
2-Evans-a (10 pgs.) | 34 | 68 | 102 | 204 | 332 | 460
3-5 | 31 | 62 | 93 | 182 | 296 | 410
NOTE: *Baily* a-4, 5; c-1-3. *Sekowsky* a-2, 4, 5; c-5.

SUSPENSE STORIES (See Strange Suspense Stories)

SUSSEX VAMPIRE, THE (Sherlock Holmes)
Caliber Comics: 1996 ($2.95, 32 pgs., B&W, one-shot)
nn-Adapts Sir Arthur Conan Doyle's story; Warren Ellis scripts | | | | | | 4.00

SUZIE COMICS (Formerly Laugh Comix; see Laugh Comics, Liberty Comics #10, Pep Comics & Top-Notch Comics #28)
Close-Up No. 49,50/MLJ Mag./Archie No. 51 on: No. 49, Spring, 1945 - No. 100, Aug, 1954
49-Ginger begins | 71 | 142 | 213 | 454 | 777 | 1100
50-55: 54-Transvestism story. 55-Woggon-a | 43 | 86 | 129 | 271 | 461 | 650
56-Katy Keene begins by Woggon | 71 | 142 | 213 | 454 | 777 | 1100
57-65 | 27 | 54 | 81 | 158 | 259 | 360
66-80 | 21 | 42 | 63 | 126 | 206 | 285
81-87,89-99 | 20 | 40 | 60 | 115 | 185 | 255
88,100: 88-Used in POP, pgs. 76,77; Bill Woggon draws himself in story. 100-Last Katy Keene | 21 | 42 | 63 | 126 | 206 | 285
NOTE: *Al Fagaly* a-49-67. Katy Keene app. in 53-82, 85-100.

SWAMP FOX, THE (TV, Disney) (See Walt Disney Presents #2)
Dell Publishing Co.: No. 1179, Dec, 1960
Four Color 1179-Leslie Nielsen photo-c | 10 | 20 | 30 | 64 | 132 | 200

SWAMP THING (See Brave & the Bold, Challengers of the Unknown #82, DC Comics Presents #8 & 85, DC Special Series #2, 14, 17, 20, House of Secrets #92, Limited Collectors' Edition C-59, & Roots of the...)

SWAMP THING
National Per. Publ./DC Comics: Oct-Nov, 1972 - No. 24, Aug-Sept, 1976
1-Wrightson-c/a begins; origin | 21 | 42 | 63 | 147 | 324 | 500
2-1st brief app. Patchwork Man (1 panel) | 8 | 16 | 24 | 56 | 108 | 160
3-1st full app. Patchwork Man (see House of Secrets #140) | 8 | 16 | 24 | 54 | 102 | 150
4-6, | 5 | 10 | 15 | 35 | 63 | 90
7-Batman-c/story | 9 | 18 | 27 | 58 | 114 | 170
8-10: 10-Last Wrightson issue | 5 | 10 | 15 | 33 | 57 | 80
11-20: 11-19-Redondo-a. 13-Origin retold (1 pg.) | 3 | 6 | 9 | 17 | 30 | 40
21-24: 22,23-Redondo-a. 23,24-Swamp Thing reverts back to Dr. Holland. 23-New logo | 3 | 6 | 9 | 19 | 30 | 40
Secret of the Swamp Thing (2005, $9.99, digest) r/#1-10 | | | | | | 10.00
NOTE: *J. Jones* a-9(assist). *Kaluta* a-9i. *Redondo* c-11-19, 21. *Wrightson* issues (#1-10) reprinted in DC Special Series #2, 14, 17, 20 & Roots of the Swamp Thing.

SWAMP THING (Saga Of The... #1-38,42-45) (See Essential Vertigo:...)
DC Comics (Vertigo imprint #129 on): May, 1982 - No. 171, Oct, 1996 (Direct sales #65 on)
1-Origin retold; Phantom Stranger series begins; ends #13; Yeates-c/a begins | 3 | 6 | 9 | 16 | 23 | 30
2-15: 2-Photo-c from movie. 13-Last Yeates-a | | | | | | 5.00
16-19: Bissette-a. | | | | | | 6.00

Surf n' Wheels #1 © CC

Surge #1 © ECL

Swamp Thing (2016 series) #3 © DC

	GD 2.0	VG 4.0	FN 6.0	VF 8.0	VF/NM 9.0	NM- 9.2
20-1st Alan Moore issue	5	10	15	30	50	70
21-New origin	4	8	12	28	47	65
21 Special Editon (5/09, $1.00) reprint with "After Watchmen" cover frame						5.00
22,23	2	4	6	9	13	16
24-JLA x-over; last Yeates-c.	3	6	9	14	19	24
25-John Constantine 1-panel cameo	5	10	15	30	50	70
26-30	1	3	4	6	8	10
31-33,35,36: 33-1st app. from House of Secrets #92						6.00
34-Classic-c	3	6	9	14	20	25
37-1st app. John Constantine (Hellblazer) (6/85)	15	30	45	100	220	340
38-40: John Constantine app.	2	4	6	8	11	14
41-52,54-64: 44-Batman cameo. 44-51-John Constantine app. 46-Crisis x-over; Batman cameo. 49-Spectre app. 50-($1.25, 52 pgs.)-Deadman, Dr. Fate, Demon. 52-Arkham Asylum-c/story; Joker-c/cameo. 58-Spectre preview. 64-Last Moore issue						4.00
53-($1.25, 52 pgs.)-Arkham Asylum; Batman-c/story						5.00
65-83,85-99,101-124,126-149,151-153: 65-Direct sales only begins. 66-Batman & Arkham Asylum x-over/story; Batman-c/story; 76-X-over w/Hellblazer #9. 79-Superman-c/story. 85-Jonah Hex app. 102-Preview of World Without End. 116-Photo-c. 129-Metallic ink on-c. 140-Millar scripts begin, end #171						4.00
84-Sandman (Morpheus) cameo.						5.00
100,125,150: 100-($2.50, 52 pgs.). 125-($2.95, 52 pgs.)-20th anniversary issue. 150 (52 pgs.)-Anniversary issue						5.00
154-171: 154-$2.25-c begins. 165-Curt Swan-a(p). 166,169,171-John Constantine & Phantom Stranger app. 168-Arcane returns						4.00
Annual 1,3,6-('82-91): 1-Movie Adaptation; painted-c. 3-New format; Bolland-c. 4-Batman-c/story. 6-Batman cameo; re-intro Brother Power (Geek),1st app. since 1968						6.00

	1	2	3	5	6	
Annual 2 (1985)-Moore scripts; Bissette-a(p); Deadman, Spectre app.						
Annual 7(1993, $3.95)-Children's Crusade						5.00
...A Murder of Crows (2001, $19.95)-r/#43-50; Moore-s						20.00
...: Earth To Earth (2002, $17.95)-r/#51-56; Batman app.						18.00
...: Infernal Triangles (2006, $19.99, TPB) r/#77-81 & Annual #3; cover gallery						20.00
...: Love and Death (1990, $17.95)-r/#28-34 & Annual #2; Totleben painted-c						18.00
...: Regenesis (2004, $17.95, TPB) r/#65-70; Veitch-s						18.00
...: Reunion (2003, $19.95, TPB) r/#57-64; Moore-s						20.00
...: Roots (1998, $7.95) Jon J Muth-s/painted-a/c						8.00
Saga of the Swamp Thing ('87, '89)-r/#21-27 (1st & 2nd print)						15.00
Saga of the Swamp Thing Book One HC (2009, $24.99, d.j.) r/#20-27; Wein intro.						25.00
Saga of the Swamp Thing Book Two HC (2009, $24.99, d.j.) r/#28-34 & Annual #2						25.00
Saga of the Swamp Thing Book Three HC (2010, $24.99, d.j.) r/#35-42; Bissette intro.						25.00
Saga of the Swamp Thing Book Four HC (2010, $24.99, d.j.) r/#43-50; Gaiman foreword						25.00
Saga of the Swamp Thing Book Five HC (2011, $24.99, d.j.) r/#51-56; Bissette intro.						25.00
...: Spontaneous Generation (2005, $19.99) r/#71-76						20.00
...: The Curse (2000, $19.95, TPB) r/#35-42; Bisley-c						20.00

NOTE: **Bissette** a(p)-16-19, 21-27, 29, 30, 34-36, 39-42, 44, 46, 50, 64: c-17i, 24-32i, 35-37p, 40p, 44p, 46-50p, 51-58, 61, 62, 63p. **Kaluta** c/a-74. **Spiegle** a-1-3, 6. **Sutton** a-98p. **Totleben** a(i)-10, 16-27, 29, 31, 34-40, 42, 44, 46, 48, 50, 53, 55i; c-25-32i, 33, 35-40i, 42i, 44i, 46-50i, 53, 55i, 59p, 64, 65, 68, 73, 76, 80, 82, 84, 89, 91-100, Annual 4, 5. **Vess** painted c-121, 129-139, Annual 7. **Williamson** 86i. **Wrightson** a-18i(r), 33r. John Constantine appears in #37-40, 44-51, 65-67, 70-77, 80-90, 99, 114, 115, 130, 134-138.

SWAMP THING
DC Comics (Vertigo): May, 2000 - No. 20, Dec, 2001 ($2.50)

1-3-Tefé Holland's return; Vaughan-s/Petersen-a; Hale painted-c.						4.00
4-20: 7-9-Bisley-c. 10-John Constantine-c/app. 10-12-Fabry-c. 13-15-Mack-c. 18-Swamp Thing app.						3.00
Preview-16 pg. flip book w/Lucifer Preview						3.00

SWAMP THING
DC Comics (Vertigo): May, 2004 - No. 29, Sept, 2006 ($2.95/$2.99)

1-29: 1-Diggle-s/Breccia-a; Constantine app. 2-6-Sargon app. 7,8,20-Corben-c/a. 21-29-Eric Powell-c						3.00
...: Bad Seed (2004, $9.95) r/#1-6						10.00
...: Healing the Breach (2006, $17.99) r/#15-20						18.00
...: Love in Vain (2005, $14.99) r/#9-14						15.00

SWAMP THING (DC New 52)
DC Comics: Nov, 2011 - No. 40, May, 2015 ($2.99)

1-Snyder-s/Paquette-a; Superman app.						8.00
1-(2nd & 3rd printing)						3.00
2-18: 2-Abigail Arcane returns. 7-Holland transforms. 10-Francavilla-c; Anton Arcane returns. 12-X-over with Animal Man #12. 13-Poison Ivy & Deadman app.; leads into Annual #1						3.00
19-23: 19-Soule-s/Kano-c begin. 19,20-Superman app. 22,23-Constantine app.						3.00
23.1 (11/13, $2.99, regular cover)						3.00
23.1 (11/13, $3.99, 3-D cover) "Arcane #1" on cover; Soule-s/Saiz-a/c; origin of Arcane						5.00
24-39: 24-Leads into Annual #2. 26-Woodrue's origin; Animal Man app. 32-Aquaman app. 39-Constantine app.						3.00
40-($3.99)						4.00

	GD 2.0	VG 4.0	FN 6.0	VF 8.0	VF/NM 9.0	NM- 9.2
#0-(11/12, $2.99) Kano-a; Arcane app.; Swamp Thing origin re-told						3.00
Annual #1 (12/12, $4.99) Flashback to 1st meeting of Alec & Abby; Cloonan-a						5.00
Annual #2 (12/13, $4.99) Soule-s/Pina-a						5.00
Annual #3 (12/14, $4.99) Soule-s/Pina-a: Etrigan app.						5.00
...: Futures End 1 (11/14, $2.99, regular-c) Five years later; Soule-s/Saiz-a; Arcane app.						3.00
...: Futures End 1 (11/14, $3.99, 3-D cover)						4.00

SWAMP THING
DC Comics: Mar, 2016 - No. 6, Aug, 2016 ($2.99)

1-6-Len Wein-s/Kelley Jones-a. 1,2-Phantom Stranger app. 2-Matt Cable returns. 3,4,6-Zatanna app.						3.00
...: Winter Special 1 (3/18, $7.99) Wein-s/Jones-a; King-s/Fabok-a; Wein script & tribute						8.00

SWAMP THING, THE
DC Comics: May, 2021 - No. 16, Oct, 2022 ($3.99, originally a 10-issue series)

1-16: 1-Ram V-s/Mike Perkins-a; intro Levi Kamei. 3,4-Poison Ivy & Alec Holland app. 5-John Constantine app.; McCrea-a. 6-8-Peacemaker & Suicide Squad app.						4.00

SWAMP THING GIANT
DC Comics: 2019 - No. 5, 2019 ($4.99, 100 pgs., squarebound, Walmart exclusive)

1-5: 1-New story Seeley-s/Perkins-a; reprints from Animal Man ('11), Swamp Thing ('11), and Shadowpact ('06). 2-New story with Joëlle Jones-a plus reprints continue						5.00
Halloween Horror Giant ('18, $4.99) Intro. Briar in new story; Capullo-a; plus reprints						5.00

SWAMP THING GIANT
DC Comics: 2019 - No. 5, 2020 ($4.99, 100 pgs., squarebound, Mass Market & Direct Market editions exist for each issue, with different covers)

1-5-New story Santucci-a & Hester-s/Mandrake-a; plus reprints						5.00

SWAMP THING: GREEN HELL
DC Comics (Black Label): Feb, 2022 - No. 3, May, 2023 ($6.99, oversized 8-1/2" x 10-3/4", lim. series)

1-3-Jeff Lemire-s/Doug Mahnke-a; John Constantine app.						7.00
1-Second printing (3/22, $6.99)						7.00

SWAN SONGS
Image Comics: Jul, 2023 - Present ($3.99)

1-6-Anthology written by W. Maxwell Prince. 1-Simmonds-a. 2-Wijngaard-a						4.00

SWASHBUCKLERS: THE SAGA CONTINUES (See Marvel Graphic Novel #14 and Swords of The Swashbucklers)
Dynamite Entertainment: 2018 - No. 5, 2018 ($3.99, limited series)

1-5-Marc Guggenheim-s/Andrea Mutti-a						4.00

SWAT MALONE (America's Home Run King)
Swat Malone Enterprises: Sept, 1955

		GD 2.0	VG 4.0	FN 6.0	VF 8.0	VF/NM 9.0	NM- 9.2
V1#1-Hy Fleishman-a		14	28	42	76	108	140

SWEATSHOP
DC Comics: Jun, 2003 - No. 6, Nov, 2003 ($2.95)

1-6-Peter Bagge-s/a; Destefano-a						3.00

SWEENEY (Formerly Buz Sawyer)
Standard Comics: No. 4, June, 1949 - No. 5, Sept, 1949

	GD 2.0	VG 4.0	FN 6.0	VF 8.0	VF/NM 9.0	NM- 9.2
4,5: 5-Crane-a	10	20	30	58	79	100

SWEE'PEA (Also see Popeye #46)
Dell Publishing Co.: No. 219, Mar, 1949

	GD 2.0	VG 4.0	FN 6.0	VF 8.0	VF/NM 9.0	NM- 9.2
Four Color 219	11	22	33	76	163	250

SWEET CHILDE
Advantage Graphics Press: 1995 - No. 2, 1995 ($2.95, B&W, mature)

1,2						4.00

SWEETHEART DIARY (Cynthia Doyle #66-on)
Fawcett Publications/Charlton Comics No. 32 on: Wint, 1949; #2, Spr, 1950; #3, 6/50 - #5, 10/50; #6, 1951(nd); #7, 9/51 - #14, 1/53; #32, 2/55; #33, 4/56 - #65, 8/62 (#1-14: photo-c)

	GD 2.0	VG 4.0	FN 6.0	VF 8.0	VF/NM 9.0	NM- 9.2
1	24	48	72	144	237	330
2	15	30	45	85	130	175
3,4-Wood-a	18	36	54	105	165	225
5-10: 8-Bailey-a	10	20	30	58	79	100
11-14: 13-Swayze-a. 14-Last Fawcett issue	9	18	27	50	65	80
32 (10/55; 1st Charlton issue)(Formerly Cowboy Love #31)						
	10	20	30	56	76	95
33-40: 34-Swayze-a	7	14	21	37	46	55
41-(68 pgs.)	8	16	24	42	54	65
42-60	3	6	9	21	33	45
61-65	3	6	9	19	30	40

SWEETHEARTS (Formerly Captain Midnight)

	GD 2.0	VG 4.0	FN 6.0	VF 8.0	VF/NM 9.0	NM- 9.2

Fawcett Publications/Charlton No. 122 on: #68, 10/48 - #121, 5/53; #122, 3/54; V2#23, 5/54 - #137, 12/73

	GD	VG	FN	VF	VF/NM	NM-
68-Photo-c begin	22	44	66	128	209	290
69,70	14	28	42	78	112	145
71-80	10	20	30	56	76	95
81-84,86-93,95-99,105	9	18	27	50	65	80
85,94,103,110,117-George Evans-a	10	20	30	56	76	95
100	10	20	30	54	72	90
101,107-Powell-a	9	18	27	52	69	85
102,104,106,108,109,112-116,118	9	18	27	47	61	75
111-1 pg. Ronald Reagan biography	12	24	36	69	97	125
119-Marilyn Monroe & Richard Widmark photo-c (1/53); also appears in story; part Wood-a	161	322	483	1030	1765	2500
120-Atom Bomb story	13	26	39	74	105	135
121-Liz Taylor/Fernando Lamas photo-c	43	86	129	271	461	650
122-(1st Charlton) 3/54)-Marijuana story	14	28	42	81	118	155
V2#23 (5/54)-28: 28-Last precode issue (2/55)	8	16	24	44	57	70
29-39,41,43,45,47-50	4	8	12	27	44	60
40-Photo-c; Tommy Sands story	4	8	12	28	47	65
42-Ricky Nelson photo-c/story	8	16	24	54	102	150
44-Pat Boone photo-c/story	4	8	12	28	47	65
46-Jimmy Rodgers photo-c/story	4	8	12	28	47	65
51-60	4	8	12	25	37	50
61-80,100	3	6	9	19	30	40
81-99	3	6	9	17	26	35
101-110	3	6	9	14	20	25
111-120,122-124,126-137	2	4	6	11	16	20
121,125-David Cassidy pin-ups	3	6	9	14	20	25

NOTE: *Photo c-68-121(Fawcett), 40, 42, 46(Charlton).* **Swayze** *a(Fawcett)-70-118(most).*

SWEETHEART SCANDALS (See Fox Giants)

SWEETIE PIE
Dell Publishing Co.: No. 1185, May-July, 1961 - No. 1241, Nov-Jan, 1961/62

Four Color 1185 (#1)	6	12	18	38	69	100
Four Color 1241	5	10	15	31	53	75

SWEETIE PIE
Ajax-Farrell/Pines (Literary Ent.): Dec, 1955 - No. 15, Fall, 1957

1-By Nadine Seltzer	14	28	42	81	118	155
2 (5/56; last Ajax?)	8	16	24	44	57	70
3-15	8	16	24	40	50	60

SWEET LOVE
Home Comics (Harvey): Sept, 1949 - No. 5, May, 1950 (All photo-c)

1	15	30	45	83	124	165
2	9	18	27	47	61	75
3,4: 3-Powell-a	8	16	24	42	54	65
5-Kamen, Powell-a	10	20	30	56	76	95

SWEET ROMANCE
Charlton Comics: Oct, 1968

1	3	6	9	14	20	25

SWEET SIXTEEN (....Comics and Stories for Girls)
Parents' Magazine Institute: Aug-Sept, 1946 - No. 13, Jan, 1948 (All have movie stars photos on covers)

1-Van Johnson's life story; Dorothy Dare, Queen of Hollywood Stunt Artists begins (in all issues); part photo-c	36	72	108	211	343	475
2-Jane Powell, Roddy McDowall "Holiday in Mexico" photo on-c; Alan Ladd story	23	46	69	136	223	310
3,5,6,8-11: 5-Ann Francis photo on-c; Gregory Peck story. 6-Dick Haymes story. 8-Shirley Jones photo on-c. 10-Jean Simmons photo on-c; James Stewart story	18	36	54	107	169	230
4-Elizabeth Taylor photo on-c	39	78	117	240	395	550
7-Ronald Reagan's life story	34	68	102	204	332	460
12-Bob Cummings, Vic Damone story	19	38	57	111	176	240
13-Robert Mitchum's life story	19	38	57	111	176	240

SWEET XVI
Marvel Comics: May, 1991 - No. 5, Sept, 1991 ($1.00)

1-5: Barbara Slate story & art						4.00

SWEET TOOTH
DC Comics (Vertigo): Nov, 2009 - No. 40, Feb, 2013 ($1.00/$2.99)

1-($1.00) Jeff Lemire-s/a	6	12	18	38	69	100
2	1	2	3	6	8	10
3-39-($2.99) 18,33-Printed sideways. 26-28-Kindt-a						3.00
40-($4.99) Final issue; two covers by Lemire and Truman						5.00
...: Animal Armies TPB (2011, $14.99) r/#12-17						15.00
...: In Captivity TPB (2010, $12.99) r/#6-11						13.00
...: Out of the Deep Woods TPB (2010, $9.99) r/#1-5						10.00

SWEET TOOTH: THE RETURN
DC Comics (Black Label): Jan, 2021 - No. 6, Jun, 2021 ($3.99, limited series)

1-6-Jeff Lemire-s/a						4.00

SWIFT ARROW (Also see Lone Rider & The Rider)
Ajax/Farrell Publications: Feb-Mar, 1954 - No. 5, Oct-Nov, 1954; Apr, 1957 - No. 3, Sept, 1957

1(1954) (1st Series)	20	40	60	117	189	260
2	13	26	39	74	105	135
3-5: 5-Lone Rider story	9	18	27	52	69	85
1 (2nd Series) (Swift Arrow's Gunfighters #4)	10	20	30	54	72	90
2,3: 2-Lone Rider begins	8	16	24	42	54	65

SWIFT ARROW'S GUNFIGHTERS (Formerly Swift Arrow)
Ajax/Farrell Publ. (Four Star Comic Corp.): No. 4, Nov, 1957

4	8	16	24	42	54	65

SWING WITH SCOOTER
National Periodical Publ.: June-July, 1966 - No. 35, Aug-Sept, 1971; No. 36, Oct-Nov, 1972

1	9	18	27	62	126	190
2,6-10: 9-Alfred E. Newman swipe in last panel	5	10	15	33	57	80
3-5: 3-Batman cameo on-c. 4-Batman cameo inside. 5-JLA cameo		10	15	34	60	85
11-13,15,19- 18-Wildcat of JSA 1pg. text. 19-Last 12¢-c	3	6	9	20	31	42
14-Alfred E. Neuman cameo	4	8	12	23	37	50
20 (68 pgs.)	5	10	15	30	50	70
21-23,25-31	3	6	9	17	26	35
24-Frankenstein-c	4	8	12	23	37	50
32-34 (68 pgs.). 32-Batman cameo. 33-Interview with David Cassidy. 34-Interview with Rick Ely (The Rebels)	4	8	12	28	47	65
35-(52 pgs.). 1 pg. app. Clark Kent and 4 full pgs. of Superman	7	14	21	49	92	135
36-Bat-signal refererence to Batman		6	9	21	33	45

NOTE: *Aragonés* a-13 (1pg.), 18(1pg.), 30(2pgs.) *Orlando* a-3, 11; c-1-11, 13. #20, 33, 34: 68 pgs.; #35: 52 pgs.

SWISS FAMILY ROBINSON (Walt Disney's...; see King Classics & Movie Comics)
Dell Publishing Co.: No. 1156, Dec, 1960

Four Color 1156-Movie-photo-c	9	18	27	62	126	190

SWITCH (Also see Witchblade titles)
Image Comics: Oct, 2015 - No. 4, Jul, 2016 ($3.99)

1-4-Stjepan Sejic-s/a; 3 covers on each						4.00

S.W.O.R.D. (Sentient World Observation and Response Department)
Marvel Comics: Jan, 2010 - No. 5, May, 2010 ($3.99/$2.99)

1-($3.99) Cassaday-s/a; Commander Brand & Henry Gyrich app.						4.00
2-5-($2.99): 2,3-Cassaday-c. 4,5-Del Mundo-c.						3.00

S.W.O.R.D. (Sentient World Observation and Response Department)
Marvel Comics: Feb, 2021 - No. 11, Feb, 2022 ($4.99/$3.99)

1-($4.99) Al Ewing-s/Valerio Schiti-a; Abigail Brand & Magneto app.						5.00
2-11-($3.99) 2,3-4- "King in Black" tie-ins. 6-Hellfire Gala tie-in						4.00

SWORD, THE
Image Comics: Oct, 2007 - No. 24, May, 2010 ($2.99/$4.99)

1-Luna Brothers-s/a						4.00
1-(2nd printing), 2-23: 12-Zakros killed						3.00
24-($4.99) Final issue						5.00

SWORD & THE DRAGON, THE
Dell Publishing Co.: No. 1118, June, 1960

Four Color 1118-Movie, photo-c	9	18	27	57	111	165

SWORD & THE ROSE, THE (Disney)
Dell Publishing Co.: No. 505, Oct, 1953 - No. 682, Feb, 1956

Four Color 505-Movie, photo-c	9	18	27	61	123	185
Four Color 682-When Knighthood was in Flower-Movie, reprint of #505; Renamed the Sword & the Rose for the novel; photo-c	7	14	21	46	86	125

SWORD DAUGHTER
Dark Horse Publishing: Jun, 2018 - No. 9, Jan, 2020 ($4.99)

1-9-Brian Wood-s/Mack Chater-a/Greg Smallwood-c						5.00

SWORD IN THE STONE, THE (See March of Comics #258 & Movie Comics & Wart and the Wizard)

SWORD MASTER
Marvel Comics: Sept, 2019 - No. 12, Jan, 2021 ($3.99)

1-12: 1-Shang-Chi & Ares app.; Shuizhu/Gunji-a. 5,6-Doctor Strange app.						4.00

SWORD OF AGES
IDW Publishing: Nov, 2017 - No. 4 ($3.99)

1-4-Gabriel Rodríguez-s/a						4.00
1 Special Edition (6/18, $6.99) bonus interview with Gabriel Rodríguez; uncolored art						7.00

SWORD OF AZRAEL
DC Comics: Oct, 2022 - No. 6, Mar, 2023 ($3.99, limited series)

1-6-Watters-s/Cizmesija-a; Bane's daughter Vengeance app.						4.00
...: Dark Knight of the Soul 1(10/22, $3.99) Prelude to the series						4.00

SWORD OF DAMOCLES
Image Comics (WildStorm Productions): Mar, 1996 - No. 2, Apr, 1996 ($2.50, limited series)

1,2: Warren Ellis scripts. 1-Prelude to "Fire From Heaven" x-over; 1st app. Sword						4.00

SWORD OF DRACULA
Image Comics: Oct, 2003 - No. 6, Sept, 2004 ($2.95, B&W, limited series)

1-6-Tony Harris-c. 1,2-Greg Scott-a						3.00
TPB (IDW, 2/05, $14.99) r/series						15.00

SWORD OF HYPERBOREA, THE
Dark Horse Comics: Jan, 2022 - No. 4, Apr, 2022 ($3.99, limited series)

1-Mike Mignola & Rob Williams-s/Laurence Campbell-a						5.00

SWORD OF RED SONJA: DOOM OF THE GODS
Dynamite Entertainment: 2007 - No. 4, 2007 ($3.50, limited series)

1-4-Lui Antonio-a; multiple covers on each						3.50

SWORD OF SORCERY
National Periodical Publications: Feb-Mar, 1973 - No. 5, Nov-Dec, 1973 (20¢)

1-Leiber Fafhrd & The Grey Mouser; Chaykin/Neal Adams (Crusty Bunkers) art; Kaluta-c		11	22	33	45	
2,3: 2-Wrightson-c(i); Adams-a(i). 3-Wrightson-i(5 pgs.)	2	4	6	9	13	16
4,5: 5-Starlin-a(p); Conan cameo	2	4	6	8	10	12

NOTE: *Chaykin* a-1-4p; c-2p, 3-5. *Kaluta* a-3i. *Simonson* a-3i, 4i, 5p; c-5.

SWORD OF SORCERY (DC New 52)
DC Comics: No. 0, Nov, 2012 - No. 8, Jun, 2013 ($3.99)

0-8: 0-Origin of Amethyst retold; Lopresti-a; Beowulf back-up; Saiz-a. 4-Stalker back-up						4.00

SWORD OF THE ATOM
DC Comics: Sept, 1983 - No. 4, Dec, 1983 (Limited series)

1-4: Gil Kane-c/a in all						4.00

Sweet Tooth #35 © Jeff Lemire

Sword Master #1 © MAR

Symbiote Spider-Man #5 © MAR

	GD	VG	FN	VF	VF/NM	NM-		GD	VG	FN	VF	VF/NM	NM-
	2.0	4.0	6.0	8.0	9.0	9.2		2.0	4.0	6.0	8.0	9.0	9.2

Special 1-3('84, '85, '88): 1,2-Kane-c/a each ... 5.00
TPB (2007, $19.99) r/#1-4 and Special #1-3 ... 20.00

SWORDQUEST (Based on the Atari game)
Dynamite Entertainment: No. 0, 2017 - No. 5, 2017 (25¢/$3.99)

0-(25¢) Bowers & Sims-s/Ghostwriter X-a; bonus game history and character art ... 3.00
1-5-($3.99) Multiple covers on each; George Perez & others ... 4.00

SWORDS OF SORROW
Dynamite Entertainment: 2015 - No. 6, 2015 ($3.99, limited series with tie-in series)

1-6-Simone-s/Davila-a; crossover of Vampirella, Red Sonja, Dejah Thoris, Lady Zorro and other female Dynamite characters; multiple covers on each ... 4.00
...: Black Sparrow & Lady Zorro Special 1 ($3.99, one-shot) Schultz-s/Zamora-a ... 4.00
...: Chaos! Prequel 1 ($3.99, one-shot) Mairghread Scott-s/Mirka Andolfo-a ... 4.00
...: Dejah Thoris & Irene Adler 1-3 ($3.99, lim. series) Leah Moore-s/Francesco Manna-a ... 4.00
...: Masquerade & Kato 1 ($3.99, one-shot) G. Willow Wilson & Erica Schultz-s ... 4.00
...: Miss Fury & Lady Rawhide 1 ($3.99, one-shot) Mikki Kendall-s/Ronilson Freire-a ... 4.00
...: Pantha & Jane Porter ($3.99, one-shot) Emma Beeby-s/Rod Rodolfo-a ... 4.00
...: Red Sonja & Jungle Girl 1-3 ($3.99, lim. series) Bennett-s/Andolfo-a/Anacleto-c ... 4.00
...: Vampirella & Jennifer Blood 1-4 ($3.99, lim. series) Nancy Collins-s/Dave Acosta-a ... 4.00

SWORDS OF TEXAS (See Scout #15)
Eclipse Comics: Oct., 1987 - No. 4, Mar, 1988 ($1.75, color, Baxter paper)

1-4: Scout app. ... 4.00

SWORDS OF THE SWASHBUCKLERS (See Marvel Graphic Novel #14)
Marvel Comics (Epic Comics): May, 1985 - No. 12, Jun, 1987 ($1.50; mature)

1-12-Butch Guice-c/a (cont'd from Marvel G.N. #14) ... 4.00

SWORN TO PROTECT
Marvel Comics: Sept, 1995 ($1.95) (Based on card game)

nn-Overpower Game Guide; Jubilee story ... 4.00

SYMBIOTE SPIDER-MAN (Takes place right after acquiring black costume in Secret Wars)
Marvel Comics: Jun, 2019 - No. 5, Oct, 2019 ($4.99/$3.99, limited series)

1-($4.99) Peter David-s/Greg Land-a; Mysterio and Felicia Hardy app. in all ... 5.00
2-5-($3.99) Kingpin & Electro app. ... 4.00
...: Marvel Tales 1 (3/21, $7.99) Reprints of notable early Symbiote apps.; Macchio intro. ... 8.00

SYMBIOTE SPIDER-MAN: ALIEN REALITY
Marvel Comics: Feb, 2020 - No. 5, July, 2020 ($4.99/$3.99, limited series)

1-($4.99) Peter David-s/Greg Land-a; Hobgoblin, Doctor Strange & Black Widow app. ... 5.00
2-5-($3.99) 2-Uncle Ben app. 3-5-Baron Mordo app. ... 4.00

SYMBIOTE SPIDER-MAN: CROSSROADS
Marvel Comics: Sept, 2021 - No. 5, Jan, 2022 ($4.99/$3.99, limited series)

1-($4.99) Peter David-s/Greg Land-a; Black Cat and Moonknight app. ... 5.00
2-5-($3.99) 2-4-Hulk & Devil Dinosaur app. 4-Eternals app. ... 4.00

SYMBIOTE SPIDER-MAN: KING IN BLACK (Tie-in to King in Black crossover)
Marvel Comics: Jan, 2021 - No. 5, May, 2021 ($4.99/$3.99, limited series)

1-($4.99) Peter David-s/Greg Land-a; The Watcher and Kang app. ... 5.00
2-5-($3.99) 2-Black Knight app. 3,4-Captain Marvel (Monica Rambeau) app. ... 4.00

SYMMETRY
Image Comics (Top Cow): Dec, 2015 - No. 8, Oct, 2016 ($3.99)

1-8-Hawkins-s/Ienco-a ... 4.00

SYMPATHY FOR NO DEVILS
AfterShock Comics: Oct, 2020 - No. 5, Feb, 2021 ($3.99)

1-5-Brandon Thomas-s/Lee Ferguson-a ... 4.00

SYN
Dark Horse Comics: Aug, 2003 - No. 5, Feb, 2004 ($2.99, limited series)

1-5-Giffen-s/Titus-a ... 3.00

SYNERGY: A HASBRO CREATORS SHOWCASE
IDW Publishing: Mar, 2019 ($7.99, one-shot)

1-Short stories and pin-ups of My Little Pony, Jem, Transformers by women creators ... 8.00

SYPHON
Image Comics (Top Cow): Jul, 2021 - No. 3, Sept, 2021 ($3.99, limited series)

1-3-Meaney & Ashraf-s/Edwards-a ... 4.00

SYPHON (Volume 2)
Image Comics (Top Cow): Nov, 2023 - No. 4, Feb, 2024 ($3.99, limited series)

1-4-Ashraf & Akanda-s/Hedglen-a ... 4.00

SYPHONS
Now Comics: V2#1, May, 1994 - V2#3, 1994 ($2.50, limited series)

V2#1-3: 1-Stardancer, Knightfire, Raze & Brigade begin ... 4.00
TPB (9/04, $15.95) B&W reprints #1-3; intro. by Tony Caputo ... 16.00

SYSTEM, THE
DC Comics (Vertigo Verite): May, 1996 - No. 3, July, 1996 ($2.95, lim. series)

1-3: Kuper-c/a ... 4.00

TAFFY COMICS (Also see Dotty Dripple)
Rural Home/Orbit Publ.: Mar-Apr, 1945 - No. 12, 1948

1-L.B. Cole-c; origin & 1st app. of Wiggles The Wonderworm plus 7 chapter WWII funny animal adventures	77	154	231	493	847	1200
2-L.B. Cole-c with funny animal Hitler; Wiggles-c/stories in #1-4	194	388	582	1242	2121	3000
3,4,6-12: 6-Perry Como-c/story. 7-Duke Ellington, 2 pgs. 8-Glenn Ford-c/story. 9-Lon McCallister part photo-c & story. 10-Mort Leav-c. 11-Mickey Rooney-c/story	20	40	60	117	189	260
5-L.B. Cole-c; Van Johnson-c/story	29	58	87	172	281	390

TAILGUNNER JO
DC Comics: Sept, 1988 - No. 6, Jan, 1989 ($1.25)

1-6 ... 4.00

TAILS
Archie Publications: Dec, 1995 - No. 3, Feb, 1996 ($1.50, limited series)

1-3: Based on Sonic, the Hedgehog video game ... 6.00

TAILS OF THE PET AVENGERS (Also see Lockjaw and the Pet Avengers)
Marvel Comics: Apr, 2010 ($3.99, one-shot)

1-Lockjaw, Frog Thor, Zabu, Lockheed and Redwing in short solo stories by various ... 4.00
...: The Dogs of Summer (9/10, $3.99) Eliopolous-s; see Avengers vs. the Pet Avengers ... 4.00

TAILSPIN
Spotlight Publishers: November, 1944

nn-Firebird app.; L.B. Cole-c	48	96	144	302	514	725

TAILSPIN TOMMY (Also see Popular Comics)
United Features Syndicate/Service Publ. Co.: 1940; 1946

Single Series 23(1940)	52	104	156	328	552	775
1-Best Seller (nd, 1946)-Service Publ. Co.	26	52	78	154	252	350

TAKIO
Marvel Comics (Icon): 2011; May, 2012 - No. 4 ($3.95/$9.95)

HC (2011, $9.95) Bendis-s/Oeming-a/c; Oeming sketch pages ... 10.00
1-4: 1-(5/12, $3.95) Bendis-s/Oeming-a/c ... 4.00

TAKION
DC Comics: June, 1996 - No. 7, Dec, 1996 ($1.75)

1-7: Lopresti-c/a(p). 1-Origin; Green Lantern app. 6-Final Night x-over ... 4.00

TALENT SHOWCASE (See New Talent Showcase)

TALE OF ONE BAD RAT, THE
Dark Horse Comics: Oct, 1994 - No. 4, Jan, 1995 ($2.95, limited series)

1-4: Bryan Talbot-c/a/scripts ... 4.00
HC ($69.95, signed and numbered) R/#1-4 ... 70.00

TALES CALCULATED TO DRIVE YOU BATS
Archie Publications: Nov, 1961 - No. 7, Nov, 1962; 1966 (Satire)

1-Only 10¢ issue; has cut-out Werewolf mask (price includes mask)	17	34	51	117	259	400
2-Begin 12¢ issues	9	18	27	63	129	195
3-6: 3-UFO cover	8	16	24	52	99	145
7-Storyline change	7	14	21	49	92	135
1(1966, 25¢, 44 pg. Giant)-r/#1; UFO cover	8	16	24	55	105	155

TALES CALCULATED TO DRIVE YOU MAD
E.C. Publications: Summer, 1997 - No. 8, Winter, 1999 ($3.99/$4.99, satire)

1-6-Full color reprints of Mad: 1-(#1-3), 2-(#4-6), 3-(#7-9), 4-(#10-12) 5-(#13-15), 6-(#16-18) ... 6.00
7,8-($4.99-c): 7-(#19-21), 8-(#22,23) ... 6.00

TALES FROM EARTH-6: A CELEBRATION OF STAN LEE (Characters from "Just Imagine Stan Lee With..." series of one-shots)
DC Comics: Feb, 2023 ($9.99, squarebound one-shot)

1-Short stories by Waid, Ordway, Maguire, Uslan, Weeks, Cloonan & others; Cheung-c ... 10.00

TALES FROM HARROW COUNTY (Also see Harrow County)
Dark Horse Comics: Dec, 2019 - No. 4, Mar, 2020 ($3.99, limited series)

1-4-Cullen Bunn-s/Naomi Franquiz-a; set 10 years after the events of Harrow County ... 4.00

TALES FROM HARROW COUNTY: FAIR FOLK

	GD 2.0	VG 4.0	FN 6.0	VF 8.0	VF/NM 9.0	NM- 9.2

Dark Horse Comics: Jul, 2021 - No. 4, Oct, 2021 ($3.99, limited series)
1-4-Cullen Bunn-s/Emily Schnall-a 4.00

TALES FROM HARROW COUNTY: LOST ONES
Dark Horse Comics: May, 2022 - No. 4, Aug, 2022 ($3.99, limited series)
1-4-Cullen Bunn-s/Emily Schnall-a 4.00

TALES FROM RIVERDALE DIGEST
Archie Publ.: June, 2005 - No. 39, Oct. 2010 ($2.39/$2.49/$2.69, digest-size)
1-39: 1-Sabrina and Josie & the Pussycats app. 11-Begin $2.49-c. 34-Begin $2.69 .... 3.00

TALES FROM THE AGE OF APOCALYPSE
Marvel Comics: 1996 ($5.95, prestige format, one-shots)
1, ...: Sinister Bloodlines (1997, $5.95) 6.00

TALES FROM THE BOG
Aberration Press: Nov., 1995 - No. 7, Nov, 1997 ($2.95/$3.95, B&W)
1-7 .... 4.00
Alternate #1 (Director's Cut) (1998, $2.95) 4.00

TALES FROM THE BULLY PULPIT
Image Comics: Aug, 2004 ($6.95, square-bound)
1-Teddy Roosevelt and Edison's ghost with a time machine; Cereno-s/MacDonald-a 7.00

TALES FROM THE CLERKS (See Jay and Silent Bob, Clerks and Oni Double Feature)
Graphitti Designs, Inc.: 2006 ($29.95, TPB)
nn-Reprints all the Kevin Smith Clerks and Jay and Silent Bob stories; new Clerks II story with Mahfood-a; cover gallery, sketch pages, Mallrats credits covers; Smith intro. 30.00

TALES FROM THE CON
Image Comics: May, 2014 ($3.50, one-shot)
...: Year 1 - Brad Guigar-s/Chris Giarrusso-a/c; comic convention humor strips 3.50

TALES FROM THE CRYPT (Formerly The Crypt Of Terror; see Three Dimensional...)
(Also see EC Archives • Tales From the Crypt)
E.C. Comics: No. 20, Oct-Nov, 1950 - No. 46, Feb-Mar, 1955

	GD 2.0	VG 4.0	FN 6.0	VF 8.0	VF/NM 9.0	NM- 9.2
20-See Crime Patrol #15 for 1st Crypt Keeper	274	548	822	2192	3496	4800
21-Kurtzman-r/Haunt of Fear #15(#1)	126	252	378	1008	1604	2200
22-Moon Girl costume at costume party, one panel	143	286	429	1144	1822	2500
23-25: 23-"Reflection of Death" adapted for 1972 TFTC film. 24-E. A. Poe adaptation	97	194	291	776	1238	1700
26-30: 26-Wood's 2nd EC-c	80	160	240	640	1020	1400
31-Williamson-a(1st at E.C.); B&W and color illos. in POP; Kamen draws himself, Gaines & Feldstein; Ingels, Craig & Davis draw themselves in this story	86	172	258	688	1094	1500
32,35-39: 38-Censored-c	69	138	207	552	876	1200
33-Origin The Crypt Keeper	109	218	327	872	1386	1900
34-Used in POP, pg. 83; classic Frankenstein Monster, Jack the Ripper-c by Davis; lingerie panels	103	206	309	824	1312	1800
40-Used in Senate hearings & in Hartford Courant anti-comics editorials-1954	109	218	327	872	1386	1900
41-45: 45-2 pgs. showing E.C. staff; anti-censorship editorial of upcoming Senate hearings	74	148	222	592	946	1300
46-Low distribution; pre-advertised cover for unpublished 4th horror title "Crypt of Terror" used on this book; "Blind Alleys" adapted for 1972 TFTC film; classic werewolf-c by Davis	149	298	447	1192	1896	2600

NOTE: *Ray Bradbury* adaptations-34, 36. *Craig* a-20, 22-24; c-20. *Crandall* a-38, 44. *Davis* a-24-46; c-29-46. *Elder* a-31, 37, 38. *Evans* a-32-34, 36, 40, 41, 43, 46. *Feldstein* a-20-23; c-21-25, 28. *Ingels* a-in all. *Kamen* a-20, 22, 25, 27-31, 33-36, 39, 41-45. *Kristgein* a-40, 42, 45. *Kurtzman* a-21. *Orlando* a-27-30, 35, 37, 39, 41-45. *Wood* a-21, 24, 25; c-26, 27. Canadian reprints known; see Table of Contents.

TALES FROM THE CRYPT (Magazine)
Eerie Publications: No. 10, July, 1968 (35¢, B&W)

	GD 2.0	VG 4.0	FN 6.0	VF 8.0	VF/NM 9.0	NM- 9.2
10-Contains Farrell reprints from 1950s	8	16	24	52	99	145

TALES FROM THE CRYPT
Gladstone Publishing: July, 1990 - No. 6, May, 1991 ($1.95/$2.00, 68 pgs.)
1-r/TFTC #33 & Crime S.S. #17; Davis-c(r) 5.00
2-6: 2,3,5,6-Davis-c(r). 4-Begin $2.00-c; Craig-c(r) 5.00

TALES FROM THE CRYPT
Extra-Large Comics (Russ Cochran)/Gemstone Publishing: Jul, 1991 - No. 6 ($3.95, 10 1/4 x13 1/4", 68 pgs.)
1-6: 1-Davis-c(r); Craig back-c(r); E.C. reprints. 2-6 ($2.00, comic sized) 5.00

TALES FROM THE CRYPT
Russ Cochran: Sept, 1991 - No. 7, July, 1992 ($2.00, 64 pgs.)
1-7 .... 5.00

TALES FROM THE CRYPT (Also see EC Archives • Tales From the Crypt)
Russ Cochran/Gemstone: Sept, 1992 - No. 30, Dec, 1999 ($1.50, quarterly)
1-4-r/Crypt of Terror #17-19, TFTC #20 w/original-c 4.00
5-30: 5-15 ($2.00)-r/TFTC #21-23 w/original-c. 16-30 ($2.50) 5.00
Annual 1-6('93-'99) 1-r/#1-5. 2- r/#6-10. 3- r/#11-15. 4- r/#16-20. 5-r/#21-25. 6- r/#26-30 .... 14.00

TALES FROM THE DARK MULTIVERSE
DC Comics: Dec, 2019 - Feb, 2021 ($5.99, series of one-shots)
...: Batman: Hush 1 (1/21) - Tommy Elliot and Batman The Silenced app. Soy-a 6.00
...: Batman: Knightfall 1 - What if Jean-Paul Valley remained as Batman; Fernandez-a 6.00
...: Blackest Night 1 - What if Sinestro kept the White Lantern power; Lobo app. Hotz-a 6.00
...: Crisis on Infinite Earths 1 (2/21) - Justice Society app.; Orlando-s/Perkins-a 6.00
...: Dark Nights Metal 1 (2/21) - What if Barbatos had won; Duke Thomas app. 6.00
...: Flashpoint 1 (2/21) - What if the Flashpoint reality was never undone; Currie-a 6.00
...: Infinite Crisis 1 - What if Blue Beetle killed Max Lord; Tynion IV-s/Lopresti-a 6.00
...: The Death of Superman 1 - What if Lois gained the Eradicator's powers; Brad Walker-a 6.00
...: Teen Titans: The Judas Contract 1 - What if Terra didn't die; Raney-a 6.00
...: Wonder Woman War of the Gods 1 (2/21) - Evil Wonder Woman; Olivetti-a 6.00

TALES FROM THE DARKSIDE
IDW Publishing: Jun, 2016 - No. 4, Sept, 2016 ($3.99, limited series)
1-4-Joe Hill-s/Gabriel Rodriguez-a. 1-Five covers. 2-4-Two covers 4.00

TALES FROM THE GREAT BOOK

Famous Funnies: Feb, 1955 - No. 4, Jan, 1956 (Religious themes)

	GD 2.0	VG 4.0	FN 6.0	VF 8.0	VF/NM 9.0	NM- 9.2
1-Story of Samson; John Lehti-a in all	14	28	42	80	115	150
2-4: 2-Joshua. 3-Joash the Boy King. 4-David	9	18	27	52	69	85

TALES FROM THE HEART OF AFRICA (The Temporary Natives)
Marvel Comics (Epic Comics): Aug, 1990 ($3.95, 52 pgs.)
1 .... 5.00

TALES FROM THE TOMB (Also see Dell Giants)
Dell Publishing Co.: Oct, 1962 (25¢ giant)

	GD 2.0	VG 4.0	FN 6.0	VF 8.0	VF/NM 9.0	NM- 9.2
1(02-810-210)-All stories written by John Stanley	21	42	63	147	324	500

TALES FROM THE TOMB (Magazine)
Eerie Publications: V1#6, July, 1969 - V7#3, 1975 (52 pgs.)

	GD 2.0	VG 4.0	FN 6.0	VF 8.0	VF/NM 9.0	NM- 9.2
V1#6	10	20	30	67	141	215
V1#7,8	8	16	24	52	99	145
V2#1-6: 4-LSD story-r/Weird V3#5. 6-Rulah-r	6	12	18	44	76	110
V3#1-Rulah-r	7	14	21	49	92	135
2-6('71),V4#1-5('72),V5#1-6('73),V6#1-6('74),V7#1-3('75)	6	12	18	37	66	95

TALES OF ASGARD
Marvel Comics Group: Oct, 1968 (25¢, 68 pgs.); Feb, 1984 ($1.25, 52 pgs.)

	GD 2.0	VG 4.0	FN 6.0	VF 8.0	VF/NM 9.0	NM- 9.2
1-Reprints Tales of Asgard (Thor) back-up stories from Journey into Mystery #97-106; new Kirby-c; Kirby-a	9	18	37	62	126	190
V2#1 (2/84)-Thor-r; Simonson-c						5.00

TALES OF ARMY OF DARKNESS
Dynamite Entertainment: 2006 ($5.95, one-shot)
1-Short stories by Kuhoric, Kirkman, Bradshaw, Sablik, Ottley, Acs, O'Hare and others 6.00

TALES OF EVIL
Atlas/Seaboard Publ.: Feb, 1975 - No. 3, July, 1975 (All 25¢ issues)

	GD 2.0	VG 4.0	FN 6.0	VF 8.0	VF/NM 9.0	NM- 9.2
1-3: 1-Werewolf w/Sekowsky-a. 2-Intro. The Bog Beast; Sparling-a. 3-Origin The Man-Monster; Buckler-a(p)	2	4	6	13	18	22

NOTE: *Grandenetti* a-1, 2. *Lieber* c-1. *Sekowsky* a-1. *Sutton* a-2. *Thorne* c-2.

TALES OF GHOST CASTLE
National Periodical Publications: May-June, 1975 - No. 3, Sept-Oct, 1975 (All 25¢ issues)

	GD 2.0	VG 4.0	FN 6.0	VF 8.0	VF/NM 9.0	NM- 9.2
1-Redondo-a; 1st app. Lucien the Librarian from Sandman (1989 series)	3	6	9	21	33	45
2,3: 2-Nino-a. 3-Redondo-a.	2	4	6	11	16	20

TALES OF G.I. JOE
Marvel Comics: Jan, 1988 - No. 15, Mar, 1989
1 ($2.25, 52 pgs.) 5.00
2-15 ($1.50): 1-15-r/G.I. Joe #1-15 .... 4.00

TALES OF HONOR (Based on the David Weber novels)
Image Comics (Top Cow): Mar, 2014 - No. 5, Oct, 2015 ($2.99)
1-5: 1-Matt Hawkins-s/Jung-Geun Yoon-a. 2-5-Sang-il Jeong-a 3.00

TALES OF HONOR VOLUME 2 (Bred to Kill on cover)
Image Comics (Top Cow): No. 0, May, 2015 - No. 4, Dec, 2015 ($3.99)
0-Free Comic Book Day giveaway; Hawkins-s/Linda Sejic-a 3.00
1-4-Hawkins-s/Linda Sejic-a 4.00

TALES OF HORROR
Toby Press/Minoan Publ. Corp.: June, 1952 - No. 13, Oct, 1954

	GD 2.0	VG 4.0	FN 6.0	VF 8.0	VF/NM 9.0	NM- 9.2
1-"This is Terror-Man"	90	180	270	576	988	1400
2-Torture scenes	57	114	171	362	619	875
3-11,13: 9-11-Reprints Purple Claw #1-3	39	78	117	231	378	525
12-Myron Fass-c/a; torture scenes	42	84	126	265	445	625

NOTE: *Andru* a-5. *Baily* a-5. *Myron Fass* a-2, 3, 12; c-1-3, 12. *Hollingsworth* a-2. *Sparling* a-6, 9; c-9.

TALES OF JUSTICE
Atlas Comics(MjMC No. 53-66/Male No. 67): No. 53, May, 1955 - No. 67, Aug, 1957

	GD 2.0	VG 4.0	FN 6.0	VF 8.0	VF/NM 9.0	NM- 9.2
53	24	48	72	142	234	325
54-57: 54-Powell-a	16	32	48	94	147	200
58,59-Krigstein-a	18	36	54	107	169	230
60-63,65: 60-Powell-a	15	30	45	88	137	185
64,66,67: 64,67-Crandall-a. 66-Torres, Orlando-a	15	30	45	90	140	190

NOTE: *Everett* a-53, 60. *Orlando* a-65, 66. *Severin* a-64; c-58, 60, 65. *Wildey* a-64, 67.

TALES OF LEONARDO BLIND SIGHT (See Tales of the TMNT Vol. 2 #5)
Mirage Publishing: June, 2006 - No. 4, Sept, 2006 ($3.25, B&W, limited series)

	GD 2.0	VG 4.0	FN 6.0	VF 8.0	VF/NM 9.0	NM- 9.2
1-Jim Lawson-s/a in all	3	6	9	21	33	45
2-4	2	4	6	10	14	18

TALES OF MOTHER F. GOOSE
AfterShock Comics: Dec, 2021 ($6.99, one-shot, oversized 8-1/2" x 10-7/8")
1-Frank Tieri-s/Joe Eisma-a 7.00

TALES OF SOPHISTICATION (Cerebus)
Aardvark-Vanaheim: Aug, 2019 ($4.00, B&W)
1-Cerebus figures with Doré artwork of Hell; cover swipe of Tales of Suspense #39 .... 4.00

TALES OF SUSPENSE (Becomes Captain America #100 on)
Atlas (WPI No. 1,2/Male No. 3-12/VPI No. 13-18)/Marvel No. 19 on:
Jan, 1959 - No. 99, Mar, 1968

	GD 2.0	VG 4.0	FN 6.0	VF 8.0	VF/NM 9.0	NM- 9.2
1-Williamson-a (5 pgs.); Heck-c; #1-4 have sci-fi/c	633	1266	1899	5381	12,191	19,000
2-Ditko robot-c	166	332	498	1370	3085	4800
3-Flying saucer-c/story	125	250	375	1000	2250	3500
4-Williamson-a (4 pgs.); Kirby/Everett-c/a	118	236	354	944	2122	3300
5-Kirby monster-c begin	96	192	288	768	1734	2700
6,8,10	75	150	225	600	1350	2100
7-Prototype ish. (Lava Man) 1 panel app. Aunt May (see Str. Tales #97)	86	172	258	688	1544	2400
9-Prototype ish. (Iron Man)	71	142	213	568	1284	2000
11,12,15,17-19: 12-Crandall-a.	57	114	171	456	1028	1600
13-Elektro-c/story	68	136	204	544	1222	1900
14-Intro/1st app. Colossus-c/sty	71	142	213	568	1284	2000

Tales From the Crypt #41 © WMG

Tales of Suspense #1 © MAR

Tales of Terror #11 © ECL

	GD 2.0	VG 4.0	FN 6.0	VF 8.0	VF/NM 9.0	NM- 9.2
16-1st Metallo-c/story (4/61, Iron Man prototype)	86	172	258	688	1544	2400
20-Colossus-c/story (2nd app.)	57	114	171	456	1028	1600
21-25: 25-Last 10¢ issue	46	92	138	368	834	1300
26,27,29,30,31,33,34,36-38: 33-(9/62)-Hulk 1st x-over cameo (picture on wall)	44	88	132	326	738	1150
28-Prototype ish. (Stone Men)	46	92	138	359	805	1250
31-Prototype ish. (Doctor Doom)	100	200	300	800	1800	2800
32-Prototype ish. (Dr. Strange) app.; "The Man and the Beehive" story, 1 month before TTA #35 (2nd Antman), came out after "The Man in the Ant Hill" in TTA #27 (1/62) (1st Antman)-Characters from both stories were tested to see which got best fan response	118	236	354	944	2122	3300
35-Prototype issue (The Watcher)	46	92	138	368	834	1300
39 (3/63)-Origin/1st app. Iron Man & begin series; 1st Iron Man story has Kirby layouts	3680	7360	12,880	25,800	58,900	92,000
40-2nd app. Iron Man (in new armor)	238	476	714	1964	4432	6900
41-3rd app. Iron Man; Dr. Strange (villain) app.	172	344	516	1419	3210	5000
42-45: 45-Intro. & 1st app. Happy & Pepper	100	200	300	800	1800	2800
46,47: 46-1st app. Crimson Dynamo	71	142	213	568	1284	2000
48-New Iron Man red & gold armor by Ditko	79	158	237	632	1416	2200
49-1st X-Men x-over (same date as X-Men #3, 1/64); also 1st Avengers x-over (w/o Captain America); 1st Tales of the Watcher back-up story & begins (2nd app. Watcher; see F.F. #13)	89	178	267	712	1606	2500
50-1st app. Mandarin	111	222	333	888	1994	3100
51-1st Scarecrow	38	76	114	285	641	1000
52-1st app. The Black Widow (4/64)	383	766	1149	3256	7378	11,500
53-Origin The Watcher; 2nd Black Widow app.	58	116	174	464	1057	1650
54,55-2nd & 3rd Mandarin app.	34	68	102	245	548	850
56-1st app. Unicorn	28	56	84	202	451	700
57-Origin/1st app. Hawkeye (9/64)	283	566	849	2335	5268	8200
58-Captain America battles Iron Man (10/64)-Classic; 2nd Kraven app. (Cap's 1st app. in this title)	68	136	204	544	1222	1900
59-Iron Man plus Captain America double feature begins (11/64); 1st S.A. Captain America solo story; intro Jarvis, Avenger's butler; classic-c	57	114	171	456	1028	1600
60-2nd app. Hawkeye (#64 is 3rd app.)	28	56	84	202	451	700
61,62,64: 62-Origin Mandarin (2/65). 64-1st Black Widow in costume	17	34	51	117	259	400
63-1st Silver Age origin Captain America (3/65)	33	66	99	238	532	825
65-G.A. Red Skull in WWII stories (also in #66-68);-1st Silver-Age Red Skull (5/65); Iron Man wears old yellow armor	38	76	114	285	641	1000
66-Origin Red Skull	27	54	81	194	435	675
67,68,70: 70-Begin alternating-c features w/Capt. America (even #'s) & Iron Man (odd #'s)	10	20	30	67	141	215
69-1st app. Titanium Man	14	28	42	97	214	330
71-74,78: 78-Col. Nick Fury app.	8	16	24	54	102	150
75-1st app. Agent 13 later named Sharon Carter; intro Batroc	25	50	75	175	388	600
76-2nd app. Batroc & 1st cover app.	9	18	27	63	129	195
77-1st app. Peggy Carter (unnamed) in WW2 flashback (see Captain America #161 & 162)	25	50	75	175	388	600
79-Begin 3 part Iron Man Sub-Mariner battle story; Sub-Mariner-c & cameo; 1st app. Cosmic Cube; 1st modern Red Skull	17	34	51	117	259	400
80-Iron Man battles Sub-Mariner story cont'd in Tales to Astonish #82; classic Red Skull-c	13	26	39	86	188	290
81-93,95,96: 82-Intro the Adaptoid by Kirby (also in #83,84). 88-Mole Man app. in Iron Man story. 92-1st Nick Fury x-over (cameo, as Agent of S.H.I.E.L.D., 8/67)	7	14	21	48	89	130
95-Capt. America's i.d. revealed	40	80	120	296	673	1050
94-Intro Modok	14	28	42	93	204	315
97-1st app Whiplash						
98-Black Panther-c/s; 1st brief app. new Zemo (son?); #99 is 1st full app.	14	28	42	96	211	325
99-Captain America story cont'd in Captain America #100; Iron Man story cont'd in Iron Man & Sub-Mariner #1	9	18	27	61	123	185
... No. 39 Facsimile Edition (11/20, $3.99) Reprints #39 with original ads	2	4	6	9	13	16
... No. 57 Facsimile Edition (8/22, $3.99) Reprints #57 (1st Hawkeye) with original ads	3	4	6	8		

Omnibus (See Iron Man Omnibus for reprints of #39-83)

NOTE: Abel a-73-81i(as Gary Michaels), J. Buscema a-1; c-3. Colan a-39, 73-99p; c(p)-73, 75, 77, 79, 81, 83, 85-87, 89, 91, 93, 95, 97, 99; Crandall a-12. Davis a-38. Ditko a-1-15, 17-44, 46, 47-49p; c-2, 10i, 13i, 23i. Kirby/Ditko a-7; c-10, 13, 22, 28, 34. Everett a-8. Forte a-5, 9. Giacoia a-82. Heath a-12. Gil Kane a-88p, 89-91; c-88, 89-91p. Kirby a(p)-2-4, 6-35, 40, 41, 43, 59-75, 77-86, 92-99; layouts-69-75, 77; c(p)4-28(most), 29-56, 58-72, 74, 76, 78, 80, 82, 84, 86, 88-89, 92, 94, 96, 98. Leiber/Fox a-42, 43, 45, 51. Reinman a-13, 25, 26, 44i, 49i, 52i, 53i. Tuska a-58, 70-74. Wood c/a-71i.

TALES OF SUSPENSE
Marvel Comics: V2#1, Jan, 1995 ($6.95, one-shot)

	GD 2.0	VG 4.0	FN 6.0	VF 8.0	VF/NM 9.0	NM- 9.2
V2#1-James Robinson script; acetate-c.	1	3	4	6	8	10

TALES OF SUSPENSE (Marvel Legacy)
Marvel Comics: No. 100, Feb, 2018 - No. 104, Jun, 2018 ($3.99)

100-104-Hawkeye & Winter Soldier team-up; Black Widow app.; Foreman-a — 4.00

TALES OF SUSPENSE: CAPTAIN AMERICA & IRON MAN #1 COMMEMORATIVE EDITION
Marvel Comics: 2004 ($3.99, one-shot)

nn-Reprints Captain America (2004) #1 and Iron Man (2004) #1 — 5.00

TALES OF SWORD & SORCERY (See Dagar)

TALES OF SYZPENSE
Image Comics: Jun, 2023 - No. 4, Dec, 2023 ($4.99)

1-4-Les Mort13 by Louise & Wood; Dreamweaver by Ryall & Daniel — 5.00

TALES OF TELLOS (See Tellos)
Image Comics: Oct, 2004 - No. 3, ($3.50, anthology)

1-3: 1-Dezago-s; art by Yates & Rousseau; Wieringo-c. 3-Porter-a — 3.50

TALES OF TERROR
Toby Press Publications: 1952 (no month)

	GD 2.0	VG 4.0	FN 6.0	VF 8.0	VF/NM 9.0	NM- 9.2
1-Fawcette-c; Ravielli-a	71	142	213	454	777	1100

NOTE: This title was cancelled due to similarity to the E.C. title.

TALES OF TERROR (See Movie Classics)

TALES OF TERROR (Magazine)
Eerie Publications: Summer, 1964

	GD 2.0	VG 4.0	FN 6.0	VF 8.0	VF/NM 9.0	NM- 9.2
1	8	16	24	52	99	145

TALES OF TERROR
Eclipse Comics: July, 1985 - No. 13, July, 1987 ($2.00, Baxter paper, mature)

	GD 2.0	VG 4.0	FN 6.0	VF 8.0	VF/NM 9.0	NM- 9.2
1	1	3	4	6	8	10

2-13: 5-1st Lee Weeks-a. 7-Sam Kieth-a. 10-Snyder-a. 12-Vampire story — 4.00

TALES OF TERROR (IDW's...)
IDW Publishing: Sept, 2004 ($16.99, hardcover)

1-Anthology of short graphic stories and text stories; incl. 30 Days of Night — 17.00

TALES OF TERROR ANNUAL
E.C. Comics: 1951 - No. 3, 1953 (25¢, 132 pgs., 16 stories each)

	GD 2.0	VG 4.0	FN 6.0	VF 8.0	VF/NM 9.0	NM- 9.2
nn(1951)(Scarce)-Feldstein infinity-c	2500	5000	7500	20,000	--	--
2(1952)-Feldstein-c	343	686	1029	2487	4200	6000
3(1953)-Feldstein bondage/torture-c	300	600	900	1950	3375	4800

NOTE: No. 1 contains three horror and one science fiction comic which came out in 1950. No. 2 contains a horror, crime, and science fiction book which generally had cover dates in 1951, and No. 3 had horror, crime, and shock books that generally appeared in 1952. All E.C. annuals contain four complete books that did not sell on the stands which were rebound in the annual format, minus the covers, and sold from the E.C. office and on the stands in key cities. The contents of each annual may vary in the same year. Crypt Keeper, Vault Keeper, Old Witch app. on all-c.

TALES OF TERROR ILLUSTRATED (See Terror Illustrated)

TALES OF TEXAS JOHN SLAUGHTER (See Walt Disney Presents, 4-Color #997)

TALES OF THE BEANWORLD
Beanworld Press/Eclipse Comics: Feb, 1985 - No. 19, 1991; No. 20, 1993 - No. 21, 1993 ($1.50/$2.00, B&W)

1-21 — 4.00

TALES OF THE BIZARRO WORLD
DC Comics: 2000 ($14.95, TPB)

nn-Reprints early Bizarro stories; new Jaime Hernandez-c — 15.00

TALES OF THE DARKNESS
Image Comics (Top Cow): Apr, 1998 - No. 4, Dec, 1998 ($2.95)

1-4: 1,2-Portacio-c/a(p). 3,4-Lansing & Nocon-a(p) — 4.00
1-American Entertainment Ed. — 4.00
#1/2 (1/01, $2.95) — 3.00

TALES OF THE DRAGON GUARD (English version of French comic title)
Marvel Comics (Soleil): Apr, 2010 - No. 3, Jun, 2010 ($5.99, limited series)

1-3: 1-Ange-s/Varanda-a. 2-Briones-a. 3-Guinebaud-a — 6.00
....: Into the Veil 1-3 (11/10 - No. 3, 1/11) 1-Briones-a. 2-Paty-a. 3-Sieurac-a — 6.00

TALES OF THE GREEN BERET
Dell Publishing Co.: Jan, 1967 - No. 5, Oct, 1969

	GD 2.0	VG 4.0	FN 6.0	VF 8.0	VF/NM 9.0	NM- 9.2
1-Glanzman-a in 1 & 5r	4	8	12	28	47	65
2-5: 5-Reprints #1	3	6	9	19	30	40

TALES OF THE GREEN HORNET
Now Comics: Sept, 1990 - No. 2, 1990; V2#1, Jan, 1992 - No.4, Apr, 1992; V3#1, Sept, 1992 - No. 3, Nov, 1992

1,2 — 5.00

	GD 2.0	VG 4.0	FN 6.0	VF 8.0	VF/NM 9.0	NM- 9.2

V2#1-4 ($1.95) — 4.00
V3#1 ($2.75)-Polybagged w/hologram trading card — 5.00
V3#2,3 ($2.50) — 4.00

TALES OF THE GREEN LANTERN CORPS (See Green Lantern #107)
DC Comics: May, 1981 - No. 3, July, 1981 (Limited series)

1-Origin of G.L. & the Guardians	2	4	6	11	16	20
2-1st app. Nekron	3	6	9	14	20	25
3	2	4	6	8	10	12
Annual 1 (1/85)-Gil Kane-c/a	2	3	5	6		8

TPB (2009, $19.99) r/#1-3 & stories from G.L. #148-151-154,161,162,164-167 ('82-'83)20.00
Volume 2 TPB (2010, $19.99) r/Annual #1 and stories from G.L. ('83-'85) — 20.00
Volume 3 TPB (2010, $19.99) r/Green Lantern #201-206 ('86) — 20.00

TALES OF THE HUMAN TARGET (Leads into 2022's Human Target #7)
DC Comics (Black Label): Oct, 2022 ($5.99, one-shot)

1-Past cases; King-s; art by Maguire, Janin, Albuquerque & Smallwood						6.00

TALES OF THE INVISIBLE SCARLET O'NEIL (See Harvey Comics Hits #59)

TALES OF THE KILLERS (Magazine)
World Famous Periodicals: V1#10, Dec, 1970 - V1#11, Feb, 1971 (B&W, 52 pg)

V1#10-One pg. Frazetta; r/Crime Does Not Pay	5	10	15	33	57	80
11-similar-c to Crime Does Not Pay #47; contains r/Crime Does Not Pay	5	10	15	30	50	70

TALES OF THE LEGION (Formerly Legion of Super-Heroes)
DC Comics: No. 314, Aug, 1984 - No. 354, Dec, 1987

314-354: 326-r-begin						4.00
Annual 4,5 (1986, 1987)-Formerly LSH Annual						5.00

TALES OF THE MARINES (Formerly Devil-Dog Dugan #1-3)
Atlas Comics (OPI): No. 4, Feb, 1957 (Marines At War #5 on)

4-Powell-a; grey tone-c by Severin	19	38	57	111	176	240

TALES OF THE MARVELS
Marvel Comics: 1995/1996 (all acetate, painted-c)

...Blockbuster 1 (1995, $5.95, one-shot), ...Inner Demons 1 (1996, $5.95, one shot), ...Wonder Years 1,2 (1995, $4.95, limited series)						6.00

TALES OF THE MARVEL UNIVERSE
Marvel Comics: Feb, 1997 ($2.95, one-shot)

1-Anthology; wraparound-c; Thunderbolts, Ka-Zar app.						4.00

TALES OF THE MYSTERIOUS TRAVELER (See Mysterious...)
Charlton Comics: Aug, 1956 - No. 13, June, 1959; V2#14, Oct, 1985 - No. 15, Dec, 1985

1-No Ditko-a; Giordano/Alascia-c	57	114	171	362	619	875
2-Ditko-a(1)	43	86	129	271	461	650
3-Ditko-c/a(1)	45	90	135	284	480	675
4-7-Ditko-c/a(3-4 stories each)	52	104	156	328	552	775
8,9-Ditko-c/a(1) each. 8-Rocke-c	42	84	126	265	445	625
10,11-Ditko-c/a(3-4 each)	48	96	144	302	514	725
12	20	40	60	114	182	250
13-Baker-a (r?)	20	40	60	120	195	270
V2#14,15 (1985)-Ditko-c/a-low print run	2	3	4	6	8	10

TALES OF THE NEW GODS
DC Comics: 2008 ($19.99, TPB)

SC-Reprints from Jack Kirby's Fourth World, Orion and Mister Miracle Special; includes previously unpublished story by Millar-s/Ditko-a						20.00

TALES OF THE NEW TEEN TITANS
DC Comics: June, 1982 - No. 4, Sept, 1982 (Limited series)

1	3	6	9	16	23	30
2-4	2	4	6	8	10	12

TALES OF THE PONY EXPRESS (TV)
Dell Publishing Co.: No. 829, Aug, 1957 - No. 942, Oct, 1958

Four Color 829 (#1) -Painted-c	6	12	18	42	79	115
Four Color 942-Title -Pony Express	5	10	15	34	60	85

TALES OF THE REALM
CrossGen Comics/MVCreations #4-on: Oct, 2003 - No. 5, May, 2004 ($2.95, limited series)

1-5-Robert Kirkman-s/Matt Tyree-a						3.00
Volume 1 HC (8/04, $39.95, dust jacket) r/#1-5; sketch pages and concept art						40.00

TALES OF THE SINESTRO CORPS (See Green Lantern and Green Lantern Corps x-over)
DC Comics: Nov, 2007 - Jan, 2008 ($2.99/$3.99, one-shots)

...: Cyborg-Superman (12/07, $2.99) Burnett-s/Blaine-a/VanSciver-c; JLA app.						3.00
...: Ion (1/08, $2.99) Marz-s/Lacombe-a/Benes-c; Sodam Yat app.						3.00
...: Parallax (11/07, $2.99) Marz-s/Melo-a; Kyle Rayner vs. Parallax						3.00
...: Superman-Prime (12/07, $3.99) Johns-s/VanSciver-c; origin re-told w/Ordway-a						4.00

TALES OF THE TEENAGE MUTANT NINJA TURTLES (See Teenage Mutant...)
Mirage Studios: May, 1987 - No. 7, Aug (Apr-c), 1989 (B&W, $1.50)

1	4	8	12	25	40	55
2-Title merges w/Teenage Mutant Ninja...	3	6	9	14	20	25
3-7	2	4	6	8	11	14

TALES OF THE TEEN TITANS (Formerly The New Teen Titans)
DC Comics: No. 41, Apr, 1984 - No. 91, July, 1988 (75¢)

41,45-49: 46-Aqualad & Aquagirl join						5.00
42,43: The Judas Contract parts 1&2 with Deathstroke the Terminator; concludes with part 4 in Annual #3.	1	2	3	5	6	8
44-Dick Grayson becomes Nightwing (3rd to Nightwing) & joins Titans; Judas Contract part 3; Jericho (Deathstroke's son) joins; origin Deathstroke	6	12	18	37	66	110
50-Double size; app. Betty Kane (Bat-Girl) out of costume	1	3	4	6	8	10
51,52,56-91: 52-1st brief app. Azrael (not same as newer character). 56-Intro Jinx. 57-Neutron app. 59-r/DC Comics Presents #26. 60-91-r/New Teen Titans Baxter series. 68-B. Smith-c. 70-Origin Kole						3.00
53-56: 53-1st full app. Azrael; Deathstroke cameo. 54,55-Deathstroke-c/stories						4.00

Annual 3(1984, $1.25)-Part 4 of The Judas Contract; Deathstroke-c/story; Death of Terra; indicia says Teen Titans Annual; previous annuals listed as New Teen Titans Annual #1,2

			1	3	8	10
Annual 4-(1986, $1.25)						4.00

TALES OF THE TEXAS RANGERS (See Jace Pearson...)

TALES OF THE THING (Fantastic Four)
Marvel Comics: May, 2005 - No. 3, July, 2005 ($2.50, limited series)

1-3-Dr. Strange app.; Randy Green-c						3.00

TALES OF THE TITANS (Teen Titans)
DC Comics: Sept, 2023 - No. 4, Dec, 2023 ($4.99, limited series)

1-4: 1-Spotlight on Starfire. 2-Spotlight on Raven. 3-Donna Troy. 4-Beast Boy						5.00

TALES OF THE TMNT (Also see Teenage Mutant Ninja Turtles)
Mirage Studios: Jan, 2004 - No. 70, May, 2010 ($2.95/$3.25, B&W)

1-7: 1-Brizuela-a						5.00
8-70: 8-Begin $3.25-c. 47-Origin of the Super Turtles						4.00

TALES OF THE UNEXPECTED (Becomes The Unexpected #105 on)(See Adventure #75, Super DC Giant)
National Periodical Publications: Feb-Mar, 1956 - No. 104, Dec-Jan, 1967-68

1	162	324	486	1337	3019	4700
2	64	128	192	512	1156	1800
3-5	42	84	126	311	706	1100
6-10: 6-1st Silver Age issue	33	66	99	238	532	825
11,14,19,20	25	50	75	175	388	600

12,13,16,18,21-24: All have Kirby-a. 16-Characters named 'Thor' (with a magic hammer) and Loki by Kirby (8/57, characters do not look like Marvel's Thor & Loki)

	29	58	87	209	467	725
15,17-Grey tone-c; Kirby-a	33	66	99	238	532	825
25-30	20	40	60	138	307	475
31-39	17	34	51	117	259	400
40-Space Ranger begins (8/59, 3rd ap.), ends #82	107	214	321	856	1928	3000
41,42-Space Ranger stories	44	88	132	326	738	1150
43-1st Space Ranger-c this title; grey tone-c	75	150	225	600	1350	2100
44-46	31	62	93	223	499	775
47-50	26	52	78	182	404	625
51-60: 54-Dinosaur-c/story	21	42	63	147	324	500
61-67: 67-Last 10¢ issue	17	34	51	117	259	400
68-82: 82-Last Space Ranger	10	20	30	66	138	210
83-90,92-99	6	12	18	40	73	105
91,100: 91-1st Automan (also in #94,97)	7	14	21	44	82	120
101-104	6	12	18	37	66	95

NOTE: *Neal Adams c-104. Anderson a-50. Brown a-50-82(Space Ranger); c-19, 40, & many Space Ranger-c. Cameron a-24, 27, 29; c-24. Heath a-49. Bob Kane a-24, 48. Kirby a-12, 13, 15-18, 21-24; c-13, 18, 22. Meskin a-15, 18, 26, 27, 35, 66. Moreira a-16, 20, 29, 38, 44. Roussos c-10. Wildey a-31.*

TALES OF THE UNEXPECTED (See Crisis Aftermath: The Spectre)
DC Comics: Dec, 2006 - No. 8, Jul, 2007 ($3.99, limited series)

1-8-The Spectre, Lapham-s/Battle-a. Dr. 13, Azzarello-s/Chiang-a. 4-Wrightson-c						4.00
1-Variant Spectre cover by Neal Adams						5.00

The Spectre: Tales of the Unexpected TPB (2007, $14.99) r/#4-8 — 15.00

TALES OF THE VAMPIRES (Also see Buffy the Vampire Slayer and related titles)
Dark Horse Comics: 2003 - No. 5, Apr, 2004 ($2.99, limited series)

1-Short stories by Joss Whedon and others. 1-Totleben-a. 3-Powell-a. 4-Edlund-c						3.00

TPB (11/04, $15.95) r/#1-5; afterword by Marv Wolfman — 16.00

TALES OF THE WEST (See 3-D...)

TALES OF THE WITCHBLADE
Image Comics (Top Cow Productions): Nov, 1996 - No. 9 ($2.95)

1/2	2	4	6	9	12	15
1/2 Gold	2	4	6	9	12	15
1-Daniel-c/a(p)	1	3	4	6	8	10
1-Variant-c by Turner	2	4	6	9	12	15
1-Platinum Edition	3	6	9	16	23	30
2,3						6.00
4-6: 6-Green-c						5.00
7-9: 9-Lara Croft-c						4.00
7-Variant-c by Turner	1	2	3	4	6	8

Witchblade: Distinctions (4/01, $14.95, TPB) r/#1-6; Green-c — 15.00

TALES OF THE WITCHBLADE COLLECTED EDITION
Image Comics (Top Cow): May, 1998 - No. 2 ($4.95/$5.95, square-bound)

1,2: 1-r/#1,2. 2-($5.95) r/#3,4						6.00

TALES OF THE WIZARD OF OZ (See Wizard of OZ, 4-Color #1308)

TALES OF THE ZOMBIE (Magazine)
Marvel Comics Group: Aug, 1973 - No. 10, Mar, 1975 (75¢, B&W)

V1#1-Reprint/Menace #5; origin Simon Garth	8	16	24	54	102	150
2,3: 2-2nd app. of Brother Voodoo; Everett biog. & memorial	5	10	15	31	53	75
V2#1(#4)-Photos & text of James Bond movie "Live & Let Die"	4	8	12	25	40	55
5-10: 8-Kaluta-a	3	6	9	18	28	38
Annual 1(Summer,'75)(#11)-B&W; Everett, Buscema-a	3	6	9	20	31	42

NOTE: *Brother Voodoo app. 2, 5, 6, 10. Alcala a-7-9. Boris c-1-4. Colan a-2r, 6. Heath a-5r. Reese a-2. Tuska a-2r.*

TALES OF VOODOO
Eerie Publications: V1#11, Nov, 1968 - V7#6, Nov, 1974 (Magazine)

V1#11	9	18	27	62	126	190
V2#1(3/69)-V2#4(9/69)	6	12	18	41	76	110
V3#1-6('70): 4- "Claws of the Cat" redrawn from Climax #1						
	5	10	15	33	57	80
V4#1-6('71), V5#1-7('72), V6#1-6('73), V7#1-6('74)	5	10	15	33	57	80
Annual 1	5	10	15	37	60	85

NOTE: *Bondage-c-V1#10, V2#4, V3#4.*

Tales of the Titans (2023 series) #1 © DC

Tales to Astonish #38 © MAR

Talon #12 © DC

	GD 2.0	VG 4.0	FN 6.0	VF 8.0	VF/NM 9.0	NM- 9.2

TALES OF WELLS FARGO (TV)(See Western Roundup under Dell Giants)
Dell Publishing Co.: No. 876, Feb, 1958 - No. 1215, Oct-Dec, 1961

	2.0	4.0	6.0	8.0	9.0	9.2
Four Color 876 (#1)-Photo-c	9	18	27	62	126	190
Four Color 968 (2/59), 1023, 1075 (3/60), 1113 (7-9/60)-All photo-c. 1075,1113-Both have variant edition, back-c comic strip	8	16	24	54	102	150
Four Color 1167 (3-5/61), 1215-Photo-c	7	14	21	48	89	130

TALESPIN (Also see Cartoon Tales & Disney's Talespin Limited Series)
Disney Comics: June, 1991 - No. 7, Dec, 1991 ($1.50)

1-7						3.00

TALES TO ASTONISH (Becomes The Incredible Hulk #102 on)
Atlas (MAP No. 1/ZPC No. 2-14/VPI No. 15-21/Marvel No. 22 on: Jan, 1959 - No. 101, Mar, 1968

	2.0	4.0	6.0	8.0	9.0	9.2
1-Jack Davis-a; monster-c.	667	1334	2000	5700	12,850	20,000
2-Ditko flying saucer-c (Martians); #2-4 have sci-fi-c.	155	310	465	1279	2890	4500
3,4	132	264	396	1056	2378	3700
5-Prototype issue (Stone Men); Williamson-a (4 pgs.); Kirby monster-c begin	100	200	300	800	1800	2800
6-Prototype issue (Stone Men)	107	214	321	856	1928	3000
7-Prototype issue (Toad Men)	75	150	225	600	1350	2100
8-10	71	142	213	568	1284	2000
11,12,14,17-20	57	114	171	456	1028	1600
13-(11/60) 1st app. Groot (Guardians of the Galaxy) by Kirby-cvr/sty; swipes story from Menace #8	1590	3180	4770	11,500	20,250	29,000
15-Prototype issue (Electro)	64	128	192	512	1156	1800
16-Prototype issue (Stone Men) named "Thorr"	68	136	204	544	1222	1900
21-(7/61)-Hulk prototype	71	142	213	568	1284	2000
22-26,28-31,33,34	44	88	132	326	738	1150
27-1st Ant-Man app. (1/62); last 10¢ issue (see Strange Tales #73,78 & Tales of Suspense #32)	1290	2580	5160	15,800	40,400	65,000
32-Sandman prototype	50	100	150	400	900	1400
35-(9/62)-2nd app. Ant-Man, 1st in costume; begin series & Ant-Man-c	535	1070	1605	4600	11,800	19,000
36-3rd app. Ant-Man	107	214	321	856	1928	3000
37,39,40	55	110	165	440	995	1550
38-1st app. Egghead	61	122	183	488	1094	1700
41-43	46	92	138	388	834	1300
44-Origin & 1st app. The Wasp (6/63)	449	898	1347	3278	5799	8300
45-47	32	64	96	230	515	800
48-Origin & 1st app. The Porcupine	35	70	105	252	564	875
49-Ant-Man becomes Giant Man (11/63)	61	122	183	488	1094	1700
50,51,53-56,58: 50-Origin/1st app. Human Top (alias Whirlwind). 58-Origin Colossus	21	42	63	147	324	500
52-Origin/1st app. Black Knight (2/64)	44	88	132	326	738	1150
57-Early Spider-Man app. (7/64)	44	88	126	311	706	1100
59-Giant Man vs. Hulk feature story (9/64); Hulk's 1st app. this title; 1st mention that anger triggers his transformation	40	80	120	296	673	1050
60-Giant Man & Hulk double feature begins	37	74	111	274	612	950
61,64-69: 61- Ditko issue; 1st app. of Glenn Talbot; 1st mailbag. 65-New Giant Man costume. 68-New Human Top costume. 69-Last Giant Man	15	30	45	105	233	360
62-1st app./origin The Leader; new Wasp costume; Hulk pin-up page missing from many copies	44	88	132	326	738	1150
63-Origin Leader continues	37	74	111	274	612	950
70-Sub-Mariner & Incredible Hulk begins (8/65)	29	58	87	209	467	725
71-81: 72-Begin alternating-c features w/Sub-Mariner (even #'s) & Hulk (odd #'s). 79-Hulk vs. Hercules-c/story. 81-1st app. Boomerang	8	16	24	55	105	155
82-Iron Man battles Sub-Mariner (1st Iron Man x-over outside The Avengers & TOS); story cont'd from Tales of Suspense #80	10	20	30	64	132	200
83-89,94-99: 97-X-Men cameo (brief)	7	14	21	44	82	120
90-1st app. The Abomination	38	76	114	285	641	1000
91-The Abomination debut continues & 1st cover	19	38	57	133	297	460
92-1st Silver Surfer x-over (outside of Fantastic Four, 6/67); 1 panel cameo only	9	18	27	62	126	190
93-Hulk battles Silver Surfer-c/story (1st full x-over)	50	100	150	400	900	1400
100-Hulk battles Sub-Mariner full-length story	10	20	30	68	144	220
101-Hulk story cont'd in Incredible Hulk #102; Sub-Mariner story continued in Iron Man	10	20	30	69	147	225

NOTE: Ayers c(i)-9-12, 16, 18, 19. Berg a-1. Burgos a-62-64p. Buscema a-85-87p. Colan a(p)-70-76, 78-82, 84, 85, 101; c(p)-71-76, 78, 80, 82, 84, 86, 88, 90. Ditko a-1, 3-48, 50i, 60-67p; c-2, 7i, 8i, 14i, 17i. Everett a-78, 79i, 80-84, 85-90i, 94i, 95, 96; c(i)-79-81, 83, 86, 88. Forte a-75, 88-91; c-89, 91. Kane a-75, 88-91; c-89, 91. Kirby a(p)-1, 5-34-40, 44, 49-51, 68-70, 82, 83; layouts-71-84; c(p)-1, 3-48, 50-70, 72, 73, 75, 77, 78, 79, 81, 85, 90. Kirby/Ditko a-7, 8, 12, 13, 50; c-7, 8, 10, 13. Leiber/Fox a-47, 48, 50, 51. Powell a-65-69p, 73, 74. Reinman a-6, 36, 45, 46, 54i, 56-60i.

TALES TO ASTONISH (2nd Series)
Marvel Comics Group: Dec, 1979 - No. 14, Jan, 1981

	GD 2.0	VG 4.0	FN 6.0	VF 8.0	VF/NM 9.0	NM- 9.2
V1#1-Reprints Sub-Mariner #1 by Buscema	3	6	9	17	26	35
2-14: Reprints Sub-Mariner #2-14	1	3	4	6	8	10

TALES TO ASTONISH
Marvel Comics: V3#1, Oct, 1994 ($6.95, one-shot)

V3#1-Peter David scripts; acetate, painted-c						7.00

TALES TO HOLD YOU SPELLBOUND (See Spellbound)

TALES TO OFFEND
Dark Horse Comics: July, 1997 ($2.95, one-shot)

1-Frank Miller s/a, EC-style cover						4.00

TALES TOO TERRIBLE TO TELL (Becomes Terrology #10, 11)
New England Comics: Wint, 1989-90 - No. 11, Nov-Dec.1993 ($2.95/$3.50, B&W with cardstock covers)

	2.0	4.0	6.0	8.0	9.0	9.2
1-($2.95) Reprints of non-EC pre-code horror; EC-style cover by Bissette	2	4	6	8	10	12
1-($3.50, 5-6/93) Second printing with alternate cover not by Bissette						6.00
2-8-($3.50) Story reprints, history of the pre-code titles and creators; cover galleries (B&W) inside & on back-c (color)						4.00
9-11-($2.95) 10,11-"Terrology" on cover						4.00

TALKING KOMICS
Belda Record & Publ. Co.: 1947 (20 pgs, slick-c)
Each comic contained a record that followed the story - much like the Golden Record sets. Known titles: Chirpy Cricket, Lonesome Octopus, Sleepy Santa, Grumpy Shark, Flying Turtle, Happy Grasshopper

with records…	5	10	15	31	53	75

TALLY-HO COMICS
Swappers Quarterly (Baily Publ. Co.): Dec, 1944

nn-Frazetta's 1st work as Giunta's assistant; Man in Black horror story; violence; Giunta-a	90	180	270	576	988	1400

TALULLAH (See Comic Books Series I)

TALON (From Batman Court of Owls crossover)
DC Comics: No. 0, Nov, 2012 - No. 17, May, 2014 ($2.99)

0-17: 0-Origin of Calvin Rose; March-a. 7-11-Bane app.						3.00

TAMMY, TELL ME TRUE
Dell Publishing Co.: No. 1233, 1961

	2.0	4.0	6.0	8.0	9.0	9.2
Four Color 1233-Movie	8	16	24	56	108	160

TANGENT COMICS
.../ THE ATOM, DC Comics: Dec, 1997 ($2.95, one-shot)

1-Dan Jurgens-s/Jurgens & Paul Ryan-a						4.00

.../ THE BATMAN, DC Comics: Sept, 1998 ($1.95, one-shot)

1-Dan Jurgens-s/Klaus Janson-a						4.00

.../ DOOM PATROL, DC Comics: Dec, 1997 ($2.95, one-shot)

1- Dan Jurgens-s/Sean Chen & Kevin Conrad-a						4.00

.../ THE FLASH, DC Comics: Dec, 1997 ($2.95, one-shot)

1-Todd Dezago-s/Gary Frank & Cam Smith-a						4.00

.../ GREEN LANTERN, DC Comics: Dec, '97 ($2.95, one-shot)

1-James Robinson-s/J.H. Williams III & Mick Gray-a						4.00

.../ JLA, DC Comics: Sept, 1998 ($1.95, one-shot)

1-Dan Jurgens-s/Banks & Rapmund-a						4.00

.../ THE JOKER, DC Comics: Dec, 1997 ($2.95, one-shot)

1-Karl Kesel-s/Matt Haley & Tom Simmons-a						4.00

.../ THE JOKER'S WILD, DC Comics: Sept, 1998 ($1.95, one-shot)

1-Kesel & Simmons-s/Phillips & Rodriguez-a						4.00

.../ METAL MEN, DC Comics: Dec, 1997 ($2.95, one-shot)

1-Ron Marz-s/Mike McKone & Mark McKenna-a						4.00

.../ NIGHTWING, DC Comics: Dec, 1997 ($2.95, one-shot)

1-John Ostrander-s/Jan Duursema-a						4.00

.../ NIGHTWING: NIGHTFORCE, DC Comics: Sept, 1998 ($1.95, one-shot)

1-John Ostrander-s/Jan Duursema-a						4.00

.../ POWERGIRL, DC Comics: Sept, 1998 ($1.95, one-shot)

1-Marz-s/Abell & Vines-a						4.00

.../ SEA DEVILS, DC Comics: Dec, 1997 ($2.95, one-shot)

1-Kurt Busiek-s/Vince Giarrano & Tom Palmer-a						4.00

.../ SECRET SIX, DC Comics: Dec, 1997 ($2.95, one-shot)

1-Chuck Dixon-s/Tom Grummett & Lary Stucker-a						4.00

.../ THE SUPERMAN, DC Comics: Sept, 1998 ($1.95, one-shot)

	GD	VG	FN	VF	VF/NM	NM-
	2.0	4.0	6.0	8.0	9.0	9.2

1-Millar-s/Guice-a ... 4.00

.../ TALES OF THE GREEN LANTERN, DC Comics: Sept, 1998 ($1.95, one-shot)
1-Story & art by various ... 4.00

.../ THE TRIALS OF THE FLASH, DC Comics: Sept, 1998 ($1.95, one-shot)
1-Dezago-s/Pelletier & Lanning-a ... 4.00

.../ WONDER WOMAN DC Comics: Sept, 1998 ($1.95, one-shot),
1-Peter David-s/Unzueta & Mendoza-a ... 4.00
... Volume One TPB (2007, $19.99) r/The Atom, Metal Men, Green Lantern, The Flash, Sea
Devils one-shots; intro and new cover by Jurgens ... 20.00
... Volume Two TPB (2008, $19.99) r/Batman, Doom Patrol, Joker, Nightwing and Secret Six
one-shots; new cover by Jurgens ... 20.00
... Volume Three TPB (2008, $19.99) r/The Superman, Wonder Woman, Nightwing: Nightforce,
The Joker's Wild, The Trials of the Flash, Tales of the Green Lantern, Powergirl, and
JLA one-shots; new cover by Jurgens ... 20.00

TANGENT: SUPERMAN'S REIGN
DC Comics: May, 2008 - No. 12, Apr, 2009 ($2.99, limited series)
1-12-Jurgens-s; Flash & Green Lantern app.; back-up histories of Tangent heroes ... 3.00
Volume 1 TPB (2009, $19.99) r/#1-6 & Justice League of America #16 ... 20.00
Volume 2 TPB (2009, $19.99) r/#7-12 ... 20.00

TANGLED (Disney movie)
IDW Publishing: Jan, 2018 - No. 3, Mar, 2018 ($3.99)
1-3: 1-Three covers. 2,3-Two covers ... 4.00
...: The Series: Hair and Now 1-3 (3/19 - 5/19, $3.99) Katie Cook-s ... 4.00
...: The Series: Hair It Is (3/19, $4.99, one-shot) Short stories by various ... 5.00
...: The Series: Hair-Raising Adventures 1-3 (9/18 - 11/18, $3.99) 1-Katie Cook-s ... 4.00

TANGLED WEB (See Spider-Man's Tangled Web)

TANKERS
Bad Idea: May, 2021 - No. 3, Aug, 2021 ($5.99, limited series)
1-3-Venditti-s/Ryp-a; back-ups by various. 3-Hank Howard, Pizza Detective app. ... 6.00

TANK GIRL
Dark Horse Comics: May, 1991 - No. 4, Aug, 1991 ($2.25, B&W, mini-series)

	GD	VG	FN	VF	VF/NM	NM-
1-Contains Dark Horse trading cards	9	18	27	58	114	170
2,3	3	6	9	14	19	24
4	3	6	9	21	33	45

...: Dark Nuggets (Image Comics, 12/09, $3.99) Martin-s/Dayglo-a ... 8.00
...: Dirty Helmets (Image Comics, 4/10, $3.99) Martin-s/Dayglo-a ... 12.00
...: Hairy Heroes (Image Comics, 8/10, $3.99) Martin-s/Dayglo-a ... 10.00

TANK GIRL ALL STARS
Titan Comics: Jul, 2018'- No. 4, Oct, 2018 ($3.99, limited series)
1-4: Alan Martin-s; art by Hewlett, Bond, Mahfood, Parson & others; bonus pin-ups ... 4.00

TANK GIRL: APOCALYPSE
DC Comics: Nov, 1995 - No. 4, Feb, 1996 ($2.25, limited series)
1-4 ... 6.00

TANK GIRL FULL COLOUR CLASSICS
Titan Comics: Jun, 2018 - Present ($6.99, limited series)
1-3.1-Newly colored reprints of original stories from Deadline Magazine; bonus photos ... 7.00

TANK GIRL: MOVIE ADAPTATION
DC Comics: 1995 ($5.95, 68 pgs., one-shot)

	GD	VG	FN	VF	VF/NM	NM-
nn-Peter Milligan scripts	2	4	6	8	10	12

TANK GIRL ONGOING
Titan Comics: Jan, 2019 - No. 8, Dec, 2019 ($3.99, limited series)
1-4-Action Alley - Martin-s/Parson-a; multiple covers and centerfold poster on each ... 4.00
5-8-Forever - Martin-s/Parson-a; multiple covers and centerfold poster on each ... 4.00

TANK GIRL: TANK GIRL GOLD
Titan Comics: Sept, 2016 - No. 4, Mar, 2017 ($3.99, limited series)
1-4: Alan Martin-s/Brett Parson-a. 2-MAD spoof ... 4.00

TANK GIRL: THE GIFTING
IDW Publishing: May, 2007 - No. 4, Aug, 2007 ($3.99, limited series)
1-4: 1-Ashley Wood-a/c; Alan Martin-s; 3 covers ... 6.00

TANK GIRL: THE ODYSSEY
DC Comics: May, 1995 - No.4, Oct, 1995 ($2.25, limited series)

	GD	VG	FN	VF	VF/NM	NM-
1-4: Peter Milligan scripts; Hewlett-a	1	3	4	6	8	10

TANK GIRL: THE ROYAL ESCAPE
IDW Publishing: Mar, 2010 - No. 4, Jun, 2010 ($3.99, limited series)
1-4: Alan Martin-s/Rufus Dayglo-a/c ... 4.00

TANK GIRL: 21ST CENTURY TANK GIRL
Titan Comics: Jul, 2015 - No. 3, Sept, 2015 ($3.99, limited series)
1-3: Alan Martin-s; art by Hewlett, Bond, Mahfood, Parson & others ... 4.00

TANK GIRL 2
Dark Horse Comics: June, 1993 - No. 4, Sept, 1993 ($2.50, lim. series, mature)

	GD	VG	FN	VF	VF/NM	NM-
1-4: Jamie Hewlett & Alan Martin-s/a	1	3	4	6	8	10
TPB (2/95, $17.95) r/#1-4						18.00

TANK GIRL: TWO GIRLS, ONE TANK
Titan Comics: Jun, 2016 - No. 4, Sept, 2016 ($3.99, limited series)
1-4: Alan Martin-s/Brett Parson-a ... 4.00

TAPPAN'S BURRO (See Zane Grey & 4-Color #449)

TAPPING THE VEIN (Clive Barker's...)
Eclipse Comics: 1989 - No. 5, 1992 ($6.95, squarebound, mature, 68 pgs.)
Book 1-5: 1-Russell-a; Bolton-c. 2-Bolton-a. 4-Die-cut-c ... 7.00
TPB (2002, $24.95, Checker Book Publ. Group) r/#1-5 ... 25.00

TARANTULA (See Weird Suspense)

TARGET: AIRBOY
Eclipse Comics: Mar, 1988 ($1.95)

	GD	VG	FN	VF	VF/NM	NM-
	2.0	4.0	6.0	8.0	9.0	9.2

1 ... 4.00

TARGET COMICS (...Western Romances #106 on)
Funnies, Inc./Novelty Publications/Star Publ.: Feb, 1940 - V10#3 (#105), Aug-Sept, 1949

	GD	VG	FN	VF	VF/NM	NM-
V1#1-Origin & 1st app. Manowar, The White Streak by Burgos, & Bulls-Eye Bill by Everett; City Editor (ends #5), High Grass Twins by Jack Cole (ends #4), T-Men by Joe Simon (ends #9), Rip Rory (ends #4), Fantastic Feature Films by Tarpe Mills (ends #39), & Calling 2-R (ends #14) begin; marijuana use story	476	952	1428	3475	6138	8800
2-Everett-c/a	284	568	852	1818	3109	4400
3,4-Everett, Jack Cole-a	194	388	582	1242	2121	3000
5-Origin The White Streak in text; Space Hawk by Wolverton begins (6/40) (see Blue Bolt & Circus)	481	962	1443	3511	6206	8900
6-The Chameleon by Everett begins (7/40, 1st app.); White Streak origin cont'd. in text; early mention of comic collecting in letter column; 1st letter column in comics? (7/40)	290	580	870	1856	3178	4500
7-Wolverton Spacehawk-c/story (scarce)	1440	2880	4320	10,600	20,300	30,000
8-Classic sci-fi cover (scarce)	411	822	1233	2877	5039	7200
9-White Streak-c	245	490	735	1568	2684	3800
10-Intro/1st app. The Target (11/40); Simon-c; Spacehawk-c; text piece by Wolverton	331	662	993	1617	3709	5800
11-Origin The Target & The Targeteers	213	426	638	1363	2332	3300
12-(1/41) Target & The Targeteers-c	161	322	483	1030	1765	2500
V2#1-Target by Bob Wood; Uncle Sam flag-c	123	246	369	787	1344	1900
2-Ten part Treasure Island serial begins; Harold Delay-a; reprinted in Catholic Comics	84	168	252	538	919	1300
V3#1-10 (see Key Comics)						
3-5: 4-Kit Carter, The Cadet begins	77	154	231	493	847	1200
6-9: Red Seal with White Streak in #6-10	71	142	213	454	777	1100
10-Classic-c	161	322	483	1030	1765	2500
11,12: 12-10-part Last of the Mohicans serial begins; Delay-a	65	130	195	416	708	1000
V3#1-3,5-7,9,10: 10-Last Wolverton issue	53	106	159	334	567	800
4-V for Victory-c	97	194	291	621	1061	1500
8-Hitler, Tojo, Flag-c; 6-part Gulliver Travels serial begins; Delay-a	155	310	465	992	1696	2400
11,12	24	48	72	140	230	320
V4#1-4,7-12: 8-X-mas-c	18	36	54	103	162	220
5-Classic Statue of Liberty-c	39	78	117	231	378	525
6-Targetoons by Wolverton	22	44	66	132	216	300
V5#1-8	15	30	45	90	140	190
V6#1-4,6-10	15	30	45	85	130	175
5-Classic Tojo hanging/Buy War Bonds WWII-c	103	206	309	659	1130	1600
V7#1-12	14	28	42	81	118	155
V8#1,3-5,8-9,11,12	13	26	39	74	105	135
2,6,7-Krigstein-a	14	28	42	81	118	155
10-L.B. Cole-c	32	64	96	188	307	425
V9#1,4,6,8,10-L.B. Cole-c	32	64	96	188	307	425
2,3,5,7,9,11, V10#1	13	26	39	74	105	135
12-Classic L.B. Cole-c	371	742	1113	2600	4550	6500
V10#2,3-L.B. Cole-c	34	68	102	199	325	450

NOTE: Certa c-V8#9, 11, 12, V9#5, 9, 11, V10#1. Jack Cole a-1-8. Everett a-1-9; c(signed Blake)-1, 2. Al Fago c-V6#8. Sid Greene c-V2#9, 12, V3#3. Walter Johnson c-V5#6, V6#4. Tarpe Mills a-1-4, 6, 8, 15, V3#1. Rico a-V7#4, 10, V8#5, 6, V9#3; c-V7#6, 8, 10, V8#2, 4, 6, 7. Simon a-2. Bob Wood c-V2#2, 3, 5, 6.

TARGET: THE CORRUPTORS (TV)
Dell Publishing Co.: No. 1306, Mar-May, 1962 - No. 3, Oct-Dec, 1962 (All have photo-c)

	GD	VG	FN	VF	VF/NM	NM-
Four Color 1306(#1), #2,3	5	10	15	35	63	90

TARGET WESTERN ROMANCES (Formerly Target Comics; becomes Flaming Western Romances #3)
Star Publications: No. 106, Oct-Nov, 1949 - No. 107, Dec-Jan, 1949-50

	GD	VG	FN	VF	VF/NM	NM-
106(#1)-Silhouette nudity panel; L.B. Cole-c	36	72	108	214	347	480
107(#2)-L.B. Cole-c; lingerie panels	30	60	90	177	289	400

TARGITT
Atlas/Seaboard Publ.: March, 1975 - No. 3, July, 1975

	GD	VG	FN	VF	VF/NM	NM-
1-3: 1-Origin; Nostrand-a in all. 2-1st in costume. 3-Becomes Man-Stalker	2	4	6	10	14	18

TAROT
Marvel Comics: Mar, 2020 - No. 4, May, 2020 ($4.99, limited series)
1-4-Alan Davis-s/Paul Renaud-a; Defenders & Avengers vs. Diablo ... 5.00

TAROT: WITCH OF THE BLACK ROSE
Broadsword Comics: Mar, 2000 - Present ($2.95/$3.99, mature)

	GD	VG	FN	VF	VF/NM	NM-
1-Jim Balent-s/c/a; at least two covers on all issues	4	8	12	27	44	60
1-Second printing (10/00)	1	2	3	5	6	8
2	2	4	6	13	18	22
3-20	1	2	3	5	6	8
21-40						5.00
41-121: 84,113-The Krampus app. 90-Crossover with School Bites characters						3.00
122/Alternate Paths: Raven Hex #1 - Raven Hex as the Swordmaiden						3.00
123/Alternate Paths: Raven Hex #2 ($12.50, sold online)						12.50
123/Alternate Paths: Raven Hex #2 (7/21, $3.99)						4.00
124,125/Alternate Paths: Boo-Cat #1,2 ($3.99)1- Boo-Cat on vacation. 2-Krampus app.						4.00
126-142 ($3.99)						4.00

TARZAN (See Aurora, Comics on Parade, Crackajack, DC 100-Page Super Spec., Edgar Rice Burroughs'..., Famous Feature Stories #1, Golden Comics Digest #4, 9, Jeep Comics, Jungle Tales of..., Limited Collectors' Edition, Popular, Sparkler, Sport Stars #1, Tip Top & Top Comics)

TARZAN
Dell Publishing Co./United Features Synd.: No. 5, 1939 - No. 161, Aug, 1947
Large Feature Comic 5 ('39)-(Scarce)-By Hal Foster; reprints 1st dailies from 1929

	GD	VG	FN	VF	VF/NM	NM-
	271	542	813	1734	2967	4200
Single Series 20 ('40)-By Hal Foster	213	426	639	1363	2332	3300
Four Color 134 (2/47)-Marsh-c/a	61	122	183	488	1094	1700
Four Color 161 (8/47)-Marsh-c/a	48	96	144	374	862	1350

TARZAN (...of the Apes #138 on)
Dell Publishing Co./Gold Key No. 132 on: 1-2/48 - No. 131, 7-8/62; No. 132, 11/62 - No. 206, 2/72

Tangled #2 © DIS

Tarot: Witch of the Black Rose #111 © Jim Balent

Tarzan #219 © ERB

	GD	VG	FN	VF	VF/NM	NM-
	2.0	4.0	6.0	8.0	9.0	9.2

	GD 2.0	VG 4.0	FN 6.0	VF 8.0	VF/NM 9.0	NM- 9.2
1-Jesse Marsh-a begins	107	214	321	856	1928	3000
2	44	88	132	326	738	1150
3-5	34	68	102	245	548	850
6-10: 6-1st Tantor the Elephant. 7-1st Valley of the Monsters	27	54	81	189	420	650
11-15: 11-Two Against the Jungle begins, ends #24. 13-Lex Barker photo-c begin	20	40	60	138	307	475
16-20	16	32	48	110	243	375
21-24,26-30	13	26	39	86	188	290
25-1st "Brothers of the Spear" episode; series ends #156,160,161,196-206	15	30	45	103	227	350
31-40	10	20	30	68	144	220
41-54: Last Barker photo-c	8	16	24	56	108	160
55-60: 56-Eight pg. Boy story	7	14	21	49	92	135
61,62,64-70	6	12	18	41	76	110
63-Two Tarzan stories, 1 by Manning	7	14	21	46	86	125
71-79	6	12	18	37	66	95
80-99: 80-Gordon Scott photo-c	5	10	15	34	60	85
100	6	12	18	38	69	100
101-109	5	10	15	33	57	80
110 (Scarce)-Last photo-c	6	12	18	38	69	100
111-120	5	10	15	31	53	75
121-131: Last Dell issue	5	10	15	30	50	70
132-1st Gold Key issue	5	10	15	31	53	75
133-138,140-154	4	8	12	25	40	55
139-(12/63)-1st app. Korak (Boy); leaves Tarzan & gets own book (1/64)	6	12	18	42	79	115
155-Origin Tarzan; text article on Tarzana, CA	5	10	15	31	53	75
156-161: 157-Banlu, Dog of the Arande begins, ends #159, 195. 169-Leopard Girl app.	3	6	9	21	33	45
162,165,168,171 (TV)-Ron Ely photo covers	4	8	12	22	35	48
163,164,166,167,169,170: 169-Leopard Girl app.	3	6	9	20	31	42
172-199,201-206: 178-Tarzan origin-r/#155; Leopard Girl app., also in #179, 190-193	3	6	9	18	28	38
200	3	6	9	21	33	45
Story Digest 1-(6/70, G.K., 148pp.)(scarce)	6	12	18	41	76	110

NOTE: *#162, 165, 168, 171* are TV issues. *#1-153* all have *Marsh* art on. *#154-161, 163, 164, 166, 167, 172-177* all have *Manning* art on Tarzan. *#178, 202* have *Manning* Tarzan reprints. No "Brothers of the Spear" in *#1-24, 157-159, 162-195. #162-195* have *Russ Manning* art on "Brothers of the Spear". *#39-126, 128-156* all have *Russ Manning* B.O.T.S. reprints; *#25-38, 127* all have Jesse Marsh art on B.O.T.S. *#206* has a Marsh B.O.T.S. reprint. *Gollub c-8-12. Marsh c-1-7. Doug Wildey* a-162, 179-187. Many issues have front and back photo covers.

TARZAN (Continuation of Gold Key series)
National Periodical Publications: No. 207, Apr, 1972 - No. 258, Feb, 1977

	GD 2.0	VG 4.0	FN 6.0	VF 8.0	VF/NM 9.0	NM- 9.2
207-Origin Tarzan by Joe Kubert, part 1; John Carter begins (origin); 52 pg. issues thru #209	3	6	11	35	63	90
208,209-(52 pgs.): 208-210-Parts 2-4 of origin. 209-Last John Carter	3	6	9	21	33	45
210-220: 210-Kubert-a. 211-Hogarth, Kubert-a. 212-214: Adaptations from "Jungle Tales of Tarzan". 213-Beyond the Farthest Star begins, ends #218. 215-218,224,225-All by Kubert. 215-part Foster-r. 219-223: Adapts "The Return of Tarzan" by Kubert	3	6	9	14	20	25
221-229: 221-223-Continues adaptation of "The Return of Tarzan". 226-Manning-a	2	4	6	10	14	18
230-DC 100 Page Super Spectacular; Kubert, Kaluta-a(p); Korak begins, ends #234; Carson of Venus app.	4	8	12	25	40	55
231-235-New Kubert-a.: 231-234-(All 100 pgs.)-Adapts "Tarzan and the Lion Man"; Rex, the Wonder Dog app. #232, 233. 235-(100 pgs.)-Last Kubert issue.	4	8	12	23	37	50
236,237,239-258: 240-243 adapts "Tarzan & the Castaways." 250-256 adapts "Tarzan the Untamed." 252,253-r/#213	2	4	6	8	10	12
238-(68 pgs.)	2	4	6	13	18	22
Digest 1-(Fall, 1972, 50¢, 164 pgs.)(DC)-Digest size; Kubert-c; Manning-a	4	8	12	25	40	55

NOTE: *Anderson* a-207, 209, 217, 218. *Chaykin* a-216. *Finlay* a(r)-212. *Foster* strip-r #207-209, 211, 212, 221. *Heath* a-230i. *G. Kane* a(r)-232p, 233p. *Kubert* a-207-225, 227-235, 257r, 258r; c-207-249, 253. *Lopez* a-250-255p; c-250p, 251, 252, 254. *Manning* strip-r 230-235, 238. *Morrow* a-208. *Nino* a-231-234. *Sparling* a-230, 231. *Starr* a-233r.

TARZAN (Lord of the Jungle)
Marvel Comics Group: June, 1977 - No. 29, Oct, 1979

	GD 2.0	VG 4.0	FN 6.0	VF 8.0	VF/NM 9.0	NM- 9.2
1-New adaptions of Burroughs stories; Buscema-a	3	6	9	17	26	35
1-(35¢-c variant, limited distribution)(6/77)	8	16	24	54	102	150
2-29: 2-Origin by John Buscema. 9-Young Tarzan. 12-14-Jungle Tales of Tarzan.	1	3	4	6	8	10
25-29-New stories	1	3	4	6	8	10
2-5-(35¢-c variants, limited distribution)(7-10/77)	5	10	15	35	63	90
Annual 1-3: 1-(1977). 2-(1978). 3-(1979)	1	3	4	6	8	10

NOTE: *N. Adams* c-11i, 12i. *Alcala* a-9i, 10i; c-8i, 9i. *Buckler* c-25-27p, Annual 3p. *John Buscema* a-1-3, 4-18p, Annual 1; c-1-7, 8p, 9p, 10, 11p, 12p, 13, 14-19p, 21p, 22, 23p, 24p, 28p, Annual 1. *Mooney* a-22i. *Nebres* a-22i. *Russell* a-29i.

TARZAN
Dark Horse Comics: July, 1996 - No. 20, Mar, 1998 ($2.95)

1-20: 1-6-Suydam-c						4.00

TARZAN / CARSON OF VENUS
Dark Horse Comics: May, 1998 - No. 4, Aug, 1998 ($2.95, limited series)

1-4-Darko Macan-s/Igor Kordey-a						4.00

TARZAN FAMILY, THE (Formerly Korak, Son of Tarzan)
National Periodical Publications: No. 60, Nov-Dec, 1975 - No. 66, Nov-Dec, 1976

	GD 2.0	VG 4.0	FN 6.0	VF 8.0	VF/NM 9.0	NM- 9.2
60-62-(68 pgs.): 60-Korak begins; Kaluta-r	2	4	6	11	16	20
63-66 (52 pgs.)	2	4	6	9	12	15

NOTE: *Carson of Venus-r 60-65. New John Carter-62-64, 65r, 66r. New Korak-60-66. Pellucidar feature-66. Foster strip-r 60(9/4/32-10/16/32), 62(6/29/32-7/31/32), 63(10/11/31-12/13/31). Kaluta Carson of Venus-60-65. Kubert a-61, 64; c-60-64. Manning strip-r 60-62, 64. Morrow a-66r.*

TARZAN/JOHN CARTER: WARLORDS OF MARS
Dark Horse Comics: Jan, 1996 - No. 4, June, 1996 ($2.50, limited series)

1-4: Bruce Jones scripts in all. 1,2,4-Bret Blevins-c/a. 2-(4/96)-Indicia reads #3						4.00

TARZAN KING OF THE JUNGLE (See Dell Giant #37, 51)

TARZAN, LORD OF THE JUNGLE
Gold Key: Sept, 1965 (Giant) (25¢, soft paper-c)

	GD 2.0	VG 4.0	FN 6.0	VF 8.0	VF/NM 9.0	NM- 9.2
1-Marsh-r	7	14	21	48	89	130

TARZAN: LOVE, LIES AND THE LOST CITY (See Tarzan the Warrior)
Malibu Comics: Aug. 10, 1992 - No. 3, Sept, 1992 ($2.50, limited series)

1-($3.95, 68 pgs.)-Flip book format; Simonson & Wagner scripts						5.00
2,3-No Simonson or Wagner scripts						4.00

TARZAN MARCH OF COMICS (See March of Comics #82, 98, 114, 125, 144, 155, 172, 185, 204, 223, 240, 252, 262, 272, 286, 300, 332, 342, 354, 366)

TARZAN OF THE APES
Metropolitan Newspaper Service: 1934? (Hardcover, 4x12", 68 pgs.)

	GD 2.0	VG 4.0	FN 6.0	VF 8.0	VF/NM 9.0	NM- 9.2
1-Strip reprints	29	58	87	172	281	390

TARZAN OF THE APES
Marvel Comics Group: July, 1984 - No. 2, Aug, 1984 (Movie adaptation)

1,2: Origin-r/Marvel Super Spec.						4.00

TARZAN ON THE PLANET OF THE APES
Dark Horse Comics: Sept, 2016 - No. 5, Jan, 2017 ($3.99, limited series)

1-5-Seeley & Walker-s/Dagnino-a. 1-Cornelius & Zira adopt young Tarzan on Earth						4.00

TARZAN'S JUNGLE ANNUAL (See Dell Giants)

TARZAN'S JUNGLE WORLD (See Dell Giant #25)

TARZAN: THE BECKONING
Malibu Comics: 1992 - No. 7, 1993 ($2.50, limited series)

1-7						4.00

TARZAN: THE LOST ADVENTURE (See Edgar Rice Burroughs' ...)

TARZAN-THE RIVERS OF BLOOD
Dark Horse Comics: Nov, 1999 - No. 8 ($2.95, limited series)

1-4: Kordey-c/a						4.00

TARZAN THE SAVAGE HEART
Dark Horse Comics: Apr, 1999 - No. 4, July, 1999 ($2.95, limited series)

1-4: Grell-c/a						4.00

TARZAN THE WARRIOR (Also see Tarzan: Love, Lies and the Lost City)
Malibu Comics: Mar, 19, 1992 - No. 5, 1992 ($2.50, limited series)

1-5: 1-Bisley painted pack-c (flip book format-c)						4.00
1-2nd printing w/o flip-c by Bisley						4.00

TARZAN VS. PREDATOR AT THE EARTH'S CORE
Dark Horse Comics: Jan, 1996 - No. 4, June, 1996 ($2.50, limited series)

1-4: Lee Weeks-c/a; Walt Simonson scripts						4.00

TASK FORCE Z
DC Comics: Dec, 2021 - No. 12, Nov, 2022 ($3.99)

Edgar Rice Burroughs' Tarzan The Joe Kubert Years - Volume One HC (Dark Horse Books, 10/05, $49.95, dust jacket) recolored r/#207-214; intro. by Joe Kubert — 50.00
Edgar Rice Burroughs' Tarzan The Joe Kubert Years - Volume Two HC (Dark Horse Books, 2/06, $49.95, dust jacket) recolored r/#215-224; intro. by Joe Kubert — 50.00
Edgar Rice Burroughs' Tarzan The Joe Kubert Years - Volume Three HC (Dark Horse Books, 6/06, $49.95, dust jacket) recolored r/#225,227-235; Kubert intro. and sketch pages — 50.00

	GD 2.0	VG 4.0	FN 6.0	VF 8.0	VF/NM 9.0	NM- 9.2

1-12-Red Hood leads a team of zombies; Bane, Man-Bat, Mr. Bloom, Deadshot app. — 4.00

TASKMASTER
Marvel Comics: Apr, 2002 - No. 4, July, 2002 ($2.99, limited series)
1-4-Udon Studio-s/a. 1-Iron Man app. — 3.00

TASKMASTER
Marvel Comics: Nov, 2010 - No. 4, Feb, 2011 ($3.99, limited series)
1-4-Van Lente-s/Palo-a; Hydra & A.I.M. app. — 4.00

TASKMASTER
Marvel Comics: Jan, 2021 - No. 5, May, 2021 ($3.99, limited series)
1-5-MacKay-s/Vitti-a; Nick Fury and Black Widow app. 2-Hyperion app. 3-White Fox app. — 4.00

TASMANIAN DEVIL & HIS TASTY FRIENDS
Gold Key: Nov, 1962 (12¢)
1-Bugs Bunny, Elmer Fudd, Sylvester, Yosemite Sam, Road Runner & Wile E. Coyote x-over — 18 — 36 — 54 — 128 — 284 — 440

TATTERED BANNERS
DC Comics (Vertigo): Nov, 1998 - No. 4, Feb, 1999 ($2.95, limited series)
1-4-Grant & Giffen-s/McMahon-a — 4.00

TATTERED MAN
Image Comics: May 2011 ($4.99, one-shot)
1-Justin Gray & Jimmy Palmiotti-s/Norberto Fernandez-a; covers by Fernandez & Conner — 5.00

TEAM AMERICA (See Captain America #269)
Marvel Comics Group: June, 1982 - No. 12, May, 1983
1,12: 1-Origin; Ideal Toy motorcycle characters. 12-Double size — 5.00
2-11: 9-Iron Man app. 11-Ghost Rider app. — 4.00
NOTE: There are 16 pg. variants known for most issues, possibly all. The only ad is on the inside front cover.

TEAM HELIX
Marvel Comics: Jan, 1993 - No. 4, Apr, 1993 ($1.75, limited series)
1-4: Teen Super Group. 1,2-Wolverine app. — 4.00

TEAM ONE: STORMWATCH (Also see StormWatch)
Image Comics (WildStorm Productions): June, 1995 - No. 2, Aug, 1995 ($2.50, lim. series)
1,2: Steven T. Seagle scripts — 4.00

TEAM ONE: WILDC.A.T.S (Also see WildC.A.T.S)
Image Comics (WildStorm Productions): July, 1995 - No. 2, Aug, 1995 ($2.50, lim. series)
1,2: James Robinson scripts — 4.00

TEAM 7
Image Comics (WildStorm): Oct, 1994 - No.4, Feb, 1995 ($2.50, limited series)
1-4: Dixon scripts in all, 1-Portacio variant-c — 4.00

TEAM 7 (DC New 52)
DC Comics: No. 0, Nov, 2012 - No. 8, Jul, 2013 ($2.99)
0-8: 0-Merino-a/Lashley-c; Slade Wilson, John Lynch, Grifter and others assemble team.
3,4-Eclipso returns. 7-Pandora & Majestic app. — 3.00

TEAM 7-DEAD RECKONING
Image Comics (WildStorm): Jan, 1996 - No. 4, Apr, 1996 ($2.50, limited series)
1-4: Dixon scripts in all — 4.00

TEAM 7-OBJECTIVE HELL
Image Comics (WildStorm): May, 1995 - No. 3, July, 1995 ($1.95/$2.50, limited series)
1-($1.95)-Newstand; Dixon scripts in all; Barry Smith-c — 4.00
1-3: 1-($2.50)-Direct Market; Barry Smith-c, bound-in card — 4.00

TEAM SONIC RACING
IDW Publishing: Oct, 2018; May, 2019 ($4.99/$5.99, one-shots)
1-Caleb Goellner-s/Adam Bryce Thomas-a; videogame tie-in — 5.00
... Deluxe Turbo Championship Edition (5/19, $5.99) Goellner-s/Thomas-a — 6.00

TEAM SUPERMAN
DC Comics: July, 1999 ($2.95, one-shot)
1-Jeanty-a/Stelfreeze-c — 4.00
...Secret Files 1 (5/98, $4.95)Origin-s and pin-ups of Superboy, Supergirl and Steel — 5.00

TEAM TITANS (See Deathstroke & New Titans Annual #7)
DC Comics: Sept, 1992 - No. 24, Sept, 1994 ($1.75/$1.95)
1-Five different #1s exist w/origins in 1st half & the same 2nd story in each: Kilowat, Mirage, Nightrider w/Netzer/Pérez-a, Redwing, & Terra w/part Pérez-p; Total Chaos Pt. 3 — 5.00
2-24: Total Chaos Pt 6. 11-Metallik app. 24-Zero Hour x-over — 4.00
Annual 1,2 ('93, '94, $3.50, 68 pgs.): 2-Elseworlds tory — 5.00

TEAM X/TEAM 7
Marvel Comics: Nov, 1996 ($4.95, one-shot)
1 — 5.00

TEAM X 2000
Marvel Comics: Feb, 1999 ($3.50, one-shot)
1-Kevin Lau-a; Bishop vs. Shi'ar Empire — 4.00

TEAM YOUNGBLOOD (Also see Youngblood)
Image Comics (Extreme Studios): Sept, 1993 - No. 22, Sept, 1995 ($1.95/$2.50)
1-22: 1-9-Liefeld scripts in all: 1,2,4-6,8-Thibert-c(i). 1-1st app. Dutch & Masada.
3-Spawn cameo. 5-1st app. Lynx. 7,8-Coupons 1 & 4 for Extreme Prejudice #0;
Black and White Pt. 4 & 8 by Thibert. 8-Coupon #4 for E. P. #0. 9-Liefeld wraparound-c
&(p)/a(p) on Pt. 1. 16,17-Bagged w/trading card. 21-Angela & Glory-app. — 4.00

TEAM ZERO
DC Comics (WildStorm Productions): Feb, 2006 - No. 6, Jul, 2006 ($2.99, limited series)
1-6-Dixon-s/Mahnke-a — 3.00
TPB (2008, $17.99) r/#1-6 — 18.00

TEAR US APART
Dark Horse Comics: Sept, 2023 - No. 4, Jan, 2024 ($4.99, limited series)
1-4-Baruchel & Jensen-s/Micelli-a — 5.00

TECH JACKET

Image Comics: Nov, 2002 - No. 6, Apr, 2003 ($2.95)
1-6-Kirkman-s/Su-a — 3.00
Vol. 1: Lost and Found TPB (7/03, $12.95, 7-3/4" x 5-1/4") B&W r/#1-6; Valentino intro. — 13.00

TECH JACKET (2nd series)
Image Comics: Jul, 2014 - No. 12, Dec, 2015 ($2.99)
1-12-Keatinge-s/Randolph-a — 3.00

TEDDY ROOSEVELT & HIS ROUGH RIDERS (See Real Heroes #1)
Avon Periodicals: 1950
1-Kinstler-c; Palais-a; Flag-c — 24 — 48 — 72 — 142 — 234 — 325

TEDDY ROOSEVELT ROUGH RIDER (See Battlefield #22 & Classics Illustrated Special Issue)

TED MCKEEVER'S METROPOL (See Transit)
Marvel Comics (Epic Comics): Mar, 1991 - No. 12, Mar, 1992 ($2.95, limited series)
V1#1-12: Ted McKeever-c/a/scripts — 4.00

TED MCKEEVER'S METROPOL A.D.
Marvel Comics (Epic Comics): Oct, 1992 - No. 3, Dec, 1992 ($3.50, limited series)
V2#1-3: Ted McKeever-c/a/scripts — 4.00

TEENA
Magazine Enterprises/Standard Comics No. 20 on: No. 11, 1948 - No. 15, 1948; No. 20, Aug, 1949 - No. 22, Oct, 1950

	GD 2.0	VG 4.0	FN 6.0	VF 8.0	VF/NM 9.0	NM- 9.2
A-1 #11-Teen-age; Ogden Whitney-c	18	36	54	105	165	225
A-1 #12, 15	15	30	45	88	137	185
20-22 (Standard)	14	28	42	76	108	140

TEEN-AGE BRIDES (True Bride's Experiences #8 on)
Harvey/Home Comics: Aug, 1953 - No. 7, Aug, 1954

	GD 2.0	VG 4.0	FN 6.0	VF 8.0	VF/NM 9.0	NM- 9.2
1-Powell-a	15	30	45	84	127	170
2-Powell-a	10	20	30	58	79	100
3-7: 3,6-Powell-a	9	18	27	52	69	85

TEEN-AGE CONFESSIONS (See Teen Confessions)

TEEN-AGE CONFIDENTIAL CONFESSIONS
Charlton Comics: July, 1960 - No. 22, 1964

	GD 2.0	VG 4.0	FN 6.0	VF 8.0	VF/NM 9.0	NM- 9.2
1	5	10	15	34	60	85
2-10	3	6	9	21	33	45
11-22	3	6	9	16	23	30

TEEN-AGE DIARY SECRETS (Formerly Blue Ribbon Comics; becomes Diary Secrets #10 on)
St. John Publishing Co.: No. 4, 9/49; nn (#5), 9/49 - No. 7, 11/49; No. 8, 2/50; No. 9, 8/50

	GD 2.0	VG 4.0	FN 6.0	VF 8.0	VF/NM 9.0	NM- 9.2
4(9/49)-Oversized; part mag., part comic	65	130	195	416	708	1000
nn(#5)(no indicia)-Oversized, all comics; contains sty "I Gave Boys the Green Light."	63	126	189	403	689	975
6-(Reg. size) pre-fame Marilyn Monroe photo-c; Baker-a(2-3)	116	232	348	742	1271	1800
7-Digest size (Pocket Comics); Baker-a(5); same contents as #9; diff.-c	106	212	318	673	1162	1650
8-(Reg. size) Photo-c; Baker-a(2-3)	74	148	222	470	810	1150
9-Digest size (Pocket Comics); Baker-a(5); same contents as #7; diff.-c by Baker	155	310	465	992	1696	2400

TEEN-AGE DOPE SLAVES (See Harvey Comics Library #1)

TEENAGE HOTRODDERS (Top Eliminator #25 on; see Blue Bird)
Charlton Comics: Apr, 1963 - No. 24, July, 1967

	GD 2.0	VG 4.0	FN 6.0	VF 8.0	VF/NM 9.0	NM- 9.2
1	7	14	21	46	86	125
2-10	4	8	12	22	37	50
11-24	3	6	9	17	26	35

TEEN-AGE LOVE (See Fox Giants)

TEEN-AGE LOVE (Formerly Intimate)
Charlton Comics: V2#4, July, 1958 - No. 96, Dec, 1973

	GD 2.0	VG 4.0	FN 6.0	VF 8.0	VF/NM 9.0	NM- 9.2
V2#4	5	10	15	35	63	90
5-9	3	8	12	28	47	65
10(9/59)-20	3	6	9	21	33	45
21-35	3	6	9	17	26	35
36-70	3	6	9	14	20	26
71-79,81,82,85-87,90-96: 61&62-Jonnie Love begins (origin)	2	4	6	10	16	20
80,84,88-David Cassidy pin-ups	3	6	9	15	22	28
83,89: 83-Bobby Sherman pin-up. 89-Danny Bonaduce pin-up	3	6	9	15	22	28

TEENAGE MUTANT NINJA CEREBI (Reprints from Cerebus in Hell)
Aardvark-Vanaheim: 2018 ($4.00, B&W)
1-Cerebus figures placed over original Gustave Doré artwork of Hell; TMNT #1-c swipe — 4.00

TEENAGE MUTANT NINJA TURTLES (Also see Anything Goes, Donatello, First Comics Graphic Novel, Gobbledygook, Grimjack #26, Leonardo, Michaelangelo, Raphael & Tales Of The...)
Mirage Studios: 1984 - No. 62, Aug, 1993 ($1.50/$1.75, B&W; all 44-52 pgs.)
1-1st printing (3000 copies)-Origin and 1st app. of the Turtles and Splinter. Only printing to have ad for Gobbledygook #1 & 2; Shredder app. (#1-4: 7-1/2x11")

	GD 2.0	VG 4.0	FN 6.0	VF 8.0	VF/NM 9.0	NM- 9.2
	2300	4600	6900	11,500	17,250	23,000
1-2nd printing (6/84)(6,000 copies)	93	186	279	744	1672	2600
1-3rd printing (2/85)(36,000 copies)	40	80	120	296	673	1050
1-4th printing, new-c (50,000 copies)	8	16	24	54	102	150
1-5th printing, new-c (8/88-c, 11/88 inside)	8	16	24	51	96	140

1-Counterfeit. Note: Most counterfeit copies have a half inch wide white streak or scratch marks across the center of back cover. Black part of cover is a bluish black instead of a deep black. Inside paper is very white & inside cover is bright white — (no value)

	GD 2.0	VG 4.0	FN 6.0	VF 8.0	VF/NM 9.0	NM- 9.2
2-1st printing (1984; 15,000 copies)	25	50	75	175	388	600
2-2nd printing	8	16	24	55	105	155
2-3rd printing; new Corben-c/a (2/85)	4	8	12	28	47	65

2-Counterfeit with glossy cover stock (no value).

	GD 2.0	VG 4.0	FN 6.0	VF 8.0	VF/NM 9.0	NM- 9.2
3-1st printing (1985, 44 pgs.)	10	20	30	69	147	225
3-Variant, 500 copies, cover printed at different plant, has 'Laird's Photo' in white rather than light blue	68	136	204	544	1222	1900

Taskmaster #1 © MAR

Teenage Mutant Ninja Turtles #16 © Mirage

Teenage Mutant Ninja Turtles Adventures #17 © Viacom

	GD 2.0	VG 4.0	FN 6.0	VF 8.0	VF/NM 9.0	NM- 9.2
3-2nd printing; contains new back-up story	5	10	15	33	57	80
4-1st printing (1985, 44 pgs.)	10	20	30	69	147	225
4-2nd printing (5/87) all have manufacturing error	16	32	48	110	243	375
5-Fugitoid begins, ends #7; 1st full color-c (1985)	6	12	18	38	69	100
5-2nd printing (11/87)	3	6	9	19	30	40
6-1st printing (1986)	5	10	15	30	50	70
6-2nd printing (4/88-c, 5/88 inside)	2	4	6	11	16	20
7-Four pg. Eastman/Corben color insert; 1st color TMNT (1986, $1.75-c); Bade Biker back-up story	4	8	12	28	47	65
7-2nd printing (1/89) w/o color insert	6	12	18	38	69	100
8-Cerebus-c/story with Dave Sim-a (1986)	4	8	12	25	40	55
9-(9/86)-Rip In Time by Corben	3	6	9	17	26	35
10-Shredder-c	4	8	12	23	37	50
11,12,14,15	3	6	9	14	20	25
13-1st Jhanna	3	6	9	19	30	40
16-18: 18-Mark Bodé-a	2	4	6	11	16	20
18-2nd printing ($2.25, color, 44 pgs.)-New-c	1	3	4	6	8	10
19-31,33,34: 19-Begin $1.75-c. 24-26-Veitch-c/a.	2	4	6	8	10	12
32-Good Girl art-c	2	4	6	11	16	20
32-2nd printing ($2.75, 52 pgs., full color)						6.00
35-46,48,49,51: 35-Begin $2.00-c.	2	4	6	8	10	12
47-1st Space Usagi	7	14	21	48	89	130
50-Features pin-ups by Larsen, McFarlane, Simonson, etc.	2	4	6	9	12	15
52-62: 52-Begin $2.25-c	1	3	4	6	8	10
nn (1990, $5.95, B&W)-Movie adaptation	3	6	9	14	20	25
Book 1,2($1.50, B&W): 2-Corben-c	2	4	6	9	12	15
...Christmas Special 1 (12/90, $1.75, B&W, 52 pgs.)-Cover title: Michaelangelo Christmas Special; r/Michaelangelo one-shot plus new Raphael story	3	6	9	14	19	24
... Color Special (11/09, $3.25) full color reprint of issue #1	3	6	9	14	20	26
...Special: The Haunted Pizza nn (10/92, $2.25, B&W, 32 pgs.) Howarth-s/a	2	4	6	9	12	15
...Special (The Maltese Turtle) nn (1/93, $2.95, color, 44 pgs.)	2	4	6	9	12	15
...Special: "Times" Pipeline nn (9/92, $2.95, color, 44 pgs.)-Mark Bodé-c/a	2	4	6	9	12	15
Hardcover ($100)-r/#1-10 plus one-shots w/dust jackets - limited to 1000 w/letter of authenticity (1988)						300.00
Softcover ($40)-r/#1-10						45.00
TEENAGE MUTANT NINJA TURTLES						
Mirage Studios: V2#1, Oct, 1993 - V2#13, Oct, 1995 ($2.75)						
V2#1-Wraparound-c	3	6	9	15	22	28
2-13						6.00
TEENAGE MUTANT NINJA TURTLES (Volume 3)						
Image Comics (Highbrow Ent.): June, 1996 - No. 23, Oct, 1999 ($1.95-$2.95)						
1-Erik Larsen-c(i)	3	6	9	15	22	28
2-23: 2-8-Erik Larsen-c(i) on all. 10-Savage Dragon-c/app.						6.00
TEENAGE MUTANT NINJA TURTLES						
Mirage Publishing: V4#1, Dec, 2001 - No. 28, Jun, 2006 ($2.95, B&W)						
V4#1-Laird-s/a(i)/Lawson-a(p)		4	6	11	16	20
V4#2-9,11-28-Laird-s/a(i)/Lawson-a(p).						6.00
10-($3.95) Splinter dies	1	3	4	6	8	10
TEENAGE MUTANT NINJA TURTLES						
Dreamwave Productions: June 2003 - No. 7, Dec, 2003 ($2.95, color)						
1-Animated style; Peter David-s/Lesean-a	2	4	6	9		15
2-7						6.00
TEENAGE MUTANT NINJA TURTLES						
IDW Publishing: Aug, 2011 - Present ($3.99)						
1-Kevin Eastman-s & layouts; four covers by Duncan (each turtle); origin flashback	4	8	12	27	44	60
1-Variant-c by Eastman	6	12	18	38	69	100
1-Halloween Edition (10/12, no cover price) Reprints #1	1	3	4	6	8	10
2-43,45-49,52-74,76-92-Multiple variant covers on each						6.00
44-Donatello killed						20.00
50-(9/15, $7.99) Multiple variant covers; Turtles & Splinter vs. Shredder; Santolouco-a						10
51-First appearance of Jennika (mutated into Ninja Turtle in #95)						
75-(10/17, $7.99) Multiple variant covers; Trial of Krang pt. 3; Santolouco-a	4	8	12	27	44	60
	1	3	4	6	8	10
93,94,96-98-City at War. 97-Jennika dons the yellow mask						6.00
95-Jennika mutated into a Ninja Turtle	4	8	12	27	44	60
99,100-($7.99) Conclusion to City at War. 100-Splinter killed						
	1	3	4	6	8	10
101-114: 101-105-Mutanimals app.						6.00
115-148: 131-139-Armageddon Game tie-ins						6.00
Annual 2012 (10/12, $8.99) Eastman-s/a; wraparound-c						
	1	3	4	6	8	10
Annual 2014 (8/14, $7.99) Eastman-s/a; Renet app.						8.00
Annual 2021 (6/21, $6.99) Waltz-s/Maloney-a; spotlight on The Rat King						7.00
Annual 2022 (3/22, $6.99) Juni Ba-s/a						7.00
Annual 2023 (7/23, $6.99) Takes place after Armageddon Game; Walsh-s						7.00
... : Deviations (3/16, $4.99) What If... the Turtles joined Shredder; Waltz-s/Howard-a						5.00
... : FCBD (3/15, giveaway) Santolouco-a						3.00
... : Free Comic Book Day 2019 (5/19, giveaway) Wachter-a; prelude to #94; Jennika app.						3.00
... : Funko Universe One Shot (5/17, $4.99) Character rendered in Funko Pop figure style						5.00
Greatest Hits - Teenage Mutant Ninja Turtles #1 (2/16, $1.00) r/#1						3.00
... : Kevin Eastman Cover Gallery (12/13, $3.99) Collection of recent Eastman covers						4.00
... : Microseries 1-8 (11/11 - No. 8, 9/12) 1-Raphael. 2-Michelangelo. 3-Donatello. 4-Leonardo. 5-Splinter. 6-Casey Jones. 7-April. 8-Fugitoid						4.00
... : 100 Page Spectacular (4/12, $7.99) r/TMNT Adventures (1988) mini-series #1-3						8.00
... : Road to 100 (11/19, free) Story summary leading to issue #100						3.00
... : Samurai Special (7/17, no price, B&W) Stan Sakai-a; reprints Usagi Yojimbo x-overs						3.00
... : Sourcebook 1 (2/24, $7.99) Profile pages of characters, locations, storylines						8.00
... : Splintered Fate (8/23, $3.99) Henry Barajas-s/Pablo Verdugo-a						5.00
... : 30th Anniversary Special (5/14, $7.99) History and reprints from all eras; pin-ups by various; multiple covers						8.00
... : 20/20 1 (1/19, $4.99) Takes place 20 years in the future; Paul Allor-s/Nelson Daniel-a						5.00
.../ Usagi Yojimbo (7/17, $7.99) Stan Sakai-a; multiple covers						8.00
... : Villains Microseries 1-8 (4/13 - No. 8, 11/13, $3.99) 1-Krang. 2-Baxter. 8-Shredder						4.00
TEENAGE MUTANT NINJA TURTLES (Adventures)						
Archie Publications: Jan, 1996 - No. 3, Mar, 1996 ($1.50, limited series)						
1	3	6	9	14	20	26
2,3	1	3	4	6	8	10
TEENAGE MUTANT NINJA TURTLES ADVENTURES (TV)						
Archie Comics: Oct, 1988 - No. 3, Dec, 1988; Mar, 1989 - No. 72, Oct, 1995 ($1.00-$1.75)						
1-Adapts TV cartoon; not by Eastman/Laird	7	14	21	44	82	120
2,3 (Mini-series)	3	6	9	16	23	30
1 (2nd on-going series)	5	10	15	30	50	70
1-2nd printing	2	4	6	8	10	12
2	3	6	9	14	19	24
2-11: 2nd printings						4.00
3-5: 5-Begins original stories not based on TV	2	4	6	10	14	18
6-18,20-22,25-30: 14-Simpson-a(p). 22-Colan-c/a	1	2	3	5	6	8
19-1st Mighty Mutanimals (also in #20, 51-54)	3	6	9	14	20	25
20,51-54	2	4	6	10	14	18
23-1st Slash	3	6	9	14	19	24
24-2nd Slash	3	6	9	14	19	24
31-48	1	2	3	5	6	8
49-Alien Abduction-c	2	4	6	11	16	20
50-Poster by Eastman/Laird	1	3	4	6	8	10
55-60	1	2	3	5	6	8
61-66: 62-w/poster	2	4	6	10	12	14
67,69-"Moon Eyes Saga" chapters 1,3	2	4	6	11	16	20
68-"Moon Eyes Saga" chapter 2	3	6	9	19	30	40
70-"Moon Eyes Saga" chapter 4 conclusion	4	8	12	27	44	60
71-Turtles origin	6	12	18	37	66	95
72- Last issue	6	12	18	42	79	115
nn (1990, $2.50)-Movie adaptation	2	4	6	11	16	20
nn (Spring, 1991, $2.50, 68 pgs.)-(Meet Archie)	1	3	4	6	8	10
nn (Sum, 1991, $2.50, 68 pgs.)-(Movie II)-Adapts movie sequel	2	4	6	9	12	15
...Meet the Conservation Corps 1 (1992, $2.50, 68 pgs.)	1	3	4	6	8	10
...III The Movie: The Turtles are Back...In Time (1993, $2.50, 68 pgs.)	2	4	6	9	12	15
Special 1,4,5 (Sum/92, Spr/93, Sum/93, 68 pgs.)-1-Bill Wray-c	1	2	3	5	6	8
Giant Size Special 6 (Fall/93, $1.95, 52 pgs.)						6.00
Special 7-9 (Win/93-Sum/94, 52 pgs.): 9-Jeff Smith-c						5.00
Special 10 (Fall/94, 52 pgs.) Last Giant	1	3	4	6	8	10

NOTE: There are 2nd printings of #1-11 w/B&W inside covers. Originals are color.

TEENAGE MUTANT NINJA TURTLES AMAZING ADVENTURES
IDW Publishing: Aug, 2015 - No. 14, Sept, 2016 ($3.99)

	GD 2.0	VG 4.0	FN 6.0	VF 8.0	VF/NM 9.0	NM- 9.2

1-14-All-ages animated-style stories; two covers ... 5.00
... Carmelo Anthony Special One-Shot (5/16, $5.99) Turtles meet the NBA player ... 6.00

TEENAGE MUTANT NINJA TURTLES AMAZING ADVENTURES: ROBOTANIMALS
IDW Publishing: Jun, 2017 - No. 3, Sept, 2017 ($3.99, limited series)
1-3-All-ages animated-style stories; three covers on each; Goellner-s/Thomas-a ... 4.00

TEENAGE MUTANT NINJA TURTLES BEBOP & ROCKSTEADY DESTROY EVERYTHING
IDW Publishing: Jun, 2016 - No. 5, Jun, 2016 ($3.99, weekly limited series)
1-5-Dustin Weaver-s; art by various; interlocking covers ... 4.00

TEENAGE MUTANT NINJA TURTLES BEBOP & ROCKSTEADY HIT THE ROAD
IDW Publishing: Jun, 2018 - No. 5, Aug, 2018 ($3.99, weekly limited series)
1-5-Dustin Weaver & Ben Bates-s/a; interlocking covers ... 4.00

TEENAGE MUTANT NINJA TURTLES: CASEY AND APRIL
IDW Publishing: Jun, 2015 - No. 4, Sept, 2015 ($3.99, limited series)
1-4-Mariko Tamaki-s/Irene Koh-a; two covers on each ... 4.00

TEENAGE MUTANT NINJA TURTLES CLASSICS DIGEST (TV)
Archie Comics: Aug, 1993 - No. 8, Mar, 1995? ($1.75)

| 1-8: Reprints TMNT Advs. | 1 | 3 | 4 | 6 | 8 | 10 |

TEENAGE MUTANT NINJA TURTLES COLOR CLASSICS
IDW Publishing: May, 2012 - Mar, 2016 ($3.99)

| 1-11-Colored reprints of the original 1984 B&W series | 1 | 2 | 3 | 5 | 6 | 8 |

...: Donatello Micro-Series One-Shot (3/13, $3.99) r/Donatello, TMNT #1 (1986) ... 5.00
... Leonardo Micro-Series One-Shot (4/13, $3.99) r/Leonardo, TMNT #1 ... 5.00
... Michaelangelo Micro-Series One-Shot (12/12, $3.99) r/Michaelangelo, TMNT #1 ... 5.00
... Raphael Micro-Series One-Shot (8/12, $3.99) r/Raphael #1 (1985) ... 5.00
... Volume 2 (11/13 - No. 7, 5/14, $3.99) 1-7: 1-Reprints TMNT #12 (1987) ... 4.00
... Volume 3 (1/15 - No. 15, 3/16, $3.99) 1-15: 1-Reprints TMNT #48 (1992) ... 4.00

TEENAGE MUTANT NINJA TURTLES: DIMENSION X
IDW Publishing: Aug, 2017 - No. 5, Aug, 2017 ($3.99, weekly limited series)
1-5-Takes place during the Trial of Krang (between TMNT #73 & 74); multiple-c on each ... 4.00

TEENAGE MUTANT NINJA TURTLES/FLAMING CARROT CROSSOVER
Mirage Publishing: Nov, 1993 - No. 4, Feb, 1994 ($2.75, limited series)

| 1-4: Bob Burden story | 1 | 3 | 4 | 6 | 8 | 10 |

TEENAGE MUTANT NINJA TURTLES / GHOSTBUSTERS
IDW Publishing: Oct, 2014 - No. 4, Jan, 2015 ($3.99, limited series)
1-4-Burnham & Waltz-s/Schoening-a; multiple covers on each ... 4.00
... #1 Director's Cut (5/15, $5.99) r/#1 with creator commentary; bonus script pages ... 6.00

TEENAGE MUTANT NINJA TURTLES / GHOSTBUSTERS 2
IDW Publishing: Nov, 2017 - No. 5, Nov, 2017 ($3.99, limited series)
1-5-Burnham & Waltz-s/Schoening-a; multiple covers on each ... 4.00

TEENAGE MUTANT NINJA TURTLES MACRO-SERIES
IDW Publishing: Sept, 2018 - Dec, 2018 ($7.99, limited series)
... #1 Donatello; Paul Allor-s/Brahm Revel-a; four covers; Metalhead app. ... 8.00
... #2 Michelangelo; Ian Flynn-s/Michael Dialynas-a; four covers ... 8.00
... #3 Leonardo; Sophie Campbell-s/a; four covers ... 8.00
... #4 Raphael; Kevin Eastman-s/Eastman and Ben Bishop-a; four covers ... 8.00

TEENAGE MUTANT NINJA TURTLES MUTANIMALS
IDW Publishing: Feb, 2015 - No. 4, May, 2015($3.99, limited series)
1-4-Paul Allor-s/Andy Kuhn-a; two covers ... 4.00

TEENAGE MUTANT NINJA TURTLES NEW ANIMATED ADVENTURES
IDW Publishing: Jul, 2013 - No. 24, Jun, 2015 ($3.99)
1-24-Multiple covers on each ... 4.00
... Free Comic Book Day (5/13) Burnham-s/Brizuela-a ... 3.00

TEENAGE MUTANT NINJA TURTLES PRESENTS: APRIL O'NEIL
Archie Comics: Mar, 1993 - No. 3, June, 1993 ($1.25, limited series)
1-3 ... 6.00

TEENAGE MUTANT NINJA TURTLES PRESENTS: DONATELLO AND LEATHERHEAD
Archie Comics: July, 1993 - No. 3, Sept, 1993 ($1.25, limited series)
1-3 ... 6.00

TEENAGE MUTANT NINJA TURTLES PRESENTS: MERDUDE
Archie Comics: Oct, 1993 - No. 3, Dec, 1993 ($1.25, limited series)
1-3-See Mighty Mutanimals #7 for 1st app. Merdude ... 6.00

TEENAGE MUTANT NINJA TURTLES SATURDAY MORNING ADVENTURES
IDW Publishing: Oct, 2022 - No. 4, Jan, 2023 ($3.99, limited series)
1-4-Burnham-s/Lattie-a ... 4.00

TEENAGE MUTANT NINJA TURTLES: SATURDAY MORNING ADVENTURES
IDW Publishing: May, 2023 - Present ($3.99, limited series)
1-10: 1-Burnham-s/Lattie-a; Rat King app. ... 4.00
... – Halloween Special 1 (10/23, $6.99) Burnham-s/Schoening-a ... 7.00

TEENAGE MUTANT NINJA TURTLES/SAVAGE DRAGON CROSSOVER
Mirage Studios: Aug, 1995 ($2.75, one-shot)
1 ... 6.00

TEENAGE MUTANT NINJA TURTLES: SHREDDER IN HELL
IDW Publishing: Jan, 2019 - No. 5, Jun, 2019 ($3.99, limited series)
1-5-Mateus Santolouco-s/a; 3 covers ... 4.00
1-Director's Cut (4/19, $4.99) Reprints #1 with uncolored art and commentary ... 5.00

TEENAGE MUTANT NINJA TURTLES: THE ARMAGEDDON GAME
IDW Publishing: Sept, 2022 - No. 8, Jul, 2023 ($3.99/$4.99, limited series)
1,8-($5.99) Waltz-s/Federici-a ... 6.00
2-7-($4.99) ... 5.00
... Alliance 1-6 (11/22 - No. 6, 4/23, $3.99) Spotlight on Oroku Karai ... 4.00
... Opening Moves 1,2 (7/22, 8/22, $5.99) Prelude to the series ... 6.00

TEENAGE MUTANT NINJA TURTLES: THE LAST RONIN – LOST YEARS
IDW Publishing: Jan, 2023 - No. 5, Aug, 2023 ($4.99, limited series)

1-5-Waltz & Eastman-s/Gallant-a ... 5.00
1-Director's Cut (4/23, $5.99) Reprints #1 with sketch art and cover designs ... 6.00
... The Lost Day Special 1 (7/23, $7.99) Spotlight on April ... 8.00

TEENAGE MUTANT NINJA TURTLES: THE SECRET HISTORY OF THE FOOT CLAN
IDW Publishing: Dec, 2012 - No. 4, Mar, 2013 ($3.99, limited series)
1-4-Santolouco-a/Santolouco & Burnham-s ... 4.00

TEENAGE MUTANT NINJA TURTLES: TURTLES IN TIME
IDW Publishing: Jun, 2014 - No. 4, Sept, 2014 ($3.99, limited series)
1-4: 1-Paul Allor-s/Ross Campbell-a; Renet app.; three covers. 2-4-Two covers each ... 4.00

TEENAGE MUTANT NINJA TURTLES UNIVERSE
IDW Publishing: Aug, 2016 - No. 25, Aug, 2018($4.99)
1-25: 1-Allor-s/Couceiro-a; Eastman & Sienkiewicz-a; multiple covers on each ... 4.00

TEENAGE MUTANT NINJA TURTLES: URBAN LEGENDS
IDW Publishing: May, 2018 - No. 26, Aug, 2020 ($3.99)
1-26-Reprints the 1996 B&W series in color; multiple covers on each ... 4.00

TEENAGE MUTANT NINJA TURTLES/USAGI YOJIMBO: WHEREWHEN
IDW Publishing: Apr, 2023 - No. 5, Jul, 2023 ($4.99, limited series)
1-5-Stan Sakai-s/a ... 5.00
1-Director's Cut (10/23, $5.99) Reprints #1 in B&W with bonus script and layout art ... 6.00

TEENAGE MUTANT NINJA TURTLES UTROM EMPIRE
IDW Publishing: Jan, 2014 - No. 3, Mar, 2014 ($3.99, limited series)
1-3-Paul Allor-s/Andy Kuhn-a; two covers on each ... 4.00

TEENAGE MUTANT NINJA TURTLES VS. STREET FIGHTER
IDW Publishing: Jun, 2023 - No. 5, Nov, 2023 ($3.99, limited series)
1-5-Paul Allor-s/Ariel Medel-a ... 4.00

TEENAGE MUTANT NINJA TURTLES X STRANGER THINGS
IDW Publishing/Dark Horse Comics: Jul, 2023 - No. 4, Oct, 2023 ($3.99, limited series)
1-4-Set in 1985; Chittock-s/c ... 4.00
1-Director's Cut (11/23, $5.99) Reprints #1 in B&W; bonus script and thumbnail pages ... 6.00

TEEN-AGE ROMANCE (Formerly My Own Romance)
Marvel Comics (ZPC): No. 77, Sept, 1960 - No. 86, Mar, 1962

	GD 2.0	VG 4.0	FN 6.0	VF 8.0	VF/NM 9.0	NM- 9.2
77-83	8	16	24	56	108	160
84-86-Kirby-c. 84-Kirby-a(2 pgs.). 85,86-(3 pgs.)	9	18	27	59	117	175

TEEN-AGE ROMANCES
St. John Publ. Co. (Approved Comics): Jan, 1949 - No. 45, Dec, 1955 (#3,7,10-18,21 are 1/2 inch taller than other issues)

	GD 2.0	VG 4.0	FN 6.0	VF 8.0	VF/NM 9.0	NM- 9.2
1-Baker-c/a(1)	206	412	618	1318	2259	3200
2,3: 2-Baker-c/a. 3-Baker-c/a(3)	226	452	678	1446	2473	3500
4,5,7,8-Photo-c; Baker-a(2-3)	53	106	159	334	567	800
6-Photo-c; part magazine; Baker-a (10/49)	54	108	162	343	574	825
9-Baker-c/a; Kubert-a	343	686	1029	2400	4200	6000
10-12,20-Baker-c/a(2-3) each	258	516	774	1651	2826	4000
13-19,21,22-Complete issues by Baker	245	490	735	1568	2684	3800
23-25-Baker-c/a(2-3) each	206	412	618	1318	2259	3200
26,27,33,34,36,37,39,40,42: Baker-c/a. 33,40-Signed story by Estrada. 42-r/Cinderella Love #9; last pre-code (3/55)	81	162	243	518	884	1250
28-30-No Baker-a. 28-Estrada-a; painted-c	22	44	66	132	216	300
31,32-Baker-c/a. 31-Estrada-s	129	258	387	826	1413	2000
35-Baker-c/a (16 pgs.)	116	232	348	742	1271	1800
38-Baker-c/a; suggestive-c	206	412	618	1318	2259	3200
41-Baker-c; Infantino-a(r); all stories are Ziff-Davis-r	103	206	309	659	1130	1600
43-45-Baker-c/a	110	220	330	704	1202	1700

TEEN-AGE TALK
I.W. Enterprises: 1964

	GD 2.0	VG 4.0	FN 6.0	VF 8.0	VF/NM 9.0	NM- 9.2
Reprint #1	2	4	6	11	16	20
Reprint #5,8,9: 5-r/Hector #? 9-Punch Comics #?; L.B. Cole-c reprint from School Day Romances #1	2	4	6	10	14	18

TEEN-AGE TEMPTATIONS (Going Steady #10 on)(See True Love Pictorial)
St. John Publishing Co.: Oct, 1952 - No. 9, Aug, 1954

	GD 2.0	VG 4.0	FN 6.0	VF 8.0	VF/NM 9.0	NM- 9.2
1-Baker-c/a; has story "Reform School Girl" by Estrada	252	504	756	1613	2757	3900
2,4-Baker-c	194	388	582	1242	2121	3000
3,5-7,9-Baker-c/a	194	388	582	1242	2121	3000
8-Teenagers smoke reefer; Baker-c/a	226	452	678	1446	2473	3500

NOTE: *Estrada*-a-1, 3-5.

TEEN BEAM (Formerly Teen Beat #1)
National Periodical Publications: No. 2, Jan-Feb, 1968

	GD 2.0	VG 4.0	FN 6.0	VF 8.0	VF/NM 9.0	NM- 9.2
2-Superman cameo; Herman's Hermits, Yardbirds, Simon & Garfunkel, Lovin Spoonful, Young Rascals app.; Orlando, Drucker-a(r); Monkees photo-c	16	32	48	112	249	385

TEEN BEAT (Becomes Teen Beam #2)
National Periodical Publications: Nov-Dec, 1967

	GD 2.0	VG 4.0	FN 6.0	VF 8.0	VF/NM 9.0	NM- 9.2
1-Photos & text only; Monkees photo-c; Beatles, Herman's Hermits, Animals, Supremes, Byrds app.	20	40	60	136	303	470

TEEN COMICS (Formerly All Teen; Journey Into Unknown Worlds #36 on)
Marvel Comics (WFP): No. 21, Apr, 1947 - No. 35, May, 1950

	GD 2.0	VG 4.0	FN 6.0	VF 8.0	VF/NM 9.0	NM- 9.2
21-Kurtzman's "Hey Look"; Patsy Walker, Cindy (1st app.?), Georgie, Margie app.; Syd Shores-a begins, and #23	39	78	117	231	376	525
22,23,25,27,29,31-35: 22-(6/47)-Becomes Hedy Devine at #22 (8/47)?	28	56	84	165	270	375
24,26,28,30-Kurtzman's-"Hey Look". 30-Has anti-Wertham editorial	29	58	87	172	281	390

TEEN CONFESSIONS
Charlton Comics: Aug, 1959 - No. 97, Nov, 1976

	GD 2.0	VG 4.0	FN 6.0	VF 8.0	VF/NM 9.0	NM- 9.2
1	10	20	30	64	132	200
2	6	12	18	37	66	95

Teenage Mutant Ninja Turtles: Dimension X #2 © Viacom

Teen-Age Romances #18 © STJ

Teen Titans #43 © DC

	GD 2.0	VG 4.0	FN 6.0	VF 8.0	VF/NM 9.0	NM- 9.2
3-10	4	8	12	27	44	60
11-30	3	6	9	21	33	45
31-Beatles-c	13	26	39	89	195	300
32-36,38-55	3	6	9	16	24	32
37 (1/66)-Beatles Fan Club story; Beatles-c	12	24	36	81	176	270
56-58,60-76,78-97: 89,90-Newton-c	2	4	6	11	16	20
59-Kaluta's 1st pro work? (12/69)	3	6	9	20	31	42
77-Partridge Family poster	3	6	9	14	20	26

TEENIE WEENIES, THE (America's Favorite Kiddie Comic)
Ziff-Davis Publishing Co.: No. 10, 1950 - No. 11, Apr-May, 1951 (Newspaper reprints)

	GD	VG	FN	VF	VF/NM	NM-
10,11-Painted-c	25	50	75	150	245	340

TEEN-IN (Tippy Teen)
Tower Comics: Summer, 1968 - No. 4, Fall, 1969

	GD	VG	FN	VF	VF/NM	NM-
nn(#1, Summer, 1968)(25¢) Has 3 full pg. B&W photos of Sonny & Cher, Donovan and Herman's Hermits; interviews and photos of Eric Clapton, Jim Morrison and others	9	18	27	62	126	190
nn(#2, Spring, 1969),3,4	6	12	18	37	66	95

TEEN LIFE (Formerly Young Life)
New Age/Quality Comics Group: No. 3, Winter, 1945 - No. 5, Fall, 1945 (Teenage magazine)

	GD	VG	FN	VF	VF/NM	NM-
3-June Allyson photo on-c & story	17	34	51	98	154	210
4-Duke Ellington photo on-c & story	15	30	45	85	130	175
5-Van Johnson, Woody Herman & Jackie Robinson articles; Van Johnson & Woody Herman photos on-c	17	34	51	98	154	210

TEEN LOVE STORIES (Magazine)
Warren Publ. Co.: Sept, 1969 - No. 3, Jan, 1970 (68 pgs., photo covers, B&W)

	GD	VG	FN	VF	VF/NM	NM-
1-Photos & articles plus 36-42 pgs. new comic stories incl.; Frazetta-a	8	16	24	52	99	145
2,3: 2-Anti-marijuana story	5	10	15	35	63	90

TEEN ROMANCES
Super Comics: 1964

	GD	VG	FN	VF	VF/NM	NM-
10,11,15-17-Reprints	2	4	6	10	14	18

TEEN SECRET DIARY (Nurse Betsy Crane #12 on)
Charlton Comics: Oct, 1959 - No. 11, June, 1961

	GD	VG	FN	VF	VF/NM	NM-
1	6	12	18	41	76	110
2	4	8	12	25	40	55
3-11	3	6	9	19	30	40

TEEN TALK (See Teen)

TEEN TITANS (See Brave & the Bold #54,60, DC Super-Stars #1, Marvel & DC Present, New Teen Titans, New Titans, Official...Index and Showcase #59)
National Periodical Publ./DC Comics: 1-2/66 - No. 43, 1-2/73; No. 44, 11/76 - No. 53, 2/78

	GD	VG	FN	VF	VF/NM	NM-
1-(1-2/66)-Titans join Peace Corps; Batman, Flash, Aquaman, Wonder Woman cameos	44	88	132	326	738	1150
2	14	28	42	96	211	325
3-5: 4-Speedy app.	9	18	27	62	126	190
6-10: 6-Doom Patrol app.; Beast Boy x-over; readers polled on him joining Titans	7	14	21	49	92	135
11-18: 11-Speedy app. 13-X-Mas-c	6	12	18	40	73	105
19-Wood-i; Speedy begins as regular	7	14	21	46	86	125
20-22: All Neal Adams-a. 21-Hawk & Dove app.; last 12¢ issue. 22-Origin Wonder Girl	9	18	27	61	123	185
23-Wonder Girl dons new costume	9	18	27	59	117	175
24-31: 25-Flash, Aquaman, Batman, Green Arrow, Green Lantern, Superman, & Hawk & Dove guests; 1st app. Lilith who joins T.T. West in #50. 29-Hawk & Dove & Ocean Master app. 30-Aquagirl app. 31-Hawk & Dove app.	5	10	15	30	50	70
32-34,40-43: 34-Last 15¢ issue	3	6	9	19	30	40
35-39-(52 pgs.): 36,37-Superboy-r. 38-Green Arrow/Speedy-r; Aquaman/Aqualad story. 39-Hawk & Dove-r.	4	8	12	22	35	48
44-(11/76) Dr. Light app.; Mal becomes the Guardian	3	6	9	16	23	30
45,47,49,51,52	3	6	9	14	19	24
46-Joker's daughter begins (cont'd in Batman Family)	4	8	12	23	37	50
48-Intro Bumblebee; Joker's daughter becomes Harlequin	4	8	12	28	47	65
50-1st revival original Bat-Girl; intro. Teen Titans West (Bat-Girl, Golden Eagle, Hawk & Dove, Lilith and Beast Boy)	4	8	12	30	40	55
53-Origin retold	3	6	9	17	26	35

... Lost Annual 1 (3/08, $4.99) Sixties-era story by Bob Haney; Jay Stephens & Mike Allred-a; President Kennedy app.; Nick Cardy-a and sketch pages ... 5.00

NOTE: *Aparo* a-36. *Buckler* c-46-53. *Cardy* a(p)-1-5, 7, 13, 14, 16, 17, 25, 26, 28-30, 32, c-1-43. *Kane* a(p)-19, 22-24, 39r. *Tuska* a(p)-31, 36, 38, 39. DC Super-Stars #1 (3/76) was released before #44.

TEEN TITANS (Also see Titans Beat for series preview)

DC Comics: Oct, 1996 - No. 24, Sept, 1998 ($1.95)

1-Dan Jurgens-c/a(p)/scripts & George Pérez-c/a(i) begin; Atom forms new team (Risk, Argent, Prysm, & Joto); 1st app. Loren Jupiter & Omen; no indicia. 1-3-Origin. ... 6.00
2-24: 4,5-Robin, Nightwing, Supergirl, Capt. Marvel Jr. app. 12-"Then and Now" begins w/original Teen Titans-c/app. 15-Death of Joto. 17-Capt. Marvel Jr. and Fringe join. ... 4.00
19-Millennium Giants x-over. 23,24-Superman app.
Annual 1 (1997, $3.95)-Pulp Heroes story ... 5.00

TEEN TITANS (Also see Titans/Young Justice: Graduation Day)
DC Comics: Sept, 2003 - No. 100, Late Oct, 2011 ($2.50/$2.99/$3.99)

	GD	VG	FN	VF	VF/NM	NM-
						5.00
1-McKone-c/a;Johns-s						15
1-Variant-c by Michael Turner	2	4	6	9	12	15

1-2nd and 3rd printings ... 3.00
2-Deathstroke app. ... 5.00
2-2nd printing ... 4.00
3-15: 4-Impulse becomes Kid Flash. 5-Raven returns. 6-JLA app.
16-33: 16-Titans go to 31st Century; Legion and Fatal Five app. 17-19-Future Titans app. ... 3.00
21-23-Dr. Light. 24,25-Outsiders #24,25 x-over. 27,28-Liefeld-a. 32,33-Infinite Crisis
34-49,51-71: 34-One Year Later begins; two covers by Daniel and Benes. 36-Begin $2.99-c. 40-Jericho returns. 42-Kid Devil origin; Snejbjerg-a. 43-Titans East. 48,49-Amazons Attack x-over; Supergirl app. 51-54-Future Titans app. ... 3.00
50-($3.99) Art by Pérez (4 pgs.), McKone (6 pgs.), Nauck and Green; future Titans app. ... 4.00
72-88: 72-Begin $3.99-c; Ravager back-up features. 77,78-Blackest Night. 83-87-Coven of Three back-up; Naifeh-a. 88-Nicola Scott-a begins ... 4.00
89-99-($2.99) 89-Robin (Damian) joins. 93-Solstice app. 98 Superboy-Prime returns ... 3.00
100-($4.99) Nicola Scott-a; pin-ups by various ... 5.00
Annual 1 (4/06, $4.99) Infinite Crisis x-over; Benes-c ... 5.00
Annual 2009 (6/09, $4.99) Deathtrap x-over prelude; McKeever-s ... 5.00
... And Outsiders Secret Files and Origins 2005 (10/05, $4.99) Daniel-c ... 6.00
...: Cold Case (2/11, $4.99) Captain Cold and the Rogues app.; Sean Murphy-a ...
.../Legion Special (11/04, $3.50) (cont'd from #16) Reis-a; leads into 2005 Legion of Super-Heroes series; LSH preview by Waid & Kitson ... 4.00
#1/2 (Wizard mail offer) origin of Ravager; Reis-a ... 8.00
.../Outsiders Secret Files 2003 (12/03, $5.95) Reis & Jimenez-a; pin-ups by various ... 6.00
...: A Kid's Game TPB (2004, $9.95) r/#1-7; Turner-c from #1; McKone sketch pages ... 10.00
...: Beast Boys and Girls TPB (2005, $9.99) r/#13-15 and Beast Boy #1-4 ... 10.00
...: Changing of the Guard TPB (2009, $14.99) r/#62-69 ... 15.00
...: Child's Play TPB (2010, $14.99) r/#71-78 ... 15.00
...: Deathtrap TPB (2009, $14.99) r/#70, Annual #1, Titans #12,13, Vigilante #4-6 ... 15.00
...: Family Lost TPB (2004, $9.95) r/#8-12 & #1/2 ... 10.00
...: Life and Death TPB (2006, $14.99) r/#29-33 and pages from Infinite Crisis x-over ... 15.00
...: On the Clock TPB (2008, $14.99) r/#55-61 ... 15.00
.../ Outsiders: The Death and Return of Donna Troy (2006, $14.99) r/Titans/Young Justice: Graduation Day #1-3, Teen Titans/Outsiders Secret Files 2003 and DC Special: The Return of Donna Troy #1-4; cover gallery ... 15.00
.../ Outsiders: The Insiders (2006, $14.99) r/Teen Titans/ #24-26 & Outsiders #24,25,26 ... 15.00
...: Ravager - Fresh Hell TPB (2010, $14.99) r/#71-76,79-82 & Faces of Evil: Deathstroke ... 15.00
...: Spotlight: Cyborg TPB (2009, $19.99) r/DC Special: Cyborg #1-6 ... 20.00
...: Spotlight: Raven TPB (2008, $14.99) r/DC Special: Raven #1-5 ... 15.00
...: The Future is Now (2005, $9.99) r/#15-23 & Teen Titans/Legion Special ... 10.00
...: The Hunt For Raven (2011, $17.99) r/#79-87 ... 18.00
...: Titans Around the World TPB (2007, $14.99) r/#34-41 ... 15.00
...: Titans of Tomorrow TPB (2008, $14.99) r/#50-54 ... 15.00

TEEN TITANS (DC New 52)
DC Comics: Nov, 2011 - No. 30, Jun, 2014 ($2.99)

1-14,17-23: 1-Lobdell-s/Booth-a/c; Red Robin assembles a team; Kid Flash, Wonder Girl app. ... 3.00
5-Superboy app. 9-The Culling conclusion. 13,14-Wonder Girl origin; Garza-a ... 5.00
15,16-"Death of the Family" tie-in. 15-Die-cut Joker mask cover. 16-Red Hood app. ... 3.00
23.1, 23.2 (11/13, $2.99, regular covers) ... 5.00
23.1 (11/13, $3.99, 3-D cover) "Trigon #1" on cover; app; Wolfman-s/Cafu-a

	GD	VG	FN	VF	VF/NM	NM-
23.1 (11/13, $3.99, 3-D cover) "Trigon #1" on cover; flashback; Deathblow app.	1	2	3	5	6	8

23.2 (11/13, $3.99, 3-D cover) "Deathstroke #1" on cover; flashback; Deathblow app.
24-29: 24-Leads into Annual #2. 25,26-Origin of Kid Flash ... 3.00
30-($3.99) Last issue; origin of Skitter; Kirkham-a ... 4.00
#0 (11/12, $2.99) Origin of Red Robin; Kirkham-a ... 5.00
Annual 1 (7/12, $4.99) The Culling x-over part 1; Legion Lost members app. ... 5.00
Annual 2 (12/13, $4.99) Future Titans app.; Lobdell-s/Kitson-a ... 5.00
... Earth One Volume One HC (2014, $22.99) Lemire-s/Dodson-a/c; new origin story ... 23.00

TEEN TITANS (DC New 52)
DC Comics: Sept, 2014 - No. 24, Nov, 2016 ($2.99)

1-24: 1-Pfeifer-s/Rocafort-a/c; Manchester Black app. 5-Hepburn-a; new Power Girl app. ... 3.00
15-Robin War tie-in; Professor Pyg app. 18,19-Wonder Woman app. ... 3.00
Annual 1 (6/15, $4.99) Superboy returns; Borges & St. Claire-a; March-c

	GD 2.0	VG 4.0	FN 6.0	VF 8.0	VF/NM 9.0	NM- 9.2

Annual 2 (8/16, $4.99) Lobdell-s/Cory Smith-a/Jonboy Meyers-c; Sister Blood app. 5.00
...: Futures End 1 (11/14, $2.99, regular-c) Five years later; Andy Smith-a 3.00
...: Futures End 1 (11/14, $3.99, 3-D cover) 4.00

TEEN TITANS (DC Rebirth)
DC Comics: Nov, 2016 - No. 47, Jan, 2021 ($2.99/$3.99)

1-6: 1-Percy-s/Meyers-a; Ra's al Ghul app. 3-6-Pham-a. 6-Intro. Aqualad (Jackson Hyde) 3.00
7-11,13-24-($3.99) 7-Aqualad joins; Black Manta cameo. 8-Lazarus Contact x-over; Titans & Deathstroke app. 9-11-Black Manta app. 15-Future adult Superboy (Conner), Wonder Girl (Cassie) and Kid Flash (Bart) app. 20-New team with Crush, Roundhouse, Djinn 4.00
12-Dark Nights: Metal tie-in; 1st full app. The Batman Who Laughs, Harley Quinn app. 50.00
25-($4.99) Origin of Crush; Rocha-a; Roundhouse back-up story 5.00
26-47: 26-32-Chang-a. 28-30-Crossover with Deathstroke #42-44. 31-33,35-37-Lobo app. 5.00
Annual 1 (7/17, $4.99) Conclusion of Lazarus Contact x-over; Titans & Deathstroke app. 5.00
Annual 1 (3/19, $4.99) Red Hood app.; intro. Joystick 5.00
Annual 2 (10/20, $4.99) Batman app.; leads into #45; Crush becomes leader; Fernandez-a 5.00
...: Endless Winter Special 1 (2/21, $3.99) Part 6 of crossover event; Merino-a 5.00
...: Rebirth 1 (11/16, $2.99) Meyers-a; Robin, Raven, Starfire, Beast Boy, Kid Flash app. 3.00
...: Special 1 (8/18, $4.99) Glass-s/Rocha-a; Harley Quinn & Black Mask app. 5.00

TEEN TITANS ACADEMY
DC Comics: May, 2021 - No. 15, Jul, 2022 ($3.99)

1-15: 1-Sheridan-s/Sandoval-a; original Titans mentoring the next gen of heroes. 2,3-Peacemaker app. 7-Grodd app. 8-Roy Harper returns. 13-War For Earth-3 4.00

TEEN TITANS GIANT (Continues in Titans Giant #1)
DC Comics: 2018 - No. 7, 2019 ($4.99, 100 pgs., squarebound, Walmart exclusive)

1-New story Jurgens-s/Eaton-a; reprints from Teen Titans ('03), Super Sons #1 ('17), and Sideways ('18) 8.00
2-7-New story Jurgens-s/Eaton-a plus reprints continue 5.00

TEEN TITANS GO! (Based on Cartoon Network series)
DC Comics: Jan, 2004 - No. 55, Jul, 2008 ($2.25)

1-12,14-55: 1,2-Nauck-a/Bullock-c/J. Torres-s. 8-Mad Mod app. 14-Speedy-c. 28-Doom Patrol app. 31-Nightwing app. 36-Wonder Girl. 38-Mad Mod app.; Clugston-a 3.00
1-(9/04, Free Comic Book Day giveaway) r/#1; 2 bound-in Wacky Packages stickers 4.00
13-($2.95) Bonus pages with Shazam! reprint 4.00
Jam Packed Action (2005, $7.99, digest) adaptations of two TV episodes 8.00
... Vol 1: Truth, Justice, Pizza! (2004, $6.95, digest-size) r/#1-5 7.00
... Vol 2: Heroes on Patrol (2005, $6.99, digest-size) r/#6-10 7.00
... Vol 3: Bring It On! (2005, $6.99, digest-size) r/#11-15 7.00
... Vol 4: Ready For Action! (2006, $6.99, digest-size) r/#16-20 7.00
... Vol 5: On The Move! (2006, $6.99, digest-size) r/#21-25 7.00
... Titans Together TPB (2007, $12.99) r/#46-52 13.00

TEEN TITANS GO! (Based on the 2013 Cartoon Network series)
DC Comics: Feb, 2014 - Present ($2.99)

1-36: 1-Fisch-s. 2-Brotherhood of Evil app. 4-HIVE Five app. 13-Aqualad app. 3.00
... FCBD Special Edition 1 (6/14, giveaway) r/#1 3.00
... FCBD Special Edition 1 (6/15, giveaway) flipbook with Scooby-Doo! Team Up 3.00
... Giant 1 (2019, $4.99) Two new stories plus reprints 5.00

TEEN TITANS SPOTLIGHT
DC Comics: Aug, 1986 - No. 21, Apr, 1988

1-21: 7-Guice's 1st work at DC. 14-Nightwing; Batman app. 15-Austin-c(i). 18,19-Millennium x-over. 21-($1.00-c)-Original Teen Titans; Spiegle-a 4.00
Note: Guice a-7p, 8p; c-7,8. Orlando c/a-11p. Perez c-1, 17i, 19. Sienkiewicz c-10

TEEN TITANS YEAR ONE
DC Comics: Mar, 2008 - No. 6, Aug, 2008 ($2.99, limited series)

1-6-The original five form a team; Wolfram-s/Kerschl-a 3.00
TPB (2008, $14.99) r/#1-6; bonus pin-up 15.00

TEEN WOLF: BITE ME (Based on the MTV series)
Image Comics (Top Cow): Sept, 2011 - No. 3, Nov, 2011 ($3.99, limited series)

1-3: 1-Tischman-s/Mooney-a/c 4.00

TEEPEE TIM (...Heap Funny Indian Boy)(Formerly Ha Ha Comics)(Also see "Cookie")
American Comics Group: No. 100, Feb-Mar, 1955 - No. 102, June-July, 1955

100-102 | 9 | 18 | 27 | 50 | 65 | 80

TEGRA JUNGLE EMPRESS (Zegra Jungle Empress #2 on)
Fox Feature Syndicate: August, 1948

1-Blue Beetle, Rocket Kelly app.; used in SOTI, pg. 31 | 110 | 220 | 330 | 704 | 1202 | 1700

TEK JANSEN (See Stephen Colbert's...)

TEKKEN: BLOOD FEUD (Based on the Bandai Namco video game)
Titan Comics: Jun, 2017 - No. 4, Sept, 2017 ($3.99, limited series)

1-4-Cavan Scott-s/Andie Tong-a; multiple covers on each 4.00

TEKNO COMIX HANDBOOK
Tekno Comix: May, 1996 ($3.95, one-shot)

1-Guide to the Tekno Universe 4.00

TEKNOPHAGE (See Neil Gaiman's...)

TEKNOPHAGE VERSUS ZEERUS
BIG Entertainment: July, 1996 ($3.25, one-shot)

1-Paul Jenkins script 4.00

TEKWORLD (William Shatner's... on-c only)
Epic Comics (Marvel): Sept, 1992 - Aug, 1994 ($1.75)

1-Based on Shatner's novel, TekWar, set in L.A. in the year 2120 5.00
2-24 4.00

TELARA CHRONICLES (Based on the videogame Rift: Planes of Telara)
DC Comics (WildStorm): Jan, 2010; Nov, 2010 - No. 4, Feb, 2011 ($3.99, limited series)

0-(1/10, free) Preview of series 3.00
1-4-Pop Mhan-a/Drew Johnson-c 4.00
TPB (2011, $17.99) r/#0-4; background info on Telara 18.00

TELEPATHS

Artists, Writers & Artisans, Inc.: Sept, 2021 - No. 6, Feb, 2022 ($3.99, limited series)

1-6-Straczynski-s/Epting-a 4.00

TELEVISION (See TV)

TELEVISION COMICS (Early TV comic)
Standard Comics (Animated Cartoons): No. 5, Feb, 1950 - No. 8, Nov, 1950

5-1st app. Willy Nilly | 15 | 30 | 45 | 83 | 124 | 165
6-8: #6 on inside has #2 on cover | 11 | 22 | 33 | 62 | 86 | 110

TELEVISION PUPPET SHOW (Early TV comic) (See Spotty the Pup)
Avon Periodicals: 1950 - No. 2, 1950

1-1st app. Speedy Rabbit, Spotty The Pup | 32 | 64 | 96 | 188 | 307 | 425
2 | 20 | 40 | 60 | 120 | 195 | 270

TELEVISION TEENS MOPSY (See TV Teens)

TELL IT TO THE MARINES
Toby Press Publications: Mar, 1952 - No. 15, July, 1955

1-Lover O'Leary and His Liberty Belles (with pin-ups), ends #6; Spike & Bat begin, end #6 | 41 | 82 | 123 | 250 | 418 | 585
2-Madame Cobra-c/story; headlights-c | 97 | 194 | 291 | 621 | 1061 | 1500
3,5 | 23 | 46 | 69 | 136 | 223 | 310
4-Headlights-c | 65 | 130 | 195 | 416 | 708 | 1000
6-12,14,15: 7-9,14,15-Photo-c | 19 | 38 | 57 | 111 | 176 | 240
13-John Wayne photo-c | 27 | 54 | 81 | 162 | 266 | 370
I.W. Reprint #9-r/#1 above | 3 | 6 | 9 | 17 | 26 | 35
Super Reprint #16(1964)-r/#4 above | 2 | 4 | 6 | 11 | 16 | 20

TELLOS
Image Comics: May, 1999 - No. 10, Nov, 2000 ($2.50)

1-Dezago-s/Wieringo-a 4.00
1-Variant-c ($7.95) 8.00
2-10: 4-Four covers 4.00
...: Maiden Voyage (3/01, $5.95) Didier Crispeels-a/c 6.00
...: Sons & Moons (2002, $5.95) Nick Cardy-c 6.00
...: The Last Heist (2001, $5.95) Rousseau-a/c 6.00
Prelude ($5.00, AnotherUniverse.com) 5.00
Prologue ($3.95, Dynamic Forces) 4.00
...Collected Edition 1 (12/99, $8.95) r/#1-3 9.00
...: Colossal, Vol. 1 TPB (2008, $17.99) r/#1-10, Prelude, Prologue, Scatterjack-s from Section Zero #1, cover gallery, Wieringo sketch pages; Dezago afterword 18.00
...: Kindred Spirits (2/01, $17.95) r/#6-10, Section Zero #1 (Scatterjack-s) 18.00
...: Reluctant Heroes (2/01, $17.95) r/#1-5, Prelude, Prologue; sketchbook 18.00

TELOS (See Convergence)
DC Comics: Dec, 2015 - No. 6, May, 2016 ($2.99)

1-6: 1,2-King-s/Pagulayan-a. 1-Brainiac app. 2-Arak, Son of Thunder and Validus app. 3-6-Hal Jordan Parallax app. 3.00

TEMPEST (See Aquaman, 3rd Series)
DC Comics: Nov, 1996 - No. 4, Feb, 1997 ($1.75, limited series)

1-4: Formerly Aqualad; Phil Jimenez-c/a/scripts in all 4.00

TEMPLARS (Assassin's Creed)
Titan Comics: Apr, 2016 - No. 9, Feb, 2017 ($3.99)

1-9-Black Cross; set in 1927; Van Lente-s/Calero-a 4.00

TEMPUS FUGITIVE
DC Comics: 1990 - No. 4, 1991 ($4.95, squarebound, 52 pgs.)

Book 1,2: Ken Steacy painted-c/a & scripts 6.00
Book 3,4-($5.95-c) 6.00
TPB (Dark Horse Comics, 1/97, $17.95) 18.00

TEN COMMANDMENTS (See Moses the... and Classics Illustrated Special)

TENDER LOVE STORIES
Skywald Publ. Corp.: Feb, 1971 - No. 4, July, 1971 (Pre-code reprints and new stories)

1 (All 25¢, 52 pgs.) | 9 | 18 | 27 | 63 | 129 | 195
2-4 | 6 | 12 | 18 | 38 | 69 | 100

TENDER ROMANCE (Ideal Romance #3 on)
Key Publications (Gilmour Magazines): Dec, 1953 - No. 2, Feb, 1954

1-Headlight & lingerie panels; B. Baily-c | 39 | 78 | 117 | 231 | 378 | 525
2-Bernard Baily-c | 20 | 40 | 60 | 120 | 195 | 270

TEN GRAND
Image Comics (Joe's Comics): May, 2013 - No. 12, Jan, 2015 ($2.99)

1-12: 1-4-Straczynski-s/Templesmith-a. 1-Multiple variant covers. 2-Two covers 3.00

TENSE SUSPENSE
Fago Publications: Dec, 1958 - No. 2, Feb, 1959

1 | 15 | 30 | 45 | 90 | 140 | 190
2 | 12 | 24 | 36 | 69 | 97 | 125

TEN STORY LOVE (Formerly a pulp magazine with same title)
Ace Periodicals: V29#3, June-July, 1951 - V36#5(#209), Sept, 1956 (#3-6: 52 pgs.)

V29#3(#177)-Part comic, part text; painted-c | 24 | 48 | 72 | 142 | 234 | 325
4-6(1/52) | 15 | 30 | 45 | 90 | 140 | 190
V30#1(3/52)-6(1/53) | 15 | 30 | 45 | 90 | 140 | 190
V31#1(2/53),V32#2(4/53)-6(12/53) | 15 | 30 | 45 | 85 | 130 | 175
V33#1(1/54)-3(#54, #195),V34#4(7/54, #196)-6(10/54, #198) | 15 | 30 | 45 | 83 | 124 | 165
V35#1(12/54, #199)-3(4/55, #201)-Last precode | 14 | 28 | 42 | 82 | 121 | 160
V35#4-6(9/55, #201-204),V36#1(11/55, #205)-3, 5(9/56, #210) | 14 | 28 | 42 | 81 | 118 | 155
V36#4-L.B. Cole-a | 14 | 28 | 42 | 80 | 115 | 150
 | 15 | 30 | 45 | 88 | 137 | 185

TENTH, THE
Image Comics: Jan, 1997 - No. 4, June, 1997 ($2.50, limited series)

1-4-Tony Daniel-c/a, Beau Smith-s 5.00
Abuse of Humanity TPB ($10.95) r/#1-4 12.00
Abuse of Humanity TPB (10/98, $11.95) r/#1-4 & 0(8/97) 12.00

Teen Titans Go! (2014 series) #11 © DC

Ten Grand #7 © Studio JMS

Terminator: 2029 #2 © Studio Canal

	GD 2.0	VG 4.0	FN 6.0	VF 8.0	VF/NM 9.0	NM- 9.2

TENTH, THE
Image Comics: Sept, 1997 - No. 14, Jan, 1999 ($2.50)

0-(8/97, $5.00) American Ent. Ed.						6.00
1-Tony Daniel-c/a, Beau Smith-s						6.00
2-9; 3,7-Variant-c						5.00
10-14						4.00
...Configuration (8/98) Re-cap and pin-ups						4.00
...Collected Edition 1 ('98, $4.95, square-bound) r/#1,2						5.00
...Special (4/00, $2.95) r/#0 and Wizard #1/2						4.00
Wizard #1/2-Daniel-s/Steve Scott-a						10.00

TENTH, THE (Volume 3) (The Black Embrace)
Image Comics: Mar, 1999 - No. 4, June, 1999 ($2.95)

1-4-Daniel-c/a						4.00
TPB (1/00, $12.95) r/#1-4						13.00

TENTH, THE (Volume 4) (Evil's Child)
Image Comics: Sept, 1999 - No. 4, Mar, 2000 ($2.95, limited series)

1-4-Daniel-c/a						4.00

TENTH, THE (Darkk Dawn)
Image Comics: July, 2005 ($4.99, one-shot)

1-Kirkham-a/Bonny-s						5.00

TENTH, THE : RESURRECTED
Dark Horse Comics: July, 2001 - No. 4, Feb, 2002 ($2.99, limited series)

1-4: 1-Two covers; Daniel-s/c; Romano-a						3.00

10th MUSE
Image Comics (TidalWave Studios): Nov, 2000 - No. 9, Jan, 2002 ($2.95)

1-Character based on wrestling's Rena Mero; regular & photo covers						3.00
2-9: 2-Photo and 2 Lashley covers; flip book Dollz preview. 5-Savage Dragon app.; 2 covers by Lashley and Larsen. 6-Tellos x-over						3.00

TEN WHO DARED (Disney)
Dell Publishing Co.: No. 1178, Dec, 1960

Four Color 1178-Movie, painted-c; cast member photo on back-c	7	14	21	46	86	125

10 YEARS TO DEATH
AfterShock Comics: Sept, 2021 ($6.99, oversized 8-1/2" x 10-7/8", one shot)

1-Aaron Douglas-s/Cliff Richards-a						7.00

TERMINAL CITY
DC Comics (Vertigo): July, 1996 - No. 9, Mar, 1997 ($2.50, limited series)

1-9: Dean Motter scripts, 7,8-Matt Wagner-c						4.00
TPB ('97, $19.95) r/series						20.00

TERMINAL CITY: AERIAL GRAFFITI
DC Comics (Vertigo): Nov, 1997 - No. 5, Mar, 1998 ($2.50, limited series)

1-5: Dean Motter-s/Lark-a/Chiarello-c						4.00

TERMINAL HERO
Dynamite Entertainment: 2014 - No. 6, 2015 ($2.99, limited series)

1-6-Milligan-s/Kowalski-a/Jae Lee-c						3.00

TERMINATOR, THE (See Robocop vs. ... & Rust #12 for 1st app.)
Now Comics: Sept, 1988 - No. 17, 1989 ($1.75, Baxter paper)

1-Based on movie	2	4	6	10	14	18
2-5						6.00
6-11,13-17						4.00
12-($2.95, 52 pgs.)-Intro. John Connor						5.00
Trade paperback (1989, $9.95)						15.00

TERMINATOR, THE
Dark Horse Comics: Aug, 1990 - No. 4, Nov, 1990 ($2.50, limited series)

1-Set 39 years later than the movie	1	2	3	5	6	8
2-4						4.00

TERMINATOR, THE
Dark Horse Comics: 1998 - No. 4, Dec, 1998 ($2.95, limited series)

1-4-Alan Grant-s/Steve Pugh-a/c						4.00
...Special (1998, $2.95) Darrow-c/Grant-s						4.00

TERMINATOR, THE: ALL MY FUTURES PAST
Now Comics: V3#1, Aug, 1990 - V3#2, Sept, 1990 ($1.75, mini-series)

V3#1,2						4.00

TERMINATOR, THE: ENDGAME
Dark Horse Comics: Sept, 1992 - No. 3, Nov, 1992 ($2.50, limited series)

1-3: Guice-a(p); painted-c						4.00

TERMINATOR, THE: ENEMY OF MY ENEMY
Dark Horse Comics: Feb, 2014 - No. 6, Oct, 2014 ($3.99, limited series)

1-6-Jolley-s/Igle-a; set in 1985						4.00

TERMINATOR, THE: HUNTERS AND KILLERS
Dark Horse Comics: Mar, 1992 - No. 3, May, 1992 ($2.50, limited series)

1-3						4.00

TERMINATOR, THE: 1984
Dark Horse Comics: Sept, 2010 - No. 3, Nov, 2010 ($3.50, limited series)

1-3: Takes place during and after the 1st movie; Zack Whedon-s/Andy MacDonald-a						3.50

TERMINATOR, THE: ONE SHOT
Dark Horse Comics: July, 1991 ($5.95, 56 pgs.)

nn-Matt Wagner-a; contains stiff pop-up inside						6.00

TERMINATOR, THE: REVOLUTION (Follows Terminator 2: Infinity series)
Dynamite Entertainment: 2008 - No. 5, 2009 ($3.50, limited series)

1-5-Furman-s/Antonio-a. 1-3-Two covers						3.50

TERMINATOR / ROBOCOP: KILL HUMAN
Dynamite Entertainment: 2011 - No. 4, 2011 ($3.99, limited series)

1-4: 1-Covers by Simonson, Lau & Feister. 2-4-Three covers on each						4.00

TERMINATOR: SALVATION MOVIE PREQUEL
IDW Publishing: Jan, 2009 - No. 4, Apr, 2009 ($3.99, limited series)

1-4: Alan Robinson/Dara Naraghi-s						4.00
0-Salvation Movie Preview (4/09) Mariotte-s/Figueroa-a						4.00

TERMINATOR SALVATION: THE FINAL BATTLE
Dark Horse Comics: Dec, 2013 - No. 12, Dec, 2014 ($3.99, limited series)

1-12-Straczynski-s/Woods-a						4.00

TERMINATOR, THE: SECONDARY OBJECTIVES
Dark Horse Comics: July, 1991 - No. 4, Oct, 1991 ($2.50, limited series)

1-4: Gulacy-c/a(p) in all						4.00

TERMINATOR SECTOR WAR
Dark Horse Comics: Aug, 2018 - No. 4 ($3.99, limited series)

1-3-Brian Wood-s/Jeff Stokely-a; a different Terminator in 1984 New York City						4.00

TERMINATOR, THE: THE BURNING EARTH
Now Comics: V2#1, Mar, 1990 - V2#5, July, 1990 ($1.75, limited series)

V2#1: Alex Ross painted art (1st published work)	3	6	9	14	19	24
2-5: Ross-c/a in all	1	3	4	6	8	10
Trade paperback (1990, $9.95)-Reprints V2#1-5						18.00
Trade paperback (ibooks, 2003, $17.95)-Digitally remastered reprint						18.00

TERMINATOR, THE: THE DARK YEARS
Dark Horse Comics: Aug, 1999 - No. 4, Dec, 1999 ($2.95, limited series)

1-4-Alan Grant-s/Mel Rubi-a; Jae Lee-c						4.00

TERMINATOR, THE: THE ENEMY WITHIN
Dark Horse Comics: Nov, 1991 - No. 4, Feb, 1992 ($2.50, limited series)

1-4: All have Simon Bisley painted-c						4.00

TERMINATOR, THE: 2029
Dark Horse Comics: Mar, 2010 - No. 3, May, 2010 ($3.50, limited series)

1-3: Kyle Reese before his time-jump to 1984; Zack Whedon-s/Andy MacDonald-a						3.50

TERMINATOR 2: CYBERNETIC DAWN
Malibu: Nov, 1995 - No.4, Feb, 1996; No. 0. Apr, 1996 ($2.50, lim. series)

0 (4/96, $2.95)-Erskine-c/a; flip book w/Terminator 2: Nuclear Twilight						4.00
1-4: Continuation of film.						4.00

TERMINATOR 2: INFINITY
Dynamite Entertainment: 2007 - No. 7 ($3.50)

1-7: 1-Furman-s/Raynor-a; 3 covers. 6,7-Painkiller Jane x-over						3.50

TERMINATOR 2: JUDGEMENT DAY
Marvel Comics: Early Sept, 1991 - No. 3, Early Oct, 1991 ($1.00, lim. series)

1-3: Based on movie sequel; 1-3-Same as nn issues						4.00
nn (1991, $4.95, squarebound, 68 pgs.)-Photo-c						6.00
nn (1991, $2.25, B&W, magazine, 68 pgs.)						5.00

TERMINATOR 2: NUCLEAR TWILIGHT
Malibu: Nov, 1995 - No.4, Feb, 1996; No. 0, Apr, 1996 ($2.50, lim. series)

0 (4/96, $2.95)-Erskine-c/a; flip book w/Terminator 2: Cybernetic Dawn						4.00
1-4:Continuation of film.						4.00

	GD 2.0	VG 4.0	FN 6.0	VF 8.0	VF/NM 9.0	NM- 9.2

TERMINATOR 3: RISE OF THE MACHINES (... BEFORE THE RISE on cover)
Beckett Comics: July, 2003 - No. 6, Jan, 2004 ($5.95, limited series)
1-6: 1,2-Leads into movie; 2 covers on each. 3-6-Movie adaptation — — — — — 6.00

TERM LIFE
Image Comics (Shadowline): Jan, 2011 ($16.99, graphic novel)
SC-Lieberman-s/Thornborrow-a/DeStefano-l — — — — — 17.00

TERRA (See Supergirl {2005 series} #12)
DC Comics: Jan, 2009 - No. 4, Feb, 2009 ($2.99, limited series)
1-4-Conner-a/c. 1,2,4-Power Girl app. 2-4-Geo-Force app. — — — — — 4.00
TPB (2009, $14.99) r/#1-4 & Supergirl #12 — — — — — 15.00

TERRAFORMERS
Wonder Color Comics: April, 1987 - No. 2, 1987 ($1.95, limited series)
1,2-Kelley Jones-a — — — — — 4.00

TERRA OBSCURA (See Tom Strong)
America's Best Comics: Aug, 2003 - No. 6, Feb, 2004 ($2.95)
1-6-Alan Moore & Peter Hogan-s/Paquette-a — — — — — 3.00
TPB (2004, $14.95) r/#1-6 — — — — — 15.00

TERRA OBSCURA VOLUME 2 (See Tom Strong)
America's Best Comics: Oct, 2004 - No. 6, May, 2005 ($2.95)
1-6-Alan Moore & Peter Hogan-s/Paquette-a; Tom Strange app. — — — — — 3.00
TPB (2005, $14.99) r/#1-6 — — — — — 15.00

TERRARISTS
Marvel Comics (Epic): Nov, 1993 - No. 4, Feb, 1994 ($2.50, limited series)
1-4-Bound-in trading cards in all — — — — — 4.00

TERRIFIC COMICS (Also see Suspense Comics)
Continental Magazines: Jan, 1944 - No. 6, Nov, 1944

	2.0	4.0	6.0	8.0	9.0	9.2
1-Kid Terrific; opium story	394	788	1182	2758	4829	6900
2-1st app. The Boomerang by L.B. Cole & Ed Wheelan's "Comics" McCormick, called the world's #1 comic book fan begins	326	652	978	2284	3991	5700
3-Diana becomes Boomerang's costumed aide; L.B. Cole-c	284	568	852	1818	3109	4400
4-Classic war-c (Scarce)	703	1406	2109	5132	9266	13,000
5-The Reckoner begins; Boomerang & Diana by L.B. Cole; Classic Schomburg bondage & hooded vigilante-c (Scarce)	3170	6340	9510	19,000	37,500	65,000
6-L.B. Cole-c/a	271	542	813	1734	2967	4200

NOTE: *L.B. Cole a-1, 2(2), 3-6. Fuje a-5, 6. Rico a-2; c-1. Schomburg c-2, 5.*

TERRIFIC COMICS (Formerly Horrific; Wonder Boy #17 on)
Mystery Publ.(Comic Media)/(Ajax/Farrell): No. 14, Dec, 1954; No. 16, Mar, 1955 (No #15)

	2.0	4.0	6.0	8.0	9.0	9.2
14-Art swipe/Advs. into the Unknown #37; injury-to-eye-c; pg. 2, panel 5 swiped from Phantom Stranger #4; surrealistic Palais-a; Human Cross story; classic-c	123	246	369	787	1344	1900
16-Wonder Boy-c/story (last pre-code)	39	78	117	240	395	550

TERRIFICS, THE
DC Comics: Apr, 2018 - No. 27, Jun, 2020 ($2.99/$3.99)
1-13: 1-Mr. Terrific, Metamorpho, Phantom Girl & Plastic Man team; Lemire-s/Reis-a. 7-10-Tom Strong app. 8,9-Swamp Thing app. — — — — — 3.00
14-24,26,29-($3.99) 18-23-Bizarro & The Terribles app. 27-Simon Stagg dies — — — — — 4.00
25-($4.99) Choose Your Adventure; Harley Quinn & Poison Ivy cameo; Yang-s/Mora-a — — — — — 5.00
Annual 1 (12/18, $4.99) Yang-s/Bennett-a; Tom Strong back-up story — — — — — 5.00

TERRIFYING TALES (Formerly Startling Terror Tales #10)
Star Publications: No. 11, Jan, 1953 - No. 15, Apr, 1954

	2.0	4.0	6.0	8.0	9.0	9.2
11-Used in POP, pgs. 99,100; all Jo-Jo-r	106	212	318	673	1162	1650
12-Reprints Jo-Jo #19 entirely; L.B. Cole splash	90	180	270	576	988	1400
13-All Rulah-r; classic devil-c	219	438	657	1402	2401	3400
14-All Rulah reprints	71	142	213	454	777	1100
15-Rulah, Zago-r; used in SOTI-r/Rulah #22	68	136	204	435	743	1050

NOTE: *All issues have L.B. Cole covers; bondage covers-No. 12-14.*

TERROR ILLUSTRATED (Adult Tales of...)
E.C. Comics: Nov-Dec, 1955 - No. 2, Spring (April on-c), 1956 (Magazine, 25¢)

	2.0	4.0	6.0	8.0	9.0	9.2
1-Adult Entertainment on-c	40	80	120	246	411	575
2-Charles Sultan-a	25	50	75	150	245	340

NOTE: *Craig, Evans, Ingels, Orlando art in each. Crandall c-1, 2.*

TERROR INC. (See A Shadowline Saga #3)
Marvel Comics: July, 1992 - No. 13, July, 1993 ($1.75)
1-8,11-13: 6,7-Punisher-c/story. 13-Ghost Rider app. — — — — — 4.00
9,10-Wolverine-c/story — — — — — 5.00

TERROR INC.
Marvel Comics (MAX): Oct, 2007 - No. 5, Apr, 2008 ($3.99, limited series)
1-5-Lapham-s/Zircher-a; origin of Mr. Terror retold — — — — — 4.00

TERROR INC. - APOCALYPSE SOON
Marvel Comics (MAX): July, 2009 - No. 4, Sept, 2009 ($3.99, limited series)
1-4: 1-Lapham-s/Turnbull-a — — — — — 4.00

TERRORS OF DRACULA (Magazine)
Modern Day Periodical/Eerie Publ.: Vol. 1 #3, May, 1979 - Vol. 3 #2, Sept, 1981 (B&W)

	2.0	4.0	6.0	8.0	9.0	9.2
Vol. 1 #3 (5/79, 1st issue)	4	8	12	27	44	60
#4(8/79), #5(11/79)	3	6	9	20	31	42
Vol. 2 #1-3: 1-(2/80). 2-(5/80). 3-(8/80)	3	6	9	17	25	34
Vol. 3 #1 (5/81), #2 (9/81)	3	6	9	19	30	40

TERRORS OF THE JUNGLE (Formerly Jungle Thrills)
Star Publications: No. 17, 5/52 - No. 21, 2/53; No. 4, 4/53 - No. 10, 9/54

	2.0	4.0	6.0	8.0	9.0	9.2
17-Reprints Rulah #21, 1st issue; used in SOTI; L.B. Cole bondage-c	194	388	582	1242	2121	3000
18-Jo-Jo-r	194	388	582	1242	2121	3000
19,20(1952)-Jo-Jo-r; Disbrow-a	77	154	231	493	847	1200
21-Jungle Jo, Tangi-r; used in POP, pg. 100 & color illos.	81	162	243	518	884	1250

	2.0	4.0	6.0	8.0	9.0	9.2
4-10: All Disbrow-a. 5-Jo-Jo-r. 8-Rulah, Jo-Jo-r. 9-Jo-Jo-r; Disbrow; Tangi by Orlando 10-Rulah-r	71	142	213	454	777	1100

NOTE: *L.B. Cole c-all; bondage c-17, 19, 21, 5, 7.*

TERROR TALES (See Beware Terror Tales)

TERROR TALES (Magazine)
Eerie Publications: V1#7, 1969 - V6#6, Dec, 1974; V7#1, Apr, 1976 - V10, 1979? (V1-V6: 52 pgs., V7 on: 68 pgs.)

	2.0	4.0	6.0	8.0	9.0	9.2
V1#7	9	18	27	62	126	190
V1#8-11('69): 9-Bondage-c	7	14	21	44	82	120
V2#1-6('70), V3#1-6('71), V4#1-7('72), V5#1-6('73), V6#1-6('74), V7#1,4('76) (no V7#2), V8#1-3('77)	5	10	15	35	63	90
V7#3-(7/76) LSD story-r/Weird V3#5	5	10	15	35	63	90
V9#2-4, V10#1(1/79)	6	12	18	37	66	95

TERROR TITANS
DC Comics: Dec, 2008 - No. 6, May, 2009 ($2.99, limited series)
1-6: 1-Ravager and Clock King at the Dark Side Club; Bennett-a. 3-Static app. — — — — — 3.00
TPB (2009, $17.99) r/#1-6 — — — — — 18.00

TERRORWAR
Image Comics: Apr, 2023 - No. 9, Feb, 2024 ($3.99)
1-9-Saladin Ahmed-s/Dave Acosta-a — — — — — 4.00

TERRY AND THE PIRATES (See Famous Feature Stories, Merry Christmas From Sears Toyland, Popular Comics, Super Book #3,5,9,16,28, & Super Comics)

TERRY AND THE PIRATES
Dell Publishing Co.: 1939 - 1953 (By Milton Caniff)

	2.0	4.0	6.0	8.0	9.0	9.2
Large Feature Comic 2(1939)	123	246	369	787	1344	1900
Large Feature Comic 6(1938)-r/1936 dailies	93	186	279	591	1021	1450
Four Color 9(1940)	90	180	270	576	988	1400
Large Feature Comic 27('41), 6('42)	74	148	222	470	810	1150
Four Color 44('43)	32	64	96	230	515	800
Four Color 101('45)	20	40	60	135	300	465
Family Album(1942)	21	42	63	122	199	275

TERRY AND THE PIRATES (Formerly Boy Explorers; Long John Silver & the Pirates #30 on) (Daily strip-r) (Two #26's)
Harvey Publications/Charlton No. 26-28: No. 3, 4/47 - No. 26, 4/51; No. 26, 6/55 - No. 28, 10/55

	2.0	4.0	6.0	8.0	9.0	9.2
3(#1)-Boy Explorers by S&K; Terry & the Pirates begin by Caniff; 1st app. The Dragon Lady	40	80	120	246	411	575
4-S&K Boy Explorers	22	44	66	132	216	300
5-11: 11-Man in Black app. by Powell	13	26	39	72	101	130
12-20: 16-Girl threatened with red hot poker	10	20	30	56	76	95
21-26(4/51)-Last Caniff issue & last pre-code issue	10	20	30	54	72	90
26-28('55)(Formerly This Is Suspense)-No Caniff-a	9	18	27	47	61	75

NOTE: *Powell a-1 (Tommy Tween)-5-10, 12, 14; 15-17(1/2 to 2 pgs. each).*

TERRY BEARS COMICS (TerryToons, The... #4)
St. John Publishing Co.: June, 1952 - No. 3, Mar, 1953

	2.0	4.0	6.0	8.0	9.0	9.2
1-By Paul Terry	15	30	45	84	127	170
2,3	10	20	30	54	72	90

TERRY-TOONS ALBUM (See Giant Comics Edition)

TERRY-TOONS COMICS (1st Series) (Becomes Paul Terry's Comics #85 on; later issues titled "Paul Terry's...")
Timely/Marvel No. 1-59 (8/47)(Becomes Best Western No. 58 on?, Marvel)/St. John No. 60 (9/47) on: Oct, 1942 - No. 86, May, 1951

	2.0	4.0	6.0	8.0	9.0	9.2
1 (Scarce)-Features characters that 1st app. on movie screen; Gandy Goose & Sourpuss begin; war-c; Gandy Goose c-1-37	275	550	825	1746	3023	4300
2	97	194	291	621	1061	1500
3-5	65	130	195	416	708	1000
6,8-10: 9,10-World War II gag-c	50	100	150	315	533	750
7-Hitler, Hirohito, Mussolini-c	300	600	900	1950	3375	4800
11-20	34	68	102	204	332	460
21-37	26	52	78	154	252	350
38-Mighty Mouse begins (1st app., 11/45); Mighty Mouse-c begin. end #86; Gandy, Sourpuss welcome Mighty Mouse	290	580	870	1856	3178	4500
39-2nd app. Mighty Mouse	77	154	231	493	847	1200
40-49: 43-Infinity-c	39	78	117	231	378	525
50-1st app. Heckle & Jeckle (11/46)	81	162	243	518	884	1250
51-60: 50-Infinity-c. 60-(9/47)-Atomic explosion panel; 1st St. John issue	20	40	60	118	192	265
61-86: 85,86-Same book as Paul Terry's Comics #85,86 with only a title change; published at same time?	16	32	48	92	144	195

TERRY-TOONS COMICS (2nd Series)
St. John Publishing Co./Pines: June, 1952 - No. 9, Nov, 1953; 1957; 1958

	2.0	4.0	6.0	8.0	9.0	9.2
1-Gandy Goose & Sourpuss begin by Paul Terry	21	42	63	124	202	280
2	12	24	36	69	97	125
3-9	10	20	30	56	76	95
Giant Summer Fun Book 101,102-(Sum, 1957, Sum, 1958, 25¢, Pines)(TV) CBS Television Presents...; Tom Terrific, Mighty Mouse, Heckle & Jeckle Gandy Goose app.	15	30	45	85	130	175

TERRYTOONS, THE TERRY BEARS (Formerly Terry Bears Comics)
Pines Comics: No. 4, Summer, 1958 (CBS Television Presents...)

	2.0	4.0	6.0	8.0	9.0	9.2
4	9	18	27	47	61	75

TESSIE THE TYPIST (Tiny Tessie #24; see Comedy Comics, Gay Comics & Joker Comics)
Timely/Marvel Comics (20CC): Summer, 1944 - No. 23, Aug, 1949

	2.0	4.0	6.0	8.0	9.0	9.2
1-Doc Rockblock & others by Wolverton	295	590	885	1888	3244	4600
2-Wolverton's Powerhouse Pepper	103	206	309	659	1130	1600
3-(3/45)-No Wolverton	50	100	150	315	533	750
4,5,7,8-Wolverton-a. 4-(Fall/45)	55	110	165	352	601	850
6-Kurtzman's "Hey Look", 2 pgs. Wolverton-a	57	114	171	362	619	875
9-Wolverton's Powerhouse Pepper (8 pgs.) & 1 pg. Kurtzman's "Hey Look"	58	116	174	371	636	900
10-Wolverton's Powerhouse Pepper (4 pgs.)	60	120	180	381	653	925

Terra Obscura #4 © ABC

Terrifics #7 © DC

Thanos (2016 series) #18 © MAR

	GD	VG	FN	VF	VF/NM	NM-
	2.0	4.0	6.0	8.0	9.0	9.2

	GD	VG	FN	VF	VF/NM	NM-
	2.0	4.0	6.0	8.0	9.0	9.2

11-Wolverton's Powerhouse Pepper (8 pgs.) — 63, 126, 189, 403, 689, 975
12-Wolverton's Powerhouse Pepper (4 pgs.) & 1 pg. Kurtzman's "Hey Look" — 57, 114, 171, 362, 619, 875
13-Wolverton's Powerhouse Pepper (4 pgs.) — 57, 114, 171, 362, 619, 875
14,15: 14-Wolverton's Dr. Whackyhack (1 pg.); 1-1/2 pgs. Kurtzman's "Hey Look".
15-Kurtzman's "Hey Look" (3 pgs.) & 3 pgs. Giggles 'n' Grins — 40, 80, 120, 246, 411, 575
16-18-Kurtzman's "Hey Look" (?, 2 & 1 pg.) — 37, 74, 111, 218, 354, 490
19-Annie Oakley story (8 pgs.) — 31, 62, 93, 182, 296, 410
20-23: 20-Anti-Wertham editorial (2/49) — 29, 58, 87, 172, 281, 390
NOTE: Lana app.-21. Millie The Model app.-13, 15, 17, 21. Rusty app.-10, 11, 13, 15, 17.

TESTAMENT
DC Comics (Vertigo): Feb, 2006 - No. 22, Mar, 2008 ($2.99)
1-22: 1-5-Rushkoff-s/Sharp-a. 6,7-Gross & Erskine-a — 3.00

TEXAN, THE (Fightin' Marines #15 on; Fightin' Texan #16 on)
St. John Publishing Co.: Aug, 1948 - No. 15, Oct, 1951
1-Buckskin Belle — 37, 74, 111, 222, 361, 500
2 — 17, 34, 51, 98, 154, 210
3,10: 10-Oversized issue — 18, 36, 54, 103, 162, 220
4,5,7,15-Baker-c/a — 194, 388, 582, 1242, 2121, 3000
6,9-Baker-a — 43, 86, 129, 271, 461, 650
8,11,13,14-Baker-c/a(2-3) each — 50, 100, 150, 315, 533, 750
12-All Matt Baker-c/a; Peyote story — 55, 110, 165, 352, 601, 850
NOTE: Matt Baker c-4-9, 11-15. Larsen a-4-6, 8-10, 15. Tuska a-1, 2, 7-9.

TEXAN, THE (TV)
Dell Publishing Co.: No. 1027, Sept-Nov, 1959 - No. 1096, May-July, 1960
Four Color 1027 (#1)-Photo-c — 9, 18, 27, 57, 111, 165
Four Color 1096-Rory Calhoun photo-c — 7, 14, 21, 46, 86, 125

TEXAS CHAINSAW MASSACRE
DC Comics (WildStorm): Jan, 2007 - No. 6, Jun, 2007 ($2.99, limited series)
1-6: 1-Two covers by Bermejo & Bradstreet; Abnett & Lanning-s — 3.00
....: About a Boy #1 (9/07, $2.99) Abnett & Lanning-s/Gomez-a/Robertson-c — 3.00
....: Book Two TPB (2009, $14.99) r/one shots & New Line Cinema's Tales of Horror story — 15.00
....: By Himself #1 (10/07, $2.99) Abnett & Lanning-s/Craig-a/Robertson-c — 3.00
....: Cut! #1 (8/07, $2.99) Pfeiffer-s/Raffaele-a/Robertson-c — 3.00
....: Raising Cain 1-3 (7/08 - No. 3, 9/08, $3.50) Bruce Jones-s/Chris Gugliotti-a — 3.50

TEXAS JOHN SLAUGHTER (See Walt Disney Presents, 4-Color #997, 1181 & #2)

TEXAS KID (See Two-Gun Western, Wild Western)
Marvel/Atlas Comics (LMC): Jan, 1951 - No. 10, July, 1952
1-Origin; Texas Kid (alias Lance Temple) & his horse Thunder begin; Tuska-a — 34, 68, 102, 204, 332, 460
2 — 18, 36, 54, 105, 165, 225
3-10 — 15, 30, 45, 83, 124, 165
NOTE: Maneely a-1-4; c-1, 3, 5-10.

TEXAS RANGERS, THE (See Jace Pearson of... and Superior Stories #4)

TEXAS RANGERS IN ACTION (Formerly Captain Gallant or Scotland Yard?)
Charlton Comics: No. 5, Jul, 1956 - No. 79, Aug, 1970 (See Blue Bird Comics)
5 — 9, 18, 27, 52, 69, 85
6,7,9,10 — 7, 14, 21, 35, 43, 50
8-Ditko-a (signed) — 10, 20, 30, 56, 76, 95
11-(68 pg. Giant) Williamson-a (5&8 pgs.); Torres/Williamson-a (5 pgs.) — 10, 20, 30, 56, 76, 95
12-(68 pg. Giant, 6/58) — 6, 12, 18, 28, 34, 40
13-Williamson-a (5 pgs); Torres, Morisi-a — 8, 16, 24, 42, 54, 65
14-20 — 5, 10, 15, 23, 28, 32
21-30 — 3, 6, 9, 15, 22, 28
31-59: 32-Both 10¢ & 15¢-c exist — 3, 6, 9, 14, 19, 24
60-Riley's Rangers begin — 3, 6, 9, 13, 18, 22
61-65,68-70 — 2, 4, 6, 8, 11, 14
66,67: 66-1st app. The Man Called Loco. 67-Origin — 2, 4, 6, 9, 13, 16
71-79: 77-(4/70) Ditko-c & a (8 pgs.) — 1, 3, 4, 6, 8, 10
76 (Modern Comics-r, 1977) — 6.00

TEXAS SLIM (See A-1 Comics)

TEX DAWSON, GUN-SLINGER (Gunslinger #2 on)
Marvel Comics Group: Jan, 1973 (20¢)(Also see Western Kid, 1st series)
1-Steranko-c; Williamson-r (4 pgs.); Tex Dawson by Romita(3) from 1955; Tuska-r — 4, 8, 12, 25, 40, 55

TEX FARNUM (See Wisco)

TEX FARRELL (...Pride of the Wild West)

D. S. Publishing Co.: Mar-Apr, 1948
1-Tex Farrell & his horse Lightning; Shelly-c — 20, 40, 60, 117, 189, 260

TEX GRANGER (Formerly Calling All Boys; see True Comics)
Parents' Magazine Inst./Commended: No. 18, Jun, 1948 - No. 24, Sept, 1949
18-Tex Granger & his horse Bullet begin — 15, 30, 45, 83, 124, 165
19 — 12, 24, 36, 67, 94, 120
20-24: 22-Wild Bill Hickok story. 23-Vs. Billy the Kid; Tim Holt app. — 9, 18, 27, 52, 69, 85

TEX MORGAN (See Blaze Carson and Wild Western)
Marvel Comics (CCC): Aug, 1948 - No. 9, Feb, 1950
1-Tex Morgan, his horse Lightning & sidekick Lobo begin — 36, 72, 108, 214, 347, 480
2 — 22, 44, 66, 132, 216, 300
3-6: 3,4-Arizona Annie app. 5-Blaze Carson app. — 15, 30, 45, 83, 124, 165
7-9: All photo-c. 7-Captain Tootsie by Beck. 8-18 pg. story "The Terror of Rimrock Valley"; Diablo app. — 20, 40, 60, 117, 189, 260
NOTE: Tex Taylor app. 2-6, 7, 9. Brodsky c-6. Syd Shores c-2, 5.

TEX RITTER WESTERN (Movie star; singing cowboy; see Six-Gun Heroes and Western Hero)
Fawcett No. 1-20 (1/54)/Charlton No. 21 on: Oct, 1950 - No. 46, May, 1959; photo front/back-c begin
1-Tex Ritter, his stallion White Flash & dog Fury begin; photo front/back-c begin — 43, 86, 129, 271, 461, 650
2 — 21, 42, 63, 124, 202, 280
3-5: 5-Last photo back-c — 16, 32, 48, 94, 147, 200
6-10 — 14, 28, 42, 80, 115, 150
11-19 — 10, 20, 30, 58, 79, 100
20-Last Fawcett issue (1/54) — 11, 22, 33, 62, 86, 110
21-1st Charlton issue; photo-c (3/54) — 14, 28, 42, 80, 115, 150
22-B&W photo back-c begin, end #32 — 9, 18, 27, 52, 69, 85
23-30: 23-25-Young Falcon app. — 8, 16, 24, 42, 54, 65
31-38,40-45 — 8, 16, 24, 42, 54, 65
39-Williamson-a; Whitman-c (1/58) — 9, 18, 27, 47, 61, 75
46-Last issue — 8, 16, 24, 44, 57, 70

TEX TAYLOR (...The Fighting Cowboy on-c #1, 2)(See Blaze Carson, Kid Colt, Tex Morgan, Wild West, Wild Western, & Wisco)
Marvel Comics (HPC): Sept, 1948 - No. 9, March, 1950
1-Tex Taylor & his horse Fury begin; Blaze Carson app. — 37, 74, 111, 222, 361, 500
2-Blaze Carson app. — 20, 40, 60, 114, 182, 250
3-Arizona Annie app. — 19, 38, 57, 111, 176, 240
4-6: All photo-c; Blaze Carson app. 4-Anti-Wertham editorial — 20, 40, 60, 117, 189, 260
7-9: 7-Photo-c;18 pg. Movie-Length Thriller "Trapped in Time's Lost Land!" with sabretoothed tigers, dinosaurs; Diablo app. 8-Photo-c; 18 pg. Movie-Length Thriller "The Mystery of Devil-Tree Plateau!" with dwarf horses, dwarf people & a lost miniature Inca type village; Diablo app. 9-Photo-c; 18 pg. Movie-Length Thriller "Guns Along the Border!" Captain Tootsie by Schreiber; Nimo the Mountain Lion app.; Heth-a — 22, 44, 66, 128, 209, 290
NOTE: Syd Shores c-1-3.

THANE OF BAGARTH (Also see Hercules, 1967 series)
Charlton Comics: No. 24, Oct, 1985 - No. 25, Dec, 1985
24,25-Low print run — 6.00

THANOS
Marvel Comics: Dec, 2003 - No. 12, Sept, 2004 ($2.99)
1-12: 1-6-Starlin-s/a(p)/Milgrom-i; Galactus app. 7-12-Giffen-s/Lim-a — 5.00
Annual 1 (7/14, $4.99) Starlin-s/Lim-a/Keown-c — 5.00
....: The Final Threat (11/12, $4.99) r/Avengers Ann. #7 & Marvel Two-In-One Ann. #2 — 5.00
Vol. 4: Epiphany TPB (2004, $14.99) r/#1-6 — 15.00
Vol. 5: Samaritan TPB (2004, $14.99) r/#7-12 — 15.00

THANOS (Also see Cosmic Ghost Rider series)
Marvel Comics: Jan, 2017 - No. 18, Jun, 2018 ($3.99)
1-Lemire-s/Deodato-a; Starfox & Thane app. — 2, 4, 6, 9, 12, 15
2-12: 2-6-Lemire-s/Deodato-a. 2-Nebula app. 3-Imperial Guard app. 7-12-Peralta-a — 4.00
13-1st app. Cosmic Ghost Rider — 5, 10, 15, 34, 60, 85
14-Cosmic Ghost Rider app. — 2, 4, 6, 9, 12, 15
15-Cosmic Ghost Rider revealed as Frank Castle — 3, 6, 9, 18, 27, 36
16-18: 16-Origin Cosmic Ghost Rider. 17,18-Death app. — 5.00
Annual 1 (6/18, $4.99) Short stories by various; hosted by Cosmic Ghost Rider — 5.00
....: Legacy 1 (11/18, $4.99) Cates & Duggan-s; Cosmic Ghost Rider app. — 5.00

THANOS
Marvel Comics: Jun, 2019 - No. 6, Nov, 2019 ($3.99, limited series)

	GD 2.0	VG 4.0	FN 6.0	VF 8.0	VF/NM 9.0	NM- 9.2

1-($4.99) Tini Howard-s/Ariel Olivetti-a; retells Thanos' first meeting with Gamora — 5.00
2-6-($3.99) — 4.00
...: Death Notes 1 (1/23, $4.99) Backstory on Thanos; art by various incl. Lim — 5.00

THANOS (Return of the Mad Titan)
Marvel Comics: Jan, 2024 - Present ($4.99/$3.99)

1-($4.99) Cantwell/Pizzari-a — 5.00
2,3-($3.99) 2-Hulk app. 3-Illuminati app. — 4.00

THANOS: A GOD UP THERE LISTENING
Marvel Comics: Dec, 2014 - No. 4, Dec, 2014 ($3.99, weekly limited series)

1-4-Thane and Ego The Living Planet app. — 4.00

THANOS IMPERATIVE, THE
Marvel Comics: Aug, 2010 - No. 6, Jan, 2011 ($3.99, limited series)

1-6-Abnett & Lanning-s/Sepulveda-a; Vision and Silver Surfer app. — 4.00
...: Devastation (3/11, $3.99) Sepulveda-a; leads into The Annihilators #1 — 4.00
...: Ignition (7/10, $3.99) Walker-a; prequel to series — 4.00
Thanos Sourcebook (8/10, $3.99) profiles/history of Thanos and Nova Corps members — 4.00

THANOS QUEST, THE (See Capt. Marvel #25, Infinity Gauntlet, Iron Man #55, Logan's Run, Marvel Feature #12, Marvel Universe: The End, Silver Surfer #34 & Warlock #9)
Marvel Comics: 1990 - No. 2, 1990 ($4.95, squarebound, 52 pgs.)

1,2-Both have Starlin scripts & covers (both printings) 3 6 9 17 25 34
1-(3/2000, $3.99) r/material from #1&2 — 5.00
1-(11/12, $7.99) r/#1&2, new cover by Andy Park — 8.00
...: Marvel Tales 1 (7/21, $7.99) r/#1 & 2; intro. by Ralph Macchio — 8.00

THANOS: THE INFINITY FINALE (Conclusion to The Infinity Entity series)
Marvel Comics: 2016 ($24.99, HC original graphic novel)

HC - Jim Starlin/Ron Lim-a; Adam Warlock & Annihilus app. — 25.00

THANOS: THE INFINITY REVELATION (Prelude to The Infinity Entity series)
Marvel Comics: 2014 ($24.99, HC original graphic novel)

HC - Jim Starlin-s/a; Adam Warlock & Silver Surfer app. — 25.00

THANOS VS. HULK
Marvel Comics: Feb, 2015 - No. 4, May, 2015 ($3.99, limited series)

1-Jim Starlin-s/a/c; Annihilus, Pip the Troll and Iron Man app. 2 4 6 9 12 15
2-4 — 4.00

THAT DARN CAT (See Movie Comics & Walt Disney Showcase #19)

THAT'S MY POP! GOES NUTS FOR FAIR
Bystander Press: 1939 (76 pgs., B&W)

nn-by Milt Gross (Rare) 43 86 129 271 461 650

THAT TEXAS BLOOD
Image Comics: Jun, 2020 - Present ($3.99)

1-20-Chris Condon-s/Jacob Phillips-a — 4.00

THAT WILKIN BOY (Meet Bingo…)
Archie Publications: Jan, 1969 - No. 52, Oct, 1982

1-1st app. Bingo's Band, Samantha & Tough Teddy 5 10 15 35 63 90
2-5 3 6 9 17 26 35
6-11 2 4 6 9 13 18 22
12-26-Giants. 12-No # on-c 3 6 9 14 20 26
27-40(1/77) 2 4 6 8 10 12
41-49 1 2 3 4 5 7
50-52 (low print) 2 4 6 8 10 12

THB
Horse Press: Oct, 1994 - 2002 ($5.50/$2.50/$2.95, B&W)

1 ($5.50) Paul Pope-s/a in all 4 8 12 27 44 60
1 (2nd Printing)-r/#1 w/new material — 6.00
2 ($2.50) 3 6 9 16 23 30
3-5 2 4 6 9 12 15
69 (1995, no price, low distribution, 12 pgs.)-story reprinted in #1 (2nd Printing) 2 4 6 11 16 20
Giant THB-($4.95) 3 6 9 14 20 25
Giant THB 1 V2-(2003, $6.95) 2 4 6 9 12 15
..M3/THB: Mars' Mightiest Mek #1 (2000, $3.95) 2 4 6 9 12 15
..6A: Mek-Power #1, 6B: Mek-Power #2, 6C: Mek-Power #3 (2000, $3.95) 1 3 4 6 8 10
.. 6D: Mek-Power #4 (2002, $4.95) 2 4 6 8 10 12

T.H.E. CAT (TV)
Dell Publishing Co.: Mar, 1967 - No. 4, Oct, 1967 (All have photo-c)

1 4 8 12 25 40 55
2-4 3 6 9 18 27 36

THERE'S A NEW WORLD COMING
Spire Christian Comics/Fleming H. Revell Co.: 1973 (35/49¢)

2 4 6 10 14 18

THEY ALL KISSED THE BRIDE (See Cinema Comics Herald)

THEY'RE NOT LIKE US
Image Comics: Dec, 2014 - No. 16, Oct, 2017 ($2.99)

1-16-Stephenson-s/Gane-a/c — 3.00

THIEF OF BAGHDAD
Dell Publishing Co.: No. 1229, Oct-Dec, 1961 (one-shot)

Four Color 1229-Movie, Crandall/Evans-a, photo-c 6 12 18 41 76 110

THIEF OF THIEVES
Image Comics: Feb, 2012 - No. 43, Jul, 2019 ($2.99/$3.99)

1-Kirkman & Spencer-s/Martinbrough-a/c 3 6 9 16 23 30
1-Second printing 1 2 3 5 6 8
2,4 1 3 4 6 8 10
7-37: 8-13-Asmus-s 1 2 3 5 6 8
38-43-($3.99) — 3.00
 — 4.00

THIMK (Magazine) (Satire)
Counterpoint: May, 1958 - No. 6, May, 1959

1 14 28 42 82 121 160
2-6 10 20 30 54 72 90

THING!, THE (Blue Beetle #18 on)
Song Hits No. 1,2/Capitol Stories/Charlton: Feb, 1952 - No. 17, Nov, 1954

1-Weird/horror stories in all; shrunken head-c 155 310 465 992 1696 2400
2,3 97 194 291 621 1061 1500
4,6,8,10: 6-Classic decapitation story 90 180 270 576 988 1400
5-Severed head-c; headlights 168 336 504 1075 1838 2600
7-Injury to eye-c & inside panel 129 258 387 826 1413 2000
9-Used in SOTI, pg. 388 & illo "Stomping on the face is a form of brutality which modern children learn early" 155 310 465 992 1696 2400
11-Necronomicon story; Hansel & Gretel parody; Injury-to-eye panel; Check-a 194 388 582 1242 2121 3000
12-1st published Ditko-c; "Cinderella" parody; lingerie panels. Ditko-a 290 580 870 1856 3178 4500
13,15-Ditko-c/a(3 & 5) 168 336 504 1075 1838 2600
14-Extreme violence/torture; Rumpelstiltskin story; Ditko-c/a(4) 181 362 543 1158 1979 2800
16-Injury to eye panel 39 78 117 231 378 525
17-Ditko-c; classic parody "Through the Looking Glass"; Powell-r/Beware Terror Tales #1 recolored 123 246 369 787 1344 1900
NOTE: Excessive violence, severed heads, injury to eye are common No. 5 on. Al Fago c-4. Forgione c-1i, 2, 6, 8, 9. All Ditko issues #14, 15. Giordano a-6.

THING, THE (See Fantastic Four, Marvel Fanfare, Marvel Feature #11,12, Marvel Two-In-One and Startling Stories:... - Night Falls on Yancy Street)
Marvel Comics Group: July, 1983 - No. 36, June, 1986

1-Life story of Ben Grimm; Byrne scripts begin 3 6 9 18 27 36
2-5: 5-Spider-Man, She-Hulk and Spider-Man app. — 6.00
6-10: 7-1st app. Goody Two-Shoes. 8-She-Hulk app. 10-Secret Wars tie-in — 5.00
11-36 — 4.00
NOTE: Byrne a-2i, 7; c-1, 7, 36i; scripts-1-13, 19-22. Sienkiewicz c-13i.

THING, THE (Fantastic Four)
Marvel Comics: Jan, 2006 - No. 8, Aug, 2006 ($2.99)

1-8: 1-DiVito-a/Slott-s. 4-Lockjaw app. 6-Spider-Man app. 8-Super-Hero poker game — 3.00
...: Idol of Millions TPB (2006, $20.99) r/#1-8; Divito sketch page — 21.00

THING, THE (Fantastic Four)
Marvel Comics: Jan, 2022 - No. 6, Jun, 2022 ($4.99/$3.99)

1-($4.99) Walter Mosley-s/Tom Reilly-a; set in the classic era; Hercules cameo — 5.00
2-6-($3.99) 4-Silver Surfer app. 5,6-Doctor Doom app. — 4.00

THING & SHE-HULK: THE LONG NIGHT (Fantastic Four)
Marvel Comics: May, 2002 ($2.99, one-shot)

1-Hitch-c/a(pg. 1-25); Reis-a(pg. 26-39); Dezago-s — 3.00

THING, THE (From Another World)
Dark Horse Comics: 1991 - No. 2, 1992 ($2.95, mini-series, stiff-c)

1,2-Based on Universal movie; painted-c/a — 5.00

THING CALLED TRUTH, A
Image Comics: Nov, 2021 - No. 5, Mar, 2022 ($3.99)

1-5-Iolanda Zanfardino-s/Elisa Romboli-a — 4.00

THING, THE: FREAKSHOW (Fantastic Four)
Marvel Comics: Aug, 2002 - No. 4, Nov, 2002 ($2.99, limited series)

1-4-Geoff Johns-s/Scott Kolins-a — 3.00
TPB (2005, $17.99) r/#1-4 & Thing & She-Hulk: The Long Night one-shot — 18.00

THING FROM ANOTHER WORLD: CLIMATE OF FEAR, THE
Dark Horse Comics: July, 1992 - No. 4, Dec, 1992 ($2.50, mini-series)

1-4: Painted-c — 4.00

THING FROM ANOTHER WORLD: ETERNAL VOWS
Dark Horse Comics: Dec, 1993 - No. 4, 1994 ($2.50, mini-series)

1-4-Gulacy-c/a — 4.00

THINK TANK (Also see Eden's Fall)
Image Comics (Top Cow): Aug, 2012 - No. 12, Feb, 2014 ($3.99)

1-12-Hawkins-s/Ekedal-a — 4.00

THINK TANK: ANIMAL
Image Comics (Top Cow): Mar, 2017 - No. 3 ($3.99)

1-3-Hawkins-s/Ekedal-a — 4.00

THINK TANK: CREATIVE DESTRUCTION
Image Comics (Top Cow): Apr, 2016 - No. 4, Jul, 2016 ($3.99, limited series)

1-4-Hawkins-s/Ekedal-a — 4.00

THIRTEEN (…Going on 18)
Dell Publishing Co.: 11-1/61-62 - No. 25, 12/67; No. 26, 7/69 - No. 29, 1/71

1 6 12 18 40 73 105
2-10 4 8 12 28 47 65
11-25 4 8 12 23 37 50
26-29-r 3 6 9 17 26 35
NOTE: John Stanley script-No. 3-29; art?

13: ASSASSIN
TSR, Inc.: 1990 - No. 8, 1991 ($2.95, 44 pgs.)

1-8: Agent 13; Alcala-a(i); Springer back-up-a — 4.00

13th ARTIFACT, THE
Image Comics (Top Cow): Mar, 2016 ($3.99, one-shot)

1-Amit Chauhan-s/Eli Powell-a — 4.00

13th SON, THE
Dark Horse Comics: Nov, 2005 - No. 4, Feb, 2006 ($2.99, limited series)

1-4-Kelley Jones-s/a/c — 3.00

30 DAYS OF NIGHT

That Texas Blood #1 © Condon & Phillips

Thief of Thieves #14 © R. Kirkman

This is War #7 © Pines

	GD 2.0	VG 4.0	FN 6.0	VF 8.0	VF/NM 9.0	NM- 9.2

Idea + Design Works: June, 2002 - No. 3, Oct, 2002 ($3.99, limited series)

1-Vampires in Alaska; Steve Niles-s/Ben Templesmith-a/Ashley Wood-c						125.00
1-2nd printing						20.00
2						35.00
3						12.00
Annual 2004 (1/04, $4.99) Niles-s/art by Templesmith and others						8.00
Annual 2005 (12/05, $7.49) Niles-s/art by Nat Jones						7.50
... 5th Anniversary (10/07 - No. 3, $2.99) reprints original series						3.00
... Sourcebook (10/07, $7.49) Illustrated guide to the 30 Days world						7.50
... Three Tales TPB (7/06, $19.99) r/Annual 2005, ...: Dead Space #1-3, and short story from Tales of Terror (IDW's...)						20.00
Hundred Penny Press: 30 Days of Night #1 (5/11, $1.00) r/#1						5.00
... 100-Page Giant (3/19, $4.99) r/30 Days of Night: Eben & Stella #1-3						5.00
TPB (2003, $17.99) r/#1-3, foreward by Clive Barker; script for #1						18.00
The Complete 30 Days of Night (2004, $75.00, oversized hardcover with slipcase) r/#1-3; prequel; script pages for #1-3; original cover and promotional materials						75.00

30 DAYS OF NIGHT
IDW Publishing: July, 2004 (Free Comic Book Day edition)

Previews CSI: Bad Rap; The Shield: Spotlight; 24: One Shot; and 30 Days of Night						3.00

30 DAYS OF NIGHT (Ongoing series)
IDW Publishing: Oct, 2011 - No. 12, Nov, 2012 ($3.99)

1-12: 1-4-Niles-s/Kieth-a; covers by Kieth and Furno. 5-12-Niles-s						4.00

30 DAYS OF NIGHT (2017 reimagining of original series)
IDW Publishing: Dec, 2017 - No. 6, May, 2018 ($3.99, limited series)

1-6-Niles-s/Kowalski; covers by Kowalski, Wood and Templesmith						4.00

30 DAYS OF NIGHT: BEYOND BARROW
IDW Publishing: Sept, 2007 - No. 3, Dec, 2007 ($3.99, limited series)

1-3-Niles-s/Sienkiewicz-a						4.00

30 DAYS OF NIGHT: BLOODSUCKER TALES
IDW Publishing: Oct, 2004 - No. 8, May, 2005 ($3.99, limited series)

1-8-Niles-s/Chamberlain-a; Fraction-s/Templesmith-a/c						4.00
HC (8/05, $49.99) r/#1-8; cover gallery						50.00
SC (8/05, $24.99) r/#1-8; cover gallery						25.00

30 DAYS OF NIGHT: DEAD SPACE
IDW Publishing: Jan, 2006 - No. 3, Mar, 2006 ($3.99, limited series)

1-3-Niles and Wickline-s/Milx-a/c						4.00

30 DAYS OF NIGHT: EBEN & STELLA
IDW Publishing: May, 2007 - No. 3, July, 2007 ($3.99, limited series)

1-3-Niles and DeConnick-s/Randall-a/c						4.00

30 DAYS OF NIGHT: NIGHT, AGAIN
IDW Publishing: May, 2011 - No. 4, Aug, 2011 ($3.99, limited series)

1-4-Lansdale-s/Kieth-a						4.00

30 DAYS OF NIGHT: RED SNOW
IDW Publishing: Aug, 2007 - No. 3, Oct, 2007 ($3.99, limited series)

1-3-Ben Templesmith-s/a/c						4.00

30 DAYS OF NIGHT: RETURN TO BARROW
IDW Publishing: Mar, 2004 - No. 6, Aug, 2004 ($3.99, limited series)

1-6-Steve Niles-s/Ben Templesmith-a/c						4.00
TPB (2004, $19.99) r/#1-6; cover gallery						20.00

30 DAYS OF NIGHT: SPREADING THE DISEASE
IDW Publishing: Dec, 2006 - No. 5, Apr, 2007 ($3.99, limited series)

1-5: 1-Wickline-s/Sanchez-a. 3-5-Sandoval-a						4.00

30 DAYS OF NIGHT: 30 DAYS 'TIL DEATH
IDW Publishing: Dec, 2008 - No. 4, Mar, 2009 ($3.99, limited series)

1-4-David Lapham-s/a; covers by Lapham and Templesmith						4.00

THIRTY SECONDS OVER TOKYO (See American Library)

THIS DAMNED BAND
Dark Horse Comics: Aug, 2016 - No. 6, Jan, 2016 ($3.99, limited series)

1-6-Paul Cornell-s/Tony Parker-a						4.00

THIS IS SUSPENSE! (Formerly Strange Suspense Stories; Strange Suspense Stories #27 on)
Charlton Comics: No. 23, Feb, 1955 - No. 26, Aug, 1955

	GD 2.0	VG 4.0	FN 6.0	VF 8.0	VF/NM 9.0	NM- 9.2
23-Wood-a(r)/A Star Presentation #3 "Dr. Jekyll & Mr. Hyde"; last pre-code issue	34	68	102	199	325	450
24-Censored Fawcett-r; Evans-a (r/Suspense Detective #1)	18	36	54	105	165	225

	GD 2.0	VG 4.0	FN 6.0	VF 8.0	VF/NM 9.0	NM- 9.2
25,26: 26-Marcus Swayze-a	15	30	45	83	124	165

THIS IS THE PAYOFF (See Pay-Off)

THIS IS WAR
Standard Comics: No. 5, July, 1952 - No. 9, May, 1953

	GD 2.0	VG 4.0	FN 6.0	VF 8.0	VF/NM 9.0	NM- 9.2
5-Toth-a	24	48	72	140	230	320
6,9-Toth-a	17	34	51	100	158	215
7,8: 8-Ross Andru-c	14	28	42	82	121	160

THIS IS YOUR LIFE, DONALD DUCK (See Donald Duck..., Four Color #1109)

THIS MAGAZINE IS CRAZY (Crazy #? on)
Charlton Publ. (Humor Magazines): V3#2, July, 1957 - V4#8, Feb, 1959 (25¢, magazine, 68 pgs.)

	GD 2.0	VG 4.0	FN 6.0	VF 8.0	VF/NM 9.0	NM- 9.2
V3#2-V4#7: V4#5-Russian Sputnik-c parody	14	28	42	82	121	160
V4#8-Davis-a (8 pgs.)	15	30	45	84	127	170

THIS MAGAZINE IS HAUNTED (Danger and Adventure #22 on)
Fawcett Publications/Charlton No. 15(2/54) on: Oct, 1951 - No. 14, 12/53; No. 15, 2/54 - V3#21, Nov, 1954

	GD 2.0	VG 4.0	FN 6.0	VF 8.0	VF/NM 9.0	NM- 9.2
1-Evans-a; Dr. Death as host begins	116	232	348	742	1271	1800
2,5-Evans-a	65	130	195	416	708	1000
3,4: 3-Vampire-c/story	61	122	183	390	670	950
6-9,12	45	90	135	284	480	675
10-Severed head-c	148	296	444	947	1624	2300
11-Classic skeleton-c	116	232	348	742	1271	1800
13-Severed head-c/story	103	206	309	659	1130	1600
14-Classic burning skull-c	300	600	900	2010	3505	5000
15,20: 15-Dick Giordano-c. 20-Cover is swiped from panel in The Thing #16	63	126	189	403	689	975
16,19-Ditko-c. 16-Injury-to-eye panel; story-r/#1	300	600	900	1920	3310	4700
17-Ditko-c/a(4); blood drainage story	103	206	309	659	1130	1600
18-Ditko-c/a(1 story); E.C. swipe/Haunt of Fear #5; injury-to-eye panel; reprints "Caretaker of the Dead" from Beware Terror Tales & recolored	84	168	252	538	919	1300
21-Ditko-c, Evans-r/This Magazine Is Haunted #1	71	142	213	454	777	1100

NOTE: Baily a-1, 3, 4, 21r/#1. Moldoff c/a-1-13. Powell a-3-5, 11, 12, 17. Shuster a-18-20. Issues 19-21 have reprints which have been recolored from This Magazine is Haunted #1.

THIS MAGAZINE IS HAUNTED (2nd Series) (Formerly Zaza the Mystic; Outer Space #17 on)
Charlton Comics: V2#12, July, 1957 - V2#16, May, 1958

	GD 2.0	VG 4.0	FN 6.0	VF 8.0	VF/NM 9.0	NM- 9.2
V2#12-14-Ditko-c/a in all	63	126	189	403	689	975
15-No Ditko-c/a	27	54	81	158	259	360
16-Ditko-a(4).	43	86	129	271	461	650

THIS MAGAZINE IS WILD (See Wild)

THIS WAS YOUR LIFE (Religious)
Jack T. Chick Publ.: 1964 (3 1/2 x 5 1/2", 40 pgs., B&W and red)

	GD 2.0	VG 4.0	FN 6.0	VF 8.0	VF/NM 9.0	NM- 9.2
nn, Another version (5x2 3/4", 26 pgs.)	2	4	6	10	14	18

THOR (See Avengers #1, Giant-Size..., Marvel Collectors Item Classics, Marvel Graphic Novel #33, Marvel Preview, Marvel Spectacular, Marvel Treasury Edition, Special Marvel Edition & Tales of Asgard)

THOR (Journey Into Mystery #1-125, 503-on)(The Mighty Thor #413-490)
Marvel Comics Group: No. 126, Mar, 1966 - No. 502, Sept, 1996

	GD 2.0	VG 4.0	FN 6.0	VF 8.0	VF/NM 9.0	NM- 9.2
126-Thor continues (#125-130 Thor vs. Hercules); Tales of Asgard back-up stories continue through issue #145	46	92	138	359	805	1250
127-130: 127-1st app. Pluto. 129-1st Ares Olympian God of War & Tana Nile of the Rigillian Colonizers	12	24	36	79	170	260
131,135,137-140: 137-1st Ulik the Troll. 138-139-Thor vs. Ulik. 140-Kang app; 1st Growing Man	9	18	27	63	129	195
132-1st app. Ego the Living Planet	10	20	30	66	138	210
133-Thor vs. Ego	15	30	45	103	227	350
134-Intro High Evolutionary and Man-Beast	46	92	138	340	770	1200
136-(1/67) Re-intro. Sif	12	24	36	82	179	275
141-145: 142-Thor vs. Super-Skrull. 143,144-Thor vs. the Enchanters	8	16	24	55	105	155
146,147: 146-Inhumans origin; begin (early app.) in back-up stories, end #152 (see Fantastic Four #45 for 1st app.). 147-Origin continues	9	18	27	59	117	175
148-Origin Black Bolt; 1st app. Wrecker	17	34	51	117	259	400
149-Origin Black Bolt continues. 149-Origin Medusa, Crystal, Maximus, Gorgon, Karnak	10	20	30	64	132	200
150-152: Inhumans app. 150-Hela app. 151,152-Destroyer and Ulik app.	9	18	27	57	111	165
153-157,159: 154-1st Mangog. 155-157-Thor vs Mangog. 159-Origin Dr. Blake (Thor) concl.	7	14	21	49	92	135
158-Origin-r/#83; origin Dr. Blake	9	18	27	62	126	190
160-162-Galactus app.	8	16	24	55	105	155

	GD 2.0	VG 4.0	FN 6.0	VF 8.0	VF/NM 9.0	NM- 9.2
163,164-2nd & 3th brief app. Warlock (Him)	6	12	18	42	79	115
165-1st full app. Warlock (Him) (6/69, see Fantastic Four #67); last 12¢ issue; Kirby-a	107	214	321	856	1928	3000
166-2nd full app. Warlock (Him); battles Thor; see Marvel Premiere #1	16	32	48	110	243	375
167,170-179: 170-1st Thermal Man. 171-Thor vs. the Wrecker. 173-Circus of Crime app. 174-1st Crypto-Man. 176-177-Surtur app. 178-1st Buscema-a on Thor; vs the Abomination. 179-Last Kirby issue	6	12	18	44	76	110
168-Origin Galactus; Kirby-a	36	72	108	259	580	900
169-Galactus continues; Kirby-a	21	42	63	147	324	500
180,181-Neal Adams-a; Mephisto & Loki app.	6	12	18	40	73	105
182,183-Thor vs. Doctor Doom. 182-Buscema-a begins (11/70)	6	12	18	37	66	95
184-192: 184-1st Infinity & the Silent One. 187-Thor vs Odin. 188-Origin of Infinity. 189,190-Thor vs. Hela. 191-1st Durok the Demolisher. 192-Last 15¢ issue; Thor vs. Durok	5	10	15	31	53	75
193-(25¢, 52 pgs.); Silver Surfer x-over; Thor vs. Durok; last Stan Lee story as regular writer	12	24	36	80	173	265
194-199: 194-Gerry Conway stories begin (ends #238). 195-Mangog returns. 196-198-Thor vs. Mangog. 199-1st Ego-Prime; Pluto app.	4	8	12	27	44	60
200-Special Ragnarok issue by Stan Lee	6	12	18	37	66	95
201-206,208-220,222-224: 201-Pluto & Hela app. 202-vs Ego-Prime. 203-1st Young Gods. 204-Thor exiled on Earth; Mephisto app. 205-vs Mephisto; Hitler app. 206-vs. the Absorbing Man. 208-1st Mercurio the 4th Dimensional Man. 210-211-vs Ulik. 214-Mercurio the 4-D Man app.; 1st Xorr the God-Jewel. 215-Origin of Xorr; Mercurio the 4-D Man app. 216-Xorr & Mecurio app. 217-Thor vs Odin-c. 218-220-Saga of the Black Stars. 222,223-vs Pluto. 224-The Destroyer app.	3	6	9	17	26	35
207-Rutland, Vermont Halloween x-over; leads into Avengers/Defenders war	4	8	12	24	38	52
221-Thor vs. Hercules; Hercules guest stars through issue #232,234-239	3	6	9	20	31	42
225-Intro. Firelord	16	32	48	111	246	380
226-Galactus and Firelord app.	3	6	9	19	30	40
227,228,230,231: 227-228-Thor, Firelord & Galactus vs Ego the Living Planet. 228-Origin of Ego	3	6	9	14	20	25
229-Has ad for Incredible Hulk #181 (Wolverine)	6	12	18	38	69	100
229 Facsimile Edition (5/20, $3.99) Reprints 1974 issue with original ads & letter column						6.00
232,233: 232-Firelord app. 233-Numerous guest stars; Asgard invades Earth	3	6	9	15	22	28
234-245: 234-Iron Man & Firelord app. 235-1st Kamo Tharnn, Elder of the Universe. 236-Thor vs. Absorbing Man. 237-239-Thor vs. Ulik. 240-1st Egyptian Gods; Osiris & Horus; 1st Seth-Egyptian God of Death. 241-Thor vs. Seth. 242-Len Wein scripts begin; ends #271. 242-245-Thor vs. Time-Twisters; Zarko the Tomorrow Man app.	3	6	9	14	19	24
246-250-(Regular 25¢ editions)(4-8/76): 246-247-Firelord app. 249-250-Thor vs. Mangog	3	6	9	14	19	24
246-250-(30¢-c variants, limited distribution)	3	6	9	17	66	95
251-280: 251-Thor vs. Hela. 252,253-Thor vs. Ulik. 255-Re-intro Stone Men of Saturn. 257-259-Thor vs. Grey Gargoyle. 260-Thor vs. Enchantress & Executioner. 261-272-Simonson-a. 264-266-Thor vs. Loki. 265,266-The Destroyer app. 269-Thor vs. Stilt-Man. 270-Thor vs. Blastaar. 271-Iron Man x-over. 272-Roy Thomas scripts begin. 274-Death of Balder the Brave. 276-Thor vs. Red Norvell Thor. 280-Thor vs Hyperion	2	4	6	8	11	14
260-264-(35¢-c variants, limited distribution)(6-10/77)	10	20	30	64	132	200
281-299: 281-Space Phantom app. 282-Immortus app. 283,284-Celestials app. 284-286-Eternals app. 287-288-Thor vs. the Forgotten one. 291,292-Asgard vs Olympus. 292-1st Eye of Odin (as sentient being). 294-Origin Asgard & Odin	2	4	6	8	11	14
300-(12/80)-End of Asgard; origin of Odin & The Destroyer; double-size	3	6	9	16	23	30
301-Numerous pantheons (skyfathers) app.	1	3	4	6	8	10
302-304	1	3		5	6	8
305-306: 305-Airwalker app. 306-Firelord	1	3	4	6	8	10
307-331,334-336: 310-Thor vs. Mephisto. 314-Moondragon and Drax app. 315,316-Bi-Beast & Man-Beast app. 316-Iron Man x-over. 325-Mephisto app. 331-1st Crusader						6.00
332,333-Dracula app.	1	2	3	5	6	8
337-Simonson-a begins, ends #382; 1st app. of Beta Ray Bill who becomes the new Thor; intro Lorelei	10	20	30	64	132	200
338-Beta Ray Bill vs. Thor; origin Beta Ray Bill	3	6	9	19	30	40
339,340: 339-Beta Ray Bill gains Thor's powers. 340-Donald Blake returns as Thor; Beta Ray Bill app.; more facts revealed about origin	2	4	6	8	10	12
341-343,345-371,373,375-381,383,386: 341-Clark Kent & Lois Lane cameo. 345-349-Malekith the Accursed app. 350-352-Avengers app. 353-'Death' of Odin. 356-Hercules app. 363-Secret Wars II crossover. 364-366-Thor as a frog. 367-Malekith app. 373-X-Factor tie-in. 383-Secret Wars flashback						6.00
344-(6/84) 1st app. of Malekith the Accursed (Ruler of the Dark Elves)(villain in the 2013 movie Thor: The Dark World); Simonson-c/a	3	6	9	15	22	28
372-1st Time Variance Authority (Loki TV)	3	6	9	17	26	35
374-Mutant Massacre; X-Factor app.	1	2	3	5	6	8
382-($1.25)-Anniversary issue; last Simonson-a	1	2	3	5	6	8
384-Intro. Thor of the 26th century (Dargo Ktor)	1	2	3	5	6	8
385-Thor vs. Hulk by Stan Lee and Erik Larsen	2	4	6	8	10	12
387-399: Thor vs. the Celestials. 389- 'Alone against the Celestials' climax. 390-Avengers app.; Captain America lifts Mjolnir. 391-Spider-Man x-over; 1st Eric Masterson. 393-395-Daredevil app. 395-New. Earth Force. 398-399-Black Knight app.						6.00
400-($1.75, 68 pgs.)-Origin Loki	1	2	3	5	6	8
401-410,404,405-Annihilus app. 409-410-Dr. Doom app.						5.00
411-Intro New Warriors (appear in costume in last panel); Juggernaut-c/story	3	6	9	21	33	45
412-1st full app. New Warriors (Marvel Boy, Kid Nova, Namorita, Night Thrasher, Firestar & Speedball)	3	6	9	21	33	45
413-428: 413-Dr. Strange app. 419-425-Black Galaxy saga; origin Celestials 427-428-Excalibur app. 428-Ghost Rider app.						5.00
429-431: 429-Thor vs Juggernaut; Ghost Rider app. 430-Ghost Rider app.						4.00
432-(52 pgs.) Thor's 350th issue (not Loki) reprints origin and 1st app. from Journey into Mystery #83						5.00
433-449,451-467: 433-Intro. Eric Masterson as Thor. 434,435-Annihilus app. 437-Quasar app.; Tales of Asgard back-up stories begin. 438-441-Thor War; Beta Ray Bill app. 443-Dr. Strange & Silver Surfer x-over; last $1.00-c. 445,446-Operation Galactic Storm. 445-Thor vs. Gladiator. 448-Spider-Man app. 451,452-Bloodaxe app. 457-Original Thor returns. 458-Thor vs. Thor. 459-Intro Thunderstrike. 460-Starlin scripts begin. 461-Thor vs. Beta Ray Bill. 463-467-Infinity Crusade x-over. 466-Drax app.						4.00
450-($2.50, 68 pgs.)-Flip-book format; r/story JIM #85 (1st Loki) plus-c plus a gallery of past-c; gatefold-c						5.00
468,469-Blood and Thunder x-over. 468-Thor vs. Silver Surfer. 469-Infinity Watch app.						6.00
470,471-Blood and Thunder x-over. 470-Thanos and the Infinity Watch app. 471-Blood and Thunder story conclusion; Infinity Watch and Silver Surfer app.						6.00
472-474: 472-Intro the Godlings. 474-Begin $1.50-c; bound-in trading cards						4.00
475-($2.00, 52 pgs.)-Regular edition; High Evolutionary and Man-Beast app.						5.00
475-($2.50, 52 pgs.)-Collectors edition w/foil embossed-c						6.00
476-481,483,486,487,488: 476-Destroyer app. 477-Thunderstrike app. 478-Return of Red Norvell Thor. 479-Detailed Origin of Thor. 486-Kurse app.						4.00
482-($2.95, 84 pgs.)-Worldengine pt. 1						5.00
484,485,490: 484-War Machine app. 485-Thing app. 490-Absorbing Man app.; Buscema-a						5.00
489-Hulk app.						6.00
491-Warren Ellis scripts begins, ends #494; Worldengine pt.1; Deodato-c/a begins						5.00
492-494: Worldengine pt.2. 494-Reintro The Enchantress; Beta Ray Bill dies						5.00
495-499: 495-Messner-Loebs scripts begins; Isherwood-c/a. 496-Captain America app.						5.00
500-($2.50)-Double-size; wraparound-c; Deodato-c/a; Dr. Strange app.						5.00
501-Reintro Red Norvell						4.00
502-(9/96) Onslaught tie-in; Red Norvell, Jane Foster & Hela app.						5.00

NOTE: Numbering continues with Journey Into Mystery #503 (11/96)

600-up (See Thor 2007 series)

	GD 2.0	VG 4.0	FN 6.0	VF 8.0	VF/NM 9.0	NM- 9.2
Special 2(9/66)-(See Journey Into Mystery for 1st annual) Destroyer app.	15	30	45	103	227	350
Special 2 (2nd printing, 1994)	2	4	6	8	10	12
King Size Special 3 (1/71)	5	10	15	35	63	90
Special 4 (12/71)-r/Thor #131,132 & JIM #113	3	6	9	21	33	45
Annual 5 (11/76)-Asgard vs Olympus; Hercules app.	3	6	9	14	19	24
Annual 6 (10/77)-Guardians of the Galaxy app.	5	10	15	30	50	70
Annual 7,8: 7 (1978)-Eternals app. 8 (1979)-Thor vs. Zeus-c/story	2	4	6	9	13	16
Annual 9-13: 9 ('81)-Dormammu app. 10 ('82)-1st Demogorge-the God Eater. 11 ('83)-Origin of Thor expanded. 12 ('84)-Intro Vidar (Thor's brother). 13 ('85)-Mephisto app.						6.00
Annual 14-19 ('86-'94, 48 pgs.): 14-Atlantis Attacks. 15 ('90)-Terminus factor Pt. 3. 16-3 pg. origin; Guardians of the Galaxy x-over. 17 ('92)-Citizen Kang Pt. 2. 18-Polybagged w/card; intro the Flame. 19 ('94) vs. Pluto						5.00
...Alone Against the Celestials nn (6/92, $5.95)-r/Thor #387-389						6.00
...Legends Vol. 2: Walter Simonson Book 2 TPB (2003, $24.99) r/#349-355,357-359						25.00
...Legends Vol. 3: Walter Simonson Book 3 TPB (2004, $24.99) r/#360-369						25.00
...: The Eternals Saga TPB (2006, $24.99) r/#283-291 & Annual #7; profile pages						25.00
...: The Eternals Saga TPB Vol. 2 TPB (2007, $24.99) r/#292-301; Thomas & Gruenwald essays						25.00
...: Visionaries: Mike Deodato Jr. TPB (2004, $19.99) r/#491-494,498-500						20.00
...: Visionaries: Walter Simonson (Vol. 1) TPB (5/01, $24.95) r/#337-348						25.00
...: Visionaries: Walter Simonson Vol. 4 TPB (2007, $24.99) r/#371-373 & Balder the Brave #1-4						25.00
... Visionaries: Walter Simonson Vol. 5 TPB (2008, $24.95) r/#375-382						25.00
...: Worldengine (8/96, $9.95)-r/#491-494; Deodato-c/a; story & new intermission by Warren Ellis						10.00

NOTE: Neal Adams a-180,181; c-179-181. Austin a-342; 346; c-312i. Buscema a-178, 182-213, 215-226, 231-238, 241-253, 254r, 256-259, 272-278, 283-285, 370, Annual 6, 8, 11; c(p)-175, 178, 182-196, 198-200, 202-204, 206, 211, 212, 215, 219, 221, 226, 259, 261, 262, 272-278, 283, 370, Annual 6, 8. Everett a(i)-143, 170-175; c(i)-171, 172, 174, 176, 241. Gil Kane a-318p; c(p)-201, 205, 207-210, 216, 220, 222, 223, 231, 233-240, 242, 243, 318. Kirby a(p)-259; c(p)-134, 145-177; c(i)-167, 169, 171-174, 176, 177, 249-253, 255, 257, 258, Annual 5, Special 2-4. Mooney a(i)-201, 204, 214-216, 218, 322i, 324i, 325i, 327i. Sienkiewicz c-332, 333, 335. Simonson a-260-271p, 337-354, 357-367, 380, Annual 7p; c-260, 263-271, 337-355, 357-369, 371, 373-382, Annual 7. Starlin c-213.

THOR (Volume 2)
Marvel Comics: July, 1998 - No. 85, Dec, 2004 ($2.99/$1.99/$2.25)

	GD 2.0	VG 4.0	FN 6.0	VF 8.0	VF/NM 9.0	NM- 9.2
1-($2.99)-Follows Heroes Return; Jurgens-s/Romita Jr. & Janson-a; wraparound-c; battles the Destroyer	1	2	3	5	6	8
1-Variant-c	2	4	6	8	10	12
1-Rough Cut-c($2.99) Features original script and pencil pages						
1-Sketch cover						35.00
2-($1.99) Two covers; Avengers app.						5.00
3-11,13-23: 3-Assumes Jake Olson ID. 4-Namor-c/app. 8-Spider-Man-c/app. 14-Iron Man c/app. 17-Juggernaut-c						4.00
12-($2.99) Wraparound-c; Hercules appears						5.00
12-($10.00) Variant-c by Jusko						10.00
24,26-31,33,34: 24-Begin $2.25-c. 26-Mignola-c/Larsen-a. 29-Andy Kubert-a. 30-Maximum Security x-over; Beta Ray Bill-c/app. 33-Intro. Thor Girl						4.00
25-($2.99) Regular edition						5.00
25-($3.99) Gold foil enhanced cover						6.00
32-($3.50, 100 pgs.) new story plus reprints w/Kirby-a; Simonson-a						6.00
35-($2.99) Thor battles The Gladiator; Andy Kubert-a						5.00
36-49,51-61: 37-Starlin-a. 38,39-BWS-c. 38-42-Immonen-a. 40-Odin killed. 41-Orbik-c. 44-'Nuff Said silent issue. 51-Spider-Man app. 57-Art by various. 58-Davis-a; x-over with Iron Man #64. 60-Brereton-c						4.00
50-($4.95) Raney-c/a; begins app. w/Nuckols-a & Armenta-s/Bennett-a						4.00
62-84: 62-Begin $2.99-c. 64-Loki-c/app. 80-Oeming-s begins; Avengers app.						4.00
85-Last issue; Thor dies; Oeming-s/DiVito-a/Epting-c.						5.00
...1999 Annual ($3.50) Jurgens-s/a(p)						5.00
...2000 Annual ($3.50) Jurgens-s/Ordway-a(p); back-up stories						5.00
...2001 Annual ($3.50) Jurgens-s/Grummett-a(p); Lightle-c						5.00
...Across All Worlds (9/01, $19.95, TPB) r/#28-35						20.00
Avengers Disassembled: Thor TPB (2004, $16.99) r/#80-85; afterword by Oeming						17.00
...Resurrection ($5.99, TPB) r/#1,2						6.00
...: The Dark Gods (7/00, $15.95, TPB) r/#9-13						16.00
...Vol. 1: The Death of Odin (7/02, $12.99, TPB) r/#39-44						13.00
...Vol. 2: Lord of Asgard (2/03, $15.99, TPB) r/#45-50						16.00
...Vol. 3: Gods on Earth (2003, $21.99, TPB) r/#51-58, Avengers #63, Iron Man #64, Marvel Double-Shot #1; Beck-c						22.00
...Vol. 4: Spiral (2003, $19.99, TPB) r/#59-67; Brereton-c						20.00
...Vol. 5: The Reigning (2004, $17.99, TPB) r/#68-74						18.00
...Vol. 6: Gods and Men (2004, $13.99, TPB) r/#75-79						14.00

Thor #345 © MAR

Thor (2014 series) #1 © MAR

Thor: God of Thunder #14 © MAR

	GD	VG	FN	VF	VF/NM	NM-		GD	VG	FN	VF	VF/NM	NM-
	2.0	4.0	6.0	8.0	9.0	9.2		2.0	4.0	6.0	8.0	9.0	9.2

THOR (Also see Fantastic Four #538)(Resumes original numbering with #600)
Marvel Comics: Sept, 2007 - No. 12, Mar, 2009; No. 600, Apr, 2009 - No. 621, May, 2011
($2.99/$3.99) (Continues numbering as Journey Into Mystery #622) (Also see Mighty Thor #1)

1-Straczynski-s/Coipel-a/c	4.00
1-Variant-c by Michael Turner	5.00
1-Zombie variant-c by Suydam	5.00
1-Non-zombie variant-c by Suydam	5.00
1-"Marvel's Greatest Comics" edition (5/10, $1.00) r/#1	3.00
2-12: 2-Two covers by Dell'Otto and Coipel. 3-Iron Man app.; McGuinness var-c. 4-Bermejo var-c. 5-Campbell var-c. 6-Art Adams var-c. 7,8-Djurdjevic-a/c; Coipel var-c	3.00
2-Second printing with wraparound-c	3.00
7-"Marvel's Greatest Comics" edition (6/11, $1.00) r/#7	3.00

(After #12 [Mar, 2009] numbering reverted back to original Journey Into Mystery/Thor numbering with #600, Apr, 2009)

600 (4/09, $4.99) Two wraparound-c by Coipel & Djurdjevic; Coipel, Djurdjevic & Aja-a; r/Tales of Asgard from Journey Into Mystery #106,107,112,113,115; Kirby-a	5.00
601-603,611-621-($3.99) 601-603-Djurdjevic-a. 602-Sif returns. 617-Loki returns	4.00
604-610-($2.99) Tan-a. 607-609-Siege x-over. 610-Braithwaite-a; Ragnarok app.	3.00
620.1 (5/11, $2.99) Brooks-a; Grey Gargoyle app.	3.00
Annual 1 (11/09, $3.99) Suayan, Grindberg, Gaudiano-a; Djurdjevic-c	4.00
... Ages of Thunder (6/08, $3.99) Fraction-s/Zircher-a/Djurdjevic-c	4.00
... & Hercules: Encyclopaedia Mythologica (2009, $4.99) profile pages of the Pantheons	5.00
... Asgard's Avenger 1 (6/11, $4.99) profile pages of Thor characters	5.00
... By Simonson Halloween Comic Fest 2017 1 (12/17, giveaway) r/#354 & JIM #102	3.00
... Crown of Fools 1 (12/13, $3.99) Di Vito & Simonson-a	4.00
... Giant-Size Finale 1 (1/01, $3.99) Dr. Doom app.; r/origin from JIM #83	4.00
... God-Size Special (2/09, $3.99) story of Skurge the Executioner re-told; art by Brereton, Braithwaite, Allred and Sepulveda; plus reprint of Thor #362 (1985)	4.00
... Goes Hollywood 1 ('11, $3.99) Collection of movie-themed variant Thor covers	4.00
... Man of War (1/09, $3.99) Fraction-s/Mann & Zircher-a/Djurdjevic-c	4.00
... Reign of Blood (8/08, $3.99) Fraction-s/Evans & Zircher-a/Djurdjevic-c	4.00
... Spotlight (10/11, $3.99) movie photo-c; movie preview; creator interviews	4.00
... The Rage of Thor (10/10, $3.99) Milligan-s/Suayan-c/a	4.00
... The Trial of Thor (2008, $3.99) Milligan-s/Nord-c/a	4.00
... Truth of History (12/08, $3.99) Thor and crew in ancient Egypt; Alan Davis-s/a/c	4.00
... Where Walk the Frost Giants 1 (12/17, $3.99) Macchio-s/Nauck-a; plus r/JIM #112	4.00
... Whosoever Wields This Hammer 1 (6/11, $4.99) recolored r/J.I.M. #83,84,88	5.00
... Wolves of the North (2/11, $3.99) Carey-s/Perkins-a	4.00
... By J. Michael Straczynski Vol. 1 HC (2009, $19.99) r/#1-6; variant cover gallery	20.00

THOR (Female Thor)
Marvel Comics: Dec, 2014 - No. 8, Jul, 2015 ($3.99)

1-Aaron-s/Dauterman-a/c; Thor, Odin and Malekith app.	10.00
2-8 2-4-Malekith app. 4-Thor vs. Thor. 5-Molina-a. 8-Identity revealed	4.00
Annual 1 (4/15, $4.99) Female Thor, King Thor stories; Young Thor by CM Punk-s	5.00

THOR (Odinson back as Thor)(Leads into King Thor series)
Marvel Comics: Aug, 2018 - No. 16, Oct, 2019 ($5.99/$3.99)

1-($5.99) Aaron-s/Del Mundo-a/c; Juggernaut and Loki app.	6.00
2-16-($3.99) 2-4-Skurge & Hela app. 5,6-Ward-a; future Doctor Doom app. 7-Tony Moore-a. 8-10,12,13,15,16-Del Mundo-a. 12-14-War of the Realms tie-ins. 16-Wraparound-c	4.00

THOR (Odinson as King Thor)
Marvel Comics: Mar, 2020 - No. 35, Aug, 2023 ($4.99/$3.99)

1-($4.99) Cates-s/Klein-a; Galactus, Silver Surfer and Loki app.	5.00
2-8: 2-6-($3.99) Thor as the Herald to Galactus; Beta Ray Bill app. 4,5-Sif app. 7,8-Kuder-a; intro. Adam Aziz	4.00
9-Donald Blake returns	4.00
10-23,26-30: 10-14-Beta Ray Bill & Sif app. 15-Capt. America app. 17-Angela app.	4.00
24-($8.99) Legacy issue #750; funeral for Odin; art by Klein, Simonson, Coipel, Garbett	9.00
25-($5.99) Hulk vs. Thor; Banner of War; Avengers app.	6.00
31-($4.99) Bonus story with Black Panther	5.00
32-35: 32-34-Doctor Doom app. 35-Leads into Immortal Thor #1	4.00
Annual 1 (9/21, $4.99) Infinite Destinies; Aaron Kuder-a	5.00
Annual 1 (9/23, $4.99) Prelude to Immortal Thor #1; M.O.D.O.K. app.	5.00
...: Lightning and Lament 1 (8/22, $3.99) Nauck-a	4.00
...: The Worthy 1 (2/20, $4.99) Short stories with Beta Ray Bill, Thunderstrike, Sif	5.00

THOR ADAPTATION (MARVEL'S...)
Marvel Comics: Mar, 2012 - No. 2, Apr, 2012 ($2.99, limited series)

1,2-Adaptation of 2012 movie; Gage-s/Medina-a; photo-c	3.00

THOR AND THE WARRIORS FOUR
Marvel Comics: Jun, 2010 - No. 4, Sept, 2010 ($2.99, limited series)

1-4-Thor and Power Pack team-up; Gurihiru-a; back-up with Coover-s/a	3.00

THOR: BLOOD OATH

Marvel Comics: Nov, 2005 - No. 6, Feb, 2006 ($2.99, limited series)

1-6-Oeming-s/Kolins-a/c	3.00
HC (2006, $19.99, dust jacket) r/series; afterword by Oeming	20.00
SC (2006, $14.99) r/series; afterword by Oeming	15.00

THOR CORPS
Marvel Comics: Sept, 1993 - No. 4, Jan, 1994 ($1.75, limited series)

1-4: 1-Invaders cameo. 2-Invaders app. 3-Spider-Man 2099, Rawhide Kid, Two-Gun Kid & Kid Colt app. 4-Painted-c	4.00

THOR: DOUBLE TROUBLE (All ages)
Marvel Comics: May, 2021 - No. 4, Sept, 2021 ($3.99, limited series)

1-4-Tamaki-s/Gurihiru-a; Thor, Loki, Jane Thor and Lady Loki app.	4.00

THOR: FIRST THUNDER
Marvel Comics: Nov, 2010 - No. 5, Mar, 2011 ($3.99, limited series)

1-5: 1-Huat-a; new retelling of origin; reprint of debut in JIM #83	4.00

THOR: FOR ASGARD
Marvel Comics: Nov, 2010 - No. 6, April 2011 ($3.99, limited series)

1-6-Bianchi-a/c. 1-Frost Giants app.	4.00

THOR: GOD OF THUNDER (Marvel NOW!)
Marvel Comics: Jan, 2013 - No. 25, Nov, 2014 ($3.99)

	GD 2.0	VG 4.0	FN 6.0	VF 8.0	VF/NM 9.0	NM- 9.2
1-Aaron-s/Ribic-a thru #5	2	4	6	11	16	20
2-1st Gorr the God Butcher	5	10	15	34	60	85
3-2nd app. Gorr	2	4	6	9	12	15
4-Gorr app.	2	4	6	11	16	20
5-Origin Gorr	4	8	12	23	37	50
6-(3/13) 1st Knull app. in cameo (unnamed)(see Venom #3 [6/18] for 1st full app.)	6	12	18	37	69	100
7,9-24: 6-Guice-a. 13-17-Malekith app. 19-23-Galactus app. 21-1st app. S.H.I.E.L.D. Agent Roz Solomon						4.00
8-1st Goddesses of Thunder	3	6	9	16	23	30
25-($4.99) Art by Guera, Bisley, and Ribic; Malekith app.; new female Thor cameo						5.00

THOR: GODSTORM
Marvel Comics: Nov, 2001 - No. 3, Jan, 2002 ($3.50, limited series)

1-3-Steve Rude-c/a; Busiek-s. 1-Avengers app.	4.00

THOR: HEAVEN & EARTH
Marvel Comics: Sept, 2011 - No. 4, Nov, 2011 ($2.99, limited series)

1-4: 1-Jenkins-s/Olivetti-a; Loki app. 2-Texeira-a/c. 3-Alixe-a. 4-Medina-a	3.00

THORION OF THE NEW ASGODS
Marvel Comics (Amalgam): June, 1997 ($1.95, one-shot)

1-Keith Giffen-s/John Romita Jr.-c/a	4.00

THORS (Secret Wars Battleworld tie-in)
Marvel Comics: Aug, 2015 - No. 4; Jan, 2016 ($3.99, limited series)

1-4: Police squad of Thors on Doomworld; Aaron-s/Sprouse-a. 2,3-Sudzuka-a	4.00

THOR: SON OF ASGARD
Marvel Comics: May, 2004 - No. 12, Mar, 2005 ($2.99, limited series)

1-12: Teenaged Thor, Sif, and Balder; Tocchini-a. 1-6-Granov-c. 7-12-Jo Chen-c	3.00
... Vol. 1: The Warriors Teen (2004, $7.99, digest) r/#1-6	8.00
... Vol. 2: Worthy (2005, $7.99, digest) r/#7-12	8.00

THOR: TALES OF ASGARD BY STAN LEE & JACK KIRBY
Marvel Comics: 2009 - No. 6, 2009 ($3.99, limited series)

1-6-Reprints back-up stories from Journey Into Mystery #97-120; new covers by Coipel	4.00

THOR: THE DEVIANTS SAGA
Marvel Comics: Jan, 2012 - No. 5, May, 2012 ($3.99, limited series)

1-5-Rodi-s/Segovia-a; Ereshkigal app.	4.00

THOR: THE DARK WORLD PRELUDE (MARVEL'S...)
Marvel Comics: Aug, 2013 - No. 2, Aug, 2013 ($2.99, limited series)

1,2-Prelude to 2013 movie; Eaton-a; photo-c	3.00

THOR: THE LEGEND
Marvel Comics: Sept, 1996 ($3.95, one-shot)

nn-Tribute issue	4.00

THOR THE MIGHTY AVENGER
Marvel Comics: Sept, 2010 - No. 8, Mar, 2011 ($2.99, limited series)

1-8-Re-imagining of Thor's origin; Langridge-s/Samnee-a. 1-Mr. Hyde app.	3.00
Free Comic Book Day 2011 (giveaway) Captain America app.	3.00

THOR: VIKINGS

	GD 2.0	VG 4.0	FN 6.0	VF 8.0	VF/NM 9.0	NM- 9.2

Marvel Comics (MAX): Sept, 2003 - No. 5, Jan, 2004 ($3.50, limited series)
1-5-Garth Ennis-s/Glenn Fabry-a/c — 3.50
TPB (2004, $13.99) r/series — 14.00

THOSE MAGNIFICENT MEN IN THEIR FLYING MACHINES (See Movie Comics)

THREE
Image Comics: Oct, 2013 - No. 5, Feb, 2014 ($2.99)
1-5-Spartans 100 years after the Battle of Thermopylae; Ryan Kelly-a/Kieron Gillen-s — 3.00

THREE CABALLEROS (Walt Disney's...)
Dell Publishing Co.: No. 71, 1945
Four Color 71-by Walt Kelly, c/a — 75 · 150 · 225 · 600 · 1350 · 2100

THREE CHIPMUNKS, THE (TV) (Also see Alvin)
Dell Publishing Co.: No. 1042, Oct-Dec, 1959
Four Color 1042 (#1)-(Alvin, Simon & Theodore) — 12 · 24 · 36 · 79 · 170 · 260

THREE COMICS (Also see Spiritman)
The Penny King Co.: 1944 (10¢, 52 pgs.) (2 different covers exist)
1,3,4-Lady Luck, Mr. Mystic, The Spirit app. (3 Spirit sections bound together); Lou Fine-a (Rare) — 47 · 94 · 141 · 296 · 498 · 700
NOTE: No. 1 contains Spirit Sections 4/9/44 - 4/23/44, and No. 4 is also from 4/44.

3-D (NOTE: The prices of all the 3-D comics listed include glasses. Deduct 40-50 percent if glasses are missing, and reduce slightly if glasses are loose.)

3-D ACTION
Atlas Comics (ACI): Jan, 1954 (Oversized, 15¢)(2 pairs of glasses included)
1-Battle Brady; Sol Brodsky-c — 68 · 136 · 204 · 435 · 743 · 1050

3-D ALIEN TERROR
Eclipse Comics: June, 1986 ($2.50)
1-Old Witch, Crypt-Keeper, Vault Keeper cameo; Morrow, John Pound-a, Yeates-c — 1 · 2 · 3 · 5 · 6 · 8
...in 2-D: 100 copies signed, numbered(B&W) — 3 · 9 · 15 · 22 · 28

3-D ANIMAL FUN (See Animal Fun)

3-D BATMAN (Also see Batman 3-D)
National Periodical Publications: 1953 (Reprinted in 1966)
1953-(25¢)-Reprints Batman #42 & 48 (Penguin-c/story); Tommy Tomorrow story; came with pair of 3-D Bat glasses — 126 · 252 · 378 · 806 · 1378 · 1950
1966-Reprints 1953 issue; new cover by Infantino/Anderson; has inside-c photos of Batman & Robin from TV show (50¢) — 23 · 46 · 69 · 164 · 362 · 560

3-D CIRCUS
Fiction House Magazines (Real Adventures Publ.): 1953 (25¢, w/glasses)
1 — 31 · 62 · 93 · 184 · 300 · 415

3-D COMICS (See Mighty Mouse, Tor and Western Fighters)

3-D DOLLY
Harvey Publications: December, 1953 (25¢, came with 2 pairs of glasses)
1-Richie Rich story redrawn from his 1st app. in Little Dot #1; shows cover in 3-D on inside — 27 · 54 · 81 · 158 · 259 · 360

3-D-ELL
Dell Publishing Co.: No. 1, 1953; No. 3, 1953 (3-D comics) (25¢, came w/glasses)
1-Rootie Kazootie (#2 does not exist) — 26 · 52 · 78 · 154 · 252 · 350
3-Flukey Luke — 24 · 48 · 72 · 142 · 234 · 325

3 DEVILS
IDW Publishing: Mar, 2016 - No. 4, Jun, 2016 ($3.99, limited series)
1-4-Bo Hampton-s/a/c — 4.00

3-D EXOTIC BEAUTIES
The 3-D Zone: Nov, 1990 ($2.95, 28 pgs.)
1-L.B. Cole-c — 3 · 6 · 9 · 15 · 22 · 28

3-D FEATURES PRESENTS JET PUP
Dimensions Publications: Oct-Dec (Winter on-c), 1953 (25¢, came w/glasses)
1-Irving Spector-a(2) — 34 · 68 · 102 · 199 · 325 · 450

3-D FUNNY MOVIES
Comic Media: 1953 (25¢, came w/glasses)
1-Bugsey Bear & Paddy Pelican — 37 · 74 · 111 · 222 · 361 · 500

THREE-DIMENSION ADVENTURES (Superman)
National Periodical Publications: 1953 (25¢, large size, came w/glasses)
nn-Origin Superman (new art) — 110 · 220 · 330 · 704 · 1202 · 1700
Reprint (1997) Regular size, bagged with glasses — 1 · 2 · 3 · 5 · 6 · 8

THREE DIMENSIONAL ALIEN WORLDS (See Alien Worlds)
Pacific Comics: July, 1984 (1st Ray Zone 3-D book)(one-shot)
1-Bolton-a(p); Stevens-a(i); Art Adams 1st published-a(p) — 2 · 4 · 6 · 9 · 12 · 15

THREE DIMENSIONAL DNAGENTS (See New DNAgents)

THREE DIMENSIONAL E. C. CLASSICS (Three Dimensional Tales From the Crypt No. 2)
E. C. Comics: Spring, 1954 (Prices include glasses; came with 2 pair)
1-Stories by Wood (Mad #3); Krigstein (W.S. #7), Evans (F.C. #13), & Ingels (CSS #5); Kurtzman-a (rare in high grade due to unstable paper) — 142 · 284 · 426 · 909 · 1555 · 2200
NOTE: Stories redrawn to 3-D format. Original stories not necessarily by artists listed. CSS: Crime SuspenStories; F.C.: Frontline Combat; W.S.: Weird Science.

THREE DIMENSIONAL TALES FROM THE CRYPT (Formerly Three Dimensional E. C. Classics)(Cover title: ...From the Crypt of Terror)
E. C. Comics: Spring, 1954 (Prices include glasses; came with 2 pair)
2-Davis (TFTC #25), Elder (VOH #14), Craig (TFTC #24), & Orlando (TFTC #22) stories; Feldstein-c (rare in high grade) — 129 · 258 · 387 · 826 · 1413 · 2000
NOTE: Stories redrawn to 3-D format. Original stories not necessarily by artists listed. TFTC: Tales From the Crypt; VOH: Vault of Horror.

3-D LOVE
Steriographic Publ. (Mikeross Publ.): Dec, 1953 (25¢, came w/glasses)
1 — 42 · 84 · 126 · 265 · 445 · 625

3-D NOODNICK (See Noodnick)

3-D ROMANCE
Steriographic Publ. (Mikeross Publ.): Jan, 1954 (25¢, came w/glasses)
1 — 39 · 78 · 117 · 240 · 395 · 550

3-D SHEENA, JUNGLE QUEEN (Also see Sheena 3-D)
Fiction House Magazines: 1953 (25¢, came w/glasses)
1-Maurice Whitman-c — 84 · 168 · 252 · 538 · 919 · 1300

3-D SUBSTANCE
The 3-D Zone: July, 1990 ($2.95, 28 pgs.)
1-Ditko-c/a(r) — 5.00

3-D TALES OF THE WEST
Atlas Comics (CPS): Jan, 1954 (Oversized) (15¢, came with 2 pair of glasses)
1 (3-D)-Sol Brodsky-c — 53 · 106 · 159 · 334 · 567 · 800

3-D THREE STOOGES (Also see Three Stooges)
Eclipse Comics: Sept, 1986 - No. 2, Nov, 1986; No. 3, Oct, 1987; No. 4, 1989 ($2.50)
1-4: 3-Maurer-r. 4-r/"Three Missing Links" — 5.00
1-3 (2-D) — 5.00

3-D WHACK (See Whack)

3-D ZONE, THE
The 3-D Zone (Renegade Press)/Ray Zone: Feb, 1987 - No. 20, 1989 ($2.50)
1,3,4,7-9,11,12,14,15,17,19,20: 1-r/A Star Presentation. 3-Picture Scope Jungle Advs. 4-Electric Fear. 7-Hollywood 3-D Jayne Mansfield photo-c. 8-High Seas 3-D. 9-Redmask-r. 11-Danse Macabre; Matt Fox c/a(r). 12-3-D Presidents. 14-Tyranostar. 15-3-Dementia Comics; Kurtzman-c, Kubert, Maurer-a. 17-Thrilling Love. 19-Cracked Classics. 20-Commander Battle and His Atomic Submarine — 1 · 3 · 4 · 6 · 8 · 10
2,5,6,10,13,18: 2-Wolverton-r. 5-Krazy Kat-r. 6-Ratfink. 10-Jet 3-D; Powell & Williamson-r. 13-Flash Gordon. 18-Spacehawk; Wolverton-r — 1 · 2 · 4 · 6 · 8 · 12
16-Space Vixens; Dave Stevens-c/a — 11 · 22 · 33 · 76 · 163 · 250
NOTE: Davis r-19. Ditko r-17. Elder r-19. Everett r-19. Feldstein r-17. Frazetta r-17. Heath r-19. Kamen r-17. Severin r-19. Ward r-17,19. Wolverton r-2,18,19. Wood r-1,17. Photo c-12

3 GEEKS, THE (Also see Geeksville)
3 Finger Prints: 1996 - No. 11, Jun, 1999 (B&W)
1,2 -Rich Koslowski-s/a in all — 1 · 2 · 3 · 5 · 8
1-(2nd printing) — 4.00
3-7, 9-11 — 4.00
8-(48 pgs.) — 5.00
10-Variant-c — 4.00
...48 Page Super-Sized Summer Spectacular (7/04, $4.95) — 5.00
...Full Circle (7/03, $4.95) Origin story of the 3 Geeks; "Buck Rodinski" app. — 5.00
How to Pick Up Girls If You're a Comic Book Geek (color)(7/97) — 4.00
When the Hammer Fallls TPB (2001, $14.95) r/#8-11 — 15.00

3 GEEKS: SLAB MADNESS!
3 Finger Prints: Sept, 2008 - No. 3, Mar, 2009 ($2.99, B&W, limited series)
1-3-Rich Koslowski-s/a; intro. The Cee-Gee-Cee — 3.00

3 GUNS
BOOM! Studios: Aug, 2013 - No. 6, Jan, 2014 ($3.99)
1-6-Steven Grant-s/Emilio Laiso-a — 4.00

300 (Adapted for 2007 movie)
Dark Horse Comics: May, 1998 - No. 5, Sept, 1998 ($2.95/$3.95, limited series)
1-Frank Miller-s/c/a; Spartans vs. Persians war — 3 · 6 · 9 · 18 · 28 · 38
1-Second printing — 5.00
2-4 — 2 · 4 · 6 · 8 · 10 · 12
5-($3.95-c) — 2 · 4 · 6 · 8 · 10 · 12
HC ($30.00) -oversized reprint of series — 30.00

3 LITTLE KITTENS
BroadSword Comics: Aug, 2002 - No. 3, Dec, 2002 ($2.95, limited series)
1-3-Jim Balent-s/a; two covers — 3.00

3 LITTLE PIGS (Disney)(...and the Wonderful Magic Lamp)
Dell Publishing Co.: No. 218, Mar, 1949
Four Color 218 (#1) — 13 · 26 · 39 · 89 · 195 · 300

3 LITTLE PIGS, THE (See Walt Disney Showcase #15 & 21)
Gold Key: May, 1964; No. 2, Sept, 1968 (Walt Disney)
1-Reprints Four Color #218 — 3 · 6 · 9 · 19 · 30 · 40
2 — 3 · 6 · 9 · 15 · 21 · 26

THREE MOUSEKETEERS, THE (1st Series)(See Funny Stuff #1)
National Per. Publ.: 3-4/56 - No. 24, 9-10/59; No. 25, 8-9/60 - No. 26, 10-12/60
1 — 25 · 50 · 75 · 175 · 388 · 600
2 — 12 · 24 · 36 · 79 · 170 · 260
3-5,7,9,10 — 8 · 16 · 24 · 56 · 108 · 160
6,8-Grey tone-c — 10 · 20 · 30 · 69 · 147 · 225
11-26: 24-Cover says 11/59, inside says 9-10/59 — 7 · 14 · 21 · 49 · 92 · 135
NOTE: Rube Grossman a-1-26. Sheldon Mayer a-1-8; c-1-7.

THREE MOUSEKETEERS, THE (2nd Series) (See Super DC Giant)
National Periodical Publications: May-June, 1970 - No. 7, May-June, 1971 (#5-7: 68 pgs.)
1-Mayer-r in all — 6 · 12 · 18 · 40 · 73 · 105
2-4: Doodles Duck begins (1st app.) — 4 · 8 · 12 · 25 · 40 · 55
5-7:(68 pgs.) 5-Dodo & the Frog, Bo Bunny begin — 5 · 10 · 15 · 31 · 53 · 75

THREE MUSKETEERS, THE (Also see Disney's The Three Musketeers)
Gemstone Publishing: 2004 ($3.95, squarebound, one-shot)
nn-Adaptation of the 2004 DVD movie; Petrossi-c/a — 4.00

THREE NURSES (Confidential Diary #12-17; Career Girl Romances #24 on)
Charlton Comics: V3#18, May, 1963 - V3#23, Mar, 1964
V3#18-23 — 5 · 10 · 15 · 30 · 50 · 70

THREE RASCALS

Three #1 © Gillen & Kelly

Threshold #6 © DC

Thrilling Comics #19 © Pines

	GD 2.0	VG 4.0	FN 6.0	VF 8.0	VF/NM 9.0	NM- 9.2

I. W. Enterprises: 1958; 1963

I.W. Reprint #1,2,10: 1-(Says Super Comics on inside)-(M.E.'s Clubhouse Rascals) DeCarlo-a.
#2-(1958). 10-(1963)-r/#1

	3	6	9	14	19	24

THREE RING COMICS
Spotlight Publishers: March, 1945

1-Funny animal

	22	44	66	132	216	300

THREE RING COMICS (Also see Captain Wizard & Meteor Comics)
Century Publications: April, 1946

1-Prankster-c; Captain Wizard, Impossible Man, Race Wilkins, King O'Leary, & Dr. Mercy app.

	45	90	135	271	461	675

THREE ROCKETEERS (See Blast-Off)

THREE STOOGES (See Comic Album #18, Top Comics, The Little Stooges, March of Comics #232, 248, 268, 280, 292, 304, 316, 336, 373, Movie Classics & Comics & 3-D Three Stooges)

THREE STOOGES
Jubilee No. 1/St. John No. 1 (9/53) on: Feb, 1949 - No. 2, May, 1949; Sept, 1953 - No. 7, Oct, 1954

1-(Scarce, 1949)-Kubert-a; infinity-c	206	412	618	1318	2259	3200
2-(Scarce)-Kubert, Maurer-a	116	232	348	742	1271	1800
1(9/53)-Hollywood Stunt Girl by Kubert (7 pgs.)	103	206	309	659	1130	1600
2(3-D, 10/53, 25¢)-Came w/glasses; Stunt Girl story by Kubert	50	150	150	315	533	750
3(3-D, 10/53, 25¢)-Came w/glasses; has 3-D-c	45	90	135	284	480	675
4(3/54)-7(10/54): 4-1st app. Li'l Stooge?	45	90	135	284	480	675

NOTE: All issues have **Kubert-Maurer** art & **Maurer** covers. 6, 7-Partial photo-c.

THREE STOOGES
Dell Publishing Co./Gold Key No. 10 (10/62) on: No. 1043, Oct-Dec, 1959 - No. 55, June, 1972

Four Color 1043 (#1)	23	46	69	161	356	550
Four Color 1078,1127,1170,1187	11	22	33	76	163	250
6(9-11/61) - 10: 6-Professor Putter begins; ends #16	9	18	27	58	114	170
11-14,16,18-20	7	14	21	48	89	130
15-Go Around the World in a Daze (movie scenes)	8	16	24	51	96	140
17-The Little Monsters begin (5/64)(1st app.?)	8	16	24	51	96	140
21,23-30	6	12	18	38	69	100
22-Movie scenes from "The Outlaws Is Coming"	6	12	18	41	76	110
31-55	5	10	15	31	53	75

NOTE: All Four Colors, 6-50, 52-55 have photo-c.

THREE STOOGES IN 3-D, THE
Eternity Comics: 1991 ($3.95, high quality paper, w/glasses)

1-Reprints Three Stooges by Gold Key; photo-c ... 5.00

THREE STOOGES
American Mythology Prods.: 2016 - Present (series of one-shots)

...: April Fools' Day Special (2017, $3.99) Check-s/Fraim brothers-a; 5 covers ... 4.00
...: Astro-Nuts 1 (2019, $3.99, B&W) Check-s/Fraim brothers-a; reprint from FC #1078 ... 4.00
...: Curly Celebration 1 (2022, $3.99) Check-s/Fraim brothers-a; Kuhoric-s ... 4.00
...: Curse of the Frankenstooge (2016, $4.99) Check-s/Fraim brothers-a; reprint from #24; 5 covers ... 5.00
...: Dell 1959 Edition 1 (2019, $3.99) Reprints Four Color #1043 from 1959 ... 4.00
...: Halloween Hullabaloo (2016, giveaway) New stories by various; Ropp-c ... 3.00
...: Halloween Stoogetacular (2017, $3.99) Check-s/Fraim brothers-a; 4 covers ... 4.00
...: Jubilee Reprint (2022, $3.99) Reprints #1 from 1949; Mauer-s/a ... 4.00
...: Matinee Madness (2018, $3.99, B&W) New stories; Wolfer-s/Shanover-a ... 4.00
...: Merry Stoogemas (2016, $3.99) New stories and reprint from #7; 5 covers ... 4.00
...: Monsters & Mayhem (2018, $3.99, B&W) Check-s/Fraim brothers-a; reprint from #2 ... 4.00
...: Red, White, & Stooge (2016, $3.99) New story and reprint from #44; 4 covers ... 4.00
...: Shemptastic Shemptacular (2017, $3.99) Check-s/Fraim brothers-a; reprint from #1; 4 covers ... 4.00
...: Slaptastic Special (2018, $3.99) Check-s/Fraim brothers-a; reprint from #7 ... 4.00
...: Stooge-A-Palooza 1 (2016, $4.99) New stories and reprint from FC #1170; 3 covers ... 5.00
...: The Boys are Back (2016, $3.99) New stories and reprint from FC #1170; 4 covers ... 4.00
...: Thru the Ages (2021, $3.99) Check-s/Fraim brothers-a; 2 covers ... 4.00
...: TV Time Special (2017, $3.99) Check-s/Fraim brothers-a; 4 covers ... 4.00
...: Vs. Cthulhu (2023, $4.99) Goldberg & Rodionoff-a/Tapie-a; 4 covers ... 5.00

3 WORLDS OF GULLIVER
Dell Publishing Co.: No. 1158, July, 1961 (2 issues exist with diff. covers)

Four Color 1158-Movie, photo-c

	6	12	18	42	79	115

THRESHOLD
DC Comics: Mar, 2013 - No. 8 ($3.99)

1-8-Anthology. 1-5-Back-up Larfleeze stories. 5,6-Brainiac app. ... 4.00

THRILL COMICS (See Flash Comics, Fawcett)

THRILLER
DC Comics: Nov, 1983 - No. 12, Nov, 1984 ($1.25, Baxter paper)

1-12: 1-Intro Seven Seconds; Von Eeden-c/a begins. 2-Origin. 5,6-Elvis satire ... 4.00

THRILLING ADVENTURE HOUR, THE
BOOM! Studios: Jul, 2018 - No. 4, Oct, 2018 ($3.99, limited series)

1-4-Acker & Blacker-s/Erickson-a/Case-c ... 4.00

THRILLING ADVENTURE HOUR PRESENTS:...
Image Comics: ($3.50)

... Beyond Belief 1-3 (4/15 - No. 3, 3/16) Acker & Blacker-s/Hester-a ... 3.50
... Sparks Nevada: Marshal on Mars 1-4 (2/15 - No. 4, 7/15) Acker & Blacker-s/Bone-a ... 3.50

THRILLING ADVENTURES IN STAMPS COMICS (Formerly Stamp Comics)
Stamp Comics, Inc. (Very Rare): V1#8, Jan, 1953 (25¢, 100 pgs.)

V1#8-Harrison, Wildey, Kiefer, Napoli-a

	97	194	291	621	1061	1500

THRILLING ADVENTURE STORIES (See Tigerman)
Atlas/Seaboard Publ.: Feb, 1975 - No. 2, Aug, 1975 (B&W, 68 pgs.)

1-Tigerman, Kromag the Killer begin; Heath, Thorne-a; Doc Savage movie photos of Ron Ely	3	6	9	21	33	45
2-Heath, Toth, Severin, Simonson-a; Adams-c	4	8	12	25	40	55

THRILLING COMICS
Better Publ./Nedor/Standard Comics: Feb, 1940 - No. 80, April, 1951

1-Origin & 1st app. Dr. Strange (37 pgs.), ends #?; Nickie Norton of the Secret Service begins	423	846	1269	3088	5444	7800
2-The Rio Kid, The Woman in Red, Pinocchio begins	284	568	852	1818	3109	4400
3-The Ghost & Lone Eagle begin	226	452	678	1446	2473	3500
4-6,8,9: 5-Dr. Strange changed to Doc Strange	187	374	561	1197	2049	2900
7-Classic-c	476	952	1428	3475	6138	8800
10-1st WWII-c (Nazi)(11/40)	206	412	618	1318	2259	3200
18-20	187	374	561	1197	2049	2900
19-Origin & 1st app. The American Crusader (8/41), ends #39,41; Schomburg Nazi WWII-c	252	504	756	1613	2757	3900
21-26,28-30: 24-Intro. Mike, Doc Strange's sidekick (1/42). 29-Last Rio Kid	142	284	426	909	1555	2200
27-Robot-c	181	362	543	1158	1979	2800
31-35,37,39,40: 39-Nazi WWII-c. 40-Japan WWII-c	126	252	378	806	1378	1950
36-Commando Cubs begin (7/43, 1st app.)	135	270	405	864	1482	2100
38-Classic Nazi bondage-c	300	600	900	2010	3605	5400
41-Classic Hitler & Mussolini WWII-c	730	1460	2190	5329	9415	13,500
42-Classic Schomburg Japanese WWII-c	187	374	561	1197	2049	2900
43,46-51: 51(12/45)-Last WWII-c (Japanese)	110	220	330	704	1202	1700
44-Hitler WWII-c by Schomburg	427	854	1281	3117	5509	7900
45-Hitler pict. on-c	161	322	483	1030	1765	2500
52-Classic Schomburg hooded bondage-c; the Ghost ends	119	238	357	762	1306	1850
53,54: 53-The Phantom Detective begins. The Cavalier app. in both; no Commando Cubs in either	77	154	231	493	847	1200
55-The Lone Eagle ends	57	114	171	362	619	875
56 (10/46)-Princess Pantha begins (not on-c), 1st app.	81	162	243	518	884	1250
57-Doc Strange-c; 2nd Princess Pantha	63	126	189	403	689	975
58-66: All Princess Pantha jungle-c, w/Doc Strange #59, his last-c. 61-Ingels-a; The Lone Eagle app. 65-Last Phantom Detective & Commando Cubs. 66-Frazetta text illo	61	122	183	390	670	950
67,70,71-Last jungle-c; Frazetta-a(5-7 pgs.) in each	71	142	213	454	777	1100
68,69-Frazetta-a(2), 8 & 6 pgs.; 9 & 7 pgs.	71	142	213	493	847	1200
72,73: 72-Buck Ranger, Cowboy Detective c/stys begin (western theme), end #80; Frazetta-a(5-7 ps.) in each	50	100	150	315	533	750
74-Last Princess Pantha; Tara app.	37	74	111	222	361	500
75-78: 75-All western format begins	21	42	63	124	202	280
79-Krigstein-a	22	44	66	128	209	290
80-Severin & Elder, Celardo, Moreira-a	22	44	66	128	209	290

NOTE: Bondage c-5, 9, 13, 20, 22, 27-30, 38, 41, 52, 54, 70. Kinstler a-45. **Leo Morey** a-7. **Schomburg** (sometimes signed as **Xela**) c-7, 9-19, 36-80 (airbrush 62-71). **Tuska** a-62, 63. Woman in Red not in #19, 23, 31-33, 39-45. No. 45 exists as a Canadian reprint but numbered #48. No. 72 exists as a Canadian reprint with photo-c. **Frazetta** story. American Crusader c-20-24. Buck Ranger c-72-80. Commando Cubs c-37, 39, 41, 43, 45, 47, 49, 51. Doc Strange c-1-19, 25-36, 38, 40, 42, 44, 46, 48, 50, 52-57, 59. Princess Pantha c-58, 60-71.

THRILLING COMICS (Also see All Star Comics 1999 crossover titles)
DC Comics: May, 1999 ($1.99, one-shot)

1-Golden Age Hawkman and Wildcat; Russ Heath-a ... 4.00

THRILLING CRIME CASES (Formerly 4Most; becomes Shocking Mystery Cases #50 on)
Star Publications: No. 41, June-July, 1950 - No. 49, July, 1952

	GD 2.0	VG 4.0	FN 6.0	VF 8.0	VF/NM 9.0	NM- 9.2

41   47   94   141   296   498   700

42-45: 42-L. B. Cole-c/a (1); Chameleon story (Fox-r)
            40   80   120   246   411   575

46-48: 47-Used in POP, pg. 84
            39   78   117   231   378   525

49-(7/52)-Classic L. B. Cole-c
            394   788   1182   2758   4829   6900

NOTE: *L. B. Cole c-all; 42-45p, 45p, 46p, 49(2 pgs.). Disbrow a-48. Hollingsworth a-48.*

THRILLING ROMANCES
Standard Comics: No. 5, Dec, 1949 - No. 26, June, 1954

5   28   56   84   168   274   380
6,8   17   34   51   100   158   215
7-Severin/Elder-a (7 pgs.)   19   38   57   111   176   240
9,10-Severin/Elder-a; photo-c   19   38   57   109   172   235
11,14-21,26: 14-Gene Tierney & Danny Kaye photo-c from movie "On the Riviera".
   15-Tony Martin/Janet Leigh photo-c   16   32   48   92   144   195
12-Wood-a (2 pgs.); Tyrone Power/ Susan Hayward photo-c
            20   40   60   117   189   260
13-Severin-a   16   32   48   94   147   200
22-25-Toth-a   18   36   54   105   165   225
NOTE: *All photo-c. Celardo a-9, 16. Colletta a-23, 24(2). Toth text illos-19. Tuska a-9.*

THRILLING SCIENCE TALES
AC Comics: 1989 - No. 2 ($3.50, 2/3 color, 52 pgs.)

1,2: 1-r/Bob Colt #6(saucer); Frazetta, Guardineer (Space Ace), Wood, Krenkel, Orlando, Williamson-r; Kaluta-c. 2-Capt. Video-r by Evans, Capt. Science-r by Wood, Star Pirate-r by Whitman & Mysta of the Moon-r by Moreira   5.00

THRILLING TRUE STORY OF THE BASEBALL...
Fawcett Publications: 1952 (Photo-c, each)

...Giants-photo-c; has Willie Mays rookie photo-biography; Willie Mays, Eddie Stanky & others photos on-c   69   138   207   442   759   1075
...Yankees-photo-c; Yogi Berra, Joe DiMaggio, Mickey Mantle & others photos on-c
       77   154   231   493   847   1200

THRILLING WONDER TALES
AC Comics: 1991 ($2.95, B&W)

1-Includes a Bob Powell Thun'da story   4.00

THRILLKILLER
DC Comics: Jan, 1997 - No. 3, Mar, 1997($2.50, limited series)

1-3-Elseworlds Robin & Batgirl; Chaykin-s/Brereton-c/a   4.00
...'62 ('98, $4.95, one-shot) Sequel; Chaykin-s/Brereton-c/a   5.00
TPB-(See Batman: Thrillkiller)

THRILLOGY
Pacific Comics: Jan, 1984 (One-shot, color)

1-Conrad-c/a   4.00

THRILL-O-RAMA
Harvey Publications (Fun Films): Oct, 1965 - No. 3, Dec, 1966

1-Fate (Man in Black) by Powell app.; Doug Wildey-a(2); Simon-c
            5   10   15   33   57   80
2-Pirana begins (see Phantom #46); Williamson 2 pgs.; Fate (Man in Black) app.; Tuska/Simon-c   3   6   9   21   33   45
3-Fate (Man in Black) app.; Sparling-c   3   6   9   18   28   38

THRILLS OF TOMORROW (Formerly Tomb of Terror)
Harvey Publications: No. 17, Oct, 1954 - No. 20, April, 1955

17-Powell-a (horror); r/Witches Tales #7   37   74   111   222   361   500
18-Powell-a (horror); r/Tomb of Terror #1   18   36   54   107   169   230
19,20-Stuntman-c/stories by S&K (r/from Stuntman #1 & 2); 19 has origin & is last pre-code (2/55)   37   74   111   222   361   500
NOTE: *Kirby c-19, 20. Palais a-17. Simon c-18?*

THROBBING LOVE (See Fox Giants)

THROUGH GATES OF SPLENDOR
Spire Christian Comics (Flemming H. Revell Co.): 1973, 1974 (36 pages) (39-49 cents)

nn-1973 Edition   3   6   9   14   19   24
nn-1974 Edition   2   4   6   9   13   16

THULSA DOOM (Robert E. Howard character)
Dynamite Entertainment: 2009 - No. 4, 2009 ($3.50, limited series)

1-4-Alex Ross-c/Lui Antonio-a   3.50

THUMPER (Disney)
Dell Publishing Co.: No. 19, 1942 - No. 243, Sept, 1949

Four Color 19-Walt Disney's...Meets the Seven Dwarfs; reprinted in Silly Symphonies
       54   108   162   432   966   1500
Four Color 243-...Follows His Nose   15   30   45   105   233   360

THUN'DA (...King of the Congo)
Magazine Enterprises: 1952 - No. 6, 1953

1(A-1 #47)-Origin; Frazetta c/a; only comic done entirely by Frazetta; all Thun'da stories, no Cave Girl   300   600   900   2010   3505   5000
2(A-1 #56)-Powell-c/a begins, ends #6; Intro/1st app. Cave Girl in filler strip (also app. in 3-6)
       40   80   120   246   411   575
3(A-1 #73), 4(A-1 #78)   28   56   84   168   274   380
5(A-1 #83), 6(A-1 #86)   29   58   87   172   281   390

THUN'DA
Dynamite Entertainment: 2012 - No. 5, 2012 ($3.99, limited series)

1-5-Napton-s/Richards-a/Jae Lee-c. 1-4-Bonus reprints of Thun'da #1 (1952) Frazetta-a   4.00

THUN'DA TALES (See Frank Frazetta's...)

THUNDER AGENTS (See Noman and Dynamo)
Tower Comics: 11/65 - No. 17, 12/67; No. 18, 9/68, No. 19, 11/68, No. 20, 11/69 (No. 1-16: 68 pgs.; No. 17 on: 52 pgs.)(All are 25¢)

1-Origin & 1st app. Dynamo, Noman, Menthor, & The Thunder Squad; 1st app. The Iron Maiden   20   40   60   140   310   480
2-Death of Egghead; A-bomb blast panel   10   20   30   64   132   200
3-5-Guy Gilbert becomes Lightning who joins Thunder Squad; Iron Maiden app.

6-10: 7-Death of Menthor. 8-Origin & 1st app. The Raven
       7   14   21   49   92   135
11-15: 13-Undersea Agent app.; no Raven story   6   12   18   38   69   100
16-19   5   10   15   35   63   90
       5   10   15   34   60   85
20-Special Collectors Edition; all reprints   4   8   12   27   44   60
...Archives Vol. 1 (DC Comics, 2003, $49.95, HC) r/#1-4, restored and recolored   50.00
...Archives Vol. 2 (DC Comics, 2003, $49.95, HC) r/#5-7, Dynamo #1   50.00
...Archives Vol. 3 (DC Comics, 2003, $49.95, HC) r/#8-10, Dynamo #2   50.00
...Archives Vol. 4 (DC Comics, 2004, $49.95, HC) r/#11, Noman #1,2 & Dynamo #3   50.00
NOTE: *Crandall a-1, 4p, 5p, 18, 20r; c-18. Ditko a-6, 7p, 12p, 13?, 14p, 16, 18. Giunta a-6. Kane a-1, 5p, 6p?, 14, 16p; c-14, 15. Reinman a-13. Sekowsky a-6. Tuska a-1p, 7, 8, 10, 13-17, 19. Whitney a-9p, 10, 13, 15, 17, 18; c-17. Wood a-1-11, 15(w/Ditko-12, 18), (inks-#9, 13, 14, 16, 17), 19, 20r; c-1-8, 9i, 10-13(#10 w/ Williamson(p)), 16.*

T.H.U.N.D.E.R. AGENTS (See Blue Ribbon Comics, Hall of Fame Featuring the..., JCP Features & Wally Wood's...)
JC Comics (Archie Publications): May, 1983 - No. 2, Jan, 1984

1,2: 1-New Manna/Blyberg-a. 2-Blyberg-c   6.00

T.H.U.N.D.E.R. AGENTS
DC Comics: Jan, 2011 - No. 10, Oct, 2011 ($3.99/$2.99)

1-3-($3.99): 1-Spencer-s/Cafu-a/Quitely-c. 3-Chaykin-a (5 pgs.)   4.00
4-10-($2.99): 4-Pérez-a (5 pgs.). 7-10-Grell & Dragotta-a   3.00
1-Variant-c by Darwyn Cooke   8.00

T.H.U.N.D.E.R. AGENTS
DC Comics: Jan, 2012 - No. 6, Jun, 2012 ($2.99, limited series)

1-6-Spencer-s/Craig-a. 1-Andy Kubert-c. 3-Craig & Simonson-a   3.00

T.H.U.N.D.E.R. AGENTS
IDW Publishing: Aug, 2013 - No. 8, Apr, 2014 ($3.99)

1-8: 1-4-Hester-s/Di Vito-a. 1-Four interlocking covers by Di Vito. 5-8-Roger Robinson-a   4.00

THUNDER BIRDS (See Cinema Comics Herald)

THUNDERBOLT (See The Atomic...)

THUNDERBOLT (Peter Cannon...; see Crisis on Infinite Earths, Peter Cannon, Captain Atom and Judomaster)
Charlton Comics: Jan, 1966; No. 51, Mar-Apr, 1966 - No. 60, Nov, 1967

1-Origin & 1st app. Thunderbolt   7   14   21   46   86   125
51-(Formerly Son of Vulcan #50)   4   8   12   25   40   55
52-Judomaster story   3   6   9   16   23   30
53-Captain Atom story, 2 pgs.   3   6   9   16   23   30
54-59: 54-Sentinels begin. 59-Last Thunderbolt & Sentinels (back-up story)
       3   6   9   14   19   24
60-Prankster only app.   3   6   9   15   21   26
57,58 ('77)-Modern Comics-r   1   3   4   6   8   10
NOTE: *Aparo a-60. Morisi a-1, 51-56, 58; c-1, 51-56, 58, 59.*

THUNDERBOLT JAXON (Revival of 1940s British comics character)
DC Comics (WildStorm): Apr, 2006 - No. 5, Sept, 2006 ($2.99, limited series)

1-5-Dave Gibbons-s/John Higgins-a   3.00
TPB (2007, $19.99) r/#1-5; intro. by Gibbons; cover gallery   20.00

THUNDERBOLTS (Title re-named Dark Avengers with #175)(Also see New Thunderbolts and Incredible Hulk #449)
Marvel Comics: Apr, 1997 - No. 81, Sept, 2003; No. 100, May, 2006 - No. 174, Jul, 2012 ($1.95-$2.99)

1-($2.99)-Busiek-s/Bagley-c/a   2   4   6   10   14   18
1-2nd printing; new cover colors   4.00
2-4: 2-Two covers. 4-Intro. Jolt   6.00
5-11: 9-Avengers app.   4.00
12-($2.99)-Avengers and Fantastic Four-c/app.   5.00
13-24: 14-Thunderbolts return to Earth. 21-Hawkeye app.   4.00
25-($2.99) Wraparound-c   5.00
26-38: 26-Manco-a   3.00
39-($2.99) 100 Page Monster; Iron Man reprints   5.00
40-49: 40-Begin $2.25-c; Sandman-c/app. 44-Avengers app. 47-Captain Marvel app.
   49-Zircher-a   3.00
50-($2.99) Last Bagley-a; Captain America becomes leader   4.00
51-74,76,77,80,81: 51,52-Zircher-a; Dr. Doom app. 80,81-Spider-Man app.   4.00
75-($3.50) Hawkeye leaves the team; Garcia-a   4.00
78,79-($2.99-c) Velasco-a begins   4.00
(See New Thunderbolts for #82-99)
100 (5/06, $3.99) resumes from New Thunderbolts #18; back-up origin stories   4.00
101-109: 103-105-Civil War x-over   3.00
110-New team begins including Bullseye, Venom and Norman Osborn; Ellis-s/Deodato-a   4.00
111-136,138-149: 111-121-Ellis-s/Deodato-a. 112-Stan Lee cameo. 123-125-Secret Invasion x-over. 128-Dark Reign begins. 130,131-X-over with Deadpool #8,9. 141-143-Siege   3.00
137-(12/09, $3.99) Iron Fist and Luke Cage app.   4.00
150-(1/11, $4.99) Thunderbolts vs. Avengers; r/#1; storyline synopsis of #1-150   5.00
151-158,160-163, 163.1, 164-174-($2.99) 151-153-Land-c. 155-Satana joins. 158-162-Fear Itself tie-in. 163-165-Thunderbolts in WWII; Invaders app.   3.00
159-($4.99) Fear Itself tie-in/ Juggernaut app.; short stories of escape from The Raft   5.00
Annual '97 ($2.99)-Wraparound-c   5.00
Annual 2000 ($3.50) Breyfogle-a   4.00
...: Breaking Point (1/08, $2.99, one-shot) Gage-s/Denham-a/Djurdjevic-c   3.00
...: By Warren Ellis Vol. 1 HC (2007, $24.99, dustjacket) r/#110-154, ...: Desperate Measures and stories from Civil War: Choosing Sides and The Initiative   25.00
...: By Warren Ellis Vol. 1: Faith in Monsters SC (2008, $19.99) same contents as HC   20.00
Civil War: Thunderbolts TPB (2007, $13.99) r/#101-105   14.00
...: Desperate Measures (9/07, $2.99, one-shot) Jenkins-s/Steve Lieber-a   3.00
...: Distant Rumblings (#1-) (7/97, $1.95) Busiek-s   5.00
First Strikes (1997, $4.99,TPB) r/#1,2   5.00
...: From the Marvel Vault (6/11, $3.99) Jack Monroe app.; Nicieza-s/Aucoin-a   4.00
...: Guardian Protocols (2007, $10.99) r/#106-109   11.00
...: International Incident (4/08, $2.99, one-shot) Gage-s/Oliver-a/Djurdjevic-c   3.00
...: Life Sentences (7/01, $3.50) Adlard-a   4.00
...: Marvel's Most Wanted TPB ('98, $16.99) r/origin stories of original Masters of Evil   17.00

Thun'da #3 © ME

Thunderbolts (2014 series) #27 © MAR

The Tick #101 © Ben Edlund

	GD	VG	FN	VF	VF/NM	NM-
	2.0	4.0	6.0	8.0	9.0	9.2

...: Reason in Madness (7/08, $2.99, one-shot) Gage-s/Oliver-a/Djurdjevic-c — 3.00
Wizard #0 (bagged with Wizard #89) — 3.00

THUNDERBOLTS (Marvel NOW!)
Marvel Comics: Feb, 2013 - No. 32, Dec, 2014 ($2.99)
1-32: 1-Punisher, Red Hulk, Elektra, Venom & Deadpool team; Dillon-a. 7-11-Noto-a. — 3.00
14-18-Infinity tie-ins; Soule-s/Palo-a. 20-Ghost Rider joins — 5.00
Annual 1 (2/14, $4.99) Dr. Strange & Elsa Bloodstone app.; Lolli-a

THUNDERBOLTS
Marvel Comics: Jul, 2016 - No. 12, Jun, 2017 ($3.99)
1-9,11,12: 1-Bucky Barnes leads the team of Kobik, Atlas, Fixer, Moonstone, & Mach-X. — 4.00
4-Squadron Supreme app. 5-Spider-Man (Miles) app. 11,12-Secret Empire tie-ins
10-($4.99) 20th Anniversary Special; prologue by Busiek-s/Bagley-a; Jolt returns — 5.00

THUNDERBOLTS
Marvel Comics: Oct, 2022 - No. 5, Feb, 2023 ($4.99/$3.99)
1-($4.99) Jim Zub-s/Sean Izaaksa-a; Hawkeye, America Chavez, John Walker app. — 5.00
2-5-($3.99) Kingpin & White Widow app. 3-Shang-Chi app. — 4.00
...: Marvel Tales 1 (10/22, $7.99) r/Thunderbolts (1997) #1,2, Inc. Hulk #449 — 8.00

THUNDERBOLTS
Marvel Comics: Feb, 2024 - Present ($4.99/$3.99)
1-($4.99) Lanzing & Kelly-s/Borges-a; Bucky Barnes, Red Guardian, Red Skull app. — 5.00
2,3-($3.99) 2-Kingpin & White Widow app. 3-Shang-Chi app. — 4.00

THUNDERBOLTS PRESENTS: ZEMO - BORN BETTER
Marvel Comics: Apr, 2007 - No. 4, July, 2007 ($2.99, limited series)
1-4-Origin of Baron Zemo; Nicieza-s/Grummett-a/c — 3.00
TPB (2007, $10.99) r/#1-4 — 11.00

THUNDERBUNNY (See Blue Ribbon Comics #13, Charlton Bullseye & Pep Comics #393)
Red Circle Comics: Jan, 1984 (Direct sale only)
WaRP Graphics: Second series No. 1, 1985 - No. 6, 1985
Apple Comics: No. 7, 1986 - No. 12, 1987
1-Humor/parody; origin Thunderbunny; 2 page pin-up by Anderson — 5.00
(2nd series) 1,2-Magazine size — 4.00
3-12-Comic size — 4.00

THUNDERCATS (TV)
Marvel Comics (Star Comics)/Marvel #22 on: Dec, 1985 - No. 24, June, 1988 (75¢)

	GD	VG	FN	VF	VF/NM	NM-
1-Mooney-c/a begins	8	16	24	51	96	140
2-(65¢ & 75¢ cover exists)	2	4	6	11	16	20
3-20: 12-Begin $1.00-c. 18-20-Williamson-i	2	4	6	8	10	12
21-24: 23-Williamson-c(i)	2	4	6	8	11	14

THUNDERCATS (TV)
DC Comics (WildStorm): No. 0, Oct, 2002 - No. 5, Feb, 2003 ($2.50/$2.95, limited series)
0-($2.50) J. Scott Campbell-c/a — 4.00
1-5-($2.95) 1-McGuinness-a/c; variant cover by Art Adams; rebirth of Mumm-Ra — 4.00
.../ Battle of the Planets (7/03, $4.95) Kaare Andrews-s/a; 2 covers by Campbell & Ross — 5.00
...: Origins-Heroes & Villains (2/04, $3.50) short stories by various — 3.50
...Reclaiming Thundera TPB (2003, $12.95) r/#0-5 — 13.00
... Sourcebook (1/03, $2.95) pin-ups and info on characters; art by various; A. Adams-c — 4.00

THUNDERCATS: DOGS OF WAR
DC Comics (WildStorm): Aug, 2003 - No. 5, Dec, 2003 ($2.95, limited series)
1-5: 1-Two covers by Booth & Pearson; Booth-a/Layman-s. 2-4-Two covers — 3.00
TPB (2004, $14.95) r/#1-5 — 15.00

THUNDERCATS: ENEMY'S PRIDE
DC Comics (WildStorm): Aug, 2004 - No. 5 ($2.95, limited series)
1-5-Vriens-s/Layman-s — 3.00
TPB (2005, $14.99) r/#1-5 — 15.00

THUNDERCATS: HAMMERHAND'S REVENGE
DC Comics (WildStorm): Dec, 2003 - No. 5, Apr, 2004 ($2.95, limited series)
1-5-Avery-s/D'Anda-a. 2-Variant-c by Warren — 3.00
TPB (2004, $14.95) r/#1-5 — 15.00

THUNDERCATS: THE RETURN
DC Comics (WildStorm): Apr, 2003 - No. 5, Aug, 2003 ($2.95, limited series)
1-5: 1-Two covers by Benes & Cassaday; Gilmore-s — 3.00
TPB (2004, $12.95) r/series — 13.00

THUNDERCATS VOLUME 1
Dynamite Entertainment: 2024 - Present ($4.99)
1-Declan Shalvey-s/Drew Moss-a; multiple covers — 5.00

THUNDER MOUNTAIN (See Zane Grey, Four Color #246)

THUNDERSTRIKE (See Thor #459)
Marvel Comics: June, 1993 - No. 24, July, 1995 ($1.25)
1-($2.95, 52 pgs.)-Holo-grafx lightning patterned foil-c; Bloodaxe returns — 5.00
2-24: 2-Juggernaut-c/s. 4-Capt. America app. 4-6-Spider-Man app. 8-bound-in trading card
sheet. 18-Bloodaxe app. 24-Death of Thunderstrike — 4.00
Marvel Double Feature...Thunderstrike/Code Blue #13 ($2.50)-Same as
Thunderstrike #13 w/Code Blue flip book — 5.00

THUNDERSTRIKE
Marvel Comics: Jan, 2011 - No. 5, Jun, 2011 ($3.99, limited series)
1-5-DeFalco-s/Frenz-a. 1-Back-up origin retold; Nauck-a — 4.00

TICK, THE (Also see The Chroma-Tick)
New England Comics Press: June, 1988 - No. 12, May, 1993
($1.75/$1.95/$2.25; B&W, over-sized)

	GD	VG	FN	VF	VF/NM	NM-
Special Edition 1-1st comic book app. serially numbered & limited to 5,000 copies						
	12	24	36	80	173	265
Special Edition 1-(5/96, $5.95)-Double-c; foil-c; serially numbered (5,001 thru 14,000)						
& limited to 9,000 copies	3	6	9	16	23	30
Special Edition 2-Serially numbered and limited to 3000 copies						
	5	10	15	35	63	90
Special Edition 2-(8/96, $5.95)-Double-c; foil-c; serially numbered (5,001 thru 14,000)						
& limited to 9,000 copies	1	2	3	5	6	8
1-Regular Edition 1st printing; reprints Special Ed. 1 w/minor changes						
	7	14	21	46	86	125
1-2nd printing	1	3	4	6	8	10
1-3rd-5th printing						5.00
2-Reprints Special Ed. 2 w/minor changes	3	6	9	16	23	30
2-8-All reprints						4.00
3-5: 4-1st app. Paul the Samurai	2	4	6	8	10	12
6,8 ($2.25)						6.00
7-1st app. Man-Eating Cow	1	3	4	6	7	10
8-Variant with no logo, price, issue number or company logos.						
	3	6	9	17	26	35
9-12 ($2.75)						5.00
12-Special Edition; card-stock, virgin foil-c; numbered edition						
	3	6	9	14	19	24
100: The Tick Meets Invincible (6/12, $6.99) Invincible travels to Tick's universe						7.00
101: The Tick Meets Madman (11/12, $6.99) Bonus publishing history of the Tick						7.00
Pseudo-Tick #13 (11/00, $3.50) Continues story from #12 (1993)						5.00
Promo Sampler-(1990)-Tick-c/story	1	2	3	5	6	8

TICK, THE (One shots)
... Big Back to School Special 1-(10/98, $3.50, B&W) Tick & Arthur undercover in H.S. — 4.00
... Big Cruise Ship Vacation Special 1-(9/00, $3.50, B&W) — 4.00
... Big Father's Day Special 1-(6/00, $3.50, B&W) — 4.00
... Big Halloween Special 1-(10/99, $3.50, B&W) — 4.00
... Big Halloween Special 2000 (10/00, $3.50) — 4.00
... Big Halloween Special 2001 (9/01, $3.95) — 4.00
... Big Mother's Day Special 1-(4/00, $3.50, B&W) — 4.00
... Big Red-N-Green Christmas Spectacle 1-(12/01, $3.95) — 4.00
... Big Romantic Adventure 1-(2/98, $2.95, B&W) Candy box-c with candy map on back — 4.00
... Big Summer Annual 1-(7/99, $3.50, B&W) Chainsaw Vigilante vs. Barry — 4.00
... Big Summer Fun Special 1-(8/98, $3.50, B&W) Tick and Arthur at summer camp — 4.00
... Big Tax Time Terror 1-(4/00, $3.50, B&W) — 4.00
... Big Year 2000 Spectacle 1-(3/00, $3.50, B&W) — 4.00
FCBD Special Edition (5/10) - reprints debut from 1988; Ben Edlund-s/a — 3.00
Free Comic Book Day 2013 (6/13) - New stories; McClelland-s/Redhead-a — 3.00
Free Comic Book Day 2014 (6/14) - New stories; McClelland-s/Redhead-a — 3.00
Free Comic Book Day 2015 (6/15) - New stories; McClelland-s/Redhead-a — 3.00
Free Comic Book Day 2016 (6/16) - New stories; McClelland-s/Redhead-a; Nichols-a — 3.00
Free Comic Book Day 2017 (6/17) - New stories; McClelland-s/Redhead-a — 3.00
Free Comic Book Day 2018 (6/18) - New stories; McClelland-s/Nichols-a — 3.00
Free Comic Book Day 2019 (6/19) - New stories; Nichols-s/a — 3.00
...: Halloween Comicfest 2017 (11/17, giveaway) r/#1 (1988) in color — 3.00
... Incredible Internet Comic 1-(7/01, $3.95, color) r/New England Comics website story — 4.00
Introducing the Tick 1-(4/02, $3.95, color) summary of Tick's life and adventures — 4.00
The Tick's Back #0 -(8/97, $3.50, B&W) — 4.00
The Tick's Comic Con Extravaganza-(6/07, $3.95, color) Wang-c — 4.00
The Tick's 20th Anniversary Special Edition #1 (5/07, $2.95, B&W) short stories by various;
history of the character; creator profiles; 2 covers by Suydam & Bisley — 6.00

--MASSIVE SUMMER DOUBLE SPECTACLE
1,2-(7,8/00, $3.50, B&W) — 5.00

TICK & ARTIE
1-(6/02, $3.50, color) prints strips from Internet comic — 4.00

	GD 2.0	VG 4.0	FN 6.0	VF 8.0	VF/NM 9.0	NM- 9.2

2-(10/02, $3.95) — 4.00

TICK AND ARTHUR, THE
New England Comics: Feb, 1999 - No. 6 ($3.50, B&W)

1-6-Sean Wang-s/a — 4.00

TICK BIG BLUE DESTINY, THE
New England Comics: Oct, 1997 - No. 9 ($2.95)

1-4: 1-"Keen" Ed. 2-Two covers — 4.00
1-($4.95) "Wicked Keen" Ed. w/die cut-c — 5.00
5-($3.50) — 4.00
6-Luny Bin Trilogy Preview #0 (7/98, $1.50) — 4.00
7-9: 7-Luny Bin Trilogy begins — 4.00

TICK BIG BLUE YULE LOG SPECIAL, THE
New England Comics: Dec, 1997; 1999 ($2.95, B&W)

1-"Jolly" and "Traditional" covers; flip book w/"Arthur Teaches the Tick About Hanukkah"
...1999 ($3.50) — 4.00 / 5.00
Tick Big Yule Log Special 2001-(12/00, $3.50, B&W) — 5.00

TICK, THE : CIRCUS MAXIMUS
New England Comics: Mar, 2000 - No. 4, Jun, 2000 ($3.50, B&W)

1-4-Encyclopedia of characters from Tick comics — 4.00
Giant No. 1 (8/03, $14.95) r/#1-4, Redux — 15.00
Redux No. 1 (4/01, $3.50) — 4.00

TICK, THE - COLOR
New England Comics: Jan, 2001 - No. 6 ($3.95)

1-6: 1-Marc Sandroni-a — 4.00

TICK, THE : DAYS OF DRAMA
New England Comics: July, 2005 - No. 6, June, 2006 ($4.95/$3.95, limited series)

1-($4.95) Dave Garcia-a; has a mini-comic attached to cover — 5.00
2-6-($3.95) — 4.00

TICK, THE - HEROES OF THE CITY
New England Comics: Feb, 1999 - No. 6 ($3.50, B&W)

1-6-Short stories by various — 4.00

TICK KARMA TORNADO (The…)
New England Comics Press: Oct, 1993 - No. 9, Mar, 1995 ($2.75, B&W)

1-($3.25) — 5.00
2-9: 2-$2.75-c begins — 4.00

TICK NEW SERIES (The…)
New England Comics: Dec, 2009 - No. 8 ($4.95)

1-8 — 5.00

TICK'S BIG XMAS TRILOGY, THE
New England Comics: Dec, 2002 - No. 3, Dec, 2002 ($3.95, limited series)

1-3 — 4.00

TICK'S GOLDEN AGE COMIC, THE
New England Comics: May, 2002 - No. 3, Feb, 2003 ($4.95, Golden Age size)

1-3-Facsimile 1940s-style Tick issue; 2 covers — 5.00
Giant Edition TPB (9/03, $12.95) r/#1-3 — 13.00

TICK'S GIANT CIRCUS OF THE MIGHTY, THE
New England Comics: Summer, 1992 - No. 3, Fall, 1993 ($2.75, B&W, magazine size)

1-(A-O). 2-(P-Z). 3-1993 Update — 5.00

TICK 2017, THE
New England Comics: Sept, 2017 - No. 4, Jun, 2018 ($3.99)

1-4: 1-Bunn & JimmyZ-s/Paszkiewicz-a — 4.00

TICKLE COMICS (Also see Gay, Smile, & Whee Comics)
Modern Store Publ.: 1955 (7¢, 5x7-1/4", 52 pgs)

| 1 | 11 | 22 | 33 | 62 | 86 | 110 |

TICK TOCK TALES
Magazine Enterprises: Jan, 1946 - V3#33, Jan-Feb, 1951

1-Koko & Kola begin	28	56	84	168	274	380
2	15	30	45	85	130	175
3-10	14	28	42	76	108	140
11-33: 19-Flag-c. 23-Muggsy Mouse, The Pixies & Tom-Tom the Jungle Boy app.						
24-X-mas-c. 25-The Pixies & Tom-Tom app.	12	24	36	69	97	125

TIGER (Also see Comics Reading Libraries in the Promotional Comics section)
Charlton Press (King Features): Mar, 1970 - No. 6, Jan, 1971 (15¢)

| 1 | 3 | 6 | 9 | 14 | 20 | 26 |
| 2-6: 3-Ad for life-size inflatable doll | 2 | 4 | 6 | 8 | 11 | 14 |

TIGER BOY (See Unearthly Spectaculars)

TIGER DIVISION
Marvel Comics: Jan, 2023 - No. 5, May, 2023 ($3.99)

1-5-Emily Kim-s/Creees Lee-a — 4.00

TIGER GIRL
Gold Key: Sept, 1968 (15¢)

1(10227-809)-Sparling-c/a; Jerry Siegel scripts; advertising on back-c
| | 5 | 10 | 15 | 35 | 63 | 90 |
| 1-Variant edition with pin-up on back cover | 6 | 12 | 18 | 41 | 76 | 110 |

TIGERMAN (Also see Thrilling Adventure Stories)
Seaboard Periodicals (Atlas): Apr, 1975 - No. 3, Sept, 1975 (All 25¢ issues)

| 1-3: 1-Origin; Ernie Colón-c. 2,3-Ditko-p in each | 2 | 4 | 6 | 11 | 16 | 20 |

TIGER WALKS, A (See Movie Comics)

TIGRA (The Avengers)
Marvel Comics: May, 2002 - No. 4, Aug, 2002 ($2.99, limited series)

1-4-Christina Z-s/Deodato-c/a — 3.00

TIGRESS, THE
Hero Graphics: Aug, 1992 - No. 6?, June, 1993 ($3.95/$2.95, B&W)

1,6: 1-Tigress vs. Flare. 6-44 pgs. — 5.00
2-5: 2-$2.95-c begins — 4.00

TILLIE THE TOILER (See Comic Monthly)
Dell Publishing Co.: No. 15, 1941 - No. 237, July, 1949

Four Color 15(1941)	81	162	243	518	884	1250
Large Feature Comic 30(1941)	47	94	141	296	498	700
Four Color 8(1942)	29	58	87	209	467	725
Four Color 22(1943)	20	40	60	138	307	475
Four Color 55(1944), 89(1945)	14	28	42	96	211	325
Four Color 106('45),132('46): 132-New stories begin	10	20	30	70	150	230
Four Color 150,176,184	10	20	30	66	138	210
Four Color 195,213,237	9	18	27	57	111	165

TIMBER WOLF (See Action Comics #372, & Legion of Super-Heroes)
DC Comics: Nov, 1992 - No. 5, Mar, 1993 ($1.25, limited series)

1-5 — 4.00

TIM DRAKE: ROBIN (Also see DC Pride: Tim Drake Special)
DC Comics: Nov, 2022 - No. 10, Aug, 2023 ($3.99)

1-10: 1-Fitzmartin-s/Rossmo-a; Darcy Thomas app. 8-Batwoman app. — 4.00

TIME BANDITS
Marvel Comics Group: Feb, 1982 (one-shot, Giant)

1-Movie adaptation — 4.00

TIME BEAVERS (See First Comics Graphic Novel #2)

TIME BEFORE TIME
Image Comics: May, 2021 - No. 29, Nov, 2023 ($3.99)

1-29-Declan Shalvey & Rory McConville-s/Joe Palmer-a. 6-Shalvey-a — 4.00

TIME BOMB
Radical Comics: Jul, 2010 - No. 3, Dec, 2010 ($4.99, limited series)

1-3-Palmiotti & Gray-s/Gulacy-a/c — 5.00

TIMECOP (Movie)
Dark Horse Comics: Sept, 1994 - No. 2, Nov, 1994 ($2.50, limited series)

1,2-Adaptation of film — 4.00

TIME FOR LOVE (Formerly Romantic Secrets)
Charlton Comics: V2#53, Oct, 1966; Oct, 1967 - No. 47, May, 1976

V2#53(10/66) Herman-s Hermits app.	4	8	12	23	37	50
1-(10/67)	4	8	12	25	40	55
2-(12/67) -10	3	6	9	15	21	26
11,12,14-20	2	4	6	11	16	20
13-(11/69) Ditko-a (7 pgs.)	3	6	9	16	23	30
21-27	2	4	6	9	13	16
28,29,31: 28-Shirley Jones poster. 29-Bobby Sherman pin-up. 31-Bobby Sherman pin-up						
	2	4	6	11	16	20
30-(10/72)-David Cassidy full page poster	3	6	9	16	24	32
32-47	2	4	6	8	11	14

TIMELESS
Marvel Comics: Feb, 2022 ($5.99, one-shot)

1-Spotlight on Kang the Conqueror; MacKay-s/Walker, Land & Bagley-a — 6.00

TIMELESS
Marvel Comics: Feb, 2023 ($5.99, one-shot)

1-Kang in search of the Missing Moment; MacKay-s/Land, Zircher & Larroca-a — 6.00

TIMELESS
Marvel Comics: Feb, 2024 ($6.99, one-shot)

1-Luke Cage in the future vs. The Immortal Moon Knight; Lanzing & Kelly-s/Cabal-a — 7.00

TIMELESS TOPIX (See Topix)

TIMELY COMICS... (Reprints of recent Marvel issues)
Marvel Comics: Aug, 2016 ($3.00)

...: All-New, All-Different Avengers (8/16) r/#1-3; Alex Ross-c — 3.00
...: All-New Inhumans (8/16) r/#1-3; Caselli-c — 3.00
...: Carnage (8/16) r/#1-3; Del Mundo-c — 3.00
...: Daredevil (8/16) r/#1-3; Garney-c — 3.00
...: Doctor Strange (8/16) r/#1-3; Bachalo-c — 3.00
...: Drax (8/16) r/#1-3; Hepburn-c — 3.00
...: Invincible Iron Man (8/16) r/#1-3; Marquez-c — 3.00
...: Moon Girl and Devil Dinosaur (8/16) r/#1-3; Reeder-c — 3.00
...: New Avengers (8/16) r/#1-3; Sandoval-c — 3.00
...: Scarlet Witch (8/16) r/#1-3; Aja-c — 3.00
...: Squadron Supreme (8/16) r/#1-3; Alex Ross-c — 3.00
...: The Totally Awesome Hulk (8/16) r/#1-3; Cho-c — 3.00
...: Ultimates (8/16) r/#1-3; Rocafort-c — 3.00
...: Uncanny Inhumans (8/16) r/#1-3; McNiven-c — 3.00
...: Venom: Space Knight (8/16) r/#1-3; Olivetti-c — 3.00
...: Web Warriors (8/16) r/#1-3; Tedesco-c — 3.00

TIMELY PRESENTS: ALL WINNERS
Marvel Comics: Dec, 1999 ($3.99)

1-Reprints All Winners Comics #19 (Fall 1946); new Lago-c — 5.00

TIMELY PRESENTS: HUMAN TORCH
Marvel Comics: Feb, 1999 ($3.99)

1-Reprints Human Torch Comics #5 (Fall 1941); new Lago-c — 5.00

TIME MACHINE, THE
Dell Publishing Co.: No. 1085, Mar, 1960 (H.G. Wells)

Four Color 1085-Movie, Alex Toth-a; Rod Taylor photo-c
| | 18 | 36 | 54 | 124 | 275 | 425 |

TIME MASTERS
DC Comics: Feb, 1990 - No. 8, Sept, 1990 ($1.75, mini-series)

1-8: New Rip Hunter series. 5-Cave Carson, Viking Prince app. 6-Dr. Fate app. — 4.00
TPB (2008, $19.99) r/#1-8 and Secret Origins #43; intro. by Geoff Johns — 20.00

Tillie the Toiler FC #176 © DELL

Time Tunnel #1 © 20Fox

Tiny Titans #4 © DC

	GD	VG	FN	VF	VF/NM	NM-
	2.0	4.0	6.0	8.0	9.0	9.2

TIME MASTERS: VANISHING POINT (Tie-in to Batman: The Return of Bruce Wayne)
DC Comics: Sept, 2010 - No. 6, Feb, 2011 ($3.99, limited series)

1-6-Jurgens-s/a/c; Rip Hunter, Superman, Green Lantern & Booster Gold app.						4.00
TPB (2011, $14.99) r/#1-6						15.00

TIMESLIP COLLECTION
Marvel Comics: Nov, 1998 ($2.99, one-shot)

1-Pin-ups reprinted from Marvel Vision magazine						4.00

TIMESLIP SPECIAL (The Coming of the Avengers)
Marvel Comics: Oct, 1998 ($5.99, one-shot)

1-Alternate world Avengers vs. Odin						6.00

TIMESTORM 2009/2099
Marvel Comics: June, 2009 - No. 4, Oct, 2009 ($3.99, limited series)

1-4-Punisher 2099 transports Spider-Man to 2099; Wolverine app.; Battle-a						4.00
...: Spider-Man One Shot (8/09, $3.99) Reed-s/Craig-a/Renaud-c						4.00
...: X-Men One Shot (8/09, $3.99) Reed-s/Irving-a/Renaud-c						4.00

TIME TO RUN (Based on 1973 Billy Graham movie)
Spire Christian Comics (Fleming H. Revell Co.): 1975 (39¢)

nn-By Al Hartley	2	4	6	13	18	22

TIME TUNNEL, THE (TV)
Gold Key: Feb, 1967 - No. 2, July, 1967 (12¢)

1-Photo back-c on both issues	8	16	24	54	102	150
2	5	10	15	33	57	80

TIME TWISTERS
Quality Comics: Sept, 1987 - No. 21, 1989 ($1.25/$1.50)

1-21: Alan Moore scripts in 1-4, 6-9, 14 (2 pg.). 14-Bolland-a (2 pg.). 15,16-Guice-c						4.00

TIME 2: THE EPIPHANY (See First Comics Graphic Novel #9)

TIMEWALKER (Also see Archer & Armstrong)
Valiant: Jan, 1994 - No. 15, Oct, 1995 ($2.50)

1-15,0(3/96): 2-"JAN" on-c, February, 1995 in indicia.						4.00
Yearbook 1 (5/95, $2.95)						4.00

TIME WARP (See The Unexpected #210)
DC Comics, Inc.: Oct-Nov, 1979 - No. 5, June-July, 1980 ($1.00, 68 pgs.)

1	2	4	6	13	18	22
2-5	2	4	6	8	11	14

NOTE: *Aparo a-1. Buckler a-1p. Chaykin a-2. Ditko a-1-4. Kaluta c-1-5. G. Kane a-2. Nasser a-4. Newton a-1-5p. Orlando a-2. Sutton a-1-3.*

TIME WARP
DC Comics (Vertigo): May, 2013 ($7.99, one-shot)

1-Short story anthology by various incl. Lindelof, Simone; covers by Risso & Jae Lee						8.00

TIME WARRIORS: THE BEGINNING
Fantasy General Comics: 1986 (Aug) - No. 2, 1986? ($1.50)

1,2-Alpha Track/Skellon Empire						4.00

TIM HOLT (Movie star) (Becomes Red Mask #42 on; also see Crack Western #72, & Great Western)
Magazine Enterprises: 1948 - No. 41, April-May, 1954 (All 36 pgs.)

1-(A-1 #14)-Line drawn-c w/Tim Holt photo on-c; Tim Holt, His horse Lightning & sidekick Chito begin	55	110	165	352	601	850
2-(A-1 #17)(9-10/48)-Photo-c begin, end #18	28	56	84	168	274	380
3-(A-1 #19)-Photo back-c	21	42	63	122	199	275
4(1-2/49),5: 5-Photo front/back-c	15	30	45	88	137	185
6-(5/49)-1st app. The Calico Kid (alias Rex Fury), his horse Ebony & Sidekick Sing-Song (begin series); photo back-c	30	60	90	177	289	400
7-10: 7-Calico Kid by Ayers. 8-Calico Kid by Guardineer (r-in/Great Western #10). 9-Map of Tim's Home Range	30	60	90	177	289	400
	30	45	85	130		175
11-The Calico Kid becomes The Ghost Rider (origin & 1st app.) by Dick Ayers (r-in/Great Western I.W. #8); his horse Spectre & sidekick Sing-Song begin series	194	388	582	1242	2121	3000
12-16,18-Last photo-c	14	28	42	81	118	155
17-Frazetta Ghost Rider-c	168	336	504	1075	1838	2600
19,22,24: 19-Last Tim Holt-c; Bolle line-drawn-c begin; Tim Holt photo on covers #19-28, 30-41. 22-interior photo-c	14	28	42	76	108	140
20-Tim Holt becomes Redmask (origin); begin series; Redmask #20-on	19	38	57	111	176	240
21-Frazetta Ghost Rider/Redmask-c	53	106	159	334	567	800
23-Frazetta Redmask-c	37	74	111	222	361	500
25-1st app. Black Phantom	24	48	72	142	234	325
26-30: 28-Wild Bill Hickok, Bat Masterson team up with Redmask. 29-B&W photo-c						

	13	26	39	72	101	130
31-33-Ghost Rider ends	11	22	33	62	86	110
34-Tales of the Ghost Rider begins (horror)-Classic "The Flower Women" & "Hard Boiled Harry!"	17	34	51	100	158	215
35-Last Tales of the Ghost Rider	14	28	42	76	108	140
36-The Ghost Rider returns, ends #41; liquid hallucinogenic drug story	16	32	48	94	147	200
37-Ghost Rider classic "To Touch Is to Die!", about Inca treasure	16	32	48	94	147	200
38-The Black Phantom begins (not in #39); classic Ghost Rider "The Phantom Guns of Feather Gap!"	16	32	48	94	147	200
39-41: All 3-D effect c/stories	18	36	54	107	169	230

NOTE: *Dick Ayers a-7, 9-41. Bolle a-1-41; c-19, 20, 22, 24-28, 30-41.*

TIM McCOY (Formerly Zoo Funnies; Pictorial Love Stories #22 on)
Charlton Comics: No. 16, Oct, 1948 - No. 21, Aug, 1949 (Western Movie Stories)

16-John Wayne, Montgomery Clift app. in "Red River"	39	78	117	236	388	540
17-21: 17-Allan "Rocky" Lane guest stars. 18-Rod Cameron guest stars. 19-Whip Wilson, Andy Clyde guest star; Jesse James story. 20-Jimmy Wakely guest stars. 21-Johnny Mack Brown guest stars	30	60	90	177	289	400

TIMMY
Dell Publishing Co.: No. 715, Aug, 1956 - No. 1022, Aug-Oct, 1959

Four Color 715 (#1)	6	12	18	41	76	110
Four Color 823 (8/57), 923 (8/58), 1022	5	10	15	34	60	85

TIMMY THE TIMID GHOST (Formerly Win-A-Prize?; see Blue Bird)
Charlton Comics: No. 3, 2/56 - No. 44, 10/64; No. 45, 9/66; 10/67 - No. 23, 7/71; V4#24, 9/85 - No. 26, 1/86

3(1956) (1st Series)	15	30	45	90	140	190
4,5	10	20	30	54	72	90
6-10	3	6	9	21	33	45
11,12(4/58,10/58)-(100 pgs.)	6	12	18	38	69	100
13-20	3	6	9	19	30	40
21-45(1966): 27-Nazi story	3	6	9	15	22	28
1(10/67, 2nd series)	3	6	9	16	24	32
2-10	2	4	6	10	14	18
11-23: 23 (7/71)	1	3	4	8	10	12
24-26 (1985-86): Fago-r (low print run)						6.00

TIM TYLER (See Harvey Comics Hits #54)

TIM TYLER (Also see Comics Reading Libraries in the Promotional Comics section)
Better Publications: 1942

1	20	40	60	117	189	260

TIM TYLER COWBOY
Standard Comics (King Features Synd.): No. 11, Nov, 1948 - No. 18, Aug, 1950

11-By Lyman Young	14	28	42	76	108	140
12-18: 13-15-Full length western adventures	9	18	27	52	69	85

TINKER BELL (Disney, TV)(See Walt Disney Showcase #37)
Dell Publishing Co.: No. 896, Mar, 1958 - No. 982, Apr-June, 1959

Four Color 896 (#1)-The Adventures of...	14	28	42	96	211	325
Four Color 982-The New Advs. of...	10	20	30	70	150	230

TINY FOLKS FUNNIES
Dell Publishing Co.: No. 60, 1944

Four Color 60	18	36	54	124	275	425

TINY TESSIE (Tessie #1-23; Real Experiences #25)
Marvel Comics (20CC): No. 24, Oct, 1949 (52 pgs.)

24	22	44	66	128	209	290

TINY TIM (Also see Super Comics)
Dell Publishing Co.: No. 4, 1941 - No. 235, July, 1949

Large Feature Comic 4('41)	55	110	165	352	601	850
Four Color 20(1941)	50	100	150	315	533	750
Four Color 42(1943)	19	38	57	133	294	460
Four Color 235	8	16	24	52	99	145

TINY TITANS (Teen Titans)
DC Comics: Apr, 2008 - No. 50, May, 2012 ($2.25/$2.50/$2.99)

1-29-All ages stories of Teen Titans in Elementary school; Baltazar & Franco-s/a						3.00
1-(6/08, Free Comic Book Day giveaway) r/#1; Baltazar & Franco-s/a						3.00
30-50: 30-Begin $2.99-c. 37-Marvel Family app. 44-Doom Patrol app.						3.00

TINY TITANS / LITTLE ARCHIE (Teen Titans) (Digest-size reprint in World of Archie Double Digest Magazine #5)

	GD 2.0	VG 4.0	FN 6.0	VF 8.0	VF/NM 9.0	NM- 9.2

DC Comics: Dec, 2010 - No. 3, Feb, 2011 ($2.99, limited series)
1-3-Character crossover; Baltazar & Franco-s/a. 2-Josie and the Pussycats app. 3.00

TINY TITANS: RETURN TO THE TREEHOUSE
DC Comics: Aug, 2014 - No. 6, Jan, 2015 ($2.99, limited series)
1-Baltazar & Franco-s/a in all; Brainiac app. 6.00
2-6: 3-Marvel Family app. 4.00

TINY TOT COMICS
E. C. Comics: Mar, 1946 - No. 10, Nov-Dec, 1947 (For younger readers)

1(nn)-52 pg. issues begin, end #4	71	142	213	454	777	1100
2 (5/46)	37	74	111	218	354	490
3-10: 10-Christmas-c	32	64	96	188	307	425

TINY TOT FUNNIES (Formerly Family Funnies; becomes Junior Funnies)
Harvey Publ. (King Features Synd.): No. 9, June, 1951
9-Flash Gordon, Mandrake, Dagwood, Daisy, etc. 10 | 20 | 30 | 58 | 79 | 100

TINY TOTS COMICS
Dell Publishing Co.: 1943 (Not reprints)
1-Kelly-a(2); fairy tales .... 45 | 90 | 135 | 284 | 480 | 675

TIPPY & CAP STUBBS (See Popular Comics)
Dell Publishing Co.: No. 210, Jan, 1949 - No. 242, Aug, 1949

Four Color 210 (#1)	9	18	27	60	120	180
Four Color 242	7	14	21	44	82	120

TIPPY'S FRIENDS GO-GO & ANIMAL
Tower Comics: July, 1966 - No. 15, Oct, 1969 (25¢)

1	10	20	30	69	147	225
2-5,7,9-15: 12-15 titled "Tippy's Friend Go-Go"	6	12	18	41	76	110
6-The Monkees photo-c	9	18	27	62	126	190
8-Beatles app. on front/back-c	12	24	36	81	176	270

TIPPY TEEN (See Vicki)
Tower Comics: Nov, 1965 - No. 25, Oct, 1969 (25¢)

1	13	26	39	89	188	290
2-4,6-10	6	12	18	40	73	105
5-1 pg. Beatles pin-up	8	16	24	51	96	140
11-20: 16-Twiggy photo-c	6	12	18	37	66	95
21-25	5	10	15	34	60	85
Special Collectors' Editions nn-(1969, 25¢)	6	12	18	37	66	95

TIPPY TERRY
Super/I. W. Enterprises: 1963

Super Reprint #14('63)-r/Little Groucho #1	2	4	6	8	10	16
I.W. Reprint #1 (nd)-r/Little Groucho #1	2	4	6	8	10	16

TIP TOP COMICS
United Features #1-188/St. John #189-210/Dell Publishing Co. #211 on:
4/36 - No. 210, 1957; No. 211, 11-1/57-58 - No. 225, 5-7/61

1-Tarzan by Hal Foster, Li'l Abner, Broncho Bill, Fritzi Ritz, Ella Cinders, Capt. & The Kids begin; strip-r (1st comic book app. of each)	1080	2160	3240	6600	12,300	18,000
2-Tarzan-c (6/36)	226	452	678	1446	2473	3500
3-Tarzan-c (7/36)	219	438	657	1402	2401	3400
4-(8/36)	116	232	348	742	1271	1800
5-8,10: 7-Photo & biography of Edgar Rice Burroughs. 8-Christmas-c	87	174	261	553	952	1350
9-Tarzan-c (1/37)	123	246	369	787	1344	1900
11,13,16,18-Tarzan-c: 11-Has Tarzan pin-up	87	174	261	553	952	1350
12,14,15,17,19,20: 20-Christmas-c	61	122	183	390	670	950
21,24,27,30-(10/38)-Tarzan-c	71	142	213	454	777	1100
22,23,25,26,28,29	42	84	126	265	445	625
31,35,38,40	39	78	117	240	395	550
32,36-Tarzan-c: 32-1st published Jack Davis-a (cartoon). 36-Kurtzman panel (1st published comic work)	71	142	213	454	777	1100
33,34,37,39-Tarzan-c	61	122	183	390	670	950
41-Reprints 1st Tarzan Sunday; Tarzan-c	71	142	213	454	777	1100
42,44,46,48,49	37	74	111	218	354	490
43,45,47,50,52-Tarzan-c. 43-Mort Walker panel	47	94	141	296	498	700
51,53	34	68	102	204	332	460
54-Origin Mirror Man & Triple Terror, also featured on cover	45	90	135	284	480	675
55,56,58: Last Tarzan by Foster	30	60	90	177	289	400
57,59-62-Tarzan by Hogarth	37	74	111	222	361	500
63-80: 65,67-70,72-74,77,78-No Tarzan	20	40	60	117	189	260
81-90	16	32	48	94	147	200
91-99	15	30	45	85	130	175
100	15	30	45	88	137	185
101-140: 110-Gordo story. 111-Li'l Abner app. 118, 132-No Tarzan. 137-Sadie Hawkins Day story	13	26	39	72	101	130
141-170: 145,151-Gordo stories. 153-Fritzi Ritz lingerie panels. 157-Last Li'l Abner; lingerie panels	10	20	30	56	76	95
171,172,174-183: 171-Tarzan reprints by B. Lubbers begin; end #188	10	20	30	58	79	100
173-(3/52) Ties with United Comics #21 for first app. of Peanuts in comics; reprints Peanuts dailies 2/06/51 & 3/05/51 (also see Tip Topper Comics)	423	846	1269	3088	5444	7800
184-Peanuts app. (1-2/54)	29	58	87	172	281	390
185-188-Peanuts stories with Charlie Brown & Snoopy on the covers. 185-(3-4/54)	333	666	999	2000	2500	3000
189,191-225-Peanuts apps.(4 pg. to 8 pg stories) in most						
Issues with Peanuts	17	34	51	100	158	215
Issues without Peanuts	11	18	27	50	65	80
190-Peanuts with Charlie Brown & Snoopy partial-c (comic strip at bottom of cover)	42	84	126	265	445	625
Bound Volumes (Very Rare) sold at 1939 World's Fair; bound by publisher in pictorial comic boards (also see Comics on Parade)						
Bound issues 1-12 (Rare)	400	800	1200	2800	4900	7000
Bound issues 13-24	194	388	582	1242	2121	3000

Bound issues 25-36	168	336	504	1075	1838	2600

NOTE: *Tarzan-r by Foster-#1-40, 44-50; by Rex Maxon-#41-43; by Burne Hogarth-#57, 59, 62.*

TIP TOPPER COMICS
United Features Syndicate: Oct-Nov, 1949 - No. 28, 1954

1-Li'l Abner, Abbie & Slats	34	68	102	204	332	460
2	14	28	42	80	115	150
3-5: 5-Fearless Fosdick app.	11	22	33	64	90	115
6-10: 6-Fearless Fosdick app.	10	20	30	56	76	95
11-15	9	18	27	52	69	85
16(4-5/52)-2nd app. of Peanuts (2 pgs.) by Schulz in comics (See United Comics #21 for 1st app. & #22 for 5-6/52 app.)(Also see Tip Top Comics #173)	129	258	387	826	1413	2000
17(6-7/52)-4th app. of Peanuts by Schulz, 2 pgs.	57	114	171	362	619	875
18-28: 18-24,26-28-Early Peanuts (2 pgs.). 25-Early Peanuts (3 pgs.) 26-28-Twin Earths	21	42	63	122	199	275

NOTE: *Many lingerie panels in Fritzi Ritz stories.*

'TIS THE SEASON TO BE FREEZIN'
DC Comics: Feb, 2022 ($9.99, 80 pages, one-shot)
1-Winter-themed short story anthology by various incl. Dini, Franklin, Hetrick, Mhan 10.00

TITAN A.E.
Dark Horse Comics: May, 2000 - No. 3, July, 2000 ($2.95, limited series)
1-3-Movie prequel; Al Rio-a 3.00

TITANS (Also see Teen Titans, New Teen Titans and New Titans)
DC Comics: Mar, 1999 - No. 50, Apr, 2003 ($2.50/$2.75)
1-Titans re-form; Grayson-s; 2 covers 5.00
2-11,13-24,26-50: 2-Superman-c/app. 9,10,21,22-Deathstroke app. 24-Titans from "Kingdom Come" app. 32-36-Asamiya-c. 44-Begin $2.75-c 4.00
12-($3.50, 48 pages) 5.00
25-($3.95) Titans from "Kingdom Come" app.; Wolfman & Faerber-s; art by Pérez, Cardy, Grummett, Jimenez, Dodson, Pelletier 5.00
Annual 1 ('00, $3.50) Planet DC; intro Bushido 5.00
...: East Special 1 (1/08, $3.99) Winick-s/Churchill-a; continues in Titans #1 (2008) 5.00
...: Secret Files 1,2 (3/99, 10/00, $4.95) Profile pages & short stories 5.00

TITANS (Also see Teen Titans)
DC Comics: Jun, 2008 - No. 38, Oct, 2011 ($3.50/$2.99)
1-($3.50) Titans re-form again; Winick-s/Churchill-a; covers by Churchill & Van Sciver 4.00
2-38: 2-4-Trigon returns. 6-10-Jericho app. 24-Deathstroke & Luthor app. 3.00
Annual 1 (9/11, $4.99) Justice League app.; Jericho returns; Richards-a 5.00
...: Villains For Hire Special 1 (4/11, $3.99) Deathstroke's team; Atom (Ryan Choi) killed 5.00
...: Fractured TPB (2010, $17.99) r/#14,16-22 .... 18.00
...: Lockdown TPB (2009, $14.99) r/#7-11 .... 15.00
...: Old Friends HC (2008, $24.99) r/#1-6 & Titans East Special 25.00
...: Villains For Hire TPB (2011, $14.99) r/#24-27 & Villains For Hire Special 1 .... 15.00

TITANS (DC Rebirth)(Follows Titans Hunt series)
DC Comics: Aug, 2016 - No. 36, Jun, 2019 ($2.99/$3.99)
1-9: Abnett-s/Booth-a; Abra Kadabra returns. 7-Superman app. 3.00
10-24,26-36-($3.99) 10-Fearsome Five app. 11-Lazarus Contract x-over; Teen Titans & Deathstroke app. 12-Rocafort-a. 28-"Drowned Earth" tie-in. 30-34-Kyle Rayner app. 4.00
25-($4.99) Peterson, March & Medri-a 5.00
Annual 1 (5/17, $4.99) Justice League and The Key app.; Abnett-s/Jung-a 5.00
Annual 2 (6/18, $4.99) Abnett-s/Grummett & Derenick-a; Monsieur Mallah & the Brain app. 5.00
...: Rebirth 1 (8/16, $2.99) Abnett-s/Booth-a; Wally West reunites with the Titans 3.00
...: Special 1 (8/18, $4.99) Abnett-s/art by various; Justice League app. 5.00

TITANS (Dawn of DC)(Follows Dark Crisis)
DC Comics: Jul, 2023 - Present ($3.99)
1-8: 1-5-Tom Taylor-s/Nicola Scott-a; Peacemaker app. 2-Brother Blood returns 4.00

TITANS: BEAST WORLD (Teen Titans)
DC Comics: Jan, 2024 - No. 6, Mar, 2024 ($5.99/$4.99, limited series)
1,6-($5.99) 1-Taylor-s/Reis-a; Justice League app.; intro Doctor Hate 6.00
2-5-($4.99) 2-5-Peacemaker & Amanda Waller app. 5.00
...: Evolution 1 (1/24, $7.99) Beast Boy reprints from Teen Titans ('66) #6, Tales of the New Teen Titans #3, Action Comics #1051; Brad Walker-c 8.00
...: Tour: Atlantis 1 (3/24, $5.99) Grace-s/Federici-a/Janin-c; Mera app. 6.00
...: Tour: Central City 1 (2/24, $5.99) Irey, Jai, Kid Flash, Pied Piper app. 6.00
...: Tour: Gotham 1 (2/24, $5.99) s/a by Zdarsky, Maggs, Starks, Kelley Jones & others 6.00
...: Tour: Metropolis 1 (2/24, $5.99) Jon Kent, Dreamer, Supergirl, Bibbo app. 6.00
...: Tour: Star City 1 (2/24, $5.99) Green Arrow, Black Canary, Stargirl app. 6.00
...: Waller Rising 1 (2/24, $5.99) Val-Zod, Black Manta, Vixen, Dr. Mist app. 6.00

TITANS BEAT (Teen Titans)
DC Comics: Aug, 1996 (16 pgs., paper-c)
1-Intro./preview new Teen Titans members; Pérez-a 4.00

TITANS: BURNING RAGE (Teen Titans)(Reprints new story from Walmart exclusive)
DC Comics: Oct, 2019 - No. 7, Apr, 2020 ($4.99, limited series)
1-7-Jurgens-s/Eaton-a. 6-Mento app. 7-Blackfire and Mongul app. 4.00

TITANS GIANT (Continued from Teen Titans Giant #7)
DC Comics: 2019 - No. 7, 2019 ($4.99, 100 pgs., squarebound, Walmart exclusive)
1-7: 1-New story Jurgens-s/Eaton-a; reprints from Teen Titans ('03), Super Sons #1 ('17), and Sideways ('18) continue (Issues #8-on) 8.00

TITANS GIANT
DC Comics: 2020 - No. 2, 2020 ($4.99, 100 pgs., squarebound, Mass Market & Direct Market editions exist for each issue, with different covers)
1,2-New stories plus 1st series Teen Titans, Starfire & Super Sons reprints 5.00

TITANS HUNT (Also see DC Universe: Rebirth)
DC Comics: Dec, 2015 - No. 8, Jun, 2016 ($3.99, limited series)
1-7: 1-Abnett-s/Siqueira-a; 1970s-era Titans app. incl. Lilith & Gnarrk. 2,4-Segovia-a 4.00
8-Titans vs. Mr. Twister 4.00

TITANS/ LEGION OF SUPER-HEROES: UNIVERSE ABLAZE
DC Comics: 2000 - No. 4, 2000 ($4.95, prestige format, limited series)

Tippy Teen #23 © Tower

Titans: Beast World #1 © DC

TMNT: Jennika II #6 © Viacom

	GD	VG	FN	VF	VF/NM	NM-
	2.0	4.0	6.0	8.0	9.0	9.2

1-4-Jurgens-s/a; P. Jimenez-a; teams battle Universo 5.00

TITAN SPECIAL
Dark Horse Comics: June, 1994 ($3.95, one-shot)
1-($3.95, 52 pgs.) 5.00

TITANS: SCISSORS, PAPER, STONE
DC Comics: 1997 ($4.95, one-shot)
1-Manga style Elseworlds; Adam Warren-s/a(p) 5.00

TITANS SELL-OUT SPECIAL
DC Comics: Nov, 1992 ($3.50, 52 pgs., one-shot)
1-Fold-out Nightwing poster; 1st Teeny Titans 5.00

TITANS UNITED (Teen Titans)
DC Comics: Nov, 2021 - No. 7, May, 2022 ($3.99, limited series)
1-7: 1-Cavan Scott-s/Jose Luis-a. 3,4-Blackfire app. 5-Black Zero returns 4.00

TITANS UNITED: BLOODPACT (Teen Titans)
DC Comics: Nov, 2022 - No. 6, Apr, 2023 ($3.99, limited series)
1-6-Cavan Scott-s/Lucas Meyer-a; Brother Blood & Mother Mayhem app. 4.00

TITANS/ YOUNG JUSTICE: GRADUATION DAY
DC Comics: Early July, 2003 - No. 3, Aug, 2003 ($2.50, limited series)
1,2-Winick-s/Garza-a; leads into Teen Titans and The Outsiders series. 2-Lilith dies 3.00
3-Death of Donna Troy (Wonder Girl) 3.00
TPB (2003, $6.95) r/#1-3; plus previews of Teen Titans and The Outsiders series 7.00

TITHE, THE (Also see Eden's Fall)
Image Comics (Top Cow): Apr, 2015 - No. 8 ($3.99, limited series)
1-7-Hawkins/Ekedal-a; multiple covers on each. 5-7-Sevy-a 4.00

T-MAN (Also see Police Comics #103)
Quality Comics Group: Sept, 1951 - No. 38, Dec, 1956

	GD 2.0	VG 4.0	FN 6.0	VF 8.0	VF/NM 9.0	NM- 9.2
1-Pete Trask, T-Man begins; Jack Cole-a	63	126	189	403	689	975
2-Crandall-c	37	74	111	222	361	500
3,7,8: Ali Crandall-c	32	64	96	188	307	425
4,5-Crandall-c/a each	34	68	102	199	325	450
6-"The Man Who Could Be Hitler" c/story; Crandall-c	53	106	159	334	567	800
9,10-Crandall-c	28	56	84	168	274	380
11-Used in POP, pg. 95 & color illo.	25	50	75	150	245	340
12,13,15-19,22-26: 23-H-Bomb panel. 24-Last pre-code issue (4/55). 25-Not Crandall-a	19	38	57	111	176	240
	37	74	111	222	361	500
14-Hitler-c	25	50	75	150	245	340
20-H-Bomb explosion-c/story	25	50	75	150	245	340
21- "The Return of Mussolini" c/story	25	50	75	150	245	340
27-33,35-38	18	36	54	107	169	230
34-Hitler-c	48	96	144	302	514	725

NOTE: Anti-communist stories common. **Crandall** c-2-10p. **Cuidera** c(i)-1-38. Bondage c-15.

TMNT... (Also see Teenage Mutant Ninja Turtles and related titles)
Mirage Publishing: March 2007 ($3.25/$4.95, B&W, one-shots)
...: Raphael Movie Prequel 1; ...: Michelangelo Movie Prequel 2; ...: Donatello Movie Prequel 3; ...: April Movie Prequel 4; ...: Leonardo Movie Prequel 5; back-story for movie 5.00
...: The Official Movie Adaptation ($4.95) adapts 2007 movie; Munroe-c 5.00

TMNT: BEST OF...
IDW Publishing: Sept, 2020 - Oct, 2023 ($5.99/$6.99)
... April O'Neil (10/21) Reprints TMNT #2 (1984), Micro-Series #7 ('11) TMNT #118 .... 6.00
... Baxter Stockman (8/22) Reprints TMNT #2 (1984) & #2 (2003), Micro-Series 6.00
... Bebop & Rocksteady (10/23) Reprints TMNT #25 Advs., Micro-Series #7 ('11) & others 7.00
... Casey Jones (7/21) Reprints TMNT #14 & #48 (1984), Micro-Series #6 ('11) 6.00
... Donatello (11/20) Reprints Donatello #1 (1986), Micro-Series #3 ('11) Macro-Series #1 .... 6.00
... Jennika (2/22) Reprints TMNT #52 (2011) and early apps. 6.00
... Karai (7/23) Reprints TMNT #56 (1984) and recent apps. 6.00
... Leatherhead (2/22) Reprints Tales of the TMNT #6, TMNT #45 ('84) & TMNT #56 ('11) 6.00
... Leonardo (1/21) Reprints Leonardo #1 (1986), Micro-Series #4 ('11) Macro-Series #3 .... 6.00
... Michelangelo (3/21) Reprints Michelangelo #1 (1986), Micro-Series #2 ('11) Macro-Series #2 .... 6.00
... Raphael (9/20) Reprints Raphael #1 (1985), Micro-Series #1 ('11) Macro-Series #4 .... 6.00
... Rat King (5/22) Reprints Tales of the TMNT #4, TMNT Advs. #11 and #36 ('11) 6.00
... Shredder (12/21) Reprints TMNT #1 (1984), Villain Micro-Series #8 ('13), TMNT: Shredder In Hell #1 ('19) 6.00
... Splinter (5/21) Reprints TMNT Advs #45, Tales of TMNT V2 #2, TMNT #5 ('11), and Micro-Series #5 ('11) 6.00

TMNT: JENNIKA
IDW Publishing: Feb, 2020 - No. 3, Apr, 2020 ($4.99, limited series)

1-3-Brahm Revel-s/a 5.00

TMNT: JENNIKA II
IDW Publishing: Nov, 2020 - No. 6, Apr, 2021 ($4.99)
1-6: 1-3-Brahm Revel-s/a. 4-Ronda Pattison-s/Jodi Nishijima-a 5.00

TMNT MUTANT UNIVERSE SOURCEBOOK
Archie Comics: 1992 - No. 3, 1992? ($1.95, 52 pgs.)(Lists characters from A-Z)

	GD 2.0	VG 4.0	FN 6.0	VF 8.0	VF/NM 9.0	NM- 9.2
1-3: 3-New characters; fold-out poster	1	3	4	6	8	10

TMNT: THE LAST RONIN
IDW Publishing: Oct, 2020 - No. 5, Feb, 2022 ($8.99, oversized 7" x 10-7/8", squarebound)

	GD 2.0	VG 4.0	FN 6.0	VF 8.0	VF/NM 9.0	NM- 9.2
1-One Turtle in the future; Waltz & Eastman-s/Eastman & Esau-a; Oroku Hiroto app.	5	10	15	30	50	70
1-Director's Cut (3/21, $10.99) r/#1 with layout pages, characters designs, story outline						
2-April O'Neil app.; intro. Casey Marie Jones	3	6	9	14	20	25
3-5	3	6	9	14	20	25
	1	3	4	6	8	10

...: Design Archive (11/21, $8.99) Eastman sketch art for characters, settings, vehicles 9.00

TMNT: THE LAST RONIN
IDW Publishing: Nov, 2023 - No. 5, Dec, 2023 ($4.99, 7" x 10-7/8", not squarebound)
1-5-Reprints 2020 series 5.00

TNT COMICS
Charles Publishing Co.: Feb, 1946 (36 pgs.)

	GD 2.0	VG 4.0	FN 6.0	VF 8.0	VF/NM 9.0	NM- 9.2
1-Yellowjacket app.	47	94	141	296	498	700

TOBY TYLER (Disney, see Movie Comics)
Dell Publishing Co.: No. 1092, Apr-June, 1960

	GD 2.0	VG 4.0	FN 6.0	VF 8.0	VF/NM 9.0	NM- 9.2
Four Color 1092-Movie, photo-c	6	12	18	41	76	110

TODAY'S BRIDES
Ajax/Farrell Publishing Co.: Nov, 1955; No. 2, Feb, 1956; No. 3, Sept, 1956; No. 4, Nov, 1956

	GD 2.0	VG 4.0	FN 6.0	VF 8.0	VF/NM 9.0	NM- 9.2
1	15	30	45	86	133	180
2-4	11	22	33	64	90	115

TODAY'S ROMANCE
Standard Comics: No. 5, March, 1952 - No. 8, Sept, 1952 (All photo-c?)

	GD 2.0	VG 4.0	FN 6.0	VF 8.0	VF/NM 9.0	NM- 9.2
5-Photo-c	17	34	51	98	154	210
6-Photo-c; Toth-a	18	36	54	103	162	220
7,8	15	30	45	85	130	175

TODD, THE UGLIEST KID ON EARTH
Image Comics: Jan, 2013 - No. 8, Jan, 2014 ($2.99)
1-8-Perker-a/Kristensen-s 3.00

TOE TAGS FEATURING GEORGE A. ROMERO
DC Comics: Dec, 2004 - No. 6, May, 2005 ($2.95/$2.99)
1-6-Zombie story by George Romero; Wrightson-c/Castillo-a 3.00

TOIL AND TROUBLE
BOOM! Studios (Archaia): Sept, 2015 - No. 6 ($3.99)
1-6-Mairghread Scott-s/Kelly & Nicole Matthews-a 4.00

TOKA (Jungle King)
Dell Publishing Co.: Aug-Oct, 1964 - No. 10, Jan, 1967 (Painted-c #1,2)

	GD 2.0	VG 4.0	FN 6.0	VF 8.0	VF/NM 9.0	NM- 9.2
1	4	8	12	28	47	65
2	3	6	9	17	26	35
3-10	3	6	9	15	22	28

TOKYO GHOST
Image Comics: Sept, 2015 - No. 10, Aug, 2016 ($3.99)
1-10-Rick Remender-s/Sean Murphy-a 4.00

TOKYO STORM WARNING (See Red/Tokyo Storm Warning for TPB)
DC Comics (Cliffhanger): Aug, 2003 - No. 3, Dec, 2003 ($2.95, limited series)
1-3-Warren Ellis-s/James Raiz-a 3.00

TOMAHAWK (Son of... on-c of #131-140; see Star Spangled Comics #69 & World's Finest Comics #65)
National Periodical Publications: Sept-Oct, 1950 - No. 140, May-June, 1972

	GD 2.0	VG 4.0	FN 6.0	VF 8.0	VF/NM 9.0	NM- 9.2
1-Tomahawk & boy sidekick Dan Hunter begin by Fred Ray	194	388	582	1242	2121	3000
2-Frazetta/Williamson-a (4 pgs.)	77	154	231	493	847	1200
3-5	42	84	126	265	445	625
6-10: 7-Last 52 pg. issue	37	74	111	222	361	500
11-20	25	50	75	150	245	340
21-27,30: 30-Last precode (2/55)	22	44	66	132	216	300
28-1st app. Lord Shilling (arch-foe)	24	48	72	142	234	325

	GD 2.0	VG 4.0	FN 6.0	VF 8.0	VF/NM 9.0	NM- 9.2
29-Frazetta-r/Jimmy Wakely #3 (3 pgs.)	27	54	81	162	266	370
31-40	20	40	60	114	182	250
41-50	10	20	30	67	141	215
51-56,58-60	9	18	27	61	123	185
57-Frazetta-r/Jimmy Wakely #6 (3 pgs.)	10	20	30	67	141	215
61-77: 77-Last 10¢ issue	9	18	27	57	111	165
78-85: 81-1st app. Miss Liberty. 83-Origin Tomahawk's Rangers	7	14	21	49	92	135
86-99: 96-Origin/1st app. The Hood, alias Lady Shilling	6	12	18	37	66	95
100	6	12	18	38	69	100
101-110: 107-Origin/1st app. Thunder-Man	5	10	15	31	53	75
111-115,120,122: 122-Last 12¢ issue	5	10	15	30	50	70
116-1st Neal Adams cover on title (5/68)	24	48	72	168	372	575
117-119,121,123-130-Neal Adams-c. 118-Origin of the Rangers	7	14	21	44	82	120
131-Frazetta-r/Jimmy Wakely #7 (3 pgs.); origin Firehair retold	3	6	9	21	33	45
132-135: 135-Last 15¢ issue	3	6	9	16	24	32
136-138,140 (52 pg. Giants)	3	6	9	19	30	40
139-Frazetta-r/Star Spangled #113	3	6	9	21	33	45

NOTE: *Fred Ray* c-1, 2, 8, 11, 30, 34, 35, 40-43, 45, 46, 82. Firehair by *Kubert*-131-134, 136. *Maurer* a-138. *Severin* a-135. *Starr* a-5. *Thorne* a-137, 140.

TOM AND JERRY (See Comic Album #4, 8, 12, Dell Giant #21, Dell Giants, Golden Comics Digest #1, 5, 8, 13, 15, 18, 22, 25, 28, 35, Kite fun Book & March of Comics #21, 46, 61, 70, 88, 103, 119, 128, 145, 154, 173, 190, 207, 224, 281, 295, 305, 321,333, 345, 361, 365, 388, 400, 444, 451, 463, 480)

TOM AND JERRY (...Comics, early issues) (M.G.M.)
(Formerly Our Gang No. 1-59) (See Dell Giants for annuals)
Dell Publishing Co./Gold Key No. 213-327/Whitman No. 328 on: No. 193, 6/48; No. 60, 7/49 - No. 212, 7-9/62; No. 213, 11/62 - No. 291, 2/75; No. 292, 3/77 - No. 342, 5/82 - No. 344, 6/84

	GD 2.0	VG 4.0	FN 6.0	VF 8.0	VF/NM 9.0	NM- 9.2
Four Color 193 (#1)-Titled "M.G.M. Presents…"	36	72	108	259	580	900
60-Barney Bear, Benny Burro cont. from Our Gang; Droopy begins	13	26	39	89	195	300
61	9	18	27	61	123	185
62-70: 66-X-Mas-c	7	14	21	49	92	135
71-80: 77,90-X-Mas-c. 79-Spike & Tyke begin	6	12	18	40	73	105
81-99	5	10	15	35	63	90
100	6	12	18	37	66	95
101-120	5	10	15	31	53	75
121-140: 126-X-Mas-c	4	8	12	28	47	65
141-160	4	8	12	25	40	55
161-200	4	8	12	23	37	50
201-212(7-9/62)(Last Dell issue)	3	6	9	21	33	45
213,214-(84 pgs.)-Titled "…Funhouse"	5	10	15	35	63	90
215-240: 215-Titled "…Funhouse"	4	8	12	16	24	32
241-270	2	4	6	11	16	20
271-300: 286- "Tom & Jerry"	2	4	6	8	11	14
301-327 (Gold Key)	1	3	4	6	8	10
328,329 (Whitman)	2	4	6	8	11	14
330(8/80),331(10/80), 332-(3-pack only)	4	8	12	27	44	60
333-341: 339(2/82), 340(2-3/82), 341(4/82)	2	4	6	9	10	12
342-344 (All #90058, no date, date code, 3-pack): 342(6/83), 343(8/83), 344(6/84)	3	6	9	16	24	32
Mouse From T.R.A.P. 1(7/66)-Giant, G. K.	4	8	12	28	47	65
Summer Fun 1(7/67, 68 pgs.)(Gold Key)-Reprints Barks' Droopy from Summer Fun #1	4	8	12	28	47	65

NOTE: *#60-87, 98-121, 268, 277, 289, 302 are 52 pgs.. Reprints-#225, 241, 245, 247, 252, 254, 266, 268, 270, 292-327, 329-342, 344.*

TOM & JERRY
Harvey Comics: Sept, 1991 - No. 18, Aug, 1994 ($1.25)

	GD 2.0	VG 4.0	FN 6.0	VF 8.0	VF/NM 9.0	NM- 9.2
1-18: 1-Tom & Jerry, Barney Bear-r by Carl Barks						4.00
50th Anniversary Special 1 (10/91, $2.50, 68 pgs.)-Benny the Lonesome Burro-r by Barks (story/a)/Our Gang #9						5.00

TOMB OF DARKNESS (Formerly Beware)
Marvel Comics Group: No. 9, July, 1974 - No. 23, Nov, 1976

	GD 2.0	VG 4.0	FN 6.0	VF 8.0	VF/NM 9.0	NM- 9.2
9	4	8	12	28	47	65
10-23: 11,16,18-21-Kirby-a. 15,19-Ditko-r. 17-Woodbridge-r/Astonishing #62; Powell-r.						
20-Everett Venus-r/Venus #19. 23-Everett-r	4	8	9	16	23	30
20,21-(30¢-c variants, limited distribution)(5,7/76)	11	22	33	72	154	235

TOMB OF DRACULA (See Giant-Size Dracula, Dracula Lives, Nightstalkers, Power Record Comics & Requiem for Dracula)
Marvel Comics Group: Apr, 1972 - No. 70, Aug, 1979

	GD 2.0	VG 4.0	FN 6.0	VF 8.0	VF/NM 9.0	NM- 9.2
1-1st app. Dracula & Frank Drake; Colan-p in all; Neal Adams-c	42	84	126	311	706	1100
1-Facsimile Edition (12/22, $3.99) Reprints #1 with original ads						5.00
2	10	20	30	67	141	215
3-6: 3-Intro. Dr. Rachel Van Helsing & Inspector Chelm. 6-Neal Adams-c	8	16	24	51	96	140
7-9	6	12	18	38	69	100
10-1st app. Blade the Vampire Slayer (who app. in 1998, 2002 and 2004 movies)	141	282	423	1142	2571	4000
10-Facsimile Edition (1/20, $3.99) Reprints #10 with original ads						
	2	4	6	10	14	18
11,14-16,20:	5	10	15	31	53	75
12-2nd app. Blade; Brunner-c(p)	13	26	39	89	195	300
13-Origin Blade	21	42	63	147	324	500
17,19: 17-Blade bitten by Dracula. 19-Blade discovers he is immune to vampire's bite.						
1st mention of Blade having vampire blood in him	7	14	21	44	82	120
18-Two-part x-over cont'd in Werewolf by Night #15	10	20	30	70	150	230
21,24-Blade app.	5	10	15	34	60	85
22,23,26,27,29	3	6	9	21	33	45
25-1st app. & origin Hannibal King	14	28	42	96	211	325
25-2nd printing (1994)	2	4	6	9	12	15
28-Blade app. on-c & inside as an illusion	5	10	15	33	57	80
30,41,42,44,45-Blade app. 45-Intro. Deacon Frost, the vampire who bit Blade's mother						

	GD 2.0	VG 4.0	FN 6.0	VF 8.0	VF/NM 9.0	NM- 9.2
31-40	4	8	12	27	44	60
31-40	3	6	9	18	28	38
43-Wrightson-c; Blade app.	5	10	15	34	60	85
43-45-(30¢-c variants, limited distribution)	9	18	27	62	126	190
46,47-(Regular 25¢ editions)(4-8/76)	3	6	9	16	23	30
46,47-(30¢-c variants, limited distribution)	9	18	27	62	126	190
48,49,51-57,59,60: 57,59,60-(30¢-c)	3	6	9	15	22	28
50-Silver Surfer app.	7	14	21	44	82	120
57,59,60-(35¢-c variants)(6-9/77)	12	24	36	82	179	275
58-All Blade issue (Regular 30¢ edition)	6	12	18	38	69	100
58-(35¢-c variant)(7/77)	13	26	39	91	201	310
61-69	3	6	9	15	22	28
70-Double size	5	10	15	30	50	70

NOTE: *N. Adams* c-1, 6. *Colan* a-1-70p; c(p)-8, 38-42, 44-56, 58-70. *Wrightson* c-43.

TOMB OF DRACULA, THE (Magazine)
Marvel Comics Group: Oct, 1979 - No. 6, Aug, 1980 (B&W)

	GD 2.0	VG 4.0	FN 6.0	VF 8.0	VF/NM 9.0	NM- 9.2
1,3: 1-Colan-a; features on movies "Dracula" and "Love at First Bite" w/photos.						
3-Good girl cover-a; Miller-a (2 pg. sketch)	1	2	4	8	11	16	20
2,6: 2-Ditko-a (36 pgs.). 6-Nosferatu movie feature. 6-Lilith story w/Sienkiewicz-a	2	4	6	8	11	14
4,5: Stephen King interview	2	4	6	13	18	22

NOTE: *Buscema* a-4p, 5p. *Chaykin* c-5, 6. *Colan* a(p)-1, 3-6. *Miller* a-3. *Romita* a-2p.

TOMB OF DRACULA
Marvel Comics (Epic Comics): 1991 - No. 4, 1992 ($4.95, 52 pgs., squarebound, mini-series)

	GD 2.0	VG 4.0	FN 6.0	VF 8.0	VF/NM 9.0	NM- 9.2
Book 1-4: Colan/Williamson-a; Colan painted-c						5.00

TOMB OF DRACULA
Marvel Comics: Dec, 2004 - No. 4, Mar, 2005 ($2.99, limited series)

	GD 2.0	VG 4.0	FN 6.0	VF 8.0	VF/NM 9.0	NM- 9.2
1-4-Blade app.; Tolagson-a/Sienkiewicz-c						3.00

TOMB OF DRACULA PRESENTS: THRONE OF BLOOD
Marvel Comics: Jun, 2011 ($3.99, one-shot)

	GD 2.0	VG 4.0	FN 6.0	VF 8.0	VF/NM 9.0	NM- 9.2
1-Story of Raizo Kodo in 1585 Japan; Parlov-a; Hitch-c						4.00

TOMB OF LEGEIA (See Movie Classics)

TOMB OF TERROR (Thrills of Tomorrow #17 on)
Harvey Publications: June, 1952 - No. 16, July, 1954

	GD 2.0	VG 4.0	FN 6.0	VF 8.0	VF/NM 9.0	NM- 9.2
1	90	180	270	576	988	1400
2	53	106	159	334	567	800
3-Bondage-c; atomic disaster story	63	126	189	403	689	975
4-12: 4-Heart ripped out. 8-12-Nostrand-a	45	90	135	284	480	675
13-Special S/F issue (1/54) White letter shadow-c	90	180	270	576	988	1400
13-Logo variant-c (striped letter shadow)	100	200	300	635	1093	1550
14-Classic S/F-c; Check-a	110	220	330	704	1202	1700
15-S/F issue; c-shows face exploding	757	1514	2271	5526	9763	14,000
16-Special S/F issue; horror-c; Nostrand-a	194	388	582	1242	2121	3000

NOTE: *Edd Cartier* a-13? *Elias* c-2, 5-16. *Kremer* a-1, 7; c-1. *Nostrand* a-8-12, 15r 16. *Palais* a-2, 3, 5-7. *Powell* a-1, 3, 5, 9-16. *Sparling* a-12, 13, 15.

TOMB OF TERROR
Marvel Comics: Dec, 2010 ($3.99, B&W, one-shot)

	GD 2.0	VG 4.0	FN 6.0	VF 8.0	VF/NM 9.0	NM- 9.2
1-Short stories of Man-Thing, Son of Satan, Werewolf By Night & The Living Mummy						4.00

TOMB RAIDER (Also see Lara Croft and The Frozen Omen)
Dark Horse Comics: Feb, 2014 - No. 18, Jul, 2015 ($3.50/$3.99)

	GD 2.0	VG 4.0	FN 6.0	VF 8.0	VF/NM 9.0	NM- 9.2
1-18: 1-6-Gail Simone-s/Nicolás Daniel Selma-a. 13-Begin $3.99-c						4.00

TOMB RAIDER
Dark Horse Comics: Feb, 2016 - No. 12, Jan, 2017 ($3.99)

	GD 2.0	VG 4.0	FN 6.0	VF 8.0	VF/NM 9.0	NM- 9.2
1-12-Mariko Tamaki-s/Phillip Sevy-a						4.00

TOMB RAIDER (one-shots)
Image Comics (Top Cow Prod.)

	GD 2.0	VG 4.0	FN 6.0	VF 8.0	VF/NM 9.0	NM- 9.2
…: Arabian Nights (8/04, $5.99) Avery-s/Tan-a/c						6.00
… Cover Gallery 2006 (4/06, $2.99) artist galleries and series gallery; pin-ups						3.00
…The Darkness Special 1 (2001, TopCowStore.com)-Wohl-s/Tan-a						3.00
Epiphany 1 (8/03, $4.99)-Jurgens-s/Banks-a/Haley-c; preview of Witchblade Animated						5.00
Takeover 1 (1/04, $2.99)-Benefiel-a/Daniel-c						3.00
… Vs. The Wolf-Men: Monster War 2005 (7/05, $2.99) 2nd part of Monster War x-over						3.00
…/Witchblade/Magdalena/Vampirella #1 (8/05, $2.99, B&W) three covers; Chin-a						3.00

TOMB RAIDER: INFERNO
Dark Horse Comics: Jun, 2018 - No. 4, Oct, 2018 ($3.99, limited series)

	GD 2.0	VG 4.0	FN 6.0	VF 8.0	VF/NM 9.0	NM- 9.2
1-4-Lanzing & Kelly-s/Sevy-a						4.00

TOMB RAIDER: JOURNEYS
Image Comics (Top Cow Prod.): Jan, 2002 - No. 12, May, 2003 ($2.50/$2.99)

	GD 2.0	VG 4.0	FN 6.0	VF 8.0	VF/NM 9.0	NM- 9.2
1-12: 1-Avery-s/Drew Johnson-a. 1-Two covers by Johnson & Hughes						3.00

TOMB RAIDER: SURVIVOR'S CRUSADE
Dark Horse Comics: Nov, 2017 - No. 4, Apr, 2018 ($3.99, limited series)

	GD 2.0	VG 4.0	FN 6.0	VF 8.0	VF/NM 9.0	NM- 9.2
1-4-Lanzing & Kelly-s/Ashley Woods-a						4.00

TOMB RAIDER: THE GREATEST TREASURE OF ALL
Image Comics (Top Cow Prod.): 2002; Oct, 2005 ($6.99)

	GD 2.0	VG 4.0	FN 6.0	VF 8.0	VF/NM 9.0	NM- 9.2
Prelude (2002, 16 pgs., no cover price) Jusko-c/a						3.00
1-(10/05, $6.99) Jusko-a/Jurgens-s; sketch pages, reference photos, art in progress						7.00

TOMB RAIDER: THE SERIES (Also see Witchblade/Tomb Raider)
Image Comics (Top Cow Prod.): Dec, 1999 - No. 50, May, 2005 ($2.50/$2.99)

	GD 2.0	VG 4.0	FN 6.0	VF 8.0	VF/NM 9.0	NM- 9.2
1-Jurgens-s/Park-a; 3 covers by Park, Finch, Turner						5.00
2-24,26-29,31-50: 21-Black-c w/foil. 37-Flip book preview of Stryke Force						5.00
25-Michael Turner-c/a; Witchblade app. Endgame x-over with Witchblade #60 & Evo #1						4.00
30-($4.99) Tony Daniel-a						5.00
#0 (6/01, $2.50) Avery-s/Ching-a/c						3.00
#1/2 (10/01, $2.95) Early days of Lara Croft; Jurgens-s/Lopez-a						3.00
…: Chasing Shangri-La (2002, $12.95, TPB) r/#11-15						13.00
Free Comic Book Day giveaway - (5/02) r/#1 with "Free Comic Book Day" banner on-c						3.00
… Gallery (12/00, $2.95) Pin-ups & previous covers by various						3.00
… Magazine (6/01, $4.95) Hughes-c; r/#1,2; Jurgens interview						5.00

Tomb of Dracula #4 © MAR

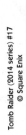

Tomb Raider (2014 series) #17 © Square Enix

Tom Strong #6 © ABC

	GD	VG	FN	VF	VF/NM	NM-		GD	VG	FN	VF	VF/NM	NM-
	2.0	4.0	6.0	8.0	9.0	9.2		2.0	4.0	6.0	8.0	9.0	9.2

...: Mystic Artifacts (2001, $14.95, TPB) r/#5-10 ..... 15.00
...: Saga of the Medusa Mask (9/00, $9.95, TPB) r/#1-4; new Park-c 10.00
... Vol. 1 Compendium (11/06, $59.99) r/#1-50; variant covers and pin-up art 60.00

TOMB RAIDER/WITCHBLADE SPECIAL (Also see Witchblade/Tomb Raider)
Top Cow Prod.: Dec, 1997 (mail-in offer, one-shot)

1-Turner-s/a(p); green background cover	2	4	6	11	16	20
1-Variant-c with orange sun background	2	4	6	11	16	20
1-Variant-c with black sides	3	6	9	14	19	24
1-Revisited (12/98, $2.95) reprints #1, Turner-c						4.00
...: Trouble Seekers TPB (2002, $7.95) rep. T.R./W & W/T.R. & W/T.R. 1/2; new Turner-c						8.00

TOMBSTONE TERRITORY
Dell Publishing Co.: No. 1123, Aug, 1960

Four Color 1123	7	14	21	49	92	135

TOM CAT (Formerly Bo; Atom The Cat #9 on)
Charlton Comics: No. 4, Apr, 1956 - No. 8, July, 1957

4-Al Fago-c/a	9	18	27	50	65	80
5-8	7	14	21	35	43	50

TOM CLANCY'S SPLINTER CELL: ECHOES
Dynamite Entertainment: 2014 - No. 4, 2014 ($3.99)

1-4-Nathan Edmonson-s/Marc Laming-a 4.00

TOM CLANCY'S THE DIVISION: EXTREMIS MALIS
Dark Horse Comics: Jan, 2019 - No. 3, Apr, 2019 ($3.99, limited series)

1-3-Christofer Emgard-s/Fernando Baldó-a 4.00

TOM CORBETT, SPACE CADET (TV)
Dell Publishing Co.: No. 378, Jan-Feb, 1952 - No. 11, Sept-Nov, 1954 (All painted covers)

Four Color 378 (#1)-McWilliams-a	20	40	60	140	315	490
Four Color 400,421-McWilliams-a	12	24	36	79	170	260
4(11-1/53) - 11	8	16	24	56	108	160

TOM CORBETT SPACE CADET (See March of Comics #102)

TOM CORBETT SPACE CADET (TV)
Prize Publications: V2#1, May-June, 1955 - V2#3, Sept-Oct, 1955

V2#1-Robot-c	40	80	120	246	411	575
2,3-Meskin-c	32	64	96	188	307	425

TOM, DICK & HARRIET (See Gold Key Spotlight)

TOM LANDRY AND THE DALLAS COWBOYS
Spire Christian Comics/Fleming H. Revell Co.: 1973 (35/49¢)

nn-35¢ edition	3	6	9	17	26	35
nn-49¢ edition	3	6	9	14	19	24

TOM MIX WESTERN (Movie, radio star) (Also see The Comics, Crackajack Funnies, Master Comics, 100 Pages Of Comics, Popular Comics, Real Western Hero, Six Gun Heroes, Western Hero & XMas Comics)
Fawcett Publications: Jan, 1948 - No. 61, May, 1953 (1-17: 52 pgs.)

1 (Photo-c, 52 pgs.)-Tom Mix & his horse Tony begin; Tumbleweed Jr. begins, ends #52,54,55	54	108	162	343	574	825
2 (Photo-c)	25	50	75	150	245	340
3-5 (Painted/photo-c): 5-Billy the Kid & Oscar app.	19	38	57	111	176	240
6-8: 6,7 (Painted/photo-c). 8-Kinstler tempera-c	16	32	48	94	147	200
9,10 (Paint/photo-c) 9-Used in **SOTI**, pgs. 323-325	15	30	45	90	140	190
11-Kinstler oil-c	14	28	42	82	121	160
12 (Painted/photo-c)	14	28	42	78	112	145
13-17 (Painted-c, 52 pgs.)	14	28	42	78	112	145
18,22 (Painted-c, 36 pgs.)	12	24	36	69	97	125
19 (Photo-c, 52 pgs.)	13	26	39	74	105	135
20,21,23 (Painted-c, 52 pgs.)	12	24	36	69	97	125
24,25,27-29 (52 pgs.): 24-Photo-c begin, end #61. 29-Slim Pickens app.	11	22	33	60	83	105
26,30 (36 pgs.)	10	20	30	56	76	95
31-33,35-37,39,40,42 (52 pgs.): 39-Red Eagle app.	10	20	30	56	76	95
34,38 (36 pgs. begin)	9	18	27	52	69	85
41,43-60: 57-(9/52)-Dope smuggling story	8	16	24	40	50	60
61-Last issue	9	18	27	47	61	75

NOTE: Photo-c from 1930s Tom Mix movies (he died in 1940). Many issues contain ads for Tom Mix, Rocky Lane, Space Patrol and other premiums. Captain Tootsie by **C.C. Beck** in #6-11, 20.

TOM MIX WESTERN
AC Comics: 1988 - No. 2, 1989? ($2.95, B&W w/16 pgs. color, 44 pgs.)

1-Tom Mix-r/Master #124,128,131,102 plus Billy the Kid-r by Severin; photo front/back/inside-c 4.00
2-($2.50, B&W)-Gabby Hayes-r; photo covers 4.00

...Holiday Album 1 (1990, $3.50, B&W, one-shot, 44 pgs.)-Contains photos & 1950s Tom Mix-r; photo inside-c 5.00

TOMMY GUN WIZARDS (Titled Machine Gun Wizards for #4)
Dark Horse Comics: Aug, 2019 - No. 4, Nov, 2019 ($3.99, limited series)

1-4-Christian Ward-s/Sami Kivelä-a; Prohibition era magicians in 1931 Chicago 4.00

TOMMY OF THE BIG TOP (Thrilling Circus Adventures)
King Features Synd./Standard Comics: No. 10, Sep, 1948 - No. 12, Mar, 1949

10-By John Lehti	15	30	45	83	124	165
11,12	10	20	30	56	76	95

TOMMY TOMORROW (See Action Comics #127, Real Fact #6, Showcase #41,42,44,46,47 & World's Finest #102)

TOMOE (Also see Shi: The Way Of The Warrior #6)
Crusade Comics: July, 1995 - No. 3, June, 1996($2.95)

0-3: 2-B&W Dogs o' War preview. 3-B&W Demon Gun preview						4.00
0 (3/96, $2.95)-variant-c.						4.00
0-Commemorative edition (5,000)	2	4	6	8	10	12
1-Commemorative edition (5,000)	2	4	6	9	12	15
1-($2.95)-FAN Appreciation edition						4.00
TPB (1997, $14.95) r/#0-3						15.00

TOMOE: UNFORGETTABLE FIRE
Crusade Comics: June, 1997 ($2.95, one-shot)

1-Prequel to Shi: The Series 4.00

TOMOE-WITCHBLADE/FIRE SERMON
Crusade Comics: Sept, 1996 ($3.95, one-shot)

1-Tucci-c 5.00
1-($9.95)-Avalon Ed. w/gold foil-c 10.00

TOMOE-WITCHBLADE/MANGA SHI PREVIEW EDITION
Crusade Comics: July, 1996 ($5.00, B&W)

nn-San Diego Preview Edition 5.00

TOMORROW
Dark Horse Comics (Berger Books): Feb, 2020 - No. 5 ($3.99, limited series)

1,2-Peter Milligan-s/Jesús Hervás-a 4.00

TOMORROW KNIGHTS
Marvel Comics (Epic Comics): June, 1990 - No. 6, Mar, 1991 ($1.50)

1-($1.95, 52 pgs.) 5.00
2-6 ..... 4.00

TOMORROW STORIES
America's Best Comics: Oct, 1999 - No. 12, Aug, 2002 ($3.50/$2.95)

1-Two covers by Ross and Nowlan; Moore-s 4.00
2-12-($2.95) 6-1st app. Splash Brannigan 3.00
... Special (1/06, $6.99) Nowlan-c; Moore-s; Greyshirt tribute to Will Eisner 7.00
... Special 2 (5/06, $6.99) Gene Ha-c; Moore-s; Promethea app. 7.00
Book 1 Hardcover (2002, $24.95) r/#1-6 ..... 25.00
Book 1 TPB (2003, $17.95) r/#1-6 ..... 18.00
Book 2 Hardcover (2004, $24.95) r/#7-12 ..... 25.00
Book 2 TPB (2005, $17.99) r/#7-12 ..... 18.00

TOM SAWYER (See Adventures of... & Famous Stories)

TOM SKINNER-UP FROM HARLEM (See Up From Harlem)

TOM STRONG (Also see Many Worlds of Tesla Strong)
America's Best Comics: June, 1999 - No. 36, May, 2006 ($3.50/$2.95/$2.99)

1-Two covers by Ross and Sprouse; Moore-s/Sprouse-a 4.00
1-Special Edition (9/09, $1.00) reprint with "After Watchmen" cover frame 3.00
2-36: 4-Art Adams-a (8 pgs.). 13-Tribute app. by Sprouse, Baker, Heath 20-Origin of Tom Stone. 21-Ordway-a. 31,32-Moorcock-a. 3.00
...: Book One HC ('00, $24.95) r/#1-7, cover gallery and sketchbook 25.00
...: Book One TPB ('01, $14.95) r/#1-7, cover gallery and sketchbook 15.00
...: Book Two HC ('02, $24.95) r/#8-14, sketchbook 25.00
...: Book Two TPB ('03, $14.95) r/#8-14, sketchbook 15.00
...: Book Three HC ('04, $24.95) r/#15-19, sketchbook 25.00
...: Book Three TPB ('04, $17.95) r/#15-19, sketchbook 18.00
...: Book Four HC ('04, $24.95) r/#20-25, sketch pages 25.00
...: Book Four TPB ('05, $17.99) r/#20-25, sketch pages 18.00
...: Book Five HC ('05, $24.99) r/#26-30, sketch pages 25.00
...: Book Five TPB ('06, $17.99) r/#26-30, sketch pages 18.00
...: Book Six HC ('06, $24.99) r/#31-36 ..... 25.00
...: Book Six TPB ('08, $17.99) r/#31-36 ..... 18.00
...: The Deluxe Edition Book One (2009, $39.99, d.j.) r/#1-12; Moore intro.; sketch-a 40.00
...: The Deluxe Edition Book Two (2010, $39.99, d.j.) r/#13-24; sketch-a 40.00

	GD 2.0	VG 4.0	FN 6.0	VF 8.0	VF/NM 9.0	NM- 9.2

TOM STRONG AND THE PLANET OF PERIL
DC Comics (Vertigo): Sept, 2013 - No. 6, Feb, 2014 ($2.99, limited series)

1-6-Hogan-s/Sprouse-a/c. 2-Travel to Terra Obscura						3.00

TOM STRONG AND THE ROBOTS OF DOOM
DC Comics (WildStorm): Aug, 2010 - No. 6, Jan, 2011 ($3.99, limited series)

1-6-Hogan-s/Sprouse-a. 1-Covers by Sprouse & Williams						4.00
TPB (2011, $17.99) r/#1-6						18.00

TOM STRONG'S TERRIFIC TALES
America's Best Comics: Jan, 2002 - No. 12 ($3.50/$2.95)

1-Short stories; Moore-s; art by Art Adams, Rivoche, Hernandez, Weiss						3.50
2-12-($2.95) 2-Adams, Ordway, Weiss-a; Adams-c. 4-Rivoche-a. 5-Pearson, Aragonés-a						
11-Timm-a						3.00
... Book One HC ('04, $24.95) r/#1-6, cover gallery and sketch pages						25.00
... Book One SC ('05, $17.99) r/#1-6, cover gallery and sketch pages						18.00
... Book Two HC ('05, $24.95) r/#7-12, covers						25.00

TOM TERRIFIC! (TV)(See Mighty Mouse Fun Club Magazine #1)
Pines Comics (Paul Terry): Summer, 1957 - No. 6, Fall, 1958
(See Terry Toons Giant Summer Fun Book)

	GD	VG	FN	VF	VF/NM	NM-
1-1st app.?; CBS Television Presents...	28	56	84	165	270	375
2-6-(scarce)	21	42	63	122	199	275

TOM THUMB
Dell Publishing Co.: No. 972, Jan, 1959

	GD	VG	FN	VF	VF/NM	NM-
Four Color 972-Movie, George Pal	8	16	24	56	105	160

TOM-TOM, THE JUNGLE BOY (See A-1 Comics & Tick Tock Tales)
Magazine Enterprises: 1947 - No. 3, 1947; Nov, 1957 - No. 3, Mar, 1958

	GD	VG	FN	VF	VF/NM	NM-
1-Funny animal	16	32	48	94	147	200
2,3(1947): 3-Christmas issue	13	26	39	74	105	135
Tom-Tom & Itchi the Monk 1(11/57) - 3(3/58)	7	14	21	37	46	55
I.W. Reprint No. 1,2,8,10: 1,2,8-r/Koko & Kola #?	2	4	6	11	16	20

TONGUE LASH
Dark Horse Comics: Aug, 1996 - No. 2, Sept, 1996 ($2.95, lim. series, mature)

1,2: Taylor-c/a						4.00

TONGUE LASH II
Dark Horse Comics: Feb, 1999 - No. 2, Mar, 1999 ($2.95, lim. series, mature)

1,2: Taylor-c/a						4.00

TONKA (Disney)
Dell Publishing Co.: No. 966, Jan, 1959

	GD	VG	FN	VF	VF/NM	NM-
Four Color 966-Movie (Starring Sal Mineo)-photo-c	8	16	24	56	108	160

TONTO (See The Lone Ranger's Companion)

TONY STARK: IRON MAN (Leads into Iron Man 2020 #1)
Marvel Comics: Aug, 2018 - No. 19, Feb, 2020 ($4.99/$3.99)

1-($4.99) Slott-s/Schiti-a; Fin Fang Foom & The Controller app.						5.00
2-19-($3.99) 3-Machine Man app. 4,6-8-Janet Van Dyne app. 5-Arno Stark app.						
12,13-War of the Realms tie-ins; Simone-s. 14-Capt. Marvel app. 16-19 Ultron app.						4.00

TONY TRENT (The Face #1,2)
Big Shot/Columbia Comics Group: No. 3, 1948 - No. 4, 1949

	GD	VG	FN	VF	VF/NM	NM-
3,4: 3-The Face app. by Mart Bailey	23	46	69	136	223	310

TOODLES, THE (The Toodle Twins with #1)
Ziff-Davis (Approved Comics)/Argo: No. 10, July-Aug, 1951; Mar, 1956 (Newspaper-r)

	GD	VG	FN	VF	VF/NM	NM-
10-Painted-c, some newspaper-r by The Baers	17	34	51	98	154	210
...Twins 1(Argo, 3/56)-Reprints by The Baers	10	20	30	54	72	90

TOO MUCH COFFEE MAN
Adhesive Comics: July, 1993 - No. 10, Dec, 2000 ($2.50, B&W)

	GD	VG	FN	VF	VF/NM	NM-
1-Shannon Wheeler story & art	2	4	6	9	12	15
2,3	1	2	3	5	7	9
4,5						6.00
6-10						4.00
Full Color Special-nn($2.95),2-(7/97, $3.95)						4.00

TOO MUCH COFFEE MAN SPECIAL
Dark Horse Comics: July, 1997 ($2.95, B&W)

nn-Reprints Dark Horse Presents #92-95						4.00

TOO MUCH HOPELESS SAVAGES
Oni Press: June, 2003 - No. 4, Apr, 2004 ($2.99, B&W, limited series)

1-4-Van Meter-s/Norrie-a						3.00
TPB (8/04, $11.95, digest-size) r/series						12.00

TOOTH & CLAW (See Autumnlands: Tooth & Claw)

TOOTS AND CASPER
Dell Publishing Co.: No. 5, 1942

	GD	VG	FN	VF	VF/NM	NM-
Large Feature Comic 5	27	54	81	158	259	360

TOP ADVENTURE COMICS
I. W. Enterprises: 1964 (Reprints)

	GD	VG	FN	VF	VF/NM	NM-
1-r/High Adv. (Explorer Joe #2); Krigstein-r	2	4	6	13	18	22
2-Black Dwarf-r/Red Seal #22; Kinstler-c	3	6	9	14	20	25

TOP CAT (TV)(Hanna-Barbera)(See Kite Fun Book)
Dell Publ.Co./Gold Key No. 4 on: 12-2/61-62 - No. 3, 6-8/62; No. 4, 10/62 - No. 31, 9/70

	GD	VG	FN	VF	VF/NM	NM-
1 (TV show debuted 9/27/61)	15	30	45	105	233	360
2-Augie Doggie back-ups in #1-4	9	18	27	58	114	170
3-5: 3-Last 15¢ issue. 4-Begin 12¢ issue; Yakky Doodle app. in 1 pg. strip.						
5-Touché Turtle app.	6	12	18	37	66	95
6-10	5	10	15	30	50	70
11-20	4	8	12	23	37	50
21-31-Reprints	3	6	9	18	28	38

TOP CAT (TV) (Hanna-Barbera)(See TV Stars #4)
Charlton Comics: Nov, 1970 - No. 20, Nov, 1973

	GD	VG	FN	VF	VF/NM	NM-
1	7	14	21	54	82	120
2-10	3	6	9	19	30	40
11-20	3	6	9	16	24	32

NOTE: #8 (1/72) went on sale late in 1972 between #14 and #15 with the 1/73 issues.

TOP COMICS
K. K. Publications/Gold Key: July, 1967 (All reprints)

	GD	VG	FN	VF	VF/NM	NM-
nn-The Gnome-Mobile (Disney-movie)	3	6	9	14	20	25
1-Beagle Boys (#7), Beep Beep the Road Runner (#5), Bugs Bunny, Chip 'n' Dale, Daffy Duck (#50), Flipper, Huey, Dewey & Louie, Junior Woodchucks, Lassie, The Little Monsters (#71), Moby Duck, Porky Pig (has Gold Key label - says Top Comics on inside), Scamp, Super Goof, Tom & Jerry, Top Cat (#21), Tweety & Sylvester (#7), Walt Disney C&S (#322), Woody Woodpecker known issues; each character given own book	2	4	6	9	13	16
1-Donald Duck (not Barks), Mickey Mouse	2	4	6	13	18	22
1-Flintstones	4	8	12	23	37	50
1-Huckleberry Hound, Yogi Bear (#30)	3	6	9	14	19	24
1-The Jetsons	5	10	15	30	50	70
1-Tarzan of the Apes (#169)	3	6	9	16	23	30
1-Three Stooges (#35)	3	6	9	16	23	30
1-Uncle Scrooge (#70)	3	6	9	19	30	40
1-Zorro (r/K. Zorro #7 w/Toth-a; says 2nd printing)	3	6	9	14	19	24
2-Bugs Bunny, Daffy Duck, Mickey Mouse (#114), Porky Pig, Super Goof, Tom & Jerry, Tweety & Sylvester, Walt Disney's C&S (r/#325), Woody Woodpecker	2	4	6	9	12	15
2-Donald Duck (not Barks), Three Stooges, Uncle Scrooge (#71)-Barks-c, Yogi Bear (#30), Zorro (r/#8; Toth-a)	2	4	6	11	16	20
2-Snow White & 7 Dwarfs(6/67)(1944-r)	2	4	6	11	16	20
2-Donald Duck	2	4	6	11	16	20
3-Uncle Scrooge (#72)	2	4	6	13	18	22
3,4-The Flintstones	3	6	9	21	33	45
3,4: 3-Mickey Mouse (r/#115), Tom & Jerry, Woody Woodpecker, Yogi Bear. 4-Mickey Mouse, Woody Woodpecker	2	4	6	9	12	15

NOTE: Each book in this series is identical to its counterpart except for cover, and came out at same time. The number in parentheses is the original issue it contains.

TOP COW (Company one-shots)
Image Comics (Top Cow Productions)

... Book of Revelations (7/03, $3.99)-Pin-ups and info; art by various; Gossett-c						4.00
... Convention Sketchbook 2004 (4/04, $3.00, B&W) art by various						3.00
... Holiday Special Vol. 1 (12/10, $12.99) Flip book with Jingle Belle						13.00
... Preview Book 2005 (3/05, 99¢) Preview pages of Tomb Raider, Darkness, Rising Stars						3.00
... Productions, Inc./Ballistic Studios Swimsuit Special (5/95, $2.95)						
...'s Best of: Dave Finch Vol. 1 TPB (8/06, $19.99) r/issues of Cyberforce, Aphrodite IX, Ascension and The Darkness; art & cover gallery						20.00
...'s Best of: Michael Turner Vol. 1 TPB (12/05, $24.99) r/Witchblade #1,10,12,18,19,25 & Witchblade/Tomb Raider chapters 1&3; Tomb Raider #25; art & cover gallery						25.00
... Secrets: Special Winter Lingerie Edition 1 (1/96, $2.95) Pin-ups						3.00
... 2001 Preview (no cover price) Preview pages of Tomb Raider; Jusko-a; flip cover & pages of Inferno						3.00

TOP COW CLASSICS IN BLACK AND WHITE
Image Comics (Top Cow): Feb, 2000 - Jan, 2003 ($2.95, B&W reprints)

...: Aphrodite IX #1(9/00) B&W reprint						3.00
...: Ascension #1(4/00) B&W reprint plus time-line of series						3.00
...: Battle of the Planets #1(1/03) B&W reprint plus script and cover gallery						3.00
...: Darkness #1(3/00) B&W reprint plus time-line of series						3.00
...: Fathom #1(5/00) B&W reprint						3.00
...: Magdalena #1(10/02) B&W reprint plus time-line of series						3.00
...: Midnight Nation #1(9/00) B&W preview						3.00
...: Rising Stars #1(7/00) B&W reprint plus cover gallery						3.00
...: Tomb Raider #1(12/00) B&W reprint plus back-story						3.00
...: Witchblade #1(2/00) B&W reprint plus back-story						3.00
...: Witchblade #25(5/01) B&W reprint plus interview with Wohl & Haberlin						3.00

TOP DETECTIVE COMICS
I. W. Enterprises: 1964 (Reprints)

	GD	VG	FN	VF	VF/NM	NM-
9-r/Young King Cole #14; Dr. Drew (not Grandenetti)	2	4	6	11	16	20

TOP DOG (See Star Comics Magazine, 75¢)
Star Comics (Marvel): Apr, 1985 - No. 14, June, 1987 (Children's book)

1-14: 10-Peter Parker & J. Jonah Jameson cameo						5.00

TOP ELIMINATOR (Teenage Hotrodders #1-24; Drag 'n' Wheels #30 on)
Charlton Comics: No. 25, Sept, 1967 - No. 29, July, 1968

	GD	VG	FN	VF	VF/NM	NM-
25-29	3	6	9	16	23	30

TOP FLIGHT COMICS: Four Star Publ.: 1947 (Advertised, not published)

TOP FLIGHT COMICS
St. John Publishing Co.: July, 1949

	GD	VG	FN	VF	VF/NM	NM-
1(7/49, St. John)-Hector the Inspector; funny animal	14	28	42	82	121	160

TOP GUN (See Luke Short, 4-Color #927 & Showcase #72)

TOP GUNS OF THE WEST (See Super DC Giant)

TOPIX (...Comics)(Timeless Topix-early issues) (Also see Men of Battle, Men of Courage & Treasure Chest)(V1-V5#1,V7 on-paper-c)
Catechetical Guild Educational Society: 11/42 - V10#15, 1/28/52
(Weekly - later issues)

	GD	VG	FN	VF	VF/NM	NM-
V1#1(8 pgs..8x11")	25	50	75	150	245	340
2,3(8 pgs..8x11")	14	28	42	82	121	160
4-8(16 pgs..8x11")	12	24	36	69	97	125
V2#1-10(16 pgs..8x11"): V2#8-Pope Pius XII	10	20	30	58	79	100
V3#1-10(16 pgs..8x11"): V3#1-(9/44)	10	20	30	56	76	95
V4#1-10: V4#1-(9/45)	10	20	30	56	76	95
V5#1(10/46,52 pg..2(11/46),no #3),4(1/47)-9(6/47),10(7/47), no #13,4(10/47), 14(11/47),15(12/47)	8	16	24	42	54	65
11(8/47),12(9/47)-Life of Christ editions	10	20	30	56	76	95
V6#1(1/48),5(2/48),7(3/48),8(4/48),9(5/48),10(6/48),11(7/48)-14 (no #1-3,6)	7	14	21	35	43	50

Top Cat #17 © H-B

Top-Notch Comics #18 © ACP

Top 10 #7 © ABC

	GD	VG	FN	VF	VF/NM	NM-
	2.0	4.0	6.0	8.0	9.0	9.2

V7#1(9/1/48)-20(6/15/49), 36 pgs. — 6 12 18 29 36 42
V8#1(9/19/49)-3,5-11,13-30(5/15/50) 30-Hitler app. — 6 12 18 28 34 40
4-Dagwood Splits the Atom(10/10/49)-Magazine format
  — 8 16 24 42 54 65
12-Ingels-a — 10 20 30 56 76 95
V9#1(9/25/50)-11,13-30(5/14/51) — 6 12 18 27 33 38
12-Special 36 pg. Xmas issue, text illos format — 6 12 18 28 34 40
V10#1(10/1/51)-15: 14-Hollingsworth-a — 6 12 18 27 33 38

TOP JUNGLE COMICS
I. W. Enterprises: 1964 (Reprint)

1(nd)-Reprints White Princess of the Jungle #3, minus cover; Kintsler-a
  — 3 6 9 18 28 38

TOP LOVE STORIES (Formerly Gasoline Alley #2)
Star Publications: No. 3, 5/51 - No. 19, 3/54

3(#1) — 37 74 111 222 361 500
4,5,7-9: 8-Wood story — 30 60 90 177 289 400
6-Wood-a — 34 68 102 204 332 460
10-16,18,19-Disbrow-a — 27 54 81 158 259 360
17-Wood art (Fox-r) — 28 56 84 165 270 375
NOTE: All have L. B. Cole covers.

TOP-NOTCH COMICS (...Laugh #28-45; Laugh Comix #46 on)
MLJ Magazines: Dec, 1939 - No. 45, June, 1944

1-Origin/1st app. The Wizard; Kardak the Mystic Magician, Swift of the Secret Service
  (ends #3), Air Patrol, The Westpointer, Manhunters (by J. Cole), Mystic (ends #2) &
  Scott Rand (ends #3) begin; Wizard covers begin, end #8
  622 1244 1866 4541 8021 11,500
2-(1/40)-Dick Storm (ends #8), Stacy Knight M.D. (ends #4) begin; Jack Cole-a;
  1st app. Nazis swastika on-c — 300 600 900 1980 3440 4900
3-Bob Phantom, Scott Rand on Mars begin; J. Cole-a
  232 464 696 1485 2543 3600
4-Origin/1st app. Streak Chandler on Mars; Moore of the Mounted only app.; J. Cole-a
  206 412 618 1318 2259 3200
5-Flag-c; origin/1st app. Galahad; Shanghai Sheridan begins (ends #8); Shield cameo;
  Novick-a; classic-c — 239 478 717 1530 2615 3700
6-Meskin-a — 161 322 483 1030 1765 2500
7-The Shield x-over in Wizard; The Wizard dons new costume
  194 388 582 1242 2121 3000
8-Origin/1st app. The Firefly & Roy, the Super Boy (9/40, 2nd costumed boy hero after
  Robin?); also see Toro in Human Torch #1 (Fall/40)
  206 412 618 1318 2259 3200
9-Origin & 1st app. The Black Hood; 1st Black Hood-c & logo (10/40); Fran Frazier begins
  (Scarce) — 811 1622 2433 5920 10,460 15,000
10-2nd app. Black Hood — 271 542 813 1734 2967 4200
11-3rd Black Hood — 200 400 600 1280 2190 3100
12-15 — 155 310 465 992 1696 2400
16-18,20 — 142 284 426 909 1555 2200
19-Classic bondage-c — 181 362 543 1158 1979 2800
21,23-30: 23-26-Roy app. 24-No Wizard. 25-Last Bob Phantom. 27-Last Firefly; Nazi war-c.
  28-1st app. Suzie; Pokey Oakey begins. 29-Last Kardak
  106 212 318 673 1162 1650
22-Archie cameo in ad (12/41) same date as Pep Comics #22
  703 1406 2109 5132 9066 13,000
31-44: 33-Dotty & Ditto by Woggon begins (2/43, 1st app.). 44-Black Hood series ends
  58 116 174 371 636 900
45-Last issue — 77 154 231 493 847 1200
NOTE: J. Binder a-1-3. Meskin a-2, 3, 6, 15. Bob Montana a-30; c-28-31. Harry Sahle c-42-45. Woggon a-33-
40, 42. Bondage c-17, 19. Black Hood also appeared on radio in 1944. Black Hood app. on c-9-34, 41-44. Roy the
Super Boy app. on c-8, 9, 11-27. The Wizard app. on c-1-8, 11-13, 15-22, 24, 25, 27. Pokey Oakey app. on c-28-
43. Suzie app. on c-44-on.

TOPPER & NEIL (TV)
Dell Publishing Co.: No. 859, Nov, 1957

Four Color 859 — 8 16 21 51 96 140

TOPPS COMICS: Four Star Publications: 1947 (Advertised, not published)

TOPS
July, 1949 - No. 2, Sept, 1949 (25¢, 10-1/4x13-1/4", 68 pgs.)
Tops Magazine, Inc. (Lev Gleason): (Large size-magazine format; for the adult reader)

1 (Rare)-Story by Dashiell Hammett; Crandall/Lubbers, Tuska, Dan Barry, Fuje-a;
  Biro painted-c — 300 600 900 2070 3635 5200
2 (Rare)-Crandall/Lubbers, Biro, Kida, Fuje, Guardineer-a
  276 552 828 1753 3027 4300

TOPS COMICS
Consolidated Book Publishers: 1944 (10¢, 132 pgs.)

2000-(Color-c, inside in red shade & some in full color)-Ace Kelly by Rick Yager, Black Orchid,
  Don on the Farm, Dinky Dinkerton (Rare) — 60 120 180 381 653 925
NOTE: This book is printed in such a way that when the staple is removed, the strips on the left side of the book
correspond with the same strips on the right side. Therefore, if strips are removed from the book, each strip can be
folded into a complete comic section of its own.

TOPS COMICS
Consolidated Book Publs. (Lev Gleason): 1944 (7-1/4x5" digest-size, 32 pgs.)

2001-Origin The Jack of Spades (costumed hero) — 39 78 117 231 378 525
2002-Rip Raider — 24 48 72 142 234 325
2003-Red Birch (gag cartoons) — 14 28 42 82 121 160
2004-"Don't Bother to Dry Off" (gag cartoons) — 23 46 69 136 223 310

TOP SECRET
Hillman Publ.: Jan, 1952

1 — 30 60 90 177 289 400

TOP SECRET ADVENTURES (See Spyman)

TOP SECRETS (...of the F.B.I.)
Street & Smith Publications: Nov, 1947 - No. 10, July-Aug, 1949

1-Powell-c/a — 47 94 141 296 498 700
2-Powell-c/a — 32 64 96 188 307 425
3-6,8,10-Powell-a — 28 56 84 165 270 375
9-Powell-c/a — 29 58 87 172 281 390
7-Used in SOTI, pg. 90 & illo. "How to hurt people"; used by N.Y. Legis. Comm.;
  Powell-a — 42 84 126 265 445 625
NOTE: Powell c-1-3, 5-10.

TOPS IN ADVENTURE
Ziff-Davis Publishing Co.: Fall, 1952 (25¢, 132 pgs.)

1-Crusader from Mars, The Hawk, Football Thrills, He-Man; Powell-a; painted-c
  57 114 171 362 619 875

TOPS IN HUMOR
Remington Morse Publ. (Harry A. Chesler, Jr.): No date (1944) (7-1/4x5" digest size,
64 pgs., 10¢)

1-WWII serviceman humor (scarce) — 32 64 96 188 307 425
2-(Wise Publ.) WWII serviceman humor — 19 38 57 111 176 240

TOP SPOT COMICS
Top Spot Publ. Co.: 1945

1-The Menace, Duke of Darkness app. — 58 116 174 371 636 900

TOPSY-TURVY (Teenage)
R. B. Leffingwell Publ.: Apr, 1945

1-1st app. Cookie — 39 78 117 231 398 525

TOP TEN
America's Best Comics: Sept, 1999 - No. 12, Oct, 2001 ($3.50/$2.95)

1-Two covers by Ross and Ha/Cannon; Alan Moore-s/Gene Ha-a — 4.00
2-11-($2.95) — 3.00
12-($3.50) — 3.50
Hardcover ('00, $24.95) Dust jacket with Gene Ha-a; r/#1-7 — 25.00
Softcover ('00, $14.95) new Gene Ha-c; r/#1-7 — 15.00
Book 2 HC ('02, $24.95) Dust jacket with Gene Ha-a; r/#8-12 — 25.00
Book 2 SC ('03, $14.95) new Gene Ha-c; r/#8-12 — 15.00
...: The Forty-Niners HC (2005, $24.99, dust jacket) prequel set in 1949; Moore-s/Ha-a — 25.00

TOP TEN: BEYOND THE FARTHEST PRECINCT
America's Best Comics: Oct, 2005 - No. 5, Feb, 2006 ($2.99, limited series)

1-5-Jerry Ordway-a/Paul DiFilippo-s — 3.00
TPB (2006, $14.99) r/series; cover sketch pages — 15.00

TOP TEN SEASON TWO
America's Best Comics: Dec, 2008 - No. 4, Mar, 2009 ($2.99, limited series)

1-4-Cannon-s/Ha-a — 3.00
... Special (5/09, $2.99) Cannon-s/Daxiong-a/Ha-c — 3.00

TOR (Prehistoric Life on Earth) (Formerly One Million Years Ago)
St. John Publ. Co.: No. 2, Oct, 1953; No. 3, May, 1954 - No. 5, Oct, 1954

3-D 2(10/53)-Kubert-c/a — 15 30 45 90 140 190
3-D 2(10/53)-Oversized, otherwise same contents — 15 30 45 83 124 165
3-D 2(11/53)-Kubert-c/a — 15 30 45 83 124 165
3-5-Kubert-c/a: 3-Danny Dreams by Toth; Kubert 1 pg. story (w/self portrait)
  21 42 63 122 199 275
NOTE: The two October 3-D's have same contents and Powell art; the October & November issues are titled 3-D
Comics. All 3-D issues are 25¢ and came with 3-D glasses.

TOR (See Sojourn)
National Periodical Publications: May-June, 1975 - No. 6, Mar-Apr, 1976

	GD 2.0	VG 4.0	FN 6.0	VF 8.0	VF/NM 9.0	NM- 9.2
1-New origin by Kubert	2	4	6	11	16	20
2-6: 2-Origin-r/St. John #1	1	2	3	5	6	8

NOTE: *Kubert a-1, 2-6r; c-1-6. Toth a(p)-3r.*

TOR (3-D)
Eclipse Comics: July, 1986 - No. 2, Aug, 1987 ($2.50)

1,2: 1-r/One Million Years Ago. 2-r/Tor 3-D #2						5.00
...2-D: 1,2-Limited signed & numbered editions	2	4	6	11	16	20

TOR
Marvel Comics (Epic Comics/Heavy Hitters): June, 1993 - No. 4, 1993 ($5.95, lim. series)

1-4: Joe Kubert-c/a/scripts						6.00

TOR (Joe Kubert's...)
DC Comics: Jul, 2008 - No. 6, Dec, 2008 ($2.99, limited series)

1-6-New story; Joe Kubert-c/a/scripts						3.00
...: A Prehistoric Odyssey HC (2009, $24.99, DJ) r/#1-6; Roy Thomas intro.; sketch-a						25.00
...: A Prehistoric Odyssey SC (2009, $14.99) r/#1-6; Roy Thomas intro.; sketch-a						15.00

TOR BY JOE KUBERT
DC Comics: 2001 - 2003 ($49.95, hardcovers with dust jacket)

Volume 1 (2001) r/One Million Years Ago #1 & 3-D Comics #1&2 in flat color; script pages, sketch pages, proposals for TV and newspapers strips; intro. by Roy Thomas						50.00
Volume 2 (2002) r/Tor (St. John) #3-5; Danny Dreams; portfolio section						50.00
Volume 3 (2003) r/Tor (DC '75) #1; (Marvel '93) #1-4; portfolio section						50.00

TORCH, THE
Marvel Comics (with Dynamite Ent.): Nov, 2009 - No. 8, Jul, 2010 ($3.99, limited series)

1-8-Thinker resurrects the Golden Age Human Torch; Toro app; Alex Ross-c on all; Berkenkotter-a. 3-5-Namor app.						4.00

TORCH OF LIBERTY SPECIAL
Dark Horse Comics (Legend): Jan, 1995 ($2.50, one-shot)

1-Byrne scripts						4.00

TORCHWOOD (Based on the BBC TV series)
Titan Comics: Sept, 2010 - No. 6, Jan, 2011 ($3.99)

1-6: 1-Barrowman-s/Edwards-a; Churchill and photo-c. 2-Art by Yeowell & Grist						4.00

TORCHWOOD (Based on the BBC TV series)
Titan Comics: Aug, 2016 - No. 4, Jan, 2017; Vol. 2: Mar, 2017 - No. 4, Jun, 2017; Vol. 3: Nov, 2017 - No. 4, Mar, 2018 ($3.99)

1-4-John & Carole Barrowman-s/Fuso & Qualano-a; multiple covers						4.00
Vol. 2 1-4-John & Carole Barrowman-s/Edwards-a; multiple covers						4.00
Vol. 3 1-4-John & Carole Barrowman-s/Edwards-a; multiple covers; Capt. John Hart app.						4.00

TORCHY (...Blonde Bombshell) (Dollman, Military, & Modern)
Quality Comics Group: Nov, 1949 - No. 6, Sept, 1950

1-Bill Ward-c, Gil Fox-a	265	530	795	1694	2897	4100
2,3-Fox-c/a	135	270	405	864	1482	2100
4-Fox-c/a(3), Ward-a (9 pgs.)	181	362	543	1158	1979	2800
5,6-Ward-c/a, 9 pgs; Fox-a(3) each	174	348	522	1114	1907	2700
Super Reprint #16(1964)-r/#4 with new-c	9	18	27	62	126	190

TO RIVERDALE AND BACK AGAIN (Archie Comics Presents...)
Archie Comics: 1990 ($2.50, 68 pgs.)

nn-Byrne-c, Colan-a(p); adapts NBC TV movie	2	4	6	8	10	12

TORMENTED, THE (Becomes Surprise Adventures #3 on)
Sterling Comics: July, 1954 - No. 2, Sept, 1954

1-Good Girl torture-c	290	580	870	1856	3178	4500
2-Devil's circus-c	103	206	309	659	1130	1600

TORNADO TOM (See Mighty Midget Comics)

TORRENT
Image Comics: Feb, 2023 - No. 5, Jul, 2023 ($3.99)

1-5-Guggenheim-s/Greenwood-a						4.00

TORSO (See Jinx: Torso)

TOTAL ECLIPSE
Eclipse Comics: May, 1988 - No. 5, Apr, 1989 ($3.95, 52 pgs., deluxe size)

Book 1-5: 3-Intro/1st app. new Black Terror. 4-Many copies have upside down pages and are mis-cut						5.00

TOTAL ECLIPSE
Image Comics: July, 1998 (one-shot)

1-McFarlane-c; Eclipse Comics character pin-ups by Image artists						4.00

TOTAL ECLIPSE: THE SERAPHIM OBJECTIVE
Eclipse Comics: Nov, 1988 ($1.95, one-shot, Baxter paper)

1-Airboy, Valkyrie, The Heap app.						4.00

TOTAL JUSTICE
DC Comics: Oct, 1996 - No. 3, Nov, 1996 ($2.25, bi-weekly limited series) (Based on toyline)

1-3						4.00

TOTALLY AWESOME HULK, THE (Amadeus Cho as The Hulk)(Continues in Inc. Hulk #709)
Marvel Comics: Feb, 2016 - No. 23, Nov, 2017 ($4.99/$3.99)

1-($4.99) Frank Cho-a/Greg Pak-s; She-Hulk and Spider-Man (Miles) app.						5.00
2,4-23-($3.99) 2-Fin Fang Foom and Lady Hellbender app. 5,6-Mike Choi-a. 7,8-Alan Davis-a. 9-11-Civil War II tie-in. 9-Del Mundo-a. 10-12-Black Panther app. 13-15-Jeremy Lin app. 19-22-Crossover with Weapon X #5,6 and Weapons of Mutant Destruction: Alpha #1; Old Man Logan & Sabretooth app. 23-Frank Cho-c						4.00
3-1st Kid Kaiju; Fin Fang Foom & Lady Hellbender app.	2	4	6	9	12	15
#1.MU (5/17, $4.99) Monsters Unleashed tie-in; art by Templeton, Ortiz, Lindsay						5.00

TOTAL RECALL (Movie)
DC Comics: 1990 ($2.95, 68 pgs., movie adaptation, one-shot)

1-Arnold Schwarzenegger photo-c						6.00

TOTAL RECALL (Continuation of movie)
Dynamite Entertainment: 2011 - No. 4, 2011 ($3.99, limited series)

1-4-Quaid and Melina on Mars following the movie; Razek/Robertson-c						4.00

TOTAL WAR (M.A.R.S. Patrol #3 on)
Gold Key: July, 1965 - No. 2, Oct, 1965 (Painted-c)

1-Wood-a in both issues	7	14	21	49	92	135
2	5	10	15	34	60	85

TOTEMS (Vertigo V2K)
DC Comics (Vertigo): Feb, 2000 ($5.95, one-shot)

1-Swamp Thing, Animal Man, Zatanna, Shade app.; Fegredo-c						6.00

TO THE HEART OF THE STORM
Kitchen Sink Press: 1991 (B&W, graphic novel)

Softcover-Will Eisner-s/a/c						20.00
Hardcover ($24.95)						30.00
TPB-(DC Comics, 9/00, $14.95) reprints 1991 edition						15.00

TO THE LAST MAN (See Zane Grey Four Color #616)

TOUCH OF SILVER, A
Image Comics: Jan, 1997 - No. 6, Nov, 1997 ($2.95, B&W, bi-monthly)

1-6-Valentino-s/a; photo-c: 5-color pgs. w/Round Table						4.00
TPB ($12.95) r/#1-6						13.00

TOUGH KID SQUAD COMICS
Timely Comics (TCI): Mar, 1942

1-(Scarce)-Origin & 1st app.The Human Top & The Tough Kid Squad; The Flying Flame app.	1000	2000	3000	7600	13,800	20,000

TOWER OF SHADOWS (Creatures on the Loose #10 on)
Marvel Comics Group: Sept, 1969 - No. 9, Jan, 1971

1-Romita-c, classic Steranko-a; Craig-a(p)	8	16	24	52	99	145
2,3: 2-Neal Adams-a. 3-Barry Smith, Tuska-a	5	10	15	31	53	75
4,6: 4-Marie Severin-c. 6-Wood-a	4	8	12	28	47	65
5-B. Smith-a(p), Wood-a; Wood draws himself (1st pg., 1st panel)	5	10	15	30	50	70
7-9: 7-B. Smith-a(p), Wood-a. 8-Wood-a; Wrightson-c. 9-Wrightson-c; Roy Thomas app.	5	10	15	31	53	75
Special 1(12/71, 52 pgs.)-Neal Adams-a; Romita-c	4	8	12	28	47	65

NOTE: *J. Buscema a-1p, 2p, Special 1r. Colan a-3p, 6p, Special 1. J. Craig a(r)-1p. Ditko a-6, 8, 9r, Special 1. Everett a-9(r)r; c-5i. Kirby a(p)-2, 5p, 6. Severin c-5p, 6. Steranko a-3. Wood a-5-8. Issues 1-9 contain new stories with some pre-Marvel age reprints in 6-9. H. P. Lovecraft adaptation-9.*

TOWN CALLED TERROR, A
Image Comics: Apr, 2022 - Present ($3.99)

1-6-Steve Niles-s/Szymon Kudranski-a						4.00

TOXIC AVENGER (Movie)
Marvel Comics: Apr, 1991 - No. 11, Feb, 1992 ($1.50)

1-Based on movie character	3	6	9	21	33	45
2-11: 3,10-Photo-c						4.00

TOXIC CRUSADERS (TV)
Marvel Comics: May, 1992 - No. 8, Dec, 1992 ($1.25)

1-8: 1-3,8-Sam Kieth-c; based on USA Network cartoon						4.00

TOXIN (Son of Carnage)
Marvel Comics: June, 2005 - No. 6, Nov, 2005 ($2.99, limited series)

1-Milligan-s/Robertson-a in all; Spider-Man app.	3	6	9	14	20	25
2-6	1	3	4	6	8	10
...: The Devil You Know TPB (2006, $17.99) r/#1-6						18.00

TOYBOY
Continuity Comics: Oct, 1986 - No. 7, Mar, 1989 ($2.00, Baxter paper)

1-7						4.00

NOTE: *N. Adams a-1; c-1, 2,5. Golden a-7p; c-6,7. Nebres a(i)-1,2.*

TOYLAND COMICS
Fiction House Magazines: Jan, 1947 - No. 2, Mar, 1947; No. 3, July, 1947

1-Wizard of the Moon begins	36	72	108	214	347	480
2,3-Bob Lubbers-c. 3-Tuska-a	20	40	60	120	195	270

NOTE: *All above contain strips by Al Walker.*

TOY STORY (Disney/Pixar movies)
BOOM! Entertainment (BOOM! KIDS): No. 0, Nov, 2009 - No. 7, Sept, 2010 ($2.99)

0-Three covers	1	3	4	6	8	10
1-Three covers	2	4	6	9	12	15
2-7-Two covers on each						4.00
Free Comic Book Day Edition (5/10, giveaway) r/#0 The Return of Buzz Lightyear						3.00
...: The Return of Buzz Lightyear (10/10, Halloween giveaway, 8-1/2" x 5-1/4")						3.00

TOY STORY (Disney/Pixar movies)
Marvel Comics: May, 2012 - No. 4, 2012 ($2.99, limited series)

1-Master Woody	1	3	4	6	8	10
2-4: 2-A Scary Night. 3-To The Attic. 4-Water Rescue						3.00

TOY STORY: MYSTERIOUS STRANGER (Disney/Pixar movies)
BOOM! Entertainment (BOOM! KIDS): May, 2009 - No. 4, July, 2009 ($2.99)

1-4-Jolley-s/Moreno-a. 1-Three covers. 2-4-Two covers						3.00

TOY STORY: TALES FROM THE TOY CHEST (Disney/Pixar movies)
BOOM! Entertainment (BOOM! KIDS): July, 2010 - No. 4, Oct, 2010 ($2.99)

1-4-Snider-s/Luthi-a. 1-Two covers. 2-4-One cover						3.00

TOY TOWN COMICS
Toytown/Orbit Publ./B. Antin/Swapper Quarterly: 1945 - No. 7, May, 1947

1-Mertie Mouse; L. B. Cole-c/a; funny animal	50	100	150	315	533	750
2-L. B. Cole-a	27	54	81	162	266	370
3-7-L. B. Cole-a. 5-Wiggles the Wonderworm-c	22	44	66	132	216	300

TRAGG AND THE SKY GODS (See Gold Key Spotlight, Mystery Comics Digest #3,9 & Spine Tingling Tales)
Gold Key/Whitman No. 9: June, 1975 - No. 8, Feb, 1977; No. 9, May, 1982 (Painted-c #3-8)

1-Origin	3	6	9	14	19	24

Torchwood #1 © BBC

Toy Story (2012 series) #1 © DIS/Pixar

Toy Story (2012 series) #1 © DIS/Pixar

Transformers (2019 series) #1 © Hasbro

MASTER WOODY

	GD	VG	FN	VF	VF/NM	NM-		GD	VG	FN	VF	VF/NM	NM-
	2.0	4.0	6.0	8.0	9.0	9.2		2.0	4.0	6.0	8.0	9.0	9.2

2-8: 4-Sabre-Fang app. 8-Ostellon app.	2	4	6	8	11	14		
9-(Whitman, 5/82) r/#1	1	2	3	5	7	9		

NOTE: *Santos* a-1, 2, 9r; c-3-7. *Spiegel* a-3-8.

TRAILBLAZER
Image Comics: June 2011 ($5.99, one shot, graphic novel)
nn-Gray & Palmiotti-s/Daly-a; covers by Johnson and Conner ... 6.00

TRAIL BLAZERS (Red Dragon #5 on)
Street & Smith Publications: 1941; No. 2, Apr, 1942 - No. 4, Oct, 1942
(True stories of American heroes)

1-Life story of Jack Dempsey & Wright Brothers	48	96	144	302	514	725
2-Brooklyn Dodgers-c/story; Ben Franklin story	29	58	87	172	281	390
3,4: 3-Fred Allen, Red Barber, Yankees stories	25	50	75	150	245	340

TRAIL COLT (Also see Extra Comics, Manhunt! & Undercover Girl)
Magazine Enterprises: 1949 - No. 2, 1949
nn(A-1 #24)-7 pg. Frazetta-a r-in Manhunt #13; Undercover Girl app.; The Red Fox by
L. B. Cole; Ingels-c; Whitney-a (Scarce)(Republished as Manhunt #12 with a different-c)

	47	94	141	296	498	700
2(A-1 #26)-Undercover Girl; Ingels-c; L. B. Cole-a (6 pgs.)						
	36	72	108	211	343	475

TRAILER PARK BOYS (Based on the TV show)
Devil's Due Comics: Jul, 2021; Jun, 2022 (series of one-shots)
... Get A F#¢*!ng Comic Book 1-(7/21, $7.99) Short stories by various ... 8.00
... House of 1000 Conkys 1-(6/22, $4.99) Halloween-themed story; Molloy-s/Rogers-a ... 5.00

TRAIN CALLED LOVE, A
Dynamite Entertainment: 2015 - No. 10, 2016 ($3.99)
1-9-Garth Ennis-s/Mark Dos Santos-a ... 4.00
10-($5.99) Last issue ... 6.00

TRANSFORMERS, THE (TV)(See G.I. Joe and...)
(Continues in Transformers: Regeneration)
Marvel Comics Group: Sept, 1984 - No. 80, July, 1991 (75¢/$1.00)

1-Based on Hasbro Toys	9	18	27	59	117	175
1-2nd & 3rd printing	3	6	9	14	20	26
2-5: 2-Golden-c. 3-(1/85) Spider-Man (black costume)-c/app. 4-Texeira-c; brief app. of						
Dinobots	3	6	9	19	30	40
2-10: 2nd & 3rd prints						4.00
6,7,9: 6-1st Josie Beller. 9-Circuit Breaker 1st full app.						
	2	4	6	9	13	16
8-Dinobots 1st full app.	5	10	15	30	50	70
10-Intro. Constructicons	3	6	9	17	26	35
11,14: 11-1st app. Jetfire. 14-Jetfire becomes an Autobot; 1st app.? of Grapple, Hoist,						
Smokescreen, Skids, and Tracks	2	4	6	8	11	14
12,13,15,17,18,20-24,26-49: 17-1st app. of Blaster, Powerglide, Cosmos, Seaspray,						
Warpath, Beachcomber, Preceptor, Straxus, Kickback, Bombshell, Shrapnel, Dirge, and						
Ramjet. 21-1st app. of Aerialbots; 1st Slingshot; Circuit Breaker app. 22-Retells origin of						
Circuit Breaker, 1st Stunticons. 23-Battle at Statue of Liberty. 24-1st app. Protectobots,						
Combaticons; Optimus Prime killed. 26-Intro The Mechanic, Prime's Funeral. 27-Grimlock						
named new Autobot leader. 28-The Mechanic app. 29-Intro Scraplets, 1st app. of Triple						
Changers	1	2	3	5	6	8
16-Plight of the Bumblebee	3	6	9	14	20	26
19-1st Omega Supreme	2	4	6	11	16	20
25-1st Predacons	2	4	6	13	18	22
50-60: 53-Jim Lee-c. 54-Intro Micromasters. 60-Brief 1st app. of Primus						
	2	4	6	8	10	12
61-70: 61-Origin of Cybertron and the Transformers, Unicron-c; app. of Primus, creator of						
the Transformers. 62-66 Matrix Quest 5-part series. 67-Jim Lee-c						
	2	4	6	10	14	18
71-77: 75-($1.50, 52 pgs.) (Low print run)	3	6	9	19	30	40
78,79 (Low print run)	4	8	12	28	47	65
80-Last issue	6	12	18	37	66	95

NOTE: Second and third printings of most early issues (1-9?) exist and are worth less than originals.
Was originally planned as a four issue mini-series. *Wrightson* a-64i(4 pgs.).

TRANSFORMERS
IDW Publishing: No. 0, Oct, 2005 (99¢, one-shot)
0-Prelude to Transformers: Infiltration series; Furman-s/Su-a; 4 covers ... 4.00

TRANSFORMERS
IDW Publishing: Nov, 2009 - No. 31, Dec, 2011 ($3.99)

1-Multple covers	1	3	4	6	8	10
2-31: Multple covers on each, 21-Chaos arc begins						4.00
...: Continuum (11/09, $3.99) Plot synopsis of recent Transformers storylines						4.00
...: Death of Optimus Prime (12/11, $3.99) Roche-a						4.00

Hundred Penny Press: Transformers Classics #1 (6/11, $1.00) r/#1 (1984 Marvel series) ... 3.00
Hundred Penny Press (3/14, $1.00) r/#1 (1984 Marvel series) ... 3.00

TRANSFORMERS (See Transformers: Robots in Disguise for #1-34)
IDW Publishing: No. 34, Nov, 2014 - No. 57, Sept, 2016 ($3.99)

35-49: 39-42-Combiner Wars x-over						4.00
50-($7.99, squarebound) Barber-s/Griffith-a						8.00
51-57: 51-55-All Hail Optimus. 56-Revolution tie-in						4.00
Annual 2017 (2/17, $7.99) Barber-s/Tramontano-a; bonus character profile pages						8.00
...: Deviations (3/16, $4.99) What If... Optimus Prime never died; Easton-s; 2 covers						5.00
...: First Strike 1 (10/17, $3.99) Part of Hasbro character crossover						4.00
...: Historia (12/18, $5.99) Text history of the Transformers with comic panels						6.00
...: Holiday Special (12/15, $5.99) Covers by Coller & Garbowska						6.00
...: Requiem of the Wreckers Annual (5/18, $7.99) Roche-s/a						8.00
...: Revolution 1 (10/16, $3.99) Revolution tie-in; Barber-s/Griffith-a; multiple covers						4.00
...: Salvation One Shot (6/17, $7.99) Barber-s/Ramondelli-a; 2 covers						8.00
...: Titans Return (7/16, $4.99) Road to Revolution; Ramondelli-a						5.00

TRANSFORMERS (Rise of the Decepticons on cover #19-24; War World on cover #25-30)
IDW Publishing: Mar, 2019 - No. 43, May, 2022 ($3.99)

1-24,26-42: 1-Intro Rubble; Ruckley-s. 7,8-Polybagged w/Transformers card game pack						4.00
25-($7.99) Ruckley-s/Malkova-a); Orion Pax becomes Optimus Prime						8.00
43-($5.99) Story concludes in Transformers: Fate of Cybertron Special						6.00
Annual 2021 (5/21, $5.99) Ruckley-s/Milne-a						6.00
...: Best of Arcee One-Shot (10/22, $6.99) Reprints character highlights						7.00
...: Best of Bumblebee One-Shot (9/22, $6.99) Reprints character highlights						7.00
...: Best of Grimlock One-Shot (11/22, $6.99) Reprints character highlights						7.00
...: Best of Hot Rod One-Shot (5/22, $6.99) Reprints of 6 stories						7.00
...: Best of Megatron One-Shot (3/22, $6.99) Reprints Transformers #70 and other stories						7.00
...: Best of Optimus Prime One-Shot (1/22, $6.99) Reprints of 5 stories						7.00
...: Best of Shockwave One-Shot (11/22, $6.99) Reprints character highlights						7.00
...: Best of Starscream One-Shot (9/22, $6.99) Reprints character highlights						7.00
...: Best of The Beasts One-Shot (7/22, $6.99) Highlights of characters from Beast Wars						7.00
...: Best of The Rarities One-Shot (8/22, $6.99) Highlights of characters from Beast Wars						7.00
...: Best of Windblade One-Shot (12/22, $6.99) Reprints character highlights						7.00
...: Fate of Cybertron Special (6/22, $7.99) Conclusion of title's storyline; follows #43						8.00
...: Halloween Special 2021 (9/21, $5.99) Dan Watters-s/Beth McGuire-Smith-a						6.00
...: 100-Page Giant: Power of the Predacons (1/20, $5.99) Reprints from UK & US comics						6.00
...: Valentine's Day Special (2/20, $3.99) Story of Glyph & Tap-Out						4.00

TRANSFORMERS (Also see Void Rivals series)
Image Comics (Skybound): Oct, 2023 - Present ($3.99)
1-($4.99) Daniel Warren Johnson-s/Mike Spicer-a ... 5.00
2-5-($3.99) 2-Bonus preview of Duke #1. 3-Cobra Commander #1 preview ... 4.00

TRANSFORMERS (Free Comic Book Day Editions)
Dreamwave Productions/IDW Publishing
... Animated (IDW, 5/08) Free Comic Book Day Edition; from the Cartoon Network series ... 3.00
... Armada (Dreamwave Prods., 5/03) Free Comic Book Day Edition ... 3.00
.../Beast Wars (Dreamwave, 2006) Free Comic Book Day Edition; flip book ... 3.00
.../G.I. Joe (IDW, 2009) Free Comic Book Day Edition; flip book ... 3.00
... Movie Prequel (IDW, 5/07) Free Comic Book Day Edition; Figueroa-c ... 3.00

TRANSFORMERS: ALL HAIL MEGATRON
IDW Publishing: Jul, 2008 - No. 16, Oct, 2009 ($3.99, limited series)

1-McCarthy-s/Guidi-a; 2 covers	1	3	4	6	8	10
2-16: 2-8,10-12-McCarthy-s/Guidi-a; 2 covers						4.00

TRANSFORMERS: ALLIANCE (Prequel to 2009 Transformers 2 movie)
IDW Publishing: Dec, 2008 - No. 4, Mar, 2009 ($3.99, limited series)
1-4-Milne-a; 2 covers ... 5.00

TRANSFORMERS ANIMATED: THE ARRIVAL
IDW Publishing: Sept, 2008 - No. 5, Dec, 2008 ($3.99, limited series)
1-5-Brizuela-a; 2 covers ... 4.00

TRANSFORMERS ARMADA (Continues as Transformers Energon with #19)
Dreamwave Productions: July, 2002 - No. 18, Dec, 2003 ($2.95)
1-Sarracini-s/Raiz-a; wraparound gatefold-c ... 6.00
2-18 ... 4.00
Vol. 1 TPB (2003, $13.95) r/#1-5 ... 14.00
Vol. 2 TPB (2003, $15.95) r/#6-11 ... 16.00

TRANSFORMERS ARMADA: MORE THAN MEETS THE EYE
Dreamwave Productions: Mar, 2004 - No. 3, May, 2004 ($4.95, limited series)
1-3-Pin-ups with tech info; art by Pat Lee & various ... 5.00

TRANSFORMERS / BACK TO THE FUTURE
IDW Publishing: Oct, 2020 - No. 4, Jan, 2021 ($3.99, limited series)

	GD 2.0	VG 4.0	FN 6.0	VF 8.0	VF/NM 9.0	NM- 9.2

1-4-Cavan Scott-s/Juan Samu-a; multiple covers on all — 4.00

TRANSFORMERS: BEAST WARS
IDW Publishing: Feb, 2021 - No. 17, Jun, 2022 ($5.99/$3.99, limited series)
1-($5.99) Maximals and Predacons app.; Erik Burnham-s/Josh Burcham-a — 6.00
2-17 ($3.99) — 4.00
Annual 2022 (4/22, $5.99) Three short stories by various — 6.00

TRANSFORMERS, BEAST WARS: THE ASCENDING
IDW Publishing: Aug, 2007 - No. 4, Nov, 2007 ($3.99, limited series)
1-4-Furman-s/Figueroa-a; multiple covers on all — 4.00

TRANSFORMERS, BEAST WARS: THE GATHERING
IDW Publishing: Feb, 2006 - No. 4, May, 2006 ($2.99, limited series)
1-4-Furman-s/Figueroa-a; multiple covers on all — 4.00
TPB (8/06, $17.99) r/series; sketch pages & gallery of covers and variants — 18.00

TRANSFORMERS: BUMBLEBEE
IDW Publishing: Dec, 2009 - No. 4, Mar, 2010 ($3.99, limited series)
1-Zander Cannon-s; multiple covers on all — 1 · 3 · 4 · 6 · 8 · 10
2-4 — 4.00
... – Go For the Gold (12/18, $3.99) Asmus-s/Ferreira-a — 4.00

TRANSFORMERS: BUMBLEBEE MOVIE PREQUEL
IDW Publishing: Jun, 2018 - No. 4, Sept, 2018 ($3.99, limited series)
1-4: Bumblebee assisting a British spy in 1964; Barber-s/Griffith-a; multiple covers — 4.00

TRANSFORMERS COMICS MAGAZINE (Digest)
Marvel Comics: Jan, 1987 - No. 10, July, 1988
1,2-Spider-Man-c/s — 2 · 4 · 6 · 11 · 16 · 20
3-10 — 2 · 4 · 6 · 8 · 11 · 14

TRANSFORMERS: DARK CYBERTRON
IDW Publishing: Nov, 2013 ($3.99)
1-Part 1 of a 12-part crossover with Transformers: More Than Meets the Eye #23-27 and Transformers: Robots in Disguise #23-27; multiple covers — 4.00
1-Deluxe Edition ($7.99, squarebound) r/#1 with bonus script and B&W art pages — 8.00
... Finale (3/14, $3.99) Three covers — 4.00

TRANSFORMERS: DARK OF THE MOON MOVIE ADAPTATION (2011 movie)
IDW Publishing: Jun, 2011 - No. 4, Jun, 2011 ($3.99, weekly limited series)
1-4-Barber-s/Jimenez-a — 4.00

TRANSFORMERS: DEFIANCE (Prequel to 2009 Transformers 2 movie)
IDW Publishing: Jan, 2009 - No. 4, Apr, 2009 ($3.99, limited series)
1-4-Mowry-s; 2 covers — 4.00

TRANSFORMERS: DEVASTATION
IDW Publishing: Sept, 2007 - No. 6, Feb, 2008 ($3.99, limited series)
1-6-Furman-s/Su-a; multiple covers on all — 4.00

TRANSFORMERS: DRIFT
IDW Publishing: Sept, 2010 - No. 4, Oct, 2010 ($3.99, limited series)
1-4-McCarthy-s/Milne-a; multiple covers on all — 4.00

TRANSFORMERS: DRIFT – EMPIRE OF STONE
IDW Publishing: Nov, 2014 - No. 4, Feb, 2015 ($3.99, limited series)
1-4-McCarthy-s/Guidi & Ferreira-a; multiple covers on all — 4.00

TRANSFORMERS '84
IDW Publishing: No. 0, Aug, 2019 - No. 4, Oct, 2021 ($3.99, limited series)
0 (8/19, $4.99) New story in art style of 1984 comics; Furman-s/Guidi-a — 5.00
1-4-Furman-s/Guidi-a; multiple covers — 4.00
...: Legends & Rumors (2/21, $7.99, 100 pgs) r/Transformers #1, ... UK #9-12 & ... '84 #0 — 8.00

TRANSFORMERS ENERGON (Continued from Transformers Armada #18)
Dreamwave Productions: No. 19, Jan, 2004 - No. 30, Dec, 2004 ($2.95)
19-30-Furman-s — 4.00

TRANSFORMERS: ESCALATION
IDW Publishing: Nov, 2006 - No. 6, Apr, 2007 ($3.99, limited series)
1-6-Furman-s/Su-a; multiple covers — 4.00

TRANSFORMERS ESCAPE
IDW Publishing: Dec, 2020 - No. 5, Apr, 2021 ($3.99, limited series)
1-5-Brian Ruckley-s/Beth McGuire-Smith; multiple covers on all — 4.00

TRANSFORMERS: EVOLUTIONS - HEARTS OF STEEL
IDW Publishing: June, 2006 - No. 4, Sept, 2006 ($2.99, limited series)
1-4-Bumblebee meets John Henry in 1880s railroad times — 4.00

TRANSFORMERS: FOUNDATION (Prequel to 2011 Transformers: Dark of the Moon movie)
IDW Publishing: Feb, 2011 - No. 4, May, 2011 ($3.99, limited series)
1-4-Barber-s/Griffith-a; 2 covers — 4.00

TRANSFORMERS: GALAXIES
IDW Publishing: Sept, 2019 - No. 12, Oct, 2020 ($3.99)
1-12: 1-Tyler Bleszinski-s/Livio Ramondelli-a; Constructicons app. — 4.00

TRANSFORMERS: GENERATION 1
Dreamwave Productions: Apr, 2002 - No. 6, Oct, 2002 ($2.95)
Preview- 6 pg. story; robot sketch pages; Pat Lee-a — 3.00
1-Pat Lee-a; 2 wraparound covers by Lee — 5.00
2-6: 2-Optimus Prime reactivated; 2 covers by Pat Lee — 4.00
...Vol. 1 HC (2003, $49.95) r/#1-6; black hardcover with red foil lettering and art — 50.00
...Vol. 1 TPB (2002, $17.95) r/#1-6 plus six page preview; 8 pg. preview of future issues — 18.00

TRANSFORMERS: GENERATION 1 (Volume 2)
Dreamwave Productions: Apr, 2003 - No. 6, Sept, 2003 ($2.95)
1-6: 1-Pat Lee-a; 2 wraparound gatefold covers by Lee — 4.00
1-($5.95) Chrome wraparound variant-c — 6.00
...Vol. 2 TPB (IDW Publ., 3/06, $19.99) r/#1-6 plus cover gallery — 20.00

TRANSFORMERS: GENERATION 1 (Volume 3)
Dreamwave Productions: No. 0, Dec, 2003 - No. 10, Nov, 2004 ($2.95)

0-10: 0-Pat Lee-a. 1-Figueroa-a; wrapaound-c — 4.00

TRANSFORMERS: GENERATION 2
Marvel Comics: Nov, 1993 - No. 12, Oct, 1994 ($1.75)
1-($2.95, 68 pgs.)-Collector's ed. w/bi-fold metallic-c 2 — 4 · 6 · 8 · 11 · 14
1-11: 1-Newsstand edition (68 pgs.). 2-G.I. Joe app., Snake-Eyes, Scarlett, Cobra Commander app. 5-Red Alert killed, Optimus Prime gives Grimlock leadership of Autobots.
6-G.I. Joe app. — 1 · 2 · 3 · 4 · 5 · 7
12-($2.25, 52 pgs.) — 1 · 3 · 4 · 6 · 8 · 10

TRANSFORMERS: GENERATIONS
IDW Publishing: Mar, 2006 - No. 12, Mar, 2007 ($1.99/$2.49/$3.99)
1,2: 1-R/Transformers #7 (1985); preview of Transformers, Beast Wars. 2-R/#13 — 4.00
3-10-($2.49) 3-R/Transformers #14 (1986). 4-6-Reprint #16-18. 7-R/#24 — 4.00
11,12-($3.99) — 4.00
Volume 1 (12/06, $19.99) r/#1-6; cover gallery — 20.00

TRANSFORMERS / GHOSTBUSTERS
IDW Publishing: Jun, 2019 - No. 5, Oct, 2019 ($3.99, limited series)
1-5-Burnham-s/Schoening-a; Ghostbusters vs. ghost of Starscream — 4.00

TRANSFORMERS/G.I. JOE
Dreamwave Productions: Aug, 2003 - No. 6, Mar, 2004 ($2.95/$5.25)
1-Art & gatefold wraparound-c by Jae Lee; Ney Rieber-s; variant-c by Pat Lee — 1 · 2 · 3 · 5 · 6 · 8
1-($5.95) Holofoil wraparound-c by Norton — 2 · 4 · 6 · 8 · 10 · 12
2-6-Jae Lee-a/c — 4.00
TPB (8/04, $17.95) r/#1-6; cover gallery and sketch pages — 18.00

TRANSFORMERS/G.I. JOE: DIVIDED FRONT
Dreamwave Productions: Oct, 2004 ($2.95)
1-Art & gatefold wraparound-c by Pat Lee — 4.00

TRANSFORMERS: HEADMASTERS
Marvel Comics Group: July, 1987 - No. 4, Jan, 1988 ($1.00, limited series)
1-Springer, Akin, Garvey-a — 2 · 4 · 6 · 9 · 12 · 15
2-4-Springer-c on all — 6.00

TRANSFORMERS: HEART OF DARKNESS
IDW Publishing: Mar, 2011 - No. 4, Jun, 2011 ($3.99, limited series)
1-4-Abnett & Lanning-s/Farinas-a — 4.00

TRANSFORMERS: INFESTATION (Crossover with Star Trek, Ghostbusters & G.I. Joe)
IDW Publishing: Feb, 2011 - No. 2, Feb, 2011 ($3.99, limited series)
1,2-Abnett & Lanning-s/Roche-a; covers by Roche & Snyder III — 4.00

TRANSFORMERS: INFILTRATION
IDW Publishing: Jan, 2006 - No. 6, June, 2006 ($2.99, limited series)
1-6-Furman-s/Su-a; multiple covers on all — 4.00
... Cover Gallery (8/06, $5.99) — 6.00

TRANSFORMERS: IRONHIDE
IDW Publishing: May, 2010 - No. 4, Aug, 2010 ($3.99, limited series)
1-4: Mike Costa-s; multiple covers on all — 4.00

TRANSFORMERS: KING GRIMLOCK
IDW Publishing: Aug, 2021 - No. 5, Feb, 2022 ($4.99, limited series)
1-5-Steve Orlando-s/Agustin Padilla-a; multiple covers on all — 5.00

TRANSFORMERS: LAST BOT STANDING
IDW Publishing: May, 2022 - No. 4, Aug, 2022 ($5.99, limited series)
1-4-Nick Roche-s/Roche & E.J. Su-a; multiple covers on each — 6.00

TRANSFORMERS: LAST STAND OF THE WRECKERS
IDW Publishing: Jan, 2010 - No. 5, May, 2010 ($3.99, limited series)
1-5-Nick Roche-s/a; two covers — 4.00

TRANSFORMERS: LOST LIGHT
IDW Publishing: Dec, 2016 - No. 25, Oct, 2018 ($3.99)
1-15: 1-7-Roberts-s/Lawrence-a; multiple covers on each. 8,9-Tramontano-a — 4.00

TRANSFORMERS: MAXIMUM DINOBOTS
IDW Publishing: Dec, 2008 - No. 5, Apr, 2009 ($3.99, limited series)
1-5-Furman-s/Roche-a; 2 covers for each — 4.00

TRANSFORMERS: MEGATRON ORIGIN
IDW Publishing: May, 2007 - No. 4, Sept, 2008 ($3.99, limited series)
1-4-Alex Milne-a; 2 covers — 4.00

TRANSFORMERS: MICROMASTERS
Dreamwave Productions: June, 2004 - No. 4 ($2.95, limited series)
1-4-Ruffolo-a; Pat Lee-c — 4.00

TRANSFORMERS: MONSTROSITY
IDW Publishing: Jun, 2013 - No. 4, Sept, 2013 ($3.99)
1-4: 1-Three covers; Ramondelli-a — 4.00

TRANSFORMERS: MORE THAN MEETS THE EYE
Dreamwave Productions: Apr, 2003 - No. 8, Nov, 2003 ($5.25)
1-8-Pin-ups with tech info on Autobots and Decepticons; art by Pat Lee & various — 5.25
Vol. 1,2 (2004, $24.95, TPB) 1-r/#1-4. 2-r/#5-8 — 25.00

TRANSFORMERS: MORE THAN MEETS THE EYE
IDW Publishing: Jan, 2012 - No. 57, Sept, 2016 ($3.99)
1-49: 1-Five covers; Roche-a. 2-Three covers; Milne-a. 23-27-Dark Cybertron x-over. 26-1st app. of Windblade — 4.00
50-(2/16, $7.99) "The Dying of the Light" begins; five covers — 8.00
51-57: 51-55-The Dying of the Light. 56,57-Titans Return — 4.00
Annual 2012 (8/12, $7.99) Salgado & Cabaltierra-a; three covers — 8.00
...: Revolution 1 (11/16, $3.99) Revolution tie-in; Roche-s/Roberts-a; multiple covers — 4.00

TRANSFORMERS: MOVIE ADAPTATION (For the 2007 live action movie)
IDW Publishing: June, 2007 - No. 4, June, 2007 ($3.99, weekly limited series)
1-4: Wraparound covers on each; Milne-a — 4.00

Transformers: Devastation #1 © Hasbro

Transformers: Primacy #2 © Hasbro

Transformers: Sector 7 #1 © Hasbro

	GD	VG	FN	VF	VF/NM	NM-		GD	VG	FN	VF	VF/NM	NM-
	2.0	4.0	6.0	8.0	9.0	9.2		2.0	4.0	6.0	8.0	9.0	9.2

TRANSFORMERS: MOVIE PREQUEL (For the 2007 live action movie)
IDW Publishing: Feb, 2007 - No. 4, May, 2007 ($3.99, limited series)

1-4: 1-Origin of the Transformers on Cybertron; multiple covers on each	4.00
Special (6/08, $3.99) 2 covers	4.00
TPB (6/07, $19.99) r/series; gallery of covers and variants	20.00

TRANSFORMERS: NEFARIOUS (Sequel to Transformers: Revenge of the Fallen movie)
IDW Publishing: Mar, 2010 - No. 6, Aug, 2010 ($3.99, limited series)

1-6: Furman-s; multiple covers on all	4.00

TRANSFORMERS: PRIMACY
IDW Publishing: Aug, 2014 - No. 4, Nov, 2014 ($3.99, limited series)

1-4-Metzen & Dille-s/Ramondelli-a; Omega Supreme app.; multiple covers on each	4.00

TRANSFORMERS: PRIME
IDW Publishing: Jan, 2011 - No. 4, Jan, 2011 ($3.99, weekly limited series)

1-4: 1-Mike Johnson-s/E.J. Su-a	4.00

TRANSFORMERS: PRIME: BEAST HUNTERS
IDW Publishing: May, 2013 - No. 8, Dec, 2013($3.99, limited series)

1-8-Agustin Padilla-a	4.00

TRANSFORMERS: PRIME: RAGE OF THE DINOBOTS
IDW Publishing: Nov, 2012 - No. 4, Feb, 2013 ($3.99, limited series)

1-4: 1-Mike Johnson-s/Agustin Padilla-a	4.00

TRANSFORMERS: PUNISHMENT
IDW Publishing: Jan, 2015 ($5.99, squarebound, one-shot)

1-Windblade app.; Barber-s/Ramondelli-a	6.00

TRANSFORMERS: REDEMPTION
IDW Publishing: Oct, 2015 ($7.99, squarebound, one-shot)

1-Dinobots app.; John Barber-s/Livio Ramondelli-a	8.00

TRANSFORMERS: REGENERATION ONE (Continues story from Transformers #80 (1991))
IDW Publishing: No. 80.5, May, 2012 - No. 100, Mar, 2014 ($3.99)

80.5 (5/12, Free Comic Book Day giveaway) Furman/Wildman-a	3.00
81-99 ($3.99) 81-92-Furman-s/Wildman-a; multiple covers on all	4.00
100-($5.99) Six covers; Furman-s/Wildman, Senior & Guidi-a; bonus cover gallery	6.00
#0 (9/13, $3.99) Hot Rod in the timestream; various artists; 4 covers	4.00
... 100-Page Spectacular (7/12, $7.99) Reprints Transformers #76-80 (1991)	8.00

TRANSFORMERS: REVENGE OF THE FALLEN OFFICIAL MOVIE ADAPTATION
(For the 2009 live action movie sequel)
IDW Publishing: May, 2009 - No. 4, June, 2009 ($3.99, weekly limited series)

1-4: Furman-s; 2 covers on each	4.00

TRANSFORMERS: RISING STORM (Prequel to 2011 Transformers: Dark of the Moon movie)
IDW Publishing: Feb, 2011 - No. 4, May, 2011 ($3.99, limited series)

1-3-Barber-s/Magno-a; 2 covers	4.00

TRANSFORMERS: ROBOTS IN DISGUISE (Re-titled Transformers #35-on)
IDW Publishing: Jan, 2012 - No. 34, Oct, 2014 ($3.99)

1-34: 1-Five covers; Griffith-a. 2-27-Three covers. 23-27-Dark Cybertron x-over	4.00

TRANSFORMERS: ROBOTS IN DISGUISE (Based on the animated series)
IDW Publishing: No. 0, May, 2015 - No. 5, Dec, 2015 ($3.99)

0-Free Comic Book Day Edition; Barber-s/Tramontano-a; Bumblebee & Strongarm app.	3.00
1-5: 1-Georgia Ball-s/Priscilla Tramontano-a	4.00

TRANSFORMERS: SAGA OF THE ALLSPARK (From the 2007 live action movie)
IDW Publishing: Jul, 2008 - No. 4, Oct, 2008 ($3.99, limited series)

1-4-Launch of the Allspark into outer space; Furman-s/Roche-c	4.00

TRANSFORMERS: SECTOR 7 (From the 2007 live action movie)
IDW Publishing: Sept, 2010 - No. 5, Jan, 2011 ($3.99, limited series)

1-5-Barber-s	4.00

TRANSFORMERS: SHATTERED GLASS
IDW Publishing: Aug, 2021 - No. 5, Dec, 2021 ($3.99, limited series)

1-5-Danny Lore-s/Guido Guidi-a; multiple covers on all	4.00

TRANSFORMERS: SHATTERED GLASS II
IDW Publishing: Aug, 2022 - No. 5, Dec, 2022 ($3.99, limited series)

1-5-Danny Lore-s/Marcelo Matere-a; multiple covers on all	4.00

TRANSFORMERS: SINS OF THE WRECKERS
IDW Publishing: Nov, 2015 - No. 5, May, 2016 ($3.99, limited series)

1-5-Roche-s/Burcham-a	4.00

TRANSFORMERS: SPOTLIGHT

IDW Publishing: Sept, 2006 - May, 2013 ($3.99, multiple covers on each)

... Arcee (2/08); ... Blaster (1/08); ... Blurr (11/08); ... Bumblebee (3/13); ... Cliffjumper (6/09);	
... Cyclonus (6/08); ...Doubledealer (8/08); ...Drift (4/09); ...Galvatron (7/07);...Grimlock (3/08);	
...Hardhead (7/08); ... Hoist (5/13); ... Hot Rod (11/06); ... Jazz (3/09); ... Kup (4/07);	
... Megatron (2/13); ... Metroplex (7/09); ... Mirage (3/08); ... Nightbeat (10/06);	
... Orion Pax (12/12); ... Prowl (4/10);... Ramjet (11/07); ... Shockwave (9/06); ... Sideswipe	
(9/08); ... Sixshot (12/06); ... Soundwave (3/07); Thundercracker (1/13); ... Trailcutter (4/13);	
... Ultra Magnus (1/07)	4.00
... Optimus Prime: 3-D (11/08, $5.99, with glasses) Furman-s/Figueroa-a	6.00

TRANSFORMERS: STORMBRINGER
IDW Publishing: Jul, 2006 - No. 4, Oct, 2006 ($2.99, limited series)

1-4-Furman-s/Figueroa-a; multiple covers on all	4.00
TPB (2/07, $17.99) r/series; cover gallery and sketch pages	18.00

TRANSFORMERS SUMMER SPECIAL
Dreamwave Productions: May, 2004 ($4.95)

1-Pat Lee-a; Figueroa-a	1	2	3	5	6	8

TRANSFORMERS: TALES OF THE FALLEN
IDW Publishing: Aug, 2009 - No. 6 ($3.99, limited series)

1-6: 2,4-Furman-s mulitple covers on all	4.00

TRANSFORMERS: TARGET 2006
IDW Publishing: Apr, 2007 - No. 5, Aug, 2007 ($3.99, limited series)

1-5-Reprints from 1980s series; multiple covers on all	4.00

TRANSFORMERS: THE ANIMATED MOVIE
IDW Publishing: Oct, 2006 - No. 4, Jan, 2007 ($3.99, limited series)

1-4-Adapts animated movie; Don Figueroa-a	4.00

TRANSFORMERS, THE MOVIE
Marvel Comics Group: Dec, 1986 - No. 3, Feb, 1987 (75¢, limited series)

1-3-Adapts animated movie	2	4	6	10	14	18

TRANSFORMERS: THE REIGN OF STARSCREAM
IDW Publishing: Apr, 2008 - No. 5, Aug, 2008 ($3.99, limited series)

1-5-Continuation of the 2007 movie; Milne-a; multiple covers	4.00

TRANSFORMERS: THE WAR WITHIN
Dreamwave Productions: Oct, 2002 - No. 6, Mar, 2003 ($2.95)

1-6-Furman-s/Figueroa-a. 1-Wraparound gatefold-c	4.00
TPB (2003, $15.95) r/#1-6; plus cover gallery	16.00

TRANSFORMERS: TILL ALL ARE ONE
IDW Publishing: Jun, 2016 - No. 12, Jul, 2017 ($3.99)

1-12-Road to Revolution; Mairghread Scott-s; multiple covers on all	4.00
Annual 2017 (12/17, $7.99) Mairghread Scott-s/Pitre-Durocher-a	
...: Revolution 1 (10/16, $3.99) Revolution tie-in; Windblade app.; multiple covers	4.00

TRANSFORMERS: UNICRON (Crossover with Optimus Prime & Transformers: Lost Light)
IDW Publishing: Jul, 2018 - No. 6, Oct, 2018 ($4.99)

1-6-Barber-s/Milne-a; multiple covers on all; Rom app.	5.00
#0 (5/18, FCBD giveaway) Barber-s/Milne-a; Rom app.	3.00

TRANSFORMERS UNIVERSE
Marvel Comics Group: Dec, 1986 - No. 4, Mar, 1987 ($1.25, limited series)

1-4-A guide to all characters	2	4	6	8	11	14
TPB-r/#1-4						15.00

TRANSFORMERS VS. G.I. JOE
IDW Publishing: No. 0, May, 2014 - No. 13, Jun, 2016 ($3.99)

Free Comic Book Day #0 (5/14, giveaway) Tom Scioli-a; Scioli & John Barber-s	3.00
1-12-Tom Scioli-a; Scioli & John Barber-s; multiple covers on each; creator commentary	4.00
13-($7.99, squarebound) Last issue; bonus commentary; 3 covers	5.00
...: The Movie Adaptation (3/17, $4.99) Tom Scioli-s/a; 4 covers; bonus sketch-a	5.00

TRANSFORMERS VS. VISIONARIES
IDW Publishing: Dec, 2017 - No. 5, Apr, 2018 ($3.99, limited series)

1-5-Vissagio-s/Ossio-a	4.00

TRANSFORMERS: WAR'S END
IDW Publishing: Feb, 2022 - No. 4, May, 2022 ($3.99/$5.99, limited series)

1-3-($3.99) Ruckley-s/Lawrence-a; multiple covers on all	4.00
4-($5.99) Concludes in Transformers: Fate of Cybertron #1; multiple covers	6.00

TRANSFORMERS WAR WITHIN: THE AGE OF WRATH
Dreamwave Productions: Sept, 2004 - No. 6, limited series)

1-3-Furman-s/Ng-a	4.00

	GD	VG	FN	VF	VF/NM	NM-
	2.0	4.0	6.0	8.0	9.0	9.2

TRANSFORMERS WAR WITHIN: THE DARK AGES
Dreamwave Productions: Oct, 2003 - No. 6 ($2.95)

1-6: 1-Furman-s/Wildman-a; two covers by Pat Lee & Figueroa						4.00
TPB (2004, $17.95) r/#1-6; plus cover gallery and design sketches						18.00

TRANSFORMERS: WINDBLADE (See Transformers More Than Meets the Eye #26)
IDW Publishing: Apr, 2014 - No. 4, Jul, 2014 ($3.99, limited series)

1-4-Mairghread Scott-s/Sarah Stone-a; three covers on each						4.00
Vol. 2 (3/15 - No. 7, 9/15, $3.99) 1-7-Scott-s; multiple covers on each. 1-Stone-a						4.00

TRANSFORMERS: WRECKERS – TREAD & CIRCUITS
IDW Publishing: Oct, 2021 - No. 4, Jan, 2022 ($3.99, limited series)

1-4-David Mariotte-s/Jack Lawrence-a; multiple covers on each						4.00

TRANSIT
Vortex Publ.: March, 1987 - No. 5, Nov, 1987 (B&W)

1-5-Ted McKeever-s/a	1	2	3	5		8

TRANSLUCID
BOOM! Studios: Apr, 2014 - No. 6, Sept, 2014 ($3.99)

1-6-Sanchez & Echert-s/Bayliss-a; multiple covers on each						4.00

TRANSMETROPOLITAN
DC Comics (Helix/Vertigo): Sept, 1997 - No. 60, Nov, 2002 ($2.50)

1-Warren Ellis-s/Darick Robertson-a(p)	5	10	15	35	63	90
1-Special Edition (5/09, $1.00) r/#1 with "After Watchmen" cover frame						5.00
2,3	2	4	6	8	10	12
4-8						5.00
9-60: 15-Jae Lee-c. 25-27-Jim Lee-c. 37-39-Bradstreet-c						3.00
Back on the Street ('97, $7.95) r/#1-3						10.00
Back on the Street ('09, $14.99) r/#1-6; intro. by Garth Ennis						15.00
Dirge ('03/'10, $14.95/$14.95) r/#43-48						15.00
Filth of the City ('01, $5.95) Spider's columns with pin-up art by various						6.00
Gouge Away ('02/'09, $14.95/$14.99) r/#31-36						15.00
I Hate It Here ('00, $5.95) Spider's columns with pin-up art by various						6.00
Lonely City ('01/'09, $14.95/$14.99) r/#25-30; intro. by Patrick Stewart						15.00
Lust For Life ('98, $14.95) r/#4-12						20.00
Lust For Life ('09, $14.99) r/#7-12						15.00
One More Time ('04, $14.95) r/#55-60						15.00
One More Time ('11, $19.99) r/#55-60 & Filth of the City & I Hate It Here one-shots						20.00
Spider's Thrash ('02/'10, $14.95/$14.99) r/#37-42; intro. by Darren Aronofsky						15.00
Tales of Human Waste ('04, $9.95) r/Filth of the City, I Hate It Here & story from Vertigo						
Winter's Edge 2						10.00
The Cure ('03/'11, $14.95/$14.95) r/#49-54						15.00
The New Scum ('00, $12.95) r/#19-24 & Vertigo: Winter's Edge #3						15.00
The New Scum ('09, $14.99) r/#19-24 & Vertigo: Winter's Edge #3						15.00
Year of the Bastard ('99, $12.95)('09, $12.99) r/#13-18						13.00

TRANSMUTATION OF IKE GARUDA, THE
Marvel Comics (Epic Comics): July, 1991 - No. 2, 1991 ($3.95, 52 pgs.)

1,2						5.00

TRAPPED!
Periodical House Magazines (Ace): Oct, 1954 - No. 4, April, 1955

1 (All reprints)	14	28	42	80	115	150
2-4: 4-r/Men Against Crime #4 in its entirety	9	18	27	50	65	80

NOTE: Colan a-1, 4. Sekowsky a-1.

TRASH
Trash Publ. Co.: Mar, 1978 - No. 4, Oct, 1978 (B&W, magazine, 52 pgs.)

1,2: 1-Star Wars parody. 2-UFO-c	3	6	9	14	28	38
3-Parodies of KISS, the Beatles, and monsters	3	6	9	19	30	40
4-(84 pgs.)-Parodies of Happy Days, Rocky movies	3	6	9	21	33	45

TRAVELER, THE (Developed by Stan Lee)
BOOM! Studios: Nov, 2010 - No. 12, Oct, 2011 ($3.99)

1-12-Waid-s/Hardin-a; three covers on each						4.00

TRAVELING TO MARS
Ablaze Publishing: 2022 - No. 11, 2024 ($3.99)

1-11-Mark Russell-s/Roberto Meli-a						4.00

TRAVELS OF JAIMIE McPHEETERS, THE (TV)
Gold Key: Dec, 1963

1-Kurt Russell photo on-c plus photo back-c	4	8	12	27	44	60

TREASURE CHEST (Catholic Guild; also see Topix)
George A. Pflaum: 3/12/46 - V27#8, July, 1972 (Educational comics)
(Not published during Summer)

V1#1	37	74	111	222	361	500
2-6 (5/21/46): 5-Dr. Styx app. by Baily	15	30	45	88	137	185
V2#1-20 (9/3/46-5/27/47)	11	22	33	60	83	105
V3#1-5,7-20 (1st slick cover)	10	20	30	54	72	90
V3#6-Jules Verne's "Voyage to the Moon"	14	28	42	80	115	150
V4#1-20 (9/48-5/31/49)	9	18	27	47	61	75
V5#1-20 (9/6/49-5/31/50)	8	16	24	44	57	70
V6#1-20 (9/14/50-5/31/51)	8	16	24	42	54	65
V7#1-20 (9/13/51-6/5/52)	8	16	24	40	50	60
V8#1-20 (9/11/52-6/4/53)	7	14	21	37	46	55
V9#1-20 ('53-'54), V10#1-20 ('54-'55)	7	14	21	35	43	50
V11('55-'56), V12('56-'57)	6	12	18	29	36	42
V13#1,3-5,7,9-20-V17#1 ('57-'63)	6	12	18	27	33	38
V13#2,6,8-Ingels-a	5	10	15	35	63	90
V17#2- "This Godless Communism" series begins(not in odd #'d issues); cover shows						
hammer & sickle over Statue of Liberty; 8 pg. Crandall-a of a family						
life under communism (9/28/61)	20	40	60	138	307	475
V17#3,5,7,9,11,13,15,17,19	3	6	9	17	26	35
V17#4,6,14- "This Godless Communism" stories	15	30	45	105	233	360
V17#8-Shows red octopus encompassing Earth, firing squad; 8 pg. Crandall-a (12/21/61)						
	18	36	54	128	284	440
V17#10- "This Godless Communism" - how Stalin came to power, part I; Crandall-a						

	16	32	48	108	239	370
V17#12-Stalin in WWII, forced labor, death by exhaustion; Crandall-a						
	16	32	48	108	239	370
V17#16-Kruschev takes over; de-Stalinization	16	32	48	108	239	370
V17#18-Kruschev's control; murder of revolters, brainwash, space race by Crandall						
	16	32	48	108	239	370
V17#20-End of series; Kruschev-people are puppets, firing squads hammer &						
sickle over Statue of Liberty, snake around communist manifesto by Crandall						
	20	40	60	136	303	470
V18#1,3,4,6-10,12-20, V19#11-20, V20#1-20(1964-65): V20#6-JFK photo-c & story.						
V20#16-Babe Ruth-c & story by Sinnott	3	6	9	19	30	40
V18#2-Kruschev on-c (9/27/62)	4	8	12	23	37	50
V18#5- "What About Red China?" - describes how communists took over China						
	9	18	27	61	123	185
V18#11-Crandall draws himself & 13 other artists on cover (1/31/63)						
	4	8	12	25	40	55
V19#1-10- "Red Victim" anti-communist series in all	9	18	27	61	123	185
V21, V22 #1-16,18-20,V23-V25(1965-70)-(two V24#5's 11/7/68 & 11/21/68) (no V24#6):						
	3	6	9	14	19	24
V22#17-Flying saucer wraparound-c	3	6	9	17	26	35
V26, V27#1-8 (V26,27-68 pgs.)	3	6	9	15	22	28
Summer Edition V1#1-6('66), V2#1-6('67)	3	6	9	16	23	30

NOTE: Anderson a-V18#13. Borth a-V7#10-19 (serial), V8#8-17 (serial), V9#1-10 (serial), V13#2, 6, 11, V14-V25 (except V22#1-3, 11-13), Summer Ed. V1#3-6. Crandall a-V16#7, 9, 12, 14, 16-18, 20; V17#1, 2, 4-6, 10, 12, 14, 16-18, 20; V18#1, 2, 3(2 pg.), 7, 9-20; V19#4, 11, 13, 16, 19, 20; V20#1, 2, 4, 6, 8-10, 12, 14-16, 18, 20; V21#1-5, 8-11, 13, 16-18; V22#2, 3, 7, 9-11, 14; V23#3, 6, 9, 16, 18; V25#8, 16; V25#8, Summer Ed. V1#2 (back c-V1#2-5). Powell a-V10#11. V19#11, 15, V10#13, V13#6, 8 all have wraparound covers.

TREASURE CHEST OF THE WORLD'S BEST COMICS
Superior, Toronto, Canada: 1945 (500 pgs., hard-c)
Contains Blue Beetle, Captain Combat, John Wayne, Dynamic Man, Nemo, Li'l Abner;
contents can vary - represents random binding of extra books; Captain America on-c

	181	362	543	1158	1979	2800

TREASURE COMICS
Prize Publications? (no publisher listed): No date (1943) (50¢, 324 pgs., cardboard-c)

1-(Rare)-Contains rebound Prize Comics #7-11 from 1942 (blank inside-c)						
	420	840	1260	2940	5170	7400

TREASURE COMICS
Prize Publ. (American Boys' Comics): June-July, 1945 - No. 12, Fall, 1947

1-Paul Bunyan & Marco Polo begin; Highwayman & Carrot Topp only app.; Kiefer-a						
	60	120	180	381	653	925
2-Arabian Knight, Gorilla King, Dr. Styx begin	39	78	117	231	378	525
3,4,9,12: 9-Kiefer-a	31	62	93	182	296	410
5-Marco Polo-c; Krigstein-a	36	72	108	214	347	480
6,11-Krigstein-a; 11-Krigstein-c	36	72	108	211	343	475
7,8-Frazetta-a (5 pgs. each). 7-Capt. Kidd Jr. app.	48	96	144	302	514	725
10-Simon & Kirby-c/a	48	96	144	302	514	725

NOTE: Barry a-9-11; c-12. Kiefer a-3, 5, 7; c-2, 6, 7. Roussos a-11.

TREASURE ISLAND (See Classics Illustrated #64, Doc Savage Comics #1, King Classics, Movie Classics & Movie Comics)
Dell Publishing Co.: No. 624, Apr, 1955 (Disney)

Four Color 624-Movie, photo-c	9	18	27	62	126	190

TREASURY OF COMICS
St. John Publishing Co.: 1947 - No. 2, July, 1947 - No. 4, Sept, 1947; No. 5, Jan, 1948

nn(#1)-Abbie an' Slats (nn on-c, #1 on inside)	20	40	60	114	182	250
2-Jim Hardy Comics; featuring Windy & Paddles	14	28	42	80	115	150
3-Bill Bumlin	11	22	33	62	86	110
4-Abbie an' Slats	13	26	39	74	105	135
5-Jim Hardy Comics #1	13	26	39	74	105	135

TREASURY OF COMICS
St. John Publishing Co.: Mar, 1948 - No. 5, 1948 (Reg. size); 1948-1950 (Over 500 pgs., $1.00)

1	21	42	63	122	199	275
2(#2 on-c, #1 on inside)	14	28	42	78	112	145
3-5	12	24	36	67	94	120
1-(1948, 500 pgs., hard-c)-Abbie & Slats, Abbott & Costello, Casper, Little Annie Rooney, Little Audrey, Jim Hardy, Ella Cinders (16 books bound together) (Rare)						
	213	426	639	1363	2332	3300
1(1949, 500 pgs.)-Same format as above	168	336	504	1075	1838	2600
1(1950, 500 pgs.)-Same format as above; different-c; (also see Little Audrey Yearbook)						
(Rare)	168	336	504	1075	1838	2600

TREASURY OF DOGS, A (See Dell Giants)

TREASURY OF HORSES, A (See Dell Giants)

TREEHOUSE OF HORROR (Bart Simpson's...)
Bongo Comics: 1995 - 2017 ($2.95/$2.50/$3.50/$4.50/$4.99, annual)

1-(1995, $2.95)-Groening-a; Allred, Robinson & Smith stories						
	3	6	9	19	30	40
2-(1996, $2.50)-Stories by Dini & Bagge; infinity-c by Groening						
	2	4	6	11	16	20
3-(1997, $2.50)-Dorkin-s/Groening-c	2	4	6	8	10	12
4-(1998, $2.50)-Lash & Dixon-s/Groening-c	2	4	6	8	10	12
5-(1999, $3.50)-Thompson-s; Shaw & Aragonés-s/a; TenNapel-a						
	2	4	6	8	10	12
6-(2000, $4.50)-Mahfood-s/a; DeCarlo-a; Morse-s/Kuper-s/a						8.00
7-(2001, $4.50)-Hamill-s/Morrison-a; Ennis-s/McCrea-a; Sakai-s/a; Nixey-s/a; Brereton back-c						8.00
8-(2002, $3.50)-Templeton, Shaw, Barta, Simone, Thompson-s/a						8.00
9-(2003, $4.99)-Lord of the Rings-Brereton-a; Dini, Naifeh, Millidge, Boothby, Noto-s/a						8.00
10-(2004, $4.99)-Monsters of Rock w/Alice Cooper, Gene Simmons, Rob Zombie and Pat Boone; art by Rodriguez, Morrison, Morse, Templeton						15.00
11-(2005, $4.99)-EC style w/art by John Severin, Angelo Torres & Al Williamson and flip book with Dracula by Wolfman/Colan and Squish Thing by Wein/Wrightson						8.00
12-(2006, $4.99)-Terry Moore, Kyle Baker, Eric Powell-s/a						8.00

Treehouse of Horror #22 © Bongo

The Trials of Ultraman #1 © MAR

Trinity #3 © DC

	GD	VG	FN	VF	VF/NM	NM-
	2.0	4.0	6.0	8.0	9.0	9.2

13-(2007, $4.99)-Oswalt, Posehn, Lennon-s; Guerra, Austin, Barta, Rodriguez-a — 8.00
14-(2008, $4.99)-s/a by Niles & Fabry; Boothby & Matsumoto; Gilbert Hernandez — 8.00
15-(2009, $4.99)-s/a by Jeffrey Brown, Tim Hensley, Ben Jones and others — 8.00
16-(2010, $4.99)-s/a by Kelley Jones, Evan Dorkin and others; Mars Attacks homage — 15.00
17-(2011, $4.99)-s/a by Gene Ha, Jane Wiedlin and others; Nosferatu homage — 12.00
18-(2012, $4.99)-s/a by Jim Valentino, Phil Noto and others; Rosemary's Baby spoof — 8.00
19-(2013, $4.99)-s/a by Len Wein, Dan Brereton and others; Cthulhu spoof — 8.00
20-(2014, $4.99)-All Zombie issue, including The Walking Ned — 8.00
21-(2015, $4.99)-Gremlins & Metropolis spoofs — 8.00
22-(2016, $4.99)-Ghostbusters & Gossamer spoofs — 8.00
23-(2017, $4.99)-Spoofs of Stephen King stories: It, Dreamcatcher and Thinner — 12.00

TREES
Image Comics: May, 2014 - No. 14, Aug, 2016 ($2.99)
1-14-Warren Ellis-s/Jason Howard-a — 3.00

TREES: THREE FATES
Image Comics: Sept, 2019 - No. 5, Jan, 2020 ($3.99, limited series)
1-5-Warren Ellis-s/Jason Howard-a — 4.00

TREKKER (See Dark Horse Presents #6)
Dark Horse Comics: May, 1987 - No. 6, Mar, 1988 ($1.50, B&W)
1-6: Sci/Fi stories — 4.00
Color Special 1 (1989, $2.95, 52 pgs.) — 5.00
Collection ($5.95, B&W) — 6.00
Special 1 (6/99, $2.95, color) — 4.00

TRENCHCOAT BRIGADE, THE
DC Comics (Vertigo): Mar, 1999 - No. 4, Jun, 1999 ($2.50, limited series)
1-4: Hellblazer, Phantom Stranger, Mister E, Dr. Occult app. — 4.00

TRENCHER (See Blackball Comics)
Image Comics: May, 1993 - No. 4, Oct, 1993 ($1.95, unfinished limited series)
1-4: Keith Giffen-c/a/scripts. 3-Supreme-c/story — 4.00

TRIAGE
Dark Horse Comics: Sept, 2019 - No. 5, Jan, 2020 ($3.99, limited series)
1-5-Phillip Sevy-s/a/c; variant covers for each — 4.00

TRIAL OF THE AMAZONS (See Wonder Woman #785,786)
DC Comics: May, 2022 - No. 2, Jun, 2022 ($4.99, limited series)
1,2: 1-First part of 7-part storyline; death of Hippolyta. 2-Conclusion of story — 5.00

TRIAL OF THE AMAZONS: WONDER GIRL (Yara Flor)
DC Comics: May, 2022 - No. 2, Jun, 2022 ($3.99, limited series)
1,2-Two covers form one image: 1-Part 4 of 7-part storyline. 2-Part 6 of 7 — 4.00

TRIALS OF SHAZAM!
DC Comics: Oct, 2006 - No. 12, May, 2008 ($2.99)
1-12: 1-Winick-s/Porter-a. 9-11-Caccioli-a. 10-Shadowpact app. 12-JLA app. — 3.00
... Volume 1 TPB (2007, $14.99) r/#1-6 and story from DCU Brave New World #1 — 15.00
... Volume 2 TPB (2008, $14.99) r/#7-12 — 15.00

TRIALS OF ULTRAMAN, THE (Also see The Rise of Ultraman)
Marvel Comics: May, 2021 - No. 5, Oct, 2021 ($4.99/$3.99)
1-($4.99) Main story by Higgins & Groom-s/Manna-a; back-up w/Gurihiru-a — 5.00
2-5-($3.99) — 4.00

TRIB COMIC BOOK, THE
Winnipeg Tribune: Sept. 24, 1977 - Vol. 4, #36, 1980 (8-1/2"x11", 24 pgs., weekly) (155 total issues)

V1# 1-Color pages (Sunday strips)-Spiderman, Asterix, Disney's Scamp, Wizard of Id, Doonesbury, Inside Woody Allen, Mary Worth, & others (similar to Spirit sections)	2	4	6	10	14	18
V1#2-15, V2#1-52, V3#1-52, V4#1-33	1	3	4	6	8	10
V4#34-36 (not distributed)	2	4	6	11	16	20

NOTE: All issues have Spider-Man. Later issues contain Star Trek and Star Wars. 20 strips in ea. The first newspaper to put Sunday pages into a comic book format.

TRIBE (See WildC.A.T.S #4)
Image Comics/Axis Comics No. 2 on: Apr, 1993; No. 2, Sept, 1993 - No. 3, 1994 ($2.50/$1.95)
1-By Johnson & Stroman; gold foil & embossed on black-c — 5.00
1-($2.50)-Ivory Edition; gold foil & embossed on white-c; available only through the creators — 5.00
2,3: 2-1st Axis Comics issue. 3-Savage Dragon app. — 4.00

TRIBUTE TO STEVEN HUGHES, A
Chaos! Comics: Sept, 2000 ($6.95)
1-Lady Death & Evil Ernie pin-ups by various artists; testimonials — 7.00

TRICK 'R TREAT
DC Comics (WildStorm): 2009 ($19.99,SC)
nn-Short Halloween-themed story anthology; Andreyko-s; art by Huddleston & others — 20.00

TRIGGER (See Roy Rogers'...)

TRIGGER
DC Comics (Vertigo): Feb, 2005 - No. 8, Sept, 2005 ($2.95/$2.99)
1-8-Jason Hall-s/John Watkiss-a/c — 3.00

TRIGGER TWINS
National Periodical Publications: Mar-Apr, 1973 (20¢, one-shot)

1-Trigger Twins & Pow Wow Smith-r/All-Star Western #94,103 & Western Comics #81; Infantino-r(p)	2	4	6	13	18	22

TRILLIUM
DC Comics (Vertigo): Oct, 2013 - No. 8, Jun, 2014 ($2.99)
1-8-Jeff Lemire-s/a. 1-Flip-book — 3.00

TRINITY (See DC Universe: Trinity)

TRINITY
DC Comics: Aug, 2008 - No. 52, July, 2009 ($2.99, weekly series)
1-52-Superman, Batman & Wonder Woman star; Busiek-s/Bagley-a. 52-Wraparound-c — 3.00
Vol. 1 TPB (2009, $29.99) r/#1-17 — 30.00
Vol. 2 TPB (2009, $29.99) r/#18-35 — 30.00
Vol. 3 TPB (2009, $29.99) r/#36-52 — 30.00

TRINITY (DC Rebirth)
DC Comics: Nov, 2016 - No. 22, ($2.99/$3.99)
1-7: 1-Superman, Batman & Wonder Woman; Manapul-s/a. 3-Mann-a. 4-6-Mongul app. — 3.00
8-22-($3.99): 9-11-Manapul-s/a; Justice League app. 12-15-Zatanna, Constantine & Deadman app.; Marion-a. 16-Deadshot app. 17-19,21,22-Warlord of Skartaris app. — 4.00
Annual 1 (7/17, $4.99) Ra's al Ghul, Circe and Etrigan app.; Guillem March-a/c — 5.00

TRINITY ANGELS
Acclaim Comics (Valiant Heroes): July, 1997 - No. 12, June, 1998 ($2.50)
1-12-Maguire-s/a(p). 4-Copycat-a — 4.00

TRINITY: BLOOD ON THE SANDS
Image Comics (Top Cow): July, 2009 ($2.99, one-shot)
1-Witchblade, The Darkness and Angelus in the 14th century Arabian desert — 3.00

TRINITY OF SIN (DC New 52)
DC Comics: Dec, 2014 - No. 6, May, 2015 ($2.99)
1-6-Pandora, The Question and Phantom Stranger; Guichet-a — 3.00

TRINITY OF SIN: PANDORA (DC New 52)
DC Comics: Aug, 2013 - No. 14, Oct, 2014 ($2.99)
1-14: 1-Fawkes-s; origin re-told. 1-3-Trinity War tie-ins. 4-9-Forever Evil tie-ins — 3.00
...: Futures End 1 (11/14, $2.99, regular-c) Five years later; Pandora vs. 7 Deadly Sins — 3.00
...: Futures End 1 (11/14, $3.99, 3-D cover) — 4.00

TRINITY OF SIN: THE PHANTOM STRANGER (See Phantom Stranger 2012 series)

TRINITY SPECIAL
DC Comics: Mar, 2024 ($5.99, one-shot)(Reprints back-ups from Wonder Woman #2-5 (2024))
1-Future stories with Jon Kent, Damian Wayne and Wonder Woman's daughter — 6.00

TRIO (Continues in Triple Helix #1)
IDW Publishing: May, 2012 - No. 4, Aug, 2012 ($3.99, limited series)
1-4-John Byrne-s/a/c — 4.00

TRIPLE GIANT COMICS (See Archie All-Star Specials under Archie Comics)

TRIPLE HELIX (Also see Trio)
IDW Publishing: Oct, 2013 - No. 4, Jan, 2014 ($3.99, limited series)
1-4-John Byrne-s/a/c; The Trio app. — 4.00

TRIPLE THREAT
Special Action/Holyoke/Gerona Publ.: Winter, 1945

1-Duke of Darkness, King O'Leary	41	82	123	256	428	600

TRISH OUT OF WATER
Aspen MLT: Oct, 2013 - No. 5, Mar, 2014 ($1.00/$3.99)
1-($1.00) Vince Hernandez-s/Giuseppe Cafaro-a; multiple covers — 3.00
2-5-($3.99) Multiple covers on each — 4.00

TRIUMPH (Also see JLA #28-30, Justice League Task Force & Zero Hour)
DC Comics: June, 1995 - No. 4, Sept, 1995 ($1.75, limited series)
1-4: 3-Hourman, JLA app. — 4.00

TRIUMPHANT UNLEASHED

	GD	VG	FN	VF	VF/NM	NM-
	2.0	4.0	6.0	8.0	9.0	9.2

Triumphant Comics: No. 0, Nov, 1993 - No. 1, Nov, 1993 ($2.50, lim. series)

0-Serially numbered, 0-Red logo, 0-White logo (no cover price; giveaway),
1-Cover is negative & reverse of #0-c 4.00

TROJAN
Artist, Writers & Artisans, Inc.: Jan, 2023 - No. 4, Apr, 2023 ($3.99, limited series)

1-4-Daniel Kraus-s/Laci-a 4.00

TROJAN WAR (Adaptation of Trojan war histories from ancient Greek and Roman sources)
Marvel Comics: July, 2009 - No. 5, Nov, 2009 ($3.99, limited series)

1-5-Roy Thomas-s/Miguel Sepulveda-a/Dennis Calero-c 4.00

TROLL (Also see Brigade)
Image Comics (Extreme Studios): Dec, 1993 ($2.50, one-shot, 44 pgs.)

1-1st app. Troll; Liefeld scripts; Matsuda-c/a(p) 5.00
Halloween Special (1994, $2.95)-Maxx app. 5.00
...Once A Hero (8/94, $2.50) 5.00

TROLLORDS
Tru Studios/Comico V2#1 on: 2/86 - No. 15, 1988; V2#1, 11/88 - V2#4, 1989 (1-15: $1.50, B&W)

1-First printing 5.00
1-Second printing, 2-15: 6-Christmas issue; silver logo 4.00
V2#1-4 ($1.75, color, Comico) 4.00
Special 1 ($1.75, 2/87, color)-Jerry's Big Fun Bk. 4.00

TROLLORDS
Apple Comics: July, 1989 - No. 6, 1990 ($2.25, B&W, limited series)

1-6: 1-"The Big Batman Movie Parody" 4.00

TROLL PATROL
Harvey Comics: Jan, 1993 ($1.95, 52 pgs.)

1 ..... 5.00

TROLL II (Also see Brigade)
Image Comics (Extreme Studios): July, 1994 ($3.95, one-shot)

1 ..... 4.00

TRON (Based on the video game and film)
Slave Labor Graphics: Apr, 2006 - No. 6 ($3.50/$3.95)

1-6: 1-DeMartinis-a/Walker & Jones-s. 5,6-($3.95) 5.00

TRON: BETRAYAL
Marvel Comics: Nov, 2010 - No. 2, Dec, 2010 ($3.99, limited series)

1,2-Prequel to Tron Legacy movie; Larroca-c 4.00

TRON: ORIGINAL MOVIE ADAPTATION
Marvel Comics: Jan, 2011 - No. 2, Feb, 2011 ($3.99, limited series)

		3	4	6	8	10
1,2-Peter David-s/Mirco Pierfederici-a/Greg Land-c						

TROUBLE
Marvel Comics (Epic): Sept, 2003 - No. 5, Jan, 2004 ($2.99, limited series)

1-5-Photo-c; Richard and Ben meet Mary and May; Millar-s/Dodson-a 3.00
1-2nd printing with variant Frank Cho-c 5.00

TROUBLED SOULS
Fleetway: 1990 ($9.95, trade paperback)

nn-Garth Ennis scripts & John McCrea painted-c/a 10.00

TROUBLEMAKERS
Acclaim Comics (Valiant Heroes): Apr, 1997 - No. 19, June, 1998 ($2.50)

1-19: Fabian Nicieza scripts in all. 1-1st app. XL, Rebound & Blur; 2 covers. 8-Copycat-c.
12-Shooting of Parker 4.00

TROUBLE SHOOTERS, THE (TV)
Dell Publishing Co.: No. 1108, Jun-Aug, 1960

		6	12	18	42	79	115
Four Color 1108-Keenan Wynn photo-c						

TROUBLE WITH GIRLS, THE
Malibu Comics (Eternity Comics) #7-14/Comico V2#1-4/Eternity V2#5 on:
8/87 - #14, 1988; V2#1, 2/89 - V2#23, 1991? ($1.95, B&W/color)

1-14 ($1.95, B&W, Eternity)-Gerard Jones scripts & Tim Hamilton-c/a in all 3.00
V2#1-23-Jones scripts, Hamilton-c/a 3.00
Annual 1 (1988, $2.95) 4.00
Christmas Special 1 (12/91, $2.95, B&W, Eternity)-Jones scripts, Hamilton-c/a 4.00
Graphic Novel 1,2 (7/88, B&W)-r/#1-3 & #4-6 ..... 8.00

TROUBLE WITH GIRLS, THE: NIGHT OF THE LIZARD
Marvel Comics (Epic Comics/Heavy Hitters): 1993 - No. 4, 1993 ($2.50/$1.95, lim. series)

1-Embossed-c; Gerard Jones scripts & Bret Blevins-c/a in all 5.00
2-4: 2-Begin $1.95-c. 4.00

TROVER SAVES THE UNIVERSE (Based on the video game by Justin Roiland)
Image Comics (Skybound): Aug, 2021 - No. 5, Dec, 2021 ($3.99, limited series)

1-5-Tess Stone-s/a 4.00

TRUE ADVENTURES (Formerly True Western)(Men's Adventures #4 on)
Marvel Comics (CCC): No. 3, May, 1950 (52 pgs.)

	GD	VG	FN	VF	VF/NM	NM-
3-Powell, Sekowsky, Maneely-a; Brodsky-c	30	60	90	177	289	400

TRUE ANIMAL PICTURE STORIES
True Comics Press: Winter, 1947 - No. 2, Spring-Summer, 1947

	GD	VG	FN	VF	VF/NM	NM-
1	15	30	45	88	137	185
2	14	28	42	76	112	145

TRUE AVIATION PICTURE STORIES (Becomes Aviation Adventures & Model Building #16 on)
Parents' Mag. Institute: 1942; No. 2, Jan-Feb, 1943 - No. 15, Sept-Oct, 1946

1-(#1 & 2 titled ...Aviation Comics Digest)(not digest size)

	GD	VG	FN	VF	VF/NM	NM-
	20	40	60	120	195	270
2	13	26	39	74	105	135
3-14: 3-10-Plane photos on-c. 11,13-Photo-c	10	20	30	58	79	100
15-(Titled "True Aviation Adventures & Model Building")						
	10	20	30	54	72	90

TRUE BELIEVERS

Marvel Comics: Sept, 2008 - No. 5, Jan, 2009 ($2.99, limited series)

1-5-Cary Bates-s/Paul Gulacy-a. 1,2-Reed Richards app. 3-Luke Cage app. 4.00

TRUE BELIEVERS...
Marvel Comics: Jun, 2015 - Present ($1.00, series of one-shot reprints)

	1	2	3		6	8
...: Absolute Carnage – Carnage 1 - Reprints Amazing Spider-Man #361; Bagley-a						

...: Absolute Carnage – Carnage, U.S.A. 1 - Reprints Carnage, U.S.A. #1; Crain-a 6.00
...: Absolute Carnage – Mania 1 - Reprints Venom #1 (2003); Herrera-a 3.00
...: Absolute Carnage – Maximum Carnage 1 - Reprints Spider-Man Unlimited #1 ..... 6.00

	1		4		8	10
...: Absolute Carnage – Mind Bomb 1 - Reprints Carnage: Mind Bomb #1; Hotz-a						

...: Absolute Carnage – Planet of the Symbiotes 1 - R/ Amaz. Spider-Man Super Special 3.00
...: Absolute Carnage – Savage Rebirth 1 - Reprints Amazing Spider-Man #430 ..... 5.00
...: Absolute Carnage – Separation Anxiety 1 - Reprints Venom: Separation Anxiety #1 ..... 3.00

	1		4		8	10
...: Absolute Carnage – She-Venom 1 - Reprints Venom: Sinner Takes All #3						

...: Absolute Carnage – Venom vs. Carnage 1 - Reprints Venom vs. Carnage #1 ..... 3.00

	3	6	15	16	23	30
...: Age of Apocalypse 1 - Reprints X-Men: Alpha #1; Cruz & Epting-a; wraparound-c						

...: Age of Ultron 1 - Reprints Age of Ultron #1; Bendis-s/Hitch-a 3.00
...: All-New, All-Different Avengers - Cyclone 1 - Reprints issue #4; Waid-s/Asrar-a 3.00
...: All-New Wolverine 1 - Reprints issue #1; Taylor-s/Lopez-a 6.00
...: Amazing Spider-Man 1 - Reprints Amazing Spider-Man #1 ..... 5.00
...: Amazing Spider-Man - The Dark Kingdom 1 - Reprints Amazing Spider-Man #6 ..... 3.00
...: Annihilation – Annihilus 1 - Reprints Fantastic Four #140 ..... 3.00
...: Annihilation – Mantis 1 - Reprints Avengers #112; Heck-a 3.00
...: Annihilation – Man-Wolf in Space 1 - Reprints Marvel Premiere #45 ..... 3.00
...: Annihilation – Moondragon 1 - Reprints Iron Man #54; Sub-Mariner app. 3.00
...: Annihilation – Nova 1 - Reprints Nova #1; John Buscema-a 3.00
...: Annihilation – Odinpower 1 - Reprints Thor #349; Simonson-s/a 3.00
...: Annihilation – Omega the Unknown 1 - Reprints Omega the Unknown #1 ..... 3.00
...: Annihilation – Quasar 1 - Reprints Incredible Hulk #234; Sal Buscema-a 3.00
...: Annihilation – Super-Adaptoid 1 - Reprints Tales of Suspense #82 & 84; Kirby-a 3.00
...: Annihilation – Super-Skrull 1 - Reprints Thor #142; Kirby-a 3.00
...: Ant-Man and Hawkeye - Avengers Assemble 1 - Reprints Avengers #223 ..... 3.00
...: Ant-Man and the Wasp - On the Trail of Spider-Man 1 - Reprints Tales to Astonish #57 ..... 3.00
...: Ant-Man and the Wasp - Birth of Giant-Man 1 - Rep. Tales to Astonish #35 & 49 ..... 3.00
...: Ant-Man and the Wasp - 'Til Death Do Us Part 1 - Reprints Avengers #60 ..... 3.00
...: Ant-Man Presents Iron Man - The Ghost and the Machine 1 - Reprints Iron Man #219 ..... 3.00

		3	4	6	8	10	12
...: Ant-Man - The Incredible Shrinking Doom 1 - Reprints Marvel Feature #4							3.00

...: Armor Wars 1 - Reprints Iron Man #225; Michelinie-s/Bright & Layton-a 3.00
...: Astonishing X-Men 1 - Reprints Astonishing X-Men #1 (2004); Whedon-s/Cassaday-a 3.00
...: Avengers – Endgame 1 - Reprints Avengers #71; Sal Buscema-a 3.00
...: Avengers Forever 1 - Reprints Avengers Forever #1; Busiek-s/Pacheco-a 3.00
...: Avengers – Nebula 1 - Reprints Avengers #260; John Buscema-a 3.00
...: Avengers - Rocket Raccoon 1 - Reprints Rocket Raccoon #1; Mignola-a 3.00
...: Avengers - Ronin 1 - Reprints New Avengers #30; Bendis-s/Yu-a 3.00
...: Avengers - Stormbreaker 1 - Reprints Thor #339; Simonson-s/a 3.00
...: Avengers – Thanos & Gamora 1 - Reprints Warlock and the Infinity Watch #9 ..... 3.00
...: Avengers – Thanos: The Final Battle 1 - Reprints Infinity Gauntlet #6; Starlin-s/Lim-a 3.00
...: Avengers – Thanos vs. The Marvel Universe 1 - Reprints Infinity Gauntlet #4 ..... 3.00
...: Avengers – The Gatherers Saga 1 - Reprints Avengers #343; Epting-a 3.00
...: Avengers vs. Thanos 1 - Reprints Avengers #125; Buscema & Cockrum-a 3.00
...: Black Widow – Amazing Adventures 1 - Reprints Black Widow #1 (2014); Edmondson-s/Noto-a 3.00
...: Black Widow – Amazing Adventures 1 - Reprints stories from Amazing Advs. #1,2 ..... 3.00
...: Black Widow & Daredevil 1 - Reprints Daredevil #81 (1971); Conway-s/Colan-a 3.00
...: Black Widow & The Avengers 1 - Reprints Avengers #111 (1973); Magneto app. 3.00
...: Black Widow & The Thing 1 - Reprints Marvel Two-In-One #10 (1975); Brown-a 3.00
...: Black Widow – Champions 1 - Reprints Champions #7 (1976); Tuska-a 3.00
...: Black Widow, Introducing The... 1 - Reprints Tales of Suspense #52-53 (1964) 3.00
...: Black Widow – Red Guardian 1 - Reprints Avengers #43 (1967); John Buscema-a 3.00
...: Black Widow – Taskmaster 1 - Reprints Avengers #196 (1980); origin; Pérez-a 3.00
...: Black Widow – Yelena Belova 1 - Reprints Black Widow #1 (1999); J.G. Jones-a 3.00
...: Cable & The New Mutants 1 - Reprints New Mutants #87; L. Simonson-s/Liefeld-a 3.00
...: Captain Marvel 1 - Reprints Captain Marvel #1 (2014); DeConnick-s/Lopez-a 3.00
...: Captain Marvel - Avenger 1 - Reprints Avengers #183; Michelinie-s/Byrne-a 3.00
...: Captain Marvel - Betrayed! 1 - Reprints Avengers Annual #10; Claremont-s/Golden-a 3.00
...: Captain Marvel - Binary 1 - Reprints Uncanny X-Men #164; Claremont-s/Cockrum-a 3.00
...: Captain Marvel - Earth's Mightiest Hero 1 - Reprints Captain Marvel #1 (2012) 3.00
...: Captain Mar-vell 1 - Reprints Marvel Super-Heroes #12 & Marvel Fanfare #24 ..... 3.00
...: Captain Marvel - Ms. Marvel 1 - Reprints Ms. Marvel #1 (1977); Buscema-a 3.00
...: Captain Marvel - Spider-Man and Ms. Marvel 1 - Reprints Marvel Team-Up #62 ..... 3.00
...: Captain Marvel - The Kree/Skrull War 1 - Reprints Avengers #89; Rick Jones app. 3.00
...: Captain Marvel - The New Ms. Marvel 1 - Reprints Ms. Marvel #20 (1978); Cockrum-a 3.00
...: Captain Marvel vs. Ronan 1 - Reprints Captain Marvel #41 (1975); Milgrom-a 3.00
...: Carol Danvers 1 - Reprints Marvel Super-Heroes #13; 1st app. Carol Danvers 3.00
...: Chewbacca 1 - Reprints Chewbacca #1; Duggan-s/Noto-a 3.00

		3		4	6	8	10
...: Civil War 1 - Reprints Civil War #1; Millar-s/McNiven-a							

...: Conan - Curse of the Golden Skull! 1 - Reps Conan the Barbarian #37; Neal Adams-a 3.00
...: Conan - Queen of the Black Coast! 1 - Reps Conan the Barbarian #58; Bêlit app. 3.00
...: Conan - Resurrection 1 - Reprints Conan the Barbarian #187; Buscema-a 3.00
...: Conan - Serpent War #0 – The Valley of the Worm - Reprints Supernatural Thrillers #3 ..... 3.00
...: Conan - Swords in the Night! 1 - Reprints Conan the Barbarian #23; Barry Smith-a 3.00
...: Conan the Barbarian 1 - Reprints Conan the Barbarian #1; Barry Smith-a 3.00
...: Conan - The Devil-God of Bal-Sagoth! 1 - Reprints Conan the Barbarian #17; Kane-a 3.00
...: Conan - The Secret of Skull River 1 - Reprints Savage Tales #5; Starlin-a 3.00
...: Conan - The Tower of the Elephant 1 - Reprints Conan the Barbarian #4; B. Smith-a 3.00
...: Daredevil - Practice to Deceive 1 - Reprints Daredevil #6 (2016); Soule-s/Buffagni-a 3.00
...: Darth Vader 1 - Reprints Darth Vader #1; Gillen-s/Larroca-a 3.00

		1		3	4	6	8	10
...: Deadpool 1 - Reprints 1st app. from New Mutants #98 (1991); Liefeld-a							

				4		6	8	10
...: Deadpool - Deadpool vs. Sabretooth 1 - Reprints Deadpool #8 (2016)							3.00

Trojan War #3 © MAR

True Believers: Droids #1 © Lucasfilm

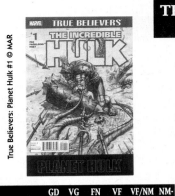

True Believers: Planet Hulk #1 © MAR

	GD	VG	FN	VF	VF/NM	NM-
	2.0	4.0	6.0	8.0	9.0	9.2

...: Deadpool Origins 1 - Reprints Wolverine Origins #25; Dillon-a — 3.00
...: Deadpool The Musical 1 - Reprints Deadpool #49.1; McCrea-a — 3.00
...: Deadpool Variants 1 - Gallery of variant covers — 3.00
...: Death of Phoenix 1 - Reprints New X-Men #150 — 3.00
...: Detective Deadpool 1 - Reprints Cable & Deadpool #13; Nicieza-s/Zircher-a — 3.00
...: Doctor Strange - The Last Days of Magic 1 - Reprints Doctor Strange #6 (2015) — 3.00
...: Droids 1 - Reprints Droids #1; Star Wars C-3PO & R2-D2 app.; John Romita-a — 3.00
...: Empyre – Anelle 1 - Reprints Fantastic Four #37 (1965) intro Princess Anelle — 3.00
...: Empyre – Galactus 1 - Reprints Fantastic Four #257 (1983) Byrne-s/a — 3.00
...: Empyre – Hulkling 1 - Reprints Young Avengers #11 (2006) Cheung-a — 3.00
...: Empyre – Lyja 1 - Reprints Fantastic Four #357 (1991) Paul Ryan-a — 3.00
...: Empyre – Mantis 1 - Reprints Avengers #133 (1975) origin of Mantis; Sal Buscema-a — 3.00
...: Empyre – Mar-Vell 1 - Reprints Avengers #89 (1971) Kree/Skrull war begins — 3.00
...: Empyre – Quoi 1 - Reprints Avengers Celestial Quest #3 (12003) Englehart-s — 3.00
...: Empyre – She-Hulk 1 - Reprints Savage She-Hulk #1 (1980) John Buscema-a — 6.00
...: Empyre – Swordsman 1 - Reprints Avengers #19 (1965) Swordsman's debut; Heck-a — 3.00
...: Empyre – Vision 1 - Reprints Giant-Size Avengers #4 (1974) Dormammu app. — 3.00
...: Enter – The Phoenix 1 - Reprints X-Men #100-101 (1976) Cockrum-a — 3.00
...: Evil Deadpool 1 - Reprints Deadpool #45; Espin-a — 3.00
...: Exiles 1 - Reprints Exiles #1 (2001); Winick-s/McKone-a — 3.00
...: Extraordinary X-Men - The Burning Man 1 - Reprints issue #6; Ibañez-a — 3.00
...: Fantastic Four - Blastaar 1 - Reprints Fantastic Four #62; Kirby-a; Inhumans app. — 3.00
...: Fantastic Four By John Byrne 1 - Reprints Fantastic Four #232; Diablo app. — 3.00
...: Fantastic Four By Walter Simonson 1 - Reprints Fantastic Four #337 — 3.00
...: Fantastic Four - Dragon Man 1 - Reprints Fantastic Four #35; Kirby-a — 3.00
...: Fantastic Four - Frightful Four 1 - Reprints Fantastic Four #36; Kirby-a — 3.00
...: Fantastic Four - Galactus Hungers 1 - Reprints Fantastic Four #175; Buscema-a — 3.00
...: Fantastic Four - Hulk vs. Thing 1 - Reprints Fantastic Four #112; Buscema-a — 3.00
...: Fantastic Four - Klaw 1 - Reprints Fantastic Four #53; Kirby-a; Black Panther app. — 3.00
...: Fantastic Four - Mad Thinker & Awesome Android 1 - Reprints Fantastic Four #15 — 3.00
...: Fantastic Four - Molecule Man 1 - Reprints Fantastic Four #20; Kirby-a; Watcher app. — 3.00
...: Fantastic Four - Puppet Master 1 - Reprints Fantastic Four #8; Kirby-a; intro. Alicia — 3.00
...: Fantastic Four - Ronan & The Kree 1 - Reprints Fantastic Four #65; Kirby-a — 3.00
...: Fantastic Four - Skrulls 1 - Reprints Fantastic Four #2; Kirby-a — 3.00
...: Fantastic Four - Super-Skrull 1 - Reprints Fantastic Four #18; Kirby-a — 3.00
...: Fantastic Four - The Birth of Valeria 1 - Reprints Fantastic Four #54 (2002) — 3.00
...: Fantastic Four - The Coming of Galactus 1 - Reprints Fantastic Four #48 — 3.00
...: Fantastic Four - The Coming of H.E.R.B.I.E. 1 - Reprints Fantastic Four #209 — 3.00
...: Fantastic Four - The Wedding of Reed & Sue 1 - Reprints Fantastic Four Annual #3 — 3.00
...: Fantastic Four vs. Doctor Doom 1 - Reprints 1st app. in Fantastic Four #5 — 3.00

	1	3	4	6		8	10

...: Fantastic Four vs. the New Fantastic Four 1 - Reprints Fantastic Four #374 — 3.00
...: Generation X 1 - Reprints Generation X #1; Lobdell-s/Bachalo-a — 3.00

	1	2	3	5		6	8

...: Guardians of the Galaxy - Galaxy's Most Wanted 1 - Reprints GOTG #6 (2015) — 3.00
...: House of M 1 - Reprints House of M #1; Bendis-s/Coipel-a — 3.00

	1	3	4	6		8	10

...: Hulk - Devil Hulk 1 - Reprints Incredible Hulk #13 (2000); Jenkins-s/Garney-a — 3.00
...: Hulk - Grey Hulk Returns 1 - Reprints Incredible Hulk #324; Milgrom-s/a — 3.00

	1	2	3	5		6	8

...: Hulk - Head of Banner 1 - Reprints Incredible Hulk #6; Stan Lee-s/Steve Ditko-a — 3.00
...: Hulk - Intelligent 1 - Reprints Incredible Hulk #272; Mantlo-s/Sal Buscema-a — 3.00
...: Hulk - Joe Fixit 1 - Reprints Incredible Hulk #347; David-s/Purves-a — 3.00
...: Hulk - Mindless Hulk 1 - Reprints Incredible Hulk #299; Mantlo-s/Sal Buscema-a — 3.00
...: Hulk - Professor Hulk 1 - Reprints Incredible Hulk #377; David-s/Keown-a — 3.00
...: Hulk - Red Hulk 1 - Reprints Hulk #1 (2008); Loeb-s/McGuinness-a — 3.00
...: Hulk - The Other Hulks 1 - r/Journey Into Mystery #62 (Xemnu) & Strange Tales #75 — 3.00
...: Infinity Gauntlet 1 - Reprints Infinity Gauntlet #1; Starlin-s/Pérez-a

	1	3	4	6		8	10

...: Infinity Incoming! 1 - Reprints Avengers #1 (2013); Hickman-s/Opeña-a — 3.00
...: Infinity War 1 - Reprints Infinity War #1; Starlin-s/Lim-a — 3.00
...: Invincible Iron Man - The War Machines 1 - Reprints Invincible Iron Man #6 — 3.00
...: Iron Man 2020 - Albert & Elsie-Dee 1 - Reprints Wolverine #37 (1988); Silvestri-a — 3.00
...: Iron Man 2020 - Arno Stark 1 - Reprints Machine Man #2 (1984); Trimpe-a — 3.00
...: Iron Man 2020 - Jocasta 1 - Reprints Avengers #162; Ultron app.; Perez-a — 3.00
...: Iron Man 2020 - Pepper Potts 1 - Reprints Tales of Suspense #45; Heck-a — 3.00
...: Iron Man 2020 - War Machine 1 - Reprints Iron Man #118 (1979); Byrne-a — 3.00
...: Kanan 1 - Reprints Kanan #1; Star Wars; Weisman-s/Larraz-a

	2	4	6	11	16	20

...: King Conan 1 - Reprints King Conan #1; Buscema-a — 3.00
...: King in Black – Beta Ray Bill 1 - Reprints Mighty Thor #337; 1st app. Bill; Simonson-s/a — 3.00
...: King in Black – Black Cat 1 - Reprints 1st app. in Amazing Spider-Man #194 — 3.00
...: King in Black – Black Knight 1 - Reprints Avengers #48 (1968); 1st app.; Tuska-a — 3.00
...: King in Black – Black Panther 1 - Reprints Fantastic Four #52 (1966); 1st app. — 3.00

...: King in Black – Franklin Richards 1 - Reprints Fantastic Four #245; Byrne-s/a — 3.00
...: King in Black – Gamma Flight's Doc Samson 1 - Reprints Incredible Hulk #141; origin — 3.00
...: King in Black – Iron Man/Doctor Doom 1 - Reprints Iron Man #149; Romita Jr.-a — 3.00
...: King in Black – Monsterworld 1 - Reprints Venom Super Special #1 (1995); Hotz-a — 3.00
...: King in Black – Thunderbolts 1 - Reprints Incredible Hulk #449; Deodato Jr.-a — 3.00
...: King in Black – Valkyrie 1 - Reprints Avengers #83 (1970); origin.; Buscema-a — 3.00
...: Kitty Pryde and Wolverine 1 - Reprints Kitty Pryde and Wolverine #1; Milgrom-a — 3.00
...: Lando 1 - Reprints Lando #1; Star Wars; Soule-s/Maleev-a — 3.00
...: Marvel Knights 20th Anniversary – Black Widow By Grayson & Jones 1 - r/#1('99) — 3.00
...: Marvel Knights 20th Anniversary – Daredevil and the Defenders 1 - r/Daredevil #80 — 3.00
...: Marvel Knights 20th Anniversary – Daredevil By Bendis & Maleev 1 - r/Daredevil #26 — 3.00
...: Marvel Knights 20th Anniversary – Daredevil By Lee & Everett 1 - r/Daredevil #1 ('98) — 3.00
...: Marvel Knights 20th Anniversary – Daredevil By Smith, Quesada & Palmiotti 1 - r/#1 ('98) — 3.00
...: Marvel Knights 20th Anniversary – Hellcat: The First Appearance 1 - r/Avengers #144 — 3.00
...: Marvel Knights 20th Anniversary – Iron Fist By Thomas & Kane 1 - r/Marvel Prem. #15 — 3.00
...: Marvel Knights 20th Anniversary – Jessica Jones: Alias By Bendis & Gaydos 1 - r/Alias #1 — 3.00
...: Marvel Knights 20th Anniversary – Luke Cage, Hero For Hire 1 - r/Hero For Hire #1 — 3.00
...: Marvel Knights 20th Anniversary – Power Man and Iron Fist 1 - r/Power Man #48 — 3.00
...: Marvel Knights 20th Anniversary – Punisher: The First Appearance 1 - r/AS-M #129

	1	3	4	6		8	10

...: Marvel Knights 20th Anniversary – Punisher By Ennis, Dillon & Palmiotti 1 - r/#1 ('00) — 3.00
...: Marvel Knights 20th Anniversary – Punisher By Grant & Zeck 1 - r/Punisher #1 ('86) — 3.00
...: Marvel Knights 20th Anniversary – Punisher War Journal By Potts & Lee 1 - r/#1 ('88) — 3.00
...: Marvel Tails Starring Peter Porker, The Spectacular Spider-Ham 1 - Reprints #1 — 3.00
...: Marvel Zombies 1 - Reprints Marvel Zombies #1; Bendis-s/Phillips-a

	2	4	6	8	10	12

...: Mighty Thor - The Strongest Viking There Is 1 - Reprints Mighty Thor #6 — 3.00
...: Miles Morales 1 - Reprints Ultimate Comics Spider-Man #1; Bendis-s/Pichelli-a

	1	3	4	6		8	10

...: Ms. Marvel 1 - Reprints Ms. Marvel #1 (2014); Wilson-s/Alphona-a — 3.00
...: New Mutants 1 - Reprints New Mutants #1; Claremont-s/McLeod-a — 3.00
...: Old Man Logan 1 - Reprints Wolverine #66 (2008); Millar-s/McNiven-a; wraparound-c — 5.00
...: Phoenix – Bizarre Adventures 1 - Reprints Bizarre Adventures #27; Buscema-a — 3.00
...: Phoenix Classic 1 - Reprints Classic X-Men #13 & 18; Bolton-a — 3.00
...: Phoenix Origins 1 - Reprints X-Men Origins: Jean Grey; Mayhew-a — 3.00
...: Phoenix Presents Cyclops & Marvel Girl 1 - Reprints X-Men #48 & 57 (1968,1969) — 3.00
...: Phoenix Presents Jean Grey vs. Sabretooth 1 - Reprints X-Men #28 (1994) — 3.00
...: Phoenix Presents The Wedding of Scott Summers & Jean Grey 1 - Reprints X-Men #30 — 3.00
...: Phoenix Returns 1 - Reprints Fantastic Four #286; Byrne-s/a — 3.00
...: Phoenix – What If? 1 - Reprints What If? #27 (Phoenix Had Not Died?) — 3.00
...: Planet Hulk 1 - Reprints Incredible Hulk #92 (2006); Pak-s/Pagulayan-a — 3.00
...: Princess Leia 1 - Reprints Princess Leia #1; Waid-s/Dodson-a — 6.00
...: Rebirth of Thanos 1 - Reprints Silver Surfer #34 (1990); Starlin-s/Lim-a — 3.00
...: Scott Lang, The Astonishing Ant-Man 1 - Reprints Marvel Premiere #47; Byrne-a — 3.00
...: Shattered Empire 1 - Reprints Journey to Star Wars: The Force Awakens – Shattered Empire #1; Rucka-s/Checchetto-a — 3.00
...: She-Hulk 1 - Reprints She-Hulk #1 (2014); Soule-s/Pulido-a — 6.00
...: Silk 1 - Reprints Silk #1 (2015); Thompson-s/Stacey Lee-a; Spider-Man app. — 3.00
...: Spider-Gwen 1 - Reprints Spider-Gwen #1 (2015); Latour-s/Robbi Rodriguez-a

	1	3	4	6		8	10

...: Spider-Man – Morbius 1 - Reprints Amazing Spider-Man #101; Gil Kane-a

	1	3	4	6		8	10

...: Spider-Man – Spider-Armor 1 - Reprints Web of Spider-Man #100; Saviuk-a — 3.00
...: Spider-Man – Spidey Fights in London 1 - Reprints Amazing Spider-Man #95 — 3.00
...: Spider-Man – The New Spider-Man 1 - Reprints Marvel Team-Up #141 — 3.00
...: Spider-Man – The Wedding of Aunt May & Doc Ock 1 - Reprints ASM #131 — 3.00
...: Spider-Man vs. Hulk 1 - Reprints Amazing Spider-Man #328; McFarlane-a — 3.00
...: Spider-Man vs. Mysterio 1 - Reprints debut in Amazing Spider-Man #13 — 3.00
...: Spider-Woman 1 - Reprints Spider-Woman #5 (2015); Hopeless-s/Javier Rodriguez-a — 3.00
...: Star Wars 1 - Reprints Star Wars #1 (2015); Aaron-s/Cassaday-a — 6.00
...: Star Wars – According to the Droids 1 - Reprints Droids #6 — 3.00
...: Star Wars – Classic 1 - Reprints Star Wars #1 (1977); Roy Thomas-s/Howard Chaykin-a — 6.00
...: Star Wars Covers 1 - Gallery of variant covers for Star Wars #1 (2015) — 3.00
...: Star Wars – Darth Maul 1 - Reprints Star Wars: Darth Maul – Son of Dathomir #1

	1	3	4	6		8	10

...: Star Wars – Darth Vader 1 - Reprints Darth Vader #1

	1	3	4	6		8	10

...: Star Wars – Dead Probe 1 - Reprints Star Wars #45 (1977); Infantino-a — 6.00
...: Star Wars – Ewoks 1 - Reprints Ewoks #1; Kremer-a

	1	3	4	6		8	10

...: Star Wars – Hutt Run 1 - Reprints Star Wars #35 (2015); Larroca-a — 3.00
...: Star Wars – Rebel Jail 1 - Reprints Star Wars #16 (2015); Doctor Aphra app.; Yu-a — 3.00
...: Star Wars – Skywalker Strikes 1 - Reprints Star Wars #1 (2015); Aaron-s/Cassaday-a — 3.00
...: Star Wars – The Ashes of Jedha 1 - Reprints Star Wars #38 (2015); Larroca-a — 3.00
...: Star Wars – The Hunter 1 - Reprints Star Wars #16 (1977); Simonson-a — 3.00
...: Star Wars – The Original Marvel Years No. 107 - Reprints Star Wars #107 (1986) — 3.00

	GD 2.0	VG 4.0	FN 6.0	VF 8.0	VF/NM 9.0	NM- 9.2

...: Star Wars – Thrawn 1 - Reprints Star Wars: Thrawn #1; Luke Ross-a — 1 3 4 6 8 10

...: Star Wars – Vader vs. Leia 1 - Reprints Star Wars #48 (1977); Infantino-a — 1 3 4 6 8 10

...: Thanos the First 1 - Reprints Iron Man #55 (1973); 1st app. Thanos & Drax — 1 3 4 6 8 10

...: Thanos Rising 1 - Reprints Thanos Rising #1; Aaron-s/Bianchi-a — 3.00
...: The Criminally Insane - Absorbing Man 1 - Reprints Journey Into Mystery #114 — 3.00
...: The Criminally Insane - Bullseye 1 - Reprints debut in Daredevil #131 — 3.00
...: The Criminally Insane - Bushman 1 - Reprints Moon Knight #1 (1980) — 3.00
...: The Criminally Insane - Dracula 1 - Reprints Tomb of Dracula #24; Colan-a — 3.00
...: The Criminally Insane - Green Goblin 1 - Reprints debut in Amazing Spider-Man #14 — 3.00
...: The Criminally Insane - Gypsy Moth 1 - Reprints Spider-Woman #10; Infantino-a — 3.00
...: The Criminally Insane - Klaw 1 - Reprints Black Panther #14 (1977) — 3.00
...: The Criminally Insane - Mandarin 1 - Reprints Tales of Suspense #50 & 55 — 3.00
...: The Criminally Insane - Masters of Evil 1 - Reprints Avengers #6 (1963) — 3.00
...: The Criminally Insane - Purple Man 1 - Reprints Daredevil #4 (1964) — 3.00
...: The Groovy Deadpool - Reprints Deadpool #13 (2013) 1970s art style — 3.00
...: The Meaty Deadpool 1 - Reprints Deadpool #11 (2008) Bullseye (as Hawkeye) app. — 3.00
...: The Sinister Secret of Spider-Man's New Costume 1 - Rep. Amaz. Spider-Man #258 — 3.00
...: The Unbeatable Squirrel Girl 1 - Reprints The Unbeatable Squirrel Girl #1 (2015) — 3.00
...: The Wedding of Deadpool 1 - Reprints Deadpool #27 (2013) wraparound-c — 3.00
...: Thor 1 - Reprints Thor #1 (2014); debut of female Thor; Aaron-s/Dauterman-a — 6.00
...: Uncanny Avengers - The Bagalia Job 1 - Reprints Uncanny Avengers #5 — 3.00
...: Uncanny Avengers 1 - Reprints Cable & Deadpool #38; Nicieza-s/Brown-a — 3.00
...: Vader Down 1 - Reprints Star Wars: Vader Down #1; Aaron-s/Deodato-a — 3.00
...: Venom - Agent Venom 1 - Reprints Venom #1 (2011) Remender-s/Moore-a — 3.00
...: Venom - Carnage 1 - Reprints Amazing Spider-Man #363 (1992) Bagley-a — 3.00

(1 3 4 6 8 10)
...: Venom - Dark Origin 1 - Reprints Venom: Dark Origin #3 (2008) Wells-s/Medina-a — 3.00
...: Venom - Flashpoint 1 - Reprints Amazing Spider-Man #654.1 (2011) Ramos-a — 3.00
...: Venom - Homecoming 1 - Reprints Venom #6 (2017) Costa-s/Sandoval-a — 3.00
...: Venom - Lethal Protector 1 - Reprints Venom: Lethal Protector #1; Bagley-a — 3.00

(1 3 4 6 8 10)
...: Venom - Shiver 1 - Reprints Venom #1 (2003) Way-s/Herrera-a — 3.00
...: Venom - Symbiosis 1 - Reprints Web of Spider-Man #1 (1985) Larocque-a — 3.00
...: Venom - Toxin 1 - Reprints Venom #17 (2011) Remender & Bunn-s/Walker-a — 3.00
...: Venom vs. Spider-Man 1 - Reprints Amazing Spider-Man #300 (1988) McFarlane-a — 3.00

(2 4 6 8 10 12)
...: What If Conan the Barbarian Walked the Earth Today? 1 - Reprints What If? #13 — 3.00
...: What If Doctor Doom Had Become a Hero? 1 - Reprints What If? #22 — 3.00
...: What If Jane Foster Had Found the Hammer of Thor? 1 - Reprints What If? #10 — 3.00
...: What If Kraven the Hunter Had Killed Spider-Man? 1 - Reprints What If? #17 — 3.00
...: What If Legion Had Killed Magneto? 1 - Reprints What If? #77; Gomez-a — 3.00
...: What If Spider-Man Had Rescued Gwen Stacy? 1 - Reprints What If? #24; Kane-a — 3.00

(2 4 6 8 10 12)
...: What If Spider-Man Joined the Fantastic Four? 1 - Reprints What If? #1 — 3.00
...: What If The Alien Costume Had Possessed Spider-Man? 1 - Reprints What If? #4 — 4.00
...: What If The Avengers Had Fought Evil During the 1950s? 1 - Reprints What If? #9 — 3.00
...: What If The Fantastic Four Had Different Super-Powers? 1 - r/What If? #1 — 3.00
...: What If The Fantastic Four Had Not Gained Their Super-Powers? 1 - r/What If? #36 — 3.00
...: What If The Silver Surfer Possessed the Infinity Gauntlet? 1 - Reprints What If? #49 — 5.00
...: Wolverine - Reprints Wolverine #1 (1982) Claremont-s/Miller-a — 3.00
...: Wolverine and the X-Men 1 - Reprints #1; Aaron-s/Bachalo-a — 3.00
...: Wolverine – Blood Hungry 1 - Reprints Marvel Comics Presents #85-87; Kieth-a — 3.00
...: Wolverine – Enemy of the State 1 - Reprints Wolverine #20 (2003); Millar-a/Romita Jr.-a — 3.00
...: Wolverine – Evolution 1 - Reprints Wolverine #50 (2007); Loeb-s/Bianchi-a — 3.00
...: Wolverine – Fatal Attractions 1 - Reprints X-Men #25 (1993); Nicieza-s/Andy Kubert-a — 3.00
...: Wolverine – Old Man Logan 1 - Reprints Old Man Logan #1; Bendis-s/Sorrentino-a — 3.00
...: Wolverine – Origin 1 - Reprints Wolverine: The Origin #1; Andy Kubert-a — 3.00
...: Wolverine – Save the Tiger 1 - Reprints Marvel Comics Presents #1-3; Buscema-a — 3.00
...: Wolverine – Sword Quest 1 - Reprints Wolverine #1 (1988); Claremont-s/Buscema-a — 3.00
...: Wolverine – The Brothers 1 - Reprints Wolverine #1 (2003); Rucka-s/Robertson-a — 3.00
...: Wolverine – The Dying Game 1 - Reprints Wolverine #90 (1995); Adam Kubert-a — 3.00
...: Wolverine vs. Hulk 1 - Reprints Incredible Hulk #181; Wein/Trimpe-a — 6.00
...: Wolverine vs. Sabretooth 1 - Reprints Wolverine #10 (1989); Buscema-a — 3.00
...: Wolverine vs. Venom 1 - Reprints Venom: Tooth and Claw #1; Hama-s/St. Pierre-a — 5.00
...: Wolverine – Weapon X 1 - Reprints Marvel Comics Presents #72-74 — 3.00
...: Wolverine – X-23 1 - Reprints X-23 #1; Craig Kyle-s/Billy Tan-a — 3.00
...: X-Factor - Mutant Genesis 1 - Reprints X-Factor #71; David-s/Stroman-a — 3.00
...: X-Force 1 - Reprints X-Force #1; Liefeld-s/a; Nicieza-a — 3.00
...: X-Men 1 - Reprints X-Men #1 (1963); Stan Lee-s/Jack Kirby-a — 3.00
...: X-Men - Apocalypse 1 - Reprints X-Factor #6; Louise Simonson-s/Jackson Guice-a — 3.00
...: X-Men - Betsy Braddock 1 - Reprints from Captain Britain #8-10 — 3.00
...: X-Men - Bishop 1 - Reprints debut in Uncanny X-Men #282; Portacio-a — 3.00
...: X-Men Blue 1 - Reprints X-Men #1 (1991); Chris Claremont-s/Jim Lee-a — 3.00
...: X-Men - Cypher - Reprints New Mutants #13; Chris Claremont-s/Sal Buscema-a — 3.00
...: X-Men - Empath - Reprints New Mutants #16; Chris Claremont-s/Sal Buscema-a — 3.00
...: X-Men Gold 1 - Reprints Uncanny X-Men #81; Byrne-s/Portacio-a — 3.00
...: X-Men - Greycrow - Reprints Uncanny X-Men #211; Claremont-s/Romita Jr.-a — 3.00
...: X-Men - Havok - Reprints X-Men #58; Roy Thomas-s/Neal Adams-a — 3.00
...: X-Men - Jubilee 1 - Reprints debut in Uncanny X-Men #244; Silvestri-a — 3.00
...: X-Men - Karima Shapandar, Omega Sentinel 1 - Reprints X-Men Unlimited #27 — 3.00
...: X-Men - Kitty Pryde & Emma Frost 1 - Reprints debuts in X-Men #129; Byrne-a — 3.00
...: X-Men - Kwannon 1 - Reprints debut in X-Men #17 (1992); Andy Kubert-a — 3.00
...: X-Men - Magik - Reprints Magik #1; Chris Claremont-s/John Buscema-a — 3.00
...: X-Men - Mister Sinister - Reprints Uncanny X-Men #221; Claremont-s/Silvestri-a — 3.00
...: X-Men - Moira MacTaggert 1 - Reprints debut in X-Men #96 — 3.00
...: X-Men - Nanny & Orphan Maker - Reprints X-Factor #35; Louise Simonson-s — 3.00
...: X-Men - Pyro 1 - Reprints debut in Uncanny X-Men #141; Byrne-a — 3.00
...: X-Men - Rictor 1 - Reprints debut in X-Factor #17; Simonson-a — 3.00
...: X-Men - Saturnyne - Reprints Marvel Super Heroes UK #380-383; Captain Britain — 3.00
...: X-Men - Soulsword - Reprints Uncanny X-Men #171; Claremont-s/Simonson-a — 3.00
...: X-Men - Wild Child - Reprints Alpha Flight #11 & Marvel Comics Presents #51 — 3.00

TRUE BELIEVERS: KIRBY 100TH
Marvel Comics: Oct, 2017 ($1.00, one-shot reprints celebrating Jack Kirby's 100th birthday)

... – Ant-Man and The Wasp #1 - Reprints Tales to Astonish #27 & #44 — 3.00
... – Avengers: Captain America Lives Again! #1 - Reprints Avengers #4; bonus pin-ups — 3.00
... – Black Panther #1 - Reprints Black Panther #1 — 6.00
... – Captain America #1 - Reprints Captain America Comics #1 & Tales of Suspense #63 — 3.00
... – Devil Dinosaur #1 - Reprints Devil Dinosaur #1; cover gallery & letter columns — 3.00
... – Eternals #1 - Reprints Eternals #1; pin-ups & letter columns — 3.00
... – Groot #1 - Reprints Tales to Astonish #13 & Journey Into Mystery #62 (Hulk/Xemnu) — 3.00

(1 3 4 6 8 10)
... – Inhumans #1 - Reprints Amazing Adventures #1,2; bonus pin-ups — 3.00
... – Introducing... The Mighty Thor #1 - Reprints Journey Into Mystery #83,85 — 3.00
... – Iron Man #1 - Reprints Tales of Suspense #40,41 — 3.00
... – Nick Fury #1 - Reprints Strange Tales #135,141 — 3.00
... – Thor vs. Hulk #1 - Reprints Journey Into Mystery #112 — 6.00

TRUE BLOOD (Based on the HBO vampire series)
IDW Publishing: Aug, 2010 - No. 6, Dec, 2010 ($3.99)
1-Messina-a; 4 covers by Messina, Campbell, Currie and Corroney — 5.00
2-6-Multiple covers on each — 4.00
...: Legacy Edition (1/11, $4.99) r/#1, cover gallery; full script — 5.00

TRUE BLOOD (2nd series)(Based on the HBO vampire series)
IDW Publishing: May, 2012 - No. 14, Jun, 2013 ($3.99)
1-14-Gaydos-a in most; 2 covers (photo & Bradstreet-c) on each. 5-Manfredi-a — 4.00

TRUE BLOOD: TAINTED LOVE (Based on the HBO vampire series)
IDW Publishing: Feb, 2011 - No. 6, Jul, 2011 ($3.99, limited series)
1-4: 1,2,4,5-Corroney-a; multiple covers. 3-Molnar-a — 4.00
... Legacy Edition 1 (7/11, $4.99) r/#1 with full script and cover gallery — 5.00

TRUE BLOOD: THE FRENCH QUARTER (Based on the HBO vampire series)
IDW Publishing: Aug, 2011 - No. 6, Jan, 2012 ($3.99, limited series)
1-6-Huehner & Tischman-s; multiple covers. 3-Molnar-a — 4.00

TRUE BLOOD: THE GREAT REVELATION (Prequel to the 2008 HBO vampire series)
HBO/Top Cow: July, 2008 (no cover price, one shot continued on HBO website)
1-David Wohl-s/Jason Badower a/c — 4.00

TRUE BRIDE'S EXPERIENCES (Formerly Teen-Age Brides)
(True Bride-To-Be Romances No. 17 on)
True Love (Harvey Publications): No. 8, Oct, 1954 - No. 16, Feb, 1956

	GD 2.0	VG 4.0	FN 6.0	VF 8.0	VF/NM 9.0	NM- 9.2
8-"I Married a Farmer"	14	28	42	76	108	140
9,10: 10-Last pre-code (2/55)	9	18	27	47	61	75
11-15	8	16	24	40	50	60
16-Last issue	9	18	27	47	61	75

NOTE: **Powell** a-8-10, 12, 13.

TRUE BRIDE-TO-BE ROMANCES (Formerly True Bride's Experiences)
Home Comics/True Love (Harvey): No. 17, Apr, 1956 - No. 30, Nov, 1958

	GD 2.0	VG 4.0	FN 6.0	VF 8.0	VF/NM 9.0	NM- 9.2
17-S&K-c; Powell-a	13	26	39	74	105	135
18-20,22,25-28,30	8	16	24	40	50	60
21,23,24,29-Powella. 29-Baker-a (1 pg.)	8	16	24	42	54	65

TRUE COMICS (Also see Outstanding American War Heroes)
True Comics/Parents' Magazine Press: April, 1941 - No. 84, Aug, 1950

	GD 2.0	VG 4.0	FN 6.0	VF 8.0	VF/NM 9.0	NM- 9.2
1-Marathon run story; life story Winston Churchill	41	82	123	256	428	600
2-Red Cross history; Everett-a	20	40	60	120	195	270
3-Baseball Hall of Fame story; Chiang Kai-Shek-c/s	18	36	54	109	172	235
4,5: 4-Story of American flag "Old Glory". 5-Life story of Joe Louis	15	30	45	86	133	180
6-Baseball World Series story	16	32	48	98	154	210
7-10: 7-Buffalo Bill story. 10,11-Teddy Roosevelt	14	28	42	76	108	140
11-14,16,18-20: 11-Thomas Edison, Douglas MacArthur stories. 13-Harry Houdini story. 14-Charlie McCarthy story. 18-Story of America begins, ends #26. 19-Eisenhower-c/s	11	22	33	62	86	110
15-Flag-c; Bob Feller story	14	28	42	80	115	150
17-Brooklyn Dodgers story	15	30	45	83	124	165
21-30: 24-Marco Polo story. 28-Origin of Uncle Sam. 29-Beethoven story. 30-Cooper Brothers baseball story	9	18	27	52	69	85
31-Red Grange "Galloping Ghost" story	8	16	24	44	57	70
32-46: 33-Origin/1st app. Steve Saunders, Special Agent of the FBI, series begins. 35-Mark Twain story. 38-General Bradley-c/s. 39-FDR story. 44-Truman story. 46-George Gershwin story	9	18	27	47	61	75
47-Atomic bomb issue (c/story, 3/46)	15	30	45	85	130	175
48-(4/46) "Hero Without a Gun" Desmond Doss story; inspired 2016 movie Hacksaw Ridge	10	20	30	54	72	90
49-54,56-65: 49-1st app. Secret Warriors. 53-Bobby Riggs story. 58-Jim Jeffries (boxer) story; Harry Houdini story. 59-Bob Hope story; pirates-c/s. 60-Speedway Speed Demon-c/story.	8	16	24	40	50	60
55-(12/46)-1st app. Sad Sack by Baker (1/2 pg.)	61	122	183	390	670	950
66-Will Rogers-c/story	8	16	24	42	54	65
67-1st oversized issue (12/47); Steve Saunders, Special Agent begins	10	20	30	54	72	90
68-70,74-77,79: 68-70,74-77-Features Steve Sanders True FBI advs. 68-Oversized; Admiral Byrd-c/s. 69-Jack Benny story. 74-Amos 'n' Andy story	8	16	24	40	50	60
71-Joe DiMaggio-c/story.	10	20	30	58	79	100
72-Jackie Robinson story; True FBI advs.	10	20	30	58	79	100
73-Walt Disney's life story	10	20	30	54	72	90
78-Stan Musial-c/story; True FBI advs.	10	20	30	50	65	80
80-84-(Scarce)-All distr. to subscribers through mail only; paper-c. 80-Rocket trip to the moon story. 81-Red Grange story. 84-Wyatt Earp app. (1st app. in comics?); Rube Marquard story	22	44	66	132	216	300

(Prices vary widely on issues 80-84)
NOTE: **Bob Kane** a-7. **Palais** a-80. **Powell** c/a-80. #80-84 have soft covers and combined with Tex Granger, Jack Armstrong, and Calling All Kids. #68-78 featured true FBI adventures.

TRUE COMICS AND ADVENTURE STORIES
Parents' Magazine Institute: 1965 (Giant) (25¢)
1,2: 1-Fighting Hero of Viet Nam; LBJ on-c — 4 8 12 25 40 55

TRUE COMPLETE MYSTERY (Formerly Complete Mystery)

True Believers: X-Men - Greycrow #1 © MAR

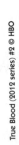

True Blood (2012 series) #2 © HBO

True Secrets #17 © PMI

	GD 2.0	VG 4.0	FN 6.0	VF 8.0	VF/NM 9.0	NM- 9.2

Marvel Comics (PrPI): No. 5, Apr, 1949 - No. 8, Oct, 1949

5-Criminal career of Rico Mancini	39	78	117	240	395	550
6-8: 6-8-Photo-c	27	54	81	158	259	360

TRUE CONFIDENCES
Fawcett Publications: 1949 (Fall) - No. 4, June, 1950 (All photo-c)

1-Has ad for Fawcett Love Adventures #1, but publ. as Love Memoirs #1 as Marvel published the title first; Swayze-a	21	42	63	122	199	275
2-4: 3-Swayze-a. 4-Powell-a	15	30	45	83	124	165

TRUE CRIME CASES (...From Official Police Files)
St. John Publishing Co.: 1951 (25¢, 100 pg. Giant)

nn-Matt Baker-c	116	232	348	742	1271	1800

TRUE CRIME COMICS (Also see Complete Book of...)
Magazine Village: No. 2, May, 1947; No. 3, July-Aug, 1948 - No. 6, June-July, 1949; V2#1, Aug-Sept, 1949 (52 pgs.)

2-Jack Cole-c/a; used in **SOTI**, pgs. 81,82 plus illo. "A sample of the injury-to-eye motif" & illo. "Dragging living people to death"; used in **POP**, pg. 105; "Murder, Morphine and Me" classic drug propaganda story used by N.Y. Legis. Comm.	300	600	900	1980	3440	4900
3-Classic Cole-c/a; drug story with hypo, opium den & with drawing addict	271	542	813	1734	2967	4200
4-Jack Cole-c/a; c-taken from a story panel in #3 (r-2) **SOTI** & **POP** stories/#2?)	142	284	426	909	1555	2200
5-Jack Cole-c, Marijuana racket story (Canadian ed. w/cover similar to #3 exists w/out drug story)	123	246	369	787	1344	1900
6-Not a reprint, original story (Canadian ed. reprints #4 w/different coloring on-c)	110	220	330	704	1202	1700
V2#1-Used in **SOTI**, pgs. 81,82 & illo. "Dragging living people to death"; Toth, Wood (3 pgs.), Roussos-a; Cole-r from #2	135	270	405	864	1473	2100

NOTE: *V2#1 was reprinted in Canada as V2#9 (12/49); same-c & contents minus Wood-a.*

TRUE FAITH
Fleetway: 1990 ($9.95, graphic novel)

nn-Garth Ennis scripts	1	3	4	6	8	10
Reprinted by DC/Vertigo ('97, $12.95)						13.00

TRUE GHOST STORIES (See Ripley's...)

TRUE LIFE ROMANCES (...Romance on cover)
Ajax/Farrell Publications: Dec, 1955 - No. 3, Aug, 1956

1	18	36	54	107	169	230
2	14	28	42	78	112	145
3-Disbrow-a	14	28	42	82	121	160

TRUE LIFE SECRETS
Romantic Love Stories/Charlton: Mar-April, 1951 - No. 28, Sept, 1955; No. 29, Jan, 1956

1-Photo-c begin, end #3?	26	52	78	154	252	350
2	15	30	45	90	140	190
3-11,13-19	15	30	45	88	124	165
12-"I Was An Escort Girl" story	37	74	111	222	361	500
20-22,24-29: 25-Last precode (3/55)	14	28	42	81	118	155
23-Classic-c	53	106	159	334	567	800

TRUE LIFE TALES (Formerly Mitzi's Romances #8?)
Marvel Comics (CCC): No. 8, Oct, 1949 - No. 2, Jan, 1950 (52 pgs.)

8(#1, 10/49), 2-Both have photo-c	20	40	60	114	182	250

TRUE LIVES OF THE FABULOUS KILLJOYS
Dark Horse Comics: Jun, 2013 - No. 6, Jan, 2014 ($3.99)

1-6-Gerald Way & Shaun Simon-s/Becky Cloonan-a; covers by Cloonan & Bá						4.00

TRUE LIVES OF THE FABULOUS KILLJOYS: NATIONAL ANTHEM
Dark Horse Comics: Oct, 2020 - No. 6, Mar, 2021 ($3.99, limited series)

1-6-Gerald Way & Shaun Simon-s/Leonardo Romero-a						4.00

TRUE LOVE
Eclipse Comics: Jan, 1986 - No. 2, Jan, 1986 ($2.00, Baxter paper)

1-Love stories reprinted from pre-code Standard Comics; Toth-a(p); Dave Stevens-c	2	4	6	11	16	20
2-Toth-a; Mayo-a						4.00

TRUE LOVE CONFESSIONS
Premier Magazines: May, 1954 - No. 11, Jan, 1956

1-Marijuana story	27	54	81	158	259	360
2	16	32	48	92	144	195
3-11	15	30	45	86	133	180

TRUE LOVE PICTORIAL
St. John Publishing Co.: Dec, 1952 - No. 11, Aug, 1954

1-Only photo-c	42	84	126	285	445	625

2-Baker-c/a	194	388	582	1242	2121	3000
3-5(all 25¢, 100 pgs.): 4-Signed story by Estrada. 5-(4/53)-Formerly Teen-Age Temptations; Kubert-a in #3; Baker-c/a in #3-5	155	310	465	992	1696	2400
6,7: Baker-c/a; signed stories by Estrada	168	336	504	1075	1838	2600
8,10,11-Baker-c/a	168	336	504	1075	1838	2600
9-Baker-c	129	258	387	826	1413	2000

TRUE LOVE PROBLEMS AND ADVICE ILLUSTRATED (Becomes Romance Stories of True Love No. 45 on)
McCombs/Harvey Publ./Home Comics: June, 1949 - No. 6, Apr, 1950; No. 7, Jan, 1951 - No. 44, Mar, 1957

V1#1	20	40	60	117	189	260
2-Elias-c	14	28	42	78	112	145
3-10: 3,4,7-9-Elias-c	9	18	27	52	69	85
11-13,15-23,25-31: 31-Last pre-code (1/55)	8	16	24	44	57	70
14,24-Rape scene	9	18	27	52	69	85
32-37,39-44	8	16	24	40	50	60
38-S&K-c	11	22	33	62	86	110

NOTE: *Powell a-1, 2, 7-14, 17-25, 28, 29, 33, 40, 41. #3 has True Love... on inside.*

TRUE MOVIE AND TELEVISION (Part teenage magazine)
Toby Press: Aug, 1950 - No. 3, Nov, 1950; No. 4, Mar, 1951 (52 pgs.)(1-3: 10¢)

1-Elizabeth Taylor photo-c; Gene Autry, Shirley Temple app.	90	180	270	576	988	1400
2-(9/50)-Janet Leigh/Liz Taylor/Ava Gardner & others photo-c; Frazetta John Wayne illo from J.Wayne Adv. Comics #2 (4/50)	58	116	174	371	636	900
3-June Allyson photo-c; Montgomery Cliff, Esther Williams, Andrews Sisters app.; Li'l Abner featured; Sadie Hawkins' Day	39	78	117	240	395	550
4-Jane Powell photo-c (15¢)	27	54	81	158	259	360

NOTE: *16 pgs. in color, rest movie material in black & white.*

TRUE SECRETS (Formerly Our Love?)
Marvel (IPS)/Atlas Comics (MPI) #4 on: No. 3, Mar, 1950; No. 4, Feb, 1951 - No. 40, Sept, 1956

3 (52 pgs.)(IPS one-shot)	27	54	81	162	266	370
4,5,7-10	18	36	54	105	165	225
6,22-Everett-a	20	40	60	115	185	255
11-20	16	32	48	92	144	195
21,23-28: 24-Colletta-c. 28-Last pre-code (2/55)	15	30	45	88	137	185
29-40: 34,36-Colletta-a	15	30	45	85	130	175

TRUE SPORT PICTURE STORIES (Formerly Sport Comics)
Street & Smith Publications: V1#5, Feb, 1942 - V5#2, July-Aug, 1949

V1#5-Joe DiMaggio-c/story	39	78	117	240	395	550
6-12 (1942-43): 12-Jack Dempsey story	22	44	66	128	209	290
V2#1-12 (1943-45): 7-Stan Musial-c/story; photo story of the New York Yankees	20	40	60	120	195	270
V3#1-12 (1946-47): 7-Joe DiMaggio, Stan Musial, Bob Feller & others back from the armed service story. 8-Billy Conn vs. Joe Louis-c/story	20	40	60	117	189	260
V4#1-12 (1947-49), V5#1,2: v4#8-Joe Louis on-c	19	38	57	111	176	240

NOTE: *Powell a-V3#10, V4#1-4, 6-8, 10-12; V5#1, 2; c-V3#10-12, V4#2-7, 9-12. Ravielli c-V5#2.*

TRUE STORIES OF ROMANCE
Fawcett Publications: Jan, 1950 - No. 3, May, 1950 (All photo-c)

1	19	38	57	111	176	240
2,3: 3-Marcus Swayze-a	15	30	45	83	124	165

TRUE STORY OF JESSE JAMES, THE (See Jesse James, Four Color 757)

TRUE SWEETHEART SECRETS
Fawcett Publs.: 5/50; No. 2, 7/50; No. 3, 1951(nd); No. 4, 9/51 - No. 11, 1/53 (All photo-c)

1-Photo-c; Debbie Reynolds?	21	42	63	124	202	280
2-Wood-a (11 pgs.)	23	46	69	136	223	310
3-11: 4,5-Powell-a. 8-Marcus Swayze-a. 11-Evans-a 15	30	45	85	130	175

TRUE TALES OF LOVE (Formerly Secret Story Romances)
Atlas Comics (TCI): No. 22, April, 1956 - No. 31, Sept, 1957

22	18	36	54	105	165	225
23-24,26-31-Colletta-a in most:	14	28	42	78	112	145
25-Everett-a; Colletta-a	14	28	42	81	118	155

TRUE TALES OF ROMANCE
Fawcett Publications: No. 4, June, 1950

4-Photo-c	14	28	42	82	121	160

TRUE 3-D
Harvey Publications: Dec, 1953 - No. 2, Feb, 1954 (25¢)(Both came with 2 pair of glasses)

1-Nostrand, Powell-a	5	10	15	35	63	90
2-Powell-a	6	12	18	37	66	95

NOTE: *Many copies of #1 surfaced in 1984.*

TRUE-TO-LIFE ROMANCES (Formerly Guns Against Gangsters)
Star Publ.: #8, 11-12/49; #9, 1-2/50; #3, 4/50 - #5, 9/50; #6, 1/51 - #23, 10/54

	GD	VG	FN	VF	VF/NM	NM-
	2.0	4.0	6.0	8.0	9.0	9.2

	GD	VG	FN	VF	VF/NM	NM-
8(#1, 1949)	40	80	120	244	402	560
9(#2),4-10	30	60	90	177	289	400
3-Janet Leigh/Glenn Ford photo on-c plus true life story of each	32	64	96	190	310	430
11,22,23	26	52	78	154	252	350
12-14,17-21-Disbrow-a	28	56	84	168	274	380
15,16-Wood & Disbrow-a in each	31	62	93	182	296	410

NOTE: **Kamen** a-13. **Kamen/Feldstein** a-14. All have **L.B. Cole** covers.

TRUE WAR EXPERIENCES
Harvey Publications: Aug, 1952 - No. 4, Dec, 1952

	GD	VG	FN	VF	VF/NM	NM-
1-Korean War	10	20	30	68	144	220
2-4	6	12	18	38	69	100

TRUE WAR ROMANCES (Becomes Exotic Romances #22 on)
Quality Comics Group: Sept, 1952 - No. 21, June, 1955

	GD	VG	FN	VF	VF/NM	NM-
1-Photo-c	24	48	72	144	237	330
2-(10/52)	15	30	45	86	133	180
3-10: 3-(12/52). 8,9-Whitney-a	14	28	42	80	115	150
11-21: 20-Last precode (4/55). 14-Whitney-a	13	26	39	74	105	135

TRUE WAR STORIES (See Ripley's...)

TRUE WESTERN (True Adventures #3)
Marvel Comics (MMC): Dec, 1949 - No. 2, March, 1950

	GD	VG	FN	VF	VF/NM	NM-
1-Photo-c; Billy The Kid story	23	46	69	136	223	310
2-Alan Ladd photo-c	26	52	78	154	252	350

TRUMP
HMH Publishing Co.: Jan, 1957 - No. 2, Mar, 1957 (50¢, magazine)

	GD	VG	FN	VF	VF/NM	NM-
1-Harvey Kurtzman satire	32	64	96	188	307	425
2-Harvey Kurtzman satire	24	48	72	142	234	325

NOTE: **Davis, Elder, Heath, Jaffee** art-#1,2; **Wood** a-1. Article by Mel Brooks in #2.

TRUMPETS WEST (See Luke Short, Four Color #875)

TRUTH ABOUT CRIME (See Fox Giants)

TRUTH ABOUT MOTHER GOOSE (See Mother Goose, Four Color #862)

TRUTH & JUSTICE
DC Comics: Apr, 2021 - No. 7, Oct, 2021 ($4.99, printing of digital first anthology series)

	GD	VG	FN	VF	VF/NM	NM-
1-7: 1-Vixen. 2-Superman. 3-Constantine. 4-Jason Todd. 5-Batwoman. 7-Zatanna						5.00

TRUTH BEHIND THE TRIAL OF CARDINAL MINDSZENTY, THE (See Cardinal Mindszenty in the Promotional Comics section)

TRUTHFUL LOVE (Formerly Youthful Love)
Youthful Magazines: No. 2, July, 1950

	GD	VG	FN	VF	VF/NM	NM-
2-Ingrid Bergman's true life story	20	40	60	117	189	260

TRUTH RED, WHITE & BLACK
Marvel Comics: Jan, 2003 - No. 7, Jul, 2003 ($3.50, limited series)

	GD	VG	FN	VF	VF/NM	NM-
1-Kyle Baker-a/Robert Morales-s; the testing of Captain America's super-soldier serum	3	6	9	19	30	40
2-7: 3-Isaiah Bradley 1st dons the Captain America costume	1	3	4	6	8	10
TPB (2004, $17.99) r/series						18.00

TRY-OUT WINNER BOOK
Marvel Comics: Mar, 1988

	GD	VG	FN	VF	VF/NM	NM-
1-Spider-Man vs. Doc Octopus	4	8	12	23	37	50

TSR WORLD (...Annual on cover only)
DC Comics: 1990 ($3.95, 84 pgs.)

	GD	VG	FN	VF	VF/NM	NM-
1-Advanced D&D, ForgottenRealms, Dragonlance & 1st app. Spelljammer						5.00

TSUNAMI GIRL
Image Comics: 1999 - No. 3, 1999 ($2.95)

	GD	VG	FN	VF	VF/NM	NM-
1-3-Sorayama-c/Paniccia-s/a						4.00

TUBBY (See Marge's...)

TUFF GHOSTS STARRING SPOOKY
Harvey Publications: July, 1962 - No. 39, Nov, 1970; No. 40, Sept, 1971 - No. 43, Oct, 1972

	GD	VG	FN	VF	VF/NM	NM-
1-12¢ issues begin	17	34	51	117	256	400
2-5	7	14	21	44	82	120
6-10	5	10	15	31	53	75
11-20	4	8	12	23	37	50
21-30: 29-Hot Stuff/Spooky team-up story	3	6	9	16	23	30
31-39,43	2	4	6	13	18	22
40-42: 52 pg. Giants	3	6	9	14	20	25

TUFFY
Standard Comics: No. 5, July, 1949 - No. 9, Oct, 1950

	GD	VG	FN	VF	VF/NM	NM-
5-All by Sid Hoff	13	26	39	72	101	130
6-9	9	18	27	50	65	80

TUFFY TURTLE
I. W. Enterprises: No date

	GD	VG	FN	VF	VF/NM	NM-
1-Reprint	3	6	9	14	20	25

TUG & BUSTER
Art & Soul Comics: Nov, 1995 - No. 7, Feb, 1998 ($2.95, B&W, bi-monthly)

	GD	VG	FN	VF	VF/NM	NM-
1-7: Marc Hempel-c/a/scripts						4.00
1-(Image Comics, 8/98, $2.95, B&W)						4.00

TUKI
Cartoon Books: Jul, 2014 - No. 4, Jan, 2016 ($3.99)

	GD	VG	FN	VF	VF/NM	NM-
1-4-Jeff Smith-s/a/c; story reads sideways						4.00

TURF
Image Comics: Apr, 2010 - No. 2 ($2.99, limited series)

	GD	VG	FN	VF	VF/NM	NM-
1,2-Jonathan Ross-s/Tommy Lee Edwards-a						3.00

TUROK
Acclaim Comics: Mar, 1998 - No. 4, Jun, 1998 ($2.50)

	GD	VG	FN	VF	VF/NM	NM-
1-4-Nicieza-s/Kayanan-a						4.00

	GD	VG	FN	VF	VF/NM	NM-
..., Child of Blood 1 (1/98, $3.95) Nicieza-s/Kayanan-a						6.00
... Evolution 1 (8/02, $2.50) Nicieza-s/Kayanan-a	3	6	9	14	19	24
..., Redpath 1 (10/97, $3.95) Nicieza-s/Kayanan-a						5.00
... / Shadowman 1 (2/99, $3.95) Priest-s/Broome & Jimenez-a	2	4	6	8	10	12
...: Spring Break in the Lost Land 1 (7/97, $3.95) Nicieza-s/Kayanan-a						4.00
...: Tales of the Lost Land 1 (4/98, $3.95)						6.00
...: The Empty Souls 1 (4/97, $3.95) Nicieza-s/Kayanan-a; variant-c						4.00

TUROK (Volume 1) (Also see Sovereigns and Magnus)
Dynamite Entertainment: 2017 - No. 5, 2017 ($3.99)

	GD	VG	FN	VF	VF/NM	NM-
1-5: 1-Wendig-s/Sarraseca-a; Doctor Spektor back-up serial with other Sovereigns titles						4.00

TUROK, DINOSAUR HUNTER (See Magnus Robot Fighter #12 & Archer & Armstrong #2)
Valiant/Acclaim Comics: June, 1993 - No. 47, Aug, 1996 ($2.50)

	GD	VG	FN	VF	VF/NM	NM-
1-($3.50)-Chromium & foil-c						5.00
1-Gold foil-c variant						20.00
0, 2-47: 4-Andar app.-5-Death of Andar. 7-9-Truman/Glanzman-a. 11-Bound-in trading card. 16-Chaos Effect						4.00
Yearbook 1 (1994, $3.95, 52 pgs.)						5.00

TUROK: DINOSAUR HUNTER
Dynamite Entertainment: 2014 - No. 12, 2015 ($3.99)

	GD	VG	FN	VF	VF/NM	NM-
1-12: 1-5-New version; Greg Pak-s/Mirko Colak-a; Sears-c. 6-8-Miyazawa-a						4.00
1-12-Variant-c by Jae Lee						4.00

TUROK, SON OF STONE (See Dan Curtis, Golden Comics Digest #31, Space Western #45 & March of Comics #378, 399, 408)
Dell Publ. Co. #1-29(9/62)/Gold Key #30(12/62)-85(7/73)/Gold Key or Whitman #86(9/73)-125(1/80)/Whitman #126(3/81) on: No. 596, 12/54- No. 29, 9/62; No. 30, 12/62 - No. 91, 7/74; No. 92, 9/74 - No. 125, 1/80; No. 126, 3/81 - No. 130, 4/82

	GD	VG	FN	VF	VF/NM	NM-
Four Color 596 (12/54)(#1)-1st app./origin Turok & Andar; dinosaur-c. Created by Matthew H. Murphy; written by Alberto Giolitti	181	362	543	1158	1979	2800
Four Color 656 (10/55)(#2)-1st mention of Lanok	42	84	126	311	706	1100
3(3-5/56)-5: 3-Cave men	22	44	66	154	340	525
6-10: 8-Dinosaur of the deep; Turok enters Lost Valley; series begins.						
9-Paul S. Newman-s (most issues thru end)	15	30	45	103	227	350
11-20: 17-Prehistoric Pygmies	11	22	33	76	163	250
21-29	9	18	27	58	114	170
30-1st Gold Key. 30-33-Painted back-c.	9	18	27	60	120	180
31-Drug use story	9	18	27	58	114	170
32-40	7	14	21	46	86	125
41-50	6	12	18	37	66	95
51-57,59,60	5	10	15	34	60	85
58-Flying Saucer c/story	5	10	15	35	63	90
61-70: 62-12¢ & 15¢ covers. 63,68-Line drawn-c.	5	10	15	30	50	70
71-84: 84-Origin & 1st app. Hutec	4	8	12	27	44	60
85-99: 93-r-c/#19 w/changes. 94-r-c/#28 w/changes. 97-r-c/#31 w/changes.						
98-r/w/o spaceship & spacemen on-c. 99-r-c/#52 w/changes.	4	8	12	23	37	50
100	4	8	12	28	47	65
101-129: 114,115-(52 pgs.). 129(2/82)	4	8	12	23	37	50
130(4/82)-Last issue	5	10	15	35	63	90
Giant 1(30031-611) (11/66)-Slick-c; r/#10-12 & 16 plus cover to #11	10	20	30	68	144	220
Giant 1-Same as above but with paper-c	11	22	33	73	157	240

NOTE: Most painted-c; line-drawn #63 & 130. **Alberto Giolitti** a-24-27, 30-119, 123; painted-c No. 30-129. **Sparling** a-117, 120-130. Reprints-#36, 54, 57, 75, 112, 114(1/3), 115(1/3), 118, 121, 125, 127(1/3), 128, 129(1/3), 130(1/3), Giant 1. Cover r-93, 94, 97-99, 126(all different from original covers).

TUROK, SON OF STONE
Dark Horse Comics: Oct, 2010 - No. 4, Oct, 2011 ($3.50)

	GD	VG	FN	VF	VF/NM	NM-
1-4: 1-Shooter-s/Francisco-a/Swanland-c; back-up reprint of debut in Four Color 596						3.50
1-Variant-c by Francisco						3.50

TUROK THE HUNTED
Acclaim Comics (Valiant): Mar, 1996 - No. 2, Mar, 1996 ($2.50, limited series)

	GD	VG	FN	VF	VF/NM	NM-
1,2-Mike Grell & Simon Furman-s/Mike Deodato & Mozart Couto-a						4.00

TUROK, TIMEWALKER
Acclaim Comics (Valiant): Aug, 1997 - No. 2, Sept, 1997 ($2.50, limited series)

	GD	VG	FN	VF	VF/NM	NM-
1,2-Nicieza story						5.00

TUROK 2 (Magazine)
Acclaim Comics: Oct, 1998 ($4.99, magazine size)

	GD	VG	FN	VF	VF/NM	NM-
...Seeds of Evil - Nicieza-s/Broome & Benjamin-a; origin back-up story						8.00
#2 Adon's Curse - Mack painted-c/Broome & Benjamin-a; origin pt. 2						8.00

TUROK 3: SHADOW OF OBLIVION
Acclaim Comics: Sept, 2000 ($4.95, one-shot)

	GD	VG	FN	VF	VF/NM	NM-
1-Includes pin-up gallery	1	3	4	6	8	10

TUROK VOLUME 4
Dynamite Entertainment: 2019 - No. 5, 2019 ($3.99)

	GD	VG	FN	VF	VF/NM	NM-
1-5-Ron Marz-s/Roberto Castro-a						4.00

TURTLE SOUP
Mirage Studios: Sept, 1987 ($2.00, 76 pgs., B&W, one-shot)

	GD	VG	FN	VF	VF/NM	NM-
1-Featuring Teenage Mutant Ninja Turtles	2	4	6	11	16	20

TURTLE SOUP
Mirage Studios: Nov, 1991 - No. 4, 1992 ($2.50, limited series, coated paper)

	GD	VG	FN	VF	VF/NM	NM-
1-4: Features the Teenage Mutant Ninja Turtles						6.00

TV CASPER & COMPANY
Harvey Publications: Aug, 1963 - No. 46, April, 1974 (25¢ Giants)

	GD	VG	FN	VF	VF/NM	NM-
1- 68 pg. Giants begin; Casper, Little Audrey, Baby Huey, Herman & Catnip, Buzzy the Crow begin	10	20	30	66	138	210
2-5	6	12	18	37	66	95
6-10	4	8	12	28	47	65
11-20	4	8	12	23	37	50
21-31: 31-Last 68 pg. issue	3	6	9	17	26	35
32-46: All 52 pgs.	3	6	9	16	23	30

Turok V4 #3 © RH

The Twelve #4 © MAR

2020 Force Works #1 © MAR

	GD	VG	FN	VF	VF/NM	NM-		GD	VG	FN	VF	VF/NM	NM-
	2.0	4.0	6.0	8.0	9.0	9.2		2.0	4.0	6.0	8.0	9.0	9.2

NOTE: *Many issues contain reprints.*

TV FUNDAY FUNNIES (See Famous TV…)

TV FUNNIES (See New Funnies)

TV FUNTIME (See Little Audrey)

TV LAUGHOUT (See Archie's…)

TV SCREEN CARTOONS (Formerly Real Screen)
National Periodical Publ.: No. 129, July-Aug, 1959 - No. 138, Jan-Feb, 1961

129-138 (Scarce) Fox and the Crow	6	12	18	42	79	115

TV STARS (TV) (Newsstand sales only)
Marvel Comics Group: Aug, 1978 - No. 4, Feb, 1979 (Hanna-Barbera)

1-Great Grape Ape app.	4	8	12	25	40	55
2,4: 4-Top Cat app.	3	6	9	15	22	28
3-Toth-c/a; Dave Stevens inks	3	6	9	16	24	32

TV TEENS (Formerly Ozzie & Babs; Rock and Rollo #14 on)
Charlton Comics: V1#14, Feb, 1954 - V2#13, July, 1956

V1#14 (#1)-Ozzie & Babs	15	30	45	86	133	180
15 (#2)	10	20	30	54	72	90
V2#3(6/54),4, 6-Don Winslow	9	18	27	52	69	85
5(10-11/54) Headlight/groping-c by Chic Stone	47	94	141	296	498	700
7-13-Mopsy. 8(7/55). 9-Paper dolls	9	18	27	50	65	80

TWEETY AND SYLVESTER (1st Series) (TV) (Also see Looney Tunes and Merrie Melodies)
Dell Publishing Co.: No. 406, June, 1952 - No. 37, June-Aug, 1962

Four Color 406 (#1)	15	30	45	103	227	350
Four Color 489,524	9	18	27	61	123	185
4 (3-5/54) - 20	5	10	15	35	63	90
21-37	5	10	15	31	53	75
(See March of Comics #421, 433, 445, 457, 469, 481)						

TWEETY AND SYLVESTER (2nd Series)(See Kite Fun Book)
Gold Key No. 1-102/Whitman No. 103 on: Nov, 1963; No. 2, Nov, 1965 - No. 121, Jun, 1984

1	8	16	24	54	102	150
2-10	4	8	12	23	37	50
11-30	3	6	9	14	20	25
31-50	2	4	6	9	12	15
51-70	1	3	4	6	8	10
71-102	1	2	3	5	6	8
103,104 (Whitman)	1	3	4	6	8	10
105(9/80),106(10/80),107(12/80) 3-pack only	4	8	12	28	47	65
108-116: 113(2/82),114(2-3/82),115(3/82),116(4/82)	2	4	6	10	12	10
117-121 (All # 90094 on-c; nd, nd code): 117(6/83). 118(7/83). 119(2/84)-r(1/3). 120(5/84).						
121(6/84)	3	6	9	17	26	35
Digest nn (Charlton/Xerox Pub., 1974) (low print run)	3	6	9	16	23	30
Mini Comic No. 1(1976, 3-1/4x6-1/2")	1	3	4	6	8	10

TWELVE, THE (Golden Age Timely heroes)
Marvel Comics: No. 0; 2008; No. 1, Mar, 2008 - No. 12, Jun, 2012 ($2.99, limited series)

0-Rockman, Laughing Mask & Phantom Reporter intro. stories (1940s); series preview						4.00
1/2 (2008, $3.99) r/early app. of Fiery Mask, Mister E and Rockman; Weston-c						5.00
1-12-Straczynski-s/Weston-a; Timely heroes re-surface in the present						4.00
... Must Have 1 (4/12, $3.99) r/#7,8						4.00
...: Spearhead 1 (5/10, $3.99) Weston-s/a; Phantom Reporter in WW2; Invaders app.						5.00

12 O'CLOCK HIGH (TV)
Dell Publishing Co.: Jan-Mar, 1965 - No. 2, Apr-June, 1965 (Photo-c)

1- Sinnott-a	5	10	15	35	63	90
2	4	8	12	28	47	65

TWELVE REASONS TO DIE
Black Mask Studios: 2013 - No. 6, 2014 ($3.50)

1-6: 1-Five covers; created by Ghostface Killah	3.50

2099
Marvel Comics: Jan, 2020 - Feb, 2020 ($4.99, bookends for series of one-shots)

... Alpha 1 (1/20) Spencer-s/Bogdanovic-a; Miguel O'Hara and Herbie app.	5.00
... Omega 1 (2/20) Spencer-s/Sandoval-a; Doom and the Watcher app.	5.00

2099 A.D.
Marvel Comics: May, 1995 ($3.95, one-shot)

1-Acetate-c by Quesada & Palmiotti	4.00

2099 APOCALYPSE
Marvel Comics: Dec, 1995 ($4.95, one-shot)

1-Chromium wraparound-c; Ellis script	5.00

2099 GENESIS
Marvel Comics: Jan, 1996 ($4.95, one-shot)

1-Chromium wraparound-c; Ellis script	5.00

2099 MANIFEST DESTINY
Marvel Comics: Mar, 1998 ($5.99, one-shot)

1-Origin of Fantastic Four 2099; intro Moon Knight 2099					
	4	8	12	23	37	50

2099 UNLIMITED
Marvel Comics: Sept, 1993 - No. 10, 1996 ($3.95, 68 pgs.)

1-10: 1-1st app. Hulk 2099 & begins. 1-3-Spider-Man 2099 app. 9-Joe Kubert-c; Len Wein & Nancy Collins scripts	5.00

2099 WORLD OF DOOM SPECIAL
Marvel Comics: May, 1995 ($2.25, one-shot)

1-Doom's "Contract w/America"	4.00

2099: WORLD OF TOMORROW
Marvel Comics: Sept, 1996 - No. 8, Apr, 1997 ($2.50) (Replaces 2099 titles)

1-8: 1-Wraparound-c. 2-w/bound-in card. 4,5-Phalanx	4.00

20XX
Image Comics: Dec, 2019 - No. 6 ($3.99, B&W)

1-6-Jonathan Luna-s/a; Lauren Keely-s	4.00
...: Transport 1 (8/22, $3.99, full color) Jonathan Luna-s/a	4.00

21
Image Comics (Top Cow Productions): Feb, 1996 - No. 3, Apr, 1996 ($2.50)

1-3: Len Wein scripts	4.00
1-Variant-c	4.00

21 DOWN
DC Comics (WildStorm): Nov, 2002 - No. 12, Nov, 2003 ($2.95)

1-12: 1-Palmiotti & Gray-s/Saiz-a/Jusko-c	3.00
...: The Conduit (2003, $19.95, TPB) r/#1-7; intro. by Garth Ennis	20.00

24 (Based on TV series)
IDW Publishing: Apr, 2014 - No. 5, Aug, 2014 ($3.99, limited series)

1-5-Brisson-s/Gaydos-a; multiple covers on each	4.00

24 (Based on TV series)
IDW Publishing: July, 2004 - July, 2005 ($6.99/$7.49, square-bound, one-shots)

...: Midnight Sun (7/05, $7.49) J.C. Vaughn & Mark Haynes-s; Renato Guedes-a	7.50
...: One Shot (7/04, $6.99)-Jack Bauer's first day on the job at CTU; Vaughn & Haynes-s; Guedes-a	7.50
...: Stories (1/05, $7.49) Manny Clark-a; Vaughn & Haynes-s	7.50

24: LEGACY – RULES OF ENGAGEMENT (Based on TV series)
IDW Publishing: Apr, 2017 - No. 5, Aug, 2017 ($3.99, limited series)

1-5-Early days of Eric Carter in DC & Iraq; Farnsworth-s/Fuso-a; art and photo-c	4.00

24: NIGHTFALL (Based on TV series)
IDW Publishing: Nov, 2006 - No. 5, Mar, 2007 ($3.99, limited series)

1-5-Two years before Season One; Vaughn & Haynes-s; Diaz-a; two covers	4.00

28 DAYS LATER (Based on the 2002 movie)
Boom! Studios: July, 2009 - No. 24, Jun, 2011 ($3.99)

1-Covers by Bradstreet and Phillips	6.00
2-24	4.00

2020 FORCE WORKS
Marvel Comics: Apr, 2020 - No. 3, Oct, 2020 ($3.99, limited series)

1-3-Rosenberg-s/Ramirez-a; War Machine and Mockingbird app.	4.00

2020 IRON AGE
Marvel Comics: May, 2020 ($4.99, one-shot)

1-Machine Man, Alkhema, & Doctor Shapiro in short stories by various	5.00

2020 iWOLVERINE
Marvel Comics: Sept, 2020 - No. 2, Oct, 2020 ($3.99, limited series)

1,2-Larry Hama-s/Roland Boschi-a; Wolverine android copy; Tyger Tiger app.	4.00

2020 MACHINE MAN
Marvel Comics: Apr, 2020 - No. 2, May, 2020 ($4.99, limited series)

1,2-Ties in with Iron Man 2020 series; Jocasta & X-52 app.	5.00

2020 RESCUE
Marvel Comics: Apr, 2020 - No. 2, Jun, 2020 ($3.99, limited series)

1,2-Schwartz-s/Burrows-a; Pepper Potts in the Rescue armor	4.00

2020 VISIONS
DC Comics (Vertigo): May, 1997 - No. 12, Apr, 1998 ($2.25, limited series)

1-12-Delano-s: 1-3-Quitely-a. 4-"la tormenta"-Pleece-a	4.00

20,000 LEAGUES UNDER THE SEA (Movie)(See King Classics, Movie Comics)

	GD 2.0	VG 4.0	FN 6.0	VF 8.0	VF/NM 9.0	NM- 9.2

& Power Record Comics)
Dell Publishing Co.: No. 614, Feb, 1955 (Disney)

	GD	VG	FN	VF	VF/NM	NM-
Four Color 614-Movie, painted-c	10	20	30	69	147	225

TWICE TOLD TALES (See Movie Classics)

TWIG
Image Comics: May, 2022 - No. 5, Sept, 2022 ($3.99, limited series)

1-5-Skottie Young-s/Kyle Strahm-a						4.00

TWILIGHT
DC Comics: 1990 - No. 3, 1991 ($4.95, 52 pgs., lim. series, squarebound, mature)

1-3: Tommy Tomorrow app.; Chaykin scripts, Garcia-Lopez-c/a						5.00

TWILIGHT CHILDREN, THE
DC Comics (Vertigo): Dec, 2015 - No. 4, Mar, 2016 ($4.99, limited series)

1-4-Gilbert Hernandez-s/Darwyn Cooke-a/c						5.00

TWILIGHT EXPERIMENT
DC Comics (WildStorm): Apr, 2004 - No. 6, Sept, 2005 ($2.95, limited series)

1-6-Gray & Palmiotti-s/Santacruz-a						3.00
TPB (2011, $17.99) r/#1-6						18.00

TWILIGHT GUARDIAN (Also see Pilot Season: Twilight Guardian)
Image Comics (Top Cow): Jan, 2011 - No. 4, Apr, 2011 ($3.99, limited series)

1-4-Hickman-s/Kotean-a						4.00

TWILIGHT MAN
First Publishing: June, 1989 - No. 4, Sept, 1989 ($2.75, limited series)

1-4						4.00

TWILIGHT ZONE, THE (TV) (See Dan Curtis & Stories From...)
Dell Publishing Co./Gold Key/Whitman No. 92: No. 1173, 3-5/61 - No. 91, 4/79; No. 92, 5/82

Four Color 1173 (#1)-Crandall-c/a	24	48	72	168	372	575
Four Color 1288-Crandall/Evans-c/a	12	24	36	83	182	280
01-860-207 (5-7/62-Dell, 15¢)	10	20	30	66	138	210
12-860-210 on-c; 01-860-210 on inside(8-10/62-Dell)-Evans-a/c (3 stories); art by Frazetta & Crandall	10	20	30	64	132	200
1(11/62-Gold Key)-Crandall/Frazetta-a (10 & 11 pgs.); Evans-a	18	36	54	124	275	425
2	8	16	24	55	105	155
3-11: 3(11 pgs.),4(10 pgs.),9-Toth-a	6	12	18	37	66	95
12-15: 12-Williamson-a. 13,15-Crandall-a. 14-Orlando/Crandall/Torres-a	5	10	15	31	53	75
16-20	4	8	12	25	40	55
21-25: 21-Crandall-a(r). 25-Evans/Crandall-a(r); Toth-r/#4; last 12¢ issue	3	6	9	19	30	40
26,27: 26-Flying Saucer-c/story; Crandall, Evans-a(r). 27-Evans-r(2)	3	6	9	18	28	38
28-32: 32-Evans-a(r)	3	6	9	16	24	32
33-51: 43-Celardo-a. 51-Williamson-a	2	4	6	13	18	22
52-70	2	4	6	10	14	18
71-82,86-91: 71-Reprint	2	4	6	8	11	14
83-(52 pgs.)	3	6	9	14	20	25
84-(52 pgs.) Frank Miller's 1st comic book work	13	26	39	91	201	310
85-Frank Miller-a (2nd)	6	12	18	37	66	95
92-(Whitman, 5/82) Last issue; r/#1.	2	4	6	9	13	16
Mini Comic #1(1976, 3-1/4x6-1/2")	2	4	6	8	10	12

NOTE: **Bolle** a-13(w/**McWilliams**), 50, 55, 57, 59, 77, 78, 80, 83, 84. **McWilliams** a-59, 78, 80, 82, 84. **Miller** a-84, 85. **Orlando** a-15, 19, 20, 22, 23. **Sekowsky** a-3. **Simonson** a-50, 54, 55, 83r. **Weiss** a-39, 79r(#39). (See Mystery Comics Digest 3, 6, 9, 12, 15, 18, 21, 24). Reprints-26(1/3), 71, 73, 79, 83, 84, 86, 92. Painted c-1-91.

TWILIGHT ZONE, THE (TV)
Now Comics: Nov, 1990 ($2.95); Oct, 1991; V2#1, Nov, 1991 - No. 11, Oct, 1992 ($1.95); V3#1, 1993 - No. 4, 1993 ($2.50)

1-(11/90, $2.95, 52 pgs.)-Direct sale edition; Neal Adams-a, Sienkiewicz-c; Harlan Ellison scripts						6.00
1-(11/90, $1.75)-Newsstand ed. w/N. Adams-c						5.00
1-Prestige Format (10/91, $4.95)-Reprints above with extra Harlan Ellison short story						5.00
1-Collector's Edition (10/91, $2.50)-Non-code approved and polybagged; reprints 11/90 issue; gold logo, 1-Reprint ($2.50)-r/direct sale 11/90 version, 1-Reprint ($2.50)-r/newsstand 11/90 version each:						5.00
V2#1-Direct sale & newsstand ed. w/different-c						4.00
V2#2-8,10-11						4.00
V2#9-($2.95)-3-D Special; polybagged w/glasses & hologram on-c						5.00
V2#9-($4.95)-Prestige Edition; contains 2 extra stories & a different hologram on-c; polybagged w/glasses						5.00
V3#1-4, Anniversary Special 1 (1992, $2.50)						4.00
Annual 1 (4/93, $2.50)-No ads						5.00
...Science Fiction Special (3/93, $3.50)						5.00

TWILIGHT ZONE, THE (TV)
Dynamite Entertainment: 2014 - No. 12, 2015 ($3.99)

1-12-Straczynski-s/Vilanova/Francavilla-c						4.00
#1959 (2016, $5.99) Short stories set in 1959; Valiente & Worley-a; Lau-c						6.00
Annual 2014 ($7.99) Three short stories; Rahner-s/Valiente, Malaga, Menna-a						8.00

TWILIGHT ZONE THE SHADOW (TV)
Dynamite Entertainment: 2016 - No. 4, 2016 ($3.99, limited series)

1-4-Avallone/Acosta-a/Francavilla-c; Shiwwan Khan app.						4.00

TWILIGHT ZONE, THE: SHADOW & SUBSTANCE (TV)
Dynamite Entertainment: 2015 - No. 4, 2015 ($3.99)

1-4-Rahner/Menna-a; multiple covers on each						4.00

TWINKLE COMICS
Spotlight Publishers: May, 1945

1	33	66	99	194	317	440

TWIST, THE
Dell Publishing Co.: July-Sept, 1962

01-864-209-Painted-c	13	26	39	89	195	300

TWISTED TALES (See Eclipse Graphic Album Series #15)
Pacific Comics/Independent Comics Group (Eclipse) #9,10: 11/82 - No. 8, 5/84; No. 9, 11/84; No. 10, 12/84 (Baxter paper)

1-9: 1-B. Jones/Corben-c; Alcala-a; nudity/violence in al. 2-Wrightson-c; Ploog-a						5.00
10-Wrightson painted art; Morrow-a	1	2	3	4	5	7

NOTE: **Bolton** painted c-4, 6, 7; a-7. **Conrad** a-1, 3, 5; c-1i, 3, 5. **Guice** a-8. **Wildey** a-3.

TWO BIT THE WACKY WOODPECKER (See Wacky…)
Toby Press: 1951 - No. 3, May, 1953

1	15	30	45	84	127	170
2,3	9	18	27	50	65	80

TWO FACE: YEAR ONE
DC Comics: 2008 - No. 2, 2008 ($5.99, squarebound, limited series)

1,2-Origin re-told; Sable-s/Saiz & Haun-a						6.00

TWO-FISTED TALES (Formerly Haunt of Fear #15-17)
(Also see EC Archives • Two-Fisted Tales)
E. C. Comics: No. 18, Nov-Dec, 1950 - No. 41, Feb-Mar, 1955

18(#1)-Kurtzman-c	131	262	393	1048	1674	2300
19-Kurtzman-c	86	172	258	688	1094	1500
20-Kurtzman-c	57	114	171	456	728	1000
21,22-Kurtzman-c	47	94	141	376	601	825
23-25-Kurtzman-c	37	74	111	256	473	650
26-29,31-Kurtzman-c. 31-Civil War issue	29	58	87	232	366	500
30-Classic Davis-c	37	74	111	256	473	650
32-34: 33- "Atom Bomb" by Wood	29	58	87	232	366	500
35-Classic Davis Civil War-c/s	40	80	120	320	510	700
36-41: 41-Contains "In Memoriam" editorial about the ending of EC War titles	23	46	69	184	297	410
Two-Fisted Annual (1952, 25¢, 132 pgs.)	155	310	465	992	1696	2400
Two-Fisted Annual (1953, 25¢, 132 pgs.)	123	246	369	787	1344	1900

NOTE: **Berg** a-29. **Colan** a-30,39p. **Craig** a-18, 19, 32. **Crandall** a-35, 36. **Davis** a-20-36, 40; c-30, 34, 35, 41, Annual 2. **Estrada** a-30. **Evans** a-28. **Feldstein** a-18. **Krigstein** a-41. **Kubert** a-32, 33. **Kurtzman** a-18-25; c-18-29, 31, Annual 1. **Severin** a-26, 28, 29, 31, 34-41 (No. 37-39 are all-**Severin** issues); c-36-39. **Severin/Elder** a-19-29, 31, 33, 36. **Wood** a-18-28, 30-35, 41; c-32, 33. Special issues: #26 (ChanJin Reservoir), 31 (Civil War), 35 (Civil War). Canadian reprints known; see Table of Contents. #25-Davis biog. #27-Wood biog. #28-Kurtzman biog.

TWO-FISTED TALES
Russ Cochran/Gemstone Publishing: Oct, 1992 - No. 24, May, 1998 ($1.50/$2.00/$2.50)

1-24: 1-4r/Two-Fisted Tales #18-21 w/original-c						4.00

TWO GRAVES
Image Comics: Nov, 2022 - No. 6, Apr, 2023 ($3.99)

1-6-Genevieve Valentine-s/Ming Doyle & Annie Wu-a						4.00

TWO-GUN KID (Also see All Western Winners, Best Western, Black Rider, Blaze Carson, Kid Colt, Western Winners, Wild West, & Wild Western)
Marvel/Atlas (MCI No. 1-10/HPC No. 11-59/Marvel No. 60 on): 3/48(No mo.) - No. 10, 11/49; No. 11, 12/53 - No. 59, 4/61; No. 60, 11/62 - No. 92, 3/68; No. 93 - No. 70 - No. 136, 4/77

1-Two-Gun Kid & his horse Cyclone begin; The Sheriff begins	181	362	543	1158	1979	2800
2	65	130	195	416	708	1000
3,4: 3-Annie Oakley app.	48	96	144	302	514	725
5-Pre-Black Rider app. (Wint. 48/49); Anti-Wertham editorial (1st?)	53	106	159	334	567	800
6-10(11/49): 8-Blaze Carson app. 9-Black Rider app.	41	82	123	256	428	600
11(12/53)-Black Rider app.; 1st to have Atlas globe on-c; explains how Kid Colt became an outlaw	37	74	111	222	361	500
12-Black Rider app.	32	64	96	188	307	425
13-20: 14-Opium story	27	54	81	158	259	360
21-24,26-29	24	48	72	142	234	325
25,30: 25-Williamson-a (5 pgs.). 30-Williamson/Torres-a (4 pgs.)	26	52	78	154	252	350
31-33,35,37-40	13	26	39	89	195	300
34-Crandall-a	14	28	42	96	211	325
36,41,42,48-Origin in all	14	28	42	97	214	330
43,44,47	12	24	36	83	182	280
45,46-Davis-a	13	26	39	89	195	300
49,50,52,53-Severin-a(2/3) in each	12	24	36	81	176	270
51-Williamson-a (5 pgs.)	13	26	39	86	188	290
54,55,57,59-Severin-a(3) in each. 59-Kirby-a; last 10¢ issue (4/61)	12	24	36	83	182	280
56	12	24	36	82	179	275
58-New origin; Kirby/Ayers-c/a "The Monster of Hidden Valley" cover/story (Kirby monster-c)	36	72	108	259	580	900
60-New origin	82	164	246	656	1478	2300
60-Edition w/handwritten issue number on cover	89	178	267	712	1606	2500
61,62-Kirby-a	17	34	51	117	259	400
63-74: 64-Intro. Boom-Boom	9	18	27	62	126	190
75,76-Kirby-a (reprint)	10	20	30	64	132	200
77-Kirby-a (reprint); Black Panther-esque villain	27	54	81	194	435	675
78-89	6	12	18	37	66	95
90,95-Kirby-a	6	12	18	37	66	95
91,92-Last story; last 12¢ issue	5	10	15	33	57	80
93,94,96-99	3	6	9	19	30	40
100-Last 15¢-c	3	6	9	19	30	40
101-Origin retold/#58; Kirby-a	3	6	9	19	30	40
102-120-reprints	3	6	9	17	26	35
121-136-reprints. 129-131-(Regular 25¢ editions)	3	6	9	14	20	25
129-131-(30¢-c variants, limited distribution)(4-8/76)	13	26	39	60	120	180

NOTE: **Ayers** a-13, 24, 26, 27, 63, 66. **Davis** c-45-47. **Drucker** a-28. **Everett** a-82, 91. **Fuje** a-13. **Heath** a-3(2), 4(3), 5(2), 7; c-13, 21, 23, 53. **Keller** a-16, 19, 28, 42. **Kirby** a-54, 55, 57-62, 75-77, 90, 95, 101, 119, 120, 129; c-10, 52, 54-65, 67-72, 74-76, 116. **Maneely** a-20; c-11, 12, 16, 19, 20, 24-28, 30, 35, 41, 42, 49. **Powell** a-38, 102, 104. **Severin** a-9, 29, 51, 55, 57, 99r(3); c-9, 39, 51. **Shores** c-1-8, 11. **Trimpe** c-99. **Tuska** a-11, 12. **Whitney** a-87, 89-92, 98-113, 124, 129; c-87, 89, 91, 113. **Wildey** a-21. **Williamson** a-110r. Kid Colt in #13, 14, 16-21.

TWO GUN KID: SUNSET RIDERS
Marvel Comics: Nov, 1995 - No. 2, Dec, 1995 ($6.95, squarebound, lim. series)

Two-Face: Year One #1 © DC

UFOlogy #6 © Tynion IV & Yuenkel

Ultimate Black Panther #1 © MAR

	GD	VG	FN	VF	VF/NM	NM-
	2.0	4.0	6.0	8.0	9.0	9.2

1,2: Fabian Nicieza scripts in all. 1-Painted-c. — — — — — 7.00

TWO GUN WESTERN (1st Series) (Formerly Casey Crime Photographer #1-4? or My Love #1-4?)
Marvel/Atlas Comics (MPC): No. 5, Nov, 1950 - No. 14, June, 1952
5-The Apache Kid (Intro & origin) & his horse Nightwind begin by Buscema
    37   74   111   222   361   500
6-10: 8-Kid Colt, The Texas Kid & his horse Thunder begin?
    26   52   78   154   252   350
11-14: 13-Black Rider app.   19   38   57   111   176   240
NOTE: *Maneely a-6, 7, 9; c-6, 11-13. Morrow a-9. Romita a-8. Wildey a-8.*

2-GUN WESTERN (2nd Series) (Formerly Billy Buckskin #1-3; Two-Gun Western #5 on)
Atlas Comics (MgPC): No. 4, May, 1956
4-Colan, Ditko, Severin, Sinnott-a; Maneely-c   22   44   66   128   209   290

TWO-GUN WESTERN (Formerly Two-Gun Western)
Atlas Comics (MgPC): No. 5, July, 1956 - No. 12, Sept, 1957
5-Return of the Gun-Hawk-c/story; Black Rider app.   22   44   66   132   216   300
6,7   15   30   45   94   147   200
8,10,12-Crandall-a   16   32   48   98   154   210
9,11-Williamson-a in both (5 pgs. each)   17   34   51   103   162   220
NOTE: *Ayers a-9. Colan a-5. Everett c-12. Forgione a-5, 6. Kirby a-12. Maneely a-6, 8, 12; c-5, 6, 8, 11. Morrow a-9, 10. Powell a-7, 11. Severin c-10. Sinnott a-5. Wildey a-9.*

TWO MINUTE WARNING
Ultimate Sports Ent.: 2000 - No. 2 ($3.95, cardstock covers)
1,2-NFL players & Teddy Roosevelt battle evil — — — — — 4.00

TWO MOONS
Image Comics: Feb, 2021 - Present ($3.99)
1-10-Arcudi-s/Giangiordano-a; set during the Civil War — — — — — 4.00

TWO MOUSEKETEERS, THE (See 4-Color #475, 603, 642 under M.G.M.'s...;

TWO ON A GUILLOTINE (See Movie Classics)

TWO-STEP
DC Comics (Cliffhanger): Dec, 2003 - No. 3, Jul, 2004 ($2.95, limited series)
1-3-Warren Ellis-s/Amanda Conner-a — — — — — 3.00
TPB (2010, $19.99) r/#1-3; sketch pages; script for #1 with B&W art — — — — — 20.00

2000 A.D. MONTHLY/PRESENTS (Showcase #25 on)
Eagle Comics/Quality Comics No. 5 on: 4/85 - #6, 9/85; 4/86 - #54, 1991 ($1.25-$1.50, Mando paper)
1-6,1-25:1-4 r/British series featuring Judge Dredd; Alan Moore scripts begin.
1-25 ($1.25)-Reprints from British 2000 AD — — — — — 4.00
26,27/28, 29/30, 31-54: 27/28, 29/30,31-Guice-c — — — — — 4.00

2001, A SPACE ODYSSEY (Movie) (See adaptation in Treasury edition)
Marvel Comics Group: Dec, 1976 - No. 10, Sept, 1977 (30¢)
1-Kirby-c/a in all   4   8   12   23   37   50
2-7,9,10   2   4   6   9   12   15
7,9,10-(35¢-c variants, limited distribution)(6-9/77)   9   18   27   63   129   195
8-Origin/1st app. Machine Man (called Mr. Machine) 6   12   18   41   76   110
8-(35¢-c variant, limited distribution)(6,8/77)   20   40   60   140   310   480
...Treasury 1 ('76, 84 pgs.)-All new Kirby-a   3   6   9   16   23   30

2010 (Movie)
Marvel Comics Group: Apr, 1985 - No. 2, May, 1985
1,2-r/Marvel Super Special movie adaptation. — — — — — 4.00

TYPHOID (Also see Daredevil)
Marvel Comics: Nov, 1995 - No. 4, Feb, 1996 ($3.95, squarebound, lim. series)
1-4: Typhoid Mary; Van Fleet-c/a — — — — — 4.00

TYPHOID FEVER
Marvel Comics: Dec, 2018 - Feb, 2019 ($4.99, limited series)
...: Iron Fist 1 (2/19, $4.99) Typhoid Mary conclusion; Chapman-s/Villanelli-a — — — — — 5.00
...: Spider-Man 1 (12/18, $4.99) Typhoid Mary returns; Chapman-s/Landini-a — — — — — 5.00
...: X-Men 1 (1/19, $4.99) Spider-Man app.; Chapman-s/Robson & Beyruth-a — — — — — 5.00

U & I
Artists, Writers & Artisans, Inc.: Feb, 2024 - No. 6 ($3.99)
1-Straczynski-s/Choi-a — — — — — 4.00

ÜBER
Avatar Press: No. 0, Mar, 2013 - No. 27, Jul, 2015 ($3.99)
0-27: 0-11-Kieron Gillen-s/Caanan White-a. 12-14-Andrade-a — — — — — 4.00
... FCBD 2014 (2/14, Free Comic Book Day giveaway) Text synopsis of early storyline — — — — — 3.00
... Special 1 (3/14, $5.99) Andrade-a — — — — — 6.00

UFO & ALIEN COMIX
Warren Publishing Co.: Jan, 1978 (B&W magazine, 84 pgs., one-shot)
nn-Toth-a, J. Severin-a(r); Pie-s   3   6   9   14   20   25

UFO & OUTER SPACE (Formerly UFO Flying Saucers)
Gold Key: No. 14, June, 1978 - No. 25, Feb, 1980 (All painted covers)
14-Reprints UFO Flying Saucers #3   1   3   4   6   8   10
15,16-Reprints   1   3   4   6   8   10
17-25: 17-20-New material. 23-McWilliams-a. 24-(3 pg.-r). 25-Reprints UFO Flying Saucers #2 w/cover   1   3   4   6   8   10

UFO ENCOUNTERS
Western Publishing Co.: May, 1978 ($1.95, 228 pgs.)
11192-Reprints UFO Flying Saucers   5   10   15   31   53   75
11404-Vol.1 (128 pgs.)-See UFO Mysteries for Vol. 2   4   8   12   27   44   60

UFO FLYING SAUCERS (UFO & Outer Space #14 on)
Gold Key: Oct, 1968 - No. 13, Jan, 1977 (No. 2 on, 36 pgs.)
1(30035-810) (68 pgs.)   8   16   24   51   96   140
2(1/70), 3(11/72), 4(11/74)   4   8   12   23   37   50
5(2/75)-13: Bolle-a #4 on   3   6   9   14   20   25

UFOLOGY
BOOM! Studios: Apr, 2015 - No. 6, Nov, 2015 ($3.99, limited series)
1-6-James Tynion IV & Noah J. Yuenkel-s/Matthew Fox-a — — — — — 4.00

UFO MYSTERIES
Western Publishing Co.: 1978 ($1.00, reprints, 96 pgs.)
11400-(Vol.2)-Cont'd from UFO Encounters, pgs. 129-224   5   10   15   35   63   90

ULTIMAN GIANT ANNUAL (See Big Bang Comics)
Image Comics: Nov, 2001 ($4.95, B&W, one-shot)
1-Homage to DC 1960's annuals — — — — — 5.00

ULTIMATE... (Collects 4-issue alternate titles from X-Men Age of Apocalypse crossovers)
Marvel Comics: May, 1995 ($8.95, trade paperbacks, gold foil covers)
Amazing X-Men, Astonishing X-Men, Factor-X, Gambit & the X-Ternals, Generation Next, X-Calibre, X-Man — — — — — 9.00
Weapon X — — — — — 10.00

ULTIMATE ADVENTURES
Marvel Comics: Nov, 2002 - No. 6, Dec, 2003 ($2.25)
1-6: 1-Intro. Hawk-Owl; Zimmerman-s/Fegredo-a. 3-Ultimates app. — — — — — 3.00
One Tin Soldier TPB (2005, $12.99) r/#1-6 — — — — — 13.00

ULTIMATE ANNUALS
Marvel Comics: 2006; 2007 ($13.99, SC)
Vol. 1 (2006, $13.99) r/Ult. FF Ann. #1, Ult. X-Men Ann. #1, Ult S-M #1, Ultimates Ann #1 14.00
Vol. 2 (2007, $13.99) r/Ult. FF Ann. #2, Ult. X-Men Ann. #2, Ult S-M #2, Ultimates Ann #2 14.00

ULTIMATE ARMOR WARS (Follows Ultimatum x-over)
Marvel Comics: Nov, 2009 - No. 4, Apr, 2010 ($3.99, limited series)
1-4-Warren Ellis-s/Steve Kurth-a/Brandon Peterson-c. 1-Variant-c by Kurth — — — — — 4.00

ULTIMATE AVENGERS (Follows Ultimatum x-over)
Marvel Comics: Oct, 2009 - No. 18 ($3.99)
1-6-Mark Millar-s/Carlos Pacheco-a/c; Red Skull app. — — — — — 4.00
1-Variant Red Skull-c by Leinil Yu — — — — — 8.00
7-12-(Ultimate Avengers 2 #1-6 on cover) Yu-a; Punisher joins. 10-Origin Ghost Rider — — — — — 4.00
7-Variant Ghost Rider-c by Silvestri — — — — — 8.00
13-18-(Ultimate Avengers 3 #1-6 on cover) Dillon-a; Blade and a new Daredevil app. — — — — — 4.00

ULTIMATE AVENGERS VS. NEW ULTIMATES (Death of Spider-Man tie-in)
Marvel Comics: Apr, 2011 - No. 6, Sept, 2011 ($3.99, limited series)
1-6: 1-Millar-s/Yu-a/c; variant covers by Cho & Hitch. 3-6-Punisher app. — — — — — 4.00

ULTIMATE BLACK PANTHER (Follows Ultimate Invasion series)
Marvel Comics: Apr, 2024 - Present ($5.99/$4.99)
1-($5.99) Bryan Hill-s/Stefano Caselli-a — — — — — 6.00
2-($4.99) — — — — — 5.00

ULTIMATE CAPTAIN AMERICA
Marvel Comics: Mar, 2011 - No. 4, Jun, 2011 ($3.99)
1-4: 1-Aaron-s/Garney-a; 2 covers by Garney & McGuinness — — — — — 4.00
Annual 1 (12/08, $3.99, one-shot) Origin of the Black Panther; Djurdjevic-a — — — — — 4.00

ULTIMATE CIVIL WAR: SPIDER-HAM (See Civil War and related titles)
Marvel Comics: March, 2007 ($2.99, one-shot)
1-Spoof of Civil War series featuring Spider-Ham; art by various incl. Olivetti, Severin — — — — — 5.00

ULTIMATE COMICS IRON MAN
Marvel Comics: Dec, 2012 - No. 4, Mar, 2013 ($3.99, limited series)
1-4-Edmonson-s/Buffagni-a/Stockton-c — — — — — 4.00

ULTIMATE COMICS SPIDER-MAN (See Ultimate Spider-Man 2011 series)

ULTIMATE COMICS ULTIMATES (See Ultimates 2011 series)

	GD 2.0	VG 4.0	FN 6.0	VF 8.0	VF/NM 9.0	NM- 9.2

ULTIMATE COMICS WOLVERINE
Marvel Comics: May, 2013 - No. 4, Jul, 2013 ($3.99, limited series)

1-4: 1-Bunn-s/Messina-a/Art Adams-c; Wolverine app. in flashback — 4.00

ULTIMATE COMICS X-MEN (See Ultimate X-Men 2011 series)

ULTIMATE DAREDEVIL AND ELEKTRA
Marvel Comics: Jan, 2003 - No. 4, Mar, 2003 ($2.25, limited series)

1-4-Rucka-s/Larroca-c/a; 1st meeting of Elektra and Matt Murdock — 3.00
... Vol.1 TPB (2003, $11.99) r/#1-4, Daredevil Vol. 2 #9; Larroca sketch pages — 12.00

ULTIMATE DOOM (Follows Ultimate Mystery mini-series)
Marvel Comics: Feb, 2011 - No. 4, May, 2011 ($3.99, limited series)

1-4-Bendis-s/Sandoval-a; Fantastic Four, Spider-Man, Jessica Drew & Nick Fury app. — 4.00

ULTIMATE ELEKTRA
Marvel Comics: Oct, 2004 - No. 5, Feb, 2005 ($2.25, limited series)

1-5-Carey-s/Larroca-c/a. 2-Bullseye app. — 3.00
... : Devil's Due TPB (2005, $11.99) r/#1-5 — 12.00

ULTIMATE END (Secret Wars Battleworld tie-in)
Marvel Comics: Jul, 2015 - No. 5, Feb, 2016 ($3.99, limited series)

1-5-Bendis-s/Bagley-a; Spider-Man & Earth-616 Avengers & Ultimate Universe app. — 4.00

ULTIMATE ENEMY (Follows Ultimatum x-over)(Leads into Ultimate Mystery)
Marvel Comics: Mar, 2010 - No. 4, July, 2010 ($3.99, limited series)

1-4-Bendis-s/Sandoval-a 1-Covers by McGuinness and Pearson — 4.00

ULTIMATE EXTINCTION (See Ultimate Nightmare and Ultimate Secret limited series)
Marvel Comics: Mar, 2006 - No. 5, July, 2006 ($2.99, limited series)

1-5-The coming of Gah Lak Tus; Ellis-s/Peterson-a — 3.00
TPB (2006, $13.99) r/#1-5 — 13.00

ULTIMATE FALLOUT (Follows Death of Spider-Man in Ultimate Spider-Man #160)
Marvel Comics: Sept, 2011 - No. 6, Oct, 2011 ($3.99, weekly limited series)

1-Bendis-s/Bagley-a/c	3	6	9	16	23	30
2,5,6: 2-6-Hitch-a-c. 5-Andy Kubert-c						5.00
3-Ad for Miles Morales; Andy Kubert-c	4	8	12	27	44	60
4-Debut of Miles Morales as the new Spider-Man; polybagged	21	42	63	147	324	500

Ultimate Comics Fallout No. 4 Facsimile Edition (11/21, $3.99) reprint with original ads — 6.00

ULTIMATE FANTASTIC FOUR (Continues in Ultimatum mini-series)
Marvel Comics: Feb, 2004 - No. 60, Apr, 2009 ($2.25/$2.50/$2.99)

1-Bendis & Millar-s/Adam Kubert-a/Hitch-c — 5.00
2-20: 2-Adam Kubert-a/c; intro. Moleman 7-Ellis-s/Immonen-a begin; Dr. Doom app. 13-18-Kubert-a. 19,20-Jae Lee-a. 20-Begin $2.50-c — 3.50
21-Marvel Zombies; begin Greg Land-c/a; Mark Millar-s; variant-c by Land — 5.00
22-29,33-59: 24-26-Namor app. 28-President Thor. 33-38-Ferry-a. 42-46-Silver Surfer — 3.00
30-32-Marvel Zombies; Millar-s/Land-a; Dr. Doom app. — 5.00
30-32-Zombie variant-c by Suydam — 6.00
50-White variant-c by Kirkham — 5.00
60-($3.99) Ultimatum crossover; Kirkham-a — 4.00
Annual 1 (10/05, $3.99) The Inhumans app.; Jae Lee-a/Mark Millar-s/Greg Land-c — 4.00
Annual 2 (10/06, $3.99) Mole Man app.; Immonen & Irving-a/Carey-s — 4.00
... MGC #1 (6/11, $1.00) r/#1 with "Marvel's Greatest Comics" logo on cover — 3.00
.../Ult. X-Men Annual 1 (11/08, $3.99) Continued from Ult. X-Men; F.F. Annual #1 — 4.00
.../X-Men 1 (3/06, $2.99) Carey-s/Ferry-a; continued from Ult. X-Men/Fantastic Four #1 — 3.00
... Vol. 1: The Fantastic (2004, $12.99, TPB) r/#1-6; cover gallery — 13.00
... Vol. 2: Doom (2004, $12.99, TPB) r/#7-12 — 13.00
... Vol. 3: N-Zone (2005, $12.99, TPB) r/#13-18 — 13.00
... Vol. 4: Inhuman (2005, $12.99, TPB) r/#19,20 & Annual #1 — 13.00
... Vol. 5: Crossover (2006, $12.99, TPB) r/#21-26 — 13.00
... Vol. 6: Frightful (2006, $14.99, TPB) r/#27-32; gallery of cover sketches & variants — 15.00
... Vol. 7: God War (2007, $16.99, TPB) r/#33-38 — 17.00
... Vol. 8: Devils (2007, $12.99, TPB) r/#39-41 & Annual #2 — 13.00
... Vol. 9: Silver Surfer (2007, $13.99, TPB) r/#42-46 — 14.00
Volume 1 HC (2005, $29.99, 7x11", dust jacket) r/#1-12; introduction, proposals and scripts by Millar and Bendis; character design pages by Hitch — 30.00
Volume 2 HC (2006, $29.99, 7x11", dust jacket) r/#13-20; Jae Lee sketch page — 30.00
Volume 3 HC (2007, $29.99, 7x11", dust jacket) r/#21-32; Greg Land sketch pages — 30.00
Volume 4 HC (2007, $29.99, 7x11", dust jacket) r/#33-41, Annual #2, Ultimate FF/X-Men and Ultimate X-Men/FF; character design pages — 30.00
Volume 5 HC (2008, $34.99, 7x11", dust jacket) r/#42-53 — 35.00

ULTIMATE FF
Marvel Comics: Jun, 2014 - No. 6, Oct, 2014 ($3.99)

1-6: 1-Team of Sue Storm, Iron Man, Falcon, Machine Man. 4,5-Spider-Ham app. — 4.00

ULTIMATE GALACTUS TRILOGY
Marvel Comics: 2007 ($34.99, hardcover, dustjacket)

HC-Oversized reprint of Ultimate Nightmare #1-5, Ultimate Secret #1-4, Ultimate Vision #0, and Ultimate Extinction #1-5; sketch pages and cover galery — 35.00

ULTIMATE HAWKEYE (Ultimate Comics)
Marvel Comics: Oct, 2011 - No. 4, Jan, 2012 ($3.99, limited series)

1-4: 1-Hickman-s/Sandoval-a/Andrews-c; polybagged. 2-4-Hulk app. — 4.00
1-Variant-c by Neal Adams — 6.00
1-Variant-c by Adam Kubert — 8.00

ULTIMATE HULK
Marvel Comics: Dec, 2008 ($3.99, one-shot)

Annual 1 (12/08, $3.99) Zarda battles Hulk; McGuinness & Djurdjevic-a/Loeb-s — 4.00

ULTIMATE HUMAN
Marvel Comics: Mar, 2008 - No. 4, Jun, 2008 ($2.99, limited series)

1-4-Iron Man vs. The Hulk; The Leader app.; Ellis-s/Nord-a — 3.00
HC (2008, $19.99) r/#1-4 — 20.00

ULTIMATE INVASION
Marvel Comics: Aug, 2023 - No. 4, Nov, 2023 ($8.99/$5.99, limited series)

1,4-($8.99) Hickman-s/Hitch-a. 1-Escape of The Maker (Ultimate Reed Richards) — 9.00

2,3-($5.99) Howard Stark app. — 6.00

ULTIMATE IRON MAN
Marvel Comics: May, 2005 - No. 5, Feb, 2006 ($2.99, limited series)

1-Origin of Iron Man; Orson Scott Card-s/Andy Kubert-a; two covers — 4.00
1-2nd & 3rd printings; each with B&W variant-c — 3.00
2-5-Kubert-a — 3.00
Volume 1 HC (2006, $19.99, dust jacket) r/#1-5; rough cut of script for #1, cover sketches — 20.00
Volume 1 SC (2006, $14.99) r/#1-5; rough cut of script for #1, cover sketches — 15.00

ULTIMATE IRON MAN II
Marvel Comics: Feb, 2008 - No. 5, July, 2008 ($2.99, limited series)

1-5-Early days of the Iron Man prototype; Orson Scott Card-s/Pasqual Ferry-a/c — 3.00

ULTIMATE MARVEL FLIP MAGAZINE
Marvel Comics: July, 2005 - No. 26, Aug, 2007 ($3.99/$4.99)

1-11-Reprints Ultimate Fantastic Four and Ultimate X-Men in flip format — 4.00
12-26-($4.99) — 5.00

ULTIMATE MARVEL MAGAZINE
Marvel Comics: Feb, 2001 - No. 11, 2002 ($3.99, magazine size)

1-11: Reprints of recent stories from the Ultimate titles plus Marvel news and features. 1-Reprints Ultimate Spider-Man #1&2. 11-Lord of the Rings-c — 4.00

ULTIMATE MARVEL SAMPLER
Marvel Comics: 2007 (no cover price, limited series)

1-Previews of 2008 Ultimate Marvel story arcs; Finch-c

ULTIMATE MARVEL TEAM-UP (Spider-Man Team-up)
Marvel Comics: Apr, 2001 - No. 16, July, 2002 ($2.99/$2.25)

1-Spider-Man & Wolverine; Bendis-s in all; Matt Wagner-a/c — 5.00
2,3-Hulk; Hester-a — 3.50
4,5,9-16: 4,5-Iron Man; Allred-a. 9-Fantastic Four; Mahfood-a. 10-Man-Thing; Totleben-a. 11-X-Men; Clugston-Major-a. 12,13-Dr. Strange; McKeever-a.14-Black Widow; Terry Moore-a. 15,16-Shang-Chi; Mays-a — 3.00
6-8-Punisher; Sienkiewicz-a. 7,8-Daredevil app. — 4.00
TPB (11/01, $14.95) r/#1-5 — 15.00
... Ultimate Collection TPB ('06, $29.99) r/#1-16 & Ult. Spider-Man Spec.; sketch pages — 30.00
HC (8/02, $39.99) r/#1-16 & Ult. Spider-Man Special; Bendis afterword — 40.00
...: Vol. 2 TPB (2003, $11.99) r/#9-13; Mahfood-c — 12.00
...: Vol. 3 TPB (2003, $12.99) r/#14-16 & Ultimate Spider-Man Super Special; Moore-c — 13.00

ULTIMATE MYSTERY (Follows Ultimate Enemy)(Leads into Ultimate Doom)
Marvel Comics: Sept, 2010 - No. 4, Dec, 2010 ($3.99, limited series)

1-4-Bendis-s/Sandoval-a; Rick Jones returns; Captain Marvel app. 1-3-Campbell-c — 4.00

ULTIMATE NEW ULTIMATES (Follows Ultimatum x-over)
Marvel Comics: May, 2010 - No. 5, Mar, 2011 ($3.99, limited series)

1-5: 1-Jeph Loeb-s/Frank Cho-a; 6-page wraparound-c by Cho; Defenders app. — 4.00
1-Villains variant-c by Yu — 8.00

ULTIMATE NIGHTMARE (Leads into Ultimate Secret limited series)
Marvel Comics: Oct, 2004 - No. 5, Feb, 2005 ($2.25, limited series)

1-5: Ellis-s; Ultimates, Nick Fury app. 1,2,4,5-Hairsine-a/c. 3-Epting-a — 3.00
Ultimate Galactus Book 1: Nightmare TPB (2005, $12.99) r/Ultimate Nightmare #1-5 — 13.00

ULTIMATE ORIGINS
Marvel Comics: Aug, 2008 - No. 5, Dec, 2008 ($2.99, limited series)

1-5-Bendis-s/Guice-a. 1-Nick Fury origin in the 1940s. 2-Capt. America origin — 3.00

ULTIMATE POWER
Marvel Comics: Dec, 2006 - No. 9, Feb, 2008 ($2.99, limited series)

1-9: 1-Ultimate FF meets the Squadron Supreme; Bendis-s; Land-a/c. 2-Spider-Man, X-Men and the Ultimates app. 6-Doom app. — 3.00
1-Variant sketch-c — 5.00
1-Director's Cut (2007, $3.99) r/#1 and B&W pencil and ink pages; covers to #2,3 — 4.00
HC (2008, $34.99) oversized r/series; profile pages; B&W sketch art — 35.00

ULTIMATES, THE (Avengers of the Ultimate line)
Marvel Comics: Mar, 2002 - No. 13, Apr, 2004 ($2.25)

1-Intro. Capt. America; Millar-s/Hitch-a & wraparound-c	1	2	3	5	6	8
2-Intro. Giant-Man, the Wasp and 1st app. Nick Fury modeled after Samuel L. Jackson	2	4	6	8	10	12
3-12: 3-1st Capt. America in new costume. 4-Intro. Thor. 5-Ultimates vs. The Hulk. 8-Intro. Hawkeye						3.00
13-($3.50)						4.00

... MGC #1 (5/11, $1.00) r/#1 with "Marvel's Greatest Comics" logo on cover — 3.00
... Saga (2007, $3.99) Re-caps 1st 2 Ultimates series; new framing art by Charest; prelude to Ultimates 3 series; Brooks-c — 4.00
... Volume 1 HC (2004, $29.99) oversized r/series; commentary pages with Millar & Hitch; cover gallery and character design pages; intro. by Joss Whedon — 30.00
... Volume 1: Super-Human TPB (8/02, $12.99) r/#1-6 — 13.00
... Volume 2: Homeland Security TPB (2004, $17.99) r/#7-13 — 18.00

ULTIMATES (Ultimate Comics) (Continues in Hunger)
Marvel Comics: Oct, 2011 - No. 30, Nov, 2013 ($3.99)

1-30: 1-Hickman-s/Ribic-a/Andrews-c; polybagged. 4-Reed Richards returns — 4.00
1-Variant-c by Esad Ribic — 6.00
#18.1 (2/13, $2.99) Eaglesham-a; Stark gets the Iron Patriot armor — 3.00
Ultimate Comics Ultimates Must Have 1 (2/12, $4.99) r/#1-3 — 5.00

ULTIMATES (Follows Secret War event)
Marvel Comics: Jan, 2016 - No. 12, Dec, 2016 ($3.99)

1-12: 1-Ewing-s/Rocafort-a; team of Capt. Marvel, Blue Marvel, Black Panther, Spectrum, and Ms. America; Galactus app. 5,7-11-Thanos app. 6,12-Christian Ward-a. 8-12-Civil War II tie-ins — 4.00

ULTIMATES 2
Marvel Comics: Feb, 2005 - No. 13, Feb, 2007 ($2.99/$3.99)

1-Millar-s/Hitch-a; Giant-Man becomes Ant-Man — 4.00
2-11: 6-Intro. The Defenders. 7-Hawkeye shot. 8-Intro The Liberators — 3.00

Ultimate Fallout #1 © MAR

Ultimate Invasion #1 © MAR

Ultimate Spider-Man #125 © MAR

	GD	VG	FN	VF	VF/NM	NM-
	2.0	4.0	6.0	8.0	9.0	9.2

12,13-($3.99) Wraparound-c; X-Men, Fantastic Four, Spider-Man app. 4.00
13-Variant white cover featuring The Wasp 15.00
Annual 1 (10/05, $3.99) Millar-s/Dillon-a/Hitch-c; Defenders app. 4.00
Annual 2 (10/06, $3.99) Deodato-a; flashback to WWII with Sook-a; Falcon app. 4.00
HC (2007, $34.99) oversized r/series; commentary pages with Millar & Hitch; cover gallery,
  sketch and script pages; intro. by Jonathan Ross 35.00
... Volume 1: Gods & Monsters TPB (2005, $15.99) r/#1-6 16.00
... Volume 2: Grand Theft America TPB (2007, $19.99) r/#7-13; cover gallery w/sketches 20.00

ULTIMATES 2
Marvel Comics: Jan, 2017 - No. 9, Sept, 2017; No. 100, Oct. 2017 ($3.99)

1-9: 1-Ewing-s/Foreman-a; team of Capt. Marvel, Blue Marvel, Black Panther, Spectrum,
  and Ms. America. 7,8-Secret Empire tie-ins; Koch-a. 8,9-Ego the Living Planet app. 4.00
100-(10/17, $4.99) The original Ultimates app. 5.00

ULTIMATES 3
Marvel Comics: Feb, 2008 - No. 5, Nov, 2008 ($2.99)

1-Loeb-s/Madureira-a; two gatefold wraparound covers by Madureira; Scarlet Witch shot 4.00
1,2-Second printings 1-Wraparound cover by Madureira. 2-Madureira-a 3.00
2-5: 2-Spider-Man app. 3-Wolverine app. 5-Two gatefold wraparound-c (Heroes & Ultron) 3.00
2-Variant Thor cover by Turner 8.00
3-Variant Scarlet Witch cover by Cho 8.00
4-Variant Valkyrie cover by Finch 4.00

ULTIMATE SECRET (See Ultimate Nightmare limited series)
Marvel Comics: May, 2005 - No. 4, Dec, 2005 ($2.99, limited series)

1-4-Ellis-s; Captain Marvel app. 1,2-McNiven-a. 2,3-Ultimates & FF app. 3.00
Ultimate Galactus Book 2: Secret TPB (2006, $12.99) r/#1-4 13.00

ULTIMATE SECRETS
Marvel Comics: 2008 ($3.99, one-shot)

1-Handbook-styled profiles of secondary teams and characters from Ultimate universe 4.00

ULTIMATE SIX (Reprinted in Ultimate Spider-Man Vol. 5 hardcover)
Marvel Comics: Nov, 2003 - No. 7, June, 2004 ($2.25) (See Ultimate Spider-Man for TPB)

1-The Ultimates and Spider-Man team-up; Bendis-s/Quesada & Hairsine-c; Cassaday-c 5.00
2-7-Hairsine-a; Cassaday-c 3.00

ULTIMATE SPIDER-MAN
Marvel Comics: Oct, 2000 - No. 133, June, 2009 ($2.99/$2.25/$2.99/$3.99)

	GD	VG	FN	VF	VF/NM	NM-
1-Bendis-s/Bagley & Thibert-a; cardstock-c; introduces revised origin and cast separate from our regular Spider-continuity	7	14	21	44	82	120
1-Variant white-c (Retailer incentive)	9	18	27	62	126	190
1-Dynamic Forces Edition	5	10	15	35	63	90
1-Kay Bee Toys variant edition	2	4	6	9	12	15
2-Cover with Spider-Man on car	3	6	9	18	27	35
2-Cover with Spider-Man swinging past building	3	6	9	18	27	35
3,4: 4-Uncle Ben killed	2	4	6	10	14	18
5-7: 6,7-Green Goblin app.	2	4	6	9	12	15
8-13: 13-Reveals secret to MJ	1	3	4	6	8	10

14-21: 14-Intro. Gwen Stacy & Dr. Octopus 5.00
22-($3.50) Green Goblin returns 4.00
23-32 6.00

	GD	VG	FN	VF	VF/NM	NM-
33-1st Ultimate Venom-c; intro. Eddie Brock	1	3	4	6	8	10

34-38-Ultimate Venom 6.00
39-49,51-59: 39-Nick Fury app. 43,44-X-Men app. 46-Prelude to Ultimate Six; Sandman app.
  51-53-Elektra app. 54-59-Doctor Octopus app. 3.00
50-($2.99) Intro. Black Cat 4.00

	GD	VG	FN	VF	VF/NM	NM-
60-Intro. Ultimate Carnage on cover	1	2	3	5	6	8

61-Intro Ben Reilly; Punisher app. 5.00
62-Gwen Stacy killed by Carnage 5.00
63-92: 63,64-Carnage app. 66,67-Wolverine app. 68,69-Johnny Storm app. 78-Begin $2.50-c.
  79-Debut Moon Knight. 81-85-Black Cat app. 90-Vulture app. 91-94-Deadpool 3.00
93-99: 93-Begin $2.99-c. 95-Morbius & Blade app. 97-99-Clone Saga 3.00
100-($3.99) Clone Saga; re-cap of previous issues 4.00
101-103-Clone Saga continues; Fantastic Four app. 102-Spider-Woman origin 3.00
104-($3.99) Clone Saga concludes; Fantastic Four and Dr. Octopus app. 4.00
105-132: 106-110-Daredevil app. 111-Last Bagley art; Immonen-a (6 pgs.) 112-Immonen-a;
  Norman Osborn app. 118-Liz Allen ignites. 123,128-Venom app. 129-132-Ultimatum 3.00
133-($3.99) Ultimatum crossover; Spider-Woman app. 4.00
(Issues #150-up. see second series) 4.00
Annual 1 (10/05, $3.99) Kitty Pryde app.; Bendis-s/Brooks-a/Bagley-c 4.00
Annual 2 (10/06, $3.99) Punisher, Moon Knight and Daredevil app.; Bendis-s/Brooks-a 4.00
Annual 3 (12/08, $3.99) Mysterio app.; Bendis-s/Lafuente-a 4.00
Collected Edition (1/01, $3.99) r/#1-3 3.00
Free Comic Book Day giveaway (5/02) - r/#1 with "Free Comic Book Day" banner on-c 3.00
... MGC #1 (5/11, $1.00) r/#1 with "Marvel's Greatest Comics" logo on cover 3.00
...Special (7/02, $3.50) art by Bagley and various incl. Romita, Sr., Brereton, Cho, Mack,
  Sienkiewicz, Phillips, Pearson, Oeming, Mahfood, Russell 4.00
Ultimate Spider-Man 100 Project (2007, $10.00, SC, charity book for the HERO Initiative)

collection of 100 variant covers by Romita Sr. & Jr., Cho, Bagley, Quesada and more 10.00
...: Venom HC (2007, $19.99) r/#33-39 20.00
...(Vol. 1): Power and Responsibility TPB (4/01, $14.95) r/#1-7 15.00
...(Vol. 2): Learning Curve TPB (12/01, $14.95) r/#8-13 15.00
...(Vol. 3): Double Trouble TPB (6/02, $17.95) r/#14-21 18.00
Vol. 4: Legacy TPB (2002, $14.99) r/#22-27 15.00
Vol. 5: Public Scrutiny TPB (2003, $11.99) r/#28-32 12.00
Vol. 6: Venom TPB (2003, $15.99) r/#33-39 16.00
Vol. 7: Irresponsible TPB (2003, $12.99) r/#40-45 13.00
Vol. 8: Cats & Kings TPB (2003, $17.99) r/#47-53 18.00
Vol. 9: Ultimate Six TPB (2004, $17.99) r/#46 & Ultimate Six #1-7 18.00
Vol. 10: Hollywood TPB (2004, $12.99) r/#54-59 13.00
Vol. 11: Carnage TPB (2004, $12.99) r/#60-65 13.00
Vol. 12: Superstars TPB (2005, $12.99) r/#66-71 13.00
Vol. 13: Hobgoblin TPB (2005, $15.99) r/#72-78 16.00
Vol. 14: Warriors TPB (2005, $17.99) r/#79-85 18.00
Vol. 15: Silver Sable TPB (2006, $15.99) r/#86-90 & Annual #1 16.00
Vol. 16: Deadpool TPB (2006, $19.99) r/#91-96 & Annual #2 20.00
Vol. 17: Clone Saga TPB (2007, $24.99) r/#97-105 25.00
Vol. 18: Ultimate Knights TPB (2007, $13.99) r/#106-111 14.00
Vol. 19: Death of a Goblin TPB (2008, $14.99) r/#112-117 15.00
Hardcover (3/02, $34.95, 7x11", dust jacket) r/#1-13 & Amazing Fantasy #15;
  sketch pages and Bill Jemas' initial plot and character outlines 35.00
Volume 2 HC (2003, $29.99, 7x11", dust jacket) r/#14-27; pin-ups & sketch pages 30.00
Volume 3 HC (2003, $29.99, 7x11", dust jacket) r/#28-39 & #1/2; script pages 30.00
Volume 4 HC (2004, $29.99, 7x11", dust jacket) r/#40-45, 47-53; sketch pages 30.00
Volume 5 HC (2004, $29.99, 7x11", dust jacket) r/#46,54-59, Ultimate Six #1-7 30.00
Volume 6 HC (2005, $29.99, 7x11", dust jacket) r/#60-71; sketch page 30.00
Volume 7 HC (2006, $29.99, 7x11", dust jacket) r/#72-85; sketch & profile pages 30.00
Volume 8 HC (2007, $29.99, 7x11", dust jacket) r/#86-96 & Annual #1&2; sketch page 30.00
Volume 9 HC (2008, $39.99, 7x11", dust jacket) r/#97-111; sketch pages 40.00
Volume 10 HC (2009, $39.99, 7x11", dust jacket) r/#112-122; sketch pages 40.00

Wizard #1/2	1	3	4	6	8	10

ULTIMATE SPIDER-MAN (2nd series)(Follows Ultimatum x-over)
Marvel Comics: Oct, 2009 - No. 15, Dec, 2010; No. 150, Jan, 2011 - No. 160, Aug, 2011 ($3.99)

1-15: 1-Bendis-s/Lafuente-a/c; new Mysterio. 1-Variant-c by Djurdjevic. 7,8-Miyazawa-a.
  9-Spider-Woman app. 4.00
150-($5.99) Resumes original numbering; wraparound-c by Lafuente; Bendis-s with art
  by Lafuente, Pichelli, Joëlle Jones, McKelvie & Young; r/Ult. S-M Special #1 6.00
150-Variant wraparound-c by Bagley 10.00
151-159: 151-154-Black Cat & Mysterio app. 157-Spider-Man shot by Punisher 4.00
159-159-variant covers. 153-155-Pichelli. 157-McGuinness. 158-McNiven. 159-Cho 8.00
160-Black Polybagged; Bagley cover inside; Death of Spider-Man part 5 4.00
160-Red Polybagged variant; Kaluta cover inside; Death of Spider-Man part 5 20.00

ULTIMATE SPIDER-MAN (3rd series)(with Miles Morales)(See Ultimate Fallout #4 for debut)
Marvel Comics: Nov, 2011 - No. 28, Dec, 2013 ($3.99)

	GD	VG	FN	VF	VF/NM	NM-
1-Polybagged, with Kaare Andrews-c; Bendis-s/Pichelli-a; origin	10	20	30	64	132	200
1-Variant Pichelli-c with unmasked Spider-Man	17	34	51	117	259	400
1-Variant Pichelli-c with Spider-Man & city bkgrd	17	34	51	117	259	400
2	3	6	9	19	30	40
3-Spider-Woman app.	3	6	9	14	20	25
4-Spider-Woman app.	3	6	9	17	26	35
5-Origin of suit; Spider-Woman, Nick Fury & Ultimates app.	3	6	9	19	30	40

6-28: 6-Samnee-a. 19-22-Venom War; Pichelli-a. 23-Cloak and Dagger app. 28-Leads into
  Cataclysm 5.00
#16.1 (12/12, $2.99) Marquez-a; Venom returns 6.00

	GD	VG	FN	VF	VF/NM	NM-
200-(6/14, $4.99) Art by Marquez and others; 2 interlocking covers by Bagley & Marquez	2	4	6	9	12	15

Ultimate Comics Spider-Man Must Have 1 (2/12, $4.99) r/#1-3 50.00

ULTIMATE SPIDER-MAN (4th series, with older Peter Parker)(Follows Ultimate Invasion series)
Marvel Comics: Mar, 2024 - Present ($5.99/$4.99)

1-($5.99) Hickman-s/Checchetto-a; intro. older married Peter Parker 6.00
2-($4.99) Kingpin and The Shocker app. 5.00

ULTIMATE SPIDER-MAN (Based on the animated series)(See Marvel Universe...)

ULTIMATE TALES FLIP MAGAZINE
Marvel Comics: July, 2005 - No. 26, Aug, 2007 ($3.99/$4.99)

1-11-Each reprints 2 issues of Ultimate Spider-Man in flip format 4.00
12-26-($4.99) 5.00

ULTIMATE THOR
Marvel Comics: Dec, 2010 - No. 4, Apr, 2011 ($3.99, limited series)

1-4: 1-Hickman-s/Pacheco-a; two covers by Pacheco & Choi; origin story 4.00

ULTIMATE UNIVERSE (Follows Ultimate Invasion series)

	GD	VG	FN	VF	VF/NM	NM-		GD	VG	FN	VF	VF/NM	NM-
	2.0	4.0	6.0	8.0	9.0	9.2		2.0	4.0	6.0	8.0	9.0	9.2

Marvel Comics: Jan, 2024 - Present ($5.99)

1-($6.99) Hickman-s/Caselli-a ... 7.00

ULTIMATE VISION
Marvel Comics: No. 0, Jan, 2007 - No. 5, Jan, 2008 ($2.99, limited series)

0-Reprints back-up serial from Ultimate Extinction and related series; pin-ups ... 3.00
1-5: 1-(2/07) Carey-s/Peterson-a/c ... 3.00
TPB (2007, $14.99) r/#0-5; design pages and cover gallery ... 15.00

ULTIMATE WAR
Marvel Comics: Feb, 2003 - No. 4, Apr, 2003 ($2.25, limited series)

1-4-Millar-s/Bachalo-c/a; The Ultimates vs. Ultimate X-Men ... 3.00
Ultimate X-Men Vol. 5: Ultimate War TPB (2003, $10.99) r/#1-4 ... 11.00

ULTIMATE WOLVERINE VS. HULK
Marvel Comics: Feb, 2006 - No. 6, July, 2009 ($2.99, limited series)

1,2-Leinil Yu-a/c; Damon Lindelof-s: 2-(4/06) ... 4.00
1,2-(2009) New printings ... 3.00
3-6: 3-(5/09) Intro. She-Hulk. 4-Origin She-Hulk ... 3.00

ULTIMATE X (Follows Ultimatum x-over)
Marvel Comics: Apr, 2010 - No. 5, Aug, 2011 ($3.99)

1-5: 1-Jeph Loeb-s/Art Adams-a; two covers by Adams. 5-Hulk app. ... 4.00

ULTIMATE X-MEN
Marvel Comics: Feb, 2001 - No. 100, Apr, 2009 ($2.99/$2.25/$2.50)

1-Millar-s/Adam Kubert & Thibert-a; cardstock-c; introduces revised origin and cast separate from regular X-Men continuity	3	6	9	14	19	24
1-DF Edition	3	6	9	15	22	28
1-DF Sketch Cover Edition	3	6	9	17	25	34

1-Free Comic Book Day Edition (7/03) r/#1 with "Free Comic Book Day" banner on-c ... 3.00

| 2 | 2 | 4 | 6 | 9 | 12 | 15 |
| 3-6 | 1 | 3 | 4 | 6 | 8 | 10 |

7-10 ... 6.00
11-24,26-33: 13-Intro. Gambit. 18,19-Bachalo-a. 23,24-Andrews-a ... 4.00
25-($3.50) leads into the Ultimate War mini-series; Kubert-a ... 4.00
34-Spider-Man-c/app.; Bendis-s begin; Finch-a ... 5.00
35-74: 35-Spider-Man app. 36,37-Daredevil-c/app. 40-Intro. Angel. 42-Intro. Dazzler. 44-Beast dies. 46-Intro. Mr. Sinister. 50-53-Kubert-a; Gambit app. 54-57,59-63-Immonen-a. 60-Begin $2.50-c. 61-Variant Coipel-c. 66-Kirkman-s begin. 69-Begin $2.99-c ... 3.00
61-Retailer Edition with variant Coipel B&W sketch-c ... 10.00
75-($3.99) Turner-c; intro. Cable; back-up story with Emma Frost's students ... 4.00
76-99: 76-Intro. Bishop. 91-Fantastic Four app. 92-96-Phoenix app. 96-Spider-Man app. 99-Ultimatum x-over ... 3.00
100-($3.99) Ultimatum x-over; Brooks-a ... 4.00
Annual 1 (10/05, $3.99) Vaughan-s/Raney-a; Gambit & Rogue in Vegas ... 4.00
Annual 2 (10/06, $3.99) Kirkman-s/Larroca-a; Nightcrawler & Dazzler ... 4.00
.../Fantastic Four 1 (2/06, $2.99) Carey-s/Ferry-a; concluded in Ult. Fantastic Four/X-Men ... 3.00
... MGC 1 (6/11, $1.00) r/#1 with "Marvel's Greatest Comics" logo on cover ... 3.00
.../Ult. Fantastic Four Ann. 1 (11/08, $3.99) Continues in Ult. F.F./Ult. X-Men Annual #1 ... 3.00
.../Fantastic Four TPB (2006, $12.99) reprints Ult X-Men/Ult. FF x-over and Official Handbook of the Ultimate Marvel Universe #1-2 ... 13.00
... No. 1 Facsimile Edition (2/23, $3.99) r/#1 with original ads ... 4.00
... Ultimate Collection Vol. 1 (2006, $24.99) r/#1-12 & #1/2; unused Bendis script for #1 ... 25.00
... Ultimate Collection Vol. 2 (2007, $24.99) r/#13-25; Kubert cover sketch pages ... 25.00
... (Vol. 1) The Tomorrow People TPB (7/01, $14.95) r/#1-6 ... 15.00
...: (Vol. 2) Return to Weapon X TPB (4/02, $14.95) r/#7-12 ... 15.00
Vol. 3: World Tour TPB (2002, $17.99) r/#13-20 ... 18.00
Vol. 4: Hellfire and Brimstone TPB (2003, $12.99) r/#21-25 ... 13.00
Vol. 5 (See Ultimate War)
Vol. 6: Return of the King TPB (2003, $16.99) r/#26-33 ... 17.00
Vol. 7: Blockbuster TPB (2004, $13.99) r/#34-39 ... 13.00
Vol. 8: New Mutants TPB (2004, $12.99) r/#40-45 ... 13.00
Vol. 9: The Tempest TPB (2004, $10.99) r/#46-49 ... 11.00
Vol. 10: Cry Wolf TPB (2005, $8.99) r/#50-53 ... 9.00
Vol. 11: The Most Dangerous Game TPB (2005, $9.99) r/#54-57 ... 10.00
Vol. 12: Hard Lessons TPB (2005, $12.99) r/#58-60 & Annual #1 ... 13.00
Vol. 13: Magnetic North TPB (2006, $12.99) r/#61-65 ... 13.00
Vol. 14: Phoenix? TPB (2006, $14.99) r/#66-71 ... 15.00
Vol. 15: Magical TPB (2007, $11.99) r/#72-74 & Annual #2 ... 12.00
Vol. 16: Cable TPB (2007, $14.99) r/#75-80; sketch pages ... 15.00
Vol. 17: Sentinels TPB (2008, $17.99) r/#81-88 ... 18.00

Volume 1 HC (8/02, $34.99, 7x11", dust jacket) r/#1-12 & Giant-Size X-Men #1; sketch pages and Millar and Bendis' initial plot and character outlines						35.00
Volume 2 HC (2003, $29.99, 7x11", dust jacket) r/#13-25; script for #20						30.00
Volume 3 HC (2003, $29.99, 7x11", dust jacket) r/#26-33 & Ultimate War #1-4						30.00
Volume 4 HC (2005, $29.99, 7x11", dust jacket) r/#34-45						30.00
Volume 5 HC (2006, $29.99, 7x11", dust jacket) r/#46-57; Vaughan intro.; sketch pages						30.00
Volume 6 HC (2006, $29.99, 7x11", dust jacket) r/#58-65, Annual #1 & Wizard #1/2						30.00
Volume 7 HC (2007, $29.99, 7x11", dust jacket) r/#66-74, Annual #2						30.00
Wizard #1/2	2	4	6	9	12	15

ULTIMATE X-MEN (Ultimate Comics X-Men) (See Cataclysm)
Marvel Comics: Nov, 2011 - No. 33, Dec, 2013 ($3.99)

1-Spencer-s/Medina-a/Andrews-c; polybagged ... 4.00
1-Variant-c by Mark Bagley ... 6.00
2-33: 2-Rogue returns. 6-Prof. X returns. 21-Iron Patriot app. ... 4.00
#18.1 (1/13, $2.99) Andrade-a/Pichelli-c ... 3.00
Ultimate Comics X-Men Must Have 1 (2/12, $4.99) r/#1-3 ... 5.00

ULTIMATUM
Marvel Comics: Jan, 2009 - No. 5, July, 2009 ($3.99, limited series)

1-5-Loeb-s/Finch-a; Ultimate heroes vs. Magneto ... 4.00
1-5-Variant covers by McGuinness ... 8.00
5-Double gatefold variant-c by Finch ... 4.00
March on Ultimatum Saga ('08, giveaway) text and art panel history of Ultimate universe ... 3.00
...: Fantastic Four Requiem 1 (9/09,$3.99) Pokaski-s/Atkins-a; Dr. Strange app. ... 4.00
...: Spider-Man Requiem 1,2 (8/09, 9/09,$3.99) Bendis-s/Bagley & Immonen-a ... 4.00
...: X-Men Requiem 1 (9/09,$3.99) Coleite-s/Oliver-a/Brooks-c ... 4.00

NOTE: Numerous variant covers and 2nd & 3rd printings exist.

ULTRA
Image Comics: Aug, 2004 - No. 8, Mar, 2005 ($2.95, limited series)

1-8: 1-Intro. Ultra/Pearl Penalosa; Luna Brothers-s/a ... 3.00
Vol. 1: Seven Days TPB (4/05, $17.95) r/#1-8; sketch pages ... 18.00

ULTRAFORCE (1st Series) (Also see Avengers/Ultraforce #1)
Malibu Comics (Ultraverse): Aug, 1994 - No. 10, Aug, 1995 ($1.95/$2.50)

0 (9/94, $2.50)-Perez-c/a. ... 5.00
1-($2.50, 44 pgs.)-Bound-in trading card; team consisting of Prime, Prototype, Hardcase, Pixx, Ghoul, Contrary & Topaz; Gerard Jones scripts begin, ends #6; Pérez-c/a begins ... 5.00

| 1-Ultra 5000 Limited Silver Foil Edition | 1 | 2 | 3 | 5 | 6 | 8 |
| 1-Holographic-c, no price | 1 | 2 | 3 | 6 | 8 | 10 |

2-5: Perez-c/a in all. 2 (10/94, $1.95)-Prime quits, Strangers cameo. 3-Origin of Topaz; Prime rejoins. 5-Pixx dies. ... 4.00
2 ($2.50)-Florescent logo; limited edition stamp on-c ... 5.00
6-10: 6-Begin $2.50-c, Perez-c/a. 7-Ghoul story, Steve Erwin-a. 8-Marvel's Black Knight enters the Ultraverse (last seen in Avengers #375); Perez-c. 9,10-Black Knight app.; Perez-c. 10-Leads into Ultraforce/Avengers Prelude ... 4.00
Malibu "Ashcan": Ultraforce #0A (6/94) ... 4.00
.../Avengers Prelude 1 (8/95, $2.50)-Perez-c. ... 4.00
.../Avengers 1 (8/95, $3.95)-Warren Ellis script; Perez-c/a; foil-c ... 5.00

ULTRAFORCE (2nd Series) (Also see Black September)
Malibu Comics (Ultraverse): Infinity, Sept, 1995 - V2#15, Dec, 1996 ($1.50)

Infinity, V2#1-15: Infinity-Team consists of Marvel's Black Knight, Ghoul, Topaz, Prime & redesigned Prototype; Warren Ellis scripts begin, ends #3; variant-c exists. 1-1st app.Cromwell, Lament & Wreckage. 2-Contains free encore presentation of Ultraforce #1; flip book "Phoenix Resurrection" Pt. 7. 7-Darick Robertson, Jeff Johnson & others-a. 8,9-Intro. Future Ultraforce (Prime, Hellblade, Angel of Destruction, Painkiller & Whipslash); Gary Erskine-c/a. 9-Foxfire app. 10-Len Wein scripts & Deodato Studios-c/a begins. 10-Lament back-up story. 11-Ghoul back-up story by Pander Bros. 12-Ultraforce vs. Maxis (cont'd in Ultraverse Unlimited #2); Exiles & Iron Clad app. 13-Prime leaves; Hardcase returns ... 4.00
Infinity (2000 signed) ... 5.00
.../Spider-Man ($3.95)-Marv Wolfman script; Green Goblin app.; 2 covers exist. ... 5.00

ULTRAGIRL
Marvel Comics: Nov, 1996 - No. 3 Mar, 1997 ($1.50, limited series)

1-1st app.; Barbara Kesel-s/Leonard Kirk-a ... 6.00
2,3-New Warriors app. ... 4.00

ULTRA KLUTZ
Onward Comics: 1981; 6/86 - #27, 1/89, #28, 4/90 - #31, 1990? ($1.50/$1.75/$2.00, B&W)

1 (1981)-Re-released after 2nd #1 ... 4.00
1-30: 1-(6/86). 27-Photo back-c ... 4.00
31-($2.95, 52 pgs.) ... 5.00

ULTRAMAN (Also see The Rise of Ultraman and The Trials of Ultraman)
Nemesis Comics: Mar, 1994 - No. 4, Sept, 1994 ($1.75/$1.95)

1-($2.25)-Collector's edition; foil-c; special 3/4 wraparound-c ... 5.00
1-($1.75)-Newsstand edition ... 4.00
2-4: 3-$1.95-c begins ... 4.00
#(-1) (3/93) ... 4.00

ULTRAMAN: THE MYSTERY OF ULTRASEVEN
Marvel Comics: Oct, 2022 - No. 5, Mar, 2023 ($4.99/$3.99)

1-($4.99) Higgins & Groom-s; art by Tinto & Lopez; back-up with Gurihiru-a ... 5.00
2-5-($3.99): 3-Ultraman vs. Ultraseven ... 4.00

ULTRAMAN TIGA
Dark Horse Comics: Aug, 2003 - No. 10, June, 2004 ($3.99)

1-10-Khoo Fuk Lung-a/Tony Wong-s ... 4.00

ULTRAMEGA
Image Comics (Skybound): Mar, 2021 - Present ($7.99, squarebound)

1-4-James Harren-s/a ... 8.00

ULTRAVERSE DOUBLE FEATURE
Malibu Comics (Ultraverse): Jan, 1995 ($3.95, one-shot, 68 pgs.)

1-Flip-c featuring Prime & Solitaire. ... 5.00

ULTRAVERSE: FUTURE SHOCK
Malibu Comics (Ultraverse): Feb, 1997 ($2.50, one-shot)

1-Paniccia-s ... 4.00

ULTRAVERSE ORIGINS
Malibu Comics (Ultraverse): Jan, 1994 (99¢, one-shot)

1-Gatefold-c; 2 pg. origins all characters ... 4.00
1-Newsstand edition; different-c, no gatefold ... 4.00

ULTRAVERSE PREMIERE
Malibu Comics (Ultraverse): 1994 (one-shot)

0-Ordered thru mail w/coupons ... 5.00

ULTRAVERSE UNLIMITED
Malibu Comics (Ultraverse): June, 1996; No. 2, Sept, 1996 ($2.50)

1,2: 1-Adam Warlock returns to the Marvel Universe; Rune-c/app. 2-Black Knight, Reaper & Sierra Blaze return to the Marvel Universe ... 4.00

ULTRAVERSE YEAR ONE
Malibu Comics (Ultraverse): Sept, 1994 ($4.95, one-shot)

1-In-depth synopsis of the first year's titles & stories. ... 5.00

ULTRAVERSE YEAR TWO
Malibu Comics (Ultraverse): Aug, 1995 ($4.95, one-shot)

1-In-depth synopsis of second year's titles & stories ... 5.00

ULTRAVERSE YEAR ZERO: THE DEATH OF THE SQUAD
Malibu Comics (Ultraverse): Apr, 1995 - No. 4, July, 1995 ($2.95, lim. series)

1-4: 3-Codename: Firearm back-up story. ... 4.00

ULTRON (See Age of Ultron series)
Marvel Comics: Jun, 2013 ($3.99, one-shot)

	GD	VG	FN	VF	VF/NM	NM-		GD	VG	FN	VF	VF/NM	NM-
	2.0	4.0	6.0	8.0	9.0	9.2		2.0	4.0	6.0	8.0	9.0	9.2

1AU-Victor Mancha from the Runaways (son of Ultron); K. Immonen-s/Pinna-a — 4.00

UMBRAL
Image Comics: Nov, 2013 - No. 12, Jan, 2015 ($2.99)
1-12-Johnston-s/Mitten-a — 3.00

UMBRELLA ACADEMY (Also see Hazel & Cha Cha Save Christmas)
Dark Horse Comics: Apr, 2007
1-Free Comic Book Day Edition - previews of the upcoming series; James Jean-c;
Zero Killer & Pantheon City on back-c — 3 6 9 19 30 40

UMBRELLA ACADEMY: APOCALYPSE SUITE
Dark Horse Comics: Sept, 2007 - No. 6, Feb, 2008 ($2.99, limited series)
1-Origin of the Umbrella Academy; Gerald Way-s/Gabriel Bá-a/James Jean-c
— 3 6 9 19 30 40
1-White variant-c by Bá — 4 8 12 23 37 50
1-Variant-c by Gerald Way — 6 12 18 42 79 115
1-2nd printing with variant-c by Bá — 1 3 4 6 8 10
2-6 — 2 4 6 8 10 12
...: One for One (9/10, $1.00) r/#1 with red cover frame
— 2 4 6 9 12 15
Vol.1: Apocalypse Suite TPB (7/08, $17.95) r/#1-6, FCBD story and web shorts; design art;
Grant Morrison intro.; cover gallery — 3 6 9 18 24 32

UMBRELLA ACADEMY: DALLAS
Dark Horse Comics: Nov, 2008 - No. 6, May, 2009 ($2.99, limited series)
1-6-Gerald Way-s/Gabriel Bá-a/c — 2 4 6 8 10 12
1-Wraparound variant-c by Jim Lee — 3 6 9 19 30 40

UMBRELLA ACADEMY: HOTEL OBLIVION
Dark Horse Comics: Oct, 2018 - No. 7, Jun, 2019 ($3.99, limited series)
1-Gerald Way-s/Gabriel Bá-a/c in all — 1 3 4 6 8 10
2-7 — 4.00

UNBEATABLE SQUIRREL GIRL, THE
Marvel Comics: Mar, 2015 - No. 8, Oct, 2015 ($3.99)
1-Doreen Green and Tippy-Toe at college; North-s/Henderson-a; Kraven app.
— 2 4 6 9 12 15
2-8: 3,4-Galactus app. 7-Avengers cameo. 8-Lady Thor, Odinson & Loki app. — 4.00

UNBEATABLE SQUIRREL GIRL, THE
Marvel Comics: Dec, 2015 - No. 50, Jan, 2020 ($3.99)
1-25,27-50: 1-North-s/Henderson-a. 2-Doreen goes to the 1960s; Doctor Doom app.
6-Crossover with Howard the Duck #6. 10-Mole Man app. 13,14-Scott Lang app.
16-25th Anniverary issue; origin re-told; Hulk app. 23-25-Dinosaur Ultron app.
43-46-War of the Realms tie-ins. 43-Intro. Ratatoskr. 48-50-Iron Man app. — 4.00
26-"Zine" issue; includes Silver Surfer/Galactus by Garfield's Jim Davis (2 pgs.) — 4.00
... Beats Up The Marvel Universe (2016, $24.99, HC) original graphic novel; North-s;
Henderson-a; Spider-Man & Avengers app.; bonus game pages and design art — 25.00
...: You Choose the Story No. 1 Halloween Comic Fest 2016 (giveaway, 12/16) r/#7 — 3.00

UN-BEDABLE VARK, THE (Reprints from Cerebus in Hell)
Aardvark-Vanaheim: Jun, 2018 ($4.00, B&W)
1-Cerebus figures over original Gustave Doré artwork of Hell; Inc. Hulk #1-c swipe — 4.00

UNBELIEVABLE GWENPOOL, THE (Also see Gwenpool Special)
Marvel Comics: Jun, 2016 - No. 25, Apr, 2018 ($3.99)
1-($4.99) Hastings-s/Gurihiru-a; MODOK app. — 2 4 6 9 12 15
2-25-($3.99) 2-Thor (Jane) app. 3-Doctor Strange app. 5,6,19,20-Spider-Man (Miles) app.
13-Deadpool app. 14,15-Hawkeye & Ghost Rider app. 22,23-Doctor Doom app. — 4.00
#0-(7/16, $4.99) Reprints apps. in Howard the Duck #1-3 & Gwenpool Special #1
— 2 4 6 9 12 15

UNBELIEVABLE UNTEENS, THE (From Black Hammer)
Dark Horse Comics: Aug, 2021 - No. 4, Nov, 2021 ($3.99)
1-4-Jeff Lemire-s/Tyler Crook-a; main cover by Crook; variant-c for each — 4.00

UNBIRTHDAY PARTY WITH ALICE IN WONDERLAND (See Alice In Wonderland, Four Color #341)

UNBREAKABLE RED SONJA
Dynamite Entertainment: 2022 - No. 5, 2023 ($3.99)
1-5: 1-Jim Zub-s/Giovanni Valletta-a — 4.00

UNCANNY
Dynamite Entertainment: 2013 - No. 6, 2014 ($3.99)
1-6-Andy Diggle-s/Aaron Campbell-a — 4.00

UNCANNY, (SEASON TWO)
Dynamite Entertainment: 2015 - No. 6, 2015 ($3.99)
1-6-Andy Diggle-s/Aaron Campbell-a — 4.00

UNCANNY AVENGERS (Marvel NOW!)
Marvel Comics: Dec, 2012 - No. 25, Dec, 2014 ($3.99)

1-25: 1-Capt. America, Thor, Scarlet Witch, Wolverine, Havok & Rogue team; Remender-s/
Cassaday-a; Red Skull app. 5-Coipel-a. 14-Rogue & Scarlet Witch die. 24,25-Axis — 4.00
8AU-(7/13, $3.99) Age of Ultron tie-in; Adam Kubert-a — 4.00
Annual 1 (6/14, $4.99) Remender-s/Renaud-a/Art Adams-c; Mojo app. — 5.00

UNCANNY AVENGERS
Marvel Comics: Mar, 2015 - No. 5, Aug, 2015 ($3.99)
1-5: 1-Capt. America (Sam Wilson), Vision, Scarlet Witch, Quicksilver, Sabretooth, Rogue &
Doctor Voodoo team; Remender-s/Acuna-a — 4.00

UNCANNY AVENGERS
Marvel Comics: Dec, 2015 - No. 30, Feb, 2018 ($3.99)
1-($4.99) Steve Rogers, Spider-Man, Deadpool, Human Torch, Quicksilver, Rogue,
Synapse & Doctor Voodoo team; Duggan-s/Stegman-a — 5.00
2-20,26-30-($3.99) 2-5-Cable app. 5,6-Pacheco-a. 7,8-Pleasant Hill Standoff tie-ins.
13,14-Civil War II tie-in. 16,17-Hulk returns. 24-Secret Empire tie-in. 26-Scarlet Witch joins.
29-Juggernaut app. — 4.00
25-($4.99) Secret Empire tie-in; Shocker & Scorpina app.; Zub-s/Jacinto-a — 5.00
Annual 1 (1/16, $4.99) Robinson-s/Laming & Giles-a/Deodato-c; Emerald Warlock app. — 5.00

UNCANNY AVENGERS
Marvel Comics: Oct, 2023 - No. 5, Feb, 2024 ($4.99/$3.99, limited series)
1-($4.99) Steve Rogers, Deadpool, Psylocke, Quicksilver, Rogue, Penance team — 5.00
2-5 ($3.99) Black Widow and Hydra Steve Rogers app. — 4.00

UNCANNY AVENGERS: ULTRON FOREVER
Marvel Comics: Jul, 2015 ($4.99)(Continued from New Avengers: Ultron Forever)
1-Part 3 of 3-part crossover with Avengers and New Avengers; Ewing-s/Alan Davis-a;
team-up of past, present and future Avengers vs. Ultron — 5.00

UNCANNY INHUMANS
Marvel Comics: No. 0, Jun, 2015; No. 1, Dec, 2015 - No. 20, May, 2017 ($4.99/$3.99)
0-Soule-s/McNiven-a/c; Black Bolt, Medusa & Kang the Conqueror app. — 5.00
1-($4.99) Johnny Storm, Beast & Kang the Conqueror app. — 5.00
2-19-($3.99) 2-4-Kang app. 5-Mad Thinker and The Leader app. 11-14-Civil War II tie-in — 4.00
20-($4.99) Leads into Inhumans Prime #1 — 5.00
#1.MU (4/17, $4.99) Monsters Unleashed tie-in; Allor-s/Level-a — 5.00
Annual 1 (10/16, $4.99) Soule-s/Kev Walker-a — 5.00

UNCANNY ORIGINS
Marvel Comics: Sept, 1996 - No. 14, Oct, 1997 (99¢)
1-14: 1-Cyclops. 2-Quicksilver. 3-Archangel. 4-Firelord. 5-Hulk. 6-Beast. 7-Venom.
8-Nightcrawler. 9-Storm. 10-Black Cat. 11-Black Knight. 12-Dr. Strange. 13-Daredevil.
14-Iron Fist — 4.00

UNCANNY SKULLKICKERS (See Skullkickers #19)

UNCANNY SPIDER-MAN
Marvel Comics: Nov, 2023 - No. 5, Feb, 2024 ($4.99/$3.99, limited series)
1-($4.99) Nightcrawler in a spider-suit; Spurrier-s/Garbett-a — 5.00
2-5 ($3.99) Mystique and Silver Sable app. — 4.00

UNCANNY TALES
Atlas Comics (PrP/PPI): June, 1952 - No. 56, Sept, 1957

	GD	VG	FN	VF	VF/NM	NM-
1-Heath-a; horror / weird stories begin	174	348	522	1114	1907	2700
2	84	168	252	538	919	1300
3-5	74	148	222	470	810	1150
6-Wolvertonish-a by Matt Fox	81	162	243	518	884	1250
7-10: 8-Atom bomb story; Tothish-a (by Sekowsky?). 9-Crandall-a	65	130	195	416	708	1000
11-20: 17-Atom bomb panels; anti-communist story; Hitler story. 19-Krenkel-a.	55	110	165	352	601	850
20-Robert Q. Sale-c	71	142	213	454	777	1100
21-Zombie cover	50	100	150	315	533	750
22-25,27: 25-Nostrand-a	50	100	150	315	533	750
26-Spider-Man prototype c/story	100	200	300	635	1093	1550
28-Last precode issue (1/55); Kubert-a; #1-28 contain 2-3 sci/fi stories each	50	100	150	315	533	750
29-41,43-49,51: 29-Variant-c exists with Feb. blanked out and Mar. printed on. Regular version just has Mar.	39	78	117	231	378	525
42,54,56-Krigstein-a	39	78	117	240	395	550
50,53,55-Torres-a	39	78	117	231	378	525
52-Oldest Iron Man prototype (2/57)	47	94	141	296	498	700

NOTE: Andru a-15, 27. Ayers a-14, 22, 28, 37. Bailey a-51. Briefer a-19, 20. Brodsky c-1, 3, 4, 8, 12-16, 19. Brodsky/Everett c-9. Cameron a-47. Colan a-11, 16, 17, 49, 52. Drucker a-37, 42, 45. Everett a-2, 9, 12, 32, 36, 39, 48; c-7, 11, 17, 39, 41, 50, 52, 53. Fass a-9, 10, 15, 24. Forte a-18, 27, 33-35, 52, 53. Heath a-13, 14; c-5, 10, 18. Keller a-3. Lawrence a-14, 17, 19, 23, 27, 28, 35. Maneely a-4, 8, 10, 16, 29, 35; c-2, 22, 26, 33, 38. Moldoff a-23. Morisi a-48, 52. Morrow a-46, 51. Orlando a-49, 50, 53. Powell a-12, 18, 34, 46. Reinman a-3, 13. Reinman a-12, 36. Romita a-10. Roussos a-8. Sale a-34, 47, 53; c-20. Sekowsky a-25. Sinnott a-14, 15, 38, 52. Torres a-53. Tothish-a by Andru-27. Wildey a-22, 48.

UNCANNY TALES
Marvel Comics Group: Dec, 1973 - No. 12, Oct, 1975

	GD 2.0	VG 4.0	FN 6.0	VF 8.0	VF/NM 9.0	NM- 9.2

	GD 2.0	VG 4.0	FN 6.0	VF 8.0	VF/NM 9.0	NM- 9.2
1-Crandall-r/Uncanny Tales #9('50s)	5	10	15	31	53	75
2-12: 7,12-Kirby-a	3	6	9	19	30	40

NOTE: *Ditko* reprints-#4, 6-8, 10-12.

UNCANNY X-FORCE
Marvel Comics: Dec, 2010 - No. 35, Feb, 2013 ($3.99)

1-17: 1-Wolverine, Psylocke, Archangel, Fantomex & Deadpool team; Opeña-a; Ribic-a						4.00
1-Variant-c by Clayton Crain						10.00
5.1 (5/11, $2.99) Albuquerque-a/Bianchi-c; Lady Deathstrike app.						3.00
18-Polybagged; Dark Angel Saga conclusion						4.00
19-35: 19-Grampa-c. 20-Yu-c						4.00
19.1 (3/12, $2.99) Remender-s/Tan-a; other-dimension X-Men vs. Apocalypse						3.00
...: The Apocalypse Solution 1 (5/11, $4.99) r/#1-3						5.00

UNCANNY X-FORCE (Marvel NOW!)
Marvel Comics: Mar, 2013 - No. 17, Mar, 2014 ($3.99)

1-17: 1-Storm, Psylocke, Spiral, Fantomex & Puck team; Bishop app.; Garney-a						4.00

UNCANNY X-MEN, THE (See X-Men, The, 1st series, #142-on)

UNCANNY X-MEN (2nd series) (X-Men Regenesis)
Marvel Comics: Dec, 2010 - No. 20, Dec, 2012 ($3.99)

1-10: 1-3-Gillen/Pacheco-a/c; Mr. Sinister app. 4-Peterson-a. 5-8-Land-a						4.00
1-Variant-c by Keown						6.00
11-20: 11-19-Avengers vs. X-Men x-over						4.00

UNCANNY X-MEN (3rd series) (Marvel NOW!)
Marvel Comics: Apr, 2013 - No. 35, Sept, 2015 ($3.99)

1-24,26-35: 1-Cyclops, Emma Frost, Magneto, Magik team; Bendis-s/Bachalo-a. 2,3-Avengers app. 5-7,10,11-Irving-a. 8,9,12,13,16,17,19,20-22,25,27-32-Bachalo-a. 12,13-Battle of the Atom. 23,24-Original Sin tie-in						4.00
25-($4.99) Original Sin tie-in						5.00
#600-(1/16, $5.99) Stories by various incl. Bendis, Pichelli, Immonen; Bachalo-a						6.00
Annual 1 (2/15, $4.99) Story of Eva Bell; Bendis-s/Sorrentino-a						5.00
Special 1 (8/14, $4.99) Death's Head & Iron Man app.; Ackins-a						5.00

UNCANNY X-MEN (4th series) (After Secret Wars)
Marvel Comics: Mar, 2016 - No. 19, May, 2017 ($3.99)

1-5: 1-Bunns-s/Land-a; Magneto, Psylocke, Sabretooth, M, and Archangel team						4.00
6-($4.99) Apocalypse Wars x-over; Lashley-a						5.00
7-19: 7-10-Apocalypse Wars x-over; Lashley-a. 11-14-Land-a; Hellfire Club app.						4.00
Annual 1 (1/17, $4.99) Bunn-s/Lashley-a; Elixir returns						5.00

UNCANNY X-MEN (5th series)
Marvel Comics: Jan, 2019 - No. 22, Sept, 2019 ($7.99/$3.99)

1-($7.99) Asrar-a; Apocalypse app.						8.00
2-9,12-22-($3.99) 2-Silva-a; Legion returns. 4-Nate Grey returns. 12-16,20-22-Larroca-a						4.00
10-($4.99) Leads into Uncanny X-Men Annual #1						5.00
11-($7.99) Cyclops returns; Captain America app.; Wolverine returns; McCrea-a						8.00
22-($4.99) Leads into Age of X-Man (2019 series); Larrocca-a						5.00
Annual 1 (3/19, $4.99) Cyclops saved by Cable; leads into #11; Carlos Gomez-a						5.00
...: Winter's End 1 (5/19, $4.99) Grace-s/Stockman-a; future Iceman app.						5.00

UNCANNY X-MEN AND THE NEW TEEN TITANS (See Marvel and DC Present...)

UNCANNY X-MEN: FIRST CLASS
Marvel Comics: Sept, 2009 - No. 8, Apr, 2010 ($2.99)

1-8: 1-The X-Men #94 (1975) team; Cruz-a; Inhumans app.						3.00
... Giant-Size (8/09, $3.99) short stories by various; Scottie Young-c						4.00

UNCENSORED MOUSE, THE
Eternity Comics: Apr, 1989 - No. 2, Apr, 1989 ($1.95, B&W)(Came sealed in plastic bag)
(Both contain racial stereotyping & violence)

1,2-Early Gottfredson strip-r in each	2	4	6	11	16	20

NOTE: *Both issues contain unauthorized reprints. Series was cancelled. Win Smith r-1, 2.*

UNCHARTED (Based on the video game)
DC Comics: Jan, 2012 - No. 6, Jun, 2012 ($2.99, limited series)

1-Williamson-s/Sandoval-a in all; Harris-c	4	8	12	25	40	55
2-6: 2,3-Harris-c	2	4	6	9	12	15

UNCLE CHARLIE'S FABLES (Also see Adventures in Wonderland)
Lev Gleason Publ.: Jan, 1952 - No. 5, Sept, 1952 (All have Biro painted-c)

1-Peter Pester by Hy Mankin begins, ends #5. Michael the Misfit by Kida; Janice & the Lazy Giant by Maurer, Lawrence the Fortune Teller app.; has photo of Biro	22	44	66	132	216	300
2-Fuje-a; Biro photo	14	28	42	81	118	155
3-5: 5-Two Who Built a Dream, The Blacksmith & The Gypsies by Maurer, The Sleepy King by Hubbel; has photo of Biro	13	26	39	72	101	130

NOTE: *Kida a-1. Hubbell a-5. Hy Mankin a-1-5. Norman Maurer a-1, 5. Dick Rockwell a-1.*

UNCLE DONALD & HIS NEPHEWS DUDE RANCH (See Dell Giant #52)

UNCLE DONALD & HIS NEPHEWS FAMILY FUN (See Dell Giant #38)

UNCLE GRANDPA (Based on the Cartoon Network series)
BOOM! Studios (kaboom!): Oct, 2014 - No. 4, Jan, 2015 ($3.99)

1-4-Short stories and gag pages; multiple covers on each						4.00
...: Good Morning Special 1 (4/16, $4.99) Short stories and gag pages; back-c mask						5.00
...: Pizza Steve Special 1 (6/15, $4.99) Short stories and gag pages						5.00

UNCLE JOE'S FUNNIES
Centaur Publications: 1938 (B&W)

1-Games, puzzles & magic tricks, some interior art; Bill Everett-c	290	580	870	1856	3178	4500

UNCLE MILTY (TV)
Victoria Publications/True Cross: Dec, 1950 - No. 4, July, 1951 (52 pgs.)(Early TV comic)

1-Milton Berle photo on-c of #1,2	61	122	183	390	670	950
2	39	78	117	240	395	550
3,4	34	68	102	199	325	450

UNCLE REMUS & HIS TALES OF BRER RABBIT (See Brer Rabbit, 4-Color #129, 208, 693)

UNCLE SAM
DC Comics (Vertigo): 1997 - No. 2, 1997 ($4.95, limited series)

	GD 2.0	VG 4.0	FN 6.0	VF 8.0	VF/NM 9.0	NM- 9.2
1,2-Alex Ross painted c/a. Story by Ross and Steve Darnell	1	2	3	5	6	8
Hardcover (1998, $17.95)						18.00
Softcover (2000, $9.95)						10.00

UNCLE SAM AND THE FREEDOM FIGHTERS
DC Comics: Sept, 2006 - No. 8, Apr, 2007 ($2.99, limited series)

1-8-Acuña-a/c; Gray & Palmiotti-s. 3-Intro. Black Condor						3.00
TPB (2007, $14.99) r/#1-8 and story from DCU Brave New World #1						15.00

UNCLE SAM AND THE FREEDOM FIGHTERS
DC Comics: Nov, 2007 - No. 8, Jun, 2008 ($2.99, limited series)

1-8-Gray & Palmiotti-s/Arlem-a/Johnson-c						3.00
...: Brave New World TPB (2008, $14.99) r/#1-8						15.00

UNCLE SAM QUARTERLY (Blackhawk #9 on)(See Freedom Fighters)
Quality Comics Group: Autumn, 1941 - No. 8, Autumn, 1943 (see National Comics)

1-Origin Uncle Sam; Fine/Eisner-c, chapter headings, 2 pgs. by Eisner; (2 versions: dark cover, no price; light cover with price sticker); Jack Cole-a	377	754	1131	2639	4620	6600
2-Cameos by The Ray, Black Condor, Quicksilver, The Red Bee, Alias the Spider, Hercules & Neon the Unknown; Eisner, Fine-c/a	168	336	504	1075	1838	2600
3-Tuska-c/a; Eisner-a(2)	135	270	405	864	1482	2100
4-Hitler app.	129	258	387	826	1413	2000
5,7-Hitler, Mussolini & Tojo-c	271	542	813	1734	2967	4200
6,8	90	180	270	576	988	1400

NOTE: *Kotzky (or Tuska) a-3-8.*

UNCLE SCROOGE (Disney) (Becomes Walt Disney's... #210 on) (See Cartoon Tales, Dell Giants #33, 55, Disney Comic Album, Donald and Scrooge, Dynabrite, Four Color #178, Gladstone Comic Album, Walt Disney's Comics & Stories #98, Walt Disney's ...)
Dell #1-39/Gold Key #40-173/Whitman #174-209: No. 386, 3/52 - No. 39, 8-10/62; No. 40, 12/62 - No. 209, 7/84

Four Color 386(#1)-in "Only a Poor Old Man" by Carl Barks; r-in Uncle Scrooge & Donald Duck #1('65) & The Best of Walt Disney Comics ('74). The 2nd cover app. of Uncle Scrooge (see Dell Giant Vacation Parade #2 (7/51) for 1st-c)	195	390	585	1600	4200	6800
1-(1986)-Reprints F.C. #386; given away with lithograph "Dam Disaster at Money Lake" & as a subscription offer giveaway to Gladstone subscribers	3	6	9	15	20	24
Four Color 456(#2)-in "Back to the Klondike" by Carl Barks; r-in Best of U.S. & D.D. #1('66) & Gladstone C.A. #4	95	190	285	760	1955	3150
Four Color 495(#3)-r-in #105	60	120	180	480	1240	2000
4(12-2/53-54)-r-in Gladstone Comic Album #1	48	96	144	374	862	1350
5-r-in Gladstone Special #2 & Walt Disney Digest #1	38	76	114	285	641	1000
6-r-in U.S. #106,165,233 & Best of U.S. & D.D. #1('66)	38	76	114	285	641	1000
7-The Seven Cities of Cibola by Barks; r-in #217 & Best of D.D. & U.S. #2 ('67)	32	64	96	230	515	800
8-10: 8-r-in #111,222. 9-r-in #104,214. 10-r-in #67	27	54	81	194	435	675
11-20: 11-r-in #237. 17-r-in #215. 19-r-in Gladstone C.A. #1. 20-r-in #213	23	46	69	161	356	550
21-30: 24-X-Mas-c. 26-r-in #211	16	32	48	112	249	385
31-35,37-40: 34-r-in #228. 40-X-Mas-c	13	26	39	91	201	310
36-1st app. Magica De Spell; Number one dime 1st identified by name	17	34	51	117	259	400
41-60: 48-Magica De Spell-c/story (3/64). 49-Sci-fi-c. 51-Beagle Boys-c/story						
(8/64)	11	22	33	73	157	240
61-63,65,66,68-71: 71-Last Barks issue w/original story (#71-he only storyboarded the script)	9	18	27	60	138	210
64-(7/66) Barks Vietnam War story "Treasure of Marco Polo" banned for reprints by Disney from 1977-1989 because of its Third World revolutionary war theme. It later appeared in the hardcover Carl Barks Library set (4/89) and Walt Disney's Uncle Scrooge Adventures #42 (1/97)	17	34	51	119	265	410
67,72,73: 67,72,73-Barks-r	8	16	24	51	86	120
74-84: 74-Barks-r(1pg.). 75-81,83-Not by Barks. 82,84-Barks-r begin	7	14	21	44	82	120
85-100	6	12	18	38	69	100
101-110	5	10	15	33	57	80
111-120	4	8	12	27	44	60
121-141,143-152,154-157	3	6	9	21	33	45
142-Reprints Four Color #456 with-c	4	8	12	22	35	48
153,158,162-164,166,168-170,178,180: No Barks	3	6	9	15	22	28
159-Whitman edition	3	6	9	17	26	35
159-160,165,167	3	6	9	17	26	35
161(r/#14), 171(r/#1), 177(r/#16),183(r/#6)-Barks-r	3	6	9	16	23	30
172(1/80),173(2/80)-Gold Key. Barks-a	3	6	9	17	26	35
174(3/80),175(4/80),176(5/80)-Whitman. Barks-a	4	8	12	22	35	48
177(6/80),178(7/80)	4	8	12	23	37	50
179(9/80)(r/#9)-(Very low distribution)	42	84	126	311	706	1100
180(11/80),181(12/80), r/#4-Barks. (r/#4)	8	16	24	51	96	140
182-195: 182-(50¢-c). 184,185,187,188-Barks-a. 182,186,191-194-No Barks. 189(r/#5), 190(r/#4), 195(r/o-Color #386)	3	6	9	16	23	30
182(1/81, 40¢-c) Cover price error variant	4	8	12	22	35	48
196(4/82),197(5/82): no Barks (r/#13)	3	6	9	17	26	35
198-209 (All #90038 on-c; pre-pack; no date or date code): 198(4/83), 199(5/83), 200(6/83), 201(6/83), 202(7/83), 203(7/83), 204(8/83), 205(8/83), 206(4/84), 207(5/83), 208(6/84), 209(7/84). 198-202,204-206: No Barks. 203(r/#12), 207(r/#93,92), 208(r/U.S. #18), 209(r/U.S. #21)-Barks-r	4	8	12	25	40	55
Uncle Scrooge & Money(G.K.)-Barks-r/from WDC&S #130 (3/67)						
	10	15	31	53	75	
Mini Comic #1(1976)(3-1/4x6-1/2")-r/U.S. #115; Barks-c						
	2	4	6	8	10	12

NOTE: *Barks c-Four Color 386, 456, 495, #4-37, 39, 40, 43-71.*

UNCLE SCROOGE (See Walt Disney's Uncle Scrooge for previous issues)
Boom Entertainment (BOOM! Kids): No. 384, Oct, 2009 - No. 404, Jun, 2011 ($2.99/$3.99)

384-399: 384-Magica de Spell app.; 2 covers. 392-399-Duck Tales						3.00
400-(2/11, $3.99) "Carl Barks" appas. as Scrooge story-teller; Rosa wraparound-c						4.00

Uncanny X-Men (2013 series) #8 © MAR

Uncle Scrooge (2015 series) #35 © DIS

Underwinter #5 © Fawkes & Snow

	GD 2.0	VG 4.0	FN 6.0	VF 8.0	VF/NM 9.0	NM- 9.2

400-$6.99) Deluxe Edition with Barks painted cover of Four Color #386 cover image — 7.00
401-404: 401-($3.99)-Rosa-s/a — 4.00
...: The Mysterious Stone Ray and Cash Flow (5/11, $6.99) reprints; Barks-s/a; Rosa-s/a — 7.00

UNCLE SCROOGE
IDW Publishing: Apr, 2015 - No. 54 ($3.99/$4.99)
1-Legacy numbered #405; art by Scarpa and others; multiple covers — 4.00
2-43-English translations of Dutch, Norwegian & Italian stories; multiple covers on each — 4.00
44-49,51-54 ($4.99) — 5.00
50-($5.99) Magica de Spell app. — 6.00

UNCLE SCROOGE AND DONALD DUCK
Gold Key: June, 1965 (25¢, paper cover)
1-Reprint of Four Color #386(#1) & lead story from Four Color #29 ... 9 / 18 / 27 / 60 / 120 / 180

UNCLE SCROOGE COMICS DIGEST
Gladstone Publishing: Dec, 1986 - No. 5, Aug, 1987 ($1.25, Digest-size)
1,3 ... 1 / 2 / 3 / 5 / 6 / 8
2,4 ... 6.00
5 (low print run) ... 1 / 2 / 3 / 5 / 7 / 9

UNCLE SCROOGE GOES TO DISNEYLAND (See Dell Giants)
Gladstone Publishing Ltd.: Aug, 1985 ($2.50)
1-Reprints Dell Giant w/new-c by Mel Crawford, based on old cover ... 2 / 4 / 6 / 8 / 10 / 12
...Comics Digest 1 ($1.50, digest size) ... 2 / 4 / 6 / 8 / 11 / 14

UNCLE SCROOGE IN COLOR
Gladstone Publishing: 1987 ($29.95, Hardcover, 9-1/4"X12-1/4", 96 pgs.)
nn-Reprints "Christmas on Bear Mountain" from Four Color 178 by Barks; Uncle Scrooge's Christmas Carol (published as Donald Duck & the Christmas Carol, A Little Golden Book), reproduced from the original art as adapted by Norman McGary from pencils by Barks; and Uncle Scrooge the Lemonade King, reproduced from the original art, plus Barks' original pencils ... 4 / 8 / 12 / 25 / 40 / 55
nn-Slipcase edition of 750, signed by Barks, issued at $79.95 ... 350.00

UNCLE SCROOGE: MY FIRST MILLIONS
IDW Publishing: Sept, 2018 - No. 4, Dec, 2018 ($3.99, limited series)
1-4-English version of Italian comics; Vitaliano-s; multiple covers — 4.00

UNCLE SCROOGE THE LEMONADE KING
Whitman Publishing Co.: 1960 (A Top Top Tales Book, 6-3/8"x7-5/8", 32 pgs.)
2465-Storybook pencilled by Carl Barks, finished art adapted by Norman McGary ... 33 / 66 / 99 / 238 / 532 / 825

UNCLE WIGGILY (See March of Comics #19) (Also see Animal Comics)
Dell Publishing Co.: No. 179, Dec, 1947 - No. 543, Mar, 1954
Four Color 179 (#1)-Walt Kelly-c ... 17 / 34 / 51 / 114 / 252 / 390
Four Color 221 (3/49)-Part Kelly-c ... 10 / 20 / 30 / 68 / 144 / 220
Four Color 276 (5/50), 320 (#1, 3/51) ... 7 / 14 / 21 / 49 / 92 / 135
Four Color 349 (9-10/51), 391 (4-5/52) ... 6 / 12 / 18 / 41 / 76 / 110
Four Color 428 (10/52), 503 (10/53), 543 ... 5 / 10 / 15 / 34 / 63 / 90

UNDATEABLE VARK, THE (Reprints from Cerebus in Hell)
Aardvark-Vanaheim: May, 2018 ($4.00, B&W)
1-Cerebus figures over Gustave Doré artwork of Hell; Uncanny X-Men #141-c swipe — 4.00

UNDEAD, THE
Chaos! Comics (Black Label): Feb, 2002 ($4.99, B&W)
1-Pulido-s/Denham-a — 5.00

UNDERCOVER GIRL (Starr Flagg) (See Extra Comics, Manhunt! & Trail Colt)
Magazine Enterprises: No. 5, 1952 - No. 7, 1954
5(#1)(A-1 #62)-Fallon of the F.B.I. in all ... 74 / 148 / 222 / 470 / 810 / 1150
6(A-1 #98), 7(A-1 #118)-All have Starr Flagg ... 63 / 126 / 189 / 403 / 689 / 975
NOTE: *Powell* c-6, 7. *Whitney* a-5-7.

UNDERDOG (TV)(See Kite Fun Book, March of Comics #426, 438, 467, 479)
Charlton Comics/Gold Key: July, 1970 - No. 10, Jan, 1972; Mar, 1975 - No. 23, Feb, 1979
1 (1st series, Charlton)-1st app. Underdog ... 23 / 46 / 69 / 161 / 356 / 550
2-10 ... 6 / 12 / 18 / 38 / 69 / 100
1 (2nd series, Gold Key) ... 7 / 14 / 21 / 44 / 82 / 120
2-10 ... 4 / 8 / 12 / 23 / 37 / 50
11-20: 13-1st app. Shack of Solitude ... 3 / 6 / 9 / 18 / 28 / 38
21-23 ... 3 / 6 / 9 / 19 / 30 / 40

UNDERDOG
Spotlight Comics: 1987 - No. 3?, 1987 ($1.50)
1-3 — 4.00

UNDERDOG (Volume 2)
Harvey Comics: Nov, 1993 - No. 5, July, 1994 ($2.25)
1-5 — 4.00
Summer Special (10/93, $2.25, 68 pgs.) — 4.00

UNDERDOG
American Mythology Productions: Apr, 2017 - No. 3, 2018 ($3.99)
1-3: 1-New stories and reprint #1 (1970); multiple covers incl. Action #1 swipe — 4.00
...and Pals 1-3 (2019, $3.99) New stories and reprint; 2 covers on each — 4.00
... 1975 #1 (2017, $3.99) Reprints stories from #23 (1979) and unpublished #24 — 4.00

UNDERHEIST
BOOM! Studios: Dec, 2023 - Present ($4.99)
1-Maria & David Lapham-s/David Lapham-a — 5.00

UNDERSEA AGENT
Tower Comics: Jan, 1966 - No. 6, Mar, 1967 (25¢, 68 pgs.)
1-Davy Jones, Undersea Agent begins ... 9 / 18 / 27 / 59 / 117 / 175
2-6: 2-Jones gains magnetic powers. 5-Origin & 1st app. of Merman. 6-Kane/Wood-c(r) ... 5 / 10 / 15 / 35 / 63 / 90
NOTE: *Gil Kane* a-3-6; c-4, 5. *Moldoff* a-2i.

UNDERSEA FIGHTING COMMANDOS (See Fighting Undersea...)
I.W. Enterprises: 1964
I.W. Reprint #1,2('64): 1-r/#? 2-r/#1; Severin-c ... 2 / 4 / 6 / 11 / 16 / 20

UNDERTAKER (World Wrestling Federation)(Also see WWE Undertaker)
Chaos! Comics: Feb, 1999 - No. 10, Jan, 2000 ($2.50/$2.95)
Preview (2/99) — 5.00
1-10: Reg. and photo covers for each. 1-(4/99) — 4.00
1-($6.95) DF Ed.; Brereton painted-c ... 2 / 4 / 6 / 11 / 16 / 20
...Halloween Special (10/99, $2.95) Reg. & photo-c ... 1 / 3 / 4 / 6 / 8 / 10
Wizard #0 — 6.00

UNDERWATER CITY, THE
Dell Publishing Co.: No. 1328, 1961
Four Color 1328-Movie, Evans-a ... 7 / 14 / 21 / 49 / 92 / 135

UNDERWINTER
Image Comics: Mar, 2017 - No. 6, Aug, 2017 ($3.99)
1-6-Ray Fawkes-s/a/c. 1-Lemire var-c. 2-Nguyen var-c. 3-Zdarsky var-c — 4.00

UNDERWINTER: A FIELD OF FEATHERS
Image Comics: Oct, 2017 - No. 5, Feb, 2018 ($3.99)
1-4-Ray Fawkes-s/a/c. 1-Fawkes var-c — 4.00

UNDERWORLD (...True Crime Stories)
D.S. Publishing Co.: Feb-Mar, 1948 - No. 9, June-July, 1949 (52 pgs.)
1-Moldoff (Shelly)-c; excessive violence ... 63 / 126 / 189 / 403 / 689 / 975
2-Moldoff (Shelly)-c; Ma Barker story used in SOTI, pg. 95; female electrocution panel; lingerie art ... 55 / 110 / 165 / 352 / 601 / 850
3-McWilliams-c/a; extreme violence, mutilation ... 48 / 96 / 144 / 302 / 514 / 725
4-Used in Love and Death by Legman; Ingels-a ... 55 / 110 / 165 / 352 / 601 / 850
5-Ingels-a ... 31 / 62 / 93 / 182 / 296 / 410
6-9: 8-Ravielli-a. 9-R.Q. Sale-a ... 24 / 48 / 72 / 140 / 230 / 320

UNDERWORLD
DC Comics: Dec, 1987 - No. 4, Mar, 1988 ($1.00, limited series, mature)
1-4 — 4.00

UNDERWORLD (Movie)
IDW Publishing: Sept, 2003; Dec, 2005 ($6.99)
1-Movie adaptation; photo-c — 7.00
... Evolution (12/05, $7.49) adaptation of movie sequel; Vazquez-a — 7.50
TPB (7/04, $19.99) r/#1 and Underworld:Red in Tooth and Claw #1-3 — 20.00

UNDERWORLD
Marvel Comics: Apr, 2006 - No. 5, Aug, 2006 ($2.99, limited series)
1-5: Staz Johnson-a. 2-Spider-Man app. 3,4-Punisher app. — 3.00

UNDERWORLD CRIME
Fawcett Publications: June, 1952 - No. 7, Sept, 1953
1 ... 41 / 82 / 123 / 256 / 428 / 600
2 ... 26 / 52 / 78 / 154 / 252 / 350
3-6 ... 22 / 44 / 66 / 132 / 216 / 300
7-(9/53)-Red hot poker/bondage/torture-c ... 730 / 1460 / 2190 / 5329 / 9415 / 13,500

UNDERWORLD: RED IN TOOTH AND CLAW (Movie)
IDW Publishing: Feb, 2004 - No. 3, Apr, 2004 ($3.99, limited series)
1-3-The early days of the Vampire and Lycan war; Postic & Marinkovich-a — 5.00

UNDERWORLD: RISE OF THE LYCANS (Movie)
IDW Publishing: Nov, 2008 - No. 2, Nov, 2008 ($3.99, limited series)
1,2-Greviour-s/Huerta-a — 4.00

	GD 2.0	VG 4.0	FN 6.0	VF 8.0	VF/NM 9.0	NM- 9.2

UNDERWORLD STORY, THE (Movie)
Avon Periodicals: 1950

	GD	VG	FN	VF	VF/NM	NM-
nn-(Scarce)-Ravielli-c	40	80	120	246	411	575

UNDERWORLD UNLEASHED
DC Comics: Nov, 1995 - No. 3, Jan, 1996 ($2.95, limited series)

1-3: Mark Waid scripts & Howard Porter-c/a(p)					4.00
...: Abyss: Hell's Sentinel 1-($2.95)-Alan Scott, Phantom Stranger, Zatanna app.					4.00
...: Apokolips-Dark Uprising 1 ($1.95)					4.00
...: Batman-Devil's Asylum 1-($2.95)-Batman app.					4.00
...: Patterns of Fear-($2.95)					4.00
TPB (1998, $17.95) r/#1-3 & Abyss-Hell's Sentinel					18.00

UNDISCOVERED COUNTRY
Image Comics: Nov, 2019 - Present ($3.99)

1-28-Snyder & Soule-s/Camuncoli-a					4.00
...: Destiny Man 1 (6/22, $3.99) Snyder & Soule-s/Camuncoli-a					4.00

UNEARTH
Image Comics: Jul, 2019 - No. 10, Mar, 2021 ($3.99)

1-10-Bunn & Strahm-s/Rivas-a					4.00

UNEARTHLY SPECTACULARS
Harvey Publications: Oct, 1965 - No. 3, Mar, 1967

	GD	VG	FN	VF	VF/NM	NM-
1-(12¢)-Tiger Boy; Simon-c	4	8	12	27	44	60
2-(25¢ giants)-Jack Q. Frost, Tiger Boy & Three Rocketeers app.; Williamson, Wood, Kane-a; r-1 story/Thrill-O-Rama #2	5	10	15	30	50	70
3-(25¢ giants)-Jack Q. Frost app.; Williamson/Crandall-a; r-from Alarming Advs. #1,1962	5	10	15	30	50	70

NOTE: *Crandall* a-3r. *G. Kane* a-2. *Orlando* a-3. *Simon, Sparling, Wood* c-2. *Simon/Kirby* a-3r. *Torres* a-1?. *Wildey* a-1(3). *Williamson* a-2, 3r. *Wood* a-2(2).

UNETHICAL SPIDER-VARK, THE (Cerebus in Hell)
Aardvark-Vanaheim: Jul, 2021 ($4.00, B&W)

1-Cerebus figures placed over Gustave Doré artwork; Amaz. Spider-Man #129-c swipe					4.00

UNEXPECTED, THE (Formerly Tales of the...)
National Per. Publ./DC Comics: No. 105, Feb-Mar, 1968 - No. 222, May, 1982

	GD	VG	FN	VF	VF/NM	NM-
105-Begin 12¢ cover price	7	14	21	44	82	120
106-113: 113-Last 12¢ issue (6-7/69)	5	10	15	33	57	80
114,115,117,118,120-125	4	8	12	23	37	50
116 (36 pgs.)-Wrightson-a	4	8	12	25	40	55
119-Wrightson-a, 8pgs.(36 pgs.)	5	10	15	31	53	75
126,127,129-136-(52 pgs.)	4	8	12	22	35	48
128(52 pgs.)-Wrightson-a	5	10	15	31	53	75
137-156	3	6	9	15	22	28
157-162-(100 pgs.)	4	8	12	28	47	65
163-188: 187,188-(44 pgs.)	2	4	6	11	16	20
189,190,192-195 ($1.00, 68 pgs.): 189 on are combined with House of Secrets & The Witching Hour	2	4	6	13	18	22
191-Rogers-a(p) ($1.00, 68 pgs.)	3	6	9	14	19	24
196-222: 200-Return of Johnny Peril by Tuska. 205-213-Johnny Peril app.						
210-Time Warp story. 222-Giffen-a	2	4	6	8	10	12

NOTE: *Neal Adams* a-110, 112-115, 118, 121, 124. *J. Craig* a-195. *Ditko* a-189, 221p, 222p, c-222. *Drucker* a-107r, 132r. *Giffen* a-219, 222. *Kaluta* c-203, 212. *Kirby* a-127r, 162. *Kubert* c-204, 214-216, 219-221. *Mayer* a-217p, 220, 221p. *Moldoff* a-136r. *Moreira* a-133. *Mortimer* a-212p. *Newton* a-204p. *Orlando* a-202; c-191. *Perez* a-217p. *Redondo* a-155, 166, 195. *Reese* a-145. *Sparling* a-107, 205-209p, 212p. *Spiegle* a-217. *Starlin* c-198. *Toth* a-126r, 127r. *Tuska* a-127, 132, 134, 136, 139, 152, 180, 200p. *Wildey* a-128r, 193. *Wood* a-122i, 133i, 137i, 138i. *Wrightson* a-161r(2 pgs.). Johnny Peril in #106-114, 116, 117, 200, 205-213.

UNEXPECTED, THE
DC Comics: Dec, 2011 ($7.99, one-shot)

1-Short horror stories by various incl. Gibbons, Thompson, Lapham, Fialkov; 2 covers				8.00	

UNEXPECTED, THE (Follows events of Dark Nights: Metal)
DC Comics: Aug, 2018 - No. 8, Mar, 2019 ($2.99)

1-8: 1-Orlando-s/Sook & Nord-a; intro. Firebrand, Bad Samaritan & Neon the Unknown. 4-Huntress app. 4-8-Hawkman app.					3.00

UNEXPECTED ANNUAL, THE (See DC Special Series #4)

UNFOLLOW
DC Comics (Vertigo): Jan, 2016 - No 18, Jun, 2017 ($3.99)

1-18: 1-Rob Williams-s/Mike Dowling-a. 6-R.M. Guéra-a. 7-Marguerite Sauvage-a					4.00
... Special Edition 1 (3/16, $4.99) r/#1&2					5.00

UNHOLY BASTARDS (Characters from The Goon)
Albatross Funnybooks: 2020 ($3.99, one-shot)

1-Eric Powell-c/Sniegoski-s/Mannion & Brown-a; The Goon and Franky app.					4.00

UNHOLY GRAIL
AfterShock Comics: July, 2017 - No. 5, Dec, 2017 ($3.99)

1-5-Cullen Bunn-s/Mirko Colak-a. 1-Multiple covers. 2-Covers by Colak & Francavilla					4.00

UNHOLY UNION
Image Comics (Top Cow): July, 2007 ($3.99, one-shot)

	GD	VG	FN	VF	VF/NM	NM-
1-Witchblade & The Darkness meet Hulk, Ghost Rider & Doctor Strange; Silvestri-c			1	3	4	6	8	10

UNIDENTIFIED FLYING ODDBALL (See Walt Disney Showcase #52)

UNION
Image Comics (WildStorm Productions): June, 1993 - No. 0, July, 1994 ($1.95, lim. series)

0-(7/94, $2.50)					4.00
0-Alternate Portacio-c (See Deathblow #5)					5.00
1-($2.50)-Embossed foil-c; Texeira-c/a in all					5.00
1-($1.95)-Newsstand edition w/o foil-c					4.00
2-4: 4-(7/94)					4.00

UNION
Image Comics (WildStorm Prod.): Feb, 1995 - No. 9, Dec, 1995 ($2.50)

1-3,5-9: 3-Savage Dragon app. 6-Fairchild from Gen 13 app.					4.00
4-($1.95, Newsstand)-WildStorm Rising Pt. 3					4.00
4-($2.50, Direct Market)-WildStorm Rising Pt. 3, bound-in card					5.00

UNION, THE (Tie-in series to The King in Black crossover event)
Marvel Comics: Feb, 2021 - No. 5, Jul, 2021 ($3.99)

1-5-Grist-s/Di Vito-a; team of Britannia, Snakes, Kelpie and The Choir; Union Jack app.					4.00

UNION: FINAL VENGEANCE
Image Comics (WildStorm Productions): Oct, 1997 ($2.50)

1-Golden-c/Heisler-s					4.00

UNION JACK
Marvel Comics: Dec, 1998 - No. 3, Feb, 1999 ($2.99, limited series)

1-3-Raab-s/Cassaday-s/a					4.00

UNION JACK
Marvel Comics: Nov, 2006 - No. 4, Feb, 2007 ($2.99, limited series)

1-4-Gage-s/Perkins-c/a					3.00
...: London Falling TPB (2007, $10.99) r/#1-4; Perkins sketch page					11.00

UNITED COMICS (Formerly Fritzi Ritz #7; has Fritzi Ritz logo)
United Features Syndicate: Aug, 1940; No. 8, 1950 - No. 26, Jan-Feb, 1953

	GD	VG	FN	VF	VF/NM	NM-
1(68 pgs.)-Fritzi Ritz & Phil Fumble	36	72	108	214	347	480
8-Fritzi Ritz, Abbie & Slats	16	32	48	92	144	195
9-20: 20-Strange As It Seems; Russell Patterson Cheesecake-a	14	28	42	82	121	160
21-(3-4/52) 2 pg. early Peanuts by Schulz; ties with Tip Top Comics #173 for 1st app. of Peanuts in comics. (Also see Tip Topper Comics)	343	686	1029	2400	4200	6000
22-(5-6/52) 2 pgs. early Peanuts by Schulz (3rd app.)	57	114	171	362	619	875
23-26: 23-(7-8/52). 24-(9-10/52). 25-(11-12/52). 26-(1-2/53). All have 2 pgs. early Peanuts by Schulz	34	68	102	199	325	450

NOTE: *Abbie & Slats* reprinted from Tip Top.

UNITED NATIONS, THE (See Classics Illustrated Special Issue)

UNITED STATES AIR FORCE PRESENTS: THE HIDDEN CREW
U.S. Air Force: 1964 (36 pgs.)

	GD	VG	FN	VF	VF/NM	NM-
nn-Schaffenberger-a	3	6	9	14	20	25

UNITED STATES FIGHTING AIR FORCE (Also see U.S. Fighting Air Force)
Superior Comics Ltd.: Sept, 1952 - No. 29, Oct, 1956

	GD	VG	FN	VF	VF/NM	NM-
1	20	40	60	120	195	270
2	14	28	42	78	112	145
3-10	10	20	30	56	76	95
11-29	9	18	27	52	69	85

UNITED STATES MARINES
William H. Wise/Life's Romances Publ. Co./Magazine Ent. #5-8/Toby Press #7-11: 1943 - No. 4, 1944; No. 5, 1952 - No. 8, 1952; No. 7 - No. 11, 1953

	GD	VG	FN	VF	VF/NM	NM-
nn-Mart Bailey-c/a; Marines in the Pacific theater	43	86	129	271	461	650
2-Bailey-a; Tojo classic-c	155	310	465	992	1696	2400
3-Classic WWII Tojo-c	142	284	426	909	1555	2200
4-WWII photos; Tony DiPreta-a; grey-tone-c	28	56	84	165	270	375
5(A-1 #55)-Bailey-a; 6(A-1 #60), 8(A-1 #72)	16	32	48	94	147	200
7(A-1 #68) Flamethrower with burning bodies-c	245	490	735	1568	2684	3800
7-11 (Toby)	15	30	45	85	130	185

NOTE: *Powell* a-5-7.

UNITED STATES OF CAPTAIN AMERICA, THE
Marvel Comics: Aug, 2021 - No. 5, Dec, 2021 ($4.99)

1-5: 1-1st app. Aaron Fischer. 2-Intro. Nichelle Wright. 3-Intro. Joe Gomez					5.00

UNITED STATES OF MURDER INC., THE
Marvel Comics (Icon): May, 2014 - No. 6, Feb, 2015 ($3.99)

1-6-Bendis-s/Oeming-a					4.00

UNITED STATES OF MURDER INC.
DC Comics (Jinxworld): Nov, 2018 - No. 6, Apr, 2019 ($3.99)

1-6-Bendis-s/Oeming-a; second story arc					4.00

UNITY
Valiant: No. 0, Aug, 1992 - No. 1, 1992 (Free comics w/limited dist., 20 pgs.)

	GD	VG	FN	VF	VF/NM	NM-
0 (Blue)-Prequel to Unity x-overs in all Valiant titles; B. Smith-c/a. (Free to everyone that bought all 8 titles that month.)	1	3	4	6	8	10
0 (Red)-Same as above, but w/red logo (5,000)	5	10	15	30	50	70
1-Epilogue to Unity x-overs; B. Smith-c/a. (1 copy available for every 8 Valiant books ordered by dealers.)						5.00
1 (Gold), 1-(Platinum)-Promotional copy.	2	4	6	9	12	15
...: The Lost Chapter 1 (Yearbook) (2/95, $3.95)-"1994" in indicia						6.00

UNITY
Valiant Entertainment: Nov, 2013 - No. 25, Dec, 2015 ($3.99)

1-24: Multiple covers on each. 1-Kindt-s/Braithwaite-a. 5,6-Cafu-a					4.00
25-($4.99) Short stories by various incl. Kindt, Asmus, Kano, Jordan, Schkade					5.00
#0 (10/14, $3.99) Kindt-s/Nord-a; the story of Unit Y in WW One					4.00

UNITY 2000 (See preludes in Shadowman #3,4 flipbooks)
Acclaim Comics: Nov, 1999 - No. 3, Jan, 2000 ($2.50, unfinished limited series planned for 6 issues)

Preview -B&W plot preview and cover art; paper cover					4.00
1-3-Starlin-s/Shooter-s					4.00

UNIVERSAL MONSTERS
Dark Horse Comics: 1993 ($4.95/$5.95, 52 pgs.)(All adapt original movies)

	GD	VG	FN	VF	VF/NM	NM-
Creature From the Black Lagoon nn-($4.95)-Art Adams/Austin-c/a	2	4	6	9	12	15
Dracula nn-($4.95), Frankenstein nn-($3.95)-Painted-c/a, The Mummy nn-($4.95)-Painted-c	1	2	3	4	5	7
...: Cavalcade of Horror TPB (1/06, $19.95) r/one-shots; Eric Powell intro. & cover						20.00

UNIVERSAL MONSTERS: DRACULA
Image Comics: Oct, 2023 - No. 4, Jan, 2024 ($4.99, limited series)

1-4-Tynion IV-s/Simmonds-a; adaptation of the Tod Browning's 1931 film					5.00

UNIVERSAL PICTURES PRESENTS DRACULA-THE MUMMY & OTHER STORIES
Dell Publishing Co.: Sept-Nov, 1963 (one-shot, 84 pgs.) (Also see Dell Giants)

The Unexpected #159 © DC

Unity (2013 series) #19 © VAL

Unnatural #1 © Mirka Andolfo

	GD 2.0	VG 4.0	FN 6.0	VF 8.0	VF/NM 9.0	NM- 9.2

02-530-311-r/Dracula 12-231-212, The Mummy 12-437-211 & part of Ghost Stories No. 1
16 32 48 108 239 370

UNIVERSAL SOLDIER (Movie)
Now Comics: Sept, 1992 - No. 3, Nov, 1992 (Limited series, polybagged, mature)
1-3 ($2.50, Direct Sales) 1-Movie adapatation; hologram on-c (all direct sales editions have painted-c) — 5.00
1-3 ($1.95, Newsstand)-Rewritten & redrawn code approved version; all newsstand editions have photo-c — 4.00

UNIVERSE
Image Comics (Top Cow): Sept, 2001 - No. 8, July, 2002 ($2.50)
1-7-Jenkins-s — 3.00
8-($4.95) extra shorts by Jenkins; pin-up pages — 5.00

UNIVERSE X (See Earth X)
Marvel Comics: Sept, 2000 - No. 12, Sept, 2001 ($3.99/$3.50, limited series)
0-Ross-c/Braithwaite-a/Ross & Krueger-s — 4.00
1-12: 5-Funeral of Captain America — 4.00
... Beasts (6/00, $3.99) Yeates-a/Ross-c — 4.00
... Cap (Capt. America) (2/01, $3.99) Yeates & Totleben-a/Ross-c; Cap dies — 4.00
... 4 (Fantastic 4) (10/00, $3.99) Brent Anderson-a/Ross-c — 4.00
... Iron Men (9/01, $3.99) Anderson-a/Ross-c; leads into #12 — 4.00
... Omnibus (6/01, $3.99) Ross B&W sketchbook and character bios — 4.00
Sketchbook- Wizard supplement; B&W character sketches and bios — 3.00
...Spidey (1/01, $3.99) Romita Sr. flashback-a/Guice-a/Ross-c — 4.00
...X (11/01, $3.99) Series conclusion; Braithwaith-a/Ross wraparound-c — 4.00
Volume 1 TPB (1/02, $24.95) r/#0-7 & Spidey, 4, & Cap; new Ross-c — 25.00
Volume 2 TPB (6/02, $24.95) r/#8-12 &X, Beasts, Iron Men and Omnibus — 25.00

UNKINDNESS OF RAVENS, AN
BOOM! Studios: Sept, 2020 - No. 5, Jan, 2021 ($3.99, limited series)
1-5-Dan Panosian-s/Marianna Ignazzi-a — 4.00

UNKNOWN, THE
BOOM! Studios: May, 2009 - No. 4, Aug, 2009 ($3.99)
1-4-Mark Waid-s/Minck Oosterveer-a; two covers on each — 4.00
...: The Devil Made Flesh 1-4 (9/09 - No. 4, 12/09, $3.99) Waid-s/Oosterveer-a — 4.00

UNKNOWN MAN, THE (Movie)
Avon Periodicals: 1951
nn-Kinstler-c 40 80 120 246 411 575

UNKNOWN SOLDIER (Formerly Star-Spangled War Stories)
National Periodical Publications/DC Comics: No. 205, Apr-May, 1977 - No. 268, Oct, 1982 (See Our Army at War #168 for 1st app.)
205 3 6 9 19 30 40
206-210,220,221,251: 220,221 (44pgs.). 251-Enemy Ace begins
3 6 9 14 19 24
211-218,222-247,250,252-264 2 4 6 11 16 20
219-Miller-a (44 pgs.) 3 6 9 16 23 30
248,249,265-267: 248,249-Origin. 265-267-Enemy Ace vs. Balloon Buster.
2 4 6 11 16 20
268-Death of Unknown Soldier 3 6 9 21 33 45
NOTE: *Chaykin* a-234. *Evans* a-265-267; c-235. *Kubert* c-Most. *Miller* a-219p. *Severin* a-251-253, 260, 261, 265-267. *Simonson* a-254-256. *Spiegle* a-258, 259, 262-264.

UNKNOWN SOLDIER (Also see Brave &the Bold #146)
DC Comics: Winter, 1988-'89 - No. 12, Dec, 1989 ($1.50, maxi-series, mature)
1-12: 8-Begin $1.75-c — 5.00

UNKNOWN SOLDIER
DC Comics (Vertigo): Apr, 1997 - No 4, July, 1997 ($2.50, mini-series)
1-Ennis-s/Plunkett-a/Bradstreet-c in all — 6.00
2-4 — 4.00
TPB (1998, $12.95) r/#1-4 — 13.00

UNKNOWN SOLDIER
DC Comics (Vertigo): Dec, 2008 - No. 25, Dec, 2010 ($2.99)
1-25: 1-Dysart-s/Ponticelli-a; intro. Lwanga Moses; two covers by Kordey and Corben. 2-20,22-25-Ponticelli-a. 21-Veitch-a — 3.00
...: Beautiful World TPB (2011, $14.99) r/#21-25; Dysart afterword; sketch/design art — 15.00
...: Dry Season TPB (2010, $14.99) r/#15-20; war history — 15.00
...: Easy Kill TPB (2010, $17.99) r/#7-14; war history — 18.00
...: Haunted House TPB (2009, $9.99) r/#1-6; glossary — 10.00

UNKNOWN WORLD (Strange Stories From Another World #2 on)
Fawcett Publications: June, 1952
1-Norman Saunders painted-c 148 296 444 947 1624 2300

UNKNOWN WORLDS (See Journey Into...)

UNKNOWN WORLDS

American Comics Group/Best Synd. Features: Aug, 1960 - No. 57, Aug, 1967
1-Schaffenberger-c 27 54 81 189 420 650
2-Dinosaur-c/story 12 24 36 79 170 260
3-5 9 18 27 61 123 185
6-11: 9-Dinosaur-c/story. 11-Last 10¢ issue 7 14 21 49 92 135
12-19: 12-Begin 12¢ issues?; ends #57 6 12 18 38 69 100
20-Herbie cameo (12-1/62-63) 8 16 24 51 96 140
21-35: 27-Devil on-c. 31-Herbie one pagers thru #39 5 11 15 30 50 70
36-"The People vs. Hendricks" by Craig; most popular ACG story ever
6 12 18 38 69 100
37-46 4 8 12 28 47 65
47-Williamson-a r-from Adventures Into the Unknown #96, 3 pgs.; Craig-a
5 10 15 30 50 70
48-57: 53-Frankenstein app. 4 8 12 27 44 60
NOTE: *Ditko* a-49, 50p, 54. *Forte* a-3, 6, 11. *Landau* a-56(2). *Reinman* a-3, 9, 13, 20, 22, 23, 36, 38, 54. *Whitney* c/a-most issues. John Force, Magic Agent-35, 36, 48, 50, 52, 54, 56.

UNKNOWN WORLDS OF FRANK BRUNNER
Eclipse Comics: Aug, 1985 - No. 2, Aug, 1985 ($1.75)
1,2-B&W-r in color — 4.00

UNKNOWN WORLDS OF SCIENCE FICTION
Marvel Comics: Jan, 1975 - No. 6, Nov, 1975; 1976 ($1.00, B&W Magazine)
1-Williamson/Krenkel/Torres/Frazetta-r/Witzend #1, Neal Adams-r/Phase 1; Brunner & Kaluta-r; Freas/Romita-c 3 6 9 21 33 45
2-6: 5-Kaluta text illos 3 6 9 14 20 26
Special 1(1976,100 pgs.)-Newton painted-c 3 6 9 18 28 38
NOTE: *Brunner* a-2; c-4, 6. *Buscema* a-Special 1p. *Chaykin* a-5. *Colan* a(p)-1, 3, 5, 6. *Corben* a-4. *Kaluta* a-2, Special 1(text illos); c-2. *Morrow* a-3, 5. *Nino* a-3, 6, Special 1. *Perez* a-2, 3. Ray Bradbury interview in #1.

UNLIMITED ACCESS (Also see Marvel Vs. DC)
Marvel Comics: Dec, 1997 - No. 4, Mar, 1998 ($2.99/$1.99, limited series)
1-Spider-Man, Wonder Woman, Green Lantern & Hulk app. — 5.00
2,3-($1.99): 2-X-Men, Legion of Super-Heroes app. 3-Original Avengers vs. original Justice League — 4.00
4-($2.99) Amalgam Legion vs. Darkseid & Magneto — 5.00

UN-MEN, THE
DC Comics (Vertigo): Oct, 2007 - No. 13, Oct, 2008 ($2.99)
1-13-Whalen-s/Hawthorne-a/Hanuka-c — 3.00
...: Children of Paradox TPB (2008, $19.99) r/#6-13 — 20.00
...: Get Your Freak On! TPB (2008, $9.99) r/#1-5; cover gallery — 10.00

UNNATURAL
Image Comics: Jul, 2018 - No. 12, Aug, 2019 ($3.99)
1-12-Mirka Andolfo-s/a; English version of a 2016 Italian comic series — 4.00

UNNATURAL: BLUE BLOOD
Image Comics: May, 2022 - Present ($3.99)
1-5-Mirka Andolfo-s/a; Bidarella-a — 4.00

UN/SACRED
Ablaze Publishing: 2019 - No. 7, 2020 ($3.99)
1-7-Mirka Andolfo-s/a; multiple covers on each — 4.00
Vol. 2 (2020 - No. 6, 2021) 1-6-Mirka Andolfo-s/a — 4.00

UNSANE (Formerly Mighty Bear #13, 14? or The Outlaws #10-14?)(Satire)
Star Publications: Dec, 1954
15-Disbrow-a(2); L. B. Cole-c 41 82 123 256 428 600

UNSEEN, THE
Visual Editions/Standard Comics: No. 5, 1952 - No. 15, July, 1954
5-Horror stories in all; Toth-a 84 168 252 538 919 1300
6,7,9,10-Jack Katz-a 53 106 159 334 567 800
8,11,13,14 45 90 135 284 480 675
12,15-Toth-a. 12-Tuska-a 57 114 171 362 619 875
NOTE: *Nick Cardy* c-12. *Fawcette* a-13, 14. *Sekowsky* a-7, 8(2), 10, 13, 15.

UNSTOPPABLE DOOM PATROL
DC Comics: May, 2023 - No. 7, Dec, 2023 ($3.99)
1-7-Culver-s/Burnham-a. 1-Batman & Peacemaker app. — 4.00

UNSTOPPABLE WASP, THE
Marvel Comics: Mar, 2017 - No. 8, Oct, 2017 ($3.99)
1-8: 1-6-Whitley-s/Charretier-a. 1-Ms. Marvel & Mockingbird app. 2,3-Moon Girl app. — 4.00

UNSTOPPABLE WASP, THE
Marvel Comics: Dec, 2018 - No. 10, Sept, 2019 ($3.99)
1-10: Whitley-s. 1-5,8-10-Gurihiru-a. 7-Winter Soldier and Young Avengers app. — 4.00

UNTAMED
Marvel Comics (Epic Comics/Heavy Hitters): June, 1993 - No. 3, Aug, 1993 ($1.95, lim. series)

Grade columns: **GD 2.0 · VG 4.0 · FN 6.0 · VF 8.0 · VF/NM 9.0 · NM- 9.2**

	GD 2.0	VG 4.0	FN 6.0	VF 8.0	VF/NM 9.0	NM- 9.2
1-($2.50)-Embossed-c						5.00
2,3						4.00

UNTAMED LOVE (Also see Frank Frazetta's Untamed Love)
Quality Comics Group (Comic Magazines): Jan, 1950 - No. 5, Sept, 1950

	GD 2.0	VG 4.0	FN 6.0	VF 8.0	VF/NM 9.0	NM- 9.2
1-Ward-c, Gustavson-a	48	96	144	302	514	725
2,4: 2-5-Photo-c	28	56	84	165	270	375
3,5-Gustavson-a	39	78	117	231	378	525

UNTOLD LEGEND OF CAPTAIN MARVEL, THE
Marvel Comics: Apr, 1997 - No. 3, June, 1997 ($2.50, limited series)
1-3 ... 5.00

UNTOLD LEGEND OF THE BATMAN, THE (Also see Promotional section)
DC Comics: July, 1980 - No. 3, Sept, 1980 (Limited series)

	GD 2.0	VG 4.0	FN 6.0	VF 8.0	VF/NM 9.0	NM- 9.2
1-Origin; Joker-c; Byrne's 1st work at DC	3	6	9	14	20	25
2,3	2	4	6	8	10	12

NOTE: *Aparo* a-1i, 2, 3. *Byrne* a-1p.

UNTOLD ORIGIN OF THE FEMFORCE, THE (Also see Femforce)
AC Comics: 1989 ($4.95, 68 pgs.)
1-Origin Femforce; Bill Black-a(i) & scripts ... 6.00

UNTOLD TALES OF BLACKEST NIGHT (Also see Blackest Night crossover titles)
DC Comics: Dec, 2010 ($4.99, one-shot)
1-Short stories by various incl. Johns, Benes, Booth; 2 covers by Kirkham & Van Sciver ... 5.00

UNTOLD TALES OF CHASTITY
Chaos! Comics: Nov, 2000 ($2.95, one-shot)
1-Origin; Steven Grant-s/Peter Vale-c/a ... 5.00
1-Premium Edition with glow in the dark cover ... 10.00

UNTOLD TALES OF I HATE FAIRYLAND (Also see I Hate Fairyland)
Image Comics: Jul, 2023 - No. 5, Nov, 2023 ($3.99, limited series)
1-5-Anthology by Skottie Young and guest creators. 1-Conley; Rankine-s/a ... 4.00

UNTOLD TALES OF LADY DEATH
Chaos! Comics: Nov, 2000 ($2.95, one-shot)

	GD 2.0	VG 4.0	FN 6.0	VF 8.0	VF/NM 9.0	NM- 9.2
1-Origin of Lady Death; Cremator app.; Kaminski-s	1	3	4	6	8	10

1-Premium Edition with glow in the dark cover by Steven Hughes ... 15.00

UNTOLD TALES OF PUNISHER MAX
Marvel Comics: Aug, 2012 - No. 5, Dec, 2012 ($4.99/$3.99, limited series)
1-($4.99) Anthology; Starr-s/Boschi-a/c ... 5.00
2-5-($3.99) 2-Andrews-c. 3-Ribic-c. 5-Skottie Young-c/Del Mundo-c ... 4.00

UNTOLD TALES OF PURGATORI
Chaos! Comics: Nov, 2000 ($2.95, one-shot)
1-Purgatori in 57 B.C.; Rio-a/Grant-s ... 3.00
1-Premium Edition with glow in the dark cover ... 10.00

UNTOLD TALES OF SPIDER-MAN (Also see Amazing Fantasy #16-18)
Marvel Comics: Sept, 1995 - No. 25, Sept, 1997 (99¢)
1-Kurt Busiek scripts begin; Pat Olliffe-c/a plus #9. ... 5.00
2-22, -1(7/97), 23-25: 2-1st app. Batwing. 4-1st app. The Spacemen (Gantry, Orbit, Satellite & Vacuum). 8-1st app. The Headsman; The Enforcers (The Big Man, Montana, The Ox & Fancy Dan) app. 9-Ron Frenz-a. 10-1st app. Commanda. 16-Reintro Mary Jane Watson. 21-X-Men-c/app. 25-Green Goblin ... 4.00
...'96-(1996, $1.95, 46 pgs.)-Kurt Busiek scripts; Mike Allred-c/a; Kurt Busiek & Pat Olliffe app. in back-up story; contains pin-ups ... 5.00
...'97-(1997, $1.95)-Wraparound-c ... 5.00
...: Strange Encounters ('98, $5.99) Dr. Strange app. ... 6.00

UNTOLD TALES OF THE NEW UNIVERSE (Based on Marvel's 1986 New Universe titles)
Marvel Comics: May, 2006 ($2.99, series of one-shots)
...: D. P. 7 - Takes place between issues #4 & 5 of D. P. 7 series; Bright-a/Cebulski-s ... 3.00
...: Justice - Peter David-s/Carmine Di Giandomenico-a ... 3.00
...: Nightmask - Takes place between issues #4 & 5 of Nightmask series; The Gnome app. ... 3.00
...: Psi-Force - Tony Bedard-s/Russ Braun-a ... 3.00
...: Star Brand - Romita & Romita Jr.-c/Pulido-a ... 3.00
TPB (2006, $15.99) r/one-shots & stories from Amaz. Fantasy #18,19 & New Avengers #16 ... 16.00

UNTOUCHABLES, THE (TV)
Dell Publishing Co.: No. 1237, 10-12/61 - No. 4, 8-10/62 (All have Robert Stack photo-c)

	GD 2.0	VG 4.0	FN 6.0	VF 8.0	VF/NM 9.0	NM- 9.2
Four Color 1237(#1)	18	36	54	124	275	425
Four Color 1286	13	26	39	89	195	300
01-879-207, 12-879-210(01879-210 on inside)	9	18	27	59	117	175

UNTOUCHABLES
Caliber Comics: Aug, 1997 - No. 4 ($2.95, B&W)
1-4: 1-Pruett-s; variant covers by Kaluta & Showman ... 4.00

UNUSUAL COMICS
Bell Features: No date (1940s)(10¢)
8-Zago Jungle Princess ... (a VG copy sold in 2018 for $185)

UNUSUAL TALES (Blue Beetle & Shadows From Beyond #50 on)
Charlton Comics: Nov, 1955 - No. 49, Mar-Apr, 1965

	GD 2.0	VG 4.0	FN 6.0	VF 8.0	VF/NM 9.0	NM- 9.2
1-Horror stories	41	82	123	256	428	600
2	22	44	66	128	209	290
3-5	18	36	54	103	162	220
6-Ditko-c only	26	52	78	154	252	350
7,8-Ditko-c/a. 8-Robot-c	37	74	111	222	361	500
9-Ditko-a (20 pgs.)	39	78	117	231	378	525
10-Ditko-c/a	39	78	117	231	378	525
11-(3/58, 68 pgs.)-Ditko-a(4)	39	78	117	231	395	550
12,14-Ditko-a	24	48	72	142	234	325
15-Ditko-c/a	9	18	27	57	111	165
13,16-20	34	68	102	204	332	460
21,24,28	7	14	21	48	89	130
22,23,25-27,29-Ditko-a/c	11	22	33	73	157	240
30-49	6	12	18	38	69	100

NOTE: *Colan* a-11. *Ditko* c-22, 23, 25-27, 31(part).

UNWORTHY THOR, THE (See Original Sin)
Marvel Comics: Jan, 2017 - No. 5, May, 2017 ($3.99)
1-5-Aaron-s/Coipel-a; multiple covers; Beta Ray Bill app. 2-Thanos app. ... 4.00

UNWRITTEN, THE
DC Comics (Vertigo): July, 2009 - No. 54, Dec, 2013 ($1.00/$2.99)
1-($1.00) Intro. Tommy Taylor; Mike Carey-s/Peter Gross-a; two covers (white & black) ... 3.00
2-16,18-31,(31.5), 32, (32.5), 33, (33.5), 34, (34.5), (35.5), 36-49-($2.99): 31.5-Art by Gross, Kaluta, Geary & Talbot. 37-Series re-cap ... 3.00
17-($3.99) Story printed sideways; Pick-a-Story format ... 4.00
35-($4.99) ... 5.00
50-(8/13, $4.99) Fables characters app.; Carey & Willingham-s; Gross & Buckingham-a ... 5.00
51-54-Fables characters app. ... 3.00
...: Dead Man's Knock TPB (2011, $14.99) r/#13-18; intro. by novelist Steven Hall ... 15.00
...: Inside Man TPB (2010, $12.99) r/#6-12; intro. by Paul Cornell ... 13.00
...: Tommy Taylor and the Bogus Identity TPB (2010, $9.99) r/#1-5; sketch art; prose ... 10.00

UNWRITTEN, THE: APOCALYPSE
DC Comics (Vertigo): Mar, 2014 - No. 12, Mar, 2015 ($3.99)
1-11-Mike Carey-s/Peter Gross-a ... 4.00
12-($4.99) Mike Carey-s/Peter Gross-a ... 5.00

UP FROM HARLEM (Tom Skinner...)
Spire Christian Comics (Fleming H. Revell Co.): 1973 (35/49¢)

	GD 2.0	VG 4.0	FN 6.0	VF 8.0	VF/NM 9.0	NM- 9.2
nn-(35¢ cover)	3	6	9	15	22	28
nn-(49¢ cover)	2	4	6	10	14	18

UP-TO-DATE COMICS
King Features Syndicate: No date (1938) (36 pgs.; B&W cover) (10¢)

	GD 2.0	VG 4.0	FN 6.0	VF 8.0	VF/NM 9.0	NM- 9.2
nn-Popeye & Henry cover; The Phantom, Jungle Jim & Flash Gordon by Raymond, The Katzenjammer Kids, Curley Harper & others. Note: Variations in content exist.	39	78	117	240	395	550

UP YOUR NOSE AND OUT YOUR EAR (Satire)
Klevart Enterprises: Apr, 1972 - No. 2, June, 1972 (52 pgs., magazine)

	GD 2.0	VG 4.0	FN 6.0	VF 8.0	VF/NM 9.0	NM- 9.2
V1#1,2	3	6	9	15	22	28

URTH 4 (Also see Earth 4)
Continuity Comics: May, 1989 - No. 4, Dec, 1990 ($2.00, deluxe format)
1-4: Ms. Mystic characters. 2-Neal Adams-c(i) ... 4.00

URZA-MISHRA WAR ON THE WORLD OF MAGIC THE GATHERING
Acclaim Comics (Armada): 1996 - No. 2, 1996 ($5.95, limited series)

	GD 2.0	VG 4.0	FN 6.0	VF 8.0	VF/NM 9.0	NM- 9.2
1,2	2	4	6	11	16	20

U.S. (See Uncle Sam)

USA COMICS
Timely Comics (USA): Aug, 1941 - No. 17, Fall, 1945

	GD 2.0	VG 4.0	FN 6.0	VF 8.0	VF/NM 9.0	NM- 9.2
1-Origin Major Liberty (called Mr. Liberty #1), Rockman by Wolverton; 1st app. The Whizzer by Avison; The Defender with sidekick Rusty & Jack Frost begin; The Young Avenger only app.; S&K-a plus 1 pg. art	1220	2440	3660	8540	16,770	25,000
2-Origin Captain Terror & The Vagabond; last Wolverton Rockman; Hitler-c	649	1298	1947	4738	8369	12,000
3-No Whizzer	423	846	1269	3088	5444	7800
4-Last Rockman, Major Liberty, Defender, Jack Frost, & Capt. Terror; Corporal Dix app.; "Remember Pearl Harbor" small cover logo	411	822	1233	2877	5039	7200
5-Origin American Avenger & Roko the Amazing; The Blue Blade, The Black Widow & Victory Boys; Gypo the Gypsy Giant & Hills of Horror only app.; Sergeant Dix begins; no Whizzer; Hitler, Mussolini & Tojo-c	730	1460	2190	5329	9415	13,500
6-Captain America (ends #17); The Destroyer, Jap Buster Johnson, Jeep Jones begin; Terror Squad only app.	1350	2700	4050	10,300	18,650	27,000
7-Captain Daring, Disk-Eyes the Detective by Wolverton app.; origin & last app. Marvel Boy (3/43); Secret Stamp begins; no Whizzer; Sergeant Dix; classic Schomburg-c	2250	4500	6750	17,100	31,050	45,000
8-Classic Japanese WWII bondage/torture-c	1300	2600	3900	9900	17,950	26,000
9-Last Secret Stamp; Hitler-c; classic-c	1350	2700	4050	10,300	18,650	27,000
10-The Thunderbird only app.; Schomburg Japanese WWII-c	1100	2200	3300	8360	15,180	22,000
11-13: 11-No Jeep Jones. 13-No Whizzer; Jeep Jones ends; Schomburg Japanese WWII-c	530	1060	1590	3869	6835	9800
14-17: 15-No Destroyer; Jap Buster Johnson ends	290	580	870	1856	3178	4500

NOTE: *Brodsky* c-14. *Gabrielle* c-4. *Schomburg* c-6, 7, 10, 12, 13, 15-17. *Shores* a-1, 4; c-9, 11. *Ed Win* a-4. Cover features: 1-The Defender; 2, 3-Captain Terror; 4-Major Liberty; 5-Victory Boys; 6-17-Captain America & Bucky.

USA COMICS 70TH ANNIVERSARY SPECIAL
Marvel Comics: Sept, 2009 ($3.99, one-shot)
1-New story of The Destroyer; Arcudi-s/Ellis-a; r/All Winners #3; two covers ... 5.00

U.S. AGENT (See Jeff Jordan...)

U.S. AGENT
Marvel Comics: June, 1993 - No. 4, Sept, 1993 ($1.75, limited series)
1-4 ... 4.00

U.S. AGENT
Marvel Comics: Aug, 2001 - No. 3, Oct, 2001 ($2.99, limited series)
1-3: Ordway-s/a(p)/c. 2,3-Captain America app. ... 3.00

U.S.AGENT (John Walker)(See Captain America #354 for 1st app.)
Marvel Comics: Jan, 2021 - No. 5, Jun, 2021 ($3.99)
1-5-Priest-s/Jeanty-a ... 4.00

USAGI YOJIMBO (See Albedo, Doomsday Squad #3 & Space Usagi)
Fantagraphics Books: July, 1987 - No. 38 ($2.00/$2.25, B&W)

	GD 2.0	VG 4.0	FN 6.0	VF 8.0	VF/NM 9.0	NM- 9.2
1	8	16	24	54	102	150
1,8,10-2nd printings						5.00
2	2	4	6	11	16	20
3-9	2	4	6	10		12
10-Leonardo app. (TMNT)	5	10	15	33	57	80
11-Aragonés-a	3	6	9	14	19	24
12-29						5.00

The Unwritten #7 © Carey & Gross

USA Comics #8 © MAR

Usagi Yojimbo #119 © Stan Sakai

	GD	VG	FN	VF	VF/NM	NM-
	2.0	4.0	6.0	8.0	9.0	9.2

	GD	VG	FN	VF	VF/NM	NM-
	2.0	4.0	6.0	8.0	9.0	9.2

30-38: 30-Begin $2.25-c — 6.00
Color Special 1 (11/89, $2.95, 68 pgs.)-new & r ... 3 6 9 14 20 25
Color Special 2 (10/91, $3.50) ... 2 4 6 8 10 12
Color Special #3 (10/92, $3.50)-Jeff Smith's Bone promo on inside-c
   2 4 6 8 10 12
Summer Special 1 (1986, B&W, $2.75)-r/early Albedo issues
   3 6 9 17 26 35

USAGI YOJIMBO (Volume 2)
Mirage Studios: V2#1, Mar, 1993 - No. 16, 1994 ($2.75)
V2#1-Teenage Mutant Ninja Turtles app. ... 3 6 9 15 22 28
2-16 — 5.00

USAGI YOJIMBO (Volume 3)
Dark Horse Comics: Apr, 1996 - No. 165, Jan, 2018 ($2.95/$2.99/$3.50, B&W)
V3#1-Stan Sakai-c/a in all ... 2 4 6 10 14 18
2-10 — 6.00
11-99,101-116: Stan Sakai-c/a — 4.00
100-(1/07, $3.50) Stan Sakai roast by various incl. Aragonés, Wagner, Miller, Geary
   2 4 6 8 10 12
117-150-($3.50) 136-Variant-c. 141-"200th issue" — 3.50
151-165-($3.99) 152-The River Rising — 4.00
...: One For One (8/10, $1.00) Reprints #1 — 4.00
Color Special #4 (7/97, $2.95) "Green Persimmon" — 4.00
Color Special #5: The Artist (7/14, $3.99) Bonus preview of Usagi Yojimbo: Senso — 4.00
Daisho TPB ('98, $14.95) r/Mirage series #7-14 — 15.00
Demon Mask TPB ('01, $15.95) — 16.00
Glimpses of Death TPB (7/06, $15.95) r/#76-82 — 16.00
Grasscutter TPB ('99, $16.95) r/#13-22 — 17.00
Gray Shadows TPB ('00, $14.95) r/#23-30 — 15.00
Seasons TPB ('99, $14.95) r/#7-12 — 15.00
Shades of Death TPB ('97, $14.95) r/Mirage series #1-6 — 15.00
The Brink of Life and Death TPB ('98, $14.95) r/Mirage series #13,15,16 &
   Dark Horse series #1-6 — 15.00
The Shrouded Moon TPB (1/03, $15.95) r/#46-52 — 16.00

USAGI YOJIMBO (Volume 4)
IDW Publishing: Jun, 2019 - Present ($3.99, color)
1-31-Stan Sakai-c/a in all. 17-Cover swipe of Creepy #4 by Frazetta — 4.00

USAGI YOJIMBO: COLOR CLASSICS
IDW Publishing: Jan, 2020 - No. 7, Sept, 2020 ($3.99, color)
1-7-Reprints early Fantagraphics B&W issues with added color; Stan Sakai-c/a in all — 4.00

USAGI YOJIMBO: DRAGON BELLOW CONSPIRACY
IDW Publishing: Jun, 2021 - No. 6, Nov, 2021 ($3.99, color)
1-6-Reprints #13-18 (1989) with new color; Stan Sakai-c/a — 4.00

USAGI YOJIMBO: ICE AND SNOW
Dark Horse Comics: Sept, 2023 - No. 5 ($4.99, color)
1-Stan Sakai-c/a — 5.00

USAGI YOJIMBO: LONE GOAT AND KID
IDW Publishing: Jan, 2022 - Present ($3.99, color)
1-6-Reprints #19-24 (1989) with new color; Stan Sakai-c/a — 4.00

USAGI YOJIMBO: SENSO
Dark Horse Comics: Aug, 2014 - No. 6, Jan, 2015 ($3.99, B&W)
1-Stan Sakai-s/c/a; Martian invasion set 20 years later; wraparound-c on each ... 1 3 4 6 8 10
2-6 — 4.00

USAGI YOJIMBO: THE HIDDEN (Doubles as issues #166-172 for Volume 3)
Dark Horse Comics: Mar, 2018 - No. 7, Oct, 2018 ($3.99, B&W)
1-7-Stan Sakai-s/c/a — 4.00

USAGI YOJIMBO: WANDERER'S ROAD
IDW Publishing: Nov, 2020 - No. 6, Apr, 2021 ($3.99, color)
1-6: 1-Reprints #7 (3/88) with new color; Stan Sakai-c/a. 2-6-Reprint #8-#12 — 4.00

U.S. AIR FORCE COMICS (Army Attack #38 on)
Charlton Comics: Oct, 1958 - No. 37, Mar-Apr, 1965
1 ... 9 18 27 59 117 175
2 ... 5 10 15 33 57 80
3-10 ... 4 8 12 25 40 55
11-20 ... 4 8 12 23 37 50
21-37 ... 3 6 9 19 30 40
NOTE: *Glanzman* c/a-9, 10, 12. *Montes/Bache* a-33.

USA IS READY
Dell Publishing Co.: 1941 (68 pgs., one-shot)
1-War propaganda ... 103 206 309 659 1130 1600

U.S. AVENGERS (Also see Avengers #675 -678)
Marvel Comics: Mar, 2017 - No. 12, Jan, 2017 ($3.99)
1-3-Ewing-s/Medina-a; team of Squirrel Girl, Cannonball, Iron Patriot, Enigma, Red Hulk.
   5-9-Secret Empire tie-ins. 11,12-Archie Riverdale spoof; Skrulls app. — 4.00

U.S. BORDER PATROL COMICS (Sgt. Dick Carter of the...) (See Holyoke One Shot)

USER
DC Comics (Vertigo): 2001 - No. 3, 2001 ($5.95, limited series)
1-3-Devin Grayson-s; Sean Phillips & John Bolton-a — 6.00

U.S. FIGHTING AIR FORCE (Also see United States Fighting Air Force)
I. W. Enterprises: No date (1960s?)
1,9(nd): 1-r/United States Fighting...#?. 9-r/#1 ... 3 6 9 14 20 25

U.S. FIGHTING MEN
Super Comics: 1963 - 1964 (Reprints)
10-r/With the U.S. Paratroops #4(Avon) ... 2 4 6 9 13 16
11,12,15-18: 11-r/Monty Hall #10. 12,16,17,18-r/U.S. Fighting Air Force #10,3,?&?
15-r/Man Comics #11 ... 2 4 6 9 13 16

U.S. JONES (Also see Wonderworld Comics #28)
Fox Feature Syndicate: Nov, 1941 - No. 2, Jan, 1942
1-U.S. Jones & The Topper begin; Nazi-c ... 314 628 942 2198 3849 5500
2-Nazi-c ... 326 652 978 2282 3991 5700

U.S. MARINES
Charlton Comics: Fall, 1964 (12¢, one-shot)
1-1st app. Capt. Dude; Glanzman-a ... 5 10 15 31 53 75

U.S. MARINES IN ACTION
Avon Periodicals: Aug, 1952 - No. 3, Dec, 1952
1-Louis Ravielli-c/a ... 30 60 90 177 289 400
2,3: 3-Kinstler-c ... 16 32 48 94 147 200

U.S. 1
Marvel Comics Group: May, 1983 - No. 12, Oct, 1984 (7,8: painted-c)
1-12: 2-Sienkiewicz-c. 3-12-Michael Golden-c — 4.00

U.S. PARATROOPS (See With the...)

U.S. PARATROOPS
I. W. Enterprises: 1964?
1,8: 1-r/With the U.S. Paratroops #1; Wood-c. 8-r/With the U.S. Paratroops #6; Kinstler-c
   3 6 9 14 20 25

U.S. TANK COMMANDOS
Avon Periodicals: June, 1952 - No. 4, Mar, 1953
1-Kinstler-c ... 19 38 57 111 176 240
2-4: Kinstler-c ... 15 30 45 85 130 175
I.W. Reprint #1,8: 1-r/#1. 8-r/#3 ... 3 6 9 15 22 28
NOTE: *Kinstler* a-I.W. #1; c-1-4, I.W. #1, 8.

U.S. WAR MACHINE (Also see Iron Man and War Machine)
Marvel Comics (MAX): Nov, 2001 - No. 12, Jan, 2002 ($1.50, B&W, weekly limited series)
1-12-Chuck Austen-s/a/c — 3.00
TPB (12/01, $14.95) r/#1-12 — 15.00

U.S. WAR MACHINE 2.0
Marvel Comics (MAX): Sept, 2003 - No. 3, Sept, 2003 ($2.99, weekly, limited series)
1-3-Austen-s/Christian Moore-CGI art — 3.00

"V" (TV)
DC Comics: Feb, 1985 - No. 18, July, 1986
1-Based on TV movie & series (Sci/Fi) — 5.00
2-18: 17,18-Denys Cowan-c/a — 4.00

VACATION COMICS (Also see A-1 Comics)
Magazine Enterprises: No. 16, 1948 (one-shot)
A-1 16-The Pixies, Tom Tom, Flying Fredd & Koko & Kola
   14 28 42 80 115 150

VACATION DIGEST
Harvey Comics: Sept, 1987 ($1.25, digest size)
1 ... 1 2 3 5 6 8

VACATION IN DISNEYLAND (Also see Dell Giants)
Dell Publishing Co./Gold Key (1965): Aug-Oct, 1959; May, 1965 (Walt Disney)
Four Color 1025-Barks-a ... 15 30 45 103 227 350
1(30024-508)(G.K., 5/65, 25¢)-r/Dell Giant #30 & cover to #1 ('58); celebrates
   Disneyland's 10th anniversary ... 5 10 15 31 53 75

VACATION PARADE (See Dell Giants)

VALEN THE OUTCAST

	GD	VG	FN	VF	VF/NM	NM-
	2.0	4.0	6.0	8.0	9.0	9.2

BOOM! Studios: Dec, 2011 - No. 8, Jul, 2012 ($1.00/$3.99)
1-($1.00) Nelson-s/Scalera-a; eight covers ... 3.00
2-8-($3.99) 2-4-Six covers on each. 5-8-Five covers on each ... 4.00

VALERIA THE SHE BAT
Continuity Comics: May, 1993 - No. 5, Nov, 1993
1-Premium; acetate-c; N. Adams-a/scripts; given as gift to retailers

	GD	VG	FN	VF	VF/NM	NM-
1-Premium	1	3	4	6	8	10

5 (11/93)-Embossed-c; N. Adams-a/scripts ... 5.00
NOTE: *Due to lack of continuity, #2-4 do not exist.*

VALERIA THE SHE BAT
Acclaim Comics (Windjammer): Sept, 1995 - No.2, Oct, 1995 ($2.50, limited series)
1,2 ... 4.00

VALHALLA MAD
Image Comics: May, 2015 - No. 4, Aug, 2015 ($3.50, limited series)
1-4-Joe Casey-s/Paul Maybury-a ... 3.50

VALIANT, THE (Leads into Bloodshot Reborn series)
Valiant Entertainment: Dec, 2014 - No. 4, Mar, 2015 ($3.99, limited series)
1-4-Lemire & Kindt-s/Rivera-a; Eternal Warrior & Bloodshot app. ... 4.00

VALIANT...
Valiant Entertainment: May, 2012 - Present (giveaways)
... Bloodshot FCBD 2019 Special (5/19) Previews Bloodshot & Fallen World; Brereton-c ... 3.00
... Comics FCBD 2012 Special 1 (5/12) Previews X-O Manowar, Harbinger and other Valiant 2012 titles; creator interviews ... 3.00
... FCBD 2013 Special #1 (5/13) Previews Harbinger Wars, X-O Manowar and others ... 3.00
... FCBD 2014 Armor Hunters Special #1 (5/14) Previews Armor Hunters and others ... 3.00
... FCBD 2014 Valiant Universe Handbook #1 (5/14) Character profiles ... 3.00
... FCBD 2015 Valiant 25th Anniversary Special (5/15) Previews Bloodshot and Ninjak ... 3.00
... FCBD 2021 Special (8/21) Previews Ninjak, X-O Manowar, Shadowman & Harbinger ... 3.00
... : 4001 A.D. FCBD Special (5/16) Prelude to the 4001 A.D. series; Crain-c ... 3.00
... : Masters: 2013 Showcase Edition #1 (5/13) Samples of hardcover volume offerings ... 3.00
... : Shadowman FCBD 2018 Special (5/18) Short stories of Shadowman, X-O Manowar, Harbinger Wars ... 3.00
... Universe Handbook 2015 Edition #1 (5/15, $2.99) Character profiles ... 3.00
... Universe Handbook 2016 Edition #1 (8/16, $2.99) Character profiles ... 3.00
... Universe Handbook 2019 Edition #1 (6/19, $3.99) Character profiles; Massafera-c ... 4.00
... : X-O Manowar 2017 FCBD Special (5/17) Short stories of X-O Manowar, Secret Weapons, Bloodshot Salvation ... 3.00

VALIANT HIGH
Valiant Entertainment: May, 2018 - No. 4, Aug, 2018 ($3.99, limited series)
1-4-Valiant heroes as high-schoolers; Kibblesmith-s/Charm-a ... 4.00

VALKYRIE (See Airboy)
Eclipse Comics: May, 1987 - No. 3, July, 1987 ($1.75, limited series)
1-3: 2-Holly becomes new Black Angel ... 5.00

VALKYRIE
Marvel Comics: Jan, 1997; Nov, 2010 ($2.95/$3.99, one-shots)
1-(1/97, $2.95) w/pin-ups ... 4.00
1-(11/10, $3.99) Origin re-told; Winslade-a/Glass-s; Anacleto-c ... 4.00

VALKYRIE!
Eclipse Comics: July, 1988 - No. 3, Sept, 1988 ($1.95, limited series)
1-3 ... 4.00

VALKYRIE: JANE FOSTER (See the 2016 Mighty Thor series and War of the Realms Omega)
Marvel Comics: Sept, 2019 - No. 10, Oct, 2020 ($3.99)
1-10: 1,2-Aaron & Ewing-s/Cafu-a; Bullseye & Heimdall app. 4-7-Dr. Strange app. ... 4.00

VALLEY OF THE DINOSAURS (TV)
Charlton Comics: Apr, 1975 - No. 11, Dec, 1976 (Hanna-Barbera)

	GD	VG	FN	VF	VF/NM	NM-
1-W. Howard-i	3	6	9	18	28	38
2,4-11: 2-W. Howard-i	2	4	6	8	11	14
3-Byrne text illos (early work, 7/75)	2	4	6	10	14	18

VALLEY OF THE DINOSAURS (Volume 2)
Harvey Comics: Oct, 1993 ($1.50, giant-sized)
1-Reprints ... 5.00

VALLEY OF GWANGI (See Movie Classics)

VALOR
E. C. Comics: Mar-Apr, 1955 - No. 5, Nov-Dec, 1955

	GD	VG	FN	VF	VF/NM	NM-
1-Williamson/Torres-a; Wood-c/a	43	86	129	344	547	750
2-Williamson-c/a; Wood-a	30	60	90	240	383	525
3,4: 3-Williamson, Crandall-a. 4-Wood-c	24	48	72	192	309	425
5-Wood-c/a; Williamson/Evans-a	23	46	69	184	292	400

NOTE: *Crandall* a-1, 4. *Ingels* a-1, 2, 4, 5. *Krigstein* a-1-5. *Orlando* a-3, 4; c-3. *Wood* a-1, 2, 5; c-1, 4, 5.

VALOR
Gemstone Publishing: Oct, 1998 - No. 5, Feb, 1999 ($2.50)
1-5-Reprints ... 4.00

VALOR (Also see Legion of Super-Heroes & Legionnaires)
DC Comics: Nov, 1992 - No. 23, Sept, 1994 ($1.25/$1.50)
1-22: 1-Eclipso The Darkness Within aftermath. 2-Vs. Supergirl. 4-Vs. Lobo. 12-Lobo cameo. 14-Legionnaires, JLA app. 17-Austin-c(i); death of Valor. 18-22-Build-up to Zero Hour ... 4.00
23-Zero Hour tie-in ... 4.00

VAMPI (Vampirella's...)
Harris Publications (Anarchy Studios): Aug, 2000 - No. 25, Feb, 2003 ($2.95/$2.99)
Limited Edition Preview Book (5/00) Preview pages & sketchbook ... 4.00
1-(8/00, $2.95) Lau-a(p)/Conway-s ... 6.00
1-Platinum Edition ... 20.00
2-25: 17-Barberi-a ... 4.00
2-25-Deluxe Edition variants ($9.95): 4-Finch-c. 5-Wieringo-c. 6-Cha-c ... 10.00
...Digital 1 (11/01, $2.95) CGI art; Haberlin-s ... 4.00
...Digital Preview (Anarchy Studios, 7/01, $2.95) preview of CGI art ... 4.00

Switchblade Kiss HC (2001, $24.95) r/#1-6 ... 25.00
Vicious Preview Ed. (Apr, 2003, $1.99) Flip book w/ Xin: Journey of the Monkey King Preview Ed. ... 4.00
Wizard #1/2 (mail order, $9.95) includes sketch pages ... 10.00

VAMPIRE BITES
Brainstorm Comics: May, 1995 - No. 2, Sept, 1996 ($2.95, B&W)
1,2:1-Color pin-up ... 4.00

VAMPIRE DIARIES, THE (Based on the CW television series)
DC Comics: Mar, 2014 - No. 6, Aug, 2014 ($3.99, printings of online comics)
1-6: 1,3-Doran-s/Shasteen-a. 5-Calero-a. 6-Doran-s/a ... 4.00

VAMPIRE LESTAT, THE
Innovation Publishing: Jan, 1990 - No. 12, 1991 ($2.50, painted limited series)

	GD	VG	FN	VF	VF/NM	NM-
1-Adapts novel; Bolton painted-c on all	2	4	6	10	14	18

1-2nd printing (has UPC code, 1st prints don't) ... 4.00
1-3rd & 4th printings ... 4.00

	GD	VG	FN	VF	VF/NM	NM-
2-1st printing	1	2	3	5	6	8

2-2nd & 3rd printings ... 4.00
3-5 ... 5.00
3-6,9-2nd printings ... 4.00
6-12 ... 4.00

VAMPIRELLA (Magazine)(See Warren Presents)(Also see Heidi Saha)
Warren Publishing Co./Harris Publications #113: Sept, 1969 - No. 112, Feb, 1983; No. 113, Jan, 1988? (B&W)

	GD	VG	FN	VF	VF/NM	NM-
1-Intro. Vampirella in original costume & wings; Frazetta-c/intro. page; Adams-a; Crandall-a	139	278	417	1112	2506	3900
2-1st app. Vampirella's cousin Evily-c/s; 1st/only app. Draculina, Vampirella's blonde twin sister	15	30	45	103	227	350
3 (Low distribution)	20	40	60	140	310	480
4,6	9	18	27	59	117	175
5,7,9: 5,7-Frazetta-c. 9-Barry Smith-c; Boris/Wood-c-9	9	18	27	60	120	180
8-Vampirella begins by Tom Sutton as serious strip (early issues-gag line)	10	20	30	66	138	210
10-No Vampi story; Brunner, Adams, Wood-a	6	12	18	42	79	115
11-Origin & 1st app. Pendragon; Frazetta-c	8	16	24	56	108	160
12-Vampi by Gonzales begins	8	16	24	56	108	160
13-15: 14-1st Maroto-a; Ploog-a	7	14	21	48	89	130
16,22,25: 16-1st full Dracula-a/app. 22-Color insert preview of Maroto's Dracula. 25-Vampi on cocaine-s	7	14	21	46	86	125
17,18,20,21,23,24: 17-Tomb of the Gods begins by Maroto, ends #22. 18-22-Dracula-s	6	12	18	41	76	110
19 (1973 Annual) Creation of Vampi text bio	7	14	21	46	86	125
26-35,38-40,45: 26,28,34,35,39,40-All have 8 pg. color inserts. 27-(1974 Annual) New color Vampi-s; mostly-r. 28-Board game inside covers. 30-Intro. Pantha; Corben-a(color). 31-Origin Luana, the Beast Girl. 32-Jones-a. 33-Wrightson-a. 34,35-1st Fleur the Witch Woman. 38-2nd Vampi as Cleopatra/Blood Red Queen of Hearts; 1st Mayo-a. 39,40-Color Dracula-s. 40-Wrightson bio	5	10	15	33	57	80
36,37: 36-1st Vampi as Cleopatra/Blood Red Queen of Hearts; issue has 8 pg. color insert. 37-(1975 Annual)	7	14	21	44	82	120
41-44,47,48: 41-Dracula-s	5	10	15	30	50	70
46-(10/75) Origin-r from Annual 1	5	10	15	34	60	85
49-1st Blind Priestess; The Blood Red Queen of Hearts storyline begins; Poe-s	5	10	15	33	57	80
50-Spirit cameo by Eisner; 40 pg. Vampi-s; Pantha & Fleur app.; Jones-a	5	10	15	34	60	85
51-57,59-63,65,66,68,75,79-89: 54-Vampi-s (42 pgs.); 8 pg. color Corben-a. 55-All Gonzales-a(r). 60-62,65,66-The Blood Red Queen of Hearts app. 60-1st Blind Priestess-c. 63-10 pgs. Wrightson-a	4	8	12	23	37	50
58,70,72: 58-(92 pgs.) 70-Rook app.	5	10	15	30	50	70
64,73: 64-(100 pg. Giant) All Mayo-a; 70 pg. Vampi-s. 73-69 pg. Vampi-s; Mayo-a	5	10	15	31	53	75
67,69,71,74,76-78-All Barbara Leigh photo-c	4	8	12	28	47	65
'90-99: 90-Toth-a. 91-All-r; Gonzales-a. 93-Cassandra St. Knight begins, ends #103; new Pantha series begins, ends #108	4	8	12	23	37	50
100 (96 pg. r-special)-Origin reprinted from Ann. 1; mostly reprints; Vampirella appears topless in next 21 pg. story	7	14	21	44	82	120
101-104,106,107: All lower print run. 101,102-The Blood Red Queen of Hearts app.	5	10	15	34	60	85
107-All Maroto reprint-a issue	5	10	15	34	60	85
105,108-110: 108-Torpedo series by Toth begins; Vampi nudity splash page. 110-(100 pg. Summer Spectacular)	5	10	15	34	60	85
111,112: Low print run. 111-Giant Collector's Edition ($2.50) 112-(84 pgs.) last Warren issue	5	10	15	34	60	85
113 (1988)-1st Harris Issue; very low print run		16	24	52	99	145
Annual 1(1972)-New definitive origin of Vampirella by Gonzales; reprints by Neal Adams (from #1), Wood (from #3)	22	44	66	154	340	525
Special 1 (1977) Softcover (color, large-square bound)-Only available thru mail order	15	30	45	103	227	350
Special 1 (1977) Hardcover (color, large-square bound)-Only available through mail order (scarce)(500 produced, signed & #'d)	30	60	90	216	483	750

#1 1969 Commemorative Edition (2001, $4.95) reprints entire #1 ... 10.00
#1 (1969) Facsimile Edition (2/20, $9.99) reprints entire #1; mosiac variant of Frazetta-c ... 10.00
#30 (1974) Facsimile Edition (2020, $6.99) reprints entire #30 ... 25.00
...Crimson Chronicles Vol. 1 (2004, $19.95, TPB) reprints stories from #1-10 ... 20.00
...Crimson Chronicles Vol. 2 (2005, $19.95, TPB) reprints stories from #11-18 ... 20.00
...Crimson Chronicles Vol. 3 (2005, $19.95, TPB) reprints stories from #19-28 ... 20.00
...Crimson Chronicles Vol. 4 (2005, $19.95, TPB) reprints stories from #29-41 ... 20.00
NOTE: *Ackerman* s-1-3. *Neal Adams* a-1, 10p, 19p(r/#10), 44(1 pg.), Annual 1. *Alcala* a-78, 90, 93. *Bodé/Todd* c-3. *Bodé/Jones* c-4. *Boris/Wood* c-9. *Brunner* a-10. *Corben* a-30, 31, 33, 36, 54; c-30, 31, 33, 54. *Crandall* a-1, 19(r/#1). *Frazetta* c-1, 5, 7, 11, 31. *Heath* a-58, 61, 67, 76-78, 83. *Infantino* a-57-62. *Jones* a-5, 9, 12, 27, 32 (color), 33(2-pg.), 54. *Krigstein* a-57. *Maroto* c-46; a-16-26. *Nebres* a-84, 88-90, 92-96. *Nino* a-59i, 61i, 67, 76, 85, 90. *Ploog* a-14. *Barry Smith* a-9. *Starlin* a-78. *Sutton* a-1-5, 7-11, Annual 1. *Toth* a-90i, 108, 110. *Wood* a-1, 2; c-9-g(partial). *Wrightson* a-33(w/Jones), 40(Bio cameo) 63r. All reprint issues-19, 74, 83, 91, 105, 107, 109, 111. Annuals from 1973 on are included in regular numbering. Later annuals are same format as regular issues. Color inserts (8 pgs.) in 22, 25-28, 30-35, 39, 40, 45, 46, 49, 54, 55, 67, 72. 16 pg color insert in #36.

VAMPIRELLA (Also see Cain/... & Vengeance of...)
Harris Publications: Nov, 1992 - No. 5, Nov, 1993 ($2.95)

Valkyrie #1 © MAR

Vampirella #53 © Warren

Vampirella (2013 series) #35 © DYN

	GD 2.0	VG 4.0	FN 6.0	VF 8.0	VF/NM 9.0	NM- 9.2
0-Bagged	1	3	4	6	8	10
0-Gold	3	6	9	19	30	40
1-Jim Balent inks in #1-3; Adam Hughes c-1-3	3	6	9	17	26	35
1-2nd printing						5.00
1-(11/97) Commemorative Edition	1	3	4	6	8	10
2	2	4	6	13	18	22
3-5: 4-Snyder III-c. 5-Brereton painted-c	1	3	4	6	8	10
Trade paperback nn (10/93, $5.95)-r/#1-4; Jusko-c	1	3	4	6	8	10

NOTE: Issues 1-5 contain certificates for free *Dave Stevens* Vampirella poster.

VAMPIRELLA (THE NEW MONTHLY)
Harris Publications: Nov, 1997 - No. 26, Apr, 2000 ($2.95)

1-3-"Ascending Evil"-Morrison & Millar-s/Conner & Palmiotti-a. 1-Three covers		
by Quesada/Palmiotti, Conner, and Conner/Palmiotti		5.00
1-3-($9.95) Jae Lee variant covers		10.00
1-($24.95) Platinum Ed.w/Quesada-c		25.00
4-6-"Holy War"-Small & Stull-a. 4-Linsner variant-c		4.00
7-9-"Queen's Gambit"-Shi app. 7-Two covers. 8-Pantha-c/app.		4.00
7-($9.95) Conner variant-c		10.00
10-12-"Hell on Earth"; Small-a/Coney-s. 12-New costume		4.00
10-Jae Lee variant-c	1	3	4	6	8	10
13-15-"World's End" Zircher-p; Pantha back-up, Texeira-a		4.00
16,17: 16-Pantha-c;Texeira-a; Vampi back-up story. 17-(Pantha #2)		4.00
18-20-"Rebirth"; Jae Lee-c on all. 18-Loeb/s-Sale-a. 19-Alan Davis-a. 20-Bruce Timm-a		4.00
18-20-($9.95) Variant covers: 18-Sale. 19-Davis. 20-Timm		12.00
21-26: 21,22-Dangerous Games; Small-a. 23-Lady Death-c/app.; Cleavenger-a. 24,25-Lau-a.		
26-Lady Death & Pantha-c/app.; Cleavenger-a.		4.00
0-(1/99) also variant-c with Pantha #0; same contents		4.00
TPB ($7.50) r/#1-3 "Ascending Evil"		8.00
Ascending Evil Ashcan (8/97, $1.00)		3.00
...: Grant Morrison/Mark Millar Collection TPB (2006, $24.95) r/#1-6; interviews		25.00
Hell on Earth Ashcan (7/98, $1.00)		3.00
... Presents: Tales of Pantha TPB (2006, $19.95) r/stories from #13-17 & one-shots		20.00
... The End Ashcan ($3/00, $6.00)		6.00
...30th Anniversary Celebration Preview (7/99) B&W preview of #18-20		10.00

VAMPIRELLA
Harris Publications: June, 2001 - No. 22, Aug, 2003 ($2.95/$2.99)

1-Four covers (Mayhew w/foil logo, Campbell, Anacleto, Jae Lee) Mayhew-a;		
Mark Millar-s		5.00
2-22: Two covers (Mayhew & Chiodo). 3-Timm var-c. 4-Horn var-c. 7-10-Dawn Brown-a;		
Pantha back-up w/Texeira-a. 15-22-Conner-c		4.00
Giant-Size Ashcan (5/01, $5.95) B&W preview art and Mayhew interview		6.00
...: Halloween Trick & Treat (10/04, $4.95) stories & art by various; three covers		5.00
...: Nowheresville Preview Edition (3/01, $2.95)- previews Mayhew art and photo models		4.00
...Nowheresville TPB (1/02, $12.95) r/#1-3 with cover gallery		13.00
... Summer Special #1 (2005, $5.95) Batman Begins photo-c and 2 variant-c		6.00
...: 2006 Halloween Special (2006, $2.95) Conner-c; Hester-s/Segovia-a; 4 covers		4.00

VAMPIRELLA
Dynamite Entertainment: 2010 - No. 38, 2014 ($3.99)

1-Four covers (Campbell, Madureira, J. Djurdjevic, Alex Ross swipe of Frazetta's #1)	4.00
1-Variant-c of blood-soaked Vampirella by Alex Ross	8.00
2-37: 2-6-Trautmann-s/Wagner Reis-a; four covers. 7-Geovani-a	4.00
38-($4.99, 40 pgs.) Pantha and Dracula app.	5.00
Annual 1 (2011, $4.99) Jerwa-s/Casalos-a; reprint with Alan Davis-a	5.00
Annual 2 (2012, $4.99) Rahner-s/Kyriazis-a; reprint with Pantha app.; Linsner-c	5.00
Annual 2013 ($4.99) Rahner-s/Valiente-a/Bolson-c	5.00
...: NuBlood (2013, $4.99) Spoof of True Blood; Rahner-s/Razek-a/c; back-up w/Timm-a	5.00
... Vs. Fluffy (2012, $4.99) Spoof of Buffy the Vampire Slayer; Bradshaw-c	5.00

VAMPIRELLA (Volume 2)
Dynamite Entertainment: 2014 - No. 13, 2015 ($3.99)

1-12: Multiple covers on each. 1-Nancy Collins-s/Berkenkotter-a	4.00
13-($4.99) Lord Drago app.; Collins-s/Berkenkotter-a; 3 covers	5.00
#100 (2015, $7.99) Short stories by various incl. Tim Seeley; multiple covers	8.00
#1969 (2015, $7.99) Short stories by various incl. Hester & Worley; 2 covers	8.00
Annual 2015 ($5.99) Collins-s/Aneke-a/Anacleto-c	6.00
...: Prelude to Shadows (2014, $7.99) Collins-s/Zamora-a; r/Vampirella #13 w/new color	8.00

VAMPIRELLA (Volume 3)
Dynamite Entertainment: 2016 - No. 6, 2016 ($3.99)

1-6: Multiple covers on each. 1-Kate Leth-s/Eman Casallos-a; new costume	4.00

VAMPIRELLA (Volume 4)
Dynamite Entertainment: 2017 - No. 11, 2018 ($3.99)

#0-(25¢) Multiple covers; Cornell-s/Broxton-a	3.00
1-11-($3.99) Vampirella in the far future. 1-5-Cornell-s/Broxton-a. 6-10-Belanger-a	4.00
... Halloween Special One-Shot (2018, $4.99) Reilly Brown-c	5.00
... Valentine's Day Special (2019, $4.99) Williams-s/Sanapo-a	5.00

VAMPIRELLA (Volume 5)
Dynamite Entertainment: 2019 - No. 25, 2021 ($3.99)

0-(2019 Free Comic Book Day giveaway) Priest-s/Gündüz-a; reprint with Art Adams-a	3.00
1-25-Vampirella's mother Lilith app.; Priest-s/Gündüz-a; multiple covers on each.	
25-Vampirella marries Dracula	4.00
...: Fairy Tales (2022, $4.99) Soo Lee-s/Emiliana Pinna-a; Red Riding Hood homage	5.00
...: Holiday Special (2021, $4.99) Robson-s/a; Federici-s/a; Carratu-s/a; Krampus app.	5.00
...: 1992 (2021, $4.99) Bemis-s/Castro & Ramos-a	5.00
...: Trial of the Soul (2020, $4.99) Intro. Prester John; Willingham-s/Cafaro-a	5.00
...: Valentine's Day Special (2021, $4.99) Marcos Ramos-a; Dracula app.	5.00
...: Valentine's Day Special (2022, $4.99) Sozomaika main-c	5.00

VAMPIRELLA (Volume 6)
Dynamite Entertainment: No. 666, 2024 - Present ($4.99)

666-Priest-s/Gündüz-a; multiple covers	5.00

VAMPIRELLA / ALIENS
Dynamite Entertainment: 2015 - No. 6, 2016 ($3.99, limited series)

1-Corinna Bechko-s/Javier Garcia-Miranda-a; multiple covers on each					
	2	4	6	9	12	15
2-6						4.00

VAMPIRELLA & PANTHA SHOWCASE
Harris Publications: Jan, 1997 (one-shot)

1-Millar-s/Texeira-c/a; flip book w/"Blood Lust"; Robinson-s/Jusko-c/a	4.00

VAMPIRELLA & THE BLOOD RED QUEEN OF HEARTS
Harris Publications: Sept, 1996 ($9.95, 96 pgs., B&W, squarebound, one-shot)

nn-r/Vampirella #49,60-62,65,66,101,102; John Bolton-c; Michael Bair back-c					
	1	3	4	6	8	10

VAMPIRELLA AND THE SCARLET LEGION
Dynamite Entertainment: 2011 - No. 5 ($3.99)

1-5: 1-Three covers (Campbell, Chen and Tucci); Malaga-a	4.00

VAMPIRELLA / ARMY OF DARKNESS
Dynamite Entertainment: 2015 - No. 4, 2015 ($3.99, limited series)

1-4-Ash meets Vampirella in 1300 AD; Mark Rahner-s/Jeff Morales-a	4.00

VAMPIRELLA: BLOODLUST
Harris Publications: July, 1997 - No. 2, Aug, 1997 ($4.95, limited series)

1,2-Robinson-s/Jusko-painted c/a	6.00
1-(2022, $4.99) Reprints 1997 issue	5.00

VAMPIRELLA CLASSIC
Harris Publications: Feb, 1995 - No. 5, Nov, 1995 ($2.95, limited series)

1-5: Reprints Archie Goodwin stories.	5.00

VAMPIRELLA COMICS MAGAZINE
Harris Publications: Oct, 2003 - No. 9 ($3.95/$9.95, magazine-sized)

1-9-($3.95) 1-Texiera-c; b&w and color stories, Alan Moore interview; reviews. 2-KISS	
interview. 4-Chiodo-c. 6-Brereton-c	4.00
1-9-($9.95) 1-Three covers (Model Photo cover, Palmiotti-c, Wheatley Frankenstein-c)	10.00

VAMPIRELLA: CROSSOVER GALLERY
Harris Publications: Sept, 1997 ($2.95, one-shot)

1-Wraparound-c by Campbell, pinups by Jae Lee, Mack, Allred, Art Adams,					
Quesada & Palmiotti and others	1	3	4	6	8	10

VAMPIRELLA: DEAD FLOWERS
Dynamite Entertainment: 2023 - No. 4, 2023 ($3.99, limited series)

1-4-Sara Frazetta & Bob Freeman-s/Alberto Locatelli-a; multiple covers on each	4.00

VAMPIRELLA: DEATH & DESTRUCTION
Harris Publications: July, 1996 - No. 3, Sept, 1996 ($2.95, limited series)

1-3: Amanda Conner-a(p) in all. 1-Tucci-c. 2-Hughes-c. 3-Jusko-c	4.00
1-($9.95)-Limited Edition; Beachum-c	10.00

VAMPIRELLA / DEJAH THORIS
Dynamite Entertainment: 2018 - No. 5, 2019 ($3.99, limited series)

1-5-Erik Burnham-s/Ediano Silva-a; multiple covers on each; Vampirella on Barsoom	4.00

VAMPIRELLA/DRACULA & PANTHA SHOWCASE
Harris Publications: Aug, 1997 ($1.50, one-shot)

1-Ellis, Robinson, and Moore-s; flip book w/"Pantha"	4.00

VAMPIRELLA / DRACULA: RAGE
Dynamite Entertainment: 2023 - No. 5, 2024 ($3.99, limited series)

1-5-Priest-s/Rosado-a; multiple covers on each	4.00

VAMPIRELLA/DRACULA: THE CENTENNIAL
Harris Publications: Oct, 1997 ($5.95, one-shot)

1-Ellis, Robinson, and Moore-s; Beachum, Frank/Smith, and Mack/Mays-a	

	GD 2.0	VG 4.0	FN 6.0	VF 8.0	VF/NM 9.0	NM- 9.2

	NM- 9.2
Bolton-painted-c	6.00

VAMPIRELLA DRACULA UNHOLY (Follows their wedding in Vampirella #25)
Dynamite Entertainment: 2021 ($3.99)

| 1-6: 1-Priest-s/Hadiwidjaja-a; main cover by Adam Hughes | 4.00 |

VAMPIRELLA: FEARY TALES
Dynamite Entertainment: 2014 - No. 5, 2015 ($3.99, limited series)

| 1-5: Anthology of short stories by various; multiple covers on each | 4.00 |

VAMPIRELLA: INTIMATE VISIONS
Harris Publications: 2006 ($3.95, one-shots)

| ..., Amanda Conner 1 - r/Vampirella Monthly #1 with commentary; interview; 2 covers | 4.00 |
| ..., Joe Jusko 1 - r/Vampirella; Blood Lust #1 with commentary; interview; 2 covers | 4.00 |

VAMPIRELLA: JULIE STRAIN SPECIAL
Harris Publications: Sept, 2000 ($3.95, one-shot)

| 1-Photo-c w/yellow background; interview and photo gallery | 4.00 |
| 1-Limited Edition ($9.95); cover photo w/black background | 10.00 |

VAMPIRELLA/LADY DEATH (Also see Lady Death/Vampirella)
Harris Publications: Feb, 1999 ($3.50, one-shot)

| 1-Small-a/Nelson painted-c | 6.00 |
| 1-Valentine Edition ($9.95); pencil-c by Small | 10.00 |

VAMPIRELLA: LEGENDARY TALES
Harris Publications: May, 2000 - No. 2, June, 2000 ($2.95, B&W)

| 1,2-Reprints from magazine; Cleavenger painted-c | 4.00 |
| 1,2-($9.95) Variant painted-c by Mike Mayhew | 10.00 |

VAMPIRELLA LIVES
Harris Publications: Dec, 1996 - No. 3, Feb, 1997 ($3.50/$2.95, limited series)

1-Die cut-c; Quesada & Palmiotti-c, Ellis-s/Conner-a	6.00
1-Deluxe Ed.-photo-c	6.00
2,3-($2.95)-Two editions (1 photo-c): 3-J. Scott Campbell-c	5.00

VAMPIRELLA: MINDWARP
Dynamite Entertainment: 2022 - No. 5, 2022 ($3.99, limited series)

| 1-5-Jeff Parker-s/Benjamin Dewey-a | 4.00 |

VAMPIRELLA: MORNING IN AMERICA
Harris Publications/Dark Horse Comics: 1991 - No. 4, 1992 ($3.95, B&W, lim. series, 52 pgs.)

	GD 2.0	VG 4.0	FN 6.0	VF 8.0	VF/NM 9.0	NM- 9.2
1,2-All have Kaluta painted-c	2	4	6	8	10	12
3,4	2	4	6	8	10	12

VAMPIRELLA OF DRAKULON
Harris Publications: Jan, 1996 - No. 5, Sept, 1996 ($2.95)

| 0-5: All reprints. 0-Jim Silke-c. 3-Polybagged w/card. 4-Texeira-c | 4.00 |

VAMPIRELLA/PAINKILLER JANE
Harris Publications: May, 1998 ($3.50, one-shot)

| 1-Waid & Augustyn-s/Leonardi & Palmiotti-a | 4.00 |
| 1-($9.95) Variant-c | 10.00 |

VAMPIRELLA PIN-UP SPECIAL
Harris Publications: Oct, 1995 ($2.95, one-shot)

| 1-Hughes-c, pin-ups by various | 5.00 |
| 1-Variant-c | 5.00 |

VAMPIRELLA QUARTERLY
Harris Publications: Spring, 2007 - Summer, 2008 ($4.95/$4.99, quarterly)

| Spring, 2007 - Summer, 2008-New stories and re-colored reprints; five or six covers | 5.00 |

VAMPIRELLA / RED SONJA
Dynamite Entertainment: 2019 - No. 12, 2020 ($3.99, limited series)

| 1-12: 1-Set in 1969; Jordie Bellaire-s/Drew Moss-a; multiple-c on each. 7,8-1920s NY | 4.00 |

VAMPIRELLA: RETRO
Harris Publications: Mar, 1998 - No. 3, May, 1998 ($2.50, B&W, limited series)

| 1-3: Reprints; Silke painted covers | 4.00 |

VAMPIRELLA: REVELATIONS
Harris Publications: No. 0, Oct, 2005 - No. 3, Feb, 2006 ($2.99, one-shot)

| 0-3-Vampirella's origin retold, Lilith app.; Carey-s/Lilly-a; two covers on each | 4.00 |
| ... Book 1 TPB (2006, $12.95) r/series; Carey interview, script for #1, Lilly sketch pages | 13.00 |

VAMPIRELLA: ROSES FOR THE DEAD
Dynamite Entertainment: 2018 - No. 4, 2019 ($3.99, limited series)

| 1-4-Kristina Deak-Linsner-s/Joseph Linsner-a; covers by Linsner & Tucci; Evily app. | 4.00 |

VAMPIRELLA: SAD WINGS OF DESTINY
Harris Publications: Sept, 1996 ($3.95, one-shot)

| 1-Jusko-c | 6.00 |

VAMPIRELLA: SECOND COMING
Harris Publications: 2009 - No. 4 ($1.99, limited series)

| 1-4: 1-Hester-s/Sampere-a; multiple covers on each. 3,4-Rio-a | 4.00 |

VAMPIRELLA/SHADOWHAWK: CREATURES OF THE NIGHT (Also see Shadowhawk)
Harris Publications: 1995 ($4.95, one-shot)

| 1 | 5.00 |

VAMPIRELLA/SHI (See Shi/Vampirella)
Harris Publications: Oct, 1997 ($2.95, one-shot)

| 1-Ellis-s | 6.00 |

	GD 2.0	VG 4.0	FN 6.0	VF 8.0	VF/NM 9.0	NM- 9.2
1-Chromium-c		1	2	3	5	8

VAMPIRELLA: SILVER ANNIVERSARY COLLECTION
Harris Publications: Jan, 1997 - No. 4 Apr, 1997 ($2.50, limited series)

| 1-4: Two editions: Bad Girl by Beachum, Good Girl by Silke | 5.00 |

VAMPIRELLA: SOUTHERN GOTHIC
Dynamite Entertainment: 2013 - No. 5, 2014 ($3.99)

| 1-5-Nate Cosby-s/José Luis-a; regular & photo-c on each | 4.00 |

VAMPIRELLA'S SUMMER NIGHTS

Harris Publications: 1992 (one-shot)

	GD 2.0	VG 4.0	FN 6.0	VF 8.0	VF/NM 9.0	NM- 9.2
1-Art Adams infinity cover; centerfold by Stelfreeze	2	4	6	10	14	18

VAMPIRELLA STRIKES
Harris Publications: Sept, 1995 - No. 8, Dec, 1996 ($2.95, limited series)

1-8: 1-Photo-c. 2-Deodato-c; polybagged w/card. 5-Eudaemon-c/app; wraparound-c; alternate-c exists. 6-(6/96)-Mark Millar script; Texeira-c; alternate-c exists. 7-Flip book	4.00
1-Newsstand Edition; diff. photo-c., 1-Limited Ed.; diff. photo-c	4.00
Annual 1-(12/96, $2.95) Delano-s; two covers	5.00

VAMPIRELLA STRIKES
Dynamite Entertainment: 2013 - No. 6, 2013 ($3.99)

| 1-6: 1-Five covers (Turner, Finch, Manara, Desjardins & photo); Desjardins-a | 4.00 |

VAMPIRELLA STRIKES (Follows events of Vengeance of Vampirella #25)
Dynamite Entertainment: 2022 - No. 13, 2023 ($3.99)

| 1-13: 1-Sniegoski-s/Lau-a | 4.00 |

VAMPIRELLA: THE DARK POWERS
Dynamite Entertainment: 2020 - No. 5, 2021 ($3.99)

| 1-5-Vampirella joins Project Superpowers team; Abnett-s/Davidson-a. 3-The Flame app. | 4.00 |

VAMPIRELLA THE RED ROOM
Dynamite Entertainment: 2012 - No. 4, 2012 ($3.99)

| 1-4-Three covers on each; Brereton-s/Diaz-a | 4.00 |

VAMPIRELLA: 25TH ANNIVERSARY SPECIAL
Harris Publications: Oct, 1996 ($5.95, squarebound, one-shot)

	1	2	3		5	6	8
nn-Reintro The Blood Red Queen of Hearts; James Robinson, Grant Morrison & Warren Ellis scripts; Mark Texeira, Michael Bair & Amanda Conner-a(p); Frank Frazetta-c	1	3	4		6	8	10
nn-($6.95)-Silver Edition							

VAMPIRELLA VERSUS PURGATORI
Dynamite Entertainment: 2020 - No. 5, 2021 ($3.99, limited series)

| 1-5-Fawkes-s/Sarraseca-a; multiple covers on each; Lilith & Hel app. | 4.00 |

VAMPIRELLA VERSUS RED SONJA
Dynamite Entertainment: 2022 - No. 5, 2023 ($3.99, limited series)

| 1-5-Abnett-s/Ranaldi-a; multiple covers on each | 4.00 |

VAMPIRELLA VERSUS THE SUPERPOWERS
Dynamite Entertainment: 2023 - No. 6, 2024 ($3.99, limited series)

| 1-6-Abnett-s/Qualano-a; multiple covers on each | 4.00 |

VAMPIRELLA VS. DRACULA
Dynamite Entertainment: 2012 - No. 6, 2012 ($3.99)

| 1-6-Harris-s/Rodriguez-a/Linsner-c | 4.00 |

VAMPIRELLA VS. HEMORRHAGE
Harris Publications: Apr, 1997 ($3.50)

| 1 | 6.00 |

VAMPIRELLA VS. PANTHA
Harris Publications: Mar, 1997 ($3.50)

| 1-Two covers; Millar-s/Texeira-c/a | 4.00 |

VAMPIRELLA VS. REANIMATOR
Dynamite Entertainment: 2018 - No. 4, 2019 ($3.99, limited series)

| 1-4-Herbert West app.; Cullen Bunn-s/Blacky Shepherd-a; multiple covers on each | 4.00 |

VAMPIRELLA/WETWORKS (See Wetworks/Vampirella)
Harris Publications: June, 1997 ($2.95, one-shot)

| 1 | 4.00 |
| 1-($9.95) Alternate Edition; cardstock-c | 10.00 |

VAMPIRELLA/WITCHBLADE
Harris Publications: 2003; Oct, 2004; Oct, 2005 ($2.99, one-shots)

1-Brian Wood-s/Steve Pugh-a; 3 covers by Texeira, Conner and Pugh	4.00
...: The Feast (10/05, $2.99) Joyce Chin-a; covers by Chin, Conner, Rodriguez	4.00
...: Union of the Damned (10/04, $2.99, one-shot) Sharp-a; three covers	4.00
Trilogy TPB (2006, $12.95) r/one-shots; art gallery and gallery of multiple covers	13.00

VAMPIRELLA YEAR ONE
Dynamite Entertainment: 2022 - No. 6, 2023 ($3.99, limited series)

| 1-6-Priest-s/Gündüz-a | 4.00 |

VAMPIRE, PA (Also see Al Capone, Vampire)
Moonstone: 2010 - No. 3, Oct, 2010 ($3.99)

| 1-3: 1-Intro. Vampire Hunter Dean; J.C. Vaughn-s/Brendon & Brian Fraim-a; three covers. 3-Zombie Proof back-up; Spencer-a | 4.00 |
| ...: Bite Out of Crime (American Mythology, 7/19, $3.99) Vaughn-s/Fraims-a; six covers | 4.00 |

VAMPIRE'S CHRISTMAS, THE (Also see Dark Ivory)
Image Comics: Oct, 2003 ($5.95, over-sized graphic novel)

| nn-Linsner-s/a; Dubisch-painted-a | 6.00 |

VAMPIRE SLAYER, THE (See the Buffy the Vampire Slayer titles)
BOOM! Studios: Apr, 2022 - No. 16, Jul, 2023 ($4.99)

| 1-16: 1-Sarah Gailey-s/Michael Shelfer-a; alternate reality where Willow is the Slayer | 5.00 |

VAMPIRE STATE BUILDING
Ablaze Publishing: 2019 - No. 4, 2020 ($3.99)

| 1-4-Charlie Adlard-a; Ange & Renault-s | 4.00 |

VAMPIRES: THE MARVEL UNDEAD
Marvel Comics: Dec, 2011 ($3.99, one-shot)

| 1-Handbook-style profiles of vampire characters in the Marvel Universe; Seeley-c | 4.00 |

VAMPIRE TALES
Marvel Comics Group: Aug, 1973 - No. 11, June, 1975 (75¢, B&W, magazine)

	GD 2.0	VG 4.0	FN 6.0	VF 8.0	VF/NM 9.0	NM- 9.2
1-Morbius, the Living Vampire begins by Pablo Marcos (1st solo Morbius series & 5th Morbius app.)	10	20	30	64	132	200
2-Intro. Satana; Steranko-r	19	38	57	133	297	460

Vampirella: Roses for the Dead #1 © DYN

Vampire, PA #2 © Vaughn & Solof

Vault of Horror #23 © WMG

	GD 2.0	VG 4.0	FN 6.0	VF 8.0	VF/NM 9.0	NM- 9.2

3,5,6: 3-Satana app. 5-Origin Morbius. 6-1st full Lilith app. in this title (continued from Giant-Size Chillers #1)
5 · 10 · 15 · 34 · 60 · 85
4,7: 4-1st Lilith cameo app. on inside back-c
5 · 10 · 15 · 33 · 57 · 80
8-1st solo Blade story (see Tomb of Dracula)
9 · 18 · 27 · 57 · 111 · 165
9-Blade app.
5 · 10 · 15 · 33 · 57 · 80
10,11
4 · 8 · 12 · 23 · 37 · 50
Annual 1(10/75)-Heath-r/#9
4 · 8 · 12 · 27 · 44 · 60
NOTE: *Alcala* a-6, 8, 9i. *Boris* c-4, 6. *Chaykin* a-7. *Everett* a-1r. *Gulacy* a-7p. *Heath* a-9. *Infantino* a-3r. *Gil Kane* a-4, 5r.

VAMPIRE VERSES, THE
CFD Productions: Aug, 1995 - No. 4, 1995 ($2.95, B&W, mature)
1-4 ... 4.00

VAMPIRONICA (Archie Comics' Veronica)(Continues in Jughead The Hunger vs Vampironica)
Archie Comic Publications: May, 2018 - No. 5, Feb, 2019 ($3.99, limited series)
1-5: 1-Veronica becomes a vampire; Greg & Meg Smallwood-s/Greg S.-a; multiple covers.
4,5-Greg Scott-a ... 4.00

VAMPIRONICA: NEW BLOOD (Archie Comics' Veronica)
Archie Comic Publications: Jan, 2020 - No. 4, Aug, 2020 ($3.99, limited series)
1-4: 1-Tieri & Moreci-s/Mok-a; multiple covers. 3-Story of Sir Francis Lodge ... 4.00

VAMPIVERSE (Vampirella)
Dynamite Entertainment: 2021 - No. 6, 2022 ($3.99, limited series)
1-6-Sniegoski & Acheson-s/Maine-a; multiple covers on each. 1-Main-c by Hughes ... 4.00
... Presents: The Vamp 1 (2022, $4.99) ... 5.00

VAMPI VICIOUS
Harris Publications (Anarchy Studios): Aug, 2003 - No. 3, Nov, 2003 ($2.99)
1-3: 1-McKeever-s/Dogan-a; 3 covers by Dogan, Lau & Noto. 3-Kau-a ... 4.00

VAMPI VICIOUS CIRCLE
Harris Publications (Anarchy Studios): Jun, 2004 - No. 3, Sept, 2004 ($2.99/$9.95)
1-3: B. Clay Moore-s ... 4.00
1-3-($9.95) Limited Edition w/variant-c. 1-Noto-c. 2-Norton-c. 3-Lucas-c ... 10.00

VAMPI VICIOUS RAMPAGE
Harris Publications (Anarchy Studios): Feb, 2005 - No. 2, Apr, 2005 ($2.99)
1,2: Raab-s/Lau-a; two covers on each ... 4.00

VAMPI VS. XIN
Harris Publications (Anarchy Studios): Oct, 2004 - No. 2, Jan, 2005 ($2.99)
1,2-Faerber-s/Lau-a; two covers ... 4.00

VAMPS
DC Comics (Vertigo): Aug, 1994 - No. 6, Jan, 1995 ($1.95, lim. series, mature)
1-6-Bolland-c ... 4.00
Trade paperback ($9.95)-r/#1-6 ... 10.00

VAMPS: HOLLYWOOD & VEIN
DC Comics (Vertigo): Feb, 1996 - No. 6, July, 1996 ($2.25, lim. series, mature)
1-6: Winslade-c ... 4.00

VAMPS: PUMPKIN TIME
DC Comics (Vertigo): Dec, 1998 - No. 3, Feb, 1999 ($2.50, lim. series, mature)
1-3: Quitely-c ... 4.00

VANDROID
Dark Horse Comics: Feb, 2014 - No. 5, Jun, 2014 ($3.99, limited series)
1-5-Tommy Lee Edwards & Noah Smith-s/Dan McDaid-a/Edwards-c ... 4.00

VANGUARD (...Outpost: Earth) (See Megaton)
Megaton Comics: 1987 ($1.50)
1-Erik Larsen-c(p) ... 4.00

VANGUARD (See Savage Dragon #2)
Image Comics (Highbrow Entertainment): Oct, 1993 - No. 6, 1994 ($1.95)
1-6: 1-Wraparound gatefold-c; Erik Larsen back-up-a; Supreme x-over. 3-(12/93)-Indicia says December 1994. 4-Berzerker back-up. 5-Angel Medina-a(p) ... 4.00

VANGUARD (See Savage Dragon #2)
Image Comics: Aug, 1996 - No. 4, Feb, 1997 ($2.95, B&W, limited series)
1-4 ... 4.00

VANGUARD: ETHEREAL WARRIORS
Image Comics: Aug, 2000 ($5.95, B&W)
1-Fosco & Larsen-a ... 6.00

VANGUARD ILLUSTRATED
Pacific Comics: Nov, 1983 - No. 11, Oct, 1984 (Baxter paper)(Direct sales only)
1,3,6-8,11: 1-Nudity scenes ... 5.00
2-1st app. Stargrazers (see Legends of the Stargrazers); Dave Stevens-c
3 · 6 · 9 · 14 · 20 · 26

7-1st app. Mr. Monster (r-in Mr. Monster #1); nudity scenes ... 6.00
NOTE: *Evans* a-7. *Kaluta* c-5, 7p. *Perez* a-6; c-6. *Rude* a-1-4; c-4. *Williamson* c-3.

VANGUARD: STRANGE VISITORS
Image Comics: Oct, 1996 - No.4, Feb, 1997 ($2.95, B&W, limited series)
1-4: 3-Supreme-c/app. ... 4.00

VAN HELSING: FROM BENEATH THE RUE MORGUE (Based on the 2004 movie)
Dark Horse Comics: Apr, 2004 ($2.99, one-shot)
1-Hugh Jackman photo-c; Dysart-s/Alexander-a ... 3.00

VANISH
Image Comics: Sept, 2022 - No. 8, Jun, 2023 ($3.99)
1-8-Cates-s/Stegman-a ... 4.00

VANITY (See Pacific Presents #3)
Pacific Comics: Jun, 1984 - No. 2, Aug, 1984 ($1.50, direct sales)
1,2: Origin ... 4.00

VARIANTS, THE
Marvel Comics: Aug, 2022 - No. 5, Feb, 2023 ($3.99, limited series)
1-5-A Jessica Jones mystery; Gail Simone-s/Phil Noto-a. 2,3-She-Hulk app. ... 4.00

VARIETY COMICS (The Spice of Comics)
Rural Home Publ./Croyden Publ. Co.: 1944 - No. 2, 1945; No. 3, 1946
1-Origin Captain Valiant
39 · 78 · 117 · 240 · 395 · 550
2-Captain Valiant
20 · 40 · 60 · 120 · 195 · 270
3(1946-Croyden)-Captain Valiant
18 · 36 · 54 · 105 · 165 · 225

VARIETY COMICS (See Fox Giants)

VARKING DEAD (Cerebus)
Aardvark-Vanaheim: Mar, 2020 ($4.00, B&W)
1-Walking Dead homage; Cerebus figures placed over original Doré artwork of Hell ... 4.00

VARK THING (Cerebus)
Aardvark-Vanaheim: Dec, 2019 ($4.00, B&W)
1-Swamp Thing homage figures placed over original Gustave Doré artwork of Hell ... 4.00

VARK WARS (Cerebus)
Aardvark-Vanaheim: Nov, 2019 ($4.00, B&W)
1-Cerebus figures placed over original Gustave Doré artwork of Hell ... 4.00

VARSITY
Parents' Magazine Institute: 1945
1 ... 14 · 28 · 42 · 82 · 121 · 160

VAULT OF CEREBUS (Imagery from Glamourpuss & Cerebus in Hell)
Aardvark-Vanaheim: Oct, 2020 ($4.00, B&W)
1-Cerebus figures placed over Doré artwork and zombies; Vault of Horror #19-c swipe ... 4.00

VAULT OF EVIL
Marvel Comics Group: Feb, 1973 - No. 23, Nov, 1975
1 (1950s reprints begin)
6 · 12 · 18 · 42 · 79 · 115
2-23: 3,4-Brunner-c. 11-Kirby-a
6 · 9 · 19 · 30 · 40
NOTE: *Ditko* a-14r, 15r, 20-22r. *Drucker* a-10r(Mystic #52), 13r(Uncanny Tales #42). *Everett* a-11r(Menace #2), 13r(Menace #4); c-10. *Heath* a-5r. *Gil Kane* c-1, 6. *Kirby* a-11. *Krigstein* a-20r(Uncanny Tales #54). *Reinman* r-1. *Tuska* a-6r.

VAULT OF HORROR (Formerly War Against Crime #1-11) (Also see EC Archives)
E. C. Comics: No. 12, Apr-May, 1950 - No. 40, Dec-Jan, 1954-55
12 (Scarce)-ties w/Crypt Of Terror as 1st horror comic; classic horror story "Terror Train" reprinted by popular demand in Haunt of Fear #20
1000 · 2000 · 3000 · 8000 · 12,750 · 17,500
13-Morphine scene
177 · 354 · 531 · 1416 · 2258 · 3100
14-Classic horror story "The Strange Couple" redrawn in 3-D Tales of Terror #2
137 · 274 · 411 · 1096 · 1748 · 2400
15- "Terror in the Swamp" is same story w/minor changes as "The Thing in the Swamp" from Haunt of Fear #15
126 · 252 · 378 · 1008 · 1604 · 2200
16
89 · 178 · 267 · 712 · 1131 · 1550
17-Classic werewolf-c
103 · 206 · 309 · 824 · 1312 · 1800
18,19
77 · 154 · 231 · 616 · 983 · 1350
20-25: 22-Frankenstein-c & adaptation. 23-Used in POP, pg. 84; Davis-a(2); Ingels bio.
60 · 120 · 180 · 480 · 765 · 1050
24-Craig bio.
86 · 172 · 258 · 688 · 1094 · 1500
26-B&W & color illos in POP
27-29,31,33,34,36: 31-Ray Bradbury bio. 36- "Pipe Dream" classic opium addict story by Krigstein; "Twin Bill" cited in articles by T.E. Murphy, Wertham
56 · 112 · 168 · 448 · 712 · 975
30-Classic severed arm-c
131 · 262 · 393 · 1048 · 1674 · 2300
32-Censored-c
91 · 182 · 273 · 728 · 1164 · 1600
35-X-Mas-c; "And All Through the House" adapted for 1972 Tales From The Crypt film
263 · 526 · 789 · 2104 · 3352 · 4600
37-1st app. Drusilla, a Vampirella look alike; Williamson-a

	GD	VG	FN	VF	VF/NM	NM-
	2.0	4.0	6.0	8.0	9.0	9.2

	GD 2.0	VG 4.0	FN 6.0	VF 8.0	VF/NM 9.0	NM- 9.2
	80	160	240	640	1020	1400
38	56	112	168	448	712	975
39-Classic Craig woman in bondage/torture-c	103	206	309	824	1312	1800
40-Low distribution	80	160	240	640	1020	1400

NOTE: *Craig* art in all but No. 13 & 33; c-12-40. *Crandall* a-33, 34, 39. *Davis* a-17-38. *Evans* a-27, 28, 30, 32, 33. *Feldstein* a-12-16. *Ingels* a-13-20, 22-40. *Kamen* a-15-22, 25, 29, 35. *Krigstein* a-36, 38-40. *Kurtzman* a-12, 13. *Orlando* a-24, 31, 40. *Wood* a-12-14. #22, 29 & 31 have Ray Bradbury adaptations. #16 & 17 have H. P. Lovecraft adaptations.

VAULT OF HORROR, THE
Gladstone Publ.: Aug, 1990 - No. 6, June, 1991 ($1.95, 68 pgs.)(#4 on: $2.00)

1-Craig-c(r); all contain EC reprints						6.00
2-6: 2,4,6-Craig-c(r). 3-Ingels-c(r)						5.00

VAULT OF HORROR
Russ Cochran/Gemstone Publishing: Sept, 1991 - No. 5, May, 1992 ($2.00); Oct, 1992 - No. 29, Oct, 1999 ($1.50/$2.00/$2.50)

1-29: EC reprints. 1-4r/VOH #12-15 w/original-a						4.00

VAULT OF SPIDERS (Tie-ins to the Spider-Geddon x-over)
Marvel Comics: Dec, 2018 - No. 2, Jan, 2019 ($4.99)

1,2-Short stories of alternate Spider-Verse super-heroes; s/a by various						5.00

V...—COMICS (Morse code for "V" - 3 dots, 1 dash)
Fox Feature Syndicate: Jan, 1942 - No. 2, Mar-Apr, 1942

	GD 2.0	VG 4.0	FN 6.0	VF 8.0	VF/NM 9.0	NM- 9.2
1-Origin V-Man & the Boys; The Banshee & The Black Fury, The Queen of Evil, & V-Agents begin; Nazi-c	331	662	993	2317	4059	5800
2-Nazi bondage/torture-c	303	606	909	2121	3711	5300

VECTOR
Now Comics: 1986 - No. 4, 1986? ($1.50, 1st color comic by Now Comics)

1-4: Computer-generated art						4.00

VEIL
Dark Horse Comics: Mar, 2014 - No. 5, Oct, 2014 ($3.50)

1-5-Greg Rucka-s/Toni Fejzula-a/c						3.50

VEILS
DC Comics (Vertigo): 1999 ($24.95, one-shot)

Hardcover-($24.95) Painted art and photography; McGreal-s						25.00
Softcover ($14.95)						15.00

VELOCITY (Also see Cyberforce)
Image Comics (Top Cow Productions): Nov, 1995 - No. 3, Jan, 1996 ($2.50, limited series)

1-3: Kurt Busiek scripts in all. 2-Savage Dragon-c/app.						4.00
...: Pilot Season 1 (10/07, $2.99) Casey/Maguire-a						4.00
Vol. 2 #1-4 (6/10 - No. 4, 4/11, $3.99) Rocafort-a/Marz-s; multiple covers						4.00

VELVET
Image Comics: Oct, 2013 - No. 15, Jul, 2016 ($3.50/$3.99)

1-14-Brubaker-s/Epting-a/c. 5-$2.99-c						3.50
15-($3.99)						4.00

VENGEANCE
Marvel Comics: Sept, 2011 - No. 6, Feb, 2012 ($3.99, limited series)

1-6-Casey-s/Dragotta-a. 1-Magneto and Red Skull app. 4-Loki cover						4.00

VENGEANCE OF THE MOON KNIGHT
Marvel Comics: Nov, 2009 - No. 10, Sept, 2010 ($3.99/$2.99)

	GD 2.0	VG 4.0	FN 6.0	VF 8.0	VF/NM 9.0	NM- 9.2
1,9: 1-($3.99) Hurwitz/Opeña-a; covers by Yu, Ross & Finch; back-up r/Moon Knight #1 ('80) 9-Spider-Man & Sandman app.; Campbell-c	2	4	6	8	10	12
2-8,10: 2-Sentry app. 5-Spider-Man app. 7,8-Deadpool app. 10-Secret Avengers app.						5.00

VENGEANCE OF THE MOON KNIGHT
Marvel Comics: Mar, 2024 - Present ($5.99/$4.99)

1-($5.99) MacKay-s/Cappuccio-a; Tigra app.						6.00
2-($4.99)						5.00

VENGEANCE OF VAMPIRELLA (Becomes Vampirella: Death & Destruction)
Harris Comics: Apr, 1994 - No. 25, Apr, 1996 ($2.95)

	GD 2.0	VG 4.0	FN 6.0	VF 8.0	VF/NM 9.0	NM- 9.2
1-($3.50)-Quesada/Palmiotti "bloodfoil" wraparound-c	2	4	6	8	10	12
1-2nd printing; blue foil-c						4.00
1-Gold						24.00
2-8: 8-Polybagged w/trading card						5.00
9-25: 10-w/coupon for Hyde -25 poster. 11,19-Polybagged w/ trading card. 25-Quesada & Palmiotti red foil-c						4.00
...: Bloodshed (1995, $6.95)						7.00

VENGEANCE OF VAMPIRELLA (Volume 2)
Dynamite Entertainment: 2019 - No. 25, 2021 ($3.99)

1-25: 1-Set 25 years in the future; Sniegoski-s/Sta. Maria-a; multiple covers on each						4.00

VENGEANCE OF VAMPIRELLA: THE MYSTERY WALK
Harris Comics: Nov, 1995 ($2.95, one-shot)

	GD 2.0	VG 4.0	FN 6.0	VF 8.0	VF/NM 9.0	NM- 9.2
0	1	2	3	5	6	8

VENGEANCE SQUAD
Charlton Comics: July, 1975 - No. 6, May, 1976 (#1-3 are 25¢ issues)

	GD 2.0	VG 4.0	FN 6.0	VF 8.0	VF/NM 9.0	NM- 9.2
1-Mike Mauser, Private Eye begins by Staton	2	4	6	11	16	20
2-6: Morisi-a in all	1	3	4	6	8	10
5,6 (Modern Comics-r, 1977)	1	2	3	5		8

VENOM
Marvel Comics: June, 2003 - No. 18, Nov, 2004 ($2.25/$2.99)

	GD 2.0	VG 4.0	FN 6.0	VF 8.0	VF/NM 9.0	NM- 9.2
1-Herrera-a/Way-s	2	4	6	9	12	15
2-15: 2-7-Herrera-a/Way-s. 6,7-Wolverine app. 8-10-Wolverine-c/app.; Kieth-c. 11-Fantastic Four app.						5.00
16-18	1	2	3	5	6	8
... Vol. 1: Shiver (2004, $13.99, TPB) r/#1-5						14.00
... Vol. 2: Run (2004, $19.99, TPB) r/#6-13						20.00
... Vol. 3: Twist (2004, $13.99, TPB) r/#14-18						14.00

VENOM (See Amazing Spider-Man #654 & 654.1)(Also see Secret Avengers)
Marvel Comics: May, 2011 - No. 42, Dec, 2013 ($3.99/$2.99)

	GD 2.0	VG 4.0	FN 6.0	VF 8.0	VF/NM 9.0	NM- 9.2
1-Flash Thompson with the symbiote; Remender-s/Tony Moore-a/Quesada-c	3	6	9	15	22	28
2-Cover swipe of ASM #300; Kraven app.	3	6	9	17	25	34
3-12-($2.99) 3-Deodato-c. 6-8-Spider Island						4.00
13-($3.99) Circle of Four; Red Hulk, X-23, and Ghost Rider app.						4.00
13.1, 13.2, 13.3, 13.4, 14-($2.99) Circle of Four parts 2-6						3.00
15-27, 27.1, 28-42: 15-Secret Avengers app. 16,17-Toxin app. 26,27-Minimum Carnage. 38-1st app. Mania. 42-Mephisto app.						4.00
...: Flashpoint 1 (2011, $4.99) r/Amazing Spider-Man #654, 654.1 and Venom 2	3	6	9	14	20	25

VENOM (Also see Amazing Spider-Man: Venom Inc.)
Marvel Comics: Jan, 2017 - No. 6, Jun, 2017; No. 150, Jul, 2017 - No. 165, Jun, 2018 ($3.99)

	GD 2.0	VG 4.0	FN 6.0	VF 8.0	VF/NM 9.0	NM- 9.2
1-Mike Costa-s/Gerardo Sandoval-a; intro. Lee Price; Mac Gargan app.	1	3	4	6	8	10
2-6						4.00

[Title switches to legacy numbering after #6 (6/17)]

150-($5.99) Eddie Brock as Venom; Spider-Man app.; Tradd Moore-a; cover gallery						6.00
151-165: 152,153-Moon Girl and Devil Dinosaur app. 155-158-Kraven app.; Bagley-a. 159-Venom Inc. part 3; Sandoval-a. 160-Venom Inc. part 5						4.00

VENOM (Follows Venomized series)
Marvel Comics: Jul, 2018 - No. 35, Aug, 2021 ($4.99/$3.99)

	GD 2.0	VG 4.0	FN 6.0	VF 8.0	VF/NM 9.0	NM- 9.2
1-($4.99) Cates-s/Stegman-a; Eddie Brock with the symbiote; intro. Rex Strickland	2	4	6	9	12	15
2,4-24,26-34 ($3.99) 2-5-Spider-Man (Miles Morales) app. 4-Origin of Knull. 13-15-War of the Realms tie-ins. 17-20-Absolute Carnage tie-ins. 21-24-Venom Island; Bagley-a. 31-34-King In Black						4.00
3-1st full app. Knull (6/18)	6	12	18	38	69	100
25-($5.99) 1st app. Virus; Cates-s/Bagley-a; Carnage app.; back-up w/Michelinie-s/Lim-a	6.00
35-($9.99) 200th Legacy issue; Venom gets a new host; bonus cover gallery						10.00
Annual 1 (12/18, $4.99) Short stories by various incl. Cates, Michelinie, Lim, Stokoe						5.00
Annual 1 (9/19, $4.99) Cady-s/Di Meo-a; Lady Hellbender app.; back-up origin; Ibáñez-a						5.00
...: The End 1 (3/20, $4.99) Warren-s/Cruz-a; Venom's last story in the far future						5.00
... 2099 #1 (2/20, $4.99) Tie-in to 2099 x-over; Venom's new host; Houser-s						5.00

VENOM
Marvel Comics: Dec, 2021 - Present ($5.99/$3.99)

1-($5.99) Ewing & Ram V-s/Hitch-a; Dylan Brock with the symbiote						6.00
2-24,26-30-($3.99) 8,9-Kang app.; Ewing's. 13-16-Dark Web tie-ins						4.00
25-($7.99) Doctor Doom app.						8.00
Annual 1 (11/23, $4.99) Deadpool app.						5.00

VENOMIZED
Marvel Comics: Jun, 2018 - No. 5, Jul, 2018 ($4.99/$3.99, weekly limited series)

1-($4.99) Bunn-s/Coello-a; X-Men vs. the Poisons						5.00
2-5-($3.99) 2,3,5-Bunn-s/Coello-a. 4-Libranda-a						4.00

VENOM: LETHAL PROTECTOR
Marvel Comics: Feb, 1993 - No. 6, July, 1993 ($2.95, limited series)

	GD 2.0	VG 4.0	FN 6.0	VF 8.0	VF/NM 9.0	NM- 9.2
1-Red holo-grafx foil-c; Bagley-c/a in all	4	8	12	25	40	55
1-Gold variant sold to retailers	16	32	48	111	246	380
1-Black-c	104	208	312	832	1866	2900

NOTE: Counterfeit copies of the black-c exist and are valueless

	GD 2.0	VG 4.0	FN 6.0	VF 8.0	VF/NM 9.0	NM- 9.2
2,4-6: Spider-Man app. in all	2	4	6	10	14	18
5-1st app. Phage, Lasher, Riot & Agony	3	6	9	17	26	35

VENOM: LETHAL PROTECTOR
Marvel Comics: May, 2022 - No. 5, Oct, 2022 ($4.99/$3.99, limited series)

1-($4.99) Michelinie-s/Fiorelli-a; set in the early days with Eddie Brock						5.00
2-5-($3.99) 5-Taskmaster app.						4.00

VENOM: LETHAL PROTECTOR II
Marvel Comics: May, 2023 - No. 5, Sept, 2023 ($4.99/$3.99, limited series)

1-($4.99) Michelinie-s/Karami-a; Silver Sable and The Wild Pack app.						5.00
2-5-($3.99) 4,5-Doctor Doom app.						4.00

VENOM: SPACE KNIGHT
Marvel Comics: Jan, 2016 - No. 13, Dec, 2016 ($3.99)

1-13: 1-Robbie Thompson-s/Ariel Olivetti-a. 8-10-Jacinto-a. 11,12-Civil War II tie-in						4.00

VENOM: Marvel Comics (Also see Amazing Spider-Man #298-300)

... ALONG CAME A SPIDER, 1/96 - No. 4, 4/96 ($2.95)-Spider-Man & Carnage app.

	GD 2.0	VG 4.0	FN 6.0	VF 8.0	VF/NM 9.0	NM- 9.2
		2	4	6	9	12	15

... CARNAGE UNLEASHED, 4/95 - No. 4, 7/95 ($2.95)

	GD 2.0	VG 4.0	FN 6.0	VF 8.0	VF/NM 9.0	NM- 9.2
	1	3	4	6	8	10

... DARK ORIGIN, 10/08 - No. 5, 2/09 ($2.99) 1-5-Medina-a

						6.00

.../DEADPOOL: WHAT IF?, 4/11 ($2.99) Remender-s/Moll-a/Young-c; Galactus app.

	GD 2.0	VG 4.0	FN 6.0	VF 8.0	VF/NM 9.0	NM- 9.2
	13	26	39	89	195	300

... DEATHTRAP: THE VAULT, 3/93 ($6.95) r/Avengers: Deathtrap: The Vault

	GD 2.0	VG 4.0	FN 6.0	VF 8.0	VF/NM 9.0	NM- 9.2
	1	3	4	6	8	10	12

... FIRST HOST, 10/18 - No. 5, 11/18 ($3.99) 1-Costa-s/Bagley & Lim-a

	GD 2.0	VG 4.0	FN 6.0	VF 8.0	VF/NM 9.0	NM- 9.2
	1	3	4	6	8	10
2-5						4.00

... FUNERAL PYRE, 8/93- No. 3, 10/93 ($2.95)-#1-Holo-grafx foil-c; Punisher app. in all

	GD 2.0	VG 4.0	FN 6.0	VF 8.0	VF/NM 9.0	NM- 9.2
	1	3	4	6	8	10

... LICENSE TO KILL, 6/97 - No. 3, 8/97 ($1.95)

	GD 2.0	VG 4.0	FN 6.0	VF 8.0	VF/NM 9.0	NM- 9.2
	1	3	4	6	8	10

... NIGHTS OF VENGEANCE, 8/94 - No. 4, 11/94 ($2.95), #1-Red foil-c

	GD 2.0	VG 4.0	FN 6.0	VF 8.0	VF/NM 9.0	NM- 9.2
	1	3	4	6	8	10

... ON TRIAL, 3/97 - No. 3, 5/97 ($1.95)

	GD 2.0	VG 4.0	FN 6.0	VF 8.0	VF/NM 9.0	NM- 9.2
	1	3	4	6	8	10

... SEED OF DARKNESS, 7/97 ($1.95) #(-1) Flashback

	GD 2.0	VG 4.0	FN 6.0	VF 8.0	VF/NM 9.0	NM- 9.2
	1	3	4	6	8	10

... SEPARATION ANXIETY, 12/94- No. 4, 3/95 ($2.95) #1-Embossed-c

	GD 2.0	VG 4.0	FN 6.0	VF 8.0	VF/NM 9.0	NM- 9.2
	1	3	4	6	8	10

... SIGN OF THE BOSS, 3/97 - No. 2, 10/97 ($1.99)

	GD 2.0	VG 4.0	FN 6.0	VF 8.0	VF/NM 9.0	NM- 9.2
	1	3	4	6	8	10

... SINNER TAKES ALL, 8/95 - No. 5, 10/95 ($2.95) 1,2,4,5

Velvet #8 © Basement Gang

Venom (2017 series) #1 © MAR

Veronica #202 © ACP

	GD	VG	FN	VF	VF/NM	NM-
	2.0	4.0	6.0	8.0	9.0	9.2

	GD 2.0	VG 4.0	FN 6.0	VF 8.0	VF/NM 9.0	NM- 9.2
3-1st time Ann Weying app. as female Venom	1	3	4	6	8	10
	6	12	18	38	69	100
... SUPER SPECIAL, 8/95($3.95) #1-Flip book	2	4	6	11	16	20
... THE ENEMY WITHIN, 2/94 - No. 3, 4/94 ($2.95)-Demogoblin & Morbius app.						
1-Glow-in-the-dark-c	2	4	6	11	16	20
... THE FINALE, 11/97 - No. 3, 1/98 ($1.99)	1	3	4	6	8	10
... THE HUNGER, 8/96- No. 4, 11/96 ($1.95)	1	3	4	6	8	10
... THE HUNTED, 5/96-No. 3, 7/96 ($2.95)	1	3	4	6	8	10
... THE MACE, 5/94 - No. 3, 7/94 ($2.95)-#1-Embossed-c	1	3	4	6	8	10
... THE MADNESS, 11/93- No. 3, 1/94 ($2.95)-Kelley Jones-c/a(p).						
1-Embossed-c; Juggernaut app.	1	3	4	6	8	10
... TOOTH AND CLAW, 12/96 - No. 3, 2/97 ($1.95)-Wolverine-c/app.						
	1	3	4	6	8	10
... VS. CARNAGE, 9/04 - No. 4, 12/04 ($2.99)-Milligan-s/Crain-a; Spider-Man app.						
	1	3	4	6	8	10
TPB (2004, $9.99) r/#1-4						10.00

VENOMVERSE
Marvel Comics: Nov, 2017 - No. 5, Dec, 2017 ($4.99/$3.99, weekly limited series)

1-($4.99) Bunn-s/Coello-a; Venoms vs. The Poisons						5.00
2-5-($3.99) Bunn-s/Coello-a						4.00
...: War Stories 1 (11/17, $4.99) Multiverse of Venoms; short stories by various						5.00

VENTURE
AC Comics (Americomics): Aug, 1986 - No. 3, 1986? ($1.75)

1-3: 1-3-Bolt. 1-Astron. 2-Femforce. 3-Fazers						4.00

VENTURE
Image Comics: Jan, 2003 - No. 4, Sept, 2003 ($2.95)

1-4-Faerber-s/Igle-a						3.00

VENUS (See Agents of Atlas, Marvel Spotlight #2 & Weird Wonder Tales)
Marvel/Atlas Comics (CMC 1-9/LCC 10-19): Aug, 1948 - No. 19, Apr, 1952 (Also see Marvel Mystery #91)

	GD 2.0	VG 4.0	FN 6.0	VF 8.0	VF/NM 9.0	NM- 9.2
1-Venus & Hedy Devine begin; 1st app. Venus; Kurtzman's "Hey Look"	389	778	1167	2723	4762	6800
2	181	362	543	1158	1979	2800
3,5	113	226	339	718	1234	1750
4-Kurtzman's "Hey Look"	181	362	543	1158	1979	2800
6-9: 6-Loki app. 7,8-Painted-c. 9-Begin 52 pgs.; book-length feature "Whom the Gods Destroy!"	100	200	300	635	1093	1550
10-S/F-horror issues begin (7/50)	142	284	426	909	1555	2200
11-S/F end of the world (11/50)	155	310	465	992	1696	2400
12-Colan-a	100	200	300	635	1093	1550
13-16-Venus by Everett, 2-3 stories each; covers-#13,15,16; 14-Everett part cover (Venus).	174	348	522	1114	1907	2700
17-Classic Everett horror & skeleton/bondage-c (scarce)	541	1082	1623	3950	6975	10,000
18-Classic Everett horror-c	423	846	1289	3088	5444	7800
19-Classic Everett skeleton Good Girl-c	1500	3000	4500	11,400	20,700	30,000

NOTE: Berg s/f story-13. Everett c-13, 14(part; Venus only), 15-19. Heath s/f story-11. Maneely s/f story 10(3pg.), 16. Morisi a-19. Syd Shores c-6.

VENUS
BOOM! Studios: Dec, 2015 - No. 4, Mar, 2016 ($3.99)

1-4-Loverd-s/Danlan-a						4.00

VERI BEST SURE FIRE COMICS
Holyoke Publishing Co.: No date (circa 1945) (Reprints Holyoke one-shots)

	GD 2.0	VG 4.0	FN 6.0	VF 8.0	VF/NM 9.0	NM- 9.2
1-Captain Aero, Alias X, Miss Victory, Commandos of the Devil Dogs, Red Cross, Hammerhead Hawley, Capt. Aero's Sky Scouts, Flagman app.; same-c as Veri Best Sure Shot #1	58	116	174	371	636	900

VERI BEST SURE SHOT COMICS
Holyoke Publishing Co.: No date (circa 1945) (Reprints Holyoke one-shots)

	GD 2.0	VG 4.0	FN 6.0	VF 8.0	VF/NM 9.0	NM- 9.2
1-Capt. Aero, Miss Victory by Quinlan, Alias X, The Red Cross, Flagman, Commandos of the Devil Dogs, Hammerhead Hawley, Capt. Aero's Sky Scouts; same-c as Veri Best Sure Fire #1	60	120	180	381	653	925

VERMILLION
DC Comics (Helix): Oct, 1996 - No. 12, Sept, 1997 ($2.25/$2.50)

1-12: 1-4: Lucius Shepard scripts. 4,12-Kaluta-c						4.00

VERONICA (Also see Archie's Girls, Betty &...)
Archie Comics: Apr, 1989 - No. 210, Feb, 2012

	GD 2.0	VG 4.0	FN 6.0	VF 8.0	VF/NM 9.0	NM- 9.2
1-(75¢-c)	3	6	9	14	19	24
2-10: 2-(75¢-c)						5.00

	GD 2.0	VG 4.0	FN 6.0	VF 8.0	VF/NM 9.0	NM- 9.2
11-18,20-22,24-27,29-38						4.00
19-Money-c	2	4	6	9	12	15
23-Pot of Gold bikini-c (9/92)	3	6	9	21	33	45
28-Bikini-c	6	12	18	38	69	100
39-Love Showdown pt. 4, Cheryl Blossom	1	2	3	5	6	8
40-67,69,70: 34-Neon ink-c						4.00
68,103,115-Bikini-c	1	2	4	7	11	16
71-102,104-114,116-201,203-206: 134-Begin $2.19-c. 152,155-Cheryl Blossom app.						3.00
163-Begin $2.25-c						
202-Intro. Kevin Keller, 1st openly gay Archie character; cover has blue background	3	6	9	14	19	24
202-Second printing; cover has black background	1	3	4	6	8	10
207-210-Kevin Keller mini-series						3.00

VERONICA'S PASSPORT DIGEST MAGAZINE (Becomes Veronica's Digest Magazine #3 on)
Archie Comics: Nov, 1992 - No. 6 ($1.50/$1.79, digest size)

1						6.00
2-6						4.00

VERONICA'S SUMMER SPECIAL (See Archie Giant Series Magazine #615, 625)

VERTICAL
DC Comics (Vertigo): 2003 ($4.95, 3-1/4" wide pages, one-shot)

1-Seagle-s/Allred & Bond-a; odd format 1/2 width pages with some 20" long spreads						5.00

VERTIGO DOUBLE SHOT
DC Comics (Vertigo): 2008 ($2.99)

1-Reprints House of Mystery (2008) #1 and Young Liars #1 in flip-book format						3.00

VERTIGO ESSENTIALS
DC Comics (Vertigo): Dec, 2013 - Feb, 2014 ($1.00, Flip book reprints with DC & Vertigo Essential Graphics novels catalog)

...: American Vampire 1 (2/14) Reprints #1; flip-c by Ryan Sook						3.00
...: Fables 1 (1/14) Reprints #1; flip-c by Ryan Sook						3.00
...: 100 Bullets 1 (2/14) Reprints #1; flip-c by Ryan Sook						3.00
...: The Sandman #1 (12/13, $1.00) Reprints Sandman #1 (1989) with flipbook						3.00
...: V For Vendetta 1 (12/13) Reprints first chapter; flip-c by Ryan Sook						3.00
...: Y: The Last Man 1 (1/14) Reprints #1; flip-c by Ryan Sook						3.00

VERTIGO: FIRST BLOOD
DC Comics (Vertigo): Feb, 2012 ($7.99, squarebound)

TPB-Reprints first issues of American Vampire, I Zombie, The Unwritten & Sweet Tooth						8.00

VERTIGO: FIRST CUT
DC Comics (Vertigo): 2008 ($4.99, TPB)

TPB-Reprints first issues of DMZ, Army@Love, Jack of Fables, Exterminators, Scalped, Crossing Midnight, and Loveless; preview of Air						5.00

VERTIGO: FIRST OFFENSES
DC Comics (Vertigo): 2005 ($4.99, TPB)

TPB-Reprints first issues of The Invisibles, Preacher, Fables, Sandman Mystery Theater, and Lucifer						5.00

VERTIGO: FIRST TASTE
DC Comics (Vertigo): 2005 ($4.99, TPB)

TPB-Reprints first issues of Y: The Last Man, 100 Bullets, Transmetropolitan, Books of Magick: Life During Wartime, Death: The High Cost of Living, and Saga of the Swamp Thing #21 (Alan Moore's first story on that title)						5.00

VERTIGO GALLERY, THE: DREAMS AND NIGHTMARES
DC Comics (Vertigo): 1995 ($3.50, one-shot)

1-Pin-ups of Vertigo characters by Sienkiewicz, Toth, Van Fleet & others; McKean-c						4.00

VERTIGO JAM
DC Comics (Vertigo): Aug, 1993 ($3.95, one-shot, 68 pgs.)(Painted-c by Fabry)

1-Sandman by Neil Gaiman, Hellblazer, Animal Man, Doom Patrol, Swamp Thing, Kid Eternity & Shade the Changing Man						5.00

VERTIGO POP! BANGKOK
DC Comics (Vertigo): July, 2003 - No. 4, Oct, 2003 ($2.95, limited series)

1-4-Camuncoli-c/a; Jonathan Vankin-s						3.00

VERTIGO POP! LONDON
DC Comics (Vertigo): Jan, 2003 - No. 4, Apr, 2003 ($2.95, limited series)

1-4-Philip Bond-c/a; Peter Milligan-s						3.00

VERTIGO POP! TOKYO
DC Comics (Vertigo): Sept, 2002 - No. 4, Dec, 2002 ($2.95, limited series)

1-4-Seth Fisher-a; Jonathan Vankin-s						3.00
Tokyo Days, Bangkok Nights TPB (2009, $19.99) r/#1-4 & Vertogo Pop! Bangkok #1-4						20.00

VERTIGO PREVIEW
DC Comics (Vertigo): 1992 (75¢, one-shot, 36 pgs.)

	GD 2.0	VG 4.0	FN 6.0	VF 8.0	VF/NM 9.0	NM- 9.2
1-Vertigo previews; Sandman story by Neil Gaiman					4.00	

VERTIGO QUARTERLY CMYK
DC Comics (Vertigo): Jun, 2014 - No. 4, Mar, 2015 ($7.99, limited series)

	GD 2.0	VG 4.0	FN 6.0	VF 8.0	VF/NM 9.0	NM- 9.2
1-4-Color themed short story anthology. 1-Cyan. 2-Magenta. 3-Yellow. 4-Black					8.00	

VERTIGO QUARTERLY SFX
DC Comics (Vertigo): Jun, 2015 - No. 4, Mar, 2016 ($7.99, limited series)

1-4-Sound effect-themed short story anthology. 1-"Pop!". 2-"Slam!". 3-"Krak!". 4-"Bang"				8.00	

VERTIGO RAVE
DC Comics (Vertigo): Fall, 1994 (99¢, one-shot)

1-Vertigo previews 4.00

VERTIGO RESURRECTED: ...
DC Comics (Vertigo): Dec, 2010 - Feb, 2012 ($7.99, squarebound, reprints)

The Extremist 1 (1/11, 12/13) r/The Extremist #1-4 ..... 8.00
Finals 1 (5/11) r/Finals #1-4; Jill Thompson-a 8.00
Hellblazer 1 (2/11) r/Hellblazer #57,58,245,246 ..... 8.00
Hellblazer - Bad Blood 1 (6/11) r/Hellblazer Special: Bad Blood #1-4 ..... 8.00
Jonny Double 1 (10/11) r/Jonny Double #1-4; Azzarello-s/Risso-a 8.00
My Faith in Frankie 1 (1/12) r/My Faith in Frankie #1-4; Carey/s 8.00
Sandman Presents - Petrefax 1 (8/11) r/Sandman Presents: Petrefax #1-4 ..... 8.00
Sgt. Rock: Between Hell and a Hard Place 1,2 (1/12, 2/12) r/the 2003 HC 8.00
Shoot 1 (12/10) r/short stories by various incl. Quitely, Sale, Bolland, Risso, Jim Lee 8.00
The Eaters 1 (12/11) r/Vertigo Visions - The Eaters and other short stories 8.00
Winter's Edge 1 (2/11) r/Vertigo's Winter Edge #1-3; Bermejo-a 8.00

VERTIGO SECRET FILES
DC Comics (Vertigo): Aug, 2000 ($4.95)

...: Hellblazer 1 (8/00, $4.95) Background info and story summaries 5.00
...: Swamp Thing 1 (11/00, $4.95) Back stories and origins; Hale-c 5.00

VERTIGO VERITE: THE UNSEEN HAND
DC Comics (Vertigo): Sept, 1996 - No. 4, Dec, 1996 ($2.50, limited series)

1-4: Terry LaBan scripts in all 4.00

VERTIGO VISIONS
DC Comics (Vertigo): June, 1993 - Sept, 1998 (one-shots)

Dr. Occult 1 (7/94, $3.95) 4.00
Dr. Thirteen 1 (9/98, $5.95) Howarth-s 6.00
Prez 1 (7/95, $3.95) 4.00
The Geek 1 (6/93, $3.95) 4.00
The Eaters ($4.95, 1995)-Milligan story 5.00
The Phantom Stranger 1 (10/93, $3.50) 4.00
Tomahawk 1 (7/98, $4.95) Pollack-s 5.00

VERTIGO WINTER'S EDGE
DC Comics (Vertigo): 1998, 1999 ($7.95/$6.95, square-bound, annual)

1-Winter stories by Vertigo creators; Desire story by Gaiman/Bolton; Bolland wraparound-c 8.00
2,3-($6.95)-Winter stories: 2-Allred-a. 3-Bond-c; Desire by Gaiman/Zulli 7.00

VERTIGO X ANNIVERSARY PREVIEW
DC Comics (Vertigo): 2003 (99¢, one-shot, 48 pgs.)

1-Previews of upcoming titles and interviews; Endless Nights, Shade, The Originals 4.00

VERY BEST OF DENNIS THE MENACE, THE
Fawcett Publ.: July, 1979 - No. 2, Apr, 1980 (95¢/$1.00, digest-size, 132 pgs.)

	GD 2.0	VG 4.0	FN 6.0	VF 8.0	VF/NM 9.0	NM- 9.2
1,2-Reprints	2	4	6	8	10	12

VERY BEST OF DENNIS THE MENACE, THE
Marvel Comics Group: Apr, 1982 - No. 3, Aug, 1982 ($1.25, digest-size)

	GD 2.0	VG 4.0	FN 6.0	VF 8.0	VF/NM 9.0	NM- 9.2
1-3: Reprints	2	3	4	6	8	10
1,2-Mistakenly printed with DC logo on cover	2	4	6	9	12	15

NOTE: *Hank Ketcham c-all. A few thousand of #1 & 2 were printed with DC emblem.*

VERY VALIANTINE'S SPECIAL, A
Valiant Entertainment: Feb, 2024 ($12.99, square-bound, one-shot)

1-Short Valentine's stories by various; Bloodshot, Doctor Mirage, Ninjak, Faith, Archer app. 13.00

VERY VICKY
Meet Danny Ocean: 1993? - No. 8, 1995 ($2.50, B&W)

1-8, ...: Calling All Hillbillies (1995, $2.50) 4.00

VERY WEIRD TALES (Also see Slithiss Attacks!)
Oceanspray Comics Group: Aug, 2002 - No. 2, Oct, 2002 ($4.00)

	GD 2.0	VG 4.0	FN 6.0	VF 8.0	VF/NM 9.0	NM- 9.2
1-Mutant revenge, methamphetamine, corporate greed horror stories	3	6	9	16	23	30
2-Weird fantasy and horror stories	2	4	6	9	12	15

NOTE: *Created in prevention classes taught by Jon McClure at the Oceanspray Family Center in Newport, Oregon, and paid for by the Housing Authority of Lincoln County. All books are b&w with color covers. Issues #1-2 penciled and inked by various artists. All comics feature characters created by students and are signed and numbered by Jon McClure. Issues #1-2 have print runs of 100 each.*

VEXT
DC Comics: Mar, 1999 - No. 6, Aug, 1999 ($2.50, limited series)

1-6-Giffen-s. 1-Superman app. 4.00

V FOR VENDETTA
DC Comics: Sept, 1988 - No. 10, May, 1989 ($2.00, maxi-series)

	GD 2.0	VG 4.0	FN 6.0	VF 8.0	VF/NM 9.0	NM- 9.2
1-Alan Moore scripts in all; David Lloyd-a	4	8	12	28	47	65
2-10	2	4	6	8	10	12

HC (1990) Limited edition 60.00
HC (2005, $29.99, dustjacket) r/series; foreward by Lloyd; promo art and sketches 30.00
Trade paperback (1990, $14.95) 20.00

VICE
Image Comics (Top Cow): Nov, 2005 - No. 5 ($2.99)

1-5-Coleite-s/Kirkham-a. 1-Three covers 3.00
1-Code Red Edition; variant Benitez-c 3.00

VIC FLINT (Crime Buster...)(See Authentic Police Cases #10-14 & Fugitives From Justice #2)
St. John Publ. Co.: Aug, 1948 - No. 5, Apr, 1949 (Newspaper reprints; NEA Service)

	GD 2.0	VG 4.0	FN 6.0	VF 8.0	VF/NM 9.0	NM- 9.2
1	37	74	111	222	361	500
2	17	34	51	100	158	215
3-5	15	30	45	85	130	175

VIC FLINT (Crime Buster...)
Argo Publ.: Feb, 1956 - No. 2, May, 1956 (Newspaper reprints)

	GD 2.0	VG 4.0	FN 6.0	VF 8.0	VF/NM 9.0	NM- 9.2
1,2	12	24	36	67	94	120

VICIOUS CIRCLE, A
BOOM! Studios: Dec, 2022 - No. 3 ($9.99, oversized 10.875" x 8.5")

	GD 2.0	VG 4.0	FN 6.0	VF 8.0	VF/NM 9.0	NM- 9.2
1,2-Tomilin-s/Bermejo-a	1	3	4	6	8	10

VIC JORDAN (Also see Big Shot Comics #32)
Civil Service Publ.: April, 1945

	GD 2.0	VG 4.0	FN 6.0	VF 8.0	VF/NM 9.0	NM- 9.2
1-1944 daily newspaper-r; WWII-c	28	56	84	165	270	375

VICKI (Humor)
Atlas/Seaboard Publ.: Feb, 1975 - No. 4, Aug, 1975 (No. 1,2: 68 pgs.)

	GD 2.0	VG 4.0	FN 6.0	VF 8.0	VF/NM 9.0	NM- 9.2
1,2-(68 pgs.)-Reprints Tippy Teen; Good Girl art	5	10	15	35	63	90
3,4 (Low print)	6	12	18	37	66	95

VICKI VALENTINE (...Summer Special #1)
Renegade Press: July, 1985 - No. 4, July, 1986 ($1.70, B&W)

1-4: Woggon, Rausch-a; all have paper dolls. 2-Christmas issue 4.00

VICKY
Ace Magazine: Oct, 1948 - No. 5, June, 1949

	GD 2.0	VG 4.0	FN 6.0	VF 8.0	VF/NM 9.0	NM- 9.2
nn(10/48)-Teenage humor	17	34	51	98	154	210
4(12/48), nn(2/49), 4(4/49), 5(6/49): 5-Dotty app.	14	28	42	80	115	150

VICTOR CROWLEY'S HATCHET HALLOWEEN TALES (Based on the 2007 movie)
American Mythology Productions: 2019, 2020 ($3.99)

1-Short stories by Pell-s/Mesarcia-a; Check-s/Bonk-a, Kuhoric-s/Calzada-a; 4 covers 4.00
... II (2020) Short stories by Kuhoric-s/Cantada-a, Pell-s/Miracolo-a, Green-s/Hoey-a 4.00

VICTORIAN UNDEAD
DC Comics (WildStorm): Jan, 2010 - No. 6, Jun, 2010 ($2.99)

1-6-Sherlock Holmes vs. Zombies; Edginton-s/Fabbri-a. 1-Two covers (Moore, Coleby) 3.00
...: Sherlock Holmes vs. Jekyll and Hyde (12/10, $4.99) Dominguez-a/Van Sciver-c 5.00
...: Sherlock Holmes vs. Zombies TPB (2010, $17.99) r/#1-6; character design sketch art 18.00
... Volume 2 (1/11 - No. 5, 5/11) 1-3-($3.99) "Sherlock Holmes vs. Dracula" on-c; Fabbri-a 4.00
... Volume 2 - 4,5-($2.99) "Sherlock Holmes vs. Dracula" on-c; Fabbri-a 3.00

VICTORIES, THE
Dark Horse Comics: Aug, 2012 - No. 5, Dec, 2012 ($3.99 limited series)

1-5-Michael Avon Oeming-s/a/c 4.00
...Volume 2: Transhuman 1-15 (6/13 - No. 15, 9/14) Oeming-s/a/c. 11-15 Metahuman 4.00

VIC TORRY & HIS FLYING SAUCER (Also see Mr. Monster's...#5)
Fawcett Publications: 1950 (one-shot)

	GD 2.0	VG 4.0	FN 6.0	VF 8.0	VF/NM 9.0	NM- 9.2
nn-Book-length saucer story by Powell; photo/painted-c	77	154	231	493	847	1200

VICTORY
Topps Comics: June, 1994 ($2.50, unfinished limited series)

1-Kurt Busiek script; Giffen-c/a; Rob Liefeld variant-c exists 4.00

VICTORY (From Vampirella)
Dynamite Entertainment: 2023 - No. 5, 2023 ($3.99, limited series)

1-5-David Walker-s/Brett Weldele-a 4.00

VICTORY COMICS
Hillman Periodicals: Aug, 1941 - No. 4, Dec, 1941 (#1 by Funnies, Inc.)

	GD 2.0	VG 4.0	FN 6.0	VF 8.0	VF/NM 9.0	NM- 9.2
1-The Conqueror by Bill Everett, The Crusader, & Bomber Burns begin; Conqueror's origin in text; Everett-c	411	822	1233	2877	5039	7200
2-Everett-c/a	226	452	678	1446	2473	3500
3,4-WWII Japanese-c	194	388	582	1242	2121	3000

VIC VERITY MAGAZINE
Vic Verity Publ.: 1945; No. 2, Jan?, 1946 - No. 7, Sept, 1946 (A comic book)

	GD 2.0	VG 4.0	FN 6.0	VF 8.0	VF/NM 9.0	NM- 9.2
1-C. C. Beck-c/a	50	100	150	315	533	750
2-Beck-c	36	72	108	211	343	475
3-7: 6-Beck-a. 7-Beck-c	34	68	102	199	325	450

VIDEO JACK
Marvel Comics (Epic Comics): Nov, 1987 - No. 6, Nov, 1988 ($1.25)

1-5 ..... 4.00
6-Neal Adams, Keith Giffen, Wrightson, others-a 5.00

VIETNAM JOURNAL
Apple Comics: Nov, 1987 - No. 16, Apr, 1991 ($1.75/$1.95, B&W)

1-16: Don Lomax-c/a/scripts in all, 1-2nd print 4.00
...: Indian Country Vol. 1 (1990, $12.95)-r/#1-4 plus one new story 13.00

VIETNAM JOURNAL: VALLEY OF DEATH
Apple Comics: June, 1994 - No. 2, Aug, 1994 ($2.75, B&W, limited series)

1,2: By Don Lomax 4.00

VIGIL, THE (Dawn of DC)
DC Comics: Jul, 2023 - No. 6, Jan, 2024 ($3.99)

1-6: 1-Ram V-s/Lalit Kumar Sharma-a 4.00

VIGILANTE, THE (Also see New Teen Titans #23 & Annual V2#2)
DC Comics: Oct, 1983 - No. 50, Feb, 1988 ($1.25, Baxter paper)

	GD 2.0	VG 4.0	FN 6.0	VF 8.0	VF/NM 9.0	NM- 9.2
1-Origin	1	3	4	6	8	10

2-16,19-49: 3-Cyborg app. 4-1st app. The Exterminator; Newton-a(p). 6,7-Origin. 20,21-Nightwing app. 35-Origin Mad Bomber. 47-Batman-c/s 4.00
17,18-Alan Moore scripts 5.00
50-Ken Steacy painted-c 5.00
Annual nn, 2 ('85, '86) 5.00

VIGILANTE
DC Comics: Nov, 2005 - No. 6, Apr, 2006 ($2.99, limited series)

1-6-Bruce Jones-s. 1,2,4-6-Ben Oliver-a 3.00

Victory #1 © DYN

Vikings: Uprising #1 © TM Prods.

UPRISING

The Vision (2016 series) #16 © MAR

	GD 2.0	VG 4.0	FN 6.0	VF 8.0	VF/NM 9.0	NM- 9.2

VIGILANTE
DC Comics: Feb, 2009 - No. 12, Jan, 2010 ($2.99)
1-12: 1-Wolfman-s/Leonardi-a. 3-Nightwing app. 5-X-over with Titans and Teen Titans ... 3.00

VIGILANTE: CITY LIGHTS, PRAIRIE JUSTICE (Also see Action Comics #42, Justice League of America #78, Leading Comics & World's Finest #244)
DC Comics: Nov, 1995 - No. 4, Feb, 1996 ($2.50, limited series)
1-4: James Robinson scripts/Tony Salmons-a/Mark Chiarello-c ... 4.00
TPB (2009, $19.99) r/#1-4 ... 20.00

VIGILANTE 8: SECOND OFFENSE
Chaos! Comics: Dec, 1999 ($2.95, one-shot)
1-Based on video game ... 5.00

VIGILANTES, THE
Dell Publishing Co.: No. 839, Sept, 1957
Four Color 839-Movie ... 8 | 16 | 24 | 54 | 102 | 150

VIGILANTE: SOUTHLAND
DC Comics: Dec, 2016 - No. 3, Feb, 2017 ($3.99, unfinished series originally set for 6 issues)
1-3-Phillips-s/Casagrande-a; intro. Donny Fairchild ... 4.00

VIKING PRINCE, THE
DC Comics: 2010 ($39.99, hardcover with dustjacket)
HC-Recolored reprints of apps. in Brave and the Bold #1-5, 7-24 & team-up with Sgt. Rock in Our Army at War #162,163; new intro. by Joe Kubert ... 40.00

VIKINGS, THE (Movie)
Dell Publishing Co.: No. 910, May, 1958
Four Color 910-Buscema-a, Kirk Douglas photo-c ... 9 | 18 | 27 | 59 | 117 | 175

VIKINGS: GODHEAD (Based on the History Channel series)
Titan Comics: May, 2016 - No. 4, Sept, 2016 ($3.99)
1-4: 1-Cavan Scott-s/Staz Johnson-a; 3 covers ... 4.00

VIKINGS: UPRISING (Based on the History Channel series)
Titan Comics: Oct, 2016 - No. 4, Jan, 2017 ($3.99)
1-4: 1-Cavan Scott-s/Daniel Indro-a. 1-Five covers. 2-4-Three covers ... 4.00

VILLAINS AND VIGILANTES
Eclipse Comics: Dec, 1986 - No. 4, May, 1987 ($1.50/$1.75, limited series, Baxter paper)
1-4: Based on role-playing game. 2-4 ($1.75-c) ... 4.00

VILLAINS FOR HIRE
Marvel Comics: No. 0.1, Jan, 2012; No. 1, Feb, 2012 - No. 4, May, 2012 ($2.99)
0.1-Misty Knight, Silver Sable, Black Panther app.; Arlem-a ... 3.00
1-4-Abnett & Lanning-s/Arlem-a; Misty Knight app. ... 3.00

VILLAINS GIANT
DC Comics: 2019 ($4.99, 100 pgs., square-bound)
1-Three new short stories and three reprints; Joker, Harley, Deathstroke, Darkseid app. ... 5.00

VILLAINS UNITED (Leads into Infinite Crisis)
DC Comics: July, 2005 - No. 6, Dec, 2005 ($2.95/$2.50, limited series)
1-6-Simone-s/JG Jones-c. 1-The Secret Six and the "Society" form ... 3.00
...: Infinite Crisis Special 1 (6/06, $4.99) Simone-s/Eaglesham-a ... 5.00

VILLAINY OF DOCTOR DOOM, THE
Marvel Comics: 1999 ($17.95, TPB)
nn-Reprints early battle with the Fantastic Four ... 18.00

VIMANARAMA
DC Comics (Vertigo): Apr, 2005 - No. 3, June, 2005 ($2.95, limited series)
1-3-Grant Morrison-s/Philip Bond-a ... 3.00
TPB (2005, $12.99) r/#1-3 ... 13.00

VINDICATION
Image Comics: Feb, 2019 - No. 4, May, 2019 ($3.99, limited series)
1-4-MD Marie-s/Carlos Miko-a ... 4.00

VINTAGE MAGNUS (...Robot Fighter)
Valiant: Jan, 1992 - No. 4, Apr, 1992 ($2.25, limited series)
1-4: 1-Layton-c; r/origin from Magnus R.F. #22 ... 4.00

VINYL
Image Comics: Jun, 2021 - No. 6, Nov, 2021 ($3.99, limited series)
1-6-Doug Wagner-s/Daniel Hillyard-a ... 4.00

VINYL UNDERGROUND
DC Comics (Vertigo): Dec, 2007 - No. 12, Nov, 2008 ($2.99)
1-12: 1-Spencer-s/Gane & Stewart-a/Phillips-c ... 3.00
...: Pretty Dead Things TPB ('08, $17.99) r/#6-12 ... 18.00
...: Watching the Detectives TPB ('08, $9.99) r/#1-5; David Laphan intro. ... 10.00

VIOLATOR (Also see Spawn #2)
Image Comics (Todd McFarlane Prods.): May, 1994 - No. 3, Aug, 1994 ($1.95, lim. series)
1-Alan Moore scripts in all ... 5.00
2,3: Bart Sears-c(p)/a(p) ... 4.00

VIOLATOR VS. BADROCK
Image Comics (Extreme Studios): May, 1995 - No. 4, Aug, 1995 ($2.50, limited series)
1-4: Alan Moore scripts in all. 1-1st app Celestine; variant-c (3?) ... 4.00

VIOLENT, THE
Image Comics: Dec, 2015 - No. 5, Jul, 2016 ($2.99)
1-5-Brisson-s/Gorham-a ... 3.00

VIOLENT LOVE
Image Comics: Nov, 2016 - No. 10, Dec, 2017 ($3.99)
1-10-Frank Barbiere-s/Victor Santos-a/c ... 4.00

VIOLENT MESSIAHS (...: Lamenting Pain on cover for #9-12, numbered as #1-4)
Image Comics: June, 2000 - No. 12 ($2.95)
1-Two covers by Travis Smith and Medina ... 4.00
1-Tower Records variant edition ... 5.00
2-8: 5-Flip book sketchbook ... 3.00
9-12-Lamenting Pain; 2 covers on each ... 3.00
...: Genesis (12/01, $5.95) r/'97 B&W issue, Wizard 1/2 prologue ... 6.00
...: The Book of Job TPB (7/02, $24.95) r/#1-8; Foreward by Gossett ... 25.00

VIP (TV)
TV Comics: 2000 ($2.95, unfinished series)
1-Based on the Pamela Lee (Anderson) TV show; photo-c ... 3.00

VIPER (TV)
DC Comics: Aug, 1994 - No. 4, Nov, 1994 ($1.95, limited series)
1-4-Adaptation of television show ... 4.00

VIRGINIAN, THE (TV)
Gold Key: June, 1963
1(10060-306)-Part photo-c of James Drury plus photo back-c ... 4 | 8 | 12 | 27 | 44 | 60

VIRTUA FIGHTER (Video Game)
Marvel Comics: Aug, 1995 (2.95, one-shot)
1-Sega Saturn game ... 4.00

VIRUS
Dark Horse Comics: 1993 - No. 4, 1993 ($2.50, limited series)
1-4: Ploog-c ... 4.00

VISION, THE
Marvel Comics: Nov, 1994 - No. 4, Feb, 1995 ($1.75, limited series)
1-4 ... 4.00

VISION, THE (AVENGERS ICONS: ...)
Marvel Comics: Oct, 2002 - No. 4, Jan, 2003 ($2.99, limited series)
1-4-Geoff Johns-s/Ivan Reis-a ... 4.00
...: Yesterday and Tomorrow TPB (2005, $14.99) r/#1-4 & Avengers #57 (1st app.) ... 15.00

VISION (From the Avengers)
Marvel Comics: Jan, 2016 - No. 12, Dec, 2016 ($3.99)
1-Tom King-s/Gabriel Walta-a; the Vison and his new synthezoid family ... 3 | 6 | 9 | 16 | 23 | 30
2-4,7-12 ... 4.00
5-Low print run ... 2 | 4 | 6 | 9 | 12 | 15
6-1st Sparky the Dog ... 2 | 4 | 6 | 9 | 12 | 15
... Director's Cut 1-6 (8/17 - No. 6, 1/18, $6.99) r/2 issues each with script and bonus art ... 7.00

VISION AND THE SCARLET WITCH, THE (See Marvel Fanfare)
Marvel Comics Group: Nov, 1982 - No. 4, Feb, 1983 (Limited series)
1-Mantlo-s/Leonardi-a ... 2 | 4 | 6 | 11 | 16 | 20
2-4: 2-Nuklo & Future Man app. ... 5.00

VISION AND THE SCARLET WITCH, THE
Marvel Comics Group: Oct, 1985 - No. 12, Sept, 1986 (Maxi-series)
V2#1-Retells origin; 1st app. in Avengers #57 ... 2 | 4 | 6 | 9 | 12 | 15
2-11: 2-West Coast Avengers x-over ... 5.00
12-Birth of Wiccan & Speed ... 3 | 6 | 9 | 14 | 20 | 25

VISIONS
Vision Publications: 1979 - No. 5, 1983 (B&W, fanzine)
1-Flaming Carrot begins (1st app?); N. Adams-c ... 24 | 48 | 72 | 188 | 372 | 575
2-N. Adams, Rogers-a; Gulacy back-c; signed & numbered to 2000 ... 9 | 18 | 27 | 60 | 120 | 180
3-Williamson-c(p); Steranko back-c ... 4 | 8 | 12 | 25 | 40 | 55

	GD 2.0	VG 4.0	FN 6.0	VF 8.0	VF/NM 9.0	NM- 9.2

4-Flaming Carrot-c & info. ... 4 / 8 / 12 / 27 / 44 / 60
5-1 pg. Flaming Carrot ... 3 / 6 / 9 / 21 / 33 / 45
NOTE: *Eisner* a-4. *Miller* a-4. *Starlin* a-3. *Williamson* a-5. After #4, Visions became an annual publication of The Atlanta Fantasy Fair.

VISITOR, THE
Valiant/Acclaim Comics (Valiant): Apr, 1995 - No. 13, Nov, 1995 ($2.50)
1-13: 8-Harbinger revealed. 13-Visitor revealed to be Sting from Harbinger ... 4.00

VISITOR, THE
Valiant Entertainment: Dec, 2019 - No. 6, Jul, 2021 ($3.99)
1-6-Paul Levitz-s. 1-4,6-MJ Kim-a. 5-Soo Lee-a ... 4.00

VISITOR: HOW AND WHY HE STAYED, THE (Character from Hellboy)
Dark Horse Comics: Feb, 2017 - No. 5, Jul, 2017 ($3.99, limited series)
1-5-Mignola & Roberson-s/Grist-a/c; Hellboy app. ... 4.00

VISITOR VS. THE VALIANT UNIVERSE, THE
Valiant: Feb, 1995 - No. 2, Mar, 1995 ($2.95, limited series)
1,2 ... 4.00

VIXEN: RETURN OF THE LION (From Justice League of America)
DC Comics: Dec, 2008 - No. 5, Apr, 2009 ($2.99, limited series)
1-5-G. Willow Wilson-s/Cafu-a; Justice League app. ... 3.00
TPB (2009, $17.99) r/#1-5 ... 18.00

VOGUE (Also see Youngblood)
Image Comics (Extreme Studios): Oct, 1995 - No.3, Jan, 1996 ($2.50, limited series)
1-3: 1-Liefeld-c, 1-Variant-c ... 4.00

VOID INDIGO (Also see Marvel Graphic Novel)
Marvel Comics (Epic Comics): Nov, 1984 - No. 2, Mar, 1985 ($1.50, direct sales, unfinished series, mature)
1,2: Cont'd from Marvel G.N.; graphic sex & violence ... 4.00

VOID RIVALS (Takes place in Skybound's Transformers/G.I. Joe universe)
Image Comics (Skybound): Jun, 2023 - Present ($3.99)
1-6-Kirkman-s/De Felici-a ... 4.00

VOLCANIC REVOLVER
Oni Press: Dec, 1998 - No. 3, Mar, 1999 ($2.95, B&W, limited series)
1-3: 1-Scott Morse-s/a ... 4.00
TPB (12/99, $9.95, digest size) r/#1-3 and Oni Double Feature #7 prologue ... 10.00

VOLITION
AfterShock Comics: Aug, 2018 - No. 6, Jun, 2019 ($3.99)
1-6: 1-Ryan Parrott-s/Omar Francia-a ... 4.00

VOLTRON (TV)
Modern Publishing: 1985 - No. 3, 1985 (75¢, limited series)
1-Ayers-a in all; Jim Fry-c ... 5 / 10 / 15 / 35 / 63 / 90
2,3 ... 2 / 4 / 6 / 11 / 16 / 20

VOLTRON (Volume 1)
Dynamite Entertainment: 2011 - No. 12, 2013 ($3.99)
1-12: 1-Padilla-a; covers by Alex Ross, Sean Chen & Wagner Reis. 2-5-Two covers ... 4.00

VOLTRON: A LEGEND FORGED (TV)
Devils Due Publishing: Jul, 2008 - No. 5, Apr, 2009 ($3.50)
1-5-Blaylock-s/Bear-a; 4 covers ... 3.50

VOLTRON: DEFENDER OF THE UNIVERSE (TV)
Image Comics: No. 0, May, 2003 - No. 5, Sept, 2003 ($2.50)
0-Jolley-s/Brooks-a; character pin-ups with background info ... 3.00
1-5-($2.95) 1-Three covers by Norton, Brooks and Andrews; Norton-a ... 3.00
...: Revelations TPB (2004, $11.95, digest-sized) r/#1-5; cover gallery ... 12.00

VOLTRON: DEFENDER OF THE UNIVERSE (TV)
Image Comics: Jan, 2004 - No. 11, Dec, 2004 ($2.95)
1-11: 1-Jolley-s; wraparound-c ... 3.00

VOLTRON: FROM THE ASHES
Dynamite Entertainment: 2015 - No. 6, 2016 ($3.99)
1-6: 1-Cullen Bunn-s/Blacky Shepherd-a ... 4.00

VOLTRON: YEAR ONE
Dynamite Entertainment: 2012 - No. 6, 2012 ($3.99, limited series)
1-6: 1-Two covers; Brandon Thomas-s/Craig Cermak-a ... 4.00

VOODA (Jungle Princess) (Formerly Voodoo) (See Crown Comics)
Ajax-Farrell (Four Star Publications): No. 20, April, 1955 - No. 22, Aug, 1955
20-Baker-c/a (r/Seven Seas #6) ... 77 / 154 / 231 / 493 / 847 / 1200
21,22-Baker-a plus Kamen/Baker story, Kimbo Boy of Jungle, & Baker-c(p) in all. ... 22-Censored Jo-Jo-r (name Powaa) ... 71 / 142 / 213 / 454 / 777 / 1100
NOTE: #22 each contain one heavily censored-r of South Sea Girl by Baker from Seven Seas Comics with name changed to Vooda. #20-r/Seven Seas #6; #21-r/#4; #22-r/#3.

VOODOO (Weird Fantastic Tales) (Vooda #20 on)
Ajax-Farrell (Four Star Publ.): May, 1952 - No. 19, Jan-Feb, 1955
1-South Sea Girl-r by Baker ... 206 / 412 / 618 / 1318 / 2259 / 3200
2-Rulah story-r plus South Sea Girl from Seven Seas #2 by Baker (name changed from Alani to El'nee) ... 142 / 284 / 426 / 909 / 1555 / 2200
3-Bakerish-a; man stabbed in face ... 110 / 220 / 330 / 704 / 1202 / 1700
4,8-Baker-r. 8-Severed head panels ... 116 / 232 / 348 / 742 / 1271 / 1800
5-Nazi death camp story (flaying alive) ... 90 / 180 / 270 / 576 / 968 / 1400
6,7,9,10: 6-Severed head panels ... 74 / 148 / 222 / 470 / 810 / 1100
11-18: 14-Zombies take over America. 15-Opium drug story-r/Ellery Queen #3. 16-Post nuclear world story.17-Electric chair panels ... 71 / 142 / 213 / 454 / 777 / 1100
19-Bondage-c; Baker-r(2)/Seven Seas #5 w/minor changes & #1, heavily modified; last pre-code; contents & covers change to jungle theme ... 77 / 154 / 231 / 493 / 847 / 1200
Annual 1(1952, 25¢, 100 pgs.)-Baker-a (scarce) ... 730 / 1460 / 2190 / 5329 / 9415 / 13,500

VOODOO

Image Comics (WildStorm): Nov, 1997 - No. 4, Mar, 1998 ($2.50, lim. series)
1-4: 1-Alan Moore-s in all; Hughes-c. 2-4-Rio-a ... 5.00
1-Platinum Ed ... 10.00
Dancing on the Dark TPB ('99, $9.95) r/#1-4 ... 10.00
...-Zealot: Skin Trade (8/95, $4.95) ... 5.00

VOODOO (DC New 52) (Also see Grifter)
DC Comics: Nov, 2011 - No. 12, Oct, 2012 ($2.99)
1-12: 1-Marz-s/Basri-a/c. 3-Green Lantern (Kyle) app. ... 3.00
#0 (11/12, $2.99) Origin of Voodoo; Basri-a/c ... 3.00

VOODOO (See Tales of...)

VOODOO CHILD (Weston Cage & Nicolas Cage's...)
Virgin Comics: July, 2007 - No. 6, Dec, 2007 ($2.99)
1-6: 1-Mike Carey-s/Dean Hyrapiet-a; covers by Hyrapiet & Templesmith ... 3.00
Vol. 1 TPB (1/08, $14.99) r/#1-6; variant covers; intro by Weston Cage & Nicolas Cage ... 15.00

VOODOOM
Oni Press: June, 2000 ($4.95, B&W)
1-Scott Morse-s/Jim Mahfood-a ... 5.00

VORTEX
Vortex Publs.: Nov, 1982 - No. 15, 1988 (No month) ($1.50/$1.75, B&W)
1 ($1.95)-Peter Hsu-a; Ken Steacy-c; nudity ... 1 / 3 / 4 / 6 / 8 / 10
2,12: 2-1st app. Mister X (on-c only). 12-Sam Kieth-a ... 6.00
3-11,13-15 ... 4.00

VORTEX
Comico: 1991 - No. 2? ($2.50, limited series)
1,2: Heroes from The Elementals ... 4.00

VOTE LOKI
Marvel Comics: Aug, 2016 - No. 4, Nov, 2016 ($3.99, limited series)
1-Loki runs for President; Hastings-s/Foss-a ... 2 / 4 / 6 / 9 / 12 / 15
2-4: 2-McCaffrey-a ... 6.00

VOYAGE TO THE BOTTOM OF THE SEA (Movie, TV)
Dell Publishing Co./Gold Key: No. 1230, Sept-Nov, 1961; Dec, 1964 - #16, Apr, 1970 (Painted-c)
Four Color 1230 (1961) ... 12 / 24 / 36 / 83 / 182 / 280
10133-412(#1, 12/64)(Gold Key) ... 10 / 20 / 30 / 69 / 147 / 225
2(7/65) - 5: Photo back-c, 1-5 ... 6 / 12 / 18 / 41 / 76 / 110
6-14 ... 4 / 8 / 12 / 28 / 47 / 65
15,16-Reprints ... 3 / 6 / 9 / 18 / 27 / 36

VOYAGE TO THE DEEP
Dell Publishing Co.: Sept-Nov, 1962 - No. 4, Nov-Jan, 1964 (Painted-c)
1 ... 5 / 10 / 15 / 35 / 63 / 90
2-4 ... 4 / 8 / 12 / 25 / 40 / 55

VOYAGIS
Image Comics: Nov, 2022 - No. 5, Apr, 2023 ($3.99, limited series)
1-5-Sumeyye Kesgin-s/a ... 4.00

VS
Image Comics: Feb, 2018 - No. 5, Jul, 2018 ($3.99)
1-5-Ivan Brandon-s/Esad Ribic-a ... 4.00

V-WARS
IDW Publishing: Apr, 2014 - No. 11, Mar, 2015 ($3.99)
1-11: 1-Vampire epidemic; Jonathan Maberry-s/Alan Robinson-a ... 4.00
...: God of Death One-Shot (4/19, $4.99) Maberry-s/Milne-a ... 5.00

WACKO
Ideal Publ. Corp.: Sept, 1980 - No. 3, Oct, 1981 (84 pgs., B&W, magazine)
1-3 ... 2 / 4 / 6 / 9 / 13 / 16

WACKY ADVENTURES OF CRACKY (Also see Gold Key Spotlight)
Gold Key: Dec, 1972 - No. 12, Sept, 1975
1 ... 3 / 6 / 9 / 14 / 20 / 26
2 ... 2 / 4 / 6 / 10 / 14 / 18
3-12 ... 2 / 4 / 6 / 8 / 10 / 12
(See March of Comics #405, 424, 436, 448)

WACKY DUCK (...Comics #3-6; formerly Dopey Duck; Justice Comics #7 on)(See Film Funnies)
Marvel Comics (NPP): No. 3, Fall, 1946 - No. 6, Summer, 1947; Aug, 1948 - No. 2, Oct, 1948
3 ... 40 / 80 / 120 / 246 / 411 / 575
4-Infinity-c ... 31 / 62 / 93 / 182 / 296 / 410
5,6(1947)-Becomes Justice comics ... 29 / 58 / 87 / 172 / 281 / 390
1(1948) ... 31 / 62 / 93 / 182 / 296 / 410
2(1948) ... 21 / 42 / 63 / 122 / 199 / 275
I.W. Reprint #1,2,7('58): 1-r/Wacky Duck #6 ... 3 / 6 / 9 / 15 / 22 / 28
Super Reprint #10(I.W. on-c, Super-inside) ... 3 / 6 / 9 / 14 / 19 / 24

WACKY QUACKY (See Wisco)

WACKY RACELAND (Update of Hanna-Barbera's Wacky Races)
DC Comics: Aug, 2016 - No. 6, Jan, 2017 ($3.99)
1-6: 1-Pontac-s/Manco-a; multiple covers; Penelope Pitstop & Dick Dastardly app. ... 4.00

WACKY RACES (TV)
Gold Key: Aug, 1969 - No. 7, Apr, 1972 (Hanna-Barbera)
1 ... 8 / 16 / 24 / 54 / 102 / 150
2-7 ... 4 / 8 / 12 / 23 / 37 / 50

WACKY SQUIRREL (Also see Dark Horse Presents)
Dark Horse Comics: Oct, 1987 - No. 4, 1988 ($1.75, B&W)
1 ... 1 / 3 / 4 / 6 / 8 / 10
2,3 ... 4.00
4-Superman parody with Action #1 cover homage ... 2 / 4 / 6 / 9 / 12 / 15
Halloween Adventure Special 1 (1987, $2.00) ... 1 / 2 / 3 / 5 / 6 / 8
Summer Fun Special 1 (1988, $2.00) ... 4.00

WACKY WITCH (Also see Gold Key Spotlight)

Voodoo (2011 series) #3 © DC

Wakanda #5 © MAR

The Walking Dead #75 © Kirkman

	GD 2.0	VG 4.0	FN 6.0	VF 8.0	VF/NM 9.0	NM- 9.2
Gold Key: March, 1971 - No. 21, Dec, 1975						
1	4	8	12	25	40	55
2	3	6	9	14	20	26
3-10	2	4	6	10	14	18
11-21	2	4	6	8	10	12
(See March of Comics #374, 398, 410, 422, 434, 446, 458, 470, 482)						

WACKY WOODPECKER (See Two Bit the…)
I. W. Enterprises/Super Comics: 1958; 1963

I.W. Reprint #1,2,7 (nd-reprints Two Bit…): 7-r/Two-Bit, the Wacky Woodpecker #1.						
	3	6	9	14	20	25
Super Reprint #10('63): 10-r/Two-Bit, The Wacky Woodpecker #?						
	2	4	6	11	16	20

WAGON TRAIN (1st Series) (TV) (See Western Roundup under Dell Giants)
Dell Publishing Co.: No. 895, Mar, 1958 - No. 13, Apr-June, 1962 (All photo-c)

Four Color 895 (#1)	10	20	30	67	141	215
Four Color 971(#2),1019(#3)	6	12	18	41	76	110
4(1-3/60),6-13	5	10	15	34	60	85
5-Toth-a	6	12	18	37	66	95

WAGON TRAIN (2nd Series)(TV)
Gold Key: Jan, 1964 - No. 4, Oct, 1964 (All front & back photo-c)

1-Tufts-a in all	5	10	15	30	50	70
2-4	4	8	12	23	37	50

WAITING PLACE, THE
Slave Labor Graphics: Apr, 1997 - No. 6, Sept, 1997 ($2.95)

1-6-Sean McKeever-s						4.00
Vol. 2 - 1(11/99), 2-11						4.00
12-($4.95)						5.00

WAITING ROOM WILLIE (See Sad Case of…)

WAKANDA (Black Panther anthology)
Marvel Comics: Dec, 2022 - No. 5, Apr, 2023 ($4.99/$3.99)

1-($4.99) Focus on Shuri; back-up story with history of the Black Panthers						5.00
2-5 ($3.99) 2-M'Baku. 3-Killmonger. 4-Tosin. 5-Okoye						4.00

WAKANDA FOREVER (See Amazing Spider-Man: Wakanda Forever for part 1)
Marvel Comics: Sept, 2018 - Oct, 2018 ($4.99, limited series)

… Avengers (10/18) Part 3; Capt. America, She-Hulk, Black Panther, Storm, Rogue app.						5.00
… X-Men (9/18) Part 2; Storm, Rogue, Nightcrawler app.						5.00

WAKE, THE
DC Comics (Vertigo): Jul, 2013 - No. 10, Sept, 2014 ($2.99)

1-Scott Snyder-s/Sean Murphy-a/c						5.00
1-Variant-c by Andy Kubert						8.00
1-Director's Cut (10/13, $4.99) B&W version, behind-the-scenes production content						5.00
2-10: 6-Story jumps 200 years ahead; Leeward app.						3.00
… Part One TPB (2/14, $9.99) r/#1-5						10.00

WAKE THE DEAD
IDW Publishing: Sept, 2003 - No. 5, Mar, 2004 ($3.99, limited series)

1-5-Steve Niles-s/Chee-a						4.00
TPB (6/04, $19.99) r/series; intro. by Michael Dougherty; embossed die cut cover						20.00

WALK IN (Dave Stewart's …)
Virgin Comics: Dec, 2006 - No. 6, May, 2007 ($2.99)

1-6: 1-5-Parker-s/Padlekar-a. 6-Parker-a						3.00

WALKING DEAD, THE (Inspired the 2010 AMC television series)(Also see Negan Lives!)
Image Comics: Oct, 2003 - No. 193, July, 2019 ($2.95/$2.99, B&W)

1-Robert Kirkman in all/Tony Moore-a; 1st app. Rick Grimes, Shane, Morgan & Duane						
	48	96	138	359	805	1250
1 Special Edition (5/08, $3.99) r/#1; Kirkman afterword; original script and proposal						
	3	6	9	16	23	30
2-Tony Moore-a through #6	16	32	48	111	246	380
3	9	18	27	61	123	185
4	8	16	24	52	99	145
5,6: 6-Shane killed	6	12	18	41	76	110
7-Charlie Adlard-a begins; 1st app. Tyreese	5	10	15	31	53	75
8-10	4	8	12	25	40	55
11-18,20: 1-Prison arc begins	3	6	9	16	23	30
19-1st app. Michonne	10	20	30	69	147	225
21-26,28-47,49,50: 25-Adlard covers begin. 28-Rick loses his hand. 46-Tyreese killed.						
	2	4	6	9	12	15
27-1st app of The Governor	7	14	21	46	86	125
48-Lori, Herschel, others killed	4	8	12	25	40	55
50-Variant wraparound superhero-style cover by Erik Larsen						
	5	10	15	34	60	85

	GD 2.0	VG 4.0	FN 6.0	VF 8.0	VF/NM 9.0	NM- 9.2
51,52,54-60: 58-Morgan returns	2	4	6	8	10	12
53-1st app. Abraham & Rosita	5	10	15	33	57	80
61-Preview of Chew; 1st app. Gabriel	4	8	12	25	40	55
62,64-74: 66-Dale dies. 70-1st Douglas Monroe	1	3	4	6	8	10
63-Flip book with B&W reprint of Chew #1	3	6	9	16	24	32
75-(7/10, $3.99) Orange background-c; back-up alien/sci-fi "fantasy" in color; TV series preview with cast photos	2	4	6	9	12	15
75-Variant-c homage to issue #1	3	6	9	21	33	45
76-91: 85-Flip book w/Witch Doctor #0. 86-Flip book w/Elephantmen						
	1	3	4	6	8	10
92-Intro. Paul Monroe (Jesus)	3	6	9	17	26	35
93-96						6.00
97-99,101-114: 97-"Something to Fear" pt. 1. 98-Abraham killed. 107-Intro Ezekiel						5.00
100-(7/12, $3.99) 1st app. Negan; Glen killed; multiple covers by Adlard, Silvestri, Quitely, McFarlane, Phillips, Hitch, & Ottley	3	6	9	16	23	30
100-Wraparound-c by Adlard	2	4	6	9	12	15
106-Variant wraparound-c by Adlard for his 100th issue						
	2	4	6	10	14	20
115-"All Out War" begins; 10 connecting covers by Adlard						
	1	2	3	5	6	8
116-126-"All Out War"						4.00
127-(5/14) Intro. Magna; bonus preview of Outcast	2	4	6	8	10	12
128-174: 132-1st Whisperers attack. 135-Intro. Lydia. 138-Intro. Alpha. 139-Michonne returns 144-Death of Ezekiel and Rosita and others. 150-Six covers. 156-Death of Alpha. 157-162-Whisper War; 2 covers (Adlard & Art Adams). 163-(25¢-c). 167-Death of Andrea.						4.00
171-Intro Princess						4.00
175-191-($3.99) 175-1st app. The Commonwealth. 185-Flip book with Outpost Zero #1						4.00
192-Death of Rick Grimes						5.00
193-($3.99, 84 pgs.) Final issue; afterword by Kirkman; fake cover art for #194-196						4.00
193-2nd printing ($3.99, 84 pgs.)						4.00
… FCBD 2013 Special (5/13, giveaway) reprints bonus stories from Michonne Special and The Governor Special; new Tyreese background story						3.00
Image Firsts: The Walking Dead #1 (3/10, $1.00) reprints #1						
	2	4	6	13	18	22
…: Michonne Special (10/12, $2.99) Reprints debut from #19 and story from Playboy						
	1	3	4	6	8	10
…: Michonne Special - 2nd printing (3/13, $2.99)						3.00
… #1 Tenth Anniversary Special (10/13, $5.99) reprints #1 with color; Kirkman's original cover proposal; Kirkman interview	2	4	6	8	11	14
"The Alien" (2020, $19.99, HC) New story taking place in Barcelona; Brian K. Vaughan-s/ Marcos Martin-a; bonus character sketches, page layouts and cover concepts						20.00
…: The Governor Special (2/13, $2.99) Reprints debut from #27 and story from CBLDF Liberty Annual 2012						6.00
…: Tyreese Special (10/13, $2.99) Reprints debut from #7 and story from FCBD 2013						4.00
… Book 1 HC (2006, $29.99) r/#1-12; sketch pages, cover gallery; Kirkman afterword						45.00
… Book 2 HC (2006, $29.99) r/#13-24; sketch pages, cover gallery						40.00
… Book 3 HC (2007, $29.99) r/#25-36; sketch pages, cover gallery						35.00
… Book 4 HC (2008, $29.99) r/#37-48; sketch pages, cover gallery						35.00
… Book 5 HC (2010, $29.99) r/#49-60; sketch pages, cover gallery						35.00
… Book 6 HC (2010, $34.99) r/#61-72; sketch pages, cover gallery						35.00
… Book 7 HC (2011, $34.99) r/#73-84; sketch pages, cover gallery						35.00
… Book 8 HC (2012, $34.99) r/#85-96; sketch pages, cover gallery						35.00
… Book 9 HC (2013, $34.99) r/#97-108; sketch pages, cover gallery						35.00
… Book 10 HC (2014, $34.99) r/#109-120; sketch pages, cover gallery						35.00
… Book 11 HC (2015, $34.99) r/#121-132; sketch pages, cover gallery						35.00
…Vol. 1: Days Gone Bye (5/04, $9.95, TPB) r/#1-4						20.00
…Vol. 2: Miles Behind Us (10/04, $12.95, TPB) r/#7-12						18.00
…Vol. 3: Safety Behind Bars (2006, $12.95, TPB) r/#13-18						18.00
…Vol. 4: The Heart's Desire (2005, $12.99, TPB) r/#19-24						18.00
…Vol. 5: The Best Defense (2006, $12.99, TPB) r/#25-30						18.00
…Vol. 6: This Sorrowful Life (2007, $12.99, TPB) r/#31-36						15.00
…Vol. 7: The Calm Before (2007, $12.99, TPB) r/#37-42						15.00
…Vol. 8: Made to Suffer (2008, $14.99, TPB) r/#43-48						15.00
…Vol. 9: Here We Remain (2009, $14.99, TPB) r/#49-54						15.00
…Vol. 10: The Road Ahead (2009, $14.99, TPB) r/#55-60						15.00
…Vol. 11: Fear the Hunters (2010, $14.99, TPB) r/#61-66						15.00
…Vol. 12: Life Among Them (2010, $14.99, TPB) r/#67-72						15.00
…Vol. 13: Too Far Gone (2010, $14.99, TPB) r/#73-78						15.00
…Vol. 14: No Way Out (2011, $14.99, TPB) r/#79-84						15.00
…Vol. 15: We Find Ourselves (2011, $14.99, TPB) r/#85-90						15.00
…Vol. 16: A Larger World (2012, $14.99, TPB) r/#91-96						15.00
…Vol. 17: Something to Fear (2012, $14.99, TPB) r/#97-102						15.00
…Vol. 18: What Comes After (2013, $14.99, TPB) r/#103-108						15.00
…Vol. 19: March To War (2013, $14.99, TPB) r/#109-114						15.00
…Vol. 20: All Out War Part 1 (2014, $14.99, TPB) r/#115-120						15.00
…Vol. 21: All Out War Part 2 (2014, $14.99, TPB) r/#121-126						15.00
…Vol. 22: A New Beginning (2014, $14.99, TPB) r/#127-132						15.00
…Vol. 23: Whispers Into Screams (2015, $14.99, TPB) r/#133-138						15.00

	GD	VG	FN	VF	VF/NM	NM-
	2.0	4.0	6.0	8.0	9.0	9.2

...Vol. 24: Life and Death (2015, $14.99, TPB) r/#139-144 ... 15.00
...Vol. 25: No Turning Back (2016, $14.99, TPB) r/#145-150 ... 15.00
...Vol. 26: Call to Arms (2016, $14.99, TPB) r/#151-156 ... 15.00
...Vol. 27: The Whisperer War (2017, $14.99, TPB) r/#157-162 ... 15.00
...Vol. 28: A Certain Doom (2017, $16.99, TPB) r/#163-168 ... 17.00
...Vol. 29: Lines We Cross (2018, $16.99, TPB) r/#169-174 ... 17.00
...Vol. 30: New World Order (2018, $16.99, TPB) r/#175-180 ... 17.00
...Vol. 31: The Rotten Core (2018, $16.99, TPB) r/#181-186 ... 17.00
...Vol. 32: Rest in Peace (2019, $16.99, TPB) r/#187-193 ... 17.00

WALKING DEAD DELUXE, THE
Image Comics: Oct, 2020 - Present ($3.99)
1-83-Newly colored reprints of original issues with Kirkman commentary and bonus "cutting room floor" content; multiple variant covers on each ... 4.00

WALKING DEAD SURVIVORS' GUIDE, THE
Image Comics: Apr, 2011 - No. 4 ($2.99, B&W)
1,2-Alphabetical listings of character profiles, first (and last) apps. and current status

	GD	VG	FN	VF	VF/NM	NM-
		2	4	6	11	16	20
3,4	1	3	4	6	8	10

WALKING DEAD WEEKLY, THE (Reprints)
Image Comics: Jan, 2011 - No. 52, Dec, 2011 ($2.99, B&W, weekly)
1-Reprints issues with original letter columns; new Kirkman afterword

	GD	VG	FN	VF	VF/NM	NM-
1	3	6	9	21	33	45
1-Arizona Comic Con variant-c	3	6	9	16	23	30
2-4,7	2	4	6	9	12	15
5-Death of Amy	4	8	12	27	44	60
6-Death of Shane	3	6	9	19	30	40
8-18,20-26,28-52	1	2	3	5	6	8
19-r/1st Michonne	6	12	18	38	69	100
27-r/1st app. The Governor	3	6	9	16	23	30

WALK THROUGH HELL, A
AfterShock Comics: May, 2018 - No. 12, Jul, 2019 ($3.99)
1-12-Garth Ennis-s/Goran Sudzuka-a ... 4.00

WALL·E (Based on the Disney/Pixar movie)
BOOM! Studios: No. 0, Nov, 2009 - No. 7, Jun, 2010 ($2.99)
0-7: 0-Prequel; J. Torres-s ... 4.00

WALLER VS. WILDSTORM
DC Comics (Black Label): May, 2023 - No. 4, Feb, 2024 ($5.99, oversized 8-1/2" x 10-3/4", lim. series)
1-4-Ackerman & Narcisse-s/Merino-a; Deathstroke & Lois Lane app. ... 6.00

WALLY (Teen-age)
Gold Key: Dec, 1962 - No. 4, Sept, 1963

	GD	VG	FN	VF	VF/NM	NM-
1	4	8	12	25	40	55
2-4	3	6	9	17	26	35

WALLY THE WIZARD
Marvel Comics (Star Comics): Apr, 1985 - No. 12, Mar, 1986 (Children's comic)
1-12: Bob Bolling a-1,3; c-1,9,11,12 ... 5.00
1-Variant with "Star Chase" game on last page and inside back-c

	GD	VG	FN	VF	VF/NM	NM-
	2	4	6	9	12	15

WALLY WOOD'S T.H.U.N.D.E.R. AGENTS (See Thunder Agents)
Deluxe Comics: Nov, 1984 - No. 5, Oct, 1986 ($2.00, 52 pgs.)
1-5-Jerry Ordway-a in Wood style ... 6.00
NOTE: Anderson a-2i, 3i. Buckler a-4. Ditko a-3, 4. Giffen a-1p-4p. Perez a-1p, 2, 4; c-1-4.

WALT DISNEY CHRISTMAS PARADE (Also see Christmas Parade)
Whitman Publ. Co. (Golden Press): Wint, 1977 (75¢, cardboard-c, 224 pgs.)
11191-Barks-r/Christmas in Disneyland #1; Dell Christmas Parade #9 & Dell Giant #53

	GD	VG	FN	VF	VF/NM	NM-
	4	8	12	27	44	60

WALT DISNEY COMICS DIGEST
Gold Key: June, 1968 - No. 57, Feb, 1976 (50¢, digest size)

	GD	VG	FN	VF	VF/NM	NM-
1-Reprints Uncle Scrooge #5; 192 pgs.	8	16	24	51	96	140
2-4-Barks-r	5	10	15	33	57	80
5-Daisy Duck by Barks (8 pgs.); last published story by Barks (art only) plus 21 pg. Scrooge-r by Barks	7	14	21	46	86	140
6-13-All Barks-r	3	6	9	21	33	45
14,15	3	6	9	16	23	30
16-Reprints Donald Duck #26 by Barks	3	6	9	20	31	42
17-20-Barks-r	3	6	9	17	26	35
21-31,33,35-37-Barks-r; 24-Toth Zorro	3	6	9	16	23	30
32,41,45,47-49	2	4	6	11	16	20

34,38,39: 34-Reprints 4-Color #318. 38-Reprints Christmas in Disneyland #1. 39-Two Barks-r/WDC&S #272, 4-Color #1073 plus Toth Zorro-r

	GD	VG	FN	VF	VF/NM	NM-
	3	6	9	16	23	30
40-Mickey Mouse-r by Gottfredson	2	4	6	13	18	22
42,43-Barks-r	2	4	6	13	18	22

44-(Has Gold Key emblem, 50¢)-Reprints 1st story of 4-Color #29,256,275,282

	GD	VG	FN	VF	VF/NM	NM-
	5	10	15	30	50	70

44-Republished in 1976 by Whitman; not identical to original; a bit smaller, blank back-c, 69¢

	GD	VG	FN	VF	VF/NM	NM-
	3	6	9	16	23	30
46,50,52-Barks-r. 52-Barks-r/WDC&S #161,132	2	4	6	11	16	20
51-Reprints 4-Color #71	3	6	9	16	23	30

53-55: 53-Reprints Dell Giant #30. 54-Reprints Donald Duck Beach Party #2. 55-Reprints Dell Giant #49

	GD	VG	FN	VF	VF/NM	NM-
	2	4	6	10	14	18
56-r/Uncle Scrooge #32 (Barks)	2	4	6	13	18	22
57-r/Mickey Mouse Almanac('57) & two Barks stories	2	4	6	11	16	20

NOTE: Toth a-52r, #1-10, 196 pgs.; #11-41, 164 pgs.; #42 on, 132 pgs. Old issues were being reprinted & distributed by Whitman in 1976.

WALT DISNEY GIANT (Disney)
Bruce Hamilton Co. (Gladstone): Sept, 1995 - No. 7, Sept, 1996 ($2.25, bi-monthly, 48 pgs.)
1-7: 1-Scrooge McDuck in "Hearts of the Yukon"; Rosa-c/a/scripts plus r/F.C. #218; Scrooge & Glittering Goldie-c. 2-Uncle Scrooge-r by Barks plus 17 pg. text story. 3-Donald the Mighty Duck; Barks & Rosa-r. 4-Mickey and Goofy; new-a (story actually stars

Goofy. Mickey Mouse by Caesar Ferioli; Donald Duck by Giorgio Cavazzano (1st in U.S.).
6-Uncle Scrooge & the Jr. Woodchucks; new-a and Barks-r. 7-Uncle Scrooge-r by Barks plus new-a ... 5.00
NOTE: Series was initially solicited as Uncle Walt's Comicology. Issue #8 was advertised, but later cancelled.

WALT DISNEY PAINT BOOK SERIES
Whitman Publ. Co.: No dates; circa 1975 (Beware! Has 1930s copyright dates) (79¢-r, 52 pgs. B&W, treasury-sized) (Coloring books, text stories & comics-r)

	GD	VG	FN	VF	VF/NM	NM-
#2052 (Whitman #886-r) Mickey Mouse & Donald Duck Gag Book	3	6	9	20	31	42
#2053 (Whitman #677-r)	3	6	9	20	31	42
#2054 (Whitman #670-r) Donald-c	4	8	12	22	35	48
#2055 (Whitman #627-r) Mickey-c	3	6	9	20	31	42
#2056 (Whitman #660-r) Buckey Bug-c	3	6	9	18	28	38
#2057 (Whitman #887-r) Mickey & Donald-c	3	6	9	20	31	42

WALT DISNEY PRESENTS (TV)(Disney)
Dell Publishing Co.: No. 997, 6-8/59 - No. 6, 12-2/1960-61; No. 1181, 4-5/61 (All photo-c)

	GD	VG	FN	VF	VF/NM	NM-
Four Color 997 (#1)	8	16	24	51	96	140
2(12-2/60)-The Swamp Fox(origin), Elfego Baca, Texas John Slaughter (Disney TV show) begin	5	10	15	33	57	80
3-6: 5-Swamp Fox by Warren Tufts	4	8	12	28	47	65
Four Color 1181-Texas John Slaughter	6	12	18	42	79	115

WALT DISNEY'S CHRISTMAS PARADE (Also see Christmas Parade)
Gladstone: Winter, 1988; No. 2, Winter, 1989 ($2.95, 100 pgs.)

	GD	VG	FN	VF	VF/NM	NM-
1-Barks-r/painted-c	2	4	6	8	10	12
2-Barks-r	1	2	3	5	7	9

WALT DISNEY'S CHRISTMAS PARADE
Gemstone Publishing: Dec, 2003; 2004, 2005, 2006, 2008 ($8.95/$9.50, prestige format)
1-4: 1-Reprints and 3 new European holiday stories. 2-All reprints. 3-Reprints and 2 new stories, 4-Reprints and 5 new stories ... 9.00
5-($9.50) R/Uncle Scrooge #47 and European stories ... 9.50

WALT DISNEY'S COMICS AND STORIES (Cont. of Mickey Mouse Magazine)
(#1-30 contain Donald Duck newspaper reprints) (Titled "Comics And Stories" #264 to #?; titled "Walt Disney's Comics And Stories" #511 on)
Dell Publishing Co./Gold Key #264-473/Whitman #474-510/Disney Comics #548-585/Gladstone #586-633/Gemstone Publishing #634-698/Boom! Kids #699-720/IDW Publishing #721-on: 10/40 - #263, 8/62; #264, 10/62 - #510, 7/84; #511, 10/86 - #633, 2/99; #634, 7/03 - #698, 11/08; #699, 10/09 - #720, 6/11; #721, 7/15 - No. 743, 7/18
NOTE: The whole number can always be found at the bottom of the title page in the lower left-hand or right hand panel.

	GD	VG	FN	VF	VF/NM	NM-
1(V1#1-c; V2#1-indicia)-Donald Duck strip-r by Al Taliaferro & Gottfredson's Mickey Mouse begin	2500	5000	7500	17,500	37,750	57,500
2	890	1780	2670	6200	13,350	20,500
3	396	792	1188	2772	5936	9100
4-Christmas-c; 1st Huey, Dewey & Louie-c this title (See Mickey Mouse Magazine V4#2 for 1st-c ever)	348	696	1044	2436	5218	8000
4-Special promotional, complimentary issue; cover same except one corner was blanked out & boxed in to identify the giveaway (not a paste-over). This special pressing was probably sent out to former subscribers to Mickey Mouse Mag. whose subscriptions had expired. (Very rare-5 known copies)	600	1200	1800	4200	9100	14,000
5-Goofy-a	272	544	816	1741	3521	5500
6-10: 8-Only Clarabelle Cow-c. 9-Taliaferro (1st)	231	462	693	1478	2989	4500
11-14: 11-Huey, Dewey & Louie-c/app.	179	358	537	1146	2323	3500
15-17: 15-The 3 Little Kittens (17 pgs.). 16-The 3 Little Pigs (29 pgs.); Christmas-c. 17-The Ugly Duckling (4 pgs.)	149	298	447	954	1927	2900
18-21	138	276	414	883	1792	2700
22-30: 22-Flag-c. 24-The Flying Gauchito (1st original comic book story done for WDC&S). 27-Jose Carioca by Carl Buettner (2nd original story in WDC&S)	118	236	354	755	1528	2300
31-New Donald Duck stories by Carl Barks begin (See F.C. #9 for 1st Barks Donald Duck)	400	800	1200	2560	5180	7800
32-Barks-a	232	464	696	1485	2543	3600
33-Barks-a; Gremlins app. (Vivie Risto-s/a); infinity-c	181	362	543	1158	1979	2800
34-Gremlins by Walt Kelly begin, end #41; Barks-a	141	282	423	902	1576	2250
35,36-Barks-a	138	276	414	883	1542	2200
37-Donald Duck by Jack Hannah	81	162	243	518	909	1300
38-40-Barks-a. 39-X-Mas-c. 40,41-Gremlins by Kelly	88	176	264	563	982	1400
41-50-Barks-a. 43-Seven Dwarfs-c app. (4/44). 45-50-Nazis in Gottfredson's Mickey Mouse Stories. 46-War Bonds-c	78	156	234	499	875	1250
51-60-Barks-a. 51-X-Mas-c. 52-Li'l Bad Wolf begins, ends #203 (not in #55). 58-Kelly flag-c	32	64	96	230	515	800
61-70: Barks-a. 61-Dumbo story. 63,64-Pinocchio stories. 63-Cover swipe from New Funnies #94. 64-X-Mas-c. 65-Pluto story. 66-Infinity-c. 67,68-Mickey Mouse Sunday-r by Bill Wright	28	56	84	202	451	700
71-80: Barks-a. 75-77-Brer Rabbit stories, no Mickey Mouse. 76-X-Mas-c. 78-"Bark's" name on wooden box shown on cover	25	50	75	175	388	600
81-87,89,90: Barks-a. 82-Goofy-c. 82-84-Bongo stories. 86-90-Goofy & Agnes app.	20	40	60	138	307	475
89-Chip 'n' Dale story	20	40	60	138	307	475
88-1st app. Gladstone Gander by Barks (1/48)	27	54	81	194	435	675
91,97,99: Barks-a. 95-1st WDC&S Barks-c. 96-No Mickey Mouse; Little Toot begins, ends #97. 99-X-Mas-c	18	36	54	126	281	435
98-1st Uncle Scrooge app. in WDC&S (11/48)	34	68	102	245	548	850
100-(1/49)-Barks-a	23	46	69	161	356	550
101-110-Barks-a. 107-Taliaferro-c; Donald acquires super powers	16	32	48	107	236	365
111,114,117-All Barks-a	13	26	39	89	195	300
112-Drug (ether) issue (Donald Duck)	20	40	60	142	316	490
113,115,116,118-123: No Barks. 116-Dumbo x-over. 121-Grandma Duck begins, ends #168; not in #135,142,146,155	10	20	30	64	132	200
124,126-130-All Barks-a. 124-X-Mas-c	10	20	30	70	154	230
125-1st app. Junior Woodchucks (2/51); Barks-a	18	36	54	126	284	440
131,133,135-137,139-All Barks-a	10	20	30	67	141	215

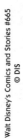

Wally Wood's T.H.U.N.D.E.R. Agents #4
© Deluxe

Walt Disney's Comics and Stories #665
© DIS

Walt Disney's Donald Duck Adventures #10 © DIS

	GD 2.0	VG 4.0	FN 6.0	VF 8.0	VF/NM 9.0	NM- 9.2
132-Barks-a(2) (D. Duck & Grandma Duck)	11	22	33	73	157	240
134-Intro. & 1st app. The Beagle Boys (11/51)	27	54	81	189	420	650
138-Classic Scrooge money story	17	34	51	114	252	390
140-(5/52)-1st app. Gyro Gearloose by Barks; 2nd Barks Uncle Scrooge-c; 3rd Uncle Scrooge cover app.	23	46	69	161	356	550
141-150-All Barks-a. 143-Little Hiawatha begins, ends #151,159	9	18	27	58	114	170
151-170-All Barks-a	8	16	24	51	96	140
171-199-All Barks-a	7	14	21	46	86	125
200	7	14	21	49	92	135
201-240: All Barks-a. 204-Chip 'n' Dale & Scamp begin	6	12	18	40	73	105
241-283: Barks-a. 241-Dumbo x-over. 247-Gyro Gearloose begins, ends #274. 256-Ludwig Von Drake begins, ends #274	5	10	15	35	63	90
284,285,287,290,295,296,309-311-Not by Barks	4	6	9	19	30	40
286,288,291-294,297,298,308-All Barks stories; 293-Grandma Duck's Farm Friends.						
297-Gyro Gearloose. 298-Daisy Duck's Diary-r	4	8	12	23	37	50
289-Annette-c & back-c & story; Barks-s	4	8	12	27	44	60
299-307-All contain early Barks-r (#43-117). 305-Gyro Gearloose	4	8	12	25	40	55
312-Last Barks issue with original story	4	8	12	25	40	55
313,315,317,327,329-334,336-341	3	6	9	15	22	28
316-Last issue published during life of Walt Disney	3	6	9	15	22	28
328,335,342-350-Barks-r	3	6	9	15	22	28
351-360-With posters inside; Barks reprints (2 versions of each with & without posters)	4	8	12	25	40	55
351-360-Without posters...	3	6	9	14	19	24
361-400-Barks-r	3	6	9	14	20	26
401-429-Barks-r	3	6	9	14	19	24
430,433,437,438,441,444,445,466-No Barks	2	4	6	8	11	14
431,432,434-436,439,440,442,443-Barks-r	2	4	6	10	14	18
440-Whitman edition	3	6	9	15	22	28
446-465,467-473-Barks-r	2	4	6	9	13	16
474(3/80),475-478 (Whitman)	3	6	9	14	19	24
479(8/80),481(10/80)-484(1/81) pre-pack only	5	10	15	30	50	70
480 (8-12/80)-(Very low distribution)	13	26	39	89	195	300
484 (1/81, 40¢-c) Cover price error variant (scarce)	6	12	18	38	69	100
484 (1/81) Regular 50¢ cover price; not pre-pack	3	6	9	19	30	40
485-499: 494-r/WDC&S #98	2	4	6	11	16	20
500-510 (all #90011 on-c; pre-packs): 500(4/83), 501(5/83), 502&503(7/83), 504-506(all 8/83), 507(4/84), 508(5/84), 509(6/84), 510(7/84). 506-No Barks	2	4	6	13	18	22
511-Donald Duck by Daan Jippes (1st in U.S.; in all through #518); Gyro Gearloose Barks-r begins (in most through #547); Wuzzles by Disney Studio (1st by Gladstone)	3	6	9	16	24	32
512,513	2	4	6	10	14	18
514-516,520	2	4	6	8	10	12
517-519,521,522,525,527,529,530,532-546: 518-Infinity-c. 522-r/1st app. Huey, Dewey & Louie from D. Duck Sunday. 535-546-Barks-r. 537-1st Donald Duck by William Van Horn in WDC&S. 541-545-52 pgs. 546,547-68 pgs. 546-Kelly-a. 547-Rosa-a						6.00
523,524,526,528,531,547: Rosa-s/a in all. 523-1st Rosa 10 pager	2	4	6	9	12	15
548-($1.50, 6/90)-1st Disney issue; new-a; no M. Mouse	1	2	3	4	5	7
549,550-551-570,572,573,577-580,581,584 ($1.50): 549-Barks-r begin, ends #585, not in #555, 556, & 564. 551-r/1 story from F.C. #29. 556,578-r/Mickey Mouse Cheerios Premium by Dick Moores. 562,563,568-570, 572, 581-Gottfredson strip-r. 570-Valentine issue; has Mickey/Minnie centerfold. 584-Taliaferro strip-r						4.00
550 ($2.25, 52 pgs.)-Donald Duck by Barks; previously printed only in The Netherlands (1st time in U.S.); r/Chip 'n Dale & Scamp from #204						5.00
571-($2.95, 68 pgs.)-r/Donald Duck's Atom Bomb by Barks from 1947 Cheerios premium						6.00
574-576,580,582,583 ($2.95, 68 pgs.)-r/1st Pinocchio Sunday strip (1939-40). 575-Gottfredson, Pinocchio-r/WDC&S #64. 580-r/Donald Duck's 1st app. from Silly Symphony strip 12/16/34 by Taliaferro; Gottfredson strip-r begin; not in #584 & 600.						
582,583-r/Mickey Mouse on Sky Island from WDC&S #1,2						5.00
585 ($2.50, 52 pgs.)-r/#140; Barks-r/WDC&S #140						5.00
586,587: 586-Gladstone issues begin again; begin $1.50-c; Gottfredson-r begins (not in #600). 587-Donald Duck by William Van Horn begins						4.00
588-597: 588,591-599-Donald Duck by William Van Horn						3.00
598,599 ($1.95, 36 pgs.): 598-r/1st drawings of Mickey Mouse by Ub Iwerks						3.00
600 ($2.95, 48 pgs.)-L.B. Cole-c(r)/WDC&S #1; Barks-r/WDC&S #32 plus Rosa, Jippes, Van Horn-r and new Rosa centerspread						4.00
601-611 ($5.95, 64 pgs., squarebound, bi-monthly): 601-Barks-c, r/Mickey Mouse V1#1, Rosa-a/scripts. 602-Rosa-a. 604-Taliaferro strip-r/1st Silly Symphony Sundays from 1932. 604,605-Jippes-a. 605-Walt Kelly-c; Gottfredson "Mickey Mouse Outwits the Phantom Blot" r/F.C. #16						6.00
612-633 ($6.95): 633-(2/99) Last Gladstone issue						7.00
634-675: 634-(7/03) First Gemstone issue; William Van Horn-c. 666-Mickey's Inferno						7.00

	GD 2.0	VG 4.0	FN 6.0	VF 8.0	VF/NM 9.0	NM- 9.2
676-681: 676-Begin $7.50-c. 677-Bucky Bug's 75th Anniversary						7.50
682-698-($7.99)						8.00
699-714: 699-(9/09, $2.99) First BOOM! Kids issue. 700-Back-up story w/Van Horn-a						3.00
715-720: 715-(1/11, $3.99) 70th Anniverary issue; cover swipe of #1 by Van Horn; Jippes, Rosa-a. 716-Barks reprints						4.00
721-738: 721-(7/15, $3.99) First IDW issue; Italian, Dutch & classic reprints						4.00
739-743-($5.99): 741-Eurasia Toft app. 743-(7/18)						6.00
... 75th Anniversary Special (10/15, $5.99) Classic short story reprints by various						6.00

NOTE: (#1-38, 68 pgs.; #39-42, 60 pgs.; #43-57, 61-134, 143-168, 446, 447, 52 pgs.; #58-60, 135-142, 169-540, 36 pgs.)

NOTE: Barks art in all issues #31 on, except where noted; c-95, 96, 104, 108, 109, 130-172, 174-178, 183, 198-200, 204, 206-209, 212-216, 218, 220, 226, 228-233, 235-238, 240-243, 247, 250, 253, 256, 260, 261, 276-283, 288-292, 295-298, 301, 303, 304, 306, 307, 309, 310, 313-316, 319, 321, 322, 324, 326, 328, 329, 331, 332, 334, 341, 342, 350, 351, 527r, 530r, 540(never before published), 546r, 557-586r(most), 596p, 601p. Kelly a-24p, 34-41, 43; r-522-524, 546, 547, 582, 583; covers(most)-34-118, 531r, 537r, 541r-543r, 562r, 571r, 605r. Walt Disney's Comics & Stories featured Mickey Mouse serials which were in practically every issue from #1 through #394 and #511 to date. The titles of the serials, along with the issues they are in, are listed in previous editions of this price guide. Floyd Gottfredson Mickey Mouse serials in issues #1-14, 18-66, 69-74, 78-100, 128, 562, 563, 568-572, 582, 583, 586-599 , 601-603, 605-present , plus "Service with a Smile" in #13; "Mickey Mouse in a Warplant" (3 pgs.), and "Pluto Catches a Nazi Spy" (4 pgs.) in #62; "Mystery Next Door", #93; "Sunken Treasure", #94; "Aunt Marissa", #95 (r in #575); "Gangland", #98 (r in #562); "Thanksgiving Dinner", #99 (r in #567); and "The Talking Dog", #100 (r in #563); "Morty's Escapade," #128. "The Brave Little Tailor", #580; "Introducing Mickey Mouse Movies", #581; Circus Roustabout, #585; "Rumplewatt the Giant", #604. Mickey Mouse by Paul Murry #152-547 except 155-57 (Dick Moore), 327-29 (Tony Strobl), 348-50 (Jack Manning), 533 (Bill Wright). Don Rosa story/a-523, 524, 526, 528, 531, 547, 601-present. Al Taliaferro Silly Symphonies in #5-"Three Little Pigs"; #13-"Birds of a Feather"; #14-"The Boarding School Mystery"; #15-"Cookieland" and "Three Little Kittens"; #16-"The Practical Pig"; #17-"The Ugly Duckling"; "The Wise Little Hen" in #580; and "Ambrose the Robber Kitten"; #19-"Penguin Isle"; and "Bucky Bug" in #20-23, 25, 26, 28 (one continuous story from 1932-34; first 2 pgs. not Taliaferro). Gottfredson strip r-562, 563, 568-572, 581, 585, 586, 590. Taliaferro strip r-584, 580. Van Horn a-537, 545, 561, 574, 587, 588, 591-on.

WALT DISNEY'S COMICS DIGEST
Gladstone: Dec, 1986 - No. 7, Sept, 1987

1	1	2	3	5	6	8
2-7						6.00

WALT DISNEY'S COMICS PENNY PINCHER
Gladstone: May, 1997 - No. 4, Aug, 1997 (99¢, limited series)

1-4						4.00

WALT DISNEY'S DONALD AND MICKEY (Formerly Walt Disney's Mickey and Donald)
Gladstone (Bruce Hamilton Co.): No. 19, Sept, 1993 - No. 30, 1995 ($1.50, 36 & 68 pgs.)

19,21,24,26-30: New & reprints. 19,21,23,24-Barks-r. 19,26-Murry-r. 22-Barks "Omelet" story r/WDC&S #146. 27-Mickey Mouse story by Caesar Ferioli (1st U.S work). 29-Rosa-c; Mickey Mouse story actually starring Goofy (does not include Mickey except on title page.)						4.00
20,25-($2.95, 68 pgs.): 20-Barks, Gottfredson-r						5.00

NOTE: Donald Duck stories are all reprints.

WALT DISNEY'S DONALD DUCK
Gemstone Publishing: 2006, 2008

... Free Comic Book Day (5/06) r/WDC&S #531; Rosa-s/a; P&S. Block-s/a; Van Horn-s/a						3.00
nn-(8-1/2"x 5-1/2", Halloween giveaway) r/"A Prank Above" -Barks-s/a; Rosa-s/a						3.00
nn-(2008, 8-1/2"x 5-1/2", Halloween giveaway) "The Halloween Huckster", Rota-s/a						3.00

WALT DISNEY'S DONALD DUCK ADVENTURES (D.D. Adv #1-3)
Gladstone: 11/87-No. 20, 4/90 (1st Series); No. 21,8/93-No. 48, 2/98(3rd Series)

1	1	2	3	5	6	8
2-r/F.C. #308						5.00
3,4,6,7,9-11,13,15-18: 3-r/F.C. #223. 4-r/FC #62. 9-r/F.C. #159, "Ghost of the Grotto". 11-r/F.C. #159, "Adventure Down Under." 16-r/FC #291; Rosa-c. 18-r/FC #318; Rosa-c						4.00
5,8: 5-Don Rosa-c/a. 8-Rosa-a						5.00
12($1.50, 52pgs)-Rosa-c/s/a; "Return to Plain Awful" story; sequel to Four Color #223 (square egg story); Barks centerfold poster						6.00
14-r/F.C. #29, "Mummy's Ring"						5.00
19($1.95, 68 pgs.)-Barks-r/F.C. #199 (1 pg.)						5.00
20($1.95, 68 pgs.)-Barks-r/F.C. #189 & cover-r; William Van Horn-a						4.00
21,22: 21-r/D.D. #46. 22-r/FC #282						4.00
23-25,27,29,31,32-($1.50, 36 pgs.): 21,23,29-Rosa-c. 23-Intro/1 app. Andold Wild Duck by Marco Rota. 24-Van Horn-a. 27-1st Pat Block-a, "Mystery of Widow's Gap". 31,32-Block-c						4.00
26,28($2.95, 68 pgs.): 26-Barks-r/F.C. #108, "Terror of the River". 28-Barks-r/F.C. #199, "Sheriff of Bullet Valley"						5.00
30($2.95, 68 pgs.)-r/F.C. #367, Barks' "Christmas for Shacktown"						5.00
33($1.95, 68 pgs.)-r/F.C. #408, Barks' "The Golden Helmet;"Van Horn-c						5.00
34-43: Resume $1.50-c. 34,35,37-Block-a/Rosa-c/a						4.00
44-48-($1.95-c)						4.00

NOTE: Barks a-1-22r, 26r, 28r, 33r, 36r; c-3r, 8r, 10r, 14r, 20r. Block a-27, 30, 34, 35, 37; c-27, 30-32, 34, 35, 37; c-27, 30, 31, 32, 34, 35, 37. Rosa a-5, 8, 12, 43; c-13, 16, 18, 21, 23, 43.

WALT DISNEY'S DONALD DUCK ADVENTURES (2nd Series)
Disney Comics: June, 1990 - No. 38, July, 1993 ($1.50)

1-Rosa-a & scripts						5.00

	GD	VG	FN	VF	VF/NM	NM-
	2.0	4.0	6.0	8.0	9.0	9.2

2-21,23,25,27-33,35,36,38: 2-Barks-r/WDC&S #35; William Van Horn-a begins, ends #20. 9-Barks-r/F.C. #178. 9,11,14,17-No Van Horn-a. 11-Mad #1 cover parody. 14-Barks-r. 17-Barks-r. 21-r/FC #203 by Barks. 29-r/MOC #20 by Barks — 4.00

22,24,26,34,37: 22-Rosa-a (10 pgs.) & scripts. 24-Rosa-a & scripts. 26-r/March of Comics #41 by Barks. 34-Rosa-c/a. 37-Rosa-a; Barks-r

NOTE: *Barks* r-2, 4, 9(F.C. #178), 14(D.D. #45), 17, 21, 26, 27, 29 , 35, 36(D.D #60)-38. *Taliaferro* a-34r, 36r.

WALT DISNEY'S DONALD DUCK ADVENTURES
Gemstone Publishing: May, 2003 (giveaway promoting 2003 return of Disney Comics)

...Free Comic Book Day Edition - cover logo on red background; reprints "Maharajah Donald" & "The Peaceful Hills" from March of Comics #4; Barks-s/a; Kelly original-c on back-c

...San Diego Comic-Con 2003 Edition - cover logo on gold background — 3.00
...ANA World's Fair of Money Baltimore Edition - cover logo on green background — 3.00
...WizardWorld Chicago 2003 Edition - cover logo on blue background — 3.00

WALT DISNEY'S DONALD DUCK ADVENTURES (Take-Along Comic)
Gemstone Publishing: July, 2003 - No. 21, Nov, 2006 ($7.95, 5" x 7-1/2")

1-21-Mickey Mouse & Uncle Scrooge app. 9-Christmas-c — 8.00

..., The Barks/Rosa Collection Vol. 2 (3/08, $8.99) reprints Donald Duck's Atom Bomb, Super Snooper & The Trouble With Dimes by Barks; The Duck Who Fell to Earth, Super Snooper Strikes Again & The Money Pit by Rosa

..., The Barks/Rosa Collection Vol. 3 (9/08, $8.99) r/FC #408 "The Golden Helmet" by Rosa & DDA #43 "The Lost Charts of Columbus" by Rosa; cover gallery and bonus art — 9.00

WALT DISNEY'S DONALD DUCK AND FRIENDS (Continues as Gladstone Donald Duck and Friends)
Gemstone Publishing: No. 308, Oct, 2003 - No. 346, Dec, 2006 ($2.95)

308-346: 308-Numbering resumes from Gladstone Donald Duck series; Halloween-c. 332-Halloween-c; r/#26 by Carl Barks — 3.00

WALT DISNEY'S DONALD DUCK AND MICKEY MOUSE (Formerly Walt Disney's Donald and Mickey)
Gladstone (Bruce Hamilton Company): Sept, 1995 - No. 7, Sept, 1996 ($1.50, 32 pgs.)

1-7: 1-Barks-r and new Mickey Mouse stories in all. 5,6-Mickey Mouse stories by Caesar Ferioli. 7-New Donald Duck and Mickey Mouse x-over story; Barks-r/WDC #51 — 4.00
NOTE: Issue #8 was advertised, but cancelled.

WALT DISNEY'S DONALD DUCK AND UNCLE SCROOGE
Gemstone Publishing: Nov, 2005 ($6.95, square-bound one-shot)

nn-New story by John Lustig and Pat Block and r/Uncle Scrooge #59 — 7.00

WALT DISNEY'S DONALD DUCK FAMILY
Gemstone Publishing: Jun, 2008 ($8.99, square-bound)

... The Daan Jippes Collection Vol. 1 - R/Barks-s re-drawn by Jippes for Dutch comics — 9.00

WALT DISNEY'S DONALD DUCK IN THE CASE OF THE MISSING MUMMY
Gemstone Publishing: Oct, 2007 ($8.99, square-bound one-shot)

nn-New story by Shelley and Pat Block and r/Donald Duck FC #29 — 9.00

WALT DISNEY'S GYRO GEARLOOSE
Gemstone Publishing: May, 2008

... Free Comic Book Day (5/08) short stories by Barks, Rosa, Van Horn, Gerstein — 3.00

WALT DISNEY SHOWCASE
Gold Key: Oct, 1970 - No. 54, Jan, 1980 (No. 44-48: 68pgs., 49-54: 52pgs.)

1-Boatniks (Movie)-Photo-c	3	6	9	19	30	40
2-Moby Duck	3	6	9	14	19	24
3,4,7: 3-Bongo & Lumpjaw-r. 4,7-Pluto-r	2	4	6	10	14	18
5-$1,000,000 Duck (Movie)-Photo-c	3	6	9	16	24	32
6-Bednobs & Broomsticks (Movie)	3	6	9	16	24	32
8-Daisy & Donald	2	4	6	11	16	20
9- 101 Dalmatians (cartoon feat.); r/F.C. #1183	3	6	9	16	24	32
10-Napoleon & Samantha (Movie)-Photo-c	3	6	9	15	22	28
11-Moby Duck-r	2	4	6	10	14	18
12-Dumbo-r/Four Color #668	2	4	6	11	16	20
13-Pluto-r	2	4	6	10	14	18
14-World's Greatest Athlete (Movie)-Photo-c	3	6	9	15	22	28
15- 3 Little Pigs-r	2	4	6	11	16	20
16-Aristocats (cartoon feature); r/Aristocats #1	3	6	9	15	22	28
17-Mary Poppins; r/M.P. #10136-501-Photo-c	3	6	9	15	22	28
18-Gyro Gearloose; Barks-r/F.C. #1047,1184	3	6	9	17	26	35
19-That Darn Cat; r/That Darn Cat #10171-602-Hayley Mills photo-c						
	3	6	9	15	22	28
20,23-Pluto-r	2	4	6	11	16	20
21-Li'l Bad Wolf & The Three Little Pigs	2	4	6	10	14	18
22-Unbirthday Party with Alice in Wonderland; r/Four Color #341						
	3	6	9	14	19	24
24-26: 24-Herbie Rides Again (Movie); sequel to "The Love Bug"; photo-c. 25-Old Yeller (Movie); r/FC #869; Photo-c. 26-Lt. Robin Crusoe USN (Movie); r/Lt. Robin Crusoe USN #10191-601; photo-c						
	2	4	6	11	16	20
27-Island at the Top of the World (Movie)-Photo-c	3	6	9	14	19	24
28-Brer Rabbit, Bucky Bug-r/WDC&S #58	2	4	6	11	16	20
29-Escape to Witch Mountain (Movie)-Photo-c	3	6	9	14	19	24
30-Magica De Spell; Barks-r/Uncle Scrooge #36 & WDC&S #258						
	3	6	9	20	31	42
31-Bambi (cartoon feature); r/Four Color #186	2	4	6	13	18	22
32-Spin & Marty-r/F.C. #1026; Mickey Mouse Club (TV)-Photo-c						
	3	6	9	14	19	24
33-40: 33-Pluto-r/F.C. #1143. 34-Paul Revere's Ride with Johnny Tremain (TV); r/F.C. #822. 35-Goofy-r/F.C. #952. 36-Peter Pan-r/F.C. #442. 37-Tinker Bell & Jiminy Cricket-r/F.C. #982,989. 38,39-Mickey & the Sleuth, Parts 1 & 2. 40-The Rescuers (cartoon feature)						
	2	4	6	9	13	16
41-Herbie Goes to Monte Carlo (Movie); sequel to "Herbie Rides Again"; photo-c						
	2	4	6	10	14	18
42-Mickey & the Sleuth	2	4	6	9	13	16
43-Pete's Dragon (Movie)-Photo-c	2	4	6	13	18	22
44-Return From Witch Mountain (new) & In Search of the Castaways-r (Movies); 68 pg. giants begin	3	6	9	14	19	24
45-The Jungle Book; r/#30033-803	3	6	9	16	24	32
46-48: 46-The Cat From Outer Space (Movie)(new), & The Shaggy Dog (Movie)-r/F.C. #985; photo-c. 47-Mickey Mouse Surprise Party-r. 48-The Wonderful Advs. of Pinocchio-r/F.C. #1203; last 68 pg. issue						
	2	4	6	9	14	18

49-54: 49-North Avenue Irregulars (Movie); Zorro-r/Zorro #11; 52 pgs. begin; photo-c. 50-Bednobs & Broomsticks-r/#6; Mooncussers-r/World of Adv. #1; photo-c. 51-101 Dalmatians-r. 52-Unidentified Flying Oddball (Movie); r/Picnic Party #8; photo-c. 53-The Scarecrow-r (TV). 54-The Black Hole (Movie)-Photo-c (predates Black Hole #1)

	2	4	6	9	13	16

WALT DISNEY SHOWCASE
IDW Publishing: Jan, 2018 - No. 6, Jun, 2018 ($3.99)

1-6-English versions of Italian Disney stories; 3 covers — 4.00

WALT DISNEY'S MAGAZINE (TV)(Formerly Walt Disney's Mickey Mouse Club Magazine)
(50¢, bi-monthly)
Western Publishing Co.: V2#4, June, 1957 - V4#6, Oct, 1959

V2#4-Stories & articles on the Mousekeeters, Zorro, & Goofy and other Disney characters & people	6	12	18	41	76	110
V2#5, V2#6(10/57)	6	12	18	37	66	95
V3#1(12/57), V3#3-5	5	10	15	34	60	85
V3#2-Annette Funicello photo-c	11	22	33	73	157	240
V3#6(10/58)-TV Zorro photo-c	7	14	21	48	89	130
V4#1(12/58) - V4#2-4,6(10/59)	5	10	15	33	57	80
V4#5-Annette Funicello photo-c, w/ 2-photo articles	11	22	33	73	157	240

NOTE: V2#4-V3#6 were 11-1/2x8-1/2", 48 pgs.; V4#1 on were 10x8", 52 pgs. (Peak circulation of 400,000).

WALT DISNEY'S MERRY CHRISTMAS (See Dell Giant #39)

WALT DISNEY'S MICKEY AND DONALD (M & D #1,2)(Becomes Walt Disney's Donald & Mickey #19 on)
Gladstone: Mar, 1988 - No. 18, May, 1990 (95¢)

1-Don Rosa-a; r/1949 Firestone giveaway						6.00
2-8: 3-Infinity-c. 4-8-Barks-r						5.00
9-15: 9-r/1948 Firestone giveaway; X-Mas-c						4.00
16($1.50, 68 pgs.)-r/FC #157						5.00
17-(68 pgs.) Barks M.M.-r/FC #79 plus Barks D.D.-r; Rosa-a; x-mas-c						6.00
18($1.95, 68 pgs.)-Gottfredson-r/WDC&S #13,72-74; Kelly-c(r); Barks-r						5.00

NOTE: Barks reprints in 1-15, 17, 18. Kelly c-13r, 14 (r/Walt Disney's C&S #58), 18r.

WALT DISNEY'S MICKEY MOUSE
Gemstone Publishing: May, 2007

... Free Comic Book Day (5/07) Floyd Gottfredson-s/a — 3.00

WALT DISNEY'S MICKEY MOUSE ADVENTURES (Take-Along Comic)
Gemstone Publishing: Aug, 2004 - No. 12 ($7.95, 5" x 7-1/2")

1-12-Goofy, Donald Duck & Uncle Scrooge app. — 8.00

WALT DISNEY'S MICKEY MOUSE AND BLOTMAN IN BLOTMAN RETURNS
Gemstone Publishing: Dec, 2006 ($5.99, squarebound, one-shot)

nn-Wraparound-c by Noel Van Horn; Super Goof back-up story — 6.00

WALT DISNEY'S MICKEY MOUSE AND FRIENDS (Becomes Mickey Mouse and Friends for #296)
Gemstone Publishing: No. 257, Oct, 2003 - No. 295, Dec, 2006 ($2.95)

257-295: 257-Numbering resumes from Gladstone Mickey Mouse series; Halloween-c. 285-Return of the Phantom Blot

WALT DISNEY'S MICKEY MOUSE AND UNCLE SCROOGE
Gemstone Publishing: June, 2004 (Free Comic Book Day giveaway)

nn-Flip book with r/Uncle Scrooge #15 and r/Mickey Mouse Four Color #79 (only Barks drawn Mickey Mouse story) — 3.00

WALT DISNEY'S MICKEY MOUSE CLUB MAGAZINE (TV)(Becomes Walt Disney's Magazine)
Western Publishing Co.: Winter, 1956 - V2#3, Apr, 1957 (11-1/2x8-1/2", quarterly, 48 pgs.)

V1#1	15	30	45	100	220	340
2-4	9	18	27	58	114	170
V2#1,2	8	16	24	51	96	140
3-Annette photo-c	13	26	39	89	195	300
Annual(1956)-Two different issues; ($1.50-Whitman); 120 pgs., cardboard covers, 11-3/4x8-3/4"; reprints	14	28	42	96	211	325
Annual(1957)-Same as above	12	24	36	79	170	260

WALT DISNEY'S MICKEY MOUSE MEETS BLOTMAN
Gemstone Publishing: Aug, 2005 ($5.99, squarebound, one-shot)

nn-Wraparound-c by Noel Van Horn; Super Goof back-up story — 6.00

WALT DISNEY'S PINOCCHIO SPECIAL
Gladstone: Spring, 1990 ($1.00)

1-50th anniversary edition; Kelly-r/F.C. #92 — 4.00

WALT DISNEY'S SEBASTIAN
Disney Comics, Inc.: 1992

1-(36 pgs.) — 4.00

WALT DISNEY'S SPRING FEVER
Gemstone Publishing: Apr, 2007; Apr, 2008 ($9.50, squarebound)

1,2: 1-New stories and reprints incl. "Mystery of the Swamp" by Carl Barks — 9.50

WALT DISNEY'S THE ADVENTUROUS UNCLE SCROOGE McDUCK
Gladstone: Jan, 1998 - No. 2, Mar, 1998 ($1.95)

1,2: 1-Barks-a(r). 2-Rosa-a(r) — 4.00

WALT DISNEY'S THE JUNGLE BOOK
W.D. Publications (Disney Comics): 1990 ($5.95, graphic novel, 68 pgs.)

nn-Movie adaptation; movie rereleased in 1990 — 6.00
nn-($2.95, 68 pgs.)-Comic edition; wraparound-c — 5.00

WALT DISNEY'S UNCLE SCROOGE (Free Comic Uncle Scrooge #1-209)
Gladstone #210-242/Disney Comics #243-280/Gladstone #281-318/Gemstone #319 on: No. 210, 10/86 - No. 242, 4/90; No. 243, 6/90 - No. 318, 2/99; No. 319, 7/03 - No. 383, 11/08

210-1st Gladstone issue; Barks-r/WDC&S #134 (1st Beagle Boys)

	2	4	6	9	13	16
211-218: 216-New story ("Go Slowly Sands of Time") plotted and partly scripted by Barks. 217-r/U.S. #7, "Seven Cities of Cibola"	2	4	6	9	12	15
219-"Son Of The Sun" by Rosa (his 1st pro work)	3	6	9	14	20	25
220-Don Rosa-a/scripts	1	2	3	5	6	8
221-223,225,228-234,236-240						4.00
224,226,227,235: 224-Rosa-c/a. 226,227-Rosa-a. 235-Rosa-a/scripts						5.00

Walt Disney's Mickey Mouse and Friends #290 © DIS

Walt Disney's Uncle Scrooge #353 © DIS

Wambi, Junge Boy #6 © FH

	GD 2.0	VG 4.0	FN 6.0	VF 8.0	VF/NM 9.0	NM- 9.2

241-($1.95, 68 pgs.)-Rosa finishes over Barks-r — 6.00
242-($1.95, 68 pgs.)-Barks-r; Rosa-a(1 pg.) — 6.00
243-249,251-260,264-275,277-280,282-284-($1.50): 243-1st by Disney Comics. 274-All Barks issue. 275-Contains centerspread by Rosa. 279-All Barks issue; Rosa-c. 283-r/WDC&S #98 — 3.00
250-($2.25, 52 pgs.)-Barks-r; wraparound-c — 4.00
261-263,276-Don Rosa-c/a — 5.00
281-Gladstone issues start again; Rosa-c — 6.00
285-The Life and Times of Scrooge McDuck Pt. 1; Rosa-c/a/scripts

1	3	4	6	8	10

286-293: The Life and Times of Scrooge McDuck Pt. 2-9; Rosa-c/a/scripts.
292-Scrooge & Glittering Goldie & Goose Egg Nugget on-c — 6.00
294-299, 301-308-($1.50, 32 pgs.): 294-296-The Life and Times of Scrooge McDuck Pt. 10-12.
295-Titanic on-c. 296-Beagle Boys & Christmas-c. 297-The Life and Times of Uncle Scrooge Pt. 0; Rosa-c/a/scripts — 3.00
300-($2.25, 48 pgs.)-Rosa-c; Barks-r/WDC&S #104 and U.S. #216; r/U.S. #220; includes new centerfold — 4.00
309-($6.95) Low print run — 3 6 9 14 20 25
310-($6.95) Low print run — 4 8 12 27 44 60
311-320-($6.95) 318-(2/99) Last Gladstone issue. 319-(7/03) First Gemstone issue; The Dutchman's Secret by Don Rosa — 2 4 6 8 10 12
321-360 — 7.00
361-366: 361-Begin $7.50-c — 7.50
367-383-($7.99) — 8.00
... Adventures, The Barks/Rosa Collection Vol. 1 (Gemstone, 7/07, $8.50) reprints Pygmy Indians appearances in U.S. #18 by Barks and WDC&S #633 by Rosa — 8.50
Walt Disney's The Life and Times of Scrooge McDuck by Don Rosa TPB (Gemstone, 2005, $16.99) Reprints #285-296, with foreword, commentaries & sketch pages by Rosa — 17.00
Walt Disney's The Life and Times of Scrooge McDuck Companion by Don Rosa TPB (Gemstone, 2006, $16.99) additional chapters, with foreword & commentaries — 17.00
NOTE: *Barks* r-210-218, 220-223, 224(2pg.), 225-234, 236-242, 245, 246, 250-253, 255, 256, 258, 261(2 pg.), 265, 267, 268, 270(2), 272-284, 299-present; c(r)-210, 212, 221, 228, 229, 232, 233, 284. scripts-287, 293. *Rosa* a-219, 220, 224, 226, 227, 235, 261-263, 268, 275-277, 285-297; c-219, 224, 231, 261-263, 276, 278-281, 285-296; scripts-219, 220, 224, 235, 261-263, 268, 276, 285-296.

WALT DISNEY'S UNCLE SCROOGE
Gemstone Publishing
nn-(5/05, FCBD) Reprints Uncle Scrooge's debut in Four Color Comics #386; Barks-s/a — 3.00
nn-(2007, 8-1/2"x 5-1/2", Halloween giveaway) Hound of the Whiskervilles; Barks-s/a — 3.00

WALT DISNEY'S UNCLE SCROOGE ADVENTURES (U. Scrooge Advs. #1-3)
Gladstone Publishing: Nov, 1987 - No. 21, May, 1990; No. 22, Sept, 1993 - No. 54, Feb, 1998
1-Barks-r begin, ends #26 — 2 4 6 8 10 12
2-4 — 5.00
5,9,14: 5-Rosa-c/a; no Barks-r. 9,14-Rosa-a — 6.00
6-8,10-13,15-19: 10-r/U.S. #18(all Barks) — 4.00
20,21 ($1.95, 68 pgs.) 20-Rosa-c/a. 21-Rosa-a — 5.00
22 ($1.50) Rosa-c; r/U.S. #26 — 5.00
23-($2.95, 68 pgs.)-Vs. The Phantom Blot-r/P.B. #3; Barks-r — 5.00
24-26,29,31,32,34-36: 24,25,29,31,32-Rosa-c. 25-r/U.S. #21 — 5.00
27-Guardians of the Lost Library - Rosa-c/a/story; origin of Junior Woodchuck Guidebook — 5.00
28-($2.95, 68 pgs.)-r/U.S. #13 w/restored missing panels — 5.00
30-($2.95, 68 pgs.)-r/U.S. #12; Rosa-c — 5.00
33-($2.95, 64 pgs.)-New Barks story — 5.00
37-54 — 4.00
NOTE: *Barks* r-1-4, 6-8, 10-13, 15-21, 23, 22, 24; c(r)-15, 16, 17, 21. *Rosa* a-5, 9, 14, 20, 21, 27, 51; c-5, 13, 14, 17(finishes), 20, 22, 24, 25, 27, 28, 51; scripts-5, 9, 14, 27.

WALT DISNEY'S UNCLE SCROOGE AND DONALD DUCK
Gladstone: Jan, 1998 - No. 2, Mar, 1998 ($1.95)
1,2: 1-Rosa-a(r) — 4.00

WALT DISNEY'S UNCLE SCROOGE ADVENTURES IN COLOR
Gladstone Publ.: Dec, 1995 - No. 56 ($8.95/$9.95, squarebound, 56 issue limited series) (Polybagged w/card) (Series chronologically reprints all the stories written & drawn by Carl Barks)
1-56: 1-(12/95)-r/FC #386. 15-(12/96)-r/US #15. 16-(12/96)-r/US #16. 18-(1/97)-r/US #18 — 10.00

WALT DISNEY'S VACATION PARADE
Gemstone Publishing: 2004 - No. 5, July, 2008 ($8.95/$9.95, squarebound, annual)
1-3: 1-Reprints stories from Dell Giant Comics Vacation Parade 1 (July 1950) — 10.00
4,5-($9.95): 4-(5/07). 5-(7/08) — 10.00

WALT DISNEY'S WHEATIES PREMIUMS (See Wheaties in the Promotional section)

WALT DISNEY'S WORLD OF THE DRAGONLORDS
Gemstone Publishing: 2005 ($12.99, squarebound, graphic novel)
SC-Uncle Scrooge, Donald & nephews app.; Byron Erickson-s/Giorgio Cavazzano-a — 13.00

WALT DISNEY TREASURES - DISNEY COMICS: 75 YEARS OF INNOVATION
Gemstone Publishing: 2006 ($12.99, TPB)
SC-Reprints from 1930-2004, including debut of Mickey Mouse newspaper strip — 13.00

WALT DISNEY TREASURES - UNCLE SCROOGE: A LITTLE SOMETHING SPECIAL
Gemstone Publishing: 2008 ($16.99, TPB)
SC-Uncle Scrooge classics from 1954-2006, including "The Seven Cities of Cibola" — 17.00

WALT DISNEY UNCLE SCROOGE AND DONALD DUCK
Fantagraphic Books: 2014 (giveaway)
Free Comic Book Day - A Matter of Some Gravity; Don Rosa-s/a — 3.00

WALTER LANTZ ANDY PANDA (Also see Andy Panda)
Gold Key: Aug, 1973 - No. 23, Jan, 1978 (Walter Lantz)
1-Reprints — 3 6 9 16 23 30
2-10-All reprints — 2 4 6 9 12 15
11-23: 15,17-19,22-Reprints — 1 2 3 5 7 9

WALT KELLY'S...
Eclipse Comics: Dec, 1987; Apr, 1988 ($1.75/$2.50, Baxter paper)
...Christmas Classics 1 (12/87)-Kelly-r/Peter Wheat & Santa Claus Funnies,
...Springtime Tales 1 (4/88, $2.50)-Kelly-r — 4.00

WALTONS, THE (See Kite Fun Book)

WALT SCOTT (See Little People)

WALT SCOTT'S CHRISTMAS STORIES (See Little People, 4-Color #959, 1062)

WAMBI, JUNGLE BOY (See Jungle Comics)
Fiction House Magazines: Spr, 1942; No. 2, Win, 1942-43; No. 3, Spr, 1943; No. 4, Fall, 1948; No. 5, Sum, 1949; No. 6, Spr, 1950; No. 7-10, 1950(nd); No. 11, Spr, 1951 - No. 18, Win, 1952-53 (#1-3: 68 pgs.)
1-Wambi, the Jungle Boy begins — 126 252 378 806 1378 1950
2 (1942)-Kiefer-c — 50 100 150 315 533 750
3 (1943)-Kiefer-c — 42 84 126 265 445 625
4 (1948)-Origin in text — 34 68 102 199 325 450
5 (Fall, 1949, 36 pgs.)-Kiefer-c/a — 22 44 66 132 216 300
6-10: 7-(52 pgs.)-New logo — 18 36 54 107 169 230
11-18 — 15 30 45 83 130 175
I.W. Reprint #8('64)-r/#12 with new-c — 3 6 9 16 23 30
NOTE: *Alex Blum* c-8. *Kiefer* c-1-5. *Whitman* c-11-18.

WANDERERS (See Adventure Comics #375, 376)
DC Comics: June, 1988 - No. 13, Apr, 1989 ($1.25) (Legion of Super-Heroes spin off)
1-13: 1,2-Steacy-a. 3-Legion app. — 4.00

WANDERING STAR
Pen & Ink Comics/Sirius Entertainment No. 12 on: 1993 - No. 21, Mar, 1997 ($2.50/$2.75, B&W)
1-1st printing; Teri Sue Wood c/a/scripts in all — 1 2 3 5 6 8
1-2nd and 3rd printings — 4.00
2-1st printing — 4.00
2-21: 2-2nd printing. 12-(1/96)-1st Sirius issue — 4.00
Trade paperback ($11.95)-r/1-7; 1st printing of 1000, signed and #'d — 18.00
Trade paperback-2nd printing, 2000 signed — 15.00
TPB Volume 2,3 (11/98, 12/98, $14.95) 2-r/#8-14, 3-r/#15-21 — 15.00

WANTED
Image Comics (Top Cow): Dec, 2003 - No. 6, Feb, 2004 ($2.99)
1-Three covers; Mark Millar-s/J.G. Jones-a; intro Wesley Gibson — 4.00
1-4-Death Row Edition; r/#1-4 with extra sketch pages and deleted panels — 3.00
1-(7/23, $4.99) 20th Anniversary Edition; bonus sketch pages and creators interview — 5.00
2-6: 2-Cameos of DC villains. 6-Giordano-a in flashback scenes — 3.00
...Dossier (5/04, $2.99) Pin-ups and character info; art by Jones, Romita Jr. & others — 3.00
Image Firsts: Wanted #1 (9/10, $1.00) reprints #1 — 3.00
... Movie Edition Vol. 1 TPB (2008, $19.99) r/#1-6 & Dossier; movie photo-c; sketch pages & cover gallery; interviews with movie cast and director — 20.00
HC (2005, $29.99) r/#1-6 & Dossier; intro by Vaughan, sketch pages & cover gallery — 30.00

WANTED COMICS
Toytown Publications/Patches/Orbit Publ.: No. 9, Sept-Oct, 1947 - No. 53, April, 1953 (#9-33: 52 pgs.)
9-True crime cases; radio's Mr. D. A. app. — 42 84 126 265 445 625
10,11: 10-Giunta-a; radio's Mr. D. A. app. — 29 58 87 172 281 390
12-Used in SOTI, pg. 277 — 31 62 93 182 296 410
13-Heroin drug propaganda story — 31 62 93 182 296 410
14-Marijuana drug mention story (2 pgs.) — 27 54 81 158 259 360
15-17,19,20 — 22 44 66 132 216 300
18-Marijuana story, "Satan's Cigarettes"; r-in #45 & retitled — 45 90 135 284 480 675
21,22: 21-Krigstein-a. 22-Extreme violence — 23 46 69 136 223 310
23,25-32,34,36-38,40-44,46-48,53 — 20 40 60 120 195 270

	GD 2.0	VG 4.0	FN 6.0	VF 8.0	VF/NM 9.0	NM- 9.2

24-Krigstein-a; "The Dope King", marijuana mention story
 — 30 60 90 177 289 400
33-Spider web-c — 53 106 159 334 567 800
35-Used in **SOTI**, pg. 160 — 28 56 84 165 270 375
39-Drug propaganda story "The Horror Weed" — 36 78 117 240 395 550
45-Marijuana story from #18 — 24 48 72 144 237 330
49-Has unstable pink-c that fades easily; rare in mint condition — 36 72 108 214 347 480
50-Has unstable pink-c like #49; surrealist-c by Buscema; horror stories — 41 82 123 256 428 600
51- "Holiday of Horror" junkie story; drug-c — 39 78 117 240 395 550
52-Classic "Cult of Killers" opium use story — 290 580 870 1856 3178 4500
NOTE: *Buscema* c-50, 51. *Lawrence* and *Leav* c/a most issues. *Syd Shores* c/a-48; c-37. *Issues 9-46 have wanted criminals with their descriptions & drawn picture on cover.*

WANTED: DEAD OR ALIVE (TV)
Dell Publishing Co.: 1102, May-July, 1960 - No. 1164, Mar-May, 1961
Four Color 1102 (#1)-Steve McQueen photo-c — 15 30 45 103 227 350
Four Color 1164-Steve McQueen photo-c — 10 20 30 69 147 225

WANTED, THE WORLD'S MOST DANGEROUS VILLAINS (See DC Special)
National Periodical Publ.: July-Aug, 1972 - No. 9, Aug-Sept, 1973 (All reprints & 20¢ issues)
1-Batman, Green Lantern (story r-from G.L. #1), & Green Arrow — 4 8 12 25 40. 55
2-Batman/Joker/Penguin-c/story r-from Batman #25; plus Flash story (r-from Flash #121) — 4 7 17 25 34
3-9: 3-Dr. Fate(r/More Fun #65), Hawkman(r/Flash #100), & Vigilante(r/Action #69). 4-Green Lantern(r/All-American #61) & Kid Eternity(r/Kid Eternity #15). 5-Dollman/Green Lantern. 6-Burnley Starman; Wildcat/Sargon. 7-Johnny Quick(r/More Fun #76), Hawkman(r/Flash #90), Hourman by Baily(r/Adv. #72). 8-Dr. Fate/Flash(r/Flash #114).
9-S&K Sandman/Superman — 3 6 9 15 22 28
NOTE: *B. Bailey* a-7r. *Infantino* a-2r. *Kane* r-1, 5. *Kubert* r-3i, 6, 7. *Meskin* r-3, 7. *Reinman* r-4, 6.

WAR (See Fightin' Marines #122)
Charlton Comics: Jul, 1975 - No. 9, Nov, 1976; No. 10, Sept 1978 - No. 47, 1984
1-Boyette painted-c — 3 6 9 14 20 26
2-10: 5-Sutton painted-c — 2 4 6 8 11 14
11-20 — 1 2 3 5 6 8
21-40 — 1 2 3 4 5 7
41,42,44-47 (lower print run): 47-Reprints — 1 2 3 5 6 8
43 (2/84) (lower print run) Ditko-a (7 pgs.) — 2 4 6 8 10 12
7,9 (Modern Comics-r, 1977) — 6.00

WAR, THE (See The Draft & The Pitt)
Marvel Comics: 1989 - No. 4, 1990 ($3.50, squarebound, 52 pgs.)
1-4: Characters from New Universe — 5.00

WAR ACTION (Korean War)
Atlas Comics (CPS): April, 1952 - No. 14, June, 1953
1 — 47 94 141 296 498 700
2-Hartley-a — 34 68 102 199 325 450
3-10,14: 7-Pakula-a/Heath-c. 14-Colan-a — 25 50 75 150 245 340
11-13-Krigstein-a. 11-Romita-a — 27 54 81 158 259 360
NOTE: *Berg* c-11. *Brodsky* a-2; c-1-4. *Heath* a-1; c-7, 14. *Keller* a-6. *Maneely* c-12. *Sale* a-7.*Tuska* a-2, 8.

WAR ADVENTURES (Korean War)
Atlas Comics (HPC): Jan, 1952 - No. 13, Feb, 1953
1-Tuska-a — 47 94 141 296 498 700
2 — 34 68 102 199 325 450
3-7,9-11,13: 3-Pakula-a. 7-Maneely-c. 9-Romita-a — 26 52 78 154 252 350
8-Krigstein-a — 27 54 81 158 259 360
12-Grey tone-c — 53 106 159 334 567 800
NOTE: *Brodsky* c-1-3, 6, 8, 11, 12. *Heath* a-2, 5, 7, 10; c-4, 5, 9, 13. *Reinman* a-13. *Robinson* a-3; c-10.

WAR ADVENTURES ON THE BATTLEFIELD (See Battlefield)

WAR AGAINST CRIME! (Becomes Vault of Horror #12 on)
E. C. Comics: Spring, 1948 - No. 11, Feb-Mar, 1950
1-Real Stories From Police Records on-c #1-9 — 219 438 657 1402 2401 3400
2,3 — 116 232 348 742 1271 1800
4-9 — 74 148 222 470 810 1150
10-1st Vault Keeper app. & 1st Vault of Horror — 314 628 942 2198 3849 5500
11-2nd Vault Keeper app.; 1st EC horror-c — 300 600 900 2010 3505 5000
NOTE: *All have Johnny Craig covers. Feldstein* a-4, 7-9. *Harrison/Wood* a-11. *Ingels* a-1, 2, 8. *Palais* a-8. *Changes to horror with #10.*

WAR AGAINST CRIME
Gemstone Publishing: Apr, 2000 - No. 11, Feb, 2001 ($2.50)
1-11: E.C. reprints — 4.00

WAR AND ATTACK (Also see Special War Series #3)
Charlton Comics: Fall, 1964; V2#54, June, 1966 - V2#63, Dec, 1967
1-Wood-a (25 pgs.) — 6 12 18 42 79 115
V2#54(6/66)-#63 (Formerly Fightin' Air Force) — 3 6 9 16 23 30
NOTE: *Montes/Bache* a-55, 56, 60, 63.

WAR AT SEA (Formerly Space Adventures)
Charlton Comics: No. 22, Nov, 1957 - No. 42, June, 1961
22 — 14 28 42 81 118 155
23-30: 26-Pearl Harbor, FDR app. — 9 18 27 52 69 85
31-42: 42-Cuba's Fidel Castro story — 5 10 15 30 50 70

WAR BATTLES
Harvey Publications: Feb, 1952 - No. 9, Dec, 1953
1-Powell-a; Elias-c — 14 28 42 96 211 325
2-Powell-a — 7 14 21 49 92 135
3,4,7-9: 3,7-Powell-a — 7 14 21 48 89 130
5-Flamethrower cover — 28 56 84 202 451 700
6-Nostrand-a — 15 30 45 103 227 350

WAR BEARS
Dark Horse Comics: Sept, 2018 - No. 3, Dec, 2018 ($4.99, limited series)
1-3-Margaret Atwood-s/Ken Steacy-a; story about creators of Canadian Whites comics in 1943 — 5.00

WAR BIRDS
Fiction House Magazines: 1952(nd) - No. 3, Winter, 1952-53
1 — 29 58 87 172 281 390
2,3 — 17 34 51 98 154 210

WARBLADE: ENDANGERED SPECIES (Also see WildC.A.T.S: Covert Action Teams)
Image Comics (WildStorm Productions): Jan, 1995 - No. 4, Apr, 1995 ($2.50, limited series)
1-4: 1-Gatefold wraparound-c — 4.00

WAR COMBAT (Becomes Combat Casey #6 on)
Atlas Comics (LBI No. 1/SAI No. 2-5): March, 1952 - No. 5, Nov, 1952
1 — 41 82 123 256 428 600
2 — 22 44 66 128 209 290
3-5 — 20 40 60 120 195 270
NOTE: *Berg* a-2, 4, 5. *Brodsky* c-1, 2, 4. *Henkel* a-5. *Maneely* a-1, 4; c-3. *Reinman* a-2. *Sale* a-5; c-5.

WAR COMICS (War Stories #5 on)(See Key Ring Comics)
Dell Publishing Co.: May, 1940 (No month given) - No. 1, April, 1941
1-Sikandur the Robot Master, Sky Hawk, Scoop Mason, War Correspondent begin; McWilliams-c; 1st war comic — 135 270 405 864 1482 2100
2-Origin Greg Gilday (5/41) — 55 110 165 352 601 850
3-Joan becomes Greg Gilday's aide — 40 80 120 246 411 575
4-Origin Night Devils — 41 82 123 256 428 600

WAR COMICS
Marvel/Atlas (USA No. 1-41/JPI No. 42-49): Dec, 1950 - No. 49, Sept, 1957
1-1st Atlas War comic — 71 142 213 454 777 1100
2 — 34 68 102 199 325 450
3-10 — 27 54 81 158 259 360
11-Flame thrower w/burning bodies on-c — 194 388 582 1242 2121 3000
12-20: 16-Romita-a — 24 48 72 140 230 320
21,23-32: 26-Valley Forge story. 32-Last pre-code issue (2/55) — 22 44 66 132 216 300
22-Krigstein-a — 23 46 69 136 223 310
33-37,39-42,44,45,47,48: 40-Romita-a — 22 44 66 128 209 290
38-Kubert/Moskowitz-a — 27 54 81 158 259 360
43,49-Torres-a. 43-Severin/Elder E.C. swipe from Two-Fisted Tales #31 — 22 44 66 132 216 300
46-Crandall-a — 24 48 72 142 234 325
NOTE: *Ayers* a-17, 32. *Berg* a-13. *Colan* a-4, 28, 34, 36, 48, 49; c-17. *Drucker* a-37, 43, 48. *Everett* a-37. *Heath* a-6-9, 16, 19, 25, 36; c-11, 16, 19, 23, 25, 26, 29-32, 36. *G. Kane* a-19. *Katz* a-34. *Lawrence* a-36. *Maneely* a-7, 9, 13, 14, 20, 23. *Orlando* a-42, 48. *Pakula* a-26, 40. *Ravielli* a-27. *Reinman* a-11, 16, 26. *Robinson* a-15; c-13. *Sale* a-28. *Severin* a-26, 27; c-48. *Shores* a-13. *Sinnott* a-27.

WARD, THE
Dark Horse Comics: Jun, 2022 - No. 4, Sept, 2022 ($3.99, limited series)
1-4-Cavan Scott-s/Andres Ponce-a — 4.00

WAR DANCER (Also see Charlemagne, Doctor Chaos #2 & Warriors of Plasm)
Defiant: Feb, 1994 - No. 6, July, 1994 ($2.50)
1-3,5,6: 1-Intro War Dancer; Weiss-c/a begins. 1-3-Weiss-a(p). 6-Pre-Schism issue — 4.00
4-($3.25, 52 pgs.)-Charlemagne app.; Billy Ballistic gains quantum powers — 5.00

WAR DOGS OF THE U.S. ARMY
Avon Periodicals: 1952
1-Kinstler-c/a — 26 52 78 154 262 350

WAREHOUSE 13 (Based on the Syfy TV series)
Dynamite Entertainment: 2011 - No. 5, 2012 ($3.99)
1-5: 1-Raab & Hughes-s/Morse-a — 4.00

WAR FOR EARTH-3
DC Comics: May, 2022 - No. 2, May, 2022 ($5.99, limited series)
1,2-Crime Syndicate, Suicide Squad & Titans app. — 6.00

WAR FOR THE PLANET OF THE APES (Prequel to the 2017 movie)
BOOM! Studios: Jul, 2017 - No. 4, Oct, 2017 ($3.99, limited series)
1-4-David F. Walker-s/Jonas Scharf-a — 4.00

WARFRAME: GHOULS (Based on the video game)
Image Comics (Top Cow): Oct, 2017 - No. 5, May, 2018 ($3.99)
1-5-Matt Hawkins & Ryan Cady-s/Studio Hive-a — 4.00

WARFRONT
Harvey Publications: 9/51 - #35, 11/58; #36, 10/65; #39, 2/67
1-Korean War — 37 74 111 222 361 500
2 — 8 16 24 54 102 150
3-10 — 6 12 18 38 69 100
11,12,14,16-20 — 5 10 15 33 57 80
13,15,22-Nostrand-a — 6 12 18 42 79 115
21,23-27,31-33,35 — 5 10 15 33 57 80
28-30,34-Kirby-c — 7 14 21 44 82 120
36-(12/66)-Dynamite Joe begins, ends #39; Williamson-a — 5 10 15 35 63 90
37-Wood-a (17 pgs.) — 5 10 15 35 63 90
38,39-Wood-a, 2-3 pgs.; Lone Tiger app. — 5 10 15 33 57 80
NOTE: *Powell* a-1-6, 9-11, 14, 17, 20, 23, 25-28, 30, 31, 34, 36. *Powell/Nostrand* a-12, 13, 15. *Simon* c-36?, 38.

WAR FURY
Comic Media/Harwell (Allen Hardy Assoc.): Sept, 1952 - No. 4, Mar, 1953
1-Heck-c/a in all; Palais-a; bullet hole in forehead-c; all issues are very violent; soldier using flame thrower on enemy — 432 864 1296 3154 5577 8000
2-4: 4-Morisi-a — 52 104 156 328 552 775

WAR GODS OF THE DEEP (See Movie Classics)

WARHAMMER 40,000: MARNEUS CALGAR (Based on the game)
Marvel Comics: Dec, 2020 - No. 5, Apr, 2021 ($4.99, limited series)
1-5-Kieron Gillen-s/Jacen Burrows-a — 5.00

WARHAMMER 40,000: SISTERS OF BATTLE (Based on the game)
Marvel Comics: Oct, 2021 - No. 5, Mar, 2022 ($4.99, limited series)

War Comics #11 © MAR

War Heroes #1 © Millar & Harris

Warlock #9 © MAR

	GD 2.0	VG 4.0	FN 6.0	VF 8.0	VF/NM 9.0	NM- 9.2
1-5-Torunn Gronbekk-s/Edgar Salazar-a						5.00

WARHAWKS
TSR, Inc.: 1990 - No. 10, 1991 ($2.95, 44 pgs.)

1-10-Based on TSR game, Spiegle a-1-6						5.00

WARHEADS
Marvel Comics UK: June, 1992 - No. 14, Aug, 1993 ($1.75)

1-Wolverine-c/story; indicia says #2 by mistake						5.00
2-14: 2-Nick Fury app. 3-Iron Man-c/story. 4,5-X-Force. 5-Liger vs. Cable. 6,7-Death's Head II app. (#6 is cameo)						4.00

WAR HEROES (See Marine War Heroes)

WAR HEROES
Dell Publishing Co.: 7-9/42 (no month); No. 2, 10-12/42 - No. 10, 10-12/44 (Quarterly)

	GD	VG	FN	VF	VF/NM	NM-
1-General Douglas MacArthur-c	48	96	144	302	514	725
2-James Doolittle and other officers-c	22	44	66	132	216	300
3,5: 3-Pro-Russian back-c; grey-tone-a. 5-General Patton-c	18	36	54	107	169	230
4-Disney's Gremlins app.; grey-tone-c	30	60	90	177	289	400
6-10: 6-Tothish-a by Discount. 6,9-Grey-tone-c	15	30	45	88	137	185

NOTE: No. 1 was to be released in July, but was delayed. Painted c-4, 6-9.

WAR HEROES
Ace Magazines: May, 1952 - No. 8, Apr, 1953

1	37	74	111	222	361	500
2-Lou Cameron-a	15	30	45	86	133	180
3-8: 6,7-Cameron-a	14	28	42	82	121	160

WAR HEROES (Also see Blue Bird Comics)
Charlton Comics: Feb, 1963 - No. 27, Nov, 1967

1,2: 2-John F. Kennedy story	5	10	15	33	57	80
3-10	3	6	9	18	28	38
11-26: 22-True story about plot to kill Hitler	3	6	9	15	22	28
27-1st Devils Brigade by Glanzman	3	6	9	18	28	38

NOTE: Montes/Bache a-3-7, 21, 25, 27; c-3-7.

WAR HEROES
Image Comics: July, 2008 - No. 6 ($2.99, limited series)

1-3-Soldiers given super powers; Mark Millar-s/Tony Harris-a/c; four covers						3.00

WAR IS HELL
Marvel Comics Group: Jan, 1973 - No. 15, Oct, 1975

1-Williamson-a(r), 5 pgs.; Ayers-a	5	10	15	33	57	80
2-8-Reprints. 6-(11/73). 7-(6/74). 7,8-Kirby-a	3	6	9	14	20	25
9-Intro Death	9	18	27	62	126	190
10-15-Death app.	3	6	9	21	33	45

NOTE: Bolle a-3r. Powell a-1. Woodbridge a-1. Sgt. Fury reprints-7, 8.

WAR IS HELL (Marvel 80th Anniversary salute to War comics)
Marvel Comics: Mar, 2019 ($3.99, one-shot)

1-Howard Chaykin-s/Alberto Alburquerque-a; Panosian-c						4.00

WAR IS HELL: THE FIRST FLIGHT OF THE PHANTOM EAGLE
Marvel Comics (MAX): May, 2008 - No. 5, Sept, 2008 ($3.99, limited series)

1-5-World War I fighter pilots; Ennis-s/Chaykin-a/Cassaday-c						4.00

WARLANDS
Image Comics: Aug, 1999 - No. 12, Feb, 2001 ($2.50)

1-9,11,12-Pat Lee-a/Adrian Tsang-s						4.00
10-($2.95) Flip book w/Shidima preview						5.00
... Chronicles 1,2 (2/00, 7.00) ($7.95) 1-r/#1-3. 2-r/#4-6						8.00
...Darklyte TPB (8/01, $14.95) r/#0,1/2,1-6 w/cover gallery; new Lee-c						15.00
...Epilogue: Three Stories (3/01, $5.95) includes r/Wizard #1/2 & AE #0						6.00
Another Universe #0						4.00
Wizard #1/2						5.00

WARLANDS: THE AGE OF ICE (Volume 2)
Image Comics: July, 2001 - No. 9, Nov, 2002 ($2.95)

#0-(2/02, $2.25)						3.00
#1/2 (4/02, $2.25)						3.00
1-9-Flip book preview of Banished Knights						3.00
TPB (2003, $15.95) r/#1-9						16.00

WARLANDS: DARK TIDE RISING (Volume 3)
Image Comics: Dec, 2002 - No. 6, May, 2003 ($2.95)

1-6: 1-Wraparound gatefold-c						3.00

WARLOCK (The Power of...)(Also see Avengers Annual #7, Fantastic Four #66, 67, Incredible Hulk #178, Infinity Crusade, Infinity Gauntlet, Infinity War, Marvel Premiere #1, Marvel Two-In-One Annual #2, Silver Surfer V3#46, Strange Tales #178-181 & Thor #165)
Marvel Comics Group: Aug, 1972 - No. 8, Oct, 1973; No. 9, Oct, 1975 - No. 15, Nov, 1976

	GD 2.0	VG 4.0	FN 6.0	VF 8.0	VF/NM 9.0	NM- 9.2
1-Origin by Gil Kane	10	20	30	67	141	215
2,3	5	10	15	31	53	75
4-8: 4-Death of Eddie Roberts	3	6	9	19	30	40
9-Starlin's 2nd Thanos saga begins, ends #15; new costume Warlock; Thanos cameo only; story cont'd from Strange Tales #178-181; Starlin-c/a in #9-15	5	10	15	35	63	90
10-Origin Thanos & Gamora; recaps events from Capt. Marvel #25-34. Thanos vs.The Magus-c/story	5	10	15	35	63	90
11-Thanos app.; Warlock dies	4	8	12	28	47	65
12-14: (Regular 25c edition) 14-Origin Star Thief; last 25c issue	5	6	9	18	28	38
12-14-(30c-c, limited distribution)	5	10	15	35	63	90
15-Thanos-c/story	5	10	15	34	60	85

NOTE: Buscema a-2p; c-8p. G. Kane a-1p, 3-5p; c-1p, 2, 3, 4p, 5p, 7p. Starlin a-9-14p, 15; c-9, 10, 11p, 12p, 13-15. Sutton a-1-8i.

WARLOCK (...Special Edition on-c)
Marvel Comics: Dec, 1982 - No. 6, May, 1983 ($2.00, slick paper, 52 pgs.)

	GD	VG	FN	VF	VF/NM	NM-
1-Warlock-r/Strange Tales #178-180.	1	3	4	6	8	10
2-6: 2-r/Str. Tales #180,181 & Warlock #9. 3-r/Warlock #10-12(Thanos origin recap).						
4-r/Warlock #12-15. 5-r/Warlock #15, Marvel Team-Up #55 & Avengers Ann. #7. 6-r/2nd half Avengers Annual #7 & Marvel Two-in-One Annual #2						5.00
Special Edition #1(12/83)						5.00

NOTE: Byrne a-5r. Starlin a-1-6r; c-1-6(new). Direct sale only.

WARLOCK
Marvel Comics: V2#1, May, 1992 - No. 6, Oct, 1992 ($2.50, limited series)

V2#1-6: 1-Reprints 1982 reprint series w/Thanos						4.00

WARLOCK
Marvel Comics: Nov, 1998 - No. 4, Feb, 1999 ($2.99, limited series)

1-4-Warlock vs. Drax						4.00

WARLOCK (M-Tech)
Marvel Comics: Oct, 1999 - No. 9, June, 2000 ($1.99/$2.50)

1-5: 1-Quesada-c. 2-Two covers						4.00
6-9: 6-Begin $2.50-c. 8-Avengers app.						4.00

WARLOCK
Marvel Comics: Nov, 2004 - No. 4, Feb, 2005 ($2.99, limited series)

1-4-Adlard-a/Williams-c						4.00

WARLOCK AND THE INFINITY WATCH (Also see Infinity Gauntlet)
Marvel Comics: Feb, 1992 - No. 42, July, 1995 ($1.75) (Sequel to Infinity Gauntlet)

	GD	VG	FN	VF	VF/NM	NM-
1-Starlin-s begin; continued from Infinity Gauntlet #6; brief origin recap; Living Tribunal app.	2	4	6	11	16	20
2-7: 2-1st app. Infinity Watch: Infinity Gauntlet broken up/ Warlock (Soul gem), Gamora (Time gem), Drax (Power gem), Moondragon (Mind gem) & Pip (Space gem). 3,4-High Evolutionary app. 5,6-Man-Beast app. 7-Re-intro Magus (dream sequence); brief Thanos app.; leads into Infinity War #1. Tom Raney-a begins						4.00
8-10: 8-Thanos teams up w/Infinity Watch; Magus app; X-Men, Avengers, Alpha Flight & Fantastic Four cameo; leads into Infinity War #4. 9-Origin Gamora; Galactus, Eternity, Thanos & Infinity app; leads into Infinity War #5. 10-Thanos vs. his doppelganger; Magus app.; continues in Infinity War #6						4.00
11-22: 11-Eternity & Living Tribunal app.; origins of the Watch. 12-1st app Maxam (brief cameo); Hulk cameo. 13-Drax vs Hulk; last Raney-a. 14-1st app. Count Abyss. 15-Eternity app. 16-1st full app. Maxam; Count Abyss app. 17-Maxam joins the Watch. 18-22-Infinity Crusade tie-ins; 18-Goddess & Reed Richards app; continued in Infinity Crusade #1. 19-X-Men, Avengers, Fantastic Four, Thanos app.; continued in Infinity Crusade #3. 20-Pip becomes master of reality; Goddess app; continued in Infinity Crusade #5. 21-Drax vs. Thor; Goddess app. 22-Goddess app; continued in Infinity Crusade #6						4.00
23,24-Blood and Thunder Pts. 4 & 8; continued from Warlock Chronicles #6; Silver Surfer & Warlock vs. Thor; continued in Thor #469. 24-Continued from Warlock Chronicles #7; Silver Surfer app.; continued in Thor #470						5.00
25-($2.95, 52 pgs.)-Die-cut and embossed double-c; Blood & Thunder Pt.12; continued from Warlock Chronicles #8; Thor, Dr. Strange, Beta Ray Bill & Silver Surfer app.; Thanos vs. Odin	2	4	6	9	12	15
26-32: 26-Avengers & Count Abyss app. 27-vs. the Avengers. 28-Avengers, Man-Beast & Count Abyss app. 29,30-Count Abyss app. 31-Origin Count Abyss; last Starlin-s. 32-Count Abyss defeats the Watch						4.00
33-35: 33-vs. Count Abyss. 34-Mole Man app.; Tyrannus cameo. 35-Mole Man & Tyrannus app.						4.00
36-Dr. Strange app.; as 'Strange'						7.00
37-39: 37-1st app Zakaius; Firelord app. 38-1st app Domitan; Zakaius app. 39-Zakaius, Domitan & Firelord app.						6.00
40,41: 40-Thanos app.; Gamora leaves the Watch; Maxam receives the Time gem. 41-Origin Maxam; Gamora joins Thanos	1	2	3	5	6	8
42-Last issue; the Watch breaks up; the Infinity Gems disappear (see Rune/Silver Surfer #1); Thanos app.	2	4	6	10	14	18

	GD	VG	FN	VF	VF/NM	NM-
	2.0	4.0	6.0	8.0	9.0	9.2

NOTE: *Austin* c/a-1-4i, 7i. *Leonardi* a(p)-3, 4. *Medina* c/a(p)-1, 2, 5; 6, 9, 10, 14, 15, 20. *Williams* a(i)-8, 12, 13, 16-19.

WARLOCK CHRONICLES
Marvel Comics: June, 1993 - No. 8, Feb, 1994 ($2.00, limited series)

1-($2.95)-Holo-grafx foil & embossed-c; Starlin/Raney-s/a; Infinity Crusade tie-in; 1st app. Darklore; origin of Warlock & the Infinity Gems; cont'd in Warlock & the Infinity Watch #18
        5.00

2-5-Infinity Crusade x-overs; 2-Cont'd from Infinity Crusade #2; Lord Order, Master Chaos, Eternity & Thanos app.; cont'd in Warlock & the Infinity Watch #19. 3-Cont'd from Infinity Crusade #3; Mephisto teams up w/Warlock & Thanos; cont'd in Warlock & the Infinity Watch #20. 4-Magus app.; cont'd in Warlock & the Infinity Watch #21. 5-Cont'd from Infinity Crusade #5; Goddess & Magus app.; cont'd in Warlock & the Infinity Watch #22
        4.00

6-Blood & Thunder Pt. 3; cont'd from Silver Surfer #86; insane Thor cameo; brief Silver Surfer app.; cont'd in Warlock & the Infinity Watch #23
        5.00

7-Blood & Thunder Pt. 7; cont'd from Silver Surfer #87; Dr. Strange, Beta Ray Bill & Silver Surfer app.; cont'd in Warlock & the Infinity Watch #24
        6.00

8-Blood & Thunder Pt. 11; cont'd from Silver Surfer #88; Thanos, Silver Surfer, Dr. Strange app.; cont'd in Warlock & the Infinity Watch #25

	1	2	3		5	8

WARLOCK 5
Aircel Pub.: 11/86 - No. 22, 5/89; V2#1, June, 1989 - V2#5, 1989 ($1.70, B&W)

1-5,7,11-Gordon Derry-s/Denis Beauvais-a thru #11. 5-Green Cyborg on-c.						
5-Misnumbered as #6 (no #6); Blue Girl on-c.						4.00
12-22-Barry Blair-a. 18-$1.95-c begins						4.00
V2#1-5 ($2.00, B&W)-All issues by Barry Blair						4.00
Compilation 1,2: 1-r/#1-5 (1988, $5.95); 2-r/#6-9						6.00

WARLOCK: REBIRTH (Continues in Silver Surfer Rebirth: Legacy)
Marvel Comics: Jun, 2023 - No. 5, Oct, 2023 ($3.99)

1-5-Ron Marz-s/Ron Lim-a; intro Eve Warlock; Gamora, Pip, Genis-Vell app.   4.00

WARLORD (See 1st Issue Special #8) (B&W reprints in Showcase Presents: Warlord)
National Periodical Publications/DC Comics #123 on: 1-2/76; No.2, 3-4/76; No.3, 10-11/76 - No. 133, Win, 1988-89

1-Story cont'd. from 1st Issue Special #8	4	8	12	27	44	60
2-Intro. Machiste	3	6	9	14	20	25
3-5	2	4	6	9	12	15
6-10: 6-Intro Mariah. 7-Origin Machiste. 9-Dons new costume						
	1	3	4	6	8	10
11-20: 11-Origin-r. 12-Intro Aton. 15-Tara returns; Warlord has son						6.00
21-36,40,41: 27-New facts about origin. 28-1st app. Wizard World. 32-Intro Shakira. 40-Warlord gets new costume						6.00
22-Whitman variant edition	3	6	9	19	30	40
37-39: 37,38-Origin Omac by Starlin; cont'd from Kamandi #59. 38-Intro Jennifer Morgan, Warlord's daughter. 39-Omac ends.						6.00
42-48: 42-47-Omac back-up series. 48-(52 pgs.)-1st app. Arak; contains free 14 pg. Arak Son of Thunder; Claw The Unconquered app.						5.00
49-62,64-99,101-132: 49-Claw The Unconquered app. 50-Death of Aton. 51-Reprints #1. 55-Arion Lord of Atlantis begins, ends #62. 91-Origin w/new facts. 114,115-Legends x-over. 125-Death of Tara. 131-1st DC work by Rob Liefeld (9/88)						4.00
63-The Barren Earth begins; free 16pg. Masters of the Universe preview						5.00
100-($1.25, 52 pgs.)						6.00
133-($1.50, 52 pgs.)						6.00
Annual 1-6 ('82-'87): 1-Grell-c,/a(i). 6-New Gods app.						5.00
The Savage Empire TPB (1991, $19.95) r/#1-10,12 & First Issue Special #8; Grell intro.						25.00

NOTE: *Grell* a1-15, 16-50p, 51r, 52p, 59p, Annual 1p; c-1-70, 100-104, 112, 116, 117, Annual 1, 5. *Wayne Howard* a-64i. *Starlin* a-37-39p.

WARLORD
DC Comics: Jan, 1992 - No. 6, June, 1992 ($1.75, limited series)

1-6: Grell-c & scripts in all   4.00

WARLORD
DC Comics: Apr, 2006 - No. 10, Jan, 2007 ($2.99)

1-10: 1-Bruce Jones-s/Bart Sears-a. 10-Winslade-a   3.00

WARLORD
DC Comics: Jun, 2009 - No. 16, Sept, 2010 ($2.99)

1-16: 1-Grell-s/Prado-a/Grell-c. 7-9,11,12,15,16-Kubik-s/a/c. 10-Hardin-a	3.00
...: The Saga SC (2010, $17.99) r/#1-6; cover gallery	18.00

WARLORD OF MARS
Dynamite Entertainment: 2010 - No. 35, 2014 ($1.00/$3.99)

1-($1.00) John Carter on Earth; Sadowski-a; covers by Ross, Campbell, Jusko, Parrillo	3.00
2-35-($3.99) Multiple covers on each. 3-Carter arrives on Mars. 4-Dejah Thoris intro.	4.00
100-($7.99, squarebound) Short stories; art by Antonio, Malaga, Luis; multiple covers	8.00
#0 (2014, $3.99) Brady-s/Jadson-a; John Carter back on Mars	4.00
... Annual 1 (2012, $4.99) Sadowski-a/Parrillo-c	5.00

WARLORD OF MARS ATTACKS
Dynamite Entertainment: 2019 - No. 5, 2019 ($3.99, limited series)

1-5-John Carter battles the Topps card Martians; Jeff Parker-s/Dean Kotz-a   4.00

WARLORD OF MARS: DEJAH THORIS
Dynamite Entertainment: 2011 - No. 37, 2014 ($3.99/$4.99)

1-36: 1-Five covers; Nakayama-s/Rafael-a. 2-5-Four covers. 6-31-Multiple covers on all	4.00
37-($4.99) Napton-s/Carita-a; Neves & Anacleto-c	5.00

WARLORD OF MARS: FALL OF BARSOOM
Dynamite Entertainment: 2011 - No. 5, 2012 ($3.99, limited series)

1-5-Napton-s/Castro-a/Jusko-c   4.00

WARLORDS (See DC Graphic Novel #2)

WARLORDS OF APPALACHIA
BOOM! Studios: Oct, 2016 - No. 4 ($3.99)

1,2-Phillip Kennedy Johnson-s/Jonas Scharf-a   4.00

WAR MACHINE (Also see Iron Man #281,282 & Marvel Comics Presents #152)
Marvel Comics: Apr, 1994 - No. 25, Apr, 1996 ($1.50)

"Ashcan" edition (nd, 75¢, B&W, 16 pgs.)	5.00
1-($2.00, 52 pgs.)-Newsstand edition; Cable app.	5.00

1-($2.95, 52 pgs.)-Collectors ed.; embossed foil-c	1	3	4	6	8	10
2-14, 16-25: 2-Bound-in trading card sheet; Cable app. 2,3-Deathlok app. 8-red logo						3.00
8-($2.95)-Polybagged w/16 pg. Marvel Action Hour preview & acetate print; yellow logo						4.00
15 ($2.50)-Flip book						4.00

WAR MACHINE (Also see Dark Reign and Secret Invasion crossovers)
Marvel Comics: Feb, 2009 - No. 12, Feb, 2010 ($2.99)

1-12: 1-5-Pak-s/Manco-a/c; cyborg Jim Rhodes. 10-12-Dark Reign	3.00
1-Variant Titanium Man cover by Deodato	6.00

WAR MAN
Marvel Comics (Epic Comics): Nov, 1993 - No. 2, Dec, 1993 ($2.50, limited series)

1,2-Chuck Dixon-s   3.00

WAR MOTHER
Valiant Entertainment: Aug, 2017 - No. 4, Nov, 2017 ($3.99, limited series)

1-4-Van Lente-s/Segovia-a; multiple covers; Ana in 4001 AD   4.00

WAR OF KINGS
Marvel Comics: May, 2009 - No. 6, Oct, 2009 ($3.99, limited series)

1-6-Pelletier-a/Abnett & Lanning-s; Inhumans vs. the Shi'Ar	4.00
... Saga (2009, giveaway) synopsis of stories involving Kree, Shi'Ar, Inhumans, etc.	3.00
...: Savage World of Skaar 1 (8/09, $3.99) Gorgon & Starbolt land on Sakaar	4.00
...: Who Will Rule? 1 (11/09, $3.99) Pelletier-a; profile pages	4.00

WAR OF KINGS: ASCENSION
Marvel Comics: June, 2009 - No. 4, Sept, 2009 ($3.99, limited series)

1-4-Alves-a/Abnett & Lanning-s; Darkhawk app.   4.00

WAR OF KINGS: DARKHAWK (Leads into War Of Kings: Ascension limited series)
Marvel Comics: Apr, 2009 - No. 2, May, 2009 ($3.99, limited series)

1,2-Cebulski-s/Tolibao & Dazo-a/Peterson-c; r/Darkhawk #1,2 (1991) origin   4.00

WAR OF KINGS: WARRIORS
Marvel Comics: Sept, 2009 - No. 2, Oct, 2009 ($3.99, limited series)

1,2-Prequel to x-over; Gage-s/Asrar & Magno-a   4.00

WAR OF THE GODS
DC Comics: Sept, 1991 - No. 4, Dec, 1991 ($1.75, limited series)

1-4: Perez layouts, scripts & covers. 1-Contains free mini posters (Robin, Deathstroke). 2-4-Direct sale versions include 4 pin-ups printed on cover stock plus different-c   4.00

WAR OF THE GREEN LANTERNS: AFTERMATH
DC Comics: Sept, 2011 - No. 2, Oct, 2011 ($3.99, limited series)

1,2: 1-Bedard-s/Sepulveda & Kirkham-a. 2-Getty & Smith-a   4.00

WAR OF THE REALMS (Tie-in issues exist in many 2019 Marvel titles)
Marvel Comics: Jun, 2019 - No. 6, Aug, 2019 ($5.99/$4.99, limited series)

1-($5.99) Aaron-s/Dauterman-a; Malekith attacks Earth; Loki eaten	1	3	4	6	8	10
2-5-($4.99) 2-Avengers, Punisher, Jane Foster app. 4-Venom app.						5.00
6-($5.99) Jane Thor app.						6.00
... Omega 1 (9/19, $4.99) Short stories; Jane Foster becomes Valkyrie; Punisher app.						5.00

WAR OF THE REALMS: JOURNEY INTO MYSTERY
Marvel Comics: Jun, 2019 - No. 5, Aug, 2019 ($3.99, limited series)

1-5-Spider-Man (Miles), Hawkeye (Kate), Wonder Man, Ares app.   4.00

WAR OF THE REALMS: NEW AGENTS OF ATLAS
Marvel Comics: Jul, 2019 - No. 4, Aug, 2019 ($3.99, limited series)

1-Greg Pak-s/Gang Hyuk Lim-a; Ms. Marvel, Silk, Shang-Chi & Amedeus Cho app.	4	8	12	23	37	50
2-1st Swordmaster	4	8	12	28	47	65
3,4						4.00

WAR OF THE REALMS STRIKEFORCE:...
Marvel Comics: Jul, 2019 ($4.99, series of one-shots)

... The Dark Elf Realm 1 - Bryan Hill-s/Yu-a; Punisher, She-Hulk, Blade, Ghost Rider	5.00
... The Land of Giants 1 - Taylor-s/Molina-a; Wolverine, Capt. America, Luke Cage app.	5.00
... The War Avengers 1 - Anindito-a; Deadpool, Namor, Capt. Marvel, Sif, Venom app.	5.00

WAR OF THE REALMS: THE PUNISHER
Marvel Comics: Jun, 2019 - No. 3, Aug, 2019 ($3.99, limited series)

1-3-Duggan-s/Ferreira-a   4.00

WAR OF THE REALMS: UNCANNY X-MEN
Marvel Comics: Jun, 2019 - No. 3, Aug, 2019 ($3.99, limited series)

1-3-Rosenberg-s/Pere Pérez-a; Cyclops, Dani Moonstar app. 2-Sabretooth app.   4.00

WAR OF THE REALMS: WAR SCROLLS
Marvel Comics: Jun, 2019 - No. 3, Aug, 2019 ($4.99, limited series)

1-Short stories by various; Daredevil serial in all w/Sorrentino-a; Alan Davis-c	1	2	3	5	6	
2,3-Alan Davis-c						5.00

WAR OF THE UNDEAD
IDW Publishing: Jan, 2007 - No. 3, Apr, 2007 ($3.99, limited series)

1-3-Bryan Johnson-s/Walter Flanagan-a	2	4	6	9	12	15

WAR OF THE WORLDS, THE
Caliber: 1996 - No. 5 ($2.95, B&W, 32 pgs.)(Based on H. G. Wells novel)

1-5: 1-Randy Zimmerman scripts begin   5.00

WARP
First Comics: Mar, 1983 - No. 19, Feb, 1985 ($1.00/$1.25, Mando paper)

1-Sargon-Mistress of War app.; Brunner-c/a thru #9	5.00
2-19: 2-Faceless Ones begin. 10-New Warp advs., & Outrider begin	4.00
Special 1-3: 1(7/83, 36 pgs.)-Origin Chaos-Prince of Madness; origin of Warp Universe begins, ends #3; Chaykin-c/a. 2,3-Silvestri-a. 2(1/84)-Lord Cumulus vs. Sargon Mistress of War ($1.00). 3(6/84)-Chaos-Prince of Madness	4.00

WARPATH (Indians on the...)
Key Publications/Stanmor: Nov, 1954 - No. 3, Apr, 1955

1	14	28	42	80	115	150

Warlord (2006 series) #5 © DC

War of the Realms #4 © MAR

Warren Presents #5 © Warren

	GD 2.0	VG 4.0	FN 6.0	VF 8.0	VF/NM 9.0	NM- 9.2			GD 2.0	VG 4.0	FN 6.0	VF 8.0	VF/NM 9.0	NM- 9.2
2,3	9	18	27	52	69	85								

WARP GRAPHICS ANNUAL
WaRP Graphics: Dec, 1985; 1988 ($2.50)
1-Elfquest, Blood of the Innocent, Thunderbunny & Myth Adventures — 5.00
1 (1988) — 4.00

WARREN PRESENTS
Warren Publications: Jan, 1979 - No. 14, Nov, 1981(B&W magazine)
1-Eerie, Creepy, & Vampirella-r; Ring of the Warlords; Merlin-s; Dax-s; Sanjulian-c

		GD	VG	FN	VF	VF/NM	NM-
		3	6	9	19	30	40

2-6(10/79): 2-The Rook. 3-Alien Invasions Comix. 4-Movie Aliens. 5-Dracula '79.

	GD	VG	FN	VF	VF/NM	NM-
6-Strange Stories of Vampires Comix	2	4	6	10	14	18
8(10/80)-r/1st app. Pantha from Vamp. #30	2	4	6	13	18	22
9(11/80) Empire Encounters Comix	2	4	6	11	16	20
13(10/81),14(11/81):13-Sword and Sorcery Comix	3	6	9	14	19	24

(#7,10,11,12 may not exist, or may be a Special below)

	GD	VG	FN	VF	VF/NM	NM-
Special-Alien Collectors Edition (1979)	3	6	9	14	20	26
Special-Close Encounters of the Third Kind (1978)	2	4	6	10	14	18
Special-Lord of the Rings (6/79)	3	6	9	19	30	40
Special-Meteor (1/80)	2	4	6	10	14	18
Special-Moonraker/James Bond (10/79)	2	4	6	10	14	18
Special-Star Wars (1977)	3	6	9	21	33	45

WAR REPORT
Ajax/Farrell Publications (Excellent Publ.): Sept, 1952 - No. 5, May, 1953

	GD	VG	FN	VF	VF/NM	NM-
1	30	60	90	177	289	400
2-Flame thrower w/burning bodies on-c	129	258	387	826	1413	2000
3,5	15	30	45	85	130	175
4-Used in POP, pg. 94	17	34	51	98	154	210

WARRIOR (Wrestling star)
Ultimate Creations: May, 1996 - No. 4, 1997 ($2.95)
1-4: Warrior scripts; Callahan-c/a. 3-Wraparound-c. 4-Warrior #3 in indicia; pin-ups — 4.00

		GD	VG	FN	VF	VF/NM	NM-
1-Variant-c		1	3	4	6	8	10

X-Mas (11/96, $3.50) listed as "No. 3" in indicia; pin-ups by various; Quesada-c — 4.00

WARRIOR COMICS
H.C. Blackerby: 1945 (1930s DC reprints)

	GD	VG	FN	VF	VF/NM	NM-
1-Wing Brady, The Iron Man, Mark Markon	32	64	96	188	307	425

WARRIOR OF WAVERLY STREET, THE
Dark Horse Comics: Nov, 1996 - No. 2, Dec, 1996 ($2.95, mini-series)
1,2-Darrow-c — 4.00

WARRIORS
CFD Productions: 1993 (B&W, one-shot)

		GD	VG	FN	VF	VF/NM	NM-
1-Linsner, Dark One-a		2	4	6	11	16	20

WARRIORS, THE: OFFICIAL MOVIE ADAPTATION (Based on the 1979 movie)
Dabel Brothers Publishing/Dynamite Ent.: Feb, 2009 - No. 5, 2010 ($3.99, limited series)
1-5: 1-Three covers plus wraparound photo-c; Dibari-a. 3-Eric Powell-c — 4.00
...: Jailbreak 1 (7/09, $3.99) Apon & Herman-a — 4.00

WARRIORS OF MARS (Also see Warlord of Mars titles)
Dynamite Entertainment: 2012 - No. 5, 2012 ($3.99, limited series)
1-5-Gulliver Jones visits Barsoom; Jusko-a — 4.00

WARRIORS OF PLASM (Also see Plasm and Dogs of War #5)
Defiant: Aug, 1993 - No. 13, Aug, 1995 ($2.95/$2.50)
1-4: Shooter-scripts; Lapham-c/a. 1-1st app Glory. 4-Bound-in fold-out poster — 5.00
5-7,10-13: 5-Begin $2.50-c. 13-Schism issue; last Defiant comic published — 4.00
8,9-($2.75, 44 pgs.) — 5.00
...Graphic Novel #1 (Home for the Holidays)(11/93, $5.95) Len Wein story; Cockrum-a; Christmas issue; story takes place between Warriors of Plasm #4 and #5 — 6.00
The Collected Edition (2/94, $9.95)-r/Plasm #0, WOP #1-4 & Splatterball

	GD	VG	FN	VF	VF/NM	NM-
	2	4	6	8	11	14

WARRIORS THREE (Fandral, Volstagg, and Hogun from Thor)
Marvel Comics: Jan, 2011 - No. 4, Apr, 2011 ($3.99, limited series)
1-4-Bill Willingham-s/Neil Edwards-a. 2,4-Conner-c — 4.00

WAR ROMANCES (See True...)

WAR SHIPS
Dell Publishing Co.: 1942 (36 pgs.)(Similar to Large Feature Comics)
nn-Cover by McWilliams; contains photos & drawings of U.S. war ships

	GD	VG	FN	VF	VF/NM	NM-
	26	52	78	154	252	350

WAR STORIES (Formerly War Comics)
Dell Publ. Co.: No. 5, 1942(nd); No. 6, Aug-Oct, 1942 - No. 8, Feb-Apr, 1943

	GD	VG	FN	VF	VF/NM	NM-
5-Origin The Whistler	39	78	117	240	395	550
6-8: 6-8-Night Devils app. 8-Painted-c	32	64	96	188	307	425

WAR STORIES (Korea)
Ajax/Farrell Publications (Excellent Publ.): Sept, 1952 - No. 5, May, 1953

	GD	VG	FN	VF	VF/NM	NM-
1	24	48	72	144	237	330
2	15	30	45	86	133	180
3-5	15	30	45	90	140	190

WAR STORIES
Avatar Press: Sept, 2014 - No. 26, Jan, 2018 ($3.99)
1-26: Garth Ennis-s in all; multiple covers on all. 1-Matt Martin-a — 4.00

WAR STORIES (See Star Spangled...)

WAR STORY
DC Comics (Vertigo): Nov, 2001 - Apr, 2003 ($4.95, series of World War II one-shots)
...: Archangel (4/03) Ennis-s/Erskine-a — 5.00
...: Condors (3/03) Ennis-s/Ezquerra-a — 5.00
...: D-Day Dodgers (12/01) Ennis-s/Higgins-a — 5.00
...: J For Jenny (2/03) Ennis-s/Lloyd-a — 5.00
...: Johann's Tiger (11/01) Ennis-s/Weston-a — 5.00
...: Nightingale (2/02) Ennis-s/Lloyd-a — 5.00
...: Screaming Eagles (1/02) Ennis-s/Gibbons-a — 5.00
...: The Reivers (1/03) Ennis-s/Kennedy-a — 5.00
Vol. 1 (2004, $19.95) r/Johann's Tiger, D-Day Dodgers, Screaming Eagles, Nightingale — 20.00
Vol. 2 (2006, $19.99) r/J For Jenny, The Reivers, Condors, Archangel; Ennis afterword — 20.00

WARSTRIKE
Malibu Comics (Ultraverse): May, 1994 - No. 7, Nov, 1995 ($1.95)
1-7: 1-Simonson-c — 4.00
1-Ultra 5000 Limited silver foil — 6.00
Giant Size 1 (12/94, $2.50, 44pgs.)-Prelude to Godwheel — 5.00

WART AND THE WIZARD (See The Sword & the Stone under Movie Comics)
Gold Key: Feb, 1964 (Walt Disney)(Characters from Sword in the Stone movie)

	GD	VG	FN	VF	VF/NM	NM-
1 (10102-402)	5	10	15	31	53	75

WAR THAT TIME FORGOT, THE
DC Comics: Jul, 2008 - No. 12, Jun, 2009 ($2.99, limited series)
1-12: 1-Bruce Jones-s/Al Barrionuevo-a/Neal Adams-c; Enemy Ace app. — 3.00

WARTIME ROMANCES
St. John Publishing Co.: July, 1951 - No. 18, Nov, 1953

	GD	VG	FN	VF	VF/NM	NM-
1-All Baker-c/a	187	374	561	1197	2049	2900
2-All Baker-c/a	129	258	387	826	1413	2000
3,4-All Baker-c/a	135	270	405	864	1482	2100
5-8-Baker-c/a(2-3) each	110	220	330	704	1202	1700
9,11,12,16,18- Baker-c/a each. 9-Two signed stories by Estrada	77	154	231	493	847	1200
10,13-15,17-Baker-c only	71	142	213	454	777	1100

WAR VICTORY ADVENTURES (#1 titled War Victory Comics)
U.S. Treasury Dept./War Victory/Harvey Publ.: Sum, 1942 - No. 3, Wint, 1943-44 (5¢/10¢)
1-(5¢)(Promotion of Savings Bonds)-Featuring America's greatest comic art by top syndicated cartoonists; Blondie, Joe Palooka, Green Hornet, Dick Tracy, Superman, Gumps, etc.; (36 pgs.); all profits were contributed to U.S.O. & Army/Navy relief funds

	GD	VG	FN	VF	VF/NM	NM-
	90	180	270	576	988	1400
2-(10¢) Battle of Stalingrad story; Powell-a (8/43); flag & WWII Japanese-c	129	258	387	826	1413	2000
3-(10¢) Capt. Red Cross-c & text only; WWII Nazi-c; Powell-a	110	220	330	704	1202	1700

WAR WAGON, THE (See Movie Classics)

WAR WINGS
Charlton Comics: Oct, 1968

	GD	VG	FN	VF	VF/NM	NM-
1	3	6	9	17	26	35

WARWORLD!
Dark Horse Comics: Feb, 1989 ($1.75, B&W, one-shot)
1-Gary Davis sci/fi art in Moebius style — 4.00

WASHABLE JONES AND THE SHMOO (Also see Al Capp's Shmoo)
Toby Press: June, 1953

	GD	VG	FN	VF	VF/NM	NM-
1- "Super-Shmoo"	23	46	69	136	223	310

WASH TUBBS (See The Comics, Crackajack Funnies)
Dell Publishing Co.: No. 11, 1942 - No. 53, 1944

	GD	VG	FN	VF	VF/NM	NM-
Four Color 11 (#1)	27	54	81	194	435	675
Four Color 28 (1943)	19	38	57	131	291	450
Four Color 53	15	30	45	103	227	350

WASP (Also see Unstoppable Wasp)
Marvel Comics: Mar, 2019 - No. 4, ($3.99, limited series)
1-4-Al Ewing-s/Kasia Nie-a; Janet Van Dyne & Nadia. 1-Whirlwind app. — 4.00

	GD 2.0	VG 4.0	FN 6.0	VF 8.0	VF/NM 9.0	NM- 9.2

WASTELAND
DC Comics: Dec, 1987 - No. 18, May, 1989 ($1.75-$2.00 #13 on, mature)

1-5(4/88), 5(5/88), 6(5/88)-18: 13,15-Orlando-a						4.00

NOTE: *Orlando a-12, 13, 15. Truman a-10; c-13.*

WASTELANDERS (The world of Old Man Logan; see Wolverine [2003] #66-72)
Marvel Comics: Feb, 2022 - Mar, 2022 ($3.99, series of one-shots)

...: Black Widow 1 (3/22) DeKnight-s/Well-Bee-a; Yelena Belova app.						4.00
...: Doom 1 (3/22) Gronbekk-s/Ohta-a; Baron Mordo app.						4.00
...: Hawkeye 1 (2/22) Sacks-s/Roberson-a; Matt Murdock & Elektra app.						4.00
...: Star-Lord 1 (2/22) Douek-s/Peeples-a; Shadow King app.						4.00
...: Wolverine 1 (2/22) DeKnight-s/Moustafa-a; Banner app.						4.00

WATCHMEN (Also see 2012-2013 Before Watchmen prequel titles)
DC Comics: Sept, 1986 - No. 12, Oct, 1987 (maxi-series)

1-Alan Moore scripts & Dave Gibbons-c/a in all	6	12	18	37	66	95
1-(2009, $1.50) Second printing						4.00
2-12	3	6	9	14	19	24
Hardcover Collection-Slip-cased-r/#1-12 w/new material; produced by Graphitti Designs						100.00
HC (2008, $39.99) recolored r/#1-12; design & promotional art; Moore & Gibbons intros						40.00
Trade paperback (1987, $14.95)-r/#1-12						25.00

WATCHVARK COMICS (Reprints from Cerebus in Hell)(Also see Aardvark Comics)
Aardvark-Vanaheim: Jan, 2018 ($4.00, B&W)

1-Cerebus figures placed over original Doré artwork of Hell; Watchmen #6-c swipe						4.00

WATER BIRDS AND THE OLYMPIC ELK (Disney)
Dell Publishing Co.: No. 700, Apr, 1956

Four Color 700-Movie	5	10	15	33	57	80

WATERWORLD: CHILDREN OF LEVIATHAN
Acclaim Comics: Aug, 1997 - No. 4, Nov, 1997 ($2.50, mini-series)

1-4						4.00

WAY OF THE RAT
CrossGeneration Comics: Jun, 2002 - No. 24, June, 2004 ($2.95)

1-24: 1-Dixon-s/ Jeff Johnson-a. 5-Whigham-a. 9,14-Luke Ross-a						3.00
Free Comic Book Day Special (6/03) reprints #1 w/features, interviews, CrossGen info						3.00
...: The Walls of Zhumar Vol. 1 (1/03, $15.95) r/#1-6						16.00
Vol. 2: The Dragon's Wake (2003, $15.95) r/#7-12						16.00

WAY OF X (X-Men)
Marvel Comics: Jun, 2021 - No. 5, Oct, 2021 ($4.99/$3.99, limited series)

1-($4.99) Spurrier-s/Quinn-a; Legion app.						5.00
2-5-($3.99) 3-Hellfire Gala						4.00

WAYWARD
Image Comics: Aug, 2014 - No. 30, Oct, 2018 ($3.50/$3.99)

1-29: 1-Jim Zub-s/Cummings-a; multiple covers. 16-Begin $3.99-c						4.00
30-($4.99) Last issue; bonus pin-up gallery						5.00

WEAPON H (See Weapon X [2017 series] #6 for debut)(See Hulkverines #1)
Marvel Comics: May, 2018 - No. 12, Mar, 2019 ($4.99/$3.99)

1-($4.99) Greg Pak-s/Cory Smith-a; Wendigo app.						5.00
2-12-($3.99) 2-Doctor Strange app. 3-7-Man-Thing app. 6,7-Captain America app.						4.00

WEAPON PLUS: WORLD WAR IV
Marvel Comics: Mar, 2020 ($4.99, one-shot)

1-Percy-s/Jeanty-a; Weapon IV app. (Man-Thing-like soldier)						5.00

WEAPONS OF MUTANT DESTRUCTION: ALPHA
Marvel Comics: Aug, 2017 ($4.99, one-shot)

1-Crossover with Weapon X #4-6 and Totally Awesome Hulk #19-22; Stryker app.						4.00

WEAPON X
Marvel Comics: Apr, 1994 ($12.95, one-shot)

nn-r/Marvel Comics Presents #72-84	3	6	9	14	20	25

WEAPON X
Marvel Comics: Mar, 1995 - No. 4, June, 1995 ($1.95)

1-Age of Apocalypse						5.00
2-4						4.00

WEAPON X
Marvel Comics: Nov, 2002 - No. 28, Nov, 2004 ($2.25/$2.99)

1-7: 1-Sabretooth-c/app.; Tieri-s/Jeanty-a						3.00
8-28: 8-Begin $2.99-c. 14-Invaders app. 15-Chamber joins. 16-18,21-25-Wolverine app.						3.00
Vol. 1: The Draft TPB (2003, $21.99) r/#1-5, #1/2 & The Draft one-shots						22.00
Vol. 2: The Underground TPB (2003, $19.99) r/#6-13						20.00
Wizard #1/2 (2002)						5.00

WEAPON X
Marvel Comics: Jun, 2017 - No. 27, Feb, 2019 ($3.99)

1-27: 1-Pak-s/Land-a; Old Man Logan & Sabretooth. 4-6-Crossover with Totally Awesome Hulk #19-22. 6-Intro. Weapon H. 17-19-Omega Red app. 23-27-Deadpool app.						4.00

WEAPON X: DAYS OF FUTURE NOW
Marvel Comics: Sept, 2005 - No. 5, Jan, 2006 ($2.99, limited series)

1-5-Tieri-s/Sears-a; Chamber, Sauron & Fantomex app.						3.00
TPB (2006, $13.99) r/#1-5						14.00

WEAPON X: FIRST CLASS
Marvel Comics: Jan, 2009 - No. 3, Mar, 2009 ($3.99, limited series)

1-3:1-Sabretooth-c/app. 2-Deadpool-c/app.						4.00

WEAPON X NOIR
Marvel Comics: May, 2010 ($3.99, one-shot)

1-Dennis Calero-s/a; C.P. Smith-c						4.00

WEAPON X: THE DRAFT (Leads into 2002 Weapon X series)
Marvel Comics: Oct, 2002 ($2.25, one-shots)

...Kane 1- JH Williams-c/Raimondi-a						3.00
...Marrow 1- JH Williams-c/Badeaux-a						3.00
...Sauron 1- JH Williams-c/Kerschl-a; Emma Frost app.						3.00

...Wild Child 1- JH Williams-c/Van Sciver-a; Aurora (Alpha Flight) app.						3.00
...Zero 1- JH Williams-c/Plunkett-a; Wolverine app.						3.00

WEAPON ZERO
Image Comics (Top Cow Productions): No. T-4(#1), June, 1995 - No. T-0(#5), Dec, 1995 ($2.50, limited series)

T-4(#1): Walt Simonson scripts in all.						5.00
T-3(#2) - T-1(#4)						4.00
T-0(#5)						4.00

WEAPON ZERO
Image Comics (Top Cow Productions): V2#1, Mar, 1996 - No. 15, Dec, 1997 ($2.50)

V2#1-Walt Simonson scripts.						5.00
2-14: 8-Begin Top Cow. 10-Devil's Reign						4.00
15-($3.50) Benitez-a						3.50

WEAPON ZERO/SILVER SURFER
Image Comics/Marvel Comics: Jan, 1997 ($2.95, one-shot)

1-Devil's Reign Pt. 1						4.00

WE ARE ROBIN (Also see Batman: Rebirth #1)
DC Comics: Aug, 2015 - No. 12, Jul, 2016 ($3.99)

1-12: 1-Bermejo-s/c; Cummings-a. 3-Batman (Gordon) app. 4-Batgirl app.; Harvey-a						4.00

WEASELGUY: ROAD TRIP
Image Comics: Sept, 1999 - No. 2 ($3.50, limited series)

1,2-Steve Buccellato-s/a						4.00
1-Variant-c by Bachalo						5.00

WEASELGUY/WITCHBLADE
Hyperwerks: July, 1998 ($2.95, one-shot)

1-Steve Buccellato-s/a; covers by Matsuda and Altstaetter						4.00

WEASEL PATROL SPECIAL, THE (Also see Fusion #17)
Eclipse Comics: Apr, 1989 ($2.00, B&W, one-shot)

1-Funny animal						4.00

WEATHERMAN, THE
Image Comics: Jun, 2018 - No. 6, Nov, 2018 ($3.99)

1-6-Jody LeHeup-s/Nathan Fox-a						4.00

WEATHERMAN, THE (Volume 2)
Image Comics: Jun, 2019 - No. 6, Jan, 2020 ($3.99)

1-6-Jody LeHeup-s/Nathan Fox-a						4.00

WEATHERMAN, THE (Volume 3)
Image Comics: Jan, 2024 - Present ($3.99)

1,2-Jody LeHeup-s/Nathan Fox-a						4.00

WEAVEWORLD
Marvel Comics (Epic): Dec, 1991 - No. 3, 1992 ($4.95, lim. series, 68 pgs.)

1-3: Clive Barker adaptation						5.00

WEB, THE (Also see Mighty Comics & Mighty Crusaders)
DC Comics (Impact Comics): Sept, 1991 - No. 14, Oct, 1992 ($1.00)

1-14: 5-The Fly x-over 9-Trading card inside						5.00
Annual 1 (1992, $2.50, 68 pgs.)-With Trading card						5.00

NOTE: *Gil Kane c-5, 9, 10, 12-14. Bill Wray a(i)-1-9, 10(part).*

WEB, THE (Continued from The Red Circle)
DC Comics: Nov, 2009 - No. 10, Aug, 2010 ($3.99)

1-10: 1-Roger Robinson-a; The Hangman back-up feature. 3-Batgirl app. 5-Caldwell-a						4.00

WEB OF BLACK WIDOW, THE
Marvel Comics: Nov, 2019 - No. 5, Mar, 2020 ($3.99, limited series)

1-5-Jody Houser-s/Stephen Mooney-a. 1,5-Iron Man app. 2-Winter Soldier app.						4.00

WEB OF CARNAGE
Marvel Comics: Sept, 2023 ($5.99, one-shot)

1-Ram V & Gage-s/Manna & Carlos-a						6.00

WEB OF EVIL
Comic Magazines/Quality Comics Group: Nov, 1952 - No. 21, Dec, 1954

1-Used in **SOTI**, pg. 388. Jack Cole-a; morphine use story	113	226	339	718	1234	1750
2-4,6,7: 2,3-Jack Cole-a. 4,6,7-Jack Cole-c/a	61	122	183	390	670	950
5-Electrocution-c/story; Jack Cole-c/a	400	800	1200	2800	4900	7000
8-11-Jack Cole-a	53	106	159	334	567	800
12,13,15,16,19-21	39	78	117	231	378	525
14-Part Crandall-c; Old Witch swipe	48	96	144	302	514	725
17-Opium drug propaganda story	45	90	135	284	480	675
18-Acid-in-face story	63	126	189	403	689	975

NOTE: *Jack Cole a(2 each)-2, 6, 8, 9. Cuidera c-1-21i. Ravielli a-13.*

WEB OF HORROR
Major Magazines: Dec, 1969 - No. 3, Apr, 1970 (Magazine)

1-Jeff Jones painted-c; Wrightson-a, Kaluta-a	13	26	39	89	195	300
2-Jones painted-c; Wrightson-a(2), Kaluta-a	10	20	30	64	132	200
3-Wrightson-c/a (1st published-c); Brunner, Kaluta, Bruce Jones-a	13	26	39	86	188	290

WEB OF MYSTERY
Ace Magazines (A. A. Wyn): Feb, 1951 - No. 29, Sept, 1955

1	129	258	387	826	1413	2000
2-Bakerish-a	53	106	159	334	567	800
3-10: 4-Colan-a	43	86	129	271	461	650
11-18,20-26: 12-John Chilly's 1st cover art. 13-Surrealistic-c. 20-r/The Beyond #1	41	82	123	256	428	600
19-Reprints Challenge of the Unknown #6 used in N.Y. Legislative Committee	45	90	135	284	480	675
27-Bakerish-a(r/The Beyond #2); last pre-code ish	42	84	126	265	445	625
28,29: 28-All-r	34	68	102	199	325	450

NOTE: *This series was to appear as "Creepy Stories", but title was changed before publication. Cameron a-6, 8, 11-13, 17-20, 22, 24, 25, 27; c-8, 13, 17. Palais a-28r. Sekowsky a-1-3, 7, 8, 11, 14, 21, 29. Tothish a-by Bill*

Wayward #30 © Zub & Cummings

Web of Spider-Man (2021 series) #5 © MAR

Wednesday Comics #1 © DC

	GD 2.0	VG 4.0	FN 6.0	VF 8.0	VF/NM 9.0	NM- 9.2

Discount #16. 29-all-r, 19-28-partial-r.

WEB OF SCARLET SPIDER
Marvel Comics: Oct, 1995 - No. 4, Jan, 1996 ($1.95, limited series)

1-Replaces "Web of Spider-Man"	2	4	6	10	14	18
2-4						4.00

WEB OF SPIDER-MAN (Replaces Marvel Team-Up)
Marvel Comics Group: Apr, 1985 - No. 129, Sept, 1995

1-Painted-c by Charles Vess (black costume app.)	4	8	12	25	40	55
2,3	2	4	6	8	10	12
4-8: 7-Hulk x-over; Wolverine splash						6.00
9-13: 10-Dominic Fortune guest stars; painted-c						5.00
14-17,19-28: 19-Intro Humbug & Solo						5.00
18-1st app. Venom (behind the scenes, 9/86)	3	6	9	19	30	40
29-Wolverine, new Hobgoblin (Macendale) app.	2	4	6	9	13	16
30-Origin recap The Rose & Hobgoblin I (entire book is flashback story); Punisher & Wolverine cameo	1	2	3	5	6	8
31,32-Six part Kraven storyline begins	2	4	6	9	12	15
33-35,37,39-47,49						4.00
36-1st app. Tombstone	3	6	9	19	30	40
38-Hobgoblin app.; begin $1.00-c						6.00
48-Origin Hobgoblin II(Demogoblin) cont'd from Spectacular Spider-Man #147; Kingpin app.	2	4	6	8	10	12
50-($1.50, 52 pgs.)						6.00
51-58						4.00
59-Cosmic Spidey cont'd from Spect. Spider-Man						5.00

60-69,89,91-99,101-106: 66,67-Green Goblin (Norman Osborn) app. as a super-hero.
69,70-Hulk x-over. 74-76-Austin-c(i). 76-Fantastic Four x-over. 78-Cloak & Dagger app.
81-Origin/1st app. Bloodshed. 84-Begin 6 part Rose & Hobgoblin II storyline; last $1.00-c.
86-Demon leaves Hobgoblin; 1st Demogoblin. 93-Gives brief history of Hobgoblin.
93,94-Hobgoblin (Macendale) Reborn-c/story, parts 1,2; Moon Knight app. 94-Venom cameo. 95-Begin 4 part x-over w/Spirits of Venom w/Ghost Rider/Blaze/Spidey vs. Venom & Demogoblin (cont'd in Ghost Rider/Blaze #5,6). 96-Spirits of Venom part 3; painted-c.
101,103-Maximum Carnage x-over. 103-Venom & Carnage app. 104-Infinity Crusade tie-in.
104-106-Nightwatch back-up stories

90-(7/92, $2.95, 52 pgs.)-Polybagged w/silver hologram-c, gatefold poster showing Spider-Man & Spider-Man 2099 (1st image of the character; pre-dates Spider-Man 2099 story debut in ASM #365 by one month)	2	4	6	8	11	14
90-2nd printing; gold hologram-c						4.00
100-($2.95, 52 pgs.)-Holo-grafx foil-c; intro new Spider-Armor						5.00
107-111: 107-Intro Sandstorm; Sand & Quicksand app.						4.00
112-116,121-124, 126-128: 116-Begin $1.50-c; bound-in trading card sheet.						4.00
113-Regular Ed.; Gambit & Black Cat app.						4.00
113-($2.95)-Collector's ed. polybagged w/foil-c; 16 pg. preview of Spider-Man cartoon & animation cel						5.00
117-($1.50)-Flip book; Power & Responsibility Pt.1						4.00
117-($2.95)-Collector's edition; foil-c; flip book						5.00
118-1st solo Scarlet Spider story; Venom app.	6	12	18	41	76	110
119-Regular edition						6.00
119-($6.45)-Direct market edition; polybagged w/ Marvel Milestone Amazing Spider-Man #150 & coupon for Amazing Spider-Man #396, Spider-Man #53, & Spectacular Spider-Man #219.	3	6	9	14	19	24
120 ($2.25)-Flip book w/ preview of the Ultimate Spider-Man						4.00
125 ($3.95)-Holodisk-c; Gwen Stacy clone						5.00
125,129: 125 ($2.95)-Newsstand. 129-Last issue						4.00
#129.1, #129.2 (both 10/12, 2.99) Brooklyn Avengers app.; Damion Scott-a						4.00
Annual 1 (1985)	1	3	4	6	8	10
Annual 2 (1986)-New Mutants; Art Adams-a	2	4	6	8	10	12

Annual 3-10 ('87-'94, 68 pgs.): 4-Evolutionary War x-over. 5-Atlantis Attacks; Captain Universe by Ditko (p) & Silver Sable stories; F.F. app. 6-Punisher back-up plus Capt. Universe by Ditko; G. Kane-a. 7-Origins of Hobgoblin I, Hobgoblin II, Green Goblin I & II & Venom; Larsen/Austin-c. 9-Bagged w/card

Super Special 1 (1995, $3.95)-flip book						5.00
NOTE: Art Adams a-Annual 2. Byrne c-3-6. Chaykin c-10. Mignola a-Annual 2. Vess c-1, 8, Annual 1, 2. Zeck a-6i, 31, 32; c-31, 32.						5.00

WEB OF SPIDER-MAN (Anthology)
Marvel Comics: Dec, 2009 - No. 12, Nov, 2010 ($3.99)

1-12: 1-Spider-Girl app. thru #7; Ben Reilly app. 2-6-Origins of villains retold. 7-Kraven origin; Paper Doll app.; Mahfood-a. 9-11-Jackpot back-up; Takeda-a. 11,12-Black Cat app.						4.00

W.E.B. OF SPIDER-MAN (All ages edition)
Marvel Comics: Aug, 2021 - No. 5, Nov, 2021 ($3.99, limited series)

1-5-Teenage Spidey with Moon Girl, Onome, Harley Keener, Squirrel Girl						4.00

WEB OF VENOM...
Marvel Comics: Oct, 2018 - Jan, 2021 ($4.99, one-shots)

	1	2	3	5	6	8
...: Carnage Born 1 (1/19) Story of Cletus Kasady; Cates-s/Beyruth-a	1	2	3	5	6	8

	GD 2.0	VG 4.0	FN 6.0	VF 8.0	VF/NM 9.0	NM- 9.2

...: Cult of Carnage 1 (6/19) Misty Knight & John Jameson app.; Tieri-s/Beyruth-a						5.00
...: Empyre's End 1 (1/21) Knull app.; Chapman-s/Vilanova-a						5.00
...: Funeral Pyre 1 (9/19) Story of Andi Benton (Mania); Carnage app.	1	2	3	5	6	8
...: The Good Son 1 (3/20) Story of Eddie Brock's son Dylan and Normie Osborn						5.00
...: Ve'Nam 1 (10/18) The first symbiote & Rex Strickland app.; Cates-s/Ramirez-a	1	2	3	5	6	8
...: Venom Unleashed 1 (3/19) Venom Dog and Carnage app.; Cates-s/Hotz & Gedeon-a						5.00
...: Wraith 1 (11/20) Origin of Wraith re-told; Cates-s/Vilanova-a						4.00

WEBSPINNERS: TALES OF SPIDER-MAN
Marvel Comics: Jan, 1999 - No. 18, Jun, 2000 ($2.99/$2.50)

	1	2	3	5	6	8
1-DeMatteis-s/Zulli-a; back-up story w/Romita Sr. art						6.00
1-($6.95) DF Edition	1	2	3	5	6	8
2,3: 2-Two covers						4.00
4-11,13-18: 4,5-Giffen-a; Silver Surfer-c/app. 7-9-Kelly-s/Sears and Smith-a. 10,11-Jenkins-s/Sean Phillips-a						4.00
12-($3.50) J.G. Jones-c/a; Jenkins-s						5.00

WEB WARRIORS
Marvel Comics: Jan, 2016 - No. 11, Nov, 2016 ($4.99/$3.99)

1-($4.99) Spider-verse characters team-up; Mike Costa-s/David Baldeon-a; alternate Black Cat app.						5.00
2-11-($3.99) 2-5-Multiple Spider-Mans vs. multiple Electros						4.00

WEDDING BELLS
Quality Comics Group: Feb, 1954 - No. 19, Nov, 1956

1-Whitney-a	27	54	81	162	266	370
2	16	32	48	94	147	200
3-9: 8-Last precode (4/55)	14	28	42	82	121	160
10-Ward-a (9 pgs.)	20	40	60	117	189	260
11-14,17	14	28	42	80	115	150
15-Baker-c	41	82	123	256	428	600
16-Baker-c/a	37	74	111	222	361	500
18,19-Baker-a each	22	44	66	132	216	300

WEDDING OF DRACULA
Marvel Comics: Jan, 1993 ($2.00, 52 pgs.)

1-Reprints Tomb of Dracula #30,45,46						5.00

WEDNESDAY COMICS (Newspaper-style, twice folded pages on 20" x 14" newsprint)
DC Comics: Sept, 2009 - No. 12, Nov, 2009 ($3.99, weekly limited series)

1-12-Superman, Batman, Kamandi, Hawkman, Deadman, Green Lantern, Flash, Teen Titans, Metamorpho, Adam Strange, Supergirl, Metal Men, Wonder Woman, The Demon with Catwoman, Sgt. Rock; s-a/ by various incl. Ryan Sook, Joe Kubert, Gaiman, Allred, Risso, Kyle Baker, Paul Pope, Conner, Simonson, Garcia-Lopez, Stelfreeze, Bermejo						4.00
HC (2010, $49.99, 17-3/4"x11-1/4") r/#1-12 plus new 1 pg. stories of Plastic Man by Dorkin-s/DeStefano-a and Beware the Creeper by Giffen-s/Canete-a; bonus sketch art						50.00

WEEKENDER, THE (Illustrated...)
Rucker Pub. Co.: V1#1, Sept, 1945? - V1#4, Nov, 1945; V2#1, Jan, 1946 - V2#3, Aug, 1946 (52 pgs.)

V#1-Same-c as Zip Comics #45 (nurse in peril), inside-c and back-c blank; Steel Sterling, Senor Banana, Red Rube and Ginger	64	128	183	390	670	950
V1#2-4: 2-Capt. Victory on-c. 3-Super hero-c; Mr. E, Dan Hastings, Sky Chief and the Echo. 4-Same-c as Punch Comics #10 (9/44); r/Hale the Magician (7 pgs.) & r/Mr. E (8 pgs.-Lou Fine? or Gustavson?) plus 3 humor strips & many B&W photos & r/newspaper articles plus cheesecake photos of Hollywood stars	53	106	159	334	567	800
V2#1-Same-c as Dynamic Comics #11; 36 pgs. comics, 16 in newspaper format with photos; partial Dynamic Comics reprints; 4 pgs. of cels from the Disney film Pinocchio; Little Nemo story by Winsor McCay, Jr.; Jack Cole-a	75	154	231	493	847	1200
V2#2,3: 2-Same-c as Dynamic Comics #9 by Raboy; Dan Hastings (Tuska), Rocket Boy, The Echo, Lucky Coyne. 3-Humor-c by Boddington?; Dynamic Man, Ima Slooth, Master Key, Dynamic Boy, Captain Glory	47	94	141	296	498	700

WEEKND PRESENTS, THE: STARBOY
Marvel Comics: Aug, 2018 ($3.99, one-shot)

1-Abel Tesfaye, La Mar Taylor & Christos Gage-s/Eric Nguyen-a/c						4.00

WE HAVE DEMONS
Dark Horse Comics: Mar, 2022 - No. 3, Jun, 2022 ($4.99, limited series)

1-3-Scott Snyder-s/Greg Capullo-a						5.00

WEIRD
Eerie Publications: V1#10, 1/66 - V8#6, 12/74; V9#1, 1/75 - V14#3, Nov, 1981 (Magazine) (V1-V8: 52 pgs.; V9 on: 68 pgs.)

V1#10(#1)-Intro. Morris the Caretaker of Weird (ends V2#10); Burgos-a	10	20	30	67	144	215
11,12	7	14	21	48	89	130
V2#1-4(10/67), V3#1(1/68), V2#6(4/68)-V2#7,9,10(12/68)	7	14	21	48	89	130

	GD	VG	FN	VF	VF/NM	NM-
	2.0	4.0	6.0	8.0	9.0	9.2

V2#8-r/Ditko's 1st story/Fantastic Fears #5

	8	16	24	56	108	160
V3#1(2/69)-V3#4	6	12	18	41	76	110

V3#5(12/69)-Rulah reprint; "Rulah" changed to "Pulah", LSD story reprinted in Horror Tales

V4#4, Tales From the Tomb V2#4, & 20	6	12	18	41	76	110

V4#1-6('70), V5#1-6('71), V6#1-7('72), V7#1-7('73), V8#4(8/74), V8#4(10/74),
(V8#5 does not exist), V8#6('74), V9#1-4(1/75-'76), V10#1-3('77), V11#1-4('78),

V12#1(2/79)-V14#3(11/81)	6	12	18	38	69	100

NOTE: There are two V8#4 issues (8/74 & 10/74). V9#4 (12/76) has a cover swipe from Horror Tales V5#1 (2/73). There are two V13#3 issues (6/80 & 9/80).

WEIRD
DC Comics (Paradox Press): Sum, 1997 - No. 4 ($2.99, B&W, magazine)

1-4: 4-Mike Tyson-c						4.00

WEIRD, THE
DC Comics: Apr, 1988 - No. 4, July, 1988 ($1.50, limited series)

1-4: Wrightson-c/a in all						5.00

WEIRD ADVENTURES
P. L. Publishing Co. (Canada): May-June, 1951 - No. 3, Sept-Oct, 1951

1- The She-Wolf Killer" by Matt Baker (6 pgs.)	84	168	252	538	919	1300
2-Bondage/hypodermic panel	63	126	189	403	689	975
3-Male bondage/torture-c; severed head story	57	114	171	362	619	875

WEIRD ADVENTURES
Ziff-Davis Publishing Co.: No. 10, July-Aug, 1951

10-Painted-c	57	114	171	362	619	875

WEIRD CHILLS
Key Publications: July, 1954 - No. 3, Nov, 1954

1-Wolverton-r/Weird Mysteries No. 4; blood transfusion-c by Baily

	300	600	900	1950	3375	4800

2-Extremely violent injury to eye-c by Baily; Hitler story

	300	600	900	1950	3375	4800
3-Bondage E.C. swipe-c by Baily	239	478	717	1530	2615	3700

WEIRD COMICS
Fox Feature Syndicate: Apr, 1940 - No. 20, Jan, 1942

1-The Birdman, Thor, God of Thunder (ends #5), The Sorceress of Zoom, Blast Bennett, Typhon, Voodoo Man, & Dr. Mortal begin; George Tuska scarce-c

	1350	2700	4050	10,260	18,630	27,000
2-Lou Fine-c	676	1352	2028	4935	8718	12,500
3,4: 3-Simon-c. 4-Torture-c	314	628	942	2198	3849	5500

5-Intro. Dart & sidekick Ace (8/40) (ends #20); bondage/hypo-c

	326	652	978	2282	3991	5700
6-Dynamite Thor app.; super hero covers begin	194	388	582	1242	2121	3000
7-Dynamite Thor app.	258	516	774	1651	2826	4000

8-Dynamo, the Eagle (11/40, early app.; see Science #1) & sidekick Buddy & Marga, the Panther Woman begin

	213	426	639	1363	2332	3300
9,10: 10-Navy Jones app.	168	336	504	1075	1838	2600

11-19: 16-The Eagle vs. Nazi battle-c/flag-c. 17-Origin The Black Rider; WWII Nazi-c

	155	310	465	992	1696	2400

20-Origin The Rapier; Swoop Curtis app; Churchill & Hitler-c

	1500	3000	4500	11,400	20,700	30,000

NOTE: Cover features: Sorceress of Zoom-4; Dr. Mortal-5; Dart & Ace-6-13, 15; Eagle-14, 16-20.

WEIRD DETECTIVE
Dark Horse Comics: Jun, 2016 - No. 5, Oct, 2016 ($3.99)

1-5-Van Lente-s/Vilanova-a						4.00

WEIRD FANTASY (Formerly A Moon, A Girl, Romance; becomes Weird Science-Fantasy #23 on)
E. C. Comics: No. 13, May-June, 1950 - No. 22, Nov-Dec, 1953

13(#1) (1950)	263	526	789	2104	3352	4600

14-Necronomicon story; Cosmic Ray Bomb explosion-c/story by Feldstein;

Feldstein & Gaines star	131	262	393	1048	1674	2300
15,16: 16-Used in SOTI, pg. 144	103	206	309	824	1312	1800
17 (1951)	80	160	240	640	1020	1400
6-Robot-c	86	172	258	688	1094	1500
7-10	69	138	207	552	876	1200

11-13 (1952): 11-Cover inspired by Chesley Bonestell painting "The End of the World" from Coronet magazine (July 1947); Feldstein bio. 12-E.C. artists cameo; Orlando bio.

	74	148	222	592	946	1300

13-Anti-Wertham "Cosmic Correspondence"

	63	126	189	504	802	1100

14-Frazetta/Williamson(1st team-up at E.C.)/Krenkel-a (7 pgs.); Orlando draws E.C. staff

	74	148	222	592	946	1300
15-Williamson/Evans-a(3), 4,3,&7 pgs.	63	126	189	504	802	1100

16-19-Williamson/Krenkel-a in all. 17-Feldstein dinosaur-c; classic sci-fi story "The Aliens".

18-Williamson/Feldstein-c; classic anti-prejudice story "Judgment Day". 19-Williamson bio.

	51	102	153	408	654	900

20-Frazetta/Williamson-a (7 pgs.); contains house ad for original, uncensored cover to Vault of Horror #32 (meat cleaver in forehead)

	66	132	198	528	839	1150
21-Frazetta/Williamson-c & Williamson/Krenkel-a	97	194	291	776	1238	1700
22-Bradbury adaptation	50	100	150	400	638	875

NOTE: Crandall a-14, 19. Feldstein a-13(#1)-8. Evans a-13(#1)-15(#1)-18 (#18 w/Williamson). 20. Harrison/Wood a-13. Kamen a-13(#1)-16, 18-22. Krigstein a-22. Kurtzman a-13(#1)-17(#5), 6. Orlando a-9-22 (2 stories in #16); c-19, 22. Severin/Elder a-18-21. Williamson a-13(#1)-14, 17(2 stories ea. in #10-13). Ray Bradbury adaptations in #13,17-22. Canadian reprints exist; see Table of Contents.

WEIRD FANTASY
Russ Cochran/Gemstone Publ.: Oct, 1992 - No. 22, Jan, 1998 ($1.50/$2.00/$2.50)

1-22: 1,2: 1,2-r/Weird Fantasy #13,14; Feldstein-c. 3-5-r/Weird Fantasy #15-17						4.00

WEIRD HORRORS (Nightmare #10 on)
St. John Publishing Co.: June, 1952 - No. 9, Oct, 1953

1-Tuska-a	97	194	291	621	1061	1500
2,3: 3-Hashish story	53	106	159	334	567	800
4,5	47	94	141	296	498	700
6-Ekgren-c; atomic bomb story	129	258	387	826	1413	2000
7-Ekgren-c; Kubert, Cameron-a	142	284	426	909	1555	2200
8,9-Kubert-c/a	61	122	183	390	670	950

NOTE: Cameron a-7, 9. Finesque a-1-5. Forgione a-6. Morisi a-3. Bondage c-8.

WEIRD MYSTERIES
Gillmor Publications: Oct, 1952 - No. 12, Sept, 1954

1-Partial Wolverton-c swiped from splash page "Flight to the Future" in Weird Tales of the Future #2; "Eternity" has an Ingels swipe

	213	426	639	1363	2332	3300

2- "Robot Woman" by Wolverton; Bernard Baily-c reprinted in Mister Mystery #18; acid in face panel

	290	580	870	1856	3178	4500
3,6: Both have decapitation-c	155	310	465	992	1696	2400

4- "The Man Who Never Smiled" (3 pgs.) by Wolverton; Classic B. Baily skull-c

	1200	2400	3600	9100	16,550	24,000

5-Wolverton story "Swamp Monster" (6 pgs.). Classic exposed brain-c

	1400	2800	4200	10,600	19,300	28,000

7-Used in SOTI, illo "Indeed", illo "Sex and blood"

	245	490	735	1568	2684	3800

8-Wolverton-c panel-r/#5; used in a '54 Readers Digest anti-comics article by T. E. Murphy entitled "For the Kiddies to Read"

	129	258	387	826	1413	2000
9-Excessive violence, gore & torture	116	232	348	742	1271	1800
10-Silhouetted nudity panel	123	246	369	787	1344	1900

11,12: 12-r/Mr. Mystery #8(2), Weird Mysteries #3 & Weird Tales of the Future #6

	103	206	309	659	1130	1600

NOTE: Baily c-2-12. Anti-Wertham column in #5. #1-12 all have 'The Ghoul Teacher' (host).

WEIRD MYSTERIES (Magazine)
Pastime Publications: Mar-Apr, 1959 (35¢, B&W, 68 pgs.)

1-Torres-a; E. C. swipe from Tales From the Crypt #46 by Tuska "The Ragman"

	19	38	57	111	176	240

WEIRD MYSTERY TALES (See DC 100 Page Super Spectacular)

WEIRD MYSTERY TALES (See Cancelled Comic Cavalcade)
National Periodical Publications: July-Aug, 1972 - No. 24, Nov, 1975

1-Kirby-a; Wrightson splash pg.	6	12	18	42	79	115
2-Titanic-c/s	3	6	9	21	33	45
3,21: 21-Wrightson-c	3	6	9	17	26	35
4-10	2	4	6	14	19	24
11-20,22-24	2	4	6	11	16	20

NOTE: Alcala a-5, 10, 13, 14. Aparo c-4. Bailey a-8. Bolle a-8?. Howard a-4. Kaluta a-4, 24; c-1. G. Kane a-10. Kirby a-1, 2p, 3p. Nino a-5, 6, 9, 13, 16, 21. Redondo a-9, 17. Sparling c-6. Starlin a-3?, 4. Wood a-23.

WEIRD ROMANCE (Seduction of the Innocent #9)
Eclipse Comics: Feb, 1988 ($2.00, B&W)

1-Pre-code horror-r; Lou Cameron-r(2)						4.00

WEIRD SCIENCE (Formerly Saddle Romances) (Becomes Weird Science-Fantasy #23 on)
(Also see EC Archives • Weird Science)
E. C. Comics: No. 12, May-June, 1950 - No. 22, Nov-Dec, 1953

12(#1) (1950)-"Lost in the Microcosm" classic-c/story by Kurtzman; "Dream of Doom" stars Gaines & E.C. artists

	337	674	1011	2646	4298	5900

13-Flying saucers over Washington-c/story, 2 years before supposed UFO sighting

	149	298	447	1192	1896	2600
14-Robot, End of the World-c/story by Feldstein	131	262	393	1048	1674	2300
15-War of Worlds-c/story (1950)	109	218	327	872	1386	1900
4-Atomic explosion-c	91	182	273	728	1164	1600
6-8,10	71	142	213	568	909	1250
9-Wood's 1st EC-c	91	182	273	728	1164	1600
11-14 (1952): 11-Kamen bio. 12-Wood bio	63	126	189	504	802	1100
15-18-Williamson/Krenkel-a in each; 15-Williamson-a. 17-Used in POP, pg. 81,82.						
18-Bill Gaines doll app. in story	57	114	171	456	728	1000

19,20-Williamson/Frazetta-a (7 pgs. each). 19-Used in SOTI, illo "A young girl on her wedding night stabs her sleeping husband to death with a hatpin..." 19-Bradbury bio.

	91	182	273	728	1164	1600

21-Williamson/Frazetta-a (6 pgs.); Wood draws E.C. staff; Gaines & Feldstein app. in story

	97	194	291	776	1238	1700

22-Williamson/Frazetta/Krenkel-a (8 pgs.); Wood draws himself in his story (last pg. & panel)

	91	182	273	728	1164	1600

NOTE: Elder a-14, 19. Evans a-12(#1)-8; c-12(#1)-8. Feldstein a-12(#1)-8, 13(#2), 5-22 (#9, 10, 12, 13 all have 2 Wood stories); c-10, 12-22. Kamen a-15. Ingels a-15. Kamen a-12(#1)-13, 15-18, 20, 21. Kurtzman a-12(#1)-7. Orlando a-10-22. Wood a-12(#1), 13(#2), 5-22 (#9, 10, 12, 13 all have 2 Wood stories); c-10, 12-22. Ray Bradbury adaptations in #17-22. Canadian reprints exist; see Table of Contents.

WEIRD SCIENCE
Gladstone Publishing: Sept, 1990 - No. 4, Mar, 1991 ($1.95/$2.00, 68 pgs.)

1-4: Wood-c(r); all reprints in each						5.00

WEIRD SCIENCE (Also see EC Archives • Weird Science)
Russ Cochran/Gemstone Publishing: Dec, 1992 - No. 22, Dec, 1997 ($1.50/$2.00/$2.50)

1-22: 1,2: r/Weird Science #12,13 w/original-c. ,4-r/#14,15. 5-7-w/original-c						4.00

WEIRD SCIENCE-FANTASY (Formerly Weird Science & Weird Fantasy)
(Becomes Incredible Science Fiction #30)
E. C. Comics: No. 23 Mar, 1954 - No. 29, May-June, 1955 (#23,24: 15¢)

23-Williamson, Wood-a; Bradbury adaptation	57	114	171	456	728	1000

24-Williamson, Wood-a; Harlan Ellison's 1st professional story, "Upheaval!", later adapted into a short story as "Mealtime", and then into a TV episode of Voyage to the Bottom of the Sea as "The Price of Doom"

	56	112	168	448	712	975

25-Williamson dinosaur-c; Williamson/Torres/Krenkel-a plus Wood-a; Bradbury adaptation and fan letter; cover price back to 10¢

	63	126	189	504	802	1100

26-Flying Saucer Report; Wood, Crandall-a; A-bomb panels

	54	108	162	432	691	950
27-Adam Link/I Robot series begins	53	106	159	424	675	925
28-Williamson/Krenkel/Torres-a; Wood-a	53	106	159	424	675	925

29-Classic Frazetta-c; Williamson/Krenkel & Wood-a; Adam Link/I Robot series concludes; last pre-code issue; new logo

	229	458	687	1832	2916	4000

NOTE: Crandall a-26, 27, 29. Evans a-26. Feldstein c-24, 26, 28. Kamen a-27, 28. Krigstein a-23-25. Orlando a-in all. Wood a-in all; c-23, 27. The cover to #29 was originally intended for Famous Funnies #217 (Buck Rogers), but was rejected for being "too violent."

WEIRD SCIENCE-FANTASY
Russ Cochran/Gemstone Publishing: Nov, 1992 - No. 7, May, 1994 ($1.50/$2.00/$2.50)

1-7: 1,2: r/Weird Science-Fantasy #23,24. 3-7 r/#25-29						4.00

WEIRD SCIENCE-FANTASY ANNUAL
E. C. Comics: 1952, 1953 (Sold thru the E. C. office & on the stands in some major cities) (25¢, 132 pgs.)

1952-Feldstein-c	429	858	1287	3432	5466	7500
1953-Feldstein-c	257	514	771	2056	3278	4500

NOTE: The 1952 annual contains books cover-dated in 1951 & 1952, and the 1953 annual from 1952 & 1953. Contents of each annual may vary in same year.

Weird Fantasy #14 © WMG

Weird Thrillers #3 © Z-D

Weird War Tales #1 © DC

	GD 2.0	VG 4.0	FN 6.0	VF 8.0	VF/NM 9.0	NM- 9.2

WEIRD SECRET ORIGINS
DC Comics: Oct, 2004 ($5.95, square-bound, one-shot)

nn-Reprints origins of Dr. Fate, Spectre, Congorilla, Metamorpho, Animal Man & others						6.00

WEIRD SUSPENSE
Atlas/Seaboard Publ.: Feb, 1975 - No. 3, July, 1975

	GD	VG	FN	VF	VF/NM	NM-
1-3: 1-Tarantula begins. 3-Freidrich-s	2	4	6	11	16	20

NOTE: *Boyette* a-1-3. *Buckler* c-1, 3.

WEIRD SUSPENSTORIES
Superior Comics (Canada): Oct, 1951 - No. 3, Dec, 1951; No. 3, no date (EC reprints)

	GD	VG	FN	VF	VF/NM	NM-
1-3,3(no date)-(Rare): Reprints Crime SuspenStories #1-3, covers & contents w/Canadian ads replacing U.S. ads	1200	2400	3600	-	-	-

NOTE: *Canada passed a law against importing crime comic books between 1949-1953, thus Crime Suspenstories became Weird Suspenstories in Canada creating a new EC title. The word "crime" was not allowed on comic books in Canada during this time.*

WEIRD TALES ILLUSTRATED
Millennium Publications: 1992 - No. 2, 1992 ($2.95, high quality paper)

1,2-Bolton painted-c. 1-Adapts E.A. Poe & Harlan Ellison stories. 2-E.A. Poe & H.P. Lovecraft adaptations						4.00
1-($4.95, 52 pgs.)-Deluxe edition w/Tim Vigil-a not in regular #1; stiff-c; Bolton painted-c						6.00

WEIRD TALES OF THE FUTURE
S.P.M. Publ. No. 1-4/Aragon Publ. No. 5-8: Mar, 1952 - No. 8, July-Aug, 1953

	GD	VG	FN	VF	VF/NM	NM-
1-Andru-a(2); Wolverton partial-c	300	600	900	1950	3375	4800
2,3-Wolverton-c/a(3) each. 2- "Jumpin Jupiter" satire by Wolverton begins, ends #5	454	908	1362	3314	5857	8400
4-(11/52) Wolverton-c from three panels of Wolverton's "Nightmare World" from issue #3 (9/52) and the girl on the cover from Mister Mystery #6 (7/52) "The Fatal Chord" by Ed Robbins, pg. 4, which was cut apart, pasted up to form the cover and partially redrawn by Harry Kantor, the editor; "Jumpin Jupiter" satire by Wolverton	200	400	600	1280	2190	3100
5-Wolverton-c/a(2); "Jumpin Jupiter" satire	508	1016	1524	3708	6554	9400
6-Bernard Baily-c	174	348	522	1114	1907	2700
7- "The Mind Movers" from the art to Wolverton's "Brain Bats of Venus" from Mr. Mystery #7 which was cut apart, pasted up, partially redrawn, and rewritten by Harry Kantor, the editor; Baily-c	400	800	1200	2800	4900	7000
8-Reprints Weird Mysteries #1(10/52) minus cover; gory cover showing heart ripped out, by B. Baily	622	1244	1866	4541	8021	11,500

WEIRD TALES OF THE MACABRE (Magazine)
Atlas/Seaboard Publ.: Jan, 1975 - No. 2, Mar, 1975 (75¢, B&W)

	GD	VG	FN	VF	VF/NM	NM-
1-Jeff Jones painted-c; Boyette-a	5	10	15	35	63	90
2-Boris Vallejo painted-c; Severin-a	6	12	18	37	66	95

WEIRD TERROR (Also see Horrific)
Allen Hardy Associates (Comic Media): Sept, 1952 - No. 13, Sept, 1954

	GD	VG	FN	VF	VF/NM	NM-
1- "Portrait of Death", adapted from Lovecraft's "Pickman's Model"; lingerie panels, Hitler story	119	238	357	762	1306	1850
2-Text on Marquis DeSade, Torture, Demonology, & St. Elmo's Fire	97	194	291	621	1061	1500
3-Extreme violence, whipping, torture; article on sin eating, dowsing	271	542	813	1734	2967	4200
4-Dismemberment, decapitation, article on human flesh for sale, Devil, whipping	219	438	657	1402	2401	3400
5-Article on body snatching, mutilation; cannibalism story	181	362	543	1158	1979	2800
6-Dismemberment, decapitation, man hit by lightning story	200	400	600	1280	2190	3100
7-Body burning in fireplace-c	258	516	774	1651	2826	4000
8,11: 8-Decapitation story; Ambrose Bierce adapt. 11-End of the world story w/atomic blast panels; Tothish-a by Bill Discount	77	154	231	493	847	1200
9,10,13: 13-Severed head panels	61	122	183	390	670	950
12-Discount-a	63	126	189	403	689	975

NOTE: *Don Heck a-most issues; c-1-13. Landau a-6. Morisi a-2-5, 7, 9, 12. Palais a-1, 5, 6, 8(2), 10, 12. Powell a-10. Ravielli a-11.*

WEIRD THRILLERS
Ziff-Davis Publ. Co. (Approved Comics): Sept-Oct, 1951 - No. 5, Oct-Nov, 1952
(#2-5: painted-c)

	GD	VG	FN	VF	VF/NM	NM-
1-Rondo Hatton photo-c	123	246	369	787	1344	1900
2-Toth, Anderson, Colan-a	87	174	261	553	952	1350
3-Two Powell, Tuska-a; classic-c; Everett-a	123	246	369	787	1344	1900
4-Kubert, Tuska-a	81	162	243	518	884	1250
5-Powell-a	77	154	231	493	847	1200

NOTE: *M. Anderson a-2, 3. Roussos a-4. #2, 3 reprinted in Nightmare #10 & 13; #4, 5 reprinted in Amazing Ghost Stories #16 & #15.*

WEIRD VAMPIRE TALES (Comic magazine)
Modern Day Periodical Pub.: V3 #1, Apr, 1979 - V5 #3, Mar, 1982 (B&W)

	GD 2.0	VG 4.0	FN 6.0	VF 8.0	VF/NM 9.0	NM- 9.2
V3 #1 (4/79) First issue, no V1 or V2	5	10	15	31	53	75
V3 #2-4	3	6	9	19	30	40
V4 #2 (4/80), V4 #3 (7/80) (no V4 #1)	3	6	9	17	26	35
V5 #1 (1/81), V5 #2 (two issues, 4/81 & 8/81)	3	6	9	17	26	35
V5 #3 (3/82) Last issue; low print	3	6	9	21	33	45

WEIRD WAR TALES
National Periodical Publ./DC Comics: Sept-Oct, 1971 - No. 124, June, 1983 (#1-5: 52 pgs.)

	GD	VG	FN	VF	VF/NM	NM-
1-Kubert-a in #1-4,7; c-1-7	22	44	66	154	340	525
2,3-Drucker-a- 2-Crandall-a. 3-Heath-a	10	20	30	64	132	200
4,5: 5-Toth-a; Heath-a	8	16	24	54	102	150
6,7,9,10: 6,10-Toth-a. 7-Heath-a	6	12	18	37	66	95
8-Neal Adams-c/a(i)	6	12	18	41	76	110
11-20	4	8	12	22	35	48
21-35	3	6	9	16	24	32
36-(68 pgs.)-Crandall & Kubert-r/#2; Heath-r/#3; Kubert-c	3	6	9	18	28	38
37-50: 38,39-Kubert-c	2	4	6	10	14	18
51-63: 58-Hitler-c/app. 60-Hindenburg-c/s	2	4	6	9	13	16
64-Frank Miller-a (1st DC work)	6	12	18	41	76	110
65-67,69-89,91,92: 89-Nazi Apes-c/s.	2	4	6	8	10	12
68-Frank Miller-a (2nd DC work)	3	6	9	21	33	45
90-Hitler app.	3	6	9	14	19	24
93-Intro/origin Creature Commandos	7	14	21	46	86	125
94-Return of War that Time Forgot; dinosaur-c/s	2	4	6	10	12	14
95,96,98,102-123: 98-Sphinx-c. 102-Creature Commandos battle Hitler. 110-Origin/1st app. Medusa. 123-1st app. Captain Spaceman	2	4	6	8	10	12
97,99,100,101,124: 99-War that Time Forgot. 100-Creature Commandos in War that Time Forgot. 101-Intro/origin G.I. Robot	2	4	6	8	11	14

NOTE: *Chaykin a-76, 82. Ditko a-95, 99, 104-106. Evans c-73, 74, 83, 85. Kane c-116, 118. Kubert c-55, 58, 60, 62, 72, 75-81, 87, 88, 90-96, 100, 103, 104, 106, 107. Newton a-122. Starlin c-89. Sutton a-91, 92, 103. Creature Commandos -93, 97, 100, 102, 105, 108-112, 114, 116-119, 121, 124. G.I. Robot - 101, 108, 111, 113, 116-118, 120, 122. War That Time Forgot - 94, 99, 100, 103, 106, 109, 120.*

WEIRD WAR TALES
DC Comics (Vertigo): June, 1997 - No. 4, Sept, 1997 ($2.50)

1-4-Anthology by various						4.00

WEIRD WAR TALES
DC Comics (Vertigo): April, 2000 ($4.95, one-shot)

1-Anthology by various; last Biukovic-a						5.00

WEIRD WAR TALES
DC Comics: Nov, 2010 ($3.99, one-shot)

1-Anthology by various incl. Cooke, Strnad, Pugh; Cooke-c						4.00

WEIRD WESTERN TALES (Formerly All-Star Western)
National Per. Publ./DC Comics: No. 12, June-July, 1972 - No. 70, Aug, 1980

	GD	VG	FN	VF	VF/NM	NM-
12-(52 pgs.)-3rd app. Jonah Hex; Bat Lash, Pow Wow Smith reprints; El Diablo by Neal Adams/Wrightson	10	20	30	64	132	200
13-Jonah Hex-c & 4th app.; Neal Adams-a	7	14	21	48	89	130
14-Toth-a	5	10	15	35	63	90
15-Adams-c/a; no Jonah Hex	4	8	12	28	47	65
16,17,19,20	4	8	12	28	47	65
18,29: 18-1st all Jonah Hex issue (7-8/73) & begins. 29-Origin Jonah Hex; 1st full app. of Quentin Turnbull	6	12	18	37	66	95
21-28,30: Jonah Hex in all	4	8	12	23	37	50
31-38: Jonah Hex in all. 38-Last Jonah Hex	3	6	9	18	28	38
39-Origin/1st app. Scalphunter & begins	2	4	6	13	18	22
40-47,50-69: 64-Bat Lash-c/story	2	4	6	8	10	14
48,49: (44 pgs.)-1st & 2nd app. Cinnamon	2	4	6	11	14	16
70-Last issue	2	4	6	9	13	16

NOTE: *Alcala a-16, 17. Evans inks-39-48; c-39i, 40, 47. G. Kane a-15, 20. Kubert c-12, 33. Starlin c-44, 45. Wildey a-26. 48 & 49 are 44 pgs..*

WEIRD WESTERN TALES (Blackest Night crossover)
DC Comics: No. 71, March, 2010 ($2.99, one-shot)

71-Jonah Hex, Scalphunter, Super-Chief, Firehair and Bat Lash rise as Black Lanterns						3.00

WEIRD WESTERN TALES
DC Comics (Vertigo): Apr, 2001 - No. 4, Jul, 2001 ($2.50, limited series)

1-4-Anthology by various						3.00

WEIRD WONDER TALES
Marvel Comics Group: Dec, 1973 - No. 22, May, 1977

	GD	VG	FN	VF	VF/NM	NM-
1-Wolverton-r/Mystic #6 (Eye of Doom)	5	10	15	30	50	70
2-10	3	6	9	17	26	35
11-22: 16-18-Venus-r by Everett from Venus #19,18 & 17. 19-22-r/Dr. Droom (re-named Dr. Druid) by Kirby. 22-New art by Byrne	3	6	9	16	23	30
15-17-(30¢-c variants, limited distribution)(4-8/76)	6	12	18	38	69	100

NOTE: *All 1950s & early 1960s reprints. Check r-1. Colan r-17. Ditko r-4, 5, 10-13, 19-21. Drucker r-12, 20. Everett r-3(Spellbound #16), 6(Astonishing #10), 9(Adv. Into Mystery #5). Heath a-13r. Heck a-1or, 14r. Gil...*

	GD	VG	FN	VF	VF/NM	NM-
	2.0	4.0	6.0	8.0	9.0	9.2

c-1, 2, 10. **Kirby** r-4, 6, 10, 11, 13, 15-22; c-17, 19, 20. **Krigstein** r-19. **Kubert** r-22. **Maneely** r-8. **Mooney** r-7p. **Powell** r-3, 7. **Torres** r-7. **Wildey** r-2, 7.

WEIRDWORLD (Secret Wars tie-in)
Marvel Comics: Aug, 2015 - No. 5, Dec, 2015 ($3.99, limited series)

1-5-Aaron-s/Del Mundo-a; Arkon, Morgan Le Fay, and Skull the Slayer app. ... 4.00

WEIRDWORLD (After Secret Wars)
Marvel Comics: Feb, 2016 - No. 6, Jul, 2016 ($3.99)

1-6-Humphries-s/Del Mundo-a; Goleta the Wizardslayer & Morgan Le Fay app. ... 4.00

WEIRD WORLD OF JACK STAFF (See Jack Staff)
Image Comics: Feb, 2010 - No. 6, Apr, 2011 ($3.50)

1-6-Paul Grist-s/a. 2-Ian Churchill-c ... 3.50

WEIRD WORLDS (See Adventures Into...)

WEIRD WORLDS (Magazine)
Eerie Publications: V1#10(12/70), V2#1(2/71) - No. 4, Aug, 1971 (52 pgs.)

V1#10-Sci-fi/horror	6	12	18	42	79	115
V2#1-4	5	10	15	35	63	90

WEIRD WORLDS (Also see Ironwolf: Fires of the Revolution)
National Periodical Publications: Aug-Sept, 1972 - No. 9, Jan-Feb, 1974; No. 10, Oct-Nov, 1974 (All 20c issues)

1-Edgar Rice Burrough's John Carter Warlord of Mars & David Innes begin						
(1st DC app.); Kubert-c	4	8	12	23	37	50
2-4: 2-Infantino/Orlando-a. 3-Murphy Anderson-c. 4-Kaluta-a						
	2	4	6	10	14	18
5-7: 5-Kaluta-c. 7-Last John Carter.	2	4	6	8	11	14
8-10: 8-Iron Wolf begins by Chaykin (1st app.)	2	4	6	8	11	14

NOTE: **Neal Adams** a-2i, 3i. John Carter by **Anderson**in r-1-3. **Chaykin** c-7, 8. **Kaluta** a-4; c-4-6, 10. **Orlando** a-4i; c-2, 3, 4i. **Wrightson** a-2i, 4i.

WEIRD WORLDS
DC Comics: Mar, 2011 - No. 6, Aug, 2011 ($3.99, limited series)

1-6-Short stories of Lobo, Garbage Man and Tanga; Ordway-a; Maguire-s/a; Lopresti-a/p/s/a 4.00

WELCOME BACK, KOTTER (TV) (See Limited Collectors' Edition #57 for unpublished #11)
National Periodical Publ./DC Comics: Nov, 1976 - No. 10, Mar-Apr, 1978

1-Sparling-a(p)	3	6	9	20	31	42
2-10: 3-Estrada-a	2	4	6	11	16	20

WELCOME SANTA (See March of Comics #63,183)

WELCOME TO RIVERDALE
Archie Comic Publications: Dec, 2023 ($3.99, one-shot)

1-Archie horror; Ginger Snapp app.; Amy Chase-s/Liana Kangas-a ... 4.00

WELCOME TO THE LITTLE SHOP OF HORRORS
Roger Corman's Cosmic Comics: May, 1995 - No. 3, July, 1995 ($2.50, limited series)

1-3	1	3	4	6	8	10

WELCOME TO TRANQUILITY
DC Comics (WildStorm): Feb, 2007 - No. 12, Jan, 2008 ($2.99)

1-12: 1-Simone-s/Googe-a; two covers by Googe and Campbell. 8-Pearson-a 3.00
...: Armageddon 1 (1/08, $2.99) Gage-s/Googe-a 3.00
...: One Foot in the Grave 1-6 (7/10 - No. 6, 2/11, $3.99) Simone-s/Domingues-a 4.00
...: One Foot in the Grave TPB (2011, $17.99) r/mini-series #1-6 18.00
... Book One TPB (2008, $19.99) r/#1-6 and variant cover gallery 20.00
... Book Two TPB (2008, $19.99) r/#7-12; sketch pages 20.00

WE LIVE
AfterShock Comics: Oct, 2020 - No. 5, Feb, 2021 ($4.99, limited series)

1-5-Inaki Miranda-s/a; Roy Miranda-s 5.00

WE LIVE VOL. 2 (Age of the Palladions on cover)
AfterShock Comics: Mar, 2022 - No. 5, Aug, 2022 ($4.99/$3.99, limited series)

1 Black -($4.99) Inaki Miranda-s/a; Roy Miranda-s 5.00
1 White -($4.99) Inaki Miranda-s/a; Roy Miranda-s 5.00
2-5-($3.99) Inaki Miranda-s/a; Roy Miranda-s 5.00

WELLS FARGO (See Tales of...)

WELLINGTON
IDW Publishing: Dec, 2019 - Present ($3.99)

1-3-Aaron Mahnke & Delilah S. Dawson-s/Piotr Kowalski-a; 2 covers on each 4.00

WENDY AND THE NEW KIDS ON THE BLOCK
Harvey Comics: Mar, 1991 - No. 3, July, 1991 ($1.25)

1-3 ... 5.00

WENDY DIGEST
Harvey Comics: Oct, 1990 - No. 5, Mar, 1992 ($1.75, digest size)

1-5 ... 4.00

WENDY PARKER COMICS
Atlas Comics (OMC): July, 1953 - No. 8, July, 1954

1	42	84	126	265	445	625
2	33	66	99	194	317	440
3-8	25	50	75	150	245	340

WENDY, THE GOOD LITTLE WITCH (TV)
Harvey Publ.: 8/60 - #82, 11/73; #83, 8/74 - #93, 4/76; #94, 9/90 - #97, 12/90

1-Wendy & Casper the Friendly Ghost begin	48	96	144	374	862	1350
2	12	24	36	84	185	285
3-5	10	20	30	64	132	200
6-10	7	14	21	48	89	130
11-20	5	10	15	34	60	85
21-30	4	8	12	27	44	60
31-50	3	6	9	17	26	35
51-64,66-69	2	4	6	13	18	22
65 (2/71)-Wendy origin.	3	6	9	16	24	32
70-74: All 52 pg. Giants	3	6	9	16	23	30
75-93	2	4	6	9	13	16
94-97 (1990, $1.00-c): 94-Has #194 on-c						5.00

(See Casper the Friendly Ghost #20 & Harvey Hits #7, 16, 21, 23, 27, 30, 33)

WENDY THE GOOD LITTLE WITCH (2nd Series)
Harvey Comics: Apr, 1991 - No. 15, Aug, 1994 ($1.00/$1.25 #7-11/$1.50 #12-15)

1-15-Reprints Wendy & Casper stories. 12-Bunny app. ... 4.00

WENDY WITCH WORLD
Harvey Publications: 10/61; No. 2, 9/62 - No. 52, 12/73; No. 53, 9/74

1-(25c, 68 pg. Giants begin)	13	26	39	89	195	300
2-5	7	14	21	44	82	120
6-10	5	10	15	33	57	80
11-20	4	8	12	27	44	60
21-30	3	6	9	21	33	45
31-39: 39-Last 68 pg. issue	3	6	9	16	24	32
40-45: 52 pg. issues	2	4	6	13	18	22
46-53	2	4	6	9	13	16

WE ONLY FIND THEM WHEN THEY'RE DEAD
BOOM! Studios: Sept, 2020 - No. 15, Dec, 2022 ($3.99)

1-15-Al Ewing-s/Simone Di Meo-a ... 4.00

WEREWOLF (Super Hero) (Also see Dracula & Frankenstein)
Dell Publishing Co.: Dec, 1966 - No. 3, April, 1967

1-1st app.	4	8	12	27	44	60
2,3	3	6	9	17	26	35

WEREWOLF BY NIGHT (See Giant-Size..., Marvel Spotlight #2-4 & Power Record Comics)
Marvel Comics Group: Sept, 1972 - No. 43, Mar, 1977

1-Ploog-a cont'd from Marvel Spotlight #4	29	58	87	209	467	725
2	8	16	24	56	108	160
3-5	5	10	15	35	63	90
6-10	5	10	15	30	50	70
11-14,16-20	4	8	12	23	37	50
15-New origin Werewolf; Dracula-c/story cont'd from Tomb of Dracula #18; classic Ploog-c	8	16	24	51	96	140
21-31	3	6	9	16	24	32
32-Origin & 1st app. Moon Knight (8/75)	370	740	1110	2220	3610	5000
33-2nd app. Moon Knight	21	42	63	147	324	500
34,36	5	10	15	35	63	90
38-43	3	6	9	14	20	26
35-Starlin/Wrightson-c	4	8	12	22	35	48
37-Moon Knight app. Wrightson-a	10	20	30	67	141	215
38,39-(30c-c variants, limited distribution)(5,7/76)	6	12	18	41	76	110
... No. 32 Facsimile Edition (9/21, $3.99) Reprints #32 with original ads & letter column	2	4	6	9	12	15
... No. 33 Facsimile Edition (10/23, $3.99) Reprints #33 with original ads & letter column						4.00

NOTE: **Bolle** a-6i. **G. Kane** a-11p, 12p; c-21, 22, 24-30, 34p. **Mooney** a-7i. **Ploog** 1-4p, 5, 6p, 7p, 13-16p; c-5-8, 13-16. **Reinman** a-8i. **Sutton** a(i)-9, 11, 16, 35.

WEREWOLF BY NIGHT (Vol. 2, continues in Strange Tales 1 (9/98))
Marvel Comics Group: Feb, 1998 - No. 6, July, 1998 ($2.99)

1-6-Manco-a; 2-Two covers. 6-Ghost Rider-c/app. ... 4.00

WEREWOLF BY NIGHT
Marvel Comics: Dec, 2020 - No. 4, Mar, 2021 ($3.99)

1-4: 1-Intro. Jake Gomez; Scot Eaton-a ... 4.00

WEREWOLF BY NIGHT
Marvel Comics: Nov, 2023 ($5.99, one-shot)

1-Elsa Bloodstone app.; Derek Landy-s/Fran Galán-a ... 6.00

WEREWOLVES & VAMPIRES (Magazine)
Charlton Comics: 1962 (One Shot)

1	9	18	27	63	129	195

WEREWOLVES ON THE MOON: VERSUS VAMPIRES
Dark Horse Comics: June, 2009 - No. 3 ($3.50, limited series)

1,2-Dave Land-s & Fillbach Brothers-s/a ... 3.50

WESLEY DODDS: THE SANDMAN
DC Comics: Dec, 2023 - No. 6, May, 2024 ($3.99, limited series)

1-6-Venditti-s/Rossmo-a; set in 1940 ... 4.00

WE STAND ON GUARD
Image Comics: Jul, 2015 - No. 6, Dec. 2015 ($2.99, limited series)

1-U.S. invasion of Canada; Vaughan-s/Skroce-a 5.00
2-6 3.00

WEST COAST AVENGERS
Marvel Comics Group: Sept, 1984 - No. 4, Dec, 1984 (lim. series, Mando paper)

1-Origin & 1st app. W.C. Avengers (Hawkeye, Iron Man, Mockingbird & Tigra)						
	3	6	9	19	30	40
2-4						6.00

WEST COAST AVENGERS (Becomes Avengers West Coast #48 on)
Marvel Comics Group: Oct, 1985 - No. 47, Aug, 1989

V2#1	3	6	9	16	24	32
2-41						5.00
42-44,46,47: 42-Byrne-a(p)/scripts begin. 46-Byrne-c; 1st app. Great Lakes Avengers						5.00
45-(6/89) 1st app. Vision in all-white exterior; cover swipe of Avengers #57	5	10	15	31	53	75
Annual 1 (1986)	1	3	4	6	8	10
Annual 2,3 (1987,1988): 3-Evolutionary War app.						6.00
Annual 4 (1989, $2.00)-Atlantis Attacks; Byrne/Austin-a						6.00

WEST COAST AVENGERS
Marvel Comics: Oct, 2018 - No. 10, Jun, 2019 ($4.99/$3.99)

1-($4.99) Hawkeye, Kate Bishop, Gwenpool, America, Kid Omega, Fuse team 5.00
2-10-($3.99) 2-4-Tigra app. 4-M.O.D.O.K. app. 6-Marvel Boy returns 4.00

WESTERN ACTION
I. W. Enterprises: No. 7, 1964

7-Reprints Cow Puncher #? by Avon	2	4	6	11	16	20

Weird Worlds (2011 series) #4 © DC

Wesley Dodds: The Sandman #1 © DC

Western Gunfighters #14 © MAR

	GD 2.0	VG 4.0	FN 6.0	VF 8.0	VF/NM 9.0	NM- 9.2

WESTERN ACTION
Atlas/Seaboard Publ.: Feb, 1975
1-Kid Cody by Wildey & The Comanche Kid stories; intro. The Renegade

| | 3 | 6 | 9 | 14 | 20 | 25 |

WESTERN ACTION THRILLERS
Dell Publishers: Apr, 1937 (10¢, square binding; 100 pgs.)
1-Buffalo Bill, The Texas Kid, Laramie Joe, Two-Gun Thompson, & Wild West Bill app.

| | 142 | 284 | 426 | 909 | 1555 | 2200 |

WESTERN ADVENTURES COMICS (Western Love Trails #7 on)
Ace Magazines: Oct, 1948 - No. 6, Aug, 1949

	GD	VG	FN	VF	VF/NM	NM-
nn(#1)-Sheriff Sal, The Cross-Draw Kid, Sam Bass begin	24	48	72	142	234	325
nn(#2)(12/48)	14	28	42	82	121	160
nn(#3)(2/49)-Used in SOTI, pgs. 30,31	16	32	48	94	147	200
4-6	13	26	39	74	105	135

WESTERN BANDITS
Avon Periodicals: 1952 (Painted-c)
1-Butch Cassidy, The Daltons by Larsen; Kinstler-a; c-part-r/paperback Avon Western Novel #1

| | 25 | 50 | 75 | 150 | 245 | 340 |

WESTERN BANDIT TRAILS (See Approved Comics)
St. John Publishing Co.: Jan, 1949 - No. 3, July, 1949

	GD	VG	FN	VF	VF/NM	NM-
1-Tuska-a; Baker-c; Blue Monk, Ventrilo app.	53	106	159	334	567	800
2-Baker-c	40	80	120	246	411	575
3-Baker-c/a; Tuska-a	45	90	135	284	480	675

WESTERN COMICS (See Super DC Giant #15)
National Per. Publ: Jan-Feb, 1948 - No. 85, Jan-Feb, 1961 (1-27: 52pgs.)

	GD	VG	FN	VF	VF/NM	NM-
1-Wyoming Kid & his horse Racer, The Vigilante in "Jesse James Rides Again" (Meskin-a), Cowboy Marshal, Rodeo Rick begin	100	200	300	635	1093	1550
2	37	74	111	222	361	500
3,4-Last Vigilante	33	66	99	194	317	440
5-Nighthawk & his horse Nightwind begin (not in #6); Captain Tootsie by Beck	32	64	96	188	307	425
6,7,9,10	21	42	63	126	206	285
8-Origin Wyoming Kid; 2 pg. pin-ups of rodeo queens	34	68	102	204	332	460
11-20	18	36	54	107	169	230
21-40: 24-Starr-a. 27-Last 52 pgs. 28-Flag-c	15	30	45	84	127	170
41,42,44-49: 49-Last precode issue (2/55)	14	28	42	82	121	160
43-Pow Wow Smith begins, ends #85	15	30	45	83	124	165
50-60	13	26	39	72	101	130
61-85-Last Wyoming Kid. 77-Origin Matt Savage Trail Boss. 82-1st app. Fleetfoot, Pow Wow's girlfriend	10	20	30	58	79	100

NOTE: G. Kane, Infantino art in most. Meskin a-1-4. Moreira a-28-39. Post a-3-5.

WESTERN CRIME BUSTERS
Trojan Magazines: Sept, 1950 - No. 10, Mar-Apr, 1952

	GD	VG	FN	VF	VF/NM	NM-
1-Six-Gun Smith, Wilma West, K-Bar-Kate, & Fighting Bob Dale begin; headlight-a	41	82	123	256	428	600
2	22	44	66	132	216	300
3-5: 3-Myron Fass-c	20	40	60	114	182	250
6-Fighting Bob Dale by Wood-a	34	68	102	204	332	460
7-Six-Gun Smith by Wood	34	68	102	204	332	460
8	18	36	54	109	172	235
9-Tex Gordon & Wilma West by Wood; Lariat Lucy app.	34	68	102	204	332	460
10-Wood-a	32	64	96	188	307	425

WESTERN CRIME CASES (Formerly Indian Warriors #7,8; becomes The Outlaws #10 on)
Star Publications: No. 9, Dec, 1951
9-White Rider & Super Horse; L. B. Cole-c

| | 29 | 58 | 87 | 172 | 281 | 390 |

WESTERNER, THE (Wild Bill Pecos)
"Wanted" Comic Group/Toytown/Patches: No. 14, June, 1948 - No. 41, Dec, 1951 (#14-31: 52 pgs.)

	GD	VG	FN	VF	VF/NM	NM-
14	20	40	60	114	182	250
15-17,19-21: 19-Meskin-a	12	24	36	67	94	120
18,22-25-Krigstein-a	13	26	39	74	105	135
26(4/50)-Origin & 1st app. Calamity Kate, series ends #32; Krigstein-a	15	30	45	90	140	190
27-Krigstein-a(2)	15	30	45	88	137	185
28-41: 33-Quest app. 37-Lobo, the Wolf Boy begins	9	18	27	47	61	75

NOTE: Mort Lawrence a-20-27, 29, 37, 39; c-19, 22-24, 26, 27. Leav c-14-18, 20, 31. Syd Shores a-39; c-34, 35, 37-41.

WESTERNER, THE
Super Comics: 1964

Super Reprint 15-17: 15-r/Oklahoma Kid #? 16-r/Crack West. #65; Severin-c; Crandall-r. 17-r/Blazing Western #2; Severin-c

| | 2 | 4 | 6 | 11 | 16 | 20 |

WESTERN FIGHTERS
Hillman Periodicals/Star Publ.: Apr-May, 1948 - V4#7, Mar-Apr, 1953 (#1-V3#2: 52 pgs.)

	GD	VG	FN	VF	VF/NM	NM-
V1#1-Simon & Kirby-c	41	82	123	256	428	600
2-Not Kirby-a	16	32	48	94	147	200
3-Fuje-c	15	30	45	83	124	165
4-Krigstein, Ingels, Fuje-a	15	30	45	86	133	180
5,6,8,9,12	11	22	33	62	86	110
7,10-Krigstein-a	14	28	42	76	108	140
11-Williamson/Frazetta-a	37	74	111	222	361	500
V2#1-Krigstein-a	14	28	42	78	112	145
2-12: 4-Berg-a	9	18	27	50	65	80
V3#1-11,V4#1,4-7	9	18	27	47	61	75
12,V4#2,3-Krigstein-a	14	28	42	78	112	145
3-D (1/53, 25¢, Star Publ.)-Came w/glasses; L. B. Cole-c	39	78	117	231	378	525

NOTE: Kinstler-rish a-V2#6, 8, 9, 12; V3#2, 5-7, 11, 12; V4#1(plus cover). McWilliams a-11. Powell a-V2#2. Reinman a-1-12, V4#3. Rowich c-5, 6i. Starr a-5.

WESTERN FRONTIER
P. L. Publishers: Apr-May, 1951 - No. 7, 1952

	GD	VG	FN	VF	VF/NM	NM-
1	19	38	57	111	176	240
2	11	22	33	62	86	110
3-7	10	20	30	54	72	90

WESTERN GUNFIGHTERS (1st Series) (Apache Kid #11-19)
Atlas Comics (CPS): No. 20, June, 1956 - No. 27, Aug, 1957

	GD	VG	FN	VF	VF/NM	NM-
20	19	38	57	111	176	240
21-Crandall-a	19	38	57	111	176	240
22-Wood & Powell-a	26	52	78	154	252	350
23,24: 23-Williamson-a. 24-Toth-a	18	36	54	105	165	225
25-27	14	28	42	76	127	170

NOTE: Berg a-20. Colan a-20, 26, 27. Crandall a-21. Heath a-25. Maneely a-24, 25; c-22, 23, 25. Morisi a-25. Morrow a-26. Pakula a-23. Severin a-20, 27. Torres a-26. Woodbridge a-27.

WESTERN GUNFIGHTERS (2nd Series)
Marvel Comics Group: Aug, 1970 - No. 33, Nov, 1975 (#1-6: 25¢, 68 pgs.)

	GD	VG	FN	VF	VF/NM	NM-
1-Ghost Rider begins; Fort Rango, Renegades & Gunhawk app.	7	14	21	46	86	125
2,3,5,6: 2-Origin Nightwind (Apache Kid's horse)	3	6	9	21	33	45
4-Barry Smith-a	4	8	12	23	37	50
7-(52 pgs) Origin Ghost Rider retold	4	8	12	25	40	55
8-13: 10-Origin Black Rider. 12-Origin Matt Slade	3	6	9	14	20	25
14-Steranko-a	3	6	9	18	27	36
15-20	4	6	10	14	19	24
21-33			5	10	13	16

NOTE: Baker r-2, 3. Colan r-2. Drucker r-3. Everett a-6i. G. Kane c-29, 31. Kirby a-1p(r), 5, 10-12; c-19, 21. Kubert r-2. Maneely r-2, 10. Morrow r-29. Severin c-10. Shores a-3, 4. Barry Smith a-4. Steranko c-14. Sutton a-1, 2i, 5, 4. Torres r-26('57). Wildey r-8, 9. Williamson r-2, 18. Woodbridge r-27('57). Renegades in #4, 5; Ghost Rider in #1-7.

WESTERN HEARTS
Standard Comics: Dec, 1949 - No. 10, Mar, 1952 (All photo-c)

	GD	VG	FN	VF	VF/NM	NM-
1-Severin-a; Whip Wilson & Reno Browne photo-c	28	56	84	165	270	375
2-Beverly Tyler & Jerome Courtland photo-c from movie "Palomino"; Williamson/Frazetta-a (2 pgs)	26	52	78	154	252	350
3-Rex Allen photo-c	18	36	54	88	137	185
4-7,10: 4-Severin & Elder, Al Carreno-a. 5-Ray Milland & Hedy Lamarr photo-c from movie "Copper Canyon". 6-Fred MacMurray & Irene Dunn photo-c from movie "Never a Dull Moment". 7-Jock Mahoney photo-c. 10-Bill Williams & Jane Nigh photo-c	14	28	42	81	118	155
8-Randolph Scott & Janis Carter photo-c from "Santa Fe"; Severin & Elder-a	14	28	42	82	121	160
9-Whip Wilson & Reno Browne photo-c; Severin & Elder-a	15	30	45	85	130	175

WESTERN HERO (Wow Comics #1-69; Real Western Hero #70-75)
Fawcett Publications: No. 76, Mar, 1949 - No. 112, Mar, 1952

	GD	VG	FN	VF	VF/NM	NM-
76(#1, 52 pgs)-Tom Mix, Hopalong Cassidy, Monte Hale, Gabby Hayes, Young Falcon (ends #78,80), & Big Bow and Little Arrow (ends #102,105) begin; painted-c begin	16	32	48	94	147	200
77 (52 pgs)	11	22	33	64	90	115
78,80-82 (52 pgs.): 81-Capt. Tootsie by Beck	11	22	33	60	83	105
79,83 (36 pgs.): 83-Last painted-c	10	20	30	54	72	90
84-86,88-90 (52 pgs.): 84-Photo-c begin, end #112. 86-Last Hopalong Cassidy	10	20	30	53	76	95
87,91,95,99 (36 pgs.): 87-Bill Boyd begins, ends #95	9	18	27	50	65	80

	GD 2.0	VG 4.0	FN 6.0	VF 8.0	VF/NM 9.0	NM- 9.2

92-94,96-98,101 (52 pgs.): 96-Tex Ritter begins. 101-Red Eagle app.

	GD 2.0	VG 4.0	FN 6.0	VF 8.0	VF/NM 9.0	NM- 9.2
100 (52 pgs.)	9	18	27	52	69	85
102-111: 102-Begin 36 pg. issues	10	20	30	56	76	95
112-Last issue	9	18	27	50	65	80

NOTE: 1/2 to 1 pg. Rocky Lane (Carnation) in 80-83, 86, 88, 97. Photo covers feature Hopalong Cassidy #84, 86, 89; Tom Mix #85, 87, 90, 92, 94, 97; Monte Hale #88, 91, 93, 95, 98, 100, 104, 107, 110; Tex Ritter #96, 99, 101, 105, 108, 111; Gabby Hayes #103.

WESTERN KID (1st Series)
Atlas Comics (CPC): Dec, 1954 - No. 17, Aug, 1957

1-Origin; The Western Kid (Tex Dawson), his stallion Whirlwind & dog Lightning begin	28	56	84	168	274	380
2 (2/55)-Last pre-code	16	32	48	94	147	200
3-8	14	48	42	80	115	150
9,10-Williamson-a in both (4 pgs. each)	14	28	42	81	118	155
11-17	13	26	39	74	105	130

NOTE: Ayers a-6, 7. Heck a-3. Maneely c-2-7, 10, 13-15. Romita a-1-17; c-1, 12. Severin c-11, 16, 17.

WESTERN KID, THE (2nd Series)
Marvel Comics Group: Dec, 1971 - No. 5, Aug, 1972 (All 20¢ issues)

1-Reprints; Romita-c/a(3)	3	6	9	21	33	45
2,4,5: 2-Romita-a; Severin-c. 4-Everett-r	3	6	9	14	20	25
3-Williamson-a	3	6	9	15	22	28

WESTERN KILLERS
Fox Feature Syndicate: nn, July?, 1948; No. 60, Sept, 1948 - No. 64, May, 1949; No. 6, July, 1949

nn(#59?)(nd, F&J Trading Co.)-Range Busters; formerly Blue Beetle #57?	32	64	96	188	307	425
60 (#1, 9/48)-Extreme violence; lingerie panel	36	72	108	211	343	475
61-Jack Cole, Starr-a	27	54	81	158	259	360
62-64, 6 (#6-exist?)	24	48	72	144	237	330

WESTERN LIFE ROMANCES (My Friend Irma #3 on?)
Marvel Comics (IPP): Dec, 1949 - No. 2, Mar, 1950 (52 pgs.)

1-Whip Wilson & Reno Browne photo-c	25	50	75	150	245	340
2-Audie Murphy & Gale Storm photo-c	21	42	63	122	199	275

WESTERN LOVE
Prize Publ.: July-Aug, 1949 - No. 5, Mar-Apr, 1950 (All photo-c & 52 pgs.)

1-S&K-a; Randolph Scott photo-c from movie "Canadian Pacific" (see Prize Comics #76)	36	72	108	211	343	475
2,5-S&K-a: 2-Whip Wilson & Reno Browne photo-c. 5-Dale Robertson photo-c	28	56	84	168	274	380
3,4: 3-Pat Williams photo-c	18	36	54	107	169	230

NOTE: Meskin a-3. Severin/Elder a-2-5.

WESTERN LOVE TRAILS (Formerly Western Adventures)
Ace Magazines (A. A. Wyn): No. 7, Nov, 1949 - No. 9, Mar, 1950

7	14	28	42	81	118	155
8,9	10	20	30	58	79	100

WESTERN MARSHAL (See Steve Donovan...)
Dell Publishing Co.: No. 534, 2-4/54 - No. 640, 7/55 (Based on Ernest Haycox's "Trailtown")

Four Color 534 (#1)-Kinstler-a	7	14	21	44	82	120
Four Color 591 (10/54), 640-All Kinstler-a	5	10	15	35	63	90

WESTERN OUTLAWS (Junior Comics #9-16; My Secret Life #22 on)
Fox Feature Syndicate: No. 17, Sept, 1948 - No. 21, May, 1949

17-Kamen-a; Iger shop-a in all; 1 pg. "Death and the Devil Pills" r-in Ghostly Weird #122	39	78	117	240	395	550
18-21	22	44	66	132	216	300

WESTERN OUTLAWS
Atlas Comics (ACI No. 1-14/WPI No. 15-21): Feb, 1954 - No. 21, Aug, 1957

1-Heath, Powell-a; Maneely hanging-c	32	64	96	188	307	425
2	16	32	48	92	144	195
3-10: 7-Violent-a by R.Q. Sale	14	28	42	78	112	145
11,14-Williamson-a in both (6 pgs. each)	14	28	42	82	121	160
12,18,20,21: Severin covers	13	26	39	74	105	135
13,15: 13-Baker-a. 15-Torres-a	14	28	42	78	112	145
16-Williamson text illo	13	26	39	74	105	135
17,19-Crandall-a. 17-Williamson text illo	14	28	42	80	115	150

NOTE: Ayers a-7, 10, 18, 20. Bolle a-21. Colan a-5, 10, 11, 17. Drucker a-11. Everett a-9, 10. Heath c-1; c-3, 4, 8, 16. Kubert a-9p. Maneely a-13, 16, 17, 19; c-1, 5, 7, 9, 10, 12, 13. Morisi a-18. Powell a-3, 16. Romita a-7, 13. Severin a-8, 16, 19; c-17, 18, 20, 21. Tuska a-6, 15.

WESTERN OUTLAWS & SHERIFFS (Formerly Best Western)
Marvel/Atlas Comics (IPC): No. 60, Dec, 1949 - No. 73, June, 1952

60 (52 pgs.) Photo-c; first Maneely Atlas work	30	60	90	177	289	400
61-65: 61-Photo-c	22	44	66	128	209	290
66-Story contains 5 hangings	22	44	66	132	216	300
67-Cannibalism story	22	44	66	132	216	300
68-72	17	34	51	98	154	210
73-Black Rider story; Everett-c	20	40	60	114	182	250

NOTE: Maneely a-60-62, 67; c-62, 69-73. Robinson a-68. Sinnott a-73. Tuska a-69-71.

WESTERN PICTURE STORIES (1st Western comic)
Comics Magazine Company: Feb, 1937 - No. 4, June, 1937

1-Will Eisner-a	290	580	870	1836	3178	4500
2-Will Eisner-a	174	348	522	1114	1907	2700
3,4: 3-Eisner-a. 4-Caveman Cowboy story	142	284	426	909	1555	2200

WESTERN PICTURE STORIES (See Giant Comics Edition #6, 11)

WESTERN ROMANCES (See Target...)

WESTERN ROUGH RIDERS
Gillmor Magazines No. 1,4 (Stanmor Publ.): Nov, 1954 - No. 4, May, 1955

1	12	24	36	69	97	125
2-4	8	16	24	44	57	70

WESTERN ROUNDUP (See Dell Giants & Fox Giants)

WESTERN SERENADE
DC Comics: May/June, 1949

---

nn - Ashcan comic, not distributed to newsstands, only for in-house use (no known sales)

WESTERN TALES (Formerly Witches...)
Harvey Publications: No. 31, Oct, 1955 - No. 33, July-Sept, 1956

31,32-All S&K-a; Davy Crockett app. in each	18	36	54	107	169	230
33-S&K-a; Jim Bowie app.	18	36	54	103	162	220

NOTE: #32 & 33 contain Boy's Ranch reprints. Kirby c-31.

WESTERN TALES OF BLACK RIDER (Formerly Black Rider; Gunsmoke Western #32 on)
Atlas Comics (CPS): No. 28, May, 1955 - No. 31, Nov, 1955

28 (#1): The Spider (a villain) dies	28	56	84	168	274	380
29-31	20	40	60	114	182	250

NOTE: Lawrence a-30. Maneely c-28-30. Severin a-28. Shores c-31.

WESTERN TEAM-UP
Marvel Comics Group: Nov, 1973 (20¢)

1-Origin & 1st app. The Dakota Kid; Rawhide Kid-r; Gunsmoke Kid-r by Jack Davis	5	10	15	23	57	80

WESTERN THRILLERS (My Past Confessions #7 on)
Fox Feature Syndicate/M.S. Distr. No. 52: Aug, 1948 - No. 6, June, 1949; No. 52, 1954?

1- "Velvet Rose" (Kamen-a); "Two-Gun Sal", "Striker Sisters" (all women outlaws issue); Brodsky-c	65	130	195	416	708	1000
2	33	66	99	194	317	440
3-6: 4,5-Bakerish-a; 5-Butch Cassidy app.	22	44	66	132	216	300
52-(Reprint, M.S. Distr.)-1954? No date given (becomes My Love Secret #53)	15	30	45	86	133	180

WESTERN THRILLERS (Cowboy Action #5 on)
Atlas Comics (ACI): Nov, 1954 - No. 4, Feb, 1955 (All-r/Western Outlaws & Sheriffs)

1	26	52	78	154	252	350
2-4	15	30	45	90	140	190

NOTE: Heath c-3. Maneely a-1; c-2. Powell a-4. Robinson a-4. Romita c-4. Tuska a-2.

WESTERN TRAILS (Ringo Kid Starring in...)
Atlas Comics (SAI): May, 1957 - No. 2, July, 1957

1-Ringo Kid app.; Severin-c	18	36	54	107	169	230
2-Severin-c	13	26	39	74	105	135

NOTE: Bolle a-1, 2. Maneely a-1, 2. Severin c-1, 2.

WESTERN TRUE CRIME (Becomes My Confessions)
Fox Feature Syndicate: No. 15, Aug, 1948 - No. 6, June, 1949

15(#1)-Kamen-a; formerly Zoot #14 (5/48)?	39	78	117	240	395	550
16(#2)-Kamen-a; headlight panels, violence	29	58	87	172	281	390
3-Kamen-a	31	62	93	182	296	410
4-6: 4-Johnny Craig-a	19	38	57	111	176	240

WESTERN WINNERS (Formerly All-Western Winners; becomes Black Rider #8 on & Romance Tales #7 on)
Marvel Comics (CDS): No. 5, June, 1949 - No. 7, Dec, 1949

5-Two-Gun Kid, Kid Colt, Black Rider; Shores-c	39	78	117	240	395	550
6-Two-Gun Kid, Black Rider, Heath Kid Colt story; Captain Tootsie by C.C. Beck	32	64	96	190	310	430
7-Randolph Scott Photo-c w/true stories about the West	32	64	96	190	310	430

WEST OF THE PECOS (See Zane Grey, 4-Color #222)

WESTWARD HO, THE WAGONS (Disney)(Also see Classic Comics #14)
Dell Publishing Co.: No. 738, Sept, 1956 (Movie)

Four Color 738-Fess Parker photo-c	8	16	24	54	102	150

WET HOT AMERICAN SUMMER (Based on the 2001 movie and Netflix series)
BOOM! Studios: Nov, 2018 ($19.99, squarebound graphic novel)

nn-Christopher Hastings-s/Noah Hayes-a; takes place after the 1st week of camp						20.00

WE3
DC Comics (Vertigo): Oct, 2004 - No. 3, May, 2005 ($2.95, limited series)

1-3-Domestic animal cyborgs: Grant Morrison-s/Frank Quitely-a						3.00
TPB (2005, $12.99) r/series						13.00

WETWORKS (See WildC.A.T.S: Covert Action Teams #2)
Image Comics (WildStorm): June, 1994 - No. 43, Aug, 1998 ($1.95/$2.50)

1- "July" on-c; gatefold wraparound-c; Portacio/Williams-c/a						5.00
1-Chicago Comicon edition						6.00
1-($4.95) "3-D Edition" w/glasses						5.00
2-4						4.00
2-Alternate Portacio-c, see Deathblow #5						6.00
5-7,9-24: 5-($2.50). 13-Portacio-c. 16,17-Fire From Heaven Pts. 4 & 11						4.00
8 ($1.95)-Newstand, Wildstorm Rising Pt. 7						4.00
8 ($2.50)-Direct Market, Wildstorm Rising Pt. 7						4.00
25-($3.95)						5.00
26-43: 32-Variant-c by Pat Lee & Charest. 39,40-Stormwatch app. 42-Gen 13 app.						4.00
Sourcebook 1 (10/94, $2.50)-Text & illustrations (no comics)						4.00
Voyager Pack (8/97, $3.50)- #32 w/Phantom Guard preview						5.00

WETWORKS
DC Comics (WildStorm): Nov, 2006 - No. 15, Jan, 2008 ($2.99)

1-15: 1-Carey-s/Portacio-a; two covers by Portacio and Van Sciver. 2-Golden var-c. 3-Pearson var-c. 4-Powell var-c						3.00
...-Armageddon 1 (1/08, $2.99) Gage-s/Badeaux-a						3.00
... Book One (2007, $14.99) r/#1-5 and stories from Eye of the storm Annual and Coup D'Etat Afterword						15.00
... Book Two (2008, $14.99) r/#6-9,13-15						15.00
...: Mutations 1 (11/10, $3.99) Grevious & Long-s/Gopez-a						4.00

WETWORKS/VAMPIRELLA (See Vampirella/Wetworks)
Image Comics (WildStorm Productions): July, 1997 ($2.95, one-shot)

1-Gil Kane-c						4.00

WHACK (Satire)
St. John Publishing Co. (Jubilee Publ.): Oct, 1953 - No. 3, May, 1954

1-(3-D, 25¢)-Kubert-a; Maurer-c; came w/glasses	34	68	102	199	325	450
2,3-Kubert-a in each, 2-Bing Crosby on-c; Mighty Mouse & Steve Canyon parodies						

Western Outlaws #16 © MAR

Wetworks #25 © WSP

What If...? (2nd) #20 © MAR

	GD 2.0	VG 4.0	FN 6.0	VF 8.0	VF/NM 9.0	NM- 9.2
3-Li'l Orphan Annie parody; Maurer-c	21	42	63	122	199	275

WHACKY (See Wacky)

WHA...HUH?
Marvel Comics: 2005 ($3.99, one-shot)

1-Humor spoofs of Marvel characters; Mahfood-a/c; Bendis, Stan Lee and others-s						4.00

WHALESVILLE X ROCKS AND MINERALS
Bad Idea: May, 2021 ($9.99, one-shot)

1-(First Printing) Kindt-s/Pollina-a; Millionaire-a	1	3	4	6	8	10
1-(Not First Printing, 8/21)	1	3	4	6	8	10

WHAM COMICS (See Super Spy)
Centaur Publications: Nov, 1940 - No. 2, Dec, 1940

1-The Sparkler, The Phantom Rider, Craig Carter and his Magic Ring, Detecto, Copper Slug, Speed Silvers by Gustavson, Speed Centaur & Jon Linton (s/f) begin	239	478	717	1530	2615	3700
2-Origin Blue Fire & Solarman; The Buzzard app.	194	388	582	1242	2121	3000

WHAM-O GIANT COMICS
Wham-O Mfg. Co. : April, 1967 (98¢, newspaper size, one-shot)(Six issue subscription was advertised)

1-Radian & Goody Bumpkin by Wood; 1 pg. Stanley-a; Fine, Tufts-a; flying saucer reports; wraparound-c	10	20	30	66	138	210

WHATEVER HAPPENED TO BARON VON SHOCK?
Image Comics: May, 2010 - No. 4, Nov, 2010 ($3.99, unfinished limited series)

1-4-Rob Zombie-s/Donny Hadiwidjaja-a						4.00

WHAT IF? (1st Series) Featuring... #13 & #?-33) (Also see Hero Initiative)
Marvel Comics Group: Feb, 1977 - No. 47, Oct, 1984; June, 1988 (All 52 pgs.)

	GD 2.0	VG 4.0	FN 6.0	VF 8.0	VF/NM 9.0	NM- 9.2
1-Brief origin Spider-Man, Fantastic Four	6	12	18	38	69	100
2-Origin The Hulk retold	3	6	9	21	33	45
3,4: 3-Avengers. 4-Invaders	3	6	9	21	33	45
5-Capt. America	2	4	6	11	16	20
6-9,13,17: 7-Betty Brant as Spider-Girl. 8-Daredevil; Spidey parody. 9-Origins Venus, Marvel Boy, Human Robot, 3-D Man. 13-Conan app.; John Buscema-c/a(p). 17-Ghost Rider & Son of Satan app.	2	4	6	8	11	14
10-(8/78) What if Jane Foster was Thor	9	18	27	62	126	190
11,12,14-16: 11-Marvel Bullpen as F.F.	2	4	6	8	11	12
18-26,29: 18-Dr. Strange. 19-Spider-Man. 22-Origin Dr. Doom retold	1	3	4	6	8	10
27-X-Men app.; Miller-c	3	6	9	16	23	30
28-Daredevil by Miller; Ghost Rider app.	3	6	9	14	19	24
30-"What If...Spider-Man's Clone Had Lived?"	2	4	6	10	14	18
31-Begin $1.00-c; featuring Wolverine & the Hulk; X-Men app.; death of Hulk, Wolverine & Magneto	5	10	15	31	53	75
32-34,36-47: 32,36-Byrne-a. 34-Marvel crew each draw themselves. 37-Old X-Men & Silver Surfer app. 39-Thor battles Conan						6.00
35-What if Elektra had lived?; Miller/Austin-a.	2	4	6	8	11	14
Special 1 ($1.50, 6/88)-Iron Man, F.F., Thor app.						6.00
... Classic Vol. 1 TPB (2004, $24.99) r/#1-6; checklist						25.00
... Classic Vol. 2 TPB (2005, $24.99) r/#7-12						25.00
... Classic Vol. 3 TPB (2006, $24.99) r/#14,15,17-20						25.00
... Classic Vol. 4 TPB (2007, $24.99) r/#21-26; checklist of all What If? series/issues						25.00

NOTE: *Austin* a-27p, 32i, 34, 35i; c-35i, 36i. *J. Buscema* a-13p, 15p; c-10, 13p, 23p. *Byrne* a-32i, 36; c-36p. *Colan* a-21p; c-17p, 18p, 21p. *Ditko* a-35. Special 1. *Golden* c-29, 40-42. *Guice* a-40p. *Gil Kane* a-3p, 24p; c(p)-2-4, 7, 8. *Kirby* a-11p; c-9p, 11p. *Layton* a-32i, 33i; c-30, 32i, 33, 34. *Mignola* a-39i. *Miller* a-28p, 32i, 34(1), 35p; c-27, 28p. *Mooney* a-8i, 30i. *Perez* a-15p. *Robbins* a-42p. *Sekiewicz* c-43-46. *Simonson* c-15p. *Starlin* a-32i. *Stevens* a-2i, 16i(part). *Sutton* a-2i, 18p, 28. *Tuska* a-5p. *Weiss* a-37.

WHAT IF...? (2nd Series)
Marvel Comics: V2#1, July, 1989 - No. 114, Nov, 1998 ($1.25/$1.50)

	GD 2.0	VG 4.0	FN 6.0	VF 8.0	VF/NM 9.0	NM- 9.2
V2#1-...The Avengers Had Lost the Evolutionary War	1	3	4	6	8	10
2,3,5: 2-Daredevil, Punisher app.						5.00
4-Alien costume had possessed Spider-Man	3	6	9	16	23	30
6-X-Men app.						6.00
7-Wolverine app.; Liefeld-c/a(1st on Wolvie?)	1	3	4	6	8	10
8,10,11,13-15,17-30: 10-Punisher app. 11-Fantastic Four app.; McFarlane-c(i).13-Prof. X; Jim Lee-c. 14-Capt. America. 15-F.F.; Capullo-c/a(p). 17-Spider-Man/Kraven. 18-F.F. 19-Vision. 20,21-Spider-Man. 22-Silver Surfer by Lim/Austin-c/a 23-X-Men. 24-Wolverine; Punisher app. 25-(52 pgs.)-Wolverine app. 26-Punisher app. 27-Namor/F.F. 28,29-Capt. America. 29-Swipes cover to Avengers #4. 30-(52 pgs.)-F.F.						5.00
9,12-X-Men						6.00
16-Wolverine battles Conan; Red Sonja app.; X-Men cameo						6.00
31-40,42,43,45,48: 31-Cosmic Spider-Man & Venom app.; Hobgoblin cameo. 32,33-Phoenix; X-Men app. 35-Fantastic Five vs. Guardians of the Galaxy. 37-Wolverine; Thibert-c(i). 38-Thor; Rogers-p(part). 40-Storm; X-Men app. 42-Spider-Man. 43-Wolverine. 45-Ghost Rider. 46-Cable. 47-Magneto						4.00
41,50: 41-(52 pgs.)-Avengers vs. Galactus. 50-(52 pgs.)-Foil embossed-c; "What If Hulk Had Killed Wolverine"	2	4	6	8	10	12
44-Venom had possessed the Punisher	3	6	9	14	20	25
49-Infinity Gauntlet w/Silver Surfer & Thanos	4	8	12	25	40	55
51-(7/93) "What If the Punisher Became Captain America" (see it happen in 2007's Punisher War Journal #6-10)	1	2	3	5	6	8
52-99,101-103: 52-Dr. Doom. 57-Punisher as Shield. 58-"What if Punisher Had Killed Spider-Man" w/cover similar to Amazing S-M #129. 59-...Wolverine led Alpha Flight. 60-X-Men Wedding Album. 61-Bound-in card sheet. 61,86,88-Spider-Man. 74,77,81,84,85-X-Men. 76-Last app. Watcher in title. 78-Bisley-c. 80-Hulk. 87-Sabretooth. 89-Fantastic Four. 90-Cyclops & Havok. 91-The Hulk. 93-Wolverine. 94-Juggernaut. 95-Ghost Rider						4.00
100-($2.99, double-sized) Gambit and Rogue, Fantastic Four	1	3	4	6	8	10
104-Silver Surfer, Thanos vs. Impossible Man	1	3	4	6	8	10
105-Spider-Girl (Peter Parker's daughter) debut; Sienkiewicz-a; (Betty Brant also app. as a Spider-Girl in What If? (1st series) #7)	9	18	27	59	117	175
106,107,109-114: 106-Gambit. 111-Wolverine. 114-Secret Wars						4.00
108-Avengers vs. Carnage	2	4	6	9	14	18
#(-1) Flashback (7/97)	1	2	3	5	6	8

WHAT IF...? (one-shots)
Marvel Comics: Feb, 2005 ($2.99)

... Aunt May Had Died Instead of Uncle Ben? - Brubaker-s/DiVito-a/Brase-c						3.00
... Dr. Doom Had Become The Thing? - Karl Kesel-s/Paul Smith-a/c						3.00
... General Ross Had Become The Hulk? - Peter David-s/Pat Olliffe-a/Gary Frank-c						3.00
... Jessica Jones Had Joined The Avengers? - Bendis-s/Gaydos-a/McNiven-c						3.00
... Karen Page Had Lived? - Bendis-s/Lark-a/c						3.00
... Magneto and Professor X Had Formed The X-Men Together? - Claremont-s/Raney-a						3.00
What If...: Why Not? TPB (2005, $16.99) r/one-shots						17.00

WHAT IF... (one-shots)
Marvel Comics: Feb, 2006 ($2.99)

... : Captain America - Fought in the Civil War?-Bedard-s/Di Giandomenico-a						3.00
... : Daredevil - The Devil Who Dares; Daredevil in feudal Japan; Veitch-s/Edwards-a						3.00
... : Fantastic Four - Were Cosmonauts?; Marshall Rogers-s; Mike Carey-s						3.00
... : Submariner - Grew Up on Land?; Pak-s/Lopez-a						3.00
... : Thor - Was the Herald of Galactus?; Kirkman-s/Oeming-a/c						3.00
... : Wolverine - In the Prohibition Era; Way-s/Proctor-a/Harris-c						3.00
What If: Mirror Mirror TPB (2006, $16.99) r/one-shots; design pages and Rogers sketches						17.00

WHAT IF ?... (one-shots altering recent Marvel "event" series)
Marvel Comics: Jan, 2007 - Feb, 2007 ($3.99)

... Avengers Disassembled; Parker-s/Lopresti-a/c						4.00
... Spider-Man The Other; Peter David-s/Khoi Pham-a; Venom app.						4.00
... Wolverine Enemy of the State; Robinson-s/DiGiandomenico/Alexander-c						4.00
... X-Men Age of Apocalypse; Remender-s/Wilkins-a/Djurdjevic-a						4.00
... X-Men Deadly Genesis; Hine-s/Yardin-a/c						4.00
What If?: Event Horizon TPB (2007, $16.99) r/one-shots; design pages and cover sketches						17.00

WHAT IF ?... (one-shots altering recent Marvel "event" series)
Marvel Comics: Dec, 2007 - Feb, 2008 ($3.99)

	GD 2.0	VG 4.0	FN 6.0	VF 8.0	VF/NM 9.0	NM- 9.2
... Annihilation; Nova, Iron Man, Captain America app.	2	4	6	9	12	15
... Civil War; 2 covers by Silvestri & Djurdjevic	1	3	4	6	8	10
... Planet Hulk; Pagulayan-c; Kirk, Sandoval & Hembeck-a; Skaar, son of Hulk app.	3	6	9	23	37	50
... Spider-Man vs. Wolverine; Romita Jr.-c; Henry-a; Nick Fury app.	2	4	6	9	12	15
... X-Men - Rise and Fall of the Shi'ar Empire; Coipel-c	2	4	6	9	12	15
What If?: Civil War TPB (2008, $16.99) r/one-shots; design pages and cover sketches						17.00

WHAT IF ?... (one-shots altering recent Marvel "event" series)
Marvel Comics: Feb, 2009 ($3.99) (Serialized sequel-w Runaways story in each issue)

... Fallen Son; if Iron Man had died instead of Capt. America; McGuinness-c						4.00
... House of M; if the Scarlet Witch had said "No more powers" instead; Cheung-c						4.00
... Newer Fantastic Four; team of Fantastic Man, Hulk, Iron Man and Wolverine						4.00
... Secret Wars; if Doctor Doom had kept the Beyonder's power; origin re-told						4.00
... Spider-Man Back in Black; if Mary Jane had been shot instead of Aunt May						4.00

WHAT IF ?... (one-shots)
Marvel Comics: Feb, 2010 ($3.99)

... Astonishing X-Men; if Ord resurrected Jean Grey; Campbell-c						4.00
... Daredevil vs. Elektra; Kayanan-a; Klaus Janson-c swipe of Daredevil #168						4.00
... Secret Invasion; if the Skrulls succeeded; Yu-c						4.00
... Spider-Man: House of M; if Gwen Stacy survived the House of M; Dodson-a						4.00
... World War Hulk; if the heroes lost the war; Romita Jr.-c						4.00

WHAT IF ?... (one-shots) (4 part Deadpool back-up story in all but #200) (Also see Venom/Deadpool: What If?)
Marvel Comics: Feb, 2011 ($3.99)

... #200 ($4.99) Siege on cover; if Osborn won the Siege of Asgard; Stan Lee back-up						5.00

	GD	VG	FN	VF	VF/NM	NM-
	2.0	4.0	6.0	8.0	9.0	9.2

... Dark Reign; if Norman Osborn was killed; Tanaka-a/Deodato-c — 4.00
... Iron Man: Demon in an Armor; if Tony Stark became Dr. Doom; Nolan-a — 4.00
... Spider-Man; if Spider-Man killed Kraven; Jimenez-c — 4.00
... Wolverine: Father; if Wolverine raised Daken; Tocchini-a; Yu-a — 4.00

WHAT IF ?... (one-shots)
Marvel Comics: Dec, 2018 ($3.99)
... Ghost Rider 1; Girner-s/Wijngaard-a; heavy metal band becomes the Ghost Rider — 4.00
... Majik 1; if Majik became Sorceror Supreme; Belasco app.; Williams-s/Andrade-a — 4.00
... Spider-Man 1; if Flash Thompson became Spider-Man; Conway-s/Olortegui-a — 4.00
... The Punisher 1; if Peter Parker became The Punisher; Potts-s/Ramírez-a — 4.00
... Thor 1; if Thor was raised by the Frost Giants; Sacks-s/Bandini-a — 4.00
... X-Men 1; X-Men in cyberspace; Hill-s/Milonogiannis & Edwards-a — 4.00

WHAT IF? AGE OF ULTRON
Marvel Comics: Jun, 2014 - No. 5, Jun, 2014 ($3.99, weekly limited series)
1-5: 1-Hank Pym's story. 2-Wolverine, Hulk, Spider-Man, Ghost Rider app. — 4.00

WHAT IF? AVX (Avengers vs. X-Men)
Marvel Comics: Sept, 2013 - No. 4, Sept, 2013 ($3.99, weekly limited series)
1-4-Palmiotti-s/Molina-a; Hope merges with the Phoenix force — 4.00

WHAT IF... ? DARK – ... (one-shots)
Marvel Comics: Sept, 2023 - Oct, 2023 ($4.99)
... Carnage; if Cortland Kasady became Carnage; Dormammu app.; Hama-s/McCrea-a — 5.00
... Loki; if Loki kept control of Mjolnir in Thor #153; Walt Simonson-s/Scot Eaton-a — 5.00
... Moon Knight; if Marlene Alraune became Moon Knight; Schultz-s/Salazar-a — 5.00
... Spider-Gwen; if Spider-Man had died in ASM #122 instead of Gwen; Bachs-a — 5.00
... Tomb of Dracula; if Dracula transformed Blade into a full vampire; Wolfman-s — 5.00
... Venom; if Ben Grimm bonded with the symbiote instead of Peter Parker — 5.00

WHAT IF ? INFINITY – ... (one-shots)
Marvel Comics: Dec, 2015 ($3.99)
... Dark Reign; if The Green Goblin stole the Infinity Gauntlet; Williamson-s/Sudzuka-a — 4.00
... Guardians of the Galaxy; if The Guardians tried to free Thanos; Copland-a — 4.00
... Inhumans; if Black Bolt betrayed Earth; Rossmo-a — 4.00
... Thanos; if Thanos joined the Avengers; Henderson-a — 4.00
... X-Men; if the X-Men were the sole survivors of Infinity; Norton-a — 4.00

WHAT IF..? MILES MORALES
Marvel Comics: May, 2022 - No. 5, Sept, 2022 ($4.99/$3.99, limited series)
1-($4.99) What if Miles became Captain America; Ziglar-s/Medina-a — 5.00
2-5-($3.99) 2-Miles becomes Wolverine. 3-Hulk. 4-Thor. 5-All team-up with Spider-Miles — 4.00

WHAT IF..? VENOM
Marvel Comics: Apr, 2024 - Present ($4.99/$3.99, limited series)
1-($4.99) What if Venom bonded to She-Hulk; Holt-s/Hervás-a — 5.00

'WHAT'S NEW? – THE COLLECTED ADVENTURES OF PHIL & DIXIE'
Palliard Press: Oct, 1991 - No. 2, 1991 ($5.95, mostly color, sq.-bound, 52 pgs.)
1,2-By Phil Foglio — 6.00

WHAT'S THE FURTHEST PLACE FROM HERE?
Image Comics: Nov, 2021 - Present ($4.99/$3.99)
1-($4.99) Boss & Rosenberg-s&a — 5.00
2-17-($3.99) — 4.00

WHAT THE--?!
Marvel Comics: Aug, 1988 - No. 26, 1993 ($1.25/$1.50/$2.50, semi-annual #5 on)
1-All contain parodies — 6.00
2-24: 3-X-Men parody; Todd McFarlane-a. 5-Punisher/Wolverine parody; Jim Lee-a. 6-Punisher, Wolverine, Alpha Flight. 9-Wolverine. 16-EC back-c parody. 17-Wolverine/Punisher parody. 18-Star Trek parody w/Wolverine. 19-Punisher, Wolverine, Ghost Rider. 21-Weapon X parody. 22-Punisher/Wolverine parody — 4.00
25-Summer Special 1 (1993, $2.50)-X-Men parody — 5.00
26-Fall Special ($2.50, 68 pgs.)-Spider-Ham 2099-c/story; origin Silver Surfer; Hulk & Doomsday parody; indica reads "Winter Special." — 5.00
NOTE: *Austin* a-8i. *Byrne* a-2, 6, 10; c-2, 6-8, 10, 12, 13. *Golden* a-22. *Dale Keown* a-8p(8 pgs.). *McFarlane* a-3. *Rogers* c-15i, 16p. *Severin* a-2. *Staton* a-21p. *Williamson* a-2i.

WHEDON THREE WAY, THE
Dark Horse Comics: Sept, 2014 ($1.00, one-shot)
1-Reprints Buffy Season 10 #1, Angel & Faith Season 10 #1, Serenity: Leaves #1 — 3.00

WHEE COMICS (Also see Gay, Smile & Tickle Comics)
Modern Store Publications: 1955 (7¢, 5x7-1/4", 52 pgs.)

	2.0	4.0	6.0	8.0	9.0	9.2
1-Funny animal	11	22	33	62	86	110

WHEEDIES (See Panic #11 -EC Comics)

WHEELIE AND THE CHOPPER BUNCH (TV)
Charlton Comics: July, 1975 - No. 7, July, 1976 (Hanna-Barbera)

	2.0	4.0	6.0	8.0	9.0	9.2
1-3: 1-Byrne text illo (see Nightmare for 1st art); Staton-a. 2-Byrne-a.						
2,3-Mike Zeck text illos. 3-Staton-a; Byrne-c/a	3	6	9	19	30	40
4-7-Staton-a	2	4	6	12	16	20

WHEN KNIGHTHOOD WAS IN FLOWER (See The Sword & the Rose, 4-Color #505, 682)

WHEN SCHOOL IS OUT (See Wisco in Promotional Comics section)

WHERE CREATURES ROAM
Marvel Comics Group: July, 1970 - No. 8, Sept, 1971

	2.0	4.0	6.0	8.0	9.0	9.2
1-Kirby/Ayers-c/a(r)	6	12	18	38	69	100
2-8: 2-5,7,8-Kirby-c/a(r). 6-Kirby-a(r)	4	8	12	23	37	50

NOTE: *Ditko* r-1-6, 7. *Heck* r-2, 5. All contain pre super-hero reprints.

WHERE IN THE WORLD IS CARMEN SANDIEGO (TV)
DC Comics: June, 1996 - No. 4, Dec, 1996 ($1.75)
1-4: Adaptation of TV show — 4.00

WHERE MONSTERS DWELL
Marvel Comics Group: Jan, 1970 - No. 38, Oct, 1975

	2.0	4.0	6.0	8.0	9.0	9.2
1-Kirby/Ditko-r; all contain pre super-hero-r	7	14	21	46	86	125
2-5,7-10: 4-Crandall-a	4	8	12	23	37	50
6-(11/70) Reprints Groot's 1st app. in Tales to Astonish #13						

	2.0	4.0	6.0	8.0	9.0	9.2
	8	16	24	54	102	150
11,13-20: 11-Last 15¢ issue. 16-Googam app. 18,20-Starlin-c	3	6	9	19	30	40
12-Giant issue (52 pgs.)	4	8	12	27	44	60
21-Reprints 1st Fin Fang Foom app.	4	8	12	23	37	50
22-37	3	6	9	16	24	32
38-Williamson-r/World of Suspense #3	3	6	9	17	26	35

NOTE: *Colan* r-12. *Ditko* a(r)-4, 6, 8, 10, 12, 17-19, 23-25, 37. *Kirby* r-1-5, 16-18, 27, 30-32, 34-36, 38; c-12? *Reinman* a-3r, 4r, 12r. *Severin* c-15.

WHERE MONSTERS DWELL (Secret Wars tie-in)
Marvel Comics: Jul, 2015 - No. 5, Dec, 2015, limited series)
1-5-Garth Ennis-s/Russ Braun-a/Frank Cho-c; The Phantom Eagle app. — 4.00

WHERE MONSTERS LIE
Dark Horse Comics: Feb, 2023 - No. 4, May, 2023 ($3.99, limited series)
1-4-Starks-s/Kowalski-a — 4.00

WHERE'S HUDDLES? (TV) (See Fun-In #9)
Gold Key: Jan, 1971 - No. 3, Dec, 1971 (Hanna-Barbera)

	2.0	4.0	6.0	8.0	9.0	9.2
1	3	6	9	18	28	38
2,3: 3-r/most #1	2	4	6	11	16	20

WHIP WILSON (Movie star) (Formerly Rex Hart; Gunhawk #12 on; see Western Hearts, Western Life Romances, Western Love)
Marvel Comics: No. 9, April, 1950 - No. 11, Sept, 1950 (#9,10: 52 pgs.)

	2.0	4.0	6.0	8.0	9.0	9.2
9-Photo-c; Whip Wilson & his horse Bullet begin; origin Bullet; issue #23 listed on splash page; cover changed to #9; Maneely-a	55	110	165	352	601	850
10,11: Both have photo-c. 11-36 pgs.; Maneely-a	33	66	99	194	317	440
I.W. Reprint #1(1964)-Kinstler-c; r-Marvel #11	3	6	9	17	26	35

WHIRLWIND COMICS (Also see Cyclone Comics)
Nita Publication: June, 1940 - No. 3, Sept, 1940

	2.0	4.0	6.0	8.0	9.0	9.2
1-Origin & 1st app. Cyclone; Cyclone-c	354	708	1062	2478	4339	6200
2,3: Cyclone-c	213	426	639	1363	2332	3300

WHIRLYBIRDS (TV)
Dell Publishing Co.: No. 1124, Aug, 1960 - No. 1216, Oct-Dec, 1961

	2.0	4.0	6.0	8.0	9.0	9.2
Four Color 1124 (#1)-Photo-c	7	14	21	49	92	135
Four Color 1216-Photo-c	7	14	21	46	86	125

WHISKEY DICKEL, INTERNATIONAL COWGIRL
Image Comics: Aug, 2003 ($12.95, softcover, B&W)
nn-Mark Ricketts-s/Mike Hawthorne-a; pin-up by various incl. Oeming, Thompson, Mack — 13.00

WHISPER (Female Ninja)
Capital Comics: Dec, 1983 - No. 2, 1984 ($1.75, Baxter paper)
1,2: 1-Origin; Golden-c, Special (11/85, $2.50) — 4.00

WHISPER (Vol. 2)
First Comics: Jun, 1986 - No. 37, June, 1990 ($1.25/$1.75/$1.95)
1-37 — 4.00

WHISPER
BOOM! Studios: Nov, 2006 ($3.99)
1-Grant-s/Dzialowski-a — 4.00

WHISPERING DARK, THE
Dark Horse Comics: Oct, 2018 - No. 4, Feb, 2019 ($3.99)
1-4-Christopher Emgård-s/Tomás Aira-a — 4.00

WHISPERS
Image Comics: Jan, 2012 - No. 6, Oct, 2013 ($2.99)
1-6-Joshua Luna-s/a — 3.00

WHITE CHIEF OF THE PAWNEE INDIANS
Avon Periodicals: 1951

	2.0	4.0	6.0	8.0	9.0	9.2
nn-Kit West app.; Kinstler-c	24	48	72	144	237	330

WHITE EAGLE INDIAN CHIEF (See Indian Chief)

WHITE FANG
Disney Comics: 1990 ($5.95, 68 pgs.)
nn-Graphic novel adapting new Disney movie — 6.00

WHITE INDIAN
Magazine Enterprises: No. 11, July, 1953 - No. 15, 1954

	2.0	4.0	6.0	8.0	9.0	9.2
11(A-1 94), 12(A-1 101), 13(A-1 104)-Frazetta-r(Dan Brand) in all from Durango Kid. 11-Powell-a	25	50	75	150	245	340
14(A-1 117), 15(A-1 135)-Check-a; Torres-a/#15	17	34	51	98	154	210

NOTE: #11 contains reprints from Durango Kid #1-4; #12 from #5, 9, 10, 11; #13 from #7, 12, 13, 16. #14 & 15 contain all new stories.

WHITEOUT (Also see Queen & Country)
Oni Press: July, 1998 - No. 4, Nov, 1998 ($2.95, B&W, limited series)
1-4: 1-Matt Wagner-c. 2-Mignola-c. 3-Gibbons-c — 4.00
TPB (5/99, $10.95) r/#1-4; Miller-c — 11.00

WHITEOUT: MELT
Oni Press: Sept, 1999 - No. 4, Feb, 2000 ($2.95, B&W, limited series)
1-4-Greg Rucka-s/Steve Lieber-a — 4.00
Whiteout: Melt, The Definitive Edition TPB (9/07, $13.95) r/#1-4; Rucka afterword — 14.00

WHITE PRINCESS OF THE JUNGLE (Also see Jungle Adventures & Top Jungle Comics)
Avon Periodicals: July, 1951 - No. 5, Nov, 1952

	2.0	4.0	6.0	8.0	9.0	9.2
1-Origin of White Princess (Taanda) & Capt'n Courage (r); Kinstler-c	97	194	291	621	1061	1500
2-Reprints origin of Malu, Slave Girl Princess from Avon's Slave Girl Comics #1 w/Malu changed to Zora; Kinstler-c/a(2)	58	116	174	371	636	900
3-Origin Blue Gorilla; Kinstler-c/a	52	104	156	328	552	775
4-Jack Barnum, White Hunter app.; r/Sheena #9	45	90	135	284	480	675
5-Blue Gorilla by McCann?; Kinstler inside-c; Fawcette/Alascia-a(3)	47	94	141	296	498	700

WHITE RIDER AND SUPER HORSE (Formerly Humdinger V2#2; Indian Warriors #7 on; also

Whisper #1 © FC

White Widow #1 © MAR

Whiz Comics #28 © FAW

	GD 2.0	VG 4.0	FN 6.0	VF 8.0	VF/NM 9.0	NM- 9.2

see Blue Bolt #1, 4Most & Western Crime Cases)
Novelty-Star Publications/Accepted Publ.: No. 4, 9/50 - No. 6, 3/51

4-6-Adapts "The Last of the Mohicans". 4(#1)-(9/50)-Says #11 on inside

	21	42	63	126	206	285

Accepted Reprint #5(r/#5),6 (nd); L.B. Cole-c

| | 10 | 20 | 30 | 56 | 76 | 95 |

NOTE: *All have* **L. B. Cole** *covers.*

WHITE SAVIOR
Dark Horse Comics: Jan, 2023 - No. 4, Apr, 2023 ($3.99, limited series)

1-4-Eric Nguyen & Scott Burman-s/Nguyen-a — 4.00

WHITE TIGER
Marvel Comics: Jan, 2007 - No. 6, Nov, 2007 ($2.99, limited series)

1-David Mack-c; Pierce & Liebe-s/Briones-a; Spider-Man & Black Widow app.

		1	3	4	6	8	10

2-6 — 4.00
...: A Hero's Compulsion SC (2007,$14.99) r/#1-6; re-cap art and profile page — 15.00

WHITE TREES: A BLACKSAND TALE
Image Comics: Aug, 2019 - No. 2, Sept, 2019 ($4.99, limited series)

1,2-Chip Zdarsky-s/Kris Anka-a/c — 5.00

WHITE WIDOW
Marvel Comics: Jan, 2024 - No. 4, Apr, 2024 ($4.99/$3.99, limited series)

1-($4.99) Spotlight on Yelena Belova; Gailey-s/Miracolo-a — 5.00
2-4-($3.99) 2-Wolverine app. 3-She-Hulk app. — 4.00

WHITE WILDERNESS (Disney)
Dell Publishing Co.: No. 943, Oct, 1958

Four Color 943-Movie

	6	12	18	37	66	95

WHITMAN COMIC BOOK, A
Whitman Publishing Co.: Sept., 1962 (136 pgs.; 7-3/4x5-3/4; hardcover) (B&W)

1-3,5,7: 1-Yogi Bear. 2-Huckleberry Hound. 3-Mr. Jinks and Pixie & Dixie. 5-Augie Doggie & Loopy de Loop. 7-Bugs Bunny-r from #47,51,53,54 & 55

	6	12	18	41	76	110

4,6: 4-The Flintstones. 6-Snooper & Blabber Fearless Detectives/Quick Draw McGraw of the Wild West

	7	14	21	44	82	120

8-Donald Duck-reprints most of WDC&S #209-213. Includes 5 Barks stories, 1 complete Mickey Mouse serial by Paul Murry & 1 Mickey Mouse serial missing the 1st episode

	7	14	21	49	92	135

NOTE: *Hanna-Barbera #1-6(TV), reprints of British tabloid comics. Dell reprints #7,8.*

WHIZ COMICS (Formerly Flash & Thrill Comics #1)(See 5 Cent Comics)
Fawcett Publications: No. 2, Feb, 1940 - No. 155, June, 1953

1-(nn on cover, #2 inside)-Origin & 1st newsstand app. Captain Marvel (formerly Captain Thunder) by C. C. Beck (created by Bill Parker), Spy Smasher, Golden Arrow, Ibis the Invincible, Dan Dare, Scoop Smith, Sivana, & James O'Casey begin

	39,600	79,200	118,800	237,600	356,300	475,000

(The only Mint copy sold in 1995 for $176,000 cash)

1-Reprint, oversize 13-1/2x10". **WARNING:** This comic is an exact duplicate reprint (except for dropping "Gangway for Captain Marvel" from-c) of the original except for its size. DC published it in 1974 with a second cover titling it as a Famous First Edition. There have been many reported cases of the outer cover being removed and the interior sold as the original edition. The reprint with the new outer cover removed is practically worthless. See Famous First Edition for value.

2-(3/40, nn on cover, #3 inside; cover to Flash #1 redrawn, pg. 12, panel 4; Spy Smasher reveals I.D. to Eve

	1200	2400	3600	9100	16,550	24,000

3-(4/40, #3 on-c, #4 inside)-1st app. Beautia

	530	1060	1590	3870	6315	9800

4-(5/40, #4 on cover, #5 inside)-Brief origin Capt. Marvel retold

	423	846	1269	3088	5444	7800

5-Captain Marvel wears button-down flap on splash page only

	389	778	1167	2723	4762	6800

6-10: 7-Dr. Voodoo begins (by Raboy-#9-22)

	297	594	891	1900	3250	4600

11-14: 12-Capt. Marvel does not wear cape

	219	438	657	1402	2401	3400

15-Origin Sivana; Dr. Voodoo by Raboy

	219	438	657	1402	2401	3400

16-18-Spy Smasher battles Captain Marvel

	245	490	735	1568	2684	3800

19-Classic shark-c

	239	478	717	1530	2615	3700

20

	142	284	426	909	1555	2200

21-(9/41)-Origin & 1st cover app. Lt. Marvels, the 1st team in Fawcett comics. In this issue, Capt. Death similar to Ditko's later Dr. Strange

	155	310	465	992	1696	2400

22-24: 23-Only Dr. Voodoo by Tuska

	116	232	348	742	1271	1800

25-(12/41)-Captain Nazi jumps from Master Comics #21 to take on Capt. Marvel solo after being beaten by Capt. Marvel/Bulletman team, causing the creation of Capt. Marvel Jr.; 1st app./origin of Capt. Marvel Jr. (part II of trilogy origin by CC. Beck & Mac Raboy); Captain Marvel sends Jr. back to Master #22 to aid Bulletman against Capt. Nazi; origin Old Shazam in text

	1000	2000	3000	7300	12,900	18,500

26-30

	77	154	231	493	847	1200

31,32: 32-1st app. The Trolls; Hitler/Mussolini satire by Beck

	66	132	198	419	722	1025

33-Spy Smasher, Captain Marvel x-over on cover and inside

	GD 2.0	VG 4.0	FN 6.0	VF 8.0	VF/NM 9.0	NM- 9.2
	87	174	261	553	952	1350

34,36-40: 37-The Trolls app. by Swayze

	53	106	159	334	567	800

35-Captain Marvel & Spy Smasher-c

	74	148	222	470	810	1150

41-50: 42-Classic time travel-c. 43-Spy Smasher, Ibis, Golden Arrow x-over in Capt. Marvel.
44-Flag-c. 47-Origin recap (1 pg.)

	43	86	129	271	461	650

51-60: 52-Capt. Marvel x-over in Ibis. 57-Spy Smasher, Golden Arrow, Ibis cameo

	37	74	111	222	361	500

61-70

	36	72	108	214	347	480

71,77-80

	33	66	99	194	317	440

72-76-Two Captain Marvel stories in each; 76-Spy Smasher becomes Crime Smasher

	36	72	108	214	347	480

81-85,87-99: 91-Infinity-c

	33	66	99	194	317	440

86-Captain Marvel battles Sivana Family; robot-c

	41	82	123	256	428	600

100-(8/48)-Anniversary issue

	43	86	129	271	461	650

101-106: 102-Commando Yank app. 106-Bulletman app.

	34	68	102	204	332	460

107-149: 107-Capitol Building photo-c. 108-Brooklyn Bridge photo-c. 112-Photo-c. 139-Infinity-c.
140-Flag-c. 142-Used in *POP*, pg. 89

	35	70	105	208	339	470

150-152-(Low dist.)

	43	86	129	271	461	650

153-155-(Scarce):154,155-1st/2nd Dr. Death stories 61

	61	122	183	390	670	950

NOTE: **C.C. Beck** *Captain Marvel-No. 25(part).* **Krigstein** *Golden Arrow-No. 75, 78, 91, 95, 96, 98-100.* **Mac Raboy** *Dr. Voodoo-No. 9-22. Captain Marvel-No. 25(part).* **M.Swayze** *a-37, 38, 59; c-38.* **Schaffenberger** *c-138-155(most).* **Wolverton** *1/2 pg. "Culture Corner"-No. 65-67, 68(2 1/2 pgs), 70-85, 87-96, 98-100, 102-109, 112-121, 123, 125, 126, 128-131, 133, 134, 136, 142, 143, 146.*

WHIZ COMICS 2 (FACSIMILE EDITION)
DC Comics: 2023 ($6.99, one-shot)

2-Reprints all of Whiz Comics #1(#2) with original 1940 ads — 7.00

WHIZ KIDS (Also see Big Bang Comics)
Image Comics: Apr, 2003 ($4.95, B&W, one-shot)

1-Galahad, Cyclone, Thunder Girl and Moray app.; Jeff Austin-a — 5.00

WHOA, NELLIE (Also see Love & Rockets)
Fantagraphics Books: July, 1996 - No. 3, Sept, 1996 ($2.95, B&W, lim. series)

1-3: Jamie Hernandez-a/scripts — 4.00

WHODUNIT
D.S. Publishing Co.: Aug-Sept, 1948 - No. 3, Dec-Jan, 1948-49 (#1,2: 52 pgs.)

1-Baker-a (7 pgs.)

	40	80	120	246	411	575

2,3-Detective mysteries

	20	40	60	114	182	250

WHODUNNIT?
Eclipse Comics: June, 1986 - No. 3, Apr, 1987 ($2.00, limited series)

1-3: Spiegle-a. 2-Gulacy-c — 4.00

WHO FRAMED ROGER RABBIT (See Marvel Graphic Novel)

WHO IS NEXT?
Standard Comics: No. 5, Jan, 1953

5-Toth, Sekowsky, Andru-a; crime stories; Strangler on the Loose-c

	271	542	813	1734	2967	4200

WHO'S MINDING THE MINT? (See Movie Classics)

WHO'S WHO IN STAR TREK
DC Comics: Mar, 1987 - #2, Apr, 1987 ($1.50, limited series)

		1	2	3	5	6	8
1,2							

NOTE: **Byrne** *a-1, 2.* **Chaykin** *c-1, 2.* **Morrow** *a-1, 2.* **McFarlane** *a-2.* **Perez** *a-1, 2.* **Sutton** *c-1, 2.*

WHO'S WHO IN THE LEGION OF SUPER-HEROES
DC Comics: Apr, 1987 - No. 7, Nov, 1988 ($1.25, limited series)

1-7 — 4.00

WHO'S WHO: THE DEFINITIVE DIRECTORY OF THE DC UNIVERSE
DC Comics: Mar, 1985 - No. 26, Apr, 1987 (Maxi-series, no ads)

1-DC heroes from A-Z — 4.00
2-26: All have 1-2 pgs-a by most DC artists — 4.00

NOTE: **Art Adams** *a-4, 11, 18, 20.* **Anderson** *a-1-5, 7-12, 14, 15, 19, 21, 23-25.* **Aparo** *a-2, 3, 9, 10, 12, 13, 14, 15, 17, 18, 21, 23.* **Byrne** *a-4, 7, 14, 16, 18i, 19, 22i, 24; c-22.* **Cowan** *a-3-5, 8, 10-13, 16-18, 22.* **Ditko** *a-15-17, 18, 23.* **Grell** *a-6, 9, 14, 20, 23.* **Evans** *a-20.* **Gil Kane** *a-1-11, 13, 14, 16, 19, 21-23, 25.* **Kirby** *a-2-6, 8-18, 20, 24.* **Kubert** *17-22, 24, 25.* **Kaluta** *a-14, 21.* **Gil Kane** *a-1-11, 13, 14, 16, 19, 21-23, 25.* **Infantino** *a-1-10, 12, 15, 22.* **Erik Larsen** *a-24.* **McFarlane** *a-10-12, 17, 19, 25, 26.* **Morrow** *a-4, 7, 25, 26.* **Orlando** *a-2, 3, 7-11, 19, 20, 25.* **Perez** *a-1-5, 8-19, 22-26; c-1-4, 13-18.* **Rogers** *a-1, 2, 5-7, 11, 12, 15, 24.* **Starlin** *a-13, 14, 16.* **Stevens** *a-4, 7, 18.*

WHO'S WHO UPDATE '87
DC Comics: Aug, 1987 - No. 5, Dec, 1987 ($1.25, limited series)

1-5: Contains art by most DC artists — 4.00

NOTE: **Giffen** *a-1.* **McFarlane** *a-1; c-4.* **Perez** *a-1-4.*

WHO'S WHO UPDATE '88
DC Comics: Aug, 1988 - No. 4, Nov, 1988 ($1.25, limited series)

1-4: Contains art by most DC artists — 4.00

NOTE: **Giffen** *a-1.* **Erik Larsen** *a-1.*

	GD 2.0	VG 4.0	FN 6.0	VF 8.0	VF/NM 9.0	NM- 9.2

WICKED, THE
Avalon Studios: Dec, 1999 - No. 7, Aug, 2000 ($2.95)

Preview-(7/99, $5.00, B&W)						5.00
1-7-Anacleto-c/Martinez-a						4.00
...: Medusa's Tale (11/00, $3.95, one shot) story plus pin-up gallery						4.00
...: Vol. 1: Omnibus (2003, $19.95) r/#0-8; Drew-c						20.00

WICKED + THE DIVINE, THE
Image Comics: Jun, 2014 - No. 45, Sept, 2019 ($3.50/$3.99)

1-25: 1-Gillen-s/McKelvie-a. 12-Kate Brown-a. 13-Lotay-a. 15-Hans-a. 23-Wada-a						3.50
26-45-($3.99)						4.00
... Christmas Annual (12/17, $3.99) Art by Anka, Clugston, McNeil						4.00
455 One-Shot (5/17, $3.99) Set in 455 AD Rome; André Araújo-a						4.00
1373 One-Shot (9/18, $3.99) Set in 1373; Ryan Kelly-a; Lucifer during the Black Death						4.00
1831 One-Shot (9/16, $3.99) Set in 1831; Stephanie Hans-a						4.00
1923 One-Shot (2/18, $4.99) Set in 1923; Aud Koch-a						5.00
...: The Funnies 1 (11/18, $3.99) Short humor stories by various incl. Zdarsky						5.00

WICKED THINGS
BOOM! Studios: Mar, 2020 - Present ($3.99)

1-5-John Allison-s/Max Sarin-a; intro. Charlotte Grote						4.00

WIDOWMAKER
Marvel Comics: Feb, 2011 - No. 4, Apr, 2011 ($3.99, limited series)

1-4-Black Widow, Hawkeye & Mockingbird app. 1,2-Jae Lee-c. 3,4-Noto-c						4.00

WIDOWMAKERS: RED GUARDIAN AND YELENA BELOVA
Marvel Comics: Jan, 2021 ($3.99, one-shot)

1-Devin Grayson-s/Michele Bandini-a						4.00

WIDOW WARRIORS
Dynamite Entertainment: 2010 - No. 4, 2010 ($3.99, limited series)

1-4-Pat Lee-a/c						4.00

WILBUR COMICS (Teen-age) (Also see Laugh Comics, Laugh Comix, Liberty Comics #10 & Zip Comics)
MLJ Magazines/Archie Publ. No. 8, Spring, 1946 on: Sum', 1944 - No. 87, 11/59; No. 88, 9/63; No. 89, 10/64; No. 90, 10/65 (No. 1-46: 52 pgs.) (#1-11 are quarterly)

1	84	168	252	538	919	1300
2(Fall, 1944)	45	90	135	284	480	675
3,4(Wint, '44-45; Spr, '45)	33	66	99	194	317	440
5-1st app. Katy Keene (Sum, '45) & begin Wilbur story same as Archie story in Archie #1 except Wilbur replaces Archie	300	600	900	2010	3505	5000
6-10: 10-(Fall, 1946)	39	78	117	231	378	525
11-20	21	42	63	124	202	280
21-30: 30-(4/50)	15	30	45	85	130	175
31-50	14	28	42	76	108	140
51-70	11	22	33	62	86	110
71-90: 88-Last 10¢ issue (9/63)	5	10	15	35	63	90

NOTE: Katy Keene in No. 5-56, 58-61, 63-69. Al Fagaly c-6-9, 12-24 at least. Vigoda c-2.

WILD
Atlas Comics (IPC): Feb, 1954 - No. 5, Aug, 1954

1	43	86	129	271	461	650
2	27	54	81	158	259	360
3-5	24	48	72	142	234	325

NOTE: Berg a-5; c-4. Burgos a-5, c-2,3. Colan a-4. Everett a-1-3. Heath a-2, 3, 5. Maneely a-1-3, 5; c-1, 5. Post a-2, 5. Ed Win a-1, 3.

WILD! (This Magazine Is...) (Satire)
Dell Publishing Co.: Jan, 1968 - No. 3, 1968 (35¢, magazine, 52 pgs.)

1-3: Hogan's Heroes, The Rat Patrol & Mission Impossible TV spoofs	3	6	9	16	23	30

WILD ANIMALS
Pacific Comics: Dec, 1982 ($1.00, one-shot, direct sales)

1-Funny animal; Sergio Aragonés-a; Shaw-c/a						4.00

WILD BILL ELLIOTT (Also see Western Roundup under Dell Giants)
Dell Publishing Co.: No. 278, 5/50 - No. 643, 7/55 (No #11,12) (All photo-c)

Four Color 278 (#1, 52 pgs.)-Titled "Bill Elliott"; Bill & his horse Stormy begin; photo front/back-c begin	15	30	45	100	220	340
2 (11/50), 3 (52 pgs.)	7	14	21	48	89	130
4-10 (10-12/52)	6	12	18	37	66	95
Four Color 472 (6/53), 520(12/53)-Last photo back-c	6	12	18	38	69	100
13 (4-6/54) - 17 (4-6/55)	5	10	15	31	53	75
Four Color 643 (7/55)	5	10	15	34	60	85

WILD BILL HICKOK (Also see Blazing Sixguns)
Avon Periodicals: Sept-Oct, 1949 - No. 28, May-June, 1956

1-Ingels-a	39	78	117	231	378	525
2-Painted-c; Kit West app.	19	38	57	111	176	240
3-5-Painted-c (4-Cover by Howard Winfield)	14	28	42	82	121	160
6-10,12: 8-10-Painted-c. 12-Kinsler-c?	14	28	42	80	115	150
11,13,14-Kinstler-c/a (#11-c & inside-f/c art only)	15	30	45	83	124	165
15,17,18,20: 18-Kit West story. 20-Kit West by Larsen	13	26	39	74	105	135
16-Kamen-a; r-3 stories/King of the Badmen of Deadwood	13	26	39	72	101	130
19-Meskin-a	12	24	36	69	97	125
21-Reprints 2 stories/Chief Crazy Horse	11	22	33	62	86	110
22-McCann-a?; r/Sheriff Bob Dixon's...	11	22	33	62	86	110
23-27: 23-Kinstler-c. 24-27-Kinstler-c/a(r) (24,25-r?)	11	22	33	62	86	110
28-Kinstler-c/a (new); r-/Last of the Comanches	11	22	33	64	90	115
I.W. Reprint #1-#2: Kinstler-c	3	6	9	13	16	
Super Reprint #10-12: 10-r/#18. 11-r/#?. 12-r/#8	2	4	6	9	13	16

NOTE: #23, 25 contain numerous editing deletions in both art and script due to code. Kinstler c-6, 7, 11-14, 17, 18, 20-22, 24-28. Howard Larsen a-1, 2, 4, 5, 6(3), 7-9, 11, 12, 17, 18, 20-24, 26. Meskin a-7. Reinman a-6, 17.

WILD BILL HICKOK AND JINGLES (TV)(Formerly Cowboy Western) (Also see Blue Bird)
Charlton Comics: No. 68, Aug, 1958 - No. 75, Dec, 1959

68,69-Williamson-a (all are 10¢ issues)	11	22	33	60	83	105

	GD 2.0	VG 4.0	FN 6.0	VF 8.0	VF/NM 9.0	NM- 9.2
70-Two pgs. Williamson-a	8	16	24	42	54	65
71-75 (#76, exist?)	6	12	18	28	34	40

WILD BILL PECOS WESTERN (Also see The Westerner)
AC Comics: 1989 ($3.50, 1/2 color, 1/2 B&W, 52 pgs.)

1-Syd Shores-c/a(r)/Westerner; photo back-c						5.00

WILD BOY OF THE CONGO (Also see Approved Comics)
Ziff-Davis No. 10-12,4-8/St. John No. 9,11 on: No. 10, 2-3/51 - No. 12, 8-9/51; No. 4, 10-11/51 - No. 9, 10/53; No. 11-#15,6/55 (No #10, 1953)

10(#1)(2-3/51)-Origin; bondage-c by Saunders (painted); used in SOTI, pg. 189; painted-c begin thru #9 (except #7)	39	78	117	240	395	550
11(4-5/51),12(8-9/51)-Norman Saunders painted-c	22	44	66	128	209	290
4(10-11/51)-Saunders painted bondage-c	20	40	60	117	189	260
5(Winter, '51)-Saunders painted-c	18	36	54	103	162	220
6,8,9(10/53): 6-Saunders-c	18	36	54	103	162	220
7(8-9/52)-Kinstler-a	20	40	60	117	189	260
11-13-Baker-c. 11-r/#7 w/new Baker-c; Kinstler-a (2 pgs.)	103	206	309	659	1130	1600
14(4/55)-Baker-c; r-/#12('51)	110	220	330	704	1202	1700
15(6/55)-Baker-c	63	126	189	403	689	975

WILD CARDS: THE DRAWING OF CARDS (George R. R. Martin)
Marvel Comics: Sept, 2022 - No. 4, Dec, 2022 ($4.99)

1-4: 1,2-Cornell-s/Hawthorne-a. 3-Balám-a						5.00

WILDCAT (See Sensation Comics #1)

WILDC.A.T.S ADVENTURES (TV cartoon)
Image Comics (WildStorm): Sept, 1994 - No. 10, June, 1995 ($1.95/$2.50)

1-10: 1,2-Templeton-c. 2,3-Templeton-a. 4,5-Joe Phillips-a. 7,9-Wieringo-c						4.00
Sourcebook 1 (1/95, $2.95) Jeff Smith-c; art by Hamner, Phillips, Staton, Stelfreeze						4.00

WILDC.A.T.S: COVERT ACTION TEAMS (Also see Alan Moore's... for TPB reprints)
Image Comics (WildStorm Productions): Aug, 1992 - No. 4, Mar, 1993; No. 5, Nov, 1993 - No. 50, June, 1998 ($1.95/$2.50)

1-1st app; Jim Lee/Williams-c/a & Lee scripts begin; contains 2 trading cards (Two diff versions of cards inside); 1st WildStorm Productions title	2	4	6	8	10	12
1-All gold foil signed edition	3	6	9	19	30	40
1-All gold foil unsigned edition	3	6	9	16	23	30
1-Newsstand edition w/o cards						4.00
1-"3-D Special"(8/97, $4.95) w/3-D glasses; variant-c by Jim Lee.						5.00
2-($2.50)-Prism foil stamped-c; contains coupon for Image Comics #0 & 4 pg. preview to Portacio's Wetworks (back-up)						5.00
2-With coupon missing						2.00
2-Direct sale misprint w/o foil-c						5.00
2-Newsstand ed., no prism or coupon						4.00
3-Lee/Liefeld-c (1/93-c, 12/92 inside)						5.00
4-($2.50)-Polybagged w/Topps trading card; 1st app. Tribe by Johnson & Stroman; Youngblood cameo						5.00
4-Variant w/red card						6.00
5-7-Jim Lee/Williams-c/a; Lee script						4.00
8-X-Men's Jean Grey & Scott Summers cameo						5.00
9-12: 10-1st app. Huntsman & Soldier; Claremont scripts begin, ends #13.						
11-1st app. Savant, Tapestry & Mr. Majestic.						4.00
11-Alternate Portacio-c, see Deathblow #5						5.00
13-19,21-24: 15-James Robinson scripts begin, ends #20. 15,16-Black Razor story.						
21-Alan Moore scripts begin, end #34; reads Apr on-c. 30-(6/96)-Fire From Heaven Pt. 7; new WildC.A.T.S team forms (Mr. Majestic, Savant, Condition Red (Max Cash), Tao & Ladytron). 22-Maguire-a						4.00
20-($2.50)-Direct Market, WildStorm Rising Pt. 2 w/bound-in card						5.00
20-($1.95)-Newsstand, WildStorm Rising Part 2						4.00
25-($4.95)-Alan Moore script; wraparound foil-c.						5.00
26-49: 29-(5/96)-Fire From Heaven Pt 7; reads Apr on-c. 30-(6/96)-Fire From Heaven Pt. 13; Spartan revealed to have transplanted personality of John Colt (from Team One: WildC.A.T.S). 31-(9/96)-Grifter rejoins team; Ladytron dies						4.00
40-($3.50)-Voyager Pack bagged w/Divine Right preview						5.00
50-($3.50) Stories by Robinson/Lee, Choi & Peterson/Benes, and Moore/Charest; Charest sketchbook; Lee wraparound-c						4.00
50-Chromium cover						6.00
Annual 1 (2/98, $2.95) Robinson-s						4.00
Compendium (1993, $9.95)-r/#1-4; bagged w/#0						15.00
Sourcebook 1 (9/93, $2.50)-Foil embossed-c						5.00
Sourcebook 1-($1.95)-Newsstand ed. w/o foil embossed-c						4.00
Sourcebook 2 (11/94, $2.50)-wraparound-c						4.00
Special 1 (11/93, $3.50, 52 pgs.)-1st Travis Charest WildC.A.T.S-a						5.00
...A Gathering of Eagles (5/97, $9.95, TPB) r/#10-12						10.00
.../ Cyberforce: Killer Instinct TPB (2004, $14.95) r/#5-7 & Cyberforce V2 #1-3						15.00
...: Gang War ('98, $16.95, TPB) r/#28-34						17.00
...: Homecoming (8/98, $19.95, TPB) r/#21-27						20.00
James Robinson's Complete Wildc.a.t.s TPB (2009, $24.99) r/#15-20,50; Annual 1, WildStorm Rising #1; Team One Wildc.a.t.s #1,2; cover and pin-up gallery						25.00

WILDCATS (3rd series)
DC Comics (WildStorm): Mar, 1999 - No. 28, Dec, 2001 ($2.50)

1-Charest-a; six covers by Lee, Adams, Bisley, Campbell, Madureira and Ramos; Lobdell-s						4.00
1-($6.95) DF Edition; variant cover by Ramos						7.00
2-28: 2-Voodoo cover. 3-Bachalo variant-c. 5-Hitch-a/variant-c. 7-Meglia-a. 8-Phillips-a begins. 17-J.G. Jones-c. 18,19-Jim Lee-c. 20,21-Dillon-a						3.00
Annual 2000 (12/00, $3.50) Bermejo-a; Devil's Night x-over						
... Battery Park ('03, $17.95, TPB) r/#20-28; Phillips-a						18.00
... Ladytron (10/00, $5.95) Origin; Casey-s/Canete-a						6.00
... Mosaic (2/00, $3.95) Tuska-a (10 pg. back-up story)						4.00
... Serial Boxes ('01, $14.95, TPB) r/#1-12; 19-c; Phillips-c						15.00
... Street Smart ('00, $24.95, HC) r/#1-6; Charest-c						25.00
...: Street Smart ('00, $14.95, SC) r/#1-6; Charest-c						15.00
...: Vicious Circles ('00, $14.95, TPB) r/#8-13; Phillips-c						15.00

WILDCATS (Volume 4)
DC Comics (WildStorm): Dec, 2006 ($2.99)

Wicked Things #5 © John Allison
WildC.A.T.s (2022 series) #2 © DC
The Wild Storm #3 © DC

	GD 2.0	VG 4.0	FN 6.0	VF 8.0	VF/NM 9.0	NM- 9.2

1-Grant Morrison-s/Jim Lee-a; Jim Lee-c — 3.00
1-Variant-c by Todd McFarlane/Jim Lee — 6.00
...: Armageddon 1 (2/08, $2.99) Gage-s/Caldwell-a — 3.00

WILDCATS (Volume 5) (World's End on cover for #1,2)
DC Comics (WildStorm): Sept, 2008 - No. 30, Feb, 2011 ($2.99)
1-30: 1-Christos Gage-s/Neil Googe-a. 5-Woods-a — 3.00
...: Family Secrets TPB (2010, $17.99) r/#8-12 — 18.00
...: World's End TPB (2009, $17.99) r/#1-7 — 18.00

WILDC.A.T.S (Volume 6)
DC Comics: Jan, 2023 - No. 12, Jan, 2024 ($3.99)
1-12: 1-Rosenberg-s/Segovia-a; Fairchild app. 5-Superman app. 10,11-Batman app. — 4.00

WILDC.A.T.S/ ALIENS
Image Comics/Dark Horse: Aug, 1998 ($4.95, one-shot)
1-Ellis-s/Sprouse-a/c; Aliens invade Skywatch; Stormwatch app.; death of Winter; destruction of Skywatch — 1 2 3 5 6 8
1-Variant-c by Gil Kane — 1 3 4 6 8 10

WILDCATS: NEMESIS
DC Comics (WildStorm): Nov, 2005 - No. 9, July, 2006 ($2.99, limited series)
1-9: 1-Robbie Morrison-s/Talent Caldwell & Horacio Domingues-a/Caldwell-c — 3.00
TPB (2006, $19.99) r/#1-9; cover gallery — 20.00

WILDC.A.T.S: SAVANT GARDE FAN EDITION
Image Comics/WildStorm Productions: Feb, 1997 - No. 3, Apr, 1997 (Giveaway, 8 pgs.) (Polybagged w/Overstreet's FAN)
1-3: Barbara Kesel-s/Christian Uche-a(p) — 4.00
1-3-(Gold): All retailer incentives — 10.00

WILDC.A.T.S TRILOGY
Image Comics Productions: June, 1993 - No. 3, Dec, 1993 ($1.95, lim. series)
1-($2.50)-1st app. Gen 13 (Fairchild, Burnout, Grunge, Freefall) Multi-color foil-c; Jae Lee-c/a in all — 6.00
1-($1.95)-Newsstand ed. w/o foil-c — 4.00
2,3-($1.95)-Jae Lee-c/a — 4.00

WILDCATS VERSION 3.0
DC Comics (WildStorm): Oct, 2002 - No. 24, Oct, 2004 ($2.95)
1-24: 1-Casey-s/Nguyen-a; two covers by Nguyen and Rian Hughes and Nguyen. 8-Back-up preview of The Authority: High Stakes pt. 3 — 3.00
...: Brand Building TPB (2003, $14.95) r/#1-6 — 15.00
...: Full Disclosure TPB (2004, $14.95) r/#7-12 — 15.00
...: Year One TPB (2010, $24.99) r/#1-12 — 25.00
...: Year Two TPB (2011, $24.99) r/#13-24 — 25.00

WILDC.A.T.S/ X-MEN: THE GOLDEN AGE (See also X-Men/WildC.A.T.S.: The Dark Age)
Image Comics (WildStorm Productions): Feb, 1997 ($4.50, one-shot)
1-Lobdell-s/Charest-a; Two covers (Charest, Jim Lee) — 5.00
1-"3-D" Edition ($6.50) w/glasses — 7.00

WILDC.A.T.S/ X-MEN: THE MODERN AGE
Image Comics (WildStorm Productions): Aug, 1997 ($4.50, one-shot)
1-Robinson-s/Hughes-a; Two covers (Hughes, Paul Smith) — 5.00
1-"3-D" Edition ($6.50) w/glasses — 7.00

WILDC.A.T.S/ X-MEN: THE SILVER AGE
Image Comics (WildStorm Productions): June, 1997 ($4.50, one-shot)
1-Lobdell-s/Jim Lee-a; Two covers(Neal Adams, Jim Lee) — 5.00
1-"3-D" Edition ($6.50) w/glasses — 7.00

WILDCORE
Image Comics (WildStorm Prods.): Nov, 1997 - No. 10, Dec, 1998 ($2.50)
1-10: Two covers (Booth/McWeeney, Charest) — 4.00
1-($3.50)-Voyager Pack w/DV8 preview — 5.00
1-Chromium-c — 5.00

WILD DOG
DC Comics: Sept, 1987 - No. 4, Dec, 1987 (75¢, limited series)
1-4 — 4.00
Special 1 (1989, $2.50, 52 pgs.) — 5.00

WILDERNESS TREK (See Zane Grey, Four Color 333)

WILDFIRE (See Zane Grey, FourColor 433)

WILDFIRE
Image Comics (Top Cow): Jun, 2014 - No. 4, Oct, 2014 ($3.99, limited series)
1-4-Matt Hawkins-s/Linda Sejic-a — 4.00

WILD FRONTIER (Cheyenne Kid #8 on)
Charlton Comics: Oct, 1955 - No. 7, Apr, 1957
1-Davy Crockett — 14 28 42 76 108 140

2-6-Davy Crockett in all — 9 18 27 47 61 75
7-Origin & 1st app. Cheyenne Kid — 10 20 30 56 76 95

WILD GIRL
DC Comics (WildStorm): Jan, 2005 - No. 6, Jun, 2005 ($2.95/$2.99)
1-6-Leah Moore & John Reppion-s/Shawn McManus-a/c — 3.00

WILDGUARD: CASTING CALL
Image Comics: Sept, 2003 - No. 6, Feb, 2004 ($2.95)
1-6: 1-Nauck-s/a; two covers by Nauck and McGuinness. 2-Wieringo var-c. 6-Noto var-c — 3.00
... Vol. 1: Casting Call (1/05, $17.95, TPB) r/#1-6; cover gallery; Todd Nauck bio — 18.00
Wildguard: Fire Power 1 (12/04, $3.50) Nauck-a; two covers — 3.50
Wildguard: Fool's Gold (7/05 - No. 2, 7/05, $3.50) 1,2-Todd Nauck-s/a — 3.50
Wildguard: Insider (5/08 - No. 3, 7/08, $3.50) 1-3-Todd Nauck-s/a — 3.50

WILD'S END
BOOM! Studios: Sept, 2014 - No. 6, Feb, 2015 ($3.99, limited series)
1-6-Dan Abnett-s/I.N.J. Culbard-a/c — 4.00

WILD'S END
BOOM! Studios: Jun, 2023 - No. 6, Nov, 2023 ($4.99, limited series)
1-6-New story; Dan Abnett-s/I.N.J. Culbard-a/c — 5.00

WILD'S END: THE ENEMY WITHIN
BOOM! Studios: Sept, 2015 - No. 6, Feb, 2016 ($3.99, limited series)
1-6-Dan Abnett-s/I.N.J. Culbard-a/c — 4.00

WILDSIDERZ
DC Comics (WildStorm): No. 0, Aug, 2005 - No. 2, Jan, 2006 ($1.99/$3.50)
0-(8/05, $1.99) Series preview & character profiles; J. Scott Campbell-a — 3.00
1,2: 1-(10/05, $3.50) J. Scott Campbell-s/a; Andy Hartnell-s — 3.50

WILDSTAR (Also see The Dragon & The Savage Dragon)
Image Comics (Highbrow Entertainment): Sept, 1995 - No. 3, Jan, 1996 ($2.50, lim. series)
1-3: Al Gordon scripts; Jerry Ordway-c/a — 4.00

WILDSTAR: SKY ZERO
Image Comics (Highbrow Entertainment): Mar, 1993 - No. 4, Nov, 1993 ($1.95, lim. series)
1-4: 1-($2.50)-Embossed-c w/silver ink; Ordway-c/a in all — 4.00
1-($1.95)-Newsstand ed. w/silver ink-c, not embossed — 4.00
1-Gold variant — 6.00

WILD STARS
Collector's Edition/Little Rocket Productions: Summer, 1984 - Present (B&W)
Vol. 1 #1 (Summer 1984, $1.50) — 5.00
Vol. 2 #1 (Winter 1988, $1.95) Foil-c; die-cut front & back-c — 5.00
Vol. 3: #1-6-Brunner-c; Tierney-s. 1,2-Brewer-a. 3-6-Simons-a — 4.00
7-($5.95) Simons-a — 6.00
TPB (2004, $17.95) r/Vol. 1-3 — 18.00

WILDSTORM
Image Comics/DC Comics (WildStorm Publishing): 1994 - 2009 (one-shots, TPBs)
... After the Fall TPB (2009, $19.99) r/back-up stories from Wildcats V5 #1-11, the Authority V5 #1-11; Gen 13 V4 #21-28, and Stormwatch: PHD #13-20 — 20.00
...Annual 2000 (12/00, $3.50) Devil's Night x-over; Moy-a — 4.00
...: Armageddon TPB (2008, $17.99) r/Armageddon one-shots in Midnighter, Welcome To Tranquility, Wetworks, Gen13, Stormwatch PHD, and Wildcats titles — 18.00
...Chamber of Horrors (10/95, $3.50)-Bisley-c — 4.00
...Fine Arts: Spotlight on Gen13 (2/08, $3.50) art and covers with commentary — 3.50
...Fine Arts: Spotlight on Jim Lee (2/07, $3.50) art and covers by Lee with commentary — 3.50
...Fine Arts: Spotlight on J. Scott Campbell (5/07, $3.50) art and covers with commentary — 3.50
...Fine Arts: Spotlight on The Authority (1/08, $3.50) art and covers with commentary — 3.50
...Fine Arts: Spotlight on WildCATs (3/08, $3.50) art and covers with commentary — 3.50
...Fine Arts: The Gallery Collection (12/98, $19.95) Lee-c — 20.00
...Halloween 1 (10/97, $2.50) Warner-c — 4.00
...Rarities 1(12/94, $4.95, 52 pgs.)-r/Gen 13 1/2 & other stories — 5.00
...Summer Special 1 (2001, $5.95) Short stories by various; Hughes-c — 6.00
...Swimsuit Special 1 (12/94, $2.95), ...Swimsuit Special 2 (1995, $2.50) — 4.00
...Swimsuit Special '97 #1 (7/97, $2.50) — 4.00
... 30th Anniversary Special 1 (1/23, $7.99) Short stories & pin-ups by various; Jim Lee-c — 8.00
...Thunderbook 1 (10/00, $6.95) Short stories by various incl. Hughes, Moy — 7.00
...Ultimate Sports 1 (8/97, $2.50) — 4.00
...Universe Sourcebook (5/95, $2.50) — 4.00
...Universe 2008 Convention Exclusive ('08, no cover price) preview of World's End x-over — 3.00

WILDSTORM!
Image Comics (WildStorm): Aug, 1995 - No. 4, Nov, 1995 ($2.50, B&W/color, anthology)
1-4: 1-Simonson-a — 4.00

WILD STORM, THE
DC Comics (WildStorm): Apr, 2017 - No. 24, Sept, 2019 ($3.99)
1-24-Warren Ellis-s/Jon Davis-Hunt-a; Zealot and the Engineer app. 19-New Apollo &

	GD 2.0	VG 4.0	FN 6.0	VF 8.0	VF/NM 9.0	NM- 9.2

Midnight 4.00

WILD STORM: MICHAEL CRAY, THE
DC Comics (WildStorm): Dec, 2017 - No. 12, Dec. 2018 ($3.99)

1-12: 1-Bryan Hill-s/N. Steven Harris-a; Oliver Queen app. 8-10,12-Constantine app. 4.00

WILDSTORM PRESENTS: ...
DC Comics (WildStorm): Jan, 2011 - Feb, 2011 ($7.99, squarebound, reprints)

1-(1/11) r/short stories by various incl. Pearson, Conner, Corben, Jeanty, Mahnke 8.00
Planetary: Lost Worlds (2/11) r/Planetary/Authority & Planetary/JLA: Terra Occulta 8.00

WILDSTORM REVELATIONS
DC Comics (WildStorm): Mar, 2008 - No. 6, May, 2008 ($2.99, limited series)

1-6-Beatty & Gage-s/Craig-a. The Authority app. 3.00
TPB (2008, $17.99) r/#1-6; cover sketches 18.00

WILDSTORM RISING
Image Comics (WildStorm Publishing): May, 1995 - No.2, June, 1995 ($1.95/$2.50)

1-($2.50)-Direct Market, WildStorm Rising Pt. 1 w/bound-in card 4.00
1-($1.95)-Newstand, WildStorm Rising Pt. 1 .... 4.00
2-($2.50)-Direct Market, WildStorm Rising Pt. 10 w/bound-in card; continues in WildC.A.T.s #21. .... 4.00
2-($1.95)-Newstand, WildStorm Rising Pt. 10 .... 4.00
Trade paperback (1996, $19.95)-Collects x-over; B. Smith-c 20.00

WILDSTORM SPOTLIGHT
Image Comics (WildStorm Publishing): Feb, 1997 - No. 4 ($2.50)

1-4: 1-Alan Moore-s 4.00

WILDSTORM UNIVERSE '97
Image Comics (WildStorm Publishing): Dec, 1996 - No. 3 ($2.50, limited series)

1-3: 1-Wraparound-c. 3-Gary Frank-c 4.00

WILDTHING
Marvel Comics UK: Apr, 1993 - No. 7, Oct, 1993 ($1.75)

1-($2.50)-Embossed-c; Venom & Carnage cameo 5.00
2-7: 2-Spider-Man & Venom. 6-Mysterio app. 4.00

WILD THING (Wolverine's daughter in the M2 universe)
Marvel Comics: Oct, 1999 - No. 5, Feb, 2000 ($1.99)

1-5: 1-Lim-a in all. 2-Two covers 4.00
Wizard #0 supplement; battles the Hulk 4.00
Spider-Girl Presents Wild Thing. Crash Course (2007, $7.99, digest) r/#0-5 .... 8.00

WILDTIMES
DC Comics (WildStorm Productions): Aug, 1999 ($2.50, one-shots)

...Deathblow #1 -set in 1899; Edwards-a; Jonah Hex app., ...DV8 #1 -set in 1944; Altieri-s/p; Sgt. Rock app., ...Gen13 #1 -set in 1969; Casey-s/Johnson-a; Teen Titans app., ...Grifter #1 -set in 1923; Paul Smith-a; ...Wetworks #1 -Waid-s/Lopresti-a; Superman app. 4.00
...WildC.A.T.s #0 -Wizard supplement; Charest-c 4.00

WILD WEST (Wild Western #3 on)
Marvel Comics (WFP): Spring, 1948 - No. 2, July, 1948

	GD	VG	FN	VF	VF/NM	NM-
1-Two-Gun Kid, Arizona Annie, & Tex Taylor begin; Shores-c	43	86	129	271	461	650
2-Captain Tootsie by Beck; Shores-c	34	68	102	199	325	450

WILD WEST (Black Fury #1-57)
Charlton Comics: V2#58, Nov, 1966

V2#58	2	4	6	11	16	20

WILD WEST C.O.W.-BOYS OF MOO MESA (TV)
Archie Comics: Dec, 1992 - No. 3, Feb, 1993 (limited series)
V2#1, Mar, 1993 - No. 3, July, 1993 ($1.25)

1-3,V2#1-3 .... 4.00

WILD WESTERN (Formerly Wild West #1,2)
Marvel/Atlas (WFP): No. 3, 9/48 - No. 57, 9/57 (3-11: 52 pgs, 12-on: 36 pgs)

	GD	VG	FN	VF	VF/NM	NM-
3(#1)-Tex Morgan begins; Two-Gun Kid, Tex Taylor, & Arizona Annie continue from Wild West	37	74	111	218	354	490
4-Last Arizona Annie; Captain Tootsie by Beck; Kid Colt app.	27	54	81	158	259	360
5-2nd app. Black Rider (1/49); Blaze Carson, Captain Tootsie (by Beck) app.	31	62	93	182	296	410
6-8: 6-Blaze Carson app; anti-Wertham editorial	18	36	54	107	169	230
9-Photo-c; Black Rider app., also in #11-19	23	46	69	136	223	310
10-Charles Starrett photo-c	25	50	75	150	245	340
11-(Last 52 pg. issue) The Prairie Kid app.	20	40	60	117	189	260
12-14,16-19: All Black Rider-c/stories. 12-14-The Prairie Kid & his horse Fury app.	21	42	63	122	199	275
15-Red Larabee, Gunhawk (origin), his horse Blaze & Apache Kid begin, end #22; Black Rider-c/story	22	44	66	132	216	300
20-30: 20-Kid Colt-c begin. 24-Has 2 Kid Colt stories. 26-1st app. The Ringo Kid? (2/53); 4 pg. story. 30-Katz-a	15	30	45	85	130	175
31-40	13	26	39	72	101	130
41-47,49-51,53,57	11	22	33	64	90	115
48-Williamson/Torres-a (4 pgs); Drucker-a	14	28	42	81	118	155
52-Crandall-a	14	28	42	76	108	140
54,55-Williamson-a in both (5 & 4 pgs), #54 with Mayo plus 2 text illos	15	30	45	84	127	170
56-Baker-a?	15	30	45	83	124	165

NOTE: Annie Oakley in #46, 47. Apache Kid in #15-22, 39. Arizona Kid in #21, 23. Arrowhead in #34-39. Black Rider in #5, 8-19, 33-44. Fighting Texan in #17. Kid Colt in #4-6, 8-11, 20-47, 51, 52, 54-56. Outlaw Kid in #43. Red Hawkins in #13, 14. Ringo Kid in #26, 39, 41, 43, 44, 46, 47, 50-56. Tex Morgan in #3, 4, 6, 9, 11. Tex Taylor in #3-6, 9, 11. Texas Kid in #3-6, 8, 9, 11, 12, 33-39, 41. Wyatt Earp in #47. Ayers-a 53, 54. Berg a-26; c-24. Colan a-49. Forte a-28, 30. Al Hartley a-16, 51. Heath a-4, 5, 8; c-34, 44. Keller a-24, 26(2), 29-40, 44-46, 48, 50. Maneely a-10, 12, 15, 16, 28, 35, 38, 40-45; c-11, 18-22, 33, 35, 36, 38-42, 45, 51, 53, 54, 56, 57. Morisi a-23, 52. Pakula a-42, 52. Powell a-51. Romita a-24(2). Severin a-46, 47; c-48. Shores a-3, 5, 30, 31, 33, 35, 36, 44. Sinnott a-34-39. Wildey a-43. Bondage c-19.

WILD WESTERN ACTION (Also see The Bravados)
Skywald Publ. Corp.: Mar, 1971 - No. 3, June, 1971 (25¢, reprints, 52 pgs.)

	GD	VG	FN	VF	VF/NM	NM-
1-Durango Kid, Straight Arrow-r; with all references to "Straight" in story relettered to "Swift"; Bravados begin; Shores-a (new)	3	6	9	16	24	32
2,3: 2-Billy Nevada, Durango Kid. 3-Red Mask, Durango Kid	2	4	6	13	18	22

WILD WESTERN ROUNDUP
Red Top/Decker Publications/I. W. Enterprises: Oct, 1957; 1960-'61

	GD	VG	FN	VF	VF/NM	NM-
1(1957)-Kid Cowboy-r	6	12	18	27	33	38
I.W. Reprint #1('60-61) r/#1 by Red Top	2	4	6	9	13	16

WILD WEST RODEO
Star Publications: 1953 (15¢)

	GD	VG	FN	VF	VF/NM	NM-
1-A comic book coloring book with regular full color cover & B&W inside	14	28	42	76	108	140

WILD WILD WEST, THE (TV)
Gold Key: June, 1966 - No. 7, Oct, 1969 (All have Robert Conrad photo-c)

	GD	VG	FN	VF	VF/NM	NM-
1-McWilliams-a	13	26	39	89	195	300
1-Variant edition with photo back-c (scarce)	14	28	42	93	204	315
2-Robert Conrad photo-c; McWilliams-a	8	16	24	56	108	160
2-Variant edition with Conrad photo back-c (scarce)	9	18	27	62	126	190
3-7	6	12	18	42	79	115
3-Variant edition with photo back-c (scarce)	8	16	24	56	108	160

WILD, WILD WEST, THE
Millennium Publications: Oct, 1990 - No. 4, Jan?, 1991 ($2.95, limited series)

1-4-Based on TV show 4.00

WILKIN BOY (See That...)

WILL EISNER READER
Kitchen Sink Press: 1991 ($9.95, B&W, 8 1/2" x 11", TPB)

nn-Reprints stories from Will Eisner's Quarterly; Eisner-s/a/c 15.00
nn-(DC Comics, 10/00, $9.95) 10.00

WILL EISNER'S JOHN LAW: ANGELS AND ASHES, DEVILS AND DUST
IDW Publ.: Apr, 2006 - No. 4 ($3.99, B&W, limited series)

1-New stories with Will Eisner's characters; Gary Chaloner-s/a 4.00

WILLIE COMICS (Formerly Ideal #1-4; Crime Cases #24 on; Li'l Willie #20 & 21)
(See Gay Comics, Laugh, Millie The Model & Wisco)
Marvel Comics (MgPC): #5, Fall, 1946 - #19, 4/49; #22, 1/50 - #23, 5/50 (No #20 & 21)

	GD	VG	FN	VF	VF/NM	NM-
5(#1)-George, Margie, Nellie the Nurse & Willie begin	65	130	195	416	708	1000
6,8,9	30	60	90	177	289	400
7(1),10,11-Kurtzman's "Hey Look"	32	64	96	188	307	425
12,14-18,22,23	27	54	81	158	259	360
13,19-Kurtzman's "Hey Look" (#19-last by Kurtzman?)	28	56	84	168	274	380

NOTE: Cindy app. in #17. Jeanie app. in #17. Little Lizzie app. in #22.

WILLIE MAYS (See The Amazing...)

WILLIE THE PENGUIN
Standard Comics: Apr, 1951 - No. 6, Apr, 1952

	GD	VG	FN	VF	VF/NM	NM-
1-Funny animal	15	30	45	85	130	175
2-6	9	18	27	50	65	80

WILLIE THE WISE-GUY (Also see Cartoon Kids)
Atlas Comics (NPP): Sept, 1957

	GD	VG	FN	VF	VF/NM	NM-
1-Kida, Maneely-a	21	42	63	122	199	275

WILLOW
Marvel Comics: Aug, 1988 - No. 3, Oct, 1988 ($1.00)

	GD	VG	FN	VF	VF/NM	NM-
1-R/Marvel Graphic Novel #36 (movie adaptation)	2	4	6	10	14	18
2,3						6.00

WILLOW (From Buffy the Vampire Slayer)
Dark Horse Comics: Nov, 2012 - No. 5, Mar, 2013 ($2.99, limited series)

1-5-Jeff Parker-s/Brian Ching-a; covers by David Mack & Megan Lara; Aluwyn app. 3.00

WILL ROGERS WESTERN (Formerly My Great Love #1-4; see Blazing & True Comics #66)
Fox Feature Syndicate: No. 5, June, 1950 - No. 2, Aug, 1950

	GD	VG	FN	VF	VF/NM	NM-
5(#1) Photo-c	34	68	102	204	332	460
2: Photo-c	28	56	84	165	270	375

WILL TO POWER (Also see Comic's Greatest World)
Dark Horse Comics: June, 1994 - No. 12, Aug, 1994 ($1.00, weekly limited series, 20 pgs.)

1-12: 12-Vortex kills Titan. 4.00
NOTE: Mignola c-10-12. Sears c-1-3.

WILL-YUM!
Dell Publishing Co.: No. 676, Feb, 1956 - No. 902, May, 1958

	GD	VG	FN	VF	VF/NM	NM-
Four Color 676 (#1), 765 (1/57), 902	5	10	15	30	50	70

WIN A PRIZE COMICS (Timmy The Timid Ghost #3 on?)
Charlton Comics: Feb, 1955 - No. 2, Apr, 1955

	GD	VG	FN	VF	VF/NM	NM-
V1#1-S&K-a; Poe adapt; E.C. War swipe	87	174	261	553	952	1350
2-S&K-a	58	116	174	371	636	900

WINDY & WILLY (Also see Showcase #81)
National Periodical Publications: May-June, 1969 - No. 4, Nov-Dec, 1969

	GD	VG	FN	VF	VF/NM	NM-
1- r/Dobie Gillis with some art changes begin	7	14	21	44	82	120
2-4	4	8	12	25	40	55

WINGS COMICS
Fiction House Mag.: 9/40 - No. 109, 9/49; No. 110, Wint, 1949-50; No. 111, Spring, 1950; No. 112, 1950(nd); No. 113 - No. 115, 1950(nd); No. 116, 1952(nd); No. 117, Fall, 1952 - No. 122, Wint, 1953-54; No. 123 - No. 124, 1954(nd)

	GD	VG	FN	VF	VF/NM	NM-
1-Skull Squad, Clipper Kirk, Suicide Smith, Jane Martin, War Nurse, Phantom Falcons, Greasemonkey Griffin, Parachute Patrol & Powder Burns begin; grey-tone-c	300	600	900	2010	3505	5000
2	138	276	414	887	1519	2150
3-5	90	180	270	576	988	1400
6-10: 8-Indicia shows #7 (#8 on cover)	69	138	207	442	759	1075

Willow #5 © 20Fox

Wings Comics #32 © FH

Winter Soldier #19 © MAR

	GD	VG	FN	VF	VF/NM	NM-
	2.0	4.0	6.0	8.0	9.0	9.2
11-15	65	130	195	416	708	1000
16-Origin & 1st app. Captain Wings & begin series	77	154	231	493	847	1200
17-20: 20-(4/42) 1st Japanese WWII-c	57	114	171	362	619	875
21-25,27-30	53	106	159	334	567	800
26-1st Good Girl WWII-c for this title	103	206	309	659	1130	1600
31-34,36-40	43	86	129	271	461	650
35-Classic Nazi WWII-c	55	110	165	352	601	850
41-50	36	72	108	211	343	475
51-60: 60-Last Skull Squad	32	64	96	192	314	435
61-67: 66-Ghost Patrol begins (becomes Ghost Squadron #71 on), ends #112?						
	30	60	90	177	289	400
68,69: 68-Clipper Kirk becomes The Phantom Falcon-origin, Part 1; part 2 in #69						
	30	60	90	177	289	400
70-72: 70-1st app. The Phantom Falcon in costume, origin-Part 3; Capt. Wings battles Col. Kamikaze in all	29	58	87	170	278	385
73-85,87,88,92,93,95-99: 80-Phantom Falcon by Larsen. 99-King of the Congo begins?						
	29	58	87	170	278	385
86-Graphic decapitation panel	36	72	108	211	343	475
89-91,94-Classic Good Girl covers	110	220	330	704	1202	1700
100-(12/48)	36	72	108	211	343	475
101-124: 111-Last Jane Martin. 112-Flying Saucer-c (1950). 115-Used in POP, pg. 89.						
121-Atomic Explosion-c. 122-Korean War	23	46	69	136	223	310

NOTE: World War II covers (Nazi or Japanese) on #1-17, 19-67. Bondage covers are common. Captain Wings battles Sky Hag-#75, 76; ...Mr. Atlantis-#85-92; ...Mr. Pupin(Red Agent)-#98-103. Capt. Wings by *Elias*-#52-64, 68, 69; by *Lubbers*-#29-32, 70-111; by *Renee*-#33-46. *Evans* a-85-106, 108-111(Jane Martin); text illos-72-84. *Larsen* a-52, 59, 64, 73-77. Jane Martin by *Fran Hopper*-#68-84; Suicide Smith by *John Celardo*-#72, 74, 76, 80-104; by *Hollingsworth*-#68-70, 105-109, 111; Ghost Squadron by *Astarita*-#67-79; by *Maurice Whitman*-#80-111. King of the Congo by *Moreira*-#99, 100. Skull Squad by *M. Baker*-#52-60; Clipper Kirk by *Baker*-#60, 61; by *Colan*-#53; by *Ingels*-(some issues?). Phantom Falcon by *Larsen*-#73-84. *Elias* c-58-72. *Fawcette* c-3-12, 16, 17, 19, 22-33. *Lubbers* c-74-109. *Tuska* a-5. *Whitman* c-110-124. *Zolnerwich* c-15, 21.

WINGS OF THE EAGLES, THE
Dell Publishing Co.: No. 790, Apr, 1957 (10¢ & 15¢ editions exist)

Four Color 790-Movie; John Wayne photo-c; Toth-a	13	26	39	89	195	300

WINKY DINK (Adventures of…)
Pines Comics: No. 75, Mar, 1957 (one-shot)

75-Marv Levy-c/a	8	16	24	42	54	65

WINKY DINK (TV)
Dell Publishing Co.: No. 663, Nov, 1955

Four Color 663 (#1)	10	20	30	64	132	200

WINNEBAGO GRAVEYARD
Image Comics: Jun, 2017 - No. 4, Sept, 2017 ($3.99)

1-4-Steve Niles/Alison Sampson-a ... 4.00

WINNIE-THE-POOH (Also see Dynabrite Comics)
Gold Key No.1-17/Whitman No. 18 on: January, 1977 - No. 33, July, 1984 (Walt Disney) (Winnie-The-Pooh began as Edward Bear in 1926 by Milne)

1-New art	12	24	36	83	182	280
2-5: 5-New material	3	6	9	16	23	30
6-17: 12-up-New material	2	4	6	9	13	16
18,19(Whitman)	2	4	6	13	18	22
20,21('80) pre-pack only	5	10	15	34	60	85
22('80) (scarcer) pre-pack only	9	18	27	61	123	185
23-28: 27(2/82), 28(4/82)	3	6	9	14	19	24
29-33 (#90299 on-c, no date or date code; pre-pack): 29(4/82), 30(5/83), 31(8/83), 32(4/84), 33(7/84)	3	6	9	21	33	45

WINNIE WINKLE (See Popular Comics & Super Comics)
Dell Publishing Co.: 1941 - No. 7, Sept-Nov, 1949

Large Feature Comic 2 (1941)	39	78	117	231	378	525
Four Color 94 (1945)	14	28	42	96	211	325
Four Color 174	9	18	27	62	126	190
1(3-5/48)-Contains daily & Sunday newspaper-r from 1939-1941						
	9	18	27	60	120	180
2 (6-8/48)	6	12	18	37	66	95
3-7	5	10	15	30	50	70

WINTER GUARD
Marvel Comics: Oct, 2021 - No. 4, Jan, 2022 ($4.99/$3.99)

1-($4.99) Cady-s/Bazaldua-a; Red Guardian & Yelena Belova app. ... 5.00
2-4-($3.99) 2,3-Dracula app. ... 4.00

WINTER MEN, THE
DC Comics (WildStorm): Oct, 2005 - No. 5, Nov, 2006 ($2.99, limited series)

1-5-Brett Lewis-s/John Paul Leon-a ... 3.00
... Winter Special (2/09, $3.99) Lewis-s/Leon-a ... 4.00

WINTER SOLDIER (See Captain America 2005 series)
Marvel Comics: Apr, 2012 - No. 19, Aug, 2013 ($2.99)

1-Black Widow app.; Brubaker-s/Guice-a/Bermejo-c	1	3	4	6	8	10
2						6.00
3-19: 3-5-Dr. Doom app.						4.00

WINTER SOLDIER
Marvel Comics: Feb, 2019 - No. 5, Jun, 2019 ($3.99)

1-5-Kyle Higgins-s/Rod Reis-a; origin re-cap; intro RJ. 3-New robot arm ... 4.00

WINTER SOLDIER: THE BITTER MARCH
Marvel Comics: Apr, 2014 - No. 5, Sept, 2014 ($3.99, limited series)

1-5: 1-Remender-s/Boschi-a/Robinson-c; set in 1966; Nick Fury app. ... 4.00

WINTER SOLDIER: WINTER KILLS
Marvel Comics: Feb, 2007 ($3.99, one-shot)

1-Flashback to Christmas Eve 1944; Toro & Sub-Mariner app.; Brubaker-s/Weeks-a ... 5.00

WINTERWORLD
Eclipse Comics: Sept, 1987 - No. 3, Mar, 1988 ($1.75, limited series)

1-3 ... 4.00

WINTERWORLD
IDW Publishing: Jun, 2014 - No. 7, Jan, 2015 ($3.99)

1-7: 1-Chuck Dixon-s/Butch Guice-a; three covers. 5-7-Giorello-a ... 4.00
#0-(3/15, $3.99) Origin of Wynn; Dixon-s/Edwards-a; covers by Edwards & Guice ... 4.00

WINTERWORLD: FROZEN FLEET
IDW Publishing: May, 2015 - No. 3, Jul, 2015 ($3.99, limited series)

1-3: 1-Chuck Dixon-s/Esteve Polls-a; three covers. 2,3-Two covers ... 4.00

WISDOM
Marvel Comics (MAX): Jan, 2007 - No. 6, July, 2007 ($3.99, limited series)

1-6: 1-Hairsine-a/c; Cornell-s. 3-6-Manuel Garcia-a ... 4.00
...: Rudiments of Wisdom TPB (2007, $21.99) r/#1-6; series pitch and sketch page ... 22.00

WISE GUYS (See Harvey...)

WISE LITTLE HEN, THE
David McKay Publ./Whitman: 1934 ,1935(48 pgs.); 1937 (Story book)

nn-(1934 edition w/dust jacket)(48 pgs. with color, 8-3/4x9-3/4") -Debut of Donald Duck (see Advs. of Mickey Mouse); Donald app. on cover with Wise Little Hen & Practical Pig; painted cover; same artist as the B&W's from Silly Symphony Cartoon, The Wise Little Hen (1934) (McKay)

Book w/dust jacket	265	530	795	1694	2897	4100
Dust jacket only	63	126	189	403	689	975
nn-(1935 edition w/dust jacket), same as 1934 ed.	152	304	456	965	1658	2350
888 (1937)(9-1/2x13", 12 pgs.)(Whitman) Donald Duck app.						
	39	78	117	231	378	525

WISE SON: THE WHITE WOLF
DC Comics (Milestone): Nov, 1996 - No. 4, Feb, 1997 ($2.50, limited series)

1-Ho Che Anderson-c/a	1	3	4	6	8	10
2-4						5.00

WIT AND WISDOM OF WATERGATE (Humor magazine)
Marvel Comics: 1973, 76 pgs., squarebound

1-Low print run	5	10	15	33	57	80

WITCHBLADE (Also see Cyblade/Shi, Tales Of The..., & Top Cow Classics)
Image Comics (Top Cow Productions): Nov, 1995 - No. 185, Nov, 2015 ($2.50/$2.99)

0	1	2	3	5	6	8
1/2-Mike Turner/Marc Silvestri-c.	3	6	9	19	30	40
1/2 Gold Ed., 1/2 Chromium-c	3	6	9	19	30	40
1/2-(Vol. 2, 11/02, $2.99) Wohl-s/Ching-a/c						3.00
1-Mike Turner-a(p)	4	8	12	19	30	45
1-Anniversary Edition (7/20, $4.99) r/#1 with creator interviews and character history						5.00
1,2-American Ent. Encore Ed.	1	2	3	4	5	7
2,3	2	4	6	11	16	20
4,5	2	4	6	8	10	12
6-9: 8-Wraparound-c. 9-Tony Daniel-a(p)	1	2	3	5	6	8
9-Sunset variant-c	2	4	6	8	10	12
9-DF variant-c	2	4	6	9	12	15
10-Flip book w/Darkness #0, 1st app. the Darkness	2	4	6	9	12	15
10-Variant-c	2	4	6	9	12	15
10-Gold logo	3	6	9	14	20	25
10-($3.95) Dynamic Forces alternate-c	1	2	3	5	6	8
11-15						5.00
16-19: 18,19-"Family Ties" Darkness x-over pt. 1,4						4.00
18-Face to face variant-c, 18-American Ent. Ed., 19-AE Gold Ed.						
	1	2	3	5	6	8
20-25: 24-Pearson, Green-a. 25-($2.95) Turner-a(p)						4.00
25 (Prism variant)						25.00
25 (Special)						10.00

	GD 2.0	VG 4.0	FN 6.0	VF 8.0	VF/NM 9.0	NM- 9.2

26-39: 26-Green-a begins 3.00
27 (Variant) 6.00
40-49,51-53: 40-Begin Jenkins & Veitch-s/Keu Cha-a. 47-Zulli-c/a 3.00
40-Pittsburgh Convention Preview edition; B&W preview of #40 3.00
49-Gold logo 5.00
50-($4.95) Darkness app.; Ching-a; B&W preview of Universe 5.00
54-59: 54-Black outer-c with gold foil logo; Wohl-s/Manapul-a 3.00
60-74,76-91,93-99: 60-($2.99) Endgame x-over with Tomb Raider #25 & Evo #1.
  64,65-Magdalena app. 71-Kirk-a. 77,81-85-Land-c. 80-Four covers. 87-Bachalo-a 3.00
75-($4.99) Manapul-a 5.00
92-($4.99) Origin of the Witchblade; art by various incl. Bachalo, Perez, Linsner, Cooke 5.00
100-($4.99) Five covers incl. Turner, Silvestri, Linsner; art by various; Jake dies 5.00
101-124,126-143: 103-Danielle Baptiste gets the Witchblade; Linsner variant-c.
  116-124,140,141-Sejic-a. 126-128-War of the Witchblades. 134-136-Aphrodite IV app.
  139-Gaydos-a. 143-Matt Dow Smith-a 3.00
125-($3.99) War of the Witchblades begins; 3 covers; Sejic-a 4.00
144-($4.99) Origin retold; wraparound-c; Sejic-a; back-up w/Sablik-s; pin-up gallery 5.00
145-149-($3.99) Sejic-a/c. 149-Angelus app. 4.00
150-($4.99) Four covers; last Marz-s; Sejic-a; cover gallery & series timeline 5.00
151-174-($2.99) Alternate reality after Artifacts #13; Seeley-s; multiple covers 3.00
175-($5.99) Three covers; Marz-s; Laura Braga-a; Temple of Shadows back-up 6.00
176-184-($5.99) 180-Hine-s/Rearte-a 4.00
185-($5.99)-Last issue; Marz & Hawkins-s; art by various; bonus preview of Switch #1 6.00
... and Tomb Raider (4/05, $2.99) Jake Lee-c; art by Lee and Texiera 3.00
...: Animated (8/03, $2.99) Magdalena & Darkness app.; Dini-s/Bone, Bullock, Cooke-a/c 3.00
...: Annual 2009 (4/09, $3.99) Basaldua-a 4.00
Annual #1 (12/10, $4.99) the Witchblade in Stalingrad 1942, Shasteen-a; Haley-a 5.00
...: Art of the Witchblade (7/06, $2.99) pin-ups by various incl. Turner, Land, Linsner 3.00
...: Bearers of the Blade (7/06, $2.99) pin-up/profiles of bearers of the Witchblade 3.00
...: Blood Oath (8/04, $4.99) Sara teams with Phenix & Sibilla; Roux-a 5.00
...: Blood Relations TPB (2003, $12.99) r/#54-58 13.00
...: Case Files 1 (10/14, $3.99) Character profiles and story summaries 4.00
...: Compendium Vol. 1 (2006, $59.99) r/#1-50; gallery of variant covers and art 60.00
...: Compendium Vol. 2 (2007, $59.99) r/#51-100; gallery of variant covers and art 60.00
...: Cover Gallery Vol. 1 (12/05, $2.99) intro. by Stan Lee 3.00
.../Darkchylde (7/00, $2.50) Green-s/a(p) 3.00
...: Dark Minds (6/04, $9.99) new story box r/Dark Minds/Witchblade #1 10.00
...: Darkness: Family Ties Collected Edition (10/98, $9.95) r/#18,19 and Darkness #9,10 10.00
...: Darkness Special (12/99, $3.95) Green-c/a 4.00
...: Day of the Outlaws (4/13, $3.99) Fialkov-s/Blake-a; Witchblade in 1878 Colorado 4.00
...: Demon 1 (2003, $6.99) Mark Millar-s/Jae Lee-c/a 7.00
...: Devi (4/08, $3.99) Basaldua-a/Land-c; continues in Devi/Witchblade 4.00
...: Distinctions (See Tales of the Witchblade)
...: Due Process (8/10, $3.99) Alina Urusov-a; Phil Smith-s 4.00
.../Elektra (3/97, $2.95) Devil's Reign Pt. 6 4.00
...: Gallery (11/00, $2.95) Profile pages and pin-up by various; Turner-c 3.00
Image Firsts: Witchblade #1 (4/10, $1.00) reprints #1 3.00
Infinity (5/99, $3.50) Lobdell-s/Pollina-c/a 3.00
.../Lady Death (11/01, $4.95) Manapul-c/a 5.00
...: Prevailing TPB (2000, $14.95) r/#20-25; new Turner-c 15.00
...: Revelations TPB (2000, $24.95) r/#9-17; new Turner-c 25.00
...The Punisher (6/07, $3.99) Marz-s/Melo-a/Linsner-c 4.00
...Tomb Raider #1/2 (7/00, $2.95) Covers by Turner and Cha 4.00
...: Unbalanced Pieces FCBD Edition (5/12, giveaway) Christopher-c 3.00
...: Vol. 1 TPB (1/08, $4.99) r/#80-85; Marz intro.; cover gallery 5.00
...: Vol. 2 TPB (2/08, $14.99) r/#86-92; cover gallery 15.00
...: Vol. 3 TPB (3/08, $14.99) r/#93-100; Edginton intro.; cover gallery 15.00
...: vs. Frankenstein: Monster War 2005 (8/05, $2.99) pt. 3 of x-over 3.00
...: Witch Hunt Vol. 1 TPB (2/06, $14.99) r/#80-85; Marz intro.; Choi afterward; cover gallery 15.00
Wizard #500 10.00
.../Wolverine (6/04, $2.99) Basaldua-c/a; Claremont-s 3.00

WITCHBLADE
Image Comics (Top Cow): Dec, 2017 - Present ($3.99)

1-18: 1-Kittredge-s/Ingranata-a; intro. Alex Underwood 4.00

WITCHBLADE/ALIENS/THE DARKNESS/PREDATOR
Dark Horse Comics/Top Cow Productions: Nov, 2000 ($2.99)

1-3-Mel Rubi-a 4.00

WITCHBLADE COLLECTED EDITION
Image Comics (Top Cow Productions): July, 1996 - No. 8 ($4.95/$6.95, squarebound, limited series)

1-7-($4.95): Two issues reprinted in each 5.00
8-($6.95) r/#15-17 7.00
...: Slipcase (10/96, $10.95)-Packaged w/ Coll. Ed. #1-4 11.00

WITCHBLADE: DEMON REBORN
Dynamite Entertainment: 2012 - No. 4, 2012 ($3.99, limited series)

1-4-Ande Parks-s/Jose Luis-a; covers by Calero & Jae Lee 4.00

WITCHBLADE: DESTINY'S CHILD
Image Comics (Top Cow): Jun, 2000 - No. 3, Sept, 2000 ($2.95, limited series)

1-3: 1-Boller-a/Keu Cha-c 3.00

WITCHBLADE: MANGA (Takeru Manga)
Image Comics (Top Cow): Feb, 2007 - No. 12, Mar, 2008 ($2.99/$3.99)

1-4-Colored reprints of Japanese Witchblade manga. 1-Three covers. 2-Two covers 3.00
5-12-($3.99) 4.00

WITCHBLADE: OBAKEMONO
Image Comics (Top Cow Productions): 2002 ($9.95, one-shot graphic novel)

1-Fiona Avery-s/Billy Tan-a; forward by Straczynski 10.00

WITCHBLADE/ RED SONJA
Dynamite Ent./Top Cow: 2012 - No. 5, 2012 ($3.99, limited series)

1-5-Doug Wagner-s/Cezar Razek-a/Alé Garza-c 4.00

WITCHBLADE: SHADES OF GRAY
Dynamite Ent./Top Cow: 2007 - No. 4, 2007 ($3.50, lim. series)

1,2: 1-Sara Pezzini meets Dorian Gray; Segovia-a; multiple covers 3.50

WITCHBLADE/ TOMB RAIDER SPECIAL (Also see Tomb Raider/...)
Image Comics (Top Cow Productions): Dec, 1998 ($2.95)

1-Based on video game character; Turner-a(p) 4.00
1-Silvestri variant-c 6.00
1-Turner bikini variant-c 10.00
1-Prism-c 12.00
Wizard 1/2 -Turner-s 10.00

WITCHCRAFT (See Strange Mysteries, Super Reprint #18)
Avon Periodicals: Mar-Apr, 1952 - No. 6, Mar, 1953

	GD 2.0	VG 4.0	FN 6.0	VF 8.0	VF/NM 9.0	NM- 9.2
1-Kubert-a; 1 pg. Check-a	142	284	426	909	1555	2200
2-Kubert & Check-a; classic skull-c	245	490	735	1568	2684	3800
3,6: 3-Lawrence-a; Kinstler inside-c	74	148	222	470	810	1150
4-People cooked alive c/story	187	374	561	1197	2049	2900
5-Kelly Freas painted-a	194	388	582	1242	2121	3000

NOTE: *Hollingsworth a-4-6; c-4, 6. McCann a-3?*

WITCHCRAFT
DC Comics (Vertigo): June, 1994 - No. 3, Aug, 1994 ($2.95, limited series)

1-3: James Robinson scripts & Kaluta-c in all 4.00
1-Platinum Edition 15.00
Trade paperback-(1996, $14.95)-r/#1-3; Kaluta-c 15.00

WITCHCRAFT: LA TERREUR
DC Comics (Vertigo): Apr, 1998 - No. 3, Jun, 1998 ($2.50, limited series)

1-3: Robinson-s/Zulli-a & Locke-a; interlocking cover images 4.00

WITCH DOCTOR (See Walking Dead #85 flip book for preview)
Image Comics: Jun, 2011 - No. 4, Nov, 2011 ($2.99, limited series)

1-4-Seifert-s/Ketner-a/c 3.00
...: Mal Practice 1-6 (11/12 - No. 6, 4/13, $2.99) Seifert-s/Ketner-a/c 3.00
...: The Resuscitation (12/11, $2.99) Seifert-s/Ketner-a/c 3.00

WITCHER, THE
Dark Horse Comics: Mar, 2014 - No. 5, Jul, 2014 ($3.99, limited series)

1-5-Tobin-s/Querio-a 4.00

WITCHER, THE: FADING MEMORIES
Dark Horse Comics: Nov, 2020 - No. 4, Mar, 2021 ($3.99, limited series)

1-4-Bartosz Sztybor-s/Amad Mir-a 4.00

WITCHER, THE: FOX CHILDREN
Dark Horse Comics: Apr, 2015 - No. 5, Aug, 2015 ($3.99, limited series)

1-5-Tobin-s/Querio-a 4.00

WITCHER, THE: OF FLESH AND FLAME
Dark Horse Comics: Dec, 2018 - No. 4, Mar, 2019 ($3.99, limited series)

1-4-Motyka-s/Strychowska-a 4.00

WITCHER, THE: THE BALLAD OF TWO WOLVES
Dark Horse Comics: Dec, 2022 - No. 4, Apr, 2023 ($3.99, limited series)

1-4-Bartosz Sztybor-s/Miki Montllo-a 4.00

WITCHER, THE: WILD ANIMALS
Dark Horse Comics: Sept, 2023 - No. 4, Feb, 2024 ($3.99, limited series)

1-4-Bartosz Sztybor-s/Nataliia Rerekina-a 4.00

WITCHER, THE: WITCH'S LAMENT
Dark Horse Comics: May, 2021 - No. 4, Aug, 2021 ($3.99, limited series)

1-4-Bartosz Sztybor-s/Vanesa Del Rey-a 4.00

WITCHES
Marvel Comics: Aug, 2004 - No. 4, Sept, 2004 ($2.99, limited series)

1-4: 1,2-Deodato, Jr-a; Dr. Strange app. 3,4-Conrad-a 3.00
... Vol. 1: The Gathering (2004, $9.99) r/series 10.00

WITCHES TALES (Witches Western Tales #29,30)
Witches Tales/Harvey Publications: Jan, 1951 - No. 28, Dec, 1954 (date misprinted as 4/55)

	GD 2.0	VG 4.0	FN 6.0	VF 8.0	VF/NM 9.0	NM- 9.2
1-Powell-a (1 pg.)	155	310	465	992	1696	2400
2-Eye injury panel	61	122	183	390	670	950
3-7,9,10	47	94	141	296	498	700
8-Eye injury panels	58	116	174	371	636	900
11-13,15,16: 12-Acid in face story	41	82	123	256	428	600
14,17-Powell/Nostrand-a. 17-Atomic disaster story	45	90	135	284	480	675
18-Nostrand-a; E.C. swipe/Shock S.S.	43	86	129	271	461	650
19-Nostrand-a; E.C. swipe/"Glutton"; Devil-c	77	154	231	493	847	1200
20-24-Nostrand-a. 21-E.C. swipe; rape story. 23-Wood E.C. swipes/Two-Fisted Tales #34	43	86	129	271	461	650
25-Nostrand-a; E.C. swipe/Mad Barber; decapitation-c	622	1244	1866	4541	8021	11,500
26-28: 27-r/#6 with diff.-c. 28-r/#8 with diff.-c	39	78	117	240	395	550

NOTE: *Check a-24. Elias c-8, 10, 16-27. Kremer a-18; c-25. Nostrand a-17-25; 14, 17(w/Powell). Palais a-1, 2, 4(2), 5(2), 7-9, 12, 14, 15, 17. Powell a-3-7, 10, 11, 19-27. Bondage-c 1, 3, 5, 6, 8, 9.*

WITCHES TALES (Magazine)
Eerie Publications: V1#7, July, 1969 - V7#1, Feb, 1975 (B&W, 52 pgs.)

	GD 2.0	VG 4.0	FN 6.0	VF 8.0	VF/NM 9.0	NM- 9.2
V1#7(7/69)	9	15	27	63	129	195
V1#8(9/69), 9(11/69)	8	16	24	51	96	140
V2#1-6('70), V3#1-6('71)	6	12	18	38	69	100
V4#1-6('72), V5#1-6('73), V6#1-6('74), V7#1	5	10	15	35	63	90

NOTE: *Ajax/Farrell reprints in early issues.*

WITCHES' WESTERN TALES (Formerly Witches Tales)(Western Tales #31 on)
Harvey Publications: No. 29, Feb, 1955 - No. 30, Apr, 1955

	GD 2.0	VG 4.0	FN 6.0	VF 8.0	VF/NM 9.0	NM- 9.2
29,30-Featuring Clay Duncan & Boys' Ranch; S&K-r/from Boys' Ranch including-c.						
29-Last pre-code	19	38	57	111	176	240

WITCHFINDER, THE
Image Comics (Liar): Sept, 1999 - No. 3, Jan, 2000 ($2.95)

1-3-Romano-a/Sharon & Matthew Scott-plot 4.00

WITCHFINDER: CITY OF THE DEAD

Witchblade #144 © TCOW

The Witching Hour #12 © DC

Wolf Moon #1 © Bunn & Haun

	GD 2.0	VG 4.0	FN 6.0	VF 8.0	VF/NM 9.0	NM- 9.2

Dark Horse Comics: Aug, 2016 - No. 5, Dec, 2016 ($3.99, limited series)
1-5-Mignola & Roberson-s/Stenbeck-a/Tedesco-c ... 4.00

WITCHFINDER: LOST AND GONE FOREVER
Dark Horse Comics: Feb, 2011 - No. 5, Jun, 2011 ($3.50, limited series)
1-5-John Severin-a; Mignola & Arcudi-s. 1-Two covers by Mignola & Severin ... 3.50

WITCHFINDER: THE GATES OF HEAVEN
Dark Horse Comics: May, 2018 - No. 5, Sept, 2018 ($3.99, limited series)
1-5-Mignola & Roberson-s/D'Israeli-c/a ... 4.00

WITCHFINDER: THE REIGN OF DARKNESS
Dark Horse Comics: Nov, 2019 - No. 5, Mar, 2020 ($3.99, limited series)
1-5-Mignola & Roberson-s/Mitten-a/c ... 4.00

WITCH HUNTER
Malibu Comics (Ultraverse): Apr, 1996 ($2.50, one-shot)
1 ... 4.00

WITCHING, THE
DC Comics (Vertigo): Aug, 2004 - No. 10, May, 2005 ($2.95/$2.99)
1-10-Vankin-s/Gallagher-a/McPherson-c. 1,2-Lucifer app. ... 3.00

WITCHING HOUR ("The ..." in later issues)
National Periodical Publ./DC Comics: Feb-Mar, 1969 - No. 85, Oct, 1978

	GD 2.0	VG 4.0	FN 6.0	VF 8.0	VF/NM 9.0	NM- 9.2
1-Toth-a, plus Neal Adams-a (2 pgs.)	20	40	60	138	307	475
2,6: 6-Toth-a	8	16	24	55	105	155
3,5-Wrightson-a; Toth-p. 3-Last 12¢ issue	8	16	24	56	108	160
4,12-Toth-a	5	10	15	34	60	85
7-11-Adams-c; Toth-a in all. 8-Adams-a	7	14	21	44	82	120
13-Neal Adams-c/a, 2pgs.	8	16	24	52	99	145
14-Williamson/Garzon, Jones-a; N. Adams-c	7	14	21	48	89	130
15	3	6	9	21	33	45
16-21-(52 pg.) Giants)	4	8	12	25	40	55
22-37,39,40	3	6	9	14	19	24
38-(100 pgs.)	5	10	15	31	53	75
41-60	2	4	6	10	14	18
61-83,85	2	4	6	8	11	14
84-(44 pgs.)	2	4	6	9	13	16

NOTE: *Combined with The Unexpected with #189. Neal Adams c-7-11, 13, 14. Alcala a-24, 27, 33, 41, 43. Anderson a-9, 38. Cardy c-4, 5. Kaluta a-7. Kane a-12p. Morrow a-10, 13, 15, 16. Nino a-31, 40, 45, 47. Redondo a-20, 23, 24, 34, 65; c-53. Reese a-23. Sparling a-1. Toth a-1, 3-12, 38r. Tuska a-11, 12. Wood a-15.*

WITCHING HOUR, THE
DC Comics (Vertigo): 1999 - No. 3, 2000 ($5.95, limited series)
1-3-Bachalo & Thibert-c/a; Loeb & Bachalo-s ... 6.00
Hardcover (2000, $29.95) r/#1-3; embossed cover ... 30.00
Softcover (2003, $19.95), (2009, $19.99) r/#1-3 ... 20.00

WITCHING HOUR, THE
DC Comics (Vertigo): Dec, 2013 ($7.99, one-shot)
1-Short story anthology by various incl. DeConnick, Doyle, Buckingham; Frison-c ... 8.00

WITHIN OUR REACH
Star Reach Productions: 1991 ($7.95, 84 pgs.)
nn-Spider-Man, Concrete by Chadwick, Gift of the Magi by Russell; Christmas stories; Chadwick-c; Spidey back-c ... 8.00

WITH THE MARINES ON THE BATTLEFRONTS OF THE WORLD
Toby Press: 1953 (no month) - No. 2, Mar, 1954 (Photo covers)

	GD 2.0	VG 4.0	FN 6.0	VF 8.0	VF/NM 9.0	NM- 9.2
1-John Wayne story	37	74	111	222	361	500
2-Monty Hall in #1,2	15	30	45	84	127	170

WITH THE U.S. PARATROOPS BEHIND ENEMY LINES (Also see U.S. Paratroops...; #2-6 titled U.S. Paratroops...)
Avon Periodicals: 1951 - No. 6, Dec, 1952

	GD 2.0	VG 4.0	FN 6.0	VF 8.0	VF/NM 9.0	NM- 9.2
1-Wood-c & inside f/c	26	52	78	154	252	350
2-Kinstler-c & inside f/c only	15	30	45	90	140	190
3-6: 5-Extreme violence. 6-Kinstler-c & inside f/c only	15	30	45	84	127	170

NOTE: *Kinstler c-2, 4-6.*

WITNESS, THE (Also see Amazing Mysteries, Captain America #71, Ideal #4, Marvel Mystery #92 & Mystic #7)
Marvel Comics (MjMe): Sept, 1948

	GD 2.0	VG 4.0	FN 6.0	VF 8.0	VF/NM 9.0	NM- 9.2
1(Scarce)-Rico-c?	354	708	1062	2478	4339	6200

WITTY COMICS
Irwin H. Rubin Publ./Chicago Nite Life News No. 2: 1945 - No. 2, 1945

	GD 2.0	VG 4.0	FN 6.0	VF 8.0	VF/NM 9.0	NM- 9.2
1-The Pioneer, Junior Patrol; Japanese war-c	43	86	129	271	461	650
2-The Pioneer, Junior Patrol	22	44	66	132	216	300

WIZARD BEACH

BOOM! Studios: Dec, 2018 - No. 5, Apr, 2019 ($3.99, limited series)
1-5-Shaun Simon-s/Conor Nolan-a ... 4.00

WIZARD OF FOURTH STREET, THE
Dark Horse Comics: Dec, 1987 - No. 2, 1988 ($1.75, B&W, limited series)
1,2: Adapts novel by S/F author Simon Hawke ... 4.00

WIZARD OF OZ (See Classics Illustrated Jr. 535, Dell Jr. Treasury No. 5, First Comics Graphic Novel, Marvel Treasury of Oz, and MGM's Marvelous...)
Dell Publishing Co.: No. 1308, Mar-May, 1962 (TV)

	GD 2.0	VG 4.0	FN 6.0	VF 8.0	VF/NM 9.0	NM- 9.2
Four Color 1308	15	30	45	103	227	350

WIZARDS OF MICKEY (Mickey Mouse)
BOOM! Studios: Jan, 2010 - No. 8, Aug, 2010 ($2.99)
1-8: 1,2-Ambrosio-s; 3 covers on each. 3-8-Two covers ... 3.00

WIZARD'S TALE, THE
Image Comics (Homage Comics): 1997 ($19.95, squarebound, one-shot)
nn-Kurt Busiek-s/David Wenzel-painted-a/c ... 20.00

WOLF & RED
Dark Horse Comics: Apr, 1995 - No. 3, June, 1995 ($2.50, limited series)

	GD 2.0	VG 4.0	FN 6.0	VF 8.0	VF/NM 9.0	NM- 9.2
1-Characters created by Tex Avery	2	4	6	11	16	20
2,3						6.00

WOLF COP
Dynamite Entertainment: 2016 - No. 3, 2016 ($3.99)
1-3-Max Marks-s/Arcana Studios-a ... 4.00

WOLFF & BYRD, COUNSELORS OF THE MACABRE (Becomes Supernatural Law with issue #24)
Exhibit A Press: May, 1994 - No. 23, Aug, 1999 ($2.50, B&W)
1-23-Batton Lash-s/a ... 4.00

WOLF GAL (See Al Capp's...)

WOLFMAN, THE (See Movie Classics)

WOLF MOON
DC Comics (Vertigo): Feb, 2015 - No. 6, Jul, 2015 ($3.99, limited series)
1-6-Bunn-s/Haun-a. 1-Covers by Jae Lee and Jeremy Haun ... 4.00

WOLFPACK
Marvel Comics: Feb, 1988 ($7.95); Aug, 1988 - No. 12, July, 1989 (Lim. series)

	GD 2.0	VG 4.0	FN 6.0	VF 8.0	VF/NM 9.0	NM- 9.2
1-(2/88) 1st app./origin (Marvel Graphic Novel #31)	2	4	6	8	10	12
1-12: 1-(8/88) Hama-s						4.00

WOLVERINE (See Alpha Flight, Daredevil #196, 249, Ghost Rider; Wolverine; Punisher, Havok &..., Incredible Hulk #180, Incredible Hulk &..., Kitty Pryde And..., Marvel Comics Presents, New Avengers, Power Pack, Punisher and..., Rampaging..., Spider-Man vs... & X-Men #94)

WOLVERINE (See Incredible Hulk #180 for 1st app.)
Marvel Comics Group: Sept, 1982 - No. 4, Dec, 1982 (limited series)

	GD 2.0	VG 4.0	FN 6.0	VF 8.0	VF/NM 9.0	NM- 9.2
1-Frank Miller-c/a(p) in all; Claremont-s	10	20	30	64	132	200
2-4	5	10	15	30	50	70
... By Claremont & Miller No. 1 Facsimile Edition (4/20, $3.99) r/#1 with original ads						4.00
... By Claremont & Miller No. 1 Facsimile Edition (2/24, $4.99) r/#1 with original ads						5.00
... By Claremont & Miller HC (2006, $19.99) r/#1-4 & Uncanny X-Men #172-173						20.00
TPB 1(7/87, $4.95)-Reprints #1-4 with new Miller-c	2	4	6	11	16	20
TPB nn (2nd printing, $9.95)-r/#1-4	2	4	6	8	10	12

WOLVERINE
Marvel Comics: Nov, 1988 - No. 189, June, 2003 ($1.50/$1.75/$1.95/$1.99/$2.25)

	GD 2.0	VG 4.0	FN 6.0	VF 8.0	VF/NM 9.0	NM- 9.2
1-Claremont-s/Buscema-a/c	6	12	18	38	69	100
2	3	6	9	18	28	38
3-5: 5-BWS back-c	2	4	6	13	18	22
6,7,9: 6-McFarlane back-c. 7-Hulk app.	2	4	6	8	10	12
8-Classic Grey Hulk-c; Hulk app.	6	12	18	38	69	100
10-1st battle with Sabretooth (before Wolverine had his claws)	4	8	12	27	44	60
11-16: 11-New costume	1	3	4	6	8	10
17-20: 17-Byrne-c/a(p) begins, ends #23	1	2	3	5	6	8
21-26,28-30: 24,25-Jim Lee-c. 26-Begin $1.75-c						6.00
27-Jim Lee-c	3	6	9	16	23	30
31-40,44,47						5.00
41-Sabretooth claims to be Wolverine's father; Cable cameo	2	4	6	11	16	20
41-Gold 2nd printing ($1.75)	2	4	6	11	16	20
42-Sabretooth, Cable & Nick Fury app.; Sabretooth proven not to be Wolverine's father	2	4	6	8	10	12
42-Gold ink 2nd printing ($1.75)	2	4	6	8	10	12
43-Sabretooth cameo (2 panels); saga ends						6.00
45,46-Sabretooth-c/stories						6.00

	GD	VG	FN	VF	VF/NM	NM-
	2.0	4.0	6.0	8.0	9.0	9.2

48,49,51-Sabretooth app. 48-Begin 3 part Weapon X sequel. 51-Sabretooth-c & app. — 6.00

50-(64 pgs.)-Die cut-c; Wolverine back to old yellow costume; Forge, Cyclops, Jubilee, Jean Grey & Nick Fury app. — 2 4 6 10 14 18

52-74,76-80: 54-Shatterstar (from X-Force) app. 55-Gambit, Jubilee, Sunfire-c/story. 55-57,73-Gambit app. 57-Mariko Yashida dies (Late 7/92). 58,59-Terror, Inc. x-over.

60-64-Sabretooth storyline (60,62,64-c) — 5.00

75-($3.95, 68 pgs.)-Wolverine hologram on-c — 1 3 4 6 8 10

81-84,86: 81-bound-in card sheet — 5.00

85-($2.50)-Newsstand edition — 5.00

85-($3.50)-Collectors edition — 6.00

87-90-($1.95)-Deluxe edition — 5.00

87-90-($1.50)-Regular edition — 4.00

91-99,101-114: 91-Return from "Age of Apocalypse," 93-Juggernaut app. 94-Gen X app. 101-104-Elektra app. 104-Origin of Onslaught. 105-Onslaught x-over. 110-Shaman-c/app.

114-Alternate-c — 4.00

100 ($3.95)-Hologram-c; Wolverine loses humanity — 2 4 6 9 13 16

100 ($2.95)-Regular-c. — 1 3 4 6 8 10

102.5 (1996 Wizard mail-away)-Deadpool app.; Vallejo-c/Buckingham-a — 150.00

115-124: 115- Operation Zero Tolerance — 5.00

125-($2.99) Wraparound-c; Viper secret — 5.00

125-($6.95) Jae Lee variant-c — 8.00

126-144: 126,127-Sabretooth app. 128-Sabretooth & Shadowcat app.; Platt-a. 129-Wendigo-c/app. 131-Initial printing contained lettering error. 133-Begin Larsen-a/ Matsuda-a. 138-Galactus-c/app. 139-Cable app.; Yu-a. 142,143-Alpha Flight app. — 4.00

145-($2.99) 25th Anniversary issue; Hulk and Sabretooth app. — 1 3 4 6 8 10

145-($3.99) Foil enhanced cover (also see Promotional section for Nabisco mail-in ed.) — 2 4 6 11 16 20

146,147-Apocalypse: The Twelve; Angel-c/app. — 1 3 4 6 8 10

148,149: 149-Nova-c/app. — 4.00

150-($2.99) Steve Skroce-s/a — 5.00

151-153,156-174,176-182,184-189: 151-Begin $2.25-c. 156-Churchill-a. 159-Chen-a begins. 160-Sabretooth app. 163-Texeira(a(p). 167-BWS-c. 172,173-Alpha Flight app. 176-Colossus app. 185,186-Punisher app. — 4.00

154,155-Deadpool app.; Liefeld-s/a. — 3 6 9 14 20 26

175,183-($3.50) 175-Sabretooth app. — 4.00

#(-1) Flashback (7/97) Logan meets Col. Fury; Nord-a — 4.00

Annual nn (1990, $4.50, squarebound, 52 pgs.)-The Jungle Adventure; Simonson scripts; Mignola-c/a — 1 3 4 6 8 10

Annual 2 (12/90, $4.95, squarebound, 52 pgs.)-Bloodlust — 6.00

Annual nn (#3, 8/91, $5.95, 68 pgs.)-Rahne of Terror; Cable & The New Mutants app.; Andy Kubert-c/a (2nd print exists) — 6.00

Annual '95 (1995, $3.95) — 5.00

Annual '96 (1996, $2.95)- Wraparound-c; Silver Samurai, Yukio, and Red Ronin app. — 5.00

Annual '97 ($2.99) - Wraparound-c — 5.00

Annual 1999, 2000 ($3.50) : 1999-Deadpool app. — 5.00

Annual 2001 ($2.99) - Tieri-s; JH Williams-c — 5.00

...Battles The Incredible Hulk nn (1989, $4.95, squarebound, 52 pg.) r/Incr. Hulk #180,181 — 2 4 6 10 14 18

Best of Wolverine Vol. 1 HC (2004, $29.99) oversized reprints of Hulk #181, mini-series #1-4, Capt. America Ann., #8, Uncanny X-Men #205 & Marvel Comics Presents #72-84 — 30.00

Black Rio (11/98, $5.99)-Casey-s/Oscar Jimenez-a — 6.00

Blood Debt TPB (7/01, $12.95)-r/#150-153; Skroce-c — 13.00

...Blood Hungry nn (1993, $6.95, 68 pgs.)-Kieth-r/Marvel Comics Presents #85-92 w/ new Kieth-c — 2 4 6 8 10 12

...: Bloody Choices nn (1993, $7.95, 68 pgs.)-r/Graphic Novel; Nick Fury app. — 8.00

... By Claremont & Buscema No. 1 Facsimile Edition (4/20, $3.99) r/#1 with original ads — 4.00

... Cable Guts and Glory (10/99, $5.99) Platt-a — 6.00

... Classic Vol. 1 TPB (2005, $12.99) r/#1-5 — 15.00

... Classic Vol. 2 TPB (2005, $12.99) r/#6-10 — 15.00

... Classic Vol. 3 TPB (2006, $14.99) r/#11-16; The Gehenna Stone Affair — 15.00

... Classic Vol. 4 TPB (2006, $14.99) r/#17-23 — 15.00

... Classic Vol. 5 TPB (2007, $14.99) r/#24-30 — 15.00

.../Deadpool: Weapon X TPB (7/02, $21.99)-r/#162-166 & Deadpool #57-60 — 22.00

... Doombringer (11/97, $5.99)-Silver Samurai-c/app. — 6.00

... Evilution (9/94, $5.95) — 6.00

... Exit Wounds 1 (8/19, $4.99) Short stories by Hama/Eaton, Claremont/Larroca; Kieth — 5.00

...: Global Jeopardy 1 (12/93, $2.95, one-shot)-Embossed-c; Sub-Mariner, Zabu, Ka-Zar, Shanna & Wolverine app.; produced in cooperation with World Wildlife Fund — 6.00

...Inner Fury nn (1992, $5.95, 52 pgs.)-Sienkiewicz-c/a — 6.00

...: Judgment Night (2000, $3.99) Shi app.; Battlebook — 6.00

...: Killing (9/93)-Kent Williams-a — 6.00

...: Knight of Terra (1995, $6.95)-Ostrander script — 7.00

... Legends Vol. 2: Meltdown (2003, $19.99) r/Havok & Wolverine: Meltdown #1-4 — 20.00

... Legends Vol. 3 (2003, $12.99) r/#181-186 — 13.00

... Legends Vol. 4,5: 4-(See Wolverine: Xisle). 5-(See Wolverine: Snikt!)

... Legends Vol. 6: Marc Silvestri Book 1 (2004, $19.99) r/#31-34, 41-42, 48-50 — 20.00

.../ Nick Fury: The Scorpio Connection Hardcover (1989, $16.95) — 25.00

.../ Nick Fury: The Scorpio Connection Softcover(1990, $12.95) — 15.00

...: Not Dead Yet (12/98, $14.95, TPB)-r/#119-122 — 15.00

...: Save The Tiger 1 (7/92, $2.95, 84 pgs.)-Reprints Wolverine stories from Marvel Comics Presents #1-10 w/new Kieth-c — 6.00

... Scorpio Rising ($5.95, prestige format, one-shot) — 6.00

.../Shi: Dark Night of Judgment (Crusade Comics, 2000, $2.99) Tucci-a — 4.00

... Triumphs And Tragedies (1995, $16.95, trade paperback) r/Uncanny X-Men #109,172,173, Wolverine limited series #4, & Wolverine #41,42,75 — 17.00

... Typhoid's Kiss (6/94, $6.95)-r/Wolverine stories from Marvel Comics Presents #109-116 — 7.00

...Vs. Sabretooth 3D 1 (3/20, $7.99) -r/Wolverine #10; bagged with 3D glasses — 8.00

...Vs. Sabretooth (3/95, $2.50) -r/Marvel Comics Presents #48-50 — 4.00

.../Witchblade 1 (3/97, $2.95) Devil's Reign Pt. 5 — 4.00

Wizard #1/2 (1997) Joe Phillips-a(p) — 10.00

NOTE: **Austin** c-3i. **Bolton** c(back)-5. **Buscema** a-1-16,25,27p; c-1-10. **Byrne** a-17-22p, 23; c-1(back), 17-22, 23p. **Colan** a-24. **Andy Kubert** c/a-51. **Jim Lee** c-24, 25, 27. **Silvestri** a(p)-31-43, 45, 46, 48-50, 52, 53, 55-57, c-31-42p, 43, 45p, 46p, 48, 49p, 50p, 52p, 53p, 55-57p. **Stroman** a-44p; c-60p. **Williamson** a-1i, 3-8i; c(i)-1, 3-6.

WOLVERINE (Volume 3) (Titled Dark Wolverine from #75-90)(See Daken: Dark Wolverine)

Marvel Comics: July, 2003 - No. 90, Oct. 2010 $2.25/$2.50/$2.99)

1-Rucka-s/Robertson-a — 2 4 6 8 10 12

2-19: 6-Nightcrawler app. 13-16-Sabretooth app. — 3.00

20-Millar-s/Romita, Jr.-a begin, Elektra app. — 4.00

20-B&W variant-c — 2 4 6 8 10 12

21-39: 21-Elektra-c/app. 23,24-Daredevil app. 26-28-Land-c. 29-Quesada-c; begin $2.50-c. 33-35-House of M. 36,37-Decimation. 36-Quesada-c. 39-Winter Soldier app. — 3.00

40,43-48: 40-Begin $2.99-c; Winter Soldier app.; Texeira-a. 43-46-Civil War; Ramos-a. 45-Sub-Mariner app. — 3.00

41,49-($3.99) 41-C.P. Smith/Stuart Moore-s — 4.00

42-Civil War — 5.00

50-($3.99) Sabretooth app.; Bianchi-a/c & Loeb-s begin; wraparound-c; McGuinness-a — 4.00

50-($3.99) Variant Edition; uncolored art and cover; Bianchi pencil art page — 4.00

51-55-(Regular and variant uncolored editions) Bianchi-a/Loeb-s; Sabretooth app. — 3.00

55-EC-style variant-c by Greg Land — 5.00

56-($3.99) Howard Chaykin-c/a — 4.00

57-65: 57-61-Suydam Zombie-c; Chaykin-a. 62-65-Mystique app. — 3.00

66-Old Man Logan begins; Millar-s/McNiven-a; McNiven wraparound-c — 3 6 9 21 33 45

66-Variant-c by Michael Turner — 6 12 18 38 69 100

66-Variant sketch-c by Michael Turner — 140.00

66-2nd printing with McNiven variant-c of Logan and Hulk gang member — 3 6 9 17 26 34

66-(5/10, $1.00) Reprint with "Marvel's Greatest Comics" cover — 3.00

67-70,72-Old Man Logan (concludes in Wolverine: Old Man Logan Giant-Sized Special). 67-Intro. Ashley, Spider-Man's granddaughter. 72-Red Skull app. — 1 3 4 6 8 10

71-Old Man Logan; Venom-ized T-Rex app. — 2 4 6 11 16 20

73,74-Andy Kubert-a — 4.00

75-($3.99) Dark Reign, Daken as Wolverine on Osborn's team; Camuncoli-a — 5.00

76-90: 76-86-Multiple covers for each. 76-Dark Reign; Yu-c. 82-84-Siege. 88,89-Franken-Castle x-over; Punisher app. — 3.00

#900 (7/10, $4.99) Short stories by various incl. Finch, Rivera, Segovia, McGuinness — 5.00

Annual 1 (12/07, $3.99) Hurwitz-s/Frusin-a — 4.00

Annual 2 (11/08, $3.99) Swierczynski-s/Deodato-a/c — 4.00

...: Blood & Sorrow TPB (2007, $13.99) r/#41,49, stories from Giant-Size Wolverine #1 and X-Men Unlimited #12 — 14.00

...: Chop Shop 1 (1/09, $2.99) Benson-s/Boschi-a/Hanuka-c — 3.00

Civil War: Wolverine TPB (2007, $17.99) r/#42-48; gallery of B&W cover inks — 18.00

... Dangerous Games 1 (8/08, $3.99) Spurrier-s/Oliver-a; Remender-s/Opena-a — 4.00

...Enemy of the State HC Vol. 1 (2005, $19.99) r/#20-25; Ennis intro.; variant covers — 20.00

...Enemy of the State HC Vol. 2 (2005, $19.99) r/#26-32 — 20.00

...Enemy of the State SC Vol. 1 (2005, $14.99) r/#20-25; Ennis intro.; variant covers — 15.00

...Enemy of the State SC Vol. 2 (2006, $16.99) r/#26-32 — 17.00

...Enemy of the State - The Complete Edition (2006, $34.99) r/#20-32; Ennis intro.; sketch pages, variant covers and pin-up art — 35.00

...: Evolution SC (2008, $14.99) r/#50-55 — 15.00

...: Flies to a Spider (2/09, $3.99) Bradstreet-c/Hurwitz-s/Opena-a — 4.00

...: Killing Made Simple (10/08, $3.99) Yost-s/Turnbull-a — 4.00

...: Enemy of the State MGC #20 (7/11, $1.00) r/#20 with "Marvel's Greatest Comics" logo — 3.00

...Japan's Most Wanted HC (2014, $34.99) printing of material that debuted online — 35.00

...: Mr. X (5/10, $3.99) Tieri-s/Diaz-a/Mattina-c — 4.00

... Old Man Logan Giant-Sized Special (11/09, $4.99) Continued from #72; cover gallery — 5.00

...: Origins & Endings HC (2006, $19.99) r/#36-40 — 20.00

...: Origins & Endings SC (2006, $13.99) r/#36-40 — 14.00

...: Origin of an X-Man Free Comic Book Day 2009 (5/09) Gurihiru/McGuinness-a — 3.00

...: Revolver (8/09, $3.99) Gischler-s/Pastoras-a — 4.00

...: Saga (9/09, giveaway) history of the character in text and comic panels — 3.00

...: Saudade (2008, $4.99) English adaptation of Wolverine story from French comic — 5.00

...: Savage (4/10, $3.99) J. Scott Campbell-c; The Lizard app. — 4.00

...: Special: Firebreak (2/08, $3.99) Carey-s/Kolins-a; Lolos-a — 4.00

...: Switchback 1 (3/09, $3.99) short stories; art by Pastoras & Doe — 4.00

...: The Amazing Immortal Man & Other Bloody Tales (7/08, $3.99) Lapham short stories — 4.00

...: The Anniversary (6/09, $3.99) Mariko flashback short stories; art by various — 4.00

...: The Death of Wolverine HC (2008, $19.99) r/#56-61 — 20.00

...: The Road to Hell (11/10, $3.99) Previews new Wolverine titles and Generation Hope — 4.00

...: Under the Boardwalk (2/10, $3.99) Coker-a — 4.00

...Vol. 1: The Brotherhood (2003, $12.99) r/#1-6 — 13.00

...Vol. 2: Coyote Crossing (2004, $11.99) r/#7-11 — 12.00

... Weapon X Files (2009, $4.99) Handbook-style pages of Wolverine characters — 5.00

...: Wendigo! 1 (3/10, $3.99) Gulacy-a; back-up with Thor — 4.00

WOLVERINE (Volume 4) (Also see Savage Wolverine)

Marvel Comics: Nov, 2010 - No. 20, Feb, 2012; No. 300, Mar, 2012 - No. 317, Feb, 2013 ($3.99/$4.99)

1-5-Jae Lee-s/Guedes-a; Wolverine Goes to Hell. 1-Back-up with Silver Samurai. — 4.00

5.1-(4/11, $2.99) Aaron-s/Palo-a/Rivera-c — 3.00

6-20: 6-Jae Lee-c/Acuña-a; X-Men & Magneto app. 20-Kingpin & Sabretooth app. — 4.00

300-(3/12, $4.99) Adam Kubert-c; Sabretooth & new Silver Samurai app. — 5.00

301-308,310-317: 301-304-Aaron-s. 302-Art Adams-c. 310-313-Bianchi-a/c — 4.00

309-($4.99) Elixir with X-Force; Albuquerque-a; Ribic-c — 5.00

#1000 ($4.99) Short stories by various incl. Palmiotti, Green, Luke Ross; Segovia-c — 5.00

Annual 1 (10/12, $4.99) Alan Davis-s/a/c; the Clan Destine app. (see Daredevil Ann. #1) — 5.00

...: Debt of Death 1 (11/11, $3.99) Lapham-s/Aja-a/c; Nick Fury app. — 4.00

.../Deadpool: The Decoy 1 (9/11, $3.99) prints online story from Marvel.com; Young-c — 4.00

WOLVERINE (5th series)

Marvel Comics: May, 2013 - No. 13, Mar, 2014 ($3.99)

1-13: 1-4-Cornell-s/Alan Davis-a/c; Nick Fury II app. 5-7-Pierfederici-a. 8-13-Killable — 4.00

... In the Flesh (9/13, $3.99) Cosentino-s/Talajic-a — 4.00

WOLVERINE (6th series)

Marvel Comics: Apr, 2014 - No. 12, Oct, 2014 ($3.99)

1-11: 1-Cornell-s/Stegman-a. 2-Superior Wolverine app. 8,9-Iron Fist app. — 4.00

12-($5.99) "1 Month To Die"; Cornell-s/Woods-a; Thor & Sabretooth app. — 6.00

Annual 1 (10/14, $4.99) Jubilee app; Nguyen-c/Kalan-s/Marks-a — 5.00

WOLVERINE (7th series)

Marvel Comics: Apr, 2020 - Present ($7.99/$3.99/$4.99)

1-($7.99) Percy-s/Adam Kubert-a; multiple covers; Dracula app. — 8.00

2-7,9-24,26-32,34-36-($3.99) 2,3-Percy-s/Adam Kubert-a. 4-6-Bogdanovic-a. 6,7-"X of Swords"

Wolverine (2008 series) #66 © MAR

Wolverine and the X-Men #17 © MAR

Wolverine: Origins #26 © MAR

	GD	VG	FN	VF	VF/NM	NM-		GD	VG	FN	VF	VF/NM	NM-
	2.0	4.0	6.0	8.0	9.0	9.2		2.0	4.0	6.0	8.0	9.0	9.2

tie-in. 13-Hellfire Gala tie-in. 20-23-Deadpool app. 24-Judgment Day tie-in 4.00
8-($4.99) 350th Wolverine issue; short stories; Kubert, Bogdanovic-a; Patch returns 5.00
25-($4.99) Judgment Day tie-in 5.00
33,37-44-($4.99) 33-Bonus back-up story with Sister Dagger. 37-Hulk app. 5.00
Annual 1 (11/19, $4.99) "Acts of Evil" tie-in; Houser-s/Borges-a; Morgan Le Fay app. 5.00
...: Through the Years Primer 1 (4/20, free) Previews #1; creator interviews; iconic covers 3.00
... vs. Blade Special (9/19, $5.99) Guggenheim-s/Wilkins-a/c; Doctor Strange app. 6.00

WOLVERINE & BLACK CAT: CLAWS 2 (See Claws for 1st series)
Marvel Comics: Aug, 2011 - No. 3, Nov, 2011 ($3.99, limited series)
1-3-Linsner-a/c; Palmiotti & Gray-s; Killraven app. 4.00

WOLVERINE & CAPTAIN AMERICA: WEAPON PLUS
Marvel Comics: Sept, 2019 ($4.99, one-shot)
1-Sacks-s/Neves-a 5.00

WOLVERINE AND JUBILEE
Marvel Comics: Apr, 2021 - No. 4, Jun, 2011 ($2.99, limited series)
1-4: 1-Vampire Jubilee; Kathryn Immonen-s/Phil Noto-a; Coipel-c

	1	2	3	5	6	8

WOLVERINE AND POWER PACK
Marvel Comics: Jan, 2009 - No. 4, Apr, 2009 ($2.99, limited series)
1-4-Sumerak-s. 1,2-GuriHiru-a. 1-Sauron app. 3-Meet Wolverine as a child; Koblish-a 3.00

WOLVERINE AND THE PUNISHER: DAMAGING EVIDENCE
Marvel Comics: Oct, 1993 - No. 3, Dec, 1993 ($2.00, limited series)
1-3: 2,3-Indicia says "The Punisher and Wolverine..." 5.00

WOLVERINE & THE X-MEN (Regenesis)(See X-Men: Schism)
Marvel Comics: Dec, 2011 - No. 42, May 2014 ($3.99)
1-8: 1-3-Aaron-s/Bachalo-a/c. 3-Sabretooth app. 4-Bradshaw-a; Deathlok-a. 4.00
9-27: 9-16,18-Avengers vs. X-Men tie-in. 17-Allred-a 4.00
27AU (6/13, $3.99) Age of Ultron tie-in; continues in Age of Ultron #6 4.00
28-41: 30-35-Hellfire Saga. 36,37-Battle of the Atom 4.00
42-($4.99) Cover swipe of X-Men #141 (1981) Graduation Day 5.00
Annual 1 (1/14, $4.99) Aaron-s/Bradshaw-a; Gladiator app. 5.00

WOLVERINE & THE X-MEN (2nd series)
Marvel Comics: May, 2014 - No. 12, Jan, 2015 ($3.99)
1-9,11,12: 1-Latour-s/Asrar-a; Fantomex app. 7-Daredevil app. 11-Spider-Man app. 4.00
10-($4.99) Follows Wolverine's death; art by various incl. Anka, Bertram, Rugg, Shalvey 5.00

WOLVERINE AND THE X-MEN: ALPHA & OMEGA
Marvel Comics: Dec, 2011 - No. 5, Jul, 2012 ($3.99, limited series)
1-5-Brooks-c/Boschi & Brooks-a; Quentin Quire vs. Wolverine 4.00

WOLVERINE: BLACK, WHITE & BLOOD
Marvel Comics: Jan, 2021 - No. 4, May, 2021 ($4.99, limited series, B&W&Red)
1-4-Short story anthology by various. 1-Duggan-s/Adam Kubert-a; Shalvey-s/a 5.00

WOLVERINE/CAPTAIN AMERICA
Marvel Comics: Apr, 2004 - No. 4, Apr, 2004 ($2.99, limited series)
1-4-Derenick-a/c 3.00

WOLVERINE: DAYS OF FUTURE PAST
Marvel Comics: Dec, 1997 - No. 3, Feb, 1998 ($2.50, limited series)
1-3: J.F. Moore-s/Bennett-a 4.00

WOLVERINE/DOOP (Also see X-Force and X-Statix)(Reprinted in X-Statix Vol. 2)
Marvel Comics: July, 2003 - No. 2, July, 2003 ($2.99, limited series)
1,2-Peter Milligan-s/Darwyn Cooke & J. Bone-a 3.00

WOLVERINE: FIRST CLASS
Marvel Comics: Mar, 2008 - No. 21, Jan, 2010 ($2.99)
1-21: 1-Wolverine and Kitty Pryde's first mission; DiVito-a. 2,9-Sabretooth app. 3.00

WOLVERINE/GAMBIT: VICTIMS
Marvel Comics: Sept, 1995 - No. 4, Dec, 1995 ($2.95, limited series)
1-4: Jeph Loeb scripts & Tim Sale-a; foil-c 5.00

WOLVERINE/HERCULES: MYTHS, MONSTERS & MUTANTS
Marvel Comics: May, 2011 - No. 4, Aug, 2011 ($2.99, limited series)
1-4-Tieri-s/Santacruz-a/Jusko-c 3.00

WOLVERINE/HULK
Marvel Comics: Apr, 2002 - No. 4, July, 2002 ($3.50, limited series)
1-4-Sam Kieth-s/a/c 4.00
Wolverine Legends Vol. 1: Wolverine/Hulk (2003, $9.99, TPB) r/#1-4 10.00

WOLVERINE: INFINITY WATCH
Marvel Comics: Apr, 2019 - No. 5, Aug, 2019 ($3.99, limited series)
1-5-Duggan-s/MacDonald-a; Loki app. 4.00

WOLVERINE: MADRIPOOR KNIGHTS
Marvel Comics: Apr, 2024 - Present ($3.99, limited series)
1-Claremont-s/Salazar-a; Captain America, Black Widow and Jubilee app. 4.00

WOLVERINE: MANIFEST DESTINY
Marvel Comics: Dec, 2008 - No. 4, Mar, 2009 ($2.99, limited series)
1-4-Aaron-s/Segovia-a 3.00

WOLVERINE MAX
Marvel Comics: Dec, 2012 - No. 15, Mar, 2014 ($3.99)
1-15: 1-5-Starr-s/Boschi-a/Jock-c; Victor Creed app. 4.00

WOLVERINE: NETSUKE
Marvel Comics: Nov, 2002 - No. 4, Feb, 2003 ($3.99, limited series)
1-4-George Pratt-s/painted-a 4.00

WOLVERINE: NOIR (1930s Pulp-style)
Marvel Comics: Apr, 2009 - No. 4, Sept, 2009 ($3.99, limited series)
1-4-C.P. Smith-a/Stuart Moore; covers by Smith & Calero; alternate Logan as detective 6.00

WOLVERINE: ORIGINS
Marvel Comics: June, 2006 - No. 50, Sept, 2010 ($2.99)
1-15: 1-Daniel Way-s/Steve Dillon-a/Quesada-c 3.00
1-10-Variant covers. 1-Turner. 2-Quesada & Hitch. 3-Bianchi. 4-Dell'Otto. 7-Deodato 4.00
16-($3.99) Captain America WW2 app.; preview of Wolverine #56; r/X-Men #268 4.00
16-Variant-c by McGuinness 4.00
17-24: 17-20-Capt. America & Bucky app. 21-24-Deadpool app.; Bianchi-c 3.00
25-($3.99) Deadpool app.; Bianchi-c; r/Deadpool's 1st app. in New Mutants #98 5.00
26-49: 26-Origin of Dakan; Way-s/Segovia-a/Land-c. 28-Hulk & Wendigo app. 3.00
50-($3.99) Last issue; Nick Fury app. 4.00
Annual 1 (9/07, $3.99) Way-s/Andrews-a; flashback to 1932 4.00
... Vol. 1 - Born in Blood HC (2006, $19.99, dustjacket) r/#1-5; variant covers 20.00
... Vol. 1 - Born in Blood SC (2007, $13.99) r/#1-5; variant covers 14.00
... Vol. 2 - Savior HC (2007, $19.99, dustjacket) r/#6-10; variant covers 20.00
... Vol. 2 - Savior SC (2007, $13.99) r/#6-10; variant covers 14.00
... Vol. 3 - Swift & Terrible HC (2007, $19.99, dustjacket) r/#11-15 20.00
... Vol. 3 - Swift & Terrible SC (2007, $13.99) r/#11-15 14.00
... Vol. 4 - Our War HC (2008, $19.99, dustjacket) r/#16-20 & Annual #1 20.00
... Vol. 4 - Our War SC (2008, $14.99) r/#16-20 & Annual #1 15.00

WOLVERINE: PATCH
Marvel Comics: May, 2022 - No. 5, Oct, 2022 ($3.99, limited series)
1-5-Larry Hama-s/Andrea Di Vito-a; Nick Fury app. 4.00

WOLVERINE/PUNISHER
Marvel Comics: May, 2004 - No. 5, Sept, 2004 ($2.99, limited series)
1-5: Milligan-s/Weeks-a 3.00
... Vol. 1 TPB (2004, $13.99) r/series 14.00

WOLVERINE, PUNISHER & GHOST RIDER: OFFICIAL INDEX TO THE MARVEL UNIVERSE
Marvel Comics: Oct, 2011 - No. 8, May, 2012 ($3.99)
1-8-Each issue has chronological synopsis, creator credits, character lists for 30-40 issues of their own titles and headlining mini-series 4.00

WOLVERINE/PUNISHER REVELATIONS (Marvel Knights)
Marvel Comics: Jun, 1999 - No. 4, Sept, 1999 ($2.95, limited series)
1-4: Pat Lee-a(p) 4.00
...: Revelation (4/00, $14.95, TPB) r/#1-4 15.00

WOLVERINES (Follows Death of Wolverine)
Marvel Comics: Mar, 2015 - No. 20, Aug, 2015 ($3.99, weekly series)
1-20: 1-Soule-s/Bradshaw-a; Sabretooth, Daken, Mystique, X-23 app. 13-Deadpool app. 4.00

WOLVERINE SAGA
Marvel Comics: Sept, 1989 - No. 4, Mid-Dec, 1989 ($3.95, lim. series, 52 pgs.)
1-Gives history; Liefeld/Austin-c (front & back) 6.00
2-4: 2-Romita, Jr./Austin-c. 4-Kaluta-c 6.00

WOLVERINE: SNIKT!
Marvel Comics: July, 2003 - No. 5, Nov, 2003 ($2.99, limited series)
1-5-Manga-style; Tsutomu Nihei-s/a 3.00
Wolverine Legends Vol. 5: Snikt! TPB (2003, $13.99) r/#1-5 14.00

WOLVERINE: SOULTAKER
Marvel Comics: May, 2005 - No. 5, Aug, 2005 ($2.99, limited series)
1-5-Yoshida-s/Nagasawa-a/Terada-c; Yukio app. 3.00
TPB (2005, $13.99) r/#1-5 14.00

WOLVERINE: THE BEST THERE IS
Marvel Comics: Feb, 2011 - No. 12, Jan, 2012 ($3.99)
1-12: 1,2-Huston-s/Ryp-a; covers by Hitch and Djurdjevic. 3-12-Hitch-c 4.00
... - Contagion 1 (6/11, $4.99) r/#1-3, cover gallery 5.00

	GD 2.0	VG 4.0	FN 6.0	VF 8.0	VF/NM 9.0	NM- 9.2

WOLVERINE: THE END
Marvel Comics: Jan, 2004 - No. 6, Dec, 2004 ($2.99, limited series)

1-5-Jenkins/Castellini-a						3.00
1-Wizard World Texas variant-c						20.00
TPB (2005, $14.99) r/#1-5						15.00

WOLVERINE: THE LONG NIGHT ADAPTATION (Based on the 2018 10-part podcast)
Marvel Comics: Mar, 2019 - No. 5, Jul, 2019 ($4.99/$3.99, limited series)

1-($4.99) Benjamin Percy-s/Marcio Takara-a; Wolverine in Alaska						5.00
2-5-($3.99)						4.00

WOLVERINE: THE ORIGIN
Marvel Comics: Nov, 2001 - No. 6, July, 2002 ($3.50, limited series)

1-Origin of Logan; Jenkins-s/Andy Kubert-a; Quesada-c						35.00
1-DF edition						25.00
2						10.00
3-6						6.00
HC (3/02, $34.95, 11" x 7-1/2") r/#1-6; dust jacket; sketch pages and treatments						35.00
HC (2006, $19.99) r/#1-6; dust jacket; sketch pages and treatments						20.00
SC (2002, $14.95) r/#1-6; afterwords by Jemas and Quesada						15.00

WOLVERINE WEAPON X
Marvel Comics: June, 2009 - No. 16, Oct, 2010 ($3.99)

1-16: 1-5,11-Aaron-s/Garney-a. -Four covers. 2,3-Two covers. 11-15-Deathlok app.						4.00

WOLVERINE: XISLE
Marvel Comics: June, 2003 - No. 5, June, 2003 ($2.50, weekly limited series)

1-5-Bruce Jones-s/Jorge Lucas-a						3.00
Wolverine Legends Vol. 4 TPB (2003, $13.99) r/ #1-5						14.00

WOMANTHOLOGY: SPACE
IDW Publishing: Sept, 2012 - No. 5, Feb, 2013 ($3.99)

1-5-Anthology of short stories by women creators						4.00

WOMEN IN LOVE (A Feature Presentation #5)
Fox Feature Synd./Hero Books: Aug, 1949 - No. 4, Feb, 1950

	GD	VG	FN	VF	VF/NM	NM-
1	55	110	165	352	601	850
2-Kamen/Feldstein-c	47	94	141	296	498	700
3	37	74	111	222	361	500
4-Wood-a	43	86	129	271	461	650

WOMEN IN LOVE (Thrilling Romances for Adults)
Ziff-Davis Publishing Co.: Winter, 1952 (25¢, 100 pgs.)

	GD	VG	FN	VF	VF/NM	NM-
nn-(Scarce)-Kinstler-a; painted-c	110	220	330	704	1202	1700

WOMEN OF MARVEL
Marvel Comics: 2006, 2007 ($24.99, TPB)

SC-Reprints 1st apps. of Dazzler, Ms. Marvel, Shanna, The Cat plus notable stories of other female Marvel characters; Mayhew-c						25.00
Vol. 2 (2007) More stories of female Marvel characters; Mayhew-c; cover process art						25.00

WOMEN OF MARVEL
Marvel Comics: Jan, 2011 - No. 2, Feb, 2011 ($3.99, limited series)

1,2-Short stories of female Marvel characters. 1-Pichelli-c. 2-Land-c						4.00
1-(6/21, $5.99) Short stories by female creators; intro by Louise Simonson						6.00
1-(5/22, $5.99) Short stories by female creators; intro by Gail Simone						6.00
1-(5/23, $5.99) Short stories by female creators; intro by Charlie Jane Anders						6.00
1-(4/24, $5.99) Short stories by female creators; intro by Angélique Roché						6.00

WOMEN OUTLAWS (My Love Memories #9 on)(Also see Red Circle)
Fox Feature Syndicate: July, 1948 - No. 8, Sept, 1949

	GD	VG	FN	VF	VF/NM	NM-
1-Used in SOTI, illo "Giving children an image of American womanhood"; negligee panels	116	232	348	742	1271	1800
2,3- 3-Kamenish-a	81	162	243	518	884	1250
4-8	63	126	189	403	689	975
nn(nd)-Contains Cody of the Pony Express; same cover as #7	36	72	108	211	343	475

WOMEN TO LOVE
Realistic: No date (1953)

	GD	VG	FN	VF	VF/NM	NM-
nn-(Scarce)-Reprints Complete Romance #1; c-/Avon paperback #165	61	122	183	390	670	950

WONDER BOY (Formerly Terrific Comics) (See Blue Bolt, Bomber Comics & Samson)
Ajax/Farrell Publ.: No. 17, May, 1955 - No. 18, July, 1955 (Code approved)

	GD	VG	FN	VF	VF/NM	NM-
17-Phantom Lady app. Bakerish-c/a	63	126	189	403	689	975
18-Phantom Lady app.	53	106	159	334	567	800

NOTE: *Phantom Lady not by Matt Baker.*

WONDER COMICS (Wonderworld #3 on)
Fox Feature Syndicate: May, 1939 - No. 2, June, 1939 (68 pgs.)

	GD	VG	FN	VF	VF/NM	NM-
1-(Scarce)-Wonder Man only app. by Will Eisner; Dr. Fung (by Powell), K-5 begins; Bob Kane-a; Eisner-c	4000	8000	12,000	28,000	49,000	70,000
2-(Scarce)-Yarko the Great, Master Magician (see Samson) by Eisner begins; 'Spark' Stevens by Bob Kane, Patty O'Day, Tex Mason app. Lou Fine's 1st-c; Fine-a (pg.); Yarko-c (Wonder Man-c #1)	1250	2500	3750	9500	17,250	25,000

WONDER COMICS
Great/Nedor/Better Publications: May, 1944 - No. 20, Oct, 1948

	GD	VG	FN	VF	VF/NM	NM-
1-The Grim Reaper & Spectro, the Mind Reader begin; Hitler/Hirohito bondage-c	429	858	1287	3132	5516	7900
2-Origin The Grim Reaper; Super Sleuths begin, end #8,17; Schomburg Nazi WWII-c	284	568	852	1818	3109	4400
3-5: All Schomburg Nazi WWII-c. 3-Indicia reads "Vol. 1, #2"	226	452	678	1446	2473	3500
6-Japanese WWII Flag-c	168	336	504	1075	1838	2600
7-10: 8-Last Spectro. 9-Wonderman begins	110	220	330	704	1202	1700
11-13: 11-Dick Devens, King of Futuria begins, ends #14. 11,12-Ingels-c & splash pg.						
12-Bondage/headlight-c by Ingels	129	258	387	826	1413	2000
14-Classic Schomburg sci-fi good girl bondage-c	206	412	618	1318	2259	3200
15-Tara begins (origin), ends #20; classic Schomburg bondage/torture-c	300	600	900	1950	3375	4800
16,18: 16-Spectro app.; last Grim Reaper. 18-The Silver Knight begins						

	GD	VG	FN	VF	VF/NM	NM-
17-Wonderman with Frazetta panels; Jill Trent with all Frazetta inks	103	206	309	659	1130	1600
19-Frazetta panels	129	258	387	826	1413	2000
20-Most of Silver Knight by Frazetta	116	232	348	742	1271	1800
	142	284	426	909	1555	2200

NOTE: *Ingels c-11, 12. Roussos a-19. Schomburg (Xela) c-1-10; (airbrush)-13-20. Bondage c-12, 13, 15. Cover features: Grim Reaper #1-8; Wonder Man #9-15; Tara #16-20.*

WONDER DUCK (See Wisco)
Marvel Comics (CDS): Sept, 1949 - No. 3, Mar, 1950

	GD	VG	FN	VF	VF/NM	NM-
1-Funny animal	30	60	90	177	289	400
2,3	20	40	60	117	189	260

WONDERFUL ADVENTURES OF PINOCCHIO, THE (See Movie Comics & Walt Disney Showcase #48)
Whitman Publishing Co.: April, 1982 (Walt Disney)

nn-(#3 Continuation of Movie Comics?); r/FC #92						6.00

WONDERFUL WIZARD OF OZ (Adaptation of the original 1900 L. Frank Baum book)
(Also see the sequels Marvelous Land of Oz, Ozma of Oz, and Dorothy & The Wizard in Oz)
Marvel Comics: Feb, 2009 - No. 8, Sept, 2009 ($3.99, limited series)

1-8-Eric Shanower/Skottie Young-a/c						4.00
1-Variant Good Witch & Dorothy wraparound cover by J. Scott Campbell						8.00
1-Variant Scarecrow & Dorothy cover by Eric Shanower						10.00
1-(4/10, $1.00) Reprint with "Marvel's Greatest Comics" on cover						3.00
... Sketchbook (2008, giveaway) Young character design sketches; Shanower intro.						3.00
HC (2009, $29.99, dustjacket) r/#1-8; Shanower intro.; cover gallery; sketch art						30.00

WONDERFUL WORLD FOR BOYS AND GIRLS
DC Comics: May, 1964

nn - Ashcan comic, not distributed to newsstands, only for in-house use					(no known sales)	

WONDERFUL WORLD OF DISNEY, THE (Walt Disney)
Whitman Publishing Co.: 1978 (Digest, 116 pgs.)

	GD	VG	FN	VF	VF/NM	NM-
1-Barks-a (reprints)	3	6	9	16	23	30
2 (no date)	2	4	6	11	16	20

WONDERFUL WORLD OF TANK GIRL
Titan Comics: Nov, 2017 - No. 4, May, 2018 ($3.99, limited series)

1-4: 1-Tank Girl Strikes Again; Martin-s/Parson-a; multiple covers						4.00

WONDERFUL WORLD OF THE BROTHERS GRIMM (See Movie Comics)

WONDER GIRL (Cassandra Sandsmark from Teen Titans)
DC Comics: Nov, 2007 - No. 6, Apr, 2008 ($2.99, limited series)

1-6-Torres-s/Greene-a. 2-6-Female Furies app. 5,6-Wonder Woman app.						3.00
Teen Titans Spotlight: Wonder Girl TPB ($17.99) r/#1-6						18.00
1-(3/11, $2.99, one-shot) Nicola Scott-c; intro. Solstice						3.00

WONDER GIRL (Yara Flor from Future State)
DC Comics: Jul, 2021 - No. 7, Mar, 2022 ($3.99, limited series)

1-7: 1-Joëlle Jones-s/a. 2-4-Jones & Melo-a. 5-7-Donna Troy app.						4.00
2022 Annual 1 (10/22, $5.99) Joëlle Jones-s; art by various						6.00

WONDERLAND (See Grimm Fairy Tales Presents Wonderland)

WONDERLAND COMICS
Feature Publications/Prize: Summer, 1945 - No. 9, Feb-Mar, 1947

	GD	VG	FN	VF	VF/NM	NM-
1-Alex in Wonderland begins; Howard Post-c	41	82	123	256	428	600
2-Howard Post-c/a(2)	22	44	66	128	209	290
3-9: 3,4-Post-c	20	40	60	117	189	260

WONDER MAN (See The Avengers #9, 151)
Marvel Comics Group: Mar, 1986 ($1.25, one-shot, 52 pgs.)

1						6.00

WONDER MAN
Marvel Comics Group: Sept, 1991 - No. 29, Jan, 1994 ($1.00)

1-29: 1-Free fold out poster by Johnson/Austin. 1-3-Johnson/Austin-c/a. 2-Avengers West Coast x-over. 4 Austin-c(i)						4.00
Annual 1 (1992, $2.25)-Immonen-a (10 pgs.)						5.00
Annual 2 (1993, $2.95)-Bagged w/trading card						5.00

WONDER MAN
Marvel Comics: Feb, 2007 - No. 5, June, 2007 ($2.99, limited series)

1-5: 1-Peter David-s/Andrew Currie-a; Beast app. 4-Nauck-a						3.00
...: My Fair Super Hero TPB (2007, $13.99) r/#1-5; Currie sketch page						14.00

WONDERS OF ALADDIN, THE
Dell Publishing Co.: No. 1255, Feb-Apr, 1962

	GD	VG	FN	VF	VF/NM	NM-
Four Color 1255-Movie	7	14	21	46	86	125

WONDER TWINS (From Superfriends)
DC Comics (Wonder Comics): Apr, 2019 - No. 12, Apr, 2020 ($3.99)

1-12: 1-Mark Russell-s/Stephen Byrne-a; Justice League and Mr. Mxyzptlk app. 3-Intro Gleek						4.00

WONDER WOMAN (See Adventure Comics #459, All-Star Comics, Brave & the Bold, DC Comics Presents, JLA, Justice League of America, Legend of..., Power Record Comics, Sensation Comics, Super Friends and World's Finest Comics #244)

WONDER WOMAN
DC Comics: Jan 1942

1-Ashcan comic, not distributed to newsstands, only for in-house use. Cover art is Sensation Comics #1 with interior being Sensation Comics #2. A CGC certified 8.5 copy sold for $17,250 in 2002. A CGC certified 8.5 copy sold for $57,668 in 2018.						

WONDER WOMAN
National Periodical Publications/All-American Publ./DC Comics:
Summer, 1942 - No. 329, Feb, 1986

	GD	VG	FN	VF	VF/NM	NM-
1-Origin Wonder Woman retold (more detailed than All Star #8); H. G. Peter-c/a begins	14,900	29,800	44,700	99,400	182,200	265,000

1-Reprint, Oversize 13-1/2x10". WARNING: This comic is an exact reprint of the original except for its size. DC published it in 1974 with a second cover titling it as a Famous First Edition. There have been many reported cases of the outer cover being removed and the interior sold as the original edition. The reprint with the new outer cover removed is practically worthless. See Famous First Edition for value.

Wonder Girl #6 © DC

Wonder Woman #45 © DC

Wonder Woman (2nd) #926 © DC

	GD 2.0	VG 4.0	FN 6.0	VF 8.0	VF/NM 9.0	NM- 9.2
2-Origin/1st app. Mars; Duke of Deception app.	975	1950	2925	7118	12,559	18,000
3	411	822	1233	2877	5039	7200
4,5: 5-1st Dr. Psycho app.	326	652	978	2282	3991	5700
6-1st Cheetah app.	1150	2300	3450	8500	15,250	22,000
7-Wonder Woman for President-c/sty	1150	2300	3450	8500	15,250	22,000
8,9: 1st app. Giganta (Sum/44)	271	542	813	1734	2967	4200
10-Invasion from Saturn classic sci-fi-c/s	277	554	831	1760	3030	4300
11-20	168	336	504	1075	1838	2600
21-30: 23-Story from Wonder Woman's childhood. 28-Cheetah and Giganta/c/app.						
	142	284	426	909	1555	2200
31-33,35-40: 37-1st app. Circe. 38-Last H.G. Peter-c						
	129	258	387	826	1413	2000
34-Robot-c	142	284	426	909	1555	2200
41-44,46-48	123	246	369	787	1344	1900
45-Origin retold	252	504	756	1613	2757	3900
49-Used in SOTI, pgs. 234,236; last 52 pg. issue	135	270	405	864	1482	2100
50-(44 pgs.)-Used in POP, pg. 97	129	258	387	826	1413	2000
51-60: 60-New logo	116	232	348	742	1271	1800
61-72: 62-Origin of W.W. i.d. 64-Story about 3-D movies. 70-1st Angle Man app. 72-Last pre-code (2/55)	110	220	330	704	1202	1700
73-90: 80-Origin The Invisible Plane. 89-Flying saucer-c/story						
	97	194	291	621	1061	1500
91-94,96,97: 97-Last H. G. Peter-a	81	162	243	518	884	1250
95-A-Bomb-c	97	194	291	621	1061	1500
98-(5/58) 1st Silver Age Wonder Woman; new origin & new art team (Andru & Esposito) begin; Kanigher-s; 1st meets Steve Trevor	676	1352	2028	4935	8718	12,500
99-New origin continues; origin Diana Prince i.d.	103	206	309	659	1130	1600
100-(8/58)	103	206	309	659	1130	1600
101-104,106,108-110	58	116	174	371	636	900
105-(Scarce, 4/59)-Wonder Woman's origin (part 3); she appears as a girl (no costume yet) (called Wonder Girl - see DC Super-Stars #1)	300	600	900	1920	3310	4700
107-1st advs. of Wonder Girl; 1st Merboy; tells how Wonder Woman won her costume						
	71	142	213	454	777	1100
111-120	43	86	129	271	461	650
121-126: 121-1st app. Wonder Woman Family. 122-1st app. Wonder Tot. 124-Wonder Woman Family app. 126-Last 10¢ issue	37	74	111	222	361	500
127-130: 128-Origin The Invisible Plane. 129-3rd app. Wonder Woman Family (#133 is 4th app.)	17	34	51	117	259	400
131-150: 132-Flying saucer-c	14	28	42	96	211	325
151-155,157,158,161-170 (1967): 151-Wonder Girl solo issue.						
	10	20	30	70	150	230
156-(8/65)-Early mention of a comic book shop & comic collecting; mentions DCs selling for $100 a copy	11	22	33	73	157	240
159-Origin retold (1/66); 1st S.A. origin?	14	28	42	98	217	325
160-1st S.A. Cheetah app.	38	76	114	285	641	1000
171-176	8	16	24	56	108	160
177-W. Woman/Supergirl battle	11	22	33	73	157	240
178-(10/68) 1st new Wonder Woman on-c only; appears in old costume w/powers inside	13	26	39	91	201	310
179-Classic-c; wears no costume to issue #203	13	26	39	86	188	290
180-195: 180-Death of Steve Trevor. 182-Last 12¢ issue. 195-Wood inks						
	6	12	18	42	79	115
196 (52 pgs.)-Origin-r/All Star #8 (6 out of 9 pgs.)	10	20	30	68	144	220
197,198 (52 pgs.)-Reprints	7	14	21	46	86	125
199-Jeff Jones painted-c; 52 pgs.	10	20	30	70	150	230
200 (5-6/72)-Jeff Jones-c; 52 pgs.	10	20	30	69	147	225
201,202-Catwoman app. 202-Fafhrd & The Grey Mouser debut.						
	6	12	18	38	69	100
203,205-210,212: 212-The Cavalier app.	4	8	12	23	37	50
204-(2/73) Return to old costume; death of I Ching; intro. Nubia						
	28	56	84	202	451	700
204 (Facsimile Edition) (1/23, $3.99) Reprints #204 with original 1973 ads						4.00
211,214-(100 pgs.)	8	16	24	54	102	150
213,215,216,218-220: 220-N. Adams assist	3	6	9	19	30	40
217: (68 pgs.)	4	8	12	28	47	65
221,222,224-227,229,230,233-236,238-240: 227-Judy Garland tribute						
	3	6	9	15	22	28
223,228,231,232,237,241,248: 223-Steve Trevor revived as Steve Howard & learns W.W.'s I.D. 228-Both Wonder Women team up & new World War II stories begin, end #243. 231,232: JSA app. 237-Origin retold. 240-G.A. Flash app. 241-Intro Bouncer; Spectre app. 248-Steve Trevor Howard dies (44 pgs.)	3	6	9	16	23	30
242-246,252-266,269,270: 243-Both W. Women team up again. 269-Last Wood a(i) for DC? (7/80)	2	4	6	9	13	16
247,249,250,271: 247,249 (44 pgs.). 249-Hawkgirl app. 250-Origin/1st app. Orana, the new Wonder Woman. 271-Huntress & 3rd Life of Steve Trevor begin						
	2	4	6	10	14	18
250-252,255-262-264-(Whitman variants, low print run, no issue # on cover)						
	3	6	9	19	30	40

	GD 2.0	VG 4.0	FN 6.0	VF 8.0	VF/NM 9.0	NM- 9.2
251-Orana dies	3	6	9	14	20	26
267,268-Re-intro Animal Man (5/80 & 6/80)	2	4	6	10	14	18
272-280,284-286,289,290,294-299,301-325	2	4	6	8	10	12
281-283: Joker-c/stories in Huntress back-ups	2	4	6	9	13	16
287,288,291-293: 287-New Teen Titans x-over. 288-New costume & logo.						
291-293-Three part epic with Super-Heroines	1	3	4	6	8	10
300-($1.50, 76 pgs.)-Anniv. issue; Giffen-a; New Teen Titans, Bronze Age Sandman, JLA & G.A. Wonder Woman app.; 1st app. Lyta Trevor who becomes Fury in All-Star Squadron #25; G.A. Wonder Woman & Steve Trevor revealed as married						
	3	6	9	14	20	26
326-328	1	3	4	6	8	10
329 (Double size)-S.A. W.W. & Steve Trevor wed	3	6	9	15	20	26
...: Chronicles Vol. 1 TPB (2010, $17.99) reprints debut in All Star Comics #8, apps. in Sensation Comics #1-9 and Wonder Woman #1						18.00
Diana Prince: Wonder Woman Vol. 1 TPB (2008, $19.99) r/#178-183						20.00
Diana Prince: Wonder Woman Vol. 2 TPB (2008, $19.99) r/#185-189, Brave and the Bold #87, and Superman's Girl Friend, Lois Lane #93						20.00
Diana Prince: Wonder Woman Vol. 3 TPB ('08, $19.99) r/#190-198, World's Finest #204						20.00
Diana Prince: Wonder Woman Vol. 4 TPB ('09, $19.99) r/#199-204, Brave & Bold #105						20.00
...: The Greatest Stories Ever Told TPB (2007, $19.99) intro. by Lynda Carter; Ross-c						20.00

NOTE: *Andru/Esposito* c-66-160(most). *Buckler* a-300. *Colan* a-288-305p; c-288-290p. *Giffen* a-300p. *Grell* c-217. *Kaluta* c-297. *Gil Kane* c-294p, 303-305, 307, 312, 314. *Miller* c-298p. *Morrow* c-233. *Nasser* a-232p; c-231p, 232p. *Bob Oksner* c(i)-39-65(most). *Perez* c-283p, 300. *Spiegle* a-312. *Staton* a(p)-241, 271-287, 289, 290, 294-299; c(p)-241, 245, 246. Huntress back-up stories 271-287, 289, 290, 294-299, 301-321.

WONDER WOMAN

DC Comics: Feb, 1987 - No. 226, Apr, 2006 (75¢/$1.00/$1.25/$1.95/$1.99/$2.25/$2.50)

	GD 2.0	VG 4.0	FN 6.0	VF 8.0	VF/NM 9.0	NM- 9.2
0-(10/94) Zero Hour; released between #90 & #91	2	4	6	10	14	18
1-New origin; Pérez-c/a begins	4	8	12	25	40	55
1 (Facsimile Edition) (12/20, 10/23, $3.99) Reprints #1 with original ads						4.00
2-5	1	3	4	6	8	10
6-20: 9-Origin Cheetah. 12,13-Millennium x-over. 18,26-Free 16 pg. story						6.00
21-49: 24-Last Pérez-a; scripts continue thru #62						5.00
50-($1.50, 52 pgs.)-More heroines, less hype						5.00
51-62: Pérez scripts. 60-Vs. Lobo; last Pérez-a. 62-Last $1.00-c						6.00
63-New direction & Bolland-c begin; Deathstroke story continued from W. W. Special #1						5.00
64-84						4.00
85-1st Deodato-a; ends #90	2	4	6	9	13	16
86-88: 88-Superman-c & app.	1	2	3	5	6	8
89-97: 90-(9/94)-1st Artemis. 91-(11/94). 93-Hawkman app. 96-Joker-c						6.00
98,99						5.00
100 ($2.95, Newsstand)-Death of Artemis; Bolland-c ends.						6.00
100 ($3.95, Direct Market)-Death of Artemis; foil-c	1	2	3	5	6	8
101-119, 121-125: 101-Begin $1.95-c; Byrne-c/a/scripts begin. 101-104-Darkseid app. 105-Phantom Stranger cameo. 106-108-Phantom Stranger & Demon app. 107,108-Arion app. 111-1st app. new Wonder Girl. 111,112-Vs. Doomsday. 112-Superman app. 113-Wonder Girl-c/app; Sugar & Spike app.						4.00
						5.00
120 ($2.95)-Perez-a						4.00
126-139: 128-Hippolyta becomes new W.W. 130-133-Flash (Jay Garrick) & JSA app. 136-Diana returns to W.W. role; last Byrne issue. 137-Priest-s. 139-Luke-s/Paquette-a begin; Hughes-c thru #146						4.00
150-($2.95) Hughes-c/Clark-a; Zauriel app.	2	4	6	8	10	12
151-158,170-Hughes-c. 153-Superboy app. 170-Lois Lane-c/app.						8.00
159-163: 159-Begin $2.25-c. 160,161-Clayface app. 162,163-Aquaman app.						4.00
164-169,171: Phil Jimenez-s/a begin; Hughes-c; Batman app. 168,169-Pérez co-plot						6.00
169-Wraparound-c						5.00
172-Our Worlds at War; Hippolyta killed						6.00
173,174: 173-Our Worlds at War; Darkseid app. 174-Every DC heroine app.						3.00
175-($3.50) Joker: Last Laugh; JLA app.; Jim Lee-c						4.00
176-199: 177-Paradise Island returns. 179-Jimenez-a. 184,185-Hippolyta-c/app.; Hughes-c. 186-Cheetah app. 189-Simonson-s/Ordway-a begin. 190-Diana's new look. 195-Rucka-s/Drew Johnson-a begin. 197-Flash-c/app. 198,199-Noto-c						3.00
200-($3.95) back-up stories in 1940s and 1950s style; pin-ups by various						4.00
201-218,220-225: 203,204-Batman-c/app. 204-Matt Wagner-c. 212-JLA app. 214-Flash app. 215-Morales-a begin. 219-Begin $2.50-c. 220-Batman app.						3.00
219-Omac tie-in/Sacrifice pt. 4; Wonder Woman kills Max Lord; Superman app.						4.00
219-(2nd printing) Altered cover with red background						3.00
226-Last issue; flashbacks to meetings with Superman; Rucka-s/Richards-a						4.00
#1,000,000 (11/98) 853rd Century x-over; Deodato-a						3.00
Annual 1,2: 1 ('88, $1.50)-Art Adams-a. 2 ('89, $2.00, 68 pgs.)-All women artists issue; Perez-c(i)/a.						5.00
Annual 3 (1992, $2.50, 68 pgs.)-Quesada-c(p)						4.00
Annual 4 (1995, $3.50)-Year One						4.00
Annual 5 (1996, $2.95)-Legends of the Dead Earth story; Byrne scripts; Cockrum-a						4.00
Annual 6 (1997, $3.95)-Pulp Heroes						4.00
Annual 7,8 ('98,'99, $2.95)-7-Ghosts; Wrightson-c. 8-JLApe, A.Adams-c						4.00
...: Beauty and the Beasts TPB (2005, $19.95) r/#15-19 & Action Comics #600						20.00
...: Bitter Rivals TPB (2004, $13.95) r/#200-205; Jones-c						14.00
...: Challenge of the Gods TPB ('04, $19.95) r/#8-14; Pérez-s/a						20.00

	GD	VG	FN	VF	VF/NM	NM-
	2.0	4.0	6.0	8.0	9.0	9.2

...: Destiny Calling TPB (2006, $19.99) r/#20-24 & Annual #1; Pérez-c & pin-up gallery — 20.00

...Donna Troy (6/98, $1.95) Girlfrenzy; Jimenez-a — 3.00

... Down To Earth TPB (2004, $14.95) r/#195-200; Greg Land-c — 15.00

... 80-Page Giant 1 (2002, $4.95) reprints in format of 1960s' 80-Page Giants

... Eyes of the Gorgon TPB ('05, $19.99) r/#206-213 — 20.00

Gallery (1996, $3.50)-Bolland-c; pin-ups by various — 4.00

... Gods and Mortals TPB ('04, $19.95) r/#1-7; Pérez-a — 20.00

... Gods of Gotham TPB ('01, $5.95) r/#164-167; Jimenez-s/a — 6.00

... Land of the Dead TPB ('06, $12.99) r/#214-217 & Flash #219 — 13.00

Lifelines TPB ('98, $9.95) r/#106-112; Byrne-c/a — 10.00

... Mission's End TPB ('06, $19.99) r/#218-226; cover gallery — 20.00

... Our Worlds at War (10/01, $2.95) History of the Amazons; Jae Lee-c — 3.00

... Paradise Found TPB (03, $14.95) r/#171-177, Secret Files #3; Jimenez-a — 15.00

... Paradise Lost TPB ('02, $14.95) r/#164-170; Jimenez-a — 15.00

Plus 1 (1/97, $2.95)-Jesse Quick-c/app. — 4.00

Second Genesis TPB (1997, $9.95)-r/#101-105

Secret Files 1-3 (1998, 7/99, 5/02; $4.95) — 5.00

Special 1 (1992, $1.75, 52 pgs.)-Deathstroke-c/story continued in Wonder Woman #63 — 7.00

...: The Blue Amazon (2003, $6.95) Elseworlds; McKeever-a — 7.00

The Challenge Of Artemis TPB (1996, $9.95) r/#94-100; Deodato-c/a — 10.00

...: The Once and Future Story (1998, $4.95) Trina Robbins-s/Doran & Guice-a — 5.00

NOTE: **Art Adams** a-Annual 1. **Byrne** c/a 101-107. **Bolton** a-Annual 1. **Deodato** a-85-100. **Perez** a-Annual 1; c-Annual 1(i). Quesada c(p)-Annual 3.

WONDER WOMAN (Also see Amazons Attack mini-series)
DC Comics: Aug, 2006 - No. 44, Jul, 2010; No. 600, Aug, 2010 - No. 614, Oct, 2011 ($2.99)

1-Donna Troy as Wonder Woman after Infinite Crisis; Heinberg-s/Dodson-a/c — 5.00

1-Variant-c by Adam Kubert — 10.00

2-44: 2-4-Giganta & Hercules app. 6-Jodi Picoult-s begins. 8-Hippolyta returns. 9-12-Amazons Attack tie-in; JLA app. 14-17-Simone-s/Dodson-a/c. 20-23-Stalker app. 26-33-Rise of the Olympian. 40,41-Power Girl app. — 3.00

14-DC Nation Convention giveaway edition — 6.00

(Title re-numbered after #44, July 2010 to cumilative numbering of #600)

600-(8/10, $4.99) Short stories and pin-ups by various incl. Pérez, Conner, Kramer, Jim Lee; intro. by Lynda Carter; debut of new costume; cover by Pérez — 5.00

600-Variant cover by Adam Hughes — 8.00

600-2nd printing with new costume cover by Don Kramer — 5.00

601-614: 601-606-Kramer-a; two covers by Kramer and Garner. 608-Borges-a — 3.00

... Annual 1 (11/07, $3.99) Story cont'd from #4; Heinberg-s/Dodson-a/c; back-up Frank-a — 4.00

...: Contagion SC (2010, $14.99) r/#40-44 — 15.00

...: Ends of the Earth HC (2009, $24.99) r/#20-25 — 25.00

...: Ends of the Earth SC (2010, $14.99) r/#20-25 — 15.00

...: Love and Murder HC (2007, $19.99) r/#6-10 — 20.00

...: Odyssey Volume One HC (2011, $22.99) r/#600-606; afterwords by Jim Lee & JMS — 23.00

...: Rise of the Olympian HC (2009, $24.99) r/#26-33 & pages from DC Universe #0 — 25.00

...: Rise of the Olympian SC (2009, $14.99) r/#26-33 & pages from DC Universe #0 — 15.00

...: The Circle HC (2008, $24.99) r/#14-19; Mercedes Lackey intro.; Dodson sketch pages — 25.00

...: The Circle SC (2009, $14.99) r/#14-19; Mercedes Lackey intro.; Dodson sketch pages — 15.00

...: Warkiller SC (2010, $14.99) r/#34-39 — 15.00

...: Who is Wonder Woman? HC (2007, $19.99) r/#1-4 & Annual #1; Vaughan intro. — 20.00

...: Who is Wonder Woman? SC (2009, $14.99) r/#1-4 & Annual #1; Vaughan intro. — 15.00

WONDER WOMAN (DC New 52)
DC Comics: Nov, 2011 - No. 52, Jul, 2016 ($2.99/$3.99)

1-Azzarello-s/Chiang-a/c | | 2 | 4 | 6 | 11 | 16 | 20

2-23: 2-4-Azzarello-s/Chiang-a/c. 5,6,9,10,13,14,17-Akins-a. 14-19,21-23-Orion app. — 3.00

23.1, 23.2 (11/13, $2.99, regular covers) — 3.00

23.1 (11/13, $3.99, 3-D cover) "Cheetah #1" on cover; origin; Ostrander-s/Ibanez-a — 5.00

23.2 (11/13, $3.99, 3-D cover) "First Born #1" on cover; origin; Azzarello-s/Aco-a — 5.00

24-35: 25-Orion app. 29-Diana becomes God of War. 35-Last Azzarello-s/Chiang-a/c — 3.00

36-40: 36-Meredith Finch-s/David Finch-a begins. 37-Donna Troy returns — 3.00

41-49,51,52: 41-New costume; begin $3.99-c. 43-Churchill-a — 4.00

50-($4.99) Finch & Desjardins-a; Ares app.; back-up Donna Troy story — 5.00

#0 (11/12, $2.99) 12 year-old Princess Diana's training; Azzarello-s/Chiang-a/c — 3.00

Annual 1 (8/15, $4.99) Concludes "War Torn" arc from #36-40; David Finch-a — 5.00

...: Futures End 1 (11/14, $2.99, regular-c) Five years later; Soule-s/Morales-a — 3.00

...: Futures End 1 (11/14, $3.99, 3-D cover) — 4.00

WONDER WOMAN (DC Rebirth)(Reverts to legacy numbering with #750)
DC Comics: Aug, 2016 - No. 83, Late Feb, 2020; No. 750, Late March, 2020 - No. 800, Aug, 2023 ($2.99/$3.99/$4.99)

1-24: 1,3,5,7-Rucka-s/Sharp-a; Cheetah app. 2,4,6,10,12,14-Year One; Nicola Scott-a — 3.00

25-($3.99) Justice League and Shaggy Man app. — 4.00

26-49: 26-Andolfo-a. 31,33-Grail & baby Darkseid app. 35-Intro. Jason. 37-Zeus vs. Darkseid. 38-40-Silver Swan app. 42-45-Darkseid app. 47-Supergirl app.; leads into Annual 2 — 3.00

50-74-($3.99): 50-Justice League app. 52,53-Aztek app. 56,57-The Witching Hour tie-in — 3.00

75-($4.99) Amazons vs. Grail; Wilson-s/Xermanico & Merino-a — 5.00

76-83-Cheetah app. (Year of the Villain) — 4.00

750-($9.99, 96 pages) Conclusion vs. Cheetah; short stories and pin-ups by various incl. Simone-a/Durana-a, Rucka-s/Scott-a, Snyder-s/Hitch-a; multiple covers — 10.00

751-769-($3.99) 751-Intro. Valda, The Iron Maiden. 758-Phantom Stranger app.

760-767-Max Lord app. 762-Intro. Liar Liar. 768-Deathstroke app. — 4.00

770-799-($4.99) 770-Afterworlds begins. 777-Justice Guild of Earth-11 app. 780-Diana returns to the living world. 781-783-Dr. Cizko app. 791,792-Cheetah app. — 5.00

800-($5.99) The Wonder Girls, Batman & Superman app. — 6.00

Annual 1 (7/17, $4.99) Retells 1st meeting with Superman & Batman; Scott-a — 5.00

Annual 2 (8/18, $4.99) The Star Sapphires app.; Putri-c/Laming, Calafiore, & Irving-a — 5.00

Annual 3 (12/19, $4.99) Gorilla Grodd app.; Orlando-s/Marion-a — 5.00

Annual 4 (10/20, $4.99) Orlando-s/Herbert-a — 5.00

2021 Annual (1/22, $5.99) Cloonan & Conrad-s/MacDonald-s; intro. Altuum — 6.00

... and Justice League Dark: The Witching Hour 1 (12/18, $4.99) Part 1 of x-over — 5.00

... 1984 (11/20, $3.99) Movie tie-in; art by Blevins & Sauvage; Steve Trevor app. — 4.00

... #1 FCBD 2017 Special Edition (5/17, giveaway) w/#2; Year One; Nicola Scott-a — 3.00

... #1 Wonder Woman Day Special Edition (12/21, giveaway) w/#1 — 3.00

...: Rebirth 1 (8/16, $2.99) Rucka-s; multiple origins; new costume — 4.00

...: 75th Anniversary Special 1 (7/99, $7.99) short stories and pin-ups by various incl. Sharp, Moon, Bolland, DeLiz, Frison, Albuquerque, Larson, Jimenez, Sauvage; Jim Lee-c — 8.00

...: Steve Trevor 1 (8/17, $3.99) Seeley-s/Duce-a — 4.00

...: Tasmanian Devil Special 1 (8/17, $4.99) Bedard-s/Kitson-a; Circe app.; cartoon-style

---

back-up with Caldwell-a; Daffy Duck & Wile E. Coyote app. — 5.00

...: The Adventures of Young Diana Special 1 (12/21, $9.99) R/back-ups from #770-779 — 10.00

...: The War of the Gods: Special Edition 1 (9/23, $4.99) Facsimile of War of the Gods #1 — 5.00

WONDER WOMAN (Dawn of DC)
DC Comics: Nov, 2023 - Present ($4.99)

1-7: 1-Tom King-s/Daniel Sampere-a. 7-Superman app. — 5.00

WONDER WOMAN: AMAZONIA
DC Comics: 1997 ($7.95, Graphic Album format, one shot)

1-Elseworlds; Messner-Loebs-s/Winslade-a | 2 | 4 | 6 | 8 | 10 | 12

WONDER WOMAN BLACK & GOLD
DC Comics: Aug, 2021 - No. 6, Jan, 2022 ($5.99, B&W&shades of gold, limited series)

1-6-Anthology of short stories from all eras. 1-Art by Sook, Reeder, Cloonan — 6.00

WONDER WOMAN: COME BACK TO ME
DC Comics: Sept, 2019 - No. 6, Feb, 2020 ($4.99, limited series)

1-6: 1-Reprints serialized story from Walmart exclusive Justice League Giant #3,4 — 5.00

WONDER WOMAN / CONAN
DC Comics: Nov, 2017 - No. 6, Apr, 2018 ($3.99, limited series)

1-6-Simone-s/Lopresti-a; meet-up in Conan's time; the Corvidae app. — 4.00

WONDER WOMAN: DEAD EARTH
DC Comics (Black Label): Feb, 2020 - No. 4, Oct, 2020 ($6.99, 10-7/8" x 8-1/2", lim. series)

1-4-Wonder Woman in post-apocalyptic future; Daniel Warren Johnson-s/a; 2 covers — 7.00

WONDER WOMAN: EARTH ONE
DC Comics: 2016; 2018 ($22.99/$24.99, HC Graphic Novel)

Volume 1 ($22.99) - Morrison-s/Paquette-a; alternate retelling of origin; bonus art — 23.00

Volume 2 ($24.99) - Morrison-s/Paquette-a; Dr. Psycho app.; bonus art — 25.00

WONDER WOMAN 80TH ANNIVERSARY 100-PAGE SUPER SPECTACULAR
DC Comics: Dec, 2021 ($9.99, squarebound, one-shot)

1-Short stories & pin-ups by various incl. García-López, Cheung, Reeder; multiple covers — 10.00

WONDER WOMAN: EVOLUTION
DC Comics: Jan, 2022 - No. 8, Sept, 2022 ($3.99, limited series)

1-8: 1-Phillips-s/Hawthorne-a; Silver Swan app. — 4.00

WONDER WOMAN GIANT (Reprint of new stories in Wonder Woman: Come Back to Me) (See Justice League Giant #1-7 for previous JL & Aquaman reprints)
DC Comics: 2019 - No. 7, 2019 ($4.99, 100 pgs., squarebound, Walmart exclusive)

1-7-New Wonder Woman story Conner & Palmiotti-s/Derenick-a; Jonah Hex app. plus reprints Justice League ('11), Wonder Woman ('06), and Aquaman ('11) in all — 5.00

WONDER WOMAN GIANT
DC Comics: 2019 - No. 4, 2020 ($4.99, 100 pgs., squarebound, Mass Market & Direct Market editions exist for each issue, with different covers)

1-4: 1-New story with Harley Quinn and reprints. 2-4-New stories and reprints — 5.00

WONDER WOMAN HISTORIA: THE AMAZONS
DC Comics (Black Label): Jan, 2022 - No. 3, Feb, 2023 ($7.99, oversized 8-1/2" x 10-3/4", lim. series)

1-3-Kelly Sue DeConnick-s. 1-Phil Jimenez-a. 2-Gene Ha-a. 3-Nicola Scott-a — 8.00

WONDER WOMAN '77
DC Comics: Jun, 2015 - No. 4, Nov, 2016 ($7.99, square-bound, printing of digital-first stories)

1-4-Stories based on the Lynda Carter series. 1-Covers by Nicola Scott-c & Phil Jimenez; Dr. Psycho app.; bonus sketch design art; afterword by Mangels. 2-(11/15) Scott-c; The Cheetah, Celsia & Solomon Grundy app. 3-Clayface app. — 8.00

WONDER WOMAN '77 MEETS THE BIONIC WOMAN (TV)
Dynamite Entertainment: 2016 - No. 6, 2017 ($3.99, limited series)

1-6-Andy Mangels-s/Judit Tondora-a; multiple covers — 4.00

WONDER WOMAN SPECTACULAR (See DC Special Series #9)

WONDER WOMAN: SPIRIT OF TRUTH
DC Comics: Nov, 2001 ($9.95, treasury size, one-shot)

nn-Painted art by Alex Ross; story by Alex Ross and Paul Dini — 10.00

WONDER WOMAN: THE HIKETEIA
DC Comics: 2002 ($24.95, hardcover, one-shot)

nn-Wonder Woman battles Batman; Greg Rucka-s/J.G. Jones-a — 25.00

Softcover (2003, $17.95) — 18.00

WONDER WOMAN: THE TRUE AMAZON
DC Comics: 2016 ($22.99, HC Graphic Novel)

HC-Retelling of childhood & origin; Jill Thompson-s/painted-a; bonus design pages — 23.00

WONDER WOMAN: THE WAR OF THE GODS: SPECIAL EDITION
DC Comics: Sept, 2023 - No. 4, Dec, 2023 ($4.99, limited series)

1-4-Reprints War of the Gods 1991 series; George Pérez-s/a Cynthia Martin-a — 5.00

WONDERWORLD COMICS (Formerly Wonder Comics)
Fox Feature Syndicate: No. 3, July, 1939 - No. 33, Jan, 1942

3-Intro the Flame by Fine; Dr. Fung (Powell-a), K-51 (Powell-a?), & Yarko the Great, Master Magician (Eisner-a) continues; Eisner/Fine-c

| | 1500 | 3000 | 4500 | 11,400 | 20,700 | 30,000 |

4-Lou Fine-c | 470 | 940 | 1410 | 3431 | 6066 | 8700

5,6,9,10: Lou Fine-c | 326 | 652 | 978 | 2282 | 3991 | 5700

7-Classic Lou Fine-c | 1750 | 3500 | 5250 | 13,300 | 24,150 | 35,000

8-Classic Lou Fine-c | 1000 | 2000 | 3000 | 7600 | 13,800 | 20,000

11-Origin The Flame | 459 | 918 | 1377 | 3350 | 5925 | 8500

12-15: 13-Dr. Fung ends; last Fine-c(p) | 258 | 516 | 774 | 1651 | 2826 | 4000

16-20 | 187 | 374 | 561 | 1197 | 2049 | 2900

21-Origin The Black Lion & Cub | 200 | 400 | 600 | 1280 | 2190 | 3100

22-27: 22,25-Dr. Fung app. | 155 | 310 | 465 | 992 | 1696 | 2400

28-Origin & 1st app. U.S. Jones (8/41); Lu-Nar, the Moon Man begins | 432 | 864 | 1296 | 3154 | 5577 | 8000

29,31: 29-Torture-c | 148 | 296 | 444 | 947 | 1624 | 2300

30-Intro & Origin Flame Girl | 187 | 374 | 561 | 1197 | 2049 | 2900

Wonder Woman #800 © DC

Wonderworld Comics #7 © FOX

World of Archie #3 © ACP

	GD	VG	FN	VF	VF/NM	NM-
	2.0	4.0	6.0	8.0	9.0	9.2

	GD 2.0	VG 4.0	FN 6.0	VF 8.0	VF/NM 9.0	NM- 9.2
32-Hitler-c	459	918	1377	3350	5925	8500
33-Last issue	400	800	1200	2800	4900	7000

NOTE: *Spies at War by* **Eisner** *in #13, 17. Yarko by* **Eisner** *in #3-11.* **Eisner** *text illos-3. Lou Fine in 15(i); text illos-4.* **Nordling** *a-4-14.* **Powell** *a-3-12. Tuska a-5-9. Bondage-c 14, 15, 28, 31, 32. Cover features: The Flame-#3, 5-31; U.S. Jones-#32, 33.*

WONDERWORLDS
Innovation Publishing: 1992 ($3.50, squarebound, 100 pgs.)

1-Rebound super-hero comics, contents may vary; Hero Alliance, Terraformers, etc.						5.00

WOODS, THE
BOOM! Studios: May, 2014 - No. 36, Oct, 2017 ($3.99)

1-36: 1-Tynion-s/Dialynas-a; multiple covers						4.00

WOODSY OWL (See March of Comics #395)
Gold Key: Nov, 1973 - No. 10, Feb, 1976 (Some Whitman printings exist)

	GD 2.0	VG 4.0	FN 6.0	VF 8.0	VF/NM 9.0	NM- 9.2
1	2	4	6	13	18	22
1-Whitman variant	3	6	9	14	20	25
2-10	2	4	6	8	10	12

WOODY WOODPECKER (Walter Lantz... #73 on?)(See Dell Giants for annuals)
(Also see The Funnies, Jolly Jingles, Kite Fun Book, New Funnies)
Dell Publishing Co./Gold Key No. 73-187/Whitman No. 188 on:
No. 169, 10/47 - No. 72, 5-7/62; No. 73, 10/62 - No. 201, 3/84 (nn 192)

	GD 2.0	VG 4.0	FN 6.0	VF 8.0	VF/NM 9.0	NM- 9.2
Four Color 169(#1)-Drug turns Woody into a Mr. Hyde						
	22	44	66	154	340	525
Four Color 188	13	26	39	86	188	290
Four Color 202,249,264,288	9	18	27	62	126	190
Four Color 232-Classic-c	23	46	69	161	356	550
Four Color 305,336,350	9	18	27	61	123	185
Four Color 364,374,390,405,416,431('52)	6	12	18	37	66	95
16 (12-1/52-53) - 30('55)	4	8	12	27	44	60
31-50	3	6	9	21	33	45
51-72 (Last Dell)	3	6	9	17	26	35
73-75 (Giants, 84 pgs., Gold Key)	5	10	15	30	50	70
76-80	3	6	9	15	22	28
81-103: 103-Last 12¢ issue	3	6	9	14	19	24
104-120	2	4	6	11	16	20
121-140	2	4	6	9	12	15
141-160: 141-UFO-c	1	3	4	6	8	10
161-187	1	2	3	5	7	9
188,189 (Whitman)	2	4	6	9	13	16
190(9/80),191(11/80)-pre-pack only	6	12	18	38	69	100
(No #192)						
193-197: 196(2/82), 197(4/82)	2	4	6	11	16	20
198-201 (All #90062 on-c, no date or date code, pre-pack): 198(6/83), 199(7/83), 200(8/83), 201(3/84)						
	3	6	9	16	24	32
Christmas Parade 1(11/68-Giant)(G.K.)	4	8	12	25	40	55
Summer Fun 1(6/66-G.K.)(84 pgs.)	4	8	12	28	47	65
nn (1971, 60¢, 100 pgs. digest) B&W one page gags	3	6	9	14	24	32

NOTE: *15¢ Canadian editions of the 12¢ issues exist. Reprints-No. 92, 102, 103, 105, 106, 124, 125, 152, 153, 157, 162, 165, 194(1/3)-200(1/3).*

WOODY WOODPECKER (See Comic Album #5,9,13, Dell Giant #24, 40, 54, Dell Giants, The Funnies, Golden Comics Digest #1, 3, 5, 8, 15, 16, 20, 24, 32, 37, 44, March of Comics #16, 34, 85, 93, 109, 124, 139, 158, 177, 184, 203, 222, 239, 249, 261, 420, 454, 466, 478, New Funnies & Super Book #12, 24)

WOODY WOODPECKER
Harvey Comics: Sept, 1991 - No. 15, Aug, 1994 ($1.25)

1-15: 1-r/W.W. #53						4.00
50th Anniversary Special 1 (10/91, $2.50, 68 pgs.)						5.00

WOODY WOODPECKER AND FRIENDS
Harvey Comics: Dec, 1991 - No. 4, 1992 ($1.25)

1-4						4.00

WOOL (Hugh Howey's...)
Cryptozoic Entertainment: Jul, 2014 - No. 6, Nov, 2014 ($3.99)

1-6-Palmiotti & Gray-s/Broxton-a/Darwyn Cooke-c						4.00

WORD WARRIORS (Also see Quest for Dreams Lost)
Literacy Volunteers of Chicago: 1987 ($1.50, B&W)(Proceeds donated to help literacy)

1-Jon Sable by Grell, Ms. Tree, Streetwolf; Chaykin-c						4.00

WORLD AROUND US, THE (Illustrated Story of...)
Gilberton Publishers (Classics Illustrated): Sep, 1958 -No. 36, Oct, 1961 (25¢)

	GD 2.0	VG 4.0	FN 6.0	VF 8.0	VF/NM 9.0	NM- 9.2
1-Dogs; Evans-a	9	18	27	52	69	85
2-4: 2-Indians; Check-a. 3-Horses; L. B. Cole-c. 4-Railroads; L. B. Cole-a (5 pgs.)						
	9	18	27	47	61	75
5-Space; Ingels-a	10	20	30	56	76	95
6-The F.B.I.; Disbrow, Evans, Ingels-a	10	20	30	56	76	95
7-Pirates; Disbrow, Ingels, Kinstler-a	9	18	27	52	69	85
8-Flight; Evans, Ingels, Crandall-a	9	18	27	52	69	85
9-Army; Disbrow, Ingels, Orlando-a	9	18	27	47	61	75
10-13: 10-Navy; Disbrow, Kinstler-a. 11-Marine Corps. 12-Coast Guard; Ingels-a (9 pgs.).
13-Air Force; L.B. Cole-c	9	18	27	47	61	75
14-French Revolution; Crandall, Evans, Kinstler-a	10	20	30	56	76	95
15-Prehistoric Animals; Al Williamson-a, 6 & 10 pgs. plus Morrow-a						
	10	20	30	58	79	100
16-18: 16-Crusades; Kinstler-a. 17-Festivals; Evans, Crandall-a. 18-Great Scientists; Crandall, Evans, Torres, Williamson, Morrow-a	9	18	27	52	69	85
19-Jungle; Crandall, Williamson, Morrow-a	10	20	30	58	79	100
20-Communications; Crandall, Evans, Torres-a	10	20	30	56	76	95
21-American Presidents; Crandall/Evans, Morrow-a	10	20	30	56	76	95
22-Boating; Morrow-a	8	16	24	44	57	70
23-Great Explorers; Crandall, Evans-a	9	18	27	52	69	85
24-Ghosts; Morrow, Evans-a	10	20	30	56	76	95
25-Magic; Evans, Morrow-a	10	20	30	56	76	95
26-The Civil War	11	22	33	62	86	110
27-Mountains (High Advs.); Crandall/Evans, Morrow, Torres-a	9	18	27	52	69	85
28-Whaling; Crandall, Evans, Morrow, Torres, Wildey-a; L.B. Cole-c	9	18	27	52	69	85
29-Vikings; Crandall, Evans, Torres, Morrow-a	10	20	30	58	79	100
30-Undersea Adventure; Crandall/Evans, Kirby, Morrow, Torres-a	10	20	30	56	76	95
31-Hunting; Crandall/Evans, Ingels, Kinstler, Kirby-a	9	18	27	52	69	85
32,33: 32-For Gold & Glory; Morrow, Kirby, Crandall, Evans-a. 33-Famous Teens; Torres, Crandall, Evans-a	9	18	27	52	69	85
34-36: 34-Fishing; Crandall/Evans-a. 35-Spies; Kirby, Morrow?, Evans-a.
36-Fight for Life (Medicine); Kirby-a	9	18	27	52	69	85

NOTE: See Classics Illustrated Special Edition. Another *World Around Us* issue entitled *The Sea* had been prepared in 1962 but was never published in the U.S. It was published in the British/European *World Around Us* series. Those series then continued with seven additional WAU titles not in the U.S. series.

WORLD BELOW, THE
Dark Horse Comics: Mar, 1999 - No. 4, Jun, 1999 ($2.50, limited series)

1-4-Paul Chadwick-s/c/a						4.00
TPB (1/07, $12.95) r/#1-4; intro. by Chadwick; gallery of sketches and covers						13.00

WORLD BELOW, THE: DEEPER AND STRANGER
Dark Horse Comics: Dec, 1999 - No. 4, Mar, 2000 ($2.95, B&W)

1-4-Paul Chadwick-s/c/a						4.00

WORLD FAMOUS HEROES MAGAZINE
Comic Corp. of America (Centaur): Oct, 1941 - No. 4, Apr, 1942 (comic book)

	GD 2.0	VG 4.0	FN 6.0	VF 8.0	VF/NM 9.0	NM- 9.2
1-Gustavson-c; Lubbers, Glanzman-a; Davy Crockett, Paul Revere, Lewis & Clark, John Paul Jones stories; Flag-c	142	284	426	909	1555	2200
2-Lou Gehrig life story; Lubbers-a	71	142	213	454	777	1100
3,4-Lubbers-a. 4-Wild Bill Hickok story; 2 pg. Marlene Dietrich story	65	130	195	416	708	1000

WORLD FAMOUS STORIES
Croyden Publishers: 1945

	GD 2.0	VG 4.0	FN 6.0	VF 8.0	VF/NM 9.0	NM- 9.2
1-Ali Baba, Hansel & Gretel, Rip Van Winkle, Mid-Summer Night's Dream	17	34	51	98	154	210

WORLD IS HIS PARISH, THE
George A. Pflaum: 1953 (15¢)

	GD 2.0	VG 4.0	FN 6.0	VF 8.0	VF/NM 9.0	NM- 9.2
nn-The story of Pope Pius XII	7	14	21	35	43	50

WORLD OF ADVENTURE (Walt Disney's...)(TV)
Gold Key: Apr, 1963 - No. 3, Oct, 1963 (12¢)

	GD 2.0	VG 4.0	FN 6.0	VF 8.0	VF/NM 9.0	NM- 9.2
1-Disney TV characters; Savage Sam, Johnny Shiloh, Capt. Nemo, The Mooncussers	3	6	9	20	31	42
2,3	3	6	9	15	21	26

WORLD OF ANIMOSITY (See Animosity)
AfterShock Comics: Sept, 2017 ($3.99, one-shot)

nn-Character profiles and series summary						4.00

WORLD OF ARCHIE, THE (See Archie Giant Series Mag. #148, 151, 156, 160, 165, 171, 177, 182, 188, 193, 200, 208, 213, 225, 232, 237, 244, 249, 456, 461, 468, 473, 480, 485, 492, 497, 504, 509, 516, 521, 532, 543, 554, 565, 574, 587, 599, 612, 627)

WORLD OF ARCHIE
Archie Comics: Aug, 1992 - No. 22 ($1.25/$1.50)

	GD 2.0	VG 4.0	FN 6.0	VF 8.0	VF/NM 9.0	NM- 9.2
1	1	2	3	5	6	8
2-15: 9-Neon ink-c						4.00
16-22						4.00

WORLD OF ARCHIE DOUBLE DIGEST MAGAZINE (World of Archie Comics Digest #41-on)
Archie Comics: Dec, 2010 - Present ($3.99/$4.99/$5.99/$6.99/$7.99/$8.99/$9.99)

1-29,31-37,39,40: 5-r/Tiny Titans/Little Archie #1-3 with sketch. 17-Archie babies						4.00

	GD 2.0	VG 4.0	FN 6.0	VF 8.0	VF/NM 9.0	NM- 9.2

30-($5.99) Double Double Digest ... 6.00
38-$4.99-c ... 5.00
41,46,51,55,60,63,67,71,73,75-91-($6.99) 41-World of Archie Double Double Digest ... 7.00
42-45,47-50,52,54,57,58,61,64,65,68-($4.99) Titled World of Archie Comics Digest ... 6.00
53,56,59,62,66,70,72,74-($5.99): 56-Winter Annual. 59,70-Summer Annual ... 6.00
92-115-($7.99): 100-Time Police app. 103-Halloween-c. 104,105-Christmas-c ... 8.00
116-125-($8.99): 116-Valentine's Day cover. 125-Christmas-c ... 9.00
126-139-($9.99) ... 10.00
World of Archie Digest, Free Comic Book Day Edition (6-7/13, giveaway) Reprints ... 3.00

WORLD OF BETTY AND VERONICA JUMBO COMICS DIGEST
Archie Comics: Feb, 2021 - Present ($7.99/$8.99/$9.99)
1-11-New story and reprints ... 8.00
12-21-($8.99) 20,21-Christmas cover ... 9.00
22-31-($9.99) ... 10.00

WORLD OF BLACK HAMMER ENCYCLOPEDIA, THE (See Black Hammer)
Dark Horse Comics: Jul, 2019 ($3.99, one-shot)
nn-Character profiles with art by various and series timeline; Sorrentino-a ... 4.00

WORLD OF FANTASY
Atlas Comics (CPC No. 1-15/ZPC No. 16-19): May, 1956 - No. 19, Aug, 1959

	GD 2.0	VG 4.0	FN 6.0	VF 8.0	VF/NM 9.0	NM- 9.2
1	103	206	309	659	1130	1600
2-Williamson-a (4 pgs.)	53	106	159	334	567	800
3-Sid Check, Roussos-a	48	96	144	302	514	725
4-7	41	82	123	256	428	600
8-Matt Fox, Orlando, Berg-a	47	94	141	296	498	700
9-Krigstein-a	41	82	123	256	428	600
10-15: 10-Colan-a. 11-Torres-a	39	78	117	231	378	525
16-Williamson-a (4 pgs.); Ditko, Kirby-a	57	114	171	362	619	875
17-19-Ditko, Kirby-a	54	108	162	343	574	825

NOTE: **Ayers** a-3. **B. Baily** a-4. **Berg** a-5, 6, 8. **Brodsky** c-3. **Check** a-3. **Ditko** a-17, 19. **Everett** a-2; c-4-7, 9, 12, 13. **Forte** a-4, 8, 18. **Heck** a-18. **Infantino** a-14. **Kirby** c-15, 17-19. **Krigstein** a-9. **Maneely** c-2, 14. **Mooney** a-14. **Morrow** a-7. **Orlando** a-8, 13, 14. **Pakula** a-4, 6. **Powell** a-4, 6. **Reinman** a-8, 10. **R.Q. Sale** a-3, 7, 9, 10. **Severin** c-1. **Sinnott** a-16,18.

WORLD OF GIANT COMICS, THE (See Archie All-Star Specials under Archie Comics)

WORLD OF GINGER FOX, THE (Also see Ginger Fox)
Comico: Nov, 1986 ($6.95, 8 1/2 x 11", 68 pgs., mature)
Graphic Novel ($6.95) ... 10.00
Hardcover ($27.95) ... 30.00

WORLD OF JUGHEAD, THE (See Archie Giant Series Mag. #9, 14, 19, 24, 30, 136, 143, 149, 152, 157, 161, 166, 172, 178, 183, 189, 194, 202, 209, 215, 227, 233, 239, 245, 251, 457, 463, 469, 475, 481, 487, 493, 499, 505, 511, 517, 523, 531, 542, 553, 564, 577, 590, 602)

WORLD OF KRYPTON, THE (World of...#3) (See Superman #248)
DC Comics, Inc.: 7/79 - No. 3, 9/79; 12/87 - No. 4, 3/88 (Both are lim. series)

	GD 2.0	VG 4.0	FN 6.0	VF 8.0	VF/NM 9.0	NM- 9.2
1-3 (1979, 40¢; 1st comic book mini-series): 1-Jor-El marries Lara. 3-Baby Superman sent to Earth; Krypton explodes; Mon-El app.	1	3	4	6	8	10

1-4 (75¢)-Byrne scripts; Byrne/Simonson-c ... 4.00

WORLD OF KRYPTON
DC Comics: Feb, 2022 - No. 6, Jul, 2022 ($3.99, limited series)
1-6: 1-Venditti-s/Oeming-a; Jor-El, Lara, and baby Kara Zor-El app. 2-Trial of Kru-El ... 4.00

WORLD OF METROPOLIS, THE
DC Comics: Aug, 1988 - No. 4, July, 1988 ($1.00, limited series)
1-4-Byrne scripts ... 4.00

WORLD OF MYSTERY
Atlas Comics (GPI): June, 1956 - No. 7, July, 1957

	GD 2.0	VG 4.0	FN 6.0	VF 8.0	VF/NM 9.0	NM- 9.2
1-Torres, Orlando-a; Powell-a?	84	168	252	538	919	1300
2-Woodish-a	37	74	111	222	361	500
3-Torres, Davis, Ditko-a	39	78	117	240	395	550
4-Pakula, Powell-a	39	78	117	240	395	550
5,7: 5-Orlando-a	37	74	111	222	361	500
6-Williamson/Mayo-a (4 pgs.); Ditko-a; Colan-a; Crandall text illo	39	78	117	240	395	550

NOTE: **Ayers** a-4. **Brodsky** c-2, 5, 6. **Colan** a-6, 7. **Everett** c-1, 3. **Pakula** a-4, 6. **Romita** a-2. **Severin** c-7.

WORLD OF SMALLVILLE
DC Comics: Apr, 1988 - No. 4, July, 1988 (75¢, limited series)
1-4-Byrne scripts. 3-Baby torture-c ... 5.00

WORLD OF SUSPENSE
Atlas News Co.: Apr, 1956 - No. 8, July, 1957

	GD 2.0	VG 4.0	FN 6.0	VF 8.0	VF/NM 9.0	NM- 9.2
1	71	142	213	454	777	1100
2-Ditko-a (4 pgs.)	41	82	123	256	428	600
3,7-Williamson-a in both (4 pgs.); #7-with Mayo	37	74	111	222	361	500
4-6,8	31	62	93	182	296	410

NOTE: **Berg** a-6. **Cameron** a-2. **Ditko** a-2. **Drucker** a-1. **Everett** a-1, 5; c-6. **Heck** a-5. **Maneely** a-1; c-1-3. **Orlando** a-5. **Powell** a-6. **Reinman** a-4. **Roussos** a-4. **Sale** a-4. **Shores** a-1.

WORLD OF TANKS
Dark Horse Comics: Aug, 2016 - No. 5, Feb, 2017 ($3.99)
1-5-Ennis-s/Ezquerra-a; set in 1944 Normandy ... 4.00

WORLD OF TANKS II: CITADEL
Dark Horse Comics: May, 2018 - No. 5, Sept, 2018 ($3.99)
1-5-Ennis-s/Holden-a; set in 1943 Russia during the Battle of Kursk ... 4.00

WORLD OF WARCRAFT (Based on the Blizzard Entertainment video game)
DC Comics (WildStorm): Jan, 2008 - No. 25, Jan, 2010 ($2.99)
1-Walt Simonson-s/Lullabi-a; cover by Samwise Didier ... 8.00
1-Variant cover by Jim Lee ... 12.00
1,2-Second printing with Jim Lee sketch cover ... 5.00
2-Two covers by Jim Lee and Samwise Didier ... 5.00
3-24: 3-14-Two covers on each ... 3.00
25-($3.99) Walt & Louise Simonson-s ... 4.00
... Special 1 (2/10, $3.99) Costa-s/Mhan-a/c ... 4.00
... Book One HC (2008, $19.99, dustjacket) r/#1-7; intro. by Chris Metzen of Blizzard ... 20.00
... Book One SC (2009, $14.99) r/#1-7; intro. by Chris Metzen of Blizzard ... 15.00
... Book Two HC (2009, $19.99, dustjacket) r/#8-14 ... 20.00
... Book Two SC (2010, $14.99) r/#8-14 ... 15.00
... Book Three HC (2010, $19.99, dustjacket) r/#15-21 ... 20.00
... Book Three SC (2011, $17.99) r/#15-21 ... 18.00

WORLD OF WARCRAFT: ASHBRINGER
DC Comics (WildStorm): Nov, 2008 - No. 4, Feb, 2009 ($3.99)
1-4-Neilson-s/Lullabi & Washington-a; 2 covers by Robinson & Lullabi ... 4.00
TPB (2010, $14.99) r/#1-4 ... 15.00

WORLD OF WARCRAFT: CURSE OF THE WORGEN
DC Comics (WildStorm #1,2): Jan, 2011 - No. 5, May, 2011 ($3.99/$2.99)
1,2-($3.99) Neilson & Waugh-s/Lullabi & Washington-a; Polidora-c ... 4.00
3-5-($2.99) ... 3.00

WORLD OF WHEELS (Formerly Dragstrip Hotrodders)
Charlton Comics: No. 17, Oct, 1967 - No. 32, June, 1970

	GD 2.0	VG 4.0	FN 6.0	VF 8.0	VF/NM 9.0	NM- 9.2
17-20-Features Ken King	3	6	9	17	26	35
21-32-Features Ken King	3	6	9	15	22	28

Modern Comics Reprint 23(1978) ... 6.00

WORLD OF WOOD
Eclipse Comics: 1986 - No. 4, 1987; No. 5, 2/89 ($1.75, limited series)

	GD 2.0	VG 4.0	FN 6.0	VF 8.0	VF/NM 9.0	NM- 9.2
1,2: 1-Dave Stevens-c. 2-Wood/Stevens-c	2	4	6	8	11	14

3-5: 5-($2.00, B&W)-r/Avon's Flying Saucers ... 5.00

WORLD OF ZORRO
American Mythology Productions: 2021 (Free Comic Book Day giveaway)
1-Sample stories from Zorro series Swords of Hell, Legendary Adventures & Flights ... 3.00

WORLD READER
AfterShock Comics: Apr, 2017 - No. 6, Sept, 2017 ($3.99, limited series)
1-6-Jeff Loveness-s/Juan Doe-a ... 4.00

WORLD'S BEST COMICS
DC Comics: Feb 1940
nn - Ashcan comic, not distributed to newsstands, only for in-house use. Cover art is Action Comics #29 with interior being Action Comics #24. One copy sold for $21,000 in 2000.

WORLD'S BEST COMICS (World's Finest Comics #2 on)
National Per. Publications (100 pgs.): Spring, 1941 (Cardboard-c)(DC's 6th annual format comics)

	GD 2.0	VG 4.0	FN 6.0	VF 8.0	VF/NM 9.0	NM- 9.2
1-The Batman, Superman, Crimson Avenger, Johnny Thunder, The King, Young Dr. Davis, Zatara, Lando, Man of Magic, & Red, White & Blue begin; Superman, Batman & Robin covers begin (inside-c is blank); Fred Ray-c; 15¢ cover price	1870	3740	5610	14,500	25,250	36,000

WORLD'S BEST COMICS: GOLDEN AGE SAMPLER
DC Comics: 2003 (99¢, one-shot, samples from DC Archive editions)
1-Golden Age reprints from Superman #6, Batman #5, Sensation #11, Police #11 ... 3.00

WORLD'S BEST COMICS: SILVER AGE SAMPLER
DC Comics: 2004 (99¢, one-shot, samples from DC Archive editions)
1-Silver Age reprints from Justice League #4, Adventure #247, Our Army at War #81 ... 3.00

WORLDS BEYOND (Stories of Weird Adventure)(Worlds of Fear #2 on)
Fawcett Publications: Nov, 1951

	GD 2.0	VG 4.0	FN 6.0	VF 8.0	VF/NM 9.0	NM- 9.2
1-Powell, Bailey-a; Moldoff-c	116	232	348	742	1271	1800

WORLDS COLLIDE
DC Comics: July, 1994 ($2.50, one-shot)

	GD 2.0	VG 4.0	FN 6.0	VF 8.0	VF/NM 9.0	NM- 9.2
1-($2.50, 52 pgs.)-Milestone & Superman titles x-over						4.00
1-($3.95, 52 pgs.)-Polybagged w/vinyl clings						5.00
1-Platinum Edition	5	10	15	31	53	75

WORLD'S FAIR COMICS (See New York...)

WORLD'S FINEST (Also see Legends of The World's Finest)
DC Comics: 1990 - No. 3, 1990 ($3.95, squarebound, limited series, 52 pgs.)
1-3: Batman & Superman team-up against The Joker and Lex Luthor; Dave Gibbons scripts & Steve Rude-c/a ... 5.00
2,3-Joker/Luthor painted-c by Steve Rude ... 5.00
TPB-(1992, $19.95) r/#1-3; Gibbons intro. ... 20.00
...: The Deluxe Edition HC (2008, $29.99) r/#1-3; Gibbons intro. from 1992; Gibbons story outline and sketches; Rude sketch pages and notes ... 30.00

WORLD'S FINEST
DC Comics: Dec, 2009 - No. 4, Mar, 2010 ($2.99, limited series)
1-4: Gates-s/two covers by Noto on each. 3-Supergirl/Batgirl team up. 4-Noto-a ... 3.00
TPB (2010, $14.99) r/#1-4, Action Comics #865 & DC Comics Presents #31 ... 15.00

WORLDS' FINEST (Also see Earth 2 series)
DC Comics: Jul, 2012 - No. 32, May, 2015 ($2.99)
1-32: 1-Huntress and Power Girl; Levitz-s/art by Pérez & Maguire. 6,7-Damian app. 19-Huntress meets Batman. 20,21-X-over with Batman/Superman #8,9. 25-Return to Earth-2. 27-29-Secret History of Earth 2. 32-Death of Lois ... 3.00
1-Variant-c by Maguire ... 5.00
#0-(11/12, $2.99) Flashback to Robin's and Supergirl's training ... 3.00
Annual 1 (3/14, $4.99) Earth 2 flashback; Wonder Woman & Fury app. ... 5.00
...: Futures End 1 (11/14, $2.99, regular-c) Five years later; Cinar-a; Deathstroke app. ... 3.00
...: Futures End 1 (11/14, $2.99, 3-D cover) ... 4.00

WORLD'S FINEST COMICS (Formerly World's Best Comics #1)
National Periodical Publ./DC Comics: No. 2, Sum, 1941 - No. 323, Jan, 1986 (#1-17 have cardboard covers)(#2-9 have 100 pgs.)

	GD 2.0	VG 4.0	FN 6.0	VF 8.0	VF/NM 9.0	NM- 9.2
2 (100 pgs.)-Superman, Batman & Robin covers continue from World's Best; (cover price 15¢ #2-70)	465	930	1395	3395	5998	8600
3-The Sandman begins; last Johnny Thunder; origin & 1st app. The Scarecrow	703	1406	2109	5132	9066	13,000
4-Hop Harrigan app.; last Young Dr. Davis	295	590	885	1888	3244	4600
5-Intro. TNT & Dan the Dyna-Mite; last King & Crimson Avenger	265	530	870	1856	3178	4500
6-Star Spangled Kid begins (Sum/42); Aquaman app.; S&K Sandman with Sandy in new costume begins, ends #7	239	478	717	1530	2615	3700
7-Green Arrow begins (Fall/42); last Lando & Red, White & Blue; S&K art	265	530	795	1694	2897	4100

World of Krypton (2022 series) #1 © DC

World's Finest Comics #231 © DC

World's Finest: Teen Titans #1 © DC

	GD 2.0	VG 4.0	FN 6.0	VF 8.0	VF/NM 9.0	NM- 9.2
8-Boy Commandos begin (by Simon(p) #12); last "Minute Man Answers the Call" promo	232	464	696	1485	2543	3600
9-Batman cameo in Star Spangled Kid; S&K-a; last 100 pg. issue; Hitler, Mussolini, Tojo-c	326	652	978	2282	3991	5700
10-S&K-a; 76 pg. issues begin	194	388	582	1242	2121	3000
11-17: 17-Last cardboard cover issue	187	374	561	1197	2049	2900
18-20: 18-Paper covers begin; last Star Spangled Kid. 19-Joker story. 20-Last quarterly issue	168	336	504	1075	1838	2600
21-30: 21-Begin bi-monthly. 30-Johnny Everyman app.	116	232	348	742	1271	1800
31-40: 33-35-Tomahawk app. 35-Penguin app.	113	226	339	718	1234	1750
41-43,45-50: 41-Boy Commandos end. 42-The Wyoming Kid begins (9-10/49), ends #63. 43-Full Steam Foley begins, ends #48. 48-Last square binding.	142	284	426	909	1555	2200
49-Tom Sparks, Boy Inventor begins; robot-c	110	220	330	704	1202	1700
44-Used in SOTI, ref. to Batman & Robin being gay, and a cop being shot in the face	142	284	426	909	1555	2200
51-60: 51-Zatara ends. 54-Last 76 pg. issue. 59-Manhunters Around the World begins (7-8/52), ends #62	106	212	318	676	1162	1650
61-Joker story	142	284	426	909	1555	2200
62-64-Capt. Compass app.	103	206	309	659	1130	1600
65-Origin Superman; Tomahawk begins (7-8/53), ends #101	168	336	504	1075	1838	2600
66-70-(15¢ issues, scarce)-Last 15¢, 68pg. issue	110	220	330	704	1202	1700
71-(10¢ issue, scarce)-Superman & Batman begin as team (7-8/54); were in separate stories until now; Superman & Batman exchange identities; 10¢ issues begin	326	652	978	2282	3991	5700
72,73-(10¢ issue, scarce)	148	296	444	947	1624	2300
74-Last pre-code issue	103	206	309	659	1130	1600
75-(1st code approved, 3-4/55)	103	206	309	659	1130	1600
76-80: 77-Superman loses powers & Batman obtains them	77	154	231	493	847	1200
81-87,89: 84-1st S.A. issue. 89-2nd Batmen of All Nations (aka Club of Heroes)	57	114	171	362	619	875
88-1st Joker/Luthor team-up	77	154	231	493	847	1200
90-Batwoman's 1st app. in World's Finest (10/57, 3rd app. anywhere) plus-c app.	90	180	270	576	988	1400
91-93,95-99: 96-99-Kirby Green Arrow. 99-Robot-c	27	54	81	194	435	675
94-New origin of Superman/Batman team	71	142	213	568	1284	2000
100 (3/59)	42	84	126	311	706	1100
101-110: 102-Tommy Tomorrow begins, ends #124	17	34	51	119	265	410
111-121: 111-1st app. The Clock King. 113-Intro. Miss Arrowette in Green Arrow; 1st Bat-Mite/Mr. Mxyzptlk team-up (11/60). 117-Batwoman-c. 121-Last 10¢ issue	13	26	39	91	201	310
122-128: 123-2nd Bat-Mite/Mr. Mxyzptlk team-up (2/62). 125-Aquaman begins (5/62), ends #139 (Aquaman #1 is dated 1-2/62)	10	20	30	68	144	220
129-Joker/Luthor team-up-c/story	10	20	30	89	195	300
130-142: 135-Last Dick Sprang story. 140-Last Green Arrow. 142-Origin The Composite Superman (villain); Legion app.	8	16	24	54	102	150
143-150: 143-1st Mailbag. 144-Clayface/Brainiac team-up. 148-Clayface/Luthor team-up; last Clayface until Action #443	8	14	21	46	86	125
151-153,157-160: 157-2nd Super Sons story; last app. Kathy Kane (Bat-Woman) until Batman Family #10; 1st Bat-Mite Jr.	6	12	18	37	66	95
154-1st Super Sons story; last Bat-Woman in costume until Batman Family #10	8	16	24	55	105	155
156-1st Bizarro Batman; Joker-c/story	16	32	48	110	243	375
161,170 (80-Pg. Giants G-28,G-40)	6	12	18	42	79	115
162-165,167,168,171,172: 168,172-Adult Legion app.	5	10	15	33	57	80
166-Joker-c/story	8	16	24	56	108	160
169-2nd app. new Batgirl(9/67)(cover and 1 panel cameo); 3rd Bat-Mite/Mr. Mxyzptlk team-up; Legion app.	10	20	30	69	147	225
173-('68)-1st S.A. app. Two-Face as Batman becomes Two-Face in story	9	18	27	62	126	190
174-Adams-c	5	10	15	35	63	90
175,176-Neal Adams-c/a; both reprint J'onn J'onzz origin/Detective #225,226	8	16	24	51	96	140
177-Joker/Luthor team-up-c/story	8	16	24	52	99	145
178-(9/68)-Intro. of Super Nova (revived in "52" weekly series); Adams-c	6	12	18	38	69	100
179-(80 Page Giant G-52) -Adams-c; r/#94	7	14	21	44	82	120
180,182,183,185,186: Adams-c on all. 182-Silent Knight-r/Brave & Bold #6. 185-Last 12¢ issue. 186-Johnny Quick-r	4	8	12	28	47	65
181,184,187: 187-Green Arrow origin-r by Kirby (Adv. #256)	4	8	12	25	40	55
188,197-(Giants G-76,G-76; 64 pages)	5	10	15	35	63	90
189-196: 190-193-Robin-r	3	6	9	21	33	45
198,199-3rd Superman/Flash race (see Flash #175 & Superman #199). 199-Adams-c	10	20	30	69	147	225
200-Adams-c	4	8	12	28	47	65
201-203: 203-Last 15¢ issue.	3	6	9	19	30	40
204,205-(52 pgs.) Adams-c: 204-Wonder Woman app. 205-Shining Knight-r (6 pgs.) by Frazetta/Adv. #153; Teen Titans x-over	4	8	12	25	40	55
206 (Giant G-88, 64 pgs.)	5	10	15	33	57	80
207,212-(52 pgs.)	3	6	9	21	33	45
208-211(25¢-c) Adams-c: 208-(52 pgs.) Origin Robotman-r/Det. #138. 209-211-(52 pgs.)	4	8	12	23	37	50
213,214,216-222,229: 217-Metamorpho begins, ends #220; Batman/Superman team-ups resume. 229-r/origin Superman-Batman team	3	6	9	14	20	25
215-(12/72-1/73) Intro. Batman Jr. & Superman Jr. (see Superman/Batman: Saga of the Super Sons TPB for all the Super Sons stories)	5	10	15	30	40	
223-228:-(100 pgs.). 223-N. Adams-r. 223-Deadman origin. 226-N. Adams, S&K, Toth-r; Manhunter part origin-r/Det. #225,226. 227-Deadman app.	5	10	15	31	53	75
230-(68 pgs.)	3	6	9	18	28	38
231-243: 231, 233, 238, 242-Super Sons	2	4	6	10	14	18
244-246-Adams-c: 244-$1.00, 84 pg. issues begin; Green Arrow, Black Canary, Wonder Woman, Vigilante app.; 246-Death of Stuff in Vigilante; origin Vigilante retold	3	6	9	16	23	30
247-252 (84 pgs.): 248-Last Vigilante. 249-The Creeper begins by Ditko, 84 pgs. 250-The Creeper origin retold by Ditko. 251-1st app. Count Vertigo. 252-Last 84 pg. issue	3	6	9	14	19	24
253-257,259-265: 253-Capt. Marvel begins; 68 pgs. begin, end #265. 255-Last Creeper. 256-Hawkman begins. 257-Black Lightning begins. 263-Super Sons. 264-Clay Face app.	2	4	6	11	13	16
258-Adams-c	3	6	9	14	20	25
266-270,272-282:-(52 pgs.). 267-Challengers of the Unknown app.; 3 Lt. Marvels return. 268-Capt. Marvel Jr. origin retold. 274-Zatanna begins. 279, 280-Capt. Marvel Jr. & Kid Eternity learn they are brothers	2	4	6	8	10	12
271-(52pgs.) Origin Superman/Batman team retold	2	4	6	8	11	14
283-299: 284-Legion app.	1	2	3	5	6	8
300-($1.25, 52pgs.)-Justice League of America, New Teen Titans & The Outsiders app.; Perez-a (4 pgs.)	1	3	4	6	8	10
301-322: 304-Origin Null and Void. 309,319-Free 16 pg. story in each (309-Flash Force 2000, 319-Mask preview)						6.00
323-Last issue	1	2	3	5	6	8

NOTE: **Neal Adams** a-230ir; c-271-c. **Austin** a-244-246i. **Burnley** a-8, 10; c-7-9, 11-14, 15p?, 16-18p, 20-31p. **Colan** a-274p, 297, 299. **Ditko** a-249-255. **Giffen** a-244-246i. **Burnley** a-8, 10; c-7-9, 11-14, 15p?, 16-18p, 20-31p. **Colan** a-274p, 297, 299. **Ditko** a-249-255. **Giffen** a-322; c-284p, 322. **G. Kane** a-38, 174r, 282, 285, 282, 289. **Kirby** a-187. **Kubert** Zatara-40-44. **Miller** c-285p. **Mooney** c-134. **Morrow** a-245-248. **Mortimer** c-16-21, 26-71. **Nasser** a(p)-244-246, 259, 260. **Newton** a-253-281p. **Orlando** a-224r. **Perez** a-300; c-271, 276, 277p, 278p. **Fred Ray** c-1-5. **Fred Ray/Robinson** c-13-16. **Robinson** a-5, 6, 9-11, 13?, 14-16; c-6. **Rogers** a-259p. **Roussos** a-212r. **Simonson** c-291. **Spiegle** a-275-278, 284. **Staton** a-262p, 273p. **Swan/Moldoff** c-126. **Swan/Mortimer** c-79-82. **Toth** a-228r. **Tuska** a-230r, 250p, 252p, 254p, 257p, 283p, 284p, 308p. Boy Commandos by **Infantino** #39-41.

WORLD'S FINEST COMICS DIGEST (See DC Special Series #23)

WORLD'S FINEST: OUR WORLDS AT WAR
DC Comics: Oct, 2001 ($2.95, one-shot)

1-Concludes the Our Worlds at War x-over; Jae Lee-c; art by various						3.00

WORLD'S FINEST: TEEN TITANS
DC Comics: Sept, 2023 - No. 6, Feb, 2024 ($3.99)

1-6-Early version of the team; Waid-s/Lupacchino-a						4.00

WORLD'S FINITE CEREBUS (Reprints from Cerebus in Hell)
Aardvark-Vanaheim: Mar, 2018 ($4.00, B&W)

1-Cerebus figures with original Gustave Doré artwork of Hell; World's Finest #7-c swipe						4.00

WORLD'S GREATEST ATHLETE (See Walt Disney Showcase #14)

WORLD'S GREATEST SONGS
Atlas Comics (Male): Sept, 1954

	GD 2.0	VG 4.0	FN 6.0	VF 8.0	VF/NM 9.0	NM- 9.2
1-(Scarce)-Heath & Harry Anderson-a; Eddie Fisher life story plus-c; gives lyrics to Frank Sinatra song "Young at Heart"	61	122	183	390	870	950

WORLD'S GREATEST STORIES
Jubilee Publications: Jan, 1949 - No. 2, May, 1949

	GD 2.0	VG 4.0	FN 6.0	VF 8.0	VF/NM 9.0	NM- 9.2
1-Alice in Wonderland; Lewis Carroll adapt.	47	94	141	296	498	700
2-Pinocchio	40	80	120	246	411	575

WORLD'S GREATEST SUPER-HEROES HOLIDAY SPECIAL
DC Comics: 2018 ($4.99, 100 pgs., squarebound, Walmart exclusive)

1-New Flash story Lobdell-s/Booth-a; plus holiday-themed reprints; Andy Kubert-c						5.00

WORLDS OF ASPEN
Aspen MLT, Inc.: 2006 - Present (Free Comic Book Day giveaways)

...: FCBD 2006, 2007, #3, #4 Editions; Fathom, Soulfire, Shrugged short stories; Turner-c						3.00
... 2010 (5/10) Previews Fathom, Mindfield, Soulfire, Executive Assistant: Iris and Dellec						3.00
... 2011 (5/11) Previews Fathom, Soulfire, Charismagic, Lady Mechanika & others						3.00
... 2012 (5/12) Previews Fathom, Homecoming, Idolized, Shrugged & others						3.00
... 2013 (5/13) Flip book; previews Fathom, Zoohunters & others						3.00

	GD	VG	FN	VF	VF/NM	NM-
	2.0	4.0	6.0	8.0	9.0	9.2

... 2014 (5/14) Flip book; previews Damsels in Excess & Zoohunters; pin-ups   3.00
... 2015 (5/15) Flip book; previews Eternal Soulfire & Fathom Blue; pin-ups   3.00
... 2016 (5/16) Prelude to Aspen Universe: Revelations; character profile pages   3.00
... 2018 (5/18) Dimension: War Eternal; Nu Way   3.00

WORLDS OF FEAR (Stories of Weird Adventure)(Formerly Worlds Beyond #1)
Fawcett Publications: V1#2, Jan, 1952 - V2#10, June, 1953

	GD	VG	FN	VF	VF/NM	NM-
V1#2	71	142	213	454	777	1100
3-Evans-a	61	122	183	390	670	950
4-6(9/52)	50	100	150	315	533	750
V2#7,8	47	94	141	296	498	700
9-Classic drowning-c (4/53)	258	516	774	1651	2826	4000
10-Saunders painted-c; man with no eyes surrounded by eyeballs-c plus eyes ripped out story	400	800	1200	2800	4900	7000

NOTE: *Moldoff c-2-8. Powell a-2, 4, 5. Sekowsky a-4, 5.*

WORLDSTORM
DC Comics (WildStorm): Nov, 2006 (Dec on cover) - No. 2, May, 2007 ($2.99)
  1,2-Previews and pin-ups for re-launched WildStorm titles.1-Art Adams-c   3.00

WORLDS UNKNOWN
Marvel Comics Group: May, 1973 - No. 8, Aug, 1974

	GD	VG	FN	VF	VF/NM	NM-
1-r/from Astonishing #54; Torres, Reese-a	4	8	12	25	40	55
2-8	5	6	9	15	22	28

NOTE: *Adkins/Mooney a-5. Buscema c/a-4p. W. Howard c/a-3i. Kane a(p)-1,2; c(p)-5, 6, 8. Sutton a-2. Tuska a(p)-7, 8; c-7p. No. 7, 8 has Golden Voyage of Sinbad movie adaptation.*

W0RLDTR33
Image Comics: Apr, 2023 - Present ($3.99)
  1-8-James Tynion IV-s/Fernando Blanco-a   4.00

WORLD WAR HULK (See Incredible Hulk #106)
Marvel Comics: Aug, 2007 - No. 5, Jan, 2008 ($3.99, limited series)

	GD	VG	FN	VF	VF/NM	NM-
1-Hulk returns to Earth; Iron Man and Avengers app.; Romita Jr.-a/Pak-s/Finch-c	2	4	6	10	14	18
1-Variant cover by Romita Jr.	2	4	6	11	16	20
2-5: 2-Hulk battles The Avengers and FF; Finch-c. 3,4-Dr. Strange app. 5-Sentry app.	1	3	4	6	8	10
2-5-Variant cover by Romita Jr.	2	4	6	11	16	20

  ...: Aftersmash 1 (1/08, $3.99) Sandoval-a/Land-c; Hercules, Iron Man app.   4.00
  ...: Gamma Files (2007, $3.99) profile pages of Hulk characters   4.00
  ...Prologue: World Breaker 1 (7/07, one-shot) Rio, Weeks, Phillips, Miyazawa-a   4.00
  TPB (2008, $19.99) r/#1-5   20.00

WORLD WAR HULK AFTERSMASH: DAMAGE CONTROL
Marvel Comics: Mar, 2008 - No. 3, May, 2008 ($2.99, limited series)
  1-3-The clean-up; McDuffie-s. 2-Romita- Jr.-c 3-Romita Sr.-c   3.00

WORLD WAR HULK AFTERSMASH: WARBOUND
Marvel Comics: Feb, 2008 - No. 5, Jun, 2008 ($2.99, limited series)
  1-5-Kirk & Sandoval-a/Cheung-c   3.00

WORLD WAR HULK: FRONT LINE (See Incredible Hulk #106)
Marvel Comics: Aug, 2007 - No. 6, Dec, 2007 ($2.99, limited series)
  1-6-Ben Urich & Sally Floyd report World War Hulk; Jenkins-s/Bachs-a   3.00
  TPB (2008, $16.99) r/#1-5 & WWH Prologue: World Breaker   17.00

WORLD WAR HULK: GAMMA CORPS
Marvel Comics: Sept, 2007 - No. 4, Jan, 2008 ($2.99, limited series)
  1-4-Tieri-s/Ferreira-a/Roux-c   3.00
  TPB (2008, $10.99) r/#1-4   11.00

WORLD WAR HULKS
Marvel Comics: Jun, 2010; Sept, 2010 ($3.99, one-shot & limited series)
  1-Short stories by various; Deadpool app.; Romita Jr.-c   4.00
  ...: Spider-Man vs. Thor 1,2 (9/10 - No. 2, 9/10) Gillen-s/Molina-a   4.00
  ...: Wolverine vs. Captain America 1,2 (9/10 - No. 2, 9/10) "Capt America vs Wolv." on-c   4.00

WORLD WAR HULK: X-MEN (See New Avengers: Illuminati and Incredible Hulk #92)
Marvel Comics: Aug, 2007 - No. 3, Oct, 2007 ($2.99, limited series)
  1-3-Gage-s/DiVito-a/McGuinness-c; Hulk invades the Xavier Institute   3.00
  TPB (2008, $24.99) r/#1-3, Avengers: The Initiative #4-5, Irredeemable Ant-Man #10, Iron Man #19-20, and Ghost Rider #12-13   25.00

WORLD WAR STORIES
Dell Publishing Co.: Apr-June, 1965 - No. 3, Dec, 1965

	GD	VG	FN	VF	VF/NM	NM-
1-Glanzman-a in all	4	8	12	28	47	65
2,3	3	6	9	17	25	34

WORLD WAR TANK GIRL
Titan Comics: May, 2017 - No. 4, Sept, 2017 ($3.99, limited series)
  1-4-Tank Girl and crew in 1944 Germany; Alan Martin-s/Brett Parson-a; multiple covers 4.00

WORLD WAR II (See Classics Illustrated Special Issue)

WORLD WAR III
Ace Periodicals: Mar, 1953 - No. 2, May, 1953

	GD	VG	FN	VF	VF/NM	NM-
1-(Scarce)-Atomic bomb blast-c; Cameron-a	245	490	735	1568	2684	3800
2-Used in POP, pg. 78 & B&W & color illos; Cameron-a	110	220	330	704	1202	1700

WORLD WAR X
Titan Comics: Jan, 2017 - No. 6, Jun, 2017 ($3.99, English version of French comic series)
  1-6-Jerry Frissen-s/Peter Snejbjerg-a; multiple covers on each   4.00

WORLD WITHOUT END
DC Comics: 1990 - No. 6, 1991 ($2.50, limited series, mature, stiff-c)
  1-6: Horror/fantasy; all painted-a   4.00

WORLD WRESTLING FEDERATION BATTLEMANIA
Valiant: 1991 - No. 5?, 1991 ($2.50, magazine size, 68 pgs.)
  1-5-Includes 2 free pull-out posters   5.00

WORST DUDES, THE
Dark Horse Comics: Jun, 2021 - No. 5, Oct, 2021 ($3.99, limited series)
  1-5-Aubrey Sitterson-s/Tony Gregori-a   4.00

WORST FROM MAD, THE (Annual)
E. C. Comics: 1958 - No. 12, 1969 (Each annual cover is reprinted from the cover of the Mad issues being reprinted)(Value is 1/2 if bonus is missing)

	GD	VG	FN	VF	VF/NM	NM-
nn(1958)-Bonus: record labels & travel stickers; 1st Mad annual; r/Mad #29-34	50	100	150	315	533	750
2(1959)-Bonus is small 33 1/3 rpm record entitled "Meet the Staff of Mad"; r/Mad #35-40	48	96	144	302	514	725
3(1960)-Has 20x30" campaign poster "Alfred E. Neuman for President"; r/Mad #41-46	16	32	48	110	243	375
4(1961)-Sunday comics section; r/Mad #47-54	14	28	42	97	214	330
5(1962)-Has 33-1/3 record; r/Mad #55-62	20	40	60	138	307	475
6(1963)-Has 33-1/3 record; r/Mad #63-70	20	40	60	138	307	475
7(1964)-Mad protest songs; r/Mad #71-76	9	18	27	61	123	185
8(1965)-Build a Mad Zeppelin	10	20	30	66	138	210
9(1966)-33-1/3 rpm record; Beatles on-c	14	28	42	97	214	330
10(1967)-Mad bumper sticker	6	12	18	40	73	105
11(1968)-Mad cover window stickers	6	12	18	37	66	95
12(1969)-Mad picture postcards; Orlando-a	6	12	18	37	66	95

NOTE: *Covers: Bob Clarke-#8. Mingo-#7, 9-12.*

WOTALIFE COMICS (Formerly Nutty Life #2; Phantom Lady #13 on)
Fox Feature Syndicate/Norlen Mag.: No. 3, Aug-Sept, 1946 - No. 12, July, 1947; 1959

	GD	VG	FN	VF	VF/NM	NM-
3-Cosmo Cat, Li'l Pan, others begin	17	34	51	98	154	210
4-12-Cosmo Cat, Li'l Pan in all	14	28	42	78	112	145
1(1959-Norlen)-Atomic Rabbit, Atomic Mouse; reprints cover to #6; reprints entire book?	9	18	27	50	65	80

WOTALIFE COMICS
Green Publications: 1959 - No. 5, 1959

	GD	VG	FN	VF	VF/NM	NM-
1-Funny animal; Li'l Pan & Tamale app.	8	16	24	44	57	70
2-5	5	10	15	24	29	34

WOW COMICS ("Wow, What A Magazine!" on cover of first issue)
Henle Publishing Co.: July, 1936 - No. 4, Nov, 1936 (52 pgs., magazine size)

	GD	VG	FN	VF	VF/NM	NM-
1-Buck Jones in "The Phantom Rider" (1st app. in comics), Fu Manchu; Capt. Scott Dalton begins; Will Eisner-a (1st in comics); Baily-a(1); Briefer-a	459	918	1377	3350	5925	8500
2-Ken Maynard, Fu Manchu, Popeye by Segar plus article on Popeye; Eisner-a	300	600	900	2070	3635	5200
3-Eisner-c/a(3); Popeye by Segar, Fu Manchu, Hiram Hick by Bob Kane, Space Limited app.; Jimmy Dempsey talks about Popeye's punch; Bob Ripley Believe it or Not begins; Briefer-a	300	600	900	2010	3635	5000
4-Flash Gordon by Raymond, Mandrake, Popeye by Segar, Tillie The Toiler, Fu Manchu, Hiram Hick by Bob Kane; Eisner-a(3); Briefer-c/a	343	686	1029	2400	4200	6000

WOW COMICS (Real Western Hero #70 on)(See XMas Comics)
Fawcett Publ.: Winter, 1940-41; No. 2, Summer, 1941 - No. 69, Fall, 1948

	GD	VG	FN	VF	VF/NM	NM-
nn(#1)-Origin Mr. Scarlet by S&K; Atom Blake, Boy Wizard, Jim Dolan, & Rick O'Shay begin; Diamond Jack, The White Rajah, & Shipwreck Roberts, only app.; 1st mention of Gotham City in comics; the cover was printed on unstable paper stock and is rarely found in fine or mint condition; blank inside-c; bondage-c by Beck	1750	3500	5250	11300	24,150	35,000
2 (Scarce)-The Hunchback begins	206	412	618	1318	2259	3200
3 (Fall, 1941)	123	246	369	787	1344	1900
4-Origin & 1st app. Pinky	142	284	426	909	1555	2200
5	81	162	243	518	884	1250
6-Origin & 1st app. The Phantom Eagle (7/15/42); Commando Yank begins	90	180	270	576	988	1400
7,8	65	130	195	416	708	1000
9-(1/6/43)-Capt. Marvel, Capt. Marvel Jr., Shazam app.; Scarlet & Pinky x-over; Mary Marvel-c/stories begins	326	652	978	2282	3991	5700
10-Swayze-c/a on Mary Marvel	300	600	900	2010	3505	5000
11-17,19,20: 15-Flag-c	65	130	195	416	708	1000
18-1st app. Uncle Marvel (10/43); infinity-c	84	168	252	538	919	1300
21-30: 23-Robot-c. 28-Pinky x-over in Mary Marvel	43	86	129	271	461	650
31-40: 32-68-Phantom Eagle by Swayze	34	68	102	199	325	450
41-50	31	62	93	182	296	410
51-58: Last Mary Marvel	28	56	84	168	274	380
59-69: 59-Ozzie (teenage) begins. 62-Flying Saucer gag-c (1/48). 65-69-Tom Mix stories (cont'd in Real Western Hero)	23	46	69	123	203	310

NOTE: *Cover features: Mr. Scarlet-#1-5; Commando Yank-#6, 7, (w/Mr. Scarlet #8); Mary Marvel-#9-56, (w/Commando Yank-#46-50), (w/Mr. Scarlet & Commando Yank #53), (w/Mr. Scarlet & Pinky #53), (w/Phantom Eagle #54, 56), (w/Commando Yank & Phantom Eagle #58); Ozzie-#59-69.*

WRAITH (Prequel to the novel NOS4A2)
IDW Publishing: Nov, 2013 (incorrect Nov, 2012 in indicia) - No. 7, May, 2014 ($3.99)
  1-7: Joe Hill-s/C.P. Wilson III-a. 5-(incorrect #4 in indicia)   4.00
  1-Director's Cut (7/14, $4.99) Includes full script   5.00

WRAITHBORN
DC Comics (WildStorm): Nov, 2005 - No. 6, July, 2006 ($2.99, limited series)
  1-6-Marcia Chen & Joe Benitez-s/a   3.00
  TPB (2007, $19.99) r/series; sketch pages and unused cover sketches   20.00

WRAITHBORN REDUX
Benitez Productions: Feb, 2016 - No. 6, Aug, 2016 ($3.99)
  1-6-Remastered printing of the 2005 series; Chen & Benitez-s/a; multiple covers   4.00
  ... HCF 2016 #1 (10/16, Halloween giveaway) r/#1   3.00

WRATH (Also see Prototype #4)
Malibu Comics: Jan, 1994 - No. 9, Nov, 1995 ($1.95)
  1-9: 2-Mantra x-over. 3-Intro/1st app. Slayer. 4,5-Freex app. 8-Mantra & Warstrike app. 9-Prime app.   4.00
  1-Ultra 5000 Limited silver foil   6.00
  Giant Size 1 (2.50, 44 pgs.)   5.00

WRATH OF THE ETERNAL WARRIOR
Valiant Entertainment: Nov, 2015 - No. 14, Dec, 2016 ($3.99)

World War Hulk #2 © MAR

Wow Comics #10 © FAW

The Wrong Earth #1 © AHOY

	GD	VG	FN	VF	VF/NM	NM-
	2.0	4.0	6.0	8.0	9.0	9.2

	GD	VG	FN	VF	VF/NM	NM-
	2.0	4.0	6.0	8.0	9.0	9.2

1-14: 1-Venditti-s/Allén-a ... 4.00

WRATH OF THE SPECTRE, THE
DC Comics: May, 1988 - No. 4, Aug, 1988 ($2.50, limited series)
1-3: Aparo-r/Adventure #431-440 ... 5.00
4-Three scripts intended for Adventure #441-on, but not drawn by Aparo until 1988

	1	2	3	5	6	8

TPB (2005, $19.99) r/series; Peter Sanderson intro. ... 20.00

WRECK OF GROSVENOR (See Superior Stories #3)

WRETCH, THE
Caliber: 1996 ($2.95, B&W)
1-Phillip Hester-a/scripts ... 4.00

WRETCH, THE
Amaze Ink: 1997 - No. 4, 1998 ($2.95, B&W)
1-4-Phillip Hester-a/scripts ... 4.00
... Vol. 1: Everyday Doomsday (4/03, $13.95) ... 14.00

WRINGLE WRANGLE (Disney)
Dell Publishing Co.: No. 821, July, 1957
Four Color 821-Based on movie "Westward Ho, the Wagons"; Marsh-a; Fess Parker photo-c

	8	16	24	51	96	140

WRONG EARTH, THE (Also see "Dragonfly & Dragonflyman")
AHOY Comics: 2018 - No. 6, 2019 ($3.99)
1-6-Tom Peyer-s/Jamal Igle-a; intro. Dragonfly & Dragonflyman ... 4.0
.... Confidence Men 1 (2022, $4.99) Mark Waid-s/Leonard Kirk-a ... 5.00
.... Fame & Fortune 1 (2022, $4.99) Mark Russell-s/Michael Montenat-a ... 5.00
.... Meat 1 (2022, $4.99) Tom Peyer-s/Greg Scott-a ... 5.00
.... Purple 1 (2022, $4.99) Stuart Moore-s/Fred Harper-a ... 5.00
.... Trapped on Teen Planet 1 (2022, $4.99) Gail Simone-s/Bill Morrison & Walter Geovani-a ... 5.00
...: We Could Be Heroes 1 (2023, $4.99) Peyer-s/Igle-a ... 5.00

WRONG EARTH, THE : NIGHT & DAY
AHOY Comics: 2020 - No. 6, 2021 ($3.99)
1-6-Dragonfly & Dragonflyman meet; Tom Peyer-s/Jamal Igle-a; Lady Dragonflyman app. ... 4.00

WRONG EARTH, THE : WE COULD BE HEROES (Leads into Wrong Earth: Dead Ringers series)
AHOY Comics: 2023 - No. 2, 2023 ($3.99)
1,2-Tom Peyer-s/Jamal Igle-a ... 4.00

WULF
Ardden Entertainment: Mar, 2011 - No. 6, Sept, 2012 ($2.99)
1-6-Steve Niles-s/Nat Jones-a/c; Lomax app. 3-6-Iron Jaw app. ... 3.00

WULF THE BARBARIAN
Atlas/Seaboard Publ.: Feb, 1975 - No. 4, Sept, 1975
1,2: 1-Origin; Janson-a. 2-Intro. Berithe the Swordswoman; Janson-a w/Neal Adams, Wood, Reese-a assists

	3	6	9	14	19	24

3,4: 3-Skeates-s. 4-Friedrich-s

	2	4	6	10	14	18

WWE (WWE Wrestling)
BOOM! Studios: Jan, 2017 - No. 25, Feb, 2019 ($3.99)
1-24: 1-4-Seth Rollins & Triple H app.; Serg Acuña-a; multiple covers. 1-Back-up w/Guillory-a. 13-Raw 25 Years. 14-17-Spotlight on the Four Horsewomen ... 4.00
25-($4.99) Hopeless-s/Serg Acuña-a; AJ Styles and Samoa Joe app. ... 5.00
... Attitude Era 2018 Special 1 (8/18, $7.99) Mick Foley & Steve Austin app. ... 8.00
...: Forever 1 (1/19, $7.99) Short stories by various; multiple covers ... 8.00
...: Royal Rumble 2018 Special 1 (1/18, $7.99) Ric Flair & Randy Savage app. ... 8.00
...: SmackDown 1 (10/19, $4.99) Short stories by various; multiple covers ... 5.00
...: Summerslam 2017 Special 1 (8/17, $7.99) Art by Guillory and others ... 8.00
...: Survivor Series 2017 Special 1 (11/17, $7.99) Shawn Michaels & Kurt Angle app. ... 8.00
...Then. Now. Forever. 1 (11/16, $3.99) Short stories by various; multiple covers ... 4.00
...: Wrestlemania 2017 Special 1 (8/17, $7.99) Art by Guillory, Corona, Mora and others ... 8.00
...: Wrestlemania 2018 Special 1 (4/18, $7.99) Art by Goode, Lorenzo and others ... 8.00
...: Wrestlemania 2019 Special 1 (3/19, $7.99) Art by Goode, Acuña and others ... 8.00

WWE HEROES (WWE Wrestling) (#7,8 titled WWE Undertaker)
Titan Comics: Apr, 2010 - No. 8 ($3.99)
1-6: 1-Two covers by Andy Smith and Liam Sharp. 5-Covers by Smith and Mayhew ... 4.00
7,8-"Undertaker" on cover; Rey Mysterio app. ... 4.00

WWE: NXT TAKEOVER (WWE Wrestling)
BOOM! Studios: Sept, 2018 ($3.99, weekly series of one-shots)
... – Into the Fire 1; Dennis Hopeless-s/Hyoenjin Kim-a; the rise of Asuka ... 4.00
... – Proving Ground 1; Dennis Hopeless-s/Kendall Goode-a; Finn Balor vs. Samoa Joe app. ... 4.00
... – Redemption 1; Hopeless-s/Lorenzo-a; Johnny Gargano & Shayna Baszler app. ... 4.00
... – The Blueprint 1; Hopeless-s/Elphick-a; Triple H & Dusty Rhodes app. ... 4.00

WWE SUPERSTARS (WWE Wrestling)
Papercutz (Super Genius): Dec, 2013 - No. 12, Feb, 2015 ($2.99/$3.99)

1-($2.99)-Mick Foley-s; John Cena, Randy Orton & CM Punk app.

	1	3	4	6	8	10

2-12: 2-($3.99) Mick Foley-s. 9-Hulk Hogan cover by Jusko ... 4.00

WWE THE NEW DAY: POWER OF POSITIVITY (WWE Wrestling)
BOOM! Studios: Jul, 2021 - No. 2, Aug, 2021 ($7.99, limited series)
1,2-Spotlight on Kofi Kingston, Big E, and Xavier Woods; Bayliss-a ... 8.00

WYATT EARP
Atlas Comics/Marvel No. 23 on (IPC): Nov, 1955 - #29, Jun, 1960; #30, Oct, 1972 - #34, Jun, 1973

	37	74	111	222	361	500
1	37	74	111	222	361	500
2-Williamson-a (4 pgs.)	18	36	54	105	165	225
3-6,8,11: 3-Black Bart app. 8-Wild Bill Hickok app.	12	24	36	69	97	125
7,12-Williamson-a, 4 pgs. ea.; #12 with Mayo	14	28	42	78	112	145
13-20: 17-1st app. Wyatt's deputy, Grizzly Grant	11	22	33	62	86	110
21-Davis-c	11	22	33	62	86	110
22-24,26-29: 22-Ringo Kid app. 23-Kid From Texas app. 29-Last 10c issue	9	18	27	52	69	85
25-Davis-a	11	22	33	62	86	110
30-Williamson-r (1972)	2	4	6	13	18	22
31-34-Reprints. 32-Torres-a(r)	2	4	6	9	13	16

NOTE: Ayers a-8, 10(2), 16(4), 17, 20(4), 26(5), 27(3), 29(3). Berg a-9. Everett c-6. Kirby c-22, 24-26, 29. Maneely a-1; c-1-4, 8, 12, 17, 20. Maurer a-2(2), 3(4), 4(4), 8(4). Severin a-4, 9(4), 10; c-2, 9, 10, 14. Wildey a-5, 7, 14, 27, 28.

WYATT EARP (TV) (Hugh O'Brian Famous Marshal)
Dell Publishing Co.: No. 860, Nov, 1957 - No. 13, Dec-Feb, 1960-61 (Hugh O'Brian photo-c)

Four Color 860 (#1)-Manning-a	11	22	33	76	163	250
Four Color 890,921(6/58)-All Manning-a	8	16	24	56	108	160
4 (9-11/58) - 12-Manning-a. 4-Variant edition exists with back-c comic strip; Russ Manning-a.						
5-Photo back-c	6	12	18	37	66	95
13-Toth-a	6	12	18	38	69	100

WYATT EARP FRONTIER MARSHAL (Formerly Range Busters) (Also see Blue Bird)
Charlton Comics: No. 12, Jan, 1956 - No. 72, Dec, 1967

12	9	18	27	50	65	80
13-19	6	12	18	31	38	45
20-(68 pgs.)-Williamson-a(4), 8,5,5,& 7 pgs.	10	20	30	56	76	95
21-(100 pgs.) Mastroserio, Maneely, Severin-a (signed LePoer)						
	5	10	15	31	53	75
22-30	3	6	9	16	23	30
31-50	2	4	6	12	16	20
51-72 (1967)	2	4	6	9	11	14

WYNONNA EARP
Image Comics (WildStorm Productions): Dec, 1996 - No. 5, Apr, 1997 ($2.50)
1-5-Beau Smith-s/Joyce Chin-a/c ... 4.00

WYNONNA EARP
IDW Publishing: Feb, 2016 - No. 8, Sept, 2016 ($3.99)
1-8: 1-Beau Smith-s/Lora Innes-a; multiple covers; bonus look at the SyFy TV series ... 4.00
...: Greatest Hits 1 (7/18, $1.00) Reprints #1 ... 3.00

WYNONNA EARP: HOME ON THE STRANGE
IDW Publishing: Dec, 2003 - No. 3, Feb, 2004 ($3.99)
1-3-Beau Smith-s/Ferreira-a ... 4.00

WYNONNA EARP LEGENDS: DOC HOLLIDAY
IDW Publishing: Nov, 2016 - No. 2, Dec, 2016 ($3.99)
1,2: 1-Beau Smith & Tim Rozon-s/Chris Evenhuis-a; multiple covers; ... 4.00

WYNONNA EARP LEGENDS: THE EARP SISTERS
IDW Publishing: No. 3, Jan, 2017 - No. 4, Feb, 2017 ($3.99)
3,4-Beau Smith & Melanie Scrofano-s/Chris Evenhuis-a; multiple covers; ... 4.00

WYNONNA EARP SEASON ZERO
IDW Publishing: Jun, 2017 - No. 5, Oct, 2017 ($3.99)
1-5-Beau Smith & Tim Rozon-s/Angel Hernandez-a; multiple covers; ... 4.00

WYNONNA EARP: THE YETI WARS
IDW Publishing: May, 2011 - No. 4, Aug, 2011 ($3.99)
1-4-Beau Smith-s/Enrique Villagran-a ... 4.00

WYRD
Dark Horse Comics: Jan, 2019 - No. 4, Sept, 2019 ($3.99, limited series)
1-4-Curt Pires-s/Antonio Fuso-a ... 4.00

WYRMS
Marvel Comics (Dabel Brothers): Feb, 2007 - No. 6, Jan, 2008 ($2.99)
1-6-Orson Scott Card & Jake Black-s. 1-3-Batista-a ... 3.00
TPB (2008, $14.99) r/#1-6 ... 15.00

WYTCHES

	GD 2.0	VG 4.0	FN 6.0	VF 8.0	VF/NM 9.0	NM- 9.2

Image Comics: Oct, 2014 - No. 6, May, 2015 ($2.99/$3.99)

1-Scott Snyder-s/Jock-a						5.00
2-5						3.00
6-($3.99) Bonus production art and Snyder afterword						4.00
...: Bad Egg Halloween Special 1 (10/18, $7.99) reprints serial from Image+ magazine						8.00
Image Firsts: Wytches (12/14, $1.00) r/#1						3.00

X (Comics' Greatest World: X #1 only) (Also see Comics' Greatest World & Dark Horse Comics #8)
Dark Horse Comics: Feb, 1994 - No. 25, Apr, 1996 ($2.00/$2.50)

1-25: 3-Pit Bulls x-over. 8-Ghost-c & app. 18-Miller-c.; Predator app. 19-22-Miller-a.						4.00
Hero Illustrated Special #1,2 (1994, $1.00, 20 pgs.)						4.00
One Shot to the Head (1994, $2.50, 36 pgs.)-Miller-c.						4.00

NOTE: *Miller* c-18-22. *Quesada* c-6. *Russell* a-6.

X (Comics' Greatest World)
Dark Horse Comics: No. 0, Apr, 2013 - No. 24, Apr, 2015 ($2.99)

0-24: 0-Swierczynski-s/Eric Nguyen-a. 13,14-Atkins-a						3.00
One For One (1/14, $1.00) r/#1						3.00

XANADU COLOR SPECIAL
Eclipse Comics: Dec, 1988 ($2.00, one-shot)

1-Continued from Thoughts & Images						4.00

XAVIER INSTITUTE ALUMNI YEARBOOK (See X-Men titles)
Marvel Comics: Dec, 1996 ($5.95, square-bound, one-shot)

1-Text w/art by various						6.00

X-BABIES
Marvel Comics: Dec, 2009 - No. 4, Mar, 2010 ($3.99, limited series)

1-4-Schigiel-s/Chabot-a; Skottie Young-c						4.00
...: Murderama (8/98, $2.95) J.J. Kirby-a						4.00
...: Reborn (1/00, $3.50) J.J. Kirby-a						4.00

X-CALIBRE
Marvel Comics: Mar, 1995 - No. 4, July, 1995 ($1.95, limited series)

1-4-Age of Apocalypse						4.00

X-CAMPUS
Marvel Comics: July, 2010 - No. 4, Nov, 2010 ($4.99, limited series)

1-4-Alternate version of X-Men; stories by European creators; Nauck-c						5.00

X-CELLENT (Characters from X-Statix)
Marvel Comics: Apr, 2022 - No. 5, Sept, 2022 ($3.99, limited series)

1-5-Milligan-s/Allred-a						4.00

X-CELLENT, THE
Marvel Comics: May, 2023 - No. 5, Sept, 2023 ($3.99, limited series)

1-5-Milligan-s/Allred-a						4.00

X-CLUB
Marvel Comics: Feb, 2012 - No. 5, Jun, 2012 ($2.99, limited series)

1-5-X-Men scientist team; Dr. Nemesis & Danger app. 1-Bradshaw-c. 2-5-Esquejo-c						3.00

X-CORP
Marvel Comics: Jul, 2021 - No. 5, Nov, 2021 ($4.99/$3.99, limited series)

1-($4.99) X-Men pharmaceutical team; Angel and Monet app.; Howard-s/Foche-a						5.00
2-5-($3.99) 2-Hellfire Gala tie-in. 3-De Landro-a						4.00

X DEATHS OF WOLVERINE (Bi-weekly series alternating with X Lives of Wolverine)
Marvel Comics: Mar, 2022 - No. 5, May, 2022 ($5.99/$4.99, limited series)

1-($5.99) Percy-s/Vicenti-a; spotlight on Moira MacTaggert; Mystique app.						6.00
2-5-($4.99) 3-5-Daken & Laura app.						5.00

XENA (TV)
Dynamite Entertainment: 2006 - 2007 ($3.50)

1-4-Three covers on each; Neves-a/Layman-s						3.50
Vol. 2 #1-4-(Dark Xena) Four covers; Salonga-a/Layman-s						3.50
Annual 1 (2007, $4.95) Three covers; Salonga-a/Champagne-s						5.00
... Vol. 2: Dark Xena TPB (2007, $14.99) r/Vol. 2 #1-4; variant cover gallery						15.00

XENA (Volume 4) (TV)
Dynamite Entertainment: 2018 - No. 10, 2018 ($3.99)

1-10: 1-Meredith Finch-s/Vicente Cifuentes-a; main covers by Cifuentes & David Finch						4.00

XENA / ARMY OF DARKNESS: WHAT...AGAIN?!
Dynamite Entertainment: 2008 - No. 4, 2009 ($3.50, limited series)

1-4-Xena, Gabrielle, & Autolycus team up with Ash; Montenegro-a; two covers on each						3.50

XENA: WARRIOR PRINCESS (TV)
Topps Comics: Aug, 1997 - No. 0, Oct, 1997 ($2.95)

	GD	VG	FN	VF	VF/NM	NM-
1-Two stories by various; J. Scott Campbell-c	1	3	4	6	8	10
1,2-Photo-c	1	3	4	6	8	10
2-Stevens-c	1	3	4	6	8	10
0-(10/97)-Lopresti-c, 0-(10/97)-Photo-c	1	2	3	5	6	8
...First Appearance Collection ('97, $9.95) r/Hercules the Legendary Journeys #3-5 and 5-page story from TV Guide						10.00

XENA: WARRIOR PRINCESS (TV)
Dark Horse Comics: Sept, 1999 - No. 14, Oct, 2000 ($2.95/$2.99)

1-14: 1-Mignola-c and photo-c. 2,3-Bradstreet-c & photo-c						4.00

XENA: WARRIOR PRINCESS (Volume 2) (TV)
Dynamite Entertainment: 2016 - No. 6, 2016 ($3.99)

1-6: 1-Valentine-s/Medel-a; main covers by Land & Frison						4.00

XENA: WARRIOR PRINCESS (Volume 3) (TV)
Dynamite Entertainment: 2018 - No. 6, 2019 ($3.99)

1-6: Vita Ayala-s; covers by David Mack and others. 1,2-Sweetman-a						4.00

XENA: WARRIOR PRINCESS AND THE ORIGINAL OLYMPICS (TV)
Topps Comics: Jun, 1998 - No. 3, Aug, 1998 ($2.95, limited series)

1-3-Regular and Photo-c; Lim-a/T&M Bierbaum-s						4.00

XENA: WARRIOR PRINCESS-BLOODLINES (TV)
Topps Comics: May, 1998 - No. 2, June, 1998 ($2.95, limited series)

1,2-Lopresti-s/c/a. 2-Reg. and photo-c						4.00
1-Bath photo-c, 1-American Ent. Ed.						5.00

XENA: WARRIOR PRINCESS / JOXER: WARRIOR PRINCE (TV)
Topps Comics: Nov, 1997 - No. 3, Jan, 1998 ($2.95, limited series)

1-3-Regular and Photo-c; Lim-a/T&M Bierbaum-s						4.00

XENA: WARRIOR PRINCESS-THE DRAGON'S TEETH (TV)
Topps Comics: Dec, 1997 - No. 3, Feb, 1998 ($2.95, limited series)

1-3-Regular and Photo-c; Teranishi-a/Thomas-s						4.00

XENA: WARRIOR PRINCESS-THE ORPHEUS TRILOGY (TV)
Topps Comics: Mar, 1998 - No. 3, May, 1998 ($2.95, limited series)

1-3-Regular and Photo-c; Teranishi-a/T&M Bierbaum-s						4.00

XENA: WARRIOR PRINCESS VS. CALLISTO (TV)
Topps Comics: Feb, 1998 - No. 3, Apr, 1998 ($2.95, limited series)

1-3-Regular and Photo-c; Morgan-a/Thomas-s						4.00

XENOBROOD
DC Comics: No. 0, Oct, 1994 - No. 6, Apr, 1995 ($1.50, limited series)

0-6: 0-Indicia says "Xenobroods"						4.00

XENOZOIC TALES (Also see Cadillacs & Dinosaurs, Death Rattle #8)
Kitchen Sink Press: Feb, 1986 - No. 14, Oct, 1996

	GD	VG	FN	VF	VF/NM	NM-
1-Mark Schultz-s/a in all	2	4	6	9	12	15
1(2nd printing)(1/89)						4.00
2-14						6.00
Volume 1 ($14.95) r/#1-6 & Death Rattle #8						15.00
Volume 2 (5/03, $14.95, TPB) B&W r/#7-14; intro by Frank Cho						15.00

XENYA
Sanctuary Press: Apr, 1994 - No. 3 ($2.95)

1-3: 1-Hildebrandt-c; intro Xenya						4.00

XERO
DC Comics: May, 1997 - No. 12, Apr, 1998 ($1.75)

1-7						4.00
8-12						4.00

XERXES: THE FALL OF THE HOUSE OF DARIUS AND THE RISE OF ALEXANDER
Dark Horse Comics: Apr, 2018 - No. 5, Aug, 2018 ($4.99, limited series)

1-5-Prequel to 300; Frank Miller-s/a						5.00

X-FACTOR (Also see The Avengers #263, Fantastic Four #286 and Mutant X)
Marvel Comics Group: Feb, 1986 - No. 149, Sept, 1998

	GD	VG	FN	VF	VF/NM	NM-
1-($1.25, 52 pgs)-Story recaps 1st app. from Avengers #263; story cont'd from F.F. #286; return of original X-Men (now X-Factor); Guice/Layton-a; Baby Nathan app. (2nd after X-Men #201)	3	6	9	17	26	35
2-4	1	3	4	6	8	10
5-1st brief app. Apocalypse (1 page)	3	6	9	18	27	36
6-1st full app. Apocalypse	8	16	24	38	69	100
7-10: 10-Sabretooth app. (11/86, 3 pgs.) cont'd in X-Men #212; 1st app. in an X-Men comic book	1	2	3	5	6	8
11-18,20-22: 13-Baby Nathan app. in flashback. 14-Cyclops vs. The Master Mold. 15-Intro wingless Angel						5.00
19-Apocalypse-c/app.	2	4	6	11	16	20
23-1st brief app. Archangel (2 pages)	2	4	6	9	13	16
24-1st full app. Archangel (now in Uncanny X-Men); Fall Of The Mutants begins; origin Apocalypse	4	8	12	28	47	65
25,26: Fall Of The Mutants; 26-New outfits	1	2	3	5	6	8
27-37,39,41-49,51-59,63-70,72-83,87-91,93-99,101: 35-Origin Cyclops. 51-53-Sabretooth app. 52-Liefeld-c(p). 54-Intro Crimson; Silvestri-c/a(p). 63-Portacio/Thibert-c/a(p) begins, ends #69. 65-68-Lee co-plots. 65-The Apocalypse Files begins, ends #68. 66,67-Baby Nathan app. 67-Inhumans app. 68-Baby Nathan is sent into future to save his life. 69,70-X-Men(w/Wolverine) x-over. 77-Cannonball (of X-Force) app. 87-Quesada-c/a(p) in monthly comic begins, ends #92. 88-1st app. Random						4.00
38,50,60-62,71,75: 38,50-(52 pgs.): 50-Liefeld/McFarlane-a. 60-X-Tinction Agenda x-over; New Mutants (w/Cable) x-over in #60-62; Wolverine in #62. 61,62-X-Tinction Agenda. 62-Jim Lee-c. 71-New team begins (Havok, Polaris, Strong Guy, Wolfsbane & Madrox); Stroman-a begins. 75-(52 pgs.)						5.00
40-Rob Liefeld-c/a (4/89, 1st at Marvel?)						5.00
60,71-2nd printing. 60-Gold ink 2nd printing. 71-2nd printing ($1.25)						4.00
84-86 -Jae Lee a(p); 85,86-Jae Lee-c. Polybagged with trading card in each; X-Cutioner's Song x-overs.						4.00
87-Facsimile Edition (10/19, $3.99) Reprints #87 with original ads and letter column						4.00
92-($3.50, 68 pgs.)-Wraparound-c by Quesada w/Havok hologram on-c; begin X-Men 30th anniversary issues; Quesada-a.						6.00
92-2nd printing						4.00
100-($2.95, 52 pgs)-Embossed foil-c; Multiple Man dies.	1	2	3	5	6	8
100-($1.75, 52 pgs.)-Regular edition						5.00
102-105,107: 102-bound-in card sheet						4.00
106-($2.00)-Newsstand edition						4.00
106-($2.95)-Collectors edition						5.00
108-124,126-148: 112-Return from Age of Apocalypse. 115-card insert. 119-123-Sabretooth app. 123-Hound app. 124-w/Onslaught Update. 126-Onslaught x-over; Beast vs. Dark Beast. 128-w/card insert; return of Multiple Man. 130-Assassination of Grayson Creed. 146,148-Moder-a						4.00
125-($2.95)-"Onslaught"; Post app.; return of Havok						5.00
149-Last issue						5.00
#(-1) Flashback (7/97) Matsuda-a						4.00
Annual 1-9: 1-(10/86-'94, 68 pgs.) 3-Evolutionary War x-over. 4-Atlantis Attacks; Byrne/Simonson-a;Byrne-c. 5-Fantastic Four, New Mutants x-over; Keown 2 pg. pin-up. 6-New Warriors app.; 5th app. X-Force cont'd from X-Men Annual #15. 7-1st Quesada-a(p) on X-Factor plus-c(p). 8-Bagged w/trading card. 9-Austin-a(i)						5.00
...Prisoner of Love (1990, $4.95, 52 pgs.)-Starlin scripts; Guice-a						5.00
... Visionaries: Peter David Vol. 1 TPB (2005, $15.99) r/#71-75						16.00
... Visionaries: Peter David Vol. 2 TPB (2007, $15.99) r/#76-78 & Incr. Hulk #390-392						16.00
... Visionaries: Peter David Vol. 3 TPB (2007, $15.99) r/#79-83 & Annual #7						16.00

NOTE: *Art Adams* a-41p, 42p. *Buckler* a-50p. *Liefeld* a-40; c-40, 50i, 52p. *McFarlane* c-50i. *Mignola* c-70. *Brandon Peterson* a-78p(part). *Whilce Portacio* c/a(p)-63-69. *Quesada* a(p)-87-92, Annual 7. c(p)-78, 79, 82,

The X-Cellent #4 © MAR

X-Factor (2008 series) #32 © MAR

The X-Files Season 10 #5 © 20Fox

	GD	VG	FN	VF	VF/NM	NM-
	2.0	4.0	6.0	8.0	9.0	9.2

Annual 7. **Simonson** c/a-10, 11, 13-15, 17-19, 21, 23-31, 33, 34, 36-39; c-12, 16. **Paul Smith** a-44-48; c-43.
Stroman a(p)-71-75, 77, 78(part), 80, 81; c(p)-71-77, 80, 81, 84. **Zeck** c-2.

X-FACTOR (Volume 2)
Marvel Comics: June, 2002 - No. 4, Oct, 2002 ($2.50)

1-4: Jensen-s/Ranson-a. 1-Phillips-c. 2,3-Edwards-c					3.00

X-FACTOR (Volume 3) (Also see All-New X-Factor)
Marvel Comics: Jan, 2006 - No. 262, Nov, 2013 ($2.99)

1-24: 1-Peter David-s/Ryan Sook-a. 8,9-Civil War. 21-24-Endangered Species back-up					3.00
25-49: 25-27-Messiah Complex x-over; Finch-c. 26-2nd printing with new Eaton-c					3.00
50-(12/09, $3.99) Madrox in the future; DeLandro-a/Yardin-c					4.00
200-(2/10, $4.99) Resumes original series numbering; 3 covers; Fantastic Four app.					5.00
201-224,224.1, 225-262 ($2.99) 201,202-Dr. Doom & Fant. Four app. 211,212-Thor app.					3.00
230-Wolverine app.; Havok & Polaris return					4.00
... Special: Layla Miller (10/08, $3.99) David-s/DeLandro-a					3.00
...: The Quick and the Dead (7/08, $2.99) Raimondi-a; Quicksilver regains powers					3.00
...: The Longest Night HC (2006, $19.99, dust jacket) r/#1-6; sketch pages by Sook					20.00
...: The Longest Night SC (2007, $14.99) r/#1-6; sketch pages by Sook					15.00
...: Life and Death Matters HC (2007, $19.99, dust jacket) r/#7-12					20.00
...: Life and Death Matters SC (2007, $14.99) r/#7-12					15.00
...: The Many Lives of Madrox SC (2007, $14.99) r/#13-17					15.00
...: Heart of Ice HC (2007, $19.99, dust jacket) r/#18-24					20.00
...: Heart of Ice SC (2008, $17.99) r/#18-24					18.00

X-FACTOR (4th series) (Leads into X-Men: The Trial of Magneto series)
Marvel Comics: Sept, 2020 - No. 10, Aug, 2021 ($4.99/$3.99)

1-($4.99) Leah Williams-s/David Baldeon-a; Northstar, Polaris, Daken app.					5.00
2,3,5-10-($3.99) 3-Shatterstar app. 10-Hellfire Gala tie-in; Scarlet Witch found dead					4.00
4-($4.99) "X of Swords" tie-in; Carlos Gomez-a					5.00

X-FACTOR FOREVER
Marvel Comics: May, 2010 - No. 5, Sept, 2010 ($3.99, limited series)

1-5-Louise Simonson-s/Dan Panosian-a; back-up origin of Apocalypse					4.00

X-51 (Machine Man)
Marvel Comics: Sept, 1999 - No. 12, Jul, 2000 ($1.99/$2.50)

1-7: 1-Joe Bennett-a. 2-Two covers					4.00
8-12: 8-Begin $2.50-c					4.00
Wizard #0					4.00

X-FILES, THE (TV)
Topps Comics: Jan, 1995 - No. 41, July, 1998 ($2.50)

-2(9/96)-Black-c; r/X-Files Magazine #1&2						5.00
-1(9/96)-Silver-c; r/Hero Illustrated Giveaway						5.00
0-($3.95)-Adapts pilot episode						4.00
0-"Mulder" variant-c	1	2	3	5	6	8
0-"Scully" variant-c	1	2	3	5	6	8
1/2-W/certificate	1	2	3	5	6	8
1-New stories based on the TV show; direct market & newsstand editions;						
Miran Kim-c on all	3	6	9	15	22	28
2	1	2	3	6	8	10
3,4						6.00
5-10: 6-Begin $2.95-c						5.00
11-41: 21-W/bound-in card. 40,41-Reg. & photo-c						4.00
Annual 1,2 ($3.95)						6.00
Afterflight TPB ($5.95) Art by Thompson, Saviuk, Kim						6.00
Classics #1: Hundred Penny Press Edition (12/13 $1.00) r/#1						3.00
Collection 1 TPB ($19.95)-r/#1-6.						20.00
Collection 2 TPB ($19.95)-r/#7-12, Annual #1.						20.00
...Fight the Future ('98, $5.95) Movie adaptation						6.00
Hero Illustrated Giveaway (3/95)	1	2	3	5	6	8
Special Edition 1-5 ($3.95/$4.95)-r/#1-3, 4-6, 7-9, 10-12, 13, Annual 1						5.00
Star Wars Galaxy Magazine Giveaway (B&W)	1	3	4	6	8	10
Trade paperback ($19.95)						20.00
Volume 1 TPB (Checker Books, 2005, $19.95) r/#13-17, #0, Season One: Squeeze						20.00
Volume 2 TPB (Checker Books, 2005, $19.95) r/#18-24, #1/2, Comics Digest #1						20.00
Volume 3 TPB (Checker Books, 2006, $19.95) r/#23-26, Fire, Ice, Hero Ill. Giveaway						20.00

X-FILES, THE (TV)
DC Comics (WildStorm): No. 0, Sept, 2008 - No. 6, Jun, 2009 ($3.99/$3.50)

0-($3.99) Spotnitz-s/Denham-a; photo-c					4.00
1-6-($3.50) 1-Spotnitz-s/Denham-a; 2 covers. 4-Wolfman-s					3.50
TPB (2009, $19.99) r/#0-6					20.00

X-FILES, THE (TV)
IDW Publishing: Apr, 2016 - Present ($3.99)

1-17: 1-Joe Harris-s/Matthew Dow Smith-a. 12,13-Flashback to Skinner in Viet Nam					4.00
... Annual 2014 (4/14, $7.99) Back-up story with Dave Sim-s/Currie-a; 2 covers					8.00
... Annual 2016 (7/16, $7.99) Greg Scott-a; Valenzuela & photo-c					8.00

...: Art Gallery (5/14, $3.99) Gallery of sketch card art by various incl. Kim & Staggs					4.00
...: Deviations (3/16, $4.99) What if... young Fox Mulder was abducted by aliens					5.00
...: Deviations 2017 (3/17, $4.99) Samantha Mulder and Scully team; Califano-a					5.00
...: Funko Universe One Shot (5/17, $4.99) Short stories with Funko Pop-styled characters					5.00
...: X-Mas Special (12/14, $7.99) Joe Harris-s/Matt Smith-a; Kesel-s/Southworth-a					8.00
...: X-Mas Special 2016 (12/16, $7.99) Joe Harris-s/Wayne Nichols-a					8.00

X-FILES, THE: CASE FILES
IDW Publishing: 2018 ($3.99, limited series)

... - Florida Man 1,2 (4/18 - No. 2, 5/18) Dawson-s/Casagrande-a					4.00
... - Hoot Goes There? 1,2 (7/18 - No. 2, 8/18) Joe & Keith Lansdale-s/Califano-a					4.00

X-FILES, THE: COMICS DIGEST, THE
Topps Comics: Dec, 1995 - No. 3 ($3.50, quarterly, digest-size)

1-3; 1,2: New X-Files stories w/Ray Bradbury Comics/r. 1-Reg. & photo-c					4.00
NOTE: **Adlard** a-1, 2. **Jack Davis** a-2r. **Russell** 1-r.					

X-FILES, THE: CONSPIRACY
IDW Publishing: Jan, 2014 - No. 2, Mar, 2014 ($3.99, limited series)

1,2-Bookends for 6-part Lone Gunmen series; Crilley-s/Stanisci-a; Kim & Corroney-c					4.00
X-Files/Ghostbusters: Conspiracy (1/14, $3.99) Part 2; Navarro-a					4.00
X-Files/Teenage Mutant Ninja Turtles: Conspiracy (2/14, $3.99) Part 3; Walsh-a					4.00
X-Files/Transformers: Conspiracy (2/14, $3.99) Part 4; Verma-a					4.00
X-Files/The Crow: Conspiracy (3/14, $3.99) Part 5; Malhotra-a					4.00

X-FILES, THE: GROUND ZERO (TV)
Topps Comics: Nov, 1997 - No. 4, March, 1998 ($2.95, limited series)

1-4-Adaptation of the Kevin J. Anderson novel					4.00

X-FILES, THE: JFK DISCLOSURE (TV)
IDW Publishing: Oct, 2017 - No. 2, Nov, 2017 ($4.99)

1,2-Tipton-s/Menton3-a					5.00

X-FILES, THE: ORIGINS (TV)
IDW Publishing: Aug, 2016 - No. 4, Nov, 2016 ($4.99)

1-4-Flipbooks with teenage Mulder and Scully					5.00

X-FILES, THE: ORIGINS – DOG DAYS OF SUMMER (TV)
IDW Publishing: Jun, 2017 - No. 4, Sept, 2017 ($3.99)

1-4-Flipbooks with teenage Mulder in 1974 and Scully in 1977					4.00

X-FILES, THE: SEASON ONE (TV)
Topps Comics: July, 1997 - July, 1998 ($4.95, adaptations of TV episodes)

1-(Pilot Episode, r/X-Files #0), 2-(Deep Throat), Squeeze, Conduit, Ice, Space, Fire, Beyond						
the Sea, Shadows	1	2	3	5	6	8

X-FILES, THE: SEASON 10 (TV)
IDW Publishing: Jun, 2013 - No. 25, Jun, 2015 ($3.99)

1-25: 1-5-Co-written by Chris Carter; multiple covers on each. 6,7-Flukeman returns.					
17-Frank Black app. 18-Doggett & Reyes app.					4.00
... #1: IDW's Greatest Hits (4/16, $1.00) r/#1					3.00

X-FILES, THE: SEASON 11 (TV)
IDW Publishing: Aug, 2015 - No. 8, Mar, 2016 ($3.99)

1-8: 1-Joe Harris-s/Matthew Smith-a					4.00

X-FILES, THE / 30 DAYS OF NIGHT
DC Comics (WildStorm)/IDW: Sept, 2010 - No. 6, Feb, 2011 ($3.99, limited series)

1-6-Steve Niles & Adam Jones-s/Tom Mandrake-a. 1-Three covers					4.00
TPB (2011, $17.99) r/#1-6; cover gallery					18.00

X-FILES, THE: YEAR ZERO (TV)
IDW Publishing: Jul, 2014 - No. 5, Nov, 2014 ($3.99)

1-5: 1-Karl Kesel-s; Greg Scott & Vic Malhotra-a; flashback to 1946					4.00

X-FORCE (Becomes X-Statix) (Also see The New Mutants #100)
Marvel Comics: Aug, 1991 - No. 129, May, 2002 ($1.00-$2.25)

1-($1.50, 52 pgs.)-Polybagged with 1 of 5 diff. Marvel Universe trading cards inside (1 each);						
6th app. of X-Force; Liefeld-c/a begins	1	3	4	6	8	10
1-1st printing with Cable trading card inside	2	4	6	11	16	20
1-1st printing with Deadpool trading card inside	2	4	6	11	16	20
1-2nd printing; metallic ink-c (no bag or card)						6.00
2-Deadpool-c/story (2nd app.)	3	6	9	14	20	26
3,4: 3-New Brotherhood of Evil Mutants app. 4-Spider-Man x-over; cont'd from						
Spider-Man #16; reads sideways; 2-pg pin-up by Mignola						5.00
5-10: 6-Last $1.00-c. 7,9-Weapon X back-ups. 8-Intro The Wild Pack (Cable, Kane, Domino						
(not Copycat), Hammer, G.W. Bridge, & Grizzly); Liefeld-c/a (4); Mignola-a. 10-Weapon X						
full-length story (part 3).						5.00
11-2nd app. the real Domino (not Copycat); Deadpool-c/story (3rd app.)						
	3	6	9	16	24	32
12-14,20-22,24,26-33						5.00
15-Cable leaves X-Force; Deadpool-c/app.	2	4	6	10	14	18

	GD 2.0	VG 4.0	FN 6.0	VF 8.0	VF/NM 9.0	NM- 9.2

16-18-Polybagged w/trading card in each; X-Cutioner's Song x-overs ... 4.00
19-1st Copycat ... 2 4 6 10 14 18
23-Deadpool-c/app. ... 6.00
25-($3.50, 52 pgs.)-Wraparound-c w/Cable hologram on-c; Cable returns ... 5.00
34-37,39-45: 34-bound-in card sheet ... 3.00
38,40-43: 38-($2.00)-Newsstand edition. 40-43 ($1.95)-Deluxe edition ... 3.00
38-($2.95)-Collectors edition (prismatic) ... 5.00
44-49,51-74: 44-Return from Age of Apocalypse. 45-Sabretooth app. 49-Sebastian Shaw app. 52-Blob app., Onslaught cameo. 55-Vs. S.H.I.E.L.D. 56-Deadpool app. 57-Mr. Sinister & X-Man-c/app. 57,58-Onslaught x-over. 59-W/card insert; return of Longshot. 60-Dr. Strange 68-Operation Zero Tolerance ... 3.00
50 ($3.95)-Gatefold wrap-around foil-c ... 4.00
50 ($3.95)-Liefeld variant-c ... 5.00
75,100-($2.99): 75-Cannonball-c/app. ... 4.00
76-99,101,102: 81-Pollina poster. 95-Magneto-c. 102-Ellis-s/Portacio-a ... 3.00
103-115: 103-Begin $2.25-c; Portacio-a thru #106. 115-Death of old team ... 3.00
116-New team debuts; Allred-c/a; Milligan-s; no Comics Code stamp on-c ... 4.00
117-129: 117-Intro. Mr. Sensitive. 120-Wolverine-c/app. 123-"Nuff Said issue. 124-Darwyn Cooke-a/c. 128-Death of U-Go Girl. 129-Fegredo-a ... 3.00
#(-1) Flashback (7/97) story of John Proudstar; Pollina-a ... 3.00
Annual 1-3 ('92-'94, 68 pgs.) 1-1st Greg Capullo-a(p) on X-Force. 2-Polybagged w/trading card; intro X-Treme & Neurtap ... 4.00
...And Cable '95 (12/95, $3.95)-Impossible Man app. ... 4.00
...And Cable '96, ...'97 ('96, 7/97) -'96-Wraparound-c ... 4.00
...And Spider-Man: Sabotage nn (11/92, $6.95)-Reprints X-Force #3,4 & Spider-Man #16 ... 7.00
.../ Champions '98 ($3.50) ... 4.00
Annual 99 ($3.50) ... 4.00
...: Famous, Mutant & Mortal HC (2003, $29.99) oversized r/#116-129; foreward by Milligan; gallery of covers and pin-ups; script for #123 ... 30.00
...New Beginnings TPB (10/01, $14.95) r/#116-120 ... 15.00
...Rough Cut ($2.99) Pencil pages and script for #102 ... 3.00
...Youngblood (8/96, $4.95)-Platt-c ... 5.00
NOTE: *Capullo* a(p)-15-25, Annual 1; c(f)-14-27. **Rob Liefeld** a-1-7, 9p; c-1-9, 11p; plots-1-12. **Mignola** a-8p.

X-FORCE
Marvel Comics: Oct, 2004 - No. 6, Mar, 2005 ($2.99, limited series)
1-6-Liefeld-c/a; Nicieza-s. 5,6-Wolverine & The Thing app. ... 3.00
X-Force & Cable Vol. 1: The Legend Returns (2005, $14.99) r/#1-6 ... 15.00

X-FORCE (Also see Uncanny X-Force)
Marvel Comics: Apr, 2008 - No. 28, Sept, 2010 ($2.99)
1-Crain-a; Wolverine & X-23 app.: two covers (regular and bloody) by Crain on #1-5 ... 4.00
2-21,23-28: 2,3-Bastion app. 4-6-Archangel app. 7-10-Choi-a. 9-11-Ghost Rider app. 26-28-Second Coming x-over; Granov-c. 26-Nightcrawler killed ... 3.00
22-($3.99) Necrosha x-over; Crain-a ... 3.00
...: Angels and Demons MGC #1 (5/11, $1.00) r/#1 with "Marvel's Greatest Comics" on-c ... 3.00
... Annual 1 (2/10, $3.99) Kirkman-s/Pearson-a/c; Deadpool back-up w/Barberi-a ... 4.00
.../Cable: Messiah War 1 (5/09, $3.99) Choi-a; covers by Andrews and Choi ... 4.00
... Special: Ain't No Dog (8/08, $3.99) Huston-s/Palo-a; Dell'Edera-a; Hitch-c ... 4.00

X-FORCE
Marvel Comics: Apr, 2014 - No. 15, Apr, 2015 ($3.99)
1-15: 1-Team of Cable, Fantomex, Psylocke & Marrow; Rock-He Kim-a. 4-6-Molina-a ... 4.00

X-FORCE
Marvel Comics: Feb, 2019 - No. 10, Sept, 2019 ($3.99)
1-10: 1-Team of Cable, Domino, Shatterstar, Warpath, Cannonball, Deathlok; Brisson-s ... 4.00

X-FORCE
Marvel Comics: Jan, 2020 - Present ($3.99)
1-($4.99) Team of Jean Grey, Wolverine, Domino, Beast, Colossus; Percy-s/Cassara-a ... 5.00
2-49-($3.99) 2-Kid Omega app. 6-Segovia-a. 13,14-"X of Swords" tie-in. 48-Beast returns ... 4.00
Annual 1 (6/22, $4.99) Shammas-s/Pimentel-a ... 5.00
...: Killshot Anniversary Special #1 (1/22, $4.99) Rob Liefeld-s/a; 7 covers ... 5.00

X-FORCE MEGAZINE
Marvel Comics: Nov, 1996 ($3.95, one-shot)
1-Reprints ... 1 2 3 5 6 8

X-FORCE: SEX AND VIOLENCE
Marvel Comics: Sept, 2010 - No. 3, Nov, 2010 ($3.99, limited series)
1-3-Dell'Otto-a/Kyle & Yost-s; Domino & Wolverine vs. The Hand & The Assassins Guild ... 6.00

X-FORCE: SHATTERSTAR
Marvel Comics: Apr, 2005 - No. 4, July, 2005 ($2.99, limited series)
1-4-Liefeld-c/s; Michaels-a ... 3.00
TPB (2005, $15.99) r/#1-4 & New Mutants #99,100 ... 16.00

X-INFERNUS
Marvel Comics: Feb, 2009 - No. 4, May, 2009 ($3.99, limited series)
1-4-Illyana Rasputin in Limbo; Cebulski-s/Camuncoli-a/Finch-c ... 4.00

XIN: JOURNEY OF THE MONKEY KING
Anarchy Studios: May, 2003 - No. 3, July, 2003 ($2.99)
Preview Edition (Apr, 2003, $1.99) Flip book w/ Vampi Vicious Preview Edition ... 3.00
1-3-Kevin Lau-a. 1-Three covers by Lau, Park and Nauck. 2-Three covers ... 3.00

XIN: LEGEND OF THE MONKEY KING
Anarchy Studios: Nov, 2002 - No. 3, Jan, 2003 ($2.99)
Preview Edition (Summer 2002, Diamond Dateline supplement) ... 3.00
1-3-Kevin Lau-a. 1-Two covers by Lau & Madureira. 2-Two covers by Lau & Oeming ... 3.00
TPB (10/03, $12.95) r/#1-3; cover gallery and sketch pages ... 13.00

X LIVES OF WOLVERINE (Bi-weekly series alternating with X Deaths of Wolverine)
Marvel Comics: Mar, 2022 - No. 5, May, 2022 ($5.99/$4.99)
1-($5.99) Percy-s/Cassara-a; Omega Red & Logan at birth of Prof. X ... 6.00
2-5-($4.99) 2-Jean Grey app. 5-Omega Red app. ... 5.00

X-MAN (Also see X-Men Omega & X-Men Prime)
Marvel Comics: Mar, 1995 - No. 75, May, 2001 ($1.95/$1.99/$2.25)
1-Age of Apocalypse ... 1 2 3 5 6 8
1-2nd print ... 4.00

2-4,25: 25-($2.99)-Wraparound-c ... 5.00
5-24, 26-28: 5-Post Age of Apocalypse stories begin. 5-7-Madelyne Pryor app. 10-Professor X app. 12-vs. Excalibur. 13-Marauders, Cable app. 14-Vs. Cable; Onslaught app. 15-17-Vs. Holocaust. 17-Onslaught Update. 18-Onslaught x-over; X-Force-c/app; Marauders app. 19-Onslaught x-over. 20-Abomination-c/app.; w/card insert. 23-Bishop app. 24-Spider-Man, Morbius-c/app. 27-Re-appearance of Aurora (Alpha Flight) ... 4.00
29-49,51-62: 29-Operation Zero Tolerance. 37,38-Spider-Man-c/app. 56-Spider-Man app. ... 4.00
50-($2.99) Crossover with Generation X #50 ... 5.00
63-74: 63-Ellis & Grant-s/Olivetti-a begins. 64-Begin $2.25-c ... 4.00
75 ($2.99) Final issue; Alcatena-a ... 4.00
#(-1) Flashback (7/97) ... 4.00
...'96, ...'97-($2.95)-Wraparound-c; '96-Age of Apocalypse ... 4.00
...: All Saints' Day ('97, $5.99) Dodson-a ... 6.00
.../Hulk '98 ($2.99) Wraparound-c; Thanos app. ... 5.00

XMAS COMICS
Fawcett Publications: 12?/1941 - No. 2, 12?/1942; (50¢, 324 pgs.)
No. 7, 12?/1947 (25¢, 132 pgs.)(#3-6 do not exist for this series, see 1949-1952 series)
1-Contains Whiz #21, Capt. Marvel #3, Bulletman #2, Wow #3, & Master #18; front & back-c by Raboy. Not rebound, remaindered comics; printed at same time as originals ... 514 1028 1542 3750 6625 9500
2-Capt. Marvel, Bulletman, Spy Smasher ... 239 478 717 1530 2615 3700
7-Funny animals (Hoppy, Billy the Kid & Oscar) ... 103 206 309 659 1130 1600

XMAS COMICS
Fawcett Publications: No. 4, Dec, 1949 - No. 7, Dec, 1952 (50¢, 196 pgs.)
4-Contains Whiz, Master, Tom Mix, Captain Marvel, Nyoka, Capt. Video, Bob Colt, Monte Hale, Hot Rod Comics, & Battle Stories. Not rebound, remaindered comics; printed at the same time as originals. Title logo and Santa's suit on cover are topped by red felt ... 148 296 444 947 1624 2300
5-7: 5-Green felt tree on-c. 6-Cover has red felt like #4. 7-Bill Boyd app.; stocking on cover is made of green felt (novelty cover) ... 116 232 348 742 1271 1800

X-MEN, THE
(See Adventures of Cyclops and Phoenix, Amazing Adventures, Archangel, Brotherhood, Capt. America #172, Classic X-Men, Exiles, Further Adventures of Cyclops & Phoenix, Gambit, Giant-Size..., Heroes For Hope..., Kitty Pryde & Wolverine, Marvel & DC Present, Marvel Collector's Edition:..., Marvel Fanfare, Marvel Graphic Novel, Marvel Super Heroes, Marvel Team-Up, Marvel Triple Action, The Marvel X-Men Collection, New Mutants, Nightcrawler, Official Marvel Index To..., Rogue, Special Edition..., Ultimate..., Uncanny..., Wolverine, X-Factor, X-Force, X-Terminators)

X-MEN, THE (1st series)(Becomes Uncanny X-Men at #142)(The X-Men #1-93; X-Men #94-141) (The Uncanny X-Men on-c only #114-141)
Marvel Comics Group: Sept, 1963 - No. 66, Mar, 1970; No. 67, Dec, 1970 - No. 141, Jan, 1981; Uncanny X-Men No. 142, Feb, 1981 - No. 544, Dec, 2011

1-Origin/1st app. X-Men (Angel, Beast, Cyclops, Iceman & Marvel Girl); 1st app. Magneto & Professor X ... 5275 10,550 21,100 48,800 119,400 190,000
2-1st app. The Vanisher ... 245 490 735 2021 4711 7100
3-1st app. The Blob (1/64) ... 166 332 498 1370 3085 4800
4-1st Quicksilver & Scarlet Witch & Brotherhood of the Evil Mutants (3/64); 1st app. Toad; 2nd app. Magneto ... 1150 2300 3450 6900 9200 11,500
5-Magneto & Evil Mutants-c/story ... 118 236 354 944 2122 3300
6-Sub-Mariner app. ... 93 186 279 744 1672 2600
7-Magneto app. ... 79 158 237 632 1416 2200
8,9,11: 8-1st app Unus the Untouchable. 9-Early Avengers app. (1/65); 1st Lucifer. 11-1st app. The Stranger ... 61 122 183 488 1094 1700
10-1st S.A. app. Ka-Zar & Zabu the zebra(3/65) ... 75 150 225 600 1350 2100
12-Origin Prof. X; Origin/1st app. Juggernaut ... 279 558 837 2302 5201 8100
13-Juggernaut and Human Torch app. ... 54 108 162 432 966 1500
14-1st app. Sentinels ... 96 192 288 768 1734 2700
15-Origin Beast ... 46 92 138 359 805 1250
16-20: 19-1st app. The Mimic (4/66) ... 22 44 66 154 340 525
21-27,29,30: 27-Re-enter The Mimic (r-in #75); Spider-Man cameo ... 15 30 45 100 220 360
28-1st app. The Banshee (1/67)(r-in #76) ... 40 80 120 296 673 1050
28-2nd printing (1994) ... 2 4 6 10 14 18
31-34,36,37,39: 34-Adkins-c/a. 39-New costumes ... 12 24 36 80 173 265
35-Spider-Man x-over (8/67)(r-in #83); 1st app. Changeling ... 42 84 126 311 706 1100
38,40: 38-Origins of the X-Men series begins, ends #57. 40-(1/68) 1st app. Frankenstein's monster at Marvel ... 12 24 36 88 185 285
41-48: 42-Death of Prof. X (Changeling disguised as). 44-1st S.A. app. G.A. Red Raven ... 11 22 33 75 160 245
49-Steranko-c; 1st Polaris ... 46 92 138 340 770 1200
50-Steranko-c/a; Polaris cover ... 44 88 132 326 738 1150
51-Steranko-c/a ... 14 28 42 96 211 325
52 ... 17 34 51 117 256 400
53-Barry Smith-c/a (his 1st comic book work) ... 12 24 36 79 170 260
54-1st app. Alex Summers who later becomes Havok; B. Smith-c ... 23 46 69 161 356 550
55-Summers discovers he has mutant powers ... 12 24 36 81 176 270
56,57,59-63,65-Neal Adams-a(p). 56-Intro Havok w/costume. 60-1st Sauron. 65-Return of Professor X. ... 12 24 36 80 173 265
58-1st app. Havok in costume; N. Adams-a(p) ... 36 72 108 259 580 900
62,63-2nd printings (1994) ... 2 4 6 8 11 14
64-1st app. Sunfire ... 32 64 96 230 515 800
66-Last new story w/original X-Men; battles Hulk ... 14 28 42 94 207 320
67-70: 67-Reprints begin, end #93. 67-70: (52 pgs.) ... 9 18 27 63 129 195
71-93: 71-Last 15¢ issue. 72: (52 pgs.). 73-86-r/#25-38 w/new-c. 83-Spider-Man-c/story. 87-93-r/#39-45 with covers ... 9 18 27 57 111 165
94 (8/75)-New X-Men begin (see Giant-Size X-Men); Colossus, Nightcrawler, Thunderbird, Storm, Wolverine, & Banshee join; Angel, Marvel Girl & Iceman resign ... 140 280 420 980 1890 2800
95-Death of Thunderbird ... 17 34 51 117 259 400
96,97 ... 12 24 36 79 170 260
98,99-(Regular 25¢ edition)(4,6/76) ... 12 24 36 82 179 275
98,99-(30¢-c variants, limited distribution) ... 29 58 87 209 467 725
100-Old vs. New X-Men; part origin Phoenix; last 25¢ issue (8/76) ... 16 32 48 111 246 380
100-(30¢-c variant, limited distribution) ... 36 72 108 259 580 900
101-Phoenix origin concludes ... 34 68 102 245 548 850

X-Force (2020 series) #39 © MAR

Xmas Comics #4 © FAW

X-Men #4 © MAR

	GD	VG	FN	VF	VF/NM	NM-
	2.0	4.0	6.0	8.0	9.0	9.2

102-104: 102-Origin Storm. 104-1st brief app. Starjammers; Magneto-c/story
| | 8 | 16 | 24 | 56 | 108 | 160 |

105-107-(Regular 30¢ editions). 106-(8/77)Old vs. New X-Men. 107-1st full app. Starjammers;
last 30¢ issue
| | 8 | 16 | 24 | 54 | 102 | 150 |

105-107-(35¢-c variants, limited distribution)
| | 36 | 72 | 108 | 259 | 580 | 900 |

108-Byrne-a begins (see Marvel Team-Up #53)
| | 8 | 16 | 24 | 56 | 108 | 160 |

109-1st app. Weapon Alpha (becomes Vindicator)
| | 15 | 30 | 45 | 103 | 227 | 350 |

110-116-Phoenix joins
| | 6 | 12 | 18 | 42 | 79 | 115 |

117-119: 117-Origin Professor X
| | 6 | 12 | 18 | 37 | 66 | 95 |

120-1st app. Alpha Flight, story line begins (4/79); app. Vindicator (formerly
Weapon Alpha); last 35¢ issue
| | 12 | 24 | 36 | 79 | 170 | 260 |

121-1st full Alpha Flight story
| | 11 | 22 | 33 | 73 | 157 | 240 |

122-128: 123-Spider-Man x-over. 124-Colossus becomes Proletarian
| | 5 | 10 | 15 | 34 | 60 | 85 |

129-Intro Kitty Pryde (1/80); last Banshee; Dark Phoenix saga begins; intro. Emma Frost
(White Queen)
| | 17 | 34 | 51 | 117 | 259 | 400 |

130-1st app. The Dazzler by Byrne (2/80)
| | 12 | 24 | 36 | 82 | 179 | 275 |

131-133: 131-Dazzler app.; 1st White Queen-c. 133-1st Wolverine solo-c
| | 5 | 10 | 15 | 34 | 60 | 85 |

134-Phoenix becomes Dark Phoenix
| | 8 | 16 | 24 | 54 | 102 | 150 |

135-1st Dark Phoenix-c
| | 6 | 12 | 18 | 42 | 79 | 115 |

136,138: 138-History of the X-Men recounted; Dazzler app.; Cyclops leaves
| | 5 | 10 | 15 | 31 | 53 | 75 |

137-Giant; death of Phoenix
| | 6 | 12 | 18 | 42 | 79 | 115 |

139-Alpha Flight app.; Kitty Pryde joins; new costume for Wolverine
| | 5 | 10 | 15 | 33 | 57 | 80 |

140-Alpha Flight app.
| | 5 | 10 | 15 | 33 | 57 | 80 |

141-"Days of Future Past" part 1; intro Future X-Men & The New Brotherhood of Evil Mutants;
1st app. Rachel (Phoenix II); Death of alt. future Franklin Richards; classic cover
| | 10 | 20 | 30 | 69 | 147 | 225 |

X-MEN: Titled THE UNCANNY X-MEN No. 142, Feb, 1981 - No. 544, Dec, 2011

142-"Days of Future Past" part 2; Rachel app.; deaths of alt. future Wolverine, Storm &
Colossus
| | 7 | 14 | 21 | 46 | 86 | 125 |

143-Last Byrne issue
| | 4 | 8 | 12 | 25 | 40 | 55 |

144-150: 144-Man-Thing app. 145-Old X-Men app. 148-1st app. Caliban; Spider-Woman,
Dazzler app. 150-Double size
| | 2 | 4 | 6 | 11 | 16 | 20 |

151-154,156,157,159-161,163,164: 161-Origin Magneto. 163-Origin Binary. 164-1st app. Binary
as Carol Danvers
| | 2 | 4 | 6 | 9 | 13 | 16 |

155-1st app of The Brood
| | 4 | 8 | 12 | 27 | 44 | 60 |

158-1st app. Rogue in X-Men (6/82, see Avengers Annual #10)
| | 4 | 8 | 12 | 25 | 40 | 55 |

162-Wolverine solo story
| | 3 | 6 | 9 | 16 | 23 | 30 |

165-Paul Smith-c/a begins, ends #175
| | 2 | 4 | 6 | 11 | 16 | 20 |

166-170: 166-Double size; Paul Smith-a. 167-New Mutants app. (3/83); same date as New
Mutants #1; 1st meeting w/X-Men; ties into N.M. #3,4; Starjammers app.; contains skin
"Tattooz" decals. 168-1st brief app. Madelyne Pryor (last page) in X-Men
(see Avengers Annual #10)
| | 2 | 4 | 6 | 8 | 11 | 14 |

171-Rogue joins X-Men; Simonson-c/a
| | 3 | 6 | 9 | 21 | 33 | 45 |

172-174: 172,173-Two part Wolverine solo story. 173-Two cover variations, blue & black.
174-Phoenix cameo
| | 2 | 4 | 6 | 8 | 11 | 14 |

175-(52 pgs.)-Anniversary issue; Phoenix returns
| | 3 | 6 | 9 | 14 | 20 | 25 |

176-185,187-192,194-199: 181-Sunfire app. 182-Rogue solo story. 184-1st app. Forge (8/84).
190,191-Spider-Man & Avengers x-over. 195-Power Pack x-over
| | 2 | 4 | 6 | 8 | 10 | 14 |

186,193: 186-Double-size; Barry Smith/Austin-a. 193-Double size; 100th app. New X-Men;
1st app. Warpath in costume (see New Mutants #16)
| | 2 | 4 | 6 | 8 | 11 | 14 |

200-(12/85, $1.25, 52 pgs.)
| | 3 | 6 | 9 | 19 | 30 | 40 |

201-(1/86)-1st app. Cable? (as baby Nathan; see X-Factor #1); 1st Whilce Portacio-c/a(i)
on X-Men (guest artist)
| | 3 | 6 | 9 | 21 | 33 | 45 |

202-204,206-209: 204-Nightcrawler solo story; 2nd Portacio-a(i) on X-Men.
207-Wolverine/Phoenix story
| | 2 | 4 | 6 | 8 | 11 | 14 |

205-Wolverine solo story by Barry Smith
| | 3 | 6 | 9 | 14 | 20 | 26 |

210,211-Mutant Massacre begins
| | 3 | 6 | 9 | 16 | 23 | 30 |

212,213-Wolverine vs. Sabretooth (Mutant Mass.)
| | 3 | 6 | 9 | 18 | 28 | 38 |

214-220,223,224: 219-Havok joins (7/87); brief app. Sabretooth.
| | 2 | 4 | 6 | 8 | 10 | 12 |

221-1st app. Mr. Sinister
| | 5 | 10 | 15 | 34 | 60 | 85 |

222-Wolverine battles Sabretooth-c/story
| | 3 | 6 | 9 | 17 | 25 | 34 |

225-242: 225-227: Fall Of The Mutants. 226-Double size. 240-Sabretooth app.
242-Double size, X-Factor app., Inferno tie-in
| | 2 | 4 | 6 | 8 | 10 | 12 |

243,245-247: 245-Rob Liefeld-a(p)
| | 2 | 4 | 6 | 8 | 10 | 12 |

244-1st app. Jubilee
| | 4 | 8 | 12 | 28 | 47 | 65 |

248-1st Jim Lee art on X-Men (1989)
| | 3 | 6 | 9 | 17 | 25 | 34 |

248-2nd printing (1992, $1.25)
| | 1 | 3 | 4 | 6 | 8 | 10 |

249-252: 252-Lee-c
| | 1 | 3 | 4 | 6 | 8 | 10 |

253-255: 253-All new X-Men begin. 254-Lee-c
| | 1 | 3 | 4 | 6 | 8 | 10 |

256-Betsy Braddock (Psylocke) 1st app. as purple-haired Asian in ninja costume; Jim Lee-c/a
| | 3 | 6 | 9 | 19 | 30 | 40 |

257-Jim Lee-c/a; Psylocke as Lady Mandarin
| | 2 | 4 | 6 | 9 | 13 | 16 |

258-Wolverine solo story; Lee-c/a
| | 2 | 4 | 6 | 9 | 13 | 16 |

259-Silvestri-c; no Lee-a
| | 1 | 3 | 4 | 6 | 8 | 10 |

260-265-No Lee-a. 260,261,264-Lee-c
| | 1 | 3 | 4 | 6 | 8 | 10 |

266-(8/90) 1st full app. Gambit (see Annual #14)-No Lee-a
| | 10 | 20 | 30 | 67 | 141 | 215 |

267-Jim Lee-c/a resumes; 2nd full Gambit app.
| | 3 | 6 | 9 | 16 | 24 | 32 |

268-Capt. America, Black Widow & Wolverine team-up; Lee-c/a
| | 3 | 6 | 9 | 21 | 33 | 45 |

268,270: 268-2nd printing. 270-Gold 2nd printing
| | 2 | 4 | 6 | 8 | 11 | 14 |

269,273,274: 269-Lee-a. 273-New Mutants (Cable) & X-Factor x-over; Golden, Byrne & Lee
part pencils
| | 1 | 3 | 4 | 6 | 8 | 10 |

270-X-Tinction Agenda begins
| | 2 | 4 | 6 | 8 | 10 | 12 |

271,272-X-Tinction Agenda
| | 2 | 4 | 6 | 8 | 10 | 12 |

275-(52 pgs.)-Tri-fold-c by Jim Lee (p); Prof. X
| | 2 | 4 | 6 | 8 | 10 | 12 |

275-Gold 2nd printing
| | | | | | | 6.00 |

276-280: 277-Last Lee-c/a. 280-X-Factor x-over
| | 1 | 2 | 3 | 5 | 6 | 8 |

281-(10/91)-New team begins (Storm, Archangel, Colossus, Iceman & Marvel Girl); Whilce
Portacio-c/a begins; Byrne scripts begin; wraparound-c (white logo)
| | 2 | 4 | 6 | 9 | 12 | 16 |

281-2nd printing with red metallic ink logo w/o UPC box ($1.00-c); does not say 2nd printing
inside
| | | | | | | 5.00 |

282-1st brief app. Bishop (cover & 1 page)
| | 3 | 6 | 9 | 21 | 33 | 45 |

282-Gold ink 2nd printing ($1.00-c)
| | 2 | 4 | 6 | 8 | 10 | 12 |

283-1st full app. Bishop (12/91)
| | 2 | 4 | 6 | 8 | 14 | 20 |

284-299: 284-Last $1.00-c. 286,287-Lee plots. 287-Bishop joins team. 288-Lee/Portacio plots.
290-Last Portacio-c/a. 294-Peterson-a(p) begins (#292 is 1 Peterson-c). 294-296 ($1.50)-
Bagged w/trading card in each; X-Cutioner's Song x-overs; Peterson/Austin-c/a on all
| | | | | | | 6.00 |
| | 13 | 26 | 39 | 89 | 195 | 300 |

297-Gold Edition
| | | | | | | 5.00 |

300-($3.95, 68 pgs.)-Holo-grafx foil-c; Magneto app.
| | 1 | 3 | 4 | 6 | 8 | |
| | | | | | | 4.00 |

301-303,305-309,311
| | | | | | | 100 |
| | 6 | 12 | 18 | 38 | 69 | |

303,307-Gold Edition
| | | | | | | |

304-($3.95, 68 pgs.)-Wraparound-c with Magneto hologram on-c; 30th anniversary issue;
Jae Lee-a (4 pgs.)
| | 2 | 4 | 6 | 8 | 10 | |
| | | | | | | 4.00 |

310-($1.95)-Bound-in trading card sheet
| | | | | | | 4.00 |

312-$1.50-c begins; bound-in card sheet; 1st Madureira
| | | | | | | 5.00 |

313-321: 318-1st app. Generation X
| | | | | | | 4.00 |

316,317-($2.95)-Foil enhanced editions
| | | | | | | 5.00 |

318-321-($1.95)-Deluxe editions
| | | | | | | 5.00 |

322-Onslaught
| | | | | | | 4.00 |

323,324,326-346: 323-Return from Age of Apocalypse. 328-Sabretooth-c. 329,330-Dr. Strange
app. 331-White Queen-c/app. 334-Juggernaut app.; w/Onslaught Update. 335-Onslaught.
338-Archangel's wings return to normal. 339-Havok vs. Cyclops; Spider-Man x-over. 341-Gladiator-c/app. 342-Deathbird
cameo; two covers. 343,344-Phalanx
| | | | | | | 4.00 |
| | | | | | | 6.00 |

325-($3.95)-Anniversary issue; gatefold-c
| | 2 | 4 | 6 | 9 | 13 | 16 |

342-Variant-c
| | | | | | | 4.00 |

347-349:347-Begin $1.99-c. 349-"Operation Zero Tolerance"
| | 2 | 4 | 6 | 10 | 14 | 18 |

350-Newsstand version
| | | | | | | 4.00 |

350-($3.99, 48 pgs.) Prismatic etched foil gatefold wraparound-c; Trial of Gambit;
Seagle-s begin
| | 2 | 4 | 6 | 11 | 16 | 20 |

351-359: 353-Bachalo-a begins. 354-Regular-c. 355-Alpha Flight-c/app.
| | | | | | | 4.00 |

356-Original X-Men-c
| | | | | | | 12 |

354-Dark Phoenix variant-c
| | | | | | | 5.00 |

360-($2.99) 35th Anniv. issue; Pacheco-c
| | | | | | | 5.00 |

360-($3.99) Etched Holo-foil enhanced-c
| | | | | | | 6.00 |

360-($3.99) DF Edition with Jae Lee variant-c
| | 2 | 4 | 6 | 8 | 10 | 12 |

361-374,378,379: 361-Gambit returns; Skroce-a. 362-Hunt for Xavier pt. 1; Bachalo-a.
364-Yu-a. 366-Magneto-c. 369-Juggernaut-c
| | | | | | | 4.00 |
| | | | | | | 6.00 |

375-($2.99) Autopsy of Wolverine
| | 1 | 3 | 4 | 6 | | 10 |

376,377-Apocalypse: The Twelve
| | | | | | | 5.00 |

380-($2.99) Polybagged w/X-Men Revolution Genesis Edition preview
| | | | | | | 5.00 |

381,382,384-389,391-393: 381-Begin $2.25-c; Claremont-s. 387-Maximum Security
| | | | | | | 4.00 |

383-($2.99)
| | | | | | | 5.00 |

390-Colossus dies to cure the Legacy Virus
| | 2 | 4 | 6 | 8 | 10 | 14 |

394-New look X-Men begins; Casey/Churchill-c/a
| | | | | | | 4.00 |

395-399-Poptopia. 398-Phillips & Wood-a
| | | | | | | 4.00 |

400-($3.50) Art by Ashley Wood, Eddie Campbell, Hamner, Phillips, Pulido and Matt Smith;
wraparound-c by Wood
| | | | | | | 6.00 |

401-421: 401-'Nuff Said issue; Garney-a. 404,405,407-409,413-415-Phillips-a. 416-Asamiya-a
begins. 421-Garney-a
| | | | | | | 4.00 |

422-($3.50) Alpha Flight app.; Garney-a
| | | | | | | 5.00 |

423-(25¢-c) Holy War pt. 1; Garney-a/Philip Tan-c
| | | | | | | 4.00 |

424-449,452-454: 425,426,429,430-Tan-a. 428-Birth of Nightcrawler. 437-Larroca-a begins.
444-New team, new costumes; Claremont-s/Davis-a begins. 448,449-Coipel-a
| | | | | | | 4.00 |

450-X-23 app.; Davis-a
| | 3 | 6 | 9 | 14 | 20 | 2 |

	GD 2.0	VG 4.0	FN 6.0	VF 8.0	VF/NM 9.0	NM- 9.2

451-X-23 app.; Davis-a — 3 6 9 14 20 25
455-459-X-23 app.; Davis-a — 6.00
460-471: 460-Begin $2.50-c; Raney-a. 462-465-House of M. 464-468-Bachalo-a. — 4.00
472-499: 472-Begin $2.99-c; Bachalo-a. 475-Wraparound-c. 492-494-Messiah Complex — 4.00
500-($3.99) X-Men new HQ in San Francisco; Magneto app.; Land & Dodson-a; wraparound covers by Alex Ross and Greg Land
500-Classic X-Men Dynamic Forces var.-c by Ross — 2 4 6 10 14 18
500-X-Men variant-c by Michael Turner — 4 8 12 22 32 40
500-X-Men sketch variant-c by Michael Turner — 14 28 42 96 211 325
500-X-Women variant-c by Dodson — 3 6 9 14 20 25
500-X-Women sketch variant-c by Dodson — 12 24 36 80 173 265
501-511,515-521,523-525: 501-Brubaker & Fraction-s/Land-a. 523-525-Second Coming — 4.00
512-514,522($3.99). 513,514-Utopia x-over. 522-Kitty Pryde returns to Earth; Portacio-a — 5.00
526-543-($3.99) 526-The Heroic Age; aftermath of Second Coming. 530-534-Land-a 540-543-Fear Itself tie-in, Juggernaut attacks; Land-a. 542-Colossus becomes the Juggernaut — 5.00
534.1 (6/11, $2.99) Pacheco-a — 4.00
544-(12/11, $3.99) Final issue; Land-a/c; Mr. Sinister app. — 2 4 6 10 14 18

#(-1) Flashback (7/97) Ladronn-c/Hitch & Neary-a — 4.00
... No. 1 Facsimile Edition (9/19, $3.99) Reprints #1 with original ads — 4.00
... No. 1 Facsimile Edition (6/23, $3.99) Reprints #1 with original ads — 4.00
... No. 4 Facsimile Edition (1/21, $3.99) Reprints #4 with original ads — 4.00
... No. 101 Facsimile Edition (9/23, $3.99) Reprints #101 with original ads and letters — 4.00
... No. 129 Facsimile Edition (12/23, $3.99) Reprints #129 with original ads and letters — 4.00
... No. 137 Facsimile Edition (9/19, $3.99) Reprints #137 with original ads and letters — 4.00
... No. 266 Facsimile Edition (1/20, $3.99) Reprints #266 with original ads and letters — 4.00
Special 1(12/70)-Kirby-c/a; origin the Stranger — 12 24 36 79 170 260
Special 2(11/71, 52 pgs.) — 8 16 24 54 102 150
Annual 3(1979, 52 pgs.)-New story; Miller/Austin-c; Wolverine still in old yellow costume — 5 10 15 30 48 65
Annual 4(1980, 52 pgs.)-Dr. Strange guest stars — 3 6 9 16 23 30
Annual 5(1981, 52 pgs.) — 2 4 6 10 14 12
Annual 6-8('82-'84 52 pgs.)-6-Dracula app. — 1 2 3 5 6 8
Annual 9,10('85, '86)-9-New Mutants x-over cont'd from New Mutants Special Ed. #1; Art Adams-a. 10-Art Adams-a — 2 4 6 8 10 12
Annual 11-13:('87-'89, 68 pgs.): 12-Evolutionary War; A.Adams-a(p). 13-Atlantis Attacks — 5.00
Annual 14(1990, $2.00, 68 pgs.)-1st app. Gambit (minor app., 5 pgs.); Fantastic Four, New Mutants (Cable) & X-Factor x-over; Art Adams-a/a(p) — 4 8 12 28 47 65
Annual 15 (1991, $2.00, 68 pgs.)-4 pg. origin; New Mutants x-over; 4 pg. Wolverine solo back-up story; 4th app. X-Force cont'd from New Warriors Annual 1 — 5.00
Annual 16-18 ('92-'94, 68 pgs.)-16-Jae Lee-c/a(p). 17-Bagged w/card — 5.00
Annual '95-(11/95, $3.95)-Wraparound-c — 5.00
Annual '96,'97-Wraparound-c — 5.00
.../Fantastic Four Annual '98 ($2.99) Casey-s — 5.00
Annual '99 ($3.50) Jubilee app. — 5.00
Annual 2000 ($3.50) Cable app.; Ribic-a — 5.00
Annual 2001 ($3.50, printed wide-ways) Ashley Wood-c/a; Casey-s — 5.00
Annual (Vol. 2) #1 (8/06, $3.99) Storm & Black Panther wedding prelude — 5.00
Annual (Vol. 2) #2 (3/09, $3.99) Dark Reign; flashback to Sub-Mariner/Emma Frost — 5.00
Annual (Vol. 2) #3 (5/11, $3.99) Escape From the Negative Zone; Bradshaw-a — 4.00
....At The State Fair of Texas (1983, 36 pgs., one-shot); Supplement to the Dallas Times Herald — 2 4 6 9 12 15
...: The Dark Phoenix Saga TPB 1st printing (1984, $12.95) — 25.00
...: The Dark Phoenix Saga TPB 2nd-5th printings — 20.00
...: The Dark Phoenix Saga TPB 6th-10th printings — 20.00
... Days of Future Past TPB (2004, $19.99) r/#138-143 & Annual #4 — 20.00
... Eve of Destruction TPB (2005, $14.99) r/#391-393 & X-Men #111-113; Churchill-c — 5.00
...:Dream's End (2004, $17.99)-r/Death of Colossus story arc from Uncanny X-Men #388-390, Cable #87, Bishop #16 and X-Men #108,110; debut pages from Giant-Size X-Men #1 — 18.00
... From The Ashes TPB (1990, $14.95) r/#168-176 — 15.00
... Future History - The Messiah War Sourcebook (2009, $3.99) Cable's files on X-Men — 4.00
... God Loves, Man Kills ($6.95)-r/Marvel Graphic Novel #5 — 7.00
... God Loves, Man Kills Extended Cut (6/20 - No. 2 10/20, $4.99) 1-Reprint with 5 new opening pages by Claremont & Anderson; creator interviews. 2-New 5-page epilogue — 5.00
... God Loves, Man Kills - Special Edition (2003, $4.99)-reprint with new Hughes-c — 5.00
... God Loves, Man Kills HC (2003, $19.99) reprint with Claremont & Anderson interviews; original artist Neal Adams' six sketch pages and interview — 20.00
...: Hope (5/10, $2.99) Collects Cable and Hope back-ups; Dillon-a — 3.00
House of M: Uncanny X-Men TPB (2006, $13.99) r/#462-465 and selections from Secrets Of The House of M one-shot — 14.00
... In The Days of Future Past TPB (1989, $3.95, 52 pgs.) — 15.00
... No More Humans HC (2014, $24.99) Carey-s/Larroca-a — 25.00
... No. 4 Facsimile Edition (3/24, $4.99) r/#4 with original ads and letters page — 5.00
... No. 141 Facsimile Edition (1/24, $4.99) r/#141 with original ads and letters page — 5.00
... Old Soldiers TPB (2004, $19.99) r/#213,215 & Ann. #11; New Mutants Ann. #2&3 — 20.00
... Poptopia TPB (10/01, $15.95) r/#394-399 — 16.00
...: Rise & Fall of the Shi'Ar Empire TPB (2007, $34.99, dustjacket) r/#475-486; bonus art — 35.00
...: Rise & Fall of the Shi'Ar Empire SC (2008, $29.99) r/#475-486; bonus art — 30.00
...: Season One HC (2012, $24.99) Origin re-told; Hopeless-s/McKelvie-a — 25.00
...: Sword of the Braddocks (5/09, $3.99) Psylocke vs. Slaymaster; Claremont-s — 4.00
...: The Complete Onslaught Epic Book 1 TPB (2007, $29.99) r/X-Men #53-54, Uncanny X-Men #334-335, Fantastic Four #414-415, Avengers #400-401, Onslaught: X-Men, Cable #34 and Incredible Hulk #444 — 30.00
...: The Complete Onslaught Epic Book 2 TPB ('08, $29.99) r/Excalibur #100, Wolverine #104, X-Factor #125-126, Amazing Spider-Man #415, Green Goblin #12, Spider-Man #72, Punisher #11, X-Man #18 & X-Force #57 — 30.00
...: The Extremists TPB (2007, $13.99) r/#487-491 — 14.00
...: The Heroic Age (9/10, $3.99) Beast, Steve Rogers and Princess Powerful app. — 4.00
Uncanny X-Men No. 142 Facsimile Edition (1/24, $4.99) r/#142 with original ads — 5.00
Uncanny X-Men No. 268 Facsimile Edition (4/24, $4.99) r/#268 with original ads — 5.00
Uncanny X-Men Omnibus Vol. 1 HC (2006, $99.99, over-sized dust jacket) r/Giant-Size X-Men #1, (Uncanny) X-Men #94-131 & Annual #3; cover gallery, promo and sketch art — 140.00
Uncanny X-Men 3D #1 (3/19, $7.99) Reprints #268 polybagged with 3-D glasses — 8.00
Vignettes TPB (9/01, $17.95) r/Claremont & Bolton Classic X-Men #1-13 — 18.00
Vignettes Vol. 2 TPB (2005, $17.99) r/Claremont & Bolton Classic X-Men #14-25 — 18.00

... Vol. 1: Hope TPB (2003, $12.99) r/#410-415; Harris-c — 13.00
... Vol. 2: Dominant Species TPB (2003, $11.99) r/#416-420; Asamiya-c — 12.00
... Vol. 3: Holy War TPB (2003, $17.99) r/#421-427 — 18.00
... Vol. 4: The Draco TPB (2004, $15.99) r/#428-434 — 16.00
... Vol. 5: She Lies with Angels TPB (2004, $11.99) r/#437-441 — 12.00
... Vol. 6: Bright New Mourning TPB (2004, $14.99) r/#435,436,442,443 & (New) X-Men #155,156; Larroca sketch covers — 15.00
...Vs. Apocalypse Vol. 1: The Twelve TPB (2008, $29.99) r/#376-377, Cable #73-76, X-Men #96,97 and Wolverine #145-147 — 30.00
... - The New Age Vol. 1: The End of History (2004, $12.99) r/#444-449 — 13.00
... - The New Age Vol. 2: The Cruelest Cut (2005, $11.99) r/#450-454 — 12.00
... - The New Age Vol. 3: On Ice (2006, $15.99) r/#455-461 — 16.00
... - The New Age Vol. 4: End of Greys (2006, $14.99) r/#466-471 — 12.00
... - The New Age Vol. 5: First Foursaken (2006, $11.99) r/#472-474 & Annual #1 — 12.00

NOTE: **Art Adams** a-Annual 9, 10p, 12p, 14p; c-218p. **Neal Adams** a-56-63p, 65p; c-56-63. **Adkins** a-34, 35p; c-31, 34, 35. **Austin** a-108i, 109i, 111-117i, 119-143i, 186i, 204i, 228i, 294-297i, Annual 3i, 7i, 9i, 13; c-109-111i, 114-122i, 123, 124-141i, 142, 143, 196i, 204i, 228i, 294-297i, Annual 3i. **J. Buscema** c-242, 43, 45. **Buscema/ Tuska** a-45. **Byrne** a(p)-108, 109, 111-143, 273; c(p)-113-116, 127, 129, 131-141. **Capullo** c-14. **Ditko** r-86, 89-91, 93. **Everett** c-73. **Golden** a-273, Annual 7p. **Guice** a-216p, 217p. **G. Kane** c(p)-33, 74-76, 79, 80, 94, 95. **Kirby** a(p)-1-17 (#12-17, 67r-layouts); c(p)-1-17, 25, 30 (18, 26-parts). **Layton** a-105i; c-112i, 113i. **Jim Lee** a(p)-248, 249, 267, 273, 275-277; c(p)-252, 254, 256-261, 264, 267, 268, 270, 275-277, 286. **Perez** a-Annual 5p; c(i)-281, 282, 284, 285. 55,56-Onslaught. **Annual 3.** **Peterson** a(p)-294-300, 304(part); c(p)-294-299. **Whilce Portacio** a(p)-281-286, 289, 290(r); c(p)-281-285p, 289p, 290; c(i)-267. **Romita, Jr.** a-300; c-300. **Rousseau** a-Annual 3-71p; c-171, 217. **B. Smith** a-53, 186p, 198p, 205, 214; c-53-55, 186p, 198, 205, 212, 214, 216. **Paul Smith** a(p)-165-170, 172-175, 278; c-165-170, 172-175, 278. **Sparling** a-78p. **Steranko** a-50p, 51p; c-49-51. **Sutton** a-106i. **Art Thibert** a(i)-281-286; c(i)-281, 282, 284, 285. **Toth** a-12p, 67p(r). **Tuska** a-40-42i, 43-46p, 88i(r); c-39-41, 77p, 78p. **Williamson** a-202i, 203i, 211i; c-202i, 203i, 206i. **Wood** c-14.

UNCANNY X-MEN AND THE NEW TEEN TITANS (See Marvel and DC Present...)

X-MEN (2nd Series)(Titled New X-Men with #114) (Titled X-Men Legacy with #210)
Marvel Comics: Oct., 1991 - No. 275, Dec, 2012 ($1.00-$2.99)

1 a-d (four different covers, $1.50, 52 pgs.)-Jim Lee-c/a begins, ends #11; new team begins (Cyclops, Beast, Wolverine, Gambit, Psylocke & Rogue); new Uncanny X-Men & Magneto app.; — 3 6 9 17 26 35
1 e ($3.95)-Double gate-fold-c consisting of all four covers from 1a-d by Jim Lee; contains all pin-ups from #1a-d plus inside-c foldout poster; no ads; printed on coated stock — 3 6 9 18 26 35
1-20th Anniversary Edition-(12/11, $3.99) r/#1 with double gatefold; Jim Lee pin-ups — 5.00
2,3,5-7- 5-Byrne scripts. 5-Sabretooth-c/story — 1 2 3 5 6 8
4-1st app. Omega Red; Wolverine back to old yellow costume (same date as Wolverine #50); last $1.00-c — 4 8 12 25 40 55
8-10: 8-Gambit vs. Bishop-c/story; last Lee-a; Ghost Rider cameo cont'd in Ghost Rider #26. 9-Wolverine vs. Ghost Rider; cont'd/G.R. #26. 10-Return of Longshot — 1 2 3 5 6 8
11-Regular edition; X-Men vs. Mojo — 3 6 9 16 23 30
11-Silver ink 2nd printing; X-Men board game — 5 10 15 33 57 80
12,13,17-24,26-29,31: 12,13-Art Thibert-c/a. 28,29-Sabretooth app. — 6.00
14-16-($1.50)-Polybagged with trading card in each; X-Cutioner's Song x-overs; 14-Andy Kubert-c/a begins — 1 2 3 5 6 8
25-($3.50, 52 pgs.)-Wraparound-c with Gambit hologram on-c; Professor X erases Magneto's mind — 3 6 9 16 23 30
25-30th anniversary issue w/B&W-c with Magneto in color & Magneto hologram & no price on-c — 5 10 15 31 53 75
25-Gold — 5 10 15 33 57 80
30-($1.95)-Wedding issue w/bound-in trading card sheet — 1 3 4 6 8 10
32-37: 32-Begin $1.50-c; bound-in card sheet. 33-Gambit & Sabretooth-c/story — 5.00
36,37-($2.95)-Collectors editions (foil-c) — 6.00
38-44,46-49,51-65: 42,43- Paul Smith-a. 46,49,53-56-Onslaught app. 51-Waid scripts begin, end #56. 54-(Reg. edition)-Onslaught revealed as Professor X. 55,56-Onslaught x-over; Avengers, FF & Sentinels app. 56-Dr. Doom app. 57-Xavier taken into custody; Byrne-c/swipe (X-Men,1st Series #138). 59-Hercules-c/app. 61-Juggernaut-c/app. 62-Re-intro. Shang Chi; two covers. 63-Kingpin cameo. 64- Kingpin app. — 5.00
45-($3.95) Annual issue; gatefold-c — 6.00
50-($2.95)-Vs. Onslaught, wraparound-c — 1 2 3 5 6 8
50-($2.95)-Vs. Onslaught, wraparound foil-c — 1 2 3 5 6 8
50-($2.95)-Variant gold-c — 4 8 12 27 44 60
50-($2.95)-Variant silver-c — 2 4 6 11 16 20
54-(Limited edition)-Embossed variant-c; Onslaught revealed as Professor X — 4 8 12 25 40 55
66-69,71-74,76-79: 66-Operation Zero Tolerance. 76-Origin of Maggott — 4.00
70-($2.99, 48 pgs.)-Joe Kelly-s begin, new members join — 5.00
75-($2.99, 48 pgs.) vs. N'Garai, wraparound-c — 5.00
80-($3.99) 35th Anniv. issue; holo-foil-c — 6.00
80-($2.99) Regular-c — 5.00
80-($6.95) Dynamic Forces Ed.; Quesada-c — 7.00
81-93,95,98,99: 82-Hunt for Xavier pt. 2. 85-Davis-a. 86-Origin of Joseph. 87-Magneto War ends. 88-Juggernaut app. — 4.00
94-($2.99) Contains preview of X-Men: Hidden Years — 5.00
96,97-Apocalypse: The Twelve — 1 2 3 5 6 8
100-($2.99) Art Adams-c; begin Claremont-s/Yu-a — 5.00
100-DF alternate-c — 2 4 6 8 11 14
101-105,107,108,110-114: 101-Begin $2.25-c. 107-Maximum Security x-over; Bishop-c/app. 108-Moira MacTaggart dies; Senator Kelly shot. 111-Magneto-c. 112,113-Eve of Destruction — 4.00
106-($2.99) X-Men battle Domina — 5.00
109-($3.50, 100 pgs.) new and reprinted Christmas-themed stories — 5.00
114-(7/01) Title change to "New X-Men," Morrison-s/Quitely-c/a begins — 4.00
114-(8/10, $1.00) "Marvel's Greatest Comics" reprint — 3.00
115-Two covers (Quitely & BWS) — 5.00
116-125,127,129-149: 116-Emma Frost joins. 117,118-Van Sciver-a. 121,122,135-Quitely-a. 127-Leon & Sienkiewicz-a. 132,139-141-Jimenez-a. 136-138-Quitely-a. 142-Sabretooth app.; Bachalo-c/a thru #145. 146-Magneto returns; Jimenez-a — 3.00
126-($3.25) Quitely-a; defeat of Cassanova — 3.00
128-1st app. Fantomex; Kordey-a — 4 8 12 23 37 50
150-($3.50) Jean Grey dies again; last Jimenez-a — 4.00
151-156: 151-154-Silvestri-c/a — 3.00
157-169: 157-X-Men Reload begins — 3.00

X-Men #500 © MAR

X-Men (2012 series) #28 © MAR

X-Men (2014 series) #21 © MAR

	GD	VG	FN	VF	VF/NM	NM-
	2.0	4.0	6.0	8.0	9.0	9.2

170-184: 171- Begin $2.50-c. 175,176-Crossover with Black Panther #8,9. 181-184-Apocalypse
returns — 3.00
185-199,201-229,231-249,251-261: 185-Begin $2.99-c. 188-190,192-194,197-199-Bachalo-a.
195,196,201-203-Ramos-a. 201-204-Endangered Species back-up. 205-207-Messiah
Complex x-over. 208-Romita Jr.-a. 210-Starts X-Men: Legacy. 228,229-Acuña-a.
235-237-Second Coming x-over. 238-The Heroic Age. 245-Age of X begins — 3.00
200-($3.99) Two wraparound covers by Bachalo & Finch; Bachalo & Ramos-a — 4.00
230-($3.99) Acuña-a; Rogue vs. Emplate — 4.00
250-($4.99) Suayan-c/Pham-a; back-up r/New Mutants #27 — 5.00
261.1-(3/12, $2.99) The N'Garai app.; Brooks-a — 3.00
262-275-Brooks-a. 266-270-Avengers vs. X-Men tie-in — 4.00
#(-1) Flashback (7/97); origin of Magneto — 5.00
Annual 1-3 ('92-'94, $2.25-$2.95, 68 pgs.) 1-Lee-c & layouts; #2-Bagged w/card — 5.00
Special '95 ($3.95) — 5.00
... '96,...'97-Wraparound-c — 5.00
.../ Dr. Doom '98 Annual ($2.99) Lopresti-a — 5.00
... Annual '99 ($3.50) Adam Kubert-c — 4.00
Annual 2000 ($3.50) Art Adams-c/Claremont-s/Eaton-a — 4.00
...2001 Annual ($3.50) Morrison-s/Yu-a; issue printed sideways — 4.00
...2007 Annual #1 (3/07, $3.99) Casey-s/Brooks-c; Cable and Mystique app. — 4.00
...Legacy Annual 1 (11/09, $3.99) Acuña-a; Emplate returns — 4.00
Animation Special Graphic Novel (12/90, $10.95) adapts animated series — 12.00
Ashcan #1 (1994, 75¢) Introduces new team members — 4.00
... Archives Sketchbook (12/00, $2.99) Early B&W character design sketches by
various incl. Lee, Davis, Yu, Pacheco, BWS, Art Adams, Liefeld — 4.00
...: Bizarre Love Triangle TPB (2005, $9.99)-r/X-Men #171-174 — 10.00
.../ Black Panther TPB (2006, $11.99)-r/X-Men #175,176 & Black Panther (2005) #8,9 — 12.00
... Blinded By the Light (2007, $14.99)-r/X-Men #188-199 — 15.00
...: Blind Science (7/10, $3.99) Second Coming x-over; Parel-c — 4.00
...: Blood of Apocalypse (2006, $17.99)-r/X-Men #182-187 — 18.00
... Day of the Atom (2005, $19.99)-r/X-Men #157-165 — 20.00
...: Decimation: X-Men - The Day After TPB (2006, $15.99) r/#177-181 & Decimation: House of
M - The Day After — 16.00
...: Declassified (10/00, $3.50) Profile pin-ups by various; Jae Lee-c — 4.00
...: Earth's Mutant Heroes (7/11, $4.99) Handbook-style profiles of mutants — 5.00
...: Endangered Species (8/07, $3.99) prologue to 17-part back-up series in X-Men titles — 4.00
...: Endangered Species HC (2008, $24.99, d.j.) over-sized 17-part series — 25.00
...: Evolutions 1 (12/11, $3.99) Collection of variant covers from May 2011 Marvel titles — 4.00
...: Fatal Attractions ('94, $17.95)-r/X-Factor #92, X-Force #25, Uncanny X-Men #304,
X-Men #25, Wolverine #75, & Excalibur #71 — 18.00
...: Golgotha (2005, $12.99)-r/X-Men #166-170 — 13.00
... Millennial Visions (8/00, $3.99) Various artists interpret future X-Men — 4.00
... Millennial Visions 2 (1/02, $3.50) Various artists interpret future X-Men — 4.00
...: Mutant Genesis (2006, $19.99)-r/X-Men #1-7; sketch pages and extra art — 20.00
New X-Men: E is for Extinction TPB (11/01, $12.95) r/#114-117 — 13.00
New X-Men: Imperial TPB (7/02, $19.99) r/#118-126; Quitely-c — 20.00
New X-Men: New Worlds TPB (2002, $14.99) r/#127-133; Quitely-c — 15.00
New X-Men: Riot at Xavier's TPB (2003, $11.99) r/#134-138; Quitely-c — 12.00
New X-Men: Vol. 5: Assault on Weapon Plus TPB (2003, $14.99) r/#139-145 — 15.00
New X-Men: Vol. 6: Planet X TPB (2004, $12.99) r/#146-150 — 13.00
New X-Men: Vol. 7: Here Comes Tomorrow TPB (2004, $10.99) r/#151-154 — 11.00
New X-Men: Volume 1 HC (2002, $29.99) oversized r/#114-126 & 2001 Annual — 30.00
New X-Men: Volume 2 HC (2003, $29.99) oversized r/#127-141; sketch & script pages — 30.00
New X-Men: Volume 3 HC (2004, $29.99) oversized r/#142-154; sketch & script pages — 30.00
New X-Men Omnibus HC (2006, $99.99) oversized r/#114-154 & Annual 2001; Morrison's
original pitch; sketch & script pages; variant covers & promo art; Carey intro. — 140.00
... No. 1 Facsimile Edition (7/23, $7.99) Reprints #1 with original ads — 8.00
... Odd Men Out (2008, $3.99) Two unpublished stories with Dave Cockrum-a — 4.00
... Original Sin 1 (12/08, $3.99) Wolverine and Daken; Deodato & Eaton-a — 4.00
... Origin: Colossus (7/08, $3.99) Yost-s/Hairsine-a; Piotr Rasputin before joining X-Men — 4.00
... Phoenix Force Handbook (9/10, $4.99) bios of those related to the Phoenix; Raney-c — 5.00
... Pixies and Demons Director's Cut (2008, $3.99) r/FCBD 2008 story with script — 4.00
... Pizza Hut Mini-comics-(See Marvel Collector's Edition: X-Men in Promotional Comics section)
... Premium Edition #1 (1993)-Cover says "Toys 'R' Us Limited Edition X-Men" — 6.00
...: Rarities (1995, $5.95)-Reprints — 4.00
...: Return of Magik Must Have (2008, $3.99) r/X-Men Unlimited #14, New X-Men #37 and
X-Men: Divided We Stand #2; Coipel-c — 4.00
...: Road Trippin' ('99, $24.95, TPB) r/X-Men road trips — 25.00
...: Supernovas ('07, $34.99, oversized HC w/d.j.) r/X-Men 188-199 & Annual #1 — 35.00
...: Supernovas ('08, $29.99, SC) r/X-Men 188-199 & Annual #1 — 30.00
...: The Coming of Bishop ('95, $12.95)-r/Uncanny X-Men #282-285, 287,288 — 13.00
...: The Magneto War (3/99, $2.99) Davis-a — 4.00
...: The Rise of Apocalypse ('98, $16.99)-r/Rise Of Apocalypse #1-4, X-Factor #5,6 — 17.00
... Visionaries: Chris Claremont ('98, $24.95)-r/Claremont-s; art by Byrne, BWS, Jim Lee — 25.00
... Visionaries: Jim Lee ('02, $29.99)-r/Jim Lee-a from various issues between Uncanny X-Men
#248 & 286; Classic X-Men #39 and X-Men Annual #1 — 30.00
... Visionaries: Joe Madureira (7/00, $17.95)-r/Uncanny X-Men #325,326,329,330,341-343;

new Madureira-c — 18.00
... Vs. Hulk (3/09, $3.99) Claremont-s/Raapack-a; r/X-Men #66 — 4.00
...: Zero Tolerance ('00, $24.95, TPB) r/crossover series — 25.00
NOTE: **Jim Lee** a-1-11p; c-1-6p, 7, 8, 9p, 10, 11p. **Art Thibert** a-6-9i, 12, 13; c-6i, 12, 13.

X-MEN (3rd series)
Marvel Comics: Sept, 2010 - No. 41, Apr, 2013 ($3.99)

1-41: 1-6-"Curse of the Mutants" x-over; Medina-a. 7-10-Spider-Man app.; Bachalo-a.
12-Continued from X-Men Giant-Size #1. 16-19-FF & Skull the Slayer app.
20-23-War Machine app. 16-Deadpool app. 28-FF & Spider-Man app. 38,39-Domino &
Daredevil team-up — 4.00
15.1 ($2.99) Pearson-c/Conrad-a; Ghost Rider app. — 3.00
...: Curse of the Mutants - Blade 1 (10/10, $3.99) Tim Green-a — 4.00
...: Curse of the Mutants - Smoke and Blood 1 (11/10, $3.99) Crain-c — 4.00
...: Curse of the Mutants Spotlight 1 (1/11, $3.99) creator profiles and interviews — 4.00
...: Curse of the Mutants - Storm and Gambit 1 (11/10, $3.99) Bachalo-a; 2 covers — 4.00
...: Curse of the Mutants - X-Men vs. Vampires 1,2 (11/10 - No. 2, 12/10, $3.99) Bradshaw-c — 4.00
...: Giant-Size 1 (7/11, $4.99) Medina & Talajic-a; cover swipe of Giant-Size X-Men #1 — 5.00
...: Regenesis 1 (12/11, $3.99) Splits X-Men into 2 teams; Tan-a/Bachalo-a — 4.00
... Spotlight 1 (7/11, $3.99) Character profiles and creator interviews — 4.00
...: With Great Power 1 (2011, $4.99) r/#7-9 — 5.00

X-MEN (4th series)
Marvel Comics: Jul, 2013 - No. 26, Jun, 2015 ($3.99)

1-26: 1-All-female team; Brian Wood-s/Olivier Coipel-a. 5,6-Battle of the Atom — 4.00
100th Anniversary Special: X-Men (9/14, $3.99) Takes place in 2061; Furth-s/Masters-a — 4.00

X-MEN (5th series)
Marvel Comics: Dec, 2019 - No. 21, Aug, 2021 ($4.99/$3.99)

1-($4.99) Hickman-s/Yu-a; follows House of X and Powers of X series; intro Serafina — 5.00
2-21-($3.99) 5-Serafina app. 3-Silva-a. 6-Mystique app.; Buffagni-a. 9-The Brood app.
10,11-Empyre tie-in. 13-15-"X of Swords" tie-in. 17-Booth-a. 21-Hellfire Gala tie-in — 4.00
...: Marvels Snapshots 1 (11/20, $4.99) Flashback to Cyclops' childhood; Alex Ross-c — 5.00

X-MEN (6th series)
Marvel Comics: Sept, 2021 - Present ($4.99/$3.99)

1-($4.99) Duggan-s/Larraz-a; new team; debut of the Treehouse — 5.00
2-24,26-31-($3.99) 4-Nightmare app. 6-Intro. Captain Krakoa. 8,22-M.O.D.O.K. app. — 4.00
25-($5.99) Follows events in X-Men: Hellfire Gala 2023 — 6.00
Annual 1 (2/23, $4.99) Foxe-s/Di Vito-a; spotlight on Firestar — 5.00
Annual 1 (11/23, $4.99) Contest of Chaos Part 7; Captain Marvel app. — 5.00
...& Moon Girl 1 (11/22, $4.99) Wolverine and Havok app. — 5.00
...: Curse of the Man-Thing 1 (7/21, $4.99) Orlando-s/Broccardo-a — 5.00
...: Hellfire Gala 1 (9/22, $7.99) 2nd gala; Immortality is revealed; new team chosen — 8.00
...: Hellfire Gala 2023 #1 (9/23, $8.99) 3rd gala; return of Ms. Marvel — 9.00
...: The Onslaught Revelation 1 (11/21, $4.99) Spurrier-s/Quinn-a; Legion app. — 5.00
...: Unforgiven 1 (5/23, $4.99) Seeley-s/Kotian-a; takes place after Spider-Man: Unforgiven — 5.00

X-MEN (Free Comic Book Day giveaways)
Marvel Comics: 2006; May, 2008

FCBD 2008 Edition #1-(5/08) Features Pixie; Carey/Land-a/c — 3.00
.../Runaways: FCBD 2006 Edition; new x-over story; Mighty Avengers preview; Chen-c — 3.00

X-MEN ADVENTURES (TV)
Marvel Comics: Nov, 1992 - No. 15, Jan, 1994 ($1.25)(Based on animated series)

1,15: 1-Wolverine, Cyclops, Jubilee, Rogue, Gambit. 15-($1.75, 52 pgs.)		2	4	6	9	12	15

2-14: 3-Magneto-c/story. 6-Sabretooth-c/story. 7-Cable-c/story. 10-Archangel guest star.
11-Cable-c/story. — 4.00

X-MEN ADVENTURES II (TV)
Marvel Comics: Feb, 1994 - No. 13, Feb, 1995 ($1.25/$1.50)(Based on 2nd TV season)

1-13: 4-Bound-in trading card sheet. 5-Alpha Flight app. — 4.00
...Captive Hearts/Slave Island (TPB, $4.95)-r/X-Men Adventures #5-8 — 5.00
...The Irresistible Force, The Muir Island Saga ($5.95, 10/94, TPB) r/X-Men Advs. #9-12 — 6.00

X-MEN ADVENTURES III (TV)(See Adventures of the X-Men)
Marvel Comics: Mar, 1995 - No. 13, Mar, 1996 ($1.50) (Based on 3rd TV season)

1-13 — 4.00

X-MEN: AGE OF APOCALYPSE
Marvel Comics: May, 2005 - No. 6, June, 2005 ($2.99, weekly limited series)

1-6-Bachalo-c/a; Yoshida-s; follows events in the "Age of Apocalypse" storyline — 4.00
... One Shot (5/05, $3.99) prequel to series; Hitch wraparound-c; pin-ups by various — 4.00
X-Men: The New Age of Apocalypse TPB (2005, $20.99) r/#1-6 & one-shot — 21.00

X-MEN ALPHA
Marvel Comics: 1994 ($3.95, one-shot)

nn-Age of Apocalypse; wraparound chromium-c	2	4	6	10	14	18
nn ($49.95)-Gold logo						55.00

	GD	VG	FN	VF	VF/NM	NM-		GD	VG	FN	VF	VF/NM	NM-
	2.0	4.0	6.0	8.0	9.0	9.2		2.0	4.0	6.0	8.0	9.0	9.2

X-MEN/ALPHA FLIGHT
Marvel Comics Group: Dec, 1985 - No. 2, Dec, 1985 ($1.50, limited series)

1,2: 1-Intro The Berserkers; Paul Smith-a — 5.00

X-MEN/ALPHA FLIGHT
Marvel Comics Group: May, 1998 - No. 2, June, 1998 ($2.99, limited series)

1,2-Flashback to early meeting; Raab-s/Cassaday-s/a — 4.00

X-MEN AND POWER PACK
Marvel Comics: Dec, 2005 - No. 4, Mar, 2006 ($2.99, limited series)

1-4-Sumerak-s/Gurihiru-a. 1-Wolverine & Sabretooth app. — 3.00
...: The Power of X (2006, $6.99, digest size) r/#1-4 — 7.00

X-MEN AND THE MICRONAUTS, THE
Marvel Comics Group: Jan, 1984 - No. 4, Apr, 1984 (Limited series)

1-4- Guice-c(a/p) in all — 5.00

X-MEN: APOCALYPSE/DRACULA
Marvel Comics: Apr, 2006 - No. 4, July, 2006 ($2.99, limited series)

1-4-Tieri-s/Henry-a/Jae Lee-c — 3.00
TPB (2006, $10.99) r/series; cover gallery — 11.00

X-MEN ARCHIVES
Marvel Comics: Jan, 1995 - No. 4, Apr, 1995 ($2.25, limited series)

1-4: Reprints Legion stories from New Mutants. 4-Magneto app. — 4.00

X-MEN ARCHIVES FEATURING CAPTAIN BRITAIN
Marvel Comics: July, 1995 - No. 7, 1996 ($2.95, limited series)

1-7: Reprints early Capt. Britain stories — 5.00

X-MEN: BATTLE OF THE ATOM
Marvel Comics: Nov, 2013 - No. 2, Dec, 2013 ($3.99, bookends for X-Men title crossover)

1,2: 1-Bendis-s/Cho-a/Art Adams-c; bonus pin-ups of the various X-teams — 4.00

X-MEN: BEFORE THE FALL
Marvel Comics: Jul, 2023 - Sept, 2023 ($4.99, series of one-shots)

... – Heralds of Apocalypse 1 (8/23) Ewing-s/Pizzari, Landini, and Pimento-a — 5.00
... – Mutant First Strike 1 (8/23) Orlando-s/Pinti-a — 5.00
... – Sinister Four 1 (9/23) Gillen-s/Medina-a — 5.00
... – Sons of X 1 (7/23) Spurrier-s/Noto-a — 5.00

X-MEN: BLACK
Marvel Comics: Dec, 2018 ($4.99, series of one-shots, back-up Apocalypse story in each)

...: Emma Frost 1 - Williams-s/Bachalo-a; Sebastian Shaw app.; Apocalypse part 5 — 5.00
...: Juggernaut 1 - Thompson-s/Crystal-a; Apocalypse part 4 — 5.00
...: Magneto 1 - Claremont-s/Talajic-a; Apocalypse part 1 — 5.00
...: Mojo 1 - Aukerman-s/Bradshaw-a; Apocalypse part 2 — 5.00
...: Mystique 1 - McGuire-s/Failla-a; Apocalypse part 3 — 5.00

X-MEN BLACK SUN (See Black Sun:...)

X-MEN: BLUE (Continued from All-New X-Men)
Marvel Comics: Jun, 2017 - No. 36, Nov, 2018 ($4.99/$3.99)

1-($4.99) Bunn-s/Molina-a; Juggernaut & Black Tom Cassidy app. — 5.00
2-24,26-36-($3.99): 4-Jimmy Hudson joins. 7-9-Secret Empire tie-ins. 13-15-"Mojo Worldwide." 18-Generation X app. 21,22-Venom app. — 4.00
25-($4.99) Bunn-s/Molina-a; Sebastian Shaw & Bastion app. — 5.00
Annual 1 (3/18, $4.99) Poison-X part 1; Venom app.; Bunn-s/Salazar-a — 5.00
... Origins 1 (1/24, $5.99) Origin of Nightcrawler; Mystique app. (see Uncanny Spider-Man) — 6.00

X-MEN BOOKS OF ASKANI
Marvel Comics: 1995 ($2.95, one-shot)

1-Painted pin-ups w/text — 4.00

X-MEN: CHILDREN OF THE ATOM
Marvel Comics: Nov, 1999 - No. 6 ($2.99, limited series)

1-6-Casey-s; X-Men before issue #1. 1-3-Rude-c/a. 4-Paul Smith-a/Rude-c. 5,6-Essad Ribic-c/a — 4.00
TPB (11/01, $16.95) r/series; sketch pages; Casey intro. — 17.00

X-MEN CHRONICLES
Marvel Comics: Mar, 1995 - No. 2, June, 1995 ($3.95, limited series)

1,2: Age of Apocalypse x-over. 1-wraparound-c — 5.00

X-MEN: CLANDESTINE
Marvel Comics: Oct, 1996 - No. 2, Nov, 1996 ($2.95, limited series, 48 pgs.)

1,2: Alan Davis-c(p)/a(p)/scripts & Mark Farmer-c(i)/a(i) in all; wraparound-c — 5.00

X-MEN CLASSIC (Formerly Classic X-Men)
Marvel Comics: No. 46, Apr, 1990 - No. 110, Aug, 1995 ($1.25/$1.50)

46-110: Reprints from X-Men. 54-(52 pgs.). 57,60-63,65-Russell-c(i); 62-r/X-Men #158 (Rogue). 66-r/#162 (Wolverine). 69-Begins-r of Paul Smith issues (#165 on). 70,79,90,97 (52 pgs.). 70-r/X-Men #166. 90-r/#186. 100-($1.50). 104-r/X-Men #200 — 4.00

X-MEN CLASSICS
Marvel Comics Group: Dec, 1983 - No. 3, Feb, 1984 ($2.00, Baxter paper)

1-3: X-Men-r by Neal Adams — 6.00
NOTE: Zeck c-1-3.

X-MEN: COLOSSUS BLOODLIINE
Marvel Comics: Nov, 2005 - No. 5, Mar, 2006 ($2.99, limited series)

1-5-Colossus returns to Russia; David Hine-s/Jorge Lucas-a; Bachalo-c — 3.00
TPB (2006, $13.99) r/#1-5 — 14.00

X-MEN: DAYS OF FUTURE PAST – DOOMSDAY
Marvel Comics: Sept, 2023 - No. 4, Dec, 2023 ($4.99/$3.99)

1-($4.99)-The events leading up to the dystopian future in Uncanny X-Men #141,142 — 5.00
2-4-($3.99) — 4.00

X-MEN: DEADLY GENESIS (See Uncanny X-Men #475)
Marvel Comics: Jan, 2006 - No. 6, July, 2006 ($3.99/$3.50, limited series)

1-($3.99) Silvestri-c swipe of Giant-Size X-Men #1; Hairsine-a/Brubaker-s — 4.00
2-6-($3.50) 2-Silvestri-c; Banshee killed. 4-Intro Kid Vulcan — 3.50
HC (2006, $24.99, dust jacket) r/#1-6 — 25.00

SC (2006, $19.99) r/#1-6 — 20.00

X-MEN: DIE BY THE SWORD
Marvel Comics: Dec, 2007 - No. 5, Feb, 2008 ($2.99, limited series)

1-5-Excalibur and The Exiles app.; Claremont-s/Santacruz-a — 3.00
TPB (2008, $13.99) r/#1-5; handbook pages of Merlyn, Roma and Saturne — 14.00

X-MEN: DIVIDED WE STAND
Marvel Comics: June, 2008 - No. 2, July, 2008 ($3.99, limited series)

1,2-Short stories by various; Peterson-c — 4.00

X-MEN: EARTHFALL
Marvel Comics: Sept, 1996 ($2.95, one-shot)

1-r/Uncanny X-Men #232-234; wraparound-c — 4.00

X-MEN: EMPEROR VULCAN
Marvel Comics: Nov, 2007 - No. 5, Mar, 2008 ($2.99, limited series)

1-5: 1-Starjammers app.; Yost-s/Diaz-a/Tan-c — 3.00
TPB (2008, $13.99) r/#1-5 — 14.00

X-MEN: EVOLUTION (Based on the animated series)
Marvel Comics: Feb, 2002 - No. 9, Sept, 2002 ($2.25)

1-9: 1-8-Grayson-s/Udon-a. 9-Farber-s/J.J.Kirby-a — 3.00
TPB (7/02, $8.99) r/#1-4 — 9.00
Vol. 2 TPB (2003, $11.99) r/#5-9; Asamiya-c — 12.00

X-MEN FAIRY TALES
Marvel Comics: July, 2006 - No. 4, Oct, 2006 ($2.99, limited series)

1-4-Re-imagining of classic stories; Cebulski-s. 2-Baker-a. 3-Sienkiewicz-a. 4-Kobayashi-a — 3.00
TPB (2006, $10.99) r/#1-4 — 11.00

X-MEN/ FANTASTIC FOUR
Marvel Comics: Feb, 2005 - No. 5, June, 2005 ($3.50, limited series)

1-5-Pat Lee-a/c; Yoshida-s; the Brood app. — 3.50
HC (2005, $19.99, 7 1/2" x 11", dustjacket) oversized r/#1-5; cover gallery — 20.00

X-MEN/ FANTASTIC FOUR
Marvel Comics: Apr, 2020 - No. 4, June, 2020 ($4.99, limited series)

1-4-Zdarsky-s/Dodson-a; Franklin recruited by X-Men; Doctor Doom app. — 5.00

X-MEN FIRST CLASS
Marvel Comics: Nov, 2006 - No. 8, Jun, 2007 ($2.99, limited series)

1-8-Xavier's first class of X-Men; Cruz-a/Parker-s. 5-Thor app. 7-Scarlet Witch app. — 3.00
... Special 1 (7/07, $3.99) Nowlan-c; Nowlan, Paul Smith, Coover, Dragotta & Allred-a — 4.00
... - Tomorrow's Brightest HC (2007, $24.99, d.j) r/#1-8; cover & character design art — 25.00
... - Tomorrow's Brightest SC (2007, $19.99) r/#1-8; cover & character design art — 20.00

X-MEN FIRST CLASS (2nd series)
Marvel Comics: Aug, 2007 - No. 16, Nov, 2008 ($2.99)

1-16: 1-Cruz-a/Parker-s; Fantastic Four app. 8-Man-Thing app. 10-Romita Jr.-c — 3.00
... Giant-Size Special 1 (12/08, $3.99) 5 new short stories; Haspiel-a; r/X-Men #40 — 4.00
... - Mutant Mayhem TPB (2008, $13.99) r/#1-5 & X-Men First Class Special — 14.00

X-MEN FIRST CLASS FINALS
Marvel Comics: Apr, 2009 - No. 4, July, 2009 ($3.99, limited series)

1-4-Cruz-a/Parker-s. 1-3-Coover-a — 4.00

X-MEN FIRSTS
Marvel Comics: Feb, 1996 ($4.95, one-shot)

1-r/Avengers Annual #10, Uncanny X-Men #266; #221; Incredible Hulk #181 — 5.00

X-MEN FOREVER
Marvel Comics: Jan, 2001 - No. 6, June, 2001 ($3.50, limited series)

1-6-Jean Grey, Iceman, Mystique, Toad, Juggernaut app.; Maguire-a — 4.00

X-MEN FOREVER
Marvel Comics: Aug, 2009 - No. 24, July, 2010 ($3.99)

1-24: 1-Claremont-s/Grummett-a/c. 7-Nick Fury app. — 4.00
... Alpha 1 (2009, $4.99) r/X-Men (1991) #1-3; 8 page preview of X-Men Forever #1 — 5.00
... Annual 1 (6/10, $4.99) Wolverine & Jean Grey romance; Sana Takeda-a/c — 5.00
... Giant-Size 1 (7/10, $3.99) Grell-a/c; Lilandra & Gladiator app.; r/(Uncanny)X-Men #108 — 4.00

X-MEN FOREVER 2
Marvel Comics: Aug, 2010 - No. 16, Mar, 2011 ($3.99)

1-16: 1-Claremont-s/Grummett-a/c. 2,3-Spider-Man app. 9,10-Grell-a — 4.00

X-MEN: GOLD
Marvel Comics: Jan, 2014 ($5.99, one-shot)

1-50th Anniversary anthology; short stories by various incl. Stan Lee, Simonson, Claremont, Thomas, Olliffe, Wein, Molina, McLeod, Larroca; Coipel-c — 6.00

X-MEN: GOLD
Marvel Comics: Jun, 2017 - No. 36, Nov, 2018 ($4.99/$3.99)

1-($4.99) Syaf-a; Storm, Nightcrawler, Old Man Logan, Colossus, Kitty Pryde team — 5.00
2-24-($3.99): 4-6-Silva-a. 7,8-Secret Empire tie-ins; Lashley-a. 13-15-"Mojo Worldwide" — 4.00
25-($4.99) Guggenheim-s/Siqueira-a; Captain Britain app. — 5.00
26-29,31-36: 26-29-Til Death Do Us Part; prelude to wedding of Kitty Pryde & Colossus — 4.00
30-($4.99) Wedding of Rogue and Gambit; leads into Mr. & Mrs. X series; Marquez-a — 5.00
Annual 1 (3/18, $4.99) Excalibur reunion; Capt. Britain app.; Martinez-a — 5.00
Annual 2 (11/18, $4.99) McGuire-s/Failla-a; 14-year-old Kitty Pryde at summer camp — 5.00

X-MEN: GRAND DESIGN
Marvel Comics: Feb, 2018 - No. 2, Mar, 2018 ($5.99, limited series)

1,2-Origins and early days of the X-Men re-told; Ed Piskor-s/a/c — 6.00

X-MEN: GRAND DESIGN - SECOND GENESIS
Marvel Comics: Sept, 2018 - No. 2, Oct, 2018 ($5.99, limited series)

1,2-Days of the X-Men from #94 (1975) to #186 (1984) re-told; Ed Piskor-s/a/c — 6.00

X-MEN: GRAND DESIGN - X-TINCTION
Marvel Comics: Jul, 2019 - No. 2, Aug, 2019 ($5.99, limited series)

1,2-Days of the X-Men from mid-'80s to early '90s re-told; Ed Piskor-s/a/c — 6.00

X-MEN: HELLBOUND
Marvel Comics: July, 2010 - No. 3, Sept, 2010 ($3.99, limited series)

X-Men Forever #18 © MAR

X-Men '92 #1 © MAR

X-Men: Red #4 © MAR

	GD	VG	FN	VF	VF/NM	NM-		GD	VG	FN	VF	VF/NM	NM-
	2.0	4.0	6.0	8.0	9.0	9.2		2.0	4.0	6.0	8.0	9.0	9.2

1-3-Second Coming x-over; Tolibao-a/Djurdjevic-c; Majik rescued from Limbo		4.00

X-MEN: HELLFIRE CLUB
Marvel Comics: Jan, 2000 - No. 4, Apr, 2000 ($2.50, limited series)

1-4-Origin of the Hellfire Club		3.00

X-MEN: HIDDEN YEARS
Marvel Comics: Dec, 1999 - No. 22, Sept. 2001 ($3.50/$2.50)

1-New adventures from pre-#94 era; Byrne-s/a(p)		5.00
2-4,6-11,13-22-($2.50): 2-Two covers. 3-Ka-Zar app. 8,9-FF-c/app.		4.00
5-($2.75)		4.00
12-($3.50) Magneto-c/app.		5.00

X-MEN: KING BREAKER
Marvel Comics: Feb, 2009 - No. 4, May, 2009 ($3.99, limited series)

1-4-Emperor Vulcan and a Shi'ar invasion; Havok, Rachel Grey and Polaris app.		4.00

X-MEN: KITTY PRYDE - SHADOW & FLAME
Marvel Comics: Aug, 2005 - No. 5, Dec, 2005 ($2.99, limited series)

1-5-Akira Yoshida-s/Paul Smith-a/c; Kitty & Lockheed go to Japan		3.00
TPB (2006, $14.99) r/#1-5		15.00

X-MEN LEGACY (See X-Men 2nd series)

X-MEN LEGACY (Marvel NOW!)
Marvel Comics: Jan, 2013 - No. 24, Apr, 2014; No. 300, May, 2014 ($2.99)

1-24: 1-Legion (Professor X's son); Spurrier-s/Huat-a. 2-X-Men app. 5,6-Molina-a		3.00
300-($4.99) Spurrier, Carey & Gage-s/Huat, Kurth & Sandoval-a; Mann-c		5.00

X-MEN LEGENDS
Marvel Comics: Apr, 2021 - No. 12, May, 2022 ($4.99/$3.99)

1-($4.99) Nicieza-s/Booth-a: the 1990s version of the X-Men & Cable app.		5.00
2-12-($3.99) 3,4,11-X-Factor; Louise Simonson-s/Walt Simonson-a. 7-9-Hama-s/Tan-a		4.00

X-MEN LEGENDS
Marvel Comics: Jul, 2022 - No. 6, Apr, 2023 ($3.99)

1-6: 1,2-Follows events of Incredible Hulk #181; Roy Thomas-s/Dave Wachter-a		4.00

X-MEN: LIBERATORS
Marvel Comics: Nov, 1998 - No. 4, Feb, 1999 ($2.99, limited series)

1-4-Wolverine, Nightcrawler & Colossus; P. Jimenez		4.00

X-MEN LOST TALES
Marvel Comics: 1997 ($2.99)

1,2-r/Classic X-Men back-up stories		4.00

X-MEN: MAGNETO TESTAMENT
Marvel Comics: Nov, 2008 - No. 5, Mar, 2009 ($3.99, limited series)

1-5-Max Eisenhardt in 1930s Nazi-occupied Poland; Pak-s/DiGiandomenico-a. 5-Back-up story of artist Dina Babbitt with Neal Adams-a		4.00

X-MEN: MANIFEST DESTINY
Marvel Comics: Nov, 2008 - No. 5, Mar, 2009 ($3.99, limited series)

1-5-Short stories of X-Men re-location to San Francisco; s/a by various		4.00
... Nightcrawler 1 (5/09, $3.99) Molina & Syaf-a; Mephisto app.		4.00

X-MEN: MESSIAH COMPLEX
Marvel Comics: Dec, 2007 ($3.99)

1-Part 1 of x-over with X-Men, Uncanny X-Men, X-Factor and New X-Men; 2 covers		4.00
... - Mutant Files (2007, $3.99) Handbook pages of x-over participants; Kolins-c		4.00
HC (2008, $39.99, oversized) r/#1, Uncanny X-Men #492-494, X-Men #205-207, New X-Men #44-46 and X-Factor #25-27		40.00

X-MEN '92 (Secret Wars tie-in)
Marvel Comics: Aug, 2015 - No. 4, Nov, 2015 ($4.99, limited series)

1-4-Koblish-a; Cassandra Nova app. 2-4-X-Force app. 4-Apocalypse cameo		5.00

X-MEN '92 (Follows Secret Wars)
Marvel Comics: May, 2016 - No. 10, Feb, 2017 ($3.99)

1-10: 1-Firmansyah-a; Omega Red & Alpha Red app. 2-U-Go Girl joins. 3,4-Dracula app. 9,10-New Mutants app.		4.00

X-MEN '92: HOUSE OF XCII
Marvel Comics: Jun, 2022 - No. 5, Nov, 2022 ($3.99, limited series)

1-5: 1-Foxe-s/Espin-a		4.00

X-MEN NOIR
Marvel Comics: Nov, 2008 - No. 4, May, 2009 ($3.99, limited series)

1-4-Pulp-style story set in 1930s NY; Van Lente-s/Calero-a		4.00
...: Mark of Cain (2/10 - No. 4, 5/10, $3.99) Van Lente-s/Calero-a		4.00

X-MEN OMEGA
Marvel Comics: June, 1995 ($3.95, one-shot)

	GD	VG	FN	VF	VF/NM	NM-
nn-Age of Apocalypse finale	2	4	6	9	13	16

nn-($49.95)-Gold edition		55.00

X-MEN: ORIGINS
Marvel Comics: Oct, 2008 - Sept, 2010 ($3.99, series of one-shots)

	GD	VG	FN	VF	VF/NM	NM-
...: Beast (11/08) High school years; Carey-s; painted-a/c by Woodward						5.00
...: Cyclops (3/10) Magneto app.; Delperdang-a/Granov-c						
		2	4	6	9	12	15
...: Deadpool (9/10) Fernandez-a/Swierczynski-s	4	8	12	25	40	55
...: Emma Frost (7/10) Moline-a; r/excerpt from 1st app. in Uncanny X-Men #129						
		2	4	6	9	12	15
...: Gambit (8/09) Mr. Sinister, Sabretooth and the Marauders app.; Yardin-a						
		3	6	9	14	20	26
...: Iceman (1/10) Noto-a						5.00
...: Jean Grey (10/08) Childhood & early X-days; McKeever-s; Mayhew painted-a/c						5.00
...: Nightcrawler (5/10) Cary Nord-a; r/excerpt from 1st app. in Giant-Size X-Men #1						5.00
...: Sabretooth (4/09) Childhood and early meetings with Wolverine; Panosian-a/c						
		1	2	3	5	6	8
...: Wolverine (6/09) Pre-X-Men days and first meeting with Xavier; Texeira-a/c						5.00

X-MEN: PHOENIX
Marvel Comics: Dec, 1999 - No. 3, Mar, 2000 ($2.50, limited series)

1-3: 1-Apocalypse app.		4.00

X-MEN: PHOENIX - ENDSONG
Marvel Comics: Mar, 2005 - No. 5, June, 2005 ($2.99, limited series)

1-5-The Phoenix Force returns to Earth; Greg Land-c/a; Greg Pak-s		3.00
HC (2005, $19.99, dust jacket) r/#1-5; Land sketch pages		20.00
SC (2006, $14.99)		15.00

X-MEN: PHOENIX - LEGACY OF FIRE
Marvel Comics: July, 2003 - No. 3, Sep, 2003 ($2.99, limited series)

1-3-Manga-style; Ryan Kinnard-s/a/c; intro page art by Adam Warren		3.00

X-MEN: PHOENIX - WARSONG
Marvel Comics: Nov, 2006 - No. 5, Mar, 2007 ($2.99, limited series)

1-5-Tyler Kirkham-a/Greg Pak-s/Marc Silvestri-c		3.00
HC (2007, $19.99, dustjacket) r/#1-5; variant cover gallery and Handbook pages		20.00
SC (2007, $14.99) r/#1-5; variant cover gallery and Handbook pages		15.00

X-MEN: PIXIE STRIKES BACK
Marvel Comics: Apr, 2010 - No. 4, July, 2010 ($3.99, limited series)

1-4-Kathryn Immonen-s/Sara Pichelli-a/Stuart Immonen-c		4.00

X-MEN: PRELUDE TO SCHISM
Marvel Comics: Jul, 2011 - No. 4, Aug, 2011 ($2.99, limited series)

1-4-Jenkins-s/Camuncoli-c. 1-De La Torre-a. 2-Magneto childhood. 3-Conrad-a		3.00

X-MEN PRIME
Marvel Comics: July, 1995 ($4.95, one-shot)

	GD	VG	FN	VF	VF/NM	NM-
nn-Post Age of Apocalypse begins		2	4	6	8	10	12

X-MEN PRIME
Marvel Comics: May, 2017 ($4.99, one-shot)

1-Preludes to X-Men: Blue #1, X-Men: Gold #1 and Weapon X #1		5.00

X-MEN RARITIES
Marvel Comics: 1995 ($5.95, one-shot)

nn-Reprints hard-to-find stories		6.00

X-MEN: RED
Marvel Comics: Apr, 2018 - No. 11, Feb, 2019 ($4.99/$3.99)

1-($4.99) Asrar-a; Jean Grey, Nightcrawler, Namor, Wolverine (X-23) team		5.00
2-11-($3.99) 4-Black Panther app.		4.00
Annual 1 (7/18, $4.99) Taylor-s/Alixe-a; Black Bolt app.		5.00

X-MEN RED
Marvel Comics: Jun, 2022 - No. 10, Mar, 2023 ($4.99/$3.99)

1-($4.99) Ewing-s/Caselli-a; new Brotherhood of Mutants is formed		5.00
2-15,17,18-($3.99) Cable app. 5-7-Judgment Day tie-ins		4.00
16-($4.99) Back-up story with Sunspot & Shark-Girl		5.00

X-MEN ROAD TO ONSLAUGHT
Marvel Comics: Oct, 1996 ($2.50, one-shot)

nn-Retells Onslaught Saga		4.00

X-MEN: RONIN
Marvel Comics: May, 2003 - No. 5, July, 2003 ($2.99, limited series)

1-5-Manga-style X-Men; Torres-s/Nakatsuka-a		3.00

X-MEN: SCHISM
Marvel Comics: Sept, 2011 - No. 5, Dec, 2011 ($4.99/$3.99, limited series)

1-($4.99) Aaron-s/Pacheco-a/c		5.00

	GD	VG	FN	VF	VF/NM	NM-
	2.0	4.0	6.0	8.0	9.0	9.2

2-5-($3.99) 2-Cho-a/c. 3-Acuña-a/c. 4-Alan Davis-a/c. 5-Adam Kubert-a — 4.00

X-MEN: SEARCH FOR CYCLOPS
Marvel Comics: Oct, 2000 - No. 4, Mar, 2001 ($2.99, limited series)
1-4-Two covers (Raney, Pollina); Raney-a — 4.00

X-MEN: SECOND COMING
Marvel Comics: May, 2010 - No. 2, Sept, 2010 ($3.99)
1-Cable & Hope return to the present; Bastion app.; Finch-a; covers by Granov & Finch — 4.00
2-Conclusion to x-over; covers by Granov & Finch — 4.00
...: Prepare (4/10, free) previews x-over; short story w/Immonen-a; cover sketch art — 3.00

X-MEN / SPIDER-MAN ("X-Men and Spider-Man" on cover)
Marvel Comics: Jan, 2009 - No. 4, Apr, 2009 ($3.99, limited series)
1-4: 1-Team-up from pre-blue Beast days; Kraven app.; Gage-s/Alberti-a — 4.00

X-MEN SPOTLIGHT ON... STARJAMMERS (Also see X-Men #104)
Marvel Comics: 1990 - No. 2, 1990 ($4.50, 52 pgs.)
1,2: Features Starjammers — 5.00

X-MEN SURVIVAL GUIDE TO THE MANSION
Marvel Comics: Aug, 1993 ($6.95, spiralbound)
1 — 7.00

X-MEN: THE COMPLETE AGE OF APOCALYPSE EPIC
Marvel Comics: 2005 - Vol. 4, 2006 ($29.99, TPB)
Book 1-4: Chronological reprintings of the crossover — 30.00

X-MEN: THE EARLY YEARS
Marvel Comics: May, 1994 - No. 17, Sept, 1995 ($1.50/$2.50)
1-16: r/X-Men #1-8 w/new-c — 4.00
17-$2.50-c; r/X-Men #17,18 — 5.00

X-MEN: THE END
Marvel Comics: Oct, 2004 - No. 6, Feb, 2005 ($2.99, limited series)
1-6-Claremont-s/Chen-a/Land-c — 3.00
... Book One: Dreamers and Demons TPB (2005, $14.99) r/#1-6 — 15.00

X-MEN: THE END - HEROES AND MARTYRS (Volume 2)
Marvel Comics: May, 2005 - No. 6, Oct, 2005 ($2.99, limited series)
1-6-Claremont-s/Chen-a/Land-c; continued from X-Men: The End — 3.00
... Vol. 2 TPB (2006, $14.99) r/#1-6 — 15.00

X-MEN: THE END (MEN & X-MEN) (Volume 3)
Marvel Comics: Mar, 2006 - No. 6, Aug, 2006 ($2.99, limited series)
1-6-Claremont-s/Chen-a. 1-Land-c. 2-6-Gene Ha-c — 3.00
... Vol. 3 TPB (2006, $14.99) r/#1-6 — 15.00

X-MEN: THE EXTERMINATED
Marvel Comics: Feb, 2019 ($4.99, one-shot)
1-Prelude to Uncanny X-Men #1 (2019); Hope and Jean Grey story; Deadpool app. — 5.00

X-MEN: THE MANGA
Marvel Comics: Mar, 1998 - No. 26, June, 1999 ($2.99, B&W)
1-26-English version of Japanese X-Men comics: 23,24-Randy Green-c — 4.00

X-MEN: THE MOVIE
Marvel Comics: Aug, 2000; Sept, 2000
Adaptation (9/00, $5.95) Macchio-s/Williams & Lanning-a — 6.00
Adaptation TPB (9/00, $14.95) Movie adaptation and key reprints of main characters; four photo covers (movie X, Magneto, Rogue, Wolverine) — 15.00
Prequel: Magneto (8/00, $5.95) Texeira & Palmiotti-a; art & photo covers — 6.00
Prequel: Rogue (8/00, $5.95) Evans & Nikolakakis-a; art & photo covers — 6.00
Prequel: Wolverine (8/00, $5.95) Waller & McKenna-a; art & photo covers — 6.00
TPB X-Men: Beginnings (8/00, $14.95) reprints 3 prequels w/photo-c — 15.00

X-MEN 2: THE MOVIE
Marvel Comics: 2003
Adaptation (6/03, $3.50) Movie adaptation; photo-c; Austen-s/Zircher-a — 4.00
Adaptation TPB (6/03, $12.99) Movie adaptation & r/Prequels Nightcrawler & Wolverine — 13.00
Prequel: Nightcrawler (5/03, $3.50) Kerschl-a; photo cover — 4.00
Prequel: Wolverine (5/03, $3.50) Mandrake-a; photo cover; Sabretooth app. — 4.00

X-MEN: THE 198 (See House of M)
Marvel Comics: Mar, 2006 - No. 5, July, 2006 ($2.99, limited series)
1-5-Hine-s/Muniz-a — 3.00
... Files (2006, $3.99) profiles of the 198 mutants who kept their powers after House of M — 4.00
Decimation: The 198 (2006, $15.99, TPB) r/#1-5 & X-Men: The 198 Files — 16.00

X-MEN: THE TIMES AND LIFE OF LUCAS BISHOP
Marvel Comics: Apr, 2009 - No. 3, June, 2009 ($3.99, limited series)
1-3-Swierczynski-s/Stroman-a. 1-Bishop's birth and childhood — 4.00

X-MEN: THE TRIAL OF MAGNETO
Marvel Comics: Oct, 2021 - No. 5, Feb, 2022 ($3.99, limited series)
1-5-Leah Williams-s/Lucas Werneck-a. 5-Thunderbird returns — 4.00

X-MEN: THE ULTRA COLLECTION
Marvel Comics: Dec, 1994 - No. 5, Apr, 1995 ($2.95, limited series)
1-5: Pin-ups; no scripts — 4.00

X-MEN: THE WEDDING ALBUM
Marvel Comics: 1994 ($2.95, magazine size, one-shot)
1-Wedding of Scott Summers & Jean Grey — 4.00

X-MEN: THE WEDDING SPECIAL
Marvel Comics: Jul, 2018 ($4.99, one-shot)
1-Prelude to wedding of Kitty Pryde & Colossus; art by Nauck, Land & Cresta — 5.00

X-MEN: TO SERVE AND PROTECT
Marvel Comics: Jan, 2011 - No. 4, Apr, 2011 ($3.99, limited series)
1-4-Short story anthology by various.1-Bradshaw-c. 2-Camuncoli-c — 4.00

X-MEN TRUE FRIENDS
Marvel Comics: Sept, 1999 - No. 3, Nov, 1999 ($2.99, limited series)
1-3-Claremont-s/Leonardi-a — 4.00

X-MEN 2099 (Also see 2099: World of Tomorrow)
Marvel Comics: Oct, 1993 - No. 35, Aug, 1996 ($1.25/$1.50/$1.95)

Description	2.0	4.0	6.0	8.0	9.0	9.2
1-($1.75)-Foil-c; Ron Lim/Adam Kubert-a begins	1	2	3		5	6	8

1-2nd printing ($1.75) — 4.00
1-Gold edition (15,000 made); sold thru Diamond for $19.40 — 20.00
2-24,26-35: 3-Death of Tina; Lim-c/a(p) in #1-8. 8-Bound-in trading card sheet. 35-Nostromo (from X-Nation) app; storyline cont'd in 2099: World of Tomorrow — 4.00
25-($2.50)-Double sized — 5.00
Special 1 ($3.95) — 5.00
...: Oasis ($5.95, one-shot) -Hildebrandt Bros.-c/a — 6.00

X-MEN ULTRA III PREVIEW
Marvel Comics: 1995 ($2.95)
nn-Kubert-a — 4.00

X-MEN UNIVERSE
Marvel Comics: Dec, 1999 - No. 15, Feb, 2001 ($4.99/$3.99)
1-8-Reprints stories from recent X-Men titles — 5.00
9-15-($3.99) — 4.00

X-MEN UNIVERSE: PAST, PRESENT AND FUTURE
Marvel Comics: Feb, 1999 ($2.99, one-shot)

Description	2.0	4.0	6.0	8.0	9.0	9.2
1-Previews 1999 X-Men events; background info	1	3	4	6	8	10

X-MEN UNLIMITED
Marvel Comics: 1993 - No. 50, Sept, 2003 ($3.95/$2.99, 68 pgs.)

Description	2.0	4.0	6.0	8.0	9.0	9.2
1-Chris Bachalo-c/a; Quesada-a.	2	4	6	8	10	12

2-11: 2-Origin of Magneto script. 3-Sabretooth-c/story. 10-Dark Beast vs. Beast; Mark Waid script. 11-Magneto & Rogue — 6.00
12-33: 12-Begin $2.99-c; Onslaught x-over; Juggernaut-c/app. 19-Caliafore-a. 20-Generation X app. 27-Origin Thunderbird. 29-Maximum Security x-over; Bishop-c/app. 30-Mahfood-a. 31-Stelfreeze-c/a. 32-Dazzler; Thompson-c/a 33-Kaluta-c — 5.00
34-37,39,40,42-($3.50) 34-Von Eeden-a. 35-Finch, Conner, Maguire-a. 36-Chiodo-c/a; Larroca, Tolleben-a. 39-Bachalo-c; Pearson-a. 41-Bachalo-c; X-Statix app. — 5.00
38-($2.25) Kitty Pryde; Robertson-a — 4.00
43-50-($2.50) 43-Sienkiewicz-c/a; Paul Smith-a. 45-Noto-c. 46-Bisley-a. 47-Warren-s/Mays-a. 48-Wolverine story w/Isanove painted-a — 4.00
X-Men Legends Vol. 4: Hated and Feared TPB (2003, $19.99) r/stories by various — 20.00
NOTE: *Bachalo* c/a-1. *Quesada* a-1. *Waid* scripts-10

X-MEN UNLIMITED
Marvel Comics: Apr, 2004 - No. 14, Jun, 2006 ($2.99)
1-14: 1-6-Pat Lee-c; short stories by various. 2-District X preview; Granov-a — 3.00

X-MEN UNLIMITED...
Marvel Comics: May, 2022 - Present ($5.99)
...: Latitude 1 (5/22, $5.99) Hickman-s/Shalvey-a — 6.00
...: X-Men Green 1,2 (7/22, 11/22, $5.99) Duggan-s/Laiso-a. 2-Sauron app. — 6.00

X-MEN VS. AGENTS OF ATLAS
Marvel Comics: Dec, 2009 - No. 2, Jan, 2010 ($3.99, limited series)
1,2-Pagulayan-a. 1-McGuinness-c. 2-Granov-c — 4.00

X-MEN VS. DRACULA
Marvel Comics: Dec, 1993 ($1.75)

Description	2.0	4.0	6.0	8.0	9.0	9.2
1-r/X-Men Annual #6; Austin-c(i)	1	2	3		5	6	8

X-MEN VS. THE AVENGERS, THE
Marvel Comics Group: Apr, 1987 - No. 4, July, 1987 ($1.50, limited series, Baxter paper)

Description	2.0	4.0	6.0	8.0	9.0	9.2
1-Silvestri-a/c	2	4	6	8	10	12

2-4: 2,3-Silvestri-a/c. 4-Pollard-a/c — 5.00

X-MEN VS. THE BROOD, THE
Marvel Comics Group: Sept, 1996 - No. 2, Oct, 1996 ($2.95, limited series)
1,2-Wraparound-c; Ostrander-s/Hitch-a(p) — 4.00
TPB ('97, $16.99) reprints X-Men/Brood: Day of Wrath #1,2 & Uncanny X-Men #232-234 — 17.00

X-MEN VISIONARIES
Marvel Comics: 1995,1996,2000 (trade paperbacks)
nn-($8.95) Reprints X-Men stories; Adam & Andy Kubert-a — 9.00
...: The Neal Adams Collection (1996) r/X-Men #56-63,65 — 30.00
...2: The Neal Adams Col. (2nd printing, 2000, $24.95) new Adams-c — 25.00

X-MEN/WILDC.A.T.S.: THE DARK AGE (See also WildC.A.T.S./X-Men...)
Marvel Comics: 1998 ($4.50, one-shot)
1-Two covers (Broome & Golden); Ellis-s — 5.00

X-MEN: WORLDS APART
Marvel Comics: Dec, 2008 - No. 4, Mar, 2009 ($3.99, limited series)
1-4-Storm and the Black Panther vs. the Shadow King. 1-Campbell-c — 4.00

X-MEN: WORST X-MAN EVER
Marvel Comics: Apr, 2016 - No. 5, Aug, 2016 ($3.99, limited series)
1-5: 1-Intro. Bailey Hoskins; Max Bemis-s/Michael Walsh-a. 3,4-Magneto app. — 4.00

X-NATION 2099
Marvel Comics: Mar, 1996 - No. 6, Aug, 1996 ($1.95)
1-($3.95)-Humberto Ramos-a(p); wraparound, foil-c — 5.00
2-6: 2,3-Ramos-a. 4-Exodus-c/app. 6-Reed Richards app — 5.00

X NECROSIA
Marvel Comics: Dec, 2009 ($3.99)
1-Beginning of X-Force/X-Men/New Mutants x-over; Crain-a; Selene returns — 4.00
...: The Gathering (2/10, $3.99) Wither, Blink, Senyaka, Mortis & Eliphas short stories — 4.00

X OF SWORDS (Marvel Event crossing over Wolverine, Cable, and the X-Men titles)
Marvel Comics: Nov, 2020 - Jan, 2021 ($6.99/$4.99)
...: Creation (11/20, $6.99) Part 1 of crossover; Hickman & Howard-s/Larraz-a — 7.00
...: Destruction (1/21, $4.99) Part 22 conclusion; Hickman & Howard-s/Larraz & Gracia-a — 5.00
...: Handbook (11/20, $4.99) Profile pages of the mutants of Krakoa — 5.00
...: Stasis (12/20, $4.99) Part 11 of crossover; Hickman & Howard-s/Larraz & Asrar-a — 5.00

X-Men 2099 #29 © MAR

X-O Manowar (2017 series) #18 © VAL

X-Ray Robot #2 © Mike Allred

	GD 2.0	VG 4.0	FN 6.0	VF 8.0	VF/NM 9.0	NM- 9.2

X-O MANOWAR (1st Series)
Valiant/Acclaim Comics (Valiant) No. 43 on: Feb, 1992 - No. 68, Sept, 1996
($1.95/$2.25/$2.50, high quality)

0-(8/93, $3.50)-Wraparound embossed chromium-c by Quesada; Solar app.; origin Aric (X-O Manowar)	1	3	4	6	8	10
0-Gold variant	3	6	9	21	33	45
1-Intro/1st app. & partial origin of Aric (X-O Manowar); Barry Smith/Layton-a; Shooter & Englehart-s	3	6	9	21	33	45
2,3: 2-B. Smith/Layton-c. 3-Layton-c(i)	2	4	6	8	10	12
4-1st app. Shadowman; Harbinger app.	4	8	12	23	37	50
5,6: 5-B. Smith-c. 6-Begin $2.25-c; Ditko-a(p)	1	2	3	5	6	8
7-15: 7,8-Unity x-overs. 7-Miller-c. 8-Simonson-c. 12-1st app. Randy Calder. 14,15-Turok-c/stories						4.00
15-Hot pink logo variant; came with Ultra Pro Rigid Comic Sleeves box; no price on-c	1	3	4	6	8	10
16-24,26-43: 20-Serial number contest insert. 27-29-Turok x-over. 28-Bound-in trading card. 30-1st app. new "good skin"; Solar app. 33-Chaos Effect Delta Pt. 3. 42-Shadowman app.; includes X-O Manowar Birthquake! Prequel						3.00
25-($3.50)-Has 16 pg. Armorines #0 bound-in w/origin						4.00
44-66: 44-Begin $2.50-c. 50-X, 50-O, 51, 52, 63-Bart Sears-c/a/scripts						3.00
67	1	2	3	5	6	8
68-Revealed that Aric's past stories were premonitions of his future	3	6	9	16	23	30
...: Birth HC (2008, $24.95) recolored reprints #0-6; script and breakdowns for #0; cover gallery; new "The Rise of Lydia" story by Layton and Leeke						25.00
Trade paperback nn (1993, $9.95)-Polybagged with copy of X-O Database #1 inside						15.00
Yearbook 1 (4/95, $2.95)						4.00

NOTE: **Layton** a-1i, 2i(part); c-1, 2i, 3i, 6i, 21i. **Reese** a-4i(part); c-26i.

X-O MANOWAR (2nd Series)(Also see Iron Man/X-O Manowar: Heavy Metal)
Acclaim Comics (Valiant Heroes): V2#1, Oct, 1996 - No. 21, Jun, 1998 ($2.50)

V2#1-21: 1-Mark Waid & Brian Augustyn scripts begin; 1st app. Donavon Wylie; Rand Banion dies; painted mirage exists. 2-Donavon Wylie becomes new X-O Manowar. 7-9-Augustyn-s. 10-Copycat-c	4.00

X-O MANOWAR (3rd series)
Valiant Entertainment: May, 2012 - No. 50, Sept 2016 ($3.99)

1-Robert Venditti-s/Cary Nord-a/Esad Ribic-c; origin re-told	4.00
1-Pullbox variant-c by Nord	5.00
1-Variant-c by David Aja	10.00
1-QR Voice variant-c by Jelena Kevic-Djurdjevic	25.00
2-24: 2-Origin continues. 2,3-Kevic-Djurdjevic-c. 5-8-Ninjak app.; Garbett-a. 9,10-Hairsine-a 11-14-Planet Death; Nord-a. 19-21-Unity tie-in	4.00
2-5,8-14-Pullbox variant covers. 2-Lozzi. 3-Suayan. 4-Kramer. 5-Tan. 14-Eight-bit art	5.00
25-($4.99) Hitch-a; Armor Hunters app., Owly & Wormy short story by Runton	5.00
26-37,39-49: 26-29-Armor Hunters tie-in. 30-32-Armorines app. 34-37-Dead Hand. 47-49-Polybagged with micro-print	4.00
38-(7/15, $4.99) Wedding of Aric and Saana; Doctor Mirage app.; flashbacks	5.00
50-(9/16, $4.99) Polybagged; wraparound-c by 50 artists; art by various	5.00
#0 (10/14, $3.99) Flashback to Aric before his kidnapping; Clay Mann-a	4.00
Annual 2016 #1 (5/16, $5.99) Art by JG Jones, Perez, McKone, Gorham, De La Torre	6.00
...: Commander Trill #0 (12/15, $3.99) Origin of Trill; Venditti-s/Portela-a	4.00
...: Valiant 25th Anniversary Special (6/15, $3.99) Origin of Shanhara; Venditti-s/Cafu-a	4.00

X-O MANOWAR (2017) (4th series)
Valiant Entertainment: Mar, 2017 - No. 26, Apr, 2019 ($3.99)

1-26: 1-Kindt-s/Giorello-a; Aric on planet Gorin. 4-6 Braithwaite-a. 7-9-Crain-a	4.00

X-O MANOWAR (5th series)
Valiant Entertainment: Mar, 2020 - No. 9, Dec, 2021 ($3.99)

1-9-Hallum-s/Laiso-a. 1-Bonus preview of Final Witness #1	4.00

X-O MANOWAR (6th series)("Unconquered" on cover)
Valiant Entertainment: Mar, 2023 - No. 6, Feb, 2024 ($3.99)

1-6-Becky Cloonan & Michael Conrad-s/Liam Sharp-a	4.00

X-O MANOWAR FAN EDITION
Acclaim Comics (Valiant Heroes): Feb, 1997 (Overstreet's FAN giveaway)

1-Reintro the Armorines & the Hard Corps; 1st app. Citadel; Augustyn scripts; McKone-c/a	5.00

X-O MANOWAR/IRON MAN: IN HEAVY METAL (See Iron Man/X-O Manowar: Heavy Metal)
Acclaim Comics (Valiant Heroes): Sept, 1996 ($2.50, one-shot)
(1st Marvel/Valiant x-over)

1-Pt 1 of X-O Manowar/Iron Man x-over; Arnim Zola app.; Nicieza scripts; Andy Smith-a	5.00

XOMBI
DC Comics (Milestone): Jan, 1994 - No. 21, Feb, 1996 ($1.75/$2.50)

0-($1.95)-Shadow War x-over; Simonson silver ink varnish-c					
	1	3	4	6	8	10

	GD 2.0	VG 4.0	FN 6.0	VF 8.0	VF/NM 9.0	NM- 9.2
1-John Byrne-c	1	2	3	5	6	8
1-Platinum	2	4	6	9	12	15
2-21						5.00

XOMBI
DC Comics: May, 2011 - No. 6, Oct, 2011 ($2.99)

1-6-Rozum-s/Irving-a/c	3.00

X-PATROL
Marvel Comics (Amalgam): Apr, 1996 ($1.95, one-shot)

1-Cruz-a(p)	4.00

X-RAY ROBOT
Dark Horse Comics: Mar, 2020 - No. 4, Nov, 2020 ($3.99)

1-4-Mike Allred-s/a. 4-Madman app.	4.00

XSE
Marvel Comics: Nov, 1996 - No. 4, Feb, 1997 ($1.95, limited series)

1-4: 1-Bishop & Shard app.	4.00
1-Variant-c	5.00

X-STATIX
Marvel Comics: Sept, 2002 - No. 26, Oct, 2004 ($2.99/$2.25)

1-($2.99) Allred-a/c; intro. Venus Dee Milo; back-up w/Cooke-a	4.00
2-9-($2.25) 4-Quitely-c. 5-Pope-c/a	3.00
10-26: 10-Begin $2.99-c; Bond-a; U-Go Girl flashback. 13,14-Spider-Man app. 21-25-Avengers app. 26-Team dies	3.00
...: Vol. 1: Good Omens TPB (2003, $11.99) r/#1-5	12.00
...: Vol. 2: Good Guys & Bad Guys TPB (2003, $15.99) r/#6-10 & Wolverine/Doop #1&2	16.00
...: Vol. 3: Back From the Dead TPB (2004, $19.99) r/#11-18	20.00
...: Vol. 4: X-Statix Vs. the Avengers TPB (2004, $19.99) r/#19-26; pin-ups	20.00

X-STATIX PRESENTS: DEAD GIRL
Marvel Comics: Mar, 2006 - No. 5, July, 2006 ($2.99, limited series)

1-5-Dr. Strange, Dead Girl, Miss America, Tike app. Milligan-s/Dragotta & Allred-a	3.00
TPB (2006, $13.99) r/series	14.00

X-TERMINATION (Crossover with Astonishing X-Men and X-Treme X-Men)
Marvel Comics: May, 2013 - No. 2, Jun, 2013 ($3.99)

1,2-Lapham-s/David Lopez-a	4.00

X-TERMINATORS
Marvel Comics: Oct, 1988 - No. 4, Jan, 1989 ($1.00, limited series)

1-1st app.; X-Men/X-Factor tie-in; Williamson-i	5.00
2-4	4.00

X-TERMINATORS
Marvel Comics: Nov, 2022 - No. 5, Mar, 2023 ($4.99, limited series)

1-($4.99)-Leah Williams-s/Carlos Gomez-a; Dazzler, Boom-Boom, Jubilee, X-23 app.	5.00
2-5-($3.99)	4.00

X, THE MAN WITH THE X-RAY EYES (See Movie Comics)

X-TINCTION AGENDA (Secret Wars tie-in)
Marvel Comics: Aug, 2015 - No. 4, Nov, 2015 ($3.99, limited series)

1-4-Guggenheim-s/Di Giandomenico-a; Havok & Wolfsbane app.	4.00

X-TREME X-MEN (Also see Mekanix)
Marvel Comics: July, 2001 - No. 46, Jun, 2004 ($2.99/$3.50)

1-Claremont-s/Larroca-c/a	4.00
2-24: 2-Two covers (Larroca & Pacheco); Psylocke killed	3.00
25-35, 40-46: 25-30-God Loves, Man Kills II; Stryker app.; Kordey-a	3.00
36-39-($3.50)	3.50
Annual 2001 ($4.95) issue opens longways	5.00
...: Vol. 1: Destiny TPB (2002, $19.95) r/#1-9	20.00
...: Vol. 2: Invasion TPB (2003, $19.99) r/#10-18	20.00
...: Vol. 3: Schism TPB (2003, $16.99) r/#19-23; X-Treme X-Posé #1&2	17.00
...: Vol. 4: Mekanix TPB (2003, $16.99) r/Mekanix #1-6	17.00
...: Vol. 5: God Loves Man Kills TPB (2003, $19.99) r/#25-30	20.00
...: Vol. 6: Intifada TPB (2004, $16.99) r/#24,31-35	17.00
...: Vol. 7: Storm the Arena TPB (2004, $16.99) r/#36-39	17.00
...: Vol. 8: Prisoner of Fire TPB (2004, $19.99) r/#40-46 and Annual 2001	20.00

X-TREME X-MEN
Marvel Comics: Sept, 2012 - No. 13, Jun, 2013 ($2.99)

1-13: 1-Pak-s/Segovia-a; Dazzler with alternate reality Wolverine, Nightcrawler, Emma 7.1-(2/12) Cyclops & The Brood app.	3.00
	3.00

X-TREME X-MEN
Marvel Comics: Jan, 2023 - Present ($3.99)

1-5-Claremont-s/Larroca-c/a	4.00

X-TREME X-MEN: SAVAGE LAND

	GD 2.0	VG 4.0	FN 6.0	VF 8.0	VF/NM 9.0	NM- 9.2

Marvel Comics: Nov, 2001 - No. 4, Feb, 2002 ($2.99, limited series)
1-4-Claremont-s/Sharpe-c/a; Beast app. 3.00

X-TREME X-POSE
Marvel Comics: Jan, 2003 - No. 2, Feb, 2003 ($2.99, limited series)
1,2-Claremont-s/Ranson-a/Migliari-c 3.00

X-23 (See debut in NYX #3)(See NYX X-23 HC for reprint)
Marvel Comics: Mar, 2005 - No. 6, July, 2005 ($2.99, limited series)

1-Origin of the Wolverine clone girl; Tan-a	3	6	9	16	24	32
1-Variant Billy Tan-c with red background	3	6	9	17	25	34
2-6-Origin continues	1	3	4	6	8	10
2-Variant B&W sketch-c	2	4	6	9	12	15

One shot 1 (5/10, $3.99) Urasov-c/Liu-s; Wolverine & Jubilee app.

	3	6	9	19	30	40
...: Innocence Lost MGC 1 (5/11, $1.00) r/#1 with "Marvel's Greatest Comics" cover logo						3.00
... Innocence Lost TPB (2006, $15.99) r/#1-6						20.00
... No. 1 Facsimile Edition (5/23, $3.99) r/#1 with original 2005 ads						4.00

X-23
Marvel Comics: Nov, 2010 - No. 21, May, 2012 ($3.99/$2.99)

1-Marjorie Liu-s/Will Conrad-a; origin retold; Luo-c	3	6	9	17	26	35
1-Djurdjevic variant-c	10	20	30	64	132	200
1-Dell'Otto variant-c	26	52	78	180	404	625
2-Luo-c	2	4	6	8	11	14
2-Mayhew variant-c	7	14	21	46	86	125
3-21: 3,10-12,17-19-Takeda-a. 8,9-Daken app. 13-16-Spider-man app.; Noto-a.						
20-Jubilee app.; Noto-a. 21-Silent issue; Noto-a						4.00

X-23
Marvel Comics: Sept, 2018 - No. 12, Jul, 2019 ($4.99/$3.99)
1-($4.99) Tamaki-s/Cabal-a; Honey Badger and the Stepford Cuckoos app. 5.00
2-12-($3.99) 7-Intro X-Assassin 4.00

X-23: DEADLY REGENESIS
Marvel Comics: May, 2023 - No. 5, Sept, 2023 ($4.99/$3.99)
1-($4.99) Schultz-s/Salazar-a 5.00
2-5-($3.99) 4,5-Kingpin app. 4.00

X-23: TARGET X
Marvel Comics: Feb, 2007 - No. 6, July, 2007 ($2.99, limited series)

1-Kyle & Yost-s/Choi & Oback-a	3	6	9	14	20	26
2-6: 6-Gallery of variant covers and sketches						6.00
TPB (2007, $15.99) r/#1-6; gallery of variant covers and sketches						16.00

X-UNIVERSE
Marvel Comics: May, 1995 - No. 2, June, 1995 ($3.50, limited series)
1,2: Age of Apocalypse 5.00

X-VENTURE (Super Heroes)
Victory Magazines Corp.: July, 1947 - No. 2, Nov, 1947
1-Atom Wizard, Mystery Shadow, Lester Trumble begin

	168	336	504	1075	1838	2600
2	74	148	222	470	810	1150

X-WOMEN
Marvel Comics: 2010 ($4.99, one-shot)
1-Milo Manara-a/Chris Claremont-s; a female X-Men adventure; Quesada afterword 5.00

XYR (See Eclipse Graphic Album Series #21)

YAK YAK
Dell Publishing Co.: No. 1186, May-July, 1961 - No. 1348, Apr-June, 1962
Four Color 1186 (#1)- Jack Davis-c/a; 2 versions, one minus 3 pgs.

	8	16	24	56	108	160
Four Color 1348 (#2)-Davis c/a	7	14	21	46	86	125

YAKKY DOODLE & CHOPPER (TV) (See Dell Giant #44)
Gold Key: Dec, 1962 (Hanna-Barbera)

1	8	16	24	56	108	160

YANG (See House of Yang)
Charlton Comics: Nov, 1973 - No. 13, May, 1976; V14#15, Sept, 1985 - No. 17, Jan, 1986
(No V14#14, series resumes with #15)

1-Origin; Sattler-a begins; slavery-s	3	6	9	14	20	25
2-13(1976)	1	2	3	6	9	10
15-17(1986): 15-Reprints #1 (Low print run)						6.00
3,10,11(Modern Comics-r, 1977)						6.00

YANKEE COMICS
Harry 'A' Chesler: Sept, 1941 - No. 7, 1942?
1-Origin The Echo, The Enchanted Dagger, Yankee Doodle Jones, The Firebrand, & The Scarlet Sentry; Black Satan app. on all covers

	271	542	813	1734	2967	4200

2-Origin Johnny Rebel; Major Victory app.; Barry Kuda begins

	123	246	369	787	1344	1900
3,4: 4-(3/42)	103	206	309	659	1130	1600

4 (nd, 1940s; 7-1/4x5", 68 pgs, distr. to the service)-Foxy Grandpa, Tom, Dick & Harry, Impy, Ace & Deuce, Dot & Dash, Ima Slooth by Jack Cole (Remington Morse publ.)

	22	44	66	132	216	300

5-7 (nd; 10¢, 7-1/4x5", 68 pgs.)(Remington Morse publ.)-urges readers to send their copies to servicemen

	20	40	60	114	182	250

YANKEE DOODLE THE SPIRIT OF LIBERTY
Spire Publications: 1984 (no price, 36 pgs)
nn-Al Hartley-s/c/a | 2 | 4 | 6 | 9 | 13 | 16 |

YANKS IN BATTLE
Quality Comics Group: Sept, 1956 - No. 4, Dec, 1956

1-Cuidera-c(i)	18	36	54	103	162	220
2-4: Cuidera-c(i)	12	24	36	67	94	120

YARDBIRDS, THE (G. I. Joe's Sidekicks)

Ziff-Davis Publishing Co.: Summer, 1952

1-By Bob Oskner	42	84	126	265	445	625

YARNS OF YELLOWSTONE
World Color Press: 1972 (50¢, 36 pgs.)

nn-Illustrated by Bill Chapman	2	4	6	9	12	15

YEAH!
DC Comics (Homage): Oct, 1999 - No. 9, Jun, 2000 ($2.95)
1-Bagge-s/Hernandez-a 4.00
2-9: 2-Editorial page contains adult language 4.00

YEAR OF MARVELS, A
Marvel Comics: ($4.99)
...: The Amazing (6/16) Spider-Man vs. the Vulture; Ant-Man 5.00
...: The Incredible (8/16) Spider-Man & D-Man story; Wolverine (X-23) & She-Hulk story 5.00
...: The Unbeatable (12/16) Nick Fury story; Rocket Raccoon & Tippy-Toe story 5.00
...: The Uncanny (2/17) Hawkeye (Kate Bishop) story; Punisher story 5.00
...: The Unstoppable (10/16) Nova & Iron Man story; Winter Soldier story 5.00

YEAR OF THE VILLAIN: HELL ARISEN
DC Comics: Feb, 2020 - No. 4, May, 2020 ($4.99, limited series)

1,2-Apex Lex vs. the Batman Who Laughs; Tynion IV-s/Epting-a. 1-Crime Syndicate app.						5.00
3-First full app. of Punchline; Joker app.	5	10	15	30	50	70
4-Perpertua app.; leads into the Death Metal series						5.00

YEAR ONE: BATMAN/RA'S AL GHUL
DC Comics: 2005 - No. 2, 2005 ($5.99, squarebound, limited series)
1-Devin Grayson-s/Paul Gulacy-a 6.00
TPB (2006, $9.99) r/#1,2 .... 10.00

YEAR ONE: BATMAN SCARECROW
DC Comics: 2005 - No. 2, 2005 ($5.99, squarebound, limited series)
1-Scarecrow's origin; Bruce Jones-s/Sean Murphy-a 6.00

YEARS OF FUTURE PAST (Secret Wars Battleworld tie-in)
Marvel Comics: Aug, 2015 - No. 5, Nov, 2015 ($4.99/$3.99, limited series)
1-($4.99) Bennett-s/Norton-a; Art Adams-c; Kitty Pryde, Wolverine, Colossus app. 5.00
2-5-($3.99) Storm, Magneto, Mystique, Blob, Sentinels app. 4.00

YEAR ZERO
AWA Studios: Apr, 2020 - No. 5, Sept, 2020; Nov, 2020 - No. 5, Mar, 2021 ($3.99)
1-5-Benjamin Percy-s/Ramon Rosanas-a 4.00
Vol. 0 (10/22 - No. 5, 2/23) 1-5-Prequel to the series; Kraus-s/Sudzuka-a 4.00
Vol. 2 (11/20 - No. 5, 3/21) 1-5-Percy-s/Ryp-a 4.00

YELLOW CLAW (Also see Giant Size Master of Kung Fu)
Atlas Comics (MjMC): Oct, 1956 - No. 4, Apr, 1957

1-Origin by Joe Maneely	290	580	870	1856	3178	4500
2-Kirby-a	181	362	543	1158	1979	2800
3-Kirby-a	161	322	483	1030	1765	2500
4-Kirby/Severin-a	168	336	504	1075	1838	2600

NOTE: *Everett* c-3. *Maneely* c-1. *Reinman* a-2i, 3. *Severin* c-2, 4.

YELLOWJACKET COMICS (Jack in the Box #11 on)(See TNT Comics)
E. Levy/Frank Comunale/Charlton: Sept, 1944 - No. 5 Jan, 1945; No. 6, Dec, 1945 - No. 10, June, 1946
1-Intro & origin Yellowjacket; Diana, the Huntress begins; "Famous Tales of Terror" begins with E.A. Poe's "The Black Cat" adaptation

	103	206	309	659	1130	1600

2-Yellowjacket-c begin, end #10; no "Famous Tales of Terror"

	65	130	195	416	708	1000

3,5: 3-"Famous Tales of Terror" with Poe's "The Pit and the Pendulum" adaptation.

5-No "Famous Tales of Terror"	58	116	174	371	636	900

4-"Famous Tales of Terror" with Poe's "Fall of the House Of Usher" adaptation; Palais-a

	61	122	183	390	670	950

6-Last "Famous Tales of Terror", with Poe's "The Tell Tale Heart" adaptation

	58	116	174	371	636	900

7-Classic Skull-c; "Tales of Terror" begins by Alan Mandel-narrated by the Ancient Witch, wearing a red cloak, stirring her bubbling cauldron at beginning and end of story just like E.C.'s Old Witch 5 years later; tells story "The Avenging Hand!" similar to "The Maestro's Hand!" in Crypt of Terror #18. (1st horror series?) Toth-a (1 pg. gag feature)

	81	162	243	518	884	1250

8-"Tales of Terror" narrated by the Old Witch; classic splash & end panel with skull & bones; early "return from the grave story"

	47	94	141	296	498	700

9,10-"Tales of Terror" in each, narrated by the Old Witch in a red cloak, w/classic splash and end panels

	47	94	141	296	498	700

NOTE: *The Old Witch in #7-10 above may have inspired creation of E.C.'s Old Witch. Her costume, dialogue, use of bubbling cauldron, skull and even the title "Tales of Terror" were possibly used.*

YELLOWSTONE KELLY (Movie)
Dell Publishing Co.: No. 1056, Nov-Jan, 1959/60

Four Color 1056-Clint Walker photo-c	6	12	18	41	76	110

YELLOW SUBMARINE (See Movie Comics)

YOGA HOSERS: A SUNDANCE SUPER SPECIAL
Dynamite Entertainment: 2016 ($10.00, one-shot)
1-Prologue to the Kevin Smith movie; Smith-s/Jeff Quigley-a 10.00
-Third printing (2017, $3.99) 4.00

YOGI BEAR (See Dell Giant #41, Golden Comics Digest, Kite Fun Book, March of Comics #253, 265, 279, 291, 309, 319, 337, 344, Movie Comics under "Hey There It's..." & Whitman Comic Books)

YOGI BEAR (TV) (Hanna-Barbera) (See Four Color #990)
Dell Publishing Co./Gold Key No. 10 on: No. 1067, 12-2/59-60 - No. 9, 7-9/62; No. 10, 10/62 - No. 42, 10/70

Four Color 1067 (#1)-TV show debuted 1/30/61	14	28	42	96	211	325
Four Color 1104,1162 (5-7/61)	9	18	27	59	117	175
4(8-9/61) - 6(12-1/61-62)	5	10	15	34	60	85
Four Color 1271(11/61)	6	12	18	40	73	105
Four Color 1349(1/62)-Photo-c	8	16	24	54	102	150
7(2-3/62) - 9(7-9/62)-Last Dell	5	10	15	33	57	80

10(10/62-G.K.), 11(1/63)-titled "Yogi Bear Jellystone Jollies" (80 pgs.); 11-X-Mas-c

X-23 (2018 series) #6 © MAR

Young Allies Comics #15 © MAR

Young Avengers #1 © MAR

	GD 2.0	VG 4.0	FN 6.0	VF 8.0	VF/NM 9.0	NM- 9.2
	6	12	18	41	76	110
12(4/63), 14-20	4	8	12	28	47	65
13(7/63, 68 pgs.)-Surprise Party	6	12	18	40	73	105
21-30	3	6	9	19	30	40
31-42	3	6	9	16	24	32

YOGI BEAR (TV)
Charlton Comics: Nov, 1970 - No. 35, Jan, 1976 (Hanna-Barbera)

1	5	10	15	31	53	75
2-6,8-10	3	6	9	16	24	32
7-Summer Fun (Giant, 52 pgs.)	4	8	12	27	44	60
11-20	3	6	9	15	22	28
21-35: 28-31-partial-r	2	4	6	11	16	20
Digest (nn, 1972, 75¢-c, B&W, 100 pgs.) (scarce)	3	6	9	18	28	38

YOGI BEAR (TV)(See The Flintstones, 3rd series & Spotlight #1)
Marvel Comics Group: Nov, 1977 - No. 9, Mar, 1979 (Hanna-Barbera)

1,7,9: 1-Flintstones begin (Newsstand sales only)	3	6	9	16	23	30
2-6	2	4	6	11	16	20

YOGI BEAR (TV)
Harvey Comics: Sept, 1992 - No. 6, Mar, 1994 ($1.25/$1.50) (Hanna-Barbera)

V2#1-6						4.00
...Big Book V2#1,2 ($1.95, 52 pgs): 1-(11/92). 2-(3/93)						5.00
...Giant Size V2#1,2 ($2.25, 68 pgs.): 1-(10/92). 2-(4/93)						5.00

YOGI BEAR (TV)
Archie Publ.: May, 1997

1						4.00

YOGI BEAR'S EASTER PARADE (See The Funtastic World of Hanna-Barbera #2)

YOGI BERRA (Baseball hero)
Fawcett Publications: 1951 (Yankee catcher)

nn-Photo-c (scarce)	84	168	252	538	919	1300

YONDU (Guardians of the Galaxy)
Marvel Comics: Jan, 2020 - No. 5, Apr, 2020 ($3.99, limited series)

1-5-Zac Thompson & Lonnie Nadler-s/John McCrea-a; future Yondu app.						4.00

YOSEMITE SAM (…& Bugs Bunny) (TV)
Gold Key/Whitman: Dec, 1970 - No. 81, Feb, 1984

1	5	10	15	34	60	85
2-10	3	6	9	16	23	30
11-20	2	4	6	11	16	20
21-30	2	4	6	9	13	16
31-50	2	4	6	8	10	12
51-65 (Gold Key)	1	2	3	5	7	9
66,67 (Whitman)	2	4	6	8	10	12
68(9/80), 69(10/80), 70(12/80) 3-pack only	5	10	15	30	50	70
71-78: 76(2/82), 77(3/82), 78(4/82)	2	4	6	9	13	16
79-81 (All #90263 on-c, no date or date code; (3-pack): 79(3/83). 80(8/83). 81(2/84)-(1/3-r)						
	3	6	9	16	24	32
(See March of Comics #363, 380, 392)						

YOSSEL
DC Comics: 2003/2011 ($14.99, B&W graphic novel)

SC-Joe Kubert-s/a/c; Nazi-occupied Poland during World War II						15.00

YOU ARE DEADPOOL
Marvel Comics: Jul, 2018 - No. 5, Jul, 2018 ($3.99, weekly limited series)

1-5-Ewing-s; interactive role-playing adventure. 3-Man-Thing app. 4-Bullseye app.						4.00

YOU ARE OBSOLETE
AfterShock Comics: Sept, 2019 - No. 5, Jan, 2020 ($3.99)

1-5-Matthew Klickstein-s/Evgeniy Bornyakov-a/Andy Clarke-c						4.00

YOU LOOK LIKE DEATH: TALES FROM THE UMBRELLA ACADEMY
Dark Horse Comics: Sept, 2020 - No. 6, Feb, 2021 ($3.99, limited series)

1-6-Gerald Way & Shaun Simon-s/I.N.J. Culbard-a; spotlight on Klaus						4.00

YOUNG ALLIES
Marvel Comics: Aug, 2010 - No. 6, Jan, 2011 ($3.99/$2.99)

1-($3.99) Wraparound-c; Nomad, Araña, Firestar, Gravity, Toro team-up; origin pages						5.00
2-6-($2.99) 2-Lafuente-c/McKeever-s/Baldeon-a. 6-Miyazawa-c; Emma Frost app.						4.00

YOUNG ALLIES COMICS (All-Winners #21; see Kid Komics #2)
Timely Comics (USA 1-7/NPI 8,9/YAI 10-20): Sum, 1941 - No. 20, Oct, 1946

1-Origin/1st app. The Young Allies (Bucky, Toro, others); 1st meeting of Captain America & Human Torch; Red Skull-c & app.; S&K-c/splash; Hitler-c; Note: the cover was altered after its preview in Human Torch #5. Stalin was shown with Hitler but was removed due to Russia becoming an ally	1480	2960	4440	10,400	20,200	30,000

2-(Winter, 1941)-Captain America & Human Torch app.; Simon & Kirby-c	470	940	1410	3431	6066	8700
3-Remember Pearl Harbor issue (Spring, 1942); Stan Lee scripts; Vs. Japanese-c/full-length story; Captain America & Human Torch app.; Father Time story by Alderman	454	908	1362	3314	5857	8400
4-The Vagabond & Red Skull, Capt. America, Human Torch app. Classic Red Skull-c	703	1406	2109	5132	9066	13,000
5-Captain America & Human Torch app.	320	640	960	2240	5420	5600
6,7: 6-Japanese/Nazi war-c	300	600	900	1950	3375	4800
8-Classic Schomburg WWII Japanese bondage-c	300	600	900	2070	3635	5200
9-Hitler, Tojo, Mussolini-c	423	846	1269	3000	5250	7500
10-Classic Schomburg Hooded Villain bondage-c; origin Tommy Tyme & Clock of Ages; ends #19	252	504	756	1613	2757	3900
11-16: 12-Classic decapitation story; Japanese war-c. 16-Last Schomburg WWII-c	181	362	543	1158	1979	2800
17-20	142	284	426	909	1555	2200

NOTE: *Brodsky* c-15. *Ferstadt* a-3. *Gabriele* a-3; c-3, 4. *S&K* c-1, 2. *Schomburg* c-5-13, 16-19. *Shores* c-20.

YOUNG ALLIES 70TH ANNIVERSARY SPECIAL
Marvel Comics: Aug, 2009 ($3.99, one-shot)

1-Bucky & Young Allies app.; Stern-s/Rivera-a; Terry Vance rep. from Marvel Myst. #14						5.00

YOUNG ALL-STARS
DC Comics: June, 1987 - No. 31, Nov, 1989 ($1.00, deluxe format)

1-31: 1-1st app. Iron Munro & The Flying Fox. 8,9-Millennium tie-ins						4.00
Annual 1 (1988, $2.00)						5.00

YOUNG AVENGERS
Marvel Comics: Apr, 2005 - No. 12, Aug, 2006 ($2.99)

1-1st app Kate Bishop; intro. Iron Lad, Patriot, Hulkling, Asgardian; Heinberg-s/Cheung-a	8	12	24	54	102	150
1-Director's Cut (2005, $3.99) r/#1 plus character sketches; original script	5	10	15	33	57	80
2-8,10,11: 3-6-Kang app. 7-DiVito-a. 9-Skrulls app.						4.00
9-1st Kate Bishop-c	3	6	9	14	19	24
12-1st Kate Bishop as Hawkeye	3	6	9	17	25	34
... Special 1 (2/06, $3.99) origins of the heroes; art by various incl. Neal Adams, Jae Lee, Bill Sienkiewicz, Gene Ha, Michael Gaydos and Pasqual Ferry						4.00
... Vol. 1: Sidekicks HC (2005, $19.99, dustjacket) r/#1-6; character design sketches						20.00
... Vol. 1: Sidekicks TPB (2006, $14.99) r/#1-6; character design sketches						15.00
... Vol. 2: Family Matters HC (2006, $22.99, dustjacket) r/#7-12 & YA Special #1						23.00
... Vol. 2: Family Matters SC (2007, $17.99) r/#7-12 & YA Special #1						18.00
HC (2008, $29.99, d.j.) oversized reprint of #1-12 and Special #1; script & sketch pages						30.00

YOUNG AVENGERS (Marvel NOW!)
Marvel Comics: Mar, 2013 - No. 15, Mar, 2014 ($2.99)

1-15: Young Avengers assembles team; Marvel Boy, Miss America app.; Gillen-s/McKelvie-a/c. 11-Loki ages back to adult. 14,15-Multiple artists						3.00
1-Variant-c by Bryan Lee O'Malley						6.00
1-Variant-c by Skottie Young						6.00

YOUNG AVENGERS PRESENTS
Marvel Comics: Mar, 2008 - No. 6, Aug, 2008 ($2.99, limited series)

1-6: 1-Patriot; Bucky app. 2-Hulkling; Captain Marvel app. 3-Wiccan & Speed. 4-Vision. 5-Stature. 6-Hawkeye; Clint Barton app.; Alan Davis-a						3.00

YOUNGBLOOD (See Brigade #4, Megaton Explosion & Team Youngblood)
Image Comics (Extreme Studios): Apr, 1992 - No. 4, Feb, 1993 ($2.50, lim. series); No. 5-(Flip book w/Brigade #4); No. 6, June, 1994 - No. 10, Dec, 1994 ($1.95/$2.50)

1-Liefeld-c/a/scripts in all; flip book format in all; 1st Image/Extreme Studios title.	2	4	6	8	10	12
1,2-2nd printing						4.00
2-(JUN-c, July 1992 indicia)-1st app. Shadowhawk in solo back-up story; 2 trading cards inside; flip book format; 1st app. Prophet, Kirby, Berzerkers, Darkthorn	2	4	6	10	14	18
3,0,4,5: 3-(OCT-c, August 1992 indicia)-Contains 2 trading cards inside (flip book); 1st app. Supreme in back-up story; 1st app. Showdown. 0-(12/92, $1.95)-Contains 2 trading cards; 2 cover variations exist, green or beige logo; w/Image #0 coupon. 4-(2/93)-Glow-in-the-dark cover w/2 trading cards; 2nd app. Dale Keown's The Pitt; Bloodstrike app. 5-Flip book w/Brigade #4						5.00
6-($3.50, 52 pgs.)-Wraparound-c						4.00
7-9: 7, 8-Liefeld-c(p)/a(p)/story. 8,9-(9/94) 9-Valentino story & art						4.00
10-Spawn story; death of Chapel	1	2	3	5	6	8
Battlezone 1 (May-c, 4/93 inside, $1.95)-Arsenal book; Liefeld-c(p)						4.00
Battlezone 2 (7/94, $2.95)						5.00
Image Firsts: Youngblood #1 (3/10, $1.00) reprints #1						4.00
...Super Special (Winter '97, $2.99) Sprouse -a						5.00
Yearbook 1 (7/93, $2.50)-Fold-out panel; 1st app. Tyrax & Kanan						5.00
Vol. 1 HC (2008, $34.99) oversized r/#1-5, recolored and remastered; sketch art and cover						

	GD 2.0	VG 4.0	FN 6.0	VF 8.0	VF/NM 9.0	NM- 9.2

gallery; Mark Millar intro. ... 35.00
TPB (1996, $16.95)-r/Team Youngblood #8-10 & Youngblood #6-8,10 ... 17.00

YOUNGBLOOD
Image Comics (Extreme Studios)/Maximum Press No. 14: V2#1, Sept, 1995 - No. 14, Dec, 1996 ($2.50)
V2#1-10,14: Roger Cruz-a in all. 4-Extreme Destroyer Pt. 4 w/gaming card. 5-Variant-c exists. 6-Angela & Glory. 7-Shadowhunt Pt. 3; Shadowhawk app. 8,10-Thor (from Supreme) app. 10-(7/96). 14-(12/96)-1st Maximum Press issue ... 4.00

YOUNGBLOOD (Volume 3)
Awesome/ Awesome-Hyperwerks #2: Feb, 1998 - No. 2, Aug, 1998 ($2.50)
1-Alan Moore-s/Skroce & Stucker-a; 12 diff. covers ... 4.00
2-(8/98) Skroce & Liefeld covers ... 4.00
...Imperial 1 (Arcade Comics, 6/04, $2.99) Kirkman-s/Mychaels-a ... 3.00

YOUNGBLOOD (Volume 4)
Image Comics: Jan, 2008 - No. 9, Sept, 2009; No. 71, May, 2012 - No. 78, Jul, 2013 ($2.99/$3.99)
1-7-Casey-s/Donovan-a; two covers by Donovan & Liefeld on each ... 3.00
8-Obama flip cover by Liefeld; Obama app. in story ... 3.00
9-(9/09, $3.99) Obama flip cover by Liefeld; Free Agent rejoins; Obama app. in story ... 3.00
71-74: 71-(5/12, $2.99) Liefeld & Malin-a; three covers ... 3.00
75-(1/13, $4.99) Five covers; Malin-a ... 5.00
76-78-($3.99) Malin-a ... 4.00

YOUNGBLOOD (Volume 5)
Image Comics: May, 2017 - No. 11, May, 2018 ($3.99)
1-11-Bowers-s/Towe-a; multiple covers on each. 1-Back-up story w/Liefeld-s/a. 4,5-Bloodstrike flip book; Liefeld-s/a ... 4.00

YOUNGBLOOD: STRIKEFILE
Image Comics (Extreme Studios): Apr, 1993 - No. 11, Feb, 1995 ($1.95/$2.50/$2.95)
1-10: 1-($1.95)-Flip book w/Jae Lee-c/a & Liefeld-c/a in #1-3; 1st app. The Allies,Giger, & Glory. 3-Thibert-i asisst. 4-Liefeld-c(p); no Lee-a. 5-Liefeld-c(p). 8-Platt-c ... 4.00
NOTE: *Youngblood: Strikefile began as a four issue limited series.*

YOUNGBLOOD/X-FORCE
Image Comics (Extreme Studios): July, 1996 ($4.95, one-shot)
1-Cruz-a(p); two covers exist ... 5.00

YOUNG BRIDES (True Love Secrets)
Feature/Prize Publ.: Sept-Oct, 1952 - No. 30, Nov-Dec, 1956 (Photo-c: V1 #1-6, V2 #1,2)

	GD 2.0	VG 4.0	FN 6.0	VF 8.0	VF/NM 9.0	NM- 9.2
V1#1-Simon & Kirby-a	55	110	165	352	601	850
2-S&K-a	34	68	102	199	325	450
3-6-S&K-a	29	58	87	172	281	390
V2#1-7,10-12 (#7-18)-S&K-a	25	50	75	150	245	340
8,9-No S&K-a	15	30	45	84	127	170
V3#1-3 (#19-21)-Last precode (3-4/55)	14	28	42	80	115	155
4,6(#22,24), V4#1,3(#25,27)	14	28	42	76	108	140
V3#5(#23)-Meskin-c	14	28	42	78	112	145
V4#2(#26)-All S&K issue	23	46	69	136	223	310
V4#4(#28)-S&K-a	20	40	60	117	189	260
V4#5,6(#29,30)	14	28	42	81	118	155

YOUNG DR. MASTERS (See The Adventures of Young Dr. Masters)

YOUNG DOCTORS, THE
Charlton Comics: Jan, 1963 - No. 6, Nov, 1963

	GD 2.0	VG 4.0	FN 6.0	VF 8.0	VF/NM 9.0	NM- 9.2
V1#1	4	8	12	28	47	65
2-6	3	6	9	16	23	30

YOUNG EAGLE
Fawcett Publications/Charlton: 12/50 - No. 10, 6/52; No. 3, 7/56 - No. 5, 4/57 (Photo-c: 1-10)

	GD 2.0	VG 4.0	FN 6.0	VF 8.0	VF/NM 9.0	NM- 9.2
1-Intro Young Eagle	22	44	66	132	216	300
2-Complete picture novelette "The Mystery of Thunder Canyon"	13	26	39	74	105	135
3-9	10	20	30	54	72	90
10-Origin Thunder, Young Eagle's Horse	9	18	27	50	65	80
3-5(Charlton)-Formerly Sherlock Holmes?	8	16	24	40	50	60

YOUNG GUNS SKETCHBOOK
Marvel Comics: Feb, 2005 ($3.99, one-shot)
1-Sketch pages from 2005 Marvel projects by Coipel, Granov, McNiven, Land & others ... 4.00

YOUNG HEARTS
Marvel Comics (SPC): Nov, 1949 - No. 2, Feb, 1950

	GD 2.0	VG 4.0	FN 6.0	VF 8.0	VF/NM 9.0	NM- 9.2
1-Photo-c	28	56	84	165	270	375
2-Colleen Townsend photo-c from movie	19	38	57	111	176	240

YOUNG HEARTS IN LOVE
Super Comics: 1964

	GD 2.0	VG 4.0	FN 6.0	VF 8.0	VF/NM 9.0	NM- 9.2
17,18: 17-r/Young Love V5#6 (4-5/62)	2	4	6	11	16	20

YOUNG HELLBOY: ASSAULT ON CASTLE DEATH
Dark Horse Comics: Jul, 2022 - No. 4, Feb, 2023 ($3.99, limited series)
1-4-Mignola & Sniegoski-s/Rousseau-a; Lobster Johnson app. ... 4.00

YOUNG HELLBOY: THE HIDDEN LAND
Dark Horse Comics: Feb, 2021 - No. 4, Jun, 2021 ($3.99, limited series)
1-4-Mignola & Sniegoski-s/Rousseau-a; Prof. Bruttenholm app. ... 4.00

YOUNG HEROES (Formerly Forbidden Worlds #34)
American Comics Group (Titan): No. 35, Feb-Mar, 1955 - No. 37, Jun-Jul, 1955

	GD 2.0	VG 4.0	FN 6.0	VF 8.0	VF/NM 9.0	NM- 9.2
35-37-Frontier Scout	14	28	42	76	108	140

YOUNG HEROES IN LOVE
DC Comics: June, 1997 - No. 17; #1,000,000, Nov, 1998 ($1.75/$1.95/$2.50)
1-1st app. Young Heroes; Madan-a ... 5.00
2-17: 3-Superman-c/app. 7-Begin $1.95-c ... 4.00
#1,000,000 (11/98, $2.50) 853 Century x-over ... 4.00

YOUNG INDIANA JONES CHRONICLES, THE
Dark Horse Comics: Feb, 1992 - No. 12, Feb, 1993 ($2.50)

1-12: Dan Barry scripts in all ... 4.00
NOTE: *Dan Barry* a(p)-1, 2, 5, 6, 10; c-1-10. *Morrow* a-3, 4, 5p, 6p. *Springer* a-1i, 2i.

YOUNG INDIANA JONES CHRONICLES, THE
Hollywood Comics (Disney): 1992 ($3.95, squarebound, 68 pgs.)
1-3: 1-r/YIJC #1,2 by D. Horse. 2-r/#3,4. 3-r/#5,6 ... 5.00

YOUNG JUSTICE (Also see Teen Titans, Titans/Young Justice and DC Comics Presents: ...)
DC Comics: Sept, 1998 - No. 55, May, 2003 ($2.50/$2.75)
1-Robin, Superboy & Impulse team-up; David-s/Nauck-a ... 6.00
2,3: 3-Mxyzptlk app. ... 4.00
4-20: 4-Wonder Girl, Arrowette and the Secret join. 6-JLA app. 13-Supergirl x-over. 20-Sins of Youth aftermath ... 4.00
21-49: 25-Empress ID revealed. 28,29-Forever People app. 32-Empress origin. 35,36-Our Worlds at War x-over. 38-Joker: Last Laugh. 41-The Ray app. 42-Spectre-c/app. 44,45-World Without YJ x-over pt. 1,5; Ramos-c. 48-Begin $2.75-c ... 3.00
50-($3.95) Wonder Twins, CM3 and other various DC teen heroes app. ... 4.00
51-55: 53,54-Darkseid app. 55-Last issue; leads into Titans/Young Justice mini-series ... 3.00
#1,000,000 (11/98) 853 Century x-over ... 3.00
...: A League of Their Own (2000, $14.95, TPB) r/#1-7, Secret Files #1 ... 15.00
...: 80-Page Giant (5/99, $4.95) Ramos-c; stories and art by various ... 5.00
...: In No Man's Land (7/99, $3.95) McDaniel-c ... 5.00
...: Our Worlds at War (8/01, $2.95) Jae Lee-c; Linear Men app. ... 4.00
...: Secret Files (1/99, $4.95) Origin-s & pin-ups ... 5.00
...: The Secret (6/98, $1.95) Girlfrenzy; Nauck-a ... 3.00

YOUNG JUSTICE (Based on the 2011 Cartoon Network series)
DC Comics: No. 0, Mar, 2011 - No. 25, Apr, 2013 ($2.99)
0-19: 1-Miss Martian joins; Joker app. 2-Joker-c/app. 5-Kid Flash & Aqualad origins ... 3.00
20-25: 20-(11/12) Starts Invasion; 5 years later ... 3.00
FCBD 2011 Young Justice Batman BB Super Sampler (7/11) Flash app. ... 3.00

YOUNG JUSTICE
DC Comics (Wonder Comics): Mar, 2019 - No. 20, Jan, 2021 ($4.99/$3.99)
1-($4.99) Robin, Wonder Girl & Impulse team; intro Jinny Hex & Teen Lantern; Bendis-s ... 5.00
2-20-($3.99): 2-Gleason & Lupacchino-a. 3-Gleason & Bogdanovic-a. 7-Capt. Carrot and the Kingdom Come Justice League app. 8-10-Earth-3 counterparts. 13-Warlord app.; art by Grell (5 pages). 20-Red Tornado app. ... 4.00

YOUNG JUSTICE: SINS OF YOUTH (Also see Sins of Youth x-over issues and Sins of Youth: Secret Files)
DC Comics: May, 2000 - No. 2, May, 2000 ($3.95, limited series)
1,2-Young Justice, JLA & JSA swap apps; David-s/Nauck-a ... 4.00
TPB (2000, $19.95) r/#1,2 & all x-over issues ... 20.00

YOUNG JUSTICE: TARGETS (Based on the 2011 Cartoon Network series)
DC Comics: Sept, 2022 - No. 6, Feb, 2023 ($3.99, limited series)
1-6: 1-Greg Weisman-s/Christopher Jones-a ... 4.00

YOUNG KING COLE (...Detective Tales)(Becomes Criminals on the Run)
Premium Group/Novelty Press: Fall, 1945 - V3#12, July, 1948

	GD 2.0	VG 4.0	FN 6.0	VF 8.0	VF/NM 9.0	NM- 9.2
V1#1-Toni Gayle begins	47	94	141	296	498	700
2	23	46	69	136	223	310
3-4	21	42	63	122	199	275
V2#1-7(8-9/46-7/47): 6,7-Certa-c	16	32	48	92	144	195
V3#1,3-6,8,9,12: 3-Certa-c. 5-McWilliams-c/a. 8,9-Harmon-c	15	30	45	89	137	185
2-L.B. Cole-a; Certa-c	22	44	66	128	209	290
7-L.B. Cole-c/a	28	56	84	168	274	380
10,11-L.B. Cole-c	33	66	99	194	317	440

YOUNG LAWYERS, THE (TV)
Dell Publishing Co.: Jan, 1971 - No. 2, Apr, 1971 (photo-c)

	GD 2.0	VG 4.0	FN 6.0	VF 8.0	VF/NM 9.0	NM- 9.2
1	3	6	9	19	30	40
2	3	6	9	14	20	25

YOUNG LIARS (David Lapham's...)(See Vertigo Double Shot for reprint of #1)
DC Comics (Vertigo): May, 2008 - No. 18, Oct, 2009 ($2.99)
1-18: 1-Intro. Sadie Dawkins; David Lapham-s/a/c in all ... 3.00
...: Daydream Believer TPB (2008, $9.99) r/#1-6; Gerald Way intro. ... 10.00
...: Maestro TPB (2009, $14.99) r/#7-12; Peter Milligan intro. ... 15.00
...: Rock Life TPB (2010, $14.99) r/#13-18; Brian Azzarello intro. ... 15.00

YOUNG LIFE (Teen Life #3 on)
New Age Publ./Quality Comics Group: Summer, 1945 - No. 2, Fall, 1945

	GD 2.0	VG 4.0	FN 6.0	VF 8.0	VF/NM 9.0	NM- 9.2
1-Skip Homeier, Louis Prima stories	26	52	78	154	252	350
2-Frank Sinatra photo on-c plus story	27	54	81	158	259	360

YOUNG LOVE (Sister title to Young Romance)
Prize(Feature)Publ.(Crestwood): 2-3/49 - No. 73, 12-1/56-57; V3#5, 2-3/60 - V7#1, 6-7/63

	GD 2.0	VG 4.0	FN 6.0	VF 8.0	VF/NM 9.0	NM- 9.2
V1#1-S&K-c/a(2)	103	206	309	659	1130	1600
2-Photo-c begin; S&K-a	43	86	129	271	461	650
3-S&K-a	31	62	93	182	296	410
4-6-Minor S&K-a	21	42	63	122	199	275
V2#1(#7)-S&K-a(2)	28	56	84	168	274	380
2-5(#8-11)-Minor S&K-a	18	36	54	107	169	230
6,8(#12,14)-S&K-c only. 14-S&K 1 pg. art	20	40	60	120	195	270
7,9-12(#13,15-18)-S&K-c/a	27	54	81	158	259	360
V3#1-4(#19-22)-S&K-c/a	24	78	72	140	230	320
5-7,9-12(#23-25,27-30)-Photo-c resume; S&K-a	20	40	60	117	189	260
8(#26)-No S&K-a	14	28	42	76	108	140
V4#1,6(#31,36)-S&K-a	18	36	54	107	169	230
2-5,7-12(#32-35,37-42)-Minor S&K-a	15	30	45	88	137	185
V5#1-12(#43-54), V6#3,7,9(#57,61,63)-Last precode	13	26	39	72	101	130
V6#1,2,4-6,8(#55,56,58-60,62) S&K-a	14	28	42	80	115	150
V6#10-12(#64-66)	10	20	30	58	79	100
V7#1-7(#67-73)	5	10	15	34	60	85
V3#5(2-3/60),6(4-5/60)(Formerly All For Love)	5	10	15	31	53	75
V4#1(6-7/60)-6(4-5/61)	5	10	15	30	50	70
V5#1(6-7/61)-6(4-5/62)	4	8	12	27	44	60
V6#1(6-7/62)-6(4-5/63), V7#1	4	8	12	28	47	65

Young Justice (2019 series) #1 © DC

Young Love #52 © DC

Young X-Men #12 © MAR

	GD	VG	FN	VF	VF/NM	NM-
	2.0	4.0	6.0	8.0	9.0	9.2

NOTE: *Meskin* a-14(2), 27, 42. *Powell* a-V4#6. *Severin/Elder* a-V1#3. S&K art not in #53, 57, 61, 63-65. Photo-c most V1 #1-6, V2 #3, V3#5-V5#11.

YOUNG LOVE
National Periodical Publ.(Arleigh Publ. Corp #49-61)/DC Comics:
#39, 9-10/63 - #120, Wint./75-76; #121, 10/76 - #126, 7/77

39	7	14	21	44	82	120
40-50	5	10	15	30	50	70
51-68,70	4	8	12	27	44	60
69-(68 pg. Giant)(8-9/68)	7	14	21	48	89	130
71,72,75-77,80	3	6	9	20	31	42
73,74,78,79-Toth-a	3	6	9	21	33	45
81-99: 88-96-(52 pg. Giants)	3	6	9	19	30	40
100	3	6	9	20	31	42
101-106,115-120	3	6	9	16	24	32
107 (100 pgs.)	8	16	24	56	108	160
108-114 (100 pgs.)	8	16	24	52	99	145
121-126 (52 pgs.)	4	8	12	28	47	65

NOTE: *Bolle* a-117. *Colan* a-107r. *Nasser* a-123, 124. *Orlando* a-122. *Simonson* c-125. *Toth* a-73, 78, 79, 122-125r. *Wood* a-109r(4 pgs.).

YOUNG LOVER ROMANCES (Formerly & becomes Great Lover…)
Toby Press: No. 4, June, 1952 - No. 5, Aug, 1952

4,5-Photo-c	16	32	48	94	147	200

YOUNG LOVERS (My Secret Life #19 on)(Formerly Brenda Starr?)
Charlton Comics: No. 16, July, 1956 - No. 18, May, 1957

16,17('56): 16-Marcus Swayze-a	18	36	54	105	165	225
18-Elvis Presley picture-c, text story (biography)(Scarce)						
	123	246	369	787	1344	1900

YOUNG MARRIAGE
Fawcett Publications: June, 1950

1-Powell-a; photo-c	19	38	57	111	176	240

YOUNG MEN (Formerly Cowboy Romances)(…on the Battlefield #12-20(4/53); … In Action #21)
Marvel/Atlas Comics (IPC): No. 4, 6/50 - No. 11, 10/51; No. 12, 12/51 - No. 28, 6/54

4-(52 pgs.)	36	72	108	211	343	475
5-11	23	46	69	136	223	310
12-23: 12-20-War format. 21-23-Hot Rod issues starring Flash Foster						
	24	48	72	142	234	325
24-(12/53)-Origin Captain America, Human Torch, & Sub-Mariner which are revived thru #28;						
Red Skull app.	486	972	1458	3550	6275	9000
25-28: 25-Romita-c/a (see Men's Advs.). 27-Death of Golden Age Red Skull						
	206	412	618	1318	2259	3200
25-2nd printing (1994)	2	4	6	10	14	18

NOTE: *Berg* a-7, 14, 17, 18, 20; c-17? *Brodsky* c-4-9, 13, 14, 16, 17, 21-25. *Burgos* c-26-28. *Colan* a-14, 15, 20. *Everett* a-18-20. *Heath* a-13, 14. *Maneely* c-10-12, 15. *Pakula* a-14, 15. *Robinson* c-18. Captain America by *Romita*-#247, 25, 26?, 27, 28. Human Torch by *Burgos*-#25, 27, 28. Sub-Mariner by *Everett*-#24-28.

YOUNG MONSTERS IN LOVE
DC Comics: Apr, 2018 ($9.99, 80 pages, one-shot)
1-Horror short stories by various; Swamp Thing, Raven, Deadman app.; Kelley Jones-c 10.00

YOUNG REBELS, THE (TV)
Dell Publishing Co.: Jan, 1971

1-Photo-c	3	6	9	14	19	24

YOUNG ROMANCE COMICS (The 1st romance comic)
Prize/Headline (Feature Publ.) (Crestwood): Sept-Oct, 1947 - V16#4, June-July, 1963 (#1-33: 52 pgs.)

V1#1-S&K-c/a(2)	194	388	582	1242	2121	3000
2-S&K-c/a(2-3)	58	116	174	371	636	900
3-6-S&K-c/a(2-3) each	41	82	123	256	428	600
V2#1-6(#7-12)-S&K-c/a(2-3) each	39	78	117	231	378	525
4-12(#16-24)-Photo-c; S&K-a	25	50	75	150	245	340
V3#1-3(#13-15): V3#1-Photo-c begin; S&K-a	25	50	75	150	245	340
4-12(#16-24)-Photo-c; S&K-a	25	50	75	150	245	340
V4#1-11(#25-35)-S&K-a	24	48	72	144	237	330
12(#36)-S&K, Toth-a	25	50	75	150	245	340
V5#1-12(#37-48), V6#4-12(#52-60)-S&K-a	24	48	72	144	237	330
V6#1-3(#49-51)-No S&K-a	15	30	45	83	124	165
V7#1-11(#61-71)-S&K-a in most	19	38	57	111	176	240
V7#12(#72), V8#1-3(#73-75)-Last precode (12-1/54-55)-No S&K-a						
	14	28	42	78	112	145
V8#4(#76, 4-5/55), 5(#77)-No S&K-a	13	26	39	72	101	130
V8#6-8(#78-80, 12-1/55-56)-S&K-a	16	32	48	92	144	195
V9#3,5,6(#81, 2-3/56, 83,84)-S&K-a	16	32	48	92	144	195
4, V10#1(#82,85)-All S&K-a	18	36	54	103	162	220
V10#2-6(#86-90, 10-11/57)-S&K-a	9	18	27	63	129	195
V11#1,2,5,6(#91,92,95,96)-S&K-a	9	18	27	63	129	195
3,4(#93,94), V12#2,4,5(#98,100,101)-No S&K	6	12	18	38	69	100

	GD	VG	FN	VF	VF/NM	NM-
	2.0	4.0	6.0	8.0	9.0	9.2

V12#1,3,6(#97,99,102)-S&K-a	9	18	27	63	129	195
V13#1(#103)-Powell-a; S&K's last-a for Crestwood	9	18	27	63	129	195
2,4-6(#104-108)	5	10	15	35	63	90
V13#3(#105, 4-5/60)-Elvis Presley-c app. only	10	20	30	64	132	200
V14#1-6, V15#1-6, V16#1-4(#109-124)	5	10	15	34	60	85

NOTE: *Meskin* a-16, 24(2), 33, 47, 50. *Robinson/Meskin* a-6. *Leonard Starr* a-11. Photo c-13-32, 34-65. Issues 1-3 say "Designed for the More *Adult* Readers of *Comics*" on cover.

YOUNG ROMANCE COMICS (Continued from Prize series)
National Periodical Publ.(Arleigh Publ. Corp. No. 127): No. 125, Aug-Sept, 1963 - No. 208, Nov-Dec, 1975

125	9	18	27	62	126	190
126-140	5	10	15	35	63	90
141-153,156-162,165-169	4	8	12	28	47	65
154-Neal Adams-c	5	10	15	34	60	85
155-1st publ. Aragonés-s (no art)	5	10	15	33	57	80
163,164-Toth-a	5	10	15	30	50	70
170-172 (68 pg. Giants): 170-Michell from Young Love ends; Lily Martin, the Swinger begins						
	5	10	15	34	60	85
173-183 (52 pgs.)	4	8	12	27	44	60
184-196	3	6	9	21	33	45
197-204-(100 pgs.)	9	18	27	58	114	170
205-208	3	6	9	19	30	40
Young Romance 125 (Facsimile Edition)(4/24, $3.99) Reprints issue with original ads						4.00

YOUNG ROMANCE: THE NEW 52 VALENTINE'S DAY SPECIAL
DC Comics: Apr, 2013 ($7.99, one-shot)
1-Short stories by various; Superman/Wonder Woman-c by Rocafort; bonus valentines 8.00

YOUNG X-MEN
Marvel Comics: May, 2008 - No. 12, May, 2009 ($2.99)
1-12: 1-Cyclops forms new team; Guggenheim-s/Paquette-a/Dodson-c. 11,12-Acuña-a 3.00

YOUR DREAMS (See Strange World of…)

YOUR HIGHNESS
Dark Horse Comics: 2011 ($7.99, one-shot)
nn-Prequel to 2011 movie; Danny McBride & Jeff Fradley-s/Phillips-a/c 8.00

YOUR PAL ARCHIE
Archie Comic Publications: Sept, 2017 - No. 5, Feb, 2018 ($3.99)
1-5-New stories with classic-style Archie gang, plus back-up reprints in #1-4 4.00

YOUR UNITED STATES
Lloyd Jacquet Studios: 1946

nn-Used in SOTI, pg. 309,310; Sid Greene-a	34	68	102	199	325	450

YOUTHFUL HEARTS (Daring Confessions #4 on)
Youthful Magazines: May, 1952 - No. 3, Sept, 1952

1- "Monkey on Her Back" swipes E.C. drug story/Shock SuspenStories #12; Frankie Laine photo on-c; Doug Wildey-a in all	50	100	150	315	533	750
2,3: 2-Vic Damone photo on-c. 3-Johnny Raye photo on-c	31	62	93	182	296	410

YOUTHFUL LOVE (Truthful Love #2)
Youthful Magazines: May, 1950

1	41	82	123	256	428	600

YOUTHFUL ROMANCES
Pix-Parade #1-14/Ribage #15 on: 8-9/49 - No. 5, 4/50; No. 6, 2/51; No. 7, 5/51 - #14, 10/52; #15, 1/53 - #18, 7/53; No. 5, Spring-No. 9, 8/54

1-(1st series)-Titled Youthful Love-Romances	42	84	126	265	445	625
2-Walter Johnson c-1-4	27	54	81	158	259	360
3-5	23	46	69	136	223	310
6,7,9-14(10/52, Pix-Parade; becomes Daring Love #15). 10(1/52)-Mel Torme photo-c/story. 12-Tony Bennett photo-c, 8pg. story & text bio.13-Richard Hayes (singer) photo-c/story; Bob & Ray photo/text story. 14-Doris Day photo/text story						
	24	48	72	142	234	325
8-Frank Sinatra photo/text story; Wood-c/a	34	68	102	199	325	450
15-18 (Ribage)-All have photos on-c. 15-Spike Jones photo-c/story. 16-Tony Bavaar photo-c/story						
	21	42	64	124	202	280
5(9/53, Ribage)-Les Paul & Mary Ford photo-c/story; Charlton Heston photo/text story						
	20	40	60	117	189	260
6-9: 6-Bobby Wayne (singer) photo-c/story. Debbie Reynolds photo/text story. 7(2/54)-Tony Martin photo-c/story; Cyd Charise photo/text story. 8(5/54)-Gordon McCrae photo/text story. (8/54)-Ralph Flanagan (band leader) photo/text story; Audrey Hepburn photo/text story						
	20	40	60	114	182	250

YTHAQ: NO ESCAPE
Marvel Comics (Soleil): 2009 - No. 3, 2009 ($5.99, limited series)
1-3-English language version of French comic; Arleston-s/Floch-a 6.00

YTHAQ: THE FORSAKEN WORLD

	GD 2.0	VG 4.0	FN 6.0	VF 8.0	VF/NM 9.0	NM- 9.2

Marvel Comics (Soleil): 2008 - No. 3, 2009 ($5.99, limited series)

1-3-English language version of French comic; Arleston-s/Floch-a						6.00

Y: THE LAST MAN
DC Comics (Vertigo): Sept, 2002 - No. 60, Mar, 2008 ($2.95/$2.99)

	GD 2.0	VG 4.0	FN 6.0	VF 8.0	VF/NM 9.0	NM- 9.2
1-Intro. Yorick Brown; Brian K. Vaughan-s/Pia Guerra-a/J.G. Jones-c	6	12	18	41	76	110
2	2	4	6	11	16	20
3-5	1	2	3	5	6	8
6-10						5.00
11-59: 16,17-Chadwick-a. 21,22-Parlov-a. 32,39-41,48,53,54-Sudzuka-a.						3.00
60-($4.99) Final issue; sixty years in the future						6.00
... Double Feature Edition (2002, $5.95) r/#1,2	2	4	6	9	12	15
... Special Edition (2009, $1.00) r/#1, "After Watchmen" trade dress on cover						3.00
... - Cycles TPB (2003, $12.95) r/#6-10; sketch pages by Guerra						13.00
... - Girl on Girl TPB (2005, $12.99) r/#32-36						13.00
... - Kimono Dragons TPB (2006, $14.99) r/#43-48						15.00
... - Motherland TPB (2007, $14.99) r/#49-54						15.00
... - One Small Step TPB (2004, $12.95) r/#11-17						13.00
... - Paper Dolls TPB (2006, $14.99) r/#37-42						15.00
... - Ring of Truth TPB (2005, $14.99) r/#24-31						15.00
... - Safeword TPB (2004, $12.95) r/#18-23						13.00
... - Unmanned TPB (2002, $12.95) r/#1-5						15.00
... - Whys and Wherefores TPB (2008, $14.99) r/#55-60						15.00
... - The Deluxe Edition Book One HC (2008, $29.99, dustjacket) oversized r/#1-10; Guerra sketch pages						30.00
... - The Deluxe Edition Book Two HC (2009, $29.99, dustjacket) oversized r/#11-23; full script to #18						30.00
... - The Deluxe Edition Book Three HC (2010, $29.99, dustjacket) oversized r/#24-36; full script to #36						30.00
... - The Deluxe Edition Book Four HC (2010, $29.99, dustjacket) oversized r/#37-48; full script to #42						30.00
... - The Deluxe Edition Book Five HC (2011, $29.99, dustjacket) oversized r/#49-60; full script to #60						30.00

Y2K: THE COMIC
New England Comics Press: Oct, 1999 ($3.95, one-shot)

1-Y2K scenarios and survival tips						6.00

YUPPIES FROM HELL (Also see Son of...)
Marvel Comics: 1989 ($2.95, B&W, one-shot, direct sales, 52 pgs.)

1-Satire						5.00

ZAGO (..., Jungle Prince) (My Story #5 on)(See Unusual Comics)
Fox Feature Syndicate: Sept, 1948 - No. 4, Mar, 1949

	GD 2.0	VG 4.0	FN 6.0	VF 8.0	VF/NM 9.0	NM- 9.2
1-Blue Beetle app.; partial-r/Atomic #4 (Toni Luck)	97	194	291	621	1061	1500
2,3-Kamen-a	87	174	261	553	952	1350
4-Baker-c	116	232	348	742	1271	1800

ZANE GREY'S STORIES OF THE WEST
Dell Publishing Co./Gold Key 11/64: No. 197, 9/48 - No. 996, 5-7/59; 11/64 (All painted-c)

	GD 2.0	VG 4.0	FN 6.0	VF 8.0	VF/NM 9.0	NM- 9.2
Four Color 197(#1)(9/48)	13	26	39	91	201	310
Four Color 222,230,236('49)	9	18	27	57	111	165
Four Color 246,255,270,301,314,333,346	6	12	18	37	66	95
Four Color 357,372,395,412,433,449,467,484	5	10	15	33	57	80
Four Color 511-Kinstler-a; Kubert-a	5	10	15	35	63	90
Four Color 532,555,583,604,616,632(5/55)	5	10	15	33	57	80
27(9-11/55) - 39(9-11/58)	4	8	12	28	47	65
Four Color 996(5-7/59)	5	10	15	33	57	80
10131-411-(11/64-G.K.)-Nevada; r/4-Color #996	3	6	9	21	33	45

ZANY (Magazine)(Satire)(See Frantic & Ratfink)
Candor Publ. Co.: Sept, 1958 - No. 4, May, 1959

	GD 2.0	VG 4.0	FN 6.0	VF 8.0	VF/NM 9.0	NM- 9.2
1-Bill Everett-c	20	40	60	117	189	260
2-4: 4-Everett-a	28	42	81	118	155

ZATANNA (See Adv. Comics #413, JLA #161, Supergirl #1, World's Finest Comics #274)
DC Comics: July, 1993 - No. 4, Oct, 1993 ($1.95, limited series)

	GD 2.0	VG 4.0	FN 6.0	VF 8.0	VF/NM 9.0	NM- 9.2
1	1	3	4	6	8	10
2-4						6.00
...: Everyday Magic (2003, $5.95, one-shot) Dini-s/Mays-a/Bolland-c; Constantine app.	4	8	12	23	37	50
Special 1(1987, $2.00)-Gray Morrow-c/a	2	4	6	10	14	18

ZATANNA
DC Comics: Jul, 2010 - No. 16, Oct, 2011 ($2.99)

	GD 2.0	VG 4.0	FN 6.0	VF 8.0	VF/NM 9.0	NM- 9.2
1-Dini-s/Roux-a/c	2	4	6	11	16	20
1-Variant-c by Bolland	3	6	9	19	30	40
2-6-Variant-c by Bolland	2	4	6	10	14	18
2-10,12: 4,5,7-Hardin-a. 7-Beechen-s. 8-Chang-a						6.00
11,13,14-Hughes-c	2	4	6	11	16	20
15-Hughes-c	5	10	15	34	60	85
16-Hughes-c	7	14	21	44	82	120
...: Shades of the Past TPB (2011, $19.99) r/#7-16; cover gallery						32.00
...: The Mistress of Magic TPB (2011, $17.99) r/#1-6; variant cover gallery						24.00

ZAWA + THE BELLY OF THE BEAST
Boom Entertainment (BOOM! Box): Nov, 2023 - Present ($4.99)

1-4-Michael Dialynas-s/a						5.00

ZAZA, THE MYSTIC (Formerly Charlie Chan; This Magazine Is Haunted V2#12 on)
Charlton Comics: No. 10, Apr, 1956 - No. 11, Sept, 1956

	GD 2.0	VG 4.0	FN 6.0	VF 8.0	VF/NM 9.0	NM- 9.2
10,11	18	36	54	107	169	230

ZEALOT (Also see WildC.A.T.S: Covert Action Teams)
Image Comics: Aug, 1995 - No. 3, Nov, 1995 ($2.50, limited series)

1-3						4.00

ZEGRA (Jungle Empress) (Formerly Tegra)(My Love Life #6 on)
Fox Feature Syndicate: No. 2, Oct, 1948 - No. 5, April, 1949

	GD 2.0	VG 4.0	FN 6.0	VF 8.0	VF/NM 9.0	NM- 9.2
2	97	194	291	621	1061	1500

	GD 2.0	VG 4.0	FN 6.0	VF 8.0	VF/NM 9.0	NM- 9.2
3-5	65	130	195	416	708	1000

ZEN INTERGALACTIC NINJA
No Publisher: 1987 -1993 ($1.75/$2.00, B&W)

	GD 2.0	VG 4.0	FN 6.0	VF 8.0	VF/NM 9.0	NM- 9.2
1	9	18	27	57	111	165
2-Copyright-Stern & Cote	3	6	9	21	33	45
3-6: Copyright-Stern & Cote	2	4	6	8	10	12
V2#1-4-($2.00)						4.00
V3#1-5-($2.95)						4.00
... :Christmas Special 1 (1992, $2.95)						4.00
... :Earth Day Special 1 (1993, $2.95)						4.00

ZEN (Intergalactic Ninja)
Zen Comics Publishing: No. 0, Apr, 2003 - No. 4, Aug, 2003 ($2.95)

0-4-Bill Maus-a/Steve Stern-s. 0-Wraparound-c						3.00

ZEN, INTERGALACTIC NINJA (mini-series)
Zen Comics/Archie Comics: Sept, 1992 - No. 3, 1992 ($1.25)(Formerly a B&W comic by Zen Comics)

1-3: 1-Origin Zen; contains mini-poster						4.00

ZEN INTERGALACTIC NINJA
Entity Comics: No. 0, June-July, 1993 - No. 3, 1994 ($2.95, B&W, limited series)

0-Gold foil stamped-c; photo-c of Zen model						5.00
1-3: Gold foil stamped-c; Bill Maus-c/a						5.00
0-(1993, $3.50, color)-Chromium-c by Jae Lee						4.00
...Sourcebook 1-(1993, $3.50)						4.00
...Sourcebook '94-(1993, $3.50)						4.00
... Spring Spectacular 1 (1994, $2.95, B&W) Gold foil logo						4.00

ZEN INTERGALACTIC NINJA: APRIL FOOL'S SPECIAL
Parody Press: 1994 ($2.50, B&W)

1-w/flip story of Renn Intergalactic Chihuahua						5.00

ZEN INTERGALACTIC NINJA COLOR
Entity Comics: 1994 - No. 7, 1995 ($2.25)

1-($3.95)-Chromium die cut-c						5.00
1, 0-($2.25)-Newsstand; Jae Lee-c; r/...All New Color Special #0						4.00
2-($2.50)-Flip book						4.00
2-($3.50)-Flip book, polybagged w/chromium trading card						5.00
3-7						4.00
Summer Special (1994, $2.95)						4.00
Yearbook: Hazardous Duty 1 (1995)						4.00
Zen-isms 1 (1995, 2.95)						4.00
Ashcan-Tour of the Universe-(no price) w/flip cover						4.00

ZEN INTERGALACTIC NINJA COMMEMORATIVE EDITION
Zen Comics Publishing: 1997 ($5.95, color)

1-Stern-s/Cote-a						6.00

ZEN INTERGALACTIC NINJA: HARD BOUNTY
1First Comics: 2015 - No. 6 ($3.99, limited series)

1-Stern-s/Mychaels-a						4.00

ZEN INTERGALACTIC NINJA MILESTONE
Entity Comics: 1994 - No. 3, 1994 ($3.95)

1-3: Gold foil logo; r/Defend the Earth						4.00

ZEN INTERGALACTIC NINJA STARQUEST
Entity Comics: 1994 - No. 6, 1995 ($2.95, B&W)

1-6: Gold foil logo						4.00

ZEN, INTERGALACTIC NINJA: THE HUNTED
Entity Comics: 1993 - No. 3, 1994 ($2.95, B&W, limited series)

1-3: Newsstand Edition; foil logo						4.00
1-($3.50)-Polybagged w/chromium card by Kieth; foil logo						5.00

ZERO GIRL
DC Comics (Homage): Feb, 2001 - No. 5, Jun, 2001 ($2.95, limited series)

1-5-Sam Kieth-s/a						3.00
TPB (2001, $14.95) r/#1-5; intro. by Alan Moore						15.00

ZERO GIRL: FULL CIRCLE
DC Comics (Homage): Jan, 2003 - No. 5, May, 2003 ($2.95, limited series)

1-5-Sam Kieth-s/a						3.00
TPB (2003, $17.95) r/#1-5						18.00

ZERO HOUR: CRISIS IN TIME (Also see Showcase '94 #8-10)
DC Comics: No. 4(#1), Sept, 1994 - No. 0(#5), Oct, 1994 ($1.50, limited series)

4(#1)-0(#5)						4.00
"Ashcan"-(1994, free, B&W, 8 pgs.) several versions exist						5.00
TPB (‘94, $9.95)						10.00

ZERO KILLER
Dark Horse Comics: Jul, 2007 - No.6, Oct, 2009 ($2.99)

1-6-Arvid Nelson-s/Matt Camp-a						3.00

ZERO PATROL, THE
Continuity Comics: Nov, 1984 - No. 2 ($1.50); 1987 - No. 5, May, 1989 ($2.00)

1,2: Neal Adams-c/a; Megalith begins						5.00
1-5 (#1,2-reprints above, 1987)						4.00

06 PROTOCOL, THE
AfterShock Comics: Sept, 2022 - No. 3 ($4.99, limited series)

1-3-Lee Turner-s/Cliff Richards-a						5.00

ZERO TOLERANCE
First Comics: Oct, 1990 - No. 4, Jan, 1991 ($2.25, limited series)

1-4: Tim Vigil-c/a(p) (his 1st color limited series)						4.00

ZIGGY PIG – SILLY SEAL COMICS (See Animal Fun, Animated Movie-Tunes, Comic Capers, Krazy Komics, Silly Tunes & Super Rabbit)
Timely Comics (CmPL): Fall, 1944 - No. 4, Summer, 1945; No. 5, Summer, 1946; No. 6, Sept, 1946

Y: The Last Man #38 © Vaughan & Guerra

Zatanna #13 © DC

Zorro New World #3 © ZPI

	GD 2.0	VG 4.0	FN 6.0	VF 8.0	VF/NM 9.0	NM- 9.2
1-Vs. the Japanese	47	94	141	296	498	700
2-(Spring, 1945)	30	60	90	177	289	400
3-5	23	46	69	136	223	310
6-Infinity-c	25	50	75	150	245	340
I.W. Reprint #1(1958)-r/Krazy Komics	5	10	15	22	26	30
I.W. Reprint #2,7,8	5	10	15	22	26	30

ZIGGY PIG – SILLY SEAL COMICS (Marvel 80th Anniversary salute)
Marvel Comics: May, 2019 ($3.99, one-shot)

1-Tieri & Cerilli-s/Chabot-a; Doctor Doom app.; Deadpool cameo						4.00

ZIP COMICS
MLJ Magazines: Feb, 1940 - No. 47, Summer, 1944 (#1-7?: 68 pgs.)

	GD 2.0	VG 4.0	FN 6.0	VF 8.0	VF/NM 9.0	NM- 9.2
1-Origin Kalathar the Giant Man, The Scarlet Avenger, & Steel Sterling; Mr. Satan (by Edd Ashe), Nevada Jones (masked hero) & Zambini, the Miracle Man, War Eagle, Captain Valor begins	486	972	1458	3550	6275	9000
2-Nevada Jones adds mask & horse Blaze	290	580	870	1856	3178	4500
3-Biro robot-c	343	686	1029	2400	4200	6000
4,5-Biro WWII-c	245	490	735	1568	2684	3800
6,7-Biro-c	219	438	657	1402	2401	3400
8-Bondage/torture-c by Biro	290	580	870	1856	3178	4500
9-Last Kalathar & Mr. Satan; classic-c	314	628	942	2198	3849	5500
10-Inferno, the Flame Breather begins, ends #13	300	600	900	2070	3635	5200
11-Inferno without costume	200	400	600	1260	2190	3100
12-Biro bondage/torture-c with dwarf ghouls	232	464	696	1485	2543	3600
13-Electrocution-c	271	542	813	1734	2967	4200
14-Biro bondage/torture guillotine-c	239	478	717	1530	2615	3700
15-Classic spider-c	245	490	735	1568	2684	3800
16-Female hanging execution-c by Biro (Rare)	284	568	852	1818	3109	4400
17-Last Scarlet Avenger; women in bondage being cooked alive-c by Biro	459	918	1377	3350	5925	8500
18-Wilbur begins (9/41, 1st app.); headlights sci-fi-c	757	1514	2271	5526	9763	14,000
19-Horror-c	290	580	870	1856	3178	4500
20-Origin & 1st app. Black Jack (11/41); Hitler-c	394	788	1182	2758	4829	6900
21-Sinister Nazi using lethal chemical weapons on the General-c	245	490	735	1568	2684	3800
22-Classic Nazi Grim Reaper w/sickle, V for Victory-c	919	1338	2757	6709	11,855	17,000
23-Nazi WWII-c	187	374	561	1197	2049	2900
24,25: 25-Last Nevada Jones	161	322	483	1030	1765	2500
26-Classic Nazi/Japanese "Remember Pearl Harbor!" WWII cover; Black Witch begins; last Captain Valor	309	618	927	2163	3782	5400
27-Intro. Web (7/42) plus-c app.; Japanese WWII-c	400	800	1200	2800	4900	7000
28-Origin Web; classic Baron Gestapo Nazi WWII-c	331	662	993	2317	4059	5800
29-The Hyena app. (scarce); Nazi WWII-c	300	600	900	2010	3505	5000
30-WWII-c	300	600	900	1950	3375	4800
31,35-WWII-c. 35-Last Zambini, Black Jack	245	490	735	1568	2684	3800
32-Classic skeleton Nazi WWII-c	703	1406	2109	5132	9066	13,000
33-Japanese war-c showing nurses bound, blindfolded, lined up at a firing squad	757	1514	2271	5526	9763	14,000
34-Japanese WWII bondage & hanging-c; 1st Applejack app.	300	600	900	2070	3635	5200
36-38: 38-Last Web issue	123	246	369	787	1344	1900
39-Red Rube begins (origin, 8/43)	90	180	270	576	988	1400
40-43	68	136	204	435	743	1050
44-46: WWII covers. 45-Wilbur ends	81	162	243	518	884	1250
47-Last issue; scarce	87	174	261	553	952	1350

NOTE: *Biro* a-5, 9, 17; c-3-17. *Meskin* a-1-3, 5-7, 9, 10, 12, 13, 15, 16 at least. *Montana* c-29, 30, 32-35. *Novick* c-18-28, 31. *Sahle* c-37, 38, 40-46. Bondage c-8, 9, 33, 34. Cover features: Steel Sterling-1-43, 47; (w/ Blackjack-20-27 & Web-27-35), 28-39; (w/Red Rube-40-43); Red Rube-44-47.

ZIP-JET (Hero)
St. John Publishing Co.: Feb, 1953 - No. 2, Apr-May, 1953

	GD 2.0	VG 4.0	FN 6.0	VF 8.0	VF/NM 9.0	NM- 9.2
1-Rocketman-r from Punch Comics; #1-c from splash in Punch #10	142	284	426	909	1555	2200
2	68	136	204	435	743	1050

ZIPPY THE CHIMP (CBS TV Presents…)
Pines (Literary Ent.)**:** No. 50, March, 1957; No. 51, Aug. 1957

	GD 2.0	VG 4.0	FN 6.0	VF 8.0	VF/NM 9.0	NM- 9.2
50,51	10	20	30	54	72	90

Z NATION (Based on the 2014 TV series on Syfy)
Dynamite Entertainment: 2017 - No. 6, 2017 ($3.99)

1-6: 1-Engler & Van Lente-s/Menna-a; multiple covers						4.00

ZODIAC STARFORCE
Dark Horse Comics: Aug, 2015 - No. 4, Feb, 2016 ($3.99, mini-series)

1-4-Kevin Panetta-s/Paulina Ganucheau-a. 2-Wada-c. 4-Babs Tarr-c						4.00

ZODIAC STARFORCE: CRIES OF THE FIRE PRINCE
Dark Horse Comics: Jul, 2017 - No. 4, May, 2018 ($3.99, limited series)

1-4-Kevin Panetta-s/Paulina Ganucheau-a						4.00

ZODY, THE MOD ROB
Gold Key: July, 1970

	GD 2.0	VG 4.0	FN 6.0	VF 8.0	VF/NM 9.0	NM- 9.2
1		3	6	9	16	23	30

ZOMBIE
Marvel Comics: Nov, 2006 - No. 4, Feb, 2007 ($3.99, limited series)

1-4-Kyle Hotz-a/c; Mike Raicht-s						4.00
...: Simon Garth (1/08 - No. 4, 4/08) Hotz-s/a/c						4.00

ZOMBIE BOY
Timbuktu Graphics/Antarctic Press: Mar, 1988 - Nov, 1996 ($1.50/$2.50/$2.95, B&W)

1-Mark Stokes-s/a						4.00
...'s Hoodoo Tales (11/89, $1.50)						4.00
... Rises Again (1/94, $2.50) r/#1 and Hoodoo Tales						4.00
1-(Antarctic Press, 11/96, $2.95) new story						4.00

ZOMBIE KING
Image Comics: No. 0, June, 2005 ($2.95, B&W, one-shot)

0-Frank Cho-s/a						5.00

ZOMBIE PROOF
Moonstone: 2007 - Present ($3.50)

1-3: 1-J.C. Vaughn-s/Vincent Spencer-a; two covers by Spencer and Neil Vokes						4.00
1-Baltimore Comic-Con 2007 variant-c by Vokes (ltd. ed. of 500)						6.00
2-Big Apple 2008 Convention Edition; Tucci-c (ltd. ed. of 250)						6.00
3-Convention Edition; Beck-c (ltd. ed. of 100)						6.00
...: Zombie Zoo #1 Virginia Comicon Exclusive Edition (2012, ed. of 150)						10.00
...: Zombie Zoo - WVPOP Exclusive Edition (2012)						10.00

ZOMBIES ASSEMBLE
Marvel Comics: Jul, 2017 - No. 3, Aug, 2017 ($4.99, B&W, manga style back to front)

1-3-English translation of Avengers Japanese manga; Komiyama-s/a						5.00
#0-(9/17) Follows Tony Stark after Avengers: Age of Ultron; Komiyama-s/a						5.00

ZOMBIES ASSEMBLE 2
Marvel Comics: Oct, 2017 - No. 4, Jan, 2018 ($4.99, B&W, manga style back to front)

1-4-Continuation of story from Zombies Assemble #1-3; Komiyama-s/a						5.00

ZOMBIES CHRISTMAS CAROL (See Marvel Zombies Christmas Carol)

ZOMBIES!: ECLIPSE OF THE UNDEAD
IDW Publ.: Nov, 2006 - No. 4, Feb, 2007 ($3.99, limited series)

1-4-Torres-s/Herrera-a; two covers						4.00

ZOMBIES!: FEAST
IDW Publ.: May, 2006 - No. 5, Oct, 2006 ($3.99, limited series)

1-5: 1-Chris Bolton-a/Shane McCarthy-s. 3-Lorenzana-a						4.00

ZOMBIES!: HUNTERS
IDW Publ.: May, 2008 ($3.99)

1-Don Figueroa-a/c; Dara Naraghi-s						4.00

ZOMBIES VS. ROBOTS
IDW Publ.: Oct, 2006 - No. 2, Dec, 2006 ($3.99, limited series)

1-Chris Ryall-s/Ashley Wood-a; two covers by Wood						18.00
2						12.00

ZOMBIES VS. ROBOTS
IDW Publ.: Jan, 2015 - No. 10, Oct, 2015 ($3.99/$4.99)

1-8-Short stories by Chris Ryall/Ashley Wood-a and others						5.00
9,10-($4.99) Two covers on each						6.00

ZOMBIES VS. ROBOTS AVENTURE
IDW Publ.: Feb, 2010 - No. 4, May 2010 ($3.99, limited series)

1-4-Short stories; Ryall-s; art by Matthews III, McCaffrey, & Hernandez; Wood-c						5.00

ZOMBIES VS. ROBOTS: UNDERCITY
IDW Publ.: Apr, 2011 - No. 3, Jun, 2011 ($3.99, limited series)

1-3-Chris Ryall-s/Mark Torres; two covers on each by Torres and Garry Brown						5.00

ZOMBIES VS. ROBOTS VS. AMAZONS
IDW Publ.: Sept, 2007 - No. 3, Dec, 2008 ($3.99, limited series)

1-3-Chris Ryall/Ashley Wood-a; two covers by Wood on each						6.00

ZOMBIE TALES THE SERIES
BOOM! Studios: Apr, 2008 - No. 12, Mar, 2009 ($3.99)

1-Niles-s; Lansdale/Barreto-a; two covers on each						5.00

ZOMBIE WAR

	GD	VG	FN	VF	VF/NM	NM-
	2.0	4.0	6.0	8.0	9.0	9.2

IDW Publishing: Oct, 2013 - No. 2, Nov, 2013 ($3.99, limited series)

1,2-Kevin Eastman & Tom Skulan-s/Eastman & Eric Talbot-a; 2 covers on each						4.00

ZOMBIE WORLD (one-shots)
Dark Horse Comics

... :Eat Your Heart Out (4/98, $2.95) Kelley Jones-c/s/a						4.00
... :Home For The Holidays (12/97, $2.95)						4.00

ZOMBIE WORLD: CHAMPION OF THE WORMS
Dark Horse Comics: Sept, 1997 - No. 3, Nov, 1997 ($2.95, limited series)

1-3-Mignola & McEown-c/s/a						4.00

ZOMBIE WORLD: DEAD END
Dark Horse Comics: Jan, 1998 - No. 2, Feb, 1998 ($2.95, limited series)

1,2-Stephen Blue-c/s/a						4.00

ZOMBIE WORLD: TREE OF DEATH
Dark Horse Comics: Jun, 1999 - No. 4, Oct, 1999 ($2.95, limited series)

1-4-Mills-s/Deadstock-a						4.00

ZOMBIE WORLD: WINTER'S DREGS
Dark Horse Comics: May, 1998 - No. 4, Aug, 1998 ($2.95, limited series)

1-4-Fingerman-s/Edwards-a						4.00

ZOO ANIMALS
Star Publications: No. 8, 1954 (15¢, 36 pgs.)

	GD	VG	FN	VF	VF/NM	NM-
8-(B&W for coloring)	10	20	30	58	79	100

ZOO FUNNIES (Tim McCoy #16 on)
Charlton Comics/Children Comics Publ.: Nov, 1945 - No. 15, 1947

	GD	VG	FN	VF	VF/NM	NM-
101(#1)(11/45, 1st Charlton comic book)-Funny animal; Al Fago-c	27	54	81	158	259	360
2(12/45, 52 pgs.) Classic-c	15	30	45	86	133	180
3-5	12	24	36	69	97	125
6-15: 8-Diana the Huntress app.	10	20	30	56	76	95

ZOO FUNNIES (Becomes Nyoka, The Jungle Girl #14 on?)
Capitol Stories/Charlton Comics: July, 1953 - No. 13, Sept, 1955; Dec, 1984

	GD	VG	FN	VF	VF/NM	NM-
1-1st app.? Timothy The Ghost; Fago-c/a	15	30	45	85	130	175
2	10	20	30	54	72	90
3-7	9	18	27	50	65	80
8-13-Nyoka app.	11	22	33	62	86	110
1(1984) (Low print run)	1	3	4	6	8	10

ZOOHUNTERS, THE
Aspen MLT: Nov, 2014 - No. 4 ($3.99, limited series)

1-4-Peter Stiegerwald-s/a; five covers on each						4.00

ZOONIVERSE
Eclipse Comics: 8/86 - No. 6, 6/87 ($1.25/$1.75, limited series, Mando paper)

1-6						4.00

ZOO PARADE (TV)
Dell Publishing Co.: #662, 1955 (Marlin Perkins)

	GD	VG	FN	VF	VF/NM	NM-
Four Color 662	6	12	18	41	76	110

ZOOM COMICS
Carlton Publishing Co.: Dec, 1945 (one-shot)

	GD	VG	FN	VF	VF/NM	NM-
nn-Dr. Mercy, Satannas, from Red Band Comics; Capt. Milksop origin retold	52	104	156	328	552	775

ZOOT (Rulah Jungle Goddess #17 on)
Fox Feature Syndicate: nd (1946) - No. 16, July, 1948 (Two #13s & 14s)

	GD	VG	FN	VF	VF/NM	NM-
nn-Funny animal only	36	72	108	214	347	480
2-The Jaguar app.	27	54	81	158	259	360
3(Fall, 1946) - 6-Funny animals & teen-age	18	36	54	107	169	230
7-(6/47)-Rulah, Jungle Goddess (origin/1st app.)	161	322	483	1030	1765	2500
8-10	97	194	291	621	1061	1500
11-Kamen bondage-c	148	296	444	947	1624	2300
12-Injury-to-eye panels, torture scene	84	168	252	538	919	1300
13(2/48)	77	154	231	493	847	1200
14(3/48)-Used in **SOTI**, pg. 104, "One picture showing a girl nailed by her wrists to trees with blood flowing from the wounds, might be taken straight from an ill. ed. of the Marquis deSade"	219	438	657	1402	2401	3400
13(4/48),14(5/48)-Western True Crime #15 on?	97	194	291	621	1061	1500
15,16	81	162	243	518	884	1250

ZORRO (Walt Disney with #882)(TV)(See Eclipse Graphic Album)
Dell Publishing Co.: May, 1949 - No. 15, Sept-Nov, 1961 (Photo-c 882 on)
(Zorro first appeared in a pulp story Aug 19, 1919)

	GD	VG	FN	VF	VF/NM	NM-
Four Color 228 (#1)	32	64	96	230	515	800
Four Color 425,617,732	13	26	39	86	188	290
Four Color 497,538,574-Kinstler-a	13	26	39	86	188	290
Four Color 882-Photo-c begin;1st TV Disney; Toth-a	15	30	45	100	220	340
Four Color 920,933,960,976-Toth-a in all	10	20	30	69	147	225
Four Color 1003('59)-Toth-a	10	20	30	69	147	225
Four Color 1037-Annette Funicello photo-c	12	24	36	81	176	270
8(12-2/59-60)	7	14	21	48	89	130
9-Toth-a	8	16	24	51	96	140
10,11,13-15-Last photo-c	7	14	21	46	86	125
12-Toth-a; last 10¢ issue	8	16	24	51	96	140

NOTE: **Warren Tufts** a-4-Color 1037, 8, 9, 10, 13.

ZORRO (Walt Disney)(TV)
Gold Key: Jan, 1966 - No. 9, Mar, 1968 (All photo-c)

	GD	VG	FN	VF	VF/NM	NM-
1-Toth-a	7	14	21	44	82	120
2,4,5,7-9-Toth-a. 5-r/F.C. #1003 by Toth	4	8	12	28	47	65
3,6-Tufts-a	4	8	12	27	44	60

NOTE: #1-9 are reprinted from Dell issues. **Tufts** a-3, 4. #1-r/F.C. #882. #2-r/F.C. #960. #3-r/#12-c & #8 inside. #4-r/#9-c & insides. #6-r/#11(all); #7-r/#14-c. #8-r/F.C. #933 inside & back-c & #976-c. #9-r/F.C. #920.

ZORRO (TV)
Marvel Comics: Dec, 1990 - No. 12, Nov, 1991 ($1.00)

1-12: Based on TV show. 12-Toth-c						4.00

ZORRO (Also see Mask of Zorro)
Topps Comics: Nov, 1993 - No. 11, Nov, 1994 ($2.50/$2.95)

			GD	VG	FN	VF	VF/NM	NM-
0-(11/93, $1.00, 20 pgs.)-Painted-c; collector's ed.								4.00
1,4,6-9,11: 1-Miller-c. 4-Mike Grell-c. 6-Mignola-c. 7-Lady Rawhide-c by Gulacy.								4.00
8-Perez-c. 10-Julie Bell-c. 11-Lady Rawhide-c								5.00
2-Lady Rawhide-app. (not in costume)								
3-1st app. Lady Rawhide in costume, 3-Lady Rawhide-c by Adam Hughes	2	4	6	9	12	15
5-Lady Rawhide app.								5.00
10-($2.95)-Lady Rawhide-c/app.								5.00
The Lady Wears Red (12/98, $12.95, TPB) r/#1-3								13.00
Zorro's Renegades (2/99, $14.95, TPB) r/#4-8								15.00

ZORRO
Dynamite Entertainment: 2008 - No. 20, 2010 ($3.50)

1-Origin retold; Wagner-s; three covers						3.50
2-20-Two covers on all						3.50

ZORRO
American Mythology Prods.: 2019; 2022 ($3.99)

...Four Color 960 Reprint (2022); art by Alex Toth						4.00
...Masters 1 (2019) Reprints Four Color #1003; art by Alex Toth						4.00
Vol. 2 1-Reprints Four Color #976 & Dell issue #12 (1960); art by Alex Toth						4.00

ZORRO BLACK & WHITE NOIR
American Mythology Prods.: 2022 ($3.99, limited series)

1-New stories in B&W plus reprint with Toth-s/a						4.00

ZORRO: FELIZ NAVIDAD
American Mythology Prods.: 2022 ($3.99, one-shot)

1-Christmas-themed short stories and reprints						4.00

ZORRO FLIGHTS
American Mythology Prods.: 2021 - Present ($3.99, limited series)

1-3-Don McGregor-s/Vincenzo Carratu-a; preview of Zorro: The Dailies						4.00

ZORRO: GALLEON OF THE DEAD
American Mythology Prods.: 2020 - No. 4, 2021 ($3.99, limited series)

1-4-Mike Wolfer-s/Alessandro Miracolo-a						4.00

ZORRO IN THE LAND THAT TIME FORGOT
American Mythology Prods.: 2020 - No. 4, 2021 ($3.99, limited series)

1-4-Mike Wolfer-s/Alessandro Ranaldi-a						4.00

ZORRO: LEGENDARY ADVENTURES
American Mythology Prods.: 2018 - Present ($3.99)

1-4-English reprints of French Zorro comics from 1975-1976; Robert Rigot-a						4.00
... Book 2 (2019 - No. 4, 2019, $3.99) 1-4-Art by Marcello & Rigot						4.00

ZORRO: MAN OF THE DEAD
Massive Publishing: Jan, 2024 - Present ($4.99, limited series)

1,2-Sean Murphy-s/a						5.00

ZORRO MATANZAS
Dynamite Entertainment: 2010 - No. 4, 2010 ($3.99, limited series)

1-4-Mayhew-a/McGregor-s						4.00

ZORRO NEW WORLD
American Mythology Prods.: 2021 - No. 4, 2022 ($3.99, limited series)

1-4-Reprints of stories from the 1990 Marvel series; Mario Capaldi-a						4.00

ZORRO RIDES AGAIN
Dynamite Entertainment: 2011 - No. 12, 2012 ($3.99)

1-12: 1-6-Wagner-s/Polls-a. 7-12-Snyder III-a. 10-Lady Zorro on cover						4.00

ZORRO: RISE OF THE OLD GODS
American Mythology Prods.: 2019 - No. 4, 2019 ($3.99, limited series)

1-4-Jason Pell-s/Puis Calzada-a. 1-Main cover by Kaluta						4.00

ZORRO: SACRILEGE
American Mythology Prods.: 2019 - No. 4 ($3.99)

1-4: 1,2-Mike Wolfer-s/Mauricio Melo-a. 1-Main cover by Kaluta. 3,4-Miracolo-a						4.00

ZORRO: SWORDS OF HELL
American Mythology Prods.: 2018 - No. 4, 2019 ($3.99, limited series)

1-4-David Avallone-s/Roy Allan Martinez-a						4.00

ZORRO TIMELESS TALES
American Mythology Prods.: 2020 ($3.99, limited series)

1,2-Nadaud-s/Marcello-a; art in the style of the Toth stories						4.00

ZOT!
Eclipse Comics: 4/84 - No. 10, 7/85; No. 11, 1/87 - No. 36 7/91 ($1.50, Baxter-p)

1						6.00
2,3						5.00
4-10: 4-Origin. 10-Last color issue						4.00
10 1/2 (6/86, 25¢, Not Available Comics) Ashcan; art by Feazell & Scott McCloud						5.00
11-14,15-35-($2.00-c) B&W issues						4.00
14 1/2 (Adventures of Zot! in Dimension 10 1/2)(7/87) Antisocialman app.						4.00
36-($2.95-c) B&W						5.00
... The Complete Black and White Collection TPB (2008, $24.95) r/#11-36 with commentary, interviews and bonus artwork						25.00

Z-2 COMICS (Secret Agent...)(See Holyoke One-Shot #7)

ZULU (See Movie Classics)

ZVRC (Zombies vs Robots Classics)
Image Comics: Mar, 2022 - No. 4, Jun, 2022 ($3.99/$5.99/$6.99, limited series)

1-($3.99)-Chris Ryall-s/Ashley Wood-a						4.00
2,4-($5.99)						6.00
3-($6.99)						7.00

Jusko Celebrates Kubert!

Acclaimed ERB Cover Artist Joe Jusko Recreates Joe Kubert's *Overstreet* #5 Cover For Its 50th Anniversary!

On Sale July 2025

LIFE CAN CHANGE IN A FLASH.

When that happens for comic shop and bookstore employees and owners, Binc is a phone call away. Support your local indie comic shop and bookstore by supporting their safety net.

BE A SUPERHERO AND CHANGE A LIFE TODAY

The **Book Industry Charitable Foundation** is the only nonprofit in the country dedicated to supporting comic shop and bookstore owners and employees through life's unexpected emergencies like ER visits, dental needs, and home fires. Support comic shops, bookstores, and the people who work there by supporting Binc. Find out more at bincfoundation.org.

binc FOUNDATION

DIRECTORY LISTINGS

Items stocked by these shops are noted at the end of each listing and are coded as follows:

(1) Golden Age Comics
(2) Silver Age Comics
(3) Bronze Age Comics
(4) New Comics & Magazines
(5) Back Issue magazines
(6) Comic Supplies
(7) Collectible Card Games
(8) Role Playing Games
(9) Gaming Supplies
(10) Manga
(11) Anime

(12) Underground Comics
(13) Original Comic Art
(14) Pulps
(15) Big Little Books
(16) Books - Used
(17) Books - New
(18) Comic Related Posters
(19) Movie Posters
(20) Trading Cards
(21) Statues/Mini-busts, etc.

(22) Premiums (Rings, Decoders)
(23) Action Figures
(24) Other Toys
(25) Records/CDs
(26) Blu-rays/DVDs/VHS
(27) Doctor Who Items
(28) Simpsons Items
(29) Star Trek Items
(30) Star Wars Items
(31) POP! Vinyls/HeroClix

ALABAMA

Quality Comix
500 Eastern Blvd.
Suite 101
Montgomery, AL 36117
PH: (800) 548-3314
info@qualitycomix.com
www.qualitycomix.com
(a-c)

CALIFORNIA

The Comic Cellar
135 W. Main St.
Alhambra, CA 91801
(626) 570-8743
comiccellar@comiccellar.com
www.comiccellar.com
(1-6, 10, 12, 13, 18, 30, 31)

ArchAngels
4629 Cass Street #9
Pacific Beach, CA 92109
(310) 480-8105
rhughes@archangels.com
www.archangels.com

CONNECTICUT

Sarge's Comics and Games
124 State St
New London, CT 06320
(860) 443-2004
sargescomics@gmail.com
(1-12, 14-18, 20-31)

FLORIDA

Emerald City Comics
4902 113th Ave. N
Clearwater, FL 33760
(727) 398-2665
email@emeraldcitycomics.com
emeraldcitycomics.com
(1-10, 12, 13, 15, 17-24, 27-31)

Classic Collectible Services
P.O. Box 4738
Sarasota, FL 34230
(855) CCS-1711
CCSpaper.com

CGC
P.O. Box 4738
Sarasota, FL 34230
PH: (877) NM-COMIC
www.CGCcomics.com

David T. Alexander Collectibles
P.O. Box 273086
Tampa, FL 33618
(813) 968-1805
davidt@cultureandthrills.com
www.dtacollectibles.com
(1-3, 5, 12-15, 18-20, 22, 24, 29,30)

Pedigree Comics, Inc.
12541 Equine Lane
Wellington, FL 33414
PH/FAX: (561) 422-1120
CELL: (561) 596-9111
E-Mail: DougSchmell
    @pedigreecomics.com
www.pedigreecomics.com

GEORGIA

Comicpresser.com
Atlanta, GA
(507) 400-0661
info@comicpresser.com
www.comicpresser.com

Dr. No's Comics & Games SuperStore
3372 Canton Road
Suite 104
Marietta, GA 30066
(770) 422-4642
manager@drnos.com
www.drnos.com
(1-7, 9, 10, 12, 17-19, 21-24, 27, 29-31)

ILLINOIS

Midgard Comics
102 West Lincoln
Charleston, IL 61920
(217) 348-8368
midgardcomics.com
(1-6, 23, 24)

Amazing Fantasy Comics and Games
20505 S. La Grange Rd.
Frankfort, IL 60423
(815) 469-5092
afbooks_frankfort
    @sbcglobal.net
www.afbooks.com
(2-10, 18, 21, 23, 24, 27-31)

INDIANA

Comics Ina Flash
P.O. Box 3611
Evansville, IN 47735-3611
(812) 589-2941
comicflash@aol.com
www.comicsinaflash.com

IOWA

Oak Leaf Comics & Collectibles
221 North Federal
Mason City, IA 50401
(641) 424-0333
miket@dustcatchers.com
www.oakleafcomics.com
(1-13, 15, 18-21, 23-26, 29-31)

KENTUCKY

The Great Escape
2945 Scottsville Road
Suites B17 & B18
Bowling Green, KY 42104
PH: (270) 782-8092
FAX: (270) 843-3090
thegreatescapebg@gmail.com
www.TheGreatEscapeOnLine.com
(1-31)

Comic Interlude
393 Waller Ave.; Ste. 10
Lexington, KY 40502
PH: (859) 321-4325
thecomicinterludeky@gmail.com

The Great Escape
2433 Bardstown Road
Louisville, KY 40205
PH: (502) 456-2216
FAX: (502) 456-5964
thegreatescapelouisville
@gmail.com
www.TheGreatEscapeOnLine.com
(1-31)

Leroy Harper
P.O. Box 212
West Paducah, KY 42086
PH: (270) 748-9364
LHCOMICS@hotmail.com

MARYLAND

Third Eye Comics
209 Chinquapin Round Rd.
Suite 200
Annapolis, MD 21401
(410) 897-0322
info@thirdeyecomics.com
http://thirdeyecomics.com
(2-12, 17-25, 27, 29, 31)

E. Gerber
1720 Belmont Ave.; Suite C
Baltimore, MD 21244

Esquire Comics.com
Mark S. Zaid, ESQ.
P.O. Box 3422492
Bethesda, MD 20827
PH: (202) 498-0011
esquirecomics@aol.com
www.esquirecomics.com
(2-11, 18, 21, 23, D, E)

Diamond Comic
Distributors
10150 York Road, Suite 300
Hunt Valley, MD 21030
PH: (443) 318-8001

Diamond International
Galleries
10720 Gilroy Rd., Suite 300
Hunt Valley, MD 21031
pokevin@DiamondGalleries.com
www.DiamondGalleries.com

Reece's Rare Comics
PO Box 399
Monrovia, MD 21770
PH: (240) 367-3662
alex@reececomics.com
www.reececomics.com
(1, 2, 3, 5, 6)

Cards Comics and
Collectibles
51 Main St.
Reisterstown, MD 21136
PH: (410) 526-7410
FAX: (410) 526-4006
cardscomicscollectibles
@yahoo.com
www.cardscomicscollectibles.com
(1-4, 6, 7, 10, 20, 23, 25)

MASSACHUSETTS

Gary Dolgoff Comics
116 Pleasant St.
Easthampton, MA 01027
PH: (413) 529-0326
FAX: (413) 529-9824
gary@gdcomics.com
www.gdcomics.com
(1-3, 5, 7, 12-16, 20, 21, 23, 24)

Federation Comics
Fulfilling orders for
Bill Cole Enterprises Inc.
3065 Cranberry Highway
Suite B17
East Wareham, MA 02538
PH: (781) 986-2653
sales@bcemylar.com
www.bcemylar.com

That's Entertainment
56 John Fitch Highway
Fitchburg, MA 01420
(978) 342-8607
dario@thatse.com
www.ThatsE.com
(1-14, 16-21, 23-31)

SuperworldComics.com
456 Main St., Suite F
Holden, MA 01520
PH: (508) 829-2259
PH: (508) UB-WACKY
Ted@Superworldcomics.com
www.Superworldcomics.com
(1-3, 13)

That's Entertainment
244 Park Avenue
Worcester, MA 01609
(508) 755-4207
pete@thatse.com
www.ThatsE.com
(1-14, 16-21, 23-31)

MICHIGAN

Harley Yee Comics
P.O. Box 51758
Livonia, MI 48151-5758
PH: (800) 731-1029
FAX: (734) 421-7928
HarleyComx@aol.com
www.HarleyYeeComics.com

NEVADA

Cosmic Comics!
3830 E. Flamingo Rd.; Ste F-2
Las Vegas, NV 89121
PH: (702) 451-6611
info@CosmicComicsLV.com
CosmicComics.vegas
(1-10, 17-19, 21, 23, 29-31)

Torpedo Comics
7300 Arroyo Crossing Pkwy
Unit 105
Las Vegas, NV 89113
PH: (702) 444-4432
BMarvelman@aol.com
(1-6, 10-15, 21, 23, 27-30)

NEW HAMPSHIRE

Rare Books & Comics
James F. Payette
P.O. Box 750
Bethlehem, NH 03574
PH: (603) 869-2097
FAX: (603) 869-3475
JimPayette@msn.com
www.JamesPayetteComics.com
(1-3, 5, 14-16)

Jetpack Comics & Games
37 North Main Street
Rochester, NH 03867
(603) 330-9636
JetpackComics@gmail.com
www.JetpackComics.com
(1-10, 12, 13, 16-18, 20, 21, 23, 24, 27-31)

NEW JERSEY

Nationwide Comics
Buying All 10¢ & 12¢
Original priced comics
Derek Woywood
Clementon, NJ 08021
PH: (856) 217-5737
dwoywood@yahoo.com
www.philadelphiacomic-con.com
(1, 2, 4-8, 13, 14, 17)

JHV Associates
(By Appointment Only)
P. O. Box 317
Woodbury Heights, NJ 08097
PH: (856) 845-4010
FAX: (856) 845-3977
JHVassoc@hotmail.com
(1, 2, 14, 19)

NEW YORK

HighGradeComics.com
17 Bethany Drive
Commack, NY 11725
PH: (631) 543-1917
FAX: (631) 864-1921
BobStorms@
  HighGradeComics.com
www.HighGradeComics.com
(1-3, 5)

Best Comics
1300 Jericho Turnpike
New Hyde Park, NY 11040
PH: (516) 328-1900
FAX: (516) 328-1909
TommyBest@aol.com
www.bestcomics.com
(1, 2, 4, 6, 13, 20, 21, 23, 29,30)

ComicConnect.com
36 West 37th St.; 6th Floor
New York, NY 10018
PH: (212) 895-3999
FAX: (212) 260-4304
support@comicconnect.com
www.comicconnect.com
(1-3, 13, 14, 19, 22)

Metropolis Collectibles
36 West 37th St.; 6th Floor
New York, NY 10018
PH: (800) 229-6387
FAX: (212) 260-4304
E-Mail: buying@
  metropoliscomics.com
www.metropoliscomics.com

Dave and Adam's
55 Oriskany Dr.
Tonawanda, NY 14150
PH: (888) 440-9787
FAX: (716) 838-9896
service@dacardworld.com
www.dacardworld.com
(1-9, 13, 18, 20, 23, 24, 27-31)

Long Island Comics
276 Little East Neck Road
West Babylon, NY 11704
(631) 321-4822
frank@licomics.com
licomics.com
(2-6, 26)

NORTH CAROLINA

Heroes Aren't Hard to Find
417 Pecan Avenue.
Charlotte, NC 28204
PH: (704) 375-7462
www.heroesonline.com

OHIO

Comics and Friends, LLC
7850 Mentor Ave.; Suite 1054
Mentor, OH 44096
PH: (440) 255-4242
comics.and.friends.store
@gmail.com
www.comicsandfriends.com
(1-7, 9, 10, 12-14, 18, 20, 21, 23-31)

Ditko Club Comics
Buying comics
North Lima, OH 44452
PH: (330) 647-5628
darren@ditkoclub.com
www.ditkoclub.com
(1, 2, 3, 13)

New Dimension Comics
Ohio Valley Mall
67800 Mall Ring Rd Unit 875
Saint Clairsville, OH 43950
PH: (740) 695-1020
ohiovalley@ndcomics.com
www.ndcomics.com

OKLAHOMA

Want List Comics
(Appointment Only)
P.O. Box 701932
Tulsa, OK 74170
PH: (918) 299-0440
E-Mail: wantlistcomics777
@gmail.com
(1-3, 13-15, 19, 20, 24, 29)

OREGON

Tasteecat Comics
2621 SE Clinton St.
Portland, OR
(503) 236-8133
@tasteecatcomics
tasteecatcomics.com

PENNSYLVANIA

New Dimension Comics
108 South Main Street
Butler, PA 16001
PH: (724) 282-5283
butler@ndcomics.com
www.ndcomics.com
(1-12, 14, 15, 18, 20, 21, 23, 24, 27-31)

New Dimension Comics – Cranberry
20550 Route 19
#20 Piazza Plaza
Cranberry Township, PA 16066
(724) 776-0433
cranberry@ndcomics.com
www.ndcomics.com
(1-4, 6-10, 12, 14, 15, 17, 18, 20-24, 27-31)

New Dimension Comics
Megastore
516 Lawrence Ave.
Ellwood City, PA 16117
PH: (724) 758-2324
ec@ndcomics.com
www.ndcomics.com
(1-12, 14, 15, 18, 20, 21, 23, 24, 27-31)

New Dimension Comics
630B East Waterfront Dr.
Homestead, PA 15120
PH: (412) 655-8661
waterfront@ndcomics.com
www.ndcomics.com
(1-12, 14, 15, 18, 20, 21, 23, 24, 27-31)

Eide's Entertainment, LLC
1121 Penn Ave.
Pittsburgh, PA 15222
PH: (412) 261-0900
eBay: Eides_Entertainment
eides@eides.com
www.eides.com
(1-31)

New Dimension Comics
Pittsburgh Mills
590 Pittsburgh Mill Circle
Tarentum, PA 15084
PH: (724) 758-1560
mills@ndcomics.com
www.ndcomics.com
(1-12, 14, 15, 18, 20, 21, 23, 24, 27-31)

Hake's Americana & Collectibles
P.O. Box 12001
York, PA 17402
PH: (866) 404-9800
www.hakes.com

SOUTH CAROLINA

Borderlands Comics and Games
410 S. Pleasantburg Dr.
Greenville, SC 29607
(864) 235-3488
BorderlandsComics@gmail.com
www.borderlands.us
(1-10, 14, 16, 18, 20, 21, 23, 24, 27-31)

TENNESSEE

The Great Escape
105 Gallatin Road North
Madison, TN 37115
PH: (615) 865-8052
FAX: (615) 865-8779
thegreatescapemadison
@gmail.com
www.TheGreatEscapeOnLine.com
(1-31)

The Great Escape
810 NW Broad St., Suite 202
Murfreesboro, TN 37129
PH: (615) 900-1937
FAX: (615) 962-9562
thegreatescapemurfreesboro
@gmail.com
www.TheGreatEscapeOnLine.com
(1-31)

The Great Escape
5400 Charlotte Avenue
Nashville, TN 37209
PH: (615) 385-2116
FAX: (615) 297-6588
contactus
@thegreatescapeonline.com
www.TheGreatEscapeOnLine.com
(1-31)

TEXAS

Comic Heaven
P.O. Box 900
Big Sandy, TX 75755
PH: (903) 539-8875
www.ComicHeaven.net

Comic Book Certification Service (CBCS)
2700 Summit Ave., Suite 100
Plano, TX 75074
www.CBCScomics.com

Heritage Auction Galleries
2801 W. Airport Freeway
Dallas, TX 75261-4127
PH: (877) 437-4827
www.HA.com

Worldwide Comics
29369 Raintree Ridge
Fair Oaks Ranch, TX 78015
PH: (830) 368-4103
stephen@wwcomics.com
wwcomics.com

William Hughes' Vintage Collectables
P.O. Box 270244
Flower Mound, TX 75027
PH: (972) 539-9190
PH: (973) 432-4070
Whughes199@yahoo.com
www.VintageCollectables.net

Lewisville Comics
2417 South Stemmons Fwy.
#106
Lewisville, TX 75067
(972) 315-3664
info@lewisville.comics.com
www.lewisville.comics.com

VIRGINIA

Dave Anderson
5192 Dawes Avenue
Alexandria, VA 22311
(703) 578-1222
danderson8991@gmail.com
(1,2,13,14)

WASHINGTON

Mill Geek Comics
17624 15th Ave SE
Suite #105a
Bothell, WA 98012
(425) 415-6666
millgeekcomics@gmail.com
www.millgeekcomics.com
(1-4, 13, 30)

Pristine Comics
2008 South 314th Street
Federal Way, WA 98003
PH: (253) 941-1986
www.PristineComics.com

Terry's Comics
Buying All 10¢ & 12¢
Original priced comics
P.O. Box 1186
Kelso, WA 98626
PH: (714) 288-8993
Cell: (360) 846-3714
info@TerrysComics.com
www.TerrysComics.com
(1, 2, 4-8, 13, 14, 17)

Fantasy Illustrated
P.O. Box 248
Silvana, WA 98287
PH: (425) 750-4513
rocketbat@msn.com
www.fantasyillustrated.net.com
(1, 2, 14, 16)

WISCONSIN

Inner Child Collectibles and Comics
5921 Sixth Avenue "A"
Kenosha, WI 53140
PH: (262) 653-0400
StevenKahn@sbcglobal.net
innerchildcomics.com
(1-6, 12-16, 18, 19, 21-24, 27-30)

CANADA

MANITOBA

Doug Sulipa's Comic World
Box 21986
Steinbach, MB., R5G 1B5
PH: (204) 346-3674
FAX: (204) 346-1632
dsulipa@gmail.com
www.dougcomicworld.com
(1-5, 8, 12, 14-20, 25, 26, 29,30)

Book Fair Winnipeg Inc.
340 Portage Ave.
Winnipeg, MB R3C 0C3
PH/FAX: (204) 957-0142
info@bookfaircomics.com
www.bookfaircomics.com
(1-10, 12, 15-18, 20, 23)

ONTARIO

Comic Cave Canada
1104 Hwy 5 West
Dundas, ON L9H 5E2
(905) 808-8185
www.comiccavecanada.com

Big B Comics
1045 Upper James St.
Hamilton, ON L9C 3A6
(905) 318-9636
mailbox@bigbcomics.com
www.bigbcomics.com
(1-7, 9, 10, 12, 13, 21-24, 27-31)

Pendragon Comics and Cards
Cloverdale Mall
181-250 The East Mall
Toronto, ON M9B 3Y8
(416) 253-6974
pendragoncomics@gmail.com
pendragoncomics.com
(1-7, 12, 14, 16, 20-24, 28-31)

INTERNET

ComicLink Auctions & Exchange
PH: (617) 517-0062
buysell@ComicLink.com
www.ComicLink.com

Get Cash For Comics
PH: (888) 440-9787; ext. 117
buying@getcashforcomics.com

MyComicShop.com
PH: (817) 860-7827
buytrade@mycomicshop.com
www.mycomicshop.com

The Comic Swap
Virginia Beach, VA
TheComicSwap.com

CGC

How the Company Has Grown and How It Works

By the CGC Grading Team

The world of comic book collecting has grown and matured considerably since the introduction of CGC (Certified Guaranty Company) in 2000. Before CGC was founded, comic book transactions required sellers to grade their own comic books, a practice that often lacked consistency and impartiality. They also had to check their books for restoration, which was limited to each seller's skills at detection. During the first decades of fandom most sales took place through mail order, as well as local comic shops or the occasional convention. The advent of the internet changed all that, allowing global buying and selling, regardless of a person's location or experience. While this greatly expanded the comic book market, it also greatly increased the potential for inaccurate grading and restoration detection.

CGC was created to help bring order and stability to comic book sales, and to put an end to the risk and the chaos that accompanied online sales. CGC is the first and largest third-party comic book grading service, totally independent and impartial. A proven and respected commitment to integrity, accuracy and consistency has made CGC the leader in its field, becoming a tool to help people with their buying and selling decisions. The universally accepted CGC Grading Scale ensures consistency and gives both dealers and collectors a sense of dependability when making purchasing decisions. With CGC certification, a collector knows what he or she is getting based on an accurate and comprehensive description that can be found on the CGC certification label.

If you've ever wondered how it's done, here's a look at how CGC came together and how a book is certified.

The Formation of the Company

In January 2000, CGC was launched as part of the Certified Collectibles Group, which includes Numismatic Guaranty Corporation (NGC), the largest third-party coin grading company in the world; Numismatic Conservation Services (NCS), the leading authority in numismatic conservation; Paper Money Guaranty (PMG), the world's leading currency certification company; Classic Collectible Services (CCS), the world's premier comic book restoration, restoration removal and pressing company; Certified Sports Guaranty (CSG), a fast-growing grading service for sports cards; Authenticated Stamp Guaranty (ASG), an expanding stamp grading service; and Collectibles Authentication Guaranty (CAG), service for preserving the authenticity and provenance of collections.

The Certified Collectibles Group sought out talented and ethical individuals to grade comic books. Experts needed a history of working with comics as well as necessary skills to verify a comic book's authenticity and to detect restoration that can affect its value. To identify these individuals, many of the most respected individuals in the hobby were consulted, and based on their recommendations, a core grading team was selected.

The members of the CGC grading team come from diverse backgrounds, and many were comic book dealers at some time in their careers. Experience in the commercial sector can be an essential ingredient in becoming familiar with market standards.

When it was time to develop a uniform grading standard, the hobby's leaders were once again called upon. Everyone agreed that the *Overstreet Guide* was the foundation of this standard, but there were a number of subjective interpretations of its published definitions. It was critical to understand how these guidelines were being applied to the everyday buying and selling of comics. To accomplish this, approximately 50 of the hobby's top experts took part in an extensive grading test. Their grades were averaged and an accurate grading standard reflecting the collective experience of the hobby's most prominent individuals was thus developed. CGC now had the best standard and the best team to apply it.

With the graders in place and the grading scale established, the next step was to develop a tamper-evident holder for the long-term storage and display of certified comics. This proved to be a technical challenge. Exhaustive material tests were conducted to determine that the holders were archival safe. To create a true first line of defense, it was determined that the comic book should be sealed in a soft inner well, then sealed again inside a tamper evident hard plastic case with interlocking ridges to enable compact storage. The CGC-certified grade appears on a label sealed inside the holder for an additional level of security.

Submitting Books

Comic books may be submitted for certification in two ways: they can be submitted by authorized dealers or by Collectors Society members. The Collectors Society is an online community with direct access to certification service from CGC, and submissions can be prepared using the CGC online submission form. Both dealers and Collectors Society members typically send their comics to CGC's offices by registered mail or through an insured express company. Submissions are also accepted at many of the comic cons that occur around the country throughout the year. CGC will grade on-site at selected shows.

Receiving the Books

CGC's Receiving Department opens packages that have arrived and verifies that the number of books in each package matches the number shown on the submitted invoice and checks the submission for any damage sustained in shipping. Once this is done, a more detailed comparison is made to ensure that their invoice descriptions correspond to the actual comics. This information is entered into a computer, and from this time forth, the comics will be traceable at all stages of the grading process by their invoice number and their line number within that invoice. Each book is checked to see that it is properly prepared for grading in an appropriately sized comic bag with backing board and then is labeled with a numbered barcode containing the pertinent data of invoice number and line-item information for quick reading by the computer.

The Grading Begins

The book is then passed on to the graders. The grading process begins by having the book's pages counted and entering into the computer any peculiarities or flaws that may affect a book's grade. Some examples of this would be "Spine Stress Lines Break Color," "Right Top Front Cover Small Crease Breaks Color," "Top Back Cover Tear with Crease" and "Staple Rusted ." This information is entered into the "Graders Notes" field and a grade is assigned. The book is also examined for restoration; if any form of restoration work is detected, this information is entered into the computer, broken down by each form of restoration found.

When other graders examine the comic, they do not see any previous assigned grades, so as to not influence their evaluation. Graders are able to view previous Graders Notes while determining their own grade. The Grader may then add to the existing commentary if he or she believes more remarks are in order. The Grading Finalizer is the last person to examine the book. He or she makes a final restoration check before determining their own grade, at which time the grades and notes entered by the previous graders are reviewed. If all grades match or are very close, they will assign the book's final grade. The book is then forwarded to the Encapsulation Department for sealing. If there is disagreement among the graders, a discussion will ensue until a final determination is made and the book can be forwarded.

Each comic book receives a restoration check and the results appear on the label.

Encapsulating the Comics

After each comic has been graded and the necessary numbers and text entered into their respective data fields, all the comics on a particular invoice are taken from the Grading Department into the Encapsulation Department. Here, appropriately color-coded labels are printed bearing the proper descriptive text, including each book's grade and identification number. This is critical, as it serves to make each certified comic unique and is also a significant deterrent to counterfeiting CGC's valued product. All of the above information is duplicated in a barcode, which also appears on the comic's label.

The newly printed labels are stacked in the same sequence as the comics to be encapsulated with them, ensuring that each book and its label match one another. The comic is now ready to be fitted inside an archival-quality interior well, which is then sealed within a transparent capsule, along with the book's color-coded label. This is accomplished through a combination of compression and ultrasonic vibration.

The Comics are Shipped

After encapsulation, all comics are sent to Quality Control for inspection. Here, they are examined to make certain that their labels are correct for both the grade and its accompanying descriptive information. Quality Control also inspects each book for any flaws in its holder, such as scuffs or nicks. CGC is careful to make certain that the comics it certifies are not only accurately graded, but attractively presented as well. When all the comics have been inspected, they are delivered to our Shipping Department for packaging. The comics are counted, and their labels checked against the original invoice to make certain that no mistakes have occurred. A Shipping Department employee then verifies the method of transport as selected by the submitter on the invoice and prepares the comics for delivery or they are held in CGC's vault for in-person pick-up by the submitter.

No matter whether the US Postal Service or a private carrier is used, the method of packaging is essentially the same. The encapsulated comics are placed inside sturdy cardboard boxes. CGC has developed a custom shipping box to enable the highest level of stability during shipping. A copy of the submitter's invoice is included before the box is sealed and heavy tape is used to prevent accidental or unauthorized opening of the box while it is in transit.

The barcode of every comic book is scanned before it is placed into its shipping box. The status of the book is changed to "shipped" in our tracking system, and we retain a record of what books were shipped in which box. This is the final crucial step of our detailed internal tracking system.

The CGC Label

Comic books certified by CGC bear color-coded labels that have different meanings. Whenever purchasing a CGC-certified comic, be certain to note not only the book's grade but also its label category. A Universal label is denoted by the color blue and indicates that a book was not found to have any qualifying defects or signs of restoration. There is one exception to this policy: At CGC's discretion, comics having a very minor amount of color touch or glue may still qualify for a Universal label provided such restoration is noted underneath the assigned grade.

As its name implies, the Restored label, identified by its purple color, is used for books found to have restoration work performed on them. The grade assigned is based on the book's appearance, with the restoration noted. The Restoration scale determines the quality (A, B, or C) and quantity (between 1 and 5) of any restoration present, and is as follows:

Quality (Aesthetic) Scale – (Determined by materials used and visual quality of work)

A (Excellent)
• Color touch using acrylic or watercolor. Color match near perfect, no bleed through
• Tear seals, reinforcement, split seals and reattachment applied with rice paper and wheat paste
• Piece fill applied with leafcasting or rice paper, seamless with correct thickness and flexibility
• Cleaning with no evidence of fading, dimensional change, excessive whiteness, ripples, cockling, or ink smudging
• Staples cleaned or replaced with vintage or rustproof staples
• Staples replaced exactly as they were
• Filled edges cut evenly
• Book feels and looks natural

B (Fine)
• Color touch using pencil, pen, crayon, or chalk. Apparent upon close inspection, but no bleed through
• Color touch using acrylic or watercolor with average color matching
• Piece fill applied with cadaver comic parts or poorly applied rice paper. Apparent upon close inspection and to the touch
• Cover cleaning exhibiting color fading, dimensional change, ink smudging, or excessive whiteness or cockling
• Interior cleaning exhibiting slight puffiness, cockling, or excessively white
• Crooked or repositioned staples
• Re-glossing agent used on cover

C (Poor)
• Color touch using pen, marker or white out. Poor color matching or bleed through evident
• Piece fill using regular paper, obvious at arm's length
• Tear seals, reinforcement, split seals and reattachment using household glue

Quality Scale – (Determined primarily by extent of piece fill and color touch)

1 (Slight)
Tear seals, spine split seals, reinforcement, piece reattachment, leafcasting, cleaning, replaced staples, re-glossing, glue. Piece fill can be no bigger than the size of two bindery chips. Color touch must be light, in small areas like spine stresses, creases or bindery chip fill.

2 (Slight/Moderate)
Piece fill can be up to ½" x ½" cumulative in size on the cover and up to 1" x 1" on the interior. Color touch can be up to 1" x 1" in area. An excessive amount of glue used on the cover or interior pages.

3 (Moderate)
Piece fill up to the size of 1" x 1" and/or color touch covering up to 2" x 2". Interior piece fill up to 2" x 2"

4 (Moderate/Extensive)
Piece fill up to the size of 2" x 2" on the cover and 4" x 4" on the interior. Color touch up to 4" x 4" in area.

5 (Extensive)
Piece fill over 2" x 2" on the cover and 4" x 4" on the interior. Color touch over 4"x 4".

The presence of trimming on a comic book will receive a CGC purple restored label. But if only trimming is present, it will not garner a quality or quantity rating, only displaying the word "apparent." If restoration is present in addition to trimming, the trimming will have no bearing on the quality or quantity assigned to the restoration.

The Conserved Label is similar to the blue Universal label but is differentiated by a silver bar across the top. Conservation is noted in a similar fashion on the label as on the purple CGC Restored Label. This label is applied to any comic book with specific, professional repairs done to improve the structural integrity and long-term preservation. These repairs include tear seals, support, staple replacement, piece reattachment, leafcasting, and certain kinds of cleaning:

Conservation Repairs

- Tear seals
- Spine split seals
- Reinforcement
- Piece reattachment
- Some cover or interior cleaning (water or solvent)
- Staples cleaned or replaced
- Leafcasting

Materials Used for Conservation Repairs:

- Rice paper
- Wheat glue
- Vintage staples
- Archival tape

The Qualified label is green, indicating one qualifying defect is present on a book, and includes detachments, missing parts, and unverified signatures. An example of such a qualifying feature would be a Marvel Value Stamp missing from an interior page that does not affect the story. If such a book appears 9.6 otherwise but would downgrade to 3.5 due to the missing stamp, assigning a grade of 3.5 does not fully represent the appearance of the comic to a collector. Through use of the green Qualified label, a comic buyer is able to make an informed decision as to what he is purchasing in terms of its overall desirability. Because of the complexity involved, green labels are seldomly assigned. In addition, high grade comic books that have an unwitnessed signature, and therefore are not eligible for the Signature Series label (see below), get the Qualified label. This is the most common use for the Qualified label and shows what the grade of the book would have been if the signature was not present. Qualified labels are always used for married parts; if no restoration is present, a comic book with a married cover, wrap or page will always receive a Qualified label.

ifying feature would be a Marvel Value Stamp missing from an interior page that does not affect the story. If such a book appears 9.6 otherwise but would downgrade to 3.5 due to the missing stamp, assigning a grade of 3.5 does not fully represent the appearance of the comic to a collector. Through use of the green Qualified label, a comic buyer is able to make an informed decision as to what he is purchasing in terms of its overall desirability. Because of the complexity involved, green labels are seldomly assigned. In addition, high grade comic books that have an unwitnessed signature, and therefore are not eligible for the Signature Series label (see below), get the Qualified label. This is the most common use for the Qualified label and shows what the grade of the book would have been if the signature was not present. Qualified labels are always used for married parts; if no restoration is present, a comic book with a married cover, wrap or page will always receive a Qualified label.

The Evolution of CGC and CCG

In October of 2003, CGC began to certify comic book related magazines. The certification process and label system for magazines is the same as for comic books. Some examples of comic book-related magazines that CGC certifies are *MAD Magazine*, *Vampirella*, *Creepy*, *Eerie* and *Famous Monsters of Filmland*.

More recently CGC introduced grading and encapsulation for *Sports Illustrated* and *Playboy* magazines, Movie Lobby Cards, Photographs and Concert Posters. In 2016, CGC launched a redesign of its holder with enhanced strength, design, clarity and tamper-proof features. In 2020, CGC launched CGC Trading Cards, a division devoted to grading the most popular TCGs, such as *Pokémon* and *Magic: The Gathering*. CGC has graded nearly 10 million collectibles to date.

In a move intended to strengthen CGC's commitment to promoting the comic collecting hobby and enhance the collecting experience, the Certified Collectibles Group acquired Classics Incorporated, the world's premier comic book restoration, restoration removal and pressing company, in 2012. Previously located in Dallas, Texas, Classics Incorporated relocated to Sarasota, Florida, to become an independent member of the Certified Collectibles Group under the new name Classic Collectible Services (CCS). Customers who wish to send books in for pressing, restoration or restoration removal are able to send them to CCS and have them transfer directly to CGC for grading — creating a synergistic relationship that saves customers time, shipping and insurance expenses.

For more information on comic book certification, pressing, restoration, and CGC's many other services, please visit our website at www.CGCcomics.com

a - Story art; **a(i)** - Story art inks; **a(p)** - Story art pencils; **a(r)** - Story art reprint.

ADULT MATERIAL - Contains story and/or art for "mature" readers. Re: sex, violence, strong language.

ADZINE - A magazine primarily devoted to the advertising of comic books and collectibles as its first publishing priority as opposed to written articles.

ALLENTOWN COLLECTION - A collection discovered in 1987-88 just outside Allentown, Pennsylvania. The Allentown collection consisted of 135 Golden Age comics, characterized by high grade and superior paper quality.

ANNUAL - (1) A book that is published yearly; (2) Can also refer to some square bound comics.

ARRIVAL DATE - The date written (often in pencil) or stamped on the cover of comics by either the local wholesaler, newsstand owner, or distributor. The date precedes the cover date by approximately 15 to 75 days, and may vary considerably from one locale to another or from one year to another.

ASHCAN - A publisher's in-house facsimile of a proposed new title. Most ashcans have black and white covers stapled to an existing coverless comic on the inside; other ashcans are totally black and white. In modern parlance, it can also refer to promotional or sold comics, often smaller than standard comic size and usually in black and white, released by publishers to advertise the forthcoming arrival of a new title or story.

ATOM AGE - Comics published from 1946-1956.

B&W - Black and white art.

BACK-UP FEATURE - A story or character that usually appears after the main feature in a comic book; often not featured on the cover.

BAD GIRL ART - A term popularized in the early '90s to describe an attitude as well as a style of art that portrays women in a sexual and often action-oriented way.

BAXTER PAPER - A high quality, heavy, white paper used in the printing of some comics.

BC - Abbreviation for Back Cover.

BI-MONTHLY - Published every two months.

BI-WEEKLY - Published every two weeks.

BONDAGE COVER - Usually denotes a female in bondage.

BOUND COPY - A comic that has been bound into a book. The process requires that the spine be trimmed and sometimes sewn into a book-like binding.

BRITISH ISSUE - A comic printed for distribution in Great Britain; these copies sometimes have the price listed in pence or pounds instead of cents or dollars.

BRITTLENESS - A severe condition of paper deterioration where paper loses its flexibility and thus chips and/or flakes easily.

BRONZE AGE - Comics published from 1970 to 1984.

BROWNING - (1) The aging of paper characterized by the ever-increasing level of oxidation characterized by darkening; (2) The level of paper deterioration one step more severe than tanning and one step before brittleness.

c - Cover art; **c(i)** - Cover inks; **c(p)** - Cover pencils; **c(r)** - Cover reprint.

CAMEO - The brief appearance of one character in the strip of another.

CANADIAN ISSUE - A comic printed for distribution in Canada; these copies sometimes have no advertising.

CCA - Abbreviation for **Comics Code Authority**.

CCA SEAL - An emblem that was placed on the cover of all CCA approved comics beginning in April-May, 1955.

CENTER CREASE - See Subscription Copy.

CENTERFOLD or CENTER SPREAD - The two folded pages in the center of a comic book at the terminal end of the staples.

CERTIFIED GRADING - A process provided by a professional grading service that certifies a given grade for a comic and seals the book in a protective **Slab**.

CF - Abbreviation for Centerfold.

CFO - Abbreviation for Centerfold Out.

CGC - Abbreviation for the certified comic book grading company, Comics Guaranty, LLC.

CIRCULATION COPY - See Subscription Copy.

CIRCULATION FOLD - See Subscription Fold.

CLASSIC COVER - A cover considered by collectors to be highly desirable because of its subject matter, artwork, historical importance, etc.

CLEANING - A process in which dirt and dust is removed.

COLOR TOUCH - A restoration process by which colored ink is used to hide color flecks, color flakes, and larger areas of missing color. Short for Color Touch-Up.

COLORIST - An artist who paints the color guides for comics. Many modern colorists use computer technology.

COMIC BOOK DEALER - (1) A seller of comic books; (2) One who makes a living buying and selling comic books.

COMIC BOOK REPAIR - When a tear, loose staple or centerfold has been mended without changing or adding to the original finish of the book. Repair may involve tape, glue or nylon gossamer, and is easily detected; it is considered a defect.

COMICS CODE AUTHORITY - A voluntary organization comprised of comic book publishers formed in 1954 to review (and possibly censor) comic books before they were printed and distributed. The emblem of the CCA is a white stamp in the upper right hand corner of comics dated after February 1955. The term "post-Code" refers to the time after this practice started, or approximately 1955 to the present.

COMPLETE RUN - All issues of a given title.

CON - A convention or public gathering of fans.

CONDITION - The state of preservation of a comic book, often inaccurately used interchangeably with Grade.

CONSERVATION - The European Confederation of Conservator-Restorers' Organizations (ECCO) in its professional guidelines, defines conservation as follows: "Conservation consists mainly of direct action carried out on cultural heritage with the aim of stabilizing condition and retarding further deterioration."

COPPER AGE - Comics published from 1984 to 1992.

COSMIC AEROPLANE COLLECTION - A collection from Salt Lake City, Utah discovered by Cosmic Aeroplane Books, characterized by the moderate to high grade copies of 1930s-40s comics with pencil

check marks in the margins of inside pages. It is thought that these comics were kept by a commercial illustration school and the check marks were placed beside panels that instructors wanted students to draw.

COSTUMED HERO - A costumed crime fighter with "developed" human powers instead of super powers.

COUPON CUT or COUPON MISSING - A coupon has been neatly removed with scissors or razor blade from the interior or exterior of the comic as opposed to having been ripped out.

COVER GLOSS - The reflective quality of the cover inks.

COVER TRIMMED - Cover has been reduced in size by neatly cutting away rough or damaged edges.

COVERLESS - A comic with no cover attached. There is a niche demand for coverless comics, particularly in the case of hard-to-find key books otherwise impossible to locate intact.

C/P - Abbreviation for **Cleaned and Pressed**. See **Cleaning**.

CREASE - A fold which causes ink removal, usually resulting in a white line. See **Reading Crease**.

CROSSOVER - A story where one character appears prominently in the story of another character. See **X-Over**.

CVR - Abbreviation for Cover.

DEALER - See **Comic Book Dealer**.

DEACIDIFICATION - Several different processes that reduce acidity in paper.

DEBUT - The first time that a character appears anywhere.

DEFECT - Any fault or flaw that detracts from perfection.

DENVER COLLECTION - A collection consisting primarily of early 1940s high grade number one issues bought at auction in Penn-

sylvania by a Denver, Colorado dealer.

DIE-CUT COVER - A comic book cover with areas or edges precut by a printer to a special shape or to create a desired effect.

DISTRIBUTOR STRIPES - Color brushed or sprayed on the edges of comic book stacks by the distributor/wholesaler to code them for expedient exchange at the sales racks. Typical colors are red, orange, yellow, green, blue, and purple. Distributor stripes are not a defect.

DOUBLE - A duplicate copy of the same comic book.

DOUBLE COVER - When two covers are stapled to the comic interior instead of the usual one; the exterior cover often protects the interior cover from wear and damage. This is considered a desirable situation by some collectors and may increase collector value; this is not considered a defect.

DRUG PROPAGANDA STORY - A comic that makes an editorial stand about drug use.

DRUG USE STORY - A comic that shows the actual use of drugs: needle use, tripping, harmful effects, etc.

DRY CLEANING - A process in which dirt and dust is removed.

DUOTONE - Printed with black and one other color of ink. This process was common in comics printed in the 1930s.

DUST SHADOW - Darker, usually linear area at the edge of some comics stored in stacks. Some portion of the cover was not covered by the comic immediately above it and it was exposed to settling dust particles. Also see **Oxidation Shadow** and **Sun Shadow**.

EDGAR CHURCH COLLECTION - See **Mile High Collection**.

EMBOSSED COVER - A comic book cover with a pattern, shape or image pressed into the cover from the inside, creating a raised area.

ENCAPSULATION - Refers to the process of sealing certified comics in a protective plastic enclosure. Also see **Slabbing**.

EYE APPEAL - A term which refers to the overall look of a comic book when held at approximately arm's length. A comic may have nice eye appeal yet still possess defects which reduce grade.

FANZINE - An amateur fan publication.

FC - Abbreviation for Front Cover.

FILE COPY - A high grade comic originating from the publisher's file; contrary to what some might believe, not all file copies are in Gem Mint condition. An arrival date on the cover of a comic does not indicate that it is a file copy, though a copyright date may.

FIRST APPEARANCE - See **Debut**.

FLASHBACK - When a previous story is recalled.

FOIL COVER - A comic book cover that has had a thin metallic foil hot stamped on it. Many of these "gimmick" covers date from the early '90s, and might include chromium, prism and hologram covers as well.

FOUR COLOR - Series of comics produced by Dell, characterized by hundreds of different features; named after the four color process of printing. See **One Shot**.

FOUR COLOR PROCESS - The process of printing with the three primary colors (red, yellow, and blue) plus black.

FUMETTI - Illustration system in which individual frames of a film are colored and used for individual panels to make a comic book story. The most famous example is DC's *Movie Comics* #1-6 from 1939.

GATEFOLD COVER - A double-width fold-out cover.

GENRE - Categories of comic book subject matter; e.g. Science Fiction,

Super-Hero, Romance, Funny Animal, Teenage Humor, Crime, War, Western, Mystery, Horror, etc.

GIVEAWAY - Type of comic book intended to be given away as a premium or promotional device instead of being sold.

GLASSES ATTACHED - In 3-D comics, the special blue and red cellophane and cardboard glasses are still attached to the comic.

GLASSES DETACHED - In 3-D comics, the special blue and red cellophane and cardboard glasses are not still attached to the comic; obviously less desirable than Glasses Attached.

GOLDEN AGE - Comics published from 1938 (*Action Comics* #1) to 1945.

GOOD GIRL ART - Refers to a style of art, usually from the 1930s-50s, that portrays women in a sexually implicit way.

GREY-TONE COVER - A cover art style in which pencil or charcoal underlies the normal line drawing, used to enhance the effects of light and shadow, thus producing a richer quality. These covers, prized by most collectors, are sometimes referred to as **Painted Covers** but are not actually painted.

HC - Abbreviation for Hardcover.

HEADLIGHTS - Forward illumination devices installed on all automobiles and many other vehicles... OK, OK, it's a euphemism for a comic book cover prominently featuring a woman's breasts in a provocative way. Also see **Bondage Cover** for another collecting euphemism that has long since outlived its appropriateness in these politically correct times.

HOT STAMPING - The process of pressing foil, prism paper and/or inks on cover stock.

HRN - Abbreviation for Highest Reorder Number. This refers to a method used by collectors of Gil-

berton's *Classic Comics* and *Classics Illustrated* series to distinguish first editions from later printings.

ILLO - Abbreviation for Illustration.

IMPAINT - Another term for **Color Touch**.

INDICIA - Publishing and title information usually located at the bottom of the first page or the bottom of the inside front cover. In some pre-1938 comics and many modern comics, it is located on internal pages.

INFINITY COVER - Shows a scene that repeats itself to infinity.

INKER - Artist that does the inking.

INTRO - Same as **Debut**.

INVESTMENT GRADE COPY - (1) Comic of sufficiently high grade and demand to be viewed by collectors as instantly liquid should the need arise to sell; (2) A comic in VF or better condition; (3) A comic purchased primarily to realize a profit.

ISSUE NUMBER - The actual edition number of a given title.

ISH - Short for Issue.

JLA - Abbreviation for Justice League of America.

JSA - Abbreviation for Justice Society of America.

KEY, KEY BOOK or KEY ISSUE - An issue that contains a first appearance, origin, or other historically or artistically important feature considered especially desirable by collectors.

LAMONT LARSON - Pedigreed collection of high grade 1940s comics with the initials or name of its original owner, Lamont Larson.

LENTICULAR COVERS or "FLICKER" COVERS - A comic book cover overlayed with a ridged plastic sheet such that the special artwork underneath appears to move when the cover is tilted at different angles perpendicular to the ridges.

LETTER COL or LETTER COLUMN

- A feature in a comic book that prints and sometimes responds to letters written by its readers.

LINE DRAWN COVER - A cover published in the traditional way where pencil sketches are overdrawn with india ink and then colored. See also **Grey-Tone Cover**, **Photo Cover**, and **Painted Cover**.

LOGO - The title of a strip or comic book as it appears on the cover or title page.

LSH - Abbreviation for Legion of Super-Heroes.

MAGIC LIGHTNING COLLECTION - A collection of high grade 1950s comics from the San Francisco area.

MARVEL CHIPPING - A bindery (trimming/cutting) defect that results in a series of chips and tears at the top, bottom, and right edges of the cover, caused when the cutting blade of an industrial paper trimmer becomes dull. It was dubbed Marvel Chipping because it can be found quite often on Marvel comics from the late '50s and early '60s but can also occur with any company's comic books from the late 1940s through the middle 1960s.

MILE HIGH COLLECTION - High grade collection of over 22,000 comics discovered in Denver, Colorado in 1977, originally owned by Mr. Edgar Church. Comics from this collection are now famous for extremely white pages, fresh smell, and beautiful cover ink reflectivity.

MODERN AGE - A catch-all term applied to comics published since 1992.

MYLAR™ - An inert, very hard, space-age plastic used to make high quality protective bags and sleeves for comic book storage. "Mylar" is a trademark of the DuPont Co.

ND - Abbreviation for **No Date**.

NN - Abbreviation for **No Number**.

NO DATE - When there is no date given on the cover or indicia page.

NO NUMBER - No issue number is given on the cover or indicia page; these are usually first issues or one-shots.

N.Y. LEGIS. COMM. - New York Legislative Committee to Study the Publication of Comics (1951).

ONE-SHOT - When only one issue is published of a title, or when a series is published where each issue is a different title (e.g. Dell's *Four Color Comics*).

ORIGIN - When the story of a character's creation is given.

over guide - When a comic book is priced at a value over *Guide* list.

OXIDATION SHADOW - Darker, usually linear area at the edge of some comics stored in stacks. Some portion of the cover was not covered by the comic immediately above it, and it was exposed to the air. Also see **Dust Shadow** and **Sun Shadow**.

p - Art pencils.

PAINTED COVER - (1) Cover taken from an actual painting instead of a line drawing; (2) Inaccurate name for a grey-toned cover.

PANELOLOGIST - One who researches comic books and/or comic strips.

PANNAPICTAGRAPHIST - One possible term for someone who collects comic books; can you figure out why it hasn't exactly taken off in common parlance?

PAPER COVER - Comic book cover made from the same newsprint as the interior pages. These books are extremely rare in high grade.

PARADE OF PLEASURE - A book about the censorship of comics.

PB - Abbreviation for Paperback.

PEDIGREE - A book from a famous and usually high grade collection - e.g. Allentown, Lamont Larson, Edgar Church/Mile High, Denver,

San Francisco, Cosmic Aeroplane, etc. Beware of non-pedigree collections being promoted as pedigree books; only outstanding high grade collections similar to those listed qualify.

PENCILER - Artist that does the pencils...you're figuring out some of these definitions without us by now, aren't you?

PERFECT BINDING - Pages are glued to the cover as opposed to being stapled to the cover, resulting in a flat binded side. Also known as **Square Back or Square Bound**.

PG - Abbreviation for Page.

PHOTO COVER - Comic book cover featuring a photographic image instead of a line drawing or painting.

PIECE REPLACEMENT - A process by which pieces are added to replace areas of missing paper.

PIONEER AGE - Comics published from the 1500s to 1828.

PLATINUM AGE - Comics published from 1883 to 1938.

POLYPROPYLENE - A type of plastic used in the manufacture of comic book bags; now considered harmful to paper and not recommended for long term storage of comics.

POP - Abbreviation for the anti-comic book volume, *Parade of Pleasure*.

POST-CODE - Describes comics published after February 1955 and usually displaying the CCA stamp in the upper right-hand corner.

POUGHKEEPSIE - Refers to a large collection of Dell Comics file copies believed to have originated from the warehouse of Western Publishing in Poughkeepsie, NY.

PP - Abbreviation for Pages.

PRE-CODE - Describes comics published before the **Comics Code Authority** seal began appearing on covers in 1955.

PRE-HERO DC - A term used

to describe *More Fun* #1-51 (pre-Spectre), *Adventure* #1-39 (pre-Sandman), and *Detective* #1-26 (pre-Batman). The term is actually inaccurate because technically there were "heroes" in the above books.

PRE-HERO MARVEL - A term used to describe *Strange Tales* #1-100 (pre-Human Torch), *Journey Into Mystery* #1-82 (pre-Thor), *Tales To Astonish* #1-35 (pre-Ant-Man), and *Tales Of Suspense* #1-38 (pre-Iron Man).

PRESERVATION - Another term for **Conservation**.

PRESSING - A term used to describe a variety of processes or procedures, professional and amateur, under which an issue is pressed to eliminate wrinkles, bends, dimples and/or other perceived defects and thus improve its appearance. Some types of pressing involve disassembling the book and performing other work on it prior to its pressing and reassembly. Some methods are generally easily discerned by professionals and amateurs. Other types of pressing, however, can pose difficulty for even experienced professionals to detect. In all cases, readers are cautioned that unintended damage can occur in some instances. Related defects will diminish an issue's grade correspondingly rather than improve it.

PROVENANCE - When the owner of a book is known and is stated for the purpose of authenticating and documenting the history of the book. Example: A book from the Stan Lee or Forrest Ackerman collection would be an example of a value-adding provenance.

PULP - Cheaply produced magazine made from low grade newsprint. The term comes from the wood pulp that was used in the paper manufacturing process.

QUARTERLY - Published every three months (four times a year).

R - Abbreviation for Reprint.

RARE - 10-20 copies estimated to exist.

RAT CHEW - Damage caused by the gnawing of rats and mice.

RBCC - Abbreviation for Rockets Blast Comic Collector, one of the first and most prominent adzines instrumental in developing the early comic book market.

READING COPY - A comic that is in FAIR to GOOD condition and is often used for research; the condition has been sufficiently reduced to the point where general handling will not degrade it further.

READING CREASE - Book-length, vertical front cover crease at staples, caused by bending the cover over the staples. Square-bounds receive these creases just by opening the cover too far to the left.

REILLY, TOM - A large high grade collection of 1939-1945 comics with 5000+ books.

REINFORCEMENT - A process by which a weak or split page or cover is reinforced with adhesive and reinforcement paper.

REPRINT COMICS - In earlier decades, comic books that contained newspaper strip reprints; modern reprint comics usually contain stories originally featured in older comic books.

RESTORATION - Any attempt, whether professional or amateur, to enhance the appearance of an aging or damaged comic book using additive procedures. These procedures may include any or all of the following techniques: recoloring, adding missing paper, trimming, re-glossing, reinforcement, glue, etc. Amateur work can lower the value of a book, and even professional restoration has now gained a negative aura in the modern marketplace from some quarters. In all cases a restored book can never be worth the same as an unrestored book in the same condition. There is no consensus on the inclusion of pressing, non-aqueous cleaning, tape removal and in some cases staple replacement in this definition. Until such time as there is consensus, we encourage continued debate and interaction among all interested parties and reflection upon the standards in other hobbies and art forms.

REVIVAL - An issue that begins republishing a comic book character after a period of dormancy.

ROCKFORD - A high grade collection of 1940s comics with 2000+ books from Rockford, IL.

ROLLED SPINE - A condition where the left edge of a comic book curves toward the front or back; a defect caused by folding back each page as the comic was read.

ROUND BOUND - Standard saddle stitch binding typical of most comics.

RUN - A group of comics of one title where most or all of the issues are present. See **Complete Run**.

S&K - Abbreviation for the legendary creative team of Joe Simon and Jack Kirby, creators of Marvel Comics' Captain America.

SADDLE STITCH - The staple binding of magazines and comic books.

san francisco collection - (see **Reilly, Tom**)

SCARCE - 20-100 copies estimated to exist.

SEDUCTION OF THE INNOCENT - An inflammatory book written by Dr. Frederic Wertham and published in 1953; Wertham asserted that comics were responsible for rampant juvenile deliquency in American youth.

SET - (1) A complete run of a given title; (2) A grouping of comics for sale.

SEMI-MONTHLY - Published twice a month, but not necessarily **Bi-Weekly**.

SEWN SPINE - A comic with many spine perforations where binders' thread held it into a bound volume. This is considered a defect.

SF - Abbreviation for Science Fiction (the other commonly used term, "sci-fi," is often considered derogatory or indicative of more "low-brow" rather than "literary" science fiction, i.e. "sci-fi television."

SILVER AGE - Comics published from 1956 to 1970.

SILVER PROOF - A black and white actual size print on thick glossy paper hand-painted by an artist to indicate colors to the engraver.

SLAB - Colloquial term for the plastic enclosure used by grading certification companies to seal in certified comics.

SLABBING - Colloquial term for the process of encapsulating certified comics in a plastic enclosure.

SOTI - Abbreviation for **Seduction of the Innocent**.

SPINE - The left-hand edge of the comic that has been folded and stapled.

SPINE ROLL - A condition where the left edge of the comic book curves toward the front or back, caused by folding back each page as the comic was read.

SPINE SPLIT SEALED - A process by which a spine split is sealed using an adhesive.

SPLASH PAGE - A **Splash Panel** that takes up the entire page.

SPLASH PANEL - (1) The first panel of a comic book story, usually larger than other panels and usually containing the title and credits of the story; (2) An oversized interior panel.

SQUARE BACK or SQUARE BOUND - See **Perfect Binding**.

STORE STAMP - Store name (and sometimes address and telephone number) stamped in ink via rubber stamp and stamp pad.

SUBSCRIPTION COPY - A comic sent through the mail directly from the publisher or publisher's agent. Most are folded in half, causing a subscription crease or fold running down the center of the comic from top to bottom; this is considered a defect.

SUBSCRIPTION CREASE - See **Subscription Copy**.

SUBSCRIPTION FOLD - See **Subscription Copy**. Differs from a **Subscription Crease** in that no ink is missing as a result of the fold.

SUN SHADOW - Darker, usually linear area at the edge of some comics stored in stacks. Some portion of the cover was not covered by the comic immediately above it, and it suffered prolonged exposure to light. A serious defect, unlike a **Dust Shadow**, which can sometimes be removed. Also see **Oxidation Shadow**.

SUPER-HERO - A costumed crime fighter with powers beyond those of mortal man.

SUPER-VILLAIN - A costumed criminal with powers beyond those of mortal man; the antithesis of **Super-Hero**.

SWIPE - A panel, sequence, or story obviously borrowed from previously published material.

TEAR SEALS - A process by which a tear is sealed using an adhesive.

TEXT ILLO. - A drawing or small panel in a text story that almost never has a dialogue balloon.

TEXT PAGE - A page with no panels or drawings.

TEXT STORY - A story with few if any illustrations commonly used as filler material during the first three decades of comics.

3-D COMIC - Comic art that is drawn and printed in two color layers, producing a 3-D effect when viewed through special glasses.

3-D EFFECT COMIC - Comic art that is drawn to appear as if in 3-D but isn't.

TITLE - The name of the comic book.

TITLE PAGE - First page of a story showing the title of the story and possibly the creative credits and indicia.

TRIMMED - (1) A bindery process which separates top, right, and bottom of pages and cuts comic books to the proper size; (2) A repair process in which defects along the edges of a comic book are removed with the use of scissors, razor blades, and/or paper cutters. Comic books which have been repaired in this fashion are considered defectives.

TTA - Abbreviation for *Tales to Astonish*.

UK - Abbreviation for British edition (United Kingdom).

UNDER GUIDE - When a comic book is priced at a value less than Guide list.

UPGRADE - To obtain another copy of the same comic book in a higher grade.

VARIANT COVER - A different cover image used on the same issue.

VERY RARE - 1 to 10 copies estimated to exist.

VICTORIAN AGE - Comics published from 1828 to 1883.

WANT LIST - A listing of comics needed by a collector, or a list of comics that a collector is interested in purchasing.

WAREHOUSE COPY - Originating from a publisher's warehouse; similar to file copy.

WHITE MOUNTAIN COLLECTION - A collection of high grade 1950s and 1960s comics which originated in New England.

X-OVER - Short for **Crossover**.

ZINE - Short for **Fanzine**.

MILLION DOLLAR SALES

It's only been 14 years since the first comic book sold for $1 million or more. *Action Comics* #1, the first appearance of Superman, is still the reigning champ for the first $1 million sale, for the highest sale ($6 million at press time), and the most $1 million or more sales.

That said, the market has come a long way since only *Action Comics* #1 and *Detective Comics* #27 held the lofty heights alone.

Since those days in 2010, observers have witnessed *All Star Comics* #8 (first appearance of Wonder Woman), *Amazing Fantasy* #15 (first appearance of Spider-Man), *Amazing Spider-Man* #1, *Batman* #1, *Captain America Comics* #1 (first appearance of Captain America), *Fantastic Four* #1 (first appearance of the Fantastic Four), *Marvel Comics* #1 (first appearances of the Human Torch and Sub-Mariner), *Superman* #1, and *Tales of Suspense* #39 (first appearance of Iron Man) all reach or eclipse the $1 million mark.

Here, starting from the most recent sale of the CGC-certified 8.5 Kansas City pedigree copy of *Action Comics* #1 at Heritage for $6 million in April and going back to that first $1 million sale by ComicConnect, is the trail of the 36 seven-figure sales. (All prices realized in auctions, unless otherwise stated.)

Action Comics #1 CGC 8.5

Kansas City pedigree

$6 million – Heritage – April 2024

Detective Comics #27 CGC 6.5

$1.8 million – ComicConnect – March 2024

Amazing Spider-Man #1 CGC 9.8

Curator pedigree

$1.3 million – Heritage – January 2024

Superman #1 CGC 7.0

$2.34 million – Heritage – January 2024

All Star Comics #8 CGC 9.4

$1.5 million – Heritage – January 2024

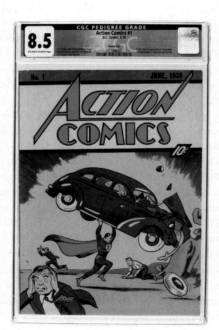

Action Comics #1
Kansas City pedigree CGC 8.5
$6,000,000
by Heritage Auctions April 2024

Tales of Suspense #39 CGC 9.8
$2 million – ComicLink – September 2023
(private sale)

Action Comics #1 CGC 3.0
$1.5 million – Goldin – June 2023

Superman #1 CGC 7.0
$1.6 million – Goldin – June 2023

Detective Comics #27 CGC 6.0
$1.74 million – Heritage – March 2023

Batman #1 CGC 8.0 (Fantast Collection)
$1.11 million – Heritage – March 2023

Action Comics #1 CGC 6.0 (rocket copy)
$3.55 million – ComicConnect
January 2023

Action Comics #1 CGC 6.0 (rocket copy)
$3.4 million – Goldin & Metropolis
September 2022

All Star Comics #8 CGC 9.4
$1.6 million – Heritage – June 2022

Detective Comics #27 CGC 6.5
$1.7 million – Goldin Auctions – May 2022

Superman #1 CGC 8.0
Edgar Church (Mile High)
$5.3 million – April 2022 (brokered sale,
reported by CGC)

Tales of Suspense #39
CGC 9.8
$2,000,000
by ComicLink   September 2023

Superman #1
Mile High copy   CGC 8.0
$5,300,000
brokered sale   April 2022

Captain America Comics #1 CGC 9.4
San Francisco pedigree
$3.1 million – Heritage – April 2022

Fantastic Four #1 CGC 9.2
$1.5 million – Heritage – April 2022

Marvel Comics #1 CGC 9.2 Pay Copy
$2.4 million – ComicConnect – March 2022

Detective Comics #27 CGC 4.5
$1.1 million – Heritage – January 2022

Action Comics #1 CGC 6.0 (rocket copy)
$3.1 million – Heritage – January 2022

Superman #1 CGC 7.0
$2.6 million – ComicConnect
December 2021

Action Comics #1 CGC 3.0
$1.6 million – ComicConnect
December 2021

Amazing Fantasy #15 CGC 9.6
$3.6 million – Heritage – September 2021

Detective Comics #27 CGC 5.0
$1.125 million – Heritage – June 2021

Action Comics #1 CGC 8.5
$3.25 million – ComicConnect – April 2021
(brokered sale)

Captain America Comics #1
San Francisco pedigree
CGC 9.4
$3,120,000
by Heritage Auctions April 2022

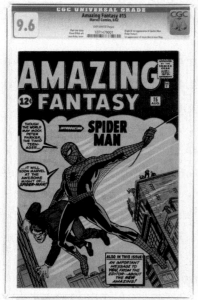

Amazing Fantasy #15
CGC 9.6
$3,600,000
by Heritage Auctions   September 2021

Batman #1 CGC 8.0
$1.2 million – ComicConnect – April 2021

Detective Comics #27 CGC 6.5
$1.2 million – ComicConnect
February 2021 (brokered sale)

Batman #1 CGC 9.4
$2.22 million – Heritage – January 2021

Detective Comics #27 CGC 7.0
$1.5 million – Heritage – November 2020

Marvel Comics #1 CGC 9.4 Windy City
$1.2 million – November 2019

Action Comics #1 CGC 8.5
$2 million – ComicConnect – June 2018

Action Comics #1 CGC 9.0
$3.2 million – Darren Adams on eBay –
August 2014

Action Comics #1 CGC 9.0
$2.1 million – ComicConnect – Dec. 2011

Amazing Fantasy #15 CGC 9.6
$1.1 million – ComicConnect – 2011

Detective Comics #27 CGC 8.0
$1 million– Heritage – February 2010

Action Comics #1 CGC 8.0
$1 million – ComicConnect – 2010

Batman #1
CGC 9.4
$2,200,000
by Heritage Auctions January 2021

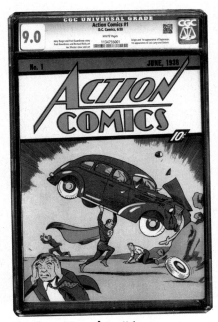

Action Comics #1
CGC 9.0
$3,200,000
by Darren Adams on eBay August, 2014

THE OVERSTREET
HALL OF FAME

The Overstreet Hall of Fame was conceived to single out individuals who have made great contributions to the comic book arts.

This includes writers, artists, editors, publishers and others who have plied their craft in insightful and meaningful ways.

While such evaluations are inherently subjective, they also serve to aid in reflecting upon those who shaped the experience of reading comic books over the years.

This year's class of inductees begins on this next page.

THE PREVIOUS INDUCTEES

Class of 2006
Murphy Anderson
Jim Aparo
Jim Lee
Mac Raboy

Class of 2007
Dave Cockrum
Steve Ditko
Bruce Hamilton
Martin Nodell
George Pérez
Jim Shooter
Dave Stevens
Alex Toth
Michael Turner

Class of 2008
Carl Barks
Will Eisner
Al Feldstein
Harvey Kurtzman
Stan Lee
Marshall Rogers
John Romita, Sr.
John Romita, Jr.
Julius Schwartz
Mike Wieringo

Class of 2009
Neal Adams
Matt Baker
Chris Claremont
Palmer Cox
Bill Everett
Frank Frazetta
Neil Gaiman
William M. Gaines

Carmine Infantino
Jack Kirby
Joe Kubert
Paul Levitz
Russ Manning
Todd McFarlane
Don Rosa
John Severin
Joe Simon
Al Williamson

Class of 2010
Sergio Aragonés
M.C. Gaines
Archie Goodwin
Winsor McCay
Mike Mignola
Frank Miller
Robert M. Overstreet
Mike Richardson
Jerry Robinson
Joe Shuster
Jerry Siegel
Jim Steranko
Wally Wood

Class of 2011
Jack Davis
Martin Goodman
Dean Mullaney
Marie Severin
Walt Simonson
Major Malcolm Wheeler-
Nicholson

Class of 2012
John Buscema
Dan DeCarlo
Jean Giraud (Moebius)

Larry Hama
Kurt Schaffenberger
Bill Sienkiewicz
Curt Swan
Roy Thomas

Class of 2013
Mark Chiarello
Mike Deodato, Jr.
Bill Finger
Jack Kamen
Bob Kane
Andy Kubert

Class of 2014
George Evans
Lou Fine
Gardner Fox
Terry Moore
Dave Sim
Jeff Smith

Class of 2015
Paul Gulacy
Don McGregor
Alex Schomburg
Mark Waid

Class of 2016
Darwyn Cooke
Russ Heath
Rob Liefeld
R.F. Outcault
Tim Truman

Class of 2017
Mike Grell
Osamu Tezuka
Jim Valentino

Mark Wheatley
Bernie Wrightson

Class of 2018
C.C. Beck
Howard Chaykin
Denny O'Neil
Katsuhiro Otomo
Marc Silvestri
Len Wein

Class of 2019
Sal Buscema
José Luis García-López
Michael Wm. Kaluta
Rumiko Takahashi

Class of 2020
Kevin Eastman
Louise Simonson
Dick Sprang

Class of 2021
Denys Cowan
David Mack
William Moulton Marston
June Tarpé Mills

Class of 2022
Ross Andru
Johnny Craig
J.G. Jones

Class of 2023
Gene Colan
Sheldon Moldoff
Christopher Priest

Ramona Fradon spent over 60 years working as a comic artist, starting with illustrating *Shining Knight* at DC. She co-created Aqualad in the Aquaman backup stories in *Adventure Comics*, and co-created Metamorpho during her time on *Brave and the Bold*. Her art appeared in *The Brave and the Bold* #59, which was the first issue to see Batman teaming up with another DC superhero. After a break from comics to raise her daughter, Fradon drew *Plastic Man*, *Freedom Fighters*, and *Super Friends* for DC and drew a fill-in issue of *Fantastic Four* and the never-published fifth issue of *The Cat* for Marvel. She began drawing the *Brenda Starr* newspaper strip in 1980, and remained on the series until 1995. In the 2010s, Fradon contributed pencils to the graphic novels *The Adventures of Unemployed Man*, *The Dinosaur That Got Tired of Being Extinct*, and the collection *The Art of Ramona Fradon*. Long after retiring from official work, Fradon continued doing commissions until her death at 97.

- Amanda Sheriff

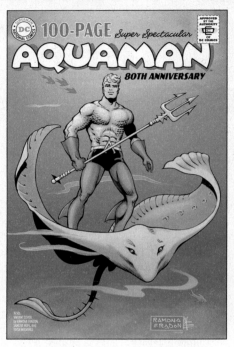

AQUAMAN 80TH ANNIVERSARY 100-PAGE SUPER SPECTACULAR
October 2021. © DC

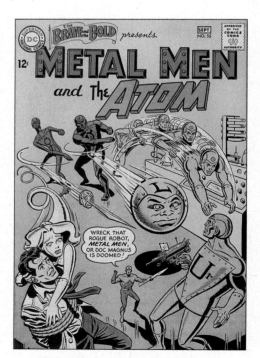

THE BRAVE AND THE BOLD #55
August - September 1964. © DC

THE BRAVE AND THE BOLD #66
June - July 1964. © DC

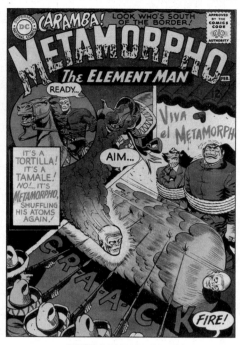

METAMORPHO #4
January - February 1966. © DC

PLASTIC MAN #20
October - November 1977. © DC

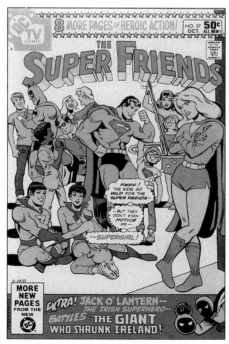

SUPER FRIENDS #37
October 1980. © DC

WONDER WOMAN #7
Variant cover. May 2024. © DC

Joe Jusko has spent a career producing realistic, expertly detailed art for book covers, comics, trading cards, and more. In his teens, he created his first cover for *Heavy Metal* magazine, and since then he has worked for most major comic publishers. Establishing his fantasy style, he had a long run as the main cover artist on *The Savage Sword of Conan*, made cover paintings for *Famous Monsters of Filmland*, and covers for John Carter and Dejah Thoris covers at Dynamite. Jusko has worked for most major publishers, creating covers of the biggest characters at DC, Marvel, and elsewhere. Outside of comic books, he is well known for his painted trading card sets that include the Marvel Masterpieces (in 1992 and 2016), the Art of Edgar Rice Burroughs set, Fleer's Ultra X-Men Wolverine Cards, Conan the Barbarian, and Vampirella. Jusko created the interior illustrations for the *Conan: Adventures in an Age Undreamed Of* roleplaying game, and in 2023 he became the first artist to ever paint the covers for all 24 books in the Tarzan series.

- Amanda Sheriff

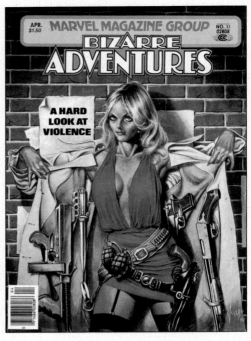

BIZARRE ADVENTURES #31
April 1982. © MAR

CAPTAIN AMERICA #8
Variant cover. September 2005. © MAR

DEATHLOK #1
July 1990. © MAR

HULK #25
February 1981. © MAR

THE SAVAGE SWORD OF CONAN #191
November 1991. © CPI

UNCANNY X-MEN #375
Variant cover. December 1999. © MAR

WARLORD OF MARS #33
2014. © ERB

Robert Kanigher worked in the comics industry as a writer and editor for five decades. He started writing for All-American Comics in 1945 and was soon promoted to editor. For over 20 years, Kanigher edited and wrote for *Wonder Woman*, taking over from creator William Moulton Marston. During that period, he co-created Black Canary, Rose and Thorn, and Harlequin. In the early 1950s, Kanigher started editing DC's war titles, and co-created Sgt. Rock in *Our Army at War*. He and Carmine Infantino co-created Barry Allen for *Showcase* #4, in what is considered the first Silver Age comic story. Kanigher and Russ Andru co-created the original Suicide Squad in *The Brave and the Bold* #25 and the Metal Men in *Showcase* #37. He created series like *Enemy Ace*, *The Losers*, and *The Unknown Soldier*. During the Bronze Age, Kanigher and Andru co-created the Rose & the Thorn backup feature in *Superman's Girlfriend, Lois Lane* #105. He introduced *Rima the Jungle Girl*, co-created Ragman with Joe Kubert, and in the early 1980s, he worked on the Creature Commandos stories in *Weird War Tales*.

- Amanda Sheriff

THE BRAVE AND THE BOLD #55
August - September 1959. © DC

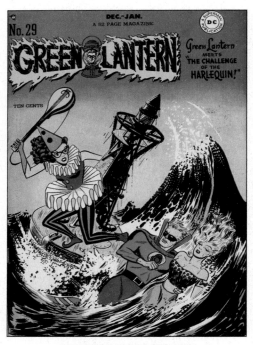

GREEN LANTERN #29
December 1947 - January 1948. © DC

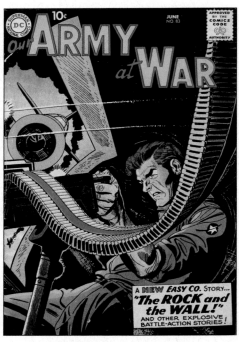

OUR ARMY AT WAR #83
June 1959. © DC

RIMA, THE JUNGLE GIRL #1
April - May 1974. © DC

SHOWCASE #37
March - April 1962. © DC

SHOWCASE #57
July - August 1965. © DC

WONDER WOMAN #141
October 1963. © DC

COWABUNGA

TEENAGE MUTANT NINJA

TURTLES

TURNS 40!

By Amanda Sheriff

Most superhero comics have a few things in common. Whether they are ordinary people with incredible skills, superpowered, or mutated individuals, the main characters are nearly all humans. They are predominately born or cultivated by the biggest comic book publishers. They're also brimming with color. And then there's the Teenage Mutant Ninja Turtles.

The comic book series created by Kevin Eastman and Peter Laird is exactly what the name implies: the story of anthropomorphic young turtles with impressive fighting skills. Named after Renaissance painters, Leonardo, Donatello, Michaelangelo, and Raphael were educated in martial arts and morality by their surrogate father Splinter, and protect their city from villains like Shredder.

Teenage Mutant Ninja Turtles (*TMNT*) is an amalgamation of comic tropes featuring mutated beings, heroes skilled in hand to hand combat, and young protagonists. The Turtles

are genuine in their pursuit of protecting people, like their contemporaries, while simultaneously being a parody of the superhero genre by utilizing the funny animal tradition instead of making the heroes human.

Once they finalized the concept, Eastman and Laird founded their own comic book company, Mirage Studios, to publish the book. They printed 3,000 copies of the first issue and advertised it in *Comics Buyer's Guide Magazine*. That small first printing debuted in May 1984, and sold out within weeks, prompting multiple printings.

It was also the start of an ongoing series that would run for 62 issues through August 1993. Eastman and Laird hired writers and artists that included Jim Lawson, Richard Corben, Michael Zulli, and Rick Veitch to work on the book. The black and white first volume ended with the 50th issue, then a few months later, the series switched to color for its second volume.

Three years into the original comic in 1987, the creators granted the toy license to Playmates Toys, who produced hundreds of action figures, vehicles, and playsets. Also that year, the Turtles made the jump from comic page to TV screens for their first animated series. The show established now-well known elements of the team, including their distinctive personalities, love of pizza, catchphrases, and color-coded masks, elbow and knee pads, and wrist bands. Aimed at kids, the animated series toned down the violence, added some silliness, and became a big success that ran for nearly a decade.

Archie published a miniseries based on the cartoon in '88, then turned it into the ongoing series, *Teenage Mutant Ninja Turtles Adventures*. It ran for 72 issues through '95, primarily written by Dean Clarrain with art by Chris Allen.

The franchise expanded to the video game market in 1989 when Konami developed the first of

several NES titles. Many *TMNT* games followed from arcade cabinets to handheld games, and across multiple video game systems.

The Turtles debuted on the big screen in 1990 with the live-action film, *Teenage Mutant Ninja Turtles*, featuring turtle costumes designed by Jim Henson's Creature Shop. The movie's tone was somewhere between the comic and the cartoon, with a serious plotline and look that was tempered by teenage energy and attitude. Two sequels were rushed to theaters in '91 and '93, each with a lighter tone than the original.

Image Comics published the next ongoing series, producing 23 issues from '96 to '99. This volume followed the Mirage continuity, with Gary Carlson on writing duties while Frank Fosco handled the art.

Mirage launched the next comic, *TMNT: Teenage Mutant Ninja Turtles*, in 2001 with Laird at the helm and Lawson on art. The

32-issue series is the third canonical title and fourth overall series, running through 2014.

The next animated show, created by 4Kids Entertainment, ran for seven seasons from 2003 to 2009. Laird worked on the production, helping to develop a show more like the original comic than the first cartoon series. The computer-animated movie *TMNT* was released in 2007, marking the first cartoon film in the franchise.

IDW Publishing kicked off a comic series in 2011 with Eastman on board as co-writer and illustrator. Many creators worked on this volume, including Dan Duncan, Mateus Santolouco, Corey Smith, David Wachter, Sophie Campbell, and several others. The ongoing title reached issue 150 in April 2024.

IDW introduced the ongoing *Teenage Mutant Ninja Turtles New Animated Adventures* in 2013, running 24 issues through 2015. The next offshoot was *Teenage Mutant Ninja Turtles Universe*, featuring 25 issues from 2016 to 2018. *Teenage Mutant Ninja Turtles: Urban Legends* was a 26-issue series published in 2018-2020.

The third animated series aired on Nickelodeon from 2012 to 2017. They returned to live-action in 2014, for the edgier movie produced by Michael Bay, followed by the sequel, *Out of the Shadows* in 2016.

The fourth animated series, *Rise of the Teenage Mutant Ninja Turtles*, aired from 2018 to 2020, then a film sequel was released two years later. In 2023, comedic actor Seth Rogen co-wrote and produced the movie *Mutant Mayhem*, which was praised for its stylized animation and humor.

THE SPIRIT OF INDEPENDENCE

30 YEARS OF

Lady Death SHI

In an industry that throws around adjectives like paper mâché boulders in a monster movie, their two characters are genuinely legitimate icons of the 1990s and modern, creator-owned comics. Brian Pulido's Lady Death and Billy Tucci's Shi celebrate their 30th anniversaries this year. And like most great success stories, the sledding across those three decades distinctly was not always easy.

Brian Pulido, a nearly lifelong comic book collector, launched his first series, *Evil Ernie*, at Eternity Comics, in 1991. He had decided, though, to venture out on his own. He launched Chaos! Comics in 1993. With its own brand of heavy metal, horror, and the supernatural, it became a home for *Evil Ernie* and other creations, which would soon follow.

Lady Death would be their breakout hit.

Billy Tucci, for his part, was just starting to break in.

"With the last of my meager savings, and stars in my eyes, I went out to the mecca of all comicdom, the San Diego Comic-Con in August of 1993 with the pages from the *Razor Annual*, (which now included my creator-owned character, Shi) and got rejected by every publisher – major and minor – except Chaos! Comics' Brian Pulido, who offered me a pin-up assignment after I visited his table in the Small Press section, Tucci said.

It would not be the last parallel in their relationship over the years.

"What struck me about Brian was that he actually spoke to me as an equal and with respect. It was a far cry from how I was treated by every other editor from every other publisher I had waited hours in line to present my work to earlier. He engaged our conversation with a passion that none of the others had shown. It was truly inspiring and literally saved what I had thought was a disastrously, soul-crushing weekend," he said.

Inspired by his meeting with Pulido, Tucci found himself committed to not only to his character, but also to going all out to make his comic book happen.

Pulido was several steps ahead of him, and now he had his lightning rod for the change he wanted to see in comics.

"I had strong women in my life, so it seemed natural to portray a female warrior. In particular, my mom, who had various careers. and my sister who was a business owner," Pulido said. "My love for horror and the dark genres is a lifelong thing. Also, I was, and am, fond of the horror hostess, Vampira. Her dark vibe spoke to me."

Lady Death had first shown up as a hallucination by Ernest Fairchild, better known as Evil Ernie, but the character developed rapidly from there. The character was born as normal mortal named Hope in medieval Sweden. Her father, outwardly pious nobleman, was truly evil. When the people rose up against him, he escaped, but Hope did not. Faced with being burned at the stake, she used an incantation of his. It started her down the road of destruction.

Fans got what Pulido was trying to do. *Lady Death* was a hit.

In the meantime, Tucci's *Shi: Way of the Warrior* #1 had come together. He had a character and he had a story. Ana Ishikawa is Shi (Japanese for "death"), a Japanese-American woman trained by her grandfather in the ways of the sohei warrior monks, who sets out on course of revenge after her family is killed. Her upbringing and her faith bring her into conflict with herself as well as the man responsible for the murders.

And it seemed like he'd found a bit of an audience, too. Against distributor orders of 37,000, he decided to print 50,000. He also deliberately planned for *Shi: Way of the Warrior* #2 to be solicited for three months later rather than the traditional two-month window, so that fans and retailers would have seen the first issue before they ordered the second.

"Then the reorders started coming in and coming and coming and then *pouring in!* They were slow at first, then within a month we had reorders for over 140,000 copies. Again, there were only 50,000 total," he said. Orders for the next issue were 80,000 rather than the normal big drop-off between the first and second issue.

Now both Pulido and Tucci had hits on their hands.

For the balance of the '90s, both creators kept things going. Pulido ran into trouble in 2002 and Chaos! Comics closed. Through various sales, Lady Death went one direction, and the other Chaos! characters went another. It would take years and legal struggles for him to control Lady Death again.

Shi was never out of Tucci's dominion, but he had interest in working on other characters. After *Shi: Ju-nen*, which was published by Dark Horse Comics in 2003, he concentrated on those other efforts, including the acclaimed *Sgt. Rock:*

The Lost Battalion.

The tide turned again in 2015 when Pulido launched Coffin Comics. Focused initially on the crowdfunding arena and then reentering the comic book specialty market, Lady Death found her fans and renewed success. Pulido and company have carried off a string of successes, including introducing new characters.

Her appeal, it seems, was undimmed. *Lady Death* was a hit again.

"My best guess is that the story and the nature of the character keep her contemporary," Pulido said. "*Lady Death* is a story about persistence against all odds. She is an aspirational character who could care less about the laws of man and that is a fantasy most of us can relate to. In the end, she follows her own moral authority."

Tucci followed a similar pattern for Shi in terms of the publishing venues. In his return to his best-known character, thought, he put a unique twist on things: he had Ana age. In the time fans hadn't seen her, Ana aged, married, had a now-teenage daughter, and got divorced.

The strategy worked. He successfully crowd-funded slates of new original stories – *Shi: Return of the Warrior, Shi: Haikyo,* and *Shi:Sakura* – and archival collections –*Shi: Way of the Warrior Omnibus, Shi: Senryaku Omnibus,* and

Shi:Way of the Warrior #1 Original Art Edition. Like *Lady Death*, the return of *Shi* to comic shops should be underway before this article sees print.

– *J.C. Vaughn*

Editor's Note: *The Lady Death and Shi covers for this year's edition,* The Overstreet Comic Book Price Guide #54, **mark only the second time in the** Guide*'s more than five decades that two covers have combined to form one **larger image.** Overstreet Advisor Scott Braden contributed to this article.*

THE SHADOW

CRIME DOES NOT PAY
(But it Makes for Great Comics)

Before he skulked about the dark and seedy corners of the crime world, The Shadow first came on the scene as the host character of Street and Smith Publications' *Detective Story* radio show in 1930. Two years later, the series was renamed *The Shadow*, and it aired on CBS, NBC and Mutual, respectively, over the next 22 years. In addition to capturing the imaginations of listeners, *The Shadow* struck into the magazine, comic strip, pulp, and film markets, as well.

In print, *The Shadow* began as a quarterly magazine. Also published by Street and Smith, the title is considered a landmark of the pulp genre. On a long string of striking covers, the Shadow's looks were hidden by his coat, hat, and scarf, leaving his piercing eyes as the character's only distinctly revealed feature.

Written by the prolific Walter B. Gibson under the alias Maxwell Grant, prose stories punctuated the radio series. And if ever "prolific" was an understatement, he wrote 282 of the 325 Shadow novels published in less than 20 years.

In the stories, The Shadow assumed the identity of wealthy, well-traveled socialite Lamont Cranston. While Cranston traveled the globe, The Shadow was free to use Cranston's status, connections, and wealth to move in and around society.

It wasn't until 1937's *The Shadow Unmasks* that readers learned he was really Kent Allard, a world renowned aviator. His supporting cast, though, was well established before that. His agents included Harry Vincent, Hawkeye, Cliff Marsland, Clyde Burke, and the beautiful Margot Lane.

In 1940, Victor Jory starred in the title role in Columbia Pictures' 15-episode serial, a Shadow comic strip ran from 1938 to 1942, and Shadow Comics first appeared in 1940 and ran for a decade. While the radio show's famous taglines – "Who knows what evil lurks in the hearts of men? The Shadow knows!" and "The weed of crime bears bitter fruit. Crime does not pay... The Shadow knows!" – became part of the lexicon and the pulps had their followers, the comic strip and comic book incarnations largely drifted from the collective pop culture memory shortly after they were published.

When the radio show ended and the pulps stopped, that could have been the end of The Shadow, but of course it wasn't. Their influence would be felt by those who'd never heard the show or read one of the stories.

"It's interesting how much the pulps influenced the early comic creators. There's a lot of callouts to The Shadow and Doc Savage in the Batman books, and even the Superman material at the start. Inspiration was coming from so many sources, and pulps were part of the creation of some of the most iconic characters and worlds I've ever known," writer-artist Frank Miller said in his foreword to *Pulp Power* by Neil McGinness.

And a revival would be just around the corner.

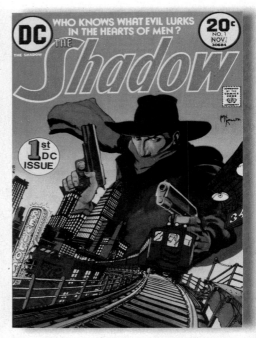

Striking covers by Steranko called attention once again to the pulp novels and old-time radio shows found new life on cassette tapes. Both found audiences willing and ready.

The first misstep came in the form of comic books in August 1964. The character was licensed to Archie, which turned him into a costume-clad superhero who had the power of ventriloquism. It raises the question of why, if you're going to pay to license a character, would you not do a familiar version of the character you licensed rather than some new interpretation of it?

"The Archie version of the Shadow is quite an enigma in the history of comics. Yet, for many reasons, I feel that it is quite collectible: certainly, it is the first time Archie licensed a property from an outside source (and one with an established track record to boot)," wrote Archie historian Paul Castiglia.[1]

It wouldn't be until 1973 that comic book readers got a chance to see The Shadow again, but it turned out to be worth the wait. DC Comics launched *The Shadow* #1 (November 1973) with writer Dennis O'Neil

and artist Michael Wm. Kaluta. Although the series only ran 12 issues and Kaluta illustrated only five of them – #1-4 and 6 – the series was foundational for many new Shadow fans and it was a character done right for many established enthusiasts.

"There were a number of immediate decisions to be made," O'Neil wrote in his introduction to the 1989 collection of his and Kaluta's work, *The Private Files of The Shadow*. "The first was: should we modernize him? I said no. It seemed to me at the time that there no point in doing the character unless we could do him as Walter Gibson had conceived him back in 1931; if we're going to cobble together just another super-doer, we might as well not use The Shadow's name and save royalty payments to Street and Smith's successor, Conde Nast Publications, and if we planned to be faithful to Gibson's vision, we had to set the stories in an earlier era – we couldn't have a lethal vigilante with his own private army marauding around modern New York saving the taxpayers court costs without offending a lot of sensibilities, including mine."

DC Comics would revive *The Shadow* again 11 years after the previous series ended in 1975, but this time writer-artist Howard Chaykin would make almost the exact opposite decision. He would transplant The Shadow – still young, vibrant, and deadly – into the 1980s with his 1930s and '40s worldview intact. The result was a thinking man's version of an origin story set against the insane backdrop of the 1980s over-the-the-top shoot-'em-up feature film genre.

"The fact is that a man of his position on a professional level, personal level, and emotional level, who was born when he was and lived when he did, would necessarily have been a sexist by today's standards. I think it's the nature of his character. It's not something I applied, it's something I extrapolated," Chaykin said in an interview with DC's Joe Orlando in the 1987 collected edition, *The Shadow: Blood & Judgement*.

Both series make compelling arguments about how The Shadow can be portrayed for modern audiences. Since then, there have been several comic book incarnations of the character.

In 1988, O'Neil and Kaluta reunited, this time with inker Russ Heath, at Marvel Comics for the graphic novel *The Shadow: Hitler's Astrologer*, which was set during World War II.

DC published *The Shadow* (1987) and *The Shadow Strikes!* (1989), set modern day and in the character's original era, respectively.

Dark Horse published a number of mini-series and one-shots, including crossovers with other characters, in the mid-1990s. A number of these issues feature art by Kaluta.

Dynamite featured the character in a number of series and mini-series beginning in 2012, including reprints of *The Shadow: Blood & Judgement* and *The Shadow: Hitler's Astrologer*, as well as new work from *Grendel* creator Matt Wagner.

– *J.C. Vaughn*

[1] ***Editor's Note:*** *If you'd like to read more about 1964's ill-fated Shadow reboot, check out Paul Castiglia's feature article, "The Shadow at Archie?" in* The Overstreet Comic Book Price Guide To Lost Universes #2, *which is now on sale. While it's easily one of the worst versions of the character, the story about it is a very interesting read.*

Introducing the

LAKE COMO COMIC ART FESTIVAL

By Joel Meadows

All photos © Joel Meadows

Imagine if you will a comic event without Stormtroopers, Funkos, and cosplayers, in an idyllic and intimate northern Italian setting. Launched back in 2018 by founders Arno Lapeyre (who runs the Pulp Comics retail chain in France as well as a former promoter of the Paris Comic Expo), and American Steve Morger (who was one of the key figures at the Big Wow! ComicFest which used to take place in San Jose, California), Lake Como is a comic festival like no other. Its tickets are capped in numbers too so it can remain an intimate affair.

Focused on original art with the cream of international artists from the United States, France, Italy, the United Kingdom and even as far afield as Australia, Lake Como has gone from strength to strength since it was created.

Lapeyre offered some insight into how Como came into being: "Each of our shows grew and we got to know each other through these events – sharing ideas and concerns in order to make each of our shows better. Sadly, both shows ended due to events beyond our control which actually was a good thing as the shows were both growing to the point that they required more and more effort. Steve was playing with the idea of an event entirely focused on comic art and artists, something that was really appealing to me as well. As much as I loved doing Paris Comics Expo and Steve enjoyed working on Big Wow!, our passion is for the art and the comic book medium. Cosplay and TV celebrities made sense in bigger and more family orientated shows, but we had no interest in these aspects of shows."

The show hosts its seventh edition in 2024, and its guest list reads like a who's who of international comics talent once again: Bill Sienkiewicz (*Batman*, *Daredevil*, *Elektra*), Alex Maleev (*Daredevil*), Charles Vess (*Sandman*), Simon Bisley (*Lobo*), David Mack (*American Gods*), and Tony Harris (*Starman*) to name just a few. Since 2018, Lake Como has attracted the likes of Art Adams (*Spider-Man*), Travis Charest (*Wildcats*), Lee Bermejo (*Joker*) and Kevin Eastman (*Teenage Mutant Ninja Turtles*) through its doors.

For its organizers, having it in Lake Como – one of the most beautiful plac-es in the world, a location that attracts millions of visitors thanks to its natural beauty and history – made perfect sense from the beginning as Lapeyre revealed. "Steve [Morger] always loved the place and acquired an apartment over there. He called me just after a trip over there and said he had found the perfect place for such a show and that I had to see it for myself as soon as possible. I was blown away. I've travelled a lot but I couldn't believe how long it took me to see such a beautiful place."

It isn't only the location that makes the Lake Como Comic Festival the perfect place either, Lapeyre continues. "It's just that the Lake itself is a true gem but the Villa Erba, where we host the convention, is the perfect location too. The villa itself is a gorgeous palace that's been used in many movies where the Friday reception event takes place and there is also a modern convention area next to it where the actual Festival is located during the weekend. I am used to older convention centers in places like Paris and Villa Erba offers a great place with all the modern amenities that you could dream of."

The show offers unparalleled access to its guests without the hours of lines waiting for the sort of brief interaction that fans and collectors are used to having at the big US shows like New York Comic Con and San Diego Comic-Con.

Como also features original art dealers like Albert Moy, Alex Ross Art, and Sal Abinanti who offer a range of comic art from classic artists like Jack Kirby, Neal Adams, and many more.

Lapeyre's enthusiasm for the show hasn't abated as he discusses who he is most excited about welcoming for 2024: "Bill

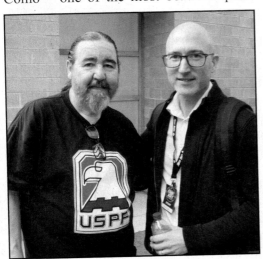

Steve Morger & Arno Lapeyre

Kevin Eastman

Joyce Chin

Sienkiewicz is returning with the best logo that we could only dream of. We were looking for a new visual identity and, my god, how fantastic his creation is. It is such an honor to have him back, and I wish he could come every year.

"David Finch, Charles Vess, David Petersen, Jordi Bernet, and John Romita Jr. are some of the new guests that I'm very glad to host, as I'm a fan of them all. I've been a fan of John Romita Jr.'s *Daredevil* run for such a long time, so it's great to finally have him in Como. Frank Quitely is also an artist who I admire and one that I've been dreaming of hosting since my show in Paris."

Simon Bisley

Liam Sharp

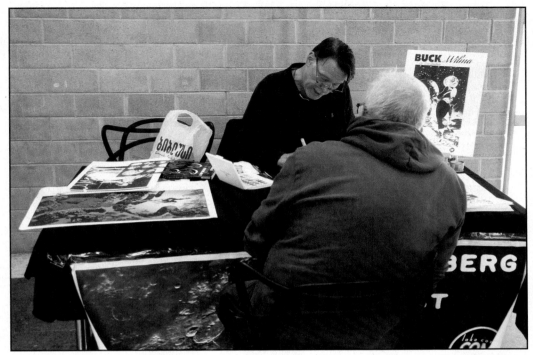

Tom Grindberg

Lake Como also has a number of returning artists who have been part of the event since it began. "We will also continue to have the best returning cast that I hope will be with us every year: Frank Cho, Juanjo Guarnido, Gabriele Dell'Otto, Sara Pichelli, Tula Lotay, Simone Bianchi, Mirka Andolfo," Lapeyre said.

The show has continued to evolve each year, as they are keen not to rest on their laurels while still maintaining its original intentions. "The main idea is still the same and we've been able to preserve the magical intimate atmosphere from its first year. We're adding more subtle touches and giveaways as well as looking into more exclusive materials. There are some artistic collaborations that can only happen in Como such as last year's pairing of Paolo Serpieri and Frank Cho," Lapeyre said.

Lapeyre continues to have a very distinct vision for the show with his partner Morger, as he describes in one short sentence what Lake Como Comic Festival is about: "A paradise for comic book lovers where you will want to return every year."

Lake Como Comic Art Festival is a comic show like no other that I have attended elsewhere and for fans of the medium and comics art, what it offers is hard to beat. The show happens every May. For further information visit its website, https://www.lccaf.com/.

Joel Meadows is the editor-in-chief of Tripwire *magazine online and in print, the UK's pre-eminent publication devoted to the worlds of comics, genre, TV, and film.*

OVERSTREET ADVISORS

DARREN ADAMS
Pristine Comics
Seattle, WA

WELDON ADAMS
Heritage Auctions
Dallas, TX

BILL ALEXANDER
Collector
Sacramento, CA

DAVID T. ALEXANDER
David Alexander
Comics
Tampa, FL

TYLER ALEXANDER
David Alexander
Comics
Tampa, FL

LON ALLEN
Heritage Auctions
Dallas, TX

DAVE ANDERSON
Want List Comics
Tulsa, OK

PETER BARBELLA
Metropolis
Collectibles, Inc.
New York, NY

L.E. BECKER
Comic*Pop Collectibles
Wixom, MI

JIM BERRY
Collector
Portland, OR

PETER BILELIS, ESQ.
Collector
South Windsor, CT

MIKE BOLLINGER
Hake's Auctions
York, PA

STEVE BOROCK
Senior Consignment Director
ComicLink
Portland, ME

SCOTT BRADEN
Comics Historian
Red Lion, PA

RUSS BRIGHT
Mill Geek Comics
Marysville, WA

IN MEMORIAM

RICHARD BROWN
Collector
Detroit, MI

MICHAEL BROWNING
Graphic Novel
Specialist

SHAWN CAFFREY
Finalizer/Modern Age
Specialist
CGC

MICHAEL CARBONARO
Dave & Adam's
New York

BRETT CARRERAS
VA Comicon
Richmond, VA

GARY CARTER
Collector
Coronado, CA

CHARLES CERRITO
Hotflips
Farmingdale, NY

JEFF CERRITO
Hotflips
Farmingdale, NY

JOHN CHRUSCINSKI
Tropic Comics
Lyndora, PA

PAUL CLAIRMONT
PNJ Comics
Winnipeg, MB
Canada

ART CLOOS
Collector/Historian
Flushing, NY

BILL COLE
Bill Cole Enterprises,
Inc.
South Dartmouth, MA

TIM COLLINS
RTS Unlimited, Inc.
Lakewood, CO

JON B. COOKE
Editor - Comic Book
Artist Magazine
West Kingston, RI

JACK COPLEY
Coliseum of Comics
Florida

ASHLEY COTTER-CAIRNS
Collector
Montreal, Canada

JESSE JAMES CRISCIONE
Jesse James Comics
Glendale, AZ

JAIME ADRIANO DAEZ
Collector/Dealer
Metro Manilla,
Philippines

BROCK DICKINSON
Collector
St. Catharines, ONT
Canada

GARY DOLGOFF
Gary Dolgoff Comics
Easthampton, MA

JOHN DOLMAYAN
Torpedo Comics
Las Vegas, NV

SHELTON DRUM
Heroes Aren't Hard
to Find
Charlotte, NC

WALTER DURAJLIJA
Big B Comics
Hamilton, ONT
Canada

KEN DYBER
Tasteecat Comics
Portland, OR

DANIEL ERTLE
Manga Specialist
CBCS
Dallas, TX

MICHAEL EURY
Author
Concord, NC

D'ARCY FARRELL
Pendragon Comics
Toronto, ONT Canada

BILL FIDYK
Collector
Annapolis, MD

PAUL FIGURA
Quality Control Specialist
CBCS
Dallas, TX

JOSEPH FIORE
ComicWiz.com
Toronto, ONT Canada

STEPHEN FISHLER
Metropolis
Collectibles, Inc.
New York, NY

DAN FOGEL
Hippy Comix LLC
Cleveland, OH

KEVIN FORBES
Comic Interlude
Lexington, KY

ERIC FOURNIER
Guardian Comics
Pickering, ON,
Canada

KEIF A. FROMM
Collector/Historian
Hillsborough, NJ

DAN GALLO
Dealer/Comic Art Con
Westchester Co., NY

JAMES GALLO
Toy & Comic Heaven
Willow Grove, PA

STEPHEN H. GENTNER
Golden Age Specialist
Portland, OR

JOSH GEPPI
Diamond Int. Galleries
Sapphire Studios
Hunt Valley, MD

STEVE GEPPI
Diamond Int.
Galleries
Hunt Valley, MD

DOUG GILLOCK
ComicLink
Portland, ME

SEAN GOODRICH
Collector
Maine, USA

TOM GORDON III
Monumental Holdings LLC
Westminster, MD

JAMIE GRAHAM
Graham Crackers
Chicago, IL

ANDY GREENHAM
Forest City Coins
London, ON Canada

ERIC J. GROVES
Dealer/Collector
Oklahoma City, OK

JOHN HAINES
Dealer/Collector
Kirtland, OH

JIM HALPERIN
Heritage Auctions
Dallas, TX

JAY HALSTEAD
International Comic
Exchange
Hamilton, ON Canada

MARK HASPEL
Finalizer/
Pedigree Specialist
CGC

JEF HINDS
Jef Hinds Comics
Madison, WI

TERRY HOKNES
Hoknes Comics
Saskatoon, SK
Canada

**GREG HOLLAND,
Ph.D.**
Collector
Alexander, AR

JOHN HONE
Collector
Silver Spring, MD

STEVEN HOUSTON
Torpedo Comics
Las Vegas, NV

BILL HUGHES
Dealer/Collector
Flower Mound, TX

ROB HUGHES
Arch Angels
Pacific Beach, CA

ROBERT ISAAC
Red Hood Comics
Las Vegas, NV

JEFF ITKIN
Elite Comic Source
Portland, OR

IN MEMORIAM

ED JASTER
Heritage Auctions
Dallas, TX

DR. STEVEN KAHN
Inner Child Comics
& Collectibles
Kenosha, WI

NICK KATRADIS
Collector
Tenafly, NJ

TERRENCE KEEGAN
Platinum Age Specialist
Phillipines

DENNIS KEUM
Fantasy Comics
Goldens Bridge, NY

IVAN KOCMAREK
Comics Historian
Hamilton, ON
Canada

ROBERT KRAUSE
Geca Comics
Lakewood Ranch, FL

TIMOTHY KUPIN
Koops Comics
Lawton, OK

BENJAMIN LABONOG
Primetime Comics
Stockton, CA

BEN LICHTENSTEIN
Zapp Comics
Wayne, NJ

STEPHEN LIPSON
Comics Historian
Mississauga, ON

PAUL LITCH
Primary Grader
CGC

DOUG MABRY
The Great Escape
Madison, TN

JOE MANNARINO
Heritage Auctions
Ridgewood, NJ

NADIA MANNARINO
Heritage Auctions
Ridgewood, NJ

BRIAN MARCUS
Cavalier Comics
Wise, VA

WILL MASON
Dave & Adam's
New York

HARRY MATETSKY
Collector
Middletown, NJ

JIM McCALLUM
Guardian Comics
Pickering, ON Canada

KELLY McCLAIN
Hake's Auctions
York, PA

JON McCLURE
Comics Historian,
Writer
Astoria, OR

TODD McDEVITT
New Dimension Comics
Cranberry Township,
PA

PETER MEROLO
Collector
Sedona, AZ

**JOHN JACKSON
MILLER**
Historian, Writer
Scandinavia, WI

BRENT MOESHLIN
Quality Comix
Montgomery, AL

STEVE MORTENSEN
Miracle Comics
Santa Clara, CA

MARC NATHAN
Cards, Comics &
Collectibles
Reisterstown, MD

JOSHUA NATHANSON
ComicLink
Portland, ME

MATT NELSON
President
CGC

TOM NELSON
Top Notch Comics
Yankton, SD

JAMIE NEWBOLD
Southern California
Comics
San Diego, CA

KAREN O'BRIEN
Comics Journalist
Dyer, IN

VINCE OLIVA
Grader
CGC

TERRY O'NEILL
Terry's Comics
Orange, CA

MICHAEL PAVLIC
Purple Gorilla Comics
Calgary, AB, Canada

JIM PAYETTE
Golden Age Specialist
Bethlehem, NH

BILL PONSETI
Fantastic Worlds
Comics
Scottsdale, AZ

SEAN PROSJE
Comic Cave Canada
Dundas, ON, Canada

RON PUSSELL
Redbeard's Book Den
Crystal Bay, NV

TOM RAUPP
POP Culture Playground
Ormond Beach, FL

ALEX REECE
Reece's Rare Comics
Monrovia, MD

AUSTIN REECE
Reece's Rare Comics
Monrovia, MD

STEVE RICKETTS
CBCS Pressing
Dallas, TX

STEPHEN RITTER
Worldwide Comics
Fair Oaks Ranch, TX

CHUCK ROZANSKI
Mile High Comics
Denver, CO

SEAN RUTAN
Hake's Auctions
York, PA

1103

BARRY SANDOVAL
Heritage Auctions
Dallas, TX

BUDDY SAUNDERS
MyComicShop.com
Arlington, TX

CONAN SAUNDERS
MyComicShop.com
Arlington, TX

MATT SCHIFFMAN
Bronze Age Specialist
Bend, OR

DOUG SCHMELL
Pedigree Comics, Inc.
Wellington, FL

BRIAN SCHUTZER
Sparkle City Comics
Neat Stuff Collectibles
North Bergen, NJ

ALIKA SEKI
Maui Comics and
Collectibles
Waiehu, HI

TODD SHEFFER
Hake's Auctions
York, PA

FRANK SIMMONS
Coast to Coast Comics
Rocklin, CA

CHRIS SIMONS
I Like Comics
Vancouver, WA

MARC SIMS
Big B Comics
Barrie, ON, Canada

LAUREN SISSELMAN
Comics Journalist
Baltimore, MD

MARK SQUIREK
Collector/Historian
Baltimore, MD

TONY STARKS
Silver Age Specialist
Evansville, IN

WEST STEPHAN
CBCS
Dallas, TX

AL STOLTZ
Basement Comics
Havre de Grace, MD

DOUG SULIPA
"Everything 1960-1996"
Manitoba, Canada

MAGGIE THOMPSON
Collector/Historian
Iola, WI

MICHAEL TIERNEY
The Comic Book Store
Little Rock, AR

TED VAN LIEW
Superworld Comics
Worcester, MA

JOE VERENEAULT
JHV Associates
Woodbury Heights, NJ

JASON VERSAGGI
Collector
Langhorne, PA

FRANK VERZYL
Long Island Comics
West Babylon, NY

BOB WAYNE
Collector
Fort Worth, TX

JEFF WEAVER
Victory Comics
Falls Church, VA

LON WEBB
Dark Adventure
Comics
Norcross, GA

RICK WHITELOCK
New Force Comics
Lynn Haven, FL

MIKE WILBUR
Diamond Int.
Galleries
Hunt Valley, MD

ALEX WINTER
Hake's Auctions
York, PA

HARLEY YEE
Dealer/Collector
Detroit, MI

ROBERT YOUNG
Borderlands Comics
and Games
Greenville, SC

MARK ZAID
EsquireComics.com
Bethesda, MD

VINCENT ZURZOLO, JR.
Metropolis
Collectibles, Inc.
New York, NY

OVERSTREET PRICE GUIDE BACK ISSUES

The Overstreet® Comic Book Price Guide has held the record for being the longest running annual comic book publication. We are now celebrating our 54th anniversary, and the demand for the Overstreet® price guides is very strong. Collectors have created a legitimate market for them, and they continue to bring record prices each year. Collectors also have a record of comic book prices going back further than any other source in comic fandom. The prices listed below are for NM condition only, with GD-25% and FN-50% of the NM value. Canadian editions exist for a couple of the early issues. Abbreviations: SC-softcover, HC-hardcover, L-leather bound.

1970

#1 White SC
$1950.00

1970

#1 Blue SC
(2nd Printing)
$1600.00

1972

#2 SC $650.00
#2 HC $1100.00

1973

#3 SC $325.00
#3 HC $950.00

1974

#4 SC $165.00
#4 HC $475.00

1975

#5 SC $155.00
#5 HC $260.00

1976

#6 SC $105.00
#6 HC $155.00

1977

#7 SC $155.00
#7 HC $230.00

1978

#8 SC $130.00
#8 HC $180.00

1979

#9 SC $130.00
#9 HC $180.00

1980

#10 SC $140.00
#10 HC $190.00

1981

#11 SC $85.00
#11 HC $115.00

1982

#12 SC $85.00
#12 HC $115.00

1983

#13 SC $85.00
#13 HC $115.00

1984

#14 SC $55.00
#14 HC $110.00
#14 L $190.00

1985

#15 SC $55.00
#15 HC $80.00
#15 L $170.00

1986

#16 SC $60.00
#16 HC $85.00
#16 L $180.00

1987

#17 SC $55.00
#17 HC $110.00
#17 L $170.00

1988

#18 SC $45.00
Art with black
background

1988

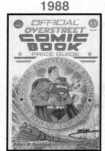

#18 HC $65.00
White background
#18 L $170.00

1989

#19 SC $50.00
#19 HC $60.00
#19 L $190.00

1990

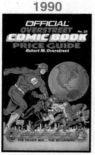

#20 SC $32.00
#20 HC $50.00
#20 L $150.00

1991

#21 SC $40.00
#21 HC $60.00
#21 L $160.00

1992

#22 SC $32.00
#22 HC $50.00

1993

#23 SC $32.00
#23 HC $50.00

1994

#24 SC $26.00
#24 HC $36.00

1995

#25 SC $26.00
#25 HC $36.00
#25 L $110.00

1996

#26 SC $20.00
#26 HC $30.00
#26 L $100.00

1997

#27 SC $22.00
#27 HC $38.00
#27 L $125.00

1997

#27 SC $22.00
#27 HC $38.00
#27 L $125.00

1998

#28 SC $20.00
#28 HC $35.00

1998

#28 SC $20.00
#28 HC $35.00

1999

#29 SC $25.00
#29 HC $40.00

1999

#29 SC $20.00
#29 HC $37.00

2000

#30 SC $22.00
#30 HC $32.00

2000

#30 SC $22.00
#30 HC $32.00

2001

#31 SC $22.00
#31 HC $32.00

2001

#31 SC $22.00
#31 HC $32.00

2001

#31 Bookstore Ed.
SC only $22.00

2002

#32 SC $22.00
#32 HC $32.00

2002

#32 SC $22.00
#32 HC $32.00

2002

#32 Bookstore Ed.
SC only $22.00

2003

#33 SC $25.00
#33 HC $32.00

2003

#33 SC $25.00
#33 HC $32.00

2003

#33 Bookstore Ed.
SC only $25.00

2004

#34 SC $25.00
#34 HC $32.00

2004

#34 SC $25.00
#34 HC $32.00

2004

#34 Bookstore Ed.
SC only $25.00

2005

#35 SC $25.00
#35 HC $32.00

2005

#35 SC $25.00
#35 HC $32.00

2005

#35 Bookstore Ed.
SC only $25.00

2006

#36 SC $25.00
#36 HC $32.00

2006	2006	2007	2007	2007	2008
#36 SC $25.00 #36 HC $32.00	#36 Bookstore Ed. SC only $25.00	#37 SC $25.00 #37 HC $32.00	#37 SC $30.00 #37 HC $35.00	#37 Bookstore Ed. SC only $30.00	#38 SC $30.00 #38 HC $35.00

2008	2008	2009	2009	2009	2010
#38 SC $30.00 #38 HC $35.00	#38 Bookstore Ed. SC only $30.00	#39 SC $30.00 #39 HC $35.00	#39 SC $30.00 #39 HC $35.00	#39 Bookstore Ed. SC only $30.00	#40 SC $30.00 #40 HC $35.00

2010	2010	2011	2011	2011	2012
#40 SC $30.00 #40 HC $35.00	#40 HERO Ed. HC only $35.00	#41 SC $30.00 #41 HC $35.00	#41 SC $30.00 #41 HC $35.00	#41 HERO Ed. HC only $35.00	#42 SC $30.00 #42 HC $35.00

2012	2012	2013	2013	2013	2014
#42 SC $30.00 #42 HC $35.00	#42 HERO Ed. HC only $35.00	#43 SC $30.00 #43 HC $35.00	#43 SC $30.00 #43 HC $35.00	#43 HERO Ed. HC only $35.00	#44 SC $30.00 #44 HC $35.00

2014

#44 SC $30.00
#44 HC $35.00

2014

#44 HERO Ed.
HC only $35.00

2015

#45 SC $30.00
#45 HC $35.00

2015

#45 SC $30.00
#45 HC $35.00

2015

#45 SC $30.00
#45 HC $35.00

2015

#45 SC $30.00
#45 HC $35.00

2015

#45 HERO Ed.
HC only $35.00

2016

#46 SC $30.00
#46 HC $35.00

2016

#46 SC $30.00
#46 HC $35.00

2016

#46 SC $30.00
#46 HC $35.00

2016

#46 HERO Ed.
HC only $35.00

2017

#47 SC $30.00
#47 HC $35.00

2017

#47 SC $30.00
#47 HC $35.00

2017

#47 SC $30.00
#47 HC $35.00

2017

#47 HERO Ed.
HC only $35.00

2018

#48 SC $30.00
#48 HC $35.00

2018

#48 SC $30.00
#48 HC $35.00

2018

#48 SC $30.00
#48 HC $35.00

2018

#48 HERO Ed.
HC only $35.00

2019

#49 SC $30.00
#49 HC $35.00

2019

#49 SC $30.00
#49 HC $35.00

2019

#49 SC $30.00
#49 HC $35.00

2019

#49 HERO Ed.
HC only $35.00

2020

#50 SC $40.00
#50 HC $50.00

2020

#50 SC $30.00
#50 HC $37.50

2020

#50 SC $30.00
#50 HC $37.50

2020

#50 HERO Ed.
HC only $37.50

2021

#51 SC $30.00
#51 HC $37.50

2021

#51 SC $30.00
#51 HC $37.50

2021

#51 HERO Ed.
HC only $37.50

2022

#52 SC $35.00
#52 HC $45.00

2022

#52 SC $35.00
#52 HC $45.00

2022

#52 SC $35.00
#52 HC $45.00

2022

#52 HERO Ed.
HC only $45.00

2022

#52 Overstreet Advisor Ed.
HC only, exclusive
print run of 200 copies

2023

#53 SC $35.00
#53 HC $45.00

2023

#53 SC $35.00
#53 HC $45.00

2023

#53 HERO Ed.
HC only $45.00

2001

#31 Big Big CBPG
$35.00

2002

#32 Big Big CBPG
$35.00

2003

#33 Big Big CBPG
$37.00

2004

#34 Big Big CBPG
$37.00

2005

#35 Big Big CBPG
$37.00

2006

#36 Big Big CBPG
$37.00

2007

#37 Big Big CBPG
$37.00

2008

#38 Big Big CBPG
$37.00

2012

#42 Big Big CBPG
$45.00

2013

#43 Big Big CBPG
$45.00

2014

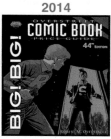

#44 Big Big CBPG
$45.00

2015

#45 Big Big CBPG
$47.50

2016

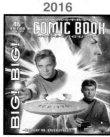

#46 Big Big CBPG
$47.50

2017

#47 Big Big CBPG
$47.50

2018

#48 Big Big CBPG
$47.50

2019

#49 Big Big CBPG
$49.50

2020

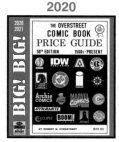

#50 Big Big CBPG
$49.50

2021

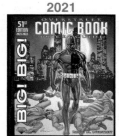

#51 Big Big CBPG
$49.50

2022

#52 Big Big CBPG
$54.95

2022

#52 Big Big CBPG
$54.95

2023

#53 Big Big CBPG
$54.95

ADVERTISERS' INDEX

THE OVERSTREET COMIC BOOK PRICE GUIDE TO
LOST UNIVERSES

2ND EDITION

BY ROBERT M. OVERSTREET & J.C. VAUGHN

1119